Chan Sin-wai

漢英 順逆序大辭典

A New Comprehensive Chinese-English Dictionary

商務印書館

漢英順逆序大辭典

A New Comprehensive Chinese-English Dictionary

作者
Author

陳善偉
Chan Sin-wai

責任編輯
Editors

黃家麗
Betty Wong

封面設計
Graphic Designer

涂　慧
Tu Hui

出版

商務印書館（香港）有限公司
香港筲箕灣耀興道 3 號東滙廣場 8 樓
http://www.commercialpress.com.hk

Published by

The Commercial Press (H.K.) Limited
8/F, Eastern Central Plaza, 3 Yiu Hing Road, Shau Kei Wan, Hong Kong
http://www.commercialpress.com.hk

發行

香港聯合書刊物流有限公司
香港新界大埔汀麗路 36 號中華商務印刷大廈 3 字樓

Distributed by

The SUP Publishing Logistics (HK) Limited
3/F, C & C Building, 36 Ting Lai Road, Tai Po, N.T., Hong Kong

印刷

中華商務彩色印刷有限公司
香港新界大浦汀麗路 36 號中華商務印刷大廈 14 字樓

Printed by

C & C Joint Printing Co., (H.K.) Ltd.
14/F, C & C Building, 36 Ting Lai Road, Tai Po, N. T., Hong Kong

版次

2016 年 1 月第 1 版第 1 次印刷

ISBN 978 962 07 0394 2
Printed in Hong Kong

Edition

First Edition, First Printing, January 2016

ISBN 978 962 07 0394 2
Printed in Hong Kong

辭典編纂 Lexicographer

陳善偉　於香港中文大學 (深圳) 人文社科學院任教，歷任香港中文大學翻譯系教授、系主任、電腦輔助翻譯碩士課程主任及翻譯科技研究中心主任。主要研究範圍為電腦輔助翻譯、雙語辭典學及漢英翻譯。曾編輯《翻譯學百科全書》，審訂《朗文當代大辭典》、《朗文簡明漢英辭典》及撰寫《翻譯科技辭典》。漢英翻譯著作有《仁學英譯》、《紫禁城宮殿》、《近代名人手札精選》、《饒宗頤書畫集》、《高陽小説選譯》及《中國古代印刷史圖冊》。英漢翻譯著作有《我的兒子馬友友》。

Chan Sin-wai　is now a professor in the School of Humanities and Social Sciences, The Chinese University of Hong Kong, Shenzhen. He was Professor and Chairman of the Department of Translation, The Chinese University of Hong Kong. He was also Director of the Master of Arts in Computer-aided Translation Programme and Director of the Centre for Translation Technology. His research interests include computer-aided translation, bilingual lexicography, and Chinese-English translation. He edited *An Encyclopaedia of Translation*, revised *Longman Dictionary of English Language and Culture (bilingual edition)* and *Longman Concise Chinese-English Dictionary* and authored *A Dictionary of Translation Technology*. His books in Chinese-English translation include *An Exposition of Benevolence, Palaces of the Forbidden City, Letters of Prominent Figures in Modern China, Paintings and Calligraphy of Jao Tsung-I, Stories by Gao Yang*, and *An Illustrated History of Printing in Ancient China*. He has also translated *My Son Yo Yo* from English into Chinese.

目錄 Table of Contents

前言 Introduction .... **i – xxxviii**

辭典正文 The Dictionary

Volume 1 (A-H) .... 1 – 1011

Volume 2 (J-S) .... 1013 – 2227

Volume 3 (T-Z) .... 2229 – 3307

筆劃索引 Stroke Index .... **3309 – 3338**

新概念、新格式、新趨勢的漢英辭典

前　言

2015年是漢英辭典誕生二百週年紀念。馬禮遜（Robert Morrison）在1815年出版第一部漢英辭典，距今剛好二百年。值此二百週年，我期望以嶄新的概念和格式出版一部別具特色，又適合語言學習、翻譯、傳譯等各種用途的大型通用漢英辭典，將漢英辭典的編纂推展到另一個階段，形成一種新趨勢，為週年誌慶。

辭典編纂是經年累月的工作，《漢英順逆序大詞典》初稿完成於2004年，經過11年的努力，不斷修訂，終於今年定稿，內容收錄超過60,000單字及多字詞條，420,000英語對應詞，2,000,000字，共計3,345頁。

辭典語料

本辭典的雙語語料主要來自七種資料，包括（1）編者早期編纂《國粵英二文三語詞典》的雙語資料；（2）編者早期負責替大學出版社編纂涉及許多門學科詞匯所建立的雙語數據庫；（3）編者負責修訂某漢英辭典的資料數據；（4）編者在過去數十年所翻譯的中譯英作品中的中英文用語，其中包括文學、建築、書法、財經、玉器、青銅器、繪畫、音樂、出版及園林藝術等不同領域；（5）編者翻譯名人傳記、作品中所處理的詞彙；（6）編者審校各類漢英、英漢辭典時所建立的資料庫；（7）詞目逆引資料包括本辭典的順序詞條及其他逆引辭典詞條。

辭典特色

本辭典在概念、格式、趨勢三方面都有其特色。

新概念

概念上，以語意關鍵字排列詞條是漢英辭典的一種突破。

一般漢英辭典內容或按分類、實用性、時代、程度而定，詞條或按拼音、部首、筆劃、四角號碼、字母排列。從來沒有一部漢英辭典在內容及排列方面是從語義相連的角度處理的。這種排列方式較諸全按條目首字的拼音排列優勝，在於根據關鍵字將相關連的條目放在同一個多字條目下，形成有意義的排列方式。

例如單字條目“是”，多字條目是“是非”，其關鍵字明顯是“是”和“非”。按順序排列“是非”，可以有“是非不分”、“是非不明”、“是非顛倒”等條目。按逆序排列，“是”“非”這兩個關鍵字可以在不同位置出現，但語義基本上屬於“是非”。設“是”為 A，“非”為 B，“是非”的位置可以有以下幾種情況：_ _AB（搬弄是非）；_ A _ B（今是昨非）；_ AB（惹是非）；AABB（是是非非）。有時 B 與 A 的次序亦會不同，例如“圖利”，“唯利是圖”（_B_A）亦屬“圖利”條目。

關鍵字對於處理語言變化很有用。(1) 成語異體：例如“大雨”，無論是“大雨傾盆”或“傾盆大雨”都會收錄於“大雨”條目下。(2) 常用字次序：例如“大”“小”，無論“大”“小”孰先孰後，如“大驚小怪”、“可大可小”、“因小失大”、“見小不見大”等等，全屬“大小”條目。(3) 句式變化：例如“對…表示…”，可以將許多不同字或詞放在虛線上，但都屬於同一條目。(4) 中綴處理：例如“做好”和“做不好”。

新格式

格式上，單字及多字條目以順逆序的方式排列是另一種突破。

一般通用漢英辭典按拼音順序排列，並無逆序排列，難以顯示條目在語言中的整體運用情況。以單字逆引的漢英辭典是存在的，但在單字及多字詞條都以順逆序的方式排列則為本辭典獨有。這種排列方式的好處是可以妥善處理前置修飾詞、前後搭配詞及量詞，令辭典的功能更為豐富。順逆序排列的優點在於 (1) 條目的意義更為整體；(2) 清楚顯示上位詞與下義詞的關係；(3) 單字與多字條目的量詞得以顯示；(4) 條目的文化意義得以表達。

新趨勢

內容上，本辭典以大型辭典的形式為漢語常用詞提供大量英語對應詞，為廣大用家提供有用的語言信息，符合近代辭典以大型辭典為主的趨勢。

一般通用漢英辭典可以分為 1,000 頁以下的小型辭典，1,000 至 1,500 頁的中型辭典，及 1,500 頁以上的大型辭典。從歷史角度看，過去二百年所出版的 81 部通用漢英辭典可分為三個時期：第一個時期由 1815 至 1965 年，出版 13 部主要是由外國人編纂的小型辭典。第二個時期由 1966 至 1986 年，出版 29 部辭典，主要是國內外學者編纂的中型辭典。第三個時期由 1987 至 2015 年，出版的 39 部辭典絕大部份為國內學者所編纂的大型辭典。本辭典是繼吳光華6,562頁的《漢英綜合大辭典》(2004) 及曹亞民4,978頁的《漢英大辭海》(2002) 後，以3,338頁成為第三部最大型漢英辭典。

結　語

本辭典注重條目的關連性與整體性，希望以新概念新格式建立漢英雙語辭典的新典範，將語言學，特別是語意學的上下義項概念，融入辭典編纂之中，有效地處理語言變化、文化內涵等問題，藉以打破二百年來單純以拼音或部首的編排方式或檢索方法，以開創雙語辭典新趨勢。

陳善偉
香港中文大學人文社科學院(深圳)

* 衷心感謝商務印書館(香港)有限公司編輯出版部黃家麗女士對本詞典出版所作的努力與支持。謹以本書獻給內子翁慧莉女士。

A New Concept, a New Format, and a New Trend in Bilingual Lexicography: Preface to *A New Comprehensive Chinese-English Dictionary*

Introduction

This year marks the bicentenary of the birth of the first Chinese-English dictionary compiled by Robert Morrison in 1815. The present work, *A New Comprehensive Chinese-English Dictionary*《漢英順逆序大詞典》, celebrates this bicentenary by introducing a new concept and format in the compilation of a general, comprehensive, new-style Chinese-English dictionary. The new concept is semantic, the new format is holistic, and our target is to produce a dictionary large enough to be of use to language professionals and translators.

Dictionary-making is a time-consuming task. It has taken me, on and off (more on than off), some eleven years to complete single-handedly this dictionary, which has incorporated the above ideas. The end product is *A New Comprehensive Chinese-English Dictionary*, which has 60,000 single-character headword entries and multiple-character sub-entries arranged in normal and reverse sequences, 420,000 English equivalents, 2 million words, and 3,345 pages.

Dictionary Corpus

The sources that formed the contents or corpus of this dictionary are several: first, the corpus I built up before 2004 when I worked on the dictionary project *A Biliterate and Trilingual Dictionary*《國粵英二文三語詞典》; second, the glossaries I consulted when commissioned by a university press to work on the terms in a number of academic disciplines; third, the data I collected when commissioned to revise and update a well-known Chinese-English dictionary; fourth, the expressions and terms I translated when rendering Chinese literature and books on Chinese culture, architecture, bronze, calligraphy, finance, economics, gardening, jade, music, painting, and printing into English; fifth, the equivalents I came across when translating works by or on high-ranking officials in China, such as Li Ruihuan and Wen Jiabao, as they were reliable translations provided by official translators in official websites; sixth, the translations I collected when revising or editing texts of English-Chinese or Chinese-English dictionaries; and seventh, the materials of the headword reverse-order entries include normal-order entries of this dictionary as well as entries in other reverse-order dictionaries.

Main Characteristics of this Dictionary

This dictionary has its own characteristics in terms of concept, format, and trend.

A New Concept

Conceptually, this dictionary has achieved a breakthrough in Chinese-English lexicography by arranging entries according to semantic interrelatedness and keywords.

The novelty of this concept can be seen from two perspectives: the content and the arrangement of entries in Chinese-English dictionaries on the market. In terms of content, most general Chinese-English dictionaries are usually organized in four different ways: (1) by classification, e.g. Li Kai-yong 李開榮《漢英百科分類詞典》(*Chinese-English Classified Encyclopedic Dictionary*) (1995); (2) by practicality, e.g. Wang Junyi 王俊怡《實用漢英詞典》(*A Practical Chinese-English Dictionary*) (1983); (3) by contemporariness, e.g. Wu Jingrong 吳景榮 and Cheng Zhenqiu 程鎮球《新時代漢英大詞典》(*New Age Chinese-English Dictionary*) (2000); and (4) by level, e.g. Walter Simon《初級中英國語字典》(*A Beginner's Chinese-English Dictionary of the National Language* (*Guoyeu*)) (1947).

In terms of the arrangement of entries, all general Chinese-English dictionaries published since 1815 have been mainly phonetic-, radical-, or alphabet-based, but not linguistic-based, and, in particular, semantic-based. Most dictionaries are based on phonetics as the major consultation method. The phonetic-based dictionaries include most of the dictionaries that use the Hanyu Pinyin Romanization system, such as《中大漢英辭典》(*Zhongda Chinese-English Dictionary*) (1999 / 2003) compiled by Leung Derun 梁德潤 and Zheng Jiande 鄭建德. Some use the Wade-Giles Romanization system, such as Robert Henry Mathews' *A Chinese-English Dictionary* (《漢英字典》(1931/1972). Still others use other Romanization systems, such as the Yale Romanization System. Some dictionaries are based on radicals, such as Liang Shih-ch'iu's 梁實秋《遠東漢英大辭典》(*Far East Chinese-English Dictionary*) (1986). Other dictionaries use alphabets, such as John DeFrancis' *ABC Chinese-English Dictionary, Alphabetically-based Computerized* (1996).

What is noticeable is that of all the general Chinese-English dictionaries published until now, none is based on the concept of semantic interrelatedness.

This new orientation towards the semantic relations of the entries arises out of the overemphasis on the use of Romanization systems as the sole or main consultation method. In fact, the use of Romanization methods in arranging entries in Chinese-English dictionaries targeted mainly at foreigners and learners of Chinese and was applied ever since the publication of Morrison's first Chinese-English dictionary. While the Romanization of the first character of an entry is a convenient way to find the word we want to look up in a dictionary, it has the disadvantage of separating semantically related entries due to the variations in the positions of the key characters, making it impossible to recognize their semantic relationship. This dictionary, therefore, arranges all entries according to the tone order of the Hanyu Pinyin Romanization for easy consultation, while it applies the method of semantic analysis in linguistics in the reverse part to arrange multiple-character sub-entries with key characters in different positions according to Hanyu Pinyin, which systematically shows the interrelatedness of the entries listed.

Taking the multiple-character entries of the single-character entry *shi* 是 as an example, the first few entries in normal order are as follows:

shi fei bu fen 是非不分 cannot tell black from white; confuse right and wrong; confuse truth and falsehood; fail to distinguish good from bad; fail to distinguish right and wrong; make no distinction between right and wrong;

shi fei bu ming 是非不明 have no sense of right or wrong; unable to tell right from wrong;

shi fei dian dao 是非顛倒 confound right and wrong;

For entries in the reverse order, the emphasis is on the key characters *shi* 是 and *fei* 非 of the multiple-character entry *shi fei* 是非 . Regardless of the positions of *shi* 是 and *fei* 非 , entries with *shi* and *fei* are semantically related to the multiple-character entry *shi fei* 是非 , and they are arranged in Hanyu Pinyin Romanization according to the tone of the first character in an entry.

The following are examples of the multiple-character entry *shi fei* 是非 in reverse order with variations in the positions of the key characters of *shi* 是 and *fei* 非 .

(1) _ _ *shi fei* 是非 (_ _ A B)

ban nong shi fei 搬弄是非 carry tales; create troubles and dissension; indulge in tittle-tattle; make mischief; make mischief through tittle-tattle; sow discord through gossip; stir up trouble by gossip; tell tales;

(2) _ *shi* 是 _ *fei* 非 (_ A _ B)

jin shi zuo fei 今是昨非 come to realize how wrong one has been all these years; realize how one has been wrong; wake up to one's past folly after realizing what is right today; things of the present are right and those of the past are wrong;

(3) _ *shi fei* 是非 (_ A B)

re shi fei 惹是非 incur unnecessary trouble; provoke a dispute; stir up ill will; stir up trouble;

(4) *shi shi fei fei* 是是非非 (AABB)

shi shi fei fei 是是非非 gossips; scandals;

Other examples that could be cited include:

(5) _ B _ A

tu li 圖利 : desire to make money; plan to make money;

wei li shi tu 唯利是圖 be bent solely on profit; be intent on nothing but profit; be interested only in personal gain; blind to all but one's own interest; care solely for profit; have an eye to the main chance; plan only how to get money; pursue profit as one's only aim; put profit-making first; scheme after nothing but gain; seek nothing but profits; seek only profit;

This keyword approach to entry treatment is useful in dealing with the following variations.

(1) Variations in an Idiom

Variations in the positions of the keywords in an idiom will not result in the separate appearances of these entries as the meanings of the expressions are the same.

Da yu qing pen 大雨傾盆, for example, means: "it is raining like billy-o; it rains cats and dogs; rain pitchforks; the rain falls in sheets; the rain is pelting; the rain teems down". This idiom can also be expressed inversely as *qing pen da yu* 傾盤大雨, or "torrential rain".

Another example is *bu shi yi ding* 不識一丁, which means "illiterate; not know a single word". This expression can also be written as *yi ding bu shi* 一丁不識 : "not know B from a battledore; not know beans; not know chalk from cheese; not know one's ABC".

(2) Variations in the Positions of the Keywords in Common Expressions

With this semantics-oriented approach, expressions with the same keywords are listed under the relevant entries. Take *da xiao* 大小 under the headword *da* 大 as an example. If A is *da* 大 , B is *xiao* 小 , then the normal sequence for *da xiao* 大小 as a compound expression can be AB_ _ , such as *da xiao bu yi* 大小不一 (not uniform in size); *da xiao he shi* 大小合適 (size to fit); *da xiao shi zhong* 大小適中 (moderate size; right size); *da xiao xiang tong* 大小相同 (of uniform size); and *da xiao you zhi* 大小由之 (can fit any size).

Entries in the reverse-order sequence of *da xiao* 大小 (AB) can have more variations.

(a) A _ B _

da chun xiao ci 大醇小疵 sound on the whole though defective in details; with great purity and small flaw;

da jing xiao guai 大驚小怪 bark at the moon; be surprised at sth normal; get excited over a little thing; great alarm at a little bogey;

make a fuss about nothing; make a great ado over sth; make a rare fuss over sth; much cry and little wool;

da ti xiao zuo 大題小做 little about a major issue; make little of; treat major issues lightly.

(b) _A _B

hua da wei xiao 化大為小 turn big issues into small ones;

ke da ke xiao 可大可小 changeable; elastic;

mei da mei xiao 沒大沒小 impertinent; impolite to an elder; imprudent; show no respect for one's elders;

yi da qi xiao 以大欺小 bully the weak for being strong; the big bullies the small;

qi da ba xiao 七大八小 objects of various sizes thrown together;

qi da jiu xiao 棄大就小 exchange the great for the small; leave big shots alone and go for the small fry;

yi da ya xiao 以大壓小 the big coerce the small;

yi da yi xiao 以大易小 exchange the great for the small;

you da you xiao 由大由小 may be large or small.

(c) _AB

yuan da xiao 原大小 life-size.

(d) _ _AB

ge zhong da xiao 各種大小 every shape and size;

jia jiao da xiao 夾角大小 corner dimension;

mo li da xiao 磨粒大小 abrasive grain sizes;

qi shi da xiao 氣室大小 air cell size;

shi wu da xiao 實物大小 life-size;

zhen ren da xiao 真人大小 life-size.

(e) _ _ _A B

chuang hu de da xiao 窗戶的大小 size of a window;

mao xi guan da xiao 毛細管大小 capillary dimension.

(f) _*B* _*A*

qi xiao jiu da 棄小就大 lose a fly to catch a trout; one has to make sacrifices in order to succeed;

wei xiao shi da 為小失大 lose a lot to save a little; lose a pound in trying to save a penny;

yi xiao bo da 以小博大 throw out a sprat to catch a herring;

yin xiao shi da 因小失大 lose a big opportunity because of a trifle consideration; lose a great deal through trying to save a little; lose much because of a small thing; lose the greater for the less; lose the main goal because of small gains; pay too big a price for mere trifles; penny-wise, pound-foolish; suffer a big loss for a little gain; try to save a little only to lose a lot;

you xiao bian da 由小變大 change from being minor to being major; from weak to strong; grow from small to big;

you xiao dao da 由小到大 grow big from being small; grow from small beginnings into a mighty force; grow from small to big; grow in size.

(g) _*B* _ _*A*

jian xiao bu jian da 見小不見大 fail to see the wood for the trees; strain at a gnat and swallow a camel.

Another example is the sub-entry *che ma* 車馬 (chariots and horses), whose reverse-order entries are as follows:

bi che nu ma 弊車駑馬 a decrepit cart drawn by a lean horse;

che shui ma long 車水馬龍 be crowded with people and vehicles; be thronged with visitors; endless stream of carriages and horses; heavy flow of traffic; heavy traffic; incessant stream of horses and carriages;

qian che wan ma 千車萬馬 a thousand coaches and ten thousand horses;

su che bai ma 素車白馬 plain cars and white horses — in a funeral procession;

xian che nu ma 鮮車怒馬 lead a luxurious life; new carriage driven by fat horses — lavish service;

xiang che bao ma 香車寶馬 fragrant carriage and precious horse — the beautiful carriage of women.

(3) Treatment of Sentence Patterns

This keyword approach allows us to treat sentence patterns in a systematic manner. The main idea is to identify the keywords in a sentence pattern and give their common collocates to form entries.

The first example is *dui ... biao shi* 對…表示 (show...to...):

dui ... biao shi fan dui 對…表示反對 declare oneself against...; show one's objection to...;

dui...biao shi tong qing 對…表示同情 express sympathy with...; show sympathy toward...;

dui ... biao shi wei wen 對…表示慰問 extend one's sympathy to...;

dui ... biao shi yi han 對…表示遺憾 proffer regret at....

The second example is *cong...dao...* 從…到… (from...to...):

cong gu dao jin 從古到今 from ancient to modern times;

cong ri chu dao ri luo 從日出到日落 from dawn till dusk;

cong shang dao xia 從上到下 from above down; from top to bottom;

cong sheng dao si 從生到死 from the cradle to the grave;

cong tou dao jiao 從頭到腳 from head to foot;

cong tou dao wei 從頭到尾 from beginning to end; from first to last;

cong wu dao you 從無到有 grow out of nothing;

cong xiao dao da 從小到大 develop gradually; expand from small to big;

cong zao dao wan 從早到晚 from dawn to dusk; from morning till night.

(4) Treatment of Infixes

This keyword approach allows entries with infixes to be placed in the same heading, such as 做好 (do sth well) and 做不好 (cannot do sth well).

(5) The Creation of New Sub-entries for Easy Consultation

For easy consultation, it is necessary to create new sub-entries to put entries with the same keywords under the relevant headwords. Take *bu zhu* 不住 as an example. 不住 can be defined as "ceaselessly; continuously;" it can also be translated as "cannot". The following are examples of the new entry *bu zhu* 不住 when used as a suffix.

ai bu zhu 挨不住 can no longer endure;

bao bu zhu 保不住 cannot be defended; there is no guarantee that;

bei bu zhu 備不住 maybe; perhaps;

beng bu zhu 綳不住 unable to bear; unable to endure;

bie bu zhu 憋不住 cannot help; cannot suppress;

bei bu zhu qi 憋不住氣 cannot hold one's anger any longer; ready to burst;

cang bu zhu 藏不住 cannot be hidden;

chi bu zhu 吃不住 unable to bear or support;

dai bu zhu 待不住 cannot stay long;

dang bu zhu 擋不住 hindering; impeding; incapable of blocking; stopping;

di bu zhu 敵不住 no match for;

jia bu zhu 架不住 (1) cannot stand the pressure; cannot stand up against; cannot sustain the weight; (2) cannot compete against; no match for;

ting bu zhu 挺不住 cannot stand it; cannot take it any more;

wu bu zhu 捣不住 cannot be concealed;

zuo bu zhu 坐不住 cannot sit still; cannot stay long; restless.

Another example of entry creation is *qi ba* 七八 [(1) seven or eight; (2) seventy or eighty per cent; (3) probably], which illustrates to some extent the use of numerals in some set expressions. The following are examples:

qi ba cheng 七八成 (1) seventy or eighty per cent; (2) extremely likely; possibly; probably;

qi ba yue de nan gua – pi lao xin bu lao 七八月的南瓜—皮老心不老 pumpkins in the seventh or eighth month of the lunar year – the skin is old but the heart is young; old in age but young at heart;

jia qi jia ba 夾七夾八 at random; cluttered; confused; incoherent; talk incoherently;

luan qi ba zao 亂七八糟 a fine kettle of fish; a glorious mess; a nice kettle of fish; a pretty kettle of fish; all in a tumble; at sixes and sevens; chaotic; higgledy-piggledy; in a clutter; in a littler; in a mess; in a muddle; in a pickle; in a state; in an awful mess; in complete confusion; in wild disorder; jumbly; make a mess of sth; make hay of; rough-and-tumble; topsy-turvy; upside down;

luan qi ba zao de 亂七八糟的 higgledy-piggledy;

luan qi ba zao shuo yi tong 亂七八糟説一通 make a chaos of utterances;

fang jian luan qi ba zao 房間亂七八糟 one's room is a dump; one's room is a mess; one's room is topsy-turvy;

gao de luan qi ba zao 搞得亂七八糟 make a mess;

jiang ji hua gao de luan qi ba zao 將計劃搞得亂七八糟 mess up one's plans; throw one's plans into confusion;

xin li luan qi ba zao 心裏亂七八糟 feel all hot and bothered; feel very perturbed;

A New Format

The second characteristic of this dictionary is its new holistic format in arranging entries in both normal and reverse sequences to give a larger context for users to understand the semantic, pragmatic, and cultural connotations of the headwords in their entirety.

So far, the only dictionary that follows this format is《漢英大辭海》(*The Chinese-English Word-ocean*) edited by Cao Yamin (2002), but the present dictionary goes further than Cao's dictionary by adopting the normal-reverse sequence at both the single and multiple headword levels.

It goes without saying that all Chinese-English bilingual dictionaries on the market, including the popular ones such as those compiled by Hui Yu 惠宇 (《新世紀漢英大詞典》(*A New Century Chinese-English Dictionary*) (2003)) and Wu Guanghua 吳光華 (《漢英綜合大辭典》(*A Comprehensive Chinese-English Dictionary*) (2004)), do not truly present the headwords in a context large enough to see how these single-character entries combine with other single or multiple characters to form character combinations that are semantically related to the headwords. In other words, the headwords and their sub-entries do not give a general background to understand the lexical, semantic, and cultural aspects of the entries. It is therefore necessary to treat headwords in bilingual dictionaries in a holistic manner.

This dictionary addresses the issue of holism through the arrangement of the single-character headwords and multiple-character sub-entries in both normal and reverse sequences. This dictionary may not be the first dictionary to put entries in reverse order (Yu et al 1986; Cao 2002), but it is probably the first dictionary to use the reverse order at multiple linguistic levels to allow the incorporation of pre- / post-modifiers, collocates, and measure words.

For single-character or headword entries, entries in the reverse order are listed after the last multiple-character entries, which are arranged in normal sequence. Taking the entry of *pai* 排 as an example, its definitions are as follows:

pai【排】

(1) arrange; arrange in order; put in order; sequence; (2) line; rank; row; (3) a clip of; a line of; a rank of; a row of; (4) platoon; (5) rehearse; (6) raft; (7) blow down; blow off; discharge; drain off; (8) discriminate against; eject; exclude; get rid of; reject; repel; shut out;

The entries of *pai* 排 in the normal sequence are as follows:

pai ban [排班] (1) fall by rank; fall in line; (2) arrange turns of work;

pai zi [排字] compose; typeset; typewrite;

pai zi gong 排字工 compositor; typesetter;

pai zi gong ren 排字工人 compositor;

pai zi ji 排字機 composing machine; compositor; typesetter; typesetting machine;

she ying pai zi ji 攝影排字機 photographic typesetter;

yi tai pai zi ji 一台排字機 a typesetting machine;

pai zi jia 排字架 composing frame;

pai zi pan 排字盤 composing stick;

dian nao pai zi 電腦排字 computerized typesetting;

The entries in the reverse sequence are as follows:

ai pai 挨排 arrange; make arrangements for;

an pai 安排 arrange; arrange for; arrangements; cuddle up; find a place for sth; fix; fix sth; fix up; lay on sth; lay out; make arrangements for; manage; plan; tee up;

bian pai 編排 arrange; lay out; make up sth;

bing pai 冰排 ice floe; ice raft.

Multiple-character sub-entries are also arranged in both normal and reverse sequences, such as *xiao hua* 消化.

xiao hua dao chu xue 消化道出血 alimentary canal haemorrhage;

xiao hua li 消化力 digestion;

xiao hua liang hao 消化良好 eupepsia;

xiao hua qi guan 消化器官 digestive organs;

xiao hua zheng chang 消化正常 eupepsia;

xiao hua ye 消化液 digestive juice;

jian xing xiao hua 鹼性消化 alkaline digestion;

ren gong xiao hua 人工消化 artificial digestion;

suan xing xiao hua 酸性消化 acid digestion;

xi jun xiao hua 細菌消化 bacterial digestion;

xu yang xiao hua 需氧消化 aerobic digestion;

yan yang xiao hua 厭氧消化 anaerobic digestion.

This normal-reverse arrangement to show headwords in a holistic manner is fully justified.

First, characters are no longer understood in a unidirectional manner. Take the character *da* 答 as an example. If entries are arranged in a normal sequence, they would be as follows:

da【答】

(1) answer; reply; (2) reciprocate; return a visit;

da an [答案] answer; key; solution;

ti gong da an 提供答案 furnish an answer; supply an answer;

zheng que da an 正確答案 correct answer;

da bai [答拜] pay a return visit; return a courtesy call;

da bian [答辯] reply in support of one's ideas; reply to a charge;

da bian quan 答辯權 right of reply;

kou tou da bian 口頭答辯 verbal defence;

zuo kou tou da bian 做口頭答辯 make verbal defence;

da ci [答詞] answering speech; reply; speech in reply; thank-you speech;

da dui [答對] answer; reply;

da fu [答覆] answer; reply;

dian hua da fu 電話答覆 answer by telephone;

han hu de da fu 含糊的答覆 dubious answer;

jian duan de da fu 簡短的答覆 brief answer;

jin shen de da fu 謹慎的答覆 cautious;

jin zao da fu 盡早答覆 make a reply as early as possible; reply at one's earliest convenience;

ju li da fu 據理答覆 give a reasonable answer;

ken ding de da fu 肯定的答覆 affirmative answer; affirmative

response;

kou tou da fu 口頭答覆 answer orally; give an answer by word of mouth; oral answer;

li ji da fu 立即答覆 immediate answer; prompt answer;

ma shang da fu 馬上答覆 make an answer straight off;

man yi de da fu 滿意的答覆 favourable answer;

ming que de da fu 明確的答覆 categorical answer; distinct answer;

mo hu liang ke de da fu 模糊兩可的答覆 ambiguous answer;

qi dai da fu 期待答覆 expect an answer;

que ding de da fu 確定的答覆 decided answer;

shan shuo qi ci de da fu 閃爍其詞的答覆 evasive answer;

shou dao da fu 收到答覆 get a reply; have a reply; receive a reply;

shu mian da fu 書面答覆 give an answer in writing;

yao qiu da fu 要求答覆 want an answer; request a reply;

zhan ding jie tie de da fu 斬釘截鐵的答覆 categorical answer;

da hua [答話] answer; reply;

da juan [答卷] answered examination paper;

wan cheng da juan 完成答卷 finish one's answer to an examination paper;

da li [答禮] return a salute;

da lu [答錄] answer and record;

da lu ji 答錄機 recorder; recording machine;

duo sheng dao da lu ji 多聲道答錄機 multichannel broadcast recorder;

li ti sheng da lu ji 立體聲答錄機 stereo recorder;

da xie [答謝] acknowledge; express appreciation; reciprocate;

da yun [答允] undertake.

When entries in the reverse order are also listed, then the lexical contents of the headword 答 are greatly enhanced.

bao da 報答 repay; requite;

bi da 筆答 reply by writing in examination papers;

chou da 酬答 (1) thank sb with a gift; (2) respond with a poem;

dui da 對答 answer; reply;

hui da 回答 answer; reply;

jie da 解答 answer; explain;

wen da 問答 question and answer;

ying da 應答 answer; reply;

zeng da 贈答 present each other with gifts, poems, etc.

Second, this holistic approach to entry presentation provides information on the semantic hierarchy of a headword. More specifically, it shows both the hypernyms and the hyponyms.

For instance, *gou* 狗 is a superordinate. Entries relating to *gou* put in the normal sequence could be *gou dan bao tian* 狗膽包天, *gou er* 狗兒, *gou fei* 狗吠, *gou gou ying ying* 狗苟蠅營, *gou jiao* 狗叫, *gou niang yang de* 狗娘養的, *gou pa shi* 狗爬式, *gou pi* 狗屁, *gou shi* 狗屎, *gou shi bu shi* 狗噬不食, *gou shou zhu ren xiu* 狗瘦主人羞, *gou tou shu qie* 狗偷鼠竊, *gou tui zi* 狗腿子, *gou wei xu diao* 狗尾續貂, *gou wo* 狗窩, *gou xue* 狗血, *gou yao* 狗咬, *gou zai dui* 狗仔隊, *gou zai zi* 狗崽子, *gou zao* 狗蚤, *gou zhang jia – chu yang xiang* 狗長角—出 [洋] (羊)[相], *gou zhi* 狗彘, and *gou zui* 狗嘴 .

With the addition of entries in the reverse order, a number of hyponyms are included, providing a large lexical context to understand the character *gou*.

ba er gou 巴兒狗 (1) lapdog; (2) Pekingese; (3) flatterer; sycophant; toady;

ba er gou 叭兒狗 (1) lapdog; (2) Pekingese;

bai gou 白狗 white dog;

ben gou 笨狗 big mastiff;

feng gou 瘋狗 mad dog; rabid dog;

ha ba gou 哈巴狗 (1) Pekingese; (2) sycophant; toady;

hai gou 海狗 fur seal; ursine seal;

kan men gou 看門狗 watchdog;

la chang gou 臘腸狗 sausage dog;

lang gou 狼狗 wolfhound;

lie gou 獵狗 hound; hunting dog;

lou shui gou 落水狗 dog in the water;

xi shi gou 西施狗 shih-tzu;

xiao gou 小狗 doggie;

xiao ling gou 小靈狗 whippet;

ye gou 野狗 wild dog;

yi tiao gou 一條狗 a dog;

yu gou 魚狗 kingfisher;

zou gou 走狗 flunkey; lackey; running dog.

Third, measure words can be treated at both the single- and multiple-character levels. Take *bu* 布 as an example. As a headword, it has:

yi ceng bu 一層布 a ply of cloth; a thickness of cloth;

yi kuai bu 一塊布 a piece of cloth;

yi kun bu 一綑布 a bale of cloth;

yi ma bu 一碼布 a yard of cloth;

yi pi bu 一匹布 a bolt of cloth; a roll of cloth.

When *bu* 布 is combined with *liao* 料, we have *bu liao* 布料, which could have the following measure words:

bu liao [布料] cloth;

yi duan bu liao 一段布料 a length of cloth; a piece of cloth;

yi fu bu liao 一幅布料 a breadth of cloth; a piece of cloth.

The display of measure words in individual entries does not mean that the measure words do not exist as independent entries.

Take *yi ceng* 一層 as an example.

yi ceng 一層 (1) one floor; one story; (2) a stratum; (3) a bed of; a blanket of; a cloak of; a coat of; a curtain of; a deck of; a film of; a flake of; a floor; a floor of; a layer; a layer of; a level of; a line of; a mantle of; a ring of; a story; a story of; a veil of.

Fourth, the cultural aspects of a character can also be shown through the reverse-order arrangement.

Shen 神 illustrates this fact. In this dictionary, there are 80 entries for *shen* 神 , including *shen bing* 神兵 , *shen bu an ti* 神不安啼 , *shen bu shou she* 神不守舍 , *shen cai* 神采 , *shen chi* 神馳 , *shen dian* 神殿 , *shen en* 神恩 , *shen feng* 神峰 , *shen feng* 神鋒 , *shen fo* 神佛 , *shen fu* 神父 , *shen gong* 神功 , *shen guai* 神怪 , *shen gui* 神龜 , *shen gui* 神鬼 , *shen han* 神漢 , *shen hu qi ji* 神乎其技 , *shen hu qi shen* 神乎其神 , *shen hua* 神化 , *shen hua* 神話 , *shen hun* 神魂 , *shen ji* 神機 , *shen ji* 神蹟 , *shen jiao* 神交 , *shen jing* 神經 , *shen kan* 神龕 , *shen li* 神力 , *shen liao* 神聊 , *shen ling* 神靈 , *shen mi* 神秘 , *shen miao* 神妙 , *shen miao* 神廟 , *shen min* 神民 , *shen ming* 神明 , *shen mou mo dao* 神謀魔道 , *shen niao* 神鳥 , *Shen Nong* 神農 , *shen nü* 神女 , *shen pin* 神品 , *shen po* 神婆 , *shen qi* 神奇 , *shen qi* 神祇 , *shen qi* 神氣 , *shenqing* 神情 , *shen quan* 神權 , *shen ren* 神人 , *shen se* 神色 , *shen shang* 神傷 , *shen sheng* 神聖 , *shen shi* 神示 , *shen shu* 神術 , *shen si* 神思 , *shen si* 神似 , *shen su* 神速 , *shen suan* 神算 , *shen sui* 神髓 , *shen tai* 神態 , *shen tong* 神通 , *shen tong* 神童 , *shen wang* 神往 , *shen wei* 神威 , *shen wei* 神位 , *shen wu* 神巫 , *shen wu* 神武 , *shen wu* 神物 , *shen wu* 神悟 , *shen xian* 神仙 , *shen xiang* 神像 , *shen xiao* 神效 , *shen xue* 神學 , *shen yi* 神醫 , *shen yi* 神異 , *shen yi* 神意 , *sheng yong* 神勇 , *shen you* 神遊 , *shen you* 神佑 , *shen yu* 神宇 , *shen yu* 神諭 , *shen zhi ren yuan* 神職人員 , *shen zhi* 神志 , *shen zhi* 神智 , and *shen zhu* 神主 .

ai shen 愛神 (1) Amor; Cupid; Eros; God of Love; (2) Goddess of Love; Venus;

an shen 安神 (1) calm one's nerves; (2) relieve uneasiness of body and mind;

ao shen 媪神 Goddess of the Earth;

bai shen 拜神 worship gods;

cai shen 財神 (1) God of Wealth; (2) money-makers;

cao shen 操神 tax on one's mind; bother; trouble;

chu shen 出神 abstractedness; abstraction; aphelxia; be lost in thought; in a trance; spellbound;

chuan shen 傳神 lifelike; vivid;

ding shen 定神 (1) collect oneself; compose oneself; pull oneself together; (2) collect one's thoughts; concentrate one's attention; take a grip on oneself;

fei shen 費神 (1) may I trouble you with sth; would you mind doing sth for me; (2) waste of energy;

fen shen 分神 give some attention to;

feng she 丰神 manner;

gui shen 鬼神 ghosts and gods; spirits; supernatural beings;

hai shen 海神 Neptune; Poseidon;

huo shen 火神 God of Fire;

jing shen 精神 (1) consciousness; mind; spirit; (2) essence; gist; spirit; substance;

lao shen 勞神 a tax on one's mind; bother; trouble;

liu shen 留神 careful; keep one's eyes on the ball; keep one's eyes peeled; look out for; look sharp; take care;

men shen 門神 door-god;

ning shen 凝神 with concentrated attention;

*n*ü *shen* 女神 goddess;

qi shen 棲神 cultivate one's mind; discipline one's mind;

qing shen 請神 call up an evil spirit;

qiu shen 求神 beg the gods;

ru shen 人神 man and God;

ru shen 如神 like god;

ru shen 入神 captivated; deeply absorbed in; enthralled; entranced; spellbound; with ecstasy;

shan shen 山神 mountain deity;

shang shen 傷神 be nerve-racking; overtax one's nerves;

shi shen 失神 (1) absent-minded; careless; inattentive; (2) in low spirits; out of sorts;

si shen 死神 Death; Mr Mose; old floorer; old man Mose; old Mr Grim; the great leveller; the great whipper-in; the graim monarch; the Grim Reaper; the Pale Rider;

si shen 祀神 worship gods;

song shen 送神 send off the gods after the offering of sacrifices;

tao shen 淘神 bothersome; trying;

ti shen 提神 arouse; elate; give oneself a lift; refresh oneself; stimulate;

tian shen 天神 deity; god;

tiao shen 跳神 sorcerer's dance in a trance;

tong shen 通神 capable of buying the gods;

wen shen 瘟神 God of the Plague;

wu shen 巫神 sorcerer; wizard;

xin shen 心神 mind; mood; state of mind;

xing shen 形神 body and spirit;

xing shen 醒神 induce resuscitation;

xiong shen 凶神 demon; evil spirit;

xiong shen 兇神 demon; fiend;

yan shen 眼神 (1) expression in one's eyes; gleams of the eyes; light; (2) eyesight;

yang shen 養神 have mental relaxation; repose; rest to attain mental tranquility;

yi shen 一神 monotheistic;

yi shen 怡神 inspire peace and harmony in one's mind;

yi shen 頤神 have mental relaxation; rest one's mind;

you shen 有神 (1) full of spirit; (2) miraculous;

zao shen 灶神 god of the kitchen;

zou shen 走神 absent-minded.

A New Trend

The third characteristic of this dictionary is the trend it sets. It is a large-scale Chinese-English dictionary with 3,338 pages, probably the third largest printed Chinese-English dictionary ever published, following those by Wu Guanghua《漢英綜合大辭典》(*A Comprehensive Chinese-English Dictionary*) (2004, 6,562 pages) and Cao Yamin (2002, 4,978 pages).

The above remark is based on the trend of bilingual lexicography in recent decades. From a historical perspective, there have been 81 general Chinese-English dictionaries published since 1815, excluding the reprints by different publishers, revised or enlarged editions, private editions, unauthorized reprints without the names of the editors, printings of the same dictionary through resetting in simplified or traditional characters, and Chinese-English dictionaries specializing in dialects.

Generally, Chinese-English dictionaries can be divided into three types: small-scale, medium-scale, and large-scale. Small-scale dictionaries are dictionaries with less than 1,000 pages; medium-scale dictionaries are dictionaries with between 1,000 and 1,500 pages, and large-scale dictionaries are dictionaries with over 1,500 pages. According to the above criteria, there are 43 small-scale dictionaries, 20 medium-scale dictionaries, and 18 large-scale dictionaries, the details of which are given below:

Small-scale CE Dictionaries (under 1,000 pages)

(1) Poletti, P. (1896) *A Chinese and English Dictionary*, 307 pages.

(2) Tsang, O.Z. (1920) *A New Complete Chinese-English Dictionary*, 756 pages.

(3) Fenn, Courtenay Hughes (1926/1940) *The Five Thousand Dictionary: A Chinese-English Pocket Dictionary and Index to the Character Cards of the College of Chinese Studies*, 696 pages.

(4) Li, Yuwen (1933 / 1966) *A New Chinese-English Dictionary*, 832 pages.

(5) Aldrich, Harry Starkey (1945) *A Topical Chinese Dictionary*, 182 pages.

(6) Chao, Yuen Ren and Yang Lien Sheng (1945) *Concise Dictionary of Spoken Chinese*, 291 pages.

(7) Wu, C.K. *et al.* (1946) *Chinese to English Dictionary: English Copy of Xinhua Zidan*, 357 pages.

(8) Simon, Walter (1947) *A Beginners' Chinese-English Dictionary of the National Language (Guoyeu)*, 880 pages.

(9) Quo, James C. (1956) *Concise Chinese-English Dictionary, Romanized*, 323 pages.

(10) Chung Hua Book Co. Ltd (1966) *General Chinese-English Dictionary*, 903 pages.

(11) Lu, Fei-zhi (1967) *Chung Hwa Chinese-English Dictionary with Supplement*, 948 pages.

(12) Wang, Fang-yu, Fred (1967) *Mandarin Chinese Dictionary: Chinese-English*, 660 pages.

(13) Huang, C.C. (1968) *A Modern Chinese-English Dictionary for Students*, 648 pages.

(14) Herring, James Alexander (1969) *The Foursquare Dictionary in Chinese and English: Based on the Four Corner Method of Classification*, 617 pages.

(15) Feng, Lang-bo (1970) *A New Chinese-English Dictionary*, 806 pages.

(16) Saphrograph Corp (1971) *Chinese-English Dictionary*, 192 pages.

(17) Anderson, Olov Bertil (1972) *A Companion Volume to R.H. Mathews' Chinese-English Dictionary*, 210 pages.

(18) Tan, Chor Eng (1973) *A Draft Copy of Modern Chinese-English Dictionary*, 333 pages.

(19) Chi, Wen-shun (1977) *Chinese-English Dictionary of Contemporary Usage*, 484 pages.

(20) Fok, Bo-choi (1977) *Chinese-English Dictionary*, 455 pages.

(21) Cosmos Books Ltd. (1978) *A Current Chinese-English Dictionary*, 750 pages.

(22) Dictionary Division, Federal Publication (1979) *Times Chinese-English Dictionary*, 564 pages.

(23) Editorial Research Division, *A Current Chinese-English Dictionary*, Beijing Language Institute (1979) *A Current Chinese-English Dictionary*, 750 pages.

(24) World Book Co. (1979) *A New Chinese-English Dictionary*, 398 pages.

(25) Wu, Jingrong (1979) *The Pinyin Chinese-English Dictionary*, 976 pages.

(26) Compiling Group, *A Classified and Illustrated Chinese-English Dictionary*, Guangzhou Institute of Foreign Languages (1981) *A Classified and Illustrated Chinese-English Dictionary*, 897 pages.

(27) Compiling Group, *A Concise Chinese-English Dictionary*, Beijing Language Institute (1982) *A Concise Chinese-English Dictionary*, 838 pages.

(28) Jiang, Jianming (1984) *A Classified Chinese-English Glossary*, 474 pages.

(29) Joint Publishing Ltd. (1984) *An Everyday Chinese-English Dictionary*, 881 pages.

(30) Wu, Chia-ch'ien (1984) *A New Chinese-English Dictionary*, 631 pages.

(31) Li, Ji et al. (1987) *A Concise Chinese-English Mini-dictionary*, 287 pages.

(32) Huang, Shouyi and Wang Wanmei (1988) *Concise Chinese-English Dictionary*, 555 pages.

(33) Chen, Pu (1989) *A New Concise Chinese-English Dictionary*, 561 pages.

(34) Editorial Committee, *The Chinese-English Dictionary* (1989) *The Chinese-English Dictionary*, 564 pages.

(35) Zeng, Zuxuan (1989) *A Practical Chinese-English Dictionary of Expressions*, 294 pages.

(36) Liu, Wei-fu (1992) *A New Practical Chinese-English Dictionary*, 824 pages.

(37) Tung, Wendy (1993) *Easy Chinese Phrasebook and Dictionary*, 256 pages.

(38) Huang, Guanfu, Huang Yongmin, and Yao Yanjin (1995) *A Practical Chinese-English Dictionary of Classified Situations*, 769 pages.

(39) DeFrancis, John (1996) *ABC Chinese-English Dictionary: Alphabetically-based Computerized*, 897 pages.

(40) Xia, Ri and Dai Zhaorong (1998) *New Practical Chinese-English Dictionary*, 608 pages.

(41) Yu, Shaosheng, Sheng Peilin, Yin Peijie, Ding Feng, Yu Rui, and Chen Yijing (1999 / 2000) *Quaille's Practical Chinese-English Dictionary*, 924 pages.

(42) Qi, Shufang (2002) *A New Chinese-English Dictionary*, 470 pages.

(43) Chan, Sin-wai (2007) *Longman Concise Chinese-English Dictionary*, 677 pages.

Medium-scale CE Dictionaries (1,000 – 1,500 pages)

(1) Wells, William, S. (1909) *A Syllabic Dictionary of the Chinese Language*, 1,056 pages.

(2) Matthews, Robert Henry (1931) *A Chinese-English Dictionary*, 1,232 pages.

(3) Wang, Junyi (1983) *A Practical Chinese-English Dictionary*, 1,388 pages.

(4) Ding, Guang-xun (1985) *A New Chinese-English Dictionary*, 1,401 pages.

(5) Yu, Yunxia (1985) *A Reverse Chinese-English Dictionary*, 1,343 pages.

(6) Dictionary Editorial Division, Foreign Languages Teaching and Research Press (1988) *A Modern Chinese-English Dictionary*, 1,219 pages.

(7) Duan, Shi-zhen (1989 / 1992) *A Modern Chinese-English Dictionary*, 1,238 pages.

(8) Editorial Committee, *A Modern Chinese-English Dictionary* (1989) *A Modern Chinese-English Dictionary*, 1,283 pages.

(9) Liu, Wen (1990) *A Chinese-English Dictionary*, 1,340 pages.

(10) Wang, Tongyi (1990) *A Chinese-English Dictionary*, 1,366 pages.

(11) Dai, Mingzhong and Dai Weidong (1991) *A Comprehensive Chinese-English Dictionary*, 1,265 pages.

(12) Wang, Youxiang and Wu Chengyuan (1992) *A Concise Chinese-English Dictionary*, 1,270 pages.

(13) Yen, Yüan-shu (1992) *Mass Modern Chinese-English Dictionary*, 1,023 pages.

(14) Hu, Xueyuan (1994) *New Chinese-English Dictionary*, 1,270 pages.

(15) Editorial Committee of Dictionary Division, English Department, Beijing Foreign Studies University *A Chinese-English Dictionary*, 1,435 pages.

(16) Bai, Yuqing (1996) *A New Chinese-English Dictionary*, 1,026 pages.

(17) Leung, Derun and Zheng Jiande (1999 / 2003) *Zhongda Chinese-English Dictionary*, 1,141 pages.

(18) Xie, Zhenqing (1997) *The New Modern Chinese-English Dictionary*, 1,253 pages.

(19) Zhu, Zumei, Jiang Shihui, and Ding Yifei (2000) *A New Practical Chinese-English Encyclopaedic Dictionary*, 1,301 pages.

(20) Yu, Baofa and Zeng Daoming (2003) *A New Century Classified Chinese-English Dictionary*, 1,335 pages.

Large-scale Dictionaries (above 1,500 pages)

(1) Morrison, Robert (1815 – 1823) *A Dictionary of the Chinese Language, in three parts*, 1,875 pages.

(2) Giles, Herbert Allen (1892) *A Chinese-English Dictionary*, 1,711 pages.

(3) Lee, S.T. (1956) *A New Complete Chinese-English Dictionary*, 1,511 pages.

(4) Lin, Yutang (1972) *Lin Yutang's Chinese-English Dictionary of Modern Usage*, 1,720 pages.

(5) Liu, Dah-jen (1978) *Liu's Chinese English Dictionary*, 1,554 pages.

(6) Liang, Shih-ch'iu (1986) *A New Practical Chinese-English Dictionary*, 2,401 pages.

(7) Chang, Fang-chieh (1992) *Far East Chinese-English Dictionary*, 1,760 pages.

(8) Wu, Guanghua (1993) *Chinese-English Dictionary*, 3,514 pages.

(9) Li, Kairong (1995) *Chinese-English Classified Encyclopedic Dictionary*, 1,657 pages.

(10) Cheng, Enhong and Zhang Yibin (1998) *A Practical Chinese-English Production Dictionary*, 1,763 pages.

(11) Pu, Yangxiang (2000) *A Chinese-English Translation Dictionary,* 1,596 pages.

(12) Wu, Jingyong and Cheng Zhenqiu (2000) *New Age Chinese-English Dictionary*, 2,176 pages.

(13) Wu, Guanghua (2001) *Chinese-English Dictionary*, 1,685 pages.

(14) Cao, Yamin (2002) *The Chinese-English Word-ocean*, 4,978 pages.

(15) Dictionary Editing Unit, Institute of Linguistic Research, Chinese Academy of Social Sciences (2002) *The Contemporary Chinese Dictionary: Chinese-English Edition*, 2,698 pages.

(16) Pan, Shaozhong (2002) *New Age Concise Chinese-English Dictionary*, 1,628 pages.

(17) Hui, Yu (2004) *A New Century Chinese-English Dictionary*, 2,258 pages.

(18) Wu, Guanghua (2004) *A Comprehensive Chinese-English Dictionary*, 6,562 pages.

A study of the development of these three types of dictionaries shows that the production of large-scale dictionaries has been the trend in recent decades. General Chinese-English dictionaries produced in the last two hundred years can be divided into three periods: the first period is from 1815 to 1965, the second period, from 1966 to 1986, and the third period, from 1987 to 2015.

The First Period: 1815-1965

During the 150 years from 1815 to 1965, dictionaries compiled by Westerners were predominant. Of the 13 dictionaries published during this period, 9 were by Westerners, accounting for 69.23%. Most notable were the dictionaries compiled by Robert Morrison (1,875 pages), Herbert Giles (1,711 pages), S.T. Lee (1,511 pages), and Robert Mathews (1,232 pages). The majority of the dictionaries edited by Westerners were small-scale dialectal dictionaries, such as dictionaries on Cantonese, Hakka, and Amoy.

(2) The Second Period: 1966-1986

During the 20 years from 1966 to 1986, 29 general Chinese-English dictionaries were published, only four of them were compiled by Westerners, accounting for 13.79 %. The large majority of Chinese-English dictionary compilers were scholars in mainland China. The Chinese-English dictionaries published during this period were of medium scale. The most popular dictionaries of this period were those by Lin Yutang (Hong Kong, 1972), Wu Jingrong (China, 1979), and Liang Shih-ch'iu (Taiwan, 1986).

(3) The Third Period: 1987-2015

During this 28-year period, 39 Chinese-English dictionaries were published. John DeFrancis's dictionary was the only dictionary compiled by a Westerner. It is noted that only one small-scale Chinese-English dictionary was published during the period between 2004 and 2014.The general trend of this period is to produce medium- to large-scale dictionaries, such as those by Wu Guanghua (3 volumes, 6,562 pages) and Cao Yamin (2 volumes, 4,978 pages).

A New Comprehensive Chinese-English Dictionary by this author follows the trend with the publication of a 3-volume dictionary.

Conclusion

It can be clearly seen that semantic interconnectedness and holism are the two major concepts of this dictionary. They offer changes to what has been practised for two centuries in the world of Chinese-English dictionaries. It is hoped that this dictionary will herald a new trend in the compilation of printed Chinese-dictionaries that are both phonetics-based and semantics-based, offering an easy consultation method and a wealth of semantic information for users to know the linguistic and cultural connotations of words in a holistic context.

Chan Sin-wai
11 November 2015

References

Aldrich, Harry Starkey (comp.) (1945) *A Topical Chinese Dictionary*, New Haven: Published for the Department of Oriental Studies by Yale University Press.

Anderson, Olov Bertil (comp.) (1972) *A Companion Volume to R. H. Mathews' Chinese-English Dictionary*, Lund: Studentlitteratur.

Bai, Yuqing 白玉清 (1996)《新編漢英詞典》(*A New Chinese-English Dictionary*), Beijing: Modern Press 現代出版社.

Cao, Yamin 曹亞民 (2002)《漢英大辭海》(*The Chinese-English Word-Ocean*), 2 volumes, Beijing: Chinese Medicine Press 中國中醫藥出版社.

Chan, Sin-wai 陳善偉 (rev.) (2007)《朗文簡明漢英詞典》(*Longman Concise Chinese-English Dictionary*), Hong Kong: Pearson Education Asia Ltd.

Chang, Fang-chieh 張芳杰 (rev.) (1992)《遠東漢英大辭典》(*Far East Chinese-English Dictionary*), Taipei: Far East Book Company 遠東圖書公司.

Chao, Yuen Ren 趙元任 and Yang Lien Sheng 楊聯陞 (comps.) (1945)《國語字典》(*Concise Dictionary of Spoken Chinese*, Cambridge: Published for the Harvard-Yenching Institute by Harvard University Press.

Chen, Pu 陳樸 (comp.) (1989)《新簡明漢英詞典》(*A New Concise Chinese-English Dictionary*), Shanghai: Shanghai Translation Publishing House 上海譯文出版社.

Cheng, Enhong 程恩洪 and Zhang Yibin 張義斌 (1998)《漢英實用表達詞典》(*A Practical Chinese-English Production Dictionary*), Beijing: Higher Education Press 高等教育出版社.

Chi, Wen-shun (comp.) (1977) *Chinese-English Dictionary of Contemporary Usage*, Berkeley, Los Angeles: University of California Press.

Chung Hua Book Co. Ltd. 中華書局(香港)有限公司 (comp.) (1966)《通用漢英辭典》(*General Chinese-English Dictionary*), Hong Kong: Chung Hua Book Co. Ltd. 中華書局(香港)有限公司.

Compiling Group, *A Classified and Illustrated Chinese-English Dictionary*, Guangzhou Institute of Foreign Languages 廣州外國語學院《漢英分類插圖詞典》編寫組 (comp.) (1981/1988)《漢英分類插圖詞典》(*A Classified and Illustrated Chinese-English Dictionary*), Guangzhou: Guangdong People's Publishing House 廣東人民出版社.

Compiling Group, *The Concise Chinese-English Dictionary*, Beijing Language Institute (1982)《簡明漢英辭典》(*A Concise Chinese-English Dictionary*), Beijing: The Commercial Press 商務印書館.

Cosmos Books Ltd. 天地圖書有限公司 (comp.) (1978)《現代漢英詞典》(*A Current Chinese-English Dictionary*), Hong Kong: Cosmos Books Ltd. 天地圖書有限公司.

Dai, Mingzhong 戴鳴鐘 and Dai Weidong 戴煒棟 (comps.) (1991)《漢英綜合辭典》(*A Comprehensive Chinese-English Dictionary*), Shanghai: Shanghai Foreign Language and Education Press 上海外語教育出版社.

DeFrancis, John (comp.) (1996) *ABC Chinese-English Dictionary, Alphabetically-based Computerized* (《漢英詞典》), Hawaii: University of Hawaii Press.

Dictionary Division, Federal Publication 聯邦出版社詞典組 (comp.) (1979) 《時代漢英詞典》(*Times Chinese-English Dictionary*), Hong Kong: The Commercial Press 商務印書館.

Dictionary Editing Unit, Institute of Linguistic Research, Chinese Academy of Social Sciences 中國社會科學院語言研究所詞典編輯室 (comp.) (2002)《現代漢語詞典：漢英雙語》(*The Contemporary Chinese Dictionary: Chinese-English Edition*), Beijing: Foreign Languages Teaching and Research Press 外語教學與研究出版社.

Dictionary Editorial Division, Foreign Languages Teaching and Research Press 外語教學與研究出版社詞典編輯室 (comp.) (1988)《現代漢英詞典》(*A Modern Chinese-English Dictionary*), Beijing: Foreign Languages Teaching and Research Press 外語教學與研究出版社.

Ding, Guang-xun 丁光訓 (comp.) (1985)《新漢英詞典》(*A New Chinese-English Dictionary*), Hong Kong: Joint Publishing Ltd. 三聯書店(香港)有限公司 ; Seattle: University of Washington Press.

Duan, Shi-zhen 段世鎮 (comp.) (1989/1992)《現代漢英詞典》(*A Modern Chinese-English Dictionary*), Hong Kong: Hai Feng Publishing Co. Ltd 海峰出版社有限公司 ; Hong Kong: Oxford University Press 牛津大學出版社.

Editorial Committee, *A Modern Chinese-English Dictionary*《現代漢英詞典》編寫組 (comp.) (1989)《現代漢英詞典》(*A Modern Chinese-English Dictionary*), Hong Kong: Hai Feng Publishing Co. Ltd. 海峰出版社 ; Singapore: Jian Wei Publications (PTE) Ltd.

Editorial Committee, *The Chinese-English Dictionary*, English Department of Beijing Foreign Studies University 北京外國語學院英語系《漢英詞典》編寫組 (comp.) (1979)《漢英詞典》(*The Chinese-English Dictionary*), Beijing: The Commercial Press 商務印書館.

Editorial Committee of Dictionary Division, English Department, Beijing Foreign Studies University 北京外國語大學英語系詞典組 (comp.) (1995)《漢英詞典》(*A Chinese-English Dictionary*), Beijing: Foreign

Languages Teaching and Research Press 外語教學與研究出版社.

Editorial Research Division, *A Current Chinese-English Dictionary*, Beijing Language Institute 北京語言學院編輯研究部《現代漢英詞典》編寫組 (comp.) (1979)《現代漢英詞典》(*A Current Chinese-English Dictionary*), Nanchang: Jiangxi People's Publishing House 江西人民出版社.

Feng, Lang-bo 馮浪波 (comp.) (1970)《全新實用漢英辭典》(*A New Chinese-English Dictionary*), Hong Kong: Ta Chia Publishers 大家出版社.

Fenn, Courtenay H. (1926/1940) *The Five Thousand Dictionary*, Cambridge, Mass: Harvard University Press.

Fok, Bo-choi 霍寶材 (comp.) (1977)《音形捷檢字典：國粵注音漢英合解》(*Chinese-English Dictionary*), Hong Kong: Fok's Press Hong Kong 霍氏出版社.

Giles, Herbert Allen (comp.) (1892) *A Chinese-English Dictionary*, Shanghai: Kelly and Walsh.

Goodrich, Chauncey (1891/1965) *A Pocket Dictionary (Chinese-English) and Pekingese Syllabary*, Hong Kong: Hong Kong University Press.

Herring, James Alexander (comp.) (1969)《漢英四角號碼字典》(*The Foursquare Dictionary in Chinese and English: Based on the Four Corner Method of Classification*), Taipei: Mei Ya Publications 美亞書版股份有限公司.

Hu, Xueyuan 胡學元 (comp.) (1994)《新漢英詞典》(*New Chinese-English Dictionary*), Haikou: Hainan Publishing House 海南出版社.

Huang, C.C. (comp.) (1968) *A Modern Chinese-English Dictionary for Students*, Lawrence: Center for East Asian Studies, University of Kansas.

Huang, Guanfu 黃關福, Huang Yongmin 黃勇民, and Yao Yanjin 姚燕瑾 (comps.) (1995)《實用漢英情景分類辭典》(*A Practical Chinese-English Dictionary of Classified Situations*), Shanghai: The World Press 世界出版社.

Huang, Shouyi 黃守義 and Wang Wanmei 王婉梅 (comps.) (1988)《簡明

漢英詞典》(*Concise Chinese-English Dictionary*), Beijing: People's Military Medical Press 人民軍醫出版社.

Hui, Yu 惠宇 (2003)《新世紀漢英大詞典》(*A New Century Chinese-English Dictionary*), Beijing: Foreign Language Teaching and Learning Publishing House 外語教學與研究出版社.

Jiang, Jianming 江建名 (comp.) (1984)《漢英分類詞匯》(*A Classified Chinese-English Glossary*), Beijing: Popular Science Press 科學普及出版社.

Joint Publishing Ltd. 三聯書店 (香港) 有限公司 (comp.) (1984)《常用漢英詞典》(*An Everyday Chinese-English Dictionary*), Hong Kong: Joint Publishing Ltd. 三聯書店 (香港) 有限公司.

Lee, S.T. 李仕德 (comp.) (1956)《最新漢英大辭典》(*A New Complete Chinese-English Dictionary*), Hong Kong: Chinese Book Publishing Company 中國圖書出版公司.

Leung, Derun 梁德潤 and Zheng Jiande 鄭建德 (eds.) (1999 / 2003)《中大漢英辭典》(*Zhongda Chinese-English Dictionary*), Hong Kong: The Chinese University Press.

Li, Ji et al. 李及等 (comps.) (1987)《簡明漢英小詞典》(*A Concise Chinese-English Mini-Dictionary*), Beijing: China Foreign Economic and Trading Press 中國對外經濟貿易出版社.

Li, Kai-rong 李開榮 (comp.) (1995)《漢英百科分類詞典》(*Chinese-English Classified Encyclopedic Dictionary*), Hong Kong: The Commercial Press 商務印書館.

Li, Yuwen 李玉汶 (1933 / 1966)《漢英新辭典》(*A New Chinese-English Dictionary*), Shanghai: The Commercial Press 商務印書館 ; Taipei: The Commercial Press 商務印書館.

Liang, Shih-ch'iu 梁實秋 (1986)《遠東漢英大辭典》(*Far East Chinese-English Dictionary*), Taipei: The Far East Book Co., Ltd. 遠東圖書公司.

Liang, Shih-ch'iu 梁實秋 (comp.) (1986)《最新實用漢英辭典》(*A New Practical Chinese-English Dictionary*), Taipei: Far East Book Co. Ltd. 遠東圖書公司.

Lin, Yutang 林語堂 (comp.) (1972)《林語堂當代漢英詞典》(*Lin Yutang's Chinese-English Dictionary of Modern Usage*), Hong Kong: The Chinese University Press 中文大學出版社.

Liu, Dah-jen 劉達人 (comp.) (1978)《劉氏漢英大辭典》(*Liu's Chinese English Dictionary*), New York: Asian Associates.

Liu, Wei-fu (comp.) (1992) *A New Practical Chinese-English Dictionary*, Taipei: Liji chubanshe 禮記出版社 .

Liu, Wen 劉聞 (comp.) (1990)《漢英通用詞典》(*A Chinese-English Dictionary*), Harbin: Heilongjiang People's Publishing House 黑龍江人民出版社 .

Lu, Fei-zhi 陸費執 (ed.) (1967)《中華漢英辭典》(*Chung Hwa Chinese-English Dictionary with Supplement*), Taipei: Chung Hwa Book Co. 中華書局 .

Mathews, Robert Henry (1931/1972) *A Chinese–English Dictionary* (《漢英字典》), Cambridge, Mass.: Harvard University Press.

Medhurst, Walter Henry (1848) *English-Chinese Dictionary*, Shanghai: Mission Press, Available from: http://archive.org/stream/englishandchine00medhgoog#page/n5/mode/1up.

Morrison, Robert (1815-1823) *A Dictionary of the Chinese Language in Three Parts*, 3 volumes, Macau: Honorable East India Company's Press.

Pan, Shaozhong 潘紹中 (comp.) (2002)《新時代精選漢英詞典》(*New Age Concise Chinese-English Dictionary*), Beijing: The Commercial Press 商務印書館 .

Poletti, P. (comp.) (1896)《華英萬字典》(*A Chinese and English Dictionary*), Shanghai: Printed at the American Presbyterian Mission Press.

Pu, Yangxiang 濮陽翔 (comp.) (2000)《漢英翻譯詞典》(*A Chinese-English Translation Dictionary*), Jinan: Shandong Friendship Press 山東友誼出版社.

Qi, Shufang 戚淑芳 (comp.) (2002)《新漢英詞典》(*A New Chinese-English Dictionary*), Haikou: South People Publishing House 南方出版社.

Quo, James C. (comp.) (1956) *Concise Chinese-English Dictionary,*

Romanized, Rutland, Vermont: Charles, E. Tuttle.

Saphrograph Corp. (comp.) (1971)《華英新辭典》(*Chinese-English Dictionary*), New York: Saphrograph Corp..

Simon, Walter (comp.) (1947)《初級中英國語字典》(*A Beginners' Chinese-English Dictionary of the National Language* (*Guoyeu*)), London: Lund Humphries.

Tan, Chor Eng 陳初榮 (ed.) (1973)《現代華語英語譯字典初稿全集》(*A Draft Copy of Modern Chinese-English Dictionary*), Kuala Lumpur: n. p..

Tsang, O.Z. 張鵬雲 (comp.) (1920)《漢英大辭典》(*A New Complete Chinese-English Dictionary*), Shanghai: Republican Press 新中國印書館.

Tung, Wendy (comp.) (1993) *Easy Chinese Phrasebook and Dictionary*, Lincolnwood, Ill.: Passport Books.

Wang, Fang-yu, Fred (comp.) (1967) *Mandarin Chinese Dictionary: Chinese-English*, South Orange, N. J.: Seton Hall University Press.

Wang, Junyi et al. 王俊怡等 (comps.) (1983)《實用漢英詞典》(*A Practical Chinese-English Dictionary*), Nanjing: Jiangsu People's Publishing House 江蘇人民出版社.

Wang, Tongyi 王同億 (comp.) (1990)《中國字典》(*A Chinese-English Dictionary*), Haikou: Sanhuan Press 三環出版社.

Wang, Youxiang 王有祥 and Wu Chengyuan 吳承遠 (comps.) (1992)《簡明漢英辭典》(*A Concise Chinese-English Dictionary*), Jinan: Shandong Education Press 山東教育出版社.

Wells, Williams, S. (1874/1909)《漢英韻府》(*A Syllabic Dictionary of the Chinese Language; Arranged according to the Wu-Fang Yuen Yin, with the Pronunciation of the Characters as Heard in Peking, Canton, Amoy, and Shanghai*), Shanghai: American Mission Press; Tung Chou: North China Union College 北通州協和書院 , available from: http://archive.org/details/syllabicdictiona00willrich.

World Book Co PTE Ltd., The, (comp.) (1979)《最新漢英辭典》(*A New Chinese-English Dictionary*), Singapore: The World Book Co PTE Ltd..

Wu, C.K. et al. 吳志鋼等 (comps.) (1946)《漢英字典：新華字典》(*Chinese to English Dictionary: English Copy of Xinhua Zidan*), Monterey: Chinese Language Research Association 中國語文研究學會.

Wu, Chia-ch'ien 吳佳倩 (comp.) (1984)《新漢英辭典》(*A New Chinese-English Dictionary*), Taipei: Yu's Press 余氏出版社.

Wu, Guanghua (comp.) (2001)《漢英辭典》(新世紀版) (*Chinese-English Dictionary*, New Century Edition), Shanghai: Jiaotong University Press 上海交通大學出版社.

Wu, Guanghua 吳光華 (comp.) (1993)《漢英大辭典》(*Chinese-English Dictionary*), 2 volumes, Shanghai: Shanghai Jiaotong University Press 上海交通大學出版社.

Wu, Guanghua 吳光華 (comp.) (2004)《漢英綜合大辭典》(*A Comprehensive Chinese-English Dictionary*), 3 volumes, Dalian: Dalian Polytechnic University Press 大連理工大學出版社.

Wu, Jingrong 吳景榮 and Cheng Zhenqiu 程鎮球 (2000)《新時代漢英大詞典》(*New Age Chinese-English Dictionary*), Beijing: The Commercial Press 商務印書館.

Wu, Jingrong 吳景榮 (1979)《漢英字典》(*The Pinyin Chinese-English Dictionary*), Hong Kong: The Commercial Press 商務印書館.

Xia, Ri 夏日 and Dai Zhaorong 戴兆榮 (1998)《最新實用漢英詞典》(*New Practical Chinese-English Dictionary*), Hankou: Hubei Education Press 湖北教育出版社.

Xie, Zhenqing 謝振清 (1997)《新現代漢英詞典》(*The New Modern Chinese-English Dictionary*), Beijing: China International Broadcasting Press 中國國際廣播出版社.

Yen, Yüan-shu 顏元叔 (comp.) (1992)《萬人現代漢英辭典》(*Mass Modern Chinese-English Dictionary*). Taipei: Wen Jen Press 萬人出版社.

Yong, Heming (2002)〈羅伯特莫禮遜其人其典〉('Robert Morrison – A Brief Biography and his Dictionary'), *Lexicographical Studies* 4: 121–125.

Yu, Baofa 俞寶發 and Zeng Daoming 曾道明 (comps.) (2003)《新世紀漢英分類詞典》(*A New Century Classified Chinese-English Dictionary*),

Shanghai: Fudan University Press 復旦大學出版社 .

Yu, Shaosheng 佘耀生, Sheng Peilin 盛培林, Yin Peijie 印丕傑, Ding Feng 丁鋒, Yu Rui 俞鋭, and Chen Yijing 陳一晴 (1999)《漢英實用辭典》(*Quaille's Practical Chinese-English Dictionary*), Hong Kong: Asia 2000 Ltd and Maison d'editions Quaille 開益出版社.

Yu, Yunxia et al. 佘雲霞等 (comps.) (1986)《漢英逆引詞典》(*A Reverse Chinese-English Dictionary*), Beijing: The Commercial Press 商務印書館.

Zeng, Zuxuan 曾祖選 (comp.) (1989)《實用漢英多種表達法詞典》(*A Practical Chinese-English Dictionary of Expressions*), Chengdu: Sichuan People's Publishing House 四川人民出版社.

Zhu, Zumei 朱祖美 , Jiang Shihui 蔣時暉, and Ding Yifei 丁一飛 (comps.) (2000)《新漢英實用百科詞典》(*A New Practical Chinese-English Encyclopaedic Dictionary*), Guangzhou: World Books Publishing Company 世界圖書出版公司.

a¹

a

【阿】 a pronunciation of 阿 ;

a

【啊】 aah; ah; alas; all right; come now; eh; ha; hah; ho; my God; now; O.K. oh; please; very well; we; what; will you; yes;

[啊哈] aha;

[啊呀] aya; ouch;

好啊 ah; aha; all right;

天啊 ah; alas; bless me; bless my heart;

a

【腌】 a pronunciation of 腌 ;

a²

a

【啊】 eh; hey; indeed; really; what; why;

a

【嗄】 what;

a³

a

【啊】 how now; I declare; indeed; my word; what;

a⁴

a

【阿】

[阿爸] dad; daddy; father; pa; papa;

[阿爹] dad; daddy; father; pa; papa;

[阿飛] teddy boy;

女阿飛 teddy girl;

小阿飛 (1) teddy boy; (2) teddy girl;

[阿哥] elder brother;

阿哥哥舞 agogo;

~方塊阿哥哥舞 square agogo;

[阿公] granddad;

[阿家阿翁] parent-in-law;

[阿舅] maternal uncle;

[阿拉伯] (1) Arab; Arabian; (2) Arabic;

阿拉伯半島 Arabian Peninsula;

阿拉伯國家 Arab countries;

阿拉伯人 Arab;

阿拉伯數字 Arabic figures; Arabic numerals;

阿拉伯語 Arabic;

[阿媽] mom;

[阿貓阿狗] average man; common man; man in the street; run of the mill; Tom, Dick and Harry;

[阿妹] little sister;

[阿婆] (1) grandma; granma; grandmamma; granny; (2) mother-in-law; (3) old granny;

[阿司匹林] aspirin;

[阿嚏] atishoo;

[阿鄉] bumpkin; country bumpkin; rustic; yokel;

[阿爺] dad; daddy; pa; papa;

[阿姨] (1) aunt; auntie; one's mother's sister; (2) childcare worker; domestic helper; maid; (3) nurse in a family; nursemaid; (4) foster mother; stepmother;

a

【錒】 actinium;

a⁵

a

【啊】 what a ... (expressing appreciation);

好啊 ah; aha; all right; attaboy; bravo;

ai¹

ai

【哀】 (1) grief; in grief; lamentable; plaintive; sad; sorrow; (2) mourn; mournful; mourning; (3) commiserate; compassion; pity; lament; sympathize;

[哀哀] deeply grieved; in deep grief; very sad;

哀哀欲絕 be overwhelmed by grief; be so distressed as if one's heart would break;

[哀不欲生] becomes so sad that one wants to end one's life;

[哀愁] grieved; lamentation; sad; sadness; sorrow; sorrowful;

解除哀愁 give relief to one's grief;

滿腹哀愁 be full of sorrow;

[哀愴] grieve; grieved; sad; sorrowful;

[哀辭] elegy; lament; plaint;

[哀悼] condole with sb upon the death of...; condolence; express one's condolences on the death of sb; grieve; grieve over sb's death; lament; lament sb's death; mourn; mourn for the dead; mourn over sb's death; mourning; wail the

A

dead;
哀悼日 day of mourning; mourning day;
哀悼者 mourner;
表示哀悼 express one's condolences; offer one's condolences;
沉痛哀悼 mourn over sb's death with deep grief;
誠摯的哀悼 sincerest condolences;
深切哀悼 deepest condolences; profound condolences;
致以哀悼 convey; extend; send one's condolences;
衷心的哀悼 heartfelt condolences;

[哀的美敦書] ultimatum;

[哀吊] (1) grieve over sb's death; (2) express deep sympathy for;

[哀調] plaintive melody;

[哀感] grief; sadness;
哀感頑艷 so sad that both the wise and the dull are moved;

[哀告] (1) beg piteously; implore; supplicate; (2) announce sb's death; (3) speak about one's grievances;
苦苦哀告 present one's case beseechingly;
四處哀告 implore everyone's commiserations;

[哀歌] (1) dirge; elegy; funeral song; lament; monody; mournful song; requiem; threnody; (2) croon plaintively;
唱哀歌 chant a dirge; sing a mournful song;
慟哭哀歌 wail forth dirges;
一曲哀歌 a mournful song;
奏哀歌 play funeral music;

[哀鴿] mournful dove;

[哀號] cry; cry bitterly; cry piteously; lament; wail; wail of woe; whine in despair;
哀號震天 the wail shakes the heaven;

[哀嚎] (1) howl; (2) cry; cry bitterly; cry piteously; lament; wail; wail of woe; whine in despair;

[哀鴻遍野] a land of wailing and despair; a land swarming with disaster victims; a land swarming with famished refugees; a place swarming with famished refugees; disaster victims moaning everywhere; everywhere are famine refugeels; famine refugees swarm the countryside; starving people fill the land; the wilderness is filled with sufferers; the wilderness is filled with suffering people; throngs of famished and homeless people are roaming the country; wretched refugees scattered all over the countryside;

[哀呼] cry piteously; cry sadly; wail;
哀呼呻吟 wail and moan;

[哀毀骨立] be consumed away with grief; be emaciated by grief;

[哀祭] mourning rite;

[哀叫] cry sadly;
嘶聲哀叫 cry sadly; wail sadly;

[哀矜] commiserate with; feel pity for; pity; sympathize;
哀矜無辜 pardon the innocent;
哀矜勿喜 feel compassion for and not be happy about sb or sth;

[哀久自滅] sorrow will die out with the passage of time;

[哀懇] beg for mercy; entreat; implore; request sorrowfully;

[哀哭] wail; weep in sorrow; whine;

[哀苦] grievous; grievous and miserable;
哀苦無依 helpless and grievous; miserable;

[哀樂] grief and joy;
哀樂相生 grief and joy is reciprocally produced;

[哀厲] heartbreaking voice;

[哀憐] commiserate; feel compassion for; have compassion for; have pity; have sympathy for; pity;
乞哀告憐 ask for pity; beg for mercy; fall on one's knees; implore bitterly; piteously beg for help; plead for compassion; throw oneself at the feet of; throw oneself on sb's mercy;
自哀自憐 wallow;

[哀涼] desolate; mournful; sad;

[哀憫] commiserate with; feel compassion for; feel pity for; pity;

[哀鳴] wail; whine;
發出哀鳴 cry with a whine;

[哀戚] be overcome with sorrow; grief; grievous; look woeful; sadness; sorrow; woe;

[哀淒] melancholy; mournful; sad; sad and wretched;

哭聲哀淒 heart-rending cry;

[哀泣] cry sorrowfully; keen; moan; sob; weep plaintively; weep with sorrow;

[哀切] sad and wretched;

[哀求] appeal pathetically; beg; beg humbly; beg piteously; beg pitifully; beseech; entreat; grovel; implore;

哀求者 suppliant;

百般哀求 resort to every means to entreat;

苦苦哀求 entreat piteously; make an earnest request of sb;

[哀勸] admonish in a tearful voice;

百般哀勸 admonish strongly and sadly; admonish strongly and tearfully;

[哀榮] posthumous honours;

[哀傷] distressed; dolour; feel grief; feel sorrow; grieve; mourn; mournful; sad; sorrowful;

哀傷的 doleful;

哀而不傷 deeply felt but not sentimental; in moderation; modest; mournful but not distressing; sorrow without self-injury; temperate; the cap fits; to a nicety; within the limits;

[哀聲] mourning;

哀聲遍地 the sound of mourning is heard everywhere;

[哀思] grief; mourning; mourning for the dead; sad feeling about the deceased; sad memories;

寄托哀思 give expression to one's grief;

[哀訴] unbosom oneself in grief; whine;

哀訴冤情 pour out one's grievances;

[哀歎] bemoan; bewail; lament; sigh in sorrow; sigh woefully;

哀歎不幸 lament a misfortune;

[哀痛] deep mourning; deep sorrow; feel the anguish of sorrow; feel the pain of grief; great sorrow; grief; profoundly grieved;

哀痛欲絕 be grieved to the extreme; broken-hearted;

萬分哀痛 immense sorrow;

無限哀痛 boundless grief;

[哀慟] extremely grieved; grief-stricken;

舉國哀慟 the entire nation is overwhelmed by sorrow;

[哀婉] pathetic; sad and moving; sadly sweet;

[哀喜交併] intermingling of grief and joy; mixed feelings of grief and joy;

[哀艷] sad and beautiful; sad but flowery; sadly touching;

哀艷動人 moving in the sad sentiment and beautiful style;

[哀怨] plaintive; sad; tragic;

纏綿哀怨 sentimental and plaintive;

[哀樂] dirge; funeral march; funeral music; lament; music of lament;

奏哀樂 play funeral music;

[哀哉] alas;

[哀子] son bereaved of his mother;

悲哀 grieved; sorrowful; woeful;

節哀 restrain one's grief;

舉哀 go into mourning; wail in mourning;

默哀 stand in silent tribute;

淒哀 sad and dreary;

榮哀 be honoured when alive and be lamented when dead;

致哀 pay one's respect to the deceased;

誌哀 express one's mourning for the deceased;

ai

【哎】 (1) but; why; (2) hey; look out;

[哎呀] ah; aiya; blast it; by Jove; damn; damned it; dear me; jeez; my eyes; my God; my word; oh; oh, dear; oh, my; oof; whoa; yahoo;

[哎喲] damn; good gracious; goodness me; great guns; hey; oh dear; oof; ouch; ow (an interjection expressing surprise or pain);

ai

【唉】 (1) ah, alas; I do not know; if only, oh; why; (2) right; well, yes;

[唉聲歎氣] heave a deep sigh; heave deep sighs; heave sighs of despair; moan and groan; mope and sigh; sigh and groan; sigh in despair;

整天唉聲歎氣 sigh all the time;

[唉呀] dear me; my god; oh;

ai

【埃】 (1) dirt; dust; fine dust; (2) angstrom;

[埃及] Egypt;

埃及金字塔 Pyramid;

埃及獅身人面像 Egyptian sphinx;

埃及學 Egyptology;

塵埃 dirt; dust;

黃埃 yellow earth; yellow soil;

A

涓埃 insignificant; negligible; tiny;

ai

【挨】 (1) according to order; by turn; follow the order; in good order; in sequence; one after another; one by one; (2) close upon; get close to; get near to; lean to; near; next to; (3) press; squeeze;

［挨挨蹭蹭］ crammed; crowded; jam-packed; packed;

［挨班］ in turn; one by one;

［挨邊］ (1) keep close to the edge; (2) close to; (3) relevant to;

［挨不上］ beside the point; extraneous; have no relations; impertinent; inapplicable; inconsequent; irrelative; irrelevant; not to the purpose;

［挨呲兒］ get a dressing down; get a tongue-lashing;

［挨次］ according to order; by turns; in order; in proper order; in sequence; in series; in succession; in turn; one after another; one by one;

挨次發言 speak according to order; speak in turn;

挨次檢查 inspect in turn;

挨次領取 get sth in turn;

挨次入場 file in;

挨次上車 get on the bus one after another;

挨次裝配 assemble in order;

按長幼挨次 by order of seniority downwards;

［挨到］ come to sb's turn;

［挨東］ in an easterly direction;

［挨風緝縫］ get some information to curry favour;

［挨個兒］ according to order; in proper order; in succession; in turn; one after another; one by one; succesively;

［挨黑］ towards evening;

［挨戶］ from door to door; from family to family; from house to house; from one house to another;

［挨擠］ be pushed here and there in a large crowd; be squeezed in a crowd;

挨擠在一起 crowd together;

［挨家］ from door to door; from family to family; from house to house; from one house to another; house-to-house;

挨家挨戶 from door to door; from family to family; from house to house; from one house to another;

~ 挨家挨戶的搜查 house-to-house search;

~ 挨家挨戶推銷 door-to-door selling;

挨家逐戶 from door to door;

［挨肩］ shoulder to shoulder;

挨肩擦背 follow closely; go in a jostling crowd; rub the shoulders; shoulder to shoulder and arm in arm;

挨肩搭背 shoulder to shoulder and arm in arm;

挨肩疊背 shoulder to shoulder and chest against back;

挨肩而過 make one's way through the crowd;

［挨近］ close by; close upon; come close to; get close to; get near to; leave a small interval; near to; steal up;

［挨靠］ (1) depend on; dependent on; lean on; rely on; rest on; rest with; (2) at the threshold of; close to; near to; next door to;

［挨滿］ be crowded together;

［挨門］ door-to-door;

挨門挨戶 door-to-door; from door-to-door; from family-to-family; from house-to-house; from one house to another; go from door-to-door; on the knocker;

~ 挨門挨戶搜索 go searching from house to house;

~ 挨門挨戶推銷 sell...from door-to-door;

~ 挨門挨戶走訪 make a house-to-house visit; pay a door-to-door visit;

~ 挨門串戶 from door-to-door; from family-to-family; from house-to-house; from one house to another;

挨門兒 from door-to-door; from family-to-family; from house-to-house; from one house to another;

挨門逐戶 from door to door; from family to family; from house to house; from one house to another;

［挨排］ arrange; make arrangements for;

［挨墻靠壁兒］ lean on the wall to avoid being kicked over;

［挨山塞海］ crammed; crowd together; packed;

［挨身］ force one's way;

挨身而入 elbow one's way in; force one's

way in; push one's way in; shoulder one's way in;
挨身過 touch in passing;
［挨晚］ towards evening;
［挨着］ close to; get close to; next to;

ai²
ai
【挨】 (1) bear; endure; suffer; (2) drag out; spend time with hardship; (3) dawdle; delay; play for time; procrastinate; put off; stall; wait; (4) same as 捱；
［挨打］ be buffeted; be licked; be spanked; come under attack; deserve a beating; get a beating; get a thrashing; get hit by someone; suffer a beating; take a beating;
挨打受餓 be beaten and starved;
挨打受罵 be beaten and cursed; put up with blows and scoldings; suffer beatings and receive scoldings;
挨打受氣 be bullied and beaten;
該挨打 deserve a beating;
受罵挨打 be scolded and beaten;
［挨凍］ (1) be frostbitten; (2) be frozen; suffer from cold;
挨凍受餓 endure cold and hunger; suffer from cold and hunger;
挨凍受冷 endure cold; suffer from cold;
［挨鬥］ be struggled against; be subjected to criticism and struggle;
［挨餓］ feel hungry; go hungry; starve; suffer from hunger; suffer from starvation;
忍饑挨餓 bear hunger; endure hunger; endure the torments of hunger; have to go hungry; stay one's stomach; suffer hunger; suffer the pangs of hunger;
受凍挨餓 suffer from cold and hunger;
［挨罰］ be fined; catch it in the neck; get a penalty; get it in the neck;
［挨光］ put for the effort in dalliances;
［挨過］ survive; weather;
挨不過 cannot endure;
［挨擠］ get pushed around;
［挨澆］ be caught in a rain; be drenched with rain; be soaked with rain; get caught in a pouring rain;
［挨剋］ (1) be reproached; be scolded; be subjected to abuse; be told off; catch it; catch it in the neck; get a dressing down; get a scolding; get a talking-to; get a tongue-lashing; get into a row; get it; receive a scolding; (2) be beaten; get a beating; take a beating;
［挨淋］ be caught in the rain; be drenched with rain; be soaked with rain; get caught in a pouring rain;
［挨罵］ be reproached; be scolded; be subjected to abuse; be told off; catch it; catch it in the neck; get a dressing down; get a scolding; get a talking-to; get a tongue-lashing; get into a row; get it; receive a scolding;
［挨磨］ (1) delay; dilly-dally; hang about; hover around; procrastinate; shilly-shally; (2) be annoyed; be pestered;
［挨批］ be criticized; be denounced; be subjected to criticism;
［挨受］ suffer;
挨受虐待 be maltreated; suffer maltreatment;
［挨推］ delay and shirk one's duty;
［挨延］ delay; procrastinate; put off;
［挨宰］ be done for; be ripped off;
［挨整］ be punished; be straightened out; be subjected to criticism and punishment; be victimized politically;
［挨揍］ (1) take a beating; (2) be defeated;
挨揍打呼嚕—裝糊塗 feign ignorance; pretend to snore while being beaten — pretend not to know;

ai
【獃】 a pronunciation of 獃；

ai
【皚】 brightly white; pure white; snow white; white and clean;
［皚皚］ brightly white; pure white;
白皚皚 brightly white; pure white;
［皚白］ brightly white; pure white;

ai
【癌】 cancer; carcinoma;
［癌棒］ cancer stick;
［癌變］ become cancerous; cancerate; canceration; cancerization; develop into cancer;
［癌病］ carcinomatosis;
［癌發生］ carcinogenesis;
［癌防治］ cancer prevention;

A

[癌化] cancerization;
[癌基因] oncogene;
[癌擴散] proliferation of cancer;
[癌瘤] cancerous tumour;
[癌魔] demon of cancer;
[癌前] precancerous;
癌前病變 precancerous lesion;
癌前狀態 precancerous condition;
[癌肉瘤] carcinosarcoma; sarcocarcinoma;
[癌細胞] cancer cell;
癌細胞溶解 carcinolysis;
[癌性] cancerous;
癌性潰瘍 cancerous ulcer;
癌性息肉 carcinopolypus;
[癌學] cancerology;
癌學家 cancerologist;
[癌症] cancer; carcinomatosis;
癌症患者 cancerous person;
得了癌症 become ill with cancer; have cancer;
發現癌症 detect a cancer;
死於癌症 die of cancer;
細菌性癌症 bacterial cancer;
征服癌症 conquer cancer;
治療癌症 treat a cancer;
[癌腫] malignant tumour;
[癌轉移] metastasis of cancer;

鼻癌 rhino-carcinoma;
鼻咽癌 cancer of nasopharynx; nasopharyngeal carcinoma;
腸癌 bowel cancer; intestinal cancer;
唇癌 cheilocarcinoma;
膽管癌 bile-duct carcinoma;
發射性癌 X-ray cancer;
防癌 prevent cancer;
肺癌 carcinoma of the lung; lung cancer; pulmonary cancer;
肺泡癌 alveolar carcinoma;
粉刺癌 comedo carcinoma;
肝癌 cancer of the liver; hepatic carcinoma; hepatocarcinoma; liver cancer;
睾丸癌 cancer of the testis;
骨癌 cancer in the bones; cancer of the bone; osteocarcinoma;
骨內癌 intraosseous carcinoma;
汗管癌 porocarcinoma;
汗腺癌 syringocarcinoma;
壺腹癌 ampullary carcinoma;
壺腹周癌 periampullary carcinoma;
環境性癌 environmental cancer;
畸胎癌 teratocarcinoma;
甲狀腺癌 thyroid cancer;
膠樣癌 colloid cancer;
接觸性癌 contact cancer;
結腸癌 colon cancer; colonic cancer;
抗癌 anticancer; repel cancer;
淋巴腺癌 cancer of the lymph glands;
慢性癌 scirrhous cancer; scirrhus;
腦癌 cancer of the brain; cerebral cancer;
腦樣癌 encephaloid cancer;
內皮癌 endothelial cancer;
膀胱癌 bladder cancer;
皮膚癌 cancer of the skin; cutaneous carcinoma; skin cancer
前列腺癌 cancer of the prostate gland;
前期癌 precancer;
乳癌 breast cancer; mammary cancer;
乳腺癌 breast cancer;
上皮癌 epithelial cancer; epithelioma;
舌癌 tongue cancer;
腎腺癌 adenocarcinoma of kidney;
食道癌 carcinoma esophagi; esophagus cancer;
食管癌 cancer of the esophagus; esophagus cancer;
胃癌 cancer of the stomach; carcinoma ventriculi gastric cancer;
腺癌 glandular cancer;
血癌 leukaemia;
眼癌 eye cancer;
胰腺癌 cancer of pancreas;
隱性癌 occult cancer;
硬癌 scirrhous cancer;
原發癌 primary cancer; primary carcinoma;
原發性骨內癌 primary intraosseous carcinoma;
原位癌 preinvasive cancer;
支氣管癌 bronchogenic carcinoma;
直腸癌 cancer of the rectum; carcinoma of the rectum; rectum cancer;
職業性癌 professional cancer;
致癌 cancer-causing; carcinogenic;
中耳癌 cancer of middle ear;
轉移癌 metastatic cancer;
子宮癌 cancer of the uterus; cancer of the womb; carcinoma uteri; uterine cancer;

ai

【騃】 foolheaded; foolish; silly; stupid; witless;

痴騃 idiotic; silly;

ai³

ai

【毐】 adulterous; be given up to lust; free

love; ill-behaved;

ai

【欸】 (1) sound of answering; (2) sigh; (3) sound of rowing a boat;

[欸乃] (1) crack of an oar; sound of rowing a boat; (2) sound of singing while oaring;

ai

【矮】 (1) dwarf; dwarfish; dwarfish; short; short in stature; short person; (2) low; low-ranking; (3) a grade lower than others;

[矮矮實實] short and sturdy; thickset;

[矮矬] low; short;
矮矬子 dwarf; short person;

[矮櫈] low bench; low stool; small trestle; taboret;

[矮篤篤] dumpy; pudgy; stumpy;
矮篤篤的身材 of dumpy build;

[矮墩墩] dumpy; pudgy; stumpy;
矮墩橔的小伙子 dumpy lad;

[矮缸] low vat;

[矮個兒] low-built person; short person;

[矮櫃] low cabinet;

[矮化] stunt; wimpify;
矮化病 dwarf disease;
矮化栽培 dwarfing culture;

[矮糠] sweet basil;

[矮林] brush; brushwood; coppice; coppice forest;

[矮趴趴] short; squat; very low;

[矮胖] dumpy; humpty-dumpty; roly-poly; short and fat; short and stout; squat; tubby;
矮胖的男人 dumpy man;
矮胖體型 dumpy type;
矮胖子 tub;
矮矮胖胖 tubby;
~矮矮胖胖的男人 tubby man;
身材矮胖 short and stout;
又矮又胖 dumpy;

[矮墻] low wall;
矮墻淺屋 a poor family with a low wall and a small house;
一堵矮墻 a low wall;

[矮人] dandiprat; dwarf; midget; short person;
矮人短秤 small men have great notions;
矮人面前莫論侏儒 one doesn't talk about midgets in front of dwarfs;

[矮瘦] short and thin;
又矮又瘦 short and thin;

[矮樹] bush; low tree;
矮樹籬笆 quickset hedge;

[矮屋] low house;

[矮小] low; low and small; short and slight; short and small; short-statured; undersized;
矮小的人 runt;
矮小症 dwarfism; nanism;
矮小綜合症 short stature syndrome;
身材矮小 microsomia; of short stature; of small bulk; short and slight; short and slight in figure; short and slight in stature; short in stature; small and slight in person; small in stature;
顯得矮小 be dwarfed by...;
又矮又小 short and small;

[矮星] dwarf;
矮星系 dwarf galaxy;
白矮星 white dwarf;

[矮型] dwarf;
矮型傢具 dwarf furniture;

[矮檐] low eave;
矮檐下 under low eaves; unfavourable condition;
矮檐之下，怎不低頭 when you are under the eaves of a low house, you have to bend your head;

[矮枝] dwarf branch;

[矮種馬] pony;

[矮桌] low table;

[矮子] dwarf; short person; shortie; shorty;
矮子矮，一肚怪 a dwarf has a bellyful of tricks;
矮子多心事 the dwarf schemes much;
矮子看戲 follow the reaction of others without an opinion of one's own; like a dwarf looking at a play — has no part to play;
矮子裏拔將軍—矮中挑長 choose a general from among the dwarfs; choose the tallest among the dwarfs; pick the best of a puny bunch; pick the best person available;
矮子騎高馬—上下兩難 difficult to advance or retreat; in a dilemma; like a dwarf riding a tall horse — has difficulty both mounting and dismounting;
矮子上樓梯—步步登高 a rise in position; like a dwarf going upstairs — rising step by step;

矮子坐高凳—夠不著 be unable to reach sth; like a dwarf trying to sit on a tall bench – not tall enough to reach it;
矮子坐末排看戲—隨人家喝彩 follow others' suit; like a dwarf watching a play from a last-row seat – applauds along with the others;
當著矮子，莫論侏儒 one should not talk about midgets in front of dwarfs;
小矮子 squirt;

高矮 height;
個子矮 short;
最矮 lowest; shortest;

ai

【噯】 come on (expressing disapproval);
[噯腐] foul breath;
[噯氣] belch; eructation;
[噯酸] acid eructation; acid rises up from the stomach;

ai

【藹】 (1) affable; amiable; friendly; gentle; kind; (2) beautiful; exuberant; lush; luxuriant; (3) dim; gloomy; hazy;
[藹藹] (1) exuberant; lush; luxuriant; (2) abundant; many; much; (3) dark; dim; gloomy; shady;
[藹彩] fresh look;
[藹甘] polite and amiable in one's manner of speech;
[藹然] (1) glossy; lustrous; luxuriant; (2) affable; amiable; amicable; friendly; gentle; kind;

菴藹 luxuriant; plentiful; prosperous; rampant; teeming;
慈藹 kind and amiable;
和藹 affable; amiable; genial; kind;
森藹 flourishing; prosperous; thriving;

ai

【靄】 (1) amiable; amicable; friendly; kind; mild; peaceful; (2) dense growth of vegetation; (3) cloudy; haze; mist; (4) a surname;
[靄靄] (1) lush; luxuriant growth; (2) abundant; numerous; (3) do one's very best; (4) cloudy; dim; dusky; (5) snowing hard;
靄靄暮雲 misty evening clouds;
[靄滴] mist droplet;

晨靄 morning haze;
暮靄 evening mist;
煙靄 mist and cloud;

ai⁴
ai

【艾】 (1) Chinese mugwort; wormwood; (2) beautiful; fair; fine; good; handsome; pretty; (3) old; (4) cease; discontinue; end; stop; (5) a surname;
[艾艾] falter; stammer; stutter;
艾艾難言 stutter and speak with difficulty;
[艾焙] cauterize with burning moxa;
[艾蒿] Chinese mugwort; moxa;
[艾虎] fitch;
[艾灸] moxibustion;
[艾酒] moxa wine;
[艾老] over fifty years old;
[艾絨] crushed dry moxa;
[艾繩] rope made of moxa;
[艾條灸] moxa roll moxibustion;
[艾窩窩] steamed cake made of glutinous rice with sweet filling;
[艾鼬] polecat;
[艾炷] moxa cone;
[艾滋病] AIDS (acronym of Acquired Immune Deficiency Syndrome);
艾滋病病毒 HIV (acronym of Human Immunodficiency virus);

苦艾 absinthe; mugwort;
蘭艾 orchid and artemisia;
蕲艾 Chinese mugwort;
耆艾 the aged; elderly people; the old;
少艾 young beauty;
怨艾 grudges; resentment;

ai

【愛】 affectionate to; affectionate towards; apt to; be gone on; be interested in; be keen on; be mashed on; be stuck on; cherish; fall for; fall in love with; fond of; get a crash on sb; give one's heart to; have a crush on sb; have a liking for; have a pash on sb; have a passion for; have an affection for; have sincere and intimate affection; keen on; like; kind to; kindness; lose

one's heart to; love; sweet on;

[愛不忍釋] love sth so much that one feels reluctant to part with it;

[愛才] cherish talent;

愛才如命 cherish talent as much as one cherishes one's life;

[愛財] avaricious; covetous; greedy for money; money-hungry; money-mad; rapacious;

愛財如命 as tight as a drum brick; close-fisted; greedy for money; love money as if it were one's own life; love money as much as one's life; love money as one loves one's life; love money like one's very life; love money more than dear life; love wealth as much as life; love wealth as though it were life itself; make an idol of wealth; misers put their back and their belly into their pockets; money rather than life; money-grubber; niggardly; skin a flea for its hide; very covetous of material things; very miserly; whip the cat;

~愛財如命的人 miser; money-grubber; old screw;

[愛巢] love nest;

[愛稱] affectionate name; diminutive; pet name; term of endearment;

[愛吃] love to eat;

愛吃好喝 love to eat, drink, and enjoy oneself;

愛吃蘿卜不吃梨—各有所好 like eating turnips, but not pears – individuals have their own preferences;

愛吃甜食 have a sweet tooth;

[愛寵] (1) bestow favour on; dote on; favour; love; (2) indulge; spoil; (3) one's beloved person;

[愛畜] pet;

[愛蝽] lovebug;

[愛戴] hold in high esteem; love and esteem; love and respect; love and support; love deeply and support; respect and support; revere;

備受愛戴 be much loved and esteemed;

很受愛戴 be much loved and esteemed;

深受愛戴 be held in deep affection; be held in great affection;

深受公眾愛戴 stand high in public love and esteem;

受到眾人愛戴 be beloved by all;

衷心愛戴 love sb from the bottom of one's heart; love wholeheartedly; love with all one's heart;

[愛服] concede willingly; submit willingly;

[愛撫] (1) love with compassion and sympathy; show tender care for; (2) canoodle; caress; fondle;

愛撫嬰兒 caress one's baby;

性愛撫 foreplay;

[愛顧] (1) take loving care of; (2) kind patronage;

[愛國] love one's country; nationalistic; patriotic;

愛國公約 patriotic pledge;

愛國華僑 patriotic overseas Chinese;

愛國熱情 patriotic enthusiasm;

愛國人士 patriot; patriotic personage;

愛國如家 love one's country like one's family;

愛國同胞 patriotic fellow-countrymen;

愛國心 patriotic feeling; patriotism;

~喚起愛國心 arouse patriotic sentiments; arouse patriotism; awaken patriotic sentiments;

~激發愛國心 inspire patriotism;

愛國者 patriot;

愛國志士 ardent patriot; dedicated patriot;

愛國主義 patriotism;

~愛國主義教育 education for patriotism;

~灌輸愛國主義 inculcate patriotism;

~極端愛國主義 jingoism;

~培養愛國主義 foster patriotism;

~頌揚愛國主義 glorify patriotism;

愛國組織 patriotic organization;

不愛國 unpatriotic;

[愛好] a favourite of; a favourite of sb; a favourite with; a friend of; a friend to; affect; after one's fancy; all for sth; an avocation; an avocation with sb; appeal to; as a hobby; be cracked about sb; be fond of; be interested in; bend one's mind to; catch sb's fancy; delight in; dote on; dote upon; drink in; enjoy; enjoy favour; enthusiastic over sth; fall for; favour; fond of; get interest in; glad of sth; go in for; have a bent for; have a fancy for; have a fondness for; have a liking for; have a liking to;

have a love for; have a love of; have a passion for; have a predilection for; have a preference for; have a soft spot for; have a taste for; have a taste in; have a weakness for; have an appetite for; have one's heart in sth; have one's likes; have partiality for; have partiality to; high on sth; hit sb's fancy; hobbies; in favour with sb; in one's favour; in one's line; keen about; keen on; love; mad on; one's cup of tea; partial to; please sb's fancy; pleased with; relish; revel in; strike sb's fancy; suit sb's fancy; take a fancy for; take a fancy to; take a liking for; take an interest in; take delight in; take pleasure in; take sb's fancy; to one's appetite; to one's fancy; to one's liking; to one's taste; with interest;
愛好廣泛 have a wide variety of hobbies;
愛好者 a follower of; a lover of; amateur; devotee; dilettante; enthusiast; fan; fancier; groupie; hobbyist; idolizer; those who are addicted to;
表示愛好 profess a liking for;
不再愛好 love one's love for;
開始愛好 develop a liking for;

[愛河] (1) river of love; (2) (Buddhism) the river of desire in which people are drowned;
愛河永浴 bathe forever in the river of love;
墮入愛河 fall head over heels in love;

[愛恨] love-hate;
愛恨交織的關係 love-hate relationship;

[愛護] care; cherish; give kind protection to; protect; safeguard; show genuine affection for; take good care of; treasure;
愛護備至 give every attention to; take good care of;
互相愛護 take care of each other;
受到愛護 receive tender attention;

[愛花狂] love flowers;
愛花狂 anthomania;

[愛火] sexual drive;

[愛己及物] extend love of oneself to others;

[愛哭] a child who cries frequently;
愛哭的人 crybaby;

[愛憐] show fondness for; show love for; show tender affection for;
惹人愛憐 arouse one's tender feelings;

[愛戀] be in love with; fall in love with; feel attached to; feel deeply attached to;

[愛侶] sweethearts;

[愛美] (1) love beauty; set great store by one's appearance; (2) be fond of making up; love to make up and wear beautiful clothes;
愛美病 pay too much attention to one's appearance;
愛美觀念 aesthetic sense;

[愛民] cherish people; love people;
愛民如子 love the people as if they were one's children;
廉正愛民 upright, honourable and have the interest of the people at heart;
擁軍愛民 support the army and cherish the people;
擁政愛民 support the government and cherish the people;

[愛莫能助] desirous but unable to help; feel sorry that one is not in a position to help; glad to but powerless to render assistance; love but have no ability to render assistance; sympathetic but unable to help; willing but powerless to help; willing but unable to help; willing to help but unable to do so;

[愛慕] admire; adoration; adore; be attached to; burn with love; dote on; fond of; have a fondness for; have a soft spot in one's heart for; like; love;
愛慕者 admirer;
愛慕之情 feeling of adoration;
互相愛慕 adore each other; affectionate to each other;
受人愛慕 be adored for;
無限的愛慕 unbounded admiration; unlimited admiration;
衷心的愛慕 heartfelt admiration; hearty admiration;

[愛昵] (1) adoring; affectionate; intimate; loving; (2) love dearly;

[愛女] one's beloved daughter; one's favourite daughter;

[愛妻] one's beloved wife;

[愛妾] one's beloved concubine;

［愛情］ affection; love; love between man and woman; romantic love;
愛情誠可貴，自由價更高 love is really to be treasured, but freedom is even more prized;
愛情的 amatory;
愛情歌曲 love song;
愛情故事 love story; romance novel;
愛情結合 love match;
愛情倫理學 ethics of love;
愛情鳥 love-bird;
愛情片 love film;
愛情騙子 love rat;
愛情生活 love life;
愛情詩 amorous poem; amorous verse; love poem;
愛情小説 amorous novel; love novel; love story; romantic fiction;
愛情專一 steadfast in love;
浪漫的愛情 romantic love;
談情説愛 be concerned with love and romance; bill and coo; chat intimately; love and romance; talk love;
甜蜜的愛情 sweet affection;
找到愛情 find love;

［愛犬］ one's beloved dog;

［愛群］ (1) congenial; gregarious; love company; sociable; (2) love the multitude;

［愛人］ (1) one's husband; (2) one's wife; (3) darling; lover; sweetheart; (4) fiance; (5) fiancee; (6) love others;
愛人如己 love a person as oneself; love others as one loves oneself;
愛人以德 love others with a due regard to what is right; love the man for his virtue;
愛人者恒愛之 those who love others are always loved in return;

［愛如己出］ love a child like one's own;

［愛上了］ be attached to; be gone on; be swept off one's feet; become attached to; become enamoured; fall head and ears in love; fall in love with; lose one's heart to; sweet on; take the fancy of; take to;

［愛神］ Amor; Cupid; Eros; God of Love; Venus;
愛神星 Eros;

［愛屋及烏］ he that loves the tree loves the branch; love me, love my dog; love one thing on account of another;

［愛物］ (1) cherished object; (2) love all creatures;
仁民愛物 love all the people and animals; love the masses and be kind to creatures;

［愛惜］ (1) cherish; hold sth dear; make good use of; make the best use of sth; prize; treasure sth; use sparingly; value; (2) miserly; niggardly; stingy;

［愛小］ go after petty advantages; greedy for small gains; keen on gaining petty advantages;

［愛心］ compassion; kindness; loving heart; strong love;
充滿愛心 fill with love;

［愛意］ love;
愛意流露 display of affection;
一陣子愛意 a flush of love;

［愛悦］ be fond of; love;

［愛樂］ philharmonic;
愛樂樂團 philharmonic orchestra;

［愛憎］ love and hate; one's likes and dislikes;
愛憎分明 clear about what to love and what to hate; clear about whom or what to love or hate; clear-cut in what one loves and hates; clear-cut on what to love and what to hate; draw a clear demarcation line between whom or what to love and whom or what to hate; draw a clear-cut line between love and hatred; have an acute sense of love and hatred; know whom to love and whom to hate; see everything in black and white; the manner of loving or hating sth is extraordinarily clear;
偏憎偏愛 one-sided in disliking and liking;

［愛重］ love and respect;
受人愛重 be loved and respected;

［愛滋病］ AIDS (acronym of Acquired Immune Deficiency Syndrome);
愛滋病病毒 AIDS virus;

［愛子］ beloved son; favourite son;

博愛 love for humanity; universal love;
寵愛 cosset; dote on; make a pet of sb;
慈愛 affection; kindness; love;
錯愛 misplaced favour; undeserved kindness;

奪愛 take away other's woman;
恩愛 affectionate; conjugal love;
夫妻之愛 conjugal love;
撫愛 caress; fondle; fondle sb sexually;
父愛 paternal love;
父母的愛 parental love;
割愛 give away what one treasures; part with what one loves;
關愛 love for others; loving care; nurturance;
互愛 reciprocal affection;
敬愛 esteem and love; respect and love;
可愛 lovable; lovely;
酷愛 be very fond of; love ardently;
憐愛 have tender affection for; love tenderly;
戀愛 in love; love; romance;
令愛 your daughter;
母愛 maternal love; mother's love;
溺愛 coddle; dote on a child; spoil a child;
偏愛 favour; partial to;
親愛 beloved; dear; loving;
情愛 affection; love;
求愛 court; pay court to; woo;
熱愛 love ardently; passionate love;
仁愛 kind-heartedness;
辱愛 receive a favour undeservingly;
示愛 show one's feeling to sb;
恃愛 presume on your kindness and affection;
素愛 frequent;
所愛 what one likes; what one loves;
疼愛 fond of; love dearly; love dearly;
痛愛 love deeply; love passionately;
偎愛 intimately in love;
喜愛 keen on; like; love;
相愛 love each other;
孝愛 filial love;
心愛 treasured;
性愛 sexual love;
雅愛 your help; your patronage;
遺愛 the benevolence left behind by a dead person;
永恒的愛 ever-lasting love;
友愛 fraternal love; friendly affection;
欲愛 love inspired by desire; passion-love;
珍愛 love dearly; treasure;
貞潔的愛 chaste love;
真愛 true love;
真摯的愛 sincere love;
鍾愛 dote on; love dearly;
自愛 (1) cherish one's good name; (2) take good care of one's health;
做愛 make love;

ai

【碍】 a simplified form of 礙;

ai

【隘】 (1) strategic pass; strategic point; (2) defile; narrow pass; narrow passageway; (3) destitute; difficult; in need; in want; (4) urgent;

［隘谷］ gully; ravine;
［隘害］ strategic pass; strategic point;
［隘口］ gap; mountain pass; notch;
［隘路］ (1) narrow passage; narrow road; (2) road flanked by water;
［隘險］ of great strategic value;
［隘巷］ alley; narrow lane;

褊隘 narrow-minded and impatient;
關隘 gate; pass;
湫隘 narrow and low-lying;
山隘 mountain pass;
狹隘 (1) narrow; (2) narrow and parochial;
險隘 dangerous; strategic pass;
要隘 key point; strategic pass;

ai

【嬡】 one's daughter;

令嬡 your daughter;

ai

【嗳】 (expressing regret) ah; dear me; my goodness; oh;

ai

【曖】 (1) dim; faint; inconspicuous; indistinct; unclear; (2) ambiguous; equivocal; obscure; vague;

［曖曖］ dark; dim; obscure; unclear;
［曖昧］ (1) ambiguous; dubious; equivocal; shady; vague; (2) improper; shady; socially unacceptable;

曖昧關係 ambiguous relationships; dishonest relations; dubious relationships; shady relationships;
～與…有曖昧關係 have a dubious relationship with sb;
曖昧行為 scandals;
答覆曖昧 give an ambiguous answer;
關係曖昧 have a dubious relationship with sb;
態度曖昧 assume an ambiguous attitude;

［曖色］ warm colour;

ai

【璦】 fine jade;

ai

【薆】 (1) luxuriant growth of vegetation; (2) cloak; conceal; cover; cover up; hide; shroud; under cover;

ai

【礙】 (1) bar; block; block up; concern; hinder; obstruct; offend; stand in the way; (2) destructive; detrimental; difficult; harmful;

［礙道］ obstruct the way;

［礙口］ find it hard to bring the matter up; too embarrassing to mention; unpleasant to talk about;

［礙目］ eyesore; offend the eye; unpleasant to look at; unpleasant to the eye;

［礙難］ find it difficult to do sth; find it inconvenient to do sth for certain reasons;

［礙事］ (1) hindrance; in the way; keep under sb's feet; obstacle; problem; (2) matter; of consequence; serious;

不礙事 do not matter;

［礙手］ hindrance; in the way;

礙手礙腳 a hindrance to sb; a nuisance to sb; an encumbrance to sb; cumbersome; cumbrous; get in the way of sb; hinder; impede; in the way; obstructive; one too many; stand in sb's way; stand in the way of;

太礙手 get in the way;

［礙眼］ (1) inconvenience; stand in the way; (2) eyesore; offend the eye; unpleasant to look at; unpleasant to the eye;

有點礙眼 be sth of an eyesore;

妨礙 encumber; hinder; obstruct;

干礙 (1) be concerned with; have to do with; (2) hinder; impede;

罣礙 worries and concerns;

掛礙 be concerned;

關礙 hinder; stand in the way;

違礙 prohibition; taboo;

無礙 all right; do not matter; no harm; not in the way;

有礙 a hindrance to; detrimental; get in way of; harmful; obstruct;

障礙 get in the way of; handicap; obstruct; obstruction;

窒礙 be obstructed; have obstacles;

滯礙 block up; obstruct;

阻礙 bar; block; hinder; obstruction;

ai

【靉】 ［靉靉］ (1) exuberant; lush; luxuriant; (2) cloudy;

［靉靆］ (1) cloudy; (2) glasses; spectacles; (3) indistinct; obscure; unclear;

an¹

【安】 (1) calm; cool; peaceful; quiescent; quiet; reposing; tranquil; (2) achieve inner harmony; calm; set at ease; set sb's mind at ease; (3) contented; pleased; rest content; satisfied; (4) good state of health; in good health; safe; secure; (5) find a place for; place in a suitable position; (6) fit; fix; instal; (7) bring a charge against sb; give sb a nickname; (8) harbour an intention; (9) how; (10) where; (11) ampere; (12) a surname;

［安邦］ bring stability to the country;

安邦定國 bring peace and stability to the country; bring peace to the country and have it settled on a firm basis; give peace and stability to the country; rule the country and give peace to the world; tranquilize the nation and settle the country;

安邦治國 effect good administration and stability for the country;

［安邊］ pacify the border area;

安邊良策 sound policy to ensure security and tranquility in the border areas;

［安泊］ put up in a hotel;

［安不忘戰］ mindful of the possibilities of war in times of peace;

［安步］ go slowly; walk slowly;

安步當車 content to go on foot instead of riding in a vehicle; foot it; hoof it; leg it; ride in the marrow-bone coach; ride on shanks' mare; ride on the horse with ten toes; tramp it; walk on one's two legs; walk over leisurely instead of riding in a carriage; walk rather than ride;

［安插］ assign to a post; get a position for a person in an organization; place sb in

a certain position; place sb in a job or position; plant sb in a place;
安插測驗 placement test;

[安常] take things as they are;
安常處順 be accustomed to a comfortable life; be content with the status quo; enjoy a tranquil and stable life; go along with things as they are; in smooth water; sail before the wind; take the peaceful world as one finds it; take things as they are; take things as they come;
襲故安常 contented with old ways and loathe to change;

[安車] cart with seats in it;

[安抵] arrive safe and sound; arrive safely;
安抵目的地 arrive at the destination safely;

[安定] (1) quiet and in order; settled; stable; steadfast; unchanging; (2) reassure; stabilize;
安定性 stabilizing ability;
安定藥 sedative; tranquilizer;

[安堵] live in peace and security;

[安頓] (1) arrange; arrange properly for; find a place for; help settle down; make proper arrangements; put in order; put sb up; (2) comfortable; keep quiet; peaceful; undisturbed;

[安放] lay; place; put in a certain place; put in a proper manner;
安放貨物 position goods;

[安分] abide by one's station in life; abide by the law and behave oneself; abide by the law in life; behave discreetly; content with one's lot; do not go beyond one's bounds; dutiful; honest and dutiful; keep to oneself; know one's place; law-abiding; let not the cobbler go beyond his last; let the cobbler stick to his last; mind one's own business; not go beyond one's bounds; not go beyond one's position; not to go beyond one's bounds; remain in one's proper sphere; stand to one's duty; stick to one's last; take one's own line; the cobbler must stick to his last; walk up to the trough, fodder or no fodder; well-disciplined;
安分得體 behave properly;
~舉止安分得體 behave properly;
安分度日 lead a sober life;
安分守法 abide by the law and behave oneself;
~安分守法做生意 do legitimate business;
安分守己 abide by law and behave oneself; abide by law and never transgress; act according to one's status; act dutifully; be contented with one's lot; behave discreetly; content with one's lot; content with things as they are; content with what one is; dutiful; keep one's nose clean; keep one's place; keep to oneself; law-abiding and well-behaved; mind one's own business; stick to one's last;
很安分 be contended with one's lot; keep to one's own line;

[安伏] calm sb down; comfort; console; give comfort to; put at ease;

[安撫] appease; console; pacify; placate; reassure; smooth down; soothe; stroke sb with the hair;
安撫政策 appeasement policy; pacification policy;
~實行安撫政策 adopt pacification policy;

[安富尊榮] be content with one's wealth and rank; enjoy wealth and honour;

[安固] fix; make fast; secure; tighten;

[安好] enjoy peace and good health; safe and sound; well;

[安魂曲] requiem;

[安家] establish residence; insure the welfare of one's family; make one's home in a place; set up a home; settle; settle down; take up one's abode; take up residence;
安家費 family allowance; settling-in allowance;
~一筆安家費 a settling-in allowance;
安家立戶 set up a home;
安家立業 make one's home and establish oneself in business; make one's home and work one's way; set up a home and establish a business; set up for oneself; settle down and start one's career; settle down to business;
安家落戶 make one's home in a place; settle; settle down in a place;

[安檢] security check;

[安靖] (1) peaceful and stable; (2) bring peace and stability;
社會安靖 peace and stability in society;

[安靜] calm; hush; peaceful; peaceful and serene; placid; quiescent; quiet; restful; resting; still; tranquil;
安靜一下 give it a rest;
安安靜靜 peaceful and serene;
保持安靜 keep quiet;
~請保持安靜 please keep quiet;
絕對安靜 absolutely quiet;
相當安靜 quite quiet;

[安居] settle down;
安居工程 affordable housing project;
安居樂業 content with one's station and happy with one's lot; enjoy a good and prosperous life; have a more secure life; lead a settled life and be content with one's work; live a good life; live a prosperous and contented life; live and work in peace and contentment; live and work in peace and happiness;

[安康] in a state of peace and good health; in good health;
祝你安康 wish you the best of health; wish you well;
祝您身體安康 I wish you the best of health;

[安瀾] (1) calm; unraffled; (2) peaceful and tranquil;
天下安瀾 peace prevails on earth;

[安老院] elderly home; home for the old people;

[安樂] comfortable; easy; free from worry; happy; peace and comfort; peace and happiness; peaceful and happy;
安樂死 euthanasia; mercy killing; painless death;
~實行安樂死 practise euthanasia; practise mercy killing;
~要求安樂死 ask to be killed painlessly; ask for mercy killing;
安樂窩 a bed of down; a bed of flowers; a bed of roses; cosy nest; cosy place; easy and comfortable life; happy retreat; love nest; place of ease and comfort; snug and cosy nest; snug den;
~經營安樂窩 feather one's cosy nest;
~營造安樂窩 make a bed of roses;
安樂鄉 (1) land of milk and honey; totus land; (2) Land of Cockaigne;
安樂椅 easy chair;
安樂之鄉 a land of milk and honey;
帶來安樂 bring peace and happiness;
生於憂患，死於安樂 life springs from sorrow and calamity; death comes from ease and pleasure; thrive in calamity and perish in soft living;
尋求安樂 find comfort;
追求安樂 seek peace and happiness;

[安良] pacify the good;
安良除暴 pacify the good and get rid of the bullies;
除暴安良 champion the good and kill tyrants; drive out the rascals and protect the people; eliminate evil and give peace to the good people; get rid of bullies and bring peace to good people; get rid of evil and give peace to the good; get rid of the cruel and pacify the good people; kill tyrants and champion the good people; remove despots and help the good people; run down the people's oppressors; weed out the tyrant and let people live in peace; weed out the wicked and let the law-abiding citizens live in peace;
除害安良 remove the evil and quiet the good;
弭盜安良 repress the bandits and pacify the people;

[安謐] peaceful; quiescent; quiet; tranquil;
安謐如常 be peaceful as usual;
環境安謐 tranquil environment;

[安眠] have a sound sleep; sleep peacefully; sleep soundly;
安眠劑 hypnotic;
安眠藥 downer; sleeping draught; sleeping pill; sleeping potion; sleeping tablet;

[安民] give peace to the people; pacify the people; quiet the people; reassure the people; reassure the public;
安民告示 notice to reassure the public;
安民政策 policies to reassure the public;
輔國安民 protect the people and bring peace to the state; serve the state and pacify the people;
護國安民 guard the state and pacify the people;

[安命] accept one's lot; content with one's lot;

[安寧] (1) peaceful; peaceful and orderly;

quiet; repose; tranquil; (2) calm; composed; free from worry;
不得安寧 be much troubled;
得到安寧 find peace;
感到安寧 free from worry;
享有安寧 have peace;

[安排] arrange; arrange for; arrangements; cuddle up; find a place for sth; fix; fix sth; fix up; lay on sth; lay out; make arrangements for; manage; plan; tee up;
安排得當 properly arranged;
安排就緒 the arrangements are complete;
安排妥當 be properly managed;
安排完畢 complete an arrangement;
必要的安排 necessary arrangements;
打亂安排 dislocate an arrangement; disturb an arrangement;
改變安排 alter one's arrangement; change an arrangement;
進一步的安排 further arrangements;
精心安排 careful arrangement; elaborate arrangement;
臨時安排 temporary arrangement;
令人不滿意的安排 unsatisfactory arrangement;
另作安排 make alternative arrangements;
巧妙的安排 clever arrangement;
取消安排 cancel an arrangement;
確定安排 finalize the arrangements;
商量安排 discuss the arrangements;
上次的安排 previous arrangement;
彈性安排 be flexibly arranged;
特殊安排 special arrangements;
調整安排 adjust an arrangement;
妥善的安排 proper arrangement;
妥為安排 make proper arrangements;
一致同意的安排 agreed arrangement;
預先安排 advance arrangement;
正式安排 formal arrangement;
自有安排 know how to deal with sb or sth;
作出安排 make an arrangement;
做好安排 make arrangements;

[安培] ampere;
安培秤 ampere balance;
~分安培秤 deci-ampere balance;
安培定理 ampere theorem;
安培定律 ampere's law;
安培計 ammeter; ampere meter;
~標準安培計 standard ammeter;
~電動式安培計 electrodynamic ammeter;
~多擋安培計 commutate ammeter;
~功率計式安培計 dynamometer;
~鉗式安培計 clamp-on ammeter;
~熱安培計 thermal ammeter;
~天線安培計 antenna ammeter;
~重力式安培計 gravity ammeter;
安培數 amperage;
安培小時 ampere-hour;
絕對安培 abampere; absolute ampere;

[安貧] contentment in poverty;
安貧樂道 be contented in poverty and devoted to things spiritual; be satisfied with one's poverty and lowly position; bend to one's lot; bow to one's fate; complacency with honest poverty; happy to lead a simple, virtuous life; lead a poor life and delight in wisdom; satisfaction with the simple life; submit to one's lot; willingness to lead a simple life;
安貧樂賤 happy to lead a simple and virtuous life;

[安琪兒] angel;

[安寢] be asleep;

[安全] (1) safe; secure; (2) safety; security;
安全板 safety guard;
安全棒 safety road; scram road;
安全保護 safeguard; safety measure;
~受到安全保護 be kept safe;
安全保證 (1) guarantee of security; safe conduct; (2) safety is guaranteed;
安全帶 safety belt; safety strap; safety strip; seat belt;
~繫好安全帶 fasten one's seat belt;
安全島 pedestrian island; safety island; traffic island;
安全燈 miner's lamp; safelight; safety lamp;
安全地 haven;
安全第一 safety first; safety is priority;
安全墊 safety pad;
安全度 degree of safety; degree of security;
安全閥 protection valve; relief valve; safe valve;
~打開安全閥 open the safe valve;
安全桿 safety rod;
安全感 safe feeling; sense of security;
安全合格牌照 safety approval plate;
安全核 security kernel;

安全檢查 safety check; safety inspection; security check;
安全簡便 safe and simple;
安全獎 safety prize;
安全獎金 accident reduction bonus;
安全角 safety angle;
安全界 safety limit;
安全卡 safety card;
安全碼 safety code;
安全帽 hard hat; head gear; safety cap; safety helmet;
~戴安全帽 wear a safety helmet;
安全門 emergency exit; fire door; theft-proof door;
安全期 safe period;
安全區 safety zone;
安全繩 safety rope;
安全閂 safety latch;
安全鎖 safety keylock;
安全套 bag; condom; joy-bag; joy-sock; rubber; safe; American sock;
安全梯 emergency staircase;
安全網 jumping net; safety net; safety netting;
安全系數 assurance coefficient; safety coefficient; safety factor;
安全系統 fail-safe system;
安全限度 safe margin; safety limit;
安全限量 threshold values;
安全線圖 safety coil;
安全銷 safety pin;
安全效應 safety effectiveness;
~安全效應影響因素 influence factors to safety effectiveness;
安全鞋 safety shoes;
安全心理 safety psychology;
~安全心理特徵 characteristic of safety psychology;
安全形勢 security situation;
安全型煙 low-tar cigarette;
安全性 safety; security;
~安全性分析 safety analysis;
~安全性維護 security maintenance;
~操作安全性 operational safety; processing safety;
~食品安全性 food safety;
~水生安全性 aquatic;
~作用安全性 work safety;
安全意識 safety awareness;
安全因數 safety factor;
安全月 safety month;
安全閘 safety brake;
安全指南 safety guide;
安全主任 safety officer;
安全裝置 security apparatus;
安全做法 safe practice;
保衛安全 safeguard the security of;
保證安全 ensure security; guarantee sb's safety;
不安全 insecure; unsafe;
~不安全感 insecurity;
不大安全 not quite safe;
操作安全 operational safety;
擔心安全 be concerned about the safety of...;
感到安全 feel secure;
絕對安全 absolute safety; as safe as houses;
確保安全 assure the safety of;
危害安全 endanger the security of; jeopardize the security of;
危及安全 endanger the safety of;
威脅安全 threaten the security of;

[安然] (1) safe and sound; safely; (2) at rest; feel at ease; free from worry; peaceful;
安然長逝 expire calmly;
安然度過難關 get through unscathed; tide over the difficulties;
安然忍受 bear stoically;
安然入睡 go to sleep peacefully;
安然逃脱 escape unscathed; get off scot-free;
安然脱險 escape scot-free; out of danger;
安然無事 free from trouble; go scot-free; meet no danger;
安然無恙 all serene; come away in a whole skin; come off with a whole skin; come through unscathed; completely free from trouble; completely uninjured; escape unscathed; fall on one's feet; get away in a whole skin; get off with a whole skin; go scot-free; in a whole skin; keep a whole skin; meet no danger; no harm done; safe and sound; sound in life and limb; unhurt; well and in good shape; with a whole skin; without mishap;
安然自愉 take the rough with the smooth;
心裏安然 feel at ease;

[安人] pacify the people;

[安忍] endure patiently;

[安設] install; set up;

A

[安身] make one's home in a place; settle; take refuge; take shelter;
安身樂業 live a peaceful and happy life;
安身立命 begin the world; enjoy peace and stability both physically and spiritually; establish oneself in a locality; find a secure job for life; find a settled place for life; get on in the world; go out into the world; nestle oneself in a place for a living; settle down and get on with one's pursuit; settle down to a quiet life; stay in;
安身為樂 glad to find a settled place for life;
安身之處 place to call home;
無處安身 have no place to stay; have nowhere to stay;

[安神] (1) calm the nerves; make sb calm and peaceful; soothe the nerves; (2) relieve tension and calm one's mind;
安神定魂 calm the nerves; soothe the nerves;
安神藥 sedative; tranquilizer;
養心安神 tone up the heart and calm the nerves;

[安生] (1) quiet; still; (2) peaceful; restful; (3) live in peace;

[安聲] quiet; silent; still;

[安適] (1) peaceful and comfortable; quiet and comfortable; (2) snug;

[安舒] leisurely and comfortably;
身心安舒 feel at ease and rested;

[安睡] sleep peacefully; sleep soundly; sleep undisturbedly; sleep well;

[安泰] healthy; in good health; safe and sound;
身心安泰 enjoy physical and mental health;

[安恬] comfortable; peaceful; undisturbed;

[安帖] feel at ease;

[安土] feel at home wherever one is;
安土重遷 be used to living in one's homeland and feel reluctant to move elsewhere;

[安妥] safe and proper; secure; well placed;

[安危] safety; safety and danger;
安危未定 hang in the balance;
安危與共 share safety and danger; share weal and woe; stick together in security and in danger;
安不忘危 be always provided against danger; in peace, do not forget danger; in peace, remember the possibilities of danger; in peacetime, do not forget the possibility of danger; mindful of possible danger in times of peace; never to relax one's vigilance while one lives in peace; watchful of possible danger in times of security;
關心國家的安危 be concerned about the safety of the country;
居安思危 be prepared for danger in times of peace; bear in mind the danger of war while living in peace; prepare for a future emergency; prepare for danger in times of peace; provide against danger while living in peace; think of danger in time of peace; vigilant in peace time;
歷盡安危 have experienced both felicity and misfortune;
無視工人的安危 ignore the safety and danger of the labourers;
轉危為安 avert a danger; become safe; out of danger; out of harm's way; pass from danger to safety; past danger; pull through; steer clear of danger to safety; take a turn for the better and be out of danger; tide over the crisis; turn from danger to safety; turn the corner;

[安慰] comfort; consolation; console; show sympathy for; soothe;
安慰的 consolatory;
安慰費 consolation fee;
安慰獎 consolation prize;
安慰賽 consolation event; consolation match;
安慰效應 placebo effects;
安慰者 comforter;
一點安慰 a modicum of comfort;
在工作中找到安慰 find consolation in one's work;

[安穩] (1) smooth and steady; steady; (2) calm; reserved in manner; serene; staid;
安安穩穩 firm and secure; secure and stable;

[安息] (1) at rest; rest in peace; (2) go to sleep; rest; sleep;
安息日 Sabbath;
安息香 benzoin;
~安息香酸 benzoic acid;

[安下] retire for rest;
安下心來 breathe again; set one's mind at rest; settle oneself down;

[安閒] enjoy leisure; leisurely; peaceful and carefree; relaxation;
安閒無事 have no work;
安閒自得 carefree and content;
安閒自在 leisurely and carefree;

[安祥] composed; peaceful; serene; undisturbed;
神態安祥 look unruffled;

[安享] enjoy; live in ease and comfort;

[安歇] (1) go to bed; (2) retire for the night; take a rest;

[安心] at ease; content and not anxious to make any change; feel at ease; have no worries; have one's heart at ease; have one's heart at rest; have peace of mind; relieved; rest assured; set one's heart at ease; set one's heart at rest; set one's mind at ease; set one's mind at rest; settle oneself down;
安心落意 feel reassured;
安心丸 sedative;
死也安心 one will die in peace;

[安逸] ease and comfort; easy; easy and comfortable; leisurely and comfortable;
安逸的生活 easy life; life of leisure;
安逸度日 pass days in indolence;
貪圖安逸 seek comfort and ease;

[安營] camp; encamp; make camp; pitch a camp;
安營紮寨 camp; encamp; make camp; pitch a camp;

[安於] be satisfied with; content with; feel contented in;

[安葬] bury the dead; entomb; lay to rest;

[安扎] camp; settle down;

[安枕] sleep in peace;
安枕無憂 rest assured without anxiety; sleep in peace; sleep without any anxiety;
夜不安枕 toss about in bed;

[安之若命] bow to one's lot; submit to one's fate;

[安之若素] as cool as a cucumber; bear hardship with equanimity; put up sth with grace; regard wrongdoings with equanimity;

[安知非福] who knows it is not a blessing in disguise;

[安置] arrange; arrange for; arrange suitable posts for; find a place for; have a good rest; help settle down; put in a proper place; settle;
安置辦 resettlement office;
安置費 settlement allowance;

[安裝] assemble; erect; fix; install; lay on; mount;
安裝步驟 installation procedure;
安裝程序 installation procedure;
安裝隊 erection group; erection team; installation gang;
安裝費 installation fee;
安裝工 erector; installer; mounter;
安裝工程 installation work;
安裝圖 installation diagram;
安裝誤差 erection error; installation error; misalignment;

[安坐] sit idly;

保安 (1) ensure public security; (2) ensure safety;
不安 (1) uncomfortable; uneasy; (2) unstable;
伏安 volt-ampere;
公安 public security;
苟安 seek momentary ease;
毫安 milliampere;
偏安 content to retain sovereignty over a part of the country;
平安 safe and sound; without mishap;
欠安 not easy at heart; unwell;
請安 inquire after an elder; pay respects to sb; wish sb good health;
日安 good day;
偷安 live in complacency; seek temporary ease;
晚安 good night;
萬安 (1) do not worry; (2) very safe;
微安 microampere;
胃安 centrine;
慰安 comfort; soothe;
問安 send greetings; wish sb good health;
午安 good afternoon;
相安 live in peace with each other;
心安 calmness of emotion; carefree; peace of mind;
宴安 feel happy and contented; live in idle comfort;
燕安 comfort; ease; peace;
永安 perpetual peace;

早安 good morning;
招安 offer amnesty and enlistment to rebels;
治安 public order; public security;

an

【桉】 eucalyptus;
［桉樹］ eucalyptus tree; gum tree;

檸檬桉 Eucalyptus citriodora;

an

【氨】 ammonia;
［氨苯喋啶］ triamterene;
［氨苯碸］ dapsone;
［氨苄青霉素］ ampicillin;
［氨草膠］ ammoniac; ammoniacum;
［氨處理］ ammonia treatment;
［氨合］ ammoniate;
氨合成法 ammonia synthesis;
氨合物 ammoniate;
氨合作用 ammoniation;
［氨化］ ammoniate; ammoniation; ammonification;
氨化劑 ammoniating agent; ammonizator;
氨化煤 ammonition coal;
氨化細菌 ammonifier;
氨化作用 ammonization;
［氨基］ amino; amino-group;
氨基苯 aminobenzene;
氨基吡啶 aminopyridine;
氨基比林 aminopyrinhe;
氨基醇 amino alcohol;
氨基多肽酶 aminopolypeptidase;
氨基二苯胺 aminodiphenylamine;
氨基甲烷 aminomethane;
氨基硫酸 aminosulfuric acid;
氨基醛 amino aldehyde;
氨基噻唑 aminothiazole;
氨基樹脂 aminoresin;
氨基塑料 aminoplastics;
氨基酸 aminoacid;
~氨基酸尿 amino aciduria;
~氨基酸型糖尿病 aminodiabetes;
氨基糖 aminosugar;
氨基酮 aminoketone;
氨基纖維素 aminocellulose;
氨基吖啶 aminoacridine;
氨基脂 aminolipid;
乙酰氨基 acetylamino;
［氨碱法］ ammonia soda process;
［氨解］ aminolysis; ammonolysis; ammonolyze;
氨解作用 ammonolysis;
［氨冷凍］ ammonia cooling;
氨冷凍機 ammonia refrigerating machine;
［氨量計］ ammoniometer;
［氨硫脲］ thiacetazone;
［氨倫］ spandex;
［氨絡］ ammine;
氨絡物 ammino-complex; ammino-compound;
［氨尿］ ammoniuria;
［氨氣］ ammonia;
氨氣滲碳 ammonia carburizing;
氨氣塔 ammonia still;
氨氣洗滌器 ammonia serubber;
氨氣壓縮機 ammonia compressor;
氨氣壓縮冷凍機 ammonia compression refrigerator;
［氨水］ ammonia spirit; ammonia water; aqua ammonia;
稀氨水 weak aqua ammonia;
［氨探漏試驗］ ammonia leak testing;
［氨轉化器］ ammonia convertor;

飽和氨 saturated ammonia;
固定氨 fixed ammonia;
合成氨 synthetic ammonia;
酒精氨 alcohol ammonia;
苛性氨 caustic ammonia;
離解氨 dissociated ammonia;
尿氨 urinary ammonia;
氣態氨 gaseous ammonia;
醛氨 aldehyde ammonia;
無水氨 anhydrous ammonia;
液態氨 liquid ammonia;
游離氨 free ammonia;

an

【庵】 (1) cottage; hut; (2) Buddhist convent; nunnery;
［庵寺］ (1) Buddhist nunnery; (2) Buddhist temple;
［庵堂］ Buddhist convent; Buddhist nunnery;
［庵子］ (1) thatched hut; (2) nunnery;

草庵 thatched hut;
尼庵 Buddhist nunnery;

an

【菴】 (1) small round hut; (2) small Buddhist monastery; small Buddhist nunnery;

small Buddhist temple; temple;
［菴廬］ hut;
［菴堂］ Buddhist monastery;

an
【鞍】 saddle;
［鞍板］ saddle plate;
［鞍鼻］ saddle nose;
［鞍部］ saddle of a hill;
［鞍點］ saddle point;
鞍點法 saddle point method;
鞍點理論 saddle point theory;
［鞍架］ saddle;
鞍架接合 saddle joint;
［鞍匠］ saddler;
［鞍具］ pommel saddlery;
［鞍馬］ (1) horse; pommel horse; side horse; (2) saddle and horse;
鞍馬畫 painting of horses;
鞍馬勞頓 be fatigued by a long journey; travel-worn;
鞍馬生活 life on horseback;
見鞍思馬 see the saddle and think of the horse — recollect by the law of association;
［鞍囊］ saddle bag;
［鞍轡］ bridle up a horse; saddle and bridle;
［鞍式］ saddle-type;
鞍式函數 saddle function;
［鞍形］ saddle;
鞍形鍵 saddle key;
鞍形填料 saddle packing;
鞍形線圈 saddle coil;
［鞍子］ saddle;

備鞍 put a saddle on a horse;
電纜鞍 cable saddle;
馬鞍 saddle;
馱鞍 packsaddle;
軸鞍 axle saddle;

an
【諳】 ability; be acquainted with; be skilled in; be versed in; familiar with; know well;
諳於書法 be skilful in calligraphy;
［諳達］ be well-versed; be familiar;
諳達世情 be familiar with the ways of the world;
［諳記］ learn by heart;
［諳練］ be skilled in; be versed in; conversant; familiar with; proficient in;
諳練老成 skilful and experienced;
［諳熟］ conservant with; proficient in; quite familiar;
諳熟歷史 be conversant with history;
［諳誦］ recite from memory;
［諳算］ calculate mentally;
［諳習］ be skilled in; be versed in; familiar with;
［諳心］ able; self-possessed;

熟諳 familiar with; good at;

an
【盦】 (1) cover of a dish; lid of a caldron; (2) same as 庵, Buddhist cloister for nuns;

an
【鮟】 anglerfish;

an
【鵪】 quail;
［鵪鶉］ quail;
一群鵪鶉 a bevy of quails;

an³
an
【俺】 (1) I; (2) we;
［俺村］ my village;
［俺爹］ my father;
［俺家］ I;
［俺們］ we;

an
【埯】 hole to dibble seeds in;

斷埯 break the rows of drilled millet;

an
【揞】 apply medicinal powder to a wound;

an
【銨】 ammonium;

磷酸銨 ammonium phosphate;
硫酸銨 ammonium sulphate;
氯化銨 ammonium chloride;
鉬酸銨 ammonium molybdate;
氫氧化銨 ammonium hydroxide;
硝酸銨 ammonium nitrate;

an⁴
【犴】 (1) jail; prison; (2) a species of dog with black mouth and nose;

A

［犴獄］ prison;

an

【犴】 (1) jail; prison; (2) a species of dog with black mouth and nose;

［犴獄］ prison;

an

【岸】 (1) bank; beach; coast; shore; (2) majestic; (3) arrogant; haughty; proud;

［岸邊］ dockside; quayside;

［岸標］ shore beacon;

［岸冰］ ice that has formed along the banks of a river or lake;

［岸畔］ path by a river;

［岸炮］ coastal artillery;

［岸然］ gravely; impressive; in a solemn manner; solemn; solemn and dignified look;

道貌岸然 assume solemn airs; one's imposing bearing; pose as a person of high morals; sanctimonious; simulate solemnity;

［岸上］ bank; shore;

岸上存倉 storage ashore;
岸上代理人 shore bailee;
岸上點數 tally ashore;
岸上管理人 shoreside superintendent;
岸上交貨 landed terms;
岸上理貨 tally ashore;

凹岸 concave bank;
傲岸 arrogant; proud;
彼岸 the other shore; yonder shore;
濱岸 alongside the sea; coast;
泊岸 anchor alongside the river;
駁岸 bank revetment;
此岸 this shore;
堤岸 embankment;
陡岸 steep coast;
對岸 the other side of the river;
海岸 coast; seacoast; seashore;
河岸 river bank;
湖岸 lakeside;
護岸 bank protection;
江岸 river bank;
近岸 inshore; nearshore;
靠岸 draw alongside the shore; pull in shore;
口岸 port; seaport;
魁岸 stalwart; tall and muscular;
離岸 offshore;
兩岸 either side of a river; either side of a strait;
攏岸 draw alongside the shore;
起岸 bring cargo from a ship to land;
上岸 go ashore; land;
隄岸 dike; embankment; levee;
凸岸 convex bank;
偉岸 big and tall; stalwart; straight and tall; tall and robust;
崖岸 haughty;
涯岸 edge; limit;
岩岸 rocky coast;
沿岸 along the bank; along the coast;

an

【按】 (1) place the hand on; press down; press with one's hand; push down; (2) examine; look into; scrutinize; (3) lay by; leave aside; push aside; put aside; put away; repress; set aside; shelve; (4) contain; control; govern; keep under control; restrain; (5) keep a tight grip on; keep one's hand on; (6) according to; by; in accordance with; in conformity with; in correspondence to; in keeping with; in line with; in the light of; on the basis of; per; (7) comment; notation; note;

［按兵不動］ be on the alert, but make no move; bide one's time; halt the troops and wait; hold back; keep back army from battle; keep immobilized; keep quiet; keep the army quiet; keep the troops in readiness, but do not send them into action; keep troops entrenched; make no move; mark time; not to make any move until an opportunity occurs; not to throw the troops into battle; phony war; play a waiting game; remain quiet; sit and do nothing; take no action;

［按步就班］ act in accordance with the prescribed order; act step by step; careful to follow the prescribed way; creep before you walk; do not run before you can walk; follow conventional procedures; follow the prescribed order; in a rut; joy along; keep the rules; keep to conventional ways of doing things; keep to fixed ways of doing things; learn to creep before you leap; learn to say before you sing; move in a groove; of gradual nature; proceed in good order; run before you leap; run in a groove; take one step at a time; work strictly by protocol;

[按成] according to percentage; proportionately;

[按次] according to order; in due order; in sequence;
按次發言 speak in due order;

[按劍] grasp one's sword;

[按鍵] push a button;
按鍵電話機 push-button telephone;
按鍵式電話 touch-tone telephone;
按鍵式數據服務 touch-tone data service;

[按揭] charge; mortgage;
按揭貸款 mortgage loan;
按揭付款 mortgage payment;
按揭購房 buy an apartment on a mortgage;
按揭利率 mortgage interest rate;
按揭業務 house-mortgaging business;
首期按揭 down payment;
再按揭 remortgage;

[按酒] dishes to go with wine;

[按勞] according to one's labour;
按勞分配 distribute according to one's labour; distribute according to work done; to each according to his work;
按勞計酬 performance-related pay;

[按理] according to common practice; according to principle; according to reason; according to simple reasoning; as things should be; be supposed to; generally speaking; in reason; in the ordinary course of events; it stands to reason; normal; normally; ought to;
按理說 according to reason; by right; in the ordinary course of events; normally;

[按例] according to precedents; as a rule;

[按鈴] ring the bell;

[按脈] feel the pulse; take the pulse;

[按摩] (1) massage; (2) masseur;
按摩護理 massage therapy;
按摩機 massager;
~足部按摩機 massager;
按摩療法 massotherapy;
按摩女郎 massage girl; masseuse;
按摩器 massager;
按摩師 masseur;
按摩醫院 massage hospital;
按摩椅 massage chair;
按摩員 massager;
~女按摩員 masseuse;
按摩院 massage parlour;
按摩中心 massage centre;
保健按摩 keep-fit massage;
徹底的按摩 thorough massage;
反射性足底按摩 foot reflexology;
空氣按摩 pneumatic massage;
輕快的按摩 brisk massage;
全身按摩 body massage;
瑞典式按摩 Swedish massage;
泰式按摩 Thai massage;
香薰按摩 aromatherapy massage;
中式傳統按摩 traditional Chinese massage;
做按摩 give a massage;

[按捺] control; hold back; press down firmly; repress; restrain; withhold;
按捺不住 beside oneself; cannot contain oneself; cannot control oneself; unable to hold back; unable to repress;
~按捺不住激動的心情 unable to hold back one's excitement;

[按耐] control; restrain; suppress;

[按年] annually; by the year; yearly;

[按鈕] push-button; push the button;
按鈕開關 push-button switch;
按鈕控制 push-button control;
安全按鈕 chicken switch;
備用按鈕 emergency button;
閉塞按鈕 block button;
返回按鈕 return push-button;

[按期] according to schedule; according to the dates specified; on schedule; on time;
按期完成 finish on schedule;

[按日] daily; every day;

[按時] according to a fixed time; according to the scheduled time; according to the time specified; at the right time; duly; in due course; in due time; in good time; in time; on schedule; on scratch; on time; punctually;

[按數] according to the number; proportionately;

[按說] according to common practice; according to common sense; in the

ordinary course of events; normally; ordinarily;
[按討] investigate a rebellion and put it down; quell an uprising;
[按圖索驥] follow clues to locate sth; follow the trail; locate sth by a chart; look for a noble steed to correspond with the one drawn; search for sth with a key-drawing; select a horse according to a picture; try to locate sth by following up a clue;
[按蚊] malarial mosquito;
[按下不表] now let us turn to;
[按序] according to the order of sequence; in sequence;
[按壓] press;
[按驗] investigate the evidence of a case;
[按語] comment; note; postscript; remark;
編者按語 editor's note;
[按月] by the month; monthly;
按月包伙 board by the month;
按月付款 pay by the month;
[按照] according as; according to; after; agreeable to; agreeably to; along; as; at; be based on; be scheduled; by; by any measure; considering; follow; from; in; in accordance with; in compliance with; in conformity to; in conformity with; in line with; in proportion as; in proportion to; in pursuance of; in the light of; on; on its merits; on the basis of; on the principle of; pursuant to; the way; to; under;
[按診] pressing;
[按址] according to the address;
[按質論價] pricing by quality;
[按住] hold up; keep under control; press down and not let go; repress; restrain; withhold;
[按資排輩] promote in order of seniority; sole regard to seniority;

編者按 editor's note; editorial note;
巡按 governor of a province;

an

【案】 (1) desk; long table; narrow and long table; table; writing table; workbench; (2) according to; be based on; following this precedent; on the basis of; on the strength of; (3) case; case at law; law case; legal case; (4) file; legal record; record; (5) plan submitted for consideration; proposal; (6) press;
[案板] chopping block; chopping board; kneading board;
案板上的肉—任人宰割 at the mercy of others; meat on a chopping block — — can be butchered by others at will;
[案秤] counter scale;
[案底] record of previous offences;
有案底 with a record of previous offences;
[案牘] official correspondence; official document;
[案犯] case criminal; convicted criminal;
[案件] case; crime; law case; legal case;
案件檔案 casebook;
案件記錄 charge sheet;
破獲案件 break the case;
容易解決的案件 open-and-shut case;
重大案件 major incident;
[案結] conclusion of a legal case;
[案酒] dish to go with wine;
[案卷] archive; dossier; file; paper; record;
[案例] case; established case; example of case; precedent;
案例分析法 case-study method;
案例研究 case study;
~案例研究法 case method;
案例摘要 digest of a case;
[案目] usher in the theatre;
[案情] details of a case; facts of a case; ins and outs of a crime; record of a case;
案情大白 details of a case have come out;
案情複雜 the details of a case are complicated;
調查案情 investigate a case;
[案頭] desktop; on one's desk; on the desk; tabletop;
案頭調研 desk research;
案頭劇 closet drama; playscript for reading only;
[案文] text;
審核案文 examine a text;
協商案文 negotiate a text;
[案驗] investigate the evidence of a case;
[案由] brief; main points of a case; summary;

[案語] comment; note;
[案證] evidence of a case;
[案桌] long narrow table;
[案子] (1) case; crime; law case; (2) counter; long wooden table;

辦案 handle a case;
報案 report a case to the police;
備案 put on record;
病案 case history;
慘案 (1) massacre; (2) murder case;
草案 draft;
查案 investigate into a case;
存案 keep on record; record;
錯案 misjudged case;
答案 answer; key; solution;
檔案 archive; dossier; file; record;
盜案 burglary; case of robbery;
定案 final decision; pass a verdict; verdict;
斷案 (1) conclusion; (2) settle a lawsuit;
對案 counterproposal;
發案 arise; break;
法案 act; bill; proposed law;
翻案 reopen a case; reverse a verdict;
犯案 be found out after committing crime;
方案 plan; programme; proposal; scheme;
伏案 bend over one's desk;
個案 case;
公案 complicated legal case;
歸案 bring to justice;
几案 small table;
積案 long-pending case;
假案 feigned case; trumped-up case;
教案 teaching notes; teaching plan;
結案 settle a lawsuit; wind up a case;
舊案 (1) long-standing court case; (2) former practice;
決議案 draft resolution;
立案 (1) put on record; (2) place a case on file for investigation and prosecution;
了案 close a case; conclude a case;
民事案 civil case;
命案 homicide case;
拍案 strike the table;
破案 crack a criminal case;
搶案 case of robbery;
竊案 burglary; theft case;
審案 try a case;
書案 writing desk;
訟案 case a law; case in court;
提案 motion; proposal;
條案 long, narrow table;
鐵案 irrevocable case of fact;
同案 codefendant;
投案 give oneself up to the police;
圖案 design; pattern;
文案 clerical; desk;
問案 hold court; try a case;
誣告案 falsely charged case; frame-up;
無頭案 case without any clues;
香案 incense burner table;
銷案 close a legal case;
刑事案 criminal case;
兇殺案 murder case;
修正案 amendment;
懸案 (1) unsettled case; (2) outstanding issue; unsettled question;
血案 murder case;
疑案 disputed case; doubtful case; mystery;
議案 bill; motion; proposal;
冤案 wronged case;
援案 in accordance with a precedent; quote a precedent;
在案 on file; on police record; on record;
專案 special case for investigation;
罪案 case; criminal case; details of a criminal case;
作案 commit a crime; commit an offence;

an

【胺】 amine;
[胺化] amination;
胺化劑 aminating agent;
胺化氧 amine oxide;
[胺霉素] amidomycin;
[胺醛樹脂] amine aldehyde resin;
[胺酸] amino acid;
[胺鹽] amine salt;

苯胺 aniline;
醇胺 alcohol amine;
丁胺 butyl amine;
蒽胺 anthryl amine;
磺胺 sulphanilamide;
己胺 hexyl amine;
甲氧胺 methoxamine;
聚酰胺 polyamide;
聯苯胺 benzidine;
氰鈷胺 cyanocobalamin;
吐根胺 emetine;
乙胺 aminoethane; ethylamine;
乙酰胺 acetylamine;
組胺 histamine;
組織胺 histamine;

A

an

【菴】 luxuriant; plentiful; prosperous; rampant; teeming;

［菴藹］ luxuriant; plentiful; prosperous; rampant; teeming;

an

【暗】 (1) black; dark; darksome; dim; dull; obscure; pitchy; unilluminated; (2) back-door; clandestine; covert; furtive; hidden; secret; slinky; sly; sneaky; stealthy; surreptitious; under the table; underground; underhanded; (3) fuzzy; hazy; indefinite; indeterminate; indistinct; obscure; unclear; vague;

［暗暗］ (1) inwardly; secretly; to oneself; (2) night-dark; pitch-dark; very dark;

［暗白］ dirty white;

［暗伴星］ dark companion;

［暗堡］ bunker; foxhole; trench;

［暗埧］ submerged dam;

［暗補］ hidden subsidy; invisible subsidy;

［暗藏］ cloak; conceal; cover up; hidden; hide; keep under cover;

［暗查］ make a secret enquiry; investigate secretly;

［暗娼］ disguised prostitute; unlicensed prostitute; unregistered prostitute;

［暗潮］ (1) undercurrent; (2) secret contention; secret strife;

［暗沉沉］ (of sky) dark;

［暗處］ dark place; hidden place;

［暗袋］ film-changing bag;

［暗淡］ bleak; dim; dismal; drab; dull; gloomy; obscure;

暗淡的光 pale light;

~發出暗淡的光 spread a pale light;

~投下暗淡的光 cast a pale light;

暗淡無光 in dim and dreary colours;

陰沉暗淡 gloomy and sullen;

［暗道］ secret passage;

［暗敵］ snake in the grass;

［暗地裏］ (1) in a secret place; (2) behind closed doors; behind sb's back; behind the scenes; clandestine; covertly; in secret; inwardly; on the quiet; on the sly; privately; secret; secretly; silently; stealthily; surreptitiously; underhand;

［暗鬥］ secret strife; secret struggle; veiled strife;

［暗渡陳倉］ act before another is aware; adultery; advance secretly along by an unknown path; do one thing under cover of another; do sth in secret; have illicit sexual relations with; hold in play; illicit affairs; pretend to prepare to advance along one path while secretly going along another; secret and illegal relations between sweethearts; secret rendezvous between lovers; steal a march on;

陳倉暗渡 do one thing under cover of another; have secret relations with one's sweetheart;

明修棧道，暗度陳倉 do one thing under cover of another; do sth behind the facade of; feign action in one place and make the real move in another; pretend to advance along one path while secretly going along another;

［暗法］ secret ways;

［暗房］ darkroom;

［暗訪］ investigate in secret; make a secret enquiry; pursue a secret investigation;

明察暗訪 observe publicly and investigate privately;

［暗諷］ allusive; implicative; insinuate; ironic;

［暗溝］ concealed drain; covered sewerage; sewer; underground drain tunnel;

［暗害］ assassinate; do secret injury to; frame up; injure secretly; kill secretly; murder; plot murder; stab in the back;

暗害人命 kill others clandestinely;

［暗含］ hint; imply; insinuate; suggest;

［暗涵］ hidden drainpipe;

［暗號］ cipher; countersign; password; secret mark; secret sign; secret signal; signal;

聯絡暗號 contact signal;

［暗合］ agree without prior consultation; coincidence in word or thought; happen to coincide; unintentional meeting of minds;

［暗河］ underground river;

一道暗河 an underground river;

［暗盒］ cartridge;

［暗黑］ deep black;

［暗紅］ dark red;

暗紅熱 dark red heat;

暗紅色 garnet;

[暗花] veiled design incised in porcelain;

[暗話] (1) code word; (2) comments made behind sb's back;

明人不説暗話 those who are open and above-board will not speak ill of people behind their back;

[暗火] (1) dying fire; smouldering fire; (2) hidden gunfire;

[暗疾] a disease one is ashamed of; unmentionable disease;

[暗計] (1) calculate in one's heart; (2) artful dodge; conspiracy; secret design; secret plot; trick;

[暗記] (1) secret mark; take note by writing in secret; (2) bear in mind; commit to memory; get by heart; learn by heart; memorize;

[暗間] inner room;

[暗箭] stab in the back; underhanded attack;

暗箭難防 a covert attack is hard to avoid; an arrow shot from hiding — a stab in the back; an unseen arrow is hard to guard against; hidden arrows are difficult to guard against; it is difficult to guard against the secret arrow; it is not easy to avoid a secret arrow;

暗箭傷人 a stab in the back; calumniate sb behind his back; hit sb below the belt; injure sb by underhand means; make a sniping attack; mill in the darkness; slander others behind their backs; stab sb in the back; wound sb with a sniping arrow; wound with a secret arrow;

放暗箭 attack by underhand means; attack sb with unfriendly remarks behind his back; snipe at sb; stab sb in the back;

謹防暗箭 guard against a hidden arrow;

明槍暗箭 an open attack or a stab in the back; an open spear thrust and an arrow in the dark; attack by overt and covert means; fight openly and snipe in the dark; open measures and covert tricks; spear thrusts in to open and arrows shot from hiding;

~明槍易躲，暗箭難防 better an open enemy than a false friend; God defend me from my friends; from my enemies I can defend myself; it is easy to repel an open attack, but difficult to defend oneself against a covert attack;

[暗礁] (1) hidden reef; hidden rock; hidden stone; submerged reef; (2) hidden danger; hidden obstacle; latent obstacle; unseen obstacle;

[暗接] secret joint;

[暗井] (1) utility hole; (2) camouflaged pit; (3) blind shaft;

[暗裏] in one's heart; inwardly; secretly;

[暗戀] love secretly;

暗戀者 secret admirer;

[暗流] (1) undercurrent; (2) undercurrent of evil social trends or ideological tendencies;

一股暗流 an undercurrent;

[暗綠] dark green;

[暗碼] secret code; secret figure; secret sign;

暗碼售貨 sell goods without price tags;

暗碼鎖 combination lock;

~裝暗碼鎖 fit a combination lock;

[暗昧] (1) clandestine; covert; stealthy; surreptitious; undercover; (2) obscure; undiscerning; unintelligible; (3) headless; ignorant; stupid; unintelligent; unreasoning;

暗昧無知 stupid and ignorant;

[暗門子] unlicensed prostitute;

[暗訥] quietly think over;

[暗盤] under-the-counter price or terms;

暗盤出賣 resale through illegal channels;

[暗泣] weep behind others' backs; weep without uttering sound;

[暗器] hidden weapon;

暗器傷人 kill sb with a hidden weapon;

身懷暗器 with arms concealed under one's clothes;

[暗槍] snipper's shot;

[暗渠] underground channel;

[暗弱] dense; stupid;

燈光暗弱 dim light;

為人暗弱 stupid and weak-willed;

[暗色] cold colours; dark colours; deep colours;

[暗殺] assassinate; assassination; waylay and kill;

暗殺隊 hit squad;

暗殺企圖 assassination attempt;

暗殺陰謀 assassination plot;

A

暗殺者 assassin;

[暗傷] (1) internal injury; invisible injury; (2) indiscernible damage; internal damage;
受暗傷 suffer from an invisible injury;

[暗哨] (1) hidden post; (2) whistle as a secret signal;
放暗哨 post a secret sentry;

[暗射] allude to; hint; hint obliquely at; insinuate; make an allusion to; throw out a hint;
暗射地圖 outline map;

[暗石] hidden rock;

[暗示] allude to; drop a hint of; drop a hint to; drop sb a hint; fall a hint of; give a hint of; give a hint to; give sb a hint; give sb an inkling of; give sb the clue; give sb to know; give sb to understand; hint; hint about; hint at; hint of; hint to sb; implicit; imply; insinuate; intimate sth; intimate to sb; let a hint of; overtone; put a bug in sb's ear; put a flea in sb's ear; suggest; suggestive of;
充滿暗示 full of suggestions;
傳遞暗示 convey a hint;
得到暗示 get hints from;
發出暗示 throw out hints;
給人暗示 drop a hint; give a hint;
公開地暗示 hint openly;
禮貌地暗示 hint politely;
清楚地暗示 hint broadly;
稍稍地暗示 hint gently;
提供暗示 furnish a hint;
小聲暗示 breathe a hint;
隱晦地暗示 hint darkly;
隱約地暗示 hint vaguely;

[暗事] clandestine action; illicit conduct; secret plot; underhand affair;
明人不做暗事 a gentleman never does anything underhand;

[暗室] dark house; darkroom;
暗室燈 darkroom lamp;
暗室濾光器 darkroom filter;

[暗算] attack by treachery; plot; plot against; plot in secret; secret plot; secretly plot against; treachery;
暗算人 plot against sb; scheme against sb;
遭人暗算 fall a prey to sb's plot;

[暗鎖] built-in lock;

[暗灘] hidden shoal;

[暗探] detective; enquire secretly; person who enquires secretly; secret agent; spy;
暗探軍情 spy on military disposition;

[暗喜] feel secretly delighted; feel secretly happy;
心中暗喜 be secretly pleased; rejoice in one's heart; secretly feel pleased;

[暗下] secretly;

[暗線] foreshadowing;
暗線光譜 dark-line spectrum;

[暗香疏影] secret fragrance and dappled shadows;

[暗箱] (1) anything shaped like a box; (2) box; case; trunk; (3) camera obscura;

[暗想] foster an idea; muse; nurse an idea; nurture an idea; ponder; secret thoughts; think in secret; turn over in one's mind;

[暗笑] chuckle; laugh behind sb's back; laugh in one's heart; laugh in one's sleeve; laugh up one's sleeve; snicker; snigger;

[暗星] dark star;
暗星雲 dark nebula;

[暗夜] dark night;

[暗影] (1) image; shadow; (2) umbra;

[暗語] (1) code word; (2) argot;
傳遞暗語 pass on the code word;

[暗喻] concealed analogy; metaphor;

[暗約] secret treaty;

[暗指] give a hint unknown to others; hint; imply; innuendo; insinuate;

[暗中] (1) in darkness; in the dark; (2) behind someone's back; clandestinely; hidden secretly; in secret; on the sly; privately; surreptitiously;

[暗自] inwardly; secretly; to oneself;

黑暗 (1) dark; dim; (2) reactionary;
灰暗 gloomy; murky gray;
晦暗 dark and gloomy;
昏暗 dim; dusky;
明暗 light and shade;
陰暗 dark; gloomy; overcast;
幽暗 dim; gloomy;

an

【闇】 (1) shut the door; (2) retire; retreat; (3) dark; lightless; obscure; pitchy; unlighted; (4) evening; fall of day; night; (5) lunar eclipse; (6) ignorant

and foolish; stupid and dull;
［闇闇］ dark and obscure;
［闇練］ familiar with; proficient in;
［闇劣］ stupid and incompetent;
［闇昧］ (1) ignorant and stupid; (2) clandestine dealings;
［闇暝］ evening; getting dark;
［闇淺］ shallow, ignorant and stupid;
［闇然］ concealed; hidden; murky; obscure;
［闇弱］ benighted; ignorant, stupid and cowardly; irresolute;
稟性闇弱 naturally weak;
［闇室］ dark room;
［闇誦］ commit to memory; recite in silence;

庸闇 ignorant; stupidity;
悠闇 far and dim;

an
【黯】 (1) black; dark; dim; pitch-dark; (2) dismal; gloomy; lamentable; miserable;
［黯黯］ gloomy; sad; sombre;
［黯慘］ dismal; gloomy;
［黯淡］ dim; dismal; dull; gloomy;
黯淡無光 dismal; gloomy; sombre;
［黯黑］ (1) dark; (2) dim;
［黯然］ (1) dim; faint; gloomy; (2) dejected; depressed; downcast; low-spirited; sad;

深黯 dark; dark and obscure;

ang¹
ang
【腌】 dirty; filthy; foul; unclean;
［腌臢］ dirty; filthy; foul; good-for-nothing; greasy; unclean;
腌臢貨 filthy person; lousy fellow; vicious fellow;
腌臢潑才 dirty fellow; filthy rascal;

ang
【骯】 dirty; filthy; foul;
［骯髒］ dirty; filthy; foul; sordid; skanky; squalid;
骯髒話 dirty words;
骯髒錢 lucre;
骯裏骯髒 filthy, dirty, and foul;

ang²
ang
【昂】 (1) hold one's head high; raise; (2) high; soaring; (3) costly; dear; exorbitant; expensive; high-priced;
［昂昂］ brave-looking; high-spirited; in high spirits;
昂昂然 high-spirited;
昂昂自若 look exalted and composed;
氣昂昂 valiant and spirited;
［昂藏］ tall and imposing;
昂藏七尺之軀 manly man; tall strapping man;
［昂奮］ buoyant; earnest; enthusiastic; excited; fervent; full of zest; in high spirits; zealous;
［昂貴］ costly; dear; exorbitant; expensive; high-priced;
昂貴的 big ticket;
昂貴無用之物 white elephant;
［昂然］ haughtily; proud and bold; upright and fearless; upright and unafraid;
昂然而入 come in walking proudly; come walking in proudly; enter in a stately manner; step grandly into;
［昂首］ hold up one's head; raise one's head high;
昂首闊步 galumph; keep one's head high and march ahead; march forward with one's head high; prance about; step along in high spirits; stride along with one's chin up; stride forward proudly; stride forward with head held high; stride forward with one's chin up; stride proudly ahead; walk in a proud, self-important manner;
昂首挺立 stand firm with raised head; stand proudly, head erect;
昂首挺胸 chin up and chest up; fling back one's head; fling hold up one's head and throw out one's chest;
昂首望天 hold one's head high and gaze at the sky;
昂首直衝 scurry along with one's head held high;
［昂揚］ high-spirited; rise; soar;
昂揚歡快 spirited and joyous;
激越昂揚 inspired and spirited;
士氣昂揚 have high morale;

高昂 (1) high; (2) expensive;
激昂 excited and indignant; roused;
軒昂 dignified; full of vigour; imposing;

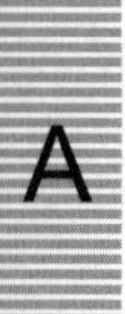

ang⁴
ang

【盎】 (1) basin; bowl; pot; (2) flourishing; full of life; in full swing; prospering; thriving; vigorous; (3) a surname;

[盎盎] abundant; ample; copious; full; plentiful;

[盎然] abundant; alive; exuberant; full; overflowing; rich;
春意盎然 spring is very much in the air;
情趣盎然 brimming with interest in nature;
趣味盎然 appealing; full of interest;
生機盎然 brimming over with vitality;
生氣盎然 full of vigour;
詩意盎然 rich in poetic flavour;
興趣盎然 burning with enthusiasm; unflagging interest;
興致盎然 full of zest;

[盎司] ounce;

ao¹
ao

【凹】 (1) concave; dented; hollow; sunken; (2) cave in; dent; sink;

[凹岸] concave bank; cutbank;

[凹板] concave;
閉式凹板 closed type concave;
槽桿式凹板 channel bar concave;
釘齒式凹板 spike-tooth concave;
復脱器凹板 rethresher concave;
柵格式凹板 grate-type concave; lattice-type concave;

[凹版] gravure; intaglio;
凹版印刷 intaglio printing;
凹版照相 heliogravure;
凹版製版 gravure plate-making;

[凹背] swayback;

[凹地] concave ground; hollow; pit;
雪蝕凹地 nivation hollow;

[凹度] concavity;

[凹痕] dent;
刻凹痕 cut a notch;
有凹痕 have a depression;

[凹進] concave; depressed; hollow; indented;

[凹鏡] concave mirror;

[凹臉蝠] hollow-faced bat; slit-faced bat;

[凹面] concavity; hollow side;
凹面鏡 concave mirror;

[凹室] alcove; cubicle;

[凹透鏡] concave lens; concave mirror;

[凹凸] concave-convex;
凹凸版 an intaglio and relief printing plate;
凹凸不平 bumpy; full of bumps and holes; full of lumps; lumpy; scraggy; uneven;
~凹凸不平的地形 accidented topography;
凹凸透鏡 meniscus; meniscus lens;
~發散凹凸透鏡 divergent meniscus;
~校正凹凸透鏡 correction meniscus;
~球面凹凸透鏡 spherical meniscus;
凹凸軋花 embossing;
凹凸印 embossing;
凹凸印刷 die stamping; embossing;

[凹紋] intaglio design;

[凹陷] (1) depressed; hollow; sunken; (2) cave in; sink;
凹陷骨折 depressed fracture;
地面凹陷 the ground caves in;
地形凹陷 the ground caves in;
面頰凹陷 have hollow cheeks; have sunken cheeks; hollow cheeks; sunken cheeks;
雙眼凹陷 have sunken eyes;
眼眶凹陷 sunken eyes;

[凹穴] hollow;
條盒凹穴 barrel hollow;

[凹眼] (1) sunken eyes; (2) celophthalmia;

耳凹 ear pit;
雙凹 double concave;
撞凹 be dented;

ao²
ao

【敖】 (1) ramble; roam; saunter; stroll; (2) idle; leisurely; (3) a surname;

[敖敖] long; tall;

[敖包] cairn;

[敖盪] fritter away one's time; idle away one's time; kill time; loaf about; while away the hours;

[敖民] idler; lazybones; loafer; lounger; time-waster;

[敖戲] frolic; make merry; play; rollick; romp;

[敖遊] travel idly; wander idly;

ao

【廒】 granary;

倉厫 barn; granary; storehouse;

ao

【嗷】 cry of hunger;

［嗷嗷］ animal cry; human cry; scream with fright;

嗷嗷待哺 cry piteously for food; cry with hunger; wait to be fed with cries of hunger;

［嗷叫］ cry; scream; sing out; squeal; yell;

ao

【熬】 (1) extract by applying heat; (2) boil; cook; cook in water; decoct; seethe; simmer; stew; (3) be worn down by worries; bear; brave; dejected; despondent; endure; go through; hold out; pull through; stand; stick it out; suffer with patience; sustain; take it;

［熬菜］ cook food in water;

［熬出來］ have gone through all sorts of ordeal;

［熬過］ endure;

熬不過 cannot survive a grave illness; unable to endure;

［熬煎］ suffer through unhappy days; suffering; torture;

［熬練］ boil and smelt—strict discipline;

［熬磨］ bear; brave; endure; go through; hold out; pull through; stand; stick it out; suffer; suffer with patience; sustain; take it;

熬磨時間 find time dragging;

［熬惱］ unhappy and dejected;

［熬湯］ stew meat for broth;

［熬頭］ reward for long hardship; reward for long patience;

熬出頭來 bring an end to one's suffering;

［熬心］ angry; annoying; cross; irritated; nettled; unhappy; vexed;

［熬藥］ decoct medicinal herbs;

［熬夜］ burn the midnight oil; far into the night; keep up; sit up; sit up deep into the night; sit up far into the night; sit up late at night; stay up; stay up all night; stay up late; stop up; up for; wait up; work late into the night; work until deep into the night;

熬夜讀書 stay up reading;

［熬油］ (1) waste lamp oil by staying up at night; (2) extract oil by heating;

［熬粥］ cook congee;

大鍋熬 cook everything in a pot;

煎熬 suffering; torment; torture;

用文火熬 simmer;

ao

【獒】 large fierce dog; mastiff;

ao

【璈】 ancient musical instrument;

ao

【遨】 ramble; roam; saunter, stroll; travel for pleasure; wander;

［遨嬉］ make merry; play; ramble; travel for pleasure;

［遨遊］ ramble; roam; travel;

ao

【翱】 (1) fly; soar; take wind; (2) roam; wander;

［翱翔］ fly about; hover; soar; take wing; wheel in the air;

翱翔機 sail plane; soaring glider;

動力翱翔 dynamic soaring;

向高空翱翔 soar high into the air;

在高空翱翔 hover high;

在空中翱翔 fly freely in the sky;

ao

【聱】 (1) hard to read or understand; (2) perverse; troublesome; unreasonable; unruly; (3) lying and winding;

［聱牙］ hard to read;

ao

【螯】 chela; nippers; pincers;

［螯合］ chelate;

螯合滴定法 chelatometry; chelometry;

螯合劑 chelator; chelon;

螯合物 chelate;

～鈈螯合物 plutonium chelate;

～聚合物螯合物 polymeric chelates;

～六配位體螯合物 sexadentate chelate;

～四配位體螯合物 quadridentate chelate;

～有機螯合物 organic chelate;

螯合作用 chelation;

～生態螯合作用 ecology chelation;

［螯角］ chelicera;

［螯酶素］ chelocardin;

［螯蝎］ chelifer;

［螯足］ cheliped;

A

ao

【謷】 (1) abuse; castigate; defame; revile; slander; smear; (2) big; giant; gigantic; huge; large; massive and great;

［謷謷］ (1) abusive; calumnious; defamatory; libellous; malicious; slanderous; (2) sound of a mourning crowd;

［謷醜］ abuse; defame; slander;

ao

【鏖】 engage in fierce battle; fight hard;

［鏖兵］ engage in fierce battle; engage in hard fighting; fight a bloody battle; fight hard;

［鏖戰］ fight a pitched battle; fight hard;
徹夜鏖戰 battle fiercely all night;

ao

【鏊】 a kind of round, flat cooking plate for cakes;

［鏊子］ griddle;

ao

【鰲】 huge legendary turtle; legendary sea-tortoise;

［鰲頭］ championship; first place;
鰲頭獨佔 champion; come out at the top; come out first; come out top; head of the list of successful candidates; perch alone on the whale's head;
獨佔鰲頭 champion; come out at the top; come out first; come out top; head of the list of successful candidates; perch alone on the whale's head;
佔鰲頭 come out first; tower above the rest;

ao

【鼇】 huge sea turtle, said to support the earth;

［鼇背負山］ my indebtedness to you is as great as the load of a mountain to a turtle;

［鼇戴］ feel indebted;

ao³

ao

【抝】 bend sth so as to break it; twist sth to break it;

［抝折］ break by twisting;

ao

【媪】 (1) old woman; (2) general term for older women; (3) goddess of the earth;

［媪娘］ old maid;

［媪婆］ female examiner of corpses;

［媪神］ goddess of the earth;

乳媪 wet nurse;
翁媪 old man and woman;

ao

【襖】 Chinese-style jacket; coat; cotton-padded jacket; jacket;

花襖 flowery coat;
夾襖 lined jacket;
棉襖 cotton-padded jacket;
皮襖 fur-lined jacket;
袷襖 lined jacket;
襦襖 short jacket;

ao⁴

ao

【坳】 cavity; col; depression in a mountain range; hollow in the ground;

［坳口］ flat land between mountains;

［坳堂］ hollow in the ground;

［坳塘］ small pond;

山坳 col;

ao

【拗】 (1) break off; pluck; snap; twist; (2) obstinate; recalcitrant; stubborn; unmanageable; (3) awkward-sounding; hard to pronounce;

［拗不過］ fail to talk sb out of doing sth; unable to dissuade;

［拗斷］ break into two; break off; snap;

［拗花］ cull flowers;
拗花枝 pluck a flowery branch;

［拗口］ awkward-sounding; hard to pronounce; tongue-twisting; twist the tongue;
拗口令 tongue twister;
發音拗口 very hard to pronounce;

［拗怒］ suppress anger;

［拗強］ obstinate; pigheaded; recalcitrant;

［拗碎］ break in pieces;

［拗彎］ twist;

［拗陷］ depression;

［拗性］ obstinacy; recalcitrance; stubbornness;

違拗 defy; disobey;
執拗 pigheaded; recalcitrant; stubborn; wilful;

ao

【敖】 (1) haughty; proud; (2) make fun of;

[敖敖] (1) long; tall; (2) smear someone's reputation;

[敖慢] haughty; overbearing; proud;

[敖弄] make fun of; poke fun at;

ao

【傲】 (1) arrogant; conceited; haughty; overbearing; proud; (2) brave; refuse to yield to; (3) despise; disdain; look down on; (4) rash and impatient;

[傲岸] haughty; proud; proud and aloof;

傲岸不群 proud and aloof;

傲岸平生 maintain one's pride and dignity throughout one's life;

[傲骨] lofty and unyielding character; self-esteem; spirit of loftiness;

傲骨天生 gifted bone of haughtiness;

[傲慢] arrogant; haughty and overbearing; hauteur; hoity-toity; hubris; impudent; insolent;

傲慢的 uppity;

傲慢無禮 arrogant and insolent; insolate and rude;

傲慢自大 arrogant and disdainful; overweening;

傲慢自得 haughty and complacent;

表情傲慢 look arrogant;

對人傲慢 arrogant to sb;

輕視傲慢 (1) contempt and pride; (2) despise and be haughty;

生性傲慢 immodest personality; imperious by nature;

態度傲慢 adopt an arrogant attitude; put on airs;

~ 對下級態度傲慢 be bumptious over one's inferiors;

性格傲慢 of haughty nature;

樣子傲慢 have a lofty appearance;

[傲睨] air of arrogant; look down on; turn one's nose at;

傲睨群雄 look down on other men of valour;

傲睨自若 look immensely proud and complacent; look supercilious;

[傲氣] air of arrogance; conceit; haughtiness;

傲氣鬼 whippersnapper;

傲氣凌人 humiliate sb with one's haughty airs;

傲氣十足 extremely haughty; full of arrogance;

殺一殺傲氣 take sb down a buttonhole lower; take the frills out of sb;

一股傲氣 arrogance;

[傲然] iron-willed and unyielding; loftily; proud; unyieldingly;

傲然挺立 stand proudly erect;

傲然屹立 like a stone wall; rise majestically; stand firmly and proudly; stand rock-firm and towering; stand unshakably; tower proudly into the skies;

傲然自大 big with pride;

[傲世] lofty-minded; look down on the world;

[傲視] despise; regard superciliously; scorn; show disdain for; treat with disdain; turn up one's nose at;

傲視權勢 hold power and authority in disdain;

傲視一切 despise everybody and everything;

[傲物] haughty; insolent; overbearing; rude;

恃才傲物 act in undue confidence of one's ability and look down upon others; arrogant because of one's ability; conceited and contemptuous; inordinately proud of one's ability; proud and insolent because of one's talent; self-conceited and insolent on account of one's ability;

[傲性] proud temperament;

高傲 arrogant; haughty; insolent; stiff-backed; supercilious;

孤傲 proud and aloof;

驕傲 arrogant; conceited; proud; uppish;

兀傲 haughty; supercilious;

瀟傲 leisurely and carefree;

嘯傲 talk and behave in a carefree manner;

自傲 arrogant; self-conceited;

ao

【奧】 (1) abstruse; difficult to understand; hard to understand; mysterious; obscure; profound; (2) secret cabin; (3) Austria;

[奧博] (1) extensive in meaning; profound; (2) wealthy; (3) widely read;

文辭奧博 abstruse in language;

蘊意奧博 profound in implication;

[奧秘] mystery; profound mystery; secret;

subtle;
奧秘莫測 be veiled in mystery;
解開奧秘 solve a mystery;
解釋奧秘 elucidate a mystery;
探索奧秘 probe into a mystery;

[奧妙] abstruse and subtle; marvellous; mysterious; mystic; profound; secret; secret power; subtle; what is behind it;
奧妙精深 profound and abstruse;
奧妙無窮 extremely subtle;
極其奧妙 marvellous to the utmost degree;

[奧甜] sweet and luscious;

[奧衍] deep; profound;

[奧義] profound meaning; subtle meaning;
深文奧義 abstruse; hard to understand;

[奧援] ally; moral or material support;
結成奧援 form an alliance;

[奧旨] main theme;
奧旨難明 the hidden meaning is hardly understandable;
採摭奧旨 glean the essence of sth;

古奧 archaic and abstruse;
深奧 abstruse; profound; unfathomable;
樞奧 confidential affairs; confidential information;
潭奧 deep; profound;
堂奧 (1) the innermost recess of a hall; (2) hinterland; (3) profundity of thought;
玄奧 (1) abstruse and subtle; difficult to comprehend; (2) mysteries; profundities;

ao

【懊】 (1) regret; regretful; remorseful; (2) angry; annoyed; vexed;

[懊恨] resentful;
懊恨不已 know no end of regret;

[懊悔] feel remorse; regret; regretful; repent; reproach oneself; upset;
一絲懊悔 a slight twinge of remorse;
一陣懊悔 a fit of remorse;

[懊悶] eat one's heart out; pine away;

[懊憹] annoyed; dejected; displeased; dissatisfied;

[懊惱] be chagrined; chagrin; feel annoyed; feel remorseful and angry; upset; vexed;
懊惱萬分 much to one's chagrin;
感到懊惱 be chagrined; be vexed at;

[懊喪] dejected; depressed; despondent; sorrowfully;
變得懊喪 fall in despondency;
非常懊喪 in great dejection;
面露懊喪 show one's dejection;
心情懊喪 in a state of depression;

[懊糟] upset; vexed;

ao

【澳】 bay; deep waters; inlet of the sea;

ao

【燠】 sweltering; very hot;

[燠熱] very hot;

ao

【隩】 (1) bend of a stream; cove; (2) warm; (3) inhabitable land;

ao

【驁】 (1) fine horse; (2) untamed horse; (3) arrogant; conceited; haughty; look down one's nose at; overbearing; proud; turn up one's nose at;

[驁放] very haughty and unrestrained;

ba¹
ba

【八】 eight;

[八百] eight hundred;
八百錢掉在井裏—難摸哪一吊 eight hundred coins falling into a well – hard to get hold of any particular string; have a hard time understanding what sb is talking about or wants;

[八寶] eight treasures;
八寶菜 assorted soy sauce pickles;
八寶飯 eight-treasure rice pudding;
~八寶飯摻漿糊—糊塗到一塊兒了 eight-treasure steamed rice pudding mixed with paste – all muddled up together;
八寶箱 treasure chest;

[八倍] octuple; eight times; eightfold;
八倍體 octoploid;

[八邊形] octagon;

[八成] (1) eighty per cent; (2) most likely; most probably; very likely;
八成熟 not quite well done;
八成新 practically new;

[八重] eightfold;
八重唱 octet;
八重奏 octet;

[八達通] octopus card;

[八帶魚] octopus;

[八斗] exceptional ability;
八斗之才 gifted person; person of great talent; person of many gifts; person with exceptional ability; talent of talents;
才儲八斗 exceedingly talented;

[八度] octave;
八度笛 octave flute;

[八段錦] eight trigram boxing;

[八方] all directions; all quarters; eight points of the compass;
八方呼應 act in co-operation; respond from all sides; seek response far and wide; take concerted action;
八方受困 be hard pressed from all sides; in a difficult position; in trouble;
八方響應 enthusiastic response from all quarters;
八方支援 aid comes from everywhere; help comes from all quarters;
八方桌 octagonal table;
耳聽八方 extraordinarily alert;

[八分儀] octant;

[八哥兒] myna; mynah; mynah bird;
八哥兒學舌—裝人腔 a myna learning to speak – pretend to sound human;
八哥兒啄柿子—挑軟的欺 a myna pecks only soft persimmons – pick the soft one; bully the weak; one only bullies the weak;

[八股] eight-legged essay; eight-part essay;
洋八股 foreign stereotyped writing;

[八卦] (1) the Eight Diagrams; (2) meddlesome
八卦教 Eight Trigram Society;
八卦婆 meddlesome woman;
八卦掌 eight-trigram boxing;
八卦陣 eight-trigram battle array;
鬼八卦 wicked idea;

[八行] eight-lined;
八行詩 octave;
八行書 eight-line letter;
八行紙 letter paper with eight vertical lines;

[八荒] outlying areas on all sides;

[八級] eighth-grade;
八級風 force eight wind; fresh gale;
八級工 eighth-grade worker; top-grade worker;
~八級工拜師父—精益求精 a top-grade worker taking a teacher – keep improving;
~八級工資制 eight-grade wage scale;

[八極管] octode;

[八角] (1) Chinese aniseed; star aniseed; (2) aniseed; (3) octagonal;
八角楓 alangium;
八角鼓 octagonal drum;
八角帽 octagonal hat;
八角亭 octagonal pavilion;
八角形 octagon; octagonal;

[八節] eight solar terms;

[八進] octal; octonary;
八進法 octonary scale;
八進制 octal system;

[八開] octavo;
八開本 octavo;

[八面] (1) octa-; (2) all sides; (3) eight sides;
八面鋒 (1) smooth and slick; (2) incisive; sharp;
八面光 smooth and slick all around; worldly wise;
八面體 octahedron;
~正八面體 regular octahedron;

[八旗] Eight Banners;
八旗制度 Banners System;
[八十] eighty;
八十歲學吹打 an old dog learning new tricks; learn to pie and drum at the age of eighty; never too old to learn;
[八仙] the Eight Immortals;
八仙過海一各顯神通 like the Eight Immortals crossing the sea, each one display his ability; try to outshine each other; vie with each other;
八仙桌 square table for eight people;
[八弦琴] octachord;
[八言] poem of eight-character lines;
[八佾] eight rows of pantomimes;
[八音] every sound of music;
八音盒 music box;
[八月] (1) August; (2) eighth month of the lunar calendar;
八月的荷花——時鮮 a lotus flower in the eighth month – fleeting beauty;
八月的棉花一越老越紅 cotton seeds in the eighth month – the older, the redder; one gets more progressively minded as one gets older;
八月節 Mid-autumn Festival;
八月十五的月餅——盆子來一盆子去 moon-cakes at the Mid-Autumn Festival – one plateful being brought in and one being taken away; things come and go;
[八折] twenty per cent discount;
[八珍] eight delicacies;
八珍蛇羹 snake potage with eight delicacies;
[八柱式] octastyle;
八柱式建築物 octastylos;
八柱式門廊 octastyle;
[八爪魚] octopus;
[八字] (1) character "eight"; (2) Eight Character (fortune telling); (3) horoscope;
八字還沒一撇 nothing has been done so far; nothing is definite yet; there is not the slightest sign of success yet; there is not the slightest sign yet;
八字鬍 moustache;
八字腳 splay-foot;
八字眉 slanted eyebrows; splay-eyebrow;
八字形拱 splayed arch;
問八字 consult a fortune teller;

二八 sixteen years of age;
臘八 eighth day of the twelfth lunar month;
七八 seven or eight;
丘八 soldier;
十八 eighteen;
王八 (1) tortoise; turtle; (2) cuckold; (3) person who works in a brothel;
望八 expect the eightieth birthday very soon;

ba

【巴】 (1) hope earnestly; wait anxiously for; (2) cling to; stick to; (3) climb physically and socially; (4) close to; next to; (5) bar; (6) a surname;
[巴巴] (1) anxiously; (2) especially; (3) slapping sound;
巴巴結結 speak haltingly;
乾巴巴 dry as dust; dull and dry; insipid;
急巴巴 in too much of a hurry;
急急巴巴 anxious; impatient;
緊巴巴 (1) rather tight; tight; (2) hard up; short of money; straitened;
可憐巴巴 very piteous;
老實巴巴 honest;
眼巴巴 (1) with steady gaze; (2) anxiously; eagerly; expectantly; (3) helplessly;
[巴答] sound of a slap;
巴答一聲 slapping sound;
[巴豆] croton;
巴豆霜 defatted croton seed powder;
巴豆中毒 croton oil poisoning;
[巴兒狗] (1) lapdog; (2) Pekingese; (3) flatterer; sycophant; toady;
[巴高望上] have the ambition to rise in society; seek advancement; strive to raise one's social status; want to rise in the world and become a person of importance;
[巴高枝兒] (1) play up to people of power and influence; (2) marry above one's station;
[巴結] be all over sb; bootlick; brown-nose; buddy up; butter up sb; cotton up to; cozy up to; curry favour with sb; fawn on; flatter; get in with sb; lay on the butter; lay the butter on; lick sb's boots; lick sb's shoes; make up to; play up to;

polish the apple; soak sb down; stand in with sb; suck up to; toady to sb; try hard to please;
[巴山] mountains in Sichuan;
巴山蜀水 mountains and rivers of Sichuan and Chongqing;
巴山夜雨 hope of reunion among friends;
[巴士] bus;
巴士服務 bus services;
~穿梭巴士服務 shuttle bus services;
巴士站 bus stop;
穿梭巴士 shuttle bus;
觀光巴士 tour bus;
~敞篷觀光巴士 open-topped bus;
空中巴士 aerobus;
[巴蜀] another name for the Sichuan Province;
巴蜀文化 the culture of Sichuan;
[巴松管] bassoon;
[巴望] await anxiously; be eager to; expect; hope anxiously for; look forward to;
巴望高昇 seek promotion;
有巴望 sth to look forward to;
[巴西] brazil;
巴西果 brazil;
巴西粟 brazil;
[巴想] await anxiously; hope anxiously;
[巴掌] (1) palm of the hand; (2) slap;
拍巴掌 clap one's hands;
撒巴掌 let go; let go one's hold;
一巴掌 slap;
~挨一巴掌 get a slap;
~打一巴掌 give sb a slap;

阿米巴 amoeba;
大巴 coach; large bus;
淡巴巴 insipid; tasteless;
嘎巴 crack;
乾巴 dry up; shrivel; wither;
鍋巴 rice crust;
毫巴 millibar;
急巴巴 impatient;
結巴 (1) stammer; stumble; stutter; (2) stammerer; stutterer;
緊巴巴 (1) taut; tight; (2) hard up;
磕巴 stammer; stutter;
淋巴 lymph;
倫巴 rumba;
泥巴 mire; mud;
蕎巴 buckwheat cake;
揉巴 crumple; knead; rub;
瘦巴 lean; skinny;
望巴巴 anxious; apprehensive;
微巴 microbar;
尾巴 tail;
下巴 (1) lower jaw; (2) chin;
小巴 minibus;
眩巴 blink;
啞巴 dumb person; mute;
鹽巴 table salt;
眼巴巴 (1) with steady gaze; (2) anxiously; eagerly; expectantly; (3) helplessly;
眨巴 blink;
皺巴巴 creased; crumpled; wrinkled;
嘴巴 cakehole; mouth;

ba
【叭】 trumpet;
[叭兒狗] (1) lapdog; (2) Pekingese;

喇叭 (1) suona; (2) brass wind instrument; horn; trumpet; (3) hooter; loudspeaker;

ba
【扒】 (1) claw; strip off; take off; (2) climb; scale; (3) dig; dig up; pull down; rake; (4) catch hold of; cling to; hold on to; (5) push aside; scratch; (6) demolish; pull down; tear down;
[扒車] cramp; jump onto a slow-moving vehicle;
[扒釘] cramp;
[扒房] pull down a house;
[扒緊] hold firmly;
扒緊欄杆 hold firmly to the rail;
[扒開] push aside;
扒開草棵 push the grass aside;
[扒拉] (1) move; push aside; push lightly; (2) sauté;
扒拉開人群 push one's way through a crowd;
[扒皮] peel off the skin;
扒皮鬼 skinny person;
[扒住] cling to; hold on to;

ba
【吧】 mimetic word;
[吧吧] loquacious;
吧兒吧兒 clear, flowing-voiced;
[吧嗒] (1) smack one's lips; (2) pull at;
吧嗒嘴 (1) smack one's lips over food, drink, etc; (2) envious of others; greedy;

B

［吧噠棍］ six-foot stick, used in fighting;
［吧唧］ move one's jaws up and down as in eating;
［吧孃］ bar girl;
［吧女］ bar girl; barmaid;
［吧枱］ bar;
免費吧枱 open bar;
［吧呀］ (1) big-mouthed (2) quarrel;

果汁吧 juice bar;
酒吧 bar; bar-room; cocktail bar; lounge; pub; watering hole;
網吧 Internet café;

ba

【芭】 (1) fragrant plant; rush; (2) flower; (3) palmetto; plantain;
［芭蕉］ banana; Chinese banana; plantain;
芭蕉結果一緊相抱 a banana tree bears fruit – closely clustered; clasping or embracing tightly;
芭蕉扇 palm-leaf fan;
雨打芭蕉 raindrops come pattering ceaselessly on the banana leaves; raindrops drum rhythmically against the banana leaves;
［芭蕾舞］ ballet;
芭蕾舞狂 balletomania;
芭蕾舞迷 balletomane;
芭蕾舞女演員 ballerina;
芭蕾舞裙 ballet-skirt; tutu;
芭蕾舞團 ballet; ballet ensemble; ballet troupe;
芭蕾舞鞋 ballet shoes;
芭蕾舞演員 ballerina; ballet dancer;
芭蕾舞組曲 ballet suite;
冰上芭蕾舞 ice ballet;
古典芭蕾舞 classical ballet;
水上芭蕾舞 water ballet;
［芭籬］ fence of bamboo; hedge of underbrush;
［芭棚］ screen of straw for barring wind;

ba

【疤】 (1) scar; (2) birthmark;
［疤痕］ pit; scar; spot; sore;
［疤瘌］ scar;
疤瘌眼 scarred eyelids;
~疤癩眼兒照鏡子一自找難看 person with a scarred eyelid looking into a mirror – expose one's own defects;
［疤臉］ scarred face;

瘡疤 (1) scar; (2) pain;
痘疤 smallpox scabs;
結疤 (1) become scarred; (2) scab;
牛痘疤 vaccination scar;
傷疤 scar;
一塊疤 a scar;

ba

【捌】 elaborate form of 八, eight;

ba

【笆】 bamboo fence; basketry;
［笆斗］ willow basket for holding grains; round-bottomed basket;
［笆簍］ basket;

籬笆 bamboo fence; hedge; hurdle; wattle;
竹笆 bamboo basket;

ba

【粑】 salted meat;

ba

【豝】 female hog; female pig; sow;

ba²

ba

【八】 a pronunciation of 八;

ba

【拔】 (1) pull out; pull up; uproot; (2) promote; (3) draw; suck out; (4) destroy; eradicate; smash up; (5) choose; pick; select; (6) lift; raise; (7) outstanding; remarkable; (8) stand out among; surpass; (9) attack and take; capture; seize; (10) cool sth in water;
［拔白］ dawn; daybreak;
［拔步］ march forward; move forward quickly; take to one's heels; walk with big and quick strides;
［拔草］ pull up weed; weed;
拔草引蛇一自討苦吃 pluck weeds to stir the snakes – suffer from one's own actions;
［拔城］ capture a city; take a city;
［拔出］ draw out; extract; pull out;
［拔除］ eradicate; pluck; pull out; remove; uproot; weed out; wipe out;
難以拔除 too difficult to be eradicated;
［拔萃］ out of the common run; outstanding among the select best; stand out from one's fellows;

拔萃出群 far above the common; outstanding; stand head and shoulders above others;

出類拔萃 among the select best; cap all; distinguished from one's kind; far above the average; fill the bill; out of the common run; outstanding; pre-eminent; rise above the common herd; stand above the rest; stand out from one's fellows; stand out from the rest; stand out in the crowd; stick out; top all of the others; tower above the rest; tower over;

[拔刀] draw one's sword;

拔刀相向 draw one's sword against; draw upon sb; pull a knife on sb;

拔刀相助 draw a sword and render help; help another for the sake of justice; take up the cudgels against an injustice;

[拔地] rise from level ground; tower;

拔地參天 tall and spreading;

拔地而起 rise abruptly out of the ground; rise straight from the ground;

~拔地而起的高樓 towering buildings;

~大山拔地而起 the mountain rises from the plain;

~萬丈高樓拔地而起 high buildings rise abruptly out of the ground;

拔地孤峰 solitary cliff soaring into the sky;

拔地擎天 remarkable and outstanding;

[拔掉] (1) pluck out; (2) capture; seize;

[拔釘] pull out a nail;

拔釘錘 claw hammer;

拔釘斧 claw hatchet;

拔釘鉗 nail drawer;

[拔頂] (1) topping; (2) go bald;

拔頂裝置 topping plant;

[拔毒] draw out pus;

[拔份兒] (1) demonstrate one's power and courage over others; show off one's strength or power; (2) act violently; dominate;

[拔縫] come apart at the seam;

[拔付] pay by instalments;

[拔高] (1) lift; raise; (2) overrate;

[拔根] uproot;

拔根汗毛，比別人腰粗 one hair from one's body is thicker than sb's waist;

[拔河] tug-of-war;

比賽拔河 have a tug-of-war;

[拔尖] (1) first-class; outstanding; the very best; tip-top; top-notch; topflight; (2) feel one is superior to others; push oneself forward; push oneself to the front;

拔尖的學生 tip-top student;

拔尖兒 come off first; get the best position; top-notch;

拔尖人才 top-notch talent;

[拔劍] draw a sword; whip out a sword;

拔劍自刎 draw one's sword to slay oneself;

[拔薦] promote ahead of others; recommend for a post;

[拔腳] (1) lift the foot; take a step; (2) extricate oneself;

拔腳就走 get off at once; leave at once; scurry away; scuttle off;

[拔毛] pluck out hairs;

拔毛機 plucker;

雁過拔毛 he rooks everyone he can get his claws into;

[拔錨] haul in an anchor; unmoor; weigh an anchor;

[拔膿] draw out the pus;

[拔起] uproot;

連根拔起 lift sth out by its roots; pull up by the roots; tear up by the roots; uproot;

[拔取] choose; draw off; select;

拔取人才 select and employ talented people;

[拔群] outstanding; stand out;

[拔山] pull up mountains;

拔山蓋世 towering and unrivalled;

拔山舉鼎 herculean in strength; strong enough to pull up mountains and raise tripods;

拔山扛鼎 herculean in strength; strong enough to pull up mountains and raise tripods;

[拔身] break away from busy schedule; escape; get away;

[拔絲] candied floss;

拔絲蘋果 hot candied apple;

[拔俗] free from vulgarity; outstanding and unique; rise far above the common lot;

拔俗超群 far above the common and

exceed the crowd;
超塵拔俗 (1) overcome material desires; (2) tower over the rest;
耿介拔俗 straightforward and outstanding, not like ordinary people;

[拔腿] lift the foot and begin to run; take to one's heels;
拔腿就跑 beat it as fast as one can; immediately take to one's heels; make the best use of one's legs; show a clean pair of heels; start running away at once; take to one's legs; take to one's legs as fast as one can; turn and scamper off;
拔腿就追 give instant chase;

[拔牙] extract a tooth; have a tooth out; pull out a tooth;
拔牙後出血 haemorrhage following tooth extraction;
選擇性拔牙 selected extraction;

[拔秧] pull up seedlings;

[拔營] break camp; decamp; strike camp;

[拔寨] (1) break camp; decamp; strike camp; (2) capture; storm;
攻城拔寨 take cities and fortified camps by storm;

[拔招] rescind a false move (in a chess game);

[拔幟易幟] (1) replace sb; take sb's place; (2) triumph by force of arms;

[拔撞] (1) win honour for sb; (2) back sb up; (3) boast one's moral; pump up one's courage;

[拔擢] promote; raise; select and promote the best;
拔擢人才 pick out and promote talents;
拔擢賢能 raise the good and able;

超拔 outstanding;
海拔 elevation; height above sea level;
簡拔 select and promote;
開拔 move; set out;
拉拔 (1) draw; (2) help sb advance;
冷拔 cold drawing;
峭拔 (1) high and steep; precipitous; (2) vigorous;
清拔 distinguished;
熱拔 hot drawing;
識拔 appreciate and promote;
提拔 promote;
挺拔 (1) tall and straight; (2) forceful;
鞋拔 shoe lifter; shoehorn;
秀拔 fine style of calligraphy;
選拔 choose; select; select from candidates;
英拔 distinguished; outstanding; prominent; surpassing;
甄拔 select;
振拔 free or extricate oneself from a predicament and brace oneself up to action;
自拔 free or extricate oneself (from pain or evildoing);

ba

【茇】 (1) grass root; (2) thatch;

ba

【跋】 (1) cross mountains; travel; trudge over mountains; (2) epilogue; afterword; postscript; (3) trample;

[跋扈] bossy; domineering; high-handed; overbearing rampant in defiance of authority;
飛揚跋扈 domineer over sb;
很跋扈 throw one's weight about;
專橫跋扈 imperious and despotic;

[跋剌] make a splashing noise;

[跋山] trek across mountains;
跋山涉水 across mountains and rivers; over the hills and through the rivers; scale mountains and ford streams; travel across mountains and rivers; travel by climbing up hills and wading over rivers; travel over land and water; travel over mountains and rivers; trek across mountains and rivers; trudge across mountains and rivers;
跋山涉野 roam over hills and dales;
跋山越谷 go up hill and down dale; roam over hill and dale;

[跋涉] make a long, tiring journey; make a weary journey; tramp; travel over land and water; trek; trudge; wade;
跋涉之苦 the hardship of journeying over land and water;
跋涉之勞 the hardship of journeying over land and water;
長途跋涉 make a long and difficult journey;
徒步跋涉 trudge along;

[跋文] postscript;

[跋語] postscript;

[跋躓] defeat; failure; setback;

題跋 colophon; preface and postscript;

序跋 preface and postscript;

ba

【鈸】 cymbals;

ba³

ba

【把】 (1) grasp; hold; hold in one's hand; take hold of; (2) handle; hold; (3) control; dominate; monopolize; (4) guard; hold; keep hold of; keep under surveillance; watch over; (5) carry; handle; (6) a bunch of; a bundle of; a fistful of; a grasp of; a handful of; a sheaf of; a wisp of; (7) about; approximately; around; more or less; or so;

[把臂] arm in arm; holding arms;

[把柄] give sb a handle against oneself;
抓住把柄 seize on sb's vulnerable point;
~讓人抓住把柄 give others a handle against oneself;

[把場] (1) direct from behind the scenes; (2) control things behind the scene;

[把持] (1) control; keep in one's hands; keep under control; (2) dominate; monopolize;
把持包辦 control and monopolize; keep everything in one's own hands;
把持一切 (1) seize control of everything; (2) control; keep everything under control;

[把舵] at the helm; hold the helm; hold the rudder; steer; take the helm;

[把風] be on the lookout; keep watch;
在外面把風 be on the lookout outside; keep watch outside;

[把關] (1) guard a pass; hold the pass; (2) check on; check up; ensure; guarantee; guard against mistakes; (3) gatekeeping;
把關守隘 guard the passes;
層層把關 make quality checks at all levels;
嚴格把關 make a careful check;
最後把關 make a final check;

[把酒] drink; fill a wine cup for sb; hold a wineglass; raise one's wine up;
把酒暢談 take up the wine cup and chat merrily;
把酒高歌 take up the wine cup and sing happily;
把酒澆愁 drown one's worries in drink;
把酒接風 pour out the wine of welcome;
把酒消愁 drown one's worries in drink; take to drinking to forget one's sorrows;
把酒言歡 take up the wine cup and chat merrily — union of friends;

[把卷] hold a book in one's hand to read;

[把攬] control; dominate; monopolize;
把攬一切 monopolize everything;

[把牢] dependable; safe and secure; strong;
不把牢 (1) not solid; (2) not reliable;

[把脈] feel the pulse;

[把袂] holding sleeves—in loving friendship;
把袂之交 bosom friend; very intimate friendship;

[把門] guard a door; stand watch at a door; watch the door;
養狗把門 keep a dog to guard the door;

[把弄] (1) fiddle with; (2) control and manipulate;

[把勢] (1) martial art; (2) person skilled in martial arts; (3) skill; technique;
老把勢 expert; old hand;

[把手] (1) grid; handle; handlebar; knob; (2) person;
搭把手 lend me a hand;
二把手 number-two person; second in command;
~第二把手 number two person; second in command;
當第二把手 play second fiddle to sb;
環狀把手 ringlike handle;
活動把手 flexible handle;
門把手 door handle; doorknob;
~黃銅門把手 brass door knob;
~球形門把手 doorknob;
球形把手 doorknob; knob;
水龍頭把手 cocket handle;
調節把手 adjusting handle;
銅把手 copper knob;
一把手 number one person; top dog;
~第一把手 number one person; top dog;
應急把手 abort handle;
轉動把手 turn the handle;

[把守] guard; watch;
把守邊關 guard the frontiers;
把守城門 guard a city gate;
把守大門 on guard at the door;

把守關隘 guard the passes;
把守關口 hold the pass;
分兵把守 divide up one's forces for defence;
[把頭] gangmaster; labour contractor;
[把玩] fondle;
把弄玉器 fondle jadewares appreciatively;
[把穩] dependable; firm; hold fast; sure about; trustworthy;
老成把穩 experienced and trustworthy;
[把握] (1) grasp; hold; seize; (2) assurance; certainty;
把握不住 lose control of;
有把握 be assured of; certain of; confident of success; sure that;
有成功的把握 the cards are in one's hands;
[把晤] meet; meet and shake hands;
[把細] careful; cautious; mindful;
做事很把細 careful in everything one does;
[把戲] (1) acrobatics; (2) cheap trick; game; scheme; trick;
變把戲 play a trick;
搞把戲 play tricks;
鬼把戲 dirty trick; sinister plot;
~耍鬼把戲 play a dirty trick; play underhand tricks;
看把戲 watch an acrobatic show;
~看穿把戲 see through sb's trick;
老把戲 old trick;
耍把戲 (1) juggle with; (2) be up to one's tricks; do tricks; play tricks;
玩把戲 juggle; play little tricks;
[把盞] raise a winecup;
[把捉] (1) grasp; (2) assess;
把捉不定 difficult to assess;
[把子] (1) bundle; (2) weapons used in operas; (3) a handful; (4) gang; group;
拜把子 become sworn brothers;

草把 a bundle of straw;
倒把 engage in profiteering; speculate;
翻把 (1) take the upper hand again; (2) deny what one has said;
鍋把 pan handle;
火把 torch;
拿把 put on airs; strike a pose in order to enhance one's own importance;
掐把 (1) hold fast; (2) treat harshly;
槍把 pistol grip;
剎把 brake clank;
順把 obedient;
笤把 long straw broom;
拖把 mop; swab;
一把 a bunch of; a bundle of; a handful of; a pair of; a wisp of;
盈把 a handful of;

ba

【鈀】 palladium;
[鈀金合金] palladium gold;
[鈀銅合金] palladium copper;

ba

【靶】 (1) target; (2) splashboard of a chariot;
[靶標] target;
[靶場] firing range; range; shooting range;
[靶船] target ship;
[靶心] bull's-eye;
擊中靶心 hit the bull's-eye;
正中靶心 hit the bull's-eye;
[靶紙] target sheet;
[靶子] target;
把箭對準靶子 aim one's arrow at the target;
活靶子 live target;

打靶 shoot at a target; have target practice;
環靶 round target;
活動靶 manoeuvring target;
空靶 air target;
射中靶 hit the target;

ba⁴

ba

【吧】 ba (a sentence-final particle).

ba

【把】 (1) handle; subject for ridicule; (2) grip;
[把兒] handle;
把兒掉了 the handle breaks off;
把兒弄斷 break the handle;
[把子] handle; handle trace;

車把 handlebar;
鍋把 pan handle;
門把 door handle; door knob;

ba

【爸】 dad; father; pa;
[爸爸] (1) dad; daddy; father; pa; papa; pater;

(2) one's husband's father;

阿爸 dad; daddy; father; pa; pap; papa;
乾爸 foster father; godfather;
老爸 dad; father;

ba

【耙】 a pronunciation of 耙;
[耙出] rake out;
耙出煤灰 rake out the coal ashes;
[耙掉] rake off;
耙掉落葉 rake off the fallen leaves;
[耙平] rake smooth;
把土耙平 rake the soil smooth;
[耙鬆] harrow up;
耙鬆土地 harrow up a field;
[耙田] harrow a field;

釘齒耙 spike-tooth harrow;
耥耙 paddy-field harrow;
圓齒耙 disc harrow;

ba

【罷】 (1) cease; end; finish; stop; to be done with; (2) discharge; dismiss;
[罷筆] stop writing;
[罷兵] suspend hostilities;
罷兵媾和 withdraw troops and negotiate for peace;
[罷黜] (1) ban; reject; (2) dismiss from office; fire; remove from office;
[罷工] come out on strike; go on strike; hit the bricks; launch a strike; lay down tools; on strike; organize a strike; stage a strike; strike; walk out;
罷工結束 end a strike;
罷工行動 strike action;
罷工者 striker;
~罷工者己經復工 the strikers resume work;
參加罷工 join in a strike;
持續罷工 rolling strike;
大罷工 general strike;
對抗罷工 resist the strike;
發動罷工 call a strike;
防止罷工 avert a strike;
鼓動罷工 agitate for a strike;
繼續罷工 continue a strike;
結束罷工 call off a strike; end a strike;
~強迫結束罷工 break a strike;
經濟罷工 economic strike;
舉行罷工 come out on strike; go on strike;
~號召舉行罷工 call a strike;
開始罷工 begin a strike; start a strike;
抗議性罷工 protest walkout;
破壞罷工 break up a strike;
取消罷工 call off a strike;
全國性罷工 national strike; nationwide strike;
閃電式罷工 lightning strike;
同情性罷工 sympathetic walkout;
野貓式罷工 wildcat strike;
在罷工 on strike;
鎮壓罷工 put down a strike;
政治罷工 political strike;
總罷工 general strike;
組織罷工 bring about a strike; organize a strike; stage a strike;
[罷官] be dismissed from office; be removed from office;
罷官歸田 remove sb from office and banish him to his family estate in the country; resign from office and go home;
[罷教] teachers' strike;
組織罷教 bring about a teachers' strike;
[罷課] boycott classes; students' strike;
舉行罷課 students are out on strike;
[罷了] might as well; nothing but; only; that is all; that is enough;
倒也罷了 it would have been better if;
[罷論] abandoned idea;
概作罷論 drop the matter altogether; let no more be said about it altogether;
[罷免] dismiss; recall; remove;
罷免權 right of recall;
罷免職務 dismiss from office; removal of sb from his position;
要求罷免 demand the dismissal of;
[罷妻] divorce a wife;
[罷市] cease trade; close up shop; shopkeepers' strike;
[罷手] discontinue an action; give up; pause; stop;
[罷閒] out of work;
[罷休] cease; give up; let the matter drop; stop;
就此罷休 leave the matter at that;
決不罷休 never be reconciled to the matter;
善罷甘休 leave the matter at that; let it go at that; stop quarreling with others; willing to give up; willing to let go;

誓不罷休 swear not to rest; swear not to stop;

［罷業］ go on strike; shopkeepers' strike; strike;

［罷職］ dismiss; remove from office;

也罷 (1) never mind; no matter whether; (2) all right; (3) let it be;

作罷 abdicate; drop; give up; relinquish;

B

ba

【霸】 (1) overlord; (2) bully; despot; tyrant; (3) hegemonist power; hegemonism; hegemony; (4) dominate; lord it over; tyrannize over;

［霸持］ dominate; occupy forcibly;

霸持文壇 dominate the literary circles;

［霸道］ overbearing; high-handed; rule by force;

逞兇霸道 throw one's weight about;

很霸道 very high-handed;

橫行霸道 act against law and reason, like a tyrant; act in a tyrannous manner; act like an overlord; act outrageously and ferociously; act unreasonably; be unbridled in one's truculence; lord it over; play the bully; play the tyrant; ride roughshod over; run wild; swagger about; trample on; tyrannize over;

性格霸道 have a domineering personality;

做事霸道 do things in a high-handed manner;

［霸地］ occupation of land;

非法霸地 illegal occupation of land;

［霸氣］ hegemony;

霸氣十足 very domineering;

［霸權］ hegemony; supremacy;

霸權政策 hegemonic policy;

霸權主義 hegemony; supremacy;

~霸權主義路線 hegemonic course;

地區性霸權 regional hegemony;

反對霸權 oppose hegemony;

海上霸權 maritime hegemony;

建立霸權 establish hegemony;

擴張霸權 spread one's hegemony;

謀求霸權 seek hegemony;

世界霸權 world hegemony;

爭奪霸權 contend for hegemony;

［霸王］ despot; overlord;

霸王車 ride a bus without a ticket;

~坐霸王車 ride a bus without a ticket;

霸王精 zygofabagine;

土霸王 cock of the dunghill;

［霸業］ accomplishment of obtaining a dominant position;

［霸佔］ occupy forcibly; seize; usurp;

［霸政］ hegemonism; oligarchy; rule by force;

［霸主］ hegemon; overlord;

稱霸 dominate; seek hegemony;

窗霸 windows blaster;

獨霸 dominate exclusively; monopolize;

惡霸 bully; local despot; local tyrant;

王霸 kings and hegemons;

漁霸 fishing despot;

爭霸 contend for hegemony; strive for supremacy;

ba

【壩】 dam; dike; embankment;

［壩工］ dam construction works;

［壩基］ base of a dam;

多用壩 multipurpose dam;

防洪壩 checking dam; flood water dam;

分水壩 diverting dam;

拱壩 arch dam;

混凝土壩 concrete dam;

活板壩 shutter dam;

活動壩 movable dam;

積水壩 splash dam;

空心壩 hollow dam;

空心重力壩 hollow gravity dam;

攔衝壩 diversion dam;

連拱壩 multi-arch dam;

門壩 wicket dam;

水壩 dam;

碎石壩 debris dam;

隄壩 dikes and dams;

填石壩 rock-fill dam;

跳越壩 jump dam;

透水壩 filter dam;

土壩 earth dam; earth-filled dam;

圍壩 box dam;

溢流壩 spillway dam; weir dam;

閘壩 gate dam;

支墩壩 buttress dam;

重力壩 gravity dam; solid gravity dam;

ba

【灞】 a river in Shensi;

［灞橋折柳］ bid farewell; part with friends;

ba5

ba

【吧】 (1) crack; snap; (2) draw on one's pipe;

［吧嗒］ pull at a pipe; smack; smoke a pipe;
吧嗒着嘴 smack one's lips; with a smack of the lips;

ba

【罷】 cease; done with; finish; stop;

bai1

bai

【掰】 (1) break off a friendship; break up; (2) pull apart with one's hands;

［掰開］ pull apart with one's hands;

［掰了］ at outs; on bad terms; on the outs;

［掰碎］ break sth into pieces with one's fingers;

［掰文兒］ find a fault;

bai2

bai

【白】 (1) white; (2) blank; clear; empty; plain; pure; (3) misspelled; wrongly written; (4) mispronounced; (5) for nothing; in vain; to no avail; to no end; to no purpose; waste efforts; without results; (6) free of charge; gratis; without charge; (7) spoken part in an opera; (8) a surname;

［白皚皚］ dazzlingly white; pure white; white and clean;

［白白］ (1) for nothing; fruitless; in vain; of no avail; to no avail; to no purpose; (2) free of charge; gratis; without charge;
白白送掉 give away;

［白斑］ leukoplakia; leukoplasia; white patch; white specks; white spots;
白斑病 leukoderma; vitiligo;
頸部白斑病 leukoderma colli;
~梅毒性白斑病 syphilitic leukoderma;
~外陰白斑病 leukoplakia vulvae;
~炎症後白斑病 postinflammatory leukoderma;
~職業性白斑病 occupational leukoderma;

［白板］ white board;
白板筆 white board marker;

［白璧］ white jade;
白璧微瑕 flaw in an otherwise perfect character; fly in the ointment; little fault; little imprefection; minor defect; no silver without its dross; slight blemish; slight flaw in a white jade; slur on one's reputation; spot in the sun; trivial flaw in a jade;
白璧無瑕 as innocent as a babe unborn; as innocent as a new born babe; clean sheet; faultless; flawless white jade; impeccable moral integrity; perfect; pure and noble; pure and spotless jade; untainted and untarnished; without a spot on one's reputation; without blemish;

［白菜］ cabbage;
白菜幫 out leaf of a cabbage;
白菜心 cabbage heart;
大白菜 Chinese cabbage;
海白菜 ulva lactuca;
小白菜 Chinese cabbage;
洋白菜 cabbage;
圓白菜 cabbage;

［白吃］ eat free of charge;
白吃白喝 free food and drink; free meals;
白吃一頓飯 have a free meal;

［白痴］ cretin; idiot; turd;
你這個白痴 you idiot; you stupid turd;
天生的白痴 congenital idiot;

［白搭］ fruitless; futile; have no use; in vain; no good; no use; of no use; spend effort in vain; to no purpose; useless;

［白帶］ leukorrhoea; whites;
白帶魚 bandfish;

［白道］ lunar orbit; moon's orbit;

［白癜瘋］ vitiligo;

［白丁］ common people; commoner;

［白豆］ white beans;

［白髮］ grey hair; white hair;
白髮白眉 have frosty white hair and eyebrows;
白髮白鬚 have white hair and a hoary beard;
白髮蒼蒼 grey-haired; grey-headed; hoary-haired; white-haired; white-headed;
白髮蒼髯 have white hair and a hoary beard;
白髮紅顏 marry a woman many years younger than oneself; an old man marrying a young lady;
白髮皤然 white-haired;
白髮齊眉 remain a devoted couple to the

B

end of their lives, with white hair and white eye-brows;
白髮偕老 a married couple reaching old age together; live to a ripe old age in conjugal bliss; remain a devoted couple to the end of their lives;
白髮銀髯 with silvery hair and beard;
白髮症 (1) canities; (2) poliosis;
拔掉白髮 pluck gray hairs; pluck out some gray hairs;
滿頭白髮 have grey hair; have snowy hair;
一頭白髮 have a head of grey hair;
有些白髮 have some grey hairs;

［白飯］ cooked white rice; plain cooked rice;
吃白飯 be supported by others; eat for free;

［白費］ in vain; spend without profit; use up without profit; waste;
白費蠟 be wasted; go down the drain;
白費辛苦 go on a wild goose chase; expend labour for nothing; it is labour lost; plough the sand;

［白狗］ white dog;
白狗吃肉，黑狗當災 the white dog eats the meat and the black dog bears the blame;

［白骨］ bones of the dead;
日骨頂 coot;

［白圭］ white jade;
白圭微瑕 a flaw in a precious stone; a slight blemish in a precious stone;
白圭有瓚 a flaw in a jade baton; a spot on white jade; there are lees to every wine;
白圭之瓚 a flaw in a jade baton; a spot on white jade;

［白果］ gingko; gingko nut;

［白鶴］ white crane;
雲中白鶴 person of unimpeachable integrity;

［白喉］ diphtheria;
白喉毒素 diphtheria toxin;
白喉膜 diphtheritic membrane
白喉性扁桃體炎 diphtherial tonsillitis;
白喉性潰瘍 diphtheritic ulcer;
白喉性麻痺 diphtheritic paralysis;
白喉性咽炎 diphtheritic pharyngitis;
假白喉 diphtheroid; pseudodiphtheria;
皮膚白喉 cutaneous diphtheria;

［白狐］ arctic fox;

［白花］ (1) white flower; (2) waste;
白花花 shining white;
錢沒白花 get one's money's worth;

［白化］ albinic;
白化病 albinism;
~白化病患者 albino;
~後天白化病 acquired albinism;
~局部白化病 partial albinism;
~全身白化病 total albinism;
白化體 albino;
白化現象 albinism;
白化症 albinism;

［白話］ colloquial Chinese; spoken Chinese; vernacular Chinese;
白話詩 vernacular Chinese poetry; verses in vernacular Chinese;
白話文 vernacular style of writing; writings in vernacular Chinese;
白話文學 vernacular literature;
白話小說 novels in vernacular Chinese;

［白樺］ white birch;

［白晃晃］ glaring; gleaming; shining and bright;

［白灰］ (1) lime; (2) whitewash;
一層白灰 a coat of whitewash;

［白肌］ white muscle;
白肌病 white muscle disease;

［白金］ platinum;

［白酒］ spirit; white spirit;

［白駒］ white colt;
白駒過隙 a glimpse of a white colt flashing past a chink in a wall; gone in a moment; how time flies; life is short like the white pony's shadow across a crevice; the stream of time; time flies like a white colt passing a crack; time flies like the shadow of the sun passing through a crevice; time is like a fleet horse passing by a crevice;

［白卷］ blank examination paper;
交白卷 completely fail to accomplish a task; hand in a blank examination paper; hand in an examination paper unanswered; have nothing to report;

［白軍］ white army;

［白蘭地］ brandy;
白蘭地酒杯 snifter;
一口白蘭地 a swallow of brandy;
一小口白蘭地 a sip of brandy;
一小桶白蘭地 a keg of brandy;

[白蘭瓜] honeydew melon;

[白浪] breaker; whitecap; white horses;

白浪翻滾 the waves roll and foam;

白浪滔滔 crashing waves; whitecaps surging;

白浪滔天 the white waves rise as high as heaven; waves heave to the skies; white breakers leap to the sky; white breakers leap skywards;

[白臉] white face;

唱白臉 coerce; play the villain; pretend to be harsh and severe; wear the white make-up of the stage villain;

小白臉 boy toy; cream puff; handsome young man with effeminate features;

[白領] white collar;

白領犯罪 white-collar crime;

白領工人 white-collar worker;

白領工作 white-collar job;

白領階層 white-collar workers;

白領階級 white-collar class;

白領文化 white-collar culture;

[白鹿] white deer;

[白鷺] egret;

小白鷺 little egret;

一行白鷺 a flight of egrets;

[白忙] busy oneself to no purpose;

白忙半天 go to a lot of trouble for nothing;

[白茫茫] in an endless whiteness; vast expanse of whiteness; white and misty;

白茫茫一片 vast expanse of whiteness;

到處白茫茫 everywhere is white and misty;

[白毛風] blizzard; snowstorm;

[白蒙蒙] (1) vast expanse of whiteness; (2) hazy; misty;

[白米] white polished rice;

[白麵] (1) flour; wheat flour; (2) heroin;

[白描] (1) simple, straight forward style of writing; (2) line drawing in traditional ink and brush style;

[白沫] frothy saliva;

口吐白沫 froth at the mouth;

[白內障] cataract;

初發白內障 incipient cataract;

初期白內障 incipient cataract;

創傷性白內障 traumatic cataract;

低鈣血性白內障 hypocalcemic cataract;

過熟白內障 hypermature cataract; overripe cataract;

黑色白內障 black cataract;

繼發性白內障 secondary cataract;

藍斑白內障 blue dot cataract;

藍色白內障 blue cataract;

老年白內障 senile cataract;

老年性白內障 senile cataract;

膜性白內障 membranous cataract;

囊性白內障 capsular cataract;

皮質性白內障 cortical cataract;

青光眼性白內障 glaucomatous cataract;

全白內障 total cataract;

糖尿病白內障 diabetic cataract;

糖尿病性白內障 diabetic cataract;

特應性白內障 atopic cataract;

外傷性白內障 traumatic cataract;

完全白內障 complete cataract;

炎症後白內障 postinflammatory cataract;

營養缺乏性白內障 nutritional deficiency cataract;

幼年型白內障 juvenile cataract;

原發性白內障 primary cataract;

早產兒白內障 cataracts of prematurity;

早老性白內障 presenile cataract;

腫脹期白內障 intumescent cataract;

中毒性白內障 toxic cataract;

[白嫩] (of skin) delicate; fair and clear;

[白皮書] official government report; White Paper;

[白旗] white flag;

[白切雞] sliced steamed chicken;

[白區] white area;

[白熱] glow; white glow; white heat; white-hot;

白熱化 bring sth to fever pitch; reach the climax; reach the white-hot point; turn white-hot;

[白人] (1) white man; (2) white race; (3) white woman;

偏袒白人 discriminate in favour of the white people;

優待白人 discriminate in favour of the whites;

[白刃] naked blade; naked sword; naked weapon; sharp knife;

[白日] (1) daylight; daytime; (2) sun;

白日不做虧心事，半夜敲門也不驚 a clear conscience is a sure card; a clear conscience laughs at false accusations; a good conscience is a constant feast; a good conscience is a soft pillow; a

quiet conscience sleeps in thunder; a safe conscience makes a sound sleep;
白日點燈 burn daylight;
白日惡夢 daymare;
白日鬼 burglar; cheater; swindler; trickster;
白日見鬼 have a fantasy; have pure fantasy; see a ghost in broad daylight; something impossible;
白日夢 daydream; pipe dream; waking dream;
白日説夢話 rave in broad daylight;
白日撞見鬼 see ghosts in broad daylight;
白日做夢 build castles in the air; cherish a pipe dream; daydream; dream daydreams; have a pure fancy; have a sheer illusion; have a walking dream; indulge in wishful thinking;
~ 開了眼睛説夢話—白日做夢 talking in one's sleep with one's eyes open — daydream;
大天白日 in broad daylight;

[白肉] plain boiled pork;

[白如寒霜] as white as winter frost;

[白色] white; white colour;
白色革命 white revolution;
白色據點 white stronghold;
白色恐怖 white terror;
白色農業 white agriculture;
白色人情 transparent relations;
白色人種 White race;
白色收入 legitimate income;
白色消費 funeral expenses; white consumption;
白色政權 White regime;
熾白色 dazzling white;
帶白色的 whitish;
乳白色 cream colour;
~ 淺乳白色 magnolia;

[白生生] as white as snow; white and delicate;

[白食] free meal;
白食的人 person who gets a free meal;
~ 吃白食的人 freeloader;
吃白食 be supported by others; eat for free;

[白市] legitimate market;

[白事] funeral;

[白首] hoary head;
白首窮經 continue to study even in old age;

[白鼠] white mouse;

[白薯] sweet potato;

[白霜] hoarfrost;
一層白霜 a hoarfrost;

[白水] plain water;

[白説] speak in vain; waste one's breath;

[白松] white pine;

[白送] give away;

[白糖] powdered sugar; refined white sugar;

[白天] day; daytime;
白天的 diurnal;
~ 白天的工作 day job;
白天黑夜 bright day and black night; day and night;

[白頭] (1) grey hair; hoary head; (2) old age;
白頭到老 live to a ripe old age in conjugal bliss; remain a devoted couple to the end of their lives;
~ 不能白頭到老 unable to live together until old age;
白頭如新 maintain an old acquaintanceship having no real understanding with each other;
白頭翁 (1) grackle; grey starling; (2) anemone;
白頭偕老 live to a hoary age as husband and wife; live to a ripe old age in conjugal bliss; remain a devoted couple to the end of their lives; stick to each other till old age; stick to each other to the end of their lives;
~ 祝你們白頭偕老 wish you two will live together till you are old and grey;
少白頭 (1) prematurely grey; (2) young person with greying hair;

[白玩兒] easy to do; not difficult; not hard;

[白熊] polar bear; white bear;

[白雪] snow; white snow;
白雪皚皚 an expanse of white snow; the snow is dazzlingly white;
一片白雪 a blanket of snow;

[白血病] leukaemia;
放射性白血病 radiation leukaemia;
急性白血病 acute leukaemia;
假白血病 pseudoleukaemia;
慢性白血病 chronic leukaemia;
皮膚白血病 leukaemia cutis;

[白血球] leucocyte; white blood cell;
白血球增多 leucocytosis;
嗜酸性白血球 eosinophilic leucocyte;

[白眼] (1) white of the eyes; (2) contemptuous

look; supercilious look; (3) contempt; disdain;

白眼看人 look upon people with disdain; treat people superciliously;

白眼狼 heartless snob; ingrate; treacherous and ruthless person; yellow dog;

白眼相看 despise; look down on; turn up the white of one's eyes upon;

白眼珠 white of the eye;

吃白眼 be given the cold shoulder; be looked down on;

翻白眼 (1) show the white of one's eyes; turn up the white of one's eyes; (2) in a dying situation;

給人白眼 look upon people with disdain; treat people superciliously;

青白眼 esteem or look down;

遭人白眼 be treated with disdain; receive a cold disdainful look; receive a cold stare;

[白雁] white wild goose;

[白楊] white poplar;

綿白楊 cottonwood;

銀白楊 abele;

[白衣] (1) white clothes; (2) clothes of the common people; (3) commoner;

白衣天使 angels in white – hospital nurses;

白衣戰士 medical worker; warrior in white;

[白蟻] termite; white ant;

[白銀] silver;

[白玉] white jade;

白玉無瑕 flawless white jade;

[白雲] white clouds;

白雲蒼狗 now sunny and then cloudy; so the world wags; the vicissitudes of fortune; white clouds change into gray dogs;

白雲朵朵 the sky is dotted with white clouds;

白雲藍天 white clouds drift through the blue sky;

白雲母 white mica;

白雲親舍 remembrance of one's parents;

白雲石 dolomite;

白雲舒捲 the white clouds mass and scatter;

蒼狗白雲 changeable world; vicissitudes of fortune;

一朵白雲 a white cloud;

[白紙] blank paper;

白紙黑字 black characters on white paper; commit sth to writing; in black and white; words printed on paper;

~白紙黑字，鐵證如山 these ironclad details are irrefutable proof in black and white;

~白紙黑字，有案可查 be written down and recorded;

一張白紙 a blank sheet of paper; a piece of blank paper;

[白種] white race;

白種人 white; white people;

~非白種人 non-white;

白種移民 béké;

[白晝] daylight; daytime;

白晝點燈 burn in broad daylight; do work of no avail;

白晝見鬼 have a fantasy; see a ghost in broad daylight;

白晝宣淫 indulge in lascivious acts in broad daylight;

明如白晝 as clear as daylight;

[白字] wrongly written or mispronounced characters;

白字連篇 full of wrongly written words; make a great number of mistakes in spelling; pages and pages of wrongly written characters;

唸白字 mispronounce a Chinese character;

寫白字 write a wrong Chinese character in mistake for one that resembles it;

用白字 misuse a word for another to which it bears resemblance;

皚白 brightly; pure white; white;

暗白 dirty white;

拔白 dawn; day break;

斑白 greying; grizzled;

頒白 (1) grey; (2) white;

邊白 margin;

辨白 (1) distinguish clearly; identify clearly; (2) account for;

辯白 offer an explanation;

表白 bare one's heart; vindicate;

稟白 report to a superior;

慘白 (1) dim; faint; gloomy; (2) pale;

黪白 gray;

蒼白 (1) pale; pallid; wan; (2) feeble; pale and weak;

葱白 scallion;

粹白 pure white;
大白 become known;
蛋白 (1) egg white; (2) protein;
道白 spoken parts in an opera;
靛白 indigo white;
獨白 monologue; soliloquy;
對白 dialogue;
發白 become white; grow white; turn pale; turn white;
飛白 (in calligraphy) flying-white;
告白 public notice;
黑白 (1) black and white; (2) right and wrong;
紅白 red and white;
花白 grey; grizzled;
黃白 (1) lunar orbit; (2) yellow and white;
灰白 ashen; greyish white; pale;
茭白 wild rice stem;
潔白 (1) pure white; spotless; white; (2) pure;
開場白 opening remarks; prologue;
空白 blank space;
露白 show one's belongings; show one's money;
卵白 albumen; egg white;
明白 bring sth home to one; catch sth; catch the drift of argument; clear; comprehend; dawn on sb; follow; get the drift of; grasp; intelligible; know; make out; make sense of; see; see the drift of; twig; understand;
內白 words spoken by an actor from offstage;
涅白 opaque white;
旁白 voice-over;
漂白 bleach;
平白 for no reason; gratuitously;
剖白 explain or vindicate oneself;
鉛白 white lead;
淺白 plain; simple;
搶白 rebuke;
清白 pure; stainless;
乳白 milky white; of cream colour;
煞白 deathly pale; ghastly pale;
刷白 pale; white;
説白 spoken parts in operas;
坦白 (1) candid; frank; honest; (2) confess; tell the truth;
提白 prompt;
顯白 (1) make clear; show; (2) clear; evident;
鋅白 zinc white;
鋅鋇白 lithopone;
雪白 snow-white;
眼白 white of the eye;
銀白 silvery white;
魚白 (1) silver-grey; (2) fish sperm; milt;
魚肚白 whitish colour of a fish's belly;
月白 bluish white; very pale blue;
皂白 (1) black and white; (2) right and wrong;
貞白 chastity; integrity;
自白 confession; explain oneself; make a personal statement; make clear one's position; vindicate oneself;

bai³
bai

【百】 (1) hundred; (2) all kinds of; many; numerous; (3) all; (4) always; very;

［百拜］ much courtesy;

［百般］ all sorts; by all manner of means; by every means; every kind; in a hundred and one ways; in every possible way;

［百寶箱］ jewel box; jewel case;

［百倍］ a hundred fold; a hundred times;
信心百倍 feel full of confidence;

［百弊］ (1) all kinds of maladies; all the ill effects; (2) many disadvantages; many drawbacks;
百弊叢生 all kinds of corruption creep in; all kinds of troubles grow up; all sorts of abuses are prevalent; all the ill effects appear;

［百病］ all kinds of diseases;
百病纏身 disease-ridden;
百病叢生 all kinds of diseases and ailments breaking out; all kinds of troubles arise;
百病回春 able to cure sb of all diseases;
包治百病 guarantee to cure all diseases;

［百步］ a hundred paces;
百步穿楊 a dead shot; have good marksmanship; hit a willow branch at a distance of one hundred steps by an arrow; hit a willow twig at a hundred paces; hit virtually any target within a hundred steps; pierce a willow leaf at a hundred paces; shoot an arrow through a willow leaf a hundred paces away; shoot with great precision; superior marksmanship;

［百城坐擁］ have a large number of books; library;

［百出］ full of; numerous; plenty of;
機變百出 with a thousand tricks up in the sleeves;

［百川歸海］ a hundred rivers find their way to

the sea; all rivers flow into the sea; all rivers meet in the sea; all things tend in one direction; everyone turns to sb for guidance;

[百端] all kinds of matters; all kinds of thoughts; all matters;

百端待舉 a hundred things wait to be done; a thousand things to be done; have one hundred and one things to attend to; numerous tasks remain to be undertaken;

百端待決 a thousand and one problems are crying for solution;

百端交集 all kinds of thoughts crowded in together; many thoughts crowded in upon sb;

[百發百中] a hundred hits for a hundred shots; a hundred shots, a hundred bull's eyes; crack shot; every shot goes home; every shot hits the target; fire at the target a hundred times without a single miss; fire with unerring aim; get a hundred hits out of a hundred shots; hit one's mark every single time and never miss; hit one's target every time one shoots; hit the bull's eye every time; hit the mark every time; infallible; make every shot tell; not miss once in a hundred shots; shoot with devastating accuracy; shoot with unfailing accuracy; shoot without fail;

[百廢] a hundred abandoned things;

百廢待舉 a hundred abandoned things wait to be done; a thousand things wait to be restored; all neglected matters call for attention; all that has been left undone is to be done; all unfinished work requires attention; so many broken things crying out to be done;

百廢俱興 all neglected tasks are being undertaken; full-scale reconstruction is under way;

[百分] (1) per cent; (2) a hundred marks;

百分比 percentage;

百分點 percentage point;

百分法 percentage;

百分號 percentage symbol (%);

百分率 (1) per cent; (2) percentage;

~ 毛利百分率 gross profit percentage;

~ 磨損百分率 percentage of wear;

~ 損失百分率 percentage of damage;

百分數 per cent; percentage;

~ 清晰度百分數 percentage of articulation;

百分之 per cent;

百分之百 absolutely; hundred per cent; out and out; thorough-going; totally;

~ 百分之百錯誤 absolutely wrong;

~ 百分之百的謊言 out-and-out lie;

~ 百分之百失敗 fail utterly;

百分制 hundred-mark system; one-hundred-point scale;

~ 實行百分制 adopt a hundred-mark system;

[百福駢臻] may all blessings join together;

[百工] all classes of artisans;

[百官] officials of all ranks and descriptions;

[百果] all kinds of fruits;

[百合] lily; lily bulb;

百合花 lily;

復活節百合 easter lily;

海百合 crinoid; sea lily;

麝香百合 white trumpet

聖母百合 madonna lily;

天香百合 goldband lily;

野百合 rattlebush;

[百花] all sorts of flowers;

百花凋零 all flowers are withering; the flowers have faded;

百花開放，滿園溢香 the flowers are in bloom and perfumes scent the garden;

百花齊放 a variety of flowers are in bloom; all flowers are in bloom; all flowers bloom at once;

百花齊放，百家爭鳴 let a hundred flowers blossom and a hundred schools of thought contend;

百花齊放，推陳出新 let a hundred flowers bloom, weed through the old to bring forth the new;

百花怒放 hundreds of flowers are blooming in profusion;

百花盛開 a blaze of flowers; a hundred flowers in bloom; a variety of flowers are in full bloom; all flowers bloom together; flowers of every kind are in bloom;

百花爭春 all plants struggle to come out in spring;

百花爭妍 a hundred flowers blossom with a great variety of shows; flowers

B

are vying with each other in beauty; flowers compete in splendour; flowers vie with each other in splendour;

[百喙莫辯] a hundred mouths cannot explain it away; even a hundred mouths cannot absolve guilt; no one can argue it away;

[百貨] general merchandise;
百貨大樓 department store;
百貨公司 department store;
百貨批發商 general line wholesaler;
百貨商場 emporium;
百貨商店 department shop; department store;

[百家] (1) various families; (2) various schools of thinkers;
百家樂 baccarat;
百家爭鳴 contention of a hundred schools of thought;
~百家齊放，百家爭鳴 let a hundred flowers blossom and a hundred schools of thought contend;
諸子百家 various schools of thought and their exponents;

[百結衣] ragged clothing;
百結鶉衣 clothes of a hundred patches, ragged as a quail's tail;

[百科全書] encyclopaedia;
百科全書編纂者 encyclopaedist;
大百科全書 macropaedia;
兒童百科全書 children's encyclopaedia;
活百科全書 walking encyclopaedia;
簡明百科全書 concise encyclopaedia;
教育百科全書 educational encyclopaedia;
圖解百科全書 illustrated encyclopaedia;
小百科全書 micropaedia;

[百口莫辯] beyond dispute; inexcusable; there is no room for verbal defense;

[百禮] all ceremonies;

[百煉] repeated tempering;
身經百煉 have gone through the mill;

[百僚] all the officials;

[百靈鳥] lark;

[百美圖] picture showing a large number of beautiful women;

[百年] (1) century; hundred years; (2) one's lifetime; one's whole life;
百年不遇 be rarely met in a century; not occur even in a hundred years; on very rare occasions; once in a blue moon; rare; scarce;
百年大計 fundamental task for generations to come; long-term measure of fundamental importance; project of vital and far-reaching importance; project of vital and lasting importance; question of primary and lasting importance;
百年好合 have a long and harmonious married life;
百年後 after death;
百年紀念 centenarian;
百年老店 century-old shop;
百年樹人 education of people takes many many years to bear fruits; it takes a hundred years to rear people;
~十年樹木，百年樹人 it takes ten years to cultivate trees, but a hundred years to cultivate people;
百年偕老 a happy union of a hundred years;
百年一遇 be found once in a hundred years;
百年之後 after one's death; when one passes away;

[百鳥] all species of birds;
百鳥朝鳳 a hundred birds are paying homage to a phoenix;
百鳥爭鳴 a hundred birds contend in singing;

[百人吃百味] everyone to his own taste; tastes differ;

[百忍] great endurance; great forbearance;

[百日] hundredth day after one's death;
百日紅 crape myrtle;
~花無百日紅 no flower can bloom for a hundred days; the fairest rose withers at last; the fairest rose ends in a hip;
百日咳 pertussis; whooping cough;
~輕百日咳 parapertussis;

[百善孝為先] filial piety is the most important of all virtues;

[百十] hundred or so;

[百世] period of a hundred generations; very long period of time;
留芳百世 go down in history; have a niche in the temple of fame; leave a good name for posterity; leave a sweet memory behind; leave one's mark on history; perpetuate one's name;

[百事] all sorts of things; everything;
百事不管 keep one's nose out of

everything;
百事大吉 everything is fine;
～百事大吉，天下太平 everything will be fine and all will be right with the world;
百事俱廢 all sorts of things are abandoned; everything goes to ruin; everything is neglected; nothing constructive has been achieved;
百事順吉 everything goes right;
百事通 all-round person; expert in everything; jack of all trades; know-all; knowledgeable person; Mr. Know-all;
百事興旺 all things flourish and grow;

［百歲］ one hundred years old;
百歲老人 centenarian;
人活百歲不嫌多 nobody's is so old that he does not hope for another year of life;

［百萬］ million;
百萬富婆 millionairess;
百萬富翁 millionaire;
百萬雄獅 mighty army; million bold warriors;
千百萬 millions; millions upon millions;

［百無］ not one out of a hundred;
百無一長 good for nothing; skilled in nothing; without a single talent;
百無一精 not particularly skilled in any trade;
百無一能 have no skill in any of a hundred ways;
百無一失 absolutely sure; cannot fail under any circumstances; cannot possibly go wrong; no danger of anything going wrong; no possibility of failure; no risk at all; not a chance of any error; perfectly safe; there is not a single miss in a hundred tries;
百無一是 all in the wrong; good for nothing; have no merits at all; worthless;

［百物］ all things;

［百姓］ common people; people;
百姓百心 many men, many minds;
百姓百樣 it takes all sorts to make a world;
百姓父老 elders of the people;
百姓生活富足 the people are well off;
安撫百姓 appease the people; pacify the people;
老百姓 civilians; common people; folks; ordinary people;
～小老百姓 little people;
平民百姓 common people;
欺壓百姓 ride roughshod over the common people;

［百葉窗］ blinds; shutters; window-blinds; window-shades;
百葉窗固定器 blindfast;
活動百葉窗 Venetian blinds;

［百憂］ all sorrows; all worries;

［百戰］ fight a hundred battles;
百戰百勝 a hundred battles, a hundred victories; come out victorious in every battle; emerge victorious in every battle; ever-triumphant; ever-victorious; invincible; victorious in every battle;
～知己知彼，百戰百勝 know the enemy and know yourself, and then you will be ever-victorious;
百戰不殆 fight a hundred battles with no danger of defeat;
身經百戰 have experienced many battles; have fought countless battles; seasoned fighter; veteran of many wars;

［百折］ repeated setbacks;
百折不回 advance bravely and never withdraw; keep on fighting in spite of all setbacks; pushing forward despite repeated frustrations; with indomitable fortitude;
～百折不回的精神 intestinal fortitude;
百折不撓 assiduous in; bob up like a cork; indomitable; keep on fighting in spite of all setbacks; never say die; persistent efforts; put up a stiff resistance against great odds; unbending; undaunted by repeated setbacks; unflinching despite repeated setbacks; unrelenting; unremitting; unshakable; unswerving; unyielding despite reverses;
～百折不撓，再接再勵 indomitable; through one's dauntless and persistent efforts;

［百足］ centipede;
百足蟲 centipede;
百足之蟲，死而不僵 a centipede dies but never falls; a centipede does not topple over even when dead; old institutions die hard;

八百 eight hundred;
半百 fifty; fifty years of age; half a hundred;
好幾百 hundreds of;
幾百 hundreds; several hundred;
千百 hundreds and thousands;
三百 three hundred;
什百 tenfold or hundredfold;
四百 four hundred;
一百 a hundred;

B

bai
【柏】 a pronunciation of 柏 ;

bai
【捭】 (1) open; spread out; (2) strike with both hands;
[捭闔縱橫] suave and ingenious persuasion;

bai
【擺】 (1) arrange; display; place; put; set in order; (2) lay bare; state clearly; talk about; (3) assume; put on; show off; (4) swing; wag; wave; (5) pendulum;
[擺撥] dismiss from attention; put aside;
[擺佈] arrange; manipulate; push about; push around;
任憑處境擺佈 at the mercy of the circumstances;
任憑風浪擺佈 rove adrift at the mercy of;
任人擺佈 allow oneself to be ordered about; at the mercy of others;
受命運擺佈 be the puppet of fate;
受人擺佈 a puppet in the hands of others; in leading strings;
聽人擺佈 allow oneself to be ordered about; at sb's disposal;
[擺出] (1) take out for display; (2) assume; put on;
擺出來 take out for display;
[擺搭] distinguish oneself; show off;
[擺動] flicker; oscillate; sway; swing; wobbling;
愛擺動 waggy;
很快的擺動 swing fast;
經常擺動 swing constantly;
來回擺動 swing to and fro;
慢慢地擺動 swing slowly;
前後擺動 swing back and forth;
輕輕地擺動 swing gently;
向一側擺動 swing aside;
迎風擺動 swing in the breeze;
左右擺動 play pendulum sway from side to side;
[擺渡] cross a river on a ferry; ferry; ferryboat;
擺渡乘客 ferry passenger;
擺渡船 ferryboat;
擺渡過河 ferry across the river;
[擺飯] lay the table for a meal;
[擺供] offer sacrifices;
[擺好] place properly; set properly;
擺好姿勢 be posed; pose;
把…擺好 set in order;
~ 把工具擺好 set the tools in order;
~ 把碗筷擺好 lay the table; set the table;
[擺件] artworks for home decoration; display pieces; knick-knacks;
[擺局] arrange a ruse;
[擺開] ostentatious and extravagant; show off one's wealth;
擺不開 (1) there is no room to place sth; (2) the business in hand cannot be shaken off;
[擺闊] parade one's wealth;
擺闊氣 ostentatious and extravagant; parade one's wealth;
愛擺闊 ostentatious;
[擺列] display in neat rows; place in order;
[擺賣] sell from a stand;
[擺弄] (1) move back and forth; fiddle with; play with; toy with; (2) manipulate; order about; (3) make fun of; trick;
受人擺弄 be dalled with;
瞎擺弄 fool about with; fool around; fuck around;
[擺平] treat fairly;
[擺譜] go in for extravagance; keep up appearances; show off one's wealth; take pains to show off; try to appear rich and elegant;
[擺齊] place in neat order;
[擺設] furnish and decorate a place;
擺設得很… be...furnished;
~ 擺設得很豪華 be luxuriously furnished;
~ 擺設得很雅致 be tastefully furnished;
簡單的擺設 simple furnishings;
精致的擺設 elaborate furnishings;
俗氣的擺設 silly ornaments;
[擺手] swing one's arms; wave one's hand;
搖頭擺手 wag the head and wave the hand;
[擺攤] (1) operate a stall; set up a stall in the

street; set up a stall in the market; (2) maintain a large organization;

擺攤維生 make one's living as a vendor;

[擺脱] break away from; break from; break off; break loose; cast off; clear of; clear off; clear sb of sth; cut loose from; do away with; extricate oneself from; find freedom from; free from; free of; free oneself from; free sth of; get rid of; get sth off one's hands; get out; get over; give sb a miss; give sth a miss; give sb the go-by; give sth the go-by; rid; rid of; rid oneself of; see the back of sb; shake off; wash one's hands of;

[擺尾] (1) shopkeepers' strike; (2) flick the tail; wag the tail;

擺尾飛行 fishtail;

擺尾乞憐 beg like a dog; wag one's tail and beg for pity;

擺尾行駛 fishtail;

[擺下] (1) put down; (2) arrange;

擺不下 there is no place to put sth;

[擺針] oscillating needle;

[擺陣] deploy troops;

[擺鐘] pendulum clock;

落地大擺鐘 grandfather clock;

單擺 simple pendulum;

符合擺 coincidence pendulum;

復擺 compound pendulum;

回擺 backswing; oscillation;

揭擺 bring to light;

停擺 come to a standstill;

下擺 (1) lower hem of a gown; (2) width of the hem of a gown;

顯擺 reveal; show off;

搖擺 oscillate; rock; sway; swing; swing to and fro; vacillate;

鐘擺 pendulum;

bai

【襬】 lower part of a Chinese long gown;

bai⁴

bai

【拜】 (1) do obeisance; pay respects to; prostrate oneself; salute; worship; (2) appoint; (3) call at; call on; make a courtesy call; pay a visit to; visit; (4) establish a relationship formally; (5) a surname;

[拜拜] (1) bye-bye; (2) break off a relationship;

[拜別] say farewell; say goodbye; take leave;

[拜茶] ask a guest to come in and have tea;

[拜辭] say goodbye; take leave;

[拜倒] fall on one's knees; grovel; prostrate oneself;

拜倒石榴裙下 at one's feet; fall head over heels for a woman; throw oneself at sb's feet;

拜倒在地 be bowed to the ground;

拜倒足下 grovel at sb's feet; lie prostrate before sb; prostrate oneself and kowtow at sb's feet; prostrate oneself before sb; throw oneself at sb's feet;

[拜讀] have the honour to read; read with respect;

拜讀大作 have the honour to read; have the pleasure of perusing your work; read with respect your work;

[拜訪] call around sb's house; call at; call at sb's house; call on sb; call over; call round; call to see; call upon sb; come around; drop in; drop in on sb; drop in to see sb; give a visit to sb; give sb a visit; go to see; look in on sb; look sb up; make a visit to sb; make sb a visit; on a visit; pay a visit to sb; pay an official call; pay sb a call; see; visit; visit with sb; wait on sb;

拜訪某人 give sb a look-in; pay sb a visit;

拜訪親友 call on relatives and friends; visit relatives and friends;

拜訪時間 time for a visit;

~確定拜訪時間 fix a time for a call;

登門拜訪 pay a visit at sb's house; visit sb at his/her residence;

非正式拜訪 informal visit;

告別拜訪 farewell call;

很少拜訪 seldom visit;

經常拜訪 make frequent calls;

禮節性拜訪 courtesy call; courtesy visit;

親自拜訪 make a personal visit;

特意拜訪 come on a visit;

正式拜訪 formal visit;

專程拜訪 make a special trip to call on sb;

[拜佛] prostrate oneself before the image of Buddha; worship Buddha;

吃齋拜佛 take vegetarian food and worship Buddha;

求神拜佛 pray to Buddha for help;
［拜服］ greatly admire;
［拜官］ be appointed to a public office;
［拜跪］ kneel and kowtow;
［拜賀］ congratulate; offer congratulations;
［拜候］ call on; visit;
［拜會］ call on; make an official visit; pay a courtesy call; pay an official call;
告別拜會 pay a farewell call;
禮節拜會 make a courtesy call;
私人拜會 personal visit;
~ 進行私人拜會 pay a personal visit;
［拜見］ (1) call to pay respect; pay a formal visit; (2) meet one's senior or superior;
［拜節］ extend holiday greetings; pay a visit on holidays;
［拜金］ worship money;
拜金主義 Mammonism; money worship; worship of gold; worship of Mammon;
［拜爵］ be knighted;
［拜客］ call on; pay a visit; visit;
［拜懇］ beg humbly; implore; request;
［拜領］ accept with thanks;
［拜門］ (1) pay thanks by personal visit; (2) become a pupil or apprentice to a master;
［拜盟］ become sworn brothers;
［拜廟］ worship at a temple;
［拜墓］ worship at a grave;
［拜年］ make a New Year call; pay a New Year call; wish sb a Happy New Year;
給長輩拜年 make a New Year call to one's elders;
［拜神］ worship gods;
［拜師］ sit at sb's feet; take sb as one's teacher;
拜人為師 acknowledge sb as one's tutor; sit at sb's feet and be his new pupil;
拜師求學 pay respect to a master and seek for knowledge;
［拜壽］ congratulate an elderly person on his/her birthday; offer birthday felicitations;
［拜堂］ perform formal bows by bride and groom in the old custom in China; perform the formal wedding ceremony;
［拜帖］ visiting card;
［拜託］ request sb to do sth;
［拜望］ call on; call to pay one's respects; visit;
拜望…人 call on sb; call on sb to pay one's respect;
［拜物教］ fetishism;
［拜相］ be appointed prime minister;
封侯拜相 be conferred a rank of nobility and become a minister;
［拜謝］ express one's thanks; thank humbly ;
［拜星］ worship famous stars blindly;
［拜謁］ (1) call to pay respects; pay a formal visit; (2) pay homage;
拜謁某人 pay sb a visit of civility;
詣府拜謁 come to your house for a call;
［拜印］ be appointed to a public office;
［拜祖］ ancestor worship;

百拜 much courtesy;
參拜 formally call on; make a formal visit to; pay a courtesy call; pay respects to;
朝拜 pay respects to; worship;
崇拜 adore; worship;
答拜 pay a return visit;
跪拜 worship on bended knees;
回拜 pay a return visit;
結拜 become sworn brothers or sisters;
叩拜 kowtow;
禮拜 (1) ceremonial observances in general; ceremony; rite; (2) week; (3) day of the week; (4) Sunday; (5) weekend;
膜拜 prostrate; worship;
趨拜 hurry on to pay respects to;
團拜 have a party to exchange New Year greetings to each other;
下拜 bow;
遙拜 worship from a distance;
揖拜 make a bow with the folding in front;
再拜 bow twice;
展拜 visit;

bai

【敗】 (1) be defeated; lose; (2) beat; defeat; (3) fail; (4) corrupt; ruin; spoil; (5) bad; decayed; declined; withered; (6) counteract;
［敗北］ lose a battle; suffer defeat;
［敗筆］ (1) faulty stroke in caligraphy or painting; (2) faulty expression in writing; (3) disappointment; let-down;
［敗兵］ army in flight; defeated army; defeated troops;
敗兵殘卒 defeated broken ranks;
［敗德］ evil conduct; licentious behaviour;
［敗敵］ crush the enemy; defeat the enemy;

[敗而不餒] be undismayed by failure; not be discouraged by failure;
[敗壞] corrupt; debase; deteriorate; ruin; spoil; spoilage; undermine;
[敗火] relieve inflammation; relieve internal heat;
[敗績] be routed; defeat; suffer a defeat;
首遭敗績 suffer the first defeat;
[敗家] dissipate the family fortune; squander the family fortune;
敗家蕩產 squander a patrimony and ruin the family;
敗家子 black sheep; disgrace to the family; prodigal son; spendthrift; wastrel;
敗家子弟 children who ruin the family;
[敗將] defeated general;
[敗局] lost battle; lost game;
敗局已定 the game is as good as lost;
挽回敗局 restore a losing battle; save the day;
[敗軍] defeated army;
敗軍殘馬 defeated troops and ruined steeds;
敗軍折將 the army is defeated and the generals have been slain;
敗軍之將 a general without an army; defeated general; routed officer; underdog;
敗軍之將不可言勇 a general whose army is defeated cannot count himself brave;
敗不成軍 the army is completely routed;
[敗類] black sheep; degenerate; dregs of society; riff-riff; scum of a community;
民族敗類 degenerates of the nation;
社會敗類 scum of the society;
~鏟除社會敗類 eliminate the scum of the society;
斯文敗類 polished scoundrels;
[敗露] be brought to light; be uncovered; become known; fall through and stand exposed;
事情敗露 bring the matter to light;
陰謀敗露 expose sb's plot to the public; lay bare one's plot;
[敗落] decline in wealth or position; fall into a decline; go down;
家道敗落 suffer a fall in one's family fortune;
~造成家道敗落 cause the family's decline;
逐漸敗落 be on the decline; decline gradually;
[敗盟] break a covenant;
[敗名] disgrace oneself; tarnish one's reputation;
[敗群] endanger the whole group;
[敗肉] spoiled meat;
[敗事] bungle a matter; spoil a matter;
[敗訴] lose a lawsuit;
敗訴方 defeated party; losing party;
[敗歲] year of bad crops;
[敗退] retreat after defeat; retreat in defeat;
[敗亡] be defeated and overthrown;
[敗胃] spoil one's appetite;
[敗興] dampen one's enthusiasm; dampen one's interest; disappointed; frustrated; lessen one's pleasure;
敗興而歸 come back disappointed; return in low spirits;
敗興而回 come back disappointed; get home dejected; go back with a sour face; go home a disappointed man; go home in low spirits; return crestfallen; return home with a broken interest; return with a sour face; return with one's tail between one's legs;
感到敗興 be disappointed;
使人敗興 disappointing;
[敗絮] waste cotton—a dry and useless thing;
敗絮其中 foul inside;
[敗血] poisonous blood;
敗血病 septicaemia;
~膿毒敗血病 septicopyemia;
~隱性敗血病 cryptogenic septicemia;
敗血膿毒症 septicopyemia;
敗血性休克 septic shock;
敗血症 septicemia; vanquished blood;
產後敗血症 puerperal septicemia;
出血性敗血症 haemorrhagic septicemia;
膿毒敗血症 septicopyemia;
~轉移性敗血症 metastasizing septicemia;
[敗葉] fallen leaves;
[敗仗] lose a battle; suffer a defeat;
吃敗仗 suffer a defeat;
打敗仗 be defeated in battle; lose a battle; suffer a defeat;
[敗陣] be beaten in a contest; be defeated on the battlefield;

敗陣撤退 be outmatched and retreat;
敗陣而歸 return defeated;
敗陣而逃 lose the field and take flight;
敗下陣來 lose a battle;
連吃敗陣 suffer one defeat after another;

［敗走］ flee after defeat;

必敗 be bound to lose; be doomed to failure; will certainly be defeated; will certainly fail;
不敗 invincible; unbeatable;
殘敗 (1) wrack; (2) wipeout;
慘敗 abysmal failure; body blow; crushing defeat; disastrous defeat; fiasco; lose heavily; suffer a crushing defeat; suffer a terrible defeat;
成敗 success or failure;
挫敗 (1) suffer a setback; (2) defeat; frustrate;
打敗 (1) beat; defeat; (2) be defeated; suffer a defeat;
大敗 (1) defeat utterly; (2) suffer a crushing defeat;
腐敗 (1) decayed; rotten; (2) decadent; degenerate; (3) corrupt; rotten;
擊敗 beat; defeat;
潰敗 be defeated; be routed;
破敗 dilapidated; ruined;
橈敗 defeated as troops;
喪敗 decline and fall; suffer a downfall;
勝敗 success or failure; victory or defeat;
失敗 a kick in the teeth; come a cropper; come unstuck; defeat; fail; fail to do sth; failure; fall down; fall through; fizzle out; flop; get a cropper; go to the wall; licking; never come to anything; pluck in sth;
衰敗 at a low ebb; decline;
酸敗 turn sour;
頹敗 decadent; declining;
朽敗 decayed and rotten;
淹敗 be routed; damaged by water;
一敗 a defeat;
窳敗 corrupt; rot;
詐敗 feign defeat;
戰敗 (1) be vanquished; lose a battle; suffer a defeat; (2) defeat; vanquish;

bai

【稗】 (1) barnyard grass; (2) little; small; (3) folk; unofficial;

［稗販］ hawker; peddler;
［稗官］ low-ranking official;
稗官野史 historical novels; unofficial historical writings;
［稗記］ books of anecdotes;
［稗史］ historical romance; unofficial history;
［稗説］ novels; stories;
［稗子］ barnyard grass; barnyard millet;

bai

【粺】 polished rice;

ban¹

ban

【扳】 (1) pull; turn; (2) count;

［扳倒］ pull down;
［扳機］ trigger;
扣扳機 pull the trigger;
［扳開］ pull open;
［扳平］ equalize the score;
［扳手］ (1) spanner; wrench; (2) lever;
管子扳手 bulldog wrench;
活動扳手 adjustable spanner; adjustable wrench;
螺栓扳手 bolt spanner;
套筒扳手 box wrench; carriage wrench;
彎頭扳手 bent spanner; bent wrench;
斜口扳手 angle wrench;
［扳指兒］ heavy ring;
［扳轉］ (1) turn around; (2) tip the scale; turn the tide;
［扳子］ spanner;
活扳子 monkey wrench;
活動扳子 monkey wrench;

ban

【班】 (1) grade; seat; (2) class; company; group; team; (3) duty; shift; (4) squad; (5) regular; scheduled; (6) distribute; (7) return; (8) a surname;

［班白］ gray-headed;
［班班］ (1) clear and apparent; (2) the noise of moving wagons;
［班車］ regular bus service;
沒趕上班車 behind schedule;
［班次］ (1) number of runs; number of flights; (2) order of classes or grades at school;
［班底］ ordinary members of a theatrical troupe, etc.;
［班機］ airliner; regular air service;
乘坐班機 fly a scheduled airliner;
商務班機 commercial airliner;
誤了班機 miss a flight;
［班級］ classes and grades in school;
［班列］ relative ranks;

[班門弄斧] a foolish display of axe before the master carpenter's home; offer to teach fish to swim; preach to be wise; show off one's proficiency with the axe before Lu Ban, the master carpenter; show off one's slight skill in the presence of an expert; teach a dog to bark; teach one's grandmother to suck eggs; wielding an axe before the door of Lu Ban the master carpenter－show off in the presence of an expert;

輔導班 auxiliary class;

[班師] (1) return after victory; (2) withdraw troops from the front;
班師而歸 make a triumphant return;
班師回朝 lead one's army and the captives in triumph back to the capital;

[班長] (1) class monitor; monitor; (2) squad leader; (3) team leader;

[班組] class; team;
班組層次管理 management through gradation of teams;

挨班 in turn; one by one;
白班 day shift;
本班 this class;
畢業班 graduating class;
編班 assign students to various classes; form the classes; group into classes;
補習班 continuation class; make-up class; reinforcement class;
插班 join a class in the middle of the course;
唱詩班 choir;
初學班 beginner's class;
炊事班 cook-house;
搭班 (1) join a group in order to help in a task; (2) join a theatrical troupe temporarily;
當班 on duty by turn;
倒班 work in shifts;
頂班 work full time;
短期學習班 sessional class;
短期訓練班 short-term training class;
短訓班 short-term training course;
蹲班 stay down;
分班 (1) divide into classes; (2) divide into squads;
輔導班 auxiliary class;
附設班 supplementary class;
高級班 advanced class;
跟班 (1) join a regular shift or class; (2) attendant; footman;
函授班 correspondence class;
航班 flight number; scheduled flight;
換班 (1) change shifts; (2) relieve a person on duty;
集訓班 training course;
加班 extra shift; work an extra shift; work extra hours; work overtime;
講習班 opportunity class; study class;
降班 fail to go up to the next grade; stay down;
交班 hand over to the next shift; pass work on to the next shift; turn over one's duty;
接班 carry on; succeed; take one's turn on duty; take over from;
進修班 class for advanced studies;
科班 regular professional training;
領班 lead; the head of;
留班 stay down;
輪班 on duty by turns;
落後班 backward class;
慢班 adjustment class;
模範班 example class;
拿班 assume great airs; put on airs; strike a pose;
年齡班 age class;
排班 (1) fall by rank; fall in line; (2) arrange turns of work;
平衡班 parallel class;
全班 whole class; whole squad;
全日班 all-day class;
日班 day shift;
上班 go on duty; go to office; go to work; on duty; start work;
昇班 (1) go up one grade in school; (2) advance to a higher grade; be promoted;
實驗班 experimental class;
識字班 literacy class;
暑期補習班 summer make-up class;
速成班 accelerated class; express class;
替班 take over another's shift;
跳班 skip a grade in school;
通訊班 signal squad;
同班 (1) classmate; (2) be in the same class;
推廣班 extension class;
脱班 (1) late for work; (2) behind schedule;
晚班 night shift;
戲班 theatrical troupe;
下班 go off work; knock off; off duty;
校外班 extramural classes;
歇班 have time off; off duty;
新生班 freshman class;
學習班 study class;

訓練班 training class; training course;
夜班 night shift;
業餘班 part-time class;
一班 (1) a class; a group; a squad; a troupe; (2) a class of; a group of; a squad of; a troupe of;
嬰兒班 baby class; nursery class;
幼兒班 children's class;
早班 morning shift;
站班 on duty; stand guard;
值班 on duty;
職業班 professional class;
中班 (1) the middle class in a kindergarten; (2) middle shift; swing shift;
重點班 major work class;
作業班 work team;

ban

【般】 (1) a kind of; a sort of; a type of; a way of; (2) alike in; as; like; (3) a surname;

［般般］ (1) colourful; (2) gorgeous; (3) all kinds; every sort;

［般配］ match each other; well matched;

百般 by every means; in a hundred and one ways; in every possible way;
全般 all; the entire amount;
恁般 to such an extent;
萬般 (1) all; all the different kinds; every; in many different ways; various; (2) extremely; utterly;
一般 (1) as a rule; common; generally; usually; (2) just like; same as;
這般 like this; so such;
諸般 all kinds; all sorts;

ban

【斑】 (1) specks; speckles; spots; stains; stripes; (2) spotted; striped;

［斑白］ grizzled; graying;

［斑斑］ full of spots; full of stains; mottled; spotted;
斑斑點點 mottled; speckled; spotted;
淚痕斑斑 be bathed in tears; tear-stained; wet with tears;
鏽迹斑斑 have rusty stains;
血淚斑斑 full of blood and tears; with spots of tears and blood;
血漬斑斑 blood-stained;

［斑鬢］ gray hair at the temples;

［斑病］ spot;
黑斑病 black spot;

［斑駁］ motley;
斑駁陸離 mixed colours; motley and chopped in appearance; of different colours; variegated;

［斑點］ dot; fleck; freckle; mottle; speckle; spot; stain;
電弧斑點 arc spot;
灰斑點 gray speck;
冷端斑點 cold-end specks;
滿臉斑點 freckled-faced;
沒有斑點 speckless;
細菌性斑點 bacterial spot;
血斑點 blood spot;
有很多斑點 be badly specked;

［斑痕］ blackspot;

［斑鳩］ turtledove;
斑鳩吃螢火蟲—肚裏明 a turtledove eating up a firefly — bright in the belly; have a clear understanding of things;

［斑斕］ bright-coloured; multicoloured;
斑斕彩色 beautifully coloured; variegated-coloured;
色彩斑斕 brightly-coloured; variegated coloured;

［斑馬］ pinto; zebra;
斑馬紋 zebra-stripe;
斑馬線 zebra crossing;
一匹斑馬 a zebra;

［斑蝥］ cantharides; Chinese blister beetle;

［斑紋］ streaks; stripes;
黑色斑紋 dark stripes;

［斑疹傷寒］ typhus; typhus fever;
地方性斑疹傷寒 endemic typhus;
典型斑疹傷寒 classic typhus;
流行性斑疹傷寒 epidemic typhus;

［斑竹］ mottled bamboo;

白斑 leucoma; eucoplakia; leukoplasia; white specks; white spots;
豹斑 leopard's spots;
鬢斑 hair turning gray at the temples;
耳斑 ear plaque;
光斑 facula;
果斑 fruit spots;
汗斑 (1) sweat stain; (2) tinea versicolour;
黑白斑 melanoleukoderma;
黑斑 freckle;
紅斑 blotch;
花斑 piebald;
花斑斑 flowery;
黃斑 macula lutea; yellow spot;

黃褐斑 chloasma;
藍斑 blue spot;
老年斑 senile lentigo;
老人斑 age-mark;
淋病性斑 macula gonorrhoea;
霉斑 mildew;
譜斑 flocculus;
青斑 blue spot;
雀斑 freckle;
日斑 sunspot;
乳白斑 milk spot;
曬斑 sunburn;
傷寒斑 typhoid spot;
神經炎性斑 neuritic plaques;
石斑 bass; grouper;
壽斑 senile plagues;
死斑 livor;
聽斑 acoustic spot;
蘚斑 patches of lichen;
血斑 blood stains;
耀斑 solar flare;
一斑 (1) a spot; (2) a tiny part;
硬斑 induration;
淤斑 ecchymosis;
瘀斑 ecchymosis;
紫斑 petechia;
紫血斑 purpura;

ban

【搬】 (1) move; remove; take away; (2) move house; move things; (3) apply indiscriminately; copy mechanically; (4) rake in money;

［搬兵］ ask for help; call in reinforcement;

［搬動］ move; shift;

［搬家］ change one's residence; make a move; move; move house; pull up stakes; up sticks;
搬家車 moving van;
搬家公司 home-moving company;
經常搬家 move house frequently;
孔夫子搬家一淨輸 Confucius moving to a new location — all loss;

［搬進］ move in;
搬進來 move in;
搬進新辦公室 move in new offices;
搬進新居 move into a new house;

［搬空］ evacuate;

［搬弄］ (1) fiddle with; move sth about; (2) display; show off;

［搬配］ unequally matched marriage;

［搬遷］ make a removal; move; move out; move to a new location; relocate;
搬遷啟示 removal notice;

［搬移］ move;

［搬用］ (1) apply indiscriminately; (2) copy mechanically;

［搬運］ carry; move; transport;
搬運費 handling charge; transportation charges;
搬運工 docker; porter;
~ 車站搬運工 porter; redcap;
搬運公司 moving company; transportation company;
搬運貨物 transport goods;
搬運行李 carry luggage;

［搬磚砸腳］ drop a brick on one's own foot;

［搬走］ move away; move out;

硬搬 copy everything mechanically; transplant mechanically;
運搬 move; transport;
照搬 copy mechanically; imitate indiscriminately;

ban

【頒】 (1) award; bestow on; confer on; grant; (2) distribute; issue; send out; (3) make public; proclaim; promulgate;

［頒白］ gray; white;

［頒布］ issue; promulgate; publish;

［頒發］ (1) issue; promulgate; (2) award; bestow; confer;

［頒獎］ hand out a prize; hand out an award; prize-giving;
頒獎典禮 award ceremony; prize-giving ceremony;
頒獎鼓勵 encourage by awards of prize;
頒獎日 award day;
頒獎儀式 awards ceremony;

［頒行］ issue for enforcement; make public and put into practice; promulgate and enforce;

ban

【斒】 (1) motley; variegated; (2) gorgeous; resplendent;

［斒斕］ (1) gorgeous; resplendent; (2) multicoloured; variegated colour;

ban

【瘢】 freckle; scar;

［瘢點］ (1) black spot on the skin; (2) scar;
［瘢痕］ cicatrix; scar;
惡性瘢痕 vicious cicatrix;
肥厚性瘢痕 hypertrophic scar;

ban
【癍】 blotch; fleck; rash on skin; unhealthy marks on the skin;

B

ban³
ban
【坂】 hillside; slope;

ban
【阪】 (1) hillside; slope of a hill; (2) hillside farm field;
［阪田］ (1) hillside farm field; (2) rugged and stony field;

ban
【板】 (1) board; plank; plate; (2) shutter; (3) bat; (4) ban clappers; (5) (in traditional Chinese music) accented beat; measure; time; (6) hard; (7) rigid; stern; stiff; straight; unnatural; (8) look serious; stop smiling;
［板板六十四］ inflexible; rigid; stick to rules strictly; unaccommodating;
版版六十四 conservative; inflexible;
［板本］ books printed with types;
［板壁］ wooden partition;
［板擦兒］ eraser;
［板材］ plate;
［板蕩］ time of turmoil; world of disorder; social confusion and chaos;
板蕩識忠臣 the true and faithful can be easily spotted in time of trouble;
［板櫈］ bench; wooden stool;
冷板櫈 (1) indifferent post; (2) be given the cold shoulder; cold reception;
～坐冷板櫈 (1) hold a position with little power; (2) be given the cold shoulder; be kept waiting long; be left on the bench; be left out in the cold;
小板櫈 low stool; small stool;
［板兒］ board; plate;
板兒寸 hush-top; closely cropped hair;
板兒爺 pedicab man;
［板斧］ hatchet;
［板塊］ plate;
板塊構造學 plate tectonics;
板塊運動 plate movement;
［板皮］ slab;
［板球］ cricket;
板球運動 cricket;
～板球運動員 cricketer;
［板刷］ scrub brush; scrubbing brush;
［板條］ lath;
板條材 lathwood;
板條花房 lathhouse;
板條箱 crate;
船底板條 bottom lath;
金屬板條 metallic lath;
石膏板條 gypsum lath;
［板鴨］ pressed dried salted duck;
［板岩］ slate;
矾板岩 alum slate;
泥質板岩 argillaceous slate;
黏板岩 adhesive slate;
碳質板岩 carbonaceous slate;
［板眼］ method; orderliness;
有板有眼 in methodical order; rhythmic; well presented;
做事沒板眼 lack method in one's work; lack orderliness in what one does;
［板印］ print with engraved blocks;
［板子］ (1) board; plank; (2) birch; punishing bamboo;
挨板子 be punished; suffer a criticism; suffer punishment;
打板子 flog with a birch;

案板 (1) chopping board; (2) kneading board;
鞍板 saddle plate;
凹板 concave;
白板 white board;
刨花板 shaving board;
壁板 wallboard;
臂板 arm;
玻璃板 glass plate;
薄板 sheet;
測繪板 plotting board;
測圖板 surveying panel;
插接板 plugboard;
搓板 wash board;
牀板 bed plank;
大板 plank;
呆板 inflexible; rigid; stiff;
單板 veneer;
擋板 shroud;
擋泥板 fender; mudguard;
導板 guide;
底板 negative;

地板 (1) floor board; (2) floor;
頂板 roof;
帆板 sailboard; windsurfer;
封檐板 caves board;
浮板 bodyboard;
甘蔗板 cane fibre board;
乾板 dry plate;
鋼板 steel plate;
隔板 bulkhead; partition;
隔聲板 sound insulating board;
隔音板 sound insulating board;
古板 old-fashioned and inflexible;
鼓板 clappers;
呱嗒板 bamboo clappers;
關板 close down; go bankrupt;
光板 (1) worn-out fur; (2) a kind of copper cash;
軌枕板 concrete slab sleeper;
夯板 tamping plate;
黑板 blackboard;
滑板 slide;
滑雪板 skis;
畫板 drawing board;
繪圖板 drawing board;
急板 presto;
極板 plate;
夾板 splint;
甲板 deck;
簡板 bamboo clappers;
瞼板 tarsus;
槳板 paddle board;
膠合板 plywood; veneer board;
刻板 (1) inflexible; mechanical; (2) cut blocks for printing;
籃板 backboard;
老板 boss;
樓板 floor; floor-slab;
鋁板 aluminium sheet;
門板 (1) door plank; (2) shutters;
模板 (1) shuttering; (2) pattern plate;
模型板 mould plate;
木板 board; plank;
木絲板 wood wool board;
拍板 (1) clappers; (2) beat time with clappers; (3) rap the gravel; (4) give the final verdict; have the final say;
平板 dull and stereotyped; flat;
鋪板 bed board; bed plank;
七巧板 tangram;
七色板 seven colour disk;
企口板 tongue-and-groove board;
縴板 tracking yoke;
蹺蹺板 seesaw; teeterboard;
翹翹板 seesaw;
球板 paddles;
柔板 adagio;
三板 sampan;
三合板 plywood; three-ply board;
三角板 set square;
舢板 sampan;
舌板 lingual plate;
石板 flag; flagstone; slabstone;
石棉板 asbestos board;
壽板 coffin;
死板 inflexible; rigid; still;
松板 deal board;
踏板 (1) footboard; footrest; treadle; (2) footstool; (3) pedal;
檀板 hardwood clappers;
踢腳板 skirting board;
天花板 ceiling;
調色板 palette;
跳板 (1) gang-plank; (2) diving board; springboard;
鐵板 iron plate; iron sheet;
鐵腳板 iron soles;
聽板 auditory plate;
銅板 (1) copper coin; (2) copper clappers;
圖板 (1) drawing board; (2) printing plate;
托灰板 hawk;
拖板 (1) mop; (2) extension board;
望板 roof boarding;
屋面板 roof boarding;
五合板 five-ply board;
洗衣板 wash-board;
纖維板 fibre-board;
響板 castanets;
鑲板 panel; paneling;
鋅板 zinc plate; zincograph;
行板 andante;
型板 template; templet;
雪板 skis;
血小板 platelet;
壓舌板 depressor;
壓制板 pressboard;
樣板 (1) sample plate; (2) template; (3) example; model; prototype;
腰板 (1) back; (2) build; physique;
一板 mechanical;
儀表板 dashboard; instrument panel;
硬紙板 cardboard; hard-board;
熨衣板 ironing board;
造型板 mould board;
閘板 (1) sluice; (2) wooden panel protecting the window;

遮板 curtain board; sunshade;
遮熱板 insulation board;
遮陽板 sun-shading board;
砧板 chopping block;
椹板 chopping board;
指板 finger-board;
指示板 indicator board;
紙板 cardboard; paperboard;
紙漿板 pulp board;
中板 medium plate;
竹板 bamboo clappers;
走板 (1) out of tune; sing out of rhythm; (2) speak beside the point; wander from the subject;

ban

【版】 (1) printing block; printing plate; (2) edition; (3) page;

[版本] edition;

[版次] edition series;

[版畫] block print; print; woodcut;

[版刻] carving; engraving;

[版框] chase;
浮動版框 floating chase;
機器版框 machine chase;
零件印刷版框 jobbing chases;
螺絲版框 screw chases;
鑄鉛版框 foundry chase;

[版面] (1) space of a whole page; (2) layout of a printed sheet;
版面編輯 make-up editor;
版面設計 layout;
版面閱讀量 page traffic;
中心頁跨頁版面 centerfold;

[版權] copyright;
版權法 copyright law;
~ 採用版權法 adopt the copyright law;
~ 實施版權法 administer the copyright law;
~ 制定版權法 make the copyright law;
版權所有 all rights reserved; copyright reserved;
版權頁 copyright page;
侵犯版權 infringement of copyright;

[版稅] royalty;
借書版稅 lending royalties;
著者版稅 author's royalty;

[版圖] domain; territory;
版圖遼闊 vast in territory;
納入…版圖 be annexed to the territory of...;
屬於…版圖 be in the domain of...;
中國版圖 territory of China;

凹版 gravure; intaglio;
碑版 stele; stone tablet;
玻璃版 collotype;
重版 republish;
出版 come off the press; publish; see the light of day;
初版 first edition;
盜版 piracy;
盜印版 pirated edition;
第一版 first edition;
底版 negative; photographic plate;
電鑄版 electrotype;
雕版 cut blocks for printing;
翻版 reprint; reproduction;
腐蝕版 etched plate;
國外版 foreign edition;
海外版 overseas edition;
航空版 airmail edition;
活版 typography; letterpress;
活字版 movable type;
膠版 offset plate;
絕版 out of print;
珂羅版 collotype;
刻版 cut blocks for printing;
蠟版 mimeograph stencil; stencil plate;
末版 back page;
木版 block;
排版 compose; typeset;
平版 lithographic plate;
普及版 popular edition;
鉛版 stereotype;
三版 third edition;
三色版 three-colour block; three-colour halftone;
石版 stone plate;
套版 colourplate; process plate;
套色版 colourplate; process plate;
謄寫版 stencil;
頭版 (1) front page; (2) first edition;
銅版 copperplate;
凸版 relief printing plate;
圖版 plate;
網版 printing screen;
新版 new edition;
橡皮版 rubber plate;
修訂版 revised edition;
印版 printing plate;
原版 original edition;
再版 (1) second edition; (2) reprint; republish;
照相版 process plate;

紙版 paper matrix; paper mould;
制版 plate making;

ban
【舨】 sampan;

舢舨 sampan;

ban
【蝂】 small insect which can move things many times its weight;

ban
【闆】 boss; owner;

ban⁴
ban
【半】 (1) half; semi-; (2) halfway; in the middle; (3) the least bit; very little; (4) about half; partly;

［半百］ fifty; fifty years of age; half a hundred;
年過半百 above fifty; already past fifty; over fifty; over fifty years of age;

［半…半］ half...half; part...part; partly...partly;
半賣半送 sell goods at rock-bottom prices;
半送半賣 sell goods at rock-bottom prices;
半推半就 feign to resist; give way after making a show of declining; half refusal and half consent; half refusing and half accepting; half rejecting and half yielding; half yield and half deny; partly refusing and partly consenting; yield while pretending to reject; yield with a show of reluctance;
半文半白 half literary, half vernacular;
半信半疑 half believe; half believe, half doubt; half-believing, half-doubting; half in doubt; not quite convinced; take sth with a grain of salt; with a pinch of salt;
～對…半信半疑 dubious about...;
半醒半睡 half awake and half asleep; slumberous;
半醒半醉 half sober and half drunk;

［半包兒］ dirty trick;

［半飽］ half full;
半飢半飽 half-starving; underfed;

［半壁］ a slice of territory; half;
半壁江山 half of the country; half of the national territory;

［半邊］ half of sth;
半邊天 (1) half the sky; (2) women of the new society;

［半…不］ half-; more...than...;
半明不滅 not very bright;

［半場］ half of a game;
後半場 second half;
前半場 first half;
上半場 first half; first half of the game; half-time;
下半場 second half of the game;

［半打］ half a dozen; six;
半打裝 six pack;

［半島］ peninsula;

［半點］ (1) the least bit; (2) half an hour;
一星半點 a tiny bit;

［半吊子］ (1) dabbler; smatterer; (2) tactless and impulsive person;

［半價］ fifty per cent discount; half price;

［半節］ half a section;

［半截］ half;
矮半截 inferior to others; worse than others;
涼了半截 one's heart is chilled with disappointment; one's heart sinks;
留下半截 leave over half of;
事做半截 give up the work
心涼半截 be stricken to the heart;

［半徑］ radius;
半徑範圍 radius;
基圓半徑 base radius;
平均半徑 average radius;
彎曲半徑 bending radius;
原子半徑 atomic radius;

［半句］ half the utterance;
話到舌邊留半句 hold back part of what one has to say when one is about to say it;

［半拉］ half;
半半拉拉 incomplete; unfinished;

［半路］ halfway; in progress; midway; on the way;
半路上殺出個程咬金 an unexpected obtruder has bounced in halfway; sth unexpected popped up halfway;
半半路路 halfway; midway;

［半年］ half a year;
半年一次的 half-yearly;
未來半年 in the next six months;

［半票］ half fare; half-price ticket;

B

[半旗] half mast; half staff;
降半旗 flag flown at halfmast; fly a flag at halfmast;
下半旗 hang the flag at half mast; hoist the flag at half mast; lower the flag at half mast;

[半球] hemisphere;
半球圖 hemisphere map;
北半球 northern hemisphere;
冬半球 winter hemisphere;
東半球 eastern hemisphere;
極半球 polar hemisphere;
~近極半球 proximal hemisphere;
陸半球 land hemisphere;
南半球 southern hemisphere;
上半球 upper semi-sphere;
西半球 western hemisphere;
下半球 lower semi-sphere;

[半群] semi-group;
收縮半群 contractive semi-group;
消去半群 cancellation semi-group;
自由半群 free semi-group;

[半日] half a day; half-day;

[半晌] (1) half a day; half-day; (2) a long time; quite a long time;
前半晌 forenoon; morning;
上半晌 forenoon; morning;
下半晌 afternoon;

[半身] (1) one side of the body; (2) half of the body;
半身不遂 be half paralyzed; half-paralyzed; hemiplegia;
半身像 (1) half-length photo; (2) bust;
~照一張半身像 have one's half-length photo taken;
上半身 above the waist; upper part of the body;
下半身 lower part of the body;

[半生] (1) half a lifetime; (2) half-baked; half-raw; not well cooked;
半生不熟 half-cooked;
後半生 afternoon of one's life;
前半生 first half of one's life;

[半世] half of a person's life span;

[半熟] half-cooked;

[半數] half; half the number;
半數以上 more than half;
過半數 majority; more than half;

[半死] half-dead;
打得半死 beat sb within an inch of his life; beat someone half-dead; beat someone until he is half-dead; beat to a mummy;
累個半死 feel dog-tired; fit to drop;

[半天] (1) half of the day; half-day; (2) a long time; quite a while; (3) period of time in a day; (4) in the air; midair;
待了半天 stay for a long while;
老半天 a long time;
前半天 forenoon; morning;
上半天 forenoon; morning;
晚半天兒 late afternoon;
下半天 afternoon; last half day;
早半天 before noon; morning;

[半途] halfway; midway;
半途而返 return halfway;
半途而廢 abandon halfway; collapse halfway; do things by halves; drop by the wayside; fall by the wayside; give up halfway through; leave sth unfinished; stop halfway;
半途換馬 change horses at mid-stream; swop horses halfway;
半途散伙 part company halfway;

[半夜] in the depth of night; in the middle of the night; late at night; midnight; the dead hours;
半夜到達 arrive in the middle of the night;
半夜叫城門—碰釘子 knock on the city gate at midnight — strike against a nail;
半夜裏屙屎—等不得 have to defecate in the middle of the night — cannot wait;
半夜三更 in the depth of night; late at night; watching hour;
半夜十二點 midnight;
~半夜十二點整 on the stroke of midnight;
黑更半夜 in the dead of night;
起五更，睡半夜 retire at midnight and rise before dawn;
前半夜 from dusk till midnight; from nightfall to midnight; the first half of the night;
上半夜 before midnight; first half of the night;
深更半夜 at the dead of night; deep in the night; far into the night; in the dead of night; in the depth of night; in the middle of the night; in the small hours of the night; midnight; the midnight hours; witching hours;

下半夜 after midnight; latter half of the night; small hours; time after midnight; wee hours;

[半因…半因] what with...and what with;

[半音] semitone;

等程半音 equally tempered semitone;

花半音 chromatic semitone;

調和半音 tempered semitone;

[半圓] semicircle;

[半月] half moon;

半月刊 bimonthly; fortnightly; semi-monthly;

半月形 half moon;

上半月 first half of a month;

下半月 last half of a month;

[半載] half a year; six months;

離開一年半載 away for six months or a year;

參半 half; half-and-half;

大半 (1) most likely; most probably; very likely; (2) for the most part; more than half; most; the best part of; the great part of;

對半 (1) divide half-and-half; down the middle; fifty-fifty; go halves; half-and-half; in half; into halves; (2) double;

多半 great part; most likely; most probably;

各半 fifty-fifty; half and half;

後半 latter half; second half;

兩半 in half; in two; two halves;

強半 (1) over half; (2) the greater half;

軟半 less than a half;

太半 greater half;

泰半 more than half; the greater part; the majority;

宵半 midnight;

小半 less than half; the lesser part; the smaller part;

夜半 midnight;

一半 half; in part; moiety; one half;

月半 fifteenth day of a month;

折半 give fifty per cent discount; reduce a price by half; reduce by half; reduce to half; sell at half price;

ban

【伴】 (1) companion; partner; (2) accompany; attend;

[伴唱] (1) vocal accompaniment; (2) accompany a singer;

伴唱者 accompanist;

[伴當] servant;

[伴兒] companion;

[伴郎] best man; groomsman;

[伴侶] companion; helpmate; mate; partner;

忠實伴侶 faithful companion; faithful mate;

終身伴侶 lifelong companion;

終生伴侶 lifelong companion;

[伴娘] bridesmaid; matron of honour at a wedding;

主要伴娘 maid of honour;

[伴聲] sound accompaniment;

[伴送] escort;

[伴隨] accompany; follow;

[伴舞] dancing partner;

伴舞樂隊 dance band;

[伴奏] accompaniment; accompany; play an accompaniment;

伴奏者 accompanist;

鋼琴伴奏 piano accompaniment;

音樂伴奏 music accompaniment;

搭伴 (1) in company; join sb on a trip; travel together; (2) partner;

伙伴 companion; partner;

夥伴 companion; helpmate; partner;

結伙 go with; travel together with;

就伴 accompany sb on a journey; travel together;

老伴 one's old man; one's old woman;

旅伴 fellow traveller; travel companion;

女伴 female companion;

陪伴 keep sb company;

隨伴 accompaniment;

同伴 companion;

相伴 accompany sb;

遊伴 travel companion;

有…做伴 have to have sb's company;

與…為伴 make companion of...; companion with;

ban

【扮】 (1) be dressed up as; disguise oneself as; dress up; play the part of; (2) put on an expression;

[扮戲] (1) make up; (2) perform on stage; play a role in a play; play the part of;

[扮相] appearance of an actor or actress in costume and make-up;

[扮演] act; act sb; act the part of sb; be dressed up to represent sb; carry off one's role of sb; dress up as sb; interpret the role

B

of sb; in the character of sb; make oneself up as sb; play sb; play the role of sb; take on the role of sb;
扮演一個角色 have a role to play; take on a role;
[扮裝] (1) disguise; (2) make-up;
男扮女裝 man disguised in female attire; man dressed like a woman;
女扮男裝 girl dressed as a boy; woman disguised as a man;
[扮作] disguise as; dress up to;
扮作商人 be disguised as a merchant;

打扮 deck out; dress; dress up; have a makeover; make-up;
改扮 disguise oneself as;
假扮 camouflage; disguise oneself as; dress up as; make one pass for; masquerade; personate; play the part of; pretend;
刷扮 dress up; make up;
妝扮 doll up;
裝扮 attire; deck out; doll up; dress up;

ban
【拌】 mix; stir;
[拌和] blend; mix and stir;
[拌麵] noodles in mixed sauce;
[拌勻] mix thoroughly; mix well;
[拌嘴] bicker; quarrel; squabble; wrangle;
為小事拌嘴 bicker with each other over small matters;
與人拌嘴 bicker with sb;

攪拌 agitate; agitation; blend; mix; mixing; stir; whip;
涼拌 season cold food with sauce and condiment;
路拌 road mix;
雜拌 (1) assorted preserved fruits; (2) hotchpotch; medley; mixture;

ban
【絆】 (1) cause to stumble; cause to trip; hindrance; stumble; trip; (2) fetters; shackles;
[絆絆坷坷] stagger along;
[絆倒] stumble; trip; trip over;
被…絆倒 stumble over...;
~被繩索絆倒 trip against a rope;
[絆腳] (1) tie up sb's movements; trip; (2) fettered; hindered;
絆腳石 obstacle; stumbling block;
[絆馬索] ropes for tripping the enemy's horses;
[絆住] be detained; be held back; entangle; successfully hinder movement;

磕磕絆絆 bumpy; limping; rough;

ban
【辦】 (1) attend to; deal with; do; handle; manage; tackle; (2) establish; run; set up; (3) get sth ready; prepare; (4) bring to justice; penalize; punish; try and punish; (5) buy; purchase;
[辦案] handle a case; take care of a matter; take charge of a case;
[辦報] publish a newspaper; run a newspaper;
[辦不來] too much for one to handle;
[辦不完] too much for one to finish;
[辦差] take charge of missions;
[辦到] accomplish; get sth done;
辦得到 can be done;
[辦法] means; measures; ways;
辦法不止一種 there is more than one way to skin a cat;
不徹底的辦法 half measures;
好辦法 a good way;
老辦法 beaten path; beaten track; old ways;
沒辦法 can do nothing about it; cannot do anything about it; have no choice but; no way out; nothing can be done about it; nothing remains but; unable to find a way out;
~沒有辦法 no way to;
~拿他沒辦法 cannot do anything about him;
那不是辦法 that is not an option;
權宜的辦法 quick-fix solution;
土辦法 indigenous methods;
想辦法 think out a way to; try to find a solution; try to find a way out;
~另想辦法 try to find some other way;
~想盡辦法 explore every avenue; go out of one's way; leave no avenue unexplored; leave no stone unturned; leave nothing untried;
有辦法 (1) have a way to solve some problem; know how to do sth; (2) resourceful;
~還有辦法 have an arrow left in one's quiver;

有效的辦法 effective means;
找到辦法 find a method to;

[辦公] attend to business; do office work; handle official business; work;
辦公大樓 office block; office building;
~一棟辦公大樓 an office block;
辦公時間 business hours; office hours;
~在辦公時間 during office hours;
辦公室 office;
~辦公室派對 office party;
~辦公室勤雜工 office boy;
~辦公室設備 office equipment;
~辦公室信息系統 office information system;
~辦公室政治 office politics;
~辦公室終端 office terminal;
~辦公室主任 head of office;
~辦公室自動化 office automation;
辦公室自動化系統 office automation system;
~地震辦公室 seismology office;
~扶貧開發辦公室 poverty reduction and development office;
~家庭辦公室 home office;
~農村能源辦公室 rural energy office;
~農業綜合發展辦公室 integrated agricultural development office;
~僑務辦公室 overseas Chinese affairs office;
~人防辦公室 civil air-defence office;
~外事辦公室 foreign affairs office;
~新聞辦公室 information office;
~虛擬辦公室 virtual office;
辦公事務自動化系統 office automation system;
辦公司 set up a company;
辦公廳 office;
~辦公廳主任 head of general office;
辦公圖像系統 office pattern system;
辦公系統 office system;
辦公信息系統 office information system;
辦公椅 office chair;
辦公用品 office equipment;
到辦公室辦公 attend the office;
去辦公 go to office;

[辦貨] make purchases; purchase supplies;
為公司辦貨 makes purchases for the company;

[辦結] deal with and finish; hand and wind up a legal case; take up and complete;

[辦理] conduct; deal with; handle; manage; take care of; transact;
辦理手續 go through the formalities; go through the procedure; proceed with the formality;
秉公辦理 handle a matter impartially;
徑行辦理 deal with the matter straight away;
據情辦理 judge by the circumstances;

[辦事] handle affairs; manage an affair; work;
辦事不力 not to pull one's weight; slack in one's work;
辦事處 agency; office;
~設立辦事處 open an office; set an office;
~設有辦事處 maintain an office;
~總辦事處 headquarters;
辦事方式 one's way of doing things;
辦事高明 play one's cards well;
辦事公道 act fairly; fair and just in handling affairs; fair and square in running affairs;
辦事公正 fair and just in handling affairs;
辦事機構 administrative body; working body;
辦事井井有條 do things in a systematic way; do things methodically; have a methodical way of doing things;
辦事謹慎 cautious at work;
辦事離譜 handle a matter in a most irregular way;
辦事麻利 neat and quick when doing things;
辦事能力 ability to get things done;
辦事認真 conscientious in one's work;
辦事拖拖拉拉 have a sluggish way of carrying out things;
辦事穩健 go about things steadily;
辦事效率 work with efficiency;
~辦事效率低下 inefficiency; low efficiency;
辦事員 clerk; office clerk; office worker;
~首席辦事員 chief clerk;
按各自方式辦事 act each in their own way;
按手續辦事 work with method;
按原則辦事 act according to principles; act on principles;
按章辦事 play fair; play the game;
按自己的方式辦事 do things in one's own way;
秉公辦事 do official business in an official way;

照章辦事 go by the rules; run things according to the rules;

[辦妥] finish doing sth properly;

[辦學] run a school;

辦學方針 guiding principle for running a school;

辦學理念 mission of the school;

辦學條件 conditions for running a school;

辦學團體 school-sponsoring bodies;

辦學興才 provide a school for fostering talents;

私人辦學 conduct a private school;

[辦罪] punish;

幫辦 (1) assist in managing; (2) deputy;

包辦 assume full responsibility for; take everything on oneself; undertake completely;

備辦 get things ready; prepare; provide;

采辦 select and purchase;

採辦 buy on a considerable scale; purchase;

操辦 handle; make arrangements; take care of;

查辦 investigate and deal with accordingly;

察辦 investigate a case and determine how to handle it;

承辦 undertake;

懲辦 punish;

籌辦 make arrangements; organize;

創辦 establish; set up;

催辦 press sb to do sth; urge sb into doing sth; urge sb to do sth;

大辦 go in for sth in a big way;

代辦 act for sb's behalf; do sth for sb;

督辦 supervise and handle;

法辦 bring to justice; punish by law;

仿辦 follow and adopt accordingly; model;

公辦 state-run;

官辦 be run by the government; government-run;

好辦 can be easily done;

合辦 jointly organize; jointly run;

緩辦 delay action;

緝辦 arrest and punish;

究辦 establish; investigate and deal with;

舉辦 conduct; hold; organize; run;

開辦 establish; open; set up; start;

聯辦 jointly organize;

買辦 comprador;

民辦 be run by the local people;

拿辦 arrest and deal with;

難辦 difficult to manage; hard to deal with; tough;

申辦 bid;

署辦 act as a deputy;

試辦 run as an experiment;

停辦 close down; discontinue; scrap; stop running; suspend;

襄辦 act as deputy; deputy manager; help manage;

協辦 do sth jointly;

新辦 newly established;

興辦 initiate; set up;

訊辦 prosecute; put on trial and convict;

嚴辦 deal with severely; punish severely; punish with severity; take a severe disciplinary measure against;

應辦 that should be handled;

照辦 act accordingly; act in accordance with; act upon; comply with; follow;

治辦 successful discharge of duties;

置辦 buy; purchase;

重辦 punish severely;

主辦 direct; sponsor;

酌辦 handle by taking actual circumstances into consideration;

遵辦 execute according to instructions;

ban

【瓣】 (1) petals of a flower; (2) section; slice; (3) clack; valve; (4) fragment; piece;

[瓣兒] (1) petal; (2) section; slice;

安全瓣 safe valve;

半月瓣 semilunar valve;

閉斷瓣 shutting clack;

二尖瓣 mitral valve;

閥瓣 valve clack;

花瓣 leaf; petal;

排氣瓣 exhaust clack;

氣瓣 air valve;

球瓣 ball clack;

三尖瓣 tricuspid valve;

舌瓣 lingual tongue flap;

蒜瓣 clove; garlic clove;

吸瓣 suction clack;

吸入瓣 inlet clack;

壓力瓣 pressure clack;

一瓣 a segment of; a petal of; a section of; a slice of;

bang¹

bang

【邦】 country; nation; state;

[邦本] foundation of a nation;

民為邦本 people are the basis of the state;

[邦國] country; nation; state;
[邦家] one's fatherland; one's nation; one's state;
邦家之光 the glory of one's fatherland;
[邦交] diplomatic relations;
[邦禁] prohibitions of a nation;
[邦聯] confederation;
[邦人] compatriot; fellow countrymen; people of a nation;
[邦土] territory of a country;
[邦域] national territory;

安邦 bring stability to the country;
城邦 (1) city-state; (2) polis;
聯邦 commonwealth; federation; union;
鄰邦 neighbouring country;
盟邦 allied country; ally;
萬邦 all nations; nations all over the world;
烏托邦 utopia;
興邦 rejuvenate a country;
異邦 foreign land;
硬邦邦 very hard; very stiff;
友邦 ally; friendly country; friendly nation;

bang
【浜】 small stream;

bang
【梆】 rattle; watchman's clapper;
[梆子] rattle; watchman's clapper;
梆子腔 clapper opera;

bang
【幫】 (1) assist; help; (2) work; (3) side of sth; (4) outer leaf of sth; (5) band; class; clique; fleet; gang; group;
[幫辦] (1) assist in managing; (2) deputy;
[幫別] (1) faction; group; (2) type;
[幫補] help out with money; subsidize;
[幫廚] help in the mess kitchen;
[幫兒] gang;
[幫扶] help; support;
[幫工] (1) help with farm work; (2) helper; servant;
在地裏幫工 help with farm work;
[幫會] secret society; underworld gang;
[幫伙] (1) store clerk; (2) clique;
結成幫伙 form gangs;
[幫教] give guidance; help and educate; help and teach;
[幫忙] aid; assist; do a good turn; do sb a favour; give a hand; help; lend a hand; put sb in the way of sth;
幫幫忙 assist; help;
幫大忙 big help; give a lot of help;
幫倒忙 kiss of death; cause trouble while trying to help; do a disservice to; more of a hindrance than a help;
給人幫忙 come to sb's help;
互相幫忙 offer help to each other;
請人幫忙 ask a favour of sb;
小罵大幫忙 a few verbal attacks but a major help in deeds; attack on minor issues and support on major ones; criticize in a small way and help in a big way; minor attack but major help; minor attacks in words but major help in deeds;
找人幫忙 come for help;
[幫派] clique; faction;
政治幫派 political gang;
[幫貧] help poor rural households;
[幫錢] help with money;
[幫腔] echo sb; chime in with sb; give verbal support to a person; speak in support of sb;
給人幫腔 keep chiming in with sb; take up the refrain of sb;
[幫人] help sb;
[幫手] assistant; helper; helpmate;
辭退幫手 lay off one's help;
得力幫手 a great help to sb;
僱幫手 engage a help;
[幫貼] subsidize;
[幫閒] hang on to and serve the rich and powerful by literary hack work;
幫閒文人 literary hack;
[幫兇] accessary; accomplice;
[幫助] assist; come to sb's aid; go to sb's aid; help; in aid of;
幫助某人做某事 aid sb in doing sth; aid sb to do sth; assist sb in doing sth; assist sb to do sth; assist sb with sth; give of oneself; give sb a helping hand to do sth; give sb a hand in doing sth; give sb a hand with sth; help sb do sth; help sb in doing sth; help sb with sth; land sb a hand in doing sth; lend sb a land with sth; lend sb a helping hand to do sth;

暗中幫助 bring secret help;
答應幫助 promise one's help;
大有幫助 help enormously;
得到幫助 get help; receive help;
互相幫助 assist mutually; help each other;
乞求幫助 cry for help;
請求幫助 ask for help;
提供幫助 give assistance; offer assistance; offer help; provide assistance; provide help;
通過…的幫助 by the aid of; with the aid of;
謝絕幫助 decline assistance;
需要幫助 need help; want help;
尋求幫助 seek assistance;

［幫嘴］ help in an altercation; speak for another;

船幫 (1) side of a ship; (2) merchant fleet;
匪幫 bandit gang;
丐幫 beggar gang;
行幫 trade association;
黑幫 reactionary gang; sinister gang;
馬幫 caravan;
青幫 a secret society in Qing China;
相幫 aid; help;
鞋幫 sides of a shoe; upper;
一幫 (1) a band; a clique; a gang; a group; a mob; (2) a band of; a clique of; a gang of; a group of; a mob of;
在幫 member of a secret society;

bang³

bang

【綁】 bind; bind sb's hands behind him; fasten; tie up;

［綁帶］ (1) bandage; (2) puttee;
［綁匪］ kidnapper;
［綁縛］ bind; tie up;
［綁架］ carry away by force; kidnap for ransoms;
綁架勒索 seize a person for extortion;
被綁架 be kidnapped;
［綁緊］ bind tight; fasten tight;
［綁票］ hold a person for ransom; kidnap; kidnap for ransoms;
［綁腿］ leg wrappings;
［綁扎］ (1) bind up; wrap up; (2) bundle up; pack; tie up;

反綁 tie one's hands behind one's back;
捆綁 bind; tie up; truss up;
鬆綁 (1) undo sth tied; untie sb; (2) relax restrictions;

bang

【榜】 (1) list of names posted up; roll; (2) announcement; notice;

［榜牌］ bulletin board;
［榜首］ top candidate of an examination;
居排行榜榜首 top the chart;
［榜樣］ example; model; pattern; role model;
崇高的榜樣 noble example;
光輝的榜樣 bright and shining example;
好榜樣 positive role model;
樹立…的榜樣 set an example of...;
效法…的榜樣 emulate the example of...;
效仿…的榜樣 imitate a model;
學習…的榜樣 take after the example;
～學習某人的榜樣 take after sb;
以…為榜樣 model oneself on...; take a leaf out of sb's book;
英勇的榜樣 heroic example;
最著名的榜樣 the most marked example;
做榜樣 make a model;

標榜 (1) advertise; flaunt; make a display of; (2) boast; excessively praise;
出榜 (1) publish a list of successful candidates or examinees; (2) put up a notice;
發榜 issue a list of successful candidates or applicants;
放榜 announcement of examination results;
光榮榜 honour roll;
紅榜 board; honour roll;
黃榜 imperial edict;
揭榜 announce the results of an examination;
選民榜 list of eligible voters;

bang

【膀】 (1) arm; upper arm; (2) shoulder; (3) wing of a bird;

［膀臂］ (1) arms; (2) capable aide; capable assistant; reliable helper; right-hand person;
［膀子］ (1) upper arm; (2) shoulder; (3) wing of a bird;
先膀子 bare-breasted; be stripped to the waist;

臂膀 arm;
翅膀 wing;
滑肩膀 sloping shoulders;

肩膀 shoulder;

bang

【膀】 (1) plaque; tablet; (2) public notice;

［膀示］ announce by putting up a notice;

bang⁴

bang

【蚌】 clam; freshwater mussel; mother-of-pearl; oyster;

［蚌胎］ pearl;

［蚌珠］ pearl;

彩蚌 painted shell;
河蚌 clam; freshwater mussel;
珠蚌 pearl oyster;

bang

【傍】 (1) approaching; at; beside; close to; draw near; towards; (2) depend on; rely on; (3) have an intimate relationship with sb; (4) love;

［傍壁籬人］ depend on others for maintenance;

［傍地走］ run closely on the ground;

［傍戶而立］ stand close to the door;

［傍家兒］ (1) lover; mistress; (2) assistant; friend; partner; (3) couple; husband and wife;

［傍近］ close to; near;

［傍晚］ at dusk; at nightfall; dusk; late in the afternoon; nightfall; toward evening; twilight;
傍晚回來 be back by nightfall;
傍晚前離開 leave before nightfall;
傍晚時出發 start when the evening begins;
傍晚時到達 arrive at nightfall;
傍晚時分 at dusk;
天已傍晚 the dusk deepens;

［傍午］ about noon; near noontime; shortly before noon;

撤傍 break off a friendship; break up with sb;
偎傍 stay close together;
依傍 (1) depend on; rely on; (2) emulate; imitate; model after; pattern after;
倚傍 emulate; pattern after;

bang

【棒】 (1) club; cudgel; stick; truncheon; (2) hit with a club; (3) excellent; fine; good; great; strong; wonderful;

［棒棒雞］ boneless chicken with heavy seasoning;

［棒棒糖］ candy cane; lollipop; lolly;

［棒冰］ frozen lollipop; ice-cream stick; ice-lolly; ice-sucker; popsicle;

［棒槌］ (1) wooden club; (2) amateur; layman;

［棒喝］ blow and shout to waken one from error;
當頭棒喝 give a timely warning; issue a strong warning;

［棒球］ baseball;
棒球場 ball park; baseball field;
棒球隊 baseball team;
棒球壘手 baseman;
棒球褸 baseball jacket;
棒球選手 baseballer;
棒球員 baseballer;
棒球運動 baseball;
~棒球運動員 ballplayer;
圓場棒球 rounders;

［棒糖］ all-day sucker; candy stick; lollipop; sucker;

［棒子］ (1) club; cudgel; stick; (2) ear of maize;
一棒子 a strike;
~一棒子打入冷宮 consign sb to limb; consign sb to the back shelf;
玉米棒子 corn on the cob;

癌棒 cancer stick;
磁棒 magnetic rod;
大棒 (1) big stick; (2) means of threat;
電棒 electric torch; flash light;
短棒 cosh;
趕牛棒 cattle prod;
杠棒 stout carrying pole;
棍棒 (1) club; cudgel; bludgeon; (2) staff; stick;
火棒 lighted torch;
接力棒 relay baton;
警棒 baton;
控制棒 controlling stick;
魔棒 magic wand;
蒲棒 the spike of cattail;
球棒 bat;
拳棒 fighting feats;
炭棒 carbon rod;
鐵棒 iron bar;
真棒 excellent;
指揮棒 baton;

bang

【磅】 (1) pound; (2) scale; (3) weigh;

［磅秤］ platform scale;

過磅 weigh (on the scales);

bang

【謗】 condemn; defame; denounce publicly; libel; slander; smear; vilify;

［謗譏］ denounce; impeach;

［謗僧］ abuse Buddhist monks;

謗僧毀道 have no respect for pious bonzes and holy Taoist priests;

謗僧罵道 abuse Buddhist and Taoist priests; attack Taoism and Buddhism;

［謗書］ defamatory writing;

［謗聞］ malicious gossip;

［謗言］ defamatory remark; libel; slander;

［謗議］ criticize; libel; slander;

讒謗 calumniate; defame; slander;

詆謗 libel;

誹謗 calumniate; defame; fling dirt at; libel; libeling; mudslinging; slander; sling mud at; throw mud at;

毀謗 calumniate; slander;

弭謗 put an end to slander;

喪謗 revile; slander; speak ill of;

訕謗 backbite; libel; slander;

誣謗 libel; slander;

息謗 silence slanders;

罾謗 be slandered by others;

虛謗 accuse groundlessly;

bang

【鎊】 pound sterling;

一鎊 a pound;

英鎊 pound sterling;

bao¹

bao

【包】 (1) pack up; wrap; (2) a bundle; a pack; a package; a packet; a parcel; (3) a bag of; a bale of; a pack of; a packet of; a sack of; (4) lump; protuberance; swelling; (5) encircle; envelop; surround; (6) contain; include; (7) undertake the whole thing; (8) assure; guarantee; (9) charter; hire; (10) a surname;

［包辦］ assume full responsibility for; do the whole job oneself; take everything on oneself; undertake completely;

包辦代替 do things in others' stead; keep everything in one's own hands; monopolize the conduct of others' affairs; run things all by oneself without consulting others; take everything into one's own hands; take everything on oneself; take on what ought to be done by others; the whole show;

包辦一切 keep everything in one's own hands;

［包庇］ cover up; cover up an evil deed; harbour; hide up; shield;

姑息包庇 tolerate and shield;

互相包庇 shield each other;

［包藏］ conceal; contain; harbour;

包藏禍心 cover up one's sinister motives; entertain a vicious scheme in mind; harbour evil intentions; harbour malicious intent; hide a malicious intent;

［包產］ make a production contract; take full responsibility for output quotas;

包產到戶 fix farm output quotas for each household;

包產合同 contract for fixed output;

包產指標 targets set in a contract for fixed output;

［包娼］ harbour call girl centres;

［包場］ book the entire place; make a block booking;

［包抄］ envelop; outflank;

兩翼包抄 outflank from both sides;

［包車］ chartered bus;

［包飯］ supply meals at a fixed rate;

按月包飯 board by the month;

［包封］ seal a package;

［包縫］ wrapseam;

包縫工 piper;

［包袱］ (1) cloth-wrapper; (2) a bundle wrapped in cloth; (3) burden; liability; load; weight;

背包袱 become a burden on one's mind; carry a bundle on one's back; have a load on one's mind; have a weight on one's mind; take on a mental burden; weigh on one's mind;

背着一個包袱 carry a bundle on one's back;

揹包袱 (1) carry a burden; carry a fardel on the back; (2) have a weight on one's mind; take on a mental burden;
打開一個包袱 untie a bundle wrapped in cloth;
丟掉包袱 drop one's burden;
放下包袱 cast off mental burdens; get rid of the baggage; lay down one's burden; put down one's burden;
減輕包袱 reduce the load;
思想包袱 weight in one's mind;
~ 解除思想包袱 lift a weight off one's mind;

[包幹] responsible for a task until it is completed;
包幹制 contract system;
~ 實行包幹制 adopt contract system;
財政包幹 be responsible for one's finance; fiscal responsibility system;
財政收支包幹 contract system on revenue and expenditure;
經費包幹 take responsibility for one's surplus or deficits;

[包工] (1) contract for a job; undertake to perform work within a time limit and according to specifications; work by contract; (2) contract worker; contractor; foreman;
包工包料 contract for labour and materials;
包工隊 contracting team;
包工頭 labour contractor;
包工運費 lump sum freight;
包工制 labour contract system;

[包管] assure; guarantee;

[包裹] (1) bind up; wrap up; (2) bundle; package; parcel;
包裹說明 docket;
保價包裹 insured parcel;
笨重的包裹 cumbersome parcel;
打開包裹 open a parcel; undo a parcel; untie a parcel;
大體積包裹 bulk parcel;
發送包裹 dispatch a package;

[包含] comprise; contain; embody; encompass; include;
包含大量信息 pack a great deal of information;
包含雙重意義 bear a double meaning;

[包涵] bear with; excuse; forgive;
包涵體 inclusion body;

[包機] chartered aeroplane; chartered flight;

[包金] cover with gold leaf; gild;

[包括] complete with; comprise; consist of; contain; cover; embody; include; inclusive of; incorporate; not excepting; ranging from...to;
不包括在內 but; except; except for; exclusive of; other than; outside of; short of; to the exclusion of; with the exception of;

[包攬] monopolize; take on everything; undertake the whole thing;
包攬大權 centralize power in one's hands;
包攬訴訟 intervene in a lawsuit; monopolize law suits;
包攬一切 make an entire monopoly;
大包大攬 monopolize the job and the responsibility; take all the responsibility on oneself;

[包羅] cover; embrace; include;
包羅很廣 cover a wide range;
包羅萬象 all-embracing; all-inclusive; cover a wide range; cover and contain everything; inclusive of everything;
~ 包羅萬象的 all-embracing;

[包絡] envelope;
絕熱包絡 adiabatic envelope;
內射包絡 injective envelope;
載波包絡 carrier envelope;

[包賠] guarantee to pay compensation;

[包皮] (1) wrapper; covering; wrapping; (2) acrobystia; foreskin; prepuce;
包皮垢 smegma;
包皮過長 redundant prepuce;
包皮結石 acrobystiolith; preputial calculus;
包皮腺 glandulae preputiales;
~ 包皮腺炎 tysonitis;
包皮炎 acrobystitis;
無包皮 aposthia;

[包容] forgive; tolerate;
包容力 capacity for taking in people;
大度包容 magnanimous and tolerant; regard with kindly tolerance;

[包圍] besiege; encircle; engulf; envelopment; hem around; hem in; hen about; lay seige to; surround;
被包圍 be compassed; be surrounded;
被敵軍包圍 be hemmed in by the enemy;
層層包圍 besiege...ring upon ring;

垂直包圍 vertical envelopment;

[包廂] box in a theatre;

[包銷] exclusive sales; have exclusive selling rights;

包銷合同 exclusive sales contract;

包銷權 exclusive selling right;

包銷協議 exclusive sales agreement;

[包心菜] cabbage;

[包修] guarantee the repair of sth;

[包爺] (1) a person who undertakes a lawsuit; (2) the go-between in business who receives a cut of the profit;

[包圓兒] (1) buy the whole lot or the remainder; (2) finish off; take on the whole thing;

[包孕] contain; embody; include;

包孕句 sentence with a clause;

[包運] transport;

[包紮] bind up; dress; pack; pack up; wrap up;

包紮東西 pack away things;

包紮傷口 bind up a wound; strap up the wound;

[包治] guarantee a cure;

[包裝] make up sth; pack; packaging; packing;

包裝不良 faulty packing; imprudent packing; poor packing; unsound packing;

包裝不完備 faulty packing;

包裝布 packing sheet;

包裝部 packaging department;

包裝材料 packaging; packing materials;

包裝費 packaging expenses;

包裝工 packer;

~包裝工人 packer;

~包裝工業 package industry;

包裝機 wrapper;

~自動包裝機 auto-wrapper;

包裝技術 packing technology;

包裝精美 beautifully packed;

包裝破損 broken package;

包裝清單 packing list;

包裝日期 date of packaging;

包裝設計 packaging design;

~包裝設計心理 psychological packaging design;

包裝條件 conditions of packing; terms of packaging;

包裝物料 packing materials;

包裝箱 packing case;

包裝要求 packing instructions;

包裝有效期 package life;

包裝紙 wrapper; wrapping; wrapping paper;

~粗包裝紙 heavy wrapping;

~防油包裝紙 grease-proof wrapping;

~辣椒包裝紙 chili wrapper;

~臘肉包裝紙 bacon wrapper;

~木絲包裝紙 excelsior wrapper;

~牛皮包裝紙 kraft wrapping;

包裝裝潢 packing and presentation;

出口包裝 export packaging; export packing;

多用途包裝 multi-purpose package;

防漏包裝 leakage-proof packing;

防漏氣包裝 air-tight packing;

防水包裝 water-proof packing;

慣常包裝 customary packing;

可拆卸包裝 dismountable package;

加固包裝 reinforced packing;

緊縮包裝 skin packaging;

可攜帶包裝 carrier package;

可折疊包裝 collapsible package;

可煮包裝 boilable pack;

零售包裝 consumer pack; retail packaging;

免費包裝 do the packing free;

內包裝 inner packaging; interior package;

軟包裝 flexible package;

商業包裝 commercial packing;

設計包裝 design a package;

特別包裝 special packing;

條形包裝 strip packing;

外包裝 exterior package; outer packaging;

外部包裝 adventitious wrappage;

無菌包裝 aseptic packaging;

現代包裝 modern packaging;

小型包裝 small packing;

硬包裝 rigid package;

原始包裝 original packing;

真空包裝 vacuum-packed;

直接包裝 immediate packing;

中性包裝 neutral packing;

[包子] steamed stuffed bun;

肉包子 meat dumplings; steamed bun with meat filling; steamed dumplings stuffed with meat;

~肉包子打狗一有去無回 pelting a dog with meat dumplings — once gone, it is never to return;

土包子 boor; clodhopper; countrified person; country bumpkin; hick; hillbilly;

[包租] (1) rent land or a house for subletting; (2) fixed rent for farmland;

背包 (1) backpack; haversack; kitbag; knapsack; rucksack; (2) blanket roll;
揹包 backpack;
閉包 closure;
草包 (1) straw bag; straw sack; (2) blockhead; good-for-nothing; idiot;
茶包 tea bag;
承包 contract;
打包 (1) bale; pack; (2) unpack;
大包 bale;
掉包 stealthily substitute one thing for another;
豆沙包 steamed bun filled with bean paste;
帆布包 canvas bag; kit bag;
佛手包 Buddha's fingers bun;
鋼包 steel ladle;
鋼水包 steel ladle;
公文包 briefcase; portfolio;
漢堡包 hamburger;
荷包 (1) pouch; small bag; (2) pocket;
紅包 (1) a red paper pocket containing money as a gift; (2) cash award; prize; (3) bribe;
紅封包 red packet;
急救包 first-aid dressing;
挎包 satchel;
旅行包 travelling bag;
麻包 gunny bag; gunnysack; sack;
蒙古包 yurt;
棉包 bale of cotton;
麵包 bread;
內包 inclusive;
膿包 (1) pustule; (2) worthless fellow; (3) good-for-nothing;
皮包 briefcase; leather handbag; portfolio;
蒲包 cattail bag; rush bag;
漆包 enamel-cover;
錢包 purse; wallet;
沙包 sandbag;
山包 hill; low hill;
手提包 bag; handbag;
受氣包 person upon whom anyone can complain;
壽桃包 peach-shaped bun;
書包 satchel; schoolbag;
湯包 steamed dumpling filled with minced meat and gravy;
糖包 steamed dumpling stuffed with sugar;
套包 collar for a horse;
提包 bag; briefcase; handbag; shopping bag; valise;
馱包 load carried by animals;
外包 contract out; outsource;
小包 packet;
小籠包 meat-filled bun cooked in a small bamboo steam;
心包 pericardium;
腰包 billfold; bum bag; money belt; pocket; purse; waist bag; wallet;
一包 (1) a bale; a box; a bundle; a pack; a package; a packet; a parcel; a sack; (2) a bale of; a box of; a bundle of; a pack of; a package of; a packet of; a parcel of; a sack of;
一個包 a bag;
衣包 canvas bag;
郵包 parcel; postal parcel;
炸藥包 explosive package;
針線包 sewing kit;
裝包 pack; packing;

bao

【孢】 spore;

[孢粉學] palynology;

[孢子] spore;

孢子被 sporocyst;
孢子蟲 sporozoite;
孢子囊 sporangium
~游動孢子囊 zoosporangium; zoosporocyst;
副孢子 accessory spore;
接合孢子 zygosperm; zygospore; zygote;
~接合孢子柄 zygosporophore;
~接合孢子囊 zygosporangium;
~多核接合孢子 zygotoid;
~游動接合孢子 zygozoospore;
烙印孢子 brand spore;
無性孢子 asexual spore;
細菌孢子 cellular spore;
游動孢子 zoosperm; zoospore;
子孢子 sporozoite; zygoblast;

bao

【炮】 (1) bake; roast; (2) dry by heat;

[炮肉] barbecue meat; roasted meat;

bao

【胞】 (1) placenta; (2) children of the same parents;

[胞弟] one's own younger brother;

[胞妹] one's own younger sister;

[胞胎] births;

三胞胎 triplets;
雙胞胎 twins;
~雙胞胎姐妹 twin sisters;
四胞胎 quadruplets;

［胞衣］ afterbirth; placenta;
［胞與為懷］ fraternity; treat all creatures like one's brothers;

肺胞 pulmonary vesicle;
管胞 tracheid;
難胞 fellow countrymen residing abroad suffering from oppression;
氣胞 air cell; respiratory hollow;
僑胞 one's fellow countrymen residing abroad; overseas Chinese;
同胞 (1) born of the same parents; (2) compatriot; fellow countryman;
細胞 cell;
芽胞 gemma;

bao
【苞】 (1) bud; (2) luxuriant; thick; (3) wrap;
［苞木］ bamboo;
［苞片］ bract;

打苞 ear up; form ears;
含苞 in bud;
花苞 bud;
栗苞 chestnut case;

bao
【剝】 peel; shell; skin; strip;
［剝開］ strip the covering off;
［剝皮］ strip off the skin;
［剝去］ strip; take off;

bao
【褒】 commend; extol; honour; praise;
［褒貶］ appraise; comment; pass judgment on; praise and disparage;
不加褒貶 make no comment; neither praise nor censure;
不置褒貶 neither praise nor criticize; utter no word of praise or blame;
有褒有貶 with criticisms and praises;
寓貶於褒 blend censure with praise; dawn with faint praise;
［褒獎］ commend and award; praise and cite; praise and honour;
［褒揚］ cite; commend; praise;
［褒義］ appreciative meaning; commendatory sense; complimentary sense;
褒義詞 meliorative word;

bao²
bao
【雹】 hail; hailstone;
［雹暴］ hailstorm;
［雹害］ hail damage;
［雹災］ disaster caused by hail;
［雹子］ hail; hailstone;

冰雹 hail; hailstone;
一陣雹 a burst of hail;

bao
【薄】 a pronunciation of 薄;

bao³
bao
【保】 (1) defend; guard; protect; shelter; (2) keep; maintain; preserve; (3) ensure; guarantee; (4) stand guarantor for sb; stand surety for sb; (5) guarantor;
［保安］ (1) ensure public security; (2) ensure safety;
保安措施 security measures;
~採取保安措施 take security measures;
保安公司 security company;
保安規程 safety regulations;
~執行保安規程 carry out safety regulations;
保安人員 bouncer; security guard; security personnel;
保安裝置 protective devices;
~利用保安裝置 use protective devices;
強化保安 increase public security;
［保鏢］ bodyguard; escort; minder;
［保不齊］ hard to avoid; may well; not sure;
［保藏］ keep in store; preservation; preserve;
食品保藏 food preservation;
妥為保藏 under lock and key;
腌製保藏 preservation by salt; salt-curing preservation;
［保持］ keep; keep up; maintain; preserve;
［保存］ conserve; keep; preserve;
保存本 reserved copy;
保存得不好 in bad keep;
保存得好 in fine preservation; in good keep;
保存完整 being fairly well preserved; in a good state of preservation;
合訂保存 keep on a file;
妥善保存 preserve well;
完整保存 preserve intact;
［保單］ (1) guaranteed warranty; warranty; (2) insurance policy;
保單無效 avoidance of policy;

保單轉讓 assignment of policy;
長期保單 long-term warranty;
單獨保單 specific policy;
短期保單 short-term warranty;

[保兑] confirm; confirmation;
保兑銀行 confirming bank;
保兑責任 confirmed engagement;

[保管] (1) put sth under one's custody; safeguard; safekeep; take care of; (2) certainly; surely;
保管得好 in good keeping;
保管人 custodian;
保管員 storekeeper;
安全保管 safekeeping;
妥善保管 safekeeping;

[保國] defend the country;
保國安民 defend the country so that the people can live and work in peace; guard the country and pacify the people; secure the state and comfort the people;
保國衛民 guard the country and protect its people;

[保護] (1) guard; protect; (2) conservation; conserve; preserve;
保護本能 protective instinct;
~具有保護本能 possess a protective instinct;
保護措施 protective measures;
保護帶 safety belt in a vehicle;
保護…的利益 defend the interests of...;
~保護人民的利益 safeguard the people's interests;
保護費 protection fee;
保護國 protectorate;
~受保護國 protectorate;
保護劑 preservative;
保護鍵 protection key;
保護令 preservation order;
~樹木保護令 tree preservation order;
~文物保護令 preservation order;
~自然保護令 preservation order;
保護器 protector;
~輸送帶保護器 conveyor belt protector;
~陰極保護器 cathodic protector;
保護區 conservation area; preserve;
~自然保護區 nature reserve;
保護人 guardian;
保護傘 protective umbrella; help and protection;
保護色 apathetic colour; protective coloration;
~具有保護色 have protective coloration;
~天然保護色 natural camouflage;
保護栓 belay;
~鎬柄保護栓 shaft belay;
~固定保護栓 fixed belay;
~肩保護栓 shoulder belay;
~靜止保護栓 static belay;
~腰保護栓 waist belay;
~移動保護栓 running belay;
~制動保護栓 dynamic belay;
保護物 protective;
保護性 protective;
~保護性措施 protective measures;
~保護性關税 protective tariff;
~保護性貿易 protective trade;
保護政策 protectionism;
保護主義 protectionism;
暗中保護 protect sb in the dark;
充分保護 adequately protect;
過度保護 overprotection;
互相保護 give mutual protection;
努力保護 strive to protect;
受到…保護 under the protectorate of...;
~受到法國政府保護 under the French protectorate;
受到…的保護 receive the protection of;
~受到充分的保護 have perfect shelter;
~受到法律的保護 be protected by law;
提供保護 furnish protection to...; give protection; offer protection; provide protection;
向…尋求保護 turn to...for protection;
~向警察尋求保護 turn to the police for protection;
需要…的保護 need the protection of...;
~需要國家的保護 need the protection of the state;
自動保護 automatic protection;

[保皇黨] royalist;

[保駕] escort the emperor; protect an important person; protect and escort;

[保價] support value;
保價包裹 insured parcel;
保價郵件 insured mail;
保價運輸 insured transportation;

[保健] health care; health protection;
保健按摩 keep-fit massage; therapeutic massage;
保健操 health exercises; setting-up exercises;

B

B

~ 眼保健操 eyerobics;
~ 做保健操 do setting-up exercises;
保健產品 health food; health product;
~ 天然保健產品 natural health product;
保健措施 hygienic measures;
保健費 health fee; health subsidy;
保健粉筆 non-toxic chalk;
保健機構 health institution;
~ 設立保健機構 establish health institutions;
保健食品 health-promoting food;
保健事業 public health work;
~ 從事保健事業 do public health work;
保健所 clinic;
保健網 health care network; health protection network;
~ 形成保健網 form a health care network;
保健箱 medical kit;
保健飲料 health drink;
保健員 health worker;
保健站 health station;
保健中心 health-care centre;
保健專家 sanitarian;
保健組織 health organization;
婦幼保健 mother and child care;
~ 開展婦幼保健 give mother and child care;

[保教] assure an education to students; guarantee education and support to children;

[保潔] keep clean;

[保齡球] (1) bowling; (2) bowling ball;
保齡球館 bowling alley;

[保留] hold over sth; preserve; reserve; with reservations;
保留數 encumbrance;
~ 內部保留數 interdepartmental encumbrance;
~ 未清償保留數 unliquidated encumbrance;
~ 支出保留數 appropriation encumbrance; expenditure encumbrance;
無保留 without reservation;
有保留 have reservations; with a hook at the end; with reservation;
~ 有所保留 with some reservation;

[保密] hold back sth; keep a secret; keep sb in the dark; keep sth in secrecy; keep sth in the dark; keep sth to oneself; keep sth under one's hat; keep sth under wraps; leave sb in the dark; leave sth in the dark; maintain secrecy; treat sth as confidential;
保密審查 inquiry on the protection of secrets;
保密條例 security regulations;
~ 實施嚴格的保密條例 enforce stringent security regulations;
保密文件 classified document;
答應保密 promise secrecy;
給予保密 be enveloped in secrecy;
絕對保密 ensure absolute secrecy; strictly confidential;
完全保密 maintain complete secrecy;
嚴格保密 strictly confidential;

[保姆] (1) nurse; (2) housekeeper; housemaid; nurse maid;
保姆的孩子—人家的 nanny's children – belong to others;
保姆市場 housemaid market;
臨時保姆 babysitter;
住家保姆 live-in nanny;

[保暖] keep warm;
保暖杯 thermos up;
保暖背心 body warmer;
保暖罩 cosy;
~ 茶壺保暖罩 tea cosy;

[保全] ensure the safety of; guard; keep intact; preserve; protect; save from damage;

[保人] (1) guarantor; (2) bail;

[保身] save one's own skin;
明哲保身 cautious in order to save one's skin; wise for the sake of personal survival; worldly-wise and play safe; stay quiet for self-protection;
~ 明哲保身，但求無過 worldly-wise and play safe and seek only to avoid blame;

[保釋] bail; release on bail;
保釋出獄 out on bail;
保釋金 bail;
~ 交納保釋金 give bail;
不准保釋 refuse bail;
得到保釋 accept bail; take bail;
獲准保釋 be allowed out on bail; be granted bail;

[保守] (1) guard; keep; (2) conservative;
保守分子 conservative;
保守觀點 conservative views;
~ 持保守觀點 maintain conservative views;

保守療法 conservative treatment;
保守秘密 guard a mystery; keep a secret;
保守思想 conservative idea;
保守主義 conservatism;
~ 保守主義者 conservative;
狂熱的保守主義者 fanatical conservative;
頑固的保守主義者 obstinate conservative;
~ 極端保守主義 extreme conservatism;
~ 老式的保守主義 old-fashioned conservatism;
~ 狹隘的保守主義 narrow-minded conservatism;
很保守 very conservative;
生來保守 naturally conservative;
思想保守 conservative;

[保帥] save the commander;
丟車保帥 sacrifice the knights in order to save the queen;
丟卒保帥 give up a rook to save the king; make a minor sacrifice to safeguard major interests; sacrifice one's pawn to save the queen; sacrifice the knights in order to save the queen;
棄車保帥 give up a rook to save the king; make minor sacrifices to safeguard major interests; sacrifice the knights in order to save the queen;
棄卒保帥 make minor sacrifices to safeguard major interests; sacrifice one's pawn to save the queen;
捨車保帥 give up a chariot to save the marshal — make minor sacrifices to safeguard major interests;

[保税] keep in bond;
保税保險 bonded insurance;
保税倉庫 bonded store;
保税工廠 bonded factory;
保税貨物 bonded goods;
保税區 bonded area; bonded zone;
保税運輸 bonded transportation;
保税制度 bonded system;

[保送] recommend sb for admission to school;

[保外] be released on bail;
保外就醫 be released on bail for medical treatment;
保外執行 serve a sentence out of the prison on bail;

[保衛] defend; guard against;
保衛科 security section;
保家衛國 protect our homes and defend our country;

[保溫] heat preservation; keep warm; preserve the temperature;
保溫杯 thermos flask; vacuum flask;
保溫材料 thermal insulation material;
保溫車 refrigerated truck;
保溫集裝箱 thermal container;
保溫瓶 flask; vacuum flask;

[保鮮] guard against spoilage of food; maintain refreshness; retain freshness;
保鮮包裝 fresh-keeping packaging;
保鮮袋 packaging to retain freshness of a product;
保鮮盒 packaging to preserve the freshness of good;
保鮮膜 cling film;
~ 塑料保鮮膜 plastic wrap;
保鮮期 length for preservation;
保鮮紙 cling film;

[保險] (1) be bound to; guarantee; sure; (2) insurance;
保險儲蓄 insured savings;
保險代理人 insurance agent;
保險單 insurance certificate; insurance policy;
~ 保險單持有人 policyholder;
~ 保險單據 insurance document;
~ 保險單退保值 surrender value;
~ 保險單有效期 policy period;
~ 海損保險單 average policy;
~ 合同保險單 contract policy;
~ 混合保險單 combination policy;
~ 貨物保險單 cargo policy;
~ 人壽保險單 life insurance policy;
~ 運費保險單 freight policy;
保險擔保書 guarantee of insurance;
保險額 amount insured;
保險法 insurance law;
保險範圍 insurance coverage; range of insurance;
保險費 insurance premium; premium;
~ 保險費回扣 premium rebate;
~ 保險費率 premium rate;
~ 保險費收據 premium receipt;
~ 初期保險費 initial premium;
~ 額外保險費 extra premium;
~ 付保險費 pay into the insurance plan;
~ 附加保險費 additional premium;
~ 基本保險費 basic premium;
~ 年度保險費 annual premium;
~ 平均保險費 average premium;

B

~ 全部保險費 in-full premium;
~ 預付保險費 deposit premium;
保險槓 bull bars; bumper;
~ 保險槓貼紙 bumper sticker;
保險公司 insurance company;
保險觀念 insurance awareness;
保險櫃 coffer; safe;
保險國有化 nationalization of insurance;
保險合同 insurance treaty;
~ 保險合同法 law of insurance contract;
保險機 safety catch;
保險集團 pool;
保險計算員 actuary;
保險鑒定人 insurance appraiser;
保險交易所 insurance exchange;
保險金 insurance;
~ 保險金額 amount insured;
~ 得到保險金 obtain the insurance;
保險經紀 insurance broker;
~ 保險經紀人 insurance broker;
保險經濟學 economics of insurance;
保險客戶 insurance policyholder;
保險庫 strongroom;
保險會計 insurance accounting;
保險類別 branch of insurance;
保險賠償 insurance indemnities; insurance proceeds;
保險批單 insurance endorsement;
保險憑證 certificate of insurance;
保險期 period of insurance;
保險器 cut-out;
~ 封閉式熔絲保險器 protected cut-out;
~ 快速熔絲保險器 quick-break cut-out;
~ 螺塞保險器 screw-plug cut-out;
~ 液浸保險器 liquid-quenched cut-out;
保險權益 insurance interest;
保險人 insurer; underwriter;
~ 保險人利益 insurer's interest;
保險事業 insurance business;
保險稅 insurance tax;
保險絲 fuse;
~ 保險絲斷了 the fuse blows out;
~ 保險絲盒 fuse box;
~ 換保險絲 change a fuse;
~ 橋接保險絲 bridge fuse;
~ 燒斷保險絲 blow a fuse;
~ 條形保險絲 band fuse;
保險索賠 insurance claim;
保險體制 social insurance system;
保險條件 insurance conditions;
保險調解人 insurance adjuster;
保險推銷員 insurance canvasser;
保險系數 level of cover given by an insurance policy;
保險箱 coffer; safe;
~ 壁上保險箱 wall safe;
~ 防火保險箱 fireproof safe;
~ 開保險箱 open a safe;
~ 強行打開保險箱 force a safe open; force upon a safe;
~ 搶劫保險箱 rob a safe;
~ 撬開保險箱 break a safe;
~ 夜間保險箱 night depository; night safe;
~ 銀行保險箱 safe-deposit box; safety-deposit box;
保險業 insurance industry;
~ 保險業務 insurance services;
保險責任 insurance liabilities;
保險賬戶 underwriting account;
保險證明書 cover note;
保險終止 termination of risk;
保險種類 kinds of insurance;
保險總額 sum insured;
駁運保險 insurance against craft;
財產保險 property insurance;
第三保險 third-party insurance;
附加保險 accessary punishment;
共同保險 co-insurance;
~ 購買共同保險 co-insure;
海損保險 maritime insurance;
航程保險 voyage policy;
航空保險 aviation insurance;
壞賬保險 bad debt insurance;
火災保險 fire insurance;
貨物保險 cargo insurance; insurance on goods;
疾病保險 health insurance;
加入保險 take a policy;
健康保險 health insurance;
絕對保險 absolute cover;
空運保險 air transport insurance;
空運貨物保險 air transportation cargo insurance;
勞動保險 labour insurance;
聯合保險 co-insurance;
旅行保險 traveller's insurance;
年金保險 annuity insurance;
農業保險 agricultural insurance;
期限保險 time policy;
汽車保險 auto insurance; automobile insurance; car insurance;
強制保險 compulsory insurance;
竊盜保險 burglary and robbery insurance;

人多保險 there is safety in numbers;
人壽保險 life insurance;
商業保險 business insurance;
社會保險 social insurance;
失竊保險 burglary insurance;
失業保險 unemployment insurance;
收成保險 crop insurance;
雙重保險 double insurance;
物產保險 property insurance;
相互保險 mutual insurance;
信用保險 credit insurance;
行李保險 baggage insurance;
養老保險 endowment insurance;
一般保險 general insurance;
意外保險 accident insurance;
意外事故保險 accident insurance;
意外死亡保險 accident death insurance;
因公傷亡保險 worker's compensation insurance;
漁業保險 fishery insurance;
原始保險 direct-writing insurance;
運輸保險 transportation insurance;
~航空運輸保險 air transportation insurance;
~陸上運輸保險 overland transportation insurance;
~郵包運輸保險 parcel post;
再保險 reinsurance;
~超額再保險 excess reinsurance;
~合約再保險 treaty reinsurance;
~臨時再保險 facultative reinsurance;
~溢額再保險 surplus reinsurance;
債務保險 liability insurance;
~僱主債務保險 employer's liability insurance;
綜合保險 all-risks insurance; comprehensive cover; comprehensive insurance; comprehensive policy;

[保修] give a service warranty; repair under warranty;
保修單 guarantee statement;
保修期 length of warranty;
~延長保修期 extend the warranty;

[保養] (1) take good care of one's health; (2) keep in good repair; maintain; maintenance;
保養得不好 in bad repair;
保養得好 be kept in proper repair;
~保養得好的人 well-preserved person;
保養費 maintenance fee;
保養維護 maintenance;

[保有] hold;
保有權 right to hold;
~永久保有權 freehold;
保有者 holder;
~永久保有者 freeholder;

[保佑] bless and protect;
靠老天保佑 rely on blessings from heaven;
祈求神靈保佑 seek the blessings of the gods;
求菩薩保佑 may Buddha bless me;

[保育] child care; child welfare;
保育意識 conservation awareness;
保育員 nurse;

[保障] ensure; guarantee; protect; safeguard;
保障措施 safety measures;
~安全保障措施 safety precautions;
加強安全保障措施 tighten up on security;

[保證] assure; ensure; give sb one's word; guarantee; pledge; pass sb one's word; pledge sb one's word; warranty;
保證金 cash deposit; earnest money; margin; surety;
~保證金額 guarantee sum;
保證人 guarantor;
保證書 letter of guaranty;
靠不住的保證 flimsy guarantee;
可靠的保證 sure guarantee;
口頭保證 make a verbal promise;
例外保證 exceptive warranty;
內在保證 implied warranty;
書面保證 sign a written pledge;
我保證 I promise you;
我無法保證 I cannot promise anything;
無條件地保證 unconditionally guarantee;
消極保證 negative assurance;
嚴肅地保證 give a solemn pledge;
作出…的保證 promise solemnly;
~作出莊嚴的保證 solemn promise;

[保值] hedge appreciation; preserve the value of sth;
保值儲蓄 inflation-proof saving deposits;
保值公債 inflation-proof government bond;
保值期限 deadline of hedge appreciation;

[保質] quality guarantee;
保質期 quality guarantee period;
保質守約 observe the contract and ensure the quality;

[保重] look after oneself; take care; take care of oneself; take care of yourself;

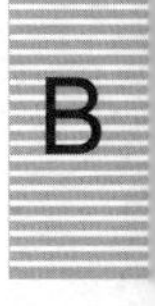

多多保重 look after yourself; take care; take good care of yourself;
善自保重 look after yourself; take good care of yourself;

[保住] keep; preserve; save;

承保 accept insurance;
擔保 assurance; bail; bet; by gum; ensure; go bail for; guarantee; surety; swear; take an oath; upon my honour; upon my name; upon my word; vouch for; vow; warrant;
分保 reinsurance;
管保 certainly; surely;
環保 environmental protection;
加保 additional insurance;
酒保 bartender;
具保 get sb to sign a guarantee for oneself;
勞保 labour insurance; labour protection;
難保 one cannot say for sure; difficult to ensure;
取保 get a guarantor; get sb to go bail for one;
確保 ensure; guarantee; insure; make certain that; make sure that; see to it that; sure to;
人保 personal guarantor;
投保 cover; insure; take out an insurance policy;
植保 crop protection; plant protection;
中保 middleman and guarantor;
准保 certainly; for sure;
準保 guarantee;
自保 self-hold; self-insurance; self-perpetuating;
作保 go bail for sb; guarantee; guarantor; sb's guarantor; sponsor sb; stand guarantee; vouch for;

bao

【堡】 (1) bulwark; fort; fortress; (2) town; walled village;

[堡壘] bastion; blockhouse; bulwark; citadel; fortress; stronghold;
堡壘戰 blockhouse warfare;
拆除堡壘 dismantle a fortress;
撤離堡壘 evacuate a fortress;
攻佔堡壘 seize a fortress;
構築堡壘 found a fort; raise a fort;
堅守堡壘 hold the fort;
砲轟堡壘 bombard the forts;
圍攻堡壘 besiege a fortress;

暗堡 bunker; foxhole; trench;
城堡 barbacan; castle; citadel; tower; town;
地堡 blockhouse;
碉堡 blockhouse; fort; pillbox; stronghold; fortification;
古堡 ancient fortification;
橋頭堡 bridge tower; bridgehead;
灘頭堡 block;
屯堡 military fortress; military outpost;

bao

【葆】 (1) hidden; not easily revealed; reserved; (2) dense growth of vegetation; (3) protect;

[葆葆] lush and luxuriant growth;
[葆真] safeguard one's divine nature－be untarnished by all desires;

bao

【飽】 (1) full; have eaten one's fill; (2) full; plump; (3) fully; to the full; (4) satisfied;

[飽飽的] glutted; stuffed with food; surfeited;
[飽餐] eat to one's heart's content;
飽餐秀色 fully enjoy the beauty; well-feasted on the beauty of;
飽餐一頓 eat and drink one's fill; eat heartily of the meal; get one's whack; take a hearty meal;
[飽嘗] experience to the fullest extent;
[飽和] saturation;
飽和點 saturation point;
~ 達到飽和點 reach the saturation point;
飽和度 saturation;
飽和汽 saturated vapour;
~ 過飽和汽 supersaturated vapour;
~ 未飽和汽 unsaturated vapour;
[飽看] feast one's eyes on; read to one's heart's content;
[飽滿] full; plump;
[飽暖] more than enough to eat and wear; well-fed and well-clad;
飽暖思淫欲 debauchery is a common vice among the wealthy; material comfort leads to sexual desire; when the belly is full, the mind is among the maids;
飽暖思淫欲，饑寒起盜心 those who are well-fed and well-clad are inclined to be lustful, whereas hunger and cold breed the temptation to steal;
吃不飽穿不暖 hardly able to keep body and soul together; lead a life of privation; not have enough food and clothing;
食飽衣暖 well fed and warmed;
[飽食] eat to one's heart's content; glut;

飽食暖衣 have ample food and clothing; in good keep; well-fed and well-clad;
飽食終日 well-fed all day;
~飽食終日，無所用心 a full belly makes a dull brain; be sated with food and led an idle life; be sated with food and remain idle; eat all day without exerting one's mind; eat one's fill and sit dozing all day long; live like a parasite; live the life of a lazy parasite; loaf all day long and do nothing; sit like a bump on a log; spend one's day in food and have an empty head;
~飽食終日，無所作為 do nothing but eat three square meals a day;

[飽受] suffer to the fullest extent;
飽受淩辱 suffer untold humiliations and insults;
飽受虛驚 suffer from nervous fears;

[飽我以德] imbue me with virtue;

[飽學] erudite; learned; scholarly; well-learned; well-versed; widely-read;
飽學之士 erudite person; learned scholar; person of learning;

[飽脹] full up to the throat; glutted; surfeited to the bursting point;

[飽醉] full and drunk;
既醉且飽 have had enough of both wine and food;

半飽 half full;
吃飽 full; have eaten one's fill;
饑飽 hunger and full stomach;
填飽 cram; feed to the full;
溫飽 adequate food and clothing; adequately fed and clothed; dress warmly and eat one's fill; have enough to eat and wear;
脹飽 fullness of the stomach from overeating;
中飽 batten on money entrusted to one's care; embezzle; line one's own pockets; pocket money to which one has no claim; squeeze;

bao

【褓】 swaddling clothes;

[褓母] babysitter; nurse;

襁褓 (1) carrying band for an infant; (2) infancy; (3) swaddling clothes;

bao

【鴇】 (1) prostitute; (2) procuress;

[鴇兒] (1) prostitute; (2) procuress;

[鴇母] procuress;

大鴇 great bustard;
老鴇 procuress;

bao

【寶】 (1) treasure; treasured object; (2) precious; treasured; valuable; (3) honourable; respectable;

[寶寶] baby; darling; poppet;
救命寶寶 saviour sibling;

[寶貝] (1) treasure; (2) cherished thing; jewel; (3) baby; darling; (4) your;
寶貝兒 poppet;
寶貝兒子 pampered child;
寶貝心肝 dear heart;

[寶刀] treasured sword;
寶刀未老 old but still vigorous in mind and body; there is life in the old dog yet;

[寶島] treasure island;

[寶典] treasury of knowledge; valuable book;

[寶貴] precious; valuable;

[寶號] your firm;

[寶盒] box of treasures; jewel box;

[寶貨] (1) money; (2) precious things; valuable articles; (3) fool; idiot;

[寶劍] double-edged sword; treasured sword;

[寶眷] your family;

[寶庫] treasure house; treasury;
史料寶庫 mine of historical data;
知識的寶庫 mine of information; storehouse of knowledge;

[寶藍] sapphire blue;

[寶墨] your most valuable handwriting;

[寶山] source of great wealth;
寶山空回 gain nothing from a rare opportunity; miss a golden chance;
如入寶山空手回 as if returning from a treasure mountain empty-handed;

[寶石] gem; jewel; precious stone;
寶石匠 lapidary;
寶石礦 gem minerals;
寶石商 jeweller;
多彩浮雕寶石 cameo;
工業寶石 industrial jewel;
古代的寶石 antique gem;
紅寶石 carbuncle; ruby;
紅綠寶石 morganite;
黃寶石 topaz;
精緻的寶石 exquisite gem;

藍寶石 sapphire;
綠寶石 emerald;
美麗的寶石 beautiful gem;
人造寶石 artificial gem; paste jewellery;
停走寶石 locking jewellery;
一盒寶石 a casket of jewels;

[寶書] treasure book;
[寶塔] pagoda;
[寶物] treasure;
[寶婺星沉] remember a deceased woman with sorrow;
[寶藏] precious deposit; treasury;
地下寶藏 buried treasure;
~發現地下寶藏 find valuable mineral deposits;
~挖掘地下寶藏 tap mineral resources; unearth buried treasure;
~珍惜地下寶藏 treasure hidden resources;
豐富的寶藏 rich precious deposit;
[寶珠] precious jewel;
[寶座] throne;
登上寶座 ascend the throne of; take the throne;
失去寶座 lose one's throne;

八寶 eight treasures;
財寶 money and valuables;
傳家寶 family heirloom;
法寶 magic weapon;
瑰寶 gem; rarity; treasure;
瓌寶 extraordinary treasure;
國寶 national treasure;
果寶 fruit juice;
海寶 tea fungus;
活寶 a bit of a clown; funny fellow; sth good;
墨寶 (1) treasured scrolls of calligraphy or painting; (2) your beautiful painting or calligraphy;
三寶 the triad of the Buddha, the dharma, and the Sangha;
瑋寶 rare treasure;
獻寶 present a treasure;
尋寶 hunt for treasure; treasure hunt;
御寶 imperial seal; seal of the emperor;
元寶 gold ingot;
珍寶 rare treasures;
之寶 the treasure of;
至寶 jewellery; pearls and jewels;
重寶 treasure of much value;
珠寶 gems; jewellery; pearls and jade;

bao⁴

bao

【刨】 plane; plane sth down;
[刨掉] plane off;
[刨花] shavings;

龍門刨 double housing planer;
牛頭刨 shaper; shaping machine;

bao

【抱】 (1) carry in one's arms; embrace; enfold; hold in one's arms; hug; (2) have one's first child or grandchild; (3) adopt a child; (4) hang together; (5) assume; bosom; cherish; entertain; foster; harbour; nourish; (6) ambition; aspiration; (7) an armful of; (8) brood; hatch eggs;

[抱冰] train oneself to endure hardships;
[抱病] ill; in bad health;
抱病不出門 be confined to one's house by illness;
抱病出席 attend a meeting despite one's illness;
抱病工作 carry on work while sick; go on working in spite of ill health;
[抱德煬和] adhere to virtue and kindness; bosom virtue and blend kindness; stick to virtue and kindness;
[抱負] ambition; aspiration;
抱負不凡 ambitious; cherish aspirations out of the common; entertain high aspirations;
宏大的抱負 generous aspirations; lofty aspirations;
實現抱負 fulfil one's ambition; realize one's aspiration;
有抱負 cherish high ambitions; have fire in one's belly; have high aspirations;
~有抱負的 ambitious; aspiring;
~有抱負者 aspirant;
~很有抱負 cherish high ambitions; have high aspirations;
[抱憾] be sorry about; deplore; regret; repent of;
抱憾終生 feel remorse for the rest of one's life; harbour a lifetime remorse; have a remorse of a lifetime; have a regret for life; regret sth to the end of one's days;

［抱恨］ have a gnawing regret; have a hatred;
抱恨終身 feel hatred all one's life;
抱恨終天 bitterly lament the non-fulfilment of one's mission; feel hatred all one's life; feel remorse for the rest of one's life; harbour an eternal sorrow; regret sth all one's life; regret forever; regret sth to the end of one's days; with a feeling of bitter frustration;
［抱節君］ bamboo;
［抱緊］ hold tightly in one's arms;
［抱愧］ feel ashamed;
抱愧認錯 blush at one's mistake; blush scarlet and apologize;
［抱念］ remember; think of;
［抱歉］ feel apologetic; feel sorry; regret; sorry;
抱歉之至 feel very sorry; very sorry;
對…感到抱歉 feel sorry for; sorry about...;
非常抱負 much to one's regret;
很抱歉 feel apologetic; very sorry;
深感抱歉 deeply regret;
［抱屈］ bear a grudge; feel wronged; harbour resentment;
抱屈含冤 be wronged and aggrieved; bear a deep grudge;
［抱首而遁］ hide one's face and beat a retreat;
［抱痛西河］ feel sorrow over the loss of one's son; mourn over the death of one's son; suffer the sorrow of losing one's son;
［抱頭］ cover one's head with one's hands;
［抱膝］ with one's arms about one's knees;
抱膝而坐 sit with one's arms about one's knees;
抱膝跳水 cannonball dive;
［抱雪向火］ do a thankless task;
［抱養］ adopt a child; adopt and raise;
［抱腰］ assist; help; lend support to;
［抱一］ stick to one principle;
［抱怨］ beef about; blow off; chew the rag about; complain; complain about; complain of; grouse; grouse about; grumble; grumble about; grumble at; grumbling; kick against; kick at; murmur against; murmur at; mutter against; mutter at; natter on about; quarrel with; rail against; rail at;
愛抱怨 querulous;
不斷地抱怨 complain constantly; make constant complaints;
大聲抱怨 complain loudly;
低聲抱怨 make a feeble complaint;
［抱着］ embrace; hold in one's arms;
抱着孩子 embrace a child in one's arms;
抱着滿腔熱情 be filled with enthusiasm;
抱着勝利的希望 hold out a hope of victory;
［抱住］ hold in one's arms; hold on to;
抱住不放 hang on; stick to;
［抱罪］ conscious of guilt; feel guilty;

拱抱 surround;
合抱 so thick that one can just get one's arms around it;
懷抱 (1) carry in one's arms; embrace; (2) cherish; keep in mind;
環抱 encircle; hem in; surround; twine around;
緊抱 hold tightly in one's arms; hug;
摟抱 embrace; hold in one's arms; hug;
襁抱 infancy;
偎抱 cuddle; hug;
一抱 an armful of;
擁抱 embrace; hold in one's arms; hug;

bao
【豹】 (1) leopard; panther; (2) a surname;
［豹斑］ leopard's spots;
［豹變］ rise from poverty to wealth;
［豹貓］ leopard cat; ocelot;
［豹鼠］ chipmunk;
［豹死留皮］ the leopard's skin survives its body;
豹死留皮，人死留名 when a leopard dies, it leaves a skin; when a man dies, he leaves a name;
［豹頭環眼］ round eyes and well-formed forehead;
［豹隱］ lead the life of a hermit; live in retirement;
［豹子］ leopard; panther;

海豹 common seal; sea dog; seal;
金錢豹 leopard;
獵豹 cheetah;
全豹 overall situation; whole picture;
土豹 buzzard;
雪豹 snow leopard;

bao
【趵】 jump; leap;
［趵趵］ noise of tramping feet;

B

bao

【報】 (1) announce; declare; inform; report; tell; (2) reciprocate; reply; respond; (3) recompense; repay; requite; show gratitude; (4) revenge; (5) retribution; reward; (6) newspaper; (7) journal; periodical; (8) bulletin; report; (9) cable; telegram;

［報案］ report a case to the police; report a case to the security authorities;

［報償］ recompense; repay;
得到報償 be repaid;

［報蟲兒］ newspaper worm;

［報仇］ avenge; be out for sb's scalp; get back at; get even with sb; get one's own back on sb; get one's revenge; get square with sb; have one's own back on sb; have one's revenge; have sb's scalp; pay back sb; pay off sb; pay out sb; revenge; serve out sb; take sb's scalp;
報仇雪恥 avenge a wrong and wipe out a humiliation; pay old scores; pay off old scores; settle an old score; take revenge and wipe out a disgrace; take revenge for an insult; wipe off old scores; wipe out an old score;
報仇雪恨 avenge a grievance; avenge oneself; get even with a hated enemy; glut one's revenge; hurt sb in return for a wrong; pay off old scores; take revenge to wreak vengeance and redress hatred;
渴望報仇 thirst for revenge;
立誓報仇 vow revenge;
企圖報仇 meditate revenge;
伺機報仇 seek every means to avenge sb; seek revenge;
為兄弟報仇 avenge one's brother;
揚言報仇 threaten with revenge;
一心要報仇 there is revenge in one's heart;
以仇報仇 take an eye for an eye;

［報酬］ pay; remuneration; reward;
報酬很低 be poorly paid;
報酬很高 be well paid;
補償報酬 compensatory payment;
不計報酬 be unconcerned with pay;
不收報酬 accept no remuneration;
不圖報酬 ask no reward;
不要報酬 ask no recompense;
額外報酬 extra pay;
分配報酬 mete out rewards;
豐厚報酬 highly paid;
各種各樣的報酬 sundry rewards;
合理報酬 just reward; reasonable recompense;
慷慨的報酬 generous remuneration;
可觀的報酬 handsome recompense;
領取報酬 draw pay;
少得可憐的報酬 beggarly pay;
特殊報酬 particular award;
無報酬 without pay;
足夠的報酬 adequate remuneration;

［報春］ proclaim the Spring Festival;
報春花 primrose;
~一束報春花 a bunch of primrose;
爆竹報春 proclaim the Spring Festival by letting off the firecrackers;

［報答］ repay another's kindness; requite;
不圖報答 expect nothing in return;

［報單］ customs form; declaration form; taxation form;

［報導］ (1) cover; report; (2) news report; story;
報導句 reporting sentence;
報導文學 reportage;
報導性文摘 information abstracts;
第一流的報導 first-rate account;
第一手報導 first-hand account;
據本報報導 as reported in this newspaper;
可靠的報導 authentic report;
全面報導 full report;
現場報導 running commentary;
詳盡報導 elaborate report;
新聞報導 news reports; press reports;
一篇報導 a report;
真實報導 true report;
直接報導 first-hand report;

［報到］ check in; register; report for duty;
報到上班 report for duty;
按時報到 report for work at the appointed time;
去報到 report oneself;

［報德］ repay another's kindness; show gratitude;
以怨報德 repay good with evil; requite kindness with ingratitude;

［報恩］ pay a debt of gratitude;
以恩報恩 requite like for like;
有恩待報 owe sb a debt of gratitude;

［報販］ seller of newspapers;

[報廢] (1) report sth as worthless; (2) discard as useless; reject; scrap;
報廢率 condemnation factor;
正常報廢 normal abandonment;

[報復] avenge; get back at sb; get one's own back on sb; have one's own back on sb; make reprisals; retaliate;
報復心 intention to revenge;
報復心切 wild for revenge;
報復行為 act of retaliation;
報復血仇 take a blood revenge;
對…進行報復 retaliate against;
發誓要報復 make a vow of vengeance;
伺機報復 seek revenge;
圖謀報復 nurse thoughts of revenge;
向…報復 retaliate against;
~向冒犯者報復 retaliate against the offender;
揚言要報復 threaten revenge;

[報告] (1) give an account of; make known; render an account of; report; (2) lecture; report; speech; talk;
報告員 reporter;
長篇報告 disquisition;
撤回報告 retract a report;
呈遞報告 present a report;
官方報告 official report;
機密報告 confidential report;
簡短報告 brief report;
接受報告 adopt a report;
絕密報告 confidential report;
考察報告 inspection report;
口頭報告 oral report;
年度報告 annual report;
起草報告 draw up a report;
親自報告 report personally;
收到報告 receive a report;
書面報告 written report;
提交報告 submit a report; turn in a report;
通過報告 pass a report;
向…報告 report to...;
~向上級報告 report to the high authorities;
向…提交報告 lay a report before...;
~向委員會提交報告 lay a report before a committee;
小報告 lodge a complaint against sb with his superior; small reports; snitch;
~打小報告 inform secretly on sb; inform on sb to superiors; tell tales; whistle-blower; write small reports;
寫報告 write a report;
~趕寫報告 dash out a report;
一份報告 a report;
正式報告 formal report;
專家報告 expert report;
準備報告 prepare a report;
做報告 make a report;

[報功] claim credit; report a victory; report an achievement;

[報關] declare sth at the customs;
報關單 customs declaration; written declaration;
報關費 customs clearance fee;
報關人 declarant;

[報館] newspaper office;

[報國] dedicate oneself to the service of one's country; devote oneself to the national cause;
報國利民 serve the state and benefit the people;
報國無門 have no opportunity to serve one's motherland;
盡心報國 devote one's energies entirely to the service of the state; do one's best for one's country;
盡忠報國 devote oneself to one's country;
精忠報國 dedicate oneself to the service of one's motherland; repay the country with supreme loyalty; serve one's country loyally; serve one's fatherland with unreserved loyalty;
許身報國 dedicate oneself to one's nation;
以身報國 devote one's life to one's country;
忠心報國 repay one's country with loyalty; work for the country heart and soul;

[報話] speak on one's walkie-talkie;
報話機 walkie-talkie;

[報夾] newspaper holder;

[報架] newspaper shelf;

[報價] quotation; quote price;
報價平穩 quoted flat;
報價有效期 valid period of an offer;
接受報價 accept an offer; take up an offer;
買方報價 bid;
收回報價 withdraw an offer;
提拱報價 give a quotation;

[報捷] announce a victory; report a success;

[報界] journalistic circles; news circles; the press;

B

B

[報警] (1) report to the police; (2) give the alarm;
報警點 place where sb reports an incident to the police;
報警服務 alerting service;
報警系統 warning system;
~ 安設報警系統 install a warning system;
報警儀 alarming equipment;
報警裝置 alarm device;
~ 安全報警裝置 safety-alarm device;
鳴鑼報警 warn by beating a gong;
鳴鐘報警 sound the alarm bell;

[報刊] newspapers and periodicals; the press;
報刊店 kiosk; newsstand;
報刊廣告 press advertising;
報刊經銷店 newsagent;
報刊經銷人 newsagent;
報刊亭 newsstand;
黃色報刊 scandal sheet; yellow press;

[報考] enter one's name for an examination; enrol for an examination; register for examination;
報考大學 apply for the entrance examination of a university;

[報名] enlist; enrol; enter one's name; sign up;
報名表格 entry form;
報名參加 enter for; put one's name down for;
報名參加比賽 enter one's name for a competition;

[報明] state clearly to the higher authorities;

[報幕] announce the items on a programme;
報幕人 announcer;
報幕員 announcer;

[報盤] make a price; make a quotation; make an offer; offer; quote a price; work out the orders;

[報批] request authorization; submit sth for approval;
層層報批 report to the higher authorities at different levels for approval;

[報請] request permission to do sth;
報請上級 report sth to the higher authorities for approval;
報請審批 submit to a higher level for examination and approval;

[報人] journalist; newspaperman; newspaperwoman;

[報喪] announce sb's death; give obituary notice;

[報社] newspaper office;
報社記者 journalist; newspaperman;
報社老闆 newspaper proprietor;

[報失] report the loss of sth to the authorities concerned;

[報時] give the correct time;
報時燈 time check lamp;
報時器 timing device;
報時信號 time signal;
報時鐘 striking clock;
在整點報時 chime the hour; strike the hour;

[報數] count off; number off;

[報稅] (1) report tax returns; (2) declare dutiable goods;
報稅表 tax return;
報稅單 duty declaration form;

[報送] select and send to sb;

[報攤] news stall; newsstand;

[報童] newsboy; newspaper delivery boy; newsy; paperboy;
女報童 papergirl;

[報頭] masthead; nameplate; newspaper heading;

[報務員] radio operator; telegraph operator;

[報喜] announce good news; report success;
報喜不報憂 report only the good news and not the bad;
爆竹報喜 announce some good news by letting off firecrackers;

[報銷] (1) submit an expense account; (2) hand in a list of expended articles; (3) wipe out; write off;
報銷花費 be reimbursed for one's expenses;
實報實銷 be reimbursed for actual expenses;
要求報銷 apply for reimbursement;

[報曉] a harbinger of dawn; announce the arrival of dawn; herald the break of day;
雞鳴報曉 cocks crow at dawn; the cocks crow for the dawning of the day; the crowing of the cock is a harbinger of dawn;

[報效] render service to repay sb's kindness;

[報信] inform; notify; report news;

[報修] request repairs;

[報業] the business of the press;
報業大王 press baron;

報業公會 newspaper association; press union;
報業巨頭 press baron;

[報以] return with sth;
報以白眼 give a black look;
報以冷笑 respond with a sneer;
報以怒目 return an angry look;
報以微笑 smile in return;
報以嘘聲 respond with hisses;
報以一笑 respond with a laugh;
報以掌聲 greet with applause;

[報應] come home to roost; judgment; retribution;
帶來報應 bring retribution;
遭到報應 suffer retribution;

[報章] (1) newspaper; (2) reply letter; return mail;
報章雜誌 newspapers and magazines;
一家報章 a newspaper;

[報帳] apply for reimbursement; render an account;

[報紙] (1) newspaper; (2) newsprint;
報紙夾 newspaper rod;
報紙銷路 circulation of the newspaper;
白報紙 newsprint;
本地報紙 local newspaper;
本國語報紙 vernacular newspaper;
編輯報紙 edit a newspaper;
出版報紙 publish a newspaper;
創辦報紙 start a newspaper;
地方報紙 local newspaper; local paper; local rag;
訂閱報紙 take in a newspaper;
讀報紙 read a newspaper;
翻開報紙 unfold a newspaper;
國內報紙 home newspaper;
姐妹報紙 sister newspaper;
寬幅報紙 broadsheet;
瀏覽報紙 scan a newspaper;
買報紙 get a newspaper;
全國性報紙 national newspaper;
投遞報紙 deliver newspapers;
外文報紙 foreign-language newspaper;
星期日報紙 Sunday papers;
嚴肅報紙 quality newspaper;
一份報紙 a copy of a newspaper; a newspaper;
一捲報紙 a roll of newspapers;
一捆報紙 a bunch of newspapers;
一張報紙 a newspaper;

板報 blackboard newspaper;
辦報 run a newspaper; publish a newspaper;
壁報 bulletin; wall newspaper; wall paper;
表報 statistical tables and reports;
稟報 report to one's senior;
播報 broadcast;
補報 (1) additional statement; (2) repay a kindness; repay favours granted;
層報 report to the immediate higher authority one level after another;
陳報 explain; report;
呈報 report a matter; submit a report;
酬報 recompense; repay; requite; reward;
黨報 party newspaper;
登報 make an announcement in newspaper;
邸報 official gazette in old China;
電報 cable; telegram;
諜報 intelligence report;
訂報 subscribe to a newspaper;
惡報 retribution for evildoing; retribution for sin;
發報 transmit a telegram;
浮報 give inflated figures in a report;
公報 bulletin; communique;
果報 retribution;
海報 playbill;
畫報 illustrated newspaper; pictorial;
謊報 give false information; lie about sth;
回報 (1) bring back a report; report back on what has been done; return for report; (2) pay back; reciprocate; repay; requite; (3) get one's own back; retaliate;
匯報 give an account of; report;
季報 quarterly report;
剪報 clippings; newspaper clippings; newspaper cuttings; scraps;
簡報 brief report; bulletin;
見報 appear in the newspaper; be reported in the newspaper;
捷報 news of victory; report of a success; victory bulletin;
警報 alarm; alert; warning;
舉報 report; report on; tip; tip-off;
據報 it is reported;
快報 bulletin; newsflash; stop-press news; wall bulletin;
漏報 fail to declare sth; fail to report sth;
賣報 sell newspapers;
年報 (1) annual report; year-book; (2) annal;
期報 dated newspaper;
祈報 rite of offering sacrifices;
啟報 report to one's superior and ask for instructions;

墻報 wall newspaper;
情報 inform; information; intelligence information;
日報 daily; daily newspaper; daily paper;
善報 reward for good deeds;
上報 (1) appear in the newspapers; (2) report to a higher body; report to the leadership;
申報 (1) report to a higher body; (2) declare sth to the Customs;
收報 receive telegrams;
書報 books and newspapers;
送報 deliver newspapers; paper round;
填報 fill in a form and submit it to the leadership;
通報 (1) circulate a notice; (2) circular; (3) bulletin; journal; (4) brief; give information with; share information with;
圖報 try to repay sb's kindness;
晚報 afternooner; evening paper;
文摘報 snippet journal;
聞報 hear it reported; learn of;
誤報 misreport; report incorrectly;
喜報 bulletin of happy tidings;
相報 serve in return;
小報 news-sheet; small newspaper; tabloid;
星期日報 Sunday newspaper;
虛報 false declaration; make a false report; misreport; report untruthfully;
學報 academic journal; journal;
旬報 ten-day report;
隱報 deceptive reporting;
預報 forecast;
月報 (1) monthly; monthly magazine; (2) monthly report;
閱報 read newspapers;
戰報 battlefield report; war bulletin;
周報 weekly;
週報 weekly newspaper;

bao

【菢】 hatch eggs; incubate;
［菢蛋］ hatch eggs;
［菢窩］ sit on the nest to hatch the eggs;

bao

【鉋】 (1) plane wood; (2) plane for carpentry;
［鉋牀］ planing machine;
［鉋凳］ carpenter's stool;
［鉋花］ shavings;
［鉋子］ plane;

bao

【暴】 (1) sharp; sudden and violent; suddenly and fiercely; (2) atrocious; brutal; cruel; fierce; harsh and tyrannical; savage; violent; (3) hot-tempered; irritable; short-tempered; (4) bulge; stand out; stick out;
［暴斃］ meet a sudden death;
［暴病］ sudden attack of a serious illness;
暴病身亡 die from a sudden illness;
得暴病 be suddenly seized with a severe illness;
［暴跌］ drop sharply; nose-dive; sharp drop in prices; slump; steep fall in prices;
市場價格暴跌 market values decline sharply;
物價暴跌 price slump; prices fall sharply;
~引起物價暴跌 bring about a heavy slump in prices;
~造成物價暴跌 result in price slumps;
銷售量暴跌 sales slump badly;
［暴動］ insurrection; rebellion; riot;
反暴動 counter-insurgency;
農民暴動 peasant insurrection;
平定暴動 put down an insurrection;
平民暴動 popular uprising;
武裝暴動 armed insurrection;
鎮壓暴動 suppress an insurrection;
［暴發］ (1) break out; erupt; (2) sudden flare-up; violent eruption; (3) suddenly become rich or important;
暴發戶 overnight millionaire; parvenu; upstart; pigs in clover;
~成為暴發戶 become an upstart;
~賣弄財富的暴發戶 codfish aristocracy;
［暴風］ squall; storm; tempest;
暴風雪 blizzard; snowstorm;
~暴風雪持續了多日 the snowstorm was protracted for several days;
~暴風雪平息了 the snowstorm raged itself out;
暴風雨 rainstorm; snow squall; storm; tempest;
~暴風雨大作 a storm blows up;
~暴風雨來臨 a storm breaks;
暴風雨肆虐 the storm raged with fury;
~暴風雨襲擊 a storm rages;
~暴風雨在醞釀 a storm is brewing;
~大的暴風雨 big storm;
~冬季暴風雨 winter storm;
~躲避暴風雨 take shelter from the storm;
~可怕的暴風雨 terrible storm;
~猛烈的暴風雨 fierce storm; severe

storm;
~ 夏季暴風雨 summer storm;
~ 嚴重的暴風雨 bad storm;
暴風雲 storm cloud;
暴風驟雨 hurricane; tempest; violent storm;
無雲暴風 white squall;

[暴富] sudden wealth;

[暴漢] bully;

[暴橫] atrocious; cruel; despotic; tyrannical;

[暴洪] flash flood; sudden and violent flood;

[暴虎馮河] brave but not resourceful;

[暴君] despot; tyrant;
暴君統治 tyrannical rule;
反抗暴君 rebel against the tyrant;

[暴侃] boast; shoot the bull; talk big;

[暴客] robber;

[暴雷] sudden clap of thunder;

[暴力] force; naked force; violence;
暴力犯罪 violent crime;
暴力革命 violent revolution;
~ 進行暴力革命 make a violent revolution;
採用暴力 resort to violence;
非暴力 non-violence;
各種暴力 different forms of violence;
濫用暴力 orgy of violence;
使用暴力 use force;
訴諸暴力 appeal to violence;
憎恨暴力 abhorrent of violence;

[暴利] sudden huge profits;
產生暴利 yield huge returns;
反對暴利 against profiteering;
獲得暴利 obtain huge profit;
牟取暴利 reap colossal profits;
~ 非法牟取暴利 make exorbitant profits illegitimately;
追求暴利 pursue huge profits;

[暴戾] brutal; cruel and fierce; despotic and tyrannical; ruthless and tyrannical;
暴戾恣睢 domineering; extremely cruel and despotic; hard and cruel; tyrannical;

[暴斂] collect illegitimate wealth; extort;
暴斂橫徵 extort and levy illegal taxes; grind the faces of the poor;

[暴烈] fierce; violent; wild;

[暴露] come to light; expose; lay bare sth; reveal; unmask;
暴露出來 disclose;
暴露老底 reveal the true story; show the inside;
暴露無遺 completely brought to light; completely exposed; completely revealed; completely unmasked; thoroughly exposed;
暴露自己 stick one's chin out;
害怕暴露 in fear of discovery;

[暴亂] rebellion; revolt; riot;
暴亂場面 riotous scenes;
發動暴亂 stage a riot;
煽動暴亂 excite rebellion; provoke a riot;
引起暴亂 lead to an outbreak;
鎮壓暴亂 suppress a revolt;

[暴民] mobs; mobsters;
暴民政治 mobocracy;

[暴怒] fury; violent rage;

[暴虐] atrocious; brutal; cruel; despotic; tyrannical;
暴虐生靈 bring violence to the people;
暴虐無道 tyrannical and inhuman;
暴虐野蠻 oppressive and brutal;

[暴棄] be abandoned; despair;
自暴自棄 abandon oneself to despair; be resigned to one's backwardness; give up on oneself; have no urge to make progress; throw oneself away;

[暴曬] under the blazing sun for a long time;

[暴食] eat too much at one meal;
暴食傷身 eating to excess is injurious to health;
暴食傷胃 eating too much is bad for the stomach;
暴食症 bulimia;

[暴死] die of a sudden disease; die suddenly; meet sudden death;

[暴徒] gangster; mob; mobster; rioter; ruffian; thug;
控制暴徒 control the mob;
驅散暴徒 disperse a mob;
一群暴徒 a gang of roughs; a mob of rioters;
鎮壓暴徒 put down the mob;
制裁暴徒 apply sanctions against rioters;

[暴行] atrocity; outrage; savage act; violent act;
犯下暴行 commit cruelties;
可怕的暴行 terrible outrage;
極端的暴行 excessive violence;
容忍暴行 tolerate cruelties;
血腥的暴行 blood-curdling cruelty;

嚴重的暴行 serious outrage;
戰爭暴行 war barbarities;

[暴雨] rainstorm; torrential rain;
暴雨成災 a heavy rain brings floods; a torrential rain brings floods; heavy showers cause a disaster;
暴雨傾盆 drenching rain; heavy rainfall; rain comes heavily and falls in torrents;
大暴雨 downpour;
飄風暴雨 hurricane; strong gale and a torrential downpour; sudden rainstorm; violent storm;
下暴雨 rain in torrents;
一陣暴雨 a blast of rain; a downpour; a heavy shower; a gust of rain; a torrent of rain;

[暴躁] irascible; irritable;
暴躁的脾氣 fiery temper;
很暴躁 person with a violent temper;
脾氣暴躁 have a fiery temper;
性格暴躁 have a violent temper;
性情暴躁 have an irascible temperament; irascible; irritable;

[暴漲] rise suddenly and sharply;
河水暴漲 the river suddenly rises;
洪水暴漲 the flood swells in volume;
物價暴漲 prices soar;
租金暴漲 rents shoot up;

[暴政] tyranny;
暴政統治 tyrannical rule;

[暴卒] die a violent death; die of a sudden illness; die suddenly;

雹暴 hailstorm;
冰暴 ice storm;
殘暴 brutal; cruel; cruel and heartless; ruthless; savage; tyrannical;
塵暴 dust storm;
磁暴 magnetic storm;
粗暴 brutal; crude; rough; rude; violent;
防暴 anti-riot;
風暴 wind storm;
橫暴 brutal and unreasonable; perverse and violent;
抗暴 fight against violent repression;
狂暴 wildly violent;
雷暴 lightning storm; thunderstorm;
強暴 brutal; ferocious; violent;
沙暴 sandstorm;
沙塵暴 dust storm;
性暴 irascible; hot-tempered;
凶暴 fierce and brutal;
兇暴 cruel and violent;
雪暴 snowstorm;
雨暴 rainstorm;
鎮暴 riot control;

bao

【鮑】 (1) abalone; (2) salted fish; (3) a surname;

[鮑人] tanner;

[鮑肆] salted fish market;
鮑魚之肆 shop that sells salted fish; salted fish market;
~入鮑魚之肆，久而不聞其臭 one is not smelt where all stink;
如入鮑魚之肆，久而不聞其臭 it is like staying in a fish market and getting used to the stink — long exposure to bad environment accustoms one to evil ways;

[鮑魚] (1) abalone; (2) salted fish;
鮑魚乾 dried abalone;
鮑魚養殖 abalone culture;
黑鮑魚 black abalone;

[鮑子知我] my good friends know me well;

bao

【瀑】 sudden shower;

bao

【爆】 (1) burst; crack; explode; pop; (2) quick-boil; quick-fry;

[爆炒] quick-fry;

[爆發] break out; burst out; erupt; explode; outbreak;
爆發力 explosive power;
大爆發 firestorm; outburst;
突然爆發 flare-up;
再次爆發 flare up again;

[爆裂] burst; crack; erupt; pop open; rupture;
爆裂開 burst open;

[爆滿] be filled to capacity; be packed; fill up; full house; have a full house; sell out;

[爆米花] popcorn; puffed rice;

[爆棚] (1) crowded; jam-packed; (2) draw a large audience; (3) in great demand; (4) full up with people;

[爆破] blast; blasting; blow up; demolish; dynamite;
爆破工 blaster; exploder;
爆破落煤 coal blasting;
爆破手 dynamiter;

爆破作用 blast action;
緩衝爆破 cushion blasting;
控制爆破 controlled blasting;
深孔爆破 long hole blasting;
水力爆破 hydraulic blasting;
水下爆破 submarine blasting;
台階式爆破 bench blasting;
用炸藥爆破 blow sth up with dynamite;
周邊爆破 periphery blasting;

[爆胎] blow-out;

[爆性] hot-tempered; quick-tempered;

[爆炸] blast; blow up; burst; detonate; explode; explosion;
爆炸力 explosive force; impact of explosion;
爆炸如雷 explode like a thunder; thundering explosion;
爆炸物 burster; explosive;
爆炸性 explosivity;
地下爆炸 subsurface explosion;
點爆炸 point blast;
發生爆炸 an explosion occurs;
粉塵爆炸 dust explosion;
過早爆炸 premature explosion;
核爆炸 nuclear burst; nuclear explosion;
一連串爆炸 a chain of explosions;
引起爆炸 cause an explosion;

[爆仗] crackers; firecrackers;

[爆竹] banger; firecrackers;
爆竹聲中辭舊歲 a year ends amidst the crepitation of firecrackers;
爆竹一聲除舊歲 a year ends amidst the crepitation of firecrackers;
爆竹迎新 firecrackers are being released to welcome the New Year;
點燃爆竹 light a firecracker;
濕水爆竹 damp squib;
櫻桃爆竹 cherry bomb;

火爆 fiery; irritable;
起爆 detonate;
試爆 test explosion;
音爆 sonic boom;
引爆 detonate; touch off;
油爆 quick-fry;

bao

【鑤】 same as 鉋;

bei¹

bei

【卑】 (1) debased; depraved; low; mean; vile; (2) inferior; (3) humble; modest;

[卑薄] poor and barren;

[卑鄙] base; contemptible; crooked; depraved; despicable; mean;
卑鄙不堪 contemptible for one's meanness;
卑鄙的人 ignoble person;
卑鄙手段 contemptible means; dirty tricks;
卑鄙齷齪 base; foul; mean; sordid;
卑鄙無恥 mean and having no sense of shame; mean and vulgar;
卑鄙行徑 sordid conduct;
行為卑鄙 guilty of a meanness;

[卑詞厚禮] humble words and handsome gifts; sweet words and lavish gifts;

[卑賤] (1) humble; lowly; (2) mean and low;
出身卑賤 of ignoble birth;

[卑劣] base; depraved; despicable; low-down; mean;
卑劣的人 scoundrel;
卑劣手法 despicable trick; mean trick;
卑劣行徑 base conduct; dishonourable behaviour; sleaze;

[卑陋] crude; inferior; low; vulgar;

[卑怯] abject; mean and cowardly;
行為卑怯 show abject behaviour;

[卑讓] defer; yield with courtesy;

[卑人] mean person;

[卑濕] dampness of low-lying land;

[卑微] humble; inferior; lowly; petty and low;

[卑污] despicable and filthy; foul;

[卑下] base; humble; low; mean;

[卑行] of the lower generation;

[卑以自牧] keep modest so as to cultivate one's moral character;

謙卑 humble; modest;
位卑 in humble station;
自卑 self-abasement;
尊卑 (1) seniors and juniors; (2) superiors and inferiors;

bei

【杯】 (1) cup; glass; goblet; mug; tumbler; (2) cup; trophy;

[杯墊] coaster; cup mat;

[杯葛] boycott;

[杯弓蛇影] extremely suspicious; imaginary fears; self-created suspicion; shy at a

shadow;
蛇影杯弓 illusion caused by suspicion; mistake the reflection of a bow in the cup for a snake;
[杯鍋] casserole; cook-and-serve vessel;
[杯酒] cup of wine;
杯酒解愁 clear worry by cups of wine;
杯酒言歡 enjoy a cup of wine with sb; take a friendly drink;
杯酒之歌 pleasure of a banquet;
杯酒之約 invitation to dinner;
[杯盤] cups and dishes;
杯盤狼籍 cups and dishes strewn in disorder; glasses and plates are scattered all over;
收拾杯盤 stack and wash up the cups and dishes;
[杯水車薪] chicken feed; completely inadequate response; too inadequate and useless; useless attempt; utterly inadequate measure;
[杯托] saucer;
[杯中物] the thing in the cup—wine; alcoholic drinks;
喜歡杯中物 be fond of the bottle;
[杯子] cup; glass; goblet; tumbler;
精緻的杯子 dainty cup;

保暖杯 vacuum flask;
玻璃杯 glass; tumbler;
茶杯 teacup;
瓷杯 china cup;
蛋杯 egg cup;
乾杯 bottoms up; cheers; crush a cup; drink a toast; drink to; let's drink up; to;
獎杯 trophy cup;
金杯 gold cup;
酒杯 goblet; wine cup; wine glass;
舉杯 raise one's cup;
爵杯 wine cup;
咖啡杯 coffee cup;
量杯 measuring glass;
滿杯 brimmer; bumper; cupful;
碰杯 clink glasses; have a drink;
啤酒杯 beer mug;
瓊杯 jade wine cup;
三杯 three cups;
燒杯 beaker;
世界杯 World Cup;
水杯 water glass;
塑料杯 plastic cup;
貪杯 addiction to the bottle; indulge in drinking; too fond of drinking;
套杯 set of cups;
巡杯 toast guests around the table;
藥杯 medicine glass;
一杯 a cup;
一大杯 a mug of; a tankard of;
銀杯 silver cup;
優勝杯 challenge trophy;
玉杯 jade cup;
紙杯 paper cup;
粥杯 porringer;

bei
【盃】 cup; tumbler;

bei
【背】 bear; carry on the back; shoulder;
[背包] (1) backpack; haversack; kitbag; knapsack; rucksack; (2) blanket roll;
背包客 backpacker;
一個背包 a backpack;
[背長] back measurement;
[背傳] back pass;
[背帶] braces; suspenders;
一副背帶 a pair of braces;
[背兒頭] (of hairstyle) all back;
[背負] bear; carry on the back; have on one's shoulder;
肩挑背負 carry on the shoulders and back;
[背上] put on the back for carrying;
騎在背上 ride on sb's back;
[背斜] anticline;
閉合背斜 closed anticline;
裂口背斜 breached anticline;
禿頂背斜 baldheaded anticline;
鹽背斜 salt anticline;
[背債] be burdened with debts; be saddled with debts; in debt;
[背着] carry on one's back;
背着孩子找孩子—頭腦昏了 look for a child while carrying him/her on one's back — be absentminded;
背着米討飯—裝窮 begging while carrying rice on one's back — pretending to be poor;
[背子] device for carrying sth on the back;

曲背 stoop;

bei
【悲】 (1) doleful; melancholy; mournful;

rueful; sad; sorrowful; woeful; (2) deplore; lament; mourn; pity; sympathize;

[悲哀] down in the blues; down in the mouth; grief; grieve; grieved; look blue; mourn; mourning; sad; sadness; sorrow; sorrow over; sorrowful; woe; woeful;
悲哀不已 be overcome with sorrow;
悲哀的 drearily;
感到悲哀 feel sorrow; sad;
令人悲哀 sad;
為…感到悲哀 sad for;
~為死者感到悲哀 grieve for the dead;
一絲悲哀 a tinge of sadness;

[悲不自勝] abandon oneself to grief; be overcome with grief; be transported with grief; unable to restrain one's grief;

[悲慘] miserable; tragic;
悲慘場面 distressing scene;
悲慘的過去 bitter past;
~回憶悲慘的過去 recall the bitter past;
悲慘的環境 miserable surroundings;
悲慘的生活 live a miserable life;
悲慘的往事 sad past;
~忘記悲慘的往事 forget the sad past;
悲慘故事 sad story;
悲慘經歷 tragic experience;
悲慘可怕 sad and terrible;
悲慘事故 grievous accident;
悲慘事件 tragedy;
悲慘遭遇 tragedy; tragic experience;
結局悲慘 conclude tragically;
死得悲慘 die in misery; meet one's death in a tragic manner;

[悲惻] sad; sorrowful;

[悲愁] heavy-hearted; low-spirited; sad;

[悲從中來] be stricken with sorrow; feel sadness welling up;

[悲悼] grieve over sb's death; mourn;

[悲調] mournful tune;

[悲憤] grief and indignation; lament and resent an injustice;
悲憤交集 with mixed feelings of grief and indignation;
悲憤填膺 be filled with grief and indignation; burning with indignation; in righteous indignation; one's breast is full of grief and anger;
悲憤欲絕 be torn by grief; give oneself up to grief;
感到悲憤 feel grievous and indignant;
慷慨悲憤 impassioned by lamentation and indignation;
滿腔悲憤 unutterable sadness fills one's heart;

[悲風] baleful sound of wind; moaning wind;

[悲夫] how sad it is;

[悲感] sense of sadness;

[悲歌] (1) sad melody; (2) dirge; elegy; (3) sing with solemn fervour;
悲歌當哭 roar out a somber song instead of crying;
悲歌慷慨 sing with solemn fervour to express one's feeling of oppression;
悲歌一曲 sing with solemn fervour;
悲歌欲哭 the song is so plaintive that it draws tears from one's eyes;
唱一曲悲歌 chant a sad melody;
含悲悲歌 sing a plaintive song;

[悲觀] pessimistic;
悲觀的態度 pessimistic attitude;
~採取悲觀的態度 assume a pessimistic attitude;
悲觀情緒 pessimism; pessimistic emotion;
悲觀喪氣 be disheartened;
悲觀失望 abandon oneself to despair; become disheartened; lose faith in;
~對人感到悲觀失望 lose faith in sb;
~陷於悲觀失望 abandon oneself to despair;
悲觀厭世 pessimism and world-weariness;
悲觀主義 pessimism;
抱悲觀 feel pessimistic; pessimistic;
變得悲觀 become disheartened; become pessimistic;
動搖悲觀 waver and grow pessimistic;
感到悲觀 feel disheartened; feel downcast;
~對將來感到悲觀 pessimistic about the future;
情緒悲觀 in a pessimistic mood;
陷於悲觀 yield to despair;
性格悲觀 of a pessimistic nature;

[悲懷] sad feelings; sorrowful mood;

[悲歡] joys and sorrows;
悲歡離合 joys and sorrows, partings and reunions — the vicissitudes of life; the sorrows of parting and the joy of

B

union in life;
~經歷悲歡離合 experience grief at separation and joy in union; suffer and rejoice;
人世間的悲歡 the sweets and bitters of life;
[悲劇] tragedy;
悲劇重演 the repeated performance of a tragedy;
悲劇演員 tragedian;
悲劇作家 tragedian;
愛情悲劇 love tragedy;
家庭悲劇 domestic tragedy;
一場悲劇 a tragedy;
[悲憐] take pity on sb;
[悲涼] desolate; dismal; sad and dreary;
感到悲涼 feel desolate;
[悲憫] have compassion for; have sympathy for; pity;
悲天憫人 be concerned over the destiny of mankind; bemoan the state of the universe and pity the fate of mankind; bewail the times and pity the people; lament the miserable state of affairs and feel pity for the suffering of all mankind;
[悲鳴] cry mournfully;
發出悲鳴 emit a plaintive cry;
風在樹梢悲鳴 the wind sighed in the treetops;
[悲淒] sorrowful;
[悲泣] weep in grief;
[悲切] mournful;
悲悲切切 full of grief; sad and touching;
[悲秋] feel sad with the coming of autumn;
[悲傷] sad; sorrowful;
悲傷的 lugubrious;
過度悲傷 be overburdened with grief;
減輕悲傷 lighten one's sorrow;
克服悲傷 get over one's sorrow;
深感悲傷 feel deeply grieved;
心裏很悲傷 sad at heart; sick at heart;
一絲悲傷 a touch of sadness; slightly sad;
引起悲傷 inspire sorrow;
[悲聲] plaintive cries; sad voice;
[悲酸] sad and bitter;
[悲歎] deplore; lament; sigh mournfully; sigh over;
悲歎不已 keep sighing with sadness;
悲歎歲月流逝 sorrow over the passing of the years;
[悲啼] cry mournfully;
[悲痛] deep sorrow; grief; grieved; lamentation; sorrowful;
悲痛萬分 be deeply grieved; be far gone in grief;
悲痛欲絕 be torn with deep sorrow; become numb with grief; carry one's grief to excess; cry one's heart out; eat one's heart out; go to pieces; the anguish of grief; wring one's heart to the very core;
化悲痛為力量 turn grief into strength;
極度悲痛 grief;
加深悲痛 intensify one's grief;
減輕悲痛 assuage grief;
深感悲痛 in bitter grief;
抑制悲痛 master one's grief;
[悲慟] lamentation; weep loudly from sorrow;
[悲喜] joy and sorrow; sad and funny;
悲喜交集 alternate between joy and grief; be joyful and sorrowful at the same time; be overcome partly with sorrow and partly with joy; have mixed feelings; have mixed feelings of grief and joy; have mingled feelings of sorrow and joy;
悲喜劇 tragicomedy; tragic-comedy;
悲喜苦樂 happiness and sorrow, bitterness and joy;
化悲為喜 turn one's sadness into joy; turn one's sorrow into happiness; turn one's sorrow into joy;
亦悲亦喜 with alternate tears and smiles;
易悲為喜 exchange grief for joy;
又悲又喜 tragicomic;
轉悲為喜 one's sorrow begins to turn to joy; turn one's sorrow into joy;
轉喜為悲 laugh on the wrong side of one's face; laugh on the wrong side of one's mouth;
[悲壯] heroic and tragic; moving and tragic; solemn and stirring; tragically heroic;

慈悲 benevolent; merciful;
可悲 lamentable; regrettable; sad;
傷悲 distress; grief;

bei
【揹】 carry on the back; piggyback; shoulder;

［揹包］ backpack;

bei

【碑】 monumental stone; stele; stone tablet; tablet;

［碑版］ stele; stone tablet;

［碑額］ head of a stone tablet; top part of a tablet;

［碑記］ inscription; inscriptional record;

［碑銘］ inscription on a stone tablet;

［碑帖］ rubbing from a stone inscription;

［碑亭］ pavilion built over a stone tablet;

［碑文］ inscription on a tablet;

［碑陰］ back of a stone tablet;

［碑誌］ inscription on a tablet;

豐碑 monument; monumental work;
紀念碑 memorial; monument;
界碑 boundary marker; boundary tablet;
鐫碑 engrave a stone tablet;
口碑 public praise;
里程碑 milestone;
墓碑 grave monument; gravestone; headstone; tombstone;
石碑 stele; stone tablet;
樹碑 erect a memorial tablet;
搨碑 take a rubbing from an inscription on a stone tablet;

bei³

bei

【北】 (1) north; northerly; northern; (2) northward; (3) be defeated;

［北邊］ (1) north; (2) northern part;

［北冰洋］ Arctic Ocean;

［北點］ north point;

［北斗星］ Big Dipper;

［北方］ (1) north; (2) northern part of a country;
北方人 northerner;

［北風］ north wind; northerly wind;
北風呼嘯 the north wind is roaring;
北風凜冽 bitter north wind howls;
北風怒號 the north wind is howling; the north wind howls angrily;
北風颼颼 the north wind is howling;

［北瓜］ bottle gourd;

［北國］ north; northern part of a country;

［北極］ Arctic Pole; North Pole;
北極光 aurora borealis;
北極圈 Arctic Circle;
北極星 polestar; Pole Star;
北極熊 polar bear;

［北京］ Beijing;
北京狗 peke; Pekingese;
北京烤鴨 Beijing roast duck;

［北里］ (1) northern village; (2) red-light district;

［北面］ north; northern part;

［北上］ go north; proceed northward;

［北緯］ northern latitude;

［北屋］ north rooms;

［北至］ summer solstice;

敗北 be defeated in a war; lose a battle or war;
奔北 flee in defeat;
磁北 magnetic north;
東北 (1) north-east; (2) north-east China;
華北 north China;
南北 (1) north and south; (2) from north to south;
窮北 extreme north; farthest north;
西北 (1) north-west; (2) north-west China;
折北 be defeated;
逐北 pursue the vanquished troops;

bei⁴

bei

【孛】 comet;

［孛孛］ radiant;

［孛星］ comet;

bei

【貝】 (1) shell; (2) precious; treasure; valuable; (3) bel; (4) a surname;

［貝幣］ shells used as money in ancient times;

［貝編］ Buddhist sutras;

［貝雕］ shell carving;
貝雕畫 shell mosaics; shell picture;

［貝殼］ seashells; shells;
貝殼學 conchology;
~貝殼學者 conchologist;

［貝類］ shellfish;
貝類罐頭 canned shellfish;
貝類學 conchology;
凍貝類 frozen shellfish;
食用貝類 edible shellfish;

［貝母］ fritillary;

寶貝 (1) treasure; treasured object; (2) baby; darling; (3) cowrie;
分貝 decibel;
乾貝 dried scallop;
拷貝 copy; replica;

笠貝 limpet;
扇貝 fan shell; scallop;
蝎貝 scorpion shell;
貽貝 mussel;
櫻貝 sea shell;
珍珠貝 pearl oyster; pearl shell;

bei

【邶】 an ancient state in today's Henan Province;

bei

【背】 (1) back of the body; (2) back of an object; (3) with the back towards; (4) abandon; cast away; give up; leave; turn away; (5) behind sb's back; hide sth from sb; (6) commit to memory; learn by heart; learn by rote; recite from memory; remember by rote; (7) act contrary to; betray; break; go against; rebel; violate; (8) hard of hearing; (9) have hard luck; unlucky;

[背包] backpack; knapsack; rucksack;

[背本] bite the hand that feeds one;

[背部] back;
背部受傷 put one's back out;
背部舒緩 back relaxation;
按摩背部 massage one's back;

[背城借一] a death struggle; fight a desperate but decisive battle; fight to the last ditch; fight with a rope round one's neck; fight with one's back to the wall; put up a desperate struggle;

[背馳] proceed in opposite directions;
背道而馳 act counter to; act in direct contravention to; be diametrically opposed to; go against; go counter to; head in opposite directions; move in the opposite directions; move in the wrong direction; proceed in opposite directions; run counter to; run in the opposite directions;
~與…背道而馳 go against...; in an opposite directions; run counter to;

[背地裏] behind one's back; on the sly; privately; secretly;
背地裏搞鬼 play a deep game;

[背對背] back to back;

[背風] leeward; on the lee side; sheltered from the wind;
背風處 lee; sheltered side;

[背光] in a poor light;
背光性 apheliotropism;

[背過臉去] turn away one's face; turn one's face away;

[背過氣] gasp for breath; out of breath; stop breathing;

[背後] (1) at the back; behind; in the background; (2) behind one's back;
躲在門背後 hide behind the door;
跟在敵人背後 hang on the rear of the enemy;
請看背後 please turn over (p.t.o.);
小心背後 watch your back;

[背脊] back;
扭傷背脊 strain one's back;

[背景] at the back of sth; backdrop; background; setting;
背景聲 background sound;
背景知識 background knowledge;
不透明背景 opaque background;
彩色背景 colour background;
反射背景 reflecting background;
放映背景 projected background;
黑背景 black background;
紅外背景 infrared background;
灰色背景 gray background;
家庭背景 family background; home background;
經濟背景 economic setting;
靜背景 static background;
可移動背景 mobile background;
空間背景 space background;
歷史背景 historical background;
墻壁背景 mural background;
時代背景 background characteristic of times;
天然背景 natural setting;
圖像背景 image background; picture background;
文化背景 cultural background;
舞台背景 stage background;
夜空背景 night sky background;
有背景 have powerful connections;
噪聲背景 background noise;
政治背景 political background;
紫外線背景 ultraviolet background;

[背靜] quiet and secluded;

[背靠] back;
背靠背 on the sly; privately;
背靠祖國 leverage on the Mainland;

[背寬] have a broad back;

[背累] burden;
[背離] depart from; deviate from;
[背理] contrary to the course of nature; go against good conscience; go against good reason;
[背盟] breach of contract; break a promise; break an agreement; violate a treaty;
背盟棄信 violate a treaty;
背盟投暗 leave the light for darkness; step out of light into darkness;
棄約背盟 abrogate the treaty and break the alliance — unfaithful to an agreement;
[背面] back side; reverse side;
讀背面 see overleaf;
在一頁的背面 overleaf;
紙的背面 back side of the paper; reverse side of the paper;
[背謬] absurd; preposterous;
[背囊] knapsack;
[背叛] apostatize; betray; defect; rebel;
背叛行為 treacherous act;
策劃背叛 plot treachery;
[背棄] betray; break faith with; renounce; turn one's back on;
[背日性] apheliotropism;
[背上] put on the back;
[背時] (1) behind the times; (2) out of luck; unlucky;
[背書] (1) recite a lesson by heart; repeat a lesson; (2) endorsement of a cheque;
背書不明 illegible endorsement;
背書人 endorser;
~後手背書人 subsequent endorser;
~前背書人 preceding endorser;
~前手背書人 prior endorser;
~通融背書人 accommodation endorser;
背書有誤 endorsement required;
代理背書 agency endorsement;
單純背書 absolute endorsement;
計名背書 full endorsement;
融通背書 accommodation endorsement;
限制背書 restrictive endorsement;
銀行背書 bank endorsement;
[背水] with one's back to the river;
背水為戰 deploy one's troops with their backs to a river;
背水一戰 fight for life or death;
背水陣 last-ditch battle;
~擺背水陣 burn the bridge; death struggle;
[背誦] recite; recitation; repeat from memory; say by heart; say by rote;
背誦如流 rattle off; reel off;
[背痛] backache; back pain; have a pain in one's back; have an ache in the back;
腰酸背痛 a sore waist and an aching back; an ache in one's waist and back; have a backache; have a pain in the back; one's back is aching;
[背心] sweater; vest; waistcoat;
汗背心 singlet; sleeveless undershirt; vest;
汗衫背心 tank top;
毛背心 sleeveless woolen sweater;
毛衣背心 tank top;
棉背心 cotton-padded waistcoat;
三角背心 halter top; halter-neck;
[背信] breach of faith; break one's promise; break one's words; faithless;
背信棄義 breach of faith; bad faith; break one's faith; break one's promise; perfidious; perfidy;
[背椅] backed chair; chair with a backrest;
[背義] renounce honour;
背義求全 renounce honour and strive for existence;
背義求生 renounce honour and strive for existence;
辜恩背義 have no sense of gratitude and justice; ungrateful to kindness;
[背陰] in the shade; obscurity;
[背影] sight of one's back;
[背泳] backstroke;
[背約] breach an agreement; break an agreement; break one's promise; fail to keep one's promise; go back on one's word;
[背運] (1) hexed; jinxed; out of luck; (2) unlucky fate;
[背窄] have a narrow back;
[背着] avoid others; in secret;
背着人 behind other's back; in secret;
背着手 with one's hands clasped behind one's back;
[背主] disloyal to one's master;

鞍背 dorsum sellae;
凹背 swayback;
背對背 back to back;
鼻背 dorsum nasi;
擦背 rub one's back; scrub one's back; touch

one's back;
赤背 backless; bare-backed; naked back;
捶背 pound sb's back;
搥背 massage the back by pounding with one's fists;
瘩背 carbuncle on the back;
刀背 back of a knife blade;
墊背 fall guy; play the scapegoat; suffer for the faults of others;
耳背 cloth ears; cloth-eared; hard of hearing;
發背 carbuncle on the back;
腹背 in front and behind;
斧背 back of an axe;
龜背 curvature of the spinal column;
脊背 back;
肩背 shoulders and the back;
見背 pass away;
腳背 instep;
頸背 nape;
揩背 scrub sb's back;
靠背 back of a chair;
空背 hollow back;
隆背 humpback;
露背 backless; sunback;
馬背 horseback;
棄背 suffer the death of one's parents; suffer the loss of one's parents;
認背 resign oneself to one's fate;
搔背 scratch the back;
舌背 dorsum of the tongue;
手背 back of one's hand;
書背 spine of a book;
駝背 (1) be humpbacked; be hunchbacked; (2) crookback; humpback; hunchback; rachiokyphosis;
違背 go against; run counter to; violate;
向背 support or oppose;
鴨背 duck's back;
椅背 back of a chair; backrest;
硬背 learn by heart; learn by rote; memorize mechanically;
紙背 back of the paper;
炙背 expose the back to the sun;
轉背 as soon as one turns one's back;
足背 acrotarsium; dorsum of the foot;

bei

【倍】 (1) -fold; times; (2) double; twice as much; (3) insubordinate; rebel;

［倍加］ double; extraordinarily; extremely; increase by one fold;
倍加努力 double one's efforts; redouble one's efforts;
倍加小心 especially careful;

［倍減］ demultiplication; demultiply;
倍減器 demultiplier;
～數字倍減器 digital demultiplier;
頻率的倍減 demultiplication of frequency;

［倍數］ multiple;

［倍壓器］ doubler;
半波倍壓器 half-wave doubler;
級聯倍壓器 cascade voltage doubler;
全波倍壓器 full-wave voltage doubler;

［倍增］ redouble;
信心倍增 redouble one's courage;

八倍 octuple; eight times; eightfold;
百倍 full of;
公倍 common multiple;
加倍 double; redouble;
兩倍 double; twofold; twice as much;
六倍 sextuple; six times; sixfold;
三倍 threefold; triple;
十倍 deca-; tenfold;
數倍 manifold; several times;
雙倍 double; twice the amount; twice the number; twofold;
四倍 quattuor;
萬倍 ten thousandfold;
一倍 double;
整倍 multiple;

bei

【悖】 (1) contrary to; go against; go counter to; revolt against; (2) erroneous; offensive; perverse;

［悖德］ immoral;

［悖理］ absurd; contrary to reason; irrational; unreasonable;

［悖禮］ contrary to etiquette; impolite; uncivil;
悖禮失檢 contrary to decorum and lacking in care;

［悖戾］ deviate from accepted rules or standards; perverse;

［悖亂］ rebellion; revolt; sedition;

［悖論］ dilemma; paradox;

［悖漫］ arrogantly impolite; disrespectful; show irreverence;

［悖謬］ absurd; irrational; preposterous; unreasonable;

［悖逆］ disloyal; rebel; revolt; treasonable;
悖逆不道 break accepted morals; defy

all laws; offensive to all established values;

[悖叛] rebel; revolt;

[悖棄] turn away from sth in revolt;

[悖情] against human nature;

[悖時] behind the times;

bei

【狽】 a kind of wolf;

狼狽 in a dilemma; in an awkward position;

bei

【被】 (1) bedding; coverlet; quilt; (2) cover; shroud; (3) reach; spread; (4) because; due to; (5) by (a passive marker); (6) a surname;

[被逼] be compelled; be forced;

[被捕] be arrested; under arrest;
犯案時被捕 be caught red-handed;

[被袋] bedding bag;

[被單] bedsheet;

[被動] inactive; passive;
被動句 passive sentence;
準被動 quasi-passive;

[被俘] be captured; be taken prisoner;

[被告] accused; defendant;
被告席 dock;
共同被告 co-respondent;

[被害] be killed; be murdered;
被害人 victim;

[被劫] be kidnapped; be robbed;

[被騙] be fooled; be swindled;

[被迫] be compelled; be constrained; be forced;

[被褥] bedclothes; bedding;

[被套] (1) bedding bag; (2) quilt cover;

[被窩] folded quilt;

[被子] comforter; quilt;
疊被鋪牀 fold the quilts and make the bed; settle the cushions and spread the covers;
疊被子 fold the quilt;
蓋被子 cover with a quilt;
一牀被子 a quilt;

百衲被 patchwork quilt;
花被 floral envelope; perianth;
馬被 horse cloth;
毛巾被 towelling coverlet;
棉被 a quilt with cotton wadding;
拼布被 patchwork quilt;
衣被 clothing and bedding;
澤被 extend benefit;
植被 vegetation; vegetation cover;

bei

【備】 (1) be equipped with; have; (2) get more things in reserve for further use; get ready; prepare; ready for; (3) guard against; prepare against; provide against; take defense measures; take precautions against; (4) equipment; (5) fully; in every possible way;

[備鞍] put a saddle on a horse;

[備案] enter in the records; keep on record; put on record; register; serve as a record;

[備辦] get things ready; prepare; provide;

[備補] next choice;

[備查] for future reference;

[備嚐] have experienced; have tasted;
備嚐憂患 have undergone much worry and hardships;

[備飯] prepare a meal;

[備份] backup; copy;
備份盤 backup disk;
備份文件 backup file;
增量備份 incremental backup;

[備耕] make preparations for ploughing;

[備荒] prepare against natural disasters;
積谷備荒 get prepared for rainy days; store up grain against a lean year;

[備件] appendage; awaiting part; part; reserve part; spare; spare part;
訂製備件 custom parts;
庫存備件 depot spare parts;
全套備件 complete spare parts;

[備考] for reference;

[備課] prepare lessons;

[備馬] saddle a horse for riding;

[備取] on the waiting list; put on reserve;

[備述] report completely;

[備忘錄] memo; memorandum;
查賬備忘錄 audit memorandum;
提交一份備忘錄 submit a memo to;
寫一份備忘錄 write a memo;
業務備忘錄 engagement memorandum;
一份備忘錄 a memo;

[備悉] know the whole story; learn sth

completely;

[備細] all the details of; in detail;

[備用] alternate; in reserve; reserve; spare;
備用電路 spare circuit;
備用款 reserve fund;
備用輪胎 spare tyre;
備用文件 duplicated file;
備用物 fallback;
備用系統 backup system;

[備戰] prepare for war;
備戰備荒 prepare against war and natural disasters;
加緊備戰 speed up war preparations;
擴軍備戰 increase armaments and prepare for war;

[備至] in every possible way; to the utmost;
關懷備至 show great consideration;
呵護備至 considerate in taking good care of sb;
頌揚備至 praise profusely;

[備種] make preparations for sowing;

[備注] notes; remarks;

必備 requisite;
不備 by surprise; not ready; off guard; unprepared;
常備 be always on the alert; be ever prepared;
籌備 arrange; prepare;
儲備 lay up; reserve; store for future use;
防備 guard against; provide against; take precautions against;
後備 reserve; spare;
兼備 have both; possess both;
戒備 guard; on the alert; take precautions against;
警備 garrison; guard;
具備 be equipped with; be provided with; have; possess;
軍備 armament; arms;
配備 (1) allocate; provide; (2) deploy; dispose; (3) equipment; outfit;
齊備 all complete; all ready; complete; everything complete; everything ready;
勤備 assiduous; diligent; hardworking; industrious;
求備 seek completeness;
設備 equipment; facilities; installation;
守備 on garrison duty; perform garrison duty;
完備 complete; perfect;
無備 unprepared; without preparation;
武備 defence preparations;
以備 ready for;
預備 do what is necessary for; prepare;
責備 blame; reproach; reprove;
戰備 combat readiness; war preparedness;
整備 reorganize and equip;
製備 prepare; preparation; provide for;
置備 purchase;
貯備 have in reserve; store up;
裝備 equip; equipment; fit out;
準備 (1) intend; plan; (2) prepare; do what is necessary for;
自備 provide for oneself;

bei

【焙】 bake; dry near a fire; heat near a fire; toast;

[焙茶] dry tea by fire;

[焙粉] baking powder;

[焙乾] dry by a fire;

[焙爐] toaster; oven;

[焙燒] bake; roast; roasting;
焙燒爐 roaster;
~ 牀式焙燒爐 hearth roaster;
~ 機械焙燒爐 mechanical roaster;
~ 流化柱焙燒爐 fluid column roaster;
粗銅焙燒 blister roasting;
脱巟焙燒 desulphurizing roasting;

[焙硬] bake;

烘焙 cure;

bei

【碚】 (1) as in 蝦蟆碚, a place in Hubei; (2) as in 碚礧, a bud;

bei

【蓓】 bud; flower bud;

[蓓蕾] flower bud;

bei

【輩】 (1) people of a certain kind; the like; (2) a generation in family; (3) life; lifetime; (4) grade; rank;

[輩出] appear one after another; come forth in large numbers; come out in succession;
人才輩出 people of talent come out in succession;
英雄輩出 a multitude of heroes come forward;

[輩兒] generation;
輩輩兒 for generations; generation after generation;

[輩份] difference in seniority; seniority in a family or clan;
[輩流] people of one's generations;
[輩名] generation name;
[輩數兒] order of seniority in the family; position in the family hierarchy;
[輩子] all one's life; lifetime;
半輩子 half a lifetime; half part of one's life;
~大半輩子 in the midst of life;
~下半輩子 latter half of one's life; the rest of one's life;
老八輩子 age-old; ancient; hackneyed; old and decayed; outworn; stale;
上八輩子 remote ancestors;
永輩子 for life; forever;
這輩子 this lifetime;

彼輩 that gang; those people;
儕輩 associates; fellows;
疇輩 people of the same generation;
此輩 people of this ilk; people of this type; such sort of people;
行輩 position in the family hierarchy;
後輩 (1) inferiors; juniors; younger generation; (2) descendants; posterity;
老輩 old people; one's elders;
老前輩 older generation; one's senior;
年輩 age and seniority;
朋輩 friends;
平輩 of the same generation;
前輩 elder; forerunners; older generation; last generation; past generation; one's senior; predecessor;
若輩 you all;
上輩 elder generation of a family;
少輩 one's juniors;
鼠輩 mean creatures; scoundrels;
同輩 of the same generation;
同行中的前輩 seniors of a profession;
晚輩 one's juniors; younger generation;
我輩 us; we;
吾輩 we;
下輩 future generation; offspring;
先輩 ancestors; elder generation;
小輩 junior;
一輩 a generation;
長輩 one's betters;
之輩 run of people;
祖輩 ancestors; forefathers;

bei

【褙】 mount;

裱褙 mount;

bei

【鋇】 barium;
[鋇餐] barium meal;
[鋇中毒] baritosis;

過氧化鋇 barium peroxide;
硫酸鋇 barium sulfate;
氯化鋇 barium chloride;
氫氧化鋇 barium hydroxide;
乙酸鋇 barium acetate;

bei

【憊】 exhausted; fatigued; tired; weary;
[憊倦] exhausted; fatigued; tired; weary;
[憊懶] tired and indolent;
[憊累] exhausted; tired; weary;
[憊色] expression of fatigue; tired look;

困憊 exhausted;
疲憊 tired out;
衰憊 feeble; weak and tired; weary;

bei

【糒】 parched rice;

bei

【臂】 a pronunciation of 臂;

胳臂 arm;

bei

【鞴】 piston;
[鞴馬] ride a horse;

鞴鞴 piston;

ben¹
ben

【奔】 (1) gallop; hasten; hurry; move quickly; run quickly; rush; rush about; (2) flee; run away; run for one's life; (3) go straight towards; head for; (4) approach; get on for; (5) elope;
[奔北] flee in defeat;
[奔波] (1) busy running about; on constant run; on the run; rush about; (2) toil; work very hard;
到處奔波 rush about hither and thither;

travel from place to place;
兩地奔波 shuttle back and forth between two places;
四處奔波 run about busily;

[奔馳] gallop; hasten; move along quickly; move fast; run quickly; speed; speed on; travel quickly;
奔馳而過 dash by;
奔馳而來 approach at full swing;
奔馳而去 gallop off;
~全速奔馳而去 gallop off at top speed;
奔馳向前 shoot forward;

[奔竄] flee about; flee and hide; scuttle off;
東奔西竄 disperse helter-skelter; flee in all directions; tear about;

[奔放] bold and unrestrained; expressive and unrestrained; moving and forceful; untrammelled;
奔放不羈 have full swing;

[奔赴] go to; hasten to; hurry off for; hurry off to; hurry to a place; rush to;
奔赴戰場 hurry to the field;

[奔競] struggle for wealth and fame;

[奔雷] thunderbolts;

[奔流] (1) flow at great speed; pour; pour out; (2) racing current; swift current;
奔流不息 flow ahead fast ceaselessly;
奔流而下 pour down;
奔流入海 flow into the sea;
奔流湍急 the flying current is rapid;

[奔馬] fleeing horses in stampede;
青銅奔馬 bronze galloping horse;

[奔忙] bustle about; busy rushing about; in a great hurry; on the move constantly; toil;
日夜奔忙 busy working day and night;
四處奔忙 bustle about everywhere; tear around;

[奔命] (1) be on the run; in a desperate hurry; run for one's life; rush about on errands; (2) do one's best; go all out;
疲於奔命 be kept constantly on the run; be tired and exhausted from urging about on missions; run off one's legs;

[奔跑] run; run in great hurry;
東奔西跑 bat about; bat around; bustle about; bustle around; bustle in and out; drive from post to pillar and from pillar to post; move from post to pillar and from pillar to post; run around here and there; run hither and thither; run this way and that; run to and fro; rush about; rush around; tear around; wander from place to place;
來回奔跑 make little runs to and fro;
拼命奔跑 run wildly;
沿路奔跑 dash along the street; fly down the street; gallop along the street; speed down the street;

[奔票] strive for a ticket;

[奔泉] gushing spring;

[奔喪] hasten home for the funeral of a parent or grandparent; hasten home on the death of one's parent;

[奔逃] flee off; run away;
奔逃進洞 scamper into a hole;
四散奔逃 flee helter-skelter;

[奔騰] (1) gallop; (2) roll on in waves; surge forward;
奔騰不息 flow on; roll ahead ceaselessly; surge ahead;
奔騰而過 rush by;
奔騰而下 roll downwards;
奔騰向前 surge ahead;
萬馬奔騰 ten thousand horses gallop;

[奔頭兒] prospect; sth to strive for;

[奔襲] long-range incursion;

[奔向] rush towards;

[奔瀉] pour down; rush down;

[奔星] meteor; shooting star;

[奔湧] surge; well up;

[奔逐] chase; run after;

[奔走] busy running about; do a job on order; run; rush about; solicit help;
奔走呼號 go around campaigning for a cause; go around crying for help; go hither and thither to call for; help;
奔走相告 lose no time in telling each other the news; pass the news from mouth to mouth; pass the news from one person to another; run around spreading the news; rush about telling the news;
東奔西走 in all directions; run about busily; run to and fro; rush hither and thither;
力疾奔走 busy oneself in running about;
四出奔走 busy travelling about; run busily around; run hither and thither;
四處奔走 run hither and thither;

出奔 flee; leave; run away; take flight;
飛奔 dash; speed along;
狂奔 run about madly; run about wildly;
裸奔 streak;
私奔 elope with one's lover;
逃奔 flee to; run away to another place;
投奔 go to a place for shelter;
淫奔 elope; elopement;

ben
【犇】 an ancient variant of 奔；

ben
【賁】 (1) forge ahead; (2) energetic; strenuous; (3) a surname;

虎賁 brave and strong person;

ben
【錛】 adze;
［錛子］ adze;

ben³
ben
【本】 (1) root of a plant; stem of a plant; (2) basis; foundation; origin; (3) capital; principal; (4) original; (5) native; one's own; (6) current; present; this; (7) according; based on; (8) book; copy; (9) edition; version;
［本班］ this class;
［本本］ book;
本本分分 not go beyond moral bounds;
本本主義 book worship; bookishness;
原原本本 from beginning to end;
源源本本 from beginning to end;
［本部］ central department; head office; headquarters;
［本草］ Chinese herbal medicine;
本草療法 phytotherapy;
［本大］ large capital;
本大利厚 a large capital brings a large profit;
本大利寬 a large capital will yield a large profit;
［本當］ ought to have; should have;
［本地］ local; locality; native; the local area;
本地詞 local word;
本地貨 local goods;
本地薑不辣 familiarity diminishes appreciation;
本地人 (1) indigenous population; (2) native of a place;
本地語 vulgar tongue;
［本兒］ a thousand yuan;
［本分］ one's duty; one's part; one's role;
安守本分 act up to one's duty; keep to one's own business; law-abiding;
不本分 go beyond what is proper;
不守本分 fail to keep to one's own line; swerve from one's duty;
各守本分 all keep to their positions; let not the cobbler go beyond his last; let the cobbler stick to his last; the cobbler should stick to his last;
盡本分 do one's bit; do one's devoir; do one's duty;
~盡其本分 do one's bit; do one's part; exhaust one's obligation; top one's part;
貓捉老鼠狗看門—本分事 a cat catching mice and a dog watching over the house — each has its own duty;
［本該］ ought to have; should have;
［本固枝榮］ when the root is firm, the branches flourish;
［本國］ one's home country; one's own country;
本國經濟 domestic economy;
本國利益 the interests of one's own country;
本國歷史 the history of one's country;
本國人 compatriot; fellow countryman; fellow countrywoman;
本國文化 national culture;
本國資源 national resources;
代表本國 represent one's country;
［本行］ one's line; one's profession; one's specialty; one's trade;
放棄本行 leave one's own profession;
非本行 off one's beat; out of one's beat;
精通本行 expert at one's trade;
三句不離本行 cadgers speak of lead saddles; talk about nothing but one's own interests; talk always about one's own line; talk shop; talk shop all the time;
［本號］ our company;
［本籍］ one's original domicile; one's permanent home address;
［本紀］ biographic sketches of emperors;
［本家］ original home;

B

B

[本屆] current; this year;

[本金] capital; principal;
本金數 capital sum;

[本科] undergraduate course; regular college course;
本科畢業 pass through college;
本科課程 undergraduate course;
本科生 undergraduate;

[本來] at first; from the beginning; in itself; in the first place; it goes without saying; original; originally; properly speaking; should have; used to be;

[本利] principal and interest;
將本求利 make money with one's capital;

[本領] ability; capacity; power; skill; talent;
本領高強 be highly skilled;
看家本領 one's special skill; one's speciality; one's trump card;
有本領 capable; have sth on the ball; resourceful; talented;

[本名] one's formal name;

[本末] (1) ins and outs; the whole course of an event from beginning to end; (2) the fundamental and the incidental;
本末倒置 confuse cause and effect; mistake the means for the end; place the effect before the cause; place the unimportant before the important; put the cart before the horse; put the incidental before the fundamental; take the branch for the root; the sauce is better than the fish;
棄本逐末 forget the important and run after the less important things;
強本弱末 strengthen the fundamental and weaken the trivial;
捨本逐末 attend to the superficial and neglect the essential; attend to the trivialities and neglect the fundamentals; attend to trifles to the neglect of essentials; concentrate on details but forget the objective; grasp the shadow instead of the essence; miss the main point and concern oneself with the insignificant; penny wise, pound foolish;
事有本末 there is a distinction between the basic essentials and the periphery;
物有本末，事有始終 there is a proper sequence of foundation and end-results; things have their root and branches; affairs have their beginning and end;
詳述本末 tell the whole story from beginning to end;
淆混本末 confound the means with the end;

[本能] inborn ability; instinct;
本能動作 instinctive action;
~ 做出本能動作 make an instinctive movement;
出於本能 by instinct;
繁衍本能 sexual drive;
攻擊本能 aggressive instinct;
喚起本能 awaken instinct;
獲得本能 acquisition instinct;
激發本能 rouse an instinct;
盲從本能 follow blindly one's instinct;
收集本能 collecting instinct;
顯示本能 show an instinct;
迎合本能 follow the instinct;

[本年] current year; present year; this year;
本年度 the current year; the present year; this year;

[本票] bank cheque; cashier's order; promissory note;

[本期] (1) this current season; this term; (2) the present class;
本期利潤 profit of the period;
本期利息 current interest;

[本錢] (1) capital; (2) ability;
小本錢 small capital;

[本人] (1) I; me; myself; (2) in person; in the flesh; oneself;

[本日] today;

[本色] distinctive character; true qualities;

[本身] in itself; itself; oneself; personally;

[本事] (1) original story; source material; (2) ability; capacity; skill; (3) able; capable;
沒本事 of no ability;
有本事 capable;
~ 有本事的人 man of ability;

[本題] main question; main subject; main theme; point at issue; subject under discussion;

[本體] noumenon; thing-in-itself;
本體論 ontology;

[本土] one's metropolitan territory; one's native country;
本土文化 indigenous culture; native culture;

[本位] (1) basis; standard; (2) one's own department or unit;
本位主義 selfish departmentalism;
金本位 gold standard;
~金本位貨幣 gold currency;
~金本位制 gold standard;
廢棄金本位制 leave the gold standard;
脫離金本位制 abandon the gold standard;
[本務] one's real duty;
[本息] principal and interest;
連本帶息 principal and interest;
[本銷] domestic sale; local sale;
[本小] small capital;
本小利大 make big profits with a small capital;
本小利微 earn profits with a small capital;
[本校] our school;
[本心] one's conscience; one's true intention;
非出本心 not one's real intention;
[本性] instincts; one's natural character; real nature;
本性不變 sb's nature never changes;
本性乖戾 sullen by nature;
本性難藏 what is bred in the bone will come out in the flesh;
本性難移 a leopard will not change its spots; it is difficult to alter one's character; one's nature cannot be altered; what is bred in the bone will come out in the flesh;
善良本性 better nature;
現其本性 appear in one's real character; come out in one's true colours;
[本業] (1) agriculture; farming; (2) original occupation;
[本意] original idea; real intention;
[本義] literal sense; original meaning;
[本應] ought to have; should have;
[本源] origin; ultimate source;
[本願] one's long cherished desire; one's real wish;
[本月] this month;
[本宅] one's own residence;
[本着] according to; based on; in conformity with; in line with; in the light of;
本着良心辦事 do things in conformity to one's conscience;
[本職] one's duty; one's job;
本職工作 one's duty; one's own job;
[本旨] real intention; real meaning;
[本質] essence; essential characteristics; essential qualities; innate character; intrinsic quality; nature;
本質上 at heart; under the skin;
事情的本質 essence of a thing;
問題的本質 essentials of a problem;
最根本的本質 by its very nature;
[本週] this week;
[本子] (1) book; notebook; script; (2) driver's license;
戲本子 script; text for a play;
[本族語] one's mother tongue; one's native language;

百衲本 collection of various editions;
板本 books printed with types;
版本 edition;
邦本 the foundation of a nation;
背本 one bites the hand that feeds one;
筆記本 notebook;
標本 (1) sample; specimen; (2) appearance and substance;
別本 replica; separate copy;
草本 herbal;
唱本 libretto; script of a ballad-singer;
抄本 hand-written book; transcript;
成本 cost; prime cost;
重版本 second edition;
抽印本 offprint;
大字本 large-character edition;
單行本 (1) article in pamphlet form; separate edition; (2) offprint;
定本 definitive edition;
讀本 (1) reader; (2) school textbook;
賭本 money to gamble with;
翻譯本 translation;
範本 model for calligraphy or painting;
父本 male parent;
副本 back-up copy; duplicate; transcript;
複本 duplicate;
改寫本 adaptation;
稿本 manuscript;
歌本 songbook;
根本 at all; essence; fundamental; not care a whit; not give it a damn; not the least; once for all; simply; thoroughly;
工本 production cost;
工作本 working copy;
夠本 make enough money to cover the cost;
孤本 the only extant copy; the only existing copy;

B

股本 capital stock;
國本 fundamental principles to administer a country;
合訂本 bound volume;
戶口本 residence booklet;
話本 script for storytelling;
還本 repay the principal;
基本 (1) base; foundation; (2) essential; main; (3) elementary; rudimentary; (4) basically; by and large; in the main; on the whole;
集注本 variorum edition;
記事本 notebook;
簡本 abridged edition; concise edition;
簡寫本 simplified edition; simplified version;
腳本 acting copy; acting script; scenario; script;
教本 textbook;
節本 abbreviated edition; abridged edition;
精裝本 deluxe edition;
劇本 (1) drama; play; (2) scenario; script;
絹本 silk scroll;
開本 book size; format;
刊本 edition of a book;
刻本 block-printed edition; carving copy;
課本 textbook;
虧本 lose one's capital; lose one's money in business;
藍本 (1) model for copying; (2) blueprint; (3) chief source; (4) original version;
撈本 recover one's losses; win back lost wagers;
老本 capital; principal;
臨本 copy;
秘本 treasured private copy of a rare book;
模本 calligraphy model; painting model;
摹本 copy; facsimile;
摹真本 facsimile;
母本 female parent;
木本 root of a tree;
賠本 run a business at a loss; sustain losses in business;
平裝本 paperback; paperbound edition;
普及本 popular edition;
槧本 a book printed by engraving;
親本 parent;
曲本 music book;
日記本 diary;
刪節本 abridged edition;
善本 good edition; reliable text;
舌本 back of the tongue; root of the tongue;
折本 get into red; lose money;
蝕本 lose money; lose one's capital;
試用本 trial edition;
書本 book;
樹本 (1) root of a tree; (2) build a good foundation for sth;
縮本 (1) abridged edition; (2) pocket size edition;
縮寫本 abridged edition; abridged version;
拓本 book of rubbings;
台本 playscript with stage directions;
謄清本 fair copy;
推本 go to the source;
忘本 (1) bite the hand that feeds one; ungrateful; (2) forget one's class origin; forget one's past suffering;
文本 text; version;
務本 attend to fundamentals;
戲本 text for a play;
下本 invest capital;
線裝本 thread-bound edition;
小本 small capital;
寫本 copy; hand-copied book; hand-written copy; transcript;
修訂本 revised edition;
袖珍本 pocket edition;
選本 anthology; selected works or writings;
血本 original capital; principal;
演出本 acting version;
贗本 spurious copy; spurious edition;
樣本 (1) sample book; (2) sample; specimen;
譯本 translation;
印本 printed copy;
油印本 mimeographed booklet;
原本 (1) master copy; original manuscript; (2) copy of the first edition; (3) original text; (4) formerly; originally;
源本 origin of an event;
再版本 second edition;
棗本 book; volume;
增補本 enlarged edition;
增訂本 revised and enlarged edition;
贈本 presentation copy;
贈閱本 complimentary copy;
張本 (1) anticipatory action; (2) anticipatory remark;
賬本 account book;
珍本 rare book; rare edition;
正本 (1) original; (2) reserved copy;
治本 deal with a trouble at the source; effect a permanent cure; get at the root; get at the root of a problem; provide fundamental solutions to the problems; take radical measures; treat a matter thoroughly;
資本 (1) capital; (2) what is capitalized on;
子本 principal and interest;

奏本 memorial;
足本 unabridged;

ben
【苯】 benzene; benzol;
［苯胺］ aniline;
苯胺黑 aniline black;
苯胺染料 aniline dye;
［苯基］ phenyl;
［苯酸銨］ ammonium benzoate;
［苯乙烯］ phenylethylene; styrene;
［苯中毒］ benzolism; poisoning by benzene;

粗苯 crude benzol;
丁苯 butylbenzene;
動力苯 motor benzol;
二毋苯 dimethylbenzene;
二戊苯 diamylbenzene;
二硝基苯 dinitro benzene;
庚基苯 heptylbenzene;
甲苯 methylbenzene; toluene;
任基苯 nonylbenzene;
三羥基苯 trihydroxybenzene;
三硝基甲苯 trinitrotoluene;
商品苯 commercial benzol;
硝化級苯 nitration grade benzene;
乙苯 ethylbenzene; phenylethane;
乙烯基苯 vinylbenzene;
異丙基苯 isopropylbenzene;
異戊基苯 isoamylbenzene;
重苯 heavy benzol;

ben
【畚】 bamboo basket for carrying earth;
［畚箕］ bamboo basket for carrying earth;

ben⁴
ben
【奔】 (1) go ahead; go straight forwards; head for; (2) towards;
［奔命］ in a desperate hurry;
［奔頭］ prospect; sth to strive for;
有奔頭 have a bright prospect;

出奔 flee; leave; run away; take flight;
飛奔 run at full speed; run like mad; run like the wind;
狂奔 run about madly; run about wildly;
裸奔 streak;
私奔 elope; run away;
逃奔 flee to; run away to;
投奔 go to sb or somewhere for shelter;

ben
【笨】 (1) dull; foolish; stupid; (2) awkward; clumsy; cumbersome; unskilful; unwieldy;
［笨伯］ clumsy fellow; fool; idiot; simpleton; slow-witted;
［笨車］ heavy cart; heavy wagon;
［笨蛋］ addle head; airhead; asshole; blubber head; bonehead; boob; booby; bozo; brack-brain; burk; charlie; chowderhead; chucklehead; chump; cretin; cunt; dipshit; duffer; fathead; fool; half-wit; idiot; knucklehead; moron; muppet; nimrod; ninny; nit; nitwit; numbskull; numptie; pillock; schnook; silly billy; stupid fellow; sucker; wanker;
大笨蛋 blamed fool; blockhead;
～十足的大笨蛋 bloody fool;
你這個笨蛋 you numbskull;
［笨工］ unskilled worker;
［笨狗］ big mastiff;
［笨瓜］ fool;
［笨漢］ clumsy fellow; fool; stupid fellow;
［笨貨］ dullard; fool; simpleton;
［笨驢］ stupid donkey;
其笨如驢 as stupid as a donkey;
［笨鳥先飛］ a slow sparrow should make an early start; clumsy birds have to start flying early; the slow need to start early;
［笨牛］ fool; stupid ox;
［笨人］ dullard; fool; idiot; nincompoop; simpleton; stupid person;
［笨賊］ stupid burglar;
［笨重］ cumbersome; heavy; unwieldly;
笨重的 clunky;
［笨拙］ awkward; clumsy; slow-witted; stupid; unskilled;
笨拙的 clumsy; lumpish;
粗魯笨拙 Outlandish; rude and clumsy;
動作笨拙 awkward in one's movements;
樣子笨拙 awkward in one's manner;

不笨 not slow-witted;
遲笨 slow;
蠢笨 clumsy; stupid;
粗笨 clumsy; unwieldy;
很笨 slow-witted;

手腳笨 have a hand like a foot; have two left hands;
愚笨 foolish; stupid;
拙笨 awkward; clumsy; unskillful;
嘴笨 clumsy of speech; inarticulate; not skilled in talking;

B

beng¹
beng

【崩】 (1) collapse; (2) die; pass away; (3) burst; (4) be hit by sth; (5) execute by shooting; shoot; shoot to death;

[崩解] collapse; crumble; disintegrate; disintegration;
光電崩解 photoelectric disintegration;
土崩瓦解 be disintegrated; break up; collapse like a house of cards; crumble; disintegrate; fall apart; fall to pieces; go to sticks and staves; in great disorder; in great tumult; in total confusion; in total disintegration; in total disorder;
陰極崩解 cathode disintegration;

[崩口] hole made by cracking;

[崩潰] breakdown; collapse; come asunder; come apart; crash; crumble; disintegrate; fall apart; fall asunder;
瀕臨崩潰 on the verge of collapse;
徹底崩潰 total collapse;
經濟崩潰 economic collapse;
精神崩潰 nervous breakdown; suffer from a nervous breakdown;
神經崩潰 shatter sb's nerves;

[崩裂] break apart; burst apart; crack;
傷口崩裂 the wound opened under the strain;

[崩漏] uterine bleeding;
崩漏帶下 uterine bleeding and vaginal discharge;
崩漏下血 uterine bleeding;

[崩塌] collapse; crumble;
橋崩塌 the bridge crumbled up;
山洞崩塌 the cave fell in;

[崩陷] cave in; collapse; fall in; sink; subside;

駕崩 (of a monarch) die;
山崩 landfall; landslide; landslip;
雪崩 snowslide; avalanche of snow;
血崩 metrorrhagia;

beng

【綳】 (1) bind; draw tight; stretch tight; (2) tighten; (3) bounce; spring;

[綳帶] bandage;
紗布綳帶 gauze bandage;
一根綳帶 a bandage;

[綳兒] extremely; so; very;

[綳簧] springs in machines;

[綳價] haggle;

[綳騙] cheat;

[綳上] tack down; tack on;
綳上衣帽 tack down a fold;

[綳針] pin;

[綳子] hoop; tambour; embroidery frame;

緊綳綳 (1) taut; tight; (2) stiffened; strained;
棕綳 wooden bed frame strung with criss-cross coir ropes;

beng²
beng

【甭】 need not; not have to; unnecessary to;

beng³
beng

【綳】 (1) taut; tense; (2) bear; endure;

[綳着臉] assume a displeased look; assume a serious look; have a straight face; have a taut face; pull a long face;

beng⁴
beng

【迸】 (1) burst forth; burst out; gush; spout; spurt; (2) explode; scatter;

[迸脆] crisp;

[迸發] burst forth; burst out;

[迸開] split open;

[迸淚] tears pouring out;

[迸裂] burst open; crack; split;

[迸流] gush; pour; spit out in all directions; spurt;

[迸散] flee in all directions;

[迸跳] jump about;

beng

【泵】 pump;

[泵房] pump room;

氣泵 air pump;
氣動泵 pneumatic pump;

氣壓泵 pneumatic pump;
水泵 water pump;
循理泵 circulating pump;

beng

【繃】 break open; burst open; crack; split open;
［繃脆］ very crisp;
［繃斷］ snap from tension;
［繃硬］ hard as a stone; stiff as a board;

緊繃繃 (1) taut; tight; (2) stiffened; strained; sullen;

beng

【蹦】 caper; jump; leap; skip; spring; trip;
［蹦跳］ bounce; jump;
蹦跳音樂 jump-up;
蹦蹦跳跳 bounce about; bouncing and vivacious; capering; cut a caper; cut capers; frolicsome; jump like parched peas; prance about to romp; romping; skipping; tripping;
歡蹦亂跳 cavort and leap; dance and skip with joy; gambol; romp;
活蹦亂跳 alive and kicking; frolic; gambol; lively; skip and jump about;
連蹦帶跳 hop and skip;
瞎蹦亂跳 up on the scamper;
一蹦三跳 hopping and jumping; very happy;
一蹦一跳 skip and hop;

bi[1]

bi

【屄】 vagina;

bi

【逼】 (1) compel; drive; force; (2) extort; press for; (3) close in on; press on towards; press up to; (4) narrow; strait; (5) annoy; harass; importune;
［逼變］ drive to revolt;
［逼供］ extort a confession;
嚴刑逼供 use torture to extort a confession;
［逼和］ win a draw;
［逼嫁］ force a woman to marry;
［逼姦］ rape;
［逼近］ approach; approximation; close in on; draw near; gain on; press on towards;
離散逼近 discrete approximation;
連續逼近 continuous approximation;
悄悄逼近 approach sth with stealthy steps;
數值逼近 digital approximation;
相容逼近 consistent approximation;
［逼勒］ blackmail; force;
［逼良為娼］ compel a female to engage in prostitution; force girls of good families to be prostitutes; force young girls of good families to prostitute themselves;
［逼鄰］ neighbouring;
［逼迫］ coerce; compel; constrain; force;
逼迫手段 coercion;
［逼前］ press forward;
［逼取］ blackmail; extort; take by forcible means;
［逼人］ pressing; threatening;
逼人太甚 push sb too hard;
［逼視］ (1) look at sth from close-up; watch intently; (2) stare at sternly;
［逼死］ hound sb to death;
［逼索］ force; obtain by force;
［逼問］ force sb to answer; press for an answer;
［逼狹］ harsh; ungenerous;
［逼肖］ bear a close resemblance to; the very image of; with striking resemblance;
［逼壓］ oppress;
［逼債］ demand payment of debt; dun; press for payment of debts;
逼債勒索 press for the repayment of debts and practise extortion;
被債主逼債 be hounded by one's creditors;
［逼真］ (1) lifelike; realistic; true to life; true to nature; (2) clearly; distinctly;
十分逼真 absolutely lifelike; remarkably to life;
形像逼真 the very image of the original;
［逼走］ force to leave;
［逼租］ press for payment of rent;

被逼 be compelled; be forced;
催逼 press for sth;
緊逼 close in one; press hard;
進逼 press on;
勒逼 coerce; force;
強逼 compel; force;
威逼 threaten by force;
追逼 (1) pursue or follow closely; (2) extort; press for;

B

bi²

bi

【荸】 water chestnut;

［荸薺］ water chestnut;

bi

B

【鼻】 nose;

［鼻癌］ rhino carcinoma;

［鼻白喉］ nasal diphtheria;

［鼻背］ dorsum nasi;

［鼻病］ rhinopathia;

［鼻部結核］ tuberculosis of nose;

［鼻出血］ nasal haemorrhage; nosebleed; pistaxie;

［鼻唇溝］ nasolabial fold;

［鼻道］ meatus of nose; nasal duct;
上鼻道 upper nasal duct;
下鼻道 lower nasal duct;
中鼻道 middle nasal duct;

［鼻竇］ paranasal sinus;
鼻竇炎 nasal sinusitis; nasosinusitis; sinusitis;
高空鼻竇炎 aerosinusitis;
航空性鼻竇炎 aerosinusitis;
化膿鼻竇炎 suppurative sinusitis;
氣壓性鼻竇炎 barosinusitis;
～全鼻竇炎 pansinuitis;

［鼻堵塞］ obstruction of the nose;

［鼻端］ tip of the nose;

［鼻反射］ nasal reflex;

［鼻峰］ bridge of the nose;

［鼻乾］ dry nose;

［鼻根］ root of the nose;

［鼻骨］ nasal bone;
鼻骨孔 nasal foramina;

［鼻喉炎］ rhinolaryngitis;

［鼻後孔］ choana;

［鼻甲］ nasal concha; turbinal;
鼻甲炎 conchitis;
全鼻甲 panturbinate;
上鼻甲 superior nasal concha;

［鼻尖］ tip of the nose;

［鼻癤］ furuncle of nose;

［鼻鏡］ rhinoscope;

［鼻疽］ glander;
日本鼻疽 Japanese glander;

［鼻科］ rhinology;
鼻科疾病 nose disease;
鼻科學家 rhinologist;
鼻科專家 rhinologist;

［鼻孔］ nares; nostrils;
鼻孔閉塞 have a blocked nose; have a stuffy nose;
鼻孔朝天 cock one's nose;
前鼻孔 prenaris;
挖鼻孔 pick one's nose;

［鼻樑］ bridge of the nose;
高鼻樑 high nose;
塌鼻樑 flat nose;

［鼻毛］ nose hair; vibrissae;

［鼻囊］ nasal sac;

［鼻黏膜］ nasal mucous membrane;

［鼻牛兒］ nose dirt; nose wax;

［鼻衄］ nosebleed; rhinorrhagia;

［鼻旁竇］ paranasal sinus;

［鼻氣管炎］ bovine rhinotracheitis;
傳染性鼻氣管炎 infectious bovine rhinotracheitis; infectious rhinotracheitis;

［鼻腔］ nasal cavity;

［鼻青臉腫］ a bloody nose and a swollen face; badly battered; beat sb black and blue; get a bloody nose;

［鼻塞］ nasal congestion; snuffles;
鼻塞不通 nasal congestion;
鼻塞欠通 nasal congestion;
鼻塞聲啞 one's nose is obstructed and one's voice hoarse;
鼻塞無歇 nasal congestion;
嬰兒鼻塞 snuffle;

［鼻石］ rhinolith;

［鼻屎］ bogey; booger; nasal secretion;

［鼻飼法］ nasal feeding;

［鼻塌嘴歪］ with a snub nose and a wry mouth;

［鼻涕］ nasal mucus; snivel;
擦鼻涕 wipe away one's mucus;
流鼻涕 have a running nose; run at the nose;
擤鼻涕 blow one's nose;

［鼻痛］ rhinalgia;

［鼻頭］ nose;
挨鼻頭 suffer a criticism;
大鼻頭 big nose;

［鼻突］ nasal process;
外側鼻突 lateral nasal process;

［鼻窩］ nasal pit;

［鼻息］ breath;
鼻息很重 heavy breather;
鼻息肉 nasal polyp;

鼻息如雷 snore like thunder;
窺人鼻息 wait on one's beck;
仰人鼻息 at sb's beck and call; cater to sb's every whim; depend on another's whims and pleasures; depend on others; dependent on the pleasure of others; dependent on the whims of others; live at sb's mercy; rely on others and have to watch their every expression; slavishly dependent on others; under sb's thumb;
~仰人鼻息的人 lap dog;

[鼻血] nasal haemorrhage; nosebleed;

[鼻咽] nasopharynx;
鼻咽癌 cancer of nasopharynx; nasopharyngeal carcinoma;
鼻咽炎 nasopharyngitis;

[鼻煙] snuff;
吸鼻煙 sniff snuff;
一撮鼻煙 a pinch of snuff;

[鼻炎] rhinitis;
鼻炎肉 nasal polyp;
變應性鼻炎 allergic rhinitis;
傳染性鼻炎 infectious coryza; infectious rhinitis;
肥厚性鼻炎 hypertrophic rhinitis;
過敏性鼻炎 allergic rhinitis;
壞疽性鼻炎 gangrenous rhinitis;
壞死性鼻炎 necrotic rhinitis;
急性鼻炎 acute rhinitis;
結核性鼻炎 tuberculous rhinitis;
慢性鼻炎 chronic rhinitis;
梅毒性鼻炎 syphilitic rhinitis;
膜性鼻炎 membranous rhinitis;
特應性鼻炎 atopic rhinitis;
萎縮性鼻炎 atrophic rhinitis;

[鼻癢] itching in the nose;

[鼻藥] nose drops;

[鼻翼] wings of the nose;

[鼻音] nasal sounds;
鼻音過少 denasality;
鼻音過重 hypernasality;
後鼻音 back nasal;
開放性鼻音 open rhinolalia;
前鼻音 front nasal;
説話帶鼻音 speak with the nose; utter with a nasal sound;

[鼻淵] deep-source nasal congestion;
鼻淵頭痛 headache due to nasosinusitis;

[鼻燥] dry nose;

[鼻直口方] have a straight nose and firm lips;

[鼻中隔] nasal septum;
鼻中隔彎曲 deviation of nasal septum;
膜性鼻中隔 membranous nasal septum;
軟骨性鼻中隔 cartilaginous nasal septum;

[鼻柱] columna nasi;

[鼻子] beezer; bugle; nose;
鼻子不靈 have a bad nose;
鼻子不是鼻子，臉不是臉 angry looks; unpleasant look;
鼻子不通 clogged-up nose; have a stuffed-up nose; stuffed-up nose;
鼻子不通氣 nasal congestion;
鼻子出血 bleed at one's nose; suffer a bleeding nose;
鼻子底下的事 trivial matter;
鼻子發炎 suffer from nasal catarrh;
鼻子靈 have a good nose;
鼻子塞住 have a stuffed-up nose; one's nose is stuffed up;
鼻子傷風 have a cold in the nose;
鼻子痛 have pain in the nose;
鼻子眼兒 nostrils;
鼻子一酸 a lump comes into one's throat;
白鼻子 crafty person; sly person;
擦鼻子 wipe one's nose;
擦破鼻子 bark one's nose;
長而高的鼻子 long, high nose;
抽鼻子 sniffle; snivel; snuffle; take a deep breath by the nose;
大鼻子 (1) big nose; bottle nose; enormous nose; high-bridged nose; (2) foreigner;
短而扁的鼻子 short, flat nose;
高鼻子 elevated nose; high nose;
刮鼻子 (1) rub sb's nose in it; rub sb's nose in the dirt; (2) be criticized; haul sb over the coals; reprimand; tell sb off;
擊中鼻子 catch sb on the nose;
夾住鼻子 clamp one's nose; pinch sb's nose;
摳鼻子 pick one's nose;
哭鼻子 snivel; weep;
老鼻子 a great number of; plenty of;
拿草棍兒戳老虎鼻子 tickle the tiger's nose with a straw — stir up trouble;
捏着鼻子 suffer patiently and silently;
氣歪鼻子 put sb's nose out of joint;
牽着鼻子走 have sb on the string; get sb on the string; keep sb on the string; lead sb by the nose;

~給牽着鼻子走 be led by the nose;
嗆鼻子 choke one's nose;
肉鼻子 dumpy nose;
蒜頭鼻子 bulbous nose;
蹋鼻子 button nose; flat nose;
擤鼻子 blow one's nose;
糟鼻子 drunkard's nose;
~糟鼻子不吃酒，枉擔虛名 have a bad reputation that one does not deserve, like a teetotaller with a red nose;
皺起鼻子 wrinkle one's nose;

［鼻祖］ earliest ancestor; founder; originator;

鞍背鼻 saddle-back nose;
鞍鼻 saddle nose;
扁蹋鼻 snub nose;
朝天鼻 short nose; upturned nose;
刺鼻 assail one's nostrils; irritate the nose; pungent;
酒糟鼻 a nose to light candles at; bottlenose; brandy nose; drunkard's nose;
酒渣鼻 coppernose; rosacea;
巨鼻 macrorhinia;
門鼻 staple;
撲鼻 assail the nostrils;
獅子鼻 pug nose; snub nose;
酸鼻 feel grieved; feel like crying;
蒜頭鼻 bulbous nose; pug nose; snub nose;
塌鼻 flat nose; snub nose;
齆鼻 blocked up nose;
象鼻 elephant trunk;
掩鼻 cover one's nose;
鷹鈎鼻 acquiline nose;
擁鼻 hold one's nose;
捉鼻 hold in contempt;

bi³

bi

【匕】 (1) ladle; spoon; (2) arrowhead; (3) dagger;

［匕首］ dagger;

bi

【比】 (1) compare; contrast; (2) compete; emulate; match; (3) compare to; draw an analogy; liken to; (4) gesticulate; gesture; (5) than; (6) proportion; ratio; (7) to;

［比比］ (1) repeatedly; time and again; (2) everywhere;
比比劃劃 gesticulate as one talks; make lively gestures; talk with lively gesticulations;
比比皆是 can be found everywhere; can be seen everywhere; such is the case everywhere;
~街頭小攤比比皆是 street stalls can be found everywhere;

［比並］ compare to; liken;

［比不上］ inferior to; no peer for; not come near; not comparable to; not hold a candle to; not so…as;

［比…大…歲］ older than sb by ...years; one is elder by ...years; ...years older than sb; ...years one's elder; ...years one's senior; ...years senior to sb;

［比得上］ bear comparison with; can compare with; compare favourably with;

［比對］ collate; compare and check; comparison;

［比方］ analogy; compare; example; for example; instance; liken;
比方說 for example; for instance;
打個比方 draw an analogy; take for example; take sth as an example;

［比分］ score;
比分是多少 what is the score;
累積比分 aggregate score; running score;
最後比分 final score;

［比附］ compare to; liken;

［比劃］ (1) gesticulate; gesture; (2) come to blows;

［比及］ by the time; till; until; when;

［比價］ compare bids; compare prices;

［比肩］ shoulder to shoulder; side by side;
比肩並進 advance shoulder to shoulder;
比肩而立 stand shoulder to shoulder; very near;
比肩而事 work together;
比肩繼踵 be overcrowded with people; follow closely one after another; one follows on the heels of another;

［比較］ by comparison; compare; compare with; comparatively; contrast; fairly; in comparison; in comparison with; in contrast to; somewhat;
比較法 (1) comparison; comparative method; (2) comparative law;
~比較法教育 the teaching of comparative law;
~比較法研究 research on comparative law;

~分析比較法 analytical comparison;
~歷史比較法 historical comparative method;
比較分析 comparative analysis;
比較格 comparative case;
比較級 the comparative degree;
比較句 comparative sentence;
比較器 comparator;
~導納比較器 admittance comparator;
~放大比較器 amplifier comparator;
~模擬比較器 analogue comparator;
~位比較器 bit comparator;
比較儀 comparator;
~電流比較儀 current comparator;
~光電比較儀 electronic optical comparator;
~體視比較儀 stereocomparator;
遞減級比較 regressive comparison;
遞增級比較 progressive comparison;
進行比較 institute a comparison;
絕對比較 absolute comparison;
累積比較 cumulative comparison;

[比快] competition of speed;

[比例] (1) proportion; ratio; (2) scale;
比例尺 proportional scale; scale;
~直線比例尺 linear scale;
比例代表制 proportional representation;
比例稅 proportional tax;
~比例稅率 proportional tax rate;
比例相等 in equal proportions;
比例相似 in similar proportion;
比例中項 mean terms of proportion;
按比例 at the ratio; in proportion; pro rata; proportionally; proportionate; on the scale of;
~按比例減少 scale down;
~按比例增加 scale up;
按照…比例 on the scale of...;
按照比例 pro rata;
不成比例 lack proportion; not in proportion to; out of proportion;
不合比例 disproportionate;
反比例 inverse proportion;
複比例 compound proportion;
改變…的比例 alter the proportions of;
更迭比例 alternate proportion;
合比例 in proportion;
進料比例 charge proportion;
佔…的很大比例 form a large proportion of...;
正比例 direct proportion;

[比量] (1) inference; (2) take rough measurements;

[比鄰] (1) neighbour; (2) near; next to;
洽比其鄰 on friendly terms with one's neighbours;
天涯比鄰 a bosom friend, though far away, is as near as one's neighbour;
天涯若比鄰 a bosom friend, though far away, is as near as one's neighbour;

[比率] proportion; rate; ratio;
促進劑比率 accelerator ratio;
平均效率比率 average efficiency ratio;
異構體比率 isomer ratio;

[比目魚] flatfish; flounder; halibut; sole;
大比目魚 halibut;

[比擬] analogy; compare; draw a parallel; liken; match; metaphor;

[比如] for example; for instance; like; such as;

[比賽] compete in a contest; competition; contest; have a race; match; tournament;
比賽場地 ring;
比賽規則 rules of the game;
比賽開始 play ball;
比賽區 playing area;
比賽取消 the game is cancelled;
安排比賽 arrange a match;
比分接近的比賽 close affair;
參加比賽 compete in a race; enter a competition; enter a contest; join in a game; run a race; take part in a competition; take part in a race;
打比賽 have a game;
打贏比賽 win a game;
發起比賽 launch a competition;
公平比賽 fair play;
觀看比賽 watch the match;
國際比賽 international tournament;
舉辦比賽 run a contest;
舉行比賽 hold a competition; hold a match; hold a race;
看比賽 see a game; watch a game;
平淡的比賽 tame affair;
取消比賽 cancel a match;
首場比賽 opener;
輸掉比賽 lose a game; lose a match; lose a race;
~故意輸掉比賽 throw a match;
一邊倒的比賽 one-sided affair;
一場比賽 a game; a match;
一次比賽 a competition;

一輪比賽 a round of matches; a round of the tournament;
一項比賽 a game;
贏得比賽 win a competition; win a race; win the match;
有獎比賽 prize competition;
中斷比賽 break off the match;
組織比賽 organize a competition;

[比色] colorimetric;
比色法 colorimetry;
比色分析 colorimetric analysis;
比色計 chromometer; colorimeter;
~吸收比色計 absorptiometer;
比色儀 colour comparator;

[比時] at that time; then;

[比試] (1) have a competition; (2) make a gesture of measuring;

[比武] demonstrate fighting skills in a tournament; joust;

[比先] formerly;

[比…小…歲] one is junior by ...years; ...years junior to sb; ...years one's junior; ...years one's younger; ...years younger than sb; younger than sb. by ...years;

[比一比] engage in a contest; have a contest; make a comparison;

[比翼] fly wing to wing;
比翼連枝 as twin birds flying side by side or trees with their branches intertwined;
比翼鳥 devoted couple; pair of lovebirds;
比翼雙飛 go together as a happy couple;

[比譯] transposition;
創造性比譯 creative transposition;

[比喻] analogy; figure of speech; metaphor; simile;
比喻意義 figurative meaning;

[比照] (1) contrast; (2) according to; in the light of;

[比值] ratio; specific value;

[比重] (1) proportion; (2) gravity; specific gravity;
比重計 hydrometer;
~化學比重計 chemical hydrometer;
~鏈式比重計 chain hydrometer;
~油比重計 oil hydrometer;
表觀比重 apparent specific gravity;
絕對比重 absolute specific gravity;
汽油比重 gasoline gravity;

[比濁計] turbidimeter;

百分比 percentage;
變速比 gear ratio;
不比 (1) different from; unlike; (2) cannot compare with; no match for;
傳動比 transmitting ratio;
打比 draw an analogy; make an analogy;
單比 simple proportion;
定比 fixed proportion;
對比 balance; compare; show by contrast;
反比 inverse ratio;
反射比 reflectance;
複比 compound ratio; double ratio;
公比 common ratio;
好比 (1) by way of example; can be compared to; for example; for instance; may be likened to; (2) just like; like;
恒比 constant proportion;
焦比 focal ratio;
較比 comparatively; fairly; relatively;
可比 comparable;
類比 analogy;
連比 continued ratio;
盧比 rupee;
倫比 equal; rival;
排比 (1) a rhetorical use of parallel constructions; (2) arrange in order; (3) parallelism;
攀比 compare unrealistically; compare with the higher; make invidious comparisons; vie with each other;
評比 appraise through comparison; compare and assess;
燃料比 fuel ratio;
透射比 transmittance;
無比 incomparable; matchless; unparalleled;
顯比 simile;
相比 compare with each other; match;
相似比 ratio of similitude;
隱比 metaphor;
正比 direct proportion; direct ratio;
質量比 mass ratio;
櫛比 placed closely side by side;
中外比 golden section;

bi

【妣】 one's deceased mother;

考妣 deceased parents;

bi

【彼】 (1) another; that; the other; those; (2) the other party; (3) there;

[彼岸] the other shore; the yonder shore of

salvation;
[彼輩] that gang; those people;
[彼蒼] the heavens;
[彼此] both parties; each other; one another; this and that; you and me;
彼此彼此 the feeling is mutual; we are in a similar position;
彼此不合 at cross purposes;
彼此之間 between two people; between you and me;
不分彼此 make no distinction between one's and another's possessions; share everything;
得此失彼 gain in one thing and lose in another; you lose on the swings what you make on the roundabouts;
非此即彼 either this or that; one or the other;
顧此失彼 attend to one thing and lose sight of another; be put in a double squeeze; cannot attend to one thing without neglecting the other; care for this and lose that; unable to attend to everything at once; unable to hit one without losing hold of the other;
忽此忽彼 hither and thither;
見此忘彼 observe this and neglect that;
無分彼此 one for all and all for one;
[彼等] those people;
[彼方] the other party; the other side;
[彼時] at that time;

bi

【秕】 (1) husks; (2) mean; no good; not qualified;
[秕糠] (1) chaff; (2) worthless stuff;
[秕謬] erroneous; go against good reasoning; mistaken;
[秕子] blighted grain;
糠秕 (1) chaff; (2) worthless stuff;

bi

【俾】 (1) in order to; so that; (2) cause; enable;
[俾眾周知] for the information of all; so as to make it known to everyone;

bi

【筆】 (1) pen; pencil; writing brush; (2) technique of writing; (3) write; (4) stroke; touch; (5) a unit of amount; (6) prose; (7) a surname;
[筆觸] (1) a brush stroke in Chinese painting and calligraphy; (2) a style of painting; (3) brushwork;
[筆牀] penholder; pen rack;
[筆答] answer in writing;
[筆調] tone of the writing; style of the writer;
筆調活潑 possess a racy style;
筆調輕鬆 write with a light touch;
優美筆調 elegant style;
[筆伐] attack in writings; chastise one with the pen; condemn in writing;
口誅筆伐 attack with the pen and punish with the mouth; criticize penetratingly;
[筆法] brushwork; calligraphy; drawing; technique of writing;
筆法剛勁 write with vigorous strokes;
筆法工整 write with neat and orderly strokes;
筆法渾遒 the strokes are bold and fluid;
粗獷筆法 rugged brushwork;
[筆鋒] (1) tip of a writing brush; (2) stroke; touch; vigorous style in writing;
筆鋒如利刃 one's pen is as keen and powerful as a sword;
筆鋒犀利 wield a pointed pen; write in an incisive style;
[筆桿] (1) penholder; (2) handle of a writing brush;
筆桿裙 pencil skirt;
筆桿子 (1) pen; writing brush; (2) effective writer;
耍筆桿 skilled in literary tricks; wield a pen;
咬著筆桿 bite one's pen;
[筆耕] make a living by writing;
筆耕不輟 keep writing;
筆耕維生 adopt writing as a profession; make a living by writing;
心織筆耕 the pen labours on the ideas of the mind;
[筆劃] number of strokes;
筆劃檢字法 indexing method for strokes;
粗筆劃 thick stroke;
細筆劃 thin stroke;
[筆記] (1) notes; (2) take down notes;
筆記本電腦 notebook computer;
筆記簿 notebook;
筆記小說 literary sketches; sketchbook;
對筆記 compare notes;

核對筆記 check notes;
記筆記 jot down notes; make notes; set down notes; take down in writing; take notes;
一批筆記 a set of notes;
整理筆記 arrange one's notes;

[筆跡] sb's handwriting;
筆跡鑒定 bibliotics;
筆跡潦草 have a bad handwriting;
筆跡難以辨認 one's writing is difficult to read; write illegibly;
筆跡漂亮 have a beautiful handwriting;
筆跡清楚 write legibly;
筆跡清晰 have a clear handwriting;
筆跡秀麗 write gracefully;
筆跡學 graphology;
鑒定筆跡 verify sb's handwriting;

[筆架] penholder; penrack;

[筆尖] (1) pen point; (2) tip of a writing brush;
筆尖生花 beautiful writing; write like an angel;
弄鈍筆尖 blunt one's pen;

[筆據] written note;

[筆力] vigour of strokes in calligraphy or drawing;
筆力蒼勁 write in bold, vigorous stroke;
筆力遒勁 every stroke of the characters is boldly and forcefully written; write with firm strokes;
筆力雄健 powerful strokes;

[筆路] style of calligraphy;

[筆錄] (1) put down in writing; take down; write down; (2) record; notes;

[筆帽] cap of a pen; cap of a writing brush;

[筆名] pen name; pseudonym;
使用筆名 use a pen name;

[筆墨] (1) pen and ink; (2) literary work; words; writing;
筆酣墨飽 joy of writing;
筆墨官司 battle of the books; battle of words; written polemics;
筆墨難罄 beyond description; hard to describe by pen and ink;
筆墨生涯 literary career; writing career;
~從事筆墨生涯 become a writer;
~結束筆墨生涯 end one's career as a writer;
~開始筆墨生涯 become a writer; take up the profession of letters;
筆墨為生 earn one's livelihood by writing; make a living with one's pen;
筆墨紙硯 writing brushes, ink sticks, paper and inkstones;
非筆墨所能形容 baffle all description; beg description; cannot be described by words; defy all description; no words can adequately describe;
和以筆墨 chime in with tendentious articles;

[筆難盡述] defy full description in writing; too much to be put down in writing;

[筆石] graptolite;

[筆勢] force of calligraphy;

[筆試] written examination;
參加筆試 take a written examination;

[筆述] narrate in writing;

[筆順] stroke order;

[筆算] (1) do a sum in writing; (2) written calculation;

[筆談] confer by writing; converse in writing;
進行筆談 talk on paper;

[筆體] handwriting;

[筆挺] (1) straight as a ramrod; very straight; (2) trim; well-ironed;

[筆筒] brush barrel; brush pot; pen container;

[筆頭兒] (1) penpoint; point of a writing brush; (2) in written form; written; (3) ability to write;

[筆誤] slip of the pen;

[筆下] wording and purport of what one writes;
筆下超生 write a lenient sentence;
筆下傳情 convey the true spirit of the subject portrayed;
筆下留情 forbear in making critical remarks; have some restraint when attacking others in writing; merciful in writing; refrain from abusing sb by writing; spare sb in making critical attacks;

[筆心] (1) pencil lead; (2) refill;
鉛筆心 pencil lead;
圓珠筆心 refill;

[筆意] (1) calligraphic style; (2) meaning of a passage;

[筆譯] written translation;

[筆友] pen pal;
網上筆友 keypal;

[筆戰] paper battle; paper warfare; polemic writing; the war of the pen; written

polemics;
筆戰一場 have written polemics;
[筆者] author; writer;
[筆直] as straight as an arrow; hold upright; in a beeline; perfectly straight;
筆直走 go straight ahead; go straight on;
挺得筆直 stand straight as a ramrod;
站得筆直 hold oneself upright;
坐得筆直 sit up straight;
[筆資] fees for writing; remuneration for writing; writer's fees;

敗筆 bad stroke;
秉筆 hold a pen;
才筆 literary talent;
彩筆 (1) brush that produces masterpieces; (2) colour pen; painting brush; colour crayons;
測電筆 test pencil;
椽筆 your masterly writing;
輟筆 stop in the middle of writing or painting;
大筆 (1) a large sum; (2) pen;
大筆耕 (1) pen; (2) your writing;
代筆 write on sb's behalf;
刀筆 writing of indictments;
動筆 put pen to paper; set pen to paper; start writing; take up the pen;
粉筆 chalk;
伏筆 foreshadowing;
附筆 additional note;
鋼筆 fountain pen; pen;
擱筆 lay down one's pen; put down the pen; stop writing either temporarily or for good;
光筆 light pen;
海筆 sea feather; sea pen;
鴻筆 great literary style; great pen;
湖筆 writing brush produced in Huzhou;
畫筆 brush; painting brush;
揮筆 write with a pen;
繪圖筆 drawing pen;
金筆 fountain pen;
絕筆 (1) last words written before one's death; (2) last work of an author or painter;
開筆 (1) begin to learn to write poems and compositions in one's life; (2) begin writing in a year;
蠟筆 colour crayon; wax crayon;
落筆 put pen to paper; start writing;
漫筆 informal essay; literary notes; ramblings;
毛筆 Chinese writing brush;
眉筆 eyebrow pencil;
命筆 set pen to paper; take up one's pen;
墨筆 Chinese writing brush;
木筆 lily magnolia;
拿起筆 take up one's pen;
拈筆 pick up a pen to write; take a pen; write;
弄筆 distort facts; exaggerate in writing;
排筆 broad brush comprising a row of pen-shaped brushes;
起筆 (1) first stroke of a Chinese character; (2) way to start each stroke in writing a Chinese character;
鉛筆 lead pencil; pencil;
親筆 (1) in one's own handwriting; (2) one's own handwriting;
曲筆 (1) distortion of the facts by an official historian to cover up the truth; (2) deliberate digression;
缺筆 missing stroke in a written character;
扔下筆 fling one's pen down;
冗筆 (1) verbosity in writing; (2) unnecessary strokes in painting;
潤筆 reward for a writer, painter, or calligrapher;
煞筆 concluding lines of an article;
涉筆 put pen to paper; set pen to paper; start writing;
石筆 slate pencil;
試電筆 test pencil;
手筆 (1) sb's own handwriting; (2) sb's own painting; (3) literary skills;
水筆 watercolour paintbrush;
俗筆 vulgar style of writing;
隨筆 informal essays; jottings; literary notes; literary rambles; miscellaneous writings;
炭筆 charcoal pencil;
韜筆 let the pen idle; write no more;
提筆 lift one's pen to write;
題筆 write;
鐵筆 stencil pen;
禿筆 (1) bald writing brush; (2) poor writing ability;
文筆 literary talent; pen; style of writing;
握筆 hold a brush; hold a pen;
誤筆 a slip of the pen;
戲筆 a poem written at will;
下筆 write;
信筆 write as fancy dictates; write freely without hesitation; write without much thought;
鴨嘴筆 drawing pen; ruling pen;
一筆 (1) a debt of; a sum of; (2) one stroke;
一大筆 a large amount of; a large sum of;
一枝筆 a pen;
銥金筆 iridium-point pen;
遺筆 writings of a deceased person;
譯筆 style of a translation;

B

B

御筆 emperor's handwriting;
援筆 take up a pen to write;
圓珠筆 ball pen; ball-point pen;
運筆 wield one's pen;
氈頭筆 felt-tip pen;
蘸筆 dip a writing brush in ink;
振筆 wield the brush;
之筆 brush;
直筆 unprejudiced writing; write in an unprejudiced way;
執筆 do the actual writing;
朱筆 Chinese writing brush dipped in red ink;
硃筆 vermilion writing brush;
主筆 editor-in-chief;
贅筆 superfluous touch;
拙筆 one's writing;
着筆 set pen to paper; start writing or painting;
自來水筆 fountain pen;
走筆 write rapidly;

bi

【鄙】 (1) base; despicable; low; mean; vulgar; (2) my; (3) despise; disdain; scorn; (4) shallow; superficial; (5) out-of-the-way; remote;
[鄙薄] (1) base; mean; (2) despise; loathe; scorn; (3) shallow; superficial;
[鄙夫] ignorant fellow; mean fellow;
[鄙見] my humble opinion;
[鄙賤] base; lowly; mean;
[鄙俚] coarse; crude; philistine; vulgar;
[鄙劣] inferior; mean;
[鄙吝] mean; miserly; niggardly; stingy; vulgar;
[鄙陋] (1) shallow; superficial; (2) base; mean;
鄙陋無知 shallow and ignorant;
[鄙棄] despise; disdain; loathe;
[鄙人] I; my humble self; your humble servant;
[鄙事] mean matters; trifles;
[鄙視] despise; disdain; look down on sb; slight;
受鄙視 be treated with disdain; be treated with scorn;
[鄙俗] low; philistine; vulgar;
鄙俗無知 shallow and ignorant;
[鄙笑] jeer; mock; ridicule; scoff at; taunt;
[鄙諺] common saying; proverb;
[鄙夷] contempt; despise; disdain; look down on sb;
[鄙意] I think; my humble opinion;
[鄙詐] deceitful; despicably untruthful;

卑鄙 (1) base; crooked; mean; (2) inferior; low;
邊鄙 border region; frontier region; frontiers;
粗鄙 coarse; vulgar;
可鄙 contemptible; despicable; mean;
猥鄙 base; despicable; mean;
蕪鄙 unsystematic and meagre;

bi⁴
bi

【必】 (1) certainly; most certainly; necessarily; surely; (2) have to; must;
[必敗] be bound to lose; be doomed to failure; will certainly be defeated; will certainly fail;
驕兵必敗 self-conceited troops are destined to fail;
驕則必敗 pride surely leads to ruin;
驕者必敗 a proud person often fails in his/her undertaking; pride goes before a fall; pride goes before destruction;
[必備] requisite;
必備條件 essential conditions; requisites;
必備資格 required qualifications;
[必不] must not;
必不得已 have no choice but to; under the necessity of;
必不可免 inevitable; no two ways about it; unavoidable;
必不可少 absolutely necessary; essential; indispensable; vital;
[必得] have to; must;
志在必得 aspire to gallop a thousand miles; cherish high aspirations;
~志在必得的人 go-getter;
[必定] bound to; sure to;
必定成功 sure of success;
必定失敗 be bound to fail; be destined to failure;
[必讀] must-read;
[必非] certainly not;
[必將] surely will; will certainly;
[必然] be bound to be; be doomed to; certain; certainly; have to be; inevitable; inevitably; necessarily; sure;
必然論 necessitarianism;
必然性 certainty; inevitability;
必然之事 a matter of necessity; what is bound to happen;

必然之勢 certainty; natural trend;
事有必然 necessary and inevitable; what is bound to happen;
勢所必然 as a matter of course; inevitable outcome; inevitably;

[必勝] cannot be defeated; cannot fail; will most certainly win;
哀兵必勝 an army burning with righteous indignation is bound to win; an army filled with righteous indignation is bound to win; an oppressed army fighting with desperate courage is sure to win; the oppressed will rise to win;
操必勝之券 certain of success; sure to win;

[必死] will certainly die; will certainly get killed;
必死之心 determination arising from a desperate situation; with one's back to the wall;

[必修課] compulsory course; obligatory course; required course;
修讀必修課 take required courses;

[必須] cannot do without; have to; it is imperative for; it is necessary that; must; ought to;

[必需] essential; indispensable;
必需品 consumer goods; daily necessities; necessaries; necessary wants; requisites;
~ 婦女必需品 feminine needs;
~ 基本必需品 bare necessities; basic necessities;
~ 家庭必需品 household necessities;
~ 簡單的必需品 simple essentials;
配置簡單的必需品 furnish with simple essentials;
~ 進口必需品 import essentials;
~ 旅行必需品 travel requirements;
~ 日常必需品 daily necessities;
~ 生活必需品 basic necessities of life;
得到生活必需品 obtain the necessities of life;
購買生活必需品 buy the necessities of life;
缺乏生活必需品 lack the necessities of life;
提供生活必需品 supply the necessities of life;
~ 應急必需品 emergency needs;

[必要] indispensable; necessary; need;
必要時 at a pinch;
必要條件 necessary condition;
不必要的 otiose; unnecessary;
有必要 necessary; there is a need for sth;
~ 沒有必要 there is no need for sth;
~ 如有必要 as the need arises; if necessary; if the need arises; if the occasion arises; when necessary; when the need arises; where necessary;

不必 need not;
何必 there is no need to; why;
諒必 most likely; probably;
是必 certainly; must be; surely;
勢必 be bound to; certainly will;
未必 may not; not always; not necessarily; not sure;
務必 must; sure to;
想必 presumably; probably;
自必 certainly; naturally; surely; unavoidably;

bi

【庇】 hide; conceal; harbour; protect; shelter; shield;

[庇短] conceal a defect; partial and willing to overlook shortcomings;

[庇護] protect; put under one's protection; shelter; shield; take under one's wing; under the aegis of;
庇護權 right of asylum;
庇護所 asylum; sanctuary;
百般庇護 shelter by all possible means;
尋求庇護 seek asylum;
政治庇護 political asylum;

[庇蔭] (1) give shade; (2) conceal; harbour; protect; shield;

[庇佑] bless; prosper; protect;
天庇神佑 be blessed by Heaven and God; be protected by Heaven and helped by God;

包庇 cover up; hide up; shield;
護庇 cover up; shelter;
曲庇 conceal by distorting facts;
袒庇 partial to; screen;
托庇 rely on one's leader for protection; seek the protection of;
翼庇 (1) patronize; (2) protect;
廕庇 harbour; protect; shelter;
蔭庇 (1) patronize; (2) protect; protect the younger generation or descendants;

B

bi

【拂】 (1) aid; assist; (2) make sth correct; make sth right;

［拂士］ straightforward adviser; wise counselor;

吹拂 stir; sway;
輕拂 flick;
拭拂 wipe, dust and clean;
照拂 attend to; care for; look after;

bi

【泌】 (1) swift and easy gushing of water; (2) a river in Henan Province;

［泌水］ the Bi River in Henan;

bi

【畀】 bestow; confer; give to;

bi

【邲】 (1) good-looking; (2) an ancient place in today's Shandong Province; (3) a surname;

bi

【毖】 (1) cautious; judicious; (2) flowing; gushing;

bi

【苾】 fragrant;

［苾苾］ aromatic; fragrant;
［苾勃］ fragrant;
［苾芬］ fragrant;

bi

【祕】 one pronunciation of 祕；

bi

【陛】 flight of steps leading to a palace hall;

［陛陛］ (1) numerous descendants; (2) everywhere;
［陛見］ have an audience with the emperor;
［陛衛］ imperial guard;
［陛下］ Her Majesty; His Majesty; Your Majesty;

bi

【狴】 (1) legendary wild dog; (2) prison;

［狴犴］ (1) legendary wild dog; (2) penitentiary; prison;
［狴牢］ jail; prison;

bi

【婢】 (1) female slave; maidservant; (2) humble term used by a girl in ancient China to refer to herself;

［婢女］ maidservant; servant-girl; slave girl;
［婢子］ maidservant;

奴婢 slaves and retainers;
侍婢 maidservant;

bi

【敝】 (1) broken; tattered; worn-out; (2) exhausted; tired; (3) my or our (self-depreciatory term);

［敝處］ my place;
［敝店］ my humble store;
［敝國］ our country;
［敝廬］ my humble house;
［敝舍］ my house;
［敝屣］ worn-out shoes; worthless thing;

敝屣虛榮 cast away vanity like a pair of worn-out shoes; despise vanity; turn one's back on worldly honours;

敝屣尊榮 turn one's back on worldly honours;

棄如敝屣 cast aside like an old shoe; cast aside sb as a pair of old shoes; cast away like a pair of worn-out shoes; discard as a squeezed lemon; give up as if it were an old sandal; reject sth as if it were worthless; throw sth on the scrapheap;

棄之如敝屣 cast aside like an old shoe; cast away as rubbish; discard sth as if it were a pair of old shoes; give sb the go-by; like throwing an old shoe; reject sth as if it were worthless;

如棄敝屣 as if casting away a pair of worn-out shoes; like throwing away an old sandal;

［敝鄉］ our village;
［敝校］ our school;
［敝姓］ my family name;
［敝友］ my friend;
［敝寓］ my residence;
［敝帚自珍］ everyone values his/her own things; my worn-out broom is a treasure to me;

凋敝 destitute;
疲敝 become inadequate; run low;

bi

【畢】 (1) accomplish; complete; end; finish; (2) all; all together; completely; entirely; fully; (3) a surname;

[畢集] assemble completely; gather completely;

[畢竟] after all; all in all; at last; in the final analysis; in the last analysis; in the long run; nevertheless; nonetheless; still; when all is said and done;

[畢露] be fully revealed;
醜態畢露 show the cloven hoof;
毒牙畢露 bare one's poison fangs;
鋒芒畢露 make a showy display of one's ability; show one's ability to the full extent;
奸心畢露 reveal one's entire scheme;
賤相畢露 one's bad countenance is flatly revealed;
馬腳畢露 show one's true colours;
窮相畢露 cut a poor figure; down-at-the-heels; out at the elbows;
兇相畢露 bare one's fangs; bear one's ferocious features; fully reveal one's atrocious features; look thoroughly ferocious; unleash all one's ferocity;
原形畢露 be revealed for what one is; be revealed in one's true colours; betray oneself; completely exposed; completely unmasked; present one's naked self; reveal one's real appearance; reveal the true nature completely; show one's true colours; show oneself in one's true colours; show the cloven hoof; show what one really is;
真情畢露 make no disguise of one's feelings; one's feelings are revealed;
真相畢露 have one's true face completely exposed; show the actual facts; show the real situation;

[畢命] die; end one's life;

[畢生] all one's life; in one's whole life; lifelong; lifetime; throughout one's lifetime;
畢生從事 be engaged in sth one's life;
畢生精力 energy throughout one's life; the energies of a lifetime;
畢生事業 an enterprise for life; lifework; the work of a lifetime;
畢生心血 the painstaking efforts of one's whole lifetime;
畢生研究 devote a lifetime to the study of sth;

[畢肖] completely alike; resemble closely; the very image of;

[畢業] be graduated; finish school; graduate;
畢業班 graduating class;
畢業答辯會 graduation oral examination;
畢業典禮 convocation; graduation ceremony;
~參加畢業典禮 attend the graduation ceremony;
~舉行畢業典禮 hold the graduation ceremony;
畢業分配 job assignment on graduation;
畢業鑒定 graduation appraisal;
畢業考試 graduation examination;
畢業論文 graduation thesis;
~寫畢業論文 write a graduation thesis;
畢業設計 graduation project;
畢業生 alum; alumnus; graduate;
~高中畢業生 high school graduate;
~女畢業生 alumna;
~校外畢業生 external graduate;
~一屆畢業生 a class of graduates;
畢業實習 graduation field work;
畢業條件 graduation requirements;
~符合畢業條件 satisfy the requirements for graduation;
畢業證書 diploma; graduation certificate;
~頒發畢業證書 issue a graduation certificate;
~獲得畢業證書 receive a diploma;
大學畢業 graduate from university;

完畢 be done; complete; end; finish;
閱畢 after reading;

bi

【閉】 (1) close; shut; (2) block up; obstruct; stop up; (3) restrain;

[閉包] closure;
背向閉包 dorsal closure;
軌道閉包 orbit closure;
緊閉包 compact closure;
耦合閉包 catenation closure;
凸閉包 convex closure;
下閉包 lower closure;
線性閉包 linear closure;
有界閉包 bounded closure;
正規閉包 normal closure;

B

自然閉包 natural closure;

[閉店] close up a shop and stop business;

[閉關] close the border;

閉關時代 period of isolationism;

閉關鎖國 avoid having contacts with other countries; close the border; cut off one's country from the outside world; lock one's doors against the world;

閉關政策 closed-door policy;

~制定閉關政策 frame a policy of seclusion; make a closed-door policy;

閉關自守 adopt a policy of isolation; close one's country to external contact; close one's doors to the rest of the world; close the border for self-sufficiency; close the country to international intercourse; shut oneself in; shut the door on the world; turn in on oneself; wall the country off from international exchanges;

[閉果] indehiscent fruit;

[閉合] close; closing; closure;

閉合線 closing line;

觸點閉合 closing of contact;

導線閉合 closing of polygon;

電路閉合 circuit closing;

接點閉合 contact closure; junction closure;

孔隙閉合 closing of pores;

仰拱閉合 invert closure;

自重閉合 gravity closing;

[閉戶] close the door;

蠡蚌閉戶 the mussel and the oyster close their shells − the wise man retires to himself;

夜不閉戶 doors are unbolted at night − law and order prevail;

[閉會] close a meeting; end a meeting; adjourn a meeting;

[閉結] constipation;

[閉經] amenorrhoea;

創傷性閉經 traumatic amenorrhoea;

垂體性閉經 pituitary amenorrhoea;

卵巢性閉經 ovarian amenorrhoea;

生理性閉經 physiologic amenorrhoea;

相對性閉經 relative amenorrhoea;

營養性閉經 dietary amenorrhoea;

原發閉經 primary amenorrhoea;

[閉口] button one's lip; shut up;

閉口不談 avoid mentioning; keep one's mouth shut; keep silent; make no mention of; keep one's tongue between one's teeth; not say a way about; never talk about; refuse to say anything about; zip your lips;

閉口不言 button one's lip; keep one's tongue between one's teeth; shut one's mouth, saying nothing;

閉口無言 be left speechless; be tongue-tied; button one's lip; keep one's mouth shut; not utter a single word; refrain from speaking; remain silent; shut one's mouth and say nothing; zip one's lip;

突然閉口 clam up;

[閉路] closed circuit;

閉路報警系統 closed alarm system;

閉路電視 closed circuit TV;

~播放閉路電視 broadcast closedcircuit television programmes;

~收費閉路電視 pay cable television;

閉路電壓 closed circuit voltage;

閉路試驗 closed-circuit test;

閉路天線 closed aerial;

閉路通訊系統 closedcircuit communication system;

[閉門] close one's door;

閉門不出 be confined in one's house; keep close at home; keep in; keep to the house; remain at home behind closed doors;

閉門不納 close the door of one's house to sb; close the door upon sb; decline to see a visitor; refuse to admit a caller; shut sb out; shut the door in sb's face;

閉門獨處 keep oneself to oneself; live in complete seclusion;

閉門讀書 study behind closed doors;

閉門羹 be denied entrance; rebuff; shut the door in sb's face;

~吃閉門羹 be denied entrance; be left out in the cold; on the wrong side of the door; slam the door in sb's face;

~饗以閉門羹 hem the door in one's face; refuse one's entrance into;

閉門思過 meditate on one's own faults behind closed doors; ponder over one's mistakes behind closed doors; reflect on one's faults or misdeeds in private; shut oneself up and ponder over one's mistakes;

閉門謝客 shut oneself up and decline

seeing visitors; sport one's oak;
閉門修養 under self-cultivation behind closed doors;
閉門造車 be isolated from reality; carry out one's idea irrespective of external circumstances; make a cart behind closed doors; work uneffectively behind closed doors;
閉門自守 isolate oneself behind closed doors;

[閉幕] (1) lower the curtain; the curtain falls; the curtain comes down; (2) close; conclude;
閉幕詞 closing address; closing speech;
~ 致閉幕詞 make a closing speech;
閉幕式 closing ceremony;
閉幕儀式 closing ceremony;
勝利閉幕 close victoriously;

[閉目] close one's eyes;
閉目沉思 shut one's eyes and meditate;
閉目合睛 shut one's eyes;
閉目枯坐 block one's ears and shut one's eyes to sth; close one's eyes and sit doing nothing;
閉目聆聽 shut one's eyes to listen;
閉目塞聽 out of touch with reality; turn a blind eye and a deaf ear to sth;
閉目閒坐 close one's eyes and sit doing nothing;
閉目養神 close one's eyes and give the mind a brief rest; close one's eyes for a rest;

[閉氣] (1) be unable to breathe; feel suffocated; (2) stop breathing;

[閉塞] (1) close up; stop up; (2) hard to get to; out-of-the-way;
自動閉塞 automatic blocking;

[閉上] close; shut;
閉上眼 close one's eyes;
閉上嘴 shut one's mouth;

[閉眼] close one's eyes;
閉眼不看事實 close one's eyes to the facts; shut one's eyes to the facts;

[閉業] wind up one's business;

[閉嘴] button one's lip; close one's mouth; hold your tongue; keep one's peace; keep one's mouth shut; shut shop; shut up; shut your mouth; shut your shop; zip one's lips;
該做就做，不然就閉嘴 put up or shut up;

倒閉 close down; go bankrupt;
封閉 (1) seal; (2) close; seal off;
關閉 (1) close; closedown; closing; closure; cut off; deactivate; gag; paralyse; shut; shut off; (2) lock up; shut in;
禁閉 confine; detain; jail;
經閉 amenorrhoea;
開閉 open and close;
密閉 airtight; hermetic;
尿閉 anuria;
啟閉 on and off; open and close; start and stop;
圈閉 shut up;
腎關閉 renal shutdown;
鎖閉 locking;
停閉 close down;
幽閉 (1) put under house arrest; (2) confine oneself indoors;
鬱閉 close;

bi

【弼】 (1) bow regulator; device for regulating bows; (2) correct; (3) aid; assist;

[弼教] assist in education;

輔弼 assist a monarch in governing a country;

bi

【愎】 obstinate; perverse; self-willed; stubborn;

[愎諫] deaf to remonstrances; reject advice;

剛愎 headstrong; self-willed;

bi

【愊】 (1) honest; sincere; (2) depressed; melancholy;

悃愊 utterly sincere;

bi

【湢】 (1) bathroom; (2) neat; orderly;

bi

【皕】 two hundred;

bi

【萆】 herb with long hard root;

bi

【詖】 (1) erroneous; unfair; wrong; (2) argue; debate;

[詖辭] biased remarks; partial statements;

[詖論] erroneous statements in which the speaker is unable to see the error;

B

［詖行］ evil behaviour; evil conduct;

bi

【賁】 (1) adorn; ornamental; (2) bright; luminous;
［賁臨］ your illustrious presence;
［賁然］ bright and brilliant;
［賁如］ brightly ornamental; richly adorned;
虎賁 brave and strong man; brave warrior;

bi

【跛】 lean; partial;
［跛依］ slanting; unbalanced;
［跛倚］ biased; partial; prejudiced;

bi

【痹】 paralysis;

bi

【辟】 (1) monarch; (2) call; summon; (3) govern; (4) avoid; escape; get rid of;
［辟世］ live in seclusion; withdraw from the world;
［辟邪］ (1) exorcise evil spirits; ward off evils; (2) a fabulous animal with two horns;
［辟言］ go away because of an offensive statement;
［辟易］ recoil; retreat;
［辟引］ appoint to office; summon to court;
復辟 restore monarchy;

bi

【逼】 a pronunciation of 逼；

bi

【鉍】 bismuth;

bi

【閟】 (1) close the door; (2) removed; secluded; secret; (3) deep; obscure;

bi

【嗶】 a character used in transliterating;
［嗶嘰］ serge;

bi

【幣】 (1) currency; legal tender; money; (2) offering; present;
［幣值］ currency value;
幣值波動 currency fluctuation;
［幣制］ currency system;
幣制改革 currency reform;
［幣重言甘］ heavy coins and sweet words;
貝幣 shells used as money in ancient times;
輔幣 fractional currency;
港幣 Hong Kong dollar;
貨幣 currency; money;
假幣 counterfeit money;
金幣 gold coin;
鎳幣 nickel; nickel coin;
錢幣 (1) coins; (2) currency; money;
人民幣 renminbi
銅幣 copper coin;
外幣 foreign currency;
偽幣 (1) counterfeit money; forged banknotes; (2) money issued by a puppet government;
贋幣 counterfeit coin;
銀幣 silver coin;
硬幣 coin;
紙幣 banknote; paper currency; paper money;
制幣 standard currency;
製幣 coin;
鑄幣 coin; specie;

bi

【弊】 (1) abuse; fraud; malpractice; (2) disadvantages; harm;
［弊病］ (1) evil; fraud; malpractice; (2) disadvantages; drawbacks;
消除弊病 remedy a drawback;
［弊端］ abuse; corrupt practice; malpractice;
弊端百出 trouble after trouble comes up;
弊端叢生 all kinds of corrupt practices prevailing; all kinds of corruptions creep in;
杜絕弊端 cut off all corruption; stop all corrupt practices;
現存的弊端 existing abuses;
嚴重弊端 gross abuses;
~根除嚴重弊端 root up gross abuses;
政治弊端 political abuses;
~根除政治弊端 wipe out political abuses;
制止弊端 check abuses;
諸多弊端 all kinds of corrupt practices;
［弊害］ harm; undesirable points;
［弊壞］ worn and damaged;
［弊絕］ free from corruption;
弊絕風清 absolutely free from corruption;
風清弊絕 absolutely free from corruption; all the malpractices have been abolished;
［弊政］ maladministration; misrule;
百弊 (1) all kinds of maladies; all the ill effects;

(2) many disadvantages; many drawbacks;
凋弊 (1) destitute; hard; (2) depressed;
積弊 age-old malpractice; long-standing abuse;
利弊 advantages and disadvantages;
流弊 corrupt practices;
情弊 dishonest practices; irregularities;
時弊 current failings; current malpractice; ills of the time;
衰弊 decadent and corrupt;
私弊 corrupt practice;
宿弊 long-standing malpractice;
舞弊 embezzlement; engage in embezzlement; fraudulent practices; malpractice; misconduct;
作弊 cheat; indulge in corrupt practices; practise fraud;

bi

【裨】 (1) aid; supplement; (2) benefit; help;
［裨補］ aid; supplement; support;
［裨益］ advantage; benefit; profit;

無裨 of no avail; of no help; useless;

bi

【碧】 (1) green jade; (2) blue; (3) bluish green; greenish blue; (4) emerald; jasper;
［碧波］ bluish waves;
碧波蕩漾 the surface of the lake ripples;
碧波粼粼 a breeze ruffles the green water; clear, blue ripples;
碧波萬頃 a boundless expanse of blue water; a boundless stretch of clear water;
［碧草］ green grass; verdant grass;
碧草如茵 a carpet of green grass;
［碧鳳］ (1) green phoenix－bamboo; (2) black hair;
［碧漢］ azure sky; blue sky;
［碧空］ azure sky; clear blue sky;
碧空如洗 cloudless blue sky;
碧空無雲 not a speck of cloud remains in the clear blue sky; the blue sky is cloudless;
［碧藍］ dark blue;
碧藍的天空 azure sky;
［碧蘭］ greenish orchid;
［碧綠］ dark green; emerald green; verdant;
［碧落］ blue realm; sky;
［碧水］ (1) blue waters; (2) green waters;
碧水蒼天 above are the blue heavens, below the green waters;
［碧桃］ flowering peach;
［碧瓦］ emerald green glazed tiles;
［碧血］ blood shed in a just cause;
碧血丹心 deep patriotism; loyal-hearted;
碧血黃沙 dark blood covered the ground;
［碧眼］ blue-eyed;
碧眼兒 person with blue eyes;
［碧玉］ jasper;
碧玉婚 jade wedding anniversary;
小家碧玉 beautiful girl from a lower family; daughter of a humble family; daughter of a middleclass family; girl out of the gutter; pretty girl of humble birth;

澄碧 clear and blue;
金碧 gold and green;
瑤碧 agate with a greenish lustre;
湛碧 jade-like colour;

bi

【箅】 bamboo frame for steaming food;
［箅子］ grate; grid;

爐箅 fire grate;
竹箅 bamboo grid;

bi

【鄙】 a pronunciation of 鄙；

bi

【蓖】 castor oil plant;
［蓖麻］ castor oil plant;
蓖麻油 castor oil;

bi

【蔽】 (1) conceal; cover; cover up; hide; shelter; (2) be hoodwinked by; (3) screen; separate;
［蔽護］ protect; shelter; take cover;
［蔽目］ blindfold; cover the eyes;
［蔽匿］ conceal; hide; lie low;
［蔽日］ cover the sun from view; dull the sunlight;
片雲足以蔽日 one cloud is enough to eclipse the sun;
［蔽體］ cover the body;
［蔽野］ cover the whole field;
［蔽障］ (1) obstacle in one's mind for understanding; (2) keep in obscurity;

B

藩蔽 barrier;
蒙蔽 cast a mist before sb's eyes; deceive; hide the truth from; hoodwink; pull the wool over sb's eyes;
屏蔽 screen; shield; shielding;
掩蔽 conceal; cover; hide; mask; screen; shelter; take cover;
蔭蔽 (1) be shaded by foliage; (2) conceal; cover;
隱蔽 conceal oneself; take cover; take shelter;
壅蔽 block up; conceal; cover;
障蔽 block; obstruct; shut out;
遮蔽 (1) hide from view; screen; (2) block; obstruct;

bi
【蓽】 (1) bamboo or wicker for making baskets; (2) Piper longum, a kind of herb growing among bamboos, used in Chinese medicine;
[蓽茇] Piper longum; long pepper;
[蓽路藍縷] firewood carts and rags—the hard life of pioneers;
[蓽門圭竇] small door of bamboo—house of a poor man;

蓬蓽 one's humble house;

bi
【篳】 bamboo or wicker that can be used to make baskets, bags, etc.;
[篳路藍縷] endure great hardships in pioneer work;
[篳門圭竇] humble dwelling;

bi
【壁】 (1) partition wall; wall; (2) sth resembling a wall; (3) cliff;
[壁板] wallboard;
[壁報] bulletin; wall newspaper; wall paper; wall poster;
壁報板 poster board; poster stand;
[壁櫥] built-in cupboard; built-in wardrobe; closet;
固定壁櫥 built-in cabinet;
[壁燈] bracket light; wall lamp;
裝壁燈 fix a wall lamp;
[壁掛] wall hanging;
[壁虎] gecko; house lizard;
[壁畫] fresco; mural; mural painting;
漢唐壁畫 murals from the Han to the Tang Dynasty;
[壁壘] barrier; breastwork; rampart;
壁壘分明 diametrically opposed; with clearly defined lines;
壁壘森嚴 (1) wall of indifference; (2) impassable barrier; closely guarded; defense is ironclad; ironclad defence; strongly fortified;
衝破壁壘 break down the barrier;
階級壁壘 barrier between classes;
~ 消除階級壁壘 abolish the barrier between classes;
貿易壁壘 trade barrier;
~ 排除貿易壁壘 remove trade barriers;
森嚴壁壘 one's defense is ironclad;
[壁立] (1) stand bolt upright; (2) poverty-stricken;
[壁爐] fireplace;
壁爐架 chimney piece;
壁爐腔 chimney breast;
壁爐枱 chimney piece;
[壁上觀] detached view; uninvolved; watch a fight without helping either party;
[壁毯] tapestry;
[壁紙] wallpaper;
吸聲壁紙 acoustic wallpaper;
[壁鐘] wall cloth;

板壁 wooden partition;
半壁 half; slice of territory;
殘壁 rubble;
艙壁 bulkhead;
陡壁 steep bank;
腹壁 abdominal wall;
戈壁 Gobi Desert;
隔壁 next door;
護壁 dado;
間壁 next door; next-door neighbour;
礁壁 reef wall;
井壁 wall of a well;
絕壁 beetling wall; bold cliff; crag; hanger; precipice;
犁壁 mouldboard;
碰壁 be obstructed; be rebuffed; run one's head against a stone wall;
墻壁 wall;
峭壁 cliff; crag; sheer cliff; steep precipice;
石壁 cliff; precipice;
四壁 the four walls of a room;
題壁 write on the wall;
體壁 body wall;

胸壁 walls of the chest;
削壁 cliff; precipice;
崖壁 precipice;
岩壁 (1) dyke; (2) cliff;
一壁 at the same time;
齦壁 gingival wall;

bi

【篦】 comb;
[篦齒兒] teeth of a comb;
[篦鷺] spoonbill;
[篦頭] comb one's hair with a fine-toothed comb;
[篦櫛] fine-toothed comb, usually made of bamboo;
[篦子] double-edged, fine-toothed comb;

梳篦 dress up one's hair;

bi

【嬖】 (1) enjoy the favour of a powerful person; (2) minion;
[嬖妾] favourite concubine;
[嬖人] favourite of the ruler;
[嬖幸] be favoured by the ruler;

bi

【觱】 (1) chilly wind; (2) leaping water;
[觱發] chilly winds;
[觱沸] spring water bubbling;

bi

【斃】 (1) die; get killed; (2) execute by shooting; shoot to death; (3) reject; veto; vote down;
[斃敵] kill enemy troops;
[斃命] get killed; meet a violent death;

暴斃 meet a sudden death;
待斃 await death;
倒斃 fall dead;
擊斃 shoot dead;
僵斃 dead and stiff;
槍斃 execute by shooting; shoot dead;
自斃 destroy oneself; self-destruction;

bi

【臂】 (1) arms; (2) upper arm;
[臂板] arm;
臂板信號機 semaphore;
~電空臂板信號機 electropneumatic semaphore;
~多臂板信號機 multiblade semaphore;
~雙臂板信號機 double-arm semaphore;
引導臂板 calling-on arm;
[臂膀] arm;
[臂部] arm;
[臂環] bracelet;
[臂節] elbow;
[臂力] strength of the arm;
一臂之力 a hand's turn; a helping hand; a lift in life; assistance; help; offer a knee to sb;
[臂章] (1) arm badge; armband; armlet; (2) shoulder emblem;
[臂助] assist; give a helping hand; help;
一臂之助 give sb a leg up; give sb a lift; lend a hand;

把臂 arm in arm; holding arms;
擺輪臂 balance arm;
膀臂 (1) arms; (2) reliable helper; right-hand person;
臂挽着臂 lock arms;
撐臂 brace;
地輪臂 bogie arm;
電橋臂 bridge arm;
斷電臂 breaker arm;
奮臂 lift one's arms; raise one's arms;
肐臂 arm;
胳臂 arm;
杠杆臂 lever arm;
工作臂 actuating arm;
關節臂 articulated arm;
橫臂 cross-beam;
護臂 armguard;
假臂 artificial arm;
交替臂 alternate arm;
校對臂 checking arm;
校準臂 calibrating arm;
巨臂 macrobrachia;
矩臂 moment arm;
力臂 arm of force;
兩臂 arms;
錨臂 anchor arm;
齧臂 bite one's arm; gnaw one's arm;
怒臂 raise one's arms in anger;
前臂 antebrachium; forearm;
屈臂 curl;
全帶臂 all-cord arm;
攘臂 push up one's sleeves and bare one's arms; roll up one's sleeves and reveal one's arms;
人造臂 artificial arm;
上臂 upper arm;

B

手臂 arm;
雙臂 one's arms;
托臂 cantilever;
握臂 grasp sb's arm;
相鄰臂 adjacent arm;
懸臂 cantilever;
搖臂 rocker arm;
右臂 (1) right arm; (2) important helper; right-hand man;
玉臂 girl's arms; pretty woman's arms;
猿臂 (1) ape's arms; (2) long arms;
紾臂 twist the arm;
振臂 raise one's arm;
重臂 short arm;
左臂 left arm;

bi

【薜】 (1) ligusticum; (2) evergreen shrub;
[薜蘿] clothing of a hermit;

bi

【避】 (1) avoid; escape; evade; shun; (2) keep away; prevent; repel;
[避彈衣] bulletproof garment; flak jacket;
[避風] (1) hide from trouble; lie low; (2) seek shelter against a strong wind;
避風港 harbour; haven;
避風頭 dodge the brunt; lie low until the critical time is over;
[避害] escape disaster; run away from a calamity;
[避寒] escape the cold; go to a winter resort;
[避諱] (1) word or phrase to be avoided as taboo; taboo; (2) dodge; evade; (3) taboo on using the personal names of emperors, one's elders, etc.;
[避火梯] fire escape;
[避靜] retreat;
[避開] avoid; bypass; evade; get away from; get out of the way; give sth a miss; keep away from; keep clear of; keep off sth; shun; stay away from; stay clear; steer clear of;
機警地避開 dodge cleverly;
謹慎地避開 abstain prudently;
靈活地避開 elude nimbly;
施計避開 elude sth by means of a trick;
小心地避開 abstain cautiously;
[避雷] lightning protection;
避雷器 lightning arrester; lightning conductor; lightning rod;
~ 電解避雷器 electrolytic arrester;
~ 多火花避雷器 multi-path arrester;
~ 多火花隙避雷器 multi-gap arrester;
~ 多級分路避雷器 graded shunt arrester;
~ 放電避雷器 discharge arrester;
~ 弧形避雷器 arc arrester;
~ 角隙避雷器 horn gap lightning arrester;
~ 鋁管避雷器 aluminium cell lightning arrester;
~ 盤形避雷器 disc type lightning arrester;
~ 旁路避雷器 by-pass arrester;
~ 氣隙避雷器 air gap lightning arrester;
~ 梳形避雷器 comb lightning arrester;
~ 水銀避雷器 mercury arrester;
~ 炭精避雷器 carbon arrester;
~ 陶瓷避雷器 ceramic arrester;
~ 丸形避雷器 pellet arreter;
~ 隙阻式避雷器 gap resistance type arrester;
~ 自動閥型避雷器 auto valve lightning arrester;
避雷針 lightning arrester; lightning conductor; lightning rod;
[避亂] run away from social upheaval;
[避免] avert; avoid; forestall; prevent sth from happening; refrain from; stave off;
可以避免 [的] avoidable;
[避面] avoid meeting a person;
[避難] evade sth difficult;
避難就易 evade the difficult and take the easy; follow the line of least resistance; shirk the hard matter and take up the easy ones;
[避難] avoid disaster; escape calamity; find refuge; seek asylum; take refuge;
避難港 harbour of refuge; haven;
避難所 bolthole; haven; refuge; sanctuary;
~ 找到避難所 find a refuge;
躲災避難 avoid the coming trouble; escape with one's life and hide from danger; hide somewhere until the evil is past;
逃災避難 seek refuge from calamities;
政治避難 political asylum;
~ 請求政治避難 ask for political asylum;
~ 尋求政治避難 seek political asylum;
[避匿] hide away; lie in hiding;
[避實] avert disasters;
避實就虛 avoid the enemy's main force and strike at its weaknesses; avoid the enemy's strongholds and strike at their

weak points;

[避世] lead a hermit's life; live as a recluse; retire from the world; retire from worldly affairs;
避世絕俗 withdraw from the society and live in solitude;
避世離俗 try to escape reality; try to keep away from this world;

[避暑] avoid the summer heat; escape the summer heat; go away for summer holidays; go to a summer resort; run away from summer heat; take a summer vacation;
避暑勝地 summer resort;

[避稅] evade duty; evade taxes; tax avoidance; tax dodge; tax evasion;
避稅天堂 tax haven;

[避蚊劑] mosquito repellent;

[避席] leave one's seat;

[避嫌] avoid arousing suspicion; avoid being suspected; avoid doing anything that may arouse suspicion; avoid suspicion;
避嫌引退 withdraw from a post to avoid suspicion;

[避凶] avoid impending disaster; flee from evil;
避凶趨吉 conduct oneself so as to avoid impending trouble and seek good luck; flee evil and strive to walk in fair fortune's way;

[避疫] escape from epidemics;

[避雨] find shelter for the rain; take shelter from rain;

[避孕] avoid pregnancy; birth control; contraception;
避孕措施 contraceptive devices;
避孕環 intrauterine contraceptive ring;
避孕栓 contraceptive pessary;
避孕套 condom;
~女用避孕套 female condom;
避孕丸 contraceptive pill;
~翌晨避孕丸 morning-after pill;
避孕藥 contraceptive; contraceptive pill;
~避孕藥具 contraceptive devices;
~避孕藥丸 birth-control pill;
~口服避孕藥 oral contraceptive;
避孕用品 contraceptives;
器具避孕 instrumental contraception;
藥物避孕 medical contraception;

[避債] avoid creditors;

[避震] shock absorption;
避震器 shock absorber;
~氣墊型避震器 air type shock absorber;

躲避 (1) avoid; evade; (2) go into hiding; hide;
規避 avoid; dodge; escapism; evade; set around;
迴避 (1) avoid meeting another person; avoidance; (2) withdraw; (3) decline an offer; (4) evade; evasion; evasive;
力避 try one's best to avoid or evade;
繞避 pass round;
閃避 dodge; sidestep;
逃避 evade, shirk, or escape from sth one is unwilling to come into contact with;
退避 keep out of the way; withdraw and keep off;
畏避 avoid sth because of fear; keep away from sth out of dread;
引避 (1) yield one's place; (2) avoid;
遠避 keep at a distance; keep far away from;
走避 evade; run away from; shun;

bi

【璧】 round piece of jade;

[璧合] perfect match;

[璧還] return with thanks;

[璧人] fine-looking person;
一對璧人 an ideal couple;

[璧謝] decline a gift with thanks;

[璧玉] round piece of jade;

[璧月] full moon;

白璧 white jade;
拱璧 large piece of jade;
合璧 (1) combine harmoniously; match well; (2) compare or refer to;

bi

【蹕】 (1) clear of traffic; (2) imperial carriage;

[蹕臨] arrive; visit;

[蹕路] clear the emperor's route of traffic;

駐蹕 (of a monarch on a tour) stay temporarily or stop over on the way;

bi

【髀】 (1) buttocks; (2) hipbone; innominate bone;

[髀骨] hip bone; innominate bone;

bi

【襞】 fold clothes;

［襞積］ lines or pleats on clothes as a result of folding;

皺襞 lines; wrinkles;

bi

【躄】 be crippled in both legs; have both legs disabled;

［躄踊］ stamp with grief;

bi

【鷩】 a kind of pheasant;

［鷩雉］ a kind of pheasant;

bian1

bian

【砭】 (1) stone probe; (2) admonish; advise; exhort; (3) pierce;

［砭骨］ pierce the bone—extremely cold or painful;

砭人肌骨 bone-piercing cold;

［砭灸］ acupuncture and cauterize;

［砭石］ stone needle;

針砭 find out and point out sb's errors in order to have them corrected;

bian

【萹】 a variety of weed or grass with narrow thick blades;

bian

【編】 (1) knit; plait; weave; (2) arrange; form; group; organize; put together; (3) compile; edit; (4) compose; write; (5) cook up; fabricate; invent; make up; (6) part of a book; part of a volume;

［編班］ assign students to various classes; form classes; group into classes;

編班考試 placement test;

［編插語］ agglomerating language;

［編程］ programme;

編程員 coder;

［編次］ order of arrangement;

［編導］ (1) write and direct; (2) playwright director;

電影編導 scenarist director;

舞劇編導 choreographer director;

戲劇編導 playwright director;

［編訂］ compile and revise;

［編隊］ organized group;

編隊特技 formation acrobatics;

［編髮］ braid hair;

［編號］ (1) arrange under numbers; number; (2) number; serial number;

按順序編號 number in order;

標有編號 bear serial numbers;

給文件編號 number the documents;

［編輯］ (1) compile; edit; editing; (2) compiler; editor;

編輯部 editorial office;

編輯程序 editorial process;

編輯工作 editing;

編輯機 editor;

～聲音編輯機 sound editor;

編輯者 editor;

編輯主任 managing editor;

編輯助理 editorial assistant;

版面編輯 make-up editor;

電訊編輯 cable editor; telegraph;

電子編輯 electronic editing;

翻譯編輯 translation editor;

高級編輯 senior editor;

稿件編輯 script editor;

故事編輯 story editor;

顧問編輯 advisory editor; consultant editor;

畫面編輯 picture editing;

技術編輯 technical editor;

～助理技術編輯 assistant technical editor;

經濟編輯 economics editor;

精心編輯 carefully edit;

連接編輯 linkage edit;

女編輯 editress;

上下文編輯 context editing;

特約編輯 contributing editor;

體育編輯 sports editor;

圖片編輯 picture editor;

文件編輯 file edit;

文字編輯 copy-editor;

新聞編輯 news editor;

譯稿編輯 translation editor;

譯文編輯 translation editor;

責任編輯 responsible editor;

政治編輯 political editor;

主任編輯 associate senior editor;

助理編輯 assistant editor; subeditor;

組合編輯 assemble editing;

自動編輯 auto edit;

總編輯 chief editor; editor-in-chief; general editor;

［編校］ edit;

[編結] knit; weave;
[編劇] (1) write a play; (2) playwright;
編劇本 write a play;
[編籃] make a basket;
編籃工 basket maker;
[編類] arrange into categories;
按科目編類 be grouped according to the subject;
[編列] arrange systematically; list;
[編碼] code; coding; encode;
編碼程序 code programme;
編碼地址 coded address; encode address;
編碼法 coding;
編碼機 code machine;
編碼寄存器 code register;
編碼器 coder; encoder;
~ 電刷編碼器 brush encoder;
~ 二進制編碼器 binary coder;
~ 高度計編碼器 altimeter coder;
~ 記時編碼器 chronometric encoder;
~ 脈衝編碼器 pulse encoder;
~ 聲頻編碼器 audio-frequency coder;
~ 聲信號編碼器 audio coder;
~ 信道編碼器 channel encoder;
編碼圖形 coded graphics;
代數編碼 algebraic coding;
二進制編碼 binary coding;
分組編碼 block encoding;
固定式編碼 fixed coding;
合成編碼 composite coding;
絕對編碼 absolute coding;
輪廓編碼 contour encoding;
數字彩色編碼 digital colour coding;
雙模式編碼 dual-mode coding;
顏色編碼 colour coding;
音頻編碼 audio encoding;
自動編碼 automatic coding;
[編目] compile a catalogue; make a catalogue;
[編內人員] in-staff;
[編年] compile annals; prepare a chronological record;
編年史 annal; chronicle;
~ 編年史作者 annalist;
編年體 annalistic style;
[編排] arrange; lay out; make up sth;
[編派] libel; vilify;
[編審] (1) read and edit; (2) copy-editor;
副編審 associate editor;
[編書] compile books; edit books;
[編述] arrange and narrate;
[編條] plait;
[編外人員] extra-organizational personnel;
[編舞] (1) choreographer; (2) choreography;
[編寫] (1) compile; (2) compose; write;
編寫歌詞 write a song;
編寫歌曲 compose a song;
編寫教科書 compile a textbook;
編寫劇本 write a play;
[編修] compile; edit;
[編選] compile; select and edit;
[編演] write and stage a play;
[編譯] (1) translate and edit; (2) compiler;
編譯程序 compiler; compiler programme;
~ 對話式編譯程序 conversational compiler;
~ 後台編譯程序 background compiler;
~ 可擴充編譯程序 extensible compiler;
~ 自動化編譯程序 automatic compiler;
編譯者 compiler;
編譯自動化 compiling automation;
[編印] compile and print; publish;
[編造] (1) compile; draw up; work out; (2) concoct; cook up; fabricate; invent; make up;
編造故事 invent a story;
編造謊言 fabricate lies;
編造假賬 falsification of an account;
編造講稿 write a lecture;
編造情節 falsify the details of an event; invent a story; make up a story;
編造預算 draw up a budget;
胡編亂造 baseless and irrational concoctions;
[編者] editor;
編者按 editor's note; editorial note;
編者的話 editor's note;
[編織] (1) knit; knitting; weaving and braiding; (2) fabricate;
編織機 knitting machine;
編織毛衣 knit a sweater;
編織品 knitting;
編織物 knitting;
編織針 knitting needle;
開始編織 take up one's knitting;
[編制] establish; establishment;
編制委員會 organization committee;
平時編制 peace establishment;
~ 減少平時編制 reduce the peace establishment;
人手編制 staffing;

縮小編制 cut down the staff; reduce the staff;
戰時編制 war establishment;
~增加戰時編制 increase the war establishment;
增加編制 augment the staff;

[編製] compile; draw up;
編製財務報告 draw up a financial report;
編製生產計劃 work out a production plan;
編製預算 draw up a budget; fix a budget; prepare a budget;

[編著] compile and write;
編著作 compiler;

[編撰] compile, write;

[編組] be grouped; group; organize into groups;
編組運輸 groupage traffic;
按能力編組 be grouped according to ability; group according to ability;
按年齡編組 be grouped according to age; group according to age;
按性別編組 be grouped according to sex; group according to sex;

[編纂] compile;
編纂者 compiler;

貝編 Buddhist sutras;
補編 supplement;
定編 establish a table of organization;
改編 (1) adapt; rearrange; revise; (2) redesignate; reorganize;
匯編 assembly; collect; collection; compilation; compile; corpus;
簡編 (1) concise edition; (2) short course;
經編 warp knitting;
擴編 enlarge the establishment;
缺編 below strength; understaffed;
收編 take in and reorganize other troops;
縮編 cut down on staff number;
緯編 weft knitting;
瞎編 pure invention; sheer concoction;
現編 extemporize;
新編 (1) newly compiled; (2) newly organized;
續編 continuation of a book; sequel;
芸編 books;
整編 reorganize;
主編 editor-in-chief;
棕編 coir-woven articles;
總編 chief editor;

bian

【蝙】 bat;

[蝙蝠] bat;
蝙蝠 bats screech;
蝙蝠類 Chiroptera;
蝙蝠衫 bat sleeved jacket;
吸血蝙蝠 vampire bat;
燕蝙蝠 bat;

bian

【箯】 bamboo sedan chair;

bian

【鞭】 (1) lash; whip; (2) pointer; (3) string of small firecrackers; (4) flog; lash; whip;

[鞭策] encourage; goad on; spur on; urge on;
鞭策落後 spur those who are backward;
加以鞭策 need the spur;

[鞭笞] flog; flogging; lashing;
鞭笞天下 flog the world;
受到鞭笞 be scourged;

[鞭蟲] whipworm;

[鞭楚] flagellate; flog; whip;

[鞭打] flagellate; flog; lash; thrash; whip;
鞭打快牛 over-demanding with those who are doing a good job;
鞭打馬 whip a horse;
用藤條鞭打 cane;
左鞭右打 pretend to strike in one direction but actually deliver the blow in another;

[鞭炮] (1) firecracker; (2) string of small firecrackers;
鞭砲齊鳴，鑼鼓喧天 the air is filled with the sound of bursting firecrackers and the din of clashing gongs and cymbals;
鞭砲聲 cracker;
~一陣鞭砲聲 a burst of crackers;
一掛鞭砲 a string of firecrackers;

[鞭辟] urge and encourage;
鞭辟入里 cut to the quick; deep-cutting; incisive; penetrating; trenchant;

[鞭撻] castigate; lash;
鞭撻社會罪惡 lash the vice of the society;

[鞭刑] flogging;

[鞭子] lash; whip;
揮動鞭子 wield a whip;

霸王鞭 (1) rattle stick used in folk dancing; (2) rattle stick dance;
教鞭 teacher's pointer;

馬鞭 horsewhip;
茸鞭 flimmer;
藤鞭 rattan whip;
仙人鞭 a kind of cactus;
執鞭 act as a coach driver for sb;
祖鞭 strive for achievements;

bian

【邊】 (1) side; (2) edge; (3) border; margin; (4) aspect; (5) as; while; (6) in; on;

[邊白] margin;

[邊…邊…] do two things at the same time;
邊吃邊談 talk while eating;
邊讀邊議 read and discuss sth the same time;
邊幹邊學 learn by doing; learn in the course of doing; learn on the job;
邊教邊學 learn while teaching;
邊哭邊說 cry between the words;
邊笑邊談 laugh over sth;
邊學邊忘 be no sooner learned than it is forgotten;
邊走邊唱 go along singing;
邊走邊考慮 walk along thinking to oneself;
邊走邊聊 stroll while chatting;

[邊帶] sideband;
獨立邊帶 independent sideband;
色度邊帶 chroma sideband;
雙邊帶 double sideband;

[邊地] border area; border district;

[邊防] border defence; frontier defence;
邊防部隊 frontier guards;
邊防檢查站 frontier inspection station;
邊防哨 border sentry;
邊防要塞 frontier strongholds;
邊防站 frontier station;
邊防證 frontier pass;
加強邊防 strengthen the frontier defences;
守邊防 keep guard on the frontiers;
削弱邊防 weaken the frontier defences;

[邊分] (of hair) side parting;

[邊幅] (1) edges; (2) appearance;
不修邊幅 be slovenly; not care about one's appearance; untidy;

[邊溝] roadside ditch;

[邊際] bound; boundary; limit;
邊際分析 marginal analysis;
邊際觀念 marginal concept;
邊際價格 marginal price;
邊際決策 marginal decision;
邊際群體 marginal group;
邊際人 marginal person;
邊際消費 marginal consumption;
邊際效率 marginal efficiency;
邊際效用 marginal utility;
安全邊際 margin of safety;
不着邊際 far off the mark; irrelevant; neither here nor there; not to the point; wide of the mark;
漫無邊際 boundless; discursive; rambling; stray far from the subject;
~漫無邊際的草原 the boundless prairie;
~漫無邊際的海洋 the immense sea;
~談話漫無邊際 discursive in one's speech;

[邊疆] border area; borderland; frontier;
邊疆地區 frontier area; frontier region;
邊疆開拓者 frontiersman; frontierswoman;
保衛邊疆 defend the frontier of the country;
開發邊疆 develop the border areas;
落戶邊疆 settle down in the frontier region;
守衛邊疆 garrison a border region; guard the frontier of a country;

[邊界] border; bound; boundary; frontier;
邊界線 boundary;
~確定邊界線 define boundaries;
邊界爭端 border dispute; boundary dispute;
~解決邊界爭端 settle a boundary dispute;
標點邊界 demarcate a boundary by setting up boundary markers;
超出邊界 beyond the boundary; exceed the bound;
穿越邊界 pass across the border;
磁極邊界 pole boundary;
反射邊界 reflecting boundary;
封鎖邊界 close the frontier;
公共邊界 common boundary;
光滑邊界 smooth boundary;
劃定邊界 demarcate the frontier; delimit the frontier; fix the boundaries;
結邊界 junction boundary;
浸水邊界 flooding boundary;
空泡邊界 cavity boundary;
理論邊界 theoretical boundary;
理想邊界 ideal boundary;
零邊界 null boundary;
判別邊界 decision boundary;
傾側邊界 tilt boundary;

全字邊界 full-word boundary;
上邊界 upper boundary;
設立邊界 set up frontiers;
踏過邊界 overstep the boundary;
逃過邊界 escape over the border;
圖象邊界 image boundary;
外邊界 outer boundary;
外推邊界 extrapolated boundary;
彎曲邊界 curved boundary;
網絡邊界 net boundary;
尾流邊界 wake boundary;
穩定性邊界 stability boundary;
相對邊界 relative boundary;
相間邊界 interphase boundary;
形成邊界 form the border;
一條邊界 a border;
越過邊界 cross the border;
正邊界 positive boundary;
自然邊界 natural boundary;

[邊境] border; frontier;
邊境安寧 peace on the borders;
邊境城鎮 border town;
邊境衝突 border clash; border conflict;
~避免邊境衝突 avoid border clashes;
邊境地帶 borderland;
邊境地區 border area; border region;
邊境管制 border controls;
邊境經濟 border economy;
~邊境經濟合作區 border economic cooperation zone;
邊境貿易 border trade; frontier trade;
~發展邊境貿易 extend border trade; extend frontier trade;
~擴大邊境貿易 increase border trade; increase frontier trade;
邊境衛兵 border guard;
邊境要塞 a fort on the frontier;
邊境爭議 border dispute;
邊境駐兵 station soldiers at the frontier;
穿越邊境 cross the border;
封鎖邊境 close the frontier; seal off the borders;
共同邊境 common border;
關閉邊境 close the border;
開放邊境 open the border;
平定邊境 pacify the frontier;
守衛邊境 guard the border;
逃過邊境 escape across the border; flee across the border;

[邊框] frame; rim;

[邊門] side door; wicket door; wicket gate;

[邊民] inhabitants of a border area;

[邊卡] border checkpoint;

[邊區] border area; border region;

[邊塞] frontier fortress;

[邊紋] fringe;
彩色邊紋 colour action fringe;
彩色動態邊紋 achromatic fringe;
近場邊紋 near-field fringes;

[邊線] sideline;
邊線裁判 linesman;
邊線球 sideline ball;
~擲邊線球 throw-in;

[邊形] number of sides of a polygon;
八邊形 octagon;
多邊形 polygon;
~凹多邊形 concave polygon;
~凸多邊形 convex polygon;
~圓內接多邊形 inpolygon;
~圓外切多邊形 circumscribed polygon;
~正多邊形 regular polygon;
九邊形 enneagon;
六邊形 hexagon;
七邊形 heptagon;
十邊形 decagon;
十二邊形 dodecagon;
十三邊形 tridecagon;
十一邊形 hendecagon;
四邊形 quadrilateral;
~平行四邊形 parallelogram;
五邊形 pentagon;

[邊沿] brim;

[邊緣] (1) border; brink; edge; fringe; limb margin; rim; skirt; (2) borderline;
邊緣地區 border district;
邊緣工業 frontier industry;
邊緣化 marginalization;
邊緣科學 borderline science; frontier science;
~邊緣科學方法 interdisciplinary approach;
邊緣事件 fringe event;
邊緣團體 fringe group;
邊緣問題 fringe issue;
邊緣效應 edge effect;
邊緣學科 borderline subject;
城市邊緣 urban fringe;
處於…的邊緣 live between…and…; on the borderline of…;
大陸邊緣 continental margin;
夾緊邊緣 clamped edge;
位錯邊緣 dislocation edge;

限下邊緣 subliminal fringe;
幀邊緣 frame edge;

[邊遠] far from the centre; outlying; remote;
邊遠的 outlying;
邊遠地區 outlying district; remote area;
~處於邊遠地區 be located in an outlying district;
~住在邊遠地區 out in the sticks;
邊遠省份 remote border provinces;

[邊註] marginal note;

挨邊 (1) keep close to the edge; (2) close to; (3) relevant to;
安邊 pacify the border area;
岸邊 dockside; quayside;
半邊 half of sth; one side of sth;
北邊 (1) north; (2) northern part;
鬢邊 temples;
船邊 alongside the vessel;
牀邊 bedside;
單邊 unilateral;
等邊 equilateral;
底邊 baseline;
東邊 east side;
多邊 multilateral;
滾邊 band; tape;
海邊 seafront; seaside;
河邊 river bank;
花邊 (1) decorative border; (2) lace; (3) fancy borders in printing;
金邊 gold-rimmed;
靠邊 keep to the side;
裏邊 inside;
兩邊 (1) both sides; (2) both directions; both places; (3) both parties; both sides;
繚邊 hem; stitch a hem;
溜邊 keep to the edge of…;
爐邊 fireside;
路邊 road side;
那邊 over there; there;
南邊 south;
旁邊 side;
上邊 (1) upper side; (2) up there;
掃邊 play a minor role in a Chinese opera;
身邊 (1) at one's side; one's immediate surroundings; one's vicinity; (2) on one; with one;
手邊 at hand; on hand;
戍邊 garrison the frontiers; guard the border; guard the frontier;
雙邊 bilateral;
朔邊 northern frontier;
四邊 four sides;
鎖邊 stitch edges;
隄邊 by the side of a levee;
天邊 (1) horizon; (2) end of the earth; remotest place;
貼邊 hem;
拓邊 open up borderlands; open up new frontiers;
外邊 (1) exterior; out; outside; (2) another place; far-away place;
無邊 boundless; brimless; rimless; vast and expansive;
徙邊 move prisoners to the border areas;
下邊 (1) as follows; following; (2) below; under;
舷邊 gunnel; gunwale;
鑲邊 rim with lace;
斜邊 (1) hypotenuse; (2) bevel edge;
沿邊 along the edge;
頁邊 margin;
一邊 (1) one side; (2) side; (3) at the same time;
右邊 on the right; the right side; the right-hand side;
緣邊 border; edge; hem; margin;
沾邊 (1) touch sth lightly; (2) close to what it should be; relevant;
褶邊 frill;
這邊 here; this side;
周邊 periphery;
嘴邊 at the tip of one's tongue;
左邊 left; left side; on the left;

bian

【鯿】 freshwater bream;
[鯿魚] bream;

bian

【籩】 bamboo container;
[籩豆] ancient food container;

bian³

bian

【扁】 (1) flat; (2) tablet; (3) a surname;
[扁擔] carrying pole;
扁擔挑燈籠—兩頭兒明 both sides understand; hanging lanterns at both ends of a carrying pole — both ends are bright;
[扁豆] hyacinth bean; lentil;
小扁豆 lentil;
[扁骨] flat bone;
[扁螺] clam;
[扁平] thin and flat;

扁平上皮 pavement epithelium;
扁平濕疣 condyloma latum; flat condyloma;
扁平濕疹 moist papule; mucous papule;
扁平台癬 lichen planus;
扁平疣 flat wart; plane wart; verruca plana; verruca plana juvenilis;

［扁蹋］ flat;
扁蹋鼻 snub nose;
扁蹋臉 flat face;

［扁桃］ (1) almond; almond tree; (2) flat peach;
扁桃體 tonsil;
~ 腭扁桃體 palatine tonsil;
~ 腺樣扁桃體 adenoid tonsil;
~ 小腸扁桃體 intestinal tonsil;
~ 小腦扁桃體 tonsil of cerebellum;
~ 咽扁桃體 pharyngeal tonsil;
~ 咽門扁桃體 faucial tonsil;
扁桃體切除 tonsillectomy;
扁桃體炎 tonsillitis;
~ 白喉性扁桃體炎 diphtherial tonsillitis;
~ 急性扁桃體炎 acute tonsillitis;
~ 鏈球菌性扁桃體炎 streptococcal tonsillitis;
~ 濾泡性扁桃體炎 follicular tonsillitis;
~ 慢性扁桃體炎 chronic tonsillitis;
~ 霉菌性扁桃體炎 mycotic tonsillitis;
~ 疱疹性扁桃體炎 herpetic tonsillitis;
~ 遷延性扁桃體炎 tonsillitis lenta;
扁桃體周圍膿腫 peritonsillar abscess;
扁桃腺 tonsil;

踮扁 trample an object flat;
踩扁 trample down;
壓扁 crush; flatten by pressure;

bian
【窆】 put the coffin in the grave;
［窆石］ stones used in gliding a coffin down a tunnel;

bian
【匾】 wooden tablet;
［匾額］ wooden tablet;

牌匾 board;

bian
【貶】 (1) degrade; demote; relegate; (2) devalue; reduce; (3) censure; condemn; depreciate; disparage; (4) dismiss; send away;
［貶斥］ demote; denounce;
［貶詞］ derogatory term; expression of censure;
［貶低］ abase; belittle; cry down; denigrate; denigration; depreciate; detract from; disparage; play down; run down;
貶低的 disparaging;
［貶官］ demote an official;
［貶價］ reduce the price;
貶價出售 sell at a reduced price;
［貶損］ (1) criticize; (2) belittle; depreciate; derogate; play down;
［貶抑］ belittle; depreciate;
［貶義］ derogatory sense;
貶義詞 derogatory term; pejorative;
~ 帶有貶義 convey a derogatory sense;
［貶責］ reprimand; reproach;
［貶謫］ banish from the court; relegate;
［貶值］ depreciate; devalue; devaluate;
貶值貨幣 depreciated currency;
貶值率 rate of depreciation;
法定貶值 official devaluation;
貨幣貶值 currency depreciation; currency devaluation;

褒貶 censure; criticize; speak ill of;
責貶 fault-finding;

bian
【稨】 lentil;

bian
【褊】 cramped; narrow; small;
［褊隘］ narrow-minded and impatient;
［褊急］ easily irritated; narrow-minded and short-tempered;
［褊陋］ cramped and crude; narrow-minded and ignorant;
［褊能］ of little ability;
［褊淺］ narrow-minded and shallow;
［褊狹］ cramped; narrow;
［褊小］ narrow; petty; small;
［褊心］ narrow-minded and impatient;

bian⁴

bian
【卞】 (1) hurriedly; rash; (2) excitable; (3) a surname;
［卞急］ irascible; testy;

bian
【弁】 (1) conical cap worn on ceremonious occasions in ancient times; (2) low-ranking military officers; (3) a surname;

[弁冕] ancient cap worn on ceremonious occasions;
[弁髦] (1) useless things; (2) despise; slight; underestimate;
弁髦法紀 despise legal orders;
弁髦榮華 spurn worldly honours;
[弁目] squad leader;
[弁言] foreword; preface; introduction;
[弁絰] a patch of coarse linen worn on the mourning cap during a funeral service;

馬弁 bodyguard;

bian
【汴】 (1) alternative name for Kaifeng in Henan; (2) ancient name of a river in Henan;

bian
【忭】 delighted; overjoyed; pleased;
[忭賀] celebrate; congratulate with joy;
[忭頌] be pleased to offer one's best wishes;
[忭躍] great joy; leap with joy; tremendous pleasure;

歡忭 glad; happy;
欣忭 happy; joyous;

bian
【抃】 applaud; cheer; clap one's hands;
[抃舞] cheer and dance; make merry;
[抃踴] cheer and dance;
[抃悅] clap one's hands for joy; cheer;
[抃掌] clap one's hands;

bian
【便】 (1) convenient; expedient; handy; (2) when an opportunity arises; when it is convenient; (3) informal; ordinary; plain; (4) relieve oneself; (5) piss or shit; urine or excrement;
[便步] walk at ease;
便步走 march at ease;
[便菜] everyday dish; ordinary dish;
[便餐] informal and ordinary meal;
電視便餐 TV dinner;
[便池] urinal;
[便當] convenient; easy; handy;
[便道] (1) shortcut; snap course; (2) pavement; sidewalk; (3) makeshift road; (4) do sth on the way;
便道過訪 drop in; look in on sb; pay an informal visit;
抄便道 take a shortcut;
走便道 walk on the pavement;
[便飯] have a light meal; have a simple meal; potluck; simple meal; take a potluck with sb;
便飯招待 treat sb with an ordinary meal;
[便服] everyday clothes; informal dress; leisurewear;
[便函] informal letter;
[便盒] lunch box;
[便壺] bed urinal; chamber pot; night-pot for urination;
[便箋] memo; memo pad; notepaper;
[便捷] easy and convenient; facility;
[便徑] quick route; shortcut;
[便覽] brief guide;
翻譯便覽 translation manual;
[便利] (1) convenient; easy; (2) accommodate; facilitate; for the convenience of;
便利查閱 facilitate consultation;
便利店 convenience store;
便利商店 convenience store;
便利設施 conveniences;
提供便利 facilitate;
提供一切便利 provide every convenience;
因利乘便 take advantage of the convenience; take the tide at the flood;
[便路] bypath; shortcut;
[便帽] cap;
[便門] access door; postern door; side door; wicket door;
[便秘] constipation; intestinal constipation;
便秘絞痛 stercoral colitis;
弛緩性便秘 atonic constipation;
痙攣性便秘 spastic constipation;
習慣性便秘 habitual constipation;
直腸性便秘 proctogenous constipation;
[便民] convenient for the people; provide for the people's convenience;
便民服務 service for the convenience of the customers;
[便溺] empty the bowels and urinate; relieve one's bowels; urinate and defecate;
[便盆] bed pan;
[便器] urinal;
[便橋] makeshift bridge; temporary bridge;
[便士] penny;
[便是] even if;

[便所] lavatory; privy; restroom; toilet;
[便條] chit; informal note; memo; note;
便條簿 notepad;
一張便條 a note;
~ 匆忙寫了一張便條 dash off a note;
[便桶] chamber pot;
座椅式便桶 commode;
[便鞋] cloth shoes; playshoes; sandal; slippers;
室內便鞋 slipper;
無帶扣便鞋 slip-on shoes; slip-ons;
[便攜式] portable;
便攜式電腦 portable computer;
便攜式電視接收機 portable television receiver;
便攜式衛星天線 portable satellite antenna;
[便血] have blood in one's stool;
[便宴] informal dinner;
[便衣] (1) civilian clothes; plain clothes; (2) plain-clothes person;
便衣警察 plainclothes policeman;
[便宜] (1) cheap; inexpensive; (2) gain advantage; (3) advantage; profit; (4) let sb off lightly;
便宜貨 bargain; schlock;
便宜沒好貨 cheapest is the dearest;
便宜行事 act as one sees fit; act at one's discretion;
很便宜 very cheap;
撿着便宜 gain an advantage from sth;
貪便宜 gain petty advantages; keen on gaining petty advantages; try to get things on the cheap;
討便宜 look for a bargain; seek for one's own benefit; seek profit in an improper way; seek undue advantage; try to gain sth at the expense of others;
小便宜 petty advantage; small advantage; small gain;
~ 佔小便宜 gain petty advantages; make small gains at other people's expense;
~ 愛佔小便宜 keen on getting petty advantages;
佔便宜 (1) gain an advantage; gain extra advantage by unfair means; get the better end of; have an advantage in; load the dice against; profit at other people's expense; (2) take advantage of a woman;
~ 佔便宜的人 freeloader;
[便於] easy to; convenient for; for the convenience of;
[便紙] toilet paper; toilet tissue;
[便中] at one's convenience; when it is convenient;
[便裝] casual wear; everyday clothes; nightgown; playsuit;

不便 (1) inappropriate; inconvenient; unsuitable; (2) hard up; short of cash;
趁便 at one's convenience; when it is convenient;
稱便 find sth a great convenience;
乘便 at one's convenience; when it is convenient;
大便 (1) defecate; discharge; dump; egest; eject; empty; empty the bowels; evacuate the bowels; expel; go boom-boom; go number one; go potty; go to the bank; have a bowel movement; loose bowels; make little soldiers; move the bowels; post a letter; relieve oneself; relieve the bowels; shit; sit on the throne; take a shit; the bowel moves; void excrement; (2) faeces; human excrement; shit; stool; turd;
得便 when it is convenient;
方便 (1) convenient; handy; (2) have money to spare or lend; (3) go to the bathroom; go to the bathroom to tidy up; go to the toilet;
糞便 dung; excrement and urine; feces; faeces; night soil; ordure; ordure pellet;
告便 excuse me;
黑便 tarry stools;
即便 even; even if; even though;
簡便 simple and convenient;
近便 close and convenient; close at hand;
就便 in passing; while you are at it; without extra effort;
兩便 convenient to both; make things easy for both;
靈便 (1) agile; nimble; (2) easy to handle; handy;
排便 defecation;
輕便 light; portable;
請便 as you please; do as you please; do as you wish; help yourself; please yourself;
取便 (1) do as one pleases without restraint; (2) facilitate; promote;
任便 as you please; do as you like;
擅便 consult one's own convenience only;
省便 convenient;
順便 at one's convenience; conveniently; in passing; while sb is about it; without extra effort; without taking extra trouble;

伺便 wait for a chance convenient for one;
俟便 when it is convenient;
溲便 urinate;
隨便 (1) careless; slipshod; (2) anyhow; wanton; wilful; (3) do as one pleases; do at one's will;
隨你的便 at your pleasure; suit yourself;
溏便 semiliquid stool;
聽便 do as one pleases; do as one sees fit;
通便 facilitate bowel movement; purging; relief of constipation;
童便 urine of boys under twelve;
未便 find it hard to; not be in a position to;
穩便 reliable and convenient;
小便 apple and pip; burn the grass; dicky-diddle; do; drain one's radiator; drain one's snake; empty one's bladder; evacuate the bladder; go tap a kidney; have a leak; have a quickie; have a run off; life his leg; make number one; make salt water; make water; micturate; pass urine; pass water; pee; piddle; pie and mash; piss; plant a sweet pea; point Percy at the porcelain; pump ship; retire; scatter; see a man about a dog; see one's aunt; shake hands with an old friend; shake the dew off the lily; shoot a lion; spend a penny; take a leak; take a quickie; tap a keg; tinkle; urinate; water the lawn; water the stock; whiz;
形便 advantages offered by terrain;
循便 be guided by expediency in performing tasks; take advantage of expediency;
要便 often; usually;
以便 (1) for the purpose of; in order that; in order to; so as to; so that; to the effect that; with the aim of; (2) for the convenience of;
遇便 at one's convenience;
自便 as one pleases; at one's convenience;

bian

【遍】 (1) all over; everywhere; throughout; (2) time;

[遍佈] all over; be found everywhere; spread all over;
遍佈全國 can be found all over the country;
遍佈全世界 spread throughout the world;

[遍地] all over the place; everywhere; throughout the land;
遍地皆是 wall to wall;

[遍訪] seek everywhere;

[遍告] announce to all; tell everyone;

[遍及] extend all over; reach everywhere; reach everywhere;
遍及全球 all over the world; extend all over the world; extend over the entire globe;
遍及世界 reach every corner of the world; spread all over the world;

[遍歷] have experienced all sorts of;

[遍身] all over the body;

[遍體] all over the body;
遍體鱗傷 a mass of bruises; beaten black and blue; covered all over with cuts and bruises; with bruises all over; with wounds all over the body;

[遍尋無着] look for sth everywhere and not be able to find it;

[遍野] scatter over the wilderness;
餓殍遍野 corpses of people who died of starvation are seen in the fields; in the fields lay people starved to death; people dying of starvation is a common sight;
屍橫遍野 dead bodies scattered over the wilderness;

傳遍 spread throughout;
訪遍 visit everywhere;
兩遍 twice;
跑遍 go around; travel all over;
普遍 common; general; universal;
踏遍 traverse the length and breadth of a place;
一遍 once; one time;
找遍 search everywhere;
周遍 all over; all round;
走遍 travel all over;

bian

【緶】 (1) narrow strip of woven material; (2) sew up a hem;

草帽緶 plaited straw;

bian

【辨】 (1) differentiate; discern; discriminate; distinguish; (2) identify; recognize;

[辨白] (1) distinguish clearly; identify clearly; (2) account for;

[辨別] differentiate; discriminate; distinguish; make out sb; make out sth;

辨別真偽 discern the false from the genuine; distinguish the true from the false;

[辨明] distinguish between;

[辨認] identify; make out; recognize;

可辨認 identifiable;

列隊辨認 identification parade; identity parade;

清楚辨認 clearly distinguishable; plainly distinguishable;

容易辨認 easily distinguishable;

[辨色] discriminate colours;

辨色測驗 colour discrimination; colour vision test;

見貌辨色 quick to see which way the wind blows;

鑒貌辨色 look at sb's face and distinguish its colour – examine sb's countenance; quick to see which way the wind blows – very shrewd; subtly react by noticing one's superior's countenance;

[辨識] identification; recognize;

錯誤辨識 false identification;

顯式辨識 explicit identification;

語言辨識 language identification;

[辨析] differentiate and analyse; discriminate;

[辨異] distinguish differences between things;

[辨證] discriminate;

分辨 (1) differentiate; discriminate; distinguish; (2) resolve;

難辨 hard to distinguish;

識辨 discern; distinguish;

思辨 (1) speculate; (2) armchair thinking; (3) analyze mentally;

bian

【辮】 braid; pigtail; plait; queue;

[辮髮] (1) plaited hair; (2) braid one's hair; plait one's hair; (3) wear a queue;

[辮子] braid; pigtail; plait; queue;

編辮子 plait one's hair;

揪辮子 capitalize on sb's vulnerable point; seize on sb's mistakes; seize sb's queue;

留辮子 wear one's hair in a pigtail;

蹺辮子 die; kick the bucket; pass away;

翹辮子 drop dead; go west; hop the stick; hop the twig; kick the bucket; turn one's toes up; turn up one's toes;

梳辮子 plait one's hair;

~梳着辮子 wear one's hair in braids;

小辮子 (1) braid; (2) little pigtail – a mistake that may be exploited by others; vulnerable point;

~抓小辮子 catch sb out; get a handle on sb; have sb by the short braids – find fault with sb; seize hold of the mistakes and shortcomings of sb;

一根辮子 a braid;

長着辮子 wear a queue;

抓辮子 capitalize on sb's vulnerable point; pull sb's leg; seize sb's queue – seize on sb's mistake;

髮辮 braid; pigtail; plait;

馬尾辮 ponytail;

小辮 pigtail; short braid;

羊角辮 bunches; ram's horns;

bian

【辯】 argue; debate; dispute;

[辯白] offer an explanation; plead innocence; try to defend oneself;

為自己辯白 proclaim one's innocence;

[辯駁] defend oneself verbally; dispute; refute;

[辯才] ability as a debater; eloquence;

辯才無礙 very eloquent;

天生辯才 be gifted with eloquence;

[辯護] apologia; argue in favour of; defend; speak in defence of; take up the gauntlet;

辯護費 defence cost; retainer;

辯護律師 defence counsel;

辯護權 right to defend;

辯護人 counsel; defender;

辯護者 apologist;

不需辯護 need no defence;

出庭辯護 defend a case in court;

口頭辯護 verbal defence;

~做口頭辯護 make verbal defence;

提出辯護 offer a defence;

為被告辯護 plead for the accused;

[辯解] apologia; argue that; provide an explanation;

辯解者 apologist;

厚着臉皮辯解 apologize for oneself with effrontery;

為自己辯解 defend oneself;

[辯口] eloquence;

[辯論] argue; debate;

辯論比賽 debate competition;

~ 時事辯論比賽 current affairs debate competition;
辯論會 debate meeting;
辯論者 debater;
擱置辯論 shelve an argument;
據理辯論 argue soundly;
公開辯論 open debate;
壓制辯論 stifle argument;
一場辯論 a debate;
終止辯論 close a debate;

[辯難] debate; defend and question; retort with challenging questions;

[辯士] (1) able speaker; gifted debater; (2) sophist;

[辯誣] defend sb falsely accused;

[辯證] (1) dialectical; (2) discriminate;
辯證法 dialectics;
~ 客觀辯證法 objective dialectics;
~ 歷史辯證法 historical dialectics;
~ 唯物辯證法 materialist dialectics;
~ 唯心辯證法 idealist dialectics;
~ 主觀辯證法 subjective dialectics;
~ 自然辯證法 natural dialectics;
辯證觀點 dialectical perspective;
辯證唯物主義 dialectical materialism;

駁辯 argue; debate; dispute;
答辯 (1) defend (2) reply;
分辯 offer an explanation to clear up a misunderstanding;
伏辯 written statement of repentance;
詭辯 sophisticate; quibble;
狡辯 indulge in sophistry; quibble;
抗辯 (1) contradict; refute; speak out in one's own defense; (2) counter-argument;
強辯 defend oneself by sophistry;
巧辯 ingenious argument; plausible argument;
善辯 skilfully debate;
申辯 argue one's case; defend oneself against a charge;
聲辯 argue; explain away; justify;
雄辯 convincing argument; forceful presentation of one's points in a debate; eloquence;
爭辯 altercation; argue; debate; dispute;
置辯 argue; defend; explain; rebut; refute;

bian

【變】 (1) become different; (2) become; change into; turn into; (3) alter; change; transform; (4) accident; misfortune; unexpected turn of events; upheaval;

[變本加厲] aggravate; be further intensified; become aggravated; exacerbate; get worse; go even further; intensify; redouble one's efforts to; step up; with redoubled efforts; worsen;

[變成] become; change into; change to; come; come off; convert into; develop into; grow; pass into; transform sth into; turn into;
把…變成 convert…into…; translate…into…;
~ 把理想變成現實 translate an ideal into reality;
從…變成… change from …into…;
~ 從液體變成固體 change from liquid into solid;
使…變成… change the transition from…to…; transform…into…;

[變稠] curdle;

[變得] become;

[變調] (1) modified tone; (2) total modification;

[變動] alter; change; vary;
必要的變動 necessary changes;

[變法] initiate political reform; political reform; reform; revise the law;
變法運動 reform movement;
變法自強 initiate political reform in quest for national strength;

[變革] change; transform;
徹底變革 complete change
~ 經歷徹底變革 undergo a complete change;

[變更] alter; change; modify;

[變故] accident; misfortune; unforeseen event;
發生變故 occurrence of an accident;

[變卦] back out; backpedal; backpedal on; backtrack; break an agreement; change one's mind; go back on one's word;

[變好] (1) become fine; clear up; (2) alter for the better; become good; change for the better; reform;

[變化] alter; change; fluctuate; vary;
變化多端 capricious; changeable; kaleidoscopic changes; multifarious changes; unpredictable;
變化很大 alter a great deal;
變化速度 pace of change;
變化萬千 change all the time; change eternally;

B

變化無常 change all the time; chop and change; hop from one thing to another;
變化無窮 with countless changes; with endless variations;
變化顯著 change noticeably;
爆炸性變化 explosive turn;
層出不窮的變化 kaleidoscopic change;
帶來變化 bring about a change;
發生變化 alter; change; produce a change;
激烈變化 violent change;
急劇變化 abrupt change; radical change;
巨大變化 might change;
可能變化 capable of variation;
可逆變化 reversible change;
可喜的變化 welcome change;
平均變化 average change;
起變化 take a turn;
千變萬化 a thousand changes and a myriad transformations; countless changes; countless variations; ever-changing; frequent changes; infinite in variety; kaleidoscopic; kaleidoscopic change; myriads of changes; unending changes;
容許變化 allowable variation;
容易變化 liable to variation;
使人振奮的變化 refreshing change;
突然變化 quick change; sudden change;
微小變化 slight change;
無窮變化 infinite variety of forms;
細微變化 slight alteration;
顯著變化 marked change; remarkable change;
引起變化 effect a change;
有益健康的變化 salutary change;

［變壞］ alter for the worse; become worse; break up; change for the worse; get worse;
圖象變壞 image deterioration;
愈變愈壞 become worse and worse; go on from bad to worse;

［變幻］ change irregularly; fluctuate;
變幻不定 keep shifting like the clouds;
變幻莫測 change irregularly;
變幻無常 change all the time; flux and reflux; hop from one thing to another;

［變換］ alternate; conversion; transform; transformation; vary;
變換策略 vary one's tactics;
變換技巧 vary one's techniques;
變換器 changer; converter;
~擋板變換器 baffle-plate converter;
~電流變換器 circuit changer;
~高度變換器 altitude converter;
~級聯變換器 cascade converter;
~極化變換器 polarization changer;
~雙極變換器 bipolar converter;
~位變換器 bit changer;
~相位變換器 phase changer;
~中頻變換器 medium-frequency changer;
變換位置 shift one's position;
變換姿勢 alter one's posture;
閉線性變換 closed linear transform;
代碼變換 code conversion;
對稱變換 symmetry transformation;
對合變換 convolution transform;
仿射變換 affine transformation;
高度變換 altitude conversion;
環變換 annular transform;
頻道變換 channel conversion;
容許變換 admissible transformation;
數據變換 data conversion;
突躍變換 abrupt transformation;
相似變換 similitude transformation;
餘弦變換 cosine transform;
座標變換 coordinate conversion;

［變節］ defect; desert a cause; make a political recantation; turn one's coat;
變節份子 recanter; turncoat;
變節事故 condescend to and serve the enemy;
變節投敵 turn one's coat and go over to the enemy;
變節者 apostate; turncoat;

［變局］ crisis; critical situation;

［變臉］ change one's countenance; get angry; suddenly turn hostile; turn angry; turn hostile; turn sulky;

［變量］ variable; variate;
伴聯變量 associated variate;
典型變量 canonical variate;
區域變量 area variable;
人為變量 artificial variable;
屬性變量 attribute variable;
作用變量 actuating variable;

［變亂］ chaos; rebellion; revolt; social upheaval; turmoil;

［變賣］ sell off sth to meet a financial need;

［變頻］ frequency conversion;
彩色變頻器 colour frequency converter;
附加變頻器 adapter converter;

寬帶變頻器 broadband converter;
色度變頻器 chroma frequency converter;

[變遷] (1) changes; vicissitudes; (2) change;
大陸變遷 continental drift;
人世變遷 the world wags;
時世變遷 the time changes;

[變色] (1) change colour; discolouration; discolour; (2) become angry; change countenance;
變色鏡 light-sensitive sunglasses; self-adjusting sunglasses;
變色龍 chamaeleon;
變色顏料 photopigment;
表面變色 surface discolouration;
~肉表面變色 meat surface discolouration;
細菌性變色 bacterial discolouration;

[變數] variable; variate;
輔助變數 auxiliary variate;
連續變數 continuous variate;
調整變數 adjusting variable;
相隨變數 concomitant variate;
有界變數 bounded variable;

[變速] change speed; gear shift; speed change;
變速車 speed-variable bike;
變速桿 gear lever; gear shift; gearstick;
變速箱 gearbox;

[變酸] turn sour;
開始變酸 on the turn;

[變態] (1) abnormal; (2) metamorphosis; (3) psychopathy;
變態發育 interrupted development;
變態人格 psychopathic personality;
變態心理學 abnormal psychology;
重演性變態 palingenesis;
後生變態 cetogenesis;
間接變態 indirect metamorphosis;
漸變態 gradual metamorphosis;
漸進變態 gradual metamorphosis;
進化變態 evolutionary metamorphosis;
全變態 complete metamorphosis;
完全變態 complete metamorphosis;
~不完全變態 incomplete metamorphosis;
細胞變態 cytomorphosis;
新性變態 caenogenesis;
脂肪變態 fatty metamorphosis;

[變體] variant; variety;
標準變體 standard variety;
詞素變體 allomorph;
電泳變體 electrophoretic variants;
風格變體 stylistic variety;
條件變體 conditional variants;
自由變體 free variants;
組合變體 combinatory variants;

[變天] (1) change of weather; (2) restoration of a reactionary rule; (3) changes of political situations;

[變通] accommodate sth to the circumstances; adapt oneself to circumstances; be flexible;
變通辦法 accommodation; adaptation;
變通辦理 do sth in a different way;
窮則變，變則通 impasse is followed by change, and change will lead to the solution; when all means are exhausted, changes become necessary;
適當變通 make appropriate adaptations;

[變味] go stale;
麵包變味 the bread went stale;

[變相] convert; in disguised form;

[變心] cease to be faithful; cease to love one's spouse; jilt a lover;

[變星] variable star;
爆發變星 explosive variable;
脈動變星 pulsation variable;
食變星 eclipsing variable;
造父變星 Cepheid;

[變形] become deformed; change shape; deform; deformation; out of shape; transfigure; transshape;
變形測定器 deformeter;
變形蟲 amoeba;
~變形蟲目 Order Amoebida;
變形性 deformability;
衝擊變形 plastic deformation;
均勻變形 affine deformation;
容許變形 allowable deformation;
體變形 body deformation;
完全變形 be badly deformed;
正在變形 be losing shape;
重心變形 barycentric deformation;
周期變形 periodical metamorphosis;

[變性] (1) degeneration; denaturation; (2) sex change;
變性人 transsexual;
變性手術 transsexual operation; transsexual surgery;
創傷性變性 traumatic degeneration;
蛋白質變性 protein denaturation;
繼發性變性 secondary degeneration;
加酸變性 acid denaturation;

可逆變性 reversible denaturation;
~ 不可逆變性 irreversible denaturation;
老年性變性 senile degeneration;
人工變性 experimental sex reversal;
水腫性變性 hydropic degeneration;
外傷性變性 traumatic degeneration;
遺傳性變性 heredodegeneration;
硬化變性 sclerotic degeneration;

[變壓器] transformer; voltage changer;
風冷式變壓器 air blast transformer;
附加變壓器 adapter transformer;
交流變壓器 alternate current transformer;
可調變壓器 adjustable transformer;
天線變壓器 aerial transformer;
自耦變壓器 autotransformer;
~ 單相自耦變壓器 single-phase autotransformer;
~ 接地自耦變壓器 earthing autotransformer;
~ 可調自耦變壓器 adjustable ratio autotransformer; variable autotransformer;
~ 零點自耦變壓器 electrical-zero autotransformer;
~ 起動自耦變壓器 starting autotransformer;
~ 三相自耦變壓器 three-phase autotransformer;
~ 昇壓自耦變壓器 step-up autotransformer;
~ 調諧自耦變壓器 tuned autotransformer;
~ 移相用自耦變壓器 phase-shifting autotransformer;
~ 儀錶用自耦變壓器 instrument autotransformer;

[變樣] change in design;
[變易] alter; change;
[變異] mutation; variation;
變異句 deviant sentence;
變異性 variability;
~ 定向變異性 directed variability;
~ 絕對變異性 absolute variability;
~ 確定變異性 definite variability;
~ 相應變異性 corresponding variability;
~ 自由變異性 free variability;
地區性變異 regional variation;
定向變異 directed variation;
對立變異 alternative variation;
抗原變異 antigenic variation;
年齡變異 age variation;
彷徨變異 fluctuation;
適應變異 adequate variation;
物種變異 mutation of species;
芽條變異 bud variation;

[變應性] allergy;
[變元] argument;
假變元 dummy argument;
實際變元 actual argument;
形式變元 formal argument;

[變造] fabricate; fill in a blank permit; forge;
[變詐] cunning means;
[變質] (1) go bad; go off; on the turn; rancid; (2) metamorphism;
變質黃油 rancid butter;
變質作用 metamorphism;
~ 低度變質作用 low-rank metamorphism;
~ 動力化學變質作用 dynamo-chemical metamorphism;
成岩變質 diagenetic metamorphism;
加物變質 additive metamorphism;
退化變質 regressive metamorphism;
蛻化變質 become morally deteriorative;

[變奏] variation;
[變阻器] rheostat;
平衡變阻器 balancing rheostat;
自動磁場變阻器 automatic field rheostat;

癌變 become cancerous; cancerate; canceration; cancerization; develop into cancer;
豹變 turn wealth from poverty;
兵變 mutiny; troops in mutiny;
病變 pathological changes;
逼變 drive to revolt;
不變 unchanged;
慘變 disastrous turn of events;
多變 changeable; changeful; varied;
改變 alter; change; transform;
肝硬變 cirrhosis of the liver;
互變 interconversion;
嘩變 mutiny;
激變 violent change;
急變 emergency;
漸變 gradual change;
巨變 tremendous change;
聚變 fusion;
劇變 change violently;
可變 changeable; variable;
量變 quantitative change;
裂變 fission;
流變 evolution;
民變 civil commotion; mass uprising; popular revolt;

叛變 betray one's country, party, etc; turn into a traitor;
切變 shear;
權變 act according to circumstances; improvise;
蠕變 creep;
色變 turn pale;
善變 apt to change; changeable;
嬗變 (1) evolve; (2) transmute;
生變 happen;
世變 changes in a situation;
事變 (1) incident; (2) emergency; exigency;
衰變 decay; disintegration;
瞬變 transient;
突變 (1) sudden change; (2) mutation; (3) leap;
蛻變 (1) change qualitatively; transform; (2) decay;
相變 phase change;
形變 deformation;
芽變 bud mutation;
衍變 develop; develop and change; evolve;
演變 develop; evolve;
一變 change;
音變 phonetic change;
應變 (1) meet an emergency; (2) strain;
災變 catastrophe; disaster;
遭變 be hit by a great misfortune; have an accident;
政變 coup d'etat;
質變 qualitative change;
驟變 abrupt change;
轉變 (1) change; transform; undergo changes; (2) change; shift; turnabout;

biao¹

biao

【彪】 (1) tiger cub; (2) tiger stripes; (3) tall and big; (4) a surname;

[彪炳] brilliant and shining achievements;
彪炳千古 shining through the ages;
彪炳事業 brilliant and glorious achievement in history;

[彪煥] brilliant and shining; outstanding and elegant;

[彪形] tall and big;
彪形大漢 bruiser; burly person; husky fellow; stalwart person; whale of a man;

[彪休] angry; wrathful;

[彪子] frolicsome creature;

虎彪彪 brave; full of vigour;

biao

【猋】 (1) gale; hurricane; (2) dogs running; (3) quick; rapid; swift;

[猋忽] gale;

biao

【摽】 (1) fall; (2) razor of a sword; (3) high; lofty; (4) strike;

[摽末] edge of a sword;

[摽旗] signal with a flag;

biao

【標】 (1) indicate; mark; put a mark on; show; sign; symbolize; (2) model; paragon; (3) label; put a mark; (4) award; prize; (5) bid; tender; (6) outward sign; superficiality; triviality;

[標榜] advertise; blow one's own trumpet; boast; flaunt; glorify oneself; parade; praise excessively;
標榜沽名 advertise oneself to seek fame;
互相標榜 boost each other;
自我標榜 advertise oneself;

[標本] (1) sample; specimen; (2) appearance and substance;
標本陳列所 specimens hall;
典型標本 typical specimen;
動物標本 zoological specimen;
活標本 living specimen;
昆蟲標本 insect specimen;
木炭標本 charcoal specimen;
真標本 original specimen;

[標兵] (1) pacemaker; pacesetter; (2) marker;
青年標兵 model youth;

[標尺] staff gauge; surveyor's rod;

[標出] scale out; section out;

[標燈] beacon; beacon light;

[標點] punctuation;
標點符號 punctuation mark;
~不用標點符號 use no punctuation marks;
~加上標點符號 put in punctuation marks;

[標定] demarcate;

[標度] scale;
標度盤 dial;
~方位標度盤 azimuth dial;
~可調標度盤 adjustable dial;
~羅盤標度盤 compass dial;
~諧波標度盤 harmonic dial;
~儀表標度盤 instrument dial;

[標封] sealed with labels;

B

[標竿] signpost;
[標高] mark up;
標高定價 mark up prices;
[標格] model; example;
[標號] grade; label; mark;
打印標號 identification mark;
公用標號 common label;
控制標號 control label;
[標記] label; labelling; mark; marker; marking; pip; sign; symbol; tag; indication;
標記詞 marked term; token word;
~無標記詞 unmarked term;
按鈕標記 button marking;
不對稱標記 asymmetric labelling;
擦去標記 rub off marks;
從句標記 clause marker;
從屬標記 dependency marker;
定義標記 defined label;
短語標記 phrase marker;
對準標記 alignment mark;
翻譯標記 translation label;
分界標記 division mark;
格標記 case label;
親合標記 affinity labelling;
調整標記 adjusting mark;
同步標記 sync pip;
外部標記 external label;
硬標記 hard label;
重標記 heavy label;
主標記 main pip;
作為標記 serve as a mark;
做個標記 put a mark on;
[標價] listed price; posted price; tag price;
標價法 quotation;
~間接標價法 indirect quotation;
直接標價 direct quotation;
[標界] mark a boundary;
[標賣] sell by tender;
[標名] label; title;
[標明] indicate; label; mark;
標明號碼 put a number on;
[標牌] label; sign;
掛標牌 hang up a sign;
一塊標牌 a sign;
載重標牌 capacity label;
[標籤] label; mark; price tag; tag; tally;
標籤翻譯 label translation;
包裹標籤 label;
成本標籤 cost tag;
加標籤 attach a label;
價格標籤 price tag;
價目標籤 price tag;
金屬標籤 metal marker tag;
盤存標籤 inventory tag;
書題標籤 book label;
説明標籤 explanatory label;
條形碼標籤 barcode label;
貼標籤 place labels on;
洗滌標籤 care label;
行李標籤 luggage label;
政治標籤 political label;
柱標籤 column tag
[標槍] javelin; lance; spear;
擲標槍 (1) javelin throw; (2) throw the javelin;
[標識] identify;
標識符 identifier;
~過程標識符 procedure identifier;
~結果標識符 resultant identifier;
~開關標識符 switch identifier;
~命令標識符 command identifier;
~設備標識符 vice identifier;
~數據使用標識符 data use identifier;
~語句標識符 statement identifier;
標識器 marker;
~撥號標識器 dial marker;
~撥號音標識器 dial tone marker;
[標示] indicate; mark; note;
結果標示器 event marker;
[標題] caption; header; heading; headline; title;
標題廣告 banner ad;
標題卡 title card;
標題欄 title bar;
標題新聞 headline;
標題頁 front page; title page;
標題音樂 programme music; signature tune;
標題語句 headline;
標題字 banner word; headletter;
倒排標題 inverted heading;
分類標題 class heading;
副標題 half-title; subheading; subtitle;
簡略標題 abbreviated title;
簡寫標題 abbreviated header;
欄外標題 running headline;
描述標題 descriptive title;
數據標題 data header;
通欄標題 banner; banner headline; streamer headline;
小標題 cross heading; subhead;

subheading;
頁標題 page header;
一個標題 a title;
章節標題 chapter heading; chapter title;
主標題 main title;

[標新立異] create sth new and original; do sth unconventional; do sth unorthodox; strain after novelty;
喜歡標奇立異 like to create sth new and original;

[標音] notation;
標音法 transcription;

[標引] index;

[標語] motto; slogan;
標語塔 slogan pylon;

[標誌] designator; hallmark; indicate; mark; marking; trappings
標誌板 marker;
~機場標誌板 aerodrome marker;
標誌器 marker;
~海灘標誌器 beach marker;
~航向標誌器 course marker;
~深度標誌器 depth marker;
安全標誌 safety sign;
交通標誌 traffic signs;
頻道標誌 channel designator;
權力標誌 trappings of power;
停車標誌 stop sign;
裝箱標誌 box marking;

[標緻] beautiful; comeliness; comely; good-looking; handsome; pretty;

[標準] criterion; standard; typical;
標準版 standard edition;
標準變體 standard variety;
標準差 standard deviation;
標準測試 standard testing;
標準程序 standard programme;
標準搭配 stock collocation;
標準代碼 standard code;
標準的 standard;
~不標準的 non-standard;
標準合同 model contract; standard contract;
標準化 standardize; standardization;
~標準化測試 standardized test;
~標準化工程 standardized project;
~標準化試題 standardized test paper;
~標準化信封 standardized envelope;
~工作標準化 work standardization;
~商品標準化 commodity standardization;
~衛生標準化 hygienic standardization;
標準接口 standardized interface;
標準理論 standard theory;
標準偏差 standardized deviation;
標準群體 standard group;
標準時 standard time;
標準數據庫 standard database;
標準圖形庫 standard graphics library;
標準文件 standard file;
標準文獻 standard document;
標準像 official photo; standard photo;
標準信封 standard size envelope;
標準信息 standard information;
標準音 standard pronunciation;
標準隱喻 standard metaphor; stock metaphor;
標準語 standard language; standard speech;
~標準語言 standard language;
~國家標準語 national standard speech;
~民族標準語 national standard speech;
標準子程序 standard subroutine;
安全標準 safety standard; standard of security;
按…的標準 by...standards;
~按我們的標準 by our standards;
保持標準 maintain the standard;
比較標準 standard of comparison;
必要標準 desirable criterion;
不夠標準 below the mark; fall short of standard; under the mark;
達到標準 come up to standard; meet a standard; reach a standard; up to scratch; up to the mark; up to the standard; secure a standard;
道德標準 moral standard;
工資標準 wage standard;
公平標準 fair criterion;
公認的標準 recognized standard;
夠標準 make the grade;
固定標準 fixed standard;
合符標準 within the mark;
降低標準 debase the standard;
接近標準 near the mark;
美的標準 standard of beauty;
評判標準 standard for judging;
確定標準 settle the standard;
設計標準 design criteria;
身高標準 standard of height;
生活標準 standard of living;
~降低生活標準 lower the standard of living;

~提高生活標準 raise the standard of living;
雙重標準 double standard;
~採取雙重標準 adopt a double standard; adopt dual criteria;
提高標準 improve standards; raise standards;
現行標準 current standards;
血糖標準 blood-sugar level;
驗收標準 acceptance criterion;
藝術標準 artistic criterion;
制定標準 establish a standard; lay down a criterion; set a standard;
最低標準 minimum standard;
最高標準 maximum standard;
最終標準 ultimate criterion;

岸標 shore beacon;
靶標 target;
測標 surveying road; measuring staff;
覘標 surveyor's beacon;
城標 city emblem; city symbol;
達標 attain a designated standard; reach a set standard; up to the standard;
導標 navigation mark;
地標 landmark;
奪標 capture prize; compete for the first prize;
風標 weathervane; weathercock;
浮標 buoy; dan; dobber; drogue; float road; floating beacon; floating mark; navigation mark; staff float;
光標 cursor;
航標 buoy; navigation mark;
錦標 prize; title; trophy;
開標 open bids; open sealed tenders;
路標 guidepost; road sign; route marking; route sign;
目標 mark; target;
商標 trademark;
書標 book label; label;
水標 watermark;
梭標 spear;
投標 make a tender; submit a bid; submit a tender;
溫標 thermometric scale;
霧標 fog buoy;
信標 beacon;
袖標 armband;
音標 phonetic symbol;
游標 vernier;
招標 invite tenders;
爭標 rival each other for a trophy;
指標 norm; quota; target;
治標 cope with the symptoms only; provide temporary solutions to the problems; take stopgap measures;
中標 win the bidding;
坐標 coordinate;

biao

【麃】 (1) cultivate fields; (2) valiant; vigorous;

biao

【鏢】 (1) dart; harpoon; javelin; (2) bodyguard; escort; guard;

［鏢局］ escort agent;
［鏢客］ armed escort;
［鏢槍］ javelin;

保鏢 bodyguard; escort; minder;
飛鏢 (1) dart; (2) dart-throwing;
走鏢 serve as a bodyguard on a journey;

biao

【臕】 fat;

［臕厚］ fat thickness;
［臕壯］ fat and strong;

biao

【飆】 gales; violent winds;

［飆車］ speed a car;
［飆忽］ gale;
［飆舉電至］ as fierce as a whirlwind;

狂飆 hurricane;

biao

【鑣】 (1) a bit for a horse; (2) ride on a horse; (3) dart; harpoon; javelin;

biao³

biao

【表】 (1) apparent; appearance; external; outside; superficial; surface; (2) announce; demonstrate; express; manifest; show; (3) example; model; (4) chart; form; list; table; (5) gauge; meter; (6) watch;

［表白］ bare one's heart; clarify; clear up; explain; express clearly; lay bare; vindicate;
表白心事 break one's mind to; open one's heart to;
自我表白 explain oneself;

[表冊] book of tables; statistical form;
[表層] surface;
表層結構 surface structure;
表層問題 superficial problem;
表層意義 surface meaning;
表層語言 adstratum;
[表達] convey; express; make known; present; voice;
表達翻譯法 expressive translation;
表達感情 give expression to one's sentiment;
表達規則 expression rules;
表達簡潔 concise in expression;
表達能力 ability of expression;
表達式 expression;
~絕對表達式 absolute expression;
~數組表達式 array expression;
~算術表達式 arithmetic expression;
表達障礙 presentation obstruction;
口頭表達 express verbally;
零表達 zero expression;
滿意地表達 express satisfactorily;
難以表達 beyond expression of words;
適當地表達 express properly;
無法表達 beyond expression;
有力地表達 express vigorously;
直率地表達 express frankly;
[表帶] watch strap; watchband;
[表弟] cousin; first cousin;
[表哥] cousin; first cousin;
[表格] form; table;
填寫表格 fill in a form; fill out a form; make out a form;
[表記] (1) mark; sign; (2) souvenir;
[表姊] cousin; first cousin;
[表決] decide by vote; vote;
表決機器 voting machine;
表決權 right to vote; vote;
~無表決權 have no right to vote;
~行使表決權 exercise the right to vote;
~有表決權 have the right to vote;
表決通過 be voted through;
表決制度 voting system;
唱名表決 vote by roll call;
重新表決 go back upon a vote;
付諸表決 be put to vote; put sth to the vote;
交付表決 put to the vote; take a vote;
進行表決 take a vote on;
舉手表決 decide it by a show of hands; take a vote by a show of hands; take a show of hands; vote by a show of hands; vote by raising hands;
口頭表決 take a voice vote;
起立表決 vote by rising; vote by sitting and standing; vote by standing;
突擊表決 snap vote;
[表裏] both sides－inside and outside;
表裏不一 act a double part; have two faces; think in one way and behave in another; think one way and act another;
~表裏不一的人 double dealer;
表裏如一 speak and act as one thinks; the same outside and inside; think and act in one and the same way; what one professes to be;
~表裏如一的人 fair dealer; plain dealer;
表裏受敵 encounter the enemy in front and behind;
表裏為奸 conspiracy with people working inside;
表裏相應 coordinated attack;
表裏一致 honest and sincere; think and act in one and the same way;
相為表裏 complementary to each other;
[表列] catalogue; list;
[表露] expose; express; make plain; reveal; show; voice;
表露感情 wear one's heart on one's sleeve;
[表妹] cousin; first cousin;
[表面] appearance; externally; face; on the surface; outwardly; superficial; surface;
表面變化 surface change;
表面粗糙 have a rough surface;
表面的 cosmetic; superficial;
表面光滑 have a smooth surface;
表面化 become apparent; come to the surface;
表面活性 surfactivity;
~表面活性劑 surfactant;
陽離子表面活性劑 cationic surfactant;
陰離子表面活性劑 anionic surfactant;
表面價值 face value;
表面判斷 judge by appearance;
表面平坦 have an even surface;
表面上 apparent; on surface; ostensible; outwardly; seeming; superficial;
表面是人，暗中是鬼 appear to be humans but be demons at heart;
表面彎曲 have a curved surface;

表面文章 assume presentable looks; emphasis on form; lip service; ostentation; specious writing; tokenism;
表面現象 superficial phenomenon;
從表面看 on the face of it; to the eye;
浮在表面 float on the surface; rise to the surface;
陸地表面 land surface;
祇重表面，不重實質 more sail than ballast;

[表明] indicate; make clear; make known; state clearly;
表明態度 make one's attitude clear;
~公開表明態度 stand up and be counted;
表明心跡 lay bare one's true feelings; show clearly one's mind;
表明意圖 disclose one's intention; show one's hand;

[表膜] outer pellicle;

[表盤] dial; dial plate;

[表皮] epidermis;
表皮發育不良 epidermodysplasia;
表皮發育不全 epidermodysplasia;
表皮傷 superficial wound;
表皮炎 epidermitis;
滲出性表皮炎 exudative epidermitis;
上表皮 epicuticle;

[表親] (1) cousin; (2) cousinship;

[表情] express one's feelings; expression; facial expression;
表情懊喪 in a state of depression;
表情悲哀 wear a sad expression;
表情達意 communicate views; convey one's ideas;
表情符號 emoticon;
表情功能 expressive function;
表情靦腆 have a sheepish look;
表情文獻 expressive text;
表情嚴肅 have a grave expression on one's face;
表情意義 emotive meaning;
表情愉快 have a happy expression;
冷漠的表情 aloof expression;
茫然的表情 vacant expression; vacuous expression;
面部表情 facial expression;
面帶…的表情 wear…expression;
~面帶困惑的表情 wear a puzzled look;
面無表情 expressionless; poker-faced;
~面無表情的 stone-faced; stony-faced;
木無表情 expressionless;
專注的表情 absorbed look;

[表示] express; indicate; manifest; representation; show;
表示感謝 express one's thanks; give expression to one's gratitude;
表示悔恨 profess regret;
表示敬意 show respect;
表示滿意 express satisfaction;
表示歉意 offer an expression of regret;
表示親熱 make a display of one's affection;
表示慶賀 express one's congratulations;
表示態度 define one's attitude;
表示同情 show sympathy;
表示同意 express one's agreement; indicate one's approval;
表示謝意 express one's gratitude; show one's appreciation;
表示願意 express one's willingness;
對…表示反對 declare oneself against; show one's objection to…;
對…表示同情 express sympathy with…; show sympathy toward;
對…表示慰問 extend one's sympathy to…;
對…表示遺憾 proffer regret at…;
對…表示異議 demur to…; make demur to…;
對…表示贊同 declare oneself for…;
公開表示 make a public demonstration of…;
基本表示 basic representation;
解析表示 analytic representation;
絕對值表示 absolute value representation;
明確地表示 conclusively show;

[表叔] uncle;

[表率] example; model; paragon;

[表態] declare oneself; declare where one stands; make known one's position towards an issue; state one's view on; take one's stand;
對…明確表態 take a clear-cut stand toward;
對…正式表態 express oneself officially on;
公開表態 make a public statement of one's attitude; openly make one's attitude known to all;
明確表態 nail one's colours to the mast;

[表顯] display; express;

[表現] acquit oneself; comport; display; express; manifest; show; show off;
表現不錯 give a good account of oneself;
表現不好 give a bad account of oneself; give a poor account of oneself; perform poorly;
表現差勁 give a poor account of oneself; have a stinker;
表現出… display; give a display of; manifest; show;
~ 表現出決心 manifest one's resolution;
~ 表現出實力 give a display of strength;
表現出色 give a good account of oneself;
的表現 the manifestation of…;
~ 民族精神的表現 the manifestation of national spirit;
表現得不光彩 behave disgracefully;
表現得不體面 make a disgraceful performance;
表現得有禮貌 behave decorously;
表現得正大光明 play fair and square;
表現很差 behave awfully; disappointing performance; put up a poor show;
表現很好 acquit oneself well; perform well;
~ 面試表現很好 acquit oneself well at the interview;
表現技巧 technique of expression;
表現力 power of expression;
表現能力 expressive power;
表現派 expressionism; impressionist school of painting;
表現手法 technique of expression;
表現勇敢 behave gallantly; behave with courage;
表現鎮靜 behave with composure;
表現主義 expressionism;
彩色表現 colour rendition;
外部表現 outer manifestation;

[表兄] cousin; elder male cousin; first cousin;
表兄弟 cousins on the maternal side;

[表演] act; demonstrate; perform; play;
表演從容 perform in a relaxed manner;
表演節目 give a performance; put on a show;
表演賽 exhibition match;
表演失手 stumble;
表演台 podium;
表演藝術 performing arts;
表演者 entertainer;
登台表演 perform on the stage;
電影表演 film acting;
即興表演 improvise;
精彩表演 cracking show; superb performance;
舉行…表演 put up…show;
~ 舉行時裝表演 put up a fashion show;
絕佳的表演 stonking performance;
平衡表演 balancing act;
拋擲表演 throwing act;
雜技表演 acrobatic performance;

[表揚] commend; praise; praise in public;
該表揚的就表揚 give credit where credit is due;
給予表揚 award praise;
受到表揚 be commended; be praised; receive praise;
值得表揚 deserve praise;

[表意] ideographic;
表意被動 notional passive;
表意符號 ideogram;
表意文字 ideogram;

[表彰] cite; commend; honour;

[表徵] superficial characteristics; surface features;

[表字] alias; courtesy name;

百分表 dial gauge; dial indicator;
報表 report form;
報關表 customs declaration; declaration form;
乘法表 multiplication table;
船期表 sailing schedule;
詞彙表 glossary; word list; vocabulary;
代表 (1) delegate; deputy; representative; (2) represent; stand for; (3) in the name of; on behalf of; on one's behalf;
調查表 list for investigation;
對數表 logarithmic table;
對照表 table of comparisons;
發表 announce; deliver; express; issue; project; publish; report; voice;
乾濕表 psychrometer;
工資表 pay sheet; payroll;
姑表 cousinship;
寒暑表 thermometer;
行情表 quotation list;
換算表 conversion table;
價目表 price list;
檢字表 character index;
進度表 progress chart;
九九表 multiplication table;
勘誤表 corrigenda; errata;
老表 (1) one's cousin; (2) one's buddies; one's

old pals;
履歷表 curriculum vitae;
量表 scale;
略語表 abbreviations;
目力表 visual chart;
年表 chronological table; chronology;
配料表 burden sheet;
其表 appearance;
汽表 steam gauge;
千分表 dial gauge; dial indicator;
阡表 grave stone; tomb tablet;
人表 person of exemplary conduct;
日程表 schedule;
生字表 list of new words;
師表 paragon worthy of emulation; person of exemplary virtue;
時間表 schedule; timetable;
收支表 balance sheet;
四表 all directions; beyond the limits of the visible world;
填表 fill in a form;
圖表 chart; diagram; figure; graph; pictogram; table;
外表 exterior; outward appearance; surface;
演員表 cast;
一覽表 schedule; table;
一張表 a form; a list;
姨表 cousinship; maternal cousins;
儀表 (1) appearance; bearing; deportment; (2) apparatus; instrument; instrumentation; meter;
意表 sth that one does not expect;
語彙表 vocabulary;
月表 monthly chronology;
運價表 tariff;
值日表 duty roster;
中表 cousinship;
周期表 periodic table;
字母表 alphabet;

biao

【婊】 prostitute; whore;

［婊子］ harlot; prostitute; scrubber; strumpet; whore;

婊子進佛堂，假裝正經人 like a prostitute going into a Buddhist temple – pretend to be a decent person;

婊子立牌坊一假正經 like a prostitute erecting a monument to her chastity – false decency;

婊子送客一虛情假意 like a prostitute seeing her customer to the door – a false display of affection;

婊子養的 you bastard; you son of a bitch;

又想當婊子，又想立牌坊 lead the life of a prostitute and expect a monument to one's chastity; lead the life of a prostitute and want a monument put up to one's chastity; wish to have a good reputation while indulging in evil practice;

biao

【裱】 (1) mount a painting; (2) scarf;

［裱褙］ mount a painting;

［裱店］ shop specialized in mounting paintings and calligraphy;

［裱工］ (1) work of mounting; (2) one who mounts artistic works; (3) charges for mounting;

［裱糊］ paste paper on;

裱糊工 paper hanger;

裱糊匠 mounting craftsman; paper hanger;

［裱畫舖］ shop for mounting Chinese paintings;

裝裱 mount a painting;

biao

【錶】 watch;

［錶帶］ band of a wristwatch; watchband; watch strap;

［錶鏈］ watch chain;

［錶盤］ face of a watch;

爆光錶 exposure meter;
撥錶 set the watch;
戴錶 wear a watch;
地溫錶 ground thermometer;
電錶 electric meter;
電流錶 galvanometer;
電壓錶 voltmeter;
防水錶 waterproof watch;
風速錶 anemometer;
乾濕錶 psychrometer;
高度錶 altimeter;
掛錶 fob watch; pocket watch;
毫安錶 milliammeter;
懷錶 fob watch; pocket watch;
計量錶 meter;
馬錶 stopwatch;
馬蹄錶 alarm clock; hoof-shaped desk clock;
秒錶 chronograph; stopwatch;

男錶 men's watch;
女錶 women's watch;
歐姆錶 ohmmeter;
跑錶 stopwatch;
氣壓錶 barometer;
晴雨錶 barometer; weatherglass;
日射錶 actinometer;
濕度錶 humidometer; hygrometer;
手錶 watch; wristwatch;
水錶 water gauge; water meter;
速度錶 speedometer;
體溫錶 thermometer;
停錶 stopwatch;
萬用錶 multi-meter;
溫度錶 (1) thermometer; (2) thermograph;
夜光錶 luminous watch;
液壓錶 hydraulic pressure gauge;
一塊錶 a watch;
儀錶 meter;
油位錶 oil gauge;
油壓錶 oil pressure gauge;
指重錶 weight indicator;
鐘錶 clocks and watches; timepiece;

biao⁴
biao

【鰾】 (1) air bladder; maw of a fish; swimming bladder; (2) fish glue;
［鰾膠］ fish glue;
魚鰾 (of fish) air bladder;

bie¹
bie

【憋】 (1) hold back; keep down; suppress the inner feelings with efforts; (2) feel oppressed; suffocate;
［憋得慌］ feel oppressed; intolerably depressing;
［憋火兒］ starter;
［憋悶］ depressed; melancholy;
［憋尿］ hold up one's urine;
［憋扭］ (1) of contrary opinion; (2) clumsy;
［憋氣］ (1) suffer breathing obstruction; (2) choke with resentment;
覺得憋氣 feel suffocated;
［憋屈］ aggrieved; nurse a grievance;
［憋暈了］ faint due to suffocation;
［憋住］ fight back; hold back; keep down;
憋住氣 (1) hold one's breath; (2) smoulder with resentment;
憋住怒氣 hold back one's anger; keep down one's anger;
憋住眼淚 fight back tears;

bie

【鱉】 freshwater turtle; mudturtle;
［鱉蛋］ bastard; turtle's egg;
［鱉甲］ turtle shells;
［鱉縮頭］ behave cowardly; hide oneself from danger;
跛鱉 lame turtle;
地鱉 ground beetle;
馬鱉 leech;
田鱉 fish killer; giant water bug;
土鱉 ground beetle;

bie²
bie

【別】 (1) leave; part; (2) another; other; (3) distinction; (4) difference; distinction; (5) differentiate; distinguish; (6) fasten with a pin or a clip; (7) stick in; (8) do not;
［別本］ replica; separate copy;
［別吵］ hold your row;
［別稱］ alternatively known as; alternative name; another name; known also by the name of; otherwise known as;
［別處］ another place; elsewhere; somewhere else;
［別的］ different; other;
別的地方 elsewhere;
［別動］ hold it;
［別幹］ do not do it;
［別管］ (1) however; no matter; whatever; (2) leave sb alone; never mind;
別管我 leave me alone;
別管閒事 butt out; mind your own business; mind your own concerns; put not your hand between the bark and the tree; send about your business;
［別館］ villa;
［別號］ alias; moniker;
［別慌］ do not be afraid;
［別解］ new interpretation;
［別久情疏］ far from eye, far from heart; long absent, soon forgotten;
［別具］ have a distinctive…; have a special…;
別具風味 have a special flavour;
別具慧心 have a special understanding;

B

別具慧眼 have a special insightful understanding;
別具匠心 have originality; show ingenuity;
別具私心 have an axe to grind;
別具一格 a class by itself; have a distinctive style; have a style of one's own; have a unique style; original in style;
別具隻眼 have an original view;

[別開生面] break a new path; break fresh ground; open up a new facet; out of the common road; start something new; with freshness and novelty;
嚐試別開生面 try to open up a fresh outlook;

[別看] despite; in spite of;

[別來] (1) since parting; (2) do not;
別來無恙 hope that you are well;

[別…了] do not; don't;
別煩了 don't you start;
別胡謅了 stop talking nonsense;
別送了 don't bother to see us off;
別忘了 do not forget;
~請別忘了 after all;

[別離] leave; parting; separation; take leave of;

[別論] another matter;
另當別論 another cup of tea; another pair of shoes; different cup of tea; horse of another colour;
又當別論 should be regarded as a different matter;
又作別論 an exception; another thing;

[別忙] do not hurry; take it easy; take your time;

[別名] alias; another name; second name;
以…為別名 under the name of;

[別人] (1) another person; sb else; (2) other people; others;
不關心別人 have no regard for others;

[別室] (1) concubine; (2) another room;

[別墅] villa;
海濱別墅 villa by the seaside;
豪華別墅 expensive villa;
私人別墅 private villa;
鄉間別墅 country cottage;
一棟別墅 a villa;

[別樹一幟] found a new school of thought; have a style of one's own; hoist separately a different banner; rise another standard to set up a new banner; start a new school;

[別耍滑] don't play tricks;

[別說] let alone;
別說了 don't tell me;

[別提] it is not necessary to say;

[別無] have no…but;
別無長物 have no valuable personal possessions; have nothing other than one's own self; not to have a penny to bless oneself with; possess nothing but;
別無出路 have no other way out;
別無所有 have no other possessions;
別無他法 have no other alternative; have no other way out; have no resource but;
別無他人 nobody else;
別無他用 there is no other use for it;
別無選擇 have no choice left;

[別緒] sorrow of parting;

[別樣] of a different kind;

[別有] have a special;
別有洞天 a world all its own; hidden but beautiful spot;
別有風味 have a distinctive flavour; have a special flavour; have a unique favour;
別有高見 have a brighter idea;
別有企圖 look one way and row another;
別有所本 be based on another source;
別有所圖 have an axe to grind; have other aims;
別有所指 imply another thing;
別有天地 like a different world; place of unique beauty; scenery of exceptional charm;
別有用心 have a hidden purpose; have an axe to grind; have an ulterior motive; have ulterior motives;

[別針] (1) brooch; (2) pin; safety pin; tack;
安全別針 safety pin;
一根別針 a pin;
裝飾別針 stickpin;

[別緻] new and unusual; unconventional; unique;

[別傳] supplementary biography;

[別字] (1) mispronounced character; wrongly written character; (2) alias;
別字連篇 plenty of characters wrongly

written;
讀別字 mispronounce a character;
寫別字 write a character wrongly;

拜別 bid farewell to; say farewell;
幫別 (1) faction; group; (2) type;
辨別 differentiate; discriminate; distinguish;
差別 difference; disparity; distinction;
辭別 bid farewell; say goodbye to;
道別 say goodbye;
分別 (1) leave each other; part; separate; (2) discriminate; differentiate; distinguish; (3) differently; (4) respectively; separately;
告別 (1) leave; part with; (2) bid farewell to; say goodbye to; (3) pay one's last respects to the deceased;
各別 (1) out of the ordinary; peculiar; (2) eccentric; odd; (3) different; distinct;
個別 (1) individual; separate; specific; (2) exceptional; one or two; very few;
話別 say a few parting words; say goodbye to each other;
級別 grade; rank; scale;
餞別 give a farewell dinner;
鑒別 differentiate; discriminate; distinguish;
界別 constituency;
訣別 bid farewell;
闊別 long parted; long separated; separated for a long time;
類別 category; classification;
離別 leave; part; separate;
臨別 at parting; just before parting;
留別 give a souvenir at parting;
派別 clique; faction; group; school;
判別 differentiate; distinguish;
區別 difference; differentiate; discriminate; distinguish;
識別 distinguish; spot; tell the difference;
殊別 different;
死別 be parted by death; part never to see each other again;
送別 (1) see sb off; wish sb bon voyage; (2) give sb a send-off party;
特別 especially; particular; particularly; special; specially; unusual;
吻別 kiss sb good-bye;
握別 shake hands and part;
惜別 reluctant to part; unwilling to part;
細別 distinguish carefully;
小別 brief separation; part for a short while;
性別 sex; sexual distinction;
敍別 have a farewell talk at parting;
揖別 bid adieu;
永別 be parted by death; die; part for good; part forever; part never to meet again;
遠別 (1) separate for a journey to a distant land; (2) part for a long time;
暫別 part for a short time; short separation;
贈別 wish sb well in parting;
甄別 (1) discriminate; examine and distinguish; (2) re-examine a case;
職別 level of position; official rank;
種別 classification;
作別 bid farewell; say goodbye; take one's leave;

bie

【蹩】 limp; sprain;

［蹩腳］ (1) lame; (2) inferior; poor; shoddy; unskilled; (3) dejected; uncomfortable;
蹩腳的 cockamamie;
蹩腳貨 dross; inferior goods; lemon; poor stuff; schlock; shoddy work;
蹩腳詩 doggerel;
蹩腳文人 hack;

bie³
bie

【癟】 flat; not full; sunken;

［癟螺痧］ cholera;

［癟子］ blow; setback;

踩癟 trample down;
乾癟 be dried and shrivelled;

bie⁴
bie

【彆】 awkward;

［彆扭］ (1) awkward; difficult; refractory; uncomfortable; (2) awkward situation;
鬧彆扭 at odds with; cut up rusty; difficult with; nasty to; sulky with; take the pet; turn rusty;

［彆氣］ silently resentful;

bin¹
bin

【邠】 ancient state in China in present-day Shaanxi Province;

［邠如］ culturally blooming; culturally flourishing;

bin

【攽】 (1) divide; (2) reduce;

bin

【彬】 (1) intelligent, refined and gentle; (2) a surname;

［彬彬］ handsome and solid; refined; urbane;
彬彬君子 refined gentleman;
彬彬有禮 refined and courteous; urbane; with a good grace;
~彬彬有禮的 courtly;
文質彬彬 elegant and refined in manner; gentle and refined in manner; quiet and scholarly; smooth in manner; urbane; well-mannered and soft-spoken; with elegant manners;

璘彬 lustre of jade in riotous profusion;

bin

【斌】 equally fine in both internal and external accomplishments;

bin

【賓】 (1) guest; visitor; (2) treat as a guest; (3) follow instructions; obey; submit; (4) a surname;

［賓待］ receive sb as a guest;

［賓服］ obey;

［賓格］ accusative; accusative case;
賓格同位語 objective appositive;
描寫性賓格 objective description;

［賓館］ guest house; hotel;
賓館餐廳 hotel restaurant;
賓館大堂 hotel lobby;
賓館服務台 hotel reception;
賓館健身房 hotel gym;
賓館經理 hotelier;
賓館酒吧 hotel bar;
賓館客房 hotel room;
賓館客人 hotel guest;
賓館老闆 hotelier;
賓館住宿 hotel accommodation;
登記入住賓館 book into a hotel; check into a hotel;
豪華賓館 luxury hotel;
經營賓館 manage a hotel; run a hotel;
兩星級賓館 two-star hotel;
三星級賓館 three-star hotel;
退房離開賓館 check out of a hotel;
住賓館 stay at a hotel; stay in a hotel;

［賓果］ bingo;

［賓客］ guest; visitor; visitors and guests;
賓客哄門 the house is full of guests;
賓客名單 gust list;
賓客盈門 the house is full of guests;
廣延賓客 keep open house;

［賓禮］ (1) courtesy on the part of a guest; (2) international courtesy;

［賓旅］ strangers and travellers;

［賓朋］ guests and friends;
賓朋滿座 the house is full of guests;

［賓天］ death of an emperor;

［賓鐵］ wrought iron;

［賓語］ object;
賓語補語 object complement;
賓語從句 object clause;
賓語格 objective case;
賓語生格 objective genitive;
賓語謂語 objective predicative;
賓語限制 object constraint; objective case;
保留賓語 retained object;
地點賓語 locative object;
複合賓語 complex object;
工具賓語 instrumental object;
換喻賓語 metonymic object;
間接賓語 indirect object;
~結果間接賓語 effected indirect object;
結果賓語 object of result;
介詞賓語 prepositional object;
同源賓語 cognate object;
形式賓語 formal object;
直接賓語 direct object;
~雙直接賓語 two direct object;
狀語性賓語 adverbial object;

［賓主］ guests and the host;
賓主盡歡 both the guests and the hosts are thoroughly enjoying themselves;
賓主就座 host and guests take their seats;
反賓為主 reverse the positions of host and guest;
強賓不壓主 a strong guest does not oppress his host; however strong the guest might be, he should not overbear his host;

酬賓 give a discount; sell at a favourable price;
動賓 verb and object;
貴賓 distinguished guest; guest of honour;
國賓 state guest;
佳賓 distinguished guest; welcome guest;
嘉賓 guest of honour; honoured guest; welcome guest;
來賓 guest; visitor;
上賓 distinguished guest; guest of honour;
外賓 foreign guest; foreign visitor;

餉賓 entertain guests with food;
迎賓 receive guests;
之賓 guest;
知賓 receptionist;
主賓 guest of honour;

bin
【儐】 a pronunciation of 儐;

bin
【濱】 (1) border on; brink; water's edge; (2) close by; near at hand; (3) low, level sea coast;
［濱岸］ alongside the sea; coast;
［濱海］ border of the sea;
濱海地區 coast; coastal region;
濱海路 cornice;
［濱近］ close to; near to;
［濱死］ dying; have one foot in the grave; near to death;
［濱危］ close to death; dying; have a close encounter with great danger;
［濱行］ on the point of going;
海濱 seashore;
河濱 streamside;
湖濱 beside the lake; lakeside; shore of a lake;
之濱 territory;
洋涇濱 pidgin;

bin
【豳】 (1) a state in the Zhou Dynasty; (2) a mountain in Shaanxi;

bin
【檳】 areca; areca nut; betel; betel nut;
［檳榔］ areca nut; betel nut;
檳榔糕 sweets made of betel nut and sugar;
［檳子］ a kind of fruit resembling an apple;

bin
【瀕】 (1) border on; close to; near; (2) on the brink of; on the point of; water's edge;
［瀕海］ along the coast; close to the sea;
［瀕河］ bank of the river; riverside;
［瀕臨］ (1) border on; close to; near; (2) on the brink of; on the point of; on the verge of;
瀕臨垂危 in a dying condition;
瀕臨大海 border on the sea;
瀕臨死亡 at death's door;
［瀕死］ near death; on the brink of death;
［瀕危］ (1) be endangered; in imminent danger; (2) critically ill; near death; terminally ill;
［瀕行］ about to leave; upon leaving;
［瀕於］ on the brink of; on the point of; on the verge of;
瀕於崩潰 verge on collapse;
瀕於餓斃 on the verge of starvation;
瀕於饑餓 on the brink of starvation;
瀕於絕境 face an impasse;
瀕於滅亡 near extinction;
瀕於破產 on the brink of bankruptcy; stand on the verge of bankruptcy; verge upon bankruptcy;
瀕於死亡 at death's door; at one's last gasp; have one foot in the grave; nearing one's doom; on one's last legs; on the brink of death; on the verge of death; totter on the brink of the grace;
瀕於災難 on the verge of disaster;
瀕於戰爭 on the brink of war;

bin
【繽】 (1) abundant; plentiful; thriving; (2) confused; disorderly;
［繽繽］ a great many; numerous;
［繽繙］ fluttering;
［繽紛］ (1) abundant; flourishing; thriving; (2) chaotic; disorderly; (3) flake beautifully;
［繽亂］ chaotic; confused; disorderly;

bin⁴

bin
【儐】 (1) entertain guests; (2) arrange; set in order; (3) guide;
［儐相］ (1) best man of a bridegroom; (2) bridesmaid;
男儐相 best man; groomsman;
女儐相 bridesmaid;
~首席女儐相 maid of honour;
［儐者］ receptionist;
男儐 best man;
女儐 bridesmaid;

bin
【擯】 (1) discard; expel; get rid of; oust; reject; (2) same as 儐;
［擯斥］ dismiss; expel; reject; repudiate;
擯斥異己 dismiss those who hold different

opinions; reject dissidents;
[擯除] discard; dispense with; get rid of;
[擯落] suffer rejection and downfall;
[擯棄] abandon; desert; cast away; discard; set aside;
擯棄不用 dismiss sb and refrain from giving him/her an appointment; throw on the scrapheap;

排擯 push aside and abandon;

bin
【殯】 carry to the grave; embalm; funeral;
[殯車] hearse;
[殯殮] funeral;
[殯喪] burial; funeral;
[殯儀] undertaking;
殯儀館 funeral parlour;
殯儀業 undertaking;
殯儀員 undertaker;
[殯葬] hold a funeral procession and bury the dead; funeral and interment;
殯葬工 undertaker;

出殯 hold a funeral procession;
送殯 attend a funeral; take part in a funeral procession;

bin
【臏】 kneecap;
[臏骨] kneecap;

bin
【鬢】 hair on the temples;
[鬢斑] hair turning gray at the temples;
[鬢邊] temples;
[鬢髮] earlock; hair on the temples;
鬢髮灰白 graying at the temples;
[鬢角] (1) temples; (2) sideburns;
[鬢腳] sideburns;
[鬢亂釵橫] hair in disorder and hairpins out of place; unkempt appearance after sleep and before makeup;
[鬢毛] hair on the temples;
[鬢霜] temples covered with white hair;

斑鬢 gray hair at the temples;
兩鬢 temples;
霜鬢 hoary hair on the temples;
玉鬢 white hair;
雲鬢 lady's thick and beautiful hair;

bin
【髕】 kneecap; kneepan;
[髕腳] ancient punishment of cutting off the kneecap;

bing¹
bing
【冰】 (1) ice; icicle; (2) ice; put on the ice; (3) feel cold; frost;
[冰雹] hail; hail stone;
在下冰雹 it is hailing;
[冰層] ice layer;
[冰場] ice stadium; skating rink;
[冰川] glacier;
冰川期 glacial epoch; ice age;
冰川甌穴 glacier mill;
冰川學 glaciology;
崩落冰川 debris glacier;
變形冰川 amoeboid glacier;
吹雪冰川 catchment glacier; drift glacier;
大陸冰川 continental glacier;
複成冰川 composite glacier;
高山冰川 alpine glacier; mountain glacier;
高原冰川 plateau glacier;
谷冰川 valley glacier;
活冰川 active glacier;
極地冰川 polar glacier;
山麓冰川 piedmont glacier;
溫帶冰川 temperate glacier;
小冰川 glacieret;
[冰袋] cool box; ice bag; ice pack;
[冰蛋] frozen egg;
[冰刀] blades of ice skates;
[冰道] ice tunnel;
[冰點] freezing point; ice point;
達到冰點 reach the freezing point;
[冰雕] ice engraving;
[冰凍] freeze; frost; frozen;
冰凍三尺，非一日之寒 the tree falls not at the first stroke;
[冰封] ice-bound;
[冰蓋] ice sheet;
[冰棍兒] frozen sucker; ice lolly; ice sucker; popsicle;
小豆冰棍兒 red-bean ice lolly;
鴛鴦冰棍兒 paired ice lolly;
[冰果店] cold drink shop;
[冰河] glacier;
流動冰河 acting glacier;
[冰盒] cool box;

[冰積] lateral moraine;

[冰晶] ice crystal;
冰晶石 cryolite;

[冰塊] ice block; ice cube; lump of ice;
小方冰塊 ice cube;

[冰冷] ice-cold;
其冷如冰 cold as charity; cold as ice;

[冰帽] ice cap;

[冰囊] ice bag;

[冰瓶] ice bucket;

[冰期] glacial epoch; glacial period; Ice Age;
第四紀冰期 Quaternary Ice Age;
間冰期 interglacial period;
小冰期 Little Ice Age;

[冰淇淋] ice cream;
冰淇淋蛋卷筒 ice cream cone;
冰淇淋店 ice cream parlour;
冰淇淋蘇打水 ice-cream soda;
冰淇淋磚 brick ice cream;
菠蘿冰淇淋 pineapple ice cream;
草莓冰淇淋 strawberry ice cream;
吃冰淇淋 like ice cream;
果仁冰淇淋 macaroon ice cream;
加酒冰淇淋 punch ice cream;
槭糖冰淇淋 maple ice cream;
巧克力冰淇淋 chocolate ice cream;
水果冰淇淋 fruit ice cream;
香草冰淇淋 vanilla ice cream;
杏子冰淇淋 apricot ice cream;
一碟冰淇淋 a dish of ice cream;
一份冰淇淋 take an ice cream;

[冰球] ice hockey; puck;

[冰人] matchmaker;

[冰山] iceberg;
衝上冰山 strike an iceberg;
島狀冰山 ice island iceberg;
風化冰山 weathered iceberg;
峰形冰山 pinnacle iceberg;
混成冰山 unconformity iceberg;
平頂冰山 table iceberg;
錐形冰山 pyramidal iceberg;

[冰上] ice;
冰上芭蕾 ice ballet;
冰上表演 ice show;
冰上曲棍球 bandy;
冰上舞蹈 ice dancing;
冰上運動 ice sports;

[冰釋] be dispelled; disappear without a trace; vanish;
冰釋前嫌 agree to forget the disagreements;
冰釋誤會 remove any misunderstanding;
煥然冰釋 all misunderstandings have now been dissipated;

[冰霜] ice and frost;
冷若冰霜 as chilly as an icicle; as cold as ice; frosty in manner; have an icy manner; severity in countenance; stern manner; treat sb coldly;
凜若冰霜 cold as ice and dew; have a forbidding manner; look severe;

[冰水] ice water; icy water;
冰水沉積 outwash;
一杯冰水 a glass of ice water;

[冰塔] serac;

[冰炭] as incompatible as ice and hot coals;
冰炭不相容 as incompatible as ice and hot coals; at loggerheads with each other;
勢同冰炭 their relations are like ice and hot charcoal — incompatible;

[冰糖] crystal sugar; rock candy;
冰糖煮黃蓮—同甘共苦 boiling crystal sugar together with the bitter Chinese gold thread — share both the bitter and the sweet;
一塊冰糖 a piece of candy;

[冰桶] ice bucket;

[冰舞] dancing on skates;

[冰箱] freezer; fridge; frig; icebox; refrigerator;
冰箱除臭劑 refrigerator deodourize;
電冰箱 electric refrigerator; freezer; fridge; icebox; refrigerator;
~半自動除霜電冰箱 semi-automatic defrosting refrigerator;
~人工除霜電冰箱 manual defrosting refrigerator;
~雙室冰箱 two-compartment type refrigerator;
~自動除霜電冰箱 automatic defrosting refrigerator;
小冰箱 minibar;

[冰消] deglaciate;
冰消瓦解 be dispelled; break down; collapse; disintegrate; dissolve like ice; melt away; melt like ice and break like tiles; vanish from the scene;
冰消霧散 dissolve like mist;
私怨冰消 a private malice is melted like ice;

[冰鞋] skating boots;

一雙冰鞋 a pair of ice skates;
[冰心] (1) chaste; virtuous; (2) not enthusiastic; somewhat indifferent;
一片冰心 a pure state of mind;
[冰雪] ice and snow;
冰雪聰明 brilliant; very bright; very clever;
[冰原] ice field;
[冰鎮] iced;
冰鎮奶茶 iced tea with milk;
冰鎮西瓜 iced watermelon;
[冰柱] icicle;
[冰磚] ice block; frozen cream;
[冰錐] icicle;
碎冰錐 ice pick;
[冰桌] glacier table;

岸冰 ice that has formed along the banks of a river or lake;
棒冰 frozen sucker; icecream stick; icelolly; icesucker; popsicle;
抱冰 train oneself to endure hardships;
刨冰 water ice;
餅冰 pancake ice;
薄冰 thin ice;
凍冰 freeze;
浮冰 floating ice;
乾冰 dry ice;
旱冰 roller skate;
黑冰 black ice;
厚厚的一塊冰 a slab of ice;
湖冰 lake ice;
滑冰 skate;
積冰 pack ice;
加冰 on the rocks;
結冰 freeze; ice over; ice up;
冷冰冰 (1) cold; frosty; (2) ice cold;
溜冰 (1) skate; slide on the ice; (2) ice-skate; ice-skating; roller-skating;
盤冰 ice pan;
人造冰 artificial ice;
碎冰 brash ice;
一層冰 a layer of ice; a sheet of ice;
一大塊冰 a block of ice; a lump of ice;
一塊冰 a block of ice; a piece of ice;
飲冰 cool oneself down by gulping ice water;

bing

【并】 Bingzhou, one of the ancient Chinese administrative divisions, consisting of parts of today's Hebei, Shaanxi;

[并州快剪] scissors made in Bingzhou – famous for having sharp blades;

bing

【兵】 (1) arms; weapons; (2) fighter; soldier; (3) army; troop; (4) pawn;
[兵敗如山倒] a beaten army is like a collapsing mountain; a rout is like a landslide; an army in flight is like a landslide;
[兵變] mutiny; troops in mutiny;
[兵柄] military command; military leadership; military power;
[兵不血刃] win victory without firing a shot; win victory without striking a blow;
[兵不厭詐] all is fair in war; deceit is not to be despised in war; nothing is too deceitful in the conduct of war; there can never be too much deception in military operations;
[兵船] man-of-war; war vessel; warship;
[兵隊] troop;
[兵法] military strategy and tactics; the art of war; warcraft;
兵法巧妙 the military tactics are skilful;
精於兵法 be accomplished in the art of war;
研究兵法 study military strategies and tactics;
[兵房] barrack;
[兵分兩路] the army branches into two columns;
[兵符] commander's seal;
[兵戈] (1) arms; weapons; (2) war; warfare;
[兵革] military weapon;
[兵工] war industry;
兵工廠 armory; arsenal;
兵工企業 arsenal; munitions factory;
[兵貴在精] it is quality that counts in an army;
[兵火] war; warfare;
[兵禍] ravages of soldiery;
兵禍連年 years of fighting;
兵連禍結 continuous war ravages; successive distresses caused by continual wars;
兵燹禍連 continuous wars and turmoil;
[兵機] military plans; military strategy; military tactics;
[兵家] (1) military strategist in ancient China;

(2) military commander; soldier;
兵家必爭之地 a place contested by all; strategic place;
兵家常事 a common occurrence with the soldier; a commonplace in military operations; ordinary things to a general;

[兵艦] warship;

[兵將] soldiers and the general;
兵不由將 disobedient soldiers; troops that do not obey orders;
兵來將擋，水來土掩 give tit for tat; measure for measure; take measures as the situation calls for; to resist invading troops, rely on generals; to stop floodwaters, use soil;
兵勇將智 the fighters displaying valour and the commanders resourcefulness;
強兵猛將 strong men and fierce chieftains; strong soldiers and able leaders;
強將手下無弱兵 give a strong and able leadership, the staff can be very efficient in their work; like master like men; the valiant general has under his command no weak soldiers; there are no inferior soldiers under a superior general — a good leader can bring about a good team; there are no poor soldiers under a good general — a capable commander leads an army of good soldiers; under a strong general, there could be no weak soldiers;
損兵折將 lose one's generals and soldiers; suffer heavy casualties; the army is defeated, the generals have been slain;
蝦兵蟹將 hopeless soldiers; ineffective troops; shrimp soldiers and crab generals — numerous underlings;

[兵力] armed forces; military strength; troops;
兵力強大 the army is in great strength;
調遣兵力 move forces;
集結兵力 gather forces;
集中兵力 concentrate forces;
加強兵力 increase military strength;
轉移兵力 transfer troops;

[兵糧] army and supplies;
兵盡糧絕 one's army is decimated and the food supplies depleted;
兵精糧足 have a large army of veterans and ample supplies; the soldiers are excellent and supplies ample;

[兵亂] disaster caused by war;

[兵馬] military forces;
兵馬未到，糧草先行 an army, like a serpent, goes on its belly; an army marches on its stomach;

[兵器] armament; arms; weaponry;
輔助兵器 secondary armament;
使用兵器 use a weapon;
攜帶兵器 carry arms;

[兵權] military leadership; military power;
運用兵權 exercise the military power;
掌兵權 command the armed forces; wield military power;
~掌握兵權 assume the power of the sword; have military leadership;
爭奪兵權 struggle for military power;

[兵戎] (1) arms; weapons; (2) warfare;
兵戎相見 cross swords with; face each other on the battleground; meet in battle; open hostilities; resort to arms;

[兵士] foot soldier; soldier;

[兵書] book on the art of war;

[兵團] large military unit; legion;
兵團農場 army farm;
一個兵團 an army corps;

[兵凶戰危] in war everybody is a loser;

[兵學] military science;

[兵役] military service;
服兵役 perform military service; serve in the army;
免服兵役 be exempt from military service;
逃避兵役 escape the military service;

[兵營] barracks; military camp;
一座兵營 an army barracks;

[兵員] soldier; troop;
兵員足額 at full strength;
招募兵員 recruit for an army;

[兵站] army service station; military depot;

[兵制] military system;

[兵種] arm of the services;
技術兵種 technical arm;

鏖兵 engage in fierce battle; engage in hard fighting; fight a bloody battle; fight hard;
罷兵 suspend hostilities;
敗兵 defeated army; defeated troops;
搬兵 ask for help; call in reinforcements;
標兵 (1) parade guards; (2) example; model; pacemaker; pacesetter;
步兵 (1) infantry; (2) foot soldier;

裁兵 disarmament;
殘兵 defeated soldiers; remnant troops;
撤兵 withdraw troops;
陳兵 deploy troops;
稱兵 start war;
出兵 dispatch troops; send out troops;
傳令兵 dispatcher; transmitter;
大兵 common soldier; soldier;
當兵 join the army; serve in the army;
刀兵 (1) arms; weapons; (2) fighting; war;
敵兵 enemy soldiers; hostile troops;
動兵 send out troops to fight;
防化兵 antichemical warfare crops;
防空兵 air defence forces;
分兵 divide forces;
伏兵 troops in ambush;
工兵 engineer troops;
工程兵 engineer troops;
官兵 government troops; officers and soldiers;
航空兵 air arm; airman;
號兵 bugler;
護兵 bodyguard;
戟兵 halberdier;
甲兵 (1) armour and weaponry; military equipment; (2) soldier in armour;
尖兵 (1) point; (2) path-breaker; pioneer; point man; vanguard;
交兵 at war; wage war;
驕兵 proud troops;
進兵 order troops to march forward;
精兵 crack troops; picked troops;
救兵 reinforcements; relief troops;
狙擊兵 sniper;
舉兵 raise an army to fight;
空降兵 air-borne force; parachute landing force;
潰兵 routed troops;
老兵 old soldier; veteran;
雷達兵 radar operator;
練兵 train troops;
列兵 private soldier;
領兵 (1) lead troops; (2) military officer;
亂兵 (1) mutinous soldiers; (2) totally undisciplined troops;
輪機兵 engineer;
民兵 (1) people's militia; (2) militiaman;
募兵 recruit soldiers;
弭兵 stop the war;
派兵 dispatch troops; send troops;
炮兵 artillery; artilleryman;
礮兵 (1) artilleryman; gunner; (2) artillery;
奇兵 ambush; attack by surprise; surprise attack; surprise raiders;
騎兵 cavalry; cavalryman;
起兵 dispatch troops; rise in arms; start a military action;
親兵 bodyguard;
寢兵 stop fighting; stop wars;
勤務兵 orderly;
冗兵 superfluous troops;
傘兵 paratrooper;
散兵 (1) skirmisher; (2) straggler;
擅兵 maintain an army without authorization;
傷兵 wounded soldier;
哨兵 guard; sentry;
神兵 divine troops;
士兵 rank-and-file soldiers; soldiers;
收兵 call off a battle; withdraw or recall troops;
水兵 bluejacket; sailor; seaman;
坦克兵 tank forces;
逃兵 (1) army deserter; (2) deserter;
特種兵 special troops;
天兵 troops from heaven – invincible army;
鐵道兵 railway corps;
通信兵 signal corps;
退兵 (1) force the enemy to retreat; (2) retreat; withdraw;
屯兵 station troops;
衛兵 bodyguard; guard;
憲兵 gendarme; military police; military policeman;
新兵 new recruit; recruit;
信號兵 signalman;
興兵 mobilize troops; open hostilities; send an army; start war;
雄兵 crack troops; powerful army;
巡邏兵 patrol;
偃兵 stop a military action;
養兵 maintain an army;
一等兵 lance corporal;
疑兵 deceptive deployment of troops;
義兵 (1) troops of justice; (2) volunteers;
陰兵 women soldiers;
誘兵 pretend to flee;
傭兵 mercenaries;
用兵 command troops; make use of troops; manipulate troops; resort to arms; use military forces;
援兵 reinforcements;
閱兵 review troops;
賊兵 enemy troops; rebel soldiers;
招兵 raise troops; recruit soldiers;
偵察兵 scout;
振兵 rally the troops;
徵兵 conscript;

知兵 be well versed in military arts;
擲彈兵 grenadier;
治兵 direct military affairs; lead troops;
重兵 a large number of troops; massive forces;
駐兵 station troops;
裝甲兵 armoured force;
追兵 pursuing troops; troops in pursuit;
子弟兵 people's own army;

bing³

bing

【丙】 (1) third of the ten "Celestial Stems"; (2) another name for fire; (3) fish's tail; (4) a surname;

[丙等] C grade; third-class;

[丙酮] acetone;
丙酮化 acetonization;
~丙酮化合物 acetonide;
丙酮基 acetonyl;
丙酮尿 acetonuria;
丙酮糖尿 acetonglycosuria;
丙酮性氣喘 acetonasthma;
丙酮血 acetonaemia;
氯丙酮 chlorinated acetone;

[丙烯] propylene;
丙烯腈 acrylonitrile;
丙烯醛 acrylaldehyde;
丙烯酸樹脂 acrylics;
丙烯酸鹽 acrylate;
丙烯酰胺 acrylamide;

[丙夜] midnight;

付丙 commit to the flames;

bing

【秉】 (1) grasp; hold in one's hand; (2) control; preside over; take charge; (3) authority; (4) a surname;

[秉筆] hold a pen;
秉筆直書 write down the truth; write the truth without fear or favour;

[秉承] in accordance with; receive;
秉承某人的旨意 act on someone's orders; at sb's beck and call; be subservient to the will of sb;

[秉持] (1) adhere to; hold on to; (2) hold in hand;

[秉賦] one's natural endowments;

[秉公] impartially; justly;
秉公辦理 handle a matter impartially;
秉公而論 in justice to;
秉公無私 handle affairs justly;
一秉至公 perfect just throughout the transaction; the utmost equity in managing affairs;

[秉國] hold political power; in power;

[秉均] in power; rule a nation;

[秉性] natural disposition; natural instincts; nature;
秉性耿直 be upright by nature;

[秉要執本] grasp the essential;

[秉正] just; upright;

[秉直] (1) frank and honest; (2) adhere to correct principles;

[秉燭] by the candlelight;
秉燭待旦 sit with the light in one's hand till morning;
秉燭而坐 sit by the light of a single candle;
秉燭夜讀 pore over one's books by the light of a candle;
秉燭夜游 be merry while one can; enjoy the short span of life;

bing

【邴】 (1) joyful; jubilant; (2) a surname;

bing

【屏】 abandon; discard; dismiss; get rid of; reject;

[屏除] banish; get rid of;
屏除不良作風 get rid of bad style;
屏除成見 remove prejudices;
屏除惡習 get rid of bad habits;

[屏跡] avoid; stay away from;

[屏居] be out of the public life; live in retirement;

[屏絕] stop having contact or intercourse with;

[屏氣] bate one's breath; hold one's breath;

[屏棄] brush aside; discard; reject; throw away;
屏棄前嫌 disregard previous enmity; end old grudges;

[屏退] order sb to retire;

[屏息] catch one's breath; hold one's breath;

[屏住] hold;
屏住呼吸 bate one's breath; catch one's breath;
屏住氣 hold one's breath;

bing

【柄】 (1) handle; (2) authority; power; (3) control; handle; operate;

B

［柄臣］ minister with full authority; powerful minister;
［柄國］ hold the political power in a nation; reign over a state;
［柄用］ be held in esteem and given authority by the monarch;
［柄政］ take the reins of government;

把柄 handle; hold;
兵柄 military command; military leadership; military power;
鍾柄 handle of a hammer;
舵柄 rudder tiller; tiller;
斧柄 axe handle;
國柄 political power of a nation;
話柄 subject for ridicule;
劍柄 handle of a sword;
句柄 handle;
竊柄 usurp the power of the state;
曲柄 crank;
權柄 authority; power;
談柄 butt; joke;
笑柄 butt; joke; laughing stock;
葉柄 leafstalk; petiole;
政柄 political power; regime;

bing

【炳】 (1) bright; luminous; (2) kindle;
［炳炳麟麟］ brilliant and glorious;
［炳然］ bright;
［炳蔚］ deep and luminous;
［炳文］ luminous style;
［炳耀］ bright and luminous;
［炳著］ eminent; renowned;
［炳燭］ by the bright candlelight;

彪炳 shinning; splendid;
較炳 clear; conspicuous; obvious;

bing

【昺】 bright; brilliant; glorious; radiant;

bing

【稟】 (1) petition; report; (2) be endowed with; receive;

［稟白］ report to a superior;
［稟陳］ report to a superior;
［稟賦］ natural endowment; talent;
稟賦聰明 be gifted with keen intelligence;
稟賦過人 possess original talents superior to other men; surpass many others in natural endowment;
自然稟賦 natural talent;
［稟告］ report to one's superior;
［稟明］ clarify a matter to a superior; explain to a superior;
［稟命］ at the behest of; by order of;
［稟受］ (1) endure; (2) nature;
［稟性］ natural disposition; natural temperament;
稟性闇弱 naturally weak;
稟性純良 simple and honest by nature;
稟性剛愎 have a perverse temper; perverse in temper;
稟性善良 frank by nature;
稟性爽直 frank by nature;
稟性溫良 of a mild disposition;

天稟 endowed by heaven; natural endowments;
異稟 extraordinary endowments; extraordinary talent;

bing

【餅】 (1) biscuits; cakes; cookies; dumplings; pastry; (2) anything roundish;
［餅餌］ steamed cakes of rice or wheat flour;
［餅分圖］ pie chart;
［餅乾］ biscuit;
餅乾壓模 cookie cutter;
薄脆餅乾 crispbread;
脆餅乾 rusk;
夾心餅乾 sandwich biscuit;
奶油餅乾 cream biscuit;
曲奇餅乾 small cookie;
維夫餅乾 wafer;
鹹餅乾 soda biscuit;
消化餅乾 digestive biscuit;
杏仁餅乾 rout biscuit;
一盒餅乾 a tin of biscuits;
一塊餅乾 a biscuit;

薄餅 pancake;
翅餅 square or round shark's fin;
豆餅 bean cake;
糕餅 cakes and biscuits; confectionery; pastry;
鍋餅 big heat cake; wheat cake;
果餅 fruitcake;
畫餅 draw a cake;
煎餅 fried pancake;
烤餅 baked cake;
枯餅 oil cake;
烙餅 a kind of pancake;
麥餅 wheat cake;
煤餅 briquette;

米餅 rice cake;
籤餅 fortune cookie;
肉餅 meat cake; meat pie;
燒餅 sesame seed cake;
柿餅 dried persimmon;
鬆餅 muffin;
酥餅 crisp biscuit;
鐵餅 (1) discus; (2) discus throw;
餡餅 meat pie; pasty; pie; tart;
杏仁餅 almond cake;
藥餅 herbal cake;
油餅 (1) deep-fried dough cake; (2) oil cake;
魚餅 fishcake;
月餅 moon cake;
折餅 toss about in bed;
蒸餅 steamed cake;

bing⁴

bing

【并】 (1) equal; even; on a level with; (2) also; and; at the same time; or; together with;

bing

【並】 (1) combine; incorporate; merge; (2) side by side; simultaneously; (3) and; moreover; (4) completely; entirely;

[並不] by no means; in no sense; not; not at all; not in any sense;

[並存] coexist; exist at the same time; exist side by side; exist simultaneously;
不能並存 can never exist side by side;
與…並存 exist with;

[並發] be complicated by; erupt simultaneously;
並發症 complication;

[並非] by no means;
並非完美 not all roses;

[並駕齊驅] abreast of; abreast with; advance at an equal pace with; get abreast of; keep abreast of each other; keep abreast of one another; keep in step with; keep pace with; match sb stride by stride; neck and neck; on a par with; run neck and neck; stay abreast of;

[並肩] abreast; shoulder to shoulder; side by side; stand beside; stand side by side;
並肩而立 stand shoulder to shoulder;
並肩而行 walk abreast; walk shoulder to shoulder; walk side by side;
並肩而坐 sit alongside of sb; sit side by side;
並肩前進 advance shoulder to shoulder; march forward shoulder to shoulder;
並肩戰鬥 fight shoulder to shoulder;
並肩作戰 fight side by side;

[並進] advance together; keep abreast of;
齊肩並進 keep abreast of; keep up with; march forward shoulder to shoulder;
齊頭並進 advance hand in hand; advance neck and neck; advance shoulder to shoulder; advance side by side; advance simultaneously; advance together; do many things at once; do several things at the same time; do sth simultaneously; go ahead together; go forward together; hank for hank; in step with; keep pace with; keep step with; march together;

[並舉] develop simultaneously;
並舉方針 policy of simultaneous development;

[並立] exist side by side; exist simultaneously;

[並聯] parallel connection;
並聯裝置 parallel arrangement;

[並列] be juxtaposed; put sth on a par with; put sth on an equal footing; put side by side; stand side by side;
並列並合詞 coordinate composite word;
並列並合句 coordinate composite sentence;
並列從句 coordinate clause;
並列第一 tie for the first place;
並列複合詞 copulative compound;
並列關係 coordination;
並列結構 coordinate construction;
並列連詞 coordinate conjunction;
並列修飾詞 coordinate modifier;
並列在一起 in juxtaposition;

[並茂] excellent in both;
文情並茂 excellent in both content and language; rich in both content and style of writing;

[並排] in a row; in the same row; side by side;
並排站在一起 stand in juxtaposition;

[並且] also; and; and also; and, moreover; as well as; besides;

[並入] amalgamate into; incorporate in; merge with;
被並入 be merged in;

[並吞] annex; merge; swallow up;
並吞別國領土 annex the territory of

another state;

[並行] (1) parallel; (2) walk side by side; (3) do two or more things at the same time;

並行不悖 both can be accomplished without coming into conflict; not to be mutually exclusive; parallel and not contrary to each other; run parallel;

並行操作 parallel operation;

~ 並行操作控制 parallel operation control;

並行查詢 parallel query;

並行程序設計 parallel programming;

並行處理 parallel processing;

並行傳輸 parallel transmission;

並行打印 parallel printing;

並行工程 concurrent engineering;

並行計算機 parallel computer;

並行控制 parallel control;

並行終端 parallel terminal;

[並重] attach equal importance to; lay equal stress;

並重方針 policy of equal emphases;

比並 compare to; liken;

相並 abreast; side by side;

B

bing

【併】 (1) equal; even; go side by side; on a level with; (2) all; entire; (3) together; (4) annex; combine;

[併發] occur at the same time;

併發症 complication;

[併合] integrate; unite;

[併肩] shoulder to shoulder;

[併攏] draw close to each other;

[併滅] destroy;

[併吞] annex and absorb; swallow up entirely;

裁併 cut down and merge;

撤併 abolish and merge;

歸併 (1) incorporate into; merge into; (2) add up; lump together; reduce;

合併 amalgamate; combine; consolidate; merge;

火併 open fight between factions;

兼併 annex;

簡併 degenerate; degeneration;

吞併 annex by force; swallow up;

一併 along with all the others; in the lump;

bing

【柄】 a pronunciation of 柄；

bing

【病】 (1) disease; illness; sickness; (2) feel unwell; ill; taken ill; (3) ill; sick; sickly; (4) defect; fault; (5) worry; (6) hate;

[病案] case history; medical record;

[病包兒] permanent invalidity;

[病變] lesion; pathological changes;

黃斑病變 maculopathy;

角膜病變 keratopathy;

尿路病變 uropathy;

皮膚病變 dermopathy;

腎病變 nephropathy;

腎小管病變 tubulopathy;

滲透性腎病變 osmotic nephrosis;

糖尿病皮膚病變 diabetic dermopathy;

營養性病變 trophic lesion;

疣樣病變 verruca;

[病病歪歪] sickly and weak;

[病殘] sick and disabled; sick and handicapped;

[病程] course of a disease;

[病牀] hospital bed; sickbed;

特殊病牀 amenity bed;

[病從口入] diseases enter by the mouth; diseases come in at the mouth; illness finds its way in by the mouth;

病從口入，禍從口出 a closed mouth catches no flies;

[病倒] come down with an illness; fall ill;

突然病倒 be suddenly seized with an illness;

[病毒] virus;

病毒病 virosis;

病毒學 inframicrobiology; virology;

蟲媒病毒 entomophilous virus;

過濾性病毒 filterable virus;

流感病毒 flu virus;

入侵性病毒 intrusive virus;

天花病毒 variola virus;

腺病毒 glandular virus;

黏病毒 mucous virus;

[病篤] critically ill; terminally ill;

[病發] fall ill;

[病房] sick room; ward;

查病房 go on rounds in the wards; make ward rounds;

產科病房 maternity ward;

隔離病房 isolation ward;

內科病房 medical ward;

外科病房 surgical ward;

[病廢] be disabled by disease;
[病夫] sick person;
[病革] about to die of an illness;
[病根] root of the trouble;
找到病根 find the root of the trouble;
[病故] die of an illness;
[病害] plant disease;
[病後] after an illness; during convalescence;
病後護理 aftercare;
病後身體虛弱 weak from one's illness;
病後休養 recuperate after illness;
[病疾] disease; illness; sickness;
[病假] sick leave;
病假工資 sick benefits; sick pay;
請病假 apply for sick leave;
休病假 be on sick leave;
[病菌] bug; germ; pathogenic bacteria;
超級病菌 superbug;
傳播病菌 spread disease germs;
帶有病菌 carry the germs of a disease;
沒有病菌 free from germs;
消滅病菌 destroy germs;
[病況] patient's condition;
[病理] pathology;
病理學 pathology;
~比較病理學 comparative pathology;
~動物病理學 zoopathology;
~教育病理學 educational pathology;
~臨牀病理學 clinical pathology;
~氣候病理學 climatic pathology;
~細胞病理學 cell pathology;
~行為病理學 behavioural pathology;
~植物病理學 phytopathology;
[病例] case;
病例記錄簿 casebook;
病例數 caseload;
[病歷] case history; medical record;
填寫病歷 fill in the medical record;
[病魔] curse of a disease; demon of ill health; serious illness;
病魔纏身 be afflicted with a lingering disease; be prone to all kinds of sicknesses;
[病情] patient's condition; state of an illness;
病情惡化 deteriorate; take a change for the worse;
病情好轉 a patient's condition takes a favourable turn; be on the mend;
病情危急 one's sickness becomes critical;
[病軀] sick body;
[病人] patient; sick person;
產科病人 obstetrical patient;
隔離病人 isolate a patient;
護理病人 nurse the sick; tend the sick;
急診病人 emergency case;
看望病人 visit an invalid;
門診病人 out-patient;
內科病人 medical patient;
外科病人 surgical patient;
一批病人 a cohort of patients;
照料病人 attend a patient; look after the sick;
治癒病人 heal the sick;
住院病人 in-patient;
自費病人 private patient;
[病容] emaciated look; sickly look;
有病容的 peaked; peaky;
[病入膏肓] be incurably ill; fatal disease; have no hope of recovery; past all hope; sick to the core;
[病弱] invalidity; sick and weak;
病弱者 invalid;
[病室] sickroom; ward;
[病逝] die of an illness;
[病勢] degree of gravity of an illness; patient's condition;
病勢危殆 dangerously ill;
[病死] die of an illness;
[病榻] sickbed;
[病態] morbid state;
病態經濟 sick economy;
病態心理學 abnormal psychology;
病態幽默 black humour; morbid humour; sick humour;
[病退] resign because of illness; retire due to illness; withdraw due to illness;
[病危] at one's last gasp; be critically ill; terminally ill;
[病象] symptoms of a disease;
[病休] sick leave; take a sick leave;
[病秧子] person in poor health; person vulnerable to illness; sick vine;
[病因] cause of a disease; origin of a disease;
病因學 aetiology;
[病癒] get well; recover from illness;
久病初癒 have just recovered from a lingering disease;
[病原] aetiology; pathogen;
病原體 pathogen;
~細菌性病原體 bacterial pathogen;

~需氧病原體 aerobic pathogen;

［病源］ cause of a disease; origin of a disease;
病源學 aetiology;
消除病源 get rid of the source of infection;

［病徵］ symptoms of a disease;

［病症］ (1) ailment; disease; (2) symptoms of a disease;
有…的病徵 have symptoms of;

［病終］ die of a disease;

［病重］ in a critical condition; seriously ill;

［病狀］ symptoms of a disease;
病狀不消 the symptoms persist;

阿米巴病 amoebiasis;
癌病 carcinomatosis;
艾滋病 AIDS (acronym of Acquired Immune Deficiency Syndrome);
愛滋病 AIDS (acronym of Acquired Immune Deficiency Syndrome);
凹背病 swayback;
白斑病 vitiligo;
白血病 leukaemia;
百病 all kinds of diseases;
斑點病 scab;
包蟲病 echinococcosis; hydatid disease;
抱病 ill; in bad health;
暴病 sudden attack of a serious disease;
鼻病 rhinopathia;
弊病 (1) abuse; evil; malady; malpractice; (2) defect; disadvantage; drawback; fault;
糙皮病 pellagra;
常見病 common ailment; common disease;
腸病 bowel disease; enteropathy;
腸熱病 enteric fever;
腸胃病 intestines and stomach trouble;
稱病 plead illness; under the pretext of being ill;
傳染病 infectious disease;
猝倒病 damping off;
大病 serious illness;
帶病 in spite of illness;
膽蛔蟲病 biliary ascariasis;
膽石病 cholelithiasis;
得病 fall ill; ill;
滴蟲病 thrichomoniasis;
地方病 endemic disease;
多病 susceptible to diseases;
多發病 frequently-occurring disease;
惡病 malignant disease;
耳病 disease of the ear; otopathy;
發病 come on;
犯病 have an attack of one's old illness;
肥胖病 obesity;
肺病 chest trouble; lung trouble; pulmonary tuberculosis; tuberculosis;
肺塵病 pneumoconoiosis;
肺吸蟲病 paragonimiasis;
風濕病 rheumatism;
扶病 do sth in spite of one's illness;
腐病 rot;
婦女病 gynaecological disease; women's disease;
肝病 hepatosis; liver ailment;
肝性腦病 hepatic encephalopathy;
高空病 altitude sickness;
高山病 mountain sickness;
工業病 industrial occupational disease;
佝僂病 rickets;
鈎蟲病 hookworm disease;
詬病 castigate; denounce;
骨病 bone disease; osteopathia; osteopathy;
骨關節病 osteoarthritis;
骨疾病 bone disease;
骨軟骨病 osteochondrosis;
骨腎病 osteonephropathy;
冠心病 coronary heart disease;
害病 ill with; fall ill; fall sick;
黑粉病 smut;
黑尿病 blackwater fever;
黑皮病 melanoderma;
黑死病 plague;
黑穗病 smut;
紅斑病 erythema;
紅眼病 pink-eye;
喉病 laryngopathy;
猴病 monkey disease;
後天病 acquired disease;
骺病 epiphysiometer;
花柳病 venereal disease;
懷鄉病 homesickness;
壞血病 scurvy;
患病 be seized with an illness; fall a victim to disease; fall ill; suffer from an illness; take disease;
肌病 myopathy;
急病 acute disease;
急性病 (1) acute disease; (2) impetuosity;
急躁病 impetuosity;
疾病 disease; illness; sickness;
寄生蟲病 parasitic disease; parasitosis;
痂病 scab;
肩垂病 drop shoulder;
腳病 pedopathy;
癤病 furunculosis;

結核病 tuberculosis;
瘧病 febrile disease;
精神病 mental disease; mental disorder;
看病 (1) see a patient; (2) consult a doctor; see a doctor;
恐水病 hydrophobia; rabies;
狂犬病 hydrophobia; rabies;
老病 chronic disease;
癆病 tuberculosis;
罹病 fall ill; suffer from an illness;
淋病 gonorrhoea;
流行病 epidemic disease;
顱病 craniopathy;
螨病 acariasis;
慢性病 chronic disease;
毛病 (1) secret trouble; (2) breakdown; mishap; trouble; (3) defect; fault; shortcoming;
酶病 enzymopathy;
霉病 mildew;
滅病 wipe out disease;
腦病 cerebral disease; cerebrosis;
囊蟲病 cysticercosis;
蟯蟲病 enterobiasis;
鬧病 fall ill; ill;
尿結石病 lithiasis;
農業病 agricultural disease;
膿疱病 impetigo;
膿皮病 pyoderma;
脾病 lienopathy;
皮膚病 dermatosis; skin disease;
貧病 sick and poor;
瞧病 (1) consult a doctor; see a doctor; (2) examine a patient; see a patient;
卻病 cure a disease; prevent a disease;
染病 be affected with a disease; catch a disease; contract a disease;
熱病 fever;
軟骨病 osteomalacia;
舌白斑病 leukoplakia lingualis;
神經病 (1) neuropathy; (2) mental disorder;
腎病 nephropathy;
生病 be ill; be taken bad; be taken ill; be taken sick; fall ill; fall sick; get sick; take ill; take sick;
濕病 disease caused by dampness;
時病 (1) malady of the age; (2) seasonal ailments;
時令病 seasonal disease;
受病 catch a disease; fall ill;
暑病 summer-heat disease;
絲蟲病 filariasis;
探病 visit the sick;
炭疽病 anthracnose;
糖尿病 diabetes;
絛蟲病 cestodiasis; taeniasis;
通病 common deficiencies; common failings; common faults; common ills;
推病 excuse oneself on the pretext of illness; feign sickness;
禿髮病 alopecia;
托病 plead illness; under the pretext of being ill;
託病 use illness as an excuse;
胃病 gastric disease; stomach trouble;
胃石病 gastrolithiasis;
瘟病 seasonal febrile diseases;
臥病 be confined to bed; be laid up; bedridden on account of illness;
無病 without an illness;
舞蹈病 chorea;
瑕病 blemish; flaw;
腺病 adenopathy;
線蟲病 nematodiasis;
相思病 lovesickness;
消渴病 diabetes;
小病 ailment; indisposition; minor ailment; minor illness;
謝病 decline office on account of illness;
心病 (1) anxiety; worry; (2) secret trouble; sore point;
心臟病 heart disease;
性病 venereal disease;
鏽病 rust;
卹病 show sympathy for the sick;
血枯病 anaemia;
血清病 serum sickness;
血友病 haemophilia;
牙病 dental disease;
牙周病 periodontal disease;
佯病 pretend to be ill;
養病 convalesce; recuperate; take rest and nourishment to regain one's health;
葉斑病 leaf spot;
一場病 a bout of illness; an illness;
醫病 cure a disease; treat a patient;
疑病 hypochondriasis;
遺傳病 hereditary disease;
疫病 epidemic disease;
癔病 hysteria;
因病 because of illness; due to illness;
銀屑病 psoriasis;
攖病 be attacked by disease;
癭病 goiter;
疣病 verrucosis;
有病 feel unwell; ill; sick;

幼稚病 (1) infantilism; (2) infantile disorder;
語病 (1) faulty wording; illogical use of words; (2) difficulty in speaking caused by vocal defects;
詐病 feign illness; malinger; pretend to be ill;
找病 look for trouble;
疹病 exanthem;
診病 diagnose a disease;
肢病 acropathy;
職業病 occupational disease;
治病 cure a sickness; treat an ailment; treat a disease;
腫瘤病 tumour;
重病 serious disease;
裝病 feign a disease; pretend to be ill; sham illness;
訾病 find fault with;
漬病 catch a disease; fall ill; get infected;
足病 foot disease;

bing
【竝】 (1) also; and; (2) combine; join;

bing
【摒】 (1) expel; get rid of; (2) arrange in order;
[摒除] get rid of; renounce;
[摒擋] arrange in order; pack up for travelling;
[摒絕] cut loose entirely;
[摒棄] abandon; get rid of;

bo¹
bo
【波】 (1) sea waves; (2) breakers; waves; (3) fluctuate; undulate; (4) affect; entangle; implicate; involve; (5) an unexpected turn of events;
[波波] on constant run;
[波長] wavelength;
波長計 wavemeter;
~定點波長計 one-point wavemeter;
~外差式波長計 heterodyne wavemeter;
~諧振腔波長計 cavity-resonator wavemeter;
臨界吸收波長 critical absorption wavelength;
天線激勵波長 antenna drive wavelength;
主波長 dominant wavelength;
[波臣] (1) denizens of water; (2) victims of drowning;
波臣肆虐 flood disaster;
[波蕩] rock; roll;
[波導] waveguide;
波導管 waveguide;
~充氣波導管 air-filled waveguide;
~螺旋狀波導管 helix waveguide;
~渦旋式波導管 coiled waveguide;
有機超導波導 organic superconducting waveguide;
[波動] fluctuate; fluctuation; rise and fall; undulate;
波動幅度 fluctuation range;
幣值波動 currency fluctuation;
不正常波動 irregular variation;
滙率波動 exchange rate fluctuation;
基線波動 baseline fluctuation;
急劇波動 sharp fluctuation;
價格波動 price fluctuation;
情緒波動 have emotional instability;
物價波動 fluctuate in price;
振動波動 amplitude fluctuation;
[波段] waveband;
寬波段 broadband;
[波峰] crest; wave crest;
[波幅] range of fluctuations; range of undulations;
波幅變化 amplitude variation;
[波谷] trough of the waves;
[波光] glistening light of waves;
波光粼粼 gleams of light are reflecting on waves in the river;
波光漪漣 the waves dance in the sunlight;
[波及] affect; extend effects to; involve; spread to;
波及很廣 spread abroad;
波及全國 affect the whole country;
[波瀾] billows; great waves;
波瀾老成 magnificently superb;
波瀾起伏 with one climax following another;
波瀾壯闊 surge ahead in powerful waves; surge forward with great momentum;
添技畫葉，故作波瀾 deliberately embellish the facts;
推波助瀾 add fuel to the fire; add fuel to the flame; aggravate a complicated situation; egg one on; fan the fire; fan the flame; help intensify the billows and waves; incite; increase trouble; instigate; intensify trouble; make a stormy sea stormier; pour oil on the flame; set the heather on fire;
[波浪] billows; breakers; waves;

波浪滾滾 the waves roll on in succession;
波浪式 (1) (of hairstyle) natural wave style; (2) wavy;
~ 波浪式前進 advance wave upon wave;
波浪滔天 billows dashing to the skies; waves running high;
波浪洶湧 the waves surge high;
清波碧浪 clear waves of the river;
掀起波浪 raise the waves;
興波作浪 stir up troubles;

[波累] involve in a trouble;

[波稜蓋] kneecap;

[波濤] billows; breakers; great waves; large waves; surge billows;
波濤怒號 the billows roar;
波濤拍岸 the waves beat upon the bank;
波濤起伏 the waves toss;
波濤聲 roar of the waves;
~ 聽到波濤聲 hear the roar of the waves;
波濤式 (of hairstyle) irregular wave style;
波濤萬頃 myriad waves;
波濤洶湧 roaring waves;
~ 波濤洶湧的海面 rough sea;

[波紋] water-ring; ripples;
波紋的 corrugated;
吹起波紋 corrugate the surface of;

[波心] (1) centre of a water-ring; (2) heart of a trouble;
風生袖底，月到波心 the breeze is playing about one's sleeves, while the moon's image sparkles in the rippling water;

[波形] waveform;
面積平衡波形 area-balanced waveform;
模擬波形 analogue waveform;
條信號波形 bar waveforms;

[波折] obstacles; obstructions; setbacks; twists and turns;

奔波 (1) busy running about; (2) toil;
碧波 bluish waves;
表面波 surface wave;
滄波 blue waves;
長波 long wave;
衝擊波 shock wave;
翠波 green waves;
地波 surface wave;
地震波 earthquake wave; seismic wave;
電波 electric wave;
電磁波 electromagnetic wave;
短波 short wave;
風波 (1) disorder; dispute; disturbance; storm in a teacup; trouble; (2) wave; wind wave;
複波 complex wave;
光波 light wave; optical wave;
海波 (1) sea waves; (2) hypo;
橫波 transverse wave;
洪波 turbulent waves;
回波 echo;
激波 shock wave;
檢波 detection; rectification;
淩波 ride the waves; walk over ripples;
濾波 filtering;
米波 metric wave;
腦電波 brainwave;
平面波 plane wave;
秋波 bewitching eyes of a woman; bright eyes of a beautiful woman;
球面波 spherical wave;
聲波 acoustic wave; sound wave;
水波 ripples of water;
彈性波 elastic wave;
濤波 billows; great waves;
天波 space radio wave;
恬波 calm waters;
微波 microwave;
消波 wave suppression;
嘯波 whistler waves;
諧波 harmonic;
行波 travelling wave;
削波 clipping;
煙波 lakes; mist and ripples; mist-covered waters;
眼波 bright-eyed; eyesight; fluid glance; vision;
揚波 swelling of waves;
漾波 ripples;
一波 a ripple; a wave;
音波 sound wave;
涌波 bore;
餘波 aftermath; aftershock; afterwinds; repercussion;
載波 carrier wave;
震波 earthquake wave; seismic wave;
中波 medium wave;
重力波 gravity wave;
周波 cycle;
皺波 ripples;
駐波 standing wave;
縱波 longitudinal wave;

bo

【缽】 (1) earthenware basin or bowl;
(2) alms bowl of a monk; Buddhist priest's rice bowl;

［鉢盂］ earthenware basin or bowl;

乳缽 mortar;
研缽 mortar;
衣缽 legacy;

B

bo

【玻】 glass;

［玻璃］ glass;
玻璃板 glass plate;
玻璃杯 glass; tumbler;
~大玻璃杯 glass tumbler;
~空玻璃杯 empties;
~水晶玻璃杯 crystal glass;
玻璃廠 glasswork;
玻璃窗 glass window;
~落地玻璃窗 French windows;
~鉛框玻璃窗 leaded lights;
~雙層玻璃窗 double-glazed window;
玻璃肥料 glass fertilizer;
玻璃粉 ground glass;
玻璃鋼 glass steel;
玻璃工 glazier;
玻璃化 vitrify;
玻璃畫 glass painting;
玻璃鏡 mirror;
~單向玻璃鏡 one-way mirror;
~明玻璃鏡 two-way mirror;
玻璃恐怖 crystallophobia;
玻璃暖房 glasshouse;
玻璃瓶 glass bottle;
~三頸玻璃瓶 three-necked bottle;
~透明玻璃瓶 clear glass bottle;
~有色玻璃瓶 stained-glass bottle;
玻璃器皿 glassware;
~光散射玻璃器皿 light-scattering glassware;
~化學玻璃器皿 chemical glassware;
~日用玻璃器皿 domestic glassware;
~信號玻璃器皿 signal glassware;
~醫藥用玻璃器皿 medical glassware;
玻璃塞瓶 glass-stoppered bottle;
玻璃碗 glass bowl;
玻璃微珠 glass microballoon;
玻璃纖維 glass fibre;
玻璃紙 glassine;
玻璃製品 glassware;
安玻璃 glaze a window;
安全玻璃 non-scatterable glass; safety glass; security glass;
~三層安全玻璃 triplex glass;
彩花玻璃 stained glass;
彩色玻璃 stained glass;
~彩色玻璃窗 stained-glass window;
窗玻璃 window glass;
磁性玻璃 magnetic glass;
擋風玻璃 windscreen; windshield;
導電玻璃 conductive glass;
~半導電玻璃 semiconductive glass;
電極玻璃 electrode glass;
雕花玻璃 cut glass;
疊層玻璃 laminated;
二元玻璃 binary glass;
防彈玻璃 bulletproof glass;
防火玻璃 fireproof glass;
浮雕玻璃 cameo glass;
鋼化玻璃 tempered glass; toughened glass;
高硅氧玻璃 Vycor glass;
高介電玻璃 superdielectric glass;
光敏玻璃 photosensitive glass;
光學玻璃 borosilicate glass;
琥珀玻璃 amber glass;
火石玻璃 flint;
~含鋇輕火石玻璃 baryta light flint;
~含硼火石玻璃 borate flint;
~特輕火石玻璃 extra light flint;
~特重火石玻璃 extra dense flint;
激光玻璃 laser glass;
夾絲玻璃 wired glass;
鏡玻璃 mirror glass;
拉玻璃 cut glass;
鋁硅玻璃 aluminosilicate glass;
濾光玻璃 filter glass;
瑪瑙玻璃 agate glass;
磨光玻璃 polished glass;
磨口玻璃 ground glass;
磨沙玻璃 frosted glass;
磨砂玻璃 frosted glass;
耐火玻璃 hard borosilicate glass;
硼硅玻璃 borosilicate glass;
片玻璃 sheet glass;
平板玻璃 plate glass;
乳白玻璃 milk glass; opal glass;
色玻璃 coloured glass; stained glass;
閃光玻璃 actinic glass;
石灰玻璃 lime glass;
石英玻璃 quartz glass;
雙重玻璃 double glazing;
特種玻璃 special glass;
透紫外線玻璃 sunalux glass;
圖案玻璃 figured plate glass;
微晶玻璃 microcrystalline glass;
吸熱玻璃 heat-absorbent glass;

雪花玻璃 alabaster glass;
壓花玻璃 embossed glass;
煙色玻璃 smoked glass;
一塊玻璃 a piece of glass; a sheet of glass;
一塊長方形的玻璃 a pane of glass;
儀器玻璃 instrument glass;
瑩光玻璃 fluorescent glass;
硬質玻璃 hard glass;

bo

【剝】 make bare; peel; peel off; shell; skin; strip;
［剝剝］ sound of pecking;
［剝奪］ deny; deprive of; divest of; expropriate; strip of; take away;
剝奪公民權 deprive one of one's civil rights;
剝奪權力 strip of power;
剝奪權利 deprive of rights;
剝奪人身自由 deprive of sb's personal liberty;
剝奪宗教自由 abridge religious freedom;
［剝極必復］ when things are at their worst, they will surely mend;
［剝蕉抽繭］ investigate deeper and deeper; press an inquiry step by step;
［剝句法］ sentence-peeling method;
［剝離］ be stripped; come off; detach; peel; separate; tear away; tear off;
［剝落］ come off; flake off; peel off;
油漆剝落 the paint flakes away;
［剝皮］ flay; peel off the skin; skin;
剝皮器 peeler;
［剝去］ strip;
［剝蝕］ corrode; denude; erode; wear away;
［剝削］ exploit;
剝削成性 exploitative by nature;
剝削階級 the exploitation class;
剝削者 exploiter;
變相剝削 covert act of exploitation;

盤剝 exploit; practise usury;
吞剝 embezzle and exploit;

bo

【般】 intelligence in Buddhism;
［般若］ wisdom (prajna);

bo

【菠】 spinach;
［菠菜］ spinach;
［菠蘿］ pineapple;
燴菠蘿 stewed pineapple;

bo

【番】 martial-like;

bo

【撥】 (1) poke; stir; turn; (2) allocate; appropriate; set aside; (3) batch; group;
［撥錶］ set the watch;
［撥充］ appropriate sth for;
［撥出］ (1) dial-out; (2) appropriate;
［撥動］ poke; stir; turn;
撥動灰土 give the ashes a stir; stir ashes;
撥動琴弦 twang strings;
用勺撥動 stir with a spoon;
［撥發］ allocate; appropriate for; issue to;
［撥付］ appropriate; make a payment;
［撥給］ appropriate;
［撥號］ dial a number;
撥號方式 dialling mode;
撥號機 dialler;
~ 機械撥號機 mechanical dialler;
~ 自動撥號機 autodialler;
撥號器 dialler;
~ 機電撥號器 electromechanical dialler;
撥號音 dial tone; dialling tone;
長途撥號 distance dialling;
單線撥號 battery dialling;
複合撥號 composite dialling;
交流撥號 alternating current dialling;
碼撥號 dialling;
用戶撥號 customer dialling;
直接撥號 direct dialling;
［撥火］ poke a fire;
［撥交］ appropriate; issue to;
［撥開］ push aside;
撥開迷霧 disperse the miasmal mist;
撥開霧霾 disperse the miasmal mist;
撥開雲霧見青天 dispel the clouds and see the sun; restore justice;
［撥款］ (1) allocate funds; (2) appropriation;
財政撥款 financial appropriation;
定額撥款 definite appropriation;
航空撥款 aviation appropriation;
計劃撥款 programme appropriation;
經常撥款 recurrent appropriation;
連續撥款 continuing appropriation;
年度撥款 annual appropriation;
提前撥款 advance appropriation;
信托基金撥款 trust fund appropriation;
預算撥款 budgetary appropriation;
專用撥款 special appropriation;

追加撥款 additional appropriation;
資本撥款 capital appropriation;

[撥拉] move; stir;

[撥浪鼓] rattle drum;

[撥馬而逃] turn one's steed and flee;

[撥弄] fiddle with; toy with;
撥弄是非 sow discord; stir things up; stir up trouble by gossip;
來回撥弄 fiddle with; move to and fro;

[撥冗] find time in the midst of pressing affairs; set aside a little time out of a tight schedule;
撥冗光臨 please spare a little time and come;

[撥絃] pluck the strings;

[撥用] appropriate; set apart for a specific use;

[撥正] correct; set right;

擺撥 dismiss from attention; put aside;
棖撥 push aside with hand;
調撥 allocate and transfer; allot;
劃撥 assign; transfer;
撩撥 (1) banter; tease; (2) incite; provoke;
提撥 (1) appropriate; (2) remind;
挑撥 arouse; cause disputes; incite; instigate; provoke; sow discord;
直撥 direct dialling service;

bo

【播】 (1) seed; sow; (2) carry; spread; (3) move; (4) abandon; cast away;

[播報] broadcast;
播報員 announcer; broadcaster;

[播出] airing; broadcast;
首次播出 first airing;

[播蕩] homeless; live in vagrancy;

[播放] be aired; broadcast; on the air; send out; transmit;
播放哀樂 broadcast the funeral music;
播放次數 airplay;
播放清單 playlist;
播放時間 airtime;

[播講] broadcast a talk;

[播客] podcast;

[播控中心] broadcasting studies;

[播弄] (1) order sb about; (2) stir up;
播弄是非 sow discord; sow dissension; stir things up; stir up trouble; tell tales;

[播棄] abandon; cast away; discard; throw away;

[播散] disseminate;

[播送] airing; airplay; beam; broadcast; transmit;
播送音樂 broadcast music;
按時播送 regular airings;
唱片播送 airplay;

[播揚] broadcast; propagate; spread;

[播音] be on the air; broadcast;
播音室 studio;
~多用途播音室 multipurpose studio;
~廣播播音室 broadcast studio;
~回聲播音室 echo studio;
~時事播音室 current affairs studio;
播音員 announcer; broadcaster;
~二級播音員 second-grade announcer;
~三級播音員 third-grade announcer;
~一級播音員 first-grade announcer;
~主任播音員 chief announcer;
播音中心 broadcasting centre;
開始播音 go on the air;
停止播音 go off the air;

[播影] broadcast on television; telecast;

[播種] plant seeds; seed; seeding; sow;
播種機 broadcaster; planter; seed sower; seeder; seeding machine; sower; sowing machine;
~飛機播種機 aerial broadcaster; aeroplane seeder;
~盤式播種機 drop plate planter;
~撒播播種機 broadcast sower;
~圓盤播種機 dish seeder;
~作壟播種機 bedder; planter;
播種面積 sown acreage;
播種期 sowing-season;
春天播種 sow in spring;
飛機播種 aerial seeding; aerial sowing;
交叉播種 criss-cross seeding;
秋天播種 sow in autumn;
在田裏播種 sow in the field;

重播 repeat programme; replay;
傳播 disseminate; dissemination; get wind; propagation; propagate; put about; spread; take wind;
春播 sow in spring;
導播 programme director;
點播 dibble;
飛播 sow seed from aircraft;
溝播 sow in furrows;
廣播 airing; broadcast; broadcasting; on the air;
連播 chain broadcast;

聯播 broadcast over a radio network; chain broadcasting; network broadcasting; radio hookup; simulcast; simultaneous broadcasting;
流播 circulate; spread;
壟播 dibble on the ridges of a field;
耬播 sow with a drill;
密播 close planting;
畦播 border method of sowing;
秋播 autumn sowing; fall sowing;
撒播 (1) broadcast; disseminate; spread; (2) sow;
散播 disseminate; spread;
條播 drill;
停播 off the air;
穴播 bunch planting;
演播 broadcast; telecast;
遠播 spread far and wide;
直播 (1) direct seeding; (2) direct broadcast; live broadcast; live telecast;
主播 presenter;
轉播 rebroadcast; relay a broadcast; relay broadcasting; retransmit; retransmission;

bo
【嶓】 a mountain in Shaanxi;

bo
【餑】 cakes; fancy baked food;

bo²

bo
【白】 a pronunciation of 白;

bo
【犮】 the way a dog walks;

bo
【百】 a pronunciation of 百;

bo
【伯】 (1) father's elder brother; uncle; (2) rank of the nobility in ancient China;

[伯伯] uncle;
[伯父] uncle;
[伯爵] count; earl;
伯爵夫人 countess;
女伯爵 countess;
[伯母] aunt;
[伯仲] brothers; older and younger brothers;
伯仲之間 about the same;
[伯祖] grandfather's elder brother; grand uncle;
伯祖母 father's aunt;

阿拉伯 Arab; Arabian; Arabic;
笨伯 clumsy fellow; fool; simpleton; idiot; slow-witted;
大伯 (1) father's elder brother; (2) uncle;
老伯 uncle;
詩伯 great poet; master in poetry;
叔伯 paternal uncles;
堂伯 paternal uncle;
姻伯 uncle by marriage;
從伯 one's father's paternal male cousins who are older than him;

bo
【帛】 (1) silk fabric; (2) property; wealth; (3) a surname;

[帛帶] silk waistband;
[帛畫] paintings on silk;
彩繪帛畫 colour painting on silk;
[帛書] letter written on silk;

布帛 cloth and silk; cotton and silk;
財帛 money; riches; valuables; wealth;
縑帛 fine silk;
粟帛 grain and cloth;
雁帛 correspondence; letters;
玉帛 (1) gems and silk; jade objects and silk fabrics; (2) friendship;
竹帛 (1) bamboo tablets and textiles; (2) books;

bo
【泊】 (1) anchor a ship; (2) lie at anchor; stay; (3) tranquil and quiet; (4) a body of water; a lake;

[泊岸] anchor alongside the river;
[泊泊] ripples of water;
[泊車] park; park a car;
泊車證 parking label;
代客泊車 valet parking;
~代客泊車服務 valet service;
[泊船] moor a boat;
泊船塢 wet dock;
[泊然] calm and at rest;
[泊位] berth;

安泊 put up in a hotel;
淡泊 lead a tranquil life without worldly desires;
澹泊 not seek fame and wealth;
碇泊 moor;
湖泊 lakes;
繫泊 moor; moor a boat;
落泊 (1) comedown; down and out; in dire straits; (2) bold and generous;

unconstrained;
漂泊 drift; lead a wandering life;
飄泊 drift; lead a wandering life;
棲泊 come to anchor; sojourn; stay temporarily;
停泊 anchor; berth;
繫泊 moor a boat;
歇泊 lie at anchor;

B

bo

【勃】 quick; sudden;

［勃勃］ flourishing; vigorous; zestful;
生氣勃勃 alive with activity; full of life; full of vitality;
興致勃勃 full of enthusiasm; in high spirits;
野心勃勃 be driven by wild ambition; overweeningly ambitious;

［勃發］ begin suddenly; break out;
游興勃發 be seized with a desire to travel;

［勃怒］ break into a rage; lose one's temper suddenly;

［勃起］ boner; erection; hard-on; have an erection; stiffy;
勃起功能障礙 erection dysfunction;
完全勃起 telotism;

［勃然］ (1) abruptly; agitatedly; excitedly; suddenly; (2) prosperously; vigorously;
勃然變色 be visibly stung; show displeasure all of a sudden; sudden change in one's countenance; turn red in the face;
勃然大怒 a wave of anger; blow a fuse; blow a gasket; blow one's lid; blow one's stack; blow one's top; bluster oneself into anger; burst into a fit of temper; burst into anger; explode with lyric wrath; fall into a rage; flame forth; flame out; flame up; flare up; fly into a passion; fly into a rage; fly off the handle; go apeshit; go off like a rocket; go off like a Roman candle; go off the top; have a mad on; hit the ceiling; hit the roof; in an awful bate; take pepper in the nose;
勃然而起 burst into activity; spring into life;
勃然色變 a sudden change in countenance; change countenance suddenly; show displeasure all of a sudden;

［勃興］ grow vigorously; rise suddenly;

苾勃 fragrant;
哈勃 Hubble;
蓬勃 exuberant; flourishing; thriving; vigorous;
舒勃 develop; expand; grow;
蓊勃 lush; luxuriant;
鬱勃 lushly; luxuriantly;

bo

【柏】 (1) cypress; (2) a surname;

［柏府］ imperial censorate;

［柏樹］ cypress;
地中海柏樹 common evergreen cypress;
日本柏樹 Japanese cypress;
西藏柏樹 Himalayan cypress;

［柏油］ asphalt; blacktop;
柏油路 bituminous road;

翠柏 bluish green cypress; incense cedar;
黃柏 golden cypress;
松柏 pine and cypress;

bo

【浡】 excited; rise;

［浡然］ excited; rising;

bo

【脖】 neck;

［脖頸］ back of the neck; nape;
光潔雪白的脖頸 alabaster neck;

［脖領兒］ neck or collar of a garment;

［脖子］ neck;
脖子僵直 have a stiff neck;
脖子歪 have a wry neck;
扯着脖子 strain the neck in shouting;
粗脖子 overgrown neck;
大脖子 goitre;
～大脖子病 goitre; struma;
勒脖子 seize sb by the throat;
摟住脖子 fall upon sb's neck;
抹脖子 cut one's own throat — commit suicide;
扭了脖子 sprain one's neck;
掐脖子 have sb by the throat;
繞脖子 beat about the bush; speak in a roundabout way;
伸長脖子 crane one's neck; stretch out one's neck;

bo

【舶】 ocean-going ship;

［舶來品］ foreign goods; imported goods;

船舶 boats and ships; shipping;

bo

【荸】 water chestnut;

［荸薺］ water chestnut;

bo

【博】 (1) extensive; wide; (2) abundant; ample; plentiful; rich; (3) erudite; knowledgeable; learned; well read; (4) barter for; exchange; (5) gamble; play games; (6) gain; win; (7) a surname;

［博愛］ love for humanity; love for mankind; universal brotherhood; universal fraternity; universal love;
提倡博愛 advocate universal love;

［博彩］ betting;
差額博彩 spread betting;

［博採］ adopt from all sides;
博採廣謀 seek advice from all sides;
博採眾長 learn widely from others' strong points;
廣謀博採 seek advice from all sides;

［博大］ broad and profound; erudite; vast;
博大精深 have both extensive knowledge and profound scholarship;

［博得］ earn; gain; obtain; win;
博得好感 gain on sb;
博得好評 have a favourable reception; obtain high praise;
博得歡心 gain on sb's heart;
博得青睞 gain in favour;
博得全場喝彩 bring the house down; carry the house; draw applause from the audience;
博得同情 win sympathy;
博得信任 win the confidence;
博得一陣又一陣的掌聲 draw rounds of applause; win round after round of applause;
博得掌聲 draw forth applause;

［博貫］ erudite; have profound and transcending knowledge of sth;

［博廣］ extensive;
博聞廣識 extensive information and learning;

［博客］ blog; video blog;
博客世界 blogosphere;
博客雜誌 blogzine;
視頻博客 vlog;

［博覽］ read extensively; well read;
博覽會 expo; fair; international exhibition; trade
~工業博覽會 industrial fair;
~國際博覽會 international fair;
~圖書博覽會 book fair;
博覽經史 read all kinds of books of classic Chinese learning;
博覽強記 be extremely well read and have a remarkable memory;
博覽群書 extensive reading of all kinds of books; read extensively; truly learned; very widely read;
~博覽群書的 well read; widely read;
空中博覽 air panorama;

［博取］ contend for; court; try to gain;
博取歡心 curry favour with sb; get on the right side of sb; wheedle one's way into favour; win sb's favour;
博取同情 enlist sb's sympathy; seek sb's sympathy; win sympathy;
博取微利 seize petty gains;
博取信任 win sb's confidence;

［博施濟眾］ help the public by bestowing generously;

［博識］ erudite; learned;

［博士］ (1) doctorate; (2) learned scholar;
博士後 postdoctoral;
~博士後研究 postdoctoral research;
博士論文 doctoral dissertation; doctoral thesis;
博士生 doctoral student;
~博士生導師 doctoral supervisor;
博士學位 doctor's degree; doctorate;
~博士學位論文答辯 doctoral dissertation defense;
~取得博士學位 receive one's doctorate;
茶博士 teahouse waiter; tearoom keeper;
法學博士 doctor of law;
工科博士 doctor of engineering;
理學博士 doctor of science;
民法博士 doctor of civil laws;
名譽博士 honorary degree;
神學博士 doctor of divinity;
文學博士 doctor of literature; Litt. D.;
醫學博士 doctor of medicine;
哲學博士 doctor of philosophy; Ph.D.;

［博通］ erudite; have a broad knowledge of;
博通淹貫 have full and ready knowledge of; have sth at one's fingertips;

［博徒］ gambler;

［博物］ natural sciences;
博物館 museum; repository;

~博物館館長 curator;
~兒童博物館 children's museum;
~教學博物館 museum of popular education;
~科學博物館 science museum;
~歷史博物館 historical museum;
~學校博物館 school museum;
博物學 natural history;
~博物學家 naturalist;
博物院 museum;

[博學] (1) erudite; knowledgeable; learned; well read; well versed; (2) wide range of studies or learning;
博學的 erudite; knowledgeable;
~博學的人 polymath;
博學多才 erudite; learned; of extensive learning; savant; well read; well read and talented;
博學多能 have extensive learning and great capacity;
博學多聞 learned and well-informed; wealthy in knowledge;
博學廣識 have a vast knowledge and have seen much of the world;
博學宏詞 extensive learning and great literary talent;
博學鴻儒 great literate of wide learning; profound scholar; well-informed scholar;
博學深世 broad of learning and wealthy in life's experience;
博學之士 polymath; savant;
博學卓識 have a vast extent of knowledge and experience;
很博學 erudite;

[博雅] erudition; learned and accomplished; well-informed and refined;
博雅之士 scholar of profound knowledge;

[博奕] play a game of chess;
閉型博奕 closed game;
標準博奕 rigid game;
商業博奕 business games;
雙人博奕 two-person game;

[博專] profound and specialized;
博而不專 know something about everything;

奧博 (1) profound; (2) erudite; learned;
賭博 gamble; gambling;
繁博 numerous and wide-ranging;
該博 broad and profound; learned;
賅博 broad and profound; learned;
廣博 erudite; extensive; wide;
洽博 of wide experience and knowledge;
淹博 erudite; wide;
淵博 broad and profound; erudite;

bo

【渤】 rising water; swelling water;

[渤海] Bohai Gulf;

bo

【搏】 (1) combat; fight; struggle; wrestle; (2) assault by preying; pounce on; (3) beat; throb;

[搏動] beat rhythmically; pulsate; throb;

[搏鬥] combat; fight; struggle; tussle with; wrestle with;
拼死搏鬥 fight desperately;
徒手搏鬥 fight barehanded;
一對一的搏鬥 single combat;
與…搏鬥 combat with; fight with; wrestle with;
- 與死神搏鬥 fight with death;

[搏擊] fight with one's hands; pound; strike; strike violently;
搏擊操 kick-boxing;

[搏殺] fight and kill;

[搏手] at the end of one's wits; powerless;

[搏影] fight a shadow;

[搏戰] box; combat; engage in hand-to-hand combat;

脈搏 pulse;
拼搏 combat against; combat with; go all out in work;
起搏 pace-making;
肉搏 close quarter fighting; fight hand-to-hand; hand-to-hand combat;
徒搏 hand-to-hand combat;
心搏 heartbeat;

bo

【鈸】 cymbals;

吊鈸 suspension cymbal;
門鈸 cymbal-shaped article with a knocker;
鐃鈸 big cymbal;
銅鈸 brass cymbal;

bo

【鉑】 (1) foil; thin sheet of metal; (2) platinum;

bo

【雹】 hail; hailstone;
[雹災] disaster caused by hail;
[雹子] hailstone; hail;

冰雹 hail; hailstone;

bo

【箔】 (1) foil; gilt; (2) curtain; (3) frame for raising silkworms;
[箔片] chaff;

蠶箔 bamboo tray for raising silkworms;
金箔 gold foil; gold leaf; rolled gold;
鋁箔 aluminium foil;
葦箔 reed matting;
錫箔 tinfoil paper;
珠箔 curtain of pearls; screen of beads;

bo

【膊】 shoulders; upper arms;
[膊膊] sound of crowing cocks;

赤膊 bare shoulders;
肐膊 arm;

bo

【駁】 (1) argue; contradict; refute; (2) barge; lighter; (3) load and unload; ship; transport by lighter;
[駁岸] low stone wall used to protect an embankment; revetment;
[駁辯] argue; debate; dispute;
[駁斥] argue against; contradict; denounce; disprove; gainsay; rebut; refute;
駁斥謬論 refute a fallacy;
[駁船] barge; lighter;
駁船船工 bargee;
非自航駁船 dumb barge;
工作駁船 utility barge;
井架駁船 derrick barge;
碼頭駁船 harbour barge;
汽油駁船 petroleum barge;
石油駁船 fuel oil barge; oil storage barge;
醫務駁船 ambulance barge;
運兵駁船 troop barge;
[駁倒] confute; defeat in a debate; demolish sb's argument; disprove; outargue; reduce sb to silence; refute; score off;
駁倒對方 refute one's opponent;
[駁還] reject;
[駁回] overrule; reject; turn down;
駁回上訴 reject an appeal;
[駁價] argue over prices; haggle over prices;
[駁詰] question persistently; refute and question;
[駁難] refute and blame; retort and blame;
[駁色] particoloured; variegated;
[駁議] dispute; refute;
[駁運] lightering; transport by lighter;
[駁雜] heterogeneous; impure; mixed;
[駁載] barge transport;
[駁正] correct by argument;
[駁子] barge; tow;

斑駁 motley; mottled;
辯駁 defend oneself verbally; dispute; refute;
反駁 confute; contradict; controvert; countercharge; counterplea; disproof; gainsay; refute; refutatrion; retort;
回駁 refute; repel; retort;
批駁 (1) criticize; refute; repel; (2) veto an opinion or a request from a subordinate body;
拖駁 barge; tugboat;
蕪駁 confused; disorderly; mixed-up;

bo

【葧】 edible roots;

bo

【踣】 (1) stumble and fall; (2) dead; stiff;

bo

【駮】 (1) a kind of fierce animal; (2) impure; mixed; (3) refute;

bo

【薄】 (1) flimsy; thin; (2) light; weak; (3) cold; lacking in warmth; (4) barren; infertile; poor; (5) meagre; slight; small; (6) mean; ungenerous; unkind; (7) belittle; despise;
[薄板] sheet;
薄板材料 sheeting;
金屬薄板 sheet metal;
[薄冰] thin ice;
如履薄冰 as though treading on thin ice; like walking on thin ice; skate on thin ice; tread as on eggs;
一層薄冰 a thin coat of ice; a thin layer of ice;
[薄餅] thin pancake;
[薄薄] (1) dilute; thin; (2) very broad;

B

B

［薄層］ flash; leaf; sheet; thin layer; thin wall;
［薄懲］ light punishment;
［薄酬］ low pay; meagre remuneration; meagre reward; small reward;
［薄脆］ crisp; fritter;
［薄待］ treat sb rather badly; treat sb ungenerously;
［薄荷］ mint;
薄荷芥末 mint mustard;
~薄荷芥末汁 mint mustard gravy;
綠薄荷 spearmint;
水薄荷 water mint;
［薄乎乎的］ thin;
［薄技］ my slight skill;
薄技養身 make a living with a little skill;
薄技在身 have a slight skill by oneself;
薄技在身，吃穿不窮 a useful trade is a mine of gold;
薄技在身，終生受用 if one could learn some skills, one would be set for life;
［薄具］ coarse food;
薄具禮物 offer slight gifts;
［薄禮］ meagre present; modest present; slight gift;
［薄利］ small profits;
薄利多銷 smaller profits but better sale; smaller profits but quicker turnover;
薄利多銷，生財有道 light gains make a heavy purse;
浮名薄利 look down fame and gain;
獲薄利 get poor profits;
賺薄利 make small profits;
［薄陋］ without ability; without talent;
［薄落］ in poor circumstances;
［薄命］ born under an unlucky star; fate is unkind to; ill-fated; ill-starred;
薄命女子負心漢 an unfortunate girl and a heartless man;
［薄膜］ film; membrane; thin film;
薄膜包裝 shrink packaging; skin pack;
導電薄膜 conductive film;
複合薄膜 coextruded film;
介電薄膜 dielectric film;
介質薄膜 dielectric membrance;
吸收薄膜 absorbing membrance;
鑄型薄膜 casting film;
［薄暮］ around sunset; dusk; evening; nightfall; twilight;
薄暮之年 approaching one's grave; old age; the sunset of life;
［薄片］ thin section; thin slice;
［薄情］ disloyal to one's love; fickle; heartless; unfaithful; ungrateful;
薄情郎 heartless lover; unfaithful husband;
薄情無義 heartless;
［薄弱］ feeble; frail; vulnerable; weak;
薄弱環節 bottleneck; vulnerable point; vulnerable sector; weak link;
基礎薄弱 on an insubstantial basis;
能力薄弱 lack in ability;
意志薄弱 have a flabby will; weak-willed;
［薄田］ barren land; unfertile land;
［薄物細故］ trifles; trivia;
［薄霧］ haze; mist; reek;
一層薄霧 a veil of mist;
［薄曉］ around sunrise; dawn;
［薄倖］ fickle; inconstant in love;
薄倖無情 inconstant in love;
負心薄倖 ungrateful and lacking in right feelings;
［薄鏽］ thin rust;
一層薄鏽 a flake of rust;
［薄紙］ thin paper;
其薄如紙 as thin as a piece of paper; paper-thin;

卑薄 poor and barren;
鄙薄 (1) base; mean; (2) despise; loathe; scorn; (3) shallow; superficial;
脆薄 shallow; thin and brittle;
悴薄 enfeebled; impoverished; weakened;
單薄 (1) little; thin; (2) frail; thin and weak; (3) flimsy; insubstantial; thin;
淡薄 (1) light; thin; (2) indifferent; (3) dim; faint;
菲薄 belittle; despise; humble; look down on; poor;
很薄 paper-thin; very thin; wafer-thin;
厚薄 thick and thin; thickness;
瘠薄 barren; infertile; unproductive;
澆薄 thoughtlessly treacherous;
刻薄 mean; unkind;
力薄 one's ability is frail;
綿薄 my humble effort; my meagre strength;
命薄 one's life is brief;
噴薄 in a gushing manner;
淺薄 meager; shallow; superficial;
磽薄 barren; hard and infertile;
峭薄 relentless; strict; unkind;
鍥薄 merciless; pitiless; unsympathetic;
輕薄 frivolous; given to philandering;

佻薄 frivolous; impudent; skittish;
微薄 meagre; scanty;
稀薄 rare; rarefied; thin; wishy-washy;
枵薄 thin and flimsy;
虛薄 poor in ability;
削薄 (of hair) thin out;
倚薄 (1) gather together; (2) come one after another;
紙薄 as thin as paper;

bo
【濼】 lake;

bo
【簙】 a kind of chess game;

bo
【鎛】 (1) a kind of ancient bell; (2) a variety of hoe;

bo
【鵓】 a kind of pigeon;
［鵓鴿］ pigeon;

bo
【檗】 half-cooked rice; parboiled rice;

bo
【欂】 square wooden block at the top of a column;

bo
【礴】 extensive; filling all space;

磅礴 majestic; permeate; powerful tremendous; spread; sweep;

bo³
bo
【跛】 crippled; lame;
［跛躄］ lame; crippled;
［跛鱉］ lame turtle;
跛鱉千里 a lame turtle can go a thousand miles by perseverance; a slow and steady pace wins the race; even a lame turtle can go a thousand miles — persistence ensures success;
［跛蹇］ lame; crippled;
［跛腳］ crippled; have a lame foot; lame; walk with a limp;
［跛蹶］ stumble and fall;
［跛腿］ crippled; lame;
［跛行］ have a limp; lameness; limp; walk lamely; walk with a limp;
跛行症 stringhalt;
間歇性跛行 intermittent claudication;
神經源性跛行 neurogenic claudication;
［跛子］ cripple; crippled; lame;
跛子爬樓梯—難上難 a cripple climbing a stairway — harder and harder;
［跛足］ crippled; crooked-foot; lame;
跛足鴨 lame duck;
~跛足鴨總統 lame duck president;

bo
【簸】 sift; winnow;
［簸蕩］ bump and sway; rock; roll;
［簸動金鑼］ strike gongs;
［簸頓］ dally with;
［簸箕］ (1) winnowing pan; (2) dustpan;
土簸箕 dustpan;
［簸弄］ (1) deceive; play jokes on; (2) spread rumours; start rumours and incite incidents; tell tales;
［簸錢］ game of casting coins;
［簸揚］ sift; winnow;

顛簸 bump; jolt; thrashing; toss;

bo⁴
bo
【亳】 seat of the government during the Shang Dynasty, located in today's Shangchiu County, Henan Province;

bo
【播】 (1) seed; sow; (2) propagate; spread; (3) move; (4) abandon; cast away;

bo
【擘】 (1) thumb; (2) break; split; tear apart;
［擘劃］ arrange; make arrangements for; plan; scheme;
擘劃精詳 arrange painstakingly; plan very carefully;
尚待擘劃 have yet to be planned;
［擘開］ break off; break open;
［擘裂］ cleave; hew apart; rend apart; split;
［擘張］ draw a bow;

巨擘 authority in a certain field; thumb;

bo
【薄】 peppermint;

bo
【蘗】 a species of oak;

bo⁵

bo

【葡】 a pronunciation of 葡;

bu¹

bu

【晡】 afternoon;
［晡時］ late afternoon;

bu

【逋】 (1) abscond; evade; flee; (2) neglect;
［逋蕩］ neglect duty and loaf;
［逋負］ neglect to pay debts;
［逋客］ (1) recluse; (2) fugitive;
［逋流］ linger; remain; stay;
［逋慢］ heedless of regulations or orders;
［逋逃］ flee from justice;
逋逃無蹤 flee away without leaving a trace;
逋逃之臣 fugitive guilty officials;
［逋亡］ abscond; escape; flee;
［逋懸］ arrears; long overdue rent;
［逋租］ neglect the payment of a rent;

宿逋 long-term overdue debt;

bu

【餔】 (1) eat; feed; (2) time for supper; (3) sunset;
［餔啜］ eat and drink;
餔啜無時 have no time to eat and drink;
［餔時］ evening; late afternoon; suppertime;

bu²

bu

【不】 a pronunciation of 不;

bu

【醭】 white specks of mildew;

白醭 mould;

bu³

bu

【卜】 (1) anticipate; foretell; predict; (2) consult the oracle; divine; (3) choose; select; (4) a surname;
［卜辭］ oracle inscriptions;
［卜骨］ oracle bones;
［卜卦］ divine by the Eight Diagrams;
［卜居］ choose a residence;
［卜課］ divine by tossing coins; practise divination;
［卜老］ choose a place for retirement;
［卜鄰］ choose neighbours;
［卜筮］ divination;
［卜數］ art of fortune telling;
［卜宅］ (1) choose a residence; (2) choose a tomb site;

問卜 consult a fortune-teller; divine;
預卜 augur; foretell; predict;
占卜 divine; practise divination;

bu

【哺】 (1) feed; nurse; (2) food in one's mouth;
［哺乳］ breastfeed; nurse; suckle;
哺乳動物 mammal;
哺乳室 nursing room;
哺乳嬰兒 breastfeed;
［哺養］ feed; rear;
哺養兒女 foster one's children;
［哺育］ (1) feed; (2) bring up; foster; nurture;
哺育兒女成長 nurture one's children;
哺育嬰兒 nurture one's baby;

bu

【捕】 (1) apprehend; arrest; catch; seize; (2) policeman in ancient China;
［捕蟲］ insect-catching;
［捕處］ arrest and punish;
［捕風捉影］ act on hearsay evidence; catch at shadows—indulge in groundless suspicion; grasp at a shadow; lay hold on the wind; run after a shadow;
純屬捕風捉影 pure speculation;
［捕狗員］ dog warden; dogcatcher;
［捕獲］ (1) acquire; arrest; capture; catch; seize; succeed in catching; (2) trapping;
難以捕獲 defy capture;
［捕集器］ catcher;
汞齊捕集器 amalgam catcher;
糖汁捕集器 juice catcher;
液滴捕集器 spray catcher;
［捕鯨］ whaling;
捕鯨船 whaler;
捕鯨者 whaler;
［捕撈］ fish for;
捕撈對蝦 catch prawns;

捕撈過度 overfishing;
捕撈鱸魚 bass fishing;
捕撈三文魚 salmon fishing;
捕撈鱒魚 trout fishing;

[捕獵] catch and hunt;

[捕拿] apprehend; arrest; capture; catch;

[捕票] arrest warrant;

[捕殺] catch and kill; capture and kill;
捕殺獵物 catch and kill animals;

[捕食] catch and feed on; prey on;
貓捕食老鼠 cats prey on mice;

[捕魚] catch fish; fishing;
淡水捕魚 freshwater fishing;
燈光捕魚 light fishing;
流網捕魚 drift fishing;
淺灘捕魚 bank fishing;
商業性捕魚 commercial fishing;
深海捕魚 deep-sea fishing;
拖網捕魚 trawler fishing;
鹹水捕魚 saltwater fishing;
遠洋捕魚 pelagic fishing;

[捕捉] catch; seize;
捕捉鏡頭 seize the right moment to take a good shot;
捕捉時機 catch an opportunity by the forelock; take time by the forelock;
捕捉者 catcher;

被捕 be arrested;
逮捕 arrest; take into custody;
兜捕 round up; surround and seize;
緝捕 arrest; seize;
拘捕 take into custody;
拒捕 resist arrest;
緝捕 capture; search and arrest;
擒捕 arrest; capture; catch; seize;
收捕 arrest;
搜捕 hunt for; manhunt; search and arrest; trace and capture; track down and arrest;
圍捕 arrest by closing in on the criminal from all sides;
誘捕 entrap; entrapment; lure a criminal out of hiding and arrest him; put a pinch of salt on sb's tail; trap;
追捕 trace and capture;

bu

【補】 (1) mend; patch; repair; (2) add to; fill; make up for; supply; (3) nourish; (4) benefit; help; make up; use; (5) appoint to a post; fill a post;

[補白] filler;

[補報] (1) repay favours granted;
(2) additional statement;

[補編] supplement;

[補差] make up the difference;

[補償] compensate; compensation; make sth good; make it up to sb; make up; make up for sth; recompense; recoup;
補償報酬 compensatory payment;
補償措施 indemnifying measures;
補償費 compensation;
補償教育 compensatory education;
補償貿易 compensatory trade;
補償器 compensator;
~冷端補償器 cold-end compensator;
~偏差補償器 deviation compensator;
~氣壓補償器 barometric compensator;
~數字式補償器 digital compensator;
~衰減補償器 attenuation compensator;
補償損失 compensate for the loss; make good for a loss; make up for the loss; compensate for a loss;
充份補償 ample compensation;
額外補償 extra compensation;
高度補償 altimetric compensation;
合理補償 fair compensation;
間隙補償 backlash compensation;
金錢補償 pecuniary compensation;
頻帶補償 band compensation;
傷殘補償 disability compensation;
衰減補償 attenuation compensation;
提供補償 afford redress;
餘輝補償 afterglow compensation;
自動低音補償 automatic bass compensation;
作為補償 by way of compensation;

[補充] add; complement; fill up; makeup; replenish; supplement;
補充成本 supplementary cost;
補充從句 amplifying clause;
補充存貨 replenish the stock;
補充供應 replenish the supplies;
補充規定 additional regulations;
補充人力 replenish manpower;
補充説明 additional remarks;
補充體力 regain one's body strength;
補充條款 supplementary terms;
補充語法 remedial grammar;

安全補充 safety supplement;
催化劑補充 catalyst make-up;
互為補充 complementary to each other;
燃料補充 fuel make-up;
溶劑補充 solvent make-up;

[補瘡] cure a boil;
挖肉補瘡 cut out a piece of one's flesh to cure a boil; rob Peter to pay Paul; resort to a remedy worse than the ailment; rob one's belly to cover one's back; sacrifice sth as makeshift to tide over a difficulty;
剜肉補瘡 cut out a piece of one's flesh to cure a boil; cut out good flesh to heal a sore; sacrifice one's interest for the advancement of another;

[補釘] darn; mend; patch;
打滿補釘 be full of darns;

[補發] pay retroactively; reissue; supply again;
補發工資 give the back pay;

[補防] filling-in;

[補鍋] tinker a pan;

[補過] make amends for mistakes; make up for a mistake;

[補好] fix up;
把牙齒補好 fix up one's teeth;

[補花] patchwork;

[補給] fitting out; provision; supply;
補給品 supplies;
~得到補給品 get supplies;
~斷絕補給品 cut off supplies;
~獲得補給品 receive supplies;
~提供補給品 furnish supplies;
補給線 supply line;
缺乏補給 go short of supplies;

[補假] take deferred holidays;

[補救] rectify; redress; remedy; repair;
補救辦法 remedy; remedial measure;
補救措施 remedial measure;
補救方法 remedy;
補救損失 repair a loss;
無可補救 beyond remedy; past remedy;

[補苴] fill; make up for; supply;
補苴罅漏 fill up the cracks and stop the leaks; make up for the shortcomings and loopholes;

[補考] make-up examination;
參加補考 take a make-up examination;

[補課] make up missed classes; make-up classes;

[補漏] stop up holes;

[補碼] complement;
二進制補碼 complement of two's;
十進制補碼 complement of ten's;
修改補碼 modified complement;

[補苗] fill the gaps with seedlings;

[補偏] remedy defects;
補偏救弊 amend defects and faults; remedy defects and rectify errors;

[補品] foods of highly nutritious value; tonic;
一種補品 a tonic;

[補氣] invigorate one's vital energy;
補氣養血 invigorate the vital energy and nourish the blood;

[補缺] fill up a vacancy; supply a deficiency;
補缺選舉 by-election;

[補身] build up one's health;

[補時] added time;
補時階段 stoppage time;
傷停補時 injury time;

[補體] complement;

[補貼] allowance; grant; subsidy;
財政補貼 grant-in-aid;
~教育支出財政補貼 grant-in-aid for education;
~收入補貼 income support;
~職能性財政補貼 functional grant-in-aid;
~住房支出財政補貼 grant-in-aid for housing;
產婦補貼 maternity allowance;
電費補貼 electricity subsidy;
國家補貼 state subsidy;
伙食補貼 food subsidy;
計時補貼 time allowance;
利息補貼 interest subsidy;
糧食補貼 grain subsidy;
日補貼 per diem;
生活補貼 living allowance;
政府補貼 government subsidy;
直接補貼 direct grants;

[補習] tutorial;
補習班 remedial class; supplementary class; tutorial class;
補習功課 take supplementary classes;
補習學校 tutorial school;

[補鞋] mend shoes; repair shoes;
補鞋匠 cobbler;

[補休] take deferred holidays;

[補修] study for a second time courses that

one has failed;
[補選] by-election;
[補血] enrich the blood;
[補牙] fill a tooth; have a tooth stopped; stop a tooth;
[補養] take a tonic or nourishing food to build up one's health;
[補藥] tonic;
一瓶補藥 a bottle of tonic;
[補遺] addendum; appendix; supplement;
[補印] reprint;
[補語] complement;
補語從句 complementary clause;
補語形式 complement form;
賓語補語 object complement;
結果補語 resultative complement;
介詞補語 prepositional complement;
[補正] additions and corrections; supplement and correct;
[補助] allowance; grant; subsidy;
補助詞 accessory word;
補助費 subsidy;
~臨時補助費 temporary subsidy;
補助金 grant; grant-in-aid; subsidy;
~國庫補助金 government subsidy;
~政府補助金 state benefit;
大筆補助 heavy subsidy;
公家補助 public subsidy;
婚喪補助 marriage and death allowance;
間接補助 indirect subsidy;
教育補助 education allowance;
生活補助 subsistence allowance;
生育補助 birth allowance;
現金補助 cash grant;
醫藥補助 medical allowance;
運輸補助 transport subsidy;
政府補助 government subsidy;
[補妝] powder one's nose; touch up one's face;
補妝室 powder room;
[補綴] (1) mend; patch; (2) patch up;
[補足] bring up to full strength; fill a gap; make complete; make up a deficiency;
補足關係 complementation;
補足物 complement;

暗補 invisible subsidy;
幫補 help with money; subsidize;
備補 the next choice;
裨補 aid; supplement; support;
抵補 compensate for; make up;
遞補 fill vacancies in the arranged order;
縫補 darn; darning; mend; sew and mend;
候補 alternate member; candicate for a post;
互補 complement each other; complementation; supplement each other;
彌補 eke out; make good; make up; make up for; remedy;
葺補 repair and mend;
熱補 vulcanize;
刪補 revise; rid superfluities and fill inadequacies;
繕補 mend;
提補 (1) select and fill a post; (2) remind;
替補 alternate;
添補 get more; put in extra;
填補 fill (a gap, a vancancy, etc.)
貼補 help with money; subsidize;
挖補 cut and mend; gouge and mend; mend by replacing the damaged part; patch up; put in repair; replace a damaged part with mending material;
無補 of no avail; of no help; to no avail;
修補 mend; patch up; repair;
增補 add to; augment; enlargement; increase and supplement; supplement;
找補 make up a deficiency;
整補 consolidate and fill up; reorganize and fill up;
織補 darn; mend;
綴補 patch up clothes;
滋補 nourish;

bu⁴
bu

【不】 no; not; negative;
[不安] (1) uneasy; uncomfortable; unpeaceful; unstable; (2) disquiet; disquietude; disturbed; restless; uneasy;
不安本分 be dissatisfied with one's post; dislike to act one's part; not content in one's station;
不安定 insecure; precarious; unsettled; unstable;
~不安定的生活 precarious life; unsettled life;
不安分 discontented with one's lot;
不安其室 be discontented with one's home;
不安心 not settle down to;
~不安心工作 not keen to stay on one's

job; not settle down to one's work;
不安於室 have extramarital relations;
不安於位 dissatisfied with one's position; not content in one's job; unsteady in one's chair;
煩躁不安 agitated; annoyed and impatient; dysphoria; have the fidgets; set one's nerves on edge; short-tempered; vexed;
感到不安 be abashed; be disturbed; feel disturbed; feel uncomfortable; not be at ease;
惶惶不安 be greatly upset; be on tenterhooks; fear and panic; go hot and cold; live in terror and uncertainty; perturbation;
惶惑不安 be lost and ill at ease; in a state of great agitation; perplexed and uneasy;
惶恐不安 be greatly alarmed; be terrified and uneasy; fear and panic; great alarm; heebie-jeebies; in a state of alarm; in a state of trepidation; panic-stricken; with one's heart going pit-a-pat;
焦急不安 flutter; in a swivet; on the anxious seat;
焦慮不安 be racked with anxiety; fret and fume; in a flutter of excitement; nail-biting; on the rack; on tenterhooks; on thorns; tear one's hair; toss about;
侷促不安 like a cat on a hot tin roof; like a cat on hot bricks; nervous; restless; uneasy;
良心不安 have an uneasy conscience;
令人不安 disquieting; distressing; disturbing;
寢處不安 restless for daily activity;
睡臥不安 restless and sleepless;
忐忑不安 all of a tremble; be overwhelmed with anxiety; feel troubled and uneasy; fidgety; fluttered; in a flutter; in a tremble; in fear and trembling; in rather a nervous state; nervous and uneasy; on nettles; on the anxious bench; on the anxious seat; on the tremble; restless; uneasy; unsettled;
心神不安 feel perturbed; feel uneasy; fidgety; have the fidgets; ill at ease; not feel easy in one's mind; suffer from the fidgets; uneasy;
於心不安 not be set at rest;
坐立不安 fidgety; have ants in one's pants; ill at ease; in terrible fidgets; lie on a bed of thorns; like a hen on a hot girdle; on hot coals; on needles and pins; on one's toes; on tenterhooks; on the anxious bench; on the jump; restless; restless with anxiety; sit on thorns;
~ 坐立不安的 antsy; fiddly;
~ 坐立不安的人 fidget;

[不敗] invincible; unbeatable;
不敗之地 a position where one will never be defeated; hold all the trumps; in an invincible position; provide with a basis of victory; put on the screw;
~ 立於不敗之地 in an impregnable position; in an invincible position; in an unassailable position; establish oneself in an unassailable position; make one's position impregnable; place in an invincible position; remain invincible; secure a firm footing; stand in an invincible position;

[不備] by surprise; not ready; off guard; unprepared;
備而不防，防而不備 it is better to get ready for nothing than be caught unprepared; preparedness averts peril;
乘其不備 catch sb flat-footed; catch sb napping; catch sb off guard; catch sb unprepared; take advantage of sb's unpreparedness; take sb napping; take sb unawares; throw sb a curve;
出其不備 before one is prepared; catch one off guard; take one unaware;
攻其不備 attack before the enemy is prepared; attack when the enemy is unprepared; catch sb napping; catch sb off his guard; catch sb on the hop; come upon sb when he is unprepared; strike where the enemy is unprepared; take sb by surprise; take sb unawares;
~ 攻其不備，出其不意 strike when the enemy is unprepared, appear where he does not expect us;
伺其不備 watch for a chance to take sb by surprise;
無一不備 everything is available; nothing is missing;

[不比] (1) different from; unlike; (2) cannot

compare with; no match for;

[不必] need not; no need to; not have to; not necessary;

不必介意 not care a rush;

不必驚慌 don't panic; there is no need to panic; there is no cause for alarm;

不必客氣 don't mention it;

不必要 dispensable; uncalled-for; unnecessary;

不必着急 there is no call for worry;

大可不必 it is not at all worth it; no call for one to;

[不變] unchanged;

不變點 fixed point, invariant point;

不變量 invariant;

~經典不變量 classical invariant;

~絕對不變量 absolute invariant;

不變式 invariant;

~代數不變式 algebraic invariant;

~基本不變式 basic invariant;

~絕對不變式 absolute invariant;

不變性 invariance;

~定向不變性 orientational invariance;

~規範不變性 gauge invariance;

~幾何不變性 geometrical invariance;

~射影不變性 projective invariance;

保持不變 remain unchanged;

以不變應萬變 cope with shifting events by sticking to a fundamental principle; meet changes with constancy;

[不便] (1) inappropriate; inconvenient; unsuitable; (2) hard up; short of cash;

大感不便 be very much put out by;

手頭不便 hard up; have little money to spare; short of cash;

造成極大的不便 be a great inconvenience;

[不別而去] go away without a leave; go away without saying goodbye; leave without notice; leave without saying a word; not utter a word before one's departure;

[不…不…] neither...nor...;

不卑不亢 neither cringing nor arrogant; neither haughty nor humble; neither haughty nor pushy; neither servile nor overbearing;

不悱不發 not explain sth to sb who is not determined to learn;

不憤不啟 not explain sth to sb unless he is desperately anxious to learn;

不驕不躁 free from arrogance and rashness; guard against self-conceit and rashness; not proud or touchy;

不亢不卑 in a happy medium between pride and humility; neither haughty nor humble; neither overbearing nor servile; neither proud nor humble; neither supercilious nor obsequious;

不倫不類 beyond standard; messy; neither fish nor fowl; neither grass nor hay; nondescript; without sense or order;

不偏不黨 fair to all; without wavering to one side or the other;

不偏不倚 avoid leaning on either side; even-handed; free from any bias; hold the scales even; impartial; take no sides; not throw one's weight either way; partial to one; show no partiality to either side; unbiased; without partiality;

[不才] without capability;

[不測] accident; contingency; disaster; misfortune; mishap; unfathomable; unpredictable;

不測之禍 unexpected calamity; unforeseen disaster;

不測之災 unexpected calamity; unexpected catastrophe; unforeseen disaster;

倘有不測 if anything untoward should happen; in case of accident;

險遭不測 barely escape an accident; escape death by a hair's breadth; have a narrow escape;

以防不測 be prepared for accidents; be prepared for any misfortune; ready against the evil day;

[不曾] never; not yet;

[不差] without difference;

不差毫髮 just right; no whit of difference; without the slightest error;

分厘不差 not make a penny's mistake; without the slightest error;

幾乎一點不差 as near as damn it;

累黍不差 not an iota of difference;

[不顫] not be afraid; not be scared;

[不成] not do;

不成材 good-for-nothing; ne'er-do-well; worthless;

不成大器 sb will never amount to much;

不成大事 cannot achieve great things;

不成功 flop; get nowhere; unsuccessful;

B

~不成功便成仁 boom or bust; determined to succeed or die;
不成敬意 just a little token to show my respect to you; just a trifle;
不成理由的理由 woman's reason;
不成器 good-for-nothing; ne'er-do-well; worthless;
不成事實 it is not a proper matter;
不成熟 immature;
不成體統 behaviour outside the bounds of propriety; downright outrageous; graceless; have no manners; in bad taste; indecent; mannerless; most improper; no sort of way; offend against good manners; out of the way; outraging decorum; unbecoming; undignified; with an ill manner;
不成文的 unwritten;
不成文法 common law; unwritten law;
不成問題 no object; no problem; out of question;
辦不成 unable to be accomplished;

[不齒] despise; hold in contempt;

[不啻] (1) not less than; (2) as; as good as; like;
不啻天地 same as the difference between heaven and earth;
不啻天壤之別 equivalent to the difference between heaven and earth;

[不愁] not to worry;
不愁衣食 need not worry oneself about clothes and food;

[不錯] (1) correct; right; (2) not bad; good; O.K.; pretty good;

[不答] make no reply;
避而不答 avoid answering a question; avoid giving an answer; avoid making any reply; be evasive; decline answering a question; parry a question; slide over without answering; take the Fifth;
笑而不答 only smile but do not answer; smile but do not reply;
置之不答 brush it aside; make no response to;

[不大] (1) not too; not very; (2) not often;
不大不小 neither too big nor too small;
不大高明 it does not amount to much;
不大容易 take some;
不大順暢 things are not going smoothly;

[不逮] incompetent;
匡我不逮 help me to overcome my shortcomings in order to make up for my deficiencies;
權所不逮 beyond one's power;
以匡不逮 correct one's mistakes; make up one's shortcomings;

[不單] (1) not the only; (2) not merely; not simply;

[不但] not only;
不但…而且 and what is more; besides; in addition; not only...but also;
不但…反而 instead;
不但如此 moreover;

[不當] (1) careless; improper; inappropriate; not appropriate; unsuitable; (2) consider sth or sb as;
不當回事 not consider sth important;
處置不當 mishandle; mismanage;
粗俗不當 harsh and inappropriate;
措辭不當 inappropriate wording; improper use of words; use the wrong words; wrong choice of words;

[不倒] tumbling;
不倒翁 Chinese tumbler; roly-poly; tumbler;
扳不倒 roly-poly;

[不到] (1) be not up to; below; (2) fail to reach;
不到長城非好漢 not stop until one's aim is attained; one who fails to reach the Great Wall is not a hero;
不到黃河心不死 not stop until one reaches one's goal; not give up hope until one comes to one's tether's end; not stop until one reaches the Huanghe River; refuse to give up until all hope is gone; until all is over, ambition never dies;
不到十八歲 under the age of eighteen;
辦不到 impossible to manage; unable to accomplish;
~逼着公雞下蛋—辦不到 forcing a rooster to lay eggs — impossible to accomplish;
見不到 nowhere in sight; nowhere to be seen;
抗傳不到 disobey the summons;
談不到 out of the question;
想不到 to one's surprise; unexpectedly;
~做夢也想不到 never in one's wildest dreams; not in one's wildest dreams;
找不到 nowhere to be found;
追不到 unable to catch up with; unable to

overtake;
走不到 unable to go as far as; unable to walk as far as;
[不得] may not; must not; not be allowed;
不得不 be bound to; be compelled to; be forced to; be obliged to; be pushed to; cannot but; cannot choose but; cannot do better than; cannot keep from; cannot help but; cannot help; cannot refrain from; have no alternative but; have no choice but; have got to; have to; must;
不得而知 can make nothing of it; cannot know; it is not for one to know; there is no knowledge; there is no way to find out; unable to find out; unknown;
不得發表 off the record;
不得翻身 have no chance to rise again;
不得好死 die in one's boots; die in one's shoes; die with one's shoes on; will die an unnatural death;
不得了 (1) desperately serious; horrible; terrible; (2) exceedingly; extremely; terrible;
~多得不得了 a jillion;
~好得不得了 out of this world;
~忙得不得了 very busy;
不得其法 do not know the right way;
不得其門而入 cannot find one's way in; cannot find the door and get in; cannot gain admission;
不得其所 in the wrong box; like a fish out of water; out of one's element; out of place; out of position;
不得人心 contrary to the will of the people; fail to gain popular support; fall into disfavour among the people; go against the will of the people; have no popular support; not enjoy popular support; unable to win popular support; unpopular;
不得人意 deep in one's black books;
不得善終 may not die a natural death;
不得要領 fail to catch one's point; fail to grasp the main points; miss the main idea; miss the point; not know what one is driving at; not see the point of sth; wide of the mark;
不得已 act against one's will; have no alternative but to; have to;
~不得已的事 necessary evil;
~不得已時 at a push;
~逼不得已 be compelled to; be forced to; have no alternative;
~勢不得已 there is no choice;
~萬不得已 as a last resort; be forced to do sth; by absolute necessity; cannot but; do sth against one's will; have no alternative; have no other choice but; out of absolute necessity; with no other alternative;
不得有誤 act without fail;
巴不得 anxious; cannot wait to; eagerly look forward to; earnestly wish; for two pins; itch for; itch to do sth; only too anxious to do sth; only wish; very anxious about sth; wish anxiously;
比不得 beyond all comparison; not to be compared;
遍索不得 search high and low for sth in vain;
吃不得 not edible;
瞅不得 not worth seeing; should not be seen;
怪不得 no wonder; so that is why; that explains why;
恨不得 itch for; itch to; how one wishes one could; long for; one would if one could; thirsty for;
見不得 (1) not be exposed to; unable to stand; (2) not fit to be seen or revealed; unpresentable;
~見不得人 cannot bear the light of day; cannot stand scrutiny; too ashamed to show up in public;
~見不得天日 cannot bear the light of day;
哭不得笑不得 not know whether to cry or laugh; at one's wits' end;
哭笑不得 find sth both funny and annoying; not know whether to laugh or to cry; unable either to laugh or to cry;
來不得 impermissible; will not do;
~來不得半點馬虎 not allow to be careless;
~來不得半點虛假 not allow to be dishonest;
~過度工作來不得 one should not work too hard;
~玩弄職守來不得 one must not neglect official obligations;
了不得 awfully; exceedingly; extraordinary; extremely; irretrievable; magnificient; proud and overweening;

serious; terrific;
~自以為了不得 become swollen-headed; cocky; get a big head; get a swollen head; give oneself airs; swell with pride; think one is the whole cheese; think oneself sth; think oneself terrific; think sth of oneself; throw one's weight about;
瞧不得 not worth seeing;
求之不得 all that one could wish for; be a godsend to; exceedingly welcome; just what one has wished for; long-cherished desire; meet one's wishes; most welcome; sth one could desire no better; the heart's desire; the very desire;
去不得 (1) should not go; (2) should not get rid of sth;
認不得 unable to recognize;
少不得 cannot do without; cannot dispense with; indispensable; not to be dispensed with;
捨不得 grudge; hate to part with; reluctant to give up; reluctant to part with;
説不得 (1) unmentionable; unspeakable; (2) scandalous;
算不得 not be regarded as;
聽不得 should not be heard;
用不得 unfit for use;
由不得 (1) beyond the control of; not be up to sb to decide; (2) cannot help;
~由不得人 be beyond one's power;
~由不得笑起來 cannot help laughing;
欲進不能，欲退不得 one cannot make any advance, neither can one retreat; unable to advance and to retreat;
怨不得 (1) cannot blame; (2) no wonder;
走不得 (1) unfit to travel; unsafe to travel; (2) not allowed to leave;
做不得 do not do it;

[不敵] be defeated; no match for;

[不第] fail in civil service examination;

[不迭] (1) cannot cope; find it too much; (2) incessantly; profusely;

[不定] (1) indefinite; indeterminate; (2) drifting; fitful; unsteady;
不定變格 indefinite declension;
不定代詞 indefinite pronoun;
不定根 adventitious roots;
~氣生不定根 aerial adventitious roots;
~水生不定根 aquatic adventitious roots;
~纖維不定根 fibrous adventitious roots;
不定冠詞 indefinite article;
不定量詞 indefinite quantitative;
不定頻度 indefinite frequency;
~不定頻度副詞 adverb of indefinite frequency;
不定期 irregularly scheduled;
不定時 irregular hours;
不定式 infinitive;
~不定式動詞 infinitive verb;
~不定式短語 infinitive phrase;
~分裂不定式 split infinitive;
~簡單不定式 simple infinitive;
~進行體不定式 progress infinitive;
~零不定式 zero infinitive;
~全現不定式 full infinitive;
~人稱不定式 personal infinitive;
~完全不定式 perfect infinitive;
不定性 ambiguity;
~信號不定性 signal ambiguity;
~噪聲不定性 noise ambiguity;
動搖不定 go see-saw; vacillate; waver;
舉棋不定 become hesitant; change one's mind often; hesitate about what move to make; in two minds; indecisive; shilly-shally; unable to make up one's mind; uncertain what to do next; vacillate between two courses of action;
説不定 you never know;
心神不定 agitated; anxious and preoccupied; confused state of mind; distracted; feel restless; have no peace of mind; ill at ease; in a state of discomposure; indisposed; out of sorts; restless mood; unstable mood; wandering in thought;

[不懂] above sb; make nothing of sth; over sb's head;
不懂人事 ignorant of the ways of the world; inexperienced in life; not to know the ways of the world;
不懂事 naive;
不懂裝懂 pretend to know sth when one does not know; smatter;
半懂不懂 not fully understand;
搞不懂 at a loss to understand; be puzzled;
裝不懂 feign ignorance;

[不動] without movement;
不動兵戈 without resorting to force;
不動產 immovable property; immovables;

real estate; realty;
不動產抵押債券 real estate mortgage bands;
不動腦筋 not take the trouble to think; not use one's brain;
不動聲色 display no sign of emotion; keep a straight face; keep one's countenance; keep one's feelings to oneself; keep one's peace and countenance; maintain one's composure; not bat an eyelid; not move a muscle; not show one's feelings; not turn a hair; shut one's pan; stay calm and collected; with a stiff upper lip; without batting an eyelash; without changing countenance;
不動心 show no interest;
背不動 too heavy to bear sth on the back;
呆立不動 stand transfixed to the ground;
伏地不動 lie still on the ground with one's face downward;
請不動 unable to make sb come by an invitation;
挑不動 unable to carry it; too heavy to carry;
馱不動 too heavy to carry on the back;
紋絲不動 absolutely still; not a wrinkle is touched; not budge an inch; not the slightest stir; not move a muscle; not stir an eyelid; not turn a hair; shut one's trap; stock-still;
兀然不動 immovable and steadfast; very determined;
坐着不動 sit still;

[不獨] not only;

[不端] dishonourable; improper;

[不斷] (1) always; continuous; (2) indecisive;
不斷地 constantly; continuously; on end; on top of each other; one following the other; steadily; unceasingly; without interruption;
不斷進步 not look back;
不斷練習 keep one's hand in;
當斷不斷 indecisive;
該斷不斷 fail to act when one should;

[不對] incorrect; wrong;
不對勁 listless; not feel well; not in harmony;
不對頭 not feel well;
對不對 is it correct;

[不二價] uniform price;
言不二價 no bargain; the prices are fixed;
真不二價 have no second price;

[不貳] royal;
不貳過 not repeat a previous mistake;
不貳其心 not be disloyal;

[不乏] there is no lack of;
不乏其人 not short of that kind of people; such people are not rare;
不乏先例 there is no lack of precedents;

[不法] illegal; lawless; unlawful;
不法份子 law breakers;
不法行為 illegal act; unlawful practice;
不法之徒 lawless person; outlaw;
橫行不法 act against law and reason; act illegally; violent and lawless;

[不凡] out of the common run; out of the ordinary;
抱負不凡 ambitious; cherish aspirations out of the common; entertain high aspirations; have great life ambition;
風度不凡 have an imposing appearance;
器度不凡 of uncommon bearing; uncommon personality;
自命不凡 delusions of grandeur; self-glorification; swollen-head;

[不妨] could as well; may as well; might as well; not matter; there is no harm in;
不妨一試 there is no harm in trying;

[不忿兒] (1) not give in to; refuse to obey; (2) not admire; not look up to;

[不符] inconsistent with; not agree with; not conform to; not square with; not tally with;

[不服] not give in to; refuse to accept as final; refuse to obey; remain unconvinced by;
不服水土 suffer from the climate;
心中不服 lack of hearty support; mutinous in one's heart;

[不該] should not;
千不該萬不該 a thousand nos; deeply regret doing sth; most emphatically not; really should not have done sth;

[不改] not change;
累教不改 refuse to correct errors; refuse to mend one's ways;
累誡不改 refuse to correct one's mistakes after repeated warnings; refuse to mend one's ways despite repeated warnings;
屢教不改 refuse to correct one's errors

despite repeated admonition; refuse to correct one's mistakes after repeated admonition; refuse to mend one's ways despite repeated admonition;
屢誡不改 fail to mend one's ways after repeated admonition; persist in doing wrong against repeated warnings; refuse to correct one's mistakes after repeated warnings;

[不甘] not resigned to; unreconciled to; unwilling;
不甘雌伏 unwilling to lie low;
不甘後人 cannot bear playing second fiddle; hate to be outdone; unwilling to let others outshine oneself; unwilling to leg behind; unwilling to take a back seat;
不甘寂寞 hate to be neglected; hate to be overlooked;
不甘落後 loathe to lag behind; unwilling to lag behind;
不甘人後 desire to be second to none; hate to be outdone; not reconcile oneself to falling behind; unwilling to lag behind; unwilling to yield to others;
不甘示弱 hate to show the white feather; refuse to admit being inferior; ill-prepared to have one's weaknesses shown; not be outdone; reluctant to show weakness; unwilling to admit oneself outdone; unwilling to be outshone;
不甘心 not reconciled to; not resigned to;

[不敢] dare not;
不敢不從 dare not disobey; dare not oppose;
不敢不服 all the more ready to obey;
不敢從命 I cannot do as you command me;
不敢當 don't mention it; I really don't deserve this; you flatter me;
~愧不敢當 be embarrassed by undeserved praise;
不敢高攀 dare not aspire to sb's acquaintance; dare not aspire to sb's company;
不敢恭維 cannot say much for;
不敢苟同 beg to differ; cannot agree with sb;
不敢後人 unwilling to fall behind others;
不敢領教 too bad to be accepted;
不敢掠美 cannot claim credit due to others;
不敢旁騖 not dare to concentrate in other endeavours;
不敢擅美 not dare to claim all the credit for oneself;
不敢説半個不字 not dare even to say no;
不敢問津 beyond the means of; not dare to ask the way to the ford; not dare to show any interest in; not dare to inquire;
不敢隱瞞 not dare to hide the truth;
不敢越雷池一步 not dare not go one step beyond the prescribed limit;
不敢造次 not dare not act rashly; not dare to venture;
不敢正視 not brave enough to look sb in the face; not dare not face up to; not dare not to look in sb's face; not dare to look straight; not dare to venture to face sb squarely;
不敢自伐 not dare to be proud of oneself;

[不幹] it is not acceptable; will not accept; will not do it;
淨説不幹 all talk and no cider; all talk and no action; all talk, no action;
撒手不幹 chuck up one's job;
洗手不幹 clear one's skirts; hang up one's axe; never do such a thing again; quit committing crimes; through with sth; wash one's hand of it once and for all; wash one's hands; wash one's hands of the matter; wash one's hands of the whole affair;

[不告而去] leave without notice; leave without saying a word;

[不公] unfair; unjust;

[不共戴天] absolutely irreconcilable; hate to live under the same sky; will not live under the same sky with one's enemy;

[不苟] careful; conscientious; not casual; not lax;
不苟言笑 discreet in speech and manner; not frivolous in talking and joking; not inclined to talk and laugh;
顰笑不苟 not frown or smile to order; natural;
作事不苟 manage things properly;

[不夠] inadequate; insufficient; not enough;

[不顧] brush aside; in contempt of; in defiance

of; in disregard of; in spite of; in the face of; in the teeth of; irrespective of; regardless of; with no respect to; without regard for; without regard to; without respect to;

不顧大局 ignore the larger issues; lack of consideration for the whole; regardless of the whole situation; show no consideration for the general interest;

不顧後果 give no heed to the consequences; reckless of the consequences;

不顧情面 have no consideration for sb's feelings;

不顧事實 disregard facts; fly in the face of the facts; have no regard for the truth; ignore the facts;

不顧他人死活 desperate; not care whether one lives or dies;

不顧體面 regardless of one's reputation;

不顧信義 guilty of bad faith;

不顧一切 desperately; neck or nothing; neck or nought; rain or shine; regardless of all consequences; stop at nothing; stick at nothing; throw caution to the wind; up hill and down dale;

掉臂不顧 walk out on sb;

墮甑不顧 not cry over the spilt milk;

悍然不顧 fly in the face of; fly in the teeth of; so audacious as to turn a deaf ear to; so rude and arrogant as to take no heed of;

棄之不顧 leave sb in the lurch;

危難時棄人於不顧 leave sb in the lurch;

置之不顧 disregard; ignore; leave out of account;

[不觀其人，但觀其友] one is known by the company one keeps;

[不關你事] it is not your business; none of your business; that is no business of yours;

[不管] all; and; any; any old how; any way; as well as; at all coasts; at all events; at all occasions; at any rate; at any events; at any price; at any terms; be it ever so; by all means; by any manner of means; by any means; by fair means or by foul; by hook or by crook; come what may; either... or; -ever; ever so; however; for love or money; for the life of me; in all events; in any case; in any event; in any sort; in any way; in either case; in spite of; independent of; independently of; irrespective of; neither...nor; no; no matter; no matter what; not on any term; not on your Nelly; on no account; on no terms; one way or another; or; regardless of; whatever; whatever happens; whether...or; whichever; whoever; without reference to; without regard to;

不管好歹 hit or miss;

不管結果如何 whatever the consequences;

不管青紅皂白 indiscriminately; irrespective of right or wrong; without finding out the truth;

不管三七二十一 casting all caution to the winds; come what may; no matter how; no matter what you may say; recklessly; regardless of the consequences;

撒手不管 refuse to have anything more to do with the matter; refuse to take any further part in the matter; relinquish one's hold on a matter; take no further interest in a matter; wash one's hands of the business;

三不管 come within nobody's jurisdiction; nobody's business;

睜眼不管 look on with folded arms;

坐視不管 sit watching;

[不光] (1) not the only one; (2) not only;

[不軌] against the law or discipline;

不軌行為 malfeasance;

合謀不軌 engage conspiratorial activities together; plot sedition together;

謀為不軌 engage in conspiratorial activities; hatch a sinister plot; plot a rebellion;

[不果] fail to attain an objective; in vain;

[不過] (1) just; merely; no more than; nothing but; only; (2) but; except that; however; nevertheless; only;

不過爾爾 just so-so; merely mediocre; only so-so;

不過份 within reason;

不過如此 nothing more than this; only so-so;

B

不過問 have no hand in; keep one's hands off; pay no attention to; not bother about; not meddle in; not meddle with; wash one's hands of;
不過意 feel apologetic; sorry;
只不過 just; merely; no more than; only;
左不過 cannot be otherwise; certainly; must be;

［不寒而慄］ blood freezes; blood runs cold; blood turns into ice; give sb the creeps; shiver all over though not being cold; shudder; tremble with fear;

［不合］ (1) not conform to; out of keeping with; unsuited to; (2) ought not; should not;
不合標準 below the mark; not up to the scratch;
不合調 off-key;
不合法 illegal; wrongful;
不合格 below grade; below proof; off-grade; off-specification; unqualified;
不合口味 not appeal to; not to one's taste; not suit the taste of;
不合理 irrational; unreasonable;
不合邏輯 illogical;
不合脾胃 not to one's liking; not suit one's taste;
不合情理 incompatible with reason; unreasonable;
不合身 bad fit;
不合時宜 ill-timed; improper to the occasion; inappropriate to the occasion; inappropriate to the season; incompatible with present needs; mistimed; not appropriate to the occasion; out of keeping with the time; out of date; out of fashion; out of season; out of time; unseasonable; untimely;
不合事實 not tally with the facts; wide of the mark;
不合適 improper; inappropriate; out of place;
不合算 it does not pay; not economical; not worth the candle; not worth the cost;
不合胃口 not suit the taste of; not to one's liking;
性情不合 uncongenial;

［不和］ at cross-purposes; at loggerheads with sb; at odds with sb; at outs with sb; at sword's points with sb; at variance with sb; bad blood; discord; disunity; get at cross-purposes; ill blood; not get along well; on bad terms;
與…不和 at odds with; at outs with sb;

［不歡而散］ break up in disagreement; break up in discord; disperse with ill feelings; end in discord; end on an unpleasant note; part in dudgeon; part on bad terms;

［不患寡而患不均］ inequality rather than want is the cause of trouble;

［不遑］ it is too late to; there is not enough time to do sth;
不遑寧處 busy; have no leisure time;
不遑暇食 so busy as to have no time for eating;
不遑置喙 too late to put in a word;

［不會］ (1) unlikely; will not; (2) have not learned to; unable to;
不會吧 who can say;
不會有好結果的 it ends in tears;
再也不會 never again;

［不諱］ frankly;
直認不諱 acknowledge openly; admit frankly; bluntly admit; confess frankly; make a full confession; plead guilty to a charge;
直言不諱 call a pikestaff a pikestaff; call a spade a spade; free one's mind; give it to sb straight; gie sb a piece of one's mind; make no secret of; mince no words; not mince words; plainspoken; speak bluntly; speak plainly and frankly; talk straight; without mincing words;
~直言不諱的 candid;

［不惑］ (1) with full self-confidence; without doubt; (2) aged forty;
年逾不惑 over forty years of age;

［不羈］ unconventional; uninhibited;
不羈之才 unconventional talent;
放誕不羈 dissipated and unrestrained; dissolute in conduct; reckless and dissipated in behaviour and speech;
放蕩不羈 have full swing; have one's fling; lead a fast life; licentious in conduct; on the loose; run riot; sow one's wild oats; take the bit between one's teeth; take one's swing; tear

around; throw off restraint and become dissolute; unconventional and unbridled; unconventional and unrestrained; uninhibited;
放縱不羈 uninhibited;
豪放不羈 vigorous and unrestrained;
落拓不羈 endowed with a romantic temperament;
倜儻不羈 unconventional; untrammelled;
心神不羈 difficult to concentrate one's mind on sth; with one's mind running wild;

[不及] (1) inferior to; not as good as; (2) find it too late;
措手不及 at a loss; attack before sb knows it; be caught unaware; be caught unprepared; be taken by surprise; cannot make an adequate defence; catch sb napping; catch sb on the wrong foot; catch sb with his pants down; have sb over the barrel; make a surprise attack on sb; put sb off his guard; spring a surprise on sb; take sb napping; throw sb off his guard; too late to do anything about it;
躲閃不及 too late to dodge;
趕不及 too late to catch;
過猶不及 do sth to excess is as bad as not to do enough; going beyond the limit is as bad as falling short; too much is as bad as too little;
匡其不及 make up for any deficiencies;
來不及 it is too late to do sth; there is not enough time to do sth;
始料不及 unexpected at the beginning;
學如不及 study as if one could never learn enough;
有過之而無不及 bear a favourable comparison with; go even farther than; outdo; with even greater; with knobs on;
遠不及 far inferior to; not a circumstance to; not a patch on; nowhere near;
知不及人 wisdom cannot equal others;

[不計] disregard; irrespective of; not take into account;
不計報酬 irrespective of pay; pay no attention to remuneration; pay no heed to whether the pay is high or low;
不計成敗 despite of success; hit or miss; indifferent about success; irrespective of success; not to take success or failure into consideration;
不計後果 ignore the possible consequences; without respect to the results;
不計毀譽 disregard praise or criticism; indifferent to people's praise or blame;
不計價 without charge; without cost; without obligation;
不計利害 regardless of gains or losses;
不計其數 countless; immeasurable; innumerable; pass counting; out of count; too many to count; too numerous to be counted; unable to find the total number of them;

[不見] (1) have not met; have not seen; (2) disappear; missing;
不見不散 don't leave until we are all there; not to leave without seeing each other;
不見得 hard to say; may not necessarily; not at all certain; not likely; not necessarily; unlikely;
不見棺材不落淚 give up only at the sight of the gallows; not shed a tear until one sees one's coffin;
不見經傳 not be found in the classics — not authoritative; unknown;
不見世面 not know anything about the world;
不見天日 live in dark oppression; live in darkness;
避而不見 avoid meeting sb; evade a meeting with sb;
瞅不見 look but unable to see; unable to see;
睹而不見 look without seeing; turn a blind eye to;
很久不見 long time no see;
視而不見 absent-minded; ignore; look at but pay no attention to; look at but pretend not to see; look without seeing; observe but not to pay attention to; see it without taking any notice; shut one's eyes to; turn a blind eye to; wink at; with unseeing eyes;
~視而不見的 unseeing;
~視而不見，聽而不聞 look at but pay no attention to, and listen to but hear nothing; look but see not, listen but hear not; see and hear it without taking any notice;

B

望不見 incapable of being seen; incapable of seeing;
佯為不見 shut one's eyes to another's faults;
一霎不見 vanished in the twinkling of an eye;
轉眼不見 in the twinkling of an eye it ceases to exist;

B

[不教而誅] deal out punishment without a period of instructions; execute without teaching; punish without prior warning;

[不解] (1) not understand; (2) puzzled; (3) indissoluble;
不解之謎 enigma; mystery; unsolved mystery; unsolved riddle;
百思不解 fail to understand even though one cudgels one's brain; incomprehensible; remain perplexed despite much thinking; remain perplexed despite much thought; remain puzzled after pondering over sth a hundred times; unable to find an answer even after much thinking;
~百思不得其解 fail to understand even though one cudgels one's brain; incomprehensible; remain perplexed despite much thinking; remain perplexed despite much thought; remain puzzled after pondering over sth a hundred times; unable to find an answer even after much thinking;
大惑不解 be greatly puzzled; be not a little bewildered; unable to make head or tail of sth;

[不禁] cannot help but; cannot help doing sth; cannot refrain from; in spite of;
不禁落淚 cannot help shedding tears; cannot help weeping;
不禁失笑 cannot forbear laughing; cannot refrain from laughing;

[不僅] (1) not the only one; (2) and not only that; and that is not all; moreover; nor is this all; not only;
不僅僅 not only;

[不盡] (1) incomplete; (2) endless;
不盡根 surd;
~二項不盡根 binomial surd;
~共軛不盡根 conjugate surds;
~同次不盡根 equiradical surd;
不盡然 not exactly so; not necessarily so;
感恩不盡 be filled with boundless gratitude;
感激不盡 exceedingly thankful; extremely grateful; have no way to express all one's gratitude; owe sb a debt of endless gratitude;
取之不盡 the supply is inexhaustible;
~取之不盡，用之不竭 abound in; abound with; abundant; an inexhaustible supply of sth; inexhaustible; inexhaustible and resourceful; inexhaustible in supply and always available for use; overflowing with milk and honey; overflowingly abundant; sufficient in every way;
説之不盡 it is too long a story to tell;
喜之不盡 supremely happy;
言無不盡 say all without reserve;

[不精] not specialized in;
無一不精 an expert in everything;

[不脛而走] gain rapid circulation; get round fast; go the round; spread far and wide; spread like wildfire;

[不久] before long; by and by; draw near; not long after; shortly afterwards; soon; very soon;
不久前 some time ago;
不久人世 not to be long for this world; one's days are numbered;
前不久 lately; of late; recently;

[不…就…] either...or; or;

[不拘] (1) not confine oneself to; not stick to; (2) whatever;
不拘禮節 dispense with formalities; neglect of social rules; not to stick to usual social rules; without ceremony;
不拘繩墨 not to stick to usual formalities;
不拘束 let loose; let loose up; turn loose up;
不拘習俗 free from old customs and habits;
不拘小節 defy trivial conventions; neglect of minor points of conduct; not bother about small matters; not stick at trifles;
不拘形式 disregard formalities; informal;
不拘一格 not stick to one pattern;

[不倦] indefatigable; tireless; untiring;
篤行不倦 work sedulously without any worries;
誨人不倦 indefatigable in teaching men; instruct without fatigue; never tired

of teaching others; teach with tireless zeal; teach without weariness; tireless in teaching others; untiring in the instruction of others;
孜孜不倦 peg away at; sedulous; work with diligence and without fatigue;

[不絕] ceaselessly; without cease;
不絕如縷 (1) almost extinct; hanging by a thread; very precarious; (2) (of sound) linger on faintly;
不絕於耳 can be heard without end; linger in one's ears;

[不覺] unconsciously; without one's knowing;

[不堪] (1) cannot bear; cannot stand; (2) extremely; utterly;
不堪回首 cannot bear to look back; find it unbearable to recall; too sad to reflect;
不堪容忍 intolerable; not to be tolerated; unbearable;
不堪入耳 disgusting; intolerable to the ear; offensive to the ear; revolting;
不堪入目 disgusting; intolerable to the eye; not a pretty sight; not fit to be seen;
不堪設想 can hardly be imagined; cannot be imagined; dreadful to contemplate; hard to imagine; unthinkable;
不堪一擊 be finished off at one blow; cannot withstand a single blow; collapse at the first blow;
不堪造就 cannot be trained; not worth getting an education;
卑鄙不堪 contemptible for one's meanness;
醜陋不堪 perfect fright;
苦不堪言 suffer unspeakably;
狼狽不堪 all in a fluster; be hard-pressed; be thrown into a panic; in a dilemma; in a desperate predicament; in a sorry plight; in an awkward predicament; in an embarrassing situation; in an extremely awkward position; in dire straits; in sore straits; in terrible stuck; in the suds; the situation is unbearable; utterly disconcerted;
潦倒不堪 have gone down in the world; in very poor circumstances;
淩亂不堪 in a fearful mess; in a state of utter confusion;
糜爛不堪 be utterly rotten;
民不堪命 living in misery; the people are hard pressed; the people cannot stand the pressure of the government;
疲憊不堪 be fatigued to the extreme; be dog-tired; be exhausted; be extremely tired; be terribly fatigued; be tired beyond endurance; be tired to death; be whacked to the wide; be worn to a frazzle; in a state of utter exhaustion;
~疲憊不堪的 fagged; fagged out;
破敗不堪 in a stare of disrepair;
破爛不堪 in rags; in shreds and patches; in tatters; ragged; tattered; torn and tattered; worn to the threads; worn-out;
憔悴不堪 pine away dreadfully;
窮困不堪 be pinched with poverty;
污穢不堪 intolerably dirty;
虛弱不堪 as weak as a cat;
擁擠不堪 crowded to capacity; packed like sardines;

[不可] be forbidden; cannot; must not; not allowed; should not;
不可避免 sure as sure can be;
不可多得 hard to come by; rare;
不可分割 indivisible; inseparable;
不可分解 undecomposable;
不可告人 hidden; not to be divulged;
不可估量 beyond measure; incalculable; inestimable;
不可忽視 not to be neglected;
不可或缺 absolutely necessary; indispensible;
不可計量 beyond count; untold;
不可見 invisible;
不可盡信 not to be believed word by word; to be taken with a grain of salt;
不可究詰 cannot explain or find out why;
不可救藥 beyond cure; beyond remedy; hopeless; incorrigible; incurable; past praying for; past remedy;
不可開交 awfully busy;
~忙得不可開交 as busy as one can possibly be; awfully busy; have one's hands full; have one's work cut out; have too much on one's plate; not to have a moment one can call one's own; terribly busy; up to one's ears in work; up to one's eyes in work; up to one's neck in work;
不可抗拒 cannot be resisted; inexorable; irresistible;
不可抗力 irresistible force;

B

不可靠 fly-by-night; unreliable;
~不可靠的人 a broken reed;
不可理解 beyond one's comprehension; incomprehensible; inscrutable;
不可理喻 cannot be brought to reason; impervious to reason; will not listen to reason;
不可彌補 irrecoverable; irredeemable; irretrievable;
不可名狀 beyond description; defy description; indescribable;
不可磨滅 can never be erased; indelible;
~不可磨滅的印象 indelible impressions;
不可能 in a pig's eye; out of the question;
不可逆料 cannot be foreseen; cannot be predicted;
不可逆性 irreversibility;
不可逆轉 irreversible; not to be turned back;
不可偏廢 cannot do one thing and neglect the other; neither can be neglected;
不可企及 beyond one's power of attainment; beyond one's reach;
不可輕視 not to be sneezed at; not to be taken lightly; not to be trifled with; not to look down on;
不可缺少 absolutely necessary; essential; indispensable; vital;
不可饒恕 cannot be excused; inexcusable;
不可勝數 beyond calculation; beyond compute; beyond counting; countless; innumerable; more than one can enumerate; more than one can shake a stick at; too many to count;
不可食的 uneatable;
不可收拾 beyond redemption; get out of hand; hopeless; irremediable; out of hand; too late to pull back; unmanageable;
不可思議 as if by magic; beyond conception; boggle the mind; inconceivable; uncanny; unimaginable;
不可同日而語 cannot be mentioned in the same breath; not to be brought into comparison; there is no comparison between;
不可推卸 bounden; inescapable;
不可挽回 irredeemable; irretrievable;
不可挽救 beyond redemption; dyed in the wool; gone case; hard case; past praying for; past redemption; without redemption;
不可想像 cannot be imagined; inconceivable; unthinkable;
不可信賴 unreliable;
不可言 beyond words;
~不可勝言 beyond description; it cannot be told;
~不可言傳 it cannot be related by language;
~糟不可言 in an indescribable mess;
不可一世 come the heavy swell over sb; consider oneself a world above others; consider oneself unexcelled in the world; insufferably arrogant; on the high ropes; ride the high horse; swagger like a conquering hero; think oneself supreme in the world;
不可譯 untranslatable;
~不可譯性 untranslatability;
不可逾越 impassable; insuperable; insurmountable; should not go beyond the limit of;
不可預見 unpredictable;
~不可預見因素 unpredictable element;
不可造次 don't hurry blindly;
不可爭辯 beyond dispute;
不可終日 in a desperate situation; unable to carry on even for a single day;
不可捉摸 difficult to ascertain; elusive; hard to grasp; intangible; unpredictable;
非…不可 be bound to; have no alternative but; have no choice but; have no option but; have to; it leaves no alternative but; must; inevitably; simply must;
非幹不可 have no option but to do it; needs must do it;
非做不可 have no choice but to;
切不可 on no account;
缺一不可 none of them can be dispensed with; not a single one can be omitted; not one of them can be excluded;
尚無不可 acceptable; passable; permissible;

［不克］ cannot; unable to;
不克分身 cannot get away; unable to leave what one is doing at the moment;
不克自持 in spite of oneself;
不克自制 cannot contain oneself; lose one's head; unable to control oneself;

［不快］ (1) displeased; in low spirits; unhappy;

(2) feel under the weather; indisposed; out of sorts;
不吐不快 have to get it out of one's chest; have to speak out;
[不愧] deserve to be called; prove oneself to be; worthy of;
不愧不怍 have neither shame nor blush;
[不賴] fine; good; not bad;
[不理] brush aside; ignore; pay no attention to; refuse to acknowledge; take no notice of;
愛答不理 get the cold shoulder; give the cold shoulder; turn a cold shoulder; reluctant to answer; show indifference; stand-offish;
愛理不理 attend to sb halfheartedly; cold and indifferent; in an unenthusiastic manner; look cold and indifferent; standoffish; with little interest;
待理不理 give the cold shoulder to sb; listen to sb; half-heartedly; show sb the cold shoulder; treat coolly;
要理不理 attend to sth halfheartedly; standoffish;
置之不理 brush aside; brush to one side; close one's eyes to; disregard; disregard it totally; fob off; ignore sth; leave alone; look the other way; pass by in silence; pass it over; pay no attention to; pay no regard to; put on one side; put sth aside and not pay attention to it; ride over; set aside; set apart; shut one's eyes to; sit idly by; take no notice of; turn a deaf ear to; turn the cold shoulder to; wave aside;
坐視不理 look on with folded arms; sit by idly and remain indifferent;
[不力] not do one's best; not exert oneself;
[不利] adverse to; bad for; count against; detrimental to; go against; go ill with; harmful to; inimical to; make against; militate against; run against; speak ill for; tell against; turn against; unfavourable for; unfavourable to; weigh against;
不利因素 drawback;
於己不利 suicidal;
[不良] bad; harmful; unhealthy;
存心不良 cherish evil designs; cherish evil thoughts; evil-minded; harbour evil intentions; have wicked intentions; have ulterior motives; ill-disposed; mean ill; with evil intent;
居心不良 harbour evil intentions; harbour hostile designs; have some dirty trick up one's sleeve; with bad intentions;
[不了] without end;
不了了之 allow sth to remain unresolved; conclude with conclusion; end up with nothing definite; settle a matter by leaving it unsettled;
辦不了 too much for one to accomplish;
錯不了 unlikely to go wrong;
大不了 (1) at the worst; if the worst comes to the worst; (2) alarming; not so remarkable; nothing serious;
管不了 none of one's business;
活不了 unlikely to survive;
~活不了多久 not long for this world; not to be long for this world;
免不了 be bound to be; hard to avoid; inevitable; it is only natural that; unavoidable;
去不了 cannot go; unable to attend; unable to go;
少不了 (1) cannot dispense with; cannot do without; (2) be bound to; unavoidable; (3) considerable;
使不了 more than one needs;
受不了 (1) cannot bear; cannot stand it; cannot take it; unable to endure; (2) too much; very much;
~壓得人受不了 get on top of sb;
~再也受不了 can't take any more;
死不了 cannot die; will not die;
算不了 not to be counted as;
~算不了甚麼 (1) not so important; nothing to be excited about; (2) not very impressive;
逃不了 inescapable from; unable to escape;
忘不了 will not forget;
醒不了 unable to wake up in time;
學到老，學不了 learning is an endless process; one is never too old to learn;
用不了 (1) have more than is needed; (2) less than;
遮不了 cannot be covered;
走不了 not able to leave; not likely to leave;
做不了 cannot do it;
[不料] to one's surprise; unexpectedly; who

B

would have thought;

[不吝] generous with; not care; not grudge; not mind; not stint;
不吝賜教 please favour me with your comments; so kind as to give me a reply;

[不靈] ineffective; not work;
不靈敏 unskilled;
冥頑不靈 stupid and obstinate;

[不論] regardless of; whether;
不論成敗 hit or miss; sink or swim; stand or fall;
不論好歹 for good and for evil;
不論真假 for what it is worth;

[不落言筌] grasp a passage without clinging to too literal an interpretation;

[不滿] disaffection; discontented; dissatisfied; resentful;
不滿現狀 discontent with things as they are;
不滿者 malcontent;
表示不滿 give sb a piece of one's mind;
發洩不滿 air one's grievances; express one's grievances;
煽動不滿 incite discontent; foment discontent;

[不忙] take one's time; there is no hurry;

[不眠] egersis;
不眠之夜 restless night; white night;

[不免] bound to be; unavoidable;

[不妙] anything but reassuring; far from good; not going well;

[不敏] not clever; not intelligent;
敬謝不敏 beg to be excused; decline a request politely; politely refuse to do sth; regret being unable to comply with your request;

[不名數] abstract number;

[不明] (1) not clear; unknown; (2) fail to understand;
不明不白 doubtful; dubious; for no clear reason whatever; obscure; unclear;
不明底蘊 have no inside information about; ignorant of the true picture;
不明飛行物體 unidentified flying object (UFO);
不明內情 out of the swim;
不明確 indeterminate;
不明事理 lack of common sense; unreasonable;
不明是非 confuse right and wrong;
不明真相 be kept in the dark; ignorant of the actual situation; ignorant of the facts; not know the truth of the matter; not understand the true situation;
不明智 ill-advised; unwise;
仍然不明 remain unknown;
身分不明 of unknown identity; one's legal identity not clarified; one's standing is not clear; unidentified;
行蹤不明 whereabouts unknown;

[不謀] without planning;
不謀而得 gain sth without looking for it;
不謀而合 act in accord, without prior deliberation; agree without prior consultation; be perfectly in harmony; happen to hold the same view;

[不能] cannot; must not; should not;
不能不 cannot but; have to;
不能不說 cannot keep silent about; feel impelled to speak;
不能得逞 be doomed to failure; cannot have one's way; cannot succeed;
不能動 like a log;
不能動彈 too tired to stir; unable to stir any more;
不能理解 beyond one's depth; out of one's depth;
不能勉強 cannot be forced;
不能批評的人 forbidden game;
不能全得，寧可全失 the whole tree or not a cherry on it;
不能容忍 cannot tolerate; have no patience with; tired of;
不能赦免 unabsolvable;
不能勝任 incompetent;
不能手軟 should not be soft-handed; show no mercy;
不能忘懷 cannot forget; cannot get sth out of one's mind;
不能忘情 be still emotionally attached;
不能相比 no true parallel can be drawn;
不能想像 unimaginable; unthinkable;
不能自拔 too deeply involved to withdraw; unable to extricate oneself;
不能自圓其說 unable to justify one's own assertion; unable to make out one's case;
不能自制 have no control over oneself;
不能奏效 cannot succeed; cannot work; not prove effective;
力不能及 beyond one's capacity; beyond

one's depth; out of one's depth; strength is not equal to duties; unequal to one's task;

力不能支 too weak to stay on one's feet; unable to stand the strain any longer;

無一不能 able to handle everything; almighty; extremely versatile;

[不寧唯是] and what is more; moreover; not only so; that is not all;

[不怕] not afraid of; not fear;

不怕低，只怕比 comparisons are odious;

不怕官，祇怕管 there is no fear of the government, but rather fear to be governed;

不怕麻煩 go out of one's way; not be afraid of trouble; not feel troublesome; spare no pains;

不怕一萬，就怕萬一 it is always wise to play safe; one cannot afford a single mishap;

天不怕，地不怕 defy heaven and earth; fear neither Heaven nor Earth; fear nothing and no one; fear nothing at all; fear nothing on earth; nothing daunted;

[不配] (1) not qualified to; unworthy of; (2) mismatch;

不配套 incompatibility between various aspects of;

[不平] (1) not level; not smooth; uneven; (2) injustice; unfairness; wrong; (3) complaint; grievance; indignant; resentful;

不平等待遇 unequal treatment;

不平等交換 unequitable exchange;

不平等條約 unequal treaty;

不平衡 imbalance; lack of balance; off-balance;

不平則鳴 where there is injustice, there will be an outcry;

抱不平 be outraged by an injustice done to another person; be the champion of the oppressed; champion the accuse of a wronged person; indignant at injustice; take up the cudgels against an injustice;

~打抱不平 champion of the weak; champion of the oppressed; champion the cause of the justice; champion the wronged party against the offender; come out in defence of the weak; defend sb against an injustice; feel injustice done to another and wish to help; interfere on behalf of the injured party; intervene in cases of injustice for the benefit of the injured party; lend a helping hand to right a wrong; play the part of a gallant knight; ready to help the wronged party to redress grievances; stand up to a bully in defense of sb; take up the cudgels against the injustice done to sb; take up the cudgels for the injured party;

~代抱不平 take up the cudgels for another;

忿忿不平 indignant and disturbed;

憤憤不平 feel aggrieved; indignant; nurse a grievance; resentful;

路見不平，拔刀相助 see injustice on the road and draw one's sword to help the victim — take up the cudgels for the injured party; take up the cudgels on behalf of the victim of injustice;

鳴不平 air grievances for; complain of unfairness; cry out against injustice;

氣不平 indignant about injustice;

[不期而遇] bump into; chance on; chance to meet; come across; happen to meet; have a chance encounter; meet sb by chance; run across; run up against; sb's paths cross;

[不起] not able to;

吃罪不起 the responsibility for the blame will be too great for sb;

擔戴不起 not able to assume the responsibility;

擔當不起 cannot bear the responsibility; unable to bear the burden;

當不起 dare not accept; unequal to a responsibility;

一病不起 die of illness; fall ill and die; fall ill and never recover; take to one's bed and never leave it again;

[不巧] as luck would have it; unfortunately;

[不屈] unbending; unyielding;

不屈不撓 carry a stiff upper lip; indomitable; keep a stiff upper lip; never give ground; refuse to submit; stick to one's guns; unyielding;

~不屈不撓的 hard-nosed; indefatigable; indomitable;

抗志不屈 adhere to high purposes and not submit to threats;

寧死不屈 would rather die than submit;
誓死不屈 vow that one would rather die than yield;
威武不屈 not to be subdued by force;
至死不屈 stick to one's principle till death;

[不全] incomplete; partial;

[不群] keep oneself aloof;
峨然不群 far excel others;
矯矯不群 excellent and outstanding; out of the ordinary;
牢落不群 bad mixer; keep oneself aloof;
挺然不群 distinguished from fellowmen; outstanding; towering over others;

[不然] but for; or; or else; otherwise;
不然的話 otherwise; or;
大謬不然 absolutely preposterous; gross error; grossly mistaken;
若不然 if not; otherwise;

[不仁] cruel;
狼戾不仁 vicious and cruel; ruthlessly cruel;
莫信直中直，須防仁不仁 do not believe all are honest who appear honest, but beware lest the semblance of goodness turn out to be the reverse;
為富不仁 rich but cruel; rich but immoral; wealthy but unkind; well off but uncharitable;

[不忍] cannot bear to; cannot endure;
不忍人 not have the heart to do;
不忍正視 hate the sight of; heartbreaking to look at;
不忍卒睹 cannot bear to finish the view; cannot bear to see; hate the sight of;
不忍卒聽 heartbreaking to hear;
不忍坐視 cannot bear to stand idly by;
小不忍則亂大謀 a little impatience spoils great plans; being unable to endure little things will upset great plans; if one is not patient in small things one will never be able to control great ventures; lack of forbearance in small matters upsets great plans; want of forbearance in small matters will spoil great plans; who cannot take small insults is liable to spoil big plans;
於心不忍 against one's conscience; cannot bear to; not to have the heart to;

[不日] in a few days; soon; within the next few days;

[不容] be not allowed;
不容耽擱 allow of no delay;
不容抵賴 brook no denial;
不容分辯 allow of no excuse; willy-nilly;
不容分說 allow no explanation; give sb no chance to argue; no time is allowed for explanation; not wait for an explanation; without wasting a word;
不容忽視 cannot be ignored;
不容懷疑 admit of no doubt;
不容諱言 it is no secret that; make no secret of;
不容冒犯 brook no offence;
不容歪曲 brook no distortion;
不容易 no cinch;
不容爭議 beyond debate; incontestable;
不容置辯 beyond dispute; indisputable; undeniable;
不容置喙 allow of no interruption; brook no intervention; refuse letting others talk;
不容置疑 above suspicion; allow of no doubt; beyond doubt; beyond question;
覆載不容 intolerable to heaven and earth — unusually wicked and evil;

[不如] (1) inferior to; not anywhere near; not as good as; not equal to; nowhere near; (2) it would be better to; not anything like; nothing like;
不如當年 beyond it; get past it; past it;
倒不如 even worse than; it's better to; no better than;
遠遠不如 be nothing near so; cannot be compared to; not a quarter as good as;
豬狗不如 worse than pigs or dogs;
自愧不如 feel ashamed of one's inferiority;
自知不如 consider oneself inferior to another; know one isn't another's equal;

[不若] no match for;
不擅詞令 lack facility in polite speech;

[不善] (1) a bad hand at; not good at; (2) bad; evil; ill; (3) quite impressive;
不善始者不善終 a bad beginning makes a bad ending;
不善應酬 socially inept;
居心不善 ill-disposed; one's heart is bent on evil;

[不捨] begrudge;

戀戀不捨 cannot bear to leave; hang about one's neck; hate to see sb go; reluctant to part with; unwilling to part with;
強聒不捨 preach tirelessly;
鍥而不捨 keep on doing sth with perseverance; keep one's nose to the grindstone; make steady efforts; peg away at it; perseverance; stick it out; stick to it; stick to sth with persistence; work with perseverance;
~鍥而不捨，金石可鏤 constant dripping wears away the stone; little strokes fell great oaks; many strokes fell down strong oaks; patience wears out stones;

[不慎] careless; headless;

[不勝] (1) cannot bear; unequal to; (2) extremely; tremendously; (3) cannot help doing sth; too...to;
不勝悲哀 overcome with sorrow;
不勝詫異 be lost in wonder; much to one's surprise;
不勝惆悵 cannot help feeling disappointed; cannot help feeling melancholy;
不勝負重 sink beneath one's burden;
不勝感激 deeply grateful; feel strongly obliged;
不勝駭異 be greatly surprised;
不勝浩歎 heave a deep sigh; sigh deeply;
不勝惶惑 be extremely perplexed and alarmed;
不勝今昔 feel quite touched by the changes of human life;
不勝驚異 be filled with wonder; be greatly surprised;
不勝枚舉 beyond calculation; cannot be counted one by one; cannot be enumerated one by one; defy enumeration; too numerous to mention one by one; uncountable;
不勝銘感 be deeply grateful;
不勝淒然 cannot help being sad;
不勝其煩 be pestered beyond endurance; cannot withstand any trouble; too troublesome;
不勝慶幸 have enough cause for rejoicing;
不勝任 incompetent; unfit for the post;
不勝榮幸 be greatly honoured; feel indebted for the honour of;
不勝惋惜 be extremely sorry for sb;
不勝羨慕 be lost in admiration;
不勝羞愧 be extremely ashamed;
不勝厭惡 be greatly disgusted with;
不勝遺憾 much to one's regret;
悲不勝悲 make one's sorrow even worse;
多不勝數 too many to enumerate;
防不勝防 cannot reckon with all eventualities; hard to guard against; impossible to defend effectively; impossible to guard against;
舉不勝舉 impossible to list; too numerous to mention;
苦不勝言 indescribable sorrow; so painstaking that it cannot be expressed in words; suffer untold misery; the suffering is indescribable;
美不勝收 feast for the eyes; too beautiful to be absorbed all at once;
美不勝言 beautiful beyond all description; too beautiful for words;
弱不勝衣 so fragile to bear the weight of clothing; too delicate to wear a coat; too feeble to bear the weight of one's clothes; too weak to bear the weight of one's clothing;
如不勝衣 as if one cannot bear clothing; humble and modest; seem scarcely strong enough to bear the trifling weight of one's clothing; so frail as to lack even the strength to bear the weight of clothing; too frail to bear the weight of one's clothes; too weak to bear the weight of one's clothes; very tender and frail;
數不勝數 beyond count; beyond number; countless; too numerous to count; without number;
無往不勝 all-conquering; ever-victorious; ever-victorious in one's forward march; invincible; victorious everywhere; win victory wherever one goes;
邪不勝正 evil can never prevail over good; the evil will not triumph over the virtuous; the upright need not fear the crooked;
讚不勝讚 above praise; beyond praise;
戰無不勝 all-conquering; ever-triumphant; ever-victorious; invincible; never to lose a battle; win in every battle;
~戰無不勝，攻無不克 one has never failed to win a battle or take a city;

B

there is no battle that one cannot win and no fortress that one cannot storm; triumph in every battle and succeed in every invasion;
指不勝屈 a great many; countless; innumerable; more than can be counted on one's fingers; too many for the fingers to calculate; too many to be counted;

[不失為] can yet be regarded as; may after all be accepted as;

[不時] at times; at whiles; between whiles; ever and again; every now and again; every now and then; from time to time; now and again; now and then; occasionally; on occasion; once in a while;
不時見到 see sth of;
不時興 go out; go out of fashion;
不時之需 a possible period of want or need;

[不識] fail to see; ignorant of; not appreciate; not know;
不識大體 fail to see the larger issue; ignore the general interest;
不識好歹 cannot tell good from bad; gullible; not know chalk from cheese; not know what is good for one;
不識趣 not know how to behave;
不識時務 (1) show no understanding of the times; (2) insensible;
不識抬舉 fail to appreciate sb's kindness; not know how to appreciate favours;
不識相 unable to see the fitness of things;
不識一丁 illiterate; not know a single word;
瞎字不識 illiterate; unable to read a single word;
一丁不識 not know B from a battledore; not know beans; not know chalk from cheese; not know one's ABC;

[不世] rare;
不世之才 rare talent;
不世之功 magnificent contributions; matchless merit;

[不是] not;
不是…而是 not...but...;
不是個兒 incapable; no good; no match;
不是開玩笑的 mean business;
不是那麼 not all that;
~他不是那麼聰明 he is not all that intelligent;
不是你死，便是我活 then one of us must die;
不是玩兒的 no joke; no kidding; not a trifling matter; serious;
不是味兒 (1) a bit off; not quite right; not the right flavour; (2) amiss; fishy; queer;
不是冤家不聚頭 enemies and lovers are destined to meet;
擔不是 take the blame;
可不是嘛 you're telling me;
派不是 lay the blame on sb; put the blame on sb; shift the blame onto sb;
賠不是 apologize; make an apology; repair a wrong;
豈不是 does it not; is it not; would it not;
認不是 admit a fault;
是不是 is it true or not;

[不適] discomfort; indisposed; malaise; out of sorts; troubled; unwell;
不適當 inadequate;
不適合 inadequate; inconvenience; unsuited;
不適時令 unfit for the season;
不適應 not adapted to; not fit to; not suited to;
略感不適 feel a bit unwell;

[不熟] (1) not yet done; still raw; (2) unacquainted with; unfamiliar with;
不熟練 unskilled;

[不爽] (1) in a bad mood; not well; out of sorts; (2) accurate; without discrepancy;
屢試不爽 as often as it is tried, it is found efficacious; as often as it is used, it proves accurate; effective every time it is used; find no fault with sth after repeated trials; prove to be successful in every test;

[不説] do not say; no comment;
不説為妙 be better left unsaid;
不説這個了 skip it;
不説自明 tell its own tale;
該説不説 button up one's lips; button up one's mouth;
笑而不説 smile and say nothing;

[不死] half dead;
不死不活 half dead; lifeless; neither dead or alive;
不死鳥 secular bird;

老不死 old bastard; old debauchee; old fart; old fellow; old fogy; old folk;

[不送] not bother to see sb out;

[不俗] not hackneyed; original; uncommon;
出語不俗 speak in a lofty manner; speak in an uncommon way;

[不遂] fail; fail to materialize;

[不談] not talk about;
避而不談 avoid any mention; avoid mentioning; draw a veil over; evade a question; keep from talking about; not to touch on the question of;
略而不談 leave unmentioned; omit to mention; skip over without reference to;

[不特] not only;

[不聽] would not listen;
屢告不聽 would not listen to repeated advice;
屢勸不聽 keep one's own course in spite of talking to him many times;

[不停] without stop;
哭個不停 go on crying;
忙個不停 on the go; on the hop; on the hump; on the trot;
~一整天忙個不停 on the trot all day;
説個不停 nineteen to the dozen;

[不通] (1) be blocked up; be obstructed; impassable; (2) illogical; not make sense; ungrammatical;
半通不通 know a little;
不通情理 impervious to reason; unreasonable;
不通水火 have no contact with others;
不通行 no thoroughfare;
此路不通 no throughfare; no throughroad; road closed;
打不通 the line is engaged;
拘泥不通 slow-witted, stubborn, and stupid;
水洩不通 even a drop of water couldn't leak out; packed; watertight;
無一不通 extremely versatile; know all;
一竅不通 a complete ignoramus; an absolute blockhead; completely ignorant; have a blind spot; impenetrably dull; it is all Greek to me; know nothing at all about sth; know nothing of; lack of slightest knowledge of; not know beans about sth; not to know anything about; not to know the ABC of; not to know the first thing; not up one's street at all; out of one's depth; out of one's element; utterly ignorant of; utterly stupid; very poor;
於理不通 improper and unreasonable; it is illogical;

[不同] different; disparity; distinct; diverse; imparity; not alike;
不同凡響 out of the common run; out of the ordinary; out of this world; outstanding;
不同流俗 against the current fashion; different from the prevalent custom;
不同意 disagree;
不同於 differ from; differ in; differ with; different from; different than; different to; differentiate; differentiate from; discern; discriminate ...from; dissimilar to; distinct from; distinguish; diverse from;
斷然不同 be not at all one and the same;
和而不同 seeking common ground while allowing differences;
完全不同 a world of difference;
與眾不同 different from all others; different from other people; different from the common run; different from the rest; distinctive; extraordinary; flaky; not like others; not the same as others; out of the common; out of the ordinary; peculiar; uncommon; unlike others; unusual;

[不妥] improper; inappropriate; not proper; not the right way;

[不外] not beyond the scope of; nothing more than;

[不忘] not forget;
戀戀不忘 affectionate remembrance; invincible attachment;
念念不忘 be always preoccupied with; be enthroned in the hearts; be obsessed with; bear in mind constantly; cling to the memory of; harp on sth; never forget sb for a moment; never forget sth for a moment; on the brain; think constantly of;
雖死不忘 I will remember it even after death;
永感不忘 grateful forever;
永矢不忘 always remember in one's

heart; vow to remain forever in one's heart;
永志不忘 bear in mind forever; enshrine in one's memory; inscribe forever in one's memory; remember forever; will always bear in mind; will always cherish the memory of sb; will never forget;

B

[不為已甚] not go too far; not push matters to extremes; refrain from going to extremes;
[不惟] not only;
[不韙] error; fault;
冒大不韙 defy the universal will of the people; defy world opinion; risk universal condemnation;
~冒天下之大不韙 against the world; defy the universal will of the people; defy world opinion; despite universal condemnation; fly in the face of the will of the people; in defiance of world condemnation; regardless of universal condemnation; risk universal condemnation;
[不畏] defy;
不畏艱險 fear neither hardship nor danger; fearless of danger and difficulty; not to shrink from hardships and crises; take the bull by the horns;
不畏強暴 defy brutal suppression; not fear brutal force;
不畏嚴寒 defy severe cold;
[不謂] to one's surprise; unexpectedly;
[不穩] insecure; unstable; unsteady;
站不穩 unable to stand firmly;
嘴不穩 fond of talking and unable to keep a secret;
坐不穩 (1) cannot sit steady; (2) unsteady;
[不問] (1) disregard; ignore; not consider pay no attention to; (2) let off;
不問好歹 come what may; no matter whether it is good or bad; whether good or bad;
不問貧富 make no distinction between the rich and the poor;
不問情由 without asking about the circumstances or causes; without first asking about what happened;
不問是非曲直 not to bother to look into the rights and wrongs of a case;
不聞不問 indifferent to sth; leave out of account; not bother to ask questions or listen to what's said; pass over in silence; pay no attention to; remain indifferent to sth; show no interest in sth;
置之不問 dismiss the subject; leave unnoticed; leave unquestioned; pass by;
[不聞] turn a deaf ear to;
充耳不聞 close one's ears to; stop one's ears to; shut one's ears to; stuff one's ears and refuse to listen; stuff up one's ears and refuse to hear; turn a deaf ear to;
塞耳不聞 turn a deaf ear to;
[不無] not without;
不無可疑 not above suspicion;
[不息] without cease;
川流不息 a continuous flow of; coming and going all the time; flow; flowing past in an endless stream; flowing without ceasing; in a steady stream; keep pouring in and out; never-ending;
[不惜] not scruple;
不惜代價 at any costs; not to balk at paying the price of; stop at no expense;
不惜工本 at all costs; go to great lengths; spare no expense;
不惜篇幅 devote a large amount of space to;
不惜犧牲 at all costs; spare no sacrifice;
不惜一切代價 at all costs; at any cost; give one's ears; give one's right arm; give the world;
[不下於] (1) as many as; no less than; (2) as good as; not inferior to; on a par with;
[不鮮] not rare;
屢見不鮮 a common occurrence; it is often seen; not rare; not uncommon; nothing new; sth that takes place again and again;
[不嫌其煩] go out of one's way;
[不祥] ill omen; inauspicious; ominous; unlucky;
不祥的開端 inauspicious start;
不祥之兆 a bad omen; an ill omen; the writing on the wall;
[不詳] (1) not in detail; (2) not quite clear;
數目不詳 an unknown number of;
語焉不詳 make only a bare of mention sth; not go into details; not speak in

detail;
源委不詳 the beginning and the end are unknown — as the details of the story are not known;

[不想] have no heart to do sth; have no stomach for;
不想要 have no heart to do sth; have no stomach for;

[不像] unlike;
不像話 (1) mere drivelling; now you are talking; unreasonable; (2) outrageous; shocking;
~太不像話 appalling; beyond all limits; simply outrageous; the height of absurdity; too preposterous; utterly not presentable; worse than a crime;
不像樣 (1) in no shape to be seen; unpresentable; (2) beyond recognition;
~太不像樣 getting out of bounds; too awful;

[不消說] it goes without saying; let alone; much less; not to mention; not to speak of; still less; to mention nothing of; to say nothing of; without mentioning the fact that;

[不孝] unfilial;

[不肖] unworthy;
不肖子孫 unworthy descendants;

[不屑] disdain to do sth; feel it beneath one's dignity to do sth;
不屑一顧 cock a snook at; fob off; beneath one's notice; not deign to take a glance; not worth sb's notice; shrug off; snap one's fingers at; wave aside; will not spare a glance for;

[不懈] unwearied;
常備不懈 always on the alert;
奮志不懈 determined and unwearied;

[不謝] it's my pleasure; not at all;

[不行] (1) be not allowed; no way; out of the question; (2) no good;
不行時 out of fashion;
那絕對不行 that will never do; that would never do;
那可不行 nothing doing;
徒法不行 good laws without enforcement are useless;

[不幸] (1) adversity; misfortune; (2) unfortunately;
不幸而言中 the prediction has unfortunately come true;
不幸中之大幸 a lucky break out of misfortune; a stroke of good luck in a stretch of bad; good fortune in the midst of bad;
哀其不幸 feel sorry for sb's misfortune; have pity on sb for his misfortune; feel sorry for sb's misfortune; have pity on sb for their misfortune;
橫遭不幸 sudden misfortune; suffer a sudden misfortune;
連遭不幸 a succession of misfortunes has befallen sb;
險遭不幸 come within an ace of death;
一連串的不幸 a chapter of accidents;
遭逢不幸 meet with misfortune;
真不幸 worse luck;

[不休] ceaselessly; endlessly;
刺刺不休 chatter like a magpie; chatter on and on; chatter without stop; gabble on and on; go nineteen to the dozen; keep on clamouring; repeat endlessly; run nineteen to the dozen; run off at the mouth; speak nineteen to the dozen; talk a leg off a dog, talk a leg off a donkey; talk a leg off a horse; talk incessantly; talk nineteen to the dozen; talk one's head off; talk without cease;
笑不休 compulsive laughing; forced laughing;

[不朽] immortal;
垂名不朽 with the name never to be forgotten;
永垂不朽 be remembered forever by posterity; eternal life; live forever; mortal; win immortality;

[不許] (1) not allow; not permit; (2) cannot;
不許干涉 hands off;

[不卹] disregard;

[不學而能] do a thing easily and naturally;

[不遜] impertinent; rude;

[不亞於] as good as; not second to;
不亞於人 bear comparison with; not inferior to anyone; second to none; stand comparison with; with the best;

[不言] keep silent; without saying;
不言而喻 it goes without saying; it is self-evident; speak for itself; taken for granted; tell its own story;
~結果不言而喻 the results speak for themselves;

杜口不言 keep silent; shut up;
妙在不言中 the charm lies in what is left unsaid;
小小不言 too small to be worth...; too trivial to talk about;
知而不言 reticent about what one knows;
知無不言 have one's say without reserve; hide nothing; say all that one knows; speak one's mind; speak without reserve; tell sb all that one knows without any reservation;
知無不言，言無不盡 say all one knows and says it without reserve; tell the truth and the whole truth;

[不厭] not mind doing sth; not object to; not tire of;
不厭其煩 go out of one's way; not mind taking all the trouble; take great pains; take the trouble; very patient;
不厭其詳 dwell at great length; go into minute details;
百讀不厭 can be read a hundred times with delight; capable of being read a hundred times without becoming stale; never get tired of reading the book a hundred times; worth reading a hundred times; worth reading again and again;
百看不厭 be at all time a great pleasure to see; be worth reading a hundred times; be worth watching a hundred times; never get tired to reading; never tire of seeing;
百聽不厭 worth hearing a hundred times; never get tired of hearing;
百問不厭 not to lose one's temper no matter how often others ask; patiently answer any questions sb asks;

[不要] don't;
不要吹牛 come off it;
不要動 hands off;
不要見外 do not treat me as a stranger; make yourself at home;
不要緊 (1) unimportant; it's nothing serious; (2) it doesn't matter; never mind; (3) it looks all right;
不要拘束 make yourself at home;
不要客氣 don't mention it; make yourself at home; you're welcome;
不要臉 have no sense of shame; shameless; what a nerve; without self-respect;
~給臉不要臉 foolish enough to reject a face-saving offer;
不要自尋麻惱 don't ask for it; don't ask for trouble; don't look for trouble; don't trouble troubles till troubles trouble you; let sleeping dogs lie; never trouble trouble till trouble troubles you;

[不藥而癒] recover for illness without medical help;

[不夜城] a city with lights turned on all night;

[不一] differ; vary;
不一定 not necessarily so; not sure; uncertain;
不一而足 by no means an isolated case; numerous;
不一致 out of accord with;
表裏不一 act a double part; have two faces; think in one way and behave in another; think one way and act another;
各說不一 each has his different version; each tells a different story;
眾說不一 there are many different versions of a story;

[不宜] inadvisable; inappropriate; not suitable;

[不已] endlessly; incessantly; unceasingly;
感奮不已 be greatly moved and inspired;
後悔不已 be overcome with regret;
嗟歎不已 sigh without ceasing;

[不以為] not to be taken as;
不以為恥 not to be ashamed of; not to think it as shameful;
不以為例 not to be taken as a precedent;
不以為然 express disapproval; not approve; object to; take exception to; think otherwise;
不以為伍 refuse to associate with sb;
不以為忤 in good spirit; take no offence;
不以為意 dismiss al anxiety from one's thoughts; indifferent to; laugh at; leave out of consideration; make little of; make nothing of; not care a pin; not care a rush; not care a straw; not pay any attention; not trouble oneself about; take no heed of;

[不亦樂乎] what a delight it would be if; will not that also be pleasant;

[不易] (1) not easy; (2) irrefutable;
不易之論 irrefutable statement;

得來不易 hard earned; it has not come easily;
~得來不易的勝利 hard-earned victory;
來之不易 be not easily won; hard to come by; hard-earned; hard-won; not come easily;

[不意] (1) to one's surprise; unexpectedly; (2) unawareness; unpreparedness;
乘其不意 take advantage of sb's ignorance;
出其不意 all of a sudden; be taken unawares; catch sb napping; catch sb unawares; catch sb with his pants down; off one's guard; surprise sb; take sb by surprise; with one's pants down;
~出其不意，攻其無備 catch a weasel asleep; catch sb unprepared; do the unexpected, attack the unprepared;
襲其不意 catch a weasel asleep; catch one unprepared;

[不義] injustice;
不義之財 crooked money; filthy lucre; ill-gotten gains; ill-gotten wealth; lucre;
多行不義必自斃 a wicked person is sure to bring about his own destruction; a wicked person is sure to bring destruction to himself; give a rogue rope enough and he will hang himself; he who is unjust is doomed to destruction; if one keeps on doing unrighteous deeds, he is bound to come to ruin; to do evil deeds frequently will bring ruin to the doer;

[不翼而飛] (1) disappear into thin air; disappear mysteriously; disappear without trace; vanish all of a sudden; (2) spread fast; spread like wildfire;

[不用] (1) need not; (2) disuse; non-utility; (3) have no intention to become;
不用客氣 don't mention it; my pleasure; you're welcome;
不用說 as a matter of course; go without saying; needless to say;
不用謝 anytime; don't mention it; no problem; not at all; that's all right;
備而不用 keep sth for possible future use;
擯而不用 reject;
擯棄不用 dismiss sb and refrain from giving him an appointment; throw on the scrap-heap;
廢而不用 fall into disuse; fall into oblivion; pass into disuse; put aside as useless; stop using;
疑人不用 if you doubt a person, do not use him/her;

[不由] cannot but; cannot help;
不由得 cannot but; cannot help;
不由分說 allowing no explanation; give no chance to explain; not allowing sb to speak; without giving sb the opportunity to explain; without listening to sb's protests; without stopping for an explanation;
不由自主 beyond one's control; cannot but; cannot help; have no control over oneself; in spite of oneself; involuntarily;
不因不由 unconsciously; unwittingly;

[不虞] (1) unexpected; (2) contingency; eventuality; (3) not worry about;
不虞匱乏 fear no shortage of material resources; freedom from want; not to worry about running out of supplies;
不虞之備 a second string to one's bow; spare parts;

[不予] deny; not give; not grant; refuse;
不予考慮 leave sb out of account; leave sb out of consideration; leave sth out of account; leave sth out of consideration; not considerate; refuse to take into consideration;
不予理睬 give no heed to; ignore; turn a deaf ear to;
不予理會 brush aside; deaf to; pay no attention to; take no notice of; turn a deaf ear to; turn one's back on;
不予批准 not grant approval;
不予受理 refuse to accept; rule sth out;
不予追究 no punishment;

[不語] without uttering a word;
低首不語 bow one's head and keep silent; hang down the head without uttering a word; hang one's head in silence;
低頭不語 lower one's head and keep quiet;

[不育] acyesis; aphoria; infertility; sterility;
不育性 self-sterility;
~雄性不育性 male sterility;
~自體不育性 self-sterility;
不育症 infertility; sterility;
胞質不育 cytoplasmic sterility;

二倍體不育 diplontic sterility;
繼發性不育 secondary sterility;
男性不育 male sterility;
女性不育 atocia;
染色體不育 chromosomal sterility;
相對性不育 relative sterility;
厭惡性不育 aphoria impercita;
陰虛性不育 aphoria impotens;
原發性不育 primary sterility;

[不願] be disinclined; reluctant; unwilling;

[不約] without previous arrangement;
不約而同 happen to coincide; in accord, without prior agreement; take the same action or view without prior consultation;
不約而遇 meet sb without previous arrangement;

[不悅] displeased; unhappy;
怫然不悅 be very much offended by; show an angry expression; show sign of displeasure;

[不孕] acyesis; dysgenesis; sterility;
不孕症 infertility;
~初發性不孕症 primary infertility;
繼發不孕 secondary infertility;
原發不孕 primary infertility;

[不再] not any more; no longer;

[不在] (1) absent; not in; out; (2) dead;
不在此例 not within the rule; that is an exception;
不在此限 not apply; not subject to the limits;
不在乎 not care a cuss; not give a cent; not give a cuss; not give a damn; not give a hang; not mind; not to care about;
不在話下 go without saying; in a cinch; nothing difficult; out of question; regard;
不在其位 not in the position;
不在眼裏 beneath one's notice; have no respect for; show one's contempt for; snap one's fingers at; think nothing of; treat with disdain;
不在意 (1) not mind; pay no attention to; take no notice of; (2) careless; negligent;

[不戰] without fighting;
不戰而退 go away without striking a blow; retreat without fighting;
不戰而降 surrender without fighting;
不戰自潰 collapse without a battle; melt away without striking a blow;
不戰自亂 become confused without even going into battle;

[不振] dejected and apathetic; in low spirits;
頹喪不振 dejected after defeat;
萎靡不振 despondent; in a dejected state; in a state of mental doldrums; lethargic; unable to pick oneself up
一蹶不振 be finished for good; collapse after one setback; curl up; never be able to recover after a setback; never to recover from a setback; unable to recover after a setback; unable to get up after a fall;

[不知] all at sea; beyond sb; have no idea of; ignorant of; in the dark; it beats me; know nothing about; not aware of; not have a clue; not hear about; not know; last person to know; without the knowledge of;
不知不覺 before one knows it; unconsciously; unwittingly; dwithout one's knowing it;
~人不知，鬼不覺 by stealth; on the sly; unknown to man or demon; unobserved; without a single soul knowing anything about it; without anyone noticing; without being noticed by anyone; without the knowledge of anybody else;
~神不知鬼不覺 be cloaked in extreme secrecy; extremely stealthy; in complete secrecy; with great secrecy; without a stir; without anybody knowing it;
不知道 all at sea; beyond sb; cannot make head or tail of sth; do not know; have no idea about; have no notion of; have not the slightest idea of; ignorant of; in the dark; it beats me; know no more than the man in the moon; know nothing about; know nothing of; make neither head nor tail of sth; not aware of; the last person to know; without the knowledge of someone;
不知底裏 know nothing of its essentials; not know the details of a matter; not know the inside story;
不知凡幾 cannot tell how many there are;
不知分寸 have no eye for proportion;

have no sense of propriety; lack tact; tactlessly;

不知分曉 not know the outcome; not understand sth at all;

不知甘苦 not know how difficult it is to make a living; unable to distinguish between sweet and bitter;

不知高低 cannot tell high from low; have no sense of propriety;

不知好歹 cannot distinguish between good and bad; not know good from bad; not know what is good for one;

不知機變 not be accommodating; wanting in tact;

不知進退 have no sense of propriety; not know where to stop; not sure whether to advance or retreat;

不知就裏 not know the inner reason; not know the inside story;

不知老之將至 not know that old age is just around the corner; not know the insidious approach of old age;

不知鹿死誰手 cannot tell who will be victor; unable to tell who will win the prize;

不知輕重 have no appreciation of thing's importance; not know the proper way; unable to distinguish between the light and heavy;

不知情 ignorant of; know nothing about;

不知去向 disappear into thin air; nowhere to be found; sb's whereabout is unknown;

不知人事 ignorant; unreasonable;

不知深淺 have no sense of propriety; not know the depth of things; not know the whole story;

不知首尾 cannot make head or tail of sth; not know the circumstances;

不知死活 act recklessly; have no idea of death or danger; heedless of consequences; regardless of danger; reckless;

不知所措 all adrift; at a loose end; at a loss; at a stand; at loose ends; at one's wit's end; at sea; be lost; be thrown into astonishment; be thrown into confusion; between the devil and the deep sea; confuse; feel oneself in a false position; feel oneself in an awkward position; hit the panic button; in perplexity; lose one's bearings; lose one's head; not know which way to turn; not know if one is coming or going; one's mind was turned; out of one's bearings; perplex; perplexed; press the panic button; scarcely know where to turn; scarcely know which way to turn; push the panic button;

不知所答 be puzzled how to answer;

不知所以 at a loss as to the why and wherefore of; can make nothing of; have no idea why it is so; cannot see the whys and wherefores; not to know why it is so;

不知所云 cannot make out what sb is driving at; make neither head nor tail of what has been said; neither rhyme nor reason; not know what is talked about; not know what it means; not know what sb is driving at; not mean a thing; not realize what one has said; not understand what sb is driving at; scarcely know what one has said; unintelligible; without rhyme or reason;

不知所終 have never been heard of since; not know the whereabouts;

不知天高地厚 not know the immensity of heaven and earth — have an exaggerated opinion of one's abilities; not know what is what;

不知下落 not know the whereabouts of sb;

不知羞恥 be lost to shame; not know what shame is; thick-skinned;

~不知羞恥的人 law-down dirty shame;

不知虛實 not know whether it is true or false; unacquainted with the actual situation; unaware of the true conditions;

不知者不罪 no blames attaches to the unconscious doer of wrong;

不知自愛 have no knowledge of self-respect;

不知自量 not know one's limits; overrate one's abilities; undertake what is beyond one's power;

不知足 greedy; insatiable;

故作不知 play dumb; pretend ignorance;

殊不知 hardly realize; little image; never dream that; really do not know; who

諉為不知 pretend not to know;

要想人不知，除非己莫為 if you do not

want anybody to know it, do not do it in the first place;
一問三不知 deny all knowledge of an event; entirely ignorant; not to know a thing;
~一問搖頭三不知 shake one's head in answer to all questions;
欲使人不知，除非己莫為 do not do it if you do not want others to know it; if you do not want a thing to be known, the only way is not to do it; the only way to keep people from knowing sth is not to do it; what is done by night appears by day;

[不值] not worth;
不值一駁 not fit to be refuted; not worth refuting;
不值一顧 beneath contempt; beneath notice; not worth a single glance; not worth notice; nothing to make a song about; out of court;
不值一擊 cannot withstand even a single blow;
不值一談 nothing to speak of;
不值一提 not much to be particular about; not worth mentioning; unworthy of being mentioned;
不值一文 not worth a button; not worth a penny; worthless;
不值一笑 beneath contempt; not worth a laugh; not worth despising;
半文不值 entirely worthless; not worth a farthing; not worth a penny;
一錢不值 completely worthless; mere trash; not worth a brass farthing; not worth a cuss; not worth a damn; not worth a penny; not worth a red cent; utterly worthless;
~貶得一錢不值 condemn as worthless;

[不止] (1) exceed; more than; not limited to; (2) incessantly; without end;

[不祇] not merely; not only;

[不忠] infidelity; unfaithful to; two-time;
懷貳不忠 double-minded and disloyal;

[不住] ceaselessly; continuously;
挨不住 can no longer endure;
保不住 cannot be defended; there is no guarantee that;
備不住 maybe; perhaps;
繃不住 unable to bear; unable to endure;
憋不住 cannot help; cannot suppress;
~憋不住氣 cannot hold one's anger any longer; ready to burst;
藏不住 cannot be hidden;
吃不住 unable to bear or support;
待不住 cannot stay long;
擋不住 hindering; impeding; incapable of blocking; stopping;
敵不住 no match for;
架不住 (1) cannot stand the pressure; cannot stand up against; cannot sustain the weight; (2) cannot compete against; no match for;
挺不住 cannot stand it; cannot take it any more;
捣不住 cannot be concealed;
坐不住 cannot sit still; cannot stay long; restless;

[不准] forbid; not allow; prohibit;
不準確 inaccurate;

[不貲] immeasurable; incalculable;

[不足] (1) deficiency; drawback; inadequate; insufficient; lack; not enough; scarcity; (2) less than; (3) beneath; not deserve; not worth; (4) cannot; need not; should not; unnecessary;
不足道 not worth mentioning; not worth saying anything of; of no consequence;
~卑不足道 beneath discussion; beneath mention; not worth mentioning; inconsiderable; insignificant; too inferior to be worth mentioning; too insignificant to be worth mentioning; trivial;
~渺不足道 insignificant; negligible; not worth mentioning; too small for mention;
不足掛齒 beneath notice; not worth mentioning; not worthy of mention; nothing to speak of; of no importance;
不足介意 beneath consideration; not worth a thought; no consequence; unworthy of consideration;
不足抗衡 not suffice to counterbalance;
不足為慮 nothing terrible; nothing to be feared; nothing to worry about; there is no need to worry;
不足為奇 all in the day's work; have nothing to be wondered at; no wonder; not anything strange; not at all surprising; not strange; not unexpected; nothing out of the

common; nothing strange; nothing to be surprised at; nothing to take exception to; small wonder;
不足為外人道 no need to let others know; not worth telling it to outsiders; off the record; strictly between ourselves;
不足為訓 not an example to be followed; not to be taken as an example;
不足徵信 not to be taken as credible and reliable;
不足之處 defects; deficiencies; downside; inadequacies; shortcomings; weak points; weaknesses;
比上不足，比下有餘 average; can pass muster; fall short of the best, but be better than the worst; worse off than some, better off than many;
補其不足 make up a deficiency;
詞匯不足 lexical inadequacy;
精力不足 deficient in energy;
勞動力不足 manpower shortage; scarcity of labour;
美中不足 a blemish in an otherwise perfect thing; a cloud on one's happiness; a fly in the ointment; an unpleasant part of a pleasant thing; beautiful yet incomplete — in want of perfection; some slight imperfection; sth left to be desired; there is a flaw in the deed;
氣流不足 air deficiency;
人手不足 shorthanded; short of hands; understaffed;
貪心不足 covetousness; greedy and dissatisfied; insatiable desire; insatiable greed;
先天不足 congenital deficiency;
需要不足 lack of demand;
學然後知不足 one discovers his ignorance only through learning; the more one learns the more he sees his ignorance;
氧不足 oxygen lack;
飲食不足 dietary dificiency;
營養不足 nutrient dificiency;
住房不足 housing shortage;
資金不足 capital scarcity; fund shortage;

必不 must not;
並不 by no means; in so sense; not; not at all; not in any sense;
慘不 be too tragic to;
從不 never ever;
還不 not yet;
毫不 devoid of; not...at all; not in the least; not the least bit; nothing; without the slightest;
好不 really; what a...;
何不 why not;
決不 never; not for all the world; not for love or money; not for love nor money; not for the world; not for worlds; over my dead body;
絕不 absolutely not; by no means; definitely not; for anything; in no circumstances; never; never in a million years; not in a million years; not in the least;
莫不 there's no one who doesn't or isn't;
豈不 doesn't that; hasn't that; isn't that; won't that; wouldn't it be; wouldn't it result in; wouldn't that;
欠不 almost;
且不 not for the time being; not going to;
時不 there is no time;
死不 stubbornly refuse to; would rather die than;
恬不 have no sense of;
無不 invariably; without exception;
要不 or; or else; otherwise;
永不 ne'er; never; never ever; will never;
再不 never again; or; or else;

bu

【布】 (1) cloth; fabric; (2) announce; declare; proclaim; publish; (3) disseminate; spread; (4) arrange; deploy; dispose;
［布帛］ cloth and silk; cotton and silk;
［布袋］ sack;
［布店］ cloth store;
［布丁］ pudding;
大米布丁 rice pudding;
海月布丁 sponge pudding;
麵包布丁 bread pudding;
牛奶布丁 milk pudding;
牛肉布丁 beef pudding;
蘋果布丁 Eve's pudding;
巧克力布丁 chocolate pudding;
聖誕布丁 plum pudding;
豌豆布丁 pease pudding;
一塊布丁 a dollop of pudding;
［布防］ organize a defence; place troops on garrison duty;
［布告］ bulletin; notice;
布告欄 bulletin board;
布告牌 bulletin board;
布告天下 make known to the world; proclaim throughout the country;

貼出布告 paste up a notice;
張貼布告 put up a notice;

［布穀］ cuckoo;
布穀鳥 cuckoo;

［布景］ setting;

［布局］ (1) distribution; layout; overall arrangement; (2) the composition of; (3) the position of;
公園的布局 layout of the park;

［布料］ cloth;
駱毛布料 camel's hair;
一段布料 a length of cloth; a piece of cloth;
一幅布料 a breadth of cloth; a piece of cloth;

［布帽］ cloth cap;

［布疋］ piece goods;

［布商］ draper;

［布條］ strip of cloth;
一截布條 a strip of cloth;

［布衣］ (1) cloth gown; (2) commoners; the common people;
布衣粗食 be clad in simple gowns and eat simple meals; live a simple life; wear clothing of coarse cloth and eat only simple food;
布衣起家 rise from cotton garments;
布衣素食 dress quietly and abstain from eating meat;
布衣之交 a friend made when one was a commoner;

［布置］ (1) arrange; decorate; fix up; (2) assign; give instructions about; make arrangements for;

頒布 issue; proclaim; promulgate;
遍布 all over; be found everywhere; everywhere;
襯布 lining cloth;
疵布 defective cloth;
粗布 coarse cloth;
墩布 mop; swab;
帆布 canvas;
飛機布 aeroplane cloth;
封面布 book cloth;
敷布 compress;
花布 cotton print; figured cloth;
畫布 canvas;
刊布 announce through printed matter;
昆布 kelp;
喇叭布 baffle cloth;
冷布 gauze;
盧布 rouble;
抹布 rag;
麻布 (1) gunny cloth; sackcloth; (2) linen;
毛布 coarse cotton cloth;
棉布 cotton cloth;
尿布 diaper; napkin;
瀑布 waterfall;
漆布 varnished cloth;
染布 colour the cloth;
絨布 cotton flannel; flannelette;
砂布 emery cloth;
紗布 gauze;
樹皮布 bark cloth;
檯布 tablecloth;
土布 homespun cloth;
吸水布 absorbent cloth;
細布 fine cloth;
夏布 grass cloth; grass linen;
一層布 a ply of cloth; a thickness of cloth;
一塊布 a piece of cloth;
一捆布 a bale of cloth;
一碼布 a yard of cloth;
一匹布 a bolt of cloth; a roll of cloth;
油布 oilcloth;
雨布 waterproof cloth;
遮羞布 fig leaf;
針布 card clothing;
織布 weave cloth;
桌布 tablecloth;

bu

【佈】 (1) announce; declare; (2) arrange;

［佈達］ notify;

［佈道］ evangelize; preach the Gospel; sermon;
佈道壇 pulpit;
一次佈道 a sermon;

［佈防］ deploy troops in anticipation of an enemy attack; organize the defense;

［佈覆］ reply;

［佈告］ bulletin; make public announcement;

［佈景］ scenery for stage;
佈景畫家 scene-painter;
佈景設計人 setting designer;
佈景員 scene-man;
搭佈景 put up a piece of scenery;
換佈景 shift the scenes;
繪製佈景 paint scenes;
舞台佈景 stage scenery;

［佈局］ layout;
用地佈局 land use distribution;

［佈滿］ be covered with;

[佈施] give money or materials to the poor; make contribution to relief fund;

[佈線] wiring;

背面佈線 back wiring;

瓷夾佈線 cleat wiring;

電燈佈線 electric light wiring;

電鈴佈線 bell wiring;

多層佈線 multilayer wiring;

[佈置] (1) make arrangements; (2) arrange; decorate;

佈置房間 fix one's room up;

佈置考究 elaborately decorated;

佈置圈套 spread one's net for sb;

佈置一新 be swept and garnished;

佈置展品 arrange exhibits;

擺佈 (1) arrange; put sth in order; (2) control; dominate; manipulate;

傳佈 disseminate; spread;

發佈 issue; release;

分佈 be dispersed; be distributed; be scattered;

公佈 announce; make public; promulgate; publish;

流佈 disseminate; spread;

密佈 be densely covered;

散佈 diffuse; disseminate; scatter;

宣佈 announce; declare; proclaim; promulgate;

bu

【步】 (1) pace; step; (2) stage; step; (3) condition; degree; situation; state; (4) go on foot; walk; (5) surname;

[步兵] (1) infantry; infantryman; (2) foot soldier;

步兵部隊 infantry;

步兵連 company of foot;

步兵團 infantry regiment;

空降步兵 airborne infantry;

[步步] at every step; step by step;

步步登高 be promoted step by step; get promotion continuously; rise step by step in the world;

步步高昇 advance degree by degree; attain eminence step by step; be promoted step by step; rise step by step;

步步緊逼 press forward steadily;

步步進逼 close in steadily; press hard;

步步留神 act with the utmost prudence and circumspection; be careful of every step; pick one's steps; watch every step;

步步退卻 give way at every step; incessant retreats;

步步為營 a bastion at every step; act cautiously; advance gradually and entrench oneself at every step; consolidate at every step; make a stand at every step; move carefully every step on the way; raise a fort at every step;

步步小心 pick one's steps;

[步程] walking distance;

數分鐘步程 minutes walking distance;

[步調] pace; step; tempo; way;

步調不一致 out of step with;

步調參差 marching orders are confused;

步調一致 in step with; keep in step; keep step;

定出步調 set the pace;

[步伐] pace; step;

步伐不一致 out of step;

步伐錯亂 fall out of step

步伐合拍 walk in step;

步伐輕快 spring in one's step;

步伐輕盈 light on one's feet;

步伐一致 keep pace with sb; keep pace with sth; walk in step with each other;

步伐滯重 have leaden feet;

改革的步伐 pace of reform;

跟上時代的步伐 keep pace with the times;

加快步伐 gather pace; quicken one's pace;

輕快的步伐 buoyant steps;

[步法] footwork; gait;

自然步法 collected gait;

[步幅] width of stride;

[步履] walk;

步履沉重 have heavy feet;

步履矯捷 fleet of foot; in great speed;

步履輕快 have a light foot; swift of foot;

步履輕盈 walk with a light step;

步履生風 stride jubilantly;

步履維艱 a little too heavy for one's feet to carry; difficult to go on foot; hard to move one's feet; have difficulty walking; hobble along; very hard to walk; walk with difficulty; walking in a difficult manner;

步履紊亂 in disorder; walk out of step — in great confusion;

步履雜亂 walk out of step;

輕盈的步履 airy step;

[步槍] rifle;
軍用步槍 service rifle;
氣步槍 air rifle;
小口徑步槍 small bore rifle;
一枝步槍 a rifle;
自動步槍 automatic rifle; machine rifle;

[步入] step into;
步入歧途 take the wrong turning;

[步速] pace;
保持步速 maintain one's pace;

[步態] gait; walk;
步態驕矜 have a proud walk;
步態裊娜 walk with a mincing step;
步態蹣跚 one's gait is unsteady; one's walk is unsteady;
步態優雅 walk gracefully;
剪形步態 scissor gait;
痙攣步態 spastic gait;
偏癱步態 hemiplegic gait;

[步行] foot it; go on foot; walk;
步行不能 abasia;
~麻痺性步行不能 paralytic abasia;
步行回家 walk back home;
步行困難 difficulty in walking; dysbasia;
步行來 come on foot;
步行前往 proceed on foot;
步行橋 footbridge;
步行上學 walk to school;
步行者 pedestrian;
長途步行 long walk;
慈善步行 charity walk;
短途步行 short walk;
俏步徐行 mincing gait;
稍稍步行 little walk;

[步驟] measure; move; procedure; step;
必要的步驟 necessary step;
採取積極步驟 take active step;
錯誤的步驟 wrong step;
大膽步驟 bold step;
果斷的步驟 decided step;
積極步驟 positive step;
決定性的步驟 decisive step;
解決問題的步驟 move towards settling a problem;
輕率步驟 rash step;
慎重步驟 prudent step;
實現目標的步驟 a step towards the realization of one's goal;
試驗性步驟 tentative step;
適當步驟 appropriate step;
下一個步驟 the next procedure;
~考慮下一個步驟 ponder on one's next move;
勇敢的步驟 courageous step;
預定的步驟 pre-arranged procedure;
重要步驟 important step;

[步子] footstep; pace; step;
步子輕快 walk with springy steps;
步子穩健 walk with firm and steady steps;
放慢步子 slacken one's pace;
加大步子 one's pace lengthens;

安步 go slowly; walk slowly;
拔步 march forward; move forward quickly; take to one's heels; walk with big and quick strides;
百步 a hundred paces;
便步 walk at ease;
側步 sidestep;
初步 initial; preliminary;
寸步 single step; tiny step;
大步 stride;
代步 ride or drive instead of walking;
地步 (1) condition; situation; state; (2) extent;
獨步 peerless; unique; unrivaled; without match;
踱步 walk with measured tread;
方步 measured steps;
放步 advance with big strides;
後步 leeway; room for manoeuvre;
狐步 foxtrot;
虎步 a great warrior's firm strides like the tiger's;
緩步 stroll; walk slowly;
換步 change step;
疾步 at full speed; go swiftly; run swiftly;
健步 walk with vigorous strides;
箭步 sudden big stride forward;
腳步 (1) space; step; (2) movement of legs in walking;
進步 advance improve; progress; progressive;
舉步 step forward; take a step forward;
跨步 stride;
快步 half step; trot;
款步 walking slowly; with deliberate steps;
跬步 half a step;
闊步 take big strides;
勞步 thank you for your visit;
斂步 hesitate to advance further; hold back from going; slow down one's steps;
留步 not bother to see me out;
邁步 step forward; take a step forward;
慢步 walking slowly; with easy step;

漫步 ramble; stroll;
跑步 march at the double; run;
七步 seven steps;
齊步 in step; march; uniform steps;
起步 (1) break the ice; start; (2) get moving; get off the mark; get started; get underway;
頃步 half a step;
覷步 spy on;
卻步 flinch from; hang back for fear; hang back from; ink back at the sight of; retreat; shrink back from; step back; step back for fear; withdraw;
讓步 back down; back out of; compromise; give in; give way; make a concession; yield;
散步 go for a stroll; go for a walk; have a stroll; have a walk; perambulation; stretch one's legs; stroll; take a ramble; take a walk;
碎步 quick short steps;
踏步 mark time;
臺步 stage walk;
停步 come to a halt;
同步 synchronization; synchronize; synchronizing; synchronous;
徒步 on foot;
退步 lag behind; leeway; retrogress; room for manoeuvre;
穩步 steadily; with steady steps;
舞步 dance steps; steps;
閒步 roam at leisure; stroll without a destination;
翔步 pace about;
小步 stroll;
信步 stroll; take a leisurely walk; walk aimlessly;
行步 go;
徐步 strolling; walk slowly;
學步 learn to walk;
雅步 leisurely and graceful steps;
一小步 small step;
移步 move one's steps; walk;
異步 asynchronous;
音步 foot;
玉步 (1) your footsteps; (2) the footsteps of a pretty girl;
躍步 galloping;
正步 goose step; parade step;
止步 go no further; halt; stand still; stop;
逐步 gradually; progressively; step by step;
縱步 bound; jump; with long steps;
走步 walk with the ball;

bu

【怖】 (1) frightened; terrified; (2) frighten; threaten;

［怖駭］ alarmed; frightened; scared;
［怖禍］ terrifying danger or calamity;
［怖畏］ afraid; dread; scared;

可怖 frightful; horrible; terrifying;
恐怖 dreadful; horrible; terrifying;
振怖 alarm;

bu

【埠】 harbour; pier; port;
［埠頭］ port; wharf;

船埠 quay; wharf;
港埠 harbour; port;
商埠 commercial port; trading port;
外埠 non-local port;

bu

【部】 (1) part; section; (2) department; unit; (3) department; headquarters; (4) ministry; (5) forces; troops; (6) volume;
［部隊］ (1) armed forces; (2) force; troops; unit;
部隊分散 the troops are dispersing;
部隊集合 the troops are assembling;
部隊退卻 the troops fall back;
邊防部隊 frontier forces;
測繪部隊 topographic troops;
導彈部隊 missile unit;
嫡系部隊 one's own troops;
地方部隊 local forces;
地雷部隊 mine forces;
地面部隊 ground forces;
調集部隊 assemble troops;
防空部隊 air defense unit;
公安部隊 public security troops;
後備部隊 reserve unit;
護航部隊 escort forces;
火箭部隊 rocket troops;
機械化部隊 mechanized troops;
集結部隊 mass troops;
檢閱部隊 inspect troops;
警察部隊 police unit;
警戒部隊 outpost;
軍需部隊 quartermaster unit;
空降部隊 airborne troops;
空中部隊 air troops;
快速部隊 mobile unit;
陸軍部隊 army unit;
陸軍地面部隊 army ground forces;
陸軍後勤部隊 army service forces;
摩托化部隊 motorized unit;

B

砲兵部隊 artillery troops;
傘兵部隊 parachute troops;
坦克部隊 tank forces;
特遣部隊 task force;
特殊部隊 special forces;
衛戍部隊 garrison forces;
武裝部隊 armed forces;
先遣部隊 advance unit;
野戰部隊 field forces;
一支部隊 a force; an army;
~建立一支部隊 build up an army;
~解散一支部隊 disband an army;
~派出一支部隊 dispatch a force;
醫療部隊 medical troops;
運輸部隊 transportation troops;
戰鬥部隊 combat unit;
整編部隊 reorganize an army;
裝甲部隊 armoured forces;
裝甲車部隊 armoured unit;

[部分] part;
天線傳動部份 antenna drive part;
組成部份 integral part;

[部份] part; portion; section;
部份合作 partial cooperation;
部份權力 a portion of the power;
大部份 the great portion of; the major portion of;
~大部份時間 for a greater part of; for the better part of the time;
導鎖部份 locking portion;
基礎部份 base component;
結晶部份 crystalline portion;
尾數部份 magnitude portion;
小部份 a small part; a small portion; the minority;
~一小部份 a tiny part of; a small minority of;
虛線部份 dotted portion;
一部份 a part of;
~一部份責任 the responsibility be in part;
增長部份 incremental portion;
重要組成部分 important part of;
主要部份 main part of;
最重要的部份 centerpiece; the meat and potatoes;

[部件] assembly; component; part;
標準部件 standardized component;
脆弱部件 vulnerable component;
電子發射部件 electron emission parts;
機器部件 parts of a machine;
靜止部件 static component;
線路部件 circuit parts;

[部將] military officers under one's command;

[部類] category; division;

[部落] tribe;
部落社會 tribal society;
部落首領 headman;
部落語 tribal language;
土著部落 native tribe;
游牧部落 nomadic tribe;

[部門] branch; class; department; section; sector;
部門化 departmentalization;
部門會議 sectoral meeting;
部門會計 segment accounting;
財政部門 financial sector;
翻譯部門 translation department;
工作部門 operative department;
局內部門 exogenous sector;
跨部門 inter-department;
行政部門 administrative department;
宣傳部門 propaganda department;
有關部門 the department concerned;
政府部門 government department;
~有關政府部門 relevant government departments;
主管部門 the department responsible for the work;
專業部門 specialized department;
綜合部門 comprehensive department;

[部首] radical;

[部署] (1) arrange; lay out; map out; (2) deploy; dispose;
部署兵力 dispose troops;
部署工作 map out the work;
部署計劃 map out the plan;
作出部署 make dispositions;

[部委] ministries and commissions of the same level;

[部位] location; place; position; region; site;
活性部位 active site;
接受部位 acceptor site;
受傷部位 injured part;
吸附部位 adsorption site;

[部下] (1) troops under one's command; (2) subordinate;

[部長] commissioner; head of a department; minister;
部長助理 assistant minister;
不管部長 minister without portfolio;

財政部部長 minister of finance;
財政部長 minister of finance;
對外貿易經濟合作部部長 minister of foreign trade and economic cooperation;
副部長 viceminister;
公安部部長 minister of public security;
國防部部長 minister of national defense;
國防部長 minister of national defense;
國家安全部部長 minister of state security;
國土資源部部長 minister of land and resources;
監察部部長 minister of supervision;
建設部部長 minister of construction;
教育部長 minister of education;
科學技術部部長 minister of science and technology;
勞動和社會保障部部長 minister of labour and social security;
民政部部長 minister of civil affairs;
農業部部長 minister of agriculture;
前部長 former minister;
人事部部長 minister of personnel;
水利部部長 minister of water resources;
司法部部長 minister of justice;
司法部長 minister of justice;
鐵道部部長 minister of railways;
外交部部長 minister for foreign affairs;
外交部長 minister for foreign affairs;
衛生部部長 minister of health;
文化部部長 minister of culture;
文化部長 minister of culture;
信息部部長 minister of the information industry;

鞍部 saddle of a hill or mountain;
北部 northern part;
背部 back;
本部 headquarters;
臂部 arm;
編輯部 editorial department;
編目部 cataloguing department;
編制部 organization bureau;
財政部 ministry of finance;
測繪部 surveying and mapping bureau;
大部 greater part;
底部 base; bottom;
地質礦產部 ministry of geology and minerals;
電力工業部 ministry of electric power industry;
電子工業部 ministry of electronic industry;
頂部 top;
東部 eastern part;
隊部 headquarters of a team; office of a team;
對外貿易經濟合作部 ministry of foreign trade and economic cooperation;
紡織工業部 ministry of textile industry;
肺部 lungs;
腹部 abdomen; belly;
幹部 cadre;
公安部 ministry of public security;
廣播電影電視部 ministry of radio, film and television;
國防部 ministry of national defense;
國家安全部 ministry of state security;
國內貿易部 ministry of internal trade;
國土資源部 ministry of land and resources;
航空航天工業部 ministry of aviation and space industry;
後勤部 logistics department;
化學工業部 ministry of chemical industry;
機械工業部 ministry of machine building;
監察部 ministry of supervision;
建設部 ministry of construction;
交通部 ministry of communications;
教育部 ministry of education;
頸部 cervix;
局部 part;
俱樂部 club;
軍部 army headquarters;
科學技術部 ministry of science and technology;
胯部 crotch; crutch;
勞動部 ministry of labour;
勞動和社會保障部 ministry of labour and social security;
連部 company headquarters;
林業部 ministry of forestry;
煤炭工業部 ministry of coal industry;
門市部 retail department; sales department;
門診部 clinic; outpatient department;
面部 face;
民政部 ministry of civil affairs;
南部 southern part;
腦部 brain;
內部 bowel; depth; indoor; internal; interior; inward; viscera;
農業部 ministry of agriculture;
批發部 wholesale department;
全部 all; complete; total; whole;
人事部 ministry of personnel;
商業部 ministry of commerce;
上部 (1) the first part; (2) the first volume;
聲部 part;
師部 division headquarters;
釋部 Buddhist sutras;

石油工業部 ministry of petroleum industry;
雙部 binomial;
水利部 ministry of water resources;
司法部 ministry of justice;
司令部 command; headquarters;
所部 troops under one's command;
鐵道部 ministry of railways;
統帥部 supreme command;
頭部 head; top;
團部 regiment headquarters;
臀部 buttocks;
外部 (1) external; (2) exterior; outside; surface;
外交部 ministry of foreign affairs;
胃部 stomach;
衛生部 ministry of public health;
文化部 ministry of culture;
膝部 knee;
下部 (1) lower part; (2) private parts;
小吃部 refreshment room; snack counter;
信息部 ministry of the information industry;
胸部 bosom; breast; bust; chest; thorax;
腰部 small of the back; waist;
冶金工業部 ministry of metallurgical industry;
陰部 private parts; pudenda;
營部 battalion headquarters;
郵電部 ministry of posts and telecommunications;
政治部 political department;
支部 branch;
中部 central section; middle part;
住院部 impatient department;
總部 general headquarters; head office; headquarters;
足部 leg;

bu

【篰】 bamboo basket;

bu

【簿】 (1) books; (2) record; register;

［簿冊］ books and files; lists;

［簿籍］ books and records;

［簿記］ bookkeeping;

簿記機 bookkeeping machine;
簿記員 accounting clerk; bookkeeper; clerk;
單式簿記 single-entry bookkeeping;
複式簿記 double-entry bookkeeping;
工廠簿記 factory bookkeeping;
工業簿記 industry bookkeeping;
規陣簿記 matrix bookkeeping;
家庭簿記 family bookkeeping;
農業簿記 agricultural bookkeeping;
商業簿記 commercial bookkeeping; merchandise bookkeeping;

［簿錄］ (1) confiscate property; (2) catalogue of books;

登記簿 register; registry;
電話簿 telephone directory;
對簿 be tried at court; confront sb with witness;
發文簿 register of outgoing dispatches;
功勞簿 record of merits;
戶口簿 residence booklet;
集郵簿 stamp album;
剪貼簿 scrapbook;
考勤簿 attendance record;
練習簿 exercise book;
留言簿 visitors' book;
拍紙簿 pad; scratch pad; writing pad;
簽到簿 attendance book;
簽名簿 visitors' book;
收據簿 receipt book;
收文簿 register of incoming dispatches;
收賬簿 account book;
意見簿 visitors' book;
賬簿 account book; accounts;
照相簿 photo album;
支票簿 cheque book;

ca[1]
ca

【嚓】 scraping sound; screech; screeching noise;

ca

【擦】 (1) chafe; rub; scrape; (2) scour; wipe; (3) apply; paint; put on; spread on; (4) brush; polish; shave; (5) scrape into shreds; (6) pass along quickly;

［擦背］ rub one's back; scrub one's back; touch one's back;

［擦邊球］ edge ball; touch ball;

［擦擦］ rub;
擦擦眼睛 rub one's eyes;

［擦掉］ abrase; erase; rub off; rub out;
擦掉記號 scrape out a mark;
擦掉泥土 scrape off dirt;
擦掉鐵鏽 rub off rust; scour the rust off;
擦掉污點 wipe out a stain;
擦掉污物 rub off the dirt;
擦掉眼淚 wipe away one's tears; wipe tears from one's eyes;
輕輕擦掉 dab off;

［擦乾］ dry; wipe dry;
擦乾盤子 mop up a plate;

［擦光］ polish; rub up;

［擦過］ brush past sb; graze;

［擦汗］ wipe the sweat away;
擦汗撣土 wipe the sweat from one's face and dust one's clothes;

［擦黑］ (1) blacken; (2) rectify errors; rectify shortcomings;
擦黑板 clean the blackboard;

［擦痕］ friction streaks; moraine scars;

［擦肩而過］ brush against sb; brush by sb; brush past sb; pass and re-pass sb;
擦身而過 brush past;

［擦淨］ clean; erase; wipe; wipe up;

［擦臉］ (1) dry one's face; (2) wash one's face;

［擦亮］ polish; rub; shine;
擦亮眼睛 become more clear-sighted; heighten one's vigilance; keep one's eyes skinned; keep one's eyes wide open; on the outlook; remove the scales from one's eyes; sharpen one's vigilance; wide the dust from one's eyes;
把鞋擦亮 give one's shoes a good shine;

［擦去］ erase; wipe off;
擦去臉上的眼淚 brush tears from one's face;

［擦傷］ abrasion; chafe; graze; scrape;
擦傷處 abrasion;
擦傷皮膚 abrade the skin;
擦傷膝蓋 graze one's knee; rub the skin off one's knee;

［擦拭］ clean; cleanse; scrub; wipe;

［擦手］ dry one's hands;
擦手巾 hand towel;

［擦損］ be damaged by friction or rubbing;

［擦痛］ chafe;

［擦洗］ clean; rinse; scrub; scrubbing;
擦洗劑 cleaner;
擦洗甲板 scrub the deck;
需要擦洗 need cleaning; want cleaning;

［擦鞋］ shoeshine;
擦鞋攤 shoeshine stand;
擦鞋油 apply shoe polish;

［擦音］ fricative;

［擦油］ apply pomade; coat with oil; oil; polish;
在皮膚上擦油 rub oil over one's skill;
在手上擦油 smear grease on one's hand;

［擦藥］ apply ointment;
需要擦藥 need an application;

［擦澡］ take a sponge bath; rub oneself down with a wet towel;

［擦子］ eraser; rubber;

板擦 blackboard eraser;
摩擦 (1) rub; (2) friction; (3) clash;
磨擦 abrade; abrase; rub;
揉擦 anatriptic;
使勁擦 rub hard;
洗擦 wash and scrub;
用布擦 use cloth to wipe with;

cai[1]
cai

【猜】 (1) conjecture; draw the bow; guess; speculate; (2) suspect;

［猜不着］ cannot guess; miss one's guess; unable to make out the right answer; unable to reach the right answer;

［猜猜猜］ scissors game; scissors and stones;

［猜測］ (1) conjecture; draw the bow; guess; guesswork; speculate; surmise; (2) suspect;
猜測秘密 guess the secret;
大膽猜測 venture a guess;

胡亂猜測 wild guess;
據猜測 at a guess;
貿然猜測 hazard a guess;
妄加猜測 hazard conjecture;
引起猜測 raise a conjecture;

做猜測 make a guess;

[猜出] dope out;
[猜到] guess;
[猜對] guess; hit it; make a correct guess; right in one's guess;
[猜度] conjecture; draw the bow; guess and assess; speculate; surmise;
猜度再三 form a judgment again and again;
[猜忌] envious; envy; jealous of; suspicious; suspicious and jealous; suspicious of and resent;
互相猜忌 suspicious and jealous of each other;
[猜枚] guessing game;
[猜謎] (1) guess a riddle; guess the answer to the riddle; solve riddles; (2) guess the real meaning;
猜謎遊戲 (1) quiz game; (2) guessing game;
[猜拳] finger-guessing drinking game; mora; play mora;
[猜透] guess correctly; make a correct guess; outguess;
猜透心思 read sb's mind;
猜不透 cannot read sb's mind; unable to guess; unable to make out;
[猜嫌] suspicious and jealous;
[猜想] guess; imagine; suppose; suspect; think;
純屬猜想 mere conjecture; pure conjecture;
胡猜亂想 make blind and disorderly conjectures; wild conjecture;
瞎想亂猜 make blind and disorderly conjectures;
[猜疑] harbour suspicions; have misgivings; suspect; suspicious;
產生猜疑 a surmise arises about;
互相猜疑 have misgiving about each other; suspicious of each other;
受到猜疑 be looked upon with suspicion; be suspected;
消除猜疑 lull sb's suspicions;
[猜中] figure answer out; guess right;
屢猜屢中 one's judgment always turns out to be right;
一猜就中 guess correctly straightway;

猜一猜 have a guess; take a guess;
無猜 childlike innocence; unsuspicious;
瞎猜 a shot in the dark; guess blindly; guess groundlessly; guess wildly; guess without ground; make a random guess; make a wild guess;
嫌猜 dislike and suspicion;
疑猜 conjecture; guess; suspect;

cai²
cai

【才】 (1) ability; gift; talent; (2) capable person; (3) just; only; then and only then; (4) just now;
[才筆] literary talent;
[才份] ability; brilliance; gift; talent;
[才幹] ability; caliber; capability; competence; management ability;
非凡才幹 exceptional ability;
很有才幹 have great ability; of considerable talent;
領導才幹 leadership ability;
~表現出領導才幹 display leadership ability;
商業才幹 business ability;
外交才幹 diplomatic ability;
顯露才幹 show one's ability;
政治才幹 political acumen;
組織才幹 talent for organization;
[才高] of great abilities;
才高八斗 be endowed with extraordinary talents; exceedingly talented; have profound learning; person of great abilities; person of great talents;
才高行潔 one's ability and virtue excel the average;
才高學廣 learned and talented; of great ability and extensive learning;
才高意廣 have a brilliant mind and a broad vision;
[才華] artistic talent; brilliance; accomplished; gifted; gifts; literary talent; rich talent; talent; talented;
才華出眾 of uncommon brilliance; of outstanding talent; possess exceptional talent; unusual talent;

才華橫溢 full of talent; full of wit; have super talent; overflowing with talent; scintillating with wit;
才華煥發 a spark of wit; scintillate with wit;
才華絕代 peerless talent; unrivalled talent;
才華俊逸 have superb talent;
才華卓越 one's talent is exceptional;
不大有才華 have not much talent;
富有才華 possess remarkable talent;
極有才華 supremely gifted;
文學才華 literary ability;
藝術才華 artistic ability;
音樂才華 gift for music;

[才盡] at the end of one's wit;
才盡詞窮 at the end of one's wit;
江郎才盡 at one's wits' end; at the end of one's rope; come to one's wit's end; feel helpless; have used up one's literary talent; one's inspiration dries up;
江淹才盡 have used up one's literary talent;

[才力] ability; talent;

[才路] a way to cultivate talent;
廣開才路 open all avenues for people of talent;

[才略] ability and sagacity; talent for scheming;

[才貌] talent and appearance; talent and beauty;
才貌超群 one's education and appearance excel the average; very talented and unusually good-looking;
才貌雙全 as wise as fair; beautiful and highly gifted; beautiful and talented; both beautiful and accomplished; both pretty and clever; endowed with both beauty and talent; have both the ability and the looks; talented and handsome;
郎才女貌 perfect match between a man and a girl;
男才女貌 ideal couple;

[才名籍甚] one's reputation for talent is well-known;

[才能] (1) ability; aptitude; capability; gift; knowledge and ability; talent; (2) only possible if;
才能表演 talent show;
才能增長規律 law of talent growth;
表現出才能 exhibit one's ability;
多方面的才能 all-round ability; manifold abilities;
非凡的才能 unusual talent;
管理才能 administrative talent;
科學才能 ability in science;
平庸才能 mediocre ability;
缺乏才能 lack ability; wanting in ability;
數學才能 ability at mathematics;
特殊才能 special ability; special talent;
文學才能 literary ability; literary talent;
寫作才能 talent for writing;
學術才能 academic aptitude;
演講才能 oratorical ability;
藝術才能 artistic ability; artistic talent;
語言才能 language ability;
組織才能 organizing ability;

[才女] a girl of many accomplishments; accomplished lady; gifted female scholar; talented woman;

[才氣] literary talent;
才氣橫溢 brilliant; brim with talent; full of talent; have superb talent; overflowing with animation; overflowing with talent; scintillating with wit;
才氣磅礴 tremendous talent;
才氣平庸 of limited ability;
才氣己盡 at one's wits' end;
有才氣 have great talent;

[才情] imaginative power; literary and artistic talent;
才情逸致 one's talent and thought are distinguished;

[才人] (1) talented person; (2) a rank of ladies-in-waiting in traditional China;

[才識] ability and insight;
才識過人 be gifted with talent and insight far beyond the average person;
才識淺陋 of small talent and shallow knowledge;

[才是] only then is...;

[才疏意廣] one's talent is inferior but his idea high; untalented but with a broad vision;

[才思] creativeness; imaginative power;
才思敏捷 acuity of wit; have a facile imagination; quick in creativeness; quick-witted;

[才望] reputation for talent;

[才學] erudition; scholarship; talent and learning;

才學出眾 excel in scholarship;
才學兼優 have both talent and learning;
才疏學淺 a person of little knowledge and ability; a person who has rather mean ability and no solid learning; a person who is but a smatterer of some kind and an apology for talent; crude and unlearned; have little talent and less learning; have slight talent and superficial learning; wanting in ability and shallow in knowledge;
很有才學 possess great talent and learning;
真才實學 genuine talent; real ability and learning; solid knowledge; solid learning; well-trained;
~有真才實學的人 man of light and leading;

[才藝] talent and skill;
才藝突出 stand out in talent and skill;
才藝卓絕 be gifted with talent and ability far beyond the average person;
才藝卓越 stand out in talent and skill;
多才多藝 able to put one's hand to many things; gifted in many ways; have ability in many different ways; have much talent; versatile; with much talent and much artistry;
~多才多藝的 versatile;
~多才多藝的人 all-rounder; person of many parts; person of many talents;

[才智] ability and wisdom; brilliance;
才智過人 tower above the rest in height of intellect;
才窮智竭 at one's wit's end; at the end of one's tether;

[才子] genius; gifted scholar;
才子佳人 a handsome scholar and a beautiful lady; genius and beauty; gifted scholars and beautiful ladies; talents and beauties;
風流才子 talented and romantic scholar;
七個才子六個癲 of seven gifted scholars, six behave madly;
一群才子 a galaxy of talent;

愛才 cherish talent;
辯才 eloquent person;
不才 worthless person;
成才 talent formation;
大才 great talent;
德才 moral character and ability;
方才 just now; only then; until;
幹才 capable person;
剛才 a moment ago; a while ago; just now;
洪才 great talent;
懷才 have talent;
忌才 jealous of other people's talent; resent people more able than oneself;
將才 talent as a field commander;
捷才 quick-wittedness in writing;
矜才 rely on one's ability;
口才 eloquence;
量才 assess one's ability;
憐才 have sympathy for talented people;
奴才 flunkey; lackey;
奇才 extraordinary talent;
喬才 (1) bad egg; bad fellow; (2) crafty; tricky;
屈才 do work unworthy of one's talents; put sb in a position that does not do him/her justice; put sb on a job unworthy of his/her talents;
全才 versatile person;
人才 person of ability; qualified personnel; talent; talented person;
適才 just now;
瑣才 person of little capability;
天才 talent;
通才 universal genius;
歪才 talent of working out crooked ideas;
文才 aptitude for writing; literary gift; literary talent;
仙才 genius;
賢才 capable and virtuous person;
謏才 limited talent;
雄才 great talent; remarkable ability and wisdom;
秀才 (1) county graduate; (2) scholar; skilful writer; (3) fine talent;
異才 extraordinary talent;
逸才 outstanding talent;
英才 gifted person; person of outstanding ability; the able and the clever;
庸才 mediocre person;
有才 gifted; talented;
育才 cultivate talents; educate people of ability;
之才 a person of; a talent of;
專才 specialist;
濁才 fool;

cai

【材】 (1) timbre; (2) materials; (3) ability; aptitude; talent; (4) capable person; (5) coffin;

[材積] volume of timbre;
[材料] (1) materials; (2) data; materials;
材料費 material cost;
材料工程師 material engineer;
材料介詞 preposition of material;
材料專家系統 expert system of materials;
包裝材料 packing material;
背景材料 background material;
~ 收集背景材料 collect background material;
參考材料 reference material;
~ 缺乏參考材料 lack reference material;
超材料 metamaterial;
處理材料 handle material;
第一手材料 primary source;
防水材料 water-proof material;
防雨材料 rainproof material;
放射性材料 active material;
複合材料 composite;
~ 高強度複合材料 high strength composite;
~ 金屬基複合材料 metal-matrix composite;
高級材料 advanced material;
高溫材料 high-temperature material;
關鍵材料 key materials;
廉價材料 cheap materials;
練習材料 practice material;
鋪路材料 paving material;
燒蝕材料 ablation material;
搜集材料 collect data; gather material;
學習材料 material for study;
陽極材料 anode material;
一種材料 a material;
易燃材料 combustible material; highly inflammable material;
真材實料 genuine material and solid substance;
[材樹] timber tree;
[材藝] ability and art;
[材質] quality of material;

板材 plate;
樗材 good-for-nothing; useless person;
春材 spring wood;
蠢材 blistering idiot; blockhead; bloody fool; bonehead; boob; booby; cabbagehead; dunce; fool; idiot; pig-headed person; pillock; stupid person;
帶材 strip;
幹材 (1) ability; capability; (2) able person; capable person;
鋼材 rolled steel; steel products;
高材 remarkable in talent;
棺材 box; burial case; casket; coffin;
管材 steel tube;
集材 log; yard;
建材 building materials;
將材 person with all the qualifications of a general;
教材 instructional material; instructional resources; teaching material;
良材 (1) good timber; (2) able person; capable person;
木材 lumber; timber; wood;
器材 equipment; equipment and materials; supplies;
翹材 person of outstanding ability;
秋材 autumn wood;
取材 collect materials; draw materials; gather materials; obtain raw materials; select material; select talent;
銓材 estimate one's ability;
人材 (1) capable person; talented person; qualified personnel; (2) handsome appearance; nice looks;
軟材 softwood;
身材 figure; stature;
壽材 coffin;
素材 source materials;
題材 subject matter; theme;
線材 wire rod;
選材 (1) select a suitable person; (2) select materials of art and literature;
藥材 medicinal materials;
軼材 outstanding talents;
軋材 rolled steel;
至材 extremely gifted; extremely talented;
中材 person of ordinary talent;
資材 materials and equipment;

cai

【財】 money; riches; wealth;
[財寶] money and valuables;
招財進寶 bring in wealth and treasure — felicitous wish of making money;
[財帛] money; riches; valuables; wealth;
[財不露眼] he that shows his purse longs to be rid of it; let not your wealth be exposed;
[財產] assets; property;
財產保護 protection of property;
~ 提供財產保護 give protection of

property;
財產保險 property insurance;
財產繼承 accession of property;
~財產繼承稅 accession tax;
財產監護人 guardian of property;
財產經營權 management right of property;
財產權 property right;
財產使用權 right to the use of property;
財產稅 property tax;
財產信托 property trust;
財產租賃 property lease;
~財產租賃收入 income from property lease;
繼承財產 come into a fortune; inherit assets; inherit property; inherit wealth; succeed a property;
出賣財產 dispose of one's property by sale;
賭輸財產 dice away one's fortune;
個人財產 personal fortune;
公司財產 company property;
公有財產 public property;
國有財產 national property; state property;
耗盡財產 consume one's fortune;
揮霍財產 dissipate one's fortune; lavish one's wealth;
沒收財產 confiscation of property;
失去財產 lose one's property;
世襲財產 hereditary property; hereditary wealth;
私人財產 goods and chattels;
私有財產 private property;
一筆財產 a fortune; a property;
一大筆財產 a large property; quite a little fortune;
~積攢一大筆財產 amass quite a little fortune;
一項財產 a piece of property;
一小筆財產 a small property;

[財大氣粗] a heavy purse gives one courage; he who has wealth speaks louder than others; self-confident owing to great wealth;

[財丁兩旺] prosper by becoming wealthy and by adding members to the family; prosperous both in family and in purse;

[財東] (1) moneybags; (2) shopowner;

[財閥] financial magnate; plutocrat; tycoon;
財閥統治 plutocracy;

[財富] mammon; riches; wealth;
財富大增 grow largely in wealth;
財富無常 riches have wings;
創建財富 build one's wealth;
創造財富 create wealth;
大量財富 a plentitude of wealth; affluent fortune;
分配財富 distribute wealth;
國家財富 national wealth;
耗盡財富 exhaust wealth;
獲得財富 acquire wealth; attain wealth;
積聚財富 amass riches; build up a fortune; heap up riches; store up wealth;
減少財富 decline largely in wealth;
金融財富 financial wealth;
累積財富 accumulated wealth;
平均財富 equalize wealth;
潛在財富 potential wealth;
輕視財富 despise riches;
人力財富 human wealth;
社會財富 wealth of society;
~侵吞社會財富 appropriate social property;
使用財富 use one's wealth;
文學財富 literary wealth;
無形財富 immaterial wealth;
炫耀財富 flaunt one's wealth; make a display of one's wealth;
擁有財富 posses wealth;
增加財富 add to one's wealth; increase wealth;
追求財富 court wealth; seek after wealth;

[財經] finance and economics;
財經紀律 financial and economic discipline;
財經記者 city editor;

[財會] (1) finance and accounting;
(2) financial accounting;

[財禮] betrothal gifts;

[財力] financial resources;
財力不缺 financial resources are never exhausted;
財力雄厚 financially strong;
財力有限 have modest financial resources;
國家財力 resources of the country;
浪費財力 waste financial resources;
削弱財力 weaken financial resources;

[財糧] money and grain;

[財路] means to gain wealth; way of earning money;

[財貿] finance and trade;

財貿工作 financial and trade work;
財貿戰線 financial and commercial front;
財貿政策 financial and trade policy;

[財迷] miser; moneygrubber;
財迷心竅 absorbed in the pursuit of wealth; befuddled by a craving for wealth; have one's head turned by greed; mad about money; money-grubbing; obsessed by lust for money;

[財氣] luck in making big money;

[財淺愁深] a light purse makes a heavy heart;

[財權] control over wealth; economic power;
掌握財權 bear the bag;

[財神] (1) God of Wealth; (2) money-makers;
財神爺 deity of wealth;
財神爺叫門—天大的好事 the God of Wealth knocking at the door − a heavenly boon;

[財勢] wealth and power;
有財有勢 have both money and power; have plenty of money and pull; rich and powerful;

[財稅] tax and finance;
財稅秩序混亂 chaos in finance and taxation;

[財團] (1) consortium; syndicate; (2) financial group;
財團法人 corporate body; juridical person;
貸款財團 loan syndicate;
金融財團 financial syndicate;

[財物] belongings; property;
財物獨立 financial autonomy;
財物混亂 chaos in bookkeeping;
財物監督 financial control;
財物整頓 put financial affairs in order; straighten out financial affairs;
財物狀況 financial situation;
公共財物 public property;
賣掉財物 sell one's belongings;
私人財物 personal belongings;
增加財物 increase one's belongings;

[財務] financial affairs;
財務安排 financial arrangements;
財務包幹 financial supply system;
~財務包幹制 financial contracted system;
財務報表 financial statements;
~財務報表審計 audit of financial statements;
財務報告 financial report;
~財務報告系統 financial reporting system;
財務大檢查 general check-up on the financial work;
財務代理人 fiscal agent;
財務公司 clearing corporation;
財務管理 financial administration; financial management;
財務經驗 experience in financial affairs;
財務會計 financial accounting;
財務困難 financial difficulties;
財務審計 financial audit;
財務實力 financial strength;
財務事項 financial transaction;
財務行政管理 financial administration;
財務主管 bursar; comptroller; financial controller;
財務總監 chief financial officer;
懂財務 know finance;

[財源] bankroll; cash cow; financial resources; source of revenue;
財源斷絕 be strapped;
財源滾滾 profits pouring in from all sides;
財源涸竭 one's resources are drained; the resources are exhausted;
財源茂盛 the source of wealth is abundant;
開發財源 exploit the sources of wealth;
開闢財源 explore more source of revenue;

[財運] bonanza; money-making luck;
財運亨通 all one touches turns to gold; the luck for wealth is prosperous; the road to wealth is wide open − wishing you prosperity;

[財政] finance;
財政包幹 financial contract;
財政撥款 financial allocation;
~財政撥款制度 financial allocation system;
財政補貼 financial subsidy; state subsidy;
~給予財政補貼 give financial subsidies;
財政赤字 financial deficit;
~消滅財政赤字 wipe out financial deficits;
財政措施 financial measure;
~採取財政措施 take financial measures;
財政的 dollars-and-cents;
財政定額包幹制 responsibility system of fixed quotas for revenue and expenditure;
財政獨立 financial autonomy;

財政法 financial law;
財政公開 make public the administration of finance;
財政關稅 revenue tariff;
財政管理控制 financial administrative control;
財政合作 financial cooperation;
~三角財政合作 triangular financial cooperation;
財政計劃 financial scheme;
~制訂財政計劃 form a financial scheme;
財政紀律 financial regulations;
財務監督 financial supervision;
~實行財務監督 exercise financial supervision;
財政檢查 financial scrutiny;
財政拮據 be financially crippled;
財政緊迫 financial stringency;
財政開支 expenditure;
~縮減財政開支 cut expenditure; reduce expenditure;
財政虧損 financial loss;
~造成財政虧損 involve a financial loss;
財政困難 financial stress;
~財政困難的 cash-trapped;
財政年度 financial year; fiscal year;
財政審計 financial audit;
財政實力 financial strength;
財政事務 fiscal matter;
財政收入 financial revenue;
財政收支 balance of revenue and expenditure;
~財政收支包幹 contract system on revenue and expenditure;
~財政收支差額 imbalance between revenue and expenditure;
~財政收支平衡 revenue and expenditure balance;
~平衡財政收支 acquire balance of revenue and expenditure;
財政稅收 fiscal levy;
~財政稅收制度 financial and taxation system;
財政體制 financial system;
財政調節 financial adjustment;
財政危機 financial crisis; fiscal crisis;
~面臨財政危機 face a financial crisis;
~引起財政危機 provoke a financial crisis;
財政信息 financial information;
財政學 finance;
~比較財政學 comparative finance;
財政預算 budget;
~國家財政預算 state budget;
財政援助 financial support;
~給予財政援助 afford a financial support;
財政災難 financial disaster;
財政政策 fiscal policy;
財政轉移支付制度 financial transferred payment system;
財政狀況 financial condition;
赤字財政 deficit financing;
懂得財政 understand finance;
改革財政 reform financial affairs;
國家財政 finances of the country;
~改善國家財政 improve the finances of the country;
調整財政 adjust the finances;
~重新調整財政 readjust the finances;
掌握財政 exercise the power of the purse;
整頓財政 order finances;

[財主] moneybags; rich person;

愛財 fond of riches;
不露財 not reveal one’s silver in pocket;
地財 valuables buried by landlords or rich peasants;
發財 get rich make a fortune;
浮財 movable property;
橫財 ill-gotten wealth or gains;
家財 family riches;
聚財 amass great fortunes;
理財 handle money;
斂財 accumulate wealth by unfair means; expropriate money; extort money;
歛財 accumulate wealth by unfair or illegal means;
謀財 strive to get money;
破財 lose money; suffer unexpected financial losses;
錢財 money; riches; wealth;
輕財 make light of wealth;
人財 life and money;
傷財 lose money; waste money;
生財 make money;
蝕財 lose money;
貪財 covet money; greedy after money; have an itching palm;
添財 become wealthy;
外財 extra income; illegal gains; windfall;
羨財 covet wealth;
小財 humble fortune;
邪財 ill-gotten wealth;

蓄財 store up wealth;
殉財 die of desire for wealth;
詐財 cheat for money;
資財 assets; capital and goods; funds and goods; riches; wealth;
貲財 money; valuables; wealth;

cai

【裁】 (1) cut into parts; (2) cut down; diminish; dismiss; reduce; (3) decide; judge; (4) check; sanction; (5) mental planning; (6) form; style; (7) kill; (8) fall; tumble;

[裁兵] (1) disarm; (2) reduce the number of soldiers;

[裁併] cut down and merge;

[裁撤] dissolve an organization;

[裁處] judge and decide;

[裁定] adjudicate; rule;
一致裁定 a unanimous verdict;

[裁斷] consider and decide;

[裁度] (1) consider and decide; (2) deduce, infer; weigh;

[裁縫] dressmaker; tailor;
裁縫的尺子—量人不量己 a tailor's ruler — measures others but not himself; apply the rules only to others;
裁縫做嫁衣—替別人歡喜 a tailor making a wedding dress — rejoice for sb else;

[裁革] abolish; cut down;

[裁剪] cut out;
裁剪衣服 cut out garments;
學習裁剪 learn tailoring;

[裁減] cut down; reduce; trim;
裁減辦公室人員 reduce the personnel of an office;
裁減軍備 make arms reduction; reduce military preparations; reduction of armaments;
裁減人員 make a personnel cut;
裁減冗員 cut down unnecessary personnel; skim away personnel fat;
裁減一半 reduce by one half;

[裁決] adjudicate; adjudication; ruling;
存疑裁決 open verdict;
多數裁決 majority verdict;
根據…裁決 judge according to...;
接受裁決 accept the ruling;
司法裁決 make a judicial decision;
推翻裁決 overturn a verdict;
無罪裁決 not guilty verdict;
宣佈裁決 announce a verdict;
依法裁決 adjudicate according to the law;
有罪裁決 guilty verdict;
作出裁決 arrive at a verdict; give a verdict; deliver a verdict; reach at a verdict;
做出裁決 make the award;

[裁軍] disarmament;
裁軍會議 disarmament conference;
裁軍談判 arm-control negotiation;
~進行裁軍談判 conduct arm-control negotiations;
裁軍協定 disarmament agreement;
~批准裁軍協定 approve a disarmament agreement;
裁軍協議 disarmament agreement;
~簽訂裁軍協議 sign a disarmament agreement;
反對裁軍 oppose disarmament;
核裁軍 nuclear disarmament;
區域性裁軍 regional disarmament;
全球裁軍 worldwide reduction of armament;
贊成裁軍 favour disarmament;

[裁判] (1) judgment; (2) judge; referee; umpire; (3) act as referee; (4) verdict;
裁判台 referee's platform, referee's stand;
裁判椅 referee's chair;
裁判員 judge; referee; umpire;
~底線裁判員 end-line judge;
~彎道裁判員 corner judge;
~終點裁判員 finishing judge;
邊線裁判 linesman;
補充裁判 additional judge;
副裁判 net umpire;
公正地裁判 judge equitably;
缺席裁判 default judgment;
主裁判 call umpire;
~主裁判員 chief referee;

[裁衣] cut cloth for making dress;
稱體裁衣 fit the dress to the figure;
就布裁衣 cut one's coat according to one's cloth;
量體裁衣 cut the garment according to the figure — act according to actual circumstances; fit the dress to the figure;
相體裁衣 decide the quantity of materials needed before proceeding to do sth;

[裁員] cut down the number of employees;

lay-off; reduce the staff;
[裁植] planting;
鏟隙裁植 notch planting;
防護帶裁植 belt planting;
建築式裁植 architectural planting;
[裁紙機] paper cutter; trimmer;
[裁制] curtail; restrict;

獨裁 dictatorship;
剪裁 (1) cut out a garment; tailor; (2) cut out unwanted material in writing; prune;
親裁 decide personally;
體裁 types of literature;
心裁 conception; idea;
制裁 take sanction against sb or sth;
仲裁 arbitrate;
酌裁 consider and decide;
自裁 commit suicide; take one's own life;
總裁 (1) governor; (2) director general;

cai
【纔】 (1) just now; just then; (2) for the first time; not until; then and only then; (3) only;
[纔到] (1) just arrived; (2) have only reached;
[纔好] just fine;
[纔來] have just arrived; have just come;
[纔是] then and only then is;

cai3
cai
【采】 (1) collect; gather; (2) pick up; select; (3) bright colours;
[采辦] select and purchase;
[采采] abundant; luxuriant;
[采集] collect; gather;
[采輯] compile;
[采色] various colours;
[采衣] bright garments; colourful garments;
[采製] collect and process;

倒采 catcall;
丰采 dashing appearance; good-looking;
風采 (1) elegant manner; graceful bearing; (2) literary grace; literary talent; (3) upright and principled style;
豐采 mien;
虹采 banner; flag;
回采 stope;
神采 countenance; expression; look;
文采 (1) rich and bright colours; (2) aptitude for writing; literary talent;
擷采 cull; gather; pick;

cai
【彩】 (1) colours; variegated colours; (2) make-up in various Chinese operas; (3) special feats or stunts in Chinese operas; (4) bright; ornamental; (5) coloured silk; variegated silk; (6) applause; cheer; (7) brilliance; splendour; variety; (8) prize; prize money; stakes in a gambling game; (9) blood from a wound;
[彩筆] (1) the brush that produces masterpieces; (2) coloured pen; painting brush; colour crayons;
[彩綢] coloured silk;
[彩帶] coloured ribbon; coloured streamer;
[彩蛋] painted eggshell;
[彩燈] coloured light;
小彩燈 fairy lights;
[彩電] (1) colour TV set; (2) colour TV;
彩電發送設備 colour TV transmitting equipment;
彩電制式 colour system;
[彩兒] delight; interest; lively atmosphere;
[彩鳳] colourful phenix;
彩鳳隨鴉 a beautiful woman married to an ugly husband; a perfect woman married to a worthless man; a pretty girl married an ugly person;
鴨學彩鳳 jackdaw in peacock's feather;
[彩虹] rainbow;
美麗的彩虹 beautiful rainbows;
七色彩虹 a rainbow of brilliant colours;
一道彩虹 a rainbow;
一抹彩虹 a rainbow;
一條彩虹 a rainbow;
[彩畫] colour painting;
[彩繪] coloured drawing; coloured pattern;
彩繪工 porcelain painter;
[彩轎] bridal sedan-chair;
[彩卷] colour film;
[彩禮] betrothal gifts;
[彩門] decorated gateway;
[彩排] dress rehearsal;
[彩棚] decorated tent; marquee;
[彩票] lottery ticket; raffle ticket;
發行彩票 institute a lottery; run a lottery;
買彩票 buy lottery tickets;

賣彩票 sell lottery tickets;

[彩旗] coloured flag;

[彩球] colourful ball;

抛彩球 toss colourful balls;

[彩券] lottery ticket;

[彩色] colour; multicolour;

彩色編碼器 colour encoder;

彩色繽紛 a riot of colour; colourful; the play of colours;

彩色打印機 colour printer;

彩色電視機 colour television;

彩色反轉片 colour reversal film;

彩色放大 colour photo enlarging;

彩色負片 colour negative film;

彩色複印機 colour copier; colour copy machine;

彩色感光材料 colour photographic material;

彩色繪圖機 colour plotter;

彩色激光式 colour laser type;

彩色膠卷 colour film;

彩色控制 colour control;

彩色片 colour film; technicolour film;

~多層彩色片 multilayer colour film;

彩色攝像機系統 colour camera system;

彩色速印機 colour duplicator;

彩色圖像信號 colour picture signal;

彩色顯示 colour display;

彩色顯像管 colour picture tube;

彩色信號 colour bar signal;

彩色印刷 colour printing;

~彩色印刷系統 colour printing system;

彩色照相紙 colour photographic paper;

彩色正片 colour positive film;

[彩聲] acclamation; applause;

彩聲四起 applause is showered; there is a storm of cheers;

[彩陶] ancient painted pottery; coloured pottery; painted pottery;

彩陶文化 painted-pottery culture;

[彩頭] auspicious sign; good luck; lucky; omen of profit; omen of victory;

討個彩頭 get an auspicious sign;

有彩頭 lucky;

[彩霞] pink clouds; rosy clouds;

[彩繡] embroidery;

五色彩繡 embroidery in five colours;

[彩印] colour printing;

[彩影] colour movie;

[彩雲] morning glow; roseate clouds; rosy clouds;

彩雲易散 bright clouds are easily scattered; good things do not last long;

一點彩雲 a speck of cloud;

[彩照] colour photo;

藹彩 fresh look;

博彩 betting;

蟾彩 moonlight;

倒彩 booing; catcall;

燈彩 (1) coloured-lantern making; (2) coloured lanterns;

粉彩 famille rose;

掛彩 be wounded in action; be wounded in battle;

光彩 glorious; honourable; lustre; radiance;

喝彩 acclaim; cheer;

虹彩 iris;

花彩 festoon;

剪彩 cut the ribbon at an opening ceremony;

結彩 adorn with festoons for festive occasions;

精彩 brilliant; splendid; wonderful;

開採 exploit; extract; mine; recover;

摸彩 draw lot to determine the prize winners in a raffle or lottery;

三彩 three-colour glazed pottery;

色彩 (1) colour; shade; (2) colour; flavour;

水彩 watercolour;

五彩 (1) the five colours (blue, yellow, red, white and black); (2) multicoloured;

異彩 extraordinary splendor;

油彩 greasepaint; paint;

雲彩 clouds illuminated by the rising or setting sun;

扎彩 hang up festoons for festive occasions;

中彩 win a prize in a lottery;

cai

【採】 (1) gather; pick; pluck; (2) extract; mine; (3) adopt; select; (4) complexion; spirit;

[採辦] buy on a considerable scale; procure; purchase;

[採茶] pick tea;

[採伐] felling;

春季採伐 spring felling;

臨時採伐 incidental felling;

掠奪式採伐 exploitation felling;

[採訪] cover; gather material;

採訪新聞 gather news;

交叉採訪 cross coverage;

面對面的採訪 face-to-face interview;

現場採訪 on-air interview;
一次採訪 an interview;

［採購］ buying; procurement; purchase;
採購代表 buying representative;
~ 常設採購代表 resident buying representative;
採購代理 buying agency; purchasing agency;
~ 採購代理人 purchasing agent;
採購供應站 purchasing and supply station;
採購員 purchasing representative;
採購站 purchasing station;
大量採購 bulk purchase;
當地採購 local purchase;
國外採購 offshore purchases;
黑市採購 black mart purchase;
就地採購 local procurement;
零星採購 hand-to-mouth buying;
商業採購 commercial procurement;
私人採購 private procurement;
投資採購 investment buying;
循環採購 circular buying;
原材料採購 material purchase;
綜合採購 basket purchase;
總價採購 lump-sum acquisition;

［採花］ pluck flowers;
採花釀蜜 make honey out of flowers;

［採集］ bring together; collect; gather;
收集者 collector;

［採金］ mine for gold;

［採礦］ drill for minerals; mining;
採礦工程 mining engineering;
露天採礦 opencast mining;

［採煤］ mine coal;
採煤業 coal mining;

［採納］ accept; adopt;
採納意見 pick sb's brains; suck sb's brains;

［採暖］ heating;

［採取］ adopt; take;
採取措施 adopt measures; sth must be done; take action; take measures; take steps;
採取攻勢 take the offensive;
採取守勢 assume the defensive; stand on the defensive;
~ 被迫採取守勢 be put on the defensive;
採取行動 make a move;
~ 按計劃採取行動 take action on a plan;
採取應急措施 take emergency action;
採取有效措施 take effective steps;
採取預防 employ prevention;
採取折衷辦法 strike a happy medium;
採取正確措施 adopt right measures;
採取主動 take the initiative;

［採石］ quarry;
採石工 quarryman;

［採收］ gather; harvest;

［採寫］ write after interviewing;

［採樣］ collect samples; sample; sampling;
採樣單位 sampling horizon;

［採藥］ gather medicinal herbs;

［採用］ adopt; employ; use;
採用…手段 use measures;
建議採用 recommend for use;

［採油］ extract oil;

［採育］ fell timber and cultivate new trees;

博採 adopt from all sides;
掇採 gather; pluck; select;
開採 extract; exploit; mine; mining; recover;
群採 prospecting by the masses;
摭採 collect;

cai

【睬】 (1) look; watch; (2) notice; pay attention to; take notice of;

瞅睬 look at or give attention;
理睬 pay attention to; show interest in;

cai

【跴】 (1) trample; tread on; (2) chase; pursue;

［跴扁］ trample an object flat;
［跴出］ tread;
［跴訪］ search and arrest a criminal;
［跴壞］ break or damage by trampling; trample and break;
［跴實］ (1) tread; tread down; (2) mat down;
［跴水］ tread water;
［跴踏］ tread;
［跴住］ keep the feet upon;

cai

【綵】 (1) motley; varicoloured silk; (2) silk festoon; varicoloured silk;

［綵結］ a woman's hair decoration;
［綵樓］ gaily decorated tower;
［綵棚］ gaily decorated wooden framework;
［綵球］ a ball wound up from varicoloured

silk;
[綵衣娛親] wear a motley to entertain one's parents;

cai
【踩】 step on; trample; tread upon;
[踩扁] trample down;
[踩乎] bully; deprecate; disparage; oppress; tread upon;
[踩實] mat; trample down;
[踩水] tread water;
[踩線] step on line;

cai⁴
cai
【采】 fief; vassalage;
[采地] fief; vassalage;
[采邑] fief; vassalage;

cai
【菜】 (1) greens; vegetables; (2) food; (3) course; dish;
[菜場] food market;
[菜單] bill of fare; menu;
一份菜單 a menu;
[菜刀] chopper; kitchen knife;
[菜地] vegetable plot;
[菜豆] bean; common bean; haricot; kidney beans; navy bean;
矮生菜豆 bush kidney beans;
白菜豆 white kidney beans;
大黑花菜豆 black coloured kidney beans;
蔓生野菜豆 trailing wild bean;
食莢菜豆 snap beans;
[菜飯] pilaf;
[菜梗] vegetable stem;
[菜瓜] snake melon;
[菜館] restaurant;
[菜花] (1) cauliflower; (2) rape flower;
[菜窖] vegetable cellar;
[菜了] be unsuccessful; fail; fall through;
[菜牛] beef cattle;
[菜農] vegetable grower;
[菜盤] serving plate;
[菜譜] recipe;
一份菜譜 a menu;
[菜色] emacciated look; famished look;
鵠面菜色 emaciated; haggard face and vegetable colour; haron face and vegetable colour — unnourished; look famished; pale;
面有菜色 have a pale, anaemic complexion; look famished;
[菜市] food market; market place;
菜市場 food market; market place;
菜市小販 food market hawker;
[菜湯] vegetable soup;
俄國菜湯 borsch;
[菜肴] cooked food;
[菜油] rape oil;
[菜園] vegetable garden;
家庭菜園 kitchen garden;
[菜站] wholesale vegetable market;
[菜籽] rapeseed;

熬菜 boil food;
八寶菜 eight-treasure pickles;
白菜 Chinese cabbage;
包心菜 cabbage;
便菜 everyday dish; ordinary dish;
菠菜 spinach;
巢菜 common vetch;
炒菜 stir-fry;
出菜 achieve sth; make sth; produce a product;
川菜 Sichuan cuisine;
春菜 spring vegetable;
蒓菜 water shield;
大菜 (1) heavy course in a dinner party; (2) Western-styled food;
淡菜 mussel;
點菜 order dishes;
冬菜 preserved dried cabbage;
髮菜 hair vegetable; hair weed;
飯菜 (1) meal; repast; (2) dishes to go with rice;
蓋菜 leaf mustard;
乾菜 dried vegetable;
瓜菜 melon and vegetable;
果菜 fruits and vegetables;
海菜 edible seaweed;
黃花菜 day lily;
葷菜 meat dishes;
蕺菜 houttuynia cordata;
薺菜 shepherd's purse;
醬菜 pickles; vegetables pickled in soy sauce;
芥菜 leaf mustard;
金花菜 bur clover;
堇菜 violet;
韭菜 Chinese chives;
酒菜 (1) food and drink; (2) food to go with wine or liquor;
捲心菜 cabbage;
蕨菜 fiddlehead;

空心菜 water spinach;
辣菜 hot pickled vegetables;
涼菜 cold dish;
買菜 buy food;
売菜 mussel;
年菜 sumptuous food and dishes prepared for the lunar New Year;
泡菜 pickled vegetables; pickles;
配菜 fixings; jardiniere; side dish;
切菜 cut vegetables;
芹菜 celery;
青菜 (1) green vegetable; greens; (2) Chinese cabbage;
上菜 (1) best dishes; (2) place dishes on the table; serve a dish;
燒菜 cook; do cooking; prepare a meal;
生菜 romaine lettuce;
蔬菜 vegetables;
熟菜 cooked food;
素菜 vegetable dish;
酸菜 pickled cabbage; pickled vegetables;
添菜 have additional dishes;
甜菜 beet; sugar beet;
西菜 Western-style food;
鹹菜 pickles; salted vegetables;
莧菜 three-coloured amaranth;
香菜 coriander;
小菜 (1) pickled vegetables; (2) common dishes; plain dishes; side dishes; (3) easy job;
荇菜 duckweed;
莕菜 kind of water plant;
芽菜 bean sprouts;
腌菜 pickled vegetables; pickles;
醃菜 pickled vegetables; pickles;
洋菜 agar;
椰菜 savoy;
野菜 edible wild herbs;
一道菜 a course;
一棵菜 a vegetable;
油菜 (1) rape; (2) Chinese cabbage;
粵菜 Cantonese food;
榨菜 hot pickled mustard tuber;
中菜 Chinese dishes; Chinese meal;
種菜 grow vegetables;
竹菜 edible plant;
主菜 main course; main dish;
煮菜 prepare dishes; prepare food;
紫菜 laver;
做菜 prepare dishes;

cai
【蔡】 (1) turtle; (2) a state in the Spring and Autumn Period in ancient China; (3) a surname;

can¹
can
【湌】 eat; meal;

can
【參】 (1) enter; get involved in; intervene; join; take part in; (2) consult together; counsel; refer; (3) collate; compare; consider; (4) call to pay one's respect to; interview; visit; (5) censure; impeach; (6) recommend;

［參拜］ formally call on; make a formal visit to; pay a courtesy call; pay respects to;
參拜祠堂 worship at the ancestral shrine;

［參半］ half; half-and-half;
好壞參半 half good and half bad;
毀譽參半 as much praised as blamed; get mixed reception; get both praise and blame;
喜憂參半 be torn between joy and sorrow; half glad and half downcast;
疑信參半 half-believe and half-doubt;

［參變元件］ parametron;
薄膜參變元件 film parametron;
磁膜參變元件 magnetic film parametron;
恒定參變元件 constant parametron;

［參禪］ practise meditation; try to reach understanding of chan;
野狐參禪 a wild fox sits absorbed in contemplation — not know the limits of one's ability, one attempts to imitate others;

［參觀］ inspect; look around; visit; visitation; watch; witness;
參觀評比 public inspection and appraisal;
參觀日 open day;
參觀學習 visit and learn from;
參觀遊覽 go on a sight-seeing tour; go sightseeing; visit places of interest;
參觀展覽 pay a visit to an exhibition;
參觀者 visitors;
~一群參觀者 a troop of visitors;
安排參觀 arrange a visit;
教室參觀 class visitation;
值得參觀 deserve a visit; worth of a visit;

［參加］ (1) attend; collaborate; enter; enter into; enter one's name for; enter oneself for; go in; go in for; have a hand in;

join; join in; partake in; partake of; participate; participate in; present; present oneself for; show up; sit for; sit in; take part in; (2) give advice;
參加會議 take part in a conference;
參加考試 sit for an examination; take an exam;
參加政黨 join a political party;
積極參加 actively take part in; take an active part in;
應邀參加 be invited to take part in;

[參見] (1) c.f.; see also; (2) pay one's respects to;

[參軍] enlist in the army; enroll oneself in the army; enter the army; go into the army; join the army; join up;

[參看] (1) c.f.; see also; (2) consult; (3) read for reference;

[參考] (1) collate; consult; (2) examine and compare; (3) read sth for reference; refer to; reference;
參考詞典 reference dictionary;
參考價格 reference price;
參考鏡 reference mirror;
參考群體 reference group;
參考手冊 reference manual;
參考書 reference books;
~參考書目 bibliography; references;
~參考書書架 reference shelf;
~一本參考書 a reference book;
~主要參考書 the Bible;
參考體系 reference system;
參考語法 reference grammar;
參考資料 reference material;
便於參考 convenient for reference;
供將來參考 for future reference;
供日後參考 for future reference;
供隨時參考 for ready reference;
僅供參考 for information only; for reference only; for your reference only; just for reference;
隨時參考 ready for reference;
隨時可供參考 readily available for reference;
現成參考 quick reference;
業務參考 business reference;

[參謀] (1) staff officer; (2) give advice; offer advice;
參謀部 general staff;
參謀長 chief of staff;
~總參謀長 chief of general staff;
作戰參謀 operational staff;

[參賽] enter a competition; participate in a competition; participate in a match; take part in match;
參賽者 entrant;

[參事] advisor; counsellor;

[參數] parameter;
地址參數 address parameter;
活化參數 activation parameter;
加速參數 acceleration parameter;
實在參數 actual parameter;
行動參數 action parameter;

[參透] understand profundities;

[參悟] understand from meditation;

[參驗] reference table;

[參謁] (1) pay one's respects to sb; (2) pay homage to sb;

[參議會] consultative council;

[參議員] senator;

[參議院] senate;

[參與] a party to; have a hand in; involvement; join; partake; participate in; participation; pitch in; take part in;
參與度 degree of participation;
參與感 sense of participation;
參與競爭 join the competition;
參與決策 participate in decision-making;
參與欺詐勾當 lend oneself to dishonest schemes;
參與其事 be involved with sth; have a finger in the pie; have a hand in the matter; participate in an activity; take art and part in sth;
參與搶劫 take part in a robbery;
參與意識 consciousness of participation; sense of participation;
參與政治 participate in politics;
公民參與 civic participation;

[參閱] consult; read sth for reference; refer to;

[參贊] counsellor;
公使銜參贊 minister-counsellor;
經濟參贊 economic counsellor;
商務參贊 commercial counsellor;
文化參贊 cultural counsellor;
~新聞文化參贊 press and cultural counselor;
政務參贊 political counselor;

[參展] participate in an exhibition;
參展商 exhibitor;

參展者 exhibitor;

[參戰] enter a war; participate in a war; take part in a war;

[參照] consult; refer to;

參照構架 frame of reference; reference frame;

參照具體情況 in the light of circumstances; in the light of the specific situation;

參照系 reference frame;

參照系數 anchoring coefficient;

參照先例 in the light of precedents;

參照依據 point of reference;

供隨時參照 for ready comparison;

相互參照 cross-refer; cross-reference;

[參政] participate in government and political affairs; take part in a government; take part in politics;

參政黨 the party participating in government and political affairs;

參政議政 participate in the deliberation and administration of state affairs;

~參政議政意識 the awareness of the need to participate in the administration and discussion of state affairs;

[參酌] consider a matter in the light of actual conditions; consult and deliberate over; deliberate;

高參 (1) senior staff officer; (2) counsellor; mentor;

海參 sea cucumber; sea slug;

互參 co-reference;

人參 ginseng;

can

【餐】 (1) eat; (2) food; (3) meal; regular meal;

[餐叉] fork;

[餐車] buffet car; diner; dining car; restaurant car;

流動餐車 chuck wagon;

自助餐車 buffet car;

[餐碟] plate;

[餐費] boarding expenses; food bill;

[餐風] feed on the wind;

餐風宿露 a hard life in the open country; endure hardships on working outdoors; endure the hardships of travelling without shelter; exposed to wind and dew; make an arduous journey braving wind and dew; suffer hardships on the road;

餐風浴雨 hardship of travel without shelter;

餐風飲露 feed on the wind and drink the dew;

[餐館] restaurant; eatery; eating house;

餐館老闆 restaurateur;

餐館文化 restaurant culture;

夫妻經營的餐館 mom-and-pop restaurant;

高檔餐館 posh restaurant; upmarket restaurant;

經營餐館 run a restaurant;

開餐館 open a restaurant;

路邊廉價餐館 truck shop;

水濱餐館 waterside restaurant;

小餐館 diner;

一家餐館 a restaurant;

運輸餐館 transport café;

[餐後] after-meal;

餐後甜品 afters;

[餐巾] napkin; serviette; table napkin;

餐巾套環 napkin ring;

餐巾紙 napkin paper;

[餐酒] dinner wine;

[餐具] cutlery; dinner set; tableware;

餐具墊 table mat;

餐具櫃 hutch;

擺餐具 lay the table; set the table;

不鏽鋼餐具 stainless steel dinner set;

收拾餐具 clear the table;

洗餐具 do the washing-up; wash up;

一堆要洗的餐具 a pile of washing-up;

[餐券] meal coupon; meal ticket;

[餐前] pre-meal;

餐前酒 aperitif;

[餐室] dining room;

[餐貼] food allowance;

[餐廳] (1) dinner room; lunchroom; (2) dining room; restaurant; (3) canteen;

茶餐廳 Hongkong-style teahouse;

高級餐廳 classy restaurant;

軍人餐廳 mess hall;

時尚餐廳 chichi restaurant;

學生餐廳 student canteen;

一家餐廳 a restaurant;

一流的餐廳 top-class restaurant;

[餐席] cover;

[餐飲] food and drink;

餐飲承辦者 caterer;

餐飲服務 catering service;
餐飲區 food court;
餐飲業 catering business;

［餐桌］ dining table;
離開餐桌 leave the table;
清理餐桌 clear the table;

飽餐 eat to one's heart's content;
鋇餐 barium meal;
便餐 informal and ordinary meal;
大餐 slap-up dinner; slap-up meal;
會餐 dine together; have a reunion dinner;
就餐 go to a dining-hall to have one's meal;
進餐 dine; have a meal;
聚餐 have a dinner party;
快餐 fast food; fast meal; quick meal; snack; fast food;
冷餐 buffet;
美餐 feast;
三餐 three meals;
聖餐 Holy Communion;
素餐 (1) vegetable meal; (2) vegetarian; (3) not work for one's living;
套餐 set menu;
晚餐 dinner; supper;
午餐 lunch;
西餐 Western food;
野餐 go on a picnic; picnic;
夜餐 midnight meal; night snack;
一餐 a meal;
用餐 take one's food;
早餐 breakfast;
中餐 Chinese food;
自助餐 buffet;
佐餐 be eaten together with rice;

can

【驂】 the two outside horses of a team of three;

［驂乘］ escorts seated on both sides in a carriage;

can²

can

【殘】 (1) damage; destroy; injure; maim; spoil; wound; (2) barbarous; cruel and fierce; ferocious; heartless and relentless; savage; (3) crippled; disfigured; (4) deficient; incomplete; (5) remaining; remnant; residue; (6) kill;

［殘敗］ (1) wrack; (2) wipeout;

［殘暴］ brutal; cruel and ferocious; cruel and heartless; ruthless; savage; tyrannical;
殘暴行為 brutality; cruelty;
殘暴罪行 cruelties;
容忍殘暴 tolerate cruelty;

［殘杯冷炙］ gravy and cold roast meat; the leavings of a dinner; what is left over from a dinner;

［殘壁］ rubble;

［殘兵］ defeated soldiers; remnant troops;
殘兵敗將 bedraggled soldiers; discomfited troops and beaten generals; remnants of a defeated army;
殘兵敗卒 remnants of a routed army; routed troops;

［殘春］ the last days of spring;

［殘次］ imperfect;
殘次品 wastrels;
殘次商品 substandard commodities;

［殘存］ remaining; remnant; surviving;
殘存物 carry-over;

［殘敵］ remnants of the enemy forces;
殲滅殘敵 annihilate remanents of the enemy forces;
肅清殘敵 mop up the remaining enemy;
追擊殘敵 closely pursue the remnants of the enemy;

［殘冬］ last days of winter;
殘冬臘月 the closing days of the year; the end of the year;

［殘匪］ remaining handful of bandits;

［殘廢］ (1) crippled; disabled; disability; disablement; maimed; (2) crippled person;
殘廢保險 disability insurance;
殘廢人士 a cripple; a maimed person;
殘而不廢 crippled but leading a useful life;
殘老不癈 handicapped but accepted and functioning in society;
局部殘廢 partial disability;
完全殘廢 total disablement;
永久殘廢 permanent disability;

［殘稿］ incomplete manuscript;
留下殘稿 leave an incomplete manuscript;

［殘羹］ leftovers;
殘羹冷炙 dinner leftovers; odds and ends of a meal; the remains of a meal;
殘羹剩飯 crumbs from the table; fag-end of lunch; leftovers; remains of a meal;

［殘骸］ wreckage;

清除殘骸 remove the wreckage;
尋找殘骸 search for the wreckage;

[殘害] cruelly injure or kill; do harm to; mutilate; mutilation; slaughter;
殘害肢體 cause bodily injury;
殘害忠良 persecute good and loyal men; persecute the faithful and honest;
遭到殘害 meet with persecution; suffer persecution;

[殘花] withered flowers;
殘花敗柳 compromise one's honour by adultery; faded beauties; fallen angels; prostitutes; women no longer pure;
殘花落葉 withered flowers and fallen leaves;
敗柳殘花 immoral women; prostitutes;

[殘毀] mutilation;

[殘貨] damaged goods; shopworn goods; substandard goods;
處理殘貨 offer shopworn goods at a bargain;

[殘疾] deformity; physical disability;
四肢殘疾 be deformed in one's limbs;

[殘局] (1) unfinished chess game; (2) aftermath of war or great upheaval;
面對殘局 face a messy situation;
收拾殘局 clear up the mess; save the situation;

[殘酷] brutal; inhuman; ruthless;
殘酷對待 be treated with savagery;
殘酷如狼 as cruel as the grave;
殘酷無情 cruel and merciless; in cold blood; merciless; relentless;
殘酷行為 cruel act;

[殘留] leftovers; remains;
植被型 vegetation form;

[殘戮] (1) massacre; (2) horrible killing;

[殘年] (1) closing days of the year; last days of the year; (2) declining years; evening of life; one's closing years;
殘年短景 at the end of the year;
殘年多病 prone to illness in failing years;
殘年餘力 remaining efforts in one's old age;
度此殘年 pass the last days of the year; spend the evening of life;
風燭殘年 have one foot in the grave; old and ailing like a candle guttering in the wind; the decline of life;
急景殘年 time slips away fast and the year is approaching its end;

[殘篇斷簡] books with missing pages, chapters, etc.; fragments of ancient texts; scraps of writing;

[殘品] damaged article; defective goods;
拒收殘品 reject defective goods;

[殘破] (1) broken; damaged; dilapidated; spoiled; (2) deficient; incomplete;

[殘缺] fragmentary;
抱殘守缺 a stickler of ancient ways and things; a traditionalist; be conservative; cherish the outmoded and preserve the outworn; cling to bygone values; retain what is old and outworn; stick to the outmoded ways;
殘缺不全 broken and incomplete; fragmentary; incomplete; not intact; with some parts broken or missing;

[殘忍] brutal; brutality; cruel; cruelty; merciless; ruthless;
殘忍好殺 bloodthirsty;
行為殘忍 cruelty; perform a cruel act;
性情殘忍 have a savage temper;

[殘殺] butchery; carnage; massacre; murder;
自相殘殺 cause death to one another; cut each other's throats; cut one another's throats; destroy each other; engage in an intramural fight; fight against each other; kill each other; mutual slaughter;

[殘生] closing years of one's life;
了此殘生 end this miserable life; get rid of this troublesome life; shake off this mortal coil;

[殘暑] lingering heat of late summer;

[殘損] damaged; spoiled;

[殘息如絲] one's breathing has dwindled to a mere thread;

[殘霞晚照] the evening glow and the rosy clouds;

[殘陽] setting sun;

[殘葉] fallen leaves;
風捲殘葉 the wind scattered fallen leaves;

[殘餘] remains; remnants; survivals;
殘餘勢力 remaining forces;

[殘月] waning moon;
殘月如弓 the waning moon resembles a bow;
曉風殘月 the morning breeze and the lingering moon;

曉星殘月 the stars are faint and the moon setting;

[殘雲] last clouds;

風捲殘雲 the wind puffed away the last clouds;

[殘渣] dregs; residual;

殘渣泛起 the dregs are stirred up;

殘渣餘孽 evil elements from the old society; the dregs and rubbish of mankind; the dregs of society and the remnant scourings of the human race; the dregs of the old society;

腐蝕殘渣 etching residual;

化學殘渣 chemical residual;

瀝青殘渣 asphaltic residual;

裂解殘渣 cracked residual;

碳質殘渣 carbonaceous residual;

製酒殘渣 distillery residual;

轉爐殘渣 converter residual;

[殘照] evening glow; setting sun;

[殘汁] dregs;

[殘燭] expiring candle;

風前殘燭 a candle before a draft; a candle before the wind; short time left for aged people;

風中殘燭 very old and near death like a candle guttering in the wind;

病殘 sick and disabled; sick and handicapped;

摧殘 damage; destroy; devastate; wreck;

傷殘 invalidity; maim; permanent disability; the wounded and disabled;

身殘 broken in body;

凶殘 bloodthirsty; fierce and cruel; merciless; savage and cruel;

自殘 autotomy;

can

【慚】 ashamed; feel ashamed; humiliated; mortified;

[慚愧] abashed; ashamed; feel ashamed;

慚愧不已 abash;

感到慚愧 be ashamed; take shame upon oneself;

深感慚愧 feel deeply ashamed;

為…感到慚愧 feel ashamed of;

- 為自己感到慚愧 be ashamed of oneself;

[慚色] look ashamed;

羞慚 ashamed;

can

【蠶】 silkworm;

[蠶豆] broad bean; fava bean; horse bean; Lima bean;

蠶豆開花—黑心 black-hearted; evil; the broad bean in bloom – black inside;

[蠶娥] silk moth;

[蠶工] sericulture; silkworm culture;

[蠶茧] silkworm cocoon;

[蠶卵] silk moth; silkworm moth;

[蠶農] sericulturist; silkworm raiser;

[蠶桑] silkworm mulberry;

[蠶食] nibble;

蠶食別國領土 nibble another country's territory away;

蠶食鯨吞 eat up by degrees; gnaw as a silkworm; gobble up; gulp down by degrees; nibble and gobble; nibble at; nibble away like a silkworm; swallow as a whale; swallow up like a whale;

蠶食政策 tactics of nibbling away;

[蠶絲] natural silk;

[蠶月] fourth lunar month;

[蠶紙] paper with worm-egg card;

[蠶子] (1) silkworm; (2) silkworm egg; silkworm seed;

蠶子牽絲—自網自 a silkworm spinning silk – entrapping itself;

孵化蠶子 hatch silkworm eggs;

地蠶 cutworm;

槐蠶 geometer; inchworm; looper;

家蠶 silkworm;

朴蠶 pseuiocampa evanida;

桑蠶 silkworm;

沙蠶 clam worm;

天蠶 giant silkworm; wild silkworm;

土蠶 larva of a noctuid;

養蠶 raise silkworms;

野蠶 wild silkworm;

蟻蠶 newly-hatched silkworm;

樟蠶 camphor silkworm;

柞蠶 tussah; silkworm;

can³

can

【慘】 (1) awkward; miserable; pitiful; sorrowful; tragic; (2) brutal; cruel; savage; (3) disastrously; to a serious degree; (4) dark; gloomy;

[慘案] (1) massacre; (2) murder case; (3) tragedy;

［慘白］ dreadfully pale; ghostly pale; pale;
［慘敗］ abysmal failure; body blow; crushing defeat; disastrous defeat; fiasco; lose heavily; suffer a crushing defeat; suffer a terrible defeat;
遭到慘敗 crash disastrously; sustain a severe defeat;
［慘不］ be too tragic to;
慘不忍睹 could not bear the sight; extremely tragic or cruel; so appalling that one could hardly bear the sight of it; so horrible that one could hardly bear to look at it; so miserable that one cannot bear seeing it; too deplorable to see; too horrible to look at;
慘不忍見 so miserable that one can't bear seeing it;
慘不忍聞 too horrified to learn; too sad and shocking to hear; too sad and shocking to the ear;
慘不忍言 too deplorable to describe;
［慘慘］ dull; melancholy; sombre;
［慘惻］ anguished; grieved;
［慘淡］ bleak; dismal; gloomy; miserable;
慘淡經營 do sth with painstaking efforts; keep an enterprise going by painstaking effort; take great pains to carry on one's work under difficult circumstances; take pains with the work;
慘淡無光 dark without light; gloomy;
日子過得很慘淡 one's life is bleak;
天色慘淡 gloomy sky; the weather looks gloomy;
新月慘淡 a waning crescent moon showed faintly;
［慘跌］ collapse;
［慘毒］ brutal and vicious; ruthless and venomous;
［慘禍］ frightful calamity; horrible disaster;
釀成慘禍 bring about frightful disaster;
招來慘禍 invite horrible disaster;
遭到慘禍 suffer a horrible calamity;
［慘叫］ give out sad shrill cries; screech;
慘叫一聲 utter a heartrending cry;
［慘境］ dire straits; miserable condition;
［慘劇］ calamity; tragedy; tragic event;
［慘苦］ miserable;
［慘酷］ cruel;
［慘烈］ desolate; miserable;
［慘然］ grieved; saddened;
［慘殺］ massacre; murder;
［慘傷］ sorrowful; tragic;
［慘死］ die a tragic death; die distressingly; meet with a tragic death;
［慘痛］ bitter; deeply grieved; grievous; painful;
慘痛教訓 bitter lesson; painful lesson;
［慘笑］ smile wanly; wan smile;
［慘遭］ meet tragically with;
慘遭不幸 die a tragic death; meet a sad end;
慘遭橫禍 meet a tragic accident; meet tragically with a disaster; meet with unexpected misfortunes;
慘遭橫死 die an unnatural death; meet a violent death;
慘遭殺害 cruelly slaughtered; killed in a cruel manner; murdered in cold blood;
慘遭殺戮 be massacred in cold blood;
［慘重］ disastrous; grievous; heavy; serious;
傷亡慘重 be defeated with terrible slaughter; suffer heavy casualties; suffer severe casualties;
［慘狀］ pitiful sight;
黯慘 dismal; gloomy;
悲慘 miserable; pitiful; tragic;
淒慘 miserable; wretched;
愀慘 sorrowful;

can

【憯】 grieved; sad; sorrowful;

can

【黲】 light bluish dark;
［黲白］ gray;
［黲淡］ dull; gloomy;

can⁴

can

【粲】 (1) beaming; bright; bright and clear; (2) beautiful; excellent; splendid; (3) laugh; smile; (4) well polished rice;
［粲粲］ bright and eye-catching;
［粲花妙舌］ gift of the tongue; glib tongue;
［粲然］ (1) beaming; bright; (2) laugh; smile;
粲然可觀 achieve a signal success;
粲然一笑 give a beaming smile; grin with delight;

can

【燦】 bright; brilliant; resplendent;

[燦爛] bright; glorious; magnificent; resplendent; splendid;

燦爛的前景 splendid prospects lie before us;

燦爛的陽光 brilliant sunshine;

燦爛奪目 brilliant; dazzling; the lustre dazzles the eye;

燦爛輝煌 bright; glorious and resplendent; magnificent; splendid;

燦爛青春 brilliant youth;

前景燦爛 have a bright future; hold out magnificent prospects;

陽光燦爛 the sun shines bright;

[燦然] brightly; brilliantly; gloriously;

燦然一新 look brand-new;

[燦若明霞] shining with a subdued pinkish hue like light morning clouds;

can

【璨】 bright and brilliant; lustrous and luminous;

[璨璨] very bright;

[璨玉] lustrous jade;

璀璨 bright; resplendent;

cang¹
cang

【倉】 (1) granary; storehouse; warehouse; (2) berth; cabin; (3) green; (4) a surname;

[倉儲] storage;

倉儲企業 storage enterprise;

[倉促] all of a sudden; hastily; hasty; hurriedly;

倉促撤退 beat a hasty retreat;

倉促到達 arrive in hot haste;

倉促防禦 hasty defence;

倉促回來 hasten back;

倉促就職 hastily assume office;

倉促離開 hasten away; hurry away with haste;

倉促退卻 retreat hastily; retreat in hot haste;

倉促行事 by ear; go off at half cock; go off half-cocked;

倉促遺逃 rout;

倉促應戰 accept a challenge in a hurry; accept battle in haste; hasty acceptance of battle; put up a flurry of resistance; take up the glove without much forethought;

[倉房] storehouse; warehouse;

[倉皇] in a flurry; in haste; in panic; scared and hasty;

倉皇撤退 bug out;

倉皇失措 all in a fluster; at a loss as to what to do; be disturbed not knowing what to do; be scared out of one's wits; disconcerted; flat-footed; lose one's head; panic-stricken; startled and at a loss what to do;

倉皇逃竄 flee helter-skelter; flee in confusion; flee in panic; skedaddle;

倉皇逃命 escape in a hurry; flee pell-mell to save one's skin; run for life; run pell-mell;

倉皇退卻 retreat in haste; withdraw in haste;

倉倉皇皇 in a great flurry; in a hurry;

臨事倉皇 be startled at a crisis;

形色倉皇 appear in a big hurry; as a fugitive; look anxious and tense;

[倉庫] depository; depot; repository; stockroom; store; storehouse; warehouse;

倉庫用地 depot and warehouse site;

備件倉庫 parts depot;

成品倉庫 goods warehouse;

海關倉庫 customs warehouse;

貨物倉庫 merchandise warehouse;

傢具倉庫 household goods warehouse;

內地倉庫 inland depot;

農業倉庫 agricultural warehouse;

清點倉庫 check a stock; take stock;

清理倉庫 check all the goods in the store;

油燃料倉庫 oil-fuel depot;

中轉倉庫 transit warehouse;

自動倉庫 automatic warehouse;

租用倉庫 hire a warehouse;

[倉廩] granary;

[倉容] warehouse capacity;

[倉租] warehouse storage charges;

倉租率 rate of storage rent expense;

穀倉 barn; breadbasket; garner; granary;

貨倉 warehouse;

虧倉 broken stowage;

糧倉 barn; grain elevator; grain silo; granary; silo;

煤倉 coal bunker;

清倉 make an inventory of warehouses;

水倉 sump;

一穀倉 barnful;
義倉 local public welfare granary;

cang
【傖】 (1) cheap; lowly; vulgar; (2) confused; disorderly;
［傖父］ vulgar person;
［傖俗］ vulgar;

cang
【滄】 azure; dark blue; green;
［滄波］ blue waves;
［滄滄涼涼］ breezy; cool;
［滄海］ ocean;
滄海孤舟 a lonely boat on an ocean;
滄海橫流 the seas are in turmoil;
滄海桑田 much water has flowed under the bridge; seas change into mulberry fields and mulberry fields into seas – time brings great changes to the world;
滄海一粟 a drop in the bucket; a drop in the ocean; a grain of millet from a granary; a grain of millet in the vast sea; a grain of wheat in a bushel of chaff; a speck in a vast ocean; one grain afloat on a vast ocean – very tiny;
滄海遺珠 unknown talented person; unnoticed talent;
［滄浪］ azure water;
［滄桑］ drastic changes;
飽經滄桑 have experienced many vicissitudes of life;
幾經滄桑 go through the mill; marked by vicissitudes;
歷盡滄桑 go through the hoops; go through the mill; have experienced many vicissitudes of life; pass through the mill;

cang
【蒼】 (1) dark green; (2) blue; (3) ashy; gray; (4) old; (5) a surname;
［蒼白］ pale; pallid; peaked; peaky; wan;
蒼白的 cadaverous;
蒼白如紙 one's face is as white as paper;
蒼白無力 feeble; pale and weak;
臉色蒼白 have a pallid complexion; have a wan complexion; look pale; one's face is as white as paper;
面色蒼白 have a pallid complexion; have a wan complexion; look pale; one's face is as white as paper;
［蒼蒼］ (1) gray; grizzled; (2) vast and hazy;
白髮蒼蒼 gray-haired;
兩鬢蒼蒼 be graying at the temples;
［蒼翠］ dark green; verdant;
蒼翠蔥蘢 luxuriantly green; verdant;
［蒼勁］ (1) old and strong; (2) bold; vigorous;
蒼勁不屈 unbending;
蒼勁古樹 hardy and old trees;
蒼勁有力 vigorous and forceful;
筆力蒼勁 paint in bold, vigorous strokes; write in bold, vigorous strokes;
［蒼老］ (1) aged; old; (2) forceful; vigorous;
蒼老了很多 have aged a lot;
面色蒼老 have an old and weathered face;
聲音蒼老 one's voice is weak and split;
顯得蒼老 be weighed down with age;
［蒼涼］ bleak; desolate;
［蒼綠］ green; verdant;
［蒼茫］ boundless and indistinct; vast and hazy;
蒼茫大地 a vast area of land; the boundless land;
雲水蒼茫 infinity of heaven and sea;
［蒼穹］ aether; firmament; vault of heaven;
蒼穹浩渺 common people;
蒼穹天空 cope of heaven;
［蒼生］ common people;
蒼生涂炭 the people are plunged into an abyss of misery;
誤盡蒼生 bring calamity to humanity; lead the masses to the road of disaster;
澤及蒼生 spread all-round benefit to all people;
［蒼松］ green pine;
蒼松翠柏 green pines and verdant cypresses;
蒼松翠竹 green pines and verdant bamboos;
蒼松茂竹 green pines and luxuriant bamboos;
［蒼天］ (1) blue sky; (2) Heaven;
蒼天保祐 May Heaven preserve us;
蒼天不負有心人 Heaven helps those who help themselves;
蒼天不容 God will repay;
蒼天在上 call Heaven to witness;
蒼天作證 Heaven knows;
感謝蒼天 Heaven be praised;
［蒼蠅］ fly;
蒼蠅拍 flyswatter;
蒼蠅嗡嗡 flies buzz; flies drone; flies hum;

捕捉蒼蠅 catch flies;
沒頭蒼蠅 do things aimlessly; headless fly;
拍蒼蠅 swat a fly;
一群蒼蠅 a swarm of flies;
一隻蒼蠅 a fly;
招蒼蠅 attract flies;

彼蒼 heavens;
莽蒼 (1) open country; (2) (of scenery) blurred; hazy; misty;
穹蒼 azure vault; dome of the sky; firmament; heavens; sky; vault of heaven;
上蒼 heaven;

cang
【艙】 (1) cabin; (2) module;
［艙室］ cabin;

船艙 cabin; ship's hold;
房艙 passenger's cabin on board a ship;
官艙 first-class cabin;
後艙 backhold;
貨艙 cargo bay;
機艙 passenger compartment;
駕駛艙 cockpit; control cabin; pilot's compartment;
客艙 cabin; main cabin; passenger cabin;
密封艙 airtight cabin; sealed cabin;
水艙 water tank;
統艙 third class steerage; tourist class;
指揮艙 command module;
座艙 cockpit;

cang
【鶬】 oriole;
［鶬鶊］ oriole;

cang²
cang
【藏】 (1) conceal; hide; (2) hoard; lay by; save; store; (3) a surname;
［藏毒］ possession of cocaine;
［藏躲］ go into hiding; hide or conceal oneself;
［藏奸］ harbour malice;
藏奸耍滑 hide one's treachery and act in a slick way; wily;
［藏經閣］ depositary of Buddhist texts;
［藏酒閣］ wine cellar;
［藏露］ hide and show; hide or show;
藏鋒露機 refrain from outspoken attack but one's intentions are revealed;
藏頭露尾 act equivocatingly; give a partial account of; show the tail but hide the head — tell part of the truth but not all of it;
［藏匿］ conceal; creep; go into hiding; hide; lurk; prowl; skulk; slink; steal;
藏匿處 hideaway; hide-out; hiding place;
［藏品］ object;
［藏起］ (1) conceal; hide; (2) hide; put out of sight; (3) superinduce over;
藏起悲傷 cloak one's sorrow;
藏起痛苦 mask one's sufferings;
［藏身］ go into hiding; hide oneself;
藏身地 bolthole; lodging;
藏身屋內 conceal oneself in a house;
藏身之處 a hole to conceal oneself in; a place to hide; a place to keep oneself out of sight; hideout; hiding place;
無處藏身 have no place to hide;
［藏書］ (1) collect books; (2) collection of books; library;
藏書癖 bibliomania;
藏書者 bibliophilist; bibliotaph;
繼承藏書 inherit a library;
交換藏書 exchange collections;
收集藏書 collect books;
整理藏書 set one's library to rights;
［藏私］ hide sth illegally;
［藏拙］ hide one's inadequacy by keeping quiet; hide one's weak points; keep one's weakness unexposed;
藏巧於拙 hide one's ingenuity in clumsiness;
掩醜藏拙 cover up shame and conceal inferiority;
［藏蹤］ conceal oneself; go into hiding;

暗藏 cloak; conceal; cover up; hidden; hide; keep under cover;
昂藏 straight and impressive looking;
包藏 conceal; harbor;
保藏 keep in store; preserve;
儲藏 (1) lay by; save and preserve; store; (2) deposit;
道藏 Daoist sutras;
典藏 book reservation;
躲藏 conceal; go into hiding; hide away;
緘藏 bear in silence; keep silent;
窖藏 cellaring; depot;
庫藏 have a storage of; have in storage; have in store;
礦藏 mineral resources;

冷藏 refrigerate;
埋藏 (1) bury; lie hidden in the earth; (2) conceal; hide;
氣藏 gas pool;
潛藏 go into hiding; hide; remain under cover;
深藏 reserved;
釋藏 Buddhist sutra;
收藏 collect; store;
帑藏 treasury;
窩藏 harbour; shelter;
掩藏 conceal; hide;
隱藏 conceal; go into hiding; hide; remain under cover; stash away;
油藏 oil deposit; oil pool;
蘊藏 contain; hold in store;
遮藏 cover up; hide;
珍藏 consider valuable and collect appropriately;
貯藏 (1) hoard; store up; (2) deposits;
捉迷藏 (1) hide-and-seek; (2) tricky and evasive; play hide-and-seek;

cang³
cang

【駔】

[駔子] mean person; rascal; ruffian;

cao¹
cao

【操】 (1) grasp; hold; (2) act; control; do; handle; manage; manipulate; operate; take up; (3) speak; (4) drill; exercise; (5) behaviour; conduct; (6) a surname;

[操辦] handle; make arrangements; take care of;
操辦婚禮 make preparations for a wedding; manage a wedding;

[操場] drill ground; playground; sports-ground;

[操持] (1) grasp; handle; manage; (2) plan and prepare;
操持家務 manage household affairs;

[操蛋] bad; disappointing; no good;

[操刀] hold a sword in one's hand;
操刀必割 as one grasps a knife, one has to use it to cut sth; sure to take advantage of chance when it comes;

[操斧伐柯] hew an ax handle with an ax handle in one's hand;

[操戈] take up arms;
同室操戈 engage in internal strife; family members drawing swards on each other; fight against one's own men; internal strife; internecine feud; internecine fight; quarrel among brothers in the same family;

[操觚] engage in writing;
操觚為生 make a living by writing;

[操勞] (1) do sth industriously; work hard; work painstakingly; (2) look after; take care;
操勞過度 overwork oneself; strain oneself; work too hard;

[操練] drill; practise;

[操切] hasty; rash;
操切從事 act with undue haste; go about impetuously;

[操神] bother; tax on one's mind; trouble;

[操守] personal integrity;
操守高潔 high-principled;
操守可信 resolute and trustworthy;

[操心] (1) be concerned over; take pains; trouble about; worry about; (2) rack one's brains;
操心工作 take pains with one's work;
為錢操心 trouble one's head about money matters;
為小事操心 worry over trifles;

[操行] (1) behaviour of a student; conduct of a student; (2) disgusting; shameful;

[操演] demonstration; drill;

[操之過急] act precipitately impulsively; act with undue haste; be overhasty; crow the mourners; go off at half cock; go off half-cocked; jump the gun; too hasty; overhastiness;

[操縱] (1) control; get sb by the balls; get sb by the short and curlies; have sb by the balls; have sb by the short and curlies; have sb on a string; operate; (2) manipulate; rig; run the show;
操縱桿 joystick;
操縱股票 manipulate the stocks;
操縱器 manipulator;
~液壓操縱器 hydraulic manipulator;
~主僕操縱器 master-slave manipulator;
操縱市場 manipulate the market; play the market; rig the market;
操蹤市價 control the market price;
操縱物價 manipulate the price;
操縱選舉 manipulate the voting;
操縱一切 boss the show; run the show;

操縱子 operon;
操縱自如 control as one likes; have an easy control in the matter; operate with facility;
暗中操縱 manoeuvre behind the scene; pull the strings from behind the screen; veiled manipulation; work the ropes;
擺脱…的操縱 break loose from;
～擺脱大國的操縱 break loose from big powers' leading strings;
急劇操縱 abrupt manoeuvre;
控制操縱 direct operation;
幕後操縱 manoeuvre behind the scenes; pull the strings;
氣動力操縱 aerodynamic manoeuvre;
手控操縱 hand-controlled manipulation;
遺傳操縱 genetic manipulation;
制動操縱 braking manoeuvre;

[操作] manipulate; manipulation; operate;
操作安全分析 operational safety analysis;
操作程序 operation sequence;
操作動詞 operative verb;
操作方法 mode of operations;
操作分析 operation analysis;
操作規程 operational regulations;
操作合理化 rationalization of operation;
操作碼 action code; function code;
操作設備 manipulator;
～顯微操作設備 micromanipulator;
操作系統 operating system;
～操作系統病毒 operating system virus;
～操作系統管理程序 operating system management programme;
～操作系統型病毒 operating system virus;
～基本操作系統 basic operating system;
操作員 operator;
～操作員信息 operator message;
～初級操作員 junior operator;
～中心操作員 centre operator;
操作指令 operational order;
安全操作 safe operation;
～安全操作規程 safe operation specification;
～安全操作區 area of safe operation;
～安全操作系統 safety operating system; security operating system;
翻譯操作 translation operation;
加快操作 speed operations;
人工操作 manual acting;
實際操作 hands-on;
手工操作 manual operation;
數據操作 data manipulation;
誤操作 incorrect manipulation;
學習操作 learn to operate;

保健操 keep-fit exercise;
兵操 military drill;
出操 go out to do exercises; go out to drill;
風操 graceful bearing and upright and honest character;
工間操 work-break setting-up exercises;
廣播操 setting-up exercises to radio music;
會操 gather together for military drill;
節操 moral integrity;
軍操 military drill;
課間操 class-break setting-up exercises;
清操 virtuous disposition and behaviour;
情操 sentiment;
上操 go out to drill; have drills;
收操 make an end of drill;
霜操 moral uprightness;
體操 exercise gymnastics;
下操 finish drilling;
早操 morning exercises;
貞操 (1) chastity; virginity; (2) loyalty; moral integrity;
志操 ambition and moral fortitude;

cao

【糙】 (1) boorish; impolite; rough; rude; uncouth; (2) course; (3) crudely made; of poor workmanship;
[糙米] brown rice; coarse rice; unpolished rice;

粗糙 (1) coarse; rough; (2) crude;

cao²

cao

【曹】 (1) plural particle; (2) a surname;
[曹白魚] Chinese herring;

爾曹 you people;
兩曹 both parties in a law suit; the plaintiff and the defendant;
市曹 marketing place;
陰曹 netherworld;

cao

【嘈】 clamorous; din; noisy;
[嘈雜] clamorous; full of confused noises; noisy and confused;
嘈雜聒耳 jar on one's ears;
嘈雜聲 clamour; din; hubbub; noise;

C

嘈嘈嘈嘈 talk rapidly and confusingly;

cao

【漕】 transport grain by water;

［漕河］ canal;

［漕糧］ tribute rice;

［漕運］ transport grain to the capital by water;

cao

【槽】 (1) manger; (2) chute; flume; trough;

［槽線］ trough line;

［槽牙］ front tooth;

齒槽 alveolus;
地槽 geosyncline;
渡槽 aqueduct;
河槽 riverbed;
流槽 launder;
溜槽 chute;
平槽 the water level of a river on the same level with the bank;
切槽 grooving;
飼槽 feeding trough;
榫槽 mortise;
掏槽 cut;
跳槽 change one's job; change one's occupation;
徒槽 chute;
洗滌槽 washing tank;
牙槽 socket of the tooth;

cao

【螬】 grub;

蠐螬 grub;

cao³

cao

【艸】 grass; straw; weeds;

cao

【草】 (1) grass; hay; straw; (2) careless; hasty; rough; (3) draft; (4) script type of Chinese calligraphy;

［草庵］ thatched hut;

［草案］ draft;
憲法草案 draft constitution;

［草包］ (1) straw bag; straw sack; (2) blockhead; good-for-nothing; idiot;

［草本］ herbal;
草本學 agrostology;

［草草］ carelessly; hastily;
草草不恭 act carelessly; finish sth roughly; hastily to prepare; in a perfunctory way; make in a hurry and without care;
草草而就 be patched up;
草草過目 cast a running glance at; give a cursory reading; ready cursorily; read through roughly; skim through;
草草結婚 rush into marriage;
草草了事 dispose of sth hastily; finish a job roughly; get through with sth any old way; give a lick and a promise;
草草收兵 beat a hasty retreat; withdraw troops in a hurry;
草草收場 hastily wind up the matter;

［草場］ meadow;

［草蟲］ grasses and insects;

［草創］ start to found;

［草袋］ straw bag;

［草地］ (1) grassland; meadow; (2) grassplot; lawn;
草地滾球 lawn bowling;
草地球場 grass court; tennis lawn;
草地網球 lawn tennis;
草地席 floor mat;
浸水草地 water meadow;
勿踩草地 don't trample on grass; keep off the grass;
一塊草地 a lawn;
一片草地 a meadow;

［草甸］ meadow;
凍原草甸 tundra meadow;
放牧草甸 grazing meadow;
高山草甸 alpine meadow;
~亞高山草甸 subalpine meadow;
旱草甸 drought meadow;
泥炭草甸 peaty meadow;
水下草甸 submerged meadow;
淹水草甸 water meadow;
永久草甸 permanent meadow;
沼澤草甸 swamp meadow;
真草甸 true meadow;

［草稿］ draft; manuscript; rough draft;
草稿紙 rough paper;
打草稿 write out a draft;
擬定草稿 prepare a draft;
修改草稿 revise a draft;
一份草稿 a draft;

［草根］ grass-root;
草根階層 grass-roots class; grass roots;
是草有根，是話有因 every blade of grass has its roots; behind every word is a thought;

[草菇] straw mushroom;
[草屐] straw sandals;
[草芥] mere nothing; trifle;
草芥不如 mere nothing; not worth a straw; trifle;
視如草芥 regard as worthless; treat like dirt;
直如草芥 as worthless as a stalk of mustard; valueless;
[草寇] bandit;
[草捆] bale;
[草莽] (1) rank growth of grass; (2) uncultivated land; wilderness;
草莽英雄 free-booting hero; greenwood hero; hero of the bush;
[草帽] straw hat;
平頂硬草帽 boater;
[草莓] strawberry;
草莓露 strawberry syrup;
大果草莓 large-fruited strawberry;
高山草莓 alpine strawberry;
麝香草莓 hautbois strawberry;
野草莓 wood strawberry;
[草昧] primeval; primitive;
[草民] common people;
[草木] flora; grass and trees; vegetation;
草木藹藹 lush vegetation;
草木常青 the grass and trees are green all the year round;
草木葱蘢 luxuriant vegetation;
草木叢生 be grown with bushes and trees; plants burst out in profusion;
草木皆兵 see an enemy behind every tree; state of extreme nervousness;
草木怒生 plants burst out in profusion;
草木知春 all plants are aware that spring will come;
草木知秋 grass and trees know the coming of every new autumn;
繁草茂木 lush growth of trees and flowers;
茂草繁木 trees and grasses grow luxuriantly;
青綠的草木 verdure;
人非草木 a person is not a stalk of grass or a tree;
一草一木 every blade of grass and every tree; every tree and bush; every tree and every blade of grass;
～愛護一草一木 cherish even the most trifling things;
依草附木 curry favour with those in power; dependent; rely on powerful friends;
倚草附木 like souls leaning on a grass or dependent on a tree;
異木奇草 rare trees and herbs;
[草擬] draft; draw up; rough out;
草擬計劃 draft a plan; sketch out a plan;
[草皮] sod; turf;
鋪草皮 lay turf;
人工草皮 turf;
一片草皮 a chunk of turf;
[草片] grass;
一葉草片 a blade of grass;
[草坪] grass-plot; greensward; lawn; sward;
修剪草坪 cut the grass on a lawn; mow a lawn;
[草簽] initial;
草簽合同 initial a contract;
草簽協定 initial an agreement;
[草裙舞] Hawaiian dance; hula-hula;
[草人] scarecrow;
[草書] cursive hand; cursive script;
[草率] careless; haste; perfunctory; rash;
草率從事 act in hasty; act rashly; act without due consideration; do a job carelessly; do one's work in a careless manner; go it blind; take hasty action;
草率了事 dispose of a matter carelessly; huddle through; huddle up;
草率輕浮 headlong and untrustworthy;
草率通過 railroad sth through;
草率行動 rash action;
[草圖] draft; outline; preliminary sketch; rough draft; rough sketch; rude drawing; scheme; sketch plan; sketching; thumbnail sketch;
草圖核准 approval of draft;
導線草圖 traverse sketch;
劃草圖 make a sketch;
目測草圖 eye sketch;
手製草圖 cartographical sketching;
現場草圖 field sketch; field sketching;
一張草圖 a sketch;
[草屋] hut;
[草席] grass mat; straw mat;
[草鞋] straw sandals;
黃帝又有草鞋親 even the emperor has poor relatives;
[草藥] herbal medicine; herbal remedies;

C

草藥商 herbalist;
草藥醫學 herbal medicine;
草藥治療法 herbal medicine;

[草葉] grass;
一片草葉 a blade of grass;

[草魚] tench;

[草原] grassland; prairie; steppe;
草原犬鼠 prairie dog;
大草原 pampas; prairie;
乾草原 steppe;
高草原 prairie;
熱帶草原 tropical grassland;
熱帶無樹大草原 llano;
熱帶稀樹草原 savanna;

[草約] draft agreement; draft treaty; protocol;

[草澤] rustic origin;
起於草澤 of rustic origin;

[草長鶯飛] the grass is tall and the nightingales are in the air;

[草織品] straw articles;

拔草 pull up weed; pull up weeds; weed;
本草 Chinese herbal medicine;
碧草 green grass; verdant grass;
柴草 firewood;
吃草 browse on grass;
除草 weed; weed out;
寸草 blade of grass;
稻草 rice straw;
燈草 rush;
毒草 (1) poisonous weeds; (2) harmful speech;
芳草 fragrant grass; green grass;
蜂草 beeweed;
甘草 liquorice root;
乾草 hay;
割草 mow the grass;
海草 seagrass; sea-plant; seaweed; wrack;
含羞草 sensitive plant;
蒿草 wormwood;
薅草 weeding;
黑麥草 ryegrass;
葒草 prince's feather;
花草 flowers and plants;
藎草 hispid arthraxon;
枯草 withered grass;
蒯草 wool grass;
狂草 cursive calligraphy;
蘭草 orchid;
糧草 army provisions; rations and forage;
潦草 (1) (of handwriting) hasty and careless; (2) sloppy; slovenly;
龍鬚草 Chinese alpine rush;
綠草 green grass;
落草 become an outlaw; take to the greenwood;
蔓草 trailing plant;
茅草 couch grass; thatch; twitch-grass;
牧草 forage grass; herbage;
起草 compose; draft; draft out; draw up; make a draft of; map out; prepare a draft; sketch; write out;
茜草 madder;
青草 green grass;
三葉草 shamrock;
蓍草 milfoil;
水草 (1) water and grass; (2) waterweeds;
四葉草 four-leaf clover;
飼草 forage grass;
蓑草 sedge;
夏枯草 selfheal;
香草 (1) sweetgrass; (2) vanilla;
萱草 daylily; tawny daylily;
諼草 daylily;
菸草 tobacco;
煙草 tobacco;
藥草 medicinal herbs;
野草 wild grasses;
一把草 a bundle of grass;
一抱草 an armful of hay;
一車草 a load of hay;
一叢草 a patch of grass;
一簇草 a tuft of grass;
一堆草 a stack of hay;
一墩草 a cluster of grass;
一根草 a blade of grass;
一棵草 a grass; a tuft of grass;
一捆草 a wisp of straw;
一綑草 a sheaf of grass;
益母草 motherwort;
櫻草 primrose;
芸草 rue; strong-scented herb;
耘草 remove weeds; weed;
雜草 rank grass;

cao

【慅】 anxious; apprehensive; uneasy;

[慅慅] anxious; apprehensive; uneasy;

cao⁴

cao

【慥】 kind-hearted; sincere;

[慥慥] sincere and honest;

ce⁴

ce

【冊】 (1) book; volume; (2) copy;
[冊封] confer titles of nobility on; invest with rank;
[冊頁] an album of calligraphy; an album of paintings;
[冊子] book; volume;

表冊 book of tables; statistical form;
簿冊 books and files; lists;
檔冊 file; record;
底冊 a bound copy of a document kept on file;
分冊 a separately published part of a book; fascicle; volume;
畫冊 album of paintings;
紀念冊 autograph book;
捐冊 a register listing donations and their donors;
名冊 register; roll;
清冊 detailed list; inventory;
史冊 annal; book of history;
手冊 directory; handbook; how-to; manual;
書冊 book;
圖冊 illustrated book;
相冊 photo album;
一冊 a copy of;
賬冊 account book;
註冊 register;

ce

【側】 (1) sideways; the side; (2) incline towards; lean; slant; (3) low and narrow-minded;
[側步] sidestep;
[側傳] side pass;
[側燈] side light;
[側翻] turn to one's side;
[側風] crosswind;
[側擊] flank attack; make a flank attack on;
[側記] sidelights;
[側流] effluent;
[側門] side door; side entrance;
[側面] aspect; flank; side;
側面 profile;
[側目] sidelong glance;
側目而視 cast a sidelong glance; give sb a sidelong glance; look askance at sb; look with a sidelong glance;
側目窺視 cast a sidelong glance at;
側目注視 give sb a sidelong glance; look at sb with a sidelong glance;
[側身] lean to one side; on one's side; sideways;
側身挨近 incline near to; lean close to; side up to;
[側室] concubine;
側室所出 offspring by a concubine;
[側視] side-looking;
[側手翻] cartwheel; lateral wheel;
做側手翻 do cartwheels; turn cartwheels;
[側躺] lie on the side;
[側聽] eavesdrop;
[側旋] sidespin;
[側影] profile; silhouette;
[側重] lay particular emphasis on; put special emphasis on;

兩側 ambo-; two flanks; two sides;
攲側 incline; slant; tilt;
清君側 rid the emperor of evil ministers;
傾側 incline; lean; lurch; tilt; vert;
翼側 flank;
右側 right; right side;
左側 left; left side;

ce

【廁】 bog; closet; lavatory; toilet; washroom;
[廁所] amenities; bog; can; cloakroom; cloaks; closet; cludge; comforts room; commode; convenience; crapper; John; lav; lavatory; lavvy; loo; lounge; marble-palace; powder room; toilet; washroom; water closet; W.C.;
廁所很骯髒 the toilet is skanky;
廁所間 toilet stall;
公共廁所 public convenience;
戶外廁所 latrine; outhouse;
男廁所 men's room;
女廁所 ladies' room; powder room; the ladies;
上廁所 answer nature's call; answer the call of nature; answer the demands of nature; answer the needs of nature; be caught short; be taken short; can I add some power; cash a cheque; check out the plumbing; do a job for oneself; do one's business; do one's duty; ease oneself; eliminate; excrete; feed a dog; find a haven of rest; fix one's

C

face; freshen up; get some fresh air; give one's bum an airing; give oneself ease; go; go feed the goldfish; go into retreat; go potty; go somewhere; go round the haystack; go to Egypt; go to one's private office; go to see one's aunt; go to see one's uncle; go to see the baby; go to stool; go to the bathroom; go to the lavatory; go to the toilet; may I be excused; natural necessity; nature is calling sb; perform certain necessary function of the body; perform one's ablutions; pluck a rose; powder one's nose; relieve bowel; relieve nature; relieve oneself; sharpen the skates; visit John; visit Lady Periam; visit the plumbing; visit the sand-box; wash one's hands; what is the geography of the house; worship at the altar;

~上廁所訓練 potty-training; toilet-training;

[廁蠅] latrine fly;

[廁紙] bog roll; toilet paper; toilet roll;

公廁 public convenience; public toilet;
溷廁 lavatory; washroom;
茅廁 latrine; latrine pit;
男廁 men's lavatory; the gents;
女廁 ladies' room; the ladies; women; women's lavatory;

ce

【惻】 feel anguish; sad; sorrowful;

[惻然] grieved; sorrowful;

[惻隱] compassion; pity;
惻隱之心 sense of pity; the milk of human kindness;
~產生惻隱之心 have compassion;
~一絲惻隱之心 a sign of sympathy for sb;

悲惻 sad; sorrowful;
慘惻 anguished; grieved;
悱惻 grieved; laden with sorrow; sad at heart;
悽惻 grieved; rueful; sad; sorrowful;
淒惻 grieved; sad; sorrowful;
隱惻 commiseration; sympathy;

ce

【測】 (1) fathom; measure; survey; (2) conjecture; infer;

[測地線] geodesic;
保形測地線 conformally geodesic;
閉測地線 closed geodesic;
仿射測地線 affine geodesic;
極小測地線 minimal geodesic;
正規化測地線 normalized geodesic;

[測定] determine; determination;
測定風向 determine the wind direction;
安全測定 safety measurement;
比色測定 colorimetric determination;
導電測定 electric conductance determination;
電流測定 amperometric determination;
絕對測定 absolute determination;
生物測定 bioassay;
水生生物測定 aquatic organism determination;

[測高] measure the height of;
測高法 altimetry;
測高計 altimeter;
~電容測高計 electric capacity altimeter;
~航空測高計 aircraft altimeter;
~激光測高計 laser altimeter;
~絕對測高計 absolute altimeter;
~雷達測高計 radar altimeter;
~脈衝測高計 pulse altimeter;
~聲學測高計 acoustic altimeter;
~調頻式測高計 frequency modulation type altimeter;
~音響測高計 echo altimeter;
~着陸測高計 landing altimeter;

[測光] photometric;
測光筆 photometric pen;
測光表 exposure meter;

[測謊器] lie detector; polygraph;

[測繪] mapping; survey and drawing;
測繪飛機 air-mapping aeroplane;
測繪衛星 cartographic satellite;

[測距] ranging;
測距器 range-finder;
~連動測距器 coupled range-finder;
測距儀 rangefinder;
~光電測距儀 geodimeter;
~雷達測距儀 tellurometer;
~脈衝激光測距儀 pulsed laser rangefinder;
~雙像測距儀 coincidence rangefinder;
~野外激光測距儀 battlefield laser rangefinder;
激光測距 laser ranging;
精密測距 fine ranging;

頻閃測距 flash ranging;
全向測距 omnidirectional ranging;

[測控] observe and control;
測控中心 measurement and control centre;

[測力計] dynamometer;
空氣磨擦測力計 air friction dynamometer;
氣力制動測力計 air brake dynamometer;
吸收測力計 absorption dynamometer;
制動測力計 brake dynamometer;

[測量] gauge; measure; measurement; measuring; survey; surveying;
測量地形 make a topographical survey; survey the topography;
測量海深 sound the sea;
測量精度 measuring accuracy;
測量器具 measuring appliance;
測量師 surveyor;
~產業測量師 property surveyor;
測量體重 take sb's weight;
測量誤差 measuring error;
測量學 grammetry; surveying;
~大地測量學 geodesy;
~天文大地測量學 astronomical geodesy;
~重力大地測量學 gravimetric geodesy;
~高低測量學 altitude surveying;
~工程測量學 engineering surveying;
~鐵路工程測量學 railroad engineering surveying;
~人體測量學 anthropometry;
~攝影測量學 photogrammetry;
~天體測量學 astrometry;
測量血壓 measure blood pressure; take blood pressure;
測量員 surveyor;
~土地測量員 land surveyor;
補充測量 additional survey;
單獨測量 measure individually ;
方位測量 azimuth measuring;
高精度測量 high-accuracy measuring;
航空測量 aerosurvey;
航空三角測量 aerotriangulation;
絕對測量 absolute measurement;
科學地測量 scientifically measure;
空中測量 aerial survey;
面積水準測量 areal levelling;
聲波測量 acoustic survey;
聲學測量 acoustic measurement;
準確地測量 measure accurately; take an accurate measurement;
仔細地測量 measure carefully;

[測深儀] bathymeter;
回聲測深儀 echo sounder;

[測試] checkout; test;
測試過程自動化 test process automation;
測試信號發生器 component test signal generator;
測試語句 test statement;
測試中心 assessment centre; test centre;
參加測試 take one's test;
初步測試 preliminary test;
接受測試 be tested;
進行測試 put sth to a test;

[測算] (1) estimate; (2) measure and calculate;

[測微計] micrometer;
方位測微計 azimuth micrometer;
氣壓測微計 air micrometer;

[測微器] micrometer;

[測向] finding;
高頻測向 high-frequency finding;
光學測向 optical direction finding;

[測驗] examination; test; trial run;
測驗不及格 fail a test; flunk a test;
測驗成績 test result; test score;
測驗卷 test paper;
測驗題 test question;
參加測驗 do a test; sit a test; take a test;
翻譯測驗 translation text;
進行測驗 have a test;
民意民驗 public opinion poll;
算術測驗 arithmetic test;
通過測驗 pass a test;
心理測驗 mental test;

[測雲器] nephoscope;
反射測雲器 reflecting nephoscope;
格柵測雲器 grid nephoscope;

[測字] fortune-telling by means of characters; glyphomancy;
賣卜測字 tell fortunes;

[測醉器] drunkometer; intoximeter;

不測 accident; mishap;
步測 pace;
猜測 conjecture; guess; infer; speculate;
草測 make a preliminary survey;
揣測 (1) conjecture; draw the bow; guess; guesswork; speculate; surmise; (2) suspect;
觀測 observe; view;
監測 monitor; survey;
檢測 check; detect; examine; test;
勘測 survey;

窺測 spy out;
蠡測 measure the sea with an oyster shell – have a shallow understanding of a person;
目測 measure with the eye; take a visual measurement;
叵測 unfathomable; unpredictable;
淺測 superficial conjecture;
探測 probe; survey;
推測 conjecture; deduce; guess; infer;
遙測 telemetering; telemetry;
臆測 conjecture; guess; surmise;
預測 calculate; forecast; predict;

ce

【策】 (1) plan; scheme; strategy; (2) whip;
[策動] enginer; instigate; stir up;
策動暴亂 incite a riot;
策動傳播 instigate communication;
策動糾紛 stir up trouble;
策動叛變 instigate rebellion;
策動政變 stage a coup d'etat;
[策反] incite defection; instigate rebellion within the enemy camp;
[策劃] engineer; plan; plot; scheme;
策劃報復 plan a revenge;
策劃陰謀 concoct a villainous scheme; engineer a plot; hatch a plot;
暗中策劃 conspire on the sly; plot in the dark;
共同策劃 plot together;
精心策劃 carefully calculated; carefully plan; deliberately design; elaborately plan; painstakingly engineer;
幕後策劃 plot behind the scenes;
[策勵] encourage; spur on;
[策略] strategy; tactic;
策略決策 strategical decision-making;
策略空間 policy space;
安全策略 security policy;
長遠的策略 long-range strategy;
翻譯策略 translation strategy;
防禦策略 defense strategy;
迴避策略 avoidance strategy;
基本策略 elementary tactics;
交際策略 communication strategy;
軍事策略 military strategy;
缺乏策略 lack in tactics;
行為策略 behaviour strategy;
政治策略 political strategy;
制定策略 devise tactics;
周密的策略 careful strategy;
[策馬] whip a horse;
策馬奔馳 ride full gallop;
策馬飛馳 fly forward on one's steed; whip the horse and ride swiftly;
策馬趕上 whip one's horse to overtake;
策馬揮戈 spur one's horse on and wield one's sword;
策馬前進 urge on a horse; whip a horse on;
策馬向前 urge a horse on;
[策士] schemer; tactician;
[策應] act in concept with each other;
[策源地] place of origin; source;
鞭策 goad on; spur on; urge on;
對策 countermeasure; countermove;
國策 national policy; the basic policy of a state;
劃策 give counsel;
計策 plan; stratagem;
決策 (1) decide a policy; make a strategic decision; make policy; (2) decision-making; policy-making;
良策 good plan; sound strategy;
妙策 brilliant scheme; excellent plan;
驅策 (1) drive; spur; whip on; urge; (2) order sb about;
上策 best plan; best policy; best stratagem; best thing to do; best way; best way out; first choice; optimal policy;
失策 bad scheming; inexpedient; miscalculate; misjudge; misstep; mistake; poor strategy; poor tactic; unwise;
下策 bad measure; bad plan; bad policy; bad strategy; stupid move; unwise decision;
獻策 make a suggestion;
遺策 (1) mistake; wrong move; (2) plan left behind by the dead;
政策 policy;
中策 the second best plan;

ce

【筴】 (1) a kind of grass used for divination in ancient times; (2) same as 策;

cen¹

cen

【參】
[參差] irregular; uneven;
參差不齊 irregular; uneven;
參差錯落 confused with errors and omission;
[參雜不醇] mixed and impure;

cen²

cen

【岑】 (1) a relatively high, pointed hill; (2) quiet; silent; still; .

［岑寂］ far removed from the hustle of life; lonely; quiet; still;

［岑樓］ a mountain-like, lofty and tapering building;

cen

【涔】 (1) puddle; (2) tearful;

［涔涔］ dripping; streaming;

涔涔淚下 in tears; tears flowing down;

淚涔涔 tears falling down abundantly;

~ 兩淚涔涔 two lines of tears keep on rolling down one's cheeks;

~ 眼淚涔涔 drip with tears; in a flood of tears; one's eyes water;

ceng²

ceng

【曾】 ever; formerly; once;

［曾經］ at one time or another;

曾經滄海 have experienced great things; have sailed the seven seas; have seen much of the world;

不曾 never;

未曾 have not;

ceng

【層】 (1) a bed of; (2) a cloak of; (3) a coat of; (4) a film of; (5) a flake of; (6) a layer of; (7) a mantle of; (8) a pile of; (9) a tier of; (10) a thickness of; (11) a veil of; (12) floor; storey;

［層層］ layer upon layer; ring upon ring; tier upon tier;

層層把關 check at each level;

層層包圍 surround ring upon ring;

層層疊疊 tier upon tier;

層層發動 mobilize level by level;

層層設防 erect defensive works in depth; set up successive lines of defense;

［層出不窮］ appear layer upon layer without end; come out thick and fast one after the other; emerge in an endless stream; spring up one after another;

［層次］ (1) administrative levels; gradation; hierarchy; (2) arrangement of ideas;

層次不清 lacking unity and coherence; not arranged systematically;

層次重疊 organizational overlapping;

層次繁多 administrations with multiplied departments;

層次分明 coherent; well arranged;

層次分析 level analysis;

層次清楚 be methodically arranged; be well organized;

層次數據庫 hierarchical data base;

層次系統 hierarchical system;

翻譯層次 level of translation;

關係層次 relational hierarchy;

學習層次 learning hierarchy;

［層疊］ stack; stack-up;

［層理］ bedding; stratification;

不對稱層理 asymmetrical bedding;

不整合層理 discordant bedding;

假層理 diagonal stratification; false bedding;

流水層理 current bedding;

傾斜層理 inclined bedding; inclined stratification;

沙丘層理 dune bedding;

水平層理 horizontal bedding;

斜層理 oblique bedding;

旋繞層理 convolute bedding;

淤泥層理 slurry bedding;

原生層理 direct stratification;

韻律層理 rhythmic stratification;

［層面］ aspects; dimension; general characteristics;

情感層面 affective dimension;

認知層面 cognitive dimension;

行為層面 action dimension;

［層壓］ laminating;

接觸加壓層壓 contact pressure laminating;

連續層壓 continuous laminating;

表層 surface;

冰層 ice layer;

薄層 flash; leaf; sheet; thin layer; thin wall;

襯層 lining;

臭氧層 ozonosphere;

單層 single-decked; single-layered;

低層 (1) lower storey; (2) low level;

底層 (1) ground floor; (2) bottom;

地層 layer; stratum;

斷層 fault;

多層 multichamber; multilayer;

分層 stratum;

蓋層 cap rock;

高層 high-level;
隔層 compartment;
冠層 canopy;
基層 basic level; primary level;
夾層 double-layered wall;
階層 stratum;
句層 sentence level;
霾層 haze layer;
煤層 coal bed; coal scam;
胚層 germinal layer;
皮層 (1) cortex; (2) cerebral cortex;
氣層 air layer;
千層 multi-layer;
上層 upper level; upper strata;
深層 (1) depth; (2) in-depth;
雙層 double-decked; double-layered;
塗層 coat; coating;
土層 soil layer;
外層 outer; outer field;
外胚層 ectoderm;
外逸層 exosphere;
下層 (1) lower layer; lower stratum; (2) low-ranking;
岩層 rock formation; rock stratum;
鹽層 salt bed; salt deposit;
一層 (1) one floor; one story; (2) a stratum; (3) a bed of; a blanket of; a cloak of; a coat of; a curtain of; a deck of; a film of; a flake of; a floor; a floor of; a layer; a layer of; a level of; a line of; a mantle of; a ring of; a story; a story of; a veil of;
油層 oil horizon; oil layer; oil reservoir;
雲層 cloud layer;
褶層 fold;
中層 medium stratum; middle level;
中膠層 mesogloea;

ceng
【嶒】 lofty; steep;

崚嶒 high mountain;

ceng⁴
ceng
【蹭】 (1) deprived of power; (2) stroll; (3) protract; (4) be smeared with;
［蹭車］ get a lift; take a bus or train without pay;
［蹭蹬］ down on one's luck; frustrated in career; meet with setbacks; run into mishaps;
［蹭兒］ (1) sth one gets for free; (2) freeloader;
［蹭癢癢］ have a good scrape against sth to relieve itching;

磨蹭 (1) dawdle; move slowly; (2) bother constantly;

cha¹
cha
【叉】 (1) cross arms; interlace fingers; (2) pierce; stab; thrust; (3) fork; prong; (4) push another's neck with one's hand;
［叉車］ fork-lift truck;
［叉開］ change;
把話題叉開 change the subject;
［叉路］ the fork of a road;
［叉燒］ barbecue pork; roast pork;
叉燒包子 barbecue pork bun;
［叉手］ folded arms;
叉手而立 stand with folded arms;
叉手拱立 stand forking one's hands together;
［叉腰］ rest the arms on the hips; stand with arms akimbo;
兩手叉腰 akimbo; with arms akimbo; with one's hands on one's hips;
［叉枝］ forked branch;
［叉子］ cross; fork; prong;
劃個叉子 mark a cross;
一把叉子 a fork;

餐叉 fork;
草叉 pitch-fork;
打叉 cross;
刀叉 knife and fork;
飛叉 flying trident;
後叉 hind fork;
交叉 (1) chiasma; crisscross; cross; cross connection; crossing; intersect; intersection; scissors; (2) overlap; (3) alternate; stagger;
母夜叉 hag;
前叉 front fork;
耍叉 make trouble;
夜叉 hideous, ferocious person;
音叉 tuning fork;
魚叉 fish fork; fish spear;
轍叉 frog;

Cha
【扠】 harpoon;
［扠腰］ stand with arms akimbo;

cha

【扱】 (1) collect; gather; (2) kneel and bow with both hands touching the ground;

［扱地］ kneel and bow with both hands touching the ground;

［扱引高賢］ gather men of wisdom;

cha

【杈】 (1) branches of a tree; (2) fish-fork; pitchfork; (3) any forklike object; (4) a kind of weapon in ancient China;

［杈枒］ branch; branching out of a tree;

cha

【差】 (1) difference; dissimilarity; (2) mistake; (3) difference;

［差別］ difference; disparity;

差別待遇 differential treatment;
差別稅率 differential tax rates;
本質上的差別 essential difference;
表面的差別 surface difference;
價格上的差別 price differentials;
絕對差別 absolute difference;
千差萬別 differ in thousands of ways; different in a thousand and one ways; have highly differentiated features; highly differentiated; immense variety; in endless variety; multifarious; the immense variety of; vary in a thousand and one ways; very different;
社會差別 social differences;
~消除社會差別 level down social differences;
社會地位的差別 difference in social status;
數量的差別 quantitative difference;
微小的差別 trifling difference;
顯著的差別 marked difference; notable difference;
質量的差別 qualitative difference;
重要的差別 serious difference;

［差池］ (1) accidents; (2) error; miscalculation;

［差錯］ (1) bodge; error; mistake; slip; (2) accident; mishap;

差錯補貼 risk money;
差錯文件 error file;
出差錯 go awry; make a slip; run awry; slip up; tread awry;
~不會出差錯 no mistake could arise;
~不小心出差錯 make a careless mistake;
~難免出差錯 slips are inevitable;
減少差錯 reduce errors;
沒有差錯 free from mistakes;
三差兩錯 a few mistakes;
消除差錯 weed out errors;
言差語錯 erroneous utterances; misunderstanding in verbal exchanges;
一差二錯 a slip somewhere; one or two mistakes; possible mistake or mishap; sth happens to;
陰錯陽差 a strange combination of circumstances; all sorts of accidental mishaps;
找出差錯 diagnose faults;

［差額］ balance; difference; margin;

差額補貼 deficiency payment;
差額選舉 contested election;
補償差額 refund the balance;
補足差額 make up the balance; make up the differences;
付足差額 pay the balance;
票據交換差額 clearing balance;
期末差額 closing balance;

［差價］ price disparities; price difference; price differentials;

差價稅 variable tax;

［差距］ (1) disparity; gap; (2) difference;

很大的差距 big gap; large gap; wide gap;
很小的差距 narrow gap;
巨大的差距 yawning gap;
彌合差距 bridge a gap;
年齡差距 age gap;

［差拍］ beat; beating;

低頻差拍 low-frequency beat;
光頻差拍 photo beat;
交叉差拍 cross beats;
空間差拍 spatial beating;
載波差拍 carrier beat;
~載波差拍干擾 intercarrier beat;
~副載波差拍 subcarrier beat;

［差誤］ error;

校正差誤 adjust the errors;

［差異］ difference; discrepancy; disparity; divergence; diversity; variance;

差異程度 degree of deviation;
差異很大 exhibit a wide range of variation;
產品差異 product differences;
成本差異 cost variance;
發現差異 find differences;
個體差異 individual difference;
基本差異 basic variance;
階級差異 class differences;

看得出差異 can see the difference; can tell the difference;
類型差異 typological difference;
年齡差異 disparity of one's sages;
調節差異 accord a difference;
文化差異 cultural differences;
顯示差異 show a difference;
顯著差異 marked difference;
消除差異 level out the differences between...and...;
性別差異 gender differences;
預算差異 budget variance;
造成差異 make a difference;
種間差異 interspecific difference;
最小差異 minimum difference;

磁差 magnetic declination;
代數差 algebraic difference;
等差 grade; place in a series;
反差 contrast;
方差 variance;
風壓差 air pressure difference;
幅度差 amplitude difference;
高度差 altitude difference;
公差 (1) common difference; (2) tolerance;
落差 (1) drop; (2) head;
逆差 adverse balance of trade;
偏差 deviation; error;
容差 tolerance;
容許壓差 allowable pressure difference;
色差 (1) chromatism; (2) off colour; off shade;
昇差 ascending difference;
時差 (1) time difference; (2) equation of time;
視差 parallax;
順差 favourable balance; surplus;
歲差 precession of the equinoxes;
溫差 difference in temperature;
誤差 error;
相角差 angular phase difference;
象差 aberration;
自差 autodyne;

cha

【喳】 sound of chattering;
[喳喳] (1) chattering sound; (2) whisper;

cha

【插】 (1) insert; put in; stick into; (2) get a word in edgeways; interpose; (3) plant; (4) take part in;
[插班] join a class in the middle of the course;
插班生 student who joins a class in the middle of the course;
[插翅] be given wings;
插翅飛走 grow wings and fly away;
插翅難飛 unable to escape even if given wings; unable to fly away, even with a pair of wings;
插翅難逃 unable to escape even if given wings;
[插隊] jump the queue; queue-jumping;
插隊的人 queue jumper;
[插管] cannula;
動脈插管 arterial cannula;
靜脈插管 venous cannula;
氣管插管 trachea cannula;
輸尿管插管 intraurethral cannula;
輸血插管 transfusion cannula;
[插花] arrange flowers; flower arrangement; flower arranging;
插花藝術 the art of arranging flowers;
[插話] (1) chime in; chip in; chuck out; interpose; interpose a remark; (2) digression; episode;
插不進話 cannot get a word in;
[插腳] (1) have a foot-hold in; participate in; step inside; take part in; (2) socket;
[插接板] plugboard;
可卸插接板 detachable plugboard;
選號插接板 selection plugboard;
[插進] dip; interject; let in; stick in; thrust into; work in;
[插科打渾] buffoonery; cut in a joke; insert dialogue for comic relief; jesting; make all manner of quips and jokes; make gags; make impromptu comic gestures and remarks;
[插柳成陰] plant a willow slip hoping to enjoy the shade of the tree;
[插曲] episode; interlude;
感人的插曲 touching episode of life;
一段插曲 an episode;
一段小小的插曲 a little episode;
[插入] break in; dig; implant; infix; inlay; insert; insertion; intercalate; interpose; intervene; plug in; run in;
插入程序 plug-in programme;
插入活動 insertion activity;
插入器 interpolator;
~ 輔助取樣插入器 subsample interpolator;
~ 行間插入器 line interpolator;
插入語 interjectional remark; parenthesis;

浮動插入 floating insertion;
微分插入 differential insertion;
消隱插入 blanking insertion;
音頻插入 audio insertion;

[插身] (1) edge in; squeeze in; (2) get involved in; take part in;

[插手] (1) lend a hand; take part; (2) have a hand in; meddle in; poke one's nose into;
插手干預 interfere in; meddle and intervene in;
插手其間 have a hand in; place oneself in;
到處插手 meddle in everything;

[插鎖] deadbolt; mortise lock;
暗插鎖 dormant bolt;

[插條] cutting;

[插頭] plug;
安全插頭 safety plug;
拔出插頭 pull the plug out of the socket;
拔去插頭 unplug;
地址插頭 address plug;
電燈插頭 plug for a lamp;
二脚插頭 two-pin plug; two-pronged plug;
三脚插頭 three-pin plug; three-pronged plug;
天線插頭 aerial plug;
彎曲插頭 angle plug;

[插圖] demonstration; figure; illustration; insert; insert map; inset; plate;
插圖畫家 illustrator;
彩色插圖 coloured illustrations;
大量插圖 be richly illustrated;
單色插圖 monochrome illustration;
繪製插圖 make illustrations;
卷首插圖 frontispiece;
全頁插圖 full page illustrations;

[插銷] bolt;

[插血為盟] lick blood and swear; smear one's mouth with blood in token of one's oath;

[插一杠子] get in the way; interfere; join in work and do more harm than good;

[插針] stick in a pin;
見縫插針 avail oneself of every opportunity; make use of every single space; seize every opportunity to do sth; stick in a pin wherever there is room;

[插枝] cutting;

[插值] interpolation;
二重插值 double interpolation;
後向插值 backward interpolation;
三次插值 cubic interpolation;

[插足] (1) put one's foot in; (2) participate in;

[插嘴] barge in; break in; break in upon; burst in; burst in on; burst in upon; butt in; butt in with a remark; chime in; chip in; chop in; cut in; cut into; get a word in; get a word in edgeways; interpolate; interpose; interrupt; put in; put in a word; snap sb up; strike in; take up;
插嘴講幾句 cut in with a few remarks;
別插嘴 don't break into our talk;
插不上嘴 cannot get a word in edgeways; cannot put a word in conversation;
老是插嘴 keep chipping in;
無法插嘴 can't get a word in edgeways;

[插座] socket;
電源插座 power point;
附插座 accessory shoe;
聲頻插座 audio socket;
天線插座 aerial socket; antenna socket;
通用插座 blanket socket;

安插 assign to a post; get a position for a person in an organization; place in a certain position; place sb in a job or position; plant sb in a place;

穿插 (1) alternate; do alternately; do in turn; (2) insert; interweave; weave; (3) episode; interlude; subplot;

扦插 cuttage; cutting;

拴插 look after the food and clothing of a child;

蹄插 shoe;

針插 (1) pin cushion; (2) stick into sth with a pin;

cha²

cha

【苴】 (1) grass floating in the water; (2) withered grass;

cha

【查】 (1) check; examine; (2) investigate; look into; (3) consult; look up; (4) wooden raft;

[查案] investigate into a case;
有案可查 a matter of record; can be checked against file; have records that can be referred to; on record;

［查辦］ investigate and deal with accordingly;
撤職查辦 dismiss a person and have him prosecuted;
嚴加查辦 be strictly prosecuted;
依法查辦 investigate and deal with according to law;

［查抄］ make an inventory of a criminal's possessions and confiscate them;
查抄賭窟 make a raid on a gambling den;
查抄沒收 make an inventory of a criminal's possessions and confiscate them;

［查出］ ferret out; trace;
查出秘密 spy out a secret;
查出詳情 search out details;
查出原因 find the cause;
查出真相 ferret out the truth;

［查處］ investigate and deal with; investigate and treat;
查處違法亂紀 check and deal with law and discipline violation;

［查點］ check the amount of sth; check the number of sth; make an inventory of;
查點存貨 make an inventory of the goods in stock; take stock;
查點貨物 check out the goods;
查點人數 check the attendants; check the number of people present;
查點損失 make an inventory of one's loss;

［查對］ check; check off; verify;
查對材料 check the data;
查對數字 check up on the figures; verify the figures;
查對無誤 examine and find it correct;
查對原文 check against the original;

［查房］ make the rounds of the wards;

［查訪］ go around and make inquiries; investigate;
查訪案情 investigate the details of a crime;
明查暗訪 conduct a thorough investigation;

［查封］ close down; seal up;
查封報館 seal up a newspaper office;
查封報紙 close down the newspaper;

［查核］ check;
查核單據 look through the vouchers;
查核事實 check the facts up;
查核無訛 audited and found correct;

［查獲］ discover and seize; ferret out; hunt down and seize; track down;
查獲犯人 ferret out a criminal;
查獲逃犯 track down a fugitive criminal;
查獲贓物 seize the loot;
查獲走私集團 track down a gang of smugglers;

［查禁］ ban; prohibit; put a ban on;
查禁賭博 search for violations of the ban against gambling;
查禁黃書 have a pornographic book banned;
查禁走私活動 search for violations of the prohibition against smuggling; suppress smuggling;

［查究］ investigate and ascertain;
查究辦理 investigate and act accordingly;
查究實情 examine the actual state of affairs; investigate the circumstances;
查究原因 find out the cause;
查究責任 find out who should be held responsible;

［查勘］ explore; prospect; survey;

［查看］ check; examine; have a look; look about; look at; look into; look over; look up; make sure; see; see about;
查看情況 observe conditions;

［查考］ do research on; examine; try to ascertain;

［查扣］ seize and hold in custody;

［查明］ ascertain; find out; prove through investigation;
查明事實真相 find out the truth of the matter;
查明屬實 prove to be true after investigation;
查明死因 find out the cause of the death;
查明有罪 find guilty;
查明真相 ascertain the facts; find out the truth;
事情尚未查明 the matter has not yet been ascertained;

［查尿］ have urine examined;

［查票］ check tickets; examine tickets;

［查破］ break a criminal case; investigate and unearth;

［查訖］ checked;

［查清］ check up on; make a thorough investigation of;

［查實］ investigate and verify;

［查收］ (1) find sth enclosed; (2) check and accept;
［查體］ physical examination;
［查問］ inquire; interrogate; question;
查問口令 demand the password;
查問證人 interrogate a witness;
查三問四 investigate thorough; make a wide-range investigation;
［查血］ have a blood test;
［查詢］ inquire about;
查詢站 enquiry station;
歡迎查詢 for enquiries;
［查驗］ check; examine;
查驗護照 examine a passport;
查驗貨物 examine goods;
查驗行李 inspect the baggage;
查驗遺囑 inspect a will;
接受查驗 submit to inspection;
［查夜］ (1) go the rounds at night; (2) night patrol;
［查閱］ consult; look up;
查閱檔案 burrow into archives;
便於查閱 facilitate consultation; for convenience of consultation;
［查帳］ audit; audit accounts; check accounts; examine accounts;
［查找］ search out;
［查照］ note;
［查證］ check and testify; investigate and verify;
查證屬實 be checked and found to be true; be verified;

暗查 make a secret enquiry; secretly investigate;
備查 for future reference;
抄查 make a raid;
澈查 investigate thoroughly;
飭查 order an investigation;
抽查 conduct a selective examination; have a spot check;
存查 file for reference;
待查 yet to be investigated;
調查 carry out a research; check into; examine into; go into; hold an inquiry into; inquire into; investigate; learn the facts about; look into; make an investigation into; make an investigation of; make an investigation on; make a survey of; search into; see into; survey;
訪查 go about making inquiries; investigate;
複查 check again; double-check; re-examine; re-investigate; review;
核查 check; examine in detail; verify;
稽查 check;
檢查 (1) check up; examine; (2) make a self-criticism;
勘查 prospecting;
考查 check; examine;
盤查 interrogate and examine;
普查 carry out a general investigation;
清查 (1) check; check up; examine; inquire into; investigate; (2) comb out; detect; ferret out; uncover; unearth;
審查 check; examine; investigate;
搜查 ransack; search;
細查 investigate thoroughly;
巡查 go on a tour of inspection; make one's rounds;
尋查 search for;
偵查 investigate;
追查 find out; trace;

cha

【臿】 (1) farming instrument; (2) same as 插；

cha

【茶】 (1) tea; (2) a certain kind of drink;
［茶包］ tea bag;
［茶杯］ teacup;
一茶杯 a cup of; a glass of; teacupful;
一套茶杯 a nest of cups;
嘴歪怪茶杯漏 a bad sheerer never had a good sickle; a bad workman always blames hit tools; a bad workman quarrels with his tools; a bungler cannot find good tools;
［茶點］ tea-flavoured food;
上午茶點 elevenses;
［茶飯］ food and drinks;
茶飯不思 have no appetite for food and drinks; lose all desire for food and drink;
不茶不飯 be laden with anxiety; neither drink nor eat; not want to eat;
殘茶剩飯 crumbs from the table; leftovers; remains of a meal;
茶餘飯後 at one's leisure; in one's leisure hours; in one's spare hours;
粗茶淡飯 bread and cheese; bread and water; cheap and simple meal; coarse beverage and simple food; homely fare; humble fare; lead a simple life;

potatoes and point; simple diet; simple fare; simple food;
~吃粗茶淡飯 have weak tea and plain food;
~喜歡粗茶淡飯 like a simple diet;

[茶館] tea house; tearoom;

[茶壺] teapot;
茶壺把 teapot handle;
茶壺墊 teapot mat;
茶壺蓋 teapot lid;
茶壺套 tea cosy;
茶壺嘴 teapot spout;
大茶壺 urn;
一把茶壺 a teapot;

[茶話會] tea party;

[茶會] tea party;

[茶几] coffee table; tea table;

[茶酒] tea and wine;
殘茶剩酒 leftovers; remains of a meal;
茶餘酒後 over a cup of tea or after a few glasses of wine — at one's leisure; teahouse and wineshop gossip;
濃茶烈酒 strong tea and spirits;

[茶具] tea set;

[茶樓] tea house;
酒肆茶樓 wine shops and teahouses;

[茶盤] tea tray;

[茶室] tearoom;

[茶托] saucer;

[茶舞] tea dance;

[茶煙] tea and cigarettes;
遞茶敬煙 serve tea and offer cigarettes to guests;
奉茶敬煙 serve tea and offer cigarettes;

[茶葉] tea; tea leaves;
茶葉罐 tea caddy; tea canister;
茶葉筒 tea tin;

[茶盅] handleless teacup;

[茶莊] tea shop;

拜茶 ask a guest to come in and have tea;
焙茶 dry tea by fire;
餅茶 cake-shaped tea;
採茶 pick tea;
春茶 spring tea;
啜茶 sip tea;
待茶 receive a guest with tea;
袋泡茶 teabag;
淡茶 weak tea;
倒茶 fill the cup with tea;
喝茶 (1) drink tea; (2) go to a restaurant;
烘茶 tea curing;
紅茶 black tea;
花茶 jasmine tea; scented tea;
緊壓茶 compressed mass of tea leaves;
敬茶 serve tea;
涼茶 herbal tea;
綠茶 green tea;
茉莉花茶 jasmine tea;
奶茶 tea with milk;
濃茶 strong tea;
泡茶 make tea;
烹茶 make tea;
普洱茶 pu'er tea;
沏茶 brew tea;
清茶 (1) green tea; (2) tea served without refreshments;
秋茶 autumn tea;
榷茶 levy tea taxes;
讓茶 offer sb tea;
山茶 camellia;
上等茶 top-grade tea; wonderful tea;
燒茶 boil tea;
受茶 receive the presents of betrothal;
沱茶 bowl-shaped compressed mass of tea leaves;
烏龍茶 oolong tea
芽茶 bud-tea;
一杯茶 a cup of tea; a cuppa;
一壺茶 a pot of tea;
一口茶 a mouthful of tea;
一小口茶 a suck of tea;
一種茶 a tea;
飲茶 drink tea;
油茶 tea-oil tree;
早茶 early tea;
斟茶 fill a cup with tea;
珠茶 a kind of green tea;
磚茶 brick tea;

cha

【搽】 apply; put sth on the skin;

[搽粉] powder;
搽粉入棺材—死要面子 powdering one's face before being put into a coffin — concerned to death with "face"; overly concerned with appearances;

[搽藥] rub on some external medicine;

[搽油] apply ointment;

輕搽 dab;

cha

【察】 examine; look into; scrutinize;

[察辦] investigate a case and determine how to handle it;
[察訪] go about to find out; go around and make inquiries; investigate; make calls and investigate;
暗中察訪 pay a secret visit; pay a surreptitious visit; make investigation quietly;
私行察訪 inquire secretly into the people's conditions;
微服察訪 go on an inspection in disguise; inquire into affairs under the disguise of a commoner;
沿街察訪 go about the street to make investigations;
[察覺] become aware; conscious of; perceive;
察覺秘密 smell out a secret;
突然察覺 suddenly discover;
未被察覺 escape detection; escape observation;
[察勘] examine; survey;
[察看] look carefully at; observe; watch;
察看地形 survey terrain;

洞察 discern; examine thoroughly; have an insight into; have penetrating insight; see clearly; see through clearly;
督察 supervise;
俯察 deign to examine;
觀察 observe;
監察 control; supervise;
檢察 prosecute;
警察 bluebottle; bobby; clodhopper; constable; cop; copper; cozzer; cozzpot; crusher; jack; jailer; John Bull; John Hop; johndarm; law enforcement agent; police; police officer; policeman; boys in blue;
糾察 (1) maintain order at a public gathering; (2) picket;
覺察 become aware of; detect;
勘察 (1) survey; (2) reconnoiter;
考察 (1) inspect; make an on-the-spot investigation; (2) observe and study;
廉察 secretly investigate;
諒察 ask sb to understand and forgive oneself;
荃察 your esteemed consideration;
審察 (1) observe carefully; (2) check; examine; investigate;
失察 fail to perform one's supervisory duties; neglect one's supervisory duties;
視察 inspect;
伺察 investigate; spy; trace secretly;
體察 experience and observe;
細察 examine thoroughly; observe carefully; observe in detail;
省察 examine oneself critically;
巡察 make an investigation;
詗察 spy;
偵察 reconnoiter; scout;
診察 examine;

cha
【槎】 (1) raft; (2) chop; cut; hew;

浮槎 floating raft;

cha
【碴】 come to blows; fight; scuffle with;
[碴架] fight; engage in a gang fight;
[碴霹] breakdance;

cha³
cha
【叉】
[叉劈] divergent;

劈叉 do the splits;

cha⁴
cha
【汊】 branch stream;
[汊港] branch point of a stream;
[汊流] tributary of a river;

港汊 branch stream;
河汊 river branch;

cha
【奼】 (1) young girls; (2) attractive; charming; seductive; (3) boast; lie; talk big;
[奼女] young maiden;
cha
【岔】 (1) branch off; diverge; fork; (2) turn off; (3) accident; trouble;
[岔開] (1) branch off; diverge; (2) diverge to; (3) stagger;
[岔路] branch; byroad; turn-off;
岔路口 turning;
三岔路 forked roads;
~三岔路口 fork in a road;
一條岔路 a byroad;
[岔子] accident; trouble;
出岔子 go awry; go off the rails; go

wrong; have an accident; lead to no good; miss one's tip; run into trouble;
找岔子 find fault with sb; nitpick; pick flaws in sth;

打岔 cut in; interrupt a conversation;
道岔 road switch; switch; turnout;
眼岔 mistake one thing for another;

cha
【杈】
［杈子］ branch of a tree;

打杈 prune;
分杈 branch;
瘋杈 branch that bears no fruit;
樹杈 crotch of a tree;
丫杈 crotch; crotched; fork of a tree; forked;
椏杈 crotch; crotched; fork of a tree; forked;
枝杈 branch; twig;

cha
【侘】 (1) boast; (2) disappointed; irresolute;

cha
【刹】 (of Buddhism) monastery; shrine; temple;
［刹那］ ksana; moment; twinkling; instant;

古刹 ancient Buddhist temple;

cha
【衩】 slits;
［衩襪］ stockings without bands;
［衩衣］ a woman's gown with slits on the sides;

褲衩 underpants; undershorts;

cha
【差】 (1) differ from; fall short of; (2) mistake; wrong; (3) missing; short of; wanting; (4) bad; inferior; not up to the standard; poor;
［差不多］ about; about and about; about the same; all but; almost; as good as; be approaching; be getting on; be nearing; just about right; near enough; nearly; similar; that's about it;
八九不離十─差不多 about right; almost correct; eight and nine followed by ten – about the same; eighty percent or more correct; most likely; most probably; mostly correct; nearly true; nine times out of ten; pretty close; quite close; ten to one; very near;
這還差不多 that's more like it; this is more like it;
［差得遠］ fall far short of; not by a long chalk; not by a long shot; not by a long sight; not by a long way;
［差勁］ bad; disappointing; no good; too bad;
差勁的 crummy;
～差勁的工作 crummy job;
表現差勁 give a poor account of oneself;

補差 make up the difference;
教養差 ill-bred;
相差 differ;
質量差 bad in quality; inferior in quality; of poor quality;
智力差 lacking in intelligence; mentally inferior; weak in intellect;

cha
【詫】 (1) surprised; wonder; (2) boast; brag; (3) cheat; deceive; (4) inform;
［詫異］ amazed; astonished; surprised;
暗自詫異 feel bewildered in one's mind;

驚詫 be astonished; be surprised;

chai¹
chai
【拆】 (1) take apart; tear open; (2) errand; job; (3) analyze; scrutinize;
［拆車］ disassemble a car;
［拆除］ demolish; dismantle; remove;
拆除騙局 expose a fraud;
拆除障礙物 remove obstacles;
軌道拆除 dismantling of tracks;
［拆穿］ expose; unmask;
拆穿謊言 nail a lie; nail a lie to the counter;
拆穿秘密 disclose a secret;
拆穿騙局 expose a fraud;
拆穿西洋鏡 expose sb's tricks; give away the show; give the show away; nail a lie; strip off the camouflage;
拆穿陰謀 lay open a plot;
［拆彈］ bomb disposal;
拆彈單位 bomb disposal unit;
拆彈小組 bomb disposal team;
拆彈專家 bomb disposal expert;

[拆股] stock split;
[拆毀] break down; demolish; destroy; dismantle; knock down; tear down;
拆毀房屋 pull down houses;
拆毀建築物 demolish buildings;
[拆伙] disband; dissolve a partnership; part company;
[拆建] dismantle and build; tear down and build;
[拆開] break up; decollate; disconnect; dismantle; open; separate; take apart; unpack;
拆開包裹 open a parcel; undo a package; unwrap a package;
拆開信封 open an envelope;
[拆零] take apart and sell separately;
[拆遷] move a building to a new site; pull down and relocate; relocate after demolition;
拆遷成本 removal cost;
拆遷範圍 length of pulling sth down;
拆遷戶 household that is being pulled down and relocated to another place;
[拆散] break up;
拆散婚姻 break the marriage tie; untie the marriage knot;
拆散市場 call loan market;
[拆台] cut the grass from under sb's feet; cut the ground from under sb's feet; pull the rug out from under sb;
拆台的貨 daredevil;
給自己拆台 cry stinking fish;
臨場拆台 pull the rug out from under; withdraw support unexpectedly;
[拆洗] strip and clean;
拆洗機器 strip and clean a machine;
[拆卸] disassemble; dismantle; dismantling; dismounting;
部份拆卸 partial dismantling; partial dismounting;
[拆信] open a letter;
拆信刀 paperknife;
[拆裝] disassemble and reassemble;

分拆 demerge; demerger;

chai

【差】 (1) dispatch; send on an errand; (2) errand person; messenger; (3) errand;
[差旅] travel on official business;
差旅費 travelling expenses;
~差旅費包幹 travelling expenses contract;
[差遣] assign; dispatch; send sb on an errand;
[差使] dispatch;
神差鬼使 a curious coincidence; as though urged by gods and demons; at the behest of supernatural powers; doings of ghosts and gods — unexpected happenings;
[差事] (1) errand; (2) dispatch;
苦差事 donkey work; fag;
[差委] appoint;

辦差 take charge of a mission;
兵差 conscript labour;
出差 away on official business; on a business trip;
當差 work as a petty official;
到差 appear for duty; arrive at post;
公差 (1) public errand; (2) person on a public errand;
官差 (1) official business; (2) government messenger;
兼差 concurrent post;
交差 report to the higher authorities after accomplishing a task;
苦差 hard and unprofitable job;
美差 cushy job;
派差 send sb on errand;
欽差 imperial commissions; imperial commissioner; imperial envoy;
撤差 dismiss from one's post;
聽差 footman; gopher;
信差 messenger;
郵差 mailman; postman; postwoman;
抓差 press sb into service;
專差 on a special mission; special mission;

chai

【釵】 hairpin;
[釵光鬢影] gathering of richly dressed women;

金釵 gold hairpin;
裙釵 woman;

chai²

chai

【柴】 (1) brushwood; firewood; (2) emaciated; hard; lean; thin; tough; (3) a surname;
[柴火] firewood;
乾柴烈火 (1) like a dry faggot on a

blazing fire; (2) be caught in a passion; irresistible to one another;
一捆柴火 a bundle of firewood;
［柴米油鹽］ fuel, rice, cooking oil and salt—the chief daily necessities;
［柴油］ diesel; diesel oil;
柴油機 diesel;
~柴油機燃料 diesel fuel;
~輔助柴油機 auxiliary diesel;
~後冷式柴油機 after-cooled diesel;
~空氣噴射式柴油機 air-injection diesel;
~氣室式柴油機 air chamber diesel;
~無氣噴射式柴油機 airless injection diesel;
柴油汽車 diesel car;
打柴 get firewood;
火柴 match;
荊柴 destitute household; poor family;
砍柴 chop firewood; cut firewood;
木柴 firewood;
劈柴 chop firewood;
拾柴 pick up sticks;
一抱柴 an armful of wood;
一捆柴 a faggot of firewood;
引柴 kindling;

chai
【豺】 (1) jackal; (2) cruel; cunning; wickedly;
［豺狼］ ravenous and cruel beasts;
豺狼成性 rapacious and ruthless; wolfish;
豺狼當道 jackals and wolves hold sway;
一群豺狼 a pack of wolves;
［豺聲］ roar as fiercely as a wild beast;

chai
【茈】 bupleurum;

chai
【儕】 (1) class; company; (2) adjunct to show plurality; (3) match;
［儕輩］ people of the same generation;
同儕 of the same generation;
吾儕 people like us; we;
友儕 peers;

chai³
chai
【茝】 angelica;

chai⁴
chai
【瘥】 cured; healed;

chai
【蠆】 a kind of scorpion;
［蠆尾］ the poisonous tail of a scorpion—a harmful thing or person;
水蠆 nymph of the dragonfly;

chan¹
chan
【摻】 adulterate;
［摻和］ commingle;
［摻假］ adulterate;
摻雜使假 mix in the inferior or fake;
［摻水］ (1) dilute; (2) fill with half truth;
摻水文憑 diploma obtained by attaining a very low standard;

chan
【襜】 (1) lower front of a gown; (2) clean and neat in appearance; (3) flapping; shaking; vibrating;

chan
【攙】 (1) help by the arm; support sb with one's hand; (2) mingle; mix; (3) add;
［攙扶］ support sb with one's hand;
攙扶老人上牀 help sb to bed;
攙扶老人下牀 help an old person down from his/her bed;
［攙合］ blend; mingle; mix;
［攙和劑］ admixture;
［攙假］ adulterate;
［攙起］ help sb stand up by giving him a hand;
［攙水］ water down;
往酒裏攙水 mingle alcohol with water;
［攙雜］ adulterate; mingle; mix;
攙雜物 adulterant;
互相攙雜 intermingle each other;

chan²
chan
【單】 chief of the Xiongnu;
［單于］ chieftain of the Xiongnu;

chan
【孱】 feeble; frail; weak;
［孱弱］ delicate; frail; weak;

chan
【嬋】 attractive; beautiful; graceful; ladylike; pretty;
［嬋娟］ attractive; beautiful; graceful; ladylike; pretty;

chan
【潺】 sound of water flowing;
［潺潺］ gurgling of flowing water; murmuring of flowing water;
潺潺流水 murmuring stream;

chan
【廛】 (1) living space; (2) shop; store;
［廛肆］ shop; store;
市廛 market; stores in a market;

chan
【澶】 (1) calm; placid; tranquil; (2) the name of a river;
［澶漫］ (1) unrestrained; (2) long and wide;
［澶州］ a political region in ancient China;

chan
【毚】 (1) crafty; cunning; (2) greedy;
［毚欲］ avarice; greed;

chan
【禪】 (1) cleanse; exorcise; (2) Buddhist;
［禪定］ deep meditation; dhyana;
［禪房］ meditation room;
參禪 practise meditation; try to reach an understanding of chan;
打禪 sit in meditation;
口頭禪 pet phrase;
受禪 receive an abdication;
悟禪 come to understand the principle of Chan;
坐禪 sit in meditation;

chan
【瀍】 a river in Henan;

chan
【蟬】 (1) cicada; (2) continuous; uninterrupted;
［蟬聯］ continue to hold a post or title;
［蟬翼］ cicada's wings;
薄如蟬翼 as thin as a cicada's wings;
寒蟬 (1) cicada; (2) cicada in winter;
沫蟬 froghopper;
秋蟬 autumn cicada;
葉蟬 leafhopper;

chan
【蟾】 toad;
［蟾彩］ moonlight;
［蟾蜍］ cane toad; toad;
蟾蜍卵素 bufovarin;
蟾蜍石 toadstone;
蟾蜍他靈 bufotalin;
蟾蜍他烯 bufotalin;
蟾蜍素 bufonin;
［蟾宮］ moon;
［蟾輪］ moon;

chan
【巉】 precipitous;
［巉巖］ crag; rock;

chan
【纏】 (1) twine; wind; (2) pester; tangle; tie up; (3) cope with; deal with; handle;
［纏綿］ exceedingly sentimental;
纏綿病榻 be bedridden with a lingering disease;
纏綿不已 lingering;
纏綿悱惻 commiserative; exceedingly sentimental; with tender and romantic sentiments;
思鄉纏綿 be tormented by nostalgia;
［纏磨］ pester;
［纏繞］ bind; twine; wind;
生纏死繞 persist in forcing one's attentions on sb;
［纏手］ difficult to deal with;
胡纏 endless bothering of another person;
絞纏 kink;
糾纏 (1) get entangled; (2) harass; nag; pester; worry;
蠻纏 harass sb with unreasonable demands; pester sb endlessly;
盤纏 coil; twine; twist; wind;
牽纏 implicate; involve;

chan
【欃】 (1) sandalwood; (2) comet;

chan
【讒】 backbite; calumniate; defame; misrepresent; slander;
［讒謗］ calumniate; defame; slander;
［讒害］ incriminate by false charges;
［讒人］ slanderer;
［讒言］ malicious talk;
讒言惹禍 slander brings trouble;
傳述讒言 give tongue to slanders;
進讒言 backbite others; speak evil of people behind their backs;
聽信讒言 lend a ready ear to slander; listen to and believe slanders;

chan
【饞】 gluttonous; greedy;

[饞鬼] gourmand;
[饞食] greedy and voracious;
[饞嘴] gluttonous;

眼饞 covetous; envious;
嘴饞 be inclined to eat greedily; fond of good food;

chan³
chan

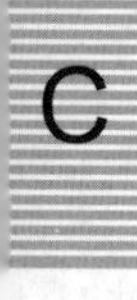

【產】 (1) deliver a baby; give birth to; (2) bring about; produce; yield; (3) produce; product; (4) estate; property;

[產出] output;
產出法 output method;
產出目標 output goal;

[產地] place of origin; place of production;
產地證明 certificate of origin;
原產地 country of origin;

[產兒] newborn infant;

[產後] postnatal;
產後檢查 postnatal check-up;
產後痛 afterpains;
產後抑鬱症 baby blues; postnatal depression;
產後憂鬱症 baby blues; postnatal depression;

[產假] maternity leave;
陪產假 paternity leave;

[產科] maternity department; obstetrical department;
產科學 obstetrics;
產科醫生 obstetrician;
產科醫院 maternity hospital;

[產量] output; yield;
產量大增 the yields have increased considerably;
產量低 yield poorly;
產量高 give a high yield; yield abundantly;
產量減少 diminish the output; fall in production;
產量會計 throughput accounting;
產量增加 increase in production;
安全產量 safe yield;
工廠產量 output of a factory;
年產量 annual output; yearly production;
日產量 daily output;
提高產量 increase the output;
削減產量 curtail the output;
月產量 monthly output;
增加產量 increase the output;
總產量 total output;

[產卵] lay eggs; spawn;
產卵力 fecundity;
產卵器 ovipositor;

[產品] product;
產品包裝 packaging of a product;
產品保險 products' insurance;
產品標準化 standardization of products;
產品測試 products testing;
產品成本 cost of manufactured goods;
~估計產品成本 estimate the cost of manufactured goods;
產品檔次 grading of products;
產品定額 required production quota;
~完成產品定額 meet one's required production quota;
~未完成產品定額 fail to fill the output quota;
產品對路 goods suited to popular tastes;
產品發明 product inventing;
產品返銷 products buy-back;
產品廣告 advertisement of products;
產品結構 product mix; product structure;
產品經濟 product economy;
~新產品經濟 economics of new products;
產品開發 product development;
產品目標 product goal;
產品批號 batch number;
產品缺陷 defects of products;
產品生命周期 product's life cycle;
產品昇級換代 upgrading and updating of products;
產品市場 product market;
產品税 product tax;
產品脱銷 shortage of products;
~長期產品脱銷 chronic shortage of products;
產品系列 product series;
~產品系列化 product serialization;
~產品系列平衡 products series balance;
產品銷路 product marketing;
產品銷售 products sale;
~產品銷售成本 cost of product marketing;
~產品銷售計劃 product and marketing plan;
產品驗收測試 product acceptance testing;
產品責任 product acceptance testing;
~產品責任法 product liability law;
產品質量 quality of the products;

~ 產品質量檢驗 product quality test;
~ 產品質量認證 product quality verification;
~ 檢查產品質量 product quality check;
~ 降低產品質量 lower the quality of products;
~ 提高產品質量 improve the quality of products;
產品專利 product patent;
安全產品 safety product;
本地產品 native products;
不對路產品 unmarketable goods;
長線產品 products in excess supply;
等外產品 off-grade product;
低檔產品 low-grade product;
附加產品 addition product;
副產品 accessory product; by-product; residual product;
鋼鐵產品 steel products;
高回報產品 high value-added products;
工廠產品 factory products;
工農業產品 industrial and agricultural products;
過剩產品 excess products;
合格產品 accepted product;
環保產品 environmentally friendly products;
混合產品 blended product;
機器產品 machine products;
積壓產品 overstocked commodities;
家禽產品 poultry products;
開發產品 develop a product;
~ 一條龍開發產品 a coordinated development of products;
礦產品 mineral product;
瀝青產品 asphaltic product;
林產品 forest product;
聯產品 joint product;
冒牌產品 fake brand-name products;
~ 出售冒牌產品 sell fake brand-name products;
名牌產品 famous brand products;
~ 優質名牌產品 famous brand quality products;
農產品 farm products;
拳頭產品 competitive products;
~ 開發拳頭產品 develop competitive products;
肉類產品 meat products;
市場產品 market product;
水產品 aquatic product;
土特產品 native product;
推銷產品 promote the sale of a product;
新產品 new product;
畜產品 livestock products;
優勢產品 competitive product;
優質產品 quality product;
漁業產品 fishery product;
原料產品 raw produce;
製造產品 manufacture a product;
中高檔產品 medium and high-grade goods;
總產品 output aggregate;
最終產品 end product;

[產婆] midwife;

[產前] prenatal;
產前的 antenatal; prenatal;
產前感染 antepartum infection;
產前檢查 prenatal check-up;

[產權] property rights;
產權保險 title insurance;
產權管理 property-rights administration;
產權交易 property-rights exchange;
~ 產權交易中心 property-rights exchange centre;
產權經濟 property-rights economy;
產權所有人 owner of title;
產權制度 property-rights system;
產權轉讓 property-rights transfer;
保護產權 protect property rights;
擁有產權 hold property rights;
知識產權 intellectual property;

[產生] (1) come into being; emerge; (2) engender; produce;
產生惡感 cause ill will;
產生反感 cause ill will;
產生副作用 have side effects; produce evil reactions;
產生結果 bear results; yield results;
產生利息 draw interest;
產生磨擦 cause friction;
產生歧義 produce ambiguity;
產生危害 do harm to sb;
產生誤會 produce misunderstandings;
產生效益 bring benefits; yield benefits;
產生需求 generate the demand;

[產物] outcome; produce; product;
年產物 annual produce;
時代的產物 product of the time;
天然產物 natural products;
主林產物 major forest products;

[產銷] production and marketing;
產銷見面 link production with sales;

產銷結合 coordination between production and marketing;
產銷兩旺 production and marketing prosper; production and marketing thrive;
產銷一體化 production integrates with marketing;
自產自銷 market one's own products; produce and market all by oneself; produce and market all on one's own;

[產需] supply and demand;
產需平衡 balance between production and demand;

[產業] (1) estate; property; (2) industry;
產業分類 industry classification;
產業革命 industrial revolution;
~ 新產業革命 new industrial revolution;
產業工人 industrial worker;
產業公會 industrial union;
產業合理化 rationalization of industry;
產業機器人 industrial robot;
產業結構 industry structure;
~ 產業結構高級化 industry structure advancement;
~ 產業結構合理化 industry structure rationalization;
~ 改革產業結構 reform the industry structure;
~ 內部產業結構 internal industry structure;
產業界 industrial circles;
產業經濟 industrial economy;
~ 產業經濟學 industrial economics;
~ 多種產業經濟 multi-industrial economy;
產業內貿易 trade inside industry;
產業昇級 upgrade industry;
產業系列化 industrial serialization;
產業心理 industrial psychology;
產業政策 industrial policy;
~ 國家產業政策 state industrial policy;
變賣產業 sell off one's property;
第二產業 secondary industry;
第三產業 tertiary industry;
第一產業 primary industry;
高技術產業 high-tech industry;
骨幹產業 pillar industries;
~ 發展骨幹產業 develop the pillar industries;
管理產業 administer one's estate;
繼承產業 accession to an estate; fall heir to an estate;
留下產業 leave an estate;
私有產業 estate; property;
衰退產業 declining industry;
支柱產業 pillar industry;
重要產業 chief industries; important industry;
主導產業 prime mover industry;
主要產業 major industry;

[產值] output value; value of output;
淨產值 net output value;
總產值 gross output value;

包產 take full responsibility for output quotas;
財產 assets; property;
超產 overfulfil a production target;
出產 manufacture; produce; production;
催產 expedite child delivery; hasten parturition;
低產 low yield;
地產 real estate;
動產 movable property; personal property;
房產 house property;
房地產 property; real estate;
豐產 bumper harvest; have a bumper harvest;
高產 high production; high yield;
公產 public property;
共產 communism; communist;
估產 estimate the yield;
官產 public property;
國產 domestic; made in one's country;
海產 marine products;
恒產 immovable property; real estate;
家產 family property;
減產 drop production; reduce production;
礦產 mineral products;
林產 forest products;
臨產 about to give birth;
流產 have an abortion; miscarriage;
名產 famous product; specialty goods;
畝產 yield per unit area;
難產 (1) difficult labour; have a difficult labour; (2) slow in coming;
逆產 traitor's property;
平產 equal in output;
破產 go bankrupt; go broke;
欠產 production shortfall; shortfall in output;
生產 (1) make; manufacture; produce; (2) give birth;
盛產 abound in; teem with;
水產 aquatic products; marine products;
順產 have a natural labour;
私產 private property;
死產 stillbirth;

嗣產 inherit a fortune;
特產 local speciality; special local product;
天產 natural products;
田產 (1) landed property; (2) farm product;
停產 stop production; suspend production;
投產 go into production;
土產 local products; native products;
脱產 be released from production;
無產 proletariat;
物產 natural resources; produce; products;
小產 abortion; miscarriage;
畜產 animal products; livestock products;
遺產 heritage; inheritance; legacy;
漁產 aquatic products;
早產 have a premature delivery;
增產 increase production;
爭產 fight for inheritance;
中產 middle class;
資產 (1) property; (2) capital; (3) assets;
祖產 ancestral estate;

chan

【剷】 (1) shovel; (2) level off; raze to the ground; shovel;
[剷除] eradicate; root out;
剷除弊病 remove evils;
剷除黃賭毒 eradicate pornography, gambling, and drug abuse;
剷除邪惡 get rid of evils;
剷除罪惡 eradicate crime; root up crime;
[剷平] level; level to the ground;
[剷子] shovel;
用剷子 use a shovel;

chan

【諂】 cringe; fawn on sb; flatter;
[諂媚] adulate; adulation; fawn on; flatter; flattery; toady;
諂媚奉承 stoop to flattery;
諂媚求寵 buy favours with flattery; flatter for favouritism; use flattery to obtain favours;
厭惡諂媚 loathe flattery;
[諂笑] ingratiating smile;
阿諛諂笑 flatter and curry favour; fulsome flattery;
[諂諛] bootlick; flatter;
諂諛者 bootlicker;

chan

【蒇】 complete; finish;
[蒇事] be completed; be finished;

chan

【鏟】 scoop; shovel;
[鏟車] forklift;
[鏟除] clear off; eliminate; uproot;
[鏟斗] bucket;
閉式鏟斗 close-type bucket;
側傾式鏟斗 side-tipping bucket;
側裝式鏟斗 side-tipping bucket;
帶齒鏟斗 tooth bucket;
底卸鏟斗 bucket;
翻轉鏟斗 reversible bucket;
後鏟斗 rear bucket;
活動底鏟斗 open-end bucket;
前裝式鏟斗 front-end bucket;
清理鏟斗 cleaning bucket;
傾翻式鏟斗 rollover bucket;
通用鏟斗 utility bucket;
挖溝鏟斗 ditching bucket;
挖土鏟斗 digging bucket; earth bucket; hoe bucket;
挖土機鏟斗 shovel bucket;
圓底鏟斗 radius bucket;
自清鏟斗 self-cleaning bucket;
[鏟雪車] snowplough;
[鏟子] scoop; shovel;
一把鏟子 a shovel;

電鏟 power shovel;
風鏟 air spade;
鍋鏟 slice;
機鏟 mechanical shovel;
煤鏟 coal shovel;
蒸汽鏟 steam shovel;

chan

【闡】 (1) elaborate; elucidate; explain; expound; make clear; (2) clear; evident;
[闡發] elucidate;
[闡明] clarify; enunciate; expound; shed light on; throw light on;
闡明觀點 clarify one's views; drive an argument home; explain one's position;
闡明理由 explain one's reasons;
闡明立場 define one's position; set forth one's position;
闡明論點 drive a point home;
[闡釋] explain; expound; interpret;
[闡述] elaborate; enunciate; expound; set forth;
闡述觀點 state one's argument;

［闡揚］ expound and propagate;

chan⁴

chan

【懺】 confess one's sin; repent;

［懺悔］ repent one's sin;

懺悔自新 repent and turn over a new leaf;

表示懺悔 express remorse; put ashes on one's head; show repentance;

跪著懺悔 kneel in confession;

臨終懺悔 deathbed repentance;

［懺禮］ a ritual for penance;

拜懺 say Mass for people;

chan

【羼】 interpolate; mix;

chan

【顫】 quiver; shake; tremble; vibrate;

［顫動］ quiver; vibrate;

在風中顫動 quiver in the wind;

在空中顫動 quiver in the air;

［顫抖］ quake; quiver; shake; shudder; tremble;

渾身顫抖 all of a tremble; tremble all over;

兩手顫抖 one's hands quiver;

嗓音顫抖 tremor in one's voice;

聲音顫抖 one's voice quivers;

手顫抖 one's hands shake;

雙手顫抖 one's hands tremble;

嘴唇顫抖 one's mouth quivers;

［顫巍巍］ falter; totter;

顫巍巍地站起來 totter to one's feet;

［顫音］ trill;

震顫 quiver; tremble;

chang¹

chang

【昌】 (1) flourishing; prosperous; (2) a surname;

［昌隆］ prosperous and flourishing;

福運昌隆 in the ascendant;

［昌明］ flourishing; thriving; well-developed;

［昌盛］ prosperous;

鼎運昌盛 the destiny of the state is prosperous;

國家昌盛 the country is prospering;

［昌亡］ prosper or perish;

得人者昌，失人者亡 those who win people prosper; those who lose them fail;

chang

【倀】 (1) ghost controlled by the tiger; (2) rash; wild;

［倀倀］ aimless wandering; bewildered;

［倀子］ exorcist;

chang

【倡】 (1) prostitute; (2) wild and unrestrained;

［倡優］ (1) prostitute; (2) actress; entertainer; musician;

chang

【娼】 prostitute; whore;

［娼妓］ prostitute; streetwalker; whore; working girl;

暗娼 unlicensed prostitute;

包娼 harbour call girl centres;

私娼 unlicensed prostitute;

夜娼 night walker;

chang

【猖】 furious; savage; unbridled; unruly;

［猖獗］ on the rampage; raging; rampant; run wild;

猖獗一時 be on the rampage for a time; run amok for a brief period; run wild for a time;

盜賊猖獗 be infested with thieves;

老鼠猖獗 be infested with rats;

土匪猖獗 be infested with bandits;

［猖狂］ furious; savage; unbridled; ungovernable; unrestrained; unruly;

說話猖狂 talk recklessly;

行為猖狂 act recklessly; behave in a disorderly manner without fear;

［猖厲］ mad and violent; wild and severe;

［猖亂］ wild and disorderly;

chang

【菖】 calamus; sweet flag;

［菖蒲］ calamus; sweet flag;

chang

【閶】 gate of a palace; gate of heaven;

［閶風］ autumn winds;

chang

【鯧】 butterfish; silvery pomfret;

烏鯧 black pomfret;

銀鯧 silvery pomfret;

chang²
chang

【長】 (1) long; length; (2) lasting; of long duration; (3) forte; strong points; (4) good at; strong in; (5) a surname;

[長把梨] pear;

[長臂猿] gibbon;

[長城] (1) Great Wall; (2) impregnable bulwark;

[長程] long-range;

[長抽] long drive;
長抽短吊 combine long drives with drop shots;

[長臭] long-winded and smelly;
又臭又長 smelly and long-winded;

[長處] best points; good points; good qualities; merits; strong points;
很多長處 many good points; many good qualities;
~ 表現出很多長處 display many good qualities;
~ 有很多長處 have many good points; possess many good qualities;

[長存] live forever;

[長凳] bench;

[長笛] flute;
長笛手 flautist;

[長度] length; longitude;
長度不等 uneven in length;
長度合適 of convenient length;
長度合要求 of desired length;
長度相等 of equal length; of the same length;
長度中等 of moderate length;
仿射長度 affine length;
絕對長度 absolute length;
實際長度 actual length;
有效長度 action length;

[長短] (1) length; (2) accident; mishap; (3) good and bad; right and wrong; strong and weak points;
長短不齊 not of uniform length; not uniform in length; uneven in length;
不爭一日之短長 not strive for only temporary superiority;
裁長補短 cut off the long and compensate the short;
長吁短歎 moan and groan; sighs and groans;
髮短心長 old in age but vigorous in mind;
飛短流長 flying rumours; spread embroidered stories and malicious gossip;
蜚短流長 flying rumours; spread embroidered stories and malicious gossip; spread rumours; talk behind sb's back; tell tales;
家長里短 small household affairs;
截長補短 cut off from the long to supply the deficiency of the short; draw on the strength of one to offset the weakness of the other; make up for each other's deficiencies; overcome one's own shortcomings by learning from another persons's strong points; take from the long to add to the short;
絕長補短 supplement insufficiency with surplus;
論長論短 talk about sb's merits and shortcomings;
七長八短 (1) of uneven lengths; of uneven sizes; (2) sth may happen; sth unfortunate;
棄短取長 eliminate the defects and adopt others' good points; forget sb's shortcomings and make use of his strong points;
取長補短 adopt others' strong points while overcoming one's weak points; draw on the strong points of others to make up for one's own weak points; learn from others' strong points to make up one's deficiencies; learn from others' strong points to offset one's weaknesses; make up each other's deficiencies; make up for one's deficiencies by learning from others; overcome one's own shortcomings by learning from the strong points of others; overcome one's weak points by learning from others' strong points;
三長兩短 anything untoward; if sth unfortunate should happen; in case of any mishap; sth unfortunate; unexpected misfortunes; unforeseen accidents; unforeseen disasters;
捨短取長 disregard the shortcomings and adopt the good points; overlook sb's shortcomings and make much of his merits; put aside the bad points and adopt the good ones;
數短論長 gossip idly; indulge in idle

gossip; make captious comments;
說長道短 backbite people; gossip about pople behind their backs; gossip idly; indulge in idle gossip; make captious comments; random talk; speak ill of a person who is absent;
~愛說長道短 delight in gossip;
說長論短 criticize others; discuss a variety of subjects; gossip idly; indulge in idle gossip; make captious comments;
說短道長 criticize others; discuss who is right and who is wrong; gossip;
天長夜短 the days are long and the nights short;
問長問短 ask a thousand and one things; ask about this and that; ask all manner of questions; ask sb about the length and breadth of various things; ask sb all sorts of questions; ask sb the whys and wherefores; inquisitive; make detailed inquiries;
夜長日短 the night gains on the day; the nights are long and the days short;
一長一短 one short, one long;
一爭短長 compete with each other; strive for mastery;
以己之長比人之短 compare one's strong points with someone else's weak points;
以己之長攻人之短 match one's advantages against other's disadvantages; use one's strong points to attack others' weak points;
有話即長，無話則短 if nothing happens, the story is short; if things happen, the story is long;
張家長，李家短 gossip about people;
紙短情長 the paper is too short to contain one's deep feelings;

［長髮］ long hair;
中長髮 medium-length hair;

［長方體］ cuboid;

［長號］ trombone;
高音長號 tenor trombone;

［長頸鹿］ giraffe;

［長久］ for a long time; permanently;
長久地等待 have a long wait; wait for ages;
長久地堅持 endure very long;
長久地忍耐 endure very long;
長久戰 long-drawn-out war;
長久之計 long-term plan; long-term policy; permanent arrangement;
~並非長久之計 just a makeshift arrangement;
~絕非長久之計 by no means a permanent arrangement;
天長地久 as long as heaven and earth endure; as long as the world lasts; enduring as the universe; everlasting and unchanging;
天長日久 after a considerable period of time; day after day; for a long, long time; for many years to come;

［長空］ vast sky;
鶴唳長空 the stork sings through the sky;

［長龍］ long line of people waiting for service;
一列長龍 a long queue; a queue stretching into the far distance;

［長毛絨］ plush;
素色平紋長毛絨 plain plush;
針織長毛絨 knitted plush;

［長矛］ lance; spear;

［長眠］ death; die; eternal sleep;
長眠不起 die; sleep the final sleep; sleep the sleep of death;
長眠地下 dead and buried; sleep eternally underground;
瞑目長眠 rest in peace;

［長命］ long life; longevity;
長命百歲 live to a ripe old age; live to be a hundred; a life of a hundred years; many happy returns; many happy returns of the day;
長命富貴 a long life of abundance and respectability; longevity with wealth and honour;

［長年］ all the year round;
長年累月 for months and years on end; month after month, year after year; over the years; year in and year out;

［長篇］ lengthy essay;
長篇大論 lengthy article; a long speech; lengthy writing; long-winded; long-winded and pompous writing; ramble on;
長篇累牘 long-drawn and tedious documents;

［長袍］ cope; robe;
家居長袍 housecoat;

［長期］ long-term; over a long period of time;
長期存在的問題 long-standing problem;

長期貸款 long-term loan;
長期的努力 efforts of many years;
長期的爭論 long-standing dispute;
長期發展 long period of growth; long-term development;
長期共存 long-term coexistence;
長期規劃 long-term programme;
長期合同 long-term contract;
長期計劃 long-term plan;
~長期計劃模型 long-range planning model;
長期決策 long-term decision;
長期虧損企業 enterprises with a long history of running at a loss;
長期生病 long illness;
長期投資 permanent investment;
長期穩定 long-term stability;
長期訓練 long practice;
~經過長期訓練 have been trained for a long time;
~需要長期訓練 require a long practice;
長期以來 for a long time; for quite some time;
長期影響 long-range effects;
長期債券 long-term bond;
長期戰爭 long war;

[長驅] make a long drive; push deep;
長驅直進 drive straight ahead; make a hasty advance;
長驅直入 advance unchecked; drive deep into; drive straight into; enter directly without resistance; penetrate inland unchecked;

[長裙] long skirt;
中長裙 midi skirt;

[長舌] fond of gossip; tongue enough for two sets of teeth;
長舌婦 garrulous woman; gossip; gossipmonger;

[長生] long life; longevity;
長生不老 enjoy a very long life without getting old; live forever and never grow old; live forever without getting old;
長生不死 live forever and never die;

[長石] feldspar;
鋇長石 barium feldspar;
鈣長石 calcium feldspar;
日長石 aventurine feldspar;

[長壽] long life; longevity;
長壽之道 the art of longevity;
長壽之家 long-lived family;

[長歎] deep sigh; sigh deeply; take a deep sigh;
長歎一聲 let out a long sigh; take a deep sigh; take a long sigh;

[長天] the vastness of heaven;

[長挑] tall and slender;

[長痛不如短痛] better a finger off than ay wagging; better eye out than always ache; better eyes out than ever to ache;

[長途] long distance;
長途跋涉 make a long and difficult journey; make a long journey on foot; trek a long way; trudge over a long distance; long and arduous journey;
長途電話 long-distance call;
~長途電話費 toll charge;
長途販運 transport goods over a long distance to sell them;
長途困頓 plod one's weary way;
長途旅行 long journey; make a long-distance travel; travel long distances;
長途汽車 coach; long-distance bus;
~長途汽車站 coach terminal;
長途運輸 long-distance transport;

[長項] forte;

[長袖善舞] resourceful;

[長夜] long night; eternal night;
長夜不寐 sleep a sleepless night; lie sleepless all night on one's pillow;
長夜難明 the long dark years under the rule of the exploiting class;

[長椅] bench;

[長於] good at;

[長遠] long-range; long-term;
長遠打算 long-term planning;
長遠利益 long-term interests;
長遠目標 long-range goal;

[長足] by leaps and bounds;
長足進步 great progress;
~取得長足進步 make great progress;
長足進展 make considerable progress;
~顯示長足進展 show vast progress;

背長 back measurement;
波長 wavelength;
抻長 lengthen;
耳長 ear length;
加長 lengthen;
見長 expert in; good at;
句長 sentence length;
拉長 drag out; draw out; elongate; prolong;

C

space out;
漫長 endless; very long;
綿長 last a long period of time;
片長 running time;
頂長 tall; tall in physique;
情長 lasting affection for one;
冗長 lengthy;
擅長 expert in; good at;
深長 profound;
瘦長 long and thin; tall and thin;
特長 speciality; strong point; what one is skilled in or expert in;
拖長 prolong;
細長 long and thin; tall and slender;
修長 slender; slim; tall and thin;
延長 extend; lengthen;
悠長 long; long-drawn-out;
周長 circumference; girth; perimeter;
專長 speciality;

chang

【常】 (1) common; normal; ordinary; (2) constant; invariable; (3) frequently; often; usually; (4) principle; rule; (5) a surname;

[常備] always on the alert; be ever prepared;
常備不懈 always on the alert; be ever prepared;
常備軍 standing army;

[常常] as often as not; frequently; generally; half the time; many a time; more often than not; often; usually;

[常規] common practice; convention; rule;
常規部隊 conventional force;
常規裁軍 conventional disarmament;
常規分組 conventional grouping;
常規化驗 routine test;
常規檢查 routine examination;
常規會計 conventional accounting;
常規科學 normal science;
常規內存 conventional memory;
常規武器 conventional weapons;
常規治療 routine treatment;
常規作戰 conventional warfare;
按常規 as a matter of course;
背離常規 different from the usual practice;
變現常規 realization convention;
打破常規 break away from convention; break old conventions; get out of the ordinary groove;
對應常規 matching convention;
蔑視常規 have contempt for old conventions;
違背常規 depart from the common practice; go against the established rules;
無視常規 disregard the established rules;
越出常規 move out of the usual rut; deviate from the common course; exceed conventional rules; off the track; out of the general road;
遵照常規 observe a usual practice;

[常軌] normal course;
恢復常軌 back on the rails;

[常會] regular meeting;

[常見] common;
常見病 common disease; common illness;
常見錯誤 common mistakes;
~避免常見錯誤 avoid common mistakes;
常見的事 common event;
常見的現象 common phenomenon;
常見現象 common phenomenon;

[常久] for a long time;

[常開] normally open;
笑口常開 grin all the time;

[常客] frequent caller;

[常理] convention; logical thinking;
有乖常理 run counter to reason;

[常禮] regular etiquette;

[常例] common practice; regular routine;

[常量] constant; regular;
常量分析 regular analysis;

[常流] average;
邁越常流 above the average; cut a conspicuous figure; surpass one's fellows; tower above the rest;

[常綠] evergreen;

[常年] (1) perennial; throughout the year; (2) year in year out;

[常青] evergreen;
常青的 evergreen;
常青樹 evergreen;
常青藤 ivy;
~一層常青藤 a mantle of ivy;
常青植物 evergreen plant;
四季常青 green all the year;

[常情] reason; sense;
合乎常情 accord with reason; stand to reason;
人之常情 common humanity; constant

occurrence in human relationships; feelings common to all human beings; human nature; it is only human nature; matter of common sense among the people; sth that is natural and normal; sth that is natural in human relationships; the way of the world;

[常人] common people; man in the street; ordinary people;
異乎常人 different from the ordinary people;

[常任] permanent; standing;
常任代表 permanent delegate; permanent representative;
常任理事 permanent council member;
常任制 permanent tenure of office;

[常設] permanent; standing;
常設機構 standing body;
常設委員會 permanent committee;

[常勝] ever-victorious;
常勝將軍 ever-victorious general;
常勝軍 ever-victorious army;

[常識] (1) general knowledge; (2) common sense;
科學常識 scientific common sense;
沒有常識 have no common sense;
缺乏常識 lack common sense;
衛生常識 knowledge of hygiene and sanitation;
一點常識 a modicum of common sense; a morsel of sense; an ounce of common sense;
運用常識 exercise common sense;

[常數] constant;
附加常數 additional constant;
活度常數 activity constant;
加速常數 acceleration constant;
絕對常數 absolute constant;
任意常數 arbitrary constant;
聲傳播常數 acoustic propagation constant;
聲相位常數 acoustic phase constant;
酸度常數 acidity constant;
吸收常數 absorption constant;

[常歲] every year;

[常談] platitude;
老生常談 banal remark; commonplace; cut and dried; home truth; mere platitude; platitudes; platitudes of an old scholar; Queen Anne is dead; stale news; standing dish; Sunday-school truth; the Dutch have taken Holland; trite remarks; truism; truth;

[常態] normal behaviour; normal conditions; normality;
保持常態 keep sth in its normal conditions;
處於常態 in the normal state;
恢復常態 back to normal conditions; back to the normal state; resume to the normal state; return to the normal;
回復常態 back to the normal state;
一反常態 act out of one's character;

[常委] member of a standing committee;

[常溫] (1) normal atmosphere;
(2) homoiothermy;
保持常溫 the temperature remains within the normal range;

[常務] day-to-day business; routine;
常務董事 managing director;
常務副市長 managing vice mayor;
常務副校長 provost;
常務工作 day-to-day business;
常務委員 member of the standing committee;

[常言] saying;
常言道 as the saying goes;
常言說得好 coin a phrase; it is well said that;

[常業] career occupation;
常業犯 habitual offender; hardened criminal; repeat offender;

[常用] in common use;
常用詞 commonly-used words;
常用語手冊 phrase book;
不常用 be hardly used; be seldom used; of little use;
很常用 be commonly used; in daily use;

[常駐] permanent; resident;
常駐巴黎 be based in Paris;
常駐代表 permanent delegate;
常駐記者 resident correspondent;
常駐使節 permanent envoy;
常駐藝術家 artist-in-residence;
常駐作家 writer-in-residence;

安常 take things as they are;
超常 above normal; superior;
反常 aberrant; abnormal; paradoxical; perverse; strange; unusual;
非常 a thousand; as blazes; as devil; as hell; as they come; awfully; badly; be burning

with; be exasperated; bloody; by half; deeply; ever and ever so; ever so; ever so much; ever such a; exceedingly; extremely; frightfully; immensely; mortally; most; no end; no end of; not half; nothing if not; one hundred percent; only too...to; simply; so much; such a; terribly; to a great extent; to death; to the bone; to the ears; to the hilt; to the world; up to the elbows; up to the handle; utterly; vastly; very; very much;

綱常 cardinal guides and constant virtues;
慣常 customary; habitual;
家常 daily life of a family;
經常 (1) always; constantly; every now and again; every now and then; every once in a while; every so often; frequent; frequently; from time to time; half the time; many's the time; more often than not; now and again; now and then; often; oftentimes; regularly; time after time; used to; (2) daily; day-to-day; everyday;
倫常 human relations;
平常 (1) ordinary; common; (2) as a rule; as usual; generally; normally; ordinarily; ordinary times; usually; (3) average; mediocre;
日常 day-to-day; routine;
如常 as usual; commonplace; ordinary;
失常 abnormal; go into a spin; go mad; not normal; odd; off form; perform below one's normal capacity;
時常 every now and again; frequently; often; oftentimes; usually;
守常 stick to tradition;
率常 usually;
素常 commonly; habitually; ordinarily; usually;
隨常 commonly; usually;
通常 generally; usually;
往常 as one used to do previously; as usual; habitually in the past; make it a rule; used to;
無常 changeable; variable;
閑常 ordinary; usually;
尋常 common; ordinary;
循常 common; ordinary; usual;
異常 (1) abnormal; unusual; (2) exceedingly; extraordinarily; extremely;
逾常 out of the ordinary; unusual;
照常 as usual;
正常 normal; regular;
中常 average; middling;

chang
【徜】 going to and fro; lingering; loitering;

chang
【場】 (1) field; ground; (2) farm; (3) scene; spot; stage; (4) stage; (5) act of a play; (6) measure word for films and plays;

［場地］ place; site; space;
場地不夠 space is insufficient;
交換場地 change sides;
練習場地 practice field;
施工場地 construction ground;
運動場地 place for sport;

［場合］ occasion; situation;
悲傷場合 sad occasion;
公開場合 public occasion;
節慶場合 festive occasion;
歷史性場合 historic occasion;
社交場合 social situation;
盛大場合 big occasion; great occasion; splendid occasion;
特殊場合 special occasion;
外交場合 diplomatic occasion;
嚴肅場合 solemn occasion;
正式場合 formal occasion;
莊重場合 solemn occasion;
宗教場合 religious occasion;

［場記］ log keeper;
女場記 continuity girl;

［場景］ situation;
工作場景 work situation;

［場論］ field theory;
經典場論 classical field theory;
量子場論 quantum field theory;
統一場論 unified field theory;

［場面］ scene; occasion;
場面背景 scenic background;
擺場面 put on splendour;
~虛擺場面 put on false splendour;
悲哀的場面 sad scene;
悲慘的場面 tragic scene;
繃繃場面 manage somehow to keep up appearances;
撐場面 keep up appearances;
動人的場面 touching scene;
憤怒的場面 angry scene;
激動人心的場面 exciting scene; moving scene;
可怕的場面 horrible scene;
控制場面 dominate the scene;

淒涼的場面 dismal scene;
使人不快的場面 unpleasant spectacle;
戲劇性場面 dramatic spectacle;
有趣的場面 entertaining spectacle;
震撼人心的場面 thrilling scene;

[場所] place; arena;
避難場所 place of refuge;
工作場所 working place;
公共集會場所 public gathering place;
公共娛樂場所 public amusement place;
空曠的場所 open space;
僻靜的場所 quiet and secluded place;
休假場所 vacation spot;
娛樂場所 amusement place;

靶場 shooting range;
把場 (1) direct from behind the scenes; (2) control things on the scene;
靶場 firing range; range; shooting range;
半場 (1) half of a game; (2) half court;
包場 book the entire place; make a block booking;
冰場 ice arena; ice stadium; skating rink;
菜場 food market;
操場 playground; sports ground;
草場 meadow;
茶場 tea plantation;
車場 car park; parking lot;
出場 (1) appear on the scene; come on the stage; make an appearance; put in an appearance; (2) enter;
憷場 feel nervous before a large audience;
詞匯場 lexical field;
磁場 magnetic field;
打場 thresh grain;
當場 dead to rights; in one's tracks; in the act of; in the mainour; off the cuff; on the dot; on the hop; on the nail; on the spot; then and there; there and then; with the mainour;
到場 present; show up; turn up;
登場 come on the stage; enter the scene;
電場 electric field;
賭場 casino; gambling house;
渡場 crossing site;
法場 execution ground; execution site;
翻場 turn over the grain on the threshing ground;
飛機場 airport;
墳場 graveyard;
工場 workshop;
穀場 yard for drying grains;
官場 official circles; officialdom;
廣場 public square; square;
過場 (1) interlude; (2) cross the stage; (3) go through the motions;
話語場 field of discourse;
滑冰場 skating rink;
會場 conference hall; meeting place;
火場 scene of fire;
貨場 freight yard; goods yard;
機場 airport;
加工場 processing workshop;
疆場 battlefield;
劇場 theatre;
開場 begin;
看場 guard the threshing ground;
考場 examination hall;
力場 field of force;
立場 position; stance; stand; standpoint;
獵場 hunting field; hunting ground;
溜冰場 skating rink;
牧場 grazing land; pastureland;
內場 infield;
農場 farm;
排場 display of splendour;
起場 gather in threshed grain on a threshing ground;
怯場 have stage fright;
球場 ball game ground;
全場 all those present; full court; whole audience;
日場 day show;
入場 enter the field;
散場 empty after the show;
沙場 battlefield; battleground;
擅場 excel in a certain field;
商場 bazaar; market;
上場 (1) appear on the stage; come on the stage; (2) enter the field; join in a contest;
市場 bazaar; market; market place;
試場 examination hall;
收場 end; end up; ending; stop; wind up;
攤場 spread harvested grain on a threshing ground;
停車場 car park; parking lot;
退場 quit the scene;
外場 behaviour of being good at social intercourse and concerned about preserving one's reputation and credibility;
晚場 evening show;
武場 percussion instruments in Chinese operas;
舞場 ballroom; dance hall;
下場 go off stage; leave the stage;
現場 (1) scene; (2) site; spot;
刑場 execution site;

C

洋場 metropolis infested with foreign adventurers;
夜場 evening show;
用場 use;
漁場 fishery; fishing ground;
浴場 outdoor bathing place;
運動場 sports ground;
在場 present at the scene;
早場 morning show;
戰場 battlefield; battleground;
終場 come to an end;
專場 special performance;

C

chang

【腸】 bowels; intestines;
[腸癌] bowel cancer; intestinal cancer;
[腸病] bowel disease; enteropathy;
腸病發生 enteropathogenesis;
缺血性腸病 ischemic bowel disease;
炎性腸病 inflammatory bowel disease;
[腸出血] enterorrhagia;
[腸穿刺] enterocentesis;
[腸穿孔] enterobrosis; intestinal perforation;
[腸道] gut; intestinal tract;
[腸動] enterokinesia;
[腸動脈] arteriae intestinales;
[腸肚] intestines and the belly;
割肚牽腸 be deeply concerned; be kept in suspense; feel anxious;
[腸斷] heartbroken; deeply grieved;
淚乾腸斷 crying one's eyes out and heartbroken;
[腸肥腦滿] with a fair round belly and swollen head;
[腸腹] intestines;
腸腹膜 intestinal peritoneum;
~膜炎 exenteritis;
撐腸拄腹 excessive eating; fill the stomach;
[腸梗阻] ileus; intestinal obstruction;
癌性腸梗阻 carcinomatous ileus;
急性腸梗阻 acute intestinal obstruction;
痙攣性腸梗阻 spastic ileus;
麻痺性腸梗阻 paralytic ileus;
阻塞性腸梗阻 occlusive ileus;
[腸絞痛] intestinal angina; tormina;
嬰兒腸絞痛 infantile colic;
[腸節] enteromere;
腸節疝 enteromerocele;
[腸結腸炎] enterocolitis;
[腸結核] tuberculosis of intestine;
[腸痙攣] enterospasm;
[腸潰瘍] enterelcosis;
[腸擴張] enterectasis;
[腸瘤] enteroncus;
[腸扭結] volvulus;
[腸熱病] enteric fever;
[腸疝] enterocele;
膀胱腸疝 cystoenterocele;
[腸神經炎] enteroneuritis;
[腸石] intestinal calculus;
腸石病 enterolithiasis;
[腸套疊] intussusception;
[腸痛] enterodynia;
[腸胃] belly; intestines and stomach;
腸胃病 digestive ailment; disease of stomach and bowels;
腸胃不好 suffer from indigestion;
腸胃不適 stomach upset;
~引起腸胃不適 upset one's stomach;
腸胃炎 gastroenteritis;
[腸炎] enteritis;
壞死性腸炎 enteritis necroticans;
節段性腸炎 segmental enteritis;
結核性腸炎 tuberculous enteritis;
結節性腸炎 enteritis nodularis;
局部性腸炎 regional enteritis;
鏈球菌性腸炎 streptococcus enteritis;
肉芽腫性腸炎 granulomatous enteritis;
息肉性腸炎 enteritis polyposa;
原蟲性腸炎 protozoan enteritis;
[腸周炎] perienteritis;
[腸子] intestines;
花花腸子 fertile imagination; many ideas;
[腸阻塞] intestinal obstruction;

愁腸 pent-up sadness;
大腸 large intestine;
肚腸 bowels;
斷腸 break the heart; extremely sad;
肥腸 pig's large intestines;
粉腸 a kind of sausage;
肝腸 liver and intestines;
灌腸 enema;
紅腸 sausage;
後腸 epigaster;
饑腸 empty stomach;
結腸 colon;
空腸 empty intestine;
枯腸 impoverished mind;
臘腸 sausage;

盲腸 caecum;
情腸 loving heart;
熱腸 ardour; enthusiastic;
胃腸 stomach intestine;
小腸 small intestine;
香腸 sausage;
心腸 (1) heart; intention; (2) mood; state of mind;
直腸 rectum;
衷腸 inner feelings; sincerer words;

chang
【嘗】 (1) taste; try the flavour of; (2) come to know; experience; taste; (3) ever; once;
[嘗嘗] have a taste; taste;
[嘗試] attempt; endeavour; take a whack at sth; try;
嘗試一下 make a try; take a try;
初次嘗試 a maiden attempt;
徒勞的嘗試 fruitless attempt;
[嘗新] taste a new delicacy;

飽嘗 experience to the fullest extent;
何嘗 it is not that but;
未嘗 (1) have not; (2) might not;

chang
【萇】 fruit of Averrhoa carambola;

chang
【霃】 snowing heavily;

chang
【嫦】
[嫦娥] goddess of the moon;
嫦娥奔月 the goddess of the moon flew to the moon;
嫦娥下凡 the goddess of the moon has left paradise and come down to the mundane world of men;
月裏嫦娥 goddess of the moon; legendary fairy of the moon;
自古嫦娥愛少年 from of old, young nymphs have preferred youth to age;

chang
【裳】 clothing; dress; garment;

chang
【償】 (1) compensate for; repay; (2) fulfil; meet; (3) offset;
[償付] pay; pay back; pay-off;
償付能力 solvency;
事後償付 ex post pay-off;
事先償付 ex ante pay-off;
[償還] pay back; pay-off; repay;
償還人情債 pay one's debt of gratitude;
償還血債 pay a debt of blood;
償還一切費用 return all costs;
償還債務 loan repayment; pay back a debt; repay a loan; repayment of a debt;
不予償還 allow no refund; make no refund;
全部償還 pay back in full;
如數償還 pay back the exact amount;
一次性償還 repay in a lump sum;
資本償還 capital pay-off;
[償命] a life for a life; pay with one's life;
以命償命 life for life;
[償清] clear off;
償清久款 pay off one's debt;
償清欠債 clear one's debt;
償清夙債 get square with one's creditors; satisfy all demands;
償清債務 clear off one's debts; liquidate one's liabilities; pay off a loan;
[償願] fulfil one's wish; get what one desires;
如願以償 achieve what one wishes; answer one's expectations; attain one's end; attain one's wish; bring about the result one wants; have one's desire gratified; have one's heart's desire; have one's way; have one's wish; have one's wishes fulfilled; get one's wish; obtain what is desired;
[償債] pay a debt;
償債基金 sinking fund;
償債能力 debt paying ability;
償債資金 sinking fund;

報償 recompense; repay;
補償 compensate for; make up; recompense;
代償 compensation;
抵償 compensate for; make good;
賠償 compensate for; make compensation;
清償 clear off; discharge; pay off;
取償 be paid back for cost or labour;
索償 claim;

chang³

chang
【昶】 (1) a long day; (2) comfortable and easy;

chang
【場】 a pronunciation of 場;

C

chang
【敞】 (1) broad; spacious; (2) open; uncovered;
[敞車] gondola;
高邊敞車 gondola;
~ 側傾卸高邊敞車 side dump gondola;
~ 平底高邊敞車 flat-bottomed gondola;
有蓋敞車 covered gondola;
[敞懷] with one's coat or shirt unbuttoned;
敞懷暢談 talk to one's content;
敞懷痛飲 drink to one's capacity;
[敞開] open wide;
敞開窗 open the window wide;
敞開大門 open the front door wide; the front door is left wide open; with the gate wide open;
敞開肚子 eat without inhibition;
敞開供應 ample supply; sufficient;
敞開門 open the door wide;
敞開門戶 open one's door wide;
敞開思想 get things off one's chest; say what is on one's mind;
[敞亮] (1) light and spacious; (2) clear in one's thinking;
[敞露] expose; open;
[敞篷車] convertible car; open car;

高敞 tall and spacious;
寬敞 spacious;
軒敞 spacious and bright;

chang
【廠】 (1) factory; mill; plant; works; (2) depot; yard;
[廠房] factory building; factory floor; mill; workshop; workshop building;
鋼架廠房 steel frame mill building;
工廠廠房 industrial building;
建廠房 construct the factory buildings;
[廠風] factory atmosphere;
[廠規] factory rules;
[廠礦] factories and mines;
廠礦企業 factory and mining enterprises;
[廠紀] factory discipline;
[廠商] firm; manufacturer;
廠商名稱 trade name of the factory;
廠商牌號 name of the firm;
廠商信息 manufacturer information;
廠商行為理論 theory of firm behaviour;
[廠史] factory history;
[廠長] factory director; factory manager;
廠長負責制 factory director responsibility system;
[廠址] site of a factory;
選廠址 choose a site for building a factory;
[廠主] factory owner;
[廠子] factory; mill;

兵工廠 arsenal;
玻璃廠 glassworks;
出廠 leave the factory;
船廠 shipyard;
工廠 factory; mill; plant; works;
建廠 start a factory;
酒廠 brewery; distillery; winery;
麵粉廠 flour mill;
釀酒廠 brewery; winery;
啤酒廠 brewery;
紗廠 cotton mill;
水泥廠 cement plant;
糖廠 sugar refinery;
五金廠 hardware factory;
下廠 go to the factory;
修理廠 repair factory;
藥廠 pharmaceutical factory;
製片場 studio;
磚廠 brickyard;

chang
【氅】 garment;
[氅衣] (1) coat; outer garment; (2) costume of a Daoist priest;

大氅 cloak; overcoat;

chang⁴
chang
【倡】 advocate; initiate; introduce; lead;
[倡導] advocate; initiate; lead;
倡導改革 advocate reforms;
倡導者 exponent; prime mover; promoter;
~ 太陽能倡導者 promoter of solar energy;
[倡亂] head a riot;
[倡始] advocate the creation of; invent;
[倡首] initiate; propose;
[倡言] initiate; propose;
[倡議] first to propose; initiate;
倡議書 initial written proposal;
提出倡議 advocate a proposal;
響應倡議 respond to a proposal;

提倡 advocate; encourage; recommend;
首倡 initiate; start;

chang

【鬯】 (1) sacrificial spirits; (2) same as 暢;
[鬯酒] sacrificial spirits;

chang

【唱】 (1) chant; sing; (2) call; crow; cry;
[唱段] aria;
主要唱段 main arias;
[唱歌] sing a song;
唱歌跳舞 singing and dancing;
唱歌自娛 amuse oneself in singing;
到甚麼山，唱甚麼歌 sail when you are on the sea and settle when you are on the land; sing different songs on different mountains;
齊聲唱歌 sing a song in unison;
[唱和] (1) one singing a song and the others joining in the chorus; (2) one person writing a poem to which one or more people reply;
此唱彼和 when one starts singing, another joins in;
千人唱萬人和 many lead the singing and many more join in; many respond;
一唱百和 meet sth with general approval; one leads, and the rest follow; one person proposes sth and a hundred others respond; when one starts singing, all the others join in;
一唱一和 chime in with each other; echo each other; in perfect harmony; join in chorus; one echoes the other; sing a duet with sb; sing in chorus with sb; sing to each other's tune;
有唱有和 echo each other;
[唱機] gramophone; phonograph; player;
電唱機 radio gramophone;
激光唱機 compact disc; compact disc player;
喇叭式唱機 acoustic gramophone;
三速唱機 triple-speed gramophone;
[唱盤] turntable;
唱盤藝術家 turntablist;
[唱片] gramophone record; record;
唱片分類學 discography;
唱片合同 recording contract;
唱片合約 record deal;
唱片排名榜 hit parade;
唱片騎師 deejay; disc jockey;
唱片製造商 disc manufacturer;
白金唱片 platinum;
~一張白金唱片 a platinum disc;
一張唱片 a record;
[唱詩班] choir;
唱詩班指揮 choirmaster;
[唱戲] act in an opera;
唱戲的喝彩—自吹自擂 actors cheering — self-glorification;
[唱針] reproducing stylus; stylus;
寶石唱針 sapphire stylus;
橢圓形唱針 elliptical stylus;
密紋唱針 microgroove stylus;
雙徑向唱針 bi-radial stylus;

伴唱 vocal accompaniment;
重唱 ensemble of two or more singers, each singing one part;
酬唱 respond;
大聲唱 sing out;
獨唱 sing a solo;
對唱 sing in antiphonal style;
高唱 (1) sing loudly; (2) call out loudly for;
歌唱 (1) sing; (2) sing in praise;
跟着一起唱 sing along;
合唱 chorus; sing in chorus;
絕唱 the peak of poetic perfection;
領唱 lead a chorus;
輪唱 sing a round;
賣唱 sing for a living;
齊唱 sing in unison;
清唱 sing opera arias without making-up and acting;
演唱 sing in a performance;
一起唱 sing together;
吟唱 chant; sing;
詠唱 chant;

chang

【悵】 disappointed; dissatisfied; frustrated; sorry;
[悵悵] disappointed; upset;
悵悵不樂 disconsolate; feel dissatisfied; feeling gloomy; heavy-hearted; in low spirits;
[悵恨] melancholy and resentful;
[悵然] disappointed; upset;
悵然而返 come away disappointed; return sorrowfully home;
悵然若失 become lost in a deep reverie; feel lost; in a despondent mood;
悵然於懷 feel dissatisfied in the bosom;

[悵惘] distracted; listless;

悁悵 disappointed; sad; sorrowful;
惆悵 disconsolate; melancholy;

chang
【暢】 (1) smooth; unimpeded; (2) free; uninhibited; (3) expanding; long; (4) a surname;

[暢達] fluent; smooth;

[暢快] carefree; free from inhibitions;
心裏暢快 have ease of mind;

[暢舒] express freely and fully;
暢舒己見 air one's view fully; assert without any restraint; express one's views freely; speak one's mind;

[暢所] freely;
暢所欲為 do exactly as the mind dictates; do whatever one wants;
暢所欲言 air one's views freely; express one's opinions freely; express oneself with zest and gusto; have one's say; pour out all that one wishes to say; say exactly as the mind dictates; say freely what one thinks without reserve; say one's say; say one's piece; say out one's say; speak one's mind freely; speak out freely; speak without any inhibitions; talk to one's heart's content;
要求暢所欲言 demand freedom to express oneself fully;

[暢談] have a delightful talk; speak glowingly of sb or sth; talk freely; talk freely and to one's heart's content;
暢談見解 air one's views fully; state one's opinion freely;
暢談無阻 there is no impediment to speaking freely;
暢談友誼 recall old friendship heartily;
互相暢談 open out to each other;
聚會暢談 meet for a good talk;

[暢通] unblocked; unimpeded;
暢通無阻 clear of traffic;
~ 道路暢通無阻 the roads are clear of traffic;
交通暢通 (1) easily accessible; (2) clear of traffic; (3) have a good transport and communication network;

[暢想] give free rein to one's imagination; give the reins to one's thoughts; pamper imagination;

[暢銷] bestseller; command a ready sale; command a good sale; enjoy a huge circulation; find a ready market; go like hot cakes; go off like hot cakes; have a good sale; have a ready market; have a ready sale; in good demand; in great demand; in great request; meet with a good sale; meet with a ready sale; sell like hot cakes; sell well; well-received;
暢銷國內外 enjoy a good market both at home and abroad; sell well both at home and abroad;
暢銷國外 sell well on foreign markets;
暢銷貨 commodities in short supply; goods in great demand; marketable products; products with a good market;
暢銷全國 sell well throughout the country;
暢銷世界 sell well all over the world;
暢銷書 bestseller;
暢銷小說 novel that sells well;
不暢銷 have a poor sale; sell poorly;
產品暢銷 create a big demand for the product;
貨物暢銷 goods are in good demand;

[暢行無阻] advance freely; can run unblocked in both directions; go off without a hitch; pass unimpeded;

[暢敘] chat cheerfully;
暢敘衷腸 pour out one's heart;

[暢飲] drink one's fill; drink to one's heart's content;
開懷暢飲 drink to one's heart's content;
邀月暢飲 drink with the moon as one's company;

[暢遊] (1) have a good swim; (2) enjoy a sightseeing tour;
暢遊各地 enjoy a sightseeing tour to many places;

充暢 richly expressive;
酣暢 (1) merry and lively; (2) sound sleep;
和暢 gentle and pleasant;
歡暢 thoroughly delighted;
寬暢 cheerful; free from worry;
流暢 easy and smooth;
明暢 lucid and smooth;
伸暢 generous with one's money;

舒暢 (1) comfortable; (2) leisurely;
順暢 smooth; unhindered;
通暢 unobstructed;
曉暢 have a good command of;

chang
【韔】 (1) wrapper or case for a bow; (2) pull an arrow;

chao¹
chao
【抄】 (1) copy; transcribe; (2) lift; plagiarize; (3) make a raid upon; search and confiscate; (4) go off with; walk off with; (5) take a shortcut; (6) fold one's arms; (7) grab; take up;
[抄本] copy; handwritten copy; transcript;
手抄本 (1) handwritten copy; manuscript; (2) codex;
[抄查] make a raid;
抄查賭場 make a raid on a gambling den;
[抄道] (1) take a shortcut; (2) shortcut;
[抄肥] block goods and take them away; profit reaping; reap profit in business; waylay;
[抄獲] ferret sth out; search and seize;
[抄家] search sb's house and confiscate one's property;
[抄件] copy; duplicate;
[抄錄] copy; make a copy;
[抄身] search sb;
[抄送] make a copy for; send a duplicate to;
[抄襲] crib; plagiarize;
抄襲行為 act of plagiarism;
抄襲者 plagiarist;
東抄西襲 plagiarize from different sources;
東襲西抄 plagiarize from different sources;
[抄寫] copy; transcribe;
抄寫錯誤 errors in transcription;
抄寫稿件 make a fair copy of the manuscript;
抄寫員 copyist; scribe;
[抄用] plagiarize;

包抄 envelop; outflank;
查抄 make an inventory of a criminal's property and confiscate it;
傳小抄 cheat in the examination;
兜抄 close in from the rear and both flanks; envelop; round up;
罰抄 assign copying out a passage as punitive homework;
史抄 extracts from history;
摘抄 (1) extract; make extracts; take passages; (2) excerpts; extracts;
照抄 copy verbatim;

chao
【弨】 bow;

chao
【超】 (1) exceed; overtake; surpass; (2) extra-; super-; (3) go beyond; transcend; (4) fly across; jump over; leap over;
[超薄型] superslim;
[超產] overfulfil a production target;
鼓勵超產 encourage overfulfilment of the production target;
[超常] above the average; superior;
超常兒童 prodigy;
[超車] overtake; overtaking;
試圖超車 try to cut in;
不要超車 do not overtake;
不准超車 no overtaking;
[超出] exceed; go beyond; overstep;
超出範圍 beyond the pale; out of the pale;
超出權限 out of bounds;
超出預算 exceed the estimate;
[超導] superconductivity;
超導存儲器 superconducting memory; superconductivity memory;
超導電纜 superconducting wire;
超導計算機 superconducting computer;
超導體 superconductor;
超導元件 superconducting component;
超導元素 superconducting element;
[超度] release souls from purgatory;
超度眾生 bring poor sinners to regeneration; save mankind from the sea of misery;
[超額] above quota; overfulfil the quota;
超額利潤 excess profit;
超額完成定額 overfulfil the quota;
[超凡] overtop the man's world;
超凡絕俗 free from worldly cares; out of this world; rise above the general run of people; tower above the rest;
超凡入化 overcome all worldly thoughts and enter sainthood;
超凡入聖 be above the common and enter the Holy Land; overcome all worldly

C

thoughts and enter sainthood;
超凡脱俗 free oneself of the concerns of secular life and become accustomed to solitude;

[超付] excess payment;

[超高] superelevate; superelevation;
煙囱超高 chimney superelevation;
曲線超高 curve superelevation;

[超過] exceed; go beyond; outstrip; surpass;
超過極限 overstep the extreme limit;
超過期限 exceed the time limit;
超過權限 exceed one's competence;
超過世界先進水平 surpass the advanced world level;
超過限度 go beyond the limit;
超過預料 exceed one's expectations;
超過正常限度 overstep the normal limit;

[超級] super;
超級大國 superpower;
超級富豪 zillionaire;
超級市場 supermarket;
~大型超級市場 hypermarket;

[超假] overstay one's leave;

[超絕] extraordinary; superb; unique;

[超齡] exceed the age; overage;

[超賣] oversell;

[超期] exceed the time limit;

[超前] lead; outstrip;

[超群] head and shoulders above all others; pre-eminent; surpassing all others;
超群出眾 cut a conspicuous figure; rise above the herd;
超群絕倫 far above the ordinary; far surpassing one's fellows; outshine all others; unequalled by contemporaries;
超倫逸群 rise above the herd; stand out from the crowd;
力大超群 excel others in strength;
技藝超群 distinguished for one's superb skill;
武功超群 one's military arts excel all;
武藝超群 excel all others in terms of strength; extremely skillful in martial arts;
智力超群 tower above the rest in height of intellect;

[超然] aloof; detached;
超然絕俗 stand aloof from the crowd;
超然世事 hold aloof from the affairs of human life;
超然態度 aloof attitude;
超然物外 above worldly considerations; hold aloof from the world;

[超人] (1) out of the common run;
(2) superhuman;
超人的記憶力 exceptionally good memory;
超人的努力 superhuman effort;
超人的忍耐力 uncommon powers of endurance;
超人的智慧 superhuman wisdom;
體力超人 superhuman in physical strength;
智力超人 superhuman in mental faculties;

[超聲] ultrasonic;
超聲波 ultrasonic wave;
~超聲波發射器 ultrasound transmitting transducer;
~超聲波發生器 ultrasonic generator;
~超聲波接收器 ultrasonic receiver;
~超聲波探傷器 ultrasonic flaw detector; ultrasonic reflectoscope;
~超聲波洗滌 ultrasonic cleaning;
超聲凝聚 ultrasonic coagulation;
超聲手術 ultrasonic operation;
超聲透鏡 ultrasonic lens;
超聲物理學 ultrasonic physics;
超聲顯微鏡 ultrasonic microscope;
超聲學 ultrasonics;
超聲醫學 ultrasound medicine;
超聲振蕩器 ultrasonicator;
超聲治療 ultrasonic therapy;
超聲鑽孔 ultrasonic drilling;

[超生] excuse from death; spare life;

[超時] overrun;
超時一小時 overrun by one hour;

[超市] supermarket;
一家超市 a supermarket;
折價超市 cut-price supermarket;

[超速] exceed the speed limit; overspeed;
超速擋 overdrive;
超速行駛 be driven above the speed limit;
駕車超速 speeding;

[超脱] (1) original; unconventional;
(2) detached; stand aloof; transcend worldliness;
超脱塵世 above worldly considerations; be detached from the world; stand aloof from this mortal life;

[超越] leapfrog; overreach; overstep; surpass; transcend;
超越極限 exceed the maximum;

超越障碍 surmount an obstacle;
超越職權 go beyond one's terms of reference; overstep one's authority;

［超載］ overladen; overload;
超載翻譯 overloaded translation;
超載的公共汽車 overladen buses;

［超支］ cost overrun; overspend;

［超知］ gifted and talented; unusually intelligent;

［超重］ (1) overload; (2) overweight;
略微超重 slightly overweight;
行李超重 excess luggage;

趕超 catch up with and overtake;
高超 excellent; remarkable; superb;

chao

【鈔】 (1) copy; transcribe; (2) banknote;

［鈔錄］ copy; transcribe;

［鈔票］ banknote;
鈔票掛帥 money in command;
發行鈔票 issue banknotes;
一疊鈔票 a sheaf of bills; a wad of banknotes;
一沓鈔票 a wad of notes;
一張鈔票 a bill; a note;
印鈔票 print paper money;

會鈔 pay a bill;
假鈔 funny money;
美鈔 greenback;
冥鈔 nether banknotes;
錢鈔 money;
偽鈔 counterfeit banknote;
現鈔 hard cash;
綃鈔 hair kerchief;

chao

【焯】 scald;

chao²

chao

【晁】 (1) an ancient form of 朝;
(2) a surname;

chao

【巢】 (1) bird's nest; living quarter in a tree;
(2) den; hideout; haunt;
(3) a surname;

［巢菜］ common vetch;
大巢菜 common vetch;

［巢居］ live in trees;

［巢穴］ den; hideout; lair; nest;

愛巢 love nest;
匪巢 bandits' lair;
蜂巢 beehive; honeycomb; nest;
老巢 den; lair; nest;
卵巢 oophoron;
蟎巢 acarodomatium;
鳥巢 bird's nest;
傾巢 sally forth; swarm out in full strength; turn out in full force;
蟻巢 ant nest;
賊巢 thieves' den;

chao

【朝】 (1) court; government; royal court;
(2) dynasty; (3) emperor's reign;
(4) have an audience with a king; make a pilgrimage to; (5) face towards;

［朝拜］ pay religious homage to; pay respects to; worship;

［朝臣］ courtier;

［朝代］ dynasty;
朝代更迭 change of dynasties;
改朝換代 change dynasties; change of government; change regimes; dynastic change; replace the old dynasty by a new one; substitute a new regime for the old;

［朝服］ court dress;

［朝貢］ pay tribute; present tribute;

［朝海］ face the sea;
房間朝海 the room faces the sea;

［朝見］ have an audience with;
朝見帝王 go to court; proceed to court;
進宮朝見 be presented at court;

［朝覲］ (1) have an audience with; (2) go on a pilgrimage;

［朝聖］ pilgrimage;

［朝天］ face the sky;
朝天放槍 fire shots in the air;
兩腳朝天 lie with one's legs pointing up;
兩眼朝了天 drop dead; kick the bucket;

［朝廷］ (1) royal court; (2) imperial government;
朝廷命官 official appointed by the imperial court; official of the government;

［朝陽］ in the morning;
鳴鳳朝陽 phoenix crying in the morning;

［朝野］ the government and the public;

C

朝野人士 public figures in and out of the government;
朝野上下 the court above and the masses below;
朝野之間 between the court and the populace;
［朝政］ affairs of the state;
皇朝 dynasty;
臨朝 hold a court audience;
上朝 go to the imperial court;
視朝 give audience; hold a court;
退朝 retire from the court;
王朝 dynasty; imperial court;
在朝 hold office at court;

chao
【嘲】 deride; jeer; mock; ridicule; scoff; sneer;
［嘲諷］ jibe; sneer at; taunt;
大聲嘲諷 cry in sarcasm;
冷嘲熱諷 cynical; disparage sb by innuendoes; give sb a dig; gloat and jeer; make sarcastic remarks against sb; rant and rave; scornful words and jeering smiles; taunt and jeer at sb;
［嘲罵］ jeer and abuse;
連嘲帶罵 taunt and jeer;
［嘲謔］ make fun of; poke fun at;
［嘲弄］ mock; poke fun at;
嘲弄宗教 scoff at religion;
忍受嘲弄 bear ridicule;
［嘲戲］ make fun of; poke fun at;
［嘲笑］ banter; chaff; deride; flout at; hold sb up to mockery; hold sth up to mockery; jeer; jeer at; jest; jibe; joke; laugh at; make a butt of; make a mockery of; make a mock of sb; mock; poke fun at; rally; ridicule; scoff at; scorn; sneer at; twist;
嘲笑宗教 sneer at religion;
暗暗嘲笑 laugh in one's beard;
百般嘲笑 heap scorn and abuse on sb;
撇嘴嘲笑 sneer with a curl of one's lips;
不怕別人嘲笑 fear no ridicule;
當面嘲笑 laugh in sb's face;
受人嘲笑 in the pillory;
引起嘲笑 arouse ridicule; bring ridicule; call forth derision; draw ridicule upon oneself; incur ridicule;
遭到嘲笑 be sneered at; incur ridicule;
譏嘲 ridicule; satirize;
解嘲 try to cover up sth ridiculed by others; try to explain things away when ridiculed;
自我解嘲 console oneself with soothing remarks; defend oneself against ridicule; explain oneself against ridicule;

chao
【潮】 (1) tide; (2) current; tide; upsurge; (3) damp; moist; (4) fashion; fashionable; (5) bad; inferior; low-grade; poor; (6) awkward; incompetent; unskilful;
［潮呼呼］ clammy; damp; dank;
［潮流］ tide; trend;
潮流受害人 fashion victim;
反潮流 countertrend; swim against the current; swim against the tide;
［潮氣］ humidity; moisture in the air;
［潮濕］ damp; humid; moist;
潮濕空氣 damp air;
潮濕天氣 wet weather;
空氣潮濕 there is dampness in the air;
氣候潮濕 have a humid climate; the climate is moist;
［潮時］ time of tide;
［潮水］ tidewater;
［潮退］ the tide goes out;
［潮汐］ morning and evening tides; tide;
潮汐會説 tidal hypothesis;
潮汐力 tidal force;
潮汐摩擦 tidal friction;
潮汐預報 tide prediction;
地方潮汐 local tide;
地區潮汐 diffusional tide;
利用潮汐 make use of the tides;
氣壓潮汐 barometric tide;
暗潮 (1) undercurrent; (2) secret contention;
赤潮 red tide;
大潮 spring tide;
大氣潮 atmospheric tide;
低潮 (1) ebb; low tide; (2) trough;
發潮 become damp; get damp;
返潮 become damp; get damp;
防潮 damp-proof;
風潮 agitation; unrest;
高潮 (1) flood; high tide; high water; (2) climax; culmination; upsurge;
工潮 labour disturbances; strike movement;
海潮 sea tide;
寒潮 cold wave; polar outbreak;

紅潮 (1) blush; flush; (2) red tide;
回潮 get damp again;
來潮 tides rise; wares rise;
浪潮 bandwagon; tide; wave;
陸潮 earth tide;
落潮 ebb;
怒潮 (1) angry tide; raging tide; (2) tidal bore;
熱潮 upsurge;
受潮 be affected with damp;
思潮 (1) trends of thought; (2) thoughts;
退潮 the tide ebbs away; the tide falls; the tide is out;
小潮 neap tide;
心潮 surge of emotions;
學潮 campus upheaval; student strike;
漲潮 (of tide) rise; incoming tide; the tide is in;

chao³
chao

【吵】 (1) make a noise; (2) quarrel; squabble; wrangle; (3) annoy; disturb;

[吵吵] make a noise; talk rapidly at the same time; twitter;
吵吵鬧鬧 create noisy disturbance; cut up; hurly-burly; in a bustle; kick up a cloud of dust; make a noise; raise a great hue and cry; raise a racket; raise jack;
吵吵嚷嚷 boisterous; clamorous; hullabaloo; in an uproar; make a noise; raise a hue and cry;

[吵架] have a row; quarrel; wrangle;
愛吵架 have a worm in one's tongue;
~ 愛吵架的人 scrapper;

[吵鬧] (1) hoo-ha; kerfuffle; pick up a row; wrangle; (2) din; hubbub;
吵鬧不休 kick up a great deal of fuss about; make a great noise;
吵鬧聲 clamour;
大聲吵鬧 make a great wrangle and quarrel;
鬼吵鬼鬧 noisy;
為小事吵鬧 kick up a dust over a small matter; make a fuss about trifles;

[吵嚷] clamour; make a racket; shout in confusion;

[吵人] disturb others by noise;

[吵嘴] bicker; quarrel;
避免吵嘴 abstain from quarrelling;

廝吵 make a fuss together;
爭吵 quarrel; squabble;

chao

【炒】 (1) fry; saute; stir-fry; (2) buy and resell at a profit; buy low and sell high; speculate; (3) select; (4) dismiss; fire; sack;

[炒菜] (1) stir-fry; (2) fried dish; (3) a dish cooked to order;

[炒飯] (1) fry rice; (2) fried rice;

[炒匯] arbitrage; buy and resell foreign currency at a profit;

[炒買] buy at a low price;
炒買炒賣 resell at a profit; speculate;

[炒賣] sell at a high profit;

[炒米] parched rice;

[炒麵] fried noodles;

[炒友] profiteer; speculator;

chao⁴
chao

【鈔】 a pronunciation of 鈔;

che¹
che

【車】 (1) vehicle; (2) bus; (3) wheeled machine or instrument; (4) machine; (5) lathe; turn;

[車蟲] bicycle fanatic;

[車窗] window of a car;
搖上車窗 roll a window up;
搖下車窗 roll a window down;

[車牀] lathe;
光軸車牀 axle finishing lathe;
台式車牀 bench lathe;
自動車牀 automatic lathe;
自動高速車牀 automatic high-speed lathe;

[車倒兒] second-hand vehicle dealer;

[車道] carriageway; cart track;
對向車道 divided highway; dual carriageway;
私人車道 driveway;

[車燈] car light;

[車頂] car roof;
車頂行李架 luggage rack; roof rack;
活動車頂 sunroof;

[車隊] cavalcade; fleet; motorcade; motor pool;

[車費] fare;

[車匪路霸] highwayman; road bandit;

［車禍］ traffic accident;
減少車禍 cut down traffic accidents;
死於車禍 die in a traffic accident;
一次車禍 a car accident;
遭到車禍 meet an automobile accident;
造成車禍 cause a traffic accident;
［車技］ artistic cycling;
［車間］ factory floor; smithy; workshop;
車間工人 factory floor;
車間設備 workshop appliance;
金工車間 machine shop;
鍛銅車間 copper smithy;
總鍛工車間 main smithy;
［車距］ distance between vehicles;
安全車距 safe distance; safe stopping distance;
~保持安全車距 remain at a safe distance from the car in front;
［車庫］ garage;
車庫自動門 automatic garage door;
地下車庫 underground garage;
雙車車庫 two-car garage;
［車輛］ car; vehicle;
車輛保養 vehicle maintenance;
車輛禁止 no vehicular access;
車輛通行 vehicular traffic;
被盜車輛 stolen vehicle;
機動車輛 automotive vehicle;
氣墊車輛 hovercraft;
重型車輛 heavy vehicle;
裝甲車輛 armoured vehicle;
［車流］ stream of traffic; stream of vehicles;
避開車流 avoid the traffic; miss the traffic;
減少車流 cut traffic; reduce traffic;
［車馬］ carts and horses;
弊車駑馬 a decrepit cart drawn by a lean horse;
車水馬龍 a heavy flow of traffic; an endless stream of carriages and horses; an incessant stream of horses and carriages; be crowded with people and vehicles; be thronged with visitors; heavy traffic;
千車萬馬 a thousand coaches and ten thousand horses;
素車白馬 plain cars and white horses — in a funeral procession;
鮮車怒馬 lead a luxurious life; new carriage driven by fat horses — lavish service;
香車寶馬 fragrant carriage and precious horses — the beautiful carriage of women;
［車門］ car door; door;
車門把手 door handle;
副駕駛車門 passenger door;
後車門 rear door;
汽車車門 car door;
鎖上車門 lock the door;
［車迷］ petrolhead;
［車牌］ licence plate; number plate; registration plate;
［車票］ ticket;
車票簿 carnet;
［車身］ bodywork; coachwork;
車身維修廠 body shop;
［車胎］ tyre;
車胎放砲 a tyre blows out;
補車胎 mend a puncture;
［車頭燈］ headlamp; headlight;
［車位］ car park; parking lot;
有蓋車位 covered car park;
［車廂］ carriage; coach; compartment;
餐臥車廂 hotel car;
火車車廂 train carriage;
列車長車廂 guard's van;
臥鋪車廂 sleeping car;
一節車廂 a coach; a railway carriage; a train;
［車削］ turning;
車削性能 turning ability;
仿形車削 copy turning;
輪廓車削 contour turning;
外圓車削 cylindrical turning;
無屑車削 chipless turning;
［車載斗量］ enough to fill carts and be measured by the dou—common and numerous;
［車站］ depot; station; stop;
到達車站 arrive at the station; get to the station;
［車照］ car licence; vehicle licence;
［車軸］ axle;
［車組］ vehicle crew;
［車子］ small vehicle;
老車子 jalopy;

安車 cart with seats in it;
扒車 cramp; jump onto a slow-moving vehicle;
班車 regular bus service;

包車 chartered bus;
殯車 hearse;
兵車 chariot;
彩車 float in a parade;
餐車 dining car; restaurant car;
鏟車 forklift;
超車 overtake a car on the road;
乘車 ride a car;
出車 (1) dispatch a vehicle; (2) be out driving a vehicle;
搭車 (1) get a lift; give sb a lift; hitchhike; (2) do sth at the same time; do sth along with someone else;
打車 by taxi; hail a cab; take a taxi;
大車 (1) cart; (2) engine driver;
單車 bicycle; bike;
倒車 back a car; back up a car; back up a locomotive; move a vehicle backward; reverse; reverse a car;
電車 (1) streetcar; tram; (2) trolley; trolleybus;
電機車 electrical locomotive;
吊車 crane; hoist;
吊裝車 sling cart;
斗車 tram; trolley;
獨輪車 wheelbarrow;
堵車 traffic congestion;
發車 outgoing train;
翻車 (1) turn over; (2) fail in doing sth;
紡車 spinning wheel;
飛車 drive at a high speed;
飛行車 aerocar;
糞車 dung cart; night cart; night-soil cart;
風車 windmill;
改裝車 hot rod;
趕車 drive a car;
高卡車 go-cart; go-kart;
公車 (1) public vehicle; (2) public bus; (3) a surname;
掛車 trailer;
罐車 tank car; tank truck;
過山車 roller coaster;
候車 wait for a bus; wait for a train; wait for a vehicle;
花車 festooned vehicle;
滑車 block; pulley; tackle;
換車 (1) change trains or buses; (2) change a vehicle;
黃包車 rickshaw;
灰漿車 grout cart;
火車 choo-choo; rail; train;
貨車 (1) freight train; goods train; (2) goods van; (3) lorry; truck;
機動車 motor-driven vehicle;
機車 engine; locomotive;
吉普車 bantam; jeep;
擠車 jam into a bus;
加車 extra buses; extra trains;
駕車 drive a vehicle;
絞車 reel cart; winch; windlass;
轎車 (1) carriage; (2) bus; car; limousine;
揭背車 hatchback;
劫車 carjack; carjacking;
警車 cop car; jam sandwich; Paddy's taxi; police car;
柩車 hearse;
舊車 old car; second-hand car; used car;
救護車 ambulance;
軍車 military vehicle;
卡車 lorry; truck;
開車 (1) set the machine going; set the machine in motion; start the machine; (2) drive a car;
客車 (1) passenger train; (2) bus;
垃圾車 dustcart; garbage truck;
拉車 pull a cart;
纜車 cable car;
列車 train;
快車 express bus; express train;
礦車 mine car; tram;
老爺車 veteran car;
靈車 hearse;
轆車 pole dolly;
驢車 donkey cart;
馬車 (1) carriage; (2) cart;
慢車 slow train;
煤車 coal car;
煤水車 tender;
摩托車 motor bicycle; motorcycle;
末班車 last bus; last train;
牛車 ox cart;
跑車 sports car; racing car;
礮車 gun carriage;
棚車 (1) box wagon; (2) covered truck;
碰碰車 bumper car; dodgem; dodgem car; Scooter car;
篷車 (1) box wagon; (2) covered truck;
平板車 flat-bottomed cart;
騎車 ride a bicycle;
汽車 automobile; motor vehicle;
前車 previous cart;
寢車 sleeper; sleeping car;
輕車 (1) light, swift chariot; (2) light cart;
囚車 prison van; prisoner's van;
驅車 drive to a place;
麴車 wine cart;

C

人力車 rickshaw;
繞線車 cable winding cart;
戎車 chariot; war vehicle;
塞車 be held up in traffic; traffic jam;
灑水車 sprinkler; watering car; watering cart;
賽車 (1) automobile race; cycle racing; motorcycle race; race car; (2) racing bicycle; racing vehicle;
三輪車 pedicab; tricycle;
掃路車 road sweeper;
剎車 brake a car;
煞車 brake;
扇車 winnowing machine;
上車 get in the car; get into a car; get into a vehicle; get on a train;
上行車 the up train;
蜃車 hearse;
試車 put a machine to a trial run; test drive;
手車 handcart; wheelbarrow;
手推車 handcart; wheelbarrow;
守車 caboose; guard's van;
水車 waterwheel;
睡車 sleeper; sleeping car;
四輪車 mule cart;
鐵甲車 armoured car; armoured vehicle;
停車 (1) stop a car; (2) stop the machine;
通車 open to traffic;
頭班車 first bus; first train;
拖車 trailer;
套車 harness an animal to a cart;
晚車 night train;
卧車 (1) sleeping carriage; (2) car; limousine; sedan;
洗車 give the car a washing;
校車 school bus;
卸車 unload sth from a vehicle;
下車 (1) get off; get out of a car; (2) take up new office;
消防車 fire engine; fire truck;
小車 cart;
校車 school bus;
卸車 unload sth from a vehicle;
行李車 baggage car; luggage van;
宣傳車 propaganda car;
雪車 sledge;
壓路車 road-roller; roller;
夜車 (1) night train; (2) work deep into the night;
一車 a load of;
驛車 courier cart;
油泵車 hydrant cart;
郵車 mail van; postal van;
輶車 light carriage;
遊覽車 tourist coach;
暈車 carsickness;
運泥車 mover;
運牛車 cattle truck;
早車 morning train;
閘車 brake;
戰車 chariot;
舟車 (1) vessels and vehicles; (2) journey;
駐車 parking;
專車 special car; special train;
轉車 transfer to another vehicle;
裝車 load a truck;
裝甲車 armoured car;
撞車 collide; traffic collision;
輜車 (1) covered wagon; (2) baggage cart;
自行車 bicycle;
坐車 ride a car;

che³
che

【尺】 foot rule; rule;

［尺寸］ dimension; measurement; size;
安裝尺寸 assembly dimensions;
邊界尺寸 boundary dimensions;
表觀尺寸 apparent size;
尺短寸長 every person has weak and strong points;
窗戶的尺寸 size of the window;
寸楮尺素 an inch of mulberry bark and a foot of white silk — a letter;
得寸進尺 give him an inch and he will take an ell; give him an inch and he will take a mile; much will have more; reach out for a yard after taking an inch; the more one gets, the more one wants;
進寸退尺 advance by an inch but retreat by a foot — lose much more than what one gets; gain little and lose much;
可調尺寸 adjustable dimension;
口徑尺寸 calibre size;
零號尺寸 size zero;
沒尺寸 rash and thoughtless;
實際尺寸 actual dimension; actuate size;
性能尺寸 characteristic dimension;
柱尺寸 column dimension;

［尺地］ small piece of land;
尺地寸土 tiny pieces of land;

［尺牘］ correspondence; letters;

［尺度］ foot measure; scale; measurement;

［尺幅］ (1) dimension; (2) small painting;

［尺碼］ (1) dimension; (2) measure; size;
尺碼多少 what is the size;

標尺 staff gauge; surveyor's rod;
丁字尺 T-square;
工尺 a traditional Chinese musical scale;
公尺 metre (m.);
矩尺 carpenter's square;
捲尺 band tape; measuring tape;
碼尺 yard measure;
軟尺 measuring tape;
三尺 three feet;
繩尺 criterion; law; rule; standard;
算尺 slide rule;
英尺 foot;
摺尺 folding ruler;
咫尺 very close;

che

【扯】 (1) pull; (2) tear; (3) buy; (4) chat; gossip;
［扯淡］ talk nonsense;
［扯掉］ tear off;
［扯謊］ lie; tell a lie;
扯謊騙錢 tell lies to swindle money out of people;
［扯了］ a lot; excessive; plenty; too much;
［扯皮］ argue back and forth; dispute over trifles; wrangle;
避免扯皮 avoid disputing over trifles;
互相扯皮 pass the buck to each other; shift responsibility;
［扯平］ make even;
［扯碎］ tear apart; tear asunder;
［扯下］ tear down;

胡扯 boloney; bosh; drivel; fiddlesticks; flimflam; hokum; rubbish; talk nonsense; talk rubbish; waffle about; wag one's tongue;
拉扯 (1) drag; pull; (2) bring up; (3) drag in; implicate; (4) chat; (5) borrow; drum up; (6) contract for;
攀扯 implicate; involve;
牽扯 implicate; involve;
瞎扯 chat aimlessly; speak nonsense; talk recklessly; talk rubbish; tell lies; waffle;
閒扯 chat; engage in chit-chat; shoot the breeze; shoot the bull;

che

【撦】 tear;
［撦破］ tear open;

che⁴

che

【坼】 (1) crack; (2) chap; rip open; tear;
［坼裂］ crack; split open;

che

【掣】 (1) pull; tug; (2) draw; (3) hinder; (4) snatch away;
［掣電］ as fast as lightning; in the twinkling of an eye;
［掣肘］ handicap; hold sb back by the elbow; impede;

牽掣 (1) hold up; impede; (2) check; pin down;

che

【徹】 penetrating; thorough;
［徹底］ through; thoroughgoing;
徹底崩潰 crash about one's ears; fall about one's ears; have had it;
徹底地 from top to bottom; good and proper; well and truly;
徹底根究 make a thorough investigation of; sift sth to the bottom;
徹底解決問題 settle a matter once and for all;
徹底決裂 make a complete break with;
徹底失敗 lay an egg;
徹底完蛋 collapse totally;
［徹骨］ to the bone;
徹骨寒冷 bitterly cold; piercingly cold;
寒風徹骨 the bitter wind chills one to the bone;
寒冷徹骨 bitterly cold; piercingly cold;
寒氣徹骨 cold strikes into one's marrow;
［徹悟］ come to a complete awakening;
大徹大悟 a great awakening; greatly discerning and apprehending;
［徹夜］ all night; all through the night;
徹夜不眠 lie awake all night; sit up all night;
徹夜燈火通明 the lights are ablaze all through the night;
徹夜工作 work all night; work through the night;
徹夜輾轉 toss about all night;

澄徹 transparently clear and limpid;
洞徹 understand thoroughly;
貫徹 carry out; implement; put into effect;
清徹 clear; crystal-clear; limpid;
通徹 understand thoroughly;

C

透徹 penetrating; thorough;
響徹 resound through; reverberate through;
瑩徹 clear and transparent;

che

【撤】 (1) remove; take away; (2) evacuate; withdraw;
[撤傍] break off a friendship; break up with sb;
[撤兵] withdraw troops;
吹號撤兵 sound a retreat;
擊鼓撤兵 the drums beat a retreat;
[撤併] abolish and merge;
[撤除] dismantle; remove;
撤除軍事設施 dismantle military installations;
[撤出] evacuate; withdraw;
撤出戰鬥 leave the field;
主動撤出 withdraw on one's own initiative;
[撤防] withdraw a garrison; withdraw from a defended position;
[撤換] dismiss and replace; recall; replace;
[撤回] recall; withdraw;
撤回成命 countermand an order; revoke an order; remove a previous order;
撤回大使 recall the ambassador home;
撤回代表 recall a representative;
撤回控告 make a retraction of a charge;
撤回命令 withdraw a command;
撤回批評 withdraw one's criticism;
撤回聲明 retract a statement;
撤回訴訟 revoke a court action; withdraw a claim;
撤回提議 withdraw an offer;
撤回邀請 withdraw an invitation;
[撤火] (1) dampen the enthusiasm of; discourage; pour cold water on; (2) extinguish a fire in a stove; stop heating;
[撤離] decamp; evacuate; leave; pull-out; withdraw from;
撤離要塞 evacuate a fortress;
[撤退] pull out; withdraw;
安全撤退 make good one's retreat;
抱恨撤退 retire full of resentment;
被迫撤退 be forced to retreat;
倉促撤退 beat a hurried retreat; make a hasty retreat;
匆匆撤退 retreat hastily;
[撤銷] cancel; rescind; revoke;
撤銷處分 annul a penalty; rescind a penalty;
撤銷法令 cancel instructions; countermand an order;
撤銷合同 cancel a contract; rescind a contract;
撤銷決議 annul a decision;
撤銷控訴 call back an accusation;
撤銷判決 recall a judgement;
撤銷上訴 abandon one's appeal;
撤銷專利 repeal a patent;
[撤職] be dismissed from office; be removed from one's office; dismiss sb from his post; remove sb from office;
撤職查辦 discharge sb from his office and prosecute him; dismiss sb and have him prosecuted; dismiss sb from his post pending further investigations; remove sb from his office and punish him;
撤職處分 be dismissed as a punishment;
被撤職 be removed from office;
[撤走] withdraw;

裁撤 dissolve an organization;

che

【澈】 (1) completely; thoroughly; (2) clear water; (3) understand;
[澈查] investigate thoroughly;
[澈底] thorough;
[澈悟] realize completely; understand thoroughly;

明澈 bright and clear; transparent;
清澈 clear; limpid;

chen¹

chen

【抻】 (1) lengthen and extenuate; (2) drag out;
[抻長] lengthen;

chen

【郴】 (1) the name of a county in Hunan; (2) a surname;

chen

【琛】 jewellry; treasures; valuables;

chen

【嗔】 (1) angry; displeased; (2) be annoyed

with sb;
[嗔怪] blame; rebuke;
[嗔怒] get angry;
[嗔色] angry look; sullen look;
微露嗔色 look somewhat displeased;

chen
【瞋】 (1) anger; angry; (2) complain; grudge; (3) open one's eyes;
[瞋目而視] glare; glare at sb in anger; stare angrily; stare at sb angrily;

chen2
chen
【臣】 (1) subject; (2) a polite address for "I"; (3) minister; official; statesman;
[臣服] acknowledge allegiance to; submit oneself to the rule of;
[臣民] subjects of a kingdom;
[臣子] officials in imperial China;
亂臣賊子 rebellious ministers and villains; rebels and traitors; traitors and villains; treacherous ministers and traitors;

柄臣 minister with full authority; powerful minister;
波臣 (1) denizens of water; (2) victims of drowning;
朝臣 courtier;
大臣 minister of a monarchy;
貳臣 turncoat official;
功臣 person who has rendered an outstanding service;
奸臣 treacherous court official;
藎臣 faithful official; loyal official;
君臣 king and ministers;
權臣 powerful minister;
人臣 minister;
侍臣 courtier;
使臣 envoy; representative of a country abroad;
守臣 king's guardians;
樞臣 chief courtier; premier; prime minister;
褻臣 intimate courtier;
幸臣 favourite at court;
朝臣 court;
忠臣 official loyal to his sovereign;
重臣 important official of the emperor;
逐臣 banished subject; vassal in exile;
柱臣 important ministers of a nation;
宗臣 (1) clan officer; (2) a respected minister of state;

chen
【忱】 sincere;
[忱辭] words from the bottom of one's heart;

寸忱 one's sincerity;
熱忱 enthusiasm and devotion;
謝忱 gratitude; thankfulness;
之忱 sincerity;
忠忱 faithfulness; loyalty;

chen
【沉】 (1) sink; submerge; (2) be addicted to; indulge; (3) keep down; lower; (4) deep; profound; (5) heavy;
[沉博絕麗] profound in substance and beautiful in style;
[沉沉] (1) heavy; (2) deep;
沉沉入睡 sink into a deep sleep;
暮靄沉沉 dusk is falling;
暮氣沉沉 apathetic;
死氣沉沉 apathetic; dead atmosphere; dead calm; deadly still; dull and despondent; hopeless and gloomy; lifeless; lifeless air; like a log; lose one's vitality; spiritless; without animation; without vitality;
[沉船] shipwreck;
[沉甸甸] heavy;
心裏沉甸甸 cloud one's heart;
[沉澱] precipitate; sedimentation;
沉澱法 precipitating method; precipitation;
沉澱器 precipitator;
~棒屏沉澱器 rod-curtain precipitator;
~熱沉澱器 thermal precipitator;
~砂濾沉澱器 permutit precipitator;
沉澱物 precipitate;
~化學沉澱物 chemical precipitates;
~晶粒沉澱物 grain precipitate;
~紫狀沉澱物 flocky precipitate;
單級沉澱 simple sedimentation;
蛋白沉澱 albumen precipitation;
二次沉澱 secondary sedimentation;
共沉澱 co-precipitation;
膠體沉澱 colloidal precipitation;
界面沉澱 interface precipitate;
聯結沉澱 coherent precipitate;
慢沉降沉澱 slow-settling precipitate;
吸附沉澱 adsorption precipitation;
載體沉澱 carrier precipitation;
[沉寂] (1) quiet; still; (2) no news;

C

沉寂無聞 unknown to the public;
打破沉寂 break the silence;
歸於沉寂 silence settles down;
死一般的沉寂 as silent as the grave;
一片沉寂 a blank silence; an oppressive silence;

[沉積] deposit; sediment; sedimentation;
沉積計 sedimentometer;
沉積速率 sedimentation rate;
沉積物 sediment;
~活性沉積物 active sediment;
~生物沉積物 biogenic sediment;
~自生沉積物 authigenic sediment;
沉積學 sedimentology;
沉積岩 sedimentary rock;
帶狀沉積 banded sediment;
淺海沉積 epicontinental sedimentation;
宇宙沉積 cosmogenous sediment;

[沉降] sedimentation;
沉降器 subsider;
~間歇式沉降器 intermittent subsider;
差示沉降 differential sedimentation;

[沉浸] immerse; steep;
沉浸於水中 be immersed in water; be steeped in water;

[沉靜] calm; quiet; serene;
神色沉靜 wear a serene look;
心情沉靜 in a placid mood;

[沉悶] (1) depressive; oppressive; (2) depressed; in low spirits;
沉悶的 dreary;
~沉悶的冬日 a dreary winter's day;
覺得沉悶 feel stuffy;
冗長沉悶 ponderous;
天氣沉悶 the weather is gloomy;
心情沉悶 feel depressed;
性格沉悶 not frank and open;

[沉迷] indulge; wallow;
沉迷不悟 indulge in error; refuse to come to one's senses;
沉迷不醒 (1) be deeply addicted; be infatuated with; (2) in a coma;
沉迷於幻想 indulge in pleasing illusion;
沉迷於女色 give oneself to female charm;
沉迷於奢侈 wallow in luxury;
沉迷於享樂 indulge in luxury;

[沉緬] be given to; wallow in;
沉緬酒色 be given to heavy drinking and sensual pleasures; indulge in wine and women; wallow in voluptuousness;
沉緬於幻想 indulge in dreams;
沉緬於回憶 indulge in reminiscences;
沉緬於酒 indulge in wine;
沉緬於酒色 overindulge oneself in wine and women;

[沉默] (1) reticent; taciturn; (2) silent;
沉默不言 keep silent;
沉默不語 as dumb as a fish; as dumb as an ox; as dumb as an oyster;
沉默的大多數 the silent majority;
沉默寡言 a person of few words; a regular oyster; a reticent person; not to be given to much speech; of few words; quiet and taciturn in disposition; scanty of words; sparingly of words;
保持沉默 bite the tongue; hush; keep a still tongue in one's head; keep mute; keep silent; mute; preserve silence; remain silent;
打破沉默 break the ice; break the silence;

[沉沒] sink;
觸礁沉沒 strike a rock and sink;

[沉溺於] abandon oneself to; be given over to; give oneself over to; indulge in; wallow;
沉溺於賭博 indulge in gambling;
沉溺於喝酒 indulge in wine;
沉溺於酒色 give oneself over to debauchery;
沉溺於享樂 be surfeited with pleasure;
沉溺於酗酒 give oneself over to drinking;

[沉實] (1) firm; powerful; weighty; (2) solid; steady;

[沉睡] be fast asleep; be sunk in sleep;
沉睡的火山 slumbering volcano;
沉睡夢鄉 sound asleep;

[沉思] be buried in thought; be lost in thought; contemplative; deliberating; in a brown study; meditate; meditative; pensive; ponder; reflective;
沉思半晌 be wrapped in thought;
沉思出神 be lost in contemplation;
沉思冥想 be in a brown study; cudgel one's brains; think long and hard;
沉思默想 in a brown study; meditate in silence; rumination;
沉思凝想 think deeply; think profoundly;
獨坐沉思 sit alone in meditation;
昏昏沉思 be deeply wrapped in one's thoughts of longing;
陷入沉思 be absorbed in contemplation; fall in reverie; sink into deep thought;

在沉思 be immersed in thought; deep in thought; in deep reverie;
皺眉沉思 wrinkle one's brows in concentration;

[沉肅] deep; grave; serious;

[沉痛] (1) deep feeling of grief or remorse; (2) bitter; deeply felt;
沉痛哀悼 mourn over sb's death with deep grief;
沉痛悼念 mourn with deep grief;
沉痛的教訓 bitter lesson;
表情沉痛 have a grievous expression on one's face;
心情沉痛 be deeply grieved;

[沉陷] cave in; landing; sink; subsidence;
地面沉陷 ground subsidence;
礦穴沉陷 mining subsidence;
射束沉陷 beam landing;
完全沉陷 full subsidence;
中心沉陷 centre landing;
最大沉陷 maximum subsidence;

[沉香] agalloch eaglewood; agarwood;
沉香樹 agallochum;

[沉箱] caisson;
沉箱套 caisson-set;
打入式沉箱 driven caisson;
防波場沉箱 breakwater caisson;
浮式沉箱 float caisson;
開口沉箱 open caisson;
木沉箱 wooden caisson;
氣壓沉箱 pneumatic caisson;
橋墩沉箱 ridge-pier caisson;
箱形沉箱 box caisson;
遙控沉箱 remote-controlled caisson;
鑽孔沉箱 drilled caisson;

[沉吟] meditate in silence; mutter to oneself; unable to make up one's mind;
沉吟半晌 meditate in perfect silence for a while; remain in deep thought for some time;
沉吟不決 hesitate; irresolute; unable to make up one's mind; undecided;
沉吟良久 mutter to oneself for a long while; ponder long in silence;
沉吟未決 hesitate; irresolute; undecided;

[沉魚落雁] dazzling beauty;

[沉鬱] depressed; gloomy;

[沉冤] gross injustice; unrighted wrong;
沉冤大白 the grievous is cleared;
沉冤莫白 a deep grievance that cannot be cleared; grievous wrongs that cannot be redressed; have no chance to right the wrong one has suffered; suffer grievous wrongs;
洗雪沉冤 wipe out a deep grievance;

[沉滯] move sluggishly; stagnate;

[沉重] (1) heavy; (2) critical serious;
沉重打擊 hard hit;
沉重的包袱 a millstone round one's neck;
沉重的擔子 heavy burden;
沉重的東西 dead weight;
沉重的壓力 extraordinary pressure;
沉重的債務 heavy debt;
沉重損失 grave losses;
病情沉重 critically ill; seriously ill;
腳步沉重 leaden feet;
心情沉重 heavy heart;

[沉住氣] hold one's horses; keep calm; keep cool; steady;
沉不住氣 blow one's cool; can hardly hold back; cannot remain calm; lose one's cool;
沉得住氣 can retain one's composure; not get excited;

[沉着] calm; composed; cool-headed; steady;
沉着病 thesaurosis;
~石棉沉着病 amianthosis;
沉着的 phlegmatic;
沉着果敢 iron nerves; nerves of iron; steel nerves;
沉着機靈 composed and smart; cool and clear;
沉着堅強 keep a stiff upper lip;
沉着冷靜 cool and composed; have a cool nerve;
沉着行事 act with composure;
沉着應變 meet the danger calmly;
沉着應試 come up for one's exam with composure;
沉着應戰 accept a challenge composedly; meet the attack calmly;
沉着勇敢 brave and steady;
沉着鎮定 presence of mind;
沉着鎮靜 steady and calm;
保持沉着 maintain composure;

[沉舟] sink the boats;
破斧沉舟 break the cauldrons and sink the boats; burn one's boats; burn the bridges behind one; cast the die; cross the Rubicon; cut off all means of retreat; go for broke; with set teeth;
沉舟破釜 break the cauldrons and sink

boats; burn one's boat;

[沉醉] become intoxicated; get drunk;

暗沉沉 (of sky) dark;
低沉 (1) overcast; lowering; (2) (of voice) low and deep; (3) downcast; low-spirited;
耳沉 hard of hearing;
浮沉 now sink, now emerge; unstable or uncertain;
黑沉沉 pitch-black; pitch-dark;
昏沉 (1) murky; (2) befuddled; dazed;
擊沉 bombard and sink; send a ship to the bottom;
浸沉 immerse; steep;
深沉 (1) dark; deep; (2) dull; (3) conceal one's real feelings;
下沉 (1) sink; submerge; subside; (2) cave in; sink; subside;
消沉 dejected; depressed; down-hearted;
血沉 erythrocyte sedimentation rate;
陰沉 cloudy; gloomy; overcast; somber;
鬱沉沉 dejected; depressed; despondent; low-spirited;

chen
【辰】 (1) early morning; (2) fortune; (3) heavenly body; (4) time;

[辰時] period of the day from 7 a.m. to 9 a.m.;
[辰星] (1) morning star; (2) Mercury;

誕辰 birthday;
忌辰 anniversary of a parent's death;
良辰 fortunate hour;
生辰 birthday;
壽辰 birthday of an elderly person;
時辰 one of the 12 two-hour periods;
星辰 stars;

chen
【宸】 (1) abode of the emperor; (2) large mansion;

[宸遊] the emperor on tour;

chen
【晨】 morning;

[晨靄] morning haze;
[晨炊] breakfast;
[晨風] morning breeze;
晨風夕月 the morning breeze and the evening moon;
[晨光] dawn; the light of the early morning sun;
晨光熹微 the dim light of dawn; the first faint rays of dawn; the first rays of the morning sun;
[晨昏] morning and night;
晨昏定省 attend to one's parents' comfort on getting up and going to bed; salute one's parents in the morning and at night; see one's parents to bed and greet them in the morning;
[晨練] morning callisthenics;
[晨曦] first rays of the morning sun;
晨曦初露 dawn breaks;
晨曦暉映 the morning sunlight is dazzling;
[晨星] (1) stars at dawn; (2) morning star;
寥若晨星 as few as stars at dawn; as rare as morning stars; as sparse as the morning stars; few and far between; scanty; sparse; very few;
[晨衣] dressing gown; morning gown;
[晨運] morning callisthenics; morning exercises;

凌晨 before dawn; in the small hours;
侵晨 approaching daybreak; early morning; towards dawn;
清晨 early morning;
霜晨 frosty morning;
嚮晨 toward dawn;
蕭晨 autumn morning;
迎晨 at dawn; at daybreak;
早晨 early morning;

chen
【陳】 (1) lay; lay out; place; put on display; (2) explain; state; (3) old; stale;

[陳報] explain; report;
[陳兵] deploy troops; mass troops;
陳兵百萬 deploy a million troops;
陳兵邊境 mass troops along the border;
[陳陳相因] follow a set routine; follow the beaten track; keep on doing the same thing over and over again; move in a rut; persist in the old ways without any change; stay in the same old groove;
[陳詞] (1) cliché; (2) explain; state;
陳詞濫調 banality; canned phrases; cliche; hackneyed and stereotyped expressions; hackneyed tune; lousy cliches; often-repeated trash; old hat; old staff; old tune; outworn and empty words; platitude; shibboleth; shop-

soiled tune; stock argument; tag; time-worn expression; trite phrases; truism; worn-out allegations;
賦詩陳詞 write poems describing occasions;
慷慨陳詞 present one's views with excitement;
冒昧陳詞 venture an opinion;

[陳風舊習] old customs and backward habits; outdated customs and habits;

[陳腐] old and decayed; outworn; stale;
陳腐搭配 stock collocation;
陳腐的 banal; cornball;
陳腐論點 moldy opinion;
陳腐隱喻 cliché metaphor;
陳腐之見 outworn opinion;
觀念陳腐 musty ideas;

[陳規] outmoded conventions; stereotyped;
陳規舊例 old rules and regulations;
陳規舊套 outdated conventions and customs;
陳規陋習 bad customs and habits; outmoded conventions and bad customs; outworn customs and bad habits;

[陳貨] old stock; shop-soiled goods;

[陳跡] thing of the past;

[陳見] outmoded ideas;

[陳酒] mellow wine; old wine;
陳酒味醇，老友情深 old friends and old wine are the best;

[陳舊] obsolete; outmoded; have come out of the Ark; old-fashioned; out-of-date;
陳舊的 antiquated; corny;
陳舊話題 weary chestnut;
陳舊過時的東西 museum piece;

[陳列] display; exhibit; set out;
陳列櫃 display case; showcase;
陳列品 exhibits;

[陳年] of many years' standing;
陳年老酒 aged wine;
世遠年陳 distant ages and olden years;

[陳皮梅] preserved prune;

[陳設] (1) display; set out; (2) furnishings;
陳設雅致 tastefully furnished;

[陳述] state;
陳述動詞 indicative verb;
陳述句 declarative sentence;
~基本陳述句 basic statement;
~間接陳述句 indirect statement;
陳述利害 explain the advantages and disadvantages;
陳述事實 state the fact;
陳述性言語行為 indicative speech act;
陳述疑問句 declarative question;
陳述語氣 indicative mood;
粗略的陳述 rough statement;
大膽的陳述 bold statement;
公正的陳述 fair and unbiased statement;
關鍵的陳述 key statement;
含蓄陳述 understatement;
客觀的陳述 objective statement;
口頭陳述 oral presentation;
籠統的陳述 general statement;
坦率的陳述 frank statement;
虛假的陳述 false statement;
真實的陳述 true statement;
做出陳述 give a statement;

[陳説] explain; state;
陳説利害 explain the advantages and disadvantages;

[陳訴] complaint; recite; state;

稟陳 report to a superior;
電陳 state or explain in a telegram;
敷陳 elaborate; state or explain in detail;
臚陳 narrate in detail; state;
縷陳 state in detail;
面陳 tell sb in person;
鋪陳 describe at great length; narrate in detail;
肆陳 exhibit;
條陳 state sth one by one;
新陳 the new and the old;
茵陳 capillary artemisia;
直陳 describe truthfully; state frankly;
自陳 state personally;

chen

【塵】 (1) dirt; dust; (2) trace; trail; (3) this world; ways of the world; (4) sensual pleasures; vice; (5) (in Daoism) lifetime;

[塵埃] dirt; dust;
大氣塵埃 atmosphere dust;
化為塵埃 crumble to dust; turn to dust and ashes;
氣載塵埃 airborne dust;
星際塵埃 interstellar dust;

[塵世] this mortal life; this world;
塵世之外 out of the dusty world;
超脱塵世 above worldly considerations; be detached from the world; stand aloof from this mortal life;

棄絕塵世 forsake human society;

[塵土] dust;

塵土飛揚 clouds of dust flying up; dust rises high in the air;

塵土濛濛 rain of ashes; storm of ashes;

拂去塵土 flick off dust;

蒙滿塵土 be covered with dust;

揚起塵土 raise a cloud of dust;

一層塵土 a film of dust;

一股塵土 a spurt of earth;

[塵霧] dust fog; fume;

毒霧迷塵 poisonous fume and blinding dust;

鹼性塵霧 alkali fume;

氧化鋅塵霧 zinc oxide fume;

[塵囂] hubbub; uproar;

承塵 a net over one's seat;

除塵 dust; dust removal;

防塵 dust-proof;

粉塵 powder-like waste;

風塵 (1) travel fatigue; (2) hardships or uncertainties in an unstable society; (3) chaos caused by war;

拂塵 fly whisk;

浮塵 floating dust; surface dust;

核塵 nuclear fallout;

紅塵 human society; material world;

後塵 footsteps;

灰塵 ash; dirt; dust;

礦塵 mine dust;

煤塵 coal dust;

前塵 (1) (in Buddhism) previous impure conditions; (2) what has happened in the past;

沙塵 fine sand flying up in the air;

洗塵 give a dinner of welcome to a visitor from afar;

纖塵 fine dust;

囂塵 (1) noise and dust; (2) the noisy, dusty world;

星塵 stardust;

血塵 blood dust; hemoconia;

煙塵 smoke and dust in the air; the smoke of battle;

岩塵 rock dust;

揚塵 raise dust;

音塵 traces; whereabouts;

原子塵 fallout;

chen

【蔯】 a variety of artemisia;

chen

【諶】 (1) candid; honest; sincere; (2) a surname;

chen⁴

chen

【趁】 (1) avail oneself of; catch up; take advantage of; (2) while; (3) possess; rich in; well-off;

[趁便] at one's convenience; when it is convenient;

[趁風] while the wind blows;

趁風起帆 hoist one's sail while the wind blows; hoist one's sail while the wind is fair; hoist one's sail by taking advantage of the wind; set sail when the wind is fair;

趁風揚土 stir up trouble;

[趁機] seize the chance; take advantage of the occasion;

趁機搗亂 seize the opportunity to make trouble; take advantage of the occasion to create a disturbance;

趁機發難 seize the chance to take action; take advantage of the opportunity to launch an attack;

趁機下手 take the good chance and begin...;

趁機造謠 seize the opportunity to spread rumours;

[趁空] avail oneself of leisure time; use one's spare time;

[趁錢] a large quantity of money;

[趁勢] take advantage of a favourable situation;

[趁心] be gratified; find sth satisfactory;

趁心如意 give one the most satisfaction; have as one wishes;

事不趁心 things look blue;

[趁虛而入] avail oneself of the opportunity to get in;

[趁早] as early as possible; before it is too late;

chen

【稱】 fit; match; suit;

[稱身] fit;

[稱心] be gratified; find sth satisfactory;

稱心如意 after one's heart; be well satisfied in accord with one's wishes; desirable; to one's heart's desire; to one's liking; to one's taste; very

gratifying and satisfactory;
不稱心 come amiss;
事事稱心 everything falls in with one's wishes;
[稱職] come up to the scratch; competent; fill a post with credit; worth one's salt;
稱職能幹 competent and efficient;
不稱職 be not fit for the task; incompetent; unfit for the job;
很稱職 fill one's position worthily;
十分稱職 highly competent;

對稱 symmetric;
相稱 match; suit;

chen
【齓】 (1) have one's milk teeth replaced with permanent teeth; (2) children;

chen
【櫬】 (1) coffin; (2) tung tree;

chen
【襯】 (1) line; place sth underneath; (2) liner; lining; (3) set off;
[襯底] substrate;
共襯底 common substrate;
互補襯底 complementary substrate;
有源襯底 active substrate;
[襯裙] petticoat; underskirt;
[襯墊] liner; lining;
尿布襯墊 nappy liner;
吸聲襯墊 acoustic lining;
[襯褲] pants; underpants;
短襯褲 short underwear;
~女用短襯褲 knickers;
男用襯褲 underpants;
女用襯褲 knickers; panties;
[襯裏] lining;
石棉襯裏 asbestos lining;
[襯料] gusset;
[襯衫] blouse; overshirt; shirt;
長袖襯衫 long-sleeved blouse;
短袖襯衫 short-sleeved blouse;
女襯衫 blouse;
脱下襯衫 take off one's shirt;
一件襯衫 a blouse;
[襯托] serve as a foil to; set off;
[襯頁] flyleaf;
[襯衣] shirt; underclothes;
[襯映] serve as a foil; set off;

背襯 back lining;
反襯 serve as a foil to; set off by contrast;
轂襯 hub plate;
爐襯 lining;
陪襯 foil; serve as a foil to; set off by contrast; set off;
映襯 relieve against; set off;
軸襯 axle bush;

chen
【讖】 (1) omen; prophecy; (2) books about omens;
[讖語] prophetic remark made casually which later comes true;
竟成讖語 this proves to be an ill omen;

圖讖 book of prophecy;

cheng1

cheng
【掌】 prop; support;

cheng
【琤】 tinkling sound;
[琤琤] (1) jangling of jade; (2) tangling of string; (3) gurgling of flowing water;
[琤瑽] tinkling of jade pendants;

cheng
【稱】 (1) call; (2) name; (3) say; state; (4) commend; praise; (5) weigh;
[稱霸] dominate; seek hegemony;
稱霸世界 dominate the world; lord it over the world;
稱霸一方 play the tyrant in a locality;
稱霸一時 hold sway for a period of time; reign supreme for a period of time;
[稱便] find sth a great convenience;
[稱病] plead illness;
稱病謝客 feign sickness and decline to receive guests;
[稱道] commend; speak approvingly of;
無足稱道 nothing commendable; nothing praiseworthy;
值得稱道 praiseworthy; worthy of praise;
[稱得起] deserve to be called; worthy of the name of;
[稱號] appellation; designation; name; title;
[稱呼] (1) address; call; (2) form of address;
稱呼系統 address system;
稱呼形式 address form; form of address;
稱呼語 address; address form;
[稱快] express one's gratification;

稱快一時 in accord with one's cheerful mind for a moment;
拍手稱快 clap and cheer; clap one's hands for joy;
~無不拍手稱快 there is no one who would not clap his hands with satisfaction;
拍掌稱快 clap one's hands in applause; clap one's hands with satisfaction;

[稱奇] express one's surprise;
暗暗稱奇 secretly admire sth; silently admire sth;

[稱觴祝嘏] pledge and implore blessings—offer birthday congratulations to the aged;

[稱賞] praise and extol; speak highly of;

[稱勢] potential;
反對稱勢 antisymmetric potential;

[稱説] name sth when speaking;

[稱頌] eulogize; extol; praise;

[稱歎] acclaim; praise;

[稱王] declare oneself king;
南面稱王 act like a king; ascend the throne;

[稱謂] appellation; title;
稱謂句 nominal sentence;

[稱羡] envy; express one's admiration;
稱羡不已 express profuse admiration;

[稱謝] express one's thanks; thank;

[稱雄] hold sway over a region; rule the roost;
稱雄一方 take forcible possession of a territory;
稱雄一時 hold sway for a period of time;
割據稱雄 break away from central authority and exercise local power;

[稱許] commendation; praise;

[稱引] quote;

[稱譽] acclaim; praise; sing the praises of;
極口稱譽 loud in one's praise of; praise lavishly; utter one's approval;
交口稱譽 be held in public esteem; be praised by one and all; praise with one voice; vie in singing the praise of sb; unanimously praise;

[稱讚] acclaim; commend; commendation; compliment; pat sb on the back; praise; slap sb on the back;
表示稱讚 express one's praise;
大加稱讚 heap praises on; shower praise on;
獲得稱讚 receive a commendation;
絕口稱讚 chant the praises of;
連聲稱讚 rain praises on;
拍手稱讚 clap one's hands in praise of;
受到稱讚 be showered with applause; receive praises;
贏得稱讚 earn praises;
值得稱讚 deserve applause; merit credit; worthy of praise;
~值得稱讚的 commendable;

愛稱 diminutive; pet name; term of endearment;
別稱 alternatively known as; an alternative name; another name; known also by the name of; otherwise known as;
代稱 antonomasia;
泛稱 be generally called; be generally termed; be generally known as; general term;
公稱 nominal;
供稱 confess; own up;
詭稱 falsely allege; pretend;
號稱 (1) be known as; (2) claim to be;
簡稱 abbreviation; shorter form;
見稱 famous for; well known for;
美稱 good name; laudatory title;
名稱 appellation; designation; name;
全稱 full name; name in full;
人稱 person;
聲稱 assert; claim; declare; proclaim;
通稱 be generally called or termed; be generally known as; general term;
俗稱 (1) commonly called ; (2) secular name of a monk;
宣稱 assert; claim; declare; profess;
職稱 title of a professional post;
著稱 celebrated; famous;
自稱 call oneself; claim to be;
尊稱 address sb respectfully;

cheng
【撐】 (1) prop up; support; (2) push or move with a pole; (3) hold out; keep up; maintain; (4) open; unfurl; (5) eat too much; fill up; make a pig of oneself; (6) ask for it; look for trouble;

[撐持] prop up; shore up; sustain;
撐持局面 shore up a shaky situation;

[撐竿] pole-vaulting;
撐竿跳 pole vault;

[撐腳] arm brace;
撐腳架 kickstand;

[撐開] open; prop up;

撐開大門 prop the gate open;
撐開帆 unfurl sails;
撐開傘 open an umbrella; unfurl an umbrella;
[撐條] stay;
鍋爐撐條 boiler stays;
角鐵撐條 angle iron stay;
[撐腰] back up; bolster up; support;
撐腰打氣 bolster and pep up; bolster and support; in an effort to back up;
有人撐腰 be backed by sb; have sb at one's back;

支撐 (1) prop up; support; (2) brace; strut;

cheng
【瞠】 stare;
[瞠乎其後] a far cry from; be left far behind; consider oneself inferior to sb; fail to secure a leading place; far behind, without any hope of catching up; feel one is not sb's equal; lag far behind; unable to catch up;
[瞠目而視] stare at with wide eyes;
[瞠視] stare at;

cheng
【赬】 red;
[赬尾] toils of a gentleman;

cheng
【檉】 tamarisk;
[檉柳] tamarisk;

cheng
【蟶】 razor clam; razor shell;
[蟶乾] dried razor clam;
[蟶子] razor clam; razor shell;

竹蟶 razor clam; razor shell;

cheng
【鐺】 (1) cauldron-like vessel with legs; heater; (2) pan for frying; shallow pot;

餅鐺 baking pan;

cheng²
cheng
【丞】 (1) aid; assist; (2) assistant to an official; deputy of an official;
[丞相] prime minister;

縣丞 county magistrate's assistant;

cheng
【成】 (1) accomplish; succeed; (2) become; turn into; (3) achievements; results; (4) fully developed; fully grown; (5) established; ready-made; (6) in considerable numbers or amounts; (7) all right; good; OK; (8) able; capable; (9) one tenth;
[成敗] success or failure;
成敗不計 not take success or failure into consideration;
成敗得失 success and failure, gain and loss;
成敗利頓 success or failure; successful or not;
成敗論人 judge a person by his success or failure;
成敗難卜 success or failure cannot be predicted;
成敗未卜 between cup and lip;
成敗興衰 wins and failures, thriving and declining;
成敗由天 chance the consequence; heaven disposes the success or failure;
成敗與共 share sb's successes and failures;
成敗在此一舉 make-or-break; sink or swim; success or failure hinges on this once action;
不管成敗 sink or swim;
不計成敗 irrespective of success or failure;
不在乎成敗 indifferent about success or failure;
成者為王，敗者為寇 losers are always in the wrong; nothing succeeds like success;
功敗垂成 a slip between the cup and the lip; abandon work near completion; between the cup and the lip; fail at the last moment; fail in a great undertaking on the verge of success; fail in the end; fail on the verge of success; fail only when nearing success; fall through when success is in sight; flop just before the finish; suffer defeat when victory is within reach;
決定成敗的 make-or-break;
事關成敗 it concerns the success or failure of the matter;

C

無論成敗 whether this will be successful or not;
坐觀成敗 a mere onlooker; sit and watch the results of; sit on the fence; wait to see what will come of sb's venture; wait to see which side wins; watch a struggle with detachment;

[成本] cost; prime cost;
成本導向 cost-oriented;
~成本導向型投資 cost-oriented investment;
成本法 law of cost;
成本分析 cost analysis;
成本估算 costing;
成本核算 cost accounting;
成本計算 costing;
~標準成本計算 standard costing;
~差異成本計算 differential costing;
~產品成本計算 product costing;
~相關成本計算 relevant costing;
~終端成本計算 terminal costing;
成本價 cost price;
~成本價格 cost price;
成本系統審計 cost system accounting;
成本效益 cost-benefit; cost-effectiveness;
~成本效益分析 cost-effectiveness analysis;
成本意識 cost-consciousness;
成本賬 cost-book;
~成本賬戶 cost account;
按成本 at cost;
變動成本 change cost;
重置成本 replacement cost;
純成本 flat cost;
單位成本 unit cost;
~平均單位成本 average unit cost;
分批成本 batch cost;
分攤成本 apportioned cost;
記賬成本 accounting cost;
間接成本 indirect cost;
降低成本 cut down the cost; lower costs;
經常成本 normal cost;
經營成本 operating cost;
全部成本 absorption cost;
人工成本 cost of labour;
生產成本 production cost;
實際成本 actual cost;
收回成本 cost-recovering;
特別成本 abnormal cost;
提高成本 raise the cost;
原始成本 aboriginal cost;
原料成本 material cost;
運銷成本 cost of marketing;
再加工成本 reprocessing cost;
直接成本 direct cost;
總成本 total cost;
主要成本 prime cost;
裝配成本 assembly cost;

[成才] talent formation;
成才動力 talent-formation force;
成才目標 talent-formation target;
~成才目標選擇 choice of talent-formation target;
不成才 good-for-nothing; worthless;

[成層岩] stratified rock;

[成仇] become enemies;
為好成仇 kill with kindness;

[成對] pair off; pair up;

[成分] component; ingredient; part;
成分詞 constituent word;
成分定義 componential definition;
成分分析 componential analysis;
~成分分析法 componential analysis;
成分介詞 preposition of ingredient;
成分結構 constituent structure;
~成分結構規則 constituent structure rules;
~成分結構語法 constituent structure grammar;
必要成分 necessary part of sth;
詞匯成分 lexical constituent;
次要成分 secondary part;
~句子次要成分 secondary parts of a sentence;
獨立成分 independent element; independent part;
~句子獨立成分 independent parts of a sentence;
輔助性成分 supplementary component;
附帶成分 incidental component;
基本成分 essential component;
基礎成分 base component;
假設成分 dummy element;
句子成分 sentence element;
絕對成分 absolute element;
區別性成分 distinctive component;
有害成分 pernicious ingredient;
主要成分 chief ingredient; main ingredient;
~句子主要成分 main parts of a sentence;

[成風] become a common practice; become the order of the day;
蔚然成風 become a common practice

which prevails throughout;
賄賂成風 bribery has become a common practice;
習沿成風 usages arise from constant practice;

[成佛] become a Buddha;
立地成佛 become a Buddha on the spot;

[成服] ready-made clothing;

[成功] get on in life; succeed;
成功的要素 factors of success;
成功立業 make one's fortune; success in life;
成功率 success rate;
成功人士 people who make it; successful people;
成功少碰壁多 meet with more setbacks than success;
成功在望 see daylight;
成功之道 avenue to success; gateway to success;
成功之路 the way to success;
巴望成功 long after success;
必然成功 sure to succeed;
不成功 failed; unsuccessful;
~不成功的演員 failed actor;
~不成功的作家 failed writer;
大獲成功 howling success; roaring success; set the world alight; set the world on fire; take somewhere by storm;
非常成功 remarkably successful;
功到事成 constant effort yields sure success; with time and patience the leaf of the mulberry becomes satin;
渴望成功 desirous of success;
獲得成功 achieve success; attain success; meet with success;
力求成功 earnest for success; strive toward achievement;
偶然成功 chance success;
取得成功 achieve success; have success; meet with success;
確保成功 assure success;
事事成功 successful in everything;
意外的成功 undreamed-of success; unhoped-for success;
祇許成功，不許失敗 succeed without fail;

[成規] established practice; groove; rut; set rules;
擺脱成規 lift out of the rut;
打破成規 break away from conventions;
墨守成規 cling to old-fashioned methods; go on in the old groove; go round like a horse in a mill;
違反成規 out of set rules;
無視成規 disregard the set rules;
因襲成規 move in a rut;
尊重成規 respect the rules laid down;
遵守成規 observe the conventionalities;

[成果] achievements; fruits; gains;
成果管理 science and technology results management;
成果獎 science and technology results award;
成果考核法 evaluation of results;
出成果 produce fruit;
鞏固成果 consolidate the gains;
科學成果 scientific fruits;
~高水平科學成果 high-level scientific fruits;
勞動成果 fruit of one's labour;
顯示成果 show the results;
學習成果 learning outcomes;
研究成果 fruit of one's research;
有成果 fruitful;
重大成果 substantial result;
最初成果 first fruits;

[成核] nucleation;
定域成核 localized nucleation;
複成核 multiple nucleation;
晶稜成核 edge nucleation;
異相成核 heterogeneous nucleation;

[成婚] get married;
奉子成婚 shotgun marriage; shotgun wedding;

[成活] survive;
成活率 survival rate;

[成績] achievements; results; success;
成績斐然 achieve splendid results; make brilliant achievements in;
成績公佈牌 results board;
成績評價 performance appraisal;
成績優異 straight A;
成績超著 achieve signal success;
創造好成績 chalk up good results;
公布成績 publish the results;
提高成績 improve results;
優秀成績 excellent results; exceptional results;

[成疾] fall ill;
積勞成疾 break down from constant

overwork; bring on an illness by overwork; fall sick from overwork;
積憂成疾 be broken by care;

[成家] get married; start one's own family; take a wife;
成家立室 get married; start a family; take a wife;
成家立業 get married and start one's career; marry and settle down;
刻苦成家 build up a family by hard work and frugality;
空手成家 build up one's fortune from scratch;

C

[成見] bias; preconceived idea; prejudice;
擺脱成見 disembarrass oneself of preconceptions;
抱有成見 adopt a prejudiced attitude; harbour prejudice; have a prejudice against sth or sb;
個人成見 personal bias;
狃於成見 a slave of preconceived ideas; look through coloured spectacles;
拋棄成見 cast aside a preconceived idea;
死抱成見 be obsessed by a fixed idea;
消除成見 put away all prejudices;
囿於成見 be bound by prejudice;

[成交] clinch a bargain; clinch a deal; close a bargain; conclude a bargain; conclude a transaction; settle a bargain; strike a bargain;
成交額 volume of business; volume of transaction;
握手成交 give one's hand on a bargain; shake hands on the bargain;

[成就] (1) accomplishments; achievements; attainment; success; (2) accomplish; achieve;
成就動機 achievement motivation;
成就感 sense of achievement;
成就傑出 outstanding achievement;
成就年齡 achievement age;
大有成就 come out on top; make good one's running; make quite a success;
東不成，西不就 fail in everything; have nothing completed;
東成西就 prosperous all round; successful in everything;
高不成，低不就 cannot have one's heart's desire but will not accept less; too choosy to succeed; unable to achieve one's heart's desire but unwilling to accept less; unfit for a higher post but unwilling to take a lower one;
輝煌成就 dazzling success;
極有成就 fly high;
~極有成就的人 high-flier; high-flyer;
了不起的成就 real accomplishment;
~是一個很了不起的成就 be quite an accomplishment;
偉大成就 a feat of mythic proportions; great achievement;
外交成就 diplomatic achievement;
學術成就 academic achievement;
藝術成就 artistic achievement;
最高成就 crowning achievement;
卓有成就 rich in accomplishment;

[成例] established customs; precedents;

[成立] (1) establish; found; set up; (2) hold water; tenable;
成立委員會 establish a committee;
成立書院 found a college;

[成龍] (1) form a dragon; (2) become a successful person;
成龍配套 form a dragon assemblage;
望子成龍 have great ambitions for one's child; hold high hopes for one's child; hope one's children will have a bright future; long to see one's child become a successful person;

[成寐] go to sleep;
睡不成寐 unable to sleep;

[成眠] fall asleep; go to sleep;

[成名] become famous; come to fame; make a name for oneself; make one's name;
成名成家 establish one's reputation as an authority;
成名作 work by which one's reputation is first made;
急於成名 anxious for fame;
期望成名 ambitious of distinction; crave for fame;
突然成名 become famous overnight;
一舉成名 achieve instant fame; be vaulted to fame; become famous overnight; bounce into fame; make one's name known at a single attempt; shoot to fame; shoot to prominence; shoot to stardom; spring into fame;
~一舉成名天下知 at one stroke one will be known all over the world;

[成命] order already issued;

[成年] (1) accession to adulthood; adulthood;

come of age; coming of age; grow up; (2) all year round; year after year; year in year out;
成年累月 for months and years; for years on end; year after year and month after month; year in, year out; year in and year out;
成年男人 man of mature age;
成年人 adult; grown-up;
成年在外 away all year;
到達成年 arrive at full age; attain full age; attain years of maturity; reach an adult age;
未成年 immaturity; not yet come to age; under age;
~尚未成年 under age;

[成批] group by group; in batches;
成批處理 batch processing;
成批加工 batch processing;
成批生產 mass production; volume production;

[成品] end product; finished product;
成品糧 processed grain;
半成品 semi-finished articles;
未成品 unfinished work;

[成器] grow up to be a useful person;
玉不琢，不成器 an uncut gem does not sparkle; gems unwrought can do nothing useful; if jade is not polished, it cannot become useful; jade cannot be made into anything without being cut and polished — one cannot become useful without being educated; nurture is above nature; the best horse needs breaking and the aptest child needs teaching; the finest diamond must be cut;

[成親] get married;

[成全] help sb to achieve his/her aim;
一力成全 spare no effort in helping sb to accomplish sth;

[成群] (1) in groups; in large numbers; (2) grouping;
成群而來 come in flocks; come trooping along;
成群結隊 band together; in crowds; in flocks; in groups; in throngs;

[成仁] die for a righteous cause;
成仁取義 die a martyr to a just cause; die for a just cause; die to preserve one's virtue intact; lay down one's life for the country;
殺身成仁 die a martyr to a noble cause; die to achieve virtue; die for a just cause; fulfil justice at the cost of one's own life; sacrifice one's life to preserve one's virtue intact;

[成人] (1) become full-grown; grow up; (2) adult; grown-up;
成人電影 adult film;
成人高等教育 adult higher education;
成人基礎教育 adult basic education;
成人教育 adult education;
成人學校 school for adults;
成人訓練 adult training;
成人之惡 help sb do sth evil;
成人之美 aid in carrying out the good designs of others; aid sb in doing a good deed; bring romance to a happy ending; help others in the completion of a worthy goal; help sb in a good cause; help sb fulfil his/her wish;
成人自學考試 adult self-taught examination;
扶養成人 bring sb up;
長大成人 be grown to adulthood;

[成聲] lose one's voice;
哽不成聲 one's voice fails one;

[成事] accomplish sth; succeed;
成事不足，敗事有餘 never make, but always mar; spoil rather than accomplish things;
酒能成事，也能敗事 matters can be either settled or ruined by wine; wine can spur action, or ruin everything;
助成其事 help to finish a business;

[成熟] maturation; mature; maturity; ripe;
成熟度 maturity;
~食用成熟度 eating maturity;
~適宜成熟度 optimum maturity;
~相對成熟度 relative maturity;
~組分成熟度 compositional maturity;
成熟過程 maturation;
成熟期 final age;
成熟社會 mature society; ripe society;
成熟性 maturity;
~社交成熟性 social maturity;
比較成熟 comparative maturity;
不成熟 immature;
發育成熟 reach full growth;
經濟成熟 economic maturity;
麵團成熟 dough maturity;

完全成熟 full maturity;
未成熟 immature; unripe;
性成熟 sexually mature;
延遲成熟 delayed maturity;

[成套] form a complete set;
成套佈置 complex;
成套課本 complete set of textbooks;
成套教材 teaching materials kit;
成套軟件 software kit;
成套設備 equipment complex;
成套引進 package deal;
成套應用軟件 applications software kit;

[成天] all day long; all the time;

[成為] become; turn into;
成為攻擊目標 at the receiving end; on the receiving end;
成為好朋友 chum up with;
成為話柄 become a subject of talk;
成為話題 become a topic for conversation;
成為泡影 end in naught; vanish like soap bubbles;
成為事實 come true;
成為笑柄 become a laughing stock;

[成文] (1) existing writings; (2) written;
成文法 common law; statute law;

[成像] imaging;
反射成像 catoptric imaging;
聲成像 acoustic imaging;
析射成像 dioptric imaging;

[成效] effects; results;
成效甚少 achieve little; yield poor results;
成效顯著 achieve remarkable success; produce a marked effect;
成效卓著 with distinguished results; with remarkable results;
初見成效 achievement of some initial successes; win initial success;
促進成效 increase effectiveness;
大見成效 achieve marked success;
立見成效 act like a charm; feel the effect immediately; have an immediate effect; produce immediate results;
顯出成效 show effect;
學習成效 learning effectiveness;
卓有成效 fruitful; highly effective; show impressive results; very effective; with outstanding success;

[成心] intentionally; on purpose; with deliberate intent;
成心作對 purposely antagonize sb;

[成形] form; shape; take shape;
爆炸成形 explosive shaping;
乾法成形 dry shaping;
冷滾成形 cold-roll forming;
手工成形 artificial forming;

[成型] forming; take shape;
氣滑成型 air-slip forming;
氣助成型 air-assist forming;
準確成型 accurate forming;

[成性] become sb's second nature; by nature;
掠奪成性 plunderous;
嗜血成性 bloodthirsty by nature;
疏庸成性 dilatory by temperament; given to delay;
貪賭成性 be given to gambling;
習久成性 long practice becomes a second nature;

[成岩] diagenesis;

[成藥] patent medicine;
成藥廣告 advertisements of patent medicine;

[成因] cause of formation; contributing factor; origin;

[成癮] be addicted; get into the habit;
賭博成癮 be addicted to gambling;
喝酒成癮 addict oneself to drinking; be addicted;
吸毒成癮 be addicted to drugs;
吸煙成癮 be addicted to smoking;

[成語] idiom;

[成員] member;
成員國 member country; member state;
創始成員 charter member; founding member;
附屬成員 associate member;
家庭成員 family member; household member; member of a family;
領導成員 leading member;
社會成員 member of society;
委員會成員 member of a committee;
增選為成員 co-opt;
重要成員 leading member;

[成災] cause disaster;
蟲害成災 be infested with insects;
泛濫成災 be flooded;

[成長] grow to maturity; grow up;
成長模式 pattern of development;
成長需要 developmental needs;
~配合成長需要 cater for developmental needs;
成長壯大 grow in strength;
鍛煉成長 be steeled and tempered and

grow up;
健康成長 healthful growth;
逐漸成長 gradually grow up;

[成竹] know what to do;
成竹在胸 have an ace up one's sleeve; have definite ideas in one's mind; have the cards in one's own hands; know what to do in the mind;
胸有成竹 everything is thought out in advance; have a card up one's sleeve; have a well-thought-out plan; know what to do in one's mind;

按成 according to percentage; proportionately;
八成 (1) eighty per cent; eighty percent; (2) most likely; most probably; very likely;
變成 become; change into; change to; come; come off; convert into; develop into; grow; pass into; transform sth into; turn into;
不成 not do;
垂成 approaching success or completion; drawing close to a successful conclusion; in sight; near completion;
促成 facilitate; favour; help to bring about; lead on to; help to materialize;
達成 achieve; conclude; reach; reach an agreement;
分成 divide into; separate into;
告成 announce the completion of sth important;
功成 achieve success;
構成 compose; constitute; make up;
合成 (1) compose; compound; (2) synthesize;
後成 epigenic;
混成 blend together; mix together;
火成 igneous;
加成 addition;
老成 experienced; steady;
禮成 (of a ceremony) end; wind up;
落成 (of a building) be completed;
釀成 breed; lead to;
守成 maintain the achievements of one's predecessors;
速成 run an accelerated educational programme or course;
完成 accomplish; complete; fulfil;
現成 ready-made;
相成 complement each other;
形成 form; take shape;
有成 succeed;
玉成 kindly help secure the success of sth;
圓成 help sb attain his aim;
贊成 agree with; approve of; endorse;
造成 bring about; cause; create;
責成 instruct;
組成 compose; form;

cheng
【呈】 (1) assume; (2) present; submit; (3) memorial; petition;

[呈報] report a matter; submit a report;
呈報上級批準 apply to the high authorities for approval;
[呈遞] present; submit;
呈遞報告 send in a report;
呈遞名片 present one's card; send in one's card;
呈遞申請書 send in one's application to;
[呈請] apply;
[呈文] (1) document submitted to a superior; (2) memorial; petition;
[呈現] appear; emerge; present;
呈現病態 assume a morbid character; take on morbid forms;
呈現眼前 come into view; rise to view;
呈現一片繁榮 have an air of prosperity;
[呈獻] respectfully present;

辭呈 resignation;
面呈 deliver sth personally;
簽呈 petition;

cheng
【承】 (1) bear; carry; hold; (2) contract to do a job; undertake; (3) be granted a favour; indebted; (4) carry on; continue;

[承辦] agree to do sth; undertake;
承辦婚禮 cater for a wedding;
承辦商 surveyor;
承辦者 promoter;
[承包] contract;
承包工程 construction contract; contract a project;
承包基數 base quota of a contract;
承包經營 contract management;
~承包經營權 right of management under contract;
~承包經營責任制 responsibility system of management under contract;
承包期 contract period;
承包企業 contract with an enterprise;
承包人 contractor;

~ 獨立承包人 independent contractor;
~ 總承包人 prime contractor;
承包商 contractor;
~ 承包商聯合體 consortium of contractors;
承包者 contractor;
承包制 contract-out system;
工程承包 project contractor;

[承保] insure;
承保人 insurer;
~ 貨物承保人 cargo insurer;
~ 責任保險承保人 liability insurer;

[承擔] assume; bear; undertake;
承擔後果 face the music; accept the consequences; underwriting the risk;
承擔精神 commitment;
承擔損失 bear losses;
承擔義務 accept the responsibility for; commitment;
承擔責任 carry the can; hold the bag; hold the sack;
承擔重任 take a heavy task upon oneself; take on heavy responsibility;

[承當] bear; take;
承當責任 bear the responsibility;

[承兌] accept; honour;
承兌滙票 accept a draft;
承兌交單 documents against acceptance;
承兌交貨 delivery against acceptance;
承兌票據 accept a note; acceptance of a bill;
承兌商號 acceptance house;
承兌市場 acceptance market;
承兌手續費 acceptance commission;
承兌信用 acceptance credit;
部份承兌 partial acceptance;
參加承兌 acceptance by intervention; acceptance for honour;
大批承兌 acceptance of batch;
附擔保承兌 collateral acceptance;
跟單承兌 documentary acceptance;
票據承兌 domestic acceptance;
票外承兌 extreme acceptance; extrinsic acceptance;
申報承兌 acceptance declaration;
無條件承兌 unconditional acceptance; unqualified acceptance;
限制承兌 qualified acceptance;
銀行承兌 bank acceptance;

[承付] assume responsibility for a payment; undertake to pay;
票據承付 acceptance of bill of exchange;

[承購] underwriting;

[承歡] do everything possible to please one's parents;
繞膝承歡 stay with one's parents in order to make them happy;
膝下承歡 please one's parents by living with them;
菽水承歡 practise great filial piety even in poverty;

[承繼] (1) be adopted as heir to one's uncle; (2) adopt one's brother's child;
承繼箕裘 step into sb's shoes and carry on from where he left off;
承繼人 heir;
~ 法定承繼人 heir at law;
~ 合法承繼人 legal heir; natural heir; right heir; true heir;
~ 假定承繼人 heir presumptive;
~ 男系承繼人 male heir;
~ 旁系承繼人 collateral heir;
~ 推定承繼人 apparent heir;
~ 限定承繼人 heir in tail
~ 直系承繼人 heir in tail;

[承建] undertake a construction;
承建商 contractor;

[承接] carry on; continue;
承接上文 continued from the preceding paragraph;
承接上頁 continued from the previous page;

[承攬] contract to do a job; hire for work;

[承蒙] be indebted; be granted a favour;
承蒙不棄 meet with your gracious consent;
承蒙錯愛 receive sb's unmerited affection; receive undeserved kindness from sb;
承蒙光臨 it is gracious of you to come;
~ 承蒙光臨，不勝榮幸 your presence is a great compliment;
承蒙過獎 be indebted to sb for his overpraise; thank sb for the undeserved compliments; you flatter me;
承蒙指教，不勝榮幸 I have the honour to receive your instructions;

[承諾] acceptance of an offer; promise to undertake; undertake to do sth;
背棄承諾 break one's promise;
信守承諾 commit oneself to a promise;

[承平] peaceful;

承平年月 piping times of peace; time of peace;
承平盛世 piping times of peace; times of peace and prosperity;

［承情］ be much obliged; owe a debt of gratitude;

［承認］ acknowledge; admit; recognize;
承認錯誤 acknowledge one's fault; admit one's mistake;
承認的 avowed;
承認失敗 admit defeat; eat boiled crow; eat crow; give up the ghost; give up the ship;
承認指控 admit the charge;
必須承認 it must be admitted that;
不承認 non-recognition;
得到廣泛承認 receive wide acceptance;
給予承認 grant sanction;
拒絕承認 refuse one's sanction to;
自己承認 by one's own admission;

［承受］ (1) bear; endure; support; (2) inherit;
承受不幸 bear misfortune;
承受負擔 bear burdens;
承受巨大壓力 bear immense pressure;
承受力 bearing capacity; holding capacity;
承受能力 capability of adapting oneself to;
承受損失 stand a loss;
好壞都能接受 take the rough with the smooth;

［承索即寄］ will be mailed upon request;

［承銷］ underwrite;
承銷人 underwriter;

［承載］ bear the weight of;
承載能力 bearing capacity; carrying ability; load absorption;
安全承載 safe bearing load;

［承租人］ leaseholder; lessee;

秉承 receive a command; take an order;
奉承 adulate; bow and scrape; fawn upon; flatter; lick the feet of sb; toady;
繼承 carry forward; carry on; come in for; come into; inherit; inherit from; receive sth by inheritance; step into sth by inheritance; succeed in; succeed to;
看承 look after; take care of;
趨承 cater to sb;
辱承 receive a favour undeservingly;
紹承 inherit; succeed to;
師承 the succession of teachings from a master to his disciples;
嗣承 succeed in line;
仰承 (1) rely on; (2) act according to sb's wish;
應承 agree; promise;
支承 bear; support;
軸承 bearing;

cheng

【城】 (1) city wall; wall; (2) city; (3) town;

［城邦］ (1) city state; (2) polis;

［城堡］ barbican; castle; citadel; tower; town;
充氣城堡 bouncy castle;
一座城堡 a castle;

［城標］ city emblem; city symbol;

［城池］ city; city wall and moat;

［城地］ cities and territories;
爭城略地 conquer cities and capture territories by force of arms;

［城防］ defence of a city;

［城府］ shrewdness; subtlety;
城府很深 shrewd and deep;
胸無城府 artless; frank; have nothing hidden in one's mind; honest; open and unreserved; simple and candid; unrestrained and frank in nature;
胸有城府 calculating; mental reservation; reticence; scheming;

［城管］ city management;

［城隍］ god of the city;
城隍廟裏內訌—鬼打鬼 an internal strife within the temple of the god of the city – devils beating devils; strife among one's enemies;

［城建］ city construction;

［城郊］ outskirts; suburb;
住在城郊 live in the suburbs of a city; live on the outskirts of a town;

［城裏］ in town; inside the city;
城裏城外 in and out of town; inside and outside the city;
城裏人 city slicker; townie;

［城樓］ gate tower;

［城門］ city gate;
城門失火，殃及池魚 in a disturbance, innocent bystanders get into trouble; when the city gate catches fire, the fish in the moat suffer;

［城牆］ city wall;
外城牆 barbican wall;

［城市］ city; town;

城市邊界 city limits;
城市病 urban disease; urban sickness;
城市佈局 city layout;
城市道路 urban road;
~城市道路網 urban road network;
~城市道路系統 urban road system;
城市定位 urban locating;
城市發展 urban development;
城市犯罪區 urban crime-committing zone;
城市房地產市場 urban real estate market;
城市分類 city classification;
城市改革 urban reform;
城市改造 city renewal; urban renewal;
城市感應 city perception;
城市規劃 city planning; urban planning;
~城市規劃學 theory of urban planning;
城市規模 city size;
~大城市規模 large city size;
城市化 urbanization; urbanize;
~城市化標準 urbanized standard;
~城市化水平 level of urbanization;
~逆城市化 counterurbanization;
城市環境 urban environment;
城市基礎建設 urban infrastructure;
城市基礎設施 urban infrastructure;
城市建設 urban construction;
城市交通管制 urban traffic control;
~城市交通管制系統 urban traffic control system;
城市經濟 urban economy;
~城市經濟管理 management of urban economy;
~城市經濟基礎 urban economic base;
~城市經濟學 urban economics;
城市景色 cityscape;
城市居民 city dweller; city slicker;
城市開發 urban development;
城市空間 urban space;
城市恐懼症 urbiphobia;
城市擴張 urban expansion; urban sprawl;
城市垃圾 municipal refuse;
城市類型 urban pattern;
城市內部結構 internal structure of a city;
城市群 urban group;
城市熱島效應 urban heat island effect;
城市商業網點 urban commercial network;
城市社會學 urban sociology;
城市設計 urban design;
~城市設計事務所 urban design office;
城市生活 city life; urban life;
~城市生活方式 urban lifestyle;
城市生態 urban ecology;
~城市生態經濟 urban ecological economy;
~城市生態系統 urban ecological system;
城市體系 urban system;
城市文化 urban culture;
城市污染 city pollution;
城市污水處理 treatment of municipal sewage;
城市系統 urban system;
城市現代化 urban modernization;
城市相互作用 city interaction;
城市學 urbanology;
城市研究 urban studies;
城市意象 city image;
城市雨島效應 urban rain island effect;
城市元老 city fathers;
城市園林規劃 city plantation planning;
城市園林綠地 urban plantation;
城市職能 urban function;
城市中心説 city central theory;
城市總體佈局 urban structure plan;
城市總體規劃 comprehensive city planning;
超級城市 supercity;
次級城市 secondary city;
重建城市 rebuild a city;
大城市 big city; large city; major city;
港口城市 port city;
工業城市 industrial city;
花園城市 garden city;
集合城市 conurbation;
家鄉城市 home city;
建造城市 found a city;
商業城市 business city; commercial city;
外向型城市 foreign-oriented city;
圍攻一座城市 beleaguer a city;
新興城市 boom city;
沿海城市 coast city;
一座城市 a city;
中心城市 central city;
主要城市 chief city;

[城下] under the city wall;
城下之盟 a humiliating treaty made under the pressure of the enemy's troops surrounding the city; a treaty concluded with an enemy who have reached the city wall; a treaty made under coercion; terms accepted under duress;
兵臨城下 the city is besieged by enemy troops; the city is under siege; the

enemy soldiers are camped outside the city walls;
直逼城下 press up to the city wall;

[城鄉] city and countryside; town and country; urban and rural;
城鄉邊緣地帶 rural-urban fringe;
城鄉結合 integration of town and countryside;
城鄉一體化 rural-urban integration;

[城垣] city wall;

[城鎮] cities and towns;
城鎮地區 urban area;
城鎮規劃 urban planning;
城鎮化 urbanization;
城鎮建設 construction of a city and town;
城鎮經濟 urban economy;
城鎮居民 townspeople;
城鎮空間發展 space development in cities and towns;
城鎮人口 urban population;
邊遠城鎮 backward town;
穿越城鎮的 cross-town;
大型城鎮 major town;

拔城 capture a city; take a city;
不夜城 a city with lights turned on all night;
長城 (1) the Great Wall; (2) impregnable bulwark;
出城 go out of town;
大學城 university town;
都城 capital;
府城 prefectural city;
鋼城 steel city;
攻城 assault a city; attack a city;
古城 ancient city;
鬼城 ghost town;
環城 around the city;
金城 strongly guarded city;
進城 go to town;
京城 capital of a country;
名城 famous city;
棄城 abandon the city;
山城 mountain city;
省城 provincial capital;
守城 defend a city;
屠城 kill all the residents of a conquered city; massacre all residents of a conquered city;
土城 a city wall made of clay;
王城 royal city;
圍城 besiege a city;
衛星城 satellite town;
縣城 county town;
小城 small town; town;
汛城 guard a city;
縋城 climb down a city wall by a rope;

cheng
【郕】 an ancient state in today's Shandong Province;

cheng
【乘】 (1) ride; (2) avail oneself of; take advantage of; (3) multiply;

[乘便] at one's convenience; when it is convenient;

[乘車] ride a car;
乘車戴笠 friendship being so profound that it does not change despite the change of social status; on intimate terms with sb; sincere friendship between rich and poor;
乘車恐怖 amaxophobia;

[乘船] ride on a boat;
乘船渡河 ride on a boat across a river;

[乘法] multiplication;
乘法表 multiplication table; times table;
乘法器 multiplier;
~ 變量乘法器 variable multiplier;
~ 模擬乘法器 analogue multiplier;
~ 振動乘法器 vibration multiplier;
二進制乘法 binary multiplication;
方括號乘法 bracket multiplication;
複數乘法 complex multiplication;
捷乘法 abridged multiplication;
邏輯乘法 logical multiplication;
模擬乘法 analogue multiplication;

[乘方] involution;

[乘號] multiplication sign;

[乘機] seize the opportunity;
乘機報復 exploit the situation to take revenge;
乘機搗亂 seize the chance to make trouble; seize the opportunity to create disturbances;
乘機而入 avail oneself of the opportunity to get in;
乘機翻案 seize the chance to reverse a verdict; take the opportunity to whitewash;
乘機反攻 seize the opportunity to counter-attack;
乘機侵入 seize the opportunity to worm one's way into…;
乘機逃脱 take a chance to escape;

乘機造謠 seize the opportunity to spread rumours;

[乘堅策肥] live in luxury;

[乘客] passenger;

乘客座椅 passenger seat;
鄰位乘客 seatmate;
免費乘客 non-revenue passenger;
年長的乘客 elderly passenger;
同船乘客 fellow passengers;
同車乘客 fellow passengers;
同機乘客 fellow passengers;
無座乘客 seatless passenger;
站立乘客 standee;

[乘涼] enjoy the cool weather; relax in a cool place;

乘涼歇息 go out into the coolness to refresh oneself; have a rest in some shade; relax in a cool place; sit in idleness in the shade; take an airing for a rest;
大樹底下好乘涼 great trees are good for shade; under the protection of people with power and influence, one can be profited;
晚上乘涼 enjoy the cool of the evening;

[乘龍快婿] proud son-in-law; handsome son-in-law;

[乘人] take advantage of;

乘人不備 take advantage of others' unpreparedness;
乘人不意 take advantage of others' ignorance;
乘人之危 capitalize on sb's difficulties; make use of sb's dilemma; take advantage of sb's precarious position;
乘人之隙 exploit sb's blunder;

[乘勝] exploit a victory; follow up a victory;

乘勝前進 advance from one victory to another; advance from victory to victory; advance in the midst of victories already won; advance on the crest of a victory; advance triumphantly; continue to march forward from an already won victory; continue one's triumphant advance; go forward in triumph; keep up the triumphant advance; march forward triumphantly; press ahead with flying colours; push on in the flush of victory;
乘勝直追 continue one's triumphant pursuit; exploit victories by hot pursuit; follow up a victory; follow up victory with hot pursuit;
乘勝追擊 continue one's victorious pursuit; exploit victories by hot pursuit; follow up a victory with hot pursuit; seize the day and pursue a routed army;

[乘時而起] emerge at favourable moments;

[乘數] multiplier;

乘數表 multiplication table;
被乘數 multiplicand;

[乘務] service;

乘務員 attendant;
~男乘務員 steward;
~女乘務員 stewardess;
~全體乘務員 cabin crew;

[乘隙] take advantage of a loophole; turn sb's mistake to one's own account;

乘隙而入 seize the opportunity and enter; get in through the crack; take advantage of the crack and enter;

[乘興] while one is in high spirits;

乘興而歸 come back looking very pleased with oneself;
乘興而來 come on an impulse;
乘興而來，敗興而歸 come in high spirits but return crestfallen; come in high spirits but go back disheartened; come in high spirits, but return in disappointment; come with great enthusiasm and return disillusioned; set out cheerfully and return disappointed; set out in high spirits and return crestfallen;

[乘虛] catch sb napping; take advantage of a weak point;

乘虛而入 break through at a weak point; get a chance to step in; hit the blot; seize the chance to get in; seize the opportunity to step in; sneak in; take advantage of an opening for a place of entrance;

[乘月夜歸] take advantage of the bright moonlight to return home;

搭乘 travel by vehicle;
大乘 Mahayana (Buddhism);
小乘 Hinayana (Buddhism);
自乘 involve; square;

cheng

【晟】 a pronunciation of 晟;

cheng

【盛】 take into a bowl or basin;

[盛飯] take boiled rice out of a cooker into a bowl;

[盛殮] place a body in a coffin;

[盛器] receptacle; vessel;

[盛湯] ladle out soup;

cheng

【程】 (1) regulation; rule; (2) order; procedure; (3) journey; stage of a journey; (4) distance;

[程度] degree; extent; level;

程度副詞 adverb of degree;

程度狀語 adverb of degree; adverb of extent;

~ 程度狀語從句 adverbial clause of degree; adverbial clause of extent;

比較程度 degree of comparison;

反應程度 extent of reaction;

教育程度 level of education;

聚合程度 extent of polymerization;

水化程度 extent of hydration;

文化程度 level of culture;

最大程度 maximum extent;

[程控] computerized; programmable; programme-controlled;

程控電話 computerized telephone;

程控電源 programmable power supply;

程控交換台 programme-controlled telephone switchboard;

程控網 programme-controlled network;

程控系統 computerized system;

[程式] (1) form; pattern; (2) programme; programming;

程式編制 programme composition;

程式員 programmer;

微程式 microprogramme;

微程式設計 microprogramming;

[程序] course; order; procedure; proceeding; process; programme; routine; sequence;

程序包 programme package; software package;

程序保護 programmed protection;

程序測試 programme test;

程序存儲器 programme storage device;

程序帶 programme tape;

程序單元 programme unit;

程序定時器 programme timer;

程序翻譯 programme translation;

程序覆蓋 programme overlay;

程序工程師 programme engineer;

程序功能鍵 programme function key;

程序管理 programme management;

~ 程序管理網絡 programme management network;

程序化決策 programmed decision;

程序檢索功能 programme search function;

程序交換 programme swap;

程序教程 programmed course;

程序教育 programmed education; programmed learning;

程序結構 programme structure;

程序開發 programme development;

~ 程序開發時間 programme development time;

程序庫 programme library;

~ 程序庫功能 programme library function;

~ 程序庫管理程序 programme library management routine;

~ 程序庫結構 programme library structure;

~ 程序庫維護 programme library maintenance;

程序塊 programme block;

程序設計 programming;

~ 程序設計管理員 programming manager;

~ 程序設計流程圖 programming flowchart;

~ 程序設計系統 programming system;

~ 程序設計語言 programming language;

程序生成程序 programme generator;

程序維護 programme maintenance;

程序文件 programme file;

程序性決策 programmed decision;

程序異常 programme exception;

程序語言 programme language;

程序員 programmer;

~ 初級程序員 junior programmer;

程序運行 programme run;

程序執行方式 programme execution mode;

報關程序 procedure of customs;

編譯程序 compile a programme;

變更程序 alter the procedure;

標準程序 standard procedure;

表決程序 voting procedure; initial programme;

存取程序 access routine;
單程序 single programme;
翻譯程序 translation procedure;
分配程序 allocation routine;
改變程序 alter the procedure;
公審程序 procedure in public trial;
關鍵程序 critical path;
記賬程序 accounting process;
檢驗程序 procedure of verification;
結束程序 wind up the procedure;
絕對地址程序 absolute address programme;
絕對程序 absolute programme;
會計程序 accounting procedure;
立法程序 legislative proceedings;
上載程序 upload;
審訊程序 trial procedure;
訴訟程序 accusatorial procedure;
調解程序 conciliation proceedings;
調整程序 alignment routine;
退出程序 exit a programme; quit a programme;
微程序 microprogramming;
~微程序控制 microprogramming control;
~微程序軟件 microprogramming software;
~微程序設計 microprogramming;
微程序設計語言 microprogramme language;
下載程序 download;
行政程序 administrative proceedings;
一般程序 usual procedure;
運行程序 run a programme;
正當法律程序 due process;
終止程序 terminate a programme;
仲裁程序 arbitral proceedings; arbitration proceedings;
主程序 main programme; master programme;
裝配程序 assembling procedure;
子程序 subprogramme; subroutine;
~操作子程序 function subprogramme;
~過程子程序 procedure subprogramme;
~匯編子程序 assembly subroutine;
~內部子程序 built-in subroutine;
~區分子程序 specification subprogramme;
~數據塊子程序 block data subprogramme;
~一級子程序 one-level subroutine;
~轉移子程序 branch subroutine;
遵循程序 follow the procedure;

刨程 planning length;
編程 programme;
病程 course of a disease;
步程 walking distance;
長程 long range;
導程 lead;
短程 short distance; short range;
方程 equation;
高程 elevation;
歸程 return journey;
過程 course; procedure; process;
海程 sea voyage;
航程 flying range; passage; voyage;
回程 (1) return trip; (2) reverse drive;
計程 (1) log; (2) taxi;
兼程 travel at double speed;
教程 course of study;
進程 progress;
近程 short-distance; short-range;
課程 course; curriculum;
里程 mileage;
歷程 course; progress;
量程 range of measuring;
療程 course of treatment;
流程 (1) flow; (2) technological process;
路程 distance travelled; journey;
旅程 itinerary; route;
啟程 set out on a journey; start off on a journey;
起程 set out on a journey; start off on a journey;
前程 future; prospect;
全程 whole course; whole journey;
日程 agenda; programme;
射程 range;
水程 journey by boat; voyage;
途程 course; road; way;
行程 (1) distance travelled; journey; (2) course; process; (3) stroke;
揚程 lift;
議程 agenda;
音程 interval;
遠程 long-distance; long-range;
章程 regulations; rules;
征程 journey;
中程 intermediate range; medium range;
專程 make a special trip;

cheng

【棖】 (1) doorpost; (2) touch;
［棖撥］ push aside with one's hand;
［棖觸］ (1) touch sth, moving it slightly; (2) move sb; stir up sb's feelings;

cheng

【誠】 (1) cordial; honest; sincere; (2) actually; indeed; really; truly;

[誠篤] cordial; sincere;

[誠服] obey willingly; submit willingly;
心悅誠服 admire sb from the heart; be completely convinced; concede willingly; feel a heartfelt admiration; submit willingly;

[誠懇] sincere;
誠懇待人 treat others with earnestness;
誠懇的 earnest; sincere;
~ 誠懇的人 person of sincerity;
~ 誠懇的態度 earnest manner;
~ 不誠懇的 cheesy;
待人誠懇 treat others with sincerity;

[誠樸] honest; sincere and simple;

[誠然] indeed; to be sure; true;

[誠實] honest;
誠實盒 honesty box;
誠實可靠 all wool and a yard wide;
誠實善良 honest and kind-hearted;
誠實做事 practise honesty;
不誠實 dishonest; dishonesty; mendacious; mendacity;

[誠心] sincere desire; wholeheartedness;
誠心誠意 wholeheartedly; with sincerity;
一片誠心 in all sincerity; straight from one's heart;

[誠信] faith; good faith;
誠信制度 honour system;
最大誠信 utmost faith;

[誠意] good faith; sincerity;
誠意合作 cooperate cordially;
表明誠意 show one's good faith;
誠心誠意 with sincerity; with the whole heart;
毫無誠意 not sincere in the least;
缺乏誠意 lack sincerity;
真心誠意 have one's heart in the right place; in earnest; in good faith; with all one's heart

[誠摯] cordial; sincere;
誠摯的朋友 sincere friend;
誠摯的慰問 sincere condolences;
誠摯的希望 earnest hope;
誠摯的謝意 sincere thanks;
誠摯的嫌意 sincere apologies;
誠摯的支持 hearty support;

赤誠 absolute sincerity;
竭誠 heart and soul; wholeheartedly;
精誠 absolutely sincere;
開誠 come into the open;
悃誠 sincere;
虔誠 devout; pious;
熱誠 cordial; earnest; warm and sincere;
輸誠 (1) capitulate; surrender; (2) show sincerity;
摅誠 frank;
投誠 sincerely surrender;
真誠 genuine; sincere;
忠誠 faithful;
專誠 for a particular purpose; specially;

cheng

【裎】 bare; naked; nude;

cheng

【酲】 hangover after heavy drinking;
解酲 relieve sb from drunkenness;

cheng

【澄】 clear; transparent;

[澄碧] clear and blue;

[澄淨] clear; pure;

[澄靜] bright eyes; clear and calm;

[澄清] clarify; clear up;
澄清池 clarifier; clarifier tank;
~ 真空澄清池 vacuum clarifier;
~ 中間澄清池 intermediate clarifier;
~ 錐形澄清池 conical type clarifier;
澄清機 clarifier;
~ 空杯澄清機 hollow-bowl clarifier;
澄清劑 clarifier;
澄清吏治 cleanse out political corruption;
澄清器 clarifier;
~ 初級澄清器 primary clarifier;
~ 迴旋澄清器 cyclone clarifier;
~ 綠液澄清器 green-liquor clarifier;
~ 潤滑油澄清器 oil clarifier;
~ 碗蓋式澄清器 disc-bowl clarifier;
澄清事實 clarify some facts; clear the air; put the record straight; set the record straight;
澄清誤會 clear a misunderstanding;
碧綠澄清 green and clear;
電泳澄清 electrophoretic clarification;
果汁澄清 juice clarification;
化學澄清 chemical clarification;
連續澄清 continuous clarification;
料液澄清 feed clarification;
綠液澄清 green liquor clarification;
油脂澄清 fat clarification;

[澄瑩] clear; transparent;

cheng
【瀓】 same as 澄;

cheng
【橙】 orange;
[橙色] orange;
鮮橙色 bright orange;
[橙汁] orange juice;
橙汁飲料 orangeade;
[橙子] orange;
一卡車橙子 a truckload of oranges;

酸橙 sour orange;
香橙 fragrant orange;

cheng
【懲】 penalize; punish;
[懲辦] punish;
依法懲辦 punish according to law;
[懲處] penalize; punish;
懲處犯人 impose a punishment on a criminal; inflict a penalty on an offender; inflict a penalty on a criminal;
懲處主義 doctrine of punishment;
隨意懲處 take the law into one's hands;
依法懲處 punish in accordance with the law;
應受懲處 deserve punishment;
[懲罰] penalize; punish; punishment;
懲罰價格 penalty prices;
懲罰條款 penalty clause;
不受懲罰 go unpublished;
減輕懲罰 mitigate a punishment;
赦免懲罰 remit a punishment;
施以懲罰 inflict a punishment;
受到懲罰 be punished; get it in the neck;
~應該受到懲罰 deserve to be punished;
逃避懲罰 escape punishment; get off scot-free;
逃脫懲罰 avoid punishment; escape being punished; escape without punishment;
嚴加懲罰 hell to pay;
嚴厲懲罰 mete out severe punishment; punish heavily;
應得的懲罰 comeuppance;
遭到懲罰 bear punishment; pay the penalty; suffer punishment; take punishment;
最高懲罰 maximum punishment;
[懲教] correction;
懲教設施 correctional facility;
[懲戒] discipline sb as a warning; punish sb to teach him a lesson; take disciplinary action against sb;
小懲大戒 a stumble may prevent a fall; petty punishment warns against a great penalty; punish sb for a little crime in order to prevent him/her from committing a bigger one;
[懲懶] punish loafers on the job;
[懲治] mete out punishment; punish;
懲治腐敗 combat corruption; crack down on corruption; fight against corruption; fight and punish corruption;
懲治犯罪 punish crime;
嚴加懲治 severe discipline;

薄懲 light punishment;
獎懲 bonus-penalty; rewards and disciplinary sanctions; rewards and penalities; rewards and punishments;
嚴懲 punish severely;
膺懲 send a punitive expedition against;
重懲 chastise severely; punish severely;

cheng³
cheng
【逞】 (1) flaunt; show off; (2) carry out an evil design; succeed in a scheme; (3) give free rein to; indulge;
[逞能] act up; parade one's ability; show off one's ability; show off one's skill;
逞能好勝 parade one's ability and strive to outshine others;
各逞其能 each one displays that in which he/she excels;
好逞能 like to show off;
人前逞能 exhibit one's prowess in the presence of sb;
[逞強] bravado; cocky; flaunt one's superiority; throw one's weight round;
逞強好勝 flaunt one's superiority and seek to criticize others; parade one's superiority and strive to outshine others;
逞強行為 bravado;
[逞凶] act violently;
逞凶霸道 throw one's weight about;
恃強逞凶 lord it over others; rely on superior brute force;
[逞勇] act recklessly;
恃才逞勇 act recklessly with undue

confidence of one's own ability;

得逞 have one's way;

cheng

【騁】 (1) gallop; (2) give free rein to;

［騁懷］ give free rein to one's thoughts and feelings;

游目騁懷 let the eye take in the landscape and please the spirit; let the eye travel over the great scene and let fancy free; rejoice one's eyes and heart

［騁目］ look into the distance;

騁目四顧 gaze in four directions; look round;

騁目遠眺 scan distant horizons;

cheng[4]

cheng

【秤】 balance; scales;

［秤錘］ balance; weight;

案秤 counter scale;

磅秤 platform balance; platform scale;

地秤 weighbridge;

電秤 electrical balance;

短秤 short weight;

杆秤 steelyard;

過秤 take the weight of; weigh;

開秤 begin business;

扭秤 torsion balance;

盤秤 steelyard with a pan;

上秤 put on the scale and weigh;

折秤 lose weight;

市秤 Chinese scale of weights;

台秤 platform balance; platform scale;

信秤 letter balance;

cheng

【稱】 balance; steelyard

［稱錘］ sliding weight of a steelyard;

［稱桿］ arm of a steelyard;

［稱盤］ pan of a steelyard;

［稱鉈］ sliding weight of a steelyard;

稱鉈落在棉花上一沒回音 the sliding weight of a steelyard falling on a pile of cotton — no echo;

chi[1]

chi

【吃】 (1) chomp on; eat; get one's teeth into; sink tooth into; take; (2) eat; have one's meal; (3) live off; live on; (4) annihilate; wipe out; (5) exhaust; strain; (6) absorb; soak up; (7) incur; suffer;

［吃飽］ full; have eaten one's fill;

吃飽穿暖 eat one's fill and wear warm clothes;

吃飽喝足 eat and drink one's fill; eat and drink to one's heart's content; eat and drink to one's satisfaction; eat and drink to the limit of one's capacity; have a good long drink of water and a hearty meal;

吃飽睡足 eat one's fill and get plenty of sleep;

［吃不開］ not in the current demand; unpopular; will not succeed; will not work;

［吃不完］ cannot be eaten out;

［吃不下］ not feel like eating; unable to eat any more;

［吃不消］ be too much for one to do sth; more than one can bear; unable to stand;

［吃穿］ food and clothing;

吃穿不愁 need not worry about food and clothing; there is plenty to eat and wear;

吃穿不盡 have as much food and clothes as one wants;

吃穿很差 be badly fed and clothed;

吃穿有餘 have more than enough to feed and clothe oneself;

愁吃愁穿 be worried about making a living; want food or clothes; worry about one's food and clothing;

愁吃穿 be worried about making a living; worry about food and clothes;

缺吃少穿 have insufficient food and clothing; not have enough food and clothing;

有吃有穿 be assured of food and clothing;

［吃醋］ jealous;

吃醋的 jealous;

~吃醋的妻子 jealous wife;

~吃醋的情人 jealous lover;

~吃醋的丈夫 jealous husband;

爭風吃醋 a storm of jealousy; fight for sb's favours; fight for the affection of a man or woman; quarrel from jealousy; start a scrap through jealousy;

［吃得］ eat like;

吃得很多 eat like a horse;

吃得極少 eat like a bird;

C

吃得講究 eat well;
吃得節約 eat sparingly;
吃得津津有味 eat with relish;
吃得開 have a big drag with; have a lot of pull; popular;
吃得苦中苦，方為人上人 a person who can bear the bitterness of hardship can then be above others; hardship increases stature; only after knowing real suffering can one have greater achievements than others;
吃得來 able to eat;
吃得滿意 eat to one's heart's content;
吃得上 (1) can afford to eat; (2) able to get a meal; in time for a meal;
吃得少 eat like a bird;
吃得下 able to eat;
吃得消 able to stand;
吃得住 able to bear or support;

[吃法] how to eat;

[吃飯] eat; eat a meal; eat meals; feed one's face; have a meal;
吃飯不給錢 eat a free meal;
吃飯了 come and get it;
吃飯時間 mealtime;
出去吃飯 go out for a meal;
看菜吃飯 fit the appetite to the dishes; regulate the appetite according to the dishes;
~看菜吃飯，量體裁衣 fit the appetite to the dishes and the dress to the figure – act according to actual circumstances; regulate the appetite according to the dishes and cut the dress according to the figure;
靠工資吃飯 live on one's wages;
靠天吃飯 at the mercy of the forces of nature; depend on Heaven for food; live at the mercy of the elements; live by what one can find; trust to Providence for one's daily food;
留下來吃飯 stay behind for dinner;
請人吃飯 entertain sb to a meal; invite sb to a meal; set sb up to a meal; stand sb a meal; treat sb to a meal;
上飯店吃飯 dine out; eat out;
同桌吃飯 eat at the same table;
想吃飯 feel like a meal;
有飯大家吃 let everyone have a finger in the pie;
用筷子吃飯 eat with chopsticks;
用碗吃飯 eat from a bowl;
在家裏吃飯 eat in;
在外面吃飯 eat out;
掙飯吃 earn a living;

[吃光] eat up;
一口吃光 eat all up in one mouthful;

[吃喝] eat and drink;
吃喝不愁 have enough to eat and drink; want neither eat nor drink; enough to live on for life;
吃喝不分 fare and share together;
吃喝過度 overindulge;
吃喝嫖賭 indulge in disgusting orgies of eating, drinking, whoring, and gambling;
吃喝痛快 eat and drink to one's heart's content;
吃喝玩樂 beer and skittles; cakes and ale; eat, drink, and be merry; feasting and revelling; gluttony and pleasure-seeking; idle away one's time in pleasure-seeking;
吃吃喝喝 eat and drink; wine and dine with sb;
好吃好喝 fond of food and drink;
會吃會喝 have a good palate for food;
濫吃濫喝 drink and eat to excess;
浪吃二喝 eating and drinking ravenously;
猛吃猛喝 eat and drink one's fill;
能吃能喝 healthy enough to enjoy food and drinks;
喜歡吃喝 fond of eating and drinking;
有吃有喝 have plenty to eat and drink;

[吃葷] eat meat and other food produced by fowls or other animals;

[吃價] very popular; well-liked;

[吃緊] critical; hard pressed;
手頭吃緊 hard up;
形勢吃緊 the situation is critical;

[吃勁] a strain; entail much effort;

[吃驚] alarmed; amazed; astonished; astound; be filled with wonder; be taken aback; freeze; give a start; in astonishment; in surprise; marvel at sth; marvel over sth; strike with wonder; surprised; take sb by surprise; to one's astonishment; with astonishment; with surprise;
瞠目吃驚 wide-eyed with horror;
大為吃驚 be greatly surprised;
令人吃驚 surprising;
猛吃一驚 be startled;

[吃苦] bear hardships;
吃苦耐勞 bear hardship and stand hard work; hardworking and able to bear hardships; inured to hardship; work hard and endure hardship;
吃苦頭 burn one's fingers; get the works; suffer; take up the gauntlet;
自討苦吃 an ass for one's pains; ask for it; ask for trouble; bring trouble upon oneself; burn one's fingers; get into hot water; kick against the pricks; make a rod for one's own back; prepare a rod for one's own back; put one's finger in the fire; ride for fall; seek out hardships; taste the bitter fruit of one's own making; walk oneself into trouble;

[吃虧] (1) come to grief; get a beating; get the worst of it; suffer losses; take a beating; (2) at a disadvantage; in an unfavourable situation;
吃虧上當 be fooled and get into trouble; have suffered and have been deceived;
吃虧學乖 a fall into the pit, a gain in your wit;
吃大虧 suffer a great loss; take a bad loss;
吃小虧佔大便宜 lose a little and gain much; take small losses for the sake of big gains; throw a sprat to catch a mackerel; venture a small fish to catch a great one;
吃啞巴虧 be cheated but unable to talk about it; be forced to keep one's grievances to oneself; be unable to speak out about one's grievances; suffer a loss but be unable to speak out;
吃眼前虧 accept a present loss; suffer loss under one's nose;
肯吃虧 willing to be taken in;

[吃力] entail strenuous effort; laborious; strain;
吃力不討好 a fool for one's pain; a thankless job; dirty work; do a hard but thankless job;
~吃力不討好的工作 thankless job; thankless task;
~趕鴨子上架—吃力不討好 drive a duck onto a perch — expend one's efforts to no good result; force a donkey to dance;
吃力的 back-breaking;
~吃力的事 real strain;
吃力地爬山 labour up a hill;
吃力地前進 labour one's way with difficulty;
吃力工作 wade through;
工作吃力 feel the strain of work; find a job difficult;
呼吸吃力 breathe with difficulty; labour for breath;
説話吃力 speak with effort;
學習吃力 have difficulty with one's lessons;

[吃膩] satiate the appetite with;
玩厭吃膩 be tired of playing and satiated with eating;

[吃請] (1) be invited to a dinner; (2) treat sb to a meal at public expense;

[吃食] feed;
幫狗吃食 help bad people to do evil things;

[吃水] (1) drinking water; (2) absorb water;

[吃素] vegetarian;
吃素的 easy; easy-going; easy to deal with;

[吃透] have a thorough grasp; understand thoroughly;
吃透兩頭 have a thorough grasp of the party's policies and a thorough understanding of the views of the masses;

[吃香] be much sought after; find favour with sb; very popular; well-liked;
很吃香 be much sought after;

[吃相] table manners;

[吃心] become suspicious; oversensitive;

[吃油] guzzle;

[吃着不盡] have as much food and clothing as one wants;

[吃着碗裏，瞧着鍋裏] take a peep at my cabbage pot, stare at my cupboard; while eating one dish, one keeps watching for the next;

[吃重] (1) arduous; strenuous; (2) carrying capacity; loading capacity;

[吃住] eat and live;
同吃同住 eat and live together with sb; live under the same roof and eat at the same table;

愛吃 love to eat;
白吃 eat without payment;
大吃 eat eagerly;
好吃 delicious; good to eat; nice; tasty;
混飯吃 just to make a living;
口吃 stammer; stutter;
零吃 between-meal nibbles;
訥吃 spasmophemia;
省吃 eat sparingly;
生吃 eat sth raw;
貪吃 eat piggishly; gluttonous;
小吃 (1) refreshment; snack; (2) cold dish; made dish;
掙飯吃 earn a living;
中吃 delicious; nice; tasty;
在家吃 eat in;
在外面吃 eat out;

chi

【蚩】 (1) a kind of worm; (2) ignorant; stupid; (3) laugh; (4) ugly;
［蚩蚩］ (1) plain and honest; (2) ignorant; uncouth;
［蚩拙］ ignorant; stupid;

chi

【郗】 (1) a town in the Zhou Dynasty; (2) a surname;

chi

【笞】 (1) bamboo whip; (2) flog; whip;
［笞刑］ flogging; whipping;
鞭笞 flog; lash;

chi

【眵】 caking of eye secretion; secretion;
［眵目糊］ caking of eye secretion;
眼眵 gum (in the eyes);

chi

【嗤】 laugh sneeringly; sneer;
［嗤笑］ laugh at; laugh sneeringly at; sneer at;
嗤嗤地笑 titter;
［嗤之以鼻］ contemptuous of; cook a snook at; despise; give a snort of contempt; make a long nose at; make a wry mouth at sb in scorn; pooh-pooh; scorn; sneeze at; sniff at; thumb one's nose at sb; treat with contempt; turn up one's nose at sb; utter a sneer through the nose to show contempt;

chi

【痴】 (1) idiotic; silly; (2) crazy about;
［痴呆］ (1) dull-witted; stupid; (2) amentia; dementia;
痴呆呆 dumbfounded;
痴呆症 dementia;
創傷後痴呆 post-traumatic dementia;
假痴假呆 pretend to be dull-witted; pretend to be stupid and silly;
酒精性痴呆 alcoholic dementia;
老年痴呆 senile dementia;
麻痺性痴呆 paralytic dementia;
如痴如呆 as if one were stupid and silly; seemingly dull-witted;
早發性痴呆 dementia praecox; schizophrenia;
早老性痴呆 presenile dementia;
中毒性痴呆 toxic dementia;
［痴肥］ abnormally fat; obese;
［痴狂］ crazy about; infatuated with;
如痴如狂 have a rat in the garret; like crazy; off one's trolley; with an air almost of idiocy;
［痴聾］ dumb and deaf;
不痴不聾 blind and deaf; indifferent; pretend not to see and hear;
［痴迷］ crazy; infatuated; obsessed;
［痴情］ blind passion; infatuated; infatuation;
痴情女子負心漢 a foolish sentimental girl and a man with a cold heart; an infatuated girl and a heartless man;
［痴人］ idiot;
痴人説夢 Alnaschar dream; fool's paradise; idiot's daydream; idiotic nonsense; lunatic ravings; sheer fantasy; talk fantastic nonsense; tell some fantastic tales; twaddle in an idiot's daydream;
痴人有福 fortune favours fools;
痴人自有痴人福 a fool has his foolish blessings; fortune favours fools;
［痴想］ illusion; wishful thinking;
［痴笑］ giggle; silly smile; titter;
［痴心］ infatuation;
痴心女子負心漢 a foolish sentimental girl deserted by a heartless man;
痴心妄想 aspire to the impossible; be infatuated with sth and indulge in vain hopes; be obsessed with wild ideas; cry for the moon; fond dream; wishful thinking;

一片痴心 sheer infatuation; strong affection;

［痴愚］ stupidity;

［痴子］ fool; idiot; simpleton;

［痴醉］ be intoxicated;

如痴如醉 delude one to folly; inebriety; lose one's mind; out of one's mind;

神痴心醉 in transports of;

似醉如痴 feel elated but rather dazed;

白痴 (1) idiocy; (2) idiot;

憨痴 idiotic;

嬌痴 childish but artless and lovely;

愚痴 feeblemindedness; imbecility;

chi

【媸】 ugly; ugly woman;

chi

【絺】 (1) fine hemp cloth; linen; (2) a surname;

chi

【摛】 (1) spread; (2) be widely known;

［摛翰］ write a composition;

［摛藻］ write in a flowery style; use poetic diction;

chi

【鴟】 (1) kite; (2) owl; (3) wine glass;

［鴟張］ stretched wings of an owl—oppressors;

chi

【螭】 hornless dragon;

［螭首］ the top of various structures adorned with a representation of the hornless dragon;

chi

【癡】 crazy; foolish; idiotic; insane; senseless; silly; stupid;

［癡肥］ very fat and looking stupid;

［癡迷］ besotted; infatuated;

［癡笑］ giggle; titter;

［癡心］ (1) blind love; blind passion; infatuation; (2) silly wish;

癡心妄想 daydreaming; silly and fantastic notions;

chi

【魑】 evil spirits;

chi

【齹】 irregular teeth; uneven teeth;

chi²

chi

【尺】 foot (a unit in Chinese linear measurement slightly longer than a foot);

［尺寸］ size;

［尺子］ ruler;

一把尺子 a ruler;

標尺 staff gauge; surveyor's rod;

公尺 metre (m.);

chi

【弛】 loosen; relax; slacken; take off;

［弛廢］ neglect;

［弛緩］ calm down; relax;

廢弛 cease to be binding;

鬆弛 (1) limp; slack; (2) lax;

chi

【池】 moat; pond; pool;

［池水］ pond water;

［池塘］ pond;

［池魚］ fish in the pond;

池魚之災 unexpected calamity;

［池沼］ pond; pool;

［池中物］ person of mediocre abilities;

非池中物 person with a promising future; person of high aspirations;

便池 urinal;

差池 (1) accident; (2) error; miscalculation;

電池 battery; cell;

糞池 cesspit; manure pit;

化糞池 digestion tank; septic tank;

臨池 practise calligraphy;

尿池 urinal;

前池 forebay;

熔池 molten bath;

水池 pond; pool; water tank;

舞池 dance floor;

嬉水池 paddling pool; wading pool;

鹽池 salt pond;

瑤池 fairyland;

游泳池 swimming pool;

魚池 fishpond;

浴池 bath pool;

chi

【持】 (1) grasp; hold; (2) maintain; support; (3) manage; run; (4) oppose;

［持刀］ hold a knife;

持刀殺人 kill a person with a knife; stab;

C

持刀威脅 at knifepoint;
持刀行凶 attack people with a knife in one's hand; grasp a knife to commit physical assault;

[持分者] stakeholder;

[持家] keep house; run one's home;
持家有方 keep house in the right way; manage the affairs of the family methodically; run one's house with the proper method;
開始持家 start housekeeping;
勤儉持家 diligently and thrifty in running the household;

[持久] enduring; lasting; protracted;
持久的 long-lasting;
持久和平 lasting peace;
~維護持久和平 maintain a lasting peace;
持久性 persistence;
~圖像持久性 image persistence;
~污染物持久性 pollutant persistence;
~熒火屏持久性 screen persistence;
持久戰 protracted war;
~打持久戰 undertake a prolonged war;
曠日持久 drag on; extend over days; last for a long time; of long duration; prolonged; waste the day and stand by;

[持卡人] cardholder;

[持論] express a view; present an argument; put a case;
持論公平 express a view impartially; state a case fairly;

[持票] bear; hold;
持票人 bearer; holder;
~付持票人 payable to bearer;
~合法持票人 lawful bearer;

[持平] unbiased; fair;
持平而論 give the devil his due;
持平之論 conciliative view; fair and square views; fair argument; unbiased view;

[持槍] hold a gun;
持槍搶劫 rob with a gun;
持槍肅立 stand at attention with rifle in hand;
持槍相峙 face each other tensely with levelled guns;
持槍走來 come this way, gun in hand;
跨馬持槍 sitting astraddle a horse with a carbine in one's hands;

[持球] carry; catch; hold;

[持身] conduct oneself;
持身涉世 exercise proper restraints in dealing with the world; maintain proper conduct in treading through the world;
持身嚴正 very exact with regard to one's personal conduct;

[持旺] continue to sell well;

[持續] continuance; continuation; continued; sustained;
持續暢銷 continue to sell briskly;
持續從屬連詞 subordinator of duration;
持續錯誤 preservation error;
持續的 continual;
持續發展論 theory of sustained development;
持續繁榮 have a continuance of prosperity;
持續教育 continuing education;
持續農業 continued agriculture;
持續評估 continuous assessment;
持續性 persistence;
~視覺持續性 eye persistence;
持續狀語 adverbial of duration;
~持續狀語從句 adverbial clause of duration;

[持有] hold;
持有不同政見 hold a different political view;
持有護照 hold a passport;
持有人 holder;
~合法持有人 lawful holder;
~債券持有人 bond holder;
~賬戶持有人 account holder;
持有相反意見 hold a contrary opinion;
持有者 possessor;
持有證件 have a certificate;
產權持有 equity holding;
股份持有 shareholding;
相互通貨持有 currency holding;

[持之以恒] have perseverance; keep it up; persevere; stick to it; perseveringly;

[持之有故] have grounds for one's views; well founded;

[持重] cautious; dignified; discreet; prudent;
持重老成 prudent and experienced;

把持 (1) control; keep in one's hands; keep under control; (2) dominate; monopolize;
霸持 dominate; forcibly occupy;
保持 keep; maintain; preserve;
秉持 (1) adhere to; hold on to; (2) hold in hand;

操持 (1) grasp; handle; manage; (2) plan and prepare;
撐持 prop up; shore up; support; sustain;
扶持 (1) offer sb a hand to support; support with the hand; (2) assist; give aid to; help to sustain; support;
護持 shield and sustain;
堅持 abide by; adhere to; adherence; assert oneself; be wedded to one's opinion; cling to; face it out; hew to; hold on; hold one's ground; hold out; hold to; insist on; keep to; keep up; maintain; persevere at; persevere in; persevere with; persist in; stand fast; stand firm; stand pat; stand to one's guns; stand up for; stick to; stick to one's guns; uphold;
僵持 be locked in a stalemate; be stalemated; in a stalemate; refuse to budge; refuse to give in;
劫持 abduct; abduction; hijack; hold under duress; kidnap;
矜持 reserved; restrained;
力持 insist on; persist in;
攝持 take proper care of one's life;
維持 keep; maintain; preserve;
相持 be locked in a stalemate; refuse to budge;
挾持 (1) seize sb on both sides by the arms; (2) hold sb under duress; kidnap;
脅持 hold sb by violence;
爭持 refuse to give in; stick to one's position;
支持 at sb's back; at the back of sb; backing; bear; buttress; countenance; for; hold out; stand up for; sustain;
主持 (1) direct; take charge of; (2) chair; preside over; (3) uphold;
住持 abbot;
自持 control oneself; exercise self-restraint; restrain oneself;

chi

【茌】 a county in Shandong;

chi

【匙】 spoon;

［匙子］ spoon;

一套匙子 a set of spoons;

茶匙 teaspoon;
羹匙 soup spoon; tablespoon;
湯匙 soup spoon; tablespoon;
一滿匙 spoonful;

chi

【馳】 (1) gallop; speed; (2) spread; (3) turn eagerly towards;

［馳騁］ gallop;

馳騁疆場 dash about in the battlefield; gallop across the battlefield;
馳騁文壇 active and aggressive in the world of letters; bestride the literary stage; make a noise in the literary stage; play an outstanding role in the literary world;
馳騁中原 gallop across the vast central plain; strive for power;
馳騁自如 ride easy;
縱橫馳騁 move about freely and swiftly; sweep through the length and breath of;

［馳口妄談］ talk at random without restrain; talk quickly and wildly;

［馳離］ depart;

［馳馬］ gallop a horse; go swiftly on horseback;

［馳名］ famous; known far and wide; renowned; well-known;

馳名世界 be renowned all over the world; world-famous;
馳名遠近 famous to all, far and near;
馳名中外 be renowned at home and abroad;
國內外馳名 be well-known at home and abroad;

［馳驅］ (1) gallop; ride fast; trot; (2) do one's utmost in sb's service; run errands; serve others;

［馳援］ rush to the rescue;

［馳驟］ gallop;

背馳 proceed in opposite directions;
奔馳 gallop; hasten; move along quickly; move fast; run quickly; speed; speed on; travel quickly;
飛馳 dart on; dash forward; go at a gallop; go at express speed; speed along;
疾馳 gallop;
名馳 one's fame spreads;
驅馳 run about busily for others;
神馳 allow the thoughts to fly to an adored person;
心馳 deep longing;
星馳 travel very fast like a shooting star;

chi

【篪】 a kind of bamboo flute;

chi

【墀】 courtyard; porch;

chi

【踟】 hesitate;

［踟躕］ hesitate; waver;

踟躕不決 remain in an undecided state;

踟躕不前 falter to press forward; hesitate to move forward;

搔首踟躕 at a loss as to what to do; hesitate; in a dilemma; in perplexity; scratch one's head in great perplexity; scratch one's head in hesitation; undecided;

C

chi

【遲】 (1) slow; tardy; (2) late;

［遲笨］ slow;

［遲遲］ slow; tardy;

遲遲不付款 tardy in one's payments;

遲遲不歸 stay away long;

遲遲不回來 late in returning;

遲遲不決 cannot make up one's mind for a long time; not make a decision after stalling for a long time;

遲遲不做決定 postpone one's decision;

［遲到］ arrive late; be late; come late;

遲到早退 arrive late and leave early; come to work late and leave early;

遲到者 latecomer;

經常遲到 constantly late;

上學遲到 arrive late for one's lessons; late at school; tardy for school;

［遲鈍］ slow; obtuse;

反應遲鈍 slow in reacting;

舉止遲鈍 blunt in one's manner;

理解力遲鈍 dull of apprehension; slow in understanding;

聽覺遲鈍 hard of hearing;

頭腦遲鈍 weak of brain;

想像力遲鈍 have a dull imagination; have a sluggish imagination;

眼神遲鈍 have glassy eyes;

語言遲鈍 slow of speech;

［遲發］ tardy;

［遲緩］ slow; sluggish; tardy;

遲緩的人 laggard;

步子遲緩 sluggish gait; with slow steps;

進展遲緩 make progress at a snail's gallop; make slow progress; the progress is slow;

行動遲緩 act slowly; slow in action;

［遲暮］ late in one's life; past one's prime;

［遲睡遲起］ keep bad hours; keep late hours;

［遲誤］ delay; procrastinate;

［遲延］ delay; drag on; postpone; retard;

不容遲延 allow of no delay;

［遲疑］ hesitate;

遲疑不決 cannot make up one's mind; hesitate; hesitate to make a decision; irresolute; undecided;

遲疑坐困 hesitate and allow oneself to be tied down; hesitate in a self-imposed predicament;

［遲早］ early or late; first or last; sooner or later;

遲出早歸 go out late and come back early;

或遲或早 sooner or later;

寧早勿遲 it is better to be too early rather than too late;

［遲滯］ slow-moving; sluggish;

幾乎太遲 not a moment too soon;

經遲 delayed menstrual cycle;

來遲 late;

凌遲 put to death by dismembering the body;

栖遲 take a rest;

棲遲 sojourn; travel and rest;

欽遲 revere; venerate;

姍姍來遲 slow in arriving; slow in coming;

事不宜遲 the matter permits no delay;

舒遲 leisurely; slow; unhurried;

睡得遲 sit up till late at night;

太少也太遲 too little, too late;

推遲 be postponed; advance; defer; delay; hold over; postpone; put off; retard;

下班遲 late from work;

醒得遲 awake late;

淹遲 dilatory; slow;

延遲 defer; delay; postpone; put off;

宜早不宜遲 it is better to be early than late;

至遲 at the latest; no later than;

最遲 at the latest;

chi³

chi

【尺】 (1) a unit of length; (2) rule; ruler; (3) an instrument in the shape of a ruler;

［尺布斗粟］ brothers at loggerheads; brothers quarrelling between themselves; disagreement between brothers;

［尺寸］ dimensions; measurements; sizes;
尺短寸長 every person is useful according to his ability; every one has his shortcoming and merits; every one has his strong and weak points;
尺有所短，寸有所長 every person has his strong and weak points; everyone has his shortcomings and merits; everyone has his weak points as well as his strong ones;
規定尺寸 set dimension;
量尺寸 make measurements;
縮小尺寸 diminish in size;
［尺度］ measurement; scale; yardstick;
［尺碼］ measures; sizes;
尺碼不同 in different sizes; of different sizes;
尺碼一樣 of a size;
各種尺碼 of all sizes;
［尺子］ rule;

丁字尺 T-square;
公尺 metre;
計算尺 slide rule;
戒尺 teacher's ruler;
進尺 footage;
矩尺 carpenter's square;
碼尺 yard measure;
米尺 metre rule;
捲尺 band tape; tape measure;
曲尺 carpenter's square;
水尺 water gauge;
算尺 slide rule;
英尺 foot;
折尺 folding ruler;
鎮尺 bronze paper weight;
直尺 straight edge;
咫尺 very close;

chi
【呎】 the foot in English measurement;

chi
【侈】 (1) extravagant; wasteful; (2) exaggerate;
［侈談］ prate about; prattle about; talk glibly about;
侈談和平 talk profusely about peace;

奢侈 extravagant; luxurious;

chi
【恥】 disgrace; humiliation; shame;
［恥骨］ (1) pubic bone; pubis; (2) sidebone;
恥骨聯合 pubic symphysis;
恥骨切開 pubiotomy;
［恥毛］ a woman's pubic hair; one's brush;
［恥辱］ disgrace; humiliation; shame;
奇恥大辱 blazing indiscretion; bring deep shame on; burning shame; crying shame; crying shame and crowning humiliation; crowning humiliation; deep disgrace; disgrace; flagrant affront; galling shame and humiliation; great insult; howling shame; humiliating disgrace; inflict unprecedented shame and humiliation on; most extreme humiliation; outrage on human dignity; profound humiliation; stinging insult; unheard-of gross indignity;
遭受奇恥大辱 be humbled to the dust;
蒙受恥辱 be humiliated;
洗雪恥辱 wipe out the disgrace;
［恥笑］ hold sb to ridicule; mock; sneer at;
［恥與為伍］ feel ashamed to associate with sb;

國恥 national humiliation;
可恥 disgraceful; ignominious; shameful;
廉恥 sense of honour; sense of shame;
榮恥 honour and dishonour;
刷恥 wipe away disgrace;
無恥 impudent; shameless;
羞恥 sense; shame; shamed;
雪恥 avenge an insult; wipe out a disgrace;
知恥 have a sense of shame;

chi
【蚇】 inchworm; looper; measuring worm;

chi
【豉】 fermented beans;

豆豉 fermented soya beans;

chi
【齒】 (1) tooth; (2) tooth-like part of anything; (3) age; (4) mention;
［齒德俱尊］ honourable both in age and in virtue;
［齒蠹］ tooth decay;
［齒洞］ cavity in a tooth;
［齒髮］ one's teeth and hair;
［齒縫］ embrasure;
［齒根］ gums; root of a tooth;

C

［齒垢］ tartar;
［齒冠］ crown of a tooth;
［齒寒］ suffer due to others' failure;
［齒擊］ clatter one's teeth in trembling;
［齒及］ mention;
［齒間留香］ leave a sweet taste in one's mouth;
［齒決］ bite off with the teeth;
［齒孔］ dental foramen;
［齒冷］ laugh sb to scorn;
［齒瘤］ odontoma;
［齒輪］ cog; gear;
齒輪傳動 gearing;
~ 行星齒輪傳動 epicyclic gearing;
~ 圓柱齒輪傳動 cylindrical gearing;
齒輪裝置 gearing;
~ 差動齒輪裝置 differential gearing;
~ 錐行星齒輪裝置 bevel planetary gearing;
安全齒輪 emergency gear;
板牙齒輪 baffle gear;
內齒輪 annular gear;
平衡齒輪 balance gear;
調節齒輪 adjusting gear;
錐齒輪 bevel gear;
［齒腔］ dental cavity; gum of the tooth; pulp cavity of tooth;
［齒齲］ tooth decay;
［齒如編貝］ very beautiful teeth;
［齒舌］ radula;
［齒髓］ dental pulp; pulp of the tooth;
齒髓炎 pulpitis;
［齒痛］ toothache;
［齒吻］ teeth and lips;
［齒齦］ dental ridge; gum of the tooth;
齒齦潰瘍 gumboil;
齒齦炎 gingivitis;
［齒質］ dentine;

刨齒 gear shaping;
不齒 despise; hold in contempt; unwilling to mention;
唇齒 lips and teeth;
對尖齒 aygodont;
掛齒 mention;
皓齒 white teeth;
珩齒 gear lapping with corundum;
劍齒 sabre-toothed;
臼齒 back teeth; molar;
鋸齒 sawtooth;
口齒 (1) enunciation; (2) ability to speak;
裂齒 carnassial tooth;
露齒 expose one's teeth;
輪齒 teeth of a cogwheel;
馬齒 horse's teeth;
門齒 front tooth; incisor;
沒齒 without teeth;
年齒 person's age;
齊齒 of the same age;
啟齒 open one's mouth; start to speak;
切齒 gnash one's teeth;
齲齒 (1) dental caries; (2) decayed tooth;
犬齒 canine tooth;
乳齒 milk tooth;
孺齒 young child;
梳齒 comb teeth;
細齒 serration;
序齒 arrange in order of age or seniority;
牙齒 tooth;
羊齒 bracken; fern;
義齒 false tooth;
智齒 wisdom tooth;
稚齒 very young;
蛀齒 decayed tooth; dental caries;

chi

【褫】 deprive; strip;
［褫奪］ deprive; strip;
［褫職］ deprive sb of his/her post; remove sb from his/her office;

chi⁴

chi

【彳】 (1) short paces; short steps; (2) a phonetic sign for "ch";

chi

【叱】 loudly rebuke; shout at; yell;
［叱喝］ bawl at; shout at;
［叱罵］ abuse; curse; scold roundly;
叱罵奸 rebuke treachery and curse slanders;
［叱責］ rebuke; scold; upbraid;
受到叱責 be scolded;

呵叱 berate; excoriate;
怒叱 rebuke; scold angrily;

chi

【斥】 denounce; reprimand; scold; upbraid;
［斥罵］ reproach; scold; upbraid;
受到斥罵 be howled out;
［斥責］ chew out; denounce; rebuke; reprimand;

大聲斥責 loudly denounce;
痛加斥責 scold sharply; take sb to task;

貶斥 (1) demote; (2) denounce;
擯斥 dismiss; expel; reject;
駁斥 contradict; denounce;
充斥 congest; flood; full of;
呵斥 berate; excoriate;
揮斥 free, bold, and unrestrained; untrammelled;
拒斥 reject;
怒斥 denounce indignantly; rebuke angrily;
排斥 reject; repel;
申斥 rebuke; reprimand; reproach;
痛斥 attack bitterly; rebuke bitterly; denounce sharply;
訓斥 rebuke; reprimand; reproach;
指斥 denounce; reprove;

chi

【赤】 (1) brownish-red colour; flesh-coloured; red; (2) naked; (3) loyal; pure; sincere; single-hearted; trustworthy;

[赤膊] barebacked;
赤膊上陣 come out into the open; come out pugnaciously; come out without any disguise; emerge into the open; go into battle stripped to the waist; go into battle with bared shoulders; step forward in person without any disguise; strip off all disguise and come to the fore; take the field oneself undisguisedly; throw away all disguise;
打赤膊 be stripped to the waist; strip down to one's underpants; strip oneself to the waist;

[赤潮] red tide;

[赤誠] absolute sincerity; singleness of heart;
赤誠待人 treat people with absolute sincerity;

[赤膽] sincere loyalty;
赤膽忠心 a red heart of complete dedication; ardent loyalty; loyalty; true devotion; utter devotion; wholehearted dedication;
忠心赤膽 wholehearted devotion;

[赤道] equator;
赤道板 equatorial plate;
赤道軌道 equatorial orbit;
赤道儀 equatorial;
地磁赤道 geomagnetic equator;
地球赤道 earth's equator;
天球赤道 celestial equator;
天文赤道 astronomical equator;
虛擬赤道 fictitious equator;

[赤豆] brown beans;

[赤鶴] brown crane;

[赤腳] barefoot;
打赤腳 (1) bare one's feet; (2) go barefoot;
赤腳走路 walk barefoot; walk barefooted;

[赤金] deep-coloured gold; pure gold;

[赤經] right ascension;
地心赤經 geocentric right ascension;
日心赤經 heliocentric right ascension;
斜交昇交點赤經 oblique ascension;

[赤佬] (1) devil; rascal; scoundrel; (2) ghost;

[赤露] bare;

[赤裸] in one's birthday suit; naked; stark naked; without a stitch of clothing;
赤裸裸 (1) stark naked; without a stitch of clothing; (2) naked; naked out and out; unadorned; undisguised;
赤裸身體 not have a stitch on one's body;

[赤米] brown rice;

[赤貧] abject poverty; destitution; dire poverty; in abject poverty;
赤貧如洗 as poor as a church mouse; as poor as a rat; as poor as Job; in dire necessity; in extreme poverty; poverty-stricken; utter destitution;

[赤熱] red heat;

[赤日] red sun;
赤日當空 red sun is hanging in the sky;
赤日炎炎 scorching sun;

[赤肉] lean pork;

[赤色] brownish-red colour; red;
赤色分子 pinko;

[赤舌燒城] a slanderous tongue can burn up a city; opinion sways the world; we are all slaves of opinion;

[赤身] naked;
赤身露體 Adam and Eve's togs; as naked as I was born; as naked as my mother bore me; in a state of nature; in one's bare skin; in the raw; naked; nature's garb; not wearing a stitch; without a piece of clothing;
赤身裸體 have not a stitch on one; in a state of nature; in one's birthday suit; in the buff; in the nude; stark naked; to the raw;

［赤手空拳］ armless; barehanded; have only empty hands; unarmed; with bare hands; with naked fists;
赤手空拳搏鬥 fight with bare fists;
［赤心］ genuine sincerity; loyalty; sincere; sincere heart; wholehearted devotion;
赤心相待 treat sb with all sincerity;
［赤子］ (1) newborn baby; (2) common people;
赤子之心 the pure heart of a newborn babe — utter innocence;
海外赤子 overseas patriots;
［赤字］ deficit;
赤字財政 deficit financing;
赤字開支 deficit spending;
財政赤字 financial deficit;
超額赤字 excess deficit;
出現赤字 go into the red; have a deficit; show a deficit;
貿易赤字 trade deficit; trade gap;
沒有赤字 out of the red;
彌補赤字 make up a deficit; meet a deficit;
石油赤字 oil-induced deficit;
現金赤字 cash deficit;
消滅赤字 get out of debt; wipe out deficits;
造成赤字 cause a deficit;
［赤足］ with bare feet;

光赤 bare; naked;
足赤 pure gold;

chi
【翅】 (1) wings; (2) fins;
［翅膀］ wings;
翅膀有力 strong on the wing;
雞翅膀 chicken wings;
拍翅膀 beat the wings; flap the wings; flutter the wings;
拍打翅膀 flap the wings;
收攏翅膀 fold the wings;
［翅餅］ square or round shark's fin;
［翅果］ samara;

雞包翅 chicken stuffed with shark's fin;
排翅 unprocessed shark's fin;
鞘翅 elytron;
魚翅 shark's fin;
展翅 get ready for a flight; spread the wings;

chi
【眙】 look in the face; stare;

chi
【敕】 (1) imperial decree; imperial order; (2) cautious;
［敕牒］ imperial order;
［敕身］ discipline oneself; prudent in conduct;

chi
【啻】 merely; only;
不啻 (1) not less than; (2) as; as good as; like;
何啻 far more than;

chi
【飭】 (1) severe; (2) careful; respectful; reverent; (3) keep in order; make ready; manage; (4) direct; instruct; order;
［飭查］ order an investigation;
［飭厲］ exhort; instruct and encourage;
［飭令］ direct; instruct; order;
［飭拿］ give orders for the arrest of sb;
［飭知］ inform a subordinate;

謹飭 cautious; prudent;
申飭 (1) admonish; warn; (2) rebuke; reprimand; reproach;
整飭 in good order; put in order; straighten out; tidy;

chi
【傺】 (1) hinder; (2) disappointed;

chi
【踟】 walk back and forth;

chi
【踅】 go on one leg;

chi
【熾】 ablaze; flaming;
［熾烈］ blazing; flaming;
醋意熾烈 burning with jealousy;
［熾熱］ blazing; red-hot;
熾熱的 blazing;
［熾盛］ ablaze; flaming; flourishing;

白熾 incandescence; white heat;
火熾 bustling with noise and excitement; lively;

chi
【鶒】 a kind of water bird;

chong¹

chong
【充】 (1) sufficient; full; (2) charge; fill; (3) act as; serve as; (4) pass sth off

as; pose as; pretend to be;

[充斥] congest; flood; full of;

充斥市場 glut the market;

充斥着小道消息 full of grapevine news;

[充當] act as; play the part of; serve as;

充當典型 serve as a model;

充當砲灰 serve as a cannon fodder;

充當調解人 act as a mediator;

充當誘餌 serve as a bait;

充當中間人 act as a go-between;

[充電] charge; charging;

充電錶 chargometer;

充電計 chargometer;

充電器 charger; recharger;

~電池組充電器 group charger;

~蓄電池充電器 battery charger;

~增壓充電器 supercharger;

充電指示燈 charge indicator;

重新充電 recharge;

恢復性充電 recovery charging;

加速充電 accelerated charging;

交流充電 alternating current charging;

粒子充電 particle charging;

平均充電 uniform charge;

蓄電池充電 accumulator charging; battery charging;

[充分] abundant; ample; full;

充分表達 give full expression to;

充分發揮 give free rein to; give the reins to;

~充分發揮聰明才智 display one's talent and wisdom to the full;

~充分發揮想像力 allow the imagination to roam free; give full play to one's imagination;

~充分發揮作用 play one's part to the full;

充分發揚 give full play to;

~充分發揚優點 develop the strong points to the full;

充分發展 fully develop;

~得到充分發展 attain full development;

充分考慮 give adequate thought to;

充分理由 abundant reason;

~有充分理由 have abundant reason;

充分利用 make much of; make the most of;

~充分利用時間 invest one's time to the best advantage;

~充分利用現有的機會 play one's hand for all it is worth;

~充分利用一切 put everything to its best use;

~充分利用這個機會 make the best of this opportunity;

~充分利用這個形勢 make the best of this situation;

充分認識 fully realize;

充分享受 enjoy sth to the full;

充分證明 bear ample testimony to;

~提供充分證明 provide ample testimony of;

充分證實 verify;

充分準備 adequate preparation;

~有充分準備 have adequate preparation;

~做充分準備 make adequate preparation;

~做好充分準備 be fully equipped for; equip oneself thoroughly for;

不充分 insufficiency;

[充公] confiscate; confiscation;

[充饑] allay one's hunger;

充饑禦寒 allay one's hunger and keep out the cold; relieve hunger and resist the cold;

充饑止渴 satisfy hunger or thirst;

畫餅充饑 a Barmecide feast; a painted cake to satisfy one's hunger — a vain promise; comfort oneself with one's imagination; draw a cake to satisfy one's hunger — feed on illusions; eat the air; have a false solution; paint a pie to satisfy one's hunger; paint a cake to satisfy one's hunger — sth impossible; satisfy hunger with pictures of cakes;

漏脯充饑 satisfy one's hunger on putrid meat — pay sole attention to the present and forget the forthcoming disasters; take poisoned meat to satisfy hunger — care only for the present regardless of future consequences;

以餅充饑 appease one's hunger with a cake;

[充軍] banish; be sent into exile; be transported to a distant place for penal servitude;

[充滿] abound in; abound with; abundant in; alive with; be filled with; be fraught with; be imbued with; be impregnated with; be permeated with; brimful of; brimming with; full of; full to the brim; crammed; fill; pervade; replete

with; swarm with; teem with;
充滿仇恨 be filled to the brim with hate;
充滿感激 full of gratitude;
充滿好奇心 full of curiosity;
充滿活力 burst with vitality;
充滿幻想 full of fantasies;
充滿夢想 full of dreams;
充滿人情味 full of human touches;
充滿殺機 be filled to the brim with the lust to kill;
充滿上進心 be filled to the brim with ambition;
充滿同情 brim over with sympathy; full of compassion; overflow with sympathy;
充滿希望 full of hope;
充滿幸福 be filled to the brim with happiness;
充滿怨氣 be filled with spleen;
充滿自豪 be filled to the brim with pride;
充滿自信 full of self-confidence;

[充沛] abundant; full of; plentiful;
感情充沛 have a big heart;
精力充沛 be charged with strength and power;
體力充沛 full of physical strength;

[充其量] at best; at most;

[充氣] inflate;
充氣屋 air house;

[充任] fill the post of; hold the position of;

[充塞] cram; fill up; full of;

[充實] (1) rich; substantial; (2) enrich; reinforce; replenish; strengthen; substantiate;
充實經驗 enrich one's experience;
充實論據 substantiate one's argument;
充實內容 enrich the content;
充實生活 enrich one's life;

[充數] make up the number; merely to take a part; serve as a stopgap;
濫竽充數 act as a stopgap; be dragged in to swell the total; fill a post without real qualifications; hold a post without qualifications; make up a number without active work; to be there just to make up the number;

[充填] fill in; fill up;

[充血] bloodshot; congestion; engorgement; hyperaemia;
充血性心臟衰竭 congestive heart failure;
肺充血 pulmonary congestion;
功能性充血 functional congestion;
脾充血 splenemphraxis;
生理性充血 physiologic congestion;
咽部充血 congestion in the throat;
眼睛充血 bloodshot eyes;
運動性充血 exercise hyperaemia;

[充溢] exuberant; full to the brim;

[充盈] full; plentiful;

[充裕] abundant; ample; plentiful;
充裕的時間 ample time;
財政充裕 financial sufficiency;

[充足] abundant; adequate; ample; plenty; sufficient;
充足資金 sufficient funds;
~提供充足資金 furnish sufficient funds;
經費充足 have ample funds; have sufficient funds;
睡眠充足 get enough sleep;
營養充足 nutritional sufficiency;
雨水充足 rainfall is plentiful;

撥充 appropriate sth for;
補充 (1) fill up; replenish; supplement; (2) additional; complementary; supplementary;
混充 palm off inferior goods; pass oneself off as;
假充 pass off as; pose as; pretended to be;
擴充 enlarge; expand; strengthen;
冒充 pass off as; pose as;
填充 (1) filling; (2) fill in the blanks;

chong

【沖】 (1) wash away; wash with running water; (2) rise rapidly; shoot up; soar; (3) infuse; pour water to make beverage; (4) empty; void; (5) clash with; dash against; (6) young; (7) make void; neutralize;

[沖沖] in a state of excitement;
怒氣沖沖 be filled with seething anger;
怒沖沖 beside oneself with rage; furious; in a rage;
氣沖沖 beside oneself with rage; furious; in a rage;
喜沖沖 be filled with gaiety; in a joyful mood; joyful and gay;
興沖沖 in the best of spirits;

[沖淡] dilute; water down;
沖淡茶水 weaken tea by adding water;
沖淡影響 cool off the effect;

[沖積] alluvial;
沖積層 alluvium;

沖積的 alluvial;
沖積分水嶺 alluvial divide;
沖積平原 alluvial plain;
沖積扇 alluvial fan;
沖積物 alluvial deposit;

[沖刷] erode; scour; wash away; wash out;
沖刷水溝 scour a ditch;

[沖洗] develop; flush; rinse;
沖洗地板 give the floor a flush; flush off the floor; wash the floor;
沖洗盤子 rinse the plates;
沖洗汽車 give the car a wash; wash down the car;

[沖走] flush away; wash away;
被河水沖走 be washed away by the rush of the current;
被激流沖走 be swept away by the rush of the current;

大沖 favourable opposition;
俯沖 dive;
謙沖 modest; unassuming;
喜沖沖 be filled with gayety; in a joyful mood; joyful and gay; look exhilarated;
興沖沖 do sth with joy and expedition; excited;
淵沖 deep but open-minded;

chong
【忡】 anxious; uneasy; worried;

[忡忡] careworn; laden with anxiety;

怔忡 palpitation;

chong
【舂】 pound grain in order to remove the husk;

[舂米] pound rice to remove the husk;
[舂藥] pound medicinal herbs in a mortar;

chong
【憧】 (1) indecisive; irresolute; (2) fatuous; muddle-headed; stupid;

[憧憧] flicker; move;
燈影憧憧 the light of a lantern flickered in;
人影憧憧 shadows of people move about;
樹影憧憧 shadows of trees are flickering;

[憧憬] look forward to; long for;
憧憬幸福的明天 long for the happy days to come;
對未來充滿憧憬 have a great longing for a bright future;

chong
【衝】 (1) important place; thoroughfare; (2) charge; dash; rush; (3) collide; clash; (4) pour boiling water on; (5) flush; rinse; (6) develop; (7) opposition;

[衝出] rush out;
衝出重圍 break through a heavy encirclement;
衝出房間 rush from the room;

[衝刺] sprint; spurt;
向終點衝刺 dash towards the goal;
最後衝刺 final dash;

[衝動] get excited; impetuous;
感情衝動 act on a momentary impulse; be carried away by one's emotions; emotional impulse; impulsive;
情感衝動 outburst of emotion;
容易衝動 get excited easily;
一時衝動 a sudden impulse; on the spur of the moment;

[衝鋒] assault; charge;
衝鋒陷陣 breach and storm the enemy's citadel; break into enemy ranks; charge against enemy fire; charge an enemy's position; charge and shatter enemy positions; charge forward; charge the enemy lines; dash bravely to the front of the battle; make frontal attacks on; press boldly forward; rush on the enemy and break the line; rush on the hostile ranks; smash into the enemy ranks; storm and break up the enemy's front; storm and shatter the enemy's position; strike into the enemy ranks;
發起衝鋒 commit an assault; perpetrate an assault;

[衝積扇] alluvial fan;

[衝擊] (1) deal a severe blow to; (2) denounce; (3) challenge; (4) impact; shock;
衝擊波 shock wave;
衝擊效應 shock effect;
電子衝擊 electron impact;
動力衝擊 dynamic impact;
負荷衝擊 load impact;
經受衝擊 experience a shock;
生態衝擊 ecological impact;
水力衝擊 hydraulic impact;
文化衝擊 culture shock;

[衝進] plunge into;
衝進房間 dart into the room; dash into the room;

C

[衝勁] enthusiasm; impulse; zeal;

[衝跨] burst; shatter;
衝跨堤防 burst the dam;

[衝口而出] blurt sth out; one's tongue runs before one's wit; say sth unthinkingly; say sth without thinking;

[衝擴] develop and enlarge;

[衝浪] surf;
衝浪板 surfboard;
衝浪褲 board shorts;
衝浪趴板 bodyboard; boogie board;
衝浪者 surfer;
人群衝浪 crowd-surf;
網上衝浪 surf the Internet; surf the Net;
~ 網上衝浪者 Internet surfer; Net surfer; Web surfer;

[衝力] impulsive force; momentum;
砲彈的衝力 impetus of a cannonball;

[衝破] breach; break through;
衝破重重障礙 surmount all sorts of obstacles;
衝破敵人防線 break through the enemy line;
衝破封鎖 break a blockade;
衝破貿易障礙 break down a trade barrier;
衝破難關 get to smooth water; reach smooth water;
衝破牢籠 shake off the bonds of;

[衝去] dash onward;
向前衝去 thrust one's way forward;

[衝入] plunge into;
衝入重圍 plunge into the press;
衝入雲霄 soar to the skies;

[衝散] break up; disperse; scatter;
衝散人群 break up the crowds; disperse the crowds;

[衝天] soaring; towering;
衝天幹勁 astonishing courage; boundless drive; heaven-storming enthusiasm; soaring enthusiasm; towering energy; unparalleled drive; with supreme energy;
衝天爐 cupola; cupola furnace;
~ 等風衝天爐 equilibrium blast cupola;
~ 計算機控制衝天爐 computerized cupola;
~ 無爐襯衝天爐 liningless cupola;
~ 小型衝天爐 cupolette;
幹勁衝天 work with soaring enthusiasm;
怒氣衝天 in a towering rage;
一飛衝天 soar up into the sky rapidly;
意氣衝天 high-spirited;
怨氣衝天 burst with anger;

[衝突] clash; conflict; confrontation;
避免衝突 avert a conflict; avoid conflicts; ward off a collision;
長期衝突 long-drawn-out conflict;
搭配衝突 collocational clash;
導致衝突 lead to a conflict;
東西方衝突 East-West conflict;
防止衝突 avoid a conflict; prevent a conflict;
感情衝突 clash of feelings; conflict of sentiments;
個性衝突 personality clash;
國際衝突 international friction;
激烈衝突 sharp conflict;
家庭衝突 domestic conflict;
階級衝突 class conflict;
利害衝突 conflict of interest;
流血衝突 bloody conflict;
內心衝突 mental conflicts;
思想衝突 conflict of thoughts;
挑起衝突 stir up a conflict;
武裝衝突 armed conflict;
小規模衝突 minor skirmishes; skirmish;
意見衝突 conflict of opinions;
與人發生衝突 come into conflict with sb; fall foul of sb; all foul with sb; have a conflict with sb; have a confrontation with sb;
應對衝突 deal with conflicts;
孕育衝突 breed a conflict;
政治衝突 political friction;
直接衝突 immediate conflict;
種族衝突 race conflict;
自相衝突 mutual conflict;

[衝撞] (1) bump; collide; ram; (2) give offence; offend;
橫衝直撞 act recklessly; barge about; barge around; clash in every direction; collide right and left; dash around madly; force one's way; go first in one direction and then another; go on the rampage; jostle and elbow one's way; push one's way by shoving; reckless action; run amok; rush and swerve about madly; veer about;

俯衝 dive;
緩衝 buffer; cushion;
脈衝 pulse;
猛衝 charge; hurl; hurtle; lunge; make a break;

onrush;
要衝 communication centre;
折衝 repulse the enemy; subdue the enemy;

chong²
chong

【重】 (1) duplicate; repeat; (2) again; once more; (3) layer;

［重播］ repeat a programme; replay;
即時重播 instant replay;

［重版］ republication;
重版書 reprint;

［重操故業］ back to the salt mines; go back to one's profession; ladle one's soup out of the old pot; resume one's old profession; return to one's old trade; start up one's old job; take up one's old trade again; turn to one's former career;

［重唱］ ensemble of two or more singers, each singing one part;
八重唱 octet;
二重唱 duet;
六重唱 sestet; sextet;
七重唱 septet;
三重唱 trio;
四重唱 quartet;
五重唱 quintet;

［重重］ layer upon layer; ring upon ring;
重重包圍 be besieged circle upon circle; be encircled ring upon ring;
重重疊疊 layer after layer; multiple series; pile one upon another; repeatedly;
重重困難 innumerable difficulties; numerous difficulties;
重重壓迫 multiple oppressions;
重重障礙 an array of barriers; all sorts of obstacles; numerous obstructions;
顧慮重重 full of worries;
困難重重 many difficulties;
疑慮重重 many misgivings;

［重疊］ one on top of another; overlap; overlapping;
重疊部份 areas of overlap;
重疊詞 reduplication
~雙韻重疊詞 female rhyme reduplications;
~頭韻重疊詞 alliterative reduplications;
~尾韻重疊詞 rhyming reduplications;
翠竹重疊 be dotted with emerald bamboo groves;
動詞重疊 reduplication of verbs;
互相重疊 overlap each other;
頻帶重疊 band overlap;
頻率重疊 frequency overlap;
普項重疊 term overlapping;

［重返］ re-enter; return;
重返工作崗位 back on the job; return to work;
重返故土 on one's native soil again;
重返家園 return to one's homeland;
重返校園 resume one's interrupted studies at school;
重返影壇 get back into the film circle;
重返政治舞台 return to the political stage;

［重犯］ repeat an offense;

［重放］ replay;
即時重放 instant replay;

［重逢］ have a reunion; meet again;
等待重逢 wait for a reunion;
久別重逢 have a reunion; meet again after a long separation; reunite with sb after a long absence; see sb after being apart for a long time;
舊友重逢 old friends hold a reunion;
意外重逢 meet again by accident;

［重覆］ duplicate; repeat; reduplicate;
重覆幾遍 repeat several times;
重覆力 repeatability;
避免重覆 avoid repetition;
不必重覆 need no repetition;
間隔重覆 epanalepsis;
連續重覆 tandem duplication;
脈衝重覆 pulse repetition;
染色體重覆 gene duplication;
圖像重覆 image repetition;
應力重覆 stress repetition;

［重歸於好］ be reconciled; renew cordial relations;

［重合］ coincidence;
多次重合 multiple coincidence;
精確重合 exact coincidence;
偶然重合 accidental coincidence; chance coincidence;
隨機重合 random coincidence;
天線重合 antenna coincidence;

［重婚］ bigamy;

［重見］ see sth again;
重見光明 see the light again;
重見青天 regain freedom;
重見天日 get freed and enjoy the sunshine

again; be released after a great injustice; see the light of day once more;

[重建] rebuild; reconstruct; re-establish;
重建家園 rebuild one's home village; rehabilitate one's homeland;
重建秩序 re-establish order;
着手重建 enter on the reconstruction of;

[重聚] be reunited;
重聚家園 be reunited with one's family; family reunion;
重聚一堂 be reunited under the same roof;

[重來] make a comeback;
捲土重來 make a comeback; make a strong effort to recover the lost ground after a defeat; renew efforts after failure; stage a comeback;

[重排] rearrange; rearrangement;
氣相重排 vapour-phase rearrangement;
數據重排 data rearrangement;
原子重排 atomic rearrangement;

[重申] reaffirm; reiterate; restate;
重申觀點 reassert one's views;
重申己見 reiterate one's views;
重申立場 reaffirm one's stand;
重申前令 reaffirm an existing decree; reiterate the previous order;

[重拾] pick up again;
重拾舊歡 revive an old romance;
墜歡重拾 pick up the fallen lover – take back the deserted wife; revive an old romance;

[重數] multiplicity;
代數重數 algebraic multiplicity;
幾何重數 geometric multiplicity;
無窮重數 infinite multiplicity;
相交重數 intersection multiplicity;

[重提] bring up again; mention again;
重提舊事 bring up an old case; rake over old coals; rake over the ashes; rake up; rake up the past; recall past events;

[重圍] tight encirclement;
殺出重圍 fight one's way out of a tight encirclement; fight one's way out of double lines of besiegers;
逃出重圍 break out from a tight siege;

[重溫] brush up; review;
重溫舊景 relive the scenes from the past;
重溫舊夢 indulge again in one's pipe dream; recall past sweet experiences; recapture the dreams one has lost; relive an old experience; renew an old romance; renew the ecstasies of sensual delight; revive an old dream; seek once more what one experienced in a dream;
重溫舊情 renew one's old friendship with sb; revive the old affection;
鴛夢重溫 reunion of old lovers after a long separation;

[重顯] rendition;
全色重顯 panchromatic rendition;

[重現] reappear; rendition;
彩色重現 colour rendering;
對比度重現 contrast rendition;
舊景重現 scenes from the past flash before one's eyes; scenes of the past keep reappearing in one's mind; scenes of the past rise up before one's eyes;

[重新] (1) again; (2) afresh; anew;
重新工作 get back into harness;
重新化裝 fix one's face;
重新開始 go back to the drawing board; start afresh; start again; make a new start; take a fresh start; weigh anchor;
重新考慮 have second thoughts; reconsider;
重新上台 come back to power; regain power; return to power; stage a comeback;
重新掌權 return to power;
重新做人 begin one's life anew; lead a new life; start one's life afresh; start with a new slate; take a fresh start in life; turn over a new leaf;

[重修] (1) rebuild; renovate; (2) retake a course after failing it;
重修舊好 become friends again; become reconciled; bury the hatchet; renew cordial relations;
重修舊情 renew one's acquaintance with sb; renew one's friendship; talk over old times;

[重演] (1) put on an old play; repeat the performance; (2) recur; repeat; (3) re-enact;

[重洋] seas and oceans;
遠隔重洋 across the seas;
遠涉重洋 cross many seas; cross the seven seas; travel across the oceans; travel all the way from across the oceans;

travel all the way from the other side of the ocean;

[重陽] Double Ninth Festival;

[重譯] retranslate;

[重印] reprint;

[重影] double image; ghost; ghost image;

彩色重影 colour ghost;

超前重影 leading ghost;

跳動重影 galloping ghost;

拖尾重影 smear ghost;

正象重影 positive ghost;

[重振] reorganize;

重振朝綱 regenerate the imperial regime;

重振精神 second breath; second wind;

重振軍威 restore the prestige of an army;

重振旗鼓 rally one's forces again; lick one's wound;

重振聲威 regain one's lost reputation;

重振信心 restore one's confidence;

[重整] reform;

重整河山 rearrange hills and streams; rearrange the mountains and rivers; reconstruct the country;

重整家園 rebuild one's homeland;

重整旗鼓 pull one's forces together and start afresh; pull oneself together; rally forces; rally one's forces again;

接觸重整 contact reform;

石油重整 petroleum reform;

[重組] recasting; recombination; reorganize; restructure;

重組技術 recombinant technique;

重組內閣 reshuffle the cabinet;

重組子 recon;

基因重組 gene recombination;

遺傳重組 genetic recombination;

資產重組 reorganization of assets;

自由重組 free recombination;

[重奏] ensemble;

二重奏 duet;

七重奏 septet;

三重奏 trio;

四重奏 quartet;

~ 弦樂四重奏 string quartet;

五重奏 quintet;

[重作馮婦] take up one's old job again; take up one's old profession;

八重 eightfold;

多重 multiple;

二重 double; dualistic;

兩重 double; dual; twofold;

三重 threefold; treble; triple; tripling;

雙重 double;

四重 quadruple;

chong

【种】 (1) naive; naivete; (2) a surname; (3) a simplified form of 種 ;

chong

【崇】 (1) high; lofty; sublime; (2) esteem; worship;

[崇拜] adore; cult; worship;

崇拜對象 cult figure;

崇拜偶像 worship idols;

崇拜英雄 have a veneration for heroes;

感恩崇拜 thanksgiving service;

個人崇拜 personality cult;

~ 反對個人崇拜 oppose personality cult;

~ 提倡個人崇拜 promote personality cult;

~ 推行個人崇拜 practise personality cult;

盲目崇拜 worship blindly;

偶像崇拜 idolatry;

人類崇拜 anthropolatry;

圖騰崇拜 totemism;

[崇奉] believe in a religion; worship;

[崇高] lofty; sublime;

崇高的思想 sublime thought;

崇高理想 a lofty ideal;

[崇敬] esteem; respect; revere;

崇敬祖先 hold ancestors in veneration;

受到崇敬 be highly esteemed; gain high esteem;

[崇尚] advocate; uphold;

崇尚勤儉 advocate industry and thrift; uphold hardworking and thrift;

崇尚真理 advocate truth;

崇尚正義 uphold justice;

[崇洋] worship foreign things;

崇洋復古 worship the foreign and revive the ancient;

崇洋恐洋 worship foreign things and be in awe of foreigners;

崇洋賣國 worship everything that is foreign and betray one's own nation;

崇洋媚外 be crazy about foreign things and obsequious to foreigners; be subservient to foreigners; worship and fawn on foreigners; worship foreign things and fawn on foreign powers; worship foreign things and toady to foreign power;

C

崇洋迷洋 have blind faith in foreign things;

欽崇 admire; adore;
推崇 esteem; have a high opinion of; have a high regard for; hold in esteem; praise highly; recommend; respect; stand in awe of; think highly of;
尊崇 esteem; hold in reverence; revere; venerate; worship;
作崇 (1) haunt; (2) cause trouble; exercise evil influence; make mischief;

chong

【蟲】 insect; worm;
［蟲害］ damage to farm crops caused by pests;
發生蟲害 be infested with insects;
［蟲牙］ carious tooth;
［蟲子］ worm;
打蟲子 cure a parasitic disease; take worm medicine;
拉蟲子 pass worms;
長蟲子 have a parasitic disease;

鼻涕蟲 slug;
鞭蟲 whipworm;
變形蟲 amoeba;
捕蟲 insect-catching;
草蟲 grasses and insects;
車蟲 bicycle fanatic;
臭蟲 bedbug;
除蟲 kill off insects;
大蟲 tiger;
滴蟲 trichomonad;
飛蟲 winged insect;
跟頭蟲 wriggler;
鉤蟲 hookworm;
害蟲 harmful insects; injurious insects;
害人蟲 evil creature; pest;
糊塗蟲 blunderer; bungler;
蝗蟲 locust;
蛔蟲 roundworm;
寄生蟲 parasitic insect;
甲蟲 beetle;
介殼蟲 scale insect;
精蟲 spermatozoon;
可憐蟲 pitiful creature;
磕頭蟲 click beetle; snapping beetle;
叩頭蟲 click beetle; snapping beetle;
昆蟲 insect;
懶蟲 idler; lazybones;
毛蟲 caterpillar;
鳴蟲 singing insects;
爬蟲 reptile;
蛆蟲 maggot;
沙蟲 siphon-worm;
絲蟲 filarial;
縮頭蟲 bamboo worm;
絛蟲 cestode; tapeworm;
跳蟲 snow flea; springtail;
吸蟲 fluke;
線蟲 nematode;
夜光蟲 noctiluca;
益蟲 beneficial insect; useful insect;
螢火蟲 firefly; glow-worm;
應聲蟲 yes-man;
幼蟲 larva;

chong³
chong

【寵】 bestow favour on; dote on; pamper; spoil;
［寵愛］ cosset; dote on; make a pet of sb; receive favour from a superior; think the world of sb; think the world of sth;
寵愛兒孫 dote on one's children;
得人寵愛 find favour in sb's eyes;
［寵兒］ blue-eyed boy; darling; fair-haired boy; favourite; minion;
老闆的寵兒 the boss's fair-haired boy;
母親的寵兒 mamma's darling;
天之寵兒 one especially blessed by Heaven;
［寵壞］ spoil;
［寵辱］ fame and humiliation;
寵辱不驚 remain indifferent whether favoured or humiliated; unmoved by official honour or disgrace;
寵辱皆忘 not at all affected by fame or humiliation;
寵辱若驚 be terrified whether granted favours or subjected to humiliation;
［寵擅專房］ be unusually favoured by a husband—said of a concubine;
［寵物］ animal companion; pet; pet animal;
寵物狗 pet dog;
~小寵物狗 lap dog;
寵物糧食 pet food;
寵物貓 pet cat;
寵物熱 pet craze;
寵物兔 pet rabbit;
寵物商店 pet shop;
養寵物 keep a pet;

[寵信] favour and trust;
[寵遇] treat as a favourite;
愛寵 (1) bestow favour on; dote on; favour; love; (2) indulge; spoil; (3) one's beloved person;
得寵 find favour with sb; in favour;
恩寵 show special favour to sb;
取寵 curry favour;
權寵 gain powers through favour from the emperor;
榮寵 glorious favour;
失寵 fall into disfavour; out of favour;
恃寵 presume on being a favourite of sb powerful;
受寵 endear oneself to; find favour in the eyes of sb; gain grace; gain upon sb's heart; gain sb's favour; get in good with sb; get on the right side of sb; in favour with sb; in good with sb; in sb's favour; in sb's good books; in sb's good graces; in with sb; make time with sb; receive favour from a superior; win sb's favour;
殊寵 special favour;
邀寵 (1) make oneself liked by a superior; (2) try to win the husband's love;
爭寵 compete for sb's favour;
專寵 monopolize the ruler's love;

chong⁴
chong
【銃】 (1) firearm; (2) joint of the metal head to the handle of an axe;

chong
【衝】 (1) head; (2) forceful; strong; (3) brave and fierce; (4) take a nap; (5) for one's sake; (6) direct one's attack toward sb;

chou¹
chou
【抽】 (1) take out; (2) take; (3) put forth; (4) obtain by drawing; (5) shrink; (6) lash; thrash; whip;
[抽查] selective examination; spot check;
[抽抽] shrink;
抽抽嗒嗒 emit intermittently; sob and sniffle; sob intermittently;
[抽出] draw out; extract; select from a lot; withdraw;
抽出時間 find time;
抽不出 cannot afford;
~抽不出時間 cannot afford the time;
[抽除] abstraction;
熱抽除 heat abstraction;
[抽搐] convulsion; tic; twitch;
抽搐病 Tourette syndrome;
肌肉抽搐 get a muscle twitch;
局部性抽搐 local tic;
面肌抽搐 facial tic;
神經性抽搐 nervous twitch;
手足抽搐 tetany;
~高空手足抽搐 altitude tetany;
四肢不斷抽搐 keep twitching one's arms and legs;
舞蹈抽搐 sleep twitching;
[抽打] (1) flog; lash; slash; thrash; whip; (2) remove dust with a towel;
被抽打 receive lashes;
[抽調] transfer;
[抽動] herky-jerky;
[抽檢] spot-check;
[抽獎] drawing; prize drawing;
[抽筋] (1) pull out a tendon; (2) charlie horse; cramp; have a cramp;
抽筋剝皮 peel off the skin and pluck out the sinews; pull out sb's tendons and tear his skin off;
[抽空] manage to find time;
抽空偷閒 spare a few moments from work; take advantage of any free time;
抽空學習 study at odd moments;
[抽立] lose money;
[抽氣機] air pump;
[抽泣] sob;
悲痛地抽泣 sob bitterly;
忍住抽泣 check one's sobs;
[抽簽] ballot; by lot; cast lots; draw cuts; draw lots;
抽籤決定 decide sth by lot;
抽籤選擇 make a choice by lot;
[抽球] drive;
反手抽球 backhand drive;
平抽球 drive;
正手抽球 forehand drive;
[抽身] get away; leave one's work;
抽身引退 leave one's work and resign; retire from active public life; withdraw from one's post;
[抽絲] (1) reel off raw silk from cocoons; (2) snag;

抽絲剝繭 make a painstaking investigation;
病來如山倒，病去如抽絲 agues come on horseback but go away on foot;
禍來如山倒，禍去如抽絲 mischiefs come by the pound and go away by the ounce;
災來如山倒，災去如抽絲 mischief comes by the pound and goes away by the ounce; misfortunes come on wings and depart on foot;

[抽水] draw water;
從河裏抽水 draw water from a river;

[抽税] levy a tax;
對煙草抽税 levy a tax on tobacco;

[抽屜] drawer;
餐具抽屜 cutlery drawer;
廚房抽屜 kitchen drawer;
頂層抽屜 top drawer;
短襪抽屜 sock drawer;
關上抽屜 shut a drawer;
拉開抽屜 open a drawer;
亂翻抽屜 ferret about in a drawer; jumble up everything in a drawer;
書桌抽屜 desk drawer;
鎖上抽屜 lock a drawer;
整理抽屜 clean out a drawer; do out a drawer;

[抽象] abstract; abstracting; abstraction;
抽象詞 abstract word;
抽象概念 abstract concept;
~ 抽象概念思維 abstract conceptual thinking;
抽象交互處理 abstract interaction handling;
~ 抽象交互處理器系統 abstract interaction handler system;
抽象名詞 abstract noun;
抽象派 abstractionism; abstractionist school;
~ 抽象派畫家 abstractionist;
~ 抽象派藝術 abstractionism;
抽象行政行為 abstract administrative action;
抽象藝術 abstract art;
抽象智力 abstract intelligence;
抽象主義 abstractionism;
~ 幾何抽象主義 geometric abstraction;
純抽象 complete abstraction;
函數抽象 functional abstraction;

[抽薪] take out the firewood;
抽薪止沸 stop the boiling by taking out the firewood; take away fuel; take away flame; take out the firewood to stop the pot boiling — take drastic measures to put sth to an end;

[抽芽] bud; sprout;
抽芽長葉 put forth leaves and put out shoots;
春天抽芽 sprout in the spring;
開始抽芽 unfold buds;

[抽煙] smoke; smoke a cigarette;
抽煙的人 smoker;
~ 不抽煙的人 non-smoker;
愛抽煙 fond of smoking;
不停地抽煙 smoke like a chimney;
老在抽煙 never stop smoking for a moment;
禁止抽煙 smoking is prohibited;
隨便抽煙 smoke freely;

[抽驗] spot check; test sample;

[抽樣] sampling;
抽樣調查 sample investigation;
~ 抽樣調查法 sampling investigation method;
抽樣檢查 take a sample for examination; sampling investigation;
抽樣均值 sample means;
重覆抽樣 duplicate sampling;
概率抽樣 probability sampling;
隨意抽樣 random sampling;
統計抽樣 statistical sampling;

[抽油煙機] smoke exhaust ventilator;

[抽脂] liposuction;

長抽 long drive;

chou

【紬】 (1) draw out; (2) collect and edit;

[紬次] collect and arrange in order;

chou

【搊】 (1) pluck stringed instruments with fingers; (2) tighten; (3) hold and support;

chou

【瘳】 (1) cured; healed; (2) harm; hurt;

chou

【篘】 (1) wine filter; (2) filter wine;

chou

【犨】 panting of an ox;

chou²

chou

【仇】 (1) enemy; foe; (2) enmity; hatred;

[仇敵] enemy; foe;

[仇惡] abhor evil;

疾惡如仇 abhor evils as deadly foes; abhor evils as if they were one's personal enemies; hate evil as much as one hates an enemy; hate injustice like poison; hate the wicked like enemies;

[仇恨] animosity; animus; enmity; grudge; hatred; hostility;

仇恨滿胸 be filled with bitter hatred;

仇恨難消 one's hatred and grief are undying;

產生仇恨 develop enmity with sb;

階級仇恨 class hatred;

滿懷仇恨 one's heart is aflame with hatred;

滿腔仇恨 be filled with an inveterate hatred; burn with hatred; see things with hatred;

千仇萬恨 a thousand and one hates; countless hatreds; innumerable hatreds;

煽動仇恨 stir up hate;

挑起仇恨 stir up enmity;

新仇舊恨 all the old and recent grudges; new hatred piled on the old;

引起仇恨 incur the enmity of sb;

招人仇恨 court hatred;

種族仇恨 race hatred;

[仇家] enemy; foe;

[仇人] personal enemy;

仇人相見，分外眼紅 meeting enemies opens old wounds; when two foes meet, there is no mistaking each other;

盻視仇人 glare at the foe;

[仇殺] kill in revenge;

[仇視] hostile to; look upon with hatred; regard as an enemy;

互相仇視 regard each other as enemies;

[仇隙] bitter quarrel; feud;

[仇英] Anglophobia;

仇英心理 Anglophobia;

仇英者 Anglophobe;

[仇怨] enmity; hatred; hostility;

舊仇宿怨 long established grudge and hatred; old feuds; old grudges; old scores;

報仇 avenge; be out for sb's scalp; get back at; get even with sb; get one's own back on sb; get one's revenge; get square with sb; have one's own back on sb; have one's revenge; have sb's scalp; pay back sb; pay off sb; pay out sb; revenge; serve out sb; take sb's scalp;

成仇 become enemies;

恩仇 debt of gratitude and revenge;

復仇 avenge; revenge;

記仇 bear grudges; harbour bitter resentment or hatred;

結仇 become enemies; start a feud;

寇仇 enemy; foe;

深仇 deep hatred;

世仇 (1) family feud; (2) bitter enemy;

私仇 personal enmity;

夙仇 old enemy;

挾仇 nurse an enmity;

冤仇 enmity; rancour;

怨仇 old enemy;

chou

【惆】 regretful; rueful;

[惆悵] regretful; rueful;

惆悵若失 in a despondent mood;

[惆然] regretful; wistful;

[惆惋] regretful; wistful;

chou

【紬】 silk fabric; thin silk goods;

chou

【愁】 anxious; worried;

[愁腸] pent-up feelings of sadness;

愁腸百結 be overwhelmed with sorrow and longing; be weighed down with anxiety; broken-hearted; suffer great agonies of the mind; with anxiety gnawing at one's heart;

愁腸寸斷 eat one's heart out; one's anxious heart is broken;

[愁煩] worried; worry;

[愁海] sea of sorrows;

[愁恨] worries and hatred;

千愁萬恨 a thousand and one worries and hatred; innumerable worries and hatred;

[愁慮交織] intense sorrow and concern are mixed in one's heart;

[愁眉] knitted brows; worried look;

愁眉不展 bend one's brows; gloom hangs upon one's brow; have a cloud

upon one's brow; have a gloomy countenance; knit one's brows; look blue; lower one's eyebrows; with a worried frown; with one's brows knitted in deep thought; with knitted brows;
愁眉蹙額 gloomy eyebrows and wrinkled forehead — knit the brows;
愁眉苦臉 a face of woe; a face shaded with melancholy; down in the dumps; down in the mouth; draw a long face; gloomy face; have a face as long as a fiddle; have a face like a fiddle; have a worried look; look blue; make a long face; pull a long face; put on a long face; wear a glum countenance; with a long face;
愁眉鎖眼 knit one's brows and cast down one's eyes in despair; knit one's brows in despair;

[愁悶] depressed; distress; feel gloomy; glum; in low spirits;
滿腔愁悶 full of care;

[愁容] anxious expression; worried look;
愁容滿面 have a mournful countenance; look extremely worried;
滿臉愁容 one's face clouds over; woebegone expression;
面帶愁容 one's face wears an anxious expression;
一片愁容 a cloud of grief; a shadow rested on one's face;

[愁色] worried expression;
面有愁色 make a glum face; one's face looks worried;

[愁思] deep longing; forlornness; melancholy;
春愁秋思 spring longings and autumn thoughts;
萬種愁思 the thousand unknown plaints and grievances;

[愁緒] feeling of sadness; gloomy mood; skein of sorrow;
愁緒滿懷 be distracted with worries; have the weight of the world on one's shoulders; one's breast filled with melancholy thoughts;
愁緒萬千 in extreme grief;
千愁萬緒 an endless stream of dreamy thoughts;
驅散愁緒 dispel one's gloomy moods;

[愁雲] cloud of sorrow; depressing clouds; heavy clouds;
愁雲慘霧 cloud of sorrow; gathering clouds and rolling mists;
愁雲滿佈 clouded with worry;
慘雨愁雲 dark clouds and chilly rain;
一絲愁雲 a cloud of sorrow; a feeling of sadness;

哀愁 sad; sorrowful;
悲愁 sad and vexed;
不愁 not worry;
發愁 anxious; worried;
犯愁 anxious; worried;
澆愁 wash away one's sorrow;
窮愁 hard up and depressed;
鄉愁 homesickness; nostalgia;
消愁 allay cares; dispel worries;
新愁 fresh sorrows;
憂愁 agony; anguish; depressed; grief; melancholy; misery; mournful; remorse; sad; sadness; woe; worried;

chou

【稠】 (1) closely; crowded; dense; (2) thick; (3) a great many; teeming; (4) a surname;

[稠度] consistence;
稠度計 consistometer;
標準稠度 standard consistence;
糊狀稠度 pasty consistence;
瀝青稠度 consistence of asphalt;
相對稠度 relative consistence;
正常稠度 normal consistence;

[稠密] crowded; dense;
居民稠密 be densely populated;
人口稠密 dense population;

[稠人廣眾] assemble in one place; large crowd of people;

[稠雲] dense clouds;

chou

【酬】 (1) propose a toast; toast; (2) payment; reward; (3) friendly exchange; (4) fulfil; realize;

[酬報] recompense; requite; reward;

[酬賓] give a discount; sell at a favourable price;

[酬答] (1) thank sb with a gift; (2) respond with a poem or speech;
酬答恩德 requite gratitude;

[酬金] commission; emolument; monetary reward; remuneration; reward; service

fees;
優厚酬金 satisfactory honorarium;

[酬勞] (1) thank sb with a gift; (2) recompense; remunerate; reward;
得到酬勞 be remunerated;

[酬謝] thank sb with a gift;

[酬應] have social intercourse with; social intercourse;

[酬酢] (1) drink toasts to each other; exchange of toasts; (2) have social intercourse with; treat with courtesy;

報酬 pay; remuneration; reward;
薄酬 low pay; meagre remuneration; small reward;
稿酬 author's remuneration; payment to an author for a book;
計酬 calculate the sum of a payment;
勸酬 urge to drink;
應酬 (1) engage in social activities; have social intercourse; (2) treat with courtesy;
重酬 handsome reward; substantial reward;

chou

【綢】 (1) silk fabric; (2) fine and delicate; (3) twine and tangle;

[綢段] silk goods;

[綢繆] (1) get prepared; (2) tender love; (3) consolidate; make strong; strengthen; (4) luxuriant growth of flowers;
綢繆繾綣 bind closely and be deeply attached;
情意綢繆 head over heels in love;
未雨綢繆 cast an anchor to windward; have an anchor to windward; have forethought; lay up for a rainy day; make provision for sth; provide against a rainy day; provide against the future; provide for a rainy day; put away for a rainy day; repair the house before it rains; save against a rainy day; take precautions before it is too late; take protective measures in advance;

[綢子] silk fabric;

波紋綢 moire; watered silk;
彩綢 coloured silk;
春綢 silk fabric with a geometric design;
紡綢 soft plain weave silk fabric;
府綢 poplin;
繭綢 pongee; tussah silk;
絹綢 silk;
綿綢 fabric made from waste silk;
絲綢 silk; silk cloth;
雲紋綢 moire;
縐綢 crepe;

chou

【裯】 (1) bed sheet; thin quilt; (2) bed curtain;

chou

【儔】 companion; company; party;

[儔侶] companion; company; party;
命儔嘯侶 call people friends and companions — gather a clique;

chou

【雔】 pair of birds;

chou

【幬】 canopy; curtain;

chou

【疇】 (1) agricultural lands; fields; (2) who; (3) formerly; previously; (4) category; class; rank;

[疇輩] people of the same generation;

[疇人] astrologist;

磁疇 magnetic domain;
範疇 ambit; category; domain; realm;
平疇 level field;
田疇 farmland; fields;

chou

【籌】 (1) chip; counter; (2) plan; plan and consider; prepare;

[籌辦] make arrangements; make preparations; organize;
籌辦會議 make preparations for a conference;

[籌備] make arrangements; make preparations; on the anvil; plan; prepare; upon the anvil;
籌備工作 preparatory work;
籌備委員會 preparatory committee;
籌備展覽 arrange an exhibition;

[籌措] financing; raise money;
籌措資金 raise funds;
貸款籌措 loan financing;
項目資金籌措 project financing;

[籌劃] plan and prepare;
周密籌劃 elaborate a plan for;

[籌集] raise money;

籌集基金 raise funds;

[籌建] prepare and establish; prepare to construct;

籌建學校 put up a school;

[籌款] fund-raising; raise funds;

籌款活動 fundraising campaign;

緊急籌款 raise funds in a hurry;

[籌碼] chip; counter;

輸光籌碼 lose all one's chips;

談判籌碼 bargaining chip;

[籌謀] plan and prepare;

[籌募] collect funds;

[籌商] consult; discuss;

籌商對策 discuss what countermeasures to take;

[籌算] count;

[籌組] plan and organize;

[籌資] financing;

籌資活動 financing activities;

黑市籌資 black market financing;

外部籌資 external financing;

藍籌 blue-chip;

統籌 plan as a whole;

一籌 a tally;

運籌 devise strategies;

chou

【躊】 (1) hesitant; (2) complacent; confident;

[躊躇] hesitate; shilly-shally;

躊躇半晌 ponder for a while;

躊躇不安 flutter; have the fidgets; in fidgets;

躊躇不決 think back and forth without end; uncertain as to what decision or action to take;

躊躇不前 hang back; hesitate to make a move; hesitate to move forward; hold back; jib at; show reluctance to go forward;

躊躇滿志 be elated with success; be self-satisfied; complacent; enormously proud of one's success; erect one's crest; feel self-satisfied; puffed up with pride; smug;

躊躇徬徨 dawdle and hesitate;

臨事躊躇 hesitate at a step;

chou

【讎】 (1) enemy; foe; rival; (2) collate; compare;

[讎敵] enemy; foe;

[讎視] hostile to; regard with hostility;

[讎問] ask difficult questions;

校讎 collate;

chou³

chou

【丑】 (1) second of the twelve Terrestrial Branches; (2) period from 1 to 3 a.m.; (3) clown; (4) a surname;

[丑表功] claim an undeserved credit;

[丑旦] comedienne; female clown;

[丑角] clown; comedian;

文丑 a kind of comedian in Chinese operas;

武丑 military comedian in Chinese operas;

小丑 (1) clown; comedian; (2) contemptible wretch;

chou

【瞅】 gaze; look; see;

[瞅睬] give attention; look at;

不瞅不睬 ignore completely; neither look or give attention; pay no attention;

互不瞅睬 pay no attention to each other;

[瞅見] see;

chou

【醜】 (1) hideous; ugly; unsightly; (2) disgraceful; scandalous; shameful;

[醜八怪] very bad-looking person; very ugly person;

[醜惡] hideous; repulsive; ugly;

[醜婦] minger;

[醜化] defame; smear; uglify; vilify;

醜化環境 uglify the environment;

[醜陋] bad-looking; hideous; ugly;

極為醜陋 hideously ugly;

[醜女] minger;

[醜事] abominable affair; disgraceful affair; scandal;

[醜態] buffoonery; ugly performance;

醜態百出 act like a buffoon; behave in a revolting manner; cut a contemptible;

[醜聞] scandal;

充滿醜聞 rife with scandals;

傳播醜聞 circulate a scandal; spread a scandal;

揑造醜聞 make up a scandal;

談論醜聞 talk about a scandal;

性醜聞 sex scandal;
一件醜聞 a scandal;
一樁醜聞 a scandal;
隱瞞醜聞 conceal a scandal;
政治醜聞 political scandals;

謷醜 abuse; defame; slander;
出醜 bring shame on oneself; make a fool of oneself; make an exhibition of oneself;
丟醜 be disgraced; lose face; make an exhibition of oneself;
家醜 family scandal;
揭醜 reveal; unmask;
獻醜 show one's incompetence; show oneself up;
遮醜 gloss over one's blemishes; hide one's shame;

chou⁴ chou

【臭】 (1) foul; smelly; stinking; (2) disgraceful; disgusting; (3) stupid; (4) bad; inferior; (5) disappointing;

[臭不可聞] a stench in everyone's nostrils; evil-smelling; give off an unbearable stink; smell to high heaven;
[臭吹] boast;
[臭蟲] bedbug;
[臭大糞] low-grade; no-good; stupid;
[臭彈] stink bomb;
[臭烘烘的] smelly; stinky;
[臭腳] stinky foot;
捧臭腳 curry favour; flatter; lick sb's boots;
[臭罵] bollocking; curse roundly; scold angrily and abusively;
臭罵一頓 skin sb alive;
一頓臭罵 give sb a good dressing down; give sb a good scolding;
[臭美] (1) beautify; dress up; make up; (2) be stuck on oneself; give oneself airs; swollen-headed;
臭美妞 fussy about her appearance;
[臭名] ill fame; infamy; notorious reputation;
臭名遠播 infamous; notorious;
臭名遠揚 create a scandal far and wide;
臭名昭著 foul reputation; infamous; notorious; of ill repute; sb's name is mud;
一身臭名 earn a very bad name for oneself;
[臭棋] hard tactics;
[臭氣] bad smell; stink;
臭氧層 ozonosphere;
臭氣衝天 stinking smell assaulting one's nostrils;
臭氣撲鼻 a strong scent irritates the nose;
臭氣熏天 stink to high heaven;
~ 廁所臭氣熏天 the toilets stink to high heaven;
發出臭氣 exhale an offensive odour; send out a bad odour;
消除臭氣 destroy foul odours;
[臭味] foul smell; odour; stink;
臭味相投 birds of a feather; two of a kind;
散發臭味 give an offensive smell;
[臭氧] ozone;
臭氧層 ozone layer;
~ 臭氧層空洞 ozone hole;
臭氧發生器 ozonizer;
臭氧計 ozone meter; ozonometer;
臭氧降解 ozone degradation;
臭氧損耗 ozone depletion;

長臭 long-winded and smelly;
除臭 deodorize;
惡臭 foul smell; offensive smell; stench; stink;
搞臭 discredit; stink; put to shame;
汗臭 stinking smell due to perspiration;
狐臭 body odour; bromhidrosis;
口臭 bad breath; foul breath; halitosis;
霉臭 musty smell;
乳臭 childishness;
腥臭 stench; stinking smell as that of rotten fish;
遺臭 infamy;

chu¹ chu

【出】 (1) come out; go out; (2) exceed; go beyond; (3) give; issue; offer; put up; (4) produce; turn out; (5) arise; happen; occur; take place; (6) put forth; vent; (7) rise well; (8) expend; pay out;

[出版] come off the press; come out; give to the world; publication; publish; publishing; see the light of day;
出版部 publishing department;
出版公司 publishing company;
出版日期 date of publication; publication date;
出版社 press; publisher; publishing

company; publishing house;
~ 編譯出版社 compilation and translation press;
~ 兵器工業出版社 ordnance industry publishing house;
~ 測繪出版社 surveying and mapping publishing house;
~ 辭書出版社 lexicographical press;
~ 檔案出版社 archives press;
~ 地圖出版社 cartographical publishing house;
~ 地質出版社 geological publishing house;
~ 電力出版社 electric power press;
~ 電影出版社 film press;
~ 電子工業出版社 electronic industry publishing house;
~ 對外經濟貿易出版社 foreign economic relations and trade press;
~ 兒童出版社 children's publishing house;
~ 法律出版社 law publishing house;
~ 法制出版社 legal system publishing house;
~ 工人出版社 workers' publishing house;
~ 工藝美術出版社 arts and crafts publishing house;
~ 古籍出版社 ancient books publishing house;
~ 廣播電視出版社 radio and television publishing house;
~ 國際廣播出版社 international radio press;
~ 畫報出版社 pictorial press;
~ 華僑出版社 overseas Chinese publishing house;
~ 環境科學出版社 environmental science press;
~ 教育出版社 education publishing house;
~ 金融出版社 finance publishing house;
~ 科技出版社 science and technology publishing house;
~ 旅遊出版社 travel and tourism press;
~ 美術出版社 fine arts publishing house;
~ 民族出版社 nationalities publishing house;
~ 青年出版社 youth publishing house;
~ 人民出版社 people's publishing house;
~ 攝影藝術出版社 photographic art publishing house;
~ 外文出版社 foreign language press;
~ 文化出版社 cultural publishing house;
~ 文史出版社 culture and history publishing house;
~ 文學出版社 literature publishing house;
~ 文獻出版社 document publishing house;
~ 文藝出版社 literature and art publishing house;
~ 一家出版社 a publishing house;
~ 譯文出版社 translation publishing house;
~ 音像出版社 music publishing house;
~ 音樂出版社 music publishing house;
~ 作家出版社 writers publishing house;
出版物 publication;
~ 大學出版物 college publication;
~ 對外出版物 external publication;
~ 外文出版物 foreign language publications;
~ 政府出版物 government publication;
出版者 publisher;
出版著作 publish a work;
出版自由 freedom of press;
不再出版 no longer in print; pass out of print;
電子出版 e-publishing; electronic publishing;
如期出版 come out on time;
首次出版 appear in print for the first time;
桌面出版 desktop publishing;
自費出版 vanity press;

[出奔] flee; leave; run away; take flight;

[出殯] carry a coffin to the cemetery; hold a funeral procession;

[出兵] dispatch troops; send an army into battle;
大舉出兵 launch a might army;
拒絕出兵 refuse to dispatch troops to;

[出彩兒] brilliant; do brilliant things; exciting; make a good show; put on a good play; splendid;

[出菜] achieve sth; make sth; produce a product;

[出操] go out to do exercises;

[出差] away on official business; on a business trip;
出差在外 on a business trip;
經常出差 a fair amount of travel;

[出產] manufacture; produce;
出產水果 teem with fruit;

[出場] (1) appear on the scene; come on the stage; make an appearance; put in an appearance; (2) enter;
被罰出場 foul out;

[出廠] leave the factory;
出廠價 ex-factory price;
出廠日期 date of production;

[出車] (1) dispatch a vehicle; (2) be out driving a vehicle;

[出醜] bring shame on oneself; make a fool of oneself; pratfall;
避免出醜 escape infamy;
大出其醜 hold sb up to ridicule; make an ass of oneself; make monkeys out of sb; put sb to shame;
當眾出醜 make a fool of oneself before others;
人前出醜 make a fool of oneself;

[出處] reference; source;
注明出處 give references; indicate the source;

[出錯] go amiss; go awry; make mistakes;

[出動] (1) set out; start off; (2) call out; dispatch; send out;
待命出動 await orders to set out;
緊急出動 come into prompt action;
提前出動 set off ahead of schedule;

[出爾反爾] back-pedal; backtrack; blow hot and cold; break one's word; contradict oneself; go back on one's word; play fast and loose;

[出發] take to the road;
出發點 origin; point of departure; starting point;
~ 基本出發點 basic point of departure;
出發日期 date of departure; departure date;
待命出發 await orders to set off; be ready for orders to set out; wait for orders to start off;

[出訪] go abroad to visit; visit a foreign country;

[出閣] get married; marry;

[出格] (1) exceed proper limits for speech or action; exceed what is proper; go too far; overdo sth; (2) differ from others; out of the ordinary;

[出工] (1) go to work; set out for work; show up for work; turn out for work; (2) supply the labour;

[出乖露丑] cut a very miserable figure; make a sight of oneself; make a spectacle of oneself;

[出軌] (1) be derailed; go off the rails; jump the rails; (2) overstep the bounds;
出軌的話 improper remarks;
火車出軌 the train left the rails; the train got off the track; the train ran off the rails;
行為出軌 commit an impropriety; step out of line;

[出國] go abroad; leave one's native land;
出國定居 go abroad to settle down there;
出國回來 return from abroad;
出國留學 go abroad to study; go abroad to further one's education;
出國旅遊 journey abroad;
出國熱 craze of going abroad;
出國深造 be sent to other countries for advanced studies; go abroad to continue one's studies; go abroad to further one's education;
出國探親 visit one's relatives abroad;
渴望出國 keen on going abroad;
因公出國 go abroad on a public errand;

[出海] go to sea; put out to sea;
出海捕魚 go fishing on the sea;
駕船出海 put to sea;
離港出海 move seaward from port;
揚帆出海 sail out to sea;

[出汗] perspire; sweat;
出汗濕透 wet with perspiration; wet with sweat;
大量出汗 desudation;
開始出汗 break into a sweat; break out in a sweat;

[出航] (1) set out on a voyage; set sail; (2) set out on a flight; take off;

[出花兒] suffer from chickenpox;

[出活] efficient; yield results at work;

[出擊] hit out; launch an attack; make a sally;
出擊部隊 attacking force;
四面出擊 hit out in all directions;
向對手出擊 hit at one's opponent;
正面出擊 make a frontal attack;
主動出擊 make an initiative sally;

[出家] become a monk or a nun;
出家人 monks and nuns;
出家皈依 give up one's home and practise

religion;
半路出家 (1) become a monk or nun late in life; (2) switch to a job half-prepared; switch to a job one is not trained for; (3) without solid foundation or training;

[出價] bid; offer a price;
出價過高 overbid;
出價合理 make a fair offer;
出價者 bidder;
撤回出價 retract one's bid;

[出嫁] get married; marry;
出嫁的姑娘—滿面春風 like a girl who is going to get married — beaming with satisfaction;

[出境] depart; emigrate; exit; leave the country;
出境簽證 exit visa;
出境手續 exit formalities;
被驅逐出境 await deportation;
被押送出境 be sent out of the country under escort;
擯逐出境 be deported from the country; oust sb from the border;
逮解出境 deportation;
遷移出境 emigrate; emigration;
驅逐出境 deport; deportation; expel;

[出鏡] come on the camera; play a role in a film;

[出口] (1) speak; utter; (2) exit; outlet; way out; (3) export;
出口按鈕 exit button;
出口補貼 export subsidy;
出口產品 export product;
~出口產品基地 base of export product;
出口成章 a ready orator whenever one speaks; have the gift of the gab; make polished impromptu speech; talk beautifully; toss off smart remarks; words flow from the mouth as from the pen of a master;
出口創匯基地 base for export and foreign exchange earning;
出口創匯企業 enterprises which are mainly intended to earn foreign exchange through exports;
出口粗野 swear like a trooper;
出口定額 export quota;
出口公司 exporter;
出口鼓勵 export promotion;
出口管制 export control;
出口國 exporter;
出口減少 decline in exports; drop in exports; fall in exports;
出口獎金 export bounty;
出口結匯 settlement;
出口謹慎 speak with reserve;
出口禁令 export ban;
出口控制 export control;
出口罵人 bawl sb out;
出口貿易 export trade;
出口配額 export quota;
出口氣 vent one's spleen on;
出口商 exporter;
~批發出口商 wholesale exporter;
出口商品 articles of export; export commodities;
出口傷人 give sb the rough side of one's tongue; offend by rude remarks; speak bitingly; use bad language to insult people;
出口市場 export market;
出口收益 export earnings; export revenue;
出口手續 export procedures;
~簡化出口手續 simplify export procedures;
出口稅 export tax;
出口退稅 export tax refund;
~出口退稅率 export tax refund rate;
~出口退稅政策 policy of tax refunds;
出口限制 export restrictions;
出口銷售 export sales;
出口信貸 export credit;
~出口信貸保險 export credit insurance;
出口信用 export trust;
~出口信用保險 export trust insurance;
出口許可證 export licence;
~出口許可證制 export-licence system;
出口增加 exports decline; exports drop; exports fall;
出口增長 growth in exports; increase in exports; rise in exports;
出口主導戰略 export-oriented strategy;
安全出口 emergency exit; fire exit;
促進出口 boost exports;
單邊出口 unilateral export;
復出口 re-export;
鼓勵出口 encourage exports;
固定出口 stationary exit;
減少出口 reduce exports;
間接出口 indirect export;
禁止出口 ban exports; prohibition on exportation;

淨出口 net export;
擴大出口 expand exports;
虧你說得出口 of all the nerve;
料倉出口 bin exit;
毛細管出口 capillary outlet;
排水出口 drain outlet;
噴嘴出口 jet exit;
說不出口 feel embarrassed to mention sth to others; hard and awkward to state;
停止出口 export suspension;
無形出口 invisible exports;
限制出口 restrict exports;
旋管出口 coil exit;
找到出口 find an exit;
暫時出口 temporary export;
直接出口 direct export;
中斷出口 cut off the export of sth;
軸出口 axial outlet;
專門出口 special export;
自由出口 free export;
總出口 general export;

[出來] come out; emerge;
迸出來 spit out; squeeze out;
變得認不出來 change beyond all recognition;
從房間出來 come out of the room;
講出來 speak up;
哭出來 burst into tears;
認不出來 be unable to recognize; fail to recognize;
掏出來 draw out; pull out;
挖出來 dig out; excavate; gouge out;
想出來 think out;

[出力] exert oneself; exert one's efforts; make great efforts; put forth one's strength;
出力不討好 do a thankless task;
為國出力 labour for the country;
有力出力 let those with strength contribute with their strength;
有錢出錢，有力出力 the rich can provide money and the strong can provide strength;

[出溜] (1) slide; slip; (2) degenerate; go downhill; sink low;

[出籠] (1) come out of the steamer; (2) appear; come forth; come out into the open;

[出路] (1) outlet; way out; (2) outlet;
打開出路 fight one's way out;
給出路 give a chance to turn over a new leaf; give a way out;
看不到出路 see no way out;
沒有出路 have nowhere to go; get nowhere;
唯一的出路 the only way out;
找出路 find a way out; find an outlet; look for a job with a future; look for a way out; seek a way out;
自謀出路 find oneself a job; find one's own means of livelihood; seek jobs on one's own; seek self-employment;
自尋出路 work out one's own salvation;

[出落] grow prettier;

[出馬] go into action; take the field; take up a matter;
親自出馬 take charge of the matter personally; take up the matter oneself;

[出賣] betray; sell out;
出賣靈魂 sell one's soul to;
出賣朋友 sell sb down the river; sell the pass;
出賣權利 barter away one's rights;
出賣榮譽 barter away one's honour;
出賣原則 barter away one's principles;
出賣自由 barter away one's freedom;
被叛徒出賣 be sold out by a traitor;

[出門] away from home; go on a journey; go out;
出門不在家 absent from home;
出門看天色，進門觀臉色 look at a man's face when you step in; look at the weather when you step out;
出門旅行 travel away from home;
出門上班 go out for work;
出門迎迓 come out to greet sb at the gate; meet sb at the gate; step out to welcome sb; welcome sb at the gate;
初次出門 first leave home;
早些出門，一路從容 an early start makes easy stages;

[出面] act in one's own capacity; appear personally; come forward;
出面人 front man;
出面調停 act as a mediator;

[出名] famous; make a name for oneself; make one's mark; make one's name; renown; rise to fame; to a proverb; well-known; win a name for oneself;
被捧出名 be lifted into fame;
渴望出名 search for fame;
開始出名 come into prominence;
人怕出名豬怕壯 a person's fame draws the envy of other people; destruction

pursues the great; fame portends trouble for people just as fattening does for pigs; great honours are great burdens; the whiter the cow, the surer it is to go to the altar;
越來越出名 gain rising fame;
以勇敢出名 have a name for bravery;

[出沒] appear and disappear; haunt;
出沒無常 appear at intervals; appear and disappear unexpectedly; come and go unexpectedly;
神出鬼沒 alert and quick; appear and disappear in quick succession; come and go like a shadow;
旋出旋沒 appear and disappear in quick succession;

[出謀獻策] give advice and suggestions; offer advice;
在背後出謀獻策 mastermind a scheme from behind the scenes;

[出納] (1) receive and pay out money or bills; (2) cashier; teller;
出納機 teller;
~自動出納機 auto-teller;
出納員 cashier; teller;
現金出納 cash handler;
銀行出納 cashier; teller;

[出票] draw;
出票人 drawer;

[出品] (1) make; manufacture; produce; (2) product;

[出奇] extraordinarily; unusually;
出奇制勝 achieve success with original ideas; defeat one's opponent by a surprise move; defeat one's opponent by surprise tactics; win by means of a surprise attack; win by novelty;
冷得出奇 unusually cold;

[出氣] blow off steam; give vent to one's anger; let off steam; vent one's spleen;
出氣筒 take it out on sb;
拿別人出氣 give vent to one's anger on others; work off one's bad temper on others;
一鼻孔出氣 breathe in the same way; conspire with sb; echo one another's opinion; hold identical opinions; in conformity with sb; in league with sb; in tune with sb; say exactly the same thing; side with sb; sing the same tune; talk exactly one like the other; toe the line of sb;

[出錢] open one's purse;

[出勤] (1) turn out for work; (2) out on duty;
出勤率 attendance rate;

[出去] get out; go out; pass out; pop out; step out;
出去了 has gone out;
出去一會兒 step out for a few minutes;
出去一下 go somewhere;
出去走走 go out for a walk;
搬出去 move out;
豁出去 go ahead regardless; ready to risk everything; shoot the works;
急忙出去 hasten out;
攆出去 drive out; oust;
氣沖沖地衝了出去 go off in a huff; leave in a huff; walk off in a huff;
踢出去 kick out;

[出缺] fall vacant;

[出讓] sell;
出讓人 transferor;
出讓土地 sell the land;
~出讓土地使用權 sell the right to use one's land;
拱手出讓 give sth away with both hands;

[出人頭地] come to the fore; fill the bill; have one's head and shoulders above others; make it to the top; make one's mark; put oneself on the map; rise head and shoulders above others; stand out among one's fellows;
靠自己的努力出人頭地 pull oneself up by one's own bootstraps; raise oneself by one's own bootstraps;

[出任] take up the post of;
出任新職 enter on the duties of one's appointment;
出任總統 take up the office as president;

[出入] (1) come in and go out; go out and come in; (2) discrepancy; divergence;
出入口 doorway;
出入上流社會 move in the best society;
出入社交界 mix in society;
出入咸亨 abroad or at home; successful in everything;
出入相抵 keep the expenses within one's income; make both ends meet;
出入相友 look for friends when one comes in and goes out — mutual help among the neighbours;

悖入悖出 evil begets evil; ill-spent;
從後門出入 enter and exit by the back door;
出雙入對 go places together as a couple; go with each other all the time as lovers;
淡入淡出 fade-in, fade-out;
鬼出電入 move in and out with lightning speed and wizard elusiveness;
量入為出 base one's expenditure upon one's income; cut one's coat according to one's cloth; in the light of one's income; keep one's expenses below one's income; keep the expenses within the limits of income; limit one's expenses by one's income; live within one's income; live within one's means; pay as you go; plan one's expenditure; put your hand no further than your sleeve will reach; stretch one's legs according to the coverlet;
略有出入 there is a slight discrepancy; vary slightly;
入不敷出 behindhand in one's circumstances; break the pale; cannot make ends meet; income falling short of expenditure; leap the pale; live beyond one's means; one's income cannot answer one's expense; outrun the constable; overrun the constable; run behind one's expenses; spend more than one earns; the income falls short; there is a deficit;
有出入 disagree; have discrepancy; inconsistent;

[出賽] compete; play in a match;

[出色] outstanding; remarkable; splendid;
出色表演 excellent performance;
出色的作品 superb work;
表現出色 behave oneself very well; make a good showing;
表演出色 give a superb performance;
不太出色 no great shakes;
幹得出色 do a remarkable job; make a wonderful showing;
工作出色 work very well;

[出身] (1) one's class origin; one's family background; (2) one's previous experience; one's previous occupation; (3) come from; rise from;
出身卑賤 spring from obscurity;
出身富貴 be born with a silver spoon in one's mouth;
出身高貴 of gentle birth; spring from a noble origin;
~出身高貴的人 person of noble birth;
出身貴族 of aristocratic origin;
出身寒賤 be born on the wrong side of the tracks; come from humble origins; emerge from obscurity; of humble origins; rise from the gutter;
出身寒門 come from a humble home; of humble origins; of mean birth; rise from obscurity;
出身好 come from a choice background; come from a good background; of excellent background;
出身名門 be born in the purple; be sprung from noble ancestors; come out of the top drawer; from the top drawer; of good ancestry; of good station;
出身貧寒 be born of poor parentage; come from an impoverished background; from a poor family;
出身清白 one's family background is clear and clean;
出身微寒 be born of low extraction;
出身微賤 one's origin is ignoble; person of obscurity; rise from humble origins; rise from obscurity;
出身顯貴 be born into the purple;
出身於 be born into; be born to; belong by birth to; come from; come of; descend from; spring from; stem from;
出身於名門 be born of a noble family; belong to a highly respectable family;
工農出身 stem from workers and peasants;
工人出身 begin life as a worker;
寒微出身 of humble birth;

[出神] abstractedness; abstraction; be lost in thought; in a trance; spellbound;
出神沉思 be buried in thought; be lost in thought;
出神入化 become spiritualized; miraculous; reach the acme of perfection; superb;
呆呆出神 be absorbed in thought; be lost in one's own thoughts; in a brown study;
聽得出神 be completely absorbed; listen with an open mouth; listen with rapt attention;

想得出神 be entranced in thought; be lost in contemplation; be lost in reverie; be lost in thought; lose oneself in thought;

[出生] be born; be sent into the world; come into the world; see the light of day;

出生地 birthplace; place of birth;

出生率 birth rate; natality;

出生日期 date of birth;

出生入死 at the risk of life and limb; at the risk of one's life; brave countless dangers; brave untold dangers; carry one's life in one's hands; defy all kinds of perils; go through fire and water; risk one's life; run the risk of life and disregard one's own safety;

出生證 birth certificate; certificate of birth;

同胎出生 be born at the same birth;

[出聲] make a sound; speak; utter a sound;

[出師] (1) finish one's apprenticeship; (2) dispatch troops to fight; send out an army;

出師不利 a bad beginning; be rebuffed in the first encounter; be thwarted at the very beginning; begin at the wrong end; get off on the wrong foot; start off on the wrong foot;

出師順利 get off on the right foot; without a hitch in the first encounter;

師出無名 dispatch troops without a just cause; do sth without proper excuse; fight a war without a just cause; fight for an unjust cause; send the army out without a righteous cause; there is no excuse for the campaign;

師出有名 a good reason for waging a war; make trouble under a certain pretext;

[出使] be sent on a diplomatic mission; serve as an envoy abroad;

[出示] produce; show;

出示證件 produce one's papers;

出示證明 produce one's proof;

出示證物 offer an exhibit;

[出世] (1) be born; come into the world; (2) be produced; come into being; (3) renounce the world; stand aloof from worldly affairs;

[出仕] become an official;

[出事] have an accident; meet with a mishap;

出事地點 site of the accident;

出事經過 story of the accident;

[出手] (1) dispose of; get off one's hands; sell; (2) skills displayed in making opening moves;

出手不凡 make skilful opening moves;

出手大方 generous with money; spend money freely;

大打出手 attack brutally; big fight; come to blows; fight brutally; get into a fight; get into a free-for-all fight; strike violently;

拿不出手 not presentable;

[出售] auction sth off; for sale; offer for sale; on offer; on sale; on the block; on the market; put sth on the market; put sth up for auction; put sth up for sale; sell; sell sth off;

出售財產 sell out one's property;

出售勞務 sales of service;

出售期貨 sell for forward delivery;

出售商品 offer goods for sale;

出售一空 be sold out;

半價出售 sell at half price;

變價出售 sell at the current price;

不准出售 sales forbidden;

成批出售 sell by bulk;

分批出售 sell by lots;

公開出售 sell openly;

減價出售 be on sale at a reduced price;

虧本出售 sell at a loss;

廉價出售 sell for a small price;

論斤出售 sell by the catty;

私下出售 dispose of sth at a private sale;

推遲出售 delay selling;

削價出售 sell at a reduction;

[出攤兒] do business; open for business;

[出逃] escape; flee; run away;

[出題] (1) assign a topic; set a question; set a theme; (2) make out questions;

[出庭] appear in court; before the court; enter an appearance;

出庭辯護 defend a case in court;

出庭受審 be brought to court for trial;

出庭作證 appear in court as a witness; serve as a witness at court;

[出頭] (1) free oneself; lift one's head; see daylight; (2) appear in public; come forward; (3) odd; slightly over; somewhat more;

出頭露角 come up in the world;
出頭露面 appear in public; in the limelight; show oneself; show one's head;
出頭之日 have one's day;
槍打出頭 common fame is seldom to blame; shoot the bird that takes the lead; the outstanding usually bears the brunt of the attack;
強出頭 interfere to mediate;
五十出頭 over fifty;

[出土] (1) be excavated; be unearthed; (2) come up;
出土文物 archaeological finds; unearthed artifacts; unearthed cultural relics;
出土文物一老古董 unearthed cultural relics — a stick-in-the-mud;

[出脫] (1) dispose of; manage to sell; (2) grow prettier; (3) absolve; acquit;

[出外] leave for another town;

[出席] attend; present;
出席會議 attend a meeting; present at a meeting;
出席人數 turnout;
出席受審 present oneself for trial;
出席宴會 attend a banquet;
出席者 attendee; attender;
抱病出席 come to the meeting despite one's illness;
扶病出席 present in spite of illness;

[出息] future; promise; prospects;
大有出息 of great promise;
沒出息 good-for-nothing; not promising;
有出息 get on in life; promising;

[出險] (1) get out of danger; (2) be threatened; in danger;

[出現] appear; appear on the scene; arise; come along; come on the scene; emerge; enter on the scene;
出現赤字 go into the red;
出現危機 reach a crisis;
重新出現 reappear; turn up;
突然出現 pop up;

[出血] (1) shed blood; (2) pay a large sum of money for sth; plunk down; (3) bleeding; haemorrhage;
出血病 bleeding disease;
出血熱 haemorrhagic fever;
~流行性出血熱 epidemic haemorrhagic fever;
出血性敗血症 haemorrhagic septicemia;
出血性壞血病 haemorrhagic scurvy;
出血性貧血 haemorrhagic anemia;
出血性心包炎 haemorrhagic pericarditis;
鼻孔出血 bleeding of the nose;
~把人打得鼻孔出血 tap sb's claret;
產後出血 post-partum haemorrhage;
產時出血 intra-partum haemorrhage;
大出血 (1) copious bleeding; bleed badly; massive haemorrhage; (2) sale;
虹膜出血 iridaemia;
喉出血 laryngorrhagia;
後鼻出血 posterior epistaxis;
結腸出血 colonorrhagia;
九竅出血 bleeding from the nine orifices;
咳出血 cough blood;
內出血 internal bleeding; internal haemorrhage;
皮下出血 subcutaneous haemorrhage;
脾出血 splenorrhagia;
氣管出血 tracheorrhagia;
前鼻出血 anterior epistaxis;
潛出血 occult bleeding;
乳頭出血 thelorrhagia;
傷口出血 wound bleeding;
滲出性出血 diapedesis;
實質性出血 parenchymatous haemorrhage;
胃出血 gastric haemorrhage;
外出血 external bleeding; external haemorrhage;
夏季出血 summer bleeding;
止住出血 arrest haemorrhage;

[出巡] (1) royal progress; (2) go out on an inspection tour; tour of inspection;

[出牙] dentia; teethe; teething; tooth eruption;
出牙不良 dysodontiasis;
出牙過早 precocious dentition;
出牙困難 dysodontiasis;
出牙延遲 retarded dentition;

[出芽] (1) budding; germinate; put forth buds; sprout; (2) budding; gemmation; prolification;

[出言] speak; talk; utter;
出言不遜 drop a clanger; make impertinent remarks; rough it; speak insolently; utter impolitely;
出言粗魯 speak in a harsh tone;
出言唐突 make a blunt remark;
出言威嚇 speak daggers to sb;
出言無狀 speak rudely; use rude

language;
何出此言 why do you utter such things;
[出洋] go abroad;
出洋相 act the ass; cut a sorry figure; cut up; lay an egg; make a fool of oneself; make a show of oneself; make a sight of oneself; make a spectacle of oneself; make an ass of oneself; make an exhibition of oneself; make oneself a laughing stock for all; play the ass; play the fool; play the monkey; show up; wear the cap and bells;
[出遊] go on a tour;
微服出遊 make a tour in disguise;
[出於] due to; out of;
出於本心 from one's heart;
出於本意 of one's own accord;
出於好心 out of good intentions;
出於好意 mean well; out of a good heart; out of good intentions; out of good will; well-intended; with the best of intentions;
出於禮貌 out of politeness;
出於憐憫 in consideration of mercy;
出於同情 out of sympathy;
出於無奈 as it cannot be helped; no other course was open to sb; only because one can do no better; out of sheer necessity;
出於無知 from ignorance; out of ignorance;
出於意外 against one's expectations; contrary to one's expectations; out of one's reckoning;
出於真心 out of sincerity;
出於直覺 on instinct;
出於自衛 out of self-defense;
出於自願 by one's own volition; of one's free will; of one's own accord; on a voluntary basis;
[出獄] be discharged from prison; be released from prison;
[出院] leave hospital;
病愈出院 be discharged from the hospital after recovery;
[出張] (mahjong) discard a tile;
[出診] make a house call; pay a home visit; visit a patient at home;
醫生出診 a doctor's visit;
[出陣] (1) go forth into battle; (2) take part in an athletic contest;

[出徵] go on an expedition; go out to battle;
[出眾] out of the ordinary; outstanding;
才不出眾 one's ability does not exceed the average;
才華出眾 of uncommon brilliance;
才藻出眾 surpassing the average in literary talent;
超群出眾 cut a conspicuous figure; rise above the herd;
口才出眾 show exceptional verbal intelligence;
能力出眾 of exceptional ability;
言不出眾，貌不驚人 neither outstanding in speech nor impressive in appearance; one's conversation does not impress anybody, nor does one's presence inspire awe;
智力出眾 with exceptional intelligence;
[出自] come from; originate; stem from;
出自肺腑 from the depths of one's heart; straight from the heart;
出自高手 come from an expert;
出自名家手筆 written by a famous writer;
出自內心 from one's heart;
[出走] flee; leave; run away;
離家出走 run away from home;
[出租] for hire; for rent; hire; hire out; let; let out; rent;
出租車 cab; hackney cab; taxi;
~出租車候客站 cab rank; cabstand;
~出租車司機 cabbie; taxi driver;
~乘出租車 take a taxi;
~叫出租車 call a taxi;
~小型出租車 minicab;
出租汽車 taxi;
出租人 leasor; lessor;
低價出租 lease at a lower rental;
廉價出租 rent sth for a song;
同意出租 grant a lease of...;

拔出 draw out; extract; pull out;
耙出 rake out;
百出 full of; numerous; plenty of;
擺出 (1) take out for display; (2) assume; put on;
輩出 come forth in large numbers;
標出 scale out; section out;
撥出 (1) dial-out; (2) appropriate;
播出 airing; broadcast;
猜出 dope out;
踩出 tread;
查出 ferret out; trace;
產出 output;

超出 exceed; overstep;
撤出 evacuate; withdraw;
衝出 rush out;
重出 reappear;
抽出 draw out; extract; select from a lot; withdraw;
淡出 fade out;
道出 speak out; voice;
得出 obtain a result; reach a conclusion;
迭出 keep coming forth;
讀出 read out;
發出 issue; send out;
放出 bleed; discharge; emit; give off; give out; go into; let out; send out; snap out; spray;
孵出 brood; hatch;
付出 expend; pay;
復出 come out again; come out of retirement again;
高出 be higher; be taller than;
搞出 achieve; produce; work out;
革出 dismiss; expel;
公出 away on official business;
供出 confess; own up;
畫出 draw up;
擠出 extrusion; force out; squeeze out;
檢出 checkout;
交出 hand over; surrender;
傑出 distinguished; outstanding; prominent; remarkable;
浸出 leaching;
進出 pass in and out;
揪出 ferret out; uncover;
舉出 cite; enumerate; itemize;
開出 draw out;
看出 become aware of; find out; make out; perceive; see;
口出 what comes out from one's mouth;
列出 enumerate; list;
流出 effusion; outflow;
留出 keep out; set apart; set aside;
露出 display; reveal; show;
賣出 sell;
娩出 be delivered (of a child);
排出 discharge; eject; exhaust; pump; squeeze; transpire; vent;
派出 send;
旁出 branch;
噴出 blowout; expulsion;
飄出 blow out;
歧出 conflicting; confusing; incoherent; inconsistent;
敲出 pound out; tap out;
取出 get out; take out;
日出 rise; sunrise;
篩出 sift out;
扇出 fan out; out fan;
伸出 extend; overhang; reach; runout;
滲出 ooze; seepage; seep out;
勝出 come out on top; end up to the better; win;
使出 exert; use;
釋出 disengage;
售出 sell; succeed in selling;
輸出 (1) export; (2) output;
算出 figure out; work out;
歲出 annual expenditures;
特出 distinguished; extraordinary; outstanding; prominent;
騰出 clear; empty; make way;
提出 advance; bring forth; bring forward; bring in; bring up; come up with; lodge; pose; pour; present; propose; put forth; put forward; rain; raise; set forth; set forward; set up; submit; suggest;
跳出 jump out; leap out;
凸出 bulge; cripling; embossment; project; protrude;
突出 (1) give prominence to; highlight; stress; (2) outstanding; remarkable;
吐出 spit out; utter;
推出 (1) push out; (2) present;
退出 quit; withdraw from;
脫出 come off; take off;
外出 go out; out of town;
喜出 be overjoyed;
顯出 appear; exhibit; express; give evidence; show;
現出 display; reveal;
想出 come up with; dope out; excogitate; think; think out;
寫出 draw up; write out;
瀉出 leak out; spurt out;
秀出 distinguished; outstanding;
選出 elect; pick out; select;
演出 perform; put on a show;
逸出 effusion; overshoot;
溢出 brim over; flow over; overflow; spill over;
譯出 translate from;
引出 draw forth; extract; elicit; lead to;
涌出 gush out; pour out;
湧出 spring out; well out;
勻出 share sth; spare sth;
搾出 squeeze out;
展出 exhibit; put on display;
長出 come into bud; come into leaf; send forth;

支出 (1) disburse; expend; pay; (2) disbursement; expenditure; outlay; payment
指出 indicate; point out;
逐出 chase sb out of; drive out; eject; expel; kick out; oust; propel;
租出 let;
做出 come to; make;
作出 make (a decision, etc.);

chu

【初】 (1) at the beginning of; in the early part of; (2) first in order; (3) for the first time; just; (4) elementary; rudimentary;

[初版] first edition;

[初步] first step; preliminary; tentative;
初步成果 initial results;
初步分析 make a preliminary analysis;
初步想法 tentative idea;
初步研究 make a preliminary study of;
初步印象 first impressions;
財政初步 the ABC of finance;

[初創] newly established;

[初春] early spring;

[初次] first time;
初次出場 make one's bow;
初次登台 appear for the first time on the stage; make a stage debut;
~初次登台成功 make a successful debut;
初次奪魁 come out of top place for the first time;

[初等] elementary; primary; rudimentary;
初等教育 elementary education; primary education;

[初冬] early winter;

[初犯] first offender;
姑念初犯 pardon for the first offence; take into consideration that it is one's first offence;

[初稿] first draft;

[初會] see sb for the first time;

[初婚] (1) first marriage; (2) newly married;

[初級] elementary; initial; junior; primary;
初級班 elementary class; junior class;
初級讀本 ABC book; abecedarium; primer;
初級教育 elementary education;
初級小學 lower primary school;
初級中學 junior middle school;

[初交] new acquaintance; recent acquaintance;

[初戀] one's first love;
少年初戀 puppy love;

[初期] early days; initial stage;
初期困難 growing pains;
發病初期 beginning of a disease; initial stage of a disease;
…世紀初期 early in the…century; in the beginning of the…century;
戰爭初期 early days of the war;

[初秋] early autumn;

[初賽] preliminary contest;

[初生] (1) primary; nascent; (2) newborn;
初生嬰兒 newborn baby;
初生之犢 newborn calf;
初生之犢不畏虎 a newborn calf does not fear the tiger; a newborn calf makes little of tigers; newborn calves are not afraid of tigers;

[初試] (1) first attempt; first try; preliminary test; (2) preliminary examination;
初試成功 successful from one's very first attempt;
初試鋒芒 display one's talent for the first time; first try of one's ability;
初試風味 have a first taste of novelty;

[初夏] early summer;

[初選] initial separation; original selection; primary election;

[初學] begin to learn;
初學書 ABC book;
初學者 abecedarian; alphabetarian; beginner; learner in the first stage; neophyte; new boy; novice; tenderfoot; tyro;
~訓練初學者 train beginners;

[初雪] first snow;

[初旬] first ten days of a month;

[初葉] (1) early years of a century; (2) primordial leaf;

[初衷] original intention;
不改初衷 not change one's original intention;
一改初衷 abandon one's original intention;
有違初衷 go back on one's original intentions;

當初 (1) at that time; at the beginning; at the outset; in the first place; originally; used to; (2) at that time; formerly; in the past;
年初 beginning of a year;

期初 beginning of a period;
起初 at first; at the outset; in the beginning; originally;
如初 as always; as it was before;
太初 beginning of the world;
往初 formerly;
月初 beginning of a month;
最初 (1) at first; at the beginning; at the outset; initial; original; (2) earliest; first;

chu

【齣】 (1) chapter; (2) numerary adjunct for plays;

chu²

chu

【芻】 (1) cut grass; mow; (2) fodder; hay; (3) feed; (4) animals that feed on grass;

[芻糧] fodder for horses and food for men;

[芻秣] fodder;

[芻牧] graze livestock; pasture livestock;

chu

【除】 (1) eliminate; get rid of; remove; (2) but; except; except for; (3) besides; in addition to; (4) divide;

[除草] weed; weed out;
除草保苗 remove weeds and protect seedling;
除草機 weeder;
~ 單行除草機 single weeder;
~ 稻田除草機 paddy field weeder;
~ 苗牀除草機 seedbed weeder;
~ 順行除草機 down-the-row weeder;
~ 旋轉除草機 spin weeder;
除草劑 herbicide;
~ 化學除草劑 chemical herbicide;
~ 石油除草劑 oil herbicide;
~ 有機除草劑 organic herbicide;

[除塵] ashing; dust abatement; dust elimination; dust precipitation; dust removal;
除塵毛刷 cleaning brush;
除塵設備 dust-cleaning apparatus;
機械除塵 mechanical ashing;
手工除塵 hand ashing;

[除蟲] kill off insects;
以蟲除蟲 use insects to fight insect pests;

[除臭] deodorize;
除臭劑 deodorant;

[除掉] get rid of; jettison; remove;
除掉心病 end a secret trouble;
除掉眼中釘 put out a thorn from one's flesh;

[除法] division;
長除法 long division;
捷除法 abridged division; short division;
輾轉相除法 division algorithm;
綜合除法 synthetic division;

[除非] given that; only if; only when; provided that; unless;

[除根] (1) dig up the roots; grub; root out; (2) cure once and for all; eradicate;
芟草除根 clear the ground of weeds and roots;
斬草除根 cut off the grass and take out the roots — eliminate the cause of sth; cut the weeds and dig up the roots — destroy root and branch; destroy evil leaving no chance of its revival; eliminate the cause of corruption; eradicate the cause throughly; pluck up the evil by the roots; stamp out the source of trouble; when pulling weeds, get rid of the root completely;
~ 斬草除根，逢春不發 a weed must be rooted out, or it will grow again in spring; if the roots are removed, the grass will not grow again; tear the weed out by the roots so that it can never grow again;
~ 斬草不除根，逢春又發青 if the grass is only cut, then the next spring it will revive;

[除害] remove an evil;
為民除害 destroy a public enemy; eliminate a public scourge; rid the people of a scourge; rid the people of an evil;

[除號] sign of division;

[除舊] get rid of the old;
除舊佈新 demolish the old and bring forth the new; do away with the old and set up the new; eliminate the old to make way for the new; get rid of the old to make way for the new; remove the old in order to build the new; ring out the old, ring in the new;
除舊更新 get rid of the old to make way for the new; replace the old with the new;
除舊立新 replace old things with new

ones; do away with the old to make way for the new;
除舊迎新 clean away the dirt and the old of the past year and usher in the new;

[除開] except;

[除了] (1) except; (2) besides; in addition to;
除了一個人以外，所有的人都到了 all but one were present;

[除名] expunge sb's name from a list; remove sb's name from the rolls; strike one's name off; take sb's name off the books;
被除名 be struck off the rolls;

[除氣] deaerate; degassing;
除氣器 deaerator;
~膨脹式除氣器 expansion deaerator;
表面除氣 open-surface degassing;
多級除氣 multi-stage degassing;
虹吸除氣 syphon degassing;
真空除氣 vacuum degassing;

[除去] blot out; eliminate; remove; work off;

[除數] divisor;
被除數 dividend;

[除外] added to; after; among other things; any other than; apart from; as well as; aside from; bar; barring; besides; beyond; but; else; except; except for; excepting; excluding; exclusive of; in addition to; independent of; independently of; into the bargain; next to; no other than; none but; not; not counting; not including; on top of; other than; otherwise; otherwise than; outside; outside of; over and above; save; save and except; save for; save that; saving; short of; than; to the exclusion of; unless; with the exception of;

[除夕] Chinese Lunar New Year's Eve;
除夕守歲 observe the year out on New Year's Eve;
除夕晚會 New Year's Eve party;
慶祝除夕 celebrate New Year's Eve;
新年除夕 New Year's Eve;

[除霜] defrosting;
除霜按鈕 defrosting button;

[除子] divisor;
標準除子 canonical divisor;
豐富除子 ample divisor;
分歧除子 branch divisor;

拔除 eradicate; pull out; remove; uproot;
擯除 discard; dispense with; get rid of;
屏除 banish; get rid of;
摒除 brush aside; get rid of; remove;
拆除 demolish; dismantle; pull down; remove;
鏟除 eradicate; root out; uproot; wipe out;
撤除 dismantle; remove;
抽除 abstraction;
滌除 do away with; eliminate; nullify; wash away;
廢除 abolish; abrogate; do away with;
祓除 exorcise;
割除 cut off; excise;
革除 (1) abolish; get rid of; (2) dismiss; expel;
根除 eliminate; exterminate; thoroughly do away with; uproot;
刮除 strike off;
化除 dispel; eliminate; remove;
剪除 annihilate; eliminate; exterminate; wipe out;
剿除 annihilate; exterminate; wipe out;
解除 dismiss; get rid of; relieve; remove; secure;
戒除 drop; give up; leave off;
蠲除 relieve from excessive burden;
開除 cast out; discharge; dismiss; expel; fire;
扣除 deduct; take off;
免除 (1) avoid; prevent; (2) exempt; relieve;
排除 (1) get rid of; remove; (2) excrete;
刨除 reduce;
破除 abolish; do away with; get rid of;
遷除 be appointed;
切除 excision; resection;
清除 clean up; clear; clear away; clear out; clear-out; discard; dump; eliminate; erase; expel; get rid of; purge; reset; sweep away; weed out;
袪除 dispel; drive away; get rid of; relieve; remove; scatter;
驅除 dispel; drive out; get rid of;
去除 abstraction; dislodge;
攘除 reject; weed out;
禳除 drive away evil spirits;
掃除 (1) have a cleaning; (2) clear away; sweep away; wipe out;
刪除 cross out; delete; strike out;
芟除 (1) cut down; mow; (2) delete;
拭除 brush sth off; wipe sth off;
歲除 New Year's Eve;
剔除 get rid of sth bad;
庭除 courtyard;
消除 eliminate; remove; wipe off;
卸除 get rid of; remove;

削除 omit; strike out; take out;
摘除 excise;
整除 be divided with no remainder;
誅除 eliminate; eradicate; root out;

chu
【滁】 a tributary of the Yangzi River;

chu
【耡】 same as 鋤;

chu
【蜍】 toad;

蟾蜍 (1) toad; (2) the fabled toad in the moon;

chu
【鉏】 (1) hoe; (2) eliminate; uproot; (3) a surname;

chu
【廚】 kitchen;
［廚房］ kitchen;
廚房用具 kitchen utensils; kitchenalia; kitchenware;
廚房用的捲紙 kitchen roll;
廚房有人好進餐，朝裏有人好做官 the influence of friends in the right place can make a person's lot much easier;
廚房鐘 kitchen clock;
飛行廚房 flight kitchen;
免費廚房 soup kitchen;
設備齊全的廚房 fully-fitted kitchen;
小廚房 kitchenette;
［廚師］ chef; cook;
廚師不好怨灶歪 a bad workman always blames his tools;
廚師長 chef;
飯店廚師 hotel cook;
糕點廚師 pastry cook;
家庭廚師 plain cook;
快餐廚師 short-order cook;
男廚師 cook;
一流的廚師 boss cook; top chef;
總廚師 head cook;
［廚餘］ food waste; kitchen scraps;
廚餘循環再造 food waste recycling;
處理廚餘 food waste management; handle food waste; treat food waste;
減少廚餘 reduce food waste;
［廚子］ cook;
廚子多了煮壞湯 too many cooks spoil the broth;

幫廚 help in the kitchen;
庖廚 kitchen;
下廚 go to the kitchen; prepare food;

chu
【鋤】 (1) hoe; (2) work with a hoe; (3) eliminate; uproot; weed out;
［鋤鏟］ shovel;
［鋤奸］ eliminate traitors; ferret out spies;
鋤奸安民 fight against evildoers and bring peace to the people;
為黨鋤奸 remove a bunch of hidden traitors from the party;
［鋤頭］ hoe;
一把鋤頭 a hoe;

掛鋤 finish hoeing; put away the hoe for the winter;
薅鋤 small short-handled hoe;
開鋤 start the year's hoeing;
悶鋤 loosen the soil and weed in order to let the seeds germinate;
耨鋤 draw hoe;

chu
【篨】 coarse bamboo mat;

籧篨 reed mat or bamboo mat in ancient times;

chu
【雛】 (1) chick; (2) fledgling; (3) small kid; toddler;
［雛鳳］ bright and promising children;
［雛菊］ daisy;
雛菊花環 daisy chain;

雞雛 chick; chicken;
鳩雛 dovelet;
育雛 brood;

chu
【幮】 bed screen; mosquito net;

chu
【櫥】 (1) cabinet; cupboard; wardrobe; (2) shop counter;
［櫥窗］ counter; display window; show window;
［櫥櫃］ cabinet; closet; cupboard; wardrobe;
［櫥子］ cabinet; sideboard;

壁櫥 built-in cupboard; built-in wardrobe;
柜櫥 cupboard;

三層櫥 three tiers of shelves;
紗櫥 screen cupboard;
書櫥 bookcase;
衣櫥 wardrobe;

chu
【躇】 hesitate;

踟躇 hesitate; waver;
躊躇 hesitate; shilly-shally;

chu
【躕】 falter; hesitate;

踟躕 hesitate; waver;

chu³
chu
【杵】 baton used to pound launders; pestle;
[杵臼之交] true friendship;

研杵 pestle; pounder;

chu
【處】 (1) get along; (2) be situated in; in a certain condition; (3) deal with; handle; manage; (4) punish; sentence;
[處變不驚] remain calm in the hour of peril; take a tense situation calmly; with presence of mind in the face of disasters;
[處罰] penalize; punish;
處罰犯人 impose a punishment upon a criminal;
不受處罰 get off;
減輕處罰 mitigate a punishment;
免除處罰 remit a punishment;
受到處罰 bear punishment; receive a punishment;
逃避處罰 escape punishment; evade punishment;
應得的處罰 condign punishment;
應受處罰 deserve punishment;
[處方] (1) prescribe; write out a prescription; (2) prescription;
不用處方 over the counter;
重複處方 repeat a prescription;
對症處方 prescribe for a complaint;
給病人處方 prescribe for a patient;
開處方 make a prescription; prescribe medicine;
[處分] punish; take disciplinary action against;
黨紀處分 disciplinary action within the Party;
法律處分 legal action;
行政處分 administrative disciplinary measure;
政紀處分 administrative disciplinary action;
[處境] circumstances one finds oneself in; plight; unfavourable situation;
處境尷尬 be awkwardly situated; be hard put to it; in a dilemma; in a pickle; in an awkward position; in an awkward situation; in difficulties; in Queer Street;
處境困難 in a difficult situation; in a predicament; in a scrape; in a sorry plight; in a spot; in a tight place; in an awkward predicament; in the soup; live in difficult circumstances;
處境危險 be in a dangerous situation; out on a limb; skate on thin ice; touch and go;
處境險惡 in a perilous position;
處境相同 in the same boat; in the same box;
處境糟糕 in a bad situation;
[處決] execute; put to death;
面臨處決 face execution;
[處理] deal with; disposal; dispose of; handle; handling; processing; treating; treatment;
處理不當 mishandle;
處理不善 mishandle; not handle properly;
處理程序 processing programme;
處理從寬 be treated with leniency; lenient in handling the cases; lenient in measures;
處理得當 deal with sth properly; run affairs in an appropriate way;
處理公務 handle official matters;
處理國家大事 conduct state affairs;
處理機 processor;
~處理機接口 processor interface;
~單處理機 monoprocessor;
~微處理機 microprocessor;
~中央處理機 central processing unit;
處理緊急事務 deal with urgent work;
處理垃圾 dispose of rubbish;
處理難局 take the bull by the horns;
處理能力 handling ability;
處理器 handler; processor; treater;

~螺旋孔處理器 bolt-hole treater;
~鋁土處理器 treater;
~設備處理器 device handler;
~數據自動處理器 handler;
~雙極化處理器 bipolar processor;
~微處理器 microprocessor;
~相聯處理器 associative processor;
~陣列處理器 array processor;
~中央處理器 central processing unit;
處理日常事務 deal with routine matters; handle day-to-day work;
處理問題 approach the problem;
處理污水 deal with effluent; dispose of sewage;
處理原則 processability principle;
爆氣處理 aeration treatment;
成批作業處理 batch job processing;
動態處理 dynamic handling;
廢水處理 effluent disposal;
廢液處理 liquid waste disposal;
分批處理 batch treatment;
分散處理 decentralized processing;
合併處理 merge application;
後處理 reprocessing;
~水法後處理 aqueous reprocessing;
~現場後處理 on-site reprocessing;
火焰處理 flame treatment;
及時處理 a stitch in time;
寬大處理 lenient treatment;
親自處理 take charge personally;
熱處理 heat treatment;
人體廢物處理 body waste disposal;
認真地處理 handle seriously; tackle seriously;
數據處理 data handling;
酸處理 acid treatment;
微處理 microprocessing;
~微處理機 microprocessor;
微處理機終端 microprocessor terminal;
~微處理器 microprocessor;
微觀處理 micromanage;
文件處理 document handling; file handling;
吸收處理 absorption treatment;
需氧處理 aerobic treatment;
嚴厲處理 get tough;
鹽水處理 brine disposal;
有利於處理 facilitate the handling of;
預處理 preprocessing;
~預處理程序 preprocessor;
酌情處理 act at one's discretion; settle a matter as one sees fit;
自動信息處理 automated information processing;

[處女] maiden; virgin;
處女的 virginal;
處女地 uncultivated land; virgin land; virgin territory;
處女航 maiden flight; maiden voyage;
處女膜 hymen; maidenhead;
處女作 first effort; maiden work;
老處女 old maid; old maiden; spinster; unappropriated blessing;

[處世] conduct oneself in society;
處世淡漠 adopt a cold attitude towards everything in the world;
處世方正 conduct oneself in society in an upright manner; fair and square in all dealings;
處世經驗 worldly experience;
~處世經驗豐富 have vast worldly experience;
處世精明 clever and smart in dealing with people;
處世老練 be versed in the ways of the world;
處世立身 begin the world with; behave oneself; start in life; ways of conducting oneself in society;
處世明智 conduct oneself wisely in the society;
處世幼稚 little more than a boy in worldly experience;
處世哲學 philosophy of living;
處世正派 fair and square in all dealings;
處世正直 fair and square in all dealings;
會處世 know the way of life; know the way of living; know the way of the world;
立身處世 conduct oneself in society; get on in life; get on in the world; ways of conducting oneself in society;

[處事] deal with affairs;
處事持重 prudent and steady in attending to business;
處事篤誠 honest in one's dealings;
處事公平 play fair; play the game;
處事公允 candid about the matter;
處事公正 candid about the matter;
處事機警 know what is what;
處事精明 clever and smart in attending to business;
處事謹慎 careful in all one does; handle

sth with kid gloves;

［處死］ executed; put to death; put to execution;
被處死 be condemned to death; be sentenced to capital punishment;
當眾處死 public execution;
絞刑處死 execution by hanging;
暫緩處死 suspend execution;

［處心積慮］ brood over a matter for a long time; intrigue all the time; plan deliberately; rack one's brains; scheme and use every kind of trick; scheme day and night; scheme incessantly; scheme sth for a long time; seek sth by all means; set one's mind on sth; work hard and deliberately at sth;

［處刑］ sentence;

［處於］ in a certain condition;
處於被動 in a passive position;
處於低潮 at a low ebb;
處於…地位 in a...position;
~處於有利地位 in an advantageous position;
處於高潮 at high tide;
處於僵局 in a stalemate;
處於靜止狀態 remain static;
處於窘境 in a tight box;
處於困境 at bay; behind the eight ball; between wind and water; get into deep waters; get into hot water; get sb into chancery; have a wolf by the ears; in a bind; in a box; in a catch-22 situation; in a cleft stick; in a dilemma; in a fix; in a hole; in a nice fix; in a scrape; in a tight box; in a tight place; in an awkward predicament; in deep waters; in hot water; in Queer Street; in rough waters; in the cart; in the soup; in the wrong box; into deep waters; on the horns of a dilemma; in troubled waters; place sb in a dilemma; put sb in a dilemma; stick in the mud; up a creek; up a gum tree; up a tree; up the pole;
處於劣勢 have the disadvantage;
處於逆境 in adverse circumstances;
處於順境 in favourable circumstances;
處於優勢 have the advantage;
處於有利地位 hold all the aces;
處於主動 take the initiative;

［處置］ (1) deal with; dispose of; handle; manage; (2) punish;
處置不當 mishandle; mismanage;
處置失當 badly managed; ill-managed; mishandle; mismanage; not properly handled;
處置失宜 handle improperly;
處置式結構 disposal construction;
斷然處置 manage resolutely; take the bull by the horns;

［處子］ maiden; virgin;
守口處子，出如脫兔 guarded as a virgin, swift as a hare;

暗處 dark place; hidden place;
敝處 my place;
別處 another place; elsewhere; somewhere else;
捕處 arrest and punish;
裁處 make a decision after consideration and then deal with it;
查處 investigate and deal with; investigate and treat;
長處 best points; good points; good qualities; merits; strong points;
懲處 penalize; punish; sentence;
共處 coexist;
困處 in a predicament; in a sorry plight; in dire straits;
論處 decide on sb's punishment;
難處 hard to deal with; hard to get along with;
判處 condemn; sentence;
善處 conduct oneself well; deal discreetly with sth;
審處 (1) try and punish; (2) deliberate and decide;
調處 arbitrate; mediate;
相處 get along with each other;
癢處 the place where it itches;
益處 advantages; benefit; good; profit;
用處 good; use;
遠處 afar off; distant; in the distance;
在處 everywhere;
雜處 live together;
住處 accommodation; domicile; dwelling; lodging; quarters; residence;
着處 everywhere;
自處 one's own position; where to place oneself;
尊處 your abode;

chu

【楮】 paper mulberry;

［楮墨］ paper and ink;

chu

【楚】 (1) clear; neat; (2) pang of pain; suffering;

[楚材楚用] use local talents;

[楚材晉用] brain drain; employ talented people from other nations; great person given an important post by another country; local talents are used by another country;

[楚楚] (1) bright and clear; neat; tidy; (2) luxuriant; (3) delicate;

楚楚動人 delicate and attractive; lovingly pathetic; moving the heart of all those who see her;

楚楚可觀 being clear and distinct, it is worth seeing;

楚楚可憐 delicate and touching; miserable;

[楚弓楚得] the bow of Chu will be found by the man of Chu—narrow-minded;

[楚河漢界] border of two opposing powers;

[楚腰] slender waist;

鞭楚 flagellate; flog; whip;

苦楚 misery; suffering;

悽楚 grievous; miserable; pathetic; pitiful; saddening; wretched;

淒楚 miserable; wretched;

齊楚 neat and smart;

翹楚 outstanding person; talented person;

清楚 (1) clear; distinct; without ambiguity; (2) clear; lucid; (3) bring sth home to; clear about; know thoroughly; understand;

酸楚 distressed; grieved;

痛楚 pain; suffering;

夏楚 ferule; rod for punishing pupils;

辛楚 sad; sorrowful;

chu

【褚】 (1) distinguish; know; recognize; (2) bag; (3) stuff a lined garment with cotton; (4) reserve; save; (5) a surname;

[褚幕] piece of red cloth for covering a coffin;

chu

【儲】 (1) save; store; (2) alternate; deputy; (3) a surname;

[儲備] (1) reserves; savings; (2) deposit money;

儲備基金 reserve fund;

儲備金 nest egg;

儲備物 fallback;

儲糧備荒 store up grain against famine;

補充儲備 replenish one's stock;

充分儲備 lay in ample stocks of;

黃金儲備 gold reserve;

留作儲備 be placed to reserve;

外匯儲備 foreign exchange reserve;

銀行儲備 bank's reserves;

[儲藏] (1) keep; lay by; save and preserve; store; (2) deposit;

儲藏室 box room; stockroom;

冷凍儲藏 keep sth in cold storage;

食品儲藏 preservation of food;

[儲存] accumulate; keep in reserve; lay in; lay up; stockpile;

儲存開關 memory switch;

儲存糧食 store grain;

儲存水果 put up stores of fruits;

儲存在記憶中 store sth in one's memory;

[儲君] crown prince;

[儲煤] coal storage;

儲煤倉 coal bunker;

儲煤庫 coal bunker; coal cellar;

儲煤室 coal bunker; coal hole;

~地下儲煤室 coal cellar;

[儲錢] save money;

儲錢罐 money box; piggy bank;

儲錢盒 money box;

[儲物] storage;

儲物空間 storage space;

儲物箱 foot locker;

[儲蓄] deposits; nest egg; savings;

儲蓄存款 money deposited as savings; savings deposit;

儲蓄防老 scrape together some money for one's age;

儲蓄公債 savings bond;

儲蓄機構 thrift institution;

儲蓄金 reserve;

~一般儲蓄金 general reserve;

儲蓄所 savings bank;

儲蓄心理 psychology of savings;

儲蓄銀行 deposit bank; savings bank;

儲蓄賬戶 savings account;

保險儲蓄 insured savings;

活期儲蓄 current savings;

~活期儲蓄賬戶 current savings account;

強迫儲蓄 forced savings;

總儲蓄 aggregate savings;

[儲運] storage and transport;

倉儲 storage;

存儲 (1) memorize; store; (2) stockpile;
皇儲 crown prince;
積儲 store up;
王儲 crown prince;

chu
【礎】 plinth;

基礎 base; basis; foundation;

chu⁴
chu
【亍】 step with the right foot;
chu
【怵】 (1) afraid; scared; timorous; (2) entice; induce; (3) coerce; intimidate;
[怵惕] scared and cautious;
chu
【畜】 animal; creature;
[畜類] domestic animals;
[畜舍] animal house;
[畜生] (1) animal; (2) beast;
[畜疫] epidemic disease of domestic animals;

愛畜 pet;
耕畜 farm animal;
公畜 male animal;
家畜 domestic animal; farm livestock;
力畜 beast of burden; draught animal;
六畜 the six domestic animals, namely, pig, ox, goat, horse, fowl, and dog;
母畜 dam; female animal;
牧畜 animal husbandry; livestock breeding;
牲畜 domestic animal; livestock;
獸畜 beast;
馱畜 pack animal;
役畜 beast of burden; draught animal;
孕畜 pregnant domestic animal;
種畜 breeding stock;
子畜 young animal;

chu
【俶】 begin;
chu
【絀】 (1) sew; (2) bend; (3) degrade; (4) deficient; wanting;

支絀 insufficient; not enough;

chu
【處】 (1) place; (2) part; point; (3) measure-word; (4) department; office;
[處處] everywhere; in all respects; right, left, and centre; right and left;
處處芳菲 everywhere, the grass grows lush and green;
處處節省 practise every conceivable economy;
處處碰壁 hit against a wall everywhere; run into snags and be foiled everywhere; run up against a wall everywhere;
處處蹴釘子 meet with rebuffs everywhere;
處處設防 set up defenses everywhere;
處處替別人着想 always consider others;
處處制肘 meet hindrance everywhere;
[處長] director of a division; head of a department; section chief;
副處長 deputy director;

暗處 dark place; secret place;
辦事處 agency; office;
保衛處 security department;
財務處 finance department;
參贊處 counsellor's office;
產業處 industries department;
長處 good points;
出處 source of a quotation; source of an allusion;
存放處 depository;
錯處 demerit; fault; mistake;
代辦處 office of the chargé d'affaires;
到處 at all places; everywhere;
登記處 registration office;
調配處 transfer department;
調研處 investigation and research department;
短處 weak points;
法制處 department of legal affairs;
公證處 notary office;
顧問處 advisory department;
掛號處 registration office;
管理處 management office;
害處 harm;
好處 (1) advantage; benefit; good; (2) gain; profit;
患處 affected part;
壞處 disadvantage; harm;
基建處 capital construction department;
機要處 confidential department;
技術合作處 technological cooperation department;
寄存處 checkroom;
寄放處 checkroom;
接待處 reception counter; reception department;
經濟處 economic department;

經銷處 agency;
開發處 development department;
科研處 science and technology department;
苦處 difficulty; hardship; suffering;
老幹部處 veteran cadres department;
離退處 retirees' affairs department;
利用外資處 foreign capital utilization department;
聯絡處 liaison department; liaison office;
落腳處 temporary lodging;
滿處 all over the place; everywhere;
秘書處 secretariat;
明處 (1) where there is light; (2) in public; in the open;
難處 difficulty; straits; trouble;
簽到處 sign-in desk;
情報處 intelligence department;
去處 (1) place to go; whereabouts; (2) place; site;
人事教育處 personnel and education department;
涉外處 foreign affairs department;
深處 depths; recesses;
審計處 auditing department;
收款處 cashier's desk;
售票處 booking office; ticket office;
四處 all round; everywhere; in all directions;
隨處 anywhere; everywhere;
停泊處 anchorage; berth;
通信處 (1) correspondence department; (2) mailing address;
痛處 sore spot; tender spot;
外經處 department of foreign economic relations and trade;
文教處 culture and education department;
物資供應處 goods and materials supply department;
下處 temporary lodging during a trip;
新聞處 office of information;
信訪處 letters and inquiries reception department;
行政處 department of administration;
宣教處 publicity and education department;
益處 advantage; benefit; good;
用處 good; use;
預算處 department of budget;
遠處 distant place;
質管處 quality control department;
註冊處 registration office;
住處 dwelling place; quarters; residence;
住院處 admissions office;
綜合事務處 general affairs department;
總務處 general affairs department;

chu

【搐】 convulsion; cramp; shake involuntarily; spasm;

[搐動] move spasmodically; twitch;
[搐縮] contract; shrink;
抽搐 tic; twitch;

chu

【歜】 furious; wrathful;

chu

【黜】 (1) dispel; reject; (2) degrade; demote; dismiss;

[黜革昏庸] dismiss the stupid and the inferior;
[黜華崇實] discard flowery words and emphasize reality; reject luxury and uphold simplicity;
[黜免] dismiss an official; remove sb from office;
罷黜 (1) dismiss from office; (2) ban; reject;
貶黜 demote; relegate;
廢黜 decrown; depose; dethrone;

chu

【觸】 (1) contact; touch; (2) bump against; hit; run against; strike; (3) touch; (4) move sb; stir up sb's feelings;

[觸點] contact;
閉塞觸點 block contact;
電刷觸點 brush contact;
輔助觸點 auxiliary contact;
燒熔觸點 burnt contact;
銜鐵觸點 armature contact;
[觸電] electric shock; get an electric shock;
觸電而死 be killed by an electric shock;
[觸動] (1) touch sth; (2) move sb; stir up sb's feelings; touch sb's heart;
觸動感情 touch the emotions;
觸動心弦 touch a chord; touch sb on a tender string; touch the right chord;
深受觸動 be deeply touched;
有所觸動 be somewhat moved;
[觸發] detonate by contact; spark; touch off; trigger;
觸發排外情緒 stimulate the anti-foreign feeling;
觸發動亂 touch off a disturbance;
觸發器 trigger;
~電容耦合觸發器 capacitance-coupled flip-flop;
~二進制觸發器 binary trigger;
~交流觸發器 alternating-current trigger;

C

~偏壓觸發器 biased flip-flop;
~雙穩態觸發器 bistable flip-flop;
~自動觸發器 automatic trigger;
觸發鄉思 provoke nostalgic longing;
一觸即發 at a simmer; imminent; may be triggered at any moment; on the simmer; on the verge of breaking out; ready to be set off at a touch; to an explosive point; touch and go;

[觸犯] go against; offend; step on sb's corns; tread on sb's toes; violate;
觸犯法律 break the law; violate the law;
觸犯公眾利益 work against the public interests;

[觸感] tactile impression; touch;

[觸機] stir up sb's feelings;
觸機即發 (1) be ready to start; (2) act on the spur of the moment; act with precipitation; do things without forethought;

[觸及] get to; touch;
觸及舊創 rip up old scores; reopen old scores;
觸及靈魂 touch sb's innermost being; touch sb to his very soul; touch sb to the quick; touch sb to the soul;
觸及傷心處 hit a nerve; touch a nerve;
觸及痛處 hit home; hit where it really hurts; strike home; touch sb on the raw; touch sb where it hurts; touch sb's sore spot; touch the tender place; touch the tender spot;
觸及問題的核心 go to the root of the problem;
觸及問題的實質 get down to the guts of a matter;
觸及爭論的焦點 touch the point at issue;

[觸礁] (1) run aground; run on rocks; strand; strike a rock; (2) run into danger;
船觸礁 the ship struck on a reef;

[觸角] antenna; feeler; tentacle;
伸出觸角 put out feelers; stretch out the feelers;
縮回觸角 draw back the feelers;
一對觸角 a pair of antennae;

[觸景] behold a view;
觸景情深 stir one's deep feelings when beholding the view;
觸景傷情 be moved by what one sees; feel moved by the prospect; memories revive at the sight of familiar places; recall old memories at familiar sights; the circumstances excite one's feelings; the scene brings back memories; the scene stirs up one's feelings; the sight strikes a chord in one's heart;
觸景生情 be moved by what one sees; be touched with memories awakened by the scene; memories revive at the sight of familiar places; recall old memories at familiar sights; stir one's deep feelings when beholding the view; the circumstances excite one's feelings; the scene brings back memories; the scene evokes memories of the past; the scene moves him to the depths; the scene touches a chord in one's heart; the sight strikes a chord in one's heart;

[觸覺] feel; feeling; sense of touch; tactile sensation; touch; touch reception;
觸覺遲鈍 amblyaphia;
觸覺過敏 hyperaphia;
觸覺減退 hypopselaphesia;
觸覺器官 touch organs;
觸覺缺失 anhaphia;
敏銳觸覺 keen touch;

[觸類] by analogy;
觸類旁通 comprehend by analogy; draw an analogy; draw parallels from inference;
觸類引伸 extend the meaning by analogy; hit on sth analogous as a means of explanation;

[觸摸] contact; feel; fumble; grope; put one's hand on sth; stroke; touch;
觸摸眼睛 touch one's eyes;
觸摸嘴巴 touch one's mouth;

[觸目] (1) meet the eye; (2) attracting attention; conspicuous; shocking; startling;
觸目皆是 a common sight; be everywhere in evidence; be seen everywhere;
觸目驚心 horrid; shocking; startling; strike the eye and rouse the mind;

[觸怒] enrage; get sb's back up; infuriate; make angry; put sb's back up; rub sb up the wrong way; set sb's back up; stroke sb's hair the wrong way;
被觸怒 be moved to anger;

[觸手] tentacle;
從輻觸手 adradial tentacle;

頂觸手 nuchal tentacle;
口觸手 buccal tentacles; oral tentacle;

［觸痛］ (1) touch a tender spot; touch sb to the quick; (2) tenderness;

筆觸 brush stroke; style of drawing or writing;
棖觸 (1) touch sth, moving it slightly; (2) move sb; stir up sb's feelings;
抵觸 conflict with; contradict;
牴觸 conflict; contradict;
點觸 pitting;
感觸 feelings; thoughts and feelings;
接觸 (1) come into contact with; engage; get in touch with; (2) contact; touch;
突觸 synapse;

chu

【矗】 (1) rising sharply; steep; (2) lofty; straight; upright; (3) luxuriant growth;

［矗立］ stand erect; stand tall and upright; tower over sth;

［矗然不誣］ be upright and practise no deception;

chua¹ chua

【欻】 word used for some sound;

［欻拉］ sizzle;

chuai¹ chuai

【搋】 (1) conceal sth in the bosom; (2) knead;

chuai³ chuai

【揣】 hide or carry in one's clothes; tuck;

［揣測］ conjecture; guess; reckon; surmise;
根據揣測 surmise from;

［揣度］ appraise; conjecture; estimate; reckon; surmise;
揣度敵情 make an appraisal of the enemy's situation;
揣情度理 consider the circumstances and judge by common sense; make a reasonable appraisal of the situation; reckon the situation; weigh the pros and cons;

［揣摩］ try to fathom; try to figure out;
揣摩話意 figure out the hidden meaning of sb's words;
細心揣摩 think of it carefully;

囊揣 pork near the pig's nipples;
掙揣 strive; struggle;

chuai⁴ chuai

【嘬】 (1) bite; (2) gobble up;

chuai

【踹】 trample; tread;

［踹踏］ trample; tread;

chuan¹ chuan

【川】 (1) river; (2) plain; (3) short for Sichuan;

［川菜］ Sichuan cuisine;

［川劇］ Sichuan opera;

［川資］ travelling expenses;
川資短缺 short of travelling expenses;

冰川 glacier;
長川 constantly; frequently;
常川 constantly; frequently;
河川 rivers; streams;
平川 flat, open country; level land; plain;
山川 mountains and rivers;

chuan

【穿】 (1) penetrate; pierce through; (2) cross; go through; pass through; (3) be dressed in; have sth on; put on; wear;

［穿插］ (1) alternate; do alternately; do in turn; (2) insert; interweave; weave; (3) episode; interlude; subplot;
穿插表演 sideshow;
穿插進行 do sth in turn;

［穿戴］ dress; apparel; clothing; what one wears;
穿戴華麗 be gorgeously appareled;
穿戴體面 in decent apparel;
穿戴整齊 be neatly dressed;

［穿得⋯］ be dressed...; be...dressed;
穿得非常時髦 be dressed to death; be dressed up to the nines;
穿得寒酸 be ill-dressed; be poorly dressed;
穿得厚實 be heavily dressed; be thickly dressed;
穿得暖和 be warmly dressed; dress oneself warmly;
穿得漂亮 be finely dressed; be nicely

dressed; be smartly dressed;
穿得輕便 be in light attire; be lightly dressed;
穿得少 wear little clothing;

[穿反了] put on sth back to front; wear sth inside out;
把襯衫穿反了 put a shirt on back to front; put one's shirt on inside out;

[穿過] cross over; pass through; passage;
穿過馬路 cross the street;
穿過沙漠 cross the desert;
從人群中穿過 thread one's way through the crowd; weave one's way through the crowd;

[穿花] go through the flowers;
穿花度柳 go through flowers and willows;
如蝶穿花 like a butterfly flying from flower to flower;

[穿舊] wear out;

[穿孔] bore a hole; perforate; pierce; punch a hole;
穿孔機 perforator; piercer; punch; puncher;
~ 邊緣穿孔機 edge-punched punch;
~ 二輥穿孔機 two-roll piercer;
~ 鍵盤穿孔機 keyboard perforator;
~ 卡片穿孔機 card puncher;
~ 盤式穿孔機 disc piercer;
~ 噴射穿孔機 jet perforator;
~ 三輥穿孔機 three-roll piercer;
~ 紙帶穿孔機 paper tape puncher;
~ 自動穿孔機 automatic puncher;
~ 自動送卡穿孔機 automatic feed punch;
穿孔卡片 punched card;
穿孔磚 air brick;
液壓穿孔 hydraulic piercing;
自動穿孔 automatic punch;

[穿林度水] through the trees and across the water;

[穿上] put on;
穿上鞋 put on one's shoes;
穿上衣服 put on one's dress;

[穿梭] shuttle back and forth;
穿梭巴士 shuttle bus;
穿梭機 space shuttle;
穿梭來往 busy comings and goings; shuttle back and forth;
穿梭外交 shuttle diplomacy;
穿梭襲擊 shuttle raid;

[穿透] pass through; penetrate; penetration; pierce through;
穿透性 penetrability;
粒間穿透 intergranular penetration;
無法穿透 impenetrable;

[穿孝] in mourning; put into mourning; wear mourning;

[穿衣鏡] dressing mirror;

[穿越] cut across; pass through;

[穿雲] break through the clouds;
穿雲觸天 penetrate the clouds to touch the sky;
穿雲而過 break through the clouds;
穿雲裂石 fly through the clouds and crack the rocks;
穿雲破霧 pierce the clouds and mist;
穿雲入海 throughout the universe;

[穿鑿] give a far-fetched interpretation; read too much into sth;
穿鑿附會 bring in by head and shoulders; distorted conclusion; fasten on an unwarranted conclusion; force words into a sense; give strained interpretations and draw far-fetched analogies; make a forced interpretation; offer a far-fetched explanation; strain the sense; stretch the meaning; twist or pervert the meaning of sth; wrest the sense;
附會穿鑿 draw far-fetched analogies and give strained interpretations; make far-fetched, unwarranted conclusions;

[穿針] thread a needle;
穿針引線 act as a go-between; act as a matchmaker; act as a middleman; act as liaison; pass the thread through the eye of a needle; try to make a match;

[穿着] apparel; dress; what one wears;
穿着打扮 dress and make-up;
~ 注意穿着打扮 care much about one's dress and make-up;
穿着大方 elegantly and gracefully dressed;
穿着得體的人 impeccable dresser;
穿着花哨 be dolled up; be dressed to kill;
穿着襤褸 be shabbily attired;
穿着樸素大方 wear plain clothes with elegance;
穿着入時的 well dressed;
~ 穿着入時的女士 well-dressed lady;
穿着奢華 be luxuriously dressed;
穿着時髦的人 fashionable dresser;
穿着素雅 be quietly dressed;

穿着體面 well dressed;
~穿着體面大方 be decently dressed;
穿着優雅入時 be elegantly dressed;
穿着整齊 be dressed up to the nines; be neatly dressed;
講究穿着 care much about one's dress; particular about one's dress; pay much attention to one's dress;

拆穿 expose; lay bare; unmask;
吃穿 food and clothing;
戳穿 (1) lay bare; puncture; (2) explode; expose;
洞穿 (1) pierce; (2) comprehend; see through;
貫穿 (1) pass through; (2) run through;
橫穿 traverse;
擊穿 break down; puncture;
揭穿 expose; lay bare; show up; unmask;
看穿 see through;
耐穿 can stand wear and tear; endurable;
身穿 attire oneself in; be attired in; be clad in; be clothed in; be dressed in; dress oneself in; have on; wear;
試穿 fit sth on; try on;
説穿 disclose; tell what sth really is;
眼穿 anxiously awaiting; eagerly expecting;

chuan²

chuan

【舡】 same as 船;

chuan

【船】 boat; ship;

[船邊] alongside the vessel;
船邊交貨 alongside delivery;
[船舶] ship; shipping;
船舶執照 ship licence;
[船東] shipowner;
[船隊] fleet; fleet of ships;
海上商船隊 maritime fleet;
商船隊 trade fleet;
漁船隊 fishing fleet;
[船帆] sail;
[船費] cost of a boat ticket;
[船夫] boatman;
[船家] boatman;
[船庫] boathouse;
[船民] boat people;
[船票] boat ticket; ship ticket;
[船期] sailing date;
[船上] on board;
[船身] hull;
金屬船身 metal hull;
水上飛機船身 seaplane hull;
油槽船船身 tanker hull;
[船體] boat hull; hull;
玻璃鋼船體 glass fibre hull;
常規船體 conventional hull;
裸船體 bare hull;
雙船體 catamaran hull;
[船塢] boatyard; dock; dockyard; shipyard;
船塢工人 docker;
浮船塢 floating dock;
乾船塢 dry dock;
油船塢 oil dock;
造船塢 building dock;
[船鞋] deck shoes;
平跟船鞋 loafer;
[船藝] seamanship;
[船員] boatman; crew; sailor; seaman;
商船船員 merchant seaman;
[船長] captain; mariner; master; shipmaster;
[船隻] ship; vessel;
拆毀船隻 scrap vessel;
改造船隻 remodel a vessel;
檢查船隻 survey ships;
停泊船隻 anchor one's vessel;
整修船隻 renovate a vessel;
指揮船隻 command a vessel;
裝備船隻 equip a ship;

靶船 target ship;
兵船 man-of-war; warship;
泊船 moor a boat;
駁船 barge; lighter;
沉船 shipwreck;
乘船 ride in a boat;
燈船 lightship; light vessel;
渡船 ferry; ferry boat;
躉船 landing stage; pontoon;
帆船 junk; sailing boat; sailing ship;
翻船 (1) shipwreck; (2) fail; suffer an upset;
飛船 airship; dirigible;
僱船 hire a boat;
海船 seagoing vessel;
航船 steamer;
划船 boating; go boating; paddle a boat; row a boat;
貨船 cargo ship; freighter;
艦船 ships and warships;
浚泥船 dredger;
開船 sail; set sail;
客船 passenger ship;
浪船 swingboat;

龍船 dragon boat;
輪船 steamer; steamship;
煤船 coaler;
木船 wooden boat;
跑船 make a living as a sailor;
破冰船 icebreaker;
汽船 steamboat; steamer;
賽船 run a boat race;
沙船 large junk;
商船 merchant ship;
上船 board a ship;
駛船 sail a ship;
雙體船 catamaran;
水翼船 hovercraft; hydrofoil craft; hydroplane;
碎冰船 icebreaker;
拖船 (1) tow boat; tug boat; (2) barge;
下船 debark; disembark; go ashore;
小船 boat; skiff;
行船 navigate; sail a boat;
搖船 row a boat;
一艘船 a ship;
一條船 a boat;
油船 oil carrier; oil tanker;
游船 pleasure boat;
遊船 cruiser; pleasure boat; yacht;
郵船 ocean liner; packet boat;
漁船 fishing boat;
暈船 seasickness;
造船 build a ship; shipbuilding;
賊船 pirate ship;
戰船 man-of-war; war vessel; warship;
櫂船 row a boat;
轉船 change to another ship;
裝船 put goods on a ship;
租船 charter; boat chartering; ship chartering;

chuan

【傳】 (1) pass; pass on; (2) hand down; (3) impart; pass on; teach; (4) spread; (5) conduct; transmit; (6) convey; express; (7) summon; (8) contagious; infectious;

［傳杯換盞］ drink after toasting to each other;

［傳遍］ spread everywhere;
傳遍各地 sound everywhere;
傳遍全城 be spread all over the town;
傳遍全校 go round the school;

［傳播］ circulate; disseminate; dissemination; pass on; propagation; propagate; put about; spread; take wind;
傳播產業 communication industries;
傳播傳染病 disseminate an infection; spread an infection;
傳播代溝 communication-generation gap;
傳播功能 function of communication;
傳播公司 communication company;
傳播理論 communication theory;
～單向傳播理論 one-way communication theory;
傳播流言蜚語 retail gossip;
傳播媒介 communication media;
傳播模式 communication model;
傳播渠道 communication channel;
傳播體 disseminule;
～具鈎傳播體 hooked disseminule;
～具毛傳播體 comate disseminule;
～傘傳播體 parachute disseminule;
傳播細菌 spread germs;
傳播先決條件 preconditions for communication;
傳播小道消息 mobilize grapevine news;
傳播效果 communication effects;
傳播新聞 disseminate news;
傳播行為 communication act;
傳播信息 diffuse information;
傳播學 communication theory;
傳播謠言 spread rumours;
傳播載體 disseminator;
傳播障礙 communication barriers;
傳播者 propagator;
爆炸傳播 propagation of detonation;
動物傳播 animal dispersal;
反常傳播 abnormal propagation; anomalous propagation;
廣為傳播 be transmitted from mouth to mouth;
疾病的傳播 transmission of a disease;
兩級傳播 two-step flow of communication;
內部傳播 internal communication;
情報傳播 information dissemination;
相關傳播 coherent propagation;
組織傳播 organizational communication;

［傳達］ communicate; convey; pass on; transmit;
傳達命令 transmit an order;

［傳代］ go down to posterity; go down to the future generation; hand from generation to generation;
代代相傳 from generation to generation; hand down from generation to generation; last from generation

to generation; transmitted through successive generations;
傳宗接代 carry on the ancestral line; continue one's family line; continue the ancestral line; inherit one's family tradition and be the authentic heir to sb;

[傳單] flyer; leaflet; handbill; propaganda sheet;
傳單廣告 circument;
廣告傳單 advertisement leaflet;
散傳單 distribute circulars;
散發傳單 hand out circulars;
宣傳傳單 propaganda leaflets;

[傳道] (1) propagate doctrines of the ancient sages; (2) deliver a sermon; preach;
傳道人 preacher;

[傳導] conduction;
傳導性 conductivity;
單極傳導 unipolar conduction;
遞減傳導 decremental conduction;
骨骼傳導 bone conduction;
激感傳導 excitory conduction;
絕緣性傳導 isolated conduction;
空穴傳導 hole conduction;
脈衝傳導 conduction of impulse;
逆向傳導 antidromic conduction;
逆行性傳導 retrograde conduction;
熱傳導 heat conduction; thermal conduction;
熱離子傳導 thermionic conduction;
神經傳導 nerve conduction;
順向傳導 orthodromic conduction;
跳躍傳導 salutatory conduction;
穩態熱傳導 steady-state conduction;
興奮傳導 conduction of excitation;
縱向熱傳導 longitudinal thermal conduction;

[傳遞] deliver; transfer; transmit;
傳遞率 transmissibility;
~變位傳遞率 displacement transmissibility;
~衝擊傳遞率 shock transmissibility;
~振動傳遞率 vibration transmissibility;
傳遞效應 transmission effect;
傳遞信息 send and receive messages;
熱傳遞 heat transfer;
依次傳遞 transmit in turn;

[傳電] conduct electricity;

[傳訛] pass on wrong reports;

[傳粉] pollination;
傳粉媒介 fertilizer; pollinator;

[傳感器] pickup; sensor;
探測傳感器 acquisition sensor;
位移傳感器 displacement sensor;

[傳給] pass to;

[傳呼] pass sb;
傳呼電話 relay telephone;
傳呼機 beeper; bleep; bleeper; pager;

[傳話] pass on a message; send word to sb;

[傳喚] summon to court;
被傳喚 be summoned;
~被傳喚出庭 be summoned to appear in court;

[傳家] hand down from generation to generation within a family;
傳家寶 cherished tradition; family heirloom; family treasure for generations; precious heritage;
一件傳家寶 a family heirloom;
詩禮傳家 cultured family; family of scholars;

[傳教] do missionary work; preach one's religion;
傳教工作 missionary work;
傳教士 missionary;

[傳經] pass on the fruits of experience;
傳經送寶 impart one's knowledge to others; pass on one's invaluable experience;

[傳開] get air; pass on;
謠言容易傳開 rumours are apt to get air;

[傳令] dispatch orders; transmit orders;
傳令官 herald;

[傳媒] disseminate; medium;
傳媒大亨 media tycoon;
傳媒學 media studies;

[傳票] summons;
發出傳票 issue a summons;

[傳奇] (1) legend; (2) verse drama;
傳奇故事 romance;
傳奇人物 legend; mythic figure;
傳奇色彩 romance;
~充滿傳奇色彩 be filled with romance;
古典傳奇 classic romance;
一段傳奇 a romance;
中古傳奇 medieval romance;

[傳情] convey one's tender feeling;
眉目傳情 cast furtive glances at; eye sb up; flash amorous glances; make eyes at; ocular intercourse; send messages

of love to sb with one's brows; send unspoken messages from the eyes; send unspoken messages of love; throw the eye at;
眉眼傳情 cast amorous glances;
秋波傳情 cast sheep's eyes; give a loving glance; give sb the glad eye; make eyes at sb; throw amorous glances at sb;
以目傳情 cast affectionate glances; convey a bewitching gleam;

[傳球] pass; pass the ball; passing;
背後傳球 around the back; back-flip pass; pass behind the body;
邊線傳球 flank pass;
側臂傳球 sidearm pass;
長傳球 long pass;
單手傳球 one-hand pass;
單手低手向前傳球 howling pass;
單手肩上傳球 baseball pass;
倒地傳球 fall-down pass;
倒手傳球 right back pass;
低傳球 low pass;
地面傳球 pass along the ground;
短傳球 short pass;
反手傳球 backhand pass; reverse pass;
反彈傳球 bounce pass;
高吊傳球 lob pass;
高挑傳球 clearing pass;
勾手傳球 hook pass;
橫傳球 cross pass; lateral pass;
弧形傳球 loop pass;
花樣傳球 fancy pass;
回傳球 return pass;
假傳球 fake-pass;
假裝投籃的傳球 fake-shot pass;
肩上傳球 shoulder pass;
交叉傳球 scissors pass;
接傳球 pick up a pass;
空中傳球 overhead pass; volley pass;
兩手交叉傳球 cross-hand pass;
凌空傳球 volley pass;
盲目傳球 phantom pass;
跑動傳球 running pass;
三角傳球 triangular pass; triangular passing;
三人傳球 three-person interpassing;
上手傳球 face pass; overhand pass;
手遞手傳球 hand-off;
手腕傳球 snap pass;
雙手低手傳球 two-hand underhand pass;
雙手胸前傳球 two-hand snap pass;
跳起傳球 jump pass;
外圍傳球 perimeter passing;
下手傳球 under pass;
胸前傳球 chest pass; push pass;
一腳傳球 one-touch passing;
張手傳球 open-hand pass;
之字形傳球 zigzag passing;
直接傳球 direct pass;
直體傳球 sitting pass;

[傳染] contagious; infect; infection; infectious;
傳染病 communicable disease; contagious disease; infectious disease;
~傳染病病房 contagious ward;
~得傳染病 catch a contagious disease; contract a contagious disease;
~接觸傳染病 contagious disease; infectious disease;
~引起傳染病 cause infectious diseases;
~預防傳染病 keep off infection; prevent infection;
傳染力 infectivity;
傳染媒介 intermediate vector;
傳染性疾病 infection;
避免傳染 keep off infection;
交叉傳染 cross infection;
接觸傳染 contagion; contagious infection;
空氣傳染 airborne infection;
疫病傳染 contagion;

[傳熱] conduct heat; heat diffusion; heat transfer;

[傳人] posterity;

[傳神] lifelike; vivid;
傳神之筆 vivid touch;

[傳聲] transmit sound;
傳聲器 mic; microphone; mike;
~廣播傳聲器 announcing microphone;
~離線傳聲器 off-mike;
~炭精傳聲器 carbon microphone;
傳聲筒 loud hailer; megaphone; sb's mouthpiece;

[傳世] be handed down from ancient times;
傳世珍寶 a treasure handed down from ancient times;
傳世之作 a piece destined to go down to posterity;

[傳授] pass on; teach;
傳授技術 impart one's technical skills; pass on one's technical skills;
傳授媒介 medium of instruction;

[傳述] it is said; they say;

[傳輸] disseminate; transmission; transmit;

傳輸能力 transmittability;
交流傳輸 alternating-current transmission;
平衡傳輸 balanced transmission;
數據傳輸 data transmission;
自動傳輸 automatic transmission;

[傳説] (1) it is said; they say; (2) legend; lore; tradition;
傳説紛繁 rumours are rife;
傳説人物 legendary personages;
當地的傳説 local legend;
古典傳説 classical legend;
古老的傳説 ancient traditions;
據傳説 according to legend;
民間的傳説 popular legend;
中古傳説 medieval legend;

[傳送] convey; deliver; transfer; transmit; transport;
傳送帶 conveyor belt;
傳送機 belt conveyer; transmitter;
~自動傳送機 auto transmitter;
傳送情報 send information to;
傳送訊息 transmit a message;

[傳頌] be on everybody's lips; be widely read;
廣為傳頌 be eulogized everywhere;
為世人所傳頌 be read with admiration by people all over the world;

[傳統] convention; tradition;
傳統導向 traditional directness;
傳統的 traditional;
~非傳統的 non-traditional;
傳統觀念 conventional ideas; traditional ideas;
~破除傳統觀念 shatter the conventional ideas;
~體現傳統觀念 embody the traditional ideas;
傳統節日 traditional festival;
~傳統節日習俗 customs of traditional festivals;
傳統看法 traditional viewpoint;
傳統手工藝 traditional craft skill;
傳統束縛 obsession with tradition;
傳統思想 traditional thought;
~中國傳統思想 Chinese traditional thought;
傳統語法 traditional grammar;
傳統政治文化 traditional political culture;
傳統主義 traditionalism;
~傳統主義者 traditionalist;
傳統做法 traditional way of doing things;
保持傳統 keep up one's tradition;
背離傳統 depart from one's tradition;
當地傳統 local tradition;
丟失傳統 lose tradition;
革命傳統 revolutionary tradition;
~光榮的革命傳統 glorious revolutionary tradition;
根據傳統 by tradition;
古老的傳統 ancient tradition; old tradition; time-honoured tradition;
過去的傳統 traditions of the past;
好傳統 good tradition;
家庭傳統 family tradition;
教育傳統 pedagogical tradition;
舊傳統 old tradition;
目的語傳統 target-language tradition;
牢固的傳統 strong tradition;
拋棄傳統 discard tradition;
文化傳統 cultural tradition;
學術傳統 academic tradition;
~優良的學術傳統 exemplary academic tradition;
優良傳統 fine traditions;
~保持優良傳統 maintain fine traditions;
~發揚優良傳統 carry forward the fine traditions;
~堅持優良傳統 uphold fine traditions;
~樹立優良傳統 build up fine traditions;
悠久的傳統 long tradition;
照傳統 by tradition;
忠於傳統 constant to tradition;
宗教傳統 religious tradition;
遵循傳統 follow a tradition;

[傳為] be passed on as;
傳為話柄 become a subject for ridicule;
傳為佳話 become a favourite tale; everybody is telling the story of;
傳為美談 be told from mouth to mouth with approbation; become an anecdote;
傳為笑柄 a laughing stock through the ages; be considered material for ridicule; it is all the more a laughing stock; pass as a proverb;
傳為笑談 become a standing joke; pass as a proverb;

[傳聞] hearsay; rumour;
傳聞失實 the rumour is unfounded;

[傳習] pass on and learn knowledge and skill;

[傳銷] pyramid selling;
非法傳銷 illegal pyramid selling;

[傳言] (1) hearsay; rumour; (2) pass on a

message; (3) make a statement; speak;
傳言非虛 it is not just hearsay;
[傳揚] spread from mouth to mouth;
傳揚四方 spread far and wide;
[傳意] communicative;
傳意翻譯 communicative translation;
[傳譯] interpret;
即時傳譯 simultaneous interpretation;
同聲傳譯 simultaneous interpretation;
[傳閱] circulate for perusal; pass round for perusal;
[傳真] fax;
傳真傳輸 facsimile transmission;
傳真通信 facsimile; fax;
傳真系統 facsimile system; fax system;
圖文傳真 fax line;
一份傳真 a fax;
[傳種] propagate; reproduce;

背傳 back pass;
側傳 side pass;
單傳 have only one son for several generations;
電傳 (1) teleprinter; (2) teleprinted message;
短傳 short pass;
訛傳 false report; groundless rumour; unfounded rumour;
二傳 set; set up;
風傳 hearsay; rumour;
哄傳 (of rumours) circulate widely;
家傳 handed down from the older generations of the family;
據傳 rumour has it that;
口傳 by word of mouth;
留傳 leave sth to pass on to later generations;
流傳 circulate; hand down; spread;
頻傳 keep pouring in;
盛傳 be widely known; be widely rumoured;
失傳 not be handed down from past generations;
世傳 be handed down through generations;
相傳 (1) according to legend; tradition has it that; (2) hand down from one to another;
心傳 pass on personal teachings to pupils;
宣傳 conduct propaganda; propagate;
言傳 explain in words;
謠傳 hearsay; rumour;
一傳 first pass;
遺傳 inherit;
祖傳 handed down from one's ancestors;

chuan
【椽】 beam; rafter;
[椽筆] your masterly writing;
[椽子] beam; rafter;

chuan
【遄】 (1) quickly; swiftly; (2) to and fro;
[遄死] die very quickly;
[遄往] go quickly;

chuan³

chuan
【舛】 (1) chaotic; confused; disorderly; messy; mixed up; (2) deviate from; disobey; oppose; run counter to;
[舛錯] mishap; mixed up; uneven;
[舛誤] error; mishap; mistake;

chuan
【喘】 (1) breathe heavily; gasp for breath; pant; (2) asthma;
[喘鳴] stridor;
喘鳴性喉痙攣 laryngismus stridulus;
喘鳴性喉炎 laryngitis stridulosa;
[喘氣] gasp; pant;
喘喘氣 pause for breath;
大口喘氣 gulp for air;
還在喘氣 be still breathing;
呼呼地喘氣 wheeze;
口不喘氣，臉不泛紅 not be out of breath or even faintly flushed;
氣得喘氣 gasp with rage;
正在喘氣 be panting for breath;
[喘息] (1) gasp for breath; pant; puff; (2) breather; breathing spell; respite;
喘息初定 just as one recovers one's breath; recover from fear and confusion;
喘息機會 a little breathing time;
喘息時間 breathing space; respite;
喘息未定 before catching one's breath; before one has a chance to catch one's breath; before one is oneself again; pant and be still out of breath;
喘息餘暇 breathing time;
[喘吁吁] puff and blow;

殘喘 lingering breath of life;
氣喘 (1) asthma; (2) breathe heavily; gasp for breath;
哮喘 (1) asthma; (2) wheeze;

chuan⁴

chuan
【串】 (1) string together; (2) a bunch; a

cluster; a string; (3) get things mixed up; (4) conspire; gang up; (5) go from place to place; go here and there; rove; run about; (6) act; play a part;

[串供] act in collusion to make each other's confessions tally; gang up to make a false confession;

[串換] change; exchange; swap;

[串講] construe;

[串街遊鄉] make one's rounds of the streets and villages;

[串烤] skewer;

[串聯] contact; establish; establish a relation with; establish ties with; link up; make contacts with;

串聯文件 sequential file;

[串門] call at sb's home; call on sb; drop around; drop in on sb; look in on sb;

串門過訪 go from house to house to talk with people;

串門几 call at sb's home; call on a friend's family; drop in on sb; drop round;

串門子 call at sb's home; drop in;

串門走戶 pass from house to house;

挨家串門 call on sb from house to house;

[串騙] gang up and swindle sb;

[串氣] collude with; gang up;

[串通] collaborate; collude; collude with; collusion; complicity; conspire with; gang up; in collusion with; work hand in glove with;

串通一氣 collaborate; collude with; gang up; hand in glove with; in cahoots with; in league with; stand in with; work in close collaboration with;

串通作弊 conspire with sb to carry out illegal acts; in collusion over corrupt practices; league together for some evil end; string together for evil purposes;

暗中串通 collude with; conspire; secret collaboration;

互相串通 conspire with each other;

~暗中互相串通 conspire with each other;

[串線] wrong number;

[串行處理] serial processing;

[串演] act the role of; play the role of;

[串音] crosstalk;

互相串音 interaction crosstalk;

間接串音 indirect crosstalk;

可懂串音 intelligible crosstalk;

路際串音 channel crosstalk;

天線串音 aerial crosstalk;

循環串音 circulating crosstalk;

直接串音 direct crosstalk;

[串遊] amble; saunter; stroll;

貫串 permeate; run through;

客串 guest performer;

一串 a bunch of; a cluster of; a rope of; a strand of; a string of;

一連串 a chain of; a round of; a series of; a streak of; a string of; a succession of; a train of; a volley of;

chuan

【釧】 bracelet; armlet;

金釧 gold bracelet;

玉釧 jade bracelet;

chuang¹
chuang

【創】 wound;

[創痕] scar;

[創傷] trauma; traumatism; vulns; wound;

創傷後營養不良 wound dystrophy;

創傷性休克 traumatic shock;

包扎創傷 dress a wound;

開放性創傷 open wound;

潛在創傷 potential trauma;

心理創傷 psychic trauma;

戰爭創傷 war scars;

[創痛] pain from an injury;

創巨痛深 be afflicted with extreme pain; in deep distress; severely wounded and deeply pained; suffer heavy losses;

草創 start to found;

初創 newly established;

chuang

【窗】 window;

[窗霸] windows blaster;

[窗格子] window lattice;

[窗戶] casement; window;

窗戶紙 camouflage; cover-up; window paper;

擦窗戶 clean a window;

打開窗戶 open the window;

打碎窗戶 break a window; crack a window; smash a window;

關窗戶 shut a window;
開窗戶 open a window;

［窗口］ (1) window; (2) wicket; (3) medium; showpiece; testing ground;
窗口功能 window function;
窗口軟件 window software;
窗口文件 window file;
窗口系統 window system;
大氣窗口 atmospheric window;
彈出式窗口 pop up; pop-up window;
接觸窗口 contact window;
輸入窗口 input window;
坐在窗口 sit at the window;

［窗框］ window frame;

［窗簾］ drapes; window curtain;
窗簾杆 curtain pole; curtain rail; curtain rod;
窗簾鈎 curtain hook;
窗簾盒 pelmet;
窗簾箱 pelmet;
關上窗簾 draw the curtains;
拉開窗簾 draw back the curtains; draw the window curtain apart; open the curtains; pull the curtains;
拉攏窗簾 draw the window curtain together; furl the window curtain;
拉上窗簾 close the curtains; draw the curtains; pull the curtains;
拉下窗簾 pull down the window curtain;
捲起窗簾 draw up the blinds;

［窗明几淨］ bright and clean; bright windows and spotless desks; with bright windows and clean tables; the windows bright and the tables clean;

［窗紗］ window gauze;

［窗台］ window sill;
扒窗台 hold on to a window sill;

［窗外］ outside the window;
看窗外 look out of the window;

［窗子］ window;
擦窗子 clean the wind;

百葉窗 blind; shutter;
車窗 window of a car;
櫥窗 (1) display window; shop window; showcase; (2) glass-fronted billboard;
吊窗 window which can be propped up;
耳窗 ear window;
後窗 rear window;
老虎窗 dormer window;
落地窗 French window;
楣窗 fanlight; transom;
門窗 doors and windows;
氣窗 fanlight; transom window;
紗窗 screen window;
視窗 window;
豎天窗 dormer window;
天窗 skylight;
鐵窗 (1) window with iron grating; (2) prison; prison bars;
同窗 schoolmate; study in the same school;
凸窗 bay window;
屋頂窗 dormer window;
舷窗 porthole;
一扇窗 a window;
芸窗 study;

chuang

【瘡】 (1) skin ulcer; sore; (2) wound;

［瘡疤］ (1) scar; (2) sore;
揭舊瘡疤 reopen old scores;
揭人瘡疤 pull the scab right off sb's sore; touch sb on the raw; touch sb's sore spot;
揭痛瘡疤 expose the real role of; touch sb on the raw;
有塊瘡疤 have a score;

［瘡痕］ wound scar;

［瘡痂］ scar;

［瘡瘍］ chronic ulcer;

［瘡痍］ (1) sores and wounds; (2) desolation after a disaster;
瘡痍滿目 distress and suffering can be seen everywhere; everywhere a scene of devastation meets the eye; wherever one looks, there is devastation;

補瘡 cure a boil;
唇瘡 cold sore; fever sore;
痤瘡 acne;
大瘡 mycotic ulcer caused by venereal disease;
疔瘡 malignant boil;
凍瘡 chilblain; perniosis;
痘瘡 smallpox;
疥瘡 scabies;
金瘡 incised wound; metal-inflicted wound;
口瘡 aphtha;
狼瘡 lupus;
氯痤瘡 chloric acne
奶瘡 mastitis;
膿瘡 running sore;
蓐瘡 (1) bedsores; (2) infantile boils;
褥瘡 bedsore;

鼠瘡 scrofula;
禿瘡 favus of the scalp;
長瘡 form a boil;
痔瘡 haemorrhoids; piles;

chuang²
chuang

【牀】 (1) bed; (2) bed-like object; (3) a bedful of;
[牀板] bed plank;
[牀邊] bedside;
[牀單] sheet; bedclothes;
換牀單 change the sheet;
曬牀單 air the sheets;
一條牀單 a bedsheet;
[牀第] (1) bed and bed mattress; (2) place of conjugal intimacies;
牀第之間 in bed or in its intimacies;
牀第之情 conjugal affection;
牀第之言 intimate words said in bed; private talks between husband and wife;
[牀墊] mattress;
充氣牀墊 airbed; air mattress;
[牀架] bedstead;
[牀上] (1) bedding; (2) on the bed;
牀上用品 bedclothes; bedding;
病在牀上 be ill abed; be sick abed;
躺在牀上 lie abed;
在牀上 in the sack;
[牀頭] bedhead; bedside; head of a bed;
牀頭按鈕 bedside button;
牀頭板 headboard;
牀頭燈 bed lamp;
牀頭櫃 (1) bedside cupboard; bedside table; nightstand; (2) henpecked husband; uxorious man;
牀頭金盡 hard up for money; find oneself in straitened circumstances; in poverty; money runs out; run out of money;
牀頭開關 bedside control;
[牀位] berth;
[牀浴] bed bath;
[牀罩] bedcover; bedspread; counterpane; spread;

刨牀 (1) planner; (2) planning machine;
冰牀 sledge;
病牀 (1) hospital bed; (2) sickbed;
糟牀 manger bed;
插牀 slotter; slotting machine;
車牀 lathe;
成對的單人牀 bunk beds;
大雙人牀 queen-size bed;
單人牀 single bed;
道牀 roadbed;
吊牀 roadbed;
帆布牀 campbed; cot;
固定牀 fixed bed;
棺牀 coffin platform;
河牀 riverbed;
活動牀 travelling bed;
機牀 machine tool;
剪牀 shearing machine;
拉牀 broaching machine;
冷牀 cold bed; cold frame;
臨牀 clinical;
靈牀 bier;
卵石牀 pebble bed;
尿牀 wet the bed;
鋪牀 make the bed;
起牀 get out of bed; get up;
曲牀 seedbed;
雙人牀 double bed;
彈簧牀 spring bed;
特大雙人牀 king-sized bed;
鐵牀 iron bed;
溫牀 (1) hotbed; (2) breeding ground;
懸浮牀 suspension bed;
岩牀 sill;
一張牀 a bed;
移植牀 transplant bed;
折疊牀 folding bed;

chuang

【幢】 (1) pennant or streamer used in ancient China; (2) stone pillar with Buddhist scripture inscriptions;
[幢幢] dancing; flickering;

經幢 a stone pillar inscribed with Buddha's name;
石幢 a stone pillar inscribed with Buddha's name;

chuang³
chuang

【闖】 (1) charge; dash; rush; (2) break through; temper oneself;
[闖蕩] make a living wandering from place to place;
闖蕩江湖 make a living wandering from

place to place; roam all over the country;

[闖關] break a blockade;
劈路闖關 carve a way through enemy lines and storm strategic passes;

[闖禍] bring disaster; get into trouble; gone and done it; lead to trouble; ride for a fall;
老是闖禍 always get into trouble;

[闖將] daring general; path-breaker;

[闖進] break in; burst in;

[闖勁] daring spirit; pioneering spirit;

[闖練] temper oneself in the world; gain experience from real life; leave home to temper oneself;

[闖入] break in; burst into; force one's way in; intrude into; rush in;
闖入會場 intrude into a meeting;
非法闖入 break in;
冒然闖入 butt in;
強行闖入 thrust oneself in;

chuang⁴
chuang

【創】 achieve; create; establish; initiate; start;

[創辦] establish; found; set up; start;
創辦報紙 start a newspaper;
創辦者 founder;
~ 創辦者之一 founder member;

[創導] initiate; propose;

[創匯] create a source for foreign exchange; earn foreign exchange;

[創見] brand-new idea; creative idea; original idea;
有創見 hold an original view;

[創建] create; creation; establish; found; set up;

[創舉] pioneering undertaking; pioneering work;
偉大的創舉 great beginning;

[創刊] begin publication; start publication;
創刊詞 inaugural statement;
創刊號 inaugural issue;

[創立] found; originate; set up; start up;
創立一種學說 establish a doctrine;
創立一家公司 start up a new company;
創立者 founder;
~ 創立者之一 founder member;
創家立業 build up one's family fortunes;

[創利] create a source of profit; create profit; make a profit;

[創設] create; establish; found; set up;

[創始] begin; initiate; open; originate; start;
創始人 founder; originator;

[創收] create a source of income; earn an income; extra income; perk;

[創新] blaze new trails; bring forth new ideas; innovate;
創新精神 spirit of innovation;
創新理論 innovative theory;
創新立異 innovative;
創新體系 innovative system;
創新性學習 creative study;
詞匯創新 lexical innovation;

[創業] do pioneering work; set up a business; start an undertaking; start up in business;
創業精神 pioneering spirit;
創業難，守業更難 keeping is harder than winning;
創業容易守業難 fortune is easy to find but hard to keep; gear is easier gained than guided; it is easy to open a shop but hard to keep it open; it is easy to start an undertaking, but hard to keep it; keeping is harder than winning; to build up a fortune is easy, but to keep it is hard;

[創意] initiative;
創意廣告 initiative advertisement;

[創優] create excellence;

[創造] bring about; create; creation; produce;
創造峰期 peak period creation;
創造工程 creation engineering;
創造好成績 produce excellent results; win excellent results;
創造力 creativity; originality;
創造美學 creativity aesthetics;
創造奇蹟 accomplish miracles; create miracles;
創造社會財富 create the wealth of society;
創造心理 creative psychology;
~ 創造心理學 psychology of creation;
創造型人才 talent of creation pattern;
創造性 creativity;
~ 創造性比譯 creative transposition;
~ 創造性順應 creative accommodation;
~ 創造性思考 creative thinking;
~ 創造性想像 creative imagination;

~創造性隱喻 creative metaphor;
創造有利條件 create favourable conditions;
創造者 creator;

[創製] create; formulate; institute;

[創作] create;
創作技巧 artistic technique;
創作經驗 creative experience;
創作美術作品 produce works of art;
創作思想 ideas guiding creation in literature and art;
創作文學作品 produce a literary work;
創作源泉 fountainhead of literary and artistic creation; source of creative writing;
創作者 creator;
劃時代的創作 epoch-making creative work;
忙於創作 busy with one's writing;
體驗創作 experiential creation;
文學創作 literary creation; literary work;
文藝創作 artistic and literary creation;

草創 found; start to establish;
初創 newly established;
獨創 original creation;
開創 initiate; pioneer; start;
始創 create; found; initiate; originate;
首創 initiate; originate; pioneer;
重創 (1) serious wound; (2) inflict a serious blow on; inflict heavy losses on; maul heavily;

chuang

【愴】 mournful; sad; sorrowful;

[愴愴欲絕] distressed to the utmost;

[愴然] sorrowful;
愴然淚下 burst into sorrowful tears;

悲愴 sad; sorrowful;
淒愴 miserable; wretched;

chui¹
chui

【吹】 (1) blow; puff; (2) play; (3) boast; brag; talk big; (4) break down; break off; break up; cut off; fail; fall through;

[吹吹打打] all the gongs and trumpets sound; all the musical instruments are being played; beating drums and blowing trumpets; piping and drumming;

[吹吹拍拍] boasting and flattering; bragging and toadying; flattering and touting; fulsome flattery;
吹吹拍拍，拉拉扯扯 boasting and toadying; resort to boasting, flattery and touting;

[吹倒] blow down;

[吹燈] break off a love affair;
鬼吹燈 disrupt furtively;

[吹風] (1) blow; catch a chill; in a draught; (2) dry hair with a blower; dry one's hair; (3) give a clue; let sb in on sth in advance; reveal information in an informal way;
吹風會 briefing;
吹風機 air blower; blow-dryer; blower; drier; hairdrier; hairdryer;

[吹拂] stir; sway;

[吹鼓手] (1) bugler; trumpeter; (2) eulogist;

[吹管] blowpipe;
吹管分析 blowpipe analysis;

[吹過] blow over; blow through;

[吹號] blare the call; blow a bugle;
各吹各的號，各唱各的調 each blows his own bugle and sings his own song — each does things in his own way;

[吹火] blow a fire;
因風吹火 make a job easy with outside help;
引風吹火 (1) fan the flame; (2) stir up trouble;

[吹開] open sth;
風把窗吹開 the wind opened the window;

[吹了] break off; break up a relationship; break up;

[吹擂] boast; brag;
大吹大擂 ballyhoo; ballyhoo for; beat the drum; blow a loud blast on the trumpet; blow one's own trumpet; blow the trumpet and beat the drum; brag; brag and blare about one's success; fuss and feathers; high-pitched loose talk; hue and cry; make a big noise; make a great fanfare; put up a big show; raise a great fanfare; talk big; trumpet loudly about;
自吹自擂 all his geese are swans; big talk; blow one's own horn; blow one's own trumpet; boast; brag; brag about; brag and boast; crack oneself up; cry

C

roast meat; indulge in self-praise; lavish praise on oneself; praise one's own wares; praise oneself; ring one's own bell; self-advertisement; self-glorification; sing one's own praise; sound one's own trumpet; tall talk; toot one's own horn; vaunt;
自吹自擂的 bumptious;
~自吹自擂的人 blowhard; boastful person; pompous person;

[吹落] blow off;
[吹毛求疵] blow aside the fur to seek for faults; blow upon the hair trying to discover a mole; captious; carp; censorious; fastidious; faultfinding; find faults deliberately; find faults with; find quarrel in a straw; hair-splitting; hypercritical; nitpick; persnickety; pettifogging; pick flaws; pick holes in; pick on sth to find fault with; picky; pull sth to pieces; split hair; squeamish; very fastidious;
吹毛求疵的 hair-splitting;
吹毛求疵的人 carper;
對別人吹毛求疵 fault-finding;
[吹滅] blow out;
[吹牛] baloney; blast; blow one's own horn; blow one's own trumpet; boast; brag; draw a long bow; eyewash; hot air; plume oneself; shoot the breeze; swing the lead; talk big; talk in high language;
吹牛大王 hot-air artist;
吹牛拍馬 boast and flatter; brag and tout;
吹牛皮 act the braggadocio; boast; brag; draw the long bow; shoot a line; shoot crap; shoot the bull; shoot the shit; stick it on; talk big; talk horse; talk in high language; talk through one's hat; tell large stories;
別吹牛 come off it; do not boast; do not brag; do not shoot a line; do not talk big; do not talk horse;
別跟我吹牛 do not give me that baloney;
[吹捧] flatter; laud to the skies; lavish praise on;
大肆吹捧 lavish an astonishing amount of praise;
互相吹捧 backslapping; flatter each other;
[吹氣如蘭] give out a fragrant smell;
[吹求] fastidious; hypercritical;
[吹去] blow away;
[吹散] blow away;
被風吹散 be blown to the four winds;
[吹熄] blow off;
[吹簫] play a flute;
吳市吹簫 beg about the streets by playing a flute;
[吹噓] advertise oneself; boast; boost up; crow about sth; profess glibly; lavish praise on oneself or others;
吹噓捧場 laud; lavish and sing praises on others;
過份吹噓 boast too much; oversell;
自我吹噓 boost oneself;
[吹影鏤塵] blow a shadow and carve on a particle of dust—without seeing any expressions or movement;
[吹奏] play wind instruments;

側吹 side-blown;
臭吹 boast;
頂吹 top-blown;
風吹 the wind blows;
告吹 fail; fall through;
鼓吹 (1) advocate; (2) advertise; preach;
蛙吹 croaks of frogs;
瞎吹 brag; make wild boasts;

chui

【炊】 cook a meal;
[炊具] cooking utensils; cookware; kitchenware;
[炊沙作飯] useless attempt;
[炊事] kitchen work;
炊事員 cook;
[炊煙] smoke from kitchen chimneys;
炊煙繚繞 smoke curling up from the kitchen chimneys; smoke from the kitchen chimney wreathing; smoke spiralling from the kitchen;
炊煙裊裊 smoke curling up from the kitchen chimneys; smoke from the kitchen chimney wreaths over the cottage;
炊煙冉上 smoke wreathed up from the kitchen chimneys;
炊煙四起 chimney smoke rises from the cottages; cooking smoke all around;
[炊帚] brush for cleaning pots and pans; pot-scouring brush;

茶炊 tea urn;
晨炊 breakfast;
野炊 cook a meal in the open;

chui² chui

【垂】 (1) droop; hang down; let fall; (2) condescend; (3) bequeath to posterity; go down; hand down; (4) approaching; nearing; on the verge of;

[垂成] approaching success or completion; drawing close to a successful conclusion;
功敗垂成 fail on the verge of success; suffer defeat when victory is in sight;
事敗垂成 fail when success is already in sight;

[垂釣] angle; angle for fish; fish with a rod and line; go angling;
垂釣者 angler;
淡水魚垂釣 coarse fishing;

[垂髮] have one's hair hang down;

[垂淚] shed tears; weep;
仰天垂淚 gaze up at the sky and let the tears roll down one's cheeks;

[垂簾] hold court from behind a screen;
垂簾聽政 administer the state from behind the curtain; attend to state affairs from behind a curtain; hold court from behind a screen; rule in place of the emperor behind a screen; supervise the emperor behind the bamboo screen;

[垂柳] weeping willow;
垂柳成行 neat rows of willows;
垂柳裊裊 the branches of the weeping willows are swaying lightly; the willow branches sway gently in the breeze;
隔岸垂柳 the weeping willows on the other bank of the river;

[垂暮] dusk; just before sunset; towards sunset;
垂暮之年 in declining years; in old age;

[垂青] look upon sb with favour; show appreciation for sb; stand high in sb's favour;

[垂手] (1) obtain sth hands down; within easy reach; (2) let the hands hang by one's sides; stand with one's hands hanging by the sides;
垂手而立 stand with one's hands hanging by the sides; stand with the hands down;
垂手可成 success would be easy and sure;
垂手可得 acquire sth easily; acquire sth with a wet finger; at one's fingertips; easy to win; get sth without lifting a finger; win sth hands down; within easy reach;
垂手侍立 stand respectfully in attendance;

[垂首] hang one's head;
垂首而立 stand with bowed head; stand with drooping head;
垂首默哀 bow one's head in silent mourning;

[垂死] at the last breath; dying; expiring; fading fast; going; going belly up; going for your tea; have one foot in the grave; knocking on heaven's door; moribund; on one's last legs; receive notice to quit; sinking; slipping;
垂死掙扎 conduct desperate struggles; deathbed struggle; flounder desperately before dying; give dying kicks; in one's death throes; in the throes of one's deathbed; make a last desperate stand; on one's last legs; put up a last-ditch fight;

[垂髫] (1) early childhood; (2) children;
垂髫之年 time of young childhood;

[垂頭] hang one's head;
垂頭餒氣 become dejected and despondent; blue about the gills; bury one's head in dejection; down at the mouth; down in the chops; down in the dumps; down in the hips; down in the mouth; hang one's head; have one's tail down; in low spirits; in the dumps; look downcast; mope oneself; one's crest falls; out of heart; out of spirits; out of sorts; sing the blues; take the heart out of sb;
~垂頭餒氣的樣子 hangdog air; hangdog look;
被打敗的公雞—垂頭喪氣 a defeated cock – dejected;

[垂危] approaching death; at one's last gasp; close to death; critically ill; near one's end; terminally ill;
垂危病人 dying patient;

C

生命垂危 at the gasp;
[垂懸] hanging;
垂懸分詞 dangling participle;
[垂涎] covet; drool over; gloat over; hanker after; slaver over;
垂涎三尺 bring the water to one's mouth; cast a covetous eye at sth; cast greedy eyes at; cannot hide one's greed; drool with envy; gape after; gape for; hanker for; have one's mouth made up for; lick one's chops; lick one's lips; make sb's mouth water; one's mouth waters after; smack one's lips;
垂涎已久 have coveted sth for a long time; one's mouth has long been watering for;
垂涎欲滴 keep a covetous eye on; make sb's mouth water;
[垂楊裊裊] weeping willows are dancing in the wind;
[垂直] perpendicular; vertical;
垂直分配系統 vertical distribution system;
垂直服務 vertical service;
垂直俯衝 dive steeply;
垂直貿易 vertical trade;
垂直起飛 make a vertical take-off;
垂直線 perpendicular line; vertical line;
[垂注] show concern;
謝謝垂注 thank you for your attention;
低垂 droop; hang low; let droop;
耳垂 earlobe; lobe of the ear; lobule; lobulus auriculae;
喉下垂 laryngoptosis;
名垂 leave a name behind; leave a name in;
肉垂 wattle;
舌下垂 glossoptosis;
腎下垂 nephroptosia;
脫垂 prolapse;
胃下垂 gastroptosis;
下垂 droop; hang down;
心下垂 cardioptosia;
懸垂 hang down;
懸雍垂 lingula; uvula;

chui
【倕】 artisan; artist; craftperson; expert craftsman;

chui
【捶】 beat; pound; thump;
[捶背] pound sb's back;
抹胸捶背 rub one's chest and massage one's back;
[捶牀搗枕] beat wildly with one's fists on the bed and the pillows;
[捶打] beat; thump;
[捶鼓] beat a drum; pound on a drum;
[捶擊] thrash; thump;
[捶門] bang on the door; pound at the door;
[捶胸] thump one's chest;
捶胸大哭 beat one's breast and weep; cry one's heart out; hit one's breast and cry;
捶胸大慟 beat one's breast and cry bitterly; clasp one's bosom in deep sorrow;
捶胸跌足 pound one's breast and stamp the ground; smite one's breast and stamp one's foot in despair; stamp one's feet, beating one's breast;
捶胸賭咒 swear and thump one's breast;
捶胸頓足 beat one's breast and stamp one's feet; beat one's breast and stamp;
捶胸拍案 beat one's breast and pound the table;

chui
【椎】 (1) bludgeon; hammer; mallet;
(2) beat; hammer; hit; strike;
[椎牛] butcher oxen; kill an ox;
椎牛宰馬 slaughter cows and horses;
[椎心泣血] deep sorrow; extreme grief;

chui
【陲】 border; frontier;
邊陲 border; frontier;

chui
【搥】 beat; pound; strike with one's fist; strike with a stick;
[搥背] massage the back by pounding with one's fists;

chui
【菙】 bramble; thorn;

chui
【槌】 hammer;
[槌鼓] beat a drum;
[槌球] croquet;
槌球球棍 mallet;
槌球遊戲 croquet;

鼓槌 drum-stick;
木槌 mallet;

chui
【箠】 (1) whip for goading horses; (2) whip; flog;

chui
【錘】 (1) weight on a steelyard; (2) ancient unit of weight; (3) a kind of ancient weapon; (4) hammer; pound;
[錘打] strike with a hammer;
[錘子] hammer;
一把錘子 a hammer;
擺錘 pendulum;
枰錘 sliding weight of a steelyard;
大錘 sledgehammer;
釘錘 claw hammer; nail hammer;
鍛錘 forging hammer;
風錘 air hammer;
銅錘 male character with his face painted;

chui
【鎚】 Same as 錘;
一把鎚子 a hammer;

chun¹
chun
【春】 (1) spring; (2) love; lust; (3) life; vitality; (4) (of mahjong) spring;
[春播] spring seeding; spring sowing;
春播季節 spring-sowing season;
春播秋收 as one sows in spring, one reaps in autumn; sow in spring and reap in autumn;
春播作物秋天成熟 the spring-sown crops ripen in autumn;
[春材] spring wood;
[春菜] spring vegetable;
[春茶] spring tea;
[春凍] spring frost;
[春肥] fertilizer applied in spring;
[春分] spring equinox; vernal equinox;
春分點 vernal equinox;
[春風] spring breeze;
春風不入驢耳 honey is not for the ass's mouth;
春風吹綠野草 when the spring wind blows, tiny shoots of grass break again through the layer of soil and shoot upwards;
春風吹綠原野 spring breezes bring greenness to the country;
春風催綠 the spring wind speeds the greening of the plants;
春風澹蕩 the spring breeze is warm and pleasant;
春風得意 extremely proud of one's success; look triumphant; ride on the crest of success; the spring breeze has obtained its wish;
春風風人 give people a timely and salutary education; the spring breeze brings people to life; the spring breeze refreshes the minds of the people;
春風拂面 a spring breeze stroking one's face;
春風和煦 balmy spring breeze;
春風花月 in the prime of spring flowers are blooming and the moon is shining;
春風化雨 the life-giving spring breeze and rain; the salutary influence of education; the stimulating influence of good teachers; the stimulating influence of a good teacher can be compared to spring atmosphere;
春風滿面 all smiles; full of joy; beaming with satisfaction; one's face is lit up with joy; radiant with happiness; smile broadly; wear a broad smile;
春風撲面 the spring wind caresses our faces;
春風秋月 the poetic spring breeze and autumn moon;
春風時雨 the spring breeze and seasonable rain;
春風送暖 the spring breeze brings warmth; the spring wind brings warm weather;
春風桃花，十里飄香 the fragrance of flowers is wafted from miles away, and the peach blossom laughs in the breeze;
春風一度 sexual intercourse;
滿面春風 all smiles; have a happy expression on one's face; one's face lit up with joy; wear a broad smile;
[春耕] spring ploughing;
春耕夏耘 plough the field in spring and till it in summer; spring ploughing and summer weeding;
[春宮圖] pornographic pictures;
[春菇] spring mushroom;

C

[春光] spring scenery;
春光和煦 beautiful and bright spring days; spring fills the air with warmth;
春光明媚 a bright and beautiful day in spring; a sunlit and enchanting scene of spring; a radiant and enchanting spring scene;
春光融融 spring fills the air with warmth;
明媚的春光 a radiant and enchanting spring scene;

[春寒] cold spell in spring; spring chill;
春寒料峭 the early spring weather is chilly; there is a chill in the air in early spring;
春寒嚴霜 the frost in early spring;

[春花] spring flower;
嬌若春花 one's face glows with the freshness of a spring flower;

[春華秋實] blossom in spring and bear fruit in autumn;

[春化] vernalization;
春化處理 vernalization;
春化作用 vernalization;

[春暉] (1) light of spring; (2) parental love;

[春季] spring; spring season; springtime;
春季學期 spring term;

[春假] spring break; spring holidays; spring vacation;

[春江] spring river;
春江花月夜 a night of flowers and moonlight by the spring river;
春江水暖鴨先知 when the river becomes warm in spring, the ducks are the first to know it;

[春節] Spring Festival;
過春節 keep the Spring Festival;
~回家過春節 spend the Spring Festival at home;
慶祝春節 celebrate the Spring Festival;

[春景] spring scenery;

[春卷] egg roll; spring roll;

[春蘭] orchid;
春蘭秋菊 everything in its season, and turnips in autumn; everything is good in its season; the orchid in spring and the chrysanthemum in autumn;

[春雷] spring thunder;
春雷動地 a clap of spring thunder shaking the earth; a spring thunder shakes the earth;

[春聯] spring couplets; Spring Festival couplets;

[春令] (1) spring; (2) spring weather;

[春麥] spring wheat;

[春夢] spring dream; transient joy;
春夢了無痕 a spring dream leaves no trace — past things vanish; spring dreams vanish without a trace;
一場春夢 a fleeting illusion; a pipe dream; an empty dream; live in a fool's paradise;

[春茗] spring feast;

[春暖] warmth of spring;
春暖花開 during the warmth of spring all the flowers bloom; in the warm spring, flowers are coming out with a rush; in the warm spring, all the blossoms are in full bloom; spring has come and the flowers are in bloom;
春暖人間 spring fills the air with warmth;

[春情] longing for love; stirrings of love;

[春秋] (1) one year; spring and autumn; (2) age; (3) annals; history;
春秋筆法 style of writing in which sublime words with deep meaning are used;
春秋代謝 changes from spring to autumn; seasonal changes;
春秋已高 advanced in years; have seen many summers;
春秋正富 in the prime of youth;
春露秋霜 the dew in spring and frost in autumn — grace and severity;
春祈秋報 pray in spring and offer thanks in fall;
傷春悲秋 grieve over the passing of spring or feel sad with the advent of autumn; shed tears over the change of seasons;

[春日] spring days;
春日遲遲 the spring days pass leisurely;

[春色] (1) spring scenery; (2) cheerful look;
春色撩人 the scenes of spring are really attractive;
春色滿園 a garden full of the beauty of spring; the garden is full of spring flowers; the garden is full of the vigour of springtime;
春色惱人 suffer from love in spring;
滿園春色 spring is in the garden;
惱人春色 suffer from love in spring;

一片春色 everywhere is a riot of spring; lie all the sights of spring;

[春山] hills in spring;

春山如笑 hills seem to be smiling in spring;

[春上] in spring;

[春樹暮雲] remembrance of a friend who is far away;

[春水] spring water;

吹皺一池春水 a slight disturbance; a spring breeze rippling the surface of the pond;

[春筍] bamboo shoots in spring;

春筍破土一節節昇 spring bamboo shoots breaking up through the ground — shooting up joint by joint;

雨後春筍 bamboo shoots after a spring rain — emerge rapidly in large numbers; mushroom like bamboo shoots after rain;

[春天] spring; springtime;

[春望] look from high up in spring;

[春夏] spring and summer;

春夏之交 at the end of spring and the beginning of summer; when spring is changing into summer;

春末夏初 in late spring and early summer; in the late spring and early summer; the end of spring and the beginning of summer;

春去夏來 spring changes into summer; spring gives place to summer; spring is gone and summer comes; summer succeeds spring;

春行夏令 exceptionally warm days in spring; summer weather in spring;

春爭日，夏爭時 in spring every day counts, in summer every hour counts;

[春宵] spring night;

春宵苦短 the night of rendezvous is always too short;

[春心] desire for love; longing for love; thoughts of love;

春心蕩漾 the surging of lustful desire;

[春藥] love potion; philtre; aphrodisiac;

[春意] (1) spring is in the air; (2) beginning of spring; (3) thoughts of love;

春意盎然 spring is very much in the air;

春意闌珊 spring is waning; the declining days of spring;

春意纏綿 spring rain falls lightly and steadily;

一絲春意 a touch of spring;

[春遊] spring outing;

[春雨] spring rains;

春雨貴如油 rain in spring is as precious as oil;

春雨如膏 spring showers fertilizing the soil like grease;

春雨瀟瀟 it is drizzling in spring;

[春裝] spring clothing;

報春 herald spring; proclaim spring;
殘春 last days of spring;
初春 early spring;
打春 beginning of spring;
懷春 become sexually awakened; begin to think of love; in love;
回春 (1) the return of spring; (2) bring back to life;
琿春 Hunchun in Jilin Province;
季春 last month of spring;
開春 beginning of spring;
立春 Beginning of Spring;
暮春 end of spring; late spring;
青春 youth; youthfulness;
三春 the three months of the spring season;
晚春 late spring;
新春 New Year;
陽春 spring time;
迎春 greet the New Year;
元春 New Year;
早春 early spring;
仲春 midspring;

chun

【椿】 (1) father; (2) Cedrela sinensis;

[椿齡] great age; venerable;

[椿庭] father;

臭椿 tree of heaven;
香椿 Chinese toon;

chun²

chun

【純】 (1) pure; unmixed; (2) simple; pure and simple; (3) practised; skilful; well versed;

[純粹] (1) complete; pure; sheer; unadulterated; (2) only; purely; solely;

純粹出於好意 only out of kindness;

[純度] purity; rate of purity;

表觀純度 apparent purity;
激發純度 excitation purity;
顏色純度 colorimetric purity;

[純化] purification;

[純潔] chaste; clean and honest; pure; virginal;
純潔的心靈 pure spirit;
純潔無辜 pure and innocent;
純潔無私 pure and unselfish;
純潔無瑕 as pure as a lily; lily-white;
品格純潔 of impeccable character; stainless character;
身心純潔 pure in body and mind;
思想純潔 pure in thought;
心地純潔 pure in heart;
心靈純潔 pure in heart; spiritual purity;
保持心靈純潔 keep one's heart pure;
行為純潔 pure in deed;

[純金] pure gold; solid gold;
純金獎盃 solid gold cup;

[純利] net profit;

[純良] simple and honest;
稟性純良 simple and honest by nature;

[純樸] honest; simple; unsophisticated;
純樸敦厚 simple and honest;
純樸爽朗 honest and frank;

[純熟] fluent; practised; skilful; well versed;
純熟技藝 exceptional skill;
技術純熟 be highly skilled in technique;

[純屬] purely; simply;
純屬揣測 mere conjecture;
純屬捏造 sheer fabrication;
純屬虛構 be made out of the whole cloth;
純屬謠言 nothing but a groundless rumour;

[純真] genuine; pure; sincere; unsophisticated;
純真的愛 pure and sincere love;
純真無邪 pure and innocent;

[純正] pure; unadulterated;
動機純正 have pure motives;

[純種] full-blooded; pedigree; purebred;
純種的 purebred;
純種馬 bloodstock;

單純 (1) pure; simple; (2) alone; merely; purely;

chun

【淳】 honest; pure;

[淳厚] pure and honest; simple and kind;
民風淳厚 people are honest and warm-hearted;

[淳樸] honest; simple, and unsophiscated;
敦實淳樸 stocky and honest;
民風淳樸 people are simple and honest;

chun

【唇】 lip;

[唇癌] cheilocarcinoma;

[唇齒] lips and teeth;
唇齒溝 labiodental sulcus;
唇齒相依 as close as lips and teeth; as close to each other as lips to teeth; as close to each other as the lips are to the teeth; as closely related as the lips and the teeth; as interdependent as lips and teeth; closely related and mutually dependent; closely related to each other like lips and teeth; interdependent; mutually depend on each other as lips and teeth;
唇紅齒白 have rosy lips and pretty white teeth;
唇亡齒寒 be immediately threatened; if one falls, the other is in danger; if the lips are gone, the teeth are exposed; the teeth are cold when the lips are cold; when the lips are lost the teeth will be exposed to the cold; share a common lot;
咬齒嚼唇 grind one's teeth and bite one's lips;

[唇瘡] cold sore; fever blister;

[唇讀] lip-read;

[唇兒] lips;

[唇發育不良] atelocheilia;

[唇發育不全] atelocheilia;

[唇反射] lip reflex;

[唇肥厚] pachycheilia;

[唇乾口燥] lips are dry and the mouth parched;

[唇乾裂] cheilosis;

[唇膏] lippy; lipstick;
亮唇膏 lip gloss;
抹點唇膏 put a bit of lippy on;
潤唇膏 lip balm;

[唇溝] labial groove;

[唇環] lip ring;

[唇尖] procheilon;

[唇角] labial angles;

[唇結節] labial tubercle;

[唇裂] cheiloschisis; cleft lip; harelip;

[唇瘤] cheiloncus;

［唇麻痺］ labial paralysis; paralysis of the lips;
［唇面］ labial surface; surface of the lips;
［唇泡疹］ cold sore; fever blister;
［唇疱疹］ herpes labialis;
［唇切開術］ cheilotomy;
［唇舌］ (1) lips and tongue; (2) argument; persuasion; plausible speech; talking round; words;
白費唇舌 speak to the wind; waste one's breath; waste one's words; whistle down the wind;
搬唇遞舌 tell tales;
唇枯舌焦 one's lips and tongue become parched;
唇枯舌爛 talk oneself hoarse;
唇槍舌劍 a battle of repartee; a battle of wits; a war of words; cross verbal swords; engage in a battle of words; exchange heated words; have a tit-for-tat argument with sharp words;
~引發唇槍舌劍 inflames a war of words;
唇槍舌戰 a battle of words; a heated dispute; go at it hammer and tongs; have a verbal battle with sb;
大費唇舌 a long harangue; exhaust one's eloquence; make a long harangue; much talking; take much talking to convince;
費唇舌 require much talking;
費盡唇舌 waste all one's breath;
費舌勞唇 talk oneself out of breath;
勞唇乏舌 waste one's words;
奴唇婢舌 have a loose-tongue like a slave or maid;
枉費唇舌 mere waste of breath; waste one's breath;
舌敝唇焦 one's tongue and lips become parched; talk oneself hoarse; talk till one's tongue and lips are parched; the tongue is weary and the lips are dry; wear oneself out in pleading;
舌枯唇焦 talk oneself hoarse;
舌劍唇槍 acrimonious words used in a quarrel;
徒費唇舌 speak to the wind; waste one's breath; waste so much breath; waste words; whistle down the wind;
搖唇鼓舌 instigate by talking; persuade sb by sweet talk; wag one's tongue;
［唇炎］ cheilitis; inflammation of the lips;
剝脫性唇炎 cheilitis exfoliative;
膿疱性唇炎 impetiginous cheilitis;
膿腫性唇炎 apostematous cheilitis;
日光性唇炎 solar cheilitis;
肉芽腫性唇炎 granulomatous cheilitis;
腺性唇炎 cheilitis glandularis;
［唇音］ labial;
［唇印］ lip print;

短唇 abnormally short lips; brachycheilia;
反唇 answer back;
關節唇 articular lip;
厚唇 abnormal thickness of the lips; pachycheilia;
絳唇 red lips;
巨唇 macrochilia;
口唇 lips;
裂唇 cleft lip;
菱唇 rhombic lip;
缺唇 cleft lip; harelip;
潤唇 moisturize the lips;
上唇 upper lip;
兔唇 cleft lip; harelip;
下唇 lower lip;
掀唇 open the mouth; speak;
陰唇 labia minora; lips of the vulva;
櫻唇 small, beautiful mouth of a woman;
魚唇 shark's lip;
沾唇 touch the lips;
朱唇 red lips;
嘴唇 lip;

chun

【醇】 (1) good wine; mellow wine; (2) pure; unmixed; (3) alcohol;
［醇和］ pure and mild;
［醇厚］ pure and honest; simple and kind;
［醇化］ (1) perfect; purify; refine; (2) alcoholization;
［醇濃］ mellow; pure; rich;
［醇香］ fragrant; rich;

膽固醇 cholesterol;
清醇 mellow; rich;

chun

【蓴】 Brasenia purpurea;
［蓴鱸］ retirement from government;
蓴鱸之思 homesickness; intention of retiring from office and going back home;

chun

【鶉】 quail;

［鶉鴿］ quail;
［鶉居］ without a fixed home;
［鶉衣］ ragged clothes;
鶉衣百結 coarse clothes with many patches;

chun³
chun
【踳】 disorderly; incongruous;
［踳踳］ disappointed; frustrated; unhappy;

chun
【蠢】 (1) boneheaded; foolish; idiotic; silly; stupid; (2) clumsy;

［蠢笨］ awkward; bog-ignorant; clumsy; foolish; stupid;
蠢笨如牛 dumb as an ox;
［蠢材］ blistering idiot; blockhead; bloody fool; bonehead; boob; booby; cabbagehead; dunce; fool; idiot; pig-headed person; pillock; stupid person;
［蠢蠢］ (1) wriggling; (2) stirring; turbulent; unrestful;
蠢蠢欲動 about to start sth; eager for action; itch for action; on the move; ready for action; restless and about to start some move;
［蠢蛋］ dumbo;
［蠢話］ blather; cobblers; foolish words; nonsense; rubbish;
［蠢貨］ blockhead; dunce; idiot; jackass; plonker;
［蠢驢］ ass; donkey; idiot; silly;
笨如蠢驢 as stupid as an ass;
［蠢人］ birdbrain; blockhead; charlie; fool; goofball; goon; imbecile; joker; moron; muppet; numpty; oaf; wiener;
［蠢事］ folly; tomfoolery;
幹蠢事 act the fool; make an ass of oneself;
做蠢事 clown;
［蠢豬］ ass; idiot; stupid swine;

愚蠢 as nutty as a fruitcake; chuckle-headed; dull; foolish; silly; stupid;

chuo¹
chuo
【戳】 (1) jab; poke; stab; (2) blunt; sprain; (3) chop; seal; stamp; (4) erect; stand sth on end; (5) back up; support;
［戳穿］ (1) pierce through; puncture; (2) expose; explode; lay bare;
戳穿謊言 nail a lie to the counter;
戳穿謬論 give the lie to the fallacy;
戳穿陰謀 lay bare a plot;
一戳就穿 be punctured with a mere stroke; one thrust and it is punctured;
［戳痕］ prod mark;
［戳記］ countermark; seal; stamp;
包裹戳記 parcel stamp;
蓋上戳記 place a stamp over;
無效戳記 non-validation stamp;
專用戳記 identification stamp;
［戳破］ break;
一戳就破 break at the slightest touch;
［戳傷］ stab; stab wound;
［戳子］ punch; seal; stamp;

猛戳 drove; jab;
手戳 private seal; signet;
郵戳 postmark;

chuo⁴
chuo
【啜】 (1) sip; suck; (2) sob;
［啜茶］ sip tea;
啜茶品茗 sip tea;
啜茶清談 sip tea as they talk;
［啜泣］ sob;
暗自啜泣 sob to oneself;
悲哀地啜泣 sob bitterly;
相偎啜泣 clasp each other and weep;

chuo
【惙】 doleful; gloomy; melancholy; mournful;
［惙惙］ gloomy; melancholy;

chuo
【綽】 ample; spacious;
［綽號］ nickname;
［綽約］ graceful;
綽約多姿 charmingly delicate; graceful and attractive;
風姿綽約 charming appearance and personality; charming in manner; graceful figure;
豐姿綽約 agreeable manners;
舞姿綽約 dance with much grace;

chuo
【輟】 cease; stop;
［輟筆］ stop in the middle of writing or

painting;
手不輟筆 write without stopping;
中途輟筆 stop in the middle of writing;
[輟工] stop work;
[輟學] discontinue one's studies; leave off one's study; stop schooling;
輟學者 dropout;

中輟 give up halfway; stop halfway;

chuo
【醱】 pour wine in libation;

chuo
【歠】 drink; sip; suck;

chuo
【齪】 (1) narrow; small; (2) dirty;

齷齪 dirty; filthy;

ci¹

ci
【差】 irregular; uneven;
[差等] classes; classification;

參差 irregular; jagged; notched; uneven;

ci
【恣】
[恣睢] (1) carefree; unbridled; (2) extremely conceited;

ci
【疵】 blemish; defect; flaw;
[疵布] defective cloth;
[疵點] blemish; defect; fault; flaw; weak spot;
[疵品] bad work;

無疵 faultless; flawless;
瑕疵 blemish; defect; flaw;
纖疵 slight error;
嫌疵 criticize; dislike;
小疵 trifling defect;

ci
【雌】 (1) female; feminine; soft; woman-like; (2) retiring; weak; (3) defeated; vanquished; (4) scold; (5) expose; show;
[雌蜂] queen bee;
[雌黃] at random;
妄下雌黃 make an arbitrary alteration; make improper comments;
信口雌黃 speak at random;
[雌貓] queen cat;
[雌威] tantrum of a shrew;
[雌性] female;
[雌雄] male and female;
雌雄同體 androgyny; hermaphrodite; hermaphroditism; monoecism;
~次體質雌雄同體 secondary somatic hermaphroditism;
~對稱雌雄同體 bilateral hermaphroditism;
~不對稱雌雄同體 unilateral hermaphroditism;
~發生雌雄同體 genetic hermaphroditism;
~機能的雌雄同體 functional hermaphroditism;
~原體質雌雄同體 somatic hermaphroditism;
雌雄同株 androgyny; monoecism;
雌雄異體 dioecism; gonochorism;
雌雄異株 dioecism;
決一雌雄 fight to see who is the master; have a showdown; slug it out;
一決雌雄 compete for the championship; fight a decisive battle; fight it out; measure strengths; see who is the winner; test the leadership; try conclusions with sb; try the test of battle;
一雄多雌 polygamy;
知雄守雌 possess strength but retain gentleness;

ci²

ci
【祠】 temple; ancestral temple;
[祠堂] ancestral hall; ancestral temple; clan hall;

家祠 ancestral temple; clan hall;
宗祠 clan hall;

ci
【茲】 a form used in 龜茲;

ci
【茨】 (1) thatch; thatched house; (2) Tribulus terrestris, a kind of thorny plant; (3) fill with earth;
[茨菰] arrowhead;

ci
【瓷】 china; porcelain;

［瓷雕］ carved porcelain; procelain carving;
［瓷婚］ china wedding;
［瓷器］ chinaware; porcelain; ware;
瓷器店 china shop;
薄胎瓷器 eggshell;
彩釉瓷器 painted china;
設計瓷器 design china;
生產瓷器 produce china;
雪花瓷器 alabaster ware;
一件瓷器 a piece of china;
一批瓷器 a trove of porcelain;
一套瓷器 a set of china;
製造瓷器 manufacture china;
［瓷土］ china clay;
［瓷碗］ china bowl;
［瓷磚］ ceramic tiles;
小瓷磚 ceramic tiles;

玻璃瓷 vitreous china;
薄瓷 eggshell china;
哥瓷 porcelain with crackled glaze;
骨瓷 bone china;
烘瓷 baked porcelain;
青瓷 blue china;
青花瓷 blue and white porcelain;
熔塊瓷 frit china;
宋瓷 Song porcelain;
搪瓷 enamel;
陶瓷 pottery and porcelain;
細瓷 fine china;
洋瓷 enamel;

ci

【詞】 (1) term; word; (2) speech; statement; (3) rhymed prose;
［詞典］ dictionary; lexicon;
詞典編輯 lexicography;
~ 單語詞典編輯 monolingual lexicography;
~ 雙語詞典編輯 bilingual lexicography;
詞典學 lexicography;
百科詞典 encyclopaedia;
~ 詞滙百科詞典 lexical encyclopaedia;
編詞典 compile a dictionary;
參考詞典 reference dictionary;
查詞典 consult a dictionary;
查閱詞典 look up a dictionary; turn up a dictionary;
初級字典 junior dictionary;
詞源詞典 etymological dictionary;
搭配詞典 collocation dictionary;
單語詞典 monolingual dictionary; unilingual dictionary;
地名詞典 dictionary of place names;
多語種詞典 multilingual dictionary;
多語種對照詞典 polylingual dictionary;
多義詞詞典 polysemantic dictionary;
兒童詞典 children's dictionary;
翻開詞典 open a dictionary;
翻閱詞典 thumb a dictionary;
方言詞典 dialect dictionary;
機器詞典 mechanical dictionary;
簡明詞典 concise dictionary;
類屬詞典 thesaurus;
類義詞典 lexicon; thesaurus;
逆序詞典 reverse dictionary;
人名詞典 biographical dictionary;
使用詞典 use a dictionary;
熟語詞典 phraseological dictionary;
雙語詞典 bilingual dictionary;
縮略語詞典 abbreviation dictionary;
微詞典 micro-dictionary;
微類屬詞典 micro-thesaurus;
修訂詞典 revise a dictionary;
袖珍詞典 pocket-size dictionary;
一本詞典 a dictionary;
增訂詞典 enlarge a dictionary;
自動翻譯詞典 automatic dictionary;
［詞鋒］ sharpness of one's tongue;
［詞幹］ stem;
動詞詞幹 verb stem;
簡單詞幹 simple stem;
派生詞幹 derivative stem;
~ 非派生詞幹 non-derivative stem;
［詞根］ stem;
詞根反義詞 base antonym;
［詞話］ notes on poetry;
［詞匯］ vocabulary;
詞匯不足 lexical inadequacy;
詞匯場 lexical field;
詞匯成份 lexical constituent;
詞匯創新 lexical innovation;
詞匯詞 lexical word;
詞匯錯誤 lexical error;
詞匯單位 lexical unit;
詞匯等級體系 lexical hierarchy;
詞匯動詞 lexical verb;
詞匯對等詞 lexical equivalent;
詞匯翻譯 lexical translation;
詞匯慣用法 lexical usage;
詞匯規則 lexical rule;
詞匯空隙 lexical gap;
詞匯控制 vocabulary control;

詞匯量 vocabulary;
~詞匯量表 lexical scale;
~擴大詞匯量 enlarge one's vocabulary; extend one's vocabulary; increase one's stock of words; increase one's vocabulary; widen one's vocabulary;
詞匯密度 lexical density;
詞匯頻度 word frequency;
詞匯歧義 lexical ambiguity;
詞匯嵌入 lexical insertion;
詞匯索引 concordance;
詞匯統計學 lexical statistics;
詞匯學 lexicology;
詞匯意義 lexical meaning;
詞匯語法 lexical grammar; lexicogrammar;
詞匯語義學 lexical semantics;
詞匯轉移 lexical transfer;
詞匯自然性 lexical naturalness;
詞匯增補 lexical expansion;
常用詞匯 minimum vocabulary;
單語詞匯 monolingual glossary;
兒童詞匯 children's vocabulary;
豐富的詞匯 copious vocabulary;
基本詞匯 basic vocabulary;
基礎詞匯 basic vocabulary;
積極詞匯 active vocabulary;
科技詞匯 scientific and technical vocabulary;
外來詞匯 exotic vocabulary;
消極詞匯 passive vocabulary;
專業詞匯 technical terms;

[詞句] expressions; words and phrases;
有力的詞句 forceful expressions;

[詞庫] lexicon;

[詞類] parts of speech;
詞類轉換 conversion in the parts of speech;
次要詞類 minor word class;
封閉性詞類 close class;
開放詞類 open word class;
開放性詞類 open class;

[詞目] headword;

[詞頻] word frequency;
詞頻表 word frequency list;
詞頻計算 word frequency count;

[詞窮] arguments exhausted; nothing more to say;
詞窮理拙 poor in expression and perverted in logic;
詞窮語塞 close one's mouth for want of words;
才盡詞窮 one's brain has now ceased to function; reach the end of one's wits;

[詞群] group;
詞群聯想 group association;

[詞素] morpheme;
詞素變體 allomorph;
詞素翻譯 morphemic translation;
詞素檢索 morpheme index;
詞素界限 morpheme boundary;
詞素序 morpheme sequence;
基本詞素 base morpheme;
連接詞素 linking morpheme;
黏附詞素 bound morpheme;

[詞條] dictionary entry;

[詞位] lexeme;
詞位教學法 word method;
詞位學 morphemics;

[詞項] lexical item;

[詞形] morphology;
詞形變化 conjugate; conjugation; declension; paradigm;
詞形翻譯 morphological translation;
詞形分類 morphological classification;
詞形分析 morphological analysis;
詞形基礎 morphological base;
詞形派生法 morphological derivation;
詞形屈折 inflection;
詞形限定 morphological specification;
詞形學 morphology;

[詞序] word order;
詞序對應 word-order correspondence;
詞序構詞法 syntactic morphology;

[詞嚴義正] severity in speech and fairness in principle; the language is stern and the reason for it is justifiable;

[詞義] word meaning;
詞義變化 change of meaning; semantic change;
詞義降格 degradation of meaning;
詞義擴大 widening of meaning;
詞義普遍化 generalization of meaning;
詞義昇格 elevation of meaning;
詞義縮小 narrowing of meaning;
詞義學 semantics;
詞義引申 extension of meaning;
詞義轉貶 degeneration of meaning;
詞義轉褒 amelioration;

[詞語] terms; words and expressions;
詞語倒裝法 anastrophe;
詞語聯想 word association;

固定的詞語 set term;
借用詞語 borrowing;
平淡的詞語 tame expression;
新造詞語 coinage;

[詞源] etymology;
詞源學 etymology;
~聯想詞源學 associative etymology;
~通俗詞源學 popular etymology;

[詞藻] flowery language; ornate diction; rhetoric;
詞藻艷麗 flowery diction;

[詞綴] affix;
詞綴法 affixation;
屈折詞綴 inflectional affix;

[詞族] word family;

[詞組] phrase; word group;
動詞詞組 verb group;
固定詞組 fixed word group; set phrases;
名詞詞組 noun group;

褒義詞 commendatory term;
閉幕詞 closing speech;
貶詞 derogatory term;
貶義詞 derogatory term;
賓詞 object; predicate;
不定冠詞 indefinite article;
常用詞 everyday words;
唱詞 libretto;
陳詞 (1) cliché; (2) explain; state;
抽象詞 abstract word;
創刊詞 foreword;
搭配詞 collocate;
答詞 speech in reply;
大詞 major term;
代詞 pronoun;
代名詞 pronoun;
單詞 (1) single-morpheme word; (2) word;
禱詞 prayer;
悼詞 memorial speech;
地點詞 local word;
疊詞 reduplicative;
定冠詞 definite article;
動詞 verb;
動名詞 gerund;
對詞 actors studying lines together;
遁詞 quibble; subterfuge;
多義詞 polysemant; polysemous word;
發刊詞 foreword;
反義詞 antonym;
方位詞 direction word; noun of locality;
分詞 participle;
分數詞 fractional numeral;
否定詞 negative; negator;
複合詞 compound;
副詞 adverb;
丐詞 beg term;
概念詞 concept word; conceptual term;
感歎詞 exclamation; interjection;
歌詞 lyrics;
功能詞 function word;
供詞 confession; statement made under examination;
構詞 form a word;
關聯詞 conjunctive word;
關係詞 rational word; relational word;
冠詞 article;
合成詞 compound word;
賀詞 congratulatory speech;
後置詞 postposition;
互補詞 complementary;
歡迎詞 welcoming speech;
混成詞 blend;
活動詞 event word;
極限詞 limit word;
簡單詞 simple word;
結構詞 structure word;
介詞 preposition;
借詞 borrowed word; loanword;
句子詞 sentence word;
開幕詞 opening speech;
科技詞 technical word;
口語詞 colloquial word;
擴詞 amplify the diction;
類別詞 classifier; generic term;
類詞 class word;
連詞 conjunction;
量表詞 scale word;
量詞 classifier; measure word;
臨時詞 nonce word;
描述詞 descriptive word;
名詞 (1) noun; (2) term; (3) name;
擬聲詞 onomatopoeic word;
逆生詞 back-formation word;
派生詞 derivative;
判詞 court verdict;
配詞 set words;
前指詞 anaphoric word;
前置詞 preposition;
遣詞 choice of words;
強調詞 emphasizer;
傾向性詞 biased word;
弱意詞 downtoner;
冗詞 superfluous words;
生詞 neologism; new word;

生造詞 coinage;
詩詞 poetry and rhymed prose;
實詞 notional word;
飾詞 excuse; pretext;
誓詞 oath; pledge;
數量詞 numeral-classifier compound;
説詞 plea; pretext; excuse;
宋詞 the ci-poetry of Song;
頌詞 (1) complimentary address; (2) speech delivered by an ambassador on presentation of his credentials;
廋詞 puzzle; riddle; enigma;
台詞 actor's lines;
臺詞 one's lines;
歎詞 exclamation; interjection;
提詞 prompt;
題詞 (1) write an inscription; (2) dedication; inscription; (3) foreword;
填詞 compose a verse to a given tune of prose-poem;
同詞 identical word;
同義詞 synonym;
同音詞 homonym;
同源詞 cognate;
托詞 find a pretext; make an excuse;
外來詞 loanword;
婉詞 euphemism; gentle words; tactful expression;
微詞 veiled words of censure;
猥詞 obscene language; salacious words;
謂詞 predicate;
蕪詞 superfluous words;
戲詞 actor's lines;
繫詞 copula;
獻詞 congratulatory message;
象聲詞 onomatopoeia
小詞 minor term;
謝詞 thank-you speech;
新詞 neologism;
新名詞 new term;
形類詞 form class word;
形容詞 adjective;
虛詞 form word; function word;
選詞 select a word group;
訓詞 admonition; instructions;
言詞 one's words; what one says;
語詞 words and phrases;
語助詞 auxiliary; expletive; grammatical particle;
讚詞 words of praise;
證詞 testimony;
致詞 deliver a speech; make a speech;
中詞 middle term;
竹枝詞 ancient folk songs with love as their main theme;
主詞 subject; subject term;
助詞 expletive;
助動詞 auxiliary verb;
祝詞 (1) congratulatory message; congratulatory speech; congratulations; (2) prayers at sacrificial rites in ancient times;
祝酒詞 toast;
狀詞 contents of an accusation;
贅詞 redundance; repetitious words; superfluous words;
作詞 write lyrics;

ci

【慈】 (1) kind; loving; (2) mother;
［慈藹］ kind and amiable;
［慈愛］ affection; gentle; gentleness; kindness; love;
父母的慈愛 parental love;
［慈悲］ benevolent; mercy;
慈悲好施 kind and fond of dispensing charity;
慈悲樂善 merciful and benevolent;
慈悲為本 compassion is the principle of life;
慈悲為懷 consider compassion as one's chief concern;
出於慈悲 out of mercy;
大慈大悲 all loving and merciful; charitable; infinitely merciful;
發慈悲 benevolent; have pity; merciful;
~大發慈悲 for mercy's sake; have pity on; show mercy;
滿懷慈悲 be filled with benevolence;
［慈父］ loving father; father;
慈父見背 my compassionate father is dead;
［慈航］ merciful ferry; way of salvation;
慈航普渡 salvation through charity to others;
［慈和］ kind and amiable;
慈和相處 live on friendly terms;
［慈母］ loving mother;
慈母多敗兒 a fond mother spoils her son;
慈母嚴父 a kind mother and a severe father;
［慈善］ benevolent; charitable; philanthropic;
慈善活動 beneficent activities; charity event;
慈善機構 charitable body;

慈善家 philanthropist;
慈善商店 charity shop; thrift shop;
慈善事業 philanthropy;
慈善為懷 cherish charity;
慈善行為 act of charity;

[慈祥] amicable; kind;
慈祥的老人 kind old man;
慈祥的面容 kind face;
慈祥的笑容 benignant smile;

仁慈 benevolent; kind; merciful;
先慈 my late mother;
孝慈 filial piety and parental tenderness;
心慈 kind; kind-hearted; soft-hearted;

C

ci

【磁】 (1) magnetism; (2) china; porcelain;

[磁北] magnetic north;

[磁場] magnetic field;
磁場強度 magnetic intensity;
產生磁場 create a magnetic field;
地球磁場 geomagnetic field;
電磁場 electromagnetic field;

[磁帶] cassette; tape;
磁帶機 magnetic tape station;
磁帶計數器 tape counter;
磁帶選擇開關 tape selector switches;
盒式磁帶 cassette tape; tape cassette;
無端磁帶 endless tape;
指令磁帶 cue tape;

[磁電機] magneto;
隔電磁電機 shielded magneto;
起動磁電機 starting magneto;
直流磁電機 direct-current magneto;

[磁法] magnetic method;

[磁鼓] drum;
磁鼓啟動器 drum starter;

[磁光盤] magneto-optic disc;
磁光盤錄音機 magnetic optical disc;

[磁化] magnetization; magnetized;
磁化杯 magnetized teacup;
磁化水 magnetized water;
反常磁化 anomalous magnetization;
反磁化 back magnetization;
絕熱磁化 adiabatic magnetization;
圓形磁化 circular magnetization;

[磁極] magnetic pole;

[磁卡] magnetic card;
磁卡電話 magnetic card telephone;

[磁控管] magnetron;
全金屬磁控管 all-metal magnetron;
射束磁控管 beam magnetron;

[磁力] magnetic force;
磁力線 magnetic line of force;
磁力懸浮式鐵路 magnetically supported railway;
磁力儀 magnetometer;

[磁療] magnetism therapy;
磁療法 magnetic treatment;
磁療戒指 magnetic ring;

[磁盤] disc; magnetic disc;
磁盤操作 disc operating;
~磁盤操作系統 disc operating systems;
磁盤初始化 disc initialization;
磁盤存儲器 disc storage;
磁盤道 disc track;
磁盤格式化 disc formatting;
磁盤記錄形式 disc record form;
磁盤控制器 disk controller;
磁盤驅動器 disk drive;
磁盤優化 disk optimization;
磁盤陣列 disk array;
軟磁盤 floppy disk;
硬磁盤 hard disk;

[磁漆] enamel;
醇酸磁漆 resin enamel;
鋁粉磁漆 aluminium enamel;
耐酸磁漆 acid-resisting enamel;
汽車磁漆 automobile enamel;

[磁強計] magnetometer;
機載磁強計 airborne magnetometer;
絕對磁強計 absolute magnetometer;

[磁石] magnet;
天然磁石 loadstone; lodestone;

[磁鐵] magnet;
磁鐵學校 magnet school;
環形磁鐵 annular magnet;
交流磁鐵 a.c. magnet;
可調磁鐵 adjustable magnet;
馬蹄形磁鐵 horseshoe magnet;
人造磁鐵 artificial magnet;
蹄形磁鐵 horseshoe magnet;
天然磁鐵 natural magnet;
條形磁鐵 axial magnet; bar magnet;
永久磁鐵 permanent magnet;

[磁條] magstripe;

[磁頭] head;
放音磁頭 playback head;
抹音磁頭 erase head;

[磁性] magnetic; magnetism;
磁性層 magnetosphere;
動物磁性 zoomagnetism;

失去磁性 lose magnetism;
視在磁性 apparent magnetism;
天然磁性 natural magnetism;
有磁性 magnetic;
自由磁性 free magnetism;

[磁學] magnetics; magnetism;

[磁針] magnetic needle;

[磁致伸縮] magnetostriction;
各向異性磁致伸縮 anisotropic magnetostriction;
逆磁致伸縮 converse magnetostriction;
強迫磁致伸縮 forced magnetostriction;
體積磁致伸縮 volume magnetostriction;
縱向磁致伸縮 longitudinal magnetostriction;
自發磁致伸縮 spontaneous magnetostriction;

[磁子] magneton;
電子磁子 electronic magneton;
核磁子 nuclear magneton;

充磁 magnetize;
電磁 electromagnetism;
防磁 antimagnetic;
消磁 degauss; degaussing; demagnetization; demagnetize;

ci

【糍】

[糍粑] glutinous rice cake;

ci

【辭】 (1) diction; phraseology; (2) rhymed prose; (3) ballad; (4) bid farewell; take leave; (5) discharge; dismiss; (6) resign; (7) decline; evade; refuse; shirk;

[辭別] bid farewell; say good-bye; take one's leave;
不辭而別 depart without saying goodbye; give one the slip; go away without saying a word; leave without saying goodbye; slip away; slip off; take French leave;

[辭不獲命] have one's resignation rejected; one's resignation is declined;

[辭呈] resignation;
撤回辭呈 withdraw one's resignation;
提交辭呈 hand in one's resignation; submit one's resignation;

[辭典] dictionary;
辭典學 lexicography;
地名辭典 geographical dictionary;
電子辭典 electronic dictionary;
慣用法辭典 usage dictionary;
教育辭典 educational dictionary;
人物傳略辭典 biographical dictionary;
圖解辭典 illustrated dictionary;
一本辭典 a dictionary;
語文辭典 language dictionary;

[辭匯] vocabulary;
辭匯缺乏 paucity of vocabulary;

[辭靈] bow to a coffin before leaving;

[辭令] a language appropriate to the occasion;
善於辭令 be gifted with a silver tongue; skilful in making statements;
外交辭令 diplomatic language;
嫻於辭令 eloquent; gifted with a silver tongue; skilled in speech;

[辭聘] discharge an appointment; refuse a job offer;

[辭去] resign;
辭去職務 resign one's position;

[辭讓] decline politely;
辭讓賢能 yield one's position to a more capable person;

[辭色] one's speech and facial expression;
不假辭色 speak bluntly; speak harshly;
辭嚴色厲 harsh speech and stern countenance;
假以辭色 bestow one's favour on sb; speak to sb encouragingly;
形於辭色 in one's speech and countenance;

[辭世] die; pass away;

[辭書] dictionary;

[辭訟] lawsuit; legal cases;

[辭歲] bid farewell to the outgoing year; celebrate the lunar New Year's Eve;

[辭退] discharge; dismiss; give sb the air; turn away;
被辭退 be discharged; be dismissed; get one's walking papers;

[辭謝] decline politely; decline with thanks; reject with thanks;
辭謝邀請 decline the invitation politely; decline the invitation respectfully;

[辭行] say goodbye to sb before setting out on a journey; take one's leave;
辭行告別 take leave of and bid farewell to;
向人辭行 bid sb goodbye; say goodbye to sb;

C

[辭嚴義正] severity in speech and fairness in principle;
[辭藻] flowery language; ornate diction; rhetoric;
辭藻華麗 flowery rhetoric;
堆砌辭藻 string together ornate phrases;
[辭章] (1) poetry and prose; prose and verse; (2) art of writing; rhetoric;
[辭職] hand in one's resignation; quit office; resign; send in one's jacket; send in one's papers; stand down; submit one's resignation;
辭職不幹 chuck one's job; chuck up one's job;
集體辭職 collective resignation;
全體辭職 resign en masse;
引咎辭職 take the blame on oneself and resign;

哀辭 elegy; lament; plaint;
拜辭 say goodbye; take one's leave;
詖辭 biased remarks;
忱辭 words from the bottom of one's heart;
讜辭 outspoken words;
告辭 farewell; take leave;
賀辭 congratulatory address;
敬辭 term of respect;
謙辭 self-depreciatory expression;
推辭 decline an invitation, offer, etc.;
托辭 excuse; give as a pretext; make an excuse; pretext;
婉辭 euphemism; tactful expression;
文辭 (1) diction; language; (2) writings;
修辭 rhetoric;
言辭 one's words; what one says;
諛辭 flattering words; flattery;
致辭 deliver a speech; make a speech;

ci3
ci

【此】 (1) this; (2) here; now;
[此輩] people of this ilk; people of this type; such sort of people;
[此地] here; this place;
此地無銀三百兩 a clumsy denial resulting in self-exposure; a poor lie which reveals the truth; protest one's innocence too much;
[此風不可長] such a tendency is not to be encouraged;
[此後] after that; after this; ever since; from now on; from then on; henceforth; hereafter;
[此間] around here; here;
[此刻] at present; at the moment; for the time being; now; this moment;
[此生] one's life;
不虛此生 not live in vain; not spend one's life in vain;
[此時] at present; for the time being; now; right now; this moment;
此時此地 here and now; under the present circumstances;
此時此刻 at this juncture; at this very moment; this hour and moment;
[此外] and; and…as well; as well as; besides; furthermore; in addition; in addition to; moreover; what with…and what with;
[此行] this trip;
不虛此行 it's been a worthwhile trip; the trip has not been made in vain; the trip has been well worthwhile;

彼此 (1) each other; one another; this and that; (2) reduplication;
從此 from now on; from then on; thereupon;
到此 so far;
據此 accordingly;
如此 so; such;
為此 for this reason; to this end;
因此 consequently; for this reason;

ci

【泚】 (1) clear water; (2) bright and brilliant; (3) sweating;

ci

【玼】 (1) blemish; flaw; (2) brilliant;

ci

【跐】 tiptoe;
[跐着腳] on tiptoe;

ci4
ci

【次】 (1) order; sequence; (2) next; second; (3) second-rate;
[次等] inferior; second-class; second-rate;
[次第] (1) order; sequence; (2) one after another;
次第入座 take seats one after another;
[次貨] inferior goods; substandard goods;
[次級] secondary;

[次毛] bad; inferior; poor in quality;
[次品] defective goods; substandard goods; substandard products;
[次數] frequency; number of times;
[次序] arrangement; order; sequence; succession;
次序顛倒 in reverse order;
次序混亂 in bad order; not in the right order; out of order;
顛倒次序 reverse the right order;
先後次序 in sequence;
[次要] less important; minor; next in importance; secondary; subordinate;
次要地位 play second fiddle; secondary position;
次要詞類 minor word-class;
次要單位 secondary unit;
次要翻譯 secondary translation;
次要功能 secondary function;
次要關係 ordering relation;
次要矛盾 secondary contradictions;
次要擬聲 secondary onomatopoeia;
次要特徵 accidental quality;
次要意義 secondary meaning;
[次於] (1) next to sth; (2) inferior to;
[次之] take second place;

挨次 according to order; by turns; in order; in proper order; in sequence; in series; in succession; in turn; one after another; one by one;
按次 according to order; in due order; in sequence;
班次 (1) order of classes; (2) number of runs or flights;
版次 the order in which editions are printed;
編次 arrange according to a certain order;
殘次 imperfect;
層次 (1) administrative levels; (2) arrangement of idea;
場次 number of performances of a play; number of showings of a film;
車次 train number;
紬次 collect and arrange in order;
初次 first time;
等次 grade; place in a series;
迭次 again and again; repeatedly; time and again;
多次 many times; on many occasions; over and over again; repeatedly; time after time; time and again;
二次 secondary;
航次 the number of flights;
架次 sortie;
漸次 gradually; little by little; one after another;
將次 about to;
累次 again and again; repeatedly;
歷次 all previous occasions;
兩次 twice;
旅次 place where one stays overnight during a journey;
屢次 repeatedly; time and again;
倫次 coherence;
每次 at every turn; every time;
名次 position in a name list;
目次 contents; table of contents;
批次 batch;
七次 septic;
其次 (1) besides; next; next in order; secondly; then; (2) next in importance; of minor importance; secondary;
遷次 (1) change of lodgings on a journey; (2) promotion to higher rank; (3) change of season;
前次 last time; previous occasion;
取次 in order; in turn; one by one;
詮次 order of arrangement;
銓次 procedures for selecting officials;
人次 person-time;
如次 as follows;
三次 ter-; tri-; three times; triple;
苫次 in mourning for one's parents;
上次 last time; previous occasion;
稍次 slightly inferior in quality;
首次 first; first time; for the first time;
數次 a few times; several times;
順次 in order; in succession; successively;
四次 four times;
梯次 phases;
途次 stopover; traveller's lodging;
位次 precedence; seating arrangement;
無數次 heaps of times;
席次 order of seats; seating arrangement;
下次 next; next time;
胸次 mood; state of mind;
許多次 many's the time;
頁次 page number;
一次 (1) once; one time; (2) liner;
依次 in proper order; in proper sequence; successively;
以次 (1) in proper order; in proper sequence; (2) the following;
因次 dimension;

印次 impression;
越次 disregard the proper order;
再次 once again; once more;
造次 (1) hasty; hurried; (2) impetuous; rash; without due consideration;
這次 current; present; this time;
逐次 each time; gradually; in succession; on each of the occasions; successive;
主次 primary and secondary;
撰次 compile;
坐次 order of seats in a meeting or feast;
座次 arrangement of seats; order of seats;

ci

【伺】 serve;
[伺候] attend upon; serve; wait upon;
伺候人吃飯 wait at table;

ci

【刺】 (1) splinter; thorn; (2) prick; stab; sting; (3) assassinate; (4) irritate; (5) stimulate; (6) detect; spy; (7) criticize;
[刺鼻] assail one's nostrils; irritate the nose; pungent;
刺鼻的氣味 pungent smell;
[刺穿] impale;
[刺刀] bayonet;
刺刀衝鋒 bayonet charge;
刺刀見紅 fight courageously at bayonet-point range;
[刺耳] ear-piercing; grating on the ear; harsh; irritating to the ear; jarring; unpleasant to the ear;
刺耳的話 harsh words; sarcastic remarks; words that irritate the ears;
刺耳的尖叫 discordant scream;
刺耳的驚叫 stunning scream;
刺耳的鬧聲 grating noise;
刺耳聲音 sudden shriek of;
[刺骨] biting; cut to the bones; piercing; piercing to the bones;
刺骨寒風 biting wind; bitter wind; cutting wind; freezing wind; piercing wind;
寒風刺骨 the wind has a sting in it;
寒冷刺骨 the cold pierced to the bone;
寒氣刺骨 cold strikes into one's marrow;
[刺激] (1) excite; incentive; stimulate; stimulation; stimulus; (2) irritate; provoke; upset;
刺激閾 stimulus threshold;
刺激介詞 preposition of stimulus;
刺激食慾 provoke the appetite;
刺激素 stimulin;
刺激作用 stimulation;
財政刺激 fiscal incentive; fiscal stimulation;
出口刺激 export incentives;
分級刺激 fractional stimulation;
複雜刺激 complex stimulus;
基本刺激 basic stimulus;
價格刺激 price incentives;
經濟刺激 economic incentive;
受到刺激 be jarred; get a jar; upset;
條件刺激 conditioned stimulus;
聽覺刺激 auditory stimulus;
暫時刺激 temporary stimulus;
[刺客] assassin;
[刺殺] assassinate;
[刺傷] stab and wound;
刺傷眼睛 the eyes are affected by;
被刺傷 be hurt by a sting; be wounded by stabbing;
[刺探] detect; make roundabout inquiries; make secret inquiries; pry; spy;
刺探軍情 gather military intelligence; pry about military intelligence; spy on the military movements; spy out military secrets;
刺探商業秘密 spy on business secrets;
[刺痛] prickle; stab;
刺痛…的心 sting sb to the quick;
一陣刺痛 a sharp sting; a tingling sensation;
[刺心] pierce the heart;
刺心之言 words that pierce the heart;
如刀刺心 feel as though a dagger were lacerating one's heart;
[刺繡] embroidery; fancywork;
刺繡畫片 needlepoint; silk embroidered picture;
刺繡技藝 skills in embroidery;
刺繡品 embroidery; needlepoint;
[刺眼] (1) dazzling; (2) offending to the eye; unpleasant to look at;
刺眼的陽光 dazzling sun;
亮得刺眼 dazzlingly bright;

拔刺 pluck a thorn;
衝刺 sprint; spurt;
穿刺 puncture;
倒刺 agnail;
粉刺 acne;

蜂刺 sting of a bee;
諷刺 mock; ridicule; satirize;
骨刺 spur;
譏刺 mock; ridicule; satirize;
馬刺 spur;
芒刺 prickle;
毛刺 burr;
謀刺 plot to assassinate;
劈刺 sabre fighting;
拼刺 (1) practise bayonets; (2) fight with bayonets;
鰭刺 base of fish fins;
鋌刺 stick;
行刺 assassinate;
一根刺 a thorn;
遇刺 be attacked by an assassin;
針刺 acupuncture;

ci
【廁】 (1) a member of; (2) mingle with;

ci
【賜】 favour; grant by a superior; honour sb by giving sth;
[賜福] blessing;
[賜覆] kindly favour us with a reply; please favour me with a reply;
[賜教] condescend to teach; grant instruction;
[賜予] bestow; grant;

恩賜 bestow charity; favour;
惠賜 bestow graciously;
見賜 be granted; be presented with;
欽賜 be bestowed by an emperor; be granted by an emperor;
辱賜 thanks for your gifts;
賞賜 grant a reward;
天賜 endowed by Heaven; given by Heaven;
御賜 bestowed by the emperor;

cong¹
cong
【匆】 hastily; hurriedly;
[匆匆] hastily; hurriedly;
匆匆不及 too much in a hurry to do sth;
匆匆出迎 hurry out and greet sb;
匆匆而來 come in great haste;
匆匆而去 hurry away; leave in a hurry; pop off; scoot off;
匆匆就座 seat oneself in haste; take a seat in haste; take one's place with a rush;
匆匆離開 bundle away; bundle off; bundle out; get up and dig; get up and dust; hurry away; hurry off; leave in a hurry; leave in haste; make away; pop off; scoot off;
匆匆忙忙 bustle up; head over heels; heels over head; jammed for time;
匆匆逃命 run for one's life;
匆匆通過議案 rush a bill through;
急匆匆 in a tearing hurry;
來去匆匆 come and go in haste;
來也匆匆，去也沖沖 come in a rush, and go with a flush;
行色匆匆 in a hurry to leave; in a rush getting ready for a journey;
[匆促] hastily; in a hurry;
匆促辦事 hurry on the business;
匆促作出決定 jump at a conclusion;
[匆猝] hastily; in a hurry;
[匆遽] hastily; hurriedly;
[匆忙] hastily; in a hurry; in haste;
匆忙回家 hasten home; hurry home;
匆忙離去 go off in a haste; hurry away; hurry off;
匆忙跑掉 make off; rush off;
匆忙下結論 hasty in drawing a conclusion; rush to a conclusion;
匆忙做出判斷 hasty in making a judgment;
不必匆忙 there is no hurry about it;

cong
【從】 (1) easy; lax; (2) abundant; plentiful; (3) persuade; strongly; urge;
[從容] calm; leisurely; unhurried;
從容不迫 by easy stages; calm and unhurried; calmly; go easy; in a leisurely manner; leisurely; pull down one's vest; take it easy; take it leisurely and unoppressively; take one's time; unhurried; with poise and ease;
從容幹好事，性急生岔子 more haste, less speed; slow and steady is the way to success;
從容堅定 stand firm and keep coolheaded;
從容就義 die a martyr to one's principle; go to one's death unflinchingly; meet one's death like a hero; tread the path of virtue calmly;
從容自若 composed;
從容自在 calm and at ease;
從從容容 leisurely; without haste;

cong
【樅】 fir; fir tree;

cong

【葱】 (1) leek; onion; scallion; (2) green;
［葱白］ scallion;
［葱翠］ fresh green; luxuriantly green;
［葱花］ chopped green onion;
［葱黃］ greenish yellow;
［葱蘢］ luxuriantly green; verdant;
［葱綠］ light green;
［葱頭］ onion;
［葱鬱］ luxuriantly green; verdant;

分葱 branched chives;
藠葱 Chinese onions;
細香葱 chives;
洋葱 onion;
一把子葱 a handful of scallions;
一根葱 a piece of green onion;

C

cong

【璁】 jade-like stone;
［璁琤］ sound of music instruments; tinkling of jades;

瓏璁 clanking sound of jade or metal;

cong

【瑽】 tinkling of jade ornaments; tinkling of jade pendants;

cong

【聰】 (1) faculty of hearing; (2) acute hearing;
［聰慧］ astute; bright; clever; intelligent;
［聰俊］ intelligent and attractive;
［聰明］ astute; bright; clever; intelligent;
聰明才智 ability and cleverness; intelligence and wisdom; wisdom and ability; wisdom and talents;
聰明的 brainy;
聰明點子 bright idea; clever idea;
聰明懂事 clever and sensible;
聰明反被聰明誤 a wise man can be ruined by his own wisdom; clever people may be victims of their own cleverness; cleverness may overreach itself; every man has a fool in his sleeve; suffer for one's wisdom;
聰明過人 cleverer than any one else; too clever by half;
聰明過頭 be ruined by one's own cleverness; too smart;
聰明好學 clear and eager to learn; intelligent and fond of study;
聰明活潑 clever and active; intelligent and lively; wise and active;
聰明伶俐 clever and quick-witted; clever and sensible; intelligent and smart; quick on the uptake;
聰明能幹 clever and capable; have a good head on one's shoulders; clever and capable;
聰明人 clever person; wise guy;
聰明人不上二次當 it is a silly fish that is caught twice with the same bait;
聰明叡智 intellectual virtues;
聰明透頂 clever to the extreme; extremely clever;
聰明賢惠 clear and virtuous;
聰明一世，糊塗一時 a clever man has his stupid moments; a lifetime of cleverness can be interrupted by moments of stupidity; clever all one's life, but stupid this once; smart as a rule, but this time a fool;
聰明一世 , 懵懂一時 wise for a lifetime but foolish at a critical moment; quick-witted throughout one's life, but bewildered for a single moment;
聰明有為 intelligent and promising;
聰明智慧 bright and intelligent; very intelligent;
聰明自誤 be ruined by one's own cleverness; too smart;
冰雪聰明 brilliant; very bright; very clever;
稟賦聰明 be gifted with keen intelligence;
事後聰明 wise after the event;
小聰明 cleverness in trivial matters; good at playing petty tricks; petty shrewdness; petty tricks; sapient; smart in a small way;
~賣弄小聰明 too clear by half;
~耍小聰明 play petty tricks;
自作聰明 act on the strength of one's own imagined cleverness; fancy oneself clever; think oneself smart; try to be smart;
［聰叡］ bright and farsighted;
［聰穎］ bright; clever; intelligent;

cong

【鏦】 (1) spear; (2) pierce with a spear; (3) clang of metal;
［鏦鏦］ clang of metal; tinkling of metal;

cong¹

【驄】 a horse with a bluish white colour;

cong²

cong

【從】 (1) follow; (2) comply with; obey; (3) be engaged in; join; (4) according to a certain principle; in a certain manner; (5) from;

[從不] never ever;

幾乎從不 hardly ever;

[從長計議] be considered slowly and carefully; be talked about at length; be treated with careful deliberation; consider careful before making a decision; give the matter further thought and discuss it later; take more time to consider; take one's time in reaching a decision; talk over at length;

[從此] from now on; from then on; from this time on; henceforth; thereupon;

[從…到…] from…to…;

從古到今 from ancient to modern times;

從日出到日落 from dawn to dusk; from sunrise to sunset; from sunup and sundown;

從上到下 from above down; from top to bottom;

從生到死 from the cradle to the grave;

從頭到腳 from head to foot;

從頭到尾 from beginning to end; from first to last;

從無到有 grow out of nothing;

從小到大 develop gradually; expand from small to big;

從早到晚 from dawn to dusk; from morning till night;

[從而] as a result; result from; so as to; so then; thereby; thus;

[從犯] accessary criminal; accomplice;

協從犯 accomplice under duress;

[從何而來] where does sth come from; where from;

[從緩] bide time; postpone; put off;

[從簡] conform to the principle of simplicity;

手續從簡 simplify the process;

一切從簡 dispense with all unnecessary formalities;

[從…角度看] from sb's point of view; from sb's standpoint; from the point of view of; from the standpoint of;

從女性的角度看 from the standpoint of women;

從商業角度看 from a business standpoint;

[從句] subordinate clause;

從句標記 clause marker;

從句翻譯 clause translation;

比較從句 comparative clause;

表語從句 predicative clause;

賓語從句 object clause;

並列從句 coordinate clause;

補充從句 amplifying clause;

程度狀語從句 adverbial clause of degree; adverbial clause of extent;

從屬從句 dependent clause;

定式從句 finite clause;

~非定式從句 non-finite clause;

定語從句 attributive clause;

獨立從句 independent clause;

對等從句 equivalent clause;

分詞從句 participial clause;

~定式分詞從句 finite participial clause;

非定式分詞從句 non-finite participial clause;

附加從句 appended clause;

關係從句 relative clause;

~名詞性關係從句 nominal relative clause;

假設從句 hypothetical clause;

接觸從句 contact clause;

絕對從句 absolute clause;

名詞從句 noun clause;

~從屬名詞從句 subordinate noun clause;

名詞性從句 nominal clause;

內容從句 content clause;

評論從句 comment clause;

同位語從句 appositive clause;

主語從句 subject clause;

狀語從句 adverbial clause;

~保留狀語從句 adverbial clause of reservation;

~比較狀語從句 adverbial clause of comparison;

~比例狀語從句 adverbial clause of proportion;

~處所狀語從句 adverbial clause of place;

~地點狀語從句 adverbial clause of place;

~結果狀語從句 adverbial clause of result;

~目的狀語從句 adverbial clause of purpose;

~偶然狀語從句 adverbial clause of

contingency;
~排除狀語從句 adverbial clause of exception;
~情況狀語從句 adverbial clause of circumstance;

[從軍] be in uniform; enlist; enter the service; join the army; take service;

[從寬] handle leniently; lenient;
從寬發落 give quarter; let up on;

[從來] all along; always; at all times; never;
從來沒有 at no period;

[從良] prostitutes getting married;

[從略] be omitted;
附錄從略 the appendix is omitted;
引文從略 the quotation is omitted;

[從命] obey an order;
礙難從命 find it hard to comply with your wish;
樂於從命 willingly comply with instructions;
不敢從命 I cannot do as you command me;
敢不從命 how dare one not obey sb's order;
勢難從命 circumstances make it difficult for me to comply with your request;
恕難從命 one is sorry but one cannot obey; regretably, one's wishes cannot be complied with; we regret that we cannot comply with your wishes;
唯命是從 accept sb's instructions without a murmur; absolutely obedient; always do as sb is told; at sb's beck and call; at sb's disposal; do sb's bidding; do whatever is told; obsequious; sign on the dotted line; unconditionally obedient; under one's thumb;
惟命是從 always do as one is told; slavishly obedient;
欣然從命 gladly comply with;

[從前] a long time ago; as of old; before; "ex-"; former; formerly; in former times; in the old days; in the past; long long ago; many years ago; old; once; once upon a time; some time ago; thousands of years ago; used to be;

[從權] as a matter of expediency;
從權處理 do what is expedient;

[從戎] enlist; enlist in the army; enter the service; join the army;

[從善] follow good advice;
從善如流 follow good advice as naturally as a river follows its course; follow good advice readily; give the ready ear to wise counsel; readily accept good advice;
擇善而從 choose and follow what is good; find the good way and follow it;

[從事] about; be bound up in; be engaged in; busy with; be occupied in; be occupied with; devote oneself to; go in for; occupy oneself with; work on; take up;
從事教育工作 take up teaching as a profession;
從事舞台藝術 go in for the stage;
從事一門手藝 be engaged in a craft;
從事著述 be engaged in writing scholarly works;
草率從事 act rashly and casually;
奮發從事 direct one's efforts to;
謹慎從事 act with discretion;
魯莽從事 throw caution to the winds;
慎重從事 act with caution; steer a cautious course;

[從屬] dependence; subordinate;
從屬詞 dependent word;
從屬從句 dependent clause;
從屬代碼 subcode;
從屬地位 in subordinate status;
從屬動詞 subordinate verb;
從屬關係 relation of dependence;
從屬規則 dependence rule;
從屬理論 dependency theory;
從屬連詞 subordinate conjunction;
從屬信用證 secondary credit;
從屬債務 secondary liability;
從屬專利 dependent patent;

[從俗] conform to conventions; follow local customs; follow traditions;

[從速] as soon as possible; at one's earliest convenience; without delay;
從速辦理 deal with the matter as soon as possible; settle the matter quickly;

[從天而降] appear out of the blue; come down from heaven; come from above; descend out of the blue; drop from the clouds; fall from the sky; sudden unexpected arrival; unexpectedly;

[從頭] (1) from the beginning; from the top; (2) anew; once again;

從頭到腳 from face to foot; from head to foot; from the sole of the foot to the crown of the head; from top to toe;

從頭到尾 all the way; at both the end and the beginning; from A to Izzard; from A to Z; from beginning to end; from cover to cover; from end to end; from first to last; from hub to tire; from soup to nuts; from start to finish; from stem to stern; from the egg to the apple; from the head to the tail; from the soul of the foot to the crown of the head; from the word go; from tip to toe; from title page to colophon; from top to bottom; from top to toe; the whole way; through and through; through the whole length;

從頭開始 a clean slate; back to square one; back to the beginning; from the jump; from the ground up; from scratch; from the word go; make a fresh start; start all over; start all over again; start anew; take a start from the head;

~再從頭開始 start afresh;

從頭做起 do it all over again; start a new life; start all over again; start all over again from the beginning; start from a clean slate; start from the beginning; turn over a new leaf;

[從未有過] break all previous records; have never occurred anywhere; have no precedent;

[從小] as a child; from childhood;

從小到大 develop gradually; expand from small to big; from small to large; man and boy;

從小看大 the child is father of the man;

[從新] afresh; again; anew;

從新學起 start learning from scratch;

從新做人 start one's life anew; start with a clean slate; turn over a new leaf;

[從心] follow one's wishes;

從心所欲 do as one pleases; follow one's heart's desire; free-wheeling;

力不從心 ability falling short of one's wishes; ability not equal to one's ambition; beyond one's power; bite off more than one can chew; lacking the ability to do what one would like to do; one's strength does not match one's ambitions; the spirit is willing but the flesh is weak; unable to do as well as one would wish;

[從嚴] on the strict side; severely; strictly;

[從業] get a job; take up an occupation;

從業員 practitioner;

~翻譯從業員 practicing translator;

[從一而終] be faithful to one's husband unto death; marry one husband in her life;

[從優] give favourable treatment to;

[從者] followers;

從者如雲 have a large following;

[從政] become a government official; enter politics; go into politics;

[從中] from among; out of; therefrom;

從中搗亂 throw a spanner into the works;

從中牟利 get advantage out of; get some advantage from the mediate position between; have an axe to grind; make a profit for oneself in some deal; make capital out of sth; play both ends against the middle; step in and take the advantage;

從中受益 get some benefit from it;

從中説合 settle through a middleman;

從中説和 play the part of a middleman;

從中挑選 make a choice among;

從中調解 act as an intermediary between...and...;

從中斡旋 in between is a person trying to mediate between the disputants;

從中漁利 cash in on; reap profits from;

從中阻礙 lie in the way;

從中作保 be sb's guarantor; go bail for; play the part of the sponsor;

從中作伐 act as a matchmaker; play the part of the go-between;

從中作梗 come between; create difficulties; hinder sb from carrying out a plan; make things difficult for sb; place obstacles in the way; put a spoke in sb's wheel;

從中作祟 do mischief surreptitiously; play tricks in secret;

服從 abide; obey; submit oneself to;

過從 have friendly intercourse with;

扈從 retainer; retinue; suite;

盲從 follow blindly; follow like sheep;

僕從 footman; henchman; servant;

騎從 servants on horseback;

曲從 obey reluctantly;

適從 head in a direction;
隨從 accompany one's superior;
聽從 comply with; obey;
無從 have no way of doing sth; not in a position to do sth;
脅從 accomplice under duress;
信從 trust and comply with;
依從 comply with; submit to; yield to;
景從 follow like a shadow;
悅從 follow willingly;
允從 promise to follow one's advice;
自從 since;
遵從 comply with; defer to; follow;

C

cong
【淙】 sound of flowing water; water flowing;
［淙淙］(1) gurgling sound of flowing water; (2) tinkling sound of metals;

cong
【琮】 an octagonal jade piece with a round hole in the centre;

cong
【叢】 (1) crowd together; (2) a clump of; a grove of; a thicket of; (3) collection; crowd;
［叢集］(1) converge; crowd together; pile up; (2) anthology; collection;
［叢林］bush; shrub; thicket;
叢林戰 bush fighting;
叢林哲學 jungle justice; the law of the jungle;
進入叢林 go into the bush;
熱帶叢林 tropical jungles;
［叢生］(1) clump; grow thickly; overgrow; (2) break out;
百病叢生 all kinds of diseases and ailments break out;
野花叢生 wild flowers grow everywhere;
雜草叢生 weed growth;
［叢書］anthology; collection; series; series of books; set;
一套文學叢書 a series of literary works;
草叢 thick growth of grass;
花叢 flowers in clusters;
灌木叢 bush;
樹叢 grove of trees;

cou⁴
cou
【湊】 (1) collect; gather together; pool; (2) happen by chance; (3) take advantage of; (4) come close to; move close to; press near;
［湊份子］(1) club together; get together; (2) bother sb;
［湊合］(1) assemble; collect; gather together; (2) improvise; (3) make do with anything;
湊湊合合 it's alright; make do with anything;
湊合湊合 make shift with what is on hand;
［湊集］scrape up; scrape together;
［湊零成整］make up an even amount;
［湊錢］pool money; raise a fund; whip-round;
湊錢買禮物 collect money to buy a present;
［湊巧］as luck would have it; fortunately; luckily;
不湊巧 as luck would have it; out of luck;
事有湊巧 as luck would have it;
［湊手］at hand; within easy reach;
［湊數］(1) make do; serve as a stopgap; (2) make up the amount; make up the number;
［湊足］get together enough;
湊足錢 scrape up enough money;
湊足人數 gather together enough people; get a quorum;
緊湊 compact; terse;
拼湊 piece together; scrape together;
生湊 mechanically put together;

cou
【腠】 texture of the muscle;

cou
【輳】 converge;
輻輳 converge;

cu¹
cu
【粗】 (1) thick; wide; (2) coarse; crude; rough; (3) gruff; husky; (4) careless; negligent; (5) rude; unrefined; vulgar; (6) slightly; roughly;
［粗暴］brutal; crude; rough; rude; violent;
粗暴對待 kick in the teeth;
粗暴舉止 crude behaviour;

粗暴行為 rude behaviour;
忿厲粗暴 angry, fierce and rough;
態度粗暴 have a rude attitude;
性格粗暴 of coarse character;

[粗笨] (1) awkward; clumsy; (2) bulky; cumbersome; heavy; unwieldy;
動作粗笨 awkward in doing things;
手腳粗笨 clumsy with one's hands;

[粗鄙] coarse; vulgar;
粗鄙的説法 vulgarity of expressions;
粗鄙的語言 vulgar language;

[粗糙] coarse; crude; rough; unpolished;
粗糙的翻譯 crude translation;
粗糙度 roughness;
~粗糙度儀 roughometer;
~壁面粗糙度 wall roughness;
~表面粗糙度 surface roughness;
~絕對粗糙度 absolute roughness;
~砂粒粗糙度 sand roughness;
表面粗糙 have a surface rough to the feel;
雙手粗糙 have rough hands;
做工粗糙 of bad workmanship; of rude workmanship;

[粗大] (1) bulky; thick; thick and big; (2) loud;
粗大的聲音 rough and loud voice;
粗大的手 big strong hand;
五大三粗 big and tall;

[粗讀] rough reading;

[粗短] humpty-dumpty;

[粗放] bold and unrestrained;
粗放耕作 extensive agriculture;

[粗嘎] gruff; loud;

[粗獷] (1) boorish; rough; rude; (2) bold and unconstrained; straightforward and uninhibited; rugged;
粗獷坦率 straightforward and candid;
性格粗獷 of straightforward and unsophisticated character;

[粗豪] forthright; straightforward;

[粗話] coarse language; obscene language; swear word; vulgar language;
別説粗話 don't use bad language;
滿口粗話 swear like a bargee;

[粗活] heavy manual work; unskilled work;
幹粗活 do menial work;
~幹粗活的人 menial;

[粗劣] cheap; of poor quality; shoddy;
粗劣作品 cheap literature;
~一件粗劣作品 a shoddy piece of work;

[粗陋] coarse and crude; rash;

[粗魯] boorish; rash; rough; rude;
粗魯笨拙 rude and clumsy; outlandish;
粗魯的 crass;
粗魯話 rough tongue;
粗魯無禮 rude;
出言粗魯 speak in a rude manner;
舉止粗魯 boorish;
説話粗魯 have a rough tongue;
態度粗魯 rude in manner; rude manners;

[粗略] rough; sketchy;
粗略地 in rough;
粗略估計 rough estimate;
粗略一看 cast a glance at; cast a look at; give a glance at; on cursory examination; take a glance at;

[粗蠻] rough; rude; unrefined;

[粗莽] reckless; rude;

[粗淺] basic; coarse and shallow; shallow; simple; superficial;

[粗人] boor; careless person; clod; clod-hopper; person of little education; rough fellow; unrefined person;

[粗食] coarse food;
粗食簡餐 have coarse rice and simple dishes for one's meals;
薄酒粗食 poor food and coarse wine;

[粗疏] inattentive;

[粗率] (1) crude and coarse; (2) careless; ill-considered; rash; rough and careless;
粗率從事 act without care;

[粗俗] coarse; uncouth; vulgar;
粗俗不當 harsh and inappropriate;
粗俗的話 gross expression; rank expressions; vulgar expressions;
粗俗的舉止 uncouth behaviour;
粗俗語 vulgarism;
舉止粗俗 crass behaviour;
説話粗俗 speak vulgarly; use low language;

[粗算] rough estimate;

[粗糖] raw sugar; unrefined sugar;

[粗通] know a little about;
粗通文墨 barely know the rudiments of writing;

[粗腿] thick leg;
抱粗腿 curry favour with; flatter; latch on to the rich and powerful; throw oneself under the protection of someone of influence;

[粗細] the rough and the refined;

粗中有細 have sth refined in one's rough ways; somewhat refined in one's rough way;
拿粗挾細 make trouble; provocative; set on; spur on;

[粗心] careless; thoughtless;
粗心大意 careless; inadvertent; negligent; remiss; scatter-brain; slipshod; thoughtless; want of care;
~粗心大意的 bumbling;
粗心的 blundering;
粗心浮氣 unthoughtful and rash;

[粗野] boorish; coarse; rough; rustic; unrefined; unpolished;
粗野的舉止 boorish manners;
粗野的趣味 boorish taste;
粗野的現象 signs of vulgarity;
粗野的語言 boorish language;
粗野態度 rustic manners;
粗野行為 vulgarity;

[粗衣] coarse clothing;
淡食粗衣 simple food and coarse clothing — live in poverty;

[粗重] (1) harsh; loud and jarring; rough; (2) big and heavy; bulky; (3) thick and heavy; (4) heavy; strenuous;

[粗壯] (1) brawny; muscular; robust; stout; sturdy; thickset; (2) thick and strong; (3) deep and resonant;
粗壯的身體 a thickset body;

[粗拙] (1) coarse; crude; (2) clumsy; unskilled;

加粗 widen;
老粗 rough and ready chap; uncouth person;
心粗 careless; thoughtless;

cu

【麤】 same as 粗;

cu²

cu

【徂】 (1) advance; go ahead; go to; (2) to; (3) die; (4) past;

[徂落] die; pass away;

cu

【殂】 death; die;

[殂沒] death; die; perish;

cu⁴

cu

【促】 (1) hurried; short; urgent; (2) promote; urge; (3) close to; near;

[促成] facilitate; favour; help to bring about; help to materialize; lead on to;
促成此事 help to accomplish the thing;

[促進] accelerate; advance; boost; encourage; facilitate; gear up; promote;
促進和平 promote peace;
促進劑 accelerator; promotor;
~附着力促進劑 adhesion promotor;
~化學促進劑 chemical promotor;
~鹹性促進劑 alkaline accelerator;
~酸性促進劑 acid accelerator;
~碳化物促進劑 carbide promotor;
~助促進劑 activating accelerator;
促進教育 give an impulse to education;
促進經濟發展 promote economic advancement;
促進貿易 give an impetus to trade;
促進器 accelerator;
促進社會發展 promote social development;
促進生長 advance growth;
促進團結 promote unity;
促進相互了解 further mutual understanding;
促進友誼 promote friendship;
反應促進 reaction promotion;
接觸促進 contact promotion;
貿易促進 trade promotion;
業務促進 business promotion;

[促使] impel; lead on to; precipitate; spur; urge;
促使政府跨台 accelerate the fall of the government;

[促膝] sit close together; sit knee to knee;
促膝談心 have a heart-to-heart talk; sit closely together and have an intimate chat; sit side by side and talk intimately; talk head and head;

[促銷] promote the sale; promotion; sales promotion;
促銷策略 promotion strategy;
促銷活動 sales campaign; sales drive; sales promotion;
促銷小姐 booth bunny;

倉促 all of a sudden; hastily; in a hurry;
匆促 hastily; in a hurry;
催促 chivvy; hasten; press; urge;
督促 press; supervise and urge;
短促 of short duration; pressed for time;

敦促 press; urge;
急促 (1) hurried; rapid; (2) (of time) pressing; short;
緊促 imminent; pressing; urgent;
窘促 (1) in dire straits; in straitened circumstances; poverty-stricken; (2) embarrassed; hard pressed;
局促 (1) cramped; narrow; (2) short;
侷促 (1) cramped; narrow; (2) short;
跼促 (1) cramped; narrow; (2) feeling constraint; nervous; showing constraint;
氣促 panting; short of breath;
偓促 dirty; filthy;

cu

【猝】 abrupt; hurried; sudden; unexpected;
[猝不及防] be caught off the guard; be caught unprepared; be taken by surprise; put off one's guard;
[猝然] abruptly; suddenly; unexpectedly;
猝然決定 make a sudden decision;
猝然一動 jerk;
[猝死] die suddenly; drop dead; sudden death;

倉猝 all of a sudden; hastily; in a hurry;
匆猝 all of a sudden; hastily; in a hurry;

cu

【趣】 same as 促;

cu

【醋】 (1) vinegar; (2) jealousy;
[醋海] jealousy;
醋海翻波 turn with jealousy;
醋海生波 a storm of jealousy; disturbance due to jealousy;
[醋壺] vinegar pot;
[醋化] acetify;
醋化器 acetifier;
醋化作用 acetification;
[醋酸] acetic acid;
醋酸測定法 acetometry;
醋酸計 acetimeter;
[醋罈子] (1) vinegar jar; (2) jealous person;
[醋味] (1) smell of vinegar; (2) jealousy;
醋味十足 very jealous;
[醋心] belching of acid from stomach;
[醋意] feeling of jealousy;
醋意熾烈 burning with jealousy;

半瓶醋 dabbler; smatterer;
陳醋 mature vinegar;
吃醋 jealous;
酒醋 wine vinegar;

cu

【蔟】 (1) same as 簇; (2) frame on which silkworms spin;

cu

【踧】 (1) reverent and nervous; (2) level and easy;
[踧爾] surprised;

cu

【簇】 (1) cluster; cluster together; crowd; (2) arrow head; (3) framework on which silkworms spin;
[簇聚] cluster together; crowd together;
[簇射] shower;
側簇射 side shower;
廣角簇射 wide-angle shower;
介子簇射 meson shower;
軟簇射 soft shower;
[簇新] brand new;
[簇擁] attended by a crowd; cluster round;
簇擁而來 press forward in a crowd;
前簇後擁 be escorted by big crowds in front and behind;

cu

【蹙】 (1) cramped; pressed; (2) knit one's brows;
[蹙額] frown; knit one's brows;
蹙額縐眉 knit one's brows; wrinkle one's brows;
愁眉蹙額 gloomy eyebrows and wrinkled forehead — knit the brows;
攢眉蹙額 bend the brows; contract the brows; frown; knit the brows;
疾首蹙額 frown in disgust; with abhorrence; with aching head and knitted brows;
顰眉蹙額 contract one's brows in a frown; knit the brows; make a wry face;
皺眉蹙額 contract one's brows in a frown; draw the brows together into wrinkles; frown; knit one's brows; one's eyebrows knit in a frown; with knitted brows; wrinkle one's brows;

顰蹙 knit the brows;
窮蹙 in dire straits; poverty-stricken;

cu

【蹴】 (1) tread on; (2) kick; (3) respectful;
[蹴踏] tread on;

cuan¹

cuan

【汆】 chafe; rinse;

［汆子］ a kind of kettle;

cuan

【攛】 (1) fling; throw; (2) do in a hurry;

［攛掇］ egg on; urge;

攛掇害人 stir up harm for everyone;

［攛弄］ egg on; urge;

cuan

【躥】 go up suddenly; hike up; leap up; rise quickly;

［躥房越脊］ jump onto the roof and descend into rooms—thief;

［躥墻］ leap over a wall;

［躥上房］ jump onto the roof;

猛地一躥 rise with a bounce;

cuan²

cuan

【攢】 assemble; collect together;

［攢聚］ crowd together; gather closely together; huddle together;

［攢眉蹙頞］ bend the brows; contract the brows; frown; knit the brows;

［攢頭接耳］ put heads together; whisper;

cuan⁴

cuan

【篡】 seize; usurp;

［篡奪］ seize; usurp;

篡奪領導權 usurp the leadership;

篡奪王位 seize the throne;

［篡改］ distort; falsify; misrepresent; tamper with;

篡改記錄 falsify accounts; tamper with the minutes;

篡改歷史 distort history;

篡改數字 juggle the figures;

篡改原則 adulterate a principle;

篡改原文 alter the original text; tamper with the text;

擅自篡改 tamper with;

［篡權］ usurp power;

篡權僭位 usurp power and the throne;

武裝篡權 seize power by armed force;

［篡弒］ commit regicide;

［篡位］ usurp the throne;

cuan

【竄】 flee; run about; scurry;

［竄犯］ intrude into; invade; make an inroad into; raid;

竄犯邊境地區 intrude the border area;

竄犯一個國家 make inroads into a country;

［竄改］ alter; falsify; manipulate; tamper with;

竄改計劃 doctor up a plan;

竄改文件 tamper with a document;

［竄擾］ harass; invade and harass;

竄擾邊境 harass the border area;

竄擾領空 intrude into the air space;

［竄逃］ flee in disorder; scurry off;

奔竄 flee; scuttle off;

點竄 polish; revise;

改竄 falsify; tamper with;

流竄 flee hither and thither;

亂竄 run helter-skelter;

鼠竄 scamper off like a frightened rat;

逃竄 flee in disorder; run away;

cuan

【爨】 (1) cook; (2) cooking stove;

［爨婦］ female cook;

［爨室］ kitchen;

分爨 divide up family property and live apart;

cui¹

cui

【衰】 (1) order; series; (2) mourning garments;

等衰 grade; place in a series;

cui

【崔】 (1) surname; (2) high and steep;

［崔巍］ lofty and steep;

［崔嵬］ (1) rocky mound; (2) high; towering;

cui

【催】 (1) hurry; press; urge; (2) expedite; hasten; speed up;

［催辦］ press for handling of a matter; press sb to do sth; urge sb into doing sth; urge sb to do sth;

［催本兒］ errand-boy;

［催逼］ hasten; press;

催逼還債 push and force for the payment of a loan;

［催產］ expedite child delivery; hasten parturition;
［催促］ chivvy; hasten; press; prompt; urge;
［催單］ reminder;
［催函］ reminder letter;
［催化］ catalyze; catalytic;
催化本領 catalytic power;
催化產品 catalyst;
催化反應 catalytic reaction;
催化活性 catalytic activity;
催化劑 catalyst; catalytic agent;
~ 二元催化劑 binary catalyst;
~ 複合催化劑 composite catalyst;
~ 活化催化劑 activating catalyst;
~ 接觸催化劑 contact catalyst;
~ 氯化催化劑 chlorination catalyst;
~ 黏土催化劑 clay catalyst;
~ 燃燒催化劑 combustion catalyst;
~ 商品催化劑 commercial catalyst;
~ 生化催化劑 biochemical catalyst;
~ 吸附催化劑 adsorption catalyst;
~ 轉化催化劑 conversion catalyst;
催化學 catalysis;
催化循環 catalytic cycle;
催化作用 catalysis; catalytic action;
~ 多種催化作用 multiple catalysis;
負催化 negative catalysis;
輻射催化 radiation catalysis;
光催化 photochemical catalysis;
膠粟催化 micellar catalysis;
均相催化 homogeneous catalysis;
酶催化 enzyme catalysis;
配位催化 coordination catalysis;
酸鹼催化 acid-base catalysis;
吸附催化 adsorption; catalysis;
氧化催化 oxidation catalysis;
異構催化 isomeric catalysis;
［催還通知］ overdue notice; recall;
［催淚彈］ lachrymatory bomb; lachrymatory shell; tear bomb; tear-gas grenade;
［催淚劑］ lachrymator;
單純催淚劑 simple lachrymator;
毒性催淚劑 toxic lachrymator;
［催眠］ hypnotize; mesmerize;
催眠療法 hypnotherapy;
催眠曲 lullaby;
催眠師 hypnotist;
催眠術 hypnotism;
催眠治療 hypnotherapy;
催眠狀態 hypnosis;
［催命］ keep pressing sb to do sth;
催命符 a written Daoist voodoo which is supposed to hasten a person's death; the final nail in one's coffin;
［催批］ press for instructions from superiors;
［催情劑］ aphrodisiac;
［催情藥］ philtre;
［催生］ expedite child delivery; hasten child delivery; hasten parturition;
［催熟］ ripening;
人工催熟 artificial ripening;
［催吐劑］ emetic;
［催瀉］ purgation;
［催債］ dun sb for payment of debt; press for payment of debt;

cui

【摧】 break; destroy; ruin;
［摧殘］ destroy; devastate; wreck;
摧殘身體 ruin one's health;
摧殘輿論 suppress public opinion;
身心受到摧殘 be physically injured and mentally affected;
受到疾病摧殘 be blighted by illness;
［摧毀］ damage; demolish; destroy; flatten; level; raze; smash; wreck;
摧毀城市 destroy a city;
摧毀敵人 cut up the enemy forces;
［摧枯］ crush dry weeds;
摧枯拉朽 as easy as crushing dry weeds and smashing rotten wood; easily overcome; make a clan sweep; smash easily like breaking dry grass and rotten wood; sweep away all obstacles in the way;
勢如摧枯 the power of something is like breaking rotten wood – invincible;
［摧折］ (1) break; snap; (2) frustrate; reverse; setback; subdue;
蘭摧玉折 the premature death of a virtuous individual;

cui

【榱】 rafter;

cui

【縗】 a piece of sackcloth worn on the breast in mourning;

cui³

cui

【璀】 bright; resplendent;
［璀璨］ bright; resplendent;
璀璨奪目 bright-coloured and dazzling;

C

dazzling; dazzling splendour; its elegance ravishes the eyes; resplendent; shine with dazzling brilliance; the dazzling brightness blinds the eyes; the lustre dazzled the eye; with dazzling brightness;

cui⁴
cui
【脆】 (1) brittle; fragile; (2) crisp; (3) clear; clear and sharp; ringing;
[脆薄] shallow; thin and brittle;
脆薄人情 thin and brittle human feeling;
[脆而不堅] brittle and easily breakable; brittle without solidity;
[脆亮] clear and melodious;
[脆怯] cowardly; timid; weak;
[脆弱] delicate; fragile; frail; frailty; tender; weak;
感情脆弱 easily upset;
神經脆弱 of weak nerves;
性格脆弱 of weak character;
[脆生] (1) crisp; (2) clear and sharp;
[脆性] brittleness; embrittlement;
衝擊脆性 impact brittleness;
低溫脆性 low-temperature brittleness;
鍍鋅脆性 galvanizing embrittlement;
高速脆性 high-speed brittleness;
高溫脆性 high-temperature brittleness;
加工脆性 work brittleness;
鹹脆性 caustic brittleness;
藍脆性 blue brittleness;
冷脆性 cold brittleness;
流動脆性 rheotropic brittleness;
切口脆性 notch embrittlement;
氫脆性 hydrogen brittleness;
缺口脆性 notch brittleness;
熱脆性 hot brittleness;
酸脆性 acid brittleness;
酸浸脆性 pickling brittleness;

迸脆 crisp;
繃脆 crisp;
乾脆 clear-cut; just; simply; straightforward;
尖脆 high and clear;
酥脆 crisp;

cui
【悴】 (1) haggard; tired out; worn-out; (2) sad; worried;
[悴薄] enfeebled; impoverished; weakened;
[悴賤] needy and lowly;

憔悴 (1) wan and sallow; (2) withered;

cui
【淬】 (1) temper iron to make swords; (2) dip into water; dye; quench; quenching; soak;
[淬火] quenching;
二重淬火 double quenching;
火焰淬火 flame quenching;
局部淬火 selective quenching;
噴射淬火 flash quenching;

cui
【啐】 (1) sip; taste; (2) spit;
啐唾沫 spit;

cui
【萃】 (1) dense growth of grass; (2) group; set; (3) congregate; gather; meet;

薈萃 assemble; gather together;
精萃 cream; pick;

cui
【毳】 (1) fine feather; (2) fine fur;
[毳幕] felt curtain;

cui
【脺】 brittle; fragile;

cui
【瘁】 (1) disease; illness; (2) over-fatigued;

勞瘁 exhausted from excessive work; worn-out;

cui
【粹】 perfect; pure; unadulterated; unmixed;
[粹白] pure white;
[粹而不雜] pure and unadulterated;

純粹 (1) pure; unadulterated; (2) merely;
國粹 quintessence of Chinese culture;
精粹 pithy; succinct; terse;

cui
【翠】 (1) green; emerald green; (2) a kingfisher;
[翠柏] bluish green cypress; incense cedar;
[翠波] green waves;
[翠柳依依] the willows swung gently gently in the breeze;
[翠綠] bluish green; emerald green; jade green;
[翠生生] fresh and green;

［翠玉］ blue jade;

蒼翠 dark green; verdant;
葱翠 fresh green; luxuriantly green;
翡翠 (1) halcyon; (2) emerald;
青翠 fresh and green; verdant; verdurous;
鮮翠 fresh and green;
珠翠 pearls and jade;

cui
【橇】 a sledge for transportation over mud or snow;

cui
【頓】 haggard;

cun¹
cun
【村】 (1) hamlet; village; (2) boorish; rustic;
［村夫］ (1) villager; (2) vulgar and coarse person;
村夫俗子 uneducated people;
村夫野老 villagers and aged rustics;
［村婦］ country woman; village woman;
村姑村婦 country girls and country women;
［村姑］ country girl; village girl;
村姑村婦 country girls and country women;
［村落］ hamlet; village;
分散村落 dispersed rural settlement;
集結村落 nucleated rural settlement;
一片村落 a village hamlet;
［村舍］ cottage;
一所村舍 a cottage;
［村社］ village community;
［村塾］ village school;
［村野］ (1) villages and fields; (2) boorish; rough;
［村寨］ stockaded village;
［村長］ village head;
［村鎮］ villages and small towns;
［村莊］ hamlet; village;
小村莊 hamlet;

俺村 my village;
農村 countryside; rural area; village;
撒村 curse; rap out; swear; talk dirty; use vulgar language;
三家村 small remote hamlet; small village;
山村 mountain village;
鄉村 country; countryside; rural area; village;
新村 new residential division;
漁村 fishing village;

cun
【皴】 (1) crack or chap of the skin; (2) the technique of representing irregular surfaces in Chinese painting;
［皴法］ the technique of representing irregular surfaces;

cun²
cun
【存】 (1) exist; live; survive; (2) keep; store; (3) accumulate; collect; (4) deposit; (5) check; leave with; (6) reserve; retain; (7) in stock; remain on balance; (8) cherish; harbour;
［存案］ keep on record; record;
存案備查 file for reference;
［存儲］ (1) memorize; store; (2) stockpile;
存儲保護 storage protection;
~存儲保護功能 memory protection function;
~存儲保護區 storage protection block;
存儲程序 stored programme;
~存儲程序方式 stored programme mode;
~存儲程序控制 stored programme control;
存儲單元 location;
存儲鍵盤 storage keyboard;
存儲器 memory; storage; storage unit;
~單片存儲器 monolithic storage;
~聲存儲器 acoustic memory;
~添加存儲器 add-on memory; add-on storage;
~相聯存儲器 associative storage;
存儲容量 storage volume;
［存檔］ file; filing; keep in a file; keep in the archives; keep on a file; place on file;
把文件存檔 file away documents; keep the documents on file;
［存而不論］ be left undiscussed; keep a problem for later discussion; leave the question open; not go into the question for the time being; put the problem away;
［存放］ (1) leave in sb's care; leave with; (2) deposit;
存放待領 be left until called for;
［存根］ counterfoil; office copy; stub;

支票存根 cheque stub;

[存貨] existing stock; goods in stock; +inventory;

存貨不足 ill-stocked;

存貨充足 be fully stocked; stocks are ample;

存貨告罄 all stock is exhausted;

存貨過多 overstock;

存貨過剩 overstocked;

期末存貨 closing inventory;

清點存貨 check a stock; make an inventory; take stock;

[存款] (1) deposit; deposit money; (2) bank savings;

存款簿 deposit pass book;

存款單 deposit slip; paying-in slip;

~存款單簿 paying-in book;

存款利率 savings interest rate;

存款利息 interest on money;

存款人 depositor;

存款收據 deposit receipt;

儲蓄存款 saving deposit;

~活期儲蓄存款 current savings account;

定期存款 fixed account; fixed deposit; time deposit;

~定期存款單 saving certificate;

活期存款 current deposit;

~活期存款賬戶 current deposit account;

~特別活期存款 special current account;

~小額活期存款 petty current account;

即期存款 deposit at call;

接受存款 take money on deposit;

金庫存款 treasury deposit;

開戶存款 open an account;

聯名存款 joint account;

生利存款 interest-bearing deposit;

~不生利存款 non-interest-bearing deposit;

提取存款 make a withdrawl of a deposit;

外幣存款 deposit in foreign currency;

現金存款 cash deposit;

信託存款 deposit in trust; trust deposit;

銀行存款 bank deposit; bank savings;

支票存款 cheque deposit;

[存歿] the dead and living;

存歿均感 both the dead and living are grateful;

[存錢] deposit money in a bank; save;

[存取] access;

存取單元 access unit;

存取方式 access mode;

存取環境 access environment;

存取控制 access control;

存取器 memory access;

存取時間 access time;

存取順序 access sequence;

存取周期 access cycle;

按序存取 sequential access;

插卡存取 card access;

成組存取 block access;

串行存取 serial access;

磁盤存取 disc access;

數據集存取 data set access;

隨意存取 arbitrary access;

直接存取 direct access;

自由存取 free access;

[存入] deposit;

[存身] make one's home; take shelter;

[存亡] live or die; survive or perish; survive and downfall;

存亡絕續 at a most critical moment; critical juncture of life and death; either continue to exist or come to an end; survive or perish; the fate is at stake;

存亡危急 at stake; at the critical juncture of life and death;

存亡未卜 to preserve or to ruin cannot be foretold;

存亡與共 throw in one's lot with;

存亡之秋 preservation or destruction crisis;

齒亡舌存 the soft and flexible lasts longer than the hard; the hard is lost, while the weak and soft endure;

共存亡 share a common destiny; stick together in life and death;

一存一亡 one has luckily survived, but the other is in the dust;

[存心] accidentally-on-purpose; cherish certain intentions; deliberately; intentionally; on purpose;

存心不良 cherish evil designs; cherish evil thoughts; evil-minded; harbour evil intentions; have ulterior motives; have wicked intentions; ill-disposed; mean ill; with evil intent;

存心搗亂 make trouble on purpose;

存心刁難 purposely to make difficulties for sb;

存心叵測 cherish unscrupulous intentions; with concealed intentions; harbour evil

intent;
存心作對 antagonize sb on purpose;
[存衣處] cloakroom;
[存疑] unanswered question; leave a question open;
[存在] (1) be; exist; (2) being; existence;
存在價值 value of being;
存在句 existential sentence;
存在詮釋學 existential hermeneutics;
存在數量詞 existential quantifier;
存在主義 existentialism;
~ 存在主義教育 existentialist education;
~ 存在主義倫理學 existentialist ethics;
~ 存在主義美學 existentialist aesthetics;
存在主語 existential subject;
不存在 non-existent;
不復存在 no longer in existence; pass out of existence;
獨立存在 exist independently;
[存折] bankbook; deposit book; passbook;

保存 conserve; keep; preserve;
并存 coexist; exist side by side;
殘存 remaining; remnant; surviving;
長存 live forever;
儲存 keep in reserve; lay in; store;
堆存 store up;
封存 seal up for safekeeping;
共存 coexist; survice together;
滚存 cumulation;
惠存 please keep sth as a souvenir;
積存 pile up; stockpile; store up;
寄存 check; deposit;
交存 deposit; hand in for safekeeping;
結存 (1) balance; cash on hand; (2) goods on hand; inventory;
庫存 inventory; reserve; stock;
留存 (1) keep preserve; (2) extant; remain;
潛存 exist in hiding;
生存 exist; live;
收存 receive and keep;
圖存 strive for survival;
慰存 comfort;
下存 remain after deduction;
現存 extant; in stock;
倖存 survive by good luck;
依存 depend on sb or sth for existence;
永存 remain forever;
貯存 keep in storage; store;

cun

【蹲】 crouch; squat;

cun³
cun

【忖】 ponder; speculate; turn over in one's mind;
[忖度] conjecture; presume; speculate; suppose; surmise;
[忖量] (1) think over; turn over in one's mind; (2) conjecture; guess;

思忖 consider; ponder;
自忖 ponder; speculate; turn over in one's mind;

cun⁴
cun

【寸】 (1) unit of length; (2) small; very little; very short; (3) coincidentally; exactly; just;
[寸步] single step; tiny step;
寸步不離 cup and can; finger and thumb; follow sb closely; keep close to; move in pairs; never move a step from; not leave by so much as an inch; not leave sb at any time; not let sb out of one's sight; not take an inch leave of sb; stay without leaving a step;
寸步不讓 dispute every inch of ground; fight every inch of the way; give not an inch; hold one's ground; never give away one inch; not bate a penny of it; not make the slightest concession; not surrender one inch of land; not yield a single step; not yield an inch; refuse to yield an inch;
寸步不移 not stir a single step;
寸步留神 watch one's step;
寸步難行 cannot do anything; cannot go a step; cannot move a single step; difficult for sb to move a single step; difficult to move even one step; find it hard to make a single move; forced into a strait; unable to do a thing; unable to move one inch forward;
寸步難移 bogged down and cannot move a step; can hardly move a step; hard to walk even an inch; in a difficult pass; stumble at every step;
[寸草] blade of grass;
寸草不留 complete devastation of land; devastated; leave not even a blade of grass; not leave even a blade of grass;
寸草不生 barren; not even a blade of grass

grows;
寸草春暉 great parental love; owe an eternal debt of gratitude to one's parents;
[寸忱] one's sincerity;
以表寸忱 as a token of one's earnest feelings; in token of one's sincerity; show one's appreciation;
[寸勁兒] accident; coincidence;
[寸絲] inch of silk;
寸絲半粟 an inch of silk and half a grain of rice – a little bit;
寸絲不掛 in a state of nature; not a stitch of clothing on; stark naked; totally nude;
[寸頭] (of hairstyle) crew cut;
[寸土] inch of land;
寸土必爭 contest every inch of ground; dispute every inch of one's ground; even an inch of land has to be fought for; fight for every inch of land;
寸土不讓 contest every inch of ground; never to yield an inch of ground; not to yield a single inch of one's land;
寸土寸金 an inch of land is worth an inch of gold;
[寸隙難留] it is impossible to stop time passing away;
[寸心] feelings;
寸心不忘 bear in mind forever; never forget;
聊表寸心 as a small token of my feelings; it is a mere proof of my regard; just to show my appreciation; just to show my gratitude;
略表寸心 as a small token of my feeling; just to show my gratitude;
[寸陰] the time indicated by a shadow moving an inch–a very short time;
寸陰尺璧 an inch of shade is equal to a foot of jade; time is money;
寸陰是惜 careful of one's time; value every spare moment;

分寸 sense of propriety in speech or action;
尺寸 dimension; size;
分寸 sense of propriety;
頭寸 (1) money market; money supply; (2) cash;
英寸 inch;

cun
【吋】 inch;

cuo¹
cuo
【搓】 (1) twist; (2) rub; rub with the hands; scrub;
[搓板兒] (1) washboard; (2) flat-chested girl; skinny person;
[搓火] feel impatient; get angry; worry;
[搓弄] rub with the hands;
[搓球] chop a ball;
[搓揉] knead; rub;
[搓手] wash one's hands with invisible soap and imperceptible water;
搓手頓腳 rub one's hands and stamp one's feet in exasperation; wring one's hands and stamp one's feet;
搓手取暖 rub one's hands together to warm them;

cuo
【撮】 (1) bring together; gather; (2) gather up; scoop up; (3) extract; summarize; (4) pinch; (5) have a meal;
[撮堆兒] goods of low quality; leftovers;
[撮合] act as a go-between; bring together; make a match;
[撮弄] (1) juggle; make a fool of; make fun of; play a trick on; tease; (2) abet; incite; instigate;
[撮土] scoop up rubbish with a dustbin;
撮土為香 burn incense in the dust in memory of;
[撮要] (1) make an abstract; outline essential points; (2) abstract; synopsis;
[撮譯] summary translation;

cuo
【磋】 polish;
[磋磨] (1) polish; (2) learn through discussions with others;
[磋商] consult; exchange views; hold a discussion;
磋商大計 discuss a great scheme;
家庭磋商 family consultation;
秘密磋商 private consultation;

切磋 learn from each other by exchanging views;

cuo
【蹉】 failure; miss;
[蹉跌] failure; mistake; slip;
[蹉跎] (1) slip and fall; (2) miss a chance;

waste time;

蹉跎歲月 dawdle one's life; dawdle one's time; fool away one's time; fritter away one's time; idle about; idle away one's time; lead an idle life; let time slip by without accomplishing anything; live an idle life; live in idleness; on the racket; profane the precious time; spend one's time in dissipation; spend one's time in frolic; trifle away one's time; waste time; while away one's time;

cuo²

cuo

【痤】 (1) boil or carbuncle on the face; (2) minor swelling;

[痤瘡] acne;

痤瘡炎 acnitis;

爆發性痤瘡 acne fulminant;

剥脱性痤瘡 excoriated acne;

充血性痤瘡 congestive acne;

傳染性痤瘡 contagious acne;

癲癇性痤瘡 epileptic acne;

碘痤瘡 iodine acne;

工業性痤瘡 trade acne;

接觸性痤瘡 contact acne;

結核性痤瘡 acne scrofulosorum;

流行性痤瘡 epidemic acne;

氯痤瘡 chloric acne;

氯萘痤瘡 halowax acne;

囊性痤瘡 cystic acne;

膿疱性痤瘡 acne pustulosa;

青年期痤瘡 adolescent acne;

丘疹性痤瘡 acne papulosa;

熱帶痤瘡 tropical acne;

萎縮性痤瘡 acne atrophica;

夏季痤瘡 acne aestivalis;

腺樣痤瘡 adenoid acne;

溴痤瘡 bromine acne;

尋常痤瘡 common acne;

嬰兒痤瘡 infantile acne;

硬結性痤瘡 acne indurate;

月經前痤瘡 premenstrual acne;

職業性痤瘡 occupational acne; trade acne;

cuo

【矬】 dwarf; shortie;

[矬子] dwarf; shortie;

cuo

【嵳】 (of mountains) high and irregular; rugged;

[嵳峨] (of mountains) high and irregular;

cuo

【瘥】 ailing; ill; sick;

cuo

【鹾】 (1) briny; salty; (2) salt;

cuo³

cuo

【脞】 little pieces; petty; tiny;

cuo

【瑳】 (1) lustre and purity of jade; (2) bright and flourishing; (3) laughing and smiling;

cuo⁴

cuo

【剉】 (1) steel file; (2) file; smooth;

cuo

【厝】 (1) place; place a coffin in a temporary shelter pending burial at a permanent site; (2) gravestone; (3) cut; engrave;

cuo

【挫】 (1) defeat; frustrate; (2) lower; subdue;

[挫敗] defeat; foil; frustrate; suffer a setback; thwart;

挫敗敵軍 defeat enemy troops;

挫敗計劃 foil one's plan; thwart one's plan;

挫敗企圖 foil one's attempt; thwart one's attempt;

挫敗陰謀 foil one's plot; thwart one's plot;

幾遭挫折 suffer repeated setbacks;

遭到挫敗 be thwarted;

一連串挫敗 a series of setbacks;

[挫傷] contusion;

[挫折] blow; frustration; reverse; setback; subdue;

挫折理論 frustration theory;

挫折雄心 check one's ambition;

大挫折 body blow;

屢經挫折 repeatedly meet with setbacks;

人有挫折河有彎 there is a crook in the lot of every one;

遇到嚴重挫折 face up serious setbacks;

遭受挫折 suffer setbacks;

頓挫 pause and transition in rhythm;

閃挫 contuse a music; sprain;

受挫 be baffled; suffer a setback;

cuo

【措】 (1) arrange; handle; manage;
(2) make plans;

［措辭］ diction; wording;
措辭不當 an improper use of words; inappropriate wording; use wrong words; wrong choice of words;
措辭得當 appropriate wording; aptly worded;
措辭得體 put it in appropriate terms; proper wording; words employed are suitable and proper;
措辭謹慎 pick one's words;
措辭精確 exact statement;
措辭欠妥 not properly worded;
措辭強硬 strongly worded;
措辭婉轉 be politely worded; put it tactfully;
措辭優美 be beautifully worded;

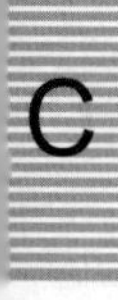

［措施］ measures; steps;
安全保障措施 safety precaution;
安全措施 accident prevention; safety measure; safety method; safety precaution; security measure;
~遵守安全措施 observe safety precautions;
保護措施 protective measure;
保健措施 hygienic measure;
必要的措施 necessary measure;
避孕措施 contraceptive devices;
補救措施 remedial measure;
採取措施 adopt measures; sth must be done; take a step; take action; take measures; take steps;
採取嚴厲措施 tighten the screws;
長期措施 long-term measure;
短期措施 short-term measure;
斷然措施 decisive measure;
鼓勵措施 incentive measure;
積極措施 vigorous measure;
及時的措施 timely measure;
急救措施 first-aid measure;
謹慎的措施 prudent measure;
緊急措施 emergency measure;
救濟措施 relief measure;
具體措施 concrete measure;
決定性措施 decisive step;
臨時措施 interim measure; make-shift measure; temporary measure;
配套措施 support measures;
強制措施 compulsory measure;
實施措施 carry out measures;
適當措施 proper measure;
衛生措施 measure of hygiene;
嚴厲的措施 drastic measure; severe measure;
一系列措施 a series of measures;
應變措施 emergency measure;
應急措施 emergency measure;
有效措施 effective measure;
預防措施 precautionary measure; preventive measure;

［措手］ deal with; manage;
措手不及 at a loss; attack before sb knows it; be caught unaware; be caught unprepared; be taken by surprise; cannot make an adequate defense; catch sb napping; catch sb on the wrong foot; catch sb with his pants down; have sb over the barrel; make a surprise attack on sb; put sb off his guard; spring a surprise on sb; take sb napping; throw sb off his guard; too late to do anything about it;

［措意］ careful; look out; pay attention to;

［措置］ arrange; handle; manage;
措置得當 be handled properly;
措置失當 mismanage; not properly handled;
措置裕如 arrange leisurely; cope with the situation successfully; deal with sth in a calm and adequate way; handle with ease; manage one's affairs easily and leisurely; manage sth in an easy and efficient way; take one's time in arranging sth;

籌措 raise money;
舉措 act; behave; move;
失措 lose one's presence of mind;

cuo

【莝】 (1) chop straw for animals;
(2) chopped hay; chopped straw;

cuo

【撮】 a pronunciation of 撮 ;

cuo

【銼】 (1) pan; (2) file; (3) file; make smooth with a file;

板銼 flat file;
扁銼 flat file;

骨銼 bone file
木銼 wood rasp;
圓銼 round file;

cuo

【錯】 (1) complex; interlocked and jagged; intricate; (2) grind; rub; (3) alternate; stagger;(4) erroneous; mistaken; wrong; (5) a demerit; a fault; (6) bad; poor;

[錯愛] misplaced favour; undeserved kindness;

[錯別字] mispronounced characters; wrongly written characters;

[錯彩鏤金] colourfully and dazzlingly embellished; elegant and refined; gilt and coloured;

[錯讀] misread;

[錯怪] blame sb wrongly; blame unjustly;
錯怪別人 bark up the wrong tree;

[錯過] let slip; miss;
錯過機會 fail to take advantage of; let the chance slip; lose a chance; miss a trick; miss an opportunity; miss the boat; miss the bus; slip through sb's fingers;
不容錯過 not to be missed; too good to miss;
無論如何也不想錯過 would not miss it for the world;

[錯話] improper remarks;

[錯角] alternate angles;
內錯角 alternate interior angle;
外錯角 alternate exterior angle;

[錯腳難返] a false step is hard to retract;

[錯覺] delusion; fallacy; false impression; illusion; misconception; phantom; wrong impression;
錯覺理論 theory of illusion;
加深錯覺 intensify the illusion;
視錯覺 optical illusion;
引起錯覺 cause an illusion; produce an illusion;
有錯覺 under an illusion;

[錯漏] errors and omissions;

[錯亂] deranged; in confusion; in disorder;
精神錯亂 be mentally deranged; have a nervous disorder; lose one's mind;

[錯落] strewn at random;
錯落不齊 at sixes and sevens; higgledy-piggledy; scattered here and there; scraggy; topsy-turvy; uneven;
錯落有致 well-proportioned;

[錯算] miscount;

[錯誤] (1) erroneous; incorrect; mistaken; wrong; (2) blunder; boo-boo; error; falsehood; fault; mistake; misstep;
錯誤百出 a lot of mistakes; full of mistakes; riddled with errors; team with blunders;
錯誤閉塞 false blocking;
錯誤的 erroneous;
錯誤分析 error analysis;
錯誤觀念 myth;
錯誤結論 wrong conclusion;
錯誤路線 erroneous line;
錯誤難免 mistakes are unavoidable;
錯誤嚴重性 error gravity;
避免錯誤 avoid errors; avoid mistakes;
不可容忍的錯誤 outrageous mistake;
不可原諒的錯誤 inexcusable mistake;
操作錯誤 operation mistake;
產生錯誤 produce errors;
常見錯誤 common error;
承認錯誤 acknowledge an error; admit an error; admit one's mistakes;
詞匯錯誤 lexical error;
持續錯誤 preservation error;
搭配錯誤 collocational error;
大錯誤 bad error; big mistake; glaring error; gross error; terrible mistake;
典型錯誤 classic mistake;
發現錯誤 find an error; notice an error; spot an error;
犯錯誤 commit an error; make a mistake; make an error;
犯愚蠢的錯誤 goof;
複製錯誤 replication mistake;
改正錯誤 correct a mistake; rectify an error;
極大的錯誤 gigantic error;
幾個錯誤 a few mistakes;
減少錯誤 reduce errors;
糾正錯誤 amend an error; correct a mistake; correct an error; redress an error; right a wrong;
局部錯誤 local error;
可怕的錯誤 hideous error;
可笑的錯誤 howler; laughable mistake; ridiculous mistake;
理解錯誤 interpretive error;

令人遺憾的錯誤 regrettable mistake;
邏輯錯誤 logical error;
明顯錯誤 conspicuous mistakes; glaring error; plain error;
認識錯誤 recognize errors;
容易犯的錯誤 easy mistake;
生長錯誤 growth mistake;
無法彌補的錯誤 irreparable error;
無可挽回的錯誤 irrecoverable error;
無心的錯誤 honest mistake;
小錯誤 minor error; mishap; peccadillo; small error;
嚴重錯誤 grave error; serious error;
有錯誤 contain an error; have an error;
語法錯誤 grammatical error;
愚蠢的錯誤 blunder; foolish mistake; silly mistake; stupid mistake;
證明錯誤 debunk;
指出錯誤 point out an error;
致命錯誤 fatal error;
重大錯誤 huge error; monumental error;
主要的錯誤 cardinal error;

[錯移] mismatch;
側向錯移 sidewise mismatch;
縱向錯移 endwise mismatch;

[錯譯] mistranslation; wrong translation;

[錯字] (1) wrongly written character; (2) misprint;
錯字連篇 a link of erroneous characters;

[錯綜] complex; intricate;
錯綜複雜 complex; complicated and confused; enough to puzzle; intricate; labyrinthic; perplexing; tangled skein; wheels within wheels;
參伍錯綜 shuffle together;

不錯 (1) correct; right; (2) not bad; pretty good;
參錯 irregular; jagged; notched; uneven;
差錯 (1) error; mistake; slip; (2) accident; mishap;
出錯 make mistakes;
舛錯 mishap; mixed up; uneven;
大錯 grave mistake;
犯錯 commit a blunder; commit a fault; commit a mistake; commit an error; do a fault; err; fall into a mistake; make a blunder; make a mistake; make a slip; make an error; mistake; pull a boner; slip a cog; slip up;
改錯 (1) correct a wrong character; (2) correct one's mistake;
搞錯 mistake;
攻錯 learn from others' strong points to offset one's weaknesses;
過錯 fault; mistake;
海錯 choice seafood; marine products; sea delicacies;
檢錯 error detection;
交錯 crisscross; entwine; interlace; interlock; intersect;
糾錯 amend an error; error correction; error recovery;
沒錯 (1) I'm quite sure; that's right; you can rest assured; (2) can't go wrong;
弄錯 make a mistake; misunderstand;
盤錯 (1) intertwining; (2) complex; complicated; intricate;
配錯 mismatch;
認錯 acknowledge a mistake; admit a fault; admit a mistake; climb-down; make an apology;
數錯 miscount;
説錯 speak incorrectly;
算錯 miscalculate;
挑錯 find fault; pick flaws;
聽錯 hear incorrectly;
位錯 dislocation;
小錯 little mistake; minor mistake;
鑄錯 commit blunders;
做錯 make mistakes;

da¹

da

【耷】 big ears;

［耷拉］ droop; hang down;

耷拉下頭 hang down one's head;
耷拉下眼皮 droop one's eyelids;
耷拉在水面上 droop over the water;
耷拉着臉 pull a long face;
耷拉着腦袋 droop one's head; hang one's head;

da

【答】 (1) answer; reply; respond; (2) reciprocate; return a visit;

［答理］ acknowledge; respond;

［答腔］ answer; respond;

［答應］ (1) answer; reply; respond; (2) accede to; agree; comply with; promise;

不答應 refuse; withhold one's consent;
~ 拒不答應 refuse firmly; refuse one's consent;
勉強答應 agree reluctantly; give a reluctant consent; promise reluctantly;
一口答應 consent without any lengthy deliberation; promise without hesitation; readily agree; readily comply with;
終於答應 finally consent;

巴答 sound of a slap;
滴答 drip; tick; ticktack; ticktock;
對答 answer; answer back; reply;
回答 reply; soft answer; answer; answer up; answer up to; in answer to; respond;
解答 answer; explain;
搶答 compete for the chance to answer;
濕答答 dripping wet;
問答 conversation; dialogue; questions and answers;
羞答答 bashful; shy;
應答 answer; answerback; reply; respond;
徵答 solicit answers to questions;
作答 answer; reply;

da

【搭】 (1) build; pitch; put up; (2) hang over; put over; (3) come into contact; join; (4) add; throw in more; (5) carry; lift sth up; (6) take; travel by;

［搭班］ (1) join a group temporarily in order to help in a task; (2) join a theatrical troup temporarily;

［搭伴］ (1) in company with; join sb on a trip; travel together; (2) partner;

［搭車］ (1) get a lift; give sb a lift; hitchhike; (2) do sth at the same time; do sth along with someone else;

搭便車 thumb a lift; thumb a ride;
搭車進城 get a lift to town;

［搭乘］ travel by...;

［搭檔］ (1) collaborate; cooperate; (2) partner; twosome;

黃金搭檔 best partner; golden pair;
老搭檔 old partner; old workmate;
雙人搭檔 duo; pair;
喜劇搭檔 comedy duo; comedy twosome;
一搭一檔 act hand in hand with sb; act in concert with sb; collaborate with each other;
一對搭檔 a pair; a twosome;
與人搭檔 partner with sb;
最佳搭檔 the best partner;

［搭蓋］ build; put up;

［搭伙］ (1) join as partner; (2) eat regularly in a place;

與人搭伙 form a partnership with sb; join sb in partnership;

［搭建］ build; put up;

［搭腳儿］ hitchhike;

［搭界］ (1) border on; (2) border; (3) have sth to do with;

［搭救］ rescue;

［搭客］ give sb a lift; passenger; take on passengers;

［搭扣］ hasp;

尼龍搭扣 Velcro;

［搭理］ acknowledge; answer; pay attention; respond; take heed;

［搭配］ (1) assort in pairs; arrange in groups; co-ordinate; combine; (2) collocation;

搭配衝突 collocational clash;
搭配詞 collocate;
搭配錯誤 collocational error;
搭配範圍 collocational range;
搭配可能性 collocational possibilities;
搭配限制 collocational restriction;
搭配意義 collocative meaning;
標準搭配 stock collocation;
常用搭配 commonly used collocation;
陳腐搭配 stock collocation;
封閉性搭配 closed collocation;
固定搭配 fixed collocation;

混合搭配 mix and match;
開放性搭配 open collocation;
內包搭配 inclusive collocation;
新搭配 new collocation;
[搭棚] (1) put up a shed; (2) build a scalfold; scalfolding;
搭棚工人 scalfolding builder;
[搭腔] (1) answer; respond; (2) talk to each other;
[搭橋] act as a go-between; bring both sides together; build bridges; mediate; put up a bridge;
搭橋鋪路 facilitate; pave the way for; remove obstacles;
搭橋牽線 bring both sides together; build bridges; mediate;
拉線搭橋 pull strings and make contacts;
[搭訕] chat up; strike up a conversation with sb;
[搭手] give a hand; help sb; render sb a service;
[搭售] make a tie-in sale;
[搭線] (1) make contact; (2) act as a go-between; act as a matchmaker;
搭錯線 make a mistake; misunderstand; wrong connection;
[搭載] carry; take on passengers;
白搭 fruitless; futile; have no use; in vain; no good; no use; of no use; spend effort in vain; to no purpose; useless;
擺搭 distinguish oneself; show off;
勾搭 (1) gang up with; (2) seduce;
花花搭搭 (1) diversified; (2) varied;
拉搭 chat; converse; talk;
配搭 accompany; supplement;

da
【嗒】 clatter;
[嗒嗒] clatter;
嗒嗒聲 clatter; strum;
~打字機的嗒嗒聲 the clatter of typewriters;

da
【褡】 (1) kerchief hung at the waist; (2) purse; tiny sack; (3) thin cloth;
[褡褳] pouch worn at the girdle;

da²
da
【打】 dozen;

da
【怛】 (1) distressed; grieved; (2) alarmed; shocked; surprised; (3) striving and toiling;
[怛怛] toiling and striving;
[怛化] (1) dead; die; (2) don't be shocked by death;
慘怛 grieved; heart-broken;

da
【妲】 a concubine of Zhou Xin, the last ruler of the Shang Dynasty;

da
【答】 (1) answer; reply; (2) reciprocate; return a visit;
[答案] answer; key; solution;
提供答案 furnish an answer; provide an answer; supply an answer;
正確答案 correct answer; true key;
[答拜] pay a return visit; return a courtesy call;
[答辯] reply in support of one's ideas; reply to a charge;
答辯權 right of reply;
口頭答辯 verbal defense;
~做口頭答辯 make verbal defense;
[答詞] answering speech; reply; speech in reply; thank-you speech;
[答對] answer; reply;
[答覆] answer; reply;
電話答覆 send an answer by telephone;
含糊的答覆 dubious answer; dubious reply;
簡短的答覆 brief answer; brief reply;
謹慎的答覆 cautious reply;
盡早答覆 make a reply as early as possible; reply at one's earliest convenience;
據理答覆 give a reasonable answer;
肯定的答覆 affirmative reply; affirmative response;
口頭答覆 answer orally; give an answer by word of mouth; oral reply;
立即答覆 immediate reply; prompt reply;
馬上答覆 reply immediately;
滿意的答覆 favourable reply;
明確的答覆 definite reply;
模糊兩可的答覆 ambiguous answer;
期待答覆 expect an answer; look forward

to the reply;
確定的答覆 confirmed reply;
閃爍其詞的答覆 evasive answer; evasive reply;
收到答覆 get a reply; have a reply; receive a reply;
書面答覆 written reply;
要求答覆 request a reply;
斬釘截鐵的答覆 categorical answer;

[答話] answer; reply;

[答卷] answer sheet;
完成答卷 complete an answer sheet in an examination;

[答禮] return a salute;

[答錄] answer and record;
答錄機 answering machine;
~多聲道答錄機 multichannel answering machine;
~立體聲答錄機 stereo answering machine;

[答謝] acknowledge; express appreciation; reciprocate; thank;

[答允] promise; undertake;

報答 repay; requite;
筆答 answer by writing in examination papers;
酬答 reciprocate;
對答 answer; reply;
回答 answer; reply;
解答 answer; explain;
問答 question and answer;
應答 answer; reply; respond;
贈答 present each other with gifts, poems, etc.;

da

【達】 (1) extend; (2) attain; amount to; reach; (3) understand thoroughly; (4) communicate; convey; deliver; express; (5) distinguished; eminent;

[達標] attain a designated standard; reach a set standard; up to the standard;

[達成] achieve; conclude; reach;
達成交易 strike a deal;
達成諒解 come to an understanding;
達成妥協 reach a compromise;
達成協議 reach an agreement;

[達旦] throughout the night; until dawn;

[達到] achieve; amount to; attain; reach; to the amount of;
達到標準 up to the mark; up to the scratch;
達到高潮 come to a climax; reach a high tide;
達到目標 achieve the goal; reach the aim;
~未達到目標 short of the goal;
達到目的 achieve one's end; attain the goal; gain one's end; win one's end;
達到水平 up to the standard;
達到指標 meet the target;
~未達到指標 fall short of the target;
有可能達到 be possible to reach;
逐步達到 work one's way through;

[達觀] optimistic; philosophical; take things philosophically;
達觀安命 take things as they come;

[達意] convey one's ideas; express one's ideas;
表情達意 express one's feeling or emotion;
詞不達意 one's word does not express one's idea; the expression does not convey the idea; the words cannot express the meaning; the words fail to convey the idea; words fail sb;
~詞不達意的 inarticulate;

諳達 be well-versed; be familiar;
表達 communicate; convey; express; voice; voice out;
佈達 notify;
暢達 fluent; smooth;
傳達 pass on; relay; transmit;
到達 arrival; arrive; arrive at; arrive in; get to; reach;
抵達 arrive; reach;
洞達 understand thoroughly;
發達 developed; flourishing; thriving;
放達 immoderate and unrestrained;
高達 reach up to; to the tune of;
豁達 broad-minded; open-minded; sanguine;
曠達 bighearted; broad-minded; open-minded;
雷達 radar;
練達 experienced and worldly-wise; mature and modest; reasonable;
遛達 stroll;
馬達 motor;
明達 reasonable; showing understanding;
窮達 obscurity or eminence; remain obscure or become distinguished;
任達 unrestrained;
上達 reach the higher authorities;
送達 deliver to; dispatch to; send to;
騰達 (1) rise; soar; (2) promote to high status; rise to power and position;

條達 (1) logical; orderly; reasonable; (2) bracelet;
通達 understand;
聞達 eminent; famous and influential; illustrious;
下達 make known to lower levels; transmit to lower levels;
先達 elder leaders;
賢達 prominent personage; the social elite; wise and virtuous; worthy;
顯達 achieve prominence in officialdom; attain high office; illustrious and influential;
直達 direct; nonstop; through;
轉達 communicate; convey; mediate; pass on; refer; transmit through another person;

da

【靼】 Tartars;

da

【韃】 Tartars;

[韃靼醬] deck out; tartare sauce;

da³

da

【打】 (1) beat; bop; hit; knock; strike; (2) break; smash; (3) attack; fight; (4) build; construct; (5) forge; make; (6) beat; mix; stir; (7) pack; tie up; (8) knit; weave; (9) draw; paint; (10) spray; spread; (11) bore; dig; open; (12) hoist; raise; (13) dispatch; emit; give out; project; send; (14) issue; (15) get rid of; remove; (16) draw; ladle; (17) collect; gather in; (18) buy; obtain; (19) catch; hunt; (20) calculate; estimate; reckon; (21) work out; (22) do; engage in; (23) play; (24) adopt; use; (25) from; since;

[打靶] practise shooting; rifle practice; target shooting practice;
練習打靶 practise shooting at a target; target practice;

[打擺子] have malaria; suffer from malaria;

[打敗] (1) beat; defeat; worst; (2) be defeated; fail; lose; suffer a defeat;
打敗敵人 defeat the enemy;
打敗敵手 defeat the opponent;
打敗仗 suffer a defeat;
徹底打敗 trounce;

[打扮] deck out; dress; dress up; makeover; make up;
打扮成…be dressed as; dress as; dress oneself up as;
~打扮成工人 be dressed as a worker;
打扮得非常漂亮的 dressed to kill;
打扮入棺材一死要面子 make up before getting in one's coffin – concerned about one's"face";
打扮整潔 brush up; neatly dressed;
精心打扮 delicate makeover;
梳洗打扮 dress up with hair dressing and bathing; freshen up;
~梳洗打扮完畢 complete freshening up;
~梳洗打扮一番 freshen oneself up;

[打包] (1) bale; bundle up; pack; (2) unpack;
打包袋 doggy bag;
打包工 packer; packing worker;
打包機 packaging machine;
打包票 guarantee; vouch;

[打比] compare; draw an analogy; make an analogy;

[打草驚蛇] act rashly and alert the enemy; beat the grass and drive the snake away; shake the bush to rouse the serpent; stir the grass and alarm the snake; to fright a bird is not the way to catch it; wake a sleeping wolf;

[打叉] cross;

[打岔] cut in; interrupt a conversation;
惱人的打岔 annoying interruption;

[打場] thresh grain; threshing;

[打車] by taxi; hail a cab; take a taxi;

[打打談談] fight and talk alternately;

[打蛋器] hand blender; hand mixer; whisk;

[打倒] down with; knock down; overthrow;
打倒法西斯 down with fascism;

[打道] clear the way;
打道回府 direct one's step toword home;

[打的] take a taxi; travel by taxi;

[打點] (1) get one's belongings ready; get ready; (2) offer a bribe; present a gift;

[打掉] destroy; drive out; eliminate; knock out; wipe out;

[打動] arouse one's feelings; move; touch;
雷打不動 determined; firm; not to be altered under any circumstances; unshakable; unyielding;

[打鬥] beating; brawl; dust-up; exchange blows; fight; fight and quarrel; tussle;
激烈的打鬥 fierce fighting;
女人之間的打鬥 catfight;

［打賭］ accept a bet; accept a wager; bet; betting; have a bet with sb; lay a wager on; lay a wager with sb; make a bet with sb; make a wager; risk money on sth; take up a bet; take up a wager; wager;
　我敢打賭 I dare to bet; I'll wager;
　喜歡打賭 fond of betting;
［打斷］ (1) break; break-in; heckle; (2) interrupt;
　打斷話頭 interrupt sb;
　打斷思路 interrupt sb's train of thought;
［打盹］ catch forty winks; doze off; nod off; snatch forty winks; take a nap;
［打呃］ hiccough; hiccup;
［打發］ (1) dispatch; send; (2) dismiss; send away; (3) while away;
　打發時光 kill time;
　打發時間 while away one's time;
［打翻］ overturn;
　打翻船 overturn a boat;
　打翻在地 beat sb down; knock down;
［打分］ (1) grade; (2) mark;
［打嗝］ burp; get hiccups; have hiccups; hiccup;
　使嬰兒打嗝 burp;
［打工］ be employed;
　打工妹 young female labourer;
　打工仔 employee; worker;
［打躬作揖］ beg humbly; bow and greet sb; do obeisance; fold the hands and make deep bows; make a deep bow; make an obeisance; salute with clasped hands; salute with folded hands again and again;
［打鈎］ tick;
　打鈎號 tick;
［打狗］ beat a dog;
　打狗看主人 in beating a dog you must consider who is the owner;
　打狗欺主 to beat the dog is to bully its owner; to humiliate the protected is to humiliate the protector;
　投石打狗 throw a stone at a dog;
［打鼓］ (1) beat a drum; drumming; play the drum; (2) feel nervous; feel uncertain;
　心裏直打鼓 one's heart is thrumping rapidly;
［打滾］ roll on the ground;
　滿地打滾 roll over and over on the floor;
　痛得打滾 tumble and toss from pain; write with pain;
　在草地上打滾 roll about on the grass;
［打鼾］ snore;
［打活結］ slipknot; tie a fast knot;
［打火］ ignite; kindle; light; strike a light;
　打火機 cigarette lighter; lighter;
［打擊］ attack; blow; crack down; deal a blow; hit; strike;
　打擊別人，抬高自己 attack others so as to build up oneself;
　打擊犯罪 crack down on crimes; fight against the crime;
　打擊名單 hit list; strike list;
　打擊貪污 hit out against corruption;
　沉重打擊 hammer blow; hard blow; hit badly; hit hard; terrible blow;
　給予嚴重打擊 strike a serious blow at;
　受到意外打擊 get an unexpected blow;
　雙重打擊 double whammy;
　先發制人的打擊 first strike;
　一陣打擊 a hail of blows;
［打家劫舍］ commit house robbery in packs; go in all directions to loot; loot; pillage and rob; plunder; raid and pillage; raid homes and plunder houses;
［打假］ anti-fake;
　打假運動 anti-fake campaign;
［打架］ come to blows; engage in a brawl; fall to cuffs; fight; go to cuffs;scuffle;
　打架鬥毆 exchange blows; fight against one another;
　打群架 engage in a gang fight; gangster fight;
［打漿］ beat; beating;
　打漿機 beater;
　～多輥打漿機 multiroll beater;
　～連續打漿機 continuous beater;
　～實驗室打漿機 experimental beater;
　～雙盤打漿機 duplex beater;
　濕打漿 wet beating;
［打攪］ (1) break; disturb; interrupt; (2) bother; trouble;
［打劫］ loot; plunder; rob;
　趁火打劫 commit robbery in the confusion of a fire; fish in troubled waters; loot a burning house; plunder a burning house; rob the owner while his house is on fire; take advantage of

sb's misfortune to do him harm;
乘火打劫 take advantage of a conflagration to loot a burning house; take advantage of sb's misfortune to do him harm;

[打緊] critical; matter; serious;
不打緊 do not matter;

[打進] make one's way into;

[打井] sink a well;

[打卡] clock; punch a card;
打卡上班 clock in; clock on; punch in;
打卡下班 clock out; punch out;
上下班打卡 clock in and out; punch in and out; punch the clock;

[打開] (1) open; unfold; untie; (2) switch on; turn on; (3) break through; (4) broaden; open up; spread; widen;
打開包裹 open up a package;
打開出路 break through an encirclement; fight a way out;
打開地圖 open out the map;
打開話匣子 begin to talk; plunge into one's spiel; start a conversation; turn on the gas;
打開僵局 break the deadlock; break the ice; break the impasse; bring the deadlock to the end; find a way out of a stalemate; find solution for a problem;
打開局面 open up a new prospect;
打開門 open the door;
打開缺口 make a breach;
打開書本 open the book;
打開天窗説亮話 come out flat-footed; frankly speaking; have a frank talk; have a straight talk; place all one's cards on the table; let's be frank and put our cards on the table; let's not mince matters; not to mince matters; speak out without the slightest hesitation; talk frankly without hedging about; talk turkey;
此處打開 open here;
強行打開 open by force;

[打孔] punch a hole;
打孔機 puncher;

[打跨] completely defeat; crush;

[打捆] bale; bind;
打捆裝置 baling apparatus; binding apparatus;

[打拉] strike and stroke;
又打又拉 strike and stroke alternately; use the stick and the carrot, either alternately or simultaneously;

[打撈] get out of water; salvage;
打撈沉船 salvage a sunken ship;
打撈船 salvage ship;
打撈費用 salvage charges;
打撈公司 salvage company;

[打雷] thunder;
乾打雷不下雨 all talk and no cider; all thunder but no rain — much noise but no action;
光打雷不下雨 all bark and no bite; all thunder and no storm; all words and no actions;

[打愣兒] in a daze; in a trance; stare blankly;

[打量] (1) look sb up and down; measure with the eye; size up; take the measure of sb; (2) reckon; suppose; think;
打量人 look sb up and down;

[打獵] hunting;
愛好打獵 fond of hunting;
去打獵 go hunting;

[打亂] disorganize; disrupt; throw into confusion; upset;
打亂計劃 disturb a plan; upset a plan; upset a scheme;
打亂交通秩序 dislocate the traffic;
打亂課堂 disturb the class;

[打馬虎眼] act dumb;

[打罵] beat and scold; maltreatment;
打人罵人 beat or scold sb; hit and swear at people; strike and curse sb;
動輒打罵 beat sb and swear at him on the least pretext;
連打帶罵 scold and beat sb at the same time; with both beating and cursing;
又打又罵 beat and curse at the same time;

[打磨] burnish; polish; shine;

[打鬧] kick up a row; quarrel and fight noisily;
打打鬧鬧 boisterous; fight in jest;
小打小鬧 fight on a small scale;

[打牌] (1) play cards; (2) play mahjong;

[打…牌] play the card;
打環保主義牌 play the environmentalism card;
打民族主義牌 play the nationalism card;
打種族牌 play the race card;

[打跑] beat away;

打跑敵人 drive away the enemy;

[打拼] try one's utmost to do sth;

敢打敢拼 dare to fight and dare to have a trail of strength; dare to fight and dare to risk all; dare to fight and dare to take on the enemy;

[打平] draw; draw a tie;

[打破] (1) break; smash; (2) break away from;

打破常規 break away from conventions; break the normal procedure; break the routine; off the beaten track;

打破沉默 break the hush;

打破醋壇子 break the jar of vinegar — burn with jealousy;

打破藩籬 break through hedging-in traditions;

打破飯碗 lose one's job; unemployed;

打破慣例 break fresh ground; break new ground;

打破寂靜 break in upon the silence of;

打破記錄 beat the record; break the record; cut the record; set a new record;

打破僵局 break a deadlock; break the ice; break the stalemate; find a way out of a stalemate;

打破界線 break down barriers;

打破框框 break away from conventions;

打破了五味瓶兒—說不出甚麼味道 breaking a Chinese five-spice bottle — can't tell what flavour it is; (fig) mixed feelings;

打破壟斷 break up a monopoly;

打破迷信 destroy superstitutions;

打破平衡 upset a balance;

打破前例 depart from precedents;

打破情面 do not attempt to spare anybody's feelings;

打破缺口 drive a wedge; make a breach; make a breakthrough;

打破沙鍋問到底 breaking an earthenware pot and it cracks to the bottom — insisting on getting to the bottom of sth; get to the bottom of sth; inquisitive; insist on getting to the bottom of a matter; keep on asking questions till one gets to the bottom of a matter; wish to know every detail of sth; interrogate thoroughly;

打破世界記錄 break the world record;

打破束縛 break the bondage of...;

打破自己飯碗 lose one's job;

[打氣] (1) inflate; pump up; (2) bolster up the morale; boost the morale; cheer up; encourage;

打氣撐腰 brace and bolster; encourage and support;

打氣筒 pump;

撐腰打氣 bolster and pep up; bolster and support; in an effort to back up;

為己隊打氣 root one's team on;

[打槍] fire with a pistol;

[打情罵俏] coquet with sb; flirt with; joke between a young couple; tease one's lover by showing false displeasure; trifle with sb in love;

[打球] play a ball game;

打球出界 overdriving, over-hitting a shot;

打球落網 net the ball;

[打趣] banter; make fun of; tease;

[打拳] box; practise boxing; shadow boxing;

[打擾] disturb; trouble;

恕我打擾 excuse me; pardon;

[打人] hit people; strike people;

嘴打人 abuse people; hurt sb with sarcastic language; ridicule people; slander people;

[打入] (1) banish to; throw into; (2) infiltrate;

打入地下 be driven underground;

打入牢獄 throw sb into prison;

打入冷宮 banish to the cold palace; be left out in the cold; consign to the back shelf; fallen into disfavour; out of favour; out in the cold; put on the back shelf; turn out in the cold;

打入悶葫蘆 throw into bewilderment;

打入十八層地獄 banish sb to the uttermost depths of hell; banish to the lowest depths of hell; condemn to eternal damnation; shut sb in the eighteenth hell;

[打散] break up; scatter; thrashing;

[打傘] hold an umbrella;

[打掃] clean up; sweep;

打掃塵土 sweep out the dust;

打掃房間 clean a room;

打掃垃圾 sweep away rubbish;

[打閃] (1) lightning; (2) flash through one's mind;

[打蛇打七吋] cut sb to the quick; hit where it hurts; touch sb's tender spot;

[打勝] bear off the palm; beat; best; carry off the palm; carry the day; conquer; defeat; down; gain the victory over; get sb down; get the better of sb; have it on sb; have it over sb; have the best of it; have the scale of; pervail over; put a head on sb; put to rout; triump over; win; win the day;
打勝仗 victorious; win a war;

[打食] (1) hunt for food; seek food; (2) help to digest and excrete; relieve indigestion with a drug;

[打手] bully; hatchet man; hired thug; hired roughneck; muscleman;

[打水漂兒] pay out, but get nothing in return; play ducks and drakes; spend in vain; with no result;

D

[打死] (1) beat to death; (2) shoot to death; (3) dispatch; (4) kill; (5) stop; (6) smite sb dead;
打死結 tie a tight knot;
一棍子打死 finish sb off with a single blow; kill with a blow; knock sb down at one stroke; shatter at one stroke;

[打算] (1) be going to; intend; have a mind to; mean; plan; think; (2) calculation; consideration;
打算盤 (1) calculate on an abacus; (2) calculating; frugal; good at budgeting;
各有打算 each has his own axe to grind; each has his own calculations; each has his own objective to pursue; each has a plan of his own; each seeks his own ends;
精打細算 accurate count; accurate in calculation; budget strictly; careful and meticulous calculation; careful calculation and strict budgeting; count every cent and make every cent count; meticulous in planning; run it fine; very careful in reckoning;
另有打算 have other plans;
另有個人打算 have a purpose of one's own; have an axe to grind;
另作打算 make some other plans; seek some other ways;
滿打滿算 at the very most; be fully prepared to;
沒有個人打算 with no consideration of personal interest;
為國家利益打算 further the interests of the state;
為自己打算 further one's own interests; take care of number one;
做最壞的打算 be prepared for the worst;

[打碎] batter; break into pieces; pound; smash;

[打胎] have an abortion;

[打探] ask about; inquire about; investigate; reconnoitre;
打探敵情 reconnoitre the enemy's position;
打探軍情 elicit military information;
打探虛實 ascertain the actual situation;

[打鐵] forge iron; work as a blacksmith;
打鐵趁熱 make hay while the sun shines; strike while the iron's hot;
趁熱打鐵 hoist sail while the wind is fair; make hay while the sun shines; strike while the iron is hot; take time by the forelock;

[打聽] ask about; find out; get a line on; inquire about;
打聽消息 ask for information; nose about for information;
挨家打聽 make enquiries from door to door;
愛打聽 (1) snoopy; (2) inquisitive; inquitorial;
到處打聽 nose about everywhere;

[打通] (1) break through; get through; open up; (2) dispel;
打通電話 get through on the phone;
打通關節 break through key links; bribe officials in charge;

[打頭] (1) take the lead; (2) from the beginning;
打頭砲 fire the first shot; lead the attack; take the lead; the first to act; the first to speak;
打頭陣 fight in the van; spearhead the attack; take the lead;

[打退] beat back; beat off; repulse;
打退堂鼓 back down; back out; back up before sth is finished; beat a retreat; chicken out; cry off; draw back; fink out; give up; haul in one's horns; retreat; take the water; withdraw from;

[打網] weave a net;

[打問] interrogate with torture; torture sb during interrogation;

[打響] (1) begin to fire; fire; open fire; start shooting; (2) get off to a good start; make a good start; win initial success;
打響頭砲 get a good start;
打響指 snap one's fingers;
槍未打響 the gun failed to shoot off;
一砲打響 make an instantaneous hit; successful for one's first attempt;

[打消] dispel; get rid of; give up; remove;
打消顧慮 dispel misgivings;
打消念頭 dismiss the idea; drop the idea; give up the idea;

[打牙涮嘴] chat; tattle;

[打眼] (1) catch the eye; draw attention; (2) beautiful; good-looking; (3) drill; punch a hole;

[打烊] close the store for the night;
打烊時間 closing time;

[打印] chop; print; printing; stamp;
打印機 printer; stamper;
~併行打印機 parallel printer;
~串行打印機 serial printer;
~帶式打印機 belt printer;
~單作用打印機 single action printer;
~點式打印機 dot printer;
~點陣打印機 array printer; dot printer; dot-matrix printer;
~電傳打印機 teleprinter; teletypewriter;
~飛擊式打印機 hit-on-the-fly printer;
~飛輪打印機 flying wheel printer;
~桿式打印機 bar printer;
~鼓式打印機 drum printer;
~行式打印機 line printer;
~激光打印機 laser printer;
~擊打式打印機 impact printer;
－非擊
－打式打印機 non-impact printer;
~鍵盤打印機 keyboard printer;
~矩陣式打印機 matrix printer;
~快速打印機 rapid printer;
~噴墨打印機 inkjet printer;
~輸出打印機 output printer;
~豎式打印機 column printer;
~數字打印機 numeric printer;
~數字記錄打印機 number record printer;
~頁式打印機 page printer;
~針式打印機 dot matrix printer;
~智能打印機 intelligent printer;
~字符打印機 character printer;
~字輪式打印機 flying drum printer;
~字盤式打印機 flying disk printer;
~終端打印機 terminal printer;
~自動打印機 automatic stamper;
打印色帶 copying ribbon;
存儲打印 storage printing;
矩陣式打印 matrix printing;
末端打印 end printing;
自動打印 automatic printing;

[打油詩] doggerel; ragged verse;
五行打油詩 limerick;

[打雜] do odds and ends; fix up odds and ends; serve as handy man;
打雜的人 dogsbody;

[打戰] shiver; shudder; tremble;
渾身打戰 shiver all over;
全身打戰 shiver all over;

[打仗] fight; fight a battle; go to war; make war;
打嘴仗 argue; dispute;
準備打仗 get ready for a war;

[打針] give an injection; have an injection;

[打中] hit; hit the mark; hit the target;
打中靶心 hit the bull's eye;
打中要害 deal a blow at the heart; hit home; hit on the vital spot; hit the mark; hit the right nail on the head; hit where it really hurts; press home; strike home; touch...to the quick; the thrust goes home;
沒打中 miss the market; miss the target; shoot beside the mark;

[打住] bring to a halt; hold on; stop;

[打轉] revolve; rotate; spin; turn round and round;

[打字] type; typewrite;
打字本 typescript;
打字錯誤 typing error;
打字打得好 type well;
打字機 typer; typewriter;
~電傳打字機 teleprinter;
~起止式電傳打字機 start-stop teleprinter;
~新聞電傳打字機 journal teleprinter;
~頁式電傳打字機 page teleprinter;
~電動打字機 electric typewriter;
~高速打字機 high-speed typewriter;
~通用打字機 general typer;
~語音打字機 phonetic typewriter;
~自動打字機 automatic typewriter;
打字員 typist;
打字組 typing pool;

[打坐] sit in meditation;

挨打 be buffeted; be beaten up; come under attack; deserve a beating; get a beating; get a thrashing; hit by someone; suffer a beating; take a beating;
半打 half a dozen; six;
鞭打 lash; thrash; whip;
抽打 (1) flog; lash; slash; thrash; whip; (2) remove dust with a towel;
吹打 play wind and percussion instruments;
捶打 beat; thump;
錘打 strike with a hammer;
單打 singles;
毒打 beat cruelly; beat savagely; beat sb up;
對打 trade blows;
攻打 assault; attack;
開打 acrobatic fight performance in Chinese opera;
拷打 beat; torture;
磕打 knock out; knock sth out of a vessel;
每打 every dozen;
扭打 grapple; wrestle;
毆打 beat up; exchange blows; hit;
拍打 beat; flutter; pat; slap;
撲打 (1) swat; (2) beat; pat;
敲打 (1) beat; knock; percuss; rap; strike; tap; (2) say sth to irritate sb;
拳打 strike with fists;
摔打 (1) beat; knock; (2) experience hardship; rough it; temper oneself;
雙打 doubles;
廝打 come to blows; fight each other with fists;
撕打 beat up; maul;
蘇打 soda;
鐵打 made-of-iron;
痛打 beat mercilessly;
武打 acrobatic fighting in Chinese opera;
相打 have a fight;
一打 a dozen;
由打 since;
責打 mete out corporal punishment; punish by flogging or lashing;
招打 invite a spanking;
找打 pick a fight;

da⁴
da

【大】 (1) big; great; large; (2) heavy; loud; strong; (3) general; major; (4) size; (5) age; old; (6) fully; greatly; (7) eldest; (8) elderly person; senior generation;
［大巴］ coach; large bus;
［大白］ become known; come out;
大白菜 Chinese cabbage;
［大敗］ (1) defeat utterly; put to rout; (2) debacle; suffer a crushing defeat;
大敗而回 suffer a crushing defeat;
大敗而逃 suffer defeat and run away;
［大板］ plank;
各打五十大板 blame both sides without discrimination; punish the innocent and the guilty alike; punish the wronged and the wrongdoer alike;
［大半］ (1) most likely; most probably; very likely; (2) for the most part; more than half; mostly; the best part of; the greater part of;
大半輩子 in the midst of life;
一大半 the better part of;
［大辦］ go in for sth in a big way;
［大包］ bale;
大包小包 with big parcels and small bags;
滾大包 steal luggage;
［大本營］ (1) headquarters; (2) base camp; home base;
［大筆］ (1) a large sum; (2) pen;
大筆的錢 a large amount of money;
大筆一揮 make a stroke with a pen; with a stroke of the pen;
［大便］ (1) defecate; dump; egest; empty the bowels; evacuate one's bowels; go boom-boom; go number two; go potty; have a bowel movement; loose bowels; make little soldiers; move the bowels; relieve oneself; relieve the bowels; shit; sit on the throne; take a shit; the bowel moves; void excrement; (2) faeces; human excrement; shit; stool; turd;
大便不通 be constipated; suffer from constipation;
大便不正常 irregular bowel movements;
大便成形 motions are well-formed;
大便乾燥 (sb's bowel motions) hard and dry;
大便困難 (1) have difficulty in passing stools; (2) dyschezia;
大便失禁 be unable to hold one's motions; faecal incontinence;
大便小便一起來一雙管齊下 both methods are adopted; defecating and urinating at the same time – doing two things at the same time;

大便正常 normal bowels movement;
按時大便 have regular bowel movements;
解大便 relieve oneself; relieve the bowel;
驗大便 stool test;
要大便 the bowels are open; the bowels move;

[大兵] soldier;

[大病] serious illness;
大病不死 give sb a new lease of life;
大病初愈 have just got over a grave illness;
大病新愈 just recovered from a serious illness;
得了大病 contract a serious illness;
患大病 suffer from a serious illness;

[大伯] (1) father's elder brother; uncle; (2) uncle (a polite from of address for an elderly man);

[大不謂然] definitely regard it as wrong; hold entirely different views; disagree strongly;

[大步] stride;
大步流星 with vigorous strides;
大步跑 run with long steps;
~笨拙地大步跑 lollop;
~輕鬆地大步跑 lope;
大步向…走去 stride toward sb;
一大步 a stride;

[大部] greater part;

[大才] great talent;
大才小用 a capable person in a job too small for his talents; a large material for petty use; an able man given a small job; cut blocks with a razor; employ a steam-engine to crack a nut; misuse of fine materials; put fine timber to petty use; shoot sparrows with artillery; use a steam-engine to crack a nut; use talented people for trivial tasks; waste of talent; waste one's talent on a petty job;
小才大用 a man of little ability in high capacity; give great responsibility to a man of common ability;

[大腸] large bowels; large intestines;
大腸癌 colorectal cancer;
大腸熱結 heat-evil accumulating in the large intestine;
大腸炎 inflammation of the large intestine;

[大吵] make a great hue;
大吵大鬧 barney; create a noisy disurbance; create a scene; cut up bad; cut up nasty; cut up rough; cut up savage; cut up stiff; cut up ugly; have a big row with sb; kick up a fuss; kick up a row; kick up a shine; kick up a stink; make a great wrangle and quarrel; make a hell of a noise; make a scene; make a stink; make a tremendous row; make the feathers fly; raise a big uproar; raise a hue and cry; raise Cain; raise havoc; raise hell; raise the devil; raise the roof; yell bloody murder;
大吵大嚷 bluster; clamour; make a great hue and cry;
大吵一場 falling-out;

[大臣] minister;

[大乘] mahayana; the great vehicle;

[大吃] eat eagerly; eat like a horse;
大吃敗仗 meet one's Waterloo;
大吃大喝 eat and drink immoderately; eat and drink to one's heart's content; excessive feasting; extravagant; make a pig of oneself; on the spree; overeating and overdrinking; pig out; spendthrift in feasting;
大吃一頓 (1) stoke; (2) have a square meal; on the spree;
大吃一驚 be astounded at; be given quite a turn; be greatly shocked; be greatly surprised; be knocked into the middle of next week; be startled at; be struck all of a heap; be taken aback; be taken completely by surprise; get a shock; jump out of one's skin; take fright at;

[大蟲] tiger;
大蟲吃小蟲 the strong bullying the weak;

[大處] (1) general goal; (2) key points;
大處落墨 concentrate on the key points; concentrate on the major problems; keep the general goal in view; lay hand on the main thing; pay attention to the important points; write on the key points;
大處著墨 write on the key points;
大處着眼 far-sighted; keep the general goal in sight; pay attention to the important points;
~從大處着眼，從小處入手 keep the general goal in view and pay attention to the details;

[大錯] grave mistake;
大錯不犯，小錯不斷 never commit serious mistakes, but have had a continuance of little faults;
大錯特錯 absolutely wrong; all wet; all wrong; as wrong as wrong can be; be gravely mistaken; be grievously mistaken; can hardly be more mistaken; commit a grave error; completely mistaken; far from being in the right; make a big mistake; make a gross error; off base; totally wrong; wide of the mark;
犯大錯 commit a gross error; make a big mistake;

[大大] enormously; greatly;
大大不然 it is quite another story;
大大超過 make rings round;
大大地 by a long way;
大大方方 frank and open; in excellent taste; very natural and poised;
大大咧咧 careless; casual;
大大小小 big or small;
大喝大嚼 eat and drink one's fill;

[大膽] audacious; bold; daring; have a nerve;
大膽嘗試 make a bold trial; take a long shot;
大膽潑辣 bold and vigorous; termagant;

[大刀] broadsword;
大刀闊斧 bold and resolute; boldly and resolutely; cut the Gordian knot; deal with a matter summarily without regard to details; doing sth in a big way; drastic; handle without gloves; handle without mittens; make bold decisions; make drastic measures; make snap decisions; put the axe in the helve;
大刀闊斧的改革 sweeping changes;
關公門前耍大刀 brandishing the sword before Guan Gong the master swordsman; show off before an expert; teaching one's grandmother how to suck eggs;

[大盜] robber;
江洋大盜 big pirate; highway robber; infamous robber;

[大道] avenue; broad road; main road;
康莊大道 bright road; broad highroad; broad highway; broad road;
林蔭大道 boulevard; tree-lined avenue;
陽關大道 straight and easy road;
拐上大道 turn to the highroad;
修大道 build an arterial road; make an arterial road;
走大道 follow the main road; take the main road;

[大德] great favours; great virtue;
大德不酬 great favours need not be requited;
深感大德 your great virtue is deeply engraved on my heart;
深銘大德 your great virtue is deeply engraved on my memory;

[大敵] archenemy; formidable enemy;
大敵當前 be confronted with a formidable enemy; be faced with a formidable foe; be faced with powerful enemies; face a formidable enemy; in the face of archenemies; with a formidable enemy right in front;
如臨大敵 as if confronted by a mortal enemy; as if faced with a formidable enemy; as if one were facing a formidable enemy; be prepared for any eventualities; like confronting a dangerous enemy; on one's guard for all possible dangers; take undue alarm;

[大抵] generally speaking; in the main; mostly; on the whole;

[大地] earth; mother earth; world;
大地測量學 geodesy;
大地春雷 like a clap of spring thunder shaking the earth;
大地構造學 geotectology;
大地回春 nature's resurrection in the spring; spring has arrived; spring is here again; spring returns to the earth; the first flush of spring;
春回大地 spring has come back to the earth; spring returns to the good earth;
~春回大地，萬象更新 spring comes round to the earth again and everything looks fresh and joyful;

[大典] grand ceremony;

[大殿] (1) audience hall; (2) main hall;

[大跌] crash; serious fall;

[大豆] soya bean;

[大都] for the most part; mostly;
大都如此 generally so;

[大度] magnanimous;
大度包容 magnanimous and tolerant;

great tolerance;
大度的 big-hearted;
豁達大度 generous; magnanimous; open-minded;

[大端] main aspects; main features; salient points;

[大隊] department;
刑偵大隊 crime inspection department;
巡警大隊 patrol police department;

[大多] for the most part; mostly;
大多數 the bulk; the great majority; the vast majority;
~團結大多數 unite with the great majority;
~佔大多數 in the great majority;

[大恩] meritorious deeds;
忘人大恩，記人小過 always forget meritorious deeds, and never overlook a minor fault;

[大而化之] do things carelessly; in a careless way; with little care and caution in doing work;

[大而無當] big but useless; large but impractical; unwieldy;

[大法] charter; fundamental law;
大法官 grand justice;

[大凡] generally; in most cases;

[大方] (1) carry oneself with ease and grace; natural; natural and poised; (2) generous; liberal; liberality; (3) in good taste; tasteful;
大方一點 be a sport; be more generous;
出手大方 generous;
穿着大方 dress in a graceful and elegant way; dress in good taste;
典雅大方 elegant and graceful;
風度大方 have an easy manner;
舉止大方 have an easy manner; natural and poised;
落落大方 dignified manners; natural and self-confident;
美觀大方 beautiful and dignified;
式樣大方 graceful in style;
用錢大方 openhanded;

[大風] gale; strong wind;
大風暴 blowdown; storm; tempest;
~大風暴肆虐 the storm runs over;
~頂住大風暴 withstand the heavy storm;
大風大浪 (1) great storms; wind and waves; (2) turbulence; upheaval;
刮大風 the wind blows hard;
一陣大風 a gale; a gust of wind;

[大副] chief officer; first mate;

[大腹便便] abdominous; as plump as a partridge; as round as a barrel; barrel-bellied; beef to the heels; big-bellied; fat and heavy belly; large belly; paunchy; potbellied; with a big belly; with a pot belly;

[大概] (1) broad outline; general idea; (2) approximate; generally; likely; more or less; most likely; or something; probably; rough;

[大綱] general outline; outline;
教學大綱 teaching programme;

[大哥] (1) eldest brother; (2) elder brother; (3) brothers;
大哥大 (1) cellular phone; mobile phone; (2) older brother;
老大哥 Big Brother;

[大功] extraordinary service; great merit;
大功告成 a project accomplished; be brought to successful conclusion; be crowned with success; ring the bell; the task is accomplished;
立下大功 make outstanding achievements;

[大狗] towser;

[大官] high-ranking official;

[大觀] grand sight; magnificent spectacle;
蔚為大觀 a sight to see; afford a magnificent view; present a splendid sight;

[大鍋] huge pot;
大鍋飯 excessive egalitarianism; reward all equally regardless of their productivity;
~吃大鍋飯 eat from the same communal pot;
~打破大鍋飯 break up a communal pot;
什錦大鍋 a casserole with different meat and vegetable;

[大國] great power; leading power; power;
超級大國 superpower;
經濟大國 econmic giant;

[大過] senior offense;
犯大過 commit a serious offense;

[大海] blue water; ocean; sea;
大海撈針 dredge for a needle in the sea; fish a needle out of the sea; fish for a

D

needle in the ocean; locate a needle at the bottom of the sea; look for a needle in a haystack; look for a needle in the ocean; search for a pin on the ocean bed;
大海怒濤 the sea throws up angry billows;
大海無垠 the sea is boundless;
被沖入大海 be swept out to sea;
濱臨大海 on the brink of the sea;
飛越大海 fly over the ocean;
橫渡大海 cross the sea;
橫跨大海 cross the ocean;
葬身大海 be lost at sea;
石沉大海 like a stone dropped into the sea; without a trace;

[大汗] profuse perspiration;
大汗淋漓 be drenched in sweat; drip sweat; sweat profusely;

[大旱] severe drought;
大旱逢甘露 rain falls in time of great drought;

[大漢] big fellow; burly fellow; hefty fellow;
梢長大漢 tall and big fellow;

[大好] beautiful; excellent; very good;
大好風光 charming scenery;
大好河山 beautiful rivers and mountains of a country; one's beloved motherland;
大好人 very good person;
大好時光 one's prime of life;
大好時機 finest hour; golden opportunity; high time; just the time for; opportune moment;
大好形勢 exceedingly favourable situation; excellent situation;

[大號] (1) large size; (2) bass horn; (3) your name;

[大河] (1) great river; (2) Yellow River;

[大亨] big shot; biggie; bigwig; magnate; mogul; tycoon;
傳媒業大亨 media mogul;
電影業大亨 movie mogul;
賭博業大亨 gambling mogul;

[大紅] bright red; royal scarlet; scarlet;
大紅大綠 gaudy; gaudy and showy; loud colours;
大紅大紫 celebrated; famous; well-known;

[大戶] (1) rich and influential family; (2) big family;
吃大戶 eat at the great households;

[大話] big talk; hot air; tall talk; boast; bragging;
説大話 boast; brag; draw a long bow; talk big; talk tall; talk through one's hat; talk wet; tell exaggerated stories;

[大會] general meeting; mass meeting;
大會代表 conventioneer;
教師大會 teachers' convention;
全國大會 national convention;

[大夥兒] everybody; we all; you all;

[大火] big fire; conflagration;

[大禍] calamity; disaster; great misfortune;
大禍臨頭 a great calamity is impending over sb; be faced with imminent disaster; disaster is hanging over sb; disaster is imminent;
闖下大禍 cause a great misfortune; make a fatal mistake; make a gross mistake;
潑天大禍 overwhelming disaster;

[大吉] (1) auspicious; (2) straightaway;
溜之大吉 beat a hasty retreat; give leg bail; make a bolt for it; make oneself scare; seek safety in flight; show a clean pair of heels; show one's heels; sling one's hook; slink away; slink off; slope off; sneak away; take it on the lam; take one's heels; take to sb's heels; take to sb's legs; top one's boom;

[大計] matter of fundamental importance;
大計小用 great scheme has only a poor result;
百年大計 important task for centuries to come;
磋商大計 discuss a major plan;
共商大計 discuss matters of vital importance;

[大家] (1) all; all and sundry; everybody; (2) we; (3) all the world and his wife; (4) authority; great master; (5) noble family;
大家閨秀 daughter of an eminent family; girl from a respectable family; young lady of a noble family;
大家庭 big family;
大家小戶 all families, rich or poor;
書法大家 great master of calligraphy;
文學大家 master in literature;

[大江] (1) great river; (2) Yangzi River;
大江不捨細流 the river takes in water from streams;

[大將] (1) senior general; (2) high-ranking military officer;
大將風度 style of a great general;
蜀中無大將，廖化作先鋒 among the blind the one-eyed man is king; in the country of the blind, the one-eyed man is king;

[大腳] big foot;
托大腳 flatter;

[大叫] (1) yell; (2) ululate;
大叫大嚷 bawl and shout; cry at the top of one's voice; make a fuss about; raise a hue and cry;
大叫救命 yell for help;
大叫一聲 give a cry; shout out loud; utter a cry;

[大街] high road; high street; main street; main thoroughfare;
大街上 on the roadside;
大街小巷 big streets and small alleys; broad avenues and back streets; high streets and back lanes; main roads and small streets; streets and alleys;
繁忙大街 busy street; lively street;

[大節] a matter of principle; political integrity; the main principles guiding one's conduct;

[大捷] great victory;

[大姐] (1) elder sister; (2) older sister (a polite form of address for a woman about one's own age); (3) alpha girl; (4) Big Sister;
大姐姐 eldest sister;

[大局] general situation; overall situation; whole situation;
大局為重 put the interest of the whole above everything else;
~以大局為重 lay store by overall situation; put store by overall situation; put the general interest first; set store by overall situation; set the general interest above everything else; take the general situation to heart;
大局已定 chips be down; the die is cast; the outcome is a foregone conclusion; the result is certain;
大局著想 have the overall situation in mind;
顧大局，識大體 bear the overall situation in mind and put the general interest above all;
~不顧大局 ignore the larger issues; lack of consideration for the whole; regardless of the whole situation; show no consideration for the general interest;
顧全大局 act with the realization that one must always place the larger group-interests above private interests; bear the whole situation in mind; consider the overall situation; consider the situation as a whole; for the sake of the general good; for the sake of larger interest; give due consideration to the overall situation; mindful of the whole situation; out of consideration for the general interest; pay attention to the interests of the whole; take into consideration the situation as a whole; take the whole situation into consideration;
了解大局 know the whole circumstances;
事關大局 it's an issue that concerns the overall situation;
縱觀大局 take a comprehensive view of the situation;

[大舉] carry out a military operation on a large scale;
大舉反攻 mount a large-scale counteroffensive;
大舉進攻 attack in force; mount a large-scale offensive; an all-out offensive; large-scale invasion;
大舉入侵 make a massive invasion into;

[大軍] (1) army; main forces; (2) large contingent;
大軍壓境 the army is bearing down in force;
百萬大軍 the army of million strong;
產業大軍 the army of industrial workers;
失業大軍 the army of the unemployed;

[大楷] (1) regular script; (2) block letters;

[大考] end-of-term examination; final examination;

[大哭] cry;
大哭不止 cry loudly and endlessly;
大哭一場 have a long heart-broken cry;
抱頭大哭 embrace and sob bitterly;
~互相抱頭大哭 weep in each other's arms;
悲慟地大哭 cry aloud in grief;

捶胸大哭 beat one's breast and weep; cry one's heart out; hit one's chest and cry;
嚎啕大哭 cry one's heart out; cry one's eyes out;
號天大哭 calling upon Heaven; weep loudly;
疼得大哭 cry loudly with pain;

[大款] (1) big wheel; rich person; (2) nouveau riche; parvenu; (3) a large sum of money;
傍大款 accompany a rich person; have an intimate relationship with a rich person;

[大浪] billows; rough sea;
大浪滔滔 surging waves;
一個大浪 a high wave;

[大佬] poohbah;

[大理石] marble;
大理石屑 marble aggregate;
大理石像 marble statue;
白雲石大理石 dolomitic marble;
風景大理石 landscape marble;
火紅大理石 fire marble;
角礫大理石 breccia marble;
石珊瑚大理石 madrepore marble;

[大力] energetically; vigorously;
大力發展教育 devote major efforts to developing education;
大力經營 devote great efforts to the development of;
大力士 man of unusual strength;
大力宣傳 conduct vigorous propaganda;
大力協助 provide great help;

[大殮] encoffining ceremony;

[大梁] mainstay;
挑大梁 play a pivotal role; play the leading role; shoulder the main responsibility; the mainstay;

[大量] a considerable amount; a great deal of; a great mass of; a great quantity; a heap of; a host of; a large number; a lot of; a number of; acres of; any amount of; coming out of one's ears; plenty of; reams;
大量財富 enormous wealth;
大量出汗 sweat profusely;
大量的 a large amount of;
大量工作 masses of work;
大量生產 high production; high-volume production; mass run; quantity production;
大量數據 a lot of data;
大量資料 a great amount of information;
寬宏大量 broad-minded; clement; have a large heart; magnanimous;

[大樓] block; building; mansion;
摩天大樓 skyscraper;
多用途大樓 multipurpose building;
一層大樓 a storey of building;

[大路] high road; main road;
大路菜 common vegetables;
大路貨 (1) cheap goods; goods at ordinary or low price; (2) popular goods;

[大陸] continent; mainland;
大陸邊緣 continental margin;
大陸坡 continental slope;
大陸架 continental shelf;
次大陸 Subcontinent;
中國大陸 mainland China;

[大略] (1) broad outline; general idea; summary; (2) bold vision; great talent;
粗枝大略 know the rough outlines;
宏才大略 a great talent and a big plan; be astute in devising great plans; be capable of doing great things; great talent and bold vision;

[大媽] auntie; granny;

[大麻] cannabis; dope; ganja; hemp; marijuana;
大麻毒品 marijuana;
大麻酚 cannabinol;
大麻素 cannabisbin;
大麻酮 cannabisbinone;
大麻烯 cannabene;
大麻中毒 cannabism;
抽大麻 smoke dope; take cannabis;

[大麻哈魚] calico salmon; salmon;
大鱗大麻哈魚 chinook salmon;
紅大麻哈魚 blueback salmon;
馬蘇大麻哈魚 cherry salmon;

[大罵] a flood of abuse; scold;
潑口大罵 give vent to a torrent of abuse; let loose a flood of abuse; pour out a torrent of abuse on;
小捧大罵 damn sb with faint praise;

[大麥] barley;
大麥茶 barley water;
大麥粒 barleycorn;
春大麥 spring barley;
發芽大麥 germinating barley;

六稜大麥 six rowed barley;
秋大麥 autumn barley;
去殼大麥 naked barley;
四稜大麥 four rowed barley;
珍珠大麥 pearl barley;

[大滿貫] (of mahjong) grand slam;

[大忙] fully occupied; very busy;
大忙特忙 in a rush;
幫了大忙 do sb a good turn;
你幫了我的大忙 you saved my life;

[大門] entrance door; front door; gate;
把大門 guard a gate;
關上大門 pull up the drawbridge;

[大夢] dream;
大夢初醒 as if one is waking from a dream;
如臨大夢 all this seems to be happening in a dream;

[大米] husked rice; rice;
一把大米 a handful of rice;

[大面兒] (1) appearance; outlook; surface; (2) face;

[大名] (1) one's formal personal name; (2) your given name;
大名鼎鼎 celebrated; enjoy a big name; enjoy great celebrity; famous; well-known; widely known;
鼎鼎大名 a great celebrity; a great reputation; celebrated; famous; very famous; well-known;
久慕大名 have long respected one's valour;
久聞大名 I have heard of your illustrious name for a long time; I have long heard of your fame; I have long heard of your name; I have long known of your great reputation;
久仰大名 I have long looked up to your name;

[大拿] (1) boss; head; a person with power; (2) able person; expert;

[大男] unmarried young men;
大男大女 unmarried people of marriageable age;
大男人主義 male chauvinism;
~大男人主義者 male chauvinist

[大難] catastrophe; disaster;
大難不死 be delivered from a great danger; escape death from a calamity; escape from death in a great catastrophe;
大難不死，必有後福 the person who does not die in great dangers will have a good fortune later on;
大難臨頭 a great calamity is at hand; be faced with imminent disaster;
逃過大難 escape from a great catastrophe;

[大腦] cerebrum; forebrain;
大腦半球 cerebral hemisphere; hemicerebrum;
~優秀大腦半球 dominant cerebral hemisphere;
大腦兩半球 brain hemispheres;
大腦病 cerebrosis;
大腦出血性中風 haemorrhagia cerebri;
大腦風濕病 cerebral rheumatism;
大腦麻痺 cerebral paralysis;
大腦死亡 cerebral death;
大腦性癱瘓 cerebral palsy;
大腦炎 cerebritis;

[大逆不道] treacherous;

[大娘] auntie; granny;

[大怒] anger;
一陣大怒 paroxysms of anger;

[大女] unmarried young women;

[大排擋] food stall;

[大牌] (1) celebrity; (2) famous;
大牌歌星 famous pop singer;
耍大牌 act like a top-billing actor;

[大砲] (1) artillery; big gun; cannon; (2) braggart;
一尊大砲 a cannon;

[大批] a smart of; large quantities;
大批生產 mass production;

[大片] a large area; a sheet;

[大票] large bill;

[大氣] (1) air; atmosphere; (2) breathe heavily; heave;
大氣層 atmosphere; atmospheric layer;
~大氣層污染 pollution of atmosphere;
~大氣層巡航 aerocruise;
~飛出大氣層 exit from the atmosphere;
~氟大氣層 fluorine atmosphere;
~居間大氣層 intervening atmosphere;
~空氣大氣層 air-like atmosphere;
~生理大氣層 physiological atmosphere;
~稀薄大氣層 rarefied atmosphere;
大氣潮 atmospheric tide;
大氣垂直穩定度 vertical stability of the atmosphere;
大氣館 atmospherium;
大氣候 climate;

大氣化 atmospherization;
大氣磅礡 grand and magnificent; great vitality; have power and range; of great momentum; powerful;
大氣探測 air sounding;
大氣壓 atmosphere;
~ 絕對大氣壓 absolute atmosphere;
~ 物理大氣壓 physical atmosphere;
~ 有效大氣壓 effective atmosphere;
大氣折射 astronomical refraction;
大氣總體 total atmosphere;
大氣阻力 atmospheric drag;
大氣作用 atmospheric action;
城市大氣 community atmosphere;
喘一口大氣 give a deep breathing;
等溫大氣 isothermal atmosphere;
地球大氣 terrestrial atmosphere;
電離層大氣 ionized atmosphere;
多元大氣 polytropic atmosphere;
高層大氣 high-level atmosphere;
高密度大氣 high-density atmosphere;
恒星大氣 stellar atmosphere;
環境大氣 ambient atmosphere;
混合氣體氣氛 mixed gas atmosphere;
火星大氣 Mars atmosphere;
金星大氣 Venus atmosphere;
靜止大氣 atmosphere at rest;
均勻大氣 homogenous atmosphere;
可感大氣 sensible atmosphere;
擴散大氣 diffusion atmosphere;
模式大氣 model atmosphere;
木星大氣 Jovian atmosphere;
擾亂大氣 rough atmosphere;
人工大氣 artificial atmosphere;
受控大氣 controlled atmosphere;
太陽大氣 solar atmosphere;
土壤大氣 soil atmosphere;
湍流大氣 turbulent atmosphere;
無塵大氣 dust-free atmosphere;
斜壓大氣 baroclinic atmosphere;
星際大氣 interplanetary atmosphere;
月球大氣 lunar atmosphere;
正壓大氣 barotropic atmosphere;
指數大氣 exponential atmosphere;
中緯度大氣 midlatitude atmosphere;
自動正壓大氣 autobarotropic atmosphere;
自由大氣 free atmosphere;
最高層大氣 extreme upper atmosphere;
座艙大氣 aircraft cabin atmosphere;

[大器晚成] late bloomer; late life success;

[大巧若拙] a great intelligent man looks dull; a man of great skill is like an idiot; great art conceals itself; great wisdom appears stupid;

[大權] authority;
大權獨攬 absolute control on; arrogate all authority to oneself; centralize power in one man's hands to deal with major issues; centralize power on major issues; grasp the central power in one's own hands; take all power into one's hands;
大權獨攬，小權分散 have absolute control on major issues, devolve power on others with respect to minor issues;
大權旁落 let power pass into others' hands; power has fallen into the hands of others;
大權在握 hold the real power in one's hands; hold the reins; the great power is within one's grasp; with power in one's hands;
把弄大權 wield power;
獨攬大權 grasp at authority by oneself; arrogate all power to oneself;
濫用大權 abuse one's power; misuse one's power;
握有生殺大權 have life and death powers;
擁有大權 possess the absolute power;
掌大權 in power;
總攬大權 have overall authority; in full power

[大人] adult; grown-up;
大人物 big boy; big cheese; big gun; big name; big noise; big shot; big wheel; bigwig; buzwig; VIP; high and mighty; somebody;
~ 成為大人物 become an important person;
尊大人 your father;

[大嫂] (1) one's elder brother's wife; one's sister-in-law; (2) one's elder sister; (3) woman;

[大廈] building; mansion;

[大蛇] serpent;

[大赦] amnesty; general pardon;
大赦犯人 grant amnesty to the criminal;
大赦天下 proclaim a general amnesty;

[大聲] in a loud voice; loud;
大聲打嗝 give a loud belch;
大聲反對 cry against...; thunder against...;

大聲喊叫 shout aloud;
大聲疾呼 call out with a loud voice; cry as loud as possible; cry out; lift up one's voice; raise a cry of warning;
大聲抗議 raise one's voice in protest;
大聲辱罵 insult loudly; shout insult at sb;
大聲喧鬧 make a racket; raise the roof;

[大師] great master; maestro; master;
大師班 masterclass;
大師課 masterclass;
大師傅 chef;
鋼琴大師 virtuoso pianist;
小提琴大師 violin virtuoso;
一流的大師 topmost masters;

[大石] megalith;
大石文化 megalithic culture;

[大使] ambassador;
大使級會議 ambassadorial-level meeting;
互派大使 exchange ambassadors;
女大使 ambassadress;
無任所大使 ambassador-at-large;
巡迴大使 ambassador-at-large; roving ambassador;

[大事] (1) great event; important matter; major event; major issue; (2) overall situation; (3) in a large scale;
大事攻擊 all-out attack; attack in a large scale; hurl wild attacks against; lash out at;
大事故 major breakdown;
大事化小 reduce a big trouble into a small one;
~大事化小，小事化無 make little of the matter and put the matter to rest;
大事揮霍 extravagant spending; launch out into extravagance;
大事記 (1) a chronicle of events; (2) a datebook;
大事件 a serious event;
大事鋪張 make much of a little; present with a great fanfare;
大事宣傳 ballyhoo; give great publicity; play up;
一樁大事 an important matter;
志小難成大事 it's difficult to achieve a great cause with small aspirations;
茲事體大 this is a big problem; this is a serious matter;
終身大事 a great event affecting one's whole life; main affair of one's life; marriage;

[大勢] general situation; general trend of events;
大勢所趨 as things are going; general course of development; general trend; irresistable trend; march of events; trend of the times;
大勢所趨，人心所向 this accords with the general trend of events and the aspirations of the people;
大勢已定 foregone conclusion; the cat jumps; the die is cast; the lot is cast;
大勢已去 be rendered powerless; it is all up with...; nothing much can be done about it now; on the decline; one's day has gone; the game is as good as lost; the situation is beyond salvation; the situation is hopeless;

[大書特書] be fully recounted; write a great deal about;

[大樹] big tree;
砍不倒大樹，弄不多柴禾 if you don't chop down the big trees, you can't get much firewood;

[大肆] recklessly; violently; wantonly; without restraint;
大肆吹捧 extol to the sky; sing the praise of;
大肆攻擊 launch an unbridled attack on;
大肆鼓吹 advocate noisily;
大肆叫囂 set up a great clamour about;
大肆誇張 exaggerate too much;
大肆蹂躪 trample on;
大肆宣傳 put on the street;
大肆宣揚 give enormous publicity to; give great publicity; trumpet with great vigour;
大肆渲染 make a big hue and cry about; play up;

[大蒜] garlic;
大蒜味 smell of garlic;
~一股大蒜味 a whiff of garlic;
一瓣大蒜 a clove of garlic;

[大堂] great hall;
萃於大堂 be gathered at one place;

[大體] (1) cardinal principle; general interest; (2) by and large; for the most part; more or less; on the whole; roughly;
大體上 by and large; for the most part; in substance; in the main; largely; on the whole; roughly;
大體相同 about the same; more or less

alike;

識大體，顧大局 have the cardinal principles in mind and take the overall situation into account; keep the whole situation in mind;

[大廳] hall; state room;

[大庭廣眾] before a big crowd of people; before a large audience; in broad daylight; in front of everybody; in public;

[大同] Great Harmony; Great Unity;

大同小異 a general resemblance with small differences; be the same in essentials while differing in minor points; differ only on minor points; much of a muchness;

~求大同，存小異 seek common ground on major issues while leaving aside the minor differences; seek common ground on major issues while reserving differences on minor points; seek common ground on major questions while reserving differences on minor ones; try to acquire a community of views on the large issues and to give up wrangling over the small ones;

[大頭] (1) big head; (2) head mask; (3) main part; (4) dupe;

大頭病 big head;

大頭朝下 (1) head over heels; upside down; (2) handstand;

大頭頭兒 big guy;

大頭照 close up;

大頭針 pin;

一根大頭針 a pin;

[大腿] thigh;

[大腕兒] big shot; celebrity; expert; famous person;

[大王] baron; magnate; king;

鋼鐵大王 steel king;

煤炭大王 coal baron;

石油大王 oil baron;

[大為] greatly; very;

大為吃驚 be greatly surprised; be quite taken aback; be utterly startled;

大為改觀 change greatly;

大為驚恐 be seized with terror; be struck with panic; in a funk;

大為惱火 fume with rage; throw a fit;

大為生色 give colour to;

大為失望 feel very disappointed;

大為遜色 not in the same street with; pale; throw sth/sb into the shade;

大為震驚 be much shaken; be terribly shocked; have a fit; have a thousand fits; throw a fit; throw a thousand fits;

[大霧] dense fog;

大霧籠罩 be enveloped by a thick fog; be wrapped in a thick fog;

常下大霧 always have a dense fog;

下起大霧 have a dark fog;

遇上大霧 experience a thick fog;

[大喜] great rejoice;

大喜過望 be delighted that things are better than one expected; be overjoyed; be pleased beyond one's expectation; rejoice beyond all expectations;

大喜臨門 great happiness is knocking at one's door;

大喜雀躍 joyful like a dancing bird;

大喜日子 red-letter day; one's wedding-day;

大喜若狂 go crazy with joy; in an ecstasy of joy;

[大顯] to full play;

大顯身手 bring one's talents into full play; come out strong; cut a dashing figure; display one's skill to the full; distinguish oneself; give a good account of oneself; give full play to one's abilities; play one's trump card; show one's best; turn one's talents to full account;

大顯神通 display all one's valour; give full play to one's remarkable skill; make the mare go; show a great miracle; show one's magic power; show what one is capable of;

[大象] elephant;

一頭大象 a big elephant; an elephant;

[大小] (1) big or small; (2) degree of seniority; (3) adults and children; (4) bulk; dimension; magnitude; scale; size; volume;

大小不一 not of uniform size;

大小合適 size to fit;

大小適中 moderate size; right size;

大小相同 of uniform size;

大小由之 can fit any size of;

窗戶的大小 size of the window;

大醇小疵 sound on the whole though defective in details; with great purity and small flaw;

大驚小怪 a tempest in a teapot; bark at the noon; get excited over a little thing; great alarm at a little bogey; make a fuss about nothing; make a great ado over sth; make a rare fuss over sth; much cry and little wool;

~大驚小怪的人 fusspot;

大題小做 little about a major issue; make little of; treat major issues light;

各種大小 every shape and size;

化大為小 turn big issues into small ones;

夾角大小 corner dimension;

見小不見大 fail to see the wood for the trees; strain at a gnat and swallow a camel;

可大可小 changeable; elastic;

毛細管大小 capillary dimension;

沒大沒小 impertinent; impolite to an elder; imprudent; show no respect for one's elders;

磨粒大小 abrasive grain sizes;

七大八小 objects of various sizes thrown together;

氣室大小 air cell size;

棄大就小 exchange the great for the small;

棄小就大 lose a fly to catch a trout; one has to make sacrifices in order to succeed;

實物大小 life-size;

為小失大 lose a pound in trying to save a penny; penny-wise and pound-foolish;

以大欺小 act in the way of the big bullying the small; bully the small by being big; bully the weak by being strong; the big bullies the small;

~以大欺小，以富壓貧 the big bullies the small and the rich oppresses the poor;

以大壓小 the big coerce the small;

以大易小 exchange the great for the small;

以小博大 bet large by small; set a sprat to catch a herring; throw out a sprat to catch a herring;

因小失大 lose a big opportunity because of a trifle consideration; lose much because of a small thing; lose the greater for the less; lose the main goal because of small gains; pay too big a price for mere trifles; penny-wise, pound-foolish; suffer a big loss for a little gain; try to save a little but lose a lot;

由大由小 may be large or small;

由小變大 change from small to big; from weak to strong; grow from small to big;

由小到大 grow big from being small; grow from small beginnings into a mighty force; grow from small to big; grow in size;

原大小 life-size; original size;

真人大小 life-size;

[大笑] guffaw; laughter;

大笑不止 in stitches;

大笑起來 break out with laughter;

大笑一聲 give a loud laugh;

阿阿大笑 guffaw; laugh a noisy laugh; laugh out loud;

胡盧大笑 roar with laughter;

開懷大笑 uninhibited laughter;

撫掌大笑 clap one's hands and laugh aloud; laugh loud and clap one's hands;

突然大笑 laugh suddenly;

仰首大笑 throw back one's head and laugh;

一聲大笑 a shout of laughter;

一陣大笑 a roar of laughter; a spate of laughing;

[大校] (1) senior captain; (2) senior colonel;

[大寫] (1) capital form of a Chinese numeral; (2) capitalization;

大寫鎖定鍵 caps lock;

大寫字母 block capital; block letter; caps; capital letter;

[大興] go in for sth in a big way;

大興土木 build many new buildings;

大興問罪之師 bring sb to book; launch a punitive campaign; point an accusing finger at sb;

[大型] large-scale;

大型公共汽車 bus;

[大熊] bear;

大熊呼嚕 bears snore;

[大選] general election;

舉行大選 go to the country;

[大學] (1) college; uni; university; (2) *The Great Learning*;

大學畢業 graduate from a university;

大學畢業生 university graduate;

大學附設部分 university extension;

大學講師 university lecturer;
大學教員 college teacher; university teacher;
大學生 college student; university student;
大學生活 university life;
大學士 grand secretary;
大學肄業生 undergraduate;
大學文憑 university diploma;
大學校長 vice-chancellor; president;
大學學位 university degree;
大學學院 university college;
大學英語 university English;
大學預科 preparatory course for college;
大學自治 university autonomy;
辦大學 run a university;
創立大學 establish a university; found a university;
電視大學 television college;
電視廣播大學 television and radio broadcasting university;
讀大學 study at a university;
分散大學 dispersed university;
古老的大學 ancient university;
工人大學 workers' college;
工業大學 polytechnic university; university of technology;
國防大學 national defense university;
國立大學 national university;
海軍大學 naval university;
海上大學 maritime university;
建立大學 build a university;
交通大學 university of communications;
進入大學 attend a university; enter a college; enter university;
~勉強進入大學 scrape into college;
軍醫大學 army medical university;
考大學 sit for university entrance examinations;
科學技術大學 university of science and technology;
空軍大學 air university;
理工大學 polytechnic university;
理工科大學 university of science and engineering;
陸軍大學 military university;
民辦大學 university run by the local people;
名牌大學 elite university;
農業大學 agricultural university;
人民大學 people's university;
認可大學 accredited university;
上大學 attend university; go to university;
~開始上大學 start college;
申請大學 apply for university;
師範大學 normal university;
市立大學 civic university;
文科大學 university of liberal arts;
喜愛的大學 one's favourite university;
野雞大學 diploma mill;
夜大學 evening college;
業餘大學 part-time college; spare-time college;
業餘工業大學 part-time engineering university;
業餘職業大學 spare-time college for staff and workers;
一所大學 a university;
醫科大學 medical university;
終身大學 lifetime university;
綜合大學 comprehensive university;
重點大學 key university; leading university;
州立大學 state university;

[大雪] (1) heavy snow; (2) Great Snow;
大雪紛飛 big snowfall;
一場大雪 a heavy fall of snow;

[大牙] (1) molar; (2) front tooth; (3) one's teeth;
笑掉大牙 double up in laughter; laugh one's head off; make one hold one's sides; make sb laugh his teeth off;

[大雅] elegance; good taste; refinement;
不登大雅之堂 not appeal to refined taste; on the margin of good taste; unpresentable; unqualified to take its place in the higher circles; unrefined;
無傷大雅 quite acceptable in high-class society;
有傷大雅 offend against good taste;

[大言不慚] biggety talk; boast without shame; brag unblushingly; brag without feeling shame; shamelessly boastful;

[大雁] wild goose;
一群大雁 a flock of wild geese;

[大要] gist; main points;

[大爺] (1) uncle; grandpa; (2) gluttonous idler; (3) lazy, arrogant, and wilful man;
闊大爺 rich man; wealthy man;

[大業] great achievement; great cause; great undertaking;
盛德大業 ethical and magnificent achievements;

[大衣] overcoat; topcoat;

穿大衣 put on one's coat;
~幫人穿大衣 help sb on with his coat;
短大衣 short overcoat; topcoat;
風雪大衣 parka;
毛皮大衣 fur coat;
皮大衣 fur overcoat;
七分長大衣 three-quarter length coat;
脱大衣 take off one's coat;
~幫人脱大衣 help sb off with his coat;
中大衣 medium-length overcoat;

[大姨] one's aunt; one's mother's eldest sister;

[大意] (1) general effect; general idea; gist; main idea; (2) careless; inattentive; negligent;
大意失荊州 suffer a major setback due to carelessness;
大意招致失敗 carelessness invites failure;
粗心大意 careless; inadvertence; inadvertent; incautious; negligence; negligent; remiss; scatter-brain; slipshod; thoughtless;
段落大意 gist of a paragraph;
講話大意 drift of the talk;
全書大意 brief outline of the book;
全文大意 outline of the text;

[大義] cardinal principles of righteousness;
大義凜然 awe-inspring righteousness; with a strong sense of righteouness;with stern righteousness;
大義滅親 kill one's blood relations to uphold justice; place righteousness above family loyalty; punish one's own relations in the cause of justice;
深明大義 have a firm grasp of what is right and wrong; know clearly the right thing to do and the principles to follow;
微言大義 subtle words with profound meanings;
曉以大義 tell sb what is right;
諭以大義 enlighten one with the general meaning of sth;

[大勇] (1) great courage; (2) courageous people;

[大油] lard;

[大有] be of great;
大有裨益 of great benefit;
大有成就 come out on top; have a good run; magnificent success;
大有出息 show great promise;
大有好處 of great benefit to; of much good;
大有進步 advance by rapid strides; have greatly improved; have taken great strides in one's progress; make great strides;
大有可觀 quite impressive; very considerable; worthwhile seeing;
大有可為 be well worth doing; can accomplish great things; have a brilliant future; have bright prospects;
大有來頭 have powerful backing; very influential socially;
大有前途 have a brilliant future;
大有區別 entirely different; poles apart;
大有人在 not the only pebble on the beach; such people are by no means rare;
大有所獲 have obtained a great deal;
大有文章 there is more to it than meets the eye; there is much more to it than appears;
大有希望 bid fair; full of hope; full of promise; give great promise; promise high hopes; show great promise; stand a chance; there is great hope for;
大有益處 very beneficial;
大有用處 of great use;
大有之年 abundant year; bumper year; good year for crops;
大有作為 able to develop one's ability to the full; go a long way; have full scope for one's talents; have great possibilities; much can be accomplished; there is plenty of room to develop one's talents to the full;

[大魚] big fish;
大魚吃小魚 big fish eat small fish; the big fish eat up the small;
放長線釣大魚 angle for a large fish with a long line; go after sth big with foresight; throw a long line to catch a big fish — adopt a long-term plan for prolonged benefits; throw out a long line to catch a big fish; trail a long line in order to catch a big fish;
小塘中的大魚 a big fish in a small pond;
要釣大魚，須放長線 to catch a big fish, you have to put out a long line;

[大於] above and beyond; bigger than; larger than;

[大雨] hale water; heavy rain; soaker;

大雨滂沱 heavy shower; it is raining cats and dogs; it is raining heavily; it rains pitchforks; pelting rain; rain in torrents; the heavy rain pours down in torrents; the rain comes down in a deluge; the rain comes down in sheets; the rain comes down in torrents; the rain comes down with a vengeance; the rain falls in sheets;

大雨瓢潑 rain buckets; the rain comes down in a splash; the rain comes down in great white sheets of water;

大雨傾盆 it is raining like billy-ho; it rains cats and dogs; rain pitchforks; the rain falls in sheets; the rain is pelting; the rain teems down; torrential rain;

大雨如注 rain in torrents; rain like fury; the heavy rain pours down in torrents; the rain comes down in sheets; the rain comes down in torrents;

瓢潑大雨 downpour; heavy fall of rain; heavy rain; torrential rain;

傾盤大雨 torrential rain;

~正在下傾盤大雨 it's pouring down; it's tipping down;

下大雨 rain cats and dogs; teem down;

~要下大雨 it's going to rain hard;

~正下大雨 it's raining heavily;

一場大雨 a deluge of rain; a downpour; a heavy rain;

一陣大雨 a downpour of rain; a flood of rain; a shower;

~好一陣大雨 what a flood of rain;

[大員] high-ranking official;

[大院] courtyard;

深宅大院 compound of connecting courtyards, a large house and a big yard; each surrounded by dwelling quarters; mansion with many courtyards and very high walls;

[大月] 31-day month;

[大約] about; almost; a matter of; approximate to; around; before or after; circa; in the neighbourhood; in the region of; in the rough; in the vicinity of; -ish; more or less; nearly; or so; or thereabout; probably; round about; some; something like; somewhere about; somewhere around; somewhere round; something like; thereabout; towards;

[大展] spread the wings;

大展鴻圖 spread one's wings;

徐圖大展 long-term plan for future development;

[大戰] (1) fierce competition; (2) big clash; large-scale fight;

大戰爆發 outbreak of war;

世界大戰 world war;

[大指] thumb;

[大志] high aims; high aspirations; lofty aims;

立大志，展宏圖 cherish high aspirations and carry out a great plan;

素有大志 have an ambition;

胸無大志 with no ambition at all; with no ideals;

[大致] (1) on the whole; roughly; (2) approximately; more or less;

大致略同 more or less alike; mostly similar; roughly the same;

大致如此 in general it is true; that's about the size of it;

[大眾] masses; people; public;

大眾傳播 mass media;

~大眾傳播功能 function of mass media;

~大眾傳播媒介 mass media;

~大眾傳播模式 models of mass media;

~大眾傳播學 mass media studies;

大眾的 demotic;

大眾歌曲 popular songs;

大眾化 popularize;

大眾科學 popular science;

大眾商品 popular commodities;

大眾社會 mass society;

大眾文化 pop culture;

大眾文藝 popular literature;

勞苦大眾 the toiling masses;

社會大眾 lowest common denominator;

團結大眾 hold the masses together;

[大專] tertiary institution;

大專生 tertiary student;

[大篆] great-seal script;

[大字] big character;

大字報 big-character poster;

大字標題 splash headline;

[大醉如泥] as drunk as a lord; blind drunk; dead drunk;

[大作] (1) your work; (2) erupt; explode;

拜讀大作 have the honour to read; have the pleasure of perusing your work; read with respect your work;

酸勁大作 burn with jealousy;

半大 medium; medium-sized;
本大 large capital;
博大 broad and profound; erudite; vast;
不大 (1) not too; not very; (2) not often;
粗大 (1) bulky; thick; thick and big; (2) loud;
膽大 audacious; bold;
放大 amplification; amplify; enlarge; enlargement; magnification; magnify;
非常大 very big; walloping big; walloping great;
肥大 (1) large; loose; (2) fat; plump; (3) hypertrophy;
肝大 hepatomegalia;
高大 (1) tall and big; (2) lofty;
光大 brighten;
廣大 (1) extensive; vast; (2) large-scale; wide-spread; (3) numerous;
浩大 huge; vast;
宏大 grand; great;
洪大 great; immense; loud; massive;
極大 very large;
加大 enlarge;
較大 relatively large;
巨大 gigantic; huge; tremendous;
開大 turn up;
誇大 exaggerate; overstate;
寬大 (1) roomy; spacious; wide; (2) lenient; magnanimous; (3) generous;
擴大 aggrandizement; amplify; broaden; dilate; enlarge; enlargement; expand; extend; multiply; swell; widening;
老大 (1) old; (2) eldest child; (3) master of a sailing vessel; (4) greatly; very; (5) don; leader of a triad society;
莫大 greatest; utmost;
拿大 give oneself airs;
女大 grown daughter;
龐大 colossal; huge; massive;
膨大 expand; inflate;
強大 formidable; powerful;
窮措大 penniless fellow assuming the air of being rich; poor scholar; poverty-stricken scholar;
人大 National People's Congress;
偌大 of such a size; so big;
盛大 grand; magnificent;
樹大 big tree;
碩大 very large;
太大 oversized;
貪大 strive for what is big;
特大 especially big; extra large; the most;
天大 as large as the heavens; extremely big;
偉大 great; mighty;
相當大 largish;
雄大 great and powerful;
一樣大 of like size;
遠大 ambitious; broad; long-range; very promising;
增大 amplify; enlargement; magnify;
張大 exaggerate; publicize widely;
長大 attain manhood; be brought up; grow; grow up; mature;
脹大 swell;
正大 aboveboard; upright;
至大 extremely large; the greatest;
志大 ambitious;
腫大 swell up;
重大 great; major; significant;
壯大 (1) grow in strength; (2) expand; strengthen;
自大 above oneself; arrogant; cocky; conceited; egotistic; hubris;
最大 biggest; greatest; largest; maximum;
坐大 emerge big and strong;
做大 put on airs;

da⁵

da

【瘩】 boil; pimple; wart;

da

【縫】 knot of a rope;

dai¹

dai

【呆】 (1) dim-witted; dull; dull of mind; dull-brained; dull-witted; slow-witted; stupid; unintelligent; (2) blank; blank-minded; empty-headed; vacuous; wooden; (3) stay;

［呆板］ (1) as dull as ditchwater; boring; dull; inflexible; rigid; stereotyped; (2) rigid; starchy; stiff;
呆板乏味 as dull as ditchwater; dull and uninteresting; very dull;
呆板公式 rigid formula;
［呆楞］ in a daze; stare blankly;
［呆驢］ stupid ass;
笨如呆驢 as stupid as an ass;
［呆木］ dazed and numb;
［呆人］ fool;
呆人有呆福 fortune favours the fools;
［呆傻］ dazed; stupefied;
［呆帳］ bad debts;
［呆怔］ in a daze; stare blankly;
呆怔怔 be dazed;

[呆滯] (1) dull; inert; lifeless; (2) dull; idle; slack; sluggish; stagnant;
表情呆滯 have a dull expression on one's face;
目光呆滯 have fishy eyes; have glassy eyes;
商業呆滯 the business slackens;
市場呆滯 it's a dull market; stagnant market;
銷路呆滯 slow in sale;
[呆子] dork; fool; idiot; oaf; plonker;
呆子幫忙—越幫越忙 a fool helps out – the more he helps, the busier one becomes;

痴呆 dull-witted; stupid;
發呆 in a trance; stare blankly;

D

dai
【待】 stay; later;
[待言] need to say;
自不待言 it goes without saying that; it is self-evident that; needless to say; self-evident; speak by itself;

dai
【獃】 (1) foolish; idiotic; silly; stupid; (2) awkward; bungling; clumsy; maladroit; (3) depressed; in low spirit;
[獃獃地] idiotically; stupidly;
[獃子] idiot;
書獃子 bookworm; pedant; studious idiot;

dai3
dai
【歹】 bad; evil;
[歹徒] brigand; evildoer; gangster; hoodlum; ruffian; scoundrel;
持槍歹徒 gunman;
一伙歹徒 a mob of gangsters;
抓住歹徒 catch the scoundrel;
[歹心] evil intent;
[歹意] evil intention; malicious intent;
心存歹意 evil-minded;
心生歹意 form malicious intention;

好歹 (1) good and bad; what's good and what's bad; (2) danger; disaster; mishap; (3) anyhow; at any rate; in any case; (4) make do with; (5) after a fashion; in some fashion;

dai
【逮】 (1) reach; (2) after; chase and make arrest; hunt;
[逮捕] make arrest;
[逮繫] arrest and detain;

不逮 incompetent;

dai4
dai
【大】
[大夫] (1) doc; doctor; medical man; physician; (2) high officials in ancient China;
蒙古大夫 charlatan; quack;
士大夫 literati and officials;

dai
【代】 (1) in place of; take the place of; (2) acting; (3) historical period; (4) era; (5) generation;
[代辦] act on sb's behalf; charge d'affairs; do sth for sb;
代辦處 agency;
~ 國外代辦處 foreign agency;
代辦所 agency;
[代筆] ghost-write; write on sb's behalf;
代筆人 ghost writer;
僱人代筆 hire a ghost;
替人代筆 ghastwrite for a person;
[代表] (1) delegate; deputy; representative; (2) represent; stand for; (3) in the name of; on behalf of; on one's behalf;
代表大會 congress;
代表人物 representative figures;
代表團 contingent; delegation; deputation; mission;
~ 代表團團長 chief of the delegation;
~ 一個代表團 a delegation;
代表性 typical;
代表作 matgnum opus;
副代表 vice-representative;
工商業代表 commercial and industrial representative;
國外代表 foreign representative;
會議代表 conference delegate;
列席代表 delegates without power to vote;
全權代表 authorized representative;
商務代表 commercial representative; trade representative;
首席代表 chief delegate;
談判代表 negotiating representative;
特別代表 special delegate;

外交代表 diplomatic representative;
委任代表 appoint a deputy;
選舉代表 elect a deputy;
營業代表 sales representative;
正式代表 official delegate;
駐地代表 resident representative;

[代步] ride instead of walk;
以車代步 take a car instead of walking;

[代償] compensation;
代償現象 compensation phenomenon;

[代稱] antonomasia;

[代詞] pronoun;
代詞同義詞 pronominal synonym;
代詞主詞 pronoun subject;
定代詞 definite pronoun;
~不定代詞 indefinite pronoun;
– 合成不定代詞 compound indefinite pronoun;
斷定代詞 assertive pronoun;
反身代詞 reflexive pronoun;
分離代詞 disjunctive pronoun;
否定代詞 negative pronoun;
關係代詞 relative pronoun;
互參代詞 coreferential pronoun;
接語代詞 clitic pronoun;
絕對代詞 absolute pronoun;
連接代詞 conjunctive pronoun;
連結代詞 syndetic pronoun;
內包代詞 inclusive pronoun;
排他代詞 exclusive pronoun;
強勢代詞 intensive pronoun;
強調勢代詞 emphatic pronoun;
人稱代詞 personal pronoun;
~非人稱代詞 impersonal pronoun;
~複合人稱代詞 compound personal pronoun;
物主代詞 possessive pronoun;
~名詞性物主代詞 nominal possessive pronoun;
相互代詞 reciprocal pronoun;
疑問代詞 interrogative pronoun;
引導代詞 anticipatory pronoun;
指示代詞 demonstrative pronoun;
自身代詞 self pronoun;

[代溝] generation gap;

[代購] act as a purchasing agent; buy on sb's behalf;

[代管] act as an agent; act for others; manage on behalf of another;
臨時代管 mind the shop; mind the store;

[代號] code; code name; designation; mark;

[代換] substitution;
倒轉代換 back substitution;
同步代換 cogradient substitution;

[代價] cost; price;
代價昂貴 cost dearly;
昂貴的代價 dear price;
不惜任何代價 at any price;
不惜一切代價 at all costs; at any cost;
付出代價 pay the price;
~付出沉重的代價 pay a severe price;
~付出很大的代價 pay big for;
~付出很高的代價 pay a high price;

[代課] take over a class for an absent teacher;
代課老師 substitute teacher; supply teacher;

[代勞] (1) ask sb to do sth for oneself; (2) do sth for sb; take trouble on sb's behalf;
拜托代勞 request to do sth for sb;
分憂代勞 share sb's sorrow and toil; share sb's worry and relieve him of work;

[代理] (1) act for sb; acting; (2) act as agent; agency; for account of;
代理地區 agent's area;
代理費 agent fee;
代理行 agency;
代理合同 agency contract;
代理機構 agency;
代理權 ; power of attorneyright of agency;
代理人 agent; deputy; proxy;
~財務代理人 fiscal agent;
~採購代理人 purchasing agent;
~獨家代理人 exclusive agent;
~輪船代理人 shipping agent;
~貿易代理人 trade agent;
~臨時代理人 locum;
~收貨代理人 receiving agent;
~訴訟代理人 agent ad litem;
~托收代理人 collection agent;
~銷售代理人 sale agent;
~佣金代理人 commission agent;
~運輸代理人 shipping agent;
~總代理人 general agent;
代理市長 acting major;
代理投票 proxy voting;
代理業務 agent service;
代理中間人 agent; middleman;
廠家代理 manufacturer's agency;
訂購代理 purchasing agency;
獨家代理 exclusive agency; sole agency; sole agent;
分代理 sub-agency;

商業代理 commercial agency;
申請代理 apply for agency;
指定代理 agency by appointment;
總代理 general agency; general agent;

[代碼] code;
代碼標準化 standardization of coding;
代碼共享 code-sharing;
代碼能力 codability;
代碼選擇 code selection;
代碼轉換 code switching;
操作代碼 operation code;
從屬代碼 sub-code;

[代名詞] (1) pronoun; (2) byword;
不定代名詞 indefinite pronoun;
絕對代名詞 absolute pronoun;
引導代名詞 anticipatory pronoun;

[代庖] act in sb's place; undertake sb's job;

[代培] train on behalf of another organization;

[代入] substitution;
代入規則 rule of substitution;

[代售] be commissioned to sell sth;

[代數] algebra;
代數和 algebraic sum;
代數式 algebraic expression;
代數數 algebraic number;
~代數數論 algebraic number theory;
代數學家 algebraist;
布爾代數 Boolean algebra;
抽象代數 abstract algebra;
初等代數 elementary algebra;
典範代數 canonical algebra;
對稱代數 symmetric algebra;
對偶代數 dual algebra;
符號代數 symbolic algebra;
高等代數 advanced algebra; higher algebra;
關係代數 relational algebra;
基本代數 basic algebra;
交錯代數 alternative algebra;
結合代數 associative algebra;
矩陣代數 matrix algebra;
量子代數 quantum algebra;
邏輯代數 logical algebra;
微分代數 differential algebra;
線性代數 linear algebra;
信息代數 information algebra;
序數代數 ordinal algebra;
餘代數 coalgebra;
~分次餘代數 graded coalgebra;
~上交換餘代數 cocommutative coalgebra;

[代替] in lieu of; replace; substitute for; take the place of;
代替人 substitute;
暫時代替 stand in;

[代銷] act as a commission agent; sell goods on a commission basis;

[代謝] metabolism; metabolize;
代謝產物 metabolite;
~初級代謝產物 primary metabolites;
~次級代謝產物 secondary metabolite;
代謝活動 metabolic activity;
代謝物 metabolite;
~抗代謝物 antimetabolite;
~真菌代謝物 fungal metabolite;
~中間代謝物 intermediate metabolites;
代謝型 metabolic type;
代謝性酸中毒 metabolic acidosis;
合成代謝 anabolism;
基礎代謝 basal metabolism;
同化代謝 assimilation;
向量代謝 vectorial metabolism;
新陳代謝 metabolism;
新舊事物的代謝 the supersession of the old by the new;
需氧代謝 aerobic metabolism;
~不需氧代謝 anaerobic metabolism;
異常代謝 abnormal metabolism;

[代行] act on sb's behalf;
代行職務 fill the breach; step into the breach;

[代序] in lieu of a preface;

[代言人] mouthpiece; spokesman;
女代言人 spokeswoman;

[代議制] representative system of government;

[代營] manage a business on sb's behalf;

[代用] substitute;
代用品 substitute; substitutor;
~合算代用品 economical substitute;
~血漿代用品 plasma substitute;

朝代 dynasty;
傳代 go down to posterity; go down to the future generation; hand from generation to generation;
當代 contemporary era; present age;
迭代 iteration;
斷代 divide history into periods;
古代 ancient times;
後代 (1) later ages; progeniture; succeeding era; (2) descendants; later generations;

offsprings; posterity; progeny;
交代 (1) account for; brief; explain; justify oneself; make clear; tell; (2) hand over; transfer; turn over;
近代 modern times;
絕代 peerless;
曠代 matchless among one's contemporaries;
歷代 past dynasties; successive dynasties;
末代 last generation;
年代 (1) age; time; years; (2) a decade of a century;
倩代 ask sb else to do sth;
求代 seek a substitute to do a duty;
取代 replace; substitute for; take for;
權代 substitute for another for the time being;
三代 three generations;
時代 (1) epoch; era; times; (2) period in one's life;
世代 (1) epoch; era; (2) for generations; from generation to generation;
替代 replace; substitute for;
下代 descendant; next generation;
現代 (1) modern times; the contemporary age; the present age; (2) contemporary; current; modern; present;
一代 a generation; a generation of;
異代 different age; different era;
昭代 enlightened age;
朝代 dynasty;
子代 filial generation;
祖代 ancestors; forbears;

dai

【岱】 Dai Mountain;

dai

【待】 (1) deal with; treat; (2) entertain; (3) await; wait for; (4) need; (5) about to; going to;

[待斃] sitting duck; await death;
坐以待斃 await one's doom; resign oneself to death; sit passively for one's end; sit still and await destruction; wait helplessly for the end; wait to be killed;

[待哺] wait for feeding;

[待茶] receive a guest with tea;

[待查] yet to be investigated;

[待產室] labour room;

[待機] await the opportune moment; bide one's time; standby;
待機而動 wait for an opportunity to make a move; wait for the right time to take action;
待機而行 wait for an opportune moment to act; wait for one's opportunity to move;
待機時間 standby time;
雌伏待機 retire and hide and wait for an opportunity to rise;

[待價而沽] sell sth for a good price; wait for the highest bid; wait for the right price to sell;

[待建] awaiting construction;

[待考] need checking; remain to be verified;

[待客] entertain guests; receive guest;
待客周到 keep a good house;

[待領] wait to be called for;

[待命] await orders;
待命出發 await orders to set off; be ready for orders to set out; wait for orders to start off;
原地待命 stand by; stay still for; pending orders;
整裝待命 ready for orders;

[待人] treat people;
待人誠懇 sincere with people; treat people sincerely;
待人很好 treat people very well;
待人接物 the manner of dealing with people; the way one conducts oneself in relation to others; the way one gets along with people; the way one treats others and handles issues;
待人寬厚 broad-minded in dealing with people;
待人刻薄 very mean toward people;
待人冷淡 treat people in a cold way;
待人禮貌 treat others with courtesy;
待人熱情 treat people warmly;
待人如己 treat others as oneself; treat others like oneself;
待人以誠 honest in dealing with people; treat people with sincerity;
待人以寬 act generously towards people;
待人友好 treat people kindly;
誠懇待人 treat others with earnestness;
赤誠待人 treat people with absolute sincerity;
接物待人 attend a matter and receive a person;
刻己待人 strict to oneself and others;

D

寬以待人 lenient; lenient toward others; treat others liberally;

[待如己出] treat a child as if he were one's own;

[待時] wait for the right moment;

待時而動 bide one's time; wait for the right time to take action;

藏器待時 store up a utensil for the right time; wait for the right moment to demonstrate one's ability;

[待續] be continued;

未完待續 to be continued;

[待業] awaiting assignment to a job; awaiting employment; wait for employment;

待業保險 unemployment insurance;

待業青年 young people awaiting employment;

待業人員 people waiting for employment;

待業者 the person for awaiting occupation;

[待用] inactive; stand-by;

[待遇] (1) treatment; (2) pay; remuneration; salary; wage;

待遇不公 unfair treatment;

待遇菲薄 a poor salary;

待遇優厚 excellent pay and conditions;

不公平的待遇 rough deal;

非平等待遇 unequal treatment;

經濟待遇 economic treatment;

平等待遇 equal treatment;

人道待遇 human treatment;

優惠待遇 preferential treatment;

政治待遇 political treatment;

最惠國待遇 most-favoured-nation treatment;

[待月西廂] have a nocturnal rendezvous with one's lover;

[待之以禮] treat with courtesy;

[待字] wait for a right man to marry;

待字閨中 a girl not betrothed yet; be still unmarried; one's daughter is still unmarried; waiting in the boudoir to be betrothed;

賓待 receive sb as a guest;

薄待 treat ungenerously;

擔待 (1) take on; take the responsibility; undertake; (2) excuse; forgive; pardon;

等待 await for; bear with; hang on; hold on; stop for; string along; wait around; wait for; wait in; wait on; wait out;

對待 (1) in a position related to another; (2) approach; treat;

鵠待 attend upon respectfully;

交待 (1) hand over; (2) explain; (3) confess;

接待 admit; receive;

看待 look upon; regard; treat;

苛待 hard on; treat harshly;

寬待 treat with leniency;

款待 entertain; treat cordially;

虧待 treat shabbily; treat unfairly;

留待 wait until;

慢待 neglect; slight;

虐待 ill-treat; maltreat;

期待 anticipate; await; expect; hope; in expectation of; look forward to; wait in hope;

恰待 just on the point of doing sth;

卻待 be just waiting to;

容待 let's wait a minute;

善待 accord sb good treatment; treat sb well;

少待 wait a moment;

徯待 expect; look forward to;

相待 treat a person;

須待 (1) have to wait until; (2) expect; look forward to;

以待 wait for;

優待 give a preferential treatment;

有待 await (to be done); remain (to be done);

欲待 intend to; want to;

招待 entertain; receive (visitors); serve (customers);

直待 (1) until; (2) up to;

坐待 sit back and wait;

dai

【怠】 idle; lazy; remiss; slack;

[怠惰] idle; indolent; lazy;

[怠工] go slow; slow down;

[怠慢] cold-shoulder; slight;

故意怠慢 willfully neglect;

受到怠慢 be treated with neglect; suffer slights;

倦怠 tired and lazy;

懈怠 slack; sluggish;

dai

【殆】 (1) dangerous; perilous; precarious; (2) tired; (3) afraid; (4) about; almost; nearly; (5) even; merely; only;

[殆無其匹] there is no equal; there is scarcely any equal;

dai

【玳】 tortoise shell;

［玳瑁］ hawksbill turtle;

dai

【迨】 by the time when; until; up until;

［迨冰未泮］ before the ice melts;

dai

【帶】 (1) band; belt; girdle; ribbon; tape; (2) tire; (3) area; belt; zone; (4) bring; take; (5) do sth incidentally; (6) bear; contain; have; (7) having sth attached; simultaneous; (8) head; lead; (9) bring up; look after;

［帶病］ in spite of illness;
帶病工作 carry on one's work in spite of illness;

［帶到］ bring; lead; take;

［帶電］ charged; electrified;

［帶動］ (1) drive; set in motion; (2) bring along; lead; spur on;
用電力帶動 be electricity-driven;

［帶教］ guidance and instruction;

［帶寬］ bandwidth;
帶寬倒數 inverse bandwidth;
倍頻程帶寬 octave bandwidth;
電視帶寬 television bandwidth;
光放大器帶寬 optical amplifier bandwidth;
開環帶寬 open-loop bandwidth;
脈衝帶寬 impulse bandwidth;
脈塞帶寬 maser bandwidth;
模擬視頻帶寬 analog video bandwidth;
逆帶寬 inverted bandwidth;
頻道帶寬 channel bandwidth;
掃描帶寬 sweep bandwidth;
聲頻帶寬 audio bandwidth;
視覺帶寬 visual bandwidth;
視頻信號帶寬 video signal bandwidth;
調制帶寬 modulation bandwidth;
響應帶寬 responsive bandwidth;
相位帶寬 phase bandwidth;
信息帶寬 intelligence bandwidth;
增益帶寬 gain bandwidth;
阻抗帶寬 impedance bandwidth;

［帶來］ bring about; produce; result in;
帶來災難 bring on a disaster;

［帶累］ implicate; involve;

［帶領］ guide; head; lead;
帶領部隊 lead an army;

［帶路］ act as a guide; lead the way; show the way;
有人給你帶路 someone will show you the way;

［帶球］ dribble;

［帶頭］ set an example; take the lead; take up the running; the first;
帶頭發言 the first to speak;
帶頭起舞 lead off a dance;

［帶孝］ in mourning; in the mourning; wear mourning for a parent or relative;

［帶羞］ look bashful; look shy;

［帶魚］ hairtail;

［帶子］ (1) video film; video tape; (2) band;
一根帶子 a band;

［帶座］ show sb to a seat;

安全帶 safety belt; seat belt;
白帶 leucorrhoea; whites;
綁帶 (1) bandage; (2) puttee;
背帶 (1) braces; suspenders; (2) sling; straps;
繃帶 bandage;
邊帶 sideband;
錶帶 watch strap; watchband;
帛帶 silk waist band;
彩帶 coloured ribbon; coloured streamer;
潮間帶 intertidal belt;
磁帶 magnetic tape;
彈帶 cartridge belt;
倒帶 rewind; rewind a cassette or a tape;
地震帶 seismic zone;
吊帶 suspender;
肚帶 bellyband; girth;
緞帶 satin ribbon;
風帶 wind belt;
帆布帶 canvas belt;
附帶 attach; include;
箍帶 strap;
拐帶 abduct; kidnap;
海帶 kelp;
寒帶 frigid zone;
盒帶 cassette tape;
夾帶 carry secretly; smuggle;
肩帶 shoulder strap;
膠帶 adhesive tape;
褲帶 trouser belt;
寬帶 broadband; wideband;
連帶 relate;
鏈帶 chain belt;
林帶 forest belt;
領帶 necktie; tie;

卵帶 chalaza;
帽帶 hatband;
面帶 wear;
磨帶 abrasive belt; grinding belt;
紐帶 bond; link; tie;
佩帶 put on;wear;
皮帶 (1) leather belt; leather girdle; (2) belt;
飄帶 ribbon; streamer;
頻帶 band;
臍帶 umbilical cord;
槍帶 sling for a rifle;
挈帶 (1) carry; take along; (2) guide; lead;
球帶 spherical zone;
裙帶 connected through one's female relations;
熱帶 torrid zone; tropics;
韌帶 ligament;
捎帶 carry; take along at one's convenience;
聲帶 (1) vocal cords; (2) sound track;
綬帶 cordon;
束帶 drawstring;
輸送帶 conveyer belt;
樹膠帶 gum tape;
順帶 conveniently; in passing;
絲帶 silk ribbon;
通帶 passband;
拖帶 (1) drag along; (2) implicate; involve;
襪帶 garters; sock suspenders;
溫帶 temperate zone;
挾帶 carry under one's arms;
携帶 carry; take along;
鞋帶 shoelaces; shoestrings;
攜帶 carry; carry with oneself; take along;
腰帶 belt; waistband;
一帶 area; surroundings;
縈帶 coil; wind around and around;
玉帶 jade belt;
雲帶 cloud band;
運輸帶 conveyor belt;
肢帶 limb girdle;
緇帶 black belt;

dai

【袋】 (1) bag; pocket; pouch; sack; (2) pocket;

[袋茶] tea bag;

[袋鼠] kangaroo;
袋鼠法庭 kangaroo court;
麝袋鼠 musk kangaroo;
一隻袋鼠 a kangaroo;

[袋裝] in bags;

[袋子] bag; sack;

暗袋 camera bag; film-changing bag;
被袋 bedding bag;
錶袋 watch pocket;
冰袋 ice bag;
布袋 sack;
草袋 straw bag;
浮袋 water wings;
箭袋 quiver;
口袋 pocket;
旅行袋 travelling bag;
麻袋 gunny-bag; gunnysack;
煤袋 coal sack;
麵袋 flour bag;
腦袋 head;
暖水袋 hot-water bottle;
皮袋 leather bag;
氣袋 airbag;
錢袋 bag; moneybag; money purse; wallet;
茄袋 wallet;
熱水袋 hot-water bottle;
沙袋 sandbag;
手袋 handbag; purse;
書袋 school bag;
睡袋 sleeping bag;
提袋 handbag;
香袋 perfume satchel;
煙袋 tobacco pipe;
眼袋 under-eye bags;
一大袋 a sack of;
一袋 a bag of; a pouch of; a sack of;
衣袋 pocket;
郵袋 mailbag; postbag;
運屍袋 body bag;
裝袋 bagging;
紙袋 paper bag;

dai

【貸】 (1) loan; (2) borrow; lend; (3) shift; shirk; (4) forgive; pardon;

[貸款] (1) extend credit to; provide a loan; (2) credit; grubstake; lending; loan;
貸款償還 loan repayment;
貸款利率 loan interest rate;
貸款條件 terms of loan;
貸款協議 loan agreement;
貸款賬戶 loan account;
長期貸款 long-term loan;
~ 對外長期貸款 long-term foreign loans;
償還貸款 pay back a loan; pay off a loan; repay a loan;
~ 可償還貸款 redeemable loan;
償清貸款 pay off a loan;

低息貸款 cheap loan; low-interest loan;
抵押貸款 secured loan;
短期貸款 short-term loan;
~對外短期貸款 short-term foreign loans;
個人貸款 personal loan;
工業貸款 industrial loan;
國外貸款 foreign lending;
過渡性貸款 bridge loan; bridging loan;
還清貸款 clear a loan;
臨時貸款 bridging loan;
免息貸款 interest-free loan;
農業貸款 agricultural loan;
企業貸款 business loan;
汽車貸款 car loan;
軟貸款 soft loan;
商業貸款 business loan; commercial loan;
無息貸款 interest-free credit; interest-free loan;
信用貸款 fiduciary loan;
學生貸款 student loan;
一筆貸款 a loan;
銀行貸款 banking lending; bank loan;
住房貸款 home loan;
專項貸款 special-purpose loan;

稱貸 borrow money;
高利貸 usurious loan; usury;
告貸 ask for a loan;
借貸 borrow money; lend money;
寬貸 forgive; pardon;
農貸 agricultural loan;
乞貸 beg for a loan;
求貸 ask for loan;
賒貸 credit;
信貸 credit;
轉貸 subloan;

dai
【逮】 reach;
[逮捕] arrest; take into custody;
非法逮捕 make a false arrest;
突然逮捕 make a surprise arrest;

dai
【戴】 (1) put on; wear; (2) have on; wear; (3) honour; respect; (4) a surname;
[戴上] don; put on;
戴上鐐銬 hangcuffing; in irons;
[戴孝] in mourning;

愛戴 hold in high esteem; love and esteem; love and respect; love and support; love deeply and support; respect and support; revere;
感戴 feel indebted;
穿戴 clothing; dress;
感戴 sincerely grateful;
推戴 nominate and support sb assuming leadership;
欣戴 gladly support;
依戴 rely on and look up to sb;
翊戴 assist and support a ruler;
翼戴 assist and support;
擁戴 support sb as leader or assuming leadership;

dai
【黛】 a black pigment used by women in ancient times to paint their eyebrows;
[黛綠] dark green;

粉黛 palace lady; young beauty;
石黛 a black pigment used by women in ancient times to paint their eyebrows;

dai
【襶】 ignorant; naive; unsophisticated;

dai
【靆】 (1) cloudy sky; (2) dark; not clear; obscure;

dan¹
dan
【丹】 (1) red; (2) pellet; powder;
[丹桂] orange osmanthus;
[丹青] painting;
丹青妙筆 superb artistry in painting; superb touch of a great painter;
妙手丹青 skilful painter;
[丹田] pubic region;
丹田之氣 deep breath controlled by the diaphragm;
[丹心] loyal heart; loyalty;
碧血丹心 deep patriotism; loyal-hearted;
一寸丹心 a loyal heart; loyalty; one's heart remains true to the end; thoroughly faithful and reliable;
一片丹心 a heart of pure loyalty; a loyal heart; a piece of loyalty;

紅丹 minium; red lead;
黃丹 yellow lead;
煉丹 make pills of immortality;
靈丹 miraculous cure; panacea;
牡丹 peony; tree peony;
秋牡丹 autumn peony;

山丹 morningstar lily;
鐵丹 ferric oxide;
仙丹 cure-all; divine pill; elixir of life; panacea;

dan
【眈】 look downward;
［眈眈］ eye gloatingly; look at greedily;
虎視眈眈 eye with hostility; hungry watchfulness; watch sb with hungry eyes;

dan
【耽】 (1) delay; (2) abandon oneself to; indulge in;
［耽擱］ (1) stay; stop over; (2) delay;
故意耽擱 make intentional delay;
在路上耽擱 tarry on the way;
［耽誤］ delay; hold up;
耽誤功夫 waste time;
耽誤時間 waste time;
［耽於］ addict; indulge in;
耽於幻想 indulge in illusion;
耽於酒色 crazy about wine and woman;
耽於逸樂 indulge in pleasure;

dan
【聃】 (1) another name for Lao Zi; (2) deformed ear;

dan
【酖】 be addicted to alcoholic drinks;

dan
【單】 (1) one; single; (2) odd; (3) alone; singly; (4) alone; only; (5) simple; (6) thin; weak; (7) flyer; (8) sheet; (9) bill; list;
［單板］ veneer;
拼接單板 edge-gluing veneer;
花紋單板 figured veneer;
中心單板 core veneer;
裝飾單板 decorative veneer;
［單薄］ (1) little; thin; (2) frail; thin and weak; (3) flimsy; insubstantial; thin;
力量單薄 weak in strength;
身體單薄 as weak as a cat; be delicately built; have a poor physique;
衣着單薄 be thinly clad; in a canty dress; wear very little clothes;
［單撥兒］ alone; single;
［單車］ bicycle; bike;
電單車 motorbike; motorcycle;
~小型電單車 scooter;
［單程］ one path; one way;
單程票 one-way ticket; single ticket;
~一張單程票 a single ticket;
單程證 One Way Permit;
［單純］ (1) pure; simple; (2) alone; merely; purely;
思想單純 innocent thought;
［單詞］ single word;
單詞動詞 single-word verb;
單詞素詞 morpheme word;
［單打］ singles;
單打邊線 side line for singles;
［單單］ alone; except; of all; only; solely;
［單調］ dull; monotonous;
單調的顏色 dull colouring; flat colour;
單調乏味 monotonous;
［單獨］ all alone; alone; by oneself; independent; on one's own; single-handed; solo;
單獨行動 take one's own line;
［單方面］ one-sided; unilateral;
單方面廢除條約 unilaterally repudiate a treaty;
單方面停火 cease-fire carried out by one side only;
［單槓］ horizontal bar;
單槓握法 grip;
［單軌］ monorail;
單軌制 monorail system;
［單花式］ (of hairstyle) wavy;
［單簧管］ clarinet;
單簧管演奏者 clarinetist;
單簧管樂師 clarinetist;
低音單簧管 bass clarinet;
~特低音單簧管 contrabass clarinet;
高音單簧管 soprano clarinet;
~超高音單簧管 sopranino clarinet;
中音單簧管 alto clarinet;
［單間］ separate room; single room;
小單間 en suite room;
［單腳跳］ hop;
［單據］ bill; invoice; receipt; voucher;
貨運單據 shipping document;
［單戀］ unrequited love;
［單親］ lone parent; single parent;
單親家庭 lone-parent family; single-parent family;
單親生殖 mongenic reproduction; monogensis;
［單人］ single;
單人牀 single bed;

單人房 single room;

[單色] monochrome; monocolour;
單色器 monochromator;
~晶體單色器 crystal monochromator;
~聚光單色器 condensing monochromator;
~彎晶單色器 bent-crystal monochromator;
單色儀 monochrometer;
~雙單色儀 double monochrometer;

[單身] (1) single; unmarried; (2) live alone;
單身獨居 live alone; live in solitude;
單身公寓 bachelor flat;
單身漢 bachelor;
~誓不結婚的單身漢 confirmed bachelor;
單身母親 single mother;
單身男子 bachelor;
單身女子 bachelorette; spinster; unmarried woman;
單身派對 bachelor party;
單身宿舍 bachelor quarters;
單身在外 live alone away from home;

[單式] single;
單式會計 single entry accounting;

[單瘦] skinny; thin;

[單數] odd number;

[單挑] challenge sb on one's own; do sth by oneself; work on one's own;

[單位] entity; unit;
單位詞 partitive;
~量度單位詞 measure partitive;
單位名詞 unit noun;
單位制 system of units;
~絕對單位制 absolute units;
抽象單位 abstract unit;
詞匯單位 lexical unit;
次要單位 secondary unit;
法人單位 impersonal entity;
翻譯單位 unit of translation;
基層單位 basic unit;
絕對單位 absolute unit;
類別單位 generic unit;
企業單位 enterprise entity; enterprise unit;
私樓單位 private flat;
事業單位 institutional unit;
吸聲單位 absorption unit;
下級單位 subordinate unit;
相連單位 combined flats;
行政單位 administrative unit;
亞單位 subunit;
~催化亞單位 catalytic subunit;
~蛋白質亞單位 protein subunit;
~核蛋白體亞單位 ribosomal subunit;
~調節亞單位 regulator subunit;

[單細] delicate; slender;

[單向] uni-direction;
單向系統 uni-directional system;

[單形] simplex;
抽象單形 abstract simplex;
絕對單形 absolute simplex;
開單形 open simplex;
有向單形 oriented simplex;
有序單形 ordered simplex;

[單行線] one way;

[單一] single; unitary;
單一翻譯 unit translation;
單一隱喻 simplex metaphor;

[單元] module; unit;
一個單元 a module;

[單字] (1) individual characters; (2) separate word;

[單座] single seat;
單座飛機 single seater aeroplane;

保單 (1) guaranteed warranty; warranty; (2) insurance policy;
保險單 insurance policy;
報單 (1) declaration form; taxation form; (2) a report of success;
被單 bed sheet; coverlet;
不單 not merely; not only; not simply;
菜單 menu;
艙單 manifest;
成績單 school report;
傳單 flyer; leaflet; handbill; propaganda sheet;
牀單 bedclothes; sheet;
催單 reminder;
存單 deposit receipt;
單單 alone; only;
點菜單 order slip;
訂單 order for goods; order form;
定單 order for goods; order form;
賭注單 betting slip;
發單 bill; receipt;
發貨單 dispatch list;
購單 purchase order;
孤單 (1) alone; (2) lonely;
掛單 put up at a temple for a short stay;
黑名單 blacklist;
回單 receipt;
貨單 manifest; waybill;

貨運單 waybill;
價目單 price list;
簡單 (1) simple; uncomplicated; (2) commonplace; (3) casual; oversimplified;
禮單 list of presents;
落單 place an order;
埋單 check the bill;
名單 name list;
憑單 voucher;
欠單 accommodation note;
衾單 blanket for covering the corpse;
清單 detailed account; detailed list; inventory; repertoire;
煢單 all alone in the whole wide world;
褥單 bed sheet;
賒單 I.O.U. receipt;
食單 menu;
書單 book list;
稅單 tax form; tax list;
索書單 book slip;
提單 bill of lading;
提貨單 bill of lading;
選單 menu;
藥單 prescription;
月結單 monthly statement;
運單 bill of lading;
棧單 warrant;
賬單 bill; check; reckoning; statement of account;
罩單 drop cloth;

dan
【儋】 (1) shoulder a burden; (2) a load of two piculs;

dan
【鄲】 (1) a county in Henan; (2) a surname;

dan
【擔】 (1) carry on a shoulder pole; (2) take on; undertake;

[擔保] assurance; bail; ensure; go bail for; guarantee; surety; swear; take an oath; upon my honour; upon my name; upon my word; vouch for; vow; warrant;
擔保承兌人 acceptor for honour;
擔保品 collateral;
擔保債權人 secured creditor;
法定擔保 statutory guarantee;
獲得擔保 get surety;
接受擔保 accept the security;
解除擔保 release of guarantee;
拒絕擔保 decline the security;
拿名譽擔保 give one's word of honour;
拿腦袋擔保 stake one's head on;
拿生命擔保 pawn one's life;
人身擔保 personal security;
雙重擔保 double securities;
提供擔保 offer the security;
投標擔保 bid guarantee;
物質擔保 material security;
無限責任擔保 unlimited guarantee;
信貸擔保 credit guarantee;
銀行擔保 bank guarantee;
政府信用擔保 government credit guarantee;

[擔待] (1) take on; take the responsibility; undertake; (2) excuse; forgive; pardon;

[擔當] assume; take on; undertake;
擔當重任 take on heavy responsibilities;
一身擔當 face everything oneself;

[擔負] be charged with; bear; shoulder; take on; undertake;
擔負部分費用 bear a part of the expense;
擔負領導工作 hold a leading post;
擔負全部費用 bear the whole expense;
擔負全部工作 undertake a full share of the job;
擔負一項艱難任務 be engaged in a difficult task; take up a difficult task;
擔負責任 shoulder one's responsibilities; take up one's responsibilities;
擔負重任 take on heavy responsibilities; undertake an important business;

[擔架] stretcher;
擔架牀 stretcher;

[擔驚受怕] afraid and on edge; feel alarmed; in a state of anxiety; in a state of apprehension;

[擔任] (1) act as; serve as; (2) assume the office of; hold the post of;
擔任裁判 act as referee; serve as referee;
擔任公職 hold public office;
擔任經理一職 hold a position as manager;
擔任領導工作 assume a leading position;
擔任要職 hold a post of great responsibility;
擔任主席 take the chair;

[擔心] apprehension; feel anxious; have apprehensions for; under the apprehension; worry;
擔心暴力行為發生 fear eruptions of violence;
擔心得要死 worry oneself to death;

表示擔心 express the worry that;
別擔心 don't worry;
不必擔心 not to worry;
極為擔心 be worried sick; sick with worry;
時刻擔心 live in constant fear of;
天天擔心 live in daily fear that;
為…擔心 worry for;
- 為別人安全擔心 worry for sb's safety;
無須擔心 need not worry;

[擔憂] anxious; worry;
為將來擔憂 feel anxious for the future;

扁擔 carrying pole;
承擔 assume; bear; shoulder; undertake;
分擔 share responsibility for;
負擔 bear a burden; shoulder burden;
挑擔 carry a load with a carrying pole;
一擔 a load of; two baskets of; two buckets of;
重擔 difficult task; heavy burden; heavy load; heavy responsibility;

dan

【殫】 exhaust; use up;
[殫悶] faint; lose consciousness; swoon;

dan

【簞】 round bamboo ware for holding cooked rice;
[簞食瓢飲] bread and water diet; lead a simple life; live an ascetic life;

dan³

dan

【疸】 jaundice;

黑疸 smut;
黃疸 jaundice;

dan

【撣】 (1) dust; (2) duster;
[撣掉] whisk off;
[撣灰] brush off dust; dust;
[撣土] brush off the dust; whisk away the dust;

dan

【膽】 (1) gallbladder; (2) courage; guts; (3) double-walled glass bottle in a vacuum flask;
[膽大] audacious; bold;
膽大包天 audacious in the extreme; without desperate daring;
膽大妄為 act in a foolhardy manner; be undaunted and reckless; daredevil; impudent; rush in where angels fear to tread; unscrupulous;
~膽大妄為的人 daredevil;
膽大心細 bold but cautious; brave but not reckless; courageous but meticulous;
沉著膽大 of steady nerve;
天生膽大 have courage in one's blood;
藝高人膽大 boldness of execution stems from superb skill;
[膽道] biliary tract;
膽道出血 bleeding in the biliary tract and gallbladder; heamatobilia;
膽道膿腫 biliary abscess;
[膽敢] dare; have the audacity to;
[膽固醇] cholesterol;
膽固醇過多 excess cholesterol; hypercholesterolia;
膽固醇結石 cholesterol calculus; cholesterol stone;
膽固醇血症 hypercholesterolemia;
低密度膽固醇 low-density lipoprotein;
高密度膽固醇 high-density lipoprotein;
總膽固醇 total cholesterol;
[膽管] bile vessels; biliary duct; bile duct; gall duct;
膽管癌 bile duct carcinoma;
膽管病 cholepathy; disease of the gallbladder;
膽管肝炎 cholangiohepatitis;
膽管結石 bile duct calculus;
膽管擴張 cholangiectasis;
膽管瘤 cholangioma;
膽管炎 cholangitis;
[膽寒] lose one's nerve;
[膽蛔蟲病] biliary ascariasis;
[膽絞痛] billary colic;
[膽結石] cholelithiasis;
[膽力] bravery; courage;
[膽量] boldness; courage; guts;
膽量過人 bolder than all the rest;
膽量很大 full of pluck; have a lot of spunk; have plenty of guts;
沒有膽量 gutless; lack courage;
有膽量 have courage; have the guts;
[膽裂] scared to death;
膽裂魂飛 be frightened out of one's wits;
魂飛膽裂 be frigtened out of one's wits; strike terror into sb's heart;
[膽略] courage and resourcefulness; daring and resolution;
膽略過人 have unusual courage and

resourcefulness;
[膽落] extremely frightened;
[膽囊] gallbladder;
膽囊病 cholecystopathy; disease of the gallbladder;
增生性膽囊病 hyperplastic cholecystosis;
膽囊動脈 cystic artery;
膽囊管 cystic duct;
膽囊結石病 cholecystolithiasis;
膽囊靜脈 cystic vein;
膽囊擴張 cholecystectasia;
膽囊淋巴結 cystic lymph node;
膽囊瘻 amphibolic fistula;
膽囊切除 cholecystectomy; removal of the gallbladder;
膽囊痛 cholecystalgia;
膽囊炎 cholecystitis; inflammation of the gallbladder;
~ 出血性膽囊炎 hemocholecystitis;
~ 濾泡性膽囊炎 follicular cholecystitis;
~ 慢性膽囊炎 chronic cholecystitis;
~ 膿氣性膽囊炎 pyopneumocholecystitis;
~ 氣腫性膽囊炎 cholecystitis emphysematosa;
膽囊移位 gallbladder displacement;
膽囊周圍炎 pericholecystitis;
膽囊周炎 pericholecystitis;
~ 氣腫性膽囊周炎 gaseous pericholecystitis;
[膽破] be frightened to death; be scared to death;
嚇破了膽 be psyched out; be scared out of one's wits; panic-stricken; strike terror into the hearts of;
[膽氣] courage;
[膽怯] cold feet; have cold feet; show the white feather;
膽怯的 diffident;
~ 膽怯的人 timid person;
膽怯起來 have a yellow belly;
克服膽怯 overcome one's timidity;
天生膽怯 timid by nature;
顯得膽怯 look coward;
心虛膽怯 apprehensive and coward; have a guilty conscience;
[膽石] cholelith; gallstone;
膽石病 biliary calculus; gallstone;
膽石切除 cholelithotomy;
膽石症 cholelithiasis; gallstone;
膽石溶解藥 anticholelithogenic;
[膽識] courage and insight;
膽識過人 exceed the rest in bravery and wisdom; surpass others in intelligence and determination;
有膽有識 courageous and knowledgeable;
[膽小] chicken-hearted; chicken-livered; cowardice; cowardliness; cowardly; timid;
膽小的 craven; lily-livered;
膽小鬼 chicken; chicken guy; chickenshit; coward; poltroon; sad coward; weakling;
膽小怕事 chicken-hearted; chicken-livered; cowardly; timid; timid and overcautious; yellow-bellied;
timid and overcautious; yellow-bellied;
膽小如鼠 afraid of one's shadow; as timid as a hare; as timid as a mouse; be a coward; chicken-hearted; mouselike timidity;
人大膽小 muscular but timid;
[膽虛] jittery; nervous; scared;
[膽汁] bile; fearless; full of courage;
苦如膽汁 as bitter as gall;
[膽壯] fearless; full of courage;
志堅膽壯 determined and brave;
[膽子] courage; nerve;
[膽總管] common bile duct;

赤膽 sincere loyalty;
大膽 bold; daring;
斗膽 bold;
放膽 act boldly and with confidence;
肝膽 (1) courage; heroic spirit; (2) open-heartedness; sincerity;
孤膽 all alone or all by oneself;
海膽 sea urchin;
苦膽 gall bladder;
瀝膽 manifest great bravery;
裂膽 extremely frightened; extremely scared;
落膽 be frightened out of one's wits; very scared;
瓶膽 glass liner for a vacuum flask;
破膽 be scared out of one's wits;
球膽 ball bladder;
喪膽 be frightened out of one's wits; disheartened; lose nerve; panic-stricken; smitten with fear; terror-stricken;
鼠膽 cowardice;
心膽 (1) heart and gall; (2) will and courage;
壯膽 embolden; screw up one's courage; strengthen one's courage;

dan

【黵】 tattoo a criminal's face;

［黵面］ ancient punishment of tattooing a criminal's face;

dan⁴

dan

【旦】 (1) dawn; daybreak; (2) day; (3) female character in Beijing opera;

［旦旦而伐］ have sexual intercourse every night;

［旦夕］ in a short while;

旦夕禍福 fortune is fickle; sudden changes of fortune; unexpected good or bad fortune;

旦夕難保 in imminent peril;

旦夕之間 in a day's time; in a short moment; overnight;

旦夕之危 immediate danger; imminent danger;

命在旦夕 death stared at one in the face; dying; in peril of one's life; on the verge of death; one's life is not worth a day's purchase;

危在旦夕 at death's door; at the last gasp; death is expected at any moment; in deadly danger; in imminent danger; not worth a day's purchase; on the verge of death; on the verge of destruction;

彩旦 young female character in Chinese operas;

丑旦 comedienne; woman clown;

達旦 until dawn;

穀旦 auspicious day;

花旦 female character in Chinese operas;

老旦 old female character in Chinese operas;

申旦 from night till morning;

武旦 female character performing martial art and swordplay in Chinese operas;

一旦 in a single day; in a very short time;

元旦 New Year's Day;

月旦 appraise people;

正旦 (1) Lunar New Year's Day; (2) female character in Chinese operas;

dan

【石】 unit of dry measure for grain;

dan

【但】 (1) but yet; (2) merely; only;

［但凡］ anybody; as long as; in every case; whatever; whenever; without exception;

［但是］ but;

［但願］ I wish; if only;

但願不會 I hope not;

但願如此 be it so; I hope so; I hope that's right; I only hope it is so; I simply wish it to be so; I wish it were true; let it be so; let's hope so; so be it;

不但 not only;

非但 not only;

豈但 not only;

dan

【啖】 eat; feed;

dan

【淡】 (1) light; thin; (2) tasteless; weak; (3) light; pale; (4) indifferent; (5) dull; off-season; slack; (6) meaningless; trivial; (7) same as 氮, nitrogen;

［淡巴巴］ insipid; tasteless;

［淡泊］ lead a tranquil and simple life;

淡泊苦難 adopt a stoic attitude in the presence of sufferings;

淡泊名利 indifferent to fame and wealth;

淡泊明志 live a simple life, showing one's aspiration;

寧定淡泊 serene;

［淡出］ fade out;

淡出淡入 fade in and fade out;

［淡淡］ light; slight;

淡淡一笑 with a faint smile;

［淡飯］ simple food;

淡飯粗茶 homely fare; plain food; simple diet; simple food and plain tea;

［淡化］ (1) desalination; (2) dilute; (3) weaken; (4) downplay; play down;

［淡黃］ light yellow;

［淡季］ dull season; low season; off season; slack srason;

在淡季 in the dull season; in the low season; in the off season;

［淡酒］ light wine;

淡酒粗菜 light wine and plain dishes — a simple meal;

［淡墨］ light ink;

［淡漠］ (1) apathetic; indifferent; nonchalant; (2) dim; faint; hazy;

淡漠視之 look at...nonchalantly;

淡漠無情 indifferent and merciless;
對人很淡漠 a cold fish;
態度淡漠 assume a nonchalant attitude; have an attitude of indifference; show an attitude of indifference;
顯得淡漠 show indifference to;
[淡然] cool; indifferent;
淡然處之 give the cold shoulder to; regard coolly; take it with indifference; take things coolly; treat with indifference; turn the cold shoulder on;
[淡弱] weak;
[淡色] delicate shade; light colour; tinge;
[淡水] fresh water;
淡水養魚 raise fresh-water fish;
淡水魚 freshwater fish;
供應淡水 provide fresh water;
[淡忘] fade from one's memory;
被人淡忘 fade out from people's memory;
[淡雅] simple and elegant;
[淡月] slack month;
淡月輕雲 glimmering moon and light clouds;

暗淡 bleak; dim; dismal; drab; dull; gloomy; obscure;
黯淡 dim; faint; gloomy;
慘淡 (1) dismal; gloomy; (2) take great pains to carry on one's work under difficult circumstances;
扯淡 talk nonsense;
沖淡 (1) dilute; (2) water down; weaken;
寡淡 boring; dull; insipid;
冷淡 (1) give the cold shoulder to; leave sb out in the cold; slight; treat coldly; turn the cold shoulder to sb; (2) cheerless; desolate; slack; (3) cold; coldness; frigid; indifferent;
平淡 dull; flat; insipid; pedestrian; prosaic; savourless; uninteresting;
清淡 (1) delicate; light; weak; (2) light; not greasy; (3) dull; slack;
輕淡 light; mild; thin;
濡淡 dye;
散淡 lead a leisure life; relax;
稍淡 relatively plain;
素淡 tint;
恬淡 indifferent to fame or gain;
雅淡 simple and elegant;

dan
【蛋】 (1) egg; (2) egg-shaped;
[蛋白] albumen; egg white;
蛋白酶 proteinase;
蛋白尿 albuminuria;
蛋白尿症 proteinuria;
心臟性蛋白尿症 cardiac proteinuria;
~殘餘蛋白尿 residual proteinuria;
~發熱性蛋白尿 febrile proteinuria;
~功能性蛋白尿 functional proteinuria;
~假蛋白尿 pseudalbuminuria;
~間歇性蛋白尿 intermittent proteinuria;
~內源性蛋白尿 intrinsic proteinuria;
~膿性蛋白尿 pyogenic proteinuria;
~輕鏈蛋白尿 light-chain proteinuria;
~腎形蛋白尿 renal proteinuria;
~生理性蛋白尿 physiologic proteinuria;
~雙蛋白尿 diploalbuminuria;
~特發性蛋白尿 essential proteinuria;
~調節性蛋白尿 regulatory preteinuria;
~痛風性蛋白尿 gouty proteinuria;
~透明蛋白尿 hyalinuria;
~消化性蛋白尿 digestive proteinuria;
~心形蛋白尿 cardiac proteinuria;
~夜蛋白尿 noctalluminuria;
~溢出性蛋白尿 overflow proteinuria;
~飲食性蛋白尿 dietetic proteinuria;
~原發性蛋白尿 essential proteinuria;
~運動性蛋白尿 athletic proteinuria;
~真性蛋白尿 true proteinuria;
~陣發性蛋白尿 paroxysmal proteinuria;
~直立蛋白尿 orthostatic proteinuria;
~自發性蛋白尿 essential proteinuria;
蛋白石 opal;
蛋白酥 meringue;
蛋白質 protein;
~蛋白質密碼學 protein cryptography;
~動物蛋白質 animal protein;
~含有豐富蛋白質 high in protein content;
~細胞蛋白質 cell protein;
~血清蛋白質 blood serum protein;
~植物蛋白質 vegetable protein;
白蛋白 albumin; white of the egg;
~卵白蛋白 egg albumin;
高蛋白 high protein;
核蛋白 nucleoprotein;
肌動蛋白 actin;
肌球蛋白 myosin;
角蛋白 keratin;
可凝蛋白 coagulable protein;
凝固蛋白 coagulated protein;
清蛋白 albumin;
球蛋白 globulin;
~抗體球蛋白 antibody globulin;

~卵球蛋白 egg globulin;
~免疫球蛋白 immune globulin;
~血清球蛋白 serum globulin;
酸性蛋白 acidic protein;
糖蛋白 glucoprotein; glycoprotein;
血漿蛋白 plasma proteins;

[蛋糕] cake;
蛋糕刀 cake knife;
蛋糕店 cake shop;
蛋糕烤盤 cake pan; cake tin;
蛋糕食譜 cake recipe;
白色蛋糕 angel cake;
磅蛋糕 pound cake;
杯形蛋糕 cupcake;
疊層大蛋糕 multi-layered cake;
果料蛋糕 fruit cake;
果仁蛋糕 nutty cake;
海綿蛋糕 sponge cake;
花生蛋糕 peanut cake;
花飾蛋糕 decoration cake;
雞蛋糕 whole-egg cake;
夾層蛋糕 sandwich cake;
結婚蛋糕 wedding cake;
精靈蛋糕 fairy cake;
卷筒蛋糕 sponge cake roll;
奶油蛋糕 butter cake;
普通蛋糕 plain cake;
巧克力蛋糕 chocolate cake;
生日蛋糕 birthday cake;
水果蛋糕 fruit cake;
鬆蛋糕 sponge cake;
仙女蛋糕 fairy cake;
小蛋糕 petit four;
一塊蛋糕 a piece of cake;
一小塊蛋糕 a silver of cake;
紙杯蛋糕 cupcake;
裝飾蛋糕 decorate a cake;
做蛋糕 bake a cake; make a cake;

[蛋盒] egg carton;
[蛋殼] eggshell;
[蛋花湯] egg-drop soup;
[蛋黃] yolk;
蛋黃醬 mayonnaise;
[蛋雞] egg-laying hen; layer;
[蛋卷] egg-roll;
[蛋殼] eggshell;
[蛋民] fisherman;
[蛋品] egg product;
[蛋清] albumen; egg white;

菢蛋 hatch eggs;
笨蛋 addlehead; airhead; asshole; blubberhead; bonehead; boob; booby; bozo; brack-brain; burk; charlie; chowderhead; chucklehead; chump; cretin; cunt; dipshit; duffer; fathead; fool; half-wit; idiot; knucklehead; moron; muppet; nimrod; ninny; nit; nitwit; numbskull; numptie; pillock; schnook; silly billy; stupid fellow; sucker; wanker;
鱉蛋 bastard; turtle's egg;
冰蛋 frozen egg;
彩蛋 painted egg;
操蛋 bad; disappointing; no good;
炒蛋 scrambled egg;
蠢蛋 dumbo;
搗蛋 (1) give sb a hard time; (2) act up; do mischief; make trouble; mischief; monkey around;
鵝蛋 goose's egg;
滾蛋 beat it; drop dead; eff off; fuck off; get away; get out; go piss up a rope; off with you; scram; sling your hook;
壞蛋 bad apple; bad egg; bad guy; bad hat; baddie; boogeyman; dirtbag; rotten apple;
混蛋 bastard;
渾蛋 blackguard; wretch;
雞蛋 hen's egg;
懶蛋 idler;
滷蛋 spiced corned egg;
皮蛋 preserved egg;
貧蛋 prater;
窮光蛋 pauper; poor wretch;
傻蛋 balmy; blockhead; bloody fool; booby; chuckle head; chump; -clod; clodhopper; clodpoll; clot; cluck; crackpot; cuckoo; daft; dead from the neck up; dense; fat-head; fool; gump; idiot; moon-raker; mug; sawney; schmo; schmuck; silly; simpleton; stupid chap;
松花蛋 preserved egg;
完蛋 all over; all up; be busted; be doomed; be done for; be finished; be ruined; busted; collapse;
下蛋 lay eggs;
鴨蛋 duck's egg;
糟蛋 egg pickled in wine;
煮蛋 boil an egg;

dan

【氮】 nitrogen;
[氮肥] nitrogenous fertilizer;
[氮氣] nitrogen; nitrogen gas;
[氮素] nitrogen;

氮素循環 nitrogen cycle;
［氮源］ origin of nitrogen;

dan

【萏】 water lily;
菡萏 lotus;

dan

【彈】 (1) ball; pellet; (2) bomb; bullet;
［彈道］ ballistic; trajectory;
彈道導彈 ballistic missile;
彈道火箭 ballistic rocket;
彈道曲線 ballistic curve;
彈道學 ballistics;
~彈道學家 ballistician;
~穿甲彈道學 penetration ballistics;
~電子彈道學 electron ballistics;
~火箭彈道學 rocket ballistics;
~內彈道學 interior ballistics;
~外彈道學 exterior ballistics;
~終段彈道學 terminal ballistics;
半射彈道 flat trajectory;
不定彈道 arbitrary ballistics;
放射彈道 ballistic trajectory;
氣動彈道 aerodynamic trajectory;
上升彈道 ascending trajectory;
下降彈道 descending trajectory;
［彈盡糧絕］ exhaust one's supplies and ammunition; expend all one's ammunition and provisions; run out of ammunition and food supplies;
［彈藥］ ammunition;
彈藥箱 caisson;
彈藥用盡 expend all one's ammunition;
供應彈藥 provide ammunition; supply with ammunition;
航空彈藥 air ammunition;
運送彈藥 transport ammunition;
［彈子］ billiards;

拆彈 bomb disposal;
臭彈 stink bomb;
催淚彈 lachrymatory bomb; lachrymatory shell; tear bomb; tear-gas grenade;
導彈 guided missile; missile;
動彈 move; stir;
防彈 bulletproof; shellproof;
飛彈 (1) missile; (2) bullet;
核彈 N-bomb; nuclear bomb;
回彈 resilience;
流彈 stray bullet;
榴彈 grenade; high explosive shell;
榴散彈 cluster bomb;
砲彈 artillery shell; bullet; cannonball; cartridge; shell;
礮彈 cannon ball; cannon shot; shell;
鉛彈 lead bullet;
槍彈 bullet; cartridge;
槍榴彈 rifle grenade;
氫彈 hydrogen bomb;
肉彈 buxom beauty; sex bomb;
實彈 live ammunition;
手榴彈 hand grenade;
鐵彈 cannonball;
投彈 (1) drop a bomb; (2) throw a hand grenade;
霰彈 canister shot; shrapnel;
械彈 weapons and ammunition;
信號彈 flare bomb;
煙幕彈 smoke bomb; smoke shell;
飲彈 be hit by a bullet;
原子彈 atomic bomb;
炸彈 bomb;
照明彈 flare; star shell;
柘彈 a slingshot made of the tree;
中彈 be struck by a bullet; get shot;
中子彈 neutron bomb;
子彈 bullet; cartridge;

dan

【憚】 fear; toil;
［憚煩］ afraid of trouble; dislike taking trouble;

忌憚 dread; fear;

dan

【誕】 (1) birth; (2) birthday; (3) absurd; fantastic;
［誕辰］ birthday;
［誕生］ be born; come into being; come into existence; come into the world; emerge;

放誕 in an absurd and wild manner;
怪誕 eccentric; odd; strange;
荒誕 absurd; ridiculous;
恢誕 exaggerated;
誇誕 boastful; exaggerative;
欺誕 cheat by exaggerating;
聖誕 Christmas;
壽誕 birthday of an elderly person;
虛誕 fantastic; preposterous; unreal;
陶誕 boastful;
迂誕 absurd; preposterous;

dan

【擔】 burden; load;

［擔擔麵］ Sichuan hot noodles;
［擔子］ burden on one's shoulder;
挑擔子 bear a load on one's shoulder;

dan

【澹】 calm; quiet;
［澹泊］ not seek for fame and wealth;
澹泊名利 indifferent towards fame and wealth;
澹泊明志 live a simple life, showing one's true goal in life;
澹泊自甘 be content with a simple life;
［澹然］ calm and tranquil;

dan

【癉】 (1) detest; hate bitterly; (2) drought; dry; (3) an illness caused by over-exhaustion;

dang[1]
dang

【當】 (1) accept; assume; face; undertake; (2) equal; well-matched; (3) the very same; (4) should; ought to;
［當班］ on duty;
［當兵］ be a soldier; serve in the army;
去當兵 enter the army; go into the army;
［當差］ work as a petty official or servant;
［當場］ dead to rights; in one's tracks; in the act of; on the dot; on the nail; on the spot; then and there; there and then;
當場被捕 be caught in the act;
當場出醜 make a spectacle of oneself; suffer embarrassment right before a crowd;
當場逮住 catch in one's tracks; catch in the act; catch red-handed;
當場付款 pay on the nail;
當場交貨 spot delivery;
當場就擒 be caught in the very act; be caught on the spot; be caught red-handed;
當場決定 decide on the spot;
當場完成 complete sth on the spot;
［當初］ (1) at that time; at the beginning; at the outset; in the first place; originally; used to; (2) at that time; formerly; in the past;
悔不當初 kick oneself; regret for a previous mistake; regret having done sth;
［當代］ the present age; the contemporary era;
當代經濟 contemporary economy;
當代科技 contemporary technology;
當代時尚 modern fashion trend;
當代外交 contemporary diplomatic relations;
當代文學 contemporary literature;
當代英語 present-day English;
當代政治 contemporary politics;
當代最偉大的詩人 greatest contemporary poet;
［當道］ (1) in power; (2) block one's way;
惡人當道 the evildoers are now in power;
［當地］ in the locality; local; this place;
當地標準時間 local standard time;
當地風土人情 local customs and mores;
當地人 the local people; the native people; the natives;
當地時間 local time;
［當關］ guard a pass;
一夫當關 hold a key position signle-handedly;
［當機立斷］ decide in the nick of time; decide on the moment; decide on the spot; decide promptly and opportunely; make a prompt decision; prompt decision at the right moment; take prompt action;
［當即］ at once; right away;
［當家］ chief cook and bottle washer; decision maker in business management; manage household affairs; play the leading role; wear the pants in the family;
當家的 person-in-charge in a family;
當家理財 take charge of household affairs and administer financial affairs;
當家作主 in power; in the driving seat; master in one's own house; rule the roast; rule the roost; the master of one's own affairs;
不當家不知柴米貴 he who takes charge knows the responsibility;
［當街］ (1) face the street; (2) in the street;
［當今］ at present; now; nowadays;
當今之世 at the present time; in the world of today;
［當局］ the authorities;
當局者迷 blunt are those concerned; men are blind in their own cause; those closely involved cannot see clearly;

當局者迷，旁觀者清 lookers-on see more than players; lookers-on see most of the game; one who is concerned in the matter has not been able to see so clearly as one who is not himself involved; standers-by see more than gamesters; the doer is not clear about what he is doing while the onlooker sees it clearly; the onlooker sees most of the game; the onlooker sees the game best; the spectators see the chess game better than the players; those involved cannot see as clearly as the outsider;

抱怨當局 make complaints against the authorities;

裁判當局 adjudicatory authority;

大學當局 the authorities of the university;

地方當局 the local authorities;

服從當局 obey the authorities;

管理當局 regulatory authority;

國家當局 the authorities of the state;

合法當局 constituted authorities;

民政當局 civil authority;

説服當局 convince the authorities;

衛生當局 health authority;

學校當局 school authority;

有關當局 appropriate authority; the authorities concerned;

政府當局 the government authorities;

主管當局 the authorities in charge;

[當空] in the sky;

皎月當空 a bright moon hung in the sky;

[當量] equivalent;

苯胺當量 aniline equivalent;

化學當量 chemical equivalent;

克當量 gram equivalent;

空氣當量 air equivalent;

[當令] in season;

[當面] face to face; in sb's presence; personally; right in one's face; to sb's face;

當面駁斥 refute sb face to face;

當面不説，背後亂説 say nothing in one's face, but gossip a lot behind one's back;

當面嘲笑 laugh in sb's face;

當面斥責 rebuke sb to his face;

當面吹捧 flatter sb to his face;

當面錯過 let the chance slip by;

當面抵賴 deny in front of sb;

當面對質 confront each other;

當面奉承 flatter sb to his face; praise sb to sb's face;

當面講清楚 straighten things out face to face;

當面叫哥哥，背後摸傢伙 a mouth that praises and a hand that kills; honey on one's lips and murder in one's heart;

當面教子，背後教妻 you may admonish your children in the presence of others, but you wife, only in privacy;

當面較量 take sb on in a face-to-face encounter;

當面鑼，對面鼓 in one's presence; right in one's face;

當面排揎 give sb a piece of one's mind;

當面捧場，背後罵娘 pay compliments to someone's face but to curse and swear at the back; praise sb to his face and abuse him behind his back;

當面取笑 laugh in one's face;

當面認錯 personally to admit one's mistakes before sb;

當面撒謊 lie in one's throat; tell a barefaced lie;

當面是人，背後是鬼 act one way in public and another in private;

當面説得好聽，背後又在搗鬼 speak fine words to sb's face while using dirty tricks behind his back; speak nice words to sb's face but resort to underhand means behind his back; speak plausibly in sb's presence but do mischief behind his back;

當面説好，背後捅刀 say nice things to sb's face, then stab him in the back;

當面説好話，背後下毒手 say nice things to sb's face, then stab him in the back;

當面説明 state clearly in sb's presence;

當面訓斥 reprove sb to his face;

當面一套，背後一套 act one way in public and another in private; act one way to sb's face and another behind sb's back; say all the proper things to sb's face but do exactly the opposite at the back;

當面造謠 lies are told point-blank; tell a barefaced lie;

當面責難 fling sth up in sb's face; throw sth in sb's face;

當面嘲笑人 laugh in sb's face;

當面直言 say sth to one's face;

當面指控 charge sb with a crime personally;

［當年］ (1) in those days; in those days gone by; in those years; (2) in one's prime;

不減當年 just like one's old self;

正當年 in one's prime;

［當前］ (1) before one; facing one; (2) current; present;

當前的重大問題 major questions at present;

當前國際形勢 current international situation;

當前政局 political situation of the day;

大敵當前 be confronted with a formidable enemy;

［當權］ hold power; in power;

［當然］ (1) as it should be; it goes without saying that; (2) certainly; of course; sure; sure thing; to be sure; without doubt;

禮所當然 etiquette requires it;

理所當然 a natural and expected development; as a matter of course; as it ought to be; in accordance with what is right; in the nature of things; it goes without saying; it stands to reason; logical and natural; natural and right; naturally; of course; what propriety requires;

想當然 assume sth as a matter of course; take for granted;

［當仁不讓］ not to decline to shoulder a responsibility; not to leave to others what one ought to do oneself; not to pass on to others what one is called upon to do; not to shirk what one's obliged to do; take sth as one's obligation;

［當時］ at that time; at the moment; at the time; just at that moment; then;

當時當地 at a given time and place; then and there; there and then;

當時得意的人 hero of the hour; man of the hour;

［當事人］ (1) the parties concerned; (2) litigant; party to a dispute;

［當頭］ (1) head on; right on sb's head; right over head; (2) imminent;

當頭砲 severe criticism;

~挨當頭砲 suffer a severe criticism;

當頭捧喝 give a timely warning; issue a strong warning;

當頭一擊 death blow;

敢字當頭 place the word daring above everything else; put daring above all else;

公字當頭 put public interest to the fore;

怕字當頭 put the fear on everything;

私字當頭 make self-interest the first consideration; put self-interest in the van;

［當下］ at once; immediately; instantly;

活在當下 live in the present;

［當先］ at the head; in the front ranks; in the van;

一力當先 try one's utmost to be ahead of others;

一馬當先 foremost in the fight; in the first flight; in the forefront; in the foremost rank; in the top flight; in the van of; lead the field; lead the van; ride the fore-horse; rush forward in front of others; take the lead; the first to do work; the first to take on the enemy;

［當心］ (1) attention; be careful; beware; heads up; look out; mind; take care; watch one's step; watch out; (2) in the centre;

當心碰頭 mind your head;

［當選］ be elected;

當選為總統 be elected as President;

以多數票當選 be elected by a plurality of votes;

以全票當選 be elected by unanimous votes;

［當政］ hold political power; in office; in power;

［當值］ on duty;

［當中］ (1) in the centre; in the middle; (2) among;

［當眾］ before the public; in front of everybody; in public; in the presence of all; openly;

當眾出醜 bring shame on oneself in public; make a fool of oneself before others; make an exhibition of oneself; pull a boner;

當眾發脾氣 lose one's temper in public;

當眾認錯 acknowledge one's mistakes in public;

當眾申斥 reprove sb in the public;

D

當眾受辱 be insulted before a large company; be insulted in the presence of others;
當眾侮辱 affront; offer an affront to; put an affront upon a person;
當眾謝罪 apologize in public;
當眾羞辱 humiliate sb in public; offer an affront to sb in public;
當眾宣佈 announce to the public;

［伴當］ (1) servant; (2) partner;

本當 should have done sth;
不當 (1) careless; improper; inappropriate; not appropriate; unsuitable; (2) consider sth or sb as;
承當 assume; bear; take on;
充當 play the part of; serve as;
擔當 assume responsibility; take on; undertake;
該當 ought to; should;
理當 naturally; of course; should;
每當 each time; every time; whenever;
爽當 agile; brisk;
相當 (1) about; considerably; fairly; quite; rather; somewhat; to a great extent; very; (2) balance; correspond to; equivalent; match; (3) appropriate; fit; suitable;
應當 naturally; ought to; should;
正當 just the time for; just when;
自當 should naturally;

dang
【噹】 a loud, resonant metallic sound;
［噹啷］ clanking sound;

叮噹 ding-dong;
響噹噹 (1) loud metal sound; (2) famous; outstanding;

dang
【璫】 (1) richly ornamented; (2) ancient headgear;

玎璫 ding-dong; jingle; tinkle;

dang
【襠】 the crotch or bottom of a pair of trousers;

褲襠 crotch (of trousers);

dang
【鐺】 (1) ear ornament; (2) clang; clank;

鈴鐺 small bell;

dang³
dang
【當】 mistake sth for another;
［當是］ mistake sth for another; think that;

dang
【擋】 impede; obstruct; resist; stop; ward off;
［擋板］ shroud;
發動機擋板 engine shroud;
［擋風］ keep off winds; keep winds away;
擋風玻璃 windscreen; windshield;
擋風條 draught excluder;
［擋橫］ block; get in the way; hinder;
擋橫兒 guard sb from violence;
［擋駕］ decline to receive a call; decline to receive a guest; turn away a visitor with some excuse;
［擋箭牌］ excuse; pretext; shield;
［擋路］ get in the way; in the way; obstruct traffic;
［擋泥］ mudguard;
擋泥板 fender; mudflap; mudguard;
~邊車擋泥板 side car mudguard;
~車首擋泥板 nose mudguard;
~前擋泥板 front mudguard;
擋泥膠皮 mudflap;
［擋眼］ obstruct one's view;
［擋雨］ keep off the rain; shelter one from the rain;
［擋住］ (1) check; halt; hamper; stop; (2) obstruct; screen; shield; (3) bar; block; stem;
擋住光線 obstruct the light;
擋住去路 block off the way;
擋主人群 hold back the crowd; keep back the crowd;
有山擋住 be blocked by hills;

摒擋 arrange in order;
抵擋 resist; stand up against; withstand;
第一擋 first gear;
風擋 windscreen; windshield;
掛擋 put into gear;
高速擋 top gear;
換擋 shift gears;
攔擋 block; obstruct; resist;
排擋 gear;
書擋 bookend;
推擋 half volley with push;
遮擋 screen; shelter from;

阻擋 block; keep out; obstruct; resist; stop;

dang

【檔】 (1) file; (2) pigeonhole; shelf; (3) wooden crosspiece;

[檔案] archive; dossier; file; record;
檔案保管員 archivist;
檔案分享 file sharing;
檔案夾子 file;
檔案館 archive; chancery;
~ 檔案館員 archivist;
檔案櫃 file cabinet; filing cabinet;
檔案名 filename;
檔案室 archive; chancery;
編輯檔案 edit a file;
儲存檔案 save a file;
傳輸檔案 transfer a file;
存取檔案 access a file;
打開檔案 open a file;
發送檔案 send a file;
翻查檔案 ransack the archives;
犯罪檔案 a criminal dossier;
複製檔案 copy a file;
附加檔案 attach a file;
個人檔案 personal file;
關閉檔案 close a file;
入檔案 file away; keep on file;
刪除檔案 delete a file;
上傳檔案 upload a file;
文件檔案 document;
下載檔案 download a file;
新建檔案 create a file;
一捆檔案 a bundle of files;
一捆捆檔案 bundles of files;
移動檔案 move a file;

[檔冊] account book; record;

[檔次] gradation; scale;
不在同一檔次 not in the same league;
夠檔次 reach a certain level; up to par; up to standard;
拉開檔次 widen the differences;

[檔卷] official files;

dang

【黨】 party;

[黨紀] party discipline;
違反黨紀 violate Party disciplines;

[黨籍] Party membership;
開除黨籍 expulsion from the Party;

[黨派] factions; party groupings; political groups; political parties;
黨派政治 party politics;
民主黨派 democratic parties;
無黨派 without political affilations;
~ 無黨派人士 persons without political affilations;

[黨員] party member;

[黨章] party constitution;

保皇黨 royalist;
保守黨 Conservative Party;
多數黨 majority party;
反對黨 opposition party;
工黨 Labour Party;
公明黨 Clean Government Party;
共產黨 Communist Party;
共黨 communist;
共和黨 Republican Party;
建黨 form a party; found a party;
民主黨 Democratic Party;
叛黨 betray the party; turn renegade from the party;
朋黨 cabal; clique; faction;
妻黨 one's wife's kinsfolk;
清黨 purge within a political party;
入黨 become a member of a political party; join a political party;
少數黨 minority party;
樹黨 form a clique;
死黨 sworn followers;
同黨 (1) of the same party; (2) member of the same party;
徒黨 band; clique; faction;
退黨 withdraw from a political party;
脱黨 give up party membership; leave a political party; quit a political party;
鄉黨 local communities;
一黨 one party;
友黨 ally;
餘黨 remnants of a party;
在野黨 opposition party;
賊黨 a gang of bandits; a group of traitors; the rebel factions;
政黨 political party;
執政黨 ruling party;
自由黨 Liberal Party;

dang

【攩】 block; hinder; impede; obstruct;

dang

【讜】 speak out boldly;

[讜辭] outspoken words;

[讜論] outspoken statements;

[讜言] outspoken remarks;

讜言高論 honest and wise counsel;

dang⁴

dang

【宕】 (1) quarryman; (2) delay; procrastinate; (3) loaf; loiter;

［宕戶］ quarryman;

dang

【當】 (1) appropriate; proper; (2) mortgage; pawn; pledge; (3) consider as; regard as; take as; (4) trap;

［當年］ that very year; the same year;

［當票］ pawn ticket;

［當鋪］ pawnbroker's shop; pawnshop; pop shop;

當鋪老闆 pawnbroker;

［當日］ that very day; the same day;

當日有效 valid on the day of issue only;

［當時］ at once; immediately; right away;

［當天］ that very day; the same day;

［當月］ the same month;

［當真］ (1) take seriously; (2) really; really true;

［當做］ look upon; regard as; treat as;

不當 inappropriate; improper; unsuitable;
不正當 improper;
的當 appropriate; proper;; suitable;
典當 mortgage; pawn;
勾當 business; deal;
鬼勾當 fishy;
精當 precise and appropriate;
快當 prompt; quick;
切當 appropriate; proper; suitable;
愜當 appropriate; proper; suitable;
確當 appropriate; correct and proper;
上當 be duped; be taken in;
失當 inappropriate; improper;
適當 appropriate; proper; suitable;
贖當 redeem sth pawned;
押當 pawnshop;
允當 appropriate; proper; suitable;
正當 rational and legitimate;

dang

【擋】 as in 摒擋 , fend off;

dang

【蕩】 (1) pond; pool; (2) cleanse; wash away; (3) move to and fro; oscillate; shake; vagrant; unsettled; (4) debauched; dissipated; licentious; of loose moral; (5) agitated; disturbed; (6) large; magnificent; vast;

［蕩侈逾檢］ lead a dissolute, extravagant life;

［蕩蕩］ (1) large; vast; (2) just; unbiased; (3) ruined; spoilt;

蕩蕩悠悠 moving to and fro; shake and move; swinging;

［蕩婦］ alley cat; easy mark; easy meat; floozie; floozy; goer; hussy; man-crazy woman; scarlet woman; slag; slapper; whore; woman of loose moral;

蕩婦淫娃 abandoned and dissolute woman; alley cats;

［蕩檢逾閑］ be broken from moral bonds; break laws and overstep bounds; licentious in conduct;

［蕩平］ clear away; quell rebellion; sweep off;

［蕩然無存］ all gone; have nothing left; nothing remaining; reduce to nothing; there is nothing left;

［蕩漾］ agitated; ripple; undulate;

春心蕩漾 the surging of lustful desire;

歌聲蕩漾 the song rose and fell like waves;

隨波蕩漾 move along with the waves;

板蕩 time of turmoil; world of disorder; social confusion and chaos;
波蕩 heave; surge;
播蕩 homeless; live in vagrancy;
簸蕩 bump and sway; rock; roll;
逋蕩 neglect duty and loaf;
沖蕩 rinse out; wash away;
闖蕩 make a living wandering from place to place;
駘蕩 comfortable; pleasant; wonderful;
滌蕩 get rid of; wash away; wipe out;
動蕩 upheaval; unrest; turbulent;
放蕩 dissipated; dissolute; loose in morals;
浮蕩 float in the air;
浩蕩 broad; magnificent; vast and mighty;
回蕩 resound; reverberate;
激蕩 agitate; surge;
空蕩蕩 deserted; empty;
曠蕩 boundless; endless;
浪蕩 dissipated; dissolute; loaf; loiter about;
流蕩 (1) flow; shift; (2) roam about; rove;
漂蕩 drift about; wander;
飄蕩 (1) drift; (2) flutter; wave;
散蕩 loaf about; play idly;
掃蕩 destroy; mop up; wipe out;
坦蕩 (1) broad and level; (2) bighearted; broad-

minded; magnanimous;
儻蕩 (1) dissipated; dissolute; (2) unconventional;
閒蕩 loaft about; stroll;
邪蕩 dissolute; obscene;
搖蕩 rock; roll; sway;
怡蕩 find pleasure in wanton ways;
軼蕩 unrestrained;
淫蕩 lascivious; lewd; licentious; loose in morals; lustful; profligate;
悠蕩 sway back and forth; swing to and fro;
遊蕩 loaf about; saunter;
振蕩 shake; shock; vibrate;
震蕩 shake; shock; vibrate;

dang
【檔】 a pronunciation of 檔;

dang
【盪】 (1) rock; swing; toss about; (2) wash;
[盪滌] wash;

dao¹
dao
【刀】 (1) blade; knife; sword; (2) knife-shaped coins of ancient China;
[刀兵] (1) arms; weapons; (2) fighting;
刀兵再起 renewal of war;
[刀叉] knife and fork;
一副刀叉 a knife and fork;
[刀鋒] blade point; edge of a knife;
[刀架] knife block;
[刀剪] cutlery;
刀剪匠 cutler;
刀剪商 cutler;
[刀劍] knives and swords;
刀光劍影 be engaged in hot battle; flashing with knives and swords; sabre-rattling; the flashes and shadows of swords; the glint and flash of cold steel;
舌非刀劍，但能傷人 the tongue is not a sword, yet it hurts people;
[刀具] cutlery;
刀具商 cutler;
[刀片] razor blade;
[刀槍] sword and spear; weapons;
刀槍不入 neither swords nor spears can enter;
刀槍如林 swords and spears are as trees in the forest;
刀對刀，槍對槍 give tit for tat;
動刀動槍 start war; take up arms;
揮刀舞槍 brandish spears and swords;
真刀真槍 in real earnest; real swords and spears — the real thing; with swords out of sheaths;
[刀刃] blade;
好鋼用在刀刃上 use the best material at the key point; use the best steel to make the blade — use material where it is needed most;
[刀山] a mountain of swords;
刀山敢上，火海敢闖 be there seas of fire and a forest of knives, one will still charge ahead;
刀山火海 most severe trials;
上刀山 climb a mountain of blades;
~上刀山下火海 climb a mountain of swords or plunge into a sea of flames; undergo the most severe trials;
[刀下] under the knife;
刀下留人 hold the execution; spare him;
[刀子] dagger; pocketknife;
白刀子入，紅刀子出 engage in killing; the knife goes in clean and comes out with blood;
刀子嘴，豆腐心 a good heart, but a sharp tongue; his bark is worse than his bite; his tongue is as sharp as a knife but his heart is as soft as bean curd; more bark than bite;
背後捅刀子 stab sb in the back;
軟刀子 a way of harming people imperceptibly; soft knife;
~軟刀子殺人 destroy people with "soft" weapons; murder with an invisible knife;

拔刀 draw one's sword;
寶刀 treasured sword;
刨刀 (1) planer tool; (2) hand plane;
冰刀 ice skate;
菜刀 kitchen knife;
操刀 hold a sword in one's hand;
插刀 slotting tool;
柴刀 chopper;
車刀 lathe tool; turning tool;
持刀 hold a knife;
吃刀 penetration of the cutting tool;
刺刀 bayonet;
銼刀 file;
大刀 broadsword;
鈍刀 blunt knife;

飛刀 flying knife;
刮刀 scraper; scraping cutter;
滾刀 hob; hobbing cutter;
尖刀 dagger; sharp knife;
剪刀 scissors; shears;
絞刀 reamer;
進刀 feed;
軍刀 sabre; soldier's sword;
開刀 (1) have an operation; operate on; perform an operation; (2) make sb the first target of attack; punish;
砍刀 chopper;
刻刀 carving tool; graver;
拉刀 broach;
鐮刀 sickle;
獵刀 hunting knife;
馬刀 sabre;
鏝刀 trowel;
美工刀 craft knife;
磨刀 keep one grind a knife; sharpen the knife; sharpen the sword;
牛刀 butcher's knife;
劈刀 (1) chopper; (2) sabre;
朴刀 sword with a long blade and a short hilt;
鉛刀 blunt knife;
槍刀 guns and swords;
韶刀 flippant; garrulous;
手術刀 scalpeol;
霜刀 sharp, shining knife;
鏜刀 boring cutter; boring tool;
剔刀 scraping knife;
剃刀 razor;
薙刀 shaving knife;
屠刀 butcher's knife;
瓦刀 cleaver;
剜刀 reamer;
銑刀 milling cutter;
小刀 (1) small sword; (2) pocket knife;
腰刀 sabrelike knife;
一把刀 a knife;
一刀 a cut of;
鏨刀 burin; graver;
閘刀 knife-switch;
鍘刀 hand hay cutter; fodder chopper;
斬肉刀 chopper;
戰刀 sabre;
折刀 folding knife; pocket knife;
摺刀 folding knife; pocket knife;
捉刀 ghostwrite;
奏刀 slither a knife;

dao

【叨】 chatterbox; garrulous; talkative;
[叨叨] chatter away; garrulous; rattle; talk on and on;
[叨登] (1) turn sth over and over; (2) harp on an old story;
[叨光] (1) thanks for a favour done; (2) get the advantage from;
[叨教] thank you for favouring us with your advice; trouble you by requesting your instructions;
[叨嘮] matter away; complain; nag; talk on and on; talkative;
愛叨嘮 gossipy; talkative;
[叨念] mutter incessantly; talk about again and again in recollection;
[叨絮] longwinded;
叨絮不休 long-winded; talk endlessly;

dao

【忉】 distressed; grieved;
[忉忉] distressed; worried;

dao

【舠】 knife-shaped boat;

dao³

dao

【倒】 (1) fall over; lie down; (2) empty; pour out; (3) and yet; but; nevertheless; on the contrary;
[倒把] engage in profiteering; speculate;
倒把者 adventurer;
~女倒把者 adventuress;
[倒班] change shifts; work by turns; work in shifts;
倒班守夜 keep watch by turns;
晝夜倒班 work in shifts round the clock;
[倒斃] fall dead;
[倒閉] close down; go bankrupt; go insolvent; go into liquidation; go out of business;
瀕臨倒閉 on the verge of bankruptcy;
[倒采] catcall;
倒采聲 catcall;
喝倒彩 boo; give a Bronx cheer; give sb the bird; hoot; make cat calls;
[倒茶] fill the cup with tea;
[倒兒] profiteer; speculator;
[倒戈] change sides in a war; mutiny; revolt against one's own side; turn one's coat;
倒戈投敵 betray to the enemy; turn

renegade; turncoat;

倒戈相向 attack one's own men; become a turncoat; revolt against constituted authority; turn one's force against one's master;

[倒匯] speculate in foreign currency;

[倒霉] (1) fall on evil days; fall on hard time; (2) bad luck; down on one's luck; hard luck; have bad luck; ill luck; just my luck; luck in a bag; off one's luck; out of luck; rough luck; tough luck; unlucky; (3) go through a bad patch; hit a bad patch; strike a bad patch;

倒霉到極點 reach the lowest pitch of bad fortune;

倒霉的 hapless; jinxed;

倒霉時期 a bad patch; a sticky patch;

僱賊看門—自找倒霉 hiring a thief to watch one's door — asking for trouble;

活該倒霉 tough luck;

爛眼睛招蒼蠅—倒霉透了 a festering eye attracts flies — bad luck;

認倒霉 take one's lump;

真倒霉 rotten luck; tough luck; worse luck;

[倒塌] cave in; collapse; come down; fall down; topple down;

[倒騰] (1) move from here to there; remove; turn sth over and over; (2) engage in buying and selling goods for profit;

[倒替] replace; substitute;

[倒挺] quite; rather;

[倒頭] lie down; touch the pillow;

倒頭便睡 fall asleep as soon as one goes to bed;

[倒下] fall down;

[倒相機] inverter;

緩衝倒相機 buffer inverter;

色度倒相機 chroma inverter;

陰極倒相機 cathode phase inverter;

[倒懸] (1) hanging upside down; (2) in a dire situation;

解民倒懸 relieve people of their sufferings; relieve the misery of the people; relieve the people's distress; rescue the people from misery; save people from deep misery;

以解倒懸 save people from a crisis;

猶解倒懸 like relieving sb hung up by the heels;

[倒運] out of luck;

[倒賬] (1) bad debts; failure to collect payment; (2) refuse to pay loans under various excuses;

拜倒 fall on one's knees; kneel; prostrate oneself;

扳倒 pull down;

絆倒 stumble; trip; trip over;

病倒 come down with an illness; fall ill;

駁倒 confute; defeat in a debate; demolish sb's argument; disprove; outargue; reduce sb to silence; refute; score off;

不倒 undefeatable;

吹倒 blow down;

打倒 down with; knock down; overthrow;

顛倒 (1) confound; invert; reverse; turn sth upside down; (2) be confused;

跌倒 fall; tip over; tumble;

官倒 bureaucratic profiteers; bureaucratic racketeering; official black-marketing; official profiteer; official racketeers; official speculation;

跪倒 grovel; prostrate oneself; throw oneself on one's knees;

轟倒 knock down by bombardment;

昏倒 faint; fall unconscious;

絕倒 roar with laughter;

砍倒 fell;

拉倒 drop it; forget about it; leave it at that; let it go at that; never mind;

潦倒 dejected; dispirited; frustrated;

難倒 baffle; beat; daunt;

攲倒 slant and fall;

傾倒 (1) collapse; topple and fall; toppl[illegible] wn; out; topple over; (2) decant; empty [illegible] oman; turn out; (3) be infatuated w[illegible] for; fall be overwhelmed with adr[illegible] for; greatly admire;

山倒 collapse of a mount[illegible]

摔倒 fall; tumble;

蹶倒 slip and fall;

躺倒 lie down; [illegible] r; (2) cancel; reverse; [illegible] le down;

推倒 (1) overt[illegible] elm; prevail over;

臥倒 drop t[illegible] in a faint; pass out;

壓倒 ove[illegible]

暈倒 f[illegible] by a bumping;

栽倒 [illegible]

撞[illegible]

dao

【島】 island; isle;

［島國］ island nation;

［島民］ islander;

［島群］ archipelago;

［島嶼］ islands and islets;

　一小群島嶼 a small group of islands;

安全島 safety island;
半島 peninsula;
寶島 treasure island;
孤島 islet;
海島 island;
荒島 desert island;
火山島 volcanic island;
列島 archipelago; chain of islands; islands;
陸邊島 continental island;
群島 archipelago; islands; isles;
珊瑚島 coral island;
小島 islet;
洋中島 oceanic island;

dao

【搗】 (1) pound with a pestle; (2) beat with stick; (3) disturb; harass;

［搗蛋］ (1) give sb a hard time; (2) act up; do mischief; make trouble; mischief; monkey around;

　存心搗蛋 be disposed for mischief;

　調皮搗蛋 mischievous;

［搗鬼］ do mischief; play tricks;

　背後搗鬼 instigate trouble at the back; play underhand tricks; plot behind the scenes; scheme behind the scenes;

［搗毀］ demolish; destroy; devastate; smash up;

［搗爛］ mash;

　把香蕉搗爛 mash the bananas;

［搗 create a disturbance; make trouble; ess about;

　搗亂 make trouble at the back; play a eep game;

　搗亂 don't make trouble with me;

　絲 throw a spanner into the works;

　瞎 ake frequent disturbance;

麻搗 hempound;

dao

【導】 a pronu

dao

【擣】 (1) beat; p

［擣爛］ pound into a pulp;

dao

【禱】 beseech; entreat; plead; pray;

［禱詞］ prayer;

［禱告］ pray; say one's prayers;

　感恩禱告 prayer of thankfulness;

　做禱告 say one's prayer;

［禱文］ prayer;

　讀誦禱文 read prayers;

［禱祝］ pray and express one's wishes;

晨禱 morning prayer;
默禱 pray in silence; say silent prayers;
祈禱 pray; say one's prayers;

dao⁴

dao

【到】 (1) arrive; get to; reach; (2) go to; leave for;

［到場］ present; show up; turn up;

　到場人數 turnout;

［到處］ all about; all over; all over the place; all over the shop; all over the show; all round; at all places; everywhere; from place to place; here, there and everywhere; here and there; high and low; hither and thither; in all directions; in every place; in every quarter; on all hands; on all sides; on every side; on every hand; right and left; up hill and down dale;

　到處奔波 rush about hither and thither; travel from place to place;

　到處插手 meddle in other's affairs everywhere; poke one's nose everywhere;

　到處打聽 ask around about; poke round;

　到處流浪 lead a vagrant life; live a vagabond life; wander from place to place;

　到處亂傳 bandy about;

　到處亂竄 poke one's nose into everywhere;

　到處謀生 go anywhere to make a living;

　到處跑 go from place to place;

　到處碰壁 get into trouble hither and thither; hit into snags everywhere; run one's head against stone walls everywhere;

　到處漂泊 drift from one place to another;

到處散佈謠言 go around circulating rumours; spread the rumour all over;
到處煽動 go around agitating;
到處伸手 ask for help at all places; reach out in all directions; reach out one's hand everywhere;
到處樹敵 make enemies everywhere; pit oneself against the people everywhere;
到處搜查 look up and down;
到處為家 can settle down everywhere; everywhere may be one's home; find oneself at home everywhere; live here, there and everywhere;
到處遊蕩 wander around;
到處找工作 go around looking for a job;
到處鑽營 worm one's way to every turn;

[到此] so far;
到此為止 leave it at that; let's call it a day; rest here; so much for; that's all for;
到此一遊 have visited this place;
到此止步 no admittance;

[到達] arrival; arrive; arrive at; arrive in; get to; reach;
到達車站 arrive at the station;
到達山頂 reach the top of the hill;
到達現場 arrive upon the scene;
到達終點 reach the end of the line;
安全到達 arrive safely;
按時到達 arrive on time;
成批到達 aggregated arrival;
批量到達 batch arrival;
平安到達 get there in one piece;
易到達［的］ accessible;
正點到達 arrive on time; arrive punctually;
準時到達 on-time arrival;

[到底] (1) to the end; to the finish; (2) after all; at last; eventually; finally; in the end; (3) indeed; (4) after all; in the final analysis; (5) what on earth; what the heck;
抵抗到底 resist up to the end;
奮戰到底 fight to the bitter end; fight to the last ditch;
堅持到底 follow through; go through with it; stick it out;
說到底 in the final analysis;
一拼到底 brave it out; fight it out; fight to a finish;
戰鬥到底 fight to the bitter end;

[到頂] reach the limit; reach the peak; reach the summit;

[到過] have been to;

[到家] excellent; perfect; reach a very high level;

[到來] arrive; come;
即將到來 in the offing;

[到期] at maturity; become due; due; expire; fall due; mature;
到期日 date due; date of expiry; expiration date; expiry date; maturity date; settlement date;
~ 平均到期日 averaging maturity; equated maturity;
到期支付 pay at maturity;
承兑到期 acceptance maturity;
兩星期到期 being due in two weeks;

[到任] assume a post; assume office; take up an official post;

[到手] come to one's hands; in one's hands; in one's possession;

[到達] arrive at; arrive in; fetch up; get into; get to; reach;

[到頭來] at last; at the end of the day; end up in; finally; in the end; result in;

[到位] reach the designated place;

[到職] arrive at one's post; assume office; take office;

挨到 come to one's turn;
辦到 accomplish ; get sth done;
報到 check in; report for duty;
不到 fail to reach;
遲到 late;
達到 achieve; attain; reach;
得到 get obtain; receive;
等到 by the time; when;
精到 precise and penetrating;
臨到 (1) just before; on the point of; (2) befall; happen to;
簽到 register one's attendance at a meeting; sign in;
收到 get; obtain; receive;
遇到 come across; encounter;
直到 (1) until; (2) up to;

dao

【倒】 inverse; place upside down;

[倒彩] applaud when a perfomer slips;
被觀眾喝倒彩 be greeted by catcalls from the audience;

被人喝倒彩 be booed;
招來倒彩 court catcalls;

[倒車] back a car; back up a car; back up a locomotive; move a vehicle backward; reverse; reverse a car;
倒車擋 reverse gear;
倒車燈 reversing light;
開倒車 pull the wheel back; put back the clock; reverse an engine; slide back; turn back the wheel of history; turn it in the opposite direction; turn the clock back;

[倒帶] rewind; rewind a cassette or a tape;
倒帶機 rewinder;
倒帶裝置 rewinder;
快速倒帶 fast rewind;
自動倒帶 automatic rewind;
~全自動倒帶 fully automatic rewind;

[倒地] fall down;
倒地傳球 fall down pass;
嚎叫倒地 fall with a howl;
哭倒於地 fall to the ground with a great cry; throw oneself on the ground and weep;

[倒掉] pour away;
把垃圾倒掉 tip out rubbish;
把剩湯倒掉 pour the rest of the soup away;

[倒反] contrary to what one expects; unexpectedly;

[倒掛] hang upside down;

[倒過頭來] turn the other way round;

[倒回] back; refund;

[倒立] (1) headstand; stand upside down; (2) balance; handstand;
倒立轉體 half-turning handstand;
擺動倒立 handstand with swing;
半屈臂倒立 low handstand;
大開臂倒立 wide arm handstand;
單臂倒立 one-arm handstand;
單手倒立 one-handed handstand'
疊椅倒立 balancing on a pyramid of chairs;
肩倒立 shoulder stand;
~側肩倒立 side shoulder balance;
~正肩倒立 front shoulder balance;
靜止手倒立 still handstand;
前臂倒立 forearm stand;
前膊倒立 arm stand;
十字倒立 inverted-cross handstand;
手倒立 hand balance; handstand;
~擺動手倒立 handstand with swing;
~單手倒立 one-handed handstand;
~慢起手倒立 handstand with press;
~頭手倒立 headstand;
胸倒立 chest stand;
椅上倒立 hand-stand on a chair;
桌上倒立 hand-stand on a table;

[倒流] backwash; backwater; flow backwards;
河水不能倒流 rivers cannot flow upward;
時光不會倒流 time that has been lost will never come again;

[倒賣] scalp; sell dear;
倒賣者 scalper;

[倒牌] lose prestige;

[倒入] decant; pour into;

[倒數] count backwards;
倒數第二 the last but one;
倒數計時 count down;

[倒貼] pay for the upkeep of a lover;

[倒退] backward motion; go backwards; fall back; retreat; retrospect; review;
反對倒退 oppose retrogression;

[倒屣] in a big hurry to welcome a guest;
倒屣相迎 a hearty welcome; greet a visitor with the shoes on back to front;
倒屣迎賓 greet a visitor with the shoes on back to front; meet friends with one's sandals upturned; put on slippers hurriedly to extend welcome; put one's shoes the wrong way in receiving one's guests; rush out in haste to receive the guests; welcome sb with the greatest deference; go out to meet one's friends in such a hurry that one puts on the sandals the wrong way;

[倒行] (1) go against the trend; (2) retroactive;
倒行干擾 retroactive interference;
倒行逆施 (1) act against the right principles; act in opposition to right principles; go against the historical trend; go against the tide of history; go against the trend of the times; push a reactionary policy; put the clock back; set back the clock; try to put the clock back; turn back the wheel of history; (2) do things in a perverse way; perverse acts;
倒行制約 retroactive inhibition;

[倒敘] take the narrative back in time from the current point in the story;

[倒影] reflection of sth in water; upside-down

image of an object in the view finder of a camera;
湖光倒影 reflection of sth or sb in the water of the lake;
湖山倒影 mountains are reflected in the lake;

[倒栽蔥] fall head over heels; fall headlong;

[倒置] anastrophe; bottom-up; inverse; inversion; invert; pend; place upside down; reversing;
倒置的 upside down;
倒置對立 inverse opposition;
本末倒置 have the order reversed; take the branches for the root;
冠履倒置 caps and shoes are upside down;
輕重倒置 place the unimportant before the important;

[倒轉] reverse; turn the other way round;
倒轉乾坤 reverse the existing state of affairs; turn around the course of events;
時運倒轉 suffer a reversal of fortune;

[倒裝] inversion; reverse; turn inverted order;
倒裝詞序 inverted word order;
倒裝逗號 inverted comma;
倒裝句 inverted sentence;
倒裝語序 inverted order;
部份倒裝 partial inversion;
全部倒裝 complete inversion; full inversion;

dao

【悼】 grieve; lament; mourn; regret;

[悼詞] memorial speech;

[悼歌] dirge; funeral hymn;

[悼念] grieve; grieve over; lament for; mourn;
沉重悼念 mourn with deep grief;

[悼痛] mourn in anguish;

[悼亡] be bereaved of one's wife;

[悼惜] deplore; lament;

哀悼 condole with sb upon the death of...; condolence; express one's condolences on the death of sb; grieve; grieve over sb's death; lament; lament sb's death; mourn; mourn for the dead; mourn over sb's death; mourning; wail the dead;
悲悼 grieve over sb's death; mourn;
傷悼 mourn or grieve over the deceased;
痛悼 grieve over the death of sb bitterly;
軫悼 mourn with deep grief;
震悼 be shocked and grieved;
誌悼 condole;
追悼 commemorate the dead; mourn over a person's death;

dao

【葤】 tall grass;

dao

【盜】 misappropriate; rob; steal;

[盜案] burglary; case of robbery;

[盜版] piracy;
盜版軟件 piracy software;

[盜伐] illegal logging;

[盜匪] bandits; robbers;
淪為盜匪 turn to banditry;
一伙盜匪 a gang of bandits;

[盜毀] steal and damage; vandalize;

[盜賣] misappropriate; steal and sell;
盜賣公物 steal and sell the public property;
盜賣國家財產 steal and sell the state property;
盜賣文物 steal and sell cultural relics;

[盜名] seek for undeserved publicity; steal glory one does not deserve;
盜名欺世 steal a reputation and deceive the world;
盜名欺世，混淆視聽 hoodwink and confuse the pubic by stealing a reputation;
盜名竊譽 seek fame by dirty means;

[盜墓] plunder graves; steal from graves; tomb raiding;

[盜騙] steal and cheat;

[盜竊] burglary; heist; pilferage; steal;
盜竊保險 burglary and robbery insurance;
盜竊國家機密 steal state secrets;
盜竊罪 bulgary charge;
~入室盜竊罪 indoor bulgary charge;
打擊盜竊 hit out against theft;
鼠竊狗盜 a petty theft; filch like rats and snatch like dogs — play petty tricks on the sly; petty thieves and small-time robbers;
誣捏盜竊 trump up a charge of burglary;
珠寶盜竊 jewelry heist;

[盜取] embezzle; steal;

[盜聽] eavesdrop; telephone tapping;

[盜用] embezzle; usurp;
盜用公款 embezzle public funds;
盜用名義 illegally use the name of; usurp

a name;

[盜運] illegal transport;

[盜賊] bandits; robbers; thieves;

盜賊猖獗 bandits are rampant;

盜賊蜂起 robbers rise up in swarms;

盜賊四起 robbers arise from all quarters;

藏賊引盜 entice thieves and vagabonds;

大盜 robber;

防盜 guard against theft;

慣盜 common thief; habitual robber; incorrigible thief;

海盜 pirate; sea rover;

緝盜 capture thieves;

強盜 bandit; robber;

竊盜 theft;

失盜 be burglarized;

偷盜 pilfer; steal;

俠盜 a robber dedicated to the cause of justice;

賊盜 brigands; thieves and robbers;

dao

【道】 (1) path; road; street; (2) way; (3) method; principle; way; (4) Daoism; (5) say; speak; (6) measure-word; (7) horizontal line; (8) from; (9) a surname;

[道別] say goodbye;

揮手道別 wave sb goodbye;

~開心的揮手道別 leave with a cheery wave;

[道不拾遺] no one picks up what is left by the wayside;

[道不同，不相為謀] there is little common ground for understanding between persons with different principles; those whose courses are different cannot lay plans for one another;

[道岔] railroad switch; switch; turnout;

扳道岔 pull railway switches;

對稱道岔 bilateral turnout; equilateral turnout;

對向道岔 facing turnout;

復式道岔 double turnout;

菱形道岔 diamond turnout;

[道出] speak out; voice;

道出心聲 give voice to sth;

[道牀] road-bed;

鬆軟道牀 soft road-bed;

整體道牀 monolithic road-bed;

[道德] ethics; moral integrity; morality; morals; virtue;

道德敗壞 be demoralized; immorality; moral turpitude; morally degenerate;

道德標準 ethics; moral standard;

道德秩序 moral order;

道德發展 moral development;

道德風尚 moral and social practices;

道德高地 moral high ground;

~佔領道德高地 claim the moral high ground; seize the moral high ground; take the moral high ground;

道德觀 moral outlook; morality;

~傳統道德觀 conventional morality; traditional morality;

~性道德觀 sexual morality;

道德觀念 moral concept; sense of morality;

道德規範 moral rule;

道德規則 moral principles;

道德家 moralist;

道德價值觀 view of moral value;

道德教育 moral education;

道德進步 moral progress;

道德境界 moral state;

道德理想 moral ideal;

道德品質 moral character;

道德評價 moral evaluation;

道德社會 moral society;

道德行為 moral conduct;

道德修養 moral cultivation;

道德意識 moral consciousness; moral sense;

道德原則 moral principle;

道德責任 moral duty;

道德哲學 moral philosophy;

道德準則 ethical code; moral code;

敗壞道德 corrupt morals;

不道德 immoral; unethical;

傳統倫理道德 the conventional ethics;

公共道德 public morality;

國民道德 national morality;

恪守道德 straight and narrow;

沒有道德 [的] amoral;

商業道德 business morality; commercial morality;

社會道德 public morals; social ethics;

~維護社會道德 safeguard public morals;

性道德 sex ethics;

有道德 with moral integrity;

政治道德 political morality;

職業道德 professional ethics;

[道地] (1) native; (2) pure; typical;

道道地地 down-right; one hundred per cent; out and out; pure and simple; through and through; to a fraction; to the core;

[道高] high morality;
道高謗至 defamation arises against the person with high morality;
道高不矮 neither too high nor too low; neither too tall nor too short;
道高一尺，魔高一丈 as virtue rises one foot, vice rises ten; the more illumination, the more temptation;

[道姑] Daoist nun;

[道賀] congratulate;

[道家] Daoist school;

[道經] Daoist scriptures;

[道具] prop; stage property;
道具管理員 property man;
道具間 property room;
道具室 property room;
大小道具 accessories;

[道口] crossing;
道口安全 crossing safety; crossing security;

[道理] (1) principle; hows and whys; the truth; (2) argument; reason; rhyme; sense;
擺事實，講道理 adduce facts and use reasoned arguments; present the facts and reason things out; set forth the facts and discuss them rationally;
不講道理 impervious to reason; not amenable to reason; not listen to reason;
大道理 general principle; great truth; major principle;
~ 少給我講大道理 say no more about unworkable theories to me;
服從道理 follow the principles;
毫無道理 nonsense;
沒道理 it's unreasonable;
是何道理 for what reason; why;
有道理 convincing; plausible; reasonable;

[道路] path; road; way;
道路安全 road safety;
~ 道路安全意識 road sense;
道路保養 maintenance of roads;
道路傳聞 inaccurate and unreliable rumours; news heard on the roads;
道路分岔 a road forks;
道路交通圖 road map;
道路結構 road structure;
道路事故 road accident;
道路試車 road test;
道路施工 roadworks;
道路收費 road pricing;
道路稅 road tax;
道路險阻 the road is dangerous and rugged;
保養道路 maintain the road;
暢通的道路 open road;
分離道路 divided road;
~ 非分離道路 undivided road;
禁停道路 clearway;
平坦的道路 smooth road;
偏僻道路 back road;
鋪平道路 pave one's path; smooth one's way;
前方道路 the road ahead;
雙層道路 double-deck road;
馱運道路 pack road;
彎曲道路 winding road;
阻塞道路 bar the path; block the road; obstruct the road;

[道破] lay bare; point out frankly; reveal;
一語道破 hit the mark with a single comment; hit the nail on the head;

[道歉] apologize; make an apology;
表示道歉 express one's apology; present one's apology;
登門道歉 call on sb at his house and apologize;
公開道歉 public apology;
立即道歉 immediate apology;
連連的道歉 many apologies;
勉強道歉 apology with a bad grace;
書面道歉 written apology;
向人道歉 apologize to sb;
欣然道歉 apology with a good grace;
要求道歉 demand an apology;
作出道歉 issue an apology;

[道士] Daoist priest;

[道統] Confucian orthodoxy;

[道喜] congratulate sb on a happy occasion;
登門道喜 come to express one's congratulation;

[道謝] express one's thanks; thank;
低聲道謝 murmur thanks;
上門道謝 come to express one's gratitude;

[道行] religious or moral attainments;
道行高潔 one's moral attainments are high;

[道學] (1) Neo-Confucianism; (2)

conservative; (3) Daoism;
道學先生 pedantic scholar;
假道學 hypocrite; sanctimonious person;

[道義] moral principles; morality and justice;
道義之交 a friendship based on principles of morality and justice;

[道藏] Daoist sutras;

礙道 obstruct the way;
暗道 secret passage;
霸道 overbearing; high-handed; rule by force of dictators;
白道 moon's path;
板道 stair path;
報道 cover; report;
鼻道 meatus of nose; nasal duct;
便道 (1) shortcut; (2) pavement; sidewalk; (3) makeshift road;
冰道 ice tunnel;
波道 wave canal;
佈道 evangelize; preach the Gospel; sermon;
岔道 branch road; side road;
產道 birth canal;
腸道 gut; intestinal tract;
抄道 shortcut;
車道 lane;
車行道 roadway;
稱道 commend; praise; speak approvingly of;
赤道 (1) equator; (2) celestial equator;
傳道 deliver a sermon; preach;
大道 avenue; main raod;
彈道 trajectory;
當道 in power;
磴道 rocky mountain path;
堤道 causeway;
地道 (1) tunnel; (2) native;
東道 (1) host; (2) one who stands treat;
耳道 auditory meatus; duct; meatus acusticus;
筏道 logway;
分道 go different ways;
婦道 woman; womenfolk;
改道 (1) change one's route; (2) (of a river) change its course;
幹道 artery; high street; main line;
給水道 waste supply canal;
公道 justice;
拱道 archway;
溝道 channel;
穀道 (1) anus; (2) attain immortality by stop eating grains;
故道 an old path;
管道 conduit; pipeline; piping;
軌道 (1) track; orbit; trajectory;
過道 corridor; passageway;
海道 sea way;
旱道 overland route;
航道 channel; course;
巷道 tunnel;
河道 river course;
黑道 gang;
護道 patrol and guard a railway;
滑道 chute; slide;
黃道 ecliptic;
夾道 flank the street;
家道 family financial situation;
假道 by way of; via;
間道 bypath; shortcut;
漿液道 serous canal;
講道 give sermons; preach;
交道 association; contact;
街道 (1) street; (2) residential district;
劫道 commit highway robbery;
近道 shortcut;
就道 start off on a journey;
開道 clear the way;
坑道 (1) gallery; (2) mine tunnel;
孔道 pass; pore canal;
廊道 gallery;
老道 Daoist priest;
樂道 keen on talking about sth;
領道 lead the way;
樓道 corridor; passageway;
路道 (1) approach; way; (2) behaviour;
馬道 avenue; road; street;
漫道 let alone; to say nothing of;
門道 (1) doorway; gateway; (2) knack; way to do sth;
墓道 path leading to a tomb; tomb passage;
難道 could it possibly be; does it mean;
黏液道 mucilage canal;
尿道 urethra;
盤道 winding mountain path;
跑道 (1) track; (2) runway;
頻道 channel; frequency;
清道 (1) clean the street; (2) clear the way for the monarch;
渠道 (1) irrigation ditch; (2) channel; medium of communication;
衢道 crossroads; side street;
取道 by way of; via;
繞道 go by a roundabout; make a detour; route;
人道 human sympathy; humanity;
柔道 judo;
入道 become a monk; become a nun;

乳汁道 latex canal;
僧道 Buddhists and Daoists;
山道 mountain pass;
師道 (1) the succession of teachings from masters to disciples; (2) the truth in learning from a master; (3) the principles a master abides by;
食道 esophagus;
世道 the manners and morals of the time;
釋道 Buddhism and Daoism;
樹膠道 gum canal;
樹脂道 resin canal;
熟道 familiar road;
恕道 the principle of forgiveness;
水道 (1) water course; (2) water route; waterway;
順道 direct route; on the way;
説道 say;
隧道 tunnel;
索道 cableway; ropeway;
鐵道 railroad; railway;
聽道 auditory canal;
通道 passage; passageway; thoroughfare;
頭道 (1) first time; (2) first;
歪道 underhand ways;
外耳道 external auditory canal;
王道 benevolent government;
味道 flavour; taste;
衛道 preserve traditional moral principles;
無道 injustice; tyrannical; unjust;
悟道 be enlightened; realize the truth;
巷道 (1) tunnel; (2) alley; back street; lane;
消化道 alimentary canal; digestive canal;
小道 branch; pass; passageway; path; pathway; trail; walkway;
孝道 the principle of filial piety;
邪道 evil ways; vice;
修道 cultivate oneself according to a religious doctrine;
穴道 acupuncture point;
殉道 a martyr for religon; die a martyr's death; die for the right cause; die in the cause of justice;
煙道 flue; smoke canal;
陽關道 broad road; thoroughfare;
妖道 witchcraft;
要道 thoroughfare;
一道 (1) alongside; on the same path; side by side; together; (2) a; one; (3) a beam of; a coat of; a flash of; a line of; a shaft of; a streak of; a trail of;
醫道 medical knowledge;
異道 (1) different path; different route; (2) different viewpoints;
溢洪道 spillway;
驛道 post road;
陰道 vagina;
銀道 galactic equator;
甬道 (1) paved path leading to a main hall or a tomb; (2) corridor;
泳道 (of a swimming pool) lane;
有道 (1) learned and virtuous; (2) lawful; reasonable; right;
魚道 fishpass; fishway;
遠道 long way;
運道 (1) fortune; luck; (2) road for grain transportation;
載道 (1) fill the streets; (2) convey principles;
窄道 narrow path;
正道 correct path; proper way; right course; right track; right way;
之道 means; way;
知道 aware of; know; realize; understand;
直道 (1) straight path; (2) talk candidly;
中道 (1) halfway; (2) doctrine of the mean;
珠孔道 micropylar canal;
轉道 go by way of; make a detour;
子道 filial duties;
走道 (1) pavement; side walk; (2) footpath; path;
祖道 entertain a parting friend with a feast;

dao

【稻】 paddy; rice;

［稻草］ rice straw;
稻草人 corn dolly; scarecrow; straw man;
撈稻草 make capital of sth; take advantage of sth;
一層稻草 a bed of straw;
一根稻草 a straw;
一捆稻草 a bundle of hay; a truss of straw;

［稻穀］ paddy; rice in the husk;
稻穀飄香 the fragrance of fresh grain drifts on the breeze from the fields;

［稻穗］ ear of rice; spike of rice;

［稻田］ paddy field; rice farm;

［稻子］ paddy; rice;
一片稻子 fields of rice;

旱稻 upland rice;
水稻 paddy; rice;
早稻 early rice;
中稻 middleseason rice;

dao

【幬】 canopy; curtain;

dao

【燾】 illuminate extensively;

dao

【蹈】 (1) step; tread; (2) skip; trip;

［蹈海］ plunge oneself into the sea to commit suicide;

［蹈襲］ follow slavishly;

蹈襲覆轍 follow the same old disastrous road; follow the tracks of an overthrown chariot;

蹈襲前人 slavishly follow one's predecessors;

蹈常襲故 follow a set routine; get into a rut; go on in the same old way;

dao

【導】 conduct; direct; guide; instruct; lead;

［導板］ guide;

帶材導板 band guide;

後導板 back guide;

可調導板 adjustable guide;

［導播］ programme director;

副導播 assistant director;

節目導播 programme director;

演員導播 casting director;

主控導播 master director;

助理導播 assistant director;

［導程］ lead;

進氣導程 admission lead;

實際導程 actual lead;

［導彈］ guided missile; missile;

導彈發射場 missile site;

導彈未中目標 the missile missed the target;

愛國者導彈 Patriot Missile;

岸艦導彈 ground-to-ship missile;

北極星導彈 polaris missile;

彈道導彈 ballistic guided missile; ballistic missile;

~ 反彈道導彈 antiballistic missile;

~ 洲際彈道導彈 transcontinental ballistic missile;

地對地導彈 surface-to-surface missile;

地對空導彈 ground-to-air missile; surface-to air missile;

地空導彈 ground-to-air missile;

反導彈 countermissile;

反潛導彈 antisubmaritime missile;

反坦克導彈 antitank missile;

防空導彈 air-defense missile; anti-aircraft missile;

核導彈 nuclear missile;

空對地導彈 air-to-ground missile; air-to-surface missile;

空對空導彈 air-to-air missile;

空對航天導彈 air-to-space missile;

空對艦導彈 air-to-ship missile;

響尾蛇導彈 side winder missile;

巡航導彈 aerodynamic missile;

遠程導彈 long-range missile;

中程導彈 medium-range missile;

洲際導彈 transcontinental missile;

主動導彈 active missile;

自控導彈 self-guided missile;

［導電］ conduction; electrical conduction;

導電圖形 conductive pattern;

電解導電 electrolytic conduction;

電子導電 electronic conduction;

固有導電 intrinsic conduction;

金屬導電 metallic electricity;

離子導電 ionic conduction;

氣體導電 gaseous conduction;

液體導電 liquid conduction;

［導管］ catheter; conduit; duct;

電纜導管 electrical cable conduit;

防冰系統導管 anti-icing duct;

光電導管 photoconductive tube;

環紋導管 annular duct;

絕緣導管 insulated conduit;

空氣導管 air conduit;

連接導管 connecting duct;

留置導管 indwelling catheter;

尿道導管 urethral catheter;

體腔導管 coelomic duct;

線路導管 circuit conduit;

泄空導管 emptying conduit;

心導管 cardiac catheter;

硬紙導管 fibre conduit;

［導航］ homing; navigate; navigation; pilot;

導航塔 beacon;

~ 無線電導航塔 radio beacon;

導航衛星 navigation satellite;

導航系統 navigation system;

~ 自動導航系統 automatic navigation system; autonavigator;

導航星 navstar;

導航儀 avigraph; navigator;

~ 軌道導航儀 orbit navigator;

~ 慣性導航儀 inertial navigator;

~ 自動天體導航儀 automatic celestial

navigator;
定角導航 constant navigation;
飛機導航 aircraft navigation;
進場導航 approach navigation;
進港導航 approach navigation;
空對空自動導航 air-to-air automatic navigation;
空中導航 avigation;
~無線電空中導航 radio navigation;
全天候導航 all-weather navigation;
聲導航 sound homing;
圓弧導航 arc navigation;
主動導航 active homing;
自動天文導航 automatic celestial navigation;

[導火線] (1) fuse; (2) direct cause of an event;
戰爭的導火線 incident that touches off a war;

[導買] (1) attract customers; (2) person whose job is to attract customers;

[導賞] guided tour;

[導師] (1) supervisor; teacher; tutor; (2) director; guide of a great cause; mentor;
導師輔導 mentoring; tutorial;
大學導師 university tutor;

[導數] derivative;
二階導數 second derivative; derivative of the second order;
反導數 antiderivative;
方向導數 directional derivative;
高階導數 derivatives of higher order;
控制導數 control derivative;
面積導數 areal derivative;
偏導數 partial derivative;
氣動導數 a erodynamic derivative;
一般導數 general derivative;
一階導數 first derivative;
阻尼導數 damping derivative;

[導體] conductor;
安培導體 ampere conductor;
半導體 semiconductor;
~半導體光電池 semiconductor photocell;
~半導體化合物 semiconducting compound;
~半導體整流器 semiconductor rectifier;
~補償半導體 compensated semiconductor;
~純半導體 intrinsic semiconductor;
~二元半導體 binary semiconductor;
~共價半導體 covalent semiconductor;
~金屬間半導體 intermetallic semiconductor;
~雜質半導體 impurity semiconductor;
不對稱導體 asymmetric conductor;
超導體 superconductor;
非導體 nonconductor;
光電導體 photoconductor;
~薄膜光電導體 film photoconductor;
~紅外光電導體 infrared photoconductor;
陽極導體 anode conductor;
有效導體 active conductor;

[導線] (1) conductor; (2) traverse;
電纜導線 cable conductor;
方位角導線 azimuth traverse;
輔助導線 auxiliary traverse;
附加導線 annexed traverse;
鋁導線 aluminium conductor;
青銅導線 bronze conductor;
雙金屬導線 bimetallic conductor;
天文導線 astronomical traverse;
天線導線 antenna conductor;
迂迴導線 by-pass conductor;

[導性] conductivity;
超導性 superconductivity;

[導言] introduction; introductory remark; preamble;

[導演] (1) direct; (2) director; film director; screen director; stage director;
電視節目導演 director of television programmes
對話導演 dialogue director;
副導演 assistant director;
剪輯導演 montage director;
錄音導演 sound recording director;
女導演 directress;
配音導演 dubbing director;
攝影導演 director of photography;
選角導演 casting director;
助理導演 assistant director;

[導引] guide; lead;
導引裝置 homing device;

[導遊] (1) guide a sight-seeing tour; (2) guide; tour guide; tourist guide;
導遊圖 tourist map;
做導遊 serve as a guide;

[導致] account for; bring about; bring on; cause; end in; end up in; give rise to; lead to; lead up to; result in;
導致革命 lead to revolution;
導致失敗 bring on a failure;
導致災難 bring on a disaster;

報導 cover; report;
編導 write and direct;
波導 waveguide;
倡導 initiate; propose;
超導 superconduction;
傳導 conduct;
電導 conductance;
督導 director; supervise and direct; supervisor;
輔導 give guidance in study;
互導 mutual conductance;
教導 enlighten; give guidance; instruct; instruction; teach; under the tutelage;
開導 enlighten; explain and make sb understand; give guidance to; help sb to see what is right or sensible; help sb to straighten out his wrong or muddled thinking;
跨導 transconductance;
利導 lead;
領導 exercise leadership; lead; leader; leadership;
蒙導 mentor;
前導 (1) lead the way; march at the head; march in front; precede; (2) guide; person who leads the way; pioneer;
勸導 advise; try to persuade;
視導 inspection;
疏導 clear the crowd; clear the traffic; dredge a river and channel the water;
順導 guide a movement along its proper course;
推導 deduce; infer;
誤導 mislead;
先導 (1) forerunner; guide; (2) precursor;
嚮導 docent; guide;
消導 cure indigestion;
宣導 guide by creating a better understanding;
訓導 instruct; teach;
引導 guide; lead;
誘導 guide; induce; induction; lead;
指導 direct; guide; instruct;
制導 control and guide;
主導 dominant; guiding; leading;

dao

【翿】 streamer for feathered dance or funeral in ancient times;

dao

【纛】 banner; streamer;

de²

de

【得】 (1) acquire; attain; effect; gain; get; obtain; (2) complacent; (3) agreement; (4) able to; can; may;

[得便] when it is convenient;
[得病] come down with an illness; fall ill; ill;
[得逞] have one's way; prevail; succeed;
得逞一時 have one's way for a time; succed for a time;
[得寵] find favour with sb; in sb's good graces;
得寵的人 fair-haired boy;
很得寵 in high favour with sb;
漸漸得寵 worm oneself into favour;
[得出] obtain a result; reach a conclusion;
得出教訓 draw a moral lesson;
得出結論 arrive at a conclusion; come at a conclusion; come to a conclusion; draw a conclusion; reach a conclusion;
[得當] appropriate; apt; proper; propriety; suitable;
安排得當 be properly arranged;
處理得當 be properly handled;
措辭得當 proper use of words and phrases;
措置得當 be handled properly;
分配得當 be properly distributed;
説話得當 speak quite apropos;
[得到] come at; gain; get; obtain; receive;
得到成功 achieve success;
得到好處 acquire benefit;
得到好評 win the praise of sb;
得到控制 get under control;
得到普遍好評 find wide-spread favour;
得到榮譽 achieve an honour;
得到深刻教訓 learn a bitter lesson;
得到優勢 gain the upper hand;
得到治療 obtain the medical treatment;
[得道多助] a just cause enjoys abundant support; one who upholds justice shall not be alone;
[得得聲] clip-clop;
[得法] do sth in the proper way; get the knack;
管理得法 manage properly;
教授得法 teach in the right way;
經商得法 have a knack for business;
使用得法 make the proper use of sth;
指導得法 proper guidance;
[得分] score;
[得過且過] drift along; let well enough alone;
得過且過的人 deadbeat;
[…得好]
幹得好 way to go; well done; well played;

說得好 well said;

[得計] succeed in one's scheme;

自以為得計 think oneself a smart fellow;

[得獎] be awarded a prize; collect a medal; win a prize;

[得勁] (1) feel well; (2) fit for use; handy;

[得救] be rescued; be saved;

[得空] be at leisure; free;

[得力] (1) benefit from; (2) get help from; (3) capable; competent; efficient;

得力助手 capable assistant; competent assistant; right-hand man;

辦事得力 do things efficiently;

工作得力 work with great efficiency;

[得隴望蜀] appetite comes with eating; give him an inch and he will take a mile; the more one gets, the more one wants;

[得其所哉] have got to the right place;

[得勝] bear away the bell; bear the bell; bring home the bacon; carry away the bell; carry off the bell; coast home; come through with flying colours; triumph; win; win a victory;

得勝回朝 return victoriously to one's palace;

得勝回營 return in triumph to one's camp;

得勝而歸 come back victorious; return in triumph; return with flying colours;

旗開得勝 gain a battle at the unfurling of the flag; make a successful beginning; start with a bang; succeed at the first try; succeed from the very start; triumphant in the first battle; win a quick victory; win in the battle; win speedy success; win victory in the first battle; win a victory the moment one's flag is unfurled;

~ 旗開得勝，馬到成功 wish you a speedy success;

[得失] (1) gain and loss; success and failure; (2) advantages and disadvantages; merits and demerits;

得失參半 half gained but half lost; success equals to failure;

得失難料 the final result is not easy to predict; whether gain or loss is beyond one's power to foresee;

得失榮枯 vicissitudes of life;

得失相當 break even; gains and losses balance each other; half loss, half gain; the gains offset the losses;

不計得失 indifferent about success or failure;

不計個人得失 regardless of personal gain or loss;

得不償失 gains cannot make up for losses; give a lark to catch a kite; it's not worth it; lose more than gain; more kicks than halfpence; pay for one's whistle; pay too dear for one's whistle; the game is not worth the candle; the loss outweighs the gain; too dear for the whistle; what is gained does not make up for what is lost;

~ 八五砲打兔子—得不償失 shooting a rabbit with a cannon — the gain is not worth the loss; the game is not worth the candle;

得東失西 you lose on the swings what you make on the roadabouts;

得而復失 lose after having got it;

得少失多 gain little and lose much;

患得患失 be anxious about personal gain and loss; be swayed by considerations of gain and loss; mindful of personal gains and losses; one is never satisfied; think in terms of personal gain and loss; worry about personal gains and losses;

雞蟲得失 inconsequential matters; matters; trifles; trivialities;

權衡得失 weigh the advantages and disadvantages of sth;

失而復得 lost and found; recover what one has lost;

旋得旋失 no sooner obtained than lost again;

易得易失 easy come, easy go; easy get; easy lose; light come, light go; quickly come, quickly go; soon gotten, soon spent; what one gets easily one parts with easily;

有得有失 you can't win them all; you win some, you lose some;

[得時] in luck;

[得勢] (1) in power; (2) ascent to power; get the upper hand; in the ascendent;

小人得勢 the tail wags the dog;

[得手] come off; do fine; go smoothly; succeed;

[得體] appropriate; befitting one's position

or suited to the occasion; decorum; propriety;

不得體 indecorous; indecorum; infelicitous; infelicity; uncomely;

措辭得體 proper wording; put it in approrpiate terms; words employed are suitable and proper;

[得天獨厚] abound in the gifts of nature; be born with a lucky star; be richly endowed by nature; enjoy exceptional advantages;

[得悉] hear of; learn about;

[得閒] at leisure; free; have leisure;

[得宜] appropriate; proper; suitable;

[得意] complacent; pleased with oneself; proud of oneself;

得意門生 one's favourite pupil;

得意傑作 one's favourite masterpiece;

得意忘形 become highly conceited; dizzy with success; elated to the degree of forgetting one's form; get dizzy with success; go wild with joy; lose all bearings in a moment of pride and satisfaction; on cloud nine; puffed up with pride;

得意洋洋 be immensely proud; be in heaven; cheerful and confident; feel oneself highly flattered; flushed; glowing with pride; have one's nose in the air; have one's tail up; jubilant; look triumphant; on the high ropes; pleased with oneself; tread on air; walk on air; with evident pride;

~得意洋洋的 cock-a-hoop;

暗暗得意 be secretly pleased with oneself;

暗自得意 be inwardly proud of oneself;

看樣子很得意 look pleased with oneself;

洋洋得意 elated; in high spirits; proud and happy; walk on air;

揚揚得意 exult over; smug and complacent; walk on air;

自鳴得意 be puffed up with pride; be very pleased with oneself; blow one's own horn; chuckle with pride; cock-a-hoop; complacent; crow over one's success; get too big for one's shoes; preen oneself; pride oneself on having done sth smart; rub one's hands in glee; self-satisfied; sing one's own praises; with stars in one's eyes;

[得益] benefit; profit;

得益非淺 enjoy great benefit; get a considerable gain; profit much;

[得魚忘筌] forget the trap as soon as the fish is caught;

[得知] be informed;

[得志] achieve one's ambition;

不得志 have little success;

少年得志 win success early in life;

小人得志 the villains are holding sway;

[得罪] cause offence to sb; cross sb; displease; give offence to sb; in sb's bad books; in sb's black books; offend; run foul of sb; step on sb's toes;

得罪人 offend sb;

~怕得罪人 afraid of giving offence; afraid of offending others;

巴不得 earnestly wish;

必得 have to; must;

變得 become;

博得 gain; obtain; win;

不得 may not; must not; not be allowed;

不由得 cannot help;

懂得 know; understand;

奪得 carry off; seize; take; win;

非得 have got to; have to; must;

分得 get a share;

購得 purchase;

恨不得 have an itch to do sth; how one wishes one could;

獲得 acquire; gain; obtain; win;

急得 anxious; worry;

記得 remember;

見得 appear; seem;

倦得 tired;

覺得 (1) feel; (2) feel; think;

虧得 fortunately; luckily; thanks to;

來得 competent;

懶得 not in the mood to;

樂得 only too glad to;

了不得 (1) extraordinary; terrific; (2) awful; dreadful; terrible;

了得 horrible; terrific;

落得 result in;

免得 so as not to; so as to avoid;

難得 hard to come by; rare;

鬧得 cause; create; raise;

氣得 with anger;

求得 obtain;

取得 achieve; acquire; gain; obtain;

惹得 arouse; provoke;
認得 know; recognize;
捨得 not grudge; willing to part with;
省得 so as to avoid; so as to save;
使得 (1) can be used; (2) feasible; workable; (3) cause; make;
睡得 sleep;
說得 what is said;
所得 (1) income; (2) what one gets; what one receives;
習得 acquisition;
顯得 appear; look; seem;
相得 friendly; harmonious;
曉得 know;
心得 what one has learned from work, study, etc.;
幸得 fortunately; thanks to;
倖得 obtain by luck;
須得 must have; should have;
焉得 how can one be...;
要得 desirable; fine; good;
一得 a good idea;
引得 index;
應得 deserved; due;
贏得 gain; win;
有得 what one has learned from work, study, etc.;
怎得 (1) how could; (2) how;
祇得 have no alternative but to; have to;
值得 deserve; worth;
自得 pleased with oneself; self-complacent; self-satisfied;
總得 bound to; have to; must; somehow;

de

【德】 (1) decency; morality; virtues; (2) favours; repay kindness; (3) behaviour; conduct; (4) German; Germany;

[德薄能鮮] lack both virtue and ability;

[德才] moral character and ability;
德才並重 equal stress on ability and moral integrity;
德才兼備 combine ability with integrity; equal stress on integrity and ability; graced with many virtues and talents; have both ability and principles; have both integrity and ability; possess integrity and professional competence;
德才兼顧 take both ability and moral character into consideration;
德薄才疏 not ethical and competent;
德廣才高 of lofty virtue and great talent;

[德望] a person's moral prestige;
德高望重 be highly respected for one's lofty virtue; be of noble character and high prestige; enjoy high prestige and command universal respect; have a high virtue and a glorious name;

[德威] display one's virtue and dignity;
彰其德威 display one's virtue and dignity;

[德行] (1) moral conduct; moral integrity; (2) disgusting; shameful;
德行差 bad moral conduct;
德行好 good moral conduct;

[德育] moral education;

[德政] benevolent rule;

[德治] rule of virtue;

敗德 evil conduct; licentious behaviour;
報德 pay a debt of gratitude; repay a kindness;
悖德 immoral;
道德 integrity; moral character; morality; morals;
恩德 favour; grace; kindness;
公德 social ethics; social morality;
功德 (1) merits and virtues; (2) benefaction; charitable and pious deeds;
穢德 debauched ways; filthy deeds;
積德 do good deeds to the doer's credit in the next world;
梏德 great virtue;
口德 propriety in one's remarks;
美德 moral excellence; moral integrity; virtue;
品德 moral character;
潛德 hidden virtues; unnoticed virtues;
全德 perfect character;
缺德 mean; villainous; wicked;
仁德 benevolence; charity; humanity; kindness; magnanimity;
上德 the highest virtue;
尚德 respect the virtuous;
世德 traditional morals;
淑德 female virtues;
樹德 establish one's virtues; examplify one's integrity;
爽德 depart from virtue; lose virtue;
順德 docile virtue;
私德 personal morals; personal virtue; private conduct;
損德 cause damage to one's virtue; injure one's virtue by misdeed;
文德 the refining influence of learning and art;
武德 soldierly virtues;

賢德 virtuous;
腥德 debauchery; dissipated ways; evil conduct;
修德 cultivate one's virtue;
醫德 medical ethics;
懿德 (1) fine virtue; (2) woman's meritorious character;
陰德 a good deed to the doer's credit in the next world;
有德 righteous; virtuous;
育德 cultivate one's virtue;
浴德 cultivate one's virtue;
之德 kindness;
至德 the highest virtue;
種德 accumulate virtuous deeds; cultivate virtues;
祖德 the cirtuous deeds of one's ancestors;

D

de⁵
de
【的】 adjectival ending;

dei³
dei
【得】 must; ought to; should;
[得饒人處且饒人] be lenient wherever it is possible; easy on people; leave room for manoeuvre;
必得 have to; must;
非得 have got to; must;
總得 be bound to; have to;

deng¹
deng
【登】 (1) ascend; climb; rise; (2) record; register; (3) employ; take; (4) board; wear;
[登報] make an announcement in the newspaper;
登報公佈 publicize in the press;
登報聲明 make a statement in the newspaper; newspaper announcement;
登報通告 put a notice in the paper;
[登場] come on the stage; enter the scene;
登場亮相 strike a pose on the stage;
粉墨登場 (1) do one's costume and appear on the stage; dress up and perform on stage; make oneself up and go on stage; mount the stage in full makeup; put on one's costume and make one's entry on the stage; put on one's makeup and go on the stage; (2) embark on a political venture; enter upon office in full preparation;
袍笏登場 dress up and go on the stage;
[登程] start off on a journey; set out on a journey;
[登峰] reach the peak;
登峰造極 at the zenith of; attain a level never known before; come to a climax; have the highest level of attainment; reach great heights; reach the limit; reach the peak of perfection; reach the summit; reach the top of the ladder;
[登高] ascend a height; climb a mountain;
登高一呼 make a clarion call; make a public appeal; mount a stone and cry;
登高遠眺 ascend a height to enjoy a distant view;
登高自卑 in order to climb to the summit, a person must begin from the bottom;
害怕登高 be afraid of heights;
[登革熱] dengue fever;
出血性登革熱 hemorrhagic dengue;
登革熱病毒 dengue virus;
[登基] accession; be enthroned;
新王登基 the accession of a new king;
[登機] board a flight; boarding;
登機卡 boarding card;
登機證 boarding pass;
[登記] check in; enter one's name; register;
登記冊 register;
~選民登記冊 electoral register;
登記結婚 register for one's marriage;
來賓登記 visitor registration;
無須登記 no registration is required;
[登科] pass civil examinations; receive government degrees;
小登科 newly wed; take a wife;
[登龍有術] very skilful in finding a powerful patron to advance one's career;
[登陸] go to debarkation; land;
登陸艇 amphibious assault ship; landing craft;
安全登陸 land safely;
成功登陸 make a successful landing;
緊急登陸 make an emergency landing;
棄舟登陸 leave the ship and go ashore;
[登門] call at sb's house;
登門拜訪 call at sb's house; call on sb in person; come on a visit to sb's house; pay sb a visit;
登門拜謝 call at sb's house to express

one's thanks; go to sb's house and offer thanks;
登門報喜 announce good news at the house door; call on sb to announce happy news; go to sb's house to report success;
登門辭別 pay a farewell call;
登門答謝 call on sb to express gratitude;
登門道賀 call on sb to offer one's congratulations; go to pay sb a congratulatory call;
登門道歉 go to sb's home and apologize;
登門道謝 go to sb's house and offer thanks;
登門吊唁 go to sb's house to offer one's condolences; pay a visit of condolence on the death of;
登門告別 call on sb to say goodbye;
登門請罪 go to sb's house and make apologies;
登門求教 call on sb for counsel; come to seek advice; go to sb for advice;
登門求醫 go to the doctor for treatment;
登門求助 come to seek help;
登門造府 call on a person at his house;
登門致歉 go to sb's house and make apology;
登門自薦 self-promotion at the door;

[登攀] climb; scale a height;

[登山] climb a mountain; climbing; mountain climbing; mountaineering; rock climbing;
登山隊 mountaineering team;
登山家 mountaineer;
登山涉水 climb mountains and wade through rivers; go over mountains and cross streams; scale mountains and cross rivers; traverse mountains and wade through rivers;
登山遠望 ascend a hill and thence to have a wide view; climb a mountain and gaze for afield;
登山運動 mountaineering;
~登山運動員 alpinist; climber; mountaineer;
渡水登山 cross rivers and go up mountains;
去登山 go climbing;

[登時] at once; immediately; then and there;

[登台] go up on the stage; mount a platform;
登台拜將 ascend the royal platform and be appointed minister;
登台表演 come on the stage; come to the stage to give one's performance;
登台獻藝 stage a performance;
登台演説 deliver a speech on the platform; give a speech on the stage;
登台演戲 play on stage; take the stage and perform;
初次登台 debut; make one's debut; one's first appearance in;
~初次登台的演員 debutant;
害怕登台 get stage fright;
首次登台 debut; make one's debut; one's first appearance in;

[登天] climb up to the sky;
難如登天 as difficult as going to heaven; as difficult as to climb up to the sky;
平步登天 have a meteoric rise to fame; make a sudden rise in social status; rise to fame suddenly; spring to the heaven from the ground; very easily come to a high position;

[登徒子] playboy;

[登仙羽化] ascend and become an immortal; becoming a god; take to the land of immortals;

[登月] land on the moon;
登月艙 lunar module;

[登載] carry; publish;
登載在頭版 be published on the front page;

叨登 (1) turn sth over and over; (2) harp on an old story;
豐登 bumper harvest;
刊登 publish in a newspaper;
摩登 fashionable; modern;
躡登 go up;
攀登 climb; scale;
縋登 climb by a rope;

deng

【燈】 burner; lamp; lantern;

[燈船] lightship; light vessel;

[燈蛾] moth; tiger moth;
燈蛾撲火 a moth flying into fire — self-destruction; a suicidal act;
燈蛾撲火，惹焰燒身 the moth flies into the flame, getting itself burnt to death;

[燈光] (1) lamplight; (2) lighting;
燈光暗淡 be dimly lit;

燈光暗下來 the lights are getting dimmer;
燈光表演 light show;
燈光閃亮 the lamp flares;
燈光師 gaffer;
燈光通明 be brightly lit;
燈光效果 lighting effect;
燈光搖曳 the lamp flickers;
暗淡的燈光 dim light;
旋大燈光 turn up a lamp; turn up the light;
旋小燈光 turn down a lamp;

[燈紅酒綠] indulge in debauchery;
燈紅酒綠，紙醉金迷 lead a luxurious life;

[燈花] ears; niggers; the snuff of a candlewick;

[燈輝如畫] the lighting of a place is as bright as daytime;

[燈會] lantern show;

[燈火] lights;
燈火輝煌 ablaze with lights; alight with lamps; be aflame with lamps; be brilliantly illuminated; be brightly lit;
燈火通明 ablaze with lights; brightly lit;
~屋子燈火通明 the house was ablaze with lights;
黑燈瞎火 blackout; dark; unlit;
一片燈火 a blaze of lights;

[燈節] Lantern Festival;

[燈籠] lantern;
燈籠褲 bloomers;
點燈籠 light a lantern;
鼓樓的燈籠—高明 a lantern on a drum tower – high brightness; (pun) high intelligence;
掛燈籠 hang up a lantern;
提燈籠 carry a lantern; hold a lantern;
紙燈籠 Chinese lantern;

[燈謎] lantern riddles; riddles written on lanterns;
猜燈謎 guess lantern riddles;

[燈泡] bulb; light bulb;
白熾燈泡 incandescent light bulb;
玻璃燈泡 glass light bulb;
充氣燈泡 gas-filled light bulb;
抽空燈泡 evacuated light bulb;
擋泥板燈泡 mudguard light bulb;
電燈泡 electric light bulb;
壞燈泡 dud light bulb;
換燈泡 change the light bulb;
漏斗形燈泡 funnel light bulb;
磨砂燈泡 frosted light bulb;
乳白燈泡 opal light bulb;
手電筒燈泡 pocket light bulb;
雙絲燈泡 double-filament bulb;
頭燈燈泡 headlight bulb;
透明玻璃燈泡 clear light bulb;
尾燈燈泡 tail-light bulb;
小燈泡 miniature light bulb;
小光燈泡 dim light bulb;
行燈燈泡 portable light bulb;
照明燈泡 lighting bulb;
縐紋燈泡 corrugated light bulb;

[燈塔] lighthouse;
一座燈塔 a lighthouse;

[燈台] lampstand;
丈八燈台—照見人家，照不見自己 like a six-foot lampstand that lights up others but stays dark itself;
丈八燈台—照遠不照近 like a ten-foot lampstand that sheds light on others but none on itstlf – see others' shortcomings while losing sight of one's own; the dark place is under candle-stick;

[燈芯絨] cord; corduroy;
燈芯絨褲 cord trousers;

[燈蕊] lampwick; wick;
燈蕊絨 ribbed velvet;

[燈油] lamp oil;

[燈罩] lampshade;

[燈座] lamp socket;

安全燈 (1) safety lamp; (2) safelight;
壁燈 backet light; wall lamp;
標燈 beacon; beacon light;
彩燈 coloured lamp; coloured lantern;
側燈 side light;
車燈 the headlight of an automobile;
車頭燈 headlamp; headlight;
牀頭燈 bedside lamp;
吹燈 break off a love affair;
大燈 head light;
電燈 electric light;
吊燈 pendent lamp;
頂燈 dome light; top light;
泛光燈 floodlight;
風燈 storm lantern;
宮燈 palace lantern;
篝燈 jack; jacklight;
關燈 snap off; switch off the light; turn off the light;

管燈 fluorescent lamp;
河燈 river lantern;
紅燈 (1) (traffic) red light; (2) red lantern;
紅綠燈 traffic light; traffic signal;
弧光燈 arc lamp;
花燈 festive lantern;
華燈 colourfully decorated lanterns; light;
幻燈 (1) slide show; (2) slide projector;
黃燈 (traffic) yellow light;
黃光燈 yellow fluorescent lamp;
腳燈 footlight;
酒精燈 alcohol burner; spirit lamp;
聚光燈 spotlight;
開燈 snap on; switch on the light; turn on the light;
立燈 floor lamp;
龍燈 dragon lantern;
路燈 road lamp; street lamp;
綠燈 (1) green light; (2) permission to go ahead with some project;
落地燈 floor lamp;
馬燈 barn lantern; lantern;
煤氣燈 gas lamp; gas light;
明燈 beacon; bright lamp;
氖燈 neon lamp;
霓虹燈 neon light;
噴燈 blowlamp; blowtorch;
汽燈 gas lamp;
氣燈 gas lamp;
前燈 headlamp; headlight;
青燈 oil lamp;
燃燈 light a lamp;
日光燈 daylight lamp; fluorescent lamp;
紗燈 gauze lantern;
閃光燈 flash lamp; photoflash;
上燈 light the lamp; light up;
上射燈 uplighter;
水銀燈 mercury-vapour lamp;
酥燈 oil lamp before the Buddha;
檯燈 desk lamp; reading lamp; table lamp;
太陽燈 sunlight lamp;
探照燈 search light;
提燈 lantern;
挑燈 raise the wick of an oil lamp;
頭燈 head lamp;
萬向燈 anglepoise lamp;
桅燈 (1) mast light; range light; (2) barn lantern;
尾燈 tail lamp; taillight;
鎢絲燈 tungsten lamp;
霧燈 fog lamp; fog light;
熄燈 put out the light; switch off the light; turn off the light;
舷燈 sidelight;
信號燈 signal lamp;
夜燈 nightlight;
一盞燈 a lamp;
螢光燈 daylight lamp; fluorescent lamp;
油燈 oil lamp;
側燈 sidelight;
桌燈 desk lamp; table lamp;
走馬燈 revolving lantern;

deng
【簦】 a kind of umbrella in ancient China;

deng
【鐙】 (1) same as 燈; (2) a kind of cooking vessel in ancient times;

deng³
deng
【等】 (1) grade; rank; (2) equal; same; (3) wait; (4) and so on; etc.;

［等邊］ equilateral;
［等次］ grade;
［等待］ await for; bear with; hang on; hold on; stop for; wait around; wait for; wait in; wait on; wait out;
等待機會到來 watch for a chance to come;
等待良機 bide one's time;
等待時機 await a favourable opportunity; bide one's time; wait for a chance; wait one's opportunity for...;
等待消息 wait for the arrival of news;
不能再等待 can't wait any longer;
激動地等待 excitedly await...;
緊張地等待 tensely await...;
靜靜地等待 silently await...;
滿懷信心地等待 wait confidently;
屏息靜氣地等待 wait in breathless expectancy;
［等到］ (1) by the time; when; (2) wait till; wait until;
等到白頭 wait until one's hair turns white;
［等等］ and all; and all that; and other things; and others; and so forth; and so on; and so on and so forth; and such like; and that; and that sort of thing; and the like; and the others; and the rest; and them; or the like; or what have you; this, that and the other; whatnot;
［等而下之］ from that grade down; lower down;

［等分］ aliquot;
等分裝藥 aliquot part of charge;
等分試樣 aliquot sample;
［等高距］ contour interval;
［等高線］ contour;
標準等高線 normal contour;
繪等高線 contouring;
精確等高線 accurate contour;
近似等高線 approximate contour;
實測等高線 instrumental contour;
指標等高線 index contour;
中間等高線 intermediate contour;
［等號］ equal sign; equals sign;
［等候］ await; expect; wait;
等候進一步指示 await for further instruction;
等候名單 waiting list; waitlist;
等候命令 await instructions; await orders;
等候室 lounge; waiting room;
焦急地等候 wait anxiously;
在家等候 wait in;
［等級］ (1) grade; rank; (2) order and degree; social estate; social stratum;
等級觀念 sense of hierarchy;
等級社會 hierarchical society;
等級森嚴 be rigidly stratified; form a strict hierarchy;
等級體系 hierarchy;
~ 等級體系對立 hierarchical opposition;
~ 等級體系結構 hierarchical structure;
等級原則 principle of hierarchy;
等級轉移 rank shift;
翻譯等級 rank of translation;
混合等級 combined grade;
絕緣等級 insulation grade;
普通等級 common grade;
社會等級 social scale;
原木等級 log grade;
［等價］ equivalence;
代數等價 algebraic equivalence;
基數等價 cardinal equivalence;
鏈式等價 chain equivalence;
同倫等價 homotopy equivalence;
［等離子］ plasma;
等離子體 plasma;
~ 電子等離子體 electron plasma;
~ 高能等離子體 energetic plasma;
~ 簡併等離子體 degenerate plasma;
~ 抗磁等離子體 diamagnetic plasma;
~ 陶瓷等離子體 ceramic plasma;
［等量齊觀］ be mentioned in the same breath; be regarded as equal; draw a parallel between; equate; equate one with the other; match; place on the same footing; put on a par;
［等人］ wait for sb;
熬夜等人 wait up;
［等容］ constant volume; isochoric;
等容過程 constant volume process; isochoric process;
［等式］ equality; equation;
不等式 inequality;
~ 條件不等式 conditional inequality;
~ 退化不等式 degenerate inequality;
~ 微分不等式 differential inequality;
恒等式 identity;
會計等式 accounting equation;
邏輯等式 logical equation;
雙積等式 dyadic equation;
條件等式 conditional equality;
向量等式 equality of vector;
［等同］ equal; equate; equative;
等同動詞 equative verb;
［等溫］ isothermal;
等溫變化 isothermal change; isothermal transprocess;
等溫高度 isothermal altitude;
等溫過程 isothermal process;
等溫條件 isothermy;
等溫線 isotherm; isothermal line;
~ 臨界等溫線 critical isotherm;
~ 吸收等溫線 absorption isotherms;
［等閒］ (1) ordinary; unimportant; (2) aimlessly; thoughtlessly; (3) for no reason; gratuitously;
等閒視之 give sb the go-by; make nothing of; regard as unimportant; treat lightly;
視作等閒 regard as a light matter; treat lightly;
［等效］ equivalent effect;
等效翻譯 equivalent-effect translation;
［等壓線］ isobar;
［等一等］ just wait a minute; just wait a moment; just wait a second; wait for a while; wait up;
最好等一等 it might be better to wait for a while;
［等於］ correspond to; equal to; equivalent to; make sth equal to; tantamount to; the equal of sth; the same as; worth;
［等震］ isoseismal;

~等震線 isoseismal line;
~等震線圖 isoseismal map;

[等着] waiting;
正等着 lurking in the wings; waiting in the wings;
~正等着晉昇 wating in the wings for promotion;

彼等 those people;
丙等 C grade; the third-class;
不等 different; not equal;
超等 exceedingly good; of superior grade;
初等 elementary; primary; rudimentary;
差等 classes; classification;
次等 second-class; second-rate;
等一等 just wait a minute; just wait a moment; just wait a second; wait a while; wait up;
低等 low grade;
對等 on an equal footing; reciprocal;
二等 second-class; second-rate;
分等 classify; grade;
高等 high;
何等 (1) how; what; (2) what kind;
恒等 identical; identically equal;
降等 degradation;
均等 equal;
老等 heron;
立等 wait on the spot until sth is done;
劣等 inferior; low-grade; of inferior quality;
躐等 skip over the normal steps;
平等 equal; equality;
親等 degree; degree of kinship; degree of relationship;
全等 congruent;
汝等 you;
三等 (1) three grades; (2) third grade;
上等 first-class; first-rate; superior;
殊等 special class;
死等 wait indefinitely without giving up hope;
特等 special class; top grade;
同等 of the same class; on an equal footing;
頭等 first-class; first-rate;
下等 inferior; low-grade;
相等 equal; equal to;
星等 apparent magnitude;
一等 first-class; first-rate;
乙等 Grade B; second grade;
異等 (1) remarkable; unusual; (2) different grade;
優等 excellent; first-class; high-class; superior;
這等 like this; such;
職等 grade of position; official rank;
中等 (1) medium; moderate; (2) secondary; (3) intermediate;
坐等 sit back and wait;

deng
【戥】 small steelyard for weighing gold, jewels, etc.;
[戥星] sliding pivot on a small steelyard;

deng⁴
deng
【凳】 bench; stool;
[凳子] stool;

矮凳 low stool;
長凳 bench;
方凳 square stool;
琴凳 music stool; piano stool;

deng
【嶝】 hill path; mountain path;

deng
【鄧】 (1) a surname; (2) an ancient state in today's Hubei;
[鄧蛾] euphonia;

deng
【瞪】 glare; stare at;
[瞪目] (1) open one's eyes wide; (2) glare; stare;
瞪目凝視 stare with wide eyes;
豎眉瞪目 raise one's eyebrows and stare in anger;
[瞪眼] (1) glare; open one's eyes wide; stare; (2) get angry with sb; glower and glare at sb;
瞪眼怒視 scowl down; stare and scowl at;
吹鬍子瞪眼 snort and stare in anger–very angry;
乾瞪眼 look on helplessly; look on in despair;
橫眉瞪眼 look angrily;
擰眉瞪眼 raise one's eyebrows and stare in anger;
死眉瞪眼 (1) with a straight face; (2) inanimate;
直眉瞪眼 be stupefied; fume; in a daze; look angry; stare blankly; stare in anger;

迷瞪 confused; dazed; perplexed; puzzled;

deng
【磴】 steps on a stone staircase;

［磴道］ mountain stairs;

deng

【蹬】 (1) step on; tread on; (2) deprived of power or influence;

［蹬技］ a variety of juggling skills;

蹭蹬 down on one's luck; in depression;

deng

【鐙】 stirrup;

馬鐙 stirrup;

di¹

di

【氐】 an ancient barbarian tribe living in the northwestern China;

di

【低】 (1) low; (2) lower;

［低層］ (1) lower storey; (2) low level;
低層語 basilect;
低層結構 underlying structure;

［低產］ low yield;
低產田 low-yielding land;

［低潮］ (1) low ebb; low tide; low water; (2) trough;
低潮時期 period of low tide;
低潮線 low water mark;
處於低潮 at a low ebb;
進入低潮 recede to a low ebb;

［低沉］ (1) overcast; (2) low and deep; (3) downcast; low-spirited;
氣氛低沉 have an atmosphere of depression;
聲音低沉 have a low and deep voice;

［低垂］ droop; hang low; let droop;
目光低垂 downcast eyes;
濃霧低垂 thick low-hanging fog;
夜幕低垂 nightfall;
烏雲低垂 cloudy;

［低擋］ low gear;
換低擋 downshift;

［低檔］ low-end; low-grade; of low quality;
低檔的 downscale;
低檔電腦 low-end computer;

［低等］ low grade;

［低地］ lowlands;

［低調］ low-key; low profile;

［低峰］ trough;

［低谷］ trough;

［低估］ disappreciation; underestimate; underrate; undervalue;
低估敵人的能力 undervalue the abilities of one's enemy;
低估對手 sell one's opponent short;
被低估的 underrated;

［低級］ (1) elementary; lower; primary; rudimentary; (2) low; vulgar;
低級趣味 bad taste; low taste; philistine taste; vulgar interests;

［低價］ at a low price;
低價租用 low cost rental;

［低賤］ low and degrading;

［低空］ low altitude;
低空飛行 low-flying;
低空特技 low-altitude aerobatics;

［低欄］ low hurdles;
200 米低欄 200-metre low hurdles;

［低廉］ cheap; low;
物價低廉 prices are low;

［低劣］ inferior; low-grade;
低劣作品 a work of poor quality;

［低落］ downcast; low;
情緒低落 down in spirits; in low spirits; in poor spirits;
士氣低落 the morale is low;
物價低落 prices have dropped to a lower level;

［低能］ feeble-mindedness; incompetent; mental deficiency; retarded;
低能兒 (1) retarded child; (2) incapable person;

［低柔］ soft and low;

［低聲］ in a low voice; in a whisper; under one's breath; with bated breath;
低聲補充 add in a low voice;
低聲咕噥 murmur in a low voice;
低聲哼唱 hum a song;
低聲說話 speak low; speak under one's voice; talk in whispers;
低聲問 ask in a whisper;
低聲細語 have a buzz of talk; in a whisper;
低聲下氣 have a servile manner; humble oneself; lower one's voice and stifle one's anger; meek and subservient; obsequious; soft-spoken and submissive; speak humbly and under one's breath; speak low and repress one's feelings of revolt;

[低首] lower one's head;
低首不語 bow one's head and keep silent; hang down the head without uttering a word; hang one's head in silence;
低首下心 bow and scrape; bow one's head in humility; humble oneself; obsequiously submissive;

[低俗] low in taste; trashy; vulgar;

[低速] low speed; low velocity; slow speed;
低速檔 bottom gear; low gear;

[低頭] (1) bow one's head; hang one's head; lower one's head; (2) submit; yield;
低頭不答 bend one's head and do not reply; bend one's head down and make no answer;
低頭不語 lower one's head and keep quiet;
低頭看書 lean over a book;
低頭默哀 lower one's head in silent mourning;
低頭認罪 hang one's head and confess one's guilt; plead guilty;
低頭掃手機 phub;
~低頭掃手機的人 phubber;
低頭歎息 hang one's head and sigh;
低頭無言 bow one's head and be silent; lower one's head and say nothing;
低頭尋思 bend one's head and try hard to remember; lower one's head in thought;
決不向困難低頭 never bow to difficulties;
人在檐下過，怎得不低頭 when one is under low eaves, one has no choice but to lower one's head;

[低窪] low-lying;
低窪地區 low-lying area;

[低微] humble; lowly;
出身低微 from a humble origin;
地位低微 in a humble position;
官職低微 hold a low official position;
收入低微 get a low salary;
職業低微 have a lowly occupation;

[低溫] cryo-; low temperature;
低溫板 cryopanel; cryoplate;
低溫泵 cryopump;
低溫層 cryosphere;
低溫電纜 cryocables;
低溫電子學 cryoelectronics; cryotronics;
低溫凍土計 cryopedometer;
低溫發生器 cryogenerator;
低溫防護劑 cryoprotector;
低溫乾燥 cryodrying;
低溫管 cryotron;
低溫恒溫器 cryostat;
低溫化學 cryochemistry;
低溫計 cryometer;
低溫晶體管 cryosistor;
低溫冷阱 cryotrap;
低溫濃縮 cryoconcentration;
低溫生物學 cryobiology;
~低溫生物學者 cryobiologist;
低溫物理學 cryophysics;
低溫學 cryoneny; cryonetics;
低溫摘除術 cryoextraction;

[低息] low interest;

[低下] low; lowly;
經濟地位低下 of low economic status;
人品低下 of abject character;
社會地位低下 lowly in social status;
智力低下 have a low grade of intelligence;

[低薪] low-paid;
低薪工人 low-paid worker;

[低胸] low-cut;

[低壓] low pressure;
低壓槽 pressure trough;
低壓等值線 meiobar;
熱帶低壓 tropical depression;

[低音] bass; low pitch;
低音部 bass part;
~低音部樂譜 bass staff;
低音大管 contra bassoon;
低音單簧管 bass clarinet;
低音歌手 bassist;
~最低音歌手 basso profundo;
低音薩克管 bass saxophone;
低音提琴 double bass;
固體低音 solid bass;
男低音 basso;
女低音 contralto;
抒情低音 basso cantante;

[低脂] low-fat;
低脂酸奶 low-fat yoghurt;
低脂飲食 low-fat diet;

[低智] below-average intelligence;

貶低 abase; belittle; cry down; denigrate; denigration; depreciate; detract from; disparage; play down; run down;

高低 (1) height; (2) difference in degree; relative inferiority; relative superiority; (3) a sense of propriety; discretion; (4) just; on any account; simply;

減低 cut; lower; reduce;
降低 become lower; cut down; drop; lower;
壓低 abate; bring down; depress; lower; reduce;
最低 the least; the lowest; the minimum;

di
【羝】 he-goat; ram;

di
【堤】 dam; dyke; embankment; levee;
［堤道］ causeway;

di
【提】 hold; take in hand;
［提溜］ hold; take in hand;
提溜著心 anxious, worried and nervous;

di
【隄】 a pronunciation of 隄 ;

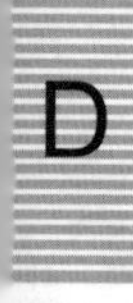

di
【滴】 (1) water drop; (2) drip;
［滴答］ drip; tick; ticktack; ticktock;
滴答聲 tick; ticking sound; ticktack; ticktock; tictac;
滴滴答答 flow in drops; pitapat; ticktack; ticktock;
［滴定］ titration;
滴定法 titration;
~ 比色滴定法 colorimetric titration;
~ 電流滴定法 amperometric titration;
~ 對抗滴定法 antagonist titration;
~ 酸鹼滴定法 acid-base titration;
~ 陽離子滴定法 cationic titration;
~ 氧化還原滴定法 oxidation- reduction titration;
滴定管 burette;
~ 標準滴定管 normal burette;
~ 橫式滴定管 horizontal burette;
~ 活栓滴定管 stopcock burette;
~ 檢定滴定管 certified burette;
~ 校準滴定管 standard burette;
~ 球滴定管 chamber burette;
~ 自動滴定管 automatic burette;
~ 自滿滴定管 zero burette;
滴定計 titrimeter;
滴定器 titrator;
~ 自動滴定器 automatic titrator;
滴定儀 titrator;
~ 連續滴定儀 continuous titrator;
回滴定 back titration;
空白滴定 blank titration;
雙安培滴定 biamperometric titration;
酸滴定 acidimetric titration;
嗅量滴定 bromometric titration;
自動滴定 automatic titration;
［滴管］ dropper;
［滴酒］ a drop of wine;
滴酒不沾 never to touch a drop of wine;
~ 滴酒不沾的 teetotal;
– 滴酒不沾的人 teetotaller;
［滴溜溜］ going round and round; round-shaped;
［滴水］ drip;
滴水板 drain board; draining board;
滴水不進 not to take even a drop of water;
滴水不漏 make sure that not a single drop leaks out;
滴水成冰 the dropping water freezes;
滴水穿石 constant dripping wears away the surface of the stone; little strokes fell great oaks;
滴水滙成河 little drops of water make a river;
［滴下］ drip;

靄滴 mist droplet;
點滴 a bit; intravenous drip;
嬌滴滴 affectedly sweet; delicately pretty; very beautiful and fascinating;
涓滴 dribble; driblet; tiny drop;
窮滴滴 destitute; poor;
數滴 a few drops; several drops;
水滴 water drops;
霧滴 fog droplet;
小滴 droplet;
一滴 a blob; a drop;
雨滴 raindrop;
雲滴 cloud droplet;

di²

di
【狄】 (1) a barbarian tribe to the north in ancient times; (2) a surname;

di
【的】 accurate; exact; proper;
［的當］ appropriate; proper; suitable;
［的確］ and no mistake; by no means; certainly; indeed; in truth; really;
的的確確 as sure as a gun; as sure as anything; as sure as death; as sure as eggs is eggs; as sure as fate; as sure as hell; as sure as nails; as sure as one lives; in all conscience; really and truly; sure enough;
［的士］ cab; taxi; taxicab;

的士司機 taxi driver;
的士站 cabstand; taxi rank; taxi stand;
打電話叫的士 call a taxi; phone for a taxi;
乘的士 get a taxi; take a taxi;
為人叫的士 call a taxi for sb;
揚招的士 hail a taxi;

di

【迪】 (1) advance; progress; (2) enlighten; teach;

啟迪 awaken; enlighten;
訓迪 enlighten and teach;

di

【笛】 flute;
［笛子］ flute;
吹笛子 play the flute;
一枝笛子 a flute;

長笛 flute;
短笛 piccolo;
風笛 bagpipe;
橫笛 bamboo flute;
鳴笛 whistle;
汽笛 air whistle; siren; steam whistle;

di

【荻】 (1) Anaphalis yedoensis; (2) Miscanthus Sacchariflorus, a kind of reed;
［荻花］ reed flower;

di

【嫡】 (1) legal wife; (2) sons born of the legal wife;
［嫡傳］ handed down in a direct line from the master;
嫡傳子弟 disciples of a master by direct line;
［嫡派］ (1) legal or official branch of a family tree; direct line of descent; (2) disciples taught by the master himself;
［嫡親］ blood relations; close paternal relations;
［嫡堂］ cousins of the same grandfather by the direct line;
［嫡系］ (1) direct line of descents; (2) closest ties of relationship; one's own clique;
［嫡子］ sons of the legal wife;

di

【滌】 (1) cleanse; wash; (2) sweep;
［滌除］ do away with; eliminate; remove; wash away;
滌除瑕穢 purge away the stains;
［滌蕩］ cleanse; get rid of; wash away; wipe out;
滌蕩無餘 rinse off without leaving a remainder;
滌瑕蕩穢 get rid of the stains; remove the flaw and wash away the dirt;

蕩滌 clean up; wash away;
洗滌 cleanse; wash;

di

【翟】 pheasant with long tail feathers;
［翟羽］ pheasant feathers;

di

【敵】 (1) enemy; foe; (2) oppose; resist;
［敵兵］ enemy soldiers; hostile troops;
［敵對］ antagonistic; antagonistism; hostile; oppose;
敵對的 antagonistic;
敵對分子 hostile element;
敵對階級 antagonistic classes;
敵對氣氛 hostile atmosphere;
敵對雙方 opposing sides;
敵對態度 hostile attitude;
~ 採取敵對態度 adopt a hostile attitude;
敵對行動 enmity; hostilities;
~ 停止敵對行動 cease the hostilities;
［敵方］ enemy; hostile forces;
［敵國］ enemy state; hostile country; hostile power;
舟中敵國 the enemy in the same boat — treacherous close friends;
［敵後］ behind the enemy; enemy's rear area;
潛伏在敵後 hide in enemy's rear area;
深入敵後 penetrate into the enemy's rear area;
［敵機］ enemy plane; hostile plane;
［敵軍］ enemy troops; hostile forces; the enemy;
［敵愾］ hatred towards the enemy;
敵愾同仇 fight against the common enemy; fight with a common hatred against the enemy; treat sb as a public enemy; wreak vengeance upon the same enemy;
［敵情］ enemy's situation; state of the enemy;
觀察敵情 observe the enemy's situation;
偵察敵情 make a reconnaissance of the enemy's situation;
［敵人］ enemy; foe;

包圍敵人 besiege the enemy;
打敗敵人 defeat the enemy;
防禦敵人 defend oneself against the enemy;
趕走敵人 drive away an enemy;
攻打敵人 attack the enemy;
攻擊敵人 attack the enemy;
孤立敵人 isolate the enemy;
擊潰敵人 rout the enemy; smash the enemy;
擊退敵人 drive back an enemy;
假想敵人 imaginary opponent;
緊逼敵人 press the enemy;
牽制敵人 keep down the enemy;
人類的敵人 the enemy of mankind;
騷擾敵人 harass the enemy;
迎戰敵人 fight against the emeny;
戰勝敵人 defeat an enemy;
主要敵人 archenemy; principal enemy;

D

[敵視] adopt a hostile attitude towards; antagonistic to; hostile to;
互相敵視 gaze at each other inimically;

[敵手] (1) adversary; antagonist; match; opponent; (2) enemy hands;
不可小覷的敵手 worthy opponent;
擊敗敵手 defeat one's antagonist;
落入敵手 fall into the enemy's hands;
淪於敵手 fall into the enemy's hands;
棋逢敵手 a good match; be equally matched in a game of chess; diamond cut diamond; equally matched; find one's match; Greek meets Greek; meet a powerful opponent; meet one's match in a contest; meet one's match in a game of chess; meet with one's equal; one is just as strong as the other; well-matched; when Greek meets Greek then comes the tug of war;
~棋逢對手，將遇良才 a chess-player meeting his match or a general coming up against a worthy foe; diamond cut diamond;
輕視敵手 belittle one's antagonist;
制服敵手 overcome one's antagonist;
挫敗敵手 foil one's antagonist;

[敵探] enemy spy;

[敵我] the enemy and the comrade;
敵我不分 can't tell friend from foe; fail to distinguish between the enemy and the comrade;
敵我矛盾 contradiction between the comrade and the enemy;
不分敵我 not to distinguish between the enemy and the comrade;
敵駐我擾 the enemy camps, we harass; when the enemy halts, we harass him;
顛倒敵我 reverse enemies and comrades; take enemies for comrades and comrades for enemies;
以我之長，攻敵之短 match one's own advantages against the enemy's disadvantages; utilize one's strong points to attack the enemy's weak points;

[敵意] animosity; enmity; hostility;
懷有敵意 harbour enmity;
沒有敵意 have no hostility;
挑起敵意 provoke hostility;

[敵友] enemies and friends;
化敵為友 convert one's enemy into one's friend;
認敵為友 regard enemies as friends; take a foe for a friend;
以友為敵 treat friends as enemies;

暗敵 a snake in the grass;
敗敵 crush the enemy; defeat the enemy;
斃敵 kill enemy troops;
不敵 be defeated; no match for;
殘敵 remnants of the enemy forces;
仇敵 enemy; foe;
讎敵 enemy; foe;
大敵 archenemy; formidable foe;
餌敵 set up a trap for the enemy;
附敵 go over to the enemy; surrender to the enemy;
赴敵 go to the battlefront;
公敵 public enemy;
殲敵 wipe out the enemy;
勁敵 formidable adversary; strong opponent;
抗敵 against the enemy;
論敵 one's opponent in a debate;
叛敵 treachery;
匹敵 equal; well matched;
前敵 front line;
強敵 formidable enemy; formidable foe; powerful enemy; powerful foe;
輕敵 take the enemy lightly; underestimate the enemy;
情敵 rival in a love affair;
卻敵 drive back the enemy; repulse the enemy;
殺敵 kill the enemy;

守敵　enemy troops on the defensive;
樹敵　make an enemy of sb; set others against oneself;
死敵　implacable foe; mortal enemy; sworn enemy;
宿敵　one's ancient antagonist;
天敵　natural enemy;
通敵　collude with the enemy;
投敵　go over to the enemy; surrender to the enemy;
退敵　drive back the enemy; repulse the enemy;
外敵　foreign enemy;
頑敵　inveterate foe; stubborn enemy;
無敵　invincible; unconquerable; unmatched;
應敵　deal with the enemy;
政敵　political opponent;

di

【嘀】 babble;

［嘀咕］ talk in whispers; whisper;

嘀嘀咕咕　babble on and on; grousing; grumbling; keep on growling; mumble to oneself; mutter to oneself;
背後嘀咕　gossip about sb behind his back;

di

【蹢】 hoof;

di

【鏑】 (1) arrowhead; (2) dysprosium;

鋒鏑　arrowhead;
鳴鏑　whistling arrow;

di

【糴】 buy grains;

［糴米］ buy rice;

di

【覿】 meet; see each other;

［覿面］ meet; see each other;

［覿儀］ presents offered at the first meeting;

di³

di

【氐】 (1) foundation; (2) same as 抵;

di

【底】 base; basis; bottom; end; foundation; underside;

［底版］ negative; photographic plate;

［底層］ ground level;

［底稿］ draft; manuscript;

［底架］ underframe;

桿式底架　bar underframe;
緩衝底架　cushion underframe;
鑄鋼底架　cast-steel underframe;

［底價］ bottom price; floor price; lowest price; rock-bottom price;

［底牌］ cards in one's hand;

［底盤］ chassis; underframe;

車子底盤　carriage underframe;
回轉底盤　reversing chassis;
平底盤　flat chassis;
汽車底盤　automobile chassis; motorcar chassis;
雙節式底盤　two-piece chassis;
坦克底盤　tank chassis;
壓鑄底盤　die-cast chassis;
自動底盤　self-propelled tool chassis;

［底片］ negative;

玻璃底片　glass negative;
分色底片　colour separation negative;
複製底片　duplicate negative;
一張底片　a negative;

［底漆］ primer; priming paint;

防鏽底漆　anti-corrosive primer;
活性底漆　active primer;
瀝青底漆　asphalt primer;
刷塗底漆　painting primer;

［底細］ exact details; ins and outs;

不明底細　ignorant of the true picture; not know the bottom of a thing; out of the swim;
了解事情的底細　in the know; know all about the matter;
明白底細　arrive at the truth; get the full picture;
問清底細　find out the exact details of the case; get to the bottom of the matter; make sure of every detail;

［底下］ below; beneath; under;

筆底下　under the sweep of a writer's pen;
私底下　privately; secretly;

［底線］ bottom line;

［底子］ (1) bottom; (2) foundation;

打底子　(1) make a rough draft of; sketch; (2) lay a foundation;

案底　record of previous offences;
班底　(1) ordinary members of a theatrical troupe; (2) ordinary members of an organization;
本底　background;
徹底　thorough; thoroughgoing;
澈底　thorough; thoroughgoing;
襯底　substrate;

打底 bottom;
到底 after all; to the end;
兜底 disclose the ins and outs; disclose the whole inside story; reveal all the details;
耳底 inner part of the ear;
肺底 base of the lung;
封底 back cover;
根底 (1) foundation; (2) cause; root;
功底 basic training for one's skill;
谷底 valley bottom; valley floor;
鍋底 bottom of a pan;
海底 bottom of the sea; sea floor; seabed;
河底 river bottom;
活底 drop bottom; false bottom;
家底 (1) family background; (2) family property accumulated over a long time; family resources;
見底 bottom out;
交底 put all one's cards on the table; tell sb one's real intentions;
腳底 sole;
揭底 disclose the inside story;
老底 sb's past;
留底 office copy; on file;
露底 betray a confidence; disclose the ins and outs; give the show away; let out the whole story; reveal the inside story;
爐底 base of a stove;
謎底 (1) answer to a riddle; (2) truth;
摸底 (1) know the real situation; (2) sound sb out;
年底 end of the year;
天底 nadir;
透底 disclose the inside story; reveal the ins and outs of the matter;
無底的 bottomless;
箱底 (1) bottom of a box; (2) one's store of valuables;
鞋底 sole of a shoe;
洩底 reveal the inside story;
心底 innermost being; heart;
有底 know the real situation;
月底 end of a month; end of the month;
知底 in the know; know the inside story;

di

【抵】 (1) prop; support; sustain; (2) resist; withstand; (3) compensate for; make for a life; (4) mortgage; (5) balance; set off; (6) equal to; (7) arrive at; reach;

[抵償] compensate for; give sth by way of payment for;
抵償損失 compensate for losses;

[抵觸] conflict; contradict; contravene; contravention; violate;

[抵達] arrive; reach;
安全抵達 safe arrival;

[抵擋] check; fend off; keep out; resist; stand up against; ward off; withstand;
抵擋敵人 keep out the enemy;
抵擋寒風 keep out cold wind;
抵擋洪水 keep the flood in check;
抵擋侵略 ward off an invasion;
抵擋危險 ward off a danger;

[抵換] substitute for; take the place of;

[抵抗] oppose; resist; stand up to;
抵抗侵略 resist aggression; stand up against aggression;
奮起抵抗 rise in resistance;
奮勇抵抗 put up an resistance;
消極抵抗 passive resistance;

[抵賴] deny; disavow; refuse to admit; renegue a promise;
抵賴事實 refuse to admit a fact;
抵賴罪行 deny one's guilt;
百般抵賴 deny by every means; try by every means to deny;
不容抵賴 brook no denial;

[抵命] atone for one's action by one's life;

[抵事] effective; serve the purpose;

[抵死] defy death; fight desperately;
抵死不從 refuse to submit, even unto death;

[抵消] cancel out; counteract; counterbalance; kill; neutralize; offset; set-off;
相互抵消 cancel out each other;

[抵押] collateral; collateralize; hock; hold in pledge; hypothecate; impawn; mortgage; pawn; pledge;
抵押貸款 mortgage bonds; mortgage loan;
~抵押貸款利率 mortgage rate;
抵押利率 mortgage rate;
抵押品 collateral;
抵押契約 mortgage deed;
抵押市場 mortgage market;
抵押債券 mortgage bonds; secured bonds;
~抵押債券資產 mortgage bonds assets;
~抵押債券資金 mortgage bonds money;
閉口抵押 closed end mortgage;
抵銷抵押 offset mortgage;
第一次抵押 first mortgage;

動產抵押 chattel mortgage;
~ 不動產抵押 real estate mortgage;
買價抵押 purchase-money mortgage;
限額抵押 closed mortgage;
信托抵押 trust mortgage;
住宅抵押 house mortgatge;

[抵禦] resist; withstand;
抵禦風雨 resist the elements;
抵禦寒冷 keep out the cold;
抵禦侵略 resist aggression;
抵禦誘惑 withstand temptation;

[抵債] pay a debt by labour; pay a debt in kind;
以實物抵債 pay one's debt in kind;
做工抵債 work out the debt;

[抵掌而談] chat leisurely; have a close, intimate talk; have a pleasant conversation;

[抵帳] repay a debt;

[抵制] boycott; resist;
抵制外國貨 press a boycott on foreign goods;

安抵 arrive safe and sound; arrive safely;
兩抵 balance each other; cancel each other;
相抵 balance; cancel each other; counterbalance; neutralize; offset;
押抵 give sth as a security for payment of a debt; mortgage;
折抵 set off against;
作抵 substitute;

di

【邸】 (1) residence of the nobility; (2) hostel; (3) screen; (4) bottom of sth; (5) a surname;

[邸報] official gazette in old China;
[邸第] residences of lords and nobility;
[邸府] manor;

府邸 mansion house of an official;
官邸 official residence; official mansion;
私邸 private residence of a high-ranking official;
宅邸 abode; hotel; residence;
朱邸 residence of a nobleman;

di

【柢】 base; foundation; root;

di

【牴】 gore; resist;

[牴獨] conflict; contradict;

di

【砥】 (1) whetstone; (2) discipline; polish;

[砥礪] (1) whetstone; (2) encourage; (3) practice;

[砥柱] mainstay;

di

【詆】 defame; slander;

[詆謗] libel;
詆謗官司 libel case;

[詆毀] calumniate; defame; slander; vilify;
詆毀人格 calumniate one's character;

醜詆 abuse; curse; slander;

di

【觝】 conflict; contradict;

[觝觸] conflict; contradict;
[觝排] get rid of; reject;
[觝牾] conflict; contradict;

di⁴

di

【地】 (1) earth; (2) land; soil; (3) fields; (4) ground; (5) locality; place; (6) position; situation; (7) background; (8) distance;

[地板] (1) floor board; (2) floor;
擦地板 scrub the floor;
沖洗地板 scour the floor;
毛地板 carcass-flooring;
鋪地板 board the floor; lay down a floor;
鑲木地板 parquet; parquet floor;
拖地板 mop the floor;

[地標] landmark;

[地步] (1) condition; plight; situation; state; (2) degree; extent; (3) leeway;
到了…的地步 reach the point where...;

[地槽] geosyncline;
大陸地槽 continental geosyncline;
原生地槽 primary geosyncline;

[地層] layer; stratum;
地層表 stratigraphic chart;
地層沉裂 subsidence break;
地層圖 stratigraphic map;
地層學 stratigraphy;
~ 地層學家 stratigrapher;
~ 動力地層學 dynamic stratigraphy;
~ 古地層學 palaeostratigraphy;
~ 幻象地層學 ghost stratigraphy;
~ 解析地層學 interpretative stratigraphy;

D

~聲波地層學 acoustic stratigraphy;
~應用地層學 applied stratigraphy;
地層油田 stratigraphic oilfields;
海相地層 marine bed;
破碎地層 crushed stratum;

[地產] real estate;
地產公司 real estate agency;
地產管理人 land agent;
房地產 property; real estate; real property;
~房地產大亨 property tycoon;
~房地產經紀人 estate agent; real estate agent;
~房地產熱 property boom;
擁有地產 hold real estate;

[地顫] earth tremor;

[地醜德齊] equal territories and similar abilities;

[地大物博] broad territory with rich natural resources; large country with great natural resources; wide area with abundant resources;
物博地大 broad territory with rich resources;

[地帶] clime; district; region; zone;
安全地帶 safety zone;
防火地帶 fire-prevention zone;
黑土地帶 black-soil belt;
緩衝地帶 buffer zone;
交戰地帶 war area;
偏遠地帶 remote region;
沙漠地帶 desert region;
山岳地帶 mountainous region;
森林地帶 forest area;
危險地帶 danger zone;
無人地帶 deserted zone; no-man's land;
心臟地帶 heartland;
要塞地帶 fortified zone;

[地道] (1) idiomatic; pure; to the backbone; typical; (2) tunnel;
地道翻譯 idiomatic translation;
地道英語 idiomatic English;
地地道道 dyed in the wool; in no less sense; one hundred percent; pure and simple; through and through; to a fraction; to the core; to the quick;
~地地道道的中國人 native Chinese;
挖地道 dig out a tunnel;

[地點] locale; place; site; venue;
地點賓語 locative object;
地點詞 place word;
地點從屬連詞 subordinator of place;
地點副詞 adverb of place;
地點附加語 place adjunct;
地點介詞 preposition of place;
地點所有格 local genitive;
地點指示詞 place deixis;
地點主語 locative subject;
地點狀語 adverbial of place;
~地點狀語從句 adverbial clause of place;
出生地點 birthplace; the place of birth;
犯罪地點 locale of a crime;
會車地點 crossing place;
集合地點 assembling place;
交貨地點 place of delivery;
納税地點 tax payment place;
起運地點 place of origin;
簽發地點 place of issue;
途中停止地點 stopping;
遠地點 apogee;
~最大遠地點 peak apogee;

[地段] a sector of an area; lot;
劃分地段 divide into sections;
相鄰地段 abutting lot;

[地盾] shield;

[地方] (1) place; room; space; (2) part; respect; (3) local;
地方保護主義 local protectionism; regional protectionism;
地方當局 local authorities;
地方風俗 local customs;
地方色彩 local colour;
地方史 local history;
地方税 local tax;
地方戲 local opera;
地方狹窄 no room to swing a cat; no room to turn in;
地方性法規 local laws and regulations;
地方議會 local council;
地方優勢 local advantage;
地方政府 local authority; local government;
地方志 local history;
地方組織 local organization;
地方主義 regionalism;
別的地方 elsewhere;
常去的地方 stamping ground;
騰出地方 make room; vacate a place;
喜歡去的地方 stomping ground;
一個地方 a place;
佔地方 occupy a place;
在恰當的時間出現在恰當的地方 in the right place at the right time;

找錯了地方 come to the wrong shop; find the wrong address; go to the wrong shop;
找對了地方 come to the right shop;

[地府] netherworld;
陰曹地府 netherworld;

[地瓜] sweet potato;

[地廣人稀] scarcely populated area; small population for a large area; vast territory with a sparse population;

[地基] foundation; ground;
打地基 lay the foundation of;

[地窖] cellar;
防風地窖 storm cellar;

[地塊] (1) patch of land; plot of land; (2) landmass;

[地曠人稀] vast territory with a sparse population; wide area with a thin population;

[地礦] geology and mineral resources;

[地老天荒] outlast even the heavn and earth; the age of earth and the extent of heaven;

[地雷] landmine; mine;
爆炸地雷 blow up a mine; explode a mine;
觸上地雷 hit a mine; strike a mine;
埋地雷 bury a mine; plant mines; lay mines; place mines;
天線控制地雷 antenna mine;
延期地雷 delayed action mine;
裝填地雷 charge a mine;

[地梨] water chestnut;

[地理] (1) geographical features of a place; (2) geography;
地理變態 geographical metamorphosises;
地理方言 geographical dialect;
地理環境 geographical envirnoment;
地理科學 geographical science;
地理民情 geographical conditions;
地理區 geographical region;
~動物地理區 zoogeographical region;
地理昇級 geographical escalation;
地理數據庫 geographical database;
地理網絡 geographical network;
地理位置 geographical position;
地理系統工程 geographical system engineering;
地理信息系統 geographical information system;
地理學 geography;
~動物地理學 animal geography; zoogeography;
~分佈區地理學 areograhic geography;
~古地理學 palaeogeography;
~歷史地理學 historical geography;
~人文地理學 anthropogeography; human geography;
~商業地理學 business geography;
~水文地理學 hydrography;
~政治地理學 political geography;
~植物地理學 phytogeography; plant geography;
~自然地理學 physical geography;
地理語言學 geographical linguistics;
非洲地理 geography of Africa;
經濟地理 economic geography;
商業地理 commercial geography;
亞洲地理 geography of Asia;
自然地理 physical geography;

[地利] (1) favourable geographical position; topographical advantages; (2) good conditions for land productivity;
地利不如人和 the spatial factors are not as decisive as human endeavours;
地利人和 favourable geographical and human conditions; favourable terrain and friendly people; the advantage of the location and human relations;
地盡其利 the soil is put to the best use;
利用地利 take the advantage of one's favourable geographical position;
佔有地利 have the advantage of location;

[地貌] land form;
地貌學 geomorphology;

[地面] floor; ground;
地面凹陷 the ground caves in;
地面高度 ground level;
地面控制 ground control;
~地面控制人員 ground controller;
地面傾斜 inclination of the ground;
地面球 grounder;
地面濕滑，敬請小心 beware of slippery floor;
地面天線 ground antenna;
地面站 earth station; ground station;
潮濕地面 damp ground;
填平地面 level the ground;

[地名] place name;
地名翻譯 translation of place names;

[地盤] domain; sphere of action; turf;

地盤之爭 turf war;
保衛地盤 defend one's turf;
串地盤 intrude into sb's sphere of influence;

[地皮] (1) land for building; (2) ground;
刮地皮 batten on people's properties;
罕有地皮 a rare piece of land;

[地痞] bully; local riffraff; local ruffian; rascal;
地痞流氓 holligans and gangsters; local bullies and loafers; local despots and thugs; local ruffians and rogues; riffraff;

[地平] ground level; horizon; horizontal plane; terrestrial horizon
地平經緯儀 altazimuth;
地平天成 all in order; everything has been arranged; everything is ready;
地平線 horizon;
~ 光學地平線 optical horizon;
~ 可見地平線 visible horizon;
~ 微波地平線 microwave horizon;
~ 有效地平線 effective horizon;

[地勤] ground service;
地勤人員 ground crew; ground staff;

[地球] earth; globe;
地球村 global village;
地球動力學 geodynamics;
地球公轉 revolution of the Earth;
地球觀察系統 earth observing system;
地球化學 geochemistry;
地球進動 precession of the Earth;
地球科學 earth science;
地球日 Earth Day (22 April);
地球同步軌道 geosynchronous orbit;
地球物理學 geophysics;
地球物理站 geophysical station;
地球儀 globe;
地球章動 nutation of the Earth;
地球植物學 geobotany;
地球資源衛星 earth resources satellite;
地球自轉 rotation of the Earth;
~ 地球自轉偏向力 deflection force of Earth rotation;
~ 地球自轉軸 rotation axis of the Earth;

[地區] area; clime; district; region;
地區差價 regional price differences;
地區代號 area code;
地區經濟學 regional economics;
地區社會 regional society;
地區申請 regional application;
地區性國家外交 regional nation's diplomacy;
地區語言 regional language;
邊疆地區 border area; border region; frontier area; frontier region;
邊界地區 boundary region;
赤道地區 equatorial region;
大片地區 immense areas; large areas; vast areas;
饑荒地區 famine area;
跨地區 inter-region;
農村地區 rural area;
貧困地區 distressed area;
平原地區 plains area;
缺糧地區 food-deficit area;
熱帶地區 tropical region;
人口稠密地區 densely-populated district;
沙漠地區 desert area;
水災地區 flood-hit area;
無人居住地區 unpopulated areas;
野蠻地區 barbaric regions;
一個地區 an area;

[地上] on the floor; on the ground;
地上打滾 roll on the floor; tumble about on the ground;
掉到地上 drop to the ground;
蹲在地上 squat down on the ground;
坐在地上 sit on the floor;

[地勢] physical features of a place; relief; terrain; topography;

[地台] platform;

[地毯] carpet; rug;
地毯編織工 carpet weaver;
地毯清掃器 carpet sweeper;
地毯拖鞋 carpet slipper;
長絨地毯 shag carpet;
寬幅地毯 broadloom;
鋪開地毯 roll out a carpet;
鋪上紅地毯 roll out the red carpet;

[地鐵] metro; subway; underground;
地鐵運輸系統 subway system; metro system;
地鐵站 metro station; tube station;
乘地鐵 take the tube; travel by tube;
坐地鐵 take the underground;

[地圖] map;
地圖冊 atlas;
地圖符號 map symbol;
地圖繪製 cartography;
地圖集 atlas;
~ 方言地圖集 dialectological atlas;

~ 國家地圖集 national atlas;
~ 歷史地圖集 historical atlas;
~ 區域性地圖集 regional atlas;
~ 一冊地圖集 an atlas;
~ 袖珍地圖集 pocket atlas;
地圖投影 map projection;
地圖學 cartography;
地圖資料庫 cartographic database;
地圖製作 map making;
裱裝地圖 mounted map;
查地圖 check a map; consult a map;
查看地圖 map-reading;
道路交通地圖 road atlas;
教學地圖 school atlas;
經濟地圖 economic map;
普通地圖 general map;
世界地圖 map of the world;
一幅地圖 a map;
一張地圖 a map;
語言地圖 linguistic atlas;
着色地圖 coloured map; tinted map;
~ 分層着色地圖 layer-tinted map;
~ 分片着色地圖 colour-patch map;
中國地圖 map of China;

[地網] counterpoise;
接地地網 grounded counterpoise;
天線地網 antenna counterpoise;

[地位] place; position; rank; standing; status;
地位低 of lower rank;
~ 地位低的人 people of lower rank;
地位高 of high standing; of upper rank;
~ 地位高的人 people of upper rank;
地位舉足輕重 of a significant rank;
地位平等 equal in status; on an equal footing;
地位無足輕重 of an insignificant rank;
卑微的地位 degraded position;
被動地位 passive position;
~ 陷於被動地位 be in a passive position;
從屬地位 subordinate position;
~ 處於從屬地位 in a subordinate position;
獨一無二的地位 unique position;
法律地位 legal status;
關鍵地位 pivotal position;
國際地位 international standing; world position;
教育地位 educational status;
傑出地位 preeminent position;
經濟地位 economic status;
屈辱的地位 humiliating position;
社會地位 social position; social standing; social status;
~ 社會地位的象徵 status symbol;
~ 很高的社會地位 high social status;
社會上的地位 the position in society;
特殊地位 privileged position;
學術地位 scholastic standing;
永久地位 permanent position;
有利的地位 advantageous position;
~ 處於有利的地位 in an advantageious position;
中心地位 central position;
重要地位 important position;
主導地位 leading position;
自貶地位 abase oneself;

[地溫] ground temperature;
地溫異常 irregular ground temperature;

[地下] (1) subterranean; underground; (2) secret; underground;
地下黨員 crypto-party member;
地下出版物 samizdat;
地下工作 underground activities; underground work;
~ 做地下工作 do underground work;
地下妓院 underground brothel;
地下教派 underground sect;
地下經濟 underground economy;
地下商場 underground shopping mall;
地下商業城 underground commercial city;
地下室 basement; cellar; undercroft;
~ 教堂地下室 crypt;
~ 一個地下室 a basement;
地下水 groundwater; underground water;
地下洞穴 cavern;
地下岩層 subterranean formation;
地下扎根 take root;
地下組織 underground organization;
被埋在地下 be buried;
打入地下 be driven into underground;
轉入地下 go underground;

[地線] ground wire;

[地形] terrain; typography;
地形凹陷 the ground caves in;
地形圖 relief map; topographic map;
地形學 topography;
~ 細部地形學 detailed topography;
地形優越 excellent terrain;
凹凸不平的地形 rough terrain;
測量地形 make a topographical survey;
成年地形 aged topography;
加積地形 accretion topography;
偵察地形 make a to pograhical

investigation;
自成地形 autogenetic topography;
[地穴] cave;
[地衣學] lichenology;
[地域] (1) district; region; (2) local;
地域生產綜合體 regional production complex;
[地獄] hell; inferno; the lower world; the nether world;
打入十八層地獄 banish sb to the uttermost depths of hell; banish to the lowest depths of hell; condemn to eternal damnation; shut sb in the eighteenth hell;
活地獄 hell on earth;
人間地獄 hell on earth; living hell;
下地獄 go to hell; perdition;
[地緣] geo-;
地緣商務 geobusiness;
地緣政治 geopolitics;
[地震] earthquake; earthshock;
地震表 seismograph;
地震波 seismic wave;
~地震波顯示儀 seismoscope;
地震帶 earthquake zone; seismic zone;
地震法 seismic method;
地震放大器 seismic amplifier;
地震構成線 seismotectonic lines;
地震計 seismometer;
~扭地震計 torsion seismometer;
地震檢波器 seismic detector;
地震警報 earthquake alarm;
地震烈度 earthquake intensity;
地震破壞 earthquake damage;
地震區 earthquake region; seismic area; seismic region;
地震台站 seismic station;
地震圖 seismogram;
地震學 seismology;
地震儀 seismograph; seismometer;
~電磁式地震儀 electromagnetic seismometer;
~電動式地震儀 electrodynamic seismometer;
~水平地震儀 horizontal seismometer;
地震預報 earthquake forecasting;
地震震級 earthquake magnitude;
地震徵兆 premonitory symptoms of earthquake;
地震中心 seismic centre;
爆裂地震 explosive earthquake;
大地震 great earthquake; violent earthquake;
斷層地震 dislocation earthquake;
感到地震 feel an earthquake;
構造地震 structural earthquake;
殼構地震 tectonic earthquake;
火山地震 volcanic earthquake;
局部地震 local earthquake;
六級地震 magnitude-six earthquake;
模擬地震 simulated earthquake;
淺源地震 shallow-focus earthquake;
強烈地震 strong earthquake;
深成地震 plutonic eqrthquake;
深源地震 deep-focus earthquake;
小地震 slight earthquake;
預報地震 forecast an earthquake; predict an earthquake;
中源地震 intermediate-focus earthquake;
[地址] address; location; site;
地址不全 incomplete address;
地址總線 address bus;
辦公地址 business address; office address;
編碼地址 coded address; encode address;
變更地址 change of address;
常住地址 fixed address; permanent address;
存儲地址 memory address;
存取地址 access address;
非法地址 illegal address;
浮動地址 floating address;
更換地址 change one's address;
固定地址 fixed address;
合法地址 legal address;
回寄地址 return address;
回信地址 return address;
機器地址 machine address;
即時地址 immediate address;
家庭地址 home address;
居住地址 residential address;
局部地址 local address;
絕對地址 absolute address;
連接地址 link address;
臨時地址 temporary address;
邏輯地址 logical address;
目的地址 destination address;
實際地址 physical address;
輸入地址 entry address;
通道地址 port address;
通訊地址 correspondence address; mailing address;
文件地址 file address;
無效地址 invalid address;

D

顯示地址 explicit address;
形式地址 formal address;
虛擬地址 virtual address;
永久地址 permanent address;
郵寄地址 postal address;
專用地址 specific address;
轉送地址 forwarding address;
轉信地址 forwarding address;
轉移地址 jump address;
字組地址 block address;
綜合地址 general address;

[地質] geology;
地質時代 geologic age; geologic period;
地質調查 geologic survey; geological survey;
地質圖 geologic map;
地質學 geology;
~構造地質學 tectonics;
~古地質學 palaeogeology;
~航空地質學 aerogeology;
~農業地質學 agrogeology;
~水文地質學 hydrogeology;
~天體地質學 astrogeology;

[地主] (1) landlord; landowner; (2) host;
地主階級 landlord class;
地主之誼 hospitality of a host;
~盡地主之誼 do the honours;
不法地主 lawless landlord;
惡霸地主 despotic landlord;
沒落地主 bankrupt landlord;
女地主 landlady;
破產地主 bankrupt landlord;

[地租] ground rent; land rent; rent;
邊際地租 marginal rent;
合同地租 contract rent;
交替地租 alternative rent;
絕對地租 absolute rent;

凹地 hollow;
拔地 rise from level ground; tower;
霸地 occupation of land;
白蘭地 brandy;
本地 local; this locality; this place;
邊地 border area; border district; borderland;
遍地 all over the place; everywhere;
采地 benefice; fief;
菜地 vegetable plot;
草地 (1) grassland; meadow; (2) lawn;
策源地 the place of origin; the source;
扱地 kneel and bow with both hands touching the ground;
產地 place of production;
場地 place; site; space;
尺地 small piece of land;
城地 cities and territories;
此地 here; this place;
赤地 barren land;
出生地 birth-place;
春地 fields for spring sowing;
此地 here; this place;
大地 (1) land; (2) earth; mother earth;
當地 at the given place; local;
低地 lowland;
甸子地 marshy grassland;
發祥地 place of origin;
發源地 place of origin; source;
翻地 turn up the soil;
防地 defence zone;
墳地 cemetery; graveyard;
坟地 cemetery; graveyard;
封地 fief; manor;
福地 place of happiness;
腹地 central region; hinterland; interior;
高地 (1) highland; upland; (2) height;
割地 cede territory;
各地 four corners of the world;
根據地 base; base area;
耕地 plough; till;
工地 construction site;
谷地 valley;
故地 old haunt;
旱地 (1) non-irrigated farm land; (2) dryland;
黑地 burnt land;
荒地 uncultivated land; wasteland;
霍地 suddenly;
迹地 slash;
基地 base;
極地 polar region;
碱地 alkaline land;
見地 insight; judgment;
接地 earthing;
階地 terrace;
近地 terrestrial;
禁地 forbidden area; out-of-bounds area; restricted area;
境地 circumstances; condition; situation;
就地 on the spot;
居留地 place of residence;
絕地 (1) dangerous place; (2) blind alley; hopeless situation; impasse;
空地 open ground;
立地 at once; immediately;
撂地 deserted land;
林地 forest land; timberland;

臨河地 frontage;
臨路地 frontage;
領地 (1) manor; (2) territory;
陸地 dry land; land;
裸地 bare area; bare land;
落地 (1) fall to the ground; (2) be born;
滿地 all over the place; everywhere;
驀地 suddenly; unexpectedly;
某地 somewhere;
牧地 grazing land; meadowland; pasture;
墓地 burial ground; cemetery; graveyeard;
內地 hinterland; inland interior;
泥地 muddy ground;
農地 agricultural land;
刨地 dig the ground;
盆地 basin;
平地 level the land; rake the land;
坡地 hillside fields; sloping fields;
穹地 elevation;
秋地 fields for autumn sowing;
泉地 oasis;
入地 (1) die; (2) sink below the surface of the earth;
掃地 (1) sweep the floor; (2) drop into the dust; reach an all-time low; reach rock bottom;
山地 (1) hilly area; mountainous region; (2) fields on a hill;
生地 uncultivated land; virgin soil;
勝地 famous scenic spot;
聖地 (1) the Holy Land; (2) sacred palace; shrine;
失地 lose territory; lost territory;
濕地 damp place; marsh; swamp;
實地 (1) on the spot; (2) in real earnest; indeed;
熟地 cultivated land
屬地 dependency; possession;
水地 (1) irrigated land; (2) paddy fields;
死地 deathtrap; fatal position;
隨地 anywhere; everywhere;
所在地 location; seat; site;
蹋地 step on the gruond;
台地 platform; tableland;
特地 for a special purpose; specially;
天地 (1) heaven and earth; world; (2) field of activity;
田地 (1) farm land; field; (2) miserable condition; plight; wretched situation;
土地 (1) land; soil; (2) territory;
拖地 mop;
拓地 expand the territory; territorial expansion;
洼地 depression; low-lying land;
窪地 depression; low-lying land; marsh land;
外地 foreign place;
旺地 good land; prosperous place;
圍地 enclosure;
席地 lie on the ground; sit on the ground;
郤地 vacant area; vacant lot;
隙地 unoccupied place;
下地 (1) go to the fields; (2) leave a sickbed; (3) give birth; (4) infertile land;
閒地 (1) public land; (2) waste land;
險地 (1) dangerous place; (2) dangerous situation; perilous position;
瀉地 cover the whole ground;
心地 (1) person's moral nature; (2) mood; state of mind;
雪地 snowfield;
養地 enrich the fertility of the soil;
要地 important place; strategic point;
野地 wild country; wilderness;
一幅地 a piece of land;
一塊地 a piece of land; a plot of land;
易地 in another person's shoes;
異地 foreign place;
陰地 (1) graveyard; (2) place where sunshine cannot reach;
營地 camping ground; campsite;
用地 land for a specific use;
餘地 leeway; margin; room;
輿地 earth; land;
原產地 country of origin; source area;
園地 (1) garden plot; (2) field; scope;
匝地 all over the ground; everywhere;
葬地 burial ground; grave;
擇地 choose a site;
宅地 croft; toft;
戰地 battlefield; battleground;
瘴地 miasmal place;
沼地 marshland;
陣地 front; position;
整地 soil preparation;
之地 place;
質地 quality of a material; texture;
擲地 throw to the ground;
重地 important place;
種地 cultivate land; go in for farming; till land;
駐地 (1) place where troops are stationed; (2) station;
墜地 (1) be born; come to this world; (2) fall; (3) failure;
着地 reach the ground; touch the ground;
坐地 (1) sit on the ground; (2) do sth on the spot; on the spot;

di

【弟】 (1) younger brother; (2) I;

［弟弟］ one's younger brother;
異父弟弟 younger stepbrother;
異母弟弟 younger stepbrother;

［弟婦］ sister-in-law; younger brother's wife;

［弟妹］ younger brother and sister;

［弟兄］ brothers;
結義弟兄 sworn brothers;

［弟子］ disciple; follower; pupil;
私淑弟子 self-proclaimed disciple;
執弟子禮 regard oneself as a pupil when treating sb one holds in high esteem;

胞弟 blood younger brother;
表弟 younger male cousin;
及弟 pass an imperial examination;
季弟 fourth or youngest brother;
老弟 my boy; young fellow; young man; younger brother;
內弟 wife's younger brother;
仁弟 my dear friend;
如弟 younger sworn brother;
弱弟 young brother;
舍弟 my younger brother;
師弟 (1) junior fellow apprentice; (2) son of one's master;
師兄弟 fellow apprentices of the same master;
堂弟 younger male cousin;
徒弟 apprentice; disciple;
小弟 (1) younger brother; (2) I;
兄弟 (1) brothers; (2) brotherly;
硯弟 junior classmate;
義弟 younger foster brother;
子弟 children; juniors;
從弟 male cousins;

di

【的】 (1) clear; manifest; (2) goal; target;

［的的］ (1) bright; lustrous; (2) certainly;

端的 (1) really; (2) after all; in the end;
目的 aim; goal; purpose;
中的 hit the mark; hit the nail on the head; hit the target;

di

【帝】 (1) God; Supreme Being; (2) emperor; (3) imperialism;

［帝國］ empire;
帝國主義 imperialism;
～反帝國主義 anti-imperialism;
～金元帝國主義 dollar imperialism;
～經濟帝國主義 economic imperialism;
～社會帝國主義 social imperialism;
～現代帝國主義 contemporary imperialism;

［帝號］ title of an emperor;

［帝王］ emperor; monarch;
帝王將相 emperors, the nobility, generals and ministers;

［帝位］ throne;

［帝制］ autocratic monarchy; imperial system; monarchy;

［帝祚］ throne;

廢帝 deposed emperor;
皇帝 emperor;
土皇帝 local despost; local tyrant;
上帝 God;
王帝 king;
望帝 cuckoo;
先帝 late emperor;
玉帝 Jade Emperor;

di

【娣】 (1) one's younger sister; (2) wife of a younger brother of one's husband;

di

【第】 (1) first; (2) residence of a high official;

［第二］ second;
第二把手 number two man; second in command;
第二產業 second industry;
第二次 second time;
第二大 second biggest;
第二代 second generation;
～第二代計算機 second-generation computer;
第二分詞 second participle;
第二經濟效益論 second economic benefits theory;
第二名 second;
～得了第二名 come second; finish second;
第二人稱 second person;
第二人稱代詞 second person pronoun;
第二語言 second language;
第二語言習得 second language acquisition;
第二職業 second job;
屈居第二 come off second best;

D

[第末] last one;

[第三] third;

第三產業 third industry;

~第三產業發展 developing the third industry;

第三產業發展政策 policies of developing the third industry;

~第三產業經濟學 economics of the third industry;

第三次浪潮 third wave;

第三代計算機 third generation computer;

第三方 third party;

~第三方責任險 third party insurance;

第三梯隊 third echelon;

第三者 adulterer; home wrecker; lover; mistress; other woman; third party; third person;

第三資源 third resources;

[第四] fourth;

第四產業 fourth industry;

第四次浪潮 fourth wave;

第四代計算機 fourth generation computer;

第四代語言 fourth generation language;

第四維 fourth dimension;

第四戰略 fourth strategy;

[第五] fifth;

第五代計算機 fifth generation computer;

[第一] first; first and foremost; for starters; foremost; primary;

第一把手 first in command; number one person;

第一步 first step;

~邁出第一步 make the first move;

first time;

~第一次的 first-ever;

第一代 first generation;

~第一代計算機 first generation computer;

第一道菜 starter;

第一流 A No.1; A1; best; classical; dandy; first-class; first-line; first-rate; first-string; foremost; in a class by itself; number one; of the best class; of the first class; of the first water; slap-up; top-flight;

~第一流的 first-rate;

第一名 first;

~考獲第一名 come out first in the examination;

第一人稱 first person;

~第一人稱代詞 first person pronoun;

the first day;

第一語言 first language; mother tongue; native language; native tongue;

獲得第一 be first; come first; come in first; finish in first place;

排名第一 come in first; finish in first place;

不第 fail in civil service examination;

牀第 (1) bed and bed mattress; (2) place of conjugal intimacies;

次第 one after another; order; sequence;

登第 pass the imperial examination;

等第 grade in an examination; grading;

邸第 residences of lords and nobility;

府第 mansion of an official or landlord;

及第 pass the imperial examination;

科第 imperial examination;

落第 fail in the imperial examination;

門第 family status;

品第 grade; rank;

上第 first-class; first-rate; superior;

私第 private residence;

覃第 (1) vast residence; (2) your house;

潭第 your residence;

下第 inferior; low-class; low-grade;

宅第 big house; mansion;

中第 pass the civil examinations;

擢第 get chosen by passing an examination;

di

【棣】 (1) kerria; mountain tree; (2) same as 弟, kid brother;

[棣華] brothers;

棠棣 (1) Chinese bush cherry; (2) a kind of white poplar;

di

【睇】 (1) take a casual look at; (2) glance; look sideways;

di

【蒂】 (1) base; footstalk of a flower; peduncle; (2) butt;

di

【遞】 (1) give; hand over; pass; (2) in the proper order; successively;

[遞補] fill vacancies in the proper order;

[遞減] decrease by degrees; decrease progressively; reduce progressively;

遞減稅 regressive tax;

D

［遞降］ be reduced by degrees; decrease gradually; go down progressively;
［遞交］ deliver; hand over; present; submit;
遞交報告 present a report;
遞交辭呈 hand in one's resignation;
遞交計劃 submit a proposal;
遞交申請書 hand in written applications;
［遞解］ escort a criminal from one place to another;
遞解出境 deportation; expel;
遞解回籍 escort a deported criminal back to his native place;
［遞進］ go forward one by one;
［遞昇］ increase progressively; rise progressively;
［遞送］ deliver; send;
遞送情報 pass on information; send information;
鄉村遞送 rural delivery;
［遞增］ increase by degrees; increase progressively;

呈遞 present; submit;
傳遞 hand over sth one after another;
寄遞 deliver a letter;
快遞 express delivery;
迢遞 far-off; faraway;
投遞 deliver;
郵遞 send by mail; send by post;
轉遞 send through another person;

di

【禘】 imperial sacrifice made once every five years;
［禘郊］ imperial sacrifice held in the countryside;

di

【締】 (1) form; (2) conclude;
［締交］ (1) establish diplomatic relations; (2) contract a friendship; form a friendship;
［締結］ conclude; establish;
締結邦交 establish diplomatic relations;
締結和約 conclude a peace treaty;
締結良緣 form marital ties;
［締約］ conclude a treaty; sign a treaty;

取締 abolish; ban; outlaw; suppress;

di

【蔕】 peduncle or footstalk of a flower or fruit;

di

【諦】 (1) attentive; careful; (2) truth;
［諦視］ examine closely; scrutinize;
凝神諦視 scrutinize with concentration;
怒目諦視 look angrily at;
［諦思］ consider carefully; ponder deeply;
凝神諦思 consider carefully with concentration;
［諦聽］ listen attentively;
屏息諦聽 listen attentively with bated breath;

di

【蝃】 rainbow;

dian¹

dian

【掂】 estimate the weight of sth by weighing it with hands;
［掂對］ weight and consider the situation;

dian

【滇】 alternative name of Yunan;

dian

【顛】 (1) crown of the head; (2) summit; top; (3) bump; jolt; (4) fall; topple down; turn over; (5) go away; run;
［顛簸］ bump; jolt; thrashing; toss;
在海洋中顛簸 welter in the sea;
一顛一簸 limp; limp along;
［顛菜］ go; leave;
［顛倒］ (1) confound; inverse; overturn; put upside down; reverse; transpose; (2) confused; disordered; get hold of the wrong end of the stick;
顛倒敵我 reverse enemies and comrades; take enemies for comrades and comrades for enemies;
顛倒過程 reverse the process;
顛倒黑白 give a false account of the truth; pretend that black is white; stand facts on their heads; swear black is white; talk black into white; turn matters upside down; transpose black and white;
顛倒乾坤 reverse heaven and earth;
顛倒是非 confound right and wrong; confuse truth and falsehood; distort the truth; give a false account of the truth; reversal of right and wrong; reverse right and wrong; stand facts on

D

their heads; turn right into wrong; turn things upside down; twist the facts;
顛倒事實 give a false account of the facts; turn things upside down;
夢魂顛倒 be infatuated; carry sb away; lose one's head;
七顛八倒 (1) a bag of nails; all in confusion; all upside down; at sixes and sevens; dilapidated; in great confusion; ramshackle, topsy-turvy; tumble-down; tumbling to pieces; upside down; (2) reel and stagger;
上下顛倒 inversion;
神魂顛倒 be infatuated; in a confused state of mind; in a state of mental confusion;
心神顛倒 go into raptures; utterly confused;

［顛覆］ overthrow; overturn; subvert;
顛覆份子 subversive;
顛覆活動 subversive activities;
顛覆性宣傳 subversive propaganda;
顛覆政府 overturn a government;
政治顛覆 political subversion;
［顛連］ (1) difficulty; hardship; trouble; (2) peak upon peak;
［顛沛］ in destitution; suffer hardship;
顛沛流離 lead a homeless life; wander from place to place, enduring many hardships;
顛沛流離，無處存身 be displaced and homeless;
［顛撲不破］ irrefutable;
顛撲不破的真理 irrefutable truth;

dian
【巔】 mountain top; peak; summit; top;
［巔峰］ peak;

dian
【攧】 fall; stumble;

dian
【癲】 insane; mentally deranged;
［癲狂］ demented; frivolous; insane; mad;
［癲癇］ epilepsy; have an attack of epilepsy;
癲癇發作 suffer an epileptic seizure;
癲癇患者 epileptic;
癲癇性痤瘡 epileptic acne;
痴笑性癲癇 gelastic epilepsy;
遲發性癲癇 late-onset epilepsy;
創傷後癲癇 post-traumatic epilepsy;
創傷性癲癇 traumatic epilepsy;
精神性癲癇 psychic epilepsy;
全身性癲癇 generalized epilepsy;
突發性癲癇 idiopathic epilepsy;

瘋癲 insane; mad;

dian³
dian
【典】 (1) canon; law; standard; (2) standard work of scholarship; (3) literary quotation; an allusion; (4) ceremony; (5) in charge of; (6) mortgage;
［典藏］ classical collection;
［典當］ hock; impawn; mortgage; pawn;
典當商 pawnbroker;
［典範］ epitome; example; model; nonesuch; paradigm;
奉為典範 look upon as a model;
傑出典範 paragon;
堪稱典範 be qualified for being a model;
樹立典範 set an example for;
效率的典範 model of efficiency;
［典故］ allusion; literary quotation;
充滿典故 be filled with classical allusions;
［典籍］ ancient books and records;
典籍故章 ancient works;
典籍浩瀚 large colloction of ancient literature;
傳統典籍 traditional literature;
故典史籍 ancient works and historical records;
［典借］ mortgage;
［典禮］ celebration; ceremonial; ceremony;
畢業典禮 graduation ceremony;
閉幕典禮 closing ceremony;
奠基典禮 cornerstone laying ceremony;
就職典禮 inaugural ceremony;
舉行典禮 hold a ceremony;
開幕典禮 opening ceremony;
開學典禮 school-opening ceremony;
入學典禮 inauguration ceremony;
~新生入學典禮 new student convocation;
下水典禮 launching ceremony;
主持典禮 host a ceremony;
［典型］ archetype; example; model; type; typical case; typical example;
典型長存 one's model will last forever;
典型的 classic; typical;
~非典型的 atypical;
典型示範 demonstrate with typical examples employ typical examples to

show the way; set up an example for all; set up typical examples for the rest to follow; show typical examples from real life;
典型性 typicality;
樹立一個典型 set an excellent example;

[典押] mortgage; pawn;

[典雅] elegant; refined;
典雅大方 elegant and graceful;
陳設典雅 be furnished elegantly;
談吐典雅 refined in speech;
舞姿典雅 dance gracefully;

[典獄] prison warden;
典獄長 chief prison warden;

[典章] decrees and regulations; institutions;
典章制度 old laws and institutions;

[寶典] treasury of knowledge; valuable book;

操典 drill book; drill regulations;
詞典 dictionary;
辭典 dictionary;
出典 source of an allusion;
大典 (1) grand ceremony; (2) body of classical writings; canon;
恩典 favour; grace; kindness;
法典 code; statute book;
古典 classical; classical allusion;
經典 (1) classics; (2) classical; scriptures;
類典 special dictionary;
慶典 ceremonial occasion; celebration;
權典 provisional law; temporary regulations;
榮典 honorary reward;
盛典 big ceremony; grand ceremony; grand occasion;
事典 encyclopaedia;
釋典 Buddhist scripture; Buddhist sutra;
祀典 religious rites;
刑典 criminal code; penal code;
藥典 pharmacopoeia;
應典 fulfil a promise;
樂典 musicological book;
重典 severe provisions;
祝典 celebration;
墜典 historical books;
字典 dictionary;

dian

【碘】 iodine;

[碘酒] iodine tincture;

dian

【點】 (1) drop; (2) dot; spot; (3) point; (4) decimal point; (5) a bit; a little; (6) place; (7) aspect; feature; (8) put a dot; (9) skim; touch on very briefly; (10) drip; (11) dibble; sow in holes; (12) check one by one; (13) choose; select; (14) hint; point out; (15) burn; light; (16) o'clock; (17) appointed time; (18) refreshments;

[點播] on demand;
點播服務 service on demand;
~點播服務系統 service on demand system;
點播節目 programme on demand;

[點菜] order dishes;

[點…成…] turn sth into;
點金成鐵 touch gold and turn it into iron — miscorrect a piece of writing;
點石成金 able to perform wonders; touch a stone and turn it into gold; work miracles;
點鐵成金 touch the metal and turn it into gold — turn a piece of poor writing into a literary gem;

[點滴] (1) a bit; a little; (2) drop;
點滴不留 not to leave a single scrap;
點滴歸公 every cent goes to the public treasury; turn over every bit to the authorities;
點點滴滴 bit by bit; bits and pieces; crumbs of; dribs and drabs; drop by drop; every bit of; in driblets; odds and ends;

[點火] (1) stir up trouble; (2) fire up; ignite; ignition; light the fire; strike a light;
點火抽煙 strike a light for a smoke;
點火管 igniter squib; squib;
~延遲點火管 time-delay squib;
點火器 lighter;
~火花點火器 spark lighter;
~雷管點火器 fuse lighter;
~油點火器 oil lighter;
點火系統 ignition system;
點火線 ignition wire;
點火裝置 ignition device;
電弧點火 arc ignition;
二次點火 reignition;
煽風點火 fan the flames; fan up flames; fan up the fire; incite trouble; inflame and agitate people; instigate; stir up trouble; stir up trouble and create splits;

~ 煽風點火的人 flame-fanner; trouble-maker;
提前點火 advanced ignition;
自動電點火 automatic electrical ignition;

[點擊] click;
點擊流 click stream;
可點擊 clickable;

[點面] points and areas;
以點帶面 fan out from point to area; promote work in all areas by drawing upon the experience gained on key points; use the experience of selected units to promote work in the entire area;
由點到面 develop from isolated points into a vast expanse; develop from isolated points to a whole area;
抓點帶面 draw experience from selected units to promote overall work; work in selected basic units to gain experience to guide and promote overall work;

[點名] (1) call the roll; keep track of one's attendance; make a roll call; (2) mention sb by name;
點名冊 attendance book; roll book;
點名批評 criticize sb by name;
不點名 name no names;
公開點名 name names;
上課點名 take attendance in class; take the attendance;

[點明] point out; put one's finger on;

[點破] bring sth out into the open; lay bare; point out bluntly; unravel;

[點球] penalty kick;
點球決勝 penalty shoot-out;

[點燃] enkindle; ignite; kindle; place a match to; put a match to; set a match to;
點燃爆竹 fire off crackers;
點燃導火線 ignite a fuse; light a fuse;
點燃火 kindle a fire;
點燃火把 light a torch;
紙易點燃 paper burns easily;

[點蝕] pitting;
表面點蝕 surface pitting;
合流點蝕 confluent pitting;
進展性點蝕 progressive pitting;
氣泡點蝕 air bubble pitting;

[點收] check and accept;

[點數] tally;
標記點數 mark tally;
吊貨點數 sling tally;

[點題] bring out the theme;

[點頭] give a nod; give permission; nod; nod assent; nod one's head;
點頭稱善 nod and express one's approval;
點頭打招呼 greet sb with a nod; nod at sb in greeting;
點頭告別 bid farewell with a nod;
點頭哈腰 bow and scrape;
點頭歡迎 welcome sb with a nod;
點頭會意 catch on and nod; nod in understanding; nod with understanding;
點頭朋友 nodding acquaintance;
點頭示意 give a nod as a signal; signal by nodding;
點頭同意 agree with a nod; give a nod of assent; nod in assent; nod one's assent; show approval by nodding;
點頭一笑 nod with a smile;
點頭允諾 promise with a nod;
點頭贊同 nod in approval;
點頭招呼 nod at sb as a greeting;
點頭之交 bowing acquaintance; have a nodding acquaintance with; incidental acquaintance;
點頭致意 nod as a greeting; nod in acknowledgement; nod in saluation;
含笑點頭 nod with a smile;
用力點頭 nod vigorously;

[點心] dessert; dim sum; light refreshments; pastry;

[點陣] lattice;
放射性點陣 radioactive lattice;
複點陣 compound lattice;
原子點陣 atomic lattice;

[點綴] (1) adorn; embellish; ornament; (2) use sth just for show;
點綴昇平 adorn the tranquil age;
略加點綴 decorate sth slightly for the sake of appearances;

[點子] idea;
鬼點子 trick; wicked idea; wicked suggestion;
想點子 work out a trick;

鞍點 saddlepoint;
斑點 speckle; spot; stain;
瘢點 black spot on the skin; scar;
半點 the least bit;
飽和點 saturation point;
北點 north point;

標點 punctuate; punctuation;
冰點 freezing point;
補給點 supply point;
茶點 refreshment; tea and pastries;
查點 check the amount of sth; check the number of sth; make an inventory of;
觸點 contact;
出發點 (1) point of departure; (2) starting point;
疵點 defect; fault; flaw;
打點 (1) get one's belongings ready; get ready; (2) offer a bribe; present a gift;
地點 place; site;
丁點 a tiny bit;
頂點 (1) acme; apex; peak; zenith; (2) vertex;
逗點 comma;
端點 end point;
耳點 auriculate; broca's point;
發火點 ignition point;
方位點 compass point;
沸點 boiling point;
分點 point of division;
浮點 floating point;
附點 dot;
糕點 cake; pastry;
拱點 apsis;
共同點 common ground;
拐點 point of inflection;
觀點 standpoint; viewpoint;
黑點 blackspot;
會合點 meeting point;
基點 (1) basic point; starting point; (2) base; (3) base point;
極點 (1) extreme; limit; utmost;
檢點 (1) check; examine; (2) cautious;
交點 (1) intersection point; point of intersection; (2) node;
焦點 (1) focal point; focus; (2) central issue; point at issue;
校點 proofread and punctuate;
接達點 access point;
接點 contact;
景點 attraction; beauty spot; scenic spot;
據點 fortified point; stronghold;
快點 be quick; bustle up; chop-chop; hurry up;
力點 power;
立腳點 (1) foothold; footing; (2) stand; standpoint;
立足點 (1) foothold; footing; (2) stand; standpoint;
亮點 bright spot;
零點 zero point;
臨界點 critical point;
留點 stationary point;
露點 dew point;
論點 argument; thesis;
落點 (1) placement; (2) point of fall;
盲點 blind spot; scotoma;
難點 difficult point; difficulty;
盤點 check; make an inventory of;
批點 comments with circles and dots on books or articles;
奇點 singularity;
歧點 bifurcation point;
起點 starting point;
敲點 prod;
切點 point of contact; point of tangency;
欽點 be designatd by the emperor;
傾點 flow point; pour point;
清點 check; make an inventory of; sort and count;
圈點 (1) punctuate; (2) mark words and phrases for special attention with dots or small circles;
缺點 defect; demerit; disadvantage; drawback; failing; fault; foible; hitch; shortcoming; vice; weak point; weakness;
燃點 (1) ignite; kindle; light; set fire to; (2) the burning point; the kindling point; the point of ignition;
溶點 melting point;
熔點 fusing point; melting point;
弱點 failing; weak point; weakness;
閃點 flash point;
始點 initial point;
試點 launch a pilot project; make experiments;
特點 characteristic; distinguishing feature; peculiarity;
提點 (1) remind; (2) official post in ancient China;
甜點 afters; confection; dessert; sweet;
完點 fixed point;
晚點 behind schedule;
位點 site;
污點 (1) spot; stain; (2) blemish; smirch;
誤點 behind schedule; overdue;
小數點 decimal point;
血點 blood splashes; blood spots; drops of blood;
眼點 eyespot; stigma;
要點 (1) gist; main points; (2) key strongpoint;
一點 (1) a few; a little; a little bit; in a way; partial; small amount; some; to some extent; (2) a bit of; a dash of; a modicum of; a morsel of; a piece of; a speck of; a sprinkling of; a stroke of; a trifle of; a whiff of; an ounce of; (3) point;

疑點 doubt point;
優點 merit; strong point; virtue;
雨點 raindrop;
原點 origin;
早點 breakfast;
正點 on schedule; on time; punctual;
支撐點 centre of resistance; strong point;
支點 fulcrum;
指點 give directions; instruct;
質點 point particle;
中點 midpoint;
中和點 neutral point;
終點 (1) destination; terminal point; (2) finish;
鐘點 hour;
重點 (1) focal point; (2) emphasis; stress; (3) weight;
逐點 point by point;
轉捩點 turning point;
轉折點 turning point;
妝點 adorn; apply makeup; dress up;
裝點 deck; decorate; dress;
濁點 cloud point;

dian

【踮】 stand on tiptoe;
[踮着腳] on tiptoe;

dian^4

dian

【佃】 (1) tenant farmer; (2) tenant a farm; (3) hunting;
[佃戶] the tenant of a farm;
[佃契] tenancy contract;
[佃農] tenant farmer;
[佃權] tenancy right;
[佃租] land rent;

承佃 rent land;
東佃 landlord and tenant;
租佃 lease or rent out land to tenants;

dian

【甸】 (1) suburbs or outskirts of the capital; (2) govern; (3) farm crops;
[甸人] ancient official title;
[甸子地] marshy grassland;

dian

【店】 (1) shop; store; (2) inn;
[店東] (1) hotel owner; (2) shop owner;
[店伙] shop assistant;
[店家] (1) hotel owner; (2) shop; store;
[店客] customer; hotel guest;
[店面] shopfront; storefront;
[店鋪] shop; store;
店鋪偵探 store detective;
店鋪裝潢 shopfitting;
一個店鋪 a shop;
一家店鋪 a shop;
照看店鋪 keep a shop; tend a store;
[店小二] waiter;
[店員] salesclerk; shop assistant;
女店員 salesgirl;
雜貨店員 grocer;
[店主] shopkeeper; storekeeper;
女店主 landlady;

敝店 my humble store;
閉店 close up shop and stop business;
裱店 shop specialized in mounting paintings and calligraphy;
冰果店 cold drink shop;
布店 cloth store; piece-goods store;
唱片店 record shop;
代銷店 commission agent;
點心店 pastry shop;
飯店 (1) hotel; (2) restaurant;
分店 branch; branch store;
分銷店 retail shop;
服裝店 boutique; clothing store;
副食店 grocer's; grocery;
黑店 blacklisted shop;
花店 florist;
寄賣店 commission shop; second hand shop;
經銷店 agency;
酒店 (1) hotel; (2) wineshop;
客店 inn;
理髮店 barbershop; hairdresser's;
糧店 grain shop;
零售店 retail shop; retail store;
旅店 hostel; inn;
帽店 millinery shop;
肉店 butcher's shop;
商店 shop; store;
食品店 food shop;
書店 bookstore;
蔬菜店 greengrocer's; vegetables shop;
水果店 green grocery;
糖果店 candy store; confectionary store;
投店 put up at an inn; seek lodging in a tavern;
文具店 stationery shop;
五金店 hardware store;
洗衣店 laundry;
小吃店 snack shop;

小店 (1) inn; lodging house; (2) small store;
鞋店 shoeshop; shoe store;
靴鞋店 bootery;
煙酒店 alcohol and tobacco shop;
藥店 chemist's; drugstore; pharmacy;
飲食店 eating house;
魚店 fishmonger's;
支店 branch; branch store;
鐘錶店 watchmaker's shop;
珠寶店 jewellery shop;

dian
【玷】 (1) flaw in a piece of jade; (2) blemish; disgrace;
［玷辱］ be a disgrace to; bring disgrace on; dishonour; humiliate;
玷辱門楣 disgrace one's family;
玷辱天地 disgraceful to the public;
玷天辱地 disgraceful to the public;
［玷污］ smear; stain; sully; tarnish;
玷污芳名 foul one's fair name;
玷污個人名譽 stain one's personal honour;
玷污家庭名聲 blacken the name of one's family;
玷污門楣 disgrace one's family;
名譽被玷污 blacken one's prestige;

瑕玷 flaw; minor fault; shortcoming;

dian
【痁】 chronic malaria;

dian
【惦】 be concerned about; remember with concern;
［惦掛］ be concerned about; worry about;
［惦記］ be concerned about; keep thinking about; remember with conern;
［惦念］ anxious about; keep thinking about; worry about;
惦念孩子 worry about one's children;

dian
【淀】 (1) sediment; (2) shallow water;
［淀粉］ starch;
酣酸淀粉 alkyd starch;
結團淀粉 aggregated starch;
同化淀粉 assimilation starch;
細菌淀粉 bacterial starch;

沉淀 precipitate; sediment;
色淀 lake;

dian
【奠】 (1) establish; settle; (2) make offerings to the spirits of the dead;
［奠定］ establish; make firm; make stable; settle;
奠定基礎 lay the foundation of...;
［奠都］ establish a capital; found a capital;
［奠基］ lay a foundation;
奠基禮 foundation stone-laying ceremony;
奠基石 foundation stone;
［奠儀］ gift of money made on the occasion of a funeral;

祭奠 hold a memorial ceremony for the deceased;

dian
【殿】 (1) hall; palace; (2) at the rear;
［殿後］ behind; bring up the rear; close the rear; follow in the rear;
［殿軍］ (1) rear guard; (2) fourth winner in a contest;
［殿試］ palace examination;
［殿下］ Your Highness;

大殿 (1) audience hall; (2) main hall of a Buddhist temple;
佛殿 hall of a Buddhist temple;
宮殿 palace;
後殿 the rear court room in a palace;
配殿 side hall;
神殿 sanctuary; temple;
聖殿 holy place;
正殿 main hall;
中殿 nave;

dian
【鈿】 filigree;
［鈿合］ filigree case;

螺鈿 mother-of-pearl inlay;

dian
【電】 (1) electricity; (2) give an electric shock; (3) cable; telegram;
［電報］ cable; telegram; telegraph; telegraphy;
電報掛號 cable address;
電報局 telegraph office;
電報用語 cablese;
電報員 telegrapher; telegraphist;

安全電報 safety telegram;
編碼電報 code telegrams;
傳真電報 facsimile telegram;
打電報 dispatch a telegram; forward a telegram; send a telegram;
發電報 issue a telegram; telegraph;
分送電報 multiple telegram;
複式電報 multiple telegrams;
公事電報 official telegram;
國際電報 international telegram;
國內電報 domestic telegram; inland telegram;
國外電報 foreign telegram;
加急電報 express telegram; urgent telegram;
明碼電報 telegram in plain language;
密碼電報 cipher telegram;
拍電報 send a telegram;
書信電報 letter telegram;
送電報 deliver a telegram;
無線電報 radio telegram; wireless telegram;
新聞電報 press telegram;
尋常電報 ordinary telegram;
一通電報 a telegram;
譯電報 decipher a telegram; decode a telegram;
音頻電報 acoustic telegraphy;
用戶電報 house telegraph;
有線電報 cablegram;
載波電報 carrier telegraph;
載波式電報 arrier current wave telegraph;
字母電報 alphabetic telegraph;

[電波] electric wave;
腦電波 brain wave;
無線電波 airwave;

[電場] electric field;
電場方向 direction of an electric field;
電場強度 electric field strength;

[電車] (1) streetcar; tram; tramcar; (2) trolleybus;
電車軌道 tram rail;
電車票 (1) tram ticket; (2) trolleybus ticket;
電車站 (1) streetcar stop; tram stop; tramcar stop; (2) trolleybus stop;
纜道電車 cablecar;
無軌電車 trackless tram; trolley bus;
有軌電車 streetcar; tram;

[電池] battery; cell; electric battery;
電池板 electropanel;
~太陽能電池板 photovoltaic panel; solar pane;
電池組 battery; group battery;
~板狀電池組 plate battery;
~併聯電池組 banked battery;
~浮充電池組 floating battery;
~乾電池組 dry-element battery;
~緩衝電池組 buffer battery; by-pass battery;
~極化電池組 polarization battery;
~鉛電池組 excide battery;
~昇壓電池組 booster battery;
~陽性電池組 anode battery;
~暫流電池組 open circuit battery;
~中央電池組 central battery;
備用電池 emergency battery; external battery; spare battery; stand-by battery;
本機電池 local battery;
便攜電池 portable battery;
操作電池 control battery;
充氣電池 aeration cell;
傳聲器電池 microphone battery;
儲備電池 reserve battery;
單電池 single battery;
多層太陽電池 multilayer solar battery;
二號電池 C-size battery;
浮充電池 boosting battery;
乾充電電池 dry-charged battery;
乾電池 aneroid battery; dry cell;
高能電池 high energy battery;
高壓電池 high tension battery;
工作電池 working battery;
光電池 photocell; photoelectric cell;
~半導體光電池 semiconductor photocell;
阻擋層光電池 blocking layer photocell;
軌道電池 track battery;
機內電池 self-contained battery;
激活電池 activated battery;
~氣體激活電池 gas-activated battery;
~熱激活電池 heat-activated battery;
加熱電池 heat battery;
檢驗電池組 testing battery;
鹼電池 alkaline cell;
校準電池 calibration battery;
結型電池 junction battery;
浸液電池 plunge battery;
空氣電池 air battery; air cell;
扣式電池 button battery;
鋰電池 lithium battery;
鋰空氣電池 lithium-air battery;
偏壓電池 bias battery;

起動器電池 starter battery;
燃料電池 fuel cell;
燃燒電池 fuel cell;
三號電池 A-size battery;
柵極電池 grid battery;
生物電池 bio-battery; biological battery;
手燈電池 lantern battery;
手電筒電池 flash-light battery; pocket lamp battery;
水電池 water battery;
酸性電池 acid cell;
太陽能電池 solar battery;
通話電池 talking battery;
無負荷電池 idle battery;
線路電池 line battery;
小型電池 compact battery;
小型核電池 penny-size nuclear battery;
信號電池 signal battery;
信號燈電池 signal-lantern battery;
蓄電池 accumulator cell; storage battery;
~ 蓄電池組 galvanic battery;
~ 車用蓄電池 car battery; vehicle battery;
~ 碱性蓄電池 alkaline storage battery;
~ 鉛蓄電池 lead storage battery;
~ 鉛鋅蓄電池 lead-zinc storage battery;
~ 用完的蓄電池 discharged battery;
氧化銀電池 silver oxide battery;
一次電池 one shot battery; primary battery;
一號電池 D-size battery;
一節電池 a battery;
已放電電池 run down battery;
原子電池 atomic battery;
重力電池 gravity battery;

[電磁] electromagnetism;
電磁波 electromagnetic wave;
電磁感應 electromagnetic induction;
電磁鐵 electromagnet;
~ 低溫電磁鐵 cryogenic electromagnet;
~ 聯鎖電磁鐵 interlocking electromagnet;
~ 馬蹄形電磁鐵 horseshoe electromagnet;
~ 條形電磁鐵 bare electromagnet;
~ 制動電磁鐵 brake electromagnet;
電磁學 electromagnetics; magnetoelectricity;
~ 航空電磁學 air-borne electromagnetics;
電磁振蕩 electromagnetic oscillation;

[電傳] (1) teleprinter; teletype; (2) teleprinted message;

[電導] conductance;
電導計 conductometer;
反向電導 back conductance;
溝道電導 channel conductance;
介質電導 dielectric conductance;
擴散電導 diffusion conductance;
特性電導 characteristic conductance;
有效電導 effective conductance;
直流電導 direct-current conductance;

[電燈] electric lamp; electric light;
電燈泡 electric bulb;

[電動] motor-driven; power-driven; power-operated;
電動車 electrically operated motor car;
電動扶梯 escalator;
電動刮臉刀 electric razor;
電動機 motor;
~ 加速電動機 acceleration motor;
~ 驅動電動機 drive motor;
電動汽車 electric vehicle;
電動勢 electromotance; electromotive force;
~ 逆電動勢 counter electromotive force;

[電鍍] electroplate;

[電法] electrical method;

[電費] electricity bill; electricity charge;
電費低 electricity charge is small;
電費高 electricity charge is high;
交電費 pay the electricity bill;
節約電費 keep down the electricity bill;
削減電費 cut down the electric ity bill;
收電費 collect charges for electricity;

[電感] inductance; induction;
充電電感 charging inductance;
可調電感 adjustable inductance;
天線電感 aerial inductance;
陰極電感 cathode inductance;

[電工] (1) electrical engineering; (2) electrician;
電工技術 electrotechnics;
電工器材廠 electrical appliances factory;
電工學 electrical engineering; electrotechnics;

[電焊] electrical soldering; electrical welding;
電焊工具 electrical soldering tool;

[電荷] electric charge;
電荷管 chargistor;
表觀電荷 apparent charge;
負電荷 negative charge;
感生電荷 induced charge;
吸收電荷 absorption charge;
陽電荷 positive charge;
陰電荷 negative charge;

正電荷 positive charge;
自由電荷 free charge;

[電賀] congratulate by telegram;

[電話] blower; call; dog and bone; phone; phone call; telephone; telephone call; telephony;

電話拜年 pay New Year phone call;
電話簿 phone book; telephone directory;
電話答錄機 answering machine;
電話訂票 order tickets by telephone;
電話斷了 the phone goes dead;
電話服務中心 call centre;
電話公司 phone company;
電話號碼 phone number; telephone number;
~電話號碼簿 telephone book; telephone directory;
~撥錯電話號碼 dial the wrong number;
電話壞了 the phone is out of order;
電話會議 telephone conference; teleconference;
~可視電話會議 videoconference;
電話機 telephone set;
~按鈕式電話機 push-button telephone;
電話間 telephone booth; telephone box; telephone kiosk;
電話交談 telephone conversation;
電話接不上 the phone is not connected;
電話局 telephone office;
電話卡 phonecard;
電話卡片 telephone card;
電話鈴響 the phone rings;
電話錄音機 answerphone;
電話熱線節目 call-in; phone-in;
電話設備 telephone plant;
電話售貨 telesales;
電話樹 phone tree;
電話聽不清 the connection is bad;
電話亭 phone booth; phone box;
~公用電話亭 call box; kiosk;
電話推銷 telemarketing;
電話網 telephone network;
電話線路 telephone line;
~電話線路不好 bad telephone line;
電話銷售 telesales;
電話竊聽 phone-tapping;
電話一點都聽不見 the line is dead;
電話應召女郎 call girl;
電話語音卡 telephone sound card;
電話佔線 the line is busy; the line is engaged; the number is engaged; the phone is busy; the phone is engaged; the phone is off the hook;
電話總機 telephone exchange;
安裝電話 fix a telephone; install a telephone; set up a telephone;
按鈕電話 push-button telephone;
辦公室電話 office telephone;
保密電話 secure telephone;
本地電話 local call;
長途電話 long-distance call;
撥出的電話 outgoing call;
撥電話 dial a telephone number; dial the telephone;
~撥電話號碼 dial the telephone number;
長途電話 long-distance call; trunk call;
程控電話 programme-controlled telephone;
傳呼電話 messenger call;
打錯電話 dial a wrong number;
打電話 call; call sb; call sb up; contact sb by phone; give sb a bell; give sb a buzz; give sb a call; give sb a ring; give sb a shout; make a call; make a phone call; phone; phone sb up; ring sb up; talk on the phone; telephone; telephone sb;
~打電話查問 enquire by telephone;
~打電話聊大天 have a long chat over the phone;
~打電話通知 inform by telephone;
~打電話者 caller;
~給我打電話 give me a call; ring me up;
~四處打電話 ring round;
打進的電話 incoming call;
打一個電話 make a phone call;
地區電話 district telephone;
電視電話 videophone; video telephone;
~彩色電視電話 colour picturephone;
~模擬電視電話 analog picturephone;
惡作劇電話 hoax call; prank call;
放下電話 put down the telephone;
付費電話 pay call;
~對方付費電話 collect call;
~受話人付費電話 collect call;
公共電話 public telephone;
~付費公共電話 pay phone;
公議電話 conference telephone;
公用電話 public telephone;
掛不通電話 can't obtain a connection;
掛斷電話 disconnect the telephone; hang up; hang up the receiver; put the phone down; ring off; ring off the telephone;

~ 別掛斷電話 hold the line;
掛個電話 give a buzz; give a call;
廣播電話 broadcasting call;
國際電話 international call;
國際無線電話 international radio telephone;
國內電話 domestic telephone;
回電話 call sb back; ring back;
~ 不必回電話 don't bother to call back;
會議電話 conference call; conference telephone;
急用電話 emergency call;
加急電話 urgent call;
簡短的電話 quick call;
郊區電話 suburban telephone;
叫人電話 person-to-person call; personal call;
叫人聽電話 call sb to answer the telephone;
叫醒電話 wake-up call;
接到電話 get a call; have a call; receive a call;
接電話 answer the phone; answer the telephone; pick up the phone; receive a call;
接聽電話 answer a call; take a call;
接通電話 put through a call;
緊急電話 emergency call;
來接電話 come to the phone;
錄音電話 answering machine;
~ 一台錄音電話 an answering machine;
免提電話 speakerphone;
拿起電話 pick up the telephone;
內線電話 housephone;
匿名電話 anonymous call;
普通電話 ordinary call;
汽車電話 car telephone;
牆上電話 wall telephone;
竊聽電話 tap a telephone;
切斷電話 cut off a telephone;
商用電話 business telephone;
市內電話 city telephone; urban telephone;
視像電話 videophone;
手提電話 cellular phone; mobile phone;
雙工電話 duplex telephony;
聽不清電話 have a bad telephone connection;
投幣式電話 coin-operated public telephone;
圖像電話 face-to-face picturephone;
衛星電話 satphone;
無線電話 radio telephone; wireless telephone;
新聞電話 press call;
一部電話 a telephone;
移動電話 mobile phone;
用電話 use the telephone;
有電話 there is a call;
有你的電話 here's a telephone call for you;
有線電話 landline telephone;
遇險電話 distress call;
預約電話 telephone appointment;
載波電話 carrier telephony;
政務電話 government telephone;
智能報盜電話 intelligent alarm telephone;
住宅電話 home telephone;
專線電話 special line telephone;
專用電話 special telephone;
桌上電話 desk telephone;
自動電話 automatic telephone; dial telephone;

[電極] electrode; pole;
電極電位 electrode potential;
二氧化碳電極 carbon dioxide electrode;
甘汞電極 calomel electrode;
接地電極 earth electrode;
毛細管電極 electrode;
同心電極 concentric electrode;
微電極 microelectrode;
~ 玻璃微電極 glass-capillary microelectrode;
~ 雙管微電極 double-barelled microelectrode;
~ 同心微電極 concentric microelectrode;

[電擊] electric shock;

[電解] electrolysis; electrolyze;
電解還原 electrolytic reduction;
電解學 electrolytics;
電解氧化 electrolytic oxidation;
電解質 electrolyte;
~ 非電解質 non-electrolyte;
~ 基底電解質 base electrolyte;
~ 膠態電解質 colloidal electrolyte;
~ 兩性電解質 amphoteric electrolyte;
~ 強電解質 strong electrolyte;
~ 弱電解質 weak electrolyte;
~ 酸電解質 acid electrolyte;
恒流電解 constant-current electrolysis;
汞法電解 mercury process electrolysis;
汞陰極電解 mercury cathode electrolysis;
鹼性電解 alkaline electrolysis;
熔鹽電解 fused-salt electrolysis;

酸性電解 acidic electrolysis;

[電晶體] transistor;
場效應電晶體 field effect transistor;
單極電晶體 unipolar transistor;
二極電晶體 diode transistor;
結型場效應電晶體 junction field effect transistor
漂移電晶體 drift transistor
三極電晶體 .triode transistor;
四極電晶體 tetrode transistor;

[電纜] cable; electric cable;
電纜船 cable ship; cablelayer;
電纜敷設船 cablelayer;
超導電纜 superconducting cable;
操作電纜 control cable;
粗電纜 thick cables;
地下電纜 underground cable;
防爆電纜 approved cable;
高架電纜 overhead cable;
高空電纜 aerial cable;
海底電纜 submarine cables; undersea cable;
合用電纜 all-in-one cable;
鋁芯電纜 aluminium cable;
衰減電纜 attenuating cable;
天線電纜 antenna cable;
通訊電纜 communications cables;
折疊電纜 accordion cable;

[電離] electrolytic dissociation; ionization;
電離層 ionosphere;
~電離層暴 ionospheric storm;
電離電勢 ionization potential;
電離電位 ionization potential;
電離度 degree of electrolytic dissociation;
電離能 ionization energy;

[電力] electric power;
電力電子學 power electronics;
電力工程 power engineering;
電力工業 power industry;
電力線 line of electric force; power line;
利用電力 use electric power;
配送電力 distribute electric power;
輸送電力 transmit electric power;

[電量計] voltameter;
本生電量計 Bunsen voltameter;
電解電量計 electrolytic voltameter;
氣體電量計 gas voltameter;
容積電量計 volume voltameter;

[電療] diathermy; electrotherapy;
接受電療 have diathermy;
實施電療 carry out electrotherapy;
使用電療 apply medical diathermy;

[電鈴] electric bell;
電鈴按鈕 bell push button;
摁電鈴 press an electric bell;

[電流] ammeter; current; electric current;
電流計 galvanometer;
~不擺電流計 aperiodic galvanometer;
~衝擊電流計 ballistic galvanometer;
~無定向電流計 astatic galvanometer;
電流密度 electric current density;
電流強度 current intensity; current strength;
安培電流 ampere currents;
安全電流 safe current;
動作電流 action current; actuating current;
反向電流 contraflow;
接通電流 complete the current;
截斷電流 break the current;
生物電流 bioelectric current;
實在電流 actual current;
天線電流 aerial current;
吸收電流 absorption current;
異常電流 abnormal current;
有效電流 active current;

[電路] circuitry; electric circuit;
電路板 circuit board;
電路圖 circuit diagram;
電路系統 circuitry;
電路學 circuitry;
~固體電路學 solid state circuitry;
~晶體管電路學 transistor circuitry;
~微波電路學 microwave circuitry;
電路中斷 a break in the circuit;
并聯電路 parallel circuit;
乘法電路 multiplying circuit;
除法電路 dividing circuit;
串聯電路 series circuit;
存取電路 access circuit;
低壓電路 low tension circuit;
動作電路 action circuit;
符合電路 coincidence circuit;
複聯電路 multiple-series circuit;
附屬電路 accessory circuit;
高壓電路 high tension circuit;
固體電路 solid state circuit;
厚膜電路 thick-film circuit;
混雜電路 sophiscated circuitry;
集成電路 integrated circuit;
積體電路 integrated circuit;
~大型積體電路 large scale integrated

circuit;
加強電路 accentuator circuit;
加速電路 accelerating circuit;
接通電路 close a circuit; complete a circuit;
模擬電路 analogue circuit;
耦合電路 coupled circuit;
切斷電路 break the circuit; open the circuit;
色調控制電路 hue control circuitry;
攝像機電路 camera circuitry;
雙工電路 duplicate circuit;
時序電路 sequential circuit;
調定電路 set-up circuitry;
微型電路 microcircuit;
~ 薄膜微型電路 film microcircuit;
~ 混合型微型電路 hybrid microcircuit;
~ 集成微型電路 integrated microcircuit;
吸收電路 absorber circuit;
印刷電路 printed circuit;
運算電路 arithmetic circuitry;
噪聲抑制電路 noise suppression circuitry;
自動彩色信號電路 automatic colour circuitry;

[電碼] code;
電碼閉塞 coded circuit blocking;

[電納] susceptance;
等效電納 equivalent susceptance;
電容性電納 capacitive susceptance;
電子電納 electronic susceptance;
反饋電納 feedback susceptance;

[電腦] computer; electronic brain;
電腦安全 computer safety;
電腦病毒 computer virus;
電腦程式 computer programme;
電腦出錯 computer error;
電腦電話 computer telephone;
電腦電視 compuvision;
電腦法學 computer jurisprudence;
電腦翻譯 computer translation;
電腦輔助 computer-aided;
~ 電腦輔助翻譯 computer-aided translation;
~ 電腦輔助設計 computer-aided design;
~ 電腦輔助製造 computer-aided manufacturing;
電腦公司 computer company;
電腦行業 computer business;
電腦鍵盤 computer keyboard;
電腦科學 computer science;
電腦可讀的 machine-readable;
電腦農業 computerized agriculture;
電腦屏幕 computer screen;
電腦軟件 computer software;
電腦設備 computing equipment;
電腦市場 computer market;
電腦死機 a computer crashes;
電腦天地 computer land;
電腦圖書館 computer library;
電腦圖像 computer graphics;
電腦網絡 computer network;
~ 電腦網絡文化 cyberculture;
電腦系統 computer system;
電腦顯示器 computer monitor;
電腦硬件 computer hardware;
電腦應用 computing;
電腦遊戲 computer game;
筆記本電腦 laptop computer; notebook;
便攜式電腦 portable computer;
超級電腦 supercomputer;
個人電腦 personal computer;
毫微極電腦 nanomachine;
機載電腦 on-board computer;
啟動電腦 boot a computer;
枱式電腦 desktop computer;
微型電腦 microcomputer;
膝上型電腦 laptop; laptop computer;
小型電腦 minicomputer;
一台電腦 a computer;
掌上電腦 handheld; handheld personal computer;
桌上型電腦 desktop computer;

[電鈕] button;
按電鈕 press a button;

[電偶] electric coupling;
熱電偶 thermocouple;
~ 充氣熱電偶 air filled thermocouple;
~ 雙金屬熱電偶 bimetallic thermocouple;

[電器] electrical appliances;
大型電器 large electrical appliances;
家用電器 domestic appliances; home appliances; household appliances; household electrical appliances;

[電氣] electrical;
電氣工程 electrical engineering;
電氣化 electrification;
~ 家庭電氣化 domestic electrification;
~ 農村電氣化 rural electrification;
~ 全盤電氣化 full electrification;

[電容] capacitance;
電容傳聲器 capacitor microphone;
電容汞弧管 mercury-arc valve;

電容率 capacitivity;
電容器 capacitor; condenser;
~補償電容器 compensation condenser;
~充電電容器 charging capacitor; charging condenser;
~儲能電容器 energy storage capacitor;
~電解質電容器 chemical condenser;
~分流電容器 bridging capacitor;
~隔直流電容器 block condenser;
~化學電容器 chemical capacitor;
~緩衝電容器 buffer capacitor;
~換向電容器 commutating condenser;
~校準電容器 calibration capacitor;
~抗干擾電容器 anti-interference condenser;
~可變電容器 adjustable capacitor;
~片形電容器 chip capacitor;
~平衡電容器 balancing capacitor;
~雙聯電容器 double capacitor;
~陶瓷電容器 ceramic condenser;
~天線耦合電容器 antenna coupling capacitor;
補償電容 compensation capacitor;
燈絲電容 filament capacitance;
等效電容 equivalent-effect capacitance;
電極電容 electrode capacitance;
電纜電容 cable capacitance;
對地電容 direct earth capacitance;
反饋電容 feedback capacitance;
固定電容 fixed capacitance;
間隙電容 gap capacitance;
接地電容 ground capacitance;
靜電電容 electrostatic capacitance;
控制電容 control capacitance;
漏電容 drain capacitance;
耦合電容 coupling capacitance;
平衡電容 balancing capacitance;
人手電容 manual capacitance;
天線電容 aerial capacitance;
線圈電容 coil capacitance;
陰極電容 cathode capacitance;
有效電容 effective capacitance;

[電熱] electric heat; electrothermal;
電熱杯 electric heating mug; electrothermal cup;
電熱廠 thermal power plant;
電熱處理 electgrothermal treatment;
電熱療法 electrothermotherapy;
電熱器 electric heater;
電熱褥 electric bedding;
電熱水器 electric heater;
電熱絲 heating wire;
電熱毯 electric blanket;
電熱學 electrothermics; electrothermy;
電熱針炙 electrothermal acupuncture;
電聲學 electroacoustics;
電聲樂器 electroacoustic musical instrument;

[電扇] electric fan;
落地電扇 stand fan;

[電視] small screen; teevee; television; TV;
電視報紙 telenewspaper; telepaper;
電視播送 telecasting;
~電視播送室 television studio;
電視採訪 television interview;
電視測試 television test;
~電視測試卡 television test card;
~電視測試信號 television test signal;
電視唱片 video disk;
電視車 television mobile unit;
電視傳播 television communication;
~電視傳播系統 teleview system;
電視電話 picture phone; video telephone;
電視電腦 teleputer;
電視電影 telecine; telecinema; telefilm;
~電視電影機 telecine; telecine projector;
~彩色電視電影機 colour telecine;
~三管式電視電影機 three-tube telecine;
~電視電影室 telecine studio;
~電視電影術 telecinematography;
電視發射 television transmission;
~電視發射台 television transmitting station;
電視觀眾 televiewer;
電視會議 teleconference; teleconferencing;
電視廣播 television broadcasting;
~電視廣播劇 teleplay;
~電視廣播事業 television industry;
~電視廣播員 telecaster; televisor;
電視廣告 television advertisement; television advertising;
電視混音室 television sound-mixing room;
電視機 box; custard and jelly; goggle box; idiot box; teevee; television set; telly; TV;
~電視機櫃 television cabinet;
~彩色電視機 colour television;
~超大電視機 large-screen television;
~超微型電視機 supermini television;
~打開電視機 turn on the television;
~黑白電視機 black-and-white television;
~落地式電視機 console television;

~數碼電視機 digital television;
~數字電視機 digital television;
~一台電視機 a television set; a TV set;
電視紀錄片 documentary television;
電視記者 television journalist; television reporter;
電視講話 televised speech; television address; television speech;
電視講演 televised speech;
電視教學 instructional television;
~電視教學節目 instructional television programme;
電視教育 television education;
電視節目 television programme;
~電視節目表 television guide;
~電視節目製作 television programme production;
~電視節目主持人 television presenter;
~長時間的電視節目 telethon;
~開放式電視節目 open access television;
電視劇 teleplay; TV drama;
~電視劇本 teleplay;
~實況電視劇 docusoap;
電視課程 telecourse;
電視連續劇 TV drama;
電視錄像轉播車 television broadcasting van;
電視迷 couch potato; telefan; TV addict;
電視明星 TV celebrity; TV star;
電視牌照 TV license;
電視屏幕 television screen;
電視頻道 television frequency channel;
電視社會 television society;
電視攝像管 television camera tube;
電視攝影機 television camera;
電視實況轉播 television live broadcast;
電視塔 television tower;
電視台 television broadcast station;
~電視台台長 television station controller;
~電視台主持人 anchorman;
~國家電視台 national television;
~有線電視台 cable television station;
電視網 television network;
電視文化 television culture;
電視文學 television literature;
電視污染 television pollution;
電視現場直播 live television;
電視現場轉播 broadcast relay; television relay;
電視小品 television sketch;
電視新聞 television news;
電視信號 television signal;
電視演播室 television studio;
電視遙控器 television remote control;
電視影片 telefilm;
電視影院 television cinema;
電視優勢論 theory of television dominance;
電視遊戲機 video game;
電視中心 television centre;
~電視中心系統 television centre system;
電視轉播 television relay;
~電視轉播車 outside broadcast vehicle;
~實況電視轉播 live broadcast; live television coverage;
電視綜合症 television syndrome;
閉路電視 CCTV; close circuit television;
彩色電視 colour television;
付費電視 pay television;
高清電視 HD television; high definition television;
工業電視 industrial television;
公眾電視 public television;
共用天線電視 communal aerial television;
黑白電視 black-and-white television; monochrome television;
機載電視 airborne television;
捲盤式電視 cartvision;
軍用電視 army television; military television;
看電視 watch television;
寬屏電視 widescreen television;
立體電視 stereoscopic television; three-dimensional television;
民用電視 public television;
模擬電視 analog television;
平板電視 flatscreen television;
上電視 be on television; go on television;
收看電視 tune in;
數碼電視 digital television;
數字電視 digital television;
水下電視 underwater television;
投幣式電視 coin-operated television;
微光電視 low light level television;
衛星電視 satellite television;
無線電電視 radio television; wireless television;
液晶電視 LCD television;
業餘電視 amateur television;
有線電視 cable television;
增強電視 enhanced television;

[電勢] electric potential; potential;
電勢差 electric potential difference

不對稱電勢 asymmetric potential;
交變電勢 alternating potential;
零電勢 zero potential;
生物電勢 bioelectric potential;
外觀電勢 appearance potential;

[電算] compute;
電算機 computer; electronic calculator;

[電台] broadcasting station; radio station;
電台節目 radio programme;
~電台節目主持人 disk jockey; radio presenter;
電台台長 radio station controller;
廣播電台 broadcasting station;
~地方廣播電台 local radio;
~對外廣播電台 overseas broadcasting station;
~國際廣播電台 international broadcasting station;
流動電台 ambulant radio station;
收聽電台 tune in;
一家電台 a radio station;
轉播電台 relay station;

[電梯] electric elevator; electrical lift; elevator; lift; passenger lift;
電梯工 liftboy; liftman;
電梯音樂 elevator music;
乘電梯 ride a lift; ride an escalator;
扶手電梯 escalator;
自動電梯 escalator;
~行人自動電梯 pedestrian escalator;

[電筒] electric flashlight; electric torch;
手電筒 electric torch; flashlight;
~手電筒—對人不對己 a flashlight (metaphorically, one who is always strict with others but never with himself);
~手電筒光 torchlight;

[電位] potential;
電位測量 measurement of electric potential;
電位差 electric potential difference;
電位計 potentiometer;
~電容電位計 capacitance potentiometer;
~平衡電位計 balancing potentiometer;
~示角電位計 angle-index potentiometer;
~雙線電位計 bifilar potentiometer;
動作電位 action potential;
加速電位 accelerating potential;
絕對電位 absolute potential;
零電位 zero potential;

[電線] electric wire; wire;
電線杆 utility pole;
電線架 electricity wire structure;
~高壓電線架 pylon;
高壓電線 high tension wires;
一捲電線 a coil of wire;

[電信] telecommunications;
電信業 telecommunications industry;
電信業務 telecommunication services;
國際電信 international telecommunications;
國內電信 domestic telecommunications;

[電學] electricity (as a science);
磁電學 magnetoelectricity;
動電學 electrokinematics;
光電學 photoelectricity;
靜電學 electrostatics;
熱電學 thermoelectricity;

[電訊] (1) telecommunications; telephone dispatch; (2) radio communication signals;

[電壓] electric voltage; voltage;
安全電壓 safe voltage; safety voltage;
端電壓 terminal voltage;
附加電壓 additional voltage;
改變電壓 change the voltage of the current;
過電壓 overvoltage;
~內部過電壓 internal overvoltage;
~調諧過電壓 resonance overvoltage;
~陽極過電壓 anodic overvoltage;
加速電壓 accelerating voltage;
降低電壓 decrease the voltage; lower the voltage; step down the voltage;
路端電壓 terminal voltage
昇高電壓 increase the voltage; raise the voltage; step up the voltage;
天線電壓 aerial voltage;
外加電壓 applied voltage;
作用電壓 active voltage;

[電影] big screen; film; flick; motion picture; movie; moving picture;
電影愛好者 cinephile;
電影編劇 scenario writer;
電影編年史 film chronicle;
電影大片 blockbuster;
電影導演 film director; movie director;
電影的 big-screen; cinematic;
電影發行公司 film distribution corporation;
電影翻譯 film translation;
電影放映機 cineprojector;

電影放映室 film projector room;
電影放映員 projectionist;
電影工作人員 movie staff;
電影工作者 cinema worker; film worker;
電影公司 film company;
電影觀眾 cinema-goer; film-goer;
電影光碟 video cassette disk (VCD);
電影技術 cinematographic technique; film technique;
電影機 movie camera;
電影剪輯機 motion picture editing machine;
電影膠片 cinefilm;
~ 電影膠片打孔機 film punching machine;
電影界 movie industry;
電影節 film festival;
~ 國際電影節 international film festival;
電影經濟學 film economics;
電影劇本 film script; scenario; script;
~ 電影劇本作者 film scenarist; scenario writer; scriptwriter;
電影劇組 film crew;
電影美學 cinema aesthetics;
電影迷 cinephile; film buff; movie fan;
電影明星 cinemaactor; film star; movie star;
電影女演員 cinemactress;
電影票 cinema ticket;
電影攝影 cinematography;
~ 電影攝影機 cinematograph; film camera;
~ 電影攝影棚 film studio;
~ 電影攝影術 cinematography;
~ 電影攝影學 cinematography;
電影攝製組 film unit;
電影生產 cinema production;
電影市場學 studies of movie market;
電影首映 film premiere;
~ 電影首映禮 film premiere; movie premiere;
電影圖書館 film library;
電影文獻 film document;
電影舞台 cinema stage;
電影演員 film actor;
電影業 film industry; filmdom; movie industry; motion picture industry;
電影藝術 cinematographic art;
電影音樂 cinema music;
電影原聲音樂 film soundtrack;
電影院 cinema; movie house; movie theatre;
~ 流動電影院 mobile cinema; road cinema;
~ 露天電影院 drive-in cinema;
~ 小汽車電影院 built-in cinema;
電影展覽 film exhibition;
電影製片廠 film studio;
電影製片人 film producer; movie producer;
電影製作人 filmmaker; moviemaker;
電影資料館 cinematheque;
彩色電影 colour cinematography; colour film; colour movies;
成人電影 adult film;
催人淚下的電影 tearjerker; weeper; weepie; weepy;
導演電影 direct a film;
電視電影 telecinema;
放映電影 release a movie; show a film;
高票房電影 box-office smash;
黑白電影 black-and-white cinematography; black-and-white film;
教育電影 educational movies;
驚險電影 thriller;
看電影 see a film; see a movie; watch a film; watch a movie;
~ 看電影的人 cinemagoer; moviegoer;
~ 去看電影 go to the films;
寬銀幕電影 wide-screen film;
~ 全景寬銀幕電影 panoramic movie;
立體電影 stereoscopic cinematography; stereoscopic film; three-dimenstional film;
~ 寬銀幕立體電影 cinerama;
美術電影 animation film studio;
~ 美術電影製片 animation film studio;
拍電影 produce a film; shoot a film;
~ 拍成電影 make a movie;
~ 拍攝電影 shoot a film;
全景電影 panorama film;
全息電影 holographic movie;
色情電影 blue movie; porno movie;
深景電影 vista-vision;
水下電影 underwater movies;
無聲電影 silent film;
懸疑兇殺電影 whodunit;
消遣性電影 pap;
小電影 (1) microfilm; mini movie; (2) porno film; skin flick;
一本電影 a reel of film;
一部電影 a film; a motion picture; a movie;
~ 發行一部電影 release a movie;

~製作一部電影 make a movie; produce a motion picture;
一場電影 a film; a show; the showing of a film;
優秀的電影 a dilly of a movie;
譯製電影 dub;
有聲電影 sound film; talkie; talking film; talking picture;
~磁錄式有聲電影 magnetic sound talkie;
~光電式有聲電影 optical sound talkie;

[電泳] electrophoresis;
電泳圖 electrophoretogram;
對流電泳 countercurrent electrophoresis;
連續紙電泳 continuous paper electrophoresis;
柱電泳 column electrophoresis;

[電郵] email;
電郵地址 email address;
電郵附件 email attachment;
電郵轟炸 mail bomb;
電郵信息 email message;
垃圾電郵 spam;
~垃圾電郵防護 spamblocking;
小心欺詐電郵 beware of fraudulent emails;

[電源] electric source; power source;
電源插座 power point;
電源組 power pack;
插上電源 plug in;
接上電源 connect the power source; wire in;
切斷電源 cut off the electric supply;

[電閘] electric gate;

[電子] (1) electron; (2) e-; electronic;
電子辦公室 electronic office;
電子報紙 electronic newspaper;
電子筆 electronic pen;
~電子筆記簿 electronic memo;
電子編輯系統 electronic editing system;
電子表格 (1) e-form; (2) spread sheet;
電子秤 electronic scales;
電子出版 electronic publishing;
~電子出版物 electronic publication;
~電子出版業 electronic publishing industry;
電子詞典 electronic dictionary;
電子存檔系統 electronic filing system;
電子打火機 electronic lighter;
電子打印機 electronic printer;
電子訂貨 electronic ordering;
~電子訂貨系統 electronic ordering system;
電子對抗技術 electronic warfare technique;
電子翻譯系統 electronic translation system;
電子工程 electronic engineering;
電子管 electron tube;
電子光學 electrooptics;
電子匯款系統 electronic funds transfer system;
電子會議系統 electronic meeting system;
電子計算機 electronic computer;
~電子計算機服務 compuserve;
電子加速器 electron accelerator
電子家庭 electronic family;
電子交換系統 electronic switching system;
電子論 electron theory;
電子媒介 electronic media;
電子秘書 electronic secretary;
電子錢包 e-purse;
電子槍 electron gun;
電子搶答器 quiz machine;
電子琴 electronic piano; electronic organ;
電子情報服務系統 electronic information service system;
電子人 cyborg;
電子商務 e-commerce;
電子商業 e-business;
電子攝影 electronic photography;
電子收款機 electronic cash register;
電子手錶 digital watch;
電子書 e-book;
電子束 electron beam;
電子數據 electronic data;
~電子數據處理 electronic data processing;
電子數據處理系統 electronic data processing system;
~電子數據交換 electronic data interchange;
電子數字 electronic digit;
~電子數字計算機 electronic digital computer;
電子鎖 electronic lock;
電子通信 electronic communication;
電子圖書 electronic books;
~電子圖書館 electronic library;
電子圖像 electronic picture;
電子顯像機 electrograph;
電子銷售 electronic marketing;
電子新聞採集 electronic news gathering;

電子信函 electronic letter;
電子信息系統 electronic information system;
電子音樂 electronic music;
電子銀行 electronic bank;
電子學 electronics;
~光電子學 photoelectronics;
~分子電子學 molecular electronics; molectronics
~生物態電子學 biostate electronics;
~天文電子學 astronomical electronics;
~通信電子學 communication electronics;
~微電子學 microelectronics;
薄膜微電子學 thin film microelectronics;
~無線電電子學 radioelectronics;
電子郵件 e-mail; electronic mail;
電子郵局 electronic mailbox;
電子郵政 electronic mail;
電子遊戲 electronic game; video game;
電子樂器 electronic musical instrument;
電子雲 electronic cloud;
電子雜誌 electronic journal;
電子戰 electronic warfare;
電子偵察 electronic reconnaissance;
~電子偵察衛星 electronic reconnaissance satellite;
電子鐘 electronic clock;
電子組件 electronic buildingbrick;
成鍵電子 bonding electrons;
加偏壓電子 biased electron;
束縛電子 binding electron;
束電子 beam electron;
水合電子 aqueous electron;
微電子 microelectronic;
~微電子編程器 microelectronic programmer;
~微電子產業 microelectronic industry;
~微電子革命 microelectronic revolution;
~微電子學 microelectronics;
陽電子 positron;
正電子 positive electron; positron;
自由電子 free electron;

[電阻] electric resistance; resistance;
電阻大 have a high resistance;
電阻率 resistivity;
~電阻率法 resistivity method;
~暗電阻率 dark resistivity;
~平均電阻率 average resistivity;
~有效電阻率 effective resistivity;
電阻器 resistor;
~分洩電阻器 bleeder resistor;
~可調電阻器 adjustable resistor;
~偏壓電阻器 bias resistor;
~陽極電阻器 anode resistor;
~鎮流電阻器 ballast resistor;
電阻箱 resistance box;
電阻小 have a low resistance;
附加電阻 adapter resistance;
光敏電阻 photoresistance;
內電阻 internal resistance;
熱敏電阻 thermal resistor; thermistor,
天線電阻 aerial resistance;
吸收電阻 absorption resistance;

彩電 (1) colour TV set; (2) colour TV;
掣電 as fast as lightning; in the twinkling of an eye;
充電 charge a battery;
觸電 get an electric shock;
傳電 conduct electricity;
大氣電 atmospheric electricity;
帶電 charged; electrified;
導電 conduct electricity;
地電 terrestrial electricity;
動電 dynamic electricity;
動物電 animal electricity;
斷電 blackout; interruption of power supply; power cut;
發電 (1) generate electricity; (2) send a telegram;
放電 discharge;
訃電 telegram of obituary;
負電 negative electricity;
復電 cable a reply;
供電 power supply;
光電 photo-electricity;
函電 letter and telegram;
賀電 message of congratulation;
回電 telephone reply;
機電 machinery and power-generating equipment;
急電 urgent cable; urgent call; urgent telegram;
集電 collect electricity;
家電 household electrical appliances;
接觸電 contact electricity;
靜電 static electricity;
來電 (1) incoming call; incoming telegram; your message; your telegram; (2) inform by telegram; send a telegram here; (3) have a phone call;
雷電 thunder and lightning;
漏電 leak electricity;
密電 cipher telegram;
跑電 leakage of electricity;
閃電 lightning;

省電 save electricity;
輸電 transmit electricity;
水電 (1) water and electricity; (2) hydro-electric power;
停電 power cut; power failure;
通電 (1) cable all concerned; (2) link with the source of an electric current; supply electricity to;
外電 dispatches from foreign news agencies;
心電 electrocardio;
唁電 cable of condolence; message of condolence;
陽電 positive electricity;
陰電 negative electricity;
用電 use electricity;
郵電 post and telecommunications;
正電 positive electricity;
直流電 direct current;
致電 (1) give a phone call; (2) send a telegram
逐電 go as quickly as a flash of lightning;
專電 special dispatch; special telegram;
走電 electric power leakage;

dian

【墊】 (1) fill up; put sth under sth else to raise it or make it level; (2) cushion; pad; (3) pay for sb and expect to be repaid later;

[墊背] fall guy; scapegoat; suffer for the faults of others;

[墊底兒] (1) underlay; (2) eat a little before dinner;

[墊付] pay for sb and expected to be repaid later;

[墊片] shim;
連桿墊片 connecting rod shim;
調整墊片 adjusting shim;
軸承墊片 bearing shim;

[墊平] level up;
墊平操場 level the playground;
把地面墊平 level up the ground;
把路墊平 level a road up;

[墊支] advance expenditure; give an advance;

[墊子] cushion; mat; mattress; pad;
一塊墊子 a pad;
椅墊子 chair cushion;
針墊子 pin cushion;

牀墊 mattress;
靠背墊 back cushion;
靠墊 cushion;
鋪墊 (1) bedding; (2) foreshadowing;
氣墊 air cushion; gas cushion;
石棉墊 asbestos cushion;
胎墊 tyre cushion;
鞋墊 insole; shoepad;
液壓墊 hydraulic die cushion;
坐墊 cushion;

dian

【澱】 (1) dregs; precipitate; sediments; (2) indigo;

[澱粉] starch;
澱粉膠 starch adhesive;
澱粉酶 amylase;

[澱積] deposition;

dian

【靛】 indigo;

[靛白] indigo white;

[靛藍] indigo;
靛藍計 indigometer;

[靛青] indigo;
靛青鳥 indigo bird;
草本靛青 Chinese indigo;
木本靛青 Indian indigo;

藍靛 (1) indigo; (2) indigo blue;

dian

【簟】 bamboo mat;

[簟竹] a variety of giant bamboo;

diao¹

diao

【刁】 (1) sly; tricky; (2) a surname;

[刁惡] rascally brutal; wicked;

[刁婦] shrew;

[刁棍] rascal;

[刁悍] crafty and fierce; cunning and ferocious; cunning and fierce; wicked and ferocious;

[刁滑] artful; crafty; cunning; foxy; sly and deceitful;
刁滑之徒 cunning and shrewd rascals; unscrupulous rogue;

[刁蠻] obstinate; unruly;

[刁難] create difficulties; deliberately put obstacles in sb's way; make things difficult;
百般刁難 create all sorts of obstacles; create obstructions of every description; keep raising objections;

put up innumerable obstacles; raise all manner of difficulties;
故意刁難 deliberately place obstacles;
受到刁難 be put in a difficult situation deliberately;
[刁詐] crafty; knavish;
刁詐凶悍 cunning and fierce; knavish and violent; tricky and savage;
[刁鑽] artful; crafty; cunning; wily;
刁鑽古怪 artful and obstinate; full of monkey tricks; sly and capricious; wily and peculiar;
刁鑽刻薄 catty;
非常刁鑽 extremely cunning;

放刁 act in a rascally manner; make difficulties for sb;
嘴刁 particular about food;

diao
【叼】 hold in the mouth;

diao
【凋】 wither;
[凋弊] (1) destitute; hard; (2) depressed;
百業凋弊 all business declines; all business languishes;
[凋零] fall and be scattered about; withered;
凋零殘敗 fall and be destroyed;
[凋落] wither and fall;
花凋葉落 the flowers dry up and the leaves fall away;
[凋萎] wither and fall;
[凋謝] (1) fade; wither and fall; wither away; (2) die of old age;
凋謝結子 go to seed;
花兒凋謝 the flowers have withered away;
老成凋謝 an experienced and accomplished person has passed away;

diao
【彫】 (1) carve; paint; tattoo; (2) emaciated; wither; (3) adorn; decorate;
[彫弓] ornamental bow;

diao
【貂】 marten; mink; sable;
[貂皮] mink; sable; sable skin;

黑貂 sable;
水貂 mink;
松貂 pine marten;
續貂 add sth bad to sth good;
紫貂 sable;

diao
【碉】 blockhouse; pillbox;
[碉堡] blockhouse; fort; pillbox; stronghold; fortification;
爆破碉堡 blow up a pillbox;
野戰碉堡 field redoubt;
炸碉堡 blast away a blockhouse;
築碉堡 build a blockhouse;
[碉樓] barbican; watchtower;

diao
【雕】 (1) carve; engrave; (2) vulture;
[雕蟲小技] clever with one's hands; insignificant skill; literary skill of no high order; small trick; the trifling skill of a scribe;
[雕工] carver; grinder;
玉雕工 jade carver; jade grinder;
[雕刻] carve; engrave; engraving;
雕刻工 engraver;
雕刻工作 carving job;
雕刻技巧 carving technique;
雕刻家 sculptor;
~女雕刻家 sculptress;
雕刻器 graver;
雕刻師 carver;
雕刻術 engraving skill;
雕刻圖案 carving illustration;
雕刻物 carving item;
雕刻藝術 art of carving;
精雕細刻 give sth careful revision; work at sth with great care; work at sth with the care and precision of a sculptor;
精於雕刻 be skilled in sculpture;
銅版雕刻 copperplate engraving;
[雕欄玉砌] carved balustrades and marble steps;
[雕器] carved objects;
玉雕器 jade carved objects;
[雕塑] carve and mould; sculpture;
雕塑家 sculptor;
~女雕塑家 sculptress;
雕塑藝術 statuary art;
雕塑作品 sculpture;
彩色雕塑 polychrome sculpture;
抽象派雕塑 abstract sculpture;
一座雕塑 a sculpture;
裝飾雕塑 ornamental sculpture;
[雕像] effigy; monument; statue;
雕刻像 statue;
大理石雕像 marble figure;

小雕像 figurine; statuette;
一座雕像 a statue;

[雕琢] (1) carve; cut and polish; sculpture; (2) embellish;
雕琢文章 polish a composition;

貝雕 shell carving;
冰雕 ice sculpture;
瓷雕 carved porcelain;
浮雕 relief;
海雕 sea eagle;
花雕 Shaoxing wine;
木雕 wood carving;
漆雕 carved lacquerware;
群雕 group sculpture; sculpture group;
石雕 (1) stone carving; (2) carved stone;
牙雕 ivory carving;
椰雕 coconut carving;
玉雕 jade carving; jade sculpture;
竹雕 bamboo carving;

diao
【鯛】 porgy; scup; sea bream;

黃鯛 yellow porgy;
雀鯛 damselfish;
真鯛 genuine porgy; red porgy;

diao
【鵰】 bird of prey;

diao⁴
diao
【弔】 (1) condole; console; mourn; (2) hang; suspend; suspended;
[弔古] think of the ancients;
[弔唁] mourning;
弔唁者 mourner;

diao
【吊】 (1) hang; suspend; (2) let down with a rope; lift up with a rope; (3) condole; mourn; (4) put in a fur lining; (5) revoke; withdraw; (6) a string of 1,000 cash; (7) crane;
[吊車] crane; hoist;
吊車手 crane operator;
臂式吊車 boom hoist;
裝卸料吊車 charge hoist;
自動吊車 power hoist;
[吊牀] hammock;
[吊燈] ceiling lamp; hanging lamp; pendant lamp;
枝形吊燈 chandelier;
[吊桿] boom;
吊桿架 derrick;
~移動式吊桿架 crab derrick;
[吊詭矜奇] try to be novel for effect;
[吊環] suspend; hand rings; rings;
擺動吊環 swinging rings;
靜止吊環 stationary rings; still rings;
[吊扣] suspend;
[吊樓] house projecting over the water;
[吊橋] drawbridge; suspension bridge;
[吊球] drop the ball;
吊高球 lob;
吊網前球 drop shot;
[吊死] hang by one's neck; hang oneself;
吊死鬼 (1) caterpillar; hanging looper; (2) ghosts of hanged people;
[吊索] halyard; sling;
電纜吊索 cable sling;
鏈式吊索 chain sling;
[吊桶] bucket;
上昇吊桶 ascending bucket;
提昇吊桶 hoist bucket;
[吊慰] express condolences;
[吊銷] revoke; withdraw;
吊銷牌照 revoke a licence;
[吊鐘] fuchsia;
[吊墜] pendant;
紀念盒吊墜 locket;

浮吊 crane vessel; floating crane;
門吊 gantry crane; overhead crane;
起吊 crane;
上吊 hang oneself;
塔吊 tower crane;

diao
【掉】 (1) come off; drop; drop off; fall; fall off; (2) lose; missing; (3) fall behind; (4) turn; (5) drop; reduce; (6) change; exchange;
[掉換] change; exchange; swap; swop;
[掉價] lower the price;
[掉淚] come to tears; tears falling;
[掉色] fade; lose colour;
[掉頭] change direction; turn about; turn round;
掉頭而去 fling off;
掉過頭來 turn about; turn around; turn back; turn one's head;

[掉下] (1) fall; (2) drop;
掉下淚來 tears roll down one's cheeks;
[掉牙] a tooth drops off;
八十歲奶奶的嘴—老掉牙 [了] the mouth of an eighty-year-old granny — toothless;
老掉牙 corny; obsolete; out of date; very old;
~ 老掉牙的話 hoary old chestnut;
[掉轉] turn about;
掉轉方向 come round; move in the opposite direction; turn round;

拔掉 (1) pluck out; (2) capture;
耙掉 rake off;
扯掉 tear off;
失掉 (1) lose; (2) miss;
挖掉 dig out; eradicate;

diao
【釣】 angle; fish with a rod and line;
[釣餌] bait;
[釣竿] angling rod; casting rod; fishing pole; fishing rod;
[釣具] fishing tackle;
釣具箱 tackle box;
[釣絲] fishing line;
[釣線] fishing line;
釣線軸 reel;
[釣魚] angle; fish; fishing; go fishing;
釣魚船 fishing boat;
~ 穩坐釣魚船 sit tight in the fishing boat; take a tense situation calmly;
釣魚消遣 divert oneself in fishing;
釣魚者 fisherman;
冰洞釣魚 ice-fishing;
冰上釣魚 ice-fishing;
喜歡釣魚 be fond of fishing;

垂釣 go angling;

diao
【銚】 (1) small pot with a handle; (2) spear;
diao
【調】 (1) shift; transfer; (2) accent; (3) key; (4) melody; tune; (5) tone; tune;
[調撥] allocate and transfer;
調撥款項 allocate funds; allocate money;
調撥物資 allocate supplies;
[調查] carry out a research; check into; examine into; go into; hold an inquiry into; inquire into; investigate; learn the facts about; look into; make an investigation into; make an investigation of; make an investigation on; make a survey of; search into; see into; survey;
調查報告 investigation report;
調查範圍 scope of investigation;
調查核實 verify through investigation;
調查情況 canvass the situation;
調查取證 obtain evidence through investigation;
調查提綱 outline for investigation;
調查團 commission; fact-finding mission;
調查研究 investigation and study;
調查員 investigator;
調查原因 investigate the cause;
調查者 investigator
調查組 investigation group;
調查罪行 investigate a crime;
暗中調查 conduct a quiet examination;
徹底調查 make a thorough investigation;
從事調查 undertake an investigation; pursue an investigation;
負責調查 in charge of the investigation;
根據仔細調查 according to careful investigation;
官方調查 official investigation;
廣泛調查 take a broad survey;
簡易調查 brief investigation;
結束調查 finish the inquiry;
經過仔細調查 on careful survey;
警方調查 police investigation;
進行調查 carry out a survey;
親自調查 make a personal inspection;
全面調查 full investigation;
深入調查 probe deeply into sth;
事故調查 accident investigation;
統計調查 statistical investigation;
推進調查 carry one's investigation forward;
系統調查 systematic investigation;
刑事調查 criminal investigation;
一項調查 a survey; an investigation;
有待調查 await investigation;
原因調查 causal investigation;
着手調查 institute a survey;
[調動] bring into play; call into play;
調動工作 be transferred to another post;
調動角色 shuffle the cards;
調動資金 mobilize financial resources;

要求調動 rrequest a transfer to another post;

[調度] (1) dispatch; (2) dispatcher; (3) control; manage; (4) scheduling;

調度室 control room;

調度有方 arrange and operate methodically; manage in the right way; skilfully arranged;

調度員 dispatcher;

~負載調度員 load dispatcher;

安全調度 security dispatching;

合理調度 rational management;

生產調度 production management; production scheduling;

順序調度 sequential scheduling;

作業調度 job scheduling;

[調虎離山] lure the tiger out of the mountains—to lure the enemy away from his base; make the tiger leave the mountain where it has entrenched itself—to make the opponent leave his advantageous position by strategem;

[調換] (1) change; exchange; swap; (2) conversion;

調換一下 swap round;

調換座位 exchange seats;

[調回] recall;

[調集] assemble; concentrate; muster;

調集兵力 assemble forces;

調集士兵 muster soldiers;

[調離] be ordered to leave; separate; transfer;

[調派] assign; dispatch; send; send out;

[調配] allocate; deploy;

調配軍隊 deploy an army;

調配勞動力 deploy manpower;

[調遣] assign; dispatch;

調遣軍隊 deploy an army;

調兵遣將 appoint commanders and deploy troops; deploy forces; dispose manpower; dispatch officers and men; maneuvre troops; move troops and dispatch generals;

靜候調遣 await quietly for the transfer of posts;

[調任] be transferred to another post;

[調入] call in;

[調頭] change direction; turn about; turn round;

調頭就跑 double back;

調個頭 end for end;

[調休] switch one's day off for a work day;

[調研] investigation and study;

調研員 investigator;

~助理調研員 assistant investigator;

調研組 investigating group;

[調轉] (1) change; switch; (2) transfer to another job;

[調子] melody; tune;

定調子 call the tune; set the tone;

改變調子 change one's tune; sing a different tune;

降低調子 play down one's tune;

哀調 plaintive melody;

悲調 mournful tune;

筆調 style; tone;

變調 (1) modified tone; (2) modulation; transposition;

步調 pace; step;

抽調 transfer;

詞調 tonal patterns and rhyme schemes of ci;

大調 major;

單調 dull; monotonous;

低調 low-key;

對調 exchange;

高調 high-sounding words; lofty tone;

格調 (1) style; (2) one's style of work;

基調 (1) fundamental key; main key; (2) keynote;

降調 falling tone;

借調 temporary transfer;

濫調 boring and unpractial words and views; hackneyed tune; worn-out theme;

老調 hackneyed theme; platitude; worn-out views;

冷調 cool colour tone; cool tone;

論調 argument; view;

腔調 (1) tune; (2) accent; intonation;

強調 emphasize; stress;

情調 emotional appeal; sentiment;

曲調 melody; tune of a song;

色調 hue; tone;

昇調 rising tone;

聲調 (1) tone; (2) tone of a Chinese character;

時調 popular song;

提調 dispatch;

外調 (1) transfer to other units; (2) carry out investigations in other units;

小調 (1) ditty; (2) minor;

選調 select and transfer;

移調 modulation; transposition;

音調 pitch;

影調 tone;
主調 homophony;
轉調 modulation; transposition;
字調 tones of Chinese characters;

die¹
die

【爹】 dad; daddy; father; pa;
[爹爹] dad; daddy; pa;
[爹娘] father and mother; ma and pa; mum and dad; parents;
呼爹叫娘 cry "mamma" in distress;
哭爹哭娘 yell inordinately;

阿爹 dad; daddy; father; pa; pap; papa;
俺爹 my father;
乾爹 one's foster father;
後爹 stepfather;

die²
die

【迭】 (1) change; (2) again and again;
[迭出] keep coming forth;
層見迭出 appear repeatedly; emerge in an endless stream; infinite changes; occur frequently;
層巒迭出 appear repeatedly; occur frequently;
[迭次] again and again; repeatedly; time and again;
迭次磋商 consult each other repeatedly;
[迭代] iteration;
反迭代 inverse iteration;
分式迭代 fractional iteration;
有限迭代 finite iteration;
[迭起] happen frequently; occur repeatedly;

更迭 alternate; change;

die
【昳】 setting sun;

die
【瓞】 small melon; unripe melon;

die
【眣】 squinting eyes;

die
【喋】 blah-blah; chatter; chirp; gibberish; incessant chattering; twitter;
[喋喋] talkative;
喋喋不休 blah-blah; chatter away; chatter like a magpie; chatter without stop; gabble on and on; gab; go nineteen to the dozen; keep clamouring; of many words; rattle away; rattle on; run nineteen to the dozen; run off at the mouth; run on; talk an arm off; talk endlessly about; talk nineteen to the dozen; talk one's head off; talk sb's arm off; talk sb's ear off;
~喋喋不休的人 chatterbox; chatterer; gasbag;
~喋喋不休地說 rattle on;
[喋血] bloodbath; bloodshed;
喋血沙場 bloodshed in battlefields;

die
【絰】 hemp hat worn in mourning for one's parents;

die
【耋】 in one's eighties;

die
【跌】 (1) fall; tumble; (2) drop;
[跌宕] (1) bold and unconstrained; free and easy; (2) flowing rhythm;
跌宕不羈 unrestrained and reckless;
[跌倒] fall; tip over; tumble;
跌倒摔傷 fall and hurt oneself;
跌倒在地 curl up on the ground;
時常跌倒 always tumbling over;
向後跌倒 fall back;
[跌份] cause yourself embarrassment; embarrass yourself;
[跌幅] range of decline;
[跌價] cut price; drop in price; fall in price; go down in price;
[跌交] (1) fall; stumble and fall; trip and fall; (2) make a mistake; meet with a setback;
[跌腳] stamp one's feet;
跌腳捶胸 stamp one's feet and beat one's breast in bitterness;
跌腳叫苦 stamp one's feet and cry out one's bitterness;
[跌落] drop; fall; go down; lapse;
[跌傷] fall and get hurt; get injured by a fall;
跌傷手臂 have a fall and hurt one's arm;
跌傷頭 fall and hurt one's head;
[跌水潭] plunge basin; plunge pool;
[跌撞] stumbling and bumping into things;
跌跌撞撞 dodder along; stagger along;

D

stumble along; totter;
前跌後撞 stagger from side to side;
[跌足] stamp one's foot;
跌足悔恨 stamp one's foot in regret;
跌足叫苦 stamp one's foot and cry out one's bitterness;
跌足歎息 stamp one's foot and sigh;

暴跌 have a steep fall; slump;
慘跌 collapse;
磋跌 slip down;
大跌 take a tumble; tumble;
回跌 fall;
看跌 be expected to fall;
撲跌 fall forward;
下跌 drop; fall; plummet; slide;
漲跌 price fluctuation;

die
【惵】 afraid; fearful; terrified;
[惵惵] afraid; fearful; terrified;
[惵息] holding breath in fear;

die
【牒】 (1) official document; (2) certificate; (3) record of family pedigree;
[牒籍] documents;
[牒文] official dispatch;
[牒狀] document pertaining to a lawsuit;

譜牒 family tree; genealogy;
通牒 diplomatic note;

die
【碟】 dish; plate;
[碟兒] dish; plate;
[碟子] saucer; small dish; small plate;

茶碟 saucer;
飛碟 frisbee;
轉碟 plate-spinning;

die
【蜨】 butterfly;

die
【蝶】 butterfly;
[蝶衣] wings of a butterfly;
[蝶泳] butterfly stroke;

蝴蝶 butterfly;

die
【諜】 (1) same as 喋; (2) espionage; spying;
[諜報] spy's report;
反諜報 counter-intelligence;
~反諜報活動 counter-intelligence;
[諜犬] setter;

間諜 secret agent; spy;

die
【蹀】 stamp one's feet;
[蹀蹀] walk in a mincing gait;
[蹀躞] (1) pace about; pace up and down; (2) walk in small steps;
[蹀足] stamp the feet;

躞蹀 (1) walk in small steps; (2) pace about;

die
【褶】 (1) riding clothes; (2) fold; pleated;
[褶裙] pleated skirt;

die
【鰈】 dab; sea dab; sole;

紅鰈 rusty dab;
黃蓋鰈 mud dab;
極光鰈 polar dab;
美首鰈 pole dab;
小頭油鰈 lemon dab;

die
【疊】 (1) pile up; repeat; (2) fold;
[疊詞] reduplicative;
疊詞法 hendiadys;
[疊韻] rhyming binomes;
[疊牀架屋] pile one bed on top of the other or build one house on top of the other—needless duplication;
[疊字] reduplication; reiterative locution;

層疊 stack; stack-up;
重疊 pile one on top of the other;
打疊 arrange things in order; get things ready;
堆疊 heap up; pile up;
一疊 a heap of; a pile of; a sheaf of; a wad of;
一厚疊 a wodge of;
折疊 fold;
摺疊 fold up; plait together;

ding¹
ding
【丁】 (1) man; (2) members of a family; population; (3) person engaged in a

certain occupation; (4) fourth of the ten Heavenly Stems; (5) fourth; (6) cube; small cubes of meat or vegetable; (7) a surname;

[丁財兩旺] be blessed with many sons and great wealth;

[丁點] a tiny bit;
丁點大的 little tiny; tiny little;

[丁香] lilac;
丁香花 lilac;
垂絲丁香 nodding lilac;
花葉丁香 Persian lilac;
華丁香 Chinese lilac;
毛丁香 hairy lilac;
羽葉丁香 pinnate lilac;
雜錦丁香 Chinese lilac;
紫丁香 lilac;
~一束紫丁香 a bunch of lilac;

[丁字] T-shaped;

白丁 common man; commoner; private;
兵丁 soldier;
布丁 pudding;
單丁 person without brothers; only son;
地丁 Chinese violet;
雞丁 diced chicken;
家丁 family servant;
拉丁 Latin;
門丁 doorman; gatekeeper;
尼古丁 nicotine;
切丁 cut into cubes; cut into dice;
親丁 blood relation; close relatives;
人丁 number of people in a family; population;
肉丁 diced meat;
添丁 have a baby;
園丁 gardener;
壯丁 able-bodied man;

ding
【仃】 lonely; solitary;

伶仃 left alone without help; lonely;

ding
【叮】 (1) bite; sting; (2) say or ask again to make sure;

[叮噹] clatter; ding-dong; fingle; ting-tang; tonk;
叮噹聲 clangour; clank;
~發出叮噹聲 clang; clank;
叮噹響 clink;
~發出叮噹響 clink;
滿瓶不響，半瓶叮噹 empty vessels make the greatest sound; empty vessels make the most noise; shallow streams make the greatest din; shallow water makes the greatest sound;

[叮嚀] exhort; repeatedly advise; urge again and again; warn;

[叮囑] exhort; repeatedly advise; urge again and again; warn;
千叮萬囑 exhort sb repeatedly; give advice repeatedly; give many exhortations to sb; warn again and again;
千叮嚀萬囑咐 enjoin repeatedly; exhort repeatedly;

ding
【玎】 jingling sound; tinkling sound;

[玎璫] clatter; ding-dong; jingle;

[玎玲] clink; jingle; tinkle;

ding
【盯】 fix one's eyes on; gaze at;

[盯梢] shadow sb; tail sb;

[盯着] fix one's eyes on; gaze at; glue one's eyes on; keep a close watch on; keep an eye on; stare at;
盯着點兒 keep an eye on;

[盯住] keep a close watch on;

ding
【町】 city block; street;

ding
【疔】 boil; carbuncle;

[疔瘡] malignant boil;

[疔毒] carbuncular infection;

ding
【釘】 (1) nail; (2) look steadily;

[釘問] question persistently;

[釘鞋釘] have a shoe nailed;

[釘掌兒] have a shoe soled and heeled;

[釘子] nail;
安釘子 drive in a nail; install a nail – put one's trusted followers in key positions;
拔釘子 pull out a nail;
拑釘子 pull out a nail;
碰釘子 be snubbed; bump one's head against a nail; get a flea in one's ear; get into trouble; get snubbed; get the bird; get the cheese; have one's offer turned down; meet rejection; meet

D

setbacks; meet with a rebuff; meet with failure; receive a serious rebuff; run into snags; run up against snags;
~自踫釘子 knock one's head against a brick;
~踫軟釘子 be tactfully rebuked; meet with a mild rebuff; meet with a polite refusal;
一顆釘子 a nail;

扒釘 cramp;
拔釘 pull out a nail;
補釘 darn; mend; patch;
釘鞋釘 have a shoe nailed;
揌釘 drawing pin;
扣釘 fastener;
螺釘 screw;
木釘 peg;
鐵釘 iron nail;
圖釘 drawing pin; thumbtack;
鞋釘 shoe nail;
眼中釘 a thorn in one's flesh;

[竹釘] bamboo peg;

ding
【靪】 (1) mend the soles of the shoes; (2) patchings;

ding³
ding
【酊】 drunk; intoxicated;

碘酊 tincture of iodine;
酩酊 dead drunk;

ding
【頂】 (1) crown; peak; (2) carry on the head; (3) butt; gore; (4) go against; (5) push from below or behind; push up; (6) retort; turn down; (7) cope with; stand up to; (8) substitute; take the place of; (9) equal; equivalent to; (10) best; the most;

[頂板] roof;
滑動頂板 sunroof;

[頂點] acme; apex; apogee; vertex; zenith;
初始頂點 initial vertex;
達到頂點 attain the zenith;
孤立頂點 isolated vertex;
角頂點 angular vertex;
升到頂點 top out;

[頂多] at best; at most; at the most;

[頂風] against the wind;
頂風而上 go against the wind;
頂風冒雪 brave blizzards; brave wind and snow; defy the wind and snow;
頂風冒雨 against the wind and rain; be undeterred by wind and rain; brave the storm; brave wind and rain; in spite of wind and rain;
頂風踏雪 brave cold winds and tread on snow;

[頂峰] apogee; crest; pinnacle; summit;
達到事業的頂峰 at the peak of one's career;
踏上頂峰 tread the summit;
征服頂峰 conquer the summit of a peak;

[頂缸] shoulder responsibilities in one's stead;
[頂呱呱] bang on; bang-up; excellent;
[頂換] replace;
[頂價] maximum price;
[頂尖] best; highest point; peak; top;
[頂抗] disobey; resist lawful orders;
[頂名] assume sb's name;
頂名冒姓 pass off sb's name as one's own; take the name of another person; use sb's name;

[頂牛儿] at loggerheads; clash;
[頂破天] at most;
[頂球] head; head the ball;
頂球入門 head in;
跳起頂球 head with a jump;

[頂少] at least;
[頂事] effective; serve the purpose; useful;
[頂替] replace; take sb's place; take the place of sb;
冒名頂替 take the name of another person;

[頂用] of help; of use; serve the purpose;
[頂障] ceiling;
無形頂障 glass ceiling;

[頂罩] canopy;
[頂職] replace a retiring parent;
[頂住] hold out against; stand up to; withstand;
頂住風浪 weather a storm;
頂住困難 stand up to difficulties;
頂住逆境 stand up against a desperate situation;
頂住壓力 withstand pressure;
頂住誘惑 withstand temptation;
頂得住 bear; endure; stand up to;

[頂撞] argue with; butt; contradict; rebut; talk back;
[頂嘴] answer back; backchat; backtalk; reply defiantly; talk back;
不許頂嘴 no backchat;
不住地頂嘴 keep answering back;

拔頂 (1) topping; (2) go bald;
朝頂 make a pilgrimage to a temple on a mountain;
車頂 car roof;
打頂 pinch;
到頂 reach the summit;
房頂 roof;
峰頂 crest; summit;
拱頂 vault;
灌頂 abhiseca;
極頂 zenith;
尖頂 tip; top;
絕頂 acme; extremely; peak; summit; utterly
帽頂 crown of a hat;
滅頂 be drowned;
沒頂 be drowned; submerge;
拿頂 stand on one's head;
篷頂 top of a tent;
坡頂 brow of a hill;
氣頂 gas cap; petrol cap;
墻頂 top of a wall;
穹頂 dome;
山頂 hilltop; mountain top; peak of a mountain; summit of a mountain;
樹頂 treetop;
塔頂 top of a pagoda;
天頂 zenith;
頭頂 top of the head;
透頂 through and through;
禿頂 bald; bald at the top of the head; bald-headed; become bald;slaphead;
屋頂 housetop; roof;
歇頂 balding; get a bit thin on top; get bald as one gets older;
秃頂 bald head; baldheaded;
圓頂 dome;
崖頂 clifftop;
雲頂 cloud top;
帳頂 top of a mosquito net;
柱頂 top part of a pillar;

ding

【鼎】 ancient cooking vessel with two loop handles and three or four legs;
[鼎沸] boiling; like a seething caldron—noisy and confused;
[鼎革] change of dynasty;
[鼎力] your kind effort;
鼎力扶持 use one's great strength to support;
鼎力相助 sb's good offices; through the good offices of sb;
鼎力玉成 help accomplish this small task with your great power;
鼎力支持 powerful support;
[鼎立] tripartite confrontation;
鼎立而三 form a trilogy with the other two;
三足鼎立 stand like the three legs of a tripod; tripartite confrontation;
[鼎盛] at the height of power and splendours; in a period of great prosperity;
鼎盛時期 a period of great prosperity; at the height of power and splendour; heyday;
[鼎新] innovate;
鼎新革故 discard the old ways of life in favour of the new; drop old habits and reform; establish the new and abolish the old;
[鼎言] weighty advice;
[鼎足] three legs of a tripod;
鼎足而立 a tripartite balance of forces;
鼎足而三 a situation dominated by three powerful rivals;
鼎足三分 a division into three parts;
鼎足之勢 a situation dominated by three powerful rivals;

遷鼎 transport the sacrificial tripod — the change of dynasty;
問鼎 inquire about the bronze tripod — covert the throne;

ding⁴ ding

【定】 (1) calm; stable; (2) decide; fix; set; (3) established; fixed; settled; (4) book; subscribe to; (5) certainly; definitely; surely;
[定案] decide on a verdict; pass a verdict; reach a conclusion on a case;
[定本] definitive edition;
[定比] fixed proportion;
定比分析 fixed proportion analysis;

[定編] establish a table of organization;
[定單] order;
下定單 place an order;
[定點] (1) fixed point; (2) fixed place; (3) fix;
定點廠家 specially-designated factory;
定點企業 specially-designated enterprise;
[定都] establish a capital;
[定奪] decide; make a final decision;
[定額] quota;
定額包幹制 system of quota and contract for fixed output;
定額管理 quota management;
定額投資基金 closed-end investment fund;
超額完成定額 overfulfill the quota;
分配定額 allot a quota; assign a quota;
勞動定額 work quota;
生產定額 production quota;
削減定額 cut a quota;
完成定額 fulfill the quota;
未完成定額 fail to fill the quota;
增加定額 add a quota;
[定稿] (1) finalize a manuscript; (2) final text;
[定購] order; place an order for; purchase by order;
歡迎定購 orders are welcome;
[定婚] be betrothed; be engaged;
慶祝定婚 celebrate one's engagement;
宣布定婚 announce one's engagement;
[定貨] place an order for goods; order goods;
定貨單 order;
~大批的定貨單 a spate of orders;
長期定貨 place standing orders;
國內定貨 domestic order;
國外定貨 foreign order;
獲得定貨 obtain orders for goods;
繼續定貨 renew an order;
交付定貨 execute orders; fill orders;
接受定貨 accept orders; take orders;
緊急定貨 urgent order;
取定貨 collect one's order;
取消定貨 cancel an order; rescind an order;
期交定貨 an order for future delivery;
生產定貨 put the order into work;
試用定貨 trial order;
送定貨 deliver orders;
早定貨 place one's order early;
[定級] establish grades;
[定價] (1) fix a price; pricing; set a price; (2) fixed price; list price;
定價策略 pricing strategy;
定價過高 overpriced;
按質定價 the price based on quality; the price of a product according to its quality;
串通定價 fix prices with one another;
公平定價 arm's length pricing;
模仿定價 imitative pricing;
人為定價 arbitrary pricing;
[定金] deposit;
付定金 pay a deposit;
[定居] cast anchor; drop anchor; put down roots; settle down; take up residence;
定居國外 live abroad;
定居鄉下 fix one's residence in the country;
[定局] (1) foregone conclusion; finality; inevitable outcome; (2) make a final decision; settle finally;
已成定局 a foregone conclusion; the die is cast; the die is thrown;
已成定局的 cut and dried;
[定理] theorem;
加法定理 addition theorem;
面積定理 area theorem;
平均值定理 average value theorem;
[定量] quantitative;
定量分析 quantitative analysis;
~定量分析法 quantitative analysis;
定量計算法 quantitative calculation;
定量社會學 quantitative sociology;
定量預測 quantitative analysis forecasting;
[定律] law;
拆射定律 law of refraction;
反射定律 law of reflection;
反作用定律 action-reaction law;
一條定律 a law;
[定論] final conclusion; final verdict;
[定評] accepted opinion; critical recognition; public acknowledgement;
[定期] (1) fix a date; set a date; (2) at regular intervals; periodical; regular;
定期儲蓄 fixed deposit; time deposit;
定期存款 fixed deposit; time deposit;
定期交貨 delivery at term;
定期貸款 fixed loan;
[定錢] deposit;
給定錢 give a deposit;
[定神] (1) collect oneself; compose oneself;

pull oneself together; (2) collect one's thoughts; concentrate one's attention; take a grip on oneself;
定定神 get one's act together;

[定時] at regular time; fixed time; timing;
定時分析 timing analysis;
定時器 timer;
~電定時器 electric timer;
~電子定時器 electronic timer;
~控制定時器 control timer;
~字母定時器 character timer;
標準定時 standard timing;
解碼器定時 decoder timing;

[定位] (1) localization; orientate; position; (2) fix; fix a position;
定位編輯 in-place editing;
定位控制 positioning control;
定位器 localizer; locator; positioner;
~比相定位器 phase localizer;
~磁頭定位器 head positioner;
~風力定位器 pneudyne positioner;
~晶片定位器 chip positioner;
~羅盤定位器 compass locator;
~熱軸定位器 hotbox locator;
~圖形定位器 pattern positioner;
~微波定位器 microwave system localizer;
定位球 place kick;
定位踢 place kick;
粗調定位 coarse positioning;
動力定位 dynamic positioning;
分角定位 split fix;
激光定位 laser positioning;
絕對定位 absolute fix;
雷達定位 radar fix;
目測定位 visual fix;
市場定位 market niche; market positioning;
雙耳定位 binaural localization;
順向定位 clockwise orientation;
天文定位 celestial fix;
外定位 outside orientation;
細胞定位 cellular localization;
自動定位 automatic positioning;

[定下] fix; set;
定下決心 be determined to do sth; make up one's mind; resolute;

[定向] bearing; clearly determined goal; directional; orientation; predetermined orientation;
定向分配 fixed direction allocation;
定向培養 directional training; fixed direction training;
定向天線 directive aerial;
定向運動 orienteering;
定向招生 directional recruitment of students;
解析定向 analytical orientation;
絕對定向 absolute orientation;
聲定向 acoustic bearing;
自我定向 ego orientation;

[定心丸] set one's mind at rest; sth capable of setting one's mind at ease; sth that soothes one's nerves;

[定型] finalize the design; stereotype; take shape;
定型產品 approved product;
定型測驗 type test;
動力定型 dynamic stereotype;

[定性] (1) determine the nature of an offence; (2) determine the chemical composition of a substance; (3) qualitative;
定性分析 qualitative analysis;
定性控制系統 qualitative control system;
定性預測 qualitative analysis forecasting;

[定義] define; definition;
定義詞匯 defining vocabulary;
不變定義 invariant definition;
操作性定義 operational definition;
成分定義 componential definition;
功能定義 functional definition;
歸納定義 inductive definition;
名詞性定義 nominal definition;
內涵定義 connotative definition;
實物定義 ostensive definition;
特徵定義 characterizing definition;
下定義 define; determine a definition; give a definition;

[定音] set the tone;
定音鼓 kettledrum; timpani;
一錘定音 set the tune with one beat of the gong – give the final word;

[定影] fixing;
定影液 fixer; fixing bath;

[定語] attribute;
定語的 attributive;
定語附加語 attributive adjunct;
定語形容詞 attributive adjective;
後置定語 post-attribute;

[定於] due to; scheduled to;

［定責］ stipulate responsibility;
［定制］ customized;
定制控制庫 custom control library;
定制貿易 tailored trade;
［定子］ stator;
定子電樞 stator armature;
活轉定子 freewheeling stator;
內定子 inner stator;
三相定子 three-phase stator;
［定罪］ convict sb for a crime; declare sb guilty;
安定 (1) quiet and in order; settled; stable; steadfast; unchanging; (2) reassure; stablize;
必定 (1) certainly; surely; (2) bound to; sure to;
標定 demarcate;
不定 (1) indefinite; indeterminate; (2) drifting; fitful; unsteady;
裁定 adjudicate; rule;
測定 measurement;
禪定 deep deditation; dhyana;
滴定 titration;
奠定 establish; make firm; settle;
斷定 decide; form a judgment;
額定 fixed; rated;
法定 legal; statutory;
否定 deny; negate;
搞定 it's settled.
更定 revise;
固定 fix; fixed; regular; regularize;
規定 formulate; regulate; regulations; rules; stipulate; stipulations;
核定 appraise and decide; check and ratify;
劃定 delimit;
既定 established; fixed; set;
假定 assume; hypothesis; presume; suppose;
堅定 firm; staunch; steadfast; strengthen;
檢定 appraise; verify;
鑒定 appraisal; appraise; identify;
界定 delimit;
決定 (1) decide; make up one's mind; resolve; (2) decision; determine; resolution;
肯定 absolute; affirm; approve; as one lives and breathes; as sure as death; as sure as eggs is eggs; as sure as fate; as sure as God made little green apples; as sure as hell; as sure as I'm standing here; as sure as you live; ascertain; certain; confident; confirm; definite; for sure; guarantee; in the affirmative; make sure; positive; sure; swear; with absolute certainty;
釐定 collate and stipulate;
立定 halt;
買定 settle a purchase;
命定 be determined by fate; be predestined;
拿定 make up one's mind;
內定 cut and dried; decide at the higher level but not officially annouced;
擬定 (1) draft; work out; (2) conjecture;
判定 decide; determine; judge;
平定 calm down; put down; suppress;
評定 appraise; assess; evaluate; pass judgement on;
前定 decided beforehand; predestined;
敲定 bang the hammer to decide; come to an agreement; fix; get down to a decision; make a final decision;
欽定 be authorized by an emperor;
確定 define; determine; fix;
認定 (1) definitely hold; firmly believe; (2) set one's mind on;
入定 enter into meditation by tranquilizing the body, mouth and mind;
商定 agree on; decide through consultation;
設定 set;
審定 check and decide; examine and approve;
説定 agree on; settle;
鎖定 lock; lock in; locking;
特定 (1) specially designated; (2) given; specific;
天定 be fixed by heaven; predestined; predetermined; preordained;
鐵定 ironclad; fixed;
推定 deduce; infer;
未定 uncertain; undecided; undefined; unfixed;
穩定 stable; stablilize; steady;
習定 enter into meditation and get rid of desires;
限定 limit; restrict;
協定 accord; agreement; reach an agreement on sth;
選定 choose and decide;
押定 sign an agreement;
咬定 insist;
一定 (1) fixed; regular; specified; (2) certain; given; particular; (3) bound to; certainly; must; surely; necessarily; (4) due; fair; proper;
已定 already fixed; already settled;
議定 arrive at a decision after discussion;
預定 fix in advance; predetermine;
約定 agree on; appoint;
站定 stand still;
暫定 arrange for the time being; tentative;
鎮定 calm; composed; cool;

指定 appoint; assign;
制定 draft; draw up; formulate; work out;
注定 be destined; be doomed;
註定 destined; doomed; predestined;
準定 definitely;
酌定 decide according to one's judgment;
坐定 be seated; take a seat;

ding
【訂】 (1) conclude; draw up; (2) book; subscribe to; (3) make corrections; (4) staple together;
［訂單］ indent; order;
長期訂單 standing order;
大宗訂單 bulk order;
接受訂單 accept an order;
確認訂單 confirm an order;
特定訂單 specific indent;
～非特定訂單 open indent;
郵購訂單 mail an order;
［訂費］ subscription;
支付訂費 pay one's subscription;
［訂購］ book; engage; order; place an order for; reserve; send for; send in orders for; speak for; subscribe for; subscribe to; take in; take;
［訂戶］ subscriber;
［訂婚］ be betrothed to; be engaged to sb; become betrothed to; betroth oneself to; engage; enter into betrothal; give one's hand to sb; plight; plight oneself to sb; promise to marry; reach an agreement to marry sb;
［訂貨］ order goods; place an order for goods;
訂貨成本 ordering cost;
訂貨合同 order contract;
訂貨記錄簿 order book;
［訂交］ become friends; form a friendship;
［訂立］ conclude; make;
［訂票］ book tickets;
訂票手續費 service fee for booking tickets;
訂票系統 reservation system;
［訂位］ booking; reservation;
［訂約］ conclude a bargain; conclude an agreement; engage; enter into an agreement;
［訂閱］ subscribe to a publication;
訂閱部 subscription department;
訂閱雜誌 take subscriptions for magazines;
繼續訂閱 renew one's subscription to…;
［訂正］ correct; make corrections; revise;
訂正印刷錯誤 correct errors in printing;
［訂製］ customize;
可訂製［的］ customizable;
［訂座］ make a reservation; reservation;
［訂做］ customize;
可訂做［的］ customizable;

編訂 compile and revise; edit and revise;
改訂 reformulate; revise;
校訂 check against the authoritative text;
考訂 do textual research; examine and correct;
擬訂 draft; draw up;
簽訂 conclude and sign;
刪訂 revise;
審訂 examine and revise;
修訂 reformulate; revise;
續訂 renew one's subscription;
議訂 negotiate;
預訂 book; place an order in advance; subscribe;
增訂 revise and enlarge;
制訂 formulate; work out; work up;
製訂 draw up; evolve; formulate; map out; work out;
裝訂 bind;
纂訂 collect and revise;

ding
【釘】 fasten with nails;
［釘書機］ stapler;
［釘死］ (1) nail securely; (2) crucify; nail to death;
［釘住］ nail securely;

ding
【飣】 (1) food items for display purposes only; (2) flowery language without substance;

ding
【碇】 anchor;
［碇泊］ moor;

起碇 set sail; weigh anchor;

ding
【錠】 (1) a kind of ancient utensil; (2) ingot of gold; (3) spindle; (4) tablet;

鋼錠 steel ingot;
紗錠 spindle;

D

銅錠 copper ingot;
銀錠 silver ingot;
鑄錠 ingot casting;

diu¹
diu

【丟】 (1) lose; mislay; (2) cast; throw; (3) lay aside; put aside;
[丟醜] be disgraced; lose face; make an exhibition of oneself;
怕丟醜 afraid of falling flat on one's face;
當眾丟醜 be disgraced in public;
給自己丟醜 disgrace oneself;
[丟掉] (1) lose; (2) cast away; discard; throw away;
丟掉幻想 cast away illusion;
丟掉壞習慣 drop a bad habit;
丟掉偏見 cast off prejudice;
丟掉偽裝 throw off one's disguise;
[丟份] disgraceful; embarrass oneself; lose face;
[丟開] forget for a while; leave it off;
[丟了] lose;
丟了肥肉啃骨頭 throw away the meat to gnaw the bone;
[丟臉] be disgraced; be humiliated; bring disgrace to; bring shame on oneself; lose face; loss of face;
[丟棄] abandon; discard; give up;
丟棄舊衣服 cast aside the old clothes;
[丟人] be disgraced; lose face;
丟人現眼 a disgrace; make a fool of oneself; make a spectacle of oneself;
[丟失] lose;
[丟手] give up; wash one's hands of;
丟不開手 cannot keep one's hands off;
[丟下] lay aside; leave behind; throw down;

diu

【銩】 thulium;

dong¹
dong

【冬】 (1) winter; (2) rat-tat; (3) (of mahjong) winter;
[冬菜] preserved, dried cabbage;
[冬…春…] winter and spring;
冬盡春初 the winter is over and the spring has come;
冬去春來 spring follows winter; spring succeeds winter; winter gives place to spring;
冬行春令 springlike winter; very mild winter;
今冬明春 this winter and next spring;
[冬耕] winter ploughing
[冬菇] dried mushroom;
[冬瓜] wax gourd; white gourd;
[冬烘] shallow but pedantic;
[冬季] winter; wintertime;
冬季運動 winter sport;
[冬令] (1) winter; (2) winter climate;
[冬眠] hibernate; hibernation; winter sleep;
冬眠場所 hibernaculum;
[冬日] winter sun; wintry day;
冬日可愛 man of kindness; the lovely sun in winter;
一個冬日 a wintry day;
[冬筍] winter bamboo shoot;
[冬天] winter; wintertime;
冬天吃冰棍一心都涼了 eating ice lolly in winter – the heart feels stone cold;
冬天吃葡萄一寒酸 eating grapes in winter – cold and sour; miserable and shabby;
冬天的大蔥一葉黃根枯心不死 a green onion in midwinter – its heart does not die with its leaves and roots (metaphorically, not dropping the idea forever);
乾冷的冬天 crisp winter;
核冬天 nuclear winter;
活過冬天 survive the winter;
暖和的冬天 open winter;
溫暖的冬天 warm winter;
嚴酷的冬天 severe winter;
陰冷的冬天 bleak winter;
[冬夏] winter and summer;
冬不借衣，夏不借扇 do not borrow from a friend things that are essential for his own well-being;
冬蟲夏草 Chinese caterpillar tungus;
冬暖夏涼 fairly mild in winter and rather cool in summer; warm in winter and cool in summer;
無冬無夏 all the year round; be it winter or summer – throughout the year; regardless of winter or summer;
[冬泳] winter swimming;
[冬至] Winter Solstice;
冬至點 winter solstice
[冬裝] winter clothes; winter dress;

殘冬 last days of winter;
初冬 early winter;
過冬 hibernate; overwinter; pass the winter; winter;
季冬 last month of winter;
款冬 coltsfoot;
立冬 Beginning of Winter;
隆冬 in the depths of winter; in the middle of the winter; midwinter; the depth of winter;
窮冬 midwinter; the depth of winter;
秋冬 autumn and winter;
忍冬 honeysuckle;
盛冬 midwinter;
夏冬 summer and winter;
嚴冬 brutal winter; severe winter;
一冬 one winter season;
越冬 live through the winter;
仲冬 second month of winter;

dong

【咚】 sound of impact caused by a falling object;

咕咚 splash; thud;

dong

【東】 (1) east; (2) master; owner; (3) host;

［東北］ (1) north-east; (2) north-east China;

［東邊］ east side;

［東牀］ one's son-in-law;
東牀快婿 one's son-in-law;
坦腹東牀 worthy son-in-law of sb;

［東道］ host;
東道國 host country;
做東道 play the host; stand treat;

［東方］ (1) east; (2) the East; the Orient; (3) a surname;
東方大白 it is bright on the eastern horizon;
東方發白 a pearly white appeared on the eastern horizon;
東方破曉 dawn breaks; dawn is breaking in the east;
東方文化 oriental culture;
東方語言 Oriental languages;
東方欲曉 dawn is breaking; soon dawn will break in the east; the east is growing light;

［東風］ (1) east wind; (2) (of mahjong) east wind;
東風帶 easterlies;
~赤道東風帶 equatorial easterlies;
~極地東風帶 polar easterlies;
~熱帶東風帶 tropical easterlies;
副熱帶東風帶 subtropical easterlies;
~深東風帶 deep easterlies;
東風過耳 go in at one ear and out at the other;
東風解凍 the eastern wind clears the cold;
東風勁吹 the east wind is blowing strong;
東風圈 (of mahjong) the east wind round;
馬耳東風 in at one ear and out at the other; pay no attention to what one says; take no heed to;

［東家］ boss; master;
少東家 young boss; young master;

［東流］ eastward-flowing streams;
付諸東流 bury in oblivion; cast to the winds; give up as impracticable; go down the plughole; go to the wall; go to the winds; go to waste; gone with the eastward-flowing streams; gone with the wind; irrevocably lost; leave a matter to chance;
滾滾東流 roll to the east;
黃河東流 the Yellow River flows east;
盡付東流 bury in oblivion; cast all to the winds; leave all to chance; all gone with the eastward stream — all in vain;
一江春水向東流 a river of spring water rolling towards the east;

［東面］ (1) east; eastern; (2) face east;
東面而坐 sit facing the east;

［東南］ south-east;
東南西北 everywhere; north, south, east, and west; on all sides;
南金東箭 the gold of the south and the arrow of the east — good talent;

［東施效顰］ copy others blindly and make oneself look foolish; crude imitation; imitate awkwardly; imitate others and make oneself foolish and ridiculous; imitate sb in certain particulars; play the sedulous ape; take a leaf out of sb's book;

［東屋］ east wing;

［東西］ (1) east and west; (2) from east to west; (3) commodity; goods; things;
東西南北 the four corners of the world;
搬東西 move things;
~東搬西搬虧了一半 a rolling stone gathers no moss;

吃東西 eat food; eat sth;
不想吃東西 not feel like eating;
~不想吃東西 go off one's food; off one's food;
東湊西補 make up deficiency by funds from elsewhere;
東倒西歪 be knocked over like ninepins; fall over like ninepins; lean crazily in all directions; waver east and west; lying on all sides; tumble down;
東扶西倒 brace up one while the other tumble down; difficult to cultivate plants;
東遛西逛 wander here and there;
東跑西竄 fool around; fool about;
東跑西顛 keep on the run; run about busily; run hither and thither;
東跑西蹓 gad about; gad around;
東瞧西望 gaze this way and that; stare about; watch out furtively to the east and west;
東嗅西聞 smell round;
好東西 good things;
~不是好東西 bad news;
壞東西 bastard; rogue; scoundrel;
借東補西 borrow from one person to pay another; cut out one piece to mend another; make up a deficiency by getting funds from elsewhere; pay off one debt by making another; rob one's belly to cover one's back; rob Peter to pay Paul; take from one person to pay another;
老東西 codger; old creature; old man;
買東西 do the shopping;
~去買東西 go shopping;
難看的東西 eyesore;
挪東補西 rob one's belly to cover one's back; rob Peter to pay Paul;
聲東擊西 feint and pretend to go east while attacking from the west; look one way and row another; make a feint to the east but attack in the west; pretend to aim at one target while shooting at another;
說東道西 chat of everything under the sun; chatter away on a variety of things; gossip; make all kinds of remarks; talk about all sorts of subjects without restraint; talk about this and that;
挑東西 carry sth on the shoulder;
偷東西 steal things;
問東問西 ask all sorts of questions;
無用的東西 dud; sth useless;
小東西 little thing;
~可憐的小東西 poor little thing;
形形色色的東西 this and that; this, that, and the other;
一包東西 a parcel;
一東一西 one east, one west; poles apart;
移東補西 pay off one debt by making another; pull down a wall in the east and use its bricks to build a wall in the west — make up a deficiency by funds from elsewhere; rob Peter to pay Paul; take from one person to pay another;
移東就西 make up a deficit in one place with a surplus from somewhere else;
有好有壞的東西 curate's egg;
髒東西 dirty thing;
摘東補西 borrow from one person to pay another; rob Peter to pay Paul; take sth from one to make up sth else;
這類東西 this kind of thing; this type of thing;
徵東徂西 attack in the east, but march west; strategic feint;
指東打西，指南打北 hit on every side; point east and strike west, point south and strike north;
指東話西 irrelevant; mislead with talk; point to east and west; talk nonsense;
指東擊西 aim at the east and hit the west; point to the east and strike the west — make a feint;
指東說西 make a concealed reference to sth; make insinuations;

[東行] eastbound;

挨東 in an easterly direction;
財東 (1) shop owner; (2) moneybags;
船東 shipowner;
店東 hotel manger; shop owner;
房東 landlord or landlady;
股東 shareholder; stockholder;
關東 northeast of China; east of Shanhaiguan;
少東 son of the master;
作東 stand treat;
做東 play the host; stand treat;

dong
【蝀】 rainbow;

dong

【鼕】 beating of a drum;

dong³
dong

【董】 (1) direct; superintend; (2) director; trustee; (3) a surname;
[董事] director; trustee;
董事會 board of directors; board of trustees; directorate;
~電視公司董事會 television directorate;
~聯合董事會 interlocking directorate;
董事長 chairman of the board;
~副董事長 vice director general;
董事職位 directorship;
董事總經理 managing director;
非執行董事 non-executive director;
女董事 directress;
執行董事 executive director;

古董 (1) antique; curio; (2) old fogey;
校董 member of the board of trustees of a college;

dong

【懂】 know; understand;
[懂得] grasp; know; understand;
[懂行] know the business;
[懂事] intelligent; reasonable; sensible;

懵懂 ignorant; muddled;

dong⁴
dong

【恫】 fear;
[恫嚇] browbeat; frighten; intimidate; scare; threaten;
不怕恫嚇 defy any threat;
武力恫嚇 sabre-rattling;
[恫疑虛喝] threaten loudly;

dong

【洞】 (1) cavity; hole; (2) penetratingly; thoroughly;
[洞察] discern; examine thoroughly; have an insight into; have penetrating insight; see clearly; see through clearly;
洞察力 clairvoyance;
洞察民情 know the popular feeling thoroughly;
洞察情勢 make a thorough investigation of the circumstances;
洞察是非 see clearly the rights and wrongs of the case;
洞察未來 see into the future;
洞察一切 have a deep insight into matters;
洞察輿情 know the public sentiment well;
[洞穿] (1) pierce; (2) comprehend; see through;
[洞達] understand thoroughly;
洞達事理 penetrating mind that grasps ideas; sensible;
[洞房] bridal chamber; nuptial chamber;
洞房花燭 wedding; wedding festivities;
[洞畫] cave painting;
[洞見] see very clearly;
洞見症結 discern clearly the crucial reason; get to the heart of the problem; see clearly the crux of the matter;
[洞口] entrance to a cave;
[洞窟] cavern;
[洞悉] know clearly; understand thoroughly;
洞悉底蘊 know the details; know the ropes;
洞悉無遺 be perfectly acquainted with; have thorough knowledge of; see and know completely; understand thoroughly;
洞悉原委 know clearly the whole story; understand thoroughly all the details;
[洞獅] cave lion;
[洞曉] have a clear knowledge of; know sth thoroughly;
[洞熊] cave bear;
[洞穴] burrow; cave; cavern;
洞穴備狗 cave hyaena;
洞穴探察 caving;
大洞穴 cavern;
~像大洞穴[的] cavernous;
小洞穴 grotto;

齒洞 cavity in a tooth;
窗洞 opening in a wall;
吹風洞 blowing cave;
地洞 hole in the ground; burrow;
風洞 wind tunnel;
涵洞 culvert;
黑洞 black hole;
呼吸洞 breathing cave;
炕洞 flue;
空洞 (1) cavity; void; (2) devoid of content; empty; hollow; vague and general; (3) hollow;
孔洞 opening in a utensil;

漏洞 (1) leak; (2) flaw; hole; loophole;
迷洞 maze cave;
橋洞 hole in a bridge;
球洞 hole;
溶洞 karst cave;
山洞 cave; cavern;
石洞 stone cave;
樹洞 tree hole;
挖洞 make a cave; make a hole;
無底洞 bottomless pit;
小洞 small leak;
岩洞 grotto;
巖洞 mountain cave;
窰洞 (1) cave dwelling; (2) opening of a kiln;
鑿洞 bore a hole; drill a hole;
蛀洞 cavity;
鑽狗洞 do evil; lead a wicked life; toady to the rich;

D

dong
【凍】 (1) freeze; (2) jelly; (3) feel very cold; freeze;

[凍冰] freeze;
[凍瘡] chilblain; frostbite; perniosis;
凍瘡紅斑 erythema pernio; suppurating frostbite;
凍瘡焦痂 eschar frostbite;
深部凍瘡 deep frostbite;
[凍結] freeze; freezing;
凍結機 freezer;
~帶式凍結機 conveyor freezer;
~接觸式凍結機 contact freezer;
~平板凍結機 plate freezer;
凍結間 freezer;
~鼓風凍結間 air-blast freezer;
~小型凍結間 walk-in freezer;
凍結器 freezer;
~柜式凍結器 cabinet freezer;
~間歇式凍結器 batch-type freezer;
~鹽水凍結器 brine freezer;
表面凍結 crust freezing;
工資凍結 wage freeze;
價格凍結 price freeze;
空氣凍結 air freezing;
普通凍結 bulk freezing;
[凍餒] cold and hunger;
凍餒而死 perish from cold and hunger;
凍餒交加 cold and hungry;
凍餒之苦 the sufferings of cold and hunger;
[凍死] die of frost; freeze and perish; freeze to death;
[凍源] tundra;
北極凍源 arctic tundra;
高山凍源 alpine tundra;
灌木凍源 fruticous tundra;
石蕊凍源 cladonia tundra;
[凍着] have a cold;

挨凍 be frostbitten; be frozen; suffer from cold;
氨冷凍 ammonia cooling;
冰凍 freeze;
春凍 spring frost;
防凍 prevent from frostbite;
果凍 jelly;
雞凍 chicken jelly;
解凍 (1) thaw; unfreeze; (2) unfreeze;
開凍 thaw;
冷凍 freeze;
凝凍 freeze;
肉凍 jelly; meat jelly;
上凍 get frozen; freeze;
受凍 suffer from cold;
速凍 quick-frozen;
霜凍 frost;

dong
【胴】 (1) large intestine; (2) body; carcass; trunk;

[胴體] body; carcass; trunk;
病畜胴體 diseased carcass;
分割胴體 dressed carcass;
四開胴體 quarter carcass;
小牛胴體 calf carcass; veal carcass;

dong
【動】 (1) move; stir; (2) act; get moving; (3) alter; change; (4) use; (5) arouse; touch; (6) eat or drink;

[動筆] put pen to paper; set pen to paper; start writing; take up the pen;
[動賓] verb and object;
動賓結構 verb-object construction;
動賓式合成詞 verb-object compound;
[動不動] at every move; at every turn; at the drop of a hat; at the slightest provocation; easily; on every occasion;
動不動就發脾氣 apt to lose one's temper;
[動詞] verb;
動詞重疊 reduplication of a verb;
動詞詞幹 verb stem;
動詞詞組 verb group;
動詞短語 verb phrase;

~ 定式動詞短語 finite verb phrase;
~ 非定式動詞短語 non-finite verb phrase;
動詞後綴 verbal suffix;
動詞化名詞 verbal noun;
動詞前綴 verbal prefix;
動詞謂語 verbal predicate;
動詞形容詞 verbal adjective;
動詞形式 form of a verb;
動詞原形 root form of a verb;
表意動詞 notional verb;
並列動詞 coordinator;
~ 準並列動詞 quasi-coordinator;
不定式動詞 infinitive verb;
不規則動詞 anomalous verb;
不完全動詞 incomplete verb;
操作動詞 operative verb;
陳述動詞 indicative verb;
抽象動詞 abstract verb;
詞匯動詞 lexical verb;
從屬動詞 subordinate verb;
代動詞 pro-verb;
單詞動詞 single-word verb;
等同動詞 equative verb;
定式動詞 finite verb;
~ 非定式動詞 non-finite verb;
動態動詞 dynamic verb;
短語動詞 phrasal verb;
~ 及物短語動詞 transitive phrasal verb;
多詞動詞 multi-word verb;
反覆性動詞 iterative verb;
反身動詞 reflexive verb;
複合動詞 compound verb;
~ 可分複合動詞 separable compound verb;
感覺動詞 verb of feeling;
感情動詞 verb of emotion;
感知動詞 verb of sensation;
關係動詞 relational verb;
規則動詞 regular verb;
~ 不規則動詞 irregular verb;
過程動詞 process verb;
及物動詞 transitive verb;
~ 不及物動詞 intransitive verb;
~ 合成及物動詞 complex transitive verb;
簡單動詞 simple verb;
介詞動詞 prepositional verb;
界限動詞 terminative verb;
~ 非界限動詞 non-terminative verb;
靜態動詞 static verb;
可分等動詞 gradable verb;
連繫動詞 linking verb;
~ 結果連繫動詞 result linking verb;
領動詞 superordinate verb;
描述動詞 descriptive verb;
片語動詞 phrasal verb;
普通動詞 ordinary verb;
起始動詞 inchoative verb;
強式動詞 strong verb;
情態動詞 modal auxiliary; modal verb;
~ 連接性情態動詞 connective modal;
趨向動詞 directional verb;
施事動詞 agentive verb;
雙體性動詞 binary verb;
特殊動詞 anomalous verb;
限定動詞 finite verb;
~ 非限定動詞 non-finite verb;
~ 合成限定動詞 complex finite verb;
主動動詞 active verb;
助動詞 auxiliary verb;
~ 被動助動詞 passive auxiliary verb;
~ 進行體助動詞 progressive auxiliary;
~ 情態助動詞 modal auxiliary;

[動盪] in a flux; turbulence; unrest; unstable; upheaval;
動盪不安 in turmoil; turbulence and intranquility; volative;
動盪不定 in a flux; unrest; unstable;
~ 動盪不定的政治局勢 volatile political situation;
動盪不穩 shaky and unstable;
大動盪 crash;
日益動盪 growing unrest;
社會動盪 social unrest;
一次動盪 a disturbance;
引起動盪 cause a commotion;
政治動盪 political unrest;

[動工] begin construction; start building;

[動畫] animation;
動畫家 animator;
動畫片 animated film;
~ 動畫片畫家 animator;
~ 一部動畫片 an animated film;

[動火] flare up; get angry; lose one's temper;

[動機] motivation; motive; intention;
動機卑鄙 one's motives are base;
動機不純 have impure motives;
成就動機 achievement motivation;
方便動機 convenience motive;
工具動機 instrumental motivation;
經濟動機 economic motivation;
利他動機 altruistic motive;
社會動機 social motive;
私利動機 interested motive;

消費動機 consumer motivation;
學習動機 academic motivation; scholastic motivation;
主要動機 chief motive;
資產動機 asset motive;
作案動機 motive for committing a crime;

[動靜] (1) sound of sth astir; (2) activities; conditions; events; happenings; movements;
百動不如一靜 keeping still is more effective than taking action;
發現可疑動靜 spot sth suspicious;
觀察動靜 watch what is going on;
久靜思動 grow weary of being quiet for a long time;

[動力] dynamic power; motive power;
動力單元 power unit;
動力工業 power industry;
動力論 dynamism;
~動力論者 dynamist;
動力學 dynamics; kinetics;
~電極動力學 electrode kinetics;
~腐蝕動力學 corrosion kinetics;
~化學動力學 chemical kinetics;
~解析動力學 analytical dynamics;
~空氣動力學 aerodynamics;
空氣動力學家 aerodynamicist;
飛機空氣動力學 aeroplane aerodynamics;
高速空氣動力學 high-speed aerodynamics;
理想空氣動力學 ideal aerodynamics;
~流體動力學 fluid kinetics; hydrodynamics;
~氣壓動力學 barodynamics; gas kinetics;
~生物動力學 biodynamics;
~束流動力學 beam dynamics;
~吸附動力學 absorption dynamics;
~宇宙航行動力學 astrodynamics;
產生動力 make power; produce power;
失去動力 run out of steam;
原動力 (1) power; (2) action;

[動量] momentum;
角動量 angular momentum;
絕對動量 absolute momentum;
正則動量 canonical momentum;
總動量 aggregated momentum;

[動亂] disturbance; turbulence; turmoil; upheaval;
動亂年代 years of upheaval;
動亂時期 time of storm and stress; time of turmoil;
社會動亂 social upheaval;
引起動亂 cause a disturbance;
政治動亂 political upheaval; political turmoil;
觸發動亂 suppress a disturbance; touch off a disturbance;

[動脈] artery;
動脈出血 arterial haemorrhage;
動脈壞死 arterionecrosis;
動脈結石 arteriolith;
動脈瘤 aneurysm;
~創傷性動脈瘤 traumatic aneurysm;
寄生蟲性動脈瘤 verminous aneurysm;
假性動脈瘤 spurious aneurysm;
梅毒性動脈瘤 syphilitic aneurysm;
偏側動脈瘤 lateral aneurysm;
蠕蟲性動脈瘤 worm aneurysm;
腎動脈瘤 renal aneurysm;
外傷性動脈瘤 traumatic aneurysm;
細菌性動脈瘤 bacterial aneurysm;
真性動脈瘤 true aneurysm;
動脈炎 arteritis;
風濕性動脈炎 rheumatic arteritis;
壞死性動脈炎 necrotizing arteritis;
結核性動脈炎 tuberculous arteritis;
梅毒性動脈炎 syphilitic arteritis;
~全身動脈炎 panarteritis;
~嬰兒動脈炎 infantile arteritis;
動脈硬化 arteriosclerosis; hardening of the walls of the arteries;
~嬰兒動脈硬化 infantile arteriosclerosis;
出球動脈 revehent artery;
腸動脈 intestinal artery;
傳導動脈 conducting arteries;
大動脈 main artery;
膽囊動脈 cystic artery;
腓動脈 peroneal artery;
肺動脈 pulmonary artery;
腹腔動脈 abdominal artery;
肝動脈 hepatic;
睪丸動脈 testicular artery;
髂內動脈 internal iliac artery;
肱動脈 brachial artery;
股動脈 femoral artery;
冠狀動脈 coronary artery;
頸動脈 carotid artery;
迷路動脈 labyrinthine artery;
面動脈 facial artery; frontal artery;
顳動脈 temporal artery;
脾動脈 arteria splenica;
前庭動脈 vestibular artery;
橈動脈 radial artery;

人造動脈 artificial artery;
腎動脈 renal artery;
輸出動脈 efferent artery;
臀上動脈 superior gluteal artery;
臀下動脈 inferior gluteal artery;
彈性動脈 elastic artery;
膝降動脈 descending genicular artery;
膝中動脈 middle genicular artery;
下唇動脈 inferior labial artery;
小腸動脈 intestinal arteries;
小動脈 arteriole;
小動脈病 arteriolopathy;
小動脈炎 arteriolitis;
小動脈硬化 arteriolar sclerosis;
陰部內動脈 internal pudendal artery;
陰道動脈 vaginal artery;
主動脈 aorta;
~主動脈弓 aortic arch;
~主動脈炎 aortitis;
風濕性主動脈炎 rheumatic aortitis;

[動能] kinetic energy;
動能武器 kinetic energy weapon;

[動怒] flare up; get angry; lose one's temper;

[動氣] become angry; get angry; lose one's temper; take offense;

[動情] (1) become excited; get worked up; (2) be enamoured; have more than a fleeting interest in sb; have one's sexual passions aroused;
動情周期 oestrous cycle;

[動人] moving; touching;
動人的 fetching;
動人耳目 make one's ears and eyes tingle;
動人肺腑 come home to sb's heart; heartening; move sb deeply; touch sb to the depths of his soul; touch sb's heart;
動人聽聞 be excited to hear about;
動人心坎 speak to one's heart;
動人心弦 deeply moving; rouse one's tender emotions; stir up one's innermost feelings; strike a chord in sb's heart; strike a deep chord in sb's heart; touch sb's feeling; touch the right chord; tug at sb's heartstrings;
楚楚動人 delicate and attractive; moving the heart of all those around her;
風采動人 cut a fine figure;
美麗動人 personable;

[動容] be visibly moved; change countenance;
為之動容 become interested and show so in one's facial expression;

[動身] begin a journey; depart; departure; go on a journey; leave for a place; set out on a journey;
提早動身 accelerate one's departure;
一早動身 make an early start;

[動手] (1) get to work; start work; (2) handle; touch;
動手打架 make motions to start a fight;
動手動腳 (1) get fresh with sb; let one's hand and foot take too great liberties; take liberties with sb; (2) make motions to start a fight;
動手工作 start on a task;
動手慢 slow in making a start;
動手術 (1) perform an operation; operate on sb; (2) be operated on; have an operation;
自己動手 do-it-yourself;

[動態] (1) cause of action; developments; general trend of affairs; tendencies; trends; (2) dynamic condition; dynamic state;
動態傳播 dynamic communication;
動態動詞 dynamic verb;
動態對等 dynamic equivalence;
動態分析法 dynamic analysis method;
動態管理 dynamic administration;
動態規劃 dynamic programming;
動態經濟 dynamic economy;
~動態經濟分析 analysis of dynamic economy;
~動態經濟學 dynamic economics;
動態連接庫 dynamic link libraries;
動態美 active beauty;
動態色彩校正 dynamic colour re-edition;
動態文化 mobile culture;
動態形容詞 dynamic adjective;
動態修辭 dynamic rhetoric;
金融動態 financial trends;

[動彈] move; stir;
動彈不得 cannot move; cannot move a step; incapable of moving;

[動聽] interesting to listen to; moving; persuasive; pleasant to listen to;
説話動聽 silver tongue;

[動武] come to blows; resort to forces; start a fight; use force;

[動物] beast; animal; zoon;
動物愛好者 animal lover;

動物愛護者 zoophile;
動物半球 animal hemisphere;
動物保護 animal protection;
動物本能 animality;
動物本性 animal nature;
動物病理學 zoopathology;
動物崇拜 zoolatry;
~動物崇拜者 zoolater;
動物傳播 zoochory;
動物傳染病 zoonosis;
~寄生蟲動物傳染病 parasitic zoonosis;
動物地理 zoogeograph;
動物地理學 zoogeography;
動物地理學家 zoogeographer;
動物動力學 zoodynamics;
動物毒素 zootoxin;
動物發生 zoogenesis;
~動物發生論 zoogeny;
動物分類學 animal taxonomy; zootaxy;
動物工藝學 zootechnics;
動物構造學 zoophysics;
動物管理員 zooman;
動物化 animalization;
動物化石 zoolith;
動物化學 zoochemistry;
動物幻視 zooscopy;
動物極 animal pole;
動物激素 zoohormone;
動物解剖 zootomy;
~動物解剖學 zootomy;
動物解剖學家 zootomist;
動物界 animal kingdom; animal world; animate nature;
動物恐怖症 zoophobia;
動物名詞 animate noun;
動物模式 zootype;
動物區系 fauna;
~海底動物區系 benthic fauna; bottom fauna;
~深海動物區系 deep-sea fauna;
~深水動物區系 deep-water fauna;
~穴居動物區系 cave fauna;
動物圈 zoosphere;
動物權益 animal rights;
動物群落 zoobiocenose; zoocoenosis;
動物生境 zootope;
動物生理學 animal physiology; zoonomy; zoophysiology;
動物實驗 zoopery;
動物數計 zoometer;
動物特徵 animal characteristic;
動物喜愛癖 zoophilism;

動物系統學 zootaxy;
動物細胞 zooblast;
動物香豆素 zoocumarin;
動物心理學 zoopsychology;
動物性 animality;
動物學 zoology;
~動物學家 zoologist;
~哺乳動物學 mammalogy;
~古動物學 palaeozoology;
~脊椎動物學 vertebrate zoology;
無脊椎動物學 invertebrate zoology;
~原生動物學 protozoology;
~植物形動物學 zoophytology;
動物移植術 zoografting;
動物園 zoo;
~動物園管理員 zookeeper;
~愛畜動物園 petting zoo;
~野生動物園 animal park; safari park;
動物誌學 zoography;
~動物誌學家 zoographer; zoographist;
動物脂肪 animal fats;
愛護動物者 zoophile;
保護動物 protect animals;
貝殼類動物 crustacean;
邊緣動物 edge animal;
變溫動物 poikilothermic animal;
哺乳動物 mammal;
常見動物 common animal;
吃草動物 herbivorous animal;
嚙齒動物 rodent;
大洋動物 pelagic fauna;
單配偶動物 monogamous animal;
單食性動物 monophagous animal;
單胎動物 monotocous animal;
單細胞動物 single-cell animal;
淡水動物 fresh-water animal;
地下動物 ground animal; subterranean animal;
底棲動物 benthic fauna; zoobenthos;
冬眠動物 hibernating animal;
對照動物 control animal;
多配偶動物 polygamous animal;
多食性動物 omnivore; polyphagous animal;
多細胞動物 multicellular animal;
多足動物 myriapod;
反芻動物 ruminant;
浮游動物 zooplankton;
~海洋浮游動物 marine zooplankton;
~食藻類浮游動物 herbivorous zooplankton;
共生動物 commensal;

廣生性動物 eurytopic animal;
廣溫動物 eurythermal animal;
海綿動物 sponge;
海洋動物 marine animal;
寒帶動物 animal of the frigid zone;
恒溫動物 homeothermal animal; warm-blooded animal;
厚皮動物 pachyderm;
化石動物 zoolite;
環節動物 annulose animal;
脊索動物 chordate;
脊椎動物 spinal animal; vertebrate;
~無脊椎動物 invertebrate;
海洋無脊椎動物 marine invertebrate;
河口無脊椎動物 estuarine invertebrate;
水生無脊椎動物 aquatic invertebrate;
寄生動物 parasitic animal; zooparasite;
~外寄生動物 ectoparasite;
甲殼動物 crustacean;
節肢動物 arthropod;
棘皮動物 echinoderm;
冷血動物 cold-blooded animal;
理性動物 rational animal;
兩棲動物 amphibian;
兩足動物 biped;
鱗尾松鼠屬動物 anomaluridae; scaly-tailed squirrel;
靈長目動物 primate;
流水動物 eotic animal;
陸生動物 terrestrial animal;
濾食性動物 filter feeder;
卵生動物 oviparous animal;
麻醉動物 anesthetized animal;
爬行動物 reptile;
~海生爬行動物 marine reptile;
~空中爬行動物 flying reptile;
腔腸動物 coelenterate;
丘腦動物 thalamic animal;
去皮質動物 decorticate animal;
去頭動物 decapitate animal;
群居動物 social animal;
熱帶動物 tropical animal;
~亞熱帶動物 subtropical animal;
軟體動物 mollusc;
蠕形動物 verme;
深海動物 abyssal fauna;
食草動物 grazing animal; herbivore; herbivorous animal;
食蟲動物 carnivorous plant; insectivore;
食腐動物 scavenger; saprophagous animal;
食肉動物 carnaria; carnivore; carnivorous animal; flesh-eating animal; predatory animal; zoophagan;
~頂極食肉動物 top carnivore;
食魚動物 piscivorous animal;
實驗動物 experimental animal;
水產動物 marine fauna;
水生動物 aquatic animal;
~多細胞水生動物 multicellular aquatic animal;
四足動物 four-legged animal; quadruped; quadrupedal animal;
胎生動物 viviparous animal;
淡水軟體動物 freshwater mollusk;
土壤動物 soil animal;
微生動物 animal cule;
溫帶動物 animal of the temperate zone;
溫血動物 warm-blooded animal;
無嗅覺動物 anosmatic animal;
吸血動物 bloodsucker;
稀有動物 rare animal;
細骨動物 fined-boned animal;
夏蟄動物 aestivator;
嗅覺不敏動物 microsmatic animal;
鴨嘴龍屬動物 anatosaurus;
穴居動物 cave animal;
延髓動物 bulbospinal animal;
野生動物 wild animal;
~野生動物保護區 wildlife reserve;
~野生動物園 wildlife park;
一群動物 a multitude of animals;
醫用動物 medical animal;
游行動物 nekton;
有毒動物 toxic animal;
有蹄動物 ungulate;
異溫動物 heterothermic animal;
原口動物 protostomia;
原生動物 protozoa;
~腸內原生動物 intestinal protozoa;
~群體原生動物 colonial protozoa;
~血內原生動物 blood protozoa;
~自由游動原生動物 free-swimming protozoa;
雜交動物 hybrid animals;
~繁育雜交動物 breeding hybrid animals;
雜種動物 cross-breed;
蜘蛛類動物 arachnid;
晝出動物 diurnal animal;

[動向] tendency; trend;
動向不明 it is uncertain which way one will go;
長期動向 long-term trend;
當代動向 current trend;

短期動向 short-term trend;
銷售動向 sales trend;

[動心] one's desire is aroused;
不動心 show no interest;

[動搖] shake; waver and falter;
動搖悲觀 waver and grow pessimistic;
動搖不定 go see-saw; vacillate; waver;
動搖決心 waver in one's determination;
動搖軍心 demoralize the army; shake the army's morale;
動搖人心 sway the mind of men;
動搖信念 waver in one's conviction;
動搖猶豫 irresolute and wavering;
地動山搖 hills topple and the earth quakes; the earth trembles and the mountains sway;
毫不動搖 impregnable; sit tight; not to waver in the least; unshaken in one's conviction; unwavering; without vacillating;

[動議] motion; move; proposal;
不信任動議 motion of no confidence;
撤回動議 withdraw a motion;
否決動議 reject a motion; turn down a motion;
附議動議 second a motion;
擱置動議 shelve a motion;
緊急動議 urgent motion;
審議動議 consider a motion;
提出動議 propose a motion; put forward a motion;
修改動議 modify a motion;
贊成動議 support a motion;

[動用] draw on; employ; put to use; resort to;
動用公款 draw on public funds;
動用一切手段 exhaust every means;

[動員] arouse; mobilize; mobilization;
動員令 mobilization order;
~頒布動員令 issue a mobilization order;
總動員 general mobilization;

[動輒] at every turn; easily; frequently;
動輒打罵 beat and swear at sb on the least pretext;
動輒得咎 be blamed for whatever one does; be constantly taken to task; get blamed for every move; liable to be blamed at every move;
動輒發怒 anger easily; prone to anger; take offence at trifles;
動輒臉紅 blush at the drop of a hat;
動輒生氣 swift to take offense;
動輒訓人 ready to lecture others; reprove others at every turn;

[動作] act; action; motion; movement; start moving;
動作被動 actional passive;
~動作被動語態 actional passive;
動作緩慢 slow in one's movements;
動作敏捷 move with alacrity; quick in one's movements;
動作一致 act in uniformity; keep strokes;
大動作 major change;
反向動作 backward action;
規定動作 compulsory exercise;
假動作 false motions; feint;
~帶球假動作 dribbling feint;
~複雜假動作 compound feint;
~兩次假動作 double feint;
~兩次身體假動作 double body feint;
~起動假動作 starting feint;
扣腕動作 cocking wrist action;
拉桿動作 fadeaway back-swing;
連續動作 consecutive action;
慢動作 micromotion; slow motion;
舞蹈動作 dance movements;
小動作 little tricks; minor manoeuvres; petty actions; petty and mean actions; petty gestures;
~搞小動作 indulge in petty and mean actions; make petty gesture; get up to little tricks;
協同動作 concerted action;
自選動作 optional exercise; voluntary exercise;
做準備動作 do warm-up exercises; have warm-up exercises;

擺動 flicker; sway; swing; wave;
搬動 move; shift;
暴動 insurrection; rebel;
被動 passive; unactive;
變動 alter; alteration; change;
別動 hold it; keep still;
波動 fluctuate; undulate; wave motion;
撥動 poke; stir; turn;
搏動 beat rhythmically; pulsate;
不動 without movement;
策動 instigate; stir up;
差動 differential;
顫動 quiver; tremble; vibrate;
腸動 enterokinesia;
衝動 get excited; impetuous;
抽動 herky-jerky;

出動 (1) set out; start off; (2) send out; (3) take action;
搐動 twitch;
觸動 (1) touch sth, moving it slightly; (2) move sb; stir up sb's feelings; touch one's heart;
傳動 drive; transmission;
蠢動 (1) wriggle; (2) create disturbances;
打動 arouse one's feelings; move sb; touch one's heart;
帶動 (1) bring along; drive; (2) lead in action;
電動 motor-driven; power-driven;
調動 (1) move; shift; transfer; (2) bring into play; mobilize;
抖動 (1) chatter; shake; tremble; vibrate; (2) agitation; joggling; whipping;
發動 (1) get going; get started; launch; (2) arouse; call into action; mobilize; (3) start a machine;
翻動 turn over and change the original position;
反動 reactionary;
風動 pneumatic;
拂動 flip; flick; whisk;
浮動 (1) drift; float; (2) fluctuate; unstable; unsteady;
改動 alter; modify;
感動 (1) be moved; be touched; (2) move sb; touch sb's heart;
更動 alter; change;
鼓動 (1) agitate; arouse; (2) incite; instigate;
滾動 roll; trundle;
撼動 rock; shake; vibrate;
哄動 cause a sensation; make a stir;
轟動 cause a sensation; make a stir;
滑動 slide;
晃動 rock; shake; sway;
揮動 brandish; flap; wave;
回動 reverse;
活動 (1) move about; exercise; (2) shaky; unstable; unsteady; (3) flexible; mobile; movable; (4) activity; manoeuvre; operation; (5) behaviour;
機動 (1) motorized; power-driven; (2) expedient; flexible; makeshift; (3) for emergency; in reserve; (4) mobile;
激動 (1) excite sb's feelings; (2) rage; surge;
攪動 mix; stir;
驚動 alarm; disturb;
舉動 activity; move; movement;
開動 (1) bring into action; bring into operation; call into action; set in motion; start; (2) march; move; on the move;
勞動 do manual labour; do physical labour; labour; work
雷動 thunderous;
流動 (1) flow; (2) go from place to place; on the move;
脈動 pulsation;
盲動 act blindly; act rashly;
萌動 germinate; put forth;
能動 active; dynamic; initiative;
扭動 wiggle;
挪動 move; shift;
拍動 beat;
飄動 float; flutter;
起動 get in motion; start; start going; start moving; start running; start working; starting;
啟動 start; switch on;
氣動 pneumatic;
牽動 affect; influence;
傾動 be infatuated; be overwhelmed;
擾動 agitate; disturb; disturbance; perturbation;
蠕動 (1) squirm; wriggle; (2) peristalsis;
搔動 become restless; commotion; disturbance;
騷動 (1) cause a commotion; disturb; (2) become restless; in a tumult;
煽動 incite; instigate; stir up;
閃動 flash; flicker; glisten; move fast; play; scintillate; twinkle; waver;
攝動 perturbation;
生動 lively; vivid;
手動 by hand; hand-driven;
受動 affected;
鬆動 become flexible;
慫動 incite; instigate;
聳動 (1) egg on; urge; (2) be alarmed; be moved;
隨動 follow-up;
所動 be swayed;
胎動 movement of the oetus causing pain in the lower abdomen;
挑動 incite; instigate; provoke; stir up;
跳動 move up and down; pulsate;
湍動 turbulence;
推動 give drive to; give impetus to; promote; push forward;
妄動 take rash actions; take reckless actions;
舞動 brandish; wave;
掀動 (1) start; (2) lift; set sth in motion;
心動 (1) palpitation of the heart; (2) become interested in sth;
行動 (1) act; move; move about; (2) behaviour; conduct; manner;
洶動 disturbed; restless; unquiet;
言動 words and conduct; speech and behaviour;

搖動 cause sth to shake; cause sth to wave;
一動 (1) a jerk; a jolt; a move; move once; (2) at every turn; easily; frequently;
移動 move; shift;
蟻動 move like ants;
異動 change; reshuffle;
引動 stir up one's feelings;
悠動 swing;
游動 go from place to place; move about;
躍動 in lively motion; move actively;
運動 (1) motion; movement; (2) exercise; sports; (3) campaign; drive;
躁動 (1) move restlessly; (2) jump incessantly;
章動 nutation;
振動 vibrate;
震動 quake; shake; shock; vibrate;
制動 apply the brake; brake;
主動 (1) initiative; (2) driving;
轉動 turn; turn round;
自動 (1) of one's own accord; voluntarily; (2) automatic;
走動 (1) walk about; (2) visit each other;

D

dong

【棟】 ridge pole;
［棟樑］ (1) important people; (2) pillar; ridge; ridge beam; ridge pole and beam;
棟樑之材 man of great ability and tremendous promise; superior talents;
雕樑畫棟 carved beams and painted rafters;
國家棟樑 pillar of the state;
畫棟雕樑 luminous coloured pillars and artistically carved beams; painted pillars and carved beams; the pillars and roof beams are richly carved; the rafters are repainted, the beams carved;
畫梁雕棟 painted beams and carved pillars;
社會棟樑 pillar of the society;
社區棟樑 pillar of the community;

dou¹
dou

【兜】 (1) bag; pocket; (2) wrap sth up in a piece of cloth; (3) move round; (4) canvass; solicit; (5) take responsibility for sth; take upon oneself;
［兜捕］ round up; surround and seize;
［兜穿而過］ thread one's way through a crowd;
［兜底］ disclose the ins and outs; disclose the whole inside story; reveal all the details;
［兜兒］ pocket;
［兜風］ (1) catch the wind; (2) go for a drive; go for a ride; go for a sail; go for a spin; take a ride;
兜風逛逛 take the air and stroll around;
駕車兜風 cruise;
去兜風 go for a drive;
偷車兜風 joyriding;
［兜個圈］ go for a ride;
［兜攬］ (1) canvass; find customers for trade; solicit; (2) take upon oneself;
兜攬生意 canvass business orders; drum up trade; find customers for trade; solicit customers; solicit for business;
［兜售］ hawk; make a sale of; peddle; tout for;
［兜銷］ find customers for trade; hawk;

褲兜 trouser pocket;
網兜 string bag;

dou

【都】 all; both; both...and; even; everything; neither; none; nothing;

dou³
dou

【斗】 (1) unit of dry measure for grain; (2) dou measure unit; (3) cup-shaped object or dipper; (4) Big Dipper;
［斗膽］ make bold; of great courage; venture;
［斗拱］ brackets;
［斗換星移］ passing of hours of the night; passing of months;
［斗篷］ cape; cloak; mantle; poncho;
［斗筲］ ancient bamboo container—narrow-mindedness;
斗筲之器 narrow-minded and short-sighted;
斗筲之人 people who are mere pecks and hampers;
［斗室］ small room;

笆斗 round-bottomed basket;
鏟斗 bucket;
鮮斗 cran;
掛斗 trailer;
戽斗 bailing bucket;
筋斗 (1) somersault; (2) fall; tumble;

料斗 hopper;
漏斗 funnel;
煤斗 coal scuttle;
墨斗 carpenter's ink marker;
香斗 incense pot;
煙斗 tobacco pipe;
一斗 hodful;
熨斗 flat iron; iron;
抓斗 grab bucket;

dou

【抖】 (1) shiver; tremble; (2) jerk; shake; (3) rouse; stir up; (4) get on in the world;

［抖掉］ shake off;

［抖動］ (1) chatter one's teeth; shake; tremble; vibrate; (2) agitation; joggle; whip;
抖動器 shaker;
~ 等幅抖動器 constant displacement shaker;
~ 慣性抖動器 inertia-type shaker;
~ 氣力抖動器 pneumatic shaker;

［抖摟］ (1) shake off; shake out of sth; (2) expose; (3) squander; waste;

［抖擻］ enliven; in high spirits; pluck up; rouse;
抖擻精神 brace up; pull oneself together;
精神抖擻 full of energy;

顫抖 quake;
發抖 shake; shiver; tremble;
擻抖抖 shivering; trembling;

dou

【蚪】 tadpole;

蝌蚪 tadpole;

dou

【陡】 (1) abruptly; suddenly; (2) precipitous; steep;

［陡岸］ steep coast;

［陡壁］ steep bank;

［陡坡］ steep slope;
爬下陡坡 clamber down the slope;

［陡度］ steepness;
地面陡度 steepness of terrain;
階躍陡度 jump steepness;
脈衝陡度 pulse steepness;

［陡峭］ abrupt; cliffy; precipitous;
陡峭的 craggy;
變得陡峭 steepen;

［陡然］ abruptly; suddenly;

［陡險］ steep and dangerous;

dou⁴
dou

【豆】 bean; pea;

［豆餅］ bean cake; soya bean cake;

［豆豉］ fermented soya beans;

［豆腐］ bean curd; tofu;
豆腐白菜，各有所愛 all men do not admire and love the same objects;
豆腐店 bean curd store;
豆腐房 bean curd mill;
豆腐乾 dried bean curd;
豆腐塊 (1) bean curd cube; (2) tiny article;
豆腐老虎 bean curd tiger;
豆腐裏挑骨頭 picky; trying to find bones in bean curd;
豆腐腦 jellied bean curd;
豆腐泡 bean curd puff;
豆腐皮 skin of soya milk;
豆腐片 thin layer of bean curd;
豆腐乳 fermented bean curd;
豆腐絲 shredded bean curd;
豆腐衣 skin of soya milk;
豆腐渣 grass dregs;
~ 豆腐渣工程 jelly-built project; shoddy construction;
豆腐嘴，刀子口一口軟心狠 with a mouth like bean curd and a heart like a knife — soft in speech, ruthless in heart;
吃豆腐 (1) eat bean curd; (2) find sexual satisfaction in touching women apart from one's wife; take advantage of women;
臭豆腐 strong-smelling fermented bean curd;
醬豆腐 fermented bean curd with soya sauce;
麻豆腐 cooking-starch residue;
燻豆腐 smoked bean curd;
糟豆腐 pickled bean curd;
炸豆腐 deep-fried bean curd;

［豆漿］ soya milk;
豆漿晶 soya bean milk powder;
熬豆漿 boil soya milk;
醬豆腐 fermented bean curd;
酸豆漿 sour soya milk;
甜豆漿 sweet soya milk;
鹹豆漿 salty soya milk;

［豆角儿］ fresh kidney beans;

［豆類］ beans;

［豆苗］ bean seedling;

[豆沙] sweetened bean paste;
豆沙包 steamed bun filled with bean paste;
豆沙餡 bean paste filling;
[豆薯] yam beans;
[豆芽] bean sprout;
[豆渣] bean dregs;
[豆子] beans;
一把豆子 a handful of beans;
一顆豆子 a bean;
一罐豆子 a can of beans; a tin of beans;

巴豆 (1) croton; (2) croton seed;
白菜豆 white kidney beans;
白豆 white beans;
籩豆 ancient food container;
扁豆 kidney bean;
菜豆 kidney bean; pea bean;
蠶豆 broad bean;
赤豆 red bean;
大豆 soya bean;
刀豆 sword bean;
黑豆 black soya bean;
黑眼豆 black-eyed bean;
紅豆 (1) ormosia; (2) love pea; red bean;
紅芸豆 red kidney bean;
紅小豆 red beans;
烘豆 baked beans;
胡豆 broad bean;
槐豆 locust bean;
黃豆 soya bean;
豇豆 cowpea;
蠟豆 wax bean;
綠豆 green gram; mung bean;
毛豆 young soya bean;
米豆 black-eyed bean;
嫩刀豆 fresh bean;
青刀豆 garden bean;
青豆 green bean; green soya bean;
觴豆 wine and food;
四季豆 garden bean;
土豆 potato;
豌豆 pea;
烏豆 black beans;
小豆 red bean;
芽豆 sprouted broad bean;
翼豆 winged bean;
鷹嘴豆 chickpea; garbanzo;
芸豆 kidney bean;
棧豆 fodder;
俎豆 sacrificial stand and pot = sacrificial rites;

dou

【鬥】 (1) fight; tussle; (2) denounce; struggle against; (3) contend with; contest with; (4) make animals fight; (5) fit together;
[鬥富] show off one's wealth by spending more money than sb else;
[鬥雞] cockfight; cockfighting;
鬥雞場 cockpit;
[鬥牛] bullfight;
鬥牛場 bullring;
鬥牛犬 bulldog;
[鬥士] fighter;
自由鬥士 free fighter;
[鬥眼] cross-eyed;
[鬥爭] combat; conflict; fight; struggle;
奮勇鬥爭 put up a struggle;
階級鬥爭 class conflict;
艱難的鬥爭 uphill struggle;
內部鬥爭 infighting;
[鬥志] fighting spirit;
鬥志昂揚 full of fight; militant; with high morale;
鼓舞鬥志 inspire the fighting spirit;
鬆懈鬥志 relax one's will to fight;
[鬥嘴] bicker; squabble; tiff;

挨鬥 be struggled against; be subjected to criticism and struggle;
暗鬥 engage in veiled strife;
搏鬥 fight; struggle; wrestle;
打鬥 beating; brawl; dust-up; exchange blows; fight; fight and quarrel; tussle;
惡鬥 ferocious battle;
奮鬥 fight; strive for; struggle;
格鬥 fist fight; grapple; wrestle;
狗鬥 dogfight;
好鬥 bellicose;
決鬥 duel;
角鬥 wrestle;
毆鬥 box; have a fist fight;
批鬥 accuse and denounce sb;
拳鬥 fist fight;
相鬥 fight against each other;
械鬥 engage in gang fighting; fight with weapons between groups of people;
戰鬥 combat; fight;
爭鬥 fight; struggle;
智鬥 vie in wisdom;

dou
【脰】 neck;

dou
【逗】 (1) play with; tease; (2) amuse; provoke laughter; (3) funny; (4) stay; stop; (5) slight pause in reading;
[逗號] comma;
倒裝逗號 inverted comma;
[逗留] stay; stick around; stop;
逗留一會兒 stick around for a while;
逗留一夜 make an overnight stop;
[逗悶子] joke with; make fun of; tease in a playful way;
[逗弄] kid; make fun of; tease;
[逗人笑] crack sb up;
[逗引] tease;
[逗嘴片子] cross words with sb; quarrel with sb;

撩逗 entice; provoke; tease;
挑逗 tantalize; tease;
引逗 entice; lure; seduce;

dou
【荳】 bean; legume; pea;
[荳蔻年華] adolescent girl; blooming girl; budding beauty; marriageable age;

dou
【痘】 smallpox;
[痘疤] smallpox scars;
[痘苗] lymph; vaccine;

出痘 have smallpox;
牛痘 (1) cowpox; (2) smallpox;
水痘 chicken pox;
羊痘 sheep pox;
種痘 vaccinate against smallpox;

dou
【鬦】 same as 鬥, struggle;

dou
【餖】 food items set out for show;

dou
【竇】 (1) burrow; cavity; hole; dig through; (2) corrupt practice; (3) a surname;

鼻竇 paranasal sinus;
疑竇 cause for suspicion; suspicion;

dou
【鬪】 same as 鬥.

dou
【讀】 pauses in a sentence;

句讀 the period and the comma; sentences and phrases;

dou
【鬭】 same as 鬥.

du¹
du
【都】 (1) all; any; any-; both; both...and; every; every-; neither; neither...nor; no matter; (2) captial; (3) big city; metropolis;
[都城] capital;
[都督] governor;
[都會] city; metropolis;
大都會 metropolis;
[都市] city; metropolis;
都市化 urbanization;
~都市化程度 degree of urbanization;
都市區域 urban area;
都市網 metropolitan area;
都市學 urban studies;
超級都市 supercity;
大都市 large city; metropolis;
~國際大都市 cosmopolitan city;
國際都市 cosmopolis; cosmopolitan city;

大都 for the most part; mostly;
奠都 found a capital;
定都 establish a capital;
古都 ancient capital;
故都 one-time capital;
國都 capital; national capital;
皇都 imperial capital;
建都 found a capital;
京都 capital of a country;
舊都 one-time capital;
遷都 move the capital to another place;
全都 all; altogether; every; everyone;
首都 capital;
行都 temporary capital;

du
【督】 superintend and direct;
[督辦] (1) supervise and handle; (2) supervisor;
[督促] press; push forward; supervise and urge;
[督導] director; supervise and direct;

D

supervisor;
督導員 warden;
~交通督導員 traffic warden;
[督軍] provincial military governor;
[督勵] spur on; urge and encourage;
[督學] school inspector;

基督 Christ;
監督 supervise;
總督 governor; governor general; viceroy;

du
【闍】 tower over a city wall;

du
【嘟】 (1) pout; (2) honk; toot;
[嘟嘟聲] beep; blare; toot;
[嘟嚕] (1) bunch; cluster; (2) trill;
[嘟囔] mumble; mutter to oneself;
嘟嘟囔囔 mumble and sputter;
[嘟噥] mumble;
嘟噥不平 complain ceaselessly; grumble
嘟嘟噥噥 mumble in whispers; mutter to oneself;

咕嚕 bubble; gurgle;

du²
du
【毒】 (1) poison; toxin; (2) narcotics; (3) noxious; poisoned; poisonous; (4) cruel; fierce; malicious; (5) kill with poison;
[毒草] (1) poisonous weeds; (2) a harmful speech;
[毒蟲] poisonous insect;
[毒打] beat cruelly; beat savagely; beat sb up;
一頓毒打 give sb a good thrashing; give sb a most terrible beating;
[毒販] drug dealer; drug pusher;
[毒害] poison sb's mind;
預謀毒害 premeditated poisoning;
[毒化] poison; spoil;
[毒計] deadly trap; insidious scheme; malicious project; venomous plot; venomous scheme; wicked plan;
[毒劑] toxic; toxicant;
[毒酒] poisonous wine;
[毒辣] diabolic; sinister;
心腸毒辣 harbour a murderous heart;
[毒理學] toxicology;
毒理學家 toxicologist;
分子毒理學 molecular toxicology;
臨牀毒理學 clinical toxicology;
農藥毒理學 pesticide toxicology;
植物毒理學 plant toxicology;
[毒謀愈肆] malicious plots become more and more brazen;
[毒品] drugs; illegal drugs; narcotic drugs;
毒品販子 drug dealer; drug trafficker; pusher;
毒品交易 drug trafficking;
毒品走私 drug smuggling; drug trafficking;
~毒品走私販 drug smuggler; drug trafficker;
化合毒品 synthetic drug;
烈性毒品 hard drugs;
人造毒品 designer drugs;
入門毒品 gateway drug;
軟毒品 soft drugs;
特製毒品 designer drugs;
吸服毒品 abuse drugs; take drugs;
消遣性毒品 recreational drugs;
硬毒品 hard drugs;
誘導性毒品 gateway drugs;
注射毒品 inject drugs;
[毒氣] poison gas; poisonous gas;
毒氣室 gas chamber;
排出毒氣 exhale a poisonous gas;
神經毒氣 nerve gas;
[毒殺] kill with poison;
[毒舌] bad tongue; biting tongue; bitter tongue; caustic tongue; dangerous tongue; have a vicious tongue; sharp tongue; sharp-tongued; venomous tongue; wicked tongue;
[毒蛇] poisonous snake;
毒蛇猛獸 venomous serpents and fierce beasts; vipers and beasts;
[毒手] murderous scheme;
下毒手 resort to violent treachery;
~背後下毒手 stab sb in the back;
險遭毒手 be nearly killed;
[毒死] kill sb with poison; poison sb;
[毒素] toxin;
產生毒素 produce toxin;
抵抗毒素 fight toxin;
動物毒素 animal toxin;
分泌毒素 excrete poison;
含有毒素 contain poison;
紅斑毒素 erythrogenic toxin;

花粉毒素 pollen toxin;
吸收毒素 absorb a poison;
細菌毒素 bacterial toxin;
中和毒素 neutralize a toxin;

[毒物] poison; toxin;
毒物學 toxicology;
~ 毒物學家 toxicologist;
~ 法醫毒物學 forensic toxicology;
~ 工業毒物學 toxicology;
~ 職業毒物學 occupational toxicology;

[毒性] toxicity;
急性毒性 acute toxicity;
接觸毒性 contact toxicity;
慢性毒性 chronic toxicity;

[毒牙] poison fang; venom fang;

[毒藥] poison; toxicant;
接觸性毒藥 contact poisons;
烈性毒藥 powerful poison; strong poison; violent poison;
慢性毒藥 slow poison;
致命的毒藥 deadly poison;

[毒癮] drug addiction; drug dependency;
戒去毒癮 give up drugs;

拔毒 draw out poison;
冰毒 crystal meth;
病毒 virus;
慘毒 brutal and vicious; ruthless and venomous;
藏毒 possession of cocaine;
丹毒 erysipelas;
惡毒 malicious; vicious;
販毒 traffic in drugs;
防毒 gas defence;
放毒 (1) poison; put poison in food; (2) make vicious remarks; spread poisonous ideas;
蜂毒 bee venom;
服毒 take poison;
狠毒 atrocious; brutal cruel; malicious; venomous; vicious;
解毒 (1) detoxicate; detoxify; (2) relieve internal heat;
戒毒 come off drugs; detox; get off drugs;
劇毒 deadly poisonous;
抗毒 antitoxic;
刻毒 harsh and venomous; mean and vicious;
流毒 baneful influence; exert a pernicious influence; pernicious influence;
梅毒 syphilis;
煤毒 coal gas; gas;
排毒 detox; detoxification;
鉛毒 lead poisoning;
染毒 contaminate;
屍毒 cadaverine;
荼毒 afflict with great suffering; cause disaster; cause injury; harm; poison; torment;
吸毒 be on drugs; become addicted to narcotics; do drugs; drug abuse; drug taking; drug use; smoke opium; take drugs; use drugs;
下毒 poison; put poison into sth;
消毒 (1) discontanminate; disinfect; disinfection; pasteurize; sterilization; sterilize; (2) degassing; (3) eliminate the pernicious influence; wipe out pernicious influence;
蝎毒 scorpion venom;
心毒 evil heart; wicked heart;
仰毒 swallow poison; take poison;
遺毒 evil legacy; pernicious influence;
陰毒 insidious; sinister;
有毒 noxious; poisonous; venomous;
餘毒 residual poison;
怨毒 enmity; hatred;
酖毒 poisoned wine;
鴆毒 poisoned wine;
腫毒 swelling; tumour;
中毒 be poisoned;

du

【頓】 as in 冒頓, name of a Tartar chieftain in the early Han Dynasty;

du

【碡】 a kind of stone roller;

du

【獨】 (1) only; single; (2) alone; by oneself; (3) childless; old people without offspring;

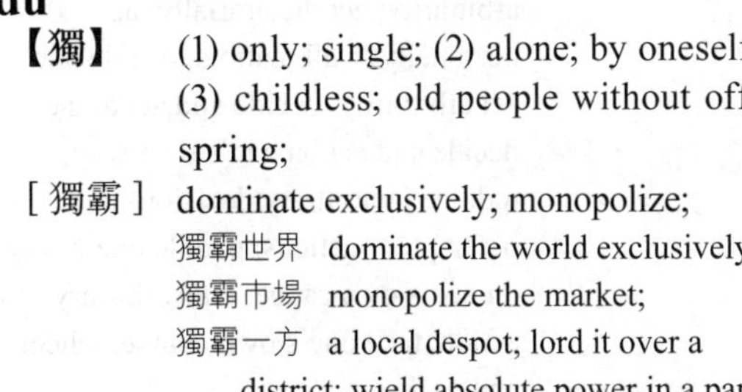

[獨霸] dominate exclusively; monopolize;
獨霸世界 dominate the world exclusively;
獨霸市場 monopolize the market;
獨霸一方 a local despot; lord it over a district; wield absolute power in a part of a country;

[獨白] monologue; soliloquy;
長篇獨白 monologue;
內心獨白 soliloquy;

[獨步] peerless; unique; unrivalled; without match;
獨步古今 have no equal in both ancient and modern times;
獨步天下 second to none; there is none to equal one on earth; there is none under heaven to equal one; unparalleled in the world;

獨步一時 have no equal in one's time; set the pace for a generation; unequalled in one's generation;

[獨裁] autocratic rule; dictatorship;

獨裁國家 dictatorship;

獨裁者 autocrat;

獨裁政府 autocracy;

獨裁政權 dictatorial regime;

獨裁政體 autocracy;

獨裁專斷 arbitrary dictation;

[獨唱] solo;

獨唱會 recital;

[獨處] privacy; solitude;

喜歡獨處 enjoy one's privacy;

想要獨處 want one's privacy;

[獨創] original creation;

獨創精神 creative spirit;

獨創性 creativity; originality;

獨創一格 create a style of one's own; have a unique style;

[獨到] original; unique;

獨到見解 original view;

獨到之處 distinctive qualities; one's own knack; special merits;

獨到之見 individual insight; original view;

[獨斷] arbitrary; dictatorial;

獨斷獨行 go one's own way; take one's own way;

獨斷專行 a law unto oneself; act arbitrarily; act dictatorially; act personally in all matters; decide and act arbitrarily; decide and act alone; decide and act on one's own way; indulge in arbitrary decisions and peremptory actions; paddle one's way on one's own canoe; take arbitrary action; take one's own course; wheel and deal;

獨斷專行，發號施令 decide and act arbitrarily and issue orders left and right; make dictatorial decisions and order others about;

做事獨斷 act dictatorially;

[獨夫] a bad ruler forsaken by all; autocrat;

獨夫民賊 the autocrat and traitor to the people;

[獨戶] isolated house;

獨戶孤門 live alone;

單門獨戶 single isolated house; live in solitude;

孤門獨戶 a solitary door and a lonely house; the only house and solitary door — live alone;

[獨家] exclusive; monopoly;

獨家出版 exclusive publishing;

獨家代理 exclusive agency; sole agency;

~獨家代理人 exclusive agent;

獨家獲利 reap the benefit alone;

獨家經營 sole agent;

獨家新聞 exclusive news report; scoop;

[獨角獸] unicorn;

[獨腳戲] one-person show;

唱獨腳戲 do sth all by oneself; go it alone; put on a one-man show;

[獨角戲] monodrama; one-man show;

女子獨角戲 one-woman show;

[獨具] possess sth special;

獨具慧心 have a special understanding;

獨具慧眼 can see what others cannot; discern what others do not; have mental discernment;

獨具匠心 have an inventive mind; have great originality; show ingenuity;

獨具一格 have a style of one's own; in a class by oneself;

[獨攬] arrogate; monopolize;

獨攬兵權 assume all the power by the sword;

獨攬大權 arrogate all powers to oneself; assume arbitrary power; concentrate the power in the hands of one individual; grasp at authority by oneself;

獨攬經濟權 assume arbitrary power in finance;

獨吞獨攬 play the hog;

[獨力] by one's own efforts; on one's own; single-handedly;

獨力地 single-handedly;

獨力扶持 give aid to sb by one's efforts; support sb single-handed;

獨力經營 manage affairs on one's own; manage with individual effort;

[獨立] (1) stand alone; (2) independence; (3) independent; on one's own;

獨立承包人 independent contractor;

獨立成分 independent element;

獨立從句 independent clause;

獨立仿真程序 stand-alone emulator;

獨立核算 independent accounting;

~獨立核算單位 independent accounting

unit;
獨立結構 absolute construction;
獨立謀生 carve out a career for oneself;
獨立思考 independent thinking; think independently; think things out for oneself;
獨立王國 independent kingdom;
獨立運動 movement for independence;
獨立系統 stand-alone system;
獨立性 independence;
~ 機械獨立性 mechanical independence;
~ 數據獨立性 data independence;
~ 完全獨立性 complete independence;
~ 裝置獨立性 device independence;
獨立終端 stand-alone terminal;
獨立自主 act independently and with the initiative in one's own hands; be one's own master; maintain independence and keep the initiative in one's own hands; stand on one's own feet; independence and initiative; to one's own right;
保持獨立 maintain independence;
財物獨立 financial autonomy;
財政獨立 fiscal independence;
得到獨立 gain independence;
地區獨立 local independence;
恢復獨立 recover one's independence; regain one's independence;
獲得獨立 achieve independence;
經濟獨立 economic independcence;
民族獨立 national independence;
取得獨立 gain independence; get independence;
失去獨立 lose one's independence;
完全獨立 absolute independence; complete independence; full independence;
享有獨立 enjoy independence;
宣佈獨立 declare independence; proclaim independence;
要求獨立 demand independence;
遺世獨立 cast aside worldly cares and live independently; forsake this world of cares and become independent; remain aloof from the world;
贏得獨立 win independence;
政治獨立 political independence;
走向獨立 move towards independence;

[獨輪車] wheelbarrow;

[獨苗儿] only son;

[獨幕劇] one-act play;

[獨木] single log;
獨木不成林 one person alone cannot accomplish much;
獨木難支 a single stick cannot prop up a big house; one person alone cannot save the situation;
獨木橋 (1) single-log bridge; single-plank bridge; (2) difficult path;
獨木舟 canoe; dugout canoe;
~ 獨木舟運動 canoeing;
~ 乘獨木舟 canoe;
~ 划獨木舟 canoe;
~ 一條獨木舟 a canoe;

[獨身] (1) separated from one's family; (2) bachelorhood; spinsterhood; state of being single; unmarried;
獨身的 celibate;
獨身女子 spinster;
獨身生活 celibacy; single blessedness; single life;
獨身終生 pass one's life unmarried; remain single all one's life;
獨身主義 to be a Diana;
獨善其身 attend to one's own virtue in solitude; be righteous alone in a community where the general moral tone is low; pay attention to one's own moral uplift without thought of others;

[獨生] the only child born into the family;
獨生女 only daughter;
獨生子 only child; only son;
~ 獨生子女 only child;
獨生子女費 only-child allowance;
獨生子女證 one-child certificate;

[獨食] domineering; selfish;
吃獨食 not share profit with others;

[獨樹一幟] create a separate school; develop a school of one's own; fly one's own colours; make a style of one's own; strike out a line for oneself;

[獨特] distinctive; original; special; unique;
獨特見解 original view;

[獨吞] pocket profit without sharing with anyone else; take exclusive possession of;
獨吞獨攬 play the hog; take exclusive possession and monopoly;

[獨舞] solo dance;

[獨享其成] reap the benefit alone;

[獨行] (1) walk alone; (2) insist on one's own ways in doing things;
獨行其是 act independently; break the herd; do what one thinks is right regardless of other's opinions; plough a lonely furrow;
獨行俠 lone wolf;
獨斷獨行 go one's own way; take one's own way;
特立獨行 one's own master; self-reliant;
~特立獨行的人 individualist;

[獨眼] one-eyed;
獨眼龍 one-eyed person;
獨眼龍看書—一目瞭然 a one-eyed person reading a book — taking everything at a glance;
獨眼龍相親—一目瞭然 a one-eyed person sizing up his prospective wife — taking everything at a glance;

[獨營] individual management; sole management;

[獨佔] have sth all to oneself; monopolize;
獨佔鰲頭 bear away the bell; bear the palm; carry off the palm; come out at the top of the list; come out first; emerge first in the examination; find the bean in the cake; head the list of successful candidates; lead the list; stand first on the list; take the first place; the champion; top the standing;
獨佔花魁 the lucky man who wins the pretty courtesan's hand;
獨佔市場 corner the market; monopolize the market;
獨佔資本 monopolize capital;
本地獨佔 local monopoly;
資本獨佔 capital monopoly;
自然獨佔 natural monopoly;

[獨資] independent investment; one's own investment; sole proprietorship;
獨資會計 single-proprietorship accounting;
獨資經營 single-proprietorship management;
獨資企業 single-proprietorship enterprise;

[獨子] only son;
單丁獨子 only son; without brothers;

[獨自] alone; by oneself; one's own;
獨自謀生 hoe one's own row; paddle one's own canoe;
獨自一人 be all alone; be oneself;
~獨自一人工作 work alone;
~獨自一人生活 live alone;

[獨奏] solo;
獨奏會 recital;
獨奏家 soloist;
~大提琴獨奏家 cello soloist;
~小提琴獨奏家 violin soloist;
獨奏曲 solo;
~鋼琴獨奏曲 piano solo;
獨奏者 soloist;
小提琴獨奏 violin solo;

[獨坐] sit all by oneself;
孤燈獨坐 sit alone in front of the lamp;

不獨 not only;
單獨 alone; by oneself; single-handed;
牴獨 conflict; contradict;
非獨 not merely;
孤獨 lonely; solitary;
惸獨 brotherless and childless; friendless; helpless and lonely;
煢獨 alone; friendless and childless;
慎獨 cautious when one is alone;
唯獨 alone; only;
惟獨 alone; only;
幽獨 lonely; solitary;

du

【瀆】 show contempt; show disrespect;

[瀆職] dereliction of duty; malfeasance;
瀆職罪 dereliction of duty; malfeasance;

溝瀆 irrigation canals and ditches;
冒瀆 annoy a superior;
褻瀆 abuse; blaspheme; pollute; profane;
自瀆 masturbate; masturbation;

du

【櫝】 (1) closet; cabinet; cupboard; sideboard; wardrobe; (2) coffin; (3) scabbard; (4) conceal; hide;

du

【牘】 (1) writing tablet; (2) archive; document; letter;

案牘 office correspondence;
公牘 official document;
書牘 correspondence; written messages;
文牘 official documents and correspondence;
讞牘 records of criminal cases;

du

【犢】 calf;

［犢不畏虎］ a newborn calf does not fear tigers;
［犢子］ calf;
產犢 calve;
牛犢 calf;

du

【讀】 (1) read; read aloud; (2) attend school;
［讀本］ reader; textbook;
初級讀本 primer;
［讀出］ read-out;
和數讀出 sum read-out;
加倍讀出 double read-out;
目視讀出 visual read-out;
直接讀出 direct read-out;
［讀書］ (1) read; study; (2) attend school; (3) read a book;
讀書會 book group; reading circle;
讀書活動 reading activities;
讀書俱樂部 book club;
讀書明禮 study and know the rules of propriety;
讀書破萬卷，下筆如有神 having pored over ten thousand volumes, one can write with godly power — ample reading produces fluent writing;
讀書須用意，一字值千金 in study, concentration is required, for every character understood is worth a thousand pieces of gold;
讀書做官 study in order to become an official;
熬夜讀書 stay up reading;
埋頭讀書 bury oneself in books; grind away;
死讀書 bookworm; study mechanically;
專心讀書 be absorbed in study;
［讀熟］ learn by heart;
［讀數］ reading;
近似讀數 approximate reading;
平均讀數 average reading;
準確讀數 accurate reading;
［讀物］ reading material;
兒童讀物 children's books;
家庭讀物 family reading;
簡易讀物 easy reading;
科普讀物 popular science readings;
課外讀物 books for outside reading;
有聲讀物 talking book;
［讀音］ pronunciation;
［讀者］ reader;
讀者反應 reader's response;
讀者服務卡 reader service card;
讀者服務站 reader service station;
讀者需要論 theory of readers' need;
目的語讀者 target language reader;
以饗讀者 offer to the readers;

拜讀 have the honour to read; read with respect;
必讀 a must for reading;
唇讀 lip-read;
粗讀 rough reading;
錯讀 misread;
泛讀 extensive reading;
工讀 work and study;
攻讀 (1) study assiduously; study diligently; (2) specialize in;
機讀 machine-readable;
校讀 proofreading;
解讀 decode;
借讀 study at a school on a temporary basis;
精讀 peruse; read carefully and thoroughly;
句讀 sentences and phrases; the period and the comma;
可讀 readable;
苦讀 study hard;
朗讀 read aloud; read loudly and clearly;
默讀 read silently;
判讀 interpretation;
審讀 check and approve;
熟讀 read carefully over and over again;
誦讀 chant; read aloud;
跳讀 skip; skip in reading; skip through;
通讀 (1) read through; (2) understand what one reads;
細讀 perusal; peruse; read carefully;
宣讀 read aloud at a gathering or meeting; read out in public;
選讀 selected readings;
一讀 first reading;
異讀 variant pronunciation;
閱讀 read;
重讀 pronounce with stress;
走讀 attend a day school;

du

【髑】 human skull;
［髑髏］ human skull;

du

【黷】 (1) act wantonly; (2) blacken; defile;
［黷武］ bellicose; militaristic; warlike;

du³

du

【肚】 Aunt Nelly; stomach; tripe;
［肚子］ stomach; tripe;

爆肚 quick-fried tripe;
魚肚 fish maw;

du

【堵】 (1) block up; stop up; (2) stifle; suffocate; (3) wall;
［堵車］ traffic congestion;
車堵車 traffic jam;
［堵擊］ intercept and attack;
東堵西擊 resist at one point and attack at another;
［堵截］ cut off;
堵截敵人 intercept the enemy;
圍追堵塞 encirclement, pursuit, obstruction and interception;
［堵塞］ (1) block up; choke; gag; jam; stop up; (2) blind; blockage; block; choke; clog; impassability; plug; plug up; stop up;
堵塞交通 block the traffic; foul up traffic; hold up the traffic;
堵塞漏洞 plug a hole; stop up a loophole;
堵塞物 blockage;
堵塞言路 stifle criticisms and suggestions;
被堵塞 gunge; gunk;
磁頭堵塞 head clogging;
過濾器堵塞 filter clogging;
交通堵塞 traffic jam; traffic is at a standstill;
~遇到交通阻塞 get stuck in a traffic jam;
油管堵塞 oil-line plugging;
油篩堵塞 oil-screen clogging;
注入井堵塞 injection-well plugging;
［堵嘴］ gag sb; shut sb's mouth; silence sb;

安堵 live in peace and contentment; settle down undisturbed;

du

【睹】 see;
［睹景傷情］ be moved by what one sees; feel depressed at the sight of the scene; the scene evokes bitter memories of the past; the sight strikes a chord in one's chord;
［睹物］ see things;
睹物生情 the sight of familiar objects fills one with infinite melancholy — think of the dead;
睹物思人 seeing the thing one thinks of the person — the thing reminds one of its owner;

目睹 eyewitness to; see with one's own eyes; witness;

du

【賭】 (1) gamble; (2) bet;
［賭本］ money to gamble with;
［賭博］ gamble; gambling;
賭博成癮 be addicted to gambling;
賭博業經營者 bookmaker;
反對賭博 against gambling;
強迫性賭博 compulsive gambling;
取締賭博 ban gambling; clap a lid on gambling; knock out gambling;
嚴懲賭博 crack down on gambling;
［賭場］ casino; gambling house;
賭場輸窮漢 the poor always lose money in gamble.
賭場煙窟 gambling houses and opium parlours;
［賭鬼］ gambler;
［賭棍］ professional gambler;
［賭局］ gambling party;
［賭具］ gambling device; gambling paraphernalia;
［賭客］ gambler;
［賭窟］ gambling den;
［賭氣］ cut off one's own nose to spite one's face; feel wronged and act rashly; get in a rage; in a fit of pique;
賭氣走開 go away in a fit of pique;
［賭錢］ gamble;
喜歡賭錢 fond of gambling;
［賭枱］ gambling table;
賭枱管理員 croupier;
［賭徒］ gambler; punter;
強迫性賭徒 compulsive gambler;
［賭友］ gambling companions;
［賭債］ gambling debt;
欠下賭債 have a gambling debt;
［賭注］ stake; wager;
賭注單 betting slip;
賭注總額 total stake;
全部賭注 all the stakes;
下賭注 ante up;

打賭 accept a bet; accept a wager; bet; betting; have a bet with sb; lay a wager; lay a wager with sb; make a bet with sb; make a wager; risk money on sth; take up a bet; take up a wager; wager;
禁賭 ban gambling; prohibition of gambling; suppress gambling;
聚賭 gather together to gamble;
牌賭 gambling by playing cards;
嗜賭 be addicted to gambling;

du
【覩】 same as 睹 , see;

du
【篤】 (1) earnest; sincere; (2) critical; serious;
[篤厚] sincere and magnanimous;
[篤實] (1) honest and sincere; (2) solid; sound;
篤實光輝 sincere and glorious;
[篤信] believe devoutly in; believe truly; believe sincerely in;
[篤學] devoted to study; diligent in study; studious;
[篤志] earnestly resolve to;
篤志力行 earnest resolution to carry sth out;
篤志於學 zealously strive to study;

矮篤篤 dumpy; stumpy;
病篤 critically ill; seriously ill; terminally ill;
誠篤 cordial; sincere;
危篤 critically ill; dying; on the point of death;

du⁴
du
【妒】 envious of; envy; jealous of;
[妒恨] envy and resent;
又妒又恨 be jealous of sth and hate sb;
[妒忌] envious of; envy; grudge; jealous of;
相互間的妒忌 mutual jealousy;
厭倦妒忌 be tired of jealousy;
一陣妒忌 a stab of envy;
招惹妒忌 invite jealousy;

嫉妒 envious; envy; jealous;

du
【杜】 (1) birch-leaf pear; (2) prevent; shut out; stop; (3) a surname;
[杜漸] destroy sth before it becomes apparent;
杜漸防萌 nip the matter in the bud;
杜漸防微 check at the outset; crush in the egg; destroy at an early stage, before any mischief is done; destroy evils before they become apparent; nip in the bud;
防微杜漸 caution against small matters; check erroneous ideas at the outset; destroy evils before they become menacing; guard against gradual creeping corruption; kill the cases at birth; nip a vice in the bud;
[杜鵑] (1) cuckoo; (2) azalea;
杜鵑花 azalea;
杜鵑自鳴鐘 cuckoo clock;
[杜絕] eradicate completely; put an end to; stop;
杜絕弊端 cut off all corruption; stop all corrupt practices;
杜絕不良現象 put an end to unhealthy phenomena;
杜絕腐敗 stop all corrupt practices;
杜絕後患 eliminate the cause of future trouble; impede a future disaster; remove seeds of future trouble;
杜絕浪費 eliminate waste; put an end to waste;
杜絕流弊 put a stop to corrupt practices; put an end to abuses;
杜絕危險 wall up the danger;
杜絕言路 not let others express their views; stifle criticism;
杜絕謠言 give a quietus to a rumour;
杜絕隱患 provide against hidden trouble;
[杜門] shut the door;
杜門不出 close the door and refrain from going out; close the door and stay home; shut the door and keep at home; shut the door without going out;
杜門卻掃 close the gate and keep oneself to oneself; sever communication with the outside world; withdraw from society and live in solitude;
杜門謝客 close one's door to visitors; close the gate and shut out visitors; live in complete seclusion; shut one's door and decline seeing visitors; sport one's oak;
杜門隱世 sever communication with the outside; withdraw from society and live in solitude;
[杜撰] fabricate; make up;

杜撰新詞 coin a phrase;

du

【肚】 abdomen; belly; stomach;

［肚飽思睡］ when the belly is full, the bones would be at rest;

［肚腸］ bowels;

掛肚牽腸 be deeply concerned; be much worried about; cause deep personal concern;

笑斷肚腸 split one's sides with laughter;

［肚量］ magnanimity; tolerance;

［肚皮］ belly;

肚皮舞 belly dance;

笑破肚皮 be overwhelmed with laughter; laugh oneself into convulsions; roll with laughter; split one's sides with laughing;

~ 笑破了肚皮 have sb in stitches; keep sb in stitches;

笑痛肚皮 in convulsions;

［肚臍］ belly button; navel; tummy button;

肚臍眼 belly button; navel;

［肚痛］ collywobbles;

［肚子］ abdomen; belly; stomach; tummy;

肚子餓 hungry;

肚子裏尋思 think within oneself;

肚子裏有數 know sth very well in one's mind;

肚子疼 bellyache; have a pain in one's belly; have a pain in one's innards; suffer from abdominal pain;

肚子痛 have a pain in the abdomen; stomach ache; tummy ache;

~ 笑得肚子痛 convulsions;

餓肚子 gaunt with hunger;

~ 餓得肚子叫 cry cupboard; have a wolf in the stomach;

~ 餓肚子過活 live on air;

餓偏肚子 gaunt with hunger;

癟着肚子 with an empty stomach;

敞開肚子 eat without inhibition;

大肚子 (1) big eater; (2) paunch; pot-bellied; pot belly;

拉肚子 give the trots; have diarrhoea; have loose bowels; suffer from diarrhoea;

滿肚子 whirlpool;

~ 滿肚子壞主意 whirlpool of evil ideas;

鬧肚子 have diarrhoea; suffer from diarrhoea;

填滿肚子 cram one's stomach;

小肚子 belly; lower abdomen;

一肚子 a stomachful of;

~ 一肚子火 a stomachful of anger;

~ 一肚子氣 a stomachful of grudge; full of complaints; full of grievances; strong emotions;

走肚子 have diarrhoea; have loose bowels;

瀉肚 have diarrhoea; have loose bowels;

du

【度】 (1) linear measure; (2) degree of intensity; (3) degree; (4) kilowatt-hour; (5) degree; extent; limit; (6) magnanimity; tolerance; (7) consideration; (8) occasion; time; (9) pass; spend;

［度過］ pass; spend;

度過一世 live out one's days;

［度假］ go on holidays; spend one's holidays;

度假安排 holiday arrangements;

度假村 holiday village; vacation community;

度假區 holiday area;

度假日 holiday; vacation day

度假勝地 holiday resort; vacation spot;

~ 一處度假勝地 a holiday resort;

度假屋 holiday home;

度假營地 holiday camp;

度假者 holidaymaker; vacationer;

國外度假 holiday abroad;

~ 在國外度假 have a holiday abroad;

海濱度假 seaside holiday;

家庭度假 family holiday;

理想的度假 dream holiday;

去度假 go on holiday; go on vacation;

全家度假 family holiday;

外出度假 away on one's holidays; out for holidays;

在鄉下度假 take a holiday in the countryside;

正在度假 on one's holidays;

［度量］ (1) magnanimity; tolerance; (2) metric;

度量大 broad-minded; magnanimous;

度量寬宏 of magnanimous bearing;

~ 度量寬宏的人 a person with a big heart;

度量小 narrow-minded;

等價度量 equivalent metric;

離散度量 discrete metric;

雙曲度量 hyperbolic metric;

同胚度量 homeomorphic metric;

[度命] drag out a miserable existence; live a miserable life;

[度日] eke out an existence; make a living; pass the day; spend the day; subsist;

度日活命 manage to keep oneself alive with;

度日如年 days wear on like years; every day seems like a year in length; every day is a year long; lead a miserable life; pass a day as if it were a year; time hangs heavily on one's hands;

度日維艱 pass the day hardly; pass the day with difficulty;

安樂度日 pass the day happily;

放蕩度日 pass the day recklessly;

靠救濟度日 live on relief;

勉強度日 eke out one's existence; get a scanty subsistence;

難以度日 have a thin time;

淫逸度日 pass days with luxurious ease;

[度外] outside one's consideration;

置之度外 care nothing about; cast out of one's mind; disregard entirely; give no thought to; have no regard for; ignore; leave out of account; leave out of consideration; not to take into account; regardless of; without regard to;

凹度 concavity;
八度 octave;
標度 dial; scale;
猜度 conjecture; draw the bow; guess and assess; speculate; surmise;
裁度 consider and decide; deduce; infer; weigh;
測度 measure;
長度 length;
超度 say prayers to release souls from purgatory;
尺度 criterion; standard;
程度 degree; extent; level;
稠度 thickness;
揣度 appraise; conjecture; estimate; reckon; surmise;
純度 pureness; purity;
忖度 conjecture; presume; speculate; suppose; surmise;
大度 magnanimous;
調度 (1) dispatch; (2) control; manage;
陡度 gradient;
額度 capacity;
法度 (1) law; (2) moral standard;
豐度 abundance;
風度 bearing; demeanour; outward behaviour;
幅度 range; scope;
剛度 rigidity;
高度 altitude; height;
光度 luminosity;
廣度 range; scope;
軌度 laws; statutes;
國度 country; nation; state;
過度 excessive; over-; undue;
合度 appropriate; proper; suitable;
厚度 thickness;
弧度 radian;
歡度 spend an occasion joyfully;
活度 activity;
極度 extreme; the utmost point; to the utmost;
季度 quarter of a year;
焦度 focal power;
角度 (1) angle; (2) point of view;
進度 (1) rate of progress; (2) planned speed; schedule;
經度 longitude;
精度 precision;
精確度 precision;
可懂度 intelligibility;
刻度 gradation;
跨度 span;
寬度 breadth; width;
揆度 conjecture; estimate; investigate and consider; observe and estimate;
力度 dynamics;
粒度 size;
量度 measurement;
亮度 brightness; brilliance;
烈度 intensity;
零度 zero;
流度 fluidity;
密度 density; thickness;
敏度 acuity;
難度 degree of difficulty; difficulty;
能見度 visibility;
撓度 deflection;
年度 year;
黏度 viscosity;
捻度 twist;
濃度 concentration; consistency; density;
頻度 frequency;
坡度 gradient; slope;
氣度 bearing; tolerance;
強度 intensity; strength;
輕度 slight;
曲度 curvature;
銓度 estimate;
權度 (1) estimate; (2) laws;

熱度 (1) degree of heat; heat; (2) fever; temperature;
熔度 fusibility;
銳度 acuity; sharpness;
色度 chromaticity;
澀度 acerbity;
攝氏度 Celsius degree; centigrade;
深度 (1) degree of depth; (2) depth; profundity;
審度 deliberate; consider the pros and cons; study and estimate;
失度 excessive; immoderate;
濕度 humidity;
適度 appropriate; moderate; proper;
速度 rate; speed;
酸度 acidity;
態度 (1) bearing; manner; (2) approach; attitude;
甜度 sweetness;
凸度 convexity;
推度 infer;
彎度 flexure;
緯度 latitude;
溫度 temperature;
無度 excessive; immoderate;
細度 fineness;
限度 limit; limitation;
斜度 obliquity;
虛度 spend time in vain; waste time;
一度 for a time; once;
逸度 elegant air; refined manner;
臆度 conjecture; guess; surmise;
硬度 hardness;
用度 expenditure; expense;
圓度 roundness;
月度 monthly;
再度 once again; second time;
則度 regulations; rules;
照度 illuminance; intensity of illumination;
制度 institution; system;
重度 serious; severe;
錐度 taper;
濁度 turbidity;

du

【渡】 (1) cross; (2) pull through; tide over; (3) ferry crossing;

［渡船］ ferry; ferry boat;
車輛渡船 car ferry;
登上渡船 board the ferry;
拉索渡船 cable ferry; rope ferry;

［渡過］ tide over; voyage;
渡過苦海 rescue from life of pains and misery and reach the other shore of salvation;
渡過難關 go through a difficult pass; go through a difficult period; pull through; tide over a difficulty; turn the corner;
渡過許多困難 through much trouble;
安全渡過 ride out;

［渡海］ sail across a sea;

［渡河］ cross a river;

［渡口］ ferry; ferry crossing; fording;

［渡輪］ ferry boat; ferry;
一班渡輪 one scheduled run of a ferry;
一艘渡輪 a ferry;

［渡線］ crossover;
對向渡線 facing point crossover;
高速渡線 high-speed crossover;
聯鎖渡線 interlocked crossover;
臨時渡線 emergency crossover;
雙叉渡線 double crossover;

擺渡 ferry; ferry boat;
過渡 interim; transition;
橫渡 cross a river or sea;
津渡 ferry crossing;
競渡 (1) have a boat race; (2) have a swimming race;
輪渡 ferry;
強渡 fight one's way across a river;
搶渡 cross a river speedily;
泅渡 swim across;
讓渡 cede; turn over;
引渡 extradite;

du

【鍍】 plating;

［鍍金］ (1) gold-plating; (2) get gilded;
鍍金相架 gilded frame;

［鍍錫］ tinning;
電鍍錫 electrolytic tinning;
接觸鍍錫 contact tinning;
冷鍍錫 cold tinning;
熱鍍錫 hot tinning;

［鍍鋅］ galvanization; galvanizing;
冷鍍鋅 cold galvanization;
普通熱鍍鋅 conventional galvanization;
熱鍍鋅 pot galvanization;
砂抹鍍鋅 sand galvanization;

du

【斁】 dislike;

du

【蠹】 (1) book-eating or cloth-eating in-

sects; (2) moth-eaten; worm-eaten;
[蠹蟲] (1) moth; (2) vermin;
[蠹魚] fishmoth; silverfish;

祿蠹 people of the exploiting class who seek rank and handsome salary;
書蠹 bookworm;

duan[1]
duan
【耑】 same as 端;
duan
【端】 (1) end; extremity; (2) beginning; (3) item; point; (4) cause; reason; (5) proper; upright; (6) carry; hold sth level with both hands;
[端的] (1) whole process from beginning to end; (2) really; (3) after all; in the end;
[端方] honest; upright;
[端服嚴容] one's dress is sober and one's face stern;
[端量] look sb up and down;
[端倪] clue; inkling;
端倪可察 have an inkling of the matter; have found a clue to sth;
端倪可見 can discern certain clues; have an inkling of the matter;
毫無端倪 not have a clue;
略察端倪 find a clue to the matter;
略有端倪 have an inkling of the matter;
已見端倪 see an indication;
[端午節] Dragon Boat Festival;
[端詳] examine; look sb up and down; scrutinize;
舉止端詳 behave with serene dignity;
細説端詳 give a full and detailed account; give full particulars;
相貌端詳 have a serene look;
[端緒] clue; inkling;
端緒顯明 the clue is evident;
千端萬緒 very complicated;
探端知緒 investigate the beginning and know the end;
[端正] (1) regular; upright; (2) correct; proper; (3) correct; rectify; straighten;
端正方向 move in the right direction;
端正思想 correct one's thinking; straighten out one's ideas;
端正態度 have a correct attitude toward…;
端端正正 regular; straight;
品貌端正 have well-shaped figure and decorous appearance;
品行端正 of good character;
人品端正 have a good personal character;
五官端正 have regular features;
坐得端正 sit up straight;
[端莊] decorum; demure; dignified; sedate;
端莊大方 dignified and magnanimous;
端莊凝重 look solemn and dignified;
端莊嫻雅 dignified and elegant;
舉止端莊 dignified conduct;

百端 all kinds of matters; all kinds of thoughts; all matters;
筆端 flow of thought in writing or drawing;
鼻端 tip of the nose;
弊端 corrupt practice; malpractice;
不端 dishonourable; improper;
大端 important points; main aspects;
頂端 (1) peak; top; (2) end; tip;
好端端 in perfectly good condition;
發端 inception; initiative; make a start;
骨端 extremitas;
禍端 cause of ruin; source of a disaster;
極端 exceeding; extreme; extremity; the utmost point;
尖端 most advanced; most sophisticated; peak; pointed end;
借端 use sth as a pretext;
開端 beginning; start;
連鍋端 destroy lock, stock and barrel; get rid of the whole lot;
兩端 both ends; either end; ends;
末端 end; tip;
起端 beginning; genesis; origin;
上端 top; upper edge; upper end; upper extreme;
事端 dispute; incident;
台端 you;
萬端 multifarious;
尾端 tail of sth;
無端 for no reason; without cause;
先端 tip of sth;
衅端 cause for a quarrel or dispute;
釁端 cause of a fight; controversial issue; dispute;
要端 essentials; main points;
一端 (1) one end; (2) one respect; one side of the matter;
異端 heresy; heterodoxy;
雲端 high in the clouds;
造端 begin; originate;
戰端 beginning of a war;

D

肇端 beginning;
爭端 conflict; dispute;
終端 terminal;

duan³
duan

【短】 (1) brief; short; (2) lack; owe; (3) fault; weak point;
[短棒] cosh;
[短波] short wave;
超短波 ultrashort wave;
中短波 medium short wave;
[短程] short distance; short range; trip;
[短秤] short weight;
[短處] bad points; defects; demerits; drawbacks; failings; faults; shortcomings; weak points; weaknesses;
彌補短處 atone for one's shortcomings;
[短促] of very short duration; pressed for time; short; swift; very brief;
呼吸短促 short of breath;
時間短促 time is short and pressing;
[短吊] drop shot;
[短髮] bobbed hair; bob-haired; hair in a bob; shingle; short hair;
齊短髮 bob cut;
[短歌] jingle;
[短見] (1) shallow knowledge; short-sighted; (2) suicide;
短見寡聞 have short sight and rare hearing; of limited experience;
尋短見 attempt suicide; commit suicide; end one's own life; take one's own life;
~自尋短見 commit suicide; seek one's own destruction; shut one's light off;
想自尋短見 intend to commit suicide;
[短劍] cutlass;
[短截線] stub;
電容性短截線 capacitive stub;
短路短截線 closed stub;
匹配短截線 matching stub;
同軸短截線 coaxial stub;
[短款] shortfall;
[短褲] shorts;
超短褲 very short shorts;
~緊身超短褲 hot pants;
平腳短褲 boxer shorts;
束腳短褲 breeches;
[短命] die young; short-lived;
[短跑] dash; short-distance running; sprint;
短跑運動員 sprinter;
[短片] short film; short videos;
觀看視頻短片 video snacking;
[短評] brief comment; short commentary;
[短期] short period; short-term;
短期而言 in the short term;
短期國庫券 short-term treasury bond;
短期記憶 short-term memory;
短期見效 bring about the effect in a short term;
短期金融市場 short-term money market;
短期決策 short-term decision;
短期投資 short-term investment;
短期信貸 short-term credit;
[短淺] narrow and shallow;
見識短淺 lack knowledge and experience; light in the head;
目光短淺 cannot see beyond one's nose; short-sighted;
眼光短淺 shortsighted;
[短球] drop shot;
[短缺] deficiency; deficit; shortage;
短缺經濟 shortage economy;
~短缺經濟學 economics of shortage;
緩解短缺 ease a shortage;
面臨短缺 face a shortage;
人力短缺 manpower shortage;
糧食短缺 food shortage;
燃油短缺 fuel shortage;
嚴重短缺 in serious shortage;
造成短缺 cause a shortage of sth; create a shortage of sth;
資金短缺 money shortage;
住房短缺 housing shortage;
[短裙] short skirt;
超短裙 mini; miniskirt;
褶襉短裙 kilt;
[短少] deficient; drought; lack; missing; short;
[短時] short time;
短時記憶 short-time memory;
[短視] (1) myopia; nearsightedness; shortsighted; (2) lack foresight;
[短途] short distance;
[短襪] socks;
翻邊短襪 bobby socks;
[短文] short essay;
[短線] goods in short supply;
短線產品 product in short supply;

[短小] short; short and small; small;
短小精悍 short and sweet; short but strong and capable; small, compactly built, and very capable; very alert and agile;
[短信] note; short letter;
一封短信 a note;
[短語] expression; phrase;
短語標記 phrase marker;
短語詞 phrasal word;
短語動詞 phrasal verb;
短語翻譯 phrasal translation;
短語介詞 phrasal preposition;
短語數詞 phrasal numeral;
短語新詞 phrasal neologism;
比較短語 comparative phrase;
并聯短語 parallel phrase;
不定式短語 infinitive phrase;
措詞精當的短語 well-turned phrase;
動詞短語 verb phrase;
動名詞短語 gerundial phrase;
分詞短語 participial phrase;
副詞短語 adverb phrase;
固定短語 set phrase;
結果短語 resultative phrase;
介詞短語 prepositional phrase;
~介詞短語狀語 prepositional adverbial;
名詞短語 noun phrase;
名詞性短語 nominal phrase;
內向短語 endocentric phrase;
前置詞短語 prepositional phrase;
所有短語 genitive phrase;
同位短語 appositive phrase;
外向短語 exocentric phrase;
限制性短語 restrictive phrase;
[短暫] brief; momentary; of short duration; transient;
人生短暫 life is short at best;

庇短 conceal a defect; partial and willing to overlook shortcomings;
長短 (1) length; (2) accident; mishap; (3) good and bad; right and wrong; strong and weak points;
粗短 humpty-dumpty;
護短 conceal one's faults; cover one's mistakes; side with a disputant who is in the wrong;
簡短 brief;
揭短 catch sb on the raw; find out sb's shortcomings; rake up sb's faults;
虧短 short of;
理短 have no justification; on the wrong side;
氣短 (1) breathe hard; short of breath; (2) be dejected; be discouraged; lose heart;
縮短 cut down; shorten;
所短 one's shortcomings or defects;
問短 make sb unable to answer;
修短 length;
最短 the shortest;

duan⁴
duan
【段】 (1) part; section; segment; (2) paragraph; passage; (3) a surname;
[段落] (1) paragraph; section; (2) conclusion of a part; phase; stage;
告一段落 be brought to a temporary close; come to the end of a stage;
過於雕飾的段落 purple passage;

波段 waveband;
唱段 aria;
綢段 silk goods;
地段 sector of an area;
分段 (1) fragment; section; (2) paragraph;
工段 (1) section of a construction project; (2) workshop section;
河段 stream segment;
階段 phase; stage;
兩段 two halves; two sections;
路段 section of a highway;
片段 section;
區段 section;
身段 (1) woman's figure; (2) posture;
時段 time interval;
手段 (1) means; measure; medium; (2) artifice; trick;
線段 line segment;
選段 selection;
一段 (1) one paragraph; one passaage; one stanza; (2) a chunk of; a leg of; a length of; a period of; a piece of; a section of; a streak of;
語段 text;
樂段 period;

duan
【緞】 satin;
[緞帶] satin ribbon;
[緞子] satin;

綢緞 silks and satin;
花緞 brocade; figured satin;
錦緞 brocade;

羅緞 tussores;
軟緞 soft silk fabric in satin weave;
羽緞 kind of satin-like cotton fabric;

duan

【鍛】 forge;

［鍛煉］ (1) have physical training; take exercise; (2) steel; temper; toughen;
鍛煉成長 be steeled and tempered and grow up;
百鍛千煉 thoroughly tempered;
堅持鍛煉 take regular exercise;
進行鍛煉 do exercise; perform physical exercise; take exercise;
久經鍛煉 long-steeled;
缺乏鍛煉 lack of exercise;
體育鍛煉 have physical training; take exercise;

［鍛造］ forging;
爆炸鍛造 explosive forging;
鋁鍛造 aluminium forging;
模型鍛造 closed die forging;

冷鍛 cold forging; cold hammering;
型鍛 swage;
壓鍛 press forging;

duan

【斷】 (1) break; snap; (2) break off; cut off; stop; (3) abstain from; give up; (4) decide; judge; (5) absolutely; decidedly;

［斷案］ (1) settle a lawsuit; (2) conclusion of a syllogism;

［斷編殘簡］ incomplete parts of ancient scripts;

［斷層］ fault;
背斜斷層 anticlinal fault;
活性斷層 active fault;
異常斷層 abnormal fault;

［斷腸］ break sb's heart; extremely sad; heart-broken;
令人斷腸 gut-wrenching;

［斷代］ divide history into periods; periods of history;

［斷檔］ (1) out of stock; (2) discontinued supply;

［斷電］ blackout; interruption of electrical power supply; power cut;

［斷定］ assertion; assertive; conclude; decide; form a judgment;
斷定代詞 assertive pronoun;
斷定句 assertive sentence;
~ 非斷定句 non-assertive sentence;
一口斷定 allege; arbitrarily assert; jump to the conclusion;

［斷斷］ absolutely;
斷斷續續 by fits and starts; by snatches; continue from time to time; disjointedly; intermittently; off and on; on and off; work in snatches;
~ 斷斷續續的 halting;
斷斷續續的關係 on-off relationship;
斷斷續續地 on and off;

［斷交］ (1) break off a friendship; (2) break off diplomatic relations; sever diplomatic relations;

［斷句］ (1) make pauses when reading unpunctuated ancient writings; (2) punctuate;

［斷絕］ break off; cut off; sever; stop;
斷絕邦交 sever diplomatic relations;
斷絕供應 cut off the supplies of; shut off the supplies of;
斷絕關係 absolve from all consequences; break off with; cut off relations; finish with; have done with; sever connections; wash one's hands of;
斷絕後患 burn one's boat; cut off one's retreat;
斷絕交通 stop traffic;
斷絕來往 break up with sb;
~ 跟人斷絕來往 break up with sb;
斷絕聯繫 sever contacts with;
斷絕外交關係 break off diplomatic relations;
斷絕往來 drop an acquaintance; finish with sb;
斷絕音信 break off contact;
斷絕友誼 sever a friendship relation;

［斷口］ break;
玻璃狀斷口 glass break;
不平整斷口 irregular break;
粗糙斷口 rough break;
晶體斷口 crystalline break;

［斷塊山］ fault-block mountain;

［斷裂］ break; breakage; disrupt; rift; rupture;
插入斷裂 insertion breakage;
脆性斷裂 brittle rupture;
底部斷裂 bottom break;
等點斷裂 isochromatic break;
等位斷裂 isolocus break;

活塞環斷裂 piston ring breakage;
鍵斷裂 bond rupture;
潛在斷裂 potential break;

[斷流] cut out the flow of an electric current; cut-out;
斷流器 cut-out;
~ 雙極斷流器 double-pole cut-out;
~ 油淬斷流器 oil-quenched cut-out;

[斷路] circuit break; cut-out;
斷路器 breaker; circuit breaker;
~ 安全斷路器 safety cut-out;
~ 備用斷路器 backup breaker;
~ 定時滯後斷路器 definite time-lag circuit breaker;
~ 對流式斷路器 convection circuit breaker;
~ 高速斷路器 high-speed circuit breaker;
~ 高壓油斷路器 high-voltage oil circuit breaker;
~ 鑒頻斷路器 frequency discriminator;
~ 角形斷路器 horn circuit breaker;
~ 空氣吹弧斷路器 airblast circuit breaker;
~ 離心式斷路器 centrifugal circuit breaker;
~ 噴氣流斷路器 air-blast circuit breaker;
~ 膨脹斷路器 expansion circuit breaker;
~ 氣動斷路器 air circuit breaker;
~ 熔絲斷路器 fusible circuit breaker;
~ 雙極斷路器 double-pole cut-out;
~ 雙投斷路器 double-throw circuit breaker;
~ 碳斷路器 carbon breaker;
~ 天線斷路器 aerial circuit breaker;
~ 壓縮空氣斷路器 compressed air breaker;
~ 延時斷路器 delay-action circuit breaker;
~ 自動斷路器 auto cut-out; automatic circuit breaker; free-handle breaker;

[斷面] profile;
平衡縱斷面 balanced profile;
凸凹形斷面 concavo-convex profile;
碴牀斷面 ballast profile;

[斷奶] wean;
斷奶食品 ablactation food;
給嬰兒斷奶 wean a baby from the breast;

[斷氣] breathe one's last breath;
斷氣身亡 with a last gasp of breath he gives up the ghost;

[斷然] (1) absolutely; categorically; flatly; simply; (2) drastic; resolute;
斷然不同 absolutely different;
斷然處置 manage resolutely; take the bull by the horns;
斷然否認 categorically deny;
斷然拒絕 dismiss peremptorily; flat refusal; refuse point-blank; reject flatly; shoot down;
斷然行動 act with decision;

[斷乳] ablactation; wean a baby;

[斷事] divide a matter;

[斷續] stop and continue;
斷弦再續 remarry after the death of one's wife;
忽斷忽續 by fits and starts;
時斷時續 off and on; on and off;

[斷送] forfeit; ruin;
斷送前程 ruin one's career;

[斷頭] be beheaded;
斷頭河 beheaded river;
斷頭台 guillotine; scaffold;

[斷尾河] betrunked river;

[斷無此理] absolutely against reason; absolutely untenable; the height of absurdity;

[斷線] (1) break off relations with sb; (2) lose continuity in tradition or accomplishments; (3) disconnection;
斷線風箏 kite with a broken line;
部份斷線 partial disconnection;
間歇斷線 intermittent disconnection;

[斷言] affirm; allege; assert categorically; aver; declare; say with certainty; state with certainty;

[斷語] conclusion; judgment;
遽下斷語 jump to conclusions;

[斷垣殘壁] broken walls; devastated houses;

[斷章取義] garble a statement; interpret out of context; make a deliberate misinterpretation out of context; quote a remark out of its context; take sth out of context;

不斷 continuous; unceasing; uninterrupted;
裁斷 consider and decide;
腸斷 heartbroken; deeply grieved;
寸斷 be broken up into very short pieces;
打斷 (1) break (one's leg, etc.); (2) cut in; cut short; interrupt;
獨斷 arbitrary; dictatorial;
割斷 chop up; cut apart; cut off; isolate; lop off;

sever;
隔斷 obstruct; separate;
公斷 (1) arbitrate; (2) make an impartial judgment;
關斷 cut off; shut off; turn off;
果斷 decisive; resolute;
機斷 act on one's own judgment in an emergency;
剪斷 cut off; nip off; shear off; snip;
間斷 be disconnected; be interrupted;
截斷 (1) block; cut off; obstruct; (2) cut in; cut short; interrupt;
決斷 make a decision; resolution; resolve;
砍斷 break apart by chopping; cut in two;
了斷 end; finish;
壟斷 monopolize;
論斷 inference; judgment;
明斷 fair judgment; pass a fair judgment;
判斷 decide; determine; judge; judgment;
片斷 extract; fragment; fragmentary; incomplete; part; passage; section;
評斷 arbitrate; judge;
掐斷 break; cut off; nip off;
切斷 break; cut; cut asunder; cut off; disconnect; key off; key out; sever; shut off; switch off; turn out;
熔斷 fuse;
掃斷 be totally eliminated;
審斷 examine and decide; pass a judgement after an examination;
摔斷 fracture;
聽斷 pass judgment after hearing the case;
推斷 deduce; infer;
枉斷 abuse law by distorting it; decide unfairly;
妄斷 jump to the conclusion;
武斷 arbitrary; subjective;
續斷 teasel root;
懸斷 judge without any sufficient basis;
訊斷 hand down a judgement;
臆斷 assume; suppose;
英斷 intelligent decision;
預斷 prejudge;
占斷 find out by practising divination;
斬斷 chop off; cleave in two;
遮斷 interdict;
折斷 break off;
診斷 diagnose; diagnosis;
中斷 break off; discontinue; suspend;
專斷 act arbitrarily;
斫斷 chop off; cut off; sever by cutting or chopping;

dui¹
dui

【堆】 (1) heap up; pile up; (2) crowd; heap; pile; sack; (3) hillock; mound;

［堆肥］ compost;
堆肥堆 compost heap;
製成堆肥 compost;
～可製成堆肥［的］ compostable;
［堆垛機］ stacker;
電力堆垛機 electric stacker;
廢板堆垛機 reject stacker;
機械堆垛機 mechanical stacker;
墜落堆垛機 down stacker;
［堆放］ pile up; stack;
［堆積］ accumulate; cumulate; heap up; pile up; upbuilding;
堆積如山 lie in a heap; pile up like a mountain;
［堆加］ accumulation;
堆加效應 accumulation effect;
［堆砌］ (1) pile up phrases and sentences; (2) pile up;
［堆石］ rockfill;
傾卸堆石 dumped rockfill; tipped rockfill;
壓實堆石 compacted rockfill; rolled rockfill;
［堆填區］ landfill;
［堆土成山］ carry earth to raise mounds; many a little makes a mickle; pile up a mound with earth;

草堆 haystack;
反應堆 reactor;
糞堆 dunghill; manure pile;
故紙堆 a heap of musty old books or papers;
沙堆 sand dune; sand hill;
石堆 cairn;
停堆 shut-down;
土堆 mound;
雪堆 snow drift;
一大堆 a big heap of; a great pile of; a large amount of;
一堆 a bank of; a bundle of; a crop of; a crowd of; a group of; a heap of; a host of; a mass of; a mountain of; a pile of; a ruck of; a tumble of;

dui⁴
dui

【兑】 (1) convert; exchange; (2) add;

[兑付] cash a cheque;
[兑換] conversion; convert; exchange; redemption;
兑換滙率 exchange rate;
兑換外幣 exchange foreign currency;
兑換現款 cash in;
自由兑換 freely convertible;
[兑匯券] foreign exchange certificate;
[兑現] (1) cash a cheque; pay cash; redemption; (2) fulfil; honour a commitment; make good a promise; make real; realize;
説話不兑現 fail to keep one's promise;
政策兑現 materialize a policy;

保兑 confirm; confirmation;
承兑 accept; honour;
匯兑 money remittance; remittance;
擠兑 (1) bully; (2) belittle;
商兑 discuss and consider;
折兑 convert; exchange gold or silver for money;

dui
【敦】 (1) container; (2) press; urge;
dui
【隊】 (1) a line of people; a row of people; (2) group; team;
[隊列] formation; queue;
隊列舞 line drawing;
[隊伍] (1) army; troops; (2) contingent; ranks;
解散隊伍 break the ranks;
率領隊伍 lead one's troops;
召集隊伍 muster in troops;
[隊形] formation;
保持隊形 keep ranks; preserve the formation;
變換隊形 change the formation;
戰鬥隊形 battle array;
[隊員] team member;
一名隊員 a team member;
[隊長] captain; chargehand; team leader;
隊長任期 captaincy;
隊長職位 captaincy;
不參加比賽的隊長 non-playing captain;
場上隊長 field caption;
擔任隊長 captain;
球隊隊長 captain; skipper;

保安隊 peace preservation corps;
編隊 form into columns; formation; organize into teams;
兵隊 troop;
部隊 (1) armed forces; army; (2) army unit; troops;
插隊 jump the queue; queue-jumping;
車隊 motorcade;
船隊 fleet; flotilla;
登山隊 mountaineering party;
掉隊 drop off; fall behind; lag behind;
分隊 military unit corresponding to the platoon or squad;
敢死隊 dare-to-die corps;
工作隊 work team; working force;
狗仔隊 paparazzo;
管樂隊 wind band;
歸隊 (1) rejoin one's unit; (2) return to the profession one was trained for;
國家隊 national team;
橫隊 rank; row;
艦隊 (1) fleet; naval force; (2) task fleet;
軍隊 armed forces; army; troops;
客隊 away team; visiting team;
拉拉隊 cheering squad; roofers;
啦啦隊 cheer squad; cheering team;
離隊 drop out of the ranks; leave one's post;
列隊 line up;
領隊 leader of a group;
男隊 men's team;
女隊 women's team;
排隊 (1) line up; queue; queue up; stand in line; (2) classify and list;
砲隊 artillery;
球隊 team;
梯隊 echelon; echelon formation;
同隊 of the same team;
團隊 team;
衛隊 armed escort; bodyguards; squad of bodyguards;
先遣隊 advance party; vanguard;
小隊 group; squad; team;
校隊 school team;
絃樂隊 string orchestra;
一大隊 an army of;
一隊 (1) a contingent; a detachment; (2) a body of; a caravan of; a column of; a fleet of; a flotilla of; a group of; a team of; a train of; a platoon of;
游擊隊 guerrilla forces;
援隊 support unit;
樂隊 band; orchestra;
運輸隊 transport corps;
站隊 line up; queue up; stand in line;
支隊 department;

主隊 home team; host team;
縱隊 column;
總隊 department;

dui

【碓】 pestle;

［碓房］ establishment for hulling grain;

dui

【對】 (1) answer; reply; (2) cope with; retreat; (3) be directed on; be trained on; (4) face to face; mutual; (5) opposing; opposite; (6) bring into contact; fit one into the other; (7) get along; suit; (8) compare; identify; (9) adjust; set; (10) correct; right; (11) add; mix; (12) divide into halves; (13) antithetical couplet; couplet; (14) couple; pair;

［對岸］ opposite bank; other side of the river;

［對白］ dialogue;

［對半］ (1) divide half-and-half; down the middle; fifty-fifty; go halves; half-and-half; in half; into halves; (2) double;
對半分 divide half and half; go halves;

［對比］ (1) balance; comparison; contrast; (2) ratio;
對比度 contrast;
~ 色對比度 colour contrast;
~ 細節對比度 detail contrast;
~ 顯色對比度 development contrast;
對比分析 contrastive analysis;
對比核心 contrastive focus;
對比話語分析 contrastive discourse analysis;
對比聯想 association by contrast;
對比率 contrast;
~ 底片對比率 film contrast;
~ 相對對比率 relative contrast;
對比語言學 contrastive linguistics;
對比重音 contrastive stress;
晶粒對比 grain contrast;
可資對比 provide a contrast;
亮度對比 brightness contrast;
派生對比 derivational contrast;
強烈的對比 strong contrast;
雙項對比 binary contrast;

［對簿］ be tried at court; confront sb with witnesses;
對簿公堂 argue with sb in the courtroom; check evidence of both parties at court; check the accounts in the court; confront at court; confront sb before a law court;

［對不起］ (1) allow me; excuse me; I am sorry; I beg your pardon; if I dare say so; if you don't mind; if you please; pardon; pardon me; sorry; will you forgive me; (2) let sb down; unfair to; unworthy of;
對不起父母 do a disservice to one's parents;
對不起麻煩你了 sorry to bother you;

［對策］ countermeasure; countermove; the way to deal with a situation;
對策論 game theory;
採取對策 take some countermeasures;
籌商對策 discuss what countermeasures to take;
毫無對策 do not have any countermeasures;

［對詞］ actors studying lines together;

［對稱］ symmetry;
對稱處理機 symmetric processor;
對稱多處理 symmetric multi-process;
對稱性方法 symmetric method;
不對稱 asymmetry;
~ 不對稱的 asymmetrical;
~ 點陣不對稱 lattice asymmetry;
~ 東西不對稱 east-west asymmetry;
~ 方位不對稱 azimuthal asymmetry;
~ 晶格不對稱 crystal lattice asymmetry;
~ 晶體不對稱 crystal asymmetry;
~ 絕對不對稱 absolute asymmetry;
~ 裂變不對稱 fission asymmetry;
~ 相對不對稱 relative asymmetry;
~ 形狀不對稱 configurational asymmetry;
~ 左右不對稱 left-right asymmetry;
電荷對稱 charge symmetry;
絕對對稱 absolute symmetry;
圓對稱 circular symmetry;
中心對稱 central symmetry;
左右對稱 bilateral symmetry; zygomorphy;

［對答］ answer; answer back; reply;
對答如流 a glib reply; answer as quickly as the flowing of water; answer fluently; answer glibly; answer readily without stopping; answer up to every question; answer without a hitch; answer without any hesitation; be ready at repartee; fluent repartee; give fluent replies; have a ready tongue;

quick in answer; ready answer; reply in a stream of eloquence; reply in a stream of eloquence;

[對打] fight each other;

[對待] approach; handle; treat;
受到不公平的對待 be treated inequitably;

[對得起] not let sb down; treat sb fairly; worthy of;

[對等] equity; on an equal footing; reciprocity;
對等詞 equivalent;
~ 比喻性對等詞 figurative equivalent;
非比喻性對等詞 non-figurative equivalent;
~ 標準對等詞 stock equivalent; standard equivalent;
~ 詞匯對等詞 lexical equivalent;
~ 法定對等詞 official equivalent;
~ 翻譯對等詞 translation equivalent;
~ 解釋性對等詞 explanantory equivalent;
~ 描述性對等詞 descriptive equivalent;
~ 目的語對等詞 target language equivalent;
對等從句 equivalent clause;
對等反應 equivalent response;
對等分布 equivalent distribution;
對等關係 equivalent relation;
部份對等 partial equivalence;
動態對等 dynamic equivalence;
風格對等 stylistic equivalence;
功能對等 functional equivalence;
潛在對等 potential equivalence;

[對對糊] (of mahjong) all-paired-tile win;

[對方] opposite side; other party; other side;

[對付] (1) cope with; deal with; tackle; (2) make do; (3) counter; oppose;
對付措施 countermeasure;
難對付 hard to handle;
- 難對付的人 hard nut; tough nut;
- 難對付的事情 a hard nut to crack;

[對合] involution;
循環對合 cyclic involution;
中心對合 central involution;

[對話] conversation; dialogue; have a conversation; have a dialogue; talk;
對話構造系統 dialogue builder system;
對話話語 dialogue discourse;
對話控制部件 dialogue control component;
多線對話 multi-threaded dialogue;
進行對話 carry on a dialogue;
平淡無奇的對話 vapid conversation;
生硬的對話 stilted conversation;
一段對話 a dialogue;

[對講] intercom; talkback;
對講電路 talkback;
~ 攝像機對講電路 camera talkback;
~ 轉播車對講電路 omnibus talkback;
對講機 intercom; walkie-talkie;
~ 無線電對講機 walkie-talkie;
對講系統 intercom system;
演講室對講 sound talkback;

[對角] diagonally; opposite angles;
對角剪開 cut diagonally;
對角線 diagonal;
~ 對角線化 diagonalization;
~ 次對角線 minor diagonal;
~ 輔對角線 auxiliary diagonal;
~ 掃描對角線 scan diagonal;
~ 體對角線 body diagonal;
~ 圖像對角線 image diagonal;
~ 主對角線 leading diagonal; principal diagonal;

[對景] seeing the scene;
對景傷情 be moved by what one sees; feel hurt at seeing the view;
對景生情 full of emotion when facing the scene;

[對勁] (1) to one's liking; suit one; (2) normal; right;

[對鏡自照] look at one's reflection in a mirror; look at oneself at a looking glass; see oneself in a looking glass;

[對句] couplet;

[對開] (1) run from opposite directions; (2) folio; (3) go fifty-fifty; (4) back-to-back;
對開利潤 halve the profit;
對開信用證 reciprocal letter of credit;
對開賬戶 back-to-back account;

[對抗] (1) antagonism; antagonize; counter; face-off; (2) oppose; resist;
對抗暴力 oppose violence;
對抗的 antagonistic;
對抗性言外功能 competitive illocutionary function;
對抗者 antagonist;
對抗作用 antagonistic action;
產生對抗 create antagonism;
敵方對抗 enemy countermeasure;
電磁對抗 electromagnetic countermeasure;
電子對抗 electronic countermeasure;

紅外對抗 infrared countermeasure;
激光對抗 laser countermeasure;
減少對抗 reduce confrontation;
平息對抗 lay an antagonism to rest;
通信對抗 communication countermeasure;
與敵人對抗 oppose resistance to the enemy;

[對口] (1) speak alternately; (2) fit in with one's speciality;
對口會談 counterpart talk;
對口形 lip-synch; lip synchronization;
~對口形錄音 lip synchronization;
對口形錄音者 lip synchronist;
對口形錄音室 lip synchronization studio;

[對了] that's right;
太對了 now you're talking;
做對了 on the right track;

[對壘] pit against each other;
兩軍對壘 the two armies throw up defenses; two armies pit against each other;
爭鋒對壘 match on the battlefield;

[對立] antagonistic to; counterpose; dichotomy; oppose; opposition; set sth against;
對立詞 opposite;
~關係對立詞 relational opposites;
對立結構 absolute construction;
對立統一 the unity of opposites;
對立者 antagonist;
部份對立 proportional opposition;
倒置對立 inverse opposition;
多邊對立 multilateral opposition;
二項對立 binary opposition;
分類對立 taxonomic opposition;
關係對立 relative opposition;
句法對立 syntactic opposition;
均等對立 equipollent opposition;
音位對立 phonological opposition;

[對聯] couplet;

[對流] convect; convection;
對流層 troposphere;
~對流層頂 tropopause;
對流放電 convective discharge;
對流換熱 convective heat transfer;
對流活動 convective activity;
對流機 convector;
電對流 electric convection;
動力對流 dynamical convection;
動態對流 dynamic convection;
環型對流 cellular convection;
空氣對流 air convection;
強制對流 forced convection;
熱對流 heat convection; thermal convection;
重力對流 gravitational convection;
自然對流 free convection;

[對路] match;
貨不對路 unwanted goods;

[對罵] abuse each other; call each other names; scold each other;

[對門] (1) face each other; (2) the building opposite; (3) face to face; (4) (mahjong) the opponent sitting opposite to one;

[對面] (1) across the way; opposite; (2) directly; right in front; (3) face to face;
對面而坐 sit opposite;
街對面 across the street; on the other side of the street;
斜對面 diagonally opposite;
在對面 on the opposite side of; on the other side;

[對內] domestic; home; internal;
對內搞活 enliven the domestic economy;

[對偶] duality; pairing;
對偶性 duality;
~部份對偶性 partial duality;
~階乘對偶性 factorial duality;
~局部對偶性 local duality;
環繞對偶 linking duality;
凸對偶 convex duality;

[對人] one's attitude towards others;
對人傲慢 arrogant to sb;
對事不對人 concern oneself with facts and not with individuals;

[對手] (1) adversary; antagonist; opponent; rival; (2) equal; match;
不堪一擊的對手 straw man;
擊倒對手 knockout;
難以戰勝的對手 nemesis;
遇到對手 meet one's match;

[對數] logarithm;
對數表 logarithmic table;
對數函數 logarithmic function;
常用對數 common logarithm;
代數對數 algebraic logarithm;
疊對數 iterated logarithms;
反對數 inverse logarithm;
複對數 complex logarithm;

積分對數 integral logarithm;
普通對數 general logarithm;
雙曲線對數 hyperbolic logarithm;
算術對數 arithmetic logarithm;
一般對數 general logarithm;
餘對數 cologarithm;
自然對數 natural logarithm;

[對台戲] rival show;
唱對台戲 act the opposite; challenge sb with opposing views; compete with sb with a countermeasure; enter into rivalry; put on a rival show; set oneself up against; set up a rival stage in opposition to;

[對頭] (1) correct; on the right track; true; (2) normal; right; (3) get on well; hit it off; on good terms with sb;
死對頭 deadly foe; sworn enemy; bitter opponents;
找對頭 look for the real adversary;

[對外] external; foreign;
對外承包工程 contract foreign projects;
對外窗口 window to the outside world;
對外服務公司 foreign service company;
對外經濟援助 foreign economic assistance;
對外開放 open to the outside world; open to the public;
~對外開放政策 open-door policy;
對外勞務人員 labour-serviceman for export;
對外貿易 external trade; foreign trade;
~對外貿易額 volume of foreign trade;
~對外貿易公司 foreign trade corporation;
~對外貿易區 foreign trade zone;
~對外貿易收入 income of foreign trade;
~對外貿易體制 structure of foreign trade;
對外投資 investments abroad;
對外政策 foreign policy;

[對位] counterpoint;
對位法 counterpoint;
複對位 double counterpoint;

[對象] (1) object; target; (2) boyfriend; girlfriend; match; prospective spouse;
對象語言 object language;
乘法對象 multiplicative object;
對偶對象 dual objects;
搞對象 be occupied with finding a match; go stead; in love;
模對象 module object;
射影對象 projective object;
同構對象 isomorphic objects;
遙控對象 remote-controlled object;
找對象 look for a mate; look for a partner in marriage;
~找錯對象 bring one's hogs to the wrong market; come to the wrong shop; knock at the wrong door; misjudge one's opponent;
子對象 sub-object;
~不可約子對象 irreducible sub-object;
~補子對象 supplementary sub-object;

[對眼] (1) cross-eyed; internal strabismus; (2) to one's liking; to one's taste;

[對應] correspondence;
對應程度 degree of correspondence;
對應詞 corresponding word;
對應賬戶 corresponding account;
邊界對應 boundary correspondence;
詞序對應 word order correspondence;
代數對應 algebraic correspondence;
漸近對應 asymptotic correspondence;
雙有理對應 birational correspondence;
目的語對應 target language correspondence;

[對於] about; for; on; to; towards; without regard to;

[對於…來説] for;
對於他來説 for him;

[對月] under the moon;
對月傷懷 give way to melancholy under moonlight;
對月寓懷 could not restrain one's fancies under the moon;

[對照] compare; contrast; cross reference;

[對陣] confront each other;
對陣戰 pitched battle;

[對症下藥] apply medicine according to th doctor's indications; do what is appropriate; prescribe medicine for a patient according to his illness—solve problems according to objective realities; prescribe the right remedy; prescribe the right remedy for an illness; suit the medicine to the illness; suit the remedy to the case;

[對證] check; verify;
死無對證 dead men tell no tales; lack of evidence because of the death of a principal witness; the dead cannot bear

witness;

［對峙］ at a stalemate; confront each other; face-off; stand facing each other; stand opposite each other;

［對趾］ zygodactylous;
對趾鳥 zygodactyle bird;
對趾型 zygodactylism;

［對撞機］ collider;

［對質］ confrontation in court;
當堂對質 confrontation of the accused with the accuser in court;

［對準］ (1) aim at; (2) align; alignment;
對準調節 alignment adjustment;
對準裝置 alignment apparatus;

［對坐］ sit opposite to each other;
憑桌對坐 sit opposite to each other at a table;

D

比對 collate; compare and check; comparison;
不對 (1) abnormal; queer; (2) inharmonious;
猜對 guess; hit it; make a correct guess; right in one's guess;
查對 check; verify;
成對 pair off; pair up;
酬對 answer; reply;
答對 answer sb's question; make a reply;
敵對 antagonistic; hostile;
掂對 weight and consider the situation;
反對 argue against; be against; be opposed to; buck against; combat; come out against; conspire against; cry against; cry out against; dead set against; declare against; decry; demonstrate against; demur at; fight; fight against; go against; have an objection to; have an opposition to; in opposition to; make an objection to; object to; objection; oppose; protest against; raise one's back against; react against; set against; set one's face against; set oneself against; show opposition to; side against; speak against; stand against; take opposition to; vote against;
核對 check;
校對 (1) calibrate; check against a standard; (2) proofread;
絕對 (1) absolute; (2) absolutely; decidedly; definitely;
面對 confront; face;
派對 gathering; party;
配對 (1) pair; (2) mate;
七對 (of mahjong) seven pairs;
全對 it's perfectly correct;
雙對 in pairs;
條對 give answers to every question asked;
輓對 elegiac couplet;
晤對 meet face to face;
線對 pair;
相對 (1) face to face; opposite; (2) relative; (3) comparatively; corresponding; relatively;
言對 (1) converse; meet and talk; (2) coupling of words;
一對 a brace; a couple; a pair;
應對 answer; reply;
擇對 select a mate; select a spouse;
針對 (1) be aimed at; be directed against; (2) in connection with; in the light of;
質對 check; verify;
屬對 search for a suitable sentence to match another;
作對 (1) act against; choose to be sb's rival; oppose; set oneself against; (2) match with another in marriage;

dui

【憝】 (1) vicious person; wicked person; (2) hate;

dui

【懟】 hate; resent;

怨懟 resent;

dun¹

dun

【惇】 generous; kind; sincere;

［惇誨］ teach kindly;

dun

【敦】 honest; sincere;

［敦促］ press; urge;

［敦厚］ honest and simple; honest and sincere;
純樸敦厚 simple and honest;
溫柔敦厚 tender and gentle;

［敦睦］ promote friendly relations;

［敦聘］ sincerely invite;

［敦請］ earnest request; earnestly invite;

［敦勸］ exhort earnestly; urge;

［敦實］ solid; stocky;
敦實淳樸 stocky and honest;

dun

【墩】 heap; mound;

橋墩 pier;
石墩 block of stone used as a seat;

樹墩 tree stump;
綉墩 garden stool;

dun
【燉】 as in 敦煌 Dunhuang, Gansu;

dun
【噸】 (1) metric ton; (2) ton;
[噸數] tonnage;
額定噸數 rated tonnage;
排水噸數 displacement tonnage;
起運噸數 originated tonnage;
總噸數 aggregate tonnage; gross tonnage;
[噸位] tonnage;
動力噸位 power tonnage;
貨物噸位 cargo tonnage;
商船噸位 merchant tonnage;
壓裝噸位 mounting tonnage;

dun
【蹲】 (1) squat on the heels; (2) stray;
[蹲班] stay down;
[蹲伏] crouch in hiding;
[蹲坐] crouch; squat on the heels;

頸後深蹲 full squat;
前深蹲 front squat;
深蹲 deep squat;
微蹲 partial squat;
胸前坐蹲 shoulder squat;

dun3
dun
【盹】 doze;
[盹睡] doze; nap; nod;

打盹 doze off; take a nap;

dun
【躉】 (1) amount; batch; (2) buy wholesale; sell wholesale;
[躉船] boat; boat warehouse;
[躉批] wholesale;
[躉售] sell wholesale;

打躉 buy in batches;

dun4
dun
【沌】 chaotic; turbid; unclear;

混沌 chaos;

dun
【炖】 fire burning intensely;

清炖 boil in clear soup;

dun
【盾】 (1) buckler; shield; (2) guilder;
[盾牌] (1) shield; (2) excuse; pretext;
防暴盾牌 riot shield;
人體盾牌 human shield;
[盾徽] coat of arms;

地盾 shield;
後盾 backing; backup force;
矛盾 contradiction; contradictory;

dun
【鈍】 (1) blunt; dull; (2) dull-witted; stupid;
[鈍兵不戰] soldiers whose moral is low will not fight;
[鈍刀] blunt knife;
鈍刀慢剮 persecute slowly, like cutting skin with a blunt knife;
鈍刀子 blunt knife; dull knife;
~ 鈍刀子割肉 cut flesh with a blunt knife;
[鈍化] passivation;
表面鈍化 surface passivation;
低溫鈍化 low-temperature passivation;
電化鈍化 electrochemical passivation;
芯片鈍化 chip passivation;
[鈍角] obtuse angle;
[鈍口拙腮] a person who does not shine in conversation; awkward in speech;
[鈍態] passivity;
電化鈍態 electrochemical passivity;
陽極鈍態 anodic passivity;
[鈍嘴拙舌] one does not shine in conversation;

遲鈍 obtuse; slow;
駑鈍 dull; stupid;
懦鈍 weak and dull;
札鈍 blunt;
頑鈍 (1) stupid; (2) having no integrity;
銖鈍 dull knives and spears;

dun
【遁】 escape; flee; fly;
[遁詞] excuse; pretext; quibble; shield; subterfuge;
[遁跡] withdraw from society and lead a

hermit's life;
遁跡空門 become a monk; conceal oneself in the holy door — become a monk; retire into a cloister; take the monastic vow;
遁跡山林 flee to the mountains — retire from official life; live the life of a hermit in a mountain;
[遁世] live in seclusion; withdraw from the world;
遁世覓道 leave the world and search for truth;
遁世隱逸 retire in seclusion;
遁世者 hermit;
懷寶遁世 possess great talent but seclude oneself from society;
棄家遁世 leave one's home and become a recluse;
[遁之夭夭] flee abroad; sneak away;

逃遁 escape; flee;

dun
【頓】 (1) pause; (2) pause in writing in order to reinforce the beginning or ending of a stroke; (3) arrange; settle; (4) touch the ground; (5) stamp; (6) immediately; suddenly; (7) fatigued; tired;
[頓挫抑揚] rising and falling of tones;
[頓號] punctuation mark placed between several proper names;
[頓開] be suddenly removed;
頓開茅塞 become enlightened immediately; be suddenly enlightened; suddenly see the light;
茅塞頓開 become enlightened at once; open sb's eyes; suddenly see the light;
[頓時] at once; forthwith; immediately; suddenly;
[頓悟] epiphany; insight;
頓悟前非 suddenly recalls to mind a previous fault;
[頓足] stamp one's feet;
頓足不前 come to a standstill;
頓足捶胸 stamp one's feet and beat one's breast; stamp one's feet and pound ones breast;
頓足號哭 cry stamping one's feet;
捶胸頓足 beat one's breast and stamp one's feet; beat the breast and stamp;

安頓 (1) arrange; arrange properly for; find a place for sb; help sb settle down; make proper arrangements; put in order; put sb up; (2) comfortable; keep quiet; peaceful; undisturbed;
簸頓 dally with;
斷頓 cannot afford the next meal; go hungry;
困頓 (1) exhausted; fatigued; tired out; weary; worn-out; (2) hard up; in financial straits; in straitened circumstances; poverty-stricken;
勞頓 fatigued; wearied;
羸頓 thin and exhausted;
魯頓 dull-witted; mentally slow; obtuse; stupid;
疲頓 exhausted; tired out;
停頓 (1) at a standstill; grind to a halt; halt; pause; stagnate; standstill; stop; suspend; (2) pause in speaking;
委頓 exhausted; tired;
一頓 (1) a pause; (2) a fit of; a meal of;
整頓 consolidate; rectify; reorganize;
躓頓 stumble and stop;

dun
【遯】 (1) escape; run off; (2) cheat; slight;

dun
【燉】 stew;
[燉熟] stew until it is done;

duo¹
duo
【多】 (1) many; much; (2) more than the correct number; too many; (3) excessive; too much; (4) odd; over; (5) far more; much more; (6) a surname;
[多半] (1) most; the greater part; (2) most likely; on the cards; probably;
[多邊] multilateral;
多邊會談 multilateral talks;
多邊會晤 multilateral meeting;
多邊貿易 multilateral trade;
多邊協議 multilateral agreement;
多邊形 polygon;
~ 凹多邊形 convex polygon;
~ 等角多邊形 equiangular polygon;
~ 配位多邊形 coordination polygon;
~ 凸多邊形 concave polygon;
~ 外切多邊形 circumscribed polygon;
~ 正多邊形 regular polygon;
[多變] changeable; changeful; varied;

多變的 mercurial;

[多病] susceptible to diseases;

[多財善賈] a wealthy person knows how to do business; it's easy to trade with much capital; plenty of capital makes it easy to trade; wealth makes a skilful merchant;

[多藏厚亡] the greater the fortune one amasses, the greater the loss one will suffer;

[多層] multichamber; multilayer;

[多重] multiple;

多重翻譯 multiple translations;

多重複合句 multiple compound sentences;

多重意義 multiple meanings;

[多愁善感] always in sorrow and melancholy; always melancholy and moody; hearts and flowers; oversensitive; sentimental;

[多次] many times; on many occasions; over and over again; repeatedly; time after time; time and again;

[多的是] plentiful;

[多得很] many; very much;

[多多] plenty;

多多益善 plenty is no plague; the more the better; the more the merrier;

~韓信將兵—多多益善 Han Xin commanding troops — the more, the better;

多彩多姿 impressive; magnificent; many-faceted; versatile;

多吃多佔 consume and take more than one's due; eat or take more than one's share; grab more than one's share; take more than one's share; take more than one is entitled to;

多見多聽 see more and hear more;

多勞多得 more pay for more work; the more one works, the more one earns;

[多方] all manners of; do everything possible; in every way; in many ways; make every effort; with various devices;

多方面 in many ways; many-faceted; many-sided;

多方譬喻 explain by all sorts of analogies;

多方設法 make every effort; try all possible means; try various devices;

多方協助 give assistance in many ways; render all manner of help;

多方阻撓 place many obstructions in the way;

[多寡] amount; number;

多寡不等 vary in amount;

裒多益寡 take from those who have too much and give to those who have too little;

[多汗] hyperhidrosis;

偏側多汗 hemihyperhidrosis;

情緒性多汗 emotional hyperhidrosis;

手掌多汗 volar hyperhidrosis;

[多角化] diversification;

集中多角化 concentric diversification;

教育多角化 diversification of education;

經營多角化 business diversification;

水平多角化 horizontal diversification;

縱向多角化 vertical diversification;

[多久] how long;

隔不多久 now and then;

沒多久 before long;

隨便多久 as long as you like;

[多款] of many designs; of many patterns;

[多虧] fortunate; lucky; owing to; thanks to;

[…多了]

喝多了 have had one too many;

[多毛症] hypertrichosis;

假多毛症 pseudohypertrichosis;

全身性多毛症 hypertrichosis universalis;

[多麼] how; what;

[多面] manifold; many-sided;

多面適應 manifold adaptation;

多面手 all-rounded person; all-rounder; Jack-of-all-trades; generalist; many-sided person; person of many abilities; versatile man;

多面體 polyhedron;

~對偶多面體 dual polyhedron;

~分格多面體 cellular polyhedron;

~原子多面體 atomic polyhedron;

[多謀] resourceful;

多謀寡成 dogs that put up many bares kill none;

多謀善斷 full of wrinkles; resourceful and decisive; sagacious and resolute;

[多年] many years;

多年積習 crusted habit;

隔別多年 be separated for years;

[多尿症] excessive urine output; polyuria;

[多情] tender and affectionate;

多情的 amatory; lovey-dovey;

~多情的一瞥 an affectionate look;

故作多情 drippy; make a pretence of affection; mawkish;
假裝多情 make a pretence of affection;
湘女多情 girls of Hunan are affectionate;
自作多情 imagine oneself as the favourite of one of the opposite sex; under the hallucination that the other party is willing;

[多色] multicolour; polychrome;
多色複印 multicolour copying;

[多少] (1) amount; number; (2) more or less; somewhat; to some extent; (3) how many; how much; (4) as much as; so much;
多少錢 how much is it;
~賣多少錢 how much do you charge for it; how much does it cost; how much is it; what's the damage; what's the price; what price do you ask;
多少也 more or less;
不多不少 just right; just the right amount; neither more nor less than; not too much and not too little; nothing more or less than;
多餐少食 have many meals but little food at each;
多多少少 in some degree; more or less; somewhat; to a certain extent; to some extent;
多聽少説 keep your mouth shut and your ears open; swift to hear, slow to speak;
多退少補 return the overcharge and demand payment of the shortage; return the surplus and charge the balance; the balances will be paid to either side as the case may be;
或多或少 in varying degrees; more or less; to a greater or lesser extent;
積少成多 a little at a time mounts up; economy in trifles ensures abundance; every little helps; every little makes; every little makes a great; from small increments comes abundance; many a little makes a mickle; many littles make a muckle; many smalls make a great; penny and penny laid up will be many; take care of the pence, and the pounds will take care of themselves;
可多可少 the amount doesn't matter;
狼多肉少 there is too little meat for so many wolves; too many looters for the limited wealth;
你要多少 how many do you want;
少食多餐 have more meals a day but less food at each;
隨便多少 as much as you like;
一共多少 how much does it come to;
以少勝多 defeat with a force inferior in number; defeat the many with the few; use a small force to defeat a large one; use the few to defeat the many;
~以少勝多，以弱勝強 defeat a numerically superior and powerful with a small and weak force;
由少到多 from few to many; from small to large numbers; grow in numbers;
僧多粥少 many monks and little gruel – not enough to go around; there are too many monks and too little gruel – there are always more round pegs than round holes;
粥少僧多 there is not enough to go around;

[多事] (1) meddlesome; (2) eventful;
多事之秋 eventful year; period of trouble; season of much trouble and anxiety; year of many troubles; troubled time;

[多手] like to try one's hand at things;

[多數] majority; most; plural; pluri-;
多數黨 majority party;
~多數黨領袖 majority leader;
多數派 majority;
~道德多數派 moral majority;
多數票 majority vote;
~絕對多數票 absolute majority;
多數統治 majority rule;
必要的多數 required majority;
沉默多數 silent majority;
簡單多數 simple majority;
絕大多數 overwhelming majority;
絕對多數 absolute majority;
少數服從多數 the minority is subordinate to the majority;
特定多數 qualified majority;
相對多數 relative majority;
壓倒性多數 overall majority; overwhelming majority;

[多態現象] polymorphism;
發育多態現象 developmental polymorphism;
平衡多態現象 balanced polymorphism;
隱藏多態現象 cryptic polymorphism;

[多頭] many aspects; many-sided; multiple;
多頭集團 bull clique;

[多聞] have wide experience;
多聞多見 widely experienced;
博洽多聞 conversant; extensive in learning; knowledgeable; well-informed;

[多項] multinominal; multiple; polynomial;
多項式 polynomial;

[多少] many and few;
多看少説 keep your mouth shut and your eyes open;

[多謝] grateful to sb; many thanks; much obliged; thank; thank you; thankful to sb; thanks a lot;

[多心] oversensitive; suspicious;

[多血] hyperaemia;
多血症 plethora;
全身多血 panhyperaemia;

[多樣] diversified; manifold; of various kinds or forms; various;
多樣翻譯 manifold translation;
多樣化 diversify; vary;
~多樣化經濟 diversified economy;
~多樣化社會 highly diverse society;
多樣性 diversity;
~絕對多樣性 absolute diversity;
~群落多樣性 community diversity;
~生物多樣性 biodiversity;

[多疑] oversensitive; suspicious;

[多義] polysemous;
多義詞 polysemant; polysemous word;
多義結構 polysemous structure;
多義性差誤 ambiguity error;

[多用櫃] multipurpose cabinet;

[多語] multilingual;
多語翻譯 multilingual translation;
多語系統 multilingual system;

[多餘] excessive; more than what is due; redundant; superfluous; surplus; uncalled for;
多餘的 otiose;

[多雨] rainy;

[多元] mutli-; plural;
多元分析 multivariate analysis;
多元化 plurality;
多元檢索 multi-aspect retrieval;
多元決定論 surdetermination;
多元論 pluralism;
多元媒介 multimedia;
多元社會 multiple society;
多元思維 multiple thinking;
多元文化 multiculturalism;
多元性 diversity; pluralism;
多元中心方式 polycentrism;

[多雲] cloudy;
多雲的 cloudy;

[多則…少則] no more than...and no less than;
多則五天，少則三天 no more than five days and no less than three;

[多種] diversified; many and various; multiple; various;
多種多樣 a great diversity of; diverse; in varied forms; manifold; many and many varied; multifarious; various;
多種經營 diverse economic undertakings; diversified economy; diversification;
多種多收 bring in bigger crops by expanding the sown area; plant more land bring in bigger crops;
原因多種 many and various reasons;

[多子] many children; many sons;
多子多孫 have many children and grandchildren; have many sons and grandsons
一胎多子 multiparous;

[多姿] varied in posture;
多姿多彩 colourful and varied in postures; varied and graceful;
~生活得多姿多彩 live life to the full;
婉孌多姿 a beauty with many countenances — young and beautiful;

[多嘴] gossipy; long-tongued; shoot off one's mouth; speak out of turn; talk out of place; talk too much;
多嘴的人 big mouth; big-mouthed person; loud mouth; loud-mouthed person;
多嘴多舌 gossipy and meddlesome; have a loose tongue; long-tongued; loquacious; run off at the mouth; shoot one's mouth off; talkative;

差不多 about; about and about; about the same; all but; almost; as good as; be approaching; be getting on; be nearing; just about right; near enough; nearly; similar; that's about it;
大多 for the most part; mostly;
頂多 at best; at the most;
繁多 in great numbers; various;
過多 excessive; too many; too much;

好多 a good deal of; a good many; a great many;
很多 oodles;
極多 abundance;
幾多 how many; how much;
加多 add; increase;
居多 in the majority;
禮多 full of courtesy;
偌多 so many; so much;
人多 a large number of people;
三多 the three abundances of blessing, longevity and sons;
甚多 very many; very much;
太多 too many; too much; overmuch;
貪多 grasp too much;
添多 add more; increase;
心多 over-suspicious;
許多 a big percentage of; a crowd of; a flock of; a good deal of; a good few of; a great deal of; a great many; a heap of; a host of; a hundred and one; a large amount of; a large body of; a large number of; a large quantity of; a lot; a lot of; a mass of; a number of; a pile of; a power of; a sight of; a store of; a thousand and one; a wealth of; a world of; all manner of; an army of; bags of; heaps of; hundreds of; in profusion; lots and lots of; lots of; many; many in number; much; no end of; not a few; numbers of; numerous; plenty; plenty of; quite a few; stacks of; the majority of; thousands of; volumes of;
益多 more and more;
增多 grow in number; increase;
至多 at the most;
眾多 multitudinous; numerous;
諸多 a good deal of; a lot of;
滋多 increase; multiply;
自多 conceited; self-satisfied;
最多 at most; the most; tops;

duo
【哆】 shiver; tremble;
［哆嗦］ shiver; tremble;
打哆嗦 (1) shiver; tremble; (2) shudder;
哆囉哆嗦 tremble with cold or fear;
渾身哆嗦 all in a tremble; feel one's skin creeping; in a tremble; on the tremble;
混身哆嗦 tremble all over;

duo[2]
duo
【多】 how;
［多好］ how nice; how wonderful;
［多美］ how beautiful; what a beauty;
［多麼］ how; what;

duo
【掇】 (1) collate; gather; (2) pirate; plagiarize; (3) pluck; select;
［掇採］ gather; pluck; select;
［掇弄］ (1) stir up conflicts; (2) gather up; repair; (3) deal with sth; handle a matter;
攛掇 egg on; urge;
掂掇 (1) think over; weigh up; (2) estimate; reckon;
拾掇 (1) put in order; tidy up; (2) fix; repair;

duo
【敠】 weigh a thing in the hand; weigh and consider a matter;

duo
【奪】 (1) seize; take by force; wrest; (2) force one's way; (3) compete for; contend for; strive for; (4) deprive; (5) decide;
［奪愛］ take away sb's woman;
橫刀奪愛 take away sb's woman by force;
［奪標］ capture prize; win the first prize; win the title;
［奪得］ carry off; seize; take; win;
［奪冠］ take the first place; win the championship;
［奪回］ recapture; retake; seize back;
奪回失去的時間 make up for lost time;
［奪魁］ contend for championship; strive for the first place;
［奪利］ scramble for gains;
爭名奪利 struggle for fame and wealth;
爭權奪利 fight for selfish gains; scramble for personal gains;
［奪目］ dazzle the eyes;
燦爛奪目 brilliant; dazzling; the lustre dazzles the eye;
璀璨奪目 bright-coloured and dazzling; dazzling; dazzling splendour; its elegance ravishes the eyes; resplendent; shine with dazzling brilliance; the dazzling brightness blinds the eyes; the lustre dazzled the eye; with dazzling brightness;
光彩奪目 dazzling with brilliance;

D

光耀奪目 dazzling;
鮮艷奪目 attractively bright-coloured; dazzlingly beautiful; resplendent; splendour blinds the eyes;
艷麗奪目 of dazzling beauty;

［奪取］ (1) capture; seize; take by force; wrest; (2) court; strive for;
奪取冠軍 capture the championship;
奪取勝利 strive for the victory;
奪取政權 seize political power;
豪奪巧取 rob by force or by trick; secure by force or trickery; forcible seizure and crafty acquisition;
強取豪奪 grab and keep; rapacity;

［奪去］ take away from;

［奪權］ seize power; take over power;
寸權必奪，寸利必得 wrest every ounce of power and every ounce of gain;

剝奪 deprive sb of sth; expropriate; strip;
裁奪 consider and decide;
褫奪 deprive sb of sth; strip;
篡奪 seize; usurp;
定奪 decide; make a final decision;
訛奪 errors and missing characters in a text;
劫奪 seize by force;
掠奪 pillage; plunder; rob;
強奪 grab; rob; snatch;
搶奪 grab; plunder; rob; seize; seize by force; snatch; wrest;
侵奪 seize; take by force;
攘奪 grab; seize;
襲奪 take over by a surprise attack;
削奪 deprive sb of power, etc.; take by force;
映奪 catch the eyes; dazzle the eyes;
與奪 giving and taking;
爭奪 enter into rivalry with sb over sth; fight for;
卓奪 your discerning decision;
酌奪 make a considered decision;

duo

【裰】 darn; mend; patch;

補裰 sew and mend;
直裰 monk's robe;

duo

【鐸】 (1) large bell; (2) a surname;

duo³

duo

【朵】 (1) bud; cluster of flowers; flower; (2) lobe of the ear;

花朵 flower;

duo

【躲】 (1) hide; (2) avoid; dodge;

［躲避］ (1) avoid; dodge; elude; (2) hide oneself;
躲避懲罰 avoid punishment;
躲避困難 dodge difficulties;
設法躲避 try to take shelter;

［躲藏］ conceal oneself; go into hiding; hide oneself;
躲藏處 hideaway; hideout; hiding place;
躲藏起來 go into hiding;
躲躲藏藏 dare not show up openly;

［躲開］ get out of the way; stay away;

［躲懶］ loaf on the job; shirk;

［躲閃］ dodge; evade; get out of the way;
躲閃不及 too late to dodge;
東躲西閃 dodge about; hide oneself from place to place; on the dodge;
躲躲閃閃 avoid being seen; dare not show up; dodge and hide; evade any direct answer; play bopeep;

［躲雨］ find shelter from the rain; get out of the rain; run for cover; run for shelter; take cover from rain;

［躲債］ avoid a creditor;

藏躲 go into hiding; hide or conceal oneself;
閃躲 dodge; evade;

duo

【垛】 (1) battlements; (2) measure word;

靶垛 butt;

duo⁴

duo

【度】 (1) instrument for measuring length; (2) degree; kilowatt-hour; (3) times; (4) system; (5) bearing; manner; (6) pass;

［度命］ make a living;

猜度 conjecture; surmise;
裁度 deduce; infer;
測度 estimate; infer;
揣度 appraise; conjecture; estimate;
忖度 conjecture; speculate; surmise;
揆度 conjecture; estimate;
審度 study and estimate;

推度 conjecture; guess; infer;
臆度 conjecture; guess; surmise;

duo
【咄】 (1) angry cry; (2) scold sb in a loud voice;
［咄咄］ tut-tut;
咄咄逼人 aggressive; arrogant; fire-eating; insolent; overbearing; overweening; pressing; pushy; threatening; truculent;
~語氣咄咄逼人 in an aggressive tone; one's tone of voice is aggressive;
咄咄怪事 astounding happenings; monstrous absurdity; out of the ordinary;
［咄嗟］ cry out;
咄嗟立辦 can be done at once;

duo
【柁】 large tie beams;

duo
【柮】 firewood;

duo
【剁】 chop; hash; mince;
［剁肉］ hash meat; mince meat;
剁肉刀 clever;
［剁碎］ hash; mince;

duo
【舵】 helm; rudder;
［舵柄］ rudder tiller; tiller;
帶鏈舵柄 chained tiller;
固定舵柄 fixed rudder;
手操舵柄 manual rudder;
小艇舵柄 boat tiller;
應急舵柄 emergency tiller;
［舵手］ cox; coxswain; helmsman; steersman;
舵手座 cockpit;

把舵 hold the helm; hold the rudder; steer;
船舵 helm; rudder;
右舵 right rudder; right standard rudder;
掌舵 at the helm; hold the rudder; steer; take the helm; take the tiller;

duo
【馱】 load carried by a pack animal;
［馱子］ load carried by a pack animal;

duo
【惰】 lazy;
［惰性］ inertia; inertness; sluggishness;

怠惰 idle; indolent; lazy;
倦惰 indolent; lazy;
懶惰 lazy; sluggish;
勤惰 diligence and negligence;

duo
【垛】 (1) heap up; pile up; (2) a heap of; a pile of;

duo
【跺】 stamp one's foot;
［跺腳］ stamp one's foot;

duo
【墮】 fall; sink;
［墮落］ decadence; degenerate; downfall; drop by the wayside; fall by the wayside; go downhill; go to the bad; go to the deuce; go to the devil; sink low;
墮落的 debauched; decadent;
~墮落的女子 fallen woman;
墮落風塵 be driven to prostitution; become a courtesan; become a prostitute;
墮落腐化 decadent and licentious; degenerate and corrupt;
墮落蛻化 demoralization and degeneration;
腐敗墮落 become corrupt and degenerate;
腐化墮落 corrupt and degenerate; corruption and degeneracy; degenerate morally; dissolute and degenerate;
自甘墮落 abandon oneself to wanton ways; abandon oneself to vice; dissolute; give up all confidence in oneself; happy in one's own degeneration; indulge in debauchery out of one's own free will; self-degradation; wallow in degeneration;
［墮馬］ fall off from a horse;
［墮入］ fall into; land oneself in; sink into;
墮入愛河 fall head over heels for sb;
墮入泥坑 fall into the pit; sink into the quagmire of;
墮入圈套 be caught in a trap;
墮入霧中 be lost in a thick fog; completely lost at sea;
墮入陷阱 be caught in a trap; fall into a trap;
墮入煙海 get lost in the fog; lose oneself in the fog;
［墮胎］ aborticide; induced abortion; forced abortion; have an induced abortion;
墮胎藥 aborticide; abortifacient;

duo

【踱】 pace; stroll;

［踱步］ walk with measured tread;

踱來踱去 be on the prowl; pace; pace back and forth; pace the floor; pace to and fro; pace up and down; scout about; tramp back and forth; walk to and fro; walking hither and thither; walk up and down;

~在房裏踱來踱去 pace the room;

e¹

e

【阿】 (1) favour; pander to; play up to; toady; (2) rely on; (3) riverbank; (4) pillar; (5) slender and beautiful; (6) a surname;

［阿附］ fawn on and echo; toady to and chime in with;

阿附權貴 attach oneself to some authority; attach oneself to the powerful and influential persons; cling to the powerful; curry favour with influential officials; curry favour with those in power; toady to and chime in with the influential officials;

［阿毛阿狗］ ordinary people; Tom, Dick and Harry;

［阿彌陀佛］ Amitabha; may Buddha preserve us; merciful Buddha－keep one's fingers crossed;

［阿諛］ curry favour with; fawn on; flatter; play up to;

阿諛奉承 act the yes-man; butter sb; butter up; compliment unduly; curry favour with sb; dance attendance on; eat sb's toads; fawn on sb; flatter and cajole; flatter and toady; flattery; ingratiate oneself into sb's favour; ingratiate oneself with sb; lay it on thick; make much of; oil one's tongue; praise insincerely in order to please another's vanity; stoop to flattery; tickle sb's ears; toady; try to get sb's favour by flattery;

阿諛人人喜，直言人人嫌 everyone is pleased by flattery but annoyed by frank statements;

阿諛諂佞 curry favour with sb;

阿諛諂笑 a fulsome flattery; flatter and curry favour;

阿諛有福，直言有禍 flattering produces good fortune and frank statements court disaster;

e

【痾】 disease; sickness;

e

【婀】 (1) elegant; graceful; (2) a surname;

［婀娜］ graceful;

婀娜多姿 gracefully slender figure; very pretty and charming;

風姿婀娜 graceful manner;

舞姿婀娜 dance gracefully;

e

【屙】 discharge excrement; discharge urine;

［屙肚］ diarrhoea;

［屙屎］ move the bowels;

e²

e

【俄】 momentarily; sudden; suddenly;

［俄而］ suddenly;

［俄然］ suddenly;

［俄雨］ shower;

e

【哦】 recite;

e

【娥】 (1) beautiful; good; (2) common name for a girl; (3) a surname;

［娥眉］ (1) beautiful eyebrows; (2) beautiful girl; girl;

娥眉本是嬋娟刀，殺盡風流世上人 beautiful women are like beautiful knives, they kill all the licentious men in the world;

娥眉月夜 on the night of a crescent moon;

淡掃蛾眉 apply a light make-up; finish pencilling one's eyebrows slightly;

皓齒蛾眉 white teeth and pretty eyebrows;

嫦娥 goddess of the moon;

宮娥 palace maid;

姮娥 goddess of the moon;

e

【峨】 lofty;

［峨峨］ looking majestic;

［峨冠博帶］ wear a high hat and broad girdles;

e

【訛】 (1) erroneous; mistaken; (2) blackmail; extort;

［訛傳］ false rumour; groundless rumour; unfounded rumour;

相信訛傳 believe the gossip;

［訛謬］ absurdness; error; mistake; slip;

［訛騙］ blackmail and swindling;

［訛人］ blackmail sb;

［訛脫］ mistakes and slips in a text;

［訛誤］ corruptions; errors in a text;

［訛詐］ blackmail; extort under false pretences; intimidate;
訛詐錢財 extort money under false pretences;
大肆訛詐 put on a good bluff;

e
【莪】 artemisia, a kind of plant with edible leaves;

e
【蛾】 moth;
［蛾眉月］ crescent moon;
［蛾子］ moth;

蠶蛾 silk moth;
燈蛾 moth;
鄧蛾 euphonia;
谷蛾 grain moth;
麥蛾 gelechiid moth;
螟蛾 snout moth;
乳蛾 acute tonsillitis;
天蛾 hawk moth; sphingidae;
夜蛾 noctuid;
衣蛾 case-making clothes moth;

e
【鋨】 osmium;

e
【額】 (1) forehead; (2) horizontal tablet; (3) specified number or amount;
［額定］ rated; specified;
額定馬力 rated horsepower;
［額度］ capacity;
保證額度 bonding capacity;
［額髮］ forelock;
［額骨］ frontal bone;
［額手稱慶］ congratulate each other by raising the hand to the brow; felicitate oneself on one's luck; overjoyed; place one's hands over one's forehead in jubilation; salute each other in a gesture of felicitation; thank one's stars;
［額頭］ brow; forehead;
擦額頭 mop one's brow; wipe one's brow;
大額頭 large forehead;
焦頭爛額 badly battered; be bruised and battered; be scorched and burned; be scorched by the flames; beat sb's head off; in a sorry plight; in a terrible fix; utterly exhausted from overwork;
寬額頭 broad forehead;
突出的額頭 protruding forehead;
窄額頭 narrow forehead;
皺起額頭 knit one's forehead; wrinkle up one's forehead;
［額外］ added; additional; extra;
額外保險費 extra premium;
額外補貼 perquisite;
額外的工作 extra work; overwork;
額外費用 extra charges; extra expenditures;
額外服務 extra service;
額外負擔 added burden;
額外津貼 extra subsidies;
額外開支 extra expenses;
額外收入 additional income;
額外投資 additional investment;
額外要求 additional demands;

碑額 top part of a tablet;
匾額 horizontally inscribed board;
差額 balance; difference; margin;
超額 above quota; overfulfil the quota;
蹙額 frown; knit one's brows;
定額 norm; quota;
份額 portion; share;
浮額 surplus number;
賦額 tax rate;
金額 amount of money;
巨額 huge sum; large amount;
空額 vacancy;
款額 amount of money;
面額 denomination;
名額 number of people assigned or allowed;
票額 denomination; face value; sum stated on a cheque or bill;
前額 forehead;
全額 full whack;
缺額 vacancy;
數額 amount; number; quota;
稅額 amount of taxes to be paid;
限額 limit; norm; quota;
薪額 pay; salary;
餘額 (1) vacancies yet to be filled; (2) remaining sum;
員額 specified number of personnel;
債額 amount of debt;
總額 total;

e
【鵝】 gander; goose;
［鵝蛋］ goose's egg;
［鵝黃］ light yellow;

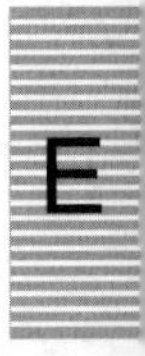

嫩柳鵝黃 the tender yellow willow turns light yellow;

［鵝頸］ gooseneck;

［鵝卵石］ cobble; cobblestone;

［鵝毛］ goose feathers;

鵝毛大雪 snowflakes;

鵝毛滿天飛，總有落地時 goose feathers may fly about in the sky, but eventually they will fall down to the ground;

鵝毛筆 goose quill pen;

［鵝行鴨步］ go as slowly as ducks and geese do; waddle along like a duck or a goose; walk with a swagger;

烤鵝 roast goose;

企鵝 penguin;

獅頭鵝 lion-headed goose;

天鵝 swan;

雄鵝 gander;

一大群鵝 a large flock of geese;

一群鵝 a flock of geese; a gaggle of geese;

E

e³

e

【噁】 disgust; scorn; sicken;

［噁心］ disgusting; feel like vomiting; feel nausea; feel sick; nauseating; repulsive; sicchasia; turn sick;

噁心的 bilious;

感到噁心 sick in the stomach;

令人噁心 disgusting; nauseating;

引起噁心 cause nausea; provoke nausea;

e

【猗】 gentle, soft, and pliant;

e⁴

e

【厄】 (1) strategic point; (2) disaster; hardship; (3) in distress;

［厄運］ adverse fate; adversity; jinx; misfortune;

一陣厄運 a spell of bad luck;

遭厄運 suffer misfortune;

困厄 difficult situation; dire straits;

險厄 strategic pass;

遭厄 meet with disaster;

e

【歹】 remains of a person;

e

【呃】 hiccough; hiccup;

［呃逆］ hiccough; hiccup;

痙攣性呃逆 spasmolygmus;

流行性呃逆 epidemic hiccup;

e

【扼】 (1) clutch; grip; (2) control; guard;

［扼亢拊背］ have a squeeze hold on an enemy; hold a strategically important terrain; hold the best strategic positions;

［扼流圈］ choke;

充電扼流圈 charging choke;

放電扼流圈 discharging choke;

共式扼流圈 common-mode choke;

換向扼流圈 commutating choke;

空心扼流圈 air choke;

聲頻扼流圈 audio-frequency choke;

天線扼流圈 aerial choke;

調幅扼流圈 amplitude modulation choke;

［扼殺］ catch sb by the throat; choke the life out of sb; have sb by the throat; hold sb by the throat; nip; nip in the bud; seize sb by the throat; smother; strangle; strangle sth in the cradle; take sb by the throat; throttle;

扼殺自由 throttle freedom;

［扼守］ guard; hold;

［扼死］ strangle; throttle;

［扼要］ to the point;

扼要重述 recapitulate; repeat the chief points of;

扼要説明 explain the main points briefly;

簡明扼要 concise and to the point;

［扼制］ check; control;

扼制通貨膨漲 control the inflation;

e

【阨】 (1) strategic position; (2) precarious position; (3) block up; obstruct; (4) destitute; difficulty; poverty-stricken;

e

【俄】

［俄國］ Russia;

［俄語］ Russian; Russian language;

e

【軛】 collar;

e

【惡】 (1) evil; vice; wickedness; (2) ferocious; fierce; vicious; (3) bad; evil; wicked;

［惡霸］ bully; local despot; local tyrant;
惡霸地主 despotic landlord;

［惡報］ retribution for evildoing;
惡有惡報 evil is rewarded with evil; evil results of evildoing; poetic justice; reap as what one has sown; sow the wind and reap the whirlwind; those who stop at no evil court their own ruin; vice will have an evil recompense; where vice is, vengeance follows;
~惡有惡報，善有善報 bad deeds, as well as good, may rebound upon the doer;

［惡病］ malignant disease;

［惡臭］ foul smell; offensive smell; stench; stink;
發出惡臭 emit a foul odour;
如惡惡臭，如好好色 dislike the ugly and like the beautiful;

［惡鬥］ ferocious battle;

［惡毒］ malicious; venomous; vicious;
惡毒攻擊 malevolent attack; malicious attack; venomous attack; vicious attack; virulent attack;
惡毒透頂 extremely wicked;
惡毒咒罵 vicious vilification;
本性惡毒 of an evil disposition;

［惡感］ hostility; ill will; resentment;
引起惡感 create ill feelings;

［惡貫滿盈］ be steeped in evil and deserve damnation; face retribution for a life of crimes; full of iniquities; guilty of countless crimes and deserve to come to judgment; have a long list of crimes; hae committed countless crimes and deserve to come to judgement; have committed one's full share of crimes; have sunk in sin with a record full of crimes and misdeeds; one's crimes are inexpiable; the measure of iniquities is full;

［惡鬼］ demon; devil; evil spirit;

［惡棍］ blackguard; bully; hoodlum; roughneck; ruffian; scoundrel; villain;
狡滑的惡棍 artful scoundrel;
可怕的惡棍 hideous devil;
十足的惡棍 consummate villain;
一群惡棍 a mob of blackguards;

［惡果］ bad results; disastrous effects; evil consequences; evil results;
惡種結惡果 no good seed can come of evil grain;
帶來惡果 bring about pernicious consequences;
惡因生惡果 sin yields bitter fruits;

［惡狠狠］ ferocious; fierce; relentless;

［惡化］ degeneration; deteriorate; exacerbate; go to the bad; take a turn for the worse; worsen;
病情惡化 one's illness takes a turn for the worse;
氣候惡化 climatic deterioration;
日益惡化 worsen daily;
使惡化 aggrevate; compound;
使事情惡化 aggravate a matter;
自然環境惡化 natural environment deterioration;

［惡疾］ foul disease; nasty disease;

［惡狼］ ferocious wolf;

［惡浪］ (1) angry waves; (2) evil tendency;

［惡劣］ abominable; adverse; bad; despicable; disgusting; evil; harsh; mean; undesirable; unfavourable; very bad;
惡劣的稟性 malignant nature;
惡劣的氣候 harsh climate;
惡劣透頂 thoroughly vile; venomous to the last degree;
惡劣行徑 disgusting conduct;
惡劣行為 mean conduct;
情緒惡劣 in a bad mood; in an ugly mood;
態度惡劣 ghastly attitude;

［惡龍難鬥地頭蛇］ even a ferocious dragon will be no match for the snake in its old haunts－a local villain won't be pushed around even by another vile creature;

［惡夢］ frightening dream; horrible dream; nightmare; paroniria;
惡夢方醒 wake up from a nightmare;
一場惡夢 a hell of a bad dream; a nightmare;
做惡夢 dream a bad dream; have a bad dream; have a nightmare;

［惡名］ bad reputation; infamy;
惡名昭著 ignominious; notorious;

［惡魔］ (1) demon; devil; evil spirit; (2) evil person;
避開惡魔 keep away the malignant

demons; ward off the malignant demons;
殺人惡魔 ruthless murderer;
召喚惡魔 invoke evil spirits;
[惡念] evil intentions;
[惡癖] bad habit;
[惡婆] harridan;
[惡人] evildoer; evil person; villain;
惡人當道 the evildoers are now in power;
惡人惡心肝 a vicious person has a vicious heart;
惡人口毒 a vicious person has a slanderous mouth;
惡人先告狀 the guilty party is the first to file the suit;
惡人心不安 a wicked person lives in his own hell;
惡人須以惡法治 to a vicious dog, a short chain;
惡人衹有惡人降 a wicked person can be dealt with only by another wicked person;
惡人自有惡人磨 a fierce person has another fierce person to torment him; a villain will encounter his match sooner or later; a wicked person will be afflicted by a person with a similar personality; an evil person will be dealt with by another evil person; bad people always find their matches; the great thieves punish the little ones; where vice is, vengeance follows;
惡人自有惡相 a wicked person has ferocious features;
鬼怕惡人 brave in face of a devil;
[惡事] misdeeds;
惡事傳千里 bad news has wings; bad news travels fast; it isn't always easy to hush up a scandal; scandal spreads apace; scandal travels fast; you can't always keep word of a disgraceful story from spreading;
~惡事傳千里，好事不出門 misdeeds always receive the maximum publicity, while good deeds are relegated to obscurity; scandal travels a thousand miles, while good deeds always stay indoors;
[惡徒] rascal; scoundrel;
[惡習] bad habits; cacoethes; evil practices; pernicious habits;
惡習難改 bad habits die hard;
擺脱惡習 break oneself of bad habits;
鏟除惡習 eradicate bad habits;
防止惡習 prevent bad habits;
克服惡習 get over bad habits; overcome bad habits;
難改的惡習 incurable vice; tenacious vice;
染惡習 take on bad habits;
~染上惡習 contract a bad habit; fall into evil ways;
~深染惡習 be accustomed to bad habits; be steeped in vice; be sunk in the depths of vice;
社會惡習 social abuses;
~改革社會惡習 reform social abuses;
[惡相] evil countenance;
[惡行] vicious behaviour;
不可饒恕的惡行 unforgivable sin;
[惡性] lethal; malignant; pernicious; vicious;
惡性貧血 pernicious anaemia;
惡性循環 vicious circle;
惡性腫瘤 malignant tumour;
[惡言] abusive words; vicious remarks;
惡言毒語 malicious language; malicious remarks;
惡言惡食 poor clothing and poor food; poor clothing, meagre meal;
惡言惡語 the rough side of the tongue;
惡言潑語 malicious remarks;
惡言傷人 make disparaging remarks about others; use bad language to insult people;
惡言相向 cast an evil eye on sb;
[惡意] evil intentions; ill will; malice;
惡意誹謗 spread vicious gossip;
惡意攻擊 bad mouth;
惡意訕謗 spread vicious gossip;
惡意行為 malicious act;
惡意中傷 malicious calumniation; vicious calumniation;
包藏惡意 harbour evil designs;
並無惡意 bear no ill will;
出於惡意 out of malice;
決非惡意 bear no ill will whatsoever; entirely without malice;
心懷惡意 malicious;
[惡運] bad luck; ill luck; misfortune;
[惡債] odious debts;
[惡戰] fierce battle; hard fighting;
[惡兆] bad omen; evil boding; ill omen;

E

[惡濁] filthy; foul;
[惡作劇] cut up; hoax; mischief; mischievous trick; monkey business; monkey trick; play a prank on sb; play a sportive trick on; play practical jokes on other people; practical joke; prank;
惡作劇報警電話 hoax calls;
惡作劇者 practical joker; prankster;
討厭惡作劇 dislike practical jokes;

仇惡 abhor evil;
醜惡 hideous; ugly;
刁惡 rascally brutal; wicked;
腐惡 corrupt and evil;
舊惡 old grievance; old wrong;
善惡 good and evil; virtue and vice;
首惡 chief criminal; principal culprit;
萬惡 absolutely vicious; diabolic; extremely evil;
為惡 do evil;
險惡 (1) dangerous; perilous; (2) malicious; sinister; wicked;
相惡 mutual inhibition;
邪惡 evil; vicious; wicked;
凶惡 brutish; fearful; ferocious;
兇惡 ferocious; fierce;
溢惡 excessively abusive;
元惡 chief criminal; principal culprit;
罪惡 crime; evil;
作惡 (1) do evil; indulge in evildoings; (2) gloomy; melancholy; sullen;

e
【愕】 astounded; stunned; startled; stunned;
[愕然] astounded; stunned;
愕然四顧 look around in astonishment;
感到愕然 be astounded by...;

錯愕 surprised;
惊愕 stunned; stupefied;

e
【鄂】 (1) brim; brink; edge; verge; (2) short for Hubei Province; (3) startled; surprised; (4) blunt; honest; (5) a surname;

e
【崿】 cliff; precipice;

e
【萼】 calyx;
[萼片] sepal;

e
【遏】 check; hold back; stop;
[遏抑] keep down; suppress;
[遏止] check; hold back; stop;
[遏制] contain; keep within limits;

沮遏 prevent; stop;
阻遏 check; stem; stop;

e
【誒】 exclamation of confirmation;

e
【餓】 (1) hungry; (2) starve;
[餓虎撲食] a hungry tiger at its prey; a hungry tiger pounces on its prey; prey on a victim like a famished tiger;
[餓死] starve to death;
餓死鬼 starveling;
餓死事小，失節事大 to be starved to death is a trifling thing, but to lose one's virtue is a serious matter;

挨餓 be starved; endure hunger; go hungry; suffer from hunger;
饑餓 hungry;
解餓 allay one's hunger; satisfy one's hunger; stay one's stomach;
有點餓 peckish;

e
【噩】 shocking; upsetting;
[噩耗] grievous news; sad news about the death of a beloved person;
[噩夢] frightening dream; nightmare;
噩夢方醒 wake up from a nightmare;
一再出現的噩夢 recurring nightmare;
做噩夢 have a bad dream;
[噩運] bad luck;
噩運連連 a run of bad luck;

渾噩 ignorant;

e
【諤】 honest speech; frank comments;
[諤諤] (1) honest; outspoken; (2) magnificent;

e
【鍔】 (1) edge of a knife; (2) lofty; towering;
[鍔鍔] lofty; towering;

e
【顎】 (1) cheekbones; jowl; (2) high-cheek-

boned; (3) reverence;
［顎骨］ jawbone;
顎骨骨折 jaw fracture;
顎骨髓炎 osteomyelitis of the jaw;
［顎裂］ cleft palate;
［顎足］ jawbone; maxilliped;

大顎 mandible; mandibular;
上顎 upper jaw;
下顎 lower jaw;

e
【鶚】 osprey; fish hawk;
［鶚視］ look fiercely;

e
【齶】 palate;

e
【鱷】 crocodile; alligator;
［鱷梨］ avocado;
［鱷魚］ crocodile;
鱷魚淚—假惺惺 crocodile tears — hypocritical;
鱷魚上岸—來者不善 a crocodile climbing up the bank — the person who comes, comes with ill intent;

ei⁴
ei
【欸】 (1) hey; (2) sigh;

en¹
en
【恩】 benevolence; charity; favour; grace; gratitude; kindness; mercy;
［恩愛］ affectionate; conjugal love;
恩愛夫妻 an affectionate couple;
~恩愛夫妻不到頭 an affectionate couple often cannot live together to the end of their lives;
兩人十分恩愛 the couple love each other tenderly;
［恩寵］ show special favour to sb;
獲得恩寵 gain grace;
［恩仇］ debt of gratitude and of revenge;
恩仇未報 have not settled old accounts with sb;
恩將仇報 bite the hand that feeds one; quit love with hate; repay kindness with ingratitude; repay love with hate; requite kindness with enmity; return evil for good; return kindness with ingratitude; treat one's benefactor as one's enemy;
~恩將仇報的人 a snake in sb's bosom;
［恩賜］ (1) bestow; (2) charity; favour;
恩賜觀點 the attitude of bestowing sth as a favour;
［恩德］ favour; grace; kindness;
報答恩德 reciprocate favours; return kindness;
大恩大德 great kindness;
以恩報德 recompense kindness for kindness;
知恩報德 return the hospitality that one has received;
［恩典］ benevolence; favour; grace; kindness;
［恩惠］ act of grace; bounty; favour; grace; kindness;
備受恩惠 load sb with favours;
小恩小惠 little deeds of kindness; petty favours; small favours;
［恩禮有加］ shower sb with favours and courtesy;
［恩情］ great kindness; love; loving-kindness;
［恩人］ benefactor;
救命恩人 the person who saved one's life;
［恩深］ one's kindness is vast;
恩深似海 one's kindness to sb has been as vast as the sea; one's mercy is deeper than the deepest sea;
恩深義重 deep favour and weighty righteousness; the spiritual debt is deep and great;
［恩師］ one's respected teacher;
［恩威］ kindness and severity;
恩威並用 apply the carrot-and-stick method judiciously; employ both kindness and severity;
恩威兼施 alternate kindness with severity; employ both kindness and severity; temper justice with mercy;
［恩義］ gratitude; spiritual debt;
辜恩背義 have no sense of gratitude and justice; ungrateful to kindness;
［恩怨］ feelings of gratitude and feelings of resentment; grievances; old scores; resentment;
恩怨分明 discriminate between love and hate; kindness and hatred are clearly distinguished; make a clear distinction between kindness and hatred;
恩多成怨 too much kindness will

eventually engender grudge;
絲恩發怨 grudge against the slightest wrong done;
[恩澤] bounties bestowed by a monarch;

報恩 pay a debt of gratitude; return sb's kindness;
大恩 meritorious deeds;
感恩 express one's gratitude; feel grateful; thankful;
開恩 bestow favours; show mercy;
施恩 bestow favours;
天恩 emperor's kindness;
忘恩 devoid of gratitude; ungrateful;

en²
en
【嗯】 (expressing doubt) what;

en³
en
【嗯】 (expressing surprise or indifference) what;

en⁴
en
【嗯】 (making a response or promise) h'm;

en
【摁】 (1) press; (2) delay; hold;
[摁釘] drawing pin;
[摁扣兒] snap fastener;

er²
er
【而】 (1) and; (2) but; (3) while; (4) when; (5) whereas; (6) if; (7) however; (8) moreover; (9) conversely; (10) with; (11) in contrast;
[而出] out;
奪眶而出 brim over; start from one's eyes;
奪門而出 force one's way out; force open the door and rush out; hasten out of the house in a great rush;
奪圍而出 burst through the investing force;
[而後] after that; then;
[而今] at present; now; nowadays;
[而立] thirty years old;
而立之年 thirty years old;
三十而立 at thirty one takes one's stand;
[而論] comment;
憑心而論 in all fairness; upon my soul and honour;
[而且] (1) and that; at that; moreover; not only…but also…; what is more; (2) and;
[而入] in;
奪門而入 force one's way into a house;
[而已] just; nothing more; only; that is all;

從而 as a result; thereby; thus;
俄而 suddenly;
反而 but; instead; on the contrary;
故而 hence; therefore;
忽而 now…, now…;
既而 afterwards; later; subsequently;
繼而 afterwards; then;
進而 going a step further; proceeding to the next step;
然而 but; however; yet; nevertheless;
甚而 even; go so far as to;
時而 from time to time; sometimes;
因而 as a result; thus; with the result that;

er
【兒】 (1) child; son; (2) youngster; youth; (3) male;
[兒歌] children's song; nursery rhyme; songs for children;
[兒科] paediatrics;
兒科學 paediatrics;
兒科醫生 paediatrician;
兒科醫院 paediatric hospital;
[兒女] children; sons and daughters;
兒女成行 sons and daughters forming a row – have many children;
兒女情長 be immersed in love; love between a man and a woman is long; the lasting affection of boys and girls;
兒女私情 love affair between a man and a woman;
膝下兒女 children surrounding their parents' knees – children living with their parents;
賣兒鬻女 sell one's children;
拋兒棄女 forsake one's children;
生兒育女 give birth to children and raise them; multiply the earth; raise children;
無兒無女 childless; have neither sons nor daughters;
[兒孫] descendants; posterity;

兒孫滿堂 have children and grandchildren;
兒孫自有兒孫福，莫為兒孫作馬牛 children are certain cares, but uncertain comforts; the children can take care of themselves when they grow up, and the parents do not have to work too hard for their future; your descendants will have blessing of their own; do not toil like a beast of burden for them;
莫為兒孫作牛馬 do no slave for your children;

[兒童] children;
兒童安全鎖 childproof lock;
兒童不宜 unsuitable for children;
兒童餐椅 highchair;
兒童成長 child development;
兒童詞典 children's dictionary;
兒童讀物 children's books;
兒童福利 child welfare;
兒童節 Chidren's Day;
兒童看護 childcare;
兒童片 children's film;
兒童期 childhood;
兒童社會化 socialization of children;
兒童社會學 children sociology;
兒童收容所 children's home;
兒童文學 children's literature; literature for children;
兒童遊樂場 children's playground;
兒童語言 child language;
兒童照管 childcare
兒童之家 children's home;
兒童座椅 child seat;
愛護兒童 bring up children with loving care; cherish children;
常態兒童 normal child;
超常兒童 exceptional child; prodigy;
超齡兒童 over-age child;
遲鈍兒童 dull child;
低常兒童 subnormal children;
低齡兒童 under-age child;
低能兒童 subnormal child;
犯罪兒童 delinquent child;
孤僻兒童 autistic child;
精神病態兒童 psychopathic child;
難管教兒童 problem child; unmanageable child;
虐待兒童 child abuse;
貧困兒童 underprivileged children;
弱智兒童 mentally retarded children;
視力不全兒童 partially seeing child;
收養兒童 adopted child;
特殊兒童 exceptional child;
天才兒童 child prodigy; gifted child;
跳級兒童 accelerated child;
聽力不全兒童 partially hearing child;
頑劣兒童 brat;
虛弱兒童 feeble child; invalid child;
學齡兒童 children of school age;
學前兒童 pre-school child;
異常兒童 abnormal child; atypical child;
優異兒童 superior child;
誘拐兒童 kidnap a child;
早熟兒童 precocious child;
智力落後兒童 retarded child;

[兒媳] daughter-in-law;

[兒戲] trifling matter;
兒戲人生 idle away one's life; trifle through all one's life;
非同兒戲 it isn't child's play; no laughing matter; sth not to be taken lightly;
視同兒戲 regard as a mere trifle;
直同兒戲 it is merely a child's play;

[兒語] baby talk;

[兒子] son;
兒子不養娘，白疼他一場 a son who does not support his mother has her affection for him wasted.
大兒子 eldest son;
乾兒子 one's adopted son;
老兒子 one's youngest son;
頭生兒子 firstborn son;
小兒子 youngest son;
一個兒子 a son;

挨呲兒 get a dressing down; get a tongue-lashing;
挨個兒 according to order; in proper order; in succession; in turn; one after another; one by one; succesively;
矮個兒 low-built person; short person;
安琪兒 angel;
拔份兒 (1) demonstrate one's power and courage over others; show off one's strength or power; (2) act violently; dominate;
把兒 handle;
掰文兒 find a fault;
白玩兒 easy to do; not difficult; not hard;
扳指兒 heavy ring;
板擦兒 eraser;
板兒 board; plate;
半包兒 dirty trick;
伴兒 companion;

E

瓣兒 (1) petal; (2) section; slice;
幫兒 gang;
傍家兒 (1) lover; mistress; (2) partner; (3) couple; husband and wife;
包圓兒 (1) buy the whole lot or the remainder; (2) finish off; take on the whole thing;
鴇兒 (1) prostitute; (2) procuress;
報蟲兒 newspaper worm;
輩兒 generation;
輩數兒 order of seniority in the family; position in the family hierarchy;
奔頭兒 prospect; sth to strive for;
本兒 a thousand yuan;
繃兒 extremely; so; very;
鼻牛兒 nose dirt; nose wax;
筆頭兒 (1) penpoint; the point of a writing brush; (2) in written form; written; (3) ability to write;
篦齒兒 teeth of a comb;
冰棍兒 frozen sucker; ice lolly; ice sucker; popsicle;
病兒 sick child;
脖領兒 neck or collar of a garment;
不忿兒 (1) not to give in to; refuse to obey; (2) not admire; not look up to;
彩兒 delight; interest; lively atmosphere;
蹭兒 (1) sth one gets for free; (2) freeloader;
產兒 newborn baby;
車倒兒 second-hand vehicle dealer;
寵兒 favourite; pet;
唇兒 lips;
催本兒 errand-boy;
寸勁兒 accident; coincidence;
搓板兒 (1) washboard; (2) flat-chested girl; skinny person;
撮堆兒 goods of low quality; leftovers;
打愣兒 in a daze; in a trance; stare blankly;
大夥兒 everybody; we all; you all;
大面兒 (1) appearance; outlook; surface; (2) face;
大腕兒 big shot; celebrity; expert; famous person;
倒兒 profiteer; speculator;
墊底兒 (1) poorest; (2) worst; (3) support; take responsibility;
碟兒 dish; plate;
釘掌兒 have a shoe soled and heeled;
兜兒 pocket;
摁扣兒 snap fastener;
法碼兒 weights of a scale;
範兒 (1) design; form; pattern; style; (2) distinguished graceful manner; standard;
房倒兒 real estate speculator;
份兒 (1) awesome; capable; cool; excellent; fine; good; skilful; (2) part; place; seat; (3) gap; room; space; (4) at the utmost; to the extent of;
縫兒 gap;
趕趟兒 have time for; in time for;
歌兒 song;
鈎兒 hook;
狗兒 dog;
夠勁兒 (1) almost too much to cope with; (2) heavy; strenuous; strong in taste;
夠味兒 pretty good; strong in taste; well-done;
孤兒 orphan;
鰥棍兒 bachelor;
罐兒 can; container; jar; jug; vessel;
蟈蟈兒 catydid; long-horned grasshopper;
孩兒 child; daughter; son;
好天兒 fine day; lovely weather;
好性兒 good temper;
患兒 sick child;
壞包兒 rascal; rogue;
混血兒 half-breed; mixed-blood; mustee; person of mixed blood;
擠眼兒 wink at;
寄兒 adopted son;
加塞兒 jump a queue; push into a queue;
假活兒 con man; swindler;
健兒 (1) athlete; (2) valiant fighter;
較勁兒 (1) have a trial of strength; (2) become worse; get worse;
較真兒 earnest; earnestly; seriously;
叫彩兒 appeal to; be warmly welcomed; welcome; win the applause of;
叫勁兒 (1) challenge; have a competition; (2) dispute; oppose;
叫針兒 (1) argue; wrangle; (2) conscientious and meticulous; finicky; inflexible;
坎兒 (1) barrier; obstacle; (2) code; enigmatic language;
空當兒 (1) break; interval; (2) gap;
摳門兒 closefisted; mean; miserly; stingy;
絝叉兒 pants or trousers reaching just above the knees; short pants; shorts;
坤角兒 actress;
老八板兒 (1) old fogy; (2) inflexible; rigid; stick to old ways;
老兒 father;
愣勁兒 dash; pep; vigour;
愣神兒 in a daze; stare blankly;
臉兒 appearance;
臉膛兒 facial contour;
零活兒 chores; odd jobs;
遛彎兒 go for a stroll; out strolling; take a walk;

E

羅鍋兒 humpback; humpbacked; hunchback; hunchbacked;
馬兒 horse;
賣勁兒 exert all one's strength; spare no effort;
沒譜兒 (1) irrelevant; unrealistic; unsettled; unsure; (2) have no idea;
沒準兒 (1) maybe; perhaps; (2) have no certainty; have no definite idea;
煤核兒 coal cinder;
悶頭兒 quietly; silently;
門兒 access;
門坎兒 threshold;
猛勁兒 (1) put on a spurt; spurt; (2) a spurt of energy; dash;
模特兒 model;
那兒 over there;
哪兒 where;
男兒 man;
猱兒 prostitutes;
腦瓜兒 head;
腦瓢兒 top of the head;
鳥兒 bird;
妞兒 girl;
弄潮兒 beach swimmer; seaman;
女兒 daughter; girl;
乳兒 nursing infant; suckling;
胎兒 embryo; foetus;
偷兒 thief;
頭兒 (1) chump; head; (2) boss; (3) ends; (4) extremes;
玩兒 play; play with; toy with;
味兒 odour; scent; smell;
細兒 young son;
纖兒 immature children;
餡兒 stuffing;
小兒 (1) child; (2) my son;
些兒 (1) a little while; (2) a little bit;
歇腿兒 (1) rest one's feet after a long walk; (2) rest at a place; stay at an inn;
歇晌兒 a rest after lunch;
歇歇兒 take a little rest; take a nap after noon;
心眼兒 (1) heart; mind; (2) intention; (3) cleverness; intelligence; (4) unfounded doubts; unnecessary misgivings;
醒盹兒 shake off drowsiness; wake up from a nap;
旋兒 circle;
學伴兒 school companion;
鴨珍兒 duck's gizzard;
壓根兒 altogether; completely; entirely; totally;
牙縫兒 space between the teeth;
芽兒 bud; shoot; sprout;
沿道兒 all along the road;
眼兒 (1) eye; (2) orifice; tiny hole;
燕雀兒 finch;
養兒 bring up children;
樣兒 appearance;
么兒 youngest son;
一丁點兒 a wee bit;
一丟點兒 just a tiny bit;
一古腦兒 completely; lock, stock and barrel; neck and crop; root and branch; the devil and all;
一忽兒 a little while; in a moment;
一晃兒 (1) flash; pass in a flash; (2) in a short period; in an instant;
一會兒 (1) a little while; a short while; in a jiffy; in a moment; presently; (2) now..., now...; one moment...the next...;
一溜兒 (1) a row; (2) neighbourhood; vicinity;
一順兒 alike; in the same direction;
嬰兒 baby; infant;
有點兒 a bit; a little; rather; some; somewhat; sort of;
有份兒 have a share; participate in;
幼兒 child; infant;
育兒 child rearing;
遭兒 (1) occasion; time; (2) complete turn; full circle;
糟錢兒 filthy lucre;
早早兒 as early as possible; well in advance;
招笑兒 funny; hilarious; incite laughter; incur ridicule;
摺兒 fold;
這兒 (1) here; (2) now; then;
胗兒 gizzard of a fowl;
胗肝兒 gizzard and liver;
針鼻兒 eye of a needle;
姪兒 nephew;
鐘兒 bell;
珠兒 beads;
抓尖兒 come off first; get the best portion;
準兒 certain; sure;
滋嘴兒 grin; smile;
髭毛兒 bristle up – get furious;
字兒 (1) character; (2) receipt;
自個兒 by oneself; oneself;
嘴兒 (1) eloquence; (2) nozzle;
昨兒 yesterday;

er

【洏】 (1) tearful; (2) cook food thoroughly;

漣洏 continual flow of tears;

er

【胹】 cooked; well-done;

er³
er

【耳】 (1) bottle of beer; ears; flaps; (2) ear of a utensil; ear-like thing; (3) flanking; on both sides; side;

［耳按摩］ auditory massage;

［耳凹］ ear pit;

［耳斑］ ear plaque;

［耳背］ cloth ears; cloth-eared; hard of hearing;

［耳鼻喉科］ department of otolaryngology;

［耳閉鎖］ aural atresia; otocleisis;

［耳邊風］ a matter of no concern; flit by like a breeze; go in at one ear and out at the other; like water off a duck's back;
- 當耳邊風 it goes in one ear and out the other; like a breeze blowing past one's ear; pay no heed of; take advice like a passing wind;
- ~把…當作耳邊風 let sth go in one ear and out the other; turn a deaf ear to sth;

［耳鬢廝磨］ close association during childhood; ear to ear and temple to temple—have always been together; have close childhood friendship;
- 耳鬢廝磨，形影不離 rubber shoulders together and cling to each other like an object and its shadow;

［耳病］ disease of the ear; otopathy;
- 耳病性眩暈 aural vertigo;
- 熱帶耳病 tropical ear;
- 游泳池耳病 tank ear;
- 游泳者耳病 swimmer's ear;

［耳部神經痛］ otic neuralgia;

［耳長］ ear length;

［耳出血］ otorrhagia;

［耳窗］ ear window;

［耳垂］ earlobe; lobe of the ear; lobule; lobulus auriculae;

［耳大神經］ great auricular nerve; nervus auricularis magnus;

［耳道］ auditory meatus; duct; meatus acusticus;
- 耳道閉合 otocleisis;
- 耳道軟骨 meatal cartilage;
- 外耳道 external auditory meatus;

［耳底］ inner part of the ear;
- 耳底骨 basiotic bone;

［耳點］ auricularе; broca's point;

［耳朵］ ear; lughole;
- 耳朵長 capable of hearing much;
- 耳朵發燒 the ears burnt;
- 耳朵根子軟 soft ear;
- 耳朵尖 have big ears; have long ears; have rabbit ears; have sharp ears;
- 耳朵靈敏 have a quick ear;
- 耳朵青腫 have a thick ear;
- 耳朵軟 be easily influenced; credulous;
- 耳朵痛 have earache; have pain in the ear;
- 耳朵嗡鳴 buzzing in one's ears;
- 擺動耳朵 waggle one's ears;
- 揪耳朵 pull one's ear;
- 開花耳朵 cauliflower ear;
- 拉長耳朵 prick up one's ears;
- 拉耳朵 drag by the ear; pull by the ear;
- 木耳朵—說不通 wooden ears – (lit) can't get through; (coll) can't be persuaded;
- 捽耳朵 pinch sb's ear;
- 豎起耳朵 prick up one's ears;
- 糖耳朵 ear-shaped twists with sugar;
- 掏耳朵 clean the ears; pick the ears;
- 挖耳朵 cleanse one's ears; pick one's ear;
- 咬耳朵 whisper; whisper in sb's ear;
- 一隻耳朵 a ear;
- 油耳朵 ceruminosis; excessive formation of cerumen;
- 扎耳朵 grate; unpleasant to the ear;

［耳風］ hearsay;

［耳高］ auricular height;

［耳垢］ cerumen; earwax;

［耳骨］ auditory ossicle; ear bones;

［耳鼓］ eardrum; tympanum;

［耳光］ a box on the ear; a clip on the ear; a slap on the face;
- 吃耳光 a slap in the face; be slapped in the face; cuff sb on the ear; slap in the face;
- 打耳光 box sb's ears; get a flap in the face; get a slap in the face; give sb a blow in the ears; give sb a box on the ears; give sb a sweet one on the ears; give sb a thick ear; hit sb in the face; slap sb across the face; slap sb in the face; slap sb on the face; slap sb's face;
- ~自打耳光 box one's own ears; contradict oneself; slap one's own face;
- 搧耳光 box the ear;
- 一記耳光 a clip on the ear; a slap in the

face; a slosh on the ear; box sb's ear; give sb a box on the ear; plant a blow on sb's ear;
一記重重的耳光 a hard blow on the ear;
［耳廓］ auricle; pinna;
耳廓反射 auricle reflex;
［耳殼］ auricle; concha;
［耳紅面赤］ be flushed; red in the face;
［耳環］ earrings;
穿孔耳環 ear stud;
戴耳環 wear earrings;
夾式耳環 clip-on earrings;
金耳環 gold earring;
圈狀耳環 hooped earrings;
珍珠耳環 pearl earrings;
鑽石耳環 diamond earrings;
［耳肌］ auricularis;
［耳機］ earphone; headphone; receiver;
耳機插座 earphone jack;
耳機話筒組 headset;
插上耳機 plug in the earphone;
高保真耳機 high-fidelity headphone;
間隔式耳機 spatial headphones;
晶體耳機 crystal earphone; crystal headphone;
寬頻帶耳機 broadband headphone;
雙耳機 double earphone;
組合耳機 combination earphone;
［耳積水］ hydrotis;
［耳癤］ ear furuncle;
［耳界］ earshot; hearing distance;
耳界清淨 free from noise; quiet;
［耳科］ otology;
耳科病症 ear diseases;
耳科醫生 ear specialist; otologist;
耳科症狀 symptoms of ear diseases;
看耳科 go to see an otologist;
［耳孔］ earhole;
［耳蠟］ earwax;
［耳力］ audition; power of hearing; sense of hearing;
［耳聆心悅］ both the ears and mind are pleased;
［耳靈眼尖］ can hear and see well; quick of hearing and sight;
［耳流膿］ discharging ear;
［耳聾］ deaf;
耳聾目眩 become both dazed and deaf;
耳聾眼花 deafness and failing eyesight; one's eyes are faded and one's ears deaf;
耳聾眼瞎 deaf and blind;
傳導性耳聾 conduction deafness;
刺激性耳聾 stimulation deafness;
非先天性耳聾 adventitious deafness;
舌敝耳聾 discussions are so numerous that the speakers' tongues are parched and the listeners' ears are deafened;
神經性耳聾 nerve deafness;
完全耳聾 as deaf as a post; as deaf as a stone; as deaf as an adder; complete deafness;
噪聲性耳聾 noise deafness;
震耳欲聾 deafening; ear-shattering; ear-splitting; enough to wake the dead; fit to wake the dead; make the ear tingle; raise the roof; split sb's ear; there is a deafening din of;
職業性耳聾 occupational deafness;
［耳漏］ otorrhea;
［耳輪］ helix;
［耳毛］ ear hair;
［耳門］ earlap; external ear; pinna;
［耳鳴］ a drumming in the ears; aurium; buzzing in the ears; have a ringing sound in the ear; have a singing in one's ear; one's ears are singing; ring in the ear; tinnitus
耳鳴目眩 one's ears rang and spots danced before one's eyes;
搏動性耳鳴 pulsatile tinnitus;
振動性耳鳴 vibratory tinnitus;
［耳膜］ eardrum;
［耳目］ (1) what one sees and hears; (2) one who spies for sb else;
耳目閉塞 ignorant; ill-informed; uninformed;
耳目不廣 not well-informed;
耳目不靈 ill-informed;
耳目清靜 free from noise and dirt;
耳目所及 from all one hears and sees; from what one knows; from what one sees and hears;
耳目一新 all is new before one's eyes – a great change for the better; find everything fresh and new; find oneself in an entirely new world; refreshing;
耳目昭彰 know to all; universally known;
耳目之娛 pleasures of the senses;
耳目眾多 all ears and eyes; eyes and ears everywhere; too many people around;

E

安插耳目 place sb's men;

~到處安插耳目 place sb's men everywhere;

避人耳目 avoid being noticed; avoid being observed; elude observation; escape the notice of others;

動人耳目 make one's ears and eyes tingle;

耳聰目明 able to see and hear clearly; can hear and see well; have good ears and eyes; have good sight and an exquisite sense of hearing; have sharp ears and eyes — have a clear understanding of the situation; quick at hearing and seeing;

耳濡目染 be coloured by what one sees and hears constantly; be influenced by what one sees and hears; osmosis;

從小耳濡目染 be influenced from childhood;

耳視目聽 use one's ears to see and one's eyes to hear;

貴耳賤目 easily accept others' words and decline to see with one's own eyes; trust one's ears rather than one's eyes — rely on hearsay;

聳人耳目 arrest public attention; deliberately exaggerate so as to create a sensation;

炫人耳目 confuse the ears and eyes of the people;

掩人耳目 cast a mist before sb's eyes; deceive others; deceive the public; hoodwink people; pull the wool over sb's eyes; throw dust in sb's eyes;

一新耳目 present a new appearance;

以耳代目 depend on hearsay instead of seeing for oneself; rely upon hearsay instead of seeing for oneself — understanding of sth not from personal investigation but from hearsay;

遮人耳目 pull the wool over the eyes of the people; throw dust in people's eyes;

[耳囊] ear vesicle; otic capsule; statocyst;

[耳內流膿] purulent ear;

[耳屏] tragus;

[耳熱] have a burning sensation in the ears; have burning ears;

[耳軟] be easily moved;

耳軟心活 credulous and pliable; easily influenced by others;

心活耳軟 easily moved; of a credulous nature;

[耳塞] cerumen; earbud; earphone; earpiece; earplug; earwax;

[耳神經] auricularis;

[耳生] strange-sounding; unfamiliar to the ear;

[耳食] believe all that one hears;

耳食不化 hear instruction without comprehending its import hearing without digesting what is heard;

[耳匙] auriscalpium; ear spoon;

[耳屎] cerumen; earwax;

[耳熟] familiar to the ear; sound familiar;

耳熟能詳 what has been often heard can be retold in detail; what is familiar to the ears is on the tip of one's tongue;

聽起來耳熟 have a familiar ring; ring a bell;

[耳屬] eavesdrop; listen with effort and attention;

[耳套] earmuffs;

[耳提面命] give earnest exhortations; pour exhortations into sb's ears; give orders personally; give personal advice sincerely; instruct with authority and sincerity; talk to sb like a Dutch uncle;

[耳痛] earache; have a pain in the ear; otalgia;

繼發性耳痛 secondary otalgia;

間歇性耳痛 intermitten otalgia;

牙性耳痛 otalgia dentalis;

[耳挖子] earpick;

[耳聞] hear about; hear of;

耳聞不如目見 seeing for oneself is better than hearing from others;

耳聞目睹 an eye finds more truth than two ears; fall under one's observation; hear with one's own ears and see with one's own eyes; hear with the ears is not so good as to see with the eyes; hearsay is not equal to observation; see and hear for oneself; seeing for oneself is better than hearing from others; seeing is believing; what is heard and seen; what one sees and hears;

耳聞為虛，眼見為實 hearing can be vague, but seeing is definite; one eyewitness is better than two hear-so's; one eyewitness is worth ten earwitness; seeing is believing; what you hear about may be false; what you

E

see is true; what you see is real, what you hear is empty words; words are but wind, but seeing's believing;
目擊耳聞 fall under one's observation; have seen with one's own eyes and heard with one's own ears; what is seen and heard; what one sees and hears;
親耳所聞 hear with one's own ears;
［耳蝸］ cochlea;
［耳息肉］ aural polyp; otic polyp;
［耳下腺］ parotid gland;
耳下腺炎 parotitis;
［耳血管炎］ angiitis;
［耳炎］ otitis;
航空性耳炎 aviation otitis;
寄生蟲性耳炎 parasitic otitis;
癤性耳炎 furuncular otitis;
氣壓性耳炎 barotitis;
全耳炎 panotitis;
脱屑性耳炎 otitis desquamativa;
［耳咽管］ auditory tube; ear canal; eustachian canal; eustachian tube;
［耳癢］ ear itching; itchy ear;
［耳溢］ otorrhea;
［耳硬化症］ otosclerosis; otospongiosis;
［耳語］ whisper; whisper in sb's ear; whispering;
［耳脂］ earwax;
［耳洽］ hear;
［耳珠］ tragus;
［耳墜］ drop earring;

刺耳 ear-piercing; grating on the ear; harsh; irritating to the ear; jarring; unpleasant to the ear;
蒼耳 the achene of Siberian cocklebur;
穿耳 pierce the ears;
刺耳 ear-piercing; grating on the ear; jarring;
鼎耳 ears of a tripod;
方面大耳 a square face with large ears; a handsome man have a dignified face and big ears;
肥頭大耳 a large head and big ears — signs of a prosperous man;
拂耳 grating on the ear;
附耳 move close to sb's ear;
貫耳 hear;
聒耳 grating on one's ears;
鍋耳 pot lug;
護耳 earflaps; earmuffs;
焦耳 joule;
口耳 mouth and ears;
兩耳 ears;
木耳 edible fungus;
內耳 inner ear;
逆耳 grate on the ar; offend the ear; unpleasant to the ear;
牛耳 ears of an ox;
親耳 with one's own ears;
人造耳 artificial ear; bionic ear;
入耳 pleasant to the ear; pleasing to the ear;
順耳 pleasant to the ear; pleasing to the ear;
擿耳 cleanse the ears – listen attentively;
俗耳 vulgar ears;
帖耳 droop one's ears like a dog — submissive;
貼耳 ready to listen;
外耳 external ear;
洗耳 clean one's ears;
小耳 congenital small ears; microtia;
心耳 auricle;
掩耳 close o plug one's ears;
銀耳 tremella;
有耳 have ears;
悦耳 pleasing to the ear; sweet-sounding;
扎耳朵 grate; unpleasant to the ear;
中耳 middle ear;

er

【洱】 (1) a lake in Yunnan; (2) a river in Yunnan;

er

【珥】 (1) ear ornament of pearl or jade; (2) insert; stick;

日珥 prominence;

er

【爾】 (1) you; your; (2) like that so; (3) that;
［爾曹］ you people;
［爾後］ subsequently; thereafter;
［爾虞我詐］ cheat and deceive each other; deceive and blackmail each other; deceive mutually; double-cross each other; each trying to cheat or outwit the other; mutual suspicion and deception; scheme against each other;

踧爾 surprised
果爾 if so;
乃爾 like this; to such an extent;
偶爾 occasional; once in a while;
率爾 hastily; rashly;

莞爾 smiling;

er

【餌】 (1) bait; (2) cake; (3) food; (4) eat;
[餌敵] set up a trap for the enemy;
[餌釣] bait fishing;
[餌料] bait;
冷凍餌料 frozen bait;

餅餌 cakes; pastry;
捕蟲餌 insect bait;
底餌 ledger bait;
釣餌 bait;
毒餌 poison bait;
果餌 confectionery;
誘餌 bait; toll bait;
魚餌 bait;

er

【鉺】 erbium;

er

【駬】 legendary swift horse;

er

【邇】 (1) lately; recently; (2) close to; near;
[邇來] recently;
[邇遠] far and near;
行遠自邇 a thousand-li journey is started by taking the first step; a thousand-li journey starts with the first step; a trip covering over 1,000 kilometers begins with the first step; no matter how distant your goal, you must start from where you are;
~行遠自邇，登高自卑 he who would climb the ladder must begin at the bottom;

遐邇 far and near;

er⁴

er

【二】 (1) two; (2) different;
[二八] sixteen years of age;
二八佳人 a beautiful girl in her sweet sixteen; a beautiful girl of sixteen years old; a beauty in her teens; a budding beauty;
二八年華 in one's teens; sixteens years old; sweet sixteen;
年方二八 just sixteen years of age;
[二百五] (1) idiot; rash person; scatterbrain; (2) smatter;
[二倍體] diploid;
單性二倍體 parthenogenetic diploid;
缺對二倍體 nullisomic diploid;
三體二倍體 trisomic diploidy;
雙二倍體 double diploid;
四二倍體 quadruple diploid;
[二遍苦] suffer for a second time;
[二茬罪] suffer for a second time;
[二重] double; dualistic;
二重唱 duet;
二重介詞 double preposition;
二重奏 duet;
[二次] secondary;
二次公式 quadratic formula;
二次曲面 quadric;
~共焦二次曲面 confocal quadric;
~絕對二次曲面 absolute quadric;
~同心二次曲面 concentric quadric;
~退化二次曲面 degenerate quadric;
[二檔] second gear;
[二等] second-class; second-rate;
二等艙 cabin class; club class;
二等公民 second-class citizen;
[二分] dichotomy;
[二鍋頭] marry for the second time;
[二合一] two in one;
二合一複數 summation plural;
[二乎] (1) retreat; withdraw; (2) hesitate; (3) have little hope; hopeless;
[二話] demur; objection;
二話不說 without further ado;
二話休提 that's flat;
八哥儿的嘴巴—專說二話 a myna's tongue — only parroting;
一家人不說二話 we need not dodge about since we are family;
[二婚] divorce; divorcee; marry for the second time;
[二極] ambipolar;
二極管 diode;
~背對背二極管 back-to-back diode;
~反對數二極管 antilog;
~反向二極管 backward diode;
~合金二極管 alloyed diode;
~吸收二極管 absorber diode;
二極體 diode;
~光電二極體 photodiode;
[二級] second-class honours;
二級二等 second-class lower; two-two;
二級一等 second-class upper; two-one;

[二價] bivalent;
二價染色體 bivalent chromosome;
~不等二價染色體 unequal bivalent;
~桿形二價染色體 rod bivalent;
二價體 bivalent;
~同形二價體 homomorphic bivalent;
~異形二價體 heteromorphic bivalent;
[二進位] binary system;
二進位運算 binary operation;
[二進制] binary; binary system;
二進制編碼地址 binary-coded address;
二進制地址 binary address;
二進制加法 binary addition;
飽和二進制 saturated binary;
標準二進制 normal binary; straight binary;
並行二進制 parallel binary;
補碼二進制 complementary offset binary;
禁止二進制 inhibit binary;
絕對二進制 absolute binary;
普通二進制 standard binary; straight binary;
中式二進制 Chinese binary;
自然二進制 natural binary;
[二聚] dimeric;
二聚物 dimer;
~環狀二聚物 cyclic dimmer;
~加成二聚物 additive dimmer;
~偶聯二聚物 coupled dimmer;
二聚性 dimerism;
二聚作用 dimerization;
丙烯二聚 propylene dimerization;
[二郎腿] with ankle on knee;
[二流] second-rate;
二流子 loafer; idler;
[二奶] mistress; illegal spouse;
二奶村 mistress village;
包二奶 keep up a mistress;
[二皮臉] brazen-faced; thick-skinned;
[二人成伴，三人不歡] two is company, three is a crowd;
[二三] two and three;
接二連三 another and yet another; coming in quick succession; in quick succession; in rapid sequence; in rapid succession; one after another; repeatedly; thick and fast; thick and threefold;
~接二連三的挫敗 a succession of defeat;
[二十分] (1) twenty marks; (2) twenty minutes past a certain clock;
[二手] second-hand;
二手貨 (1) second-hand goods; used goods; worn goods; (2) defiled woman; divorced woman;
二手煙 second-hand smoke;
~吸二手煙 passive smoking;
[二位] two-place;
二位謂項 two-place predicate;
[二五眼] (1) inferior ability; inferior quality; (2) incompetent person;
[二項] binary; binomial;
二項對立 binary opposition;
二項分類 binary taxonomy;
二項式定理 binomial theorem;
二項展開式 binomial expansion;
[二心] disloyalty; half-heartedness;
誓不二心 swear to be loyal forever;
[二氧化碳] carbon dioxide;
呼出二氧化碳 exhale carbon dioxide;
[二一] two and one;
二一添作五 divide equally; go fifty-fifty; go halves;
買二送一 buy two get one free;
[二元] binary; dual;
二元論 dualism;
二元市場 dual market;
二元體系 dual system;
~二元體系説 dual system theory;
二元性 dualism;
[二月] (1) February; (2) second month of the lunar calendar;
[二值] two-valued;
二值傾向 two-valued orientation;
二值思維 two-valued thinking;

第二 second;
店小二 waiter;
禮拜二 Tuesday;
三二 three and two;
十二 twelve;
星期二 Tuesday;
一二 one or two; just a few just a little;

er

【貳】 (1) deputy; (2) distrust; doubt; suspect; (3) separate; (4) complicated form of 二 (two); (5) a surname;
[貳臣] turncoat official;
[貳心] rebellious mind;

攜貳 at odds with the community; disloyal;

fa[1]
fa

【發】 (1) deliver; send out; (2) discharge; emit; shoot; (3) deliver a speech; express; utter; (4) develop; expand; (5) rise or expand when fermented or soaked; (6) come or bring into existence; produce; (7) discover; open up; (8) become; get into a certain state; (9) show one's feeling; (10) feel; have a feeling; (11) set out; start; (12) distribute; issue; (13) get rich;

［發案］ arise; break;

［發白］ become white; grow white; turn pale; turn white; turn whitish;
 臉色發白 turn pale;

［發榜］ issue a list of successful candidates or applicants;

［發包工程］ contract work;

［發報］ transmit messages;
 發報機 transmitter;
 發報人 sender of a telegraph;

［發表］ announce; deliver; express; issue; project; publish; report; voice;
 發表權 publication right;
 發表聲明 issue a statement;
 發表文章 publish an article;
 發表演説 deliver a speech; make a speech;
 發表意見 air one's views; express an opinion; pass on; put in one's two cents worth; state one's views;

［發病］ fall ill;
 發病率 morbidity;
 諸病併發 different diseases break out at the same time;

［發佈］ issue; release;
 發佈命令 issue orders;
 發佈消息 give out information;
 發佈新聞 release news;
 發佈正式通知 deliver a formal announcement;

［發財］ (1) clean up; get rich; make a fortune; make a pile; (2) (of mahjong) green dragon tile;
 發財致富 amass great fortunes; enrich; get rish; make one's pile;
 大發橫財 amass ill-gotten riches; get rich illegally; make staggering profits;
 發大財 achieve great wealth; strike gold;
 恭喜發財 happy Chinese new year;
 渴望發財 aspire after wealth;
 夢想發財 have visions of wealth;
 突然發財 in the money;
 想發財 desire a fortune;

［發車］ outgoing train;
 發車閉塞 outgoing train blocking;

［發愁］ anxious; become sad; sullen; vexed; worry;

［發出］ deliever; dispatch; emit; issue; send out;
 發出傳票 issue a summons;
 發出呼救信號 dispatch an SOS;
 發出緊急呼籲 send out an urgent appeal;
 發出警告 send out a warning;
 發出匣 out tray;
 發出指示 issue a directive;

［發達］ advanced; developed; flourishing; prosperous; thriving;
 發達國家 developed country; developed nation;
 不發達 underdeveloped;
 肌肉發達 have well-developed muscles;
 頭腦發達 have fully-developed mental powers;
 一朝發達 overnight riches;

［發呆］ abstractedness; dumbfounded; in a daze; in a trance; spellbound; stare blankly; stunned; stupefied;
 嚇得發呆 be frightened out of one's wits; be scared stiff;

［發電］ furnish power; generate electricity; power generation;
 發電場 mill;
 ~地熱發電場 geothermal energy plant;
 ~風力發電場 wind farm;
 發電廠 power plant; power station;
 ~地熱發電廠 geothermal power plant;
 ~火力發電廠 thermal power plant;
 ~水力發電廠 hydraulic power plant; hydroelectric power plant;
 ~原子能發電廠 atomic power plant;
 發電機 dynamo; generator;
 ~充電發電機 charging dynamo;
 ~電動發電機 dynamotor;
 ~定流發電機 constant current dynamo;
 ~感應發電機 induction generator;
 ~航空發電機 aerogenerator;
 ~交流發電機 A.C. generator; alternator;
 ~平衡發電機 equalizing dynamo;
 ~熱核發電機 thermo-nuclear generator;

~手搖發電機 hand dynamo;
~直流發電機 D.C. generator;
發電站 power plant; power station;
發電裝置 power plant;
風力發電 wind power;
核能發電 nuclear power;
水力發電 hydro-electric power;
太陽能發電 solar power;

[發動] (1) get going; get started; launch; (2) arouse; call into action; mobilize; (3) start a machine;
發動機 engine; motor;
~發動機關閉 shutdown the motor;
~發動機器 set a machine going; start a machine;
~發動機外罩 cowling;
~高空發動機 altitude engine;
~航空發動機 aeromotor;
~火箭發動機 propellant rocket engine;
固體火箭發動機 solid-propellant rocket engine;
~加速發動機 acceleration motor;
~爬昇發動機 ascent engine;
~吸氣式發動機 airbreathing motor;
~一台發動機 an engine;
~遠地點發動機 apogee motor;
發動進攻 launch an attack;
發動汽車 make the car start; start up the car;
發動群眾 arouse the masses to action; mobilize the masses;
發動戰爭 launch a war; start a war; unleash a war;
熱線發動 hot-wire;
推車發動 push-start;

[發抖] quiver; shake; shiver; tremble;
渾身發抖 all of a dither; all of a shake; all of a tremble;
冷得發抖 be pinched with cold; shake with cold; shiver with cold;
嚇得發抖 shake in one's shoes; tremble all over; tremble with fear;

[發端] inception; initiative; make a start;

[發凡] foreword; introduction; preface; preamble;

[發放] extend; give out; grant; issue; provide;
發放貸款 extend a loan; give out a loan; grant a loan;
發放護照 issue a passport;

[發奮] bestir oneself; exert oneself; make a determined effort; make a firm resolution; rouse oneself; strive resolutely; work energetically; work hard;
發奮工作 pull all one's energies into one's work; work energetically;
發奮圖強 bring oneself to make the country strong; rise in great vigour; strive for national prosperity; with firm resolve to succeed; work hard and aim high; work with a will to make the country strong;
發奮忘食 be roused to such diligence as to forget one's meals;
發奮學習 put all one's energies into one's studies; stimulate oneself to study;
發奮用功 resolve to study hard;
發奮有為 proving one's worth; with firm resolve to succeed;

[發憤] make a determined effort; make a firm resolution;
發憤求學 very eager in one's studies;
發憤忘食 so immersed in work as to forget one's meals; study hard, neglecting one's meals; work so hard as to forget to eat;

[發瘋] around the bend; become insane; drive sb crazy; go bonkers; go crazy; go mad; go nuts; go out of one's mind; inside oneself; lose one's mind; lose one's reason; lose one's senses; off one's head; off one's nut; out of one's mind; round the bend; round the twist;
發瘋的 loco; nutty;
氣得發瘋 beside oneself with fury;
嚇得發瘋 be frightened out of one's wits;

[發福] become plump; get fat; grow stout; plump; put on weight;
發福的 plump;
中年發福 middle-age spread;

[發糕] steamed sponge cake;

[發稿] send manuscripts to the press;

[發光] emit light; luminescence;
發光材料 luminescent material;
發光度 luminosity;
~絕對發光度 absolute luminosity;
~相對發光度 relative luminosity;
~最大發光度 highlight luminosity;
發光率 luminance;
發光器 light organ; luminous organ;
發光強度 luminous intensity;

發光體 luminous body;
電化學發光 electrochemical luminescence;
晶體發光 crystal luminescence;
生物發光 bioluminescence;
~ 生物發光現象 biological luminescence;
細菌發光 bacterial luminescence;
有一分熱，發一分光 contribute one's share according to one's lights; give as much light as the fuel can produce — do one's best, however little it may be;

[發汗] make one perspire;
發汗藥 diaphoretic; sudorific;
促使發汗 promote sweating;

[發黑] become black; blacken; darken; grow black; turn black;
兩眼發黑 all has turned black before one's eyes; everything turns dark before one's eyes;
眼前突然發黑 have a sudden blackout;

[發狠] (1) make a determined effort; (2) angry; be enraged; get rough; turn angry;

[發橫] become suddenly hard and harsh;
發橫財 get a windfall; get rich by foul means; ill-gotten gains; make a fortune in a devious way; strike it rich; strike oil;

[發花] be dazzled; grow dim; grow haze; grow misty; see things in a blur;
眼睛發花 dim-sighted;

[發還] give back; return sth;

[發慌] become confused; feel nervous; get flustered; get panic;
別發慌 don't get flurried;
悶得發慌 feel quite suffocated; terribly bored;
閒得發慌 be bored with little to do; be plagued with leisure; sick of doing nothing; time hangs heavily on one's hands;

[發揮] (1) bring into play; give play to; give scope to; give free rein to; (2) air; amplify; develop; elaborate; expound; express;
發揮不出自己的水平 off one's game;
發揮想像力 give the rein to one's imagination;
發揮優勢 exploit one's advantages to the full; give play to strong points;
發揮餘熱 devote one's remaining years to the service of people;
發揮專長 give full play to sb's professional knowledge;
充分發揮 use to the greatest advantage;
大加發揮 dilate;
借題發揮 give vent to one's pent-up feelings on some extraneous pretext; make an issue of; make use of a subject as a pretext for one's drawn-out talk; make use of the subject under discussion to put over one's own ideas; play on the theme of; seize on a theme as a false pretext to express one's own view; seize on an incident to exaggerate matters; seize on some pretext and make a fuss; seize on some pretext or other to distort; seize upon a pretext and give vent to one's feelings; take some pretext and make a fuss;
盡情發揮 bring into full play;
就題發揮 elaborate on the subject; talk to the point;
最佳發揮 at the top of one's game;

[發昏] (1) faint; feel giddy; (2) become confused; beside oneself; go crazy; lose one's head;
頭腦發昏 lose one's head;

[發火] be ablaze with anger; fire up; fit to be tied; flare up; get angry; get shirty; lose one's temper;
不要發火 keep one's shirt on;
動輒發火 lose one's temper easily;
好發火 apt to lose one's temper easily;
氣得發火 hot with rage;
惹人發火 put sb out of temper;
突然發火 fire up; flare up;

[發貨] consign; ship;
發貨人 consignor; shipper;

[發急] become impatient;
別發急 have patience;
等得發急 wait impatiently;

[發跡] enrich oneself; gain fame and fortune; make a career; make a fortune; make one's way; rise in the world; rise to power and position;

[發家] build up a family fortune;
發家致富 build up family fortunes; enrich one's family; enrich oneself; make one's family's fortune;
不義之財不能發家 ill-gotten wealth never

thrives;

[發價] offer;
重覆發價 repeat offer;
聯合發價 combined offer;
有效發價 effective offer;

[發酵] ferment; fermentation; zymosis;
發酵變化 fermentative change;
發酵病 zymosis;
發酵法 zymotechnics;
發酵工藝 zymotechnique;
發酵管 fermentation tube;
發酵罐 fermenter;
~ 密閉式發酵罐 closed fermenter;
~ 塔式發酵罐 tower fermenter;
~ 微型發酵罐 miniature fermenter;
發酵活性 fermentation activity;
發酵計 zymometer;
發酵菌 yeast;
發酵能力 fermentation ability;
發酵飼料 fermented fodder;
發酵學 zymology;
~ 發酵學家 zymologist;
快速發酵 accelerated fermentation;
酸性發酵 acid fermentation;
異常發酵 abnormal fermentation;

[發窘] become embarrassed; feel embarrassed; ill at ease;

[發掘] disinterment; excavate; explore; unearth;
發掘古墓 excavate an ancient burial site; unearth culture relics;
發掘人才 seek gifted people; seek talented people;

[發覺] (1) aware of; come to know; get wind of; (2) detect; discover; find; realize;

[發刊] issue; publish; start the publication of a periodical;

[發狂] delirium; flip out; go barmy; go crazy; go mad;
氣得發狂 rage with anger;

[發睏] drowsy; sleepy;

[發冷] feel chilly; feel cold;
感到手腳發冷 feel a chill both in hands and feet;
渾身發冷 a chill comes creeping over one;

[發愣] in a daze; in a trance; stare blankly;
坐在那裏發愣 sit there as if in a trance;

[發力] pull;
第二次發力 second pull;
第一次發力 first pull;

[發亮] become shiny; shine;
東方發亮 the gleam of dawn shimmered in the east;
兩眼發亮 one's eyes shone;

[發令] start;
發令槍 starting pistol;
發令員 starter;

[發落] deal with (an offender);
從輕發落 deal with sb leniently; give quarter; give sb a light sentence; let sb off lightly; reduce the term of a sentence;
聽候發落 wait for one's punishment;

[發麻] have pins and needles; numb; tingle;
兩腿發麻 have pins and needles in one's legs;

[發毛] (1) afraid of; scared; terrified; (2) lose one's temper;

[發霉] become mildewed; go mouldy; mildew; mouldiness; mustiness;
發霉的奶酪 mouldy cheese;
發霉麵包 mouldy bread;
開始發霉 gather mould;
皮鞋發霉 shoes have become mildewed;

[發蒙] teach a child to read and write;
發蒙啟滯 enlighten the young and open the minds of the dull;
發蒙振聵 awaken the blind and rouse the deaf; enlighten the benighted; enlighten the blind and stir the deaf; make a deaf man hear and a blind man see;
發蒙振落 things easily accomplished without mental effort;

[發明] invent; invention;
發明家 inventor;
~ 天才發明家 genius inventor;
發明權 right of invention;
發明人 inventor;
發明者 inventor;
發明專利 patent for invention;
促進發明 promote invention;
新發明 new invention;
一項發明 an invention;
專利發明 patented invention;
自發性發明 autonomous invention;
最新發明 latest invention;

[發難] launch an attack; rise in revolt; the first to start revolt;

[發怒] a burst of anger; act up; fit to be tied; flare up; fly into a rage; get angry;

have a black dog on one's shoulder; have one's gorge rise; lose one's rag; lose one's temper; see red
動輒發怒 get angry easily; get into a huff; go into a huff; huffy; prone to anger; take offence at trifles; touchy;
~動輒發怒的人 sorehead;
突然發怒 fit of anger; outburst of anger;

[發盤] offer; offering;
發盤人 offerer;
撤回發盤 withdraw an offer;
撤銷發盤 cancel an offer;
重新發盤 re-offer;
搭配發盤 combination offer;
電報發盤 cable offer;
獨家發盤 exclusive offer;
附樣發盤 sample offer;
接受發盤 acceptance of offer;
口頭發盤 verbal offer;
確認發盤 confirmation of offer;
特殊發盤 exceptional offer;
實盤發盤 firm offer;
婉拒發盤 declination of offer;
原發盤 original offer;
暫停發盤 withhold an offer;
轉門發盤 special offer;
綜合發盤 lump offer; offer on a lump basis;

[發胖] burst one's buttons; gain flesh; get fat; put on weight; round out;

[發砲] shoot a cannon;

[發票] bill; invoice;
商務發票 commercial invoice;
限額發票 limit bill;
現購發票 cash invoice;
銀行發票 bank invoice;

[發起] get up; initiate;
發起反攻 launch a counterattack;
發起國 sponsor nation;
發起人 initiator; sponsor;
發起宣傳攻勢 start a press campaign;

[發情] heat; oestrus; rut;
發情周期 sexual cycle;

[發球] serve; serve a ball; service;
發球裁判 foot fault judge;
發球觸網 let serve;
發球錯區 wrong court;
發球得分 ace service; serve a winner;
發球犯規 fault;
發球方 serving side;
發球搶攻 attack after service; hit the service return;
發球權 right to serve;
~失發球權 loss of service;
~無發球權 hand-out;
~有發球權 hand-in;
發球失誤 missed service; faulty service;
發球違例 service fault;
發球線 service line;
發球員 server;
重發球 let; service let;
大力發球 drive service;
~勾手大力發球 cannon-ball service;
第二發球員發球 second server;
發保險球 safe service;
發短球 short service;
發高球 lobbing service;
發飄球 floating service;
發平擊球 flat service;
發平線球 flat service; level service;
發削球 slice service;
發下墜球 drop service;
勾手發球 hook service;
過頭發球 overhead service;
合法發球 good service;
換發球 change of service; change service; service over;
接發球 return the service;
~接發球得分 kill the service;
~接發球搶攻 counter-hit the service;
拋起發球 toss-up;
巧妙的發球 tricky service;
上手發球 overhand service;
下蹲式發球 squatting service;
下手發球 underhand service;
助跑發球 running service;

[發熱] (1) generate heat; give out heat; (2) have a fever;
電機發熱 the motor feels hot;
頭腦發熱 have a hot head;
有點發熱 have a slight heat;

[發軟] become limp; soften;
腳發軟 leg turning weak;
兩腿發軟 one's legs feel like jelly; one's legs give way; weak at the knees;
周身發軟 become limp all over;

[發散] divergence;
紅外線發散 infrared beam divergence;
累積發散 accumulated divergence;
射束發散 beam divergence;

[發燒] fever; have a fever; have a temperature; run a fever; run a

temperature;
發燒友 fanatic;

[發射] discharge; emission; emit; fire; launch; launching; shoot;
發射場 launching site;
發射導彈 launch a guided missile;
發射功率 transmitted power;
發射機 transmitter;
~ 伴音發射機 aural transmitter;
~ 補點發射機 auxiliary transmitter;
~ 電弧發射機 arc transmitter;
~ 調幅發射機 amplitude-modulated transmitter;
發射極 emitter;
發射架 launcher;
發射井 silo;
發射率 emissivity;
~ 定向發射率 directional emissivity;
~ 火焰發射率 flame emissivity;
~ 熱發射率 thermal emissivity;
~ 陰極發射率 cathode emissivity;
發射能力 emissing ability;
發射砲彈 fire shells;
發射區 emitter region;
發射時間 fire time;
發射塔 launching tower;
發射台 launching pad; transmitting station;
發射體 emitter;
~ 電子發射體 electron emitter;
~ 共發射體 common emitter;
~ 陰極發射體 cathode emitter;
發射信號 transmit signals;
發射中心 transmitting centre;
發射裝置 launcher;
~ 彈帶式發射裝置 belt feed; launcher;
~ 定向發射裝置 aimed launcher;
~ 固定發射裝置 fixed launcher;
~ 自動發射裝置 automatic launcher;
伴生發射 associated emission;
反向發射 back emission;
軌道發射 orbital launch;
空中發射 air launch;
傾斜發射 oblique launching;
試驗性發射 test launching;
陰極發射 cathode emission;
正確發射 correct launch;
自動電子發射 autoelectronic emission;

[發生] arise; come about; come over; come to pass; come up; fall out; go off; go on; happen; occur; spring up; take place; turn up;
發生衝突 conflicts occur;
發生關係 establish a relationship; have an affair; have sexual intercourse; have sth to do;
發生了什麼事 what's going on;
發生爐 producer;
~ 環形發生爐 annular producer;
~ 煤氣發生爐 coal gas producer;
發生器 generator; producer;
~ 乾底發生器 dry bottom producer;
~ 回流式發生器 downdraught type producer;
~ 精密掃描發生器 accurate sweep generator;
~ 空氣煤氣發生器 air producer gas generator;
~ 氣體發生器 gas generator;
~ 聲頻信號發生器 audio signal generator;
~ 煙霧發生器 aerosol producer;
發生效力 do the trick;
重演發生 palingenesis;
即將發生 draw near; in the offing;
經常發生 frequently happen;
同時發生 coincide;
突然發生 from nowhere; out of nowhere;
細胞發生 cytogenesis;
自然發生 abiogenesis; abiogeny;
~ 自然發生論者 abiogenist;
~ 自然發生説 autogenesis; spontaneous generation;

[發聲] phonation; vocalize;
發聲過強 superenergetic phonation;
發聲過弱 subenergetic phonation;
發聲困難 dysphonia;
~ 痙攣性發聲困難 spasmodic dysphonia;
發聲器官 vocal organ;
發聲術 vocalism;
發聲無力 phonasthenia;
練習發聲 exercise one's voice; practise vocalization;

[發誓] make a vow; make an oath; pledge; swear; take an oath; vow;
發誓戒酒 swear off drinking;
發誓戒煙 swear off smoking;
發誓相互忠誠 pledge mutual fidelity;
暗自發誓 swear to oneself; swear within oneself;
對天發誓 call Heaven to witness; cross one's heart; swear an oath before Heaven; swear by Heaven; swear

F

by the heaven as witness; swear to heaven;
舉手發誓 hold up one's hand and pledge;
鄭重發誓 make a solemn vow;

[發售] put on sale; sell;

[發抒] express; voice;
發抒己見 express one's personal views;

[發送] (1) consignment; dispatch; send; sending; (2) transmit by radio;
發送的貨物 consignment;
發送器 sender;
~電碼發送器 code sender;
~受控發送器 controlled sender;
~指令發送器 command sender;
盲發送 blind transmission;
自動發送 automatic sending;

[發條] (1) clockwork spring; (2) mainspring;
發條裝置 clockwork;
變截面發條 tapered mainspring;
反轉發條 reverse mainspring;
回彈發條 resilient mainspring;
上發條 wind a toy; wind a watch;

[發問] ask a question; fire off; pose a question; put a question; raise a question;

[發現] discover; discovery; find;
發現系統 discovery system;
故障發現 fault discovery;
科學發現 scientific discovery;
良心發現 be strung by conscience; conscience-stricken;
新發現 new discovery;

[發祥] occur; prosper; rise;
發祥地 birthplace; place of origin;

[發響] make a sound;

[發笑] laugh;
暗暗發笑 chuckle to oneself; laugh up one's sleeve; smile secretively;
暗自發笑 chuckle; laugh inside oneself;
令人發笑 make sb laugh; provoke laughter; ridiculous;
忍不住發笑 cannot control the outbursts of mirth;

[發洩] give vent to; let off; let out;
發洩不滿 air one's grievances; express one's grievances;
發洩感情 relieve one's feelings; uncork one's emotion;
發洩怒火 give vent to sb's anger;
發洩心中怒火 ventilate sb's angry feeling;

[發薪] pay salary; pay wages;
發薪日 payday;
發薪水 pay salary; pay wages;

[發信] post a letter;
發信人 addresser;

[發行] distribute; issue; put on sale;
發行部 circulation department;
發行成本 floatation cost;
發行費 distribution cost;
發行股票 stock issue;
發行科 circulation department;
發行權 distribution right;
發行人 publisher;
發行日期 date of issue;
發行商 distributor;
發行網 distribution network;
發行債券 bond issue;
按市價發行 issue at the market price;
貨幣發行 monetary issue;
紙幣發行 note issue;
總發行 distributor; sole distributor;
~國內總發行 domestic distributor;
~國外總發行 overseas distributor;

[發噱] amusing; funny;

[發芽] burgeon; germinate; sprout;
發芽能力 germination ability;

[發言] make a statement; make a speech; speak; take the floor;
發言稿 address;
~起草發言稿 draft out an address;
~縮短發言稿 condense an address;
發言權 right to speak;
發言人 spokesman;
~女發言人 spokewoman;
發言中肯 hit the mark; hit the right nail on the head; speak to the point; strike the right note;
主題發言 keynote speech;

[發炎] inflame; inflammation;
急性發炎 acute inflammation;

[發揚] (1) carry forward; carry on;develop; promote; (2) bring into full play; make full use of; make the most of;
發揚成績 carry forward one's achievements;
發揚光大 bring to a greater height of development; carry forward; develop; develop and shine with greater brilliance; develop to a higher stage; enhance; foster and enhance; give full play to; give greater scope to; spread and flourish;
發揚優良傳統 carry forward the fine

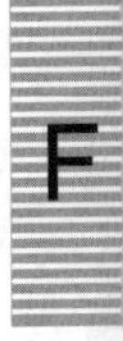

tradition;

[發癢] itch; tickle;

令人發癢 tickle;

腿發癢 one's leg is itchy;

[發瘧子] suffer from malaria;

[發音] articulate; get one's tongue round;

發音不好 pronounce badly;

發音不清 blurring articulation;

發音方法 manner of articulation;

發音方式 articulation type;

發音過強 hyperphonia;

發音過弱 hypophonia;

發音痙攣 phonatory spasm;

發音課程 lessons in pronunciation;

發音困難 dysphonia;

發音速度 rate of articulation;

發音正常 orthophony;

重複發音 iterative articulation;

公認發音 received pronunciation;

強調發音 emphatic articulation;

舌尖發音 apical articulation;

語音學發音 phonetic articulation;

正確發音 correct pronunciation;

[發育] development; engender; grow;

發育病 developmental diseases;

發育不良 maldevelopment;

表皮發育不良 epidermodysplasia;

~唇發育不良 atelocheilia;

~額鼻發育不良 frontonasal dysplasia;

~宮頸發育不良 cervical dysplasia;

~骨發育不良 anostosis;

~骨幹發育不良 diaphyseal dysplasia;

~骨骼發育不良 ostemyelodysplasia;

~骨髓發育不良 myelodysplasia;

~關節發育不良 arthrodysplasia;

~骺發育不良 epiphyseal dysplasia;

~脊柱發育不良 atelorachidia;

~口發育不良 atelostomia;

~淋巴發育不良 alymphoplasia;

~顱發育不良 atelocephaly;

~面發育不良 ateloprosopia;

~腦發育不良 atelencephalia;

~皮膚發育不良 dermatodysplasia;

~偏側發育不良 hemihypoplasia;

~軟骨發育不良 achondroplasia;

~舌發育不良 ateloglossia;

~身體發育不良 hyposomia;

~腎發育不良 renal dysplasia;

~視網膜發育不良 retinal dysplasia;

~手發育不良 atelocheiria;

~心發育不良 atelocardia;

~牙發育不良 hypodontia;

~足發育不良 atelopodia;

發育不全 agenesis; aphasia; hypoplasia; underdevelopment;

~表皮發育不全 epidermodysplasia;

~唇發育不全 atelocheilia;

~宮頸發育不全 cervical dysplasia;

~骨發育不全 dyosteogenesis;

~關節發育不全 arthrodysplasia;

~骺發育不全 epiphyseal dysplasia;

~脊柱發育不全 atelorachidia;

~口發育不全 atelostomia;

~淋巴發育不全 alymphoplasia;

~顱發育不全 atelocephaly;

~面發育不全 ateloprosapia;

~腦發育不全 atelencephalia;

~皮膚發育不全 adermogenesis;

~偏側發育不全 hemihypoplasia;

~軟骨發育不全 dyschondroplasia;

~舌發育不全 ateloglossia;

~身體發育不全 hyposomia;

~腎發育不全 renal dysplasia;

~生殖器發育不全 agenosomia;

~生殖腺發育不全 gonadal dysgenesis;

~視網膜發育不全 retinal aplasia;

~手發育不全 atelocheiria;

~心發育不全 atelocardia;

~性腺發育不全 gonadal dysgenesis;

~子宮發育不全 uterine hypoplasia;

~足發育不全 atelopodia;

發育遲緩 hypoevolutism;

~宮內發育遲緩 intrauterine growth retardation;

發育規律 developmental mechanism; law of development;

發育過度 hypergenesis;

~偏側發育過度 hemihyperplasia;

~生殖器發育過度 hypergenitalism;

發育過緩 bradygenesis;

發育過小 microgenesis;

發育均衡 eurhythmia;

發育均勻 eurhythmia;

發育力 potency;

發育良好 physically well-developed;

發育期 maturity;

發育失調 dysmaturity;

發育條件 condition for development;

發育停頓 arrested development;

發育停止 developmental arrest;

發育異常 dysplasia;

~骨幹發育異常 diaphyseal sclerosis;

發育障礙 developmental disorders;

~ 骨發育障礙 dysosteogenesis;
~ 偏側發育障礙 hemidystrophy;
~ 生殖器發育障礙 dysgenitalism;
被動發育 dependent development;
被囊發育 encapsulated development;
充分發育 reach full growth;
出生後發育 postnatal development;
出生前發育 prenatal development;
個體發育 ontogenesis; ontogeny;
會聚發育 convergent development;
漸進發育 gradual development;
卵表發育 exoblastic development;
胚胎發育 embryonic development;
系統發育 phylogenesis; phylogeny;
延緩發育 delayed development;

[發源] have its source; originate; rise;
發源地 matrix; place of origin;
~ 文化發源地 cultural matrix;

[發暈] faint; feel dizzy; feel giddy;
因饑餓發暈 feel faint through lack of food;

[發展] (1) burgeon; develop; expand; grow; (2) admit; recruit;
發展傳播學 developmental mass communications;
發展規律 law of development;
發展國民經濟 develop the national economy;
發展會員 recruit new members;
發展基金 development fund;
發展價值 causative value;
發展教育事業 promote education;
發展階段 development stage;
發展經濟 develop the economy;
~ 發展經濟學 development economics;
發展模式 mode of development;
發展權 right to development;
發展商 developer;
發展社會學 developmental sociology;
發展事業 develop one's business;
發展勢頭 momentum of development;
發展水平 development level;
~ 發展水平理論 theory of development level;
~ 發展速度 pace of development;
發展心理學 development psychology;
發展戰略 development strategy;
發展中國家 developing country;
發展中心 development centre;
發展智力 develop intelligence;
發展壯大 develop and grow in strength; expand; go from strength to strength;
發展自由貿易 expand free trade;
發展組織 expand an organization;
不平衡發展 disproportionate development; uneven development;
城市發展 urban development;
持續發展 onwards and upwards; sustainable development;
妨礙發展 hamper the development;
工業發展 industrial expansion;
國家發展 national development;
和諧發展 harmonic development;
經濟發展 economic development;
驚人的發展 alarming development; amazing development; startling development;
可持續發展 sustainable development;
課程發展 curriculum development;
平衡發展 balanced development; symmetrical development;
全球發展 global development;
全人發展 whole-person development;
順其發展 run its course;
隨著經濟發展 with the economic development of;
穩定發展 steady development;
協調發展 coordinated development;
循環發展 cyclic development;
延緩發展 delayed development;
智力發展 intellectual development;
自我發展 ego development;
最新發展 latest development;
阻礙發展 impede the development;

[發脹] swell;
頭腦發脹 have a swelled head;

[發震] occurrence of earthquake;
發震時刻 time of occurrence of earthquake;

[發作] (1) break out; show effect; (2) flare up; have a fit of anger; lose one's temper;
心悸發作 palpitation of the heart comes on;

頒發 (1) issue; promulgate; (2) award;
暴發 (1) break out; erupt; flare; (2) suddenly become rich;
爆發 (1) erupt; (2) break out; (3) burst out;
迸發 burst forth; burst out;
觱發 chilly winds;
並發 be complicated by; erupt simultaneously;
併發 be complicated by; erupt simultaneously;
病發 fall ill;

撥發 allocate; appropriate for; issue to;
播發 broadcast on the air;
勃發 (1) prosperous; thrive; (2) break out; erupt;
補發 pay retroactively; reissue; supply again;
闡發 elucidate;
遲發 tardy;
出發 (1) set out; start off; (2) proceed from; start from;
觸發 detonate by contact; touch off;
打發 (1) dispatch; send; (2) dismiss; send away; (3) while away;
單發 single shot;
點發 firing in bursts;
分發 (1) distribute; hand out; issue; (2) assign;
奮發 exert oneself; work hard and aim high;
風發 (1) as swiftly as the wind; (2) energetical; vigorous;
復發 recur; have a relapse;
告發 inform aginst; lodge an accusation against;
煥發 glow; glowing; irradiate; shine; shining;
揮發 volatilize;
彗發 coma;
擊發 percussion;
激發 (1) arouse; stimulate; (2) excitation;
揭發 bring to light; disclose; expose; ferret out; give the lie to; lay bare; lay open; reveal; show up; uncover; unmask;
進發 set out; start;
舉發 expose;
開發 develop; exploit; open up;
萌發 germinate; shoot forth; sprout;
偶發 accidental; chance; fortuitous;
拍發 send a telegram;
噴發 gush; spurt;
批發 (1) wholesale; (2) be authorized for dispatch;
啟發 enlighten; enlightenment; inspiration; inspire;
簽發 sign and issue;
散發 (1) diffuse; emit; send out; (2) distribute; give out;
沙發 settee; sofa;
閃發 shoot;
繕發 copy and deliver;
生發 breed; develop; multiply;
事發 be exposed; the story is out;
收發 receive and dispatch;
抒發 convey; express; voice;
舒發 express one's emotion;
填發 fill in and issue;
先發 attack first;
秀發 (1) blooming; (2) fine-looking; good-looking; handsome;
虛發 shoot without hitting the target;
延發 delayed action;
一發 (1) even; (2) together;
亦發 (1) all the more; (2) simply;
益發 all the more; increasingly;
引發 initiate;
印發 print and distribute;
英發 intelligent and energetic;
誘發 (1) bring out; induce; (2) cause to happen;
越發 (1) all the more; even; (2) the more...the more;
再發 have a relapse;
照發 issue as before; issue as usual;
蒸發 atmid(o)-; evaporate; evaporation; evaporization;
征發 collect; levy;
徵發 collect; levy;
轉發 transmit;
自發 spontaneous;

fa²
fa

【乏】 (1) lack; (2) tired; weary; (3) exhausted; worn-out;

［乏累］ tired; weary;
［乏力］ feeble; lacking in strength; weak;
［乏善可陳］ have nothing good to report;
［乏味］ drab; dull; insipid; lacking in flavour; lackluster; off-flavour; tasteless;
乏味的 boring; corny;
～乏味的工作 tedious job;
～乏味的書 tedious book;

不乏 there is no lack of;
承乏 unworthily fill a post;
道乏 express one's thanks; say thanks;
解乏 (1) recover from fatigue; (2) refresh;
空乏 destitute;
匱乏 deficient; short of;
困乏 exhausted; fatigued; tired; weary;
勞乏 overworked; physically exhausted; tired;
疲乏 fatigued; tired; weary;
貧乏 lacking; poor;
窮乏 destitute; poverty-stricken;
缺乏 be wanting in; lack; short of;
歇乏 have a rest;

fa

【伐】 (1) cut wood; (2) subjugate;

［伐木］ cutting; felling; logging; lumbering;
伐木工人 forest labourer; lumberjack;

lumberman;
伐木工業 lumbering;

筆伐 attack in writing;
步伐 pace; step;
盜伐 bootleg felling of trees;
口伐 attack verbally;
傘伐 shelterwood cutting;
撻伐 send armed forces to suppress;
討伐 send a punitive expedition against; send armed forces to suppress;
斬伐 fell trees;
徵伐 go on a punitive expedition;
自伐 abuse oneself;
作伐 act as matchmaker;

fa
【砝】 standard weights used in scales; steelyard weights;

fa
【筏】 raft;
［筏道］ log chute; logway;
［筏子］ raft;

fa
【罰】 penalize; punish;
［罰不當罪］ be unduly punished; have the punishment exceed the crime; punishment not in keeping with the crime;
［罰抄］ assign copying out a passage as punitive homework;
［罰金］ fine; forfeit; penalty;
處以罰金 subject to a fine;
小額罰金 light fine;
［罰款］ fine;
懲治性罰款 corrective fine;
交付罰款 pay a fine;
違者罰款 under penalty of a forfeit;
［罰球］ penalty kick; penalty shot;
罰球點 penalty spot;
罰球區 penalty area; penalty box;
罰球線 penalty line;
放棄罰球 forfeit a penalty;

挨罰 be fined; catch it in the neck; get a penalty; get it in the neck;
懲罰 penalize; punish;
處罰 penalize; punish;
獎罰 rewards or punishments;
認罰 admit that one deserves punishment;
賞罰 rewards and punishments;
受罰 be punished;
撻罰 (1) corporal punishment; flogging; (2) punish;
體罰 corporal punishment; physical punishment;
刑罰 penalty; punishment;
責罰 punish;
陟罰 promote and demote; reward and punish;
重罰 keelhaul;

fa
【閥】 (1) left wing of the window; (2) influential family, clique or bloc;

安全閥 safety valve;
財閥 financial magnate; tycoon;
黨閥 party tyrant;
軍閥 (1) warlord; (2) militarist;
門閥 family of power and influence;
學閥 scholar-tyrant;

fa³
fa
【法】 (1) laws; (2) method; way; (3) follow; model after; (4) model; standard; (5) magic arts; (6) Legalist School; (7) Buddhist doctrines; (8) a surname;
［法案］ act; bill; proposed law;
財政法案 finance bill;
減稅法案 tax-slash bill;
金融法案 money bill;
一項法案 an act;
~通過一項法案 pass an act;
政府法案 government bill;
［法寶］ magical weapon;
奉為法寶 look upon as a magical weapon;
使盡法寶 have exerted one's utmost skill;
［法不阿貴］ the law does not protect the rich people;
［法場］ execution ground; scaffold;
［法典］ statute book;
編纂法典 codify the laws;
民法法典 civil code;
刑法法典 penal code;
制定法典 formulate the laws; lay down the laws; set up the laws;
［法定］ legal; statutory;
法定城市 statutory city;
法定程序 legal procedures;
法定代理 legal agency;
~法定代理人 legal representative;

F

法定對等詞 official equivalent;
法定費用 statutory fee;
法定股本 authorized stock;
法定匯價 official quotation;
法定滙率 official rate of exchange;
法定貨幣 lawful money;
法定繼承權 legal heirship;
法定繼承人 legal successor;
法定假日 legal holiday;
法定價格 official price;
法定監護人 legal guardian; statutory guardian;
法定檢驗 legal inspection;
法定利率 official rate of interest;
法定年齡 lawful age; legal age;
法定權利 legal right; statutory right;
法定人數 quorum;
~ 不足法定人數 lack a quorum;
~ 己足法定人數 have a quorum; procure a quorum;
法定審計 legal audit;
法定稅率 national tariff;
法定信托 statutory trust;
法定語言 official language;
法定責任範圍 legal limitation of liability;
法定資本 authorized capital;

[法度] (1) law; (2) moral standard;

[法官] judge;
地方法官 magistrate;
陪審法官 associate judge;
首席法官 chief justice;
一名法官 a judge;
預審法官 preliminary judge;

[法規] bylaw; laws and regulations; ordinance;
單行法規 special regulation;
工廠法規 factory legislation;
教育法規 education legislation;
通過法規 pass a statute;
修正法規 amend legislation;
援引法規 invoke the law;

[法紀] law and discipline;
干犯法紀 break the law and violate discipline;
目無法紀 flout law and discipline;

[法家] Legalists;

[法警] judicial policeman;

[法距] length of normal;
次法距 subnormal;

[法蘭] flange;
艙壁法蘭 bulkhead flange;
成對法蘭 companion flange;
跨接法蘭 crossover flange;

[法郎] franc;
法郎區 franc zone;

[法力] supernatural power;

[法令] act; decree; laws and decrees;
法令生效 the law comes into force;
頒布法令 issue a decree; promulgate a decree;
頒布政府法令 publish the government decree;
發佈法令 issue a decree;
國有化法令 nationalization decree;
緊急法令 emergency act;
沒收法令 confiscatory decree;
違反法令 break a decree;
無視法令 ignore a decree;
現行法令 decrees in effect;
一項法令 an act;
~ 廢除一項法令 abolish an act;
遵守國家法令 obey the law of the country;

[法螺] conch;
自吹法螺 blow one's own trumpet; toot one's own horn;

[法律] (1) legal; (2) law;
法律保護 legal protection; the aegis of law;
~ 不受法律保護 outlawry;
~ 受到法律保護 under the aegis of law;
法律程序 legal procedure;
法律衝突 conflict of law;
法律地位 legal status;
法律翻譯 legal translation;
法律根據 legal basis;
法律顧問 law consultant; legal adviser; legal counsel;
~ 法律顧問處 legal consultation;
法律管轄範疇 jurisdictional boundaries;
法律規定 legal provisions; the law provides that;
法律規範 legal norm;
~ 法律規範結構 legal norm structure;
~ 法律規範模式 model of legal norm;
法律環境 legal environment;
法律監督 legal supervision;
~ 法律監督作用 role of legal supervision;
法律監護人 legal guardian;
法律糾紛 legal dispute;
法律精神 spirit of the law;
法律面前，人人平等 all are equal before

the law; all men are equal in the sight of law; everybody is equal before the law;
法律人格 legal personality;
法律適用條款 proper law clause;
法律事實 juristic facts;
法律事務所 lawyer's office;
法律手續 legal formalities; legal procedure;
法律術語 legalese;
法律體系 legal system
~法律體系總體 general legal system;
法律體制 legal system;
法律條款 legal provisions;
法律條文 the letter of law;
法律文化 legal culture;
~大眾法律文化 public legal culture;
法律文獻 legal text;
法律問題 legal question;
法律效力 legal effect;
法律協議 legal agreement;
法律心理學 psychology of law;
法律行為 legal action;
法律性 legality;
法律許可 legal authorization;
法律意見 legal advice;
法律意識 awareness of the legal system;
法律用語 legalese;
法律語言 law language; legal language;
法律預測 legal prediction;
法律援助 legal aid; legal assistance;
法律責任 legal liability;
~承擔法律責任 bear the legal liability;
法律制裁 legal sanction;
~受法律制裁 be dealt with according to law; be punished according to law;
法律制度 legal institutions; legal system;
法律中心說 doctrine of law as a centre;
法律咨詢 legal consulting;
嘲弄法律 mock the law;
成為法律 become law;
觸犯法律 go beyond the law;
廢除法律 repeal a law;
根據法律 by law;
解釋法律 interpret the law;
濫用法律 take the law into one's hands;
藐視法律 flout the law;
曲解法律 strain the law; stretch the law;
實施法律 put a law into effect;
訴諸法律 go to law;
通過法律 pass a law;
推行法律 introduce a law;
違反法律 break the law; transgress the law; violate the law;
執行法律 enforce a law;
制定法律 enact a law; formulate a law; formulate decrees; make a law;
制訂法律 institute a law; lay down a law;
最高法律 supreme law;
遵守法律 obey the law;

[法碼兒] weights of a scale;

[法盲] legally illiterate;

[法門] (1) door to enlightenment; (2) method; way;
不二法門 standard practice; the one and only way; the only correct approach to; the only proper course to take;

[法名] religious name;

[法權] legal right;
治外法權 extraterritoriality;

[法人] corporation; juridical person; legal body; legal entity; legal person;
法人財產 corporate property;
法人代表 legal representative;
法人地位 status of a legal person;
法人公司 incorporated company;
法人股 legal person share;
法人身份 status of a legal person;
法人實體 legal entity;
法人稅 corporation tax;
法人團體 corporate body; corporate group;
法人制度 legal person system;
法人資格 coporate capacity; qualification of a legal person;
法人作品 work of legal entity;
財團法人 corporate body; juridical person;
兩級法人 two-fold legal person;
普通法人 ordinary corporations;
社團法人 aggregate corporation;
營利法人 business corporation; profit-seeking corporation;
宗教法人 religious corporation;

[法師] Buddhist master;

[法事] Daoist or Buddhist rites;
做法事 perform Daoist or Buddhist rites;

[法書] (1) model calligraphy; (2) your calligraphy;

[法術] witchcraft;

[法庭] court; court of law; courtroom; law court; tribunal;

法庭副庭長 associate chief judge;
法庭記錄員 court reporter;
法庭判決 court ruling;
法庭庭長 chief judge;
法庭指令 court order;
調查法庭 court of inquiry;
兒童法庭 children's court;
國際法庭 international court;
海事法庭 admiralty court; maritime court;
海牙國際法庭 the International Court of Justice in the Hague;
交通法庭 traffic court;
經濟法庭 economic tribunal;
警察法庭 police court;
軍事法庭 military court;
民事法庭 civil court;
模擬法庭 moot court;
破產法庭 bankruptcy court;
商業法庭 commerce court;
上訴法庭 appeals court; court of appeal;
少年法庭 juvenile court;
税務法庭 tax court;
刑事法庭 criminal court;
仲裁法庭 arbitration tribunal; court of arbitration;
宗教法庭 ecclesiastical court;

[法網] arm of the law; net of justice;
法網難逃 it is difficult to escape from the meshes of the law; it is difficult to escape the arm of the law;
落入法網 be caught in the net of justice;
難逃法網 cannot escape punishment; unable to escape the net of justice;
自蹈法網 break the law out of free will; hurl oneself into the net of justice;

[法位] tagmeme;
法位學 tagmemics;

[法線] normal;
仿射法線 affine normal;
公法線 common normal;
內法線 inner normal;
外法線 exterior normal;

[法學] jurisprudence; science of law;
法學會 jurisprudence society;
法學家 juriprudent;
法學士 bachelor of law;
法學碩士 master of law;
法學院 law school;
比較法學 comparative jurisprudence;
~比較法學基礎 basics of comparative law;
研究法學 study jurisdence;
綜合法學 synthetic jurisprudence;

[法衣] cassock;

[法醫] legal medical expert;
法醫病理學家 forensic pathologist;
法醫學 forensics;
法醫專家 forensic expert;

[法院] court; court of justice; court of law; law court;
法院裁決 court decision;
法院大樓 courthouse;
法院副院長 vice-president of court;
法院院長 president of court;
法院指令 court order;
初審法院 court of first instance;
地方法院 local court;
地區法院 district court;
高等法院 high court;
高級人民法院 higher people's court;
國際法院 international court of justice;
上法院 go to court;
上訴法院 appellate court; court of appeal;
申訴法院 court of claims;
縣法院 county court;
小額錢債法院 small claims court;
行政法院 administrative court;
巡迴法院 circuit couet;
中級人民法院 intermediate people's court;
終審法院 court of final jurisdiction; court of final appeal;
仲裁法院 arbitration tribunal; court of arbitration;
州法院 state court;
最高法院 supreme court;
最高人民法院 supreme people's court;
最高上訴法院 court of last resort;

[法則] law; rule;
安全法則 safety code; safety regulations;
普遍的法則 a universal law;
維護法則 maintain the laws and regulations;
無視法則 defy the laws and regulations;
行為法則 law of honour;
自然法則 law of nature;

[法治] governed by law; government by law; rule by law;

[法制] legal system; legality;
法制觀念 legal sense;
法制建設 legal system building;
法制教育 legal education;

法制片 lega film;
法制文學 legal literature;
法制協調 legal system coordination;
法制心理學 legal psychology;

[法子] means; methods; ways;
沒法子 can do nothing about it; can't help it;
死法子 a rigid and unimaginative way of doing things;

氨碱法 ammonia soda process;
暗法 secret ways;
辦法 means; measure; way;
鼻飼法 nasal feeding;
筆法 technique of writing;
變法 initiate political reform; political reform; reform; revise the law;
兵法 art of war; military strategy and tactics;
剝句法 sentence-peeling method;
不成文法 unwritten law;
不法 illegal; unlawful;
步法 footwork;
操法 methods and rules for military drill;
成法 established law;
成文法 statute law; written law;
乘法 multiplication;
吃法 how to eat;
除法 division;
詞法 morphology;
磁法 magnetic method;
皴法 technique of representing irregular surfaces;
大法 charter; fundamental law;
得法 do sth in the right way;
電法 electrical method;
犯法 violate the law;
方法 method; way;
非法 illegal; illicit; unlawful;
分析法 analytic approach;
佛法 (1) Buddha dharma; Buddhist doctrine; (2) power of Buddha;
伏法 be executed;
服法 directions for taking medicine;
弓法 bowing;
公法 public law;
功能法 functional approach;
國法 law; national law; the law of the land;
海法 maritime law;
合詞法 compounding;
合法 lawful; legal; rightful;
畫法 technique of painting;
混成法 blending;
激將法 encourage sb to do sth by means of criticizing his ability; goading sb into action by ridicule or sarcasm; prodding sb into action;
技法 skill and method;
加法 addition;
家法 (1) domestic discipline exercised by the head of a feudal household; (2) rod for punishing children or servants in a feudal household;
漸層法 climax;
漸降法 anticlimax;
減法 subtraction;
講法 (1) a way of saying a thing; wording; (2) opinion; view;
交際法 communicative approach;
句法 (1) sentence structure; (2) syntax;
軍法 military law;
看法 a way of looking at a thing; view;
誇張法 hyperbole;
括號法 bracketing;
擴詞法 diction-amplification;
禮法 law and discipline rite;
立法 legislate;
曆法 calendar;
斂法 tax law;
療法 therapy; treatment;
民法 civil law;
魔法 conjuration; magic;
膜法 membrane method;
逆成法 back-formation;
擬人法 personification;
擬聲法 onomatopoeic method;
唸法 pronunciation;
判例法 case law;
拼法 spelling;
槍法 marksmanship;
取法 follow the example of; take as one's model;
染印法 dyeing transfer process;
熔法 melt;
篩法 sieve method;
商法 commercial law;
設法 devise a way; do what one can; think of a way; think up a method; try;
師法 (1) emulate; imitate; model after; pattern after; (2) knowledge handed down by one's master; methods taught by one's teacher;
世法 (1) tradition; traditional practices; (2) common truths;
謚法 regulations for conferring posthumous titles;
手法 (1) skill; technique; (2) gimmick; trick;

守法 abide by the law; law-abiding; observe the law;
說法 (1) a way of saying a thing; formulation; wording; (2) argument; statement;
書法 calligraphy; penmanship;
梳法 combing;
順譯法 translation in regular sequence;
税法 tariff law; tax law;
司法 judiciary;
速算法 short-cut method of counting;
算法 algorithm;
圖示法 iconography;
土法 indigenous method; local method;
玩法 toy with the law;
王法 law of the land;
枉法 abuse law; pervert the law; twist law to suit one's own purpose;
違法 break the law; illegal;
骫法 abuse the law; violate the law;
畏法 fear the law;
文法 grammar;
握法 grip;
無法 incapable; unable;
戲法 conjuring; juggling; magic; tricks;
憲法 charter; constitution;
想法 idea; opinion;
相法 physiognomy;
效法 follow the example of; learn from; model oneself on;
邪法 black magic; witchcraft;
寫法 style of writing;
新法 (1) new method; new technique; (2) new laws;
刑法 corporal punishment; criminal law; penal code; torture;
掩眼法 camouflage; cover-up;
依法 according to law; by operation of law; in conformity with legal provisions;
譯法 translation method;
用法 use; usage;
優選法 optimum seeking method;
語法 (1) grammar; (2) study of grammar;
緣法 (1) follow the old laws; (2) abide by the law;
約法 provisional constitution;
越法 illegal; transgress the law; unlawful;
增譯法 amplification method;
章法 (1) art of composition; presentation of ideas in a piece of writing; (2) methodicalness; orderly ways;
障眼法 (1) legerdemain; (2) cover-up; camouflage;
遮眼法 camouflage;
針法 stitching;
正法 execute a criminal;
政法 politics and law;
證法 demonstration;
指法 fingering;
執法 enforce the law;
製法 method of making sth;
宗法 patriarchal clan system;
作法 (1) practise magic; resort to magic arts; (2) course of action; practise; ways of doing things; (3) art of composition;
做法 course of action; practice; way of doing a thing;

fa

【髮】 hair;
［髮辮］ braid; plait; tail;
［髮菜］ hair vegetable; hair weed;
［髮髻］ bun; chignon;
黃髮垂髫 old and young; the aged and the young;
［髮際線］ hairline;
［髮夾］ bobby pin; hairgrip; hairpin;
髮夾灣 hairpin bend;
小髮夾 bobby pin; hair slide;
［髮蠟］ pomade;
［髮廊］ barber shop;
［髮妻］ first wife;
［髮乳］ hair cream;
［髮梢］ end of a hair;
髮梢分叉 split ends;
［髮式］ hair style;
［髮刷］ hairbrush;
［髮網］ hairnet;
［髮屋］ barber shop;
［髮型］ coiffure; hairdo; hairstyle;
板刷頭髮型 crew cut;
背兒頭髮型 all back;
邊分髮型 side parting;
辮子髮型 braid; pigtail; plait; queue;
波浪式髮型 natural wave style; wavy achirstyle;
波濤式髮型 irregular wave style;
長髮髮型 long hair;
單花式髮型 wavy;
短髮髮型 bob-haired; bobbed hair; short hair; hair in a bob; shingle;
髮髻髮型 bun;
飛燕式髮型 swept-back;
分頭髮型 hair partings;
風涼式髮型 cool style;

光頭髮型 shaven;
弧形式髮型 arc style;
花瓣兒式髮型 petal style;
角形式髮型 angular style;
螺旋式髮型 spiral style;
馬尾辮髮型 ponytail;
蓬鬆式髮型 bouffant style;
平頭髮型 close crop; crew cut; flat top;
平直形式髮型 smooth style;
齊短髮型 bob style;
雙花式髮型 symmetric waves;
童花式髮型 pageboy style;
學生頭髮型 student's haircut;
羊角辮髮型 ram's horns;
圓頭髮型 pudding cut; round cut;
中長髮髮型 medium-length hair;
中分髮型 centre parting;

[髮針] hairpin;

[髮指] boil with anger; bristle with anger;
令人髮指 get one's hackles up; make one bristle with anger; make one's blood boil; make one's hackles rise; make one's hair stand on end;

白髮 gray hair; white hair;
編髮 braid the hair;
辮髮 (1) plaited hair; (2) braid one's hair; plait one's hair; (3) wear a queue;
鬢髮 hair on the temples;
長髮 long hair;
齒髮 one's tooth and hair;
垂髮 have one's hair hang down;
短髮 bobbed hair; bob-haired; hair in a bob; shingle; short hair;
額髮 forelock;
毫髮 a hair; the least bit; the slightest;
鶴髮 hoary head;
鵠髮 gray hair; white hair;
華髮 gray hair;
假髮 toupee; wig;
剪髮 cut one's hair; hairdressing; have a haircut;
金髮 blonde hair;
捲髮 curly hair;
鬈髮 crimps;
理髮 cut sb's hair; dress sb's hair; have a haircut; have one's hair dressed;
燎髮 to singe hair — a thing that can be done very easily;
落髮 shave one's head;
毛髮 hair;
眉髮 eyebrows;
美髮 hairdressing;
濃髮 shock of hair;
披髮 dishevelled hair;
卷髮 (1) curly hair; (2) curl hair;
染髮 colour one's hair; dye one's hair;
鋭髮 stray hair before the ear;
束髮 reach boyhood;
甩髮 long, hanging wig;
絲髮 glossy, silky hair;
酥髮 lustrous hair;
素髮 white hair;
蒜髮 premature white hair of a young person;
胎髮 foetal hair; hair of a new born baby; lanugo;
燙髮 give a permanent; have a permanent wave; perm; wave hair;
薙髮 cut hair; haircut; shave hair;
頭髮 hair; hair on the human head;
禿髮 alopecia;
脱髮 alopecia; baldness; falling out of hair; lose one's hair; trichomadesis;
修髮 trim one's hair;
鬚髮 beard;
蓄髮 grow long hair;
削髮 shave one's head;
銀髮 silver hair;
總髮 childhood;
捽髮 grasp by the hair;

fa⁴

fa

【法】 (1) Frank; (2) France; French;

[法國] France;

fa

【珐】 enamel; enamel-ware;

[珐瑯] enamel;
珐瑯器 enamel vessels; enamel wares;
珐瑯質 enamel; porcelain enamel;

fan¹

fan

【帆】 canvas; sail; sail-cloth;

[帆板] sailboard; wind-surfer;

[帆布] canvas;
帆布包 canvas bag;
帆布鞋 canvas shoes;
~平底帆布鞋 deck shoe;
~橡皮底帆布鞋 plimsoll; sneaker;
帆布牀 campbed; cot;
防水帆布 tarpaulin;
游艇帆布 yacht canvas;

[帆船] junk; sailing boat; yacht;

帆船比賽 yacht race;
帆船運動 yachting;
大帆船 sailing ship;
高桅橫帆船 tall ship;
快速帆船 clipper;
三桅帆船 bark; barkantine;
小帆船 sailing boat;
一艘帆船 a sailing boat;

［帆傘運動］ parasailing;

fan

【番】 (1) take turns; (2) order in a series; time; (3) barbarian; (4) (of mahjong) time;

［番瓜］ pumpkin;

［番鬼］ foreign devil;

［番紅花］ crocus; crocus sativus; saffron;

［番茄］ tomato;
番茄 tomato juice;
番茄醬 catsup; ketchup; tomato ketchup;
~ 一包番茄醬 a packet of ketchup; a sachet of ketchup;
醋栗番茄 currant tomato;
罐頭番茄 canned tomatoes;
李形番茄 plum tomato;
去皮整番茄 peeled tomato; whole tomato;
櫻桃番茄 cherry tomato;

［番薯］ sweet potato;

fan

【幡】 (1) flag; pennant; pennon; streamer; (2) sudden; suddenly;

［幡然］ come to a sudden realization; suddenly;
幡然悔悟 determined to make a clean break with one's past; see the error of one's ways and repent;
幡然悔悟，改弦更張 repent and mend one's ways;

fan

【蕃】 barbarian; foreign; uncivilized;

fan

【繙】 (1) interpret; translate; (2) flutter; fly;

［繙蠻］ speak an incomprehensible local dialect;

fan

【翻】 (1) turn over; (2) cross; get over; (3) rummage; search; (4) translate; (5) reverse; (6) multiply;

［翻案］ reopen a case; reverse a case; reverse a sentence; reverse a verdict; revoke a decision;

［翻版］ reprint; reproduction;

［翻邊機］ flanger;
頸部翻邊機 necker flanger;
旋轉式翻邊機 rotary double-end flanger;
自動翻邊機 automatic flanger;

［翻車］ (1) turn over; (2) fail in doing sth;

［翻船］ (1) shipwreck; (2) fail; suffer an upset;

［翻番］ double; increase 100 percent;

［翻飛］ flit to and fro; fly up and down;
紅旗翻飛 the flag fluttered in the wind;
蝴蝶翻飛 butterflies fly up and down;

［翻覆］ overturn; turn upside down;
翻覆無常 vacillating in attitude; wavering;
翻翻覆覆 vacillating; wavering;
翻來覆去 again and again; back and forth; over and over again; repeatedly; toss about; toss and turn; toss from side to side;
~ 在牀上翻來覆去 one tossed and turned on the bed;
天翻地覆 a state of extreme confusion; almighty fuss; an extreme upheaval; earth-shaking; in sheer pandemonium; in total disorder; shake the very ground; the sky and the earth turning upside down;

［翻改］ renovate;

［翻跟頭］ loop the loop; somersault; turn a somersault;
表演翻跟頭 perform tumbles;
練習翻跟頭 practise tumbles;
在草地上翻跟頭 turn a somersault on the lawn;

［翻滾］ reverse dive; roll; somersault; toss; turn; turn over; tumble;
翻滾的波濤 the rolling waves; the tumbler of the waves;
滿地翻滾 toss on the ground;
心潮翻滾 one's mind is confused and excited; one's mind is in a tumult; one's mind is racing; thoughts tumble through one's mind;

［翻悔］ back out; go back on;

［翻看］ leaf through;

［翻臉］ fall out; suddenly turn hostile;
翻臉不認人 pretend not to know old friends; turn against a friend;
翻臉無情 a word and a blow; be treacherous and ruthless; break up an old friendship; change colour and

have no feeling; fall out with and turn a cold shoulder to sb; turn against a friend and show him no mercy;
與朋友翻臉 fall out with one's friends; turn against one's friends;

[翻領] lapel; turndown collar;

[翻錄] copy;

[翻墻越脊] climb over the walls and run on the roof; leap onto roofs and vault over walls; make one's way into a house over walls and roofs;

[翻然] change quickly and completely;
翻然改悔 make a determined effort to atone for past misdeeds;
翻然改進 change quickly and completely;
翻然改圖 repent and change course; quickly change one's plans;
翻然悔悟 be determined to make a clean break with one's past; make an effort to atone for one's misdeeds; make determined effort to make amends for past misdeeds; see the error of one's ways and repent; quickly wake up to one's error;

[翻上] swing up;
翻上向前 upward circle forward;

[翻身] (1) turn over; (2) free oneself; stand up;

[翻騰] (1) tuck dive; (2) churn; rise; seethe; (3) turn sth over and over;
翻騰的波浪 seething waves;
臂立翻騰 armstand somersault;
臂立中穿翻騰 armstand cut-through reverse somersault;
內心翻騰 one's heart is in a tumult;
思緒翻騰 thoughts are tumbling about in one's mind;
向前翻騰 forward somersault;

[翻天] overturn the heavens; shake the sky;
翻天覆地 earth-shaking; epoch-making; turn the world upside down; titantic change;
鬧翻天 raise a rumpus;

[翻箱倒篋] empty everything from the trunks; overturn the trunks and boxes; ransack boxes and chests; ransack suitcases and wardrobes; rummage through chests and cupboards; turn boxes upside down; turn everything inside out;

[翻新] make over; recondition; renovate; retrofit;

[翻修] rebuild;
翻譯工程 rebuilding work; renewal work;

[翻譯] (1) do into; interpret; put into; put one language into another language; render; render into another tongue; transcribe; translate; translate into; turn into; (2) translator;
翻譯編輯 translation editor;
翻譯便覽 translation manual;
翻譯標記 translation label;
翻譯部門 translation department;
翻譯操作 translation operation;
翻譯策略 translation strategy;
翻譯測驗 translation test;
翻譯層次 level of translation;
翻譯程序 translation procedure;
翻譯從業員 practising translator;
翻譯單位 unit of translation;
翻譯等級 rank of translation;
翻譯對等詞 translation equivalent;
翻譯法 translation method;
~表達翻譯法 expressive translation;
~拆句翻譯法 sentence-splitting translation;
~反襯翻譯法 antipode in translation;
~改詞翻譯法 word-modification method;
~構成翻譯法 compositive translation;
~加注翻譯法 annotation;
~精簡翻譯法 diction-simplificiation translation;
~逆序翻譯法 inversion method;
~駢體翻譯法 antithesis method;
~移名翻譯法 transfer of denomination;
翻譯方法 translation method;
~翻譯方法學 translation methodology;
翻譯分析 translation analysis;
翻譯服務 translation service;
~翻譯服務中心 translation service centre;
翻譯輔助 translation aids;
翻譯改編 adaptation;
翻譯工具 translation tool;
翻譯工作 translation work;
~翻譯工作量 translation workload;
~翻譯工作室 translation workshop;
翻譯公司 translation company;
翻譯規範 translation norm;
翻譯規則 translation rule;
翻譯過程 translation process;
翻譯行業 translation industry;
翻譯活動 translation activity;

翻譯機 translation machine;
翻譯機構 translation organization;
翻譯計劃 translation plan;
翻譯技巧 translation technique;
翻譯獎 translation prize;
翻譯教師 translation teacher;
翻譯教學 translation teaching;
~翻譯教學法 translation pedagogy;
翻譯教育 translation education;
~翻譯教育工作者 translation educator;
翻譯劇 translated play;
翻譯科目 translation course;
翻譯科學 science of translation;
翻譯課程 translation programme;
翻譯理論 translation theory;
~翻譯理論家 translation theorist;
~特殊翻譯理論 specific translation theory;
翻譯練習 translation exercise;
翻譯美學 translation aesthetics;
翻譯器 interpreter;
~撥號脈衝翻譯器 dial pulse interpreter;
~電子翻譯器 electronic interpreter;
翻譯軟件 translation software;
翻譯社 translation agency;
翻譯實踐 translation practice;
翻譯市場 translation market;
翻譯手冊 translation handbook;
翻譯體 translationese;
翻譯委員會 translation committee;
翻譯文獻 translated literature;
翻譯文學 translated literature;
翻譯系 translation department;
翻譯問題 translation problem;
翻譯系統 translation system;
~口語翻譯系統 voice translation system;
翻譯小組 translation team;
翻譯協會 translation association;
翻譯學 translatology;
翻譯學會 translation society;
翻譯學生 translation student;
翻譯學徒 apprentice translator;
翻譯學校 translation school;
翻譯訓練 translation training;
翻譯研究 translation studies;
翻譯藝術 art of translation;
翻譯員 translator;
~高級翻譯員 senior translator;
~公司翻譯員 staff translator;
~會議翻譯員 conference translator;
~科技翻譯員 schientific and technological translator;
翻譯原理 translation principle;
翻譯職責 translation task;
翻譯質素 translation quality;
~翻譯質素評估 translation quality assessment;
翻譯中心 translation centre;
翻譯轉換 translation shift;
翻譯準確性 accuracy in translation;
翻譯作業 translation assignment;
部份翻譯 partial translation;
傳意翻譯 communicative translation;
詞對詞翻譯 word-for-word translation;
詞匯翻譯 lexical translation;
詞素翻譯 morphemic translation;
詞形翻譯 morphological translation;
次要翻譯 secondary translation;
從句翻譯 clause translation;
單一翻譯 unit translation;
等效翻譯 equivalent effect translation;
地道翻譯 idiomatic translation;
電腦翻譯 computer translation;
電腦輔助翻譯 computer-aided translation;
電影翻譯 film translation;
短語翻譯 phrasal translation;
多重翻譯 multiple translation;
多樣翻譯 manifold translation;
多語翻譯 multilingual translation;
法律翻譯 legal translation;
服務性翻譯 service translation;
符號翻譯 symbolic translation;
符際翻譯 intersemiotic translation;
高質量翻譯 high-quality translation;
~全自動高質量翻譯 fully automatic high-quality translation;
個人翻譯 individual translation;
功能性翻譯 functional translation;
關聯的翻譯 correlative translation;
合法翻譯 legitimate translation;
機器翻譯 machine translation;
機器輔助翻譯 machine-aided translation;
機器洋涇濱翻譯 mechanical pidgin translation;
極量翻譯 maximum translation;
間接翻譯 indirect translation;
交際翻譯 communicative translation;
教學翻譯 pedagogical translation;
結構性翻譯 constructional translation;
科技翻譯 scientific and technological translation;
科學翻譯 scientific translation;
刻板翻譯 slavish translation;
口語翻譯 speech translation; voice

translation;
跨類翻譯 transmutation;
類別翻譯 generic translation;
全文翻譯 full translation;
生硬的翻譯 stilted translation;
文化翻譯 cultural translation;
~跨文化翻譯 intercultural translation;
文學翻譯 literary translation;
~非文學翻譯 non-literary translation;
逐詞翻譯 word-for-word translation;
助理翻譯 assistant translator;
自動翻譯 automatic translation;
~全自動翻譯 fully automatic translation;

[翻印] reprint; reproduce;
翻印必究 reproduction of the book will be prosecuted;

[翻閱] browse; flick through; flip through; glance over; leaf through; look over; read over;
匆匆翻閱 leaf through; thumb through;
快速翻閱 flick through;

[翻轉] overturn; turn;

側翻 turn on one's side;
側手翻 cartwheel; lateral wheel;
滾翻 roll;
瞼內翻 entropion;
瞼外翻 ectropion;
空翻 flip; somersault;
鬧翻 fall out with sb;
前滾翻 forward roll;
傾翻 tipover;
騰翻 roll;
推翻 (1) overthrow; overturn; (2) cancel; repudiate;
掀翻 throw;
足外翻 strephexopodia;

fan
【旛】 (1) flag; streamer; (2) silk pennant for hanging;

fan
【飜】 turn over;

fan²

fan
【凡】 (1) ordinary; (2) earth; mortal world; (3) all; any; every; (4) altogether;

[凡例] notes on the use of a book;
[凡人] (1) ordinary person; (2) mortal;
[凡事] everything;
凡事開頭難 a good lather is half a shave; getting things started is always difficult; it is the first step that costs; nothing is easy in the beginning; the first blow is half the battle; to begin is difficult; well begun is half done;
凡事有盛必有衰 every tide has its ebb;
凡事有因 every why has a wherefore; everything has a cause; there is a reason for everything;
凡事總有開頭 everything must have a beginning;

[凡是] all; any; every;
凡是你説得出的 you name it;

[凡庸] commonplace; ordinary;

不凡 out of the ordinary; outstanding; uncommon;
超凡 overtop the man's world;
大凡 generally; in most cases; mostly;
但凡 as long as; in every case;
發凡 state the gist of a book;
非凡 extraordinary; out of the ordinary; outstanding;
舉凡 range from…to…;
平凡 common; commonplace; ordinary; undistinguished;
思凡 have worldly thoughts;
下凡 come down to earth; descend to the world;

fan
【釩】 vanadium;

fan
【煩】 (1) annoyed; irritated; vexed; (2) tired of; (3) superfluous and confusing; (4) trouble;

[煩交] c.o. sb; care of sb; kindness of sb;
[煩勞] trouble;
不避煩勞 take the touble to;

[煩悶] unhappy; worried;
感到煩悶 feel much depressed;
令人煩悶 degress people;

[煩惱] fret over; vexed; worried;
極其煩惱 be tearing one's hair out;
忍字家中寶，不忍惹煩惱 "bear and forbear" should be the motto in every family; want of forbearance produces discord;
為小事煩惱 fret over trifles;
~為小事煩惱的人 fusspot;
自尋煩惱 ask for trouble; borrow trouble; bring trouble on oneself; fret one's

gizzard; give oneself unnecessary trouble; harass oneself; look for trouble; meet trouble half-way; seek trouble; torture oneself with unpleasant thoughts; upset oneself for no reason; vex oneself; torture oneself with unpleasant thoughts; wake a sleeping dog; work oneself up for no reason at all; worry oneself;

~自尋煩惱的人 worrywart;

~別自尋煩惱 let sleeping dogs lie;

［煩膩］ (1) bored; (2) abhor;

［煩擾］ (1) bother; (2) feel disturbed;

［煩人］ annoying; troubling; vexing;

［煩冗］ (1) diverse and complicated; (2) lengthy and tedious;

煩冗的事務 diverse and complicated affairs;

煩冗的文章 lengthy and tedious article;

［煩瑣］ be loaded down with trivial details;

煩瑣的考證 overelaborate research;

煩瑣的禮節 tedious formalities;

煩瑣的手續 overelaborate procedure; red tape; tedious formalities;

煩瑣的文章 long and wordy article;

［煩囂］ noisy and annoying;

［煩言］ complaints;

嘖有煩言 there are a lot of complaints; there are complaints all round;

［煩躁］ agitated; fidgety; in a fret; irritable;

煩躁不安 agitated; annoyed and impatient; have the fidgets; set one's nerves on edge; short-tempered; vexed;

感到煩躁 get in a fret; get the fidgets; have the fidgets; suffer from the fidgets;

燋心煩躁 being distressed and harassed;

愁煩 worried; worry;

憚煩 afraid of trouble; dislike taking trouble;

麻煩 bother sb; cumbrance; give sb trouble; inconvenience; lead sb a dance; make trouble for sb; play up on sb; play up sb; play up on sb; put sb to trouble; trouble; trouble sb;

耐煩 patient;

膩煩 (1) be bored; be fed up; (2) hate; loathe;

慳煩 avoid making trouble;

相煩 trouble sb with requests;

心煩 perturbed; vexed; worried;

絮煩 be fed up with; sick of; be tired of;

厭煩 be fed up with; sick of; be tired of;

憂煩 depressed; perturbed; worried;

fan

【樊】 (1) big cage; (2) confused; disorderly; messy; (3) a surname;

［樊籬］ (1) fence; (2) barriers; restriction;

［樊籠］ bird cage; place of confinement;

虎入樊籠 like a tiger in the cage;

逃出樊籠 break loose; escape from a cage;

fan

【蕃】 (1) flourishing; luxuriant growth; (2) increase; multiply; propagate; (3) numerous; plentiful;

［蕃昌］ luxuriant and prosperous;

［蕃衍］ increase gradually in number or quantity; multiply;

fan

【燔】 (1) roast; (2) burn;

fan

【璠】 a piece of precious jade;

fan

【膰】 cook meat for sacrifice or offering;

fan

【繁】 (1) in great numbers; numerous; (2) propagate;

［繁博］ numerous and wide-ranging;

［繁多］ various;

花樣繁多 a great variety of patterns;

［繁複］ heavy and complicated;

［繁花］ blooming flowers;

繁花似錦 carpet of flowers; flowers blooming like a piece of brocade;

滿樹繁花 the trees are in full blossom;

茂竹繁花 luxuriant bamboos and gorgeous flowers;

［繁華］ bustling; busy; flourishing; prosperous;

繁華地帶 prosperous area;

［繁簡］ the complicated and the simple;

避繁就簡 shun the complicated and tackle the simple;

捨繁就簡 take the simple, less complicated way;

由簡及繁 proceed from the simple to the complex;

［繁麗］ rich and flowery;

［繁忙］ busy;

繁忙的 bustling;

繁忙景象 a scene of bustling activity;
~一片繁忙景象 a scene of bustling activity;
工作繁忙 be busily engaged; busy with one's work;
事務繁忙 be busily engaged in business;

[繁茂] lush; luxuriant;
草木繁茂 a lush growth of trees and grass; an exuberance of foliage;

[繁密] dense;

[繁榮] (1) make sth prosper; (2) booming; flourishing; prosperous;
繁榮昌盛 a flourishing and invigorating scene; flowering; prosperity; thriving and prospering; prosperous and thriving;
繁榮富強 prosperous and powerful; prosperous and strong; rich, strong and prosperous;
繁榮經濟 bring about a prosperous enconomy; promote economic prosperity;
繁榮興旺 brisk and flourish; flourishing; prosperous; rish or vigorous;
持續繁榮 continuous prosperity;
初步繁榮 initial prosperity;
共同繁榮 common prosperity;
經濟繁榮 business prosperity; economic prosperity;

[繁盛] bloom; boom; flourishing; grow; mushroom; prosperous; sprout; thriving;

[繁瑣] many and miscellaneous with trifles;

[繁體] traditional Chinese;
繁體字 traditional Chinese character;

[繁文] empty forms;
繁文縟節 complicated rules and ceremonials; mumbo-jumbo; red tape; superfluous rules and usages; trivial formalities; unnecessary and overelaborate formalities;

[繁蕪] verbose; wordy;

[繁細] excessively detailed;

[繁星] array of stars; clusters of stars;
繁星點點 the sky is studded with stars;
繁星滿天 a starry sky; the sky is studded with stars;
多似繁星 as thick as the stars in the sky; like the stars in multitude;

[繁衍] increase gradually in number or quantity; multiply;
繁衍昌盛 multiply and be prosperous;

[繁育] breed;
雜交繁育 crossbreed;

[繁雜] miscellaneous;
繁雜的日常瑣事 daily chores of all sorts;

[繁殖] breed; propagate; reproduce;
繁殖力 fecundity; fertility; reproductive capacity;
繁殖率 breeding rate; rate of reproduction;
嫁接繁殖 propagation by grafting;
近親繁殖 close breeding; inbreeding; propagation by inbreeding;
親緣繁殖 related breeding;
無性繁殖 asexual reproduction; vegetative propagation;
有性繁殖 sexual reproduction;
雜交繁殖 interbreed;
植物繁殖 vegetative propagation; vegetative reproduction;
自體繁殖 self-reproduction;
自我繁殖 autosynthesis; self-reproduction;

[繁重] difficult; hard; heavy; onerous; strenuous;
繁重的 burdensome; onerous;

[繁滋] multiply profusely;

紛繁 many and complicated;
浩繁 vast and numerous;
頻繁 frequently; often;
刪繁 cut out what is superfluous;

fan

【藩】 barrier; boundary; fence; frontier; hedge;

[藩蔽] barrier;

[藩附] protectorate; vassal state;

[藩國] feudatory state; vassal state;

[藩籬] (1) fence; hedge; (2) anything acting as a hedge; (3) line of defense; barrier;
藩籬盡撤 all fences are removed;

[藩屏] line of defence; protective barrier;

fan

【蹯】 paws;

fan

【礬】 alum; vitriol;

[礬石] alunite;

[礬土] alumina;

明礬 alum;

fan

【蘩】 artemisia stelleriana, a kind of herb;

fan³
fan

【反】 (1) turn over; (2) in an opposite direction; in reverse; inside out; (3) on the contrary; instead; (4) rebel; revolt; (5) counter; return; (6) combat; oppose;

［反綁］ tie one's hands behind one's back;
把手反綁 tie one's hand behind one's back; with one's arm bound behind one's back;

［反比］ inverse ratio;
反比例 inverse proportion; inverse ratio; reciprocal ratio;

［反駁］ confute; contradict; controvert; countercharge; counterplea; disproof; gainsay; refute; refutation; retort;
反駁對手 refute an opponent;
反駁方式 way of refutation;

［反差］ contrast;
彩色反差 colour contrast;

［反常］ aberrant; abnormal; paradoxical; perverse; strange; unusual;
反常的 anomalous;
~反常的人 aberrant;
反常現象 anomaly;
反常行為 aberrant behaviour; eccentricity; perverse behaviour;
表現反常 behave pathologically;
感情反常 emotional abnormality;

［反唇］ answer back;
反唇相譏 answer back sarcastically; answer with sarcastic rebuttal; back talk; bicker with each other; dispute with each other; retort like for like; throw back an insinuation;
反唇相稽 answer back; rebuke with sarcastic remarks; retort; retort like for like; turn against sb in mutual recrimination;

［反調］ opposite view;
唱反調 deliberately speak or act contrary to; harp on an opposite tune; sing a different tune; strike up a tune that runs counter to;
~大唱反調 come out with a different tune; sing a different tune; strike up an entirely different tune;

［反動］ bad;
反動力量 the forces of reaction;

［反對］ argue against; be against; be opposed to; buck against; combat; come out against; conspire against; cry against; cry out against; declare against; decry; demonstrate against; demur at; fight; fight against; go against; have an objection to; have an opposition to; in opposition to; make an objection to; object to; objection; oppose; protest against; react against; set against; set one's face against; set oneself against; show opposition to; side against; speak against; stand against; take opposition to; vote against;
反對黨 opposition party;
反對者 objector;
暗中反對 make veiled resistance; resist in secret;
表示反對 indicate one's opposition; turn thumbs down;
不顧反對 in the teeth of opposition;
堅決反對 adamantly oppose; deprecate; reolutely oppose; set one's face against;
明確反對 be unequivocally opposed to;
拼命反對 make strenuous opposition;
強烈反對 be strongly against;
投票反對 vote against;

［反而］ but; instead; on the contrary; rather than;

［反腐］ combat corruption;
反腐敗 anti-corruption; fight against corruption;
反腐倡廉 combat corruption to build a clean government;

［反覆］ again and again; once and again; over and over; over and over again; iterative; time after time; time and again;
反覆辯論 argue back and forth;
反覆嘗試 make repeated attempts;
反覆解釋 explain over and over again;
反覆警告 repeatedly warn;
反覆強調 repeatedly stress;
反覆説明 explain over and over again;
反覆體 iterative aspect;
反覆無常 behave capriciously; blow hot and cold; caprice; capricious;

chameleonic; change one's mind constantly; changeable; chop and change; erratic; fickle; pitified; flighty; freakish; inconsistent; inconsisten and capricious; inconstancy; moonish; mutability; play fast and loose; repeatedly change one's attitude; volatile; wayward; whimsical; wobble;
~反覆無常的 capricious;
反覆現在式 iterative present;
反覆性動詞 iterative verb;
反覆吟詠 recite again and again in appreciation;
反反覆覆 again and again; like the burden of a song; over and over again; repeatedly;

[反感] antipathy; averse to; be disgusted with; dislike; odium;
反感的 antipathetic;
激起反感 provoke antipathy;
極其反感 be allergic to;
~對現代音樂極其反感 be allergic to modern music;
令人反感 offensive; repulsive;
消除反感 arouse antipathy;
引起反感 remove antipathy;

[反攻] counterattack; counteroffensive; strike back;
反攻倒算 counterattack to settle old scores; launch a vindictive counterattack; retaliate;
發起反攻 launch a counterattack; make a counterattack;
展開反攻 launch a counterattack;

[反顧] look back;
無所反顧 never look back;
義無反顧 duty-bound not to turn back; find it one's duty to go forward and not to turn back; never to look back for the just; proceed without hesitation;

[反光] reflect; reflection;
反光板 reflector;
反光罩 reflector;

[反過來] (1) conversely; (2) in turn;
反過來說 conversely;
反過來也一樣 it's the same the other way round;

[反話] irony;
說反話 speak an irony;

[反悔] go back on one's word;

[反擊] beat back; counterattack; counterblow; counterfire; strike back;
反擊敵人 fire back at the enemy;
進行反擊 fight back; fire back;
自衛反擊 counterattack self-defence;

[反間計] device which causes alienation among the enemies;

[反抗] contumacy; react; resist; revolt; revolt;
反抗精神 rebellious spirit; spirit of revolt;
奮力反抗 do all one can in resistance;
奮起反抗 rise in revolt;
公然反抗 be at open defiance;
挺身反抗 stand up and fight; stand up to an enemy;
消極反抗 passive resistance;

[反口相詰] ask in retort; counter with a question;

[反饋] feedback;
反饋電路 feedback loop;
反饋方法 feedback method;
反饋控制 feedback control;
反饋系統 feedback system;
反饋信號 feedback signal;
反饋信息 feedback information;
反饋型預測 feedback forecasting;
反饋裝置 positioner;

[反面] (1) back; reverse side; (2) flip side; negative side; opposite; (3) the other side of the matter;
反面教材 lesson by negative example;
反面教訓 a lesson learnt from negative experience;
反面教員 teacher by negative example;
反面啟示法 method of heuristic by the negative;
反面人物 negative character; villain;
反面無情 forget sb's help; turn a cold shoulder;
走向反面 change into one's opposite; go over to the opposite side;

[反目] fall out;
反目成仇 fall out and become enemies; quarrel with sb and then become enemies with each other;
彼此反目 on bad terms with each other;

[反派] negative character; villain;
反派人物 negative character; villain;

[反叛] mutiny; rebel; revolt;
反叛的 defiant;
反叛者 insurgent; mutineer; rebel;

[反其道而行之] act against this; act in a

diametrically opposite way; act in opposition to; do exactly the opposite; go in the opposition; run counter to this;

[反求諸己] reflect and try to find fault in oneself; seek the cause in oneself; self-examination; turn inwards and examine oneself in every point;

[反射] reflex; reflectance; reflection;
反射比 reflectance;
~表觀反射比 apparent reflectance;
~界面反射比 boundary reflectance;
反射波 reflected wave;
反射定律 law of reflection;
反射動作 reflex action;
~随意反射动作 voluntary reflex action;
不随意反射动作 involuntary reflex action;
反射法 reflection method;
反射光學 catoptrics;
反射光組 catoptric system;
反射計 reflectometer;
~光電反射計 photoelectric reflectometer;
~光學反射計 optical reflectometer;
~浸沒反射計 immersion reflectometer;
~微波反射計 microwave reflectometer;
反射角 angle of reflection;
反射鏡 catoptron;
反射療法 reflexology;
反射率 reflectivity;
~聲反射率 acoustical reflectivity;
~最佳反射率 optimum reflectivity;
反射面 catopter;
反射能力 reflecting ability;
反射器 reflector;
~角形反射器 angle reflector;
~天線反射器 antenna reflector;
反射紊亂 parareflexia;
反射物 reflector;
反射驗物鏡 catoptroscope;
反射異常 dysreflexia;
鼻反射 nasal reflex;
髕反射 patellar reflex;
不對稱反射 asymmetric reflection;
唇反射 lip reflex;
鐙骨反射 stapedial reflex;
耳廓反射 auricle reflex;
二頭肌反射 biceps reflex;
翻正反射 righting reflex;
腹壁反射 abdominal reflex;
肛門反射 anal reflex;
骨反射 bone reflex;
骨膜反射 periosteal reflex;
喉反射 laryngeal reflex;
踝反射 ankle jerk;
加速反射 acceleratory reflex;
腱反射 tendon jerk; tendon reflex;
交叉反射 crossed reflex;
角膜反射 corneal reflex;
結膜反射 conjunctival reflex;
緊張反射 tonic reflex;
近視反射 myopic reflex;
頸反射 neck reflex;
靜脈反射 venous reflux;
局部反射 local reflex;
頦反射 chin reflex;
咳嗽反射 cough reflex;
老年性反射 senile reflex;
淚反射 lacrimal reflex;
漫反射 diffuse reflection;
迷路反射 labyrinthine reflex;
面反射 facial reflex;
腦反射 cranial reflex;
腦幹反射 brain stem reflex;
內臟反射 viceral reflex;
排便反射 defecation reflex;
排尿反射 micturition reflex;
膀胱反射 micturition reflex;
皮膚反射 skin reflex;
前庭反射 vestibular reflex;
全反射 total reflection;
缺血性反射 ischemic reflex;
三頭肌反射 triceps reflex;
深層反射 deep reflex;
睡眠反射 hypnic jerk;
瞬目反射 blink reflex;
條件反射 conditional reflex;
~非條件反射 unconditioned reflex;
~無條件反射 unconditioned reflex;
聽反射 auditory reflex;
聽覺反射 acoustic reflex;
瞳孔反射 pupillary reflex;
臀反射 gluteal reflex;
外耳道反射 external auditory meatus reflex;
胃結腸反射 gastrocolic reflex;
膝反射 knee jerk; knee reflex; patellar;
心反射 heart reflex;
行為反射 behaviour reflex;
性反射 sexual reflex;
腰反射 lumbar reflex;
陰莖反射 penis reflex;
隱性反射 concealed reflex;
幼年性反射 juvenile reflex;

F

掌反射 palmar reflex;
直腸反射 rectal reflex;
指反射 digital reflex;
跖反射 plantar reflex;
肘反射 elbow reflex;
姿勢反射 postural reflex;
足背反射 dorsocuboidal reflex;
足底反射 plantar reflex;

[反身] reflexive;
反身代詞 reflexive pronoun;
反身動詞 reflexive verb;
反身關係 reflexive relation;
反身語態 reflexive voice;

[反手] backhand;
反手抽球 backhand drive;
反手擊球 backhand stroke;
反手扣殺 backhand volley;
反手握法 backhand grip;
反手握拍法 backhand grip;

[反思] introspection; self-examination; self-reflection;
反思精神 sense of self-reflection;
反思文學 reflectional literature;
自我反思 self-reflection;
~自我反思能力 the skills of self-reflection;

[反訴] countercharge;

[反胃] feel sick to one's stomach; regurgitation; sb's stomach churns; turn one's stomach;
令人反胃 stomach-churning; turn one's stomach;

[反問] (1) ask in reply; (2) rhetorical question;
反問句 echo question; rhetorical question;
- 重述性反問句 recapitulatory echo question;
- 解釋性反問句 explicatory echo interrogation;

[反響] echo; repercussion;
引起反響 arouse an echo; awake a response; meet with a response;

[反向] (1) opposite direction; (2) back; backward; counter; reversal; reverse;
反向定價 reverse price-fixing;
反向動作 backward action;
反向兼容 backwards-compatible;
反向開關 reverse switching;
反向器 reverser;
~隔離反向器 disconnecting switch reverser;
~三極反向器 triple pole reverser;
半反向 half reverse;
動力反向 power reverse;
使反向 invert;
應力反向 stress reversal;

[反省] introspection; self-examination; self-questioning;
反省社會學 reflective sociology;
反省思維 introspective thinking;
自我反省 look at home;

[反咬] invent a charge against sb;
反咬一口 make a false countercharge; make false countercharges; shift the blame to sb; trump up a countercharge against one's accuser; turn around and charge the victim;

[反意] disjunctive;
反意疑問句 disjunctive question;

[反義] antonymic;
反義詞 antonym;
~程度反義詞 graded antonym;
非程度反義詞 ungraded antonym;
~詞根反義詞 base antonym;
~互補反義詞 complementary antonym;
~派生反義詞 derivative antonym;
反義法 oxymoron;

[反映] (1) mirror; reflect; (2) make known; report;
反映意義 reflected meaning;
向上級反映 report to the higher level;
真實反映 genuine reflection;

[反應] reaction; response;
反應遲鈍 slow off the mark;
反應過激 overreact; overreaction;
反應介詞 preposition of reaction;
反應快 quick off the mark; quick on the trigger; think on one's feet;
反應冷淡 the response was indifferent;
反應靈敏 quick on the draw;
反應慢 slow off the mark;
反應能力 reactions;
反應器 reactor;
~化學反應器 chemical reactor;
~火焰反應器 flame reactor;
~色譜反應器 chromatographic reactor;
反應熱 heat of reaction; reaction heat;
反應速度 reaction velocity;
反應堆 reactor;
~反應堆裝置 reactor arrangement;
~核反應堆 nuclear reactor;
~核裂變反應堆 fission-type reactor;
~熱化反應堆 heat reactor;

~重水反應堆 heavy-water reactor;
反應物 reactant;
反應性 reactive; reactivity;
~反應性公關 reactive public relations;
~反應性趨向 response trend;
~比較反應性 comparative reactivity;
~緩發反應性 delayed reactivity;
本能反應 instinctive reaction;
變態反應 allergic response;
超敏反應 hypersensitivity;
~花粉超敏反應 pollen hypersensitivity;
~接觸性超敏反應 contact hypersensitivity;
~青霉素超敏反應 penicillin hypersensitivity;
~野葛超敏反應 poison ivy hypersensitivity;
催化反應 catalytic reaction;
對等反應 equivalent response;
放熱反應 exothermic reaction;
分解反應 decomposition reaction;
~複分解反應 double reaction;
公眾反應 public reaction;
過敏反應 anaphylactic reaction;
化合反應 combination reaction;
化學反應 chemical reaction;
假性反應 pseudoreaction;
鹼性反應 alkali reaction; alkaline reaction;
腱反應 tendon reaction;
覺醒反應 arousal response;
可逆反應 reversible reaction;
~不可逆反應 irreversible reaction;
肯定反應 affirmative response;
冷淡的反應 lukewarm response;
鏈式反應 chain reaction;
麻瘋反應 lepra reaction;
沒有引起反應 no response;
皮膚反應 cutaneous reaction;
取代反應 replacement reaction;
試探反應 fly a kite; kite-flying;
酸性反應 acid reaction;
聽覺反應 auditory response;
瞳孔反應 pupillary reflex;
吸熱反應 endothermic reaction;
一連串反應 a chain of reactions;
異常反應 strange reaction;
引起反應 induce reaction;
置換反應 displacement reaction; replacement reaction;
中和反應 neutral reaction;
中性反應 neutral reaction;
自然反應 natural reaction;
作出反應 make a response;

[反語] antiphrasis; irony;
反語法 litotes;
情景式反語 situational irony;

[反照] reflection of light;

[反正] all the same; anyhow; anyway; in any case; must; surely;

[反之] and...either; but; contrariwise; conversely; on the contrary; otherwise; the other way around;
反之亦然 and the reverse is also true; and and ...either; by vice versa;

[反轉] reverse;
反轉法 adversative method;
反轉來 turn around;
反轉片 reversal film;
反轉運動 return motion;

策反 incite defection; instigate rebellion within the enemy camp;
倒反 contrary to what one expects; unexpectedly;
謀反 conspire against the state; plot a rebellion; plot treason;
逆反 adverse; rebellious;
平反 redress; rehabilitate;
逃反 flee from chaos caused by war or gangsters;
違反 run counter to; violate;
相反 by contrast; contradictory; contrary; contrary to; go contrary to; in contrast to; in contrast with; in opposition to; on the contrary; opposed to each other; opposite; quite the contrary; run contrary to; to the contrary;
一反 a reversal of; contrary to;
隅反 assess by inference;
造反 revolt; rise in rebellion;
正反 positive and negative;
鎮反 suppress counterrevolutionaries;
自反 examine one's own conduct; introspect; self-examination;
作反 rebel; revolt; rise in revolt;

fan

【返】 return;

[返潮] get damp;

[返回] come back; go back; return; revert;
返回港口 put back to port;
返回基地 come back to the base; return to the base;
返回原地 return to the starting point;

異常返回 abnormal return;
自動快速返回 automatic fast return;

[返老還童] become young again; become youthful in one's old age; feel rejuvenated; kick up one's heels; recover one's youthful vigour; rejuvenate; rejuvenate in old age; renew one's youth; restore youth to the aged;

[返銷] resold by the state to the place of production;

重返 return;
復返 return;
遄返 return quickly;
遣返 deport; repatriate; send back; send home;
往返 arrive and depart; come and go; go there and back; journey to and fro; make a round trip; to and fro;

fan⁴

fan

【氾】 (1) fill everywhere; spread; (2) extensive; vast;

[氾論] general discussion;

fan

【犯】 (1) offend; violate; (2) criminal; (3) assail; attack; work against; (4) have a recurrence of; (5) commit;

[犯不上] not worth;

[犯愁] anxious; worry;

[犯錯] commit a blunder; commit a fault; commit a mistake; commit an error; do a fault; err; fall into a mistake; make a blunder; make a mistake; make a slip; make an error; mistake; pull a boner; slip a cog; slip up;
人人都會犯錯 we all make mistakes;

[犯得着] it is worthwhile;
犯不着 is it worthwhile; it is not worthwhile; it won't pay; unnecessary; not worthwhile;

[犯法] break the law; violate the law;
犯法的人 law-breaker; offender;
犯法行為 illegal conduct; offence against the law;
犯法者 offender;
~初次犯法者 first offender;
知法犯法 deliberately break the law; know the law and violate it; know the law but break it; knowingly violate the law; transgress a law knowingly; wilfully commit an offence;

[犯各] (1) act differently; do things in a strange or unusual manner; (2) make trouble for sb; mess with;

[犯規] (1) breach of rules; break the rules; offend; violation of rules; (2) foul;
犯規動作 foul play;
犯規握法 false grasp;
犯規線 foul line;
打人犯規 striking;
打手犯規 hacking;
故意犯規 intentional foul; professional foul;
~非故意犯規 unintentional foul;
技術犯規 technical foul;
腳步犯規 foot fault;
聚眾犯規 multiple foul;
拉人犯規 grabbing;
連續犯規 consecutive fouls;
侵人犯規 personal foul;
雙方犯規 double foul;
無球犯規 off-the-ball foul;
嚴重犯規 serious foul;
阻擋犯規 blocking;

[犯急] tetchy;
有點犯急 a bit tetchy;

[犯忌] violate a taboo;

[犯戒] break into forbidden ground;

[犯禁] break prohibition; violate a ban;

[犯科作奸] transgress the law and become a traitor;
作奸犯科 act criminally; break the law; commit crimes and act the part of a traitor; commit crimes in violation of the law; do evil; violate the law and commit crimes;

[犯人] convict; criminal; prisoner; the guilty;
假釋犯人 parole a prisoner;
一群犯人 a gang of convicts;
在押犯人 remand prisoner;
捉拿犯人 apprehend a criminal;

[犯疑] suspicious;

[犯罪] commit a crime; commit an offence; crime; offence;
犯罪標定理論 criminal labeling theory;
犯罪動機 motives of crime;
犯罪分子 criminal; offender;
犯罪高潮 crime wave;

犯罪化 criminalization;
~非犯罪化 non-criminalization;
犯罪活動 criminal activity;
犯罪集團 criminal gang;
~國際犯罪集團 international organized crime;
犯罪記錄 criminal record; rap sheet;
犯罪客體 criminal object;
犯罪控制 crime control;
犯罪率 crime rate;
犯罪模擬 crime simulation;
犯罪目標 crime target;
犯罪情景 criminal situation;
犯罪人格 personality of crime;
犯罪數字 crime figures; crime statistics;
犯罪統計學 criminal statistics;
犯罪現場 scene of the crime;
犯罪心理 mind of crime;
~犯罪心理矯治 psychological correction of crime;
~犯罪心理學 criminal psychology;
犯罪行為 criminal behavior; criminal offense;
犯罪學 criminology;
~比較犯罪學 comparative criminology;
犯罪亞文化群 criminal sub-culture group;
犯罪因果關係 criminal causation;
犯罪預測 crime forecasting;
犯罪預防 crime prevention;
犯罪再現 reproduction of crime;
犯罪主體 criminal subject;
白領犯罪 white-collar crime;
暴力犯罪 violent crime;
財產犯罪 property crime;
仇恨犯罪 hate crime;
打擊犯罪 crime-busting;
~打擊犯罪的人 crime-buster;
電腦犯罪 computer crime;
共同犯罪 joint offense;
故意犯罪 intentional offense;
過失犯罪 offense through negligence;
減少犯罪 diminish crime; reduce crime;
街頭犯罪 street crime;
立體犯罪 stereo-commission of crime;
企業犯罪 corporate crime;
汽車犯罪 car crime;
青少年犯罪 juvenile crime; teenage crime; youth crime;
情感犯罪 crime of passion;
少年犯罪 juvenile delinquency;
性犯罪 sex crime;
有組織犯罪 organized crime;
政治犯罪 political crime;
職業性犯罪 occupational crime commitment;
智能犯罪 intelligence crime;

案犯 case criminal; convicted criminal;
沖犯 affront; offend;
重犯 repeat;
初犯 commit an offence for the first time;
觸犯 go against; offend; violate;
從犯 accessary; accessary criminal; accomplice;
竄犯 make an inroad into; raid;
干犯 encroach upon; offend;
共犯 accomplice;
慣犯 habitual offender; hardened criminal;
監犯 convict; prisoner;
教唆犯 abettor;
進犯 intrude into; invade;
來犯 come to attack us; invade our territory;
累犯 commit repeated offenses;
冒犯 affront; offend;
偶犯 commit a casual offence;
竊犯 burglar; thief;
侵犯 (1) encroach upon; infringe upon; violate; (2) intrude into; invade;
囚犯 convict; prisoner;
人犯 criminal;
殺人犯 manslayer; murderer;
首犯 chief criminal;
逃犯 escaped criminal or convict;
違犯 infringe; violate;
誤犯 offend unintentionally;
嫌疑犯 suspect;
現行犯 an offender caught red-handed;
協從犯 accomplice under duress;
兇犯 one who has committed homicide or mayhem; murderer;
要犯 important criminal;
疑犯 criminal suspect;
獄犯 convict;
越獄犯 prison breaker;
再犯 (1) repeat an offense; (2) second-time offender;
戰犯 war criminal;
正犯 principal criminal;
政治犯 political offender; political prisoner;
重犯 important criminal;
主犯 prime culprit; principal criminal; principal offender;
從犯 accessory;
罪犯 criminal; offender;

fan
【汎】 (1) afloat; (2) extensive;

fan
【泛】 (1) float; (2) be suffused with; (3) flood; (4) extensive; general;
［泛讀］ extensive reading;
［泛泛］ general; not deepgoing;
泛泛而談 speak in general terms; talk in generalities;
泛泛之交 bowing acquaintance; casual acquaintance; nodding acquaintance; on speaking terms with; speaking acquaintance;
［泛光燈］ floodlight;
［泛濫］ (1) flow; overflow; in flood; (2) spread unchecked;
泛濫成災 be swamped by sth; in flood; run rampant;
河水泛濫 a river floods;
洪水泛濫 be inundated with flood;
凌汛泛濫 debacle;
任其泛濫 allow it to spread unchecked; be left unrestricted and uncurbed;
［泛指］ be used in a general sense; make a general reference; refer to sth in general;

膚泛 shallow; superficial;
浮泛 (1) float about; (2) display; reveal;
廣泛 extensive; wide-ranging; widespread;
空泛 vague and general;
寬泛 broad; covering a wide range;

fan
【范】 (1) bee; (2) a surname;

fan
【梵】 (1) clean and pure; (2) Brahman; Sanskrit; (3) anything pertaining to Buddhism;
［梵音］ the chanting of the Buddhist scriptures;

fan
【販】 (1) buy to resell; (2) dealer; monger; pedlar;
［販毒］ deal in drugs; drug trafficking; sell drugs; supply drugs; traffic in narcotics;
販毒者 drug dealer;
［販夫走卒］ pedlars and menial servants; small tradesmen and porters;
［販賣］ market; peddle; sell; traffic;
販賣軍火 traffic in arms;
販賣人口 traffic in person;
毒品販賣 drug trafficking;
人口販賣 human trafficking;
色情販賣 sexploitation;
［販私］ sell prohibited goods; traffic in smuggle goods;
［販運］ traffic; transport goods for sale;
［販子］ dealer; monger; trafficker;
毒品販子 trafficker;
二道販子 middle-man profiteer; resale monger;
票販子 ticket-monger; ticket tout;
人販子 human trader; trader in human beings;
魚販子 fishmonger;

稗販 hawker; peddler;
報販 newspaper-seller in the streets;
毒販 drug dealer; drug pusher;
肉販 butcher;
商販 pedlar; small retailer;
攤販 street pedlar;
屠販 butchers and vendors;
小販 hawker; pedlar; vendor;
行販 hawker; pedler; vender;
營販 manage sale business;
魚販 fishmonger;

fan
【笵】 (1) bamboo form; (2) same as 範, a model;

fan
【飯】 (1) cooked rice; (2) meal;
［飯煲］ rice-cooker;
電飯煲 electric rice-cooker;
［飯菜］ (1) meal; repast; (2) dishes;
熱飯熱菜 hot rice and hot dishes; rice and dishes served hot;
剩飯菜 leftover;
像樣的飯菜 proper meals;
一桌飯菜 a meal;
［飯店］ (1) hotel; (2) restaurant;
飯店管理學 restaurant management science;
飯店經理 restaurant manager;
飯店銷售學 restaurant marketing science;
飯店營銷學 restaurant management science;
飯店主人 restaurateur;

大飯店 grand hotel;
快餐飯店 fast-food restaurant;
清真飯店 Muslim restaurant;
小飯店 diner;
一家飯店 a restaurant;
自助飯店 cafeteria;

[飯館] restaurant;

[飯鍋] rice cooker;
電飯鍋 electric rice cooker;

[飯盒] lunch box; mess tin;

[飯局] dinner party; fete;

[飯量] appetite;
飯量大 eat like a horse;
飯量小 eat like a bird;

[飯杓] rice ladle;

[飯廳] dinning hall;
客飯廳 combined living and dining room;
小飯廳 dinette;

[飯桶] (1) rice bucket; (2) big eater; (3) fathead; good-for-nothing; poor tool; waster;
一無是處的飯桶 a good-for-nothing;

[飯碗] (1) rice bowl; (2) job;
保住飯碗 keep one's job;
瓷飯碗 porcelain rice bowl;
打破飯碗 lose one's job; unemployed;
丟飯碗 lose one's job;
奪人飯碗 take the bread out of sb's mouth;
金飯碗 gold rice bowl; golden bowl; well-paid occupation;
搶飯碗 grab sb's job; take the bread out of a person's mouth;
~ 搶人飯碗 grab sb's job; take the bread out of a person's mouth;
鐵飯碗 iron rice bowl; life-tenure system; secure job; steady and permanent job;
~ 端着鐵飯碗 have a lifelong job;
小飯碗 rice bowl;
砸飯碗 be fired; get fired; get the sack; lose one's job; lose one's work;
找飯碗 earn a living; hunt for a job; look for a job;

[飯友] dinner companion;

[飯桌] dining table;

八寶飯 eight-treasure rice pudding;
白飯 plain cooked rice;
擺飯 lay the table for a meal;
包飯 supply meals at a fixed rate;
備飯 prepare a meal;
便飯 potluck; have a light meal; have a simple meal; simple meal; take potluck with sb;
菜飯 pilaf;
茶飯 food and drinks;
炒飯 fried rice;
盛飯 take boiled rice out of a cooker into a bowl;
吃飯 (1) eat; have a meal; (2) keep alive; make a living;
出飯 rise well;
淡飯 simple food;
乾飯 cooked rice without gravy;
盒飯 boxed meal; lunch box;
燴飯 rice with mixed vegetable;
酒飯 food and drink;
開飯 serve a meal;
爛飯 soft rice;
撈飯 mix with rice;
冷飯 same old stuff;
糲飯 cooked unpolished rice;
燜飯 rice cooked over a slow fire;
米飯 cooked rice;
年飯 family dinner on the lunar New Year's Eve;
弄飯 cook; prepare a meal;
泡飯 cooked rice reheated in boiling; thick gruel;
噴飯 split one's sides with laughter;
偏飯 preferential treatment;
軟飯 paste-like rice;
晌飯 midday meal; lunch;
燒飯 cooking;
盛飯 ladle rice into a bowl;
剩飯 leftover rice; leftovers from a meal;
蔬飯 vegetables and rice;
熟飯 cooked rice;
送飯 bring meals;
素飯 vegetarian diet;
粟飯 coarse staple food;
湯飯 soup and cooked rice;
討飯 beggar; beg for food;
添飯 replenish rice;
摶飯 roll rice balls;
晚飯 dinner; supper;
餵飯 feed sb with rice;
午飯 lunch; midday meal;
稀飯 porridge;
下飯 (1) go with rice; (2) go well with rice;
閒飯 idle life;
要飯 beg for food;
一餐飯 a meal;
一頓飯 a meal;
一份飯 a portion of food;
一鍋飯 a pot of cooked rice;
一盆飯 a plate of cooked rice;

一團飯 a lump of cooked rice;
一碗飯 a bowl of rice;
早飯 breakfast;
齋飯 vegetarian food;
蒸飯 steamed rice;
中飯 lunch; midday meal;
粥飯 porridge and rice;
煮飯 cook meals; cook rice;
做飯 cook a meal; do the cooking; prepare a meal; prepare food;

fan

【範】 (1) pattern; (2) example; model; pattern; (3) a surname;

[範本] model for calligraphy or painting;

[範疇] ambit; category; domain; realm; scope;
範疇符號 category symbol;
抽象範疇 abstract category;
代數範疇 algebraic category;
對偶範疇 dual category;
概念範疇 conceptual category;
個人範疇 personal domain;
國家範疇 national domain;
加性範疇 additive category;
家庭範疇 family domain;
經濟範疇 economic category;
句法範疇 syntactic category;
倫理學範疇 ambit of ethics;
平衡範疇 balanced category;
社群範疇 social domain;
世界範疇 global domain;
完全範疇 complete category;
知識範疇 knowledge domain;
指示範疇 deictic category;
子範疇 subcategory;
~ 共尾子範疇 cofinal subcategory;
~ 零子範疇 null subcategory;
~ 完全子範疇 full subcategory;
~ 遺傳子範疇 hereditary subcategory;

[範兒] (1) design; form; pattern; style; (2) distinguished graceful manner; standard;

[範例] example; instance; model;

[範數] norm;
抽象範數 abstract norm;
加性範數 additive norm;
絕對範數 absolute norm;
適應範數 adaptation norm;

[範圍] ambit; boundary; confines; extent; limits; range; scope; spectrum;
範圍從屬連詞 subordinator of extent;
範圍寬廣 have a wide reach;
範圍有限 be limited in scope;
安全範圍 safe range;
搭配範圍 collocational range;
翻譯範圍 extent of translation;
方角度範圍 azimuth coverage;
航線範圍 scope of voyage;
經營範圍 scope of business;
擴大工作範圍 broaden the scope of work; enlarge the scope of work; extend the scope of work;
年齡範圍 range of age;
頻率範圍 frequency coverage;
區域範圍 area coverage;
商品範圍 commodity coverage;
勢力範圍 sphere of influence;
調整範圍 adjusting range;
通信範圍 communication range;
興趣範圍 wide range of interests;
營業範圍 business scope;
應用範圍 application range;
責任範圍 scope of cover;
作用範圍 agency coverage;

[範文] model essay;

典範 example; model to be followed;
防範 keep a lookout; on guard;
規範 norm; normal; standard; standardized;
軌範 criterion; standard;
就範 abstain from resistance to; give in; submit;
模範 fine example; model;
師範 (1) normal school; (2) a person of exemplary virtue;
示範 demonstrate; set an example;
淑範 paragon of female virtues;
體範 model; pattern;

fang¹
fang

【方】 (1) square; (2) direction; (3) party; side; (4) method; way; (5) prescription; (6) surname;

[方案] formula; outline; programme; project; proposal; scheme; suggestion;
方案預測 programme prediction;
編碼方案 code scheme;
第二方案 Plan B;
第一方案 Plan A;
放棄方案 abandon one's plan; abolish one's plan; cancel one's plan; give up one's plan; relinquish one's plan; throw up one's plan;

F

改良方案 improve a plan;
基本方案 basic scheme;
結合方案 association scheme;
解決方案 solution;
~ 和平解決方案 peaceful solution;
~ 替代解決方案 alternative solution;
~ 政治解決方案 political solution;
破壞方案 cripple a plan; frustrate a plan; ruin a plan; spoil a plan; wreck a plan;
提出方案 present a plan; propose a plan; put forward a plan; suggest a plan;
一個方案 plan; scheme;
政府方案 government programme;
執行方案 act out a plan; carry into execution a plan; carry out a plan; carry through a plan; conduct a plan; prosecute a plan; pursue a plan; put into action a plan;
制定方案 design a scheme; devise a scheme; draw up a scheme; form a scheme; formulate a scheme; frame a scheme; lay out a scheme; map out a scheme;

[方便] (1) convenient; handy; (2) go to the bathroom; go to the bathroom to tidy up; go to the toilet;
方便顧客 making things convenient for customers;
~ 方便顧客的 customer-friendly;
方便麵 instant noodle;
方便群眾 make things convenient for the people;
方便食品 fast food;
方便用戶 convenience of users;
~ 方便用戶的 user-friendly;
方便之門 a favour for sb; convenience;
~ 開方便之門 do everything to suit sb's convenience; facilitate sth; give the green light to; open the floodgates wide to sb; provide sb with easy access;
給方便 accommodate;
交通方便 have a good transport service;
說方便 speak in favour of;
行方便 accommodating; make things convenient for sb;
與人方便 accommodate others; give sb convenience;

[方步] measured steps;
踱着方步 walk leisurely;
走方步 exercise caution; prudent;

[方才] just now;
[方差] variance;
基本方差 basic variance;
加性方差 additive variance;
條件方差 conditional variance;
自方差 auto variance;

[方程] equation;
方程的根 root of an equation;
方程式 equation;
~ 變換方程式 equation of transformation;
~ 參數方程式 parametric equation;
~ 軌跡方程式 equation of a locus;
~ 絕熱方程式 adiabatic equation;
~ 相關方程式 correlative equation;
~ 預算方程式 budget equation;
~ 約束方程式 constraint equation;
不定方程 indefinite equation;
超越方程 transcendental equation;
代數方程 algebraic equation;
二次方程 quadratic equation;
~ 聯立二次方程 simultaneous quadratic equations;
~ 雙二次方程 biquadratic equation;
分式方程 fractional equation;
高次方程 equation of higher degree;
角運動方程 angular motion equation;
開度量方程 allometry equation;
聯立方程 simultaneous equations;
年齡擴散方程 age-diffusion equation;
齊次方程 homogeneous equation;
無理方程 irrational equation;
線性方程 linear equation;
~ 聯立線性方程 simultaneous linear equations
相伴方程 associated equation;
一次方程 equation of first-order; first-order equation; simple equation;
有理方程 rational equation;
有理整方程 integral rational equation;

[方寸] heart;
方寸不亂 in one's right mind; in one's sense; of sound mind; presence of mind; undisturbed;
方寸無主 confused in mind and not know what to do;
方寸已亂 one's heart is already upset; one's heart is confused; with one's mind in a turmoil;
不亂方寸 keep one's sense;

[方櫈] square stool;
[方法] device; fashion; maneuver; means;

method; methodology; plan; procedure; process; technique;
方法附加語 means adjunct;
方法介詞 preposition of means;
方法論 methodology;
~聯合成本方法論 joint-costing methodology;
方法學 methodology;
~翻譯方法學 translation methodology;
~研究方法學 research methodology;
方法研究 method study;
別的方法 a different tack;
翻譯方法 translation method;
理解方法 comprehension approach;
想方設法 by hook or by crook; do all in one's power; do everything possible; do one's best; find ways and means; in every possible way; make every effort; move heaven and earth; rack one's brains to find ways; try a thousand and one ways; try every means; try everything possible; try in every way; try various devices;
一種方法 a method; a way;
用盡方法 resort to every possible means;
有效方法 effective method;
正確方法 proper way;

［方塊］ square;
方塊舞 square dance;

［方臉突額］ have a prominent forehead and a broad face;

［方面］ (1) aspect; field; respect; side; (2) face;
方面大耳 a handsome man have a dignified face and big ears; a square face with large ears;
方面狀語 adverbial of respect;
各個方面 all over; diverse aspects of;
~考慮這個問題的各個方面 consider all sides of the problem;
~他各個方面都好 he's good all over;
許多方面 of many directions;
~在許多方面 in many respects; in many ways;
一方面 (1) one side; (2) on the one hand, on the other hand;
~一方面…另一方面 at the same time; for one thing...for another; on the one hand...on the other (hand); partly...partly; what by...what by; what with...what with;
有關方面 quarters concerned;
在其他方面 in other respects;
在這方面 in this connection; in this direction; in this respect;

［方式］ fashion; mode; pattern; way;
方式副詞 adverbial of manner;
方式附加語 manner adjunct;
方式介詞 preposition of manner;
方式狀語 adverbial of manner;
方式準則 maxim of manner;
按自己的方式 in one's own way;
存取方式 access mode;
話語方式 mode of discourse;
領導方式 style of leadership;
生活方式 life-style; mode of life; way of life;
~改變生活方式 change one's style of living;
先行方式 anticipation mode;
運輸方式 mode of transport;
指令方式 command mode;
最佳方式 best mode;

［方糖］ cube sugar; sugar cube; sugar lump;
一塊方糖 a cube of sugar; sugar cube;

［方位］ bearing; direction; placement; position; points of the compass;
方位詞 direction word;
方位點 compass point;
方位格 locative case;
方位角 azimuth;
~安全方位角 safe azimuth;
~磁頭方位角 head azimuth;
~大地方位角 geodetic azimuth;
~地理方位角 geographical azimuth;
~發射方位角 launch azimuth;
~反方位角 back azimuth; reverse azimuth;
~風向方位角 wind azimuth;
~高度方位角 altitude azimuth;
~羅盤方位角 compass azimuth;
~平面方位角 grid azimuth;
~前方位角 forward azimuth;
~球面方位角 spherical azimuth;
~射擊方位角 firing; azimuth;
~瞬時方位角 instantaneous azimuth;
~提前方位角 future azimuth;
~天體方位角 star azimuth;
~天文方位角 astronomical azimuth;
~陀螺方位角 gyro azimuth;
~修正方位角 corrected azimuth;
~儀器方位角 instrumental azimuth;
~真北方位角 true north azimuth;

~主方位角 principal azimuth;
方位結構 direction compound;
方位意義 locative meaning;
基本方位 cardinal point;
目標方位 target bearing;
全方位 comprehensiveness; omnibearing;
~全方位外交 omnibearing diplomacy;

[方向] direction; orientation;
方向附加語 direction adjunct;
方向感 sense of direction;
方向角 direction angle;
方向盤 steering wheel;
方向舵 rudder;
方向性 directionality; directivity;
~發射方向性 transmitting directivity;
~接收方向性 receiving directivity;
~豎直方向性 vertical directivity;
~豎直面方向性 directivity on vertical plane;
~水平方向性 horizontal directivity;
~天線方向性 antenna directivity;
閉塞方向 blocking direction;
辨別方向 take one's bearings;
大方向 general orientation;
搞錯方向 mistake one's bearings;
基線方向 base direction;
漸近方向 asymptotic direction;
迷失方向 lose one's orientation;
實際飛行方向 actual flight direction;
順時針方向 clockwise direction;
指明方向 give the direction; point the direction;

[方興未艾] in full swing; in the ascendant; on the upgrade; on the upward surge;

[方形] square;
方形舞 square dance;
長方形 oblong shape; rectangle;
正方形 square;

[方言] dialect; localism; patois;
方言詞語 dialecticism;
方言學 dialectology;
~方言學家 dialectician; dialectologist;
方言主義 dialectalism;
~雙方言主義 bidialectalism;
標準方言 acrolect; standard dialect;
地理方言 geographical dialect;
地區方言 local dialect;
古方言 ancient dialect;
基礎方言 root dialect;
親屬方言 related dialect;
社會方言 social dialect; sociolect;
~較低級社會方言 lower sociolect;
~較高級社會方言 higher sociolect;
視覺方言 eye dialect;

[方圓] (1) circumference; (2) neighbourhood; surrounding area;
方圓難合 square and round cannot be fixed together;
隨方就圓 accommodating; adaptable; adjustable to circumstances; easygoing; follow the square and comply with the round – adaptation to circumstances;

[方針] guiding principle; orientation; policy;
施政方針 administrative programme;
一套方針 a set of policies;
總方針 general policy; general principle;

[方正] (1) upright and foursquare; (2) upright; (3) square;

[方桌] square table;

[方子] prescription for the patient;
開方子 write a prescription for the patient;

八方 all directions;
北方 (1) north; (2) northern part of the country;
比方 analogy; compare; example; for example; instance; liken;
彼方 other party; other side;
長方 rectangular;
成方 set prescription;
乘方 (1) involution; (2) power;
處方 prescription; recipe;
船方 ship;
大方 (1) expert; scholar; (2) a kind of green tea; (3) generous; (4) natural and poised; (5) in good taste;
貸方 credit; credit side;
丹方 folk prescription; home remedy;
單方 fold prescription; home remedy;
敵方 enemy; hostile forces;
地方 (1) locality; (2) local; (3) place; space; (4) part; respect;
東方 (1) east; (2) the East; the Orient;
端方 honest; upright;
對方 the opposite side; the other party;
多方 in every way; in many ways; with various devices;
付方 credit; credit side;
官方 by the government; of the government; official;
己方 one's own side;
見方 square;

借方 debit; debit side;
軍方 the military;
勞方 labour;
良方 (1) effective prescription; good recipe; (2) good plan;
買方 buyer; the buying party;
賣方 seller; the selling party;
秘方 secret recipe;
南方 (1) south; (2) southern part of the country;
男方 bridegroom's side;
女方 bride's side;
配方 directions for producing chemicals or metallurgical products;
偏方 folk prescription;
平方 square;
前方 (1) ahead; (2) front;
收方 debit; debit side;
雙方 both sides; two parties;
朔方 north;
四方 four directions;
塌方 (1) cave in; collapse; (2) landslide; landslip;
坍方 (1) cave in; collapse; (2) landslide; landslip;
填方 fill;
萬方 all places;
無方 in the wrong way; not in the proper way; not knowing how;
五方 all directions;
西方 (1) west; (2) the West;
炎方 southern tropical area;
驗方 proved recipe;
樣方 quadrat;
藥方 prescription;
一方 (1) one side; party; (2) area; region; (3) a cubic meter of; a piece of; a square of;
醫方 medical prescription;
義方 principle of justice;
有方 in the right way; with the proper method;
圓方 the round and the square;
遠方 distant place;
正方 square;
資方 employer;
左方 on the left; to the left;

fang

【坊】 (1) community; neighbours; subdivisions of a city; (2) workshop of a trade; (3) arch-like memorial building;

[坊間] on the market;

牌坊 memorial archway;
書坊 bookshop;

fang

【妨】 (1) hinder; impede; interfere with; obstruct; (2) damage; harm; undermine;

fang

【枋】 sandal wood;

fang

【肪】 a pronunciation of 肪;

fang

【芳】 (1) fragrant; sweet-smelling; (2) good; virtuous;

[芳草] fragrant grass; green grass;
芳草鋪地 green grass carpets the ground;
芳草如茵 a carpet of green grass; the grass looks like a carpet;
十步芳草 within a distance of ten steps there must be some sweet-smelling grass – there are able men everywhere;

[芳烴] aromatic;
稠合芳烴 condensed aromatic;
高級芳烴 higher aromatic;
兩核芳烴 dinuclear aromatic;
重芳烴 heavy aromatic;

[芳香] aromatic; fragrant; sweet fragrance;
芳香馥郁 rich in fragrance;
芳香含量 aromaticity;
芳香撲鼻 feel a sharp aroma; the fragrance assailed one's nostrils;
芳香四溢 sweet perfumes are diffused all around;

[芳心] heart of a young lady;
芳心默許 a woman bestowing her favours on sb; a woman giving her heart to someone without openly admitting it; love a man silently;
贏得芳心 gain her affection; win her affections;

[芳澤] fragrance of a woman;
得親芳澤 be admitted to a lady's intimate presence;
一親芳澤 approach a woman; caress a woman; kiss a woman; sleep with a woman;

芬芳 fragrance; fragrant; sweet-smelling;
流芳 leave a good name; leave a reputation;
群芳 beautiful and fragrant flowers;

fang²

fang

【妨】 hinder; obstruct;

［妨礙］ encumber; hamper; handicap; hinder; impede; obstruct; put a crimp in; put a crimp into; stand in the way;
妨礙工作 come between sb and sth; hinder one's work;
妨礙公務 interference with public function;
妨礙交通 block the traffic; obstruct the traffic;

［妨害］ harmful to; impair; jeopardize;
妨害風化 offensive to morality;
妨害健康 harmful to one's health;
妨害社會秩序 blemish the peace;

不妨 might as well; there is no harm in;
何妨 might as well; why not;
無妨 might as well; there's no harm in;

fang

【防】 (1) guard against; provide against; (2) defend;

［防癌］ prevent cancer;

［防暴］ antiriot;
防暴警察 riot police;

［防備］ guard against; premunition;take precautions against;
防備不測 be prepared for any contingency; guard against unforseen emergencies;
防備萬一 be prepared for the worst; be ready for all eventualities;
防備災難 prepare against disaster;

［防波堤］ breakwater;

［防潮］ damp-proof;
防潮層 damp course; damp-proof course;

［防衝器］ shock absorber;
扭震防衝器 torsional shock absorber;

［防蟲］ insect prevention;

［防彈］ bulletproof;
防彈車 armoured car;
防彈的 bullet-proof;
防彈衣 body armour;

［防盜］ guard against theft; take precautions against burglars;
防盜保護 protection from theft;
~提供防盜保護 afford protection from theft;
防盜警報器 burglar alarm;

［防地］ defence sector;

［防毒］ gas defence;
防毒面具 gas mask;
防毒軟件 anti-virus software;
防毒衣 protective clothing;

［防範］ keep a lookout; keep watch; on guard;
疏於防範 neglect to take precautions;

［防風］ protect against the wind;
防風燈 hurricane lamp;

［防腐］ antiseptic;
防腐劑 preservative;
~化學防腐劑 chemical preservative;
~食品防腐劑 food preservative;
~水溶性防腐劑 waterborne preservatives;
防腐作用 antiseptic action;

［防光］ antihalation;

［防洪］ flood protection;
防洪工程 flood control works;

［防護］ defense; guard; proofing; protect; shelter; shield;
防護服 protective clothing;
防護用品 protective appliance;
安全防護 safety protection;
區域防護 area defense;

［防滑］ non-slip;
防滑釘 cleat;

［防火］ fire prevention; fire safety;
防火安全門 fire door;
防火的 fireproof;
防火服 fireproof clothing;
防火警報器 fire alarm;
防火墻 firewall;
防火線 firebreak;
防火障 firebreak;

［防空］ air defense; anti-aircraft; anti-aircraft defense;
防空部隊 air defense force;
防空導彈 air defense missile; anti-aircraft;
防空洞 air-raid shelter; bomb shelter;
防空警報 air-raid siren; air-raid warning;
防空砲 air defense artillery;
防空行動 air defence action;
防空演習 air defense exercise; air-raid drill;

［防守］ defend; defense; guard; parry;
釘人防守 close-marking defense;
對抗防守 holding parry;
複雜防守 compound defense;
混合防守 combination defense;
近台防守 close-table defense; short

defense;
擊打防守 beat parry; slinging parry;
緊密防守 tight defense;
密集防守 bunched defense; closed defense; packed defense;
人釘人防守 man to man defense;
嚴密的防守 airtight defence;
遠台防守 far-from-table defense; long defense;

[防水] waterproof;
防水的 waterproof; waterrepellent;water resistant;
防水服 waterproof clothing;

[防衛] defend;
防衛機制 defence mechanism;
正當防衛 legal defence;

[防霧] antifogging;
防霧作用 antifogging action;

[防線] line of defence;
一道防線 a line of defence;

[防疫] epidemic prevention;
衛生防疫站 sanitation and epidemic prevention station;

[防意如城] guard against one's desire as if guarding a city against an enemy; guard the thoughts of the heart as one would defend a city;

[防禦] defend; defense;
防禦工事 defensive works;
反導彈防禦 antimissile defense;
積極防禦 active defense;
正統防禦 orthodox defense;

[防震] shockproof;

[防止] avoid; forestall; guard against; prevent;
防止疾病 ward off disease;

[防撞] crashproof;
防撞護欄 crash barrier;
防撞架 bull bars;
防撞器 bumper;
~履帶防撞器 track bumper;
防撞墻 crash barrier;

邊防 border defence; frontier defence;
補防 filling-in;
布防 organize a defence; place troops on garrison duty;
佈防 organize a defence; place troops on garrison duty;
撤防 withdraw a garrison; withdraw from a defended position;
城防 defence of a city;
堤防 dike; embankment;
調防 relieve a garrison;
冬防 (1) security measures taken in winter; (2) preventive measures against winter cold;
返防 return to stations;
關防 (1) measures taken to forestall the leaking of secrets;
國防 national defence;
海防 coast defence;
河防 flood-prevention work done on rivers;
換防 relieve a garrison;
接防 relieve a garrison;
謹防 beware of; guard against; provide against;
空防 air defence;
聯防 strictly on guard against; take strict precautions against;
人防 civil air defence; people's air defence;
設防 fortify; set up defences;
消防 fire control; fire protection;
血防 prevent against nail fever;
嚴防 strictly on guard against; take strict precautions against;
移防 be shifted elsewhere for garrison duty;
預防 forestall; guard against; make provision against; nip in the bud; prepare against; prevent; prevent beforehand; take precautions against;
駐防 garrison; on garrison duty;

fang

【房】 (1) house; (2) room; (3) chamber; (4) a surname;

[房產] house property;
看房產 view a property;
擁有房產 own a house; possess a house;

[房倒兒] real estate speculator;

[房東] landlady; landlord;
女房東 landlady;

[房荒] housing shortage; lack of housing;

[房價] house price;
房價急劇上漲 a steep rise in house prices;

[房間] chamber; room; apartment;
房間整潔 the room is in order;
~保持房間整潔 keep the room in order;
朝南的房間 southward room;
出租房間 let a room out;
闖入房間 burst into the room;
打掃房間 clean a room; clear up a room; dust a room; sweep the room clean; tidy up a room;
供出租的房間 room for rent;

擠滿房間 crowd a room; throng a room;
空氣不流通的房間 airless room;
寬敞的房間 big room; commodious room; large room; spacious room;
明亮的房間 bright room; light room; well-lighted room;
舒適的房間 a snug little room;
通風的房間 airy room;
小房間 cubbyhole; cubicle;
一個房間 a room;
一間房間 a room;
一套房間 a suite of rooms;
有傢具的房間 furnished room;
有兩張單人牀的房間 twin-bed room;
有陽台的房間 a room with a balcony;
整理房間 clean a room; clear up a room; dust a room; sweep the room clean; tidy up a room;
走出房間 walk out of the room;

[房客] roomer; tenant;
現住房客 sitting tenant;
新房客 incomer;

[房事] sexual intercourse;

[房屋] buildings; houses;
房屋協會 housing association;
半獨立式房屋 semi-detached house;
代為看管房屋 housesit;
供出租的房屋 house for rent;
活動房屋 mobile home;
建成房屋 finish a house;
破舊的房屋 a shabby house;
一幢房屋 a house;
轉租房屋 sublet a house;
資助房屋 subsidized housing;

[房修] home repair; house repair;

[房子] (1) building; house; (2) room;
拆房子 pull down a house;
蓋房子 build a house;
看房子 view a house;
空房子 empty flat;
木頭房子 wooden house;
破房子 dilapidated house;
跳房子 hopscotch;
玩具房子 doll's house; dollhouse
搖搖欲墜的房子 tumbledown house;
一棟房子 a house;
~合住一棟房子 share a house;
一排房子 a row of houses;
一所房子 a house;
一幢房子 a building; a house;
一座房子 a house;
找房子 house-hunting;
整幢房子 from cellar to garret; from garret to kitchen;
走進房子 step into the house;

[房租] rent;
房租補貼 rent rebate;

[兵房] barrack;

暗房 dark room;
扒房 pull down a house;
泵房 pump room;
兵房 barrack;
病房 ward;
倉房 storehouse; warehouse;
茶房 (1) pantry; (2) steward; waiter;
查房 make the rounds of the wards;
產房 delivery room;
廠房 (1) factory building; (2) workshop;
廚房 kitchen;
洞房 bridal chamber;
堆房 storehouse; storeroom;
碓房 mill;
耳房 side room; small annex;
二房 the second branch of a family;
蜂房 beehive;
杠房 old-fashioned funeral parlour;
公房 state-owned house;
閨房 boudoir; women's quarters;
柜房 cashier;
號房 reception office;
烘房 baking oven;
花房 greenhouse;
客房 guest room;
牢房 jail; prison;
樓房 building of two or more storeys;
馬房 stable;
茅房 latrine;
民房 house owned by a citizen;
鬧房 chat and joke with the newly-wedded couple;
暖房 greenhouse; hothouse;
配房 wing; wing-room;
偏房 concubine;
平頂房 flat-roofed house;
平房 bungalow; one-storey house; single-story house;
乳房 (1) breast; (2) udder;
掃房 have a general house-cleaning;
膳房 royal dining room;
書房 study;
糖房 sugar mill;
填房 marry a man whose first wife died;

F

同房 (1) of the same branch of a family; (2) have sexual intercourse; sleep together;
瓦房 tile-roofed house;
卧房 bedroom;
心房 atrium of the heart;
新房 bridal chamber;
刑房 torture room;
行房 have sexual intercourse;
洋房 foreign-style house;
藥房 (1) chemist's shop; drugstore; pharmacy; (2) dispensary; hospital; pharmacy;
一間房 a room;
營房 barracks;
幽房 (1) secluded room; (2) grave;
遠房 distantly related;
長房 eldest branch;
賬房 (1) accountant's office; cashier's office; (2) accountant; cashier; teller; treasurer;
棧房 storehouse; warehouse;
住房 lodgings; housing;
磚房 brick house;
子房 ovary;

fang
【肪】 fat;

fang
【魴】 fresh-water bream; triangular bream;
［魴鮄］ gurnard;

fang³

fang
【仿】 copy; imitate;
［仿古］ model after an antique;
［仿建］ build in imitation of a model;
［仿冒］ counterfeit; fabricate;
仿冒名牌 counterfeit of a well-known brand;
仿冒商標 imitated trademark;
［仿若］ as if; as though;
仿若隔世 feel as if in another life; seem to belong to another world;
［仿生］ bionic;
仿生方法 bionics method;
仿生技術 bionics techniques;
仿生學 bionics;
~仿生學家 bioncist;
仿生自動機 bio-robot;
信息仿生學 information bionics;
［仿宋］ Imitation Song;
仿宋本 publications with Imitation Song typeface;
仿宋體 Imitation Song typeface;
［仿傚］ after the model of; follow the example of; imitate; model oneself upon sb; on the model of;
仿傚榜樣 example to follow; role model;
轉相仿傚 copy each other;
［仿造］ copy; counterfeit; model on;
仿造的 counterfeit;
仿造語 calque;
［仿真］ emulate; simulate;
仿真程序 emulator;
仿真技術 simulation techniques;
仿真器 emulator;
仿真網絡 emulating network;
仿真語言 simulation language;
［仿製］ be modelled;
仿製品 copy; imitation; replica;

碘仿 iodoform;
氯仿 chloroform;
摹仿 copy; imitate;
模仿 copy imitate;
相仿 more less the same; similar;
效仿 follow the example of; imitate;

fang
【彷】 like; resemble;
［彷彿］ as if; as it were; as though; seem;

fang
【昉】 (1) dawn; daybreak; (2) heaven; sky;

fang
【紡】 (1) reel; spin; (2) reeled pongee;
［紡紗］ spin cotton, etc. into yarn;
［紡織］ spinning and weaving;
紡織廠 textile mill;
紡織工業 textile industry;
紡織品 drapery;
~紡織品商 draper;
~紡織品生意 drapery business;

粗紡 rove;
乾紡 dry spinning;
混紡 blend; blending;
絹紡 silk spinning;
毛紡 wool spinning;
棉紡 cotton spinning;
濕紡 wet spinning;
細紡 finespinning;

fang
【舫】 (1) two boats lashed side by side; (2) boat; ship;

畫舫 decorated pleasure-boat;
游舫 pleasure-boat;

fang
【訪】 (1) call on; visit; (2) inquire about; look for; (3) a surname;
[訪遍] visit everywhere;
訪遍全市 visit everywhere;
[訪查] go about making inquiries; investigate;
[訪求] search for; seek;
[訪視] make a house-call;
[訪談] interview;
訪談錄 interview;
[訪問] (1) call by; call on; interview; pay a call; visit; (2) access;
訪問控制 access control;
- 訪問控制包 access control packet;
訪問學者 visiting scholar;
國事訪問 state visit;
禮節性訪問 ceremonial call; courtesy call;
頻繁的訪問 frequent visit;
事務性訪問 business call;
私交性訪問 social visit;
私人訪問 personal call;
友好訪問 friendly visit;
正式訪問 official visit;
[訪銷] sales promotion;
[訪友求賢] call on friends and seek for worthies;

暗訪 investigate in secret; make a secret enquiry; secret investigation;
拜訪 call around sb's house; call at; call at sb's house; call on sb; call over; call round; call to see; call upon sb; come around; drop in; drop in on sb; drop in to see sb; give a visit to sb; give sb a visit; go to see; look in on sb; look sb up; make a visit to sb; make sb a visit; on a visit; pay a visit to sb; pay an official call; pay sb a call; see; visit; visit with sb; wait on sb;
遍訪 seek everywhere;
採訪 gather material; have an interview with;
踮訪 search and investigate;
查訪 investigate; make inquiries;
察訪 go about to find out; go around and make inquiries; investigate; make calls and investigate;
出訪 visit a foreign country;
過訪 call on sb; visit sb;
互訪 exchange visits;
回訪 pay a return visit;
家訪 house visit; pay a visit to the parents;
來訪 come to call; come to visit;
覓訪 try to find and meet a person;
上訪 apply for an audience with the higher authorities to appeal for help;
私訪 make an inspection trip incognito;
探訪 (1) seek by inquiry or search; (2) pay a visit to; visit;
尋訪 look for; make inquiries about;
造訪 call on; pay a visit;
專訪 special report on a special visit;
咨訪 ask for advice; consult;
諏訪 ask for advice; consult; seek the advice of;
走訪 (1) have an interview with; interview; (2) go and see; pay a visit;

fang
【髣】 like; similar;

fang⁴
fang
【放】 (1) let go; release; set free; (2) give out; let off; (3) put out to pasture; (4) give way to; let oneself go; (5) lend money for interest; (6) expand; let out; (7) blossom; open; (8) place; put; (9) send away; (10) show;
[放榜] announcement of examination results;
[放出] bleed; discharge; emit; give off; give out; go into; let out; send out; snap out; spray;
[放大] amplification; amplify; enlarge; enlargement; magnification; magnify;
放大機 enlarger;
~ 檢查放大機 inspection enlarger;
~ 漫射放大機 diffusion enlarger;
放大鏡 magnifier; magnifying glass;
~ 雙合放大鏡 doublet magnifier;
~ 雙筒放大鏡 binocular magnifier;
~ 天平放大鏡 balance magnifier;
放大率 magnification; magnifying power;
~ 基線放大率 base magnification;
~ 角度放大率 angular magnification;
~ 軸向放大率 axial magnification;
放大器 amplifier; magnifier;
~ 電纜放大器 cable amplifier;
~ 混合放大器 hybrid amplifier;
~ 交流放大器 alternating-current amplifier;
~ 模擬放大器 analogue amplifier;

~平衡放大器 balanced amplifier;
~前置放大器 preamplifier;
激光前置放大器 laser preamplifier;
液壓前置放大器 hydraulic preamplifier;
音頻前置放大器 audio preamplifier;
~聲放大器 acoustic amplifier;
~音頻放大器 audiofrequency amplifier;
~原子放大器 atomic amplifier;
放大砲 brag; speak with a sharp tongue;
放大照片 enlarge a photo;
尺寸放大 size enlargement;
電子放大 electronic magnification;
動態放大 dynamic amplification;
對比度放大 contrast amplification;
級聯放大 cascade amplification;
空放大 empty magnification;
寬帶放大 broad band amplification;
生物放大 biological magnification;
聲頻放大 audio-frequency amplification;
雙重放大 dual amplification;
影像放大 image enlargement;
有效放大 effective amplification;
直接放大 straight amplification;

[放膽] act boldly and with confidence;

[放誕] wild in speech and behaviour;
放誕不羈 dissipated and unrestrained; dissolute in conduct; reckless and dissipated in behaviour and speech;
放誕不經 absurd; fantastic;
放誕風流 reckless and dissipated in behaviour and speech;
放誕無禮 guilty of a liberty;

[放蕩] (1) dissipated; dissolute; (2) unconventional;
放蕩不羈 have full swing; have one's fling; lead a fast life; licentious in conduct; on the loose; run riot; sow one's wild oats; take the bit between one's teech; take one's swing; tear around; throw off restraint and become dissolute; unconventional and unrestrained; uninhibited;
~放蕩不羈的 libertine;
~放蕩不羈的人 a bit of a lad; libertine;
放蕩的 dissipated;
~放蕩的人 swinger;
放蕩度日 pass the day recklessly;
放蕩女人 dissolute woman; fast woman; loose woman; man-eater; woman of easy virtue;
放蕩者 debauchee;
極端放蕩 run the gamut of dissipation;
生活放蕩 sow one's wild oats;

[放電] discharge;
放電叉 discharge tongs;
放電器 discharger; electrical discharger;
~鋇放電器 barium discharger;
~固定放電器 fixed discharger;
~盤式放電器 disc discharger;
大氣放電 atmospheric discharge;
電弧放電 arc discharge;
高壓放電 high voltage discharge;
尖端放電 point discharge;
交替放電 alternating discharge;
氣體放電 aerial discharge;
無聲放電 effluvium;

[放飯流歠] eat a hurried meal; hurry over one's meals;

[放風] (1) let in fresh air; (2) let prisoners out for exercise; (3) leak certain information; play the kite;
放風箏 fly a kite;

[放工] knock off;

[放過] let off; let slip;

[放虎歸山] allow a tiger to return to his lair; cause future trouble; give a man his chance; lay by trouble for the future; let the tiger escape to the mountain again; release a tiger back to the mountains; set a tiger free; set free a tiger back to the mountains;

[放話] create public opinion; spread news; spread rumours;

[放懷] to one's heart's content;

[放活] release from unnecessary constraints;

[放火] set fire on; set fire to;
放火犯 arsonist;
放火燒山 set the mountain on fire;

[放假] have a day off; have a holiday; have a vacation; on leave;

[放開] come out of one's shell; let go; lift the control over; out of one's shell;
放開手腳 have one's hands and feet unfettered;
放開膽子 pluck up courage; stop being afraid;

[放空砲] boast; brag; empty talk; fire blank shots; indulge in idle boasting; make an empty threat; spout hot air; talk big;

[放寬] relax; relax restrictions;

放寬尺度 relax the requirements;
放寬期限 extend a time limit;
放寬條件 soften the terms;
放寬胸懷 broad-minded;
放寬政策 adopt more liberal policies; implement policies more flexibly;

[放款] make loans;
放款人 lender; moneylender;
比期放款 ultima loan;
長期放款 long-term loan;
抵押放款 secured loan;
短期放款 short-term loan;
活期放款 demand loan;
商業放款 commercial loan;
生產放款 productive loan;
信用放款 credit loan;
銀行放款 bank loan;

[放浪] (1) unrestrained; (2) dissolute;
放浪形骸 abandon oneself to Bohemianism; be completely informal; given to sensual pleasures;

[放療] radiotherapy;

[放龍入海] allow the dragon to reach the sea—free the enemy;

[放慢] delay; slow;

[放牧] graze; grazing; herd; pasture; put out to pasture;
放牧牛羊 graze sheep and cattle;
家禽放牧 poultry pasture;
連續放牧 continuous grazing;
適度放牧 conservative grazing;
循環放牧 rotational grazing;
延遲放牧 deferred grazing;
正常放牧 normal grazing;
周期放牧 periodic grazing;

[放砲] (1) fire a gun; (2) let off firecrackers; (3) shoot off one's mouth;
放砲仗 let off firecrackers;

[放屁] (1) backfire; beef-hearts; break wind; break wind backwards; break wind downwards; breezer; cut one's finger; drop a rose; fart; have gas; lay fart; let one fly; make a noise; pass air; pass wind; raspberry tart; rip off a fart; set a fart; gunpowder; shoot rabbits; sneeze; there's a smell of touch bone and whistle; (2) nonsense; talk nonsense; what a crap;
放屁蟲 bombardier beetle;

[放平] (1) put sth flat on the ground; (2) knock somebody down;

[放棄] abandon; abstain from; back down; back down on; bargain away; beat a retreat; bottle out; cop out; drop; fall away; fall out of; forgo; forsake; get out of; give away; give up; lay aside sth; lay down; let down; pack in; pack up; pass up; put aside; put away; quit; render up; relinquish; renounce; resign a claim; sell the pass; send in one's resignation; surrender; throw over; throw up one's hands; wash one's hands of; wash out; whistle down;
放棄財產 relinquish one's possession;
放棄國籍 renounce one's nationality;
放棄立場 sell the pass;
放棄權利 abdicate a right;
放棄上訴權 renunciation of appeal;
放棄事業 give up one's career;
放棄訴訟 abandon an action; renounce an action; the abandonment of action;
放棄學業 withdraw one's study;
放棄要求 quit claim;
放棄原則 forsake one's principles;
放棄責任 abdicate one's responsibility;
放棄職守 desert one's post;
別輕言放棄 never say die;
暫時放棄 abandon temporarily;
自動放棄 abdicate voluntarily;

[放槍] fire with a pistol;

[放權] release authority;

[放熱] exthermal;
放熱反應 exothermal reaction; exothermic reaction;

[放任] let alone; let things drift; not interfere;
放任政策 laissez-faire policy; let-alone policy;
放任自流 adopt a let-alone policy toward sb; give free rein to; give full swing to; give up due guidance; keep a slack rein on sth; let sb do as he likes; let things drift; let things take their own course;
放任自由 on a loose rein;
自由放任 free-for-all;

[放哨] on sentry go; stand sentry;
站崗放哨 stand sentry;

[放射] radiate;
放射病 radiation sickness;
放射蟲 radiolarian;

放射光芒 send forth rays;
放射科 X-ray department;
~ 放射科技師 radiographer;
~ 放射科醫生 radiologist;
放射性 radioactivity;
~ 放射性塵埃 radioactive ash;
~ 放射性廢料 radioactive waste; radwaste;
~ 放射性雨 radioactive rain;
~ 放射性元素 radioactive element;
~ 放射性沾染 radioactive contamination;
~ 大氣放射性 atmospheric radioactivity;
~ 核放射性 nuclear activity;
~ 人工放射性 artificial radioactivity;
~ 水中放射性 waterborne radioactivity;
~ 天然放射性 natural radioactivity;
放射學 radiology;
放射治療 radiotherapy;
~ 放射治療師 radiographer;

[放生] (1) free captive animals; (2) buy captive fish or birds and set them free;

[放聲] sound reproduction;
放聲大哭 burst into loud sobbing; burst into tears; burst out crying; burst out sobbing; cry loudly and bitterly; cry without restraint; give away to a storm of weeping; life up one's voice and wail; raise one's voice in loud weeping; set up loud lamentations; sob loudly; utter a great cry; wail at the top of one's voice; weep aloud; weep in a loud voice;
放聲大笑 give a noisy laugh; guffaw; screams of laughter;
放聲歌唱 sing at the top of one's voice; sing heartily; sing loud;
放聲痛哭 raise one's voice in great weeping; utter a stifled cry of agony;

[放手] (1) let go; let go one's hold; (2) go all out; have a free hand;
放手的 hands-off;
放手放腳 with hands and feet unfettered;
放手去做 do sth with a free hand;
死不放手 hold on like grim death;

[放肆] get wise; run wild; unbridled; wanton;
放肆無忌 throw all restraint to the winds; unbridled and run amuck;
放肆無禮 frantic and rude;
極為放肆 throw all restraint to the winds;

[放鬆] chillax; loosen; relax; slacken; uncage;
放鬆點 loosen up a bit;
放鬆肌肉 loosen up one's muscles; relax one's muscles;
放鬆努力 slack up; slacken one's effort;
放鬆下來 loosen up;
放鬆學習 slack off one's studies;
放鬆音樂 chillout; chillout music;

[放送] send out;

[放下] lay down; put down;
放下包袱 cast off mental burdens; get rid of the baggage; lay down one's burden; put down one's budren;
放下不管 leave sb in the lurch;
放下臭架子 drop pretentious airs; shed the ugly mantle of pretentiousness;
放下官架子 discard bureaucratic aris; drop pretentious airs and graces;
放下架子 come off one's high horse; come off one's perch; discard one's haughty airs; pocket one's dignity;
放下手頭的工作 put aside the work on hand;
放下屠刀，立地成佛 a butcher become a Buddha the moment he drops his cleaver; drop the butcher's knife and immediately become a Buddha; lay down the butcher knife and become a Buddha; throw away one's cleaver and become a Buddha;
在火車站把我放下 drop me off at the railway station;
重重放下 plonk;

[放小] tone down;

[放心] at ease; breathe easy; feel relieved; free from cares; have one's heart at ease; put one's heart at ease; rest assured; rest one's heart; set one's mind at rest;
放心不下 be kept in suspense; feel anxious; in daily suspense;
不放心 anxious for; feel worried about;
讓人放心的 reassuring;

[放行] let sb pass;

[放學] classes are over;

[放眼] scan widely; take a broad view;
放眼世界 have the whole world in view; keep the whole world in view; open one's eyes to the whole world;
放眼未來 look far ahead into the future; look forward to the future;
放眼遠望 look far ahead into the distance;

[放一碼] forgive; have mercy on; let a person off; release;

[放映] on show; show a film;
放映電影 have a film show; show a film;
放映隊 cinema team;
~流動放映隊 mobile cinema team;
~巡迴放映隊 mobile cinema team;
放映機 projector;
~背景放映機 back projector; background projector;
~連續放映機 continuous projector;
~投影片放映機 slide projector;
~右手放映機 right-hand projector;
~字幕放映機 animatic projector; subtitle projector;
~左手放映機 left-hand projector;
放映器 projector;
~電影放映器 cine projector;
放映員 projectionist;
首輪放映 first runs; premiere;

[放債] lend money at interest; moneylending;
放債人 moneylender;

[放置] lay aside; lay up; place;

[放逐] banish; exile; send into exile;

[放恣] proud and self-indulgent; proud and undisciplined;
放恣失儀 debauched and impolite;

[放縱] connive at; indulge; let sb have his own way;
放縱不羈 uninhibited;
盡情放縱 have one's fling;
肉慾放縱 sensual decadence;
恣意放縱 reckless decadence;
自我放縱 self-abandonment;

[放走] let go; release; set free;

安放 lay; place; put in a certain place;
驁放 very haughty and unrestrained;
奔放 bold and unrestrained; expressive and unrestrained; moving and forceful; untrammelled;
播放 be aired to; broadcast; on the air; send out; transmit;
重放 replay;
粗放 bold and unrestrained;
存放 leave in sb's care; leave with;
堆放 pile up; stack;
發放 extend; grant; provide;
豪放 bold and unconstrained;
寄放 leave in the care of; leave with;
解放 emancipate; emancipation; liberate; liberation;
開放 (1) bloom; blossom; (2) lift a ban, blockade, etc.;
狂放 unruly or unrestrained; wild or undisciplined;
流放 (1) banish; send into exile; (2) float downstream;
牧放 herd; put out to pasture; tend;
怒放 in full bloom;
燃放 set off;
施放 discharge; fire;
釋放 release; set free;
停放 park or place a vehicle;
投放 (1) put in; throw in; (2) put goods on the market; put money into circulation;
頹放 decadent and dissolute;
下放 (1) transfer to a lower level; (2) transfer cadres to work at lower levels;
淫放 lustful;
追放 banish;

fei¹
fei

【妃】 (1) spouse; wife; (2) concubine of a king or an emperor; imperial concubine; (3) wife of a crown prince;

[妃色] light pink;

[妃子] imperial concubine;

貴妃 higest-ranking imperial concubine;
王妃 princess-consort;

fei

【非】 (1) wrong; (2) not conform to; run counter to; (3) no; not; (4) blame; censure; (5) have got to; simply must;

[非常] a thousand; as blazes; as devil; as hell; as they come; awfully; badly; be burning with; be exasperated; bloody; by half; deeply; ever and ever so; ever so; ever so much; ever such a; exceedingly; extremely; frightfully; immensely; mortally; most; no end; no end of; not half; nothing if not; one hundred percent; only too...to; simply; so much; such a; terribly; to a great extent; to death; to the bone; to the ears; to the hilt; to the world; up to the elbows; up to the handle; utterly; vastly; very; very much;
非常必要 high necessary;
非常沉悶 as dull as dish-water; as dull as ditch-water; be bored to death; bore sb

to tears; bore the pants off sb; dead-and-alive; deadly dull;
非常成功 go places; go to town;
非常憤怒 in high dudgeon;
非常好 very good;
非常合適 to a T; to a tee; to a tittle; to a turn;
非常健康 as fit as a fiddle; in the pink;
非常狡猾 as slippery as an eel;
非常緊張 heart in one's boots; heart in one's mouth;
非常樂意 as soon as as not;
非常齊平 very even;
非常親熱 cheek by jowl;
非常容易 as easy as ABC; dead easy; very easy;
非常時期 unusual times;
非常舒適 as snug as a bug in a rug;
非常嚴肅 as grave as a judge; as grave as an owl;
非常整潔 spick and span;
非常重視 attach great importance to;
非常重要 of great account; of high account; of much account;

[非但] not only;

[非得] have got to; have to; must;

[非法] illegal; illicit; unlawful;
非法倒賣 illegal buying and selling; profiteering;
非法活動 illegal activity; unlawful activity;
非法集會 unlawful assembly;
非法交易 illegal transaction; unlawful trading;
非法入境 illegal entry into a country;
非法收入 illicit income;
非法行為 illegal act; illicit act; lawless behaviour; unlawful act;

[非凡] extraordinary; outstanding; uncommon; neither...nor;
熱鬧非凡 very lively;

[非…非…] neither…nor…;
非親非故 a perfect stranger; be bound to sb by no times; neither hith nor kin; neither relative nor friend; not to be one's relative;
非親非鄰 not to be related by ties of kinship nor even as neighours;

[非份] overstepping one's bounds;
非份之想 an improper desire; inordinate ambitions;

[非公莫入] no admittance; no admittance except on business;

[非…即] either...or;

[非君莫屬] only you can fill the post;

[非禮] impolite;
非禮之舉 improper conduct; indecorous behaviour;

[非賣品] not for sale;

[非難] animadvert; blame; cast sth in sb's teeth; censure; fling sth in sb's teeth; reproach;
加以非難 animadvert at length;

[非人] (1) not the right person; (2) inhuman;
非人待遇 inhuman treatment;
非人生活 a miserable life disgracing humanity;
所用非人 choose the wrong person for a job;

[非同小可] it is by no means a small matter; not to be trifled with; not trivial matter; not usual; of great consequence;

[非議] censure; reproach;
背人非議 speak ill of a man behind his back;
無可非議 irreproachable;
招來非議 bring reproach; draw reproach;
非正式會議 informal meeting;

必非 certainly not;
並非 really not;
除非 (1) only if; only when; (2) unless;
莫非 can it be that; is it possible that;
豈非 wouldn't it…;
是非 (1) right and wrong; (2) dispute; quarrel;
無非 no more than; nothing but; only; simply;
遠非 far from; not anywhere near; not nearly; nowhere near;
知非 know one's mistakes;
昨非 past mistakes;

fei

【飛】 (1) fly; (2) hover or flutter in the air; (3) swiftly; (4) accidental; unexpected;

[飛白] (in calligraphy) flying-white;

[飛奔] run at full speed; run like mad; run like the wind;
飛奔而去 fly off; take a flight; take wing;
飛奔上樓 dash up a flight of stairs;
飛奔下樓 fly downstairs;
策馬飛奔 ride away at a gallop;

[飛鏢] (1) dart; (2) dart-throwing;
飛鏢遊戲 darts;
[飛播] sow seed from aircraft;
[飛叉] flying trident;
[飛車] drive at a high speed;
飛車仔 boy racer;
飛車走壁 drinve on the inner surface of a cyclindrical wall; stunt cycling;
[飛馳] dart on; dash forward; go at a gallop; go at express speed; speed along;
[飛船] airship; dirigible; spacecraft; spaceship;
人造飛船 artificial spacecraft;
行星際飛船 interplanetary spacecraft;
宇航飛船 aerospacecraft;
~人造宇宙飛船 man-made spacecraft;
~有人操縱的宇宙飛船 unmanned spacecraft;
月球飛船 lunar spacecraft;
載人飛船 inhabited spacecraft;
[飛彈] (1) missile; (2) stray bullet;
[飛刀] flying knife;
[飛碟] (1) flying saucer; (2) UFO; unidentified flying object;
[飛蛾] moth;
飛蛾撵蜘蛛—自投羅網 a moth trying to drive out a spider – casting oneself into the net;
飛蛾撲火—自找死路 a moth throwing itself toward the fire – taking the road to one's doom;
[飛過] fly across; fly over; fly pass;
從空中飛過 fly across the sky; fly through the air;
[飛黃騰達] climb up the social ladder rapidly; come into one's kingdom; come up in the world; have a meteoric rise in position; have the world at one's feet; make one's way; make rapid advance in one's career; rise high; rise in the world; sail before the wind; win one's spurs;
[飛機] aeroplane; aircraft; airplane; plane;
飛機場 aerodrome; aerotrack; airport;
~小型飛機場 aerodrome;
~一個飛機場 an airport;
飛機隊 air team;
飛機發動機 aeroengine;
飛機機身 fuselage;
飛機駕駛員 airpilot; aviator; flyboy;
飛機結構學 aerostructure;
飛機輪胎 aerotire;
飛機模型 aircraft model;
飛機噴霧器 aerosprayer model;
飛機票 air ticket; airline ticket; plane ticket;
~飛機票價 airfare;
飛機起飛 a plane takes off; take off;
~飛機起飛裝置 acircraft launching apparatus;
飛機上拉二胡—唱高調 play an erhu on board an airplane – singing a "high" tune;
飛機上聊天—空談 chatting aboard an airplane – talking in the air; empty talk;
飛機上做夢—空想 building castles in the air; dreaming on an airplane – thinking in space;
飛機失事 plane crash;
飛機墜毀 plane crash;
飛機着陸 a plane lands;
超音速飛機 supersonic plane;
測繪飛機 air-mapping aeroplance;
測量飛機 survey aircraft;
乘飛機 take a plane;
單翼飛機 monoplane;
單座飛機 single seater aeroplane;
登上飛機 board a plane; get on a plane;
低空飛機 hedge-hopper airplane;
短距起落飛機 short take-off and landing aircraft;
多用途飛機 all-can-do aircraft;
飛往北京的飛機 the plane to Beijing;
趕上飛機 catch a plane;
國際航線飛機 international airplane;
海軍飛機 naval aeroplane;
航天飛機 aerospace plane; space shuttle;
核動力飛機 nuclear-powered aircraft;
護航飛機 escort aircraft;
加油飛機 tanker;
~空中加油飛機 air tanker; aircraft tanker;
駕駛飛機 drive an aeroplane; fly a plance; pilot a plane;
劫持飛機 hijack a plane;
救護飛機 ambulance aeroplane; ambulance aircraft;
軍用飛機 military aircraft; military plane;
空投飛機 supply dropper aircraft;
空中加油飛機 air-to-air refueling aircraft;
兩棲飛機 amphibian aircraft; amphibious aeroplane;
陸上飛機 landplane;

民用飛機 civil aircraft;
農用飛機 agricultural aircraft;
噴氣飛機 jet aircraft;
輕型飛機 light aircraft;
全高度飛機 all-altitude aircraft;
上飛機 go aboard the plane; step aboard;
雙翼飛機 biplane;
水陸兩用飛機 amphibious aeroplane;
水上飛機 aeroboat; aerohydroplane; hydroplane; seaplane;
~船式水上飛機 flying boat seaplane;
~浮筒式水上飛機 floatplane;
私人飛機 private plane;
特技飛機 acrobatic aircraft;
通用飛機 general-purpose aircraft;
外伸翼飛機 overhanging aeroplane;
微型飛機 microlight;
無人駕駛飛機 drone-equipped aircraft;
下飛機 deplane; get off a plane;
消防飛機 fire airplane;
協和式飛機 concorde;
旋翼飛機 autogyro;
雪上飛機 ski-plane;
夜航飛機 night-operating aircraft;
一班飛機 a flight;
一大群飛機 a cloud of planes;
一架飛機 a plane; an aeroplane;
游覽飛機 touring aircraft;
運貨飛機 aerovan; airtruck;
直昇飛機 helicopter;
~單槳直昇飛機 single-rotor helicopter;
~嚙合槳直昇飛機 intermeshing-rotor helicopter;
~農用直昇飛機 agricopter;
~雙槳直昇飛機 dual-rotor helicopter;
~縱列槳直昇飛機 tandem-rotor helicopter;
~重型直昇飛機 heavy-duty helicopter;
中程飛機 medium-haul aircraft;
洲際飛機 intercontinental aircraft; transoceanic aircraft;
裝甲飛機 armoured aeroplane;
自動飛機 autoplane;
作戰飛機 combat plane;
坐飛機 ride in a plane;

[飛濺] splash;
浪花飛濺 the waves splash;

[飛快] (1) at lightning speed; very fast; (2) extremely sharp;
時間過得飛快 time flies;
時日過得飛快 the hours and days speed apace;

[飛輪] flywheel;
帶扇飛輪 fan flywheel;
液力飛輪 fluid flywheel;
有齒飛輪 cogged flywheel;
主導軸飛輪 capstan flywheel;

[飛毛腿] fleet-footed; fleet-footed runner; fleet of foot;

[飛跑] bolt off; dask; race; run very fast; tear;
飛跑進來 dash in;
飛跑去趕火車 bolt off to catch the train;
裸體飛跑 streaking;

[飛禽] aerial creatures; birds;
飛禽走獸 birds and animals; fowls and beasts;

[飛昇] fly up to heaven;

[飛逝] fleet away; flight; fly; pass away swiftly;
時光飛逝 time flies;

[飛速] at full speed;
飛速運轉 run at full speed;

[飛騰] fly swiftly upward;

[飛艇] aeroboat; airship; dirigible;
軟式飛艇 blimp airship; non-rigid airship;
搜索飛艇 search airship;
巡邏飛艇 patrol airship;
硬式飛艇 rigid airship;

[飛吻] blow a kiss;
給人一個飛吻 blow a kiss to sb; throw sb a kiss;

[飛舞] dance in the air;
狂飛亂舞 hunt riot; run riot;
柳絮在空中飛舞 willow catkins are fluttering in the air;
雪花飛舞 snowflakes are dancing in the air;

[飛翔] circle in the air; hover;
展翅飛翔 fly on wings; spread wings and fly; wing its flight;

[飛行] flight; flying;
飛行安全 aviation safety;
飛行表演 air show; demonstration flight;
飛行車 aerocar;
飛行記錄儀 flight recorder;
飛行家 aeroplanist;
飛行甲板 flight deck;
飛行俱樂部 aero club;
飛行路線 flight path;
飛行模擬器 flight simulator;
飛行器 aerial craft; airborne craft;

F

～航天飛行器 aerospace craft;
～月球旅行飛行器 lunar excursion craft;
飛行時間 airtime; flight time;
飛行事故 air accident; aircraft accident; flight accident; flying accident;
飛行速度 airspeed;
飛行特技 aerial aerobatics; aerobatics; aerobation;
～飛行特技表演 airshow;
飛行學 aeronautics;
飛行學校 aerie;
飛行員 aeriator; aviator; flyer; pilot;
～二級飛行員 second-grade pilot;
～海軍飛行員 naval aviator;
～陸軍航空兵飛行員 army aviator;
～民航飛行員 civil aviator;
～女飛行員 airwoman; aviatress; bird woman; lady aviator;
～三級飛行員 third-grade pilot;
～四級飛行員 fourth-grade pilot;
～一級飛行員 first-grade pilot;
翺翔飛行 soaring flight;
編隊飛行 flyover; flypast;
長途飛行 long flight;
彈道飛行 ballistic flight;
高空飛行 high altitude flying;
慣性飛行 coasting flight;
基線飛行 base-line flying;
加班飛行 extra flight;
艦上飛行 deck flying;
連續飛行 non-stop flight;
盲目飛行 blind flying;
民航飛行 civil flight;
～民航飛行事故 civil accident;
偏向飛行 declination flying;
平穩飛行 smooth flight;
～不平穩飛行 bumpy flight;
全天候飛行 all-weather flight; all-weather flying;
特技飛行 aerial acrobatics; aerobat; aerobation; fly aerobatics;
～特技飛行員 aerobat;
～滑翔機特技飛行 sailplane aerobatics;
線控飛行 fly-by-wire;
儀錶飛行 instrument flying;
越野飛行 cross country; flight;
雲中飛行 cloud-hopping;
中斷飛行 air abort;

[飛絮] floating catkins;
輕如飛絮 as light as a thistledown;

[飛檐] overhanging eaves; upturned eaves;
飛檐走壁 climb walls and leap onto roofs; fly from house to house and walk on walls; fly over the eaves and run on the walls; leap onto roofs and vault over walls; make one's way into a house over walls and roofs;

[飛燕] flying swallows;
飛燕式 (of hairstyle) swept-back;
輕如飛燕 as light as a swallow on the wing;

[飛揚] fly upward; rise;
飛揚跋扈 act like overlords; arrogant and domineering; domineer; lord it over; powerful and arrogant; throw one's weight around;
塵土飛揚 clouds of dust are flying up;
歌聲飛揚 songs are floating;
神采飛揚 exuberant in spirit; in high spirit;

[飛鷹走狗] fly one's falcons and course one's hounds; hunt wild animals; hunt with a pack of hounds or with falcons;

[飛魚] flying fish;

[飛躍] leap;
飛躍發展 advance in development by leaps and bounds;

[飛災] unexpected disaster;
飛災橫禍不入慎家之門 sudden misfortune and unexpected mischance cannot enter the family of the careful; unexpected calamity with its misery will not enter the door of the prudent;

[飛賊] cat burglar;

[飛漲] shoot up; skyrocket; soar;
物價飛漲 prices are skyroacketing;

[飛着] float in the air; not decided; unsolved;

[飛走] fly away; take wing;

阿飛 teddy boy;
單飛 solo flight;
倒飛 inverted flight;
紛飛 flutter about;
起飛 get off; get off the ground; hop off; launch; lift off; take off;
如飛 like flying; quickly; swiftly;
試飛 test flight; trial flight;
騰飛 rise rapidly; soar; take off;
停飛 grounding of aircraft;
雄飛 strive for bigger and better things;

fei

【啡】 a form used in transliterating;

咖啡 coffee;
嗎啡 morphine;

fei

【扉】 door leaf;
[扉頁] flying leaf of a book; title page;

柴扉 house door made of small pieces of wood or branches;
心扉 way of thinking;

fei

【菲】 (1) fragrant; (2) the Philippines;
[菲菲] (1) luxuriant and beautiful; (2) richly fragrant;
[菲律賓人] Filipinos;
[菲律賓語] Tagalog;

芳菲 (1) fragrance of flowers and grass; (2) flowers and grass;

fei

【緋】 red;
[緋紅] bright red; crimson;
亮緋紅 brilliant crimson;
酸性緋紅 acid crimson;
[緋聞] (1) pink journalism; (2) scandal;
散佈緋聞 spread the scandal;
製造緋聞 invent pink journalism;

fei

【蜚】 fly;
[蜚鴻滿野] distressed populace is found everywhere;
[蜚聲] become famous; make a name;
蜚聲海外 enjoy a high reputation abroad;
蜚聲鵲起 one's reputation suddenly becomes high and widespread;
蜚聲四海 become well-known all over the world;
蜚聲文壇 famous in literary circle;
[蜚英騰茂] reputed and rise up to prosperity;
[蜚語] gossip; rumours;

fei

【霏】 falling of snow and rain;
[霏霏] snow or rain hard;
雨雪霏霏 it is sleeting hard; it sleets; the sleet is falling fast;

fei

【鯡】 herring;
[鯡斗] cran;
[鯡魚] herring;
一群鯡魚 a shoal of herrings;
一桶鯡魚 a barrel of herrings;

脂眼鯡 Pacific round herring;

fei²

fei

【肥】 (1) flat; (2) fertile; rich; (3) fertilize; (4) fertilizer; manure; (5) large; loose; loose-fitting;
[肥大] (1) large; loose; (2) fat; plump; (3) hypertrophy;
肥大性肥胖 hypertrophic obesity;
肥大症 hypertrophy;
~肢端肥大症 acromegaly;
代償性肥大 compensatory hypertrophy;
單純性肥大 simple hyperthrophy;
單純指甲肥大 hyperonychia;
骨肥大 bone hypertrophy;
假肥大 false hypertrophy; pseudohypertrophy;
假性肥大 pseudohypertrophy;
良性前列腺肥大 benign prostatic hypertrophy;
腦肥大 encephalauxe;
內臟肥大 visceromegaly;
偏側肥大 hemihypertrophy;
腎肥大 nephromegaly;
生理性肥大 physiologic hypertrophy;
適應性肥大 adaptive hypertrophy;
心臟肥大 cardiac hypertrophy;
真性肥大 true hypertrophy;
指肥大 pachydactyly;
指甲肥大 onychauxis;
趾肥大 pachydactyly;
[肥厚] fleshy; plump; stout and strong;
[肥力] fertility;
海洋肥力 sea fertility;
潛在肥力 potential fertility;
土壤肥力 soil fertility;
[肥料] fertilizer; manure;
肥料等級 fertilizer grade;
肥料配合式 fertilizer formula;
肥料要素 fertility element;
粉狀肥料 powdered fertilizer;
複合肥料 compound fertilizer; compound manure;
化學肥料 chemical fertilizer;
混合肥料 compost; mixed fertilizer;
~多種混合肥料 multicomponent fertilizer;

F

簡單肥料 straight fertilizer;
間接肥料 indirect fertilizer;
抗菌肥料 antibiotic fertilizer;
顆粒肥料 granular fertilizer;
礦質肥料 mineral fertilizer;
人造肥料 artificial manure;
完全肥料 complete fertilizer;
~不完全肥料 incomplete fertilizer;
污泥肥料 sludge manure;
細菌肥料 bacterial fertilizer; bacterial manure;
液體肥料 liquid fertilizer;
一擔肥料 a bucket of fertilizer;
一堆肥料 a heap of manure;
有機肥料 organic fertilizer;
~天然有機肥料 natural organic fertilizer;
有效肥料 available fertilizer;
直接肥料 direct fertilizer;

[肥美] (1) fertile; rich; (2) fat; luxuriant; plump;

[肥膩] greasy; rich;

[肥胖] adiposity; as fat as butter; corpulent; fat; fleshiness; obesitas; obesity; polypionia; polysarcia; weight;
肥胖病學 bariatrics;
肥胖的 corpulent;
肥胖過度 hyperadiposis;
肥胖症 obesity;
成年型肥胖 adult-onset obesity;
垂體性肥胖 pituitary adiposity;
單純性肥胖 simple obesity;
肥大性肥胖 hypertrophic obesity;
肥肥胖胖 fat;
過於肥胖 too obese;
內源性肥胖 endogenous obesity;
偏側肥胖 hemiobesity;
偏身肥胖 hemiobesity;
全身性肥胖 adiposis universalis;
痛性肥胖 adiposis dolorosa;
外源性肥胖 exogenous obesity;

[肥缺] fat job; lucrative post; plum;

[肥肉] fat; fat meat; speck;
肥肉裏挑骨頭—找岔子 looking for bones in fat — nit-picking;
膩味肥肉 hate fatty pork;

[肥瘦] the fat and the lean;
肥瘦得中 good figure; half lean; round without being plump, slender without being bony;
抽肥補瘦 take from the fat to pad the lean; take from those who have too much and give to those who have too little; take from those with much and give to those with little;
環肥燕瘦 beautiful women are attractive in their own ways;
揀肥挑瘦 very choosy; very particular;
綠肥紅瘦 flourishing leaves and withering flowers; late spring; the scene of late spring;

[肥水] rich water;

[肥田] (1) enrich the soil; fertilize the soil; (2) fertile land;

[肥沃] fertile; rich;

[肥皂] soap;
肥皂粉 soap powder;
肥皂盒 soapbox;
肥皂劇 soap opera;
~紀實肥皂劇 docusoap;
肥皂泡 soap bubble;
肥皂泡末 soapsuds;
肥皂水 soapy water;
乾洗肥皂 dry cleaning soap;
乳白肥皂 curd soap;
一塊肥皂 a bar of soap; a cake of soap; a piece of soap;
一條肥皂 a bar of soap;
硬肥皂 hard soap;

[肥壯] stout and strong;
膘肥體壯 plump and sturdy;

抄肥 block goods and take them away; profit reaping; reap profit in business; waylay;
痴肥 abnormally fat; obese;
癡肥 very fat and looking stupid;
畜肥 animal manure;
春肥 fertilizer applied in spring;
催肥 fatten;
氮肥 nitrogenous fertilizer;
底肥 base fertilizer; base manure;
堆肥 compost;
分肥 divide booty; share out illgotten gains;
糞肥 dung; manure; muck;
乾肥 dried human and animal excreta;
骨肥 fertilizer made from bones;
河肥 river mud; river silt;
化肥 chemical fertilizer;
灰肥 plant ash;
基肥 base fertilizer; base manure;
積肥 collect manure;
鉀肥 potash fertilizer;
減肥 reduce weight;
廄肥 animal manure;

菌肥 bacterial manure;
粒肥 granulated fertilizer;
磷肥 phosphate fertilizer; phosphatic manure;
綠肥 green manure;
面肥 leaven; leavening dough;
泥肥 lake and river mud; silt; sludge;
尿肥 urine;
漚肥 wet compost;
施肥 apply fertilizer; spread manure;
水肥 manure of fermented night-soil mixed with water;
塘肥 pond sludge used as manure;
育肥 fatten;
雜肥 farmyard manure;
種肥 seed manure;
追肥 topdressing;
自肥 enrich oneself by unlawful means; fatten oneself; feather one's nest;

fei
【淝】 the Fei River (in Anhui);

fei
【腓】 (1) calf; (2) ill; sick; (3) avoid;

fei³

fei
【朏】 light of a crescent moon;

fei
【匪】 (1) hooliganish; loutish; rough; (2) not;
［匪幫］ bandit gang;
［匪巢］ bandits' lair;
直搗匪巢 drive straight on to the bandit's den;
［匪首］ bandit chieftain;
［匪徒］ bandit; gangster;
一幫匪徒 a band of gangsters; a mob of gangsters;
一群匪徒 a band of gangsters;

白匪 White bandits;
綁匪 kidnapper;
殘匪 remaining handful of bandits;
股匪 gang of bandits;
慣匪 hardened bandit; professional brigand;
胡匪 bandit; brigand;
土匪 bandit; brigand;

fei
【悱】 (1) inarticulate; unable to give vent to one's emotion; (2) sorrowful;
［悱惻］ laden with sorrow; sad at heart;

fei
【斐】 (1) beautiful; elegant; (2) a surname;
［斐然］ excellent; very satisfactory;
斐然成章 show striking literary talent;
斐然可觀 stately; strikingly;

fei
【菲】 (1) humble; unworthy; fragrant; (2) a kind of radish;
［菲薄］ (1) humble; poor; (2) belittle; despise;

fei
【棐】 (1) a species of yew found in North China; (2) bamboo products;

fei
【翡】 (1) kingfisher; (2) emerald;
［翡翠］ (1) halcyon; kingfisher; (2) emerald;

fei
【榧】 a species of yew;

香榧 Chinese torreya nut;

fei
【蜚】 cockroach;

fei
【誹】 slander;
［誹謗］ calumniate; defame; fling dirt at; libel; libeling; mudslinging; slander; sling mud at; throw mud at;
誹謗法 libel laws;
誹謗名譽 defamatory libel;
背後誹謗 slander people at the back;
政治誹謗 political libel;
［誹過其實］ paint the devil blacker than he is;

腹誹 unspoken criticism;

fei
【篚】 square bamboo basket;

fei⁴

fei
【吠】 bark; give tongue; throw tongue;
［吠犬不咬］ barking dogs seldom bite; great barkers are no biters;

狂吠 bark furiously; howl;

fei
【怫】 (1) inarticulate; unable to give vent to one's emotion; (2) sorrowful;
［怫憒］ sadness kept to oneself;

fei

【沸】 boil;

［沸點］ boiling point;

［沸反盈天］ cause a shocking commotion; raise hell; raise a rumpus; raise the devil;

［沸沸揚揚］ bubbling and gurgling; bubbling with noise; in a bubbub; like widlfire;

［沸泉］ boiling spring;

［沸石］ zeolite; zeolum;
- 沸石催化 zeolite catalysis;
- 沸石脂 zeolite ester;
- 紅菱沸石 acadialite;
- 紅斜方沸石 acadialite;

［沸騰］ (1) boiling; (2) boil over; seethe with excitement;
- 沸騰牀 boiling bed; bubbling bed;
- 沸騰室 boiling-house;
- 飽和沸騰 saturation boiling;
- 表面沸騰 surface boiling;
- 薄膜狀沸騰 film boiling;
- 過度沸騰 excessive boiling;
- 過冷沸騰 subcooled boiling;
- 泡核沸騰 nucleate boiling;
- 一片沸騰 a blaze of excitement;

鼎沸 boiling; like a seething cauldron; noisy and confused;

fei

【肺】 lung;

［肺癌］ caner of the lung; lung cancer; pulmonary cancer;
- 晚期肺癌 advanced lung cancer;

［肺胞］ pulmonary vesicle;

［肺病］ chest trouble; lung trouble; pulmonary tuberculosis; tuberculosis
- 限制性肺病 restrictive lung disease;
- 支氣管肺病 bronchopneumopathy;

［肺不張］ atelectasis;
- 黏連性肺不張 adhesive atelectasis;
- 盤狀肺不張 patelike atelectasis;
- 壓迫性肺不張 compression atelectasis;
- 原發性肺不張 primary atelectasis;
- 圓形肺不張 round atelectasis;
- 阻塞性肺不張 obstructive atelectasis;

［肺部］ lungs;

［肺腸炎］ pneumoenteritis;

［肺塵埃沉着病］ pneumonoconiosis chalicotica;

［肺塵病］ pneumoconoioisis;

［肺充血］ pulmonary congestion;

［肺出血］ pulmonary hemorrhage;

［肺底］ base of the lung;

［肺動脈］ pulmonary artery;
- 肺動脈瓣 pulmonary valve;
- 肺動脈栓塞 pulmonary embolism;

［肺腑］ bottom of one's heart;
- 肺腑之交 bosom friend; deep and sincere friendship;
- 肺腑之言 hearty talk; most reliable words; speak from the bottom of one's heart; talk from the heart; the words from one's heart; words from the depths of one's heart;
- 出自肺腑 from the depths of one's heart; straight from the heart;
- 動人肺腑 come home to sb's heart; heartening; move sb deeply; touch sb to the depths of his soul; touch sb's heart;
- 感人肺腑 be deeply moved by; bring home to sb's heart; come home to sb's heart; fill sb with a deep emotion; go to sb's heart; move sb deeply; pull at sb's heartstrings; touch sb deeply in the heart; touch sb to the depths of his soul; touch sb to the heart; touch the chords of sb's heart;
- 銘鐫肺腑 bear firmly in mind; engrave on one's memory;
- 銘諸肺腑 be deeply impressed; engrave on one's mind or memory;
- 沁人肺腑 gladden the heart; mentally refreshing; refreshing; seep into one's heart; touch one's heart;
- 痛徹肺腑 cut sb to the heart; deep regret;

［肺肝］ lungs and liver;

［肺梗塞］ pulmonary impaction;

［肺壞疽］ gangrene of the lung;

［肺活量］ vital capacity;

［肺尖］ apex of the lung;

［肺結核］ consumption; pulmonary tuberculosis; TB; tuberculosis;
- 肺結核病 consumption; pulmonary tuberculosis; TB; tuberculosis;

［肺靜脈］ pulmonary vein;

［肺擴張不全］ pulmonary atelectasis;

［肺癆］ consumption; phthisis; tuberculosis;

［肺門］ hilus of the lung;

肺門結核 hilus tuberculosis;
肺門淋巴結 hilar lymph nodes;

[肺膜] pleura;
肺膜炎 pulmonary pleurisy;

[肺膿腫] lung abscess; suppuration of the lung;

[肺泡] lung alveolus; pulmonary alveolus;
肺泡癌 alveolar carcinoma;
肺泡孔 lung alveolar pores;
肺泡炎 alveolitis;
變應性肺泡炎 allergic alveolitis;

[肺氣腫] emphysema; pulmonary emphysema;
大泡性肺氣腫 bullous emphysema;
局限性肺氣腫 focal emphysema;
老年肺氣腫 aging-lung emphysema; senile emphysema;
彌漫性肺氣腫 diffuse emphysema;
囊性肺氣腫 cystic emphysema;
萎縮性肺氣腫 atrophic emphysema;
小葉中心肺氣腫 centrilobular emphysema;
阻塞性肺氣腫 obstructive emphysema;

[肺切除] pneumonectomy; surgical removal of the lung;

[肺熱喘咳] dyspnea and cough due to lung-heat;

[肺軟骨] pulmonary cartilage;

[肺軟化] pneumomalacia;

[肺石] pneumolith;

[肺水腫] oedema pulmonary; pulmonary oedema;
實質肺水腫 solid pulmonary oedema;
陣發性肺水腫 paroxysmal pulmonary oedema;

[肺吸蟲病] paragonimiasis;

[肺炎] pneumonia;
白色肺炎 pneumonia alba; white pneumonia;
病毒性肺炎 viral pneumonia;
創傷性肺炎 traumatic pneumonia;
大葉性肺炎 lobar pneumonia;
得了肺炎 suffer from pneumonia;
非典型肺炎 atypical pneumonia; atypical pneumonitis;
~傳染性非典型肺炎 infectious atypical pneumonia;
~原發性非典型肺炎 primary atypical pneumonia;
風濕性肺炎 rheumatic pneumonia;
乾酪性肺炎 caseous pneamonia;
宮內肺炎 intrauterine pneumonia;
汞性肺炎 mercury pneumonitis;
過敏性肺炎 hypersensitivity pneumonitis;
壞疽性肺炎 gangrenous pneumonia;
壞死性肺炎 recrotising pneumonia;
機化性肺炎 organizing pneumonia;
急性肺炎 acute pneumonia;
繼發性肺炎 secondary pneumonia;
假肺炎 pseudopneumonia;
結核性肺炎 tuberculous pneumonia;
酒毒性肺炎 alcoholic pneumonia;
局限性肺炎 pneumonitis;
鏈球菌性肺炎 streptococcus pneumonia;
念珠菌性肺炎 candida pneumonia;
尿毒症性肺炎 uremic pneumonitis;
肉芽腫性肺炎 granulomatous pneumonitis;
蠕蟲性肺炎 verminous pneumonia;
鼠疫性肺炎 plague pneumonia;
炭宜性肺炎 anthrax pneumonia;
細菌性肺炎 bacterial pneumonia;
小葉性肺炎 lobular pneumonia;
游走性肺炎 wandering pneumonia;
支氣管肺炎 broncho-pneumonia;
脂質性肺炎 pneumonolipidosis;
中央肺炎 central pneumonia;
終末期肺炎 terminal pneumonia;
轉移性肺炎 metastatic pneumonia;
阻塞性肺炎 obstructive pneumonia;

[肺葉] lobe;
上肺葉 upper lobe;
下肺葉 lower lobe;

[肺臟] lungs;

[肺脹] emphysema;

塵肺 pneumoconiosis;
硅肺 silicosis;
脾肺 spleen and lung;
人造肺 aqualung; artificial lung;
潤肺 nourish the lung;
書肺 book lung;
矽肺 silicosis;
心病肺 cardiac lung disease;
心肺 heart and lung;
宜肺 open the inhibited lung-energy;

fei

【芾】 lush; luxuriant;

fei

【狒】 baboon;

[狒狒] mandrill;

fei

【費】 (1) charges; dues; expenses; fees; (2) cost; expend; spend; (3) wasteful; (4) a surname;

［費解］ hard to understand; obscure; unintelligible;
費解的 enigmatic;
說話令人費解 speak in riddles;

［費勁］ be strenuous; need great effort; use great effort;

［費力］ need great effort; put oneself out; strenuous;
費力不討好 a fool for one's pains; a fool to oneself; arduous but fruitless; do a hard but thankless job; exacting but unrewarding; more kicks than halfpence; put in much hard work, but get very little result; tough but thankless; undertake a thankless task; work hard but get little result;
~費力不討好的事 thankless task;
費力氣 do one's best;
不費力 at an easy rate; effortless;
~毫不費力 as slick as a whistle; effortless; like a dream; no sweat; with a wet finger; without a blow; without striking a blow; without the slightest effort;

［費錢］ cost a lot; costly;

［費神］ (1) may I trouble you to do sth; would you mind doing sth for me; (2) waste of energy;

［費時］ take time; time-consuming;
費時費力 waste time and energy;

［費事］ give a lot of trouble;

［費心］ give a lot of care; take a lot of trouble;
費心勞力 take a lot of trouble;
無需費心 need not take any trouble about; need not trouble oneself with;

［費用］ charge; cost; expense; fare; fee; freight; outlay; overhead; tip; tuition;
費用安排 financial arrangement;
費用賬 expense account;
~預付費用賬 prepaid expense account;
昂貴的費用 great expense;
~需要昂貴的費用 incur great expenses;
~支付昂貴的費用 defray enormous cost;
包裝費用 packing charges;
產生費用 incur a charge;
遞延費用 deferred expense;
額外費用 additional charge; additional expense; extra charge; extra expense;
廢棄費用 waste expense;
分攤費用 split the cost;
附加費用 loading expense;
管理費用 management expense;
國防費用 military spending;
間接費用 indirect cost;
節約費用 reduce expenses;
人事費用 personnel expense;
生活費用 living expenses;
收取費用 make a charge;
~亂收費用 arbitrary charges; collect fees arbitrarily;
推廣費用 promotion expense;
削減費用 curtail expenditure; cut expenditure; reduce expenditure; retrench expenditure; whittle down cost;
業務費用 functional expense;
應計費用 accrued expense;
支付費用 defray; meet a cost; pay a charge;
製造費用 factory overhead;

白費 in vain; spend without profit; use up without profit; waste;
報費 subscription for a newspaper;
餐費 boarding expenses; food bill;
車費 fare;
船費 cost of a boat ticket;
訂費 subscription;
港口費 port charge;
稿費 contribution fee;
公費 at public expense;
官費 funds from public coffers;
耗費 consume; cost; expend;
花費 cost; expend; expenditure; expenses;
匯費 remittance fee;
會費 membership dues;
經費 funds; outlay;
軍費 military expenditure;
曠費 waste;
浪費 extravagant; squander; waste;
路費 travelling expenses;
糜費 spend extravagantly; waste;
免費 free; free of charge;
盤費 travelling expenses;
破費 go to some expense; spend money;
膳費 board expenses;
團費 league membership dues;
枉費 of no avail; try in vain; waste;

消費 consume;
小費 gratuity; tip;
學費 tuition; tuition fees;
藥費 charges for medicine; expenses for medicine;
用費 cost; expense;
郵費 postage;
月費 monthly expenses;
運費 carriage; freight; transportation expenses;
雜費 (1) incidental expenses; (2) sundry fees;
自費 at one's own expense;
租費 rent;

fei

【痱】 heat rash; heat spot; prickly heat;
[痱子] heat rash; heat spot; prickly heat;
痱子粉 prickly-heat powder;
起痱子 have prickly heat;
長痱子 have prickly heat;

fei

【廢】 (1) abandon; abolish; give up; (2) useless; waste; (3) disabled; maimed;
[廢弛] (1) cease to be binding; (2) become lax;
[廢除] abolish; abrogate; annihilate; annul; cancel; do away with; nullify; repeal; repeal; revoke;
廢除繁文縟節 do away with tedious formalities;
依法廢除 abate by law;
[廢黜] decrown; depose; dethrone;
廢黜王位 dethrone king; forfeit the crown;
[廢話] cobblers; codswallop; crap; eyewash; guff; hokum; malarkey; nonsense; rubbish; superfluous words; talk rubbish;
廢話連篇 be full of waffle; beat one's gums; blather; empty phrases; it's all moonshine; multiply words; pages of nonsense; reams of rubbish; talk downright nonsense; talk rubbish;
別廢話 keep your breath; save your breath;
講了一堆廢話 talk a load of cobbers; talk a load of garbage; talk a lot of nonsense;
淨説廢話 only talk nonsense;
少廢話 cut the cackle; don't talk rubbish; no more nonsense;
~ 少説廢話 keep one's breath to cool one's porridge; less of your nonsense; no more nonsense; stop chattering; stop talking nonsense; stop talking rubbish;
無關痛癢的廢話 irrelevant inanities;
一大堆廢話 a load of waffle;
一堆廢話 a load of cobblers; a load of garbage;
[廢料] dross; waste;
廢料處理 waste disposal;
放射性廢料 radioactive waste;
工業廢料 industrial waste;
固體廢料 solid waste;
核廢料 nuclear waste;
化學廢料 chemical waste;
[廢氣] exhaust fumes; exhaust gas;
廢氣淨化 purification of exhaust gas;
[廢棄] abandon; cast aside; discard; disuse;
廢棄不用 fall into disuse;
廢棄品 discarded article;
廢棄條款 denounce a clause;
[廢寢忘食] lose sleep and forget to eat; neglect one's meals and sleep; too busy to eat or sleep;
[廢熱] waste heat;
[廢水] effluent; waste water;
廢水處理 waste water treatment;
~ 廢水處理方法 treatment of waste water;
電鍍廢水 electroplating effluent;
焦爐廢水 coke-oven effluent;
氯化廢水 chlorinated effluent;
[廢鐵] scrap iron;
揀拾廢鐵 scavenge pices of scrap iron;
[廢物] dreck; dud; garbage; rubbish; trash; waste material; waste substance; waster;
廢物場 wasteyard;
廢物處理 waste disposal;
廢物回收箱 recycling bin; recycling box;
廢物利用 convert waste into useful material; make good use of waste materials; productive use of cast-off things; the utilization of waste products; utilize waste materials;
處理廢物 disposal of waste;
富碳廢物 carbon-rich waste;
固體廢物 solid waste;
~ 都市固體廢物 municipal solid waste;
核廢物 nuclear waste products;
回收廢物 recycle waste;
可燃廢物 combustible waste;
瀝青化廢物 bituminized waste;

農業加工廢物 agricultural processing waste;
纖維質廢物 cellulosic waste;
原子能廢物 atomic waste;

[廢墟] debris; remainder; ruins; wastage; wasteland;
城市廢墟 ruined city;
荒草廢墟 ruins overgrown with weeds;
一片廢墟 a heap of rubble; in ruins;

[廢言] dismiss sb's statement as untrue;
以人廢言 dismiss sb's statement as untrue because of his ill reputation;
因人廢言 reject an opinion on account of the speaker;

[廢止] abolish; annul; put an end to;
廢止法令 annul a decree;
廢止婚約 annulment of the marriage;

[廢紙] broke; waste paper;
廢紙簍 circular file; waste basket; wastepaper basket;
一簍廢紙 a basket of wastepaper;

[廢置] put aside as useless;

百廢 a hundred things are put aside;
報廢 (1) report sth as worthless or invalid; (2) discard as useless; reject;
病廢 be disabled by disease;
殘廢 cripple; crippled; disabled; maimed; maimed person;
荒廢 (1) leave uncultivated; lie waste; (2) fall into disuse; (3) neglect; out of practice;
曠廢 neglect; out of practice;
偏廢 over-concentrate on one issue and neglect another; emphasize one thing at the expense of another;
頹廢 decadent; dispirited; downhearted;
作廢 become invalid; cancel; declare invalid; delete; make void; nullify;

fen¹
fen

【分】 (1) divide; part; separate; (2) assign; distribute; (3) differentiate; distinguish; (4) branch; (5) minute; (6) mark; point; (7) cent;

[分班] (1) divide into classes; (2) divide into squads;

[分保] reinsurance;
成數分保 contributory reinsurance;
集團分保 pool reinsurance;
臨時分保 facultative reinsurance;
預約分保 obligatory-facultative reinsurance;

[分貝] decibel;

[分辨] differentiate; distinguish;
分辨能力 resolving ability;
分辨是非 distinguish between right and wrong;
分辨真假 distinguish truth from falsehood;

[分辯] defend oneself; offer an explanation;
不容分辯 allow no explanation to be offered;

[分別] (1) leave each other; part; separate; (2) discriminate; differentiate; distinguish; (3) differently; (4) respectively; separately;
分別輕重 differentiate the important from the less important; distinguish the trivial from the important;
~分別輕重緩急 do things in order of importance and urgency; handle problems in the right order of priority;
分別善惡 distinguish good from evil; separate the sheep from the goats;
分別先後 distinguish according to the order of priority;
概念性分別 conceptual difference;

[分兵] divide forces;
分兵把守 divide the forces for defense;

[分佈] be dispersed; be distributed; distribute; distribution; scatter; spread;
分佈器 distributor;
~多孔板分佈器 perforated-plate distributor;
~發射機分佈器 transmitter distributor;
~強氣流分佈器 air blast distributor;
對等分佈 equivalent distribution;
互補分佈 complementary distribution;
交流分佈 alternating current distribution;
氣流分佈 air flow distribution;
徒度分佈 abrupt distribution;
速度分佈 velocity spread;
無中心分佈 acentric distribution;
振幅分佈 amplitude distribution;

[分冊] fascicles;

[分層] stratum;
分層抽樣 stratified sampling;
分層規劃 hierarchical planning;

[分拆] demerge; demerger;

[分成] divide into; separate into;
分成三份 divide into three parts;

[分詞] participle;
分詞形容詞 participial adjective;
被動分詞 passive pariticiple;
垂懸分詞 dangling participle;
第二分詞 second participle;
第一分詞 first participle;
獨立分詞 absolute pariticple;
附着分詞 adherent participle;
過去分詞 past participle;
溶合分詞 fused pariticiple;
現在分詞 present pariticiple;
主動分詞 active pariticiple;

[分寸] a sense of propriety;
不知分寸 have no sense of propriety; lack of tact;
有分寸 have a sense of propriety; know how far to go and when to stop;
~有失分寸 have a breach of propriety;
~發言有分寸 make a measured speech;
~説話有分寸 know what to say and what not to say;
~做事有分寸 act with propriety; observe proper restraint;
掌握分寸 act properly; behave oneself; exercise sound judgement; handle appropriately; speak properly;

[分擔] share the responsibility;
分擔費用 share the expenses;
分擔痛苦 participate in sb's suffering;
分擔責任 share the responsibility;
平均分擔 share and share alike; take equal shares;

[分檔] classify; grade;

[分道揚鑣] each going his own way; go by different roads; go different ways; go separate ways; jerk the reins and ride on separate routes; part company with; part ways; separate and go different ways;

[分等] classify; grade;
可分等 gradable;
~可分等動詞 gradable verb;
~可分等形容詞 gradable adjective;

[分點] point of division;

[分度圈] graduated circle;

[分段] (1) fragment; section; (2) paragraph;
分段解決 solve sth section by section;
分段製造 build in section;

[分而治之] divide and rule;

[分發] dispatch; distribute; hand out; issue; serve out;
分發證件 issue certificates individually;

[分割] break up; carve up; cut apart; section; segmentation;
分割比 ration of divison;
黃金分割 golden section;
模式分割 pattern segmentation;
市場分割 market segmentation;
字符分割 character segmentation;

[分隔] divide; separate;
分隔帶 divider;
分隔物 divider;

[分給] allot;

[分工] divide the work;
分工負責 division of labour and responsibilities; division of labour with individual responsibility;
分工合作 divide labour and join in work; share out the work and cooperate with one another; work in cooperation with a due division of labour;
社會分工 social division of labour;

[分光] (1) divide up; (2) spectrum;
分光吃光 eat up and divide everything;
分光計 spectrometer;
分光鏡 spectroscope;
分光儀 ultraviolet spectrometer;
~紫外線分光儀 ultraviolet spectrometer;

[分行] branch of a bank;
國內分行 domestic branch; home branch;
國外分行 overseas branch;

[分毫] fraction; iota;
分毫不變 not change by an iota;
分毫不差 not a tiny bit of difference; not the least portion is mistaken; perfectly exact; there is not the least difference at all;
分毫不讓 not give the slightest concession;
不差分毫 absolutely right; without the slightest error;

[分號] (1) semicolon; (2) branch of a firm;

[分紅] distribute bonus; draw extra dividends; share out bonus;
按股分紅 share profits according to contributions;
年底分紅 share out the bonus at the end of the year;
現金分紅 cash bonus;

[分化] become divided; break up; differentiation; split up;

F

分化瓦解 disintegrate; divide and demoralize; split and disintegrate;
化學分化 chemical differentiation;
階級分化 class differentiation;
兩極分化 go polarized;
適應分化 adaptive differentiation;
細胞分化 cell differentiation;

[分級] classification; classify; grade; grading;
分級管理 graded administration;
分級機 grader;
~蛋分級機 egg grader;
~玉米分級機 corn grader;
~自動分級機 automatic grader;
長度分級 length grading;
色度分級 colour grading;
自動分級 automatic grading;

[分家] break up the family and live apart;

[分件賣] sell by the piece;

[分節] segmentation;
同律分節 homonomous segmentation;
異律分節 heteronomous segmentation;

[分解] (1) decompose; resolution; resolve; (2) disclose; recount;
分解反應 decomposition reaction;
分解器 resolver;
~電磁分解器 electromagnetic resolver;
~電流分解器 current resolver;
~角分解器 angular resolver;
且聽下回分解 read the next chapter for disclosure;
標準分解 canonical decomposition;
催化分解 catalytic decomposition;
複分解 metathesis;
複譜分解 complex spectral resolution;
內射分解 injective resolution;
頻率分解 frequency resolution;
酸性分解 acid decomposition;
細菌性分解 bacterial decomposition;
直積分解 direct product decomposition;
自由分解 free resolution;

[分界] (1) have as the boundary; (2) dividing line;
分界線 borderline; boundary line; dividing line; line of demarcation;

[分居] live apart; separate without a legal divorce; separation;
分居兩地 live in two separate places;
兩地分居 live in two places;

[分開] break up; divide; isolate; part; partition; segregate; separate; sort;

[分類] classification; ledger; sort; sorting; taxonomy;
分類層次 sort hierarchy;
分類對立 taxonomic opposition;
分類公關 public relation's classification;
分類機 sorter;
~自動分類機 automatic sorter;
分類卡 classified card;
分類描述 taxonomy description;
分類器 sorter;
~字母分類器 alphabetic sorter;
分類學 systematics; taxonomy;
~動物分類學 animal taxonomy; zootaxy;
~昆蟲分類學 entomological taxonomy;
~數值分類學 numerical taxonomy;
~植物分類學 phytotaxonomy; plant taxonomy; systematic botany;
分類語言學 taxonomic linguistics;
分類賬 ledger; ledger account;
~財產分類賬 property ledger;
~輔助分類賬 auxiliary ledger; subsidiary ledger;
~進貨分類賬 purchase ledger;
~累進式分類賬 accumulative ledger;
~明細分類賬 detail ledger;
~原料分類賬 raw material ledger;
~摘要分類賬 abstract ledger;
標準分類 normal sort;
成本分類 cost classification;
詞形分類 morphological classification;
磁盤分類 disk sort;
磁心分類 core sort;
代碼分類 code classification;
對生分類 dichotomous classification;
多項分類 multiple taxonomy;
二項分類 binary taxonomy;
顧客分類 customer classification;
將…分類 classify;
交叉分類 cross classification;
兩組分類 dichotomy classification;
氣候分類 climatic classification;
群落分類 community classification;
人為分類 artificial classification;
生態分類 ecological classification;
速度分類 velocity sorting;
屬性分類 attributive classification;
數據分類 data classification;
業務活動分類 activity classification;
賬戶分類 account classification;
自動分類 automatic classification; automatic sorting;

[分離] detach; dissociate; segregation;

F

separate; separation; sever;
分離規律 law of segregation;
分離號 apostrophe;
分離器 separator;
~空氣分離器 air separator;
~頻帶分離器 band separator;
分離性副詞 adverb as dispunct;
分離主義 separatism;
~分離主義者 separatist;
分崩離析 be split and disintegrated; come apart; crumbling; disintegrate; disunited; divergence and disintegration; fall separately and split differently; fall to pieces; go to stick and staves;
幅度分離 amplitude separation;
氣流分離 air-blast separation;
無性分離 asexual segregation;
信用分類 credit classification;
永不分離 never to be separated;
有性分離 sexual segregation;
暫時分離 be separated for the present;
政教分離 divorce church from state; separate religion from politics;

[分裂] break up; cleavage; disintegrate; dissociate; disunity; divide; division; smash; split; splitting; tear;
分裂本領 disintegrating ability;
分裂繁殖 reproduction by fission;
分裂句 cleft sentence;
~假分裂句 pseudo-cleft sentence;
分裂性人格 schizoid personality;
分裂引語 broken quotation;
胞質分裂 cytokinesis;
單元分裂 cellular splitting;
複分裂 multiple fission;
核分裂 karyokinesis; nuclear division,
減數分裂 meiosis;
頻帶分裂 band splitting;
人格分裂 the disintegration of personality;
四分五裂 be rent by disunity; be smashed to bits; be split up; be torn apart; break into pieces; come apart at the seams; come to pieces; fall apart; fall to pieces; scattered and disunited; split up;
無絲分裂 amitosis;
細胞分裂 cell division;
異型分裂 allotypic division; heterolypic division;
有絲分裂 mitosis;
~有絲分裂孢子 mitospore;
~反常有絲分裂 abnormal mitosis;
~畸形有絲分裂 aberrant mitosis;
~雙星有絲分裂 amphiastral mitosis;
~無星有絲分裂 anastral mitosis;
~有星有絲分裂 astral mitosis;
直接分裂 amitosis;

[分齡] divide into age-groups;

[分流] divert into separate streams;
分流器 shunt;
~並聯分流器 parallel shunt;
~電感分流器 inductive shunt;
雙電感分流器 double inductive shunt;
~螺紋式分流器 threaded shunt;
分流人才 reassigning the talented people;

[分餾] fractionating;

[分路] shunt;
分路器 shunt;
~柔軟分路器 flexible shunt;
磁分路 magnetic shunt;
人工分路 man-made shunt;

[分門別類] arrange under categories; be arranged into sorts; be divided into classes and divisions; classify; classify according to subjects; divide into different classes; put into different categories; sort out into categories;

[分米] decimeter(dm);

[分泌] secrete;
分泌物 secretion;
分泌學 eccrinology;
~外分泌學 exocrinology;
內分泌 endocrine;
~內分泌腺 endocrine gland;

[分娩] childbearing; childbirth;
分娩過緩 bradytocia;
分娩期痛 expulsive pains;
臀部分娩 breech birth; breech delivery;
過期分娩 delayed labour;
過熟分娩 postmature delivery;
急速分娩 oxytocia;
強促分娩 accouchement force;
無痛分娩 painless delivery;
陰道分娩 vaginal delivery;
正常分娩 eutocia;
自然分娩 natural childbirth;

[分秒] minutes and seconds;
分秒必爭 cannot afford to waste a single minute; count every minute and second; every inch of time is to be contested; every moment counts; every

minute counts; every second counts; get hold of every minute; make every minute count; make use of every possible minute; seize every second; there is not a moment to be lost;
分秒不差 just in time; very punctual;

[分明] (1) clearly demarcated; distinct; (2) evidently; plainly;
愛憎分明 have a clear distinction between love and hate;
恩仇分明 make a clear distinction between kindness and wrongs done by others;
恩怨分明 discriminate between love and hate; make a clear distinction between kindness and hatred; kindness and hatred are clearly distinguished;
公私分明 scrupulous in distinguishing between public and private interests;
黑白分明 white is in sharp contrast to black;
界線分明 the division is clearly demarcated;
是非分明 clearly distinguish right from wrong;

[分母] denominator;
公分母 common denominator;
~ 最小公分母 least common denominator;
有理化分母 rationalizing denominator;

[分派] assign; distribute; dole sth out; hand out;

[分配] allot; allotment; apportion; apportionment; assign; assignment; distribute; distribution;
分配方案 distribution plan;
分配房屋 allot dwelling houses;
分配工作 share out the work;
分配股份 allotment of shares;
分配經濟學 economics of distribution;
分配器 distributor;
~ 離心分配器 centrifuging distributor;
~ 流體分配器 fluid distributor;
~ 燃料分配器 fuel distributor;
~ 飼料分配器 feed distributor;
按比例分配 proportional allotment;
按需分配 distribute according to need; to each according to his needs;
材料分配 material allotment;
財富分配 distribution of wealth;
成本分配 cost apportionment;
重新分配 redistribution;
服從組織分配 accept the job assigned by the organization;
公平分配 equitable distribution;
機場分配 airfields assignments;
金額分配 allotment of money;
糧食分配 distribution of grain;
頻率分配 frequency allotment;
平均分配 fair division;
秋收分配 distribution after autumn harvest;
設備分配 facilities assignment;
收入分配 distribution of income;
收益分配 income apportionment;
税收分配 tax apportionment;

[分批] in batches; in turn;
分批交貨 deliver the goods in batches;
分批裝運 partial shipment;

[分票] dispatch tickets;

[分期] by instalment; by stages;
分期付款 by instalments; have an easy-payment plan; hire purchase; in instalments; instalment payment; instalment plan; on easy terms; on hire purchase; on the instalment plan; on time; pay by instaments; payment on deferred terms;
分期施用 split application;
分期實施 implement by stages;
分期貸款 installment credit;

[分歧] difference; divergence; gulf;
摒棄分歧 sink one's differences;
解決分歧 settle their differences;
調和分歧 mediate their differences;
消除分歧 iron out differences;
意見分歧 differences of opinion; divergence of views;
原則分歧 a difference in principle;
製造分歧 create dissension; sow discord;

[分清] distinguish; draw a clear distinction between; draw a clear line of demarcation between;
分清敵我 draw a clear distinction between ourselves and the enemy; draw a clearcut line between the enemy and ourselves; make a distinction between ourselves and the enemy;
分清敵友 distinguish between friend and enemy; know a friend from an enemy;
分清界限 draw a clear line of demarcation;
分清良莠 differentiate; distinguish;

separate the husk from the grain;
分清是非 differentiate between truth and falsehood; distinguish between right and wrong; distinguish right from wrong; draw a clear distinction between right and wrong;
分清主次 differentiate what is primary from what is secondary;
分不清 cannot distinguish; can't tell which is which;

[分區] partition; zonation; zoning;
農業分區 agricultural zoning;
生物氣候分區 bioclimatic zonation;

[分權] separation of powers;

[分散] decentralize; dispersal; disperse; dispersion; scatter; segregation;
分散村落 dispersed rural settlement;
分解代謝 catabolism;
分散光圈 circle of confusion;
分散劑 dispersant;
~ 化學油分散劑 chemical oil dispersant;
~ 無灰分散劑 ashless dispersant;
分散精力 diffuse one's energies;
分散力 dispersancy;
分散流 dispersion train;
分散模式 dispersion pattern;
分散扇 dispersion fan;
分散性 dispersivity;
~ 分散性系數 specific dispersivity;
~ 分子分散性 molecular dispersivity;
分散暈 dispersion halo;
分散注意力 divert one's attention;
東分西散 be scattered here and there; lie scattered; lying in different directions;
適應性分散 adaptive dispersion;
炭黑分散 carbon black dispersion;
原子分散 atomic dispersion;

[分色] separation;
分色負片 separation negative;
分色片 chromatic film;

[分身] spare time from one's main work to attend to sth else;
分身不暇 unable to be in two places at a time; unable to disengage oneself;

[分神] give some attention to;

[分手] be separated; break up; drift apart; part company; say good-bye to; split up with sb;

[分數] (1) grade; mark; score; (2) fraction; fractional number;
分數詞 fractional numeral;
標準分數 criterion score;
不可約分數 irreducible fraction;
代數分數 algebraic fraction;
帶分數 mixed fraction;
繁分數 complex fraction;
負分數 negative fraction;
高分數 high score;
好分數 good mark;
及格分數 pass mark;
既約分數 reduced fraction;
假分數 improper fraction;
克分子分數 molar fraction;
連分數 continued fraction;
~ 收斂連分數 convergent continued fraction;
~ 循環連分數 recurring continued fraction;
~ 有盡連分數 terminating continued fraction;
普通分數 common fraction; vulgar fraction;
原子分數 atomic fraction;
真分數 proper fraction;
正分數 positive fraction;

[分水界] water parting;

[分水嶺] (1) dividing crest; watershed; (2) line of demarcation; watershed;
分水嶺工業 watershed industry;
地面分水嶺 surface watershed;

[分説] defend oneself; explain matters;

[分送] distribute; send;

[分攤] divide pro rata; share;
分攤成本 overhead cost;
分攤費用 share the expenses;
成本分攤 cost absorption;
平均分攤 go halves;
損失分攤 loss apportionment;

[分庭抗禮] act independently and defiantly; be pitted against each other; be received as an equal; counterpose oneself to; make rival claims as an equal; match oneself with; meet as equals; pit one's wits against; stand up to sb as an equal;

[分頭] (1) separately; several; (2) hair partings; parted hair;
分頭進行 proceed each following one assignment; proceed separately on a common objective;
分頭做備準 get preparation individually;

[分腿] straddle;
分腿騰越 vault over with straddled legs;

[分文] single cent; single penny;
分文不給 refuse to give even a cash;
分文不取 do not accept a cent; free of charge; not a cash will be charged; not to accept a penny; not to take a single cent; refuse to take any payment; will not take a penny;
分文不受 refuse to take a cent;
分文不值 not worth a farthing; not worth a fig; not worth a pin; not worth a rush; not worth a straw;
不取分文 free of charge;
身無分文 broke to the wide; flat broke; not to have a bean; penniless; stone-broke; with empty pockets; without a bean; with a cash in one's pocket; without a penny in one's pocket;

[分析] analyze;
分析報告 analytic report;
分析法 analytic approach;
~比較分析法 method of comparison analysis;
~鏈狀分析法 chain analysis;
分析化學 analytical chemistry;
分析技術 analytical skills;
分析家 analyst;
~政治分析家 political analyst;
分析科學 analytic science;
分析論 analytics;
分析命題 analytic proposition;
分析能力 analytical ability;
分析器 analyzer;
~大氣分析器 atmosphere analyzer;
~光譜分析器 spectrum analyzer;
~曲線分析器 curve analyzer;
~失真分析器 distortion analyzer;
~網絡分析器 network analyzer;
~微分分析器 differential analyzer;
~諧波分析器 harmonic analyzer;
~序列分析器 sequential analyzer;
~噪音分析器 sonic noise analyzer;
~振動分析器 vibration analyzer;
~自動電路分析器 atutomic circuit analyzer;
~座標分析器 coordinate analyzer;
分析實相 analytic truth;
分析天平 analytic balance;
分析形式 analytic form;
分析形勢 size up a situation;
分析性 analyzability;
~可分析性 analyzability;
分析學 analytics;
分析語言 analytic language;
分析員 analyst;
~系統分析員 system analyst;
安全性分析 safety analysis;
比色分析 colorimetric analysis;
不定分析 indeterminate analysis;
參量分析 parametric analysis;
成分分析 componential analysis; compositional analysis;
吹管分析 blowpipe analysis;
錯誤分析 error analysis;
帶譜分析 band spectrum analysis;
電導分析 conductometric analysis;
電解分析 electrolytic analysis;
電解液分析 electrolyte analysis;
定量分析 quantitative analysis;
定性分析 qualitative analysis;
動態分析 dynamic analysis;
翻譯分析 translation analysis;
分配性分析 distributive analysis;
概率分析 probability analysis;
構象分析 conformational analysis;
故障分析 malfunction analysis;
光度分析 photometric analysis;
光譜分析 spectrum analysis;
毫分縷析 analyze minutely; make a detailed analysis;
回歸分析 regressive analysis;
極譜分析 polarographic analysis; polarography;
幾何分析 geometric analysis;
結構分析 structural analysis;
進行分析 conduct an analysis;
精闢分析 penetrating analysis;
句法分析 syntactic analysis;
句子分析 parsing;
可靠性分析 fail-safe analysis;
可行性分析 feasibility analysis;
客觀分析 objective analysis;
臨牀分析 clinical analysis;
流向圖分析 flow graph;
爐料分析 burden analysis;
邏輯分析 logical analysis;
毛利分析 gross profit analysis;
疲勞分析 fatigue analysis;
氣候分析 climatological analysis;
氣體分析 gas analysis;
氣象分析 meteorological analysis;
器械分析 instrumental analysis;

前向誤差分析 forward error analysis;
容量分析 volumetric analysis;
熔池分析 bath analysis;
色譜分析 chromatographic analysis; chromatography;
深入細緻的分析 in-depth and careful analysis;
收支分析 income-expenditure analysis;
輸入分析 input analysis;
數學分析 mathematical analysis;
速度分析 velocity analysis;
條分縷析 analyze point by point; bring up each point in order; detailed presentation; make a careful and detailed analysis;
聽覺分析 auditory analysis;
通量分析 flux analysis;
投資分析 investment analysis;
圖樣分析 pattern analysis;
微量分析 microanalysis;
~ 微量分析器 microanalyzer;
電子探針微量分析器 electron probe microanalyzer;
~ 半微量分析 semimicroanalysis;
~ 超微量分析 supermicroanalysis;
~ 電子探針微量分析 electroprobe microanalysis;
~ 核微量分析 nuclear microanalysis;
無機分析 inorganic analysis;
系統分析 circuit analysis;
相關分析 correlation analysis;
信息流分析 information flow analysis;
要素分析 factor analysis;
陰極分析 cathode analysis;
熒光分析 fluorescence analysis;
有機分析 organic analysis;
語法分析 grammatical analysis;
元素分析 elemental analysis; elementary analysis;
整體分析 global analysis;
重量分析 gravimetric analysis;

[分享] have a share in; partake of; share; sharing;
分享經濟 share economy;
分享利潤 participate in the profits; share in profits;
分享榮華 share sb's wealth and splendour;
利潤分享 profit sharing;
平均分享 share and share alike;
權力分享 power sharing;
時間分享 time sharing;

[分銷] distribute;
分銷店 retail shop;
分銷商 distributor; distributorship;

[分曉] (1) outcome; solution; (2) understand clearly; (3) reason;
見分曉 arrive at final results; clear up; know the outcome;
~ 此事未見分曉 the outcome of the matter is still uncertain;
~ 最後才見分曉 be down to the wire; come down to the wire; go down to the wire;
直到最後才見分曉 it's not over until it's over; it's not over until the fat lady sings;
問個分曉 inquire about and get to the bottom of a matter;

[分校] branch campus;

[分心] (1) distract one's attention; divert one's attention; (2) claim attention;

[分野] dividing line;

[分陰] a moment;
惜分陰 careful not to waste even a moment; harness one's time;

[分憂] help sb to get over a difficulty; share sb's cares and burdens;
分憂代勞 share sb's sorrow and toil; share sb's worry and relieve him of work;
分憂共患 share sb's sorrows and misfortunes;
分憂解愁 relieve sb of the daily worries; share and lessen worry;
分憂解勞 a trouble shared is a trouble halved;

[分贓] divide the spoils; share the booty; share the loot;
均勻分贓 split the loot evenly;

[分支] angle tee; branch; filiation; offtake; subfield;
分支電路 chain branching;

[分至] tropic;
分至月 tropical month;

[分鐘] minute;

[分子] (1) numerator; (2) molecule;
分子重排 molecular rearrangement;
分子力 molecular force;
分子量 molecular weight;
分子論 molecular theory;
分子生物學 molecular biology;
分子式 molecular formula;

分子說 molecular theory;
分子吸附 molecular adsorption;
分子鐘 molecular clock;
締合分子 associated molecule;
高分子 high polymer;
~生物高分子 biological high polymer;
壞分子 bad element; evildoer;
活化分子 activated molecule;
積極分子 active member; activist;
克分子 gram molecule;
兩性分子 amphiphathic molecule;
強硬分子 hard core;
中堅分子 hard core;

[分租] sublease; sublet;

[分組] (1) divide into groups; (2) grouping; subgroups;
分組討論 discussion in groups; group discussion;
分組學習 study in groups;

百分 (1) per cent; percent; (2) 100 marks;
報分 call the score;
比分 score;
邊分 (of hair) side parting;
春分 the Spring Equinox;
得分 score;
等分 divide from the middle; halve;
工分 workpoint;
公分 (1) centimeter; (2) gram;
瓜分 carve up; divide up; partition;
劃分 (1) differentiate; (2) divide;
積分 integral;
記分 (1) keep the score; record the points; (2) register a student's marks; (3) record workpoints;
滿分 full marks;
平分 divide equally; share and share alike;
評分 (1) give a mark; mark; (2) decide on workpoints;
秋分 the Autumn Equinox;
區分 differentiate; discriminate; distinguish;
篩分 screen; sieve;
十分 extremely; fully; utterly; very;
時分 time;
通分 reduction of fractions to a common denominator;
萬分 extremely; very much;
微分 differential;
微積分 calculus;
學分 credit;
夜分 midnight;
約分 reduce a fraction;

fen

【吩】 direct; instruct;

[吩咐] instruct; tell;
聽候吩咐 at sb's command;
照吩咐去辦吧 do as you are told;

卟吩 porphin;
噻吩 thiophene;

fen

【氛】 air; atmosphere; prevailing mood;

[氛圍] atmosphere;
學習氛圍 learning environment;

[氛邪] evil air;

氣氛 atmosphere;

fen

【芬】 (1) fragrance; sweet smell; (2) a surname;

[芬芳] fragrant; sweet-smelling;
芬芳撲鼻 a fragrance strikes the nostrils;
芬芳郁馥 frangrant and beautiful; rich in fragrance;

fen

【紛】 (1) confused; disorderly; tangled; (2) many and various; numerous; profuse;

[紛繁] numerous and complicated;
頭緒紛繁 have too many things to take care of;

[紛紛] (1) in succession; one after another; one following the other; (2) numerous and confused;
紛紛不一 contradictory and confused;
紛紛出籠 come out in large numbers; come out of one's hiding place; keep up a steady flow; quickly raise one's ugly heads; swarm out;
紛紛四散 disperse in all directions;
紛紛逃命 flee for their lives;
紛紛揚揚 drifting profusely and disorderly;
紛紛要求發言 all clamour to take the floor;
落葉紛紛 leaves fall in profusion;
議論紛紛 provoke much discussion;
雨雪紛紛 confused falling of rain and snow;

[紛亂] chaotic; helter-skelter; numerous and disorderly;

［紛擾］ confusion; turmoil;
紛擾不休 be confused without an end;
［紛如亂絲］ like a tangled skein;
［紛紜］ diverse and confused;
紛紜舛錯 confused and disordered;
紛紜雜沓 mixed and disorderly;
聚訟紛紜 a welter of conflicting opinions; argue back and forth and cannot agree; argue back and forth without coming to an agreement; at sixes and sevens; be at variance with each other; give rise to much discussion; in a great controversy; opinions are widely divided; opinions differ widely; there are many discussions and many different opinions;
人說紛紜 the people are at loggerheads;
頭緒紛紜 be confused with too many things to attend to;
眾說紛紜 accounts differ and opinions vary; opinions are widely divided; opinions vary; public opinions are divergent;
~ 眾說紛紜，莫衷一是 as opinions vary, no devision can be reached; as opinions vary, no unanimous conclusion can be drawn; there are so many contradictory views that it is difficult to decide which is right;
［紛爭］ dispute; wrangle;
紛爭不已 endless dispute; wrangle endlessly;
內部紛爭 internal dissensions;
引起紛爭 cause dissension;
［紛至沓來］ be deluged with; come as thick as hail; come in a throng; come thick and fast; roll in;

繽紛 in riotous profusion;
糾紛 dispute; issue;

fen
【棻】 a kind of wood burnt for perfume;

fen
【雰】 fog; mist;

雰雰 heavy;

fen²

fen
【汾】 a river in Shanxi;
［汾河］ Fenhe River in Shanxi;
［汾酒］ a kind of spirit distilled in Fengyang;
［汾陽］ Fengyang, in Shanxi;

fen
【枌】 variety of elm with small seeds and white bark;

fen
【羒】 white ram;

fen
【焚】 burn; set fire to;
［焚膏繼晷］ burn the midnight oil; turn a candle to lengthen the day—sit up and study late at night;
［焚化］ cremate; incinerate; incineration;
焚化廠 incineration plant;
焚化爐 incinerator;
［焚毀］ burn down; destroy by fire;
［焚琴煮鶴］ act alike a philistine; burn a lute for fuel and cook a crane for food—offend against good taste; burn famous string instrument for fuel and cook crane for meat—offence against culture; philistine behaviour; vandalism;
［焚燒］ burn; incineration; set on fire;
焚燒爐 incinerator;
~ 低火層焚燒爐 low incinerator;
~ 工業焚燒爐 industrial incinerator;
~ 雙室焚燒爐 incinerator;
多效焚燒 multiple-effect incineration;
就地焚燒 on-site incineration;
垃圾集中焚燒 central incineration;
［焚屍］ burn sb's body;
焚屍爐 cinerator; crematory;
焚屍滅跡 burn sb's body to cover up the crime; burn the corpse in order to destroy all the traces; burn the corpse to destroy the evidence; reduce the corpse to ashes in order to destroy all traces of one's crime;
焚屍揚灰 burn sb's corpse and scatter the ashes to the winds; destroy the corpse by fire and obliterate all the traces;
［焚書坑儒］ burn books and bury Confucian scholars alive; burn books and bury the literati in pit;
［焚屋驅鼠］ burn the house to rid it of mice—foolish acts;
［焚香］ burn incense;

F

焚香拜神 burn incense to worship god;
焚香禱祝 burn incense and ask for blessings;
焚香點燭 burn incense and light candles;
焚香結盟 burn incense and pledge an oath;
焚香膜拜 burn incense before; worship at temples; prayers and incense-burning;
焚香沐浴 take a bath and burn incense preparation of a slemn prayer;
焚香載道 line the roads and burn incense in honour of;
焚香祝禱 burn incense and pray; burn incense and say a prayer;

［焚舟］ burn one's boats;
洛河焚舟 burn one's boats; draw the sword and throw away the scabbard;

自焚 burn oneself;

fen

【棼】 (1) beams on the roof of a house; (2) a kind of linen; (3) confused; disarrayed; disordered;
［棼棼］ disheveled;
［棼亂］ in confusion;

fen

【賁】 great; large;
［賁鼓］ large drums;
［賁門］ the cardia;

fen

【墳】 (1) grave; mound; (2) big; great; large;
［墳場］ graveyard;
墳場裏唱戲—給鬼看 devilish behaviour; putting on a Chinese opera in a graveyard – for ghosts to watch;
［墳地］ cemetery; graveyard;
墳地裏吹口哨—自己給自己壯膽 whistling in a graveyard – emboldening oneself;
［墳墓］ grave; one's last home; one's long home;
自掘墳墓 bring ruin upon oneself; court death; dig one's own grave; draw ruin upon oneself; work for one's own destruction;
［墳頭］ grave; mound;
［墳址］ graveside;

上墳 visit a grave to honour the memory of the dead;
祖墳 ancestral grave;

fen

【蕡】 (1) seed of hemp; (2) plants with many fruit;

fen

【鼢】
［鼢鼠］ myospalax;

fen

【豶】 male livestock;

fen³

fen

【粉】 (1) powder; (2) noodles; (3) pink; (4) white wash;
［粉白黛綠］ beauty; fair sex; heavy makeup; ladies;
［粉筆］ chalk;
粉筆畫 chalk drawing; crayon drawing;
一點粉筆 a bit of chalk;
一根粉筆 a stick of chalk;
一枝粉筆 a piece of chalk;
［粉彩］ famille rose;
粉彩畫 pastel drawing;
［粉刺］ acne; comedo; pimple;
粉刺癌 comedo carcinoma;
粉刺痣 nevus comedonicus;
黑頭粉刺 blackhead; comedo;
開放性粉刺 open comedo;
［粉蝶］ white butterfly;
菜粉蝶 cabbage butterfly;
［粉坊］ mill for making vermicelli;
［粉盒］ compact powder box; powder box; powder case;
［粉紅］ pale red; pink;
粉紅色 pink;
~珍珠粉紅色 orient pink;
鋯鐵粉紅 iron-zirconium pink;
意大利粉紅 Italian pink;
［粉領］ pink-collar;
粉領工人 pink-collar worker;
粉領工作 pink-collar job;
粉領行業 pink-collar industry;
［粉瘤］ atherome; sebaceous;
［粉末］ flour; powder; smalls; stive;
合金粉末 alloy powder;
金屬粉末 metal powder;
球磨粉末 ball-milled powder;
一層粉末 a coat of powder;

F

~薄薄的一層粉末 a film of powder;

[粉皮] sheet jelly;

粉皮捲兒 steamed flour rolls;

[粉撲] powder puff;

[粉墻] (1) whitewash a wall; (2) plastered wall; whitewashed wall;

[粉身碎骨] be beaten till one's bones are broken; be crushed to powder; be crushed to pulp; be dashed to pieces; be hacked to pieces; be smashed to pieces; die the most cruel death; grind someone's bones to powder and make mincemeat of one's flesh; have one's body pounded to pieces and one's bones ground to powder; have one's body smashed to pieces; one's ones are ground to powder;

粉身碎骨，在所不惜 not to flinch even if one is threatened with destruction;

[粉飾] gloss over; prettify; sugar up; varnish; whitewash;

粉飾錯誤 whitewash mistakes;

粉飾門面 put up a facade; serve as a window-dressing; serve as signboards; top one's fruit; whitewash the appearance; window-dressing;

粉飾事實 varnish over the facts;

粉飾太平 a false peace; present a false appearance of peace and prosperity; pretend that everything is going well; put a good face;

粉飾現實 sugar up reality;

[粉刷] brush; paint; render; whitewash;

粉刷一新 take on a new look after whitewashing;

[粉絲] vermicelli;

[粉碎] (1) crush; shatter; smash; (2) broken into pieces; shiver; shred;

粉碎叛亂 crush out a rebellion;

粉碎器 disintegrator;

~棒式粉碎器 bar disintegrator;

~超聲粉碎器 ultrasonic disintegrator;

~離心粉碎器 centrifugal disintegrator;

~土塊粉碎器 clay disintegrator;

~植物粉碎器 vegetation disintegrator;

[粉條] flat-strip vermicelli;

焙粉 baking powder;

搽粉 powder;

傳粉 pollinate;

蛋粉 egg powder;

淀粉 amylum; starch;

發粉 baking powder;

骨粉 bone dust; bone meal;

胡椒粉 ground pepper powder;

花粉 pollen;

涼粉 grass jelly;

磷粉 phosphate powder;

米粉 (1) ground rice; rice flour; (2) rice-flour noodles;

麵粉 flour; wheat flour;

奶粉 milk powder; powdered milk;

藕粉 lotus root starch;

鉛粉 lead powder;

去污粉 cleanser;

撒粉 dust;

通心粉 macaroni;

五香粉 the powder of five spices;

洗衣粉 washing powder;

牙粉 tooth powder;

胭粉 rouge;

藥粉 medicinal powder;

銀粉 silver powder;

魚粉 fish meal;

皂粉 laundry soap; powdered soap; soap powder;

脂粉 cosmetics; rouge and powder;

fen⁴
fen

【分】 (1) component; (2) what is within one's rights or duty;

[分量] weight;

固有分量 proper component;

色度分量 chromaticity component;

他說的話很有分量 what he has said carried a lot of weight;

[分內] one's duty; one's job;

分內之事 a matter within one's duties;

[分所當為] one is duty-bound to do such things;

[分外] (1) all the better; all the more; especially; extremely; more than ever; particularly; (2) beyond one's duty; not one's duty; not one's job; outside the scope of one's duty;

分外高興 particularly happy;

分外香 especially fragrant;

分外妖嬈 grow more enchanting; more beautiful than ever;

分外有趣 extremely amusing;

分外之物 undue gain;

分外之想 second inordinate ambition;

[分子] element; member;

反動分子 reactionary element;

積極分子 active member;

落後分子 laggard;

先進分子 advanced element;

知識分子 intellectual;

安分 not go beyond one's bounds;

輩分 seniority in the family;

本分 one's duty;

才分 ability; gift; talent;

充分 abundant; ample; full;

處分 take disciplinary action against; punish; punishment;

非分 improper to one's status; overstepping one's bounds; presumptuous;

過分 go too far; overdo;

名分 person's status;

情分 mutual affection;

水分 (1) moisture content; (2) exaggeration;

天分 natural gift; special endowments; talent;

養分 nutrient;

應分 part of one's job;

逾分 excessive; over; undue;

緣分 luck by which people are brought together;

職分 (1) duty; (2) official post; position;

自分 estimate one's own ability or strength;

fen

【份】 (1) portion; share; (2) measure-word;

[份額] share;

最大的份額 the lion's share;

[份兒] (1) awesome; capable; cool; excellent; fine; good; skilful; (2) part; place; seat; (3) gap; room; space; (4) at the utmost; to the extent of;

份兒飯 set-dish meal;

[份子] one's share of expenses for a joint undertaking;

等份 an equally divided part of sth;

股份 (1) share; stock; (2) shares in a partnership;

年份 (1) particular year; (2) age; time;

全份 complete set;

省份 province;

月份 month;

fen

【忿】 indignant;

[忿忿] angry; furious; indignant;

忿忿不平 indignant and disturbed;

忿忿而去 go away burning with rage; go away in ill humour; leave in a state of great anger;

不忿 not give in to; refuse to accept as final; refuse to obey;

狷忿 irascible; quick-tempered;

fen

【憤】 anger; indignation; resentment;

[憤不欲生] so angry that one does not wish to live; tire of life at the extremity of indignation; would end life in a fit of bitterness;

[憤憤] angry; furious; indignant;

憤憤不樂 upset and displeased;

憤憤不平 feel aggrieved; indignant; nurse a grievance; resentful;

~感到憤憤不平 become indignant;

[憤恨] detest; indignantly resent;

[憤慨] indignation;

憤慨的 indignant;

表示憤慨 express one's indignation;

極為憤慨 indignant beyond measure;

[憤懣] depressed and discontented; resentful;

說出心中的憤懣 speak up one's resentment;

[憤怒] anger; blow hot coals; indignation; wrath;

遏制憤怒 master one's wrath;

激起憤怒 arouse anger;

滿心憤怒 in a towering rage;

掩飾憤怒 hide one's anger;

抑制憤怒 keep down one's wrath; repress one's wrath;

[憤然] angry; indignant;

憤然離去 leave in anger; shake the dust off one's feet; walk off in a huff;

憤然作色 cynical; detest the world and its ways; feel resentful and disgusted at the living reality of society;

[憤世嫉俗] destest the world and its ways; highly critical of society; misanthropic;

憤世疾俗的 cynical;

~憤世疾俗的人 cynic;

悲憤 grief and indignation; lament and resent an injustice;

發憤 make a determined effort;

怫憤 sadness kept to oneself;

公憤 popular anger; public indignation;

激憤 enraged; indignant; wrathful;
民憤 popular indignation; the people's wrath;
氣憤 furious; indignant;
攄憤 vent one's indignation;
洩憤 give vent to one's anger;
羞憤 ashamed and resentful;
悒憤 resent; unhappy with anger;
義憤 moral indignation; righteous indignation;
憂憤 worried and indignant;
幽憤 hidden resentment;
怨憤 indignant and hate;

fen

【奮】 (1) act vigorously; exert oneself; put forth energy; resolve to; (2) lift; raise; wave;

[奮臂高呼] raise one's hand and shout;

[奮不顧身] be so dauntless as to forget one's own safety; be so eager for the safety of others as to forget about one's own; dash ahead regardless of one's safely; defy personal danger; regardless of personal danger;

[奮鬥] fight; strive; struggle;
奮鬥到底 fight to the bitter end; nail one's colours to the mast;
奮鬥目標 the objective to fight for;
奮鬥終身 battle on to the end of one's days; dedicate one's life to the struggle of...; devote oneself to the cause of ... as long as life endures.; fight all one's life for; work and fight all one's life;

[奮發] exert oneself; rouse oneself;
奮發從事 direct one's efforts to;
奮發努力 put one's back to it; put one's back into sth;
奮發圖強 go all out to make the country strong; make efforts; rise in great vigour; strive to be strong; work hard for the prosperity of the country; work with stamina and diligence;
奮發有為 enthusaiatic and press on; resolve to do some great things;

[奮進] advance bravely;
逼人奮進 spur sb on to effort;

[奮力] do all one can; spare no effort;
奮力反抗 do all one can to resist;
奮力前進 spare no effort to advance; struggle along;
奮力圖存 keep one's head above water; put forth to maintain existence;
奮力掙扎 struggle with all one's might;
奮力自救 keep one's head above water; work out one's own salvation;

[奮袂] roll up one's sleeves for action;

[奮起] make a vigorous start; rise; rise up with ardour; rise with force and spirit;
奮起反抗 rise up in resistance;
奮起抗敵 rise against the enemy;
奮起行動 rouse oneself up to action;
奮起直追 catch up assiduously; do all one can to catch up; make a high resolve to catch up with; press ahead to overtake; press forward to catch up with; pull up with a supreme effort; rise in great vigour so as to catch up with; rise up in a bouce and try to catch up with; rise up in pursuit straightaway;
奮起自衛 rise in self-defence;

[奮勇] summon up all one's courage and energy;
奮勇當先 be brave and rush to the front; fight bravely in the van;
奮勇抵抗 put up a good fight;
奮勇前進 advance bravely; forge ahead courageously; forge valiantly ahead; march forward;
奮勇殺敵 fight the enemy bravely;
奮勇戰鬥 act a good part; put up a courageous fight;
奮勇直前 screw up one's courage and push forward;
自告奮勇 come forward of one's own accord to proffer; offer one's free service; offer oneself; offer to take the responsibility upon oneself; offer to undertake a task; volunteer for one special duty; volunteer one's services for; volunteer to do sth; willingly take the responsibility on himself;

[奮戰] fight bravely; work strenuously;
奮戰到底 fight to the bitter end; fight to the last ditch;
日夜奮戰 struggle hard day and night;
英勇奮戰 fight gallantly;

昂奮 buoyant; earnest; enthusiastic; exited; fervent; full of zest; in high spirits; zealous;
發奮 (1) exert oneself; work energetically; (2) make a determined effort; make a firm resolution;
感奮 feel indignant;
激奮 be roused to action;

F

亢奮 excited; stimulated;
勤奮 assiduous; diligent; industrious;
興奮 (1) excited (2) exciting; stimulating;
振奮 (1) brace oneself up; rouse oneself; (2) inspire; spur on; stimulate;

fen

【糞】 (1) droppings; dung; excrement; faeces; (2) apply manure; (3) clear away;
[糞便] dung; excrement and urine; faeces; night soil; ordure; ordure pellet;
糞便處理 fecal treatment;
[糞池] cesspit; cesspool; manure pit;
化糞池 septic tank;
[糞肥] manure;
[糞坑遮不住臭] it isn't always easy to hush up a scandal; you can't always keep word of a disgraceful story from spreading;
[糞桶] a honey bucket; a manure bucket; a night-soil bucket;
[糞土] dung and dirt; muck;
糞土之言 a talk of refuse; valueless talk;
糞土之墻不可圬 a wall of dirty earth will not receive a trowel — hard to bring up;
棄如糞土 cast away like dirt;

臭大糞 low-grade; no good; stupid;
大糞 human excrement; night soil;
倒糞 turn over a heap of manure;
黑糞 melaena;
撒糞 defecate; empty the bowels evacuate the bowels; loose bowels; move the bowels; relieve bowels; shit; take a shit;
胎糞 meconium;
一桶糞 a tub of dung;

fen

【鱝】 eagle ray;

feng¹

feng

【丰】 (1) buxom; good-looking; (2) appearance and carriage of a person;
[丰采] dashing appearance; good-looking;
[丰神] manner;
[丰韻] charming appearance or carriage; graceful poise;
[丰姿] agreeable manners;
丰姿綽約 charming manners of a lady;

從丰 give generously;

feng

【封】 (1) seal; (2) envelope;
[封閉] (1) close; close down; (2) seal off; seal up;
封閉的市場 closed market;
封閉機場 close an airport;
封閉經濟 closed economy;
封閉人口 closed population;
封閉式管理 closed management;
封閉系統 closed system;
封閉性詞類 close class;
封閉性搭配 closed collocation;
封閉性條件 closed condition;
封閉性系統 closed system;
[封話筒] quit the airwave;
[封建] (1) enfeoffment; (2) feudalism;
封建殘餘 feudal remnants;
封建色彩 mark of feudalism;
封建社會 feudal society;
封建意識 feudal ideology;
封建制度 feudal system; feudalism;
封建主義 feudalism;
半封建 semi-feudal;
頭腦封建 feudal-minded;
[封爵] raise to the nobility;
封爵加官 raise to the nobility and rise in rank;
[封口] (1) close; seal; (2) shut up;
封口機 sealer; seamer;
~多頭封口機 multistation seamer;
封口令 gagging order;
[封面] (1) title-page; (2) front-cover of a book; (3) cover; front cover;
封面故事 cover story;
封面女郎 cover girl;
設計封面 design a cover;
[封山] close hillside; seal a mountain pass;
封山育林 close hillside to fertilitate afforestation;
[封鎖] block; blockade; seal off;
封鎖邊境 close the border;
封鎖港口 blockade a port; close a port with blockage;
封鎖線 blockade line; cordon;
封鎖消息 block the passage of information;
打破封鎖 break a blockade;
海上封鎖 naval blockade;
解除封鎖 lift a blockade;

經濟封鎖 economic blockade;
實行封鎖 enforce a blockade;

[封套] cover; envelop; jacket;
硬紙封套 digipak;

[封條] paper-strip seal;

[封網] block;

[封信] seal up a letter;

[封住] seal; seal up;
封住嘴巴 gag one's mouth; one's lips are sealed; shut one's mouth; shut sb up; silence the voice of; stop sb mouth;

[封裝] capsulation; encapsulation;
封裝電路 packaged circuit;
玻璃封裝 glass encapsulation;
機械封裝 mechanical capsulation;
塑料封裝 plastic capsulation;
真空封裝 vacuum encapsulation;

[封阻] blockade; blockage;

[封嘴錢] hush money;

包封 seal a package;
標封 sealed with labels;
冰封 icebound;
冊封 confer titles of nobility on; invest with rank;
查封 close down; seal up;
塵封 be covered with dust; dust-laden;
護封 book jacket;
加封 confer another title on sb;
密封 (1) seal up; (2) seal airtight;
啟封 break the seal; open an envelope; unseal;
賞封 tip wrapped in red paper;
襲封 receive a hereditary rank;
喜封 tip given to sb on a happy occasion;
信封 envelope;
油封 oil seal;
雁封 letters; written messages;
蟻封 ant hill;
踰封 cross the national boundary;
原封 intact; with the seal unbroken;
追封 ennoble posthumously;
自封 (1) proclaim oneself; (2) confine oneself; isolate oneself;

feng

【風】 (1) wind; (2) put out to dry or air; (3) winnow; (4) custom; practice; style; (5) scene; view; (6) information; news;

[風雹雨澇] wind, hail, rain and flood－natural calamities;

[風暴] storm; tempest; windstorm;
風暴破壞 storm damage;
風暴中心 vortex;
不畏風暴 dare to face a storm;
大風暴 great storm;
頂住風暴 brave the storm; face the storm;
革命風暴 storm of revolution;
海上風暴 a storm at sea;
黑風暴 black buran; black storm;
平息風暴 lull a storm; quiet a storm;
熱帶風暴 tropical storm;
~強熱帶風暴 severe tropical storm;
~中等熱帶風暴 moderate tropical storm;
閃電風暴 electrical storm;
旋轉風暴 revolving storm;
陣陣風暴 succession of storms;
政治風暴 political storm;

[風波] (1) disorder; dispute; disturbance; storm in a teacup; trouble; (2) wave; wind wave;
風波迭起 disturbances come up repeatedly;
東風波 easterly wave;
平地起風波 a storm out of nowhere;
平息風波 pour oil on troubled waters;
平息一場風波 quell a disturbance;
西風波 westerly wave;
一場風波 a disturbance;

[風采] elegant appearance; elegant demeanour; graceful bearing;
風采不減當年 as good-looking as as ever;
風采動人 cut a fine figure;
風采依然 one's elegance remains as before;
風采韻秀 of a most refined and prepossessing appearance;

[風操] graceful bearing and upright and honest character;

[風潮] agitation; unrest;
大風潮 great storm;
鬧風潮 agitate a strike;
一場風潮 a storm;
~平息一場風潮 still a storm;

[風車] windwill;
玩具風車 pinwheel;

[風塵] (1) travel fatigue; (2) hardships or uncertainities in an unstable society;
風塵表物 one who rises above the common herd; one who rises above the wind and dust; one who rises from rank and file; one who transcends the

secular world;
風塵碌碌 busy with worldly affairs;
風塵女子 bachelor's wife; courtesan; cousin Betty; fancy girl; fancy lady; fancy woman; lady of easy virtue; lady of pleasure; lady of the evening; prostitute; sporting lady; street girl; woman amidst winds and dust; woman of pleasure; woman of the street; woman of the town;
風塵僕僕 be fatigued with the journey; be worn out by one's journey; be travel-worn and weary; busy with travelling; endure the hardships of a long journey; endure the hardships of travel; hard journey; look travel-stained; look travelweary; worn out by a long journey;
墮落風塵 become a prostitute;
淪落風塵 be driven to prostitution;
淪入風塵 fall into professions not socially respectable;
滿面風塵 travel-stained and weary;

[風馳電掣] as swift as an arrow; as swift as lightning; as swift as thought; as swift as the wind; be going at lightning speed; burn up the road; go at a lightning speed; go by like the wind; go like a bat out of hell; pass swiftly like the wind; strike swiftly like lightning; swift as the wind and quick as lightning;

[風吹] the wind blows;
風吹草低見牛羊 sheep and oxen can be seen from the bended grasses when the wind blows;
風吹草動 the grass bends as the wind blows – a metaphor for a slight stir or a trifling upset; the mere rustle of leaves in the wind;
~一有風吹草動 at the mere rustle of leaves in the wind; every time he smells danger; in times of stress; whenever some wind stirs the grass;
風吹草伏 the grass bends low in a puff of wind;
風吹浪打 be battered by a storm; be beaten by wind and waves; the wind blows and waves beat;
風吹墻頭草一兩邊倒 the wind blowing the grass atop a wall – wavering on both sides; fence-sitting; sit on the fence; straddle the fence;
風吹日曬 expose to the weather; weather-beaten;
風吹葉落 the wind blows and the leaves fall;
風吹雨打 be battered by the wind and the rain; be ruffled by the winds and drenched by the rain; expose to wind and rain;
風吹枝曳 when the wind blows, the branches sway;
一風吹 all cancelled; cancel the whole thing; dismiss altogether; scatter to the winds;

[風帶] wind belt;
赤道無風帶 doldrums; equatorial calms;
東風帶 easterly belt;
副熱帶無風帶 horse latitudes;
西風帶 westerly belt;

[風笛] bagpipes;

[風洞] air tunnel; tunnel;
放氣式風洞 blowdown tunnel;
高空模擬風洞 altitude wind tunnel;
環狀回流式風洞 annular wind tunnel;

[風度] (1) bearing; demeanour; (2) manners; (3) tolerance;
風度不凡 have an imposing appearance;
風度大方 have an easy manner;
風度迷人 charming in manner;
風度翩翩 be dapper in appearance; dashing; graceful bearing;
風度優雅 elegance of manner;
毫無風度 no style about one;
軍人風度 military bearing;
騎士風度 chevalier manner;
紳士風度 gentleman-like manner;
一種風度 a personal style of acting;

[風發] energetic;
踔厲風發 talk eloquently and knowledgeably;

[風帆] sail;
滑浪風帆 windsurfing;

[風格] form; manner; style; touch;
風格變化 stylistic variation;
風格變體 stylistic variety;
風格導演 auteur;
風格對等 stylistic equivalence;
風格改編 stylistic adaptation;
風格清雅 in an elegant style;
風格外加語 style disjunct;

風格學 stylistics;
~比較風格學 comparative stylistics;
風格意義 stylistic meaning;
風格轉換 style shift;
古典派風格 classic style;
建築風格 architectural style;
書法風格 calligraphic style;
西洋風格 western style;
藝術風格 artistic style;

[風骨] (1) moral courage; moral fibre; moral strength; sense of honour; strength of character; (2) vigour of style;

[風光] (1) scene; sight; view; (2)enjoy a luxury life; have fame; have status;
風光明媚 radiant and enchanting scene;
風光旖旎 charming sight; exquisite scenery; lovely scene;
本地風光 local scenery;
好風光 wonderful sight;
南國風光 southern scenery; typical southern scene;
如畫的風光 picturesque view;
山區風光 mountain scenery;
田園風光 rural scene; rustic scene;

[風寒] chill; cold; wind chill; wind-cold;
抵禦風寒 resistance to colds;
受了點風寒 nothing but a chill;

[風和] gentle breeze;
風和日麗 bright sunshine and gentle breeze; the breeze is balmy and the sun warm; the wind is mild and the sunshine is warm;
風和日暖 bright sunshine and gentle breeze; the wind blows gently and the sunshine is warm;
日麗風和 the sun is beautiful and the breeze pleasant; there is a warm sun and balmy breez; with warm sunshine and gentle breezes;

[風華] elegance and talent;
風華絕代 indescribably beautiful and striking; really a most unusual and individual beauty; unparalleled manner and deportment; unsurpassed beauty of a generation;
風華正茂 at life's full flowering; at the height of one's youth and vigour; in one's prime;

[風化] (1) decency; morals and manners; (2) efflorescence; (3) weathering;
化學風化 chemical weathering;
球狀風化 spherical weathering;
日曬風化 insolation weathering;
深層風化 deep-seated weathering;
生物風化 biological weathering;
同心風化 concentric weathering;
有傷風化 an offence against decency;

[風紀] conduct and discipline; discipline; morale;
風紀蕩然 moral standards have disappeared;

[風景] landscape; scenery;
風景點 scenic spot;
風景畫 landscape painting;
風景建築學 landscape architecture;
風景旅遊點 scenic tourist spot;
風景美學 aesthetics of landscape;
風景名勝區 scenic zone;
風景區 scenic area;
風景如畫 the scenery is as beautiful as a painting;
風景遊覽城市 tourist city;
風景遊覽區 tourist spot;
殺風景 a skeleton at the feast; a wet blanket; damper interest; do sth to spoil one's enthusiasm; kill joy; make dull; ruin happiness; spoil happiness; spoil the fun; spoil the sport;
煞風景 spoil the pleasure; throw a wet blanket;
~大煞風景 dampen the spirit; disappointing; frustrating; put a wet blanket on; sink the spirits of; spoil the fun; spoil the pleasure; take all the fun out of; throw a wet blanket over;

[風靜] the wind dies down;
風靜雪止 the wind has died down and the snow ceases to fall;
風靜雨止 the wind dies down and the rain stops;
風靜月明 the wind is hushed and the moon is bright;
風靜雲閒 there is neither wind nor clouds; there is no wind and the clouds stand still;
夜涼風靜 the night is cool and windless;

[風鏡] goggles;

[風浪] (1) storm; stormy waves; wind waves; (2) difficulties; hardship;
長風破浪 brave the wind and the waves; ride the wind and cleave the waves;
乘風破浪 brave the storm; brave the wind

and the waves; plough the waves; ride the waves; ride the wind and cleave the waves; sail through wind and waves;
風大浪急 waves whipped up by the wind roll turbulently;
風過浪平 after a storm comes a calm; the wind passes and the waves calm down;
風猛浪高 the wind is strong and the waves run high;
風平浪靜 a calm sea; a gentle breeze and calm waves; all is calm; all is tranquil without storms and waves; calm and tranquil; everything goes smoothly; in smooth water;
風恬浪靜 calm and tranquil; smooth; the wind has subsided and the waves have calmed down;
風嘯浪湧 the wind howls and the waves rise; the wind roars, waves wildly toss;
黑風惡浪 a sinister storm; an evil wind and storm;
驚風駭浪 fearful winds and dreadful waves;
久經風浪 have weathered many a storm;
掀風鼓浪 make trouble; raise a strom; stir up a turmoil; stir up an upheaval;
興風作浪 become active and cause trouble; cause unrest; create a nuisance; fan the flames of disorder; incite and create trouble; incite trouble and create confusion; make trouble; make waves; raise Ned; stir up disorder; stir up trouble;
斬風劈浪 speed through wind and waves;
戰風鬥浪 battle with wind and waves;

[風雷] tempest; wind and thunder;
風雷激蕩 a storm ranging in all its fury; tempestuous;
驚風走雷 the wind howls and thunder rumbles;

[風涼] cool;
風涼話 irresponsible and sarcastic remarks; sarcastic comments;
~說風涼話 make cool, sly criticisms; make irresponsible and carping comments; make sarcastic comments; talk like an unconcerned person;
風涼式 (of hairstyle) cool style;

[風流] (1) distinguished and admirable; (2) talented and romantic; (3) amorous; dissolute; loose;
風流才子 talented and romantic scholar;
風流佳事 romance between man and woman;
風流寡婦 merry widow;
風流年少 romantic young man;
風流人物 a romantic person; an original genius; truly great and noble-hearted men; truly great men;
風流儒雅 cultured, talented and refined;
風流藪澤 the mashy place of lewdness — brothels;
風流倜儻 casual and elegant bearing;
風流瀟灑 handsome and talented; graceful but not showy;
風流雲散 be blown apart by the wind and scattered like the clouds — separated and scattered; be dispersed and evaporated into thin air; go with the wind; scatter and dissolve like wind-swept clouds; scatter like clouds before the wind; vanish without a trace;
風流蘊藉 graceful but not showy; urbanely charming;
風流韻事 amorous affairs; love affair; romantic affair; romance;
風流罪過 blemishes;
放誕風流 reckless and dissipated in behaviour and speech;

[風馬牛不相及] as different as chalk and cheese; as like as an apple to an oyster; as like as chalk and cheese; be related to one another like an apple to an oyster; beside the point; beside the question; have no relevance whatsoever with each other; have nothing in common; totally unrelated; two different unrelated things; untirely unrelated;

[風帽] cowl;

[風貌] (1) style and features; (2) scene; view;

[風靡] fashionable; popular;
風靡全國 sweep the country;
風靡一時 all the rage; become fashionable for a time; popular for a time;

[風派] fence-sitter; opportunist; people who change readily; timeserver;
風派人物 fence-sitter; opportunist;

timeserver; weather cock;

[風氣] atmosphere; common practice; ethos; fashion; general mood;
不良風氣 unhealthy custom and practice;
道德風氣 moral tone;
社會風氣 current tendencies in society;
蔚成風氣 become a common practice; become fashionable; become the order of the day; grow into a general trend;
學習風氣 climate for learning;
學校風氣 school climate;

[風琴] organ;
風琴手 organist;
大風琴 great organ;
簧風琴 harmonium; reed organ;
手風琴 accordion;
~手風琴手 accordionist;
~手風琴演奏者 accordion player; accordionist;
~六角形手風琴 concertina;
手搖風琴 hurdy-gurdy;
~手搖風琴手 organ grinder;

[風清] the breeze is light;
風清氣爽 the breeze is light and the air is clear;
風清月朗 light breeze and a bright moon

[風情] amorous feelings; flirtatious expressions;
風情萬種 (of a woman) exceedingly fascinating and charming;
風情月債 love affairs between man and woman;
不解風情 do not understand the implications in love affair;
當地風情 local conditions and customs;
賣弄風情 flirt with sb; play the coquette;
~賣弄風情的女子 coquette;
熱帶風情 tropical customs;

[風趣] humorous; witty;
風趣橫生 sauced with wit;
風趣幽默 have a fine sense of humour;
很風趣 witty and humorous;
饒有風趣 rich incident; rich joke; full of wit and humour; highly amusing; very entertaining; witty;

[風日晴和] the weather is fine;

[風柔夜暖] the breeze is soft and the night warm;

[風騷] (1) literary excellence; (2) coquettish;
風騷的 tarty;

[風掃淡雲] the wind blows away the faint clouds from the sky;

[風色] how the wind blows;
風色佳麗 bright weather;
看風色 find out how the wind blows; see how things stand; see which way the wind blows;
善觀風色 quick to see which way the wind blows — very shrewd;

[風沙] sand blown by the wind;
風沙很大 it is windy and dusty;

[風扇] (1) electric fan; (2) blower; fan; ventilator;
風扇皮帶 fan belt;
氣運風扇 conveying fan;
托架風扇 bracket fan;
圓盤風扇 disk fan;

[風尚] bandwagon; prevailing custom;
時代風尚 the vogue of the day;
眼下的風尚 fashion of the moment;
一時的風尚 a passing vogue;
異國風尚 exotic fashion;

[風神軒舉] with a distinguished air;

[風聲] (1) sound of the wind; (2) news; rumours; talks;
風聲哀厲 the wind is wailing;
風聲很緊 the situation is getting tense;
風聲淒厲 the wind is wailing;
風聲鶴唳 apprehend danger in every sound; start at the mere rustle of leaves in the wind; the whining of the wind and the cry of cranes — a fleeing army's suspicion of danger at the slighest sound;
風聲鶴唳，草木皆兵 a slight movement in the grass or a gust of wind is enough to make the enemy jittery; be scared by the sigh of the wind or the cry of the cranes; be so panic-stricken as to be scared by the whistle of the wind or the rustle of a leaf; fear ambush at every tree and tuft of grass; fear hath a quick ear; imaginary fears; take the very rustle of a leaf and the very shadow of a tree for an enemy; the moan of the wind, the cry of the cranes, the rustle of the grass, all seem like the sound of an advancing army;
風聲如吼 the wind blows hard, making a roaring noise;
不透露風聲 button up one's lip;
放出風聲 let out news;

露風聲 leak information; let a word leak out;
聽到風聲 get wind of sth;
走漏風聲 leak information;

[風濕] rheumatism; wind-damp;
風濕病 rheumatism;
~ 關節風濕病 articular rheumatism;
假風濕病 pseudorheumatism;
類風濕病 rheumatoid disease;
~ 淋病性風濕病 gonorrheal rheumatism;
~ 炎性風濕病 inflammatory rheumatism;
風濕關節炎 rheumarthritis;
風濕熱 rheumatic fever;
風濕痛 rheumatalgia;
風濕性動脈炎 rheumatic arteritis;
風濕性肺炎 rheumatic pneumonia;
風濕性肌萎縮 rheumatic atrophy;
風濕性疾病 rheumatic disease;
風濕性水腫 rheumatismal oedema;
風濕性心包炎 rheumatic pericarditis;
風濕性心肌炎 rheumatic myocarditis;
風濕性心炎 rheumatic carditis;
風濕性心臟病 rheumatic heart disease;
風濕性主動脈炎 rheumatic aortitis;
風濕性紫癜 purpura rheumatica;
風濕疹 rheumatid;

[風勢] force of wind;
風勢加大 the wind gets up; the wind picks up;
風勢減弱 the wind dies down; the wind drops;
火借風勢 there arises a mighty wind and the fire goes rolling and blazing;
火仗風勢 fanned by the wind the fire burns furiously; the wind presses and the fire becomes fast and fierce;

[風樹興悲] the wind and tree give rise to grief – unable to care for parents when they were dead;

[風霜] hardships of a journey or of one's life;
風霜之苦 suffer much from wind and frost;
飽經風霜 endure all the hardship of exposure; have experienced the hardships of life; have experienced years of wind and frost; have gone through all hardships of life; have weathered many storms; weather-beaten;
經風傲霜 become hardened in the storm and stress; weather the wind and rost;
久經風霜 have experienced all sorts of hardships; have had one's fill of hardships; seasoned; weather-beaten;

[風水] fengshui; geomancy;
風水好 of high geomantic quality;
風水師 geomancer;
風水先生 geomancer;
看風水 practise geomancy;

[風俗] customs;
風俗畫 genre painting;
風俗習慣 customs and folkways; customs and habits; customs and mores; manners and customs; mores;
風俗喜劇 comedy of manners;
地方風俗 local customs;
古老風俗 old custom;
~ 保持古老風俗 keep up an old custom;
奇風異俗 exotic customs; strange customs;
十里不同風，百里不同俗 every country has its customs; so many countries, so many customs; the customs and habits of people differ in each locality; the customs of one place differ from those of another;
移風易俗 alter old customs and habits; bring about a change in morals and mores; change existing habits and customs; change the manners and customs; improve public morals; make changes in customs and traditions; transform customs and habits; transform established traditions and practices; transform social traditions; transformation of customs and habits;

[風速] wind speed;
風速測定 anemometry;
風速風向測定 anemometry;
風速計 anemometer;
~ 擺式風速計 pendulum anemometer;
~ 磁電風速計 magneto anemometer;
~ 風琴式風速計 eolian anemometer;
~ 激光風速計 laser anemometer;
~ 接觸性風速計 contact anemometer;
~ 偏轉風速計 deflection anemometer;
~ 熱線風速計 hot-wire anemometer;
~ 聲波風速計 sonic anemometer;
~ 壓板風速計 plate anemometer;
風速記錄儀 anemograph; anemometer;
風速圖 anemogram;
風速儀 anemoscope;

F

[風停潮落] the storm dies down and the tide runs out;

[風頭] (1) the trends of events; (2) the publicity one receives; (3) the way the wind blows;

風頭人物 a man of fashion;

風頭十足 in the centre of attention; very much in the limelight;

風頭主義 showing off; striving for the limelight;

避避風頭 lie low until sth blows over;

避風頭 dodge the brunt; lie low until the critical time is over;

避開風頭 stay away from trouble;

出風頭 be in the limelight; cut a dash; cut a smart figure; cut a swatch; hold the limelight; in the spotlight; push oneself forward; seek the limelight; show off; steal the limelight;

愛出風頭 be fond of the limelight; pushing; seek the limelight; swanky;

愛出風頭的人 limelight seeker;

~不要出風頭 don't push yourself forward;

~出盡風頭 steal the limelight;

~大出風頭 be in the limelight; cut a dashing figure; cut quite a figure; enjoy great popularity go into headlines; make a great figure; make a hit;

~到處出風頭 always thrust oneself forward;

~好出風頭 fond of publicity; fond of the limelight;

看風頭 find out how the wind blows; see how things stand; see which way the wind blows;

~搶出風頭 try to outshine others; walk off with;

~喜歡出風頭 like to be in the limelight; like to be the centre of attention; seek the limelight; thirsty for publicity;

~想出風頭 seek publicity;

搶人風頭 steal sb's thunder; steal the limelight; steal the scene; steal the show;

[風土] natural conditions and social customs of a place;

風土人情 local customs and practices; local manners and feelings;

[風味] local colour; local flavour; special flavour;

風味菜 local delicacies; typical local dishes;

風味小吃 local flavour snacks;

~品嚐風味小吃 taste the food of local taste;

本地風味 native flavour;

別有風味 have a distinctive flavour;

地方風味 local cuisine;

家鄉風味 one's native flavour;

[風聞] get wind of; learn through hearsay;

風聞其事 get wind of the affair; hear the affair by rumour; learn the matter through hearsay;

[風物] scenery;

[風險] danger; hazard; risk;

風險報酬 risk premium; risk reward;

風險抵押承包 risk mortgage contract;

風險分擔 risk sharing;

風險管理 risk management;

風險合同 risk contract;

風險很大 the stakes are high;

風險基金 risk fund;

風險評審法 venture evaluation and review technique;

風險企業 risk enterprise;

風險認可 risk acceptance;

風險社會 risk society;

風險收入 risk income;

風險特徵 risk features;

風險投資 risk investment; venture capital;

風險轉移 passing of the risk;

避免風險 avoid a risk;

從屬風險 attendant risks;

擔風險 face danger; run risks; take the risk of;

~不肯擔風險 take no risks;

~不怕擔風險 always ready to face any risks;

~準備擔風險 be prepared to run risks;

低風險 low-risk;

~低風險投資 low-risk investment;

甘冒風險 stick one's chin out; willing to take risks;

高風險 high-risk;

~高風險投資 high-risk investgment;

構成風險 pose a risk;

降低風險 minimize a risk; reduce a risk;

冒風險 run a risk; run risks;

難以預測的風險 scarcely predictable dangers;

潛在風險 potential risk;

消除風險 eliminate risk;
增加風險 increase a risk;
組合風險 portfolio risk;

［風箱］ bellows;
風箱拉手 bellows handle;

［風向］ (1) wind direction; (2) turn of events;
風向變化 wind change;
風向改變 the wind changes;
風向計 registering weather vane;
風向儀 anemoscope;
觀察風向 find out how the wind blows; find out which way the wind blows; see how the gander hops; see how the land lies; see which way the cat jumps; wait for the cat to jump;
一羽示風向，一草示水流 a little straws shows which way the wind blows;

［風信子］ hyacinth;

［風行］ in fashion; in vogue; popular;
風行草偃 where the wind passes, the grass bends — the inferiors imitate the superiors;
風行一時 all the fashion; all the go; all the rage for a time; all the vogue; become a fad of the time; in fashion for a time; in vogue for a time; popular for a while;
風行於世 popular among the people;
重新風行 regain its vogue;
開始風行 come into fashion; grow into fashion;
雷厲風行 vigorously and speedily; with thunder-like violence and wind-like swiftness;

［風雪］ snowstorm; wind and storm;
風雪交加 a raging snowstorm; a snowstorm is raging;
風雪載途 whirling snow swept over the road;
暴風雪 blizzard;
大風雪 driving snow;
風花雪月 romantic themes;
風吼雪舞 the howling wind whiles snowflakes through the air;
冒着風雪 brave the wind and storm;

［風雅］ (1) grace; literary pursuit; (2) elegant; refined;
附庸風雅 hang on to the lips of men of letters;
舉止風雅 have refined manners;

［風煙滾滾］ fumes billow in the wind;

［風搖岸柳］ the wind sways willows on the banks;

［風謠］ folk rhyme; folk song;

［風衣］ wind coat;

［風雨］ the elements; trials and hardships; wind and rain;
風雨不更 no alternation on account of the weather;
風雨大作 the storm bursts in all its fury; the storm rages;
風雨改期 postpone due to the weather;
風雨晦冥 maintain one's moral integrity in adverse conditions; obscured by wind and rain; turbulent and dark society;
風雨雞鳴 fowls crow in the wind and rain; say what others dare not say;
風雨交加 it's raining and blowing hard; it's wet and windy; rain and wind come simultaneously; wind and rain coming at one and the same time;
風雨交作 a storm is raging; a storm of wind and rain; the wind howls and the rain beats down;
風雨連綿 a succession of storms; rain continuously;
風雨飄搖 beffeted by wind and rain; fluttering about in the storm; precarious; swaying in the midst of a raging storm; tossing; tottering; unstable;
風雨淒淒 chilly wind and rain; cold, cold are the wind and the rain; windy and rainy;
風雨橋 wind and rain bridge;
風雨如晦 it blows and rains like a dark night;
風雨送春 wind and rain escort spring's departure;
風雨同舟 cast one's lot with; go through storm and stress together; in the same boat; stand together through storm and stress — share a common fate; stand together through thick and thin;
風雨無阻 in all weathers; rain or shine; regardless of wind or rain; wet or fine;
風雨瀟瀟 the whistling of wind and pattering of rain;
風雨衣 mackintosh;
風雨欲來 a storm is brewing; troubles are coming;

飽經風雨 one's face furrowed by rain and wind;
蔽風避雨 shelter from the wind and rain;
蔽風雨 shelter from the wind and rain;
風大雨狂 the wind is high and the rain pours down;
風風雨雨 disturbances; rumours;
風鬟雨鬢 the wind blowing the hair knotted on the top of the head and the rain wetting the hair puffed out at the side — a distressed appearance of a woman;
風裏來，雨裏去 brave the weather; carry out one's task even in the teeth of wind and rain; come in the wind and go in the rain; through wind and rain;
風猛雨驟 the wind blows hard and the rain comes down in sheets;
風調雨順 favourable weather; good weather for the crops; propitious weather; seasonable weather; the wind and rain come in their time; timely wind and rain;
風停雨歇 the rain subsides and the wind dies down; the wind dies down and the rain stops falling;
風蕭雨淅 wind is rustling and raindrops pattering;
風止雨息 the wind has subsided and the rain stopped;
呼風喚雨 call for wind and rain — a magic; call the winds and summon the rains; call winds and cry out for rains;
喚風呼雨 call for wind and rain — a magic; call the winds and summon the rains;
箕風畢雨 everybody has his own taste; there is no accounting for tastes;
急風暴雨 a strong gale and a torrential downpour; a sudden rainstorm; hurricane; tempest; violent storms;
幾番風雨 the devastation of a few storms and gusts;
經風雨，見世面 face the world and brave the storm; see life and stand its tests;
苦風淒雨 a nipping wing and chilly rain; bitter winds and dull rain;
滿城風雨 be widely reported; become the gossip of the town; become the talk of the town; cause a big scandal; create a tremendous sensation; flood the city; give rise to a big scandal; like a storm over the whole city; raise a colossal uproar; storm the whole city; the talk of the town;
~鬧得滿城風雨 create a sensation;
沐雨櫛風 be washed by the rains and combed by the winds; rush with one's work; toil and trouble; toil constantly under the exposure to the weather; travel despite wind and rain; work very hard regardless of weather;
耐風雨 weather proof;
十風五雨 different categories of rainfall; seasonable rains and moderate winds;
五風十雨 different categories of rainfall intensity and wind scales; favourable weather for the crops;
腥風血雨 a foul wind and a rain of blood — reign of terror; winds carrying an offensive smell of blood;
雨集風馳 heavy downpour and strong wind;
雨沐風餐 toil rain or shine;
雨驟風狂 the wind blows hard and the rain comes down in sheets;
最難風雨故人來 a friend in need is a friend indeed;

[風浴] wind bath;

[風源] the source of evil influence; the source of trouble;

[風月] (1) wind and moon; (2) scene; scenery; view; (3) love affairs; romance; romantic affairs;
風月清幽 the wind and the moon happen to be in such a state as to give one a feeling of ease and quietude;
風月無邊 the wonders of natural beauty are boundless;
嘲風弄月 sport with the wind and play with the moon — seek pleasure;
擔風袖月 travel in the open; with the wind on one's back and the moonlight in one's sleeves;
光風霽月 benign and open-hearted; open and aboveboard;
批風抹月 sing in praise of the beauty of nature;
哨風傲月 whistling and swaggering in breeze and moonlight;
笑遨風月 enjoy the breeze and the moonlight; revel in the breezy moonlight;

笑風遨月 enjoy the breeze and moonlight;
吟風弄月 be devoted to the wind and the moon — write pastoral essay; sing of the moon and the wind — write sentimental verse;
祇談風月 speak all mirth and no matter;

[風雲] stormy situation; unstable situation; wind and cloud;
風雲變幻 a changeable situation; amidst the winds of change; constant change of events; rapid change; the winds and clouds chnge their colours; unexpected gathering of clouds;
~形勢風雲變幻 the situation is changeable;
風雲變色 a drastic change of a political situation;
風雲不測 a sudden change of fortune; unexpected misfortune;
風雲際會 emergence into prominence in times of crisis; the meeting of wind and clouds — riding the crest of fortune;
風雲緊急 it looks squally;
風雲人物 celebrity; influential man; man in the news; man of the moment; man of the hour; man of the day;
~當年的風雲人物 man of the year;
~當時的風雲人物 man of the moment;
風雲突變 a sudden burst of a storm; a sudden change in the situation; a sudden veer of wind and rain;
叱吒風雲 all-powerful; earthshaking; have nature at one's beck and call; have nature under one's thumb; ride the whirlwind; commanding the wind and the clouds; shaking heaven and earth;
風起雲湧 on a spectacular scale; rage like a storm; roll on with full force; spread like a storm;
風展雲開 the wind blows away the clouds in the sky;
際會風雲 riding on the crest of success;
天有不測風雲 a blustering night, a fair day; a storm may arise from a clear sky — sth unexpected may happen any time;
~天有不測風雲，人有旦夕禍福 fortune is fickle; human fortunes are unpredictable as the weather; in nature there are uneexpected storms and in life unpredictable vicissitudes; it is the unexpected that always happens; man's fate is as uncertain as the weather; nothing is so certain as the unexpected; storms gather without warning in nature, and bad luck befalls men overnight; sudden storms spring up in nature and men's fortunes may change overnight; the future is a sealed book; the weather and human life are both unpredictable;
月露風雲 the dew in the moonlight or clouds in the wind — vague and light literary composition;
雲淡風輕 the clouds are pale and the stars are without lustre;

[風韻] charm; graceful bearing;
風韻依舊 as charming as before; look still attractive; one's majesty and charm still remain;
風韻猶存 keep one's charm; still look attractive;

[風疹] nettle rash;

[風箏] kite;
風箏衝浪 kite surfing;
牀底下放風箏—不見起 flying kites underneath a bed — unable to make much progress;
一隻風箏 a kite;

[風緻] (1) charming appearance and behaviour; (2) charm and wit; special flavour;

[風姿] charm; graceful bearing;
風姿婀娜 graceful manner;
風姿娟秀 her deportment and air are refined and attractive — said of a beautiful woman;
風姿綽約 charming appearance and personality; charming in manner; graceful figure;

把風 keep watch; on the lookout;
暴風 (1) storm wind; (2) storm;
北風 north wind;
背風 leeward; on the lee side; out of the wind;
避風 take shelter from the wind; (2) stay away from trouble;
閶風 autumn winds;
廠風 factory atmosphere;
晨風 morning breeze;
趁風 while the wind blows;
成風 become a common practice; become the

order of the day;
抽風 (1) fall into convulsions; (2) draw in air with a kind of device;
吹風 (1) catch a chill; get in a draught; (2) dry with a blower; (3) let sb in on sth in advance;
春風 (1) spring breeze; (2) beaming with smiles;
大風 (1) fresh gale; (2) gale; strong wind;
擋風 keep off winds; keep winds away;
頂風 head wind;
東風 (1) east wind; (2) driving force of revolution;
兜風 (1) catch the wind; (2) go for a drive;
耳邊風 a matter of no concern; flit by like a breeze; go in at one ear and out at the other; like water off a duck's back;
耳風 hearsay;
防風 protect against the wind;
放風 (1) let in fresh air; (2) let prisoners out for exercise; (3) leak certain information; spread news;
焚風 foehn wind;
罡風 strong wind;
古風 (1) ancient customs; antiquities; (2) a form of pre-Tang poetry;
谷風 (1) east wind; (2) up-draft in a valley;
鼓風 blast air; blow;
刮風 have a storm;
颳大風 gale;
觀風 on the lookout; serve as a lookout;
海風 sea breeze; sea wind;
海陸風 land and sea breeze;
寒風 chill wind; cold wind;
穀風 valley breeze;
和風 moderate breeze; soft breeze;
湖風 lake breeze;
惠風 pretty breeze;
疾風 (1) gale; strong wind; (2) moderate gale;
季風 monsoon;
家風 family customary tradition, style of life, etc.;
接風 give a dinner for a visitor from afar;
驚風 infantile convulsions;
颶風 hurricane;
口風 one's intention as revealed in what one says;
狂風 (1) fierce wind; (2) whole gale;
冷風 negative comments spread behind sb's back;
烈風 strong gale;
臨風 (1) facing the wind; (2) with the wind;
漏風 (1) air leak; (2) speak indistinctly through having one or more front teeth missing; (3) leak out;
陸風 land breeze;
痲風 leprosy;
門風 family customary moral standards and way of life;
南風 south wind;
逆風 contrary wind; head wind;
披風 cloak;
屏風 screen;
強風 strong breeze;
輕風 light breeze;
清風 cool breeze; refreshing breeze;
秋風 autumn wind;
祛風 dispel the wind;
融雪風 snow eater;
柔風 gentle breeze;
軟風 light breeze;
山風 mountain breeze;
山谷風 mountain and valley breeze;
傷風 catch cold; have a cold;
上風 (1) windward; (2) advantage; superior position; upper hand;
世風 common practice of society; general mood of society;
順風 tail wind;
朔風 north wind;
台風 (1) stage manners; (2) typhoon;
痛風 gout;
透風 (1) let in air; ventilate; (2) dry in the air; (3) divulge a secret; leak;
土風 local custom;
頹風 degenerate practice;
歪風 evil wind; unhealthy trend;
望風 keep watch;
威風 power and prestige; domineering influence imposing; impressive;
微風 gentle breeze;
文風 style of writing;
無風 calm;
西風 west wind;
下風 (1) leeward; (2) disadvantageous position;
校風 school spirit;
信風 trade wind;
旋風 whirlwind;
學風 style of study;
巡風 keep watch;
炎風 northeast wind;
羊癲風 have an attack of epilepsy;
妖風 evil wind; noxious trend;
一股風 a blast of wind;
一級風 a force 1 wind;

一絲風 a breath of wind;
一陣風 a blast of wind; a gust of wind;
遺風 remains of a former dynasty;
義風 prevailing sense of justice;
陰風 (1) chilly winds; (2) evil winds; ill winds; sinister winds;
淫風 dissoluteness and debauchery that prevail; libidinous practices; wanton customs;
迎風 (1) face the wind; (2) down the wind; with the wind;
餘風 influence left by a person;
漲風 upward trend of prices;
招風 attract too much attention and invite trouble; catch the wind; look for trouble; provoke mischief;
著風 expose to wind;
遮風 shield from wind;
陣風 gust;
整風 rectification of incorrect style of work;
中風 have a stroke;
走風 become known; leak out; let out a secret;
作風 style; style of work; way;

feng
【峰】 (1) peak; summit; (2) peak-like thing;
［峰頂］ crest; summit;
［峰化］ peaking;
併聯峰化 shunt peaking;
串聯峰化 series peaking;
高頻峰化 high-frequency peaking;
視頻峰化 video peaking;
陰極峰化 cathode peaking;
［峰迴路轉］ the path winds along mountain ridges;
［峰巒］ ridges and peaks;
峰巒重疊 ridges and peaks rise one after another;
峰巒屏嶂 rounding ranges of hills;
千重峰巒，萬頃巨浪 cover a thousand perilous peaks, across a boundless expanse of seething waves;
［峰值］ peak;
峰值負載 peakload;
峰值論 peakology;
負載峰值 load peak;
黑色峰值 black peak;
截止峰值 cut-off peak;
吸收峰值 absorption peak;

鼻峰 bridge of the nose;
波峰 wave crest;
頂峰 (1) peak; summit; top; (2) height; peak; summit;
洪峰 flood peak;
極峰 polar front;
山峰 mountain peak;
上峰 higher authorities; upper echelon;
神峰 outstanding dignity;
險峰 perilous peak;
主峰 highest peak in a mountain range;

feng
【烽】 beacon;
［烽火］ (1) beacon-fire; (2) the flames of war;
烽火連連 continuous wars;
烽火連年 continuous wars for years;
烽火連天 flames of battle raging everywhere; the flames of war raging across the length and breath of the region;
烽火燎原 the flames of war spread far and wide;
烽火台 beacon tower;
［烽煙］ beacon; beacon-fire;
烽煙遍地 a beacon fire is found everywhere — in time of trouble;
烽煙滾滾 the flames of war are raging;
烽煙四起 a land beset by war; uprisings of war everywhere;
烽煙未熄 beacon fires are not yet extinguished; the war is still going on;

feng
【楓】 (1) maple; (2) Chinese sweet gum;
［楓樹］ maple;
［楓糖］ maple sugar;
［楓葉吐火］ maple leaves glow as red as fire;

椏楓 trident maple;

feng
【蜂】 (1) wasp; (2) bee; (3) in swarms;
［蜂草］ beeweed;
［蜂蠆］ wasp;
蜂蠆入懷，解衣去趕 if a wasp gets next to your skin, remove your coat to shake it off;
蜂蠆入懷，唯有解衣 when a wasp gets in one's bosom, one has to unfasten one's clothes;
［蜂巢］ beehive; honeycomb; nest;
［蜂蝶］ bees and butterflies;
蜂媒蝶使 the bee acts as a go-between and the butterfly as an agent;

狂蜂浪蝶 lascivious men;

[蜂糕] steamed sponge cake;

[蜂皇精] royal jelly;

[蜂聚] gather in swarms; swarm together;

[蜂蠟] beeswax;

[蜂蜜] honey;

蜂蜜拌紅糖—甜到底 honey mixed with brown sugar — thoroughly sweet;

蜂蜜加香油—又香又甜 honey plus sesame oil — both savory and sweet;

蜂蜜酒 mead;

~ 一杯蜂蜜酒 a glass of mead;

一滴蜂蜜 a blob of honey;

一罐蜂蜜 a jar of honey; a pot of honey;

[蜂鳴器] buzzer;

變調蜂鳴器 variable note buzzer;

測試蜂鳴器 test buzzer;

高鳴蜂鳴器 high-frequency buzzer;

警告蜂鳴器 warning buzzer;

[蜂目豺聲] the eyes of a wasp and the howl of a jackal—a fierce and wicked look; the eyes of a wasp and the voice of a wolf—ferocious look;

[蜂鳥] humming bird;

[蜂群] a cluster of bees; a swarm of bees;

[蜂王] (1) queen bee; (2) queen wasp;

[蜂窩] honeycomb;

[蜂箱] beehive; hive;

[蜂腰] a supple waist like a wasp

蜂腰削肩 have a supple waist like a wasp and round, gently sloping shoulders; have a supple wasplike waist and slender shoulders;

腰細如蜂 have a slender waist like a wasp;

[蜂擁] flock; swarm;

蜂擁而來 come in great numbers; come swarming; pour in; swarm forward;

蜂擁而起 rise up in swarms; like the bees rising in swarms;

蜂擁而前 rush forward in swarms; surge forward;

蜂擁而入 come pouring in through the door; crash in; stream in;

蜂擁而上 like bees pressing forward in swarms; rush on like a swarm of hornets;

蜂擁而至 come in great numbers; press forward in a crowd;

雌蜂 queen bee;

工蜂 worker bee;

胡蜂 hornet; wasp;

黃蜂 hornet; wasp;

姬蜂 ichneumon wasp;

馬蜂 hornet; wasp;

螞蜂 hornet; wasp;

蜜蜂 bee; honey-bee;

母蜂 queen bee;

樹蜂 wood wasp;

雄蜂 drone;

熊蜂 bumble bee;

養蜂 raise bees;

feng

【葑】 turnip rape;

feng

【瘋】 (1) bonkers; crackers; crazy; insane; mad; (2) spindle;

[瘋癲] crazy; insane; mad;

半瘋不癲 crazy;

瘋瘋顛顛 act like a lunatic; as daft as a brush; balmy on the crumpet; barmy on the crumpet; bats; batty; be mentally deranged; behave in a crazy manner; dotty; flighty; gesticulate wildly; go gaga; have a bee in one's bonnet; have a screw loose; have a screw missing; have bats in one's belfry; have rats in the garret; off one's crumpet; off one's head; out of one's head; out of one's senses; queer in one's garret; wrong in one's garret;

~ 有點瘋瘋癲癲 have a screw loose;

[瘋狗] mad dog; rabid dog;

[瘋話] made talk; nonsense; ravings;

狂人的瘋話 the ravings of a madman;

説瘋話 talk nonsense;

[瘋狂] (1) insane; madness; (2) frenzied; unbridled; wild abandon;

瘋狂的 crazed; demented; doolally; lunatic;

~ 瘋狂的人 lunatic;

~ 瘋狂的行為 lunatic behavior;

~ 瘋狂的咒罵 frenzied vilification;

瘋狂敵視 rabid hostility;

瘋狂反撲 a desperate counterattack; make a frenzied counterattack;

瘋狂掙扎 frenzied and desperate kicks;

近乎瘋狂 border on madness;

一時瘋狂 in a moment of madness;

[瘋牛] mad cow;

瘋牛症 mad cow disease;

［瘋人］ lunatic;

瘋人院 bedlam; bughouse; giggle factory; loony bin; lunatic asylum; madhouse;

［瘋癱］ paralysis;

［瘋子］ crackpot; crazy; crazy person; demented man; headcase; insane; lunatic; madling; madman; nutter; wacko; whacko;

胡言亂語的瘋子 raving lunatic;

女瘋子 madwoman;

十足的瘋子 absolute nutter;

一個瘋子 demented person;

白癜瘋 vitiligo;

發瘋 around the bend; become insane; drive sb crazy; go bonkers; go crazy; go mad; go nuts; go out of one's mind; inside oneself; lose one's mind; lose one's reason; lose one's senses; off one's head; off one's nut; out of one's mind; round the bend; round the twist;

酒瘋 silly behaviour of a drunkard;

麻瘋 leprosy;

撒瘋 (1) behave recklessly; (2) vent one's anger;

撒酒瘋 be drunk and act crazy; behave atrociously;

feng

【鋒】 (1) cutting edge of a sword; sharp point of a sword; (2) van; (3) front;

［鋒利］ (1) keen; sharp; (2) incisive; poignant; sharp;

鋒利潑辣 sharp and pungent;

如鋒之利，如椒之辣 as sharp as a razor and as hot as pepper;

［鋒芒］ (1) cutting edge; spearhead; (2) abilities; talent displayed;

鋒芒逼人 display one's talent in an agresive manner;

鋒芒初露 display one's talent for the first time;

鋒芒所向 the direction of an attack; the spearhead of; the target of attack;

鋒芒太露 fail to show restraint; show too much of one's ability;

鋒芒小試 display only a small part of one's talent;

鋒芒指向 direct the attack on; direct the sharp edge of struggle against; direct the spearhead against; focus the attack on;

不露鋒芒 able but modest; hide one's light under a bushel; refrain from showing one's ability;

初露鋒芒 display one's talent for the first time; make a first display of one's abilities;

挫其鋒芒 blunt the edge of one's advance;

［鋒面］ frontal surface;

鋒面霧 frontal fog;

［鋒線］ frontal line;

筆鋒 (1) tip of a writing brush; (2) vigorous of style in writing, stroke, touch;

衝鋒 assault; charge;

詞鋒 sharpness of one's tongue;

刀鋒 edge of a knife;

話鋒 thread of discourse; topic of conversation;

交鋒 cross swords; engage in a battle or contest;

冷鋒 cold front;

內鋒 inside forward;

暖鋒 warm front;

前鋒 (1) vanguard; (2) forward;

談鋒 thread of discourse;

先鋒 van; vanguard;

右鋒 right forward;

針鋒 point of a needle;

中鋒 centre; centre forward;

左鋒 left forward;

feng

【豐】 (1) abundant; plentiful; (2) great; (3) fine-looking; handsome; (4) a surname;

［豐碑］ monument; monumental work;

［豐采］ mien;

一瞻豐采 have a look at sb's beautiful appearance;

［豐產］ bumper crop; high yield;

豐產田 high yield plot;

［豐登］ bumper harvest;

豐登之年 prosperous year; year of abundance; year of abundant harvest;

［豐度］ abundance;

［豐而不肥］ plump without being fat;

［豐富］ (1) abundant; plentiful; rich; (2) enrich;

豐富的 copious;

豐富多彩 colourful; rich; show colour and variety; parti-coloured and variegated; rich and colourful; rich in variety; varied and interesting;

豐富多腔 rich in tunes;

豐富知識 enrich one's knowledge;
感情豐富 abundance of the heart;
學識豐富 a wealth of learning;
［豐厚］ (1) thick; (2) rich and generous;
［豐滿］ (1) plentiful; (2) full and round; full-grown; well-developed; well-endowed; well-equipped; well-heeled; well-loaded; well-stacked;
豐滿的身段 plump figure;
豐滿的體形 well-shaped body;
豐滿健美的 buxom;
體態豐滿 have a well filled-out figure;
羽毛豐滿 full-fledged;
［豐茂］ lush; luxuriant;
［豐美］ lush;
［豐年］ abundant year; bumper harvest year; bumper year; good year; year of abundance;
雪兆豐年 a snowfall is an omen of an abundant year;
［豐沛］ plentiful;
水源豐沛 plenty of water supply;
雨水豐沛 have plenty of rain;
［豐取刻與］ take a lot and give away little;
［豐饒］ rich and fertile;
［豐盛］ bumper; rich; sumptuous;
［豐收］ abundant harvest; bumper harvest;
豐收在望 a bumper harvest is anticipated; a good harvest is in sight; give promise of a bumper harvest;
大豐收 bumper crop; bumper harvest;
喜獲豐收 reap a bumper harvest happily;
預期豐收 anticipate a bumper harvest;
［豐碩］ plentiful and substantial;
豐碩成果 fruitful results; great successes; rich fruits;
［豐儀］ elegant demeanour;
［豐盈］ (1) have a full figure; (2) plentiful;
體態豐盈 have a full figure;
衣食豐盈 have plenty to eat and wear;
［豐腴］ full and round; have a full figure; well-developed;
［豐裕］ in plenty; well provided for;
豐裕社會 affluent society;
［豐足］ abundant; plentiful;

feng
【灃】 a river in Shaanxi;
［灃水］ Fengshui River in Shaanxi;

feng
【酆】 (1) capital of the Zhou Dynasty under Emperor Zhou Wenhuang 周文王；

feng
【蠭】 bee; wasp;
［蠭目豺聲］ eyes of a wasp and the voice of a wolf; ferocious-looking;

feng²

feng
【逢】 (1) come upon; meet; (2) a surname;
［逢場作戲］ act according to circumstance; along for the ride; find amusement when the occasion arises; join in for the fun of it; join in the fun when there is a chance; seize a chance where there is merrymaking; want only a little excitement occasionally;
［逢集］ market day;
［逢人］ meet with others;
逢人但說三分話，莫把真心一鍋端 think before you speak and then talk with reservation;
逢人且說三分話，未可全拋一片心 all truths are not to be told; all truths must not be told at all times;
逢人說項 praise a person before everybody; publish abroad a person's good acts; tell everybody of a person's virtue;
［逢迎］ curry favour with; fawn on; make up to;
逢迎巴結 bootlick; suck; suck up to sb;
逢迎阿諛 bootlick; dance attendance on; flatter and toady;
逢迎感載 bootlick; fawn on and servilely thank;
逢迎拍馬 unctuous;
逢迎上司 make up to one's senior office;
百般逢迎 bend every effort to please sb;
揣合逢迎 try by tricks to find favour; try by various tricks to find favour with;

重逢 have a reunion; meet again;
每逢 on every occasion; when;
遭逢 come across; encounter; meet with;

feng
【馮】 a surname;

feng
【縫】 sew; stitch;
［縫補］ darn; darning; mend; sew and mend;

F

縫補漿洗 mend and wash one's clothes;
縫補衣服 mend clothes;
縫補針 darning needle;
縫縫補補 make and mend; sew up;

[縫兒] gap;
鑽頭覓縫兒 look for profit by hook or by crook;

[縫合] lacing; seaming; sew up; suture;
縫合創口 sew up the wound; suture;
縫合裂縫 sew up a crip;
縫合起來 unite by a seam;
縫合切口 sew up the incision;
縫合傷口 sew up a wound; suture a wound;

[縫口] seam;
拆開縫口 undo a seam;
扯裂縫口 rip up the seams;

[縫連] mend;
縫連補綴 mend and darn;
縫縫連連 sewing and mending;

[縫紉] needlework; sew; stitch; tailor;
縫紉工 stitcher;
縫紉活 stitching;
縫紉機 sewing machine;
縫紉女工 needlewoman;
縫紉業 needle trade;

[縫衣針] sewing needle;

拔縫 come apart at the seam;
包縫 wrapseam;
裁縫 dressmaker; tailor;
齒縫 embrasure;
骨縫 sutura;
銲縫 seam; weld;
門縫 crack in the door;
瞇縫 narrow;
彌縫 gloss over faults; plug up holes;
拼縫 piece;
一道縫 a crevice;
窄縫 narrow slit;

feng³
feng

【唪】 chant; recite;

[唪經] chant liturgies; recite scriptures;

feng⁴
feng

【奉】 (1) dedicate; give with respect; present; (2) receive; (3) believe in; (4) esteem; respect; (5) attend to; serve; wait upon; (6) entrust; (7) a surname;

[奉承] adulate; bow and scrape; fawn upon; flatter; lick the feet of sb; toady;
奉承話 blarney;
奉承拍馬 apple-polish; bow the scrape; cajole sb with flattering words; kiss the hem of sb's garment; tickle sb's ears;
奉承上司 play up to one's superiors;
奉承討好 fawn upon sb; flatter; lick the feet of sb; toady;
百般奉承 flatter sedulously; sedulous flattery; servile flattery; tirelessly fawn upon;
諂媚奉承 stoop to flattery;
阿諛奉承 act the yes-man; butter sb; butter up; compliment unduly; curry favour with sb; dance attendance on; eat sb's toads; fawn on sb; flatter and cajole; flatter and toady; flattery; ingratiate oneself into sb's favour; ingratiate oneself with sb; lay it on thick; make much of; make up to; oil one's tongue; polish the apple; praise insincerely in order to please another's vanity; stoop to flattery; tickle sb's ears; toady; try to get sb's favour by flattery;
互相奉承 backslapping;
屈意奉承 studious to please;
一番奉承 a dose of flattery;

[奉告] inform; let sb know;
無可奉告 no comment;

[奉公] act for public interests;
奉公守法 carry out official duties and observe the laws; conscientious and law-abiding; dutiful and law-abiding; just and respect the law; respect justice and abide by the laws;
潔己奉公 clean oneself and perform a duty;
克己奉公 put the interest of the public above one's own;

[奉還] return sth with thanks;

[奉令承教] obey commands and observe instructions;

[奉命] act under orders; receive orders;
奉命出發 receive orders to set off;
奉命而來 come with a command from sb;
奉命唯謹 obey orders scrupulously; receive orders respectfully;

奉命行動 act pursuant to the orders;

[奉陪] keep sb company;

奉陪到底 keep sb company to the end; keep sb company and fight to the finish; take on sb to the end; take sb on right to very end;

恕不奉陪 excuse me for not keeping you company; sorry cannot keep one company;

恕未奉陪 forgive me for not having accompanied you;

[奉勸] admonish; advise; give a piece of advice;

[奉觴] offer;

奉觴進酒 offer gifts of wine;

奉觴上壽 drink a toast of longevity;

[奉上] have the honour to send;

雙手奉上 present respectfully with both hands;

[奉送] give away free; offer as a gift;

奉湯送藥 dedicate oneself with touching devotion to nurse one's sick parent;

[奉為] hold up as; look upon as; regard sth as; value;

奉為典範 look upon as a model;

奉為圭臬 hold up as a model; look up to as the standard; take sth as the pattern;

奉為經典 regard sth as canons;

奉為楷模 hold up as a model; look upon sth as a pattern; regard sth as an example;

奉為至寶 value highly;

[奉獻] offer as a tribute; present with all respect;

奉獻精神 the spirit of dedication;

[奉行] pursue a policy of;

奉行不怠 carry out without negligence;

奉行故事 act in accordance with practices and rules; follow established practice mechanically; follow the old routine;

[奉養] support and wait upon;

[奉趙不誤] return a borrowed thing without delay;

朝奉 pawnbroker; the rich;

崇奉 believe in; worship;

供奉 (1) piously worship; (2) offer respectfully;

敬奉 (1) piously worship; (2) offer respectfully;

趨奉 fawn on; toady to;

侍奉 attend upon; serve; wait upon;

祀奉 worship;

信奉 (1) believe in and worship; (2) believe and pursue;

自奉 provide the necessities of life for oneself;

遵奉 obey; observe;

feng

【風】 (1) announce; make known; (2) ridicule; satirize; (3) blow;

feng

【俸】 (1) pay; salary; (2) a surname;

[俸祿] official's salary;

薪俸 pay; salary;

feng

【鳳】 (1) phoenix; (2) a surname;

[鳳冠霞帔] a chaplet and official robes; phoenix coronet and robes of rank; the headgear and dress;

[鳳凰] Arabic bird; phoenix;

鳳凰來儀 a phoenix appears at court — an auspicious omen; a phoenix has been seen to bow; the phoenix has appeared;

鳳凰於飛 conjugal harmony; the male and female phoenix flying together — conjugal felicity; the pair fly together happily; the two phoenixes fly side by side — a wedding compliment;

鳳凰佔枝 the phoenix perches on a high branch;

[鳳梨] pineapple;

[鳳麟] phoenixes and unicorns;

鳳飛麟散 there are no wise men in the government;

鳳毛麟角 a black swan; an extraordinary and unusually excellent person; as rare as hen's teeth; as scarce as hen's teeth; phoenix feathers and unicorn horns; rare; rare and precious things;

[鳳毛濟美] complete the beauty of the plumage of the phoenix — said of an officer who has a worthy son; rare and precious things or persons;

[鳳尾魚] anchovy;

鸞鳳 husband and wife;

feng

【諷】 (1) mock; satirize; (2) chant; intone;

[諷刺] make a crack; mock; satirize;

F

諷刺詩 satirical poetry;
諷刺文 satire;
~諷刺文學 satire;
諷刺小品 satirical essay;
諷刺小說 satirica;
諷刺作家 caricaturist; satirist;
害怕諷刺 fear sarcasm;
莫大諷刺 truly ironical;
戲劇性諷刺 dramatic irony;

[諷誦] read with intonation and expression;
[諷喻] allegory; parable;

嘲諷 sneer at; taunt;
譏諷 ridicule; satirize;

feng

【縫】 (1) seam; (2) crack; crevice;
[縫隙] chink; crack; cranny; crevice; slit;
接收縫隙 receiving slit;
平行縫隙 parallel slit;
聲縫隙 sound slit;

拔縫 crack;
焊縫 weld line; welding seam;
夾縫 narrow space between two adjacent things; crack; crevice;
褲縫 seams of a trouser leg;
裂縫 crack; fissure; rift;
門縫 crack between a door and its frame;
騎縫 junction of the edges of two sheets of paper;
牙縫 crevice between teeth;

fo²
fo

【佛】 (1) Buddha; (2) Buddhism; (3) statue of the Buddha;
[佛法] (1) Buddhist dharma; Buddhist doctrines; (2) power of the Buddha;
佛法無邊 the powers of the Buddha are unlimited;
皈依佛法 follow the laws of Buddha;
[佛腳] Buddha's feet;
急來抱佛腳 ask for help at the last moment; clasp Buddha's feet when in trouble — seek help at the last moment; do nothing until the last minute; embrace Buddha's legs when in urgent need; make a frantic last-minute effort; seek help in time of emergency; the chamber of sickness is the chapel of devotion;
急時抱佛腳 pray to gods only in extremity; seek help when it is very late;
[佛教] Buddhism;
佛教徒 Buddhist;
佛教學 Buddhology;
大乘佛教 Mahayana Buddhism;
小乘佛教 Hinayana Buddhism;
[佛經] Buddhist scriptures; Buddhist sutras;
[佛門] Buddhism;
佛門子弟 Buddhists; followers of Buddhism;
[佛面] Buddha's face;
佛面上塗金一淺薄 the gilt on the face of a Buddha image — just a thin coating; (fig) shallow; superficial;
佛面蛇心 with a Buddha's face and the heart of a snake;
不看僧面看佛面 do sth for a person out of deference to sb else;
[佛事] Buddhist ceremony; Buddhist service;
[佛手] Buddha's-hand; fingered citron;
[佛塔] pagoda;
[佛頭] Buddha's head;
佛頭着糞 put night soil on Buddha's head — a black spot in a writing; smear Buddha's head with dung — desecrate;
[佛陀] Buddha;
[佛像] figure of Buddha; image of Buddha;
[佛學] Buddhism;
[佛爺] Buddha;

拜佛 prostrate oneself before the image of Buddha; worship Buddha;
成佛 become a Buddha;
活佛 Living Buddha;
念佛 chant the name of the Buddha; pray to the Buddha;
神佛 gods and Buddha;
銅佛 brazen Buddha;
浴佛 bathe Buddha's image;
玉佛 jade Buddha;

fou³
fou

【缶】 (1) amphora-like jar; crock with a narrow opening; earthen jar; (2) clay musical instrument;

fou

【否】 (1) denial; deny; negate; negation; (2) nay; no; (3) whether;

［否定］ (1) denial; deny; negate; negation; (2) negative;
否定詞 negative; negator;
~含蓄否定詞 implied negative;
否定代詞 negative pronoun;
否定句 negative sentence;
否定祈使句 negative imperative sentence;
否定條件介詞 preposition of negative condition;
否定疑問句 negative question;
否定之否定 the negation of negation;
全部否定 sheer negation;
全盤否定 throw out the baby with the baoth water;
雙重否定 double denial; double negative;
四重否定 tetra negation;
完全否定 confute;

［否決］ nix; overrule; reject; veto; vote down;
否決動議 vote down the motion;
否決權 the right of veto; veto;
~無限制否決權 absolute veto;
~行政否決權 executive veto;
否決提案 veto a proposal;

［否認］ deny; disclaim; gainsay; give a denial to sth; make a denial of; negate; repudiate;
否認謠傳 give a denial to the rumour;
否認罪責 deny one's guilt;
斷然否認 categorically deny;
無可否認 cannot be denied; it is not to be denied that; there is no denying; undeniable;
一口否認 completely deny; flatly deny; repudiate flatly;

［否則］ if not; or else; otherwise;

［否證］ falsify;

是否 if; whether; whether or not;

fu¹

fu

【夫】 (1) one's husband; (2) man; (3) person engaged in manual labour; (4) person served in forced labour;

［夫婦］ husband and wife; man and woman;
夫婦關係 connubiality;
夫婦好合 conjugal felicity; connubial happiness;
夫婦之道 the proper relation between husband and wife;
夫唱婦隨 domestic harmony; harmony between husband and wife;
結為夫婦 be conjoined in wedlock;
新婚夫婦 newly-married couple; newly-wedded couple; newlyweds;
一對夫婦 a couple; a husband and wife; a married couple;
一對年輕夫婦 a young couple;
義夫節婦 just men and decent women; men of high principles and chaste wives; righteous husbands and faithful wives;
淫夫淫婦 adulterers and adulteresses;
有夫之婦 feme covert; married woman; wife;
有婦之夫 husband; married man;
愚夫愚婦 ignorant multitude; uneducated public;
育齡夫婦 couples of child-bearing age;

［夫妻］ husband and wife; man and wife; pair;
夫妻店 mom-and-pop store;
夫妻恩愛 conjugal affection; connubial love;
夫妻恩怨 conjugal feelings;
夫妻反目 bickerings of husband and wife; quarrel between man and wife;
夫妻感情 affection between a couple;
夫妻工廠 mom-and-pop factory;
夫妻共有財產 community property;
夫妻無隔夜之仇 enmity between husband and wife doesn't last the night; lovers' quarrels are soon mended; married couples rarely sleep on a quarrel; nothing can come between husband and wife;
夫妻之愛 conjugal love;
夫妻之間的 conjugal;
半路夫妻 married when they are half way through life; or when they have reached middle age;
糟糠夫妻 bread-and-cheese marriage;
夫榮妻貴 woman of low birth may marry into the purple;
結髮夫妻 husband and wife by the first marriage;
結為夫妻 be tied to each other in bonds of matrimony;
老夫老妻 old married couple;
老夫少妻 an old man with a young wife;

那對夫妻 that pair;
少夫老妻 marry a man much younger than oneself;
艷妻醜夫 a beautiful wife and an ugly husband;
一對夫妻 a husband and wife;
一夫多妻 plural marriage; polygamy;
一夫一妻 monogamy;
~一夫一妻制 monogamy; monogyny;
一妻多夫 polyandry;

[夫人] lady; ladyship; ma'am; madam; madame;
第一夫人 first lady; president's wife;
賠了夫人又折兵 lose the bait along with the fish; suffer a double loss; throw the handle after the axe; throw the helve after the hatchet;
如夫人 concubine;
嫂夫人 your wife;
小夫人 concubine;
休閒夫人 lady of leisure;
尊夫人 your wife;

[夫婿] one's husband;

[夫子] (1) ancient form of address to a Confucian scholar; (2) pedant; (3) husband; (4) husband and children;
夫子廟前賣文章 carry water to the river; teach fish to swim;
夫子自道 one speaks of oneself; the master exposes himself; the master speaks of himself;
老夫子 tutor in a private school; unpractical scholar;
相夫教子 help the husband and teach the children;
迂夫子 impractical scholar; pedant;

悲夫 how sad it is;
鄙夫 ignorant fellow; mean fellow;
病夫 sick man;
車夫 cart driver; carter;
船夫 boatman;
村夫 (1) villager; (2) vulgar and coarse person;
大夫 doctor;
獨夫 a bad ruler forsaken by all; autocrat;
高爾夫 golf;
更夫 night watchman;
工夫 (1) time; (2) art; skill; workmanship;
功夫 (1) time; (2) art; skill; workmanship;
姑夫 uncle;
鰥夫 bachelor or widower; old wifeless man;
伙夫 cook; mess cook;
奸夫 adulterer;
腳夫 porter;
轎夫 sedan chair bearer;
姐夫 brother-in-law; elder sister's husband;
馬夫 cart driver;
妹夫 brother-in-law; younger sister's husband;
農夫 farmer;
前夫 ex-husband;
懦夫 coward; craven; weakling;
匹夫 (1) ordinary man; (2) ignorant person;
姘夫 adulterer;
前夫 ex-husband; former husband;
樵夫 woodcutter; woodman;
情夫 lover;
挑夫 porter;
屠夫 (1) butcher; (2) ruthless ruler;
武夫 (1) man of prowess; (2) military man; warrior;
役夫 labourer; servant;
姨夫 husband of one's maternal aunt; uncle;
庸夫 common people;
有夫 have a husband;
漁夫 fisher; fisherman;
丈夫 (1) husband; (2) man;
壯夫 able-bodied person; sturdy person;
拙夫 clumsy husband;

fu

【柎】 (1) calyx of a flower; (2) foot of clock or drum rack;

fu

【趺】 (1) back of the foot; (2) sit cross-legged;

[趺坐] sit cross-legged;

fu

【鈇】 hatchet; ax;

fu

【跗】 acrotarsium; instep;

[跗骨] tarsal bone; tarsus;
跗骨痛 pain in the foot; tarsalgia;
跗骨炎 inflammation of the tarsus of the foot; tarsitis;

fu

【孵】 (1) hatch eggs; incubate; (2) emerge from eggs or spawn;

[孵出] brood; hatch;

[孵化] brood; emerge from eggs; hatch; hatching; incubate; gestate; spawn;
孵化器 incubator;
孵化性 hatchability;

［孵育］ incubation;

fu

【鄜】 the name of a county in Shaanxi;

fu

【敷】 (1) apply; (2) lay out; spread; (3) sufficient for;

［敷布］ compress;
冷敷布 cold compress;
熱敷布 hot compress;
一塊敷布 a compress;

［敷料］ dressing;

［敷設］ lay; rough in;

［敷衍］ go through the motions; perfunctory; skimp; whitewash;
敷衍幾句 dismiss perfunctorily in a few words; make a few casual remarks;
敷衍了事 attend to a matter negligently; do things carelessly; do things in a perfunctory manner; finish a job carelessly; give a lick and a promise; go through the motions; make a muddle of one's work; muddle through; play at; shuffle through one's work; skimp one's work; slight over; work perfunctorily;
敷衍塞責 be halfhearted about; be perfunctory in one's work; do just enough to get by; do things perfunctorily; give a lick and a promise; make a display and evade promise; make a display and evade responsibility; make a show of doing one's duty; muddle with one's duty; perform one's duties as routine functions;
敷衍手段 a slovenly manner of attending to business;

［敷用］ apply;

冷敷 apply cold compress;
熱敷 apply hot compress;
外敷 external application;

fu

【膚】 (1) skin; surface; (2) shallow; skin-deep; superficial;

［膚泛］ shallow; superficial;
膚泛之論 shallow views;

［膚淺］ shallow; superficial;
膚淺之見 skin-deep sight;
膚淺之説 skin-deep statement;

［膚色］ colour; colour of skin; complexion; skin colour;
膚色很美 beautiful complexion;
膚色紅潤 florid complexion;
膚色障礙 colour bar; colour line;

肌膚 skin;
皮膚 skin;
切膚 keenly felt; very close to oneself;
雪膚 snow-white skin;

fu

【麩】 bran;

［麩皮］ wheat bran;

fu²

fu

【弗】 (1) not; (2) a surname;

［弗克］ unable;

［弗如］ not as good as; not equal to; worse than;

fu

【伏】 (1) bend over; (2) lie prostrate; (3) go down; subside; (4) hide; (5) admit; subdue; surrender; (6) dog days; hot season; (7) volt;

［伏案］ bend over a table; bend over one's desk;
伏案讀書 bend over one's desk reading;

［伏筆］ an anticipatory remark in a story; foreshadowing;
埋下伏筆 carries a foreshadowing of what is to follow later on;

［伏擊］ ambuscade; ambush; still-hunt; waylay;
伏擊敵人 ambush the enemy;
進行伏擊 attack from an ambush;
受到伏擊 be attacked from ambush; fall into an ambush;

［伏劍而亡］ die by the sword; fall victim to a sword;

［伏特計］ voltmeter;

［伏維尚饗］ I do hereby most respectfully ask the spirit of...to come and eat it; may you taste of this offer;

［伏罪］ admit one's guilt; plead guilty;

安伏 calm sb down; comfort; console; give comfort to; put at ease;
出伏 ending of the dog days;
蹲伏 crouch in hiding; hunker down;
倒伏 (of crops) lodge;

二伏 second of the three ten-day periods of the hot season;
俯伏 lie prostrate;
跪伏 couch;
埋伏 (1) ambush; (2) hide; lie low;
匿伏 in hiding; lurk;
起伏 rise and fall; undulate;
千伏 kilovolt;
潛伏 conceal; hide; lie low;
綣伏 curl up; huddle up; lie with the knees drawn up;
入伏 beginning of hot summer days;
設伏 lay an ambush;
收伏 bring under control; subdue;
數伏 the beginning of hot summer days;
頭伏 (1) first of the three ten-day periods of the hot season; (2) last of the first period of the hot season;
降伏 subdue; tame;
歇伏 stop work during the dog days;
隱伏 lie concealed; lie low;
兆伏 mega-electron-volt;
蟄伏 (1) hibernate; lie dormant; (2) live in seclusion;
制伏 bring under control check; subdue;
中伏 (1) second of the three ten-day periods of the hot season; (2) first day of the second period of the hot season;
終伏 (1) last of the three ten-day periods of the hot season; (2) first day of the last period of the hot season;

fu

【孚】 (1) confidence; trust; (2) spread widely;

fu

【扶】 (1) support with the hand; (2) help sb up; straighten sth up; (3) help; relieve;

［扶病］ do sth in spite of illness;
扶病出席 present in spite of illness;

［扶持］ give aid to; help sustain; place a hand on sb for support; support; support with the hand;
扶持正氣 encourage healthy trends;
持危扶傾 act as a champion of justice; uphold the tottering and support the falling;
鼎力扶持 use one's great strength to support;
相互扶持 lean on each other for support;
左扶右持 support on the left and prop on the right;

［扶箕］ planchette writing;
扶箕請仙 play a little at calling up spirits;

［扶柩歸籍］ escort sb's coffin back to his native place for burial; escort the coffin to the native place of the dead;

［扶鸞請仙］ consult spirits through the planchette;

［扶貧］ help the poor; support the poor;
扶貧工作 help-the-poor work;
扶貧計劃 aid-to-poor programme;
扶貧濟困 help poor rural households;
扶貧舉措 measures for supporting the poor;
扶貧項目 anti-poverty project;
扶貧運動 anti-poverty programme;
扶貧政策 policy for supporting the poor;
智力扶貧 help the poor with intelligence;

［扶桑］ (1) large mulberry; (2) Japan;

［扶手］ (1) balustrade; bannister; handrail; rail; (2) armrest;
扶手椅 armchair;
~一個扶手椅 an armchair;

［扶疏］ luxuriant and well-spaced;

［扶危］ help those in danger;
扶危定傾 deliver the country from distress;
扶危濟困 deliver the poor and all those who are oppressed; help poor people in distress; help the distressed and succour those in peril; help those in distress and aid those in peril; rescue the desperately poor and help those who are in difficulty; succour the poor and deliver those in distress and danger;
扶弱濟危 assist the weak and oppressed;

［扶養］ bring up; foster; provide for;
扶養成人 bring sb up;
扶養父母 support one's parents;

［扶掖］ help and support; support with one's hand;

［扶仗而行］ walk with a cane; walk on crutches; walk with the help of a staff;

［扶植］ foster; groom sb to be; prop up;
扶植親信 foster trusted followers;
扶植養育 groom and foster;

［扶助］ assist; help; support;
扶助服務 support services;

扶助老弱 help the old and the weak;

攙扶 support sb with one's hand;

fu

【佛】 as if; like; similar to;

彷佛 (1) alike; more or less the same; (2) as if; seem;

fu

【怫】 angry; depressed and discontented;

［怫而不釋］ unable to get rid of one's anxiety;

［怫然］ abruptly; angrily;

怫然不悅 be very much offended by; show angry countenance; show sign of displeasure;

fu

【拂】 (1) stroke; (2) flick; whisk; (3) go against;

［拂塵］ fly whisk;

拂塵拭埃 brush off the dust and wipeaway the dirt;

［拂淚而別］ wipe tears and leave;

［拂去］ flick away; flip; whisk;

［拂拭］ whisk off; wipe off;

［拂曉］ before dawn; break of day;

拂曉動身 set off at dawn; start at dawn;

拂曉時分 at dawn; at daybreak;

［拂袖］ give a flick of one's sleeve;

拂袖而去 flick the sleeve and go away — leave in displeasure; fling off; fling out of; go off in a huff; go out abruptly; storm out of the room; turn on one's heel;

吹拂 stir; sway;

披拂 flutter;

飄拂 flutter lightly;

輕拂 flick;

照拂 attend to; care for; look after;

fu

【服】 (1) clothes; dress; (2) take medicine; (3) serve; (4) be convinced; obey; (5) be accustomed to; (6) a surname;

［服從］ abide; be subordinated to; comply; obey; subject; submit oneself to;

服從法律 abide by the law; subject to the law;

服從命令 hew the line; hew to the line; obey orders; toe the line; toe the mark; toe the scratch;

服從判決 accept the ruling;

服從上級 yield obedience to the higher-ups;

不服從 disobey;

~拒不服從 disobey; refuse obedience; refuse to obey;

拒絕服從 refuse obedience to;

［服毒］ take poison;

服毒而死 die of poison;

服毒又上吊—死定了 taking poison and hanging oneself — sure to die;

服毒自殺 destroy oneself by taking poison; poison oneself; swallow poison purposely to commit suicide;

被迫服毒 be forced to take poison;

武大郎服毒—吃也死，不吃也死 Wu Dalang's dose of poison — sure to die if he takes it, or not;

［服法］ instructions about how to take medicine;

認罪服法 admit one's guilt and submit oneself to the law;

［服量］ dosing;

［服氣］ be convinced;

不服氣 disobedient; recalcitrant; unwilling to submit;

~暗暗不服氣 be inwardly unwilling to give in;

使人服氣 convince others;

［服人］ convince people; subdue others;

以力服人 convince people by force; dominate others by force; force people to submit; make sb submit by force; subdue others by force; use pressure to browbeat others;

以威服人 overawe sb into submission;

［服喪］ in mourning;

［服式］ line; style of dress;

［服侍］ attend; care; nurse; serve; wait; wait upon;

服侍病人 attend the patient;

服侍父母 look after one's parents;

［服飾］ biliment; costume; dress; dress and personal adornment; equipage; trappings;

服飾華麗 elegantly attired; in elegant attire;

服飾奢華 extravagant in dress;

［服輸］ acknowledge defeat; admit defeat;

不服輸 refuse to concede defeat;

[服貼] (1) docile; obedient; submissive; (2) be convinced; (3) fitting; proper; well arranged; well-done;
服服貼貼 as to leave nothing further to be desired on his part; as to meet the wishes, etc. of sb; be convinced; docile and obedient; take it lying down;

[服務] give service to; in the service of; serve;
服務標準 service standard;
服務部門 service department;
服務程序 service programme;
服務單位 service unit;
~一所服務單位 a service unit;
服務費 cover charge; service charge; service fee;
~不收服務費 no service charge accepted;
服務經濟 service economy;
~服務經濟學 service economics;
服務率 service rate;
服務貿易 service trade;
服務區 service area;
服務數據單元 service data unit;
服務台 service desk;
~服務台接待員 desk clerk;
服務態度 attitude in attending to customers;
服務協議 service agreement;
服務性翻譯 service translation;
服務性行業 service industry;
服務學習 service learning;
服務員 attendant; waiter; waitron;
~房間服務員 room waiter;
~柜台服務員 counter assistant;
~男服務員 waiter;
~女服務員 waitress;
~夜班服務員 night porter;
服務站 server;
服務質量 service quality;
服務中心 service centre;
~翻譯服務中心 translation service centre;
服務週到 offer good service; provide good service; serve hand and foot; the guests are well accommodated;
服務桌 service desk;
代理服務 agency service;
翻譯服務 translation service;
擴大服務 extend its service to;
上門服務 do door-to-door service; offer door-to-door service;
售後服務 after-sale service;
通宵服務 all-night service;
為大家服務 serve the public;
一條龍服務 conglomerative service; coordinated service; one-stop service;
優質服務 quality service;
暫停服務 out of service;
忠誠服務 loyal service;
周到的服務 satisfactory service;

[服刑] be executed; imprisonment; serve a sentence;
服刑期滿 complete a term of imprisonment;

[服藥] take medicine;
服藥過量 overdose;

[服役] (1) enlist in the army; on active service; take service; (2) do corvee labour;
服役期間 during one's term of military service; during the period of enlistment;
服役期滿 complete one's term of service;

[服膺] (1) bear in mind; (2) feel deeply convinced;

[服用] take medicine;

[服裝] apparel; clothing; costume; dress; fashion; garment;
服裝廠 clothing factory;
服裝店 clothing store;
服裝費 clothing allowance; dress allowance;
服裝行業 clothing industry;
服裝設計 dress designing; fashion design;
服裝師 dresser;
服裝業 rag trade;
服裝製造商 clothing manufacturer;
穿異性服裝 cross-dressing;
戶外服裝 outdoor clothing;
民族服裝 national costume;
名牌服裝 designer clothes;
名師設計的服裝 designer clothing;
奇裝異服 bizarre clothing; bizarre dress; peculiar dress; weird dress; an exotic dress; an outlandish dress; exotic costume; fancy clothes; fancy dresses; outlandish clothing; strange clothing; strange fashions;
全套服裝 outfit;
正式服裝 formal clothes;

[服罪] admit one's guilt; admit that one is guilty; plead quilty;

拜服 greatly admire sb;

被服 bedding and clothing;
便服 (1) everyday clothes; informal dress; (2) civilian clothes;
賓服 obey;
不服 not give in to; recalcitrate; refuse to accept as final; refuse to obey; remain unconvinced by;
拆服 (1) bring into submission; subdue; (2) be convinced; be filled with admiration;
常服 informal dress;
朝服 court dress;
成服 ready-made clothing;
臣服 acknowledge allegiance to; submit oneself to the rule of;
誠服 obey willingly; submit willingly;
防護服 protective clothing;
防水服 waterproof clothing;
袞服 the ceremonial dress of the emperor;
和服 kimono;
吉服 (1) formal dress for happy events; (2) costume for ritual ceremony;
警服 police uniform;
爵服 the degree and costume of nobility;
軍服 military uniform;
克服 (1) conquer; overcome; surmount; (2) put up with;
口服 (1) profess to be convinced; (2) take medicine orally;
禮服 ceremonial robe; full dress;
獵服 safari outfit;
男服 menswear;
內服 (of medicine) be taken orally;
佩服 have respect for sb;
平服 be convinced; stabilize;
屈服 knuckle under; surrender; yield;
喪服 mourning apparel;
懾服 (1) submit because of fear; succumb; (2) cow sb into submission;
盛服 rich dress; splendid attire;
收服 bring under control; subdue;
順服 obedient; submit;
說服 convince; persuade; talk sb over;
伺服 servo;
素服 white dress;
歎服 gasp in admiration;
帖服 docile and obedient;
推服 esteem and admire;
西服 European-style dress; Western-style clothes;
降服 surrender; yield;
孝服 mourning dress;
心服 acknowledge sincerely; be genuinely convinced;
信服 be convinced; completely accept;
壓服 force sb to submit;
洋服 Western-style clothes;
悅服 heartily admire;
運動服 sports clothing;
征服 conquer; subjugate;
制服 (1) uniform; (2) bring under control; check; subdue;

fu

【芙】 hibiscus;

［芙蓉］ (1) cottonrose hibiscus; (2) lotus; (3) confederate rose;
芙蓉出水 hibiscus rising out of water; lotus comes into bloom;
芙蓉其面，蛇蝎其心 have a fair face, but a foul heart;
出水芙蓉 pretty girl;
臉若芙蓉 with a face like hibiscus flowers;

fu

【芣】 medicinal plantago;

［芣莒］ Asiatic plantain;

fu

【芾】 lush; luxuriant;

fu

【帗】 multicoloured prop used in dancing rituals;

fu

【俘】 (1) capture; take prisoner; (2) captive; prisoner of war;

［俘獲］ (1) capture; (2) capture; entrapment; gathering; trapping;
俘獲假說 capture hypothesis;
超熱俘獲 epithermal capture;
輻射俘獲 radiative capture;
共振俘獲 resonance capture;
光磁俘獲 photomagnetic capture;
核俘獲 nuclear capture;
寄生俘獲 parasitic capture;
介子俘獲 meson capture;
空穴俘獲 hole capture;
離解俘獲 dissociative capture;
吸收俘獲 absorption capture;
信號俘獲 signal capture;
質子俘獲 proton capture;
中子俘獲 neutron capture;

［俘虜］ (1) capture; take prisoner; (2) captive; prisoner of war;

被俘 be taken prisoner;
傷俘 (1) those wounded and captured in battle; (2) wounded prisoners of war;
生俘 capture alive;
遣俘 repatriate prisoners of war;

fu

【氟】 fluorine;

fu

【枹】 drum-stick;

fu

【洑】 (1) vortex; whirlpool; (2) undercurrent;

fu

【罘】 (1) net for catching hares; (2) net for catching beasts;

［罘罳］ (1) screen partition; (2) wire netting;

fu

【茀】 (1) weedy; (2) hindrance; obstacle; rank growth of weed obstructing the way; (3) fortune; luck; (4) a surname;

fu

【苻】 (1) a kind of herb; (2) a surname;

fu

【浮】 (1) float; (2) on the surface; superficial; (3) flighty; unstable; (4) hollow; inflated; (5) excessive; surplus;

［浮板］ bodyboard;

［浮標］ buoy; dan; dobber; drogue; float road; floating beacon; floating mark; staff float;
浮標裝置 buoyage;
標誌浮標 marker buoy;
補給浮標 replenishment buoy;
沉船浮標 wreck buoy;
燈浮標 light buoy;
滴定管浮標 burette float;
電纜浮標 telegraph buoy;
冬季浮標 winter buoy;
發光浮標 lighted buoy;
港外浮標 outer buoy;
告別浮標 farewell buoy;
鼓形浮標 drum buoy;
罐形浮標 can buoy;
海界浮標 sea buoy;
航向浮標 mark buoy;
號角浮標 horn buoy;
河口浮標 outfall buoy;
環狀浮標 annular float;
江河浮標 river buoy;
進口浮標 approach buoy; entrance buoy;
抗冰浮標 ice buoy;
雷達浮標 radar buoy;
流跡浮標 drift float;
鳴笛浮標 whistle buoy;
鳴哨浮標 whistle buoy;
氣燈浮標 gas buoy;
球形浮標 globe buoy; spherical buoy;
聲響浮標 sound buoy;
失事浮標 release buoy;
水道浮標 channel buoy;
同心浮標 concentric float;
桶形浮標 cask buoy;
危險浮標 danger buoy;
無線電浮標 radio buoy;
乙炔浮標 acetylene buoy;
音響浮標 acoustic buoy;
魚網浮標 fish net buoy;
圓柱浮標 spar buoy;
指示浮標 position buoy;
中心浮標 centre buoy;
終點浮標 finishing buoy;
鐘浮標 bell buoy;
柱形浮標 pillar buoy; spar buoy;
專用浮標 special-purpose buoy;
錐形浮標 conical buoy;
組合浮標 combination buoy;

［浮冰］ floating ice;
大片浮冰 pack ice;

［浮沉］ drift along; now sink, now emerge;
半沉半浮 float half in and half out of the water;
沉李浮瓜 floating melons and plums submerge in water — pursue summer joys;
宦海浮沉 the ups and downs in officialdom; the vicissitudes of an official career;
人生的浮沉 the ups and downs of one's life; the vicissitudes of life;
與世浮沉 follow the trend; swim with the tide;
載沉載浮 bobbing up and down; now sinking, now rising again;

［浮蕩］ float in the air;

［浮點］ floating point;
浮點運算 floating point operation;

［浮雕］ boss; cameo; enchase; phalera; relief; rilievo;

浮雕玻璃 cameo glass;
浮雕模子 hollow relief;
浮雕木刻 wooden carvings in relief;
浮雕細工 embossed work;
浮雕影片 embossed film;
半浮雕 bas-relief; low relief;
對立浮雕 counter relief;
高浮雕 alto-relievo; deep relief;
高凸浮雕 high relief;
空心浮雕 concave relief;
淺浮雕 anaglyph;
深浮雕 high relief;
中浮雕 medium relief;

[浮動] (1) drift; float; ripple; (2) fluctuate; unstable; unsteady; (3) float; (4) flexibility; floating; relocatability;
浮動工資 floating wage;
浮動匯率 floating exchange rate;
~浮動匯率制度 floating exchange rate system;
浮動貨幣 floating currency;
浮動價 floating price;
~浮動價格 floating price;
聯合浮動 joint float;
無限制浮動 unlimited flexibility;
自由浮動 free float; unmanaged flexibility;

[浮而不實] an empty show; giddy and insincere; superficial and insubstantial;

[浮泛] (1) float about; (2) display; reveal; (3) superficial; too abstract; unpractical;
內容浮泛 superficial and full of generalities;
輕舟浮泛 a light boat gliding past;

[浮華] flashy; foppish rococo; ostentatious; showy; vain;
浮華不實 a flowery language which lacks content; a meretricious style of writing; attractive on the surface but of no solid value;
浮華浪蕩 frivolous;
浮華生活 showy and luxurious life;
浮華虛禮 empty show and pretentious ceremony;
文詞浮華 florid language; ornate style;

[浮誇] boastful; exaggerate; fuddy-duddy;
浮誇的 highfalutin;
~浮誇的話 fustian;
浮誇言論 bombast;
浮誇言語 boastful words;
浮誇作風 proneness to boasting and exaggeration;

[浮力] buoyance; buoyancy;
浮力計 buoyance gauge;
浮力中心 centre of buoyance;
安全浮力 safety buoyance;
儲備浮力 reserve buoyance;
負浮力 negative buoyance;
工作浮力 working buoyance;
後備浮力 reserve buoyance;
淨浮力 net buoyance;
可用浮力 available buoyance;
內部浮力 internal buoyance;
剩餘浮力 surplus buoyance;
水上浮力 buoyance in water;
外部浮力 external buoyance;
完整浮力 intact buoyance;
正浮力 positive buoyance;
中和浮力 neutral buoyance;
總浮力 gross buoyance;

[浮名] undeserved reputation;
浮名薄利 look down fame and gain;
浮名虛利 despise reputation;

[浮萍] duckweed;
浮萍尚有相逢日，人豈全無見面時 even floating weeds may come together again, so do human beings;

[浮淺] obvious; shallow; superficial;

[浮説游詞] unfounded statement;

[浮屠] pagoda;
七級浮屠 seven-storied pagoda;

[浮文] padding; verbiage;
浮文巧語 a flowery and bombastic style of writing;

[浮現] appear before one's eyes; drift; emerge; occur; raise;

[浮想] thoughts flashing across one's mind;
浮想聯翩 many thoughts flash through one's mind; thoughts thronging one's mind;

[浮艷] flowery diction but flat content; ostentious; showy but unsubstantial;

[浮游] (1) sail; swim; (2) go on a pleasure trip; roam;
浮游動物 zooplankton;
浮游生物 plankter; plankton;
浮游生物 plankton;
~半浮游生物 mesopelagic plankton;
~海洋浮游生物 marine plankton;
~空氣浮游生物 air plankton;
~淺水浮游生物 neritic plankton;
~夜浮游生物 nyctipelagic plankton;

F

浮游植物 phytoplankton;

［浮雲］ floating clouds;

浮雲富貴 look down money and powerful status;

浮雲翳日 floating clouds obscure the sun;

浮雲朝露 life is as short as passing clouds and morning dew;

［浮躁］ flighty and rash; impetuous; impulsive;

漂浮 (1) float; (2) superficial;

輕浮 fighty; frivolous; light; light-hearted; light-headed; playful;

心浮 flighty and impatient; unstable;

囂浮 frivolous;

虛浮 impractical; superficial;

fu

【祓】 (1) exorcise; offer sacrifices to Gods for getting rid of disasters and begging blessings; (2) clean; cleanse; cleanse away; wash away evil influence;

［祓除］ exorcise;

fu

【茯】 tuckahoe;

fu

【蚨】 a kind of water beetle;

青蚨 (1) copper cash in ancient times; (2) money;

fu

【郛】 outer city; suburbs;

fu

【匐】 crawl; creep; lie prostrate;

匍匐 (1) crawl; creep; (2) lie prone; lie prostrate;

fu

【涪】 (1) a river in Sichuan Province; (2) an old administrative district;

fu

【符】 (1) tally issued by a ruler to generals or envoys as credentials in ancient China; (2) symbol; (3) accord with; tally with; (4) magic figures drawn by Daoist priests to invoke or expel spirits and bring good or ill fortune; (5) a surname;

［符號］ (1) mark; notation; sign; symbol; (2) insignia;

符號翻譯 symbolic translation;

符號學 semiotics;

變音符號 diacritic mark;

標點符號 punctuation mark;

抽象符號 abstract symbol;

代數符號 algebraic sign; algebraic symbol;

地址符號 address mark;

電碼符號 code sign;

範疇符號 category symbol;

計算符號 compute sign;

絕對值符號 absolute value sign;

可變符號 variable symbol;

容許符號 admissible sign;

數學符號 mathematical sign; mathematical symbol;

習用符號 conventional sign;

斜線符號 slash;

抑音符號 grave accent;

重音符號 accent mark; acute accent; stress mark;

注音符號 phonetic symbol;

字母符號 alphabetic symbol;

［符合］ accord with; agree with; answer to; be accordant to sth; be in accordance with sth; be in conformity with; be in line with sth; bring into accord; conform to; come up to sth; consist with; correspond to; fall in with; hit off with; in accord with; jibe with; square with; tally with; tie in with sth;

符合標準 meet a criterion; up to the scratch; up to the standard;

符合實際情況 conform to reality; tally with the actual situation;

符合市場需求 accord with the demands of the market;

符合條件 be fully qualified for;

符合要求 accord with the demands; fill the bill; fit the bill; suit the need;

符合原則 conform with the principle;

不符合 inconformity;

［符節］ tally;

若合符節 as similar as the two halves of a tally; fit exactly; tally perfectly;

［符實］ conform to reality; tally with the fact;

言不符實 statements that do not tally with the facts;

言符其實 don't take a mountain out of a molehill; the statement is tally with the fact; what one speaks conforms to reality;

[符咒] amulets; charms; magic script-incantations and amulets;
驅除厄運的符咒 a charm against bad luck;

兵符 (1) commander's seal; (2) a book on the art of war;
不符 inconsistent with; not agree with; not conform to;
鬼畫符 (1) scrawly handwriting; scribble; (2) hypocritical talk;
虎符 tiger-shaped tally issued to generals as imperial authorization for troop movement in ancient China;
護符 amulet; protective talisman;
護身符 (1) amulet; protective talisman; (2) person or thing that protects one from punishment or censure; shield;
神符 magic figures or charms to invoke or expel spirits and bring good or ill fortune;
相符 agree with; conform to; correspond to;
休止符 rest;
意符 ideogram; ideograph;
音符 note;
字符 character;

fu
【紼】 (1) large rope; (2) cord or rope attached to a bier or coffin; (3) ancient ribbons;

fu
【紱】 (1) ribbon; sash; strand; (2) ceremonial dress worn during sacrificial rituals;

fu
【桴】 (1) ridge pole on a roof; (2) drumstick; (3) raft;
[桴鼓相應] echo in close coordination;

fu
【艴】 look angry;
[艴然] angry look; look angry;

fu
【莩】 membrane in stems of rushes or reeds;

fu
【幅】 (1) width of cloth; (2) size; (3) margin;
[幅度] extent; range; scope;
幅度變化 amplitude variation;
大幅度 a wide margin; by a big margin; substantially;
~大幅度上漲 rise immensely;
~大幅度下跌 drop sharply;
~大幅度優惠 a big margin of preference;
~大幅度增長 increase by a wide margin; rise by a big margin;
[幅面] width of cloth;
[幅員] size of the country;
幅員廣大 vast in territory;
幅員遼闊 broad territory; vast territory;

邊幅 (1) edges; (2) appearance;
波幅 amplitude;
步幅 width of stride;
插幅 width of furrows for sowing;
尺幅 (1) dimensions; (2) small painting;
單幅 single width;
畫幅 (1) painting; picture; (2) size of a picture;
寬幅 (of cloth) width;
雙幅 double width;
條幅 scroll;
一幅 a piece of;
漲幅 rate of increase;
振幅 amplitude (of vibration);
震幅 amplitude of an earthquake;

fu
【菔】 turnip;

fu
【袱】 bundle wrapped in cloth;

fu
【蜉】 ephemera; ephemerid; mayfly;
[蜉蝣] mayfly;
蜉蝣撼樹 a mayfly trying to shake a tree; a rash, ridiculous attempt;

蚍蜉 big ant;

fu
【鳧】 (1) mallard; wild duck; (2) swim;
[鳧脛難加] it is hard to lengthen a duck's leg; one should be content with what one has;
[鳧趨雀越] dance with joy; like ducks waddling and sparrows hopping;
[鳧燕難明] hand to distinguish between high-flying wild ducks and swallows; things easily confused;

F

棉鳧 cotton teal;
田鳧 lapwing;

fu

【福】 blessing; good fortune; happiness;
[福不徒來] happiness will not come easily;
[福地] place of happiness;
福地洞天 blessed spot; place of scenic beauty;
洞天福地 blessed spot; fairyland; the land of the fairies;
[福分] good fortune; happy lot; share of happiness allotted by destiny;
[福過災生] excessive joy brings forth misfortune; good fortune is often followed by calamity;
[福禍] good fortune and calamity;
福從禍中來 good fortune comes out of bad;
福壽禍淫 bless the good and curse the wicked; god blesses the good and punishes the evil;
福無重受日，禍有併來時 good fortune never repeats itself, but troubles come thick and fast;
福無雙至，禍不單行 blessings do not come in pairs whereas calamities never come singly; good fortune does not come in pairs and disasters do not come alone; joy comes never more than once but sorrows never come singly;
福中伏禍，禍中寓福 in good fortune lurks calamity and in calamity lies good fortune;
求福免禍 seek happiness and avoid calamity;
[福利] material benefits; welfare; well-being;
福利費 welfare expense;
福利國家 welfare state;
福利基金 welfare fund;
福利津貼 fringe benefit;
福利社會 welfare society;
兒童福利 child welfare;
附加福利 fringe benefit;
經濟福利 economic welfare;
社會福利 social welfare;
[福祿壽考] good luck and long life;
[福氣] good fortune; happy lot;
有福氣 be favoured by fortune; have abundance of blessings;
[福如東海] happiness as immense as the Donghai Sea;
福如東海，壽比南山 may your fortune be as boundless as the Donghai Sea and may you live a long and happy life;
[福壽] good fortune and long life;
福壽康寧 good fortune; long life, health and peace;
福壽綿綿 enjoy long life and good fortune; long-continued prosperity; unlimited happiness and longevity;
福壽雙全 enjoy both felicity and longevity;
多福多壽 happiness and longevity;
添福添壽 add to one's happiness and one's longevity; increase one's luck and lengthen one's life; increase of happiness and longevity;
[福無雙至] blessings do not come hand in hand; blessings never come in pairs; felicity never turns out in pairs; good fortune does not come in pairs; lightning never strikes twice in the same place; the same person does not have the same luck twice;
[福星] lucky star; mascot;
福星高照 a lucky star shines on high; be born under a lucky star; by in the ascendant; be under the smiles of fortune; bring sb good luck and success in life; come into luck; ride the high tide of good luck; have one's star in the ascendant;
[福音] (1) gospel; (2) glad tidings; good news;
傳播福音 evangelize;
[福祉] (1) blessedness; happiness; (2) betterment; well-being;
長遠福祉 long-term betterment;
謀求福祉 strive for the betterment of;
人類福祉 the betterment of mankind;

發福 grow stout; put on weight;
過福 be dissatisfied with good creature comforts one has;
洪福 good fortune; happy lot;
鴻福 good fortune; happy lot;
後福 luck in later life;
禍福 disaster and happiness; fortunes and misfortunes;
口福 gourmet's luck; the luck to get sth very nice to eat;

納福 enjoy a life of ease and comfort; enjoy the blessings of life;
祈福 pray for blessings;
清福 easy and carefree life;
托福 thanks to you;
託福 thank you;
晚福 old age bliss;
萬福 wish you all happiness; wish you good luck;
威福 punishment and reward;
惜福 make sparing use of one's wealth; refrain from leading an excessively comfortable life;
賜福 bestow happiness; bless;
遐福 great happiness; lasting blessings; lasting happiness;
享福 enjoy a happy life; live in ease and comfort;
幸福 happy; happiness; well-being;
修福 do good deeds in order to win blessings;
眼福 the good fortune of seeing sth rare or beautiful;
載福 enjoy happiness; receive blessings;
造福 benefit; bring benefit to;
招福 welcome and invite blessings;
折福 reduce blessings in one's later life because of excessive easy living;
祝福 benediction; blessing;

fu
【箙】 quiver;

fu
【韍】 leather garment worn during sacrificial rituals in ancient times;

fu
【蝠】 bat;
［蝠蛾］ bat;

凹臉蝠 hollow-faced bat; slit-faced bat;
蝙蝠 bat;
狐蝠 fox bat;

fu
【縛】 bind; tie;
［縛緊］ tie or bind tightly;

束縛 bind up; fetter; tie;
繫縛 fasten; tie;

fu
【輻】 spoke;
［輻合］ convergence;
［輻散］ divergence;
［輻射］ irradiation; radiance; radiation;
輻射安全 radiation safety;
輻射對稱 radial symmetry;
輻射防護屏 radiation shield;
輻射固化塗料 radiation curing coatings;
輻射率 radiance; radiation;
~光輻射率 luminous radiance;
輻射器 irradiator; radiator;
~理想輻射器 ideal radiator;
~聲輻射器 acoustic radiator;
輻射事故 radiation accident;
輻射損傷 irradiation damage; radiation injury;
輻射霧 radiation fog;
輻射學 radiology;
大氣輻射 atmospheric radiation;
電磁輻射 electromagnetic radiation;
反向輻射 back radiation;
光譜輻射 spectral radiance;
黑體輻射 blackbody radiation;
淨輻射 net radiance;
熱輻射 thermal radiation;
適應輻射 adaptative irradiation;
吸收輻射 absorbed radiation;
宇宙輻射 cosmic radiation;
原子輻射 atomic radiation;
［輻照］ irradiation;
分批輻照 batch irradiation;
急性輻照 acute irradiation;

輪輻 spoke of a wheel;

fu
【黻】 sacrificial robe;

fu
【鵩】 buzzard; vulture;

fu³
fu
【父】 (1) man; old man; (2) a man's courtesy name; (3) a surname;

fu
【甫】 (1) man; (2) father; (3) then and only then; (4) a short while ago; immediately after; just; (5) a surname;
［甫出龍潭，又入虎穴］ out of the frying pan into the fire;

fu
【府】 (1) government; government office; prefecture; (2) mansion; official residence; (3) your home;

F

[府邸] mansion; mansion house;
[府上] (1) your family; your home; (2) your native place;
柏府 imperial censorate;
城府 shrewdness; subtlety;
地府 the nether world;
洞府 abode of fairies and immortals;
官府 (1) local authorities; (2) feudal official;
盟府 place for safekeeping records of an alliance; repository of covenants;
幕府 governor's office;
首府 (1) prefecture where the provincial capital is located; (2) capital of a prefecture; (3) captial of a colony;
王府 prince's residence;
相府 prime minister's residence;
學府 institution of higher learning; seat of learning;
陰府 Hades; the nether world;
怨府 object of general indignation;
藏府 storage; warehouse;
造府 call on; pay a visit;
政府 government;
知府 magistrate of a prefecture;
尊府 your home;

fu
【斧】 (1) axe; hatchet; (2) chop; cut;
[斧頭] axe; hatchet;
斧頭吃鑿子，鑿子吃木頭 everything has its vanquisher; there is always one thing to conquer another;
一把斧頭 a hatchet; an axe;
[斧鉞] axe and battleaxe;
不避斧鉞 not afraid of being killed;
[斧正] make corrections;
敬請斧正 please make suggestions and corrections;
[斧子] axe; hatchet;
一把斧子 an axe;

板斧 broad axe; hatchet;
冰斧 ice axe;
採脂斧 cupping axe;
齒斧 tooth axe;
錘斧 hammer axe;
單刃斧 single-bladed axe;
丁字斧 pick axe;
剁斧 chip axe;
伐木斧 felling axe; woodcutter's axe;
鶴嘴斧 pitch axe;
掘根斧 dipping axe;
闊斧 broad axe;
兩刃斧 double-bladed axe;
木工斧 bench axe;
披斧 side axe;
劈斧 clearing axe;
樵斧 axe;
手斧 hand axe;
螳斧 ax-shaped forelegs of a mantis;
鏽斧 sharp axe;
小斧 hatchet; woodsman's axe;
修枝斧 topping axe;
月斧 round axe;
戰斧 battleaxe;
資斧 travelling expenses;

fu
【拊】 (1) pat; touch with hand lightly or tenderly; (2) slap; tap; (3) the handle of a vessel or utensil;

fu
【俯】 bow one's head;
[俯衝] dive;
俯衝轟炸 dive-bombing;
[俯瞰] look down at; overlook;
俯瞰全城 get a bird's-eye view of the city;
俯瞰攝影 boom shot; crane shot;
俯瞰圖 a bird's-eye view;
[俯視] look down at; overlook;
俯視圖 vertical view;
[俯拾皆是] all one has to do is to stoop and pick them up; be easily available; be extremely common; can be found everywhere; obtainable everywhere;
[俯首] bow one's head;
俯首方寸存心地，舉頭三尺有神明 we do nothing but in the presence of two great witnesses, God and our conscience;
俯首就範 bend one's head and sbumit to control; bow the head and conform to the rule — meekly submitting;
俯首就縛 bend the head and be tired; droop one's head and allow oneself to be bound — give no resistance;
俯首就戮 bow before the butcher's knife;
俯首屈膝 kneel down humbly;
俯首帖耳 all obedience and servility; docile and obedient; docilely obey; in complete obedience; obey with servility; servile like a dog; submissive

and obedient; subservient to;

俯首聽命 at sb's beck and call; be submission; bend one's neck; bow down to obey submissively; obey sb's order with all due submission; obey with bent head; submissively hear and obey;

甘心俯首 content to bow one's head and yield to;

[俯卧] lie flat on one's stomach;

俯卧撐 press-up; push-up;

俯臥撐推起 push-up;

[俯仰] bending of the head; lifting of the head; simple action; simple move;

俯仰無愧 not feel disgraceful in looking down and up – having a clear conscience;

俯仰由人 be at others' beck and call; be twisted round other's finger; submit oneself to other's whims and fancies;

俯仰之間 in a flash; in a short span; in a twinkling; in an instant; in the twinkling of an eye;

俯仰自得 contented and happy wherever one may be;

前俯後仰 be convulsed; bend forwards and backwards; laugh oneself into convulsions; rock forwards and backwards; stagger forward and back;

隨人俯仰 at one's beck and call; at one's mercy; live under the thumb of others; submit to others' whim and will; submit to one's beck and call; submit to one's every whim and fancy;

仰俯 look up and stoop down;

fu

【釜】 cauldron;

[釜底抽薪] adopt full measure; cut the ground from under one's foot; cut the ground on which someone stands; extract the firewood from below the cauldron so as to stop its boiling; remove burning wood from under the boiler; strike at the root of sth; take a drastic measure to deal with a situation; take away the firewood from under the cauldron;

[釜底游魚] a fish swimming in the bottom of a cauldron; a person whose fate is sealed;

[釜中] in a pot;

釜中生魚 extreme poverty; grow fish in one's cauldron;

釜中游魚 a fish in the pot – one who has been driven into an impasse and is approaching one's doom; a fish swimming in the cauldron – one's fate is sealed;

釜中之魚 a fish in the fish kettle – though living but not long; like a rat in a hole; like fish in a cauldron – without hope of escape;

fu

【脯】 (1) dried and seasoned meat; (2) preserved fruits;

果脯 candied fruit; preserved fruit;

海棠脯 preserved crabapple;

鹿脯 dried venison;

蜜桃脯 preserved peach;

蜜棗脯 candied date;

桃脯 preserved peach;

兔脯 dried hare meat;

杏脯 preserved apricot;

fu

【莆】 a kind of legendary tree with big leaves;

fu

【腑】 bowels; entrails; viscera;

肺腑 the bottom of one's heart;

六腑 the six hollow organs;

臟腑 internal organs including the heart, liver, spleen , lungs, kidneys, stomach, gall, intestines and bladder;

fu

【腐】 (1) decayed; rotten; stale; (2) bean curd;

[腐敗] (1) corrupt; (2) canker; decayed; putrid; rotten; spoilage;

腐敗墮落 become corrupt and degenerate;

腐敗分子 the corrupt;

腐敗風 rottenness;

腐敗透頂 rotten to be core;

腐敗無能 corrupt and incompetent;

腐敗現象 corruption;

產氣性腐敗 gaseous spoilage;

懲治腐敗 combat corruption;

反腐敗 anti-corruption;

~反腐敗鬥爭 anti-corruption campaign; fight against corruption;

官員腐敗 official corruption;
生化腐敗 biochemical spoilage;
食物腐敗 food spoilage;
市場腐敗 municipal corruption;
貪污腐敗 corruption;
細菌性腐敗 bacterial spoilage;
政治腐敗 political corruption;

[腐病] rot;
底腐病 bottom rot;
黑腐病 black rot;

[腐化] (1) corrupt; degenerate; dissolute; (2) decay; rot;
腐化處理 septicization;
腐化墮落 corrupt and degenerate; degenerate morally; corruption and degeneracy; dissolute and degenerate;
腐化分子 a degenerate; a depraved person;
腐化作用 putrefaction;
墮落腐化 decadent and licentious; degenerate and corrupt;
生活腐化 lead a dissolute life;
貪污腐化 graft and corruption;

[腐爛] decomposed; putrid;
腐爛透頂 rotten to the core; thoroughly decadent;
局部腐爛 partial decomposition;

[腐乳] fermented bean curd;
一塊腐乳 a lump of fermented beancurd;

[腐生] saprophytism;
腐生菌 saprophytic bacteria;
腐生物 saprophyte;
兼腐生 facultative saprophyte;

[腐屍] carrion;

[腐蝕] (1) corrode; corrosion; etch; etching; (2) corrupt;
腐蝕劑 (1) corrodent; corrosive; erodent; (2) etchant;
腐蝕性 corrosiveness;
腐蝕作用 corrosive action;
大氣腐蝕 atmospheric corrosion;
宏觀腐蝕 macro etch;
化學腐蝕 chemical etch;
加速腐蝕 accelerated corrosion;
鹼腐蝕 alkali etch;
接觸腐蝕 contact etching;
階調腐蝕 fine etching;
可控腐蝕 controlled etching;
氣體腐蝕 corrosion by gases;
酸腐蝕 acid corrosion;
陽極腐蝕 anode corrosion;

[腐熟] become thoroughly decomposed;

[腐朽] (1) decayed; rotten; (2) decadent; degenerate;
腐朽糜爛 decadent and dissolute;
腐朽沒落 decadent and moribund; decaying; rotten to the core and declining;
腐朽思想 decadent ideology;
化腐朽為神奇 make a silk purse out of a sow's ear; make the ugly beautiful; make use of discarded things; transform the corruptible into mysterious life; turn bad into good;
荒淫腐朽 lead a depraved and dissolute life; live in wanton luxury;

[腐殖土] humus soil; mould; muck;

[腐殖質] humus;

豆腐 bean curd;

fu

【輔】 assist; complement; supplement;

[輔幣] fractional currency;

[輔導] coach; counselling; give guidance in study or training;
輔導報告 guidance lecture;
輔導員 counselor;
~學生輔導員 counselor;
~政治輔導員 assistant for political and ideological work;
個別輔導 individual coaching; individual counseling;
教育輔導 educational counseling;

[輔音] consonant;
閉塞輔音 stop consonant;
重疊輔音 geminated consonant;
動輔音 kinetic consonant;
顎輔音 guttural consonant;
基輔音 supported consonant;
尖-鈍輔音 acute-grave consonant;
緊輔音 tense consonant;
靜態輔音 static consonant;
開端輔音 initial consonant;
摩擦輔音 fricative consonant;
陪輔音 supporting consonant;
清輔音 voiceless consonant;
溶合輔音 fused consonant;
軟輔音 smooth consonant; soft consonant;
弱輔音 lenis consonant; weak consonant;
首強輔音 strong beginning consonant;
雙峰輔音 double-peak consonant;

F

雙輔音 double consonant;
送氣輔音 rough consonant;
尾強輔音 strong-termination consonant;
延長輔音 prolonged consonant;
音節輔音 syllabic consonant;
硬輔音 hard consonant;
元音性輔音 vocalic consonant;
噪輔音 noise consonant;
中立輔音 neutral consonant;
濁輔音 voiced consonant;
~ 非濁輔音 non-voiced consonant;

[輔助] (1) assist; (2) auxiliary; subsidiary; supplementary;
輔助程序 secondary programme;
輔助句 supporting sentence;
輔助人員 aide; auxiliary staff members;
~ 教師輔助人員 teacher aide;
~ 教學輔助人員 school aide;
輔助武器 secondary weapon;
輔助性成分 supplementary component;
輔助語言 auxiliary language; paralanguage;
輔助資料 secondary sources;
翻譯輔助 translation aids;

畿輔 capital city and its environs;

fu
【撫】 (1) console; comfort; (2) foster; nurture; (3) stroke;
[撫愛] caress; cop a feel on sb; fondle; fondle sb sexually; touch sb sexually;
[撫摩] stroke;
[撫慰] comfort; console; soothe;
百般撫慰 try to soothe in every possible way;
[撫卹] comfort and compensate a bereaved family;
撫卹基金 pension funds;
撫卹金 consolation money; pension for the disabled or for the family of the deceased;
~ 寡婦撫卹金 widow's benefit;
~ 遺屬撫卹金 survivor benefit;
[撫養] foster; nurture; tend;
撫養成人 bring sb up; bring to maturity;
撫養費 cost of maintenance;
撫養義務 duty to provide support; duty to rear;
撫養責任 duty of care;

愛撫 show tender care for;
安撫 appease; pacify; placate;
存撫 appease; pacify; placate;
巡撫 provincial governor;

fu
【頫】 bow one's head; chin down;

fu
【簠】 ancient vessel used for holding grains in sacrifices or feasts;

fu
【黼】 a kind of embroidered design on ancient sacrificial robes;

fu⁴

fu
【父】 (1) father; (2) male relative of a senior generation;
[父本] male parent;
[父老] elders;
父老鄉親 elders and folks; fellow countrymen;
父老兄弟 elders and brethren;
羞見江東父老 be ashamed to return after defeat and be unwilling to face one's fellow-countrymen;
[父母] father and mother;
父母官 local official;
父母見背 one's parents have passed away;
父母健在 both parents are in good health; one's parents are enjoying sound health; one's parents are still living and in good health;
父母離異 divorce;
父母雙全 both of one's parents are still alive;
父母雙亡 one's parents are both dead; one has lost both one's parents;
父母之邦 one's own country;
父母之命，媒妁之言 arrange a match by parents' order and on the matchmaker's word — old-fashioned marriage; matches are arranged by go-betweens according to the wishes of the parents;
拜別父母 bid farewell to one's parents;
本生父母 the real, natural parents of an adopted son;
贍養父母 support one's parents;
生身父母 one's own parents;
同父異母 having the same father but

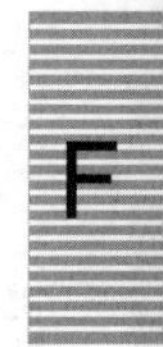

different mothers;
為人父母 being a mother or being a father;
尊敬父母 respect one's parents;
做父母 mothering and fathering;
［父親］ father; old man; pater;
父親般的 fatherly;
父親般的人 father figure;
單身父親 lone father;
兩個孩子的父親 a father of two;
［父系］ paternal line;
父系親屬 parernal relatives;
［父兄］ (1) father and elder brothers; (2) heads of a family;
［父子］ father and son;
父子關係 set membership;
父子失和 there is some soreness between father and son;
父子相傳 from father to son;
其父其子 a chip of the old block (coll);
有其父必有其子 as is the father, so is the son; he is his father's son; like father, like son;
知子莫若父 father knows his sons best; no one knows a man better than his own father;
子肖其父 a chip of the old block; the son is the very image of his father;

伯父 (1) father's elder brother; (2) uncle;
傖父 vulgar person;
慈父 father; loving father;
姑父 one's uncle-in-law;
國父 Father of a Nation;
季父 the youngest paternal uncle;
寄父 foster father;
繼父 stepfather;
舅父 mother's brother; uncle;
厥父 his or her father;
叔父 father's younger brother; uncle;
外祖父 maternal grandfather;
養父 foster father;
義父 adopted father;
岳父 father-in-law; wife's father;
祖父 paternal grandfather;

fu

【付】 (1) commit to; hand over to; (2) pay;
［付出］ pay sth off;
付出代價 pay a price;
付出生命 give one's life for;
［付費］ pay a fee;
付費電視 paid television;
［付款］ make payment; payment;
付款交單 documents against payment;
付款人 payer;
按價付款 give value for value;
按期付款 make punctual payments;
按議價付款 pay the agreed price;
擔保付款 aval;
定期付款 due payment;
分期付款 easy payment; hire purchase; payment in instalments;
貨到付款 cash on delivery (COD); payment upon receipt of goods;
經常性付款 current payments;
立即付款 immediate payment;
履行付款 make a payment;
憑票付款 payable to bearer;
憑證付款 payment voucher;
期中付款 interim payment;
日付款 daily payment;
首期付款 down payment;
先期付款 anticipate payment;
現金付款 cash payment;
延誤付款 fall behind on the payments; fall behind with the payments;
用現金付款 pay in cash;
用信用卡付款 pay by credit card;
用支票付款 pay by cheque;
預算付款 budgetary payments;
預先付款 forward payment; pay upfront; payment in advance;
［付錢］ give sb the money;
按小時付錢 be paid by the hour;
我付錢 my treat;
用支票付錢 pay by cheque;
［付清］ ante up; pay in full; pay up;
悉數付清 pay the amount in full;
［付託］ charge sb with sth; commit sth to sb; consign; entrust; leave sth to sb; leave sth with sb; put sth in sb's charge; refer sth to sb; trust sb with sth; trust sth to sb;
付託得人 have entrusted the matter to the right person;
付託重任 charge sb with a heavy responsibility; entrust sb with an important task;
［付印］ go to press;
付印清樣 pass sheet;
［付與］ pay;
［付帳］ ante up; foot the bill; pay a bill; pony up;

用支票付帳 pay the bill with a cheque;

[付之一炬] be destroyed by fire; be burnt down; commit to the flames; consign to the flames; set fire to; set to fire;

拔付 pay by instalment;
撥付 appropriate a sum of money;
償付 pay; pay back;
超付 excess payment;
承付 assume responsibility for payment; undertake to pay;
墊付 pay for sb and expect to be paid back in future;
兑付 cash a cheque;
對付 cope with; deal with; make do; tackle;
發付 (1) dispatch; send; (2) dismiss; send away;
過付 pay through an intermediary in a business deal;
交付 (1) pay; (2) consign; deliver; hand over;
拒付 refuse payment;
托付 commit sth to sb's care; entrust;
應付 (1) cope with; deal with; handle; (2) do sth after a fashion; do sth perfunctorily; (3) make do;
預付 pay in advance;
照付 pay the full amount according to the price tag;
支付 defray; pay;
止付 stop payment;

fu

【咐】 direct; instruct;

fu

【阜】 (1) mound; small hill; (2) continent; mainland; (3) abundant; big; flourishing; numerous;

fu

【附】 (1) add; attach; enclose; (2) get close to; near; (3) agree to;

[附筆] postscript; P.S.;

[附帶] include;
附帶成分 incidental component;
附帶設備 attendant equipment;
附帶條件 strings attached;

[附耳] move close to sb's ear; whisper in one's ear;
附耳低語 whisper in sb's ear;
附耳而言 speak into sb's ear; put one's mouth to sb's ear and say;
附耳授計 whisper into sb's ear secret plans;

[附睪] epididymis;
附睪切除 epidiclymectomy;
附睪丸 epididymitis;

[附函] covering letter;

[附和] chime in with; echo;
隨聲附和 agree to what other people say; chime in with others; echo this line; echo what others say; follow others' lead in voicing opinion; swell the chorus;

[附加] add; attach;
附加從句 appended clause;
附加費 surcharge;
~幣值附加費 currency surcharge;
~擁擠附加費 congestion surcharge;
附加服務 additional services;
附加工程 additional work;
附加工資 extra pay; extra salary; supplementary wages;
附加合同 accessory contract;
附加賽 play-off;
附加税 additional tax; supertax; surtax;
~進口附加税 import surcharge;
~燃油附加税 bunker surcharge;
附加條件 supplementary clause;
附加文件 appended document;
附加性副詞 adverb as adjunct;
附加樣本 additive samples;
附加疑問句 question tag;
附加語 adjunct;
~地點附加語 place adjunct;
~定語附加語 attributive adjunct;
~方法附加語 means adjunct;
~方式附加語 manner adjunct;
~方向附加語 direction adjunct;
~工具附加語 instrumental adjunct;
~觀點附加語 viewpoint adjunct;
~過程附加語 process adjunct;
~焦點附加語 focusing adjunct;
~禮節附加語 formulaic adjunct;

[附件] (1) appendix; enclosure; (2) accessories; adjunct; attachments;
仿形附件 copying attachment;
飛機附件 aircraft accessory;
光學附件 optical accessory;
合同附件 attachments to a contract;
計算附件 computing attachments;
冷卻附件 cooling attachment;
履帶附件 crawler attachment;
起重機附件 crane attachment;
切絲附件 chasing attachment;

條約的附件 annex to a treaty;
通用附件 general-purpose accessory;
壓模附件 die accessory;

[附近] around the corner; in the vicinity; neighbouring; nearby; round the corner;
附近地區 nearby regions;
在附近 a stone's throw; be within an inch of; close by; close to; down in somewhere; hard by; in the neighbourhood of somewhere; in the vicinity of; near; nearby; next to; off; within hail;
~住在附近 live close by;

[附錄] addendum; annex; appendix;

[附設] have as an attached institution;

[附屬] affiliate; attach; auxiliary; subsidiary;
附屬產品 auxiliary product;
附屬工程 appurtenant work;
附屬公司 affiliate;
附屬國 dependency;
附屬品 accessory; appendage;
附屬企業 affiliated enterprise;
附屬物 adjunct;
附屬學校 affiliated school;
附屬醫院 affiliated hospital;
附屬中學 affiliated school;

[附送] give as a bonus;
隨報附送 be distributed gratis along with the newspaper;

[附小] attached primary school;

[附議] second a motion; support a proposal;

[附庸] (1) dependence of a country; (2) appendage;
附庸風雅 artsycraftsy; mingle with men of letters and pose as a lover of culture;
附庸國 client state;

[附中] attached middle school;

[附着] adhere to; stick to;
附着分詞 adherent participle;
附着力 adhesion; adhesive force;
附着形容詞 adherent adjective;

比附 compare to; liken;
阿附 curry favour with those in power and echo; fawn on and echo;
藩附 protectorate; vassal state;
歸附 submit to the authority of another;
黏附 adhere; stick to;
攀附 play up to;
趨附 curry favour with; ingratiate oneself with;
吸附 absorb;
依附 attach oneself to; become an appendage to; depend on;

fu

【訃】 obituary;

[訃電] telegram of obituary;

[訃告] obituary notice;

[訃文] obituary;

[訃聞] obituary;

fu

【負】 (1) bear; carry on the back or shoulder; shoulder; (2) have at one's back; rely on; (3) suffer; (4) enjoy; (5) owe; (6) fail in one's duty or obligation; (7) be defeated; lose; (8) minus; negative; (9) negative;

[負擔] bear a burden; shoulder;
負擔不起 above one's weight; beyond one's capacity;
負擔費用 bear the expenses;
負擔能力 affordability;
財政負擔 financial burden;
工作負擔 work load;
共同負擔 joint burden;
加重負擔 put extra burden on;
家庭負擔 family burden;
經濟負擔 economic burden;
精神負擔 a weight on the mind;
巨大的負擔 incubus;
思想負擔 mental burden;
稅務負擔 tax burden;

[負電] negative charge;

[負號] minus sign; negative sign;

[負荷] capacity; load;
負荷分析法 load analysis method;
負荷涵義 loaded connotation;
負荷量 load capacity;
負荷重任 shoulder important responsibility;
安全負荷 safe load; safe working load;
超負荷 overload; overloaded;
~超負荷運轉 overloaded operation;
工作負荷 workload;
~安全工作負荷 safe working load;
功能負荷 functional load;
交際負荷 communication load;

[負笈] leave home to study;
負笈從師 carry one's bookcase to follow one's teacher; shoulder one's satchel and go to one's teacher — study

abroad;
負笈求師 carry one's bookcase and go abroad as a student to seek a teacher; shoulder one's bookcase to seek learned masters;
負笈遊學 pursue one's studies away from home;
負笈遠遊 carry a satchel and travel to a great distance to study; study in a place far away from home;

[負極] cathode;
[負面] flip side;
[負片] negative;
彩色負片 colour negative;
[負氣] do sth in a fit of pique;
負氣而去 leave angrily out of spite;
[負傷] be wounded;
身負重傷 be badly wounded; be seriously injured;
[負數] negative number;
[負險固守] put up a stubborn defence by relying on one's strategic position;
[負向] negative orientation;
負向強化 negative reinforcement;
負向轉移 negative transfer;
[負心] desert one's love or lover; fail to be loyal to one's love;
負心漢 love rat;
[負嵎依險] fight from high position, back to cliffside;
[負約] break one's promise;
[負載] load; loading;
負載變化 load change;
安全負載 safe bearing load; safe load; safety load;
部分負債 partial loading;
電容性負債 capacitive loading;
動力負債 power loading;
附加負載 additional load;
耦合負載 coupled load;
聲負載 acoustic load;
[負責] bear one's responsibility; in charge of; responsible for; take one's responsibility;
負責人 honcho; person in charge; responsible member;
對…負責 account for; account to; answer for; answer to; be accountable for sth; be accountable to sb; be answerable for sb; be answerable to sb; be liable for sth; be responsible for sth; be responsible to sb; take care of; take charge of; take the responsibility upon sb;
個人負責 personal responsibility;
身負全責 take up the whole responsibility; undertake the whole management;
[負債] in debt; incur debts; indebtedness; liability;
負債比率 debt ratio;
負債經營 management in debt;
負債纍纍 deeply in debt; get into debt; head over ears in debt; heavily in debt; in the red; over head and ears in debt; run in debt; up to one's eyes in debt; up to one's neck in debt; own lots of debts;
~負債纍纍的 debt-ridden;
負債賬戶 liability account;
擔保負債 funded indebtedness;
國際負債 international indebtedness;
家庭總負債 total household debt;
淨負債 net indebtedness;
實際負債 actual liabilities;
應計負責 accrued liabilities;
有債券的負債 bonded indebtedness;
[負重] carry a heavy load on one's back;
負重致遠 bear a heavy burden and cover a long distance – be able to shoulder important tasks;
忍辱負重 endure humiliation in order to carry out an important mission;
如牛負重 carry a heavy load on one's back like an ox; like an ox carrying a heavy load; like loads on the backs of oxen; like beasts of burden; overburdened; toil like a beast of burden;

抱負 ambition; aspiration;
背負 (1) bear; carry on the back; (2) have on one's shoulder;
逋負 neglect to pay debts;
擔負 bear; shoulder; undertake;
辜負 fail to live up to; let down;
肩負 bear; shoulder; take on; undertake;
虧負 let sb down; let sb suffer;
民負 people's burden;
欺負 bluff; bluster; browbeat; bulldoze; bully; coerce; insult; intimidate; oppress; overbear; push around; ride roughshod over sb; ridicule; treat sb high-handedly; treat sb

rough;
勝負 success or failure; victory or defeat;
襁負 (1) infancy; (2) a carrying band for an infant;
倚負 depend on; rely on;
正負 plus-minus; positive and negative;
重負 heavy burden; heavy load;
自負 (1) responsible for one's own action; (2) be conceited; think highly of oneself;

fu
【赴】 attend; go to;
［赴會］ attend a meeting;
孑身赴會 attend the meeting alone;
［赴難］ go to help save the country from danger; go to the aid of one's country;
［赴湯蹈火］ confront danger and death; go into boiling water and walk on fire; go through fire and water; go through hell and high water; go through the fire;
［赴宴］ attend a banquet;
［赴約］ keep an appointment;

奔赴 go to; hasten to; hurry off for; hurry off to; hurry to a place; rush to;
分赴 leave for different destinations;
趕赴 proceed to without delay; rush to;
開赴 be bound for; march to;
駛赴 be bound for;

fu
【袝】 (1) enshrine in the ancestral temple; (2) bury in the family tomb;

fu
【副】 (1) assistant; associate; deputy; vice; (2) auxiliary; secondary; subsidiary; (3) correspond to; fit;
［副本］ backup copy; copy; duplicate; duplicate copy; transcript;
不可轉讓副本 non-negotiable copy;
複寫副本 carbon copy;
硬副本 hard copy;
證明副本 attested copy;
［副詞］ adverb;
副詞短語 adverbial phrase;
副詞化 adverbialization;
不定頻度副詞 adverb of indefinite frequency;
程度副詞 adverb of degree;
持續副詞 adverb of duration;
地點副詞 adverb of place;
動副詞 action adverb;
方式副詞 adverb of manner;
分離性副詞 adverb as disjunct;
附加性副詞 adverb as adjunct;
工具副詞 instrumental adverb;
關係副詞 relative adverb;
加添副詞 additive adverb;
焦點副詞 focusing adverb;
介詞性副詞 prepositional adverb;
句子副詞 sentential adverb;
連接副詞 conjunctive adverb;
連接性副詞 adverb as conjunct;
排除副詞 adverb of exception;
頻度副詞 adverb of frequency;
普通副詞 ordinary adverb;
讓步副詞 adverb of concession; concessive adverb;
時間副詞 adverb of time;
位置副詞 adverb of position;
疑問副詞 interrogative adverb;
語氣副詞 adverb of mood;
［副歌］ chorus;
［副官］ aide;
［副刊］ (newspaper) supplement;
［副品］ substandard goods;
［副食］ non-staple food;
副食品 non-staple food;
~副食品補貼 subsidy to offset the increased prices of non-staple food;
［副手］ (1) assistant; helper; (2) deputy;
［副署］ countersign;
［副業］ auxiliary occupation; side-line occupation; subsidiary occupation;
副業生產 sideline production;
家庭副業 household sideline production;

大副 chief officer; first mate;

fu
【婦】 (1) woman; (2) married woman; (3) one's wife;
［婦道］ woman; womenfolk;
婦道人家 the fair sex; the womenfolk;
守婦道 follow female virtues;
［婦科］ gynaecology;
婦科病 gynopathy;
婦科醫生 gyrnaecologist;
［婦女］ fair sex; fairer sex; woman;
婦女病 gynaecological disease; women's ailments;
婦女節 International Women's Day (8

March);
婦女倫理學 ethics of women;
保護婦女 shield women;
憤怒的婦女 angry women;
~ 一群憤怒的婦女 a mob of angry women;
家庭婦女 housewife;
姦污婦女 rape a woman;
年輕婦女 young women;
~ 一群年輕婦女 a bevy of young women;
中年婦女 women of middle age;

[婦人] married woman;
婦人之見 view of a woman;
時髦婦人 a lady of fashion;

[婦孺] women and children;
婦孺皆知 every women and children all know it; it is known even to women and children;

[婦幼] women and children;
婦幼衛生 maternity and child hygiene;

產婦 lying-in woman;
娼婦 bitch; whore;
醜婦 minger;
爨婦 female cook;
村婦 country woman; village woman;
蕩婦 alley cat; easy mark; easy meat; floozie; floozy; goer; hussy; man-crazy woman; scarlet woman; slag; slapper; whore; woman of loose moral;
弟婦 sister-in-law; younger brother's wife;
刁婦 shrew;
夫婦 husband and wife;
寡婦 widow;
貴婦 gentlewoman; noble lady;
悍婦 battleaxe;
奸婦 adulteress;
姦婦 adulteress; paramour;
荊婦 my wife;
嫠婦 widow;
農婦 peasant woman;
姘婦 adulteress; mistress;
潑婦 fishwife; harridan; harpy; shrew; shrewish woman; vixen;
僕婦 elderly woman servant;
棄婦 abandoned woman; deserted wife;
巧婦 clever woman;
妾婦 (1) concubine referring to herself; (2) common person; inferior person;
情婦 a bit of jam; fancy woman; housekeeper; inamorata; mistress; illicit girlfriend; one's bit of nonsense; shack job; the other woman;
妊婦 pregnant woman;
少婦 young married woman;
孀婦 widow;
媳婦 daughter-in-law; son's wife;
小婦 (1) concubine; (2) young woman;
新婦 bride;
淫婦 cocotte; immoral woman; scarlet woman; slag; slapper; whore;
孕婦 pregnant woman;
貞婦 chaste woman;
侄婦 wife of brother's son;
姪婦 wife of one's nephew;
冢婦 the eldest daughter-in-law;
主婦 housewife;
子婦 (1) son and daughter-in-law; (2) daughter-in-law; one's son's wife;

fu

【傅】 (1) teach; teacher; (2) add to; be attached to; be attached with; go together with; (3) a surname;

師傅 master;

fu

【富】 (1) rich; wealthy; (2) abundant; rich in;

[富貴] riches and honour; wealth and rank;
富貴多朋友，患難見交情 prosperity gets friends, but adversity distinguishes them; prosperity makes friends and adversity tries them;
富貴浮雲 regard honour and riches as floating clouds;
富貴利達 rich and powerful; riches, honour and success;
富貴人家 rich and powerful family;
安享富貴 enjoy wealth and honour;
出身富貴 be born into wealth; be born with a silver spoon in one's mouth;
貪圖富貴 desire wealth and honour;

[富國] enrich the country;
富國利民 enrich the country and benefit the people; enrich the state and bring benefits to the people; promote national welfare and foster the happiness of the people;
富國強兵 enrich the country and increase its military force; make one's country rich and build up its military power; make the country rich and at the same

time maintain an efficient army; make the country rich and its military force efficient;

[富豪] millionaire; rich and powerful people;
超級富豪 the ultra-rich;
女富豪 millionaires;

[富集] enrichment;
次生富集 secondary enrichment;
過高富集 excessive enrichment;
陰極層富集 cathode layer enrichment;

[富家] rich family;
富家一席酒，貧漢半年糧 a rich man's banquet is a poor man's food for half a year;
富家子弟 sons of rich families;

[富民] enrich the people;
policy of enriching the people;

[富農] rich peasant;
不法富農 lawless rich peasant;
舊式富農 old-type rich peasant;
新式富農 new-type rich peasant;

[富強] prosperous and strong;
民富國強 the people live in plenty and the country is strong;

[富饒] abundant; fertile; rich in;
土地富饒 the soil is fertile;

[富人] rich people;
遊手好閒的富人 the idle rich;

[富商] millionaire businessman;
一位富商 millionaire businessman;

[富庶] rich and populous;

[富態] fat; plump; stout;

[富翁] man of wealth; moneybags; rich man;
百萬富翁 millionaire;
千萬富翁 multimillionaire;
億萬富翁 billionaire; zillionaire;

[富有] big purse; fat purse; heavy purse; long well-lined purse; rich; wealthy;
富有成效 fruitful; productive of results; to good purpose;
富有經驗 of rich experience; rich in experience; very experienced;
富有生命力 full of vitality;
富有遠見 full of farsightedness;
非常富有 roll in riches;

[富於] rich in;
富於春秋 in the prime of life; rich in years;
富於同情心 have wide sympathies;
富於營養 nourishing; rich in nutrition;

[富餘] have enough and to spare; have more than needed;

[富裕] prosperous; well-off; well-to-do;
富裕地區 areas of well-being; better-off area;
富裕濶綽的人 person of ample means;
富裕起來 become prosperous; become rich; become well-to-do; become well-off; flourish; prosper; thrive;
富裕社會 affluent society;
富裕之家 prosperous family;
繁榮富裕 prosperity and affluence;
很富裕 flush with money;
黎元富裕 the masses are prosperous — in easy circumstances;

[富足] abundant; plentiful; rich;
富足的日子 a well-to-do life;
富足社會 affluent society;

暴富 sudden wealth;
財富 riches; wealth;
鬥富 show off one's wealth by spending more money than someone else;
豐富 aboundant; enrich; plentiful; rich;
國富 national wealth;
豪富 powerful and wealthy;
宏富 abundant; rich;
露富 show one's riches;
貧富 poverty and affluence; the haves and the have-nots; the rich and the poor;
窮富 the poor and the rich;
饒富 abundant; affluence; plentiful;
首富 the richest family of a district;
新富 new money; new rich;
殷富 prosperous; rich; wealth; well-off;
淵富 rich and variegated;
乍富 from rags to riches; sudden wealth;
致富 get rich; make a fortune;

fu

【復】 (1) come back; return; (2) answer; reply; (3) recover; resume; (4) again; repeat; repeatedly; (5) a surname;

[復辟] (1) the restoration of a dethroned monarch; (2) restoration of monarchy;
復辟活動 restorationist activity;
陰謀復辟 plot to stage a comeback;

[復仇] avenge; revenge; take revenge; vengeance;
復仇心理 a desire for revenge; vindictiveness;

復仇雪恥 get even with a person to wreck out one's vengeance; take one's revenge on sb for an insult;
發誓要復仇 vow to avenge;
決心復仇 resolve on vengeance;
向敵人復仇 take vengeance on an enemy;

[復出] come out again; come out of retirement again;

[復電] cable a reply;

[復發] have a relapse; recur; relapse; return;
復發率 recurrence rate;
舊病復發 fall back again into illness; fall into one's bad old ways again; have a recurrence of an old illness; have a relapse; have a relapse of a disease; have an attack of an old illness; slip back into one's bad old ways; succumb to one's old weaknesses again;
宿病復發 repetition of an old ailment;

[復返] return;
一去不復返 be gone forever;

[復古] backswing; restore ancient ways; return to the ancients;
復古倒退 return to the old and retrogress;
復古傾向 tendency towards idolizing the ancients;
復古思想 back-to-the-ancients ideology;
崇洋復古 worship the foreign and revive the ancient;

[復工] go back to work; return to work; start operations again;

[復核] check;

[復活] (1) bring back to life; resurgence; resuscitate; revive; (2) Resurrection;
復活彩蛋 Easter egg;
復活節 Easter;
復活日 the Easter Day;

[復舊] restoration of old ways; return to the original condition; return to the past; throwback;
復舊如新 restore sth to its original state;

[復明] revival of light;
殘燈復明 the reviving flicker of an expiring lamp — the last flicker of life in a dying man;

[復命] report on completion of a mission or task;

[復任] return to one's former office; take up a position one held formerly;

[復生] become alive again;
死而復生 come back to life; resurrect; return to life after death; revive; rise from the dead;

[復蘇] (1) come back to life; resuscitate; (2) recovery;
復蘇現象 resurgence;
經濟復蘇 economic recovery;

[復位] (1) be restored to the throne; (2) replace;
骨折復位 reduction of the fracture;
脱臼復位 replace dislocated joints;

[復習] brush up; dust off; get up; go over; look over; look through; review; review lessons learned; revise; run over;
復習功課 review one's lessons;

[復現] reappear; reappearance;

[復校] reactivate a school; reactivation of a school;

[復新] make anew; make to look as new;

[復興] return to prosperity; revival;
民族復興 national rejuvenation;
文藝復興 the Renaissance;
戰後復興 postwar recovery;
宗教復興 religious revival;

[復醒] wake up again;

[復姓] resume the original family name;

[復業] resume or return to business again;

[復議] discuss a proposal or project which has been rejected or discarded previously;

[復元] as good as new;

[復原] restoration; return to original state or condition;
代數法復原 algebraic approach restoration;
非約束復原 unconstrained restoration;
自發復原 spontaneous restoration;

[復員] demobilize;
復員中心 demobilization centre;

[復診] further consultation; return visit; subsequent visit;

[復政] regain power;

[復職] reinstate an official to the former position; reinstate sb in his former office; reinstatement; resume one's post;

報復 avenge; get back at sb; get one's own back on sb; have one's own back on sb; make reprisals; retaliate;

康復 convalesce; get well; on the mend; recover;

restored to health;
克復 recapture; recover; retake;
平復 (1) be pacified; calm down; subside; (2) be cured; be healed;
收復 recapture; recover;
往復 move back and forth; reciprocate;
興復 restore; revive;
修復 (1) make as good as new; renovate; repair; restore; (2) repair;

fu

【腹】 (1) abdomen; belly; stomach; (2) protruding part of a vessel; (3) a surname;

[腹背] in front and behind;
腹背受敵 be attacked both from behind and in front; be caught between two fires; between the devil and the deep sea; between the hammer and the anvil; have enemies in front and rear;
腹背相親 very intimate;
腹背之毛 sth insignificant; trifle;

[腹部] abdomen; midriff; stomach;
腹部去脂術 abdominoplasty;
腹部疼痛 a pain in one's abdomen;
鬆弛的腹部 flabby stomach;

[腹地] hinterland;

[腹誹] unspoken criticisms;

[腹稿] draft; mental notes;

[腹肌] abdominal muscle; abs;
腹肌痛 celiomyalgia; myocelialgia;
腹肌炎 celiomyositis; laparomyitis;
鍛鍊腹肌 harden one's abs;

[腹絞痛] angina abdominis; cramps;

[腹裏藏刀] hiding a sword in the bossom; very treacherous;
腹中藏刀 a dagger hidden in the belly — a treacherous person;

[腹裂] celoschisis;

[腹瘤] celioma;

[腹鳴] borborygmus;

[腹膜] abdominal membrane;
腹膜病 peritoneopathy;
腹膜炎 peritonitis;
~產後腹膜炎 puerperal peritonitis;
~腸腹膜炎 exenteritis;
~出血性腹膜炎 hemorrhagic peritonitis;
~穿孔性腹膜炎 perforative peritonitis;
~創傷性腹膜炎 traumatic peritonitis;
~肥厚性腹膜炎 pachyperitonitis;
~假腹膜炎 pseudoperitonitis;
~結核性腹膜炎 tuberculous peritonitis;
~局限性腹膜炎 circumscribed peritoritis; localized peritonitis;
~彌漫性腹膜炎 diffuse peritonitis;
~黏連性腹膜炎 adhesive peritonitis;
~念珠菌性腹膜炎 candida peritonitis;
~膿毒性腹膜炎 septic peritonitis;
~膿氣性腹膜炎 pyopneumoperitonitis;
~氣性腹膜炎 pneumoperitonitis;
~潛伏性腹膜炎 silent peritonitis;
~細菌性腹膜炎 bacterial peritonitis;
~硬化性腹膜炎 sclerosing peritonitis;
~終期腹膜炎 terminal peritonitis;
~周期性腹膜炎 periodic peritonitis;
~子宮腹膜炎 metroperitonitis;

[腹內腫塊] abdominal mass;

[腹氣脹] tympanites;

[腹腔] abdominal cavity;
腹腔穿刺術 abdominocentesis;
腹腔鏡 abdominoscopy;

[腹熱心煎] look forward to sth very eagerly;

[腹水] ascites; ascitic fluid;
抽腹水 tap the abdomen;
早發性腹水 ascites praecox;

[腹痛] abdominal pain; stomach ache;
腹痛如絞 have an excurciating pain in the belly;

[腹外斜肌] oblique abdominal muscle;

[腹無滴墨] therre is not a single drop of ink in the bosom; utterly uneducated;

[腹瀉] diarrhoea; have lose bowels;
病毒性腹瀉 virus diarrhoea;
晨起腹瀉 morning diarrhoea;
傳染性腹瀉 infectious diarrhoea;
刺激性腹瀉 irritative diarrhoea;
機械性腹瀉 mechanical diarrhoea;
積便性腹瀉 paradoxical diarrhoea;
積糞性腹瀉 paradoxical diarrhoea;
流行性腹瀉 epidemic diarrhoea;
急性腹瀉 sudden onset of diarrhoea;
旅游者腹瀉 traveller's diarrhoea;
熱帶腹瀉 tropical diarrhoea;
滲透性腹瀉 osmotic diarrhoea;
特發性腹瀉 idiopathic steatorrhoea;
夏季腹瀉 summer diarrhoea;
消化不良性腹瀉 lienteric diarrhoea;
炎性腹瀉 inflammatory diarrhoea;
胰原性腹瀉 pancreatic diarrhoea;
嬰兒腹瀉 infantile diarrhoea;

[腹心] (1) belly and the heart; (2) true thoughts and feelings; (3) reliable

agent; trusted subordinate;
腹心之患 danger from within;
敢不腹心 make a frank statement without reservations; speak boldly from the depth of one's heart;
[腹議] criticize in one's mind;
[腹有鱗甲] harbour evil intentions and be unapproachable; one's mind is treacherous and evil; treacherous;
[腹脹] abdominal distension; meteorism;
腹脹如鼓 a well-to-do person; one's belly is tight as a drum — well fed and content;
[腹直肌] straight abdominal muscle;
[腸腹] intestines;

鼓腹 (1) eating well and living well; well-fed and unoccupied; (2) beat one's belly as a drum;
果腹 fill the stomach; satisfy one's hunger;
壺腹 ampulla;
空腹 on an empty stomach;
口腹 food;
滿腹 having one's mind filled with;
袜腹 stomacher;
捧腹 split one's sides with laughter;
剖腹 cut open the stomach; make an abdominal incision;
氣腹 pneumoperitoneum;
枵腹 empty stomach;
小腹 lower abdomen; underbelly;
心腹 (1) bosom friend; confidant; henchman; reliable agent; trusted subordinate; (2) faith; loyalty;
魚腹 fish belly;

fu

【複】 (1) double; overlapping; (2) complex; (3) reiterate; repeat; (4) lined garment;
[複本] copy;
代用複本 dummy copy;
增添複本 added copy;
[複比] compound ratio; double ratio;
複比例 compound proportion;
[複查] check again; double-check; re-examine; re-investigate; review;
[複合] complex; composite; compound; recombination;
複合詞 compound word;
~複合詞構詞法 compound word formation;
~並列複合詞 copulative compound;
~重迭式複合詞 iterative compound;
~假複合詞 improper compound;
~聚集複合詞 aggregative compound;
複合從屬連詞 compound subordinator;
複合動詞 compound verb;
複合合成句 compound complex sentence;
複合介詞 compound preposition;
複合句 complex sentence;
~并列複合句 compound sentence;
~多重複合句 multiple compound sentence;
~緊縮複合句 compressed compound sentence;
~主從複合句 complex sentence;
複合名詞 compound noun;
複合命題 compound proposition;
複合器 recombiner;
~催化複合器 catalytic recombiner;
複合人稱代詞 compound personal pronoun;
複合生產系統 complex system;
複合時 compound tense;
複合數詞 compound numeral;
複合雙語現象 compound bilingualism;
複合物 composite;
複合形容詞 compound adjective;
複合主語 compound subject;
等離子體複合 plasma recombination;
輻射複合 radiative recombination;
間接複合 indirect recombination;
線性複合 linear recombination;
誘導複合 induced recombination;
擇優複合 preferential recombination;
[複基] compound radical;
[複句] complex sentence; a compound sentence;
[複利] compound interest;
[複名數] compound number;
[複賽] intermediary heat; play-off; quarter-final; semi-final;
[複色] compound colour;
[複式] (1) double; (2) double entry;
複式會計 double entry account;
[複視] diplopia;
單眼複視 polyopia monophthalmica;
生理性複視 physiological diplopia;
同側複視 homonymous diplopia;
[複數] (1) plural number; (2) complex number; plurality;

F

共軛複數 conjugate imaginary numbers;
規則複數 regular plural;
零複數 zero plural;

[複寫] duplicate; make carbon copies; reproduce;
複寫紙 carbon paper;

[複姓] compound surname; two-character surname;

[複選] (1) election by delegates; indirect election; (2) run-off; (3) semi-final;

[複眼] compound eye;

[複葉] compound leaf;

[複印] copy; copying; duplicate; photocopy; xerox;
複印成本 copying cost;
複印費用 copying charge;
複印機 copier; copying machine;
~ 靜電複印機 electrostatic copier;
~ 智能複印機 intelligent copier;
複印速度 copying speed;

[複雜] complex; complicated; intricate; sophisticated;
複雜化 make complicated;
複雜性 complexity;
~ 計算複雜性 computational complexity;

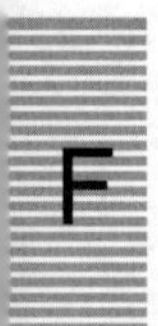

[複製] copy; copying; duplicate; replication; reproduce;
複製帶 tape copy;
複製機 duplicator;
~ 磁帶複製機 tape duplicator;
~ 卡片複製機 card duplicator;
~ 模型複製機 mold duplicator;
~ 手動複製機 manual duplicator;
複製錄音指示 dubbing indicator;
複製品 dup; duplicate; knock-off; replica;
複製者 copyist;
單向複製 unidirectional replication;
基因複製 gene replication;
文件複製 document copying;
轉環複製 swivel replication;

fu

【賦】 (1) bestow on; endow with; vest with; (2) descriptive prose; (3) compose a poem;

[賦格曲] fugue;

[賦稅] taxes;

[賦閒] unemployed;

[賦有] be endowed with; be gifted with; possess;
賦有才能 be gifted with talents;

[賦予] endow; entrust; give;
秉賦 gift; natural endowments;
稟賦 natural endowments; talent;
辭賦 rhymed composition;
貢賦 tribute and taxes;
天賦 (1) inborn; innate; (2) endowments; natural gift; talent;
田賦 taxes on agricultural land;

fu

【駙】 (1) extra horse harnessed by the side of the team; (2) swift;

[駙馬] emperor's son-in-law;

fu

【蝮】 (1) viper; (2) a surname;

[蝮蛇] adder; hagworm; water mocassin;

fu

【蚨】 a kind of small insect which can move things many times its weight;

[蚨蝂] a kind of insect mentioned in ancient literature;

fu

【輹】 pieces of wood holding the axle underneath a cart;

fu

【鮒】 carassius; gold carp;

fu

【賻】 give a gift to a bereaved family;

[賻錢] money given to a bereaved family;

[賻儀] gift to a bereaved family;

[賻贈] present a gift to a bereaved family;

fu

【覆】 (1) cover; (2) overturn; upset;

[覆巢無完卵] if a country is beaten, all it's people will suffer; when the nest falls, there are no whole eggs; when the nest is overturned, no eggs stay unbroken;
覆巢之下安得完卵 no egg stays unbroken when the nest is upset — when disaster befalls a family, no member can escape unscathed;

[覆蓋] (1) cover; overlap; (2) plant cover; vegetation; (3) cover; covering;
覆蓋率 rate of coverage;
覆蓋面積 coverage area;
覆蓋物 overlay;
薄片覆蓋 laminated covering;
程序覆蓋 programme overlay;

動態覆蓋 dynamic overlay;
基本覆蓋 basic overlay;
極大點覆蓋 maximum point covering;
極小線覆蓋 minimum line covering;
可數覆蓋 numerable covering;
瓊脂覆蓋 agar overlay;
文法覆蓋 grammar covering;
線覆蓋 line covering;
正規覆蓋 normal covering;

[覆滅] complete collapse; destruction; doom;

[覆沒] (1) capsize and sink; (2) be annihilated; be overwhelmed; be routed; be wiped out;

[覆水難收] spilled water cannot be gathered up; the mill cannot grind with the water that is past; it is no use crying over spilt milk; things done cannot be undone; what is done cannot be undone; what is lost is lost; when water's spilt you can never retrieve it—difficult for a divorced couple to remarry;

[覆亡] demise; fall;
巢覆雛亡 the nest comes down and the young birds are killed by the fall;

[覆羽] covert;
大覆羽 greater coverts;
~次級大覆羽 greater secondary coverts;
上覆羽 upper wing coverts;
中覆羽 medium coverts;
~次級中覆羽 medium secondary coverts;

[覆轍] the track of an overturned cart;
重蹈覆轍 follow the same old disastrous road; get on to the path of; go the way of; meet the same fate as that of; take the same disastrous road;
仍蹈覆轍 continue at sb's unsuccessful practices; meet with disaster by following the steps of another;

被覆 cover; covering;
顛覆 overturn; subvert; turn upside down;
翻覆 overturn; turn upside down;
傾覆 (1) capsize; overturn; topple; (2) collapse; fail; lose;

fu

【馥】 aroma; fragrance;

[馥郁] heavy perfume; strong fragrance;

芳馥 fragrance;
馥馥 fragrant;

fu

【鰒】 abalone;

ga¹

ga

【旮】 dark corner;

［旮旯］ (1) corner; nook; (2) out-of-the-way place;

ga

【咖】 transliteration of the character 咖;

［咖哩］ curry;

咖哩鯧魚 curry pomfret;
咖哩粉 curry powder;
咖哩雞 chicken curry; curried chicken;
咖哩醬 curry paste;
咖哩牛腩 brisket curry;
咖哩牛肉 beef curry;
咖哩蝦 prawn curry;
咖哩蜆 curry clams;
咖哩蟹 crab curry;
咖哩羊肉 mutton curry;
咖哩魚 fish curry;
咖哩珠蚌 curry mussels;
咖哩豬肉 pork curry;

ga²

ga

【軋】 (1) associate with; make friends with; (2) press hard against each other; push against; (3) check;

［軋頭］ dog;

［軋帳］ check the accounts;

ga

【釓】 gadolinium;

［釓合金］ godalinium alloy;

ga⁴

ga

【尬】 embarrassed; ill at ease;

gai¹

gai

【垓】 (1) far and remote places; wilds beyond the frontier; (2) boundary; limit; (3) a hundred million;

［垓下］ Gaixia, in Anhui Province;

gai

【陔】 (1) grades; order; scale; steps; storey; (2) a place near the steps;

gai

【荄】 grass roots;

gai

【該】 (1) ought to; should; (2) one's turn to do sth; (3) deserve; (4) most likely; probably; (5) owe; (6) that; the above-mentioned; the said; this;

［該當］ (1) deserve; (2) should;

該當別論 should be regarded as a different matter;
該當何罪 what punishment do you deserve; what should be the punishment;
該當如此 it should be like that; it should be so;
該當萬死 deserve to die a thousand times;

［該和則和，該嚴則嚴］ be stern when it is necessary and extremely gentle too if the occasion warrants;

［該死］ (1) damned; dang; (2) deserve to die; ought to die;

該死的 bugger; damned; for crying out loud; go to blazes; goddammit; goddamn; how tiresome;

［該帳］ in debt;

［該着］ certainly. naturally; ought to;

［該做則做］ if you find it correct then you should act;

本該 ought to have; should have;
不該 should not;
活該 not wronged at all; serve sb right;
應該 behoove; belong; bound to; deserve; do well; due; expected to; have no business to; incumbent on; it is for...to; it is time that; it is time to; merit; might; must; ought to; owe; right; shall; should; supposed to; up to; want; well;

gai

【賅】 (1) be included in; nothing left out; provided for; (2) all-inclusive; complete; comprehensive; full;

［賅括］ generalize; summarize;

gai³

gai

【改】 (1) change; transform; (2) alter; modify; revise; (3) correct; put right; rectify; (4) switch over to; (5) a surname;

［改扮］ disguise oneself as;

［改編］ (1) adapt; adaptation; convert; rearrange; revise; transcribe; (2) redesignate; reorganize;

改編本 adaptation;
~電視改編本 television adaptation;
~小說改編本 adaptation of a novel;
改編目錄 recataloguing;
改編者 adaptor;
翻譯改編 adaptation in translating;
風格改編 stylistic adaptation;

[改變] alter; change; convert; modify; mold; transform; turn;
改變調子 change one's note; change one's tune; dance to another tune; sing a different tune; sing another tune;
改變決定 think better of one's decision;
改變立場 change one's position; shift one's ground; turn one's coat;
改變生活方式 change one's style of living;
改變主意 change of heart; change one's mind;
改來變去 shift about;
作出改變 make a change;

[改步改玉] adopt different measures according to circumstances;

[改竄] falsify; tamper with;

[改錯] (1) correct a wrong word; (2) correct one's mistake;
有錯則改 once a mistake is made, one should correct it;
知錯不改 aware of one's own mistakes and make no attempt to correct them; cling to the mistake instead of correcting it;
知錯則改 if you know you have made mistakes, corrent them;

[改道] (1) change one's route; rechannel; (2) change the course of a river;
改道而行 change one's course of action;
交通改道 traffic diversions;

[改掉] drop; give up; remove;
改掉不良作風 get rid of a bad style;

[改訂] reformulate; rewrite;
改訂計劃 reformulate the plan;

[改動] alter; amend; change; improve on; modify;

[改革] reform; reformation;
改革財政 reform the financial affairs;
改革措施 reform measures;
改革方向 orientation of reform;
改革活力 vigour in reform;
~注入改革活力 inject vigour into reform;
改革家 reformer; reformist;
~徹底的改革家 all-out reformer;
改革開放 refrom and open; reform and open to the outside world; reform and open up; reform and openness;
~改革開放政策 the policy of reform and opening-up;
改革派 reform group; reform school;
改革試點 selected units for experiments in reform;
改革園地 field of reform;
改革者 reformer;
徹底改革 overhaul;
貨幣改革 currency reform;
加快改革 accelerate the reform; speed up the reform;
金融改革 financial reform;
課程改革 curriculum reform;
深化改革 deepen reform;
~全面深化改革 deepen reform comprehensively;
土地改革 agrarian reform; land reform;
信用改革 credit reform;
重大改革 step change;

[改觀] change the appearance of; change the face of; put a new face on sth;
大為改觀 change greatly;

[改過] correct one's mistakes; mend one's ways;
改過不嫌遲 it is never too late to mend;
改過遷善 change from sin to holiness; convert from a bad life to a good one; correct evil doings and revert to good deeds; reform errors and practise what is morally good;
改過自新 become a new man; convert from a bad life to a good one; correct one's errors and make a fresh start; correct one's mistakes and turn over a new leaf; live down; mend one's ways and start anew; reform oneself; repent and reform; start with a clean slate; turn over a new leaf;

[改行] change one's profession; change one's trade;
不斷改行 drift from job to job;

[改換] change; change over to;
改換地點 change the place; change the venue;
改換家門 change the status of one's family; raise the social position of one's family;

改換門庭 grow prosperous; rise in prominence;

[改悔] repent;
樂於改悔 willing to repent;

[改嫁] (of a woman) remarry;

[改建] rebuild; reconstruct; transform;
房屋改建 the alteration of the houses;

[改進] better; improve; improvement; make better; mend; perfect;
改進方法 method to remedy;
操作改進 operations improvement;
輻合改進 convergent improvement;
設備改進 capital improvement;
顯著的改進 marked improvement; noticeable improvement;
營利改進 profit improvement;
有改進 see an improvement;
重大改進 great improvement; major improvement; vast improvement;
逐步改進 gradual improvement;
總體上的改進 general improvement;

[改口] correct oneself; modify one's previous remarks; withdraw one's previous remarks;

[改良] (1) ameliorate; improve; (2) reform;
改良派 reformist;
改良主義 reformism;

[改判] amend a judgement; change the original sentence; commute;

[改期] change the date;
會議改期 change the date of the meeting;

[改任] change to another post;

[改日] another day; some other day;
改日再來 come again another day;

[改善] ameliorate; better; improve; improvement; mend; modify; perfect;
改善供應 supply more and better commodities;
改善關係 mend one's fences;
改善交通設施 improve the traffic conditions;
改善投資環境 improve the investment environment;
很大的改善 big improvement;
進一步的改善 further improvement;
經營管理改善 administrative improvement;
局部改善 local improvement;
條件改善 improvement of terms;

[改天] another day; some other day;
改天吧 take a rain check;
改天換地 change heaven and earth; change the earth's features; change the world; make nature over; remake nature; reshape nature; transform nature;

[改土] improve the soil;
改土治水 improve the soil and control the water;

[改絃] start afresh;
改絃更張 adopt new ways; change over to new ways; change the course; cut loose from the past and make a new start; make a fresh start; mend one's ways; start a thorough reform; start afresh;
改絃易轍 change one's direction; dance to another tune; make a new start; strike out on a new path;

[改寫] adapt; rewrite;
改寫員 rewriteman;

[改選] reelect;

[改元] change the designation of an imperial reign; change the title of a reign;
改元易號 change the designation of an imperial reign; change the title of a reign;

[改灶節煤] make alterations in an oven so that it will burn less coal;

[改造] reform; remake; remould; revamp; transform;
改造廚房 revamp one's kitchen;
改造社會風氣 reform the standards of social conduct;
改造世界 change the world;
改造世界觀 remould one's outlook;
改造思想 remould one's ideology;
改造自然 remake nature; transform nature; transformation of nature;
城市改造 urban renewal;
環境改造 environmental reform;
技術改造 technical reform;

[改轍] change one's course of action;

[改正] amend; correct; put right;
彩色改正 colour correction;
限期改正 correct one's mistakes with a stated timer;

[改製] customize;

[改裝] (1) change one's costume or dress; (2) repack; repackage; (3) reequip; refit;

改裝車 hot rod;
[改錐] screwdriver;
[改組] reorganize; reshuffle; shake-up;
改組內閣 reshuffle the cabinet;
[改嘴] modify one's previous remarks;

不改 not change;
纂改 distort; falsify; misrepresent;
竄改 falsify; tamper with;
翻改 renovate;
更改 alter; change;
悔改 repent and mend one's way; repent and reform;
校改 read and correct proofs;
勞改 reform through labour;
批改 correct;
悛改 reform oneself; repent of one's sin;
刪改 delete and change; delete and improve; revise;
擅改 change without authorization; revise without authorization;
塗改 alter; erase and change the wording of an article; obliterate;
挖改 cut and make changes;
修改 alter; amend; correct; emend; modification; modify; revise;

gai⁴
gai
【丐】 (1) beg for alms; (2) beggar; (3) bestow; give; grant;
[丐幫] beggar gang;
[丐詞] beg term;
[丐頭] leader of beggars;

乞丐 beggar;

gai
【溉】 (1) irrigate; water; (2) wash;

gai
【鈣】 calcium;
[鈣化] calcify;
[鈣片] calcium tablet;

氯化鈣 calcium chloride;
硫酸鈣 calcium sulphate;
乙酸鈣 calcium acetate;

gai
【概】 (1) approximate; general; general outline; (2) exemplify; generalize; typify; (3) categorically; without exception; (4) deportment; manner of carrying oneself;
[概觀] general survey; review;
[概況] basic facts; general situation; lay of the land; survey;
調查經濟概況 investigate the general economic situation;
[概括] (1) generalize; summarize; (2) briefly; in broad outline;
概括地說 generally speaking; in a nutshell; put it briefly; to sum up; to summarize;
概括人稱 generic person;
概括性 generality;
[概率] probability;
範圍概率 coverage probability;
複合概率 composite probability;
合成概率 compound probability;
絕對概率 absolute probability;
累積概率 cumulative probability;
平均概率 average probability;
條件概率 conditional probability;
吸收概率 absorption probability;
[概略] outline; summary;
[概論] introduction; outline; survey;
概論課程 survey course;
概而論之 put it briefly; put it in a nutshell; generally speaking;
[概貌] general picture;
[概莫能外] admit of no exception; it admits of no exception;
[概念] concept; conception; idea; notion;
概念詞 concept word; conceptual term;
概念翻譯 conceptual translation;
概念分類法 classification of concept;
概念功能 ideational function;
概念句 conceptual sentence;
概念論 conceptualism;
~概念論者 conceptualist;
概念形成 concept formation;
概念性分別 conceptual differene;
概念意義 conceptual meaning;
概念藝術 conceptual art;
概念語法 notional grammar;
抽象概念 abstract concept; abstract conception; abstraction;
對偶概念 dual concept;
反饋概念 feedback concept;
分段概念 fractional concept;
基本概念 fundamental conception;
絕對概念 absolute concept;

派生概念 derivational concept;
一般概念 general concept;
一種概念 an abstraction;
預算概念 budget concept;
總合概念 aggregate concept;
總括概念 all-inclusive concept;

[概述] sketch; summary; survey;

[概數] approximate number;

[概要] abstract; bare bones; essentials; general outline; general remark; lexicon; line; resume;

大概 general outline; main idea;
梗概 broad outline; general idea; gist;
氣概 heroic; lofty quality; spirit;
一概 categorically; one and all; totally; without exception;

gai

【蓋】 (1) cap; cover; lid; (2) shell; (3) canopy; (4) cover; shield; (5) affix a seal; (6) excellent; surpass; the best; top; (7) build; construct; (8) about; approximately; (9) because; for; since; (10) ace out;

[蓋菜] leaf mustard;

[蓋地而來] come in large numbers;

[蓋覆] coating;
蓋覆作用 coating action;

[蓋棺論定] a man's merits or demerits can be finally judged only after his death; call no man happy before he is dead; one's character is correctly criticized after his death;

[蓋然性] probability;

[蓋世] matchless; unparalleled;
蓋世無雙 have no equal on earth; matchless; peerless; stand without peer in one's generation; the best one in the whole world; unparalleled; without an equal in the world;
蓋世英雄 peerless hero; the greatest hero in the world; the hero of the age;
蓋世之才 unsurpassed talent;

[蓋柿] lid persimmon;
大蓋柿 lid persimmon;

[蓋寫] overwrite;

[蓋因] it is because;

[蓋印] affix one's seal;

[蓋章] affix one's seal; seal; stamp;

[蓋子] cap; cover; lid; top;
揭蓋子 bring sth into the open; take the lid off sth; uncover the facts of;
擰上蓋子 screw a lid on;
瓶蓋子 bottle top;
牙膏蓋子 toothpaste top;

冰蓋 ice sheet;
翻蓋 renovate a house;
覆蓋 cover;
鍋蓋 pot cover;
華蓋 aureola;
鋪蓋 spread out;
膝蓋 knee;
修蓋 build a house;
壓蓋 gland;
掩蓋 conceal; cover;
遮蓋 (1) cover; (2) conceal; cover up; hide

gan¹

gan

【干】 (1) harry; interfere; jam; (2) invade; offend; oppose; (3) concern; involve; (4) beseech; seek; (5) bank of a river; (6) shield; (7) how many; how much; (8) stem; (9) a surname;

[干犯] (1) encroach upon; offend; (2) invade;
干犯法紀 break the law and violate discipline;

[干戈] armed conflicts; arms; war; weapons of war;
干戈擾攘 in the tumult of war;
干戈擾擾 incessant wars and the resultant unrest;
干戈入庫，偃武修文 the sword sleeps in the scabbard;
干戈四起 civil war breaks out in the country; fighting breaks out all over the country;
干戈相見 declare war on each other;
大動干戈 get into a fight; go to war;
化干戈為玉帛 beat swords into ploughshares and spears into pruning hooks; bury the hatchet; bury the tomahawk; cease hostilities and negotiate for peace; lay aside the tomahawk; put an end to war and have peace; turn hostility into friendship; turn swords into ploughshares;
息干戈 end hostilities; stop fighting;

[干己] concern oneself;

G

[干進] seek a higher office in government; seek official promotion;
[干連] implicate; involve;
[干祿] seek an official post;
[干冒] offend intentionally; transgress;
[干求] beseech; importune; request;
[干擾] backdrop; disturb; interfere; lapse; obstruct; tamper; trouble; upset;
干擾計 interferometer;
~ 聲干擾計 acoustic interferometer;
干擾破壞 interference and sabotage;
干擾視線 interrupt the view;
干擾素 interferon;
倒行干擾 retroactive interference;
交際干擾 communicative interference;
抗干擾 anti-interference;
氣動干擾 aerodynamical interference;
順行干擾 proactive interference;
阻塞干擾 blocking interference;
[干涉] butt in on sth; butt into sth; interfere in; interfere with; intervene in; meddle in; mess in; nose into; poke one's nose into sth; poke into sth; thrust one's nose into;
干涉量度學 interferometry;
~ 按時平均干涉量度學 time average interferometry;
~ 單曝干涉量度學 single exposure interferometry;
~ 全息干涉量度學 holographic interferometry;
~ 實時干涉量度學 real-time interferometry;
干涉內政 interference in domestic affairs; meddle in a country's internal affairs;
干涉素 interferon;
干涉圖樣 interference pattern;
干涉儀 interferometer;
~ 複式干涉儀 compound interferometer;
~ 記時干涉儀 chrono interferometer;
~ 角度干涉儀 angle interferometer;
不干涉 noninterference; nonintervention;
~ 不干涉的 hands-off;
~ 互不干涉 mutual noninterference; noninterference in each other's affairs;
機身干涉 body interference;
交叉干涉 chiasma interference;
結構干涉 constructive interference;
外力干涉 external intervention;
相消干涉 destructive interference;
遠紅外干涉 far infrared interference;
[干時] seek to keep up with the times; suit the occasion;
[干世] conformity; seek to conform with the world;
[干休] bring to an end; give up;
[干預] interfere; intervene; intervention; meddle;
不干預 keep one's nose out of;
市場干預 market intervention;
政府干預 government intervention;
[干譽] seek for higher reputation;
[干政] interfere in politics;

若干 (1) how many; how much; (2) a certain number or amount;
天干 the ten Heavenly Stems;
相干 (1) be concerned with; connected; have to do with; related; (2) coherent;

gan

【甘】 (1) pleasant; sweet; (2) of one's own accord; willingly; (3) of one's own accord;
[甘草] licorice;
甘草精 liquorice;
藥裏的甘草－總有份兒 as indispensable as the licorice root in Chinese medicine;
[甘井先竭] a sweet well dries early;
[甘居人下] content to be below others; contented to occupy a position below others; willing to enslave oneself to another person;
[甘苦] (1) sweetness and bitterness; weal and woe; (2) hardships and difficulties experienced in work;
甘苦備嘗 have tasted both sweetness and bitterness; have undergone both prosperity and adversity;
甘苦與共 cast one's lot with sb; stick by sb through thick and thin;
甘苦自知 one knows best what one has gone through with;
備嚐甘苦 have experienced good fortunes and adversities; have tasted the sweet and bitter; have tasted the sweetness and bitterness of life;
分甘共苦 fare and share alike; go through thick and thin together; share comforts and hardships; share good luck and ill; share prosperity and adversity; share

the sweet and the bitter together; share weal and woe;

苦盡甘來 after suffering comes happiness; after the bitter comes the sweet; after the bitter days are gone by come the sweet ones; dawn will follow the darkness; from foul to fair; luck turns after hardship; past labour is pleasure; sweet are the fruits of labour; the bitterness ends and the sweetness begins; when bitterness is finished, sweetness begins; when sorrow is at the end, then comes joy;

歷盡甘苦 have suffered many hardships;

同甘共苦 go through thick and thin together; in weal and woe; partake in each other's joys and sorrows; share bliss and adversity together; share comforts and hardships; share happiness and sufferings; share sb's joys and sorrows; share prosperity and adversity; share weal and woe; share with sb both prosperity and adversity; stand all weathers with; stick together though thick and thin; sweets and bitters; take the rough and smooth together; through thick and thin;

同甘苦，共患難 go through storm and stress together with; share the joys and sorros of; share weal and woe with;

[甘霖] good rain after a long drought; timely rainfall;

甘霖普降 seasonable rain has fallen everywhere;

久旱逢甘霖，他鄉遇故知 meeting an old friend in a distant land is like refreshing rain after a long drought;

沛雨甘霖 a deep and great favour; an abundant and seasonable rain;

[甘露] (1) sweet dew; (2) manna;

如得甘露 as if it were the sweetest dew from heaven;

[甘美] luscious; nectavean; nectarous; sweet and refreshing;

[甘薯] sweet potato;

[甘甜] luscious;

[甘味] (1) delicious food; (2) appetite for food;

食不甘味 eat but not have any taste for it — in great worry; eat food without knowing its taste — in deep anxiety; eat without relish; have no appetite for food — in deep sorrow;

[甘心] (1) readily; willing; (2) be content with; be reconciled; resign oneself to;

甘心俯首 content to bow one's head and yield to;

甘心樂意 of one's free will; perfectly happy;

甘心瞑目 die without dissatisfaction;

甘心清貧 have a sense of pride of one's poor material life;

甘心情願 act entirely of one's own free will; perfectly willing; willingly and gladly;

甘心於 be reconciled to; reconcile oneself to;

不甘心 not reconciled to; not resigned to;

死也甘心 willing to die;

心有未甘 somewhat dissatisfied;

[甘休] give up willingly; willing to stop;

誓不甘休 swear not to give up; swear not to let the matter drop; vow never to let an offender get away with the offense;

[甘言] honeyed words;

甘言蜜語 honeyed tongue and sugary words; honeyed words;

幣重言甘 coins heavy and words sweet;

蜜語甘言 honeyed phrases and sweet words;

[甘於] happy to; ready to; willing to;

甘於清貧 to be satisfied with poverty;

甘於屈就 content oneself with a subordinate job;

[甘願] readily; willingly;

甘願受罰 ready to bear punishment;

甘願效勞 exert oneself voluntarily in the service of another; glad to do sth for sb; glad to offer one's services; render readily a service to sb; willingly serve;

甘願作出讓步 make the concession willingly;

[甘蔗] sugar cane;

甘蔗沒有兩頭甜 sugar cane is never sweet at both ends — you cannot have it both ways;

糖甘蔗 sugar cane;

一段甘蔗 a segment of sugar cane;

[甘之如飴] enjoy sth bitter as if it were malt sugar—gladly endure hardships; consume sth pleasantly as if taking sugarplums—be willing to endure in adversity;

G

謞甘 polite and amiable in one's manner of speech;
不甘 not resigned to; unreconciled to; unwilling to;
情甘 voluntary; willing;
薦甘 amiable and mild;
旨甘 dainties; delicacies;

gan
【杆】 (1) shaft of a spear; wooden pole; (2) rod; (3) balustrade; wooden fence;
[杆子] (1) pole; rod; (2) gang of bandits;
杆子頭 ringleader of a gang;

欄杆 balustrade; railing;

gan
【肝】 liver;
[肝癌] hepatocarcinoma; liver cancer;
[肝變硬] cirrhosis of the liver;
結節性肝變硬 hobnail liver;
[肝病] hepatosis; liver ailment;
肝病口臭 liver breath;
肝病面容 facies hepatica;
肝病性口臭 fetor hepaticus;
肝病性水腫 hepatic oedema;
脂肪肝病 fatty liver disease;
[肝腸] liver and intestines;
肝腸寸斷 be overwhelmed with grief; deep affliction; emotionally upset; sorrow-stricken; the liver and intestines seem broken into inches — heartbroken;
哭斷肝腸 cry as if one's heart would break; cry one's eyes out; cry one's heart out;
[肝穿刺] liver puncture;
[肝大] hepatomegalia;
[肝膽] (1) liver and gall bladder; (2) courage; heroic spirit; (3) open-heartedness; sincerity;
肝膽過人 a person of unusual courage; exceed others in courage; far surpass others in daring; unsurpassed in valour; unusually courageous;
肝膽俱裂 heartbroken; one's liver and gall bladder both seem torn from within — extremely frightened; overwhelmed with grief; terror-stricken;
肝膽濕熱 dampheat of liver and gall bladder;
肝膽相照 a genuine meeting of minds between friends; be open-hearted to each other; friends devoted to each other heart and soul; loyal-hearted; show utter devotion to a friend; treat each other with absolute sincerity;
瀝膽披肝 absolutely sincere and loyal;
披肝瀝膽 (1) bare one's heart; be open and sincere; disclose one's secret feelings; hang one's heart on one's sleeve; lay bare one's mind; lay open one's heart; open one's heart to sb; unbosom oneself to sb; unbutton one's soul; (2) loyal and faithful; show a loyal heart;
披肝露膽 lay bare one's heart; lay open one's heart to show loyalty;
剖肝瀝膽 be open and sincere; lay bare one's mind; open up one's heart; show sb one's inmost feelings; speak one's whole mind; unbosom oneself to sb; unbutton one's soul;
忠肝義膽 have good faith; virtue and patriotism;
[肝功能] liver function;
[肝管] hepatic duct;
肝管系統 hepatic duct system;
[肝壞死] hepatic necrosis;
飲食性肝壞死 dietary hepatic necrosis;
[肝昏迷] hepatic coma;
[肝火] (1) irascibility; (2) liver fire;
肝火耳鳴 tinnitus due to the dominant liver fire;
肝火旺 hot-tempered; irascible;
動肝火 in a rage;
~大動肝火 fall into a rage; fly into a rage; get into a rage; stir the gorge; thow a tantrum; up in arms;
~好動肝火 easy on the trigger;
撩動肝火 excite one's wrath; provoke agitation; stir up anger;
清肝火 clear away liver-fire;
[肝腦塗地] die the cruelest death; ready to die the cruelest death for principles; suffer any form of death; the liver and brains split on the ground—lay down one's life; willing to repay a favour with extreme sacrifice;
肝腦塗地在所不惜 would not have grudged anything, even one's life;
[肝膿腫] liver abscess;

[肝破裂] rupture of the liver;
[肝氣] liver energy;
肝氣不和 liver energy disorder;
[肝切除] hepatectomy; surgical removal of the liver;
[肝切開] hepatectomy;
[肝腎] liver and kidney;
肝腎大 hepatonephromegaly;
肝腎虧損 asthenia of the liver and kidneys;
肝腎炎 hepatonephritis;
肝腎腫大 hepatonephromegaly;
[肝石] hepatolith;
肝石病 hepatolithiasis;
[肝損傷] liver damage;
[肝痛] hepatodynia;
[肝萎縮] hepatatrophia;
[肝性腦病] hepatic encephalopathy;
[肝血] liver-blood;
肝血虛 deficiency of liver blood;
[肝炎] hepatitis;
肝炎病毒 hepatitis virus;
~丙型肝炎病毒 hepatitis C virus;
~甲型肝炎病毒 hepatitis A virus;
乙型肝炎病毒 hepatitis B virus;
爆發性肝炎 fulminant hepatitis;
丙型肝炎 hepatitis C;
病毒性肝炎 viral hepatitis;
傳染性肝炎 infective hepatitis;
膽管肝炎 cholangiohepatitis;
急性突發型肝炎 acute fulminant hepatitis;
甲型肝炎 hepatitis A;
家族性肝炎 familial hepatitis;
接種後肝炎 inoculation hepatitis;
酒精性肝炎 alcoholic hepatitis;
流行性肝炎 epidemic hepatitis;
膿氣性肝炎 pyopneumohepatitis;
輸血後肝炎 post-transfusion hepatitis;
輸血性肝炎 transfusion hepatitis;
無黃疸型肝炎 anicteric hepatitis;
血清肝炎 serum hepatitis;
乙型肝炎 hepatitis B;
脂肪肝性肝炎 fatty liver hepatitis;
脂肪肝炎 steatohepatitis;
中毒性肝炎 toxic hepatitis;
[肝樣變] hepatization;
[肝葉] hepatic lobes;
肝葉切除 hepalobectomy;
[肝胰臟] hepatopancreas;
[肝硬變] cirrhosis;
充血性肝硬變 congestive cirrhosis;
[肝硬化] cirrhosis;
充血性肝硬化 congestive cirrhosis;
酒精性肝硬化 alcoholic cirrhosis;
梅毒性肝硬化 syphilitic cirrhosis;
萎縮性肝硬化 atrophic cirrhosis;
細菌性肝硬化 bacterial cirrhosis;
心形肝硬化 cardiocirrhosis;
心源性肝硬化 cardiac cirrhosis;
脂肪性肝硬化 fatty cirrhosis;
脂性肝硬化 fatty cirrhosis;
中毒性肝硬化 toxic cirrhosis;
[肝右葉] right lobe of the liver;
[肝臟] liver;
肝臟脱出 hepatocele;
肝臟硬化 cirrhosis of the liver;
[肝腫大] enlargement of the liver; hepatomegaly
[肝左葉] left lobe of the liver;

保肝 protect the liver;
肺肝 lungs and liver;
和肝 regulate the liver-energy;
青銅色肝 bronze liver;
心肝 (1) conscience; (2) darling; deary;
養肝 nourish the liver;
脂肪肝 fatty liver;
豬肝 pork liver;

gan
【玕】 inferior jade;

琅玕 pearl-like stone;

gan
【泔】 (1) water from washing rice; (2) way of cooking; boil thick; (3) (of food) stale;
[泔水] slops; swill;

gan
【柑】 orange;
[柑橘] (1) oranges and tangerines; (2) citrus;
柑橘醬 marmalade;
柑橘學 citrology;
柑橘栽培 citriculture;
[柑子] mandarin orange;

gan
【坩】 earthen pot;
[坩堝] crucible;
瓷坩堝 ceramic crucible;

浮置坩堝 floating crucible;
過濾坩堝 filtering crucible;
環形坩堝 annular crucible;
耐火坩堝 fire-clay crucible;
石墨坩堝 black-lead crucible;
碳化物坩堝 carbide crucible;

gan

【竿】 bamboo pole; pole; rod;

[竿釣] fishing rod;

[竿頭] head of a rod;

竿頭直上 have an uninterrupted career of advancement; make constant progress in one's studies;

百尺竿頭，更進一步 break one's own record; exert greater efforts and make further progress; further improve one's work; make further progress; not be complacent, but aim at the highest achievement; one who has made the highest record should make even a greater effort; progress by working much harder; try to do still better after having achieved a fair degree of success;

[竿子] bamboo pole;

一竿子插到底 carry a task right down to the grass-roots level; carry through to the end;

標竿 guidepost;
撐竿 vaulting pole;
釣竿 angling rod; casting rod; fishing pole; fishing rod;
揭竿 raise sharpened sticks;
魚竿 fishing rod;
竹竿 bamboo cane; bamboo pole;

gan

【疳】 a kind of infantile disease caused by digestive troubles or malnutrition;

[疳積] infantile malnutrition;

[疳症] infantile malnutrition;

gan

【乾】 (1) dry; (2) dried food; (3) empty; hollow; (4) do sth for nothing; (5) have to do with;

[乾巴] dry up; shrivel; wither;

乾巴巴 deficient in moisture; dry; dry as dust; dull and dry; dull as ditchwater; insipid; parched;

~乾巴巴的講座 dull lecture;

乾巴瘦 lean; skinny; thin;

[乾草] hay;

乾草閣 hayloft;
乾草棚 hayloft;
乾草堆 hayrick; haystack;
一堆乾草 a pile of hay;
製乾草 haymaking;

[乾爸] foster father; godfather;

[乾杯] bottoms up; cheers; drink a toast; drink to; let's drink up; to;

為友誼乾杯 to our friendship, cheers;

[乾貝] dried scallop;

[乾冰] dry ice;

[乾菜] dried vegetables;

[乾處理] dry cure;

[乾脆] (1) altogether; just; simply; (2) clear-cut; not mince one's words; straightforward;

乾脆利落 come straight to the point without the slightest hesitation; crisp and clear-cut; simple and straightforward; laconic; racy;

辦事乾脆 do things neatly;

乾乾脆脆 flat and plain; without further ado;

[乾爹] foster father;

闊乾爹 sugar daddy;

[乾飯] cooked rice without gravy;

[乾果] dried fruit;

[乾旱] arid; drought; dry;

乾旱地區 arid area;
大氣乾旱 atmospheric drought;
絕對乾旱 absolute drought;
生理乾旱 physiological drought;
天大旱，人大乾 fight a big drought with redoubled energy;
土壤乾旱 soil drought;
物理乾旱 physical drought;
一陣乾旱 a dry spell;
戰勝乾旱 conquer drought;

[乾貨] dry goods;

[乾淨] (1) clean; neat and tidy; (2) all gone; completely; entirely; totally;

乾淨利落 crispy; dapper; efficient; neat; neat and tidy; neatly; smooth and clean; trim; very efficient;

~乾淨利落地 cleanly;

乾淨整齊 neat and tidy;
不乾不淨 filthy; unclean;
乾乾淨淨 as clean as a new pin; clean and

fresh; neat and tidy; spick and span;
揩乾淨 wipe clean;
掃乾淨 sweep clean;
手腳不乾淨 in the habit of stealing; light-fingered; questionable in money matters; sb's hands are not clean; seek minor illicit gains; sticky-fingered;
手腳乾淨 clean hands;
舔乾淨 lick clean;
一乾二淨 altogether; completely; lock, stock, and barrel; root and branch; thoroughly;
~ 賴得一乾二淨 deny completely; repudiate completely;
~ 忘得一乾二淨 all forgotten; cast into oblivion; cast to the winds; clean forgotten; forget completely;
嘴不乾淨 use dirty language;

[乾咳] dry cough;
短促頻繁的乾咳 hacking cough;

[乾渴] dry and thirsty;

[乾枯] desiccation; dried-up; shrivelled; withered;
乾枯面 dead and dry face;

[乾涸] dry up;
河水乾涸 a river dries up;

[乾酪] cheese;
乾酪板 cheeseboard;
乾酪蛋糕 cheesecake;
乾酪漢堡包 cheeseburger;
乾酪味的 cheesy;
乾酪味調味醬 cheesy sauces;
長方形乾酪 loaf cheese;
成熟乾酪 ripened cheese;
臭乾酪 stinking cheese;
低脂肪乾酪 low fat cheese;
加工乾酪 processed cheese;
煎乾酪 fried cheese;
酪農乾酪 cottage cheese;
酪乳乾酪 buttermilk cheese;
冷裝乾酪 cold-pack cheese;
綿羊奶乾酪 sheep cheese;
模制乾酪 moulded cheese;
奶油乾酪 cream cheese;
奶渣乾酪 cake cheese;
農家乾酪 cottage cheese; farmer cheese;
去皮乾酪 rindless cheese;
全脂奶乾酪 full-cream cheese;
全脂乳乾酪 whole milk cheese;
乳清乾酪 whey cheese;
軟乾酪 soft cheese;
山羊奶乾酪 goat's milk cheese;
脱脂乾酪 lean cheese;
未成熟乾酪 young cheese;
稀奶油乾酪 single-cream cheese;
一包乾酪 a packet of cheese;
一薄片乾酪 a slice of cheese;
一大塊乾酪 a big hunk of cheese; a loaf of cheese;
一點乾酪 a bit of cheese;
一塊乾酪 a lump of cheese;
一片乾酪 a piece of cheese;
植物性乾酪 vegetable cheese;

[乾糧] dry provisions; field rations; solid food;

[乾餾] destructive distillation; dry distillation;

[乾媽] foster mother; godmother;

[乾娘] foster mother; godmother;

[乾濕表] psychrometer;
手搖乾濕表 sling psychrometer;
通風乾濕表 aspirated psychrometer; ventilated psychrometer;

[乾洗] dry-clean;
乾洗店 cleaner's; dry-cleaner's;

[乾笑] hollow laugh; laugh without mirth;

[乾薪] draw wages without working; salary drawn for a sinecure; unemployed salary;

[乾性] dry; dryness;

[乾衣機] dryer;

[乾燥] (1) dehydration; dry; drying; (2) boring; dull;
乾燥機 dehydrator; dryer;
~ 鼓風式乾燥機 forced-air dehydrator;
~ 氣流式乾燥機 airflow dryer;
~ 人工通風乾燥機 artificial-draft dryer;
~ 水果乾燥機 fruit dehydrator;
~ 自動乾燥機 automatic dryer;
乾燥器 dehydrator; desiccator; dryer; dryer;
~ 攪拌乾燥器 agitator dryer;
~ 絕熱乾燥器 adiabatic dryer;
~ 空氣乾燥器 air dryer; atmospheric dryer;
~ 離心乾燥器 centrifuge dehydrator;
~ 速凍乾燥器 accelerated freeze dryer;
真空乾燥器 vacuum desiccator;
乾燥無味 dry and tasteless; very dull;
紅外線加熱乾燥 infrared dehydration;
化學乾燥 chemical drying;
冷凍乾燥 freeze dehydration;
離心乾燥 centrifugal drying;
日曬乾燥 sun dehydration;

直接乾燥 direct drying;

焙乾 dry by a fire;
鼻乾 dry nose;
餅乾 biscuit; cracker;
擦乾 dry; wipe dry;
蟶乾 dried razor clam;
風乾 air-dry;
涸乾 dried-up; exhausted;
烘乾 stoving;
揩乾 wipe up;
烤乾 dry sth by fire;
口乾 dry; thirst;
淚乾 one's tears dry up;
晾乾 airing; dry by airing; dry in the air; dry out;
擰乾 wring out the water;
曬乾 dry in the sun;
颼乾 make sth dry or cool by wind;
筍乾 air-dried bamboo shoots;
蝦乾 dried prawn;
陰乾 dry in the shade;
咂乾 suck dry;
炙乾 dry by applying heat;

gan

【尷】 embarrassed; ill at ease;

［尷尬］ awkward; embarrassed;

尷尬異常 be much embarrassed; look very put out;

一陣尷尬 a twinge of embarrassment;

gan³

gan

【桿】 bar; rod; shaft;

［桿菌］ bacillus;

桿菌狀 bacillus forms;

大腸桿菌 colibacillus;

痢疾桿菌 dysentery bacteria;

嗜血桿菌 haemophilus;

gan

【敢】 (1) bold; courageous; daring; (2) dare; (3) certain; have the confidence to do sth; (4) make bold; venture;

［敢…敢…］ dare to... and dare to...;

敢衝敢打 have the courage and will to fight;

敢說敢做 dare to speak and dare to act;

敢想敢幹 bold in thinking and action; dare to think and dare to act; have the courage to think and act;

敢想敢說 be bold in one's thinking and speech; dare to think and speak;

敢想敢為 dare to think and do;

［敢開牙］ dare to ask a high price;

［敢情］ (1) I say; so; why; (2) indeed; of course; really;

［敢死隊］ suicide squad;

［敢言］ speak out; vocal;

敢怒而不敢言 be forced to keep one's resentment to oneself; feel indignant but not dare to speak out; furious but not dare to say anything; choke with silent fury; not dare to express one's inner anger or discontent; suppress one's rage;

［敢於］ bold in; dare to; have the courage to;

敢於承認錯誤 admit one's mistake readily;

敢於吃苦 ready to bear hardships;

敢於講真話 dare to tell the truth;

敢於面對 bold in; dare to; face up to; have the courage to;

敢於面對現實 have the courage to face the facts;

不敢 dare not;
膽敢 dare to; have the nerve to;
果敢 brave and decisive; courageous and resolute;
焉敢 how dare...;
勇敢 brave; courageous;

gan

【稈】 stalk of grain; straw;

［稈稻］ stalk of rice;

矮稈稻 short stalk of rice;

gan

【感】 (1) feel; sense; (2) affect; move; touch; (3) grateful; obliged; (4) be affected;

［感測器］ sensor;

光感測器 optical sensor;

恒星感測器 star sensor;

［感觸］ feelings; thoughts and feelings;

忽有感觸 be seized by a sudden feeling; be unexpectedly moved or touched;

深有感觸 with deep feeling;

［感戴］ sincerely grateful;

［感到］ feel; sense;

感到不耐煩 have a feeling of impatience;

感到不舒服 feel under the weather;

感到不知所措 at a loss;

感到難受 feel sick;

G

[感動] move; touch;
感動落淚 be melted into tears; be moved to tears; in a melting mood;
深受感動 be deeply moved;

[感恩] feel grateful; thankful;
感恩不盡 everlastingly grateful;
感恩戴德 be overwhelmed with gratitude; bear a debt of gratitude; bear a debt of gratitude for past kindness; deeply grateful; feel a debt of gratitude for some kind act; feel grateful for sth; grateful for a favour; grateful for sb's kindness; thankful for sb's goodness; with one's heart overflowing with gratitude;
感恩節 Thanksgiving Day;
感恩不盡 everlastingly grateful;
感恩非淺 esteem it a great favour;
感恩莫名 not know how to express one's gratitude;
感恩圖報 feel grateful for a kind act and plan to repay it; grateful to sb and seek ways to return his/her kindness; owe a debt of gratitude and hope to requite it;
感恩終生 grateful to sb as long as one lives;
要感恩 count one's blessings;

[感奮] be fired with enthusiasm; be moved and inspired;

[感憤] feel indignant;

[感官] sense organ;

[感光] sensitization;
感光片 sensitive plate and film;

[感荷] be much obliged;

[感化] help sb to change by education and persuasion;
感化教育 reformatory education;
感化院 reformatory;
~少年感化院 borstal;

[感懷] (1) recall with emotion; (2) recollections; reflections; thoughts;
感懷往事 be moved when thinking of past affairs; recall past events with deep feeling;
詠物感懷 chant things when recollecting past memories;

[感激] feel indebted; feel grateful; thankful;
感激不盡 exceedingly thankful; extremely grateful; have no way to express all one's gratitude; owe sb a debt of endless gratitude;
感激莫名 more grateful than words can tell; my gratitude beggars description; not know how express one's gratitude;
感激涕零 be moved to tears of gratitude; bring sb to tears of gratitude; shed grateful tears; shed tears of joy and thank sb; so grateful as to shed tears; thank sb with tears; with tearful gratitude;
感激萬分 be very much obliged to sb;
深表感激 express one's deep gratitude;
無限感激 feel an immense gratitude to...;

[感覺] (1) feeling; sensation; sense; sense perception; (2) become aware of; feel; perceive;
感覺不舒服 feel under the weather;
感覺動詞 verb of feeling;
感覺剝奪 sensory deprivation;
感覺遲鈍 bradyesthesia;
~偏側感覺遲鈍 hemidysesthesia;
~深部感覺遲鈍 bathyhypesthesia;
感覺過敏 hyperaesthesia;
~偏側感覺過敏 hemihyperaesthesia;
~深部感覺過敏 bathyhyperaesthesia;
~睡夢性感覺過敏 oneiric hyperaesthesia;
感覺好多了 feel much better;
感覺減退 hypoaesthesia;
~偏側感覺減退 hemihypoaesthesia;
感覺力 aesthesia;
感覺麻痺 sensory paralysis;
感覺能力 sensibility;
感覺器官 sense organ; sensory organ;
感覺缺失 anesthesia;
~偏側感覺缺失 hemianesthesia;
~深部感覺缺失 bathyanesthesia;
~痛性感覺缺失 anesthesia dolorosa;
~外周性感覺缺失 peripheral anesthesia;
感覺適應 sensory adaptation;
感覺細胞 aesthacyte; sensory cell;
感覺消失 anesthesia;
感覺學 asethematology; asethesiology;
感覺異常 paresthesia;
~偏側感覺異常 hemiparesthesia;
~術後感覺異常 postoperative paresthesia;
感覺正常 eugnosia;
不祥的感覺 sinking feeling;
彩色感覺 colour perception;
第六感覺 sixth sense;
骨感覺 bone sensibility;
繼發感覺 secondary sensation;

G

假感覺 pseudoesthesia;
接觸感覺 contiguous sense;
前庭感覺 vestibular sense;
潛在感覺 cryptaesthesia;
全部感覺 panaesthesia;
色彩感覺 chromatic sensation; colour sense;
深部感覺 deep sensibility;
失去感覺 lose sensibility;
形式感覺 form perception;
延緩感覺 delayed sensation;
一種感覺 a feeling;
運動感覺 movement perception;

[感慨] sigh with emotion;
感慨流涕 be moved to tears;
感慨萬端 all sorts of feelings well up in one's mind; with great feeling;
感慨萬千 be filled with a thousand regrets; be filled with painful recollections;

[感冒] (1) cold; common cold; head cold; influenza; (2) catch a cold; have a cold; take cold;
感冒瘡 cold sore;
得了感冒 come down with a cold; go down with a cold; have a cold;
患感冒 catch a cold; suffer from a cold;
流行性感冒 influenza; flu;
~一陣流行性感冒 a bout of influenza;
輕微的感冒 slight cold;
重感冒 bad cold; heavy cold; nasty cold;
~得重感冒 have a bad cold;

[感念] recall with deep emotion; remember with gratitude;

[感情] emotion; feeling; sentiment;
感情衝動 act on a momentary impulse; be carried away by one's emotions; emotional impulse; impulsive;
感情脆弱 be easily upset;
感情動詞 emotive verb;
感情彌篤 have an ever deeper affection for each other;
感情豐富 abundance of heart;
感情功能 emotive function;
感情生活 affective life;
感情投資 investment in human relation;
感情外露 express one's feelings openly;
感情誤置 pathetic fallacy;
感情消費 emotional consumption;
感情用事 abandon oneself to emotion; act according to one's sentiments; act impetuously; allow emotion to sway one's judgment; be swayed by emotions; do sth in an emotional manner; give oneself over to blind emotions; give way to one's feelings; let emotions hold sway; under the sway of emotions;
感情主義 emotionalism;
表露感情 wear one's heart on one's sleeve;
發洩感情 give vent to one's emotion; relieve one's feelings;
好動感情 be easily moved to emotion;
一種感情 a feeling;
隱藏感情 conceal one's feelings;
轉移感情 transfer one's affections;

[感染] (1) be infected; infect; (2) affect; infect; influence;
感染愛滋病毒 be infected with the HIV virus; contract the HIV virus;
感染疾病 contract a disease;
感染擴散 spread of an infection;
感染力 appeal;
~藝術感染力 artistic appeal;
感染消失 clear up an infection;
產前感染 antepartum infection;
害怕受感染 be afraid of being infected;
患上感染 suffer from an infection;
機會性感染 opportunistic infection;
繼發感染 secondary infection;
寄生蟲感染 parasitization;
寄生物感染 parasitism;
交叉感染 cross infection;
精神感染 psychic contagion;
抗感染[的] antiseptic;
~抗感染藥膏 antiseptic;
流產感染 septic abortion;
內源性感染 endogenous infection;
潛伏感染 latent infection;
潛在性感染 latent infection;
蠕蟲感染 invermination;
受感染 develop an infection; get an infection; have an infection;
外源性感染 exogenous infection;
細菌感染 bacterial infection;
先天感染 congenital infection;
心理感染 psychic contagion;
隱性感染 latent infection;
隱源性感染 cryptogenic infection;
自體感染 autogenous infection;

[感人] moving; touching;
感人至深 move people deeply;

以德感人 influence others by goodness;

[感受] be affected by; experience; feel;

感受風寒 be affected by the cold; catch a cold; contract a cold;

感受器 receptor;

~皮膚感受器 cutaneous receptor;

~嗅覺感受器 olfactory receptor;

感受性 receptivity;

~靜電感受性 electrostatic receptivity;

切身感受 personal impressions and experience;

[感暑] be affected by summer heat;

[感歎] sigh with feelings;

感歎詞 exclamation; interjection;

感歎號 exclamation mark;

感歎句 exclamatory sentence;

~回聲感歎句 echo exclamation;

[感想] impressions; reflections; thoughts;

[感謝] grateful; thank;

感謝幫忙 thank you for your help;

感謝了 thank you

~太感謝了 that's very kind of you;

感謝你 thank you;

~真不知如何感謝你 I can't thank you enough;

感謝信 letter of thanks; note of thanks; thank-you letter; thank-you note;

感謝主 God be blessed;

非常感謝 many thanks; thanks a lot; thanks very much;

衷心感謝 express one's sincere thanks to sb; thank sb from the bottom of one's heart; thank sincerely;

~我衷心感謝 I am deeply grateful; I am most grateful;

[感性] perception; perceptual;

感性消費活動 perceptual consumption activities;

感性運動 nastic movement;

[感夜性] nyctinasty;

[感應] (1) interaction; reaction; response; (2) irritability; (3) induction;

感應爆炸 detonation by influence;

感應器 inductor;

~磁傾角感應器 dip inductor;

~地磁感應器 earth inductor;

感應線圈 induction coil;

感應性 irritability;

電樞感應 armature induction;

靜電感應 electrostatic induction;

有效感應 actual induction;

[感召] impel; move and inspire;

[感知] (1) perception; (2) feel; sense;

感知動詞 verb of perception;

感知器 perceptron;

哀感 grief; sadness;

悲感 sense of sadness;

觸感 tactile impression;

電感 inductance;

惡感 bad impression; ill feeling; malice;

反感 averse to; be disgusted with;

觀感 impressions on what one has seen;

好感 favourable impression; good opinion;

喝感 thirst;

快感 delight; pleasant sensation;

靈感 inspiration;

流感 flu;

美感 aesthetic feeling; sense of beauty;

敏感 sensitive; susceptible;

銘感 deeply grateful;

情感 emotion; feeling;

肉感 sensual appeal; sensuality;

善感 apt to arouse thoughts and feelings;

傷感 sentimental; sick at heart;

手感 feel; handle;

隨感 informal essay; jottings;

同感 same feelings;

痛感 feel keenly;

外感 diseases caused by external factors;

性感 sex appeal; sexy;

遙感 remote sensing;

有感 a comment on sth;

語感 linguistic feeling; linguistic sense;

預感 (1) forebode; foreboding; have a premonition; hunch; (2) premonition; presentiment;

雜感 random thoughts;

gan

【趕】 (1) catch up with; overtake; (2) make a dash for; rush for; try to catch; (3) hurry through; rush through; (4) drive; (5) drive away; expel;

[趕超] catch up with and surpass;

[趕赴] proceed to do sth without delay; rush to do sth;

[趕活兒] hasten to get the work done;

[趕集] go to a fair; go to the market;

[趕緊] at once; dash off; develop at a very rapid rate; hasten; hurry sb up; hurry up; lose no time; make haste; make

haste with; quicken; run; speed up;
趕緊叫醫生 bring the doctor in haste;
趕緊啦 shake a leg;

[趕盡殺絕] destroy entirely without remainder; drive away and exterminate everyone; kill all; make a clean sweep of; spare none; wipe out the whole lot;

[趕快] at once; get one's skates on; quickly;
趕快交卷 hand in one's paper at once;
趕快跑開 make a run for it;

[趕路] hurry on with one's journey;
繼續趕路 push on with one's journey;

[趕忙] hasten; hurry; make haste;
趕忙加快步伐 hasten one's steps;

[趕牛棒] cattle prod;

[趕巧] happen to; it so happened that;

[趕上] (1) catch up with; get up to; keep pace with; keep up with; overtake; (2) run into; (3) in time for;
趕上發達國家 catch up with the developed countries;
趕上時代 keep abreast of times;
趕不上 there's not enough time to do sth;
迎頭趕上 catch up forthwith; come up from behind; try hard to catch up;

[趕趟兒] have time for; in time for;

[趕走] drive away; drive sb out of the door; expel; hunt; kick out of; kick sb downstairs; put sb to the door; see the back of sb; send sb packing; show sb the door; throw out; turn out sb; turn sb out of doors; turn sb out of the house;

追趕 chase after; pursue; run after;

gan
【澉】 (1) wash; (2) weak; (3) a surname;

gan
【橄】 (1) olive; (2) a surname;

[橄欖] (1) Chinese olive; (2) olive;
橄欖綠 olive-green;
橄欖屁股—坐不住 bottom of a Chinese olive — cannot sit firmly; cannot sit still; hyperactive;
橄欖球 American football; Rugby;
橄欖樹 olive tree;
橄欖樹林 olive grove;
橄欖油 Florence oil; olive oil;

gan
【簳】 young bamboo;

gan⁴

gan
【旰】 (1) evening; night; (2) late;

[旰食] late meal—too busy; eat late and get up early;

宵旰 get up before dawn and eat late;

gan
【淦】 (1) water leaking into a boat; (2) a river in Jiangsi Province; (3) shallow; (4) a surname;

gan
【紺】 reddish dark colour;

[紺青] dark purple; prune purple;

發紺 cyanosis;
紫紺 cyanosis;

gan
【幹】 (1) main part; trunk; (2) cadre; (3) do; work; (4) able; capable;

[幹部] cadre;
幹部學校 cadre school;
幹部責任制 cadre responsibility system;
幹部政策 policy of cadres;
幹部終身制 lifelong tenure of leading posts;
地方工作幹部 cadres working in the locality;
高級幹部 high level cadre;
基層幹部 grass-root cadre;
離休幹部 retired veteran cadre;
領導幹部 leading cadres;
青年幹部 young cadre;
下層幹部 lower cadres;
中層幹部 middle-level cadres;

[幹不幹] do you accept;

[幹材] (1) ability; capability; (2) able person; capable person;

[幹道] artery; high street; main line;
次幹道 subsidiary road;
快速幹道 urban motorway;
主幹道 trunk road;

[幹掉] eliminate; get rid of; kill; put sb out of the way;
幹掉叛徒 get rid of the traitor;

[幹活] labour; work; work on a job;
從早到晚地幹活 drudge from dawn till dark;
加班幹活 work overtime;

G

拼命幹活 work very hard; work your fingers to the bone; work one's socks off;

［幹架］ (1) quarrel; (2) come to blows;

［幹將］ capable person; go-getter;

［幹勁］ drive; dynamism; enthusiasm; get-up-and-go; vigour;

幹勁衝天 display rousing zeal; show great enthusiasm; throw oneself with rousing enthusiasm and boundless vigour into; with soaring enthusiasm; work with untiring energy;

幹勁十足 go all out; go at sth with a will; full of drive; full of energy; full of vigour;

幹勁十足的人 fireball; go-getter;

鼓足幹勁 do one's utmost; exert the utmost efforts; give full rein to one's energy; go all out; put forth one's energy; summon up one's energy;

缺乏幹勁 lack drive;

［幹流］ trunk stream;

［幹嗎］ why;

［幹線］ artery; main line; trunk line;

主要幹線 main artery;

包幹 responsible for a task until it is completed;

別幹 don't do it;

不幹 it's not acceptable; won't accept; won't do it;

才幹 ability; competence;

詞幹 stem;

大幹特幹 go at it hammer and tongs;

高幹 senior cadre;

公幹 business trip;

骨幹 (1) diaphysis; (2) backbone; mainstay;

基幹 backbone; hard core;

精幹 (1) crack; small in number but highly trained; (2) keen-witted and capable;

苦幹 at it; bang away at; plod along; plod on; work hard;

愣幹 do things recklessly; persist in going one's own way;

蠻幹 act rashly;

盲幹 be foolhardy;

腦幹 brain stem;

能幹 able; capable; competent;

強幹 able; capable; competent;

巧幹 do things in a clever way; work skilfully;

軀幹 torso; trunk;

實幹 do solid work; steadfast in one's work;

樹幹 tree trunk; trunk;

楨幹 backbone; core member;

枝幹 the trunk and the branches;

株幹 trunk of a tree;

主幹 (1) trunk; (2) main force; mainstay;

gan

【骭】 (1) shank; shin bone; (2) rib;

gan

【榦】 railing around a well;

gan

【贛】 (1) alternative name of Jiangxi Province; (2) a river in Jiangxi Province; (3) a county in Jiangxi Province;

gan

【灨】 Gan River in Jiangxi Province;

gang[1]

gang

【杠】 (1) flagpole; flagstaff; (2) small sedan chair; (3) bridge;

［杠桿］ (1) lever; (2) leverage;

杠桿臂 lever arm;

杠桿錘 helve hammer;

杠桿定律 lever law;

杠桿閥 lever valve;

杠桿開關 lever switch;

杠桿率 leverage ratio;

杠桿收購 leveraged buyout;

杠桿效應 leverage effect;

杠桿原理 lever principle;

杠桿運動 lever motion;

杠桿作用 lever action; leverage;

~財務杠桿作用 financial leverage;

~營業杠桿作用 operating leverage;

加速器杠桿 accelerator lever;

經濟杠桿 economic leverage;

調節杠桿 adjustment lever;

外交杠桿 diplomatic leverage;

［杠鈴］ barbell;

杠鈴杆 bar;

杠鈴架 barbell stand;

杠鈴練習 barbell exercise;

杠鈴片 disc; plate;

放下杠鈴 lay down the weight; put down the weight;

單杠 horizontal bar;

高低杠 high-low bars; uneven bars; uneven parallel bars;

高杠 top bar;

雙杠 parallel bars;

gang

【肛】 anus;

［肛管］ anal canal;

［肛裂］ anal fissure;

［肛瘻］ anal fistula;

［肛門］ anus;

肛門反射 anal reflex;
肛門管 rectal pipe;
肛門鏡 anoscope;
肛門裂 anal fissure;
肛門瘙癢 pruritus ani;
肛門瘙癢症 pruritus ani;
肛門生殖器癢症 anogenital pruritus;
肛門失禁 copracrasia;
肛門瘻 anal fistula;
肛門腺 anal glands;
肛門炎 anusitis;
肛門直腸 proctitis;
肛門直腸炎 proctitis;
肛門指診 rectal touch;

［肛膜］ anal membrane;

脱肛 anal prolapse; prolapse of anus;

gang

【岡】 ridge;

青岡 oriental white oak;
山岡 hillock; low hill;

gang

【缸】 cistern; crock;

［缸瓦］ earthen ware;

［缸子］ bowl; mug;

茶缸 tea mug;
頂缸 take blame; for others;
烘缸 dryer;
醬缸 jar for preserving sauce;
金魚缸 goldfish bowl;
酒缸 wine jar;
氣缸 air cylinder; cylinder;
汽缸 cylinder;
染缸 vat dye;
水缸 water vat;
糖缸 sugar bowl;
煙灰缸 ashtray;
一口缸 a vat;
魚缸 fish tank;

gang

【剛】 (1) firm; indomitable; strong; (2) exactly; just; (3) barely; (4) only a short while ago;

［剛愎］ headstrong; self-willed;

剛愎自用 headstrong; obstinate and adhere to one's own judgement; obstinate and self-opinionated; self-willed and conceited; set in one's ways; wrong-headed;
稟性剛愎 have a perverse temper; perverse in temper;

［剛才］ a moment ago; a while ago; just now;

［剛度］ rigidity;

剛度計 rigidometer;
抗拉剛度 extensional rigidity;
抗扭剛度 anti-torsion rigidity;
抗撓剛度 flexural rigidity;
線性剛度 linear rigidity;

［剛剛］ as soon as; hardly...when; just; no sooner...when; (2) barely; merely; narrowly;

［剛好］ as it happens; chance; exactly; happen; just; just enough; just in time; on the dot; only;

［剛健］ energetic; robust; vigorous;

剛健質樸 vigorous and simple;

［剛勁］ bold; sturdy; vigorous;

剛勁有力 (of calligraphy) powerful and vigorous; vigorous and forcible;

［剛強］ firm; staunch; unyielding;

剛強不拔 steely fortitude;
剛強果斷 firm and resolute;
剛強鐵漢 man of steel;

［剛巧］ it so happened that;

［剛柔］ hardness and softness;

剛柔並濟 couple hardness with softness; exercise a combination of inflexibility and yielding; temper severity with mercy; temper toughness with gentleness; use both tough and gentle methods;
摧剛為柔 force the obstinate to yield; make the inflexible become supple;
內剛外柔 an iron hand in a velvet glove;
內柔外剛 soft inside despite one's hard shell;
能柔能剛 able to be soft and strong;
柔能克剛 gentleness can overcome strength; softness can overcome hardness; the soft can conquer the hard;
柔茹剛吐 deceive the good and be afraid

of evil; devour what is soft and spit out what is hard — bully the good-natured and fear the ferocious; fear the strong and bully the weak; feeble towards the staunch and brutal towards the weak; oppress the weak and fear the strong;

柔中有剛 an iron hand in a velvet glove; gentle but firm; firmness cloaked beneath gentleness; hard enough within in spite of one's mild exterior; there is strength as well as grace in sb/sth;

茹柔吐剛 bully the good-natured and fear the atrocious; eat the soft and spit the hard;

吐剛茹柔 avoid the strong and bully the weak;

以柔克剛 roll with a punch;

以柔制剛 soft and fair goes far;

[剛毅] resolute and steadfast;

剛毅果斷 resolute and daring;

剛毅果決 resolute and daring;

剛毅精神 fortitude;

[剛正] honourable; principled; upright;

剛正不阿 frank and straightforward; neither bribes nor pressure from above can deflect him from administering the law justly;

[剛直] upright and outspoken;

金剛 Buddha's warrior attendant;

gang

【罡】 Daoist name of the Dipper;

[罡風] strong wind;

天罡 Big Dipper;

gang

【崗】 (1) hillock; mound; (2) guard; sentry; (3) ridge;

[崗位] post; station;

崗位津貼 post subsidy;

崗位評估 post appraisal;

崗位責任制 system of job responsibility;

工作崗位 post of duty;

堅守崗位 stand fast at one's post;

擅自離開崗位 desert one's post;

[崗哨] guard;

崗哨樓 guardhouse;

撤崗 withdraw the guard;

換崗 changing of guards;

門崗 gate sentry;

沙崗 sandhill;

下崗 go off sentry duty;

站崗 on sentry duty; stand guard; stand sentry;

gang

【綱】 (1) headrope of a fishing net; (2) guiding principle; key link; (3) outline; programme; (4) class;

[綱常] cardinal guides and constant virtues;

綱常名教 cardinal guides and constant virtues; moral obligations and preachings;

三綱五常 the three cardinal guides and the five constant virtues;

[綱紀] social order and law;

綱紀國法 discipline; law and order; morale;

綱紀律法 discipline and rules of conduct; law;

綱紀四方 rule over the whole country;

[綱領] creed; guiding principle; programme;

政治性綱領 political programme;

[綱目] detailed outline;

綱舉目張 once the headrope of a fishing net is pulled up, all its meshes open; once the key link is grasped, everything falls into place; once the main rope of a net is lifted up, all the meshes of the net will open wide; when the general plan is laid out, the details are easy to arrange;

以綱帶目 grasp to key link so as to push everything else forward; use the key link to set everything else in motion;

以目代綱 use the secondary to replace the primary;

[綱要] (1) outline; sketch; (2) compendium; essentials;

大綱 outline;

紀綱 (1) law; (2) moral standard;

量綱 dimension;

乾綱 (1) emperorship; (2) the authority of a husband to his wife;

上綱 raise to the higher place of principle;

提綱 outline;

亞綱 subclass;

政綱 political programme;

總綱 general principles; general programme;

gang

【鋼】 steel;

[鋼鏰兒] coins;

[鋼筆] fountain pen; pen;
鋼筆尖 nib;
鋼筆帽 pen top;
一枝鋼筆 a pen;

[鋼鼓] steel drum;
鋼鼓樂隊 steel band;

[鋼管] steel pipe; steel pole; steel tube;
鋼管舞 pole dancing;

[鋼軌] rail;
複式鋼軌 compound rail;
寬底鋼軌 broad-base rail;
橋形鋼軌 bridge rail;

[鋼筋] reinforcement; reinforcing steel bar;
鋼筋工 steel fixer;
鋼筋鐵骨 a body strong as iron; muscles of iron; unyielding integrity;
防爆鋼筋 bursting reinforcement;
抗壓鋼筋 compression reinforcement;
聯繫鋼筋 bracing reinforcement;

[鋼片琴] celesta;

[鋼琴] piano; pianoforte;
鋼琴伴奏 with piano accompaniment;
鋼琴家 pianist;
~ 一位鋼琴家 a pianist;
鋼琴師 pianist;
鋼琴演奏者 concert pianist; pianist;
大鋼琴 concert piano; grand piano;
電鋼琴 electric piano;
電子鋼琴 electronic piano; pianotron;
古鋼琴 clavichord;
~ 擊絃古鋼琴 clavichord;
立式鋼琴 upright piano;
~ 小型立式鋼琴 spinet;
三角鋼琴 concert piano; grand piano;
豎式鋼琴 upright piano;
彈鋼琴 play the piano;
調鋼琴 tune a piano;
無聲鋼琴 dumb piano;
小鋼琴 upright piano;
一架鋼琴 a piano;
自動鋼琴 pianola;

[鋼絲] wire;
鋼絲繩 wire;
走鋼絲 tightrope walking; wire-rope dancing; wire-rope walking;

[鋼鐵] iron and steel;
鋼鐵廠 steel mill; steelworks;
鋼鐵工人 steelworker;
鋼鐵公司 steelmaker;
鋼鐵意志 iron determination;

[鋼印] steel seal;
蓋上鋼印 affix a steel seal;

扁鋼 flat steel;
槽鋼 channel iron;
出鋼 tapping of molten steel;
磁鋼 magnet steel;
帶鋼 strip steel;
煉鋼 steel-smelting; steelmaking;
一爐鋼 a cast of steel; a heat of steel;

gang³
gang

【港】 harbour; port;

[港埠] harbour; port;

[港口] harbour; port;
深水港口 deepwater harbour;

[港灣] bay; harbour;
小港灣 marina;

避風港 harbour; haven;
汊港 branching point of a stream;
出發港 port of departure;
出港 clear a port; leave port;
到達港 port of arrival;
海港 harbour; seaport;
寄泊港 port of call;
交貨港 port of delivery;
進口港 port of entry;
軍港 naval port;
良港 good harbour;
領港 pilot a ship into or out of a harbour; pilotage
目的港 port of destination;
入港 come at port; come into port;
入口港 port of entry;
商港 commercial port;
深水港 deepwater port;
外港 outport;
漁港 fishing port;
裝貨港 port of loading; port of shipment;
自由港 free port;

gang⁴
gang

【槓】 (1) carrying pole; lever; (2) sharpen; (3) argue; dispute;

[槓鈴] barbell;
槓鈴片 weights;

[槓子] (1) thick stick; (2) bar;

打槓子 loot; rob; plunder;

單槓 (1) horizontal bar; (2) horizontal bar gymnastics;
吊槓 trapeze;
高低槓 uneven bars;
撬槓 crowbar;
雙槓 parallel bars;
抬槓 argue for argument's sake; wrangle;

gao[1]

gao

【臯】 (1) marsh; swamp; (2) shore;

gao

【羔】 fawn; kid; lamb;

［羔皮］ lambskin; kidskin;

［羔羊］ lamb; yearling;

代罪羔羊 fall guy; scapegoat; whipping boy;
柔如羔羊 as meek as a lamb; as mild as a lamb;

［羔子］ fawn; kid; lamb;

產羔 kidding;
羊羔 lamb;
紫羔 Chinese blue sheep;

gao

【高】 (1) high; tall; (2) above the average; advanced; superior; (3) loud; (4) dear; expensive; high-priced; (5) a surname;

［高矮］ height;

高矮不一 differ in height; vary in height;

［高昂］ (1) hold one's head high; (2) elated; exalted; high; (3) costly; dear; exorbitant; expensive;

情緒高昂 be heightened in spirits;

［高傲］ arrogant; haughty; insolent; stiff-backed; supercilious;

高傲自大 arrogant and self-important; be stuck up; have a big head; have a swelled head; get a swollen head; too big for one's breeches;
志高氣傲 aspiring and haughty;

［高保真］ high fidelity;

高保真立體聲 hi-fi stereo;
高保真視聽系統 hi-fi audiovisual system;
高保真系統 hi-fi system;
高保真音響 hi-fi music;;

［高材］ remarkable in talent;

高材捷足 remarkable in talent and quick in movement; skilled talent works swiftly;
高材生 brilliant student; outstanding student; whiz-kid;

［高參］ (1) senior staff officer; (2) counsellor; mentor;

［高層］ high-level;

高層會議 high-level meeting;
高層領導人 high-level leader; top leader;
高層人士 high-up; higher-up; people in positions of authority;
高層人物 higher-up;
高層文化 high culture;

［高產］ high production; high yield;

［高敞］ tall and spacious;

［高唱］ (1) sing loudly; sing with spirit; (2) call out loudly for; talk glibly about;

高唱入雲 sing so loud as to reach the clouds; sing with a resounding voice;
高唱贊歌 sing out the hymn;

［高超］ exquisite; remarkable; superb;

技術高超 be skilled in technique;

［高潮］ (1) flood; high tide; high water; spring tide; (2) climax; culmination; high tide; upsurge;

高潮線 high watermark;
達到高潮 ascend to the climax; rise to a climax;
激動人心的高潮 a thrilling climax;

［高程］ elevation;

絕對高程 absolute elevation;
平差高程 adjusted elevation;
外業高程 field elevation;
制高高程 critical elevation;

［高出］ be higher than; be taller than;

［高處］ high place;

［高矗］ straight and towering;

高矗雲霄 rise into the clouds;

［高達］ reach up to; to the tune of;

高達 20 萬人民幣 to the tune of 200,000 RMB;
高達雲霄 touch the clouds;

［高大］ (1) stalwart; tall; tall and big; (2) great; high and noble; lofty;

身材高大 of a great stature;
又高又大 big and tall;

［高檔］ high-grade; of superior quality; top grade;

高檔產品 high-quality products;

高檔的 high-end; upmarket;
高檔商品 high-class goods;
高檔消費品 high-grade consumer goods;

[高蹈] (1) travel to a faraway place; (2) hermit;

[高等] advanced; higher; of a higher level;
高等級公路 high-class highway;
高等教育 higher education;
~ 高等教育管理 higher education management;
~ 高等教育院校 institution of higher education;
高等學位 advanced degree;
高等院校 colleges and universities; institutions of higher learning;

[高低] (1) height; (2) difference in degree; relative inferiority; relative superiority; (3) a sense of propriety; discretion; (4) just; on any account; simply;
高低不平 uneven;
~ 高低不平的路 bumpy road;
不分高低 equally matched;
不論職位高低 irrespective of duty status;
忽高忽低 in high spirits one moment and in low spirits the next; subject to sudden mood swings;
見高低 contest to see who is better; fight for mastery; see who is better;
難分高低 hard to tell which is better;
七高八低 bumpy and rough; uneven in height;
手高手低 small difference;
說高說低 criticize others thoughtlessly;
說話不知高低 say sth improper; speak without thought and often inappropriately;
隨高就低 adapt to circumstances; adjustable to circumstances;
一見高低 fight it out; fight with sb to victory or defeat;
爭個高低 vie with each other to see who is better;
做事不知高低 act in an improper way; behave inappropriately;

[高地] highlands; uplands;

[高調] bombastic words; high-profile; high-sounding words; lofty tone; high-pitched tone;
唱高調 affect a high moral tone; chant to bombastic words; use high-flown words;
~ 大唱高調 claim in high-sounding language; play up the theme of;

[高度] (1) altitude; elevation; height; (2) high; high degree;
高度變化 altitude variation;
高度計 altimeter;
高度評價 deserve of high praise; give a high appraisal to; pay high tribute to; praise; set a high value on; sing sb's praises; speak highly of sb; value oneself on; win high praise;
高度贊揚 speak highly of;
高度重視 attach great importance; pay great attention; set great store by;
安全高度 safe altitude; safe height;
飛行高度 flight altitude;
軌道高度 orbital altitude;
絕對高度 absolute altimeter; absolute height;
實際高度 actual height;
天體高度 astronomical altitude; celestial altitude;
天線高度 aerial height;

[高爾夫] golf;
高爾夫臂 golf arm;
高爾夫球 (1) golf; (2) golf ball;
~ 高爾夫球場 golf course; golf links;
~ 高爾夫球桿 golf club;
~ 高爾夫球球僮 caddy;
~ 高爾夫球運動 golf; golfing;
小型高爾夫球運動 crazy golf; minigolf;
~ 打高爾夫球 play golf;
~ 小場地高爾夫球 pitch-and-putt;
~ 小型高爾夫球 minigolf;
~ 一場高爾夫球 a round of golf;
~ 一局高爾夫球 a round of golf;
草地高爾夫 clock golf;

[高飛] fly high; high-flying;
奮翮高飛 flutter and soar high;

[高風亮節] exemplary conduct and nobility of character; have a strong sense of integrity; high and upright character; noble character and sterling integrity;

[高峰] climax; height; peak; summit;
高峰車 relief bus;
高峰時間 peak hours; rush hours;
高峰期 rush hour;
登上高峰 scale the heights;

[高歌] sing loudly; sing with a resounding voice;
高歌猛進 advance boldly with a song

on one's lips; advance triumphantly; stride forward singing militant songs;
高歌抒懷 express one's heart's feelings by a song;
高歌一曲 chant a melody; raise one's voice to sing a song; sing a song loudly;
引吭高歌 belt out a song; roar out a song; sing aloud; sing at the top of one's voice; sing in a spirit of utter abandonment; sing joyfully in a loud voice; sing lustily; stretch one's neck and sing loudly;

[高跟] high heels;
高跟鞋 high heels; high-heeled shoes;
~半高跟鞋 half-heeled shoe;
~穿高跟鞋 wear high-heeled shoes;

[高估] overvalue;

[高官] high official;
高官厚祿 a high position and a good pay; a high position and a large income; a high official with a high salary; high emoluments and a high position; high positions and handsome salaries; high posts with salaries to match;
高官顯爵 be honoured with high official titles; dignity;

[高貴] (1) high; honourable; noble; (2) rare; valuable; (3) elitist; highly privileged;
高貴品質 noble qualities;
出身高貴 high-born; high-born and highbred;

[高級] (1) high; high-level; high-ranking; senior; (2) advanced; high-class; high-grade;
高級班 advanced class;
高級編譯程序 advanced level compiler;
高級查詢語言 advanced query language;
高級餐廳 fashionable restaurant; high-class restaurant;
高級程序 high-level programme;
~高級程序設計語言 high-level programming language;
~高級程序員 high-level programmer;
高級的 deluxe;
高級翻譯員 senior translator;
高級官員 high-ranking official; top-level official;
高級規程 high-level protocol;
高級會議 summit meeting;
高級匯編程序 high-level assembler;
高級商店 exclusive shop;
高級生活 high life;
高級通信服務 advanced communication service;
高級信息系統 advanced information system;
高級譯員 senior translator;
高級語言 high-level language; superior language;
~高級語言程序 high-level language programme;
高級職稱 title of a senior professional post;
高級職員 senior clerk;

[高價] high price;
高價的 big ticket;
出高價 bid a high price;
極高價 an arm and a leg;

[高架橋] viaduct;

[高見] wise idea; your opinion;

[高腳] high-legged;
高腳杯 goblet;
高腳盤 compote;
高腳椅 high chair;

[高就] be promoted to a higher post;
另有高就 have a better job;

[高舉] hold aloof; hold high;
高舉遠蹈 lead a secluded life; seclude oneself and avoid all worldly cares;

[高卡車] go-cart; go-kart;

[高考] university entrance examination;
參加高考 take part in the university entrance examination;
成人高考 entrance examination to institution of higher education for adults;

[高空] high altitude; upper air; welkin;
高空鼻竇炎 aerosinusitis;
高空轟炸 high-level bombing;
高空恐怖 aerophobia;
月掛高空 the moon rides high up in the sky;

[高欄] high hurdles;
110米高欄 110-metre high hurdles;

[高利貸] usury;
放高利貸 usury;
~放高利貸者 usurer;

[高梁] grain sorghum; sorghum;
高梁地 sorghum field;
甜高梁 sweet sorghum;
雜種高梁 hybrid sorghum;

[高齡] advanced age; advanced in years; ripe old age; venerable age;
高齡產婦 lying-in woman advanced in years;
高齡老人 very old person;

[高領] high collar; polo neck; turtleneck;
高領衫 mock turtleneck;

[高樓] high building;
高樓大廈 high buildings and large mansions; high-rise buildings; many-storied buildings; tall and big buildings; tall buildings and great mansions;
百尺高樓平地起 high buildings rise from the ground — everything starts from scratch;
廣廈高樓 high and big buildings; skyscrapers;
萬尺高樓起於累土 a building ten thousand feet high must be constructed from its very base;

[高爐] blast furnace;

[高論] brilliant views; enlightening remarks;
放言高論 give a free speech and boasting; high-flown talk;

[高邁] (1) free and natural; (2) advanced in years; superannuated;

[高慢] arrogant;

[高門] rich family;

[高妙] ingenious; masterly;

[高明] (1) brilliant; clever; superior; wise; (2) brilliant people;
另請高明 ask some other person who is more capable; find sb better; find sb who is better qualified;
手段高明 play one's cards well;
手法高明 play a good game;

[高攀] make friends or claim ties of kinship with someone of a higher social position;
高攀不上 cannot be friends of a richer family; unable to claim ties of kinship with sb of higher social position; unworthy to seek connections with;
不敢高攀 dare not aspire to sb's acquaintance; dare not aspire to sb's company;
高不可攀 beyond reach; beyond the grasp of ordinary people; high and mighty; inaccessible; too high to be reached; unattainable; unreachable;

[高強] outstanding; superior;

[高蹺] stilts;
踩高蹺 walk on stilts;

[高峭] high and steep;

[高球] lob;
高球拍殺 overhead smash;

[高熱] high fever; high heat;

[高人] (1) person of high quality; (2) very capable person;
高人一等 a cut above others; a head taller than; a notch above others; regard oneself head and shoulders above others; stand head and shoulders above others; tower above the rest;
~自視高人一等 think oneself to be better than others;
高人逸士 hermits and recluses; holy hermits; one who lives secluded and does not admire wealth and high emolument;

[高僧] eminent monk;

[高山] high mountain;
高山矮曲林 elfin wood;
高山病 altitude sickness; mountain sickness;
~急性高山病 acute mountain sickness;
~慢性高山病 chronic mountain sickness;
高山景行 high moral integrity; look up to a worthy person, as one looks up to a mountain — admire the behaviour of a worthy person; show admiration for sb;
高山口 col
高山流水 (1) bosom friend; (2) refined music;
高山平地 alp;
高山仰止 admire a worthy person greatly; behold a high mountain with awe — respect a great person with admiration;
高山有好水，平地有好花 there is good water in the high mountains, there are beautiful flowers on the plain;
不上高山，不顯平地 one who has not ascended a high hill cannot appreciate the level ground;
重重高山 alps upon alps;
前有高山，後有深谷 with high mountains in front and deep ravines behind;
讓高山低頭，叫河水讓路 make the mountains bow their heads and the

rivers give way;

[高尚] high; high-minded; lofty; noble; respectable; sublimate;

高尚的道德 attainment in virtue;

高尚的目標 worthy end;

高尚的品行 lofty morality;

高尚的情操 elevated sentiments;

高尚的人 noble-minded person; the salt of the earth;

高尚的態度 noble attitude;

高尚的行為 high-minded act; noble act;

高尚嫺雅 grace; noble and refined;

靈魂高尚 nobility of soul;

情操高尚 high-minded;

行為高尚 act nobly;

[高燒] burning fever; high fever;

一陣高燒 a bout of high fever;

[高射砲] ack-ack; anti-aircraft gun;

高射砲兵 ack-acker; anti-aircraft guner;

高射砲隊 anti-aircraft artillery;

小高射砲 light anti-aircraft artillery;

中型高射砲 medium anti-aircraft artillery;

重型高射砲 heavy anti-aircraft artillery;

[高深] advanced; profound; recondite;

高深的道理 recondite principles;

高深莫測 beyond one's depth; fathomless; get out of one's depth; too profound to be understood; unfathomable;

故作高深 pretend to be profound;

莫測高深 as deep as a well; beyond one's depth; enigmatic; fathomless; too profound to be understood;

[高昇] get a promotion; get promoted;

[高聲] sing loudly; speak loudly;

高聲大笑 roar with laughter;

高聲喊 scream out;

高聲喊叫 shout at the top of one's voice;

高聲叫罵 scream abuse;

[高手] ace; hotshot; master; master hand;

外交高手 master hand at diplomacy;

游泳高手 expert swimmer;

[高壽] (1) long life; longevity; (2) your venerable age;

[高聳] ascend; cloud-capped; lofty; mount; stand tall and erect; steeple; tower; towering;

高聳入雲 cloud-kissing; reach into the sky;

高聳雲霄 cloud-kissing; raise up in the clouds; touch the clouds;

[高速] express; fast; high rate; high speed; high velocity; swift;

高速打印 high-speed printing;

~高速打印機 high-speed printer;

高速檔 top gear;

高速複印機 high-speed copier;

高速複製機 high-speed reproductor;

高速公路 expressway; highway; motorway;

高速局部網絡 high-speed local network;

高速前進 advance at the utmost speed;

高速攝影機 high-speed camera;

高速數據傳遞 high-speed data transfer;

高速閱讀器 high-speed reader;

高消費 high-level consumption;

高速增長 grow with leaps and bounds;

最高速 top speed;

[高抬貴手] will you do me a favour;

[高臺] raised platform;

高臺定車 cricus bike on a raised platform;

[高溫] high temperature;

高溫測定法 pyrometry;

高溫計 pyrometer;

~壁式高溫計 wall-type pyrometer;

~比色高溫計 constant intensity pyrometer;

~比色光學高溫計 brightness-temperature pyrometer;

~變焦點高溫計 variable-focus pyrometer;

~表面高溫計 surface pyrometer;

~插入式高溫計 insert pyrometer;

~磁高溫計 magnetic pyrometer;

~單式高溫計 monochromatic pyrometer;

~電測高溫計 electric pyrometer;

~電阻高溫計 resistance pyrometer;

~發光絲高溫計 luminous filament pyrometer;

~輻射高溫計 radiation pyrometer;

~光測高溫計 optical pyrometer;

~光測式高溫計 head radiation;

~光電高溫計 photoelectric pyrometer;

~光學高溫計 optical pyrometer;

~紅外線高溫計 infrared pyrometer;

~機械高溫計 mechanical pyrometer;

~金屬高溫計 metallic pyrometer;

~鏡式高溫計 mirror pyrometer;

~空氣高溫計 air pyrometer;

~目測高溫計 visual pyrometer;

~目視光測高溫計 visual optical pyrometer;

~氣動高溫計 pneumatic pyrometer;

~ 輕便高溫計 portable pyrometer;
~ 全輻射高溫計 total radiation pyrometer;
~ 熱電高溫計 thermoelectric pyrometer;
~ 熱電偶高溫計 potentiometer pyrometer; thermocouple pyrometer;
~ 熔化高溫計 fusion pyrometer;
~ 石墨高溫計 graphite pyrometer;
~ 收縮高溫計 contraction pyrometer;
~ 手提式高溫計 handheld pyrometer;
~ 雙色高溫計 two-colour pyrometer;
~ 透鏡高溫計 lens pyrometer;
~ 吸色高溫計 colour-extinction pyrometer;
~ 真空高溫計 vacuum superheater pyrometer;
~ 自動指示高溫計 automatic pyrometer;
~ 自記高溫計 recording pyrometer;

[高下] superiority or inferiority;
高下難分 hard to distinguish between high and low; very hard to tell which one is better;
分出高下 separate the men from the boys;
見個高下 contest and see who is better; fight for mastery; see who is better;
難分高下 hard to distinguish between high and low; very hard to tell which one is better;
一分高下 decide who is the better of the two groups;

[高小] higher primary school;

[高校] college; institution of higher education;
成人高校 institution of higher education for adults;

[高興] happy; merry;
高興得跳起來 jump for joy;
高興極了 be on top of the world;
暗暗高興 laugh in one's heart;
暗自高興 be secretly delighted;
白高興一場 have a windy joy;
不高興 unhappy;
~ 感得不高興 feel unhappy;
~ 覺得不高興 feel unhappy;
非常高興 all over oneself; be tickled pink; be tickled to death; on cloud nine; on top of the world; over the moon; very happy;
感到高興 feel happy;
高高興興 in a gleeful mood; with a good grace; with heartfelt delight; with a light heart;
很高興 be extremely delighted;
説不出的高興 unspeakable joy; unutterable delight;

[高雅] elegant and in good taste; noble and graceful;
高雅藝術 the art of refined taste and style;
措詞高雅 be worded graciously;
格調高雅 elegant style;
情趣高雅 elegant in taste;

[高壓] high; high pressure;
高壓等值線 pleiobar;
高壓電纜 high tension cable;
高壓電線 high tension wire;
高壓鍋 pressure cooker;
高壓脊 pressure ridge;
高壓球 smash;
高壓手段 high-handed measures;
~ 用高壓手段 by a stong arm; with a strong hand;
北極高壓 arctic high;
閉合高壓 closed high;
超高壓 supervoltage;
氣泡高壓 bubble high;
阻塞高壓 blocking high;

[高義薄雲] one's morality reaches up to the clouds;

[高音] (1) high pitch; (2) top;
男高音 tenor;
女高音 soprano;
~ 花腔女高音 coloratura soprano;

[高原] highlands; plateau; uplands;
黃土高原 loess plateau;

[高瞻遠矚] far-sighted; look far ahead and aim high; see far and wide; show great foresight; stand high and see far into the future; stand on a high vantage point and have a far-sighted view; take a broad and long view; transcendent view; with clear vision; with great foresight;

[高漲] rise; run high; upsurge;
情緒高漲 upsurge of emotions;
突然高漲 groundswell;
物價高漲 prices surge up;

[高招] brilliant idea; clever move; master stroke;
外交高招 master stroke in diplomacy;

[高職] high position;
出任高職 fill a high post;
就任高職 assume high office;

[高脂] fatty;

高脂食品 fatty food;

[高中] high school; secondary school;
一所高中 a high school;

[高桌] high table;
高桌晚宴 high table dinner;

[高足] your disciple; your pupil;

拔高 (1) lift; raise; (2) overrate;
標高 mark up;
才高 of great abilities;
測高 measure the height of;
超高 superelevate; superelevation;
崇高 high; lofty; sublime;
登高 ascend a height;
孤高 proud and aloof; supercilious;
加高 heighten;
淨高 clear height;
清高 of lofty moral character and aloof from politics and material pursuits;
身高 height;
昇高 go up; rise;
抬高 build up; lift; raise;
提高 enhance; heighten; improve; increase; raise;
跳高 high jump;
斜高 slant height;
音高 pitch;
增高 raise;
最高 the highest; the maximum; the supreme; the tallest; the topmost; the uppermost;

gao

【睪】 (1) smooth and glossy; (2) bank; (3) testicles;

[睪丸] achers; acres; apples; balls; ballocks; bollocks; clappers; clusters; cobblers; cods; danglers; dusters; family jewels; flowers; gollies; goolie; knackers; marbles; nads; nuts; pills; plums; testicles; testis; wedding kit; wedding tackle;
睪丸癌 cancer of the testis;
睪丸病 orchiopathy;
睪丸動脈 arteria testicularis;
睪丸瘤 testicular tumour;
睪丸膜 tunicae testis;
睪丸鞘膜炎 vaginalitis;
~肥厚性睪丸鞘膜炎 pachy vaginalitis;
~黏連性睪丸鞘膜炎 periorchitis adhaesiva;
睪丸素 testosterone;
睪丸痛 didymalgia;
睪丸突出 orchiocele;
睪丸未降 undescended testis;
睪丸萎縮 testicular atrophy;
睪丸下垂 orchidoptosis;
睪丸炎 orchitis;
~創傷性睪丸炎 traumatic orchitis;
~副睪丸炎 epididymitis;
~轉移性睪丸炎 metastatic orchitis;
睪丸硬變 orchioscirrhus;
睪丸症 orchidism;
~巨睪丸症 macro-orchidism;
睪丸腫瘤 orchiocele;
副睪丸 epididymis;
受阻睪丸 obstructed testis;
游走性睪丸 retractile testis;

附睪 epididymis;

gao

【膏】 (1) fat; grease; (2) cream; oil; ointment; paste; (3) fertile; riches; (4) region just below the heart; (5) favours; grace; (6) sweet; (7) plaster; (8) (of food and fruit) cooked to a very thick or pasty form;

[膏火] lamp oil;

[膏藥] medicated plaster; patch; plaster;
狗皮膏藥 dog skin plaster — quack medicine;
~賣狗皮膏藥 quack peddling dog skin plasters; palm things off on people; sell quack remedies;
貼膏藥 stick on a medicated plaster;
一塊膏藥 a patch;
一貼膏藥 a piece of medicated plaster;

[膏腴] fertile;
膏腴之地 fertile land; fertile soil; productive land;

唇膏 lipstick;
浸膏 extract;
軟膏 ointment; paste;
石膏 gypsum; plaster stone;
糖膏 fillmass; massecuite;
牙膏 toothpaste;
煙膏 prepared opium paste;
藥膏 ointment; salve;
油膏 ointment;
脂膏 (1) fat; grease; (2) wealth of the people;

gao

【槔】 well sweep;

桔槔 a kind of instrument to draw water;

gao

【篙】 boat-pole; pole for punting a boat;

杉篙 fir pole;

gao

【糕】 cake; pastry; steamed dumpling;

［糕餅］ cake; confectionery; pastry;

糕餅店 baker's; bakery;

糕餅師 baker;

糕餅商 confectioner;

糕餅屋 baker's;

［糕點］ cakes and pastries;

一塊糕點 a pastry;

板糕 sandwich cake topped with candied fruit;

蛋糕 cake;

發糕 steamed sponge cake;

蜂糕 steamed sponge cake;

馬拉糕 Malaysian-style sponge cake;

年糕 New Year cake;

肉糕 meat loaf;

鬆糕 sponge cake;

雪糕 ice cream;

糟糕 how terrible;

gao

【餻】 cakes; dumplings;

gao³

gao

【杲】 (1) bright as the shining sun; (2) high;

杲杲 bright;

gao

【搞】 (1) be engaged in; carry on; do; go in for; practise; (2) cause; draw up; make; produce; work out; (3) organize; set up; start; (4) get; get hold of; secure;

［搞臭］ discredit; put to shame;

［搞出］ achieve; produce; work out;

［搞錯］ mistake;

［搞掉］ do away with; get rid of; winkle out;

［搞定］ it's settled.

［搞鬼］ play a dirty trick on; play tricks; up to some mischief;

背地裏搞鬼 play a deep game;

［搞好］ (1) do well; make a good job of; (2) carry out; get sth done;

［搞壞］ botch up;

［搞活］ (1) activate; enliven; invigorate; put life into; vitalize; (2) give sb freedom to do a job; release from constraints;

搞活經濟 enliven the economy; reinvigorate the economy; stimulate the economy;

［搞垮］ break down; collapse; disrupt; do in; get down; undermine;

［搞亂］ confuse; end up in a mess; mess up; mix up; muddle up; upset;

［搞深搞透］ carry through...thoroughly and in depth; do a thorough and exhaustive job of it; in a thoroughgoing way;

［搞糟］ make a mess of; mess up;

胡搞 (1) meddle with sth; mess things up; (2) carry on an affair with sb; promiscuous;

gao

【槁】 withered;

［槁木］ withered tree;

形如槁木 as lean as a rake; thin and emaciated;

［槁項黃馘］ a withered neck and yellow face;

枯槁 (1) withered; (2) haggard;

gao

【稿】 (1) stalk of grain; straw; (2) draft; rough copy; sketch; (3) manuscript; original text;

［稿本］ manuscript;

彩色稿本 illuminated manuscript;

［稿費］ contribution fee;

［稿件］ contribution; manuscript;

［稿約］ notice to contributors;

［稿紙］ manuscript paper;

［稿子］ (1) draft; sketch; (2) contribution; manuscript;

抄稿子 copy a manuscript;

改稿子 revise a draft;

辦稿 prepare the draft of an official document;

草稿 draft; rough draft;

初稿 first draft; initial draft;

底稿 draft; original manuscript;

定稿 final version of a text; finalize a manuscript;

發稿 (1) distribute new dispatches; (2) send manuscripts to the press;

腹稿 mental notes;

G

畫稿 rough sketch;
講稿 draft of a speech; lecture notes;
來稿 contributed article; contribution;
擬稿 make a draft;
起稿 draft; make a draft;
清稿 clean copy; fair copy;
審稿 examine and approve manuscripts;
手稿 manuscript; original manuscript;
投稿 contribute; submit a piece of writing for publication;
退稿 send back the manuscript;
脱稿 complete a manuscript;
完稿 complete the manuscript; finish a piece of writing;
文稿 draft; manuscript;
寫稿 write for a magazine;
遺稿 manuscript left unpublished by the author at his/her death;
原稿 master copy; original manuscript;
約稿 make an arrangement in advance with sb for his contribution;
徵稿 solicit contributions;
撰稿 write articles;

gao

【縞】 plain white raw silk;

［縞素］ white mourning dress;
渾身縞素 dressed in the white robes of mourning;
身穿縞素 be dressed entirely in white; be dressed in mourning white;
一身縞素 be dressed in mourning white;

gao

【鎬】 hoe; pick; pickaxe;

［鎬頭］ pick; pickaxe;
一把鎬頭 a pick;

電鎬 electric pick;
風鎬 air pick; pneumatic pick;
洋鎬 mattock; pick; pickaxe;

gao

【攪】 do; handle; manage;

［攪鬼］ play underhand tricks;
暗地裏搗鬼 make trouble secretly;

［攪和］ mix evenly by stirring;

［攪亂］ mess up; screw up;

gao⁴

gao

【告】 (1) inform; notify; tell; (2) accuse; bring an action against; go to law against; sue; (3) ask for; request; solicit; (4) announce; declare;

［告白］ public notice;

［告別］ (1) leave; part with; (2) bid farewell to; say goodbye to;
告別演出 farewell performance;
告別語 valediction;
黯然告別 say goodbye with a heavy heart;
彼此告別 say goodbye to each other;
不告而別 leave without saying goodbye; take French leave;
點頭告別 nod one's farewell;
告別拜訪 farewell call;
揮淚告別 depart in tears;
揮手告別 wave away; wave farewell; wave goodbye to sb; wave off; wave one's hand to bid sb farewell; wave one's hands on departure;
灑淚告別 part in tears; pay one's last respects with tears; take a tearful leave;
握手告別 shake hands with sb in farewell;
向遺體告別 pay last respects to sb's remains;

［告成］ accomplish; complete;

［告吹］ fail; fizzle out;

［告辭］ farewell; take leave;
準備告辭 ready to leave;

［告貸］ ask for a loan;
告貸無門 have no means to borrow money; no place to borrow money from; nowhere to borrow money; nowhere to turn for loans; there is no place where the money can be borrowed from;

［告發］ blow the whistle; delate; fink on; inform against; lodge an accusation against; peach against; put the finger on; report; split on sb;
告發者 informant; informer; whistle-blower;

［告急］ ask for emergency help; in an emergency; make an urgent request for help; report an emergency;
前線告急 the front line asked for emergency help;

［告假］ ask for leave;

［告捷］ (1) win a victory; (2) announce a victory; report a victory;
首次告捷 win one's first victory;

[告解] confession;
告解神父 confessor;
告解室 confessional;
[告誡] admonish; counsel; dissuade from; enjoin; warn;
[告警] give an alarm; report an emergency;
[告竣] be completed;
[告老] retire on account of age;
告老還鄉 resign from office and return to one's native town; retire from office and return to private life; retire in one's old age; retire on account of old age and return to one's native place;
[告密] give secret information against sb; inform against sb; snitch;
告密者 snitch; whistle-blower;
[告罄] be exhausted; run out;
[告饒] ask sb's pardon; beg for mercy;
[告示] bulletin; official notice; placard;
張貼告示 post up a placard;
[告訴] inform; let know; make know; tell;
告訴你 tell you;
~我有消息要告訴你 I've news for you;
[告退] ask for leave to withdraw from a meeting, etc.;
[告知] inform; notify;
[告終] come to an end; conclude; end up;
害己告終 end up by destroying oneself;
以失敗告終 end in a failure;
[告狀] (1) bring a lawsuit against sb; file a suit; go to law against sb; indict; sue; (2) complain of one's grievances; lodge a complaint against sb with his/her superior;

哀告 (1) beg piteously; implore; supplicate; (2) announce sb's death; speak about one's grievances;
報告 (1) give an account of; make known; render an account of; report; (2) lecture; report; speech; talk;
被告 accused; defendant;
遍告 announce to all; tell everyone;
禀告 report to one's superior;
佈告 bulletin proclamation; notice;
禱告 pray;
電告 inform or report in a telegram;
奉告 inform; let sb know;
訃告 announce sb's death; obituary notice;
公告 announcement; proclamation;
廣告 advertisement;
警告 admonish; give a caution to; warn; warning;
控告 accuse; bring a charge against sb; bring a suit against sb; bring an action against sb; call an action against sb; charge; complain; enter a suit against sb; file a suit against sb; have the law of sb;; institute a suit against sb; lodge a complaint; make a charge against sb; make a complaint; take an action against sb; take the law of sb;
求告 entreat; implore; supplicate;
勸告 admonish; advise; counsel; exhort; remonstrate; urge;
上告 complain to the higher authorities or appeal to a higher court;
申告 file a complaint;
通告 announce; give public notice; public notice;
文告 announcement in writing; manifesto; message; proclamation; public notice; statement;
誣告 bring a false charge against; lodge a false accusation against;
相告 pass information; tell;
宣告 declare; proclaim;
預告 advance notice; announce in advance; herald;
原告 plaintiff; prosecutor;
詔告 proclaim;
正告 earnestly admonish; warn sternly;
忠告 admonish; advice; sincere advice; sincerely advise;
祝告 implore in prayer; invoke;
轉告 communicate; pass on; transmit;
諄告 repeatedly admonish;

gao
【郜】 (1) an ancient place in today's Shensi Province; (2) a surname;

gao
【膏】 lubricate; make glossy; make smooth;
[膏油] add lubricating oil;

gao
【誥】 (1) bestow; confer; grant; (2) enjoin; order;
[誥命] imperial mandates; royal orders;

gao
【鋯】 zirconium;

ge¹
ge
【戈】 (1) dagger-axe; javelin; lance; spear;

G

(2) surname;

［戈甲］ weapon and armour;

抛戈棄甲 throw away one's arms and cast aside one's breastplate; throw away weapon and armour;

［戈矛］ lance; spear;

操戈 take up arms;
倒戈 change sides in a war; turn one's coat;
干戈 arms; war; weapons of war;
揮戈 brandish one's weapon;
探戈 tango;
游戈 cruise; patrol;

ge

【仡】 (1) gallant; valiant; (2) majestic; stately;

［仡老族］ Gelo nationality, living in the Guizhou Province;

ge

【肐】 the arm – from armpit to wrist;

ge

【疙】 pimple; pustule; wart;

［疙瘩］ (1) lump; pimple; (2) difficulty; knot; problem;

疙疙瘩瘩 bumpy; knotty; rough;
解開疙瘩 loosen a knot;

ge

【哥】 elder brother;

［哥哥］ one's elder brother;

異父哥哥 elder stepbrother;
異母哥哥 elder stepbrother;

［哥老會］ Elder Brother Society;

阿哥 elder brother;
表哥 elder male cousin;
大哥 (1) eldest brother; (2) elder brother;
款哥 rich brother; rich man; young big buck;
鵯哥 grackle; tinkling;
堂哥 elder male cousin with the same surname;
燕八哥 starling;
鸚哥 parrot;

ge

【胳】 armpit; same as 骼, arms;

［胳臂］ arm;

［胳膊］ arm;

胳膊粗 have strong and muscular arms;
胳膊肘儿 elbow;
捋胳膊 roll up one's sleeves and show the arms;
攔胳膊 refuse one's request for help;
兩條胳膊 two arms;
伸開胳膊 put one's arm out; stretch one's arms;
抬起胳膊 lift one's arm;
抓住他的胳膊 grab him by the arm;

［胳肢］ tickle sb;

ge

【割】 cut; sever;

［割愛］ give away what one loves; give up sth that one treasures; part with a cherished possession; part with what one loves;

割愛見遺 give away one's beloved thing to another; part with sth and make a present of it;

［割草］ cut down grass; mow;

割草機 lawnmower; mower;
~雙刀割草機 double-knife mower;
~圓盤式割草機 disk mower;

［割除］ cut; cut off; cut out; excise;

［割地］ cede territory;

割地賠款 cede territory and pay indemnities;
割地求和 beg for peace by ceding part of one's territory to another country; cede one's territory and ask for peace; sacrifice part of one's territory in order to make peace;

［割斷］ chop up; cut apart; cut off; isolate; lop off; sever;

割袍斷義 break a relationship with a friend;

［割據］ set up a separatist regime by force of arms;

割據稱雄 break away from central authority and exercise local power; set up a separationist rule;

［割口］ incision;

［割裂］ carve up; cut apart; rend; separate;

［割讓］ cede; cession;

割讓領土 cession of territory;

［割肉補瘡］ cutting the flesh to cure a boil;

［割線］ secant;

分割 break up; carve up; cut apart;
交割 complete a business transaction;
臠割 carve up; slice up;
氣割 gas cutting;
切割 cut;

收割 gather in; harvest; reap;
閹割 castrate; spay;
餘割 cosecant;
宰割 invade; oppress and exploit;
正割 secant;

ge

【歌】 (1) song; (2) sing;
［歌本］ songbook;
［歌唱］ (1) sing; singing; (2) praise; sing in praise of;
歌唱比賽 singing contest;
~ 書院歌唱比賽 college singing contest;
歌唱家 singer; vocalist;
~ 男歌唱家 male singer; male vocalist;
~ 女歌唱家 female singer; female vocalist;
放聲歌唱 break into song; burst into song;
［歌詞］ libretto; lyrics; lyrics of a song;
歌詞作者 librettist; lyricist;
［歌兒］ song;
［歌喉］ singer's voice; singing voice; voice;
歌喉婉轉 sing with a beautiful voice; sweet singing; sweet voice;
一副歌喉 a voice;
［歌姬］ female entertainer; singing girl;
［歌劇］ opera;
歌劇演出 operatic performance;
歌劇演員 opera singer;
歌劇院 opera house;
大歌劇 grand opera;
輕歌劇 operetta;
小歌劇 operetta;
［歌女］ singsong girl;
［歌譜］ music of a song; music score of a song;
［歌曲］ song;
歌曲創作 songwriting;
歌曲集 songbook;
愛國歌曲 patriotic song;
愛情歌曲 love song;
標題歌曲 title track;
獨唱歌曲 song for one voice;
合唱歌曲 choral song;
抗議歌曲 protest song;
流行歌曲 pop song; popular song;
~ 流行歌曲偶像 pop idol;
輕快的歌曲 airy song;
通俗歌曲 popular song;
鄉土歌曲 rustic song;
最出名的歌曲 best-known song;
［歌聲］ singing; sound of singing;
歌聲哀厲 the song is plaintive;
歌聲嘹亮 the singing is loud and clear;
歌聲繚繞 the song lingered in the air;
歌聲繞梁 the voice of singing reverberates round the beams of a house for days;
歌聲如潮 the sound of songs rising and falling like waves;
歌聲四起 sounds of singing were heard from all around;
歌聲甜美 sweet singing voice;
歌聲盈耳 the sound of singing fills the ear;
［歌手］ singer; songster; vocalist; warbler;
伴唱歌手 backing singer;
參賽歌手 a singer who has entered a competition;
流行樂歌手 pop singer;
民歌手 folk singer;
女歌手 songstress;
天生的歌手 natural-born singer;
［歌頌］ eulogize; extol; praise; sing the praises of;
歌頌勝利 sing of victory;
歌功頌德 chant one's praises and sing of sb's virtue; eulogize sb's virtue and achievements; eulogize the deeds and virtues of; flattery and exaggerated praise; glorification of; glorify sb's character and accomplishments; heap praises on; praise and eulogy; sing the praise of; sing the praise of sb's achievements and virtue;
［歌壇］ circle of singers; song circles;
歌壇新秀 new singing star;
［歌舞］ singing and dancing; song and dance;
歌舞表演 cabaret;
歌舞隊 chorus line;
~ 歌舞隊女演員 chorus girl;
歌舞片 musical; musical film;
歌舞昇平 celebrate peace by singing and dancing; sing and dance to extol the good times; sing and dance in celebration of peace;
歌舞團 song and dance ensemble; song and dance troupe;
歌舞影片 musical; musical film;
歌伎舞娘 female singer and dancer; singsong girl and dancing hostess;
歌台舞榭 halls for the performance of songs and dances; singsong stages and dancing halls;

G

酣歌狂舞 sing and dance rapturously;
狂歌酣舞 sing and dance rapturously;
能歌善舞 be able to sing and dance; good at singing and dancing; skilled in both singing and dancing;
清歌妙舞 a good song-and-dance performance; elegant songs and refined dancing — pleasing to ears and eyes;
輕歌曼舞 cheerful songs and graceful dances; elegant songs and refined dancing; sing cheerfully and dance gracefully; sing light songs and dance with rhythmic beauty; sing merrily and dance gracefully; soft music and graceful dances; sweet singing and graceful dancing;
輕歌舞 a kind of lively dance;
載歌載舞 festively singing and dancing; now singing, now dancing; sing and dance at the same time; singing and dancing; singing and dancing joyously;

[歌星] singing star; star singer;
紅歌星 star singer;
流行音樂歌星 pop star;

[歌謠] ballad; ditty; folk song; nursery rhyme; rustic song;
短歌謠 ditty;

[歌吟] sing;

[歌詠] singing;

哀歌 (1) dirge; elegy; funeral song; keen; lament; monody; mournful song; requiem; threnody; (2) croon plaintively;
悲歌 sad melody; sing with solemn fervor;
唱歌 sing; sing a song;
對歌 sing in antiphonal style;
兒歌 children's song; nursery rhymes;
副歌 refrain;
高歌 sing loudly; sing with a resounding voice;
國歌 national anthem;
凱歌 song of triumph;
老歌 old song;
俚歌 folk song;
戀歌 love song;
錄歌 record a song;
民歌 folk song;
牧歌 madrigal;
謳歌 celebrate in song; sing the praise of;
情歌 love song;
山歌 folk song;
笙歌 play and sing;
詩歌 poems and songs;
頌歌 ode; song;
踏歌 dancing accompanied by singing;
挽歌 dirge; elegy;
寫歌 compose a song; write a song;
新歌 new song;
一首歌 a song;
漁歌 fisherman's song;
樂歌 music and songs;
贊歌 song of praise;
戰歌 battle song; fighting song;
主歌 theme song;
組歌 suite of songs;

ge

【擱】 (1) place; put; (2) lay down; leave over; put aside; shelve;

[擱筆] lay down one's pen; put down the pen; stop writing either temporarily or for good;

[擱淺] (1) aground; be grounded; be stranded; beach; go aground; ground; run aground; run ashore; (2) a deadlock; at a deadlock; be held up; be suspended; come to a deadlock; reach a deadlock;

[擱置] abeyance; fall into abeyance; hold in abeyance; in abeyance; keep in abeyance; lay aside; lay on the shelf; leave in abeyance; pigeonhole; shelve;
擱置動議 shelve a motion;
擱置不管 lay aside; shelve; toss aside;
擱置不用 lie by; lie idle;
擱置腦後 off one's mind; put out of mind; throw to the winds;
擱置一項計劃 shelve a plan;

延擱 delay; procrastinate;

ge

【鴿】 dove; pigeon;

[鴿房] dovecote;

[鴿派] dove; dove faction;
鴿派的 dovish;

[鴿舍] dovecote;

[鴿子] dove; pigeon;
鴿子咕咕 doves coo; pigeons coo;
鴿子籠 dovecote; loft; pigeon house;
一隻鴿子 a pigeon;

鵓鴿 pigeon;

G

家鴿 pigeon;
賽鴿 racing pigeon;
信鴿 carrier pigeon; homing pigeon;

ge²

ge

【革】 (1) hide; leather; (2) change; reform; transform; (3) abolish; dismiss; expel; remove from office;

［革出］ dismiss; expel;

［革除］ (1) abolish; do away with; get rid of; (2) dismiss; dispel; excommunicate; expel; remove from office;
革除不良作風 get rid of a bad style;
革除陋習 abolish irrational practices;

［革命］ revolution;
革命暴動 revolutionary outbreak;
革命化 revolutionization;
白色革命 white revolution;
大革命 great revolution;
反對革命 oppose revolution;
反革命 counter-revolution;
農業革命 agrarian revolution;
人口革命 demographic revolution;
商業革命 commercial revolution;
投身革命 join in the revolution; join the revolutionary ranks;
一場革命 start a revolution;
~爆發一場革命 a revolution breaks out;
~掀起一場革命 start a revolution;

［革新］ innovation; reform; renovation;
革新的 innovatory;
革新者 innovator;
革故鼎新 abolish the old and establish the new; abolish what is old and establish in its place the new order of things; discard the old and introduce the new; drop old habits and establish new ones; reform the set rules to create sth new;
技術革新 technical innovation; technological innovation;
教育革新 educational innovation;
學校革新 school innovation;

［革職］ discharge from a position; dismiss; remove from office; sack;
革職查抄 one is demoted and one's property confiscated;
革職留任 dismissal from sb's post while retaining his/her duties;
革職問罪 remove sb from office and punish sb for his/her crimes;

［革製品］ leather goods;

變革 change; transform;
兵革 military weapon;
病革 about to die of an illness;
裁革 abolish; cut down;
斥革 dismiss sb from office;
鼎革 change of dynasty;
改革 reform;
面革 upper leather;
皮革 hide; leather;
漆革 patent leather;
興革 start reforms; initiate the new and abolish the old;
沿革 course of change and development;
因革 evolution; successive changes; the course of change and development;
制革 process hide;
製革 tanning;

ge

【咯】 cluck;

［咯咯］ cluck;
咯咯叫 cackle;
咯咯聲 cluck;

ge

【格】 (1) check; squares formed by crossed lines; (2) pattern; standard; style; (3) division; (4) case;

［格調］ style;
明快的格調 lucid and lively style;

［格格不入］ alien to; cannot get along with others; feel out of one's element; ill-adapted to; incompatible with; jar with; like a square peg in a round hole; misfits; out of one's elements; out of tune with;

［格格笑］ cackle;

［格局］ arrangement; manner; pattern; setup; structure; style;
新格局 new pattern;

［格律］ rules and forms of classical poetic composition;

［格式］ form; format; layout; mode; style;
代碼格式 code format;
機器可讀格式 machine-readable format;
既定格式 established form;
交替格式 alternative pattern;
字符格式 character format;

［格外］ all the more; especially; exceptionally; extraordinarily;
格外高興 especially happy;
格外愜意 feel especially pleased;
格外優遇 exceptionally good treatment;
［格物致知］ investigation of things and acquisition of knowledge;
［格言］ adage; aphorism; maxim; motto; saw;

標格 model; example;
表格 form; table;
賓格 accusative; accusative case;
出格 (1) exceed proper limits for speech or action; exceed what is proper; go too far; overdo sth; (2) differ from others; out of the ordinary;
方格 check;
方位格 locative case;
風格 style;
工具格 instrumental case;
共同格 common case;
夠格 qualified; up to standard;
規格 (1) standard; (2) norms; specifications; standards;
國格 national character and morals; national dignity;
扞格 conflict; contradict;
合格 qualified; up to standard;
呼格 vocative case;
及格 pass; qualify;
價格 price;
間接格 oblique case;
降格 lower one's standard;
空格 blank space (on a form, etc.);
平行格 parallelism;
品格 (1) one's character and morals; (2) quality and style;
破格 break a rule; make an exception;
人格 (1) character; moral quality; personality; (2) human dignity;
賞格 size of a reward;
昇格 promote; upgrade;
屬格 possessive case;
體格 build; physique;
性格 disposition; nature; temperament;
嚴格 rigid; rigorous; strict; stringent;
資格 (1) qualifications; (2) seniority;

ge

【鬲】 (1) an ancient state; (2) same as 隔;
［鬲津］ Gegin River;

ge

【蛤】 clam;
［蛤殼］ clamshell;
［蛤蠣］ bivalve;

長柄蛤 dipper clam; surf clam;
魁蛤 big clam;
文蛤 clam;

ge

【葛】 (1) poplin; (2) a surname;
［葛粉］ arrowroot;
［葛薯］ yam beans;
［葛衣］ hemp cloth;

ge

【隔】 (1) lie between; partition; separate; stand between; (2) after an interval of; at a distance from; at an interval of;
［隔板］ bulkhead; partition;
波形隔板 corrugated bulkhead;
防火隔板 fireproof bulkhead;
氣密隔板 airtight bulkhead; pressure bulkhead;
［隔壁］ next door;
隔壁公寓 next-door apartment;
隔壁鄰居 neighbour; next door;
［隔層］ compartment;
獨立隔層 separate compartment;
［隔斷］ cut off; obstruct; separate;
［隔行］ interlace;
隔行如隔山 difference in profession makes one fell worlds apart;
［隔閡］ (1) estrangement; misunderstanding; (2) barrier; gulf;
思想隔閡 communication gap;
消除隔閡 remove gaps;
種族隔閡 barrier between races;
［隔間］ compartment;
頭等隔間 first-class compartment;
小隔間 cubicle;
［隔絕］ completely cut off; isolated;
隔絕期 isolation period;
完全隔絕 complete isolation;
與世隔絕 be isolated from the world;
與外界隔絕 be cut off from the outside world;
［隔離］ isolate; isolation; keep apart; segregate; severe;
隔離帶 dividing area;

G

~中央隔離帶 central reservation;
隔離器 isolator;
~蓄電池隔離器 battery isolator;
~輔助隔離器 auxiliary isolator;
隔離醫院 isolation hospital;
故障隔離 failure isolation;
生物隔離 biological isolation; biotic isolation;

[隔膜] diaphragm;
差壓隔膜 unbalanced diaphragm;
多孔隔膜 porous diaphragm;
隔板隔膜 separator diaphragm;
絕熱隔膜 adiabatic diaphragm;
星狀隔膜 stellate diaphragm;

[隔熱] heat insulation; heat-proof;
隔熱材料 lagging;

[隔聲] sound insulation;

鼻中隔 nasal septum;
分隔 divide; separate;
骨隔 scleroseptum;
間隔 intermission; separate; set apart;
暌隔 separate;
每隔 day at certain intervals; every...;
舌中隔 septum of tongue;
相隔 be separated by;
懸隔 be separated by a great distance;
遙隔 far-off;
壅隔 block up; obstruct; stop the flow of;
遠隔 distant; far; far apart; remote;
中隔 septum;
縱隔 mediastinum;
阻隔 cut off; separate;

ge

【嗝】 belch; hiccough; hiccup;

飽嗝 belch; burp;
打嗝 (1) hiccup; (2) belch; burp;
噎嗝 cancer of the esophagus;

ge

【膈】 diaphragm;

ge

【閣】 (1) pavilion; (2) cabinet;

[閣樓] attic; garret; loft;

出閣 get married; marry;
高閣 (1) large and tall pavilion; (2) rack; shelf;
閨閣 boudoir;
內閣 cabinet;
組閣 form a cabinet;

ge

【閤】 (1) small side door; (2) same as 閣, chamber, pavillion, etc.;

ge

【骼】 bone; skeleton;

骨骼 skeleton;

ge

【鎘】 cadmium;

ge

【轕】 dispute; (2) disorder;

ge³

ge

【舸】 large boat;

ge

【葛】 a surname;

ge

【蓋】 a surname;

ge⁴

ge

【各】 (1) all; each; every; (2) different; various;

[各半] fifty-fifty; half-and-half;

[各別] (1) different; distinct; separate; (2) out of the ordinary; peculiar; (3) eccentric; funny; odd;

[各處] everywhere;

[各從其類] each after its kind; every item in its proper category;

[各得其所] each gets its due; each has a role to play; each is in its proper place; each is properly provided for; each takes its proper place;

[各地] four corners;

[各個] (1) each; every; various; (2) one by one; separately;
各個擊破 conquer one after the other; defeat one after another; divide and conquer; knock down one by one; smash one by one;

[各級] all levels; different levels;

[各界] all circles; all walks of life;
各界人士 people of different circles;

[各盡其用] each answers the intended purpose;
物有所歸，各盡其用 a place for everything and everything in its place;

［各人］ each one; everyone;
各人各愛 there's no accounting for taste;
各人各心 many people, many minds; several people, several minds;
各人難處各人知 no one but the wearer knows where the shoe pinches;
各人自掃門前雪 clear the snow away only from one's own doorstep; give your own fish guts to your own seamaws; hoe one's own row; let every man skin his own skunk; mind only one's own business;
各人自掃門前雪，莫管他人瓦上霜 each one sweeps the snow from one's own doorsteps and does not bother about the frost on the neighbours' roofs; let every man skin his own skunk; mind only one's own business and not meddle in other people's affairs; sweep the snow of one's own doorsteps, leave alone the frost on other people's roofs;
［各色］ assorted; of all kinds; of every description;
各色人等 all classes of people; all kinds of people; people of every description;
［各事其主］ each serves its own master;
［各適其所］ each to his taste; every hog to his trough; everyone after its own fashion; everyone enjoys his place; let each do the things that please himself/herself;
［各位］ everybody;
［各行其是］ act as one pleases; each does in ways he thinks are right; each does what he thinks is right; each goes his own way;
［各種各樣］ all kinds of; all manner of; all sorts of; of all sorts; of every description; of every variety; of sorts; this and that; various;
［各自］ by oneself; each; respective;
各自付帳 go Dutch;
各自為戰 each fights his own battle; fight the enemy separately;
各自為政 each administers in their own way; each conducts governmental affairs in their own way; each does things in their own way; each forms an independent system of their own; everyone goes their own way; lack of coordination;
［各走各道］ each goes their own way; go different ways;

ge

【虼】 flea;
［虼螂］ dung beetle;
［虼蚤］ flea;

ge

【個】 (1) individual; (2) measure word;
［個案］ case;
個案史 case history;
個案數 caseload;
個案研究 case study;
~ 個案研究法 case study method;
［個別］ (1) individual; personal; separately; specific; (2) one or two; exceptional; rare; very few;
個別輔導 personal counselling;
個別教育計劃 individualized education programme
個別學習 personalized learning;
個別治療 individual therapy;
［個個］ each and every one;
［個人］ (1) individual; personal; (2) I;
個人財產稅 personal property tax;
個人差異論 individual differences theory;
個人成份 personal class status;
個人崇拜 cult of personality; personality cult;
個人地位 personal status;
個人電腦 individual computer;
個人獨資企業 sole proprietorship;
個人翻譯 individual translation;
個人負責 individual responsibility;
個人股 personal share;
個人化 personification;
~ 非個人化 impersonification;
個人計算機 personal computer;
個人價值 personal value;
~ 個人價值論 individual evaluation theory;
個人經歷 personal experience;
個人決策 personal decision-making;
個人空間 personal space;
個人迷信 cult of personality; personality cult;
個人權利 individual rights;
個人收入 personal income;
個人雙語現象 individual bilingualism;
個人所得稅 individual income tax;

個人特質 unique trait;
個人通訊 personal telecommunications;
個人系統 personal system;
個人習語 idiolect;
~ 個人習語歧義 idiolectal ambiguity;
個人興趣 personal preference;
個人野心家 careerist;
個人隱私 individual privacy;
個人語言 personal language;
個人賬戶 single account;
個人職業選擇 personal occupation choice;
個人主義 individualism;
每個人 one and all;

[個體] (1) individuality; personality; thing; (2) individual; particular;
個體差異 individual difference;
個體道德 individual morality;
個體工商戶 individual industrial or commercial unit;
個體戶 person engaged in an individual enterprise;
個體化 individualization;
個體經濟 individual economy;
~ 個體經濟法學 individual economy jurisprudence;
~ 個體經濟分析 individual economic analysis;
個體經營 individually-owned business;
~ 個體經營戶 individual business;
~ 個體經營者 individual operator;
個體名詞 individual noun;
個體企業 individually-owned enterprise;
個體商販 individual retailer;
個體社會學 individual sociology;
個體審美發展 individual aesthetic development;
個體審美能力 individual aesthetic capability;
個體生態學 individual ecology;
個體所有制 individual ownership;
個體行為 individual behaviour;
~ 個體行為模式 model of individual behaviour;

[個性] habit; haecceity; individual character; individuality; personality; specific character;
個性衝突 personality clash;
個性發展 personal development;
個性功能 personal function;
個性化的 individualized;
個性結構 structure of personality;
~ 個性結構理論 structure theory of personality;
個性模式 model of personality;
個性強的人 person of strong personality;
個性傾向 personality tendency;
~ 個性傾向性 personality tendentiousness;
個性軟弱 have a weak personality;
個性特徵 personality trait; trait;
個性特徵 personality characteristic; personality feature;
個性鮮明 have a striking personality;
個性心理特徵 psychological characteristics of the personality;
個性心理學 personality psychology;
保持個性 preserve one's individuality;
暴露個性 unfold personality;
發展個性 cultivate one's individuality;
剛強的個性 forceful personality;
好個性 sweet disposition;
活潑外向的個性 vivacious personality;
令人作嘔的個性 brackish personality;
難以捉摸的個性 amorphous personality;
強烈的個性 strong personality;
缺乏個性 lack of individuality;
失去個性 lose one's individuality;
突出個性 one's middle name;
抑制個性 repress individuality;
有個性 have individuality;
~ 有個性的人 person of character;
友善的個性 warm personality;
尊重個性 respect individuality;

[個中] therein;
個中奧妙 the inside story; the secret of it;
個中老手 expert in a given field; old hand;
個中能手 dab hand at; expert in a given field;
個中人 insider; person in the know;

[個子] build; height; stature;
個子不高 smallish;
個子矮 short; short in stature;
矮個子 dwarf; person of short stature; short person;
大個子 hulk;
高個子 tall person;
~ 瘦高個子 beanpole;
小個子 little chap; small fellow;

那個 that;
哪個 which one;
些個 a little;

一個 (1) a; an; one; (2) a piece of; a word of;
這個 (1) this; this one; (2) this;
真個 indeed; really; truly;
整個 entire; whole;
逐個 one by one;

ge

【硌】 damages or injuries caused by being squeezed or pressed on a rough surface;

ge

【箇】 same as 個；

ge

【鉻】 chrome; chromium;
［鉻處理］ chroming;
［鉻黃］ chrome yellow;
［鉻綠］ chrome green;

六價鉻 hexavalent chromium;
鋅鉻 zinc chromium;
乙酸鉻 chromium acetate;

gei³
gei

【給】 (1) give; grant; (2) for; for the benefit of; (3) allow; let; (4) by (passive marker);
［給錢］ give money;
［給人］ by sb; give sb; to sb;
給人補課 help sb make up lessons;
給人口實 give sb a handle;
給人騙了 be ripped off;
偷偷給人 slip sth to sb;
［給與］ give, grant, pay; render; show;
給與麻煩 give sb a hard time;

gen¹
gen

【根】 (1) root; (2) radical; (3) base; foot; root; (4) cause; origin; source; (5) completely; thoroughly;
［根本］ at all; essence; fundamental; not care a hoot; not give a damn; not the least; once for all; simply; thoroughly;
根本不同 be like chalk and cheese;
根本利益 fundamental interests;
根本原因 basic reason; root cause;
［根除］ do away with; eliminate; eradicate; exterminate; root out; uproot;
根除錯誤 root up errors;
根除惡習 do away with bad habits;
根除後患 dig up the root of future trouble; remove the cause of future trouble;
根除禍害 cut off the evil at its source;
根除迷信 extirpate superstitions;
根除貧困 uproot poverty;
根除社會罪惡 strike at the root of the social evil; strike the social evil at its source;
根除罪惡 eliminate the root of evil;
［根底］ (1) foundation; (2) cause; root; the ins and outs;
查根問底 investigate thoroughly;
追問根底 inquire into the cause of the matter;
知根知底 know the background; know the bottom; know through and through;
［根兒硬］ be backed up; have connections; have strong support;
［根基］ basis; foundation;
［根究］ get to the bottom of; make a thorough investigation of; probe into;
根究緣由 go into the whys and wherefores; probe into the cause;
［根據］ according as; according to; in accordance with; in line with; in the light of; on the basis of;
根據地 base; base area;
根據各方面所說 according to all accounts; by all accounts; from all accounts;
根據某人自己所說 by one's own account;
沒有根據 not have a leg to stand on;
［根絕］ eliminate; eradicate; exterminate; stamp out; wipe out;
根絕弊端 do away with bad practices;
根絕事故 eliminate accidents;
［根深］ be deep-rooted;
根深蒂固 be firmly established and not easily removed; become deeply ingrained in; bred-in-the-bone; deep-seated; deep-rooted; ingrained; inveterate; long-established;
~根深蒂固的觀點 long-held views;
~根深蒂固的習慣 long-standing habit;
根深葉茂 be deeply rooted and thickly covered with foliage — be well-established and have deep roots and luxuriant leaves; thick with leaves and deep-rooted;
［根源］ bottom; fountain; fountainhead; grass roots; origin; root; source;

G

究其根源 trace sth to its source;
找根源 go to the root of;

[根治] bring under permanent control; cure once and for all; fundamental solution; radical cure;

病根 (1) incompletely cured illness; old complaint; (2) root cause of trouble;
不定根 adventitious root;
側根 lateral root;
城根 sections of a city close to the city wall;
齒根 root of a tooth;
除根 remove the root;
詞根 root;
存根 counterfoil; stub;
斷根 be completely cured; effect a permanent cure;
方根 square root;
禍根 cause of ruin; root of the trouble;
假根 rhizoid;
塊根 tuberous root;
立方根 cube root;
年根 end of the year;
票根 counterfoil; stub;
平方根 square root;
起根 all along; at all time;
氣根 aerial root;
墻根 foot of a wall;
山根 foot of a hill;
舌根 base of the tongue;
生根 take root;
酸根 acid radical;
鬚根 fibrous root;
虛根 imaginary root;
牙根 fang; root of a tooth;
銀根 money; money market;
扎根 take root;
直根 taproot;
主根 main root; taproot;

gen

【跟】 (1) heel; (2) follow; (3) and;

[跟班] (1) join a regular shift or class; (2) attendant; footman;

[跟車人] patcher;

[跟骨] calcaneum; heel bone;
跟骨凹 calcaneal sulcus;
跟骨刺 calcaneal spur;
跟骨結節 calcaneal tubercle;
跟骨炎 calcaneitis;
巨跟骨 tarsomegaly;

[跟腱] Achilles tendon;
跟腱反射 Achilles reflex;
跟腱縫術 achillorrhapy;
跟腱囊炎 achillobursitis;
跟腱切斷術 achillotenotomy;
跟腱痛 achillodynia;

[跟腳] (1) (of shoes) fit well; (2) close upon sb's heels;
這鞋不跟腳 the shoes do not fit properly;

[跟進] follow-up;
跟進行動 follow-up;

[跟牌] (of mahjong) following suit;

[跟屁蟲] (1) one's shadow; (2) ass kisser; bootlicker; brown-noser; flatterer;

[跟前] close to; in front of; near; nearby;

[跟上] abreast of; catch up sb; catch up with sb; come up with; draw up with; gain on; get up to; hold pace with; keep abreast of; keep pace with; keep up with; overtake; pull up with;
跟上潮流 keep abreast with the times; keep up to date;
跟上時代 keep abreast of the times;
跟不上 unable to keep pace with; drag;

[跟隨] follow; go after;
跟隨左右 follow sb wherever that person goes;

[跟頭] somersault;
翻跟頭 turn a somersault;
摔跟頭 blunder; come a cropper; fall over; have a fall; make a blunder; trip up;

[跟頭蟲] wriggle;

[跟着] (1) follow; in the wake of; (2) at once; right away;

[跟蹤] dog sb's footsteps; dog sb's steps; follow sb's tracks; follow up the scent; shadow; tracking; trail after sb; trail sb;
跟蹤調查 follow-up survey;
跟蹤緝捕 follow a clue and put sb under arrest;
跟蹤獵物 on the track of the game;
跟蹤器 tracker;
~ 方位跟蹤器 azimuth tracker;
~ 光學跟蹤器 optical tracker;
~ 位置跟蹤器 position tracker;
~ 仰角跟蹤器 elevation tracker;
~ 自動跟蹤器 automatic tracker;
跟蹤逃犯 follow the traces of the escaped prisoner;
跟蹤小偷 track down a thief;

跟蹤者 stalker;
跟蹤追擊 follow sb's heels in hot pursuit; give chase to; go in hot pursuit of; pursue close on sb's heels;
跟蹤罪 stalking;
跟蹤罪犯 track a criminal;
邊界跟蹤 boundary tracking;
電子跟蹤 electronic tracking;
動物跟蹤 animal tracking;
方位跟蹤 azimuth tracking;
負荷跟蹤 load tracking;
光跟蹤 optical tracking;
精確跟蹤 accurate tracking;
輪廓線跟蹤 contour following;
目標跟蹤 target following;
天線跟蹤 antenna tracking;
網絡跟蹤 cyberstalking;
~網絡跟蹤者 cyberstalker;
自動跟蹤 automatic tracking;

後跟 heel;
腳跟 heel;
鞋跟 heel of a shoe;

gen³
gen

【艮】 (1) resilient; tough; (2) outspoken; straightforward; (3) simple clothing;

gen⁴
gen

【亙】 extend; stretch;
［亙古］ eternally;
亙古不變 eternally immutable;
亙古未有 hitherto unequalled;

橫亙 lie across; span;
連亙 continuous;
綿亙 stretch in an unbroken chain;
盤亙 extend; stretch;

gen

【艮】 one of the Eight Diagrams for divination;

儒艮 dugong;

gen

【茛】 rhus toxicodendron, a kind of poisonous vine;

毛茛 buttercup;

geng¹
geng

【更】 (1) change; replace; (2) experience; (3) watch;
［更杯易箸］ bring clean cups and chopsticks to renew the feast;
［更迭］ alternate; change;
［更動］ alter; change; modify;
計劃更動 a change in the plan;
稍有更動 some slight changes;
作必要的更動 make the necessary alteration;
［更番］ alternately; by turns;
更番迭次 again and again; many times; modify repeatedly;
［更夫］ night watchman;
［更改］ alter; change;
更改日期 change the date;
更改姓名 change one's name;
［更換］ alter; change; exchange; renew; replace; replacement; transpose;
更換位置 change one's position;
道碴更換 ballast replacement;
線路更換 track replacement;
需要更換 need replacement;
［更年期］ change of life; climacteric; climacterium; menopause;
男性更年期 male climacteric; male menopause;
女性更年期 female climacteric; female menopause;
早發更年期 climacterium praecox; precocious menopause;
［更僕難數］ countless; innumerable; too many to count; too numerous to count;
［更深］ in the dead of night;
更深漏殘 in the dead of night;
更深人靜 in the dead of night; it is late and everything is quiet;
更深夜靜 in the dead of night;
更深夜漏 in the deep of night;
［更生］ (1) regenerate; revive; (2) renew;
自力更生 regeneration through one's own efforts; self-reliance;
自然更生 spontaneous regeneration;
［更事］ experience in practical affairs;
更事未多 with little experience in practical affairs;
少不更事 as green as grass; green; inexperienced; still wet behind

the ears; unfledged; young and inexperienced;

[更替] replace; substitute; take turns;
更替水平 replacement level;

[更新] renew; renewal; renovate; replace; update;
更新改造 make replacements and technical innovations; transformation and renovation of;
更新換代 replace old products with new;
更新技術設備 renovate the technical equipment;
更新知識 renew one's knowledge; update one's knowledge;
軌枕更新 sleeper renewal;
局部更新 partial renewal;
線路更新 track renewal;

[更衣] change dresses; change one's clothes;
更衣室 cabana; changing room; dressing room; locker room;
~ 一間更衣室 a changing room;

[更張] change over to new ways; make a fresh start;

[更正] amend; make corrections;
更正錯誤 make corrections;

變更 alter; change; modify;
三更 third watch at night;
守更 keep watch during the night;
五更 (1) five watches of the night; (2) fifth watch of the night;
巡更 keep watch;

geng

【庚】 (1) seventh of the Ten Celestial Stems; (2) age;

長庚 ancient Chinese name for Venus;
貴庚 may I know your age;
年庚 date of birth;
同庚 born in the same year; of the same age;

geng

【耕】 plough; till;

[耕地] (1) plough; till; (2) cultivated land; farmland; field land;
耕地面積 acreage under cultivation; agricultural acreage;

[耕田] cultivate; till a field;
耕田不用牛，點燈不用油 ploughing without oxen, lighting without oil lamps;
耕者有其田 land to the tiller;
無牛捉了馬耕田 make a horse do the ploughing when there is no ox;

[耕耘] cultivation; ploughing and weeding;
莫問收獲，但問耕耘 don't ask about the harvest, but ask about the ploughing;
先有耕耘，後有收獲 one must sow before one can reap;
一分耕耘，一分收獲 one reaps no more than what one has sown; the more ploughing and weeding, the better the crop;

[耕織] farming and weaving;
男耕女織 men do farm work and women engage in spinning and weaving; men tilling the farm and women weaving;

[耕種] cultivate; plough and sow; till; work on a farm;
耕種土地 cultivate the soil;
耕種者 cultivator;

[耕作] cultivate; cultivation; farming; tillage;
耕作學 agronomics;
~ 耕作學家 agronomist;
粗放耕作 extensive agriculture; low agriculture;
大面積耕作 large-scale agriculture;
機械化耕作 mechanized agriculture;
集約耕作 intensive agriculture;
精耕細作 intensive and meticulous farming; intensive cultivation; well-cultivated;
可耕作的 cultivable;
梯田耕作 terrace agriculture;
土壤耕作 soil cultivation;

備耕 make preparations for ploughing and sowing;
筆耕 make a living by writing;
春耕 spring ploughing;
粗耕 extensive cultivation;
代耕 do farm work for a soldier's family;
冬耕 winter ploughing;
機耕 tractor ploughing;
淺耕 shallow ploughing;
秋耕 autumn ploughing;
深耕 plough deeply;
套耕 plough twice using two ploughs at the same time;
旋耕 rotary tillage;
硯耕 plough the field of the inkslab — live by writing;
中耕 intertill;

geng
【浭】 a river in Hebei;

geng
【賡】 carry on; continue;

geng
【羹】 broth; thick soup;
[羹匙] soup spoon; tablespoon;
[羹湯] broth;

閉門羹 slam the door in sb's face;
調羹 spoon;

geng
【鶊】 oriole;

鶬鶊 oriole;

geng³
geng
【哽】 choke;
[哽噎] choke;
[哽咽] choke with sobs; spasmodic;
哽咽難言 choke with sobs and be unable to speak;
哽哽咽咽 groan in sorrow and tears;

geng
【埂】 (1) cave; pit; (2) irrigation ditch;
[埂堰] ridge;

geng
【耿】 (1) honest and just; upright; (2) bright; (3) dedicated; (4) a surname;
[耿耿] (1) dedicated; devoted; (2) be troubled; have sth on one's mind;
耿耿不寐 lose sleep over sth; restless and unable to sleep because of uneasiness of mind;
耿耿此心 devoted; loyal heart;
耿耿於懷 bear sb a grudge; brood over an offence; take sth to heart; uneasy heart;
耿耿忠心 be dedicated heart and soul; dogged adherence to;
[耿直] fair and just; honest and frank; integrity; straightforward; upright;
秉性耿直 candid; upright by nature;

geng
【梗】 (1) stem of a plant; (2) prick or pierce with thorn; thorny; (3) outline; summary; synopsis; (4) block; obstruct; (5) stubborn; (6) fierce and fearless; (7) bane; distress; (8) honest; stiff; straight;
[梗概] outline; summary; synopsis;
略言梗概 give a broad outline; just tell the main points;
[梗化] hinder cultural development; obstruct education;
[梗塞] (1) block; clog; obstruct; (2) infarction;
[梗死] infarction;
假性梗死 pseudoinfarction;
囊性梗死 cystic infarct;
偏頭痛性梗死 migrainous infarction;
貧血性梗死 anaemic infarct;
心肌梗死 myocardial infarction;
~ 急性心肌梗死 acute myocardial infarction;
[梗阻] (1) block; hamper; obstruct; (2) obstruction;

花梗 pedicel;
桔梗 root of balloon flower;
頑梗 obstinate; perverse;
阻梗 block; obstruct;
作梗 create difficulties; hinder; obstruct;

geng
【綆】 rope for drawing up water;
[綆短汲深] a short rope for a deep well—one's ability is inadequate for the task; within sight but beyond reach;

汲綆 rope used for drawing water;

geng
【骾】 fishbone etc. stuck in the throat;

geng
【鯁】 (1) fishbone stuck in the throat; (2) honest; straightforward;

骨鯁 fishbone;

geng⁴
geng
【更】 (1) even more; more; still more; (2) further; furthermore; what is more;
[更多] more; still more;
[更好] all the better; better; so much the better;
不說出來更好 be better left unsaid;
[更壞] even worse; worse; worse still;

G

［更加］ all the more; even more; further; more; still more;
［更妙］ more interesting; still better;
更妙的是 to crown it all; to top it all;
［更少］ still less;
［更有甚者］ and what is more; furthermore; to top it all;

gong[1]
gong

【工】 (1) worker; workman; the working class; (2) labour; work; (3) project; (4) industry; (5) man-day; (6) craftsmanship; skills; (7) be versed in; good at;
［工本］ production cost;
［工筆畫］ painting done with fine delicate strokes;
［工場］ workhouse; workshop;
［工廠］ factory; mill; plant; works;
工廠保養 plant maintenance;
工廠倒閉 closure of a factory;
工廠管理 factory management;
工廠環境保護 factory environmental protection;
工廠經濟 factory economy;
工廠投資 factory investment;
工廠自動化 factory automation;
保税工廠 bonded factory;
兵工廠 armament factory;
停辦工廠 close down a factory;
關閉工廠 shut down a factory;
化工廠 chemical plant;
建立工廠 set up a factory;
軍需工廠 munitions factory;
無人化工廠 unmanned factory;
校辦工廠 school-run factory;
一家工廠 a factory;
自動工廠 automatic factory;
［工潮］ labour disturbances; strike movement; workers' demonstration; workers' protest movement;
［工程］ engineering; programme; project;
工程產業 engineering industry;
工程承包公司 architectural engineering company;
工程成本 engineering cost;
工程顧問 engineering adviser;
工程管理 engineering supervision;
~工程管理費 project management costs;
~工程管理人員 project manager;
~工程管理軟件 project management software;
工程浩大 gigantic project; tremendous amount of work;
工程合同 project contract;
工程計算 engineering calculation;
工程技術人員 engineers and technicians;
工程監督 project superintendent;
工程監理 construction supervision;
工程建設標準 engineering construction standard;
工程經濟 engineering economics;
~工程經濟學 engineering economics;
工程控制 engineering control;
~工程控制論 engineering cybernetics;
工程倫理學 engineering ethics;
工程期限 period of construction;
工程設計 engineering design;
工程師 engineer;
~高級工程師 senior engineer;
教授級高級工程師 professor of engineering;
~錄音工程師 sound engineer;
~隨機工程師 flight engineer;
~現場工程師 field engineer;
~選線工程師 locating engineer;
~驗收工程師 inspecting engineer;
~值班工程師 shift engineer;
~鐘錶工程師 horological engineer;
~助理工程師 assistant engineer;
~總工程師 chief engineer; engineer-in-chief;
~主任工程師 chief engineer;
工程系統工程 engineering system engineering;
工程項目 engineering project;
工程心理學 engineering psychology;
工程學 engineering;
~海岸工程學 coastal engineering;
~航空站工程學 airport engineering;
~化學工程學 chemical engineering;
~環境工程學 environmental engineering;
~生物工程學 bioengineering;
~系統工程學 systems engineering;
工程延誤 project falls behind schedule;
工程造價 project price;
安全工程 safety engineering;
安裝工程 installation work;
採礦工程 mining engineering;
地震工程 earthquake engineering;
電機工程 electrical engineering;
公共工程 public works;
航空工程 aeronautical engineering;

航空航天工程 aerospace engineering;
化學工程 chemical engineering;
機械工程 mechanical engineering;
建築工程 architectural engineering;
土木工程 civil engineering;
無線電工程 radio engineering;
石油工程 petrochemical engineering;
市政工程 municipal engineering;
水利工程 hydraulic engineering;
微型工程 microengineering;
細胞工程 cell engineering;
修路工程 roadworks;
一期工程 a phase of the project;
一項工程 a project;
造船工程 naval architecture; shipbuilding;

[工愁善病] lackadaisical;

[工地] building site; construction plant; construction site; work site;
建築工地 building site;
橋梁工地 bridge construction site;

[工讀] work and study;
半工半讀 part-work and part-study; work one's way through school; work-study programme;
工讀教育 work-study education;
工讀生 training student; work-and-study student;
工讀學校 reformatory; reformatory school; training school;

[工夫] (1) time; (2) free time; leisure;
苦工夫 painstaking effort;
煞費工夫 take much trouble;
死工夫 sheer hard work;
枉費工夫 waste time and work in vain; waste time and energy;
用工夫 practise diligently; study hard; work hard;
一眨眼工夫 in the twinkling of an eye;
用工夫 practise diligently; work hard;
有一頓飯的工夫 for about the time it would take to eat a meal;

[工會] labour union; trade union;
工會會員 union member;
工會主義 unionism;
加入工會 join a union;
教師工會 teachers' union;

[工間] break
工間操 do physical exercise during one's break;
工間休息 coffee break;

[工匠] artisan; craftsman; mechanic;
名工巧匠 experienced artificer;
能工巧匠 dab hand; skilled worker; skilful craftsman;

[工具] (1) appliances; implement; means; tool; (2) instrument;
工具包 toolkit;
工具賓語 instrumental object;
工具動機 instrumental motivation;
工具副詞 instrumental adverb;
工具附加語 instrumental adjunct;
工具格 instrumental case;
工具功能 instrumental function;
工具欄 toolbar;
工具棚 toolshed;
工具箱 tool box; toolkit;
工具主語 instrumental subject;
工具書 reference book;
電動工具 power tool;
電焊工具 electric soldering kit;
翻譯工具 translation tool;
交通工具 means of conveyance;
視聽工具 audiovisual tool;
宣傳工具 propaganda tool;
研磨工具 abrasive tool;
一般工具 general purpose tools;
一件工具 a tool;
一批工具 an array of tools;
一套工具 a set of tools;
一樣工具 a type of tool;
作案工具 tools used in a crime;

[工齡] length of service; working years;

[工農] workers and peasants;

[工錢] pay; salary; wages;

[工人] factory worker; factory-hand; worker;
工人工程師 worker engineer;
工人技術員 worker technician;
工人階級 labouring class; working class;
工人運動 labour movement;
白領工人 white-collar worker;
採煤工人 coalminer;
採石工人 quarryman;
產業工人 industrial worker;
伐木工人 forest labourer;
幹粗活的工人 navy;
鋼鐵工人 steel worker;
機械工人 mechanic;
建築工人 building worker;
局部工人 detail labourer;
藍領工人 blue-collar workers;
老工人 veteran worker;
林業工人 forester;

農業工人 farmhand;
石油工人 oil worker;
熟練工人 skilled worker;
~ 非熟練工人 unskilled worker;
退休工人 retired worker;
外籍工人 guest worker;
先進工人 advanced worker;
小工人 worker;
一大隊工人 an army of workers;
一名工人 a worker;
一批工人 a group of workers;
園林工人 park gardener;
鑄字工人 type founder;

[工日] work-day;

[工商] industry and commerce;
工商管理 business administration; business management;
~ 工商管理碩士 master of business administration;
工商界 industrial and commercial circles;
工商聯 association of industry and commerce;
工商稅 industrial and commercial tax;
工商信貸 industrial and commercial credit;
工商行政管理 industrial and commercial administration;
工商業 industry and commerce;

[工時] labour time; man-hour; task time; working hours;
工時記錄卡 time card;
工時記錄鐘 time clock;
工時模擬 working-hour simulation;
標準工時 standard labour time; standard working hours;
工程工時 engineering man-hour;

[工頭] foreman; ganger; headman; overseer;
女工頭 forewoman;

[工效] work efficiency;
工效標準 work efficiency standard;
工效學 ergonomics;

[工序] procedure; production processes; working procedure;
工序統計質量控制 statistical process control;
簡化工序 simplify working processes;

[工學] engineering;
工學士 bachelor's degree in engineering;
靜工學 electrotechnics;
熱工學 thermal engineering;

[工業] industry;
工業安全 industrial security;
工業標準 industrial standard;
~ 工業標準結構 industrial standard architecture;
工業病 industrial disease;
工業佈局 industrial arrangement;
工業部門 industrial branch;
工業產品 industrial products;
工業產權 industrial property;
~ 工業產權法 industrial property law;
~ 工業產權制度 industrial property system;
工業城市 industrial city;
工業大學 polytechnic university;
工業地理學 industrial geography;
工業地域綜合體 industrial territorial complex;
工業地域組合 territorial combination of industry;
工業動態模型 industrial dynamic model;
工業發展戰略 industrial development strategy;
工業個人計算機 industrial personal computer;
工業管理 industrial management;
~ 工業管理工程 industrial engineering;
工業國 industrial powers; industrialized country;
工業化 industrialization;
~ 工業化社會 industrialization society;
~ 後工業化 post-industrial;
~ 加快工業化 intensify industrialization;
~ 實現工業化 bring about industrialization;
~ 再工業化 reindustrialization;
工業機器人 industrial robot;
工業技術經濟 industrial-technology economy;
~ 工業技術經濟學 economics of industrial technology;
工業家 industrialist;
工業經濟 industrial economy;
~ 工業經濟管理 industrial economic management;
~ 工業經濟結構 industrial economy structure;
~ 工業經濟學 economics of industry;
工業淨產值 net production value of industry;
工業考古學 industrial archaeology;
工業會計學 industrial accounting;
工業聯合公司 joint corporation of

industry;
工業美學 industrial aesthetics;
工業企業 industrial enterprise;
~工業企業管理 industrial enterprise management;
~工業企業經營 industrial enterprise operation;
工業企業經營管理 industrial enterprise operation management;
工業企業經營學 industrial enterprise management;
工業區 industrial area;
工業圈 industrial ring;
工業人口 industrial population;
工業社會 industrial society;
~工業社會心理學 psychology of industrial society;
~工業社會學 industrial sociology;
工業設計 industrial design;
工業數據處理 industrial data processing;
~工業數據處理中心 industrial data processing centre;
工業稅 industrial tax;
工業統計 industrial statistics;
工業文明 industrial civilization;
工業心理學 industrial psychology;
工業信息 industrial information;
~工業信息綜合體 industrial information cooperative;
工業訓練中心 industrial training centre;
工業用地 industrial area;
工業園 industrial estate; industrial park; industry park;
工業戰線 industrial front;
工業主義 industrialism;
工業自動化 automation of industry;
~工業自動化總體技術 general technologies for industry automation;
工業總產量 gross industrial output;
朝陽工業 sunrise industry;
出口工業 export industry;
傳統工業 traditional industry;
地方工業 local industry;
電機工業 electrical engineering industry;
電力工業 electric power industry;
紡織工業 textile industry;
鋼鐵工業 iron and steel industry;
國內工業 home industry;
國營工業 state-operated industry;
航空工業 aviation industry;
化學工業 chemical industry;
~石油化學工業 petrochemical industry;
基本工業 basic industry;
基礎工業 basic industry;
機械工業 machine industry;
加工工業 processing industry;
建築工業 building industry;
街道工業 neighbourhood industry;
軍火工業 arms industry;
軍需工業 arms industry;
瀝青工業 bituminous industry;
沒落工業 sunset industry;
汽車工業 car industry;
輕工業 light industry;
燃料工業 fuel industry;
釀酒工業 wine industry;
乳品工業 dairy industry;
石油工業 petroleum industry;
食品工業 food industry;
手工業 handicraft industry;
塑膠工業 rubber industry;
陶瓷工業 ceramics industry;
無線電工業 radio industry;
夕陽工業 sunset industry;
現代工業 modern industry;
原材料工業 raw material industry;
原子工業 atomic industry;
造紙工業 papermaking industry;
振興工業 promote industries;
製革工業 leather-tanning industry;
製糖工業 sugar refinery industry;
重工業 heavy industry;
主要工業 main industries;

[工藝] (1) craft; industrial art; techniques; technology; workmanship; (2) handicraft; handicraft art;
工藝精湛 exquisite artisanship;
工藝課 industrial arts;
工藝美術 arts and crafts; industrial art;
~工藝美術師 industrial artist;
高級工藝美術師 senior industrial artist;
助理工藝美術師 assistant industrial artist;
~工藝美術學院 institute of arts and crafts;
~工藝美術員 handicraft painter;
工藝美學 aesthetics in arts and crafts;
工藝水準 artistic and technical level;
~高超工藝水準 high artistic and technical level;
革新工藝 renovate the technology;
直接合成工藝 direct synthesis technology;

[工友] (1) fellow worker; (2) manual worker;

G

[工於此道] be good at this kind of work;
[工餘] after hours; leisure after work;
[工欲善其事，必先利其器] a workman must sharpen his tools in order to do a good job; better tools make better work; better tools are a prerequisite to the successful execution of a job; if a workman wishes to get his work well done, he must sharpen his tools first; it is necessary to have effective tools to do good work;
[工運] labour movement;
[工整] carefully and neatly done;
字迹工整 have neat handwriting;
[工種] branch of work; kind of work; profession; type of work in production;
[工資] pay; remuneration; salary; wage;
工資變動 wage change;
工資差額 wage differences;
工資袋 pay packet;
工資單 payslip; pay stub;
工資凍結 pay freeze;
工資改革 wage reform;
工資管理系統 wage management system;
工資合同 wage contract;
工資級別 scale of wages;
工資糾紛 pay dispute;
工資率 pay rate;
工資税 pay roll tax; wage tax;
工資支票 pay cheque;
工資制 wage system;
工資總支出 payroll;
包工工資 group piecework;
保留工資 retained salaries;
病假工資 sick pay;
產假工資 maternity pay;
補發工資 give back pay;
發工資 pay salary; pay wages;
浮動工資 floating wage;
附加工資 additional wage;
高級工資 higher-grade pay;
基本工資 basic wage;
基本生活工資 living wages;
加工資 pay rise;
降低工資 reduce sb's wage;
競爭性工資 competitive wage;
絕對工資 absolute wage;
平均工資 average wages;
日工資 daily wage; per diem,
實得工資 take-home pay;
實際工資 actual wage;
提高工資 raise sb's salary; raise sb's wage;
小時工資 hourly pay;
休假工資 vacation pay;
虛構工資 fake pay;
應計工資 accrued wage;
預付工資 advance wages;
月工資 monthly wage;
最低工資 minimum wage;
[工作] (1) operation; performance; work; (2) job;
工作安定 job security;
工作安全分析 job safety analysis;
工作報酬 recompense sb's for his/her work;
工作到很晚 stay late;
工作繁忙 be up to one's shoulders;
工作範圍 operating range; operating space; scope of work;
工作方式 working style;
~改變工作方式 vary one's working style;
工作服 work uniform;
工作負荷 working load;
~安全工作負荷 safe working load;
工作夥伴 colleague;
工作環境 working atmosphere; working environment;
工作簡單化 job simplification;
工作節律 work rhythm;
工作狂 glutton for work; workaholic;
工作擴大化 job enlargement;
工作量 amount of work; throughput; workload;
~翻譯工作量 translation workload;
~最大工作量 maximum amount of work;
~最小工作量 minimum amount of work;
工作滿意度 job satisfaction;
工作帽 cloth cap;
工作迷 work addict; workaholic;
工作馬馬虎虎 slipshod in work;
工作能力 working ability;
工作前景 career prospect; job prospect;
工作區 operation area;
~安全工作區 area of safe operation; safe operating area;
工作日 weekday; working day;
~工作日夜晚 weeknight;
工作群體 work group;
工作人員 personnel; staff;
~國家機關工作人員 state personnel;
工作日 working day;

~連續工作日 running lay days;
~晴天工作日 weather working day;
工作室 workshop;
~翻譯工作室 translation workshop;
工作手套 working glove;
工作台 bench; workbench;
~焊接工作台 welding bench;
~鉗工作台 file bench;
~試驗工作台 test bench;
~小工作台 snap bench;
~裝配工作台 assembly bench;
工作條件 working condition;
~改善工作條件 ameliorate working conditions; improve the working conditions;
工作午餐 business lunch; working lunch;
工作效率 working efficiency;
工作辛苦 work very hard;
工作壓力 working pressure;
~安全工作壓力 safe working pressure;
工作站 workstation;
~智能工作站 intelligent workstation;
工作者 worker;
~教育工作者 educator;
~科學翻譯工作者 scientific translator;
~科學工作者 scientific worker;
~遠程工作者 teleworker;
工作之餘 after work; after working hours;
工作制 working system;
~八小時工作制 eight-hour working day;
工作組 task force; task group; working group;
~特別工作組 working party;
工作專業化 job specialization;
安全工作 safe operation; safe working; trouble-free service;
安心工作 keep one's mind on one's work;
按章工作 work to rule;
白天工作 work by day;
保住工作 keep one's job;
抱病工作 carry on with one's work while being sick; go on working in spite of ill health;
不費力的工作 doss;
不停地工作 work incessantly; work tirelessly;
超時工作 work overtime;
吃力工作 wade through;
辭去工作 leave one's job; quit one's job;
吹氣工作 blown work;
帶病工作 carry on with one's work in spite of illness;
單調工作 routine job;
得到工作 land a job;
丟掉工作 lose one's job;
發奮工作 pull all one's energies into one's work; work energetically;
高薪工作 well-paid job;
翻譯工作 translation work;
放棄自己的工作 quit one's job;
很多工作 much work; tons of work;
堅持工作 stick at one's work;
艱苦乏味的工作 slog;
艱難的工作 arduous task;
接受工作 take a job;
開始工作 start work;
~立刻開始工作 start working straightaway;
科學工作 scientific work;
理想的工作 niche;
忙着工作 be busy working;
埋頭工作 be absorbed in one's work; bury oneself in one's work; give oneself wholly to one's work;
沒有工作 out of a job;
努力工作 put one's shoulder to the wheel; work hard; work your fingers to the bone; work your socks off;
~開始努力工作 start to put one's shoulder to the wheel;
拋棄工作 chuck work;
拼命工作 slog one's guts out; sweat one's guts out; work like fury; work one's guts out;
鉗工工作 benchwork;
全日工作 work full-time;
~非全日工作 work part-time;
認真工作 thorough in one's work;
日常工作 day-to-day work;
日夜工作 work around the clock;
申請工作 apply for a job;
失去工作 be given the chop; lose one's job;
逃避工作 stay away from work;
~逃避工作的人 goldbrick;
文書工作 clerical work;
學術工作 academic work;
壓力大的工作 high-pressure job;
延誤工作 dally over one's work;
一大堆工作 a whole stack of work;
一點點工作 a stroke of work;
一點工作 a bit of work; a stroke of work;
一份工作 a job;
一件工作 a piece of work;

一項工作 a piece of work;
有工作 have a job;
在工作 be at one's desk;
在極其惡劣的條件下工作 work in abysmal conditions;
在家裏工作 work at home;
朝九晚五的工作 nine-to-five job;
找工作 job-hunting; look for a job;
~找到工作 find a job; get a job;
孜孜不倦地工作 work tirelessly;

罷工 come out on strike; go on strike; hit the bricks; launch a strike; lay down tools; on strike; organize a strike; stage a strike; strike; walk out;
壩工 dam construction works;
百工 all classes of artisans;
板金工 metal worker;
幫工 helper;
包縫工 seam worker;
包工 (1) contract for a job; undertake to perform work within a time limit and according to specifications; work by contract; (2) contract worker; contractor; foreman;
包裝工 packer;
保養工 fettler;
爆破工 exploder;
笨工 unskilled workman;
裱工 (1) the work of mounting; (2) one who mounts artistic works; (3) charges for mounting;
裱糊工 paper hanger;
兵工 war industry;
玻璃工 glazier;
採石工 quarryman;
蠶工 sericulture; silkworm culture;
長工 long-term employment;
車工 (1) lathe work; (2) lathe operator; lathe turner;
出工 (1) go to work; set out for work; show up for work; turn out for work; (2) supply the labour;
船工 boatman; junkman;
輟工 stop work;
打工 be employed;
怠工 go slow at work; slacken at work; slow down;
擋車工 spinner;
電工 electrician;
雕刻工 engraver;
動工 begin a construction; start building;
短工 seasonal labourer; short-term employment;
鍛工 riveter;
紡紗工 spinner;
放工 knock off;
分工 divide the work; division of labour;
鋼筋工 steel fixer;
復工 go back to work; return to work; start operations again;
僱工 (1) hire hands; hire labour; (2) hired labourer;
管道工 plumber;
管工 plumber;
焊工 welder;
河工 (1) river work; (2) labourer working on a river engineering project;
黑工 illegal worker;
化工 chemical engineering; chemical industry;
畫工 commercial painter;
換工 exchange labour;
機工 machinist;
技工 mechanician; skilled worker;
加工 processing;
監工 supervise;
刻字工 carver; punch cutter;
金工 metal working;
軍工 (1) war industry; (2) military project;
竣工 (of a project) be completed;
開工 (1) (of a factory) go into operation; (2) start;
苦工 hard work;
曠工 stay away from work without leave;
礦工 miner;
勞工 labourer;
零工 (1) odd job; (2) odd jobsman;
路面工 pavement worker;
煤氣工 gas fitter;
民工 labourer working on a public project;
模型工 VAT man;
抹灰工 plasterer;
木工 (1) woodwork; (2) carpenter; woodworker;
泥水工 mason;
釀酒工 brewer;
女工 female worker;
排版工 compositor;
刨工 planer;
漆工 (1) lacquering; (2) lacquerer;
砌磚工 brick mason;
鉗工 (1) bench worker; (2) fitter;
青工 young worker;
清潔工 dustman; sweeper;
染色工 dyer;
人工 (1) manual work; (2) manpower;
日工 (1) daywork; (2) dayworker; (3) day

labourer;
散工 casual labourer; seasonal labourer;
上工 go to work; start work;
施工 build; construct;
石工 stonecraft;
試工 on probation; try out a worker;
收工 knock off; stop work for the day;
手工 (1) handwork; (2) charge for a piece of handwork;
燙衣工 ironer; presser;
陶工 potter;
特工 secret service;
替工 temporary substitute worker;
停工 shut down; stop work;
童工 (1) child labourer; (2) child labour;
徒工 apprentice;
挖土工 excavator;
完工 complete a project; finish doing sth; get through;
屋面工 roofer;
洗衣工 laundryman;
銑工 miller;
歇工 knock off; stop work;
修版工 retoucher;
繡花工 embroider;
養路工 linesman;
冶工 blacksmith;
夜工 night job; night work;
印花工 screen printing operator;
印刷工 printer;
養路工 linesman;
義工 (1) volunteer services; (2) volunteer worker;
營工 do paid labour;
傭工 hired labourer; servant;
油漆工 painter;
釉工 glazier;
員工 personnel; staff;
月工 labourer hired by the month;
雜工 backman; handyman;
招工 employ workers; hire workers; recruit; recruit workers;
鑿岩工 driller;
造型工 moulder;
職工 (1) staff and workers; workers and staff members; (2) labour; workers;
製革工 fur worker; tanner;
製漿工 masher;
製靴工 bootmaker;
竹工 bamboo works;
鑄工 (1) foundry work; (2) foundry worker;
壯工 coolie; unskilled labourer;
拙工 a poor craftsman; an incompetent worker;
鑽井工 well-sinker;
作工 labour; work;
做工 (1) do manual work; work; (2) workmanship;

gong
【弓】 (1) bow; (2) bow-shaped object; (3) wooden land-measuring dividers; (4) old unit of length for measuring land; (5) arch; bend;

［弓法］ archery; bowing;
［弓箭］ bow and arrow;
［弓馬嫻熟］ be adept in archery and horsemanship; be an accomplished horseman and trained in the use of arms; be an expert archer and horseman; be proficient in archery and riding; be very able in archery and in riding horses; excel in horsemanship and archery ; gain proficiency in archery and riding;
［弓駑齊發］ arrows and bolts fly thick; the arrows and bolts fly forth in a sudden fierce shower;
［弓形］ (1) segment of a circle; (2) arched; bow-shaped; curved;
弓形窗 bow window;
弓形橋 humpbacked bridge;
弓形腿 bow legs;
［弓子］ bow;
一把弓子 a bow;

閉弓 closing bow;
步弓 ancient wooden bow-shaped device for measuring land;
車篷弓 roof bow;
彈弓 catapult; slingshot; spring bow;
東方弓 oriental bow;
複合弓 composite bow;
橫弓 horizontal bow;
十字弓 crossbow;
彤弓 crimson bow;
彎弓 (1) drawn bow; (2) ready to shoot the arrow; (3) arch;
挽弓 draw a bow;
引弓 draw the bow;
張弓 draw the bow;

gong
【公】 (1) collective; public; state-owned;

(2) common; general; (3) metric; (4) make public; (5) equitable; fair; impartial; just; (6) official business; public affairs; (7) duke; (8) father-in-law; (9) male; (10) a surname;

[公哀] a surname;

[公安] public security;
公安部 Ministry of Public Security;
公安部門 department of public security;
公安機關 public security unit;

[公案] complicated legal case;

[公辦] state-run;
公辦學校 state-run school;

[公報] bulletin; communique;
公報部 ministry of information;
公報私仇 abuse public power to retaliate on a personal enemy; avenge personal grudges in the name of public interests; use one's position to get even with sb for a private grudge; use the power of the state for one's own private revenge;
行業公報 industry bulletin; trade bulletin;
技術公報 technical bulletin;
聯合公報 joint communique;
每日公報 daily bulletin;
每月公報 monthly bulletin;
每周公報 weekly bulletin;
年度公報 annual bulletin;
新聞公報 news bulletin;
一份公報 a communique;
一項公報 a communique;
政府公報 government bulletin;

[公倍] common multiple;
公倍數 common multiple;
~最小公倍數 lowest common multiple;

[公比] common ratio;

[公賓] a surname;

[公伯] a surname;

[公布] announce; make public; promulgate; publish;

[公廁] public convenience; public toilet;

[公差] (1) tolerance; (2) common difference;
基本公差 basic tolerance;
角度公差 angle tolerance;
容許公差 allowable tolerance;
雙向公差 bilateral tolerance;
驗收公差 acceptance tolerance;

[公差] (1) non-combatant duty; public errand; (2) person on a public errand;
出公差 go on an official trip;

[公產] public property;

[公車] (1) a surname; (2) public vehicle; (3) public bus;
公車隊 carpool;

[公乘] a surname;

[公尺] metre (m.);

[公檮] a surname;

[公疇] a surname;

[公出] away on official business;

[公道] fair; impartial; just; reasonable;
辦事公道 fair and just; play the game;
價錢公道 reasonable in price;
主持公道 uphold justice;

[公德] (1) social ethics; social morality; (2) a surname;
公德心 public-mindedness;
~有公德心 public-spirited;
敗壞公德 corrupt social ethics;
講公德 have social morality;
損害公德 injure public morality;
維護公德 safeguard public morals;

[公敵] common enemy; public enemy;
頭號公敵 public enemy number one;

[公斷] arbitration;
付諸公斷 be submitted to arbitration; refer to arbitration;

[公法] public law;
國際公法 international law;
違抗公法 defy the public law;

[公費] at public expense; at state expense;
公費出國 go abroad at government expense;
公費留學 state-financed student studying abroad;
公費旅游 junket; travel at public expense;
公費醫療 free medical care;

[公憤] furore; popular anger; public indignation;
激起公憤 cause a furore; create a furore; excite public indignation;
平息公憤 appease public indignation; quell popular anger;
引起公憤 arouse public indignation;

[公甫] a surname;

[公父] a surname;

[公告] advisory; announcement; proclamation; notice; public announcement; public notice;
公告日期 declaration date;

G

發表公告 issue a public proclamation; issue an announcement; make an announcement;
旅遊公告 travelers' advisory;

［公共］ common; communal; public;
公共安全 public safety; public security;
公共財政學 science of public finance;
公共廁所 public toilet;
公共代碼 common code;
公共道德 public morality;
公共服務 public service;
公共關係 public relations;
~公共關係部 department of public relations;
~公共關係顧問 public relations advisor;
~公共關係學 science of public relations;
公共交通 mass transit; public transit;
公共空間接口 common air interface;
公共命令語言 common command language;
公共汽車 autobus; bus; motor bus; omnibus; public bus;
~公共汽車司機 bus driver;
公共市場業務 open-market operation;
公共事務 public affairs;
公共事業 public utilities;
公共數據網 public data network;
公共天線 communal aerial;
公共衛生 public health; public hygiene;
公共小車 minibus;
公共行政 public administration;
公共用戶系統 common user system;
公共政策 public policy;
公共組織 community organization;

［公公］ (1) father-in-law; husband's father; (2) grandfather; (3) grandad; grandpa;

［公關］ public relations;
公關部 public relations department;
公關步驟 stages of public relations;
公關道德 ethics of public relations;
公關調查 research of public relations;
公關工具 tools of public relations;
公關功能 functions of public relations;
公關顧問 public relations consultant;
公關廣告 public relations advertising;
公關活動 public relations activity;
公關計劃 plans for public relations;
公關交往 contacts of public relations;
公關角度 angle of public relations;
公關經理 public relations manager;
公關糾紛 public relations disputes;
公關禮儀 public relations etiquette;
公關媒介 public relations media;
公關模式 public relations model;
公關目標 public relations goal;
公關評估 evaluation of public relations;
公關人員 public relations staff;
公關設計學 public relations designs;
公關先生 public relations man;
公關項目 programme of public relations;
公關小姐 public relations girl;
公關心理學 psychology of public relations;
公關形象 image of public relations;
公關意識 consciousness of public relations;
公關語言 language of public relations;
公關原則 principles of public relations;
公關職能 functions of public relations;
公關主題 theme of public relations;
公關專家 expert in public relations;
公關咨詢 consultation of public relations;

［公海］ (1) high seas; international waters; (2) open sea;

［公害］ nuisance; public hazard; public nuisance;
公害經濟 economy of environmental pollution;
~公害經濟學 economics of environmental pollution;
工業公害 industrial public nuisance;
構成公害 constitute a public nuisance;
減輕公害 reduce the environmental pollution;
交通公害 traffic nuisance;

［公函］ official letter;

［公翰］ a surname;

［公戶］ a surname;

［公會］ guild;
行業公會 craft guild;
教師公會 teachers'guild;
同業公會 business guild; guild; trade guild;

［公積金］ central provident fund;

［公雞］ cock; rooster;
公雞喔喔叫 a cock crows;
公雞下蛋—沒指望 a rooster laying eggs — no hope;
鐵公雞——毛不拔 an iron cock from which not a single feather can be plucked — a miser;
小公雞 cockerel;

[公家] organization; public; state;

[公假] leave to attend to official business; official leave;

[公堅] a surname;

[公建] a surname;

[公斤] kilogramme;

[公爵] duke;

[公開] (1) open; overt; public; (2) disclosure; make known to the public; make public; open to the public;
公開的 open;
~公開的秘密 open secret;
~不公開 injustice;
不公開的 closed-door;
公開地 openly;
~不公開地 behind closed doors;
公開認錯 put on a white sheet; stand in a white sheet;
公開審判 open trial;
公開市場 open market;
~公開市場業務 open-market operations;
公開試 public examinations;
公開説出來 tell the world;
公開性 openness;
公開信 open letter;
公開宣佈 publicly proclaim;
公開招標 public bidding;
把醜事公開 give a scandal an airing;
半公開 more or less open; semi-overt;
口頭公開 oral disclosure;
書面公開 written disclosure;

[公款] government expenses; public funds; public money;
公款吃喝 enjoy banquets on public funds;
公款出國旅游 sightseeing trips abroad on public expense;
盜用公款 embezzle public funds;
侵吞公款 embezzlement of public funds;
吞公款 embezzle public funds;

[公理] (1) generally acknowledged truth; self-evident truth; (2) axiom; postulate;
公理的 axiomatic;
公理學 axiomatics;
構造性公理 constructivity axiom;
關聯公理 axiom of alignment;
合同公理 axiom of congruence;
連續性公理 continuity axiom;
維數公理 dimension axiom;
相容性公理 consistent axiomatics;
正合序列公理 exact-sequence axiom;
坐標公理 coordinate axiom;

[公里] kilometre (km.);
公里里程 kilometrage;
車輪公里 kilometres of a car;
噸公里 ton-kilometre;
~換算噸公里 ton-kilometre conversion;
~計費噸公里 charged ton-kilometre;
~淨重噸公里 net ton-kilometre;
客車公里 coach kilometre;
軸公里 axle kilometre;

[公曆] Gregorian calendar;

[公例] general rule;

[公立] public;
公立學校 public school;
~特許公立學校 charter school;

[公良] a surname;

[公路] (1) driveway; highway; (2) highroad; road;
公路幹線 arterial road; trunk road;
公路橋 highway bridge; road bridge;
公路容量 highway capacity;
公路賽 road race;
公路稅 road tax;
公路巡邏隊 highway patrol; road patral;
公路支線 feeder road; secondary road;
筆直的公路 air-line highway;
超級公路 superhighway;
地方公路 local motorway;
輻射式公路 radial road;
幹線公路 arterial main motorway; mainline motorway;
高速公路 expressway; freeway; highway; motorway; turnpike;
~超級高速公路 superhighway;
國家公路 national road;
海濱公路 coast road;
環城公路 ring road;
環心式公路 orbital road;
環行公路 ring road;
免費公路 toll-free road;
繞城公路 ring road;
收費公路 toll road;
雙車道公路 two-lane road;
雙向公路 dual carriageway;
四車道公路 four-lane road;
鄉村公路 country road;
鄉間公路 country road;
一段公路 a section of a road;
一級公路 first-class road;
側繞公路 bypass road;
州際公路 interstate road;

[公鹿] stag;

[公驢] jack; jackass; male ass; male donkey;

[公論] public opinions; verdict of the masses;

自有公論 there is always a fair public opinion;

[公馬] stallion;

[公民] citizen; civil;

公民參與 civic participation;

公民道德 civic ethics; civicism;

公民教育 civic education;

公民抗命 civil disobedience;

公民科 civics;

公民權 civil rights;

~ 剝奪公民權 forfeit civil right;

公民權利 citizenship; rights of citizens;

~ 保障公民權利 safeguard the rights of citizens;

公民身分 citizenship;

公民提名 civic nomination;

公民投票 plebiscite; referendum;

公民學 civics;

公民責任 civic responsibilities;

公民自由 civil liberty;

次等公民 second-class citizen;

普通公民 plain citizen;

全體公民 citizenry;

社會公民 citizen;

世界公民 citizen of the world; global citizen; world citizen;

守法的公民 law-abiding citizen;

[公明] surname;

[公牛] bull;

公牛吼叫 a bull bellows; a bull lows;

小公牛 bullock;

一頭公牛 a bull;

[公平] equitable; equity; fair; fairness; impartial; just;

公平待人 deal fairly with sb; give sb one's due;

公平對待 impartial to; not make chalk of one and cheese of the other;

公平合理 equitable and rational; fair and reasonable; fair and square;

公平交易 square deal; straight dealings; trade justly;

公平競爭 fair competition;

公平理論 equity theory;

公平貿易 fair trade;

公平市價 fair market value;

不公平 not cricket; unfair; unjust;

~ 我們輸得不公平 we were robbed;

處事公平 play fair; play the game;

以示公平 show fairness; show impartiality;

[公僕] public servant;

人民公僕 public servants of the people;

[公權] public rights;

[公然] brazenly; in the face of day; openly;

公然違抗命令 at open defiance with orders;

[公認] generally recognized;

公認發音 received pronunciation;

[公設] postulate;

不變性公設 invariance postulate;

定義公設 defining postulates;

完全性公設 postulate of completeness;

[公升] litre;

[公使] envoy; minister;

[公式] expression; formula;

公式化 formularize; formulistic;

安全公式 safe formula;

代數公式 algebraic formula;

積分公式 formula of integration;

假定公式 assumption formula;

近似公式 approximate formula;

數學公式 mathematical formula;

彎曲公式 bending formula;

[公事] official business; public affairs;

公事包 briefcase;

公事公辦 business is business; do official business according to official principles; public business affairs should be strictly managed;

辦公事 perform the routine;

例行公事 daily routine;

[公叔] a surname;

[公署] government office;

[公私] public and private;

公私不分 not distinguish what is one's own and what is public; not make a clean distinction between public and private interests;

公私分明 be clearly demarcated between public and private interests; scrupulous in separating public from private interests;

公私關係 relation between public and private interests; relation between the state and private sectors of the economy;

公私兼顧 give consideration to both public and private interests; take into account both public and private interests;

公私交鋒 confrontation between selfish interests and the sense of civic duty;

公私兩便 advantageous to both public and private interests;

大公無私 impartial; selfless; unselfish;

~大公無私的精神 the spirit of selflessness;

公而忘私 public business comes before private affairs; put aside selfishness in the interest of the public; selfless;

公是公，私是私 business is business and friends are friends;

化公為私 appropriate a public property; embezzle a public property; turn a public property into a private property;

假公濟私 abuse the public trust; act in the public service for one's own ends; jobbery; promote one's private interests under the guise of serving the public; use public means to satisfy private ends;

借公肥私 enrich oneself by performing public services;

借公濟私 seek for private interest through public affairs;

破私立公 overcome selfishness and foster public spirit; put aside selfishness and build up devotion to the public interest;

先公後私 public affairs precede private obligations; put public interest before self-interest; put public interests ahead of personal interests; put public interests before one's own; put public interests before private ones; subordinate one's own interests to the public good;

以公濟私 act in the public service for one's own ends; further one's private ends by means of official resources; merge private affairs into public ones;

以私廢公 allow private feelings to outweigh public duty;

以私忘公 careless of the common weal and indulge one's private feelings;

[公司] company; corporation; firm; incorporation;

公司法 company law;

公司翻譯員 staff translator;

公司會計 (1) corporate accounting; (2) corporate accountant;

公司秘書 company secretary;

公司名稱 name of the company;

公司配車 company car;

公司稅 corporation tax;

公司文化 corporate culture;

公司譯員 in-house translator;

公司債券 corporate security;

~公司債券溢價 bond premium;

~公司債券折價 bond discount;

公司章程 charter of a company;

公司政策 company policy;

公司主管 company director; company executive;

辦公司 set up a company;

保險公司 insurance company;

被接管公司 predecessor company;

超級公司 supercorporation;

成立公司 form a company; set up a company; start a company;

船公司 shipping company;

創立公司 establish a company; found a company;

大公司 big company; large company;

擔保公司 bonding company;

地產公司 real estate company;

翻譯公司 translation company;

分公司 branch office;

父公司 parent company;

附屬公司 affiliated company; auxiliary firm; subsidiary company;

工程公司 engineering company;

工業公司 industrial company;

估價公司 appraisal company;

廣告公司 advertisement company;

國營公司 national corporation;

國有公司 state-owned company;

航空公司 airline company;

合資公司 joint venture;

加入公司 join a company;

家族公司 family corporation;

~非家族公司 non-family corporation;

建築公司 building company;

姊妹公司 sister company;

經營公司 manage a company; run a company;

進出口公司 import and export company;

控股公司 holding corporation;

跨國公司 international company; multinational corporation; transnational corporation;

兩合公司 limited partnership;

貿易公司 commercial firm;

民辦公司 company run by local people;
母公司 parent company; parent corporation;
龐大的公司 mammoth corporation;
商業金融公司 commercial financial company;
商業信用公司 commercial credit company;
上市公司 listed company;
~股票上市公司 public company;
收購公司 take over a company;
私有公司 private company;
無限公司 unlimited company;
小公司 small company;
一家公司 a company; a firm;
有限公司 limited company;
~控股有限公司 holdings limited;
~私人有限公司 private limited company;
~責任有限公司 limited liability company;
專業公司 professional corporation; specialized company;
子公司 constituent company; daughter firm; fellow subsidiary; subsidiary corporation;
外國子公司 foreign subsidiary company; foreign subsidiary corporation;
總公司 head office; headquarters;

[公訴] public prosecution;
公訴權 right of prosecution;
公訴人 prosecutor;
公訴書 bill of prosecution;

[公攤] equally shared by all;

[公堂] law court; tribunal;

[公文] government documents;
公文包 briefcase;
公文保管處 chancery;
公文箱 dispatch box;
偽造公文 forge an official document;

[公物] public property;
公物還家 return public property where it belongs;
愛護公物 take good care of public property;

[公務] official business; public affairs;
公務繁冗 be overburdened with official duties;
公務羈身 be detained by official business; be tied down by one's duties;
公務員 civil servant; public functionary;
~公務員制度 civil service system;
~國家公務員 civil servant;
~國家公務員制度 system of public services;
公務在身 have some public affairs to handle;
處理公務 manage public affairs;
履行公務 perform official duty;

[公晳] a surname;

[公西] a surname;

[公夏] a surname;

[公學] public school;

[公鴨] drake;

[公演] give a public performance; perform in public;

[公冶] a surname;

[公儀] a surname;

[公意] public will;

[公義] justice;
自然公義 natural justice;

[公益] public good; public welfare;
公益廣告 common wealth advertisement;
公益事業 public welfare establishment;
熱心公益 make earnest efforts to promote public good;
~熱心公益的公民 public-spirited citizen;

[公議] public discussion;

[公營] public; state-operated; state-owned;
公營部門 public sector;
公營經濟 public sector of the economy;
公營農業 public sector of agriculture;
公營企業 public enterprise;
公營商店 state store;

[公用] communal; for public use; public;
公用程序 communal programme;
公用存儲器 communal memory;
公用電話 public telephone;
公用管理域 administration management domain;
公用計算機軟件 common computer software;
公用交換網絡 public switched network;
公用筷子 serving chopsticks;
公用勺兒 serving spoon;
公用事業 public utility;
~公用事業用地 public utility area;
公用數據網絡 public data network;
公用無繩電話 telepoint;

[公有] public; publicly-owned;
公有財產 public property;
公有化 socialization;

公有領域 public domain;
公有制 public ownership system;

[公玉] a surname;

[公寓] apartment; apartment house; flat; lodging house;
公寓房 apartment; flat;
~一套公寓房間 an apartment;
~找公寓房 flat-hunting;
公寓酒店 aparthotel;
公寓樓 apartment block;
~一排公寓樓 an apartment block;
公寓式旅館 apartment hotel;
單身公寓 bachelor apartment;
地下室公寓 basement apartment;
頂層公寓 penthouse apartment;
度假公寓 holiday apartment; vacation apartment;
豪華公寓 luxury apartment;
花園公寓 garden apartment;
看公寓 view an apartment;
買公寓 buy an apartment;
一套公寓 a flat; an apartment;
租公寓 rent an apartment;

[公元] Christian era;

[公園] park; public garden;
公園管理員 park ranger;
城市公園 metropolitan park;
管理公園 tend to a park;
國家公園 national park;
國家歷史公園 national historical park;
海濱公園 seashore park;
海洋公園 ocean park; sea park;
人工公園 artificial parks;
設計公園 lay out a park;
省立公園 provincial park;
市郊公園 out-of-city park;
市立公園 city park;
市區公園 urban park;
天然公園 landscape park;
州際公園 interstate park;
州立公園 state park;
主題公園 theme park;

[公約] (1) convention; pact; treaty; (2) joint pledge;
公約數 common divisor;
~最大公約數 greatest common divisor;

[公允] even-handed; fair and equitable; fair and just; just and sound;

[公債] government bonds; government loans; public loans; state loans;
公債經濟學 economics of bonds;
發行公債 issue government loans;
國防公債 defence bond;
建國公債 national development bond;
臨時公債 war bond;
政府公債 government bond;

[公章] common seal; official seal;
刻公章 engrave an official seal;

[公正] (1) fair; fair and square; fair-minded; impartial; just; righteous; (2) a surname;
公正誠實 play fair; play the game;
公正持平 fair and honest; just and upright;
公正待人 be just to a person;
公正的 even-handed; fair-minded;
公正合理 fair-minded and reasonable; just and equitable;
公正價格 just price;
公正無私 impartial to;
辦事公正 do one's job squarely;
處事公正 act on square;
待人公正 fair in one's dealings;

[公證] notarization; public notary;
公證處 notary public office;
公證行 notary;
公證機關 notary organ;
公證鑒定 notary survey;
公證人 notary; notary public;
公證事務 notary affairs;
~公證事務所 notary office;
公證員 notary public;
~二級公證員 second-grade notary public;
~三級公證員 third-grade notary public;
~四級公證員 fourth-grade notary public;
~一級公證員 first-grade notary public;

[公之] a surname;
公之於世 blaze sth abroad; make known to the world; reveal to the public;

[公職] public employment; public office;
公職人員 civil servant; person in public service;
辭去公職 resign from a public employment;
擔任公職 serve in public office;
開除公職 be dismissed from one's post; discharge sb from public employment;
濫用公職 misuse public office;

[公制] metric system;
公制化 metrication;

[公仲] a surname;

[公眾] public;
公眾傳播 public propagation;

公眾假期 public holiday;
公眾監察 public supervision;
~受到公眾監察 be subject to public supervision;
公眾利益 public interests;
公眾馬，公眾騎 public horses are for the public to ride;
公眾圈 public field;
公眾堂屋沒人掃 everybody's business is nobody's business;
公眾事務 public affairs;
公眾行為 public behaviour;
公眾輿論 public opinion;

[公朱] a surname;
[公豬] boar;
[公諸] make public;
公諸同好 let others with the same taste share; share enjoyment with those of the same taste;
公諸於世 give publicity to sth; give sth publicity; give to the world; make public to the world;

[公主] princess;
[公子] (1) son of a feudal prince or high official; (2) a surname;
公子哥兒 gilded youth; pampered son of a wealthy family; playboy;
花花公子 beau; buck; coxcomb; dandy; dissolute youth; dude; fop; Jack-a-dandy; man about town; playboy;
~中年花花公子 middle-aged playboy;
無腸公子 crab;
游閒公子 fop;

[公族] a surname;
[公祖] a surname;

阿公 grandpa;
辦公 attend to business; do office work; handle official business; work;
秉公 impartially;
不公 unfair; unjust;
充公 confiscate;
大公 grand duke;
奉公 act for public interests;
歸公 be made a public possession; go to the public;
郭公 cuckoo;
老公 hubby; husband; old man;
雷公 God of Thunder;
梢公 boatman;
艄公 (1) helmsman; (2) boatman;
師公 master's master;
叔公 husband's uncle; grand-uncle;
損公 injure the public interest;
太公 great-grandfather;
天公 ruler of heaven;
外公 maternal grandfather;
王公 nobility; princes and dukes; princes and nobles;
為公 for public good;
文抄公 plagiarist;
仙公 (1) male immortal; (2) venerable old man;
相公 (1) premier; (2) young gentleman;
鴨公 drake;
因公 on business; on duty;
寓公 man of wealth living as an exile;
在公 (1) as part of one's duty; (2) for the sake of the public; officially;
至公 absolutely just; absolutely unbiased;
諸公 all the gentlemen;
尊公 your father;

gong 【功】

(1) exploits; merits; meritorious service; (2) achievement; result; (3) skills;

[功臣] a person who has rendered outstanding service; meritorious statesman;
功臣自居 give oneself the airs of a hero; regard oneself as having rendered a great service to;
無名功臣 back room staff;

[功成] achieve success;
功成不居 claim no credit for one's service; disclaim all achievements one has made;
功成名立 achieve success and win recognition;
功成名遂 achieve success and acquire fame; accomplish both success and fame; make a name for oneself;
功成身退 retire after having made one's mark; retire after winning merit; retire from political life after winning tremendous success;
功成業就 be crowned with success;
功成竹帛 be recorded in history in letters of gold; one's deeds will live forever in history;
馬到功成 be accomplished instantly; carry out one's mission quickly; gain an immediate victory; meet with an instant success after the work gets

started; succeed as soon as one goes into action; win instant success; win success immediately upon arrival; win success the moment one arrives;

[功德] (1) merits and virtues; (2) benefaction; charitable and pious deeds;
功德無量 boundless beneficence; great service to mankind; kindness knows no bounds;
功德圓滿 come to a successful end; round it off;
功微德薄 my merit is small and my virtue meagre;

[功夫] (1) ability; art; skill; workmanship; (2) acrobatic fighting; martial art;
功夫片 martial arts movie;
白費功夫 draw water with a sieve; waste one's time;
~ 給死人醫病—白費功夫 giving medical treatment to the dead – a vain effort;
耽誤功夫 waste time;
下功夫 concentrate one's efforts; devote time and effort to a task; put in time and energy;
閒功夫 leisure; spare time;
要學驚人藝，須下苦功夫 no day without a line;
一番功夫 a lot of effort;
硬功夫 great proficiency; masterly skill; proficient craft;
真功夫 true accomplishment; true skill;
中國功夫 Chinese martial art;
抓功夫 find time; make good use of one's time;

[功高] meritorious;
功高不賞 unrewardable merit;
功高望重 highly meritorious and respectable;

[功過] merits and demerits;
功不補過 demerits outweigh merits;
功不抵過 no merit can wipe out one's faults; one's merit cannot wipe out one's faults;
功大過小 merits outweigh faults;
功大於過 merits outweigh demerits; one's achievements outweigh one's errors; one's deeds outweigh one's faults;
功歸人，過歸己 for accomplishment he gives other the credit; for failures, he takes all the blame;
功過不分 no distinction is made between merits and demerits;
功過相抵 merits equal demerits; merits offset faults;
功難掩過 one's merits are not enough to redeem one's offenses;
將功補過 atone for past mistakes; expiate and atone for one's wrongdoing by zealous service; make amends for one's faults by good deeds; make amends for one's previous faults by giving good service; make up for one's mistakes with new contributions;

[功績] contribution; feat; merits and achievements;
豐功偉績 gigantic contribution; great achievements; great service to the country; heroic deeds; high merit and great achievements; immense merits;

[功課] home assignment; lesson; school lesson; homework; schoolwork;
完成功課 finish one's homework;
做功課 do schoolwork;

[功虧一簣] abandon work when it is nearly completed; be just one step short of success; between the cup and the lip; fail on the eve of complete success; fail to succeed for lack of a final effort; fall short of completion by one basket of earth; fall short of success at the last stage; just one step short of final completion;
~ 為山九仞，功虧一簣 a failure is still a failure even when it comes very near to success; the lack of one basketful of earth spoils the entire effort to build a high mountain;

[功勞] contributions; credits; meritorious service;
汗馬功勞 a merit laboriously achieved; achievements in war; contributions in work; war exploits;
~ 立下汗馬功勞 perform deeds of valour in battle;

[功利] material gains; utility;
功利主義 utilitarianism;
急功近利 anxious to achieve quick success and get instant benefits; eager for quick success and instant benefits; seek quick success and instant benefits;

追求個人功利 intend one's own material gain;

[功率] horsepower; power;

電功率 electrical horsepower;

放大功率 amplifying power;

絕對功率 absolute power;

可用功率 available horsepower;

聲功率 acoustic power;

輸出功率 delivered horsepower;

有效功率 active power; actual power;

[功懋懋賞] reward one's merit as one deserves;

[功名] scholarly honour and official rank;

功名富貴 fame and fortune; fame, riches, and honours; officialdom, wealth and fame; rank, success, fame, and riches;

功名利祿 high official positions and riches;

[功能] function; functionality;

功能詞 function word;

功能定義 functional definition;

功能對等 functional equivalence;

功能法 functional approach;

功能分化 function differentiation;

功能負荷 functional load;

功能加工 functional processing;

功能鍵 function key;

~功能鍵盤 function keyboard;

功能碼 function code;

功能模擬 functional simulation;

功能評估 functional evaluation;

功能評價 functional evaluation;

功能社會學 functional sociology;

功能特性 performance characteristic;

功能系統 functional system;

功能性翻譯 functional translation;

功能性因素 functional factor;

功能意義 functional meaning;

功能語法 functional grammar;

功能語言學 functional linguistics;

功能職權 function authority;

功能主義 functionalism;

功能轉換 functional shift;

功能組織 functional organization;

表情功能 expressive function;

次要功能 secondary function;

多功能 all-in-one; multifunction; multifunctional;

概念功能 ideational function;

感情功能 emotive function;

個性功能 personal function;

工具功能 instrumental function;

呼喚功能 vocative function;

呼語功能 vocative function;

交際功能 communicative function;

校訂功能 revising function;

美學功能 aesthetic function;

描寫功能 descriptive function;

啟發功能 heuristic function;

認識功能 recognizing ability;

雙功能 dual function;

~雙功能電源 dual-function power supply;

特異功能 supernatural power;

應酬功能 phatic function;

[功同賞異] the same service receives different rewards;

[功完行滿] achieve all;

[功效] effects;

取得功效 achieve efficiency;

[功勛] exploit; feats; meritorious deeds; meritorious service;

[功業] achievements; exploits;

功業彪炳 one's achievement is distinguished; one's feat is noteworthy and successful;

[功用] function; role;

[功罪] merits;

將功贖罪 atone for a crime by good deeds; atone for a crime by meritorious actions; atone for one's guilt by devoted service; atone for one's mistakes by good acts; expiate crimes by good services; expiate one's guilt by good deeds; make amends for one's crimes by good deeds; make amends for one's misdeeds; redeem sins by good deeds; set off merit against fault;

報功 claim credit; report a victory; report an achievement;

唱功 art of singing; singing;

成功 succeed; successful;

丑表功 claim an undeserved credit;

寸功 meagre achievement; small contribution;

大功 extraordinary service; great merit;

歸功 attribute the success to; owe the credit to;

記功 cite sb for meritorious service; record a merit;

居功 claim credit for oneself;

軍功 military exploit;

苦功 hard work; painstaking effort;

立功 do a deed of merit; perform meritorious service;
練功 practise one's skill;
賣功 parade one's merits; show off what one has done;
內功 exercises to benefit the internal organs;
評功 appraise sb's merits;
奇功 outstanding service;
氣功 system of deep breathing exercises;
慶功 celebrate the achievements gained;
事功 cause and contributions;
無功 without achievements;
武功 (1) military accomplishments; (2) skill in acrobatics in Chinese operas;
敘功 assess merits;
勳功 meritorious services;
邀功 appropriate the meritorious services of others;
陰功 a good deed to the doer's credit in the next world; one's unpublicized good deeds;
用功 diligent; hardworking; studious;
有功 have performed meritorious service; have rendered great service; make contributions to;
戰功 battle achievements; meritorious military service; military exploits;
治功 achievement of managing national affairs;
奏功 achieve success; have the intended effect;

gong

【攻】 (1) attack; take the offensive; (2) accuse; charge; (3) specialize in; study;

［攻城］ attack a city;
攻城略地 attack cities and acquire lands; take cities and seize territory;
攻城為下，攻心為上 it is better to win the heart of the people than to take the city; winning a person's friendship is a greater achievement than capturing a city;

［攻打］ assail; assault; attack;
攻點打援 attack the enemy's strongholds and strike at their reinforcements;
硬攻硬打 make head-on attacks;

［攻讀］ (1) study; (2) read; specialize in;
攻讀博士學位 study for one's doctorate;

［攻擊］ (1) assault; attack; launch an offensive; (2) accuse; attack; charge; slander; vilify; (3) challenge;
攻擊艦 assault ship;
～兩棲攻擊艦 amphibious assault ship;
攻擊區 attack zone;
攻擊手 attacker; spiker;
攻擊者 assailant; attacker;
背後攻擊 rip up the back;
大事攻擊 all-out attack; attack in a big way; hurl wild attacks against; lash out at;
惡意攻擊 bad mouth;
近距離攻擊 close-in attack;
盲目攻擊 blind attack;
猛烈攻擊 tear sb limb from limb;
全面攻擊 all-out offensive;
人身攻擊 assault and battery; attacks concerning personal matters; personal abuse; personal attack;
上昇攻擊 climb attack;
受到攻擊 under fire;
迎面攻擊 head-on attack;
側向攻擊 beam attack;

［攻殲］ wipe out;

［攻堅］ assault fortified positions; storm fortifications;

［攻訐］ expose sb's past misdeeds; rake up sb's past and attack him/her;

［攻克］ capture; take;
攻克城堡 take the castle by storm;
攻無不克 all-conquering; ever-victorious; take every objective one attacks; win in every assault;

［攻苦食淡］ work hard and live plainly and frugally;

［攻破］ break through;
不攻自破 be destroyed from within; cave in by oneself; collapse of itself; fall to the ground of itself without being attacked;

［攻勢］ offensive;
攻勢淩厲 powerful offensive; swift and fierce attack;
採取攻勢 act on the offensive; take the offensive;
和平攻勢 peace offensive;
鉗形攻勢 pincers movement; two-pronged attack;
箝形攻勢 pincers movement;

［攻守］ offensive and defensive;
攻守同盟 agreement between partners in crime not to give each other away; alliance for offence and defence; offensive and defensive alliance; pact to shield each other; secret agreement

to defend each other by hiding each other's crimes;
反守為攻 turn the tables on the attackers;
可攻可守 equally valuable as a steppingstone for offensive or a strong point for defence;
能攻能守 able to charge or hold one's ground; good at offence and defence;
以攻為守 attack as a means of defence; attack in order to defend; take the offensive in a basically defensive operation; use attack as a means of defence; use offensive tactics as a means of defence; use offensive tactices for defence;
易攻難守 easy to attack but hard to defend;
易守難攻 easy to hold but hard to attack;
轉攻為守 change from the offensive to the defensive;
轉守為攻 change from the defensive to the offensive;

[攻下] capture; overcome; take;

[攻陷] capture; storm;

[攻心] attempt to demoralize sb; make a psychological attack on sb; try to persuade an offender to confess;
攻心為上 it is better to win the hearts of the people; psychological offense is the best of tactices; winning a person's friendship is the greatest achievement;

[攻佔] attack and occupy; storm and capture;

反攻 counter-attack; strike back;
火攻 fire attack;
夾攻 attack from both sides; converging attack; pincer attack; two-way attack;
進攻 assault; attack;
快攻 fast break; quick attack;
猛攻 attack by storm; attack violently; charge to; fierce attack; onslaught; storm; whale away;
強攻 take by storm;
圍攻 (1) besiege; lay siege to; (2) jointly attack sb;
佯攻 feign attack; make a feint;
主攻 main attack;
助攻 holding attack;
專攻 specialize in;
總攻 general offensive;

gong

【供】 enshrine; provide; supply;

[供給] appoint; deliver; feed; furnish; provide; supply;
保障供給 ensure supply;
削減供給 abridge supply;

[供求] supply and demand;
供求關係 supply and demand relationship;
供求經濟學 economics of supply and demand;
供不應求 demand exceeds supply; supply fails to meet the demand; supply falls short of demand; the demand outstrips the supply; the supply can hardly keep pace with the demand; the supply does not meet the demand; the supply is not adequate to the demand; the supply is unable to meet the demand;
供過於求 an excess of supply over demand; in excess of demand; pile up in excess of requirement; the supply exceeds the demand; the supply outstrips the demand;
求過於供 an excess of demand over supply; demand outstrips supply; the demand exceeds the supply;

[供水] water supply;
供水管 water pipe;
供水系統 waterworks;

[供銷] supply and marketing;
供銷科 supply and marketing section;
產供銷 supply, production, and sale;

[供需] supply and demand;

[供養] provide for one's parents; provide for the need of one's parents; support one's parents;

[供應] accommodate; supply;
供應不足 in short supply; insufficiency; undersupply;
供應充沛 the supply is sufficient to meet the demand;
供應充足 in abundant supply;
供應處 supply department;
供應方 supplier;
供應緊張 in acute shortage;
供應商 supplier;
供應站 supply station;
供應者 purveyor;
過多供應 oversupply;
過量供應 oversupply;
熱供應 heat application;

食物供應 food supply;
敞開供應 be supplied without any restriction;
增加供應 increase supply;

提供 furnish; provide; supply;

gong
【肱】 forearm;
［肱骨］ humerus;

股肱 chief assistant; right-hand man;

gong
【紅】 work; working;

gong
【宮】 (1) palace; (2) temple; (3) place for cultural activities and recreation; (4) uterus; womb; (5) a surname;
［宮車晏駕］ demise of an emperor;
［宮燈］ palace lantern;
［宮殿］ palace;
富麗堂皇的宮殿 sumptuous palace;
一座宮殿 a palace;
［宮頸］ cervix;
宮頸發育不良 cervical dysplasia;
宮頸發育不全 cervical dysplasia;
宮頸管 cervical tunnels;
宮頸積血 hematotrachelos;
宮頸裂 cervical clefts;
宮頸瘻 cervical fistula;
宮頸妊娠 cervical pregnancy;
宮頸息肉 cervical polyp;
宮頸炎 cervicitis;
~ 創傷性宮頸炎 traumatic cervicitis;
~ 肉芽腫性宮頸炎 granulomatous cervicitis;
~ 外傷性宮頸炎 traumatic cervicitis;
宮頸陰道炎 cervicovaginitis;
~ 氣腫性宮頸陰道炎 cervicocolpitis emphysematosa;
［宮內］ intrauterine;
宮內發育遲緩 intrauterine growth retardation;
宮內肺炎 intrauterine pneumonia;
宮內骨折 intrauterine fracture;
宮內輸血 intrauterine transfusion;
宮內脱位 intrauterine dislocation;
［宮廷］ (1) palace; (2) court; royal court;
宮廷內侍 chamberlain;
宮廷政變 palace coup;
［宮闈］ palace chambers;
［宮刑］ castration;
［宮苑］ palatial garden;
三宮六苑 emperor's harem;

逼宮 force the king or emperor to abdicate;
蟾宮 moon;
皇宮 palace;
迷宮 labyrinth; maze;
寢宮 emperor's resting place; imperial burial place; masoleum;
深宮 forbidden palace; harem;
天宮 heavenly palace;
王宮 palace;
行宮 abode of an emperor on a tour;
璿宮 gem-studded chamber;
子宮 uterus; womb;

gong
【恭】 (1) respectful; reverent;
(2) congratulations; greetings;
［恭賀］ congratulate;
恭賀佳節 compliments of the season;
恭賀新禧 Happy New Year;
［恭候］ await respectfully;
恭候光臨 we request the pleasure of your company; your presence is requested;
［恭謹］ respectful and cautious;
恭謹勤勞 respectful and diligent; respectful and industrious;
維恭維謹 sincere and respectful;
［恭敬］ respectful; with great respect;
恭敬不如從命 it is better to accept deferentially than to decline courteously; obedience is better than politeness; the best way to show respect is to obey; to accept is better than to stand on ceremony;
恭敬施禮 bow respectfully; make a respectful bow;
恭敬行為 deferential behaviour;
必恭必敬 extremely deferential; reverent and respectful;
畢恭畢敬 cap in hand; extremely deferential; hat in hand; in a most respectful attitude; in humble reverence; reverent and respectful; with all courtesy and respect; with excessive courtesy; with the utmost deference;
對長輩恭敬 deferential to one's superiors;
恭恭敬敬 in an attitude of respect; most

respectfully; reverently; with cap in hand;

［恭聆明誨］ I will assuredly listen most reverently to your words;

［恭順］ respectful and submissive;

［恭維］ adulation; butter sb up; compliment; flatter;

不敢恭維 cannot say much for;

受到恭維 be exposed to flattery;

似褒實貶的恭維 left-handed compliment;

［恭喜］ congratulate; congratulation;

恭喜發財 may you be happy and prosperous;

恭喜恭喜 congratulations; give you joy;

不恭 disrespectful;

出恭 go to the lavatory;

謙恭 modest and courteous; polite and modest;

gong

【蚣】 centipede;

蜈蚣 centipede;

gong

【躬】 (1) personally; (2) bend forward; bow;

［躬逢其盛］ present in person on a grand occasion;

［躬親］ attend to sth personally;

躬親其事 attend to the matter in person; undertake an affair personally;

躬親叩賀 tender one's congratulations in person;

［躬自厚而薄責於人］ require much from oneself and little from others;

背躬 aside;

鞠躬 (1) in a discreet and scrupulous manner; (2) bow;

gong

【觥】 (1) wine vessel made of horn in ancient times; (2) big; great;

［觥觥］ upright and outspoken;

gong

【龔】 (1) reverential; (2) a surname;

gong³

gong

【汞】 mercury;

［汞中毒］ mercury poisoning;

［汞柱］ mercury column;

紅汞 mercurochrome;

乙酸汞 mercury acetate;

gong

【拱】 (1) cup one hand in the other in front of the chest as a salute; (2) surround; (3) hump up; (4) arch; (5) push without using one's hands;

［拱抱］ surround;

［拱璧］ large piece of jade;

珍如拱璧 as precious as a piece of large jade; prize sth like a piece of old jade;

［拱道］ archway;

［拱肩縮背］ hunch one's shoulders and bow;

［拱立］ stand with cupped hands;

叉手拱立 stand cupping one's hands together;

［拱門］ arch; arched door; archway;

［拱橋］ arch bridge;

［拱讓］ give up submissively;

雙手拱讓 give away sth to sb with both hands;

［拱手］ (1) pay obeisance by cupping one hand in the other in front of one's chest; (2) submissively;

拱手稱謝 join one's hands together in salute and thank;

拱手出讓 give away sth to sb with both hands;

拱手而別 bid farewell in a respectful manner; take leave by saluting with both hands folded and raised in front;

拱手讓人 give away sth to sb with both hands; give up sth to others without putting up a fight; hand over sth on a silver platter; hand over with a bow; surrender sth submissively;

拱手致禮 salute with joined hands; salute with one's hands folded;

［拱衛］ surround and protect;

半圓拱 round arch;

垂拱 drop arch;

粗拱 common arch; plain arch;

大弧拱 coved arch;

等角拱 equilateral arch;

吊拱 hanging arch;

端拱 end arch;

多心拱 multicenter arch;

G

斧拱 axed arch;
虹式拱 rainbow arch;
構架拱 framed arch;
桁拱 braced arch;
橫拱 transverse arch;
環拱 ring arch;
混凝土拱 concrete arch;
假拱 dumb arch; false arch;
尖拱 acute arch; cusped arch; ogival arch;
減重拱 discharging arch;
間壁拱 curtain arch;
棱角拱 angular arch;
馬蹄拱 mosque arch;
牛眼形拱 bullseye arch;
平拱 jack arch;
平衡拱 balance arch;
平弧拱 scheme arch;
平圓拱 diminished arch; hance arch;
拋物線拱 parabolic arch;
前拱 face arch;
橋拱 bridge arch;
曲拱 arched;
全拱 full arch;
雙鉸拱 double-hinged arch;
雙葉拱 lenticular arch;
鰓拱 branchial arch;
四鉸拱 four-hinged arch;
四心拱 four-centred arch;
通航拱 fairway arch;
同心拱 concentric arch;
筒拱 barrel arch;
突拱 corbel arch;
彎拱 camber arch;
紋形拱 frilled arch;
楔形拱 extrados arch;
抑拱 inverted arch;
圓拱 circular arch;
正拱 right arch;
中心拱 centre arch;
鐘狀拱 bell arch;
主動拱 active arch;
磚拱 brick arch;

gong
【栱】 big peg or stake;

gong
【珙】 large piece of jade stone;
［珙桐］ dove tree;

gong
【鞏】 (1) consolidate; (2) a surname;
［鞏伯］ a surname;
［鞏固］ (1) consolidate; solidify; strengthen; (2) consolidated; firm; solid; stable; strong;
基礎鞏固 solid foundations;
政權鞏固 strong political power;
［鞏膜］ external covering of the eyeball; sclera;
鞏膜管 scleral canal;
鞏膜虹膜炎 scleroiritis;
鞏膜軟化 scleromalacia;
鞏膜炎 scleritis;
~ 壞死性鞏膜炎 scleritis necroticans;
~ 角膜鞏膜炎 keratoscleritis;
~ 結節性鞏膜炎 nodular scleritis;

gong4
gong
【共】 (1) common; general; (2) share; (3) together; (4) in all; (5) Communist Party;
［共產］ communism; communist;
共產黨 Communist Party;
~ 共產黨人 Communist;
~ 共產黨員 Communist;
~ 中國共產黨 Chinese Communist Party;
共產國際 Communist International;
共產主義 Communism;
~ 共產主義的 Communist;
~ 共產主義國家 Communist country;
~ 共產主義者 Communist;
~ 共產主義政權 Communist regime;
~ 共產主義制度 Communist system;
［共處］ coexist; coexistence;
晨夕共處 together in the morning and night;
和平共處 peaceful coexistence;
［共存］ coexist; coexistence; survive together;
共存共榮 coexistence and co-prosperity;
［共黨］ Communist;
［共軛］ conjugate;
共軛雙曲線 conjugate hyperbolas;
共軛軸 conjugate axis;
共軛狀態 conjugate action;
［共犯］ complicity;
［共和］ republic; republicanism;
共和國 republic;
~ 自治共和國 autonomous republic;
共和政體 republic;
［共計］ add up to; aggregate; altogether; amount to; grand total; total;
共計多少錢 how much does it come to; how much does it cost altogether; how much does that add up to; how much

is that altogether; how much is that in all;

[共濟] mutual aid;

共濟時艱 work together to solve a difficult situation;

和衷共濟 pull together for a common cause; stick together; work harmoniously; work together with one heart;

和舟共濟 help one another while travelling in the same boat — mutual help; share sb's success and failure;

[共聚] copolymerization; gather together;

共聚物 copolymer; copolymerization;

~丙烯腈共聚物 acrylonitrile copolymer;

~丙烯酰胺共聚物 acrylamide copolymer;

~共沸共聚物 azeotropic copolymer;

~恒沸共聚物 azeotropic copolymerization;

~交替共聚物 alternating copolymer;

~膠黏共聚物 adhesive copolymer;

共聚一堂 gather in the same hall; gather together;

共聚作用 copolymerization;

恒比共聚 azeotropic copolymerization; constant copolymerization;

接枝共聚 graft copolymerization;

嵌段共聚 block copolymerization;

浮液共聚 emulsion copolymerization;

[共勉] mutual encouragement;

[共鳴] sympathetic response;

引起觀眾的共鳴 awaken a responsive chord in the audience's mind;

[共謀] collude; collusion;

[共棲] symbiosis;

[共商] discuss together; hold joint discussion;

共商大計 discuss matters of vital importance;

共商國事 discuss the state affairs together;

[共生] commensalism; symbiosis;

共生生物 commensal;

共生體 symbiont;

共生現象 commensalism;

~互惠共生現象 mutualism;

[共時] synchronic;

共時語言學 synchronic linguistics;

[共識] common view; consensus;

[共事] fellow workers; work together;

共事多年 have been colleagues for many years;

[共同] common; in common; jointly; side by side;

共同成分 common component;

共同承擔責任 undertake the responsibility together;

共同點 common ground;

共同對敵 join forces to oppose the enemy; joint opposition to the enemy; oppose the enemy together; stand together against the enemy; wage a common struggle against the enemy;

共同犯罪 joint offense;

共同富裕 common prosperity; prosperity for all;

共同格 common case;

共同核心 common core;

共同交際語 contact vernacular;

共同群體 common group;

共同體 community;

共同協商 hold a mutual consultation;

共同行動 go hand in hand with;

共同語言 common language;

共同賬戶 common account;

共同之處 have sth in common;

~無共同之處 have nothing in common;

共同致富 common prosperity;

[共現] co-occurrence;

共現限制 co-occurrence restriction;

[共享] enjoy together; share; sharing;

共享甘苦 share the sweet and the bitter together;

共享空間意識 concept of shared space;

共享軟件 shareware;

共享甜頭 share benefit;

電子共享 electron sharing;

頻率共享 frequency sharing;

文件共享 file sharing;

[共用] common; sharing;

共用操作系統 share operating system;

共用存儲器 common memory; common storage;

共用天線 communal antenna;

~共用天線電視 central aerial television;

共用系統 sharing system;

公共 common; communal; public;

合共 all told; altogether; in all;

攏共 all told; altogether; in all;

廝共 in company with each other; together;

通共 all told; altogether; in all;

統共 altogether; in all;

一共 all told; altogether; in all;

與共 share...with;
總共 add up to; all together; all told; altogether; amount to; come to; count; count up to; foot up to; in all; in number; in the aggregate; knock up; number; reach a total of; sum up to; to the tune of; total; total up to;

gong
【供】 (1) lay; (2) offerings; (3) confess; confession;
[供詞] confession;
[供奉] consecrate; enshrine and worship;
[供具] sacrificial vessel;
[供品] offerings;
[供認] confess;
供認不諱 candidly confess; confess everything; make a clean breast of everything;
全部供認 make a full confession;
[供養] consecrate; enshrine and worship; make offerings to; offer sacrifices to;
[供職] hold office;
[供狀] deposition; written confession;
擺供 offer sacrifices;
逼供 extort a confession; extort a confession by force or pressure;
筆供 deposition; written confession;
串供 act in collusion to make each other's confessions tally;
翻供 take back one's testimony; withdraw a confession;
口供 statement made by the accused under examination;
攀供 implicate others in one's confession;
親供 confess in person; personal confession;
提供 furnish; offer; provide; supply;
誘供 trap a person into a confession;
招供 confess;
自供 self-confession;

gong
【貢】 (1) tribute; (2) a surname;
[貢金] aids; tributes;
[貢品] articles of tribute;
[貢獻] contribute; dedicate; devote;
劃時代的貢獻 an epoch-making contribution;
重大貢獻 monumental contribution;
作出傑出的貢獻 make outstanding contributions;
朝貢 pay tribute; present tribute;
進貢 pay tribute;
納貢 pay tribute;

gou[1]
gou
【勾】 (1) cancel; cross out; strike out; tick off; (2) delineate; draw; (3) fill up the joints of brickwork with cement; (4) thicken; (5) call to mind; induce; revoke; (6) collude with; gang up with; (7) shorter side of a right triangle; (8) surname;
[勾搭] (1) gang up with; (2) seduce;
勾勾搭搭 flirt with; gang up with; have illicit relations with; hobnob with; mix up with; team up with; work hand in glove with; work in collusion with;
[勾結] collaborate with; collude with; collusion; gang up with; hand and glove with; in league with; join in a plot;
暗中勾結 make secret deals with;
彼此勾結 play into each other's hands;
私下勾結 in league with;
相互勾結 play booty;
[勾留] break one's journey at; stay; stop over;
[勾芡] make cooking starch;
[勾手] stroke with a hook;
勾手傳球 hook pass;
勾手大力發球 cannonball service;
勾手發球 hook service;
勾手投籃 hook shot;
[勾通] collude with; join in a plot; secretly connected; work hand in glove with;
[勾銷] cancel; expunge; liquidate; strike out; wipe out; write off;
[勾心鬥角] conspire against each other; each trying to outwit the other; engage in a battle of wits; engage in petty intrigue and try to get the better of each other; jockey for position; scheme against each other; scheme and plot against one another;
[勾引] allure; entice; lure; seduce; tempt;

gou
【句】 a surname;

gou
【佝】
［佝僂］ rickets;
佝僂病 rickets;
成年佝僂病 adult rickets;
腎形佝僂病 renal rickets;

gou
【溝】 (1) channel; ditch; trench; (2) furrow; groove; rut; (3) gully; ravine;
［溝道］ channel;
［溝壑］ ravine;
［溝渠］ ditch; channel; lake; trench; irrigation canals and ditches;
［溝流］ channeling;
回流液溝流 channeling of reflux;
潤滑脂溝流 grease channeling;
［溝水］ ditchwater;
［溝通］ communicate; connect; link up;
溝通技巧 communication skills;
溝通能力 communication skills;
缺乏相互間的溝通 lack of mutual communication;

暗溝 blind ditch; covered sewerage;
地溝 underground ditch for irrigation;
分水溝 diversion ditch;
海溝 oceanic trench;
壕溝 (1) trench; (2) ditch;
河溝 brook; stream;
鴻溝 chasm; wide gap;
壟溝 field ditch; furrow;
明溝 ditch; open drain;
排水溝 drainage ditch;
山溝 gully; ravine; valley;
滲溝 sewer;
水溝 ditch; drain;
掏溝 dredge a ditch;
天溝 gutter;
挖溝 ditch up;
陽溝 ditch; open drain;
陰溝 sewer;
引水溝 feed ditch;

gou
【鈎】 hook; tick;
［鈎蟲］ hookworm;
［鈎兒］ hook;
［鈎眼扣］ hook and eye;
［鈎子］ hook;

車鈎 coupling;
秤鈎 steelyard hook;
打鈎 tick;
打一個鈎 tick;
吊鈎 hanger; hook;
釣鈎 fish hook;
掛鈎 (1) couple; (2) link up with;
鏈鈎 chain hook; sling;
帽鈎 hatrack;
撓鈎 longhand hook;
上鈎 get hooked; rise to the bait; swallow the bait;
一個鈎 a tick;
衣鈎 clothes hook;
魚鈎 fish hook;
帳鈎 bed-curtain hook;

gou
【鉤】 (1) hook; (2) investigate; probe; (3) entice; lure;

gou
【緱】 (1) cord binding on the hilt of a sword; (2) a surname;

gou
【篝】 basket; cage;
［篝燈］ jacklight;
［篝火］ bonfire; campfire;
篝火狐鳴 a rebellion is afoot; plan and prepare for an uprising;
篝火之夜 bonfire night;

gou
【韝】 armlet and glove of a falconer;

gou³
gou
【狗】 (1) dog; pooch; (2) cursed; damned;
［狗膽包天］ monstrous audacity; monstrously audacious;
［狗兒］ dog;
狗兒狂吠 dogs growl;
［狗吠］ dogs bark;
狗吠非主 the dog barks at a man who is not its master;
狗吠聲 boof; bow-wow;
驢鳴狗吠 like donkeys braying and dogs barking — poor style of writing;
［狗苟蠅營］ seek personal gain shamelessly;
［狗叫］ yelp;
［狗娘養的］ son of a bitch;
［狗爬式］ dog paddle; doggy paddle;
［狗屁］ nonsense; rubbish;

G

狗屁不通 absurd; baloney; mere trash; nonsense; unreadable rubbish;
狗屁倒灶 disorganized;

[狗屎] dog dirt; dog dung;
狗屎堆 a pile of dog dung;
狗屎做鞭子—不能文（聞）也不能武（舞） a whip made from a dog's droppings — neither a scholar nor a soldier;

[狗噬不食] not even fit for the kennel;

[狗瘦主人羞] a lean dog is a disgrace to its master; a lean dog shames its master;

[狗偷鼠竊] petty theft;

[狗腿子] henchman; hired thug; lackey;
當狗腿子 lick sb's boots;

[狗尾續貂] a wretched sequel to fine work; add a dog's tail to the sable coat—write such a deplorable sequel to a masterpiece; make an unworthy continuation of a great work;

[狗窩] doghouse; kennel;

[狗血] dog's blood;
狗血淋頭 be cursed by; pour dog's blood on;
狗血噴頭 curse at full blast; let loose a steam of abuse; pour out a flood of invective; pour out a torrent of abuse; shower blame on;

[狗咬] a dog bites;
狗咬刺蝟—下不得嘴 a dog trying to eat a hedgehog — unable to take a bite;
狗咬狗 dog-eat-dog; dogfight;
狗咬呂洞賓—不識好人心 a dog biting Lu Dongbin — bite the hand that feeds one; snarl and snap at Lu Dongbin — wrong a kind-hearted person;

[狗仔隊] paparazzo;

[狗崽子] (1) pup; puppy; (2) son of a bitch;

[狗蚤] dog flea;

[狗長角—出洋(羊)相] a dog with horns—having the appearance of a ram;

[狗彘] dogs or pigs;
狗彘不如 lewd man who has no moral principles; worthless fellow; worse than a cur; worse than a swine;
行同狗彘 behave like dogs and pigs — awful behaviour; bestial; make a beast of oneself;

[狗嘴] dog's mouth;
狗嘴裏長不出象牙 a cracked bell can never sound well; a filthy mouth cannot utter decent language; an enemy's mouth seldom speaks well; believe no tales from an enemy's tongue; no ivory will come of a dog's mouth; one does not expect ivory from a dog's mouth; what can you expect from a dog but a bark; what can you expect from a hog but a grunt; you cannot make a silk purse out of a sow's ear;

巴兒狗 (1) lapdog; Pekingese; (2) flatterer; sycophant; toady;
叭兒狗 lapdog; Pekingese;
白狗 white dog;
笨狗 big mastiff;
瘋狗 mad dog; rabid dog;
哈巴狗 (1) Pekingese; (2) sycophant; toady;
海狗 fur seal; ursine seal;
看門狗 watchdog;
狼狗 wolfhound;
臘腸狗 sausage dog;
獵狗 hound; hunting dog;
落水狗 dog in the water;
西施狗 Shih Tzu;
小狗 doggie; doggy; puppy;
小靈狗 whippet;
野狗 wild dog;
一條狗 a dog;
魚狗 kingfisher;
走狗 flunkey; lackey; running dog;

gou

【枸】 medlar;

[枸杞] goji berry; lycium chinensis; matrimony vine;
枸杞子 fruit of Chinese wolfberry;

gou

【苟】 (1) careless; indifferent; negligent; (2) if;

[苟安] content with temporary ease and comfort; seek momentary ease;
苟安一時 gain some respite for oneself; seek improper ease for a time; seek security for a time;
苟安一隅 be content to exercise sovereignty over only a part of the country; seek momentary ease in a section of the nation;
圖一時之苟安，貽百年之大患 indulging in a moment's ease only to incur a

century of suffering; one moment's false security can bring a century of calamities;

[苟合] illicit sexual relations;
苟合取容 agree without justification;

[苟活] drag out an ignoble existence; live on in degradation;

[苟且] (1) be resigned to the circumstances; muddle along; muddle through; (2) perfunctory; (3) illicit; improper;
苟且了事 dispose of sth perfunctorily; do sth carelessly; slight over;
苟且求安 be resigned to the circumstances; settle for ease and comfort;
苟且求活 preserve one's life at all costs;
苟且偷安 seek a moment's peace however one can; seek ease and comfort at the expense of principles; seek only temporary ease and comfort;
苟且偷生 a mere vegetative existence; drag out an ignoble existence; keep alive without serious ambition; live just for the sake of remaining alive;

[苟全] preserve one's life at all costs;
苟全性命 manage to stay alive with sacrifice of principles; preserve one's own life at all costs; remain alive; save one's own skin; barely manage to survive;

[苟同] agree without giving serious thought; readily subscribe to sb's views;
不敢苟同 beg to disagree; cannot agree;
~恕我不敢苟同 I beg to differ; I beg to disagree; I would beg to disagree;
未敢苟同 beg to differ; cannot agree;

[苟延] linger on;
苟延殘喘 be on one's last legs; drag out one's feeble existence; eke out a living; eke out a meagre existence; linger on in a steadily worsening condition; linger on in the last days of one's life; linger on with one's last breath of life; merely prolong one's death throes; prolong one's moribund life; prop up one's tottering ruling position; remain alive for a little while; win some time in one's deathbed struggle;
苟延殘生 linger on feebly;

G

不苟 careful; conscientious; not casual; not lax;

gou

【耇】 (1) old age; (2) the wizened face of age;

[耇老] old people;

[耇長] elders;

gou⁴

gou

【勾】 (1) mark; mark on; put a check; (2) cancel; (3) connect; join; (4) hook;

[勾當] business; deal;
曖昧勾當 dark business;
骯髒勾當 foul deed; foul practice; dirty work; evil things;
卑鄙勾當 dirty deal; mean action;
卑劣勾當 low-down trick;
鬼勾當 fishy;
幹盡勾當 do every evil things;
見不得人的勾當 shameful act;
騙人的勾當 funny business;

gou

【垢】 (1) dirt; filth; stains; (2) disgrace; shame; (3) unclean;

[垢泥] dirt on the face;

[垢膩] dirt; dirty; greasy;

[垢污] dirt; filth;
藏垢納污 all that is evil and filthy finds a home; assemble the worst elements of society; cover a multitude of sins; harbour criminals; shelter evil people and countenance evil practices;
陳垢積污 ingrained dirt;
清除垢污 get rid of the dirt;

塵垢 dust and dirt;
齒垢 tartar;
耳垢 earwax;
面垢 dirty complexion;
污垢 dirt; filth;
牙垢 dental calculus; tartar;

gou

【冓】 secluded place in a palace; secret cabinet;

gou

【夠】 (1) reach; (2) enough; sufficient;

[夠本] break even; make enough money to cover the cost;

[夠不着] beyond one's reach; cannot reach;

[夠吃夠用] just enough to eat and to meet one's needs;

[夠格] qualified; up to standard;
夠格當會計 qualify as an account;

[夠勁兒] (1) almost too much to cope with; (2) heavy; strenuous; strong in taste;

[夠戧] difficult; hard; terrible; unbearable;
累得夠戧 much exhausted;
氣得夠戧 extremely annoyed;

[夠瞧的] really awful; too much;

[夠受的] hard to bear; quite an ordeal;
天熱得夠受的 the weather is too hot to bear;

[夠數] enough; sufficient in quantity;

[夠味兒] pretty good; strong in taste; well-done;

能夠 able to; can; capable of;
足夠 ample; enough; sufficient;

gou

【媾】 (1) marry; wed; (2) reach an agreement; (3) coition;

[媾和] conclusion of peace; make peace;

[媾疫] breeding paralysis; covering disease;

交媾 have sexual intercourse;

gou

【搆】 (1) drag; pull; (2) reach; (3) implicate; (4) incur; make;

[搆陷] frame sb up; make a false charge against sb;

gou

【詬】 (1) humiliation; shame; (2) revile; talk abusively;

[詬病] castigate; denounce;
人所詬病 what people generally disapprove of;
為世詬病 become an object of public denunciation;

[詬罵] abuse; revile; vilify;

[詬誶謠諑] be whispered about and secretly discussed everywhere;

gou

【雊】 the crow of a male pheasant;

gou

【彀】 (1) draw a bow to the full; (2) rule; (3) sufficient;

[彀中] shooting range;
盡入彀中 have all come within shooting range; have all come under control; have all fallen into the trap;

gou

【構】 (1) compose; construct; form; (2) fabricate; make up;

[構成] compose; consist of; constitute; form; make up;
構成死罪 form a capital crime;

[構詞] form a word;
構詞成分 combining form;
構詞法 word formation;
~ 詞序構詞法 syntactic morphology;
~ 複合詞構詞法 compound word formation;
~ 截取構詞法 clipping;
~ 逆構詞法 back-formation;
~ 派生構詞法 derivation;

[構思] conception; work out the plot of a literary work;
大膽的構思 boldness of conception;

[構圖] composition;
構圖設計 composition design;
彩色構圖 colour composition;
動態構圖 dynamic composition;
靜態構圖 static composition;

[構陷] frame sb up; make a false charge against sb;

[構想] (1) compose; conceive; visualize; (2) blueprint; concept; idea; proposition;

[構象] conformation;
重疊構象 eclipsed conformation; opposed conformation;
船式構象 boat conformation;
鏈構象 chain conformation;
順式構象 cisoid conformation;
歪扭構象 gauche conformation;
椅式構象 chair conformation;

[構形] configuration;
代數構形 algebraic configuration;
仿射構形 affine configuration;
調和構形 harmonic configuration;

[構型] configuration;
混合式構型 compound configuration;
鏈構型 chain configuration;
柱構型 column configuration;

[構造] build; conformation; construction; makeup; structure;

[構築工事] build defences; construct field works; dig in;

G

機構 (1) mechanism; (2) organization; setup; (3) the internal structure of an organization;
結構 composition; construction; structure;
異構 isomery;

gou
【遘】 come across; encounter; meet;

gou
【購】 buy; purchase;
［購單］ buying order;
［購得］ purchase;
［購房］ buy a house or flat;
購房者 flat buyer;
~首次購房者 first-time buyer
［購股權］ stock option;
購股權證 stock option warrant;
［購貨］ purchase commodities;
［購買］ acquire; buy; buying; purchase;
購買合同 contract of purchase and sale;
購買力 purchasing power;
~購買力平價理論 purchasing power parity theory;
單邊購買 straight purchase;
單面購買 straight purchase;
大量購買 bulk buying;
大批購買 bulk purchase;
記帳購買 purchase on credit;
間接購買 indirect buying;
投機性購買 speculative buying;
現金購買 cash purchase;
直接購買 direct buying;
［購票］ buy a ticket;
排隊購票 queue up for tickets;
［購物］ shop;
購物車 cart;
購物袋 shopping bag;
~手提購物袋 carrier bag;
購物單 shopping list;
購物廣場 shopping mall;
購物狂 shopaholic;
購物籃 shopping basket;
購物區 shopping area;
~步行購物區 pedestrian mall; pedestrian precinct;
購物手推車 shopping cart; shopping trolley;
購物嚮導 shopping guide;
購物者 shopper;
~一群群購物者 groups of shoppers;
購物指南 shapping guidance;
購物中心 shopping centre; shopping mall;
~超級購物中心 supermall;
衝動購物 impulse buying; impulse shopping;
電話購物 phone purchase;
瘋狂購物 crazy about shopping; shopping spree;
網上購物 online purchase;
喜歡購物 enjoy shopping;
郵寄購物 mail purchase;
［購銷］ buying and selling; purchase and sale;
購銷價格 retail price;
購銷兩旺 both purchasing and marketing are brisk; brisk buying and selling;
統購統銷 planned purchase and marketing by the state; state monopoly for purchase and marketing; system of planned purchase and supply;
［購置］ purchase;

採購 purchase;
承購 underwriting;
代購 act as a purchasing agent; buy on sb's behalf;
訂購 order goods; place an order for sth;
函購 purchase by mail;
批購 buy goods wholesale;
搶購 rush to buy; rush to purchase;
認購 offer to buy; subscribe for bonds;
賒購 buy on credit;
收購 buy out; purchase;
套購 illegally buy up;
添購 buy in addition; buy more;
統購 monopolize the purchase of sth;
選購 pick out and buy; purchase after careful selection;
郵購 purchase by mail;
預購 purchase in advance;
徵購 requisition by purchase;

gou
【覯】 meet with;

罕覯 seldom see;

gu1
gu
【估】 appraise; estimate;
［估產］ appraise the assets; assess; crop estimate; estimate the yield;
［估計］ appraise; calculate; estimate; estimation; forecast; reckon; size up; take stock of;

G

估計量 estimator;
~輔助估計量 ancillary estimator;
~容許估計量 admissible estimator;
~有偏的估計量 biased estimator;
保守估計 conservative estimate;
不變估計 invariant estimation;
粗略估計 coarse estimate;
大致估計 approximate estimate; guesstimate;
官方估計 official estimate;
過低估計 underestimate;
過高估計 overestimate;
據估計 at a guess; by sb's reckoning;
軍費估計 army estimate;
偏誤估計 biased estimate;
容許估計 admissible estimate;
一致估計 consistent estimation;
約略估計 approximate estimate;
作估計 make an estimate;

[估價] (1) evaluate; valuation; (2) appraised price;
估價員 assessor;
比較估價 alternate valuation;
投資估價 investment appraisal;
債券估價 bond valuation;
徵税估價 rateable value;

[估量] appraise; assess; balance; estimate; ponder; value; weigh;
估量局勢 take stock of the situation;

[估摸] guess; reckon;

[估評] evaluation;

[估算] calculate roughly; estimate; reckon;
折舊估算 depreciation appraisal;

[估損] appraisal of damage; assessment of loss;

[估值] appraisement; value of assessment;

高估 overvalue;

gu

【咕】 (1) cluck; (2) coo; (3) murmur;

[咕咚] plump; splash; thud;

[咕嘟] bubble; grugle;

[咕咕] cluck; coo;

[咕嚕] roll; rumble;
咕嚕肉 sweet and sour pork;

[咕噥] grumble; mumble; murmur; mutter; throat;
低聲咕噥 murmur under one's breath;
腼腆地咕噥 murmur coyly;

[咕容] wriggle;

叨咕 grumble in an indistinct voice;
嘀咕 (1) talk in whisper; whisper; (2) have sth on one's mind;
唧咕 mutter; talk in a low voice; whisper;
嘰咕 mutter; talk in a low voice; whisper;
捅咕 (1) touch; (2) urge sb to do sth;

gu

【呱】 cry;

[呱嗒] clack; clip-clop;
呱嗒板兒 (1) bamboo clappers;

[呱呱] (1) cry of a baby; (2) quack; (3) croak; (4) caw;
呱呱墮地 be born; be born crying; be born to bed; come into the world with a cry;
呱呱叫 excellent; first-rate; gorgeous; great; superb; terrific; thumbs up; tiptop; top-notch;
~趕鴨子過河—呱呱叫 driving ducks across the river – quack-quacking; top-notch; very good;

[呱唧] clap hands;

gu

【姑】 (1) aunt; father's sister; (2) husband's sister; sister-in-law; (3) nun; (4) for the time being; tentatively;

[姑表] cousinship;

[姑布] a surname;

[姑夫] uncle-in-law;

[姑父] uncle-in-law;

[姑姑] aunt; father's sister;

[姑漫應之] just promise casually;

[姑母] aunt; father's sister;

[姑娘] (1) girl; (2) daughter;
姑娘的心—難捉摸 a lady's heart – hard to understand;
姑娘十八變 a girl changes all the time before eighteen;
~毛頭姑娘十八變 a girl changes all the time before eighteen;
大姑娘 (1) unmarried young woman; (2) eldest daughter; (3) first young lady;
~大姑娘説媒—難張口 find it hard to open one's mouth, like a young girl to act as a marriage broker;
灰姑娘 Cinderella;
俊美的姑娘 dainty girl;
老姑娘 old maid; spinster;
身材曲條的姑娘 slimly built girl;
小姑娘 lass; missy; young girl;

[姑婆] (1) husband's paternal aunt; (2) grandfather's sister;
三姑六婆 a bevy of shrewish women;
[姑且] anyhow; for the moment; might as well;
姑且不論 let's not discuss it for the present; let's not go into the question now; not to mention; simply have to leave it at that;
[姑嫂] sisters-in-law;
[姑妄] see no harm in sth;
姑妄聽之 just listen leisurely and by no means seriously; just listen to sth without taking it seriously; let him talk and let's just listen; take sth for what it is worth; take sth with a grain of salt; to hear is not to believe; to see no harm in hearing what sb has to say;
姑妄言之 just talk for talking's sake; just talk for the sake of talking; just venture an opinion; tell sb sth for what it is worth;
[姑息] appease; attention; indulge; tolerate;
姑息遷就 excessively accommodating; overlenient;
姑息養奸 excessive indulgence breeds traitors; indulge the evildoers; lenient towards villains and let them grow; overindulgence nurtures evil; pardon makes offenders; to tolerate evil is to abet it; tolerant and indulgent;
姑息養奸，縱虎為患 indulge the evildoers and connive at their crimes;
[姑爺] son-in-law;
[姑子] (1) Buddhist nun; (2) paternal aunt;
大姑子 one's eldest paternal aunt;

村姑 country girl;
道姑 Daoist nun;
尼姑 Buddhist nun;
仙姑 (1) female immortal; (2) sorceress;

gu

【孤】 (1) fatherless; orphaned; (2) isolated; solitary;
[孤傲] proud and aloof;
[孤本] only copy extant; only existing copy;
[孤雛腐鼠] a lone young bird or a decayed rat—easily be deserted; ordinary person;
[孤單] (1) alone; (2) friendless; lonely;
感到孤單 feel lonely;
孤孤單單 lonely and single; out in the cold;
孑影孤單 leave alone with one's shadow only;
異常孤單 extremely lonely;
[孤島] islet;
[孤獨] lonely; lonesome; reclusive; single; solitary;
孤獨的人 the lonely;
孤獨困苦 hopeless and alone;
孤獨無偶 all alone without a mate;
孤獨無援 alone and with no help;
孤獨症 autism;
孤眠獨宿 live and sleep alone;
孤枕獨眠 sleep alone on a single pillow;
尋找孤獨 seek solitude;
[孤犢] orphan;
孤犢觸乳 orphan-calf injures the nursing cow — ingratitude;
[孤兒] orphan;
孤兒寡婦 orphans and widows;
收養孤兒 bring up an orphan;
[孤寡] orphans and widows;
殘老孤寡 those who are disabled, old, orphaned or widowed;
稱孤道寡 act like an absolute ruler; address oneself as king; call oneself king; style oneself king;
孤家寡人 a loner; a man isolated from the masses; a man without followers; a person in solitary splendour; an elderly bachelor;
孤陋寡聞 live in a back water; ill-informed; out of touch with the outside world; rough and ignorant; solitary and inexperienced; with very limited knowledge and scanty information;
矜孤卹寡 feel for the orphan and the widow; have commiseration on the orphan and the widow; have pity on the orphan and the widow;
憐孤惜寡 compassionate towards the orphans and widows; compassionate the orphans and widows; relieve and pity orphans and widows; show solicitude for orphans and widows;
淩孤逼寡 ill-treat orphans and oppress widows;
[孤軍] isolated force;
孤軍深入 an isolated force penetrating

G

deep into the enemy's territory;
孤軍作戰 carry on the struggle single-handed; fight a lone battle; fight in isolation;

[孤立] (1) isolated; separate; solitary; (2) isolate; seclude;
孤立無援 alone and helpless; be left hgih and dry; isolated and cut off from help; isolated and helpless;
孤立語 isolating language;
孤立主義 isolationism;

[孤零零] all alone; lone; solitary;

[孤僻] odd; solitary; unsocial; unsociable and eccentric;
天生孤僻 naturally solitary; rather solitary by nature;

[孤身] lonely figure;
孤身獨坐 sit alone;
孤身赴敵 fight the enemy alone;
孤身枯坐 sit alone;
孤身一人 all on one's own;
孤身隻影 a lone man and a solitary shadow; a lone soul; all alone; all by oneself; lonely;

[孤燕不成夏] one swallow doesn't make a summer;

[孤雲野鶴] a lone cloud or a wild crane — said of the life of a carefree hermit; a wild crane in a solitary cloud — a recluse leading a carefree life;

[孤掌難鳴] a single palm cannot clap; alone and helpless; cannot clap with one hand; he who stands alone has no power; it is difficult to accomplish sth without the help of others;

[孤竹] surname;

[孤注一擲] a long shot gamble; all-or-nothing; ball the jack; bet all on a single throw; bet one's boots on; bet one's last dollar on; bet one's shirt on; bet one's bottom dollar on; cast the die; go for the gloves; go nap over; go the vole; have all one's eggs in one basket; make a last desperate effort; make a spoon or spoil a horn; make or break; make or mar; mend or mar; monkey with a buzz saw; neck or nothing; place one's efforts in a single thing; put all one's eggs in one basket; put the fate of sb/sth at a stake; risk all on a single throw; risk everything on a single venture; risk everything in one effort; send the axe after the helve; shoot one's wad; shoot the works; sink or swim; stake all one's fortune in a single throw; stake all one has; stake everything on a cast of the dice; stake everything on one last throw; stake everything on one attempt; take a great rish; venture on a single chance; venture one's fortune on a single stake; vie money on the turn of a card; win the horse or lose the saddle; win the mare or lose the halter; throw the helve after the hatchet;

托孤 entrust an orphan to sb;
遺孤 orphan;

gu
【沽】 (1) buy; (2) sell;

[沽名釣譽] angle for compliment; angle for praise; angle for undeserved fame; buy reputation and fish for praise; cater to publicity by sordid methods; chase fame; court publicity; fish for fame and compliments; fish for fame and reputation; strive for reputation;

gu
【骨】 a pronunciation of 骨;

gu
【蛄】 mole cricket;

蟪蛄 a kind of cicada;
螻蛄 mole cricket;
蝦蛄 mantis shrimp;

gu
【菰】 (1) zizania latifolia; (2) same as 菇, mushroom;

gu
【辜】 (1) crime; guilt; (2) a surname;

[辜負] disappoint; fail to live up to; let down; unworthy of;

無辜 innocent;

gu
【菇】 fungus; mushroom;

草菇 straw mushroom;
春菇 spring mushroom;

冬菇 dried mushroom;
香菇 mushroom;

gu
【觚】 (1) ancient wine vessel; (2) angle; angular; (3) corner; (4) rule; square; (5) correspondence or file, etc.;

gu
【酤】 sell or buy alcoholic drinks;

gu
【箍】 hoop;
［箍帶］ strap;
輪箍 tyre;
卡箍 band; clamp; hoop;
鐵箍 iron hoop;

gu
【鴣】 pigeon;

gu²
gu
【骨】 (1) bone; (2) frame; framework; skeleton;
［骨頭］ (1) bone; (2) person of a certain character;
骨頭鯁在喉嚨口—咽不下，吐不出 a bone wedge in one's throat – can't get rid of sth in any way;
骨頭架子 (1) skeleton; (2) bag of bones; skin and bones; skinny person;
骨頭裏搾油 squeeze fat from bones; take sth out of nothing;
骨頭輕 light bones;
骨頭痛 pain in the bones;
骨頭硬 hard bone – a dauntless, unyielding person;
含著骨頭露著肉 hesitate in speech; speak with reservation; with the bone in the mouth but the meat still visible – beat about the bush;
賤骨頭 contemptible wretch; miserable wretch; worthless creature;
接骨頭 set a fracture;
啃骨頭 gnaw a bone; pick out the residual meat on the bones with teeth;
懶骨頭 lazybone; loafer;
輕骨頭 (1) base; lowly; mean; (2) frivolous;
窮骨頭 poor person; stingy person;
耍骨頭 irritate sb with sarcastic remarks;
損骨頭 wicked person;
剔骨頭 take out bones from meat;
一塊骨頭 a bone;
硬骨頭 dauntless; hard bone; man of iron; unyielding integrity;
~ 啃硬骨頭 crack a hard nut;
賊骨頭 depravity; meanness; wickedness;
［骨質疏鬆］ osteoporosis;
骨質疏鬆症 osteoporosis;

gu³
gu
【古】 (1) ancient; (2) a surname;
［古柏參天］ the tall ancient cypress trees reach towards the sky;
［古板］ bigoted; conservative; old-fashioned and inflexible; poky; straight-arrow;
老古板 fuddy-duddy;
［古成］ surname;
［古城］ ancient city;
歷史古城 historic city;
［古代］ ancient; ancient times; antiquity; archaic;
古代傳説 old legend;
古代人 ancient people;
古代史 ancient history;
元古代 Proterozoic era;
［古道可風］ old ways;
古道可風 the old ways may be adopted and practised;
古道熱腸 considerate and warm-hearted; warm-hearted and compassionate; sympathetic;
［古典］ (1) classical; (2) classical allusions;
古典風格 classicism;
古典畫 classical painting;
~古典畫家 classical painter;
古典文學 classical literature;
古典學者 classicist;
古典藝術 classical art;
古典音樂 classical music;
古典主義 classicalism;
~ 古典主義者 classicist;
~ 新古典主義 neoclassicism;
［古調獨彈］ one's speech and behaviour not being in keeping with the time; strike up the hackneyed tunes alone;
［古董］ (1) antique; curio; (2) old fogey;
古董店 antique shop;
古董商 antique dealer;
老古董 (1) antique; museum piece; old-fashioned article; (2) fuddy-duddy; old

fogey; ultra-conservative;
稀世古董 rare antique;
一件古董 an antique;

[古都] ancient capital;

[古風] (1) ancient customs; antiquities; (2) a form of pre-Tang poetry;
古風遺俗 antiquities; customs handed down from past generations; old customs;

[古怪] bats; bizzare; cranky; eccentric; erratic; flaky; funky; gnarled; odd; ornery; quaint; queer; quizzical; strange; uncouth; wacky; wayward; whimsical; whimsy; wonder;
古怪的 bizarre;
古怪念頭 loony idea;
古怪想法 odd notions;
古怪行為 eccentricity;
古怪隱喻 bizarre metaphor;
刁鑽古怪 cranky;
古裏古怪 bizarre; eccentric; odd; peculiar; queer;

[古畫] ancient painting;

[古話] old saying;

[古蹟] ancient relics; historic sites; places of historic interest;
古蹟文物 antiquities;
歷史古蹟 historical antiquities;
名勝古蹟 places of historic interest;

[古籍] ancient books;

[古今] the ancient and the modern;
古今雜揉 a blending of the ancient and the modern;
古今中外 at all times and in all countries; both ancient and modern, Chinese and foreign; classical and modern, Chinese and foreign; in China or elsewhere, in modern or ancient times; in the past or present, in China or anywhere else in the world; past and present, at home and abroad; whether in China or other lands, in ancient or today;
博古通今 be well versed in things past and present;
崇古非今 exalt the past and disparage the present; praise the past and despise the present;
從古到今 from ancient times to the present; from ancient to modern times; from time immemorial; throughout history;
亙古亙今 from ancient times till the present; from the earliest time down to the present;
古往今來 everywhere and at all times; from ancient times; from ancient to modern times; from of old till now; in all ages; past and present; since remote antiquity; since time immemorial; throughout the ages;
古為今用 adapt ancient forms for present-day use; let the ancient serve the present; make the past serve the present-day needs;
～古為今用，洋為中用 make the past serve the present and foreign things serve China;
厚古薄今 esteem the past over the present; lay emphasis on the ancient as against the contemporary; lay more stress on the past than on the present; pay more attention to the past than to the present; stress the past, not the present; value the past and slight the present;
厚今薄古 lay more stress on the present than on the past; stress the present more than the past;
鑑古知今 learn about the present with reference to past experience;
妙絕古今 an unparalleled wonder both in ancient and modern times;
攀今攬古 discourse at random of things past and present; talk over past and present;
茹古涵今 extensive learning; well read;
釋古行今 justify one's own wishes and desires by abandoning ancient principles;
説古談今 discourse at random of things past and present; talk over past and present;
頌古非今 admire everything ancient and belittle present-day achievements; eulogize the ancient while disparaging the modern; eulogize the past and condemn the present; eulogize the past at the expense of the present; extol the past to negate the present; praise the ancient and attack the present; praise the past and deplore the present;
頌古誹今 denounce the present and extol the past; praise the past to condemn the present;

談古説今 discourse at random of things past and present; talk over past and present;
通今博古 conversant with things present and past; erudite and informed;
學貫古今 well-versed in the learning of both ancient and modern times;
淹通古今 be thoroughly acquainted with the old and modern;
以古非今 belittle the present by extolling the past; disparage the present by extolling the past; use the past to attack the present;
以古諷今 use ancient things to satirize the present;
以古況今 draw parallels from history;
震古鑠今 galvanize the world; peerless; surpass the ancients and amaze the contemporaries — earthshaking; unprecedented;
自古及今 from ancient times till now; from ancient times up to the present-day; since time immemorial;
自古至今 down the ages; from of old; in all ages; in all periods of the world;

[古井] dried-up well; old well;
古井不波 a dried-up well does not have ripples; impervious to desires and passions;
心如古井 call forth no response in sb's breast; one's heart is as tranquil as an old well;

[古鏡] ancient mirror;
[古舊] antiquated; archaic;
[古口] a surname;
[古來] since time immemorial;
[古老] ancient; antiquity; hoariness; old age;
古老的 age-old;
~古老的歌 ancient song;
古老肉 sweet and sour pork;

[古龍] (1) a surname; (2) cologne;
古龍水 cologne;

[古貌古心] dignified-looking;
[古木] ancient trees;
古木參天 ancient trees touch the sky; ancient trees tower to the skies; old trees that reach into the skies; the old trees rear their heads to the sky;
參天古木 old trees that reach into the sky; towering old trees;

[古墓] ancient tomb;
[古樸] of primitive simplicity; simple and unsophisticated;
[古錢] ancient coins;
[古人] ancients; old friend;
前無古人 have no parallel in history; no one has ever attempted anything of this kind; peerless; unknown in history; unparalleled in history; unprecedented in history; without parallel in history; without precedent in history;
~前無古人，後無來者 a record that has never been approached and will never be approached again;

[古色古香] air of antiquity; antique quaint; be beautiful in the traditional style; classic beauty; having an antique flavour; in ancient sytles; of ancient flavour; smack of sth classical in its design;
古色古香的教堂 quaint church;

[古詩] ancient poetry;
[古書] ancient books;
[古樹] ancient tree; old tree;
[古孫] surname;
[古體] old styles;
古體詩 ancient-style poetry;

[古玩] antique; curio;
仿古玩 imitation antiquities;

[古文] ancient style prose;
古文字 ancient writing;

[古物] ancient objects; antiquities; archaeology; curio;
偽造古物 forge antiquities;
一件古物 an antique;

[古稀] seventy years of age;
古稀之年 seventy years of age; three score years and ten;
年逾古稀 past seventy years of age;

[古雅] conservative; of classic beauty and in elegant taste; of classic elegance;
[古已有之] have existed since ancient times;
[古印] ancient seal;
[古裝] ancient costume; costume;
古裝電影 costume drama;
古裝劇 costume drama;
古裝戲 costume drama;

弔古 think of the ancients;
仿古 in the style of the ancients; model after an antique;
復古 backswing; return to the ancients;

G

亘古 from time immemorial down to the present day;
懷古 cherish the past; meditate on the past; reflect on an ancient event;
借古 use the past;
考古 archaeology;
曠古 from time immemorial;
摹古 model after the ancient style;
擬古 model one's artistic style on that of the ancients;
千古 (1) eternal; for all time; through the ages; (2) eternal repose to;
上古 ancient times; remote ages;
邃古 remote antiquity;
太古 remote antiquity;
萬古 eternally; forever; through the ages;
遠古 remote antiquity;
中古 medieval times; Middle Ages; middle ancient times;
終古 forever;
作古 die; pass away;

gu

【谷】 (1) ravine; valley; waterway between two mountain; (2) hollow; pit; (3) difficulty; poverty; (4) grain; (5) a surname;

[谷底] valley bottom; valley floor;
跌至谷底 hit rock bottom; reach rock bottom;
[谷風] (1) east wind; (2) up-draft in a valley;
[谷坑] valleys and ravines;
滿坑滿谷 exceedingly numerous; in every valley and ravine; in great abundance; in large numbers; in plenty;
[谷飲] live like a hermit;

苞谷 corn; maize;
波谷 trough;
布谷 cuckoo;
槽谷 trough valley;
稻谷 rice;
毒谷 poisoned grains;
河谷 river valley;
裂谷 rift valley;
平齊谷 accordant valley;
山谷 mountain valley;
五谷 (1) five cereals; (2) food crops;
峽谷 canyon; gorge;
懸谷 hanging valley;
一把谷 a handful of grain;
幽谷 deep and secluded valley;

gu

【汩】 (1) destroy; ruin; (2) confused; disorderly; (3) sound of waves;

[汩汩] gurgle;
[汩亂] cause disorder;

gu

【股】 (1) thigh; (2) section; (3) ply; strand; (4) share;

[股本] capital; capital stock; equity; stock;
[股東] shareholder; stockholder;
股東大會 general meeting of stockholders;
股東權 stockholder's equity;
~股東權利 stockholder rights;
~股東權益 stockholder's equity;
股東資本 equity capital;
無限責任股東 active partner;
有限責任股東 limited partner; sleeping partner;
[股份] allotment; share; stock;
股份保險公司 stock insurance company;
股份公司 joint-stock company;
股份合作制 joint-stock cooperative system;
股份經濟 joint-stock economy;
股份式企業 joint enterprise;
股份銀行 joint-stock bank;
股份責任公司 shareholding limited coorpation;
股份制 (1) shareholding system; (2) joint stock system;
~股份制經濟 economy of shareholding system;
~股份制企業 shareholding enterprise;
~股份制外商投資企業 shareholding of foreign-invested enterprise;
~實行股份制 introduce the shareholding system;
多數股份 majority shareholding; majority stake;
分攤股份 allot shares;
[股肱] right-hand man;
股肱耳目 bosom assistants;
股肱心腹 bosom assistant; right-hand person;
股肱之臣 the most trustworthy ministers;
[股骨] femur;
[股栗膚慄] tremble with fear and have goose-flesh;
[股民] shareholders; stockholders;

[股票] captial stock; equity security; share; share certificate; stock; stock certificate;
股票報價 quotation for stock;
股票持有人 shareholder; stockholder;
股票持有證 stock certificate;
股票公司 stock company;
股票過戶 stock transfer;
股票行情 quotations on the stock market;
~股票行情指數 index of stock price;
股票價格 share price;
股票交易 share dealing; trade in stocks;
~股票交易額 stock turnover;
~股票交易所 stock exchange;
~從事股票交易 deal in shares; trade in shares;
股票經紀 stockbroker;
股票買賣 buying and selling of stock;
股票熱 craze for stock;
股票商人 stock jobber;
股票上漲 shares go up; shares rise;
股票市場 stock market;
~股票市場指數 stock market index;
股票所有權 share ownership;
股票下跌 shares fall; shares go down;
股票有限公司 joint stock corporation;
股票證書 stock certificate;
股票指數 stock index;
股票轉讓 transfer of shares;
股票轉讓證 transfer deed;
保息股票 guaranteed stock;
超級股票 super stock;
炒股票 buy and resell stocks at a profit; engage in speculation in stock; speculate in stocks;
付息股票 cum coupon;
工業股票 industrial stock;
公司股票 shares in companies;
公用事業股票 utility stock;
購買股票 buy shares;
記名股票 registered stock;
~不記名股票 bearer shares;
借入股票 borrowed share;
面額股票 par value stock;
普通股票 ordinary share;
上市股票 listed shares;
投資股票 invest in shares;
玩股票 dabble stock;
無記名股票 bearer stock;
無面額股票 no-par value stock;
一種股票 a kind of stock;
銀行股票 bank stock;
有面值股票 par value stock;

[股權] equity; shareholding; stock right;
股權交易方式 equity transaction method;
股權資本 equity capital;

[股市] stock market;
股市指數 stocket market index;

[股息] dividend; stock divident;
股息賬戶 dividend account;
股息政策 dividend policy;
股息支票 dividend cheque;
累計股息 accumulated dividend;
推定股息 constructive dividend;
應計股息 accured dividends;

[股長] section chief;

八股 eight-legged essays;
公股 government share;
合股 (1) form a partnership; pool capital; (2) plying;
內部股 internal share;
普通股 ordinary shares;
入股 become a shareholder; buy a share;
私股 private share;
退股 withdraw a share from a company;
招股 raise capital by floating shares;

gu

【牯】 castrated bull; ox;

[牯牛] bull;

gu

【罟】 net;

gu

【骨】 (1) bone; (2) framework; skeleton; (3) character; spirit;

[骨癌] cancer of the bone; osteocarcinoma;

[骨痺] heumatism;

[骨病] bone disease; osteopathia; osteopathy;
饑餓性骨病 hunger osteopathy;
尿毒症骨病 uremic bone disease;
飲食性骨病 alimentary osteopathy;
營養不良性骨病 hypertrophic osteopathy;

[骨出血] osteorrhagia;

[骨瓷] bone china;

[骨刺] bony spur; spur;

[骨脆症] fragile fern; fragilitas ossium;

[骨銼] bone file;

[骨端] extremitas;

[骨發生] osteogenesis; ostosis;

[骨發育不良] anostosis;

[骨發育不全] dysosteogenesis;
[骨發育障礙] dysosteogenesis;
[骨反射] bone reflex;
[骨肥厚] hyperostosis;
[骨粉] bonemeal;
[骨縫] sutura;
[骨復位] reduction;
[骨感覺] bone sensitivity;
[骨幹] (1) diaphysis; (2) backbone; mainstay;
骨幹發育不良 diaphyseal dysphlasia;
骨幹發育異常 diaphyseal sclerosis;
骨幹份子 core members;
骨幹企業 key enterprises;
骨幹炎 diaphysitis;
骨幹硬化 diaphyseal sclerosis;
[骨隔] scleroseptum;
[骨骼] skeleton; ossature;
骨骼發生 skeletogenesis;
骨骼發育不良 ostemyelodysphlasia;
骨骼肌 skeletal muscle;
粗大的骨骼 massive bones;
人體骨骼 human skeleton;
外骨骼 exoskeleton;
~硬外骨骼 hard exoskeleton;
硬化骨骼 scleroskeleton;
[骨鯁] bone sticking;
骨鯁在喉 a bur in the throat; a lump in the throat; have a fishbone stuck in one's throat; having a fishbone in one's throat; having an opinion one cannot suppress; voice certain sentiments which one can no longer repress;
骨鯁之臣 outspoken minister who gives unpleasant advice;
骨鯁之氣 have the spirit of open frankness;
[骨刮] raspatory; scalprum;
[骨關節病] osteoarthritis;
[骨關節結核] osteoarticular tuberculosis;
[骨關節窩] socket;
[骨關節炎] osteoarthritis;
地方性骨關節炎 endemic osteoarthritis;
幼年性骨關節炎 osteoarthrosis juvenilis;
增殖性骨關節炎 hyperplastic osteoarthritis;
[骨骺] apophysis ossium;
骨骺發生不全 epiphyseal dysgenesis;
[骨化] ossification; sclerotization;
骨化病 osteosis;
~皮膚骨化病 osteosis cutis;
骨化不全 defective formation of bone; dysostosis;
骨化過度 excessive ossification of bone; pleonosteosis;
骨化過早 excessive ossification of bone; pleonosteosis;
骨化軟骨 ossifying cartilage;
骨化性骨炎 osteitis ossificans;
骨化性肌炎 myositis ossificans;
骨化異常 osthexy; osthexia;
骨化中心 centre of ossification;
骨膜骨化 periosteal ossification;
迷路炎性骨化 labyrinthitis ossificans;
膜內骨化 intramembranous ossification;
皮膚骨化 osteodermia;
軟骨內骨化 endochondral ossification;
異位骨化 heterotopic ossification;
[骨壞死] osteonecrosis; recrosis of bone;
[骨灰] (1) bone ash; bone char; cinder; (2) ashes of the dead; cremains;
骨灰瓷 bone china;
骨灰盒 cinerary casket;
骨灰堂 cermation hall;
骨灰甕 mortuary urn;
[骨畸形] bone malformation;
[骨疾病] bone disease;
[骨極] bone exhaustion;
[骨痂] callus; osteotylus; poroma;
暫時骨痂 provisional callus;
[骨架] (1) skeleton; (2) armature; bone; carcass; frame; framework; scaffolding;
車體骨架 body skeleton;
凝膠骨架 gel skeleton;
[骨膠] bone glue; lime glue; pastern; osseocolla;
[骨結核] bone tuberculosis; tuberculosis of bones;
[骨節] osteocomma; scleromere;
骨節粗大 gnarl;
骨節疼痛 arthralgia; pain in a joint;
[骨靜脈炎] inflammation of the veins of a bone; osteophlebitis;
[骨臼] bone socket;
[骨疽] caries; decay;
骨疽性壞死 carionecrosis;
[骨抗] fracture;
[骨科] orthopedics;
骨科醫生 orthopedist;
[骨刻] bone carving; bone sculpture;

[骨臘] bone wax;
[骨癆] bone and joint tuberculosis;
[骨聯合] synostosis;
[骨料] aggregate;
石灰骨料 calcareous aggregate;
陶瓷骨料 ceramic aggregate;
無級配骨料 ungraded aggregate;
[骨瘤] bone tumour;
皮膚骨瘤 osteoma cutis;
象牙樣骨瘤 ivory osteoma;
[骨瘻] bone fistula;
[骨顱] osteocranium;
[骨膜] periost; periosteum;
骨膜反射 periosteal reflex;
骨膜反應 periosteal reaction;
骨膜骨 periosteal bone;
骨膜骨化 periosteal ossification;
骨膜骨髓炎 periosteomyelitis;
骨膜骨炎 periostosteitis;
骨膜疾病 periosteous disease;
骨膜瘤 periosteoma;
骨膜水腫 periosteoma;
骨膜炎 periostitis;
出血性骨膜炎 hemorrhagic periostitis;
~肥厚性骨膜炎 pachyperiostitis;
~早發性骨膜炎 precocious periostitis;
~增生性骨膜炎 periostitis hyperplastica;
[骨囊腫] bone cyst;
創傷性骨囊腫 traumatic bone cyst;
[骨內癌] intraosseous carcinoma;
原發性骨內癌 primary intraosseous carcinoma;
[骨牌] dominoes;
骨牌理論 domino theory;
骨牌作用 domino effect;
[骨盆] pelvis;
骨盆骨 pelvic bone;
骨盆管 pelvic canal;
骨盆聯合 symphysis pelvis;
骨盆炎 pelvic inflammation;
長型骨盆 dolichopellic pelvis;
男性骨盆 masculine pelvis;
[骨氣] backbone; moral integrity; strength of character;
沒骨氣 have no guts; of no character;
~沒骨氣的人 person of no character;
有骨氣 adhering to moral principles; have integrity;
~有骨氣的男子漢 man with backbone;
~有骨氣的人 person of character; person of character and mettle; person of integrity; person of spine and starch;
做人很有骨氣 behave oneself like a man;
[骨肉] flesh and blood; kindred;
骨肉瘤 osteosarcoma;
~骨肉瘤病 osteosarcomatosis;
~典型性骨肉瘤 classical osteosarcoma;
骨肉情誼 feelings of kinship; kindred feelings;
骨肉同胞 kith and kin; one's own flesh and blood;
骨肉團聚 family reunion;
骨肉相連 as close and dear as blood relatives; as closely linked as flesh and blood; near to each other as bone and flesh; very closely related;
骨肉兄弟 blood brothers; one's own brothers;
骨肉之親 blood relationship; blood relationship; near of kin;
骨肉之情 family relationship and feeling; kindred feelings; the ties of blood;
骨肉至親 blood relations;
骨騰肉飛 be fascinated by sb's compelling beauty; go off into ecstasies;
親骨肉 blood kin; one's own flesh and blood;
情同骨肉 as dear to sb as one's own flesh and blood; as fast and indissoluble as flesh and bone;
情逾骨肉 as dear as one's own flesh and blood; dearer than one's own flesh and blood;
義同骨肉 have an affection for one another which surpasses that of blood brothers;
[骨軟骨病] osteochondrosis;
[骨軟骨關節炎] osteochondroarthritis;
[骨軟骨瘤] osteochondroma;
[骨軟骨炎] osteochondrosis;
剝脫性骨軟骨炎 osteochondritis dissecans;
壞死性骨軟骨炎 osteochondritis necroticans;
[骨軟化] halisteresis;
骨軟化症 osteomalacia;
創傷性骨軟化 malacia traumatica;
假骨軟化 pseudo-osteomalacia;
老年性骨軟化 senile osteomalacia;
[骨軟筋麻] enervated; one's bones are weak and one's muscles numbed; paralyzed;
[骨傷] bone fracture;

[骨神經痛] osteoneuralgia;
[骨腎病] osteonephropathy;
[骨生成] ostosis;
[骨瘦] bone-thin;
骨瘦如柴 a mere bag of bones; a mere skeleton; as thin as a lath; as thin as a rail; as thin as a rake; as thin as a threadpaper; as thin as a whipping post; as thin as sticks; bare-boned; be all skin and bone; be reduced to a skeleton; be reduced to a show; become as emaciated as a fowl; bone-thin; lean and skinny; worn to a shadow;
~骨瘦如柴的人 living skeleton; rack of bones; stack of bones; walking corpse;
骨瘦形銷 growly greatly emaciated;
[骨髓] bone marrow; marrow;
骨髓病 myelopathy;
全骨髓病 panmyelopathy;
骨髓發育不良 myelodysplasia;
骨髓化 medullization;
骨髓癆 myelophthisis;
骨髓瘤 myeloma;
局限性骨髓瘤 localized myeloma;
硬化性骨髓瘤 sclerosing myeloma;
骨髓炎 osteomyelitis;
~化膿性骨髓炎 purulent osteomyelitis;
骨髓移植 marrow transplant;
恨入骨髓 hate to the marrow of one's bones;
壞入骨髓 rotten to the core;
怨入骨髓 hate to the very marrow — cherish bitter hatred;
[骨碎裂] osteomiosis;
[骨損傷] bone injury;
[骨痛] ostalgia;
[骨頭] bone;
骨頭鯁在喉嚨口—咽不下，吐不出 a bone wedge in one's throat — can't get rid of sth in any way;
骨頭架子 (1) skeleton; (2) bag of bones; skin and bones;
骨頭裏搾油 squeeze fat from bones; take sth out of nothing;
骨頭輕 light bones;
骨頭痛 pain in the bones;
骨頭硬 dauntless, unyielding person; hard bone;
啃骨頭 gnaw on bones;
沒骨頭 have no backbone; spineless person;
一把骨頭 a bag of bones; all bones;
有骨頭 indomitable; manly;
[骨突] apophysis;
骨突病 apophysitis;
[骨歪] displacement of the fractured end of a bone;
[骨彎曲] cyrtosis;
[骨萎縮] bone atrophy;
創傷後骨萎縮 post-traumatic atrophy of bone;
[骨小管] bone canaliculus;
[骨小梁] bone trabecula;
[骨性關節炎] osteoarthritis;
[骨性瘤] osteocele;
[骨炎] inflammation of the bone; osteitis;
脆性骨炎 osteitis fragilitans;
骨化性骨炎 osteitis ossificans;
壞死性骨炎 necrotic osteitis;
急性骨炎 acute ostetitis;
慢性骨炎 chronic osteitis;
梅毒瘤性骨炎 gummatous osteitis;
全骨炎 panosteitis;
肉芽性骨炎 osteitis granulosa;
硬化性骨炎 sclerosing osteitis;
增生性骨炎 productive osteitis;
[骨硬化] osteosclerosis;
[骨折] fracture;
骨折復位 reduction of the fracture;
凹陷骨折 depressed fracture;
閉合性骨折 closed fracture;
剝離骨折 cleavage fracture;
不完全骨折 incomplete fracture;
遲發性骨折 deferred fracture;
穿孔骨折 perforating fracture;
單純性骨折 simple fracture;
粉碎性骨折 comminuted fracture;
複合骨折 compound fracture;
宮內骨折 intrauterine fracture;
骺骨折 epiphyseal fracture;
繼發性骨折 secondary fracture;
假骨折 pseudofracture;
節段性骨折 segmental fracture;
開放性骨折 open fracture;
內分泌性骨折 endocrine fracture;
疲勞骨折 fatigue fracture;
鉛管骨折 lead pipe fracture;
嵌入骨折 impacted fracture;
青枝骨折 greenstick fracture;
上頜骨折 maxillary fracture;
神經源性骨折 neurogenic fracture;

腿部骨折 fracture in the leg;
完全骨折 complete fracture;
完全性骨折 complete fracture;
萎縮性骨折 atrophic fracture;
炎性骨折 inflammatory fracture;
營養性骨折 trophic fracture;
腫瘤性骨折 neoplastic fracture;
自發性骨折 spontaneous fracture;

[骨針] spicule;

[骨整形術] osteoplasty;

[骨質軟化症] osteomalacia;

[骨質疏鬆] osteoporosis;
創傷後骨質疏鬆 post-traumatic osteoporosis;
老年性骨質疏鬆 senile osteoporosis;
骨質疏鬆症 brittle-bone disease; osteoporosis;

[骨質增生] hyperplasia;

[骨子裏] at bottom; between privates; in actuality; in one's heart and soul; in one's heart of hearts;

[骨組織] bone tissue;

傲骨 lofty and unyielding character;
白骨 bones of the dead;
鼻骨 nasal bone;
扁骨 flat bone;
髕骨 kneecap; patella;
長骨 long bone;
腸骨 ilium;
徹骨 to the bone;
尺骨 ulna;
恥骨 pubic bone; pubis;
錘骨 malleus;
刺骨 biting; piercing; piercing to the bones;
代換骨 replacement bone; replacing bone;
鐙骨 stapes; stirrup bone;
骶骨 sacrum;
蝶骨 sphenoid bone;
頂骨 parietal bone;
短骨 short bone;
額骨 frontal bone;
顎骨 jawbone; palatal bone;
腓骨 calf bone; fibula;
風骨 (1) strength of character; (2) vigour of style;
跗骨 tarsal bones; tarsus;
鋼骨 reinforcing bar;
肱骨 humerus;
枸骨 Chinese holly;
股骨 femur; round bone thigh bone;
冠狀骨 coronary bone;
骸骨 human bones; skeleton;
後腦骨 occipital bone;
滑稽骨 funny bone;
踝骨 anklebone;
肌間骨 inrtermuscular bone;
脊骨 ridge bone;
頰骨 cheek bone;
胛骨 scapula; should blade;
肩骨 flat bones;
肩胛骨 blade bone; shoulder bone;
薦骨 sacrum;
接骨 set a bone; set a fracture;
筋骨 bones and muscles; physique;
頸椎骨 neck bone;
脛骨 shank bone; shin bone; tibia;
距骨 ankle bone;
刻骨 deep-rooted; deeply-ingrained;
胯骨 hipbone; innominate bone;
髖骨 hip bone; innominate bone;
肋骨 rib bones; side bones;
龍骨 (1) a bird's sternum; (2) fossil fragments; (3) keel;
顱骨 cranical bone; skull;
露骨 barefaced; undisguised;
媚骨 obsequiousness;
密質骨 compact bone; dense bone;
面骨 facial bone;
顳骨 temporal bone;
排骨 spareribs;
炮骨 cannon bone;
顴骨 cheekbone;
氣骨 pneumatic bone;
髂骨 iliac bone; ilium;
去骨 clear bone;
橈骨 radius;
入骨 to the marrow;
軟骨 cartilage;
軟骨膜骨 perichondrial bone;
軟骨內骨 endochondral bone;
軟骨性骨 cartilaginous bone;
篩骨 ethmoid bone;
舌骨 hyoid bone;
舌頜骨 gullet bones;
舌間骨 interhyal bone;
屍骨 skeleton;
食管骨 oesophageal bone;
鬆質骨 spongy bone;
鎖骨 clavicle; collar bone;
蹄骨 coffin bone;
聽骨 auditory ossicle; ear bones;
頭骨 cranium; skull;

G

蹠骨 metatarsal bone;
外枕骨 exoccipital bone;
腕骨 carpal bones;
尾骨 coccyx;
烏賊骨 cuttle bone;
無板骨 non-lamellar bone;
無骨 clear bone;
小骨 bonelet;
胸骨 breast bone; sternum;
咽喉軟骨 gullet bones;
咽舌骨 glossohyal bone;
腰骨 pelvic bone;
翼狀骨 pterygoid bone;
隅骨 angular bone;
掌骨 metacarpal bone;
砧骨 anvil; incus;
枕骨 occipital bone;
正骨 bonesetting; set a bone;
蹠骨 metatarsal bones;
肢帶骨 girdle bone;
指骨 phalanx;
趾骨 toe bone;
舟狀骨 navicular bone;
椎骨 vertebra;
坐骨 ischium;

gu
【羖】 black ram;

gu
【詁】 (1) explain; explanatory commentary; explanatory notes; (2) transcribe the classics in everyday language;

解詁 explanations of archaic words in current language;
訓詁 explanations of words in ancient books; gloss;

gu
【賈】 (1) businessman; merchant; (2) buy; trade;

商賈 merchants;

gu
【鈷】 cobalt;

gu
【鼓】 (1) drum; (2) beat; sound; strike; (3) blow with bellows; (4) agitate; pluck up; rouse; (5) bulge; swell;

［鼓吹］ (1) advocate; speak in advocacy of; (2) advertise; agitate; play up; preach;
鼓吹非暴力主義 advocate nonviolence;
鼓吹世界和平 speak in advocacy of world peace;
鼓吹言論自由 speak in advocacy of freedom of speech;

［鼓搗］ (1) fiddle with; inker with; (2) egg on; incite;

［鼓動］ (1) actuate; agitate; arouse; promote; tickle; (2) incite; instigate;
鼓動家 agitator;
~政治鼓動家 political agitator;
鼓動者 agitator;
進行鼓動 conduct agitation;
宣傳鼓動 agitprop;
~宣傳鼓動劇 agitprop drama;

［鼓風］ blast air; blow;
鼓風機 blast blower; blower; draft blower; fan blower;
~擺旋鼓風機 cycloidal blower;
~帶動鼓風機 belt driven blower;
~單級鼓風機 single-stage blower;
~電動鼓風機 electric blower;
~高爐鼓風機 stove blower;
~高壓鼓風機 high-pressure blower;
~盒形鼓風機 cased-in blower;
~活塞式鼓風機 piston blower;
~離心式鼓風機 centrifugal blower; turbo blower;
~噴氣鼓風機 jet blower; steam jet blower;
~清除鼓風機 scavenging blower;
~熱鼓風機 hot-air blower;
~容積式鼓風機 displacement blower;
~昇壓鼓風機 booster blower;
~手搖鼓風機 hand blower;
~通用鼓風機 universal blower;
~往復式鼓風機 reciprocating blower;
~旋轉鼓風機 rotary blower;
~循環鼓風機 recycle gas blower;
~蒸汽鼓風機 steam blower;
~正鼓風機 positive blower;
~主鼓風機 main blower;
鼓風設備 blast apparatus;

［鼓鼓囊囊］ bulging; bulging out;

［鼓角齊鳴］ beat the drums and blare the trumpets; the beating of drums and the blare of trumpets come from every side;

［鼓勵］ a pat on the back; comfort; encourage; foster; incite; embolden; flatter; pat sb on the back; poke; pull for; slap sb on

the back; urge;
鼓勵的話 words of encouragement;
鼓勵競爭 encourage competition;
[鼓盆而歌] sing with a beating on a basin;
[鼓起] bag; balloon; blowup; call up; gather; muster up; pluck up; puff; rally; swell; take heart;
鼓起勇氣 get up one's courage; look up; muster up one's courage; nerve oneself; pluck up one's courage; screw up one's courage;
[鼓瑟吹笙] play flutes and blow pipe instruments;
[鼓舌] wag one's tongue;
鼓舌如簧 talk glibly; wag one's tongue with honeyed words;
鼓舌搖唇 flatter; gossip; spread rumours;
[鼓聲] drumbeat; tum;
鼓聲大作 the loud beating of the drum;
鼓聲震地 drums roll as though the earth is rending;
[鼓手] drummer;
[鼓舞] brace; embolden; fortify; gladen; hearten; impulse; infuse; inspire; kindle; nerve; support; sustain;
鼓舞斗志 inspire the fighting spirit;
鼓舞人心 gladden the people's hearts; heartening; inspiring; set the hearts of the poeple aflame;
鼓舞士氣 boost morale; enhance troop morale;
鼓舞作用 influence;
歡欣鼓舞 be filled with exultation; be gladdened; buck up; dance with pleasure; elated and inspired; exult; gladden and inspire; jubilant over; jump for joy;
[鼓樂] music accompnaied by drumbeats;
鼓樂大作 strike up the drums and trumpets;
鼓樂齊鳴，萬眾歡騰 the cheers of the jubilant crowds mingled with crescendos of music;
鼓樂喧天 a great din of drums and pipes; loud music fills the air;
[鼓噪] boil in hurly-burly; bustle in hurly-burly; clamour; make a great to-do; make an uproar; pitch in and raise an uproar; raise a hubbub; rise in a hubbub;
鼓噪而進 charge ahead shouting and beating drums;
鼓噪四起 rise in a hubbub; rise up with a great clamour;
[鼓掌] applaud; clap one's hands; handclap;
鼓掌喝彩 applaud with the hands; clap the hands in applause; ovation;
鼓掌歡呼 clap one's hands and cheer; rejoice over;
鼓掌通過 approval by acclamation;
慢吞吞的鼓掌 slow applause;
起立鼓掌 standing ovation;
熱烈鼓掌 applaud wildly; clap enthusiastically; clap with all one's might;

打鼓 (1) beat a drum; (2) feel uncertain;
大鼓 bass drum;
電子鼓 drum machine;
定音鼓 timpani;
耳鼓 eardrum; tympanic membrane;
更鼓 night watchman's drum;
花鼓 flower-drum;
擊鼓 beat a drum;
鈴鼓 tambourine;
鑼鼓 gong and drum;
石鼓 drum-shaped stone blocks;
手鼓 small drum similar to the tambourine;
銅鼓 bronze drum;
小鼓 side drum; snare drum;
腰鼓 (1) waist drum; (2) folk dance with waist drums;
戰鼓 battle drum; war drum;

gu

【嘏】 blessing; felicity; happiness; prosperity;

gu

【穀】 (1) cereals; corns; grains; (2) favourable; good; happy; lucky; (3) alive;
[穀倉] barn; breadbasket; garner; grannary;
穀倉舞會 barn dance;
一個穀倉 a barn;
[穀場] yard for drying grains;
[穀旦] auspicious day;
[穀道] (1) anus; (2) attain immortality by stop eating grains;
[穀賤傷農] cheap grain harms the peasants; low grain price hurts the farmers; low prices for grain hurt the peasants;
[穀類] cereal; grain and corn;

穀類食物 cereal;
穀類作物 cereal;
~ 春播穀類作物 spring sown cereal;
~ 秋播穀類作物 autumn sown cereal;
[穀日] the eighth day of the first moon in the lunar calendar;
[穀物] cereal; grain;
穀物交易市場 corn exchange;
膨化穀物 puffed cereals;
整粒穀物 whole grain cereal;
主要穀物 staple cereal;
[穀雨] Grain Rain (6th solar term);
[穀子] millets;

gu
【梏】 chopped pieces of wood;

gu
【蓇】 follicle;

gu
【轂】 hub of a wheel;
[轂襯] hub plate;
[轂擊肩摩] hubs hit hubs and shoulders rub shoulders; with jamming vehicles and pedestrians;
輪轂 hub;

gu
【臌】 expand; swell; swollen;
[臌脹] (1) expand; swell; (2) dropsy; edema;
水臌 ascites;

gu
【瞽】 (1) blind; (2) blind musicians; (3) having no discerning ability; lacking power of judgment;
[瞽議] groundless statements; wild talks;

gu
【鵠】 target;

gu
【盬】 (1) salt pit; (2) incompact; (3) leisure; (4) drink by sucking;

gu
【鶻】 birds of prey;
[鶻軍] swift army;
[鶻鵃] kind of bird mentioned in ancient books;

gu
【蠱】 legendary venomous insect;
[蠱惑] enchant; poison and bewitch;
蠱惑人心 agitate people by demagogy; befog the minds of the people; be guile poeple out of the right way; confuse and poison people's minds; confuse public opinion; hoodwink people with demagogy; instil poisonous suspicions into men's minds; resort to demagogy; spread false doctrines to undermine the people's morale; undermine popular morale by spreading unfounded rumours;

gu⁴

gu
【估】 sell used clothing;
[估衣] secondhand clothes;
估衣鋪 second-hand clothes store;

gu
【固】 (1) firm; solid; (2) firmly; resolutely; (3) consolidate; strengthen; (4) originally; (5) no doubt;
[固定] (1) fixed; regular; (2) fasten; fix; make fast; mount; regularize; (3) fix; fixation; fixing;
固定成本 fixed cost;
固定程序 fixed programme; fixed routine;
固定詞組 fixed word group; set phrases;
固定搭配 fixed collocation;
固定的 immobile;
固定發放比率 constant payout ratio;
固定費用 constant expenses;
固定工資 regular pay;
固定劑 fixative;
~ 丙烯固定劑 acrylic fixative;
~ 顏色固定劑 colour fixative;
固定價格 set price;
固定收入 fixed income; regular income;
固定預算 fixed budget;
固定職業 permanent occupation;
固定資產 capital assets; fixed assets; permanent assets;
~ 固定資產規模 sacle of fixed assets;
~ 固定資產投資 investment of fixed assets;
固定資金 fixed capital;
飛砂固定 dane fixation;
剛性固定 rigid fixing;
管腳固定 bayonet fixing;
化學固定 chemical fixation;
頻率固定 frequency fixing;

G

沙丘固定 sand dune fixation;
用爪固定 snap fixing;

[固化] cure; curing; solidification; solidify;
固化處理 curing process;
固化點 solidification point;
固化劑 curing agent; firming agent;
固化酒精 solidified alcohol;
固化能力 ability to cure;
固化油 solidified oil;
固化作用 solidification;
潤滑劑固化 grease solidification;
真空固化 vacuum solidification;

[固件] firmware;

[固然] indeed; it is true; of course; really;

[固若金湯] as strong as iron; secure against assult; impregnable; strongly fortified;

[固守] defend tenaciously;
固守成規 get into a rut; stick to old rules;
固守城池 tenaciously defend the city wall and moat;
固守陣地 tenaciously defend one's position;

[固體] solid; solid body;
固體火箭 solid rocket;
固體力學 solid mechanics;
固體物 solid;
~黑液固體物 black liquor solid;
充氣固體 aerated solids;
結晶固體 crystalline solid;
溶解固體 dissolved solid;

[固有] inherent; innate; intrinsic;
固有形容詞 inherent adjective;
固有種 autochthonous species;

[固執] (1) obstinate; stiff neck; stubborn; (2) cling to; persist in;
固執的 adamant;
固執己見 abide by one's opinion; adhere stubbornly to one's own ideas; have a will of one's own; hold stubbornly to one's own viewpoint; nail one's colours to the mast; stick to one's guns; stick to one's own view; stubbornly adhere to one's views;
固執如驢 as stubborn as mules;
生性固執 pertinacious; stubborn by nature;
越老越固執 grow more obstinate as one grows older;
擇善固執 choose what is good and hold fast to it;

安固 fix; make fast;
加固 consolidate; reinforce;
堅固 firm; solid; strong;
牢固 fast; firm; secure;
凝固 coagulate; congeal; solidify;
強固 consolidated; strong;
韌固 firm and strong;
穩固 firm; stable;

gu

【故】 (1) happening; incident; (2) cause; reason; (3) intentionally; on purpose; (4) consequently; for this reason; hence; therefore; (5) former; old; (6) acquaintance; friend; (7) die;

[故步自封] a standpatter and be proud of it; be satisfied with old practices; complacent and conservative; confine oneself to the old method; content with staying where one is; do not want to move a step forward; hold fast to one's established ideas; limit one's own progress; remain where one is; rest complacently on one's laurels; self-satisfaction and conservatism; self-satisfied with being a stick-in-the-mud; stand still and cease to make progress; stand still and refuse to make progress; ultraconservative and self-satisfied; unwilling to move forward; without desire to advance further;

[故此] therefore;

[故地] old haunt;
故地重遊 revisit the old haunt;

[故都] former capital; onetime capital;

[故宮] Imperial Palace;

[故技] old tactics; old tricks;
故技重演 play the same old trick; up to one's old tricks;
重施故技 play the same old trick; repeat a stock trick;

[故舊] old friends and acquaintances;
故舊不棄 not to neglect an old acquaintance; not to throw away an old friend;

[故居] former home; former residence;
故居新址 one's old homestead and new site;
名人故居 former residence of a famous person;

G

[故里] home village; native place;
重返故里 return to one's native place;
童年故里 scenes of one's childhood;

[故去] die; pass away;
安然故去 die at peace;
突然故去 leave this world suddenly;
在家中故去 breathe one's last at home;

[故人] (1) old friend; (2) ex-husband; (3) ex-wife;
故人入罪 falsely accuse sb of a crime; purposely implicate sb in crime;
已作故人 no more; have passed away; one has gone the way of all flesh;

[故世] die; pass away;

[故事] (1) old practice; routine; (2) story; tale; (3) plot;
故事梗概 synopsis;
故事片 feature film; story film;
故事情節 plot of the story; storyline;
故事書 storybook;
愛情故事 love story;
背景故事 back story;
編造故事 spin a story; spin a tale; spin a yarn; trump up a story;
動物故事 animal story;
封面故事 cover story;
奉行故事 act in accordance with practices and rules; follow established practice mechanically; follow the old routine;
鬼故事 ghost story;
荒唐故事 cock-and-bull stories; old wives' tales;
黃色故事 dirty story;
講故事 spin a yarn; tell stories;
~講故事的人 storyteller;
恐怖故事 hair-raising story; spooky story;
令人傷心的故事 tale of woe;
民間故事 folk tale;
傷感故事 sob story;
神話故事 fairy tale;
下流故事 off-colour story;
虛應故事 do sth as a mere matter of form; do sth for form's sake; do sth in a perfunctory manner; do sth perfunctorily as a mere matter of routine; do the routine things superficially and have done with it; follow a mere routine; fulfill parts of one's daily routine; go through the motions; make a virute of necessity; pass the bottle of smoke; perform a duty perfunctorily;
懸疑兇殺故事 whodunit;
一個故事 a story;
一篇故事 a story;
一則故事 a narrative; a story;
真實故事 true story;

[故態] old manners;
故態復萌 go back to one's old way of doing things; old habits come back again; play one's old tricks again; relapse into error; resume one's former manner; resume to one's old manners; return to one's old habits; return to one's old vices; revert to one's old way of life; the old vice has come upon one again;

[故土] homeland; native land;
故土難移 it is hard to go away from one's native soil; it is hard to leave one's homeland;

[故鄉] birthland; birthplace; hometown; native place;
第二故鄉 second home;
思念故鄉 miss one's native shore;
遠離故鄉 far from the land of one's birth;

[故意] by design; by intention; deliberately; go out of one's way; intentionally of set purpose; on purpose; willfully;
故意犯罪 intentional offense;
故意侵權行為 intentional tort;
故意刁難 deliberately make things difficult for others; deliberately place obstacles;
故意挑釁 trail one's coat;
故意拖延 drag one's feet; give sb the runaround;

[故障] accident; blunder; breakdown; bug; conk; defect; do not work; do not work properly; failure; fault; hitch; inaction; ineffective; malfunction; out of gear; out of order; sth wrong; stoppage; trouble;
故障按鈕 failure button;
故障率 fault frequency rate;
閉塞機故障 block instrument failure;
操作故障 operating trouble;
出故障 go out of order; malfunctioning;
~發動機出故障 develop engine trouble;
導接線故障 bond failure;
短路故障 short trouble;
機械故障 accident to the machinery;

技術故障 technical hitch;
排除故障 clear away obstacles;
線路故障 wiring troubles;
小故障 glitch;

[故轍] old track;
復蹈故轍 follow in the oldtrack; return to the old rut;
仍蹈故轍 follow in the old track; get into a rut; return to the old rut;
一改故轍 change one's customary direction thoroughly; change thoroughly one's usual way; make a new start courageously; mend one's ways; turn over a new leaf;

[故紙堆] a heap of musty old books or papers;
鑽故紙堆 bury oneself in outdated writings; delve into musty old books;

變故 an unforeseen event; misfortune;
病故 die of an illness;
大故 die;
曷故 what for; why;
借故 find an excuse for; make a pretext for; on the pretext of;
藉故 find an excuse;
如故 (1) as before; as usual; (2) like old friends;
身故 die;
世故 art of dealing with people; ways of the world;
事故 accident; mishap;
托故 give a pretext; make an excuse;
亡故 decease; die; pass away;
無故 for no reason; without cause or reason;
物故 die; pass away;
細故 trivial matter; trifle;
緣故 cause; reason;
掌故 anecdotes;

gu

【梏】 (1) hand-shackle; handcuffs; manacles; (2) insult; play joke on;

[梏亡] be fettered in mind by greed;

gu

【雇】 employ; hire;

gu

【痼】 chronic disease;

[痼疾] chronic illness; intractable disease; obstinate illness;

[痼癖] inveterate weakness;

[痼習] inveterate habit;

沉痼 deep-rooted bad habit; serious and protracted illness;
深痼 deep-rooted disease habit, prejudice, etc.;

gu

【僱】 employ; hire;

[僱船] hire a boat;

[僱工] (1) hire hands; hire labour; (2) hired labourer;

[僱傭] employ; hire;
僱傭文人 hire a scribbler;

[僱員] employee;
低級僱員 junior employee;
普通僱員 rank and file employees;
兼職僱員 part-time employee;
下級僱員 low-ranking employee;
政府僱員 government employees;

[僱主] employer;
無恥的僱主 unscrupulous employer;

解僱 discharge; fire; give sb the sack;

gu

【錮】 (1) run metal into cracks; (2) confine; keep in custody; (3) secure; sturdy;

[錮囚] occlusion;

禁錮 (1) debar from holding office; (2) keep in custody; put in prison; (3) confine; forcibly restrict;

gu

【顧】 (1) look at; turn round and look at; (2) attend to; take into consideration; (3) call on; visit; (4) a surname;

[顧及] attend to; give consideration to; take into account;

[顧忌] misgiving; qualm; scruple; stick;
無所顧忌 go all lengths; have no scruples; hesitate at no act; not to scruple to; stick at nothing; unscrupulously; without any scruple;

[顧客] client; clientele; customer; patient; punter; shopper;
顧客第一 customers first;
顧客姓名 customer name;
顧客盈門 do a land-office business;
殘障顧客 disabled patron;
年輕顧客 young clientele;
神秘顧客 mystery shopper;
招徠顧客 tout for business;
招攬顧客 solicit customers;

[顧慮] apprehension; misgiving; scruple; worry;
顧慮重重 be encumbered with personal concerns; full of worries; have no end of misgivings; have numerous scruples;
顧慮周詳 consider sth down to the minutest details; thoughtful about everything;
拋開顧慮 pay away one's scruples;
無所顧慮 free from all anxiety;
[顧盼] look around;
顧盼神飛 in one's eyes there is a look of quick intelligence and soft refinement;
顧盼生姿 look around charmingly;
顧盼自如 gaze round as one wishes; gaze round to one's heart's content;
顧盼自雄 as proud as a peacock; gaze round with great airs; look about complacently; look about in a haughty manner; preen oneself; struct about pleased with oneself;
[顧曲周郎] music connoisseur;
[顧問] adviser; consultant; counselor;
顧問團 advisory body;
顧問委員會 advisory committee;
顧問制 advisory system;
技術顧問 technical adviser;
投資顧問 investment counselor;
政治顧問 political adviser;
治療顧問 therapeutic counselor;
[顧惜] take good care of;
[顧主] client; customer; patron;

愛顧 take loving care of;
反顧 look back;
光顧 honour with; patronize;
後顧 (1) turn back; (2) look back; review;
環顧 look about; look round;
回顧 look back; review;
惠顧 patronize;
兼顧 take account of two or more things;
眷顧 regard with tenderness; take good care of;
看顧 look after; nurse; take care of;
四顧 look around;
瞻顧 look ahead and behind;
照顧 (1) attend to; give consideration to; (2) attend to; care for; look after; (3) patronize;
祇顧 be absorbed in; be engrossed in;
主顧 client; customer;

gua¹
gua

【瓜】 gourd; melon;
[瓜菜] melon and vegetable;
砍瓜切菜 cut melons and cabbages — an easy job;
[瓜蒂] melon and stem;
甘瓜苦蒂 nothing is perfect; the melon is sweet but the stalk is bitter;
瓜熟蒂落 at the right time everything comes easy; fruits fall off when ripe; things will happen when conditions are ripe; when a melon is ripe it falls off its stem — things will be easily settled when conditions are ripe; when the melon is ripe it naturally falls — at the right time everything comes easy; when the pear is ripe, it falls;
[瓜分] carve up; divide up; partition;
瓜分豆剖 divide it like a melon; split it into two like a bean;
瓜分世界 carve up the world; divide up the world;
豆剖瓜分 divide up sth just as one separates pea-pods;
瓜剖豆分 divide up sth as one cuts melons into slices or separate peapods; melon cutting;
[瓜葛] association; connection; have sth to do with sb; implication;
了無瓜葛 have no bearing on; have nothing to do with;
牽絲瓜葛 be interrelated and dependent upon one another;
有瓜葛 (1) have relations; (2) have complications;
[瓜李] melon and plum;
瓜李之嫌 the suspicion of being in the melon field and under the plum tree;
浮瓜沉李 floating melons and plums submerged in water — pursue summer joys;
[瓜皮帽] skullcap;
[瓜田] (1) melon patch; (2) a surname;
瓜田不納履 not to bend to tie shoes on a melon patch — not to compromise one's honour; not to do up one's shoe in a pumpkin field — to avoid suspicions;
瓜田不納履，李下不整冠 do not put on your shoe in a melon patch; dont

adjust your cap under a plum tree — don't do anything to arouse suspicion; don't tidy up your shoes in a melon patch, neither adjust your hat under a plum tree — to avoid being suspected;
瓜田裏抓刺蝟 catching a porcupine in a bramble patch — a thorny business;
瓜田李下 be found in a suspicious position; liable to lay oneself open to suspicion;
李下瓜田 in a melon patch or under a plum tree; liable to get into trouble; liable to lay oneself open to suspicion;

[瓜子] melon seed;
瓜子敬客——點兒心意 entertain one's guests with melon seeds — small hospitality; small but thoughtful gift;
一把瓜子 a handful of melon seeds;
用牙剥瓜子 crack melon-seeds with one's teeth;

菜瓜 snake melon;
打瓜 a kind of water melon;
地瓜 (1) yam bean; (2) sweet potato;
冬瓜 wax gourd; white gourd;
胡瓜 cucumber;
黃瓜 cucumber;
金瓜 (1) a kind of pumpkin; (2) ancient weapon;
苦瓜 balsom pear;
木瓜 (1) Chinese flowering quince; (2) papaya;
南瓜 cushaw; pumpkin;
匏瓜 a kind of gourd;
傻瓜 block-head; fool; simpleton;
蛇瓜 snake gourd;
絲瓜 dishcloth gourd; towel gourd;
笋瓜 winter squash;
糖瓜 malt sugar candy;
甜瓜 melon; muskmelon;
倭瓜 cushaw; pumpkin;
西瓜 water melon;
香瓜 melon; muskmelon;
油瓜 large-fruited hodgsonia;
越瓜 snake melon;

gua
【刮】 (1) scrape; (2) smear with; (3) extort; fleece; plunder; (4) blow; (5) shave;
[刮除] strike off;
[刮刀] slicker;
推皮刮刀 hand slicker;
小圓刮刀 bead slicker;
[刮掉] scrape;
[刮風] have a storm;
[刮痕] scratch; shear marks;
[刮臉] shave; shave the face;
刮臉刀 safety razor;
刮臉皮 rub the forefinger against one's own cheek;
[刮皮] beam;
刮皮工人 beamer;
[刮水器] windscreen wiper; windshield wiper; wiper;
手動刮水器 hand wiper;
雙刷刮水器 tandem;
自動開關刮水器 self-parking wiper;
[刮削] scrap;
刮削器 scrapper;

頂刮刮 excellent; first-rate;
搜刮 extort; loot; plunder;

gua
【括】 (1) embrace; include; (2) search for; seek; (3) restrain; tie;

gua
【栝】 same as 檜, the juniper;

gua
【适】 fast; quick; swift;

gua
【筈】 the end of an arrow;

gua
【聒】 clamorous; uproarious;
[聒耳] din in sb's ears; offensive to the ear;
多言聒耳 make a din in one's ears;
笙簫聒耳 the sound of songs and every sort of music fill the ears without ceasing;
[聒聒] clamorous; noisy; uproarious;
聒聒叫 excellent; very good; wonderful;
[聒擾] make a din;
[聒絮] keep talking noisily;
[聒噪] noisy; uproarious;

gua
【颳】 wind blowing;
[颳大風] gale;

gua
【蝸】 snail;
[蝸居] my humble house;
[蝸廬] cottage; simple dwelling;
[蝸牛] snail;

gua

【鴰】 crow;

gua³

gua

【寡】 (1) few; scant; (2) tasteless; (3) widowed;

［寡不敵眾］ be hopelessly outnumbered; be outnumbered; few cannot resist many; fight against hopeless odds; the few are no match for the many;

［寡淡］ boring; dull; insipid;

［寡二少雙］ matchless; second to none; without a peer;

［寡婦］ widow;

寡婦的心—三心二意 a widow's heart – of two minds;

寡婦門前是非多 there are many scandals laid before a widow's door – a widow is liable to lay herself open to suspicion;

寡婦養子—醜事 a widow giving birth to a baby – a shameful act;

寡婦再嫁 remarry after one's husband's death;

網絡寡婦 cyberwidow;

［寡鵠孤鸞］ a lone dove or a solitary bird—a widow;

［寡陋孤聞］ ignorant and ill-informed;

［寡欲］ have few desires;

寡欲清心 have few desires and cleanse the heart;

廉靜寡欲 pure and have few desires – pure and modest;

多寡 amount; number;

孤寡 orphans and widows;

gua⁴

gua

【卦】 (1) divine; divination; (2) one of the Eight Diagrams of the *Book of Changes*;

八卦 (1) the Eight Trigrams; (2) meddlesome;

變卦 back out; go back on one's word;

卜卦 divine by the Eight Trigrams;

打卦 tell fortune according to the divinatory symbols;

算卦 practise divination;

占卦 fortune telling by means of the Eight Trigrams;

gua

【掛】 (1) hang; put up; (2) get caught; hitch; (3) righ off; (4) call up; put sb through to; (5) be concerned about; (6) be coated with; be covered with; (7) register;

［掛錶］ fob watch; pocket watch;

［掛彩］ (1) decorate for festive occasions; decorate with coloured silk festoons; (2) be wounded in action;

［掛車］ hand car; trailer;

［掛齒］ mention;

不足掛齒 beneath notice; not worth mentioning; not worthy of mention; nothing to speak of; of no importance;

何足掛齒 don't mention it; not worth mentioning;

［掛燈結彩］ decorate with lanterns and coloured hangings; hang up lamps and festoon drapes;

［掛冠］ hang one's hat;

掛冠而去 hang one's hat on a rafter and leave – take French leave;

掛冠封印 hang up the cap and close up the seal – give up office and leave the place; resign and go home;

掛冠歸里 bow out; go to grass; hang one's cap and return to one's own district; hang up one's axe; retire;

［掛號］ (1) register; (2) send by registered mail; (3) establish a criminal record;

掛號信 registered letter;

掛號員 registrar;

排隊掛號 stand in the queue to register;

［掛曆］ wall calendar;

［掛慮］ anxious about; have sth on one's mind; worry about;

［掛麵］ dried noodles;

［掛名］ nominal; only in name; titular;

掛名差事 sinecure;

掛名夫妻 husband and wife in name only – a false couple;

［掛念］ lie at sb's heart; miss; worry about sb who is absent;

［掛拍］ give up an athlete's life; hang up one's racket; retire from professional athletics;

［掛牌］ (1) hang out one's shingle; (2) put up a tag;

G

掛牌公司 registered company;
掛牌開業 hang out one's shingle; put up one's plate in; put up one's shingle;
掛牌證券 quoted securities;

[掛屏] panel;
立體掛屏 relief panel;

[掛帥] assume command; assume leadership; in command;
鈔票掛帥 money in command;
利潤掛帥 profit in command;
政治掛帥 politics in command;

[掛心] anxious for; be concerned about; keep in mind;

[掛靴] retire from a football team;

[掛衣] coat; coating;
掛衣袋 garment bag;
掛衣架 coat rack;

[掛鐘] wall clock;

壁掛 wall hanging;
倒掛 hang upside down;
記掛 be concerned about; miss;
樹掛 frost; rime;
懸掛 fly; hang;
張掛 hang up;

gua
【罣】 (1) hindrance; obstruction; (2) sieve; (3) be concerned; be worried;

[罣礙] worries and concerns;
無罣無礙 no worry nor care;

gua
【絓】 hindered; obstructed;

gua
【詿】 (1) error; mistake; (2) cheat; deceive;

gua
【褂】 gown; jacket; overcoat; robe;

[褂子] short gown;

大褂 unlined long gown;
汗褂 undershirt;
馬褂 mandarin jacket;
小褂 shirt;

guai¹
guai
【乖】 (1) well-behaved; (2) alert; clever; shrewd;

[乖乖] (1) good; lovely; well-behaved; (2) little dear; darling; poppet; (3) good gracious;
乖乖地 tamely;
乖乖兒 goody-goody;
小乖乖 honey-bunny;

[乖蹇] unlucky;
命蹇時乖 ill-fated;
時乖運蹇 be born under an evil star; down on one's luck; have the hand of fate against one; ill fortune; luck is against one; one's luck has run out of its course; run into back luck; the time and fates are against one; unkind fate;

[乖覺] alert; nimble;

[乖戾] crusty; disagreeable; perverse; unnatural;
乖戾之氣 epidemic pathogenic factors;
語多乖戾 use absurd and offensive language;

[乖謬] abnormal; absurd;

[乖癖] distortion; eccentric; odd;

[乖僻] eccentric; odd;
乖僻的行為 eccentric behaviour;
乖僻邪謬 disagreeable; eccentric; odd;
行為乖僻 behave oddly;

[乖巧] (1) clever; (2) cute; lovely;

[乖張] eccentric and unreasonable;

賣乖 show off one's cleverness;

guai³
guai
【拐】 (1) turn; limp; (2) cane; staff for an old person; (3) crosier; crutch; walking stick; (4) decoy; kidnap; make off with; swindle; (5) abduct; kidnap;

[拐點] point of inflection;

[拐角] corner; turning;

[拐賣] abduct and traffic;
拐賣婦女 abduct and traffic women;
拐賣人口 kidnap and sell people;

[拐騙] (1) swindle; (2) abduct;
拐騙婦女 carry off women by fraud;
拐騙錢財 swindle money;
東拐西騙 swindle on all sides;
偷訛拐騙 steal, swindle and blackmail;

[拐彎] (1) turn; turn a corner; (2) pursue a new course; turn round; (3) corner; turning;
拐彎處 turning;
拐彎抹角 beat about the bush; by indirection; evasive; in a round-about

way; talk in a roundabout way; turn a corner here and there;
慢慢拐彎 go around a corner slowly;
曲裏拐彎 tortuous; winding; zigzag;
[拐杖] crutch; old person's staff;
[拐子] (1) cripple; lame person; (2) abductor;
拐子走路—左右搖擺 a cripple walking – swaying from side to side; vacillating;

向右拐 make a right turn;
向左拐 make a left turn;
誘拐 abduct;

guai⁴

guai

【夬】 one of the Eight Diagrams in the *Book of Changes*;

guai

【怪】 (1) bewildering; odd; queer; strange; (2) find sth strange; wonder at; (3) quite; rather; (4) demon; evil being; monster; (5) blame;
[怪誕] absurd; strange; weird;
怪誕不經 crazy; fantastic; droll; supernatural and unreasonable; weird and uncanny;
怪誕行為 antics;
[怪話] complaints; cynical remarks; grumbles;
好說怪話 often speak with bitter sarcasm;
[怪傑] geek;
技術怪傑 techno-geek;
[怪裏怪氣] comical; eccentric; have a screw loose; peculiar; perfect sight; queer;
[怪僻] crankery; eccentric; kink;
小怪僻 foible;
異常怪僻 highly peculiar;
[怪人] aberrant; codger; dweeb; eccentric; loon; odd ball; odd fish; oddity; peculiar person; queer bird; queer fish; quite a character; sphinx; strange fish; varietist monster; wacko; weirdo; whacko;
真是個怪人 what a queer bird;
[怪事] oddity; queer go; rum go; wonder;
[怪獸] monster;
雙頭怪獸 two-headed monster;
[怪胎] genetic freak; reak;
[怪物] (1) boogeyman; freak; monster; (2) eccentric person;
[怪相] grimace;
做怪相 draw faces; make faces; pull faces;
[怪異] monstrous; strange; unusual;

嗔怪 blame; rebuke;
錯怪 blame sb wrongly;
古怪 eccentric; odd; queer;
詭怪 odd; strange;
鬼怪 ghosts and monsters;
駭怪 astonished; shocked;
見怪 mind; take offence;
精怪 evil spirits;
魔怪 demons and monsters; fiends;
難怪 can hardly blame sb for; no wonder;
奇怪 odd; queer; strange;
無怪 no wonder; not to be wondered at;
妖怪 bogy; demon; goblin; monster;
有點怪 a bit off;
珍怪 strange happenings;
責怪 blame; fix the responsibility on;
作怪 do mischief; make trouble; play tricks;

guan¹

guan

【官】 (1) government official; officer; officeholder; (2) government-owned; official; public; (3) organ; (4) a surname;
[官兵] officers and men;
官兵團結 unity between officers and men;
官兵一致 unity between officers and men;
[官場] official circles; officialdom;
官場得意 successful in one's official career;
官場積習 tradition of official circles;
[官倒] bureaucratic profiteers; bureaucratic racketeering; official black-marketing; official profiteer; official racketeers; official speculation;
[官邸] official mansion; official residence;
[官方] authority; by the government; of the government; official;
官方牌價 official market quotation;
官方人士 official circles; official quarters;
官方消息 news coming from an official source; news from government sources; official sources;
官方語言 official language;
半官方 semi-official;
~半官方關係 semi-official relation;
非官方 unofficial;
~非官方會晤 unofficial meeting;

G

~非官方消息 information from unofficial sources;

［官房主義］ cameralism;

［官府］ (1) local authorities; (2) feudal officials;

［官話］ official dialect; officialese;

［官價］ official price; official rate;

［官階］ official ranks;

［官吏］ government officials;

濫官污吏 covetous and corrupt officers;

貪官污吏 corrupt officials; rapacious officials and corrupt functionaries; venal officials;

［官僚］ bureaucrats;

官僚政府 bureaucratic government;

官僚主義 bureaucracy; bureaucratism;

技術官僚 technocrat;

［官民］ officials and people;

諂官欺民 curry favour with the officials and oppress the people;

官逼民反 misgovernment makes the people rebel; oppressive government drives the people to rebellion; tyrants make rebels;

官出於民，民出於土 the officials depend on the people, and the people depend on the land;

賣官害民 sell offices and injure the people;

［官能］ function; sense;

官能團 functional group;

［官氣］ bureaucratic airs; official airs;

官氣十足 be puffed up with bureaucratic airs;

［官腔］ bureaucratic tones; official jargons;

打官腔 assume bureaucratic airs; speak in a bureaucratic tone; speak with official jargon; stall with official jargon; talk like a bureaucrat;

［官商］ officials and merchants;

官商作風 style of bureaucratic traders;

官督商辦 government-supervised and merchant-managed;

［官師］ a surname;

［官司］ law suit;

打筆墨官司 engage in a polemic with sb; paper polemics; polemics on paper;

打官司 engage in a lawsuit; file a suit against sb; go to court; go to law; litigation; squabble;

［官銜］ official title;

［官員］ officer; official;

高級官員 top-level official;

海關緝私官員 customs preventive officer;

任命官員 elect officers;

稅務官員 revenue officer;

選舉官員 elect officers;

政府官員 government official;

中層官員 middle-ranking official;

駐外官員 outposted officer;

［官職］ government posts; official positions;

官卑職小 petty official;

官復原職 be reinstated; be restored to one's former rank;

一官半職 official post; some official appointment;

［官制］ bureaucratic establishment;

罷官 dismiss from office;

貶官 demote an official;

大官 high-ranking official;

法官 judge; justice;

感官 sense organ; sensory organ;

高官 high official;

軍官 officer;

考官 official in charge of examination;

器官 organ;

清官 honest and upright official;

史官 historiographer; official historian;

貪官 corrupt official;

尉官 junior officer;

文官 civil official;

五官 (1) five sense organs (ears, eyes, lips, nose and tongue); (2) facial feature;

武官 (1) military officer; (2) military attaché;

校官 field grade officer; field officer;

長官 senior officer;

職官 officials;

做官 secure an official position;

guan

【冠】 (1) hat; (2) corona; crown; (3) comb; crest;

［冠層］ canopy;

樹冠層 crown canopy;

下冠層 lower canopy;

［冠蓋］ officials' caps and carriages;

冠蓋相望 caps and carriages to be seen on both sides — a gathering of dignitaries;

［冠冕］ official hat; royal crown;

冠冕堂皇 fine; have a bold and dignified bearing; high-flown; high-sounding;

G

of noble bearing; ostentatious and pretentious;
冠冕堂皇，連篇廢話 high-sounding rubbish;
小冠冕 coronet;
[冠心病] coronary disease; coronary heart disease;
急性冠心病 acute coronary disease;

鳳冠 phoenix coronet;
根冠 root cap;
桂冠 laurel;
花冠 corolla;
皇冠 imperial crown;
雞冠 cockscomb;
極冠 polar cap;
林冠 polar cap;
肉冠 comb;
樹冠 crown of a tree;
王冠 imperial crown; royal crown;
衣冠 dress; hat and clothes;
羽冠 crest of a bird;

guan
【矜】 widower;

guan
【倌】 (1) assistant in a wineshop; (2) euphemism for a prostitute; (3) groom;

馬倌 groom;
牛倌 cowherd;
堂倌 waiter;
羊倌 shepherd;
豬倌 swineherd;

guan
【莞】 scirpus lacustris, a kind of aquatic herb;

guan
【棺】 box; coffin;
[棺材] box; burial case; casket; coffin;
棺材店裏咬牙—恨人不死 gritting one's teeth in a coffin shop – laying a curse upon all who are not dying;
棺材架 bier;
棺材裏的生意—賺死人的錢 do business in a coffin – making money out of the dead; try to make money by all possible means;
棺材裏伸手—死要錢 greedy for money; money-grabber; stretch out one's hand from a coffin – after sb's blood;
棺材裏伸頭—死不要臉 dead to all feelings of shame; poke out one's head out of a coffin – not to lose one's face even in death;
棺材上畫老虎—嚇死人 be frightened to death; paint a tiger on a coffin – frighten the dead;
棺材頭上放砲—嚇死人 be frightened to death; explode firecrackers on a coffin – frighten the dead;
活棺材 living tomb;
進棺材 die; kick the bucket;
[棺牀] coffin platform;
石棺牀 coffin platform;
[棺木] coffin;

guan
【綸】 ancient cap;
[綸巾] black silk ribbon scarf; silk head dress resembling a ridged roof;

guan
【瘝】 ailing; ill; sick;

guan
【關】 (1) close; shut; (2) lock up; shut in; (3) turn off; (4) pass; (5) custom house; (6) close down; (7) barrier; critical juncture; (8) concern; involve; (9) a surname;
[關愛] love for others; loving care; nurturance;
[關隘] gate; pass; slip;
闖關過隘 break through rank after rank of the enemy's defence lines;
斬關奪隘 capture many strategic points; take pass after pass;
[關板] close down; go bankrupt;
[關閉] (1) close; closedown; closing; closure; cut off; deactivate; gag; paralyse; shut; shut off; (2) lock up; shut in;
關閉工廠 factory closure; shut down a factory;
關閉門窗 close the doors and windows;
強制關閉 forced shutdown;
自動關閉 automatic closing; self closing;
[關燈] turn off the light;
[關掉] breaking; switching;
[關東] northeast of China; east of Shanhaiguan;
[關斷] cut off; shut off; turn off;
[關懷] nurturance; show loving care for; show solicitude for;

關懷備至 be deeply concerned with; give meticulour care to sb; show every concern for sb; show the utmost solicitude;
關懷病人 attentive to the sick;
關懷青年一代 care for the younger generation;
深切關懷 be deeply concerned about; show great concern about;

[關鍵] crux; hinge; key; linchpin; lynchpin; name of the game;
關鍵詞 keyword;
~ 關鍵詞檢索 keyword search;
關鍵期 critical period;
關鍵人物 key figure; linchpin; lynchpin;
關鍵時刻 critical moment; when the chips are down;
~ 在關鍵時刻 at the crucial moment;
關鍵問題 the crux of the matter; the key to the question;
問題的關鍵 the crux of the matter;

[關節] articulus; joint; juncture; knuckle;
關節臂 articulated arm;
關節病 arthropathy; arthrosis; articular disease;
~ 關節病理學 arthropathology;
~ 開放性關節病 open joint;
~ 梅毒性關節病 syphilitic arthropathy;
~ 神經病性關節病 neuropathic arthropathy;
~ 神經性關節病 neuroarthropathy;
~ 神經源性關節病 neurogenic arthropathy;
~ 炎性關節病 inflammatory arthropathy;
~ 銀屑病性關節病 psoriatic arthropathy;
關節穿刺術 arthrocentesis;
關節發育不良 arthrodysplasia;
關節發育不全 arthrodysplasia;
關節風濕病 articular rheumatism;
~ 急性關節風濕病 acute articular rheumatism;
~ 慢性關節風濕病 chronic articular rheumatism;
關節骨折 joint fracture;
關節固定術 arthrodesis;
關節化膿 arthropyosis;
關節活動術 arthroclasia;
關節積水 hydrarthrosis;
~ 間歇性關節積水 intermittent hydrarthrosis;
關節結核 tuberculosis of joints;
關節強直 arthrodesis;
關節切除術 arthrectomy;
關節軟骨 arthrodial cartilage;
~ 關節軟骨瘤 joint chondroma;
~ 關節軟骨炎 arthrochondritis;
關節石 arthrolith;
關節水腫 arthredema;
關節鬆弛 arthrochalasis;
關節痛 arthralgia; joint pains; pain in a joint;
~ 鉛毒性關節痛 arthralgia saturnina;
關節痛風 articular gout;
關節脱位 abarticulation;
關節學 arthrology;
關節炎 arthritis; zygophophysis;
~ 變性關節炎 degenerative arthritis;
~ 病毒性關節炎 viral arthritis;
~ 腸病性關節炎 enteropathic arthritis;
~ 單關節炎 monarthritis;
~ 反應性關節炎 reactive arthritis;
~ 肥大性關節炎 hypertrophic arthritis;
~ 風濕關節炎 rheumarthritis;
~ 風濕性關節炎 rheumatic arthritis;
~ 急性風濕性關節炎 acute rheumatic arthritis;
~ 類風濕性關節炎 rheumatoid arthritis;
~ 骨性關節炎 osteoarthritis;
~ 股關節炎 coxarthrosis;
~ 化膿性關節炎 suppurative arthritis;
~ 急性關節炎 acute arthritis;
~ 肩關節炎 omarthritis;
~ 結核性關節炎 tuberculous arthritis;
~ 淋病性關節炎 gonorrheal arthritis;
~ 淋球菌性關節炎 gonococcal arthritis;
~ 梅毒性關節炎 syphilitic arthritis;
~ 霉菌性關節炎 mycotic arthritis;
~ 膿毒性關節炎 septic arthritis;
~ 皮膚病關節炎 dermatoarthritis;
~ 全身關節炎 panarthritis;
~ 少關節炎 oligoarthritis;
~ 神經病性關節炎 neuropathic arthritis;
~ 滲出性關節炎 exudative arthritis;
~ 手關節炎 cheirarthritis;
~ 痛風性關節炎 gouty arthritis;
~ 細菌性關節炎 bacterial arthritis;
~ 性病關節炎 venereal arthritis;
~ 銀屑病關節炎 psoriatic arthritis;
~ 幼年性關節炎 juvenile chronic arthritis;
~ 增生性關節炎 proliferative arthritis;
~ 增殖性關節炎 hypertrophic arthritis;
~ 肢關節炎 acroarthritis;
~ 足關節炎 podarthritis;
關節硬化 arthrosclerosis;

關節造影片 arthrogram;
關節造影術 arthrography;
關節腫大 arthrophyma;
暗通關節 bribe people in power; make secret deals with sb;
出血性關節 bleeder's joint; hemophilic joint;
打通關節 break through key links; bribe officials in charge;
單關節 simple joint;
動關節 abarticulation; abarthrosis;
假關節 false joint; pseudoarthrosis;
面關節 facet joint;

[關緊] fasten;

[關進] impound; shut; shut-in;

[關口] (1) gate; strategic position; (2) juncture;

[關聯] correlation; internection; relevance;
關聯詞 conjunctive word;
~關聯詞叢 referential cluster;
~關聯詞群 association group;
關聯的翻譯 correlative translation;
關聯連詞 correlative;
關聯序 related order;

[關龍] a surname;

[關門] (1) close; (2) refuse discussion or consideration; slam the door on sth; (3) behind closed doors;
關門閉戶 close the door;
關門打狗 beating a dog behind closed doors — unable to run away; bolt the door and beat the dog — block the enemy's retreat and then destroy him; shut the dogs up to beat them;
關門大吉 close down for good; close the door and stop doing business permanently; fold up; put up the shutters; wind up;
關門落閂 bolt the door; close the door and bolt it;
關門上鎖 close the door and lock it; lay the key under the door;
關門政策 closed-door policy;
關門捉賊 catch the thief by closing his escape routes;
你有關門計，我有跳牆法 you have your tricks, and I've got mine;
隨手關門 close the door behind one; shut the door after you;
賊去關門 lock the barn door after the horse is gone; shut the door after the horse is stolen;

[關卡] censorship; checkpoint; customs pass; screening;
一道關卡 a checkpoint;

[關切] be deeply concerned; show one's concern over;

[關山迢遞] be separated far apart; long journey;

[關上] close;
把燈關上 turn off the light;
把水龍頭關上 turn off the tap;
砰地關上 close with a bang;

[關税] customs; customs duties; duty; tariff;
關税壁壘 tariff barriers;
~非關税壁壘 non-tariff barriers;
關税及貿易總協定 General Agreement on Tariff and Trade (GATT);
關税減讓 concession of tariff;
關税配額 tariff quota;
關税區 tariff zone;
~單獨關税區 separate tariff zone;
關税水平 tariff level;
關税税則 customs tariff;
關税特惠 tariff preference;
關税政策 tariff policy;
關税自主 tariff autonomy;
保護關税 protective tariff;
~保護關税政策 policy of protective tariff;
~保護關税制度 protective tariff system;
保護性關税 protective tariff;
報復關税 retaliatory tariff;
財政關税 financial tariff; revenue tariff;
出口關税 export tariff;
單一關税 single tariff;
複合關税 compound duty; mixed duty;
複式關税 complex tariff;
國民關税 national tariff;
混合關税 compound duty; mixed duty;
歧視關税 discriminatory tariff;
~非歧視關税 nondiscriminatory tariff;
特惠關税 preferential duty; preferential tariff;
~普通特惠關税 general preferential duty;
~現存特惠關税 existing preferential tariff;
提高關税 raise the customs tariff;
協定關税 agreement tariff; conventional tariff;
修改關税 revise the tariff;
選擇關税 selective duty;
徵收關税 collection of duty;

自主關稅 autonomous tariffs; national tariff;

[關頭] juncture; moment;

存亡關頭 at a most critical moment;

緊急關頭 critical juncture;

緊要關頭 momentous crisis;

~到了緊要關頭 at the critical moment; come to the point; when it comes to the push;

~在緊要關頭 in the clutches; in the nick of time;

[關務] customs matters;

關務監理 customs supervisor;

~高級關務監理 senior customs supervisor;

~助理關務監理 assistant customs supervisor;

關務員 customs clerk; customs officer;

[關係] (1) connections; filiation; pull; ratio; regard; relevance; relation; tie; (2) bearing; impact; significance; (3) affect; concern; have a bearing on; have to do with; (5) credentials showing membership in an organization;

關係比較 relative comparative;

~關係比較級 relative comparative;

關係不和 rupture;

關係不清 ambiquity;

關係詞 rational word; relational word;

~零關係詞 zero relative;

關係從句 relative clause;

關係代詞 relative pronoun;

關係動詞 relational verb;

關係對立 relative opposition;

~關係對立詞 relational opposites;

關係副詞 relative adverb;

關係戶 relative family; special connections;

關係數據庫 relational database;

關係網 nectwork of connections; relationship network; well-connected network;

關係形容詞 relative adjective;

關係學 making connections for improper advantage; networking;

關係意義 relational meaning;

關係語法 relational grammar;

關係正常化 normalization of relations;

關係重大 count for much;

關係準則 maxim of relevance;

必然關係 inevitable connection;

~建立必然關係 build up an inevitable connection;

半官方關係 semi-official relation;

保持關係 keep up relation;

並列關係 coordination;

次序關係 ordering relation;

從屬關係 relation of dependence;

搭上關係 establish contact with; strike up a relationship with;

對等關係 equivalent relation;

反身關係 reflexive relation;

~非反身關係 inreflexive relation;

公共關係 public relations;

國際關係 international relations;

換喻關係 metonymy;

角色關係 role relationship;

拉關係 claim relationship with; cotton up to; exploit the connection; make use of connection; scrape acquaintance with sb; strike up an acquaintance with sb; try to establish a relationship with sb;

勞資關係 labour relations; labour-management relations;

類似關係 affinity;

鏈狀關係 chain relationship;

邏輯關係 logical relation;

沒關係 don't worry; forget it; it doesn't matter; it's all right; it's nothing; it's nothing serious; never mind; not at all; not in the least; skip it; that's all right;

~沒多大關係 it makes no odds;

目的語關係 target language relationship;

內包關係 inclusion;

親密關係 intimate terms;

~有親密關係 on intimate terms;

人際關係 personal relationships;

~人際關係網 social network;

~建立人際關係網 social networking;

三角關係 triangular relationship;

雙邊關係 bilateral relations;

特殊關係 special relationship;

託關係 pull strings;

脱離關係 sever relations;

外交關係 diplomatic relations;

相互關係 interrelation;

~營養相互關係 tropic interrelation;

性關係 sexual relationship;

~三角性關係 eternal triangle;

業務關係 business connections;

因果關係 causal relation;

友好關係 amicable relations; friendly

relations;
正常關係 normal relations;

[關小] turn down;
把收音機關小 turn down the radio;

[關心] be concerned about; be concerned for; be concerned with; be interested in; care about; care for; concern oneself about; concern oneself with; display deep concern for; display one's concern for; express great concern for; express one's concern for; feel concerned about; feel concerned for; give first place to; have a concern for; have a thought for; have sth at heart; have sth in one's heart; make over; make the most of; show concern for; show consideration for; show one's concern for; solicitous for; surround sb with love and care; take sth to one's heart; think of; thoughtful about;
關心疾苦 care about sb's troubles;
關心民瘼 look after the suffering of the people;
關心時事 take an interest in current affairs;
關心未來 thoughtful of the future;
不關心 be indifferent to; not concern oneself with;
毫不關心 apathetic; care nothing for; express no concern; glacial indifference; indifferent; let things go hang; nonchalant; not care a brass farthing; not care a button; not care a damn; not care a fart; not care a fuck; not care a monkey's fuck; not care a toss; not care a tuppence; not care two hoots; not give a brass farthing; not give a button; not give a damn; not give a fart; not give a fuck; not give a hoot; not give a monkey's fuck; not vie a toss; not give a tuppence; not give two hoots; take a casual attitude; totally indifferent; unconcerned;
互相關心 mutual consideration;
漠不關心 apathetic; care nothing for; express no concern; glacial indifference; indifference; indifferentism; indifferent; let things go hang; nonchalant; not care a brass farthing; not care a button; not care a damn; not care a fart; not care a fuck; not care a monkey's fuck; not care a toss; not care a tuppence; not care two hoots; not give a brass farthing; not give a button; not give a damn; not give a fart; not give a fuck; not give a hoot; not give a monkey's fuck; not vie a toss; not give a tuppence; not give two hoots; take a casual attitude; totally indifferent; unconcern; unconcerned;
事不關心 the affair does not concern me;

[關押] lock up; put behind bars; put in prison;

[關於] about; apropos of; as concerns; as far as sth goes; as far as sth is concerned; as for; as regards; as to; as touching; concerning; in connection with; in reference to; in regard to; with relation to; in respect to; in the matter of; on; on the subject of; regarding; relating to; relative to; respecting; when it comes to; with reference to; with regard to; with relation to; with respect to;

[關照] (1) keep an eye on; look after; (2) notify by word of mouth; tell;

[關注] follow with interest; pay close attention to; show solicitude for;
關注團體 interested party;
公共關注 public eye;
全力關注 undivided attention;

把關 (1) guard a pass; (2) check on strictly; gatekeep;
報關 declare sth at customs;
閉關 close the border;
邊關 frontier pass;
攻關 storm a strategic pass; tackle key problems;
過關 go through an ordeal; pass a barrier; pass a test; reach the required standard;
海關 customs;
機關 (1) mechanism; (2) body; office; organ; (3) intrigue; scheme;
交關 be interrelated;
結關 customs clearance;
開關 (1) switch; (2) valve;
難關 crisis; difficulty;
年關 end of the year;
雙關 have a double meaning;
無關 have nothing to do with;
相關 be interrelated;
攸關 concern;

有關 (1) have sth to do with; (2) concern; have a bearing on; with regard to;

guan

【觀】 (1) look at; observe; watch; (2) sight; view; (3) concept; outlook;

[觀測] observation; observe; view;
觀測機 observation aeroplane;
觀測氣象 make weather observations;
觀測器 observer;
大量觀測 mass observation;
累積觀測 cumulative observations;
偏流觀測 drift current observation;
偏心觀測 eccentric observation;
水流觀測 current observation;
子午觀測 meridian observation;

[觀察] examine; inspect; observe; survey; watch;
觀察動靜 watch what is going on;
觀察風向 find out how the wind blows; find out which way the wind blows; see how the gander hops; see how the land lies; see which way the cat jumps; wait for the cat to jump;
觀察孔 spyhole;
觀察形勢 examine the situation; observe the situation;
觀察員 observer; watcher;
~行業觀察員 industry-watcher;
觀察者 observer; viewer; watcher;
還有待觀察 it remains to be seen;
宏觀觀察 macroscopic observation;
實地觀察 actual observation;
物候觀察 phonological observation;
直接觀察 immediate observation;

[觀潮派] bystander; onlooker; person who takes a wait-and-see attitude;

[觀點] point of view; standpoint; viewpoint;
觀點不同 have a difference of opinion;
觀點附加語 viewpoint adjunct;
觀點相同 see eye to eye;
表明觀點 express one's viewpoint; lay down one's cards; lay one's cards on the table; place one's cards on the table; put one's card on the table; show one's cards; show one's colours; show one's hand;
持不同觀點 hold a different view;
持相同觀點 be of the same opinion; be of the same view;
恩賜觀點 the attitude of bestowing sth as a favour;
官方觀點 official view;
很好的觀點 good point;
堅持自己的觀點 stick to one's guns;
雙重觀點 doublethink;
說明觀點 demonstrate a point; illustrate a point;
提出觀點 make a point; raise a point;
同意你的觀點 point taken;
我接受你的觀點 I take your point;
一再重複某一觀點 belabor a point; labour a point;
有趣的觀點 interesting point;
中間觀點 middle ground;

[觀風] on the lookout;
觀風駛舵 follow the trend of the moment; see which way the wind blows; test which way the wind blows; trim one's sails; veer with the wind;
穩坐觀風 sit firmly and see which way the wind blows — sit on the fence;

[觀感] impression;
觀感所及 what one sees and what one gathers;

[觀光] go sightseeing; tour; visit;
觀光客 sightseer;
觀光團 sightseeing group;
觀光業 tourism;

[觀過知仁] after observing a person's faults and failings, one will undetrstand what he really is; understand a person by his/her faults; you can know a person by observing his/her mistakes;

[觀火] look at fire;
洞若觀火 as clear as day; as clear as looking at fire; as plain as a pikestaff; see sth as clearly as blazing fire;
隔岸觀火 be unconcerned; gloat over other's misfortune; watch a fire across the river — take a look-on attitude towards those in misfortune; watch the fire from the other bank — look on at sb's trouble with indifference; watch the fire from the other side of the river — adopt a "wait-and-see" attitude;
了如觀火 as clear as day; as clear as watching a fire;
明若觀火 as clear as day; as clear as looking at a fire; as clear-sighted as viewing a fire; clear like looking at a

fire; exceptionally clear and vivid;

[觀看] view; watch;

[觀禮] attend a celebration; attend a ceremony;

[觀摩] inspect and learn from each other's work; view and emulate;
觀摩演出 performance before fellow artists for the purpose of discussion and emulation;

[觀念] concept; idea; perception; sense;
觀念語法 notional grammar;
道德觀念 sense of morality;
等級觀念 sense of hierarchy;
轉變觀念 transition of people's conception;

[觀鳥] bird watching;
觀鳥者 bird watcher;

[觀人] judge a person;
觀人如觀玉，拙眼喜譏評 judging character is like judging jade, the uninformed like to criticize;
觀其行而知其人 a person is known by his/her behaviour; a tree is known by its fruit;
觀其友，知其人 a person is known by the company he/she keeps;

[觀賽] watch a sports contest;

[觀賞] enjoy the sight of; view and admire;

[觀望] look on; wait and see;
觀望不前 hesitate; hesitate and make no move; look about and make no move; undecided;
觀望態度 take a wait-and-see attitude;
東觀西望 look around;
徘徊觀望 wait and see;

[觀微知巨] a straw shows which way the wind blows;

[觀象台] observatory;

[觀音] Goddess of Mercy; Guanyin;
觀音菩薩一年年十八 Goddess of Mercy — eighteen years old every year; forever young;
觀音生子一天知道 Goddess of Mercy giving birth to a baby — Heaven knows;

[觀瞻] appearance of a place and the impressions it leaves; sight; view;
大失觀瞻 great loss of prestige;
以壯觀瞻 beautify the appearance; make a good appearance; strength the attraction;
有礙觀瞻 be an eyesore; be repugnant to the eye;

[觀者如堵] spectators stand round like a wall; there is a crowd of spectators;

[觀眾] audience; spectator; viewer;
觀眾大廳 auditorium;
觀眾席 auditorium; spectatory;
電視觀眾 TV viewers;
電影觀眾 film viewers;
取悦觀眾 please the crowd;
~取悦觀眾的人 crowd pleaser;
演播室現場觀眾 studio audience;
一大群觀眾 a throng of spectators;
一群觀眾 a crowd of audience; a crowd of spectators; a shoal of spectators;

悲觀 pessimistic;
壁上觀 detached view;
參觀 look around; visit;
達觀 optimistic; philosophical;
大觀 grand sight; magnificent spectacle;
改觀 change the appearance of;
概觀 general survey;
宏觀 macroscopic view;
景觀 landscape;
舊觀 former appearance; old look;
可觀 (1) worth seeing; (2) considerable; impressive; sizable;
客觀 objective;
樂觀 hopeful; optimistic;
美觀 artistic; beautiful; pleasing to the eye;
旁觀 look on;
奇觀 marvelous spectacle; wonder;
外觀 exterior appearance;
微觀 microcosmic;
雅觀 in good taste; refined;
直觀 directly perceived through the senses;
主觀 subjective;
壯觀 grand; magnificent;
綜觀 make a comprehensive survey;

guan

【鰥】 (1) kind of predatory fish; (2) widower; (3) bachelor;

[鰥夫] (1) widower; (2) bachelor;

[鰥寡] (1) old widowers and widows;
鰥寡孤獨 those who have no wives, husbands, parents or children;

[鰥棍兒] bachelor;

guan³

guan

【莞】 used in 東莞, a county in Guangdong;

guan

【脘】 inside of the stomach;

guan

【琯】 (1) jade musical tube; (2) polish preceious stones;

guan

【筦】 (1) tube; (2) key; (3) in charge; (4) wind instruments made of bamboo; (5) a surname;

guan

【管】 (1) tube; pipe; (2) wind instrument; (3) in charge of; manage; run; (4) subject sb to discipline; (5) bother about; (6) guarantee; provide; (7) tube; valve; (8) a surname;

[管胞] tracheid;
含脂管胞 resinous tracheid;
環紋管胞 annular tracheid;
纖維管胞 fibre tracheid;

[管保] (1) assure; guarantee; (2) certainly; surely;
管保令顧客滿意 perfect satisfaction is guaranteed to our customrs;

[管鮑分金] bosom friends; intimate friendship; sharing money and property with each other like Guan Zhong and Bao Shuya;

[管道] conduit; pipe;
管道工 piper;
曝氣管道 aerated conduit;
單孔管道 single duct conduit;
地線管道 ground conduit;
動力管道 power conduit;
多孔管道 multiple-duct conduit;
煤氣管道 gas conduit;
室內管道 interior conduit;
陶管管道 earthenware conduit;
污水管道 sewage conduit;
蒸汽管道 steam conduit;

[管燈] fluorescent lamp;

[管風琴] organ; pipe organ;
管風琴手 organist;
~教堂管風琴手 church organist;
管風琴演奏家 organist;

[管工] plumber;

[管護] manage and protect;

[管家] (1) butler; steward; (2) housekeep; (3) housekeeper; manager;
大管家 majordomo;
男管家 butler;

[管見] my humble opinion; my limited understanding;
管見所及 as far as I can see; as my humble view could reach; in my apprehension; in my humble opinion; in the light of my limited experience;
略陳管見 offer a few of one's humble opinions; pass a remark;

[管教] control; subject sb to discipline;
管教藝術 art of discipline and education;
不聽管教 beyond control;

[管窺] have a restricted view; look at sth through a bamboo tube;
管窺筐舉 limited outlook;
管窺蠡測 look at the sky through a tube and measure the sea with an oyster shell — a person of small experience; view the sky through a bamboo tube and measure the sea with a calabash — be restricted in vision and shallow in understanding;
管窺所及 in my humble opinion;
管窺之見 the view through a tube — limited outlook; what has been seen through a tube — one's narrow views;

[管理] administer; manage; management; regulate; rule; run; supervise;
管理不善 mismanage; poor management;
管理層 upper echelons;
~中級管理層 middle management; management office;
管理處 management department; management office;
~城市建設管理處 management office for urban development;
~公路運輸管理處 management office for highway transport ;
~航運管理處 management office for shipping;
~後勤管理處 management office for logistics;
~勞資管理處 management office for labour and capital;
~企業管理處 management office for the enterprises;
管理費 management fee;

管理工程 management engineering;
~管理工程學 management engineering;
管理工作系統 management operating system;
管理顧問 management consultant;
管理環境 management environment;
管理機構 management department;
管理機能 management function;
管理技術 management technique;
管理經濟學 managerial economics;
管理局 bureau of administration;
~電信管理局 telecommunications administration;
~國家工商行政管理局 state industrial and commercial administration;
~國家土地管理局 state bureau of land administration;
~國家外匯管理局 state administration of foreign exchange control;
~國家醫藥管理局 state bureau of medicine administration;
~國有資產管理局 strate assets administration;
~黃金管理局 gold administration;
~機關事務管理局 organization affairs bureau;
~農業機械化管理局 agriculturacl mechanization administration;
~土地管理局 land administration;
~鄉鎮企業管理局 rural enterprises administration;
醫藥管理局 medicine administration;
~郵電管理局 posts and telecommunications bureau;
管理決策過程 managerial decision-making process;
管理科學 management science;
管理會計 management accounting;
管理權 management;
~變更管理權 change of management;
管理人員 administrator; management;
~高層管理人員 high-level executive;
~中層管理人員 middle management; middle manager;
管理社會學 managerial sociology;
管理審計 management audit;
管理實踐 managerial practice;
管理世界 managerial world;
管理統計學 management statistics;
管理委員會 management committee;
管理系統 management system;
~管理系統工程 managerial system engineering;
~智能管理系統 intelligent management system;
管理現代化 management modernization;
管理心理學 managerial psychology;
管理信息動態 trends of management information;
管理信息系統 management information system;
管理行為 administrative behavior;
管理形象 managers' image;
管理學 management science; manageology;
~比較管理學 comparative management science;
管理藝術 management art;
管理預測方法 forecasting methods of management;
管理原則 principles of management;
管理員 caretaker; clerk; controller; management clerk;
~操縱台管理員 console controller;
~存貨管理員 stock clerk;
~發票管理員 invoice clerk;
~進場管理員 approach controller;
~空中交通管理員 air traffic controller;
~票據管理員 bill clerk;
管理職能 management function;
管理咨詢 management consultation;
安全管理 safety management; security management;
~安全管理目標 object of safety management;
變動管理 change management;
財務管理 financial administration;
底線管理 bottom-line management;
多頭管理 overlapping management;
多維管理 multi-dimensional management;
~多維管理結構 multi-dimensional management structure;
~多維管理目標 multi-dimensional management target;
集中管理 centralized management;
計劃管理 plan control;
經濟管理 economic management;
科學管理 scientific management;
內部管理 internal management;
日常管理 day-to-day running;
商業管理 business management;
微觀管理 micromanage;
行政管理 administrative management;

銀行管理 banking management;
預算管理 budget management;
中層管理 middle-level management;

[管事] (1) in charge; run affairs; (2) effective; of use; (3) manager; steward;
這藥不管事 this medicine doesn't work;

[管束] (1) check; control restrain; (2) pipe bundle; pipe column;
不服從管束 not submit to restraint;
嚴加管束 control vigorously; exercise strict discipline over; keep a tight rein on; keep sb under strict control; keep strict watch over;
~需要嚴加管束 need severe discipline;

[管它] forget it;
管它三七二十一 forget about it and let it rip;

[管轄] administer; have jurisdiction over;
管轄範圍 competency range;
管轄權 jurisdiction;
~海事管轄權 admiralty jurisdiction;
~沿海管轄權 coastal jurisdiction;
~諮詢管轄權 advisory jurisdiction;
行政管轄 administrative jurisdiction;

[管弦] pipes and strings;
管弦樂 orchestral music;
~管弦樂隊 orchestra;
繁弦急管 tune of music with a fast tempo;
急管繁弦 fast playing of wind and string instruments; hastening tune of music; tune of music with a fast tempo;

[管用] alive and well; bring home the bacon; effective;
對我挺管用 it works for me;

[管樂] wind music;
管樂隊 band;
管樂器 wind instruments; winds;

[管制] control;

[管中窺豹] look at a leopard through a bamboo tube—have a limited view of sth; peep at a leopard through a tube—have a small field of vision;
管中窺豹，可見一斑 conjure up the whole thing through seeing a part of it; from his claw you may know the lion; look at one spot on a leopard and you can visualize the whole animal; one may see day at a little hole; you may know by a handful the whole sack;

[管子] hose; pipe; tube;
一段管子 a length of pipe; a section of pipe;
一根管子 a pipe; a tube;
一節管子 a length of pipe; a section of pipe;

包管 assure; guarantee;
保管 (1) take care of; (2) certainly; surely;
別管 no matter (who, what, etc.); regardless of;
不管 no matter (who, what, etc.); regardless of;
監管 keep watch on;
接管 take over; take over control;
儘管 even though; in spite of;
經管 in charge of;
拘管 control; restrain;
看管 (1) attend; look after; (2) guard; watch;
氣管 trachea; wind pipe;
食管 esophagus;
試管 test tube;
信管 fuse;
血管 blood vessel;
油管 oil pipe; oil tube;
掌管 administer; in charge of;
照管 in charge of; look after; tend;
衹管 (1) by all means; (2) merely; simply;
主管 in charge of; responsible for;
總管 manager;

guan
【舘】 building; mansion;

guan
【館】 (1) accommodation for guests; (2) consulate; embassy; legation; (3) shop; (4) place for cultural activities;

[館子] eating house; restaurant;
吃館子 eat in a restaurant;

報館 newspaper office;
賓館 guesthouse;
殯儀館 funeral parlour; the undertaker's;
博物館 museum;
菜館 restaurant;
茶館 teahouse;
陳列館 exhibition hall;
大使館 embassy;
飯館 restaurant;
紀念館 memorial hall; musemum in memory of sb;
酒館 pub; public house;
領事館 consulate;
旅館 hotel;
美術館 art gallery;

G

水族館 aquarium;
體育館 gymnasium;
天文館 planetarium;
圖書館 library;
文史館 research institute of culture and history;
展覽館 exhibition hall;

guan4

guan

【冠】 (1) put on a hat; (2) crown with; precede; (3) best; first place;

［冠詞］ article;
部份冠詞 partitive article;
定冠詞 definite article;
~ 不定冠詞 indefinite article;
零冠詞 zero article;

［冠軍］ (1) champion; gold medalist; (2) a surname;
奪回冠軍 regain a championship;
獲得冠軍 get the championship;
全國冠軍 national champion;
世界冠軍 world champion;
現任冠軍 reigning champion;
總冠軍 overall champion;
~ 全場總冠軍 overall champion;

guan

【貫】 (1) pass through; pierce; (2) be linked together; follow in a continuous line; (3) birthplace; native place; (4) string of 1,000 cash; (5) a surname;

［貫徹］ carry out; implement; put into effect;
貫徹始終 always adhere to; carry through to the end; prosecute to the end;

［貫穿］ (1) penetrate; run through; (2) breakthrough; penetrate;

［貫串］ permeate; run through; string;

［貫入］ injection;
深成貫入 abyssal injection;
整合貫入 concordant injection;
~ 不整合貫入 discordant injection;

［貫通］ (1) be well versed in; have a thorough knowledge of; (2) cut through; link up; thread together;
融會貫通 achieve mastery through a comprehensive study of the subject;
一理貫通 one principle running through all;

［貫注］ (1) be absorbed in; concentrate on; (2) be connected in meaning;
全神貫注 all attention; all ears; all eyes; all eyes and ears; apply the mind to; be absorbed in; be deeply engrossed in sth; be engrossed in; be occupied with; be preoccupied with; be utterly concentrated in; be wholly absorbed in; be wrapped up in; complete mental concentration; concentrate on; concentrate one's attention on; concentrate the whole energy upon; give one's whole attention to; have sth on the brains; have sth on the mind; in complete absorption; pay undivided attention to; rapt; very attentive; with absorbed interest; with all one's mental faculties on the stretch; with all one's soul; with breathless attention; with one's heart an soul; with rapt attention; with undivided attention;

博貫 erudite;
大滿貫 grand slam;
籍貫 one's native place;
萬貫 formerly ten million cash;
一貫 all along; consistent; persistent;
魚貫 in single file; one following the other;

guan

【祼】 libation;

guan

【慣】 (1) in the habit of; used to; (2) indulge; spoil;

［慣常］ usual;
慣常做法 usual practice;

［慣盜］ common thief; habitual robber; incorrigible thief;

［慣犯］ habitual offender; hardened criminal; old lag; repeater;

［慣匪］ hardened bandit; professional brigand;

［慣技］ customary tactic; old trick;

［慣例］ common practice; convention; customary rule; customs and usages; practice; ritual; routine; usual practice;
安全慣例 safe practice;
按照慣例 by convention; go through the ritual;
打破慣例 break fresh ground; break new ground;
工作慣例 working practices;
國際慣例 international convention; international practice;
商務慣例 commercial practice;

G

商業慣例 business practice;
[慣竊] hardened thief;
[慣偷] confirmed thief; habitual thief; hardened thief;
[慣性] force of inertia; inertance; inertia; sluggishness;
慣性力 apparent force; effective force; inertial force; mass force; mass load;
慣性輪 flywheel;
慣性平衡 inertia balance;
[慣用] (1) consistently use; habitually practise; (2) customary; habitual;
慣用法 usage;
~ 慣用法層次 usage level;
~ 慣用法障礙 usage obstruction;
~ 詞匯慣用法 lexical usage;
慣用技倆 customary tactics; old tricks; usual trickery; well-worn tactics;
慣用生格 traditional genitive;
慣用手法 habitual practice;
慣用語 route;
~ 慣用語手冊 phrase book;
~ 會話慣用語 conversational routine;

看不慣 cannot bear the sight of;
習慣 be accustomed to; be used to;

guan
【摜】 (1) throw on the ground; (2) accustomed to; used to;
[摜砲] torpedo;

guan
【盥】 (1) wash hands; (2) wash;
[盥漱] wash one's face and rinse out one's mouth;
[盥洗] wash one's hands and face;

guan
【灌】 (1) irrigate; (2) fill; pour;
[灌腸] enema; clyster;
灌腸機 stuffer;
~ 活塞式灌腸機 piston-type stuffer;
~ 氣動灌腸機 compressed air stuffer; pneumatic air
~ 氣壓式灌腸機 air stuffer;
~ 雙頭灌腸機 dual-connected stuffer;
~ 水壓灌腸機 water stuffer;
小腸灌腸 small bowel enema;
[灌叢] bushwood;
灌叢地 bushland;
密灌叢 scrufo;
[灌頂] abhisenca;
[灌東] a surname;
[灌溉] irrigate; irrigation; watering;
灌溉方法 irrigation methods;
灌溉渠 channel irrigation;
灌溉用水 irrigation water;
小塊灌溉 basin irrigation;
[灌錄] cut a disc; make a tape; record;
灌錄唱片 make records;
[灌滿] tank up;
[灌米湯] bewitch sb by means of flattery; butter sb up; lay it on thick; lay the butter on;
[灌木] bush; shrub;
灌木叢 coppice; copse; shrubbery;
~ 一簇灌木叢 a clump of hushes;
常綠灌本 evergreen shrubs;
小灌本 dwarf shrub;
~ 常綠小灌木 evergreen undershrub;
遮蔭灌本 shade-giving shrub;
[灌輸] beat sth into sb's head; cram sth down sb's throat; drum sth into sb; drum sth into sb's ear; drum sth into sb's head; hammer sth into sb's head; imbue with; inculcate; indoctrinate; infuse sth into sb; infuse sth into sb's mind; instil into; put sth into sb's head; ram sth down sb's throat; thrust sth down sb's throat;
灌輸思想 inculcation; indoctrinate; indoctrination;
[灌水] pour water into sth;
[灌醉] fuddle; inebriate; make sb drunk;

春灌 irrigate in spring;
滴灌 drip irrigation; trickle irrigation;
電灌 irrigate by electric pumping;
冬灌 irrigate in winter;
溝灌 furrow irrigation;
澆灌 (1) irrigate; water; (2) pour;
井灌 irrigate with well water;
漫灌 flood irrigation;
排灌 drain and irrigate;
噴灌 sprinkle;
渠灌 canal irrigation;
淹灌 basin irrigation;

guan
【罐】 can; container; jar; jug; vessel;
[罐兒] can; container; jar; jug; vessel;
[罐籠] cage; cage conductor;

[罐頭] can; canning; tin;
罐頭船 floating cannery;
罐頭廠 cannery;
~ 肉類罐頭廠 meat cannery;
罐頭工廠 cannery;
罐頭食品廠 cannery;
密封的罐頭 airtight tin;
水產罐頭 fisheries canning;
水果罐頭 fruit can;
飲料罐頭 beverage can;
製成罐頭 can;
[罐裝] canning;
罐裝的 canned;
[罐子] can; container; jar; jug; vessel;

安全罐 safety can;
扁罐 flat can;
長方罐 rectangular can;
鋼罐 steel can;
金屬罐 metal can;
漏罐 leak can;
啤酒罐 beer can;
湯罐 pot;
衛生罐 sanitary can;
鋅罐 zinc can;
油罐 oil tank; storage tank;
易開罐 easy open convenience can;
異形罐 irregular shaped can;
圓罐 cylindrical can;
裝料罐 charge can;

guan
【觀】 (1) Daoist shrine; Daoist temple; (2) a surname;

guan
【鸛】 stork;

白鸛 white stork;
禿鸛 adjutant stork;

guang¹
guang
【光】 (1) light; ray; (2) bright; glossy; lustrous; shiny; (3) glory; honour; (4) scene; scenery; (5) polished; smooth; (6) nothing left; used up; (7) bare; naked; (8) alone; merely; only; solely;
[光筆] light pen;
光筆跟蹤 light pen tracing;
[光標] cursor;
光標控制鍵 cursor control key;
[光波] light wave; optical wave;
[光彩] (1) glittering; glow; lustre; radiance; sheen; splendour; (2) glorious; honourable;
光彩奪目 dazzling radiance; dazzlingly brilliant; its brightness dazzles the eyes; its elegance ravishes the eye; shine with dazzling brilliance; so bright and colourful that it dazzles the eye; the lustre dazzles the eye; very bright-coloured and dazzling; with dazzling brightness;
光彩奇異 fancy;
光彩炫目 blindingly bright; dazzling splendour;
光彩絢麗 brilliant lustre; splendour and gorgeous;
不光彩 disgraceful; dishonourable; ignominious; inglorious;
放光彩 iridescence;
[光大] brighten;
發揚光大 bring to a greater height of development; carry forward; develop; develop and shine with greater brilliance; develop to a higher stage; enhance; foster and enhance; give full play to; give greater scope to; spread and flourish
[光電] photoelectricity;
光電倍增管 photomultiplier;
光電管 phototube;
~ 發射光電管 emission phototube;
~ 銫光電管 caesium phototube;
光電晶體管 phototransistor;
~ 電鍍光電晶體管 electroplated phototransistor;
~ 合金型光電晶體管 alloy phototransistor;
光電率 chargeability;
光電排版 photo composition;
光電攝像管 emitron;
~ 標準光電攝像管 standard emitron;
~ 超光電攝像管 super emitron;
光電象管 .photoelectric image tube;
光電效應 photoelectric effect;
光電閱讀機 optical mark reader;
光電子產業 photoelectronic industry;
光電子技術 photoelectronic technique;
光電子學 photoelectronics;
[光碟] compact disc;

G

[光度] (1) luminosity; (2) photon;
光度計 light meter; photometer;
~對比光度計 contrast type photometer;
~分光光度計 spectrophotometer;
差比分光光度計 difference spectrophotometer;
雙束分光光度計 double-beam spectrophotometer;
熒光分光光度計 spectrophotofluorometer;
~立方體光度計 cube photometer;
~漫射光度計 diffusion photometer;
~天體光度計 astrophotometer;
~自動光度計 automatic photometer;
光度學 photometry;
~分光光度學 spectrophotometry;
~分析光度學 analytical photometry;
~雙目光度學 binocular photometry;
~天體光度學 celestial photometry;

[光復] recover;
光復舊物 recover one's lost territory; recover one's past heritage; recover what has been lost; regain possession of lost territory;

[光顧] honour with; patronize;

[光棍] hoodlum; ruffian;
光棍兒 bachelor; unmarried person;
光棍一條 a man who has lost his family; a person without a following; keep bachelor's half; one is all on one's own; one's hat covers one's family;
老光棍 old bachelor;

[光合] photosynthetic;
光合作用 photosynthesis;
~細菌光合作用 bacterial photosynthesis;

[光花] blink; brilliance; splendour;

[光華] bright; brilliance; lustre; splendour;

[光滑] glossy; sleek; slick; smooth;
光滑的 glossy;
光滑如鏡 smooth and bright like a mirror;
光滑如玉 as smooth as jade;
地面很光滑 the floor is very smooth;

[光化] actinic; photochemical;
光化層 chemosphere;
光化力 actinicity;
光化射線 actinic ray;
光化生物學 actinobiology;
光化性 actinicity; actinism;
光化學 (1) actinology; (2) actinochemistry;

[光環] aureole; corona; glory; halo; nimbus; ring of light;
光環働用 halo effect;

[光輝] blaze; brilliance; flame; fulguration; glory; luminosity; lustre; radiance; shine;
光輝燦爛 glittering; glorious and lustrous; most brilliant; radiant; shine with great splendour; shining; splendid;
光輝篇章 brilliant chapter;
光輝耀目 dazzle;
篤實光輝 sincere and glorious;
太陽的光輝 sunshine;

[光火] (1) fly into a rage; (2) light and fire;
電光石火 anything that vanishes in a flash;

[光潔] bright and clean;

[光景] (1) scene; (2) circumstances; conditions; (3) about; around; (4) quite likely; very probably;

[光可鑒人] brilliant enough to reflect one's image; so bright that it can serve as a mirror; so shining and bright that it can serve as a looking glass;

[光亮] bright; burnish; luminous; lustre; shine;
光亮帶 euphotic zone;
光亮的 lustrous;
光亮如新 show their original lustre;
一片光亮 a circle of light; a pool of light; an area of light;

[光臨] presence;
撥冗光臨 please spare a little time and come;
恭請光臨 we respectively solicit your patronage;
闔第光臨 the whole family is invited;
敬請光臨 request the honour of your presence; the favour of your presence is requested; your presence is cordially requested;

[光溜] slippery; smooth;
光溜溜的 bare; naked; smooth;

[光輪] aureole;

[光芒] light;
光芒四射 a flash of light radiating in all directions; flashing; radiate brilliant light; scattering splendour; sending out rays of light in all directions;
光芒萬丈 blazing a long way ahead; forever glorious; gloriously radiant; shining gloriously; shining with

G

boundless radiance;
永放光芒 eternally glorious; will shine forever;
[光麵] noodles;
[光明] (1) light; (2) bright; promising; (3) guileless; openhearted;
光明大道 a bright future; the right road;
光明磊落 aboveboard; completely open; frank and forthright; on the up-and-up; frank and forthright; open and aboveboard; open and upright; plain dealing; plainly and squarely;
~光明磊落的人 square shooter; straight shooter;
光明正大 aboveboard and straightforward; entirely aboveboard; fair and square; frank and righteous; just and honourable; on the square; open and aboveboard; openly and honestly; plain dealing; sporting; upright;
心地光明 clear conscience; upright;
一片光明 a flood of light; a stream of light; bright;
一線光明 a gleam of light;
[光年] light year;
[光盤] CD; compact disc; compact disk; optical disk;
一張光盤 a CD;
[光譜] spectrum;
光譜法 spectrometry;
~原子發射光譜法 atomic emission spectrometry;
~原子吸收光譜法 atomic absorption spectrometry;
光譜分析 spectrum analysis;
光譜化學 spectrochemistry;
光譜計 spectroscope;
~天體光譜計 astrospectroscope;
光譜型 spectral type;
光譜學 spectroscopy;
~激光光譜學 laser spectroscopy;
~天體光譜學 astronomical spectroscopy; astrospectroscopy;
~原子光譜學 atomic spectroscopy;
暗線光譜 dark line spectrum;
帶光譜 band spectrum;
發射光譜 emission spectrum;
激光光譜 laser spectrum;
連續光譜 continuous spectrum;
明線光譜 bright line spectrum;
太陽光譜 solar spectrum;
吸收光譜 absorption spectrum;
原子光譜 atomic spectrum;
[光球] photosphere;
[光榮] credit; glory; honour;
光榮榜 honour roll;
光榮就義 die a heroic death; prefer death to disgrace; sacrifice one's life for the sake of righteousness;
[光潤] smooth;
[光柵] grating;
光柵單元 grating unit;
光柵顯像 grating display;
光柵線 grating line;
長方形光柵 rectangular grating;
點光柵 polka-dot grating;
交叉光柵 crossed grating;
階梯光柵 echelon grating;
~小階梯光柵 echelette grating;
~中階梯光柵 echelle grating;
潔淨光柵 pure grating;
炫耀光柵 blazed grating;
衍射光柵 diffraction grating;
[光是] alone; merely; solely;
[光束] beam;
光束擺動 beam wobbling;
參考光束 reference beam;
基準光束 reference beam;
[光天化日] broad daylight; broad light of day; in broad daylight; in the open day; the harsh glare of daylight; the light of day;
在光天化日之下 in the face of day;
[光瞳] pupil;
出射光瞳 exit pupil;
入射光瞳 entrance pupil;
[光頭] bareheaded; shaven head; shaven-headed;
光頭禿額 with balding hair and shining forehead;
剃光頭 shave the head bald;
[光禿禿] bald; bare; barren; bleak;
光禿禿的山坡 the bare hillsides;
[光線] light; luminous beam; ray; ray of light;
光線不足 poor light;
避開光線 shun the light;
擋住光線 obstruct the light;
投下光線 throw a light;
一道光線 a ray of light;
一縷光線 a stream of light;
一束光線 a beam of light;

[光學] optics;
光學變化 optical change;
光學漢字識別 optical Chinese character recognition;
光學纖維 optical fibre;
大氣光學 atmospheric optics;
電光學 electrooptics;
電子光學 electrooptics;
非線性光學 non-linear optics;
幾何光學 geometrical optics;
聚光光學 light-gathering optics;
物理光學 physical optics;
應用光學 applied optics;

[光焰] flare; radiance;
光焰萬丈 cast its radiance far and wide; illuminating highly in a myriad feet;

[光耀] (1) brilliance; brilliant light; (2) glorious; honourable;
光耀奪目 dazzling;
光耀門楣 bring honour to the family name; do honour to one's family; win honour and distinction for one's family;
光耀門庭 bring honour to the family name; win honour and distinction for one's family;

[光陰] sands of time; time;
光陰駒隙 time flies like the shadow of the sun passing through a crevice; time passes quickly;
光陰冉冉 the years roll on smoothly; time passes away slowly;
光陰荏苒 day and night alternate in quick succession; the flow of time;
光陰如流水，一去不復還 lost time is never found again; time lost cannot be won again; time past cannot be recalled;
光陰如水 time passes like flowing water;
光陰似箭 the fllight of time; the swift passage of time; the time goes like lightning; time flies; time flies like an arrow;
光陰虛度 loaf away one's time; lose one's time by trifling; racket away one's time;
光陰一去不復返 all time is no time when it is past; lost time is never found again; time and tide wait for no man;
愛惜光陰 cherish time;
寸金難賣寸光陰 an inch of gold will not buy an inch of time; money can't buy time; time is money; time is money but money can never buy time; time is more precious than gold;
浪費光陰 waste the time;
虛度光陰 loaf away one's time; lose one's time by trifling; racket away one's time;
一寸光陰一寸金 an inch of time is worth an inch of gold; time is gold; time is money; time is precious; time is priceless;

[光影] shadows;
浮光泛影 the floating moonlight reflected on the water;
浮光掠影 a dim impression which vanishes easily; cursory; floating light and passing shadow; hasty and casual;

[光油] varnish;
一層光油 a coat of varnish;

[光源] light source;

[光暈] aureole;

[光澤] brilliance; burnish; gloss; lustre; sheen; shine;
光澤面 shiny side;
光澤柔和 gentle gloss;
玻璃光澤 glassy lustre;
金剛光澤 adamantine lustre;
金屬光澤 metallic lustre;
目無光澤 dull eyes; one's eyes are without lustre;
有光澤的 lustrous;

[光照人寒] the moon sends forth cold rays that make sb shudder;

[光子] photon;
可見光子 light photon;
紫外光子 ultraviolet photon;

挨光 put for the effort in dalliances;
暴光 exposure;
背光 in a poor light;
波光 glistening light of waves;
不光 (1) not the only one; (2) not only;
擦光 polish; rub up;
測光 photometric;
吃光 eat up;
春光 spring scenery;
單色光 monochromatic light
燈光 (1) the light of a lamp; (2) lighting;
地光 flashes of light preceding an earthquake;
電光 lightning;

頂光 spotlight;
多色光 heterochromatic light;
耳光 a box on the ear; a slap on the face;
發光 (1) give out light; shine; (2) luminescence;
反光 reflect light; reflected light;
風光 scene; sight; view;
感光 sensitize;
觀光 go sight-seeing; tour; visit;
黑光 black light;
弧光 arc light;
火光 blaze; flame;
激光 laser;
借光 excuse me;
金光 golden light; golden ray;
可見光 visible light;
淚光 glistening teardrops;
冷光 cold light;
亮光 light;
磷光 phosphorescence;
流光 time;
漏光 light leak;
露光 light leak;
鎂光 magnesium light;
磨光 polish;
目光 (1) sight; view; vision; (2) gaze; look;
年光 (1) time; years; (2) the year's harvest;
拋光 buff; polish;
偏光 polarized light;
平光 plain glass; zero diopter;
爆光 expose;
日光 sunbeam; sunlight; sunshine;
容光 one's facial expression; one's general appearance;
柔光 soft light;
散光 astigmatism;
色光 coloured light;
閃光 flash of light;
賞光 request the pleasure of your company;
韶光 (1) beautiful springtime; (2) glorious youth;
時光 (1) time; (2) days; times; years;
曙光 first light of morning;
死光 death ray;
叨光 much obliged to you;
天光 daylight; time of the day;
天然光 natural light;
透光 (of light) come in through;
畏光 photophobia;
霞光 rays of morning or evening sunlight;
眼光 (1) eye; (2) foresight; insight; sight; vision;
陽光 sunlight; sunshine;
耀光 sparkling;
夜光 moonlight;
一道光 a beam of light; a ray of light; a shaft of light;
一束光 a beam of light; a ray of light; a shaft of light;
瑩光 fluorescence; fluorescent light;
油光 glossy; shiny; varnished;
月光 moonbeam; moonlight;
增光 add lustre to; add to the prestige of; do credit to;
沾光 benefit from association with sb or sth;
爭光 do credit to;
燭光 candle light;

guang
【洸】 (1) a river in Shandong; (2) glitter;

guang
【胱】 bladder;

膀胱 bladder;

guang³
guang
【廣】 (1) extensive; vast; wide; (2) numerous; (3) expand; spread; (4) short for Guangzhou;

[廣播] airing; broadcast; broadcasting; on the air;
廣播大學 broadcasting university;
廣播電視大學 broadcasting and television university;
廣播電視塔 broadcast television tower;
廣播電視學 broadcasting and television studies;
廣播電台 broadcasting station;
廣播發射機 broadcasting transmitter;
廣播稿 script;
廣播工作 broadcasting job;
廣播技術 broadcasting technique;
廣播間歇 station break;
廣播講話 radio address;
廣播教材 broadcasting teaching materials;
廣播教育 broadcasting education;
廣播節目 broadcasting programme;
~ 廣播節目傳送 transmission of broadcasting programmes;
~ 次要廣播節目 minor broadcasts;
~ 主要廣播節目 major broadcasts;
廣播劇 radio drama; radio play;
廣播評論 radio commentary;
廣播權 broadcast right;
廣播軟件 telesoftware;
廣播時間 airtime; broadcasting time; on-air time;

廣播視頻技術 televideo technique;
廣播事業 broadcasting business;
廣播討論會 broadcasting seminar;
廣播體操 broadcast calisthenics;
廣播聽眾 broadcast listener;
廣播網 broadcasting network;
廣播衛 broadcasting satellite;
廣播信道 broadcast channel;
廣播學校 broadcasting school;
廣播演説 broadcast speech;
廣播業 broadcasting industry;
廣播影視 radio, film and television;
廣播語言學 broadcasting linguistics;
廣播員 broadcaster;
廣播作品 broadcastworks;
本地廣播 local broadcasting;
標準廣播 standard broadcast;
彩色電視廣播 colour television broadcasting;
超短波廣播 ultra-shortwave broadcast;
傳真廣播 facsimile broadcast;
大功率廣播 high-power broadcasting;
地方廣播 local broadcasting;
地區廣播 regional broadcasting;
電視廣播 television broadcast; television broadcasting; visual broadcast; visual broadcasting;
~電視廣播劇 teleplay;
~電視廣播員 telecaster;
定向廣播 directional broadcasting;
對外廣播 external broadcasting;
多路廣播 multiplex broadcasting;
兒童廣播 children's broadcasts;
公營廣播 public broadcasting;
國際廣播 international broadcast; international broadcasting;
國內廣播 domestic broadcasting; home broadcast;
海外廣播 overseas broadcasting;
黑白電視廣播 monochrome broadcasting;
教學廣播 school broadcast;
教育廣播 educational broadcast; educational broadcasting;
節目每天廣播 the programme airs daily;
開始廣播 get on the air; go on the air;
立體聲廣播 stereo broadcasting; stereophonic broadcast;
~兩路立體聲廣播 binaural broadcast;
氣球廣播 balloon broadcasting;
商業廣播 commercial broadcasting;
聲音廣播 sound broadcasting;
時事廣播 current affairs broadcast;
實況廣播 live broadcast; outside broadcast; outside broadcasting; remote broadcast;
~實況廣播報導 running commentary;
~實況廣播員 commentator;
室內廣播 studio broadcast;
數據廣播 datacasting;
雙重廣播 dual broadcast; dual broadcasting;
調幅廣播 amplitude-modulation broadcasting;
調頻廣播 frequency modulation broadcasting;
聽廣播 listen to the radio;
同步廣播 synchronized broadcast;
同頻廣播 common-frequency broadcasting; same frequency broadcasting;
圖文廣播 teletext;
衛星電視廣播 satellite television broadcasting;
衛星廣播 satellite broadcast;
無線電廣播 air-cast; radio broadcast; radio broadcasting;
無線廣播 wireless broadcasting;
現場廣播 live broadcast;
新聞廣播 news broadcast; newscast;
~國際新聞廣播 world news broadcast;
~國內新聞廣播 home news broadcast;
學校廣播 school broadcasting;
音樂廣播 music broadcast;
有線廣播 wire broadcasting;
正在廣播 on the air;
綜合廣播 general broadcast;

[廣博] extensive; wide;
廣博見識 extensive knowledge;
見識廣博 have extensive experience; wide in experience;
見聞廣博 have extensive knowledge; well-informed;

[廣場] piazza; plaza; public square; square;
廣場恐怖 agorphobia;
廣場恐怖症 agorphobia;
~廣場恐怖症患者 agoraphobe;

[廣大] (1) extensive; vast; wide; (2) large-scale; widespread; (3) numerous;

[廣度] extent; range; scope;

[廣泛] extensive; wide-ranging; widespread;
廣泛的 catholic;
廣泛深入 both extensively and intensively in breadth and depth; extensive and

intensive;
廣泛應用 extensive use;
興趣廣泛 catholic tastes;
[廣柑] orange;
[廣告] (1) advert; advertisement; (2) poster;
廣告刺激 adsturbation;
廣告從業人 adman; advertiser;
廣告促銷策略 promotion strategy in advertisement;
廣告代理 advertisement agency; advertising agency;
~ 廣告代理公司 advertising agency;
廣告單張 leaflet;
廣告點擊率 click-through rate;
廣告法學 advertisement jurisprudence;
廣告費 advertising fee; advertising rate;
廣告份額 shares of advertising;
廣告感染力 advertisement appeal;
廣告公司 advertising agency;
廣告攻勢 aggressive advertising;
廣告管理 advertisement management;
廣告畫 poster;
廣告活動 advertising campaign;
廣告價格 advertising rate;
廣告科 advertising department;
廣告欄 advertising columns; hoarding;
廣告媒體 advertising medium;
廣告牌 advertisement sign; billboard;
~ 三明治廣告牌 sandwish board;
廣告片 advertising film;
~ 專題廣告片 infomercial;
廣告人 adman; advertiser; advertising maker; advertising man;
廣告商 advertiser; advertising agency;
廣告商標 advertising mark;
廣告社 advertising agency;
廣告設計 advertisement design;
廣告事業 advertising career;
廣告統計 advertising statistics;
廣告文學 advertising literature;
廣告效果 advertising effectiveness;
廣告新聞 advertising news;
廣告心理學 advertising psychology;
廣告信息 advertising information;
~ 廣告信息系統 advertising information system;
廣告宣傳 advertising;
廣告顏料 poster paint;
廣告業 adand; advertising;
廣告業務 advertising affairs;
廣告用語 advertising language;
廣告源 advertising source;
廣告戰 advertising war;
廣告咨詢 advertisement consulting;
辯護性廣告 defensive advertising;
彩色廣告 colour advertising;
倡議性廣告 advocatory advertising;
車廂廣告 bus advertising;
大眾廣告 admass; masses advertising;
~ 大眾廣告文化 admass culture;
大做廣告 conduct advertising campaign;
登廣告 advertise;
~ 為商品登廣告 advertise goods;
燈光廣告 illuminated advertising; light box advertising;
電視廣告 television advertisement;;
電影廣告 cinema film advertising;
分類廣告 classified ad; classified advertisement; small ad;
廣播廣告 advertising on radio; radio advertsing;
幻燈廣告 slide advertising;
活動類廣告 advertisement of activity kind;
價格廣告 price advertising;
減少廣告 cut off advertising;
街頭廣告 outdoor advertising;
巨型廣告 gigantic advertisement;
刊登廣告 put in an advertisement;
可點擊廣告 click-through advertisement;
空中廣告 aerial advertising;
口頭廣告 word-of-mouth advertising;
賣廣告 advertise;
潛意識廣告 subliminal advertising;
區域性廣告 local advertising;
全國性廣告 national advertising;
商業廣告 commercial advertisement; commercial advertising;
社論式廣告 advertorial;
室外廣告 outdoor advertising;
彈出式廣告 pop-up advertising;
推銷廣告 sales promoting advertisement;
網絡廣告 network advertising;
無線電廣播廣告 radio advertising;
五光十色的廣告 dazzling advertisement;
小廣告 (1) classified ad; (2) small ad;
信譽廣告 prestige advertising;
銀行廣告 bank advertising;
雜誌廣告 magazine advertising;
張貼廣告 bill-posting advertising;
[廣闊] broad; expansive; extensive; spacious; vast; wide;
廣闊無垠 great distance; unmeasured vastness;

［廣漠］ vast and bare;
［廣謀從眾］ consult and follow the multitude;
［廣土眾民］ vast territory and huge population;
［廣武］ surname;
［廣義］ (1) broad sense; wide sense; (2) generalized;
廣義節能 general energy conservation;
廣義系統 pansystems;
廣義行政學 public administration in a broad sense;
廣義語境 macro-context;
廣義智能技術 general intelligence technique;
［廣種薄收］ extensive cultivation;

博廣 extensive;
深廣 far-ranging and profound;
推廣 popularize; spread;

guang
【獷】 fierce and rude; uncivilized;
［獷俗］ barbarian ways; uncivilized customs;

粗獷 (1) boorish; rough; rude; (2) bold and unconstrained; rugged; straightforward and unibhibited;

guang⁴
guang
【桄】 (1) cross beam; (2) grade;
［桄榔］ gomuti palm;

guang
【逛】 ramble; roam; stroll;
［逛蕩］ gad about; linger idly; loaf about; loiter;
［逛街］ go shopping; strolling around the streets; window-shopping;
逛大街 go shopping; strolling around the streets; window-shopping;

閒逛 ramble; saunter;
游逛 go sight-seeing; stroll about;

gui¹
gui
【圭】 jade tablet;
［圭臬］ criterion; standard;
奉為圭臬 hold up as a model; look up to as the standard; take sth as the pattern;
［圭璋］ (1) high-quality jade; (2) of noble character;

gui
【皈】 follow;
［皈依］ (1) be converted to Buddhism; (2) ceremony of proclaiming sb a Buddhist;
皈依佛法 follow the laws of Buddha;
皈依歸真 become a Buddha after death;
皈依三寶 become a Buddhist;
皈依宗教 become a believer;

gui
【邽】 (1) a county in the Han Dynasty, in today's Gansu Province; (2) a surname;

gui
【珪】 same as 圭, a jade tablet worn by feudal princes as symbol of authority;

gui
【規】 (1) compasses; dividers; (2) regulation; (3) admonish; advise; (4) map out; plan;
［規避］ avoid; dodge; escapism; evade; set around;
［規程］ regulations;
安全規程 safety code; safety procedure; safety regulations; safety rules; safety specification;
［規定］ (1) provide; stipulate; (2) fix; formulate; set; specify; (3) get-set; provision; rule; stipulation;
規定的 compulsory;
規定動作 compulsory exercise; prescribed exercises;
必不可少的規定 standard rules;
不符合規定 not in accordance with the relevant rules;
不許違反的規定 inviolable rule;
服從規定 follow a rule;
明文規定 express provision; stipulate in writing;
違反規定 break a rule; violate a rule;
現行規定 existing provision;
行政規定 administrative provisions;
執行規定 put rules into practice;
做硬性規定 lay down hard-and-fast rules;
［規範］ canon; norm; performance; specification; standard;
規範化 normalization; standardization;
規範經濟學 normative economics;
規範決策論 normative decision theory;

G

規範倫理學 normative ethics;
規範型預測 normative forecasting;
規範性決策 normative decision;
規範性預測 normative forecasting;
翻譯規範 translation norm;
軍用規範 army specifications;
目的語規範 target language norm;
配料規範 mixture specifications;
社會規範 social norms;
驗收規範 acceptance specification;

[規復] rehabilitate; restore to norm;

[規格] (1) norm; specification; standard; (2) format; requirement; standard;
規格齊全 complete in specifications;
不合規格 fall short of specification;
電纜規格 cable specification;
符合規格 fulfil quality requirements;
技術規格 the technical specifications;

[規劃] plan; planning; project; programming; schematization;
規劃方向 direction of planning;
規劃審計 programme audit;
規劃生成系統 programme production system;
規劃一般化 plan generalization;
規劃原則 principles for planning;
安全規劃 safety programme;
產業規劃 estate planning;
長期規劃 long-term planning;
長遠規劃 long-term planning;
城市規劃 city planning;
城鄉規劃 planning of town and country;
分區規劃 zoning;
環境計劃 environmental planning;
科目規劃 course planning; subject planning;
課程規劃 curriculum planning;
生產規劃 production planning;
整體規劃 integrated overall planning;
總體規劃 general planning; master plan;
綜合規劃 comprehensive planning;
作業規劃 operational planning;

[規矩] (1) custom; established practice; rule; (2) well-behaved; well-disciplined;
規矩準繩 criteria; norms; standards;
不成文規矩 an unwritten rule;
規規矩矩 as good as gold; behave oneself; law-abiding; morally; on one's good behaviour; remain orderly; well-behaved;
~ 規規矩矩的孩子 well-behaved child;
規行矩步 behave correctly and cautiously; follow the beaten track; observe due decorum; stick to convention; strictly upright and correct in one's behaviour;
規圓矩方 adhere to rules strictly;
老規矩 conventions; established custom; established practice; old rules and regulations;
立規矩 establish rules;
立下規矩 draw up a set of rules;
守規矩 abide by discipline;
中規中矩 straight and narrow;

[規律] law; regular pattern;
規律性 regularity;
~ 教育規律性 educational regularity;
~ 顯性規律性 dominant regularity;
按照事情的規律 in the nature of things;
必然規律 inevitable low;
自然規律 law of nature; rule of nature;
~ 違反自然規律 violate the rules of nature;

[規模] dimension; scale; scope;
規模宏大 broad in scale; on a grand scale;
規模經濟 economy of scale;
~ 規模經濟學 economics of scale;
規模空前 unparalleled proportions; unprecedented scale;
初具規模 begin to take shape; give signs of future shape;
粗具規模 fashion roughly; give signs of future shape; have just laid a foundation; roughly in order; roughly in shape;
大規模 extensive; in a big way; in force; large-scale; mass; massive; on a big scale; on a large scale; to a large extent;
小規模 on a small scale;

[規勸] admonish; advise; exhort; expostulate; remonstrate;
規勸朋友 remonstrate with one's friend;
娓娓規勸 soft-voiced admonition;

[規一化] normalization;

[規約] stipulations of an agreement;

[規則] (1) ordination; regulation; rule; (2) regular;
規則化 regularization;
表達規則 expression rules;
不成文的規則 unwritten rules;
不規則 inordinance; irregular; irregularity;

~不規則性 irregularity;
頻率不規則性 frequency irregularity;
循環不規則性 cyclic irregularity;
~局部不規則 local irregularities;
成分結構規則 constituent structure rules;
詞匯規則 lexical rule;
從屬規則 dependency rule;
翻譯規則 translation rule;
互參規則 rule of coreference;
交替規則 alternation rule;
交通規則 traffic rules;
會計規則 accounting rule;
頻度規則 frequency rule;
普遍規則 universal rule;
特定規則 ad hoc rule;
違反規則 break the rules;
行為規則 rules of conduct;
一套規則 a set of regulations; a set of rules;
遵守規則 stick to the rules;

[規章] regulations; rules;
規章制度 bylaw; codes and conventions; regulations and systems; rules and regulations;
一套規章 a set of rules;
遵守規章 abidance by rules;

板規 plate gauge;
常規 (1) convention; rule; (2) routine;
陳規 outmoded conventions;
成規 established; set rules;
定規 established rules and regulations; set pattern;
法規 laws and regulations;
犯規 (1) break the rules; (2) foul;
行規 guild regulations;
家規 family rules;
陋規 objectionable practices;
清規 monastic rules for Buddhists;
日規 sundial;
無規 random;
校規 school regulations;
圓規 compass;
正規 regular; standard;
子規 cuckoo;

gui

【傀】 great; wonderful;
[傀偉] great and imposing;
[傀異] rare and strange;

gui

【瑰】 marvellous; rare;
[瑰寶] gem; rarity; treasure;
[瑰麗] magnificent; surpassingly beautiful;
瑰麗多姿 elegant and magnificent; full of magnificent carriage;
[瑰瑋] (1) remarkable; (2) ornate;
[瑰意琦行] extraordinary ideas and admirable action; outstanding in thinking and action; praise of a man of high integrity;

gui

【溈】 a river in Shansi Province;

gui

【閨】 (1) small door; (2) woman's apartment; (3) feminine;
[閨房] boudoir; harem;
[閨閣] boudoir;
閨閣名媛 daughters of rich families;
閨閣千金 young lady;
閨閣綉房 boudoir; lady's private quarters;
幽閨深閣 deep, hidden boudoir;
[閨闥] woman's quarters;
[閨門] door of a boudoir; door to the women's apartments;
[閨女] (1) girl; maiden; (2) daughter;
俊閨女 pretty girl;
[閨秀] (1) young lady; (2) graceful girls; lady writer; literary woman; woman with literary talent;
閨秀淑女 yound and virtuous virgin;
[閨中膩友] woman's paramour;

深閨 boudoir;

gui

【龜】 tortoise; turtle;
[龜甲] tortoise shell;
[龜鑒] past event or incident serving as an example or warning to future generations;
[龜齡鶴算] old age;
[龜毛兔角] hair of tortoises and horns of rabbits—exist in name but not in reality; merely nominal;
[龜縮] hole up; huddle up like a turtle drawing in its head and legs; withdraw into passive defense;
龜縮一團 be huddled up;
[龜頭] balmony; glans penis;
[龜胸] pigeon-breast;

海龜 sea turtle;
神龜 supernatural tortoise;
蓍龜 tortoise divination;
烏龜 (1) tortoise; (2) cuckold;

gui

【鮭】 salmon;
[鮭魚] trout;

海鮭 bull trout; ea trout;
銀鮭 herring smelt; less silver smelt;

gui

【歸】 (1) go back to; return; (2) give back to; return sth to; (3) come together; converge; (4) put in sb's charge; turn over to; (5) division on the abacus with a one-digit divisor; (6) a surname;
[歸案] bring to justice;
歸案法辦 bring back to court for trial and punishment; bring someone to justice; bring someone to trial and mete out punishment;
[歸併] (1) incorporate into; merge into; (2) add up; lump together; reduce;
[歸程] return journey;
[歸檔] file; place on file;
把報告歸檔 file away the reports;
把文件歸檔 place the papers on file;
[歸隊] (1) rejoin one's unit; report for duty; report to the ranks; (2) return to the profession one is trained for;
[歸附] submit to the authority of another;
[歸根] in the end;
歸根到底 after all; in the final analysis; in the long run; when all is said and done;
歸根結蒂 boil down to; come down to bedrock; get down to bedrock; get to the root of the problem; in the end; in the final analysis; in the last analysis; in the long run; when all is said and done;
[歸公] be made a public possession; go to the public;
掃數歸公 the entire amount is contributed to the public; the whole amount is confiscated for the public;
[歸功於] attribute the success to; be attributed to sth; be credited with sth; credit sth to sb; give the credit to; owe to;
[歸國] return to one's country;
[歸航] homing;
被動歸航 passive homing;
定向歸航 directional homing;
跟踪歸航 racking homing;
紅外線歸航 infrared homing;
滑翔機歸航 glider homing;
自動歸航 automatic homing;
[歸化] (1) adopt the customs of; submit to the rule of; (2) be naturalized; (3) be naturalized;
[歸還] send back; give back; return; revert;
按期歸還 return on time;
[歸家] home-coming; return home;
無家可歸 be rendered homeless; homeless; without a home to go back to;
~ 無家可歸的人 derelict; down-and-out;
[歸結] (1) put in a nutshell; sum up; (2) end of a story;
歸結落空 end up in smoke; in the end get nothing;
[歸究] attribute a fault to; impute to; put the blame on;
歸究於人 ascribe a fault to others; ascribe the crime to; blame sth on others; lay the blame on sb else; put the blame on; throw the blame on;
[歸口] put under centralized management;
歸口單位 specified administrative department enterprise;
歸口管理 centralized management by specialized departments;
歸口領導 leadership under a specified administrative department;
[歸類] (1) classification; classify; sort out; (2) grouping;
把貨物歸類 arrange goods in classes;
[歸攏] put together; take in;
[歸納] conclude; induce; sum up;
歸納反駁 inductive refutation;
歸納論證 inductive argument;
歸納邏輯 inductive logic;
歸納推理 inductive inference;
歸納證明 inductive proof;
[歸寧] go back to maternal home for a visit;
[歸期] date of return;
[歸僑] returned overseas Chinese;
[歸入] classify; include;

[歸生] a surname;
[歸屬] belong to; come under the jurisdiction of;
歸屬地位 ascribed status;
歸屬感 sense of belonging;
歸屬理論 attribution theory;
[歸順] come over and pledge allegiance; pay allegaince to; yield surrender;
[歸宿] home to return to;
必然歸宿 inevitable outcome;
[歸天] die; pass away;
[歸田] resign from office and return home;
解甲歸田 quit military service and resume civilian life; take off one's armour and go home – retire from office;
解綬歸田 resign one's post to live and toil on one's own farm;
卸甲歸田 take off one's armour and go home – retire from office;
[歸途] homeward journey; one's way home;
[歸西] die; pass away;
病老歸西 die of old age; go to the paradise in the west;
駕鶴歸西 mount and ride away to Elysium – die;
撒手歸西 die; go to the western Heaven; go west; pass away; pay one's debt of nature;
一命歸西 die; pass away;
[歸降] surrender;
[歸向] incline to; turn towards;
[歸心似箭] anxious to go back home; anxious to return home as soon as possible; eager to dart homeward; impatient to get back; long to return home; return with the swiftness of an arrow;
[歸省] go home for a visit; go home to pay respects to one's parents;
歸省故里 pay a visit to one's native village;
[歸因] ascribe to; attribute to;
[歸於] (1) be attributed to; belong to; (2) end in; result in; tend to;
歸於泡影 come to naught; come to nothing; go up in smoke;
歸於無效 neutralize;
[歸著] put in order; tidy up;
[歸真] return to one's original purity;
歸真反璞 rediscover one's true self; regain nature; return to one's original purity and simplicity; return to original purity and simplicity;
返璞歸真 recover one's original simplicity; return to one's original nature;
[歸正] mend one's ways; reform oneself;
[歸置] clear away; put in order; tidy up;
[歸總] put together; sum up;
歸總一句話 in a word; to put it in a nutshell;
[歸組] grouping;
[歸罪] impute to; incriminate; inculpate; put the blame on;
歸罪於人 ascribe the crime to others; lay the blame on others; scapegoatism;

當歸 Chinese angelica;
回歸 draw; retreat;
來歸 come over and pledge allegiance; submit to the authority;
榮歸 return in glory;
同歸 get to the same destination; have the same ending;
終歸 after all; eventually; in the end;
總歸 after all; anyhow; eventually;

gui

【瓌】 (1) same as 瑰, a kind of jasper; (2) admirable; extraordinary; fabulous;
[瓌寶] extraordinary treasure;
[瓌奇] rare and precious things;

gui³

gui

【宄】 thief; traitor; treacherous fellow;

gui

【癸】 last of the Ten Celestial Stems;

gui

【軌】 (1) rail; track; (2) course; path;
[軌道] course; orbit; orbital; path; track;
軌道安全 track safety;
~ 軌道安全設備 track safety appliances;
軌道參數 orbital parameters;
軌道面 orbital plane;
軌道平面 orbital plane;
軌道傾角 orbit inclination;
軌道速度 orbital velocity;
軌道衰減 orbital decay;
軌道週期 orbital period;
閉軌道 closed orbit;
電車軌道 electric car tracks;

分子軌道 molecular orbital;
火車軌道 train rails;
既定軌道 definitive orbit;
漸近軌道 asymptotic orbit;
交替軌道 alternant orbital;
前沿軌道 frontal orbital;
上軌道 begin to work smoothly; get on the right track; well under way;
同步軌道 geostationary orbit; synchronous orbit;
一條軌道 a path;
原子軌道 atomic orbit;
圓軌道 circular orbit;
直接軌道 direct orbit;

[軌跡] (1) locus; path; way; (2) orbit;
額外軌跡 extraneous locus;
飛行軌跡 flight path;
振幅值軌跡 amplitude locus;
效率軌跡 efficiency locus;

[軌枕] sleeper; tie;
不合格軌枕 failed sleeper;
浮動軌枕 floating tie;
合成軌枕 composite sleeper;
混凝土軌枕 concrete sleeper;
硬木軌枕 hardwood sleeper;
組合軌枕 composite tie;

不軌 against the law or discipline;
常軌 normal course;
出軌 (1) be derailed; go off the rails; (2) overstep the bounds;
單軌 one-track;
鋼軌 rail;
接軌 (1) connect the rails; (2) integrate;
鋪軌 railway track;
雙軌 double track;
鐵軌 rail;
脱軌 derail;
越軌 exceed the bounds;
正軌 right path;

gui

【鬼】 (1) ghost; spirit; spook; (2) stealthy; surreptitious; (3) dirty trick; sinister plot; (4) damnable; terrible; (5) clever; quick; smart;

[鬼不招不來] ghosts do not come in unless they are invited;

[鬼城] ghost town;

[鬼怪] boogeyman; evil spirits; forces of evil; ghosts and monsters; monsters of all kinds;
驅除鬼怪 exorcise the evil spirit;
驅趕鬼怪 keep off evil spirit;

[鬼䰟] surname;

[鬼畫符] (1) scrawly handwriting; (2) hypocritical talk;

[鬼話] baloney; deceptive remarks; lies; nonsense; outright lies;
鬼話連篇 a pack of lies; tell a whole series of lies;
説鬼話 lie; tell a lie;
~見人説人話，見鬼説鬼話 double-cross; double-faced; scratch sb where he feels an itch;

[鬼魂] apparition; disembodied spirits; ghost; spectre; spirit;

[鬼混] fool about; fool around; lead an aimless or irregular existence; play about; potter about; run around;

[鬼火] jack-o'-lantern; will-o'-the wisp;

[鬼計多端] full of schemes and tricks; wily and mischievous;

[鬼節] ghost festival; spirit festival;

[鬼哭] devils weep;
鬼哭狼嚎 let loose wild shrieks and howls; set up wild shrieks and howls; utter dreary cries and screams; wail and howl in a piercing and terrifying voice; wail like ghosts and howl like wolves;
狼嚎鬼哭 blood-curdling shrieks; give dreary cries and screams; howl like wolves and wail like ghosts; pathetic cries; set up wild shrieks and howls;

[鬼臉] (1) funny face; grimace; wry face; (2) mask used as a toy;
扮鬼臉 make faces; make grimaces; mop and mow;
做鬼臉 make a face; make faces; pull a face;

[鬼靈精] clever and mischievous person;

[鬼魅] forces of evil; ghosts and goblins;

[鬼門關] danger spot; Gate of Hell; jaws of death; trying moment;
鬼門關出告示—鬼話連篇 a notice put up at the Gate of Hell — all devilish words; a pack of lies;

[鬼迷心竅] be obsessed with; be corrupted by; be possessed by ghosts; under the obsession of sth;

[鬼魔三道] indecent;
[鬼神] ghosts and gods; spirits; supernatural beings;
鬼神不測 beyond the ken of god or devil;
鬼神崇拜 demonolatry;
~鬼神崇拜者 demonologist;
鬼神恐怖 demonophobia;
鬼神學 demonology;
鬼斧神工 extraordinary as if done by the spirits; superlative craftsmanship;
鬼哭神嚎 demons weeping and spirits crying — a dreadful clamour; devils howl and spirits cry;
鬼泣神號 devilish howling; the ghosts weep and the gods howl;
鬼使神差 at the behest of supernatural powers; curious coincidence; doings of ghosts and gods; messengers of the gods and spirits; unexpected happenings;
泣鬼神 move not only men, but also the spirits and gods;
[鬼祟] dishonourable; intriguing; tricky;
鬼鬼祟祟 act secretively; behind one's back; behind the curtain; clandestinely; furtive; hole-and-corner; like a thief in the night; lurk and sneak around like a ghost; maliciously and secretly; on the cross; slinky; sneaky; stealthily; surreptitious; thievish; under the counter; up to some hanky-panky; with a hangdog expression;
~鬼鬼祟祟的 furtive;
[鬼胎] sinister design; ulterior motive;
懷鬼胎 cherish evil schemes; have a bad conscience; pregnant with evil schemes; with evil in one's heart; with ulterior motive;
~各懷鬼胎 each has his own ax to grind; each has sth up his sleeve; each one harbours his sinister designs;
~心懷鬼胎 cherish evil designs; with ulterior motives;
[鬼頭蛤蟆眼] furtive; stealthy;
[鬼物] ghost; spirit;
[鬼黠] crafty; sly;
[鬼蟹] ghost crab;
[鬼蜮] demon; spirit; treacherous person;
鬼蜮伎倆 devilish stratagem; devilish tricks; evil tactics; malicious intrigues; underhanded tricks; vicious plots;
鬼蜮為災 this calamity is caused by evil spirits;
為鬼為蜮 injure others in secret;
[鬼子] devil;
鬼子煙 imported cigarettes;
洋鬼子 foreign devil;

白鬼 whitey;
膽小鬼 coward;
搗鬼 do mischief; play tricks;
賭鬼 gambler;
短命鬼 person who dies young;
惡鬼 devil;
搞鬼 play tricks; up to some mischief;
活見鬼 it's sheer fantasy; you're imaging things;
見鬼 (1) absurd; fantastic; (2) go to hell;
酒鬼 drunkard; sot;
懶鬼 lazy bones;
厲鬼 ferocious ghost;
冒失鬼 harum-scarum;
魔鬼 devil; monster;
怕死鬼 coward;
缺德鬼 mean person;
死鬼 devil;
淘氣鬼 mischievous imp;
替死鬼 fall guy; scape goat;
吸血鬼 blood-sucker; vampire;
小鬼 (1) imp; (2) little devil;
小氣鬼 miser; niggard;
煙鬼 (1) heavy smoker; (2) opium addict;
醉鬼 drunkard; sot;
做鬼 get up to mischief; play an underhand game; play tricks;

gui

【匭】 box; casket; chest;

gui

【晷】 (1) shadows caused by the sun; (2) sundial; (3) time;
[晷影] shadows;

日晷 sundial;
餘晷 spare time;

gui

【詭】 (1) cunning; deceitful; trickly; (2) weird;
[詭辯] casuistry; quibbling; sophism; sophistry;
詭辯術 casuistry;
[詭稱] falsely allege; pretend;
[詭怪] odd; strange;

G

［詭計］ chicanery; crafty plot; cunning scheme; trick;
詭計多端 as cunning as a fox; as tricky as monkey; be up to all the dodges; bromful of mischief; crafty; foxy and wily; full of craft; full of cunning manoeuvre; full of tricks; have a bag full of tricks; have a flair for intrigue; know every sort of wicked guile; play many deceitful tricks; use every cunning trick;
~詭計多端的 crafty;
精於詭計 be skilled in deception;
識破詭計 see through a trick;
下流詭計 lousy trick;
中詭計 be caught in a trap;
［詭譎］ (1) strange and changeful; treacherous; (2) eccentric and wild;
詭譎多詐 sly and shrewd; treacherous and cunning;
波譎雲詭 beautiful turns of thought; fast, unexpected, exciting changes; sudden and perplexing changes;
［詭戾］ treacherous and perverse;
［詭秘］ secretive; surreptitious;
行動詭秘 behave queerly;
［詭特］ marvellous; remarkable;
［詭異］ strange;
［詭詐］ crafty; cunning; treacherous;
詭詐取寵 worm oneself into one's favour;
［詭諸］ surname;

雲譎波詭 fast and unexpected changes; sudden and perplexing changes;

gui
【簋】 round bamboo vessel for holding grains in ancient offerings;

gui⁴
gui
【桂】 (1) cassia; cinnamon; (2) name for Guangxi province; (3) a surname;
［桂宮］ moon;
［桂冠］ crown of laurels; laurel;
桂冠詩人 Poet Laureate;
［桂花］ sweet-scented osmanthus;
桂花陳酒 old wine fermented with osmanthus flowers;
［桂皮］ cassia bark;
［桂魚］ mandarin fish;
［桂圓］ longan;
［桂子飄香］ fragrance of the laurel blossoms fills the air;

丹桂 organge osmanthus;
肉桂 Chinese cassia tree; Chinese cinnamon;

gui
【貴】 (1) costly; dear; expensive; (2) highly valued; precious; valuable; (3) noble; of high rank; (4) your;
［貴賓］ distinguished guest; honoured guest;
款待貴賓 entertain the distinguished guests;
宴請貴賓 feast one's honoured guests;
招待貴賓 receive guests of distinction;
［貴妃］ highest-ranking imperial concubine;
［貴婦］ gentlewoman; noble lady;
貴婦狗 poodle;
［貴庚］ may I know your age;
［貴國］ your country;
［貴賤］ (1) cheap or expensive; (2) high or low;
貴賤上下 the rich, the poor, the high, and the low;
不分貴賤 irrespective of high or low birth; make no distinctions between the high and the low;
賤斂貴出 buy cheap and sell dear; purchase at low prices and offer for sale at high prices;
一貴一賤，交情乃見 prosperity gets followers, but adversity distinguishes them; prosperity makes friends, adversity tries them;
［貴精不貴多］ it is quality rather than quantity that counts; things are valued for their quality rather than their numbers;
［貴人］ (1) high-ranking government official; (2) title of a female palace official;
貴人多忘 a highly placed person is apt to be forgetful; a person of distinction always has a poor memory; a person of your eminence has a short memory; great people are apt to have short memories; important people have short memories;
達官貴人 government officials; high cockalorums; high officials and noble lords; magnates; prominent officals and eminent personages; the upper crust; VIPs;

[貴姓] your family name; your last name; your surname;
[貴恙] your illness;
[貴重] precious; valuable;
貴重商品 articles of price;
貴重物品 valuable article;
[貴冑] descendants of nobles;
黃炎貴冑 Chinese nationals; princes of the blood of Huangdi and Yandi;
[貴族] aristocrat; nobility; noble; nobleman; peer; peerage;
貴族爵位 peerage;
男貴族 nobleman;
女貴族 noblewoman; peeress;
終生貴族 life peer;

昂貴 costly; dear; expensive;
寶貴 (1) precious; treasured; valuable; (2) rich and honoured;
高貴 (1) high; noble; (2) highly privileged;
華貴 (1) costly; luxurious; sumptuous; (2) gorgeous; sumptuous;
可貴 commendable; praiseworthy;
名貴 famous and precious; rare;
親貴 monarch's close relatives or trusted followers;
權貴 influential officials;
恃貴 presume on one's high position;
顯貴 influential officials;
新貴 new money; new rich; upstart;
珍貴 precious; valuable;p
尊貴 distinguished; honourable; respectable;

G

gui
【跪】 fall on one's knees; go down on one's knees; kneel;
[跪拜] worship on bended knees; kowtow;
跪拜父母 fall at one's parents' feet to worship them;
跪拜祖先 worship one's ancestors on bended knees;
屈膝跪拜 genuflection;
[跪倒] grovel; prostrate oneself; throw oneself on one's knees;
跪倒腳下 throw oneself at sb's feet;
跪倒在地 go down on one's knees; kneel on the ground;
[跪地] kneel on the ground;
跪地哀求 kneel on the ground crying for mercy;
跪地乞命 lie in the dust pleading for one's life;
跪地乞饒 prostrate oneself before sb and beg for mercy and forgiveness; throw oneself on the ground and plead for mercy;
[跪伏] couch;
[跪落] knee drop;
[跪下] drop to one's knees; kneel;
跪下求饒 fall to one's knees, begging for mercy; kneel down begging for pardon;
[跪姿] kneeling position;
跪姿射擊 shoot from a kneeling position;

下跪 go down on one's knees; kneel down;

gui
【洼】 name of a river;

gui
【劊】 amputate; cut off;
[劊子手] (1) executioner; (2) butcher; hatchetman; slaughterman;

gui
【瞶】 dim-sighted; poor vision—sometimes as a result of old age;

gui
【檜】 a pronunciation of 檜, the Chinese cypress;

gui
【櫃】 (1) cabinet; cupboard; wardrobe; (2) counter; shop;
[櫃櫥] cupboard; showcase;
[櫃房] cashier's office;
[櫃門] wardrobe door;
[櫃台] bar; counter; desk;
櫃台服務員 desk clerk;
[櫃員] counter clerk;
櫃員機 teller machine;
~自動櫃員機 automatic teller machine; cash dispenser; cash machine;
[櫃桌] hutch table;
[櫃子] cabinet; chest; cupboard; sark;
[櫃組] group;

保險櫃 safe;
陳列櫃 showcase;
櫥櫃 cupboard;
牀頭櫃 bedside cupboard;
酒櫃 drinks cabinet;
攔櫃 shop counter;

錢櫃 money-locker;
書櫃 bookcase;
五斗櫃 chest of drawers; commode;
衣櫃 wardrobe;

gui
【鱖】 a pronunciation of 鱖 , mandarinfish;

gun³
gun
【袞】 (1) imperial robe with embroidered dragons; (2) high officials; robes of very high officials;
［袞服］ ceremonial dress of the emperor;
［袞袞］ (1) continual; (2) numerous;
袞袞諸公 high-ranking officials;

gun
【滾】 (1) roll; trundle; (2) beat it; get away; get out; (3) boil; (4) bind; hem; trim;
［滾蛋］ beat it; drop dead; eff off; fuck off; get away; get out; go piss up a rope; off with you; scram; sling out; sling your hook;
［滾刀］ hob;
滾刀肉 head meat to be chopped up — a difficult person;
鏈輪滾刀 wheel hob;
圓盤滾刀 disk hob;
錐形滾刀 conical hob;
［滾動］ rotate;
滾動承包 rolling contract;
［滾翻］ roll;
側滾翻 sideward roll;
後滾翻 backward roll;
前滾翻 forward roll;
［滾瓜爛熟］ at one's tongue's end; have sth at one's fingertip; know thoroughly by heart; rattle off with the greatest of ease; ready and smooth;
［滾滾］ billow; roll; roll on; rush on; surge;
滾滾波濤 the tumble of the waves;
滾滾而來 come in torrents; roll in;
滾滾而下 rush down in a torrent;
滾滾激流 tumbling torrent;
滾滾入海 roll to the sea;
滾滾向前 roll forward; roll on; surge forward;
白浪滾滾 white-crested waves rolled in all directions;
波濤滾滾 waves rolled on;
淚珠滾滾 tears trickled down in drops;
熱淚滾滾 warm tears streaming down one's face;
思緒滾滾 the flow of ideas;
心潮滾滾 feel an upsurge of emotion;
珠淚滾滾 one's tears fall like pearls and beans; tears pour down one's cheeks; the tears run from one's eyes in torrents;
［滾開］ bog off; bugger off; buzz off; fuck off; get lost; get out; go away; go piss up a rope; go to hell; naff off; piss off; scram;
［滾石不生苔］ a rolling stone gathers no moss;
［滾水］ boiling water;
［滾湯熱菜］ boiling soup and hot dishes; hot food;
［滾筒］ cylinder; roll;
［滾削］ hobbing;
對角線滾削 diagonal hobbing;
徑向滾削 radial hobbing;
切向滾削 tangential hobbing;
旋昇滾削 climb hobbing;
［滾油澆心］ mental anguish;
［滾珠］ ball; steel ball;
滑動滾珠 advance ball;
軸承滾球 bearing ball;

打滾 roll about; roll on the ground;
翻滾 roll; toss; tumble;

gun
【鯀】 (1) large fish; (2) father of the legendary ruler Yu 禹 ;

gun⁴
gun
【棍】 (1) club; cane; cudgel; stick; truncheon; (2) rascal; ruffian; villain;
［棍棒］ (1) club; cudgel; bludgeon; (2) staff; stick;
揮舞棍棒 brandish a club;
使用棍棒 use the rod;
［棍術］ cudgel play;
［棍水果糖］ rock;
［棍子］ rod; stick;
打棍子 criticize; punish;
倔巴棍子 rude fellow;
一根棍子 a stick;

賭棍 hardened gambler;
惡棍 bully; rascal; scoundrel;

拐棍 walking stick;
光棍 hoodlum; ruffian;
警棍 policeman's baton;
悶棍 staggering blow with a cudgel;
土棍 local ruffian; village bully;
淫棍 immoral man;

guo¹

guo

【郭】 (1) outer wall of a city; (2) outer part of anything; (3) a surname;
［郭公］ cuckoo;
［郭公蟲］ clerid;
［郭外］ beyond the outer city wall; outside the city;

城郭 city walls; inner and outer city walls;
耳郭 auricle;

guo

【渦】 a surname;
［渦河］ the Guohe River in Anhui;

guo

【過】 a surname;
［過福］ be dissatisfied with good creature comforts one has;
［過熱］ overheat; superheat; superheating;
過熱的 overheated;
過熱器 superheater;
~ 對流式過熱器 convection superheater;
~ 接觸過熱器 contact superheater;
~ 螺旋管過熱器 spiral superheater;
~ 外置式過熱器 external superheater;
核過熱 nuclear superheating;
經濟過熱 economic overheat;

guo

【蟈】 (1) frog; (2) mole cricket;
［蟈蟈兒］ catydid; long-horned grasshopper;

guo

【鍋】 (1) cooking pan; pan; pot; (2) a boiler of; a caldron of; a pan of; a pot of;
［鍋巴］ rice crust;
油炸鍋巴 oil-fried rice crust;
［鍋把］ pan handle;
［鍋餅］ wheat cake;
［鍋鏟］ fish slice; shovel slice; turner;
［鍋底］ bottom of a pan;
鍋底朝天 no rice at all in the pot; nothing to eat in the house;
黑如鍋底 as black as a crow; as black as the bottom of a frying pan;
［鍋墊］ tablemat;
［鍋耳］ pot lug;
［鍋蓋］ lid of a cooking pot;
鍋蓋把 knob of a pan lid;
［鍋裏滿才有碗裏滿］ there will be more in one's own bowl only if the pot is full;
［鍋爐］ boiler;
鍋爐房 boiler room;
鍋爐間 boiler room;
對流式鍋爐 convection boiler;
複合式鍋爐 composite boiler;
複式鍋爐 combination boiler;
橫管鍋爐 cross tube boiler;
回焰鍋爐 back-flame boiler;
逆流式鍋爐 counterflow boiler;
盤管鍋爐 coil boiler;
汽包鍋爐 drum boiler;
燒煤鍋爐 coal-fired boiler;
雙頭鍋爐 double-ended boiler;
順流鍋爐 concurrent boiler;
循環鍋爐 circulation boiler;
~ 複合循環鍋爐 combined circulation boiler;
~ 受控循環鍋爐 controlled circulation boiler;
一個鍋爐 a boiler;
一座鍋爐 a boiler;
直焰式鍋爐 direct-flame boiler;
鑄鐵鍋爐 cast-iron boiler;
錐形鍋爐 conical boiler;
［鍋台］ kitchen range surface; top of a kitchen range;
［鍋貼］ fried dumpling;
［鍋子］ (1) pot; (2) chafing pot;
涮鍋子 chafing-pot meal;

扒鍋 stick to the pot;
不黏鍋 non-stick pan;
炒菜鍋 cooking pot;
炒鍋 frying pan;
單柄鍋 saucepan;
飯鍋 pot for cooking rice; rice cooker;
高壓鍋 pressure cooker;
回鍋 cook again;
火鍋 hot pot;
汽鍋 steamer;
沙鍋 earthenware cooking pot;
湯鍋 slaughterhouse; stockpot;
一個鍋 a pan;
一口鍋 a pan;

G

蒸鍋 steamer;
煮魚鍋 fish kettle;

guo²
guo

【國】 (1) country; nation; state; (2) national; of the state; (3) Chinese; of our country; (4) a surname;
出國 go abroad;

[國寶] national treasure;

[國本] fundamental principles to administer a country;

[國賓] state guest;

[國柄] political power of a nation;

[國策] basic policy of a state; national policy;
基本國策 basic state policy;

[國產] domestic; made in one's country;

[國恥] national humiliation;

[國粹] quintessence of Chinese culture;

[國都] capital; national capital;

[國度] country; nation; state;

[國法] law; national law; law of the land;
國法無情 the law is no respecter of persons;

[國防] national defence;
國防部 ministry of national defence;
國防地理學 national defence geography;
國防發展戰略 strategy of national defence development;
國防費用 military spending;
國防工業 national defence industry;
國防計量學 national defence metrology;
國防建設 national defence construction; the building up of national defence;
國防教育 national defence education;
~國防教育法 laws of national defence;
國防經濟 economy of national defence;
~國防經濟學 economics of national defence;
國防軍 national defence force;
國防力量 defence capability;
國防潛力 national defence potential;
國防人口 national defence population;
國防生產 defence production;
國防體制 national defence structure;
國防通信衛星 national defence satellite communications system;
國防現代化 modernization of national defence;
國防線 national defence line;
國防心理學 psychology of national defence;
國防政策 national defence policy;
國防支出 defence spending;

[國父] father of a nation;

[國富] national wealth;
國富民強 the nation is prosperous and the people are strong and powerful;
國富民殷 the people are noble and the country prosperous;
民殷國富 the people are noble and the country prosperous; the people live in plenty and the country prospers;

[國歌] national anthem;
唱國歌 sing the national anthem;
典禮開始前先奏國歌 the ceremony commenced with national anthem;

[國格] national character and morals; national dignity;

[國故] ancient learning; national cultural heritage;

[國號] title of a reigning dynasty;

[國花] national flower;

[國畫] traditional Chinese painting;
國畫技巧 technique in the traditional Chinese painting;

[國徽] national emblem;
懸掛國徽 hang the national emblem;

[國會] congress; parliament;
國會女議員 congresswoman;
國會委員會 congressional committee;
國會議員 congressman;

[國魂] national genius; soul of a nation;

[國籍] nationality;
國籍不明 unknown nationality;
保留國籍 retain nationality;
剝奪國籍 denationalization; deprivation of nationality;
出生國籍 nationality by birth;
多重國籍 plural nationality;
放棄國籍 renunciation of nationality;
改變國籍 change one's nationality;
恢復國籍 regain one's nationality; restoration of nationality;
喪失國籍 lose one's nationality;
雙重國籍 double nationality; dual nationality;
退出國籍 renounce one's nationality;
無國籍 stateless;
隱瞞國籍 disguise one's nationality;

[國際] international;
國際安定 international stability;
~破壞國際安定 destroy international stability;
國際版權公約 Universal Copyright Convention;
國際保護 international protection;
國際保險市場 international insurance market;
國際標準化組織 international standards organization;
國際標準集裝箱 ISO freight container;
國際標準期刊號 International Standard Serials Number;
國際標準書號 International Standard Book Number;
國際博覽會 international fair;
國際財政學 international public finance;
國際長途電話 international call;
國際長途直撥電話 international direct distance call;
國際承包工程 international contract project;
國際傳播 international communication;
國際電話 overseas telephone;
國際電匯 international telegraphic transfer;
國際法 international law;
國際公共關係 international public relations;
國際關係 international relations;
~國際關係學 international relations discipline;
國際慣例 customary international practice;
國際合作 international cooperation;
國際化 internationalization;
~國際化經營 internationalized operation;
國際交往 international intercourse;
國際結算 international clearing;
國際金融學 science of international finance;
國際經濟 international economics;
~國際經濟法學 science of international economic law;
~國際經濟關係 international economic relations;
~國際經濟新秩序 new international economic order;
~國際經濟一體化 international economic integration;
~國際經濟政策 international economic policies;
~國際經濟制裁 international economic sanction;
~國際經濟組織 international economic organization;
國際經營 international operation;
國際競爭力 international competition capability;
國際局勢 international situation;
國際恐怖活動 international terror activities;
國際恐怖主義 international terrorism;
國際會計 international accounting;
~國際會計準則 international accounting standards;
國際勞務 international labour;
~國際勞務合同 international labour contract;
~國際勞務合作 international labour cooperation;
~國際勞務貿易 international labour trade;
國際貿易 international trade;
~國際貿易地區 international trade district;
~國際貿易法 international trade law;
~國際貿易工程 international trade engineering;
~國際貿易慣例 practice of international trade;
~國際貿易經濟 international trade economy;
~國際貿易系統 international trade system;
~國際貿易學 science of international trade;
~國際貿易證書 certificate of international trade;
~國際貿易支付方式 mode of payment in international trade;
~國際貿易值 value of international trade;
國際票匯 international remittance by bank draft;
國際企業 international enterprise;
國際遷移 international migration;
國際商事仲裁 international commercial arbitration;
國際社會 international community; international society;
~國際社會保障 international social security;
國際申請 international application;
國際生態學 international ecology;
國際市場 international market;

G

~ 國際市場學 science of international marketing;
國際事務 international affairs; international matters;
~ 國際事務專家 expert in international affairs;
國際視野 horizons of the world;
~ 開拓國際視野 broaden horizons of the world;
國際收支 balance of international payments;
~ 國際收支逆差 balance of international payments deficit;
~ 國際收支平衡 equilibrium of balance of international payments;
~ 國際收支順差 balance of international payments surplus;
~ 國際收支危機 balance of international payments crisis;
國際稅法 international tax law;
國際稅收 international taxation;
國際跳棋 checkers; draughts;
~ 國際跳棋棋盤 draughtboard;
國際通信衛星 international telecommunication satellite;
國際投資 international investment;
~ 國際投資法 international investment law;
~ 國際投資法學 science of international investment law;
國際托收 international collection;
國際象棋 chess;
國際協定 international agreement;
國際信匯 international mail transfer;
國際刑法 international criminal law;
國際行政法學 study of international administrative law;
國際學校 international school;
國際義務 international obligation;
國際銀行信貸 international bank credit;
國際營銷學 international operating and marketing techniques;
國際有限招標 limited international bidding;
國際輿論 world opinion;
國際債券 international bond;
國際展覽中心 international exhibition centre;
國際戰略 international strategy;
國際爭端 international disputes;
國際政治 international politics;
~ 國際政治環境 international political environment;
~ 國際政治經濟 international political economy;
國際直接投資 international direct investment;
國際主義 internationalism;
國際專利 international patent;
~ 國際專利分類法 international patent classification;
國際資金 international fund;
國際租賃制 international leasing system;
國際組織 international organizations;
蜚聲國際 be internationally known;

[國家] country; nation; state;
國家安全 national security;
~ 危及國家安全 threaten the national security;
國家財政 state finance;
國家出口產品 national export products;
國家地位 nationhood;
國家隊 national team;
國家發明 state invention;
~ 國家發明獎 state award for invention;
國家發展 national development;
國家法人 legal person of a state;
國家高新技術區 state high and new tech zone;
國家公務員制度 system of public service;
國家觀念 concepts of the state;
國家核安全局 national nuclear safety board;
國家環保局 national environment protection bureau;
國家活力 national vitality;
國家機構 national organization;
國家機關 state agency; state organ;
~ 國家機關工作人員 state employees;
國家機密 state secrets;
~ 洩漏國家機密 betrayal of state secrets;
國家機器 state apparatus;
國家級 national level;
~ 國家級鑒定 national-level appraisal;
~ 國家級企業 national-grade enterprise;
國家開發銀行 national development bank;
國家牌價 price set by the state;
國家賠償 state compensation;
~ 國家賠償法 state compensation liability;
國家書目 national bibliography;
國家稅收 state tax;
國家衛生城市 national hygienic city;
國家興亡，匹夫有責 all people share a

common responsibility for the fate of their country; every person alive has a duty to his/her country; every person has a share of responsibility for the fate of his/her country; the rise and fall of the nation is the concern of every citizen;
國家預算 national budget;
國家元首 head of state;
國家責任 national responsibility;
國家戰略 national strategy;
國家至上 national interest comes above enverything else;
國家主權 national sovereignty;
~維護國家主權 safeguard national sovereignty;
保衛國家 safeguard one's country;
報效國家 serve the nation;
背叛國家 betray one's country;
不結盟國家 non-aligned nations;
大陸法國家 civil law country;
代表國家 represent the country;
獨立國家 independent country;
發達國家 advanced country; developed country;
~半發達國家 semi-developed nation;
~不發達國家 underdeveloped nation;
~超級發達國家 superdeveloped country;
~欠發達國家 underdeveloped country;
發展中國家 developing country;
法治國家 legal state;
福利國家 welfare state;
共產主義國家 communist country;
國破家亡 the country is defeated and the home lost;
結盟國家 aligned nations;
~不結盟國家 non-aligned nations;
傀儡國家 puppet state;
聯邦國家 federal state;
領導國家 lead the country;
民主國家 democratic country;
全民福利國家 welfare state;
説英語的國家 English-speaking world;
逃離國家 flee the country;
統治國家 rule a country;
完整的國家 undivided country;
西方國家 Western nations;
友好國家 friendly nation;
治理國家 over the country; run the country;
主權國家 sovereign state;
專制國家 authoritarian state;

資本主義國家 capitalist country;
資源豐富的國家 a country abundant with resources;
自由國家 free country;
自由主義國家 free nation;
自治國家 autonomous state;

[國交] diplomatic relations between nations;

[國教] state religion;

[國界] national boundaries;
超越國界 overstep national boundaries;
劃定國界 fix national boundaries;
確定國界 define national boundaries;

[國境] frontier; territory;
守衛國境 guard the border;
逃越國境 escape over the border;

[國舅] maternal uncle of a prince;

[國君] monarch;

[國庫] exchequer; national treasury;
國庫券 treasury bill; treasury bond; treasury note;

[國力] national capabilities; national power; national strength;
國力評價 national strength assessment;
國力雄厚 have solid national strength;
超越國力 go beyond the state's capability;
綜合國力 overall national strength; overall strength of the country;
~提高綜合國力 improve the overall national strength;

[國立] national; state-maintained; state-run;
國立大學 national university;

[國民] (1) national; (2) the state and the people;
國民教育 national education;
國民經濟 national economy;
~國民經濟管理學 management science of national economy;
~國民經濟核算體系 system of national accounts;
~國民經濟計劃 national economic plan;
~國民經濟良性循環 fair circulation of national economy;
國民生產淨值 net national product;
國民生產總值 gross national product;
國民生計 national economy and the people's livelihood;
國民收入 national income; national revenue;
本生國民 natural-born citizen;
病國病民 injure both the state and the people;

病國殃民 injure both the state and the people;
歸化國民 naturalized national;
國泰民安 the country is prosperous and the people are at peace;
害國殃民 a scourge of the country and the people; harm the nation and the country; play havoc with the nation and the people; wreck the country and ruin the people;
禍國殃民 a bane to the country and the people; bring calamity to the country and people; bring misfortune to the whole nation; bring untold suffering and damage to the state and the people; cause serious harm to the state and the people; compromise the state and bring misfortune upon the people; damage the country and bring calamity to the people; do harm to the country and people; injure the country and bring calamity to the people; play havoc with the nation and the poeple; ruin a country and bring sorrow to its people; wreck the country and bring ruin to the people;
利國利民 benefit the nation and the people; bring profit to one's country and the people;
為國為民 for the state and the people;
貽殃國民 bring misfortune to the people;
憂國憂民 anxious about the destiny of the state and the people; be concerned about one's country and one's people; be concerned over the fate of the nation; worry about the fate of one's country and the people; worry for the country and the people;
淤國害民 do harm to the nation and the people; pollute the state and oppress the people;

[國難] national calamity;
國難當頭 the country is facing a crisis;
國難方殷 the nation is facing a great danger;
國難深重 serious national calamity;
共赴國難 call for united efforts to save the nation; play citizen's part when nation calls;

[國內] domestic; home; internal;
國內貿易 domestic trade; internal trade;
國內生產總值 gross domestic product;
國內市場 domestic market; home market;
國內事務 home affairs;
國內特快專遞 domestic express mail;

[國旗] national flag;
降國旗 haul down the national flag; lower the national flag;
昇國旗 put up the national flag; raise the national flag;

[國情] national conditions; conditions of a country; situations of the country;
國情國策 national situation and policy;
國情經濟學 economics of national conditions;
國情咨文 State of the Union Address;
了解國情 understand the situations of the country;
我國國情 our own national conditions;

[國慶] National Day;

[國人] compatriots; countrymen; fellow countrymen;
同國人 compatriot;

[國色] national beauty;
國色天香 celestial beauty; national beauty and heavenly fragrance;
國色天姿 celestial beauty; woman of great beauty; possess surpassing beauty;
天香國色 a woman of great beauty; heaven fragrance and national beauty;

[國殤] national martyr;

[國史] national history;

[國事] national affairs;

[國是] national affairs;

[國勢] (1) national power; (2) national situation at a given moment;

[國筬] a surname;

[國手] national champion;

[國書] letter of credence; credential;

[國術] traditional Chinese boxing and fencing;

[國帑] national funds; public funds;

[國體] (1) state system; (2) national prestige;

[國土] land; territory;
國土安全 homeland security;
國土規劃 territorial programme;
～國土規劃局 territorial programme;
國土經濟學 economics of territory;
國土整治 territory renovation;
～國土整治規劃 territory renovation planning;
～國土整治戰略 territory renovation strategy;

國土資源 land resources;

[國外] abroad; external; overseas;

國外工作 work overseas;

國外銷售 overseas sales;

在國外 be abroad;

~住在國外 live abroad;

[國王] king;

國王身分 kingship;

[國威] national prestige;

[國文] Chinese as the national language;

[國務] affairs of the state; national affairs;

國務大臣 minister of state;

國務委員 state councilor;

國務院 State Council;

處理國務 conduct state affairs;

[國璽] broad seal; great seal; the seal of the state;

[國學] studies of Chinese ancient civilization;

[國宴] state banquet;

[國藥] traditional Chinese medicine;

[國醫] (1) traditional Chinese medical science; (2) doctor of traditional Chinese medicine;

[國音] standard Chinese pronunciation approved by the government;

[國營] state-operated; state-run;

國營的 state-run;

國營經濟 state economy; state-owned economy;

國營企業 state-owned enterprise;

[國有] belong to the state; nationalized;

國有大型企業 state-owned big enterprise;

國有公司 state-owned corporation;

國有國法，家有家法 a country has its laws and a family its rules;

國有化 nationalization;

~非國有化 non-nationalization;

國有經濟 state-owned economy;

~非國有經濟 non-state-owned economy;

國有民營 nation-owned and people-operated way;

國有企業 state-owned enterprise;

~國有企業法 law of state-owned enterprise;

國有銀行 state-owned bank;

~國有銀行資產 asset of national bank;

國有專業銀行 state specialized bank;

國有資本 government capital;

國有資產 state-owned assets;

~國有資產淨值 state-owned assets net value;

~國有資產流失 loss of state-owned assets;

~國有資產評估 state-owned assets valuation;

~國有資產授權經營 authorized management of state-owned assets;

收歸國有 nationalize;

[國語] (1) national language used by the people at large; (2) Chinese textook for students of primary or secondary school;

國語羅馬字 national Romanization;

[國樂] traditional Chinese music;

[國葬] state funeral;

[國賊] traitor;

國賊祿鬼 time-servers and place-seekers;

[國債] government loan; national debt;

國債貨幣化 monetization of national debts;

愛國 love one's country; patriotic;

報國 dedicate oneself to the service of one's country;

本國 one's own country;

秉國 hold political power; in power;

出國 go abroad;

島國 island country;

敵國 enemy state;

帝國 empire;

東道國 host country;

獨立國 independent country;

發送國 forwarding country;

複本位國 double standard country;

共和國 republic;

故國 one's motherland;

歸國 return to one's country;

合眾國 United States;

建國 (1) found a state; (2) build up a country;

交戰國 belligerent powers;

金本位國 gold standard country;

金幣國 gold reserve country;

救國 save the country;

捐贈國 donor country;

舉國 whole nation;

開國 found a state;

理想國 utopia;

聯合國 United Nations;

列國 various countries;

賣國 betray one's country; turn traitor to one's country;

盟國 allied countries; ally;
農業國 agrarian country;
叛國 betray one's country; commit treason;
強國 power; powerful nation;
竊國 usurp state power;
酋長國 Sheikhdom;
全國 whole country;
弱國 weak country;
山國 mountainous country;
受惠國 benefit country;
受援國 assisted country;
輸出國 exporting country;
屬國 dependent state; vassal state;
鎖國 close the country to international intercourse;
通國 whole country; whole nation;
同盟國 allied nations;
外國 foreign country;
亡國 (1) conquered nation; (2) subjugate a nation;
王國 (1) kingdom; (2) domain; realm;
協約國 Entente states;
殉國 die for one's country;
異國 foreign country;
債權國 creditor nation;
債務國 debtor nation;
戰敗國 defeated nation;
戰勝國 victorious nation;
澤國 (1) land that abounds in rivers and lakes; (2) inundated area;
治國 administer a country; manage state affairs; run a country;
中立國 neutral state;
主權國 sovereign state;
祖國 home country; homeland; native land; one's country;

guo
【幗】 woman's headdress;

巾幗 (1) ancient woman's headdress; (2) woman;

guo
【摑】 box; slap another on his face;

guo
【虢】 name of an ancient feudal state;
［虢射］ a surname;

guo
【馘】 cut off the ear;

guo³
guo
【果】 (1) fruit; (2) consequence; result; (3) determined; resolute; (4) as expected; really; sure enough; (5) if indeed; if really;
［果斑］ fruit spots;
［果寶］ fruit juice;
［果餅］ fruitcake;
［果不其然］ as expected; indeed; not unexpectedly;
［果菜］ fruits and vegetables;
［果凍］ jelly;
果凍粉 jelly powder;
仿製果凍 imitation fruit jelly;
雜錦果凍 mixed fruit jelly;
［果斷］ decisive; resolute;
果斷的 assertive;
果斷的人 person of decision;
剛強果斷 firm and resolute;
生性果斷 have great decision of character;
行動果斷 act decisively; behave with resolution;
［果爾］ if so;
［果蝠］ fruit bat;
［果脯］ preserved fruit;
果脯膩人 the preserved fruit is too sweet;
［果腹］ fill the stomach; satisfy one's hunger;
食不果腹 have little food to eat; have not enough to eat; have not sufficient food to eat; insufficient food at meals; not to have enough food to eat;
~食不果腹，衣不蔽體 have not enough food and clothes;
［果敢］ courageous and resolute;
果敢行為 courageous and resolute action;
沉着果敢 iron nerves; nerves of iron; nerves of steel; steel nerves;
［果醬］ jam; marmalade; squish;
馬茉蘭果醬 marmalade;
~橙皮馬茉蘭果醬 orange marmalade;
~甜馬茉蘭果醬 sweet marmalade;
一層果醬 a layer of jam;
一罐果醬 a jar of jam;
［果酒］ fruit wine;
［果決］ firm and resolute;
剛毅果決 resolute and daring;
態度果決 hardball;
［果盤］ fruit basket; fruit tray;
［果皮］ peel; pill; rind; skin; skin of fruit;
內果皮 endocarp;
外果皮 exocarp;

G

中果皮 mesocarp;
[果品] fruit;
[果然] as expected; if indeed; if really; really; sure enough;
[果實] (1) fruit; (2) gains;
結果實 fruit;
[果蔬] fruits and vegetables;
[果樹] fruiter; fruit tree;
[果心] fruit pith;
去掉果心 core;
~去掉果心的刀 corer;
[果芽] fruit bud;
[果蠅] fruit fly;
[果園] garden; orchard;
[果真] as expected; if indeed; if really; really; sure enough;
[果枝] (1) fruit branch; fruit-bearing shoot; (2) ball-bearing branch of the cotton plant;
[果汁] fruit juice; juice;
果汁吧 juice bar;
罐頭果汁 canned fruit juice;
混合果汁 blended fruit juice;
濃縮果汁 fruitade;
瓶裝果汁 bottled juice;
桶裝果汁 barreled juice;
一盒果汁 a carton of fruit juice;
[果子] fruit;
果子凍 jelly;
果子狸 masked civet;
果子露 fruit syrup;

白果 ginkgo;
成果 achievement; fruit; gain; positive result;
惡果 bad result; evil consequence;
乾果 (1) dry fruit; (2) dried fruit;
黑果 huckleberry;
後果 aftermath; consequence;
堅果 nut;
漿果 berry;
結果 (1) bear fruit; (2) result;
蠟果 wax furit;
芒果 mango;
杧果 mango;
蘋果 apple;
肉果 nutmeg;
如果 if; in case;
水果 fruit;
碩果 great achievements; rich fruits;
糖果 candyh; sweetmeats; sweets;
鮮果 fresh fruit;
效果 (1) effect; result; (2) sound effects;
腰果 cashew;
野果 wild fruit;
因果 (1) cause and effect; (2) kara; pre-ordained fate;
戰果 results of battle;
真果 true fruit;
正果 the spiritual state of an immortal reached by practicing Buddhism;
坐果 bear fruit;

guo
【猓】 a tribe that spreads over Yunnan, Guizhou and Sichuan provinces;
[猓子] fried twisted dough sticks;

guo
【菓】 fruits and nuts;

guo
【裹】 bind; wrap;
[裹腳] foot-binding;
[裹脅] coerce; force to take part;
[裹足] (1) bind the feet of women; (2) hesitate for fear of danger;
裹足不前 come to a standstill; drag one's feet; halt in hesitation; hesitate to move forward; hesitate to proceed; mark time; not step forward; put down one's feet; refuse to go further; stop from proceeding; unwilling to go further;
~買主裹足不前 buyers are standing aloof;

裝裹 dress a corpse; wrap a corpse in a shroud;

guo
【蜾】 a kind of wasp;

guo
【槨】 outer coffin;

棺槨 inner and outer coffins;

guo
【餜】 cakes and dumplings;
[餜子] twisted fritters;

guo⁴
guo
【過】 (1) cross; pass; (2) across; over; past; through; (3) pass time; spend time; (4) after; past; (5) go over; go through; undergo a process; (6) exceed; go

G

beyond; (7) excessively; unduly; (8) fault; mistake;

[過磅] weigh in; weigh on the scales;
重新過磅 re-weigh;

[過不去] (1) cannot get through; impassable; unable to get by; (2) embarrass; find fault with; hard on; make it difficult for;
存心與人過不去 at cross purposes;

[過場] (1) interlude; (2) cross the stage; (3) go through the motions;
走過場 do sth as a mere formality; do sth perfunctorily; go through the motion; make a gesture to give the impression of doing sth; make sth a sham;
~ 走走過場 do sth perfunctorily or superficially;

[過程] course; in the course of; procedure; process;
過程分析法 method of process analysis;
過程控制 process control;
~ 過程控制工程 process control engineering;
~ 過程控制系統 process control system;
~ 過程控制語言 process control language;
過程咨詢 process consultation;
過程自動化 process automation;
翻譯過程 translation process;
活化過程 activated process;
適應過程 adaptive process;
調整過程 adjustment process;
吸收過程 absorption process;

[過秤] take the weight of; weigh on a steelyard;

[過從] associate; have a friendly relationship;
過從甚密 in close association with; in constant and close contact with; on very intimate terms with;

[過錯] fault; mistake;
過錯方 guilty party;
掩飾過錯 palliate a sin;

[過道] avenue; corridor; gangway; passageway;
一條過道 a passageway;

[過得去] (1) able to pass; can get through; crack a crust; may pass in a crowd; might pass in a crowd; would pass in a crowd; (2) not too bad; passable; so-so; tolerable;

[過得硬] able to stand all tests; become truly proficient in sth; have a good mastery of; have superb skill;

[過冬] hibernate; overwinter; pass the winter; winter;

[過度] ana-; excessively; hyper-; over-; too much; undue; without restraint;
過度緊張 supertension;
發展過度 overdeveloped;
淫慾過度 abandon oneself to passion;
用力過度 exert oneself too strenuously;

[過渡] transition;
過渡理論 theory of transition;
~ 大過渡理論 theory of great transition;
過渡時期 period of transition;
和平過渡 peaceful transition;
黑白過渡 black-to-white transition;
平穩過渡 smooth transition; stable transition;
吸收過渡 absorptive transition;

[過多] superabundant; too many; too much;
吃得過多 overeat; overfeed;
充電過多 be overcharged with electricity;
餵得過多 overfeed;

[過分] carry sth too far; excessively; go too far; overdo; overkill; overstep the mark; too much; undue;
過分苛求 overdemanding;
過分慷慨 generous to a fault;
過分熱心 excess of enthusiasm;
做得過分 run sth into the ground;

[過高] excessively high;
過高估計 overestimate;
期望過高 put one's expectations too high;
自視過高 hoity-toity; think too highly of oneself;

[過關] (1) go through an ordeal; pass a barrier; (2) pass a test; reach a standard;
過關斬將 overcome all the difficulties in the way;
過五關，斬六將 experience many hardships; surmount numerous difficulties;

[過海] cross the sea;
瞞天過海 cross the sea by a trick; try to deceive everybody; try to get away with it under pretence;
漂洋過海 go abroad; sail across the ocean; travel far away across the sea;
飄洋過海 sail across the seas; swept the seas;

[過河] cross the river;
過河拆橋 kick down the ladder; pull down the bridge after crossing the river; tear down the bridge after crossing the river; the danger past and God forgotten; the river past over, the saint forgotten; ungrateful;
過河棄舟 set adrift the boat once the river is crossed;
[過後] afterwards; later;
[過話] (1) exchange words; talk with one another; (2) pass on a message;
[過活] live; make a living;
一個人過活 live by oneself;
[過火] go to extremes; go too far; overdo;
[過激] extreme; radical; too drastic;
[過繼] (1) adopt a young relative; (2) have one's child adopted by a relative;
[過獎] overpraise; undeserved compliment;
[過節] (1) celebrate a festival; celebrate festivities; (2) after the festivities;
逢年過節 at every festival and at New Year; at the holidays and New Year; on New Year's Day and other festivals;
逢時過節 at every festival; during festivals;
[過境] in transit; pass through the territory of a country;
過境處 border crossing;
過境貿易 transit trade;
過境稅 transit tax;
[過客] passing traveller; transient guest;
[過來] come here; come over; come up;
過來人 experienced hand; person who has had the experience;
~ 欲知河淺深，須問過來人 he who has waded through the water knows it best;
倒過來 turn sth upside down;
[過勞] overwork;
[過梁] lintel;
安全過梁 safety lintel;
焦渣過梁 breeze lintel;
門過梁 door lintel;
[過量] excessive; overage; overdose;
吃過量 eat to excess; overeat;
服藥過量 overdose; take an overdose;
[過路] pass by on one's way;
[過慮] overanxious; worry unnecessarily;
[過濾] filter; leach; screen;
過濾嘴 filter tip;
[過門] move into one's husband's household upon marriage;
過門不入 pass one's own house without entering it;
[過敏] allergic; have an allergic reaction to; hypersensitive; irritable;
過敏的 allergic;
過敏性 allergy;
~ 過敏性反應 allegic reaction; allergy;
~ 過敏性皮疹 allergic rash;
過敏原 allergen;
過敏症 allergy; anaphylaxis;
對牛奶過敏 be allergic to milk;
對青霉素過敏 have an allergy to penicillin;
花粉過敏 pollen allergy;
農藥過敏 pesticide allergy;
皮膚過敏 skin allergy;
[過目] go over; look over;
過目不忘 gifted with an extraordinarily retentive memory; have a retentive memory;
過目成誦 able to recite sth after reading it over once;
草草過目 cast a running glance at; give a cursory reading;
略一過目 run over;
[過年] celebrate the Lunar New Year; celebrate the Spring Festival;
過年娶媳婦 one's son getting married while celebrating the Lunar New Year — a double blessing descends upon the house;
天天過年 hold Spring Festival-like celebrations every day;
王小二過年，一年不如一年 get more rundown every year; go from bad to worse every year; on the decline;
[過期] exceed the time limit; expire; overdue;
過期利息 overdue interest;
過期未還 overdue;
過期賬款 past due account;
過期支票 overdue cheque;
[過謙] over modest; too modest;
[過去] (1) antecedent; formerly; in the past; of the past; once; past; previously; (2) go over; go pass; pass by;
過去的 bygone;
~ 過去的事就讓它過去吧 let bygones be bygones;

過去分詞　past participle;
過去幾天　in the past few days;
過去將來進行式　past future continuous tense;
過去將來式　past future tense;
過去將來完成進行式　past future perfect continuous tense;
過去將來完成式　past future perfect tense;
過去進行式　past continuous tense;
過去了　die; pass away;
過去式　past form; past tense;
~ 簡單過去式　simple past tense;
過去完成進行式　past perfect continuous tense;
過去完成式　past perfect tense;
回顧過去　look back to the past; review the past;
昏過去　faint; fall down in a faint; fall into a swoon; lose consciousness; pass out;
混過去　muddle through;
~ 混不過去　unable to fool others;
跑過去　run past;
讓人過去　let sb pass;
説不過去　cannot be explained away; cannot be justified; doesn't make sense; hardly justifiable; have no excuse;
搪不過去　unable to parry;
挺過去　tough it out;
忘掉過去　bury one's past; forget one's past;
一個人的過去　antecedents of a person;
在過去　in the past;
再現過去　reconstruct the past; recreate the past;
走過去　walk past;
~ 走不過去　not able to go over;

[過人] (1) excel; surpass; (2) beating;
過人之處　sb's forte; things as which sb excels;
稟賦過人　possess original talents superior to other people; surpass many others in natural endowment;
技術過人　surpass others in skill;
記憶力過人　surpass others in memory;
口才過人　have no equal in eloquence;
氣力過人　surpass others in strength;
體力過人　person with supernatural physical strength;
學識過人　have few superiors in knowledge;
勇力過人　braver and stronger than most men; the boldest of the bold, the strongest of the strong;
勇氣過人　have no superior in courage;
智慧過人　excel in wisdom;
智力過人　possess intellectual superiority over other people;

[過山車] roller coaster;

[過少] too few; too little;

[過甚] exaggerate; overstate;
過甚其詞　give an exaggerated account; overstate the case; stretch the truth;

[過剩] excess; redundancy; surplus;
彩色過剩　colour excess;
界面過剩　interfacial excess;
精力過剩　overflow energy;
人口過剩　surplus population;
需求過剩　demand surplus;
中子過剩　neutron excess;

[過失] (1) error; fault; misconduct; (2) negligence; offense;
過失犯罪　unpremeditated crime;
~ 過失犯罪心理　mind of a negligent crime;
不可挽回的過失　irrecoverable error;
改正過去　amend one's fault;
共同過失　concurrent negligence; contributory negligence;
雙重過失　double fault;
小過失　peccadillo;
掩蓋過失　cover up faults;
一般過失　ordinary negligence;
重大過失　culpable negligence;

[過時] (1) behind the times; go out; go out of fashion; obsolete; out of date; out of fashion; out of style; outdated; (2) past the appointed time;
過時不候　not wait after the set time; not wait for sb if he/she comes late;
過時的　antediluvian; antiquated; cornball; dated; out-dated;
~ 不會過時的　future-proof;
~ 永不過時的　ageless;
隔年的黃曆—過時了　last year's almanac — out of date;
設備過時　the equipment is behind the times;

[過手] handle; receive and distribute; take in and give out;

[過頭] go beyond the limit; overdo;
過頭話　make thoughtless statements;
~ 説過頭話　make thoughtless statements;

煮過頭 overcook; overdone;
～煮過頭的雞肉 cooked chicken;
做得過頭 overleap one's shoulders;

[過往] (1) come and go; (2) associate with; have friendly intercourse with;
過往甚密 as thick as thieves; in with sb;

[過午] afternoon;

[過細] careful; meticulous;

[過夜] overnight;
活不過夜 unable to keep overnight;
一起過夜 spend the night together;

[過意不去] feel apologetic; feel sorry;

[過硬] able to pass the stiffest test; have a perfect mastery of sth; really up to the mark;

[過癮] do sth to one's heart's content; enjoy oneself to the full; satisfy a craving;

[過於] by half; excessively; too; unduly;
過於寬容 lenient to a fault;
過於輕率 unduly reckless;
過於自信 overconfident;

[過譽] overpraise;

[過雲雨] shower;

[過早] premature; untimely;
過早樂觀 count one's chickens before they hatch out;

[過載] overload;
動態過載 dynamic overload;
容許過載 permissible overload;
瞬時過載 instantaneous overload;

[過重] excess weight; overcharge;
工作過重 be overburdened with work;

挨過 survive; weather;
補過 make amends for one's mistakes;
不過 but; except that; only;
擦過 brush past sb;
穿過 cross over;
度過 pass; spend;
改過 correct one's mistakes; mend one's ways;
功過 achievements and errors;
好過 (1) have an easy time; in easy circumstances; (2) feel well;
悔過 repent one's error;
記過 record a demerit;
經過 go through; pass; undergo;
路過 pass by a place; pass through a place;
掠過 skim over; sweep past;
難過 hard up; lead a hard life;
賽過 better than; exceed; overtake; surpass;
勝過 better than; excel; surpass;
通過 (1) get past; pass through; (2) adopt; carry; pass;
委過 put the blame on sb else; shift the blame onto others;
謝過 apologize for having done sth wrong;
越過 cross; negotiate; surmount;
知過 realize one's mistakes;

ha¹
ha
【哈】 (1) blow; blow one's breath; breathe out; exhale; (2) (expressing satisfaction) aha; ha; (3) (sound of laughter) ha ha; (4) bow;
[哈巴狗] Pekingese;
[哈勃] Hubble;
[哈哈] ha ha; haw haw;
哈哈大笑 burst into hearty laughter; burst out into a fit of violent laughter; give a loud guffaw; laugh heartily; roar with laughter;
哈哈鏡 distorting mirror; magic mirror;
打哈哈 crack a joke; joke; joke about; make fun; poke fun at;
[哈蜜瓜] Hami melon;
[哈欠] yawn;
打哈欠 give a yawn; yawn;
忍住哈欠 stifle a yawn; suppress a yawn;
[哈腰] (1) bend one's back; stoop; (2) bow slightly in greeting;
哈腰告辭 bow oneself out of the apartment;
哈腰曲背 humble oneself in serving a master;
點頭哈腰 bow and scrape;
低頭哈腰 humble oneself in serving a master;

笑哈哈 laughingly; with a laughter;

ha²
ha
【蛤】 toad;
[蛤蟆] toad;
疥蛤蟆 toad;

ha
【蝦】 shrimps;
[蝦米] small dried shrimps;

ha³
ha
【哈】 (1) rebuke; reprimand; (2) a surname;
[哈巴狗] Pekinese dog; Pekingese;

hai¹
hai
【咳】 (expressing surprise, sorrow, etc.) hey;

hai
【嗨】 (expressing surprise) heave-ho;

hai²
hai
【孩】 child;
[孩兒] child; daughter; son;
孩兒臉 baby face;
[孩裹孩氣] childish;
[孩提] early childhood; infancy;
[孩子] (1) child; (2) one's son or daughter;
孩子般的 childish;
孩子出生 a child is born;
孩子離開娘，瓜兒離開秧 when a child leaves his/her mother, it is like a melon torn off the vine;
孩子氣 childish; childishness;
~ 一臉的孩子氣 have a childish look;
孩子王 (1) head of children; (2) teacher;
孩子長大 a child grows up;
抱孩子 carry a baby in one's arms; hold a baby in one's arms;
不守規矩的孩子 unruly child;
不聽話的孩子 disobedient child;
誠實的孩子 truthful child;
寵壞孩子 spoil one's child;
膽小的孩子 timid child;
管教孩子 manage one's children;
好孩子 good child;
懷孩子 with child;
壞孩子 bad child;
教養孩子 educate one's children;
看孩子 look after the children;
沒規矩的孩子 pert child;
男孩子 boys;
~ 一群男孩子 a crowd of boys;
難管教的孩子 unruly children;
溺愛孩子 honour one's child;
女孩子 girl;
~ 逗女孩子 tease girls;
~ 一班女孩子 a group of young girls;
~ 一個女孩子 a girl;
~ 一群女孩子 a bevy of girls; a group of girls;
排行中間的孩子 middle child;
任性的孩子 wilful child;
三歲以下的孩子 children under three;
生孩子 be brought to bed of sb; be delivered of sb; bear a child; bearing; bring forth sb; bring sb into the world; give birth to a child; send sb into the world;

收養孩子 adopt a child;
私孩子 illegitimate child;
討人喜歡的孩子 lovable child;
討厭的孩子 annoying child; pesky kids;
撫愛孩子 caress a child;
撫養孩子 bring up one's child; raise a child;
想要個孩子 try for a baby;
小孩子 kids; mite; small child;
~靜不下來的小孩子 restless kids; squirrelly kids;
許多孩子 many a child;
許許多多孩子 a great many children;
野孩子 street urchin; urchin;
一幫孩子 a group of children;
一大群孩子 a host of children; a whole passel of kids;
一伙孩子 a gang of children;
一群孩子 a gang of kids; a group of children; a troop of children;
一群十歲的孩子 a group of ten-year-olds;
照看孩子 babysit;
縱容孩子 indulge one's children;
最大的孩子 eldest child; oldest child;
最小的孩子 youngest child;
坐立不安的孩子 a restless child;

男孩 boy;
女孩 girl;
小孩 child;
嬰孩 baby; infant;

hai
【頦】 chin;

hai
【骸】 (1) skin and bone; (2) skeleton;
[骸骨] human bones; skeleton;

病骸 ailing body;
殘骸 remains; wreckage;
屍骸 skeleton;
形骸 human body; human skeleton;
遺骸 body; corpse; remains;

hai
【還】 (1) after all; still; yet; (2) even more; still more; (3) also; as well; besides; in addition; too; (4) fairly; passably; (5) even;
[還不] not yet;
還不晚 it's not too late;
[還好] (1) not bad; passable; (2) fortunately; luckily;
還好呢 that would be even better;
感覺還好 not feeling too bad;
[還沒] not yet;
還沒有 not yet;
[還是] after all; all the same; else; had better; indeed; might as well; more; nevertheless; or; really; still; yet;
[還要] (1) even more; still more; (2) still want to;
[還有] (1) there is still some left; (2) furthermore; in addition;

hai³
hai
【海】 (1) big lake; sea; (2) a great number of things; a huge number of people; (3) extra large; plenty; of great capacity; (4) willy-nilly; without a goal; (5) a surname;
[海岸] coast; seaboard; sea coast; seashore;
海岸地區 coastal area;
海岸警衛隊 coastguard;
海岸砲 coastal artillery;
~海岸砲兵 coastal artillery;
海岸線 coastline; shoreline;
~一段海岸線 a stretch of coastline;
~縱式海岸線 concordant coastline;
開闊海岸 open coast;
平直海岸 regular coast;
上昇海岸 elevated coast;
灣型海岸 estuary coast;
下沉海岸 submerged coast;
懸崖海岸 cliffed coast;
一段海岸 a stretch of coast;
[海拔] elevation; height; height above sea level;
海拔高度 altitude;
[海報] bill; playbill; poster;
海報兒童 poster child;
海報宣傳 poster campaign;
貼出海報 paste up a poster;
貼海報 put up a poster;
張貼海報 put up posters;
[海豹] canimal seal; sea dog; seal;
海豹皮 sealskin;
捕獵海豹 sealing;
~捕獵海豹者 sealer;
[海邊] seafront; seaside;
在海邊 at the seaside;
住在海邊 live beside the sea;

[海濱] (1) strand; (2) seafront; seashore; seaside;
海濱別墅 beach house;
海濱地區 seafront area;
海濱房屋 seafront house;
海濱風景 beachscape;
海濱服務員 beach boy;
海濱巨浪 beachcomber;
海濱旅館 seaside hotel;
海濱線 shoreline;
~ 負海濱線 negative shoreline;
~ 珊瑚海濱線 coral shoreline;
~ 視海濱線 apparent shoreline;
~ 正海濱線 positive shoreline;
海濱小道 coastal path;
海濱浴場 bathing beach;
在海濱 at the seaside;

[海波] (1) sea waves; (2) hypo;
薄海騰波 cheers from all over the country;
海不揚波 the sea is calm – peace in the country;

[海菜] edible seaweed;

[海草] seagrass; seaweed; wrack;

[海產] marine product;

[海潮] sea tide;

[海程] sea voyage;

[海船] seagoing vessel;

[海牀] ocean floor; seabed;

[海錯] choice seafood; marine products; sea delicacies;
海錯蠻珍 delicacies from the sea and barbarians – rare and delicate food;
山珍海錯 feast of fat things; a sumptuous repast; all kinds of costly food; dainties of all lands and seas; dainties of every kind; delicacies; exotic food from mountains and seas; nice dishes of every kind; table delicacies from land and sea;

[海帶] (1) kelp; (2) sea zone; sea-tangle; sea-tent;
濱海帶 littoral zone;
~ 亞濱海帶 sublittoral zone;
淺海帶 neritic zone;

[海膽] sea chestnut; sea hedgehog; sea urchin;

[海島] island;
一群海島 a clump of islands; a multitude of islands;

[海道] seaway;

[海盜] pirate;

[海堤] coastal levee; sea embankment; sea wall;

[海底] bottom of the sea; ocean floor; seabed;
海底地形 submarine topography;
海底電纜 submarine cable;
海底谷 sea valley;
海底火山 submarine volcano;
海底撈月 ask for the moon; cry for the moon; dredge for the moon in the sea; strive for an illusion; strive for the impossible; try to fish out the moon from the bottom of the sea;
海底撈針 dredge for a needle from the bottom of the sea; find a needle in a haystack; fish for a needle in the ocean; hunt for a needle in a haystack; impossible task; try to recover a needle from the bottom of the sea; vain effort;
海底生物 benthos;
海底探險 undersea exploration;
海底資源 seabed resources;
遨遊海底 roam deep under the sea;
冤沉海底 unable to get one's wrongs redressed;

[海雕] sea eagle;

[海法] maritime law;

[海防] (1) Haiphong; (2) coastal defences;

[海風] sea breeze;
冷鋒狀海風 cold-front-like sea breeze;

[海港] dock; harbour; seaport;
封鎖海港 blockade a harbour;
建造海港 construct a seaport;

[海溝] oceanic trench;
克馬德克海溝 Kermadec Trench;
馬里亞納海溝 Marianas Trench;
秘魯海溝 Peru Trench;
日本海溝 Japan Trench;
深海溝 deep-sea trench;
湯加海溝 Tonga Trench;
智利海溝 Chile Trench;

[海狗] fur seal; seal; ursine seal;

[海怪] sea monster;

[海關] custom house; customs;
海關登記 customs registration;
海關法 customs law;
海關關長 customs commissioner;
海關規則 customs regulations;
海關監督 customs supervision;
海關監管 customs supervision and control;

海關檢查 customs inspection;
海關人員 customs officer; customs official;
海關税率 customs tariff;
海關税收 customs revenue;
海關税則 customs tariff;
海關手續 customs formalities;
海關文件 customs papers;
海關總署 general customs administration;
通過海關 go through customs;

[海鮭] bull trout; sea trout;

[海龜] sea turtle;

[海國] maritime country;

[海涵] forgive shortcomings; magnanimous enough to forgive or tolerate; tolerate shortcomings;

[海貨] marine products;

[海疆] coastal areas and territorial seas;

[海角] cape; promontory;
海角天涯 back of beyond; corners of the sea and the end of the sky; corners of the world; remotest corners of the earth; utmost ends of the earth;

[海禁] ban on maritime intercourse with foreign countries;

[海景] waterscape;
海景單位 seaview apartment;
海景悦目 the sea view pleases the eyes;
遼闊海景 sweeping sea view;
壯麗海景 magnificent sea view; stunning sea view;

[海鳩] guillemot;

[海軍] navy; sea service;
海軍飛機 naval aeroplane;
海軍軍官 naval officer;
海軍軍士 petty officer;
海軍基地 naval bastion;
海軍藍 navy blue;
海軍陸戰隊 marine crops;
海軍強國 sea power;
海軍上將 admiral;
海軍實力 sea power;
參加海軍 join the navy;

[海空] aeronaval;
海空基地 aeronaval base;
海空救援 air-sea rescue;

[海口] (1) seaport; (2) big talk; boast about sth; brag; (3) Haikou;

[海枯石爛] I shall love you for ever and ever; I shall love you to the end of time no matter what happens; until the seas dry up and the rocks decay;

[海葵] sea anemone;

[海闊] the sea is wide;
海闊從魚躍，天高任鳥飛 the wide sea allows the fish to leap about and the vast sky allows the birds to fly;
海闊天空 as boundless as the sea and sky; without limit; without restriction;

[海浪] sea wave;

[海狸] beaver;
海狸鼠 (1) coypu; (2) nutria;

[海里] mile; nautical mile; sea mile;
國際海里 international nautical mile;
雷達海里 radar nautical mile;
平均海里 mean nautical mile;

[海立雲垂] the sea stands and the clouds hang down;

[海蠣子] oyster;

[海量] (1) magnanimity; (2) have a hollow leg;

[海嶺] submarine ridge;

[海流] ocean current; seawater;
海流板 drogue;
北赤道海流 north equatorial current;
風海流 wind current;
南赤道海流 south equatorial current;

[海龍] (1) sea otter; (2) pipefish;

[海路] sea route; seaway;

[海陸] sea and land;

[海輪] seagoing vessel;

[海螺] conch;
海螺殼 conch;

[海洛因] heroin; scag; skag;
海洛因癮君子 heroin addict;
吸食海洛因 heroin; take heroin; use heroin;

[海馬] seahorse;

[海鰻] conger eel; conger pike;

[海米] dried shrimps;

[海綿] (1) sponge; (2) foam rubber;
海綿冰 sludge;
海綿擦 sponge;
海綿蛋糕 sponge cake;
海綿墊 foam-rubber cushion;
海綿拍 sponge bat;
海綿排水孔 osculum;
海綿橡膠 sponge rubber;
海綿學 spongiology;
海綿硬蛋白 spongin;
穿孔海綿 boring sponge;

H

陶瓷海綿 ceramic sponge;
一塊海綿 a sponge;

[海面] bosom of the sea; sea level; surface of the sea;

[海難] marine perils; perils of the sea;
遭遇海難 shipwreck;

[海內] the world; throughout the country; within the four seas;
海內景仰 be held in deep respect throughout the country;
海內名士 the most distinguished people of the country;
海內清平 the country is in peace and good order;
海內人望 the cynosure of the whole country;
海內外 inside and outside the country;
海內無雙 unequalled or peerless in the whole country;
海內晏如 peace reigns throughout the land; peace reigns within the four seas; the country is in peace;
海內知名 be known throughout the country;
海內宗仰 be admired in the entire country; be held in esteem throughout the country;

[海鳥] sea crow; seabird; sea fowl;
海鳥糞 guano;

[海牛] manatee; sea cow; sea slug;

[海鷗] gull; mew; seagull;

[海派] (1) Shanghai style; (2) people who put up a big front;

[海區] sea area;

[海鰓] sea feather; sea pen;

[海沙] sea sand;

[海山] seamount;

[海鱔] moray; moray eel;

[海上] at sea; maritime; on the sea; seaborne;
海上城市 marine city;
海上航行 a voyage at sea;
海上力量 sea power;
海上無魚蝦自大 among the blind the one-eyed man is king;
遨遊海上 go cruising in the sea;

[海蛇] sea snake;

[海參] sea cucumber;

[海神] Neptune; Poseidon;

[海獅] sea lion;

[海蝕] marine corrosion;

[海市] mirage;
海市蜃樓 castles in Spain; castles in the air; cities and buildings seen in a mirage; flyaway; illusions that cannot be realized; mirage; shadow of a shade;

[海事] maritime affairs;
海事衛星 marine satellite; maritime satellite;

[海水] seawater; the sea;
海水不可斗量 seawater is immeasurable – great minds cannot be fathomed; the sea cannot be measured with a bushel – men are not to be measured by inches;
海水測溫儀 bathy thermograph;
海水浴 seawater bath; sea bathing;
海水浴場 seawater bath;
海水澡 sea bathing; shore bathing;

[海說神聊] talk aimlessly;

[海損] cargo damage; ship damage;
海損查勘人 average surveyor;
海損理算人 average adjuster;
單獨海損 particular average;
國外共同海損 foreign general average;
普通海損 common average;
小海損 petty averages;

[海獺] sea otter;

[海苔] sea moss;

[海灘] beach; coastal beach;
並列海灘 apposition beach;
風暴海灘 storm beach;
卵石海灘 cobble beach;
上昇海灘 raised beach;
硬底海灘 hard beach;
障礙海灘 barrier beach;

[海棠] Chinese flowering apple; crab apple;
海棠花 Chinese flowering apple;
蜜餞海棠 sweetened crab apple;
秋海棠 begonia;
西府海棠 mini crab apple;
野海棠 begonia;
一樹梨花壓海棠 be married to a woman many years younger than oneself;

[海塘] sea well;

[海濤] billow; ocean wave;
海濤洶湧 dashing of billows;

[海天] the sea and the sky;
海天相接 the great ocean stretches away to meet the sky;
海天一色 the sea and the sky merged into

one; the sea melted into the sky;

[海圖] marine chart; nautical chart; sea chart;

[海豚] dolphin;
寬吻海豚 bottlenose dolphin;
鼠海豚 porpoise;

[海外] abroad; overseas;
海外版 overseas edition;
海外辦事處 overseas branch;
海外關係 overseas relationships;
海外華僑 Chinese citizens abroad; overseas Chinese;
海外歸來 return from abroad;
海外留學人員 Chinese students and scholars studying abroad;
海外奇談 cock and bull story; curious tale; strange tale from over the seas; tall story; traveller's tale;
海外僑胞 Chinese residing abroad;
海外同胞 compatriots residing abroad;
海外投資 overseas investment;
海外移民 overseas emigrant;
定居海外 reside abroad permanently;

[海灣] arm of the sea; bay; gulf; sea loch;
開展海灣 bight;
小海灣 cove;
一個海灣 a bay;

[海碗] big bowl; huge bowl; large bowl;

[海王星] Neptune;

[海味] choice seafood; marine food products; seafood;

[海霧] sea fog; sea smoke;

[海峽] channel; gullet; narrows; pass; strait;
海峽兩岸 both sides of the Taiwan Straits; Cross-Straits;
~ 海峽兩岸關係 Cross-Straits relations;

[海鮮] seafood;
海鮮餐廳 seafood restaurant;

[海象] walrus;

[海嘯] bore; seaquake; tidal waves; tsunami;
風嚎海嘯 the wind howls and the sea roars;
海嘯風狂 the sea roars and the wind rages;
金融海嘯 financial tsunami;

[海蟹] sea crab;

[海星] sea star; starfish;

[海熊] fur seal; ursine seal;

[海崖] sea cliff;

[海鹽] sea salt;

[海燕] petrel;

[海洋] ocean; seas and oceans;
海洋沉積 marine deposit; marine sediment;
海洋磁力儀 marine magnetometer;
洋地質研究 marine geological research;
海洋動物 marine animals;
海洋法 maritime law;
海洋工程 ocean engineering;
海洋公約 maritime convention;
海洋觀測站 oceanographic station;
海洋環境 marine environment;
~ 海洋環境科學 marine environmental science;
海洋經濟 marine economy;
~ 海洋經濟產業 marine economic industry;
~ 海洋經濟地理 marine economic geography;
~ 海洋經濟學 ocean economics;
海洋開發 ocean development;
~ 海洋開發產業 ocean development industry;
海洋考察船 oceanographic vessel;
海洋空間 ocean space;
海洋氣象船 an ocean weather ship;
海洋生物 marine organisms;
海洋水流 ocean current;
海洋污染 marine pollution;
海洋性氣候 oceanic climate; maritime climate;
海洋學 oceanography;
~ 海洋學院 oceanology college;
海洋研究 oceanographic research;
海洋漁業 sea fishery;
海洋運輸經濟 marine transportation economy;
海洋重力儀 sea gravimeter;
海洋資源 marine resources;
海洋作業台 offshore platform;
原始海洋 primordial seas;

[海妖] enchantress; siren;

[海郵] by sea; sea mail;

[海隅] seaside nook;

[海域] maritime space; sea area;

[海員] mariner; sailor; seaman;
海員用語 nautical expression;

[海運] ocean carriage; ocean shipping; sea transportation; transport by sea;
海運界 ocean shipping circles;
海運學院 institute of marine transport;

[海葬] sea burial;

［海藻］ kelp; marine algae; sea wrack; seaweed;
［海棗］ date; date palm;
［海賊］ sea poacher;
［海戰］ naval battle; sea warfare;
［海蜇］ jellyfish;
海蜇皮 dried jellyfish strips;
涼拌海蜇 shredded jellyfish with soya sauce;
［海震］ seaquake;

拔海 elevation (above sea level);
濱海 border on the sea;
瀕海 along the coast; close to the sea;
渤海 Bohai, a gulf of the Yellow Sea;
滄海 the blue sea; the sea;
朝海 face the sea;
澄海 Sea of Serenity;
愁海 a sea of sorrows;
出海 go to sea; put out to sea;
醋海 jealousy;
大海 ocean; sea; the blue water; the sea;
蹈海 plunge oneself into the sea to commit suicide;
渡海 sail across a sea;
豐富海 Sea of Fertility;
公海 high seas;
過海 cross the sea;
航海 navigate;
河海 the river and the sea;
恨海 deep hatred;
湖海 lakes and seas;
寰海 the whole earth;
宦海 official circles; officialdom;
火海 a sea of fire;
近海 coastal waters; inshore; offshore;
靜海 Mare Tranquillitatis; Sea of Tranquillity;
酒海 Mare Nectaris; Sea of Nectar;
苦海 abyss of misery; sea of bitterness;
冷海 Mare Frigoris; Sea of Cold;
林海 immense forest;
領海 territorial sea; territorial waters;
墨海 inkslab; inkstone;
腦海 brain; mind;
內海 (1) inland sea; (2) continental sea;
汽海 Mare Vaporum; Sea of Vapours;
人海 a huge crowd of people; a sea of faces;
濕海 Sea of Moisture;
四海 the four seas; the whole country; the whole world;
危海 Sea of Crises;
下海 (1) go to sea; put out to sea; (2) go fishing on the sea;
血海 sea of blood;
煙海 huge and voluminous; vast sea of fog;
沿海 along the coast; costal; littoral;
瀛海 ocean; sea;
雨海 Mare Imbrium; Sea of Rains;
慾海 sea of passions;
淵海 (1) deep pool and big ocean; (2) broad and profound;
願海 profound wish;
雲海 sea of clouds; Sea of Clouds;

hai
【醢】 (1) minced and hashed meat; (2) mince;

hai⁴
hai
【亥】 (1) last of the twelve Terrestrial branches; (2) period of the day between 9 and 10 p.m.;

hai
【咳】 (expressing regret, remorse, sorrow, disgust, etc.) blast it; damn it; oh;

hai
【害】 (1) bane; calamity; evil; harm; (2) destructive; harmful; injurious; (3) cause trouble to; do harm to; harm; impair; injure; (4) kill; murder; (5) contract a disease; contract an illness; suffer from; (6) feel ashamed;
［害病］ ill with; fall ill; fall sick;
［害蟲］ destructive insects; injurious insects;
消滅害蟲 eliminate destructive insects;
［害處］ harm;
［害命］ kill; murder; take sb's life;
謀財害命 commit murder out of greed; murder sb for his/her money;
圖財害命 murder sb for money;
［害鳥］ harmful bird;
［害怕］ afraid for sth; afraid of sb; be frightened; be overcome by fear; be overcome with fear; be scared of; can't say boo to a goose; dread; dreadful; fear; fearful; fly the white feather; for fear of; frighten; frightful; get cold feet; have a dread of; have cold feet; in dread of sb; in dread of sth; in fear of; make one's blood run cold; make one's

hair stand on end; quail; shake in one's boots; show the white feather; strike fear into; tremble in one's shoes;
害怕死 afraid of death; fear to die; in fear of death;
暗自害怕 be secretly afraid;
不害怕 unafraid;
非常害怕 break into a sweat; break out in a sweat; intensely afraid of;
極其害怕 be mortally afraid of;
覺得害怕 feel afraid;

[害群] bring disgrace to the group;
害群敗類 black sheep;
害群之馬 a horse that spoils the whole herd; bad apple that spoils the barrel; bad egg of the community; black sheep; evil member of the herd; person who brings disgrace to the group; pests of society; public enemy; rotten apple; there is a black sheep in every flock;

[害人] victimization;
害人不淺 cause deep injury to people; cause infinite harm to people; do people great harm; injure the people deeply; no small harm is done; very harmful to people;
害人蟲 evil creature; pest; vermin;
害人害己 bite off one's own head; curses come home to roost; harm set, harm get; harm watch, harm catch; he who bites others gets bitten himself;
害人利己 benefit oneself at the expense of another person;
害人之心 malice;
害人終害己 curses come home to roost; harm set, harm get; harm watch; harm catch; he that mischief hatches mischief catches; hoist with one's own petard; one will injure oneself in injuring others; the damage recoils upon one's own head;
攛掇害人 stir up harm for everyone;

[害臊] bashful; feel ashamed;
不知害臊 have no sense of shyness;

[害獸] harmful animal; vermin;

[害喜] (of pregnant woman) feel morning sickness; pregnant;

[害羞] bashful; shy;
害羞的 coy;
害羞赧顏 blush a scarlet red; feel ashamed;
不害羞 unabashed; shameless;
天生害羞 have ingrained shyness;
在生人面前害羞 get shy in the presence of strangers;

[害眼] have eye trouble;

[害意] interfere with the sense;
以詞害意 allow language to interfere with the thought; let the form of expression interfere with the meaning of the text; let the words interfere with the sense; sacrifice clarity in the use of wrong words for expression;

隘害 strategic pass; strategic point;
暗害 assassinate; do secret injury to; frame up; injure secretly; kill secretly; murder; plot murder; stab in the back;
雹害 hail damage;
被害 be killed; be murdered;
弊害 harm; undesirable points;
避害 escape disaster; run away from a calamity;
病害 disease; plant disease;
殘害 cruelly injure or kill; do harm to; mutilate; mutilation; slaughter;
讒害 incriminate by false charges;
虫害 insect pest;
除害 remove an evil;
毒害 poison sb;
妨害 harmful to; impair; put in danger;
公害 nuisance; public hazard; public nuisance;
禍害 (1) curse; disaster; scourge; (2) damage; destroy;
加害 do harm to; injure;
坑害 entrap; lead into a trap; scheme to do harm;
澇害 damage caused by waterlogging;
利害 (1) advantages and disadvantages; (2) formidable; terrible;
厲害 (1) cruel; fierce; severe; sharp; (2) formidable; serious; terrible;
謀害 (1) plot to murder; (2) plot a frame-up against sb;
迫害 oppress cruelly; persecute;
戕害 harm; hurt; injure;
侵害 encroach on; make inroads on;
擾害 harass and injure;
殺害 kill; murder; slaughter;
傷害 harm; hurt; injure;
受害 be affected; be afflicted; be damaged; be victimized; fall victim; suffer injury; suffer losses;
霜害 frost injury;

損害 damage; harm; injure;
危害 endanger; harm;
為害 cause damage;
誣害 calumniate; defame sb; frame sb;
無害 do no harm to; harmless; innocuous; innoxious;
陷害 calumniate; make a false charge against; plot a frame-up;
要害 (1) crucial point; vital part; (2) strategic point;
貽害 leave a legacy of trouble;
遺害 cause troubles;
有害 detrimental; harmful; pernicious;
遇害 be killed; be murdered;
災害 calamity; disaster;
遭害 be assassinated; be killed; be murdered;
糟害 damage; make havoc of;
賊害 cause harm to another;

hai

【氦】 helium;

hai

【駭】 astonished; shocked;
[駭詫無似] in incomparable amazement;
[駭怪] astonished; shocked;
[駭然] gasping with astonishment; struck dumb with amazement;
駭然不知所措 dumb with astonishment; be paralyzed with amazement;
[駭人] appalling; astounding; horrendous; horrifying; shocking; terrifying;
駭人報導 horror story;
駭人聽聞 appalling; astounding; frightful to the ear; horrifying; shocking; terrifying;
~駭人聽聞的謀殺 shocking murder;
~駭人聽聞的屠殺 horrifying killing;
[駭異] astonished; shocked;

han1

han

【蚶】 clam;
[蚶子] blood clam;

han

【酣】 (1) drink to one's heart's content; (2) fully; heartily; heatedly; in the heat of;
[酣暢] (1) merry and lively; (2) sound sleep; (3) with ease and verve;
酣暢淋漓 heartily; to one's heart's content;
[酣夢] sweet dream;
[酣適] sound sleep;
[酣睡] dead to the world; fall into a deep sleep; fast asleep; sleep like a log; sleep soundly;
[酣飲] drink to the full;
[酣戰] be engaged in a fierce battle; fight a fierce battle; fight fiercely;
[酣醉] dead drunk;

han

【頇】 (1) foolish and slow; (2) thick;
[頇實] thick and solid;

han

【憨】 (1) foolish; silly; (2) naive; simple and honest; straightforward;
[憨痴] idiotic;
[憨厚] simple and honest; straightforward and good-natured;
[憨實] (1) stalwart; sturdy; (2) simple-hearted;
[憨態] silly appearance;
憨態可掬 charmingly naive;
[憨笑] simper; smile fatuously;
[憨直] honest and straightforward; honest and upright;
[憨子] fool; idiot; nincompoop; ninny; simpleton;

嬌憨 childish but artless and lovely;

han

【鼾】 snore;
[鼾齁如雷] snore like thunder; thunderous snores;
[鼾孔] snore-hole;
[鼾聲] snore; sound of snoring;
鼾聲大作 drive one's pigs to the market; snore terribly; stertorous breathing;
鼾聲呼吸 a stertorous breathing;
鼾聲如雷 one's snores drone like the distant roll of thunder; snore like thunder; snore thunderously; thunderous snores;
鼾聲如豬 snore like a pig;
鼾聲響得嚇人 snore horribly;
打鼾聲 snore; ZZZ;
[鼾睡] heavy sleep; snore away soundly; sound, snoring sleep;
整個下午都在鼾睡 snore away the whole afternoon;

[鼾音] sonorous rale;

打鼾 snore;

han²

han

【汗】 khan, as in 可汗 ;

han

【含】 (1) hold sth in the mouth; keep in the mouth; (2) contain; hold back; (3) cherish; harbour; nurse; (4) a feeling that is implied rather than revealed outright;

[含苞] in bud;

含苞待放 a bud ready to burst; be in a bud; in early puberty; the buds are getting ready to burst;

含苞未放 the budding blossoms waiting to burst forth;

[含哺鼓腹] feed food and fill the stomach to the full − a scene of light-heartedness in times of peace; with food in the mouth and a well-filled belly;

[含垢] bear disgrace;

含垢忍辱 bear disgrace and insults with patience; bear insult and obloquy patiently; bear shame and humiliation; eat dirt;

忍尤含垢 able to endure disgrace and hardships; accept insults and humiliations passively; suffer shame and obloquy; swallow insults;

[含毫吮墨] moisten the tip of the writing brush with one's lips; pause to think when writing;

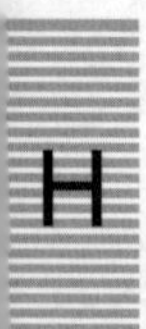

[含恨] harbour hatred;

含恨長逝 die unavenged;

含恨在心 harbour resentment in the heart; harbour hatred against sb; nurse hatred;

含恨終天 die with deep regret;

[含糊] (1) ambiguous; vague; unclear; (2) careless; perfunctory; sloppy;

含糊不明 muddled and unclear;

含糊不清 ambiguous and vague; imprecise; unclear;

~含糊不清地說話 bumble;

含糊答應 mutter a vague assent;

含糊敷衍 gloss things over;

含糊了事 finish a job carelessly; settle a case carelessly;

含糊其詞 ambiguous; equivocate; hum and haw; make sth very vague; mention vaguely; mince matters; mince one's words; prevaricate; slur over a matter; weasel word;

不含糊 (1) unambiguous; unequivocal; (2) not ordinary; really good;

~毫不含糊 clear-cut; explicit; in no uncertain terms; in terms; unambiguous; unequivocal; unmistakable; well-defined;

含含糊糊 ambiguous; befuddled; evasive; of doubtful meaning; uncertain; vague;

[含混] ambiguous; equivocal; indistinct; vague;

[含金量] gold content; gold parity;

[含淚] with tears in one's eyes;

含淚哀求 implore with tears in one's eyes;

滿目含淚 one's eyes are filled with tears; one's eyes are full of tears;

眼中含淚 one's eyes are swimming with tears;

[含量] content;

酒精含量 alcohol content;

空氣含量 air content;

瀝青含量 asphalt content;

酸含量 acid content;

細菌含量 bacterial content;

[含蓼問疾] ask after the people's sufferings with deep concern; console the people with deep concern;

[含怒] contain one's anger;

含怒不言 hold one's tongue sulkily;

[含情] cherish affection; exude love;

含情脈脈 full of tender affection; with loving eyes;

~含情脈脈地說 say gently;

眉目含情 her eyes wear an expression of coquetry;

脈脈含情 eyes quietly sending the message of love;

笑臉含情 one's smiling face exudes love;

[含容巽順] forbearing and retiring;

[含辱忍苦] eat the leek; swallow the leek;

[含沙射影] attack by innuendo; attack by insinuation; hurt others maliciously; insinuate; make insinuations;

[含笑] grin; have a smile on one's face; smilingly; wearing a smile; with a

smile;
含笑不語 smile without speaking;
含笑地下 die with satisfaction;
含笑回答 reply with a smile;
含笑九泉 die with satisfaction; smile in one's grave;
含笑作答 laugh in reply;
滿臉含笑 all smiles;

[含羞] bashful; be overcome by shyness; shy; with a shy look;
含羞不語 go into one's shell; silent with shame;
含羞草 mimosa; sensitive plant;
含羞嬌嗔 pout prettily in embarrassment;
含羞自盡 commit suicide out of shame;
抱慚含羞 be overcome by shame;
嬌嗔含羞 pout prettily with shame;

[含蓄] (1) contain; embody; (2) implicit; suggestive rather than explicit; veiled; (3) reserved; restrained;
含蓄不露 containing much but revealing little;
含蓄的批評 implicit criticism;
性格含蓄 have a reserved character;

[含血噴人] cast malicious words to injure sb; do wrong to sb; fling mud at; make slanderous accusations; make slanderous charges against others; make vicious attacks; mud-slinging; sling mud at; slur sb's good name; smite with the tongue; spit poison; throw dirt at sb; throw mud at;

[含飴弄孫] a life of leisure in one's old age; hold candy in one's mouth and play with one's grandchild; lead a carefree life in one's old age;

[含義] implication; import; meaning; message; sense;
含義深長 with a deep implication;
會話含義 conversational implicature;
具更深的含義 have deeper implication;
具有深刻的含義 have a profound meaning;
雙重含義 double meaning;
~具有雙重含義 bear a double meaning;
一種含義 a meaning;

[含有] contain; have; import;

[含冤] suffer a wrong; victim of a false charge;
含冤而死 die uncleared of an unjust charge;
含冤負屈 be wronged on a false charge; cherish grievance and bear injustice; suffer an iniquitous wrong; suffer an unjust grievance;
含冤莫白 be falsely accused and condemned; bear an injury with no hope of being revenged; suffer unjust accusation with no chance to clear one's name;
含冤去世 die uncleared of a false charge; die with one's name uncleared; die with regret;
含冤吞聲 suffer injustice patiently without protest;
含冤終天 die with one's name uncleared;
抱屈含冤 be wronged and aggrieved; hold a deep grudge;

[含怨] hold a grudge; nurse a grievance;
含怨忍辱 accept insults and humiliations passively;
含怨受屈 be accused falsely;

暗含 imply; insinuate;
包含 contain; embody; include;
飽含 full of;
隱含 implication;
蘊含 contain; include;

han

【函】 (1) case; envelope; (2) letter;

[函件] correspondence; letters;

[函授] correspondence course; give a correspondence course; lessons by correspondence; run a correspondence course; teach by correspondence;
函授班 correspondence class;
函授部 department of correspondence instruction;
函授大學 correspondence college; correspondence university;
函授輔導 correspondence coaching;
函授講座 correspondence courses;
函授教材 correspondence materials;
函授教育 correspondence education;
函授學校 correspondence school;

[函數] (maths) function;
被積函數 integrand;
初等超越函數 elementary transcendental function;
單調函數 monotone function; monotonic function;

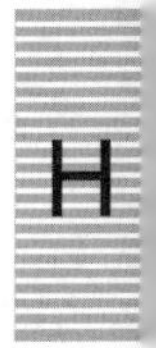

~嚴格單調函數 strictly monotonic function;
導出函數 derivative function;
遞減函數 decreasing function;
遞增函數 increasing function;
對數函數 logarithmic function;
二次函數 quadratic function;
反函數 inverse function;
合成函數 composite function;
匯出函數 derivative function; derived function;
絕對函數 absolute function;
連續函數 continuous function;
~不連續函數 discontinuous function;
邏輯函數 logical function;
冪函數 power function;
酸度函數 acidity function;
下降函數 decreasing function;
顯函數 explicit function;
線性函數 linear function;
象差函數 aberration function;
樣條函數 spline;
~逼近樣條函數 approximating spline;
~基數樣條函數 cardinal splines;
一次函數 linear function;
隱函數 implicit function;
餘函數 cofunction;
原函數 primitive function;
指數函數 exponential function;
周期函數 periodic function;

［函索即寄］ send upon request by mail;
［函約］ make an appointment by letter;

便函 informal letter;
公函 official letter;
賀函 congratulatory letter;
來函 incoming letter;
謝函 thank-you letter;
修函 write a letter;
唁函 letter of condolence;
致函 send a letter;
專函 special letter;

han

【邯】 (1) a county in Hebei Province; (2) a river in Jinghai; (3) a hill in Hebei;

［邯鄲］ (1) Handan in Hebei; (2) a surname;
邯鄲夢覺 rude awakening; unrealized ambition;
邯鄲學步 imitate another without success and lose what used to be one's own ability; imitate others and thus lose one's own individuality; take a leaf out of another person's book;

han

【涵】 (1) wet, damp, and marshy; (2) contain; (3) show nothing; (4) lenient and broad-minded;

［涵洞］ culvert;
涵洞 culvert;
~蛋形涵洞 egg-shaped culvert;
~副涵洞 secondary culvert;
~管道涵洞 pipe culvert;
~橫向涵洞 cross culvert;
~虹吸涵洞 siphon culvert;
~卵形涵洞 oval culvert;
~木質涵洞 timber culvert;
~鐵路涵洞 railway culvert;
~筒形涵洞 barrel culvert;
~瓦管涵洞 tile culvert;
~圓形涵洞 circular culvert;
~縱向涵洞 longitudinal culvert;

［涵蓋］ contain; contain completely; cover;
［涵容］ bear with; forgive;
［涵養］ (1) forbearance; self-control; self-restraint; the ability to control oneself; the virtue of patience; (2) conserve;
涵養功夫 forbearance; self-culture
涵養萬物 nourish all things;
［涵義］ connotation; implication; meaning;
負荷涵義 loaded connotation;

包涵 bear with; excuse; forgive;
海涵 magnanimous enough to forgive or tolerate;
內涵 connotation; intension;
蘊涵 contain;

han

【崡】 a checkpoint located in today's Henan;

han

【寒】 (1) cold; (2) afraid; tremble with fear; (3) needy; poor; (4) humble;

［寒不可支］ unbearably cold;
［寒不擇衣］ a person who feels cold is not choosy about clothing; any port in a storm; one who is cold does not select his/her clothing;
［寒潮］ cold wave; polar outbreak;
寒潮期 cold spell;
一陣寒潮 a cold spell; a spell of cold weather;

H

[寒帶] cold zone; frigid zone;
北寒帶 north frigid zone;
南寒帶 south frigid zone;
[寒風] bleak wind; cold wind;
寒風徹骨 a breath of wind chills sb to the bone; the bitter wind cuts sb to the very bone; the cold wind cuts sb to the marrow;
寒風刺骨 a cold wind cutting through one's bones; the cold wind chills one to the bone; the cold wind penetrates one's bones; the wind is piercingly cold;
寒風江洌 piercing cold wind; the wind is piercingly cold;
寒風透骨 the icy wind penetrates to the very bones;
寒風自北吹來 a cold wind blows from the north;
刺骨寒風 biting wind; piercing wind;
凜冽的寒風 piercing wind;
一股寒風 a cold wind;
[寒假] winter vacation;
[寒噤] shiver with cold;
打寒噤 shudder with cold; tremble with cold;
[寒苦] destitute; in financial straits; poverty-stricken;
[寒冷] cold; frigid;
寒冷徹骨 be chilled to the marrow; cold strikes one to the marrow; in shivering cold;
寒冷的 chill; chilly;
~寒冷的夜晚 a chilly night;
寒冷難熬 the bitter cold is unbearable;
極為寒冷 extremely cold;
[寒涼] cold and cool;
[寒流] cold current; cold wave;
寒流到來 the presence of the cold wave;
[寒露] Cold Dew (17th solar term);
[寒毛] fine hair on the human body;
[寒梅] winter plum;
寒梅斗雪 the plum trees in full bloom are braving the snow;
寒梅吐幽 the winter plum trees exude a fragrant smell;
[寒門] humble family; of humble origins;
[寒暖] cold and warm;
寒暖適宜 the land has a varied climate;
送暖偷寒 have affectionate concern for each other;
問寒問暖 ask about sb's needs; ask after sb's health with deep concern; inquire with concern about sb's well-being; see to the comfort of sb; solicitous for sb's welfare;
嘘寒問暖 ask after sb's needs; inquire after sb's well-being; show a kind concern for sb's comfort; show great concern for sb's well-being; solicitous about sb's health;
乍暖還寒 after suddenly getting warmer, the weather has turned cold again;
[寒氣] cold air; cold draught;
寒氣逼人 there is a cold nip in the air;
寒氣刺骨 be chilled to the bone; nip to the bone; the cold pierces one to the bone;
寒氣侵肌 the cold air encroaches one's muscles;
寒氣襲人 the chill enters into the very flesh of people;
趕去寒氣 take the chill off;
一股寒氣 a chill; a nip of cold air;
[寒峭] piercingly cold; there is a nip in the air;
[寒熱] chills and fever;
[寒色] cool colour;
[寒舍] my humble dwelling;
歡迎光臨寒舍 welcome to my humble dwelling;
[寒濕] cold dampness;
[寒士] poor scholar;
[寒暑] cold and hot seasons;
寒暑表 thermometer;
寒暑無間 all the year round;
寒暑相推 the seasonal changes hurry on;
寒來暑往 as summer goes and winter comes — as time passes; as the years roll on; cold and heat alternate; cold and heat succeed each other; the vicissitude of the seasons; with the passage of time;
冒暑憋寒 put up with cold and heat;
數易寒暑 go through many changes of seasons;
[寒素] destitute; poor;
[寒酸] miserable and shabby; shabby; sorry; scrubby;
寒酸瑣褻 poverty-stricken and contemptible;
寒酸相 miserable and shabby appearance;
衣著寒酸 be shabbily dressed;
[寒微] of low station;

寒微身世 of poor origins;

［寒心］ (1) be bitterly disappointed; (2) afraid; fearful; feel the blood running cold;

令人寒心 bitterly disappointing; cast a chill over sb;

使人感到寒心 strike a chill to one's heart;

［寒喧］ (1) exchange of compliments; exchange of conventional greetings; (2) pass the time of day with sb;

寒喧問好 conversation about the weather; exchange of conversational greetings;

寒喧語 greeting;

~定式寒喧語 conventional greeting;

彼此寒喧 greet one another;

一番寒喧 an exchange of compliments; an exchange of polite remarks; an exchange of polite remarks upon meeting;

［寒夜］ chilly night; cold night;

［寒衣］ winter clothing;

［寒意］ a chill in the air; a nip in the air;

感到寒意 feel the cold;

［寒顫］ shake; shiver; shiver with cold;

嚇得直打寒顫 shake with terror; shiver all over with fear;

避寒 escape cold; go to a winter resort;

齒寒 suffer due to failure of the other;

春寒 cold spell in spring;

大寒 Great Cold (period);

單寒 (1) thin; (2) thinly clad; (3) poor;

膽寒 be strucked with terror; be terrified;

風寒 chill; cold;

饑寒 hunger and cold;

苦寒 bitter cold;

酷寒 severely cold;

耐寒 cold-resistant;

貧寒 poor; poverty-stricken;

清寒 (1) in straitened circumstances; poor; (2) cold and clear;

傷寒 (1) typhoid; typhoid fever; (2) diseases caused by harmful cold factors; febrile disease;

受寒 catch a chill; catch cold;

惡寒 aversion to cold;

小寒 Slight Cold (period);

心寒 be bitterly disappointed;

嚴寒 bitter cold; severely cold;

陰寒 cold and humid;

禦寒 protect oneself from cold; take precautions against cold;

沾寒 catch cold; suffer from a cold;

中寒 be attacked by cold; catch cold;

han

【榦】 rail around a well;

han

【蜬】 a checkpoint during the Qin and Han dynasties, located in today's Henan;

han

【韓】 (1) a state in the Zhou Dynasty; (2) a state of the Warring States Period; (3) a surname;

［韓侯］ a surname;

［韓籍］ a surname;

［韓楬］ a surname;

［韓言］ a surname;

［韓嬰］ a surname;

［韓餘］ a surname;

han³

han

【罕】 rarely; seldom; uncommon; unusual;

［罕父］ a surname;

［罕見］ rare; seldom seen;

罕見的笑容 rare smiles;

罕見文物 rare relics;

極為罕見 a rarity;

史上罕見 be rarely seen in history;

［罕井］ a surname;

［罕事］ rare event; rare thing;

［罕聞］ rarely or seldom heard of;

［罕用］ seldom used;

［罕有］ exceptional; rare; unusual;

罕有現象 exceptional phenomenon;

納罕 surprised;

稀罕 rare and precious;

han

【喊】 (1) cry out; shout; yell; (2) call;

［喊倒好］ shout catcalls;

［喊話］ shout through a loudspeaker;

［喊叫］ cry out; shout; yell;

大聲喊叫 lift up a cry; yell one's head off;

高聲喊叫 yell loudly;

拼命喊叫 shout with the utmost strength;

［喊聲］ hubbub; yell;

喊聲連天 the battle cry reaches the heaven;

喊聲震天 make the welkin ring;

高喊 shout loudly;
呼喊 call out; shout;
叫喊 howl; shout; yell;
空喊 indulge in empty shouting;
哭喊 cry and shout;
吶喊 cry out; shout loudly;

han

【闞】 (1) growl; tiger's roar; (2) brave;

han⁴

han

【汗】 perspiration; sweat;

［汗斑］ (1) sweat stain; (2) tinea versicolour;
［汗孔］ sweat pores;
［汗淋淋］ wet with sweat;
［汗流］ sweat;
汗流浹背 all of a sweat; be running with sweat; be soaked with sweat; drip with perspiration; perspire all over; pouring with sweat; stream with sweat; sweat like a pig; sweat like a trooper; wet through with perspiration; wringing wet;
汗流滿面 one's face streaming with perspiration; perspire all over one's face; sweat dripped from one's face; sweat like a trooper; sweat stream down one's face;
汗流如雨 the perspiration pours down one's face;
汗流如珠 the perspiration drips off sb like falling pearls;
汗流如注 the perspiration runs off sb like a waterfall;
汗流雙頰 sweat comes trickling down one's cheeks;
［汗毛］ fine hair on the human body;
［汗牛充棟］ an immense number of books;
［汗青］ (1) sweating green bamboo strips; (2) annals; chronicles; historical records;
［汗衫］ T-shirt;
無袖汗衫 singlet;
［汗水］ perspiration; sweat;
［汗味］ stink with perspiration;
［汗腺］ apocrine sweat gland; sweat gland;
汗腺癌 syringocarcinoma;
汗腺管 sudoriferous duct; sweat duct;
汗腺炎 hydradenitis;
［汗顏］ feel abashed;
愧赧汗顏 blush with blame;
［汗液］ perspiration; sweat;
［汗珠］ beads of perspiration; beads of sweat;
汗珠直淌 beads of sweat have broken out profusely; the sweat rolls off in big drops;
汗珠子 beads of sweat;
顆顆汗珠 beads of sweat;

擦汗 wipe the sweat away;
出汗 perspire; sweat;
盜汗 night sweat;
發汗 induce perspiration;
愧汗 be ashamed to the extent of sweating;
瀾汗 vast expanse of water;
冷汗 cold sweat;
流汗 all of a sweat; dripping with sweat; in a sweat; sweat; sweat pour off sb; sweat streaming;
冒汗 perspire; sweat;
尿汗 uridrosia;
捏一把汗 be seized with anxiety; be seized with deep concern; break into a sweat with fright; breathless with anxiety; breathless with tension; in a sweat; have one's heart in one's mouth; with one's heart in one's mouth;
虛汗 abnormal sweating due to general debility;
血汗 blood and sweat; sweat and toil;
一把汗 breathless with anxiety;
一頭汗 a sweat-covered head;
止汗 check sweating;
珠汗 beads of perspiration;
自汗 spontaneous perspiration;

han

【扞】 (1) obstruct; oppose; resist; (2) defend; guard; withstand;

［扞格］ conflict; incompatible;

han

【旱】 (1) drought; dry spell; (2) dry land; (3) on land;

［旱冰］ roller skate;
旱冰場 ice rink; rink; skating rink;
旱冰鞋 roller skate;
［旱地］ dry farm;
［旱瓜澇桃］ melon is good in drought and peach in wet days;
［旱季］ dry season; dry summer;
［旱井］ (1) water-retention well; (2) dry well;
［旱澇］ drough and flood;
旱澇保收 give stable yields despite

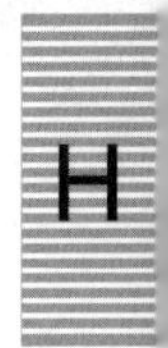

drought or floods;
［旱路］ overland route;
［旱苗逢雨］ a sweet rain falls on the parched seedlings; it is like rain upon parched rice plants;
［旱年］ year of drought;
［旱芹］ celery;
［旱情］ crops damaged by drought;
［旱天］ drought; dry days; dry weather;
［旱田］ dry farmland; dry land; upland field;
［旱象］ signs of drought;
［旱災］ drought;
［旱作］ dry farming;

伏旱 drought during hot summer days; summer drought;
乾旱 arid; dry;
亢旱 severe drought;
抗旱 combat drought; fight a drought;
起旱 take an overland route;
受旱 be drought-stricken; suffer from drought;

han
【悍】 (1) bold; brave; (2) ferocious; fierce;
［悍婦］ battleaxe;
悍潑婦人 shrew;
［悍然］ brazenly; flagrantly; outrageously;
悍然不顧 so audacious as to turn a deaf ear to; so rude and arrogant as to pay no heed to;

刁悍 cunning and fierce; wicked and ferocious;
獷悍 tough and intrepid;
精悍 (1) capable and vigorous; (2) pithy and poignant;
剽悍 agile and brave; quick and fierce;
慓悍 agile and brave; quick and fierce;
強悍 dauntless; intrepid; valiant;
兇悍 ferocious and tough; fierce and tough;
勇悍 brave and fierce;

han
【捍】 defend; guard;
［捍格不入］ conflicting; mutually conflicting; not mesh; obstructed;
［捍衛］ defend; guard; protect; safeguard; take up the cudgels for; uphold;

han
【豻】 (1) wild dog; (2) lock-up;

han
【菡】 another name of water lily or lotus flower;
［菡萏］ lotus;

han
【漢】 (1) Chinese; (2) man; (3) Han nationality;
［漢白玉］ white marble;
［漢奸］ traitor;
漢奸賣國賊 traitor and collaborator;
［漢人］ the Han people; the Hans;
［漢學］ (1) Han school of classical philology; (2) Sinology;
［漢語］ Chinese; Chinese language;
漢語信息處理 Chinese information processing;
［漢藏語］ Sino-Tibetan language;
［漢字］ Chinese character;
漢字編碼技術 Chinese character coding technique;
漢字編排系統 Chinese character editing and typesetting system;
漢字標準交換碼 Chinese character standard exchange code;
漢字操作系統 Chinese character disk operating system;
漢字工作站 Chinese character work station;
漢字管理程序 Chinese character service programme;
漢字庫 Chinese character bank;
漢字識別 Chinese character recognition;
~漢字識別系統 Chinese character recognition system;
漢字數據庫 Chinese character database;
漢字通信系統 Chinese character communication system;
漢字信息處理 Chinese character information processing;
~漢字信息處理工程 Chinese character information processing engineering;
漢字信息檢索系統 Chinese character information retrieval system;
漢字語音合成 Chinese character speech synthesis;
漢字語音識別 Chinese character speech recognition;
一行漢字 a line of Chinese characters;
［漢子］ (1) fellow; man; (2) one's husband;
偷漢子 (said of a married woman) have a lover; have an affair with a man other than one's own husband;

[漢族] Han nationality;

暴漢 bully;
笨漢 clumsy fellow; fool; stupid fellow;
碧漢 azure sky; blue sky;
大漢 big fellow;
單身漢 bachelor;
好漢 brave man; hero; true man;
懶漢 idler; lazybones; sluggard;
老漢 old man;
羅漢 arhat;
門外漢 layman; uninitiated;
男子漢 man;
鐵漢 man of iron;
閑漢 bum; idler; vagrant;
閒漢 bum; jobless person; vagrant;
霄漢 heavens; the firmament; the sky;
星漢 Milky Way; stars;
兇漢 gangster; hoodlum; violent person;
硬漢 dauntless, unyielding man; man of iron;
雲漢 Milky Way;
醉漢 drunkard; drunken man;

han

【銲】 solder; weld;

[銲縫] seam; weld;
承載銲縫 strength weld;
對接銲縫 butt weld;
多道銲縫 multiple-pass weld;
間斷銲縫 intermittent weld;
曲線銲縫 curve welding seam;

[銲工] solderer; welder;

[銲機] welder;
電銲機 arc welder;
縫銲機 seam welder;
激光銲機 laser welder;

[銲接] seal; brazing; soldering; weld; welding;
爆炸銲接 explosive weld;
不鏽剛銲接 austenite welding;
高頻銲接 high-frequency soldering;
減少焊接 reduce the number of soldered connections;
流體銲接 flow soldering;
射頻銲接 radio-frequency induction brazing;
特形銲接 contour welding;
氧氣銲接 oxygen welding;
真空銲接 vacuum brazing;

[銲料] solder;
鎘銲料 cadmium solder;
合金銲料 alloy solder;
鉛銲料 coarse solder;
銅銲料 copper solder;

[銲住] fix with a solder;

銅銲 brazing; copper brazing;

han

【暵】 dry; expose to sunshine;

han

【憾】 regret;

[憾事] matter for regret; pity;
一生中最大的憾事 the great regret of one's life;
真正的憾事 a real pity;

抱憾 regret; repent of;
缺憾 defect; imperfection;
遺憾 regretful; repentant; sorry;

han

【撼】 shake;

[撼動] rock; shake; vibrate;
撼動人心 move one's heart; shake people's faith;
撼天動地 cause a great sensation; shake both the heaven and the earth;
~撼天動地的英雄氣概 earth-shaking heroism;

搖撼 shake to the root;
震撼 rock; shake; shock;

han

【翰】 (1) white horse; (2) feather; (3) piece of writing; (4) writing brush;

han

【頷】 (1) chin; (2) nod;

[頷首] nod;
頷首會意 nod one's comprehension;
頷首示意 give a nod as a signal;
頷首微笑 nod smilingly;
頷首讚許 nod approvingly;
頷首之交 nodding acquaintance;

han

【馯】 fierce; wild;

han

【瀚】 expansive; vast;

浩瀚 vast;

hang¹

hang

【夯】 (1) burden; heavy load; (2) raise with

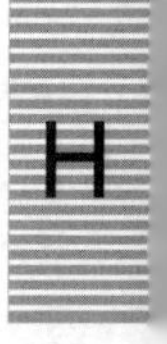

force; (3) fill cracks and leakages with earth;

[夯板] tamping plate;

[夯錘] rammer;

氣動夯錘 air rammer;

[夯鎬] tamping pick;

[夯歌] rammers' chant;

[夯棍] tamping bar; tamping rod;

[夯漢] person who carries heavy loads on the shoulder;

[夯貨] a husky but foolish person;

[夯具] rammer;

[夯路機] tamping plate roadpacker;

[夯土] rammed earth;

夯土壩 rammed earth dam;

夯土機 ramming machine;

夯土建築 house with tamped clay walls;

[夯砣] heavy end of a rammer;

打夯 drill piles in construction; tamp;

機動夯 power rammer;

木夯 wooden rammer;

hang²
hang
【行】 (1) line; row; single file; (2) elder among brothers and sisters; (3) line of business; profession; trade; (4) branch of a trade; (5) business firm; (6) a column of; a line of; a row of; a stream of;

[行幫] trade association;

[行輩] a position in the family hierarchy; seniority in the family;

[行當] (1) line of business; profession; trade; (2) a type of role in traditional Chinese operas;

邪惡的行當 one's vicious trade;

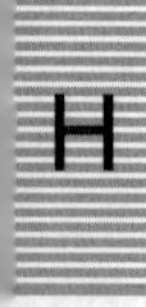

[行道] profession; trade;

[行販] pedlar;

[行規] guild regulations;

[行話] cant; jargon;

行話市語 the language of every trade and business;

[行會] guild;

[行貨] goods which are not carefully processed;

[行家] cognoscente; connoisseur; expert; professional;

老行家 veteran;

事怕行家 he who knows his trade works best;

[行列] (1) line of people; rank; (2) determinant;

行列式 determinant;

~ 加邊行列式 bordered determinant;

~ 交錯行列式 alternate determinant;

~ 線路行列式 circuit determinant;

~ 相關行列式 correlation determinant;

~ 軸對稱行列式 axisymmetric determinant;

[行情] conjuncture; market quotations; the market price;

行情記錄 quotation record;

行情堅挺 the market is strong;

行情上漲 in a rising market;

行情下跌 in a falling market;

一分行情一分貨 nothing for nothing, and very little for a halfpenny;

影響行情 affect the market;

[行市] (1) market; (2) quotation;

行市不振 the market is weak;

行市好轉 the market is improving;

行市活躍 the market is active;

行市堅挺 the market is firm;

行市堅穩 the market is steady;

行市堅硬 the market is strong;

行市疲軟 the market is easy;

行市平靜 the market is quiet;

行市上昇 the market is picking up;

行市死寂 the market is still;

行市閒散 the market is idle;

行市興隆 the market is brisk;

[行業] biz; branch of a trade; calling; industry; line of business; line of work; profession; trade;

行業不正之風 evil winds in business;

行業暗語 lingo;

行業發展 growth of an industry;

行業分析師 industry analyst;

行業國有化 nationalize an industry;

行業領頭羊 industry leader;

行業私有化 privatize an industry;

行業衰退 decline of an industry;

行業專家 industry expert;

翻譯行業 profession of translation;

服務性行業 service industry; service trades;

服裝行業 apparel industry; rag trade;

各行各業 all fields of endeavour; all

professions and trades; all walks of life; different trades and callings; different walks of life; every field of work;
~各行各業的人 all walks of life; the butcher, the baker, the candlestick-maker;
跨行業 cross-industry;
衰落的行業 declining industry;
選擇行業 choose a trade;
增長的行業 growing industry;
逐行逐業 trade by trade;

[行長] president of a bank;
銀行副行長 vice president of a bank;
銀行行長 president of a bank;

本行 one's line; one's own profession;
懂行 know the business; know the ropes;
發行 sell wholesale;
分行 branch;
改行 change one's profession;
內行 adept; expert;
排行 list according to seniority;
商行 commercial firm; trading company;
同行 of the same occupation; of the same trade;
外行 lay; unprofessional;
洋行 foreign firm;
銀行 bank;
在行 expert at sth; know a trade well;
支行 sub-branch;

hang
【沆】 ferry;

hang
【杭】 (1) Hangzhou; (2) same as 航, to sail; cross a stream; navigate;
[杭育] heave ho;
[杭州] Hangzhou;

hang
【迒】 (1) animal tracks; (2) path; road; way;

hang
【航】 (1) boat; ship; (2) navigate;

[航班] flight number; scheduled flight;
航班號 flight number;
航班取消 the flight is cancelled;
航班延誤 the flight is delayed;
常規航班 routine flight;
出發航班 departures;
~出發航班告示板 departures board;
定期航班 scheduled flight;
訂航班 get a flight;
國際航班 international flight;
國內航班 cross-country flight; domestic flight; internal flight;
廉價航班 cheap flights;
取消航班 cancel a regular flight;
銜接航班 connecting flight;
預訂航班 book a flight;
洲際航班 intercontinental flight;

[航標] buoy;

[航程] air-range; flying range; passage; range; sail; voyage;
不同航程 different voyage;
第一航程 first voyage;
拖帶航程 towing voyage;
往返航程 round voyage;

[航道] channel; course; fairway; lane; passage; waterway;
海上航道 shipping lane;
天然航道 natural navigable waterway;

[航海] navigation; voyage;
航海安全 navigation safety;
~危及航海安全 jeopardize the safety of navigation;
航海裝備 nautical equipment;
梯山航海 scale mountains and cross seas;
棧山航海 climb up high mountains and cross vast seas; have long and hard journeys;

[航空] aviation; voyage;
航空愛好者 aerophile;
航空安全 air safety;
航空保險 aviation insurance;
航空表演 air show;
航空兵 aerial army; aviation;
~岸基航空兵 land-based aviation;
~部隊輸送航空兵 troop-carrier aviation;
~敵航空兵 hostile aviation;
~輔助航空兵 auxiliary aviation;
~觀察航空兵 observational aviation;
~海軍航空兵 fleet air army; marine aviation;
~轟炸航空兵 bombardment aviation;
~輕型轟炸航空兵 light bombardment aviation;
~重型轟炸航空兵 heavy bombardment aviation;
~艦基航空兵 ship-based aviation;
~艦載航空兵 carrier aviation;
~近程轟炸航空兵 short-range bombardment;

~ 陸軍航空兵 army aviation;
~ 陸軍運輸航空兵 army transport aviation;
~ 空降突擊航空兵 assault aviation;
~ 強擊航空兵 attack aviation;
~ 訓練航空兵 tactical aviation;
~ 遠程航空兵 long-range aviation;
~ 戰鬥航空兵 fighter aviation;
~ 戰術航空兵 tactical aviation;
~ 偵察航空兵 reconnaissance aviation;
校射偵察航空兵 spotting and reconnaissance aviation;
前線偵察航空兵 surveillance aviation;
~ 支援航空兵 support aviation;
~ 直昇機航空兵 helicopter aviation;
~ 中程航空兵 medium-range transport aviation;
航空病 aeropathy;
船空測量 aerial survey; aerosurvey;
航空地質學 aerogeology;
航空電子設備 avionics;
~ 超小型化航空電子設備 microminiaturized avionics;
~ 高性能航空電子設備 high-performance avionics;
~ 機載航空電子設備 aircraft avionics;
~ 軍用航空電子設備 military avionics;
~ 全天候航空電子設備 all weather avionics;
航空電子學 avionics;
航空發動機 aeroengine;
航空發電機 aerogenerator;
航空港 airport;
航空公司 airline; airline company;
~ 地方航空公司 local-service airline;
~ 國際航空公司 international airline;
~ 貨運航空公司 cargo airline;
~ 私營航空公司 private airline;
航空顧問 aviation adviser;
航空航天 aerospace;
~ 航空航天公司 aerospace company;
~ 航空航天研究 aerospace research;
航空化學 aerochemistry;
航空技術 aerotechnics; technical aeronautics;
航空狂熱 aeromania;
航空力學 aeromechanics;
~ 理論航空力學 theoretical aeromechanics;
~ 應用航空力學 applied aeromechanics;
航空流體 aerofluid;
航空輪胎 aerotire;
航空母艦 aeroplane carrier; aircraft carrier; carrier; flat-top; floating aerodrome;
航空疲勞 aeronautical fatigue;
航空器構架 airframe;
航空人身保險 aviation personal accident insurance;
航空三角測量 aerotriangulation;
航空攝影 airphoto;
~ 航空攝影術 aerial photography; aerophotography;
航空時代 air age;
航空聲學 aeroacoustics;
航空事業 aviation industry;
航空物理學 aerophysics;
航空武器 air armament;
航空無線電 aeroradio;
航空小姐 air hostess;
航空信 (1) air letter; (2) airmail;
~ 航空信件 aerogramme;
~ 一封航空信 a letter by airmail;
航空學 aeronautics;
~ 高速航空學 high-speed aeronautics;
~ 海上航空學 naval aeronautics;
~ 民用航空學 civil aeronautics;
航空醫學 aeromedicine;
航空郵遞 airmail;
航空郵寄 airmail; par avion;
航空郵簡 aerogramme;
航空郵件 airmail;
航空郵政 airmail;
航空員 aerator;
航空運輸地理 geography of air transportation;
航空炸彈 aerial bomb; aerobomb;
航空展覽 aeroshow; air show;
航空站 aerodrome; aeroport; airport;
~ 備用航空站 alternature airport;
~ 民用航空站 civil airport;
~ 全天候航空站 all-weather airport;
~ 入境航空站 airport of entry;
航空照片 aerophotography;
航空照相機 aerocamera;
航空支線 feeder airline;
民用航空 civil aviation;

[航路] airway; waterway;
國際航路 international airway;
環球航路 global airway;
人造航路 artificial navigable waterway;

[航天] aerospace; space flight;
航天測控 spacecraft tracking, telemetering, and controlling;

~航天測控網 spacecraft tracking, telemetering, and controlling network;
~航天測控系統 spacecraft tracking, telemetering, and controlling system;
~航天測控站 spacecraft tracking, telemetering, and controlling station;
航天測量船 spacecraft tracking, telemetering, and controlling ship;
航天發射場 space launching field;
航天飛機 space shuttle;
航天工程 space engineering;
航天環境 space environment;
航天計算機 aerospace computer;
航天技術 space technology;
航天救生 rescue in space flight;
航天科技 aerospace technology;
航天控制中心 space flying control centre;
航天器 spacecraft; space vehicle;
航天器對接 spacecraft docking;
~航天器發射 spacecraft launching;
航天拖船 space tug;
航天武器 astro weapon;
航天系統工程 space system engineering;
航天學 astronautics; space aeronautics;
航天醫學工程 space medico-engineering;
航天員 astronaut;
~航天員訓練機 astrotrainer;
航天站 space station;

[航線] air route; itinerary; navigation route; route; way;
常規航線 air lane;
定期短途航線 commuter air lane;
定期航線 scheduled flight;
國際航線 international air lane;
國內航線 domestic air lane; internal air lane;
海上航線 sea lane;
貨運航線 cargo airline;
一條航線 a route;

[航行] navigate by water; sail; seaway; voyage
航行中 on a voyage;
國際航行 international voyage;
~長途國際航行 long voyage;
環球航行 circumnavigation of the world;

[航運] shipping; transportation by water;
航運商 shipper;

出航 (1) set out on a voyage; set sail; (2) set out on a flight; take off;
處女航 maiden voyage;
慈航 merciful ferry; way of salvation;
導航 guide navigation; pilot;
返航 return to base; return to port;
歸航 home;
護航 convoy; escort;
開航 (1) become open for navigation; (2) set sail;
領航 navigate; pilt;
迷航 drift off course; get lost;
民航 civil aviation;
起航 set sail;
試航 trial trip; trial voyage;
停航 suspend air service;
通航 open to navigation;
續航 fly continuously;
巡航 cruise;
夜航 night flight;
引航 pilot;
遠航 ocean-going voyage;

hang

【桁】 rack for hanging clothes;

hang

【頏】 contest; match; well matched;

頡頏 (1) (of birds) fly up and down; (2) contend with each other; match;

hang⁴

hang

【沆】 (1) vast expanse of water; (2) fog; mist; (3) flowing;

[沆瀣] evening mist;
沆瀣一氣 act in collusion with sb; collaborate in evildoing; conspire with sb;

hao¹

hao

【蒿】 (1) plants of the mugwort or artemisia family; (2) rising vapour;

[蒿草] wormwood;

[蒿目] gaze far; gaze into the distance;
蒿目時艱 foresee and worry about worldly troubles; look with anxiety at the world's ills; survey the country's situation with concern; survey the world with concern;

[蒿子稈兒] wormwood;

灌木蒿 sagebrush;

hao

【嗃】 give forth sound; sound;

[嗃矢] (1) arrow with a whistle attached; (2)

beginning; (3) forerunner; harbinger; precursor;

嚆矢維艱 the beginning is difficult;

hao

【薅】 root out; weed;

［薅草］ weeding;

［薅鋤］ small short-handled hoe;

hao²

hao

【毫】 (1) fine long hair; (2) writing brush; (3) at all; in the last; (4) milli-;

［毫不］ devoid of; not...at all; not in the least; not the least bit; nothing; without the slightest;

毫不動容 not change countenance; not move a muscle;

毫不動搖 impregnable; not waver in the least; sit tight; unshaken in one's conviction; unwavering; without vacillating;

毫不費力 as slick as a whistle; at one blow; like a dream; no sweat; with a wet finger; without the slightest effort;

毫不關心 be not in the last concerned about sth;

毫不含糊 clear-cut; explicit; in no uncertain terms; unambiguous; unequivocal; unmistakable; well-defined;

毫不諱言 call a spade a spade; candid; confess freely; declare in no uncertain terms; make no attempt to conceal the truth; make no secret of; outspoken; put it bluntly;

毫不介意 not care a fig; not care a straw; not care at all; not matter a farthing; not mind; pay no attention to; take no notice of;

毫不拘束 not feel restrained in the least;

毫不客氣 without ceremony;

毫不利己，一心為公 devote oneself to serving the public without any selfish thoughts;

毫不留情 act in cold blood; give no mercy; give no quarter; in spades; relentlessly; show no mercy; take off the gloves; with the gloves off; without gloves;

毫不氣餒 without flagging;

毫不容情 make absolutely no allowance; mercilessly; not make any allowance; not pull any punches;

毫不示弱 not give any impression of weakness; not take sth lying down;

毫不畏懼 without a trace of fear;

毫不相干 have nothing to do with; have nothing to say to; irrelevant;

毫不相容 utterly incompatible with;

毫不遜色 with the best of them;

毫不掩飾 make no bones about; make no secret of; not mince words; totally undisguised; undisguisedly;

毫不隱諱 outspokenly; with great candour; without any reservation;

毫不猶疑 every time; straight away; straight off; unhesitatingly; without the least hesitation;

毫不在乎 completely unperturbed; like it is going out of style; make nothing of; not care a bean; not care a bit; not care a cuss; not care a hang; not care a pin; not care a row of beans; not care a stiver; not care at all; not give a damn; not mind at all; think little of; without the slightest compunction;

毫不在意 not care a bit; not care a dump; not care a rap; not care a whoop;

毫不知恥 have the impudence to; lose all sense of shame;

毫不足怪 not at all surprising;

毫不足奇 not at all strange; there is no surprise; there is nothing strange;

毫不足取 not worth taking;

［毫髮］ a hair; the least bit; the slightest;

毫髮不差 exactly the same; not deviate a hair's breadth; perfectly accurate; without a shade of difference; without the least difference; without the slightest difference;

毫髮不爽 exact to a tee; exact to a tittle; not the least error; not to deviate a hair's breath; perfectly accurate; there is not a fraction of difference; to a hair; to a hair's breadth; to the turn of a hair; without the slightest error;

毫髮之差 turn of a hair;

不差毫髮 exactly the same; not deviate a hair's breadth; perfectly accurate; without a shade of difference; without the least difference; without the slightest difference;

［毫厘］ an iota; the least bit;

毫厘不差 exactly; just right; not the least loss; there is not the slightest error; to a nicety; to a tittle; without a shade of difference; without the slightest difference;

毫厘千里 the difference of a little leads a thousand li astray — a warning against carelessness;

不失毫厘 just right; perfectly accurate;

差之毫厘，謬以千里 a slight discrepancy leads to a gigantic error; a small discrepancy leads to a great error; an error with the breadth of a single hair can lead sb a thousand miles astray; one false step will make a great difference;

失之毫厘，差之千里 a little error may lead to a large discrepancy; a slight discrepancy leads to a gigantic error; a small discrepancy leads to a great error; a slight mistake will result in a great error in the end; an error with the breadth of a single hair can lead sb a thousand miles astray; one false step will make a great difference; the slightest deviation leads one far astray;

[毫毛] hair;

不敢動人一根毫毛 dare not touch a hair of sb;

不傷毫毛 not hurt a hair of sb's head;

一根毫毛 a hair; a single hair of one's head; the least little bit;

[毫米] millimetre;

[毫秒] millisecond;

[毫末] tiny;

毫末之利 the least profit;

合抱之木，生於毫末 a huge tree grows from a tiny seedling; great oaks from little acorns grow;

[毫升] millilitre;

[毫無] by no means; devoid of; not in the least; without the least;

毫無把握 have nothing to catch hold of; cannot be sure; unable to guarantee; uncertain of success;

毫無辦法 at a complete loss as to what to do; at one's wits' end; can do nothing about; no way out; on the ropes; there is no help for; there is nothing one can do about;

毫無保留 outspoken; without reservation;

~毫無保留的 unreserved;

~毫無保留地 unreservedly;

毫無差異 six of one and half a dozen of the other; without the slightest difference between two alternatives;

毫無誠意 an utter absence of honest intentions; not sincere in the least;

毫無出路 have no way out at all;

毫無道理 for no reason whatever; utterly unjustifiable;

毫無二致 as like as two peas; be entirely at one with; be identical with; exactly the same; no difference between the two at all; there is no difference at all; without the least difference;

毫無改悔之意 absolutely unrepentant;

毫無感覺 completely numb;

毫無根據 absolutely unfounded; baseless; for no valid reason; groundless; there is absolutely no ground; utterly groundless; without book;

毫無顧忌 have no scruples; make no bones about; make no scruple; stick at nothing; stop at nothing; without scruple;

毫無顧慮 free from all anxiety; throw all caution to the winds; without any misgivings whatsoever; without the slightest hesitancy;

毫無悔意 unrepentant;

毫無價值 count for nothing; not worth a brass farthing; not worth a button; not worth a continental; not worth a damn; not worth a farthing; not worth a snap; not worth a straw; not worth a toss; not worth two hoots; of no value; of no worth;

毫無結果 for nothing;

毫無進展 in circles;

毫無懼色 maintain a bold front; not at all afraid; show no sign of fear; never change colour; without the least sign of fear;

毫無倦意 not feel tired at all;

毫無可能 out of the question;

毫無可取 not a single merit; not have the slightest good point; totally worthless;

毫無例外 every one of them; every time; most and least; without exception;

毫無牽掛 free from care;

毫無權利 have no manner of right;

毫無生氣 have the vitality sapped;

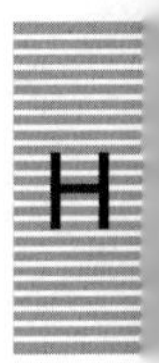

lifeless; without any vitality;
毫無希望 entirely hopeless; not have the slightest hope; there is not a ray of hope;
毫無效果 like a lead balloon;
毫無遜色 by no means inferior; by no means weaker; every bit as good as; not a whit inferior; not in the least inferior;
毫無頭緒 in a hopeless tangle;
毫無疑問 as sure as a gun; as sure as fate; beyond all question; beyond any shadow of doubt; beyond dispute; beyond doubt; beyond question; doubtless; for sure; go without saying; it is not a question; it leaves little doubt as to; it stands to reason that; no doubt; no two ways about it; out of question; past question; sure enough; there can be very little doubt about; there is no doubt that; there is no question that; there is no question of; there is no room for doubt; without any doubt; without question;
毫無疑義 beyond all doubt; there is not a shadow of doubt; there is not the slightest doubt;
毫無異議 no objection at all; there is no objection to;
毫無用處 as much use as a headache; good-for-nothing; not at all useful; of no earthly use; of no use at all; utterly useless;
毫無原則 a total lack of principles;
毫無怨言 not utter a single complaint;
毫無指望的人 gone coon; goner; hopeless person;
毫無著落 nowhere to be found;
毫無蹤影 leave without a trace;
毫無主見 have no mind of one's own;
毫無作用 like water off a duck's back;

［毫子］ silver coin;

分毫 fraction; iota;
揮毫 draw a picture with a brush; wield one's writing brush;
秋毫 autumn hair; newly-grown down; sth so small as to be almost indiscernible;
潤毫 pay for services rendered;
絲毫 a bit; a particle; a shred; an iota; the least bit; the slightest amount; the slightest degree; the tiniest;
兔毫 writing brush;
纖毫 every small detail; extremely minute; minute; tiny parts of things; tiny things; very little;
羊毫 writing brush made of goat's hair;

hao

【嗥】 frantic barks of dogs or wolves;

［嗥鳴］ howl;
嗥鳴雷動 roar like a thunderpeal;

hao

【號】 howl; wail; yell;

［號叫］ howl; yell;
號叫求救 yell for help;
大聲號叫 yell one's head off;

［號哭］ blubber; cry loudly; wail;
大聲號哭 set up a howl;
號天哭地 bewail loudly; weep and wail, calling on heaven and earth; weep to the very heaven and to the very earth;
拼命號哭 howl horribly;

［號喪］ cry at a funeral;

［號啕］ cry loudly; wail;
號啕大哭 cry one's heart out; wail aloud;
號啕痛哭 bewail mournfully; burst into a storm of tears; cry loudly; cry one's eyes out; cry one's heart out; utter a loud cry; wail loudly; weep and wail; weep with complete abandon;

哀號 cry; cry bitterly; cry piteously; lament; wail; wail of woe; whine in despair;
暗號 cipher; countersign; password; secret mark; secret sign; secret signal; signal;
百分號 percent sign;
寶號 your firm;
本號 our company;
編號 (1) arrange under numbers; number; (2) number; serial number;
標號 grade; label; marking;
別號 alias; moniker;
撥號 dial a number;
長號 trombone;
參見號 index;
稱號 appellation; designation; name; title;
乘號 multiplication sign;
除號 sign of division;
吹號 blare the call; blow a bugle;
綽號 nickname;
大括號 braces;
大號 (1) large size; (2) bass horn; (3) your name;
代號 code; code name; designation; mark;

代字號 swung dash;
單引號 single quotation marks;
等號 equal sign; equals sign;
帝號 title of an emperor;
逗號 comma;
頓號 punctuation mark placed between several proper names;
方括號 square brackets;
分號 semicolon;
分離號 apostrophe;
符號 (1) mark; sign; symbol; (2) insignia;
負號 minus sign; negative sign;
感歎號 exclamation mark;
隔音號 syllable-dividing mark;
掛號 (1) register; (2) send by registered mail; (3) establish a criminal record;
國號 the title of a reigning dynasty;
和號 "and" sign;
呼號 cry out in distress; wail;
徽號 title of honour;
諢號 nickname;
或號 "or" sign;
尖括號 angle brackets;
件號 part number; piece number;
劍號 dagger sign;
箭號 arrow sign;
井號 pound key; pound sign;
句號 full stop; period;
軍號 bugle;
口號 shibboleth; slogan; watchword;
括號 brackets;
連字號 hyphen;
聯號 chain store;
溜號 slink off; sneak away;
冒號 colon;
廟號 dynastic title;
鳴號 sound the bugle; trumpet;
年號 reign title;
怒號 howl; roar;
牌號 (1) mark; shop sign; (2) make; trademark; (3) name of a product;
批號 batch number;
撇號 apostrophe;
平行號 parallels;
破折號 dash;
譜號 clef;
旗號 army signal; banner; flag; standard;
竊號 usurp the name of the emperor;
商號 business entity; business establishment; corporate name; firm; shop; store;
昇號 sharp;
省略號 ellipsis; ellipsis dots;
省字號 apostrophe;
時號 time signal;
謚號 posthumous title;
書號 book number; call number;
書名號 book title brackets;
雙方括號 double brackets;
雙劍號 double dagger;
雙引號 double quotation marks;
索書號 call number;
脱字號 caret;
外號 nickname;
問號 (1) a question mark; an interrogation mark; (2) unknown factor; unsolved problem;
小號 (1) trumpet; (2) small size;
斜線號 slant;
信號 signal; signaling;
星號 asterisk;
型號 marker; model; model number; type; marking;
押號 sign; stamp;
雅號 your gracious name;
銀號 banking house;
引號 inverted comma; quotation mark; speech mark;
魚尾號 bold square brackets;
圓號 French horn; horn;
圓括號 parenthesis;
猿號 ape's call; gibbon's howls;
章節號 section;
正號 plus sign;
中音號 althorn;
專號 special issue;
字號 name of a shop;

hao

【貉】 (1) name of a northern barbarian tribe; (2) quiet;

［貉絨］ racoon dog fur;

［貉子］ racoon dog;

hao

【豪】 (1) person of extraordinary powers of endowments; (2) bold and unconstrained; forthright; unrestrained; (3) bullying; despotic;

［豪放］ bold and unconstrained;

豪放不羈 bold and uninhibited; vigorous and unrestrained;

文筆豪放 write in a bold and unconstrained style;

性格豪放 vigorous and unrestrained;

［豪富］ (1) powerful and wealthy; (2) powerful

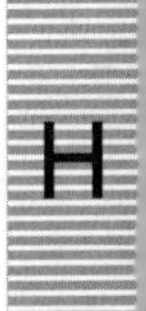

rich; rich and powerful;
豪富狂 plutomania;
豪富妄想 plutomania;
[豪光焕目] dazzling glory agreeable to the eye;
[豪橫] bullying; despotic;
[豪華] luxurious; sumptuous;
豪華成癖 be addicted to extravagance; love extravagance;
豪華的 deluxe; luxurious;
豪華酒店 luxury hotel; plush hotel;
豪華生活 luxurious life;
生活豪華 live in splendour;
[豪傑] hero; heroine; person of exceptional ability;
豪傑之士 hero; person of exceptional ability;
女中豪傑 heroine;
英雄豪傑 hero;
[豪舉] (1) bold move; (2) munificent act;
[豪客] gallant person;
大豪客 big spender;
[豪邁] great; not petty; valiant;
豪邁性情 magnanimous disposition;
[豪門] rich and powerful family; wealthy and influential clan;
豪門大族 wealthy and influential clan;
豪門富戶 rich and powerful families; wealthy and influential clan;
豪門貴族 powerful family and honourable clan;
豪門巨室 rich and powerful families;
豪門子弟 children of the rich;
出身豪門 be born in a rich and powerful family;
嫁入豪門 marry into money; marry money;
[豪氣] heroic spirit; heroism;
[豪強] (1) despotic; tyrannical; (2) bully; despot;
[豪情] lofty sentiments;
豪情滿懷 be filled with boundless pride; full of pride and enthusiasm; full of spirit;
豪情壯志 lofty sentiments and aspirations; lofty spirit and soaring determination;
滿懷豪情 be filled with boundless pride; full of pride and enthusiasm; full of spirit;
抒發豪情 give off one's lofty sentiments;
[豪紳] bullying gentry; despotic gentry;
[豪爽] forthright; noble-minded and forthright; straightforward; virile vigour;
性格豪爽 of a generous nature;
[豪俠] (1) gallant; (2) gallant person;
[豪興] exhilaration; exuberant spirits; keen interest; overflowing spirits;
[豪飲] drink to the limit of one's capacity;
[豪雨] heavy rain; torrential rain;
[豪語] brave words;
[豪宅] luxury property;
豪宅價格 luxury property prices;
[豪壯] bold; daring; grand and heroic;

粗豪 forthright; unconstrained;
富豪 rich and powerful people;
人豪 hero; the ablest and bravest of men;
土豪 local tyrant;
文豪 great writer; literary giant;
邑豪 village bully;
英豪 have a proper sense of pride or dignity;
自豪 feel proud of; have a proper sense of pride; pride oneself on; proud of; take pride in;

hao

【嚎】 howl; wail;
[嚎哭] wail;
神哭鬼嚎 heartbreaking crying; the wailings of demons and moans of ghosts; weird and horrible;
[嚎啕] cry loudly; wail;
嚎啕大哭 a rain of tears; a storm of tears; break into violent lamentations; burst into loud sobs; burst into tears; crack up; cry aloud; cry bitter tears; cry loudly with abandon; wail at the top of one's voice; wail bitterly;

hao

【壕】 ditch around a city wall; moat;
[壕溝] (1) ditch; (2) trench;
加固壕溝 fortify trenches;
填平壕溝 fill up moats;
跳過壕溝 jump a ditch;

城壕 moat;
反坦克壕 anti-tank ditch;
坦克壕 tank ditch;
戰壕 entrenchment; trench;

hao

H

【濠】 ditch; moat; trench;

hao

【蠔】 oyster;

［蠔油］ oyster sauce;

hao

【鶴】 a pronunciation of 鶴 , crane;

hao³

hao

【好】 (1) fine; good; having the desired quality; nice; well; (2) friendly; kind; on good terms; (3) of a high level; (4) beneficial; efficient; useful; (5) get well; healthy; in good health; sound; (6) convenient; easy; (7) so as to; so that; (8) in proper order;

［好啊］ ah; aha; all right; attaboy; bravo; capital; excellent; good; great stuff; ho; hurrah; hurray; now you're talking; oh; that's champion; that's the style; that's the way; well; well done; well run; wonderful; yippee;

［好辦］ can be easily done;
好辦好辦 it can be easily done;

［好比］ (1) by way of example; can be compared to; for example; for instance; may be likened to; (2) just like; like;

［好不］ really; what a...;
好不害臊 for shame;
好不講理 utterly impervious to reasoning;
好不容易才 by the skin of one's teeth; go to a lot of trouble; have a hard time; it takes a lot of time to; not easy at all; with much difficulty;
好不知羞恥 brazen;

［好吃］ delicious; good to eat; nice; palatable; tasty; toothsomeness;
不好吃 not good to eat;

［好處］ easy to get along with;

［好處］ (1) advantage; benefit; (2) gains; profits;
從好處看 on the plus side;
獲得好處 obtain an advantage;
~獲得雙重好處 secure a double benefit;
撈好處 benefit from; obtain an advantage; take advantage of sth;
恰到好處 do just the thing needed; do the thing mentioned to the right and proper degree; do the very thing desired; hit the spot; just perfect; just right; neither too much nor too little; perfect; say the right thing at the right moment; strike the happy medium; the cap fits; to a fit; to a nicety; to a T; to a tee; to a tittle; to a turn; to the point;
往好處想 think of the better possibilities of a situation;
有好處 it pays; useful;
~大有好處 of great benefit to; of much good;
~對健康有好處 of real benefit to health;

［好歹］ (1) good and bad; what's good and what's bad; (2) danger; disaster; mishap; (3) anyhow; at any rate; in any case; (4) make do with; (5) after a fashion; in some fashion;
好歹試試 let's try, anyhow; take one's chance;
不知好歹 not appreciate a favour; unable to tell what's good or bad for one;
分清好歹 know good from evil;
好説歹説 do a lot of talking to convince sb; plead with sb in every way one could; try every possible way to persuade sb;
是好是歹 for good or for evil; for good or ill; whether it is good or bad;
嫌好道歹 fastidious in every way; nitpick in many ways;
做好做歹 play the good or crook; try every way possible to persuade sb into doing sth;

［好端端］ in perfectly good condition; when everything is all right;

［好多］ (1) a good deal; a good many; a great many; a lot of; (2) how many; how much;
胖了好多 put on much weight;
瘦了好多 thin down a lot;

［好感］ favourable impression; liking;
保持好感 preserve one's good feeling;
對…有好感 be well-disposed towards sb;
給人好感 give sb a good impression;

［好過］ (1) have an easy time; in easy circumstances; (2) feel well;
不好過 have a hard time;

［好漢］ brave man; determined and brave man; hero; true man;
好漢不吃眼前虧 a wise man does not fight against impossible odds; a

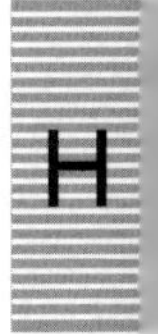

wise man does not fight when the odds are against him; a wise man knows when to retreat; a wise man never deliberately runs his head against a brick wall; a wise man never fights at a disadvantage; a wise man will extricate himself from a disadvantageous position wherever possible; a wise man will not fight when the odds are obviously against him; better bend the back than bruise the forehead; call the bear "uncle" till you are safe across the bridge; discretion is the better part of valour; one pair of heels is often worth two pairs of hands;

好漢不提當年勇 a hero is silent about his past glories;

好漢上場，一人頂兩 a host in oneself;

好漢做事好漢當 a true man has the courage to accept the consequences of his own actions;

充好漢 play the hero; pose as a hero;

[好好兒] (1) all out; to one's heart's content; well; (2) in good condition; in good shape; in perfect good condition; when everything is all right; (3) properly; thoroughly;

[好花] good flower;

好花不常開，好景不常在 Christmas comes but once a year; the morning sun never lasts a day;

好花插在牛糞上—白糟蹋了 sticking a good flower in cow dung – wasted;

[好話] (1) a good word; word of praise; (2) fine words;

好話説盡，壞事做絕 go to all lengths to flatter as well as commit the worst crime; mouth the nicest things while committing the most outrageous crimes; say all the fine things while doing all the vilest actions; say all the nice things while stopping at no crime; say every fine word and do every foul deed;

輕信好話 swallow flattery;

討好話 fish for compliments;

為人講句好話 put in a good word for sb; put in a good word on sb's behalf;

[好壞] the good and the bad;

好壞不分 good or bad work makes no difference; no difference is made between those who do a good job and those who do soddy work; not know chalk from cheese; not distinguish the good from the bad;

好壞不一 patchy;

辨別好壞 differentiate between good and evil;

不好不壞 neither better nor worse;

不論天氣好壞 rain or shine;

分清好壞 separate the wheat from the chaff;

時好時壞 now good, now bad; up and down;

[好景] good time;

好景不常 a good time never lasts long; a sweet dream is short-lived; Christmas comes but once a year; good times don't last long; happy days are soon over; not every day is Sunday; pleasant hours fly fast; the longest day must have an end; the morning sun never lasts a day; the morning sun never lasts long;

[好久] a dog's age; for a long time; long;

好久不見 haven't seen you for a long time; haven't seen you in ages;

等了人很久 wait for sb for a long time;

[好看] (1) good-looking; handsome; nice; (2) interesting; (3) be honoured; do credit to; (4) deliberately embarrass sb; in a fix; in an embarrassing situation; on the spot;

好看的 good-looking;

要好看 not show due respect to sb;

[好了] stop; that's enough;

好了瘡疤忘了痛 forget the bitter past when released from one's suffering; forget the pain after the wound is healed; when the sore is well, the pain is forgotten;

[…好了] really;

太好了 you're a star; what a star;

[好料] honest materials;

[好夢] beautiful

好夢不長 beautiful dreams are soon to be interrupted;

一場好夢 a beautiful dream;

做個好夢 sweet dreams;

[好評] favourable comments; good review; high opinion of;

好評如潮 rave reviews;
博得普遍好評 find widespread favour;
受到新聞界的好評 get a good press; have a good press;
贏得公眾的好評 win the good opinion of the public;

[好球] bravo; good shot; well played;

[好人] (1) fine person; good person; goodie; goody; (2) healthy person; (3) a person who tries to get along with everyone;
好人多磨難 good people usually suffer much;
好人好事 fine people and fine deeds; good people and good deeds; good people doing good deeds;
好人難做 it is difficult to be a nice guy;
老好人 a benign and uncontentious person who is indifferent to matters of principle; one who tries never to offend anybody;
冤枉好人 wrong an innocent person;
一個好人 a grand fellow;
做好人 play the role of the good guy;

[好生] (1) exceedingly; quite; (2) carefully; properly;

[好使] convenient to use; work well;

[好事] (1) good deeds; good turn; (2) an act of charity; good works; (3) happy event;
好事不出門，壞事傳千里 bad news has wings; bad news travels fast; good deeds always stay indoors, while scandals travel a thousand miles; good deeds are never heard of outside the door, but bad deeds are proclaimed for three hundred miles; ill news comes apace; ill news flies fast; misdeeds always receive the maximum publicity, while good deeds are relegated to obscurity; news of good works seldom go beyond the threshold of the house, but reports of evil deeds are quickly circulated for a thousand miles around; when I did well, I heard it never; when I did ill, I heard it ever;
好事成雙 good things should be in pairs;
好事多磨 good things are a long time in coming; love's course seldom runs smooth; the course of true love never did run smooth; the course of worthy projects never did run smooth; the realization of good things is usually preceded by rough goings; the road to happiness is strewn with setbacks;
好事過頭，反成壞事 too much of a good thing;
一點好事 a bit of good;
做好事 do a good deed; do good; do good things;

[好手] adept at; capable person; good hand; past master;
理財好手 good at managing money matters;
烹調好手 excellent in cooking;
一把好手 adroit at; a good hand at;

[好受] feel better; feel more comfortable;
不好受 feel uncomfortable;
~感覺不大好受 not feel very well;
~很不好受 feel quite uncomfortable;
~心中感到不好受 sad in one's heart;

[好書] good book;
好書不厭百回讀 not get tired of reading a good book a thousand times;
好書如摯友，情誼永不渝 a good book is the best of friends, the same today and forever;

[好睡] good night;

[好說好說] it's nice for you to say so;

[好說話兒] amiable; easy to deal with; easy to get along with; good-natured;

[好似] like; look like; seem;

[好天兒] fine day; lovely weather;
晴朗的好天兒 clear and fine weather;

[好聽] (1) pleasant to hear; pleasant to listen to; pleasing to the ear; (2) high-sounding;
好聽的歌 pleasant songs;
好聽的聲音 a dulcet sound;
好聽的音樂 melodious music;
唱得很好聽 sing beautifully;
說的比唱的好聽 make empty promises; mouth high-sounding words;
說得倒好聽 that is very pretty talking;

[好玩] amusing; funny; interesting;
出於好玩 for a laugh; for fun; for laughs;

[好聞] pleasant to smell; smell good;
很好聞 smell nice;

[好戲] (1) good play; (2) great fun;
好戲不厭百回看 a good take is none the worse for being twice told;
好戲賣座 a good play draws well;
好戲在後頭 the best is behind; the best

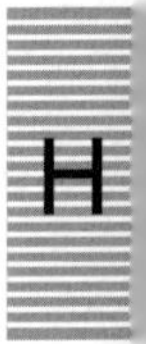

part is still behind; the last act crowns the play;
壓軸好戲 the last but best one of a series of performances;

[好險] near thing;

[好像] appear; as if; as it were; look; look as if; look like; seem; seemingly;

[好笑] funny; laughable; ridiculous;
好笑之至 utterly ridiculous;
暗自好笑 feel very much amused;
荒謬得好笑 laughably ridiculous;
荒唐好笑 absurdly ridiculous;
令人感到好笑 have a funny effect on sb;
十分好笑 screamingly funny;
愚蠢得好笑 foolishly ridiculous;

[好些] a good deal of; quite a lot;

[好心] good intentions;
好心好意 for the best; good-willed and well-intentioned; have one's heart in the right place; kind-hearted; with good intentions; with goodwill;
好心人 person of good intentions;
好心有好報 good-heartedness often meets with recompense; one good turn deserves another; your charity would be rewarded;
出於好心 with good intentions;
一片好心 with the best of intentions;
~出於一片好心 with the best of intentions;

[好性兒] good temper;

[好言] nice words;
好言相勸 plead with tactful words;
好言相慰 say sth nice to comfort sb; soothe the sb with fair words;

[好樣兒的] fine example; good person; good sort; great fellow;

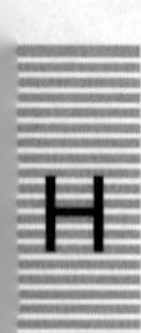

[好意] good intentions; goodwill; kindness;
好意規勸 give well-intentioned advice; offer well-meaning advice;
好意思 have the nerve;
報答人家的好意 repay the kindness;
不懷好意 after no good; bear ill-will; harbour evil designs; harbour malicious intentions; have bad intentions; not have good intentions; not with the best of intentions; up to no good; with bad intentions;
出於好意 mean well; out of a good heart; out of good intentions; out of good will; well meaning; well-intended; with the best of intentions;
~出於好意的 well-meant;
好心好意 for the best; have one's heart in the right place; good-willed and well-intentioned; kind-hearted; with good intentions; with goodwill;
一番好意 a piece of kindness; a show of hospitality; good will; well-intentioned;
一片好意 a piece of kindness; a show of hospitality; an atmosphere of goodwill;
真心好意 good intentions;

[好友] buddy; close friend; friend;
好友名單 buddy list; friend list;
諸親好友 relatives and close friends;

[好運] a piece of luck; a stroke of luck; good luck;
好運連連 a run of good luck;
交好運 have good luck; luck is on sb's side; lucky;
一點好運 an element of luck;
祝你好運 all the best; good luck to you; good wishes; wish you luck; wish you the best of luck;
祝下次好運 better luck next time;

[好在] fortunately; luckily; lucky enough;
好在天晴了 as luck would have it the weather cleared up;

[好中選好] sort out the best from among the good;

[好轉] alter for the better; improve; take a favourable turn; take a turn for the better;
經濟好轉 economic upturn;
開始出現好轉 begin to show improvement;
正在好轉 on the mend; on the up;

[好字] good handwriting;
寫一手好字 write a good fist;
一筆好字 good handwriting;

[好自為之] conduct oneself well; go ahead; try to do your best;

安好 safe and sound; well;
擺好 place properly; set properly;
變好 (1) become fine; clear up; (2) alter for the better; become good; change for the better; reform;
補好 fix up;
纔好 just fine;

大好 (1) beautiful; excellent; (2) (of an illness) completely recovered;
多好 how nice; how wonderful;
剛好 (1) exactly; just; (2) happen to; it so happens that;
和好 become reconciled;
搞好 (1) do well; make a good job of; (2) carry out; get sth done;
更好 all the better; better; so much the better;
還好 (1) not bad; passable; (2) fortunately; luckily;
和好 become reconciled;
極好 bodacious;
見好 get better;
交好 have good relations with; on friendly terms with;
叫好 applaud;
良好 good; well;
美好 fine; glorious; happy;
恰好 as luck would have it;
討好 (1) curry favour with; ingratiate oneself with; play up to; (2) be rewarded with a fruitful result; have one's labour rewarded;
通好 have friendly relations;
完好 in good condition; intact;
問好 say hello to; send one's regards to;
相好 (1) on intimate terms; (2) have an affair with; (3) intimate friend; (4) lover; mistress;
行好 perform charitable deed;
幸好 fortunately; luckily;
修好 foster cordial relations between states;
學好 improve oneself; learn from good examples;
要好 (1) on good terms; (2) eager to improve oneself;
友好 amicable; friendly;
祇好 be forced to; have to;
至好 best friend; most intimate friend;
最好 it would be best; had better;

hao

【郝】 (1) an ancient place in today's Shaanxi Province; (2) a surname;

［郝骨］ a surname;

hao⁴

hao

【好】 (1) fond of; like; love; (2) apt to; liable to; likely to;

［好吃懶做］ caring for nothing but eating; eat one's head off; fond of eating and averse to work; gluttonous and lazy; lazy and fond of good food; like to eat but not to work;

［好大喜功］ ambitious for great achievements; attempt to do sth overambitious and unrealistic; be ambitious; crave after greatness and success; flamboyant; have a fondness for the grandiose; like to do grandiose things to impress people;

［好鬥］ bellicose;
好鬥的 combative;
生性好鬥 bellicose disposition;
性剛好鬥 obstinate and fond of fighting;

［好高騖遠］ aim at the moon; aim too high; bite off more than one can chew; crave after sth high and out of reach; reach for sth that is beyond one's grasp; run after far-off things; try to run before one can walk;

［好潔成癖］ excessive fondness for cleanliness;

［好酒］ fond of the bottle; fond of the cup;
好酒廢事 be given to wine and neglect one's business;
好酒貪杯 be fond of the bottle; on the bottle; take to the bottle;

［好客］ hospitable; hospitality; keep open house;
好客的人 hospitable person;
不好客 inhospitable; inhospitality;
極為好客 be overwhelmingly hospitable;

［好哭］ apt to cry;

［好名］ be fond of fame; take a fancy to fame;
顧臉好名 care for one's face and be fond of fame;
嗜權好名 greedy for honour and power;

［好謀善斷］ resourceful and decisive; sagacious and resolute;

［好謀無斷］ fond of grandiose schemes but unable to take a decision; fond of scheming but fail to make a decision;

［好奇］ curious; full of curiosity;
好奇心 curiosity;
～保持好奇心 keep one's curiosity alive;

［好強］ aspiring; eager to do well in whatever one does;

［好色］ fond of women; lust for women;
好色的 lascivious; lewd;
好色之徒 lustful man;

~他是個好色之徒 he's an animal;
貪淫好色 debauched and sensual;

[好善樂施] always glad to give to charities; always ready to help in a worthy cause; be interested in charities; do good naturally and happily; happy in doing good; love to do philanthropic work; prodigal of benefactions;

[好尚] love and uphold;

[好勝] have a desire to excel; seek to do others down; try to be pre-eminent;
好勝的人 emulative person;
好勝心強 loving to excel others;
逞強好勝 flaunt one's superiority and seek to pull others down; parade one's superiority and strive to outshine others;

[好事] meddlesome; officious;
好事的人 busybody;
好事之徒 busybody; nosy parker;
太好事 meddle too much;

[好問] great curiosity to ask all sorts of questions;

[好惡] likes and dislikes; taste;

[好賢禮士] appreciate talented people;

[好學] bookish; diligent; educated; fond of learning; learned; scholarly; studious;
好學不倦 be devotedly attached to learning and never get wearied; insatiable of learning;
好學不厭 insatiable of learning;
好學心 acquisitive mind;
沉潛好學 quiet and studious;
敏而好學 intelligent and studious;
虛心好學 modest and eager to learn;

[好勇喜鬥] fond of bravery and fighting;

[好戰] bellicose; warlike;
好戰成性 warlike;
好戰份子 war hawk;

[好整以暇] remain calm and composed while handling pressing affairs; take things easy;

愛好 a bee in one's bonnet; a favourite of; a favourite of sb; a favourite with; affect; a friend of; a friend to; after one's fancy; all for sth; an avocation; an avocation with sb; appeal to; as a hobby; be cracked about sb; be fond of; be interested in; bend one's mind to; catch sb's fancy; delight in; dote on; dote upon; drink in; enjoy; enjoy favour; enthusiastic over sth; fall for; favour; fond of; get interest in; glad of sth; go in for; have a bent for; have a fancy for; have a fondness for; have a liking for; have a liking to; have a love for; have a love of; have a passion for; have a predilection for; have a preference for; have a soft spot for; have a taste for; have a taste in; have a weakness for; have an appetite for; have one's heart in sth; have one's likes; have partiality for; have partiality to; high on sth; hit sb's fancy; hobbies; in favour with sb; in one's favour; in one's line; keen about; keen on; love; mad on; one's cup of tea; partial to; please sb's fancy; pleased with; relish; revel in; strike sb's fancy; suit sb's fancy; take a fancy for; take a fancy to; take a liking for; take an interest in; take delight in; take pleasure in; take sb's fancy; to one's appetite; to one's fancy; to one's liking; to one's taste; with interest;
癖好 favourite hobby;
嗜好 (1) hobby; (2) habit; (3) addiction;
同好 people of the same taste or hobby;
喜好 be fond of; be keen on; like; love;

hao

【昊】 (1) summertime; (2) heaven; sky;

[昊天] (1) heaven; (2) parents' great, good kindness; (3) summer;
昊天不吊 heaven does no favours; heaven does not give a hand; heaven does not help;

hao

【浩】 grand; great; vast;

[浩大] great; huge; vast;
浩大的工程 a huge project;
聲勢浩大 gigantic;

[浩蕩] broad; magnificent; vast and mighty;
浩浩蕩蕩 enormous and powerful; in force; in a formidable array; in massive, streaming columns; in mighty formation; in proud array; vast and mighty; with greatness and vigour;
皇恩浩蕩 infinite royal graciousness;

[浩繁] vast and numerous;
部帙浩繁 voluminous works;
卷帙浩繁 voluminous works;

[浩瀚] vast;
浩瀚如海 vast as the ocean;

浩瀚無垠 immensity; vast and boundless;
浩瀚無際 immensity;
一片浩瀚 a vast expanse of water;

[浩劫] catastrophe; great calamity; havoc; holocaust; scourge;
紅羊浩劫 the catastrophe of war and rampage of bandits; the country suffers a great calamity;

[浩闊] extensive; vast;

[浩淼] extending into the distance; vast;
煙波浩淼 mist and waves stretched far into the distance;

[浩氣] noble spirit;
浩氣長存 a noble spirit that will never perish;
浩氣凜然 awe-inspiring noble spirit;
浩氣凌雲 display one's noble spirit fully;

[浩然而去] go away quickly; leave at once without hesitation;

[浩生] a surname;

[浩歎] heave a deep sigh;

[浩星] a surname;

hao

【耗】 (1) consume; cost; (2) dawdle; waste time; (3) bad news;

[耗費] consume; cost; expend;
耗費公款 squander public funds;

[耗竭] exhaust; use up;

[耗盡] burn up; consume; deplete; exhaust; impoverish; use up;
耗盡感情 exhaust one's emotions;
耗盡人力 drain away manpower;
耗盡心血 exhaust all one's energies;
體力耗盡 be completely exhausted;

[耗散] dissipation;
功率耗散 power dissipation;
屏極耗散 plate dissipation;
熱耗散 heat dissipation;
陽極耗散 anode dissipation;

[耗損] consume; deplete; lose; waste;
儲備耗損 stock depletion;
偶然耗損 random depletion;

[耗資] consume funds;
耗資巨大 entail an enormous cost;

[耗重] expendable weight;

[耗子] mouse; rat;
耗子逗貓—沒事找事 a mouse teasing a cat – asking for trouble; look for trouble;
耗子見到貓 as terrified as a mouse confronting a cat;
耗子進書房—咬字 a rat entering a library – eating characters;
耗子舔貓鼻子—找死 a mouse licking a cat's nose – courting one's own death;
耗子尾巴長瘡—沒多少膿血 a boil on a rat's tail – there's a small amount of pus;
耗子鑽水溝—各有各的路 rats passing through a sewer – each going its own way;
狗拿耗子 a dog catching mice – meddle in sb else's business;
~狗拿耗子，多管閒事 poke one's nose into other people's business;
瞎貓逮死耗子—碰運氣 a blind cat caught a dead mouse – merely a lucky hit; a dead rat falling into a blind cat's clutches – sheer luck;

噩耗 sad news;
空耗 consume for nothing; expend in vain;
虧耗 lose by a natural process;
煤耗 coal consumption;
磨耗 wear and tear;
損耗 lose; spoilage; wastage; wear and tear;
消耗 consume; expend; use up;
凶耗 news of sb's death;

hao

【涸】 dried up; dry up; exhaust;

hao

【晧】 (1) daybreak; (2) bright and brilliant;

hao

【皓】 (1) white; (2) bright; luminous;

[皓齒] white teeth;
皓齒蛾眉 white teeth and pretty eyebrows;
皓齒朱唇 have pearly white teeth and crimson lips; one's teeth are very white and one's lips vermillion; white teeth and red lips;
明眸皓齒 have bright eyes and white teeth;

[皓首] hoary head;
皓首窮經 a hoary head does research in the classics; continue to study even in old age; live and learn;

[皓月] bright moon;
皓月當空 the bright moon is shining in the sky; the bright moon hangs high in

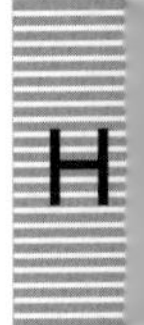

the sky; the round, snow-white moon is suspended in the sky;

皓月清空 a crystal moon hangs high in the cloudless sky; the full moon hangs in the clear sky;

hao

【號】 (1) name; (2) alternative name; assumed name; (3) business house; (4) mark; sign; signal; (5) number; (6) size; (7) date; (8) order; (9) any brass-wind instrument; (10) sth that is used as a horn; (11) call made on bugle; bugle call; (12) measure word for business transactions;

[號稱] (1) be known as; (2) claim to be;

[號角] (1) bugle; horn; trumpet; (2) bugle call;

高山號角 alpenstock;

[號令] order; verbal command; whistle;

號令槍 starter's pistol

發號施令 boss; call the shots; call the tune; call the turn; command; dictate; dictate one's terms to; give law to; give orders; issue orders; lay down the law; order people about; order sb as one fancies;

[號碼] number;

號碼牌 license plate; number plate;

號碼鎖 combination lock;

房間號碼 room number;

街道號碼 street number;

中獎號碼 winning numbers for the lottery;

座位號碼 seat number;

[號脈] feel sb's pulse; take sb's pulse;

[號聲] clarion calls sound from all sides;

[號手] bugler; trumpeter;

[號數] number;

[號外] extra of a newspaper;

叫賣號外 scream an extra;

[號召] appeal; call; draw;

[號嘴] mouthpiece;

暗號 cipher; countersign; secret signal;

編號 serial number;

標號 number;

別號 alias;

不等號 sign of inequality;

長號 trombone;

稱號 designation; name; title;

乘號 multiplication sign;

除號 division sign;

綽號 nickname;

大號 one's given name;

大括號 braces;

代號 code name;

等號 equal sign; equality sign;

調號 (1) tone mark; (2) key signature;

逗號 comma;

短號 cornet;

對號 check mark; tick;

方括號 square brackets;

符號 (1) mark; symbol; (2) insignia;

負號 negative sign;

感歎號 exclamation mark;

根號 radical sign;

掛號 (1) register; (2) send by registered mail;

國號 name of a state;

呼號 (1) call sign; (2) catchword;

徽號 title of honour;

諢號 nickname;

加號 plus sign;

尖括號 angle brackets;

減號 minus sign;

句號 full stop; period;

口號 slogan; watchword;

括號 brackets;

流水號 serial number;

冒號 colon;

名號 name and alias;

年號 title of an emperor's reign;

拍號 time signature;

牌號 (1) shop sign; (2) trademark;

批號 batch number; lot number;

旗號 banner;

商號 business establishment; shop; store;

時號 time signal;

書名號 editorial marks for books or articles;

雙號 even numbers;

外號 nickname;

斜線號 slash (/);

圓號 French horn;

圓括號 brackets; parentheses;

專號 special issue;

着重號 mark of emphasis;

字號 name of a shop;

hao

【鄗】 a town in ancient China in today's Hebei Province;

hao

【滈】 radiance of gems;

hao

【皜】 bright; white;

hao
【鎬】 hoe;
hao
【顥】 bright; hoary; luminous; white;
hao
【灝】 bean soup;

he¹
he
【呵】 (1) breathe out; exhale; (2) scold;
[呵呵] ho ho; laugh;
呵呵大笑 a horse laugh; be convulsed in laughter; burst into peals of laughter; laugh a great ho-ho; laugh loudly; roar out a great ho-ho of laughter; roar with laughter;
呵呵傻笑 cackle foolishly;
樂呵呵 cheerful and joyful; happy and joyful;
傻呵呵 simple-minded;
笑呵呵 cheerful and joyful; happy and joyful;
[呵護] (1) protect; (2) take good care of;
百般呵護 give painstaking care to sb;
[呵欠] yawn;
打了個呵欠 yawn;
忍住呵欠 stifle a yawn; suppress a yawn;
[呵責] give sb a dressing-down; scold sb severely;

叱呵 bawl at; shout at;

he
【渴】 wish;
[渴望] ache for; aspire; be all agog to; be eager about; be eager after; be eager for; hanker after; hanker for; long for; pine for; thirst for; yearn after; yearn for;
渴望有個孩子 yearn for a child;
非常渴望 sb would give the world to do sth;

he
【喝】 (1) drink; (2) drink alcoholic liquor;
[喝茶] (1) drink tea; (2) go to a restaurant;
喝茶抽煙 drink tea and smoke;
喝茶聊天 chat over a cup of tea; gossip over a cup of tea; sip tea and chat;
[喝感] thirst;
喝感過少 adipsia;
喝感減退 abnormal absence of thirst; adipsia;
喝感正常 eudipsia; ordinary normal thirst;
[喝光] drain; drink off; drink up;
[喝酒] boozing; drink wine; drinking; knock over a drink; moisten one's clay; moisten one's lips; moisten one's throat;
喝酒猜拳 drink and play the finger game;
喝酒的人 tippler;
喝酒解愁 drown one's sorrows in wine;
喝酒太多 bend one's elbow; crook the elbow; lift the elbow; raise the elbow;
不讓喝酒 keep sb from the bottle;
大量喝酒 cane;
請人喝酒 can I buy you a drink; stand sb a drink;
[喝水] (1) drink water; (2) suffer losses in business;
喝水不忘掘井人 don't forget the well-diggers when you drink from this well; when you drink the water, think of those who dug the well;
牛不喝水，按不低牛頭 one may lead a horse to the water, but twenty cannot make it drink; you can take a horse to the water, but you cannot make it drink;
牛不喝水強按頭 try to make an ox drink by forcing its head into the water — try to impose one's will on sb;
[喝粥] eat porridge;
[喝醉] drunk; have a drop too much; intoxicated; pissed; sottish; the worse for wear; tipsy;
喝醉酒的 bevvied up; crocked; intoxicated; sloshed; sozzled; stewed;

喝醉了 in one's cup;
大口地喝 swig; take a long swig of sth;

he
【訶】 blame in a loud voice; scold in a loud voice;
[訶子] myrobalan fruit;

he²
he
【禾】 (1) grains still on the stalk; (2) rice plant;
[禾束] sheaf;
he

【合】 (1) close; shut; (2) combine; join; (3) whole; (4) agree; right; suit; (5) add up to; equal to;

[合辦] jointly organize; jointly run;

[合璧] (1) combine harmoniously; match well; (2) compare; refer to;

[合併] amalgamate; coalesce; combine; consolidate; consolidation; fold; merge; merger;
合併處理 merge application;
合併提議 merger proposal;
工業合併 industrial consolidation;
購買合併 consolidation by purchase;
股票合併 share consolidation;
吸收合併 consolidation by merger;
銀行合併 bank merger;
租借合併 consolidation by lease;

[合博] a surname;

[合唱] chorus; ensemble;
合唱隊 chorus;
~合唱隊人員 theatre chorus;
~合唱隊指揮 chorus master;
合唱歌曲 part-song;
合唱曲 chorus;
~四部合唱曲 quartet;
合唱團 choir; chorus; glee club;
~合唱團指揮 chorus master;
~男聲合唱團 male-voice choir;
~學生合唱團 student's chorus;
合唱組 glee club;
大合唱 cantata; chorus;
混聲合唱 mixed chorus;
男聲合唱 male chorus; men's chorus;
女聲合唱 female chorus; women's chorus;
童聲合唱 children's chorus;
無伴奏合唱 unaccompanied chorus;

[合成] (1) compose; (2) compound; (3) synthesis; synthesize;
合成詞 compound; portmanteau word;
~動賓式合成詞 verb-object compound;
合成句 complex sentence;
~複合合成句 compound complex sentence;
合成器 synthesizer;
~諧波合成器 harmonic synthesizer;
~語音合成器 voice synthesizer;
合成性 complexity;
合成作用 synthesis;
~化能合成作用 chemosynthesis;
加色法合成 additive colour synthesis;
生物合成 biosynthesis;
陽極合成 anodic synthesis;
有機合成 organic synthesis;

[合詞法] compounding;

[合得來] get along well with people; hit it off;
合不來 unable to get along with;

[合訂本] bound volume;

[合而為一] be made one; be united as one; come together as one; merge into a single whole; unite many into one;

[合法] lawful; legal legitimate; rightful;
合法財產 lawful property;
合法地位 legal status;
合法翻譯 legitimate translation;
合法化 legalize;
合法繼承人 rightful heir;
合法經營 lawful business operation;
合法權利 legitimate right;
合法權益 lawful rights and interests;
合法收入 lawfully earned income;
合法性 legality;

[合格] measure up; on test; qualified; up to grade; up to standard; up to the scratch;
合格標誌 mark of conformity;
合格產品 qualified goods;

[合共] all told; altogether; in all;

[合股] (1) form a partnership; (2) joint-stock; pool capital; (3) ply;
合股公司 joint-stock company;

[合乎] accord with; agree with; come up to; conform to; correspond to; meet; suit; tally with;
合乎標準 up to the mark; up to the standards; within the mark;
合乎道理 in accordance with reason;
合乎規定 conform with the regulations;
合乎規格 come up to the standard; up to standard; up to the specifications;
合乎國情 conform with the national conditions;
合乎民意 conformable to the will of the people;
合乎情理 reasonable; sensible; stand to reason;
合乎實際 conform to the actual situation; conform with reality; correspond with reality;
合乎事實 tally with the facts;
合乎要求 meet the requirements;

[合歡] (1) happy get-together; happy reunion; (2) meet and enjoy; (3) silk tree;

金合歡 acacia; sweet acacia;
~澳大利亞金合歡 wallaby acacia;
銀合歡 hedge acacia;

[合伙] (1) form a partnership; (2) partnership;
合伙家庭 aggregate family;
合伙經營 run a business in partnership;
合伙會計 partnership accounting;
合伙企業 partnership;
合伙人 partner; trading partner;
~出面合伙人 public partner;
~掛名合伙人 nominal partner; ostensible partner;
~普通合伙人 ordinary partner;
~主要合伙人 predominant partner;
合伙組建公司 organize a firm in partnership;
家庭合伙 family partnership;
商業合伙 commercial partnership;
隱名合伙 sleeping partnership;

[合夥] form a partnership;
合夥用車 carpool;

[合擊] make a joint attack on;

[合計] add up to; amount to; total;

[合家] whole family;
合家歡 photograph of the whole family;
合家團聚 reunion of the whole family;

[合金] alloy;
合金工藝 alloy technology;
超合金 superalloy;
耐火合金 refractory alloy;
耐磨合金 abrasion-resistant alloy;
鐵鋁合金 ferro-aluminium alloy;

[合巹] drink the nuptial cup—get married;
合巹交杯 drink the nuptial wine cup;

[合刊] combined issue;

[合口] heal;
笑不合口 keep on laughing; laugh to the extent of being unable to close one's mouth;

[合理] (1) equitable; (2) rational; reasonable;
合理化 rationalization;
~合理化建設 rationalization proposal;
~產業合理化 rationalization of the industry;
~生產合理化 rationalization of the production;
合理使用人才 use one's talents rationally;
合理調整 reasonable readjustment;

[合力] join forces; pool efforts; make a concerted effort;
合力同心 make a united effort; unite in a concerted effort; work in full co-operation and with unity of purpose; work together with one will; with concerted effort;
齊心合力 unite efforts; with concerted effort;

[合謀] (1) conspire; plot together; (2) conspiracy;
合謀不軌 engage in conspiratorial activities together; plot sedition together;
暗中合謀 in league with sb;

[合拍] in harmony; in time;
一拍即合 become good friends after a brief contact; click with; fit in readily;

[合群] (1) get on well with others; (2) gregarious;
合群的 clubbable;
不合群 asocial;

[合上] close; shut;
合上詞典 shut the dictionary;
合上書 shut the book;

[合身] a good fit; fit; fit well;
不合身 ill-fitting; unbecoming; unfitting;
完全合身 perfect fit;
衣服不合身 bad fit of clothes;

[合十] put one's palms together;
合十虔誠 put one's hands together in prayer;
雙手合十 put one's palms together devoutly;

[合適] appropriate; becoming; right; suitable;
非常合適 that'll do nicely;
最合適 most suitable;

[合算] deserving; worthwhile;

[合體字] mixed character;

[合同] agreement; contract; contractual agreement; covenant;
合同保證金 contract bond;
合同草案 draft a contract;
合同持有人 holder of the contract;
合同法 contract law;
合同附件 appendix to a contract;
合同各方 all parties of a contract;
合同格式 contract form;
合同管理 contract management;
合同規定 contract specifications; contract stipulation;
合同號碼 contract number;
合同價 contract price;
合同金額 contract value;

合同糾紛 contract dispute;
合同類型 type of contract;
合同期 contract period;
~合同期滿 contract expiry;
合同市場 contract market;
合同雙方 both parties of a contract;
合同税 tax on a contract;
合同條件 conditions of a contract;
合同文本 contract version;
合同義務 contractual obligations;
合同有效期 duration of a contract; term of a contract;
合同責任 contractual liabilities;
合同正本 original copy of a contract;
合同制 contract system;
合同仲裁機構 contract arbitration organization;
合同作家 contract writer;
包銷合同 exclusive sales contract;
保管合同 storage contract;
保險合同 insurance contract;
背棄合同 back out of contract;
標準合同 standard contract;
長期合同 long-term contract;
承兑合同 acceptance contract;
撤銷合同 cancel a contract;
到岸價合同 cost, insurance, and freight contract;
得到合同 get a contract;
締結合同 conclude a contract;
訂立合同 enter into a contract;
獨家代理合同 sole agency contract;
分保合同 reinsurance contract;
格式合同 model contract;
更改合同 alter a contract;
供貨合同 supply agreement;
購貨合同 purchase contract;
僱用合同 contract of employment; employment contract;
互惠合同 reciprocal contract;
集體勞動合同 collective labour agreement;
結束合同 end a contract;
接受合同 agree to a contract;
~同意接受合同 accept a contract;
解除合同 terminate a contract;
經銷合同 distribution contract;
經營合同 operating agreement;
離岸價合同 free on board contract;
履行合同 carry a contract; comply with an agreement; discharge a contract; fulfil a contract; honour a contract; implement a contract;
貿易合同 commercial contract;
破壞合同 break a contract;
期貨合同 forward contract;
起草合同 draw up a contract;
簽訂合同 make a contract; sign a contract;
簽合同 conclude a contract; sign a contract;
取消合同 cancel a contract;
認股合同 subscription agreement;
商業代理合同 commission contract;
生產合同 production agreement;
~合作生產合同 co-production agreement;
書面合同 written contract;
撕毀合同 tear up a contract;
違反合同 breach of contract; break a contract; violate a contract;
無效合同 void contract;
銷售合同 sales contract;
協商合同 negotiate a contract;
賒銷合同 credit sale contract;
信守合同 abide by a contract;
修改合同 amend a contract;
一年合同 one-year contract;
贏得合同 win a contract;
有合同 have a contract;
有效合同 valid contract;
運輸合同 transportation contract;
運送合同 affreightment contract;
運載合同 carriage contract;
中標合同 contract awarded;
中止合同 suspension of a contract;
終止合同 terminate a contract; termination of a contract;
遵守合同 abide by the contract;

[合演] put on joint performances;

[合頁] hinge;

[合宜] appropriate; proper; suitable;

[合意] to one's liking; to one's taste;

[合營] jointly operate; jointly own;

[合影] group photo; take a group photo;
合影留念 have a group photo taken to mark the occasion;

[合用] (1) share; (2) fit for use; meet the requirement; serve the purpose;

[合約] contract; treaty;
多邊合約 multilateral agreement;
一年合約 one-year contract;
遵守合約 adhere to a contract;

[合則留，不合則去] free to quit if conditions

are not suitable; stay if the conditions are agreeable and leave if they are not;

[合奏] ensemble;

[合著] co-author; write in collaboration with;

[合資] combined investment;

合資經營 joint venture;

~合資經營企業 joint venture enterprise;

合資企業 joint venture enterprise;

合資銀行 joint venture bank;

[合子] (1) zygocyte; zygote; (2) zygosperm;

合子核 zygotonucleus;

合子期 zygophase;

合子形成 zygogenesis;

合子植物 zygophyte;

[合作] between; collaborate; collaborate with; collaboration; cooperate; cooperate with; cooperation; join hands with; play ball with; work together;

合作教育 cooperative education;

合作經濟 cooperative economy;

合作經營 joint operation;

~合作經營企業 companionship enterprise;

合作開發 cooperative development;

合作潛力 potential for cooperation;

合作融洽 work together in complete harmony;

合作社 co-op; cooperative; cooperative society;

~合作社社員 cooperator;

~辦合作社 run a cooperative;

~保險合作社 insurance cooperative;

~初級合作社 elementary cooperative;

~高級合作社 advanced cooperative;

~供銷合作社 marketing cooperative; purchasing cooperative; trading cooperative;

~建立合作社 establish a cooperative;

~農業合作社 agricultural co-op;

~生產合作社 producers' cooperative;

~手工業合作社 handicraft cooperative;

~消費合作社 consumers' cooperative; users' cooperative;

~信用合作社 credit cooperative;

合作生產 joint production;

合作條件 cooperative conditions;

合作無間 work in perfect harmony;

合作原則 cooperative principle;

安全合作 security cooperation;

發展合作 develop cooperation;

熱情合作 cooperate enthusiastically;

通力合作 make concerted efforts; work in concert;

願意合作 ready to cooperate;

氨合 ammoniate;

暗合 agree without prior consultation; an unintentional meeting of minds; coincidence in word or thought; happen to coincide;

螯合 chelate;

百合 lily;

閉合 close;

璧合 perfect match;

併合 integrate; unite;

不合 (1) not conform to; out of keeping with; unsuited to; (2) ought not; should not;

攙合 blend; mingle; mix;

參合 consult and sum up;

場合 occasion; situation;

重合 coincide;

湊合 (1) assemble; collect; gather together; (2) improvise; (3) make do;

撮合 (1) act as a go-between; (2) make a match;

鈿合 filigree case;

對合 involution;

縫合 sew up; suture;

符合 accord with; agree with; answer to; be accordant to sth; be in accordance with sth; be in conformity with; be in line with sth; bring into accord; conform to; come up to sth; consist with; correspond to; fall in with; hit off with; in accord with; jibe with; square with; tally with; tie in with sth;

輻合 convergence;

複合 complex; composite; compound; recombination;

苟合 have illicit sexual relations;

寡合 aloof from people; have few friends;

光合 photosynthetic;

化合 chemical combination;

回合 bout; round;

滙合 converge; join;

會合 assemble; converge; join; meet;

混合 blend; mingle; mix;

集合 assemble; call together; collect; gather; muster;

膠合 glue together;

接合 bonding; copulation; joint; jointing; juncture; zygosis;

結合 (1) combine; integrate; link; unite; (2) be married; be united in wedlock;

糾合 gather together;

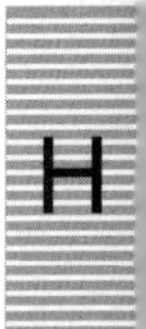

聚合 (1) get together; (2) polymerization;
勘合 stamp the edges of two separate documents with a seal for being identified;
離合 be separated and reunited; be separated and recombined;
聯合 (1) ally; unite; (2) combined; joint;
六合 the six directions: east, west, north, south, heaven and earth; the world or universe;
貌合 seemingly in harmony;
彌合 bridge; close;
黏合 adhere; bind; bond;
捏合 (1) act as go-between; mediate; (2) fabricate; make up;
偶合 coincide;
耦合 coupling;
配合 cooperate; coordinate;
契合 accord with; conform to; tally with;
巧合 coincide; coincidence;
切合 fit in with; suit;
溶合 mix by solution;
熔合 alloy; fuse; merge; mix together;
融合 blend; fuse; merge; mix together;
揉合 blend; combine; incorporate; merge;
糅合 form a mixture; mix;
適合 appropriate for; apt for; becoming; calculate for; fit; fit for; fit in with; sit sb like a glove; good for; just the job for; perfect for; proper; right for sb; suit; suitable for;
水合 hydrate;
説合 (1) bring two parties together; (2) discuss; talk over;
縮合 condensation;
沓合 pile one upon another; superimpose;
投合 (1) agree; get along; (2) cater to;
脗合 be identical; tally with;
霧合 gather together like the mist;
翕合 join together; put together;
相合 agree with; conform to;
迎合 cater to; pander to; play up to;
遇合 (1) meet and get along well; (2) meet;
愈合 heal;
折合 amount to; convert into;
整合 conformity;
宙合 all embracing; all encompassing;
綴合 join together; put together;
綜合 (1) synthesize; (2) composite; comprehensive; multiple; synthetical;
組合 (1) association; combination; (2) compose; constitute; make up;

he

【何】 (1) how; (2) when; (3) where; (4) who; (5) why not; (6) a surname;
［何必］ there is no need; why;
何必小題大做 there is no need to fuss;
［何不］ not see any harm in; why not;
［何嘗］ no question; not that;
何嘗不可 why would sth be impossible;
何嘗不是 how can it be otherwise;
［何啻］ (1) far more than; (2) not different from; the same as;
何啻萬千 more than thousands and myriads;
［何處］ where;
往何處 whither;
［何等］ (1) how; what; (2) what kind;
［何妨］ might as well; there is no harm in; why not;
何妨一試 why not give sth a try; you might as well have a try;
［何幹］ what relation;
［何苦］ not worth; not worth the trouble; why bother; why trouble;
［何況］ let alone; much less; not to mention; to say nothing of;
［何樂而不為］ one would be only too glad to do it; what is there against it; why not go ahead with it;
［何其］ how; what;
［何邱］ a surname;
［何如］ (1) how about; (2) wouldn't it be better;
［何時］ at what time; when;
何時何地 at what time and under what circumstances; when and where;
曾幾何時 before long; in a short space of time; not long after; not long afterwards; not long since; not so long after; not take very long for; only a short while ago;
［何事］ what matter;
干卿何事 it has nothing to do with you; it is no concern of yours; what has that to do with you;
［何謂］ what is meant by; what is the meaning of;
［何以］ how; why;
何以見得 what makes you think so;
［何止］ far more than; not only;
［何足］ not worth;
何足掛懷 not worth thinking about;

何足為怪 there is nothing to be surprised at;
何足為奇 nothing wonderful;

幾何 (1) geometry; (2) how many; how much;
奈何 (1) do sth to sb; (2) how; to no avail;
任何 any; whatever; whichever;
如何 how; what;
若何 how; what;
為何 for what reason; why;
因何 for what reason; why;
緣何 why;
云何 how; why;

he

【劾】 accuse; charge;

he

【和】 (1) gentle; kind; mild; (2) harmonious; on good terms; (3) peace; (4) draw; tie; (5) together with; (6) and; (7) a sum; (8) a surname;

[和藹] affable; amiable; genial; kind;
和藹可親 affable; amiable; courteous and accessible; genial;
~ 和藹可親的人 affable person;
和藹謙虛 gentle and unassuming;

[和璧隋珠] sth rare and very valuable, like jade and pearls;

[和暢] gentle and pleasant;

[和風] (1) soft breeze; (2) moderate breeze;
和風拂面 a gentle breeze caressing one's face; a soft breeze stroking the face;
和風甘霖 soft breeze and timely rainfall; gentle breezes and good rain;
和風麗日 gentle breeze and bright sun – fine weather;
和風習習 a pleasant breeze blows gently;
和風細雨 gentle breeze and light rain – in a gentle and mild way; as mild as drizzle and as gentle as breeze – moderate in attitude; gentle breeze and fine drizzle; gentle breeze and mild rain; not be rough;

[和服] kimono;

[和光同塵] drift with the current; not to distinguish oneself in;

[和好] become reconciled;
和好如初 become friends again as before; on good terms again; restore good relations;

[和緩] (1) gentle; mild; (2) ease up; relax;
和緩之計 a strategy to play for time by conceding a little;
局勢和緩 the situation is improving;
態度和緩 mild of manner;
藥性和緩 this medicine is mild;

[和會] peace conference;

[和解] amicable settlement; become reconciled; compromise; conciliate; reconciliate;
達到和解 come to an accommodation;
庭外和解 settle out of court;

[和局] draw; drawn game; tie;

[和了] draw;
和了滿貫 (in gambling) slam;

[和樂] harmonious and happy;

[和睦] (1) amity; concord; harmony; (2) friendly; harmonious; in amity with; peaceful;
和睦相處 live in amity; live in harmony; live side by side peacefully and friendly; live together in a friendly way; live together in peace; live together in unity; on friendly terms;
保持和睦 preserve harmony;
夫妻和睦 conjugal harmony;
和和睦睦 in harmony;
家庭和睦 peace in the family;
上和下睦 those who are above and those who are below are all on good terms;

[和暖] genial; pleasantly warm;

[和盤托出] come clean; disclose the whole secret; emerge in its totality; empty the bag; let out the whole story; let the whole truth be known; make a clean breast of; make the whole thing known without the slightest concealment; pour it all out; reveal everything;
把秘密和盤托出 make a clean breast of a secret;
把事實真相和盤托出 reveal the whole truth;

[和平] (1) peace; (2) mild;
和平共處 coexist peacefully; live in peace alongside each other; live in peace with; live together in peace; live with...in peace; peaceful coexistence;
和平建設 peaceful construction;
和平進程 peace process;
和平禮物 peace offering;
和平力量 forces of peace;

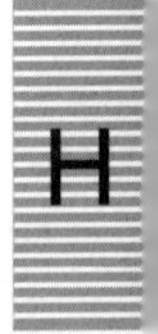

和平時期 peacetime;
和平統一 peaceful reunification;
和平相處 peaceful coexistence;
和平效益 peace dividend;
和平演變 peaceful evolution;
~ 和平演變戰略 peaceful evolution strategy;
和平運動 peace movement;
和平主義 pacifism;
~ 和平主義者 pacifist;
愛好和平 love peace; peace-loving;
愛和平 love peace; peace-loving;
安定和平 stability and peace;
~ 需要安定和平 need stability and peace;
保衛和平 defend peace; preserve peace; protect peace; safeguard peace;
持久和平 lasting peace;
促進和平 promote peace;
渴望和平 desire peace;
內心和平 one's heart is full of peace;
全面和平 overall peace;
世界和平 world peace;
態度和平 amicable; friendly; peaceful attitude;
危及和平 endanger the peace;
維持和平 keep the peace;
宣告和平 declare peace;
尋求和平 seek for peace;
主張和平 stand for peace;

[和氣] (1) gentle; kind; polite; (2) amiable; friendly; harmonious; (3) friendship; harmonious relations;
和氣生財 amiability attract riches; an even temper brings wealth; friendliness is conducive to business success; harmony brings wealth; peace breeds wealth;
和氣翔洽 a spirit of peace and harmony;
和氣致祥 good-naturedness leads to propitiousness; peaceful disposition brings blessing;
彼此很和氣 polite to each other;
和和氣氣 polite and amiable;
~ 對下屬和和氣氣 affable to one's juniors;

[和親] make peace with rulers of minority nationalities in the border areas by marriage;

[和善] genial; kind and gentle;
和善的 companionable;
和善仁慈 affable and kind;
和善態度 genial manner;
性情和善 of a kindly disposition;

[和尚] bronze; Buddhist monk;
和尚打傘—無法（髮）無天 a Buddhist monk opens an umbrella – no hair, no sky; (pun) lawless and godless;
和尚廟裏借梳子—走錯門了 asking a monk in a temple for a comb – getting into the wrong way;
和尚腦袋上塗油—滑頭 putting oil on a monk's shaven head – slippery head; (coll) slippery fellow;
和尚念經—老一套 a monk chanting scriptures – the same old story;
和尚生子—豈有此理 a monk has a son – how can this be? (coll) outrageous;
當一天和尚撞一天鐘 as long as one remains a monk, one keeps ringing the bell;
跑了和尚跑不了廟 the monk may run away, but the temple cannot – one simply can't get away;
三個和尚沒水喝 everybody's business is nobody's business;
做一天和尚撞一天鐘 do just enough to get by; follow a routine; go on tolling the bell as long as one is a monk;

[和事老] conciliator; mediator; peacemaker;

[和順] amiable; gentle;

[和談] peace negotiations; peace talks;

[和婉] mild;

[和絃] chord;

[和諧] accord; harmonious; harmony; melodious; tuneful;
和諧共處 get along;
和諧相處 get with it;
不和諧 discord; disharmony; incompatibility;
彩色和諧 colour harmony;
夫妻和諧 concord between husband and wife;
集體和諧 collective harmony;
勞資和諧 industrial harmony;
社會和諧 social harmony;
斜線和諧 diagonal harmony;

[和煦] genial; pleasantly warm;
天氣和煦 it is mild and warm;

[和衣而臥] go to bed in one's clothes; sleep in one's clothes; sleep without undressing;

[和以處眾] make oneself agreeable to everybody;

[和易] gentle; mild;
和易近人 person who is gentle and easy to approach;
[和議] peace negotiations;
[和約] peace treaty;
締結和約 conclude a peace treaty;
簽訂和約 sign a peace treaty;
違反和約 break a treaty of peace; violate a peace treaty;
[和悦] amiable; kind;

拌和 blend; mix and stir;
飽和 saturate;
逼和 force a draw;
不和 at cross-purposes; at loggerheads with sb; at odds with sb; at outs with sb; at sword's points with sb; at variance with sb; bad blood; discord; disunity; get at cross-purposes; ill blood; not get along well; on bad terms;
摻和 commingle;
唱和 (1) one singing a song and the others joing in the chorus; (2) one person writing a poem to which one or more other people reply;
醇和 pure and mild;
慈和 amiable; kind;
共和 republic; republicanism;
媾和 make peace;
緩和 alleviate; mitigate; relax;
講和 become reconciled; bury the hatchet; make peace;
平和 gentle; mild; moderate;
謙和 modest amiable;
晴和 warm and fine;
求和 sue for peace;
勸和 offer services for reconciliation;
柔和 gentle; mild; soft;
失和 become estranged; fail to keep on good terms;
順和 soothing;
調和 (1) mediate; reconcile; (2) compromise; make concessions;
溫和 (1) mild; moderate; temperate; (2) gentle;
協和 bring into line; concert; harmonize;
諧和 concordant; harmonious;
言和 become reconciled; make peace;
陽和 balmy; warm;
怡和 delightful harmony; on very pleasant terms;
議和 conduct peace negotiations; make peace; negotiate peace;
應和 echo; work in concert with;
雍和 harmony;
勻和 evenly distributed;
戰和 war or peace;
中和 neutralize;
主和 advocate peace;
總和 sum; sum total; total;

he

【河】 river; stream;
[河岸] riverbank;
一個河岸 a riverbank;
一條河岸 a riverbank;
[河蚌] clam; freshwater mussel;
[河北] Hebei Province;
[河邊] riverbank;
河邊賣水—取之不盡 selling water at the riverside — the source is inexhaustible;
河邊陡岸 riverside bluff;
在河邊 by the side of the river;
~久在河邊走，沒有不濕鞋 the pitcher goes often to the well but is broken at last; go often to the waterside cannot avoid wetting one's shoes;
[河濱] streamside;
[河川] river; stream;
河川徑流 stream flow;
[河牀] bed; riverbed;
[河道] river channel; river course; streamway;
改河易道 change the river course;
[河燈] river lantern;
放河燈 floating river lanterns;
[河堤] dyke; river embankment; river levee;
[河底] river bottom;
[河東獅吼] lioness's roar; outburst of a virago; the shrew scolding her husband;
[河段] stream segment;
[河肥] river mud; river silt;
[河港] river port;
[河工] (1) river work; (2) labourer working on a river engineering project;
[河溝] brook; stream;
[河谷] river valley;
[河海] the river and the sea;
河海不擇細流 profound learning is an accumulation of bits of knowledge;
海晏河清 the sea is quiet and the river clear — peace and tranquility;
河落海乾 not leave a bit;

河清海晏 peacetime; times of peace; the Yellow River is clear and the seas are calm — perfect tranquility under heaven; the world is at peace; time of peace and prosperity;

［河漢］ Galaxy; Milky Way;
河漢斯言 statements that are too far-fetched to gain credulity;

［河口］ estuary; firth; river mouth;
河口灣 estuary;

［河流］ rivers; streams;
河流坡降 stream gradient;
河流改道 diversion;
河流乾涸，田地荒蕪 streams dry up and fields lie neglected;
河流襲奪 river capture; stream piracy;
三大河流 Three Great Rivers;

［河馬］ hippo; hippopotamus;

［河鰻］ river eel;

［河南］ Henan (Province);

［河泥］ canal mud; river mud; river silt;

［河鳥］ dipper;

［河清］ the river is clear;
河清難俟 it is hard to wait till the Yellow River is clear — it takes too long to wait for sth to happen;
笑比河清 to make sb smile is as difficult as to purify the river;

［河山］ rivers and mountains;
河山帶礪 an everlasting country with strong boundaries; an oath of everlasting fealty; endure the test of time, not change one's mind under any upheaval;
寸寸河山 every inch of territory;
改山易河 reshape the mountains and rivers;
還我河山 let's restore our lost land; recover our lost territories;
血染河山 blood dyes the mountains and rivers red;
壯闊河山 natural beauty of the country;

［河水］ river water;
河水不犯井水 each minds its own business; the river water does not intrude into the well water;
河水流淌 a river flows; a river runs;
河水浼浼 smooth-flowing river;
河深水急 the water is deep and swift;

［河套］ bend of a river;

［河豚］ balloonfish; globefish; puffer fish;

［河蝦］ river prawn; shrimp;

［河蟹］ river crab;

［河魚腹疾］ have loose bowels; stomach ailment; suffer from diarrhoea;

［河源］ headwaters; river source;

［河運］ river transport;

［河豬］ river hog;

［河宗］ a surname;

愛河 (1) the river of love; (2) (Budd) the river of desire in which people are drowned;
暗河 underground river;
拔河 tug of war;
瀕河 on the bank of the river; riverside;
冰河 glacier;
漕河 canal;
大河 (1) great river; (2) the Yellow River;
渡河 cross a river;
斷尾河 betrunked river;
過河 cross the river;
護城河 city moat; moat;
黃河 Yellow River;
江河 river;
界河 boundary river;
老年河 old river;
內河 inland river; inland waters;
馮河 cross a river without a boat; reckless;
山河 mountains and rivers; the land of a country;
天河 the Galaxy; the Milky Way;
跳河 jump into the river to drown oneself;
投河 commit suicide by throwing oneself into the river; drown oneself;
先河 a forerunner; a harbinger; anything that is advocated earlier; the beginning of sth; the saying that the river is the source of the sea;
小河 brook; rivulet;
星河 the Milky Way;
懸河 (1) pour continually; (2) speak eloquently;
沿河 along the river;
一道河 a river;
一條河 a river;
陰河 underground river;
銀河 the Milky Way;
幼年河 young river;
運河 canal;
壯年河 mature river;

he

【曷】 (1) what; (2) why not;

［曷故］ what for; why;

he

【紇】 (1) silk of an inferior quality; (2) a barbarian tribe, the ancestor of Xiongnu;

he

【核】 (1) pit; stone; (2) nucleus; (3) check; examine; (4) nuclear-powered;

[核安全] nuclear safety;

[核爆炸] nuclear explosion;

[核不擴散條約] Nuclear Non-proliferation Treaty;

[核查] check; examine in detail; verify;

[核塵] nuclear fallout;

[核打擊] nuclear striking;
核打擊目標 nuclear striking target;

[核彈] nuclear bomb;

[核電] nuclear power;
核電廠 nuclear power plant;
核電站 nuclear power station;

[核定] appraise and decide; check and ratify;

[核對] check; collate; verify;
核對數字 check the figures;
核對賬目 check accounts;

[核反應] nuclear reaction;
核反應堆 nuclear reactor;
熱核反應 thermonuclear reaction;

[核防護] nuclear defence;

[核輻射] nuclear radiation;

[核苷] nucleoside;
核苷酸 nucleotide;

[核力] nuclear force;

[核能] nuclear power;
核能安全 nuclear energy security;

[核配合] karyogamy;

[核批] examine and give comments and instruction;

[核潛艇] nuclear submarine;

[核燃料] nuclear fuel;

[核仁] (1) nucleolus; (2) kernel of a fruit-stone;

[核設施] nuclear facilities;

[核實] check; verify;
核實事實 check up on the facts;
核實數字 check up on the figures;
核實一下電話 verify the call;
調查核實 verify through investigation;
自動核實 autoverify;

[核事故] nuclear accident;

[核試驗] nuclear test;

[核素] nuclide;
關鍵核素 critical nuclide;
裂變核素 fissile nuclide;
重核素 heavy nuclide;

[核酸] nucleic acid;
核糖核酸 ribonucleic acid;
脫氧核糖核酸 deoxyribonucleic acid;

[核算] adjust accounts; business accounting; check computation;
班組核算 accounting in work groups;
成本核算 cost accounting;
經濟核算 business accounting;

[核桃] walnut;
核桃殼 walnut shell;
核桃仁 walnut meat;

[核武器] nuclear weapon;
核武器擴散 proliferation of nuclear weapons;

[核心] centre; core; crux; heart; kernel; nucleus;
核心程序 nucleus core programme;
核心家庭 core family;
核心句 kernel sentence;
~ 雙核心句 two-nucleus sentence;
核心課程 core curriculum;
核心力量 force at the core; hard core;
核心人物 key figure;
核心網絡 nucleus network;
核心語言 kernel language;
對比核心 contrastive focus;
共同核心 common core;
領導核心 core of leadership;
問題的核心 the heart of the matter; the very core of a subject;

[核准] (1) approval; examine and approve; (2) check and approve; ratify;
核准賬目 account approval;
草圖核准 approval of a draft;
放款核准 loan approval;
預先核准 prior approval;

[核子] (1) nuclear; (2) nucleon;
核子科學 nuclear science;

查核 check; examine;
大核 macronucleus;
覆核 (1) check; (2) review a case;
稽核 check; examine;
結核 tuberculosis;
考核 assess; check; examine;
審核 check; examine and verify;
小核 micronucleus;

he

【盍】 (1) what; (2) why not; (3) correspond; match;

he

【涸】 dried up; dry up; exhausted;

［涸竭］ dry up;

河涸魚竭 when rivers dry up, the fish die;

［涸轍］ in dire poverty;

［涸鮒］ in dire poverty;

［涸乾］ dried-up; exhausted;

［涸澤］ dried-up lake; dry up a lake;

乾涸 dry up; run dry;

he

【盒】 case; small box;

［盒帶］ cassette tape;

［盒飯］ lunch box;

［盒蓋］ cover;

磁帶盒蓋 cassette cover;

電池盒蓋 battery cover;

鬧條盒蓋 alarm barrel cover;

［盒式］ cassette;

盒式磁帶 cassette tape;

盒式錄音帶 cassette tape;

盒式錄音機 cassette recorder;

［盒裝］ boxed;

［盒子］ box; case; casket;

一套盒子 a nest of boxes;

［盒座］ cassette holder;

暗盒 cassette; magazine;

飯盒 dinner pail; lunch box;

花盒 fireworks;

墨盒 ink box;

煙盒 cigarette case;

印盒 seal box;

H

he

【荷】 lotus;

［荷包］ (1) pouch; small bag; (2) pocket;

荷包蛋 (1) fried eggs; (2) poached eggs;

［荷爾蒙］ hormone;

男性荷爾蒙 androgen;

女性荷爾蒙 female sex hormone;

［荷花］ lotus; lotus flower;

荷花出水 a lotus rising from the water;

［荷蘭］ Holland; the Netherlands;

荷蘭盾 guilder;

［荷馬］ Homer;

［荷塘竹徑］ lotus flower pools and bamboo lined paths;

［荷葉］ lotus leaf;

風捲荷葉 make a clean sweep;

［荷載］ load;

安全容許荷載 safety allowable load;

he

【貉】 (1) badger; fox-like animal nocturnal in habit; (2) racoon dog;

［貉藻］ water bug trap;

he

【蓋】 why not; would it not be better to;

he

【閤】 (1) close doors; (2) all; whole;

［閤府］ your whole family;

he

【閡】 (1) blocked; obstructed; separated; (2) prevent; shut out;

he

【鉿】 hafnium;

he

【褐】 (1) coarse cloth; (2) brown;

［褐煤］ brown coal;

［褐色］ brown; brown colour;

茶褐色 dark brown;

赤褐色 dark brown;

淡褐色 ecru;

紅褐色 reddish brown;

黃褐色 yellow brown;

深褐色 seal brown;

中褐色 medium brown;

紫褐色 puce;

he

【翮】 shaft of a feather;

he

【闔】 (1) entire; whole; (2) close; shut;

［闔府］ your whole family;

［闔家］ whole family;

闔家大小 old and young members of a family; whole family,

闔家團圓 one's family is united; reunion of a family after a temporary separation;

he

【鞨】 (1) as in 靺鞨, the Tungusic tribe in ancient China; (2) rough sandals; shoes;

he

【齕】 gnaw;

齮齕 (1) bite; gnaw; (2) envy and hate sb out of jealousy;

he

【覈】 (1) examine; investigate; test; (2) deep; deeply; (3) stone of a fruit;

he

【鶡】 (1) a sort of nightingale; (2) a sort of pheasant;

he

【龢】 same as 和 , harmonious; peaceful;

he⁴

he

【和】 (1) harmonize; match; (2) knead; make dough; mix;

［和麵］ knead flour;

［和弄］ knead; make dough;

［和詩］ compose verses to match those written by others;

酬和 respond to a poem with a poem;

附和 echo; repeat what others say;

應和 echo; work in concert with;

he

【郝】 (1) ancient place in today's Shaanxi province; (2) a surname;

he

【荷】 (1) carry sth on one's shoulder or back; (2) burden; responsibility;

［荷負］ bear a burden; be burdened;

［荷載］ load; loading;

不規則荷載 abnormal load;

反對稱荷載 antisymmetrical load;

周期荷載 cyclic loading;

組合荷載 combined loading;

［荷重］ loading;

電荷 electric charge;

負荷 load;

感荷 be much obliged;

載荷 load;

he

【喝】 shout loudly;

［喝彩］ acclaim; cheer;

喝彩叫好 a shout of applause; applaud to the echo;

喝倒彩 boo; boo and hoot; give sb the bird; shout booing; shout catcalls;

~被喝倒彩 be greeted with hisses;

滿場喝彩 bring down the house; universal applause;

拍手喝彩 clap one's hands and applaud;

為主隊喝彩 root for the home team;

叱喝 bawl at; shout at;

呵喝 shout loudly;

he

【黑】 a pronunciation of 黑 , black;

he

【賀】 (1) congratulate; (2) a surname;

［賀詞］ congratulatory address; greeting; speech of congratulation;

聖誕賀詞 Christmas greetings;

新年賀詞 New Year message;

致賀詞 offer one's congratulations;

［賀電］ congratulatory telegram; message of congratulation;

發賀電 send a congratulatory message;

收到賀電 receive a message of greetings;

［賀卡］ greeting card;

［賀禮］ gift;

節日賀禮 festive gift;

結婚賀禮 wedding gift;

［賀年］ extend New Year greetings; pay a New Year call;

賀年卡 New Year card;

登門賀年 make a New Year call at sb's house;

［賀喜］ congratulate sb on a happy occasion;

［賀信］ congratulatory letter; letter of congratulation;

道賀 congratulate;

電賀 congratulate sb by sending a telegram;

恭賀 congratulate;

慶賀 celebrate; congratulate;

致賀 extend one's congratulations;

祝賀 congratulate;

he

【赫】 (1) conspicuous; (2) hertz; (3) a surname;

［赫赫］ illustrious;

赫赫有名 have a great reputation; highly acclaimed; illustrious; well-renowned;

赫赫戰功 brilliant achievements in war; impressive military success; illustrious military exploits;

［赫然］ (1) awesomely; impressively; (2) terribly angry;

馬赫 Mach;
千赫 kilohertz;
顯赫 celebrated; illustrious; impressive; powerful;
煊赫 of great renown and influence;
兆赫 megahertz;

he

【爀】 angry;

he

【嚇】 (1) intimidate; threaten; (2) sound of laughter;

he

【豁】 bright and spacious;
［豁亮］ bright and spacious;

he

【壑】 (1) pool; (2) a narrow ravine at the foot of a hill; gully;

he

【鶴】 crane;
［鶴髮］ hoary head;
鶴髮雞皮 a hoary head with wrinkled skin; white hair and wrinkled skin;
鶴髮童顏 a hoary head and a fresh boyish complexion; hale and hearty; healthy and aged; healthy in old age; one's hair is white and one's complexion is like that of a child;
［鶴骨］ crane's bone;
鶴骨雞膚 like a crane's bone and a fowl's skin – thin and weak;
鶴骨松姿 a crane's bone and a pine's appearance – lean and shrivelled;
［鶴立雞群］ a crane among a brood of chickens—a distinguished man in a common crowd; a giant among dwarfs; like a crane standing among chickens – stand head and shoulders above others; stand out in a crowd; stand out like a stork in a flock of fowls; the flower of the flock;
［鶴鳴九皋］ the crane screams in the middle of the marsh;
［鶴勢螂形］ a crane's appearance and a mantis' figure; the aspect of a crane and the appearance of a mantis – said of a tall and lively woman;
［鶴嘴］ crane's beak;
鶴嘴鋤 pickaxe;

白鶴 white crane;
紅鶴 flamingoes;
灰鶴 common crane;
仙鶴 red-crowned crane;

hei¹

hei

【黑】 (1) black; (2) dark; (3) secret; shady; (4) avaricious; greedy; (5) crafty; evil-minded; sinister; wicked;
［黑暗］ (1) dark; dim; (2) reactionary;
黑暗地獄 a hell of darkness – in which there is no ray of light;
黑暗時代 the dark ages;
黑暗世界 a dark world;
暴露黑暗 expose the dark;
寫黑暗 write about the dark;
一片黑暗 a mantle of darkness;
［黑白］ (1) black and white; (2) right and wrong;
黑白不分 black and white mixed together; confound right and wrong; not distinguish between right and wrong;
黑白電視 black-and-white television;
黑白電視機 black-and-white television set;
黑白電影 motion picture in black and white;
黑白分明 a clear distinction between black and white; as clear as black and white; draw a clear demarcation line between right and wrong; in sharp contrast; with black and white sharply contrasted;
黑白監視器 black-and-white monitor;
黑白片 black-and-white film;
黑白相間 be chequered with black and white; black alternating with white; in black and white check;
黑白相同 black alternating with white;
黑白尋像器 black-and-white viewfinder;
白黑分明 make a clear distinction between black and white; with black and white sharply contrasted;
顛倒黑白 call black white;
汩陳黑白 confuse black and white;
黑中有白 the devil is not as black as he is

painted;
混淆黑白 mix up black and white;
認黑作白 prove that black is white; talk black into white;
説黑道白 criticize others thoughtlessly; practise groundless criticism;
以白為黑 confound black and white; confuse right and wrong; take white for black;
有白必有黑，有甜就有苦 every white has its black, and every sweet its sour;
知白守黑 know and observe all but stay obscure; know the white and keep the black — a person must yield when it is necessary;
指黑道白 call black white; point to black and say it is white;

[黑板] blackboard;
黑板擦 blackboard eraser;
黑板抹布 blackboard cloth;
電視黑板 tele-board;
滑動黑板 sliding blackboard;
一塊黑板 a blackboard;

[黑幫] reactionary gang; sinister gang;
黑幫成員 gangster;

[黑便] tarry stools;

[黑冰] black ice;

[黑不溜秋] having a dark complexion; very dark in appearance; swarthy;

[黑沉沉] very dark;

[黑道] gang;

[黑點] black spot;
交通黑點 accident black spot;

[黑洞] black hole;
黑洞洞 pitch-dark;

[黑度] blackness;
相對黑度 relative blackness;

[黑粉病] smut;
桿黑粉病 flag smut;
假黑粉病 false smut;
玉米黑粉病 corn smut;

[黑糞] melena;
假性黑糞 melena spuria;
真性黑糞 melena vera;

[黑咕隆咚] dark and gloomy; pitch-dark; very dark;

[黑工] illegal worker;

[黑鬼] coon; darkie; nigger;

[黑鍋] black pot;
背黑鍋 be made a scapegoat; be unjustly blamed; carry the can; hold the bag; take the blame for another person; take the consequences on one's own;
揹黑鍋 be made the scapegoat for sth; take blame for sb;

[黑盒] block box;

[黑黑的] black;

[黑糊糊] (1) black; blackened; (2) dusky; rather dark; (3) indistinctly observable in the distance;

[黑話] (1) argot; cant; (2) doublespeak; double-talk; malicious words;

[黑貨] (1) contraband; smuggled goods; (2) rubbish; sinister stuff; trash;

[黑家白日] all the days; daily; every day;

[黑客] hacker;
政治黑客 hacktivist;

[黑裏泛紅] tanned and glowing;

[黑馬] dark horse;

[黑麥] rye;
黑麥草 ryegrass;
黑麥麵包 rye bread;

[黑矇] amaurosis;

[黑幕] inside story of a plot; shady deal;
黑幕重重 curtains behind a black curtain — inside secrecy;

[黑尿病] blackwater fever;

[黑皮病] melanoderma;
寄生性黑皮病 parasitic melanoderma;
老年性黑皮病 senile melanoderma;

[黑皮炎] melanodermatitis;

[黑漆漆] pitch-dark;

[黑人] black man; black person; blackamoor; blackie; darkie; darky; eggs and spoons; the Black people;
黑人英語 Black English;

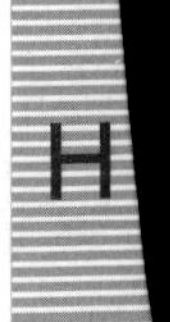

[黑色] black; black colour;
黑色經濟 black economy;
黑色素 melanin;
黑色人種 black race;
黑色喜劇 black comedy;
黑色幽默 black humour;
深黑色 blue-black;

[黑市] black market;
黑市匯率 black market exchange rate;
黑市價格 black market price;
黑市交易 black market bargain;
黑市經濟 black economy;
黑市商人 black marketer;

[黑手] evil backstage manipulator; vicious

person who manipulates sb or sth from behind the scenes;
黑手黨 Mafia;
~黑手黨成員 Mafioso;
［黑死病］ the plague;
［黑穗病］ smut;
堅黑穗病 covered smut;
絲黑穗病 head smut;
［黑體］ black body;
黑體輻射 black body radiation;
［黑天］ night;
黑天摸地 grope in the dark; so dark that nothing is discernible;
月黑天 moonless night;
［黑霜］ black frost;
［黑心］ black heart; evil mind;
［黑信］ anonymous letter from a hostile pen; poison pen letter;
［黑熊］ black bear;
［黑壓壓］ a dense mass of;
［黑眼豆］ black-eyed bean;
［黑夜］ blind man's holiday; dark night; night;
寒冬黑夜 it is a dark night in the dead of winter;
［黑黝黝］ (1) shiny black; (2) dark; dim;
［黑油油］ glossy black; jet-black; shiny black;
［黑魚］ snakehead;
［黑子］ sunspot;
黑子周 sunspot cycle;
後隨黑子 following sunspot;
前導黑子 leading sunspot;
太陽黑子 sunspot;

挨黑 towards evening;
暗黑 deep black;
黯黑 (1) dark; (2) dim;
擦黑 (1) blacken; (2) rectify errors; rectify shortcomings;
非常黑 pitch-dark;
骨炭黑 bone black;
昏黑 dark; dusky;
焦黑 burned black;
黎黑 (of complexion) dark;
黧黑 (of complexion) dark;
亮黑 brilliant black;
抹黑 blacken sb's name; bring shame on; smear;
墨黑 pitch-dark;
漆黑 pitch-black; pitch-dark;
黢黑 pitch-black; pitch-dark;
碳黑 carbon black;
鐵黑 (1) iron black; (2) iron oxide black;
烏黑 jet-black; pitch-black;
象牙黑 abaiser;
黝黑 dark; dark-complexioned; swarthy;

hei

【嘿】 hey; why;
［嘿嘿］ hey;

hen[2]
hen

【痕】 mark; trace;
［痕跡］ mark; trace; vestige;
不落痕跡 leave no trace;
不着痕跡 leave no trace;
電弧痕跡 arc trace;
模糊痕跡 blurred trace;
磨擦痕跡 abrasion mark;

凹痕 dent;
疤痕 scar; sore;
斑痕 black-spot;
瘢痕 cicatrix; scar;
潮痕 tidemark;
創痕 scar;
斧痕 axe mark;
刻痕 mark engraved with a knife;
淚痕 tear stains;
裂痕 crack; fissure; rift;
傷痕 bruise; scar;
條痕 streak;
印痕 mark; trace;
折痕 line made by folding;

hen[3]
hen

【很】 (1) quite; (2) very; (3) cruel; fierce; (4) disobedient; intractable; quarrelsome; truculent;
［很多］ a lot of;
［很乖］ as good as gold;
［很好］ very good;
［很久］ for ages; for an age; very long;
很久以前 since Adam was a boy;
［很睏］ very sleepy;
［很悶］ (1) sultry; (2) boring;
［很少］ (1) rarely; (2) few; little;

hen

【狠】 (1) relentless; ruthless; (2) harden; suppress; (3) firm; resolute;
［狠毒］ atrocious; brutal; cruel; malicious; venomous; vicious;

［狠狠］ (1) cruel; ferocious; ruthless; (2) determined; firm; resolute;
狠狠打擊 hit hard at;
狠狠地 brutally; cruelly; in cold blood; mercilessly; severely;
惡狠狠 ferocious; fierce; relentless;
［狠戾］ atrocious; cruel; vicious;
［狠命］ make a desperate effort; use all one's strength;
［狠心］ cruel-hearted; heartless;

發狠 (1) make a determined effort; (2) be angry; be enraged;
心狠 cruel; merciless;
兇狠 cruel; fiendish; fierce and malicious;

hen⁴
hen

【恨】 (1) hate; (2) regret;
［恨海］ deep hatred;
恨海難填 the sea of hatred is hard to fill up;
［恨人］ misanthrope; person who hates humankind;
［恨如頭醋］ as sour as the sourest vinegar—extremely sour;
［恨事］ matter for regret; regrettable thing;
引為恨事 much to one's regret;
［恨鐵不成鋼］ be exasperated at sb's failure to make good; regret that one's offspring does not live up to one's expectations;

愛的反面是恨 the antipode of love is hatred;
愛恨 love-hate;
懊恨 resentful;
暗恨 harbour resentment in one's heart; hate sb in one's heart;
抱恨 be regretful; have a gnawing regret;
悵恨 melancholy and resentful;
仇恨 enmity; hatred; hostility;
憤恨 indignantly resentful;
懷恨 bear a grudge; nurse hatred;
悔恨 be bitterly remorseful; regret deeply;
嫉恨 envy and hate; hate out of jealousy;
記恨 bear a grudge against sb; bear sb a grudge; harbour hatred for sb;
解恨 have one's hatred slaked; vent one's hatred;
惱恨 hate; resent;
痛恨 hate bitterly; utterly detest;
銜恨 bear a grudge; harbour resentment;
挾恨 hold a grudge; harbour hatred;
雪恨 get even;
遺恨 eternal regret;
飲恨 harbour resentment; nurse a grievance;
怨恨 harbour hatred for sb; hold a grudge against sb;
憎恨 detest; harbour hatred for sb; hate;

heng¹
heng

【亨】 go smoothly;
［亨通］ go smoothly; prosperous;
官運亨通 have a successful official career;
老運亨通 have good luck in old age;

大亨 big shot; bigwig; magnate;

heng

【哼】 (1) but; (2) h'm; (3) humph; (4) ugh; (5) yes;
［哼哧］ puff hard;
［哼哈］ hum and haw;
哼几哈几 hum and haw;
［哼哼］ groan continually;
哼哼哈哈 hum and haw;
哼哼唧唧 groan and moan;
［哼唧］ make inaudible sounds; mumble; whisper;
［哼聲］ heave ho; hum; yo-heave-ho; yo-ho;

heng²
heng

【恒】 (1) lasting; permanent; (2) perseverance; (3) common; constant; usual;
［恒比］ constant proportion;
［恒等式］ identity;
對數恒等式 logarithmic identity;
循環恒等式 cyclic identity;
［恒河沙數］ as numerous as the grains of sand in the Ganges River; innumerable;
［恒勁］ persistent power; persistent strength; stamina; staying power;
［恒久］ constant; endurable; forever; lasting;
［恒溫］ constant temperature;
恒溫器 incubator; thermostat;
～電熱恒溫器 electrically-heated thermostat;
～冷凍恒溫器 freezing thermostat;
～氣動恒溫器 air-operated thermostat;
［恒心］ constancy of purpose; perseverance;
［恒星］ fixed star; star;
恒星年 sidereal year;

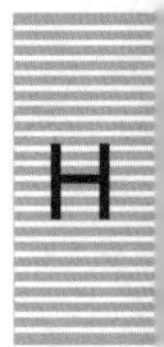

恒星日 sidereal day;
恒星時 sidereal time;
恒星世界 stellar universe;
恒星月 sidereal month;
恒星自行 proper motion of stars

守恒 conservation;
逾恒 go beyond the regular practice;

heng
【桁】 rack for hanging clothes;
［桁架］ truss;
拱形桁架 arch truss;
纜索桁架 cable truss;
曲弦桁架 broken-chord truss;
組合桁架 built-up truss;

heng
【珩】 top gem of a pendant;
［珩齒］ gear lapping with corundum;

heng
【橫】 (1) horizontal; transverse; (2) across; sideways; (3) move crosswise; traverse; (4) turbulently; unrestrainedly; (5) fiercely; violently;
［橫穿］ traverse;
［橫渡］ cross; traverse; sail across;
［橫幅］ banner; streamer;
橫幅廣告 banner ad;
［橫貫］ traverse;
橫貫大陸的 transcontinental;
［橫過］ (1) across; (2) cross; traverse;
橫過馬路 cross the street;
［橫加］ flagrantly; violently;
橫加白眼 look upon with contempt;
橫加干涉 flagrantly interfere; interfere wantonly;
橫加迫害 persecute wilfully;
橫加梗阻 obstruct unreasonably; obstruct wilfully;
橫加誣蔑 slander wildly;
橫加指責 hurl abuses at; make an arbitrary attack on; make unwarranted charges;
橫加阻撓 obstruct wilfully;
［橫街］ bystreet; side street;
［橫跨］ stretch across; stretch over;
［橫梁］ crossbar; cross-beam;
［橫列］ arrange in a horizontal line;
［橫流］ (1) (of tears) gush; stream; (2) (of water) flow in all directions;
老淚橫流 tears flowing from the aged eyes; tears and mucus flowing down rapidly;
眼淚橫流 stream with tears;
［橫脈］ crossvein;
臂橫脈 anal crossvein; posterior crossvein;
分橫脈 sectorial crossvein;
結後橫脈 postcubital crossvein;
徑中橫脈 ordinary crossvein;
前橫脈 discoidal crossvein;
中橫脈 medial crossvein;
中肘橫脈 mediocubital crossvein;
［橫眉］ frown; scowl;
橫眉瞪眼 look angrily at;
橫眉怒目 face others with furrowed brows and angry eyes; furrow one's eyebrows and stare in anger; straighten the eyebrows and raise the eyes — angry looks;
橫眉豎眼 put on a fierce look;
［橫木］ crossbar;
［橫目］ angry eyes; look angrily at;
橫目斜睨 cross the eyes and look askance;
［橫肉］ fierce-looking;
［橫掃］ make a clean sweep of; sweep away;
橫掃千軍 make a clean sweep of the enemy; sweep all before one; sweep aside large numbers of enemy troops; sweep away the millions of enemy troops;
～橫掃千軍如捲席 sweep aside the enemy like rolling up a mat;
［橫生］ (1) grow wild; (2) happen unexpectedly;
橫生是非 complicate an issue deliberately; raise obstacles;
橫生枝節 branch out; bring up unexpected troubles; deliberately complicate an issue; raise obstacles; side issues unexpectedly crop up; trouble arising on every hand;
妙趣橫生 full of wit and humour; rich in wisecracks; sparkle with wit; very witty
［橫是］ maybe; perhaps; probably;
［橫豎］ anyhow; anyway; at any rate; in any case; since;
橫七豎八 at random; at sixes and sevens; higgledy-piggledy; in disorder; lying this way and that; spread all across in

confusion; topsy-turvy;
橫三豎四 in disarray; lying this way and that;
橫説豎説 exhaust oneself with persuasion; persuade repeatedly and insistantly;
橫挑鼻子豎挑眼 find faults in a petty manner; look for flaws; nitpick; pick faults right and left; pick faults with sb in various ways; pick holes in;
七橫八豎 at sixes and sevens;

[橫向] crosswise; horizontal;
橫向地 crabwise;
橫向公平 horizontal equity;
橫向交流 lateral exchange;
橫向經濟聯合 lateral economic tie;
橫向經濟聯繫 lateral economic contact;
橫向思維 lateral thinking;
橫向行政組織 horizontal administrative organization;
橫向學科 horizontal discipline;
橫向研究 cross-sectional study;
橫向一體化 horizontal integration;

[橫心] (1) become desperate; (2) steel one's heart;
橫心辭職 take a firm resolution to quit one's job;
橫了心 dead determined; in desperation; steel one's heart;
橫下心來 harden one's heart; steel oneself to do sth;

[橫行] on a rampage; run amuck; run wild;
橫行霸道 act against law and reason, like a tyrant; act in a tyrannous manner; act like an overlord; act outrageously and ferociously; act unreasonably; be unbridled in one's truculence; lord it over; play the bully; play the tyrant; ride roughshod over; run wild; swagger about; trample on; tyrannize over;
橫行不法 act against law and reason; act illegally; violent and lawless;
橫行介士 one who walks sideways – another name for "crab";
橫行無忌 act outrageously without scruple; run amuck; run wild;
橫行一時 run amuck for a certain time; run wild for a time;

[橫越] overstep; traverse;

[橫徵暴斂] bleed the people white with taxes; extort heavy taxes; extort illegal taxes; levy exorbitant taxes; oppressive taxes; ruthless taxation;

打橫 sit in the inferior seat at a square table;
縱橫 (1) in length and breadth; vertically and horizontally; (2) freely; with great ease;

heng
【衡】 (1) graduated arm of a steelyard; (2) weighing apparatus; (3) judge; measure; weigh;

[衡量] appraisal; judge; measure; measure up; weigh;
衡量得失 weigh up the gains and losses;
衡量利害 weigh choices;
全面衡量 all-round appraisal;
仔細衡量 mull;

常衡 avoirdupois;
杜衡 wild ginger;
度量衡 length, capacity, and weight;
均衡 balanced; harmonious; proportionate;
抗衡 contend with; enter into rivalry with; match;
平衡 balance; equilibrium;
權衡 balance; weigh;
盱衡 (1) lift one's eyebrows and look up; (2) survey;
爭衡 be in rivalry with; scramble for supremacy; vie for superiority;

heng
【蘅】 Asarum blumei, a fragrant plant;

杜蘅 wild ginger;

heng⁴
heng
【橫】 (1) harsh and unreasonable; perverse; (2) unexpected;

[橫暴] perverse and violent;

[橫財] ill-gotten wealth; windfall;
發橫財 get a windfall;

[橫話] harsh words; stiff and stern language;

[橫禍] sudden misfortune; unexpected calamity; unexpected disaster;
飛來橫禍 sudden misfortune; unexpected disaster; unforeseen disaster;

[橫蠻] harsh and unreasonable; perverse;
橫蠻無理 arrogant and high-handed; become high-handed in one's behaviour towards; truculent and

unreasonable;

[橫逆] effrontery; insult; unreasonable behaviour;

[橫死] die a violent death; meet with a sudden death; violent death;

[橫夭] an unnatural death;

[橫議] extreme views; far-fetched arguments; radical statements;

暴橫 atrocious;
擋橫 get in the way;
發橫 become suddenly hard and harsh;
強橫 brutal and unreasonable; despotic; tyrannical;
兇橫 brutal and tyrannical; fierce and arrogant;
專橫 arbitrary; domineering; imperious;

hong¹

hong

【哄】 (1) roars of laughter; (2) hubbub;

[哄傳] circulate widely;

[哄動] cause a sensation; make a stir;
哄動一時 cause a sensation; sensational;

[哄喊] shout at;

[哄騙] bamboozle; blandish; cajole; coax; humbug; wheedle;

[哄搶] gang-loot; rush in and grab;

[哄然] boisterous; uproarious;
哄然而散 disperse with great noise and hubbub;
哄然起笑 go off into laughter;

[哄抬] drive up; force up;
哄抬物價 force up prices; rig prices;

[哄堂] bring the room down; fill the room with laughter;
哄堂大笑 a volley of laughter; burst into a guffaw; burst into uproarious laughter; fall about laughing; laugh uproariously; roar with laughter; the whole room bursts out laughing; the whole room rocking with laughter;
哄堂絕倒 all break out into a fit of laughter; the entire house is convulsed with laughter;

hong

【訇】 (1) loudly; stentorian; (2) a surname;

hong

【烘】 (1) dry or warm by the fire; (2) set off;

[烘焙] cure; dry over the fire;
真空烘焙 vacuum baking;

[烘茶] tea curing;

[烘瓷] baked porcelain;

[烘豆] baked beans;

[烘乾] (1) dry over the fire; (2) oven dry;
烘乾機 dryer;

[烘烘] blazing;
臭烘烘 foul-smelling; stinking;
毛烘烘 furry; hairy;
暖烘烘 nice and warm;
熱烘烘 very warm;

[烘焦] get partially burned because of overheating near the fire;

[烘烤] bake; baking; burn off; dry by the fire; roast; toast; warm by the fire;
烘烤盤 baking sheet;
低溫烘烤 low-temperature baking;
電熱烘烤 electric baking;
高溫烘烤 high-temperature baking;
麵包烘烤 bread baking;
微波烘烤 microwave baking;

[烘暖] warm by the fire;

[烘托] (1) add shading around an object to make it stand out; (2) set off by contrast;

[烘箱] oven;

冬烘 shallow and pedantic;

hong

【魟】 rays;

[魟魚] skate;

hong

【薨】 (1) death of a feudal lord; (2) loud buzzing of insects in flight;

hong

【轟】 (1) bang; boom; (2) bombard; explode; (3) rumble; (4) drive off;

[轟倒] knock down by bombardment;

[轟動] cause a sensation; create a sensation; create a stir; earth-shaking; make a noise in the world; make a stir; rouse a furore;
轟動全城 get the whole city astir;
轟動全國 make a sensation throughout the country;
轟動一時 create a great sensation; make a noise in the world;
引起轟動 set the world alight; set the world on fire;

引起巨大轟動 create a wonderful sensation;

[轟轟] (1) booming sound; roaring sound; (2) in a grand fashion; with grandeur;

轟轟烈烈 amid fire and thunder; magnificent and victorious; on a grand and spectacular scale; stirring and seething; stormy and heroic; with vigour and vitality;

[轟擊] bombard; bombardment;

電子轟擊 electron bombardment;
電子束轟擊 beam bombardment;
高通量轟擊 high-flux bombardment;
海上轟擊 naval bombardment;
核轟擊 nuclear bombardment;
交叉轟擊 cross bombardment;
空中轟擊 aerial bombardment;
砲火轟擊 artillery bombardment;
陰極轟擊 cathode bombardment;
重離子轟擊 heavy ion bombardment;

[轟雷擊頂] as if a thunderbolt has struck sb right on the top of the head;

[轟隆] roar; roll; rumble; thunder;

轟隆一聲 with a crash;
大轟隆 big talk but no action;
雷聲轟隆 rolling of a thunder;

[轟鳴] growl; roll; roar; thunder;

轟鳴而過 roar past;

[轟然] with a loud crash;

[轟響] thunder;

[轟炸] bomb; bombardment; bombing;

轟炸機 bomber; bomb-carrying aeroplane; bombing aeroplane; bombing plane;
~俯衝轟炸機 dive bomber;
~核轟炸機 nuclear bomber;
~殲擊轟炸機 attack bomber;
~輕轟炸機 light bomber;
~無人駕駛轟炸機 robot bomber;
~巡邏轟炸機 patrol bomber;
~魚雷轟炸機 torpedo bomber;
~遠程轟炸機 long-distance bombardment aeroplane; long-range bomber;
~戰鬥轟炸機 fighter bomber;
~重轟炸機 heavy bombardment aeroplane;
~重型轟炸機 heavy bomber;
~晝間轟炸機 day bomber;
轟炸航程 bombing run;
轟炸瞄準器 bombsight;
~雷達轟炸瞄準器 radar bombsight;
飽和轟炸 saturation bombing;
編隊轟炸 formation bombing;
低空轟炸 low-level bombing;
地氈式轟炸 carpet-bombing;
俯衝轟炸 dive-bomb;
高空轟炸 high-altitude bombing;
空襲轟炸 aerial bombardment; air bombardment;
狂轟濫炸 wanton and indiscriminate bombing;
攔阻轟炸 interdiction bombing;
雷達轟炸 radar bombing;
連續轟炸 train bombing;
密集轟炸 density bombing;
面積轟炸 area bombing;
區域轟炸 area bombing;
水平轟炸 level bombing;
跳彈轟炸 skip bombing;
一陣轟炸 a hail of bombs;
有效轟炸 functional bombing;
遠程轟炸 long-range bombardment;
雲上轟炸 overcast bombing;
戰略轟炸 strategic bombing;

砲轟 bombard; shell;

hong²

hong

【弘】 great; immense; magnanimous;

[弘大] great; immense;

[弘道] expand one's teachings; immense; promote;

[弘量] huge capacity for forgiveness; liberal-minded; magnanimous;

[弘論] informed opinion; intelligent view;

[弘誓大愿] great determination and aspiration;

[弘圖] grand prospect; great plan;

[弘揚] propagate;

[弘遠] far and wide;

[弘願] great ambition; great wish; noble ambition;

[弘旨] main theme of an article;

[弘志] great ambition;

恢弘 develop; encourage; generous;

hong

【宏】 great; grand; magnificent;

[宏大] grand; great;

宏大的抱負 generous aspirations;
宏大的計劃 grand plan;

規模宏大 gigantic scale;

[宏富] abundant; rich;

[宏觀] macroscopic view;
宏觀分配學 macrodistribution studies;
宏觀管理 macromanagement;
宏觀教育 macroeducation;
宏觀結構 macrostructure;
宏觀經濟 macroeconomy;
~宏觀經濟分析 macroeconomic analysis;
~宏觀經濟管理 macroeconomic management;
~宏觀經濟規劃 macroeconomic planning;
~宏觀經濟決策 macroeconomic decision;
~宏觀經濟效益 macroeconomic results;
~宏觀經濟學 macroeconomics;
宏觀控制 macrocontrol;
~宏觀控制體制 macroeconomic control system;
宏觀能源需求預測 macro energy demand forecasting;
宏觀人口投資 macroscopic population investment;
宏觀社會 macrosociety;
宏觀市場 macromarket;
宏觀調整 macroeconomic regulation;
宏觀統計學 macrostatistics;
宏觀系統 macrosystem;
宏觀效應 macro effect;
宏觀語言 macrolanguage;
宏觀指導 macro direction;

[宏亮] loud and clear; sonorous;

[宏論] informed opinion; intelligent view;
大發宏論 express one's intelligent views freely; get on one's soapbox; pour forth wisdom;

[宏圖] grand prospect; great plan;
大展宏圖 extend one's great plans far and wide;

[宏偉] grand; magnificent;
宏偉的建築物 imposing building;
宏偉的禮堂 grand cathedrals;
宏偉目標 ambitious goal; magnificent target;
宏偉前景 grand prospects;
宏偉事業 magnificent cause;

[宏揚] disseminate;
宏揚民族精神 disseminate the national spirit;

[宏業] great achievement;

[宏願] great aspirations; noble ambition;
胸懷宏願 cherish a high aspiration; entertain a high ambition;

[宏旨] leading idea of an article; main theme;

[宏壯] great and solid;

寬宏 large-minded; magnanimous;

hong

【泓】 (1) clear, deep water; (2) a stream in Henan Province;

hong

【洪】 (1) big; vast; (2) flood; (3) a surname;

[洪波] turbulent waves;
洪波滾雪 the wind whips the waves into a snowy foam;

[洪才] great talent;

[洪大] great; immense; loud; massive;

[洪峰] flood crest; flood peak; high point of a flood;

[洪福] blessing; bliss; good luck; great happiness;
洪福齊天 have great luck; one's vast happiness is as high as heaven; supremely fortunate;

[洪荒] chaotic; primitive;

[洪量] (1) generosity; magnanimity; (2) great capacity for liquor;

[洪亮] loud and clear; resonant; sonorous;

[洪流] flood current; mighty torrent; powerful current;
奔騰的洪流 rushing torrents;
順應時代洪流 go with the powerful current of times;

[洪爐] great furnace;

[洪儒] great scholar;
洪儒碩彥 great scholar and eminent talent;

[洪水] deluge; flood; torrent; waterflood;
洪水暴發 immense floods prevail;
洪水暴漲 the flood swelled in volume;
洪水連天 the deluge extends far and wide; the flood reaches the horizon;
洪水猛獸 dreadful monster – vast evil;
~視作洪水猛獸 regard sth as dangerous as floods and wild beasts;
洪水滔滔 the flood spreads wide;
洪水退了 the flood has subsided;
洪水在上漲 the flood is rising;
大洪水 deluge; flood;

堵住洪水 stem the flood;
控制洪水 check the floods;
秋汛洪水 autumn flood;
設計洪水 design flood;
特大洪水 catastrophic flood;

[洪災] flood;

[洪鐘] large bell;
聲如洪鐘 have a stentorian voice; have good lungs; sb's voice sounds like a roaring bell;

暴洪 flash flood; sudden, violent flood;
防洪 control floods; prevent floods;
分洪 flood diversion;
抗洪 fight a flood;
山洪 mountain floods;
蓄洪 store floodwater;
治洪 flood control;

hong

【紅】 (1) red; (2) revolutionary; (3) bunting or red cloth used on festive occasions; (4) symbol of success; (5) bonus; dividend;

[紅白] red and white;
紅白事 weddings and funerals;
~紅白大事 happy and unhappy events;
白裏透紅 peaches and cream; white touched with red;
~白裏透紅的膚色 peach-and-cream complexion;
批紅判白 graft plants of various colours in order to produce new varieties;
外紅內白 red in the outside and white in the inside;

[紅斑] blotch; erythema;
紅斑點 rash;
紅斑狼瘡 lupus erythematosus;
皮膚紅斑狼瘡 cutaneous lupus erythematosus;
深部紅斑狼瘡 lupus erythematosus profundus;
系統性紅斑狼瘡 system lupus erythematosus;
增殖性紅斑狼瘡 hypertrophic lupus erythematosus;
腫脹性紅斑狼瘡 lupus erythematosus tumidus;
紅斑性濕疹 eczema erythematosum;
邊緣性紅斑 erythema marginatum;
擦爛紅斑 erythema intertrigo;
凍瘡紅斑 erythema pernio; suppurating frostbite;
多形紅斑 erythema multiforme;
壞死性紅斑 erythema necroticans;
結節性紅斑 erythema nodosum;
粒狀紅斑 pellagra;
鏈球菌性紅斑 erythema streptogenes;
流行性紅斑 epidemic erythema;
尿布紅斑 napkin erythema;
熱激性紅斑 erythema caloricum;
手掌紅斑 palmar erythema;
硬結性紅斑 erythema induratum;
游走性紅斑 erythema migrans;
暫時性紅斑 erythema fugax;
增殖性紅斑 erythroplasia;
肢端紅斑 acral erythema;
中毒性紅斑 toxic erythema;

[紅榜] board; honour roll;

[紅包] (1) red paper pocket containing money as a gift; (2) cash award; prize; (3) bribe;
討紅包 ask for red packets;

[紅不稜登] red;

[紅茶] black tea;

[紅腸] sausage;

[紅潮] (1) blush; flush; (2) red tide; red water;

[紅塵] human society; material world; secular world; world of mortals;
看破紅塵 be disillusioned with the mortal world; see through the vanity of life;

[紅得發紫] at the height of one's power and influence; at the zenith of one's fame; enjoying great popularity; extremely popular;

[紅燈] (1) (traffic) red light; (2) red lantern;
紅燈區 red-light district;
闖紅燈 go through a red light; hit the red light; ignore a red light; jump the red light; run the red light; run through a red light;
開紅燈 give the red light to;

[紅豆] (1) red bean; (2) love pea;
紅豆相思 red beans that inspire the memory of one's love;

[紅粉] (1) the fair sex; women; (2) rouge and powder;
紅粉佳人 gaily dressed beauty; young beauty;

[紅封包] red packet;

[紅果] haw;
紅果露 haw syrup;

[紅黑] red and black;
捧紅踏黑 snobbish;
[紅乎乎的] red;
[紅花] red flower;
紅花綠葉 red blossoms and green leaves; the green leaves set off the flower;
紅花雖好，綠葉扶持 with all its beauty, the red flower needs the green of its leaves to set it off;
[紅火] flourishing; having a run of luck; prosperous;
生意紅火 the business is flourishing;
[紅角] famous actor or actress;
[紅利] bonus; dividend; extra dividend; yield;
紅利分配 profit sharing;
紅利賬戶 bonus account;
紅利賬目 bonus account;
紅利儲備金 dividend cover;
附有紅利 cum bonus;
股票紅利 share bonus;
和平紅利 peace dividend;
累積紅利 accumulated bonus;
年中紅利 interim dividend;
年終紅利 final dividend; year-end dividend;
總紅利 total dividend;
[紅臉] (1) blush; (2) flush with anger; get angry;
唱紅臉 play the hero; pretend to be harsh and severe; wear the red make-up of the stage hero;
~又唱紅臉又唱白臉 play the role of a gentleman and villain;
[紅亮] glow;
[紅綠] red and green;
紅綠燈 traffic light; traffic signal;
紅綠相映 green and red set each other off;
穿紅著綠 gaily dressed;
淡紅淺綠 pale red and light green;
紛紅駭綠 luxuriant growth of flowers and sway of vegetation;
紅男綠女 fashionably dressed men and women; gaudily dressed men and women; men and women in gay dresses; young men and women in holiday dress;
嬌紅翠綠 tender blossoms and delicate leaves;
酒紅燈綠 a scene of debauchery with red lanterns and green wine; indulge in gay life and debauchery;
披紅戴綠 be gaily dressed;
稚綠嬌紅 a profusion of flowers of all colours;
萬綠叢中一點紅 a single red flower in the midst of thick foliage;
[紅鸞] lucky star of love;
紅鸞星動 a marriages is coming;
[紅莓] red berry;
一簇紅莓 a cluster of red berries;
[紅木] rosewood;
[紅娘] (1) go-between for lovers; matchmaker; (2) expediter;
做紅娘 play cupid;
[紅牌] red card;
[紅牆碧瓦] red walls and green tiles;
[紅人] favourite of sb in power; blue-eyed boy; fair-haired boy; favourite person; hotshot;
[紅日] red sun
紅日高照 the red sun shines brightly;
紅日西沉 the red sun sinks in the west;
一輪紅日 a red sun;
[紅潤] rosy; ruddy; smooth; tender and rosy;
紅潤的面孔 high-coloured cheeks;
紅潤的面色 blooming complexion;
紅潤的面頰 florid cheeks;
紅潤的雙頰 ruddy cheeks;
紅潤的嘴唇 rosy lips;
[紅色] (1) blush; blusher; (2) red; (3) revolutionary;
暗紅色 garnet;
粉紅色 pink;
~鮮艷的粉紅色 shocking pink;
亮紅色 pillar-box red;
玫瑰紅色 rose;
梅紅色 plum colour;
品紅色 magenta;
深紅色 dark red;
桃紅色 pink;
鮮紅色 bright red; cerise; pillar-box red;
洋紅色 carmine; magenta;
棗紅色 claret;
朱紅色 vermillion;
磚紅色 brick red;
紫紅色 purplish red;
[紅燒] braise in soy sauce;
[紅事] happy occasion;
[紅視症] erythropsia;
[紅薯] sweet potato;
[紅糖] brown sugar;

[紅彤彤] bright red; glowing;
紅彤彤的晚霞 flames of sunset;
秋林一片紅彤彤 the autumn woods flamed with colour;
[紅頭文件] red-tapism;
[紅外] infrared; infrared ray;
紅外跟蹤 infrared tracking;
紅外通信 infrared communication;
~ 遠紅外通信 far-infrared communication;
紅外線 infrared ray;
~ 紅外線攝影 infrared photography;
~ 紅外線效應 effect of infrared rays;
~ 測距紅外線 range-measurement infrared;
~ 短波紅外線 short infrared;
~ 近紅外線 near infrared;
~ 前視紅外線 forward-looking infrared;
~ 遠紅外線 infrared;
紅外遙感技術 infrared remote sensing technique;
[紅杏出墻] unfaithful to one's husband;
[紅顏] beauty; rosy countenance;
紅顏白髮 young lady married to an old man;
紅顏白骨 beauty is but skin-deep;
紅顏薄命 a beautiful girl often has an unfortunate life; beautiful women are the prey of evil designs;
紅顏易老 beauty is a fragile good;
[紅眼] (1) bloodshot eye; pink eye; (2) jealous of sb; (3) become infuriated; see red;
紅眼病 (1) pink eye; red eye disease; (2) jealousy; resentment;
[紅艷艷] brilliant red;
[紅陽] surname;
[紅藥水] mercurochrome;
[紅葉] red leaf;
紅葉題詩 a good match met by chance; a happy match is fixed by heaven;
[紅運] good luck;
紅運高照 born under a fortunate star; have fortune on one's side; lucky star shines bright;
[紅暈] blush; flush;
臉上微微泛出紅暈 flush slightly;
[紅中] (of mahjong) red dragon tile;
[紅腫] red and swollen;
又紅又腫 red and swollen;
[紅裝] clad in red;
紅裝素裹 clad in white, adorned in red (said of a sunset snow scene);

暗紅 dark red;
潮紅 blush; flush;
赤紅 crimson;
大紅 bright red; scarlet;
緋紅 crimson;
粉紅 pink;
火紅 fiery; flaming; red as fire;
口紅 (1) lipstick; (2) rouge;
梅紅 plum colour;
深紅 deep red;
通紅 red through and through; very red;
鮮紅 bright red; scarlet;
猩紅 bloody red; scarlet;
杏紅 apricot pink;
血紅 blood red;
殷紅 blackish red;
胭脂紅 carmine;
嫣紅 bright red;
眼紅 (1) be envious; be jealous; covet; (2) furious;
洋紅 carmine;
一串紅 scarlet sage;
銀紅 pale rose colour;
棗紅 jujube red;
朱紅 bright red; vermilion;
紫紅 purplish red;
棕紅 brownish red;

hong

【虹】 rainbow;
[虹采] banner; flag;
[虹彩] iridescence;
[虹光花] rainbow shower;
[虹橋] arched bridge; rainbow-shaped bridge;
[虹膜] iris;
虹膜閉鎖 atresia iridis;
虹膜病 iridopathy;
虹膜出血 iridaemia;
虹膜肥厚 iridauxesis;
虹膜角 angulus iridis;
~ 虹膜角膜炎 iridokeratitis;
虹膜掃瞄 iris scan;
虹膜撕裂 iridorhexis;
虹膜痛 iridalgia; pain in the iris of the eye;
虹膜炎 inflammation of the iris of the eye; iritis;
~ 角膜虹膜炎 corneoiritis;
~ 濾泡性虹膜炎 follicular iritis;

~ 丘疹性虹膜炎 iritis papulosa;
~ 糖尿病性虹膜炎 diabetic iritis;
~ 痛風虹膜炎 gouty iritis;

[虹吸管] siphon;
玻璃虹吸管 glass siphon;
酸虹吸管 acid siphon;
自動虹吸管 automatic siphon;

hong
【訌】 confusion; discord; quarrel;

hong
【紘】 (1) hat string fastened under the chin; (2) spacious; vast;

hong
【翃】 flying insects;

hong
【閎】 rich;
[閎中肆外] profound ideas and a good style of writing; rich in substance and graceful in style;

hong
【葒】 polygonum orientale;
[葒草] prince's feather;

hong
【鴻】 (1) swan goose; (2) letter; (3) grand; great;
[鴻筆] great literary style; great pen;
[鴻飛] go away for some great undertakings;
鴻飛冥冥 avoid and keep far away from; run away without leaving any trace behind; the wild goose flies to the unseen world — one's whereabouts are unknown;
[鴻福] great blessing; great luck;
鴻福齊天 one's vast happiness is as high as the sky;
[鴻溝] chasm; gulf; wide gap;
社會鴻溝 social gulf;
數碼鴻溝 digital divide;
數字鴻溝 digital divide;
[鴻鵠] large swan;
鴻鵠之志 great ambition; high aspirations;
[鴻毛] goose feather — sth very light or insignificant;
輕如鴻毛 as light as a feather; as light as a thistledown;
輕於鴻毛 (1) as light as a feather; lighter than a goose feather; (2) of little significance; of little value; trivial;
[鴻蒙] before the universe was formed; primordial world;
[鴻篇巨製] monumental masterpiece;
[鴻儒] learned scholar;
碩學鴻儒 eminent scholar; erudite and wise scholar; great learned literate; profound scholar;
[鴻圖] great plan;
鴻圖大展 carry out one's great plan; ride on the crest of success;
大展鴻圖 carry out one's great plan; realize one's ambition; ride on the crest of success;
[鴻雁] (1) swan goose; (2) letter; mail;
鴻雁哀鳴 the wild geese are crying mournfully — the refugees are moaning sorrowfully;
鴻雁傳書 deliver a message through wild swans; mail a letter; messenger of a letter;
鴻雁來書 letter from afar;
[鴻業] achievements of a ruler;
[鴻運] good luck;
鴻運高照 bread buttered on both sides; bring sb good luck and success in life; having good luck; in luck;
[鴻爪] traces left over by past events;

hong
【黌】 school;

hong³
hong
【哄】 (1) humbug; (2) coax;
[哄騙] cajole; cheat; hoodwink; humbug;
哄騙別人同意 coax consent out of others;
[哄搶] create a disturbance and rob; gang robbery;
[哄勸] persuade or coax sb into doing sth;
鬧哄 (1) make a noise; (2) (of many people) be busy doing sth;
起哄 (1) gather together to create a disturbance; (2) boo and hoot one or two people;

hong⁴
hong
【汞】 mercury;

hong
【鬨】 (1) boisterous; clamour; noise; uproar; uproarious; (2) dispute; quarrel;

hou¹

hou
【齁】 (1) snoring; (2) snorting;
[齁齁熟睡] lie gently breathing in a sound sleep;
[齁聲] snore; sound of snoring;

hou²
hou
【侯】 (1) marquis; (2) nobleman or high official; (3) a surname;
[侯服玉食] live in extreme luxury;
[侯岡] a surname;
[侯爵] marquess; marquis;
侯爵夫人 marchioness;
[侯麗] a surname;
[侯門] gate of a noble house;
侯門似海 the gate of a noble house is like the sea — impassable to the common man; the mansions of the nobility are inaccessible to the common man; the threshold of a noble house is deeper than the sea;
身入侯門 marry into the purple;
[侯史] a surname;
[侯叟] a surname;

王侯 princes and marquises; the nobility;
諸侯 dukes or princes under an emperor;

hou
【矦】 (1) marquis; (2) bull's-eye; (3) beautiful; (4) why; (5) a surname;

hou
【喉】 larynx; throat;
[喉白喉] laryngeal diphtheria;
[喉斑點] stigma;
[喉病] laryngopathy;
[喉出血] laryngorrhagia;
[喉竇] laryngeal sinus;
[喉惡性腫瘤] malignant tumour of larynx;
[喉反射] laryngeal reflex;
[喉結] Adam's apple; laryngeal prominence;
喉結核 laryngeal tuberculosis; tuberculosis of larynx;
[喉痙攣] laryngismus;
喘鳴性喉痙攣 laryngismus stridulus;
麻痺性喉痙攣 laryngismus paralyticus;
[喉科專家] laryngologist;
[喉良性腫瘤] benign tumour of larynx;
[喉嚨] gullet; throat;
喉嚨發癢 have a tickle in one's throat; ticklish throat;
割喉嚨 slit sb's throat;
口大喉嚨小 bite off more than one can chew;
掐喉嚨 choke; seize by the throat;
[喉麻痺] laryngoplegia;
[喉門] glottis;
[喉膿腫] laryngeal abscess;
[喉氣管炎] laryngotracheitis;
傳染性喉氣管炎 infectious laryngotracheitis;
[喉腔] cavitas laryngis;
[喉舌] (1) throat and tongue; (2) mouthpiece;
費盡喉舌 do a lot of talking; waste all one's breath;
為民喉舌 speak for the people;
[喉軟骨] cartilagines laryngeales;
[喉痛] laryngalgia; sore throat;
[喉頭] larynx;
喉頭炎 laryngitis;
哽在喉頭 stick in sb's throat;
[喉突] laryngeal prominence;
[喉息肉] laryngeal polyp;
[喉下垂] laryngoptosis;
[喉狹窄] laryngeal stenosis;
[喉咽] laryngopharynx;
喉咽腔 laryngopharyngeal cavity;
[喉炎] laryngitis;
喘鳴性喉炎 laryngitis stridulosa;
肥厚性喉炎 hypertrophic laryngitis;
壞疽性喉炎 gangrinous laryngitis;
壞死性喉炎 necrotic laryngitis;
急性喉炎 acute laryngitis;
慢性喉炎 chronic laryngitis; clergyman's throat;
梅毒性喉炎 syphilitic laryngitis;
膜性喉炎 membranous laryngitis;
前庭喉炎 vestibular laryngitis;
萎縮性喉炎 atrophic laryngitis;
[喉異物] foreign body in the larynx;
[喉音] guttural sound;
[喉阻塞] laryngeal obstruction;

白喉 diphtheria;
歌喉 singing voice; voice;
結喉 Adam's apple;
人造喉 artificial larynx;
咽喉 (1) pharynx and larynx; (2) key link; strategic passage;

hou

【猴】 (1) monkey; (2) clever boy; smart chap;

[猴病] monkey disease;

[猴急] very impatient;

[猴精] clever and mischievous person;

[猴快] quick as a monkey;

[猴賴] mischievous;

[猴皮筋] rubber band;

[猴猻] monkey;

[猴頭猴腦] silly; silly-faced;

[猴戲] monkey show;

[猴子] monkey;

猴子穿衣—假充人 a monkey wearing clothes – pretend to be a human being;

猴子看書—假斯文 a monkey reading a book – pretend to be refined in manner;

猴子撈月亮—空忙一場 a monkey trying to fish the moon out of the water – a vain attempt;

猴子唧唧 monkey's chatter;

一大群猴子 a barrel of monkeys;

一群猴子 a troop of monkeys;

一隻猴子 a monkey;

恒河猴 rhesus monkey;

狐猴 lemur;

懶猴 loris;

獼猴 macaque;

熊猴 Assamese macaque;

葉猴 leaf monkey;

猿猴 apes and monkeys;

hou

【篌】 musical instrument like a lute;

hou

【骺】 epiphysis;

[骺病] epiphysiometer;

[骺發育不良] epiphyseal dysplasia;

[骺發育不全] epiphyseal dysplasia;

[骺骨折] epiphyseal fracture;

[骺炎] epiphysitis;

青少年骺炎 epiphysitis juvenilis;

hou

【餱】 dry provisions;

hou³

hou

【吼】 howl; roar;

[吼喊] shout at;

[吼猴] howling monkey;

[吼叫] bellow;

吼叫如牛 roar like a bull;

低聲吼叫 growl;

[吼聲] roaring cry;

吼聲如雷 roar like a thunder; roar with rage;

怒吼 howl; roar;

hou⁴

hou

【后】 (1) empress; (2) god of the earth; (3) same as 後, after; behind;

[后妃] empress and imperial concubines;

[后冠] tiara;

[后土] the earth;

皇后 empress;

太后 empress dowager; queen mother;

王后 queen; queen consort;

hou

【厚】 (1) thick; (2) deep; profound; (3) kind; magnanimous; (4) generous; large; (5) rich or strong in flavour; (6) favour; stress;

[厚愛] great kindness; treat very kindly and generously;

[厚薄] thick and thin;

厚此薄彼 biased; discriminate against one and favour the other; discriminate against some and favour others; favour one and be prejudiced against the other; give handsome treatment to one and niggardly treatment to the other; give a royal welcome to one and cold reception to the other; give too much to one and too little to the other; liberal to one and stingy to the other; make chalf of one and cheese of the other; make fish of one and flesh of the other; make invidious distinctions; partial to one while neglecting the other; say turkey to one and buzzard to the other; the treatment accorded to one is out of all proportion to that accorded to the other; treat one warmly and another

H

coldly; treat with partiality;
物薄情厚 the gift is of small value but the thoughtfulness behind it is immense;

[厚道] honest and kind; virtuous and sincere;

[厚德載福] great virtue carries happiness with it; virtue and happiness are mother and daughter;

[厚度] (1) depth; (2) thickness;
大氣厚度 atmospheric depth;
當量厚度 equivalent depth;
切屑厚度 chip thickness;
樹冠厚度 crown depth;
弦齒厚度 chordal thickness; tooth thickness;

[厚望] great expectations;
不負厚望 live up to sb's expectations; not to let sb down;

[厚意] kindness;
多謝厚意 thank one's kindness;

膘厚 fat thickness;
薄厚 thickness;
淳厚 pure and honest; simple and kind;
醇厚 (1) mellow; (2) pure and honest; simple and kind;
篤厚 sincere, honest, and kind; sincere and magnanimous;
敦厚 honest and simple; honest and sincere;
肥厚 fleshy; plump;
豐厚 (1) thick; (2) rich and generous;
憨厚 simple and honest;
渾厚 (1) simple and honest; sincere; (2) simple and vigorous;
加厚 thicken;
寬厚 (1) wide and thick; (2) generous; generous and kind; magnanimous;
濃厚 (1) dense; thick; (2) pronounced; strong; (3) (of interest) great;
仁厚 kind-hearted and generous;
深厚 (1) deep; profound; (2) deep-seated; solid;
溫厚 gentle and kind; good-natured;
雄厚 abundant; rich; solid;
優厚 favourable; liberal; munificent;
忠厚 honest and tolerant; sincere and kind;

hou

【後】 (1) back; behind; rear; (2) after; afterwards; later; (3) offspring;

[後半] latter half; second half;
後半部 latter portion of a book or film;

[後輩] (1) inferiors; juniors; younger generation; (2) descendants; posterity;

[後備] reserve; spare;
後備保護 backup protection;
後備幹部 bacup cadres; cadres in reserve;
後備工業 supporting industry;
後備力量 reserve forces;
後備軍 reserve forces;

[後步] room for maneuvre;

[後腸] epigaster;
後腸管 metagaster;
後腸門 posterior intestinal portal;

[後成] epigenic;
後成説 epigenesis;
後成質 metaplasm;

[後塵] footsteps;
步人後塵 dog the steps of others; follow in sb's footsteps; follow in the wake of; step into sb's shoes; trail along behind others; tread in the footsteps of;
踵其後塵 follow sb's footsteps;

[後窗] rear window;

[後代] (1) later ages; succeeding era; (2) descendants; later generations; offspring; posterity; progeniture; progeny;
後代不昌 posterity is not prosperous;
後代測試 progeny test;
傳至後代 go down to posterity;
單性後代 unisexual progeny;
雙傾後代 biparental progeny;
無性後代 vegetative progeny;
有性後代 sexual progeny;
雜種後代 hybrid progeny;
直系後代 lineal descent;
種子後代 seed progeny;
自交後代 self-bred progeny;

[後殿] rear court room in a palace;

[後爹] stepfather;

[後發制人] gain mastery by striking only after the enemy strikes;

[後方] rear;
大後方 rear area;

[後福] the blessings to follow; the good days to come;
後福無窮 your future happiness is unlimited;

[後跟] heel;
腳後跟 heel;

[後宮] (1) imperial harem; (2) concubines of a

monarch;

[後顧] (1) turn back; (2) look back to the past;

後顧前瞻 look back to the past and ahead into the future; look behind and forward;

後顧無憂 looking behind, there is no anxiety;

後顧之憂 fear of attack from behind; fear of disturbance in the rear; family considerations that cause delay in decision; trouble back at home;

[後果] aftermath; consequence;

後果自負 accept the consequences oneself; at one's own risk;

不顧後果 give no heed to the consequences; reckless of the consequences;

產生後果 have consequences;

長期後果 long-term consequences;

承擔後果 accept the consequences; take the consequences;

~必須承擔後果 have to abide by the consequences;

化學後果 chemical consequence;

考慮後果 consider the consequences;

可怕的後果 terrible consequences;

面對後果 face the consequences; suffer the consequences;

逃避後果 escape the consequences;

嚴重後果 serious consequences;

~帶來嚴重後果 involve fateful consequences;

~留下嚴重後果 leave serious consequences;

直接後果 immediate consequence;

[後漢] (1) Eastern Han Dynasty; (2) Later Han Dynasty;

[後患] future trouble;

後患堪虞 further trouble is to be worried; there will be the deuce to pay;

後患無窮 bring sb evil consequences unceasingly; bring sb trouble without end; constant source of future troubles; lead to endless trouble; no end of trouble for the future; source of endless trouble; there will be the deuce to pay;

~打蛇不死—後患無窮 beat a snake without killing it — leave the door open to endless troubles in the future;

杜絕後患 eliminate the cause of future trouble; impede a future disaster; remove seeds of future trouble;

而毖後患 provide against future troubles;

免致後患 avoid causing future trouble;

以杜後患 forestall future trouble; prevent any future complications; provide against future troubles;

以防後患 guard against a future evil;

以絕後患 avoid trouble later on; guard against future evil; spare all later trouble;

以彌後患 in order to forestall calamities;

[後悔] regret; remorse; repent;

後悔不已 be overcome with regret;

後悔失言 bite off one's tongue; bite one's tongue off;

後悔無益 it is no use crying over spilt milk; repentance is of no avail;

表示後悔 show repentance;

當取不取，過後莫悔 if one does not take what one ought to take, one must not regret it afterwards;

毫不後悔 have no regrets;

[後會有期] I am sure we shall meet soon; there will be time for us to meet again; we'll meet again some day; we'll meet some other day; we shall meet again; we will meet each other later;

[後稷] god of agriculture;

[後記] afterword; postscript;

編後記 afterword; postscript;

[後繼] carry on; succeed;

後繼乏人 have no qualified successors; lack a worthy successor; leave no successor; there is no successor;

後繼無人 have no qualified successors; lack a worthy successor; leave no successor; there is no successor;

後繼有人 have qualified successors; there's another generation to carry on; there is no lack of successors to carry on; there will be people who can carry on;

[後街] backstreet;

後街小巷 backstreet;

[後進] backward; lagging behind; less advanced;

後進趕先進 the less advanced striving to catch up with the more advanced;

後進先出 last in, first out;

受提攜的後進 protégé;

[後勁] (1) after-effect; delayed effect; (2) gather more and more momentum; (3) ability to make further progress; stamina; reserve one's strength;
積蓄後勁 accumulate and preserve strength; accumulate and store up strength;

[後來] afterwards; eventually; later; later on; subsequently;
後來居上 catch up from behind; newcomers gain the upper hand on the old; successors excel the predecessors; the latecomers become the first; the latecomers get ahead of others; the latecomers get to the top; the latecomers surpass the early starters; the latecomers surpass the old-timers;
後來者 latecomer;

[後浪推前浪] each wave pushing at the one ahead; the waves behind drive on those before; waves urge waves;

[後路] (1) route to retreat; (2) room for manoeuvre; way of escape;
抄後路 turn the enemy's rear;
留後路 keep a way open for retreat; leave a way open for the future; leave a way out;
~留有後路 leave oneself enough leeway for...;

[後媽] stepmother;

[後門] (1) back door; (2) back-door influence; backdoorism;
後門成風 the malpractice of going in for back door deals becomes common;
後門貨 goods illegally obtained and sold;
後門交易 back-door deal;
後門送舊，前門迎新 send away the old clients at the back door, admit the new ones at the front gate;
開後門 open the back door; resort to backstairs influence;
走後門 enter by the back door; get in by the back door; get in through the back door; pull strings; secure advantages through influence; take the back door;

[後面] (1) at the back; behind; in the rear; (2) later;
跟在後面 follow in the rear;
坐在車後面 sit on the back seat of the car;

[後母] stepmother;

[後腦] hindbrain;
後腦勺留鬍子—隨便（辮）beard growing on the back of one's head — as you please;
後腦勺子 the back of one's head;
後腦勺子上長瘡，自己看不見 one has a boil on the back of one's head, one can't see it oneself;

[後年] the year after next;
大後年 three years from now;

[後娘] stepmother;

[後怕] fear after an event;

[後排] back row;
後排隊員 backcourt player; backline player;
後排右 right back;
後排中 centre back;
後排左 left back;

[後期] later period; later stage;

[後妻] second wife;

[後起] of new arrivals; of the younger generation;
後起之秀 coming man; new star; promising youngster; up-and-coming youngester; up-and-comer;

[後勤] rear service; logistics;
後勤部門 back office;
後勤指揮自動化 automation of logistical command;

[後區] back zone;

[後人] descendants; futurity; later generations; posterity;
不甘後人 cannot bear playing second fiddle; hate to be outdone; not willing to let others outshine oneself; unwilling to lag behind; unwilling to take a back seat;
不敢後人 unwilling to fall behind others;

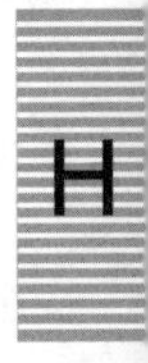

[後任] successor to an office;

[後身] (1) back of a person; (2) back of a garment;

[後生] lad; young man;
後生可畏 a ragged colt may make a good horse; every oak has been an acorn; the young are to be regarded with awe; the younger generation will grow up one day to surpass the older; youth are to be regarded with respect;
後生小子 lad; young man; naive youngsters;

[後世] (1) later ages; (2) later generations;
傳諸後世 bequeath to later ages; hand down to posterity; pass down to latter generations; transmit to posterity;
垂法後世 set an example for future generations; set an example for posterity;
名傳後世 hand down one's name to posterity;
名留後世 leave a fine reputation to future ages;

[後事] (1) what happened afterwards; (2) funeral affairs;
辦後事 arrange matters for the deceased;
欲知後事如何，且聽下回分解 if you want to know what happens afterwards, read the next chapter;

[後視] back vision;
後視鏡 rear-view mirror;
~ 側後視鏡 side-view mirror; wing mirror;
~ 內後視鏡 rear-view mirror;

[後手] room for sth;
後手翻 flip-flop;
留後手 leave room for manoeuvre;

[後嗣] descendants; offspring;

[後台] (1) backstage; (2) backstage supporter; behind-the-scenes backer;
後台老板 backstage boss; behind-the-scenes boss; paymaster; wirepulling boss; wirepulling master;
找後台 seek the backstage boss;

[後天] (1) the day after tomorrow; (2) acquired; postnatal;
大後天 three days from now;

[後退] back away; backlash; draw back; fall back; recess; retreat; retrograde;
後退一步 take a step back;

[後腿] hind leg;
扯後腿 a drag on sb; a hindrance to sb; hold sb back from action; pull sb back from action;
拉後腿 a drag on sb; a hindrance to sb; hinder sb; hold sb back; pull sb back;
拖後腿 a drag on sb; hinder sb; hold sb back;

[後衛] guard;

[後效] (1) after-effect; (2) future performance;
彈性後效 elastic after-effect;
以觀後效 observe how the offender behaves; see how the offender behaves;
有限後效 limited after-effect;

[後續] follow-up;
後續產品 follow-up product;
後續工作 follow-up;
後續篇 follow-up;
後續任務 follow-up task;
後續投資 follow-up investment;
後續行動 follow-up;

[後學] pupil of young age; scholar of young age;

[後頁] back page;
請閱後頁 please turn over (p.t.o);

[後遺症] sequel;

[後裔] descendants; offsprings; posterity; progeny; scion;

[後援] backing; backup force; reinforcements; support;

[後院] backyard;

[後者] the latter;

[後置] postposition;
後置詞 postposition;
後置定語 post-attribute;
後置介詞 postposed preposition;
後置修飾詞 postmodifier;

[後綴] postfix; suffix;
褒義後綴 meliorative suffix;
動詞後綴 verbal suffix;
派生後綴 derivational suffix;
屈折後綴 inflectional suffix;
使役後綴 factitive suffix;

[後座] back seat;

背後 (1) at the back; behind; in the rear; (2) behind sb's back;
病後 after an illness;
餐後 after-meal;
此後 after this; henceforth; hereafter;
敵後 enemy's rear area;
斷後 (1) bring up the rear; cover a retreat; (2) have no male offspring; have no male progeny;
而後 after that; then;
爾後 subsequently; thereafter;
過後 afterwards; later; later on; some time later;
婚後 after wedding;
今後 from now on; henceforth; in the days to come;
久後 long afterwards;
絕後 (1) have no progeny; without offspring; (2)

never to be seen again;
落後 backward; fall behind; lag behind;
末後 finally;
幕後 backstage; behind the scenes;
前後 (1) about; round; (2) altogether; from beginning to end;
然後 after that; afterwards; then;
日後 in the future;
善後 deal with problems arising from an accident, etc.;
身後 after one's death;
事後 after an event; afterwards;
書後 postscript;
嗣後 hereafter; later on; subsequently;
隨後 soon afterwards;
退後 fall back; fall behind; step back;
往後 from now on; in the future; later on;
午後 afternoon;
先後 one after another; order; priority; successively;
以後 after; afterwards; hereafter; later;
預後 prognosis;
最後 final; last; ultimate;

hou
【候】 (1) await; wait; (2) inquire after; (3) season; time;
[候補] alternate; candidate for a vacancy;
候補委員 substitute member of a committee;
[候車] wait for a bus; wait for a train;
[候光] await the honour of your presence;
[候機] waiting;
候機大樓 airport terminal;
候機室 airport lounge; airport waiting room; departure lounge;
~中轉候機室 transit lounge;
[候駕] wait to welcome sb's presence;
[候教] await your instructions;
潔樽候教 look forward to the pleasure of your company;
[候客室] antechamber; reception room;
[候命] await your instructions;
[候鳥] (1) bird of passage; migratory bird; (2) visitant;
冬候鳥 winter resident;
[候任] designate;
候任董事 director designate;
[候審] await trial;
[候選人] candidate;
候選人資格 candidacy;
提名候選人 nominate a candidate;
[候訊] await court trial or cross-examination;
[候診] wait for one's turn to see a doctor; wait to see the doctor;
候診室 waiting room;

拜候 call on; visit;
測候 astronomical and meteorological observation;
斥候 reconnoitre;
伺候 serve; wait upon;
等候 await; expect; wait;
恭候 await respectfully;
花候 flowering season;
火候 (1) duration and degree of heating, etc.; (2) level of attainment; (3) crucial moment;
立候 wait on the spot and leave until sth is done;
氣候 (1) climate; (2) situation;
稍候 wait a moment;
少候 wait a moment;
時候 (1) a duration of time; (2) a point in time;
侍候 attend upon; look after; wait upon;
守候 (1) expect; wait; (2) keep watch;
天候 weather;
聽候 wait for...;
問候 extend greetings to; greetings; send one's regards;
迎候 await the arrival of;
徵候 sign;
症候 (1) disease; (2) symptom;

hou
【逅】 come across; meet unexpectedly; run into;

邂逅 meet by chance; meet unexpectedly; run into sb;

hou
【鱟】 king crab;

hu¹
hu
【乎】 (1) at; from; in; than; (2) interrogative particle; (3) exclamatory particle;
斷乎 absolutely;
關乎 concern; involve;
合乎 conform with; correspond to;
幾乎 almost; nearly; practically;
近乎 be close to; be little short of;
類乎 be similar to;
全乎 all in readiness; complete;
確乎 indeed; really;

似乎 as if; it seems; seemingly;
在乎 (1) depend on; (2) care about; mind; take to heart;
不在乎 not care; not mind;

hu

【呼】 (1) breathe out; exhale; (2) shout; (3) call;
[呼哧] sound of puffing and blowing;
呼哧直喘 puff and blow;
[呼叱] shout at;
[呼格] vocative case;
[呼庚呼癸] request for financial help;
[呼喊] call out; holler; shout;
扯着嗓子呼喊 shout at the top of one's voice;
高聲呼喊 give a loud yell; lift up one's voice; yell loudly;
[呼號] cry out in distress; wail;
[呼喝] bawl at;
[呼呼] (1) snore; (2) howling of the wind;
呼呼大睡 snore loudly in one's sleep;
呼呼入睡 sink into a deep sleep;
呼呼聲 birr; flurr; whir; whirr;
呼呼作響 whir; whirr;
[呼喚] call; shout to;
呼喚功能 vocative function;
呼喚機 bleeper;
~無線電呼喚機 bleeper;
呼喚語 call;
千呼萬喚 a thousand calls; be called again and again; be called and called;
[呼叫] (1) call out; shout; (2) call; ring;
呼叫按鈕 call circuit button;
呼叫信號 call letters; call sign;
編碼呼叫 code call;
長途呼叫 trunk call;
錯號呼叫 wrong number call;
大呼小叫 shout and wrangle;
燈光呼叫 lamp call;
定時呼叫 fixed time call;
分鈴呼叫 extension call;
蜂音呼叫 buzzer call;
緊急呼叫 emergency call;
狂呼亂叫 scream aloud;
普通呼叫 ordinary call;
全忙呼叫 overflow call;
市內呼叫 exchange call; local call;
手搖呼叫 manual call;
順序呼叫 sequence call;
完成呼叫 complete call;
未接通的呼叫 loss call;
無線電呼叫 radio call;
延遲呼叫 delayed call;
音響呼叫 audible call;
優先呼叫 preference call;
有效呼叫 effective call;
預約呼叫 advance call;
振鈴呼叫 bell call;
直接呼叫 direct call;
自動中斷呼叫 automatic trunk call;
[呼酒荐饌] call for wine and food;
[呼救] call for help;
呼救無門 nowhere to turn for help;
呼救信號 distress signal; emergency pulses; signal for help; SOS;
尖聲呼救 scream for help;
[呼號] give password; shout slogans;
[呼拉舞] hula dance;
[呼嚕] snore;
呼嚕聲 snore;
打呼嚕 snore;
[呼門] call for opening the door;
[呼名] address sb by name;
直呼其名 address a person without an honorific title; address sb disrespectfully by his name;
[呼朋引類] gang up; gather a clique; summon one's friends and pals;
[呼氣] breath; breathe out; expiration;
呼氣測試 breath test;
[呼扇] (1) shake; (2) fan;
[呼哨] whistle;
[呼聲] cry voice;
呼聲甚高 be favoured to win; great popular demand for sb to be elected;
呼聲震天 rend the air;
[呼損] call loss;
[呼吸] breathe; breath; respiration; respire;
呼吸不足 hypopnea;
呼吸遲緩 oligopnea;
呼吸過度 hyperpnea;
呼吸過緩 bradypnea;
呼吸過慢 bradypnea;
呼吸緩慢 bradypnea;
呼吸急促 breathe raggedly; polypnea;
呼吸減弱 hypopnea;
呼吸結構 respiratory structure;
呼吸困難 breathe with difficulty; breathing difficulties; have difficulty in breathing;
~腎形呼吸困難 renal dyspnea;

~心形呼吸困難 cardiac dyspnea;
~心臟性呼吸困難 cardiac dyspnea;
~夜發性呼吸困難 nocturnal dyspnea;
~直立性呼吸困難 orthostatic dyspnea;
呼吸孔 blow-hole;
呼吸器 breathing apparatus;
~水中呼吸器 aqualung;
呼吸商 respiratory quotient;
呼吸系統 respiratory system;
~呼吸系統疾病 respiratory disease;
呼吸相通 be intimately bound up with; their views are in accord and their interests are linked together;
呼吸自由的空氣 breathe the breath of liberty;
呼吸作用 respiration;
長吸呼吸 apneustic breathing;
腹式呼吸 abdominal breathing;
負壓呼吸 negative pressure breathing;
加壓呼吸 pressure breathing;
均勻呼吸 regular breathing;
空中呼吸 respiration in air;
困難的呼吸 laboured breathing;
內呼吸 internal respiration;
屏住呼吸 bate one's breath; catch one's breath;
淺深吸 shallow breathing;
強力呼吸 forced respiration;
人工呼吸 artificial respiration; rescue breathing;
~進行人工呼吸 practise artificial respiration; try artificial respiration;
~口對口人工呼吸 mouth-to-mouth resuscitation;
~嘴對嘴人工呼吸 mouth-to-mouth breathing;
深呼吸 breathe deeply; deep breath; deep breathing;
水中呼吸 respiration in water;
停止呼吸 cease breathing;
同呼吸，共命運 breathe the same air and share the same fate; identify oneself heart and soul with; share a common fate; share weal and woe; throw in one's lot with sb; their hearts beating as one and sharing the rough and smooth;
外呼吸 external respiration;
無呼吸 apnoea;
需氧呼吸 aerobic respiration;
有節奏呼吸 rhythmic breathing;
周期性呼吸 periodic breathing;

[呼嘯] howl; roar; scream; whistle; whizz;
呼嘯而過 roar past; whizz pass;
呼嘯而去 peel out;
[呼延] a surname;
[呼應] act in cooperation with each other; echo; work in concert with;
呼應句 pair;
~緊接呼應句 adjacency pair;
呼應所指 anaphoric reference;
彼此呼應 act in concert with each other; act in coordination with each other; support each other;
此呼彼應 act in coordination with each other; echo each other; echo one another; react on each other; respond to each other; take concerted actions;
前呼後應 act in cooperation; take concerted actions;
遙相呼應 coordinate with each other from afar; echo each other at a distance; echo from afar;
[呼語] direct address; vocative expression;
呼語功能 vocative function;
呼語語段 vocative text;
[呼籲] appeal; call on;
發出呼籲 issue an appeal; launch an appeal; make an appeal;
公開呼籲 public appeal;
急切呼籲 desperate appeal;
緊急呼籲 urgent appeal; urgent call;
親自呼籲 personal appeal;
向政府呼籲 address an appeal to the government;
再次呼籲 renew an appeal;
直接呼籲 direct appeal;
[呼冤] call for justice;
呼冤喊屈 complain about an injustice; complain and call for redress; cry out for justice;
[呼噪] make loud, confused noise;
[呼之欲出] almost certain; obvious; seem ready to come out at one's call;

哀呼 cry piteously; cry sadly; wail;
潮呼呼 clammy; damp; dank;
稱呼 address; call; form of address;
傳呼 pass on a message left by phone;
高呼 shout loudly;
歡呼 acclaim; cheer; hail;
嗚呼 alack; alas;
招呼 (1) call; (2) greet; hail; say hello to; (3)

notify; tell; (4) take care of;

hu

【忽】 (1) neglect; overlook; (2) suddenly;

［忽地］ abruptly; suddenly;

［忽而］ now..., now...;

忽而哭，忽而笑 cry and laugh intermittently;

忽而這麼説，忽而那麼説 say one things one moment and another thing the next;

［忽發奇想］ have a strange idea suddenly;

［忽...忽］ alternatively; in turn; now..., now....; sth today, another thing tomorrow;

［忽忽不樂］ be discouraged and unhappy; in an absent-minded and depressed mood; in low spirits; in the dismals; suffer from the mopes; unhappy at sth; with a heavy heart;

［忽略］ elude; ignore; lose sight of; neglect; overlook;

忽略健康 neglect one's health;

［忽然］ all of a sudden; suddenly; unexpectedly;

忽然間 all of a sudden; suddenly; unexpectely;

［忽閃］ flash; glisten; twinkle;

［忽視］ blank sb; disregard; give a cold shoulder; ignore; look down on; neglect; overlook;

忽視事實 blink the fact;

被上司忽視 be ignored by one's superiors;

遭到忽視 be left out in the cold;

［忽聞］ hear suddenly; learn of sth unexpectedly;

［忽悠］ flicker;

忽忽悠悠 careless; indifference to the passing of time;

［忽作忽止］ by fits and starts;

飄忽 (1) fleet; move swiftly; (2) float; wave to and fro;

倏忽 in the twinkling of an eye; swiftly;

玩忽 neglect; take things lightly; trifle with;

奄忽 quickly; suddenly;

悠忽 lazy and idle;

hu

【惚】 absent-minded; entranced;

恍惚 (1) absent-minded; in a trance; (2) dimly; faintly; seemingly;

hu

【淴】 sound of flowing water;

［淴浴］ bathe; have a bath;

hu

【虖】 cry; howl; roar; shout;

hu

【欻】 abruptly; suddenly;

hu

【滹】 a river flowing through Hebei;

hu

【歑】 blow mildly, as breeze;

hu

【戲】 ah; alas; oh;

hu²

hu

【圀】 entire; whole;

［圀圇］ entire; whole;

圀圇吞咽 psomophagy;

圀圇吞棗 gulp down without thought; lap up information without digesting it; read without understanding; swallow an entire date; swallow at a gulp without chewing; swallow whole dates — read hastily and without thinking;

hu

【弧】 (1) wooden bow; (2) segment of a circle;

［弧度］ radian;

［弧光燈］ arc lamp;

水銀弧光燈 mercury arc lamp;

［弧圈球］ loop;

［弧線］ arc;

［弧形］ arc; curve;

弧形式 (of hairstyle) arc style;

電弧 electric arc;

劣弧 minor arc;

優弧 major arc;

hu

【狐】 (1) fox; (2) a surname;

［狐步舞］ foxtrot;

［狐臭］ body odour; bromhidrosis;

［狐蝠］ flying fox;

［狐猴］ lemur;

［狐狸］ fox; lowrie;

狐狸吵架——派胡言 foxes quarreling —

sheer nonsense;

狐狸精 fox spirit; seductive woman; temptress; woman of easy virtue;

狐狸雖狡，難逃獵手 however sly a fox may be, it is no match for a good hunter; the craftiest fox can't escape the skilled hunter;

狐狸尾巴 a fox's tail — sth that gives away a person's real character or evil intentions;

狐狸尾巴藏不住 a fox cannot hide its tail; the tail doth often catch the fox;

狐狸似的 vulpine;

狐狸穴 foxhole;

老狐狸 (1) old fox; (2) crafty scoundrel;

~狡猾的老狐狸 sly old fox;

一群狐狸 a skulk of foxes;

一隻狐狸 a fox;

玉面狐狸 a pretty woman of loose morals;

[狐埋狐滑] change one's mind constantly; hesitant to achieve success; suspicious and indecisive like a fox; the fox buries it and the fox digs it up;

[狐媚] bewitch with cajolery; charm with flattery; sycophantic;

狐媚淫態 attractive looks and seductive manners;

[狐憑鼠伏] in hiding; lie in ambush;

[狐裘] fox fur robe;

狐裘羔袖 fox fur robe with lambskin sleeves — good on the whole but not perfect;

[狐犬] fox dog;

[狐群狗黨] a bad lot; a bunch of rascals; a company of evildoers; a gang of scoundrels; a pack of rogues; an evil banch; despicable gang;

[狐死兔悲] when the fox dies the hare grieves — grieve for one's kind;

[狐仙] fairy fox;

[狐疑] doubt; suspicion;

狐疑不決 indecisive in one's mind; suspicious and undecided; wavering and unable to decide;

心中狐疑 with one's stomach heaving with torturing doubts;

心中有些狐疑 slight misgivings found place in one's mind;

赤狐 red fox;

紅狐 red fox;

火狐 red fox;

沙狐 corsac fox;

玄狐 a kind of black fox;

銀狐 silver fox;

hu

【胡】 (1) non-Han nationalities living in the north and west in ancient times; (2) introduced from the northern and western nationalities or from abroad; (3) outrageously; recklessly; wantonly; (4) why; (5) beard; moustache; whiskers; (6) a surname;

[胡纏] bothering sb endlessly; harass;

[胡扯] baloney; bosh; drivel; fiddlesticks; flimflam; hokum; rubbish; talk nonsense; talk rubbish; waffle on about; wag one's tongue;

別胡扯 come off it; get off it; stop waffling;

[胡打海摔] not pampered;

[胡非] a surname;

[胡匪] bandit; brigand;

[胡蜂] hornet; vespid; wasp;

[胡搞] (1) meddle with sth; mess things up; (2) carry on an affair with sb; promiscuous;

胡搞蠻纏 argue tediously and vexatiously; harass sb with unreasonable demands; pester sb endlessly;

胡搞一通 make a mess of things;

[胡瓜] cucumber;

小胡瓜 courgette;

[胡話] ravings; wild talk;

滿口胡話 rave in delirium;

[胡混] fool around; loaf about;

[胡椒] black pepper; pepper;

胡椒粉 pepper;

~白胡椒粉 white pepper;

~黑白胡椒粉 black pepper;

~一撮胡椒粉 a pinch of pepper;

胡椒粒 peppercorn;

胡椒麵 ground pepper;

胡椒瓶 pepper pot;

胡椒研磨器 pepper mill;

少許胡椒 a dash of pepper;

一點胡椒 a dash of pepper;

[胡攪] (1) behave randomly; mess around; mischievous; pester sb; screw around; (2) argue tediously and vexatiously;

wrangle;
胡攪蠻纏 argue tediously and vexatiously; harass sb with unreasonable demands; pester sb endlessly;

[胡來] make trouble; mess things up; run wild;

[胡聊] chat;

[胡嚕] (1) rub; (2) scrape together; sweep away;

[胡亂] at random; carelessly; casually;
胡亂猜測 make wild guesses;
胡亂發脾氣 lose one's temper for nothing;
胡亂花錢 careless with one's money;
胡花亂用 spend money extravagantly and recklessly;

[胡母] a surname;

[胡鬧] cause disturbance without obvious reasons; kick up a row; make a row; mischievous; raise a row; run riot; run wild;
不要胡鬧 don't be absurd;
瞎胡鬧 behave in a foolish and excited way; play the giddy goat; mischievous;
小胡鬧 naughty child; urchin;

[胡哨] whistle;

[胡琴] two-string bow instrument;
拉胡琴 play the two-string Chinese violin;
~老西兒拉胡琴－自顧自 a Shanxi man playing the *huqin* – self-care;

[胡說] baloney; bilge; blather; bullshit; cobblers; cod; codswallop; cut the nonsense; don't talk rot; fiddlesticks; guff; horseshift; humbug; nonsense; rats; rot it; rubbish; shit; stuff and nonsense; what crap;
胡說八道 a pile of shit; all baloney; all my eye; apple sauce; banana oil; broad nonsense; cobblers; cod; drool; flubdub and gulf; full of hops; haver; hooey; lie in one's teeth; lie in one's throat; mere humbug; prate nonsense; pure rubbish; rats; rubbish; sheer nonsense; sling the bull; speak through the back of one's neck; stuff and nonsense; talk bosh; talk foolishly; talk gibberish; talk nonsense; talk rot; talk rubbish; talk sheer nonsense; talk through one's hat; talk through the back of one's neck; talk wet; talk without truth; throw the bull;
~完全胡說八道 arrant nonsense;
胡說亂道 speak wildly like a fool; talk foolishly and wildly; talk in a wild disorderly manner; talk without restraint;
信口胡說 make irresponsible remarks; wag one's tongue too freely;

[胡桃] walnut;
胡桃木 walnut tree;

[胡同] alley; alleyway; lane; side road;
胡同裏扛木頭－直來直去 walking in a lane with a plank on one's shoulder – taking an arrow-straight course;
小胡同 by-street;
死胡同 blind alley; cul-de-sac; dead end; impasse;
~鑽入死胡同 push into a dead end;

[胡為] act recklessly; act like a bully;

[胡言] rave; talk nonsense;
胡言亂語 babble; blather; clotted nonsense; codswallop; delirium; flimflam; full of hops; maunder; muck; nonsense; punk; ramble in one's speech; rave; ravings; rigmarole; shoot off one's mouth; shoot the bull; sling the bull; speak at a venture; talk foolishly; talk through one's hat; talk wildly; throw the bull; wander in one's speech; wander in one's talk; wanderings;
一派胡言 a bunch of malarkey; a load of codswallop; a load of hogwash; a load of rubbish; a lot of eyewash; a lot of malarkey; a pack of lies; a pack of nonsense; complete nonsense; gross nonsense; sheer rubbish;

[胡謅] cook up; fabricate wild tales;
信口胡謅 fabricate wild tales; speak thoughtlessly; speak wildly; talk at random; talk nonsense; talk recklessly;

二胡 erhu, a bowed two-stringed instrument;
高胡 two-stringed instrument;
京胡 Beijing opera fiddle;

hu

【斛】 (1) dry measure 10 or 5 times that of 斗; (2) a surname;

hu

【壺】 jug; pot; wine-vessel; (2) any potbellied container with a small opening; (3) surname;

[壺腹] ampulla;
壺腹癌 ampullary carcinoma;
壺腹炎 ampullitis;
壺腹周癌 periampullary carcinoma;
便壺 bed urinal; chamber pot; night-pot for urination;
茶壺 teapot;
醋壺 vinegar pot;
咖啡壺 coffee pot;
漏壺 clepsydra; hourglass; water clock;
暖壺 thermos bottle; thermos flask;
噴壺 sprinkling can; watering can;
水壺 (1) kettle; (2) canteen; (3) watering can;
湯壺 vacuum flask;
懸壺 practise medicine;
夜壺 chamber pot;
油壺 oilcan; oiler;

hu

【湖】 lake; lough;
[湖岸淺灘] shoal lake;
[湖濱] beside the lake; lakeside; shore of a lake;
[湖冰] lake ice;
[湖風] lake breeze;
[湖港] lake port;
[湖海] lakes and seas;
湖海之士 person with a great mind;
五湖四海 all corners of the country; every corner of the country; everywhere in the world;
[湖面] lake surface;
湖面如鏡 the smooth surface of the lake is like a mirror; the surface of the lake is tranquil like a mirror;
[湖泥] lake mud;
[湖畔] beside the lake; lakeside;
[湖泊] lakes;
[湖區] lake district;
[湖山] lakes and mountains;
湖山秀色 the beauty of lakes and mountains;
湖光山色 a landscape of lakes and mountains; the natural beauty of lakes and mountains;
湖光山影 the mountains are reflected in the lake; the still water of the lake mirrors the mountains;
[湖水] lake water;
[湖心] middle of a lake;
[湖煙] mist on a lake;
[湖澤] lakes and marshes;
[湖沼] lakes and marshes;
淡水湖 freshwater lake;
低鹽湖 brackish lake;
斷層湖 fault lake;
火口湖 crater lake;
江湖 (1) rivers and lakes; (2) all corners of the country;
苦湖 bitter lake;
內陸湖 interior lake;
人工湖 man-made lake;
鹹水湖 saline lake; salt lake;
瀉湖 lagoon;
鹽湖 salt lake;

hu

【猢】 monkey;
[猢猻] macaque;
猢猻屁股—坐不住 a macaque's bottom — can't sit still; hyperactive;
猢猻入布袋 submit to discipline reluctantly — the ape goes into the pocket — lose one's freedom;
猢猻王 king of the monkeys;
樹倒猢猻散 once the tree falls, the monkeys on it flee helter-skelter — when the chief falls from fortune, his followers disperse all at once; rats desert a falling house; rats leave a sinking ship; when a tree comes down, all the monkeys on it disperse; when the tree falls, the monkeys scatter — when the boss falls from power, his lackeys disperse;

hu

【瑚】 (1) person of virtue and quality; (2) coral;
[瑚璉] vessels of grain at ancestral temples;

hu

【葫】 bottle gourd; calabash;
[葫蘆] bottle gourd; calabash;
沒嘴的葫蘆 one who is not gifted in tongue;
悶葫蘆 (1) enigma; puzzle; riddle; sealed book; (2) bewilderment;
~打悶葫蘆 be thrown into bewilderment; guess sb's riddles; puzzle one's head over sb's silly riddles;
~悶嘴葫蘆 silent person;

水裏的葫蘆－兩邊擺 a calabash shell in water sways in every direction;
依樣畫葫蘆 ape others; copy mechanically; follow others' example; follow suit; imitate; mimic; mimicry; slavish imitation; stick closely to the pattern given;
油葫蘆 fat person;
照葫蘆畫瓢 draw a dipper with a gourd as a model － copy; imitate;

[葫蔓藤] graceful jesamine;
[葫蒜] garlic poison hemlock;

hu

【煳】 burnt;

hu

【糊】 (1) be burnt; be singed; (2) paste;
[糊口] eke out a living; make a living to feed the family;
糊口謀生 eke out the barest of livings; make a living;
糊口之道 means to live by;
僅以糊口 live from hand to mouth;
勉強糊口 hand-to-mouth; live from hand to mouth; scrape by;
[糊弄] (1) cheat; deceive; fool; (2) do sth lackadaisically; go through the motions;
[糊塗] bewildered; confused; muddled;
糊塗蟲 addle-brained; airhead; nitwit;
糊塗東西 fool; idiot;
糊塗了事 finish a job carelessly; wind up a case carelessly;
糊塗一世 dream away one's life;
糊塗一時 every man has a fool in his sleeve;
搞糊塗了 get confused;
糊裏糊塗 act stupidly; bewildered; in disorderly fashion; mixed-up; muddle-headed; puzzled;
老糊塗 dotard;
頭腦糊塗 be confused in mind;
稀里糊塗 not know what one is about; muddle-headed; unwitting;
一時糊塗 in a moment of aberration; suddenly take leave of one's sense;
一塌糊塗 a fine kettle of fish; a hell of a mass; a mess of; a fine kettle of fish; a nice kettle of fish; a pretty kettle of fish; here's the very devil to pay; in a complete mess; in a great mess; in a muddle; in an awful state; in utter disorder; it is complete chaos; make a pig's ear out of; topsy-turvy;
～搞得一塌糊塗 make a mess of sth; muddle sth together;
裝糊塗 feign ignorance; play the fool; pretend not to know;

裱糊 paste paper on;
眵目糊 caking of eye secretion;

hu

【蝴】 butterfly;
[蝴蝶] butterfly;
蝴蝶穿花 butterflies are flitting through the flowers;
蝴蝶結 bowknot;
蝴蝶雙飛 two butterflies are flapping in the wind;
一群蝴蝶 a cluster of butterflies; a swarm of butterflies;

hu

【槲】 a species of oak;
[槲鶇] missel thrush; mistle thrush;
[槲實] acorn;

hu

【衚】 lane; side street; sublane;
[衚衕] alley; lane;

hu

【縠】 crepe;

hu

【醐】 as in 醍醐, clarified butter;

hu

【斛】 (1) a measure for volume in ancient time; (2) barren; poor;
[斛觫] trembling from fear;

hu

【餬】 (1) congee; gruel; porridge; (2) paste;
[餬口] eke out one's living; keep body and soul together;

hu

【鵠】 target;
[鵠待] attend to sb respectfully;
[鵠髮] gray hair; white hair;
[鵠候] await respectfully;
[鵠立] be on the lookout for;
[鵠面鳩形] emaciated from hunger; haggard;
[鵠望] eagerly look forward to;

hu

【鬍】 beard;

[鬍刷] shaving brush;
[鬍鬚] beard; beard and moustache; moustache;
鬍鬚花白 have a grizzled beard;
鬍鬚結霜 one's beard frosts in the piercing winter wind;
鬍鬚滿腮 whiskers cover one's cheeks;
留着鬍鬚 keep a moustache;
翹八字鬍鬚 handlebar moustache;
修剪鬍鬚 clip one's beard;
[鬍子] beard;
鬍子拉碴的 much-bearded;
鬍子沾屎—開不得口 a beard sticky with dung — can't open one's mouth;
吹鬍子瞪眼睛 blow a fuse; blow a gasket; fall into a rage; foam with rage; froth at the mouth and glare with rage; scowl and growl; snort and stare in anger;
大鬍子 (1) full beard; long beard; (2) heavily-bearded man;
刮鬍子 shave;
黑鬍子 dark beard;
灰白鬍子 gray beard;
假鬍子 false beard;
捋鬍子 stroke one's beard;
連鬢鬍子 full beard;
留鬍子 grow a beard; wear a beard;
絡腮鬍子 whiskers;
濃而短的鬍子 thick and short beard;
山羊鬍子 goatee;
小鬍子 moustache;
~剃去小鬍子 shave off one's moustache;
羊排絡腮鬍子 mutton chop whiskers;
一撇鬍子 a moustache;
長鬍子 grow a beard;

八字鬍 a pair of moustaches;

hu

【鶘】 pelican;

hu

【鶻】 a kind of bird of prey;
[鶻突] bewildered; confused; muddled;
鶻突而來 pounce down like a hawk;

hu³

hu

【虎】 (1) tiger; (2) brave; vigorous;
[虎背熊腰] boxer's sinuous posture; of a stocky and imposing build; strong as a bear in the hips and with a back supple as a tiger's strapping; thick, powerful back and shoulders; tiger-backed and bear-loined—stalwart;
[虎賁] brave and strong man; brave warrior;
[虎步] a great warrior's firm strides like the tiger's;
虎步龍驤 walk like a tiger and prance like a dragon;
[虎膽] as brave as a tiger;
[虎毒不食子] all men, good or bad, rarely illtreat their own children; even a vicious tiger would not eat its cubs — no one is capable of hurting his own children;
[虎而冠者] cruel person who borrows power from another is like a dressed-up tiger;
[虎骨] tiger-bone;
虎骨酒 tiger-bone liquor;
[虎將] brave general;
[虎勁] dash; dauntless drive;
[虎鯨] killer whale;
[虎口] (1) a tiger's mouth; jaws of death; (2) the part of the hand between the thumb and the index finger;
虎口拔牙 pull a front tooth from the jaw of the tiger — provoke sb who is far superior in power; pull a tooth from the tiger's mouth — to dare the greatest danger;
虎口奪食 snatch food from the jaws of a tiger;
虎口捋鬚 pull the tiger's whiskers;
虎口覓食 be engaged in a hazardous task; snatch food from the tiger's mouth;
虎口餘生 be snatched from the jaws of death; escape by the skin of one's teeth; escape from a very dangerous situation; escape from the tiger's jaws; escape narrowly from danger; have a hairbreadth escape; out of the jaws of death; survive a disaster;
逃出虎口 escape from a dangerous situation; escape from a tiger's mouth;
羊落虎口 the sheep falls into the tiger's mouth — be in a hopeless situation;
羊入虎口 a sheep in a tiger's mouth;
[虎狼] tigers and wolves;
虎狼成性 wolfish disposition;
虎狼在前 with the wolf and tiger

confronting us;
虎狼之國 nation of savages;
虎狼之性 a tiger-like, wolfish disposition; beastly nature; violent nature; voracious;
餓如虎狼 hungry as a hawk;
虎窟狼窩 a nest of tigers and wolves;
拒狼防虎 guard against a tiger while repelling the wolf;
前怕狼，後怕虎 anxious about a possible wolf in front and a possible tiger behind; be reduced to inaction by overcaution; fear the wolf in front and the tiger behind; in constant fear of wolves ahead and tigers behind — full of misgivings;
前有狼，後有虎—進退維谷 with a wolf ahead and a tiger behind — in a dilemma;

[虎鹿不同行] tigers and deer do not walk together;

[虎落平陽] tigers come down to the plain;
虎落平陽被犬欺 a tiger down on the plain is set at naught by a dog; hares may pull dead lions by the beard; if the tiger went down to level land, it would be insulted by dogs — a person who loses position and influence may be subjected to much indignity;

[虎門無犬種] everyone is brave in a general's family; you won't find a puppy in a tiger's den;

[虎皮] tiger skin;
虎皮鸚鵡 budgerygan;
虎死留皮 a tiger leaves its skin behind;
拉大旗作虎皮 drape oneself in a flag to impress people; hoist a banner such as the tiger's skin to intimidate others; ride on sb's coat-tails; use the great banner as a tiger skin — deck oneself out and intimidate people;
驢蒙虎皮 a donkey in a tiger's skin — frighten people; empty show of strength;
羊質虎皮 a sheep in a tiger's skin — a dressed-up weakling; outwardly strong but inwardly weak;

[虎鉗] jaw vice; vice;
活塞虎鉗 piston vice;
平行虎鉗 parallel vice;
台虎鉗 leg vice;

[虎石蛇杯] imaginary fear;

[虎士] brave warrior;

[虎視眈眈] cast covetous eyes on; eye covetously; glare like a tiger eyeing its prey; with a covetous look;

[虎視鷹瞵] strong powers are waiting on all sides;

[虎體熊腰] lithe and yet powerfully built;

[虎頭] tiger's head;
虎頭虎腦 looking dignified and strong;
虎頭拍蠅 beat a fly on the head of a tiger — unwise provocation, very daring;
虎頭蛇尾 a brave beginning and weak ending; a tiger's head and a snake's tail; begin well but fall off towards the close; begin with tigerish energy but peter out towards the end; come out at the small end of the horn; fine start and poor finish; in like a lion, out like a lamb; start out well but not continue; with a fine start but a poor finish;
虎頭抓蒼蠅 catch flies on the tiger's head — unwise provocation;
虎頭捉虱 catch lice on a tiger's head — unwise provocation; louse on a tiger's head — be in a precarious position;
搔虎頭，弄虎鬚 offend the mighty and powerful;

[虎威] the frightful appearance of a tiger;
狐假虎威 a donkey in a lion's hide; a fly sits upon the axletree of the chariot-wheel and says "what a dust do I raise!"; a fox putting on tiger's skin — a man assuming self-importance by his connections; an ass in a lion's skin; assume someone else's authority as one's own; assume the dignity of another; browbeat others by virtue of others' position; jack-in-office; lion's skin; rely on one's master's might to bully others; take advantage of the influence of others; take advantage to someone else's power to throw one's weight about; the fox assumes the majesty of the tiger — rely on someone else's power to bully people; the fox "borrowing" the awe of the tiger; the fox borrows the tiger's fierceness — to swagger about in borrowed plumes; the fox borrows the tiger's terror — to bully people by

flaunting one's powerful connections; the fox makes himself feared by walking in tiger's company – to assume someone else's authority to bowbeat others;

[虎尾] tiger's tail;
虎尾春冰 in a precarious position; like treading on a tiger's tail or on spring ice – very cautious;
若蹈虎尾 like treading on a tiger's tail; very dangerous;

[虎嘯] tigers roar;
虎嘯風生 great men appear in response to the call of the times; tigers howl with the rise of winds;
虎嘯狼嗥 the roar of tigers and the howls of wolves; the tigers roar and the wolves howl;
虎嘯龍吟 roars of dragons and tigers;
虎嘯猿啼 tigers roar and monkeys yell;

[虎鬚] tiger's whiskers;
虎頷捋鬚 pluck the tiger's whiskers – do sth to offend the powerful;
捋虎鬚 offend the powerful; pluck the tiger's whiskers;

[虎穴] tiger's den;
虎穴除奸 enter the enemy's territory and killed the traitor;
虎穴狼窩 tiger's den;
虎穴龍潭 tiger's den and dragon's lair – a dangerous spot; the tiger's den and the dragon's liar – a hazardous spot;
虎穴追蹤 track the tiger to its den;
不入虎穴，焉得虎子 he who would search for pearls must dive below; how can you catch tiger cubs without entering the tiger's lair; if one does not dare to enter the tiger's lair, how can one obtain tiger cubs; nothing is achieved without effort; nothing venture, nothing gain;
才脱虎穴，又入龍潭 from one danger into a greater danger; from the smoke into the smother; jump out of the frying pan into the fire; misfortunes never come alone; one misfortune comes on the neck of another;
勉從虎穴 constrain oneself to lodge in the tiger's lair;

艾虎 fitch;
壁虎 gecko; house lizard;
燈虎 lantern riddles;
蜂虎 bee-eater;
老虎 tiger;
母虎 tigress;
貔虎 bold and powerful troops;
騎虎 ride on a tiger's back;
如虎 like a tiger;
獅虎 lions and tigers;
詩虎 riddles in poetry form;
為虎 assist the tiger;
文虎 lantern riddles;
笑面虎 a friendly-looking villain; a smiling tiger – an outwardly kind but inwardly cruel person; a tiger with a smiling face – a wicked person with a hypocritical smile; a treacherous fellow; a wolf in sheep's clothing;
蝎虎 gecko; house lizard;
臙脂虎 shrew;
與虎 with the tiger;
縱虎 let loose a tiger;

hu

【唬】 (1) intimidate; scare; (2) roar of a tiger;

[唬人] bluff; cheat; deceive;

嚇唬 frighten; intimidate; scare;

hu

【琥】 (1) jade ornament in the shape of a tiger; (2) amber;

[琥珀] amber; lynx stone;
琥珀耳環 amber earrings;
琥珀色 amber;
人造琥珀 amberoid;

hu

【滸】 (1) watergate; (2) shore;

hu⁴

hu

【互】 each other; mutual;

[互補] complement each other; complementation; supplement each other;
互補詞 complementary;
互補分布 complementary distribution;
互補性 complementarity;
互補原則 complementarism;
基因間互補 interallelic complentation;
順反子內互補 intracistron complementation;

線粒體互補 mitochondrial complementation;
隱性互補 recessive complementarity;

［互參］ coreference;
互參規則 rule of coreference;

［互動］ interactive;
互動分析 interaction analysis;
互動系統模式 interaction system model;
互動作用體系 interaction system;

［互訪］ exchange visits;

［互…互…］ each other; mutual;
互幫互學 help each other and learn from each other;
互敬互惠 mutual respect and mutual benefit;
互諒互讓 mutual understanding and mutual accommodation; two-way street;
互勉互助 encourage and help each other;

［互換］ interchange; mutual exchange;
互換俘虜 exchange prisoners;
互換禮物 exchange gifts;
互換名片 exchange cards;
互換性 interchangeability;
~ 尺寸互換性 dimensional interchangeability;
~ 磁帶互換性 tape interchangeability;
~ 功能互換性 functional interchangeability;
~ 燃料互換性 interchangeability of fuels;
~ 選擇互換性 selective interchangeability;
互換座位 exchange seats;

［互惠］ mutually beneficial; reciprocal;
互惠關税 reciprocal tariff;
互惠合作 cooperate to obtain mutual benefits; mutual benefit and collaboration;
互惠貿易 reciprocal trade;
互惠許可合同 cross-licence;

［互忌］ jealous of each other;

［互利］ mutually beneficial; of mutual benefit;
互利共贏 mutually beneficial;
互利合作 mutually beneficial cooperation;
互利互惠 mutual benefit and reciprocity;

［互聯］ interconnect;

［互讓］ make mutual accommodation;

［互相］ mutual; each other; hand in glove with;
互相愛慕 mutual love and admiration;
互相包庇 shield each other;
互相標榜 boost each other; exchange excessive praise; praise each other in public; put up placards for each other; scratch one another's backs; mutual admiration and eulogy;
互相殘殺 cut each other's throats;
互相拆台 undermine each other's work;
互相扯皮 argue back and forth over trifles; buck-passing; endless disputes over trifles; engage in endless haggling and buck-passing; engage in endless haggling and shifts of responsibility;
互相仇視 regard each other as enemies;
互相促進 help each other forward;
互相吹捧 flatter each other;
互相抵觸 contradict each other;
互相砥礪 encourage each other;
互相對照 check one against another;
互相攻擊 run foul of each other;
互相勾結 act in collusion; work hand and glove with each other;
互相貫通 interpenetrate;
互相呼應 take concerted action;
互相輝映 add radiance and beauty to each other; add splendour to each other; increase the brilliant display; shine by reflected glory;
互相激勵 interanimation;
互相監督 mutual supervision;
互相交換 intercourse;
互相介紹 introduce each other;
互相敬愛 mutually respect and love;
互相利用 each using the other for their own ends;
互相謾罵 slanting match;
互相埋怨 blame one another;
互相勉勵 encourage each other;
互相排斥 mutual exclusion; mutual repulsion;
互相配合 work in coordination;
互相捧場 cheer each other;
互相遷就 give in to each other; mutually make a compromise;
互相牽連 interrelated; involve each other;
互相牽累 drag in one another; implicate each other; involve each other;
互相牽制 hold each other up;
互相切磋 improve each other by active discussion;
互相傾心 become greatly attached to each other;
互相傾軋 fight each other for power;
互相讓步 give and take;

互相滲透 interpenetrate;
互相適應 co-adaptation;
互相痛恨 hate each other like poison;
互相推諉 make excuses to each other;
互相信賴 mutual trust;
互相揖讓 bow to each other complaisantly;
互相依存 depend on each other for their existence;
互相印證 corroborate each other;
互相制約 condition each other; interact; mutual conditioning;
互相掣肘 hold each other back;
互相轉化 mutual transformation;
互相尊重 think highly of each other;

［互爭雄長］ fight for hegemony; fight for leadership;

［互助］ cooperation; help each other; mutual aid;
互助合作 mutual aid and cooperation;
互助互讓 help each other and make mutual concessions;
互助會 friendly society;

交互 (1) each other; mutually; (2) alternately;
相互 each other; mutual; reciprocal;

hu

【戶】 (1) door; (2) family; household; (3) account; (4) family status;

［戶告人曉］ every family circulates and everyone knows;

［戶籍］ (1) census register; household register; (2) one's registered permanent residence;

［戶口］ (1) number of households; (2) one's registered permanent residence;
報戶口 apply for a residence permit;

［戶名］ name in an account book;

［戶內］ indoor;
戶內學習 indoor activity;
戶內運動 indoor games;

［戶樞］ door hinge; door pivot;

［戶外］ outdoors;
在戶外 in the open;

［戶限］ threshold;
戶限為穿 a threshold worn low by visitors — an endless flow of visitors; even the threhold is spoilt — have many visitors; the threshold is bored through — numerous guests or customers;

［戶牖］ door; doors and windows;

［戶政］ administration concerning residents and residency;

［戶主］ head of a household;

挨戶 from door to door; from family to family; from house to house; from one house to another;
閉戶 close the door;
窗戶 casement; window;
儲戶 depositor;
船戶 boatman; one who owns a boat and makes a living as a boatman;
存戶 depositor;
佃戶 tenant farmer;
訂戶 subscriber;
開戶 open an account;
獵戶 hunter; huntsman;
門戶 (1) door; (2) gateway; important passageway; (3) faction; sect; (4) family status;
農戶 peasant household;
棚戶 slum dwellers; shack dwellers;
鋪戶 shop;
欠戶 debtor;
屠戶 butcher;
小戶 (1) small family; (2) family of limited means and without powerful connections;
雁戶 wanderer;
業戶 owner of property;
陰戶 female reproductive organ; vagina;
用戶 consumer; user;
牖戶 window and door;
債戶 debtor;
賬戶 bank account;
珠戶 pearl divers;
住戶 household; resident;
莊戶 farmer; peasant household;
租戶 (1) tenant; (2) hirer;

hu

【怙】 (1) presume on; rely on; (2) one's father;

［怙惡不悛］ irreclaimable; persist in evil and not repent; remain impenitent; steeped in evil and refuse to repent;

［怙惡淩人］ intimidate and oppress others;

hu

【戽】 bucket; pail;

［戽斗］ bailing bucket; bucket;

［戽索］ bucket rig;

風戽 pneumatic bailer;

hu
【祜】 blessing;

hu
【笏】 tablet held by a civil official during an audience with the monarch;
[笏石英] sceptre-quartz;

hu
【扈】 (1) follow as escort or retinue; (2) impertinent; insolent;
[扈從] retainer; retinue; suite;
跋扈 bossy; bullying; domineering;

hu
【瓠】 calabash; gourd;
[瓠果] pepo;
[瓠犀] melon seed;
[瓠子] a kind of edible gourd;

hu
【楛】 (1) crude and easy to break; (2) name of a plant;

hu
【滬】 alternative name of Shanghai;
[滬劇] Shanghai opera;

hu
【護】 (1) guard; protect; shield; (2) partial to; shield from censure;
[護岸] bank protection;
[護臂] armguard; bracer;
[護庇] cover up; shelter;
[護兵] military guards;
[護城壕溝] moat;
[護城河] city moat; moat;
[護持] shield and sustain;
[護短] conceal one's faults; cover one's mistakes; side with a disputant who is in the wrong;
[護耳] ear flaps; earmuffs;
[護航] convoy; escort;
護航艦 frigate;
[護己] defend oneself;
[護駕] escort the emperor;
[護欄] guard rail; side barrier;
防撞護欄 guard rail;
[護理] care; nurse; nursing; tend and protect;
護理部 nursing department;
~護理部主任 nursing department;
護理工作 nursing;
護理員 assistant nurse; caregiver; care worker; orderly;
護理院 care home; residential home;
保健護理 health care;
~初級保健護理 primary care; primary health care;
產後護理 postnatal care;
產前護理 prenatal care;
精心護理 nurse with the best of care;
面部護理 facial;
~緊膚排毒面部護理 firming and deterring facial;
~抗壓面部護理 anti-stress facial;
~男士面部護理 facial for men;
~香薰面部護理 aroma facial;
面部美白護理 whitening facial treatment;
奶鹽護理 milk salt scrub;
皮膚護理 skincare;
上門護理 home service care;
手部護理 hand care;
術後護理 post-operative care;
塑身角質護理 exfoliating body scrub;
住院護理 residential care;
[護籠] cage;
安全護籠 safety cage;
[護膜] cuticle;
[護目鏡] goggles; protective goggles; safety goggles;
安全護目鏡 safety goggles;
[護目罩] eye guard; eye shield; head shield;
[護身] protect one's body;
護身法寶 protective talisman;
護身符 (1) amulet; protective talisman; (2) person that protects one from punishment or censure; shield;
[護士] nurse;
護士長 charge nurse; head nurse; sister;
~病房護士長 ward sister;
病房護士 ward nurse;
從業護士 nurse practitioner;
當護士 work as a nurse;
高級護士 senior nurse;
精神病院護士 psychiatric nurse;
男護士 male nurse;
日班護士 day nurse;
社區護士 community nurse; district nurse;
實習護士 student nurse;
手術室護士 operating theatre nurse;
夜班護士 night nurse;

助理護士 assist nurse;
~ 手術助理護士 scrub nurse;

[護手] handguard; hand protector;

[護送] convoy; escort;

[護腿] boothose; gaiter; legging; shin guard;

[護腕] armguard; bracer; wrister; wrist guard;

[護衛] guard; protect;
護衛艦 frigate;

[護膝] kneecap; patella;

[護胸] chest plate; chest protector;
護胸甲 breastplate;

[護養] (1) cultivate; nurse; (2) maintain;

[護運] ship sth under guard;

[護罩] shroud;
氣球護罩 balloon shroud;

[護照] passport;
護照持有人 passport holder;
護照檢查 passport inspection;
~ 護照檢查處 passport control;
護照申請 passport application;
護照照片 passport photo;
更新護照 renew one's passport;
公務護照 service passport;
官員護照 official passport;
假護照 fake passport; false passport; forged passport;
拿到護照 get a passport; obtain a passport;
取得護照 get one's passport;
申請護照 apply for a passport;
特別護照 special passport;
外交護照 diplomatic passport;
一本護照 a passport;

[護柱] bollard; post;

愛護 care; cherish; give kind protection to; protect; safeguard; show genuine affection for; take good care of; treasure;

保護 (1) guard; protect; (2) conservation; conserve; preserve;

庇護 protect; put under one's protection; shelter; shield; take under one's wing; under the aegis of;

蔽護 protect; shelter; take cover;

辯護 (1) argue in favour of; speak in defence of; (2) (of a lawyer) defend a case in court;

防護 protect; shelter;

呵護 bless and protect;

回護 cover up; harbour; shield;

監護 place sb under guardianship;

救護 give first aid; relieve a sick or injured person; rescue;

看護 look after; nurse;

偏護 be partial to and side with;

守護 defend; guard;

袒護 be partial to; give unprincipled protection to; shield from censure;

調護 nurse;

維護 defend; safeguard; uphold;

衛護 guard; protect; safeguard;

掩護 camouflage; cover; screen; shield;

養護 conserve; maintain;

醫護 health care;

翼護 shelter and protect;

擁護 endorse; support; uphold;

照護 attend; look after; nurse; tend;

hua¹
hua

【花】 (1) bloom; blossom; flower; (2) anything resembling a flower; (3) design; pattern; (4) coloured; multicoloured; variegated; (5) blurred; dim; (6) cotton; (7) smallpox; (8) wound; (9) bleed sb dry; expend; spend; (10) fancy; flowery; showy; (11) lecherous; randy; (12) fireworks; (13) a surname;

[花白] gray; grizzled;
變花白 change to gray;

[花斑斑] flowery;

[花瓣] leaf; petal;
花瓣兒式 (of hairstyle) petal style;
一片花瓣 a petal;

[花苞] bud;

[花邊] (1) decorative border; (2) lace; (3) fancy borders in printing;
花邊新聞 box news; colour news; follow-up; titbits;
爛花花邊 burnt-out lace;
梭結花邊 bobbin lace;
蛛網花邊 arraignee lace;

[花布] cotton print; figured cloth; print;

[花不稜登] variegated;

[花彩] festoon;

[花草] flowers and plants;
拈花惹草 chase after loose women; dally with women; enjoy oneself with women; frequent houses of courtesans; have many love affairs; have promiscuous relations with women; sow one's wild oats;

琪花瑤草 blossoms and vegetation in the fairyland; jade-like flowers of the fairy land;
惹草拈花 have one love affair after another; have promiscuous relations with women; stir bushes and pick flowers — have a fancy for prostitutes;
閑花野草 disreputable women; promiscuous women;
閒花野草 promiscuous women;
遺花殘草 discarded flowers and trampled grass;
沾花惹草 fool around with women; promiscuous in sex relations;
[花茶] jasmine tea;
[花傳風信] flowers show the wind blows;
[花叢] flowering shrubs; flowers in clusters;
花叢穿蝶 butterflies flutter about among the flowers;
[花簇] inflorescence;
[花旦] female role in Chinese opera;
[花道] flower way;
[花燈] festive lantern;
[花癲] erotomania;
[花店] florist's shop; flower shop;
花店店員 florist;
花店主人 florist;
[花雕] high-grade Shaoxing wine;
[花緞] (1) brocade; (2) damask; (3) figured satin;
[花朵] flower; inflorescence;
[花萼] calyx;
[花房] garden house; glasshouse; greenhouse;
[花費] (1) cost; expend; spend; (2) money spent; expenditures; expenses;
花費金錢 expend money;
不必要的花費 unnecessary expenses;
不惜花費 spare no expense;
[花粉] pollen;
花粉計數 pollen count;
傳授花粉 pollinate;
[花崗石] granite;
[花崗岩] granite;
花崗岩精 granitic ichor
帶狀花崗岩 banded granite;
假花崗岩 bastard granite;
塊狀花崗岩 blocky granite;
雙雲母花崗岩 binary granite;
[花骨朵] flower bud;
[花冠] corolla;
不整齊花冠 irregular corolla;
重瓣花冠 multiple corolla;
蝶形花冠 papilionaceous corolla;
唇形花冠 labiate corolla;
合瓣花冠 gamopetalous corolla;
假面狀花冠 personate corolla;
周位花冠 perigynous corolla;
[花光] wipe out; bleed sb; bleed sb dry; bleed sb white;
[花果] flowers and fruit;
先花後果 blossom flowers first and bear fruits afterwards — first have daughters, then sons;
[花紅] crab apple;
花紅柳綠 a profusion of garden flowers; bright red blossoms and green willows; red flowers and green willow;
花紅樹 crab apple;
[花候] flowering season;
[花花綠綠] brightly coloured; in colour; colourful; garish; multicoloured; varicoloured;
[花花搭搭] diversified; varied;
[花環] floral hoop; garland; torse; wreath;
[花卉] (1) flowers and plants; (2) painting of flowers and plants in traditional Chinese style;
奇花異卉 exotic flowers and rare herbs; marvelous flowers and rare plants; rare flowers and grasses; strange flowers and grasses;
[花甲] cycle of sixty years;
年逾花甲 over sixty; past sixty years of age;
[花箋] fancy stationery;
[花匠] floriculturist; gardener;
[花轎] bridal sedan chair;
[花酒] dinner party with singsong girls;
吃花酒 drink and eat at a girlie restaurant;
[花開] flowers bloom;
花開並蒂 two flowers growing from the same base — symbol of marital luck;
花開不謝一長春 ever-blooming flowers — forever spring;
花開富貴 rich and honoured, being in full bloom;
花開花落 flowers bloom and fade;
花開堪析直須折，莫待無花空折枝 when flowers bloom and are worthy of picking, one must pick them; do not

wait until the branches are empty of flowers;

[花魁] (1) plum flower; winter plum; (2) the most popular courtesan;

[花籃] (1) basket of flowers; (2) gaily decorated basket;

[花蕾] flower bud;

[花裏胡哨] (1) garish; gaudy; in a gaudy dress; (2) showy; without solid worth;

[花臉] male character in Chinese opera with a painted face;

[花柳] (1) flowers and willows; (2) brothel; (3) prostitute; (4) venereal disease;

花柳病 venereal disease;

傍花隨柳 enjoy flowers on a spring outing;

傍柳隨花 prostitutes;

摧花拆柳 break a tree, climbing for flowers;

花嬌柳媚 flowers are charming and willows fascinating;

花街柳巷 disreputable quarter of the city; a red-light district; house of ill fame; stews;

花門柳戶 bagnio; bawdy house; bordellos; brothel; house of ill fame; house of prostitution;

花說柳說 speak false and sweet words;

花遮柳掩 evasive; hide oneself among flowers and willows; slip;

階柳庭花 the willow beside the steps and the flowers in the courtyard;

路柳墻花 harlots; indecent women; loose women picked up by men; prostitutes; singsong girls; street girls; women of easy virtue; women of the streets;

眠花宿柳 go whoring; use the services of prostitutes;

攀花折柳 injure flowers and willows – use the services of prostitutes;

庭柳階花 willows in the courtyard and flowers alongside the terrace steps;

尋花問柳 frequent brothels; frequent houses of courtesans; go about in the hope of finding girls; go round singsong houses; go to houses of professional gaiety; promiscuous in sex relations; rove among flowers and willows – visit houses of ill fame; seek carnal pleasure; spend one's time with prostitutes; take a step along the primrose path; visit brothels;

[花落] flowers fall;

花落人亡 the flowers fall and the maiden dies;

花落葉黃 the flowers fall off and the leaves turn yellow;

[花蜜] (1) honey; (2) nectar;

花中取蜜 extract honey from flowers;

[花苗] flower seedling;

[花木] flowers and trees;

花木掩映 be sheltered by trees and flowers;

繁花茂木 a lush growth of trees and grass;

攀花折木 break off flowers and branches;

奇花異木 exotic flowers and rare trees; rare flowers and uncommon trees;

異花奇木 rare flowers and trees;

移花接木 cheat by sleight of hand; graft and transplant; graft flowers on a tree – place a substitute by subterfuge; graft one twing on another – stealthily substitute one thing for another; graft the flower of one tree onto another – palm off the spurious for the genuine;

~移花接木，金蟬脫殼 escape running into danger only at the expense of other innocent people;

栽花植木 plant flowers and trees;

[花鳥] painting of flowers and birds in traditional Chinese style;

花鳥畫 flower-bird works;

[花農] flower grower;

[花牌] court card;

[花盆] flowerpot;

[花棚] flower stand;

[花瓶] flower vase; vase;

花瓶兒 pretty and coquettish woman;

一對花瓶 a pair of vases;

[花圃] flower nursery;

[花錢] spend; spend money;

花錢的人說了算 the person who pays the piper calls the tune;

花錢買氣 spend money only to get annoyed;

花錢似水 spend money like water;

避免花錢 avoid spending money;

很花錢 cost an arm and a leg; costly; expensive;

濫花錢 go to town;

亂花錢 spend money with abandon;

[花槍] trickery;

耍花槍 cheat; dishonest; perform a sleight of hand;

［花腔］ (1) coloratura; (2) florid ornamentation in Chinese opera singing; (3) guileful talk;

花腔音樂 coloratura;

耍花腔 speak guilefully;

［花青素］ (1) anthocyanidin; (2) cyaniding;

［花圈］ floral wreath; torse;

［花拳］ fancy boxing;

［花容］ woman's face;

花容失色 (said of a woman or girl) turn pale;

花容月貌 fair as a flower and beautiful as the moon — beautiful face of a woman; one's face is like flowers and one's features like the moon — said of a woman or maiden;

［花蕊］ (1) pistil; (2) stamen;

［花色］ (1) designs and colours; (2) a variety of designs;

花色繁多 a great variety; a wide selection of colours and designs;

花色品種 assortment; colours and patterns; variety of colours and designs; variety of designs and specifications;

花色齊備 have a rich assortment of goods;

花色入時 fashionable patterns;

花色素淨 pattern in quiet colours;

［花生］ earth chestnut; groundnut; peanut;

花生殼 peanut shell;

花生醬 peanut butter;

花生米 peanut kernel;

花生皮 peanut coat;

花生糖 peanut brittle;

花生油 peanut oil;

剝花生 shell peanuts;

帶殼花生 monkey nut;

烤花生 roasted peanut;

~一袋烤花生 a packet of roasted peanuts;

一把花生 a handful of groundnuts;

一粒花生 a peanut;

一捧花生 a double handful of peanuts;

［花市］ flower fair; flower market;

［花鼠］ chipmunk;

［花束］ bunch of flowers;

裝飾花束 corsage;

小花束 posy;

［花絲］ (1) filament (2) filigree;

［花壇］ flower bed;

一層花壇 a tier of flower beds;

［花廳］ drawing room; parlour;

［花頭］ artifice; fresh ideas; ruses; tricks;

［花團錦簇］ a carpet of flowers; a company of gorgeously dressed ladies; a conglomeration of splendid and beautiful things; a mass of rich silks and brocades—very ornamental; bouquets of flowers and piles of brocades—rich multicoloured decorations;

［花紋］ decorative pattern; figure;

花紋繁縟 variegated in pattern;

隆起花紋 raised flower pattern;

細條花紋 pinstripe;

自然花紋 natural pattern;

［花香］ fragrance of a flower;

花香撲鼻 the scent of flowers assails the nostrils;

花香郁馥 the flowers smell sweet;

風動花香 the scent of the flowers is wafting through the breeze;

風送花香 the breeze wafts the fresh scent of flowers; the fragrant perfume of the flowers are borne towards sb by the breeze;

室雅何須大，花香不在多 a clean chamber does not need to be large, the flowers can still provide scent even if they are few;

［花消］ (1) cost; expense; (2) commissions; taxes and levies;

［花形］ floral pattern;

花形圖案 floral pattern;

［花序］ inflorescence;

不定花序 adventitious inflorescence;

離心花序 centrifugal inflorescence;

上昇花序 ascending inflorescence;

腋生花序 axillary inflorescence;

有限花序 definite inflorescence;

［花絮］ interesting sidelights; titbits;

花花絮絮 (1) different sidelights; (2) muddled and ill-assorted; variegated;

［花樣］ (1) floral designs; models; patterns; varieties; (2) tricks;

花樣翻新 innovations in pattern; the same old thing in a new guise; the tricks vary;

花樣繁多 a great variety; of all shapes and

colours;
花樣滑冰 fancy skating;
花樣騎術賽 dressage;
百般花樣 resort to a hundred tricks;
搞花樣 play tricks;
起花樣 play tricks; resort to scheming;
耍花樣 use tricks;
耍新花樣 play new tricks;
玩花樣 cheat; play tricks;
小花樣 little stunt;

[花藥] anther;

[花藝] floriculture;

[花園] garden;
花園城市 garden city;
後花園 back garden;
前花園 front garden;
御花園 imperial garden; the emperor's garden;
走進花園 walk into the garden;

[花月] flowers and the moon;
閉月羞花 dazzling beauty;
花好月圓 blooming flowers and full moon — perfect conjugal bliss; the flowers are in full bloom and the moon is full;
花痕月影 the shadow of the moon and flowers;
花前月下 in front of the flowers and under the moon — ideal setting for a couple in love; under the moon and surrounded by flowers;
羞花閉月 so beautiful that causes the flower to blush and the moon to hide — an incomparable beauty;

[花展] flower show;

[花招] (1) flourish; (2) showy movement in Chinese martial art; (3) game; gimmick; hocus-pocus; legerdemain; sleight of hand trick;
廣告花招 advertising gimmick;
耍花招 manoeuvre; perform a sleight of hand; play tricks; trickish; try it on; up to one's tricks; up to sth;
~別耍花招 none of your games; none of your tricks;
玩花招 play tricks;
政治花招 political manoeuvre;

[花枝] flowering branches;
花枝輕曳 blossoming branches sway gently in the breeze;
花枝招展 as gaudy as a butterfly; as gaudy as a peacock; be gorgeously dressed; freshly made up and as pretty as a flower; like a bed of beautiful flowers;
掐花折枝 break off flowers from the stem;

[花鐘] floral clock;

[花種] flower seed;
外來花種 adventive flower seed;

[花燭] fancy candles lit in the bridal chamber at the wedding;
花燭夫妻 formally married couple;
花燭之喜 nuptial bliss;
花燭之夜 the wedding night;

[花柱] style;
頂生花柱 terminal style;
基生花柱 basilar style;
側生花柱 lateral style;

暗花 veiled design incised in porcelain or woven in fabric;
拗花 cull flowers;
白花 (1) white flower; (2) waste;
百合花 lily;
百花 all sorts of flowers;
刨花 wood shavings;
鉋花 wood shavings;
爆米花 popcorn; puffed rice;
壁花 wallflower;
補花 patchwork;
採花 pluck flowers;
菜花 (1) cauliflower; (2) rape flower;
殘花 withered flowers;
插花 arrange flowers; flower arrangement; flower arranging;
茶花 camellia;
長春花 periwinkle;
穿花 go through the flowers;
串花 (of crops) cross-breed; hybridize;
窗花 paper-decorations for windows;
春花 spring flowers;
葱花 chopped green onion;
燈花 snuff (of a candle wick);
荻花 reed flower;
雕花 carve patterns or designs on woodwork; carving;
發花 be dazzled; grow dim; grow haze; grow misty; see things in a blurr;
番紅花 crocus; crocus sativus; saffron;
翻花 magic flower;
繁花 blooming flowers;
飛花 flying flower;
鳳仙花 garden balsam;
鋼花 spray of molten steel;

掛花 be wounded in action;
光花 blink; brilliance; splendour;
桂花 sweet-scented osmanthus;
國花 national flower;
好花 good flower;
荷花 (1) lotus; (2) lotus flower;
紅花 safflower;
虹光花 rainbow shower;
蝴蝶花 fringed iris;
槐花 sophora flower;
黃花 (1) chrysanthemum; (2) day lily; (3) virgin;
謊花 fruitless flower;
火花 spark;
昏花 dim-sighted;
雞冠花 cockscomb;
假花 artificial flower;
薑花 gingerlily;
交際花 social butterfly;
澆花 water flowers;
金銀花 honeysuckle;
菊花 chrysanthemum;
絹花 silk flower;
開花 (1) bloom; blossom; (2) break apart; explode; (3) burst with joy; (4) rise; spring up;
看花 look at flowers;
刻花 engrave designs;
葵花 sunflower;
拉花 latte-art;
喇叭花 morning glory;
蠟花 snuff (of a candlewick);
蘭花 (1) orchid; (2) fragrant thoroughwort;
浪花 (1) spray; (2) specific phenomenon;
老花 presbyopia;
烙花 pyrography;
淚花 tears in one's eyes;
梨花 pear blossom;
禮花 fireworks display;
蓮花 (1) lotus; (2) lotus flower;
零花 pocket money; small amount of money for minor expenses;
鏤花 engrave designs;
蘆花 reed catkins;
落花 flower drop;
麻花 fried dough twist;
帽花 insignia on a cap;
玫瑰花 rose;
梅花 plum blossom;
棉花 cotton;
茉莉花 jasmine;
木花 wood chips;
盆花 potted flower;
牽牛花 morning glory;
絨花 velvet flowers;
如花 like a flower;
山花 mountain flower;
賞花 enjoy the sight of flowers;
生花 fresh flower;
蒔花 grow flowers;
霜花 frostwork;
貪花 indulge in carnal passion;
曇花 orchid cactus; broad-leaved epiphyllum;
唐花 hothouse flower;
桃花 peach blossom;
題花 title design;
天花 (1) smallpox; (2) ceiling;
挑花 cross-stitch work;
貼花 appliqué;
頭花 headdress flower;
五花 (1) streaky; (2) streaky pork;
鮮花 flower; fresh flower;
獻花 present a bouquet of flowers;
香花 (1) fragrant flower; (2) writings, artistic works, etc. that are beneficial to people;
校花 campus queen; queen of the college; school belle;
杏花 apricot blossoms;
胸花 boutonniere;
雄花 male flower; staminate flower;
繡花 do embroidery; embroider;
雪花 snow flake;
血花 spurt of blood;
軋花 cotton ginning;
煙花 firework;
鹽花 a pinch of salt;
眼花 have blurred vision; have dim eyesight;
楊花 poplar blossoms; poplar filaments;
養花 grow flower;
腰花 (1) scalloped pork; (2) lamb kidneys;
野花 wild flower;
一把花 a bunch of flowers;
一朵花 a flower;
一棵花 a flower;
一盆花 a pot of flowers;
一束花 a bunch of flowers;
一枝花 a flower;
一株花 a flower;
印花 stamp;
櫻花 cherry blossom; oriental cherry;
鶯花 prostitute;
迎春花 jasminum nudiflorum;
油花 blobs of fat;
魚花 (1) fish fry; (2) minnows;
育花 cultivate flowers;

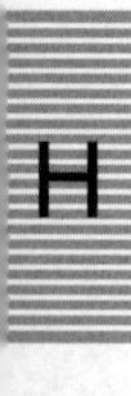

芫花 lilac daphne;
簪花 stick a flower on one's cap; wear a flower;
摘花 pluck flowers;
紙花 paper flower;
螽花 spikelet;
種花 cultivate flowers; grow flowers; raise flowers;
州花 state flower;
燭花 snuff (of a candle wick);
着花 blossom; flower;
紫花 lucerne;

hua

【華】 same as 花 , flowers;

hua

【嘩】 sound of a massive object falling to pieces;

[嘩啦] with a crash;
嘩啦一聲 with a thunderous noise;

hua²

hua

【划】 oar; row;

[划船] boating; go boating; paddle a boat; row a boat;
划船比賽 boat race;
划船運動 boating; rowing;
划船機 rowing machine;

[划得來] worthwhile;
划不來 not worthwhile;

[划手] oarsman;
女划手 oarswoman;

[划水] arm pull;

[划算] deserving; worthwhile;
在心裏划算 calculate mentally;

[划艇] (1) canoe; (2) rowboat;
划艇隊 rowing team;
划艇運動 canoeing;

[划行] paddle; row gently;

hua

【華】 (1) magnificent; splendid; (2) flourishing; prosperous; (3) best part; cream; (4) extravagant; flashy; (5) China; (6) Chinese; (7) corone;

[華燈] colourfully decorated lanterns; light;
華燈初上 when the evening lights are lit;

[華而不實] arty and crafty; flashy and without substance; have all one's goods in the window; have everything in the window; flashiness without substance; gewgaw; gimcrack; meretricious; pomposity; showy but not substantial;
華而不實的章句 purple passage; purple patch;

[華髮] gray hair;

[華貴] costly; gorgeous; luxurious; sumptuous;
雍容華貴 graceful and poised; regal;

[華麗] gorgeous; magnificent; resplendent;
華麗的詞藻 flowers of speech;
華麗的宮殿 gorgeous palace;
華麗臻美 beautiful and charming;
華麗奪目 (1) dazzling with resplendence; (2) glitter;
衣着華麗 dress colourfully;

[華僑] overseas Chinese;

[華人] Chinese;

[華氏] Fahrenheit;

[華文] Chinese;

[華夏] ancient name for China;

[華裔] foreign citizens of Chinese origin;

[華語] Chinese language;

[華冑] (1) descendants of a nobleman; (2) Chinese people; people of Chinese ancestry;

才華 literary or artistic talent;
繁華 bustling; flourishing; prosperous;
紛華 (1) rich and splendid; (2) glorious;
風華 elegance and talent; elegance and brilliance;
浮華 ostentatious; showy; vain;
光華 brilliance; splendour;
豪華 luxurious; sumptuous;
菁華 cream; quintessence;
精華 cream; essence; the best part;
硫華 sublimed sulphur;
年華 time; years;
凝華 sublimate;
榮華 glory, prosperity and a high position;
韶華 glorious youth;
奢華 extravagant; luxurious; sumptuous;
昇華 (1) sublimate; (2) distillate; raise things to a higher level;
瑤華 (1) blossoms as white and pure as jade; (2) precious; treasurable;
英華 (1) luxuriant beauty; (2) fame; glory; honour;
月華 (1) moonlight; (2) lunar corona;
中華 China;

hua

【滑】 (1) slippery; smooth; (2) slide; slip; (3) crafty; cunning;

［滑板］ skateboard; slide; slide board; slider;
滑板運動場地 skatepark;
倒滑滑板 fakie;
風箏滑板 kite boarding; kitesurfing;
回輪滑板 revolving slider;
炮身滑板 gun slide; pistol slide;
氣動滑板 air slide;
山地滑板 mountain board;
水上滑板 wakeboard;
遮光滑板 dark slide;

［滑冰］ ice-skating; skate; skating;
滑冰場 ice-skating rink; skating rink;
花樣滑冰 figure skating;
～單人花樣滑冰 single skating;
～雙人花樣滑冰 pair skating;
速度滑冰 speed skating;
自由式滑冰 free skating;

［滑車］ block; block and tackle; pulley; pulley block; tackle;
滑車組 burton;
～單滑車組 single burton;
～三併滑車組 tackle burton;
～雙滑車組 double Spanish burton;
滑車裝置 block and tackle;
差動滑車 differential tackle;
吊貨滑車 cargo block;
吊艇滑車 sailboat pulley;
翻身滑車 cant pulley;
複滑車 compound pulley;
固定滑車 fixed pulley;
滑動滑車 movable pulley;
減摩滑車 anti-friction block;
配重滑車 counterweight pulley;
起重滑車 gun tackle; hoisting tackle;
水平滑車 fleeting tackle;
移動滑車 movable tackle;
裝車滑車 loading tackle;

［滑道］ chute;

［滑動］ sliding;
滑動關稅 sliding duties;

［滑乎乎的］ slippery;

［滑稽］ (1) amusing; comical; funny; (2) comic talk;
滑稽可笑 absurd and ridiculous;
滑稽演員 comedian; funny man;
～女滑稽演員 comedienne; funny woman;
滑天下之大稽 be a laughing stock of the world; make a laughing stock of oneself; object of universal ridicule; the biggest joke in the world;

［滑溜］ slippery; smooth;
滑溜溜的 slippery; smooth;

［滑輪］ pulley;
安全滑輪 safety pulley;
固定滑輪 fixed pulley;
主動滑輪 feed pulley;

［滑跑］ skating;
彎道滑跑 curve skating;
直道滑跑 straight skating;

［滑坡］ (1) landslide; (2) go steadily downhill; slide downhill;

［滑潤］ lubricant; smooth; well-lubricated;

［滑石］ talc;
塊滑石 block talc; steatite talc;
雲母滑石 mica talc;

［滑鼠］ mouse;

［滑爽］ smooth and comfortable;

［滑水］ water ski;
滑水板 aquaplane;
滑水運動 water skiing;
風箏滑水 kite surfing;

［滑梯］ chute; slide;
螺旋滑梯 helter-skelter;
水上滑梯 water slide;

［滑頭］ (1) cunning person; fox; slippery person; sly person; (2) sly customer; (3) slick; slippery;
滑頭話 weasel word;
滑頭滑腦 artful; crafty; slick;
大滑頭 big operator;
老滑頭 old artful person;
耍滑頭 act in a slick way; at fast and loose; play fast and loose; try to shirk responsibility;
小滑頭 little fox; naughty urchin;

［滑翔］ glide;
滑翔機 aerodone; glider;
～滑翔機機場 gliderport;
～初級滑翔機 primary type glider;
～電動滑翔機 motor glider;
～高超音速滑翔機 hypersonic glider;
滑翔力學 aerodonetics;
滑翔運動 gliding;

［滑行］ coast; freewheel; freewheeling; slide;
滑行痕跡 skid mark;
風箏滑行 kite boarding; kitesurfing;
雙腳滑行 two-footed skating;
在冰上滑行 slide on ice;

［滑雪］ ski; skiing;

滑雪板 ski;
~一副滑雪板 a pair of skis;
滑雪鏡 ski goggles;
滑雪坡 ski slope;
滑雪勝地 ski resort;
滑雪鞋 ski boots;
滑雪運動 skiing;
滑雪者 skier;
道外滑雪 off-piste skiing;
狗拉滑雪 skijoring;
滑降滑雪 downhill skiing;
去滑雪 go skiing;
速降滑雪 downhill skiing;
越野滑雪 cross-country skiing;
直升機滑雪 heli-skiing;

[滑移] glide; slip;
複滑移 multiple glide;
基礎面滑移 basal-plane slip;
離合器滑移 clutch slip;
錨定滑移 anchorage slip;
頻率滑移 frequency slip;
雙滑移 double glide;
彎曲滑移 flexural glide;
易滑移 easy glide;

打滑 slide; slip;
刁滑 artful; crafty; cunning;
光滑 glossy; sleek; smooth;
狡滑 cunning; sly; tricky;
平滑 level and smooth; smooth;
潤滑 lubricate;
耍滑 act in a slick way;
油滑 foxy; slippery;
圓滑 slick and sly; smooth and evasive;

hua

【猾】 crafty; cunning; shrewd;

hua

【嘩】 clamour; hubbuh; uproar;

[嘩然] outcry; uproar;
舉座嘩然 the audience burst into an uproar;

hua

【劃】 (1) paddle; row gently; (2) cut the surface of; scratch; (3) to one's profit; (4) cross; erase;

[劃不來] it does not pay to do sth;

[劃掉] delete;

[劃痕] scratch;
一道劃痕 a scratch;

[劃破] lacerate;
被碎玻璃劃破 be lacerated by a broken glass;

hua

【譁】 clamour; noise;

[譁變] mutiny;
一場譁變 a mutiny;

[譁然] in an uproar; in commotion;
譁然起哄 rising up in an uproar;
舉國譁然 trigger a domestic outcry;
輿論嘩然 cause an uproar;

[譁笑] roar with laughter; uproarious laughter;

hua

【驊】 legendary fine horse;

[驊騮] famous horse;

hua⁴

hua

【化】 (1) change; transform; turn into; (2) convert; influence; (3) dissolve; melt; (4) digest; (5) burn up; (6) -ify; -ize;

[化除] dispel; eliminate; remove;

[化廢] turn waste materials into;
化廢為寶 change waste material into things of value; turn waste into assets; turn waste into useful things;
化廢為利 turn waste materials into sth useful;

[化糞池] septic tank;

[化工] chemical engineering; chemical industry;
化工廠 chemical plant;

[化害為利] turn a disadvantage into an advantage; turn harm into good;

[化合] chemical combination;
化合反應 combination reaction;
化合價 valence;
化合量 combining weight;
化合物 chemical compound;
~飽和化合物 saturated compound;
~不飽和化合物 unsaturated compound;
~芳族化合物 aromatic compound;
~高分子化合物 high molecular compound;
~加成化合物 addition; compound;
~金剛化合物 adamantine compound;
~離子化合物 ionic compound;
~兩性化合物 amphoteric compound;
~偶氮化合物 azo compound;
~碳環化合物 carbocyclic compound;
~碳水化合物 carbohydrate;

~無環化合物 acyclic compound;
~無機化合物 inorganic compound;
~無水化合物 anhydrous compound;
~吸水化合物 absorption compound;
~有機化合物 organic compound;
~人造有機化合物 man-made organic compound;
~有機金屬化合物 organometallic compound;
~雜環化合物 heterocyclic compound;
~脂肪族化合物 aliphatic compound;
~重氮化合物 diazo compound;

[化境] perfection; sublimity;

[化療] chemotherapy;

[化名] alias; false name; pass by the name of; pass under the name of; use an assumed name;
化名潛逃 change one's name and run away; flee under the name of;
使用化名 adopt a false name; take an alias;

[化募] collect alms;

[化身] embodiment; incarnate; incarnation;
仁慈的化身 embodiment of kindness;
智慧的化身 incarnation of wisdom;

[化石] fossil;
化石層 fossil bed;
化石學 palaeontology;
~植物化石學 phytopalaeontology
標準化石 index fossil; leading fossil;
化學化石 chemical fossil;
活化石 living fossil;
人類化石 human fossil;
植物化石 fossil plant;
指帶化石 zone fossil;
轉生化石 derived fossils;
踪迹化石 trace fossil;

[化痰] reduce phlegm;
消食化痰 eliminate indigestion and phlegm;

[化外] outer fringes of civilization;

[化險為夷] come safely out of danger; emerge safely out of danger; fall on one's feet; get out of the jaws of danger; land on one's feet; pass through a dangerous crisis safely; head off a disaster; save the situation; turn danger into safety; turn peril into safety;

[化學] chemistry;
化學變化 chemical change;
化學成份 chemical composition;
化學電離 chemical ionization;
化學雕版術 chemigraphy;
化學發光 chemiluminescence;
~電致化學發光 electrogenerated chemiluminescence;
化學反應 chemical reaction;
~化學反應式 chemical equation;
化學方程式 chemical equation;
化學分化 chemical differentiation; chemodifferentiation;
化學分解 chemical analysis; chemolysis;
化學分類學 chemotaxonomy;
化學分析 chemical analysis;
化學風化 chemical weathering;
化學符號 chemical symbol;
化學腐蝕凸板 chemigraph;
化學工程 chemical engineering;
~化學工程學 chemical engineering;
化學固化 chemical setting; chemosetting;
化學合成 chemical synthesis; chemosynthesis;
化學化 chemization;
化學計量學 chemical metrology; chemometrics;
化學家 chemist;
化學進化 chemical evolution; chemoevolution;
化學絕育劑 chemosterilant;
化學抗性 chemoresistance;
化學療法 chemotherapy;
~化學療法專家 chemotherapist;
化學化變學 chemorheology;
化學硫化 chemicure;
化學免疫學 chemoimmunology;
化學敏感性 chemosensitivity;
化學凝固法 chemocoagulation;
化學品 chemical;
~產生臭氣的化學品 odour-causing chemicals;
~有毒化學品 toxic chemicals;
化學平衡 chemical equilibrium;
化學熱力學 chemical thermodynamics;
化學蠕變 chemocreep;
化學殺菌作用 chemosterilization;
化學滲透作用 chemosmosis;
化學生態學 chemecology;
化學生物動力學 chemobiodynamics;
化學式 chemical formula;
化學受體 chemoreceptor;
~化學受體瘤 chemodectoma;
化學梯度 chemogradient;

化學天平 chemical balance;
化學外科 chemosurgery;
化學穩定器 chemostat;
化學武器 chemical weapon;
化學物 chemical;
~無機汞化學物 inorganic mercury chemicals;
~營養化學物 nutrient chemical;
~有機砷化學物 organoarsenic chemicals;
化學物理 chemical physics; chemisophysics;
~化學物理學 chemisophysics;
化學吸附 chemisorption;
~化學吸附劑 chemical sorbent;
~化學吸附作用 chemisorption;
化學吸收 chemisorption;
化學箱 chemistry set;
化學向性 chemotactism;
化學性質 chemical property;
化學儀器 chemical apparatuses;
化學誘變 chemomorphosis;
化學運動性 chemokinesis;
化學戰 chemical warfare;
~化學戰爭 chemical warfare;
化學質體 chemical plasmid;
化學治療藥 chemotherapeutant;
化學製版 chemitype;
化學專家系統 expert system of chemistry;
化學自養 chemautotrophy;
~化學自養菌 chemoautotgroph;
化學作用 chemical action; chemism;
表面化學 capillary chemistry; surface chemistry;
病理化學 pathological chemistry;
磁化學 magnetochemistry;
代謝化學 metabolic chemistry;
等離子體化學 plasma chemistry;
地球化學 geochemistry;
地外化學 extraterrestrial chemistry;
地質化學 geological chemistry;
電化學 electrochemistry;
動物化學 zoochemistry;
毒物化學 toxicological chemistry;
法醫化學 forensic chemistry;
發酵化學 fermentation chemistry;
仿生化學 biomimetic chemistry;
放射化學 radiation chemistry; radiochemistry; radiological chemistry;
分析化學 analytical chemistry;
~電分析化學 electroanalytical chemistry;
~光分析化學 photoanalytical chemistry;
輻射化學 radiation chemistry;
高分子化學 high polymer chemistry;
工程化學 engineering chemistry;
固體化學 solid chemistry;
~缺陷固體化學 defect solid chemistry;
光化學 actinic chemistry; actinochemistry; photochemistry;
光譜化學 spectrochemistry;
海洋化學 oceanographic chemistry;
航空化學 aerochemistry;
核化學 nuclear chemistry;
激發態化學 excited state chemistry;
激光化學 laser chemistry;
計算量子化學 computational quantum chemistry;
膠體化學 colloidal chemistry;
結構化學 structural chemistry;
晶體化學 crystal chemistry;
考古化學 archaeological chemistry;
礦物化學 mineralogical chemistry;
理論化學 pure chemistry; theoretical chemistry;
立體化學 space chemistry; spatial chemistry; stereochemistry;
量子化學 quantum chemistry;
酶化學 zymochemistry;
農業化學 agricultural chemistry; agrochemistry;
~農業化學加工學 chemurgy;
配位化學 coordination chemistry;
普通化學 general chemistry;
氣動熱化學 aerothermochemistry;
熱化學 thermochemistry;
熔鹽化學 fused salt chemistry;
森林化學 forest chemistry;
生理化學 chemophysiology; physiological chemistry;
生物化學 biochemistry; biological chemistry;
生物物理化學 biophysical chemistry;
石油化學 chemofining;
食品化學 food chemistry;
示蹤化學 tracer chemistry;
同位素化學 isotope chemistry;
土壤化學 soil chemistry;
衛生化學 hygienic chemistry; sanitary chemistry;
無機化學 abiochemistry; inorganic chemistry;
~生物無機化學 bio-inorganic chemistry;
無生化學 abiochemistry;
物理化學 physical chemistry;

~海洋物理化學 marine physical chemistry;
稀有元素化學 rare element chemistry;
冶金化學 metallurgical chemistry;
應用化學 applied chemistry; practical chemistry;
有機化學 organic chemistry;
有機金屬化學 organometallic chemistry;
宇宙化學 cosmochemistry
原子核化學 atom nuclear chemistry;
雜環化學 heterocyclic chemistry;
照相化學 photographic chemistry;
植物化學 vegetable chemistry;
重化學 heavy chemistry;
組織化學 histological chemistry;

[化驗] chemical examination; laboratory test; test;
化驗員 laboratory technician;

[化油器] carburetor;

[化緣] beg alms;

[化整為零] break up the whole into parts;
化零為整 assemble the parts into a whole; gather parts into a whole;

[化裝] (1) make up; (2) disguise oneself;
化裝服 fancy dress;
化裝師 make-up artist;
化裝室 dressing room;
化裝遊戲 dress-up; dressing-up;

[化妝] apply cosmetics; make up; put on make-up; wear make-up;
化妝間 powder room;
化妝鏡 dressing-table mirror;
化妝品 cosmetics;
~化妝品商店 cosmetics shop;
~浮液化妝品 emulsion cosmetic;
~含汞化妝品 mercury cosmetic;
~使用化妝品 use make-up;
~液質化妝品 beauty wash;
化妝師 make-up artist;
化妝術 beauty art;
化妝香水 beauty water;
化妝油彩 greasepaint;

氨化 ammoniate; ammoniation;
胺化 amination;
變化 change; vary;
春化 vernalize;
純化 purify;
惡化 deteriorate; worsen;
分化 become divided; break up; split up;
焚化 cremate; incinerate;
風化 decency; morals and manners;
副詞化 adverbialization;
腐化 (1) corrupt; degenerate; dissolute; (2) decay; rot;
鈣化 calcify;
感化 help sb change by education, persuasion, etc.;
骨化 ossify;
固化 solidify;
光化 actinic; photochemical;
歸化 (1) adopt the customs of; submit to the rule of; (2) be naturalized;
幻化 change and disappear;
磺化 sulfonation;
活化 activate;
火化 cremate;
機化 organize;
激化 become acute; intensify; sharpen;
極化 polarize;
簡化 simplify;
僵化 become rigid; ossify;
焦化 coke;
教化 help to change by education, persuasion, etc.;
進化 evolve;
淨化 purify;
開化 (1) become civilized; (2) thaw;
老化 age;
綠化 make a place green;
氯化 chlorinate; chlorination;
煤化 coalification;
美化 beautify; embellish; prettify;
名詞化 nominalization;
奴化 enslave;
歐化 Europeanize;
氣化 gasify;
汽化 vaporize;
強化 consolidate; intensify; strengthen;
氫化 hydrogenate;
氰化 cyanide;
全球化 globalization;
勸化 (1) urge sb to do good; (2) collect alms;
溶化 (1) dissolve; (2) fuse; melt;
融化 melt; thaw;
乳化 emulsify;
軟化 (1) soften; (2) win over by soft tactics; (3) bate;
燒化 (1) cremate; (2) burn;
深化 deepen;
神化 deify;
生化 biochemistry;
熟化 familiarize;

水化 hydrate;
酸化 acidize;
碳化 carbonize;
糖化 saccharify;
同化 assimilate;
退化 (1) degenerate; (2) deteriorate; retrograde;
蛻化 (1) exuviate; slough off; (2) degenerate;
文化 (1) civilization; culture; (2) education; schooling;
物化 die; pass away;
消化 digest;
硝化 nitration;
馴化 domesticate; tame;
衍化 develop; evolve;
演化 evolve;
氧化 oxidize;
異化 (1) alienate; (2) dissimilate;
硬化 harden;
轉化 change; transform;

hua

【畫】 (1) draw; paint; (2) painting; picture; (3) be decorated with paintings or pictures; (4) stroke;

［畫板］ drawing board;

［畫報］ illustrated magazine; pictorial;

［畫筆］ brush; painting brush;
畫筆敲鼓—有聲有色 beating a drum with a painting brush — full of sound and colour; vivid and dramatic;
一枝畫筆 a painting brush;

［畫餅］ (1) draw a cake; (2) titular;
盡成畫餅 fall to the ground; fruitless; in vain;
空成畫餅 but a sham;
終成畫餅 fall to the ground; result in failure;

［畫布］ canvas;
成形畫布 shaped canvas;
棉質油畫布 cotton canvas;

［畫冊］ picture album;
一本畫冊 a book of drawings;

［畫出］ draw up;

［畫地］ draw a circle on the ground;
畫地為牢 draw a circle on the ground as a house of detention for sb; draw a circle on the ground to serve as a prison — restrict sb's activities to a designated area;
畫地自限 impose a restriction on oneself;

［畫法］ brushwork; technique of drawing; technique of painting;

［畫舫］ painted pleasure boat;

［畫幅］ (1) painting; picture; (2) size of a picture;

［畫符］ draw magical characters;
畫符念咒 draw magical characters and recite incantations;

［畫稿］ (1) rough sketch; (2) endorse the draft of a document;

［畫工］ painter;

［畫鬼易，畫人難］ it is easier to paint a ghost than to paint a person;

［畫虎］ draw a tiger;
畫虎不成反類犬 try to draw a tiger and end up with the picture of a dog;
畫虎畫皮難畫骨 in drawing a tiger, you show its skin but not its bones; it is easy to draw a tiger's skin but hard to draw its bones; you may sketch a tiger's skin, but you cannot sketch its bones;
畫虎類犬 paint a tiger but result in the picture of a cub — to attempt sth overambitious and end in failure; set out to be tigers but end up as dogs — fail to achieve what one sets out to do; try to draw a tiger and end up with the picture of a dog — make a poor imitation;
照貓畫虎 draw a tiger with a cat as a model — copy sth without catching its spirit;

［畫家］ artist; painter;
壁畫家 muralist;
當代畫家 contemporary painter;
風景畫家 landscape painter; landscapist;
宮廷畫家 court painter;
廣告畫家 poster artist;
廣告牌畫家 sign painter;
海景畫家 marine painter;
流行藝術畫家 pop artist;
路邊畫家 sidewalk artist;
馬路畫家 pavement artist;
漫畫家 caricaturist; cartoonist;
色彩派畫家 colour painter;
未來派畫家 futurist painter;
寫實派畫家 realistic painter;
行動派畫家 action painter;
業餘畫家 spare-time artist; Sunday painter;
印象派畫家 impressionist painters;

油畫家 oil painter;
拙劣的畫家 daubster painter;

[畫架] easel;
輕便畫架 lightweight easel;
寫生畫架 sketching easel;

[畫匠] (1) artisan painter; (2) inferior painter;

[畫境] picturesque scene;
如入畫境 feel as though one were in a landscape painting;

[畫具] painter's paraphernalia;

[畫卷] picture scroll; scroll painting;

[畫刊] (1) pictorial section of a newspaper; (2) pictorial;

[畫框] frame;

[畫廊] (1) painted corridor; (2) art gallery; gallery; salon;

[畫龍] paint a dragon;
畫龍點睛 add an apt word to clinch the point; add an eyeball to the picture of a dragon – add the finishing touch; bring the painted dragon to life by putting in the pupils in its eyes – to add the touch that brings a work of art to life; put in the eyeballs in a painted dragon – add the critical touch; put the finishing touches on one's work; round off a picture;
畫龍畫虎難畫骨，知人知面不知心 in knowing a man, you may know his face, but not his heart; when painting a tiger, its skin is shown but its bones are not; when one paints a tiger, one paints its skin; it is difficult to paint its bones; when you know a person, you may know his face but not his heart;

[畫眉] babbling thrush;
山畫眉 song thrush;

[畫謎] picture puzzle;

[畫面] (1) general appearance of a picture; (2) frame;
畫面結構 composition of a picture; tableau composition;
暗淡的畫面 gloomy picture;

[畫皮] disguise of an evildoer; mask of an evildoer;

[畫片] picture postcard; printed picture;

[畫屏] painted screen;

[畫譜] book on the art of painting; picture copybook;

[畫蛇添足] add legs to one's sketch of a serpent–spoil sth by taking it to extremes; do sth superfluous; draw a snake and add feet to it–ruin the effect by adding sth superfluous; gild the lily; over-egg; over-egg the pudding; paint the lily;

[畫師] painter;

[畫室] studio;

[畫線] draw a line;

[畫像] (1) draw a portrait; portray; (2) portrait; portrayal;
半身畫像 half-length portrait;
全身畫像 full-length portrait;
一張畫像 a portrait;
自畫像 self-portrait;

[畫押] make one's cross; make one's mark; sign;

[畫展] art exhibition; art show;
參觀畫展 visit an exhibition of paintings;
舉辦畫展 run an art exhibition;
主辦畫展 organize a painting exhibition;

[畫脂鏤冰] draw on butter or carve ice–a futile undertaking;

[畫紙] drawing paper;
一張畫紙 a piece of drawing paper;

[畫中有詩] there is poetry in a painting;

[畫作] painting;
一幅畫作 a painting;

版畫 picture printed from an engraved plate;
筆畫 strokes of a Chinese character;
壁畫 fresco; mural;
帛畫 painting on silk;
擘畫 arrange; plan;
插畫 illustration;
扉畫 illustrations before the text of a book;
風景畫 landscape painting;
風情畫 genre painting;
風俗畫 genre painting;
工筆畫 traditional Chinese realistic painting;
國畫 traditional Chinese painting;
花鳥畫 flower-and-bird painting;
繪畫 drawing; painting;
靜物畫 still life;
絹畫 classical Chinese painting on silk;
刻畫 depict; portray;
裸體畫 nude painting;
漫畫 caricature; cartoon;
描畫 describe; draw; paint;
木炭畫 charcoal painting;

年畫 Spring Festival pictures;
漆畫 lacquer painting;
人物畫 figure painting;
入畫 picturesque; suitable for a painting;
山水畫 landscape painting;
書畫 painting and calligraphy;
水彩畫 watercolour painting;
水墨畫 ink and wash; wash painting;
炭筆畫 charcoal drawing;
炭畫 charcoal drawing;
鐵畫 iron picture;
圖畫 drawing; painting; picture;
西圖 Western painting;
寫生畫 sketch;
寫意畫 freehand brushwork;
一筆畫 one-stroke painting;
一幅畫 a painting; a picture;
一批畫 a batch of paintings;
一張畫 a picture;
油畫 oil painting;
指畫 point at; point to;
字畫 calligraphy and painting;

hua

【華】 (1) brilliancy; glory; lustre; splendour; (2) a surname;

［華陽］ surname;

hua

【話】 (1) talk; word; (2) speak about; talk about;

［話本］ script for story-telling;

［話別］ say a few parting words; say goodbye;
與父母話別 say goodbye to one's parents;
與朋友話別 bid farewell to one's friends;

［話柄］ subject of ridicule;
從不留下話柄 never become an object of ridicule;

［話不成意］ the words make no sense;

［話不離宗］ speak exclusively of one's own business; talk shop;

［話不虛傳］ that remark is true;

［話多不甜］ too much talk is unpleasant;

［話鋒］ thread of a discourse; topic of a conversation;

［話舊］ reminisce; talk about the old days; talk about old times;

［話劇］ drama; play;

［話裏］ in one's words
話裏帶刺 hidden barbs in one's words; one's words carry a sting; there is a touch of irony in one's speech;
話裏帶骨 hidden barbs in one's words;
話裏套話 touch upon other matters when discussion is centered on one topic;
話裏有話 have one's tongue in one's cheek; speak with tongue in cheek; the words mean more than they say; there is an insinuation in that remark; there is more to it than meets the ear; there is more to it than what is said; tongue-in-cheek;
話裏有因 there is sth more than what is said;

［話梅］ candied plum; preserved plum;

［話少禍少］ the least said, the soonest mended;

［話説］ (1) it is said that; (2) words spoken;
話説半截 finish half of what one has to say;
話説三遍淡如水 a tale twice told is cabbage twice sold; don't take your harp to the party; it is not good to harp on the same string;

［話題］ subject matter; subject of a talk; talking point; topic of a conversation;
話題介詞 preposition of subject matter;
改變話題 change the subject;
複雜的話題 complex subject;
街頭巷議的話題 talk of the town;
熱門話題 hot button; hot issue; hot topic;
日常話題 everyday topics;
談老話題 one's hobby horse; one's preoccupation or favourite topic;
有趣的話題 interesting subject;

［話筒］ (1) microphone; mike; (2) telephone speaker; (3) megaphone;
隨身話筒 body mike;
無載話筒 dead mike;
桌上用話筒 desk microphone;

［話頭］ thread of a discourse;
打斷話頭 break the thread;
拾起話頭 pick up the thread of a conversation;

［話音］ (1) one's voice in speech; (2) implication; tone;
話音剛落 as soon as one stops; before the sound of one's voice has died away; hardly had one's voice faded away;
話音識別 voice recognition;
話音未落 when one has hardly finished speaking;
話音信息系統 voice message system;

話音郵件 voice mail;
話還沒落音 just in the middle of a sentence;

[話語] (1) utterance; (2) discourse;
話語場 field of discourse;
話語方式 mode of discourse;
話語分析 discourse analysis;
~對比話語分析 contrastive discourse analysis;
話語結構 discourse structure;
話語能力 discourse competence;
話語性質 tenor of discourse;
話語指示詞 discourse deixis;
程序性話語 procedural discourse;
督促性話語 hortatory discourse;
對答話語 response utterance;
對話話語 dialogue discourse;
會話話語 conversational discourse;
記敍性話語 narrative discourse;
講解性話語 expository discourse;
口頭話語 the spoken word;
描寫性話語 descriptive discourse;
巧辯性話語 repartee discourse;
最小話語 minimum utterance;

[話中] in one's words;
話中見情 feelings expressed in one's words;
話中有刺 hidden barbs in one's words;
話中有話 with tongue in cheek;
話中有因 sth left unsaid;

白話 (1) empty promise; groundless talk; (2) vernacular;
插話 (1) chip in; (2) digression;
傳話 pass on a message;
串話 crosstalk;
蠢話 foolish words; nonsense; rubbish;
詞話 notes on poetry;
粗話 vulgar language;
錯話 improper remarks;
答話 answer; reply;
大話 big talk; boast;
電話 (1) phone; telephone; (2) phone call;
對話 dialogue;
二話 demur; objection;
反話 irony;
廢話 nonsense; rubbish; superfluous words;
費話 do a lot of talking;
古話 old saying;
怪話 complaint; grumble;
官話 official dialect;
鬼話 lie;
喊話 communicate by tele-equipment;
行話 cant; jargon;
好話 fine words; good words;
黑話 (1) argot; (2) double-talk; (3) malicious words;
胡話 ravings; wild talk;
壞話 malicious remarks; vicious talk;
謊話 falsehood; lie;
回話 answer; reply;
會話 have a conversation;
記住我的話 mark my words;
佳話 deed praised far and wide;
假話 falsehood; lie;
講話 lecture; speech; talk;
空話 empty talk; idle talk;
老話 (1) adage; old saying; (2) remarks about the old days;
冷話 biting remarks; bitter words; cold, sarcastic remarks;
留話 leave a message;
漫話 have an informal discussion;
夢話 (1) words uttered in one's sleep; (2) daydream;
賠話 make an apology;
屁話 nonsense; rubbish; shit;
普通話 colloquial;
情話 lovers' prattle;
趣話 wisecrack; witticism; witty remark;
如果我沒有記錯的話 if I remember correctly; to the best of my recollection;
如果一切順利的話 if everything goes smoothly;
神話 fairy tale; myth; mythology;
詩話 notes on poets and poetry;
實話 truth;
史話 historical narrative;
説不該説的話 speak out of turn; talk out of turn;
説該説的話 talk the talk;
説話 (1) say; speak; talk; (2) chat; chatter; gossip; tittle-tattle;
説下流話 talk dirty;
私話 strictly confidential talk;
俗話 common saying; proverb;
談話 (1) chat; conversation; talk; (2) statement;
套話 politeness formula;
聽話 obedient;
通話 communicate by telephone;
童話 children's stories; fairy tales;
土話 local dialect;
外話 words of an outsider;
瞎話 lie; untruth;
閒話 (1) digression; (2) complaint; (3) gossip;

H

訓話 give an admonitory talk to subordinates;
一句話 a sentence; a word; in a word; in brief; in one word; in short;
一連串的話 a fusillade of words;
一席話 a conversation; a speech; a talk; what one says during a conversation;
逸話 anecdote;
硬話 big talk; defiant talk;
真話 truth;
直話 frank speech; outspoken remarks;
準話 honest words;
走話 divulge secrets;

hua

【劃】 (1) delimit; differentiate; (2) assign; transfer; (3) plan; (4) delineate; draw; mark; (5) a stroke;
[劃定] delimit; designate;
劃定年齡範圍 delimit the range of ages;
[劃分] (1) compartmentalize; divide; partition; repartition; (2) differentiate;
劃分階級 determine classes;
[劃歸] incorporate into; put under;
[劃框框] place restrictions; set limits;
[劃清] distinguish; draw a clear line of demarcation; make a clear distinction;
劃清界限 draw a clear line between; draw a dividing line; make a clean break with sb; make a clear distinction between;
[劃圈] draw a circle;
[劃一] standardized; uniform;
劃一不二 fixed; hard and fast; rigid; unalterable;

比劃 gesticulate;
筆劃 number of strokes;
籌劃 plan and prepare;
規劃 plan; programme;
計劃 map out; plan; programme; project;
謀劃 plan; scheme;

hua

【樺】 birch;
[樺木] birch;
樺木傢具 birch furniture;
[樺皮舟] birchbark;
[樺樹] birch; birch wood;

矮樺 dwarf birch;
白樺 Japanese birch; white birch;
紅樺 red birch;
黃樺 yellow birch;
加拿大樺 yellow birch;
歐洲白樺 drooping birch;
歐洲樺 common birch; European birch;
山樺 mahogany birch;
西方樺 black birch;
疣皮樺 silver birch;
紙皮樺 canoe birch; paper birch;

huai²

huai

【徊】 (1) hesitating; indecisive; irresolute; (2) move to and fro; walk around;

徘徊 (1) pace up and down; (2) hesitate; waver;

huai

【淮】 name of a river;
[淮劇] Huai opera;
[淮夷] a surname;

huai

【槐】 acacia; locust tree (Sophora japonica);
[槐蚕] inchworm; measuring worm;
[槐豆] locust bean;
[槐花] sophora flower;
[槐樹] ash-tree; Chinese scholar tree; locust; locust tree; pagoda tree;

刺槐 locust;
國槐 Chinese scholar tree;
洋槐 locust;

huai

【踝】 ankle;
[踝反射] ankle jerk reflex;
[踝骨] ankle bone;
[踝關節] ankle joint;
[踝子骨] ankle bone;

內踝 internal malleolus;
外踝 external malleolus;
右踝 right ankle;
左踝 left ankle;

huai

【懷】 (1) bosom; (2) mind; (3) cherish; keep in mind; (4) think of; yearn for; (5) conceive a child;
[懷寶迷邦] possess great talent but not render a service to one's country;
[懷抱] (1) carry in the arms; embrace; (2)

bosom; (3) cherish; keep in mind;
投懷送抱 behave like a man-chaser; overtly aggressive in love affairs;

［懷璧其罪］ the precious stone lands its innocent possessor in jail－an innocent person gets into trouble because of his wealth;

［懷錶］ fob watch; pocket watch;

［懷才］ have talent;
懷才不露 modest about one's talent; refrain from showing one's ability;
懷才不遇 able as they were, they had no chance to carry out their ideals; be frustrated, for all one's talent; have a soul above buttons; have abilities too good for one's present employment; have talent but no opportunity to use it; have unrecognized talents; one's talents remain unrecognized;

［懷春］ become sexually awakened; begin to think of love; in love;
有女懷春 there is a girl in love;

［懷古］ cherish the past; meditate on the past; reflect on an ancient event;
懷古憑吊 evoke a sense of the past by looking at old historical places;

［懷恨］ bear a grudge; conceive a hatred for; harbour resentment; nurse a hatred for;
懷恨在心 bear sb a grudge; cherish a secret resentment against; full of rancour against sb; harbour a grudge against; harbour resentment in one's heart; have a spite against; have resentment rankling on one's mind; nourish feeling of hatred; nurse hatred in one's heart; nurse rancour against;

［懷瑾握瑜］ carrying gems in one's bosom and grasping valuables in one's hands－a person of scholarly virtue;

［懷舊］ recollect the good old days; remember old acquaintances; remember past times;

［懷裏］ in sb's arm;
倒在懷裏 fall into sb's arms; lie back on sb's breast;

［懷戀］ look back nostalgically; think fondly of;

［懷念］ cherish the memory of; think of;
懷念父親 cherish the memory of one's father;
深切懷念 dearly cherish the memory of;

［懷柔］ make a show of conciliation in order to bring other nationalities or states under control;

［懷胎］ conceive; in the family way; pregnant;

［懷鄉］ homesick;
懷鄉病 homesickness; nostalgia;

［懷想］ think about with affection; yearn for;

［懷疑］ call into question; doubt; have a suspicion that; suspect; suspicious about; suspicious of; there is reason to suspect;
抱有懷疑 foster suspicion;
表示懷疑 express doubt; voice doubt;
產生懷疑 create suspicion; raise doubts;
毫無懷疑 there is not a shadow of a doubt;
加深懷疑 strengthen one's suspicion;
令人懷疑 cause suspicion;
受到懷疑 fall under suspicion;
絲毫不懷疑 have no doubt;
消除懷疑 allay suspicion; disarm suspicion;
一絲懷疑 a flicker of doubt; a shadow of a doubt; an element of doubt;
～沒有一絲懷疑 not the slightest doubt; without a shadow of a doubt;
引起懷疑 arouse suspicion; wake suspicion;
有懷疑 have doubts;
招致懷疑 incur suspicion;

［懷有］ cherish; harbour;
懷有敵意 hostile to;
懷有殺機 have a thirst for blood;
懷有野心 harbour wild ambitions of;
懷有異心 harbour disloyal thoughts;

［懷孕］ anticipating; be big with child; become impregnated; become pregnant; beget; clucky; conceive a child; enceinte; expectant mother; expecting; have a hump in the front; have one on the way; heavy with child; in a delicate condition; in an interesting condition; in the family way; in the pudding club; infanticipating; mother-to-be; mum-to-be; pregnant; swallow a watermelon seed; waiting woman; with child;
剛懷孕 beginning of the pregnancy;
少女懷孕 teenager pregnancy;
意外懷孕 unplanned pregnancy;
再次懷孕 undergo another pregnancy;

[懷着] be filled with; cherish; harbour;
懷着鬼胎 fearful with a guilty conscience; have sinister designs; with evil in one's heart; with one's heart full of evil and fear;

悲懷 a sorrowful mood; sad feelings;
敞懷 with one's coat or shirt unbuttoned;
騁懷 give free rein to one's thoughts and feelings;
放懷 to one's heart's content;
感懷 recall with emotion;
掛懷 be concerned about; have a weight on one's mind;
關懷 show loving care for; show solicitude for;
襟懷 (1) bosom; (2) mind;
開懷 to one's heart's content;
空懷 barren;
滿懷 (1) be imbued with; be full of; have one's heart filled with; (2) chest;
緬懷 cherish the memory of; recall;
愜懷 satisfied;
情懷 feelings;
抒懷 express one's feelings;
忘懷 dismiss from one's mind; forget;
下懷 one's heart's desire;
心懷 (1) intention; purpose; (2) mood; state of mind;
胸懷 heart; mind;
雅懷 generous heart; refined taste and disposition;
縈懷 occupy one's mind;
軫懷 sorrowfully cherish sb's memory;
衷懷 inner feelings;
追懷 recall; reminisce;

huai⁴
huai

【壞】 (1) bad; (2) go bad; spoil; (3) awfully; badly; very; (4) dirty trick; evil idea; (5) broken; damaged; torn; worn-out;

[壞包兒] rascal; rogue;

[壞處] disadvantage; harm;
往壞處想 think of the unfavourable possibilities of a situation;

[壞蛋] bad apple; bad egg; bad guy; baddie; bogeyman; dirtbag; rotten apple;
小壞蛋 little brat; little rascal;

[壞話] vicious talk; malicious remarks; speak ill of sb;
壞話傳千里 bad news has wings;
背後講人壞話 speak ill of sb behind sb's back; tell tales;
到處説別人壞話 do dirt to; flig dirt about;
説壞話 bad-mouth sb;

[壞疽] gangrene;
壞疽性壞死 gangrenous necrosis;
壞疽性潰瘍 cancrum;
壞疽性牛痘 vaccinia gangrenosa;
老年性壞疽 senile gangrene;
氣性壞疽 gas gangrene;
糖尿病壞疽 diabetic gangrene;
外傷性壞疽 traumatic gangrene;
壓迫性壞疽 pressure gangrene;
炎性壞疽 inflammatory gangrene;
原發性壞疽 primary gangrene;

[壞人] bad person; evildoer; scoundrel; villain;
壞人不臭，好人不香 bad people are not looked down on and good people are not looked up to;
壞人當道 bad people in power; evildoers hold sway;
壞人當道，百姓遭殃 a bad man in office causes mischief to the public;
壞人當道，好人受氣 bad eggs wield power while good people are oppressed; bad elements hold sway while good people are pushed around; when evildoers are in power, good people suffer misdeeds;
壞人壞事 bad people and bad things; evildoers and evil deeds; evildoers and wrongdoings;
包庇壞人 hide up an evildoer;
一小撮壞人 a handful of bad people;

[壞事] (1) bad things; evil deeds; (2) make things worse; ruin sth;
壞事丑事 foul and evil things; wicked and shameless things;
壞事成雙 double whammy;
壞事做絕 commit every evil; commit terrible crimes without end; do all kinds of evil things; do all manner of evil; perpetrate every kind of villainy; stop at no crimes; stop at nothing in committing all kinds of evil;
幹壞事 do evil;
幹盡壞事 commit every evil deed; do all manner of evil; do every evil; perpetrate every conceivable evil; stop at no evil;
難免的壞事 necessary evil;

做壞事 commit a wicked deed;

［壞死］ necrosis;

播散性壞死 diaspironecrosis;

播散性漸進性壞死 diaspironecrobiosis;

動脈壞死 arterionecrosis;

肝壞死 hepatic necrosis;

骨壞死 osteonecrosis;

骨疽性壞死 carionecrosis;

壞疽性壞死 gangrenous necrosis;

漸進性壞死 bionecrosis;

進行性壞死 necrosis progrediens;

局部壞死 local death;

梅毒性壞死 syphilitic necrosis;

膿毒性壞死 septic necrosis;

貧血性壞死 anemic necrosis;

全部壞死 total necrosis;

缺血性壞死 avascular necrosis; ischemic necrosis;

韌皮壞死 phloem necrosis;

網狀壞死 net necrosis;

細胞壞死 cell necrosis;

小動脈壞死 arteriolonecrosis;

壓迫性壞死 pressure necrosis;

牙壞死 odontonecrosis;

疹性壞死 exanthematous necrosis;

脂肪壞死 adiponecrosis; fat necrosis;

周圍性壞死 peripheral necrosis;

［壞透壞絕］ shockingly bad;

敗壞 damage; ruin; spoil; undermine;

弊壞 worn and damaged;

變壞 alter for the worse; become bad; break up; change for the worse; get worse;

踊壞 break or damage by trampling; trample and break;

寵壞 spoil;

搞壞 botch up;

更壞 even worse; wrose; wrose still;

好壞 the good and the bad;

毀壞 damage; destroy; ruin;

教壞 lead astray; misguide;

磨壞 grind away;

薦壞 treacherous;

弄壞 make a mess of; put out of order; ruin;

破壞 (1) destroy; do great damage to; ruin; wreck; (2) change; (3) violate;

氣壞 beside oneself with rage;

使壞 (1) play a dirty trick; up to mischief; (2) destroy;

損壞 damage; injure;

替壞 decay; decline; deteriorate;

朽壞 decay; decayed; rot; rotten;

壓壞 damaged by high pressure;

撞壞 damage by bumping;

最壞 the meanest; the most vicious; the worst;

huan¹

huan

【懽】 glad; happy; joyous;

huan

【貛】 (1) he-wolf; male wolf; werewolf; (2) wild boar; (3) badger;

［貛油］ badger fat;

一隻貛 a badger;

huan

【歡】 (1) joyous; jubilant; merry; (2) in full swing; vigorously; with great drive;

［歡暢］ elated; thoroughly delighted;

心情歡暢 be filled with joy; in high spirits;

［歡度］ spend an occasion joyfully;

歡度佳節 celebrate a festival with jubilation; celebrate a joyous festival;

歡度節日 indulge in a holiday; joyously celebrate a festival; spend a holiday joyfully;

［歡呼］ acclaim; acclamation; cheer; hail; holler; jubilate;

歡呼雀躍 shout and jump for joy;

歡呼聲 cheering;

～一陣歡呼聲 a roar of cheering;

瘋狂歡呼 wildly acclaim;

鼓掌歡呼 clap one's hands and cheer; rejoice over;

［歡聚］ a happy get-together; a happy reunion;

歡聚一堂 be gathered happily in the same hall; be together on a happy occasion; happy gathering; have a joyous gathering;

合家歡聚 a happy family reunion;

［歡快］ cheerful and light-hearted; in a merry mood;

歡快的 cheery;

［歡樂］ (1) happy; jollity; jolly; joyous; (2) hilarity; mirth;

充滿歡樂 be filled with joy; full of joy;

感到歡樂 experience joy; feel joy;

盡情歡樂 make merry to one's heart's content;

黎庶歡樂 people are happy;

窮歡樂 find moments of rejoicing in

poverty;
享盡歡樂 drink the cup of joy;
一片歡樂 a scene of great joy;
一陣歡樂 an agony of joy;
[歡鬧] jollity; jollification;
[歡慶] celebrate joyously;
歡慶勝利 celebrate victory;
[歡聲] cheers;
歡聲遍野 gladness fills the countryside;
歡聲動地 the sound of rejoicing fills the land;
歡聲歌唱 sing with joy;
歡聲雷動 break into deafening cheers; break into thunderous applause; cheers rend the air like thunder; cheers resound like peals of thunder; give thunderous cheers; loud acclamation;
歡聲笑語 cheering and laughing;
[歡送] see off; send off;
歡送會 send-off;
盛大的歡送 royal send-off;
[歡騰] great rejoicing; jubilation; rejoice;
一片歡騰 a great cheer; a scene of great rejoicing; astir with jubilation; jubilation reigns everywhere;
[歡喜] (1) delighted; happy; joyful; (2) delight in; fond of; like;
歡喜雀躍 skip and jump about with joy; tread on air;
歡喜若狂 (1) gleeful; gloat over; (2) frantic with joy; tread on air;
歡喜冤家 quarrelsome and loving couple; quarrelsome lovers;
暗自歡喜 laugh up one's sleeve;
歡歡喜喜 delightedly; happily; joyfully;
歡天喜地 be filled with great joy; be greatly pleased; dance for joy; elated and happy; extremely delighted; full of joy; go into raptures about; in an ecstasy of joy; in seventh heaven; one's happiness knows no bounds; overjoyed; tread on air; wild with joy; with boundless joy;
皆大歡喜 all is gas and gaiters; everybody is happy; to the satisfaction of all;
空歡喜 be let down; rejoice too soon;
~貓咬尿泡空歡喜 an empty dream; baseless rejoicings;
滿心歡喜 delighted; full of joy; very pleased; with heartfelt delight;
千歡萬喜 very glad;
[歡笑] hilarity; laugh heartily; laughter; mirth;
歡笑聲 laughter;
買笑追歡 abandon oneself to pleasures; look for distractions; seek pleasures; visit prostitutes;
強作歡笑 force a smile; with a forced smile;
引起歡笑 evoke mirth;
陣陣歡笑 a gale of laughter;
縱情歡笑 laugh a hearty laugh;
[歡欣] be filled with joy; elated; jubilation;
歡欣鼓舞 be filled with exultation; buck up; dance with pleasure; elated and inspired; exult; jubilant over; jump for joy;
[歡心] favour; liking; love;
博取歡心 curry favour;
[歡顏] happy appearance; happy looks;
安得廣廈千萬間，大庇天下寒士俱歡顏 if only there were thousands and more spacious houses, it would bring joy to the poor;
假意歡顏 affected cheerfulness;
[歡宴] entertain at a banquet on some happy occasion;
歡宴作樂 make merry;
[歡迎] (1) greet; welcome; (2) receive favourably;
歡迎參觀 visitors are welcome;
歡迎辭 welcoming speech;
歡迎回家 welcome home;
歡迎回來 welcome back;
歡迎惠顧 welcome sb; welcome to enjoy sb's service;
歡迎午宴 welcoming lunch;
歡迎者 welcomer;
~一群歡迎者 a troop of welcomers;
點頭歡迎 nod sb a welcome; welcome sb with a nod;
熱忱的歡迎 hearty welcome;
熱情歡迎 glad-hand; warm welcome;
受歡迎 be a favourite with sb; be favourably received; be in favour with sb; be in sb's favour; be popular with sb; be sought after; catch on; find favour in sb's eyes; find favour with sb; go over big with sb; go with a bang;
~備受歡迎 be very popular; enjoy great popularity;
~不受歡迎 not welcome;

不受歡迎的人 persona non grata; person who is not welcome;
~大受歡迎 be in vogue; very popular;
大受歡迎的節目 top-rated show;
~廣受歡迎的 acclaimed;
微笑歡迎 welcome sb with a smile;
夾道歡迎 line the streets to welcome sb;

[歡娛] happiness; joy and pleasure;
[歡愉] happy; joyful;
[歡躍] dance with joy; jump for joy;

悲歡 joys and sorrows;
承歡 do everything to please one's parents;
合歡 (1) happy get-together; happy reunion; (2) silk tree;
狂歡 hold a carnival; rejoice with wild excitement; revel;
聯歡 have a get-together;
喜歡 (1) be fond of; be keen on; like; (2) be filled with joy; be happy; feel delighted;
新歡 new sweetheart;
追歡 pursue pleasure;

huan
【讙】 (1) clamorous; noisy; (2) same as 歡, rejoice;

huan
【貛】 (1) he-wolf; male wolf; werewolf; (2) wild boar; (3) badger;

狗貛 badger;
狼貛 glutton;
沙貛 sand badger;
豬貛 hog badger;

huan
【驩】 same as 歡, have joy;

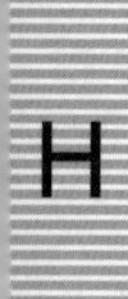

huan²
huan
【桓】 (1) tree with leaves similar to those of a willow and a white bark; (2) a surname;

huan
【寰】 large domain; vast space;
[寰海] the whole world;
名震寰海 one's name has spread over the whole world;
[寰球] the earth; the whole world;
[寰宇] the earth; the whole world;
寰宇無雙 there is no equal in the world;

塵寰 this moral life; this world;
人寰 human world; the world;
瀛寰 the world over;

huan
【環】 (1) hoop; ring; (2) link; (3) encircle; hem in; surround;
[環保] environmental protection;
環保產品 environmentally friendly products;
環保主義 environmentalism;
[環抱] encircle; hem in; surround;
峰環水抱 be surrounded by hills and water;
[環城] around the city;
[環顧] look around;
環顧四周 look all around; look around;
環顧左右 look to the left and right;
[環化] cyclization; cyclize;
環化脫胺酶 cyclodeaminase;
環化脫水酶 cyclohydrase;
環化脫水作用 cyclodehydration;
環化脫氫作用 cyclodehydrogenation;
環化作用 cyclization;
催化環化 catalytic cyclization;
還原性環化 reductive cyclization;
烯烴環化 cyclization of olefines;
氧化環化 oxidative cyclization;
原油環化 crude-oil cyclization;
[環節] (1) link; (2) segment;
關鍵的環節 key link;
缺失環節 missing link;
[環境] circumstances; environment; surroundings;
環境保護 environmental conservation; environmental protection;
~環境保護法 environmental protection law;
~環境保護論者 environmentalist;
~環境保護稅 environmental protection tax;
~環境保護主義者 environmentalist;
環境標準 environmental standard;
環境工程 environmental engineering;
環境公害 environmental hazard;
環境管理 environmental management;
環境規劃 environmental programme;
環境監測 environmental monitoring;
環境教育 environmental education;
環境結構 environmental structure;
環境經濟學 environmental economics;

環境敬語 situational honorifics;
環境科學 environmental science;
環境控制 environmental control;
環境療法 milieutherapy;
環境美化 landscaping;
環境美學 aesthetics of the environment;
環境能源 environmental energy;
環境寧靜 quiet environment;
環境評價 environmental appraisal;
環境破壞 environmental damage;
環境權 environmental rights;
環境社會學 environmental society;
環境設計 environmental design;
環境損害 environmental damage;
環境衛生 environmental health; environmental hygiene;
~環境衛生標準 environmental health standards;
環境文化 environmental culture;
環境問題 environmental problems;
環境污染 environmental pollution;
環境系統 environmental system;
~環境系統分析 environmental system analysis;
~環境系統工程 environmental system engineering;
~環境系統科學 environmental system science;
環境現狀評價 assessment of the environmental status;
環境效應 environmental effect;
環境心理學 environmental psychology;
環境學家 environmentalist;
環境要素 environmental element;
環境醫學 environmental medicine;
環境異常 environmental abnormality;
環境藝術 environmental art;
環境影響 environmental impact;
~環境影響分析 environmental impact analysis;
~環境影響評價 environmental impact assessment;
環境語境 context of a situation;
環境戰 environmental warfare;
環境質量 environmental quality;
~環境質量標準 environmental quality standard;
~環境質量評價 environmental quality evaluation;
~環境質量指數 environmental quality index;
~環境質量綜合評價 environmental quality comprehensive assessment;
環境足跡 environmental footprint;
保護環境 conserve the environment; protect the environment;
不衛生的環境 unhygienic conditions; unsanitary conditions;
典型環境 typical environment;
改善環境 improve the environment;
工作環境 working environment;
航空航天環境 aerospace environment;
毀壞環境 destroy the environment;
控制環境 control the environment;
美化環境 beautify the environment;
目的語環境 target language setting;
破壞環境 damage the environment;
軟環境 soft environment;
社會環境 social environment;
~生物社會環境 biosocial environment;
深海環境 abyssal environment;
生物環境 biological environment;
損害環境 harm the environment;
污染環境 pollute the environment;
硬環境 hard environment;
整治環境 clean up the environment;
致癌環境 carcinogenic environment;
周圍環境 surrounding circumstances;
自然環境 natural environment;
~保護自然環境 preservation of the natural environment;

[環流] circulation;
大氣環流 atmospheric circulation; general circulation;
反環流 counter circulation;
高空環流 upper-air circulation;
海洋環流 ocean circulation;
近岸環流 nearshore circulation;
徑向環流 meridional circulation;
局部環流 local circulation;
逆環流 indirect circulation;
全球環流 global circulation;
熱島環流 heat-island circulation;
潤滑油環流 lubricating-oil circulation;
三級環流 tertiary circulation;
外環流 outside circulation;
緯向環流 zonal circulation;
小環流 minor circulation;
行星環流 planetary circulation;
壓力環流 forced circulation;
一級環流 primary circulation;
永久環流 permanent circulation;

[環球] (1) round the world; (2) the earth; the

whole world;
環球安全 global safety;
行銷環球 sell well all over the world;
[環繞] embrace; encircle; revolve around; surround;
[環蝕] annular eclipse;
[環視] look around;
環視房間 look round the room;
[環烷] naphthene;
三環環烷 tricyclic naphthene;
烷化環烷 alkylated naphthene;
五碳環烷 five-cardon ring naphthene;
[環形] loop-like; ring-shaped;
環形島 roundabout;
環形山 crater;
~柏拉圖環形山 crater Plato;
~第穀環形山 crater Tycho;
~碟形環形山 saucer crater;
~哥白尼環形山 crater Copernicus;
~溝紋環形山 rill crater;
~開普勒環形山 crater Kepler;
~碗形環形山 bowl crater;
~相接環形山 contiguous crater;
~月面環形山 lunar crater;
環形效應 doughnut effect;

臂環 bracelet;
吊環 rings;
耳環 earrings;
光環 a ring of light; halo;
花環 floral hoop; garland;
連環 chain of rings;
套環 set of connected rings;
鐵環 iron hoop;
循環 circulate; cycle;
玉環 jade ring;
指環 (finger) ring;

H

huan

【還】 (1) come back; go back; (2) give back; repay; return; (3) give or do sth in return;
[還本] repayment of principal;
還本付息 pay back the capital plus interest; repay the capital with interest;
[還魂] (1) return from the grave; revive after death; (2) reprocessed;
[還擊] (1) counter-attack; fight back; return fire; (2) riposte;
合法還擊 good return;
[還籍] return to one's native place;
[還價] counter-bid; counter-offer;
討價還價 haggle over prices;
[還口] answer back; retort; talk back;
[還禮] (1) return a salute; (2) present a gift in return;
[還盤] counter-offer; make a counter-offer;
[還清] meet one' debt; pay off a debt; wipe off a debt;
還清欠債 clear a debt incurred;
還清債務 clear one's debts;
[還手] hit back; strike back;
打不還手 not strike back when attacked;
[還俗] resume one's secular life;
[還鄉] return to one's native place;
[還原] recovery; reduction; restore; return to the original condition or shape;
還原劑 reducing agent;
還原能力 reducing ability;
還原焰 reducing flame;
還原作用 reduction;
~分子內還原作用 internal reduction;
~酸性還原作用 acid reduction;
催化還原 catalytic reduction;
碱性還原 alkaline reduction;
碳熱還原 carbon thermal reduction;
自動還原 automatic recovery;
[還愿] (1) redeem a vow to a god; (2) fulfil one's promise;
[還債] pay one's debt; repay a debt;
還債高峰期 peak debt repayment period;
父債子還 a dutiful son is obliged to pay his father's debts; it is the custom for a son to pay his father's debts;
無力還債 unable to discharge one's debts;
做工還債 work out one's debt;
[還帳] pay bills; pay one's debt; repay a debt; settle an account on credit sales;
[還政於民] hand the state power back to the people; return the power of government to the hands of the people;
[還嘴] answer back; come back at sb; retort; talk back;
善於還嘴 quick at retort;

壁還 (1) return; (2) decline a gift with thanks;
駁還 reject;
發還 give back; return sth to sb;
奉還 return sth with thanks;
歸還 give back; return; revert;
交還 give back; return;

清還 clear a debt; pay off a debt; pay up a debt;
生還 return alive;
送還 give back; return;
討還 get sth back;
退還 give back; return;
往還 have social dealings with; keep in contact;
擲還 please return to me;

huan
【鍰】 (1) ancient unit of weight; (2) cash; money;

huan
【繯】 (1) noose; (2) death by hanging; hang sb to death;

huan
【鐶】 ring;

huan
【闤】 wall around a marketplace;

huan
【鬟】 (1) bun; dress the hair in a coiled knot; (2) female servant; maid;

huan³
huan
【浣】 rinse; wash;
[浣衣] wash clothes;
[浣熊] coon; raccoon;

huan
【緩】 (1) slow; unhurried; (2) delay; postpone; put sth off; (3) not tense; relaxed; (4) come to; regain consciousness; revive;
[緩辦] delay an action; put off a project;
[緩步] stroll; walk slowly;
緩步當車 have a slow walk instead of riding on a carriage;
緩步而行 walk at a foot's pace; walk at a snail's pace; walk unhurriedly;
[緩衝] (1) buffer; buffering; cushion; dampen; (2) slow down attack;
緩衝地帶 buffer zone;
緩衝器 (1) buffer; (2) bumper;
~彈簧緩衝器 spring bumper;
~地址緩衝器 address buffer;
~空氣緩衝器 air buffer;
~槍托緩衝器 butt buffer;
~色度緩衝器 chroma buffer;
~數據緩衝器 data buffer;
~通信緩衝器 communication buffer;
~橡膠緩衝器 rubber bumper;
~中心緩衝器 central buffer;
~字符緩衝器 character buffer;
緩衝物 cushioning;
緩衝作用 buffer action; buffer reaction;
動態緩衝 dynamic buffering;
更換緩衝 exchange buffering;
簡單緩衝 simple buffering;
數據緩衝 data buffering;
專用緩衝 dedicated buffering;
[緩和] allay; calm; diffuse; ease up; mitigate; relax;
緩和步伐 slacken the pace;
緩和語氣 moderate one's tone;
[緩緩] gradually; little by little; slowly; step by step;
[緩急] (1) degree of urgency; (2) emergency;
緩急相通 help each other on need;
緩急相助 give mutual help in an emergency; help each other in case of need;
緩不濟急 a slow action cannot save a critical situation; a slow remedy cannot meet an urgency;
事有緩急 there are both deferred and urgent matters;
[緩解] alleviate;
[緩慢] slow;
緩慢地走 walk slowly;
進展緩慢 slow in progress;
行動緩慢 slow in action;
[緩期] delayed schedule; postpone a deadline; suspend;
[緩氣] get a breathing space; have a respite;
[緩限] extend the time limit; put off the deadline;
[緩刑] imprisonment with a suspension of sentence; suspended sentence;
緩刑一年 one-year suspended sentence;
判了緩刑 be given a suspended sentence;
[緩議] defer the discussion;

弛緩 calm down; relax;
遲緩 slow; sluggish; tardy;
從緩 bide time; postpone; put off;
和緩 ease up; gentle; mild; relax;
減緩 retard; slow down;
平緩 gentle; mild; placid;
舒緩 leisurely;
死緩 stay of execution;
坦緩 level; smooth;
徐緩 slow;

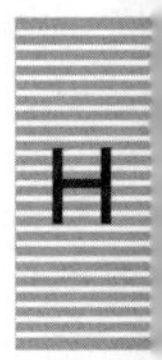

延緩 delay; postpone; put sth off;
迂緩 dilatory; slow to act;
暫緩 defer; postpone; put sth off;
展緩 extend; postpone; prolong;
暫緩 defer; hold for a while; postpone for a while; put off;

huan
【澣】 wash;

huan⁴
huan
【幻】 (1) illusory; imaginary; unreal; (2) magical;
［幻燈］ (1) slide show; (2) magic lantern; slide projector;
幻燈機 magic lantern; slide projector;
~ 投影幻燈機 overhead projector;
幻燈片 filmstrip; lantern slide; slide; transparency;
~ 一張幻燈片 a slide;
幻燈影片 filmstrip;
［幻景］ blaze; illusion; mirage;
［幻境］ dreamland; fairyland;
［幻覺］ delusion; hallucination; illusion;
幻覺發生 hallucinogenesis;
幻覺空間 illusory space;
幻覺症 hallucinosis;
~ 酒精性幻覺症 alcoholic hallucinosis;
~ 器質性幻覺症 organic hallucinosis;
殘肢幻覺 stump hallucination;
產生幻覺 has an illusion; see things;
貨幣幻覺 money illusion;
假性幻覺 pseudo-hallucination;
色幻覺 colour illusion;
外匯幻覺 foreign exchange illusion;
振動幻覺 oscillating vision;
自發幻覺 autokinetic illusion;
［幻夢］ daydream; dream; fantasy; illusion;
［幻滅］ vanish into thin air;
［幻視］ optical illusion; vision; visual hallucination;
藍光幻視 cyanophose;
藍幻視 indicophose;
振動幻視 oscillopsia;
［幻想］ fancy; fantasy; illusion; make-belief; square the circle;
幻想曲 fantasia;
不抱幻想 cherish no illusions; not to cherish fancies;
充滿幻想 full of fancies;
丟掉幻想 cast away illusions;
追求幻想 chase a rainbow;
［幻像］ ghost; mental image; mirage; phantom; vision;
［幻影］ ghost; phantom; rainbow; unreal image;
虛景幻影 castles in the air;

變幻 change irregularly; fluctuate;
空幻 illusory; imaginary; visionary;
夢幻 dream; illusion;
奇幻 bizarre; queer; strange;
虛幻 illusory; imaginary; unreal;

huan
【奐】 (1) leisurely; (2) brilliant; colourful; gay; lively; (3) elegant; (4) many; numerous; (5) a surname;

huan
【宦】 (1) official; (2) eunuch; (3) a surname;
［宦官］ eunuch;
［宦海］ official circles; officialdom;
宦海浮沉 the ups and downs in officialdom; the vicissitudes of official life;
［宦途］ official career;
［宦游］ leave one's home and take up a government job;

官宦 officials;
紳宦 retired government official;

huan
【患】 (1) disaster; peril; trouble; (2) anxiety; worry; (3) contract a disease; suffer from a disease;
［患病］ get ill; get sick; suffer from an illness;
［患處］ affected part; wounded part;
［患難］ adversity; trials and tribulations; troubles;
患難得救 be dragged in out of the rain;
患難弟兄 brothers in affliction;
患難見棄 leave sb to hold the bag;
患難見人心 a friend is never known until one has need of him; calamity is the touchstone of a person;
患難見真情 a friend in need is a friend indeed;
患難同舟 comrades in misfortune;
患難相處 have borne many troubles

together;
患難相棄 desert sb in his misfortunes; fail sb in need; leave sb in the lurch;
患難相依 share sb's hardships through thick and thin; share weal and woe;
患難相助 help sb in distress; help sb in need; help sb in trouble; help sb in his hour of need;
患難與共 come together through thick and thin; go through thick and thin together; share each other's hardships; share weal and woe; stand together in times of need;
安於患難 reconcile oneself with adversity;

[患者] patient; sufferer;
精神病患者 person who suffers from mental troubles;

匪患 banditry; the evil of banditry;
後患 future trouble;
禍患 calamity; disaster;
疾患 disease; illness;
內患 internal troubles;
傷患 sicked and wounded;
水患 flood; inundation;
外患 foreign aggression;
隱患 hidden trouble; latent danger; lurking peril;
憂患 hardship; misery; suffering;
災患 calamity; disaster;

huan

【喚】 call sb out;

[喚起] (1) arouse; call; call to mind; recall; summon sth up; (2) evocation;

[喚醒] awaken; rouse; wake up;

傳喚 summon to court;
呼喚 call; shout to;
叫喚 (1) call out; cry out; (2) (of animals) cry;
使喚 (1) order about; (2) handle;
召喚 call; summon;

huan

【換】 (1) barter; exchange; (2) change;

[換班] (1) change shifts; (2) relieve a person on duty;

[換車] change trains or buses; transfer;

[換乘] change; transfer;

[換擋] shift gears;
換擋桿 gear lever; gear shift;

[換崗] changing of guards;

[換工] change one's job; exchange labour;
換工作 change one's job;

[換貨] exchange goods;
換貨憑單 credit note;

[換季] change into a dress proper for the season;

[換句話說] in other words; put it in another way; say sth in other words; that is to say;

[換課] change class;

[換氣] (1) take a breath (in swimming); (2) change of air;
換氣裝置 scavenging arrangement;

[換錢] (1) change money; (2) barter goods for money;

[換取] exchange sth for; get in return;

[換熱器] heat interchanger; interchanger;
板式換熱器 plate heat interchanger;
盤式換熱器 disc heat interchanger;

[換人] substitution of players;

[換算] conversion;
換算賬戶 conversion account;

[換位] change of positions; transposition;
換位反義詞 conversive;
換位作用 metathesis;

[換文] exchange of notes;

[換向] commutation;
換向器 commutator;
~磨損過深換向器 undercut commutator;
~遙測系換向器 telemetering commutator;
~主換向器 prime commutator;
典型換向 canonical commutation;
電壓換向 voltage commutation;
電阻換向 resistance commutation;
強制換向 forced commutation;

[換性] transsexual;
換性手術 transsexual surgery;

[換血] bring in new blood;

[換喻] metonymy;
換喻賓語 metonymic object;
換喻關係 metonymy;
換喻性意義 metonymic meaning;
本來換喻 original metonymy;
標準換喻 stock metonymy;

變換 alternate; vary;
撤換 dismiss and replace; recall; replace;
串換 exchange;
倒換 (1) rotate; take turns; (2) rearrange; replace;
抵換 substitute sb; take the place of sb;

調換 change; exchange; swap;
掉換 change; exchange; swap;
兌換 convert; exchange;
改換 change; change over to;
更換 change; replace;
互換 exchange;
交換 exchange; swop;
輪換 rotate; take turns;
貼換 trade sth in; trade-in;
偷換 substitute sth stealthily;
退換 exchange a purchase; replace a purchase;
置換 displace;
轉換 change; transform;

huan
【渙】 melt away; vanish;
［渙渙］ overflowing;
［渙然］ disappear; melt away; scatter; vanish;
渙然冰釋 be instantly dispelled; be instantly dissipated; be instantly removed; clear away; disappear; melt away; vanish;
［渙散］ lax; slack;
渙散意志力 sap sb's willpower;
工作渙散 slack in one's work;
學習渙散 slack in one's study;

huan
【逭】 (1) avoid; (2) escape from; flee; get away from; run away;

huan
【煥】 glow; shine;
［煥發］ glow; irradiate; shine;

huan
【豢】 (1) feed animals with grains; (2) entice people with profit or gains; tempt; (3) domesticated animals;
［豢龍］ a surname;
［豢養］ feed; keep support;
豢養家禽 feed poultry;

huan
【瘓】 paralysis;
癱瘓 (1) palsy; paralysis; (2) be at a standstill; be paralysed;

huan
【漶】 wear out beyond recognition;
［漶漫］ illegible;
漫漶 illegible;

huan
【擐】 put on; wear;
［擐甲持戈］ don one's armour; take one's spear and prepare to fight;
［擐甲執鋭］ clad in armour and grasping a spear — ready to fight;

huan
【轘】 tear an offender apart using vehicles (an ancient form of punishment);

huang1
huang
【肓】 (1) region between the heart and the diaphragm; (2) vitals;

huang
【荒】 (1) waste; (2) uncultivated land; wasteland; (3) barren; desolate; (4) crop failure; famine; (5) out of practice; (6) scarcity; shortage;
［荒誕］ absurd; incredible; unbelievable;
荒誕不經 absurd; fantastic; most absurd and irrational; nonsensical; preposterous; wild and fanciful;
荒誕劇 absurd play; fantasy play;
荒誕派 absurdism;
~荒誕派戲劇 absurd theatre;
~荒誕派作家 absurdist;
荒誕無稽 absurd; absurd and groundless; fantastic; incredible; preposterous;
~荒誕無稽的故事 cock and bull story;
荒誕小説 absurd novel;
荒誕主義 absurdism;
［荒島］ barren island; desert island; uninhabited island;
杳無人跡的荒島 desert island;
［荒地］ no man's land; wasteland;
改良荒地 improve the wasteland;
開墾荒地 bring land into cultivation;
一塊荒地 a piece of wasteland;
一片荒地 a barren; a heath;
［荒廢］ fall into disuse; fall into disrepair; lie waste; out of practice;
荒廢學業 neglect one's studies;
［荒郊］ desolate place outside a town; wild countryside; wilderness;
一片荒郊 a vast expanse of wasteland; a deserted wilderness;
［荒涼］ bleak and desolate; wild;
荒涼寥落 lonely and pathetic sight;
荒涼滿目 waste and destitution meet the

eye;

滿目荒涼 a scene of desolation meets the eye on every side — the sight of an area in war;

一片荒涼 a scene of desolation;

~一片荒涼的景象 a picture of bleak desolation;

[荒亂] in great disorder; in turmoil;

兵荒馬亂 disorder caused by continuous military operations; in the tumult of a raging war; the turmoil and chaos of war;

蝦荒蟹亂 an evil omen of great disturbance;

陷入一片荒亂 fall into general disorder;

[荒謬] absurd; preposterous;

荒謬的 cockamamie; cockeyed;

荒謬絕倫 absolutely preposterous; absurd to the highest degree; absurd without comparison; absurd without equal; height of absurdity;

荒謬透頂 the height of absurdity; utterly absurd;

極端荒謬 utterly absurd;

[荒漠] desert;

荒漠群落 deserts;

北極荒漠 arctic desert;

黏土荒漠 argillaceous desert;

熱帶荒漠 tropical desert;

鹽土荒漠 solonchak desert;

[荒年] famine year; lean year;

[荒僻] deserted; desolate and out-of-the-way;

[荒歉] crop failure; famine;

[荒腔脱板] sing out of key;

[荒沙] barren sand;

[荒山] barren hills; waste mountains;

荒山野村 a desolate mountain village; a village in the barren mountains; bleak mountains and remote villages; remote mountain villages;

[荒時暴月] lean year; time of dearth; year of famine; hard times;

[荒疏] out of practice; rusty;

棋藝荒疏 rusty in chess;

[荒唐] absurd; fantastic; preposterous;

荒唐不經 absurd and unreasonable; fantastic; unbelievable;

荒唐的 ludicrous;

荒唐故事 cock and bull stories; old wives' tales;

荒唐可笑 absurd and ridiculous; how absurd;

荒唐透頂 absolutely ridiculous; cap the climax of absurdity; most illogcial; preposterous to the extreme; utterly absurd;

荒唐無稽 frivolous and unfounded; most absurd;

[荒蕪] aridity; go out of cultivation; lie waste;

[荒野] the wilds; the wilderness;

開拓荒野 pioneer wilderness;

[荒淫] debauched; dissolute; licentious;

荒淫腐朽 lead a depraved and dissolute life; live in wanton luxury;

荒淫無恥 dissipated and unashamed; licentious and decadent; profligate and shameless; shameless dissipation; shamelessly dissipated;

荒淫無道 be a dissolute person and lack principles; be a profligate and devoid of principles;

荒淫無度 be vicious beyond measures; indulge in sensual excesses; excessive indulgence in lewdness; given to sexual pleasures; immeasurably dissolute;

[荒原] wasteland; wilderness;

石楠荒原 heath;

[荒政] neglect affairs of the state;

[荒冢] abandoned graves; neglected graves;

八荒 outlying areas on all sides;

備荒 prepare against natural disasters;

草荒 farmland running to weeds;

房荒 housing shortage;

放荒 set fire to woods and grass in a mountainous area;

洪荒 primitive;

飢荒 (1) crop failure; famine; (2) debt;

救荒 send relief to a famine area;

開荒 start to develop the wasteland;

墾荒 start to cultivate the virgin soil;

落荒 take to the wild;

錢荒 short of money;

沙荒 sandy wasteland;

燒荒 burn the grass on the wasteland;

生荒 uncultivated land; virgin soil;

拾荒 glean and collect scraps;

熟荒 abandoned land;

逃荒 flee from famine; get away from a famine-stricken area;

拓荒 start to cultivate the virgin soil; reclaim wasteland;

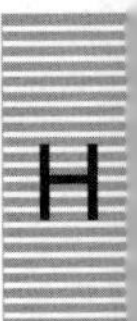

災荒 famine due to crop failure;

huang
【慌】 (1) confused; flurried; flustered; (2) awfully; unbearably;

［慌亂］ alarmed and bewildered; flurried; hurry and confusion; hurry-scurry;
引起慌亂 cause sb flutter;

［慌忙］ hurriedly; in a flurry; in a great rush; rush to;
不慌不忙 calmly; deliberately; keep a level head; keep one's head; leisurely; neither alarmed nor excited; take one's time; unhurried; with full composure; without haste or confusion; without hurry or bustle;
慌慌忙忙 hurriedly; in a rush;

［慌張］ confused; flurried; flustered; trepidation;
慌張離去 hurry off in great confusion;
非常慌張 be covered with confusion;
慌慌張張 be covered with confusion; hastily; helter-skelter; in a flurried manner; in a flurry; in an abrupt manner;
慌裏慌張 all in a fluster; higgledy-piggledy; in a hurried and confused manner; in a rush; lose one's head; on the rush;

別慌 don't be afraid;
驚慌 alarmed; panic-stricken; scared;
恐慌 panic; terrified;
心慌 flustered; nervous;
着慌 become flustered; get alarmed;

huang²
huang
【皇】 emperor; sovereign;

［皇儲］ crown prince;

［皇帝］ emperor;
皇帝的媽媽—太厚 mother of the emperor — the dowager empress; too thick;
三皇五帝 three emperors and five sovereigns;
土皇帝 local chieftain; local despot; local tyrant; the king of the countryside;

［皇都］ imperial capital;

［皇甫］ a surname;

［皇父］ a surname;

［皇宮］ imperial palace; palace; royal palace;
一座皇宮 a royal palace;

［皇冠］ crown;
一頂皇冠 a crown;

［皇家］ imperial family;
皇家園林 imperial garden;

［皇陵］ imperial mausoleum;

［皇權］ imperial authority; imperial power;

［皇上］ His Majesty;

［皇室］ imperial family; imperial household; royal household;

［皇天］ heaven;
皇天不負有心人 God helps those who help themselves; heaven helps those who help themselves; keep your shop, and your shop will keep you; providence does not let down a person who does his best;
皇天后土 the great heaven and earth; heaven and earth;

［皇族］ imperial family; imperial kinsmen; people of imperial lineage;

［皇祖］ imperial ancestors preceeding the founder of a dynasty;

倉皇 in a flurry; in panic;
教皇 pontiff; Pope;
女皇 empress;
沙皇 tsar;
太上皇 supreme ruler;
天皇 (1) emperor; (2) emperor of Japan;
張皇 alarmed; flurried; flustered; scared;

huang
【凰】 phoenix, a legendary bird in Chinese mythology;
鳳凰 phoenix;

huang
【徨】 (1) agitated; alarmed; (2) irresolute;

huang
【惶】 anxiety; fear; trepidation;

［惶惶］ alarmed; in a state of anxiety; on tenterhooks;
惶惶不安 be greatly upset; go hot and cold; in fear and panic; live in terror and uncertainty; on tenterhooks;
惶惶不可終日 in a constant state of tension; in a constant state of anxiety; in a state of constant nervousness;

on edge and alarmed all day; on tenterhoods all the time; sit on thorns;
惶惶如喪家之犬 as frightened as a mouse; as frightened as a rabbit; as frightened as a stray dog;
惶惶無主 panic and not know what to do;
惶惶欲淚 close to tears; tears are very near to one's eyes;

[惶惑] apprehensive; perplexed and alarmed;
惶惑不安 be lost and ill at ease; in a state of great agitation; perplexed and uneasy;

[惶遽] frightened; scared;

[惶恐] frightened; scared; terrified;
惶恐不安 be greatly alarmed; be terrified and uneasy; great alarm; in a state of alarm; in a state of trepidation; in fear and panic; panic-stricken; with one's heart going pit-a-pat;
惶恐萬狀 be frightened out of one's senses; be seized with fear;
惶恐無措 be stumped; in a situation too difficult to manage; up a stump;
誠惶誠恐 be struck with awe; in fear and trepidation; with reverence and awe;

驚惶 alarmed; panic-stricken; scared;

huang

【湟】 (1) mean, dirty place; (2) name of a river;

[湟里] a surname;

huang

【黃】 (1) sallow; yellow; (2) short for the Huanghe River; (3) fall through; fizzle out; (4) a surname;

[黃白] (1) lunar orbit; (2) yellow and white;
黃白交角 inclination of the lunar orbit;
數黃道白 coax with sweet words; speak honeyed words;

[黃柏] golden cypress;

[黃斑] macula lutea; yellow spot;
黃斑病變 maculopathy;
黃斑點疾病 macular degeneration;
假性黃斑 false macula;
結膜黃斑 pinguicula;

[黃榜] imperial edict;

[黃包車] rickshaw;

[黃疸] jaundice;
傳染性黃疸 infectious jaundice;
機械性黃疸 mechanical jaundice;
流行性黃疸 epidemic jaundice;
潛伏性黃疸 latent jaundice;
溶血性黃疸 hemolytic jaundice;
生理性黃疸 physiologic jaundice;
隱性黃疸 latent jaundice;
早發性黃疸 icterus praecox;
中毒性黃疸 toxic jaundice;
阻塞性黃疸 obstructive jaundice;

[黃道] eliptic;
黃道帶 zodiac;
黃道光 zodiacal light;
黃道吉日 auspicious day; lucky day; propitious date; red-letter day;
黃道十二宮 12 signs of the zodiac;
黃道圖 ecliptic diagram;
黃道坐標系 ecliptic system of coordinates;

[黃澄澄] glistening yellow; golden;

[黃燈] (traffic) yellow light;

[黃豆] soy; soya; soya bean; soybean;
黃豆芽 soy-bean sprouts;

[黃蜂] hornet; wasp;
大黃蜂 (1) bumblebee; (2) hornet;
~ 兇猛的大黃蜂 angry hornet;

[黃公] a surname;

[黃瓜] cucumber; green cucumber;
伏季黃瓜 summer cucumber;
秋黃瓜 autumn cucumber;
酸黃瓜 dill pickle;
溫室黃瓜 forcing cucumber;
小黃瓜 gherkin;
一根黃瓜 a cucumber;
一片黃瓜 a slice of cucumber;

[黃光燈] yellow fluorescent lamp;

[黃河] Yellow River;
跳進黃河洗不清 cannot clean oneself even if one jumps into the Yellow River; even if one jumps into the Yellow River one could never clean oneself; unable to clean oneself even if one plunges into the Yellow River — find it hard to clear oneself of a charge;

[黃鶴] yellow crane;
杳如黃鶴 gone as the yellow crane — gone forever; disappear like the yellow crane — nowhere to be found; leave like the yellow crane — leave never to return;

[黃黑] yellow and black;
說黃道黑 criticize others; tell lies about

this and that person; slander others;

[黃乎乎的] yellow;

[黃花] yellow-weed;

黃花菜 dried lily flowers;

黃花閨女 virgin;

黃花後生 celibate man;

黃花晚節 integrity in one's later life;

黃花魚 yellow croaker;

一枝黃花 a yellow-weed;

[黃化現象] aetiolation;

[黃昏] dusk; gloaming;

黃昏前 before dark;

黃昏時分 at dusk; at sunset;

黃昏後 after dark; after dusk;

從黎明到黃昏 from dawn till dusk;

[黃禍] Yellow Peril;

[黃醬] fermented soya bean paste;

[黃金] aurum; gold;

黃金流動 gold movements;

黃金內流 gold influx;

黃金入球 golden goal;

黃金時代 the best years of one's life; the golden age; the most flourishing period of a person;

黃金輸出 gold export;

黃金輸入 gold import;

黃金雙價 dual gold price;

黃金條款 gold clause;

黃金外匯儲備 gold and foreign currency reserves;

黃金外流 gold efflux;

黃金未為貴，安樂值錢多 pleasure is worth more than gold;

黃金總庫 gold pool;

黃金儲備 gold reserve;

黃金儲蓄 gold holdings; gold reserve; gold stock;

搶購黃金 gold rush;

遍地黃金 the streets are paved with gold;

一塊黃金 a lump of gold; a piece of gold;

[黃酒] Shaoxing wine; yellow rice wine;

[黃臘] beeswax;

臉如黃臘 ashen-faced; one's face turns waxen;

[黃鸝] oriole;

黃鸝喚春 the nightingale hails the spring — the return of spring;

[黃蓮] bitter wort;

黃蓮樹下拉胡琴—苦中作樂 play a fiddle under a bitter wort tree — seeking pleasure under adverse circumstance;

不嚐黃蓮苦，怎知蜜糖甜 a person who has never tasted bitterness before cannot know what sweetness is;

吃黃蓮 swallow a bitter pill;

苦如黃蓮 as bitter as bile;

苦似黃蓮 as bitter as wormwood;

[黃臉婆] yellow-faced woman—one's wife;

[黃綠] yellow and green;

回黃轉綠 from the yellow autumn to the green spring;

[黃麻] jute;

黃麻袋 gunnysack;

黃麻纖維 jute;

[黃梅] (1) folk melody of the Anhui Province; (2) rainy season;

黃梅調 folk melody originated from Anhui Province;

黃梅天 rainy season;

黃梅雨 intermittent drizzles in the rainy season;

[黃米] glutinous millet;

[黃牛] (1) ox; (2) ticket tout;

黃牛過河—各顧各 oxen crossing a river — each one taking care of himself;

老黃牛 (1) willing ox; (2) person who serves the people heart and soul;

[黃袍] imperial robe;

黃袍加身 be draped with the imperial yellow robe by one's supporters — be acclaimed emperor;

[黃泉] netherworld;

黃泉之下 dwelling place of the dead;

命赴黃泉 set out on one's journey to the Yellow Spring — be dying;

[黃雀] golden oriole;

黃雀伺蟬 the golden oriole waits upon the cicada — carelessness for a coming disaster;

[黃色] (1) yellow; (2) erotic; obscene; pornographic;

黃色報刊 scandal sheet; yellow press;

黃色電影 pornographic film;

黃色錄相 blue video; pornographic video;

黃色人種 yellow race;

黃色書刊 pornographic books and periodicals;

黃色小說 pornographic novel; sex novel;

黃色新聞 yellow journalism;

黃色音樂 decadent music; vulgar music;

橙黃色 orange;

淡黃色 beige-yellow; canary yellow; lemon yellow;
鉻黃色 chrome yellow;
薑黃色 gingery;
~ 薑黃色的貓 ginger cat;
略帶黃色 yellowy;
米黃色 beige;
檸檬黃色 lemon yellow;
土黃色 yellowish brown;
鮮黃色 bright yellow;

[黃鱔] (1) finless eel; (2) ricefield eel;

[黃鼠] ground squirrel; souslik;

[黃鼠狼] yellow weasel;
黃鼠狼給雞拜年—不懷好意 a weasel giving new year's greetings to a hen has ulterior motives; a yellow weasel goes to pay New Year's call to a hen – not with the best of intentions; the weasel goes to pay its respects to the hen – not with the best of intentions;

[黃松] yellow pine;

[黃糖] brown sugar;

[黃銅] brass; yellow metal;
黃銅板 plate brass;
黃銅工匠 brazier;
黃銅匠 brasssmith;
黃銅接頭 brazed joint;
黃銅噴漆 lacquering brass;
黃銅鑄件 brassing;
標準黃銅 standard brass;
彈殼黃銅 cartridge brass;
海軍黃銅 admiralty brass;
紅黃銅 red brass;
簧片黃銅 reed brass;
可鍛黃銅 forging brass;
鋁黃銅 aluminium brass;
鋁鎳黃銅 aluminium nickel brass;
螺絲黃銅 screwing brass;
錳黃銅 manganese brass;
鉛黃銅 lead brass;
商品黃銅 market brass;
生黃銅 cast brass;
碎黃銅 scrap brass;
特種黃銅 special brass;
鐵錳黃銅 iron manganese brass;
錫黃銅 tin brass;
壓鑄黃銅 die-cast brass;
硬黃銅 hard brass;
硬焊黃銅 brazing brass;
鐘錶黃銅 clock brass;
鑄造黃銅 casting brass;

[黃土] loess;
黃土高原 loess plateau;
一抔黃土 (1) a handful of earth; a handful of yellow soil; (2) grave; (2) sth that is utterly insignificant;

[黃胸鵐] yellow hammer;

[黃楊] Chinese littleleaf box;
黃楊厄閏 in straits;
黃楊木雕 boxwood carving;
黃楊之厄 distressed affairs of a dissipated person;

[黃鶯] oriole; yellow warbler;
黃鶯抓住鷂子的腳—扣了環 like an oriole holding the feet of a kestrel – they are locked in a clinch;

[黃油] (1) butter; (2) grease;
黃油刀 butter knife;
春季黃油 grass butter;
加工黃油 process butter;
人造黃油 margarine;
~ 一盒人造黃油 a tub of margarine;
一塊黃油 a block of butter; a gob of butter;

[黃魚] croaker; yellow croaker;
大黃魚 large yellow croaker;
小黃魚 small yellow croaker;

[黃鐘大呂] one's resonant voice rings out, clear as a bell;

蒼黃 greenish yellow;
草黃 straw colour;
橙黃 orange yellow;
雌黃 orpiment;
葱黃 greenish yellow;
淡黃 light yellow;
蛋黃 yolk;
鵝黃 light yellow;
昏黃 (1) dim; faint; (2) pale yellow;
姜黃 turmeric;
焦黃 (1) brown; (2) sallow;
金黃 golden; golden yellow;
韮黃 hotbed chives;
橘黃 orange yellow;
枯黃 withered and yellow;
蠟黃 sallow; wax yellow; waxen;
米黃 cream-coloured;
嫩黃 light yellow;
牛黃 bezoar;
鐵黃 iron oxide yellow;
土黃 yellowish brown;
蟹黃 ovaries and digestive glands of a crab;

杏黃 apricot yellow;

huang

【煌】 bright and brilliant;

[煌煌] bright; brilliant; luminous;

[煌綠] brilliant green;

huang

【遑】 (1) hurry; (2) anxious; disturbed; (3) leisurely; (4) not to;

[遑遑] hastily; in a hurry;

[遑論其他] let alone the other points;

不遑 it's too late (to do sth); there's not enough time (to do sth);

huang

【篁】 bamboo bush; bamboo grove; clump of bamboos;

huang

【蝗】 locust;

[蝗草鵐] grasshopper sparrow;

[蝗蟲] grasshopper; locust;

一大群蝗蟲 a swarm of locusts;

一群蝗蟲 a swarm of locusts;

[蝗蛹] nymph of a locust;

飛蝗 migratory locust;

土蝗 a kind of locust;

huang

【潢】 (1) lake; pond; (2) coloured paper;

裝潢 decoration; packaging;

huang

【璜】 ancient jade ornament;

裝璜 decoration; mounting; packaging;

huang

【磺】 brimstone; sulfur;

huang

【簧】 (1) metal tongue in a reed organ; (2) spring in a machine;

[簧管] reed pipe;

[簧夾] spring clip;

齒條簧夾 rack spring clip;

時輪簧夾 hour wheel spring clip;

條盒簧夾 barrel spring clip;

[簧片] reed;

綳簧 spring;

拉簧 extension spring;

盤簧 coil spring;

片簧 leaf spring;

彈簧 spring;

huang

【蟥】 horseleech;

huang³

huang

【怳】 (1) dejected; despondency; (2) mad; wild;

惝怳 (1) disappointed; let down; unhappy; (2) be at a loss; be perplexed;

huang

【恍】 all of a sudden; suddenly;

[恍惚] (1) absent-minded; in a trance; (2) dimly; faintly; seemingly;

心神恍惚 in a trance; perturbed in mind;

恍恍惚惚 confused and stupefied;

[恍然] suddenly;

恍然大悟 be suddenly enlightened; come to understand sth suddenly; it is a revelation to one; it suddenly dawns on one; scales fall from one's eyes; see the light suddenly; suddenly realize sth; suddenly become aware of sth;

恍然若失 feel like having lost bearings;

恍然興歎 give a sign of disappointment;

[恍如] as if; as it were; as though; seem;

恍如隔世 as if a generation had passed; as if one had been cut off from the outside world for ages;

恍如夢境 as if in a dream;

[恍若] as if; seem;

huang

【晃】 (1) brightness; (2) dazzling; glaring; (3) appear and disappear very quickly; (4) glimpse;

[晃眼] dazzlingly bright;

huang

【幌】 cloth screen; curtain;

[幌子] (1) guise; (2) under the pretext of sth;

打着民主的幌子 under the cover of democracy;

掛幌子 (1) put up a signboard to advertise goods; (2) give oneself away;

裝幌子 keep up appearances; maintain an outward show; put up a front;

huang

【謊】 falsehood; lie;
[謊報] give false information; lie about sth;
謊報軍情 make a false report about the military situation;
[謊花] fruitless flower;
[謊話] lie; falsehood; porky;
謊話連篇 a tissue of lies;
説謊話 tell a lie;
[謊言] (1) categorical inaccuracy; cover story; distort facts; embroider the truth; erroneous report; fiddle; flannel; humbug; misinform; mispresent the facts; prevaricate; selective facts; stretch the truth; tall tale; terminological inexactitude; with forked tongue; (2) fabrication; falsehood; fib; lie; porky; (3) bunk; eyewash; fiddle-faddle;
謊言可畏 lies are terrible; untrue statements are frightful;
謊言腿短 lies have short legs;
卑鄙的謊言 base fabrication;
駁斥謊言 refute a lie;
拆穿謊言 nail a lie to the counter;
大謊言 big lie;
各種各樣的謊言 all sorts of lies;
揭穿謊言 nail a lie;
輕信謊言 believe falsehood;
一連串謊言 a skein of lies; a string of lies;
一派謊言 a pack of lies; a tissue of lies;
一片謊言 a pack of lies;
一紙謊言 a lying document; a paper of lies;
以謊言蓋謊言 cover one lie with another;

扯謊 lie; tell a lie;
撒謊 lie; make up a story; tell a lie;
説謊 lie; tell a lie;
要謊 ask a price higher than the real cost of commodities;
圓謊 straighten out contradictions in a lie and make it plausible;

huang4
huang

【晃】 shake; sway;
[晃蕩] oscillate; rock; shake; sway;
[晃動] (1) rock sway; (2) twirl around;
晃動杯中的液體 twirl the liquid around in one's glass;
晃不動 unshakable;
突然的晃動 lurch;
[晃悠] shake from side to side; stager; wobble;
晃晃悠悠 swaying; unstable;

打晃 sway one's body before falling down;
搖晃 rock; shake; sway;
一晃 (of time) pass in a flash;

hui1
hui

【灰】 (1) ash; (2) dust; (3) mortar; (4) gray; (5) discouraged; disheartened;
[灰暗] gloomy; murky gray;
灰暗的天空 murky sky;
[灰白] ashen; grayish; hoary; pale; white;
灰白色 ash gray; grayish white;
變灰白 become gray;
臉色變得灰白 turn pale;
頭髮灰白 have grizzled hair;
[灰塵] (1) ash; dirt; dust; (2) spindrift;
打掃灰塵 sweep up the dust;
撣去灰塵 dust off;
拂去灰塵 flick the dust off;
積聚灰塵 accumulate dust; gather dust;
揚起灰塵 kick up a dust;
一層灰塵 a coat of dust; a coating of dust; a layer of dust;
~薄薄的一層灰塵 a film of dust;
一點灰塵 a speck of dust;
一粒灰 a speck of dust;
[灰燼] ashes;
化為灰燼 be consumed by a fire; commit to the flames; crumble to dust; reduced to ashes; turn to dust and ashes;
[灰溜溜] crestfallen; dejected; gloomy;
[灰蒙蒙] overcast; dusky; murky;
[灰泥] plaster;
一層灰泥 a layer of plaster;
[灰色] (1) ashy; gray; (2) gloomy; pessimistic; (3) ambiguous; obscure;
灰色決策 gray decision-making;
灰色權力 gray power;
灰色系統 gray system;
~灰色系統決策 gray system decision-making;
~灰色系統預測 gray system forecasting;
灰色消費 gray consumption;
灰色小説 gray novel;
藍灰色 bluish gray; sky gray;
鉛灰色 leaden;
淺灰色 French gray; light gray; oyster

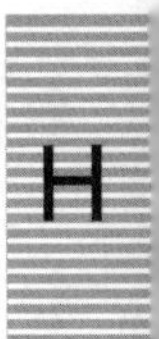

gray;
青灰色 steel gray;
深灰色 charcoal gray;
鐵灰色 gunmetal gray; iron-gray;
瓦灰色 slate gray;
銀灰色 metallic gray; silver gray;
紫灰色 purplish gray;

[灰市] gray market;
灰市場理論 theory of gray market;

[灰心] disappointed; discouraged; disheartened; lose heart;
灰心喪氣 discouraged; lose heart; utterly disheartened; yield to despair;
不灰心 keep one's chin up;

白灰 lime;
草灰 (1) ashes from grass stalks used as fertilizer; (2) grayish; yellow;
骨灰 (1) bone ash; (2) ashes of the dead;
黑灰 black ash;
爐灰 stove ash;
煤灰 coal ash;
抹灰 plaster;
砲灰 cannon fodder;
青灰 graphite;
石灰 lime;
死灰 dying embers;
香灰 incense ashes;
煙灰 cigarette ash;
洋灰 cement;
一層灰 a coat of dust;
一堆灰 a pile of ashes;
銀灰 silver gray;
油灰 putty;

hui

【恢】 extensive; vast;

[恢誕] exaggerated;

[恢復] reconstruction; recover; regain; renew; restitution; resume;
恢復健康 recover from an illness; restore one's health;
恢復交通 resume traffic;
恢復名譽 redeem sb's reputation;
恢復器 restorer;
~綠色恢復器 green restorer;
~熱電偶恢復器 thermocouple restorer;
恢復青春 regain youth;
恢復勇氣 regain one's nerve;
恢復元氣 recover one's impaired energy; recuperate; regain one's strength; rehabitate;
恢復原狀 restore to the former state;
恢復知覺 regain consciousness;
恢復職務 resume one's duties;
恢復自由 regain freedom;
部份恢復 be partially recovered;
幾何恢復 geometric reconstruction;
明顯恢復 make a remarkable recovery;
缺氧恢復 anaerobic recovery;
數據恢復 data reconstruction;
彈性恢復 elastic recovery;
~非彈性恢復 inelastic recovery;
~完全彈性恢復 perfect elastic recovery;
完全恢復 complete recovery;
信號恢復 signal reconstruction;

[恢弘] (1) broad; extensive; (2) carry forward; develop;

[恢恢] extensive; vast;
恢恢有餘 have plenty of space; roomy; very spacious;

[恢廓] (1) generous; large-minded; (2) develop; expand;

hui

【虺】 (1) diseased; ill; sick; (2) discouraged;

hui

【揮】 (1) wave; wield; (2) wipe off; (3) command; (4) disperse; scatter;

[揮斥] free, bold and unrestrained; untrammelled;

[揮動] brandish; wave;
揮動大棒 wield clubs;
揮動拳頭 shake one's fist;

[揮發] volatilize;
揮發度 volatility;
~操作揮發度 operating volatility;
~相對揮發度 relative volatility;
~有效揮發度 effective volatility;
揮發性 volatility;
~燃料揮發性 fuel volatility;

[揮戈] brandish one's weapons; lead troops to battle;

[揮汗] wipe off perspiration;
揮汗成雨 perspire to the extent to make a shower — referring to a large number of people;

[揮毫] wield one's writing brush; write with a brush;
揮毫作詩 take up the brush and write a poem; wield one's writing brush to compose a poem;

H

［揮霍］ spend freely; spend lavishly; squander;
揮霍的 spendthrift;
揮霍濫用 dip into one's purse;
揮霍浪費 play ducks and drakes with money; spend extravagantly; squander wantonly;
~避免揮霍浪費 avoid extravagance;
揮霍錢財 squander one's wealth;
揮霍無度 spend without restraint; squander wantonly;
大肆揮霍 orgy of spending; recklessly squander;
瘋狂揮霍 spending spree;

［揮軍］ lead troops to war;

［揮淚］ flick a tear; shed tears;
揮淚而別 part in tears; wipe one's tears and leave;
揮淚而讀 read sth through flowing tears;
揮淚如雨 in a storm of tears;

［揮灑］ (1) spray; sprinkle; (2) paint freely; write freely;
揮灑自如 write and draw freely as one wishes; write with a free pen;

［揮師］ command a troop;
揮師出擊 dispatch troops to fight; push troops onward to attack; send out an army to war;
揮師向前 advance the troops;

［揮手］ wave; wave one's hand;
揮手告別 wave farewell; wave goodbye; wave one's hand to bid sb farewell; wave one's hand on departure;
揮手致意 wave greetings to; wave to sb in acknowledgement;

［揮舞］ brandish; wave; wield;
揮舞武器 brandish weapons;

發揮 (1) give free rein to; give play to; (2) develop;
指揮 command; commander; conduct; conductor; direct; director;

hui
【撝】 (1) brandish; wave; (2) humble; modest;

hui
【暉】 bright; radiant; sunshine;

春暉 (1) light of spring; (2) parental love;
斜暉 oblique sunlight;
朝暉 morning sunlight;

hui
【詼】 (1) tease; (2) mock;

［詼諧］ humorous; jocular;
詼諧曲 scherzo;

hui
【輝】 (1) brightness; splendour; (2) shine;

［輝光］ glow;
反常輝光 abnormal glow;
藍輝光 blue glow;
氖輝光 neon glow;
陽極輝光 anode glow;
陰極輝光 negative glow;

［輝煌］ brilliant; glorious; magnificent; splendid;
輝煌的戰績 brilliant achievement in a war;
輝煌歲月 glory days;

［輝映］ emit and reflect light; shine;
輝映成趣 cast beautiful reflections;
交相輝映 add radiance and beauty to each other; contrast finely with; enhance each other's beauty; sort well with;

光輝 brilliance; glory; radiance;

hui
【麾】 (1) banner; flag; standard; (2) command; lead;

［麾下］ (1) commander; general; (2) those under one's command;

hui
【翬】 (1) fly; (2) multicoloured pheasant;

hui
【褘】 ceremonial gowns of a queen;

hui
【徽】 (1) good and beautiful; honourable; (2) stops on a lute; (3) flag; pennant, streamer; (4) badge; emblem; (5) another name for Anhui;

［徽號］ title of honour;

［徽章］ badge; insignia;
圓形徽章 medallion;

盾徽 coat of arms;
國徽 national emblem;
軍徽 army emblem;
團徽 league badge;
校徽 school badge;

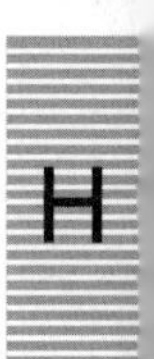

hui
【隳】 destroy; dishearten; ruin;

hui²
hui
【回】 (1) circle; (2) go back; return; (3) turn round; (4) answer; reply; (5) chapter;
[回擺] (1) backswing; (2) oscillation;
[回拜] pay a return visit;
[回報] (1) bring back a report; report back on what has been done; return for report; (2) pay back; reciprocate; repay; requite; (3) get one's own back; retaliate;
回報恩惠 requite an obligation;
帶來回報 bring rewards;
獲得回報 receive one's reward;
收獲回報 reap rewards;
物質回報 material rewards;
[回波] echo;
回波定位 echolocation;
電纜回波 cable echo;
相干回波 coherent echo;
雜散回波 angel echo;
[回嗔作喜] forget one's anger and be placated; one's anger has turned into joy; overcome one's anger and smile;
[回程] return trip; reverse drive;
[回春] (1) return of spring; (2) bring back to life; (3) rejuvenate;
回春乏術 nothing can be done to save the dying; the sickness is too deeply rooted in the body for doing anything;
回春靈藥 miraculous cure; wonderful remedy;
大地回春 spring has returned;
妙手回春 a quick cure by a clever doctor; bring a patient back to life; bring life back to a patient; the magic hand that restores health; use a miraculous cure and bring the dying back to life;
[回答] reply; answer; answer up; in answer to; respond;
回答正確 right answer;
不能接受否定的回答 not take no for an answer;
肯定的回答 affirmative reply;
含糊的回答 vague reply;
據理回答 give a reasonable answer; make a fair answer;
以微笑表示回答 respond with a smile;
[回彈] resilience;
回彈能 energy resilience;
剪切回彈 shearing resilience;
[回跌] fall;
技術性回跌 technical reaction;
[回訪] pay a return visit;
[回復] (1) answer; reply; (2) recoil; reflex;
[回顧] look back; retrospect; review;
回顧過去 look back on the past; review the past;
回顧一生 pass one's life in review;
回顧展 retrospective;
[回歸] (1) flyback; (2) recurrence; regression; (3) return of sovereignty;
回歸測試 regression test;
回歸分析 regressive analysis; regressive education;
回歸教育 recurrent education;
回歸線 tropic;
~北回歸線 Tropic of Cancer;
回歸以後 since the return of sovereignty;
對角回歸 diagonal regression;
反序回歸 antitonic regression;
曲線回歸 curvilinear regression;
虛回歸 dummy regression;
[回合] (1) bout; round; (2) rally;
打贏一回合 winning a rally;
勝一回合 win a bout;
[回話] answer; reply;
[回環] circle;
大回環 giant circle;
~向前大回環 giant circle forward;
[回回] Hui people; Huis;
[回火] temper; tempering;
回火處理 tempering;
空氣中回火 air tempering;
軟化回火 soft temper;
彈簧回火 spring temper;
完全回火 complete tempering;
油回火 oil temper;
直接回火 direct tempering;
中溫回火 average tempering;
[回擊] counter-attack; fight back; hit back; retaliate; return fire; return stroke;
[回家] go home; return home;
趕緊回家 hurry home;
立刻回家 go straight home;
送人回家 walk sb home;
[回見] catch you later;

H

[回教] Islam; Mohammedanism;
[回叫] call back;
[回敬] do sth in return; return a compliment; return the salute;
回敬一杯 drink a toast in return;
照樣回敬 return a compliment;
[回絕] decline; refuse;
斷然回絕 resolutely decline;
[回扣] (1) kickback; (2) rebate; (3) sales commission;
扣除回扣 deduct a commission;
按比例回扣 prorated rebate;
保險回扣 insurance rebate;
利息回扣 interest rebate;
運費回扣 freight rebate;
[回來] back; come back; go back; on one's return from; return; turn one's steps back;
搬回來 move back;
從國外回來 return from abroad;
從幾分鐘回來 be back in a few minutes;
趕不回來 unable to get sth back;
收不回來 impossible to get sth back; impossible to recover;
下班回來 return from work;
找回來 recover;
[回禮] (1) return a salute; (2) present a gift in return;
作為回禮 in reply to a salute;
[回流] circulation reflux; reflux;
冷回流 cold reflux;
實際回流 actual reflux;
循環回流 circulating reflux;
[回路] loop;
冷回路 cold loop;
循環回路 circulation loop;
陽極回路 anode loop;
陰極回路 cathode;
[回落] fall after rise;
[回馬槍] (1) back thrust; (2) Parthian shot; parting shot;
殺回馬槍 give a back thrust; make a backward thrust at one's pursurer; wheel around and hit back;
[回描] retrace;
水平回描 horizontal retrace;
帖回描 retrace;
[回暖] get warm again after a cold spell;
[回聘] re-employment;
[回請] give a return banquet; return hospitality;
[回球] make a return;
回球失誤 make a faulty return;
[回去] back; go back; return;
[回聲] echo;
回聲測定 echolocation;
回聲測跑儀 echometer;
回聲測深儀 echometer;
回聲感歎句 echo exclamation;
回聲室 echo studio;
回聲説 echoism;
仿真回聲 artificial echo;
胎兒回聲 foetal echo;
諧和回聲 harmonic echo;
胸內回聲 echophony;
[回生] (1) bring back to life; (2) forget through lack of practice; get rusty;
回生乏術 it is beyond mortal power to bring the dead to life;
起死回生 bring the dying back to life; rise from the grave;
[回昇] pick up; rise again;
技術性回昇 technical rally;
價格回昇 recovery in price;
銷售回昇 sales picked up;
[回師] return in triumph;
[回收] reclaim; recover; recovery; retrieve;
回收設備 recovery apparatus;
回收系統 recovery system;
回收站 collection depot;
回收總量 total recovery;
水煮回收 water cooked reclaim;
酸回收 acid recovery;
餘熱回收 waste heat recovery;
[回首] (1) turn one's head; turn round; (2) call to mind; look back; recollect;
回首前塵 look back upon the past; recall past events;
不堪回首 cannot bear to look back; find it unbearable to recall; too sad to remember;
[回述] recount past events;
[回溯] look back on; recall sth;
[回天] save a desperate situation;
回天乏術 nothing can be done to revive the dead; powerless to save a desperate situation; unable to save the situation;
回天之力 power that is capable of saving a desperate situation; tremendous power that overcomes difficulties;

［回頭］ (1) turn about; turn one's head; turn round; (2) later;
回頭見 cheerio; laters; see you later;
回頭路 the road back to one's former position;
～走回頭路 backtrack; put retrace one's steps; take the road back; turn the clock back;
回頭是岸 it is never too late to mend one's misdeeds; just repent and salvation is at hand; never too late to mend one's misdeeds; repentance is never too late; repentance is salvation; repentance is the only way out; repentance never comes too late; the shore is just behind one; there is time for one to mend one's ways; turn back to safety; turn from one's evil ways; turn one's head and the shore is at hand — to repent and be saved;
回頭一看 glance over one's shoulder; look back; turn one's head and look;
回頭一想 on second thoughts;
敗子回頭 return of the prodigal son;
好馬不吃回頭草 a good horse does not graze twice on the same ground;
十步九回頭 hesitate; look back nine times every ten steps; waver ;

［回味］ (1) aftertaste; recollect the pleasant flavour of; (2) call sth to mind and ponder over it; enjoy in retrospect;
回味無窮 lead sb to endless aftertastes; the more one recalls sth the sweeter it becomes;

［回鄉］ return to one's home town;

［回翔］ circle round; wheel;

［回想］ (1) recall; recollect; think back; (2) anamnesis;

［回信］ (1) reply to sb's letter; write back; write in reply; (2) letter in reply;

［回敘］ (1) recount past events; (2) flashback;

［回憶］ call to mind; dredge up memories; recall; recollect;
回憶對比 recall the past and contrast it with the present;
回憶錄 memoirs; reminiscences;
回憶往事 cast one's mind back;
對童年的回憶 memory of one's childhood;
痛苦的回憶 painful recollection;

［回譯］ back translation;
回譯測試法 back translation test;

［回音］ (1) echo; (2) reply; response; (3) turn;
立候回音 an immediate reply is requested; awaiting you prompt reply; hoping for an immediate reply;

［回游］ migration;
取食回游 alimental migration;
索餌回游 feeding migration;
溯河回游 anadromous migration;
魚類回游 fish migration;

［回贈］ give a gift in return;
現金回贈 cash rebate;

［回嘴］ (1) answer back; retort ; (2) backchat ;

駁回 overrule; reject; turn down;
撤回 recall; retract; revoke; withdraw;
返回 come back; go back; return;
叫回 recall;
來回 (1) go to a place and come back; make a return journey; make a round trip; (2) back and forth; to and fro; (3) a cycle;
領回 get back; take back;
收回 (1) recall; (2) get back; regain; (3) countermand; withdraw an order;
彈回 rebound;
退回 (1) return; send back; (2) go back;
挽回 (1) redeem; retrieve; (2) reverse an unfavourable state of affairs;
下回 next time;
一回 (1) a chapter; (2) once; one time; (3) a round; an occasion;
漲回 rises and corrections;
招回 recall;
召回 recall;
折回 turn back (halfway);
轉回 return; turn back;
追回 recover; retrieve;

hui

【徊】 (1) hesitating; indecisive; irresolute; (2) move to and fro; walk around;

［徊徨］ hesitate; walk back and forth;

hui

【洄】 whirl (said of water);

［洄游］ migration;
洄游魚 migratory fish;

潆洄 swirl;

hui

【茴】 aniseed; (2) fennel;
[茴芹] anise;
[茴香] fennel;
茴香菜 fennel;
茴香酒 anisette;
茴香子 aniseed;

hui
【迴】 (1) revolve; rotate; turn; (2) winding; zigzag; (3) return;
[迴避] (1) avoid meeting another person; avoidance; (2) withdraw; (3) decline an offer; (4) evade;
迴避策略 avoidance strategy;
迴避挑戰 evade challenge;
迴避制度 withdrawal system;
[迴腸] ileum;
迴腸蕩氣 agitated in mind; deeply affect sb's emotions; heartrending; inspiring; soulstirring; thrilling;
迴腸九轉 dejected and vexed without peace; one's mind is burning with grief;
蕩氣迴腸 deeply affects one's emotions; heart-rending; soul-stirring; thrilling;
[迴光反照] a reflected ray of the setting sun—the transient reviving of a dying person; an illumination before death; the last radiance of the setting sun—moment of consciousness just before death; the sun's reflected light at the evening—brief glow of health before passing away;
[迴形針] paper clip;
[迴旋] roundabout;
迴旋燈 praxinoscope;
迴旋曲 rondo;
迴旋餘地 elbow room; room for freedom of action; room for manoeuvre;

輪迴 transmigration;
旋迴 cycle;
巡迴 go the rounds; make a circuit of;
迂迴 (1) circuitous; roundabout; (2) outflank;

hui
【蛔】 ascarid; roundworm;
[蛔蟲] roundworm;
蛔蟲病 ascariasis;

hui³
hui
【虺】 a kind of venomous snake;
[虺蝮之行] sneaky, contemptible ways, like snakes;

hui
【悔】 regret; repent;
[悔改] repend and mend one's ways;
不思悔改 make no attempt to correct one's own mistakes; remain impenitent; show no sign of repentance;
死不悔改 unrepentant;
痛自悔改 show deep repentance;
真心悔改 sincerely repent and earnestly reform oneself;
[悔過] penitence; repent one's error; repentant;
悔過從善 acknowledge one's errors and become a good person;
悔過自新 express one's repentance and determination to turn over a new leaf; repent and make a fresh start; repent and start anew; repent and start with a clean slate; repent and turn over a new leaf;
具結悔過 write a statement of repentance;
~責令具結悔過 instruct sb to write a statement of repentance;
[悔恨] bitterly remorseful; regret deeply;
悔恨交加 mixed feelings of remorse and shame; regret mingled with self-reproach;
悔恨莫及 cry over split milk;
悔恨終身 have a secret regret all one's life; nurse a secret regret all one's life; regret sth all one's life;
[悔愧] regret and shame;
悔愧交織 be torn by self-recrimination and repentance;
[悔悟] awake from sin; repent;
悔悟的 contrite;
頓然悔悟 be suddenly awakened to one's errors; suddenly realize one's error and show repentance;
幡然悔悟 determined to make a clean break with one's past; see the error of one's ways and repent;
翻然悔悟 repent and mend one's ways;
真心的悔悟 sincere repentance;
[悔之已晚] it is now too late to repent; it is no use regretting it now; repentance is too late; it is no use crying over spilt milk; too late for regrets; too late to regret;

[悔之無及] it is useless to repent now; rue sth in vain; too late for remorse; too late to repent;

[悔罪] show penitence; show repentance;
悔罪的 contrite;

懊悔 be regretful; feel remorse; repent of;
懺悔 (1) repent of; (2) confess;
翻悔 back out; go back on one's word;
反悔 back out; go back on one's word;
改悔 repent;
後悔 regret; remorse;
嗟悔 regret and lament;
失悔 regret;
痛悔 deeply regret;
追悔 feel remorse; regret; repent of;

hui

【毀】 (1) damage; destroy; ruin; (2) burn up; (3) defame; slander; (4) make over;

[毀謗] calumniate; malign; slander;
惡毒的毀謗 wicked slander;
荒謬的毀謗 absurd slander;
缺德的毀謗 unprincipled slander;
策劃毀謗 set up a slander;

[毀壞] break; damage; decay; destroy; ravage; ruin;
遭到毀壞 receive damage;

[毀滅] destroy; exterminate; ruin;
毀滅前途 ruin one's prospects;
免於毀滅 escape destruction;
招致毀滅 court destruction;
遭到毀滅 meet destruction;

[毀棄] annul; scrap;
毀棄契約 annul a contract;
黃鐘毀棄 employ incapable people instead of able people;

[毀容] disfigure;

[毀傷] damage; hurt; injure;

[毀屍滅跡] burn the corpse to destroy the evidence; bury the corpse in order to destroy all traces of one's crime; chop up a corpse and obliterate all traces; reduce the corpse to ashes in order to destroy all traces of one's crime;

[毀損] breakage; damage; impair;

[毀形滅性] ruin one's figure and destroy one's disposition through grief;

[毀譽] praise or blame;
毀譽參半 be as much censured as praised; be as much praised as blamed; get both praise and blame; have a mixed reception;
毀譽失當 get the boot on the wrong foot; inappropriate in giving praise;
毀譽圖利 prostitute one's own honour for personal gains;
不計毀譽 indifferent to people's praise or blame;
面譽背毀 praise openly and slander secretly; praise sb to his face and abuse him behind his back;
無毀無譽 neither criticism nor praise; passable;

[毀約] (1) break one's promise; (2) scrap a contract;

殘毀 mutilation;
摧毀 destroy; smash; wreck;
搗毀 crush; destroy; smash;
盜毀 steal and damage;
詆毀 defame; smear; vilify;
焚毀 burn down; destroy by fire;
擊毀 destroy; shatter; smash;
燒毀 burn down; destroy by fire;
撕毀 tear sth to pieces;
銷毀 destroy sth by burning or melting;
墜毀 crash; fall and break;
訾毀 defame; slander; vilify;
自毀 self-destruction;

hui

【會】 brief period of time; moment;

hui

【燬】 (1) blaze; fire; (2) burn down; destroy by fire;

hui⁴

hui

【卉】 (1) general term for plants; (2) myriads of;

花卉 flowers and plants;

hui

【恚】 anger; rage;

hui

【彗】 (1) broom; (2) comet;

[彗發] coma;

[彗頭] head of a comet;

[彗尾] tail of a comet;

多重彗尾 multiple comet tail;
反常彗尾 anomalous comet tail;
曲彗尾 curved comet tail;
直彗尾 straight comet tail;

[彗星] comet;
彗星群 comet group;
恩克彗星 Encke's Comet;
哈雷彗星 Halley's Comet;
海王族彗星 comet of Neptune family;
木族彗星 comet of Jupiter family;
天王族彗星 comet of Uranus family;
土族彗星 comet of Saturn family;

交食彗 eclipse comet;
母彗星 parent comet;

hui

【晦】 (1) last day of a lunar month; (2) dark; (3) gloomy; obscure; (4) night;

[晦暗] dark and gloomy;
晦暗呆滯 dull and glazed;

[晦蒙] dark; gloomy; obscure;

[晦冥] dark and gloomy;

[晦匿] retire into obscurity;

[晦氣] bad luck; unlucky;
十分晦氣 in hard luck; in ill luck;
自認晦氣 accept bad luck without complaint; grin and bear bad luck;

[晦澀] hard to understand; obscure; unclear in meaning;

霾晦 (of sky) overcast by dust;
韜晦 conceal one's true features or intentions; lie low;
隱晦 obscure; vague; veiled;

hui

【喙】 (1) beak; bill; (2) snout;

[喙魚] billfish;

置喙 chip in; interrupt;

hui

【惠】 benefit; favour; kindness;

[惠賜] bestow sth graciously; kind enough to give;

[惠存] please keep it as a souvenir;

[惠而不費] a kind act which does not cost much; be beneficent without great expenditure; give sb a pleasure which costs one nothing;

[惠風] fair wind; pleasant breeze;
惠風和暢 a gentle and pleasant breeze; a gentle breeze is blowing;

[惠顧] one's patronage; patronize;
荷蒙惠顧 thank you for your patronage;

[惠臨] your gracious presence;

[惠然肯來] be so kind as to come; honour me with your presence;

[惠聲] reputation for kindness;

[惠音] your esteemed letter;

[惠贈] so kind as to give;

[惠政] benevolent rule or administration;

恩惠 favour; kindness;
互惠 mutually beneficial; reciprocal benefit;
口惠 empty promise; lip service;
柔惠 gentle and kind;
實惠 material benefit; solid benefit; substantial benefit;
碩惠 great indebtedness;
特惠 special offer;
賢惠 virtuous;
小惠 petty favour;
優惠 favourable; preference; preferential;

hui

【匯】 (1) converge; (2) gather together; (3) assemblage; collection; (4) remit;

[匯報] give an account of; report;

[匯編] assembly; collect; collection; compilation; compile; corpus;
匯編程序 assembly programme;
匯編命令 assembler command;
匯編器 assembler;
匯編語言 assembly language;
匯編指令 assembly command; assembler instruction;

[匯兑] remittance;
國內匯兑 domestic remittance;
國外匯兑 foreign remittance;

[匯合] confluence; converge; fusion; join;
匯合點 confluence; junction;

[匯集] (1) collect; compile; (2) assemble; come together; converge;
匯集情報 pool of information;
資源匯集 pool of resources;

[匯寄] remit;

[匯價] conversion rate; exchange rate;

[匯聚] collect; conjuncture; converge; gather in one place;

[匯款] (1) make a remittance; remit money;

(2) remittance;
匯款方式 form of remittance;
匯款人 remitter;
匯款通知 remittance note;
匯款用途 purpose of remittance;
電報匯款 telegraphic remittance;
家庭匯款 family remittance;
普通匯款 general remittance;
推遲匯款 delayed remittance;
外僑匯款 immigrant's remittance;
銀行匯款 bank remittance;
郵政匯款 postal remittance;
支票匯款 remittance by cheque;

[匯流] confluence; converge; flow together;
匯流點 confluence; junction;

[匯率] conversion rate; exchange rate;
匯率機制 exchange rate mechanism;
單匯率 single exchange rate;
單一匯率 single exchange rate;
電匯匯率 rate of mail transfer;
法定匯率 official exchange rate;
浮動匯率 floating exchange rate;
複匯率 multiple exchange rate;
固定匯率 fixed exchange rate;
間接匯率 indirect exchange rate;
開盤匯率 opening exchange rate;
聯繫匯率 linked exchange rate;
名義匯率 nominal exchange rate;
商業匯率 commercial exchange rate;
市場匯率 market exchange rate;
~實際市場匯率 actual market exchange rate;
收盤匯率 closing exchange rate;
雙檔匯率 dual exchange rate;
現行匯率 current exchange rate;
銀行匯率 bank exchange rate;
應付匯率 payable exchange rate;
遠期匯率 forward exchange rate;
中間匯率 mid-point exchange rate;
中心匯率 central exchange rate;
自由匯率 free exchange rate;

[匯票] (1) bank draft; (2) bill of exchange; (3) money order; order; (4) remittance;
匯票到期 bill to fall due;
匯票展期 prolongation of a bill;
本國貨幣匯票 home currency bill;
長期匯票 long draft; long-term bill;
承兑匯票 acceptance bill;
~銀行承兑匯票 banker's acceptance bill;
出口匯票 export bill;
單張匯票 sola draft bill;
定期匯票 fixed remittance; period remittance; term bill;
短期匯票 short-term bill;
附息匯票 interest bill;
跟單匯票 documentary bill;
國內匯票 inland bill;
即期匯票 (1) demand draft; (2) sight draft;
間接匯票 indirect bill;
進口匯票 import bill;
見期匯票 bill at sight; sight bill;
來人匯票 bearer draft;
旅行社匯票 express money order;
通融匯票 accommodation draft;
退匯匯票 return bill;
托收匯票 bill of collection;
未付匯票 outstanding bill;
一張匯票 a draft;
銀行匯票 bank bill; bank draft;
郵政匯票 postal money order;
遠期匯票 forward remittance;

[匯演] joint performance;

[匯印成書] put together one's articles and publish them in book form;

[匯展] collective exhibition;

炒匯 change money on the black market;
電匯 telegraphic money order;
套匯 arbitrage;
外匯 foreign exchange;
信匯 mail transfer;
郵匯 remit by post;
語匯 vocabulary;

hui

【彙】 (1) categorize; category; class; classify; series; (2) collect;

[彙報] give an account of; report;

詞彙 vocabulary; words and phrases;
字彙 glossary; lexicon;

hui

【會】 (1) assemble; get together; (2) meet; see each other; (3) conference; gathering; get-together; meeting; party; (4) association; society; union; (5) temple fair; (6) association of people who regularly contribute to a common fund and draw from it by turns; (7) capital; chief city; (8) occasion; opportunity; (9) grasp; understand; (10) able to; can; (11) good at; skillful

H

in; (12) likely to; sure to; (13) pay a bill; (14) moment;
[會餐] dine together; have a dinner party;
[會操] gather together for military drill;
[會場] (1) conference hall; (2) meeting place;
[會費] membership dues; membership fees;
[會逢其適] happen to be present on the occasion;
[會館] country guild; guild hall; provincial guild;
[會海文山] too many meetings to attend and documents to handle;
[會合] assemble; converge; join; meet; rendezvous;
軌道會合 orbital rendezvous;
深空會合 in-space rendezvous;
送入軌道 injecting into orbit;
[會話] (1) colloquy; conversation; (2) session;
會話分析 conversational analysis;
會話慣用語 conversational routine;
會話含義 conversational implicature;
會話話語 conversational discourse;
會話準則 conversational maxim;
[會籍] membership;
[會集] assemble; gather together;
[會見] interview; meet with;
[會刊] (1) proceedings of a conference; (2) journal of an association;
[會考] general public examination;
[會客] receive a visitor;
[會面] come together; meet;
[會商] hold a conference;
[會審] (1) joint hearing; joint trial; (2) make a joint check-up;
[會師] join forces;
[會試] metropolitan examination;
[會談] conversation; talk;
打斷會談 interrupt a conversation;
對口會談 counterpart conversation;
繼續會談 continue a conversation;
結束會談 close a conversation;
進行會談 carry out talks;
開始會談 commence a conversation; open a conversation; start a conversation;
停止會談 drop a conversation;
一度會談 a talk;
一輪會談 a round of talks;
圓桌會談 round-table talk;
中止會談 break off a conversation;
[會堂] assembly hall; hall;
[會通] master; understand thoroughly;
[會晤] meet;
定期會晤 meet regularly;
要求會晤 request an interview;
[會務] club affairs; committee affairs;
[會悟] realize the truth;
[會心] know; understand;
會心微笑 smile in understanding;
[會要] compendium of government and social institutions;
[會意] (1) knowing; understanding; (2) associative compounds;
點頭會意 nod in understanding; nod understandingly; nod with understanding;
頷首會意 nod one's comprehension;
[會議] conference; convention; meeting;
會議桌 conference table;
會議翻譯員 conference translator;
會議旅遊 conference tourism;
會議口譯員 conference interpreter;
會議日程表 daily programme of a meeting;
會議廳 conference hall;
會議召集人 congregant; convener;
會議中心 conference centre; convention centre;
會議綜述 summaries of meetings;
安排會議 arrange a meeting;
參加會議 attend a meeting; go to a conference; take part in a meeting;
出席會議 attend a meeting;
大使級會議 ambassadorial-level meeting;
電話會議 conference call; teleconference;
~電話會議網 teleconferencing network;
成功的會議 successful conference;
~非常成功的會議 highly successful conference;
國際會議 international conference;
和平會議 peace conference;
家長會議 parents' meeting;
教務會議 senate meeting;
舉行會議 hold a conference; hold a meeting;
~按期舉行會議 hold the meeting as scheduled;
理事會議 council meeting;
聯席會議 joint conference;
秘密會議 clandestine meeting; closet consultation; conclave; hush-hush

meeting; secret meeting;
全體會議 plenary session;
視頻會議 video conferencing;
首腦會議 summit;
現場會議 on-the-spot meeting;
學術會議 academic conference;
業務會議 business conference; business meeting;
一次會議 a meeting;
一屆會議 one session;
圓桌會議 round-table conference; round-table meeting;
召集會議 call a meeting; convene a meeting; convoke;
召開會議 call a meeting; convene a meeting;
正式會議 official meeting
~不正式會議 unofficial meeting;
重要會議 important meeting;
主持會議 preside over a meeting;
組織會議 organize a conference; organize a meeting;

[會員] member;
會員國 member state;
非會員 non-member;
名譽會員 honorary member;
吸收會員 admit members;
預備會員 probationary member;
正式會員 full member;
終身會員 life member;

[會章] (1) constitution of an association; (2) emblem of an association;

[會長] chairman; president;
副會長 vice president;
女會長 chairwoman;

[會賬] pay a bill;

[會診] collective solution; group consultation;

[會址] (1) address of an association; (2) site of a conference;

拜會 call on; make an official visit; pay a courtesy call; pay an official call;
幫會 secret society; underworld gang;
閉會 close a meeting; end a meeting; adjourn a meeting;
博覽會 exposition; fair;
不會 (1) unlikely; will not; (2) have not learned to; unable to;
財會 (1) finance and accounting; (2) financial accounting;
參議會 consultative council;
茶話會 tea party;
茶會 tea party;
常會 regular meeting;
初會 see sb for the first time;
大會 (1) plenary session; (2) mass meeting;
董事會 board of directors; board of trustees;
都會 large city; metropolis;
分會 branch; chapter;
附會 draw a far-fetched analogy; make a strained interpretation;
赴會 attend a meeting;
復會 resume a session;
工會 labour union; trade union;
國會 congress; parliament;
和會 peace conference;
花會 flower fair;
歡送會 farewell meeting; farewell party; send-off meeting;
歡迎會 welcoming party;
基金會 foundation;
機會 chance; opportunity;
集會 assembly; gathering; hold a mass rally; meeting; rally;
紀念會 commemoration meeting;
檢討會 self-criticism meeting;
交易會 commodities fair; trade fair;
教會 church;
酒會 cocktail party;
雞尾酒會 cocktail party;
聚會 get together; meet;
開會 (1) attend a meeting; (2) hold a meeting;
理會 (1) comprehend; understand; (2) pay attention to; take notice of;
理事會 board of directors; council;
例會 regular meeting;
莅會 be present at a meeting;
聯歡會 get-together;
領會 comprehend; grasp; understand;
流會 (of a meeting) fail to be convened for lack of a quorum;
廟會 fair; temple fair;
年會 annual conference; annual meeting;
全會 plenary meeting; plenary session;
群英會 gathering of heroes;
融會 blend; fuse; merge; mix together;
散會 be over; break up;
商會 chamber of commerce;
社會 society;
省會 provincial capital;
盛會 distinguished gathering;
誓師會 oath-taking rally;
體會 experience; know from experience; realize;

understand;
同鄉會 association of fellow provincials or townspeople;
晚會 evening party;
委員會 commission; committee;
舞會 dance ball; dancing party;
誤會 misconstrue; mistake; misunderstand;
小組會 group meeting;
協會 association; society;
休會 adjourn;
學會 learned society;
學生會 student association; student union;
研討會 seminar;
演奏會 instrumental performances;
宴會 banquet; dinner party; feast;
夜總會 nightclub;
議會 legislative assembly; parliament;
意會 sense; understand by insight;
音樂會 concert;
營火會 campfire party;
幽會 (of lovers) meet;
遊藝會 carnival;
與會 participate in a conference;
園遊會 garden party;
約會 appointment; date; engagement;
運動會 athletic meeting; games; sports meet;
運會 international situations; trends of the time;
再會 goodbye; see you soon;
展覽會 exhibition;
展銷會 commodities fair;
招待會 reception;
早會 morning assembly;
照會 (1) present a note to a government; (2) diplomatic memorandum; diplomatic note;
知會 notify orally;
執委會 executive committee;
周會 weekly assembly;
轉會 transfer;
追悼會 memorial meeting;
總會 (1) assemblage; collection; conglomeration; (2) bound to; inevitable; sure to happen;
座談會 forum; symposium;

hui

【賄】 bribe;

［賄賂］ bribe; bung; buy over; buy sb off; give a bribe to sb; grease sb's hand; grease sb's palm; hand out a bribe to sb; offer a bribe to sb; oil sb's palm; pay off;

賄賂成風 bribery has become a common practice;

賄賂公行 bribery is openly practised; bribery is practised in public; commit bribery undisguisedly; give and take bribes openly; give sb a backhander; give sb an inducement; practise bribery publicly;

賄賂金 payola;

賄賂貪官 bribe a corrupt official;

不受賄賂 proof against bribery;

［賄賣］ buy over;

賄上賣下 send bribes to the upper and lower officials;

［賄托］ ask sb to do sth for a consideration;

［賄選］ get elected by bribery; practise bribery at an election;

納賄 (1) take bribes; (2) offer bribes;
受賄 accept bribes;
索賄 extort bribes;
行賄 bribe; offer bribes;

hui

【誨】 instruct; teach;

［誨淫誨盜］ debauch people and turn them into gangsters; inculcate sex and robbery; propagate sex and violence; stir up the base passions;

教誨 instruction; teaching;
訓誨 instruct; teach;

hui

【慧】 bright; intelligent;

［慧根］ root of wisdom that can lead one to the truth;

［慧光］ wisdom that, like the light, pierces darkness;

［慧劍］ the sword of wisdom that cuts through illusions of the material world;

慧劍斬情絲 cut the thread of carnal love with the sword of wisdom;

［慧力］ power of intelligence;

［慧目］ discerning eyes;

［慧黠］ clever and artful; shrewd;

［慧心］ clear, alert mind;

別具慧心 have a special understanding;

［慧性］ intelligence;

靈心慧性 intelligent and talented;

［慧眼］ eyes of wisdom;

慧眼獨具 can see what others cannot;

慧眼識人 develop a sharp eye for discovering able people;

慧眼識英雄 discerning eyes can tell greatness from mediocrity;
獨具慧眼 can see what others cannot; discern what others do not; have mental discernment;

［慧中］ intelligent inside;
慧中秀外 clever in mind and beautiful in appearance; intelligent within and beautiful without;

聰慧 bright; clever; intelligent;
敏慧 clever; sharp-witted;
穎慧 bright; clever; intelligent;
智慧 intelligence; wisdom;

hui
【櫘】 small coffin;

hui
【蕙】 (1) a species of fragrant grass with red flowers and black seeds in early autumn; (2) a species of fragrant orchid;
［蕙蘭］ a species of orchid;
［蕙心］ pure heart;
［蕙質］ good and pure quality of a person;
蕙質蘭心 pure heart and spirit;

hui
【諱】 (1) avoid as taboo; (2) forbidden word; taboo;
［諱忌］ forbidden;
諱忌詞 forbidden word; taboo;
諱疾忌醫 conceal a malady for fear of taking medicine; conceal one's ailment and refuse to consult the doctor; hide one's sickness for fear of the treatment; refuse to face the harsh reality;
［諱莫如深］ guard a secret closely; conceal in a most careful way — keep a closely guarded secret; not breathe a word to a soul; not utter a single word about sth;
［諱飾］ conceal the truth; make a deceptive display;
［諱言］ avoid mentioning sth; dare not speak up;
諱言其事 forbid to mention an affair;
毫不諱言 make no attempt to conceal the truth;
無可諱言 cannot avoid mentioning;
無容諱言 not mince words; straightforward;

避諱 taboo on using personal names of emperors, one's elders, etc.;
忌諱 (1) taboo; (2) avoid as taboo;
隱諱 avoid mentioning; cover up;

hui
【濊】 water plentifully;

hui
【燴】 (1) put together and cook; (2) serve with a topping of meat and vegetables in a gravy;
［燴飯］ mixed rice;
魚蛋燴飯 kedgeree;

雜燴 (1) hotchpotch; (2) medley; miscellany; mixture;

hui
【篲】 broom;

hui
【薈】 (1) a luxuriant growth of vegetation; (2) conceal; cover;
［薈萃］ assemble; gather together;
薈萃一堂 a distinguished gathering;
［薈蔚］ abundant; massive;

hui
【穢】 (1) vile; wicked; (2) dirty; filthy; (3) obscene; (4) ugly and abominable; (5) weeds on a farm;
［穢德］ debauched ways; filthy deeds;
［穢名］ notorious reputation;
［穢氣］ foul air;
［穢土］ (1) dirty earth; (2) (Buddhism) the human world;
［穢物］ filth;
［穢語］ dirty words; obscene language;
淫詞穢語 obscenities;

污穢 filthy; foul;
蕪穢 overgrown with weed;
淫穢 obscene; pornographic;

hui
【繢】 same as 繪, draw; make a sketch of;

hui
【蟪】 a kind of bright-coloured cicada;
［蟪蛄］ a kind of cicada;

hui

【繪】 draw; paint;
[繪畫] drawing; painting;
繪畫板 drawing board;
繪畫技巧 draughtsmanship;
繪畫能力 draughtsmanship;
繪畫繡花 paint a picture or do embroidery;
繪畫紙 drawing paper;
愛好繪畫 have a bent for painting;
彩色繪畫 polychrome painting;
業餘繪畫 amateur painting;
展出繪畫 exhibit paintings;
[繪景] scenic painting;
[繪圖] draw; sketch;
繪圖員 draughtsman;
[繪像] draw portraits;
[繪影繪聲] sketch the shadow and describe the voice — true to reality;
[繪製] draw;

彩繪 coloured drawing; coloured pattern;
草繪 draft;
測繪 map; survey and draw;
描繪 describe; portray;
清繪 delineation;

hui
【闠】 gate of a market;
hui
【靧】 shy; timid;
hui
【翽】 sound of wings flapping;

hun¹
hun
【昏】 (1) dusk; (2) dark; dim; (3) confused; muddled; (4) faint; lose consciousness;
[昏暗] dim; dusky;
半昏半暗 in a semi-comatose;
臨邊昏暗 limb darkening;
天昏地暗 a murkey sky over a dark earth; dark all round; heaven and earth are enveloped in gloom; in a state of chaos and darkness;
天昏地暗，日月無光 murkiness which neither moonlight nor sunlight can penetrate;
[昏沉] (1) murky; (2) befuddled; dazed;
暮色昏沉 murky twilight;
[昏倒] faint; fall down in a faint; fall unconscious;
[昏定晨省] attend to one's parents personally; visit one's parents day and night;
[昏黑] dark; dusky;
[昏花] dim-sighted;
餓得兩眼昏花 feel that one is going to faint with hunger;
[昏黃] (1) dim; faint; (2) pale yellow;
[昏昏] dizzy; drowsy;
昏昏沉沉 dizzy and sleepy; have a dizzy spell; one's mind is in a whirl;
～喝酒喝得昏昏沉沉 be bemused with drink;
昏昏好夢 dream pleasant dreams;
昏昏迷迷 half unconscious;
昏昏入睡 go to a lethargic sleep; sink into a deep sleep;
昏昏欲睡 drowse; drowsy; feel sleepy; heavy with sleep; one's eyes draw straws; sleepy;
[昏厥] faint; swoon;
一陣昏厥 a fainting spell;
[昏君] fatuous and self-indulgent ruler;
[昏聵] decrepit and muddleheaded;
昏聵龍鍾 with a dim vision and the dullness of senility;
昏聵無能 decrepit and incompetent; decrepit and muddle-headed;
昏聵愚昧 being stupefied and foolish;
[昏亂] befuddled; dazed and confused;
神志昏亂 delirious; delirium;
[昏迷] coma; in a coma; knockdown; muzziness; stupor;
昏迷不省 in a coma;
昏迷不醒 in an adject state of mental confusion; remain unconscious;
昏迷的 comatose;
半昏迷 semicoma;
肝昏迷 hepatic coma;
假昏迷 pseudocoma;
酒精性昏迷 alcoholic coma;
尿毒症昏迷 uremic coma;
輕昏迷 semicoma;
糖尿病昏迷 diabetic coma;
糖尿病性昏迷 diabetic coma;
陷入昏迷 fall into a coma;
永久高溫昏迷 permanent heat stupor;
暫時低溫昏迷 temporary cold stupor;
暫時高溫昏迷 temporary heat stupor;
[昏睡] lethargic sleep; trance;
昏睡病 sleeping sickness;

[昏霧蔽天] the sky becomes overcast with heavy clouds;
[昏眩] dizzy; giddy;
[昏庸] fatuous; imbecile; muddleheaded; stupid;

晨昏 morning and night;
發昏 (1) feel dizzy; (2) become confused; lose one's head;
黃昏 dusk; evening;

hun

【婚】 (1) marry; wed; (2) marriage; wedding;
[婚後] after marriage; after wedding;
婚後生活 married life;
婚後姓 married name;
[婚嫁] marriage; take a wife or marry a man; wed;
男婚女嫁 a man should take a wife and a woman should take a husband;
[婚禮] wedding ceremony;
婚禮彌撒 nuptial mass;
白色婚禮 white wedding;
參加婚禮 attend a wedding; go to a wedding;
大型婚禮 big wedding;
奉子成婚的婚禮 shotgun wedding;
公證婚禮 civil wedding;
教堂婚禮 church wedding;
舉行婚禮 perform marriages;
普通婚禮 civil wedding;
世俗婚禮 civil ceremony;
主持婚禮 conduct a wedding;
[婚齡] marriageable age;
[婚期] wedding day;
[婚前] before marriage; premarital;
婚前不睜眼，婚後傻了眼 marry in haste, repent at leisure;
婚前健康檢查 premarital consultation;
婚前姓 maiden name;
[婚紗] wedding dress;
婚紗照 wedding photography;
[婚生子] son born in wedlock;
婚生子女 children born in wedlock;
~ 非婚生子女 children born out of wedlock;
非婚生子 adulterine son;
[婚事] marriage; wedding;
安排婚事 make up a marriage;
協商婚事 negotiate marriage;
[婚外] extramarital;
婚外戀 extramarital affair; extramarital relations;
婚外情 double life; extramarital affair; extramarital flirtations; extramarital love;
[婚宴] wedding banquet;
[婚姻] marriage; matrimony;
婚姻長久 have a long marriage;
婚姻大事 marriage is a big event in one's life; the great affair of marriage;
婚姻道德 morality of marriage;
婚姻合法年齡 age of consent;
婚姻幻滅 marital disillusion;
婚姻家庭 marriage and family;
~ 婚姻家庭道德 morality of marriage and family;
婚姻介紹所 dating agency; marriage agent;
婚姻糾紛 matrimonial dispute;
婚姻美滿 connubial bliss; have a happy marriage; nuptial bliss;
婚姻破裂 a marriage breaks down; a marriage breaks up; bust-up of one's marriage; marital breakdown; marriage breakdown; marriage on the rocks; marriage split;
婚姻社會學 marriage sociology;
婚姻調解 matrimonial dispute mediation;
婚姻指導 marriage guidance;
婚姻狀況 marital status;
婚姻自由 freedom of marriage;
婚姻自主 marry the partner of one's own choice;
包辦婚姻 arranged marriage;
第二次婚姻 second marriage;
第一次婚姻 first marriage;
教會婚姻 canonical marriage;
開放式婚姻 open marriage;
買賣婚姻 mercenary marriage;
美滿的婚姻 happy marriage;
強迫婚姻 shotgun marriage; shotgun wedding;
權宜婚姻 marriage of convenience;
同性婚姻 same-sex marriage;
虛假婚姻 sham marriage;
[婚約] engagement; marriage contract;
毀棄婚約 breach of promise;
解除婚約 break off one's engagement; dissolve a marriage contract;
取消婚約 call off an engagement;

[婚贈] nuptial gift; wedding gift;

逼婚 force sb to get married;
成婚 get married;
重婚 bigamy;
瓷婚 China wedding;
訂婚 be engaged;
二婚 divorce;
結婚 get married; marry;
金婚 golden wedding;
抗婚 refuse to marry;
離婚 divorce;
求婚 make an offer of marriage; propose;
群婚 communal marriage; group marriage;
逃婚 run away from wedding;
通婚 be related by marriage; intermarry;
退婚 break off an engagement;
完婚 get married; marry;
晚婚 marry at a mature age;
未婚 single; unmarried;
新婚 newly-married;
已婚 married;
銀婚 silver wedding;
再婚 marry again; remarry;
早婚 marry too early;
證婚 chief witness at a wedding ceremony;

hun

【惛】 (1) confused; (2) senile;

hun

【葷】 (1) meat and fish diet; (2) strong smelling foods; (3) obscene or dirty language;

[葷腥] meat or fish;

[葷油] lard;
葷油蒙了心 befuddled; with one's mind in a haze;

開葷 begin or resume a meat diet;
冷葷 cold buffet; cold meat;

hun

【閽】 (1) door; gate; palace-gate; (2) gate-keeper;

[閽者] gatekeeper; janitor;

叩閽 go to the royal court to complain about one's wrong;

hun²

hun

【混】 muddy; not clear; turbid;

[混充] palm off inferior goods; pass oneself off as sb;

[混蛋] bloody fool; cocksucker;

[混雙] mixed doubles;

[混一色] (of mahjong) mixed tiles with one suit of characters;

[混音桌] mixing desk;

糊塗地混 bumble;

hun

【渾】 (1) muddy; turbid; (2) foolish; stupid; (3) simple and natural; (4) all over; whole;

[渾蛋] bastard; blackguard; bleeder; scoundrel; skunk; wretch;
搬弄是非的渾蛋 poisonous bastard;

[渾厚] (1) simple and honest; sincere; (2) simple and vigorous;

[渾渾噩噩] in a nebulous state; listlessly; muddle along; muddle-headed and ignorant; simple-minded; with one's mind in a haze;
渾渾噩噩地生活 lead an aimless existence; live in a state of ignorance;

[渾家] (1) the whole family; (2) one's wife;

[渾括] include;

[渾名] agnomen; nickname;

[渾樸] simple and honest;

[渾球] brazen-faced person; scatterbrain;

[渾然] (1) completely; without leaving a trace; (2) integral and indivisible;
渾然不覺 not aware at all; not feel at all;
渾然天成 like nature itself – highest quality of art;
渾然一體 a unified entity; all blend into one harmonious whole; an integral whole; an unseparable whole; one integrated mass;
渾然一新 everything made new;

[渾人] unreasonable fellow;

[渾身] all over; from head to foot;
渾身臭汗 be covered with smelly sweat; be in a muck of sweat; reek with sweat;
渾身打戰 shiver all over; shiver convulsively; shiver from head to foot; tremble like leaves;
渾身大汗 all of a muck of sweat; all of a sweat; be covered with sweat; be in a sweat all over; be steeped in sweat;
渾身哆嗦 all in a tremble; feel one's skin

creeping; in a tremble; on the tremble;
渾身發抖 all of a dither; all of a shake; tremble all over; tremble from head to foot; tremble in every limb; tremble like an aspen leaf;
渾身發冷 a chill comes creeping over one;
渾身發癢 itch all over;
渾身縞素 dressed in the white robes of mourning;
渾身解數 all one's skill; employ all one's skill to; every means of solution; exert oneself to the utmost to; try every means of solution; usc all one's skill;
渾身冷汗 a cold sweat breaks forth on one's whole body; be bathed in a cold and clammy perspiration;
渾身流汗 one's whole body is dripping with sweat;
渾身青紫 be beaten black and blue;
渾身肉顫 feel one's skin creeping;
渾身傷痕 all one's body is covered with bruises;
渾身上下 from top to toe;
渾身濕透 be drenched; be soaked; be soaked to the skin; be wet to the skin; be wet through; get a thorough souse; have not a dry thread on; wet as a drowned rat; wet to the skin;
渾身是膽 be filled with courage; every inch a hero; full of courage; one's whole body is valour; the very embodiment of valour;
渾身是汗 be covered with sweat; be steeped in sweat; in a sweat all over;
渾身是勁 alive every fibre; brimming with energy;
渾身是傷 be covered with wounds;
渾身是血 be covered all over with blood;
渾身素裹 be dressed all in white;
渾身酸軟 one fells at fagged out;
渾身酸痛 ache all over; the whole body aches;
~他渾身酸痛 he has aches all over;
渾身疼痛 have pains all over;

[渾水] muddy water;
渾水摸魚 fish in troubled waters;
[渾似] as if; as though; just like;
[渾俗和光] in harmony with the rest of the world;
[渾天儀] (1) armil; armillary sphere; (2) celestial globe;
[渾象] celestial globe;
[渾儀] armillary sphere;
[渾圓] perfectly round;
[渾濁] muddy; opacitas; turbid;
雄渾 forceful; vigorous and firm;
圓渾 (1) sweet and mellow; (2) profound and natural;

hun

【琿】 a kind of precious jade;
[琿春] Hunchun in Jilin Province;

hun

【魂】 (1) soul; (2) lofty spirit of a nation; (3) mood; spirit;
[魂不附體] as if the soul has left the body; be entranced with fear; be frightened out of one's wits; be scared out of one's wits; be scared to death;
嚇得魂不附體 scare sb out of his wits; scare sb still; scare the daylights out of sb
[魂不守舍] be in a dream; lose one's presence of mind; one's mind is somewhat unhinged; out of one's mind;
[魂離軀存] one's spirit has departed and only one's body remains;
[魂靈] ghost; soul; soul of the departed;
[魂夢] in one's dreams;
魂夢不安 on tenterhooks;
魂夢為勞 be troubled with dreams; remember ... even in one's dreams;
魂牽夢繞 be carried away into a region of dreams; be lost in a reverie; in a disturbed state of mind; in a state of mental confusion;
[魂魄] psyche; soul; the spirits and animal forces of man;
丟魂失魄 distracted;
勾魂攝魄 do execution; have the power to make men crazy; hook soul and arrest spirit; summon spirits;
魂飛魄散 be frightened out of one's wits; one's heart almost stands still;
魂飛魄喪 in extreme fright; make the soul of sb almost leave his body in horror;
魂迷魄蕩 bewitched; fascinated;
魂消魄散 it seems that their souls have melted away or evaporated like a mist;
魄散魂飛 be frightened out of one's wits;

喪魂落魄 be battered out of one's senses; be driven to distraction; be frightened out of one's wits; be frightened to distraction; be shaken to the core; beside oneself with fear; in panic; lose one's nerve; out of one's life; out of one's senses; out of one's wits; panic-stricken; terror-stricken;

鬼魂 ghost; spirit;
國魂 soul of the nation;
驚魂 fright;
靈魂 soul; spirit;
神魂 state of mind;
失魂 be frightened; be out of one's wits; be stricken;
亡魂 soul of a deceased person;
消魂 feel transported;
陰魂 soul; spirit;
英魂 spirit of the brave departed;
幽魂 ghost;
冤魂 the ghost of one who was wrongly accused;
招魂 call back the spirit of the dead;

hun²
hun
【餛】 ravioli; stuffed dumpling with delicate flour wrapping;
[餛飩] dumpling soup; huntun; wonton;

hun⁴
hun
【混】 (1) confuse; mix; (2) pass for; pass off as; (3) drift along; muddle along; (4) get along with sb;
[混成] blend together; mix together;
混成詞 blend; portmanteau word;
混成法 blending;
[混充] palm sth off as; pass oneself off as; pretend to be sb else;
混充內行 pretend to be an expert;
[混沌] (1) chaos; the chaotic world in prehistoric times; (2) ignorant and dumb; (3) a surname;
混沌初開 at the dawn of civilization innocent as a child;
分子混沌 molecular chaos;
[混飯吃] just to make a living;
[混合] admix; blend; commingle; mingle; mix; mix-up; mixing; mixture;
混合公司 mixed corporation;
混合家庭 blended family;
混合價 mixed price;
混合經濟論 theory of mixed economy;
混合林 mixed forest;
混合能力 mixed ability;
混合品 blend;
混合器 mixer;
~ 分批混合器 batch mixer;
~ 孔徑混合器 aperture mixer;
~ 錨式混合器 anchor mixer;
~ 平衡光電混合器 balanced photoelectric mixer;
混合稅 mixed duties;
混合體 amalgam;
~ 善與惡的混合體 amalgam of good and evil;
混合物 combo; composite; mélange; mixture;
~ 苯混合物 benzol mixture;
~ 基礎混合物 basic mixture;
~ 一種混合物 a mixture;
混合信貸 government mixed credit;
混合許可證 mixed licence;
混合岩 migmatite;
混合語 mixed language;
混合賬戶 combined account;
混合作用 migmatization
分批混合 batch mixing;
冷混合 cold mixing;
軸向混合 axial mixing;
[混混] (1) blackened; blurred; dark; opague; (2) drift along; drift through;
[混進] infiltrate; sneak into; worm one's way into;
[混亂] chaos; confusion; disorder; foul-up; havoc; muddledness;
混亂不堪 in utter disorder; utter disorder prevails; utterly chaotic;
混亂狀態 a state of disorder;
避免混亂 avoid confusion;
財務混亂 financial chaos;
大混亂 chaotic confusion; mayhem;
結束混亂 end the confusion;
一片混亂 a complete confusion; a great confusion; a lot of confusion; a scene of chaos; a scene of confusion; a state of chaos; in a litter; in a whirlpool; in complete shambles; in utter confusion;
造成混亂 create the confusion;
[混凝土] concrete;
混凝土工 concreter;
混凝土攪拌機 concrete mixer;
混凝土殼 concrete-shell;

鋼筋混凝土 armoured concrete; reinforced concrete;
加氣混凝土 aerated concrete; aeroconcrete;
焦渣混凝土 breeze concrete;
瀝青混凝土 asphaltic concrete;
耐酸混凝土 acid resisting concrete;
橋面板混凝土 bridge deck concrete;
石碴混凝土 ballast concrete;
一塊混凝土 a slab of concrete;

[混入] absorption; get into an organization without going through the proper procedures; mix oneself inside a body of people; sneak into; worm one's way into;
填料混入 filler absorption; filler acceptance;

[混事] drift along; muddle along;

[混同] combine; confuse; merge; mix up;

[混為一談] be confused; be identified with; confuse sth with sth else; confuse the issue; equate...with...; umble together; lump...together; mix up; place sth on a par with sth else; put on the same plane;

[混響] reverberation;
電子混響 electronic reverberation;
人工混響 artificial reverberation;
最佳混響 optimum reverberation;

[混淆] blur; confound; confuse; mingle; mix up;
混淆敵友 confuse friend with foe;
混淆黑白 call white black; juggle black and white; mix up black and white; obliterate the difference between black and white; obliterate the difference between good and bad; the confounding of black and white; to call black white; turn black into white; turn things upside down;
混淆是非 call right wrong and wrong right; confound the right with the wrong; confuse right and wrong; confuse the right with the wrong; confound the right with the wrong; confuse right and wrong;
混淆是非界線 blur out distinctions between right and wrong;
混淆視聽 call black white; confuse the people; confuse the public; confuse the public opinion; lead the public opinion astray; mislead the people; mislead the public; throw dust in sb's eyes;
混淆陣線 blur the alignments; mix up the fronts;

[混血兒] half-breed; mixed-blood; mustee; person of mixed blood;

[混雜] confounding; mingle; mix;

[混戰] confused fighting; melee; tangled warfare; wild war;

[混賬] bastard; scoundrel;

[混濁] (1) muddy; turbid; (2) nubecula;

[混子] quack;

鬼混 fool around;
含混 ambiguous; indistinct; vague;
蒙混 deceive and swindle;
閒混 idle about;

hun

【渾】 chaotic; confused; messy;

[渾沌] chaos; confusion; mess;
渾沌初開 when the universe was taking shape;
渾渾沌沌 dark and chaotic;

[渾天儀] armillary sphere; celestial globe;

hun

【溷】 (1) dirty; (2) messy;

hun

【慁】 (1) distress; disturb; (2) disgrace; (3) worry;

hun

【諢】 derision; ridicule;

[諢號] nickname;

[諢名] nickname;

打諢 indulge in raillery; mock in fun;

hun

【鯇】 grass carp;

huo¹

huo

【豁】 (1) break; crack; slit; (2) give up; sacrifice;

[豁口] breach; break; opening;
杯子上的豁口 a crack in the cup;

[豁命] at the expense of one's life; risk one's life;
豁出命幹 work as hard as anything;
豁出命拼 fight sth tooth and nail;

H

［豁子］ breach; opening;
［豁嘴］ cleff lip;

huo²
huo

【活】 (1) live; (2) alive; living; (3) save; (4) lively; vivid; (5) movable; moving; (6) exactly; simply; (7) work; (8) product;

［活寶］ a bit of a clown; funny fellow; sth good;
家有一老，黃金活寶 an old man in house is a good sign; that house is happy which smells of an old man;

［活不長了］ one's days are numbered;

［活到老學到老］ a man should study till his dying day; it is never too old to learn; keep on learning as long as you live; live and learn; never too old to learn; one is never too old to learn;

［活底］ drop bottom; false bottom;

［活動］ (1) exercise; move about; (2) shaky; unsteady; (3) mobile; movable; (4) activity; going-ons; maneuvre; (5) use personal influence or irregular means; (6) behaviour;
活動策劃人 campaign manager;
活動詞 event word;
活動名詞 event noun;
活動目標 moving target;
活動站 activity station;
活動資金 campaign funds; campaign money;
暗中活動 carry on surreptitious activities;
插入活動 insertion activity;
慈善活動 philanthropic activity;
代謝活動 metabolic activity;
對流活動 convective activity;
翻譯活動 translation activity;
非法活動 illegal activities;
戶外活動 outdoor activities;
競選活動 election campaign;
課堂活動 classroom activity;
課外活動 extracurricular activities;
幕後活動 the behind-the-scenes activities;
腦電波活動 brain electrical activity;
破壞活動 destructive activitity;
社會活動 social activities;
社交活動 social affair;
實踐活動 practical activity;
適應活動 adaptive activity;
文娛活動 recreational activities;
校外活動 after-school activities;
宣傳活動 propaganda activity;
學術活動 academic activity;
學習活動 learning activities;
演講活動 lecturing activity;
一連串活動 an orgy of activities;
一項活動 an activity;
整理活動 warming-down exercise;
準備活動 warming-up exercise;
作息活動 work-and-rest system;

［活度］ activity;
活度常數 activity constant;
絕對活度 absolute activity;
離子活度 ionic activity;
雙重活度 double activity;

［活泛］ quick-witted;

［活佛］ Living Buddha;

［活該］ have only oneself to thank; not wronged at all; serve sb right; that's tough; tough; tough shit;
活該倒霉 destined to come to grief; tough luck;
活該如此 deserve whatever one gets; get what one deserves; it serves you right; serves you right;
你活該 it serves you right;

［活化］ activation;
活化劑 activator;
活化碳 activated carbon;
共活化 coactivate;
光化活化 photochemical activation;
還原活化 reduction activation;
基因活化 gene activation;
極性活化 polar activation;
疏水活化 hydrophobic activation;
質子活化 proton activation;
中子活化 neutron activation;

［活活］ alive; live; living; while still alive;

［活計］ (1) handicraft work; manual labour; (2) handiwork; work;
針線活計 needlework;

［活劇］ drama in real life; living drama;

［活口］ (1) survivor of a murder attempt; (2) prisoner who can furnish information;
養家活口 look after one's family and a living to earn;

［活力］ activity; brio; energy; juice; light; lust; verve; vigour; vitality;
活力充沛 of great vitality; sprightly;

保持活力 maintain vigour;
充滿活力 full of life; full of piss and vinegar; full of vitality; have an exuberant vitality; in full activity; lively; spry; with lots of zing;
很有活力 has a lot of bounce;
恢復活力 renew vigour; restore vigour;
青春的活力 vagour of youth;
缺乏活力 lack energy; lack vigour;
攝食活力 feeding activity;
顯示活力 show vigour;
有無窮的活力 possess inexhaustible vitality;
增加活力 enhance vigour;

[活靈活現] bear a living resemblance to; lifelike; living image of; tone it up with colour and life; vivid;
說得活靈活現 give a vivid description;

[活路] (1) means of subsistence; way out; way to make a living; (2) workable method;

[活絡] adroit in thinking;
手腳活絡 dexterous and quick in action;
頭腦活絡 quick-witted;

[活埋] bury alive;

[活命] (1) earn a bare living; eke out an existence; scrape along; (2) save sb's life; (3) life;
活命之恩 indebtedness to sb for saving one's life;
度日活命 manage to keep oneself alive with;

[活潑] (1) active; full of life; lively; sprightly; vivacious; vivid; (2) reactive;
活潑的 brisk; frisky;
活潑輕快 breezy; vivacious and light-hearted;
活潑有趣 amusing; lively; vivacious;
性格很活潑 vivacious disposition;

[活期] current;
活期存款 current deposit;

[活氣] vigorous atmosphere;

[活人] living person; person who is still alive;

[活塞] piston;
活塞環 piston ring;
減震活塞 damping piston;
控制活塞 control piston;
平衡活塞 balancing piston;
鑄鐵活塞 cast-iron piston;
組合活塞 assembled piston; built-up piston;

[活生生] (1) actual; alive; alive and kicking; in real life; living; real; (2) while still alive;
活生生打死 beat a person to death;
活生生的例子 living example;
活生生的事實 real fact;

[活水] flowing water; fresh current; running water;

[活套] flexible; free; unconstrained;

[活現] appear vividly; come alive;

[活像] a model of sb; an exact replica of sb; bear a strong resemblance to sb; favour sb; have a look of sb; have a strong resemblance to sb; look as if indeed; look exactly like sb; remarkably alike; resemble sb; show a strong resemblance to sb; take a strong resemblance to; take after sb; the double of sb; the living image of sb; the spit and image of; the very image of sb; the very picture of sb;
活像自己的母親 the replica of one's mother;

[活性] activated; active; activity;
活性氮 active nitrogen;
活性染料 reactive dye;
活性炭 active carbon;
活性吸附 activated adsorption;
催化活性 catalytic activity;
發酵活性 fermentation activity;
界面活性 interfacial activity;
毛細活性 capillary activity;
生物活性 biological activity;

[活學活用] creatively study and apply; learn and apply with full vigour;

[活頁] leaflet; loose-leaf;
活頁本 loose-leaf note-book;
活頁夾 binder; loose-leaf binder; ring binder;
活頁文檔 loose-leaf file;
活頁紙 paper for a loose-leaf notebook;

[活用] make flexible use of;

[活魚] live fish;

[活躍] (1) active; brisk; dynamic; (2) animate; enliven; invigorate;
活躍的 frisky;
活躍份子 live wire;
過度活躍 overactive;
市場很活躍 the market is lively;

[活捉] capture alive; catch alive;
[活罪] hardship; suffering;

長活 long-term job;
成活 survive;
出活 efficient; yield results in work;
粗活 heavy manual labour; unskilled work;
放活 release from unnecessary constraints;
復活 bring back to life; revive;
幹活 work; work on a job;
苟活 drag out an ignoble existence;
過活 live; make a living;
快活 cheerful; happy; satisfied;
靈活 (1) agile; nimble; quick; (2) elastic; flexible;
輕活 light work; soft job;
生活 (1) life; (2) livelihood;
死活 life and death;
鐵活 ironwork;
細活 skilled work;
養活 (1) feed; support; (2) raise; (3) give birth to;
夜活 night work;
圓活 (1) clever and active; energetic; flexible; nimble; quick-minded; (2) a rich and round voice;
雜活 odd jobs;
重活 heavy work;
自己活也讓別人活 live and let live;
作活 work for one's living;
做活 do manual labour; work;

huo³
huo

【火】 (1) fire; (2) ammunition; firearm; (3) anger; temper; (4) pressing; urgent; (5) fiery; flaming; (6) internal heat;

[火把] torch;
[火爆] fiery; irritable;
火爆的脾氣 volcanic temper;
性情火爆 of impetuous temper;
性子火爆 have a hot temper; have a quick temper; have a short temper;
[火併] open fight between factions;
[火柴] match;
火柴桿 matchstick;
火柴棍 matchstick;
火柴盒 matchbox;
火柴人 matchstick figures; matchstick men;
安全火柴 safety match;
擦根火柴 strike a match;
劃火柴 strike a match;
一包火柴 a box of matches;
一根火柴 a match;
一盒火柴 a box of matches;
紙夾火柴 matchbook;
[火車] choo-choo; rail; train;
火車出發 a train departs; a train leaves;
火車出站 a train pulls out of a station;
火車到達 a train arrives;
火車進站 a train pulls into a station;
火車開到馬路上一越軌 a train running onto the highway — transgressing the tracks; (coll) exceeding the bounds;
火車輪渡 train ferry;
火車旅行 a journey on a train;
火車票 train ticket;
~一張火車票 a rail ticket;
火車票價 train fare;
火車事故 train accident;
火車司機 train driver;
火車頭 locomotive;
火車脱軌 the train was derailed;
火車相撞事故 train crash; train wreck;
火車站 railway station; train station;
~火車站站長 station master;
乘火車 by train; get a train; ride on a train; take a train; travel in a train;
搭火車 aboard a train;
單軌火車 monorail;
當心火車 beware of trains;
等火車 wait for a train;
電氣火車 electric train;
調度火車 dispatch a train;
趕火車 catch a train;
開火車 operate a train; run a train;
開往北京的火車 the train for Beijing;
聯運火車 boat train;
沒趕上火車 miss a train;
上火車 get into a train; get on a train;
玩具火車 train set;
誤了火車 miss one's train;
下火車 get off a train; get out of a train;
懸浮火車 aerotrain;
一列火車 a train;
一趟火車 a train;
走下火車 step down from a train;
坐火車 go by train; ride on a train; travel by train;
[火成] igneous;
火成碎屑岩 pyroclastic rock;
火成岩 igneous rock;

[火耕水耨] burn straws and weeds and water the land－primitive method of farming;
[火攻] fire attack;
[火光] blaze; flame; flare; the glow of fire; the light of fire;
火光衝天 be all afire; flames leap to the sky; flames spring up to heaven; the falmes light up the sky;
火光明亮 burn bright;
火光耀眼 burn with a glaring light;
火光燭天 leaping flames light up the sky;
火光灼天 flames redden the sky; flames rise high toward the sky; the fire illuminates the sky; the flames leap to heaven; the sky is lit with flames; the sky is reddened with the flames;
遍地火光 flames scorch the earth far and wide;
一片火光 in a blaze;
[火鍋] chafing dish;
吃火鍋 chafing-pot meal;
[火海] sea of fire;
一片火海 a sea of flame; a sheet of flames; an ocean of fire; be speedily covered with fire;
葬身火海 perish in flames;
[火紅] fiery; firelight; flaming; red as fire;
火紅的年代 fiery years;
[火候] (1) duration and degree of heating or cooking; (2) the level of attainment;
未到火候 not yet up to the required standard;
[火狐] red fox;
[火花] cremation; spark; spark discharge;
火花放電 spark discharge;
火花隙 spark-gap;
火花室 spark chamber;
火花四濺 sparks flying off in all directions;
電刷火花 brush spark;
斷路火花 break spark;
分化火花 branched spark;
生命的火花 spark of life;
天才的火花 a spark of genius;
[火化] cremate; cremation;
[火雞] turkey;
火雞咯咯叫 a turkey gobbles;
公火雞 gobbler;
烤火雞 roast turkey;
一隻火雞 a turkey;
[火急] pressing; urgent;
[火箭] bird; fire arrow; rocket;
火箭彈 rocket;
火箭發動機 rocket engine; rocket motor;
火箭基地 rocket base;
火箭探空儀 rocketsonde;
火箭推進 rocket propulsion;
~火箭推進劑 rocket propellant;
火箭武器 rocket armament;
火箭專家 rocket scientist;
單級火箭 one-stage rocket;
彈道火箭 ballistic rocket;
~州際彈道火箭 intercontinental ballistic rocket;
多級火箭 multi-stage rocket;
防空火箭 anti-aircraft rocket;
航空火箭 aircraft rocket;
航天火箭 space rocket;
核火箭 nuclear rocket;
減速火箭 retrorocket;
兩級火箭 two-stage rocket;
氣象火箭 meteorological rocket;
嵌火箭 carrier rocket; launch vehicle;
三級火箭 three-stage rocket;
微調火箭 vernier rocket;
一枚火箭 a rocket;
宇宙火箭 cosmic rocket;
運載火箭 carrier rocket; launch vehicle;
~發射運載火箭 launch a carrier rocket;
主級火箭 sustainer rocket;
助推火箭 booster rocket;
[火警] fire alarm; fire police;
火警出口 fire exit;
報火警 report a fire;
一起火警 a case of fire alarm;
[火炬] torch; torch light;
火炬賽跑 torch race;
火炬手 torch bearer;
[火坑] fiery pit;
復墮火坑 out of the frying-pan into the fire;
救出火坑 save sb from an abyss of suffering;
[火辣辣] burning;
火辣辣的大熱天 a broiling hot day;
[火烙] burnt;
火烙畫 burnt picture; poker work;
[火力] fire; firepower;
低伸火力 grazing fire;
防空火力 antiaircraft fire;

交叉火力 crossfire;

[火爐] furnace; stove;
火爐用具 fire iron;

[火冒三丈] burst into a fury; flare up; fly into a rage; fly into a towering passion; hit the ceiling; hit the roof; in the fury; in a towering rage; lose one's rag; see red;

[火帽] primer;

[火鳥] firebird;

[火砲] armament; artillery; cannon; gun;
火砲操作 gunnery;
火砲射擊術 gunnery;
固定火砲 fixed armament;
強擊火砲 assault artillery;
移動火砲 mobile artillery;

[火盆] brazier; fire basket; fire pan; fired devil;

[火氣] (1) internal heat; (2) anger; temper;
火氣很大 be possessed of a fiery temper;
按下火氣 keep down one's anger;
抑制自己的火氣 restrain one's temper;

[火槍] musket;
火槍手 fusilier; musketeer;

[火球] fireball;
一團火球 a fireball;

[火熱] (1) burning hot; fervent; fiery; (2) intimate;
火熱的眼睛 burning eyes;
火熱的語言 words of fire;
打得火熱 as thick as thieves; be infatuated with sb; be passionately attached to each other; carry on intimately with; cheek by jowl; chum up with; fraternize with; hobnob with; join in a love feast; on terms of intimacy; thick with each other;

[火山] burning mountain; volcano;
火山爆發 the volcano burst into eruption; volcanic eruption;
火山帶 volcanic belt;
火山彈 volcanic bomb;
火山地震 volcanic earthquake;
火山灰 volcanic ash;
火山角礫岩 volcanic breccia;
火山口 crater;
～爆裂火山口 explosion crater;
～寄生火山口 adventive crater;
火山筒 pipe;
火山學 volcanology;
火山岩 volcanic rocks;
火山雲 volcanic cloud;
火山渣錐 cinder core;
火山錐 cone;
爆裂火山 erupting volcano;
盾形火山 shield volcano;
海底火山 submarine volcano;
複合火山 compound volcano;
複式火山 composite volcano;
海底火山 oceanic volcano;
活火山 acting volcano; active volcano;
泥火山 mud volcano;
氣火山 air volcano;
熔岩火山 lava volcano;
死火山 extinct volcano;
體眠火山 dormant volcano;
休眠火山 dormant volcano;
周期性火山 periodic volcano;

[火上] to the fire;
火上加油 add fuel to the fire; add oil to the flames; aggravate the problem; inflame one's anger; pour oil on the fire; pour oil over the flames; stir things up; throw the fat in the fire;
火上添薪 feed fresh fuel to the fire; give fuel to fire;

[火燒] (1) burn; (2) baked wheaten cake;
火燒芭蕉一心不死 burning a banana — the heart is not dead; unwilling to give up;
火燒火燎 burn like fire; burn with a feeling; feeling terribly hot; restless with anxiety;
火燒眉毛 a matter of the utmost urgency; fire catches the eyebrows — in imminent danger;
火燒屁股—急煞人 fire burning one's buttocks — extremely nervous;
火燒旗桿—長歎(炭) burning a flagpole — a long piece of charcoal;
開花兒火燒 split-top baked wheaten cake;
糖火燒 baked wheaten cake with sugar;
糖酥火燒 sweet and crisp baked cake;

[火舌] fireflow; licking flame; tongues of fire;

[火神] god of fire;

[火石] fire-stone; flint;

[火樹銀花] bonfires display; fiery trees and silver flowers — dazzling displays of fireworks and a sea of lanterns;

[火速] at top speed; posthaste;

[火炭] live charcoal;

[火燙] (1) scalding; very hot; (2) have one's

hair permed; perm;

[火頭] (1) flame; (2) duration and degree of heating or cooking; (3) anger; blaze of temper; fit of anger; flare-up;
火頭兒上 at the height of one's anger;

[火腿] gammon; ham;
帶骨火腿 bone-in ham;
方火腿 square ham;
冷盤火腿 cold ham;
碎火腿 chopped ham;
圓火腿 round ham;

[火險] (1) fire insurance; (2) fire danger;

[火星] (1) flake; spark; sparkle; spunk; (2) Mars;
火星表面學 aerography;
火星人 aliens from the Mars; Martian;
火星衛星 the Martian satellites;
火星學 aerography;
打出火星 strike out sparks;
發出火星 emit sparks;

[火焰] blaze; flame;
火焰衝天 flames mount to heaven;
火焰清理 scarfing;
~機動火焰清理 machine scarfing;
~手動火焰清理 hand scarfing;
~自動火焰清理 automatic scarfing;
柴多火焰高 more logs make a bigger fire;
輔助火焰 booster flame;
明亮火焰 clear flame;
撲不滅的火焰 quenchless flame;
撲滅火焰 extinguish the flames; put out the flames; put the blaze out;
煽動火焰 fan the flame;
碳化火焰 carbonizing flame;
突然冒出火焰 flame out;
一陣火焰 a burst of flame;

[火藥] gunpowder; powder;
火藥爆炸 gun-powder explosion;
火藥桶 powder keg;
火藥味 the smell of gundpowder;
發明火藥 invent gunpowder;
慢性火藥 slow-burning punpowder;
無煙火藥 cordite; smokeless gunpowder;

[火災] conflagration; fire;
火災破壞 fire damage;
火災學 fire science;
森林火災 forest fire;
一場火災 a fire;

[火葬] cremate; cremation;
火葬場 crematory;
提倡火葬 advocate cremation;

[火中取栗] a cat's-paw; pull sb's chestnuts out of the fire;

[火燭] things that may cause a fire;
小心火燭 beware of fire;

[火嘴] nozzle;

愛火 sexual drive;
暗火 dying fire;
敗火 relieve internal heat;
兵火 war; warfare;
撥火 poke a fire;
柴火 faggot; firewood;
淬火 quench;
燈火 lights;
點火 (1) kindle the flames; light a fire; start a fire; (2) stir up trouble;
發火 (1) catch fire; ignite; (2) detonate; go off; (3) flare up; get angry; lose one's temper;
防火 fire prevention; fireproof;
放火 (1) set fire to; set on fire; (2) create disturbances;
烽火 (1) beacon; beacon fire; (2) flame of war;
肝火 irascibility;
膏火 lights;
鬼火 jack-o'-lantern; will-o'-the-wisp;
過火 go to extreme; go too far; overdo;
紅火 flourishing; prosperous;
回火 back fire;
活火 fire;
交火 be at war; fight; wage war;
接火 start to exchange fire;
借火 ask for a light;
救火 fight a fire;
舉火 (1) light a fire; (2) light a stove;
軍火 arms and ammunition;
開火 open fire;
烤火 warm oneself by a fire;
烈火 raging fire; raging flames;
磷火 phosphorescent light;
流火 erysipelas on the leg;
榴火 garnet;
爐火 furnace fire; stove fire;
慢火 gentle heat; slow fire;
冒火 burn with anger; flare up; get angry;
滅火 extinguish a fire; put out a fire;
惱火 feel irritated;
怒火 flames of fury; fury;
砲火 artillery fire; gunfire;
起火 (of fire) break out;
去火 reduce internal heat;
熱火 tremendously enthusiastic;
上火 suffer from excessive internal heat;

H

燒火 light a fire; make a fire; tend the kitchen fire;
生火 light a fire; make a fire;
失火 a fire breaks out; be on fire; catch fire;
炭火 charcoal fire;
停火 cease fire;
退火 anneal;
玩火 play with fire;
微火 slow fire;
文火 gentle heat; slow fire;
武火 high heat;
熄火 put out the fire;
香火 burning incense; burning joss sticks;
心火 internal heat;
星火 (1) spark; (2) meteor; shooting star;
煙火 (1) smoke and fire; (2) cooked food;
焰火 fireworks;
洋火 matches;
野火 bush fire; prairie fire; wildfire;
一層火 a ring of fire;
一肚子火 have a stomachful of anger;
一團火 a ball of fire;
引火 draw fire;
營火 campfire;
漁火 lights on fishing boats;
戰火 flames of war;
着火 be on fire; catch fire;
縱火 commit arson; set on fire;

huo

【伙】 (1) board; meal; mess; (2) company; partnership; (3) mate; partner; (4) band; crowd; group; (5) combine; join;

[伙伴] companion; partner;
好伙伴 worthy companion;
合適的伙伴 fit companion;
競選伙伴 running-mate;

[伙房] kitchen;

[伙夫] cook; mess cook;

[伙計] (1) business associate; partner; (2) fellow; mate; (3) salesman; shop assistant; shop clerk; waiter; (4) farm labourer;
小伙計 young chap;

[伙食] board; fare; food; meal; mess; table;
自理伙食 board oneself;

[伙同] gang up with sb; in collusion with; in league with; work in collusion with; work in league with;

[伙子] company; partnership;
小伙子 chap; chappy; kiddo; lad; laddie; laddy; little fellow; sonny; stripling; young chap; young fellow; young lad; young man; youngster;
~小伙子似的 laddish;
~小伙子文化 culture of laddism;
~矯健的小伙子 a dapper little fellow;
~魁梧的小伙子 a strapping young lad;
~前途無量的小伙子 a young lad with the world at his feet;
~瘦長的小伙子 a slip of a boy;
~瘦高的小伙子 lanky young man;

包伙 board;
拆伙 dissolve a partnership; part company;
搭伙 (1) join as partner; (2) eat regularly in (a mess, etc.);
合伙 form a partnership;
入伙 (1) join a gang; join in partnership; (2) join a mess;
散伙 disband; dissolve;

huo

【鈥】 holmium;

huo

【夥】 (1) lots of; many; much; plenty; (2) assistant; companion; company; partner; (3) clerk; waiter;

[夥伴] companion; helpmate; partner; the lads;
貿易夥伴 trading partner;
童年夥伴 childhood friend;

[夥計] clerk; matey; waitor;

[夥同] gang up with; in league with;

[夥頤] many;

[夥友] business associate;

huo⁴

huo

【或】 (1) maybe; perhaps; probably; (2) either...or; or; (3) some people; someone;

[或…或] either...or; or;

[或是] or;

[或許] likely; maybe; might; perhaps; possible; would;

[或者] maybe; perhaps; or;

即或 even; even if; even though;
間或 occasionally; now and then; once in a while; sometimes;
容或 maybe; perhaps; possibly;
設或 if; supposing;

甚或 even; go so far as to; so much so that;
倘或 if; in case;
抑或 or;

huo
【砉】 cracking sound; splitting sound;

huo
【貨】 (1) commodity; goods; (2) money;

[貨幣] currency; money;
貨幣貶值 devaluation of currency;
貨幣單位 monetary unit;
貨幣改革 monetary reform;
貨幣供應 money supply;
~貨幣供應量 money supply;
貨幣購買力 purchasing power of currency;
貨幣回籠 withdrawal of currency from circulation;
貨幣經濟學 economics of money;
貨幣均衡論 monetary equilibrium;
貨幣流通 currency circulation;
~貨幣流通管理 current circulating management;
貨幣平價 currency parity;
貨幣期貨 currency future;
貨幣昇值 currency appreciation;
貨幣市場 money market;
貨幣條款 currency clause;
貨幣投放 money supply;
貨幣危機 monetary crisis;
貨幣信用 confidence in the currency;
貨幣債務 monetary liabilities;
貨幣戰 currency war;
貨幣政策 monetary policy;
貨幣制度 coinage;
~十進制貨幣制度 decimal coinage;
貨幣周轉 money turnover;
貨幣主義 monetarism;
~貨幣主義者 monetarist;
貨幣責任 dollar responsibility;
保管貨幣 custody of money;
本位貨幣 monetary money; standard money;
儲備貨幣 reserve currency;
單一貨幣 single currency;
電子貨幣 e-money; electronic currency; electronic money;
兌換貨幣 money changing;
法定貨幣 legal tender;
干預貨幣 intervention currency;
基本貨幣 basic monetary unit;
~基本貨幣供應額 basic money supply;
金屬貨幣 metallic currency; metallic money;
可兌換貨幣 convertible currency;
流通貨幣 money in circulation;
~流通貨幣量 volume of money in circulation;
內部貨幣 inside money;
歐洲貨幣 Euro-currency;
強勢貨幣 hard currency;
軟貨幣 soft currency;
十進制貨幣 decimal currency;
世界貨幣 world currency;
外國貨幣 foreign currency;
中性貨幣 neutral money;
周轉貨幣 vehicle currency;

[貨倉] warehouse;
迷你貨倉 mini-warehouse;

[貨暢其流] facilitate commodity interflow; smooth flow of goods;

[貨車] (1) freight trains; goods trains; (2) freight car; goods van; (3) goods wagon; lorry; road wagon; truck; wagon;
貨車車廂 freight car;
大型貨車 juggernaut;
小貨車 pick up truck;
小型貨車 panel truck; van;
~小型貨車 van driver;
一列貨車 a cargo train;
有蓋貨車 boxcar;
運煤貨車 coal truck;
載重貨車 heavy goods vehicle;

[貨船] cargo ship; cargo vessel; freighter;

[貨到即提] delivery on arrival;

[貨櫃] (1) counter; (2) container;

[貨價] commodity prices; prices of goods;
減低貨價 mark down goods;
穩定貨價 squeeze the price of commodity;

[貨郎] itinerant pedlar; street vendor;

[貨輪] cargo vessel; freighter;

[貨品] kinds of goods; quality of product;

[貨色] goods; kinds and quality of goods;
貨色齊全 goods of every description are available;
好貨色 excellent goods;
上等貨色 first-class goods;

[貨攤] shopboard; stall; stand;

[貨物] cargo; commodity; goods; merchandize; stock of goods;
貨物出門，概不退換 products sold are

H

non-refundable;
貨物稅 commodity tax;
貨物說明 docket;
包裝貨物 bale cargo; packed cargo;
保價貨物 insured cargo;
保稅貨物 bonded cargo;
爆炸性貨物 explosive cargo;
笨大貨物 bulky goods;
採辦貨物 buy goods on a large scale;
殘損貨物 damaged cargo;
艙面貨物 deck cargo;
艙內貨物 under-deck cargo;
超長貨物 long goods;
超程貨物 distance freight;
超量貨物 excess cargo;
超重貨物 heavy package;
出口貨物 export cargo; export commodities; outward cargo;
儲藏箱貨物 locker cargo;
待領貨物 unclaimed cargo;
袋裝貨物 bag cargo;
腐蝕性貨物 corrosive cargo;
穀類貨物 grain cargo;
貴重貨物 valuable goods;
過境貨物 transit cargo;
合時貨物 seasonal goods;
混裝貨物 consolidated cargo;
集裝箱運貨物 containerized cargo;
進口貨物 import cargo; import commodities;
均質貨物 homogenous cargo;
空運貨物 air cargo; air freight;
漏卸 overcarried cargo;
免稅貨物 duty-free goods;
同盟貨物 conference cargo;
退關貨物 shut out cargo;
危險貨物 dangerous cargo;
未經申報的貨物 undeclared cargo;
無人領取的貨物 unclaimed cargo;
銷售貨物 market the goods;
一般貨物 general cargo;
一批貨物 a batch of goods; a load of goods; a shipment of goods; an assortment of goods;
易燃貨物 inflammable;
異質貨物 heterogenous cargo;
運載貨物 carry cargo;
轉手貨物 switch cargo;
轉運貨物 transshipment cargo;
裝艙貨物 hold cargo;
自由貨物 open cargo;

[貨箱] container;
木製大貨箱 packing case;

[貨樣] sample;
小包貨樣 small sample;

[貨源] a source of goods; a supply of goods;
貨源充足 an ample supply of goods;
開闢貨源 open up new sources of goods;

[貨運] freight transport;
貨運單 waybill;
貨運量 volume of freight;
貨運列車 freight train; goods train;

[貨載] transport a cargo;
放棄貨載 abandonment of a cargo;

[貨主] owner of a cargo;

百貨 general merchandise;
包裝貨 packed cargo;
北貨 goods or produce from the North;
殘貨 damaged goods; shopworn goods; substandard goods;
艙內貨 inboard cargo;
炒貨 roasted seeds and nuts;
陳貨 old stock; shopworn goods;
暢銷貨 popular goods;
出口貨 export cargo; outward cargo;
蠢貨 blockhead; dunce; idiot;
次貨 inferior goods; substandard goods;
存貨 existing stock; goods in stock;
訂貨 order goods; plan an order for goods;
發貨 deliver goods; send out goods;
乾貨 dried food and nuts; dry cargo;
國貨 Chinese goods;
海貨 marine products;
行貨 goods which are not carefully processed;
好貨 clean cargo;
黑貨 (1) contraband; smuggled goods; (2) sinister stuff; trash;
換貨 exchange goods;
加載貨 additional cargo;
賤貨 (1) cheap goods; (2) base woman;
交貨 deliver goods;
進貨 replenish one's stock;
進口貨 import cargo; inward cargo;
舊貨 junk; secondhand goods;
冷凍貨物 frozen cargo; refrigerated cargo;
冷貨 dull goods; goods not much in demand;
理貨 tally;
名牌貨 goods of a famous brand;
南貨 delicacies from the South;
年貨 special purchases for the Spring Festival;
盤貨 take stock;
皮貨 fur; pelt;
期貨 futures;

散貨 bulk cargo;
散裝貨 bulk cargo;
上貨 exhibit goods for sale;
剩貨 surplus goods;
識貨 know all about the goods; know what's what;
售貨 sell goods;
私貨 contraband goods; smuggled goods;
提貨 pick up goods; take delivery of goods;
通貨 currency; current money;
土貨 local products; native produce;
外貨 foreign goods; imported goods;
未到貨 floating cargo; pending cargo;
稀貨 goods badly in need; rare goods;
鮮貨 (1) fresh fruit; (2) fresh aquatic food; (3) perishable cargo;
現貨 live cargo; merchandise on hand; spot cargo; spot goods;
卸貨 discharge cargo; unload; unload a cargo;
洋貨 foreign goods; imported goods;
雜貨 groceries; sundry goods;
載貨 load a cargo;
滯銷貨 slow-selling goods;
裝貨 load cargo;

huo

【惑】 (1) beguile; confuse; delude; misguide; mislead; (2) doubt; suspect;

[惑亂] confuse; delude; puzzle;

[惑術] deceitful tricks; guile; ruse;

[惑志] doubt; suspicion;

[惑眾] delude or confuse people;

左道惑眾 delude the people by heretical doctrines;

蠱惑 (1) poison; (2) confuse; delude;
惶惑 apprehensive; perplexed and alarmed;
困惑 perplexed; puzzled;
煽惑 agitate; incite;
淆惑 bewilder; confuse; mislead;
疑惑 feel uncertain; not be convinced;
熒惑 confuse; dazzle; mislead;
誘惑 (1) entice; lure; seduce; (2) allure; attract;

huo

【禍】 (1) calamity; disaster; misfortune; (2) bring disaster upon; ruin;

[禍不單行] an evil chance seldom comes alone; an Illiad of woes; bad events rarely come singly; disasters do not come alone; disasters pile up on one another; it never rains but it pours; misery loves company; misfortunes never come singly; one misfortune calls upon another; one misfortune comes on the neck of another; one woe doth tread upon another's heels; when it rains it pours; when sorrows come, they come not single spies, but in battalions;

[禍不妄至] disaster never strikes without cause; woes never come without reason;

[禍從天降] a calamity descends from the sky; an unexpected affliction; disaster comes from the sky; misfortune drops from heaven, and falls on sb;

[禍端] cause of a disaster; cause of a misfortune; cause of ruin; source of the disaster;

[禍福] disaster and happiness; fortunes and misfortunes;

避禍趨福 pursue good fortune and avoid disaster;

禍福淳淳 misfortune and happiness alternate;

禍福共之 independent of good or evil fortune;

禍福難卜 misfortunes cannot be foretold;

禍福榮枯 the shifts and changes of life;

禍福同當 share weal and woe; throw in one's lot with sb;

禍福同門，利害為鄰 as to advantages and disadvantages, they are closely linked; weal and woe come from the same source;

禍福無門 God's even-handed justice; happiness and woe are two things to which there is no open door;

禍福無門，唯人自招 misery and happiness have no door, but men bring them upon themselves; there is no highroad to happiness or misfortune, every man brings them on himself;

禍福與共 go through thick and thin together; share thick and thin with sb; share weal and woe;

旦夕禍福 fortune is fickle; sudden changes of fortune; unexpected good or bad fortune;

~人有旦夕禍福 man's fate is as uncertain

as the weather; men's fortunes may change overnight;

化禍為福 turn bad luck into a blessing; turn disaster into good luck;

禍兮福所倚，福兮禍所伏 good fortune lieth within bad, bad fortune lurketh within good; in calamity lies good fortune and in good fortune lurks calamity;

禍中得福 good comes out of evil; good luck sometimes comes out of a calamity;

禍中寓福，福中伏禍 in calamity lies good fortune and in good forune lurks calamity;

因禍得福 a blessing in disguise; a fault on the right side; an alliction works out a blessing; derive gain from misfortune; get good out of misfortune; good comes out of evil; profit by misfortune; profit from a misfortune;

轉禍為福 turn a disaster into a blessing; turn bad luck into a blessing; turn calamity into blessing; turn disaster into happiness;

[禍根] bane; curse; seeds of misfortune; source of disaster; the cause of ruin; the root of the trouble;

拔除禍根 eradicate the root of trouble;

種下禍根 sow seeds of calamity;

[禍害] (1) canker; curse; disaster; scourge; (2) bane; curse; scourge;

禍害莊稼 damage the crops;

根除禍害 cut off the evil at its source;

極大的禍害 deadly evils;

戰爭的禍害 the scourge of war;

[禍患] calamity; disaster;

禍患無窮 constant cause of trouble; incessant calamities; with consequences of maximum seriousness;

銷弭禍患 dispel misgivings — avoid a calamity;

[禍亂] curse; disaster;

[禍事] calamity; disaster; mishap;

[禍首] arch-criminal; chief culprit; chief offender;

[禍水] force compared to flood, causing trouble;

禍水妞 jailbait;

[禍胎] cause of the disaster; root of the trouble;

[禍心] evil intent; evil intention; malice;

暗藏禍心 conceal one's evil intent;

[禍殃] calamity; catastrophe; disaster;

兵禍 ravages of soldiery;

怖禍 terrifying calamity;

車禍 traffic accident;

闖禍 bring disaster; get into trouble;

匪禍 banditry; the evil of banditry;

橫禍 sudden misfortune; unexpected calamity;

嫁禍 put the blame on sb else; shift the blame onto others;

巨禍 calamity; disaster; ruin;

罹禍 suffer from misfortune;

惹禍 cause trouble; court disaster; stir up trouble;

遺禍 leave behind disaster and cause people to suffer;

災禍 calamity; catastrophe; disaster;

戰禍 disaster of war;

召禍 cause trouble; court disaster;

肇禍 cause an accident; cause trouble;

huo

【霍】 (1) quickly; suddenly; (2) a surname;

[霍地] in a flash; suddenly; very quickly;

[霍霍] (1) scrape of a sword; (2) flash;

[霍亂] (1) cholera; (2) acute gastroenteritis;

霍亂爆發 cholera outbreak;

[霍然] (1) quickly; rapidly; suddenly; (2) be cured quickly;

霍然大怒 bluster oneself into anger; burst into a passion; flare up; fly into a rage; one's anger flares up; suddenly burst into a fit of temper; suddenly grow very angry;

霍然痊愈 one recovers from an illness suddenly;

霍然雲消 the clouds disperse hastily;

揮霍 spend freely; squander;

huo

【壑】 (1) channel for water; gully; (2) narrow ravine at the foot of a hill;

[壑溝] ditch; narrow strip of water; the moat around a city wall;

huo

【擭】 (1) snare; trap; (2) catch; seize;

huo
【濩】 turbulent water;

huo
【獲】 (1) capture; catch; (2) obtain; reap; win;
[獲得] achieve; acquire; acquisition; earn; gain; obtain; win;
獲得成功 attain success;
獲得冠軍 take the crown;
獲得特權 secure the privilege;
獲得性 acquired character;
獲得許可 secure permission;
獲得自由 gain freedom;
[獲獎] bring down the persimmon; get an award; prize-winning; receive an award; win an award; win the prize;
獲獎產品 products of awarded medal;
獲獎小說 prize-winning novel;
獲獎者 award winner;
獲獎作品 prize-winning work;
[獲救] be rescued or saved from death;
[獲利] earn profit; get profit; make a profit; obtain profit; reap profits;
[獲取] achieve; acquire; gain; obtain;
獲取知識 acquire knowledge;
[獲勝] come out on top; triumph; victorious; win victory;
獲勝歸來 return triumphantly;
大獲全勝 carry all before one; gain a complete victory; make a clean sweep; sweep the broad;
勉強獲勝 gain a victory by a slim margin;
聲稱獲勝 claim victory;
以微弱優勢獲勝 win by a neck;
[獲釋] be released; get off; set free;
平安獲釋 be released unharmed;
[獲悉] learn of an event;
[獲益] benefit;
獲益匪淺 reap no little benefit;
獲益良多 benefit a great deal;
[獲知] learn;
[獲准] obtain permission;

捕獲 capture; catch; seize;
查獲 ferret out; hunt down and seize; track down;
抄獲 ferret out; search and seize;
創獲 achievement;
俘獲 capture;
緝獲 capture;
繳獲 capture; seize;
截獲 intercept and capture;
獵獲 capture or kill in hunting;
虜獲 capture;
拿獲 apprehend;
破獲 uncover; unearth;
榮獲 have the honour to get or win;
收獲 gather in the crops; harvest;
抓獲 capture;

huo
【豁】 (1) clear; generous; open; open-minded; (2) exempt; remit;
[豁達] (1) open and clear; (2) broad-minded; generous; magnanimous; open-minded; sanguine;
豁達大度 generous and open-minded; open-minded and magnanimous;
[豁亮] (1) roomy and bright; (2) resonant; sonorous;
[豁免] exempt; remit;
豁免罰金 remit fines;
豁免債務 remit a debt;
部份豁免 partial exemption;
全部豁免 total exemption;
[豁拳行令] play rowdy drinking games;
[豁然] open and clear; suddenly enlightened;
豁然貫通 suddenly see the whole thing in a clear light; understand the thorough meaning suddenly;
豁然開朗 be suddenly enlightened; become clear-minded; suddenly see the light;

開豁 (1) open and clear; (2) with one's mental outlook broadened;
顯豁 conspicuous; obviously clear;
軒豁 open; wide;

huo
【穫】 cut grain; harvest; reap;

huo
【矱】 criterion; measure;

huo
【藿】 (1) coarse vegetables; leaves of a legume; (2) lophanthus rugosus, a kind of medicinal herb;
[藿香] wrinkled giant hyssop;

huo
【蠖】 looper; measuring worm;

尺蠖 geometer; inchworm; looper;

huo

【騞】 sound of a knife cutting sth;

huo

【鑊】 (1) wok; (2) cauldron for cooking;

Chan Sin-wai

漢英順逆序大辭典

A New Comprehensive Chinese-English Dictionary

商務印書館

目錄 Table of Contents

前言 Introduction .... **i – xxxviii**

辭典正文 The Dictionary

Volume 1 (A-H) .... 1 – 1011

Volume 2 (J-S) .... 1013 – 2227

Volume 3 (T-Z) .... 2229 – 3307

筆劃索引 Stroke Index .... **3309 – 3338**

J

ji1

ji

【几】 a pronunciation of 几；

茶几 coffee table; tea table;

ji

【乩】 divine; resolve doubts by an application to spiritual being;

ji

【肌】 flesh; muscle;

[肌病] myopathy;

脂質性肌病 lipid myopathy;

[肌膚] skin and muscle;

冰肌雪膚 delicate skin;

潤滑肌膚 lubricate the skin and muscle;

袒露肌膚 expose one's skin and muscle;

[肌腱] tendon;

[肌覺] muscle sense ; muscular sensation;

[肌瘤] muscular tumour; myama; myoma;

[肌肉] muscle;

肌肉抽搐 tic;

肌肉刺疼 have a tingling sensation in one's muscles;

肌肉發達 brawny; muscular;

肌肉痙攣 charley horse;

肌肉萎縮症 muscular dystrophy;

肌肉無力 myasthenia;

肌肉系統 musculature;

肌肉注射 intramuscular injection;

鍛煉肌肉 exercise one's muscles;

放鬆肌肉 loosen muscles;

活動肌肉 flex a muscle;

拉傷肌肉 pull a muscle;

[肌鬆弛] muscular relaxation;

[肌體] human body; organism;

肌體吸收 absorption by tissue;

[肌痛] muscular rheumatism; myalgia; pain in the muscles;

流行性肌痛 epidemic myalgia;

[肌萎縮] muscular atrophy;

風濕性肌萎縮 rheumatic atrophy;

進行性肌萎縮 progressive muscular atrophy;

缺血性肌萎縮 ischemic muscular atrophy;

神經病性肌萎縮 neuropathic atrophy;

神經炎性肌萎縮 neuritic muscular atropathy;

神經源性肌萎縮 neural atrophy;

糖尿病肌萎縮 diabetic amyotrophy;

特發性肌萎縮 idiopathic muscular atrophy;

[肌無力症] myasthenia;

[肌纖維] muscle fibres;

[肌炎] inflamation of a muscle; myositis;

膿性肌炎 pyomyositis;

實質性肌炎 parenchymatous myositis;

受寒性肌炎 myositis a frigore;

增生性肌炎 proliferative myositis;

白肌 white muscle;

背闊肌 latissimus dorsi;

比目魚肌 soleus;

表情肌 muscles of expression;

不隨意肌 involuntary muscle;

催動肌 agonistic muscle;

大圓肌 teres major;

額肌 frontal muscle; frontalis;

方形肌 musculus quadratus;

腓腸肌 gastrocnemius;

縫匠肌 sartorius;

腹肌 abdominal muscle;

腹直肌 straight abdominal muscle; transversus abdominis;

肱二頭肌 biceps; biceps brachii;

肱橈肌 trachio radialis;

肱三頭肌 triceps; triceps brachii;

股二頭肌 biceps femoris; femoral biceps;

股內肌 vastus medialis;

股四頭肌 quadriceps femoris;

股外肌 vastus lateralis;

骨骼肌 skeletal muscle;

合作肌 synergistic muscle;

橫肌 transversalis;

橫紋肌 striated muscle;

降肌 depressor muscle;

拮抗肌 antagonistic muscle;

脛骨前肌 anterior tibial muscle;

頸肌 cervical muscle;

頸闊肌 neck muscle; platysma;

咀嚼肌 masticatory muscles;

頦肌 mentalis;

口輪匝肌 orbicularis oris;

快肌 fast muscle;

擴張肌 dilator muscle;

慢肌 slow muscle;

面肌 facial muscle;

顳肌 temporal muscle; temporalis;

膀胱逼尿肌 detrusor urinae muscle;

皮肌 cutaneous muscle;

平滑肌 smooth muscle;

前鋸肌 serratus anterior;

J

前列腺肌 musculus prostaticus;
橈側腕屈肌 flexor carpi radialis;
三角肌 deltoid; deltoid muscle;
隨意肌 voluntary muscle;
臀大肌 gluteus maximus;
臀小肌 musculus gluteus minimus;
臀中肌 mesogluteus;
臀最小肌 least gluteal muscle;
外部肌 extrinsic muscle;
小圓肌 teres minor;
斜方肌 trapezius;
心肌 cardiac muscle;
胸大肌 greater pectoral muscle; pectoralis major; pectoris major;
胸肌 chest muscle; pectoral muscle;
胸鎖乳突肌 amuent muscle;
雪肌 snow-white skin;
眼肌 eye muscle;
眼輪匝肌 orbicularis oculi;
咬肌 great masticatory muscle; masseter;
魚際肌 thenar muscle;
玉肌 pure, snow-white skin of a woman;
張肌 tensor;
枕肌 occipital muscle; occipitalis;
趾長伸肌 extensor digitorum;

ji
【奇】 (1) odd number; (2) fractional amount;
［奇偶］ odd-even;
奇偶校驗 even-odd check;
［奇數］ odd number; uneven number;
［奇質量數］ odd mass number;

ji
【迹】 footprints; traces; tracks;
［迹地］ slash;
［迹象］ indications; marks; signs;

ji
【姬】 (1) charming girl; handsome girl; (2) concubine; (3) a surname;
［姬妾成群］ have troops of maids and concubines;

歌姬 singing girl;
侍姬 concubine;
舞姬 dancing girl;

ji
【屐】 clogs; patterns; wooden shoes;

草屐 straw sandals;
木屐 clogs;

ji
【飢】 (1) same as 饑, meaning hunger; hungry; starving; (2) a surname;

ji
【笄】 hairpin for fastening the hair;

ji
【基】 (1) base; foundation; (2) basic; cardinal; key; primary; (3) base; group; radical;
［基本］ (1) base; foundation; (2) essential; main; (3) elementary; rudimentary; (4) basically; by and large; in the main; on the whole;
基本成分 essential component;
基本詞素 base morpheme;
基本點 key element;
基本方向 basic direction; basic orientation;
基本高等教育 initial higher education;
基本功 basic skills; basic training; basics; essential techniques;
~基本功扎實 have a solid mastery of the basic skill;
~練好基本功 master the basic skills;
基本國策 the basic state policy;
基本好轉 turn for the better by and large;
基本建設 capital construction;
~搞好基本建設 do a good job of capital construction;
~擴大基本建設 expand capital construction;
基本句 basic sentence;
基本滿意 be satisfied in the main;
基本內容 nitty-gritty;
基本擬聲詞 primary onomatopoeia;
基本上 basically; broadly speaking; by and large; in principle; in substance; in the main; for the most part; largely; on the whole;
基本形式 base form;
基本學歷 initial qualification;
基本要點 nuts and bolts;
基本意義 essential meaning;
基本英語 basic English;
基本語素 base morpheme;
基本語文能力 initial language proficiency;
基本正確 in the main true;
基本知識 basic knowledge;

[基層] basic level;
基層單位 grassroots unit;
基層選舉 elections at the basic level;

[基礎] base; basis; cornerstone; foundation; groundwork; substructure;
基礎班 beginners' class;
基礎部份 base component;
基礎產業 basic industries;
基礎成分 base component;
基礎方言 root dialect;
基礎工資 basic wage;
基礎教育 basic education;
基礎課 basic course;
基礎設施 infrastructure; infrastructure facilities;
~物質基礎設施 physical infrastructure;
基礎形式 base form;
基礎學科 basic studies;
基礎訓練 elementary training;
基礎研究 basic research;
基礎英語 basic English;
基礎知識 fundamental knowledge;
打基礎 do spade work; lay the base; lay the foundations; lay the groundwork;
句法基礎 syntactic base;
橋梁基礎 bridge foundation;
天線基礎 antenna foundation;
有群眾基礎 have a mass basis;
組裝基礎 built-up foundation;
座板基礎 bed plate foundation;

[基地] base;
航空基地 air base;
空軍基地 air base;

[基點] basic point; starting point;
基點制 basing-point system;
提出基點 present the starting point;
證明基點 prove the basic point;

[基調] (1) fundamental key; main key; (2) keynote; mood;
定下基調 set the keynote;

[基建] capital construction; infrastructure;

[基金] foundation; fund;
基金會 foundation;
~殘疾人基金會 foundation for the disabled;
基金會計 fund accounting;
基金賬戶 fund account;
撥出基金 appropriate funds;
籌集基金 build up funds;
創立基金 create a fund;
對沖基金 hedge fund;
發放基金 distribute funds;
共同基金 mutual fund;
積累基金 accumulate funds;
領取基金 draw a fund; receive a fund;
提供基金 furnish funds;
限額基金 limit fund;
轉出基金 switched out of fund;
轉入基金 switched in of fund;

[基色] primary; primary colours;
假想基色 fictitious primaries;
攝像機基色 camera primaries;

[基石] anvil; cornerstone; footing stone; foundation stone; rock;
國家的基石 cornerstone of the state;
重要基石 foundation;

[基數] base number; cardinal number; radix;
浮點基數 floating radix;
可變基數 variable radix;

[基線] baseline;
浮動基線 floating baseline;
輔助基線 auxiliary baseline;
校核基線 check baseline;
平坦基線 flat baseline;
圖形基線 baseline of diagram;

[基岩] bedrock;

[基因] gene;
基因重組 gene recombination;
基因定位 gene mapping;
基因工程 gene engineering;
基因基礎 gene basis;
基因激素 gene-hormone;
基因庫 gene bank; gene pool;
基因流動 gene flow;
基因突變 gene mutation;
基因位點 gene locus;
基因型 genotype;
基因學說 theory of genes;
基因移植 gene transplantation;
基因組 genome;
~人類基因組 human genome;
基因組合 gene combination;
操縱基因 operator gene;
代償基因 compensator genes;
等位基因 allele; aellelomorphic gene;
對偶基因 allele;
工程基因 cyborg gene;
互補基因 complementary gene;
緩衝基因 buffering gene;
加性基因 additive gene;
結構基因 structural gene;
控制基因 control gene;

J

調節基因 regulator gene;
稀釋基因 dilution gene;
細菌基因 bacterial gene;
~ 無害細菌基因 harmless bacterial gene;
顯性基因 dominant gene;
抑制基因 inhibitory gene;
異體基因 foreign gene;
隱性基因 recessive gene;
致死基因 lethal gene;
自效基因 autarchic gene;

[基於] because of; by reason of; considering; due to; in consideration of; in view of; on account of; seeing that;
基於以上理由 for the above-mentioned reasons;
基於這種考慮 in view of this consideration;
基於這種情況 in view of the situation;

[基準] reference; standard;
基準鏡 reference mirror;
基線基準 baseline reference;
絕對基準 absolute standard;
亮度基準 luminance reference;
原子基準 atomic standard;
姿態基準 attitude reference;
資本基準 capital standard;

氨基 amino; amino-group;
壩基 base of a dam;
垻基 base of a dam;
苯基 phenyl;
登基 ascend the throne; be enthroned;
地基 foundation;
奠基 lay a foundation;
房基 foundations of a building;
根基 basis; foundation;
路基 bed; roadbed;
墻基 foundation;
色基 colour base;
烷基 alkyl;
岩基 batholith;
乙基 ethyl;
游離基 free radical;
原基 rudiment;
肇基 do the spadework; lay the foundation; pave the way;
鎡基 big hoe;

ji

【嵇】 (1) a surname; (2) a mountain in Henan;

ji

【幾】 almost; nearly;
[幾不欲生] almost despair of living; hardly care to live;
[幾乎] about; all but; almost; as good as; come close to; come near + ing; few; fit; go near; hardly; if any; it is all but done; it is all but impossible; just manage; little; much; near; nearly; next to; on the brink of; on the point of; on the verge of; only not; or thereabouts; practically; pretty much; pretty well; ready; scarcely; some; thereabout; well-nigh; within an ace of;

ji

【期】 one year;
[期年] first anniversary;

ji

【犄】 horn;
[犄角] (1) corner; (2) horn;

ji

【畸】 (1) lopsided; unbalanced; (2) abnormal; irregular;
[畸變] distortion;
平頂畸變 flat-top distortion;
時延畸變 delay distortion;
彈性畸變 elastic distortion;
[畸形] abnormal; deformation; deformity; lopsided; malformation;
畸形發育 grow in an abnormal way;
畸形發展 deformed development; lopsided development; overdevelopment;
畸形增長 abnormal increase;
畸形足 club foot;
先天畸形 congenital abnormalities; congenital malformation;

ji

【箕】 (1) sieve; winnowing basket; (2) dust basket; dustpan; garbage basket; (3) spiral lines on a finger tip; (4) a surname;
[箕踞] sit on the floor with one's legs stretched out;
[箕帚] one's wife;
願侍箕帚 glad to be a wife to sb;

ji

【嘰】 (1) mutter; whisper; (2) eat a bit; (3)

lament;

[嘰咕] mutter; talk in a low voice; whisper;

嘰嘰咕咕 babble on and on; mumble; murmur; mutter; whisper;

[嘰嘰] twee;

嘰嘰嘎嘎 cackle; creak;

嘰嘰喳喳 buzz; chirp; chirrup; jabber; twitter;

[嘰里咕嚕] gabble; jabber; talk in an indistinct manner; talk in low whispers;

[嘰里喳拉] make a confused noise;

嗶嘰 serge; soft wool fabric;

咔嘰 khaki;

ji

【畿】 (1) the areas near the capital; (2) threshold;

[畿輔] the areas near the capital;

ji

【稽】 (1) check; examine; (2) delay; procrastinate;

[稽查] check;

[稽核] audit; check; examine;

[稽考] ascertain; verify;

[稽留] delay; detain;

鈎稽 (1) examine; try to ascertain; (2) do business accounting;

滑稽 amusing; comic talk; funny;

無稽 absurd; fantastic;

ji

【觭】 (1) (said of horns of an animal) one turning up and the other turning down; (2) get; obtain; (3) same as 奇, odd;

ji

【機】 (1) engine; machine; (2) aeroplane; aircraft; airplane; plane; (3) crucial point; key link; pivot; (4) chance; occasion; opportunity; (5) organic; (6) flexible; quick-witted;

[機場] airfield; airport;

機場班車 airport shuttle;

機場大廈 air terminal;

機場候機大樓 air terminal;

機場酒店 airtel;

機場跑道 airstrip;

機場小説 airport fiction;

到達機場 arrive at an airport;

國際機場 international airport;

簡單機場 landing strip;

軍用機場 military airport;

離開機場 leave an airport;

[機車] locomotive;

電池機車 accumulator locomotive;

電力機車 electric locomotive;

輔助機車 booster locomotive;

內燃機車 internal combustion locomotive;

[機電] machinery and electrical equipments;

機電學 electromechanics;

[機動] (1) motor-driven; mororized; (2) expedient; flexible; manoeuvrable; mobile;

機動車輛 motor vehicle;

機動處置 deal with sth flexibly;

機動靈活 flexible;

[機讀] machine-readable;

機讀目錄 machine-readable catalogue;

機讀文獻 machine-readable document;

[機斷] act on one's own judgment in an emergency; adaptable to circumstances and decisive;

機斷行事 act promptly at one's own discretion;

[機輔] machine-aided;

機輔翻譯 machine-aided translation;

[機工] machinist;

熟練機工 skilled machinist;

[機構] (1) mechanism; (2) institution; organization; setup;

機構重疊 organizational overlapping;

機構改革 institutional reform;

機構設置 institutional setup;

機構臃腫 overstaffed organization;

半官方機構 semi-public organization;

辦事機構 administrative body; working body;

財政機構 fiscal institution;

重建機構 reconstruct the internal structure of an organization;

傳動機構 transmission mechanism;

慈善機構 charity organization;

存取機構 access mechanism;

翻譯機構 translation organization;

非牟利機構 non-profit organization;

分離機構 disengaging mechanism;

分支機構 affiliated organization;

福利機構 welfare organization;

官僚機構 bureaucratic administration;

管理機構 administrative organization;
國際組織機構 office of international organization;
國家機構 government organizations; state institutions;
加法機構 adding mechanism;
簡化機構 streamline an organization;
金融機構 financial institution;
領事機構 consular mission;
民間機構 non-governmental institution;
情報機構 information organization;
權力機構 organ of power;
商務機構 commercial organization;
調整機構 (1) adjust the organizational structure; (2) adjustment mechanism;
投資機構 investment institution;
下屬機構 subordinate organization;
宣傳機構 propaganda organ;
學術機構 academic institution;
政府機構 government organization;
中間機構 intermediate organization;
自治機構 autonomous organ;

[機關] (1) gear; mechanism; (2) machine-operated; (3) institution; office; organization; (4) trap;
機關敗露 one's plot fails;
機關報 authorities newspaper;
機關會計 institutional accounting;
機關砲 cannon;
~航空機關砲 aerocannon;
機關槍 machine gun;
~一挺機關槍 a machine gun;
機關失算 the scheme fell through;
機關算盡 exhaust every power of one's mind; for all one's calculations and scheming; one's schemes rack one's brains in scheming; use all sorts of intrigues and wiles; use up all one's tricks;
機關算盡，一朝覆亡 they are tricky enough, but they collapse after all;
安全機關 security organ;
國家機關 government office; state apparatus; state organ;
檢察機關 prosecution organ;
決策機關 policy-making body;
領導機關 leading bodies;
上級機關 higher authorities;
審判機關 judicial organ;
識破機關 see through a trick;
行政機關 administrative organ;
政府機關 government institution;
專政機關 organ of dictatorship;

[機會] chance; opportunity;
機會成本 opportunity cost;
機會出現 an opportunity arises;
機會費用 opportunity coast;
機會還是有的 all is not lost;
機會均等 a fair field and no favour; equal opportunity for all; equality of opportunity; the chances are even;
機會來臨 an opportunity come along;
機會難得 it's a rare chance; it's now or never; opportunities are few and far between;
機會平等 equality of opportunity;
機會主義 opportunism;
~機會主義者 bluffer; chancer; opportunist;
把握機會 seize the opportunity; seize the right time; take opportunity;
寶貴的機會 precious opportunity;
~失去寶貴的機會 lose a precious opportunity;
趁機會 take advantage of an opportunity;
錯過機會 miss a chance; miss an opportunity; miss the boat;
錯失機會 let sth slip; let sth slip through one's fingers; slip away;
丟了機會 lose one's opportunity;
好機會 good opportunity;
~失去好機會 miss a good chance;
借此機會 take the opportunity made available to me to; take this opportunity to;
看機會 look for a chance; watch for an opportunity;
利用機會 capitalize on one's opportunity; use opportunity;
覷機會 watch for a chance; watch for an opportunity;
失去機會 lose an opportunity;
學習機會 learning opportunities;
一點點機會 half a chance;
一個機會 an opportunity;
一有機會 as occasion offers; at every opportunity;
抓住機會 grasp an opportunity; leap at the chance; leap at the opportunity; seize an opportunity;

[機警] alert; on one's toes; sharp-witted; vigilant;

J

機警的 canny;
處事機警 know what's what;

[機理] mechanism;
額外機理 additional mechanism;
燒蝕機理 ablative mechanism;

[機靈] clever; intelligent; sharp; smart; up to trap;
機靈鬼 smart child;
辦事很機靈 manage things cleverly;
沉着機靈 composed and smart; cool and clear;

[機密] classified; confidential; confidentiality; private; secret;
機密的 confidential;
公開機密 make the secrets public;
洩漏機密 disclose secrets to sb;
知曉機密 know the secrets;

[機敏] alert and resourceful; touch;
機敏的 adroit;

[機謀] artifice; scheme; stratagem;
腹藏機謀 one's breast conceals tactics;

[機能] enginery; function;
機能適應 functional adaptation;
保留機能 retain a function;
恢復機能 regain the function of...;
失去機能 lose the use of;

[機票] air ticket; airplane ticket;

[機器] (1) engine; machine; machinery; (2) apparatus; organ;
機器保養 machine maintenance;
機器翻譯 machine translation; mechanical translation;
~ 機器翻譯系統 machinery translation system;
機器輔助翻譯 machine-aided translation;
機器可讀的 machine-readable;
機器可讀格式 machine readable form;
機器碼 machine code;
機器人 android; robot;
~ 機器人系統 robot system;
~ 機器人學 robotics;
~ 機器人語言 robot language;
~ 家用機器人 domestic robot;
~ 人形機器人 anthropomorphic robot;
~ 數控機器人 numerical control robot;
機器識別 machine recognition;
機器舞 body popping;
機器洋涇濱翻譯 mechanical pidgin translation;
機器運轉良好 the machine works well;
安裝機器 install a machine;
保養機器 maintain machinery;
拆卸機器 dismantle machinery;
操作機器 operate machines;
國家機器 state machinery;
檢修機器 overhaul apparatuses;
精密機器 precision machinery;
開動機器 set the machinery in motion;
兩用機器 combination machine;
設計機器 design machinery;
使用機器 use machines;
試驗機器 test a machine;
維修機器 maintain machinery;
新發明的機器 new-invented machine;
宣傳機器 propaganda machine;
一部機器 a machine;
一台機器 a machine;
~ 報廢一台機器 scrap a machine;
預熱機器 warm up machinery;
戰爭機器 war machine;
裝配機器 assemble a machine;
自動化機器 automatic machinery;

[機槍] machine gun; stutterer;
輕機槍 light machine gun;

[機體] organism;

[機械] (1) machine; machinery; (2) inflexible; mechanical; rigid;
機械工 mechanic;
機械工廠 machine shop;
機械工程 mechanical engineering;
機械化 mechanize; mechanization;
~ 機械化部隊 mechanized unit;
~ 合理機械化 rational mechanization;
~ 全盤機械化 all-round mechanization;
~ 裝卸機械化 loading and unloading mechanization;
~ 綜合機械化 comprehensive mechanization;
機械人 robot;
~ 點位機械人 point-to-point controlled robot;
~ 電動機械人 electric robot;
~ 人形機械人 android;
機械師 engineer;
~ 飛行機械師 flight engineer;
二級飛行機械師 second-grade flight engineer;
三級飛行機械師 third-grade flight engineer;
四級飛行機械師 fourth-grade flight engineer;
一級飛行機械師 first-grade flight

J

engineer;
機械手 manipulator;
~ 關節式機械手 articulated manipulator;
~ 球承機械手 ball-joint manipulator;
機械舞 body popping;
機械學習 rote learning;
機械用具 mechanical appliances;
大型機械 big machinery;
工業機械 industrial machinery;
建築機械 construction machinery;
農業機械 farm machinery;

[機心] (1) machination; (2) movement;

[機要] confidential;

[機宜] principles of action;

[機遇] favourable circumstances; opportunity;
機遇社會 society of opportunity;
錯過機遇 balk an opportunity;
等待機遇 wait one's opportunity;
挑戰與機遇 challengers and opportunities;
選擇機遇 choose an opportunity;
尋求機遇 look for the main chance;
找到機遇 find an opportunity;
抓住機遇 seize opportunity by the forelock; seize the current opportunity;

[機緣] good luck; lucky chance;
機緣湊巧 as luck would have it; by a lucky coincidence; by chance;

[機制] (1) machine-made; machine-processed; (2) mechanism;
機制轉換 mechanism transform;
改進機制 improve mechanism;
官方溝通機制 official communication mechanism;
加速機制 acceleration mechanism;
會計機制 accounting mechanism;
神經反射性機制 nervous reflex mechanism;
調節機制 adjust the mechanism of…;
轉換機制 transform the institutions;

[機智] quick-witted; resourceful;
機智沉著 composed and quick-witted; cool and resourceful;
機智果斷 flexible and resolute;
機智果敢 with resourcefulness and determination;
機智過人 have the wisdom to form unique judgements beyond the intelligence of ordinary people;
機智奸詐 wise but crafty;
機智靈活 quick-witted and elastic;
機智勇敢 brilliant and resourceful, brave and steadfast; resourceful and brave;

[機杼] loom;
別出機杼 original in conception; strike out a new path for oneself;
自出機杼 make a new departure; original in conception; original in writing; originate a fashion; originate an idea; strike out a new path for oneself;

[機組] (1) set; unit; (2) aircraft crew; aircrew; flight crew;
機組人員 aircraft crew; aircrew;

[機座] stand;
粗軋機座 breakdown stand;
寬展機座 broadside stand;

靶機 target airplane; target drone;
扳機 trigger;
班機 scheduled flight;
包機 chartered airplane; chartered flight;
兵機 military plans; military strategy; military tactics;
裁紙機 paper cutter; trimmer;
禪機 Buddhist allegorical word or gesture;
唱機 gramophone; phonograph;
趁機 seize the chance; take advantage of the occasion;
乘機 seize the opportunity;
吃角子老虎機 fruit machine; one-armed bandit; slot machine;
抽氣機 air pump;
觸機 stir up sb's feelings;
吹風機 blower;
磁電機 magnetor;
打火機 lighter;
打字機 typewriter;
待機 await an opportunity; bide one's time;
倒相機 inverter;
登機 board a flight; boarding;
敵機 enemy plane;
電機 power-driven machine;
電視機 television set;
釘書機 stapler;
動機 intention; motivation; motive;
堆垛機 stacker;
對撞機 collider;
耳機 (1) (telephone) receiver; (2) earphone;
發電機 dynamo; generator;
發動機 engine; motor;
發送機 transmitter;
翻邊機 flanger;
飛機 aeroplane; aircraft; plane;
分機 extension (telephone);

乾衣機 dryer;
攻擊機 attack plane;
銲機 welder;
夯路機 tamping plate roadpacker;
轟炸機 bomber;
候機 waiting;
護航機 escort aircraft;
滑翔機 glider;
貨機 air freighter; cargo aircraft;
計算機 computer;
加油機 tanker aircraft;
見機 according to circumstances; as the opportunity arises;
教練機 trainer aircraft; training aircraft;
軍機 (1) military plan; (2) military secret;
客機 airliner; passenger plane;
良機 good opportunity;
臨機 as the occasion requires;
靈機 brainwave; sudden inspiration;
領隊機 lead plane;
錄像機 video cassette recorder;
錄音機 recorder;
拋砂機 sandslinger;
噴碼機 ink jet printer;
鋪路機 paver;
汽機 steam engine;
汽輪機 steam turbine; turbine;
契機 juncture; moment; turning point;
槍機 trigger;
切布機 rag chopper; rag cutter;
熱燙機 blancher;
人機 man-machine;
殺機 the intention to kill;
商機 business opportunity;
攝像機 camcorder;
攝影機 camera;
神機 (1) God-given chance; (2) the divine plan;
生機 (1) lease of life; (2) life; vitality;
昇降機 elevator;
昇運機 elevator;
失機 let slip an opportunity; lose a chance;
時機 an opportune moment; opportunity;
事機 (1) confidential affairs; secret affairs; (2) circumstances; situation; trend of events;
收報機 radiotelegraphic receiver; telegraphic receiver;
收音機 radio;
手機 (1) handset; (2) mobile phone;
售貨機 vending machine;
樞機 cardinal; vital element;
司機 chauffeur; driver;
伺機 await an opportunity; watch for one's chance;
俟機 wait for an opportunity; watch for one's chance;
隨機 (1) planless; random; (2) as the situation allows;
天機 (1) nature's mystery; (2) God's design;
跳汰機 jigger;
停機 shutdown;
通風機 ventilator;
投機 agreeable; congenial;
推土機 bulldozer;
脱機 off-line;
拖拉機 tractor;
挖土機 excavator;
萬機 myriad of state affairs;
危機 crisis; critical point; crunch; precarious moment;
微機 microcomputer;
無機 inorganic;
吸塵機 vacuum cleaner;
洗片機 film-developing machine;
洗衣機 washing machine;
相機 camera;
心機 craftiness; scheming; thinking;
玄機 profound and mysterious principle;
巡邏機 patrol airplane;
尋機 look for an opportunity;
壓路機 road roller; roller;
壓縮機 compressor;
印刷機 printing machine;
有機 organic;
暈機 airsickness; have airsickness;
運輸機 transport plane;
鍘草機 chaffcutter; hay cutter;
搾果機 juicer;
戰鬥機 fighter airplane;
戰機 opportunity for combat;
照相機 camera;
偵察機 reconnaissance plane;
偵碼機 cellular phone read system;
蒸氣機 steam engine;
織機 loom;
直升機 copter; helicopter;
主機 (1) main engine; mainframe; (2) host computer;
專機 (1) special plane; (2) private plane;
轉機 a favourable turn; a turn for the better;
撞機 air crash;
墜機 plane crash;
總機 switchboard; telephone exchange;
鑽機 driller;

J

ji

【激】 (1) dash; surge; wash; (2) catch a chill; fall ill from getting wet; (3) arouse; excite; stimulate; (4) fierce; sharp; violent;

[激昂] aroused; emotionally wrought up; excited and indignant;
激昂發言 speak in excitement;
激昂慷慨 fervent and excited; in excitement; with strong emotion;
慷慨激昂 arousing; impassioned;
情緒激昂 in an emotive state; in high spirits;

[激薄停澆] use one's personality to influence others;

[激蕩] agitate; rage; surge;
激蕩人心 stir people's hearts;
心潮激蕩 one's heart leaps;

[激動] agitate; excite; sensation; stir; work up;
激動的心情 a feeling of excitement;
激動人心 arouse sb's feelings; soul-stirring;
激動萬分 beside oneself with excitement;
非常激動 be greatly excited;
過度激動 overexcited;
滿懷激動 be filled with excitement; full of excitement;
情緒激動 be heated with passion;
心情激動 excited; thrilled;
一時激動 a flicker of excitement; in the heat of the moment;
一陣激動 a flurry of excitement; a gale of excitement; a rush of excitement; a spasm of excitement;
引起激動 cause excitement; generate excitement;

[激發] arouse; set up stimulate; stir up;
激發愛心 arouse the love of sb;
激發態 excited state;

[激奮] be roused to action; be stirred into activity;

[激憤] enraged; indignant; wrathful;

[激光] laser;
激光筆 laser pen; laser pointer;
激光唱機 compact disk player;
激光唱片 compact disk (CD);
激光唱頭 laser pick-up;
激光磁盤 laser disk;
激光打印機 laser printer;
激光電影 laser film;
激光複印機 laser copier;
激光計量學 lasermetrics;
激光排版 laser typesetting;
激光器 laser;
~ 多摻激光器 alphabet laser;
~ 氣動激光器 air-breathing laser;
~ 搜索激光器 acquisition laser;
激光手術 laser surgery;
激光束 laser beam;
激光通訊 laser communication;
激光衛星 laser satellite;
激光武器 laser weapon;
激光效應 effect of laser;
激光治療 laser treatment;

[激化] become acute; flare-up; intensify; sharpen;
激化對立情緒 sharpen sb's antagonism;
激化矛盾 intensify the contradictions;

[激將法] encourage sb to do sth by means of criticizing his ability; goading sb into action by ridicule or sarcasm; prodding sb into action;

[激進] radical;
激進手段 radical measures;
~ 採取激進手段 take radical measures;

[激勵] encourage; excitation; excite; impel; inspire; put one on one's mettle; stimulate; urge;
激勵器 driver; exciter; stimulator;
~ 蜂聲激勵器 buzzer driver;
~ 晶體激勵器 crystal driver;
~ 橋路激勵器 bridge driver;
~ 圖象激勵器 video driver;
~ 自舉激勵器 bootstrap driver;
激勵性講話 pep talk;
大氣輻射激勵 airglow excitation;
聲激勵 acoustic excitation;
天線激勵 excitation;

[激烈] acute; fierce; intense; sharp; violent;
激烈的 fierce;
~ 十分激烈的 hruising;
會上爭論激烈 the meeting was aboil with contreocversy;

[激流] rapids; rush; torrent; turbulent current;
激流險灘 rapids; turbulent rivers and treacherous shoals;

[激酶] kinase;
蛋白激酶 protein kinase;
肌激酶 adenylate kinase;

[激怒] enrage; exasperate; infuriate; rile;
容易被激怒 be easily exasperated;

［激起］ arouse; evoke; set fire to; set sth on fire; stir up;
激起風波 cause a commotion;
激起公憤 arouse public indignation;
激起浪花 swash the foam of breaking waves;
激起騷亂 arouse a commotion; cause a commotion; create a commotion; produce a commotion;
［激切］ impassioned; vehement;
［激情］ enthusiasm; fervour; intense emotion; passion;
激情減弱 one's enthusiasm wanes;
表達激情 express fervor;
熾熱的激情 white-hot passion;
充滿激情 be filled with enthusiasm;
喚起激情 awaken one's intense emotions;
滿腔激情 one's breast is filled with emotion;
缺乏激情 void of enthusiasm;
燃起激情 set one's passion aflame;
一陣激情 a fit of passion;
抑制激情 suppress passion;
［激素］ hormone;
雌性激素 estrogen hormone; female hormone;
環境激素 environmental hormone;
腦激素 brain hormones;
女性激素 female hormone;
雄激素 androgen;
雄性激素 androgenic hormone;
植物激素 phytohormone; plant hormone;
［激揚］ excited; inspired;
激揚士氣 boost the morale; give a boost to the role;
［激增］ increase sharply; jump from; shoot up; soar;
體重激增 gain much weight;
［激戰］ fierce battle; fierce fighting; pitched battle;
［激震］ shock;
外施激震 applied shock;
錐形激震 applied shock;

串激 series excitation;
刺激 (1) excite; incentive; stimulate; stimulation; stimulus; (2) irritate; provoke; upset;
憤激 excited and indignant;
復激 compound excitation;
感激 be thankful; feel grateful;
過激 radical; to the extreme; too drastic;
偏激 extreme;

ji

【璣】 (1) jade and pearls which are not quite circular; (2) ancient astronomical instrument; (3) name of a constellation;
［璣衡撫辰儀］ astrological armlillary sphere;

璇璣 armillary sphere;
珠璣 gem; pearl;

ji

【緝】 (1) arrest; capture; catch; order the arrest of; seize; (2) twist and join; (3) continue; (4) hem clothing;
［緝辦］ arrest and punish;
［緝捕］ capture; search and arrest;
［緝盜］ capture thieves;
［緝獲］ arrest; capture; seize;
［緝緝翩翩］ make a lisping noise;
［緝究］ investigate and prosecute;
［緝理］ set in order;
［緝穆］ at peace with each other;
［緝拿］ apprehend; arrest;
［緝私］ arrest smugglers; antismuggling;
緝私隊 antismuggling team;
緝私人員 anti-contraband personnel;
［緝熙］ bright; brilliant;

ji

【積】 (1) accumulate; amass; store up; (2) age-old; long-pending; long-standing; (3) products;
［積案］ long-pending case;
［積弊］ age-old malpractice; long-standing abuse;
［積不相能］ always at loggerheads; have always been at variance; have never been on good terms;
［積儲］ store up;
［積存］ lay up; pile-up; stockpile; store up;
［積德］ accumulate virtue;
積德從善 accumulate virtue and follow the good; follow a virtuous path;
積德累功 accumulate virtue and merit;
［積分］ integral; integration;
積分變換 integral transformation;
積分法 integration;
~ 部分分數積分法 integration by partial fraction;

~遞化積分法 integration by successive reduction;
~分部積分法 integration by parts;
~置換積分法 integration by substitution;
積分方程 integral equation;
積分符號 sign of integration;
積分卡 loyalty card;
積分器 integrator;
~風速積分器 air-speed integrator;
~模擬積分器 analogue integrator;
~自動積分器 automatic integrator;
積分學 integral calculus;
積分之和 integral sum;
抽象積分 abstract integral;
觸發積分 activation integral;
代數積分 algebraic integral;
定積分 definite integral; definite integration;
~定積分上限 upper limit of the definite integral;
~定積分下限 lower limit of the definite integral;
~不定積分 indefinite integral; indefinite integration;
輔助積分 auxiliary integral;
漸近積分 asymptotic integration;
角積分 angular integral;
近似積分 approximate integration;
模擬積分 analogue integration;
原子積分 atomic integral;
作用積分 action integral;

[積谷防饑] accumulate grain against famine; store up grain against dearth;

[積毀銷骨] accumulated defamation melts the bones — defamation destroys a person; much reviling and slander wears the bone; rumours can kill a person; when everybody speaks against a person, it makes him tired of life;

[積極] (1) positive; (2) active; energetic; vigorous;
積極的 assertive;
積極分子 activist;
積極派 ginger group;
積極性 initiatives;
~調動積極性 bring one's initiatives into play; call one's initiatives into play; give play to one's initiatives;
~充分調動積極性 bring one's initiative into full play; call one's initiative into full play; give full play to one's initiatives;

[積久] accumulate in the course of time;
積久成習 from a habit through long-repeated practice;

[積聚] accumulate; build up; gather;
積聚財富 store up wealth;
積聚能量 gather strength;
積聚能源 gather resources;
積聚資本 accumulate capital;
癥瘕積聚 a lump in the abdomen causing distension and pain;

[積累] (1) accumulate; (2) build-up;
積累基金 build up a fund;
積累現金 amass cash;
積累知識 accumulate knowledge;
積累資本 accumulate capital;
積銖累寸 accumulate bit by bit; accumulate little by little; build up bit bu bit; build up little by little; let small amounts accumulate; save every tidy bit;
日積月累 accumulate day by day and month by month; accumulate over a long period; accumulate steadily; by slow accumulation; day after day and month after month; days and month multiplying; gradual accumulation over a long time
銖積寸累 a lump sum is the total of pennies accumulated through the years; accumulate little by little; build up bit by bit; huge capital investments come from the paltry savings of individuals; let small amounts accumulate; wealth is but small increments piling up in course of time;

[積木] building blocks; juggle;

[積年] for many years;
積年舊案 law cases which have piled up over the years; long-pending case;
積年累月 for months and years; for years on end; year after year;

[積欠] (1) have one's debts piling up; (2) arrears; outstanding debts;

[積沙成塔] many a little makes a mickle; many littles make a mickle; take care of the pence, and the pounds ill take care of themselves;

[積水] hydrops;
耳積水 hydrotis;
關節積水 hydrarthrosis;

繼發性腦積水 secondary hydrocephalus;
假性積水 hydrops spuris;
迷路積水 labyrinthine hydrops;
腦積水 hydrocephalus;
腎盂積水 nephrydrosis;

[積習] deep-rooted habits; long-standing practice; old habits;
積習成性 deep-rooted habits have become second-nature;
積習難除 a habit is very hard to shake off when once acquired;
積習難改 a settled practice is hard to reform; ingrained habits cannot be cast off overnight; it is difficult to get rid of deep-rooted habits; old habits die hard;
積習宿弊 bad old practices; ingrained vices; long-standing abuses;
狃於積習 be accustomed to old habits; stick to old customs;

[積蓄] accumulate; lay up a purse; put aside; salt away; save; save up;
積蓄力量 accumulate strength;
積蓄能源 save energy;
積蓄脂肪 accumulate fat;
積蓄資金 accumulate funds;

[積壓] keep long in stock; overstock;
積壓產品 overstocked products;
積壓的 backlog;
~積壓的工作 backlog;
積壓稿件 pile up manuscripts;
積壓工作 pile up work;
積壓物資 keep goods and materials long in stock;
積壓資金 let the funds lie idle;

[積羽沉舟] a heavy load of feathers can sink a boat — minor offences unchecked may bring disaster; a straw added breaks the camel's back — the awesome power of sheer numbers; accumulated feathers can sink a boat — tiny things may gather into a mighty force;

[積怨] accumulated rancour; piled-up grievance;
積怨成仇 be made to hate each other due to piled-up grievances;
積怨多年 store up resentment over years;
積怨甚多 have incurred widespread resentment; have many complaints against one;
發洩積怨 pour out one's accumulated rancor;
消除積怨 remove piled-up grievances;

[積雲] cumulus;
層積雲 stratocumulus;
高積雲 altocumulus;
捲積雲 cirrocumulus;
晴天積雲 fair-weather cumulus;
塔狀積雲 towering cumulus;
信風積雲 trade-wind cumulus;

[積攢] collect bit by bit; save bit by bit;
積攢零錢 save pocket money;
積攢學費 save for tuition;

[積重難返] old practice die hard; confirmed habits are hard to get rid of; ingrained habits are hard to change; long-standing practices are difficult to change; old habits are difficult to drop;

- 襞積 lines or pleats on clothes as a result of folding;
- 冰積 lateral moraine;
- 材積 volume of timber;
- 沉積 deposit;
- 乘積 product;
- 沖積 alleviation;
- 蟲積 parasitic disease;
- 地積 area; measure of land;
- 電積 electrodeposition;
- 澱積 deposition;
- 堆積 accumulate; heap up; pile up;
- 疳積 infantile malnutrition;
- 洪積 diluvial;
- 聚積 accumulate; build up;
- 累積 accumulate;
- 面積 area;
- 容積 bulk; dimension; content; dimension; holding capacity; volume;
- 山積 pile mountain high;
- 食積 dyspepsia; indigestion;
- 體積 bulk; size; volume;
- 屯積 hoard up;
- 囤積 corner the market; hoard for speculation;
- 委積 accumulate; pile up;
- 蓄積 save up; store up;
- 有積 have digestive disorders;
- 淤積 deposit; silt up;
- 鬱積 pent-up; smolder;
- 滯積 pile up;
- 貯積 accumulate; store up;

ji

【擊】 (1) beat; hit; strike; (2) assault; at-

tack;

［擊敗］ beat; defeat; vanish;
擊敗對手 beat one's opponent;
擊敗情敵 defeat one's rival;
被徹底擊敗 take a pounding;
被擊敗 come off worst;
以點數擊敗 outpoint;

［擊穿］ breakdown;
倍增擊穿 multiplicative breakdown;
表面擊穿 surface breakdown;
材料擊穿 material breakdown;
電擊穿 electrical breakdown;
電纜擊穿 cable breakdown;
電子共振擊穿 electron resonance breakdown;
反向擊穿 reverse breakdown;
隔離擊穿 isolation breakdown;
火花擊穿 spark breakdown;
介質擊穿 dielectric breakdown;
局部擊穿 localized breakdown;
絕緣擊穿 insulation breakdown;
空隙擊穿 gap breakdown;
破壞性擊穿 destructive breakdown;
軟擊穿 soft breakdown;
雪崩擊穿 avalanche breakdown;
陽極擊穿 anodic breakdown;
陰極擊穿 cathode breakdown;
硬擊穿 hard breakdown;

［擊倒］ knockdown;

［擊鼓］ beat the drum; ;
擊鼓而舞 beat the drums while dancing;
擊鼓鳴金 beat drums and clang gongs;
擊鼓鳴冤 beat the drum at court to ledge a complaint against some injustice; beat the drum outside the court and make known one's wrong;
擊鼓慶賀 beat the drums to celebrate;
擊鼓昇堂 beat the drum to start the court;
擊鼓退堂 beat the drums to dismiss the court;
擊鼓助威 beat the drums to encourage;

［擊昏］ knock sb out;
擊昏器 stunner;
~ 打擊式擊昏器 concussion stunner;
~ 電擊昏器 electrical stunner;
~ 氣動擊昏器 pneumatic stunner;

［擊劍］ fencing;
擊劍運動 fencing;
~ 擊劍運動員 fencer;
擊劍者 fencer;

［擊潰］ put to flight; rout;
擊潰敵人 put the enemy to rout;
把敵軍擊潰 rout the enemy;
被完全擊潰 in full rout;

［擊球］ hit;
擊球手 batsman; hitter;
~ 指定擊球手 designated hitter;
大力擊球 drive;
四次擊球 four-hit;
用手掌擊球 bat the ball;
正手擊球 forehand;

［擊退］ beat back; repel; repulse;
擊退進攻 beat off an attack;
擊退圍剿 repel encirclement and suppression;
被擊退 be repelled;

［擊掌］ clap one's hands;
擊掌表示祝賀 clap hands to extend congratulations;
擊掌為定 palm against palm; swear it to sb;
擊掌為罰 strike the open hand with a ruler as the punishment;
擊掌為號 clap hands as a signal;
擊掌以示安靜 clap hands for silence;
擊掌以示同意 give consent by clapping one's hands;
擊掌奏拍 clap one's hands to give the tempo;
舉手擊掌 high five;

［擊中］ hit the target;
擊中靶心 hit the bull's-eye;
擊中靶子 hit the target;
擊中目標 hit the mark;
擊中痛處 hit sb on a tender place; hit sb squarely in a sore spot; hit sb to the quick;
擊中要害 come home; cut to the quick; get home; go home; have hit at the nub of; hit close to home; hit home; hit sb's vital point; hit sb where it hurts; hit the point; shoot home; strike at the root of; strike home; touch sb's tender spot;
沒有擊中 miss the target;

搏擊 pound; strike violently;
側擊 flank attack;
齒激 clatter the teeth in trembling;
衝擊 (1) lash; pound against; (2) assault; charge;
出擊 launch an attack; start off for an attack;
搥擊 thrust; thump;
打擊 (1) hit; strike; (2) deal a blow;

堵擊 intercept and attack;
反擊 beat back; counterattack; strike back;
伏擊 ambush;
攻擊 (1) launch an offensive; assault; (2) accuse; charge;
合擊 make a joint attack on;
轟擊 (1) bombard; shell; (2) bombard;
還擊 (1) counterattack; fight back; return fire; (2) riposte;
回擊 counterattack; fight back;
夾擊 attack from both sides; make a flank attack from both sides;
殲擊 attack and destroy;
截擊 intercept;
狙擊 snipe;
抗擊 beat back; resist;
攔擊 volley;
雷擊 be struck by lightning;
連擊 double hit;
目擊 see with one's own eyes; witness;
排擊 repel and attack;
砲擊 bombard; shell;
抨擊 attack;
破擊 attack and destroy; sabotage;
掊擊 attack;
拳擊 box; boxing; pugilism;
射擊 fire; shoot; shooting;
痛擊 bitterly attack; deal a heavy blow;
突擊 (1) make a sudden and violent attack; (2) make a concentrated effort to finish a job quickly;
圍擊 besiege; lay siege to;
誤擊 mishit;
襲擊 assault; make a surprise attack on;
邀擊 intercept; waylay;
迎擊 intercept; meet and attack an advancing enemy;
游擊 carry out a guerrilla warfare;
撞擊 dash against; strike;
追擊 follow up; pursue and attack;
阻擊 block; check;

ji
【磯】 (1) rocky cliff on water's edge; water-surrounded rocks; (2) water pounding against rocks;

ji
【禨】 seek blessings from ghosts;
［禨祥］ pray to the gods for blessing;

ji
【績】 (1) spin; (2) achievements; merits;

敗績 be utterly defeated; suffer a defeat;
成績 achievement; success;
功績 contribution; merits and achievements;
考績 examine working personnel's achievement;
勞績 merits and accomplishments;
偉績 glorious achievements; great feats;
勛績 meritorious service; outstanding contribution;
業績 outstanding accomplishment;
戰績 combat gains; military exploits;
政績 achievements in one's official career;

ji
【隮】 (1) rise up; (2) rainbow; (3) fall; topple;

ji
【蹟】 footprint; trace;

古蹟 historic site;
奇蹟 miracle; wonder;
史蹟 historical relics; historical site;
事蹟 achievement; deed;
手蹟 sb's original handwriting or painting;
遐蹟 matters and stories of ancient people;
削蹟 conceal oneself from the world; lead a recluse life;
真蹟 authentic works;
字蹟 handwriting; writing;
足蹟 (1) footmarks; footprints; tracks; (2) whereabouts;

ji
【雞】 (1) chicken; (2) prostitute;
［雞脖子］ chicken neck;
［雞蛋］ hen's egg;
雞蛋變壞 eggs addle;
雞蛋茶 eggs with tea;
雞蛋羹 steamed egg custard;
雞蛋卷 egg roll;
雞蛋裏挑骨頭 find fault; find quarrel in a straw; look for a bone in an egg – for for a flaw where there is none to be found; nitpick; pick a bone in an egg – cavil at sth; pick holes;
雞蛋碰不過石頭 whether the pitcher strikes the stone, or the stone the pitcher, it is bad for the pitcher; whether the pot strikes the stone, or the stone the pot, it will be ill for the pot;
雞蛋碰石頭 like an egg dashing itself against a rock – courting destruction;

J

雞蛋挑石頭—沒茬找茬 fault-finding; nitpick; picking bones in an egg – overcritical;
雞蛋下山—滾蛋 eggs rolling down a mountain; go away; rolling eggs;
雞蛋餡烘餅 tart;
雞飛蛋打 come out empty-handed; the hen has flown away and the eggs in the coop are broken – all is lost;
一個雞蛋 an egg;
一籃雞蛋 a basket of eggs;
一箱雞蛋 a case of eggs;

[雞丁] diced chicken;
雞丁麵 noodles with diced chicken;

[雞凍] chicken jelly;

[雞狗] chicken and dogs;
雞豚狗彘 fowls, pigs, dogs and swine;
嫁雞隨雞，嫁狗隨狗 a woman must follow her husband's lot and position; once a girl has attached herself to one man, she must be faithful to him forever regardless of all circumstances;

[雞冠] cockscomb; comb;

[雞姦] paederasty; sodomy; sodomize;
雞姦者 paederast; paedophile; sodomite;

[雞腳] chicken's feet;

[雞口牛後] better to reign in hell than serve in heaven;

[雞塊] chicken cubes;

[雞欄] chicken farm;

[雞肋] chicken ribs–things of little value or interest;

[雞籠] coop;

[雞毛] chicken feathers;
雞毛撢子 feather duster;
雞毛當令箭 take a chicken feather for a warrant to give commands – take seriously a casual word dropped by a superior;
~拿著雞毛當令箭 take a chicken feather for a warrant to issue orders – treat one's superior's casual remark as an order and make a big fuss about it; treat an utterly worthless thing like an order from on high;
雞毛堵著耳朵 have chicken feathers in one's ears – unable to hear anything;
雞毛飛上天 a chicken feather flying up to heaven – do sth never done before;
雞毛蒜皮 chicken feathers and garlic skins – trifles; odds and ends; small potatoes; trivialities; worthless things;

[雞鳴] cockcrow;
雞鳴而起 rise at cockcrow;
雞鳴狗盜 crow like a cock and snatch like a dog – small tricks;
雞鳴狗吠 a few dogs are barking and some cocks crowing;

[雞皮] chicken's skin;
雞皮疙瘩 gooseflesh; make sb's flesh creep;
~起雞皮疙瘩 be gooseflesh all over; one's flesh creeps; come out in goosebumps;
雞皮鶴髮 wrinkled skin and white hair – advanced in age;

[雞犬] a dog or a cock;
雞犬不驚 not a dog or a cock is aroused – complete peace and quiet; not to wake fowls or dogs;
雞犬不留 even fowls and dogs are not spared – ruthless mass slaughter; not even a dog or a chicken would be left – utter extermination;
雞犬不寧 cause such utter confusion as to make everybody nervous; flutter the dove-cotes; each chickens and dogs are greatly upset – great disorder; even fowls and dogs are not left in peace – general turmoil;
雞犬昇天 fowls and dogs turn immortals – relatives and followers of a high official get promotion after him;
雞犬相聞 live in the neighbourhood; live nearby;
淮南雞犬 humble followers waiting for a pull from their superior;
土雞瓦犬 completely useless person; shape without soul;

[雞群一鶴] a triton among the minnows;

[雞舍] hen house;

[雞頭] chicken head;

[雞腿] chicken's leg;
雞腿打來牙齒軟 a dog will not cry if you strike him with a bone; spread the table and contention will cease;

[雞尾酒] cocktail; flip;
雞尾酒杯 cocktail glass;
雞尾酒會 cocktail party;
雞尾酒調酒器 cocktail shaker;

[雞瘟] chicken pest; fowl plague;

[雞窩] chicken coop; henhouse; roost;
雞窩裏飛出金鳳凰 phoenixes soaring out of a chicken coop — sophisticated products can be made in makeshift factories;
[雞心] chicken heart;
雞心領 V-neck;
[雞胸] chicken breast;
雞胸脯 chicken breast;
[雞血] chicken's blood;
[雞雜] chicken giblets;
[雞子] chicken;
[雞嘴猴腮] thrust out one's lips and have a chin like an ape's;

白切雞 sliced steamed chicken;
棒棒雞 boneless chicken with heavy seasoning;
蛋雞 layer;
蛋用雞 layer;
鬥雞 cock fight; cockfighting;
咖哩雞 curry chicken;
公雞 cock; rooster;
光雞 plucked chicken; pulled chicken;
黑水雞 moorhen;
活雞 live chicken;
火雞 turkey;
家雞 chicken; hen;
烤雞 roast chicken;
燜雞 stewed chicken;
母雞 hen; mother hen;
茄汁雞 chicken in tomato sauce;
去毛雞 dressed chicken;
肉用雞 meat chicken;
沙雞 sandgrouse;
山雞 pheasant;
田雞 frog;
填餡雞 stuffed chicken;
小雞 chick; chickling;
雄雞 cock; rooster;
雪雞 snow cock;
腌雞 preserved chicken;
野雞 pheasant;
一隻雞 a chicken;
炸子雞 fried young chicken;
澤雞 moorhen;
珍珠雞 guinea fowl;
子雞 young chicken;

ji

【譏】 mock; ridicule; satirize;
[譏諷] ridicule; satirize; throw out innuendoes against;
譏諷腐敗現象 ridicule corrupt dealings;
[譏笑] deride; jeer; ridicule; sneer at;
忍受譏笑 bear ridicule;
引起譏笑 provoke the derision of...;
招致譏笑 incur ridicule;

ji

【饑】 (1) famish; hungry; starve; (2) crop failure; famine;
[饑飽] hunger and full stomach;
饑飽勞碌 salve all day long with no asurance when the next meal will come;
眼飽肚饑 although one's eyes feast, one's belly starves;
[饑不納言] hungry bellies have no ears; the belly has no ears;
[饑腸] empty stomach;
饑腸轆轆 as hungry as a hawk; as hungry as a hunter; as hungry as a wolf; famishing; feel a vacuum in the lower regions; have a wolf in the stomach; one's belly is rumbling with hunger; one's inside rumbles for want of food; one's stomach cries out for food; one's stomach rumbles with hunger; so hungry that the stomach is beginning to gurgle; the belly thinks the throat is cut;
[饑餓] hunger; starvation;
饑餓病 malnutrition;
饑餓難忍 feel unbearably hungry;
饑餓痛 hunger pain hunger pangs;
饑餓性骨病 hunger osteopathy;
饑餓性水腫 hunger swelling;
飽漢不知餓漢饑 one who is in comfortable circumstances does not know the bitterness of misfortune; the well-fed don't know how the starving suffer;
飽人不知餓人饑 he who is well-fed does not know what hunger is like;
不知饑餓 not know hunger when one is hungry;
防止饑餓 ward off starvation;
感到饑餓 feel hungry;
饑鷹餓虎 a hungry vulture and tiger; as greedy as a hungry vulture and tiger;
面臨饑餓 hunger stares at sb in the face;
死於饑餓 die from hunger; die of hunger;
戰勝饑餓 conquer hunger;

J

[饑寒] hunger and cold;
饑寒交迫 a life of cold and hunger; be poverty-stricken; be pressed by hunger and cold; be wedged in between hunger and cold; go cold and hungry; lack of proper food and warmth; live in hunger and cold; suffer from cold and hunger; suffer hunger and cold;
饑寒難耐 one can hardly bear hunger and cold;
饑寒起盜心 an empty belly hears nobody; hunger and cold tempt men to steal;
饑寒所逼 be driven by hunger and cold;
號寒啼饑 cry from hunger and cold; cry out because of hunger and cold; howl for being hungry and cry for feeling cold;
啼饑號寒 cry out from hunger and cold; howl for being hungry and cry for feeling cold; lament in hunger and cold; wail with hunger and cold;

[饑荒] (1) crop failure; famine; (2) hard pressed for money; hard up; short of money; (3) debt;
拉饑荒 in debt; owe a debt; run into debt;
鬧饑荒 hard up; suffer from famine; turn short of cash;
死於饑荒 die of famine; perish with famine;
引起饑荒 cause famine;

[饑饉] crop failure; famine;
饑饉頻仍 famines occur time and again;

[饑渴] hungry and thirsty;
饑餐渴飲 eat when hungry and drink when thirsty; when one is hungry, one eats and when thirsty, one drinks;
饑名渴勢 greedy for honour and power;
如饑似渴 avidly; eagerly; hungrily; hungry for; like hunger and thirst to; thirst for; with great eagerness;
又饑又渴 hungry and thirsty; weak from hunger and thirst;

[饑民] famine refugees; famine victims;

[饑者] hungry person;
饑者甘食 the hungry think any food sweet;
饑者易為食 a good appetite is a good sauce; all food is delicious to the starving; hunger finds no fault with the cookery; hunger is the best sauce; hunger makes hard beans sweet; the cat is hungry when a crust contents her; the first dish pleases all;
~饑者易為食，渴者易為飲 the hungry man is easily satisfied with food and the thirsty man with drink;

充饑 allay one's hunger;
點饑 have a snack to stave off hunger;
搪饑 ward off hunger;

ji

【躋】 ascend; go up; rise;

ji

【齎】 (1) offer; present; (2) entertain; harbour; have in one's mind;

[齎志而歿] die without accomplishing what one has wanted; die without realizing one's ambitions;

ji

【羇】 lodge in sb's house;

ji

【虀】 minced pickle;

ji

【齏】 (1) powdered; pulverized; (2) seasoning in powdered form;

[齏粉] broken bits; fine powder;

ji

【羈】 (1) bridle; headstall; (2) control; restrain; (3) delay; detain; stay;

[羈絆] fetters; trammels; yoke;
擺脱 ... 的羈絆 shake off the yoke of...;
~擺脱感情的羈絆 get rid of restraints of emotions;

[羈留] (1) stay; stop over; (2) detain; keep in custody;

[羈旅] live in a strange land; stay long in a strange place;

[羈押] detain; take into custody;

不羈 uninhibited; unruly;

ji²

ji

【及】 (1) come up to; reach; (2) in time for; (3) and; (4) a surname;

[及弟] pass an imperial examination;

[及鋒而試] come up to the tip of a bayonet and try; strike while the iron is hot; try while the point is sharp;

[及格] pass an examination;
及格分數 pass mark;
及格賽 qualifying events; qualifying heats; qualifying rounds; qualifying trials;
考試及格 pass an examination;
考試未及格 fail to pass the examination;
不及格 clutch the gunny; fail; fail in an examination;
~考試不及格 fail in an examination;

[及瓜而代] a promoise to relieve sb from a difficult job before long; as soon as the melons are ripe one will be relieved — to be replaced from a job;

[及笄] (of a girl) come of age;
及笄之年 a woman of marriageable age;
年方及笄 bud into womanhood; just of marriageable age (said of a girl);
年事及笄 bud into womanhood;

[及齡] reach a required age;

[及難] encounter disaster; encounter calamity;

[及時] at a most opportune moment; at the right time; in due course; in due time; in good season; in good time; in season; in the nick of time; in time; promptly; timely; without delay;
及時趕到 arrive in the very nick of time;
及時滙報 report without delay;
及時糾正錯誤 correct a mistake promptly;
及時賞春 enjoy the spring while it lasts;
及時行樂 enjoy pleasure in good time; enjoy the pleasure of life here and now; enjoy the sweet of life while one is young; make merry while one can;
及時雨 a much-needed rain; a seasonable rain; a timely help; a timely rain; an opportune rain; help rendered in the nick of time;
~如及時雨 spread benefit to the people as rain benefits the fields;

[及位] ascend throne; ascend to power; assume position; assume reign;

[及物] transitive;
及物動詞 transitive verb;
及物短語動詞 transitive phrasal verb;
及物性 transitivity;

[及早] as soon as possible; at an early date; before it is too late;
及早回頭 lose no time in mending one's ways; make haste to reform; mend one's ways without delay; repent before it is too late;
及早準備 make preparations as soon as possible;
及早作出安排 make arrangements before it is too late;

[及至] until; up to;

埃及 Egypt;
比及 by the time; when;
遍及 extend all over; spread all over;
波及 affect; involve;
不及 (1) inferior to; not as good as;
齒及 mention;
觸及 touch;
顧及 give consideration to; take into account;
累及 implicate; involve;
料及 anticipate; expect;
旁及 take up;
普及 disseminate; popularize;
涉及 involve; relate to; touch upon;
提及 mention; refer to;
推及 analogize…to; spread…to;
危及 endanger; imperil;
無及 it's too late (to do sth); there's not enough time (to do sth);
言及 mention; talk about; touch on;
殃及 bring disaster to;
以及 along with; and; as well as;
憶及 call to mind; recollect; remember;
又及 postscript;
贅及 (1) add to; append to; (2) postscript;

ji

【伋】 (1) deceptive; (2) the name of Zisi, a grandson of Confucius;

ji

【吉】 (1) auspicious; lucky; propitious; (2) a surname;

[吉卜賽] gipsy;
吉卜賽人 Gypsy;
吉卜賽舞 the gipsy dance;

[吉光片羽] a fragment of a highly treasured relic; a fragment of an ancient literary work; cultural relics;

[吉利] auspicious; lucky; propitious;
吉利的 auspicious;
大吉大利 big fortune and great profit; good luck;
討個吉利 ask for sth as a token of good omen; for good luck;

J

[吉普車] bantam; jeep;
電視吉普車 television jeep;
井下吉普車 mine jeep;
水陸兩用吉普車 amphibian jeep;
[吉期] wedding day;
[吉慶] auspicious; happy; propitious;
[吉人天相] a charmed life; a life full of lucky escapes; bear a charmed life; blessed are the good men; God bless the good man; heaven always provides for good people; heaven keeps the good out of harm's way;
[吉他] guitar;
吉他獨奏 guitar solo;
吉他手 guitarist;
~首席吉他手 lead guitarist;
電吉他 electronic guitar;
彈吉他 play the guitar;
夏威夷吉他 Hawiian guitar;
[吉祥] auspicious; lucky; propitious;
吉祥卜鳳 lucky harmony and choice of a good son-in-law;
吉祥的 auspicious;
吉祥如意 good fortune as one wishes; good luck and happiness to you; may your good luck be as you would like it;
吉祥物 good luck charm; mascot;
[吉星高照] a lucky star shines on; be born under a lucky star; bring sb good luck and success in life; the lucky star shines bright;
[吉凶] good or ill luck;
吉凶未卜 cannot predict the outcome, good or bad; no one knows how it will turn out; not to know whether it will turn out good or bad; one's fate is in the balance;
吉凶相救，患難相扶 the victims of misfortune aid each other and those in trouble support each other;
趨吉避凶 pursue good fortune and avoid disaster; pursue good fortune and shun the course of calamity; strive for a friendly settlement and avoid conflict;
[吉兆] a good omen; a propitious sign;
遇到吉兆 come across a propitious sign;

大吉 (1) auspicious; (2) straightaway;
凶吉 the portentous and propitious;
擇吉 pick an auspicious day;
諏吉 pick an auspicious day;

ji

【吃】 stammer; stutter;
[吃吃] the sound of giggling;

ji

【即】 (1) approach; near; reach; (2) assume; undertake; (3) at present; in immediate future; (4) be prompted by the occasion;
[即便] even; even if; even though;
[即或] even; even if; even though;
[即將] about to; in no time; on the horizon; on the point of; soon;
即將到來 upcoming;
即將到手 at hand; between cup and lip;
即將來臨 about to come; impending arrival; it will soon be; upcoming;
[即景] be inspired by what one sees;
即景生情 the landscape evokes memories of the past;
[即刻] at once; before long; directly; immediately; instantly; presently; promptly; quickly; right away; shortly;
[即來] come at once;
召之即來 assemble as soon as summoned; come as soon as called; on call; ready to assemble at the first call;
[即離] familiar or distant;
不即不離 keep sb at arm's length; neither too familiar nor too distant;
若即若離 hold oneself slightly aloof; keep sb at arm's length; neither close nor distant; neither friendly nor aloof; neither to accept nor reject; partly accepting, partly rejecting;
[即令] even; even if; even though;
[即鹿無虞] act without due consideration and end up in failure;
[即年] current year;
即年指標 present index;
[即期] immediate; on demand; spot;
即期外匯業務 spot exchange;
[即日] (1) that very day; this very day; (2) within the next few days;
自即日起 as from today; as of today; beginning from this day;
[即若] even; even if; even though;
[即時] forthwith; immediacy; immediately; real-time; simultaneous;

即時傳譯 simultaneous interpretation;
[即食] ready to eat instantly;
即食餐點 ready meal;
即食麵 instant noodles;
[即使] even; even when; if; in spite of; notwithstanding; though; very; when;
即使如此 even so;
[即位] (1) take one's place; (2) ascend to; accession to the throne; come to; mount; take the throne;
[即席] extemporaneous; impromptu; off the cuff; offhand;
即席表演 give a show on the spur of the moment;
即席發言 make an impromptu speech; offhand speech; speak off the cuff; speak offhand;
即席之作 extempore; impromptu; improvisation;
[即興] extemporaneous; impromptu;
即興的 impromptu;
即興賦詩 dash off a poem; hit off a poem; write poems on the spur of the moment;
即興講話 improvisational speech;
即興曲 impromptu;
即興音樂會 impromptu concert;
即興之作 improvisation;
即興做 improvise;

當即 at once; right away;
立即 at once; immediately;
俟即 as soon as; when...then;
隨即 immediately; presently;
遂即 then; thereupon;
迅即 at once; immediately;
亦即 i.e.; namely; that is; viz.;
在即 near at hand; soon;

ji

【岌】 lofty; towering;
[岌岌] precarious;
岌岌不可終日 live in constant fear; live precariously;
岌岌可危 be placed in jeopardy; between the beetle and the block; extremely hazardous; hang by a hair; hang by a single thread; in a critical situation; in a precarious situation; in a tottering position; in great peril; in imminent danger;

ji

【汲】 draw water;
[汲汲] anxious; avid;
汲汲皇皇 in a haste;
汲汲名利 crave fame and gain; restlessly seeking for fame and riches;
汲汲於名 not free from anxiety about achieving celebrity;
[汲取] derive; dip; draft; draw;
汲取歡樂 derive pleasure from...;
汲取教訓 take a lesson from...;
~從經驗中汲取教訓 learn a lesson from experience;
汲取經驗 draw on the experience of...;
汲取營養 draw nourishment from...;
[汲深綆短] the well is deep and the rope short — beyond one's reach;
[汲水] draw water;
從井裏汲水 draw water from a well;

ji

【亟】 pressing; urgent;
[亟欲] very anxious to do sth;

ji

【急】 (1) anxious; impatient; (2) worry; (3) annoyed; irritated; (4) fast; rapid; violent; (5) pressing; urgent; (6) emergency; urgency;
[急巴巴] impatient;
急急巴巴 anxiously;
[急病] acute disease;
[急不可待] be all agog for; can scarcely wait; extremely anxious; in too much of a hurry to wait; on edge; too impatient to wait;
[急不暇擇] any port in a storm; catch at a straw; in emergency there is no time to choose; no choice in emergency;
[急促] (1) hurried; rapid; (2) pressing; short;
時間急促 time is pressing; time is running short;
[急得] worry;
急得大哭 be so worried that one bursts into tears;
急得跺腳 make sb jump up with nervousness; stamp one's foot with worry;
急得上火 so worried that one gets angry;
急得說不出話來 be too worried to speak;
急得團團轉 so agitated that one is like an

ant on a hot pan;
急得要發瘋 be so agitated that one is about to be crazy;
急得要哭 be worried and about to cry;
急得要命 in a mortal hurry; worried to death;
急得要死 get into a flap; in a flap; worried to death;
急得語無倫次 ramble in one's statement for anxiety;

[急電] urgent cable; urgent telegram;

[急公好義] public-spirited; zealous for public interests; zealous for the common weal ready to stand up for justice; public-spirited;

[急緩]
急事緩處 make haste slowly;

[急擊] attack fiercely; attack furiously;

[急件] urgent document;

[急驚風] acute infantile convulsions;
急驚風偏遇慢郎中 an urgent case receiving slow treatment; deferred action taken in cases requiring prompt attention;

[急救] first aid; give first aid treatment;
急救包 first aid kit;
急救車 emergency ambulance;
急救隊 rescue brigade;
急救盒 first aid kit;
急救室 emergency room;
急救箱 first aid kit;
急救用品 first-aid appliance;
急救員 first aider;
急救站 first-aid station;
急救中心 emergency centre; first-aid centre;

[急就章] a composition completed in haste; a hurriedly-written essay; a piece of hasty work; improvisation;

[急劇] rapid; sharp; sudden;

[急遽] rapid; sharp; sudden;
急遽直下 the situation takes a sharp turn for the worse;

[急流] (1) rapid stream; rapids; rush; torrent; (2) jet flow; jet stream;
急流險灘 rapids and shoals;
急流勇進 advance through the rapids; forge ahead against a swift current; press on in the teeth of difficulties;
急流勇退 draw back wisely in face of overwhelming odds; leave off while the play is good; make a quick retreat before a crisis; resign at the height of one's prosperity; resolutely retire at the height of one's official career; retire when in gigh office; retreat heroically before a rushing torrent;

[急忙] hurry; in a hurry; in great haste; in one's hurry; make a dash; quickly; rush;
急忙走去 hasten to; hurriedly set out for; hurry away; hurry to; in a hurry; leave in haste; run; run off with haste; rush;
急急忙忙 harried and busy; hurriedly; in a hurry; in a rush; in great haste; on the rush;

[急難] (1) grave danger; misfortune; (2) anxious to help those in grave danger;
急難相助 help in a crisis;

[急迫] imperative; pressing; urgent;
情況急迫 the situation is urgent;
任務急迫 the task is pressing;
時間急迫 time is pressing;
事情急迫 the business is pressing;

[急起直追] do one's utmost to catch up with; do one's utmost to overtake; endeavour to overtake others; jump up and run straight after sb; make a dash; make every endeavour to catch up; rouse oneself to cathc up; spring up and give chase;

[急切] (1) eager; impatient; imperative; urgent; (2) in a hurry; in haste;
急切難辦 hard to do in a hurry;

[急死] sudden death;

[急速] at high speed; rapidly; very fast;
急速趕往現場 make haste to the scene;

[急灘] rapids;

[急湍] swift current;

[急彎] (1) sharp turn; (2) turn suddenly; (3) elbow;

[急務] urgent task;
不急之務 a matter of no great urgency;
先務之急 first things first;

[急性] acute;
急性病 acute disease;

[急需] (1) badly in need of; (2) urgent need;
急需救濟 in dire need of relief;
急需救治 need treatment and cure badly;
急需要錢 there is a great need of money;

急需援助 in urgent need of help;
緩解急需 relieve urgent needs;
滿足急需 satisfy the pressing need;
以備急需 save against a rainy day;
以應急需 in order to answer an urgent need; meet a crying need;

[急用] urgent need;
以備急用 save against a rainy day;

[急於] all eagerness; anxious; burning to; impatient; itch for; long for;
急於表態 eager to state one's position;
急於表現自己 anxious to show off;
急於成親 impatient to get married;
急於求成 a rush for quick results; avoid eagerness for quick results; be anxious for success; be anxious to accomplish one's purpose; be impatient for success; hope to achieve quick results; overanxious to make achievements; rush things through to completion;
急於求利 eager to draw quick profit;
急於討好 anxious to please sb;
急於完成任務 eager to fulfill a task;
急於要走 impatient to go;

[急躁] (1) irascible; irritable; testy; (2) impatient; impetuous; rash;
急躁冒進 impetuous and rash; rush things through;
變得急躁 become irritated;
克服急躁 restrain oneself from losing one's temper;
顯得急躁 exhibit impatience;

[急診] emergency call; emergency treatment;

[急症] emergency;

[急智] nimbleness of mind in dealing with emergencies; quick-wittedness;
急智多謀 quick-witted and resourceful;
急智風趣 nimble and humorous;
急中生智 a clever idea occurs to one's mind at the crucial moment; have a brainwave when in danger; have a sudden flash of inspiration; have quick wits in emergency; hit upon a plan in desperation; show resourcefulness in an emergency; suddenly hit on a way out of a predicament; wit comes to their rescue when people are in a critical situation;

[急走] hotfoot;

褊急 narrow-minded and short-tempered;
卞急 impetuous;
不用急 ther's no rush;
發急 become impatient;
乾急 be anxious, but unable to do anything;
告急 (1) be in an emergency; (2) ask for emergency help;
緩及 of greater or lesser urgency;
火急 pressing; urgent;
濟急 relieve sb in need;
焦急 anxious; worried;
緊急 critical; urgent;
救急 help meet an urgent need;
狷急 impetuous; impulsive; quick-tempered; rash;
峻急 (of water currents) rapid; torrential;
內急 want to go to the toilet badly;
氣急 flustered and exasperated;
情急 in a moment of desperation;
特急 extra urgent;
湍急 (of a current) rapid; torrential;
萬急 very urgent;
危急 hazardous; in a desperate situation; in a state of emergency; pressing; urgent;
心急 impatient; short-tempered;
性急 hot-tempered; impatient; short-tempered;
迅急 speedy; swift; ver fast;
應急 meet an emergency; meet an urgent need;
躁急 restless; uneasy;
着急 feel anxious; worry;
至急 extremely urgent; most urgent;
嘴急 eager to eat;

ji
【革】 anxious; dangerous; urgent;

ji
【唧】 (1) pump; (2) buzzing sound;

ji
【疾】 (1) disease; illness; sickness; (2) difficulty; pain; suffering; (3) abhor; hate; (4) fast; quick;

[疾病] disease; illness; sickness;
疾病纏身 be eaten up with diseases;
疾病叢生 be infested with all diseases;
疾病津貼 sick benefit;
疾病虧身 illness makes one weak;
擺脱疾病 throw off one's illness;
常見疾病 common ailment;
傳播疾病 pass on a disease; spread disease; transmit a disease;
傳染性疾病 infectious disease;
防治疾病 prevention and treatment of

disease;
功能性疾病 functional disease;
加重疾病 aggravate disease;
減少疾病 reduce disease;
局部性疾病 local disease;
恐懼疾病 afraid of a disease;
腦血管疾病 cerebro-vascular disorder;
器質性疾病 parenchymal disease;
全身性疾病 systemic disease;
染上疾病 be seized with an illness;
熱帶疾病 tropical diseases;
系統性疾病 systemic disease;
細菌性疾病 bacteriosis;
心血管疾病 cardiovascular disease;
一種疾病 a sickness;
引起疾病 cause a disease;
隱性疾病 pseudodisease;
預防疾病 prevent a disease;ward off disease;
戰勝疾病 triumph over illness;
診斷疾病 diagnose an illness;
征服疾病 conquer a stubborn disease;
治療疾病 treat a disease;
治愈疾病 cure a disease;
周期性疾病 periodic disease;
主要疾病 principal disease;
滋生疾病 germinate disease;

[疾馳] gallop at full speed;
疾馳而過 shoot past; speed past; whirl away;
騁足疾馳 run quickly — in a quick manner;

[疾風] gale; strong wind;
疾風暴雨 hurricane; tempest; violent storm;
疾風掃落葉 like a strong wind sweeping away dead leaves — carrying everything before one;
疾風迅雷 swift wind and sudden clap of thunder;
疾風迅雨 there is strong wind and torrential rain;
疾風知勁草 adversity is the best testing ground for moral stamina; adversity tries a friend; separate the men from the boys;
疾風知勁草，患難見交情 calamity is man's true touchstone; the strong wind reveals sturdy grass, and in calamity one meets true friends;
疾風知勁草，烈火見真金 sturdy grass withstands high winds, true gold stands the test of fire;

[疾苦] difficulties; hardships; sufferings;
關心疾苦 care about sb's troubles;
忍受疾苦 endure pain; endure sufferings;

[疾趨而過] hurry past;

[疾如飛矢] as swift as an arrow;

[疾善如仇] hate good folks as if they were enemies; hate goodness as one does one's enemies;

[疾書] write swiftly;
握管疾書 hold a pen and write swiftly;
縱筆疾書 write with a running pen;

[疾走] trot;
疾走如飛 run so fast as if flying; speed on flying feet;

[疾足先登] one who acts fast will succeed first; the hasty foot gets there first;

暗疾 a disease one is ashamed of; unmentionable;
惡疾 foul disease;
殘疾 disability;
痼疾 chronic illness;
宿疾 chronic complaint; old trouble;
問疾 visit and console a patient;
心疾 (1) illness caused by deep worries; (2) mental ailment;
迅疾 impetuous; quick; rapid; speedy; swift;
眼疾 (1) eye ailment; eye disease; eye trouble; (2) keen-eyed;
引疾 take illness as a reason for resignation;
隱疾 unmentionable disease;
嬰疾 catch illness; fall sick;

ji

【級】 (1) grade; level; rank; (2) class; course; form; grade; (3) step; (4) stage; (5) degree;

[級別] grade; level; rank; rating; scale; sort;
屬於不同級別 in a different league;

[級數] array; progression; series;
級數解 series solution;
級數值 value of series;
等比級數 geometric progression; geometrical series;
等差級數 arithmetic series; arithmetic progression;
附貼級數 adherent series;
幾何級數 geometric progression; geometrical series;
算術級數 arithmetic series; arithmetic

progression;
泰勒級數 Taylor series;
調和級數 harmonic progression; harmonious series;
無限級數 infinitive progression;
有限級數 finite progression;

ji
【脊】 (1) spinal column; spine; (2) ridge;
[脊背] back;
[脊梁] back of the human body;
脊梁骨 backbone; spine;
[脊膜脊髓炎] meningomyelitis;
[脊膜炎] spinal meningitis;
[脊髓] spinal cord; spinal marrow;
脊髓病 myelopathy;
出血性脊髓病 hemorrhagic myelopahty;
創傷性脊髓病 traumatic myelopathy;
壞死性脊髓病 necrotizing myelopathy;
外傷性脊髓病 traumatic myelopathy;
系統性脊髓病 systemic myelopathy;
壓迫性脊髓病 compression myelopathy;
脊髓灰質炎 poliomyelitis;
脊髓麻醉 spinal anaesthesia;
脊髓軟化 spondylomalacia;
~創傷性脊髓軟化 spondylomalacia traumatica;
脊髓神經 spinal nerve;
脊髓炎 myelitis;
病毒性脊髓炎 viral arthritis;
播散性脊髓炎 disseminated myelitis;
脊膜脊髓炎 meningomyelitis;
接種後脊髓炎 postvaccinal myelitis;
慢性脊髓炎 chronic myelitis;
梅毒性脊髓炎 syphilitic myelitis;
彌散性脊髓炎 diffuse myelitis;
壓迫性脊髓炎 compression myelitis;
震蕩性脊髓炎 concussion myelitis;
[脊柱] spine; vertebral column;
~脊柱病 rachiopathy;
脊柱發育不良 atelorachidia;
脊柱發育不全 atelorachidia;
脊柱痛 rachialgia;
脊柱炎 rachitis;
裂脊柱 cleft spine;
[脊椎] vertebrae;
脊椎病 spondylopathy;
脊椎骨 spine; vertebra;
脊椎痛 spondylitis;
脊椎炎 spondylitis;
~創傷後脊椎炎 post-traumatic spondylitis;
~創傷性脊髓炎 traumatic spondylitis;
~肥大性脊椎炎 hypertrophic spondylitis;
創傷性脊椎病 traumatic spondylopathy;

裏脊 fillet; tenderloin;
通脊 loin and rib;

ji
【笈】 bamboo bookcase;

ji
【寂】 (1) quiet; serene; silent; still; (2) lonely; lonesome; solitary; (3) death of a Buddhist monk or nun;
[寂靜] hush; quiet; silent; still;
寂靜無嘩 silent and still; very quiet;
寂靜無聲 silent and still;
沉悶的寂靜 lifeless quiet;
打破寂靜 shatter the silence;
極度寂靜 the utmost silence;
死沉沉的寂靜 dead silence;
死一般的寂靜 deathlike silence;
[寂寥] emptiness;
[寂寞] lonely; lonesome;
寂寞無聊 be bored by idleness and loneliness;
不甘寂寞 hate to be neglected; hate to be overlooked;
感到寂寞 feel lonely; have the feeling of loneliness;

岑寂 lonely; quiet; still;
沉寂 (1) quiet; still; (2) no news;
孤寂 lonely;
枯寂 dull and lonely;
冷寂 quiet and lonely;
熱寂 heat death;
死寂 deathly stillness;
幽寂 secluded and lonely;
圓寂 (of Buddhist monks) pass away;

ji
【棘】 (1) buckthorns; thorny brambles; (2) difficult; troublesome; urgent; (3) a surname;
[棘手] difficult to handle; knotty; thorny; ticklish; troublesome;
棘手的事情 ticklish;
棘手的問題 knotty problem; thorny question; ticklish question;
[棘爪] pawl; ratchet;
棘爪簧 pawl spring;
保護棘爪 pawl maintaining;

衝擊棘爪 impulse ratchet;
傳動棘爪 driving ratchet;
打點棘爪 strike ratchet;
連接簧片棘爪 coupling spring ratchet;
起鬧棘爪 alarm ratchet;
日曆調整棘爪 date corrector ratchet;
上條棘爪 winding ratchet;
條輪棘爪 power wheel ratchet;
張力棘爪 tension ratchet;
自動簧片棘爪 automatic spring ratchet;

荊棘 brambles; thistles and thorns;

ji

【集】 (1) assemble; collect; gather; (2) (墟) country fair; market; (3) anthology; collection; (4) part; volume; (5) a surname;

[集成] integrated;
集成電路 integrated circuit;
~集成電路計算機 computer of integrated circuit;
~集成電路卡 circuit card;
~大規模集成電路 large-scale integration;
集成服務 integrated service;
~集成服務數字網 integrated service digital network;
集成化 intergrated;
~集成化技術 integrated technology;
集成曲 medley;
集成生產 integrated production;
~集成生產系統 integrated manufacture system;
~集成生產線 integrated production line;
集成製造系統 intetrated manufacturing system;
集大成 a comprehensive expression of; an agglomeration of; epitomize; the culmination of;

[集電] collect electricity;
集電極 collector;
集電區 collector region;

[集合] assemble; call together; gather; muster;
集合城市 conurbation;
集合名詞 collective noun;
集合賬戶 collective account;

[集會] assembly; gathering; meeting; rally;
集會自由 freedom of assembly;
安排集會 arrange an assembly;
籌劃集會 plan and prepare for a rally;
舉行集會 hold a rally;
抗議集會 protest meeting;
取消集會 cancel a gathering;

[集結] build up; concentrate; mass;
集結待命 assemble and wait orders;
集結軍隊 build up one's military forces;

[集錦] collection of choice specimens;

[集居] reside collectively;

[集句] poem made up of lines from various poets;

[集聚] (1) assemble; collect; gather; (2) concentration; (3) grouping;

[集料] aggregate;
合成集料 synthetic aggregate;
耐火集料 fireproof aggregates;
特製集料 special aggregate;
填隙集料 interstital aggregate;
吸水集料 absorbent aggregate;
吸油集料 blotter aggregate;

[集納] collect; gather;

[集權] centralization of state power; concentration of power;
中央集權制 centralism;

[集群] colony; en masse; in swarms; schooling;

[集市] bazaar; country fair; fair; market; rural fair;
錯過集市 miss the market;
檢查集市 check on the market;
開闢集市 open up markets;

[集書狂] bibliomania;

[集水] catchment;
集水面積 catchment area;
集水區 catchment area;

[集思廣益] benefit by mutual discussion; draw on collective wisdom and absorb all useful ideas; draw upon all useful opinions; gather opinions from all sides and thus make it possible to reap greater benefits; good at listening to all useful opinions; much benefit can be derived from listening to all opinion; pool collective wisdom and get better results in the work; pool the wisdom of the masses; put heads together so as to get better results; two heads are better than one;

[集體] (1) collectively; (2) collective ownership; (3) collective; community; group; team;

集體創作 collective efforts in artistic creation;
集體的 collective;
集體化 collectivization;
集體經濟 collective economy;
集體領導 collective leadership;
集體企業 collective enterprise;
集體所有制 collective ownership;
集體智慧 collective wisdom;
集體主義 collectivism;
關心集體 show concern for the collective;

[集團] bloc; circle; clique; group; ring;
集團標準 group standard;
集團公司 group corporation;
集團購買力 group purchasing power;
集團訴訟 group action;
集團消費 institutional purchase;
金融集團 financial clique;
軍事集團 military bloc;
小集團 clique; coterie; in-crowd; in-group;
~小集團的 clannish; cliquey; cliquish;

[集訓] assemble for training;
參加集訓 take part in the assemblage for training;

[集腋成裘] collect bits of fur under the fox's forelegs to make a robe; every little makes a mickle; make a fur coat from many pieces of felt — get the benefit of many opinions; little and often fills the purse; many a little makes a mickle; make a mickle makes a muckle; many drops of water make an ocean; many small things put together make a great deal; the bits of fur from the axillae of many foxes take together will make a robe;

[集郵] philately; stamp collecting;
集郵簿 stamp album;

[集苑集枯] every man to his taste; everybody has his likes and dislikes; some gather on the pastures and some on the branches — the political attitude of men differ; tastes differ;

[集約] intensive;
集約耕作 intensive agriculture;
集約灌溉農業 intenstive irrigated agriculture;
集約經營 intensive management;

[集智] collective wisdom;

[集中] amass; centralize; concentrate; focus; put together;
集中兵力 gather the troops;
集中點 focal point;
集中管理 centralized management;
集中監控系統 centralized monitoring system;
集中控制 centralized control; centralization of control;
集中力量 concentrate forces;
集中器 concentrator;
~數據集中器 data concentrator;
~自動集中器 automatic concentrator;
集中數據庫 integrated database;
集中思維 convergent thinking;
集中營 concentration camp;
集中制 centralism; centralization;
~財政集中制 fiscal centralization;
~民主集中制 democratic centralism;
電報集中 telegraphy centralization;
異常集中 abnormal concentration;
資本集中 centralization of capital;

[集裝箱] container;
集裝箱船 container ship;
集裝箱碼頭 container terminal;
集裝箱運輸 container traffic;
半集裝箱 semi-container;
加熱集裝箱 heated container;
絕熱集裝箱 adiabatic container;
空氣調節集裝箱 air-conditioned container;
空運集裝箱 air container;
汽車集裝箱 auto container;
箱型集裝箱 box-type container;

[集資] collect funds; collect money; concentrate funds; pool resources; raise funds;

畢集 assemble completely; gather completely;
岔集 gather at a place;
別集 anthology of an author's works;
采集 collect; gather;
採集 collect; gather;
籌集 raise money;
叢集 collection; converge; pile up; series of books;
湊集 gather together;
調集 assemble; concentrate;
逢集 on market day;
趕集 go to a fair; go to market;
匯集 (1) collect; gather together; (2) assemble; come together; crowd together;

J

會集 assemble;
交集 (1) intersection; (2) with mixed feelings;
結集 (1) concentrate; mass; (2) collect articles into a volume;
糾集 get together; muster;
鳩集 get together; muster;
聚集 assemble; gather;
麇集 flock together; swarm;
密集 concentrated; crowded together;
募集 collect; raise;
凝集 agglutinate;
齊集 assemble;
全集 collected works; complete works;
詩集 collection of poems; poetry anthology;
市集 (1) fair; (2) small town;
收集 collect; gather;
搜集 collect; gather;
文集 collected works;
續集 sequel;
選集 anthology; selected works;
邀集 call together; invite to meet together;
影集 photograph album;
約集 call together; meet by appointment;
雲集 converge; crowd together; gather;
召集 call together; convene;
徵集 (1) collect; (2) call up; draft; recruit;
總集 an anthology of works by various authors;

ji

【嫉】 (1) envious; jealous; (2) detest; hate;
[嫉妒] envy; jealous of;
嫉妒心 jealousy;
出於嫉妒 out of jealousy;
一絲嫉妒 a slight twinge of jealousy;
一陣嫉妒 a rush of jealousy;

ji

【戢】 cease; fold; put away or store up;
[戢暴除強] run down the people's oppressors;

ji

【極】 (1) extreme; the utmost point; (2) pole; (3) exceedingly; extremely;
[極板] plate;
負極板 negative plate;
陽極板 positive plate;
陰極板 negative plate;
正極板 positive plate;
[極大] maximum;
負極大 negative maximum;
局部極大 local maximum;
條件極大 conditional maximum;
真實極大 true maximum;
正常極大 proper maximum;
[極點] apotheosis; culminating point; limit; perfoot; the extreme; the utmost; top;
感動到極點 be extremely moved;
氣憤到極點 be enraged to the utmost;
興奮到極點 be extremely excited;
[極度] exceeding; extreme; to the utmost; to the world;
極度不安 be extremely anxious about;
極度悲傷 be extremely sad;
極度疲勞 be overcome with fatigue;
極度痛苦 in extreme pain;
極度危險 in extreme danger;
極度興奮 be exceedingly elated;
[極端] (1) extremes; (2) exceeding; extreme;
極端分子 extremist; lunatic fringe;
極端腐敗 be rotten to the core;
極端困難 exceedingly difficult;
極端貧困 in dire poverty;
極端組織 extremist group;
走極端 go to excess; go to extremes; run to an extreme;
~避免走極端 avoid the extremes;
[極多] abundance;
[極光] aurora;
[極化] polarization;
偶極極化 dipole polarization;
陰極極化 cathodic polarization;
原子極化 atomic polarization;
[極簡主義] minimalism;
[極了] very;
好極了 like a dream; wonderful;
妙極了 most enjoyable; wonderful;
[極力] do one's utmost; spare no effort;
極力反對 oppose actively; oppose stoutly;
極力鼓吹 vigorously publicize;
極力勸阻 do one's utmost to dissuade sb from doing sth;
極力阻撓 try one's best to stand in the way of;
[極量] maximum amount;
極量翻譯 maximum translation;
[極目] look as far as the eye can see;
極目了望 look afar;
極目四眺 survey all that is spread before one; take a panoramic view from some vantage point;
極目遠眺 gaze into the distance; look far into the distance; strain one's eyes to look at the distance;
[極品] best quality; highest grade;

官居極品 official of the highest rank;

[極譜] polarography;

極譜法 polarography;

~ 放射極譜法 radiometric polarography;

~ 快速掃描極譜法 rapid-scan polarography;

極譜分析 polarographic analysis; polarography;

極譜儀 polarography;

[極其] exceedingly; extremely; most; very;

極其荒唐 absolutely ridiculous;

極其困難 extremely difficult;

極其懶惰 very lazy;

極其耐心 extremely patient;

極其努力 work with utmost efforts;

極其認真 very serious;

極其容易 as easy as ABC;

極其傷心 feel extremely heartbroken;

極其失望 be exceedingly disappointed;

極其有用 exceedingly useful;

[極權主義] totalitarianism;

[極少] hardly any; scarcely any;

[極盛] the highest point of development

極盛時期 acme; heyday; zenith;

達到極盛 reach the height of;

[極限] (1) extremity; limit; maximum; ultimate limit; (2) limit;

極限詞 limit word;

極限點 limiting point;

極限科學技術 ultimate science-technique;

極限明信片 maximum post card;

極限位置 extreme position;

超出極限 go beyond the limit of; overstep the limit of;

超越極限 beyond the limits;

達到極限 be stretched to the limit; reach the limit;

確立極限 establish a maximum;

允許極限 allowable limit;

[極小] minimum;

極小的 extremely small; liliputian; little tiny; tiny little;

局部極小 local minimum;

弱相對極小 weak relative minimum;

正常極小 proper minimum;

[極性] polar; polarity;

極性對立 polar opposition;

偏轉極性 deflection polar;

時鐘極性 clock polarity;

[極值] extreme; extremum;

極值點 extreme point; extremum point;

北極 the Arctic Pole; the North Pole;

磁極 magnetic pole;

電極 electrode;

二極 ambipolar;

負極 cathode;

骨極 bone exhaustion;

窮極 (1) extremely; in the extreme; (2) abjectly poor; hard up;

柵極 grid;

盛極 reach the peak;

雙極 dipole;

天極 celestial pole;

罔極 (1) infinite; (2) transgress;

消極 (1) negative; (2) inactive; passive; pessimistic;

陽極 anode; positive pole;

陰極 cathode; negative pole;

銀極 galactic pole;

至極 extremely; the most; to the utmost degree;

終極 end; finality; ultimate

ji

【楫】 oar;

[楫師篙工] all kinds of boatmen;

舟楫 vessel;

ji

【殛】 put to death;

ji

【蒺】 caltrop;

ji

【瘠】 (1) emaciated; lean; thin; (2) infertile; sterile; unproductive;

[瘠薄] barren; unproductive;

[瘠田] barren land;

貧瘠 barren; infertile; poor;

ji

【踖】 trample; tread upon;

ji

【輯】 (1) collect; compile; edit; (2) division; part; volume;

[輯錄] compile;

輯錄辭典 compile dictionaries;

[輯要] abstract; summary;

編輯 compile; compiler; edit; editor;

剪輯 (1) film; montage; (2) edit and rearrange;

邏輯 logic;

裒輯 compile;

特輯 (1) special issue of a periodical; (2) special

J

collection of short films;
選輯 compile; edit;
纂輯 edit and compile;
綴輯 compose;

ji
【蕺】 houttuynia cordata, a smelly but edible vegetable with light yellow flowers in summer;

ji
【蹐】 small step; walk at a small pace;

局蹐 confined; constraint; nervous;
跼蹐 confined; nervous;

ji
【藉】 confusion; disorder;

狼藉 in total disarray; in total disorder; scattered about in a mess;

ji
【籍】 (1) book; (2) registry; roll; (3) native place; (4) membership;
[籍貫] one's native place;
[籍邱] a surname;

本籍 one's original domicile; one's permanent home address;
薄籍 account books;
廠籍 factory membership;
黨籍 party membership;
典籍 ancient books;
古籍 ancient books;
國籍 nationality;
戶籍 (1) household register; (2) registered permanent residence;
還籍 return to one's native place;
會籍 membership of an association;
寄籍 domicile;
入籍 be naturalized;
史籍 historical records;
書籍 books;
圖籍 map of territory and census register;
土籍 the land where a family has lived for generations;
團籍 league membership;
外籍 foreign nationality;
學籍 studentship;
原籍 ancestral home;
載籍 books;
祖籍 ancestral home;

ji
【鶺】 wagtail;

ji³
ji
【几】 (1) bench; small table; (2) same as 幾；

ji
【己】 (1) oneself; (2) one's own; personal;
[己見] one's own opinion;
暢舒己見 air one's view fully; assert without any restraint; express one's views freely; speak one's mind;
發抒己見 express one's personal views;
各持己見 each holds his own opinion; each sticks to his own view; there is no meeting of the minds;
~同意各持己見 agree to differ;
各抒己見 each airs his own views; each has his say; each one expresses his own views; everybody expresses his views freely; everybody sets forth his own views;
孤行己見 act in disregard of other people's opinion; be hell-bent on having one's way; follow one's bigoted course; insist on having one's own way;
堅持己見 hold on to one's own views;
偏執己見 bigoted in one's opinion; stick to one's own opinion;
直抒己見 express one's views freely; plainspoken in one's remarks; state one's views frankly;
[己人] self and others;
瘠人肥己 exhaust others to enrich oneself;
己所不欲，勿施於人 do not impose on others what you yourself do not desire;
己欲立而立人 being able to establish oneself, one should help others to do so;
恕己恕人 forgive others as you do to yourself;
恕人恕己 forgive others as you do yourself;
推己及人 consider others by putting oneself in their places; consider others in one's own place; considerate; do unto others what you would do unto yourself; extend one's own feelings to others; put oneself in the place of

another; treat other people as you would like to be treated;

[己任] one's duty;
引為己任 regard as one's duty; take as one's own responsibility;

[己說] what one preaches;
躬行己說 practise what one preaches;

干己 concern oneself;
護己 defend oneself;
克己 be strict with oneself;
人己 others and the self;
捨己 sacrifice oneself;
私己 (1) privately; (2) one's own benefits;
梯己 (1) intimate; (2) private savings of a family member;
為己 for personal interest;
虛己 humble; open-minded;
一己 oneself;
異己 alien; dissident;
知己 bosom friend;
自己 (1) oneself; (2) closely related; own;

ji

【庋】 (1) closet; cupboard; (2) put away; put into a cupboard; put into the proper place;

ji

【脊】 (1) backbone; spine; (2) ridge;

[脊梁] back of the human body;
脊梁骨 backbone; spine;
~斷了脊梁骨 break one's spine;
~扭了脊梁骨 wrench one's spine;
光着脊梁 bare-backed;
國家的脊梁 backbone of a country;
挺着脊梁 straighten one's back;

[脊神經] spinal nerve;
抽脊髓 draw spinal cord;
移植脊髓 transplant spinal cord;

背脊 back of the human body;
海脊 ridge;
山脊 ride of a mountain;
書脊 spine of a book;
屋脊 ridge of a roof;

ji

【掎】 drag; draw aside;

ji

【幾】 (1) how many; (2) a few; several; some;

[幾多] how many; how much;

[幾分] a bit; quite some; rather; slight; something; somewhat;

[幾何] (1) how many; how much; (2) geometry;
幾何加法 geometric addition;
幾何圖形 geometric figure;
幾何紋 geometric pattern;
幾何學 geometry;
~幾何學基礎 foundations of geometry;
~解析幾何學 analytic geometry;
~立體幾何學 solid geometry;
~平面幾何學 plane geometry;
幾何元素 geometric element;
幾何作圖 geometric construction;
代數幾何 algebraic geometry;
解析幾何 analytic geometry;
絕對幾何 absolute geometry;
黎曼幾何 Riemannian geometry;
立體幾何 solid geometry;
歐幾里得幾何 Euclidean geometry;
平面幾何 plane geometry;
球面幾何 spherical geometry;
網絡幾何 network geometry;
微分幾何 differential geometry;
星形幾何 astral geometry;

[幾十] dozens;
幾十個人 dozens of people;

[幾時] what time; when;
最快幾時 how soon;

[幾歲] how old;
三十幾歲 thirty something;

[幾天] a few days;
前幾天 a few days ago; the other day;

[幾許] how many; how much;

ji

【戟】 two-pronged spear;

[戟兵] halberdier;

ji

【給】 (1) provide; supply; (2) ample; well provided for;

[給養] rations; provisions;
給養不足 short of provisions;
給養充足 be abundantly provisioned;
補充給養 replenish the provisions;
削減給養 cut down provisions;

[給予] afford; give; offer; render;
給予幫助 render assistance to sb;
給予充分肯定 approve of sth;
給予法律保護 give legal protection;
給予鼓勵 give sb encouragement;

J

給予紀律處分 take disciplinary measures to sb;
給予滿意答覆 make a satisfactory reply;
給予認真考慮 give careful consideration to sth;
給予同情與支持 give support to and show sympathy for sb;
給予協助 render assistance to sb;
給予嚴厲打擊 deliver powerful attack on sb;
給予嚴重警告 give serious warning to sb;

補給 supply;
供給 furnish; provide; supply;
配給 ration out;
取給 draw;
薪給 pay; salary;
仰給 rely on the support of others;
自給 self-supporting; self-sufficient;

ji

【麂】 moschus chinensis, an animal resembling the deer but without antlers;
［麂皮］ chamois leather;
［麂子］ barking deer;

ji

【踦】 the shin;

ji

【擠】 (1) cram; crowd; pack; throng; (2) push against; (3) press; squeeze;
［擠車］ jam into a bus;
［擠出］ extrusion; force out; squeeze out;
［擠兑］ (1) bully; force to; (2) belittle; insult;
［擠擠插插］ jamed together; packed like sardines; packed tight; very crowded;
［擠滿］ alive with; be crammed with; be crowded with; be filled with; be jammed with; be packed out; be packed with; flow with; full of; swarm with;
［擠奶］ milk;
擠奶房 milking parlour;
擠奶工人 dairyman;
擠奶機 milking machine;
擠奶女工 dairymaid; milkmaid;
［擠入］ squeeze into;
［擠壓力］ compressional force;
［擠眼兒］ wink at;

排擠 edge out; squeeze out;
壓擠 extrude;
擁擠 be packed; crowd; push and squeeze;

ji

【濟】 (1) aid; relieve; (2) cross a stream; (3) succeed; up to standard; (4) benefit;
［濟濟］ many; numerous;
濟濟一堂 a gathering of many people; a great assemblage of people in a hall; a large gathering in an auditorium; congregate in this hall; fill the hall; gather together under the same roof; the house is packed with people;
人材濟濟 full of men of talents;there is a galaxy of talents;

ji

【蟣】 (1) larvae of lice; (2) leeches;
［蟣子］ nit; egg of a louse;

ji4

ji

【旡】 choke in eating;

ji

【伎】 ability; skills; talent;
［伎爾止此］ one's cleverness stops here;
［伎倆］ foul means; intrigue; tactics; trick;
慣用伎倆 customary tactics;

ji

【即】 (1) since; (2) already; de facto; (3) finish; (4) a surname;

ji

【妓】 (1) prostitute; street girl; streetwalker; whore; (2) songstress in old China;
［妓女］ bimbo; bluefoot; bride; business girl; cookie; early door; edie; flat-backer; floosie; harlot; ho; hustler; jane; laced mutton; lady of the town; prostitute; scrubber; shawl; slag; slapper; street girl; streetwalker; strumpet; tart; tom; tool; troller; trollop; whore; woman of the street; working girl;
當妓女 walk the streets;
高級妓女 courtesan;
［妓院］ bawdy house; bordello; brothel; cathouse; whorehouse;

娼妓 prostitute;
男妓 gigolo;
狎妓 indulge in dallying with prostitutes;

J

ji

【忌】 (1) envy; jealous; jealous of; (2) dread; fear; scruple; shun; (3) abstain from; avoid; shun; (4) give up; quit; (5) death anniversary of one's parents or grandparents;

[忌才] jealous of other people's talent; resent people more able than oneself;

[忌憚] dread; fear; scruple;
毫無忌憚 scruple at nothing;
肆無忌憚 act outrageously; act recklessly and care for nobody; afraid of nothing; behave in a disroderly manner without fear; have no scruples at all; have no respect for anything; in an unrestrained way; indulgent and reckless; make no scruple; reckless and unbridled; run riot; scruble at nothing; stop at nothing; unbridled; unscrupulous; without restraints of any kind; without scruple;
無所忌憚 without restraint;

[忌妒] envy; jealous;
引起忌妒 stir jealousies;

[忌諱] (1) taboo; (2) avoid as taboo; (3) abstain from; avoid as harmful;
忌諱生冷油膩 avoid raw, cold or greasy food;
犯忌諱 violate a taboo;

[忌刻] jealous and malicious; jealous and mean;

[忌口] avoid certain food; on a diet;

[忌食] avoid certain food;
忌食辛辣 avoid pungent food;

[忌嘴] avoid certain food; on a diet;

避忌 be suspicious and jealous of;
猜忌 be envious; envy;
妒忌 be jealous of; envy;
犯忌 violate a taboo;
互忌 jealous of each other;
戒忌 (1) abstain from; avoid; (2) be on one's guard against what one avoids;
禁忌 (1) taboo; (2) contraindication;
鉗忌 jealous and unfriendly;
疑忌 be suspicious and jealous of;

ji

【技】 ability; skill; technique; trick;

[技工] artificer; artisan; mechanic; mechanician; skilled worker; technician;

[技擊] art of attack and defence in Chinese martial art;

[技倆] manoeuvring;
外交技倆 diplomatic maneuverings;

[技能] art; mastery of a skill; skill; technical ability; technique;
技能分析 skills analysis;
技能工資 skill wage;
技能訓練 safety skill training;
~安全技能訓練 safety skill training;
電腦技能 computer skills;
多工種技能 multskilling;
發展技能 develop a skill;
高超的技能 great skill;
管理技能 management skills;
很好的技能 good skills;
基本技能 basic skills; fundamental skills;
技術技能 technical skill;
就業技能 employability skill;
利用技能 use a skill;
實用技能 practical skills;
提高技能 upgrade one's skills;
聽説技能 audiolingual skills;
寫作技能 writing skills;
學習技能 acquire a skill; learn a skill;
閱讀技能 reading skills;
專門技能 expertise;

[技巧] artifice; skill; technique; craftsmanship; know-how; mechanics; mechanism; workmanship;
技巧生疏 one's skill is out of practice;
技巧嫻熟 consummate skill;
技巧運動 acrobatic gymnastics;
翻譯技巧 translation technique;
工作技巧 job skill;
溝通技巧 communication skills;
繪畫技巧 drawing skill;
精湛技巧 virtuosity;
賣弄技巧 show off one's skill;
求職技巧 job-seeking skills;
調解技巧 mediation skills;
與人打交道的技巧 social skills;

[技窮] at one's wits' end;
黔驢技窮 a fool's bolt is soon shot; at one's wit's end; at the end of one's rope; have exhausted one's bag of tricks; have exhausted one's cheap tricks; have no card left up one's sleeve; have no more arrow left in one's quiver; have no other tricks left

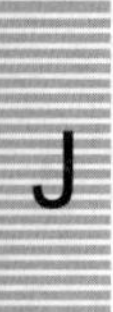

to play; have shot one's bolt; show feet of clay;
梧鼠技窮 at one's wits' end; at the end of one's rope; can do nothing more;

[技師] artificer; mechanic; technician;
放射科技師 radiographer;
主管技師 technician-in-charge;
主任技師 senior technician;
~副主任技師 associate senior technician;

[技術] skill; technic; technique; technology;
技術報告 technical report;
技術產業 technological industries;
~技術產業開發區 new technological industries developing zone;
~新技術產業 new technological industries;
技術成果 technological achievements;
技術城市 city of technology;
技術出口 export of technology;
技術創新 technological innovation;
技術動向 trend of technology;
技術發明 technological invention;
技術法規 technical laws and regulations;
技術服務 technical service;
~技術服務合同 technical service contract;
技術改造 technological renovation;
技術革命 technological revolution;
~新技術革命 new technological revolution;
技術革新 technical innovations;
技術更新 technological updating;
技術工藝 technology;
~成組技術工藝 group technology;
技術故障 technical glitch;
技術顧問 technical advisor;
技術規範 technical manual; technical regulations; technical specifications;
技術合同 technology contract;
~技術合同條款 clauses of technology contract;
~技術合同形式 forms of technology contract;
~技術合同主體 subject of technology contract;
技術合作 technological cooperation;
技術檢查 technical inspection;
技術鑒定 technology appraisal;
技術教育 technical education;
技術進步 technological progress;
技術進口 import of technology;
技術經濟 technical economy;
~技術經濟分析 technical economic analysis;
~技術經濟決策 technical economic decision-making;
~技術經濟情報 technical economic information;
~技術經濟效益 technical economic profit;
~技術經濟學 economics of technology;
~技術經濟指標 technological and economic index;
技術決定論 technological determinism;
技術開發 technical development;
~技術開發公司 technical development company;
~技術開發管理 technical development management;
~技術開發合同 contract of technical development;
~技術聯營 technical association;
技術恐懼 technophobia;
~技術恐懼者 technophobe;
~技術恐懼症 technophobia;
技術困難 technical difficulties;
技術壟斷 practise a monopoly of techniques;
技術貿易 technology trade;
~技術貿易機構 organization of technology trade;
技術美學 aesthetics in technology;
技術培訓 technical training;
技術評價 technology assessment;
~技術評價法 technological assessment;
技術人員 technician;
~技術人員結構 technical personnel structure;
~圖書館技術人員 library technician;
~文職技術人員 civilian technician;
技術軟件 software of technology;
技術商品化 technology commercialization;
技術社會 technical society;
技術生命 technology life;
~技術生命周期 technology-life period;
技術市場 technology market;
~技術市場管理 management of technology market;
技術輸出 technological export;
技術水平 technical level;
技術推廣 technological push;
技術委員會 technical committee;
技術項目 technology project;

~轉讓技術項目 transferred technology project;
技術依托 technical backstopping;
技術引進 introduction of technology;
技術預測 technology forecasting;
技術員 technician;
~信號技術員 signal technician;
~鐘錶技術員 watch technician;
技術支持 technical assistance;
技術職稱 technical title;
技術指導 (1) technical guidance; technological guidance; (2) technical adviser;
技術中介 technological intermediary;
技術轉讓 technical transformation; technology transfer; transfer of skill; transfer of technology;
~技術轉讓合同 contract of technology transfer;
~技術轉讓項目 technological transfer projects;
~技術轉讓協議 technological transfer agreement;
技術專家 technologist;
技術咨詢 technology consultation;
~技術咨詢合同 technology consultation contract;
安全技術 safety engineering technique;
~安全技術措施 technical safety measure;
超導技術 superconducting technology;
超微技術 ultramicro technique;
登山技術 alpine skill;
低技術 low-tech;
分離技術 isolation technics;
高技術 high-tech; high-technology;
~高技術產業 high-tech enterprise;
~高技術風險投資 high-tech risk investment;
~高技術企業 high-tech enterprise;
~高技術人 high-tech man;
~高技術社會 high-tech society;
~高技術園區 high-tech park;
~高技術戰爭 high-tech war;
高新技術 new and high tech;
~高新技術產業化 industrialization of new and high tech;
~高新技術企業 new and high tech enterprise;
~高新技術園區 new and high tech area;
國防技術 defense technology;
機械技術 mechanical skill;
尖端技術 high technology;
控球技術 ball playing skill;
民用技術 civilian technology;
模擬技術 analogue technique;
農業技術 agricultural technology;
深海技術 deep-sea technology;
提高技術 develop skill;
鐵路技術 railway technology;
微電子技術 microelectronics;
無菌技術 aseptic technique;
先進技術 advanced techniques; advanced technology;
修理技術 service technique;
遙感技術 remote sensing techniques;
一項技術 a technique;
掌握技術 master a skill;
專有技術 know-how;

[技癢] have a whim to exercise one's skill;
技癢難熬 a whim to make a parade of one's skill;
技癢欲試 a whim for a try;
暗暗技癢 a whim for a chance to show off;
不覺技癢 a whim to have a go; a whim to have a try;

[技藝] artistry; skills;
技藝超群 distinguished for one's superb skill;
技藝高超 superb skills;
技藝精湛 highly skilled; masterly;
技藝拙劣 show clumsy mastery of sth;
精湛技藝 bravura;
切磋技藝 swap pointers;
商討技藝 discuss skill and technique;
提高技藝 improve one's skills;

薄技 my slight skill;
車技 trick-cycling;
蹬技 juggling with feet;
故技 old trick;
慣技 customary tactic; old trick;
競技 athletics; sports;
絕技 unique skill;
科技 science and technology;
口技 vocal imitation; vocal mimicry;
特技 (1) stunt; trick; (2) special effects;
獻技 show one's skill;
演技 acting; acting skill;
雜技 acrobatics;
展技 demonstrate one's ability to the fullest extent;
奏技 skill in performing;

J

ji

【季】 (1) season; (2) crop; yield of a product in one season;

[季報] quarterly report;

[季度] quarter of a year;

季度報告 quarterly report;

[季風] monsoon;

[季節] season; time;

季節更迭 change of seasons;
季節調整 seasonal adjustment;
季節往返 seasons follow each other in rotation;
季節性 seasonality;
~季節性工作 seasonal job;
登山季節 climbing season;
放牧季節 grazing season;
歡樂季節 festive season;
交配季節 mating season;
旅遊季節 tourist season;
農忙季節 busy farming season;
農閒季節 slack farming season;
生物季節 biological season;
收獲季節 harvest time;

[季軍] second runner-up; third place; third winner in contest;

[季刊] quarterly; quarterly publication;

[季末] the end of the season;

[季相] aspect; aspection; seasonal aspect;

冬季相 winter aspect;
秋季相 autumnal aspect;
夏季相 aestival aspect;
~盛夏季相 aestival aspect;
中秋季相 serotinal aspect;
組合季相 combined aspect;

[季雨] monsoon; seasonal rain;

季雨林 monsoon forest; seasonal rain forest;
~常綠季雨林 evergreen seasonal forest;

春季 spring; springtime;
淡季 off season; slack season;
冬季 winter;
旱季 dry season;
換季 change of seasons;
秋季 autumn;
暑季 summer time;
旺季 busy season; peak season;
夏季 summer;
雨季 rainy season;
月季 Chinese rose;

ji

【芰】 water caltrop;

[芰實] water caltrop;

ji

【洎】 (1) up to; till; until; (2) meat broth; soup; (3) drench; soak;

[洎今] till now;

ji

【紀】 (1) discipline; (2) put down in writing; record; (3) age; epoch; (4) period;

[紀綱] legal and political order; legal institutions; rules of conduct;

[紀律] discipline;

紀律處分 disciplinary punishment; disciplinary sanction; take disciplinary actions;
紀律渙散 lax in discipline;
紀律鬆弛 lax in discipline;
紀律嚴明 be highly disciplined; observe strict discipline; strict in discipline; the discipline is stern and clear;
~紀律嚴明的人 disciplinarian;
財經紀律 financial and economic discipline;
財務紀律 financial discipline;
破壞紀律 undermine the discipline; violate the discipline;
繩以紀律 enforce discipline upon sb;
守紀律 behave in accordance with the regulations; observe the rules;
~必須守紀律 have to abide by discipline;
違反紀律 breach of discipline;
無紀律 indiscipline;
學校紀律 school discipline;
自覺紀律 conscious discipline;

[紀年] (1) way of numbering the years; (2) annals; chronological record of events;

[紀念] as a token of; commemorate; commemoration; in commemoration of; in honour of; in memory of; in remembrance of; in token of; mark; observe; to the memory of;

紀念幣 commemorative coin;
紀念碑 cenotaph; monument;
~一塊紀念碑 a monument;
紀念冊 autograph album; autograph book; commemorative album; souvenir album;
~題字紀念冊 autograph album;

紀念封 commemorative envelope;
紀念館 memorial hall; monument;
紀念刊 memorial volume;
紀念品 keepsake; memento; memorabilia; souvenir; token;
~紀念品商店 souvenir shop;
~小紀念品 memento;
紀念日 memorial day;
~國定紀念日 national day;
紀念塔 monument;
紀念堂 commemoration hall; mausoleum; memorial hall;
紀念郵票 commemorative stamp;
紀念章 souvenir badge;
百周年紀念 centenary; centenary celebration;
豎碑紀念 erect a monument for commemoration;

[紀實] on-the-spot report; record of actual events;
紀實文學 documentary literature;

[紀事] record events;

[紀要] summary; summary of minutes;
報告紀要 summary of reports;
編年紀要 chronological summary;
會談紀要 summary of conversations;
座談會紀要 summary of a forum;

[紀元] (1) beginning of an era; (2) epoch; era;
新紀元 new epoch; new era;

[紀傳體] history presented in a series of biographies;

本紀 biographic sketches of emperors;
廠紀 factory discipline;
黨紀 party discipline;
法紀 law and discipline;
風紀 conduct and discipline;
綱紀 social order and law;
經紀 (1) manage; (2) agent; broker; handle; manage; run;
軍紀 military discipline;
年紀 age;
世紀 century;

ji

【計】 (1) calculate; compute; count; number; (2) gauge; meter; (3) idea; plan; stratagem;

[計步器] pedometer;

[計策] plan; stratagem;
採用計策 adopt a stratagem;
改進計策 improve one's plan;
提出計策 propose the idea of;
竊取計策 steal an idea of;
制定計策 make a plan;

[計程] (1) log; (2) taxi;
計程表 odometer; taximeter;
計程車 cab; hackney cab; taxi; taxi-cab;
~計程車司機 cabbie; cabby; taxi driver;
~叫計程車 hail a cab; hail a taxi;
計程器 taximeter;
計程儀 log;
~計程儀誤差 log error;
計程運價 mileage tariff of transportation;
計程裝置 log arrangement;

[計酬] calculate payment; work out payment;
按工計酬 pay according to work;
不計酬 without pay;
~服務不計酬 render service without pay;
~工作不計酬 work without being paid;
~授課不計酬 conduct classes without pay;
論件計酬 payment by the piece;
以…計酬
~以小時計酬 calculate payment by the hour;
~以星期計酬 work out payment by the week;
~以月計酬 compute payment by the month;

[計費] charge;
計費時間 charges period;
按分計費 per minute billing;

[計工] according to the quanity of work done;
按件計工 pay according to the quantity of work done;

[計劃] design; map out; plan; planning; plot; programme; project;
計劃風險 calculated risk; planned risk;
計劃管理 project management;
計劃計量學 planning metrology;
計劃經濟 planned economy;
~計劃經濟學 economics of planning;
計劃決策 planning decision;
計劃評估法 programme evaluation and review technique;
計劃生產 planned production;
~計劃生產指標 planned production quota;
計劃生育 birth control; family planning;
~計劃生育協會 association of family planning;

計劃調整 planned regulation;
計劃外懷孕 unscheduled pregnancy;
計劃未來 map out one's future;
計劃協調技術 plan coordination technique;
計劃語言 planned language;
計劃職能 programme function;
安全計劃 safety programme;
變更計劃 modify a plan;
不切實際的計劃 airy-fairy plan;
翻譯計劃 translation plan;
放棄計劃 abandon a plan; scrap a plan;
否決計劃 reject a plan;
改變計劃 change one's plan;
概述計劃 outline a plan;
擱置計劃 hung up a plan;
國家計劃 state plan;
合作計劃 cooperative plan;
經濟計劃 economic planning;
課程計劃 curriculum planning;
秘密計劃 secret plan;
批准計劃 approve a plan;
披露計劃 unveil a plan;
破壞計劃 upset the apple cart;
取消計劃 cancel a plan;
生產計劃 production plan;
實施計劃 carry out a plan; put a plan into action;
實行計劃 act out one's plan;
事先計劃 plan sth ahead;
試驗性計劃 pilot scheme;
討論計劃 discuss plans;
提出計劃 set forth a plan;
完成計劃 carry a plan to completion; carry through a plan;
現行計劃 operative;
想出計劃 come up with a plan;
行動計劃 action projects;
宣佈計劃 announce a plan;
一攬子計劃 package plans; total plans;
有計劃 have a plan;
遠景計劃 long-term plan;
制定計劃 make a plan;
周密計劃 plan sth out;
轉出計劃 transfer out of scheme;
轉入計劃 transfer into scheme;
贊成計劃 favour the plan;
贊助計劃 sponsor a plan;
增資計劃 capital increase plan;
資助計劃 sponsor a plan;
自動化計劃 automation plan;
遵守計劃 keep to a plan; stick to a plan;

[計較] bother about; fuss about; haggle over; keep account of; split hairs;
別計較 don't fuss about;
不為小事計較 not particular about trifles;
斤斤計較 calculating and unwilling to make the smallest sacrifice;

[計量] calculate; estimate; measure;
計量尺寸 take dimensions;
計量法 quantitative law;
計量技術 measurement technique;
計量經濟學 econometrics;
計量器 meter;
計量學 metrology;
~ 法制計量學 legal metrology;
~ 工程計量學 engineering metrology;
~ 應用計量學 applied metrology;
不可計量 inestimable;
無法計量 immeasurable;

[計謀] plot; scheme; stratagem;
策劃計謀 concoct a ruse;
放棄計謀 abandon the idea of;
實現計謀 carry out one's idea;

[計窮] at the end of one's rope;
計窮才竭 at the end of one's row; at the end of one's tether; come to the end of one's tether;
計窮力竭 at the end of one's rope; come to the end of one's tether; one's schemes are poor and his strength is exhausted; with nothing much left up one's sleeves;
計窮慮極 helpless and in the greatest straits;
計窮智盡 at one's wit's end; on one's beam-ends;

[計圈器] lap-counting apparatus;

[計日] count in days; reckon by the day;
計日程功 estimate exactly how many days are needed to complete a project; estimate exactly how much time is needed to complete a project; have the completion of a project well in sight; the day is not far off; the time required to complete sth can be counted in days;
計日而待 able to achieve the goal according to schedule;

[計時] chronography; reckon by time; timing;
計時付酬 pay fees by the hour;
計時卡 time card;
計時器 adjustable timer; chronograph;

timer;
~打印式計時器 printing chronograph;
~多用途計時器 multiple-purpose chronograph;
~防水計時器 water-tight chronograph;
~分計時器 minute chronograph;
~航海計時器 navigational chronograph;
~積分計時器 integral timer;
~計算器計時器 computer chronograph;
~日曆計時器 calendar chronograph;
~睡眠計時器 sleep timer;
~自記計時器 registering chronograph;
計時收費 charge by the hour;
計時儀 chronograph;
計時員 timekeeper;
計時運價 time tariff of transportation;
操作定時 function timing;
倒計時 countdown;
開始計時 start the clock;
脈衝計時 pulse timing;
停止計時 stop the clock;

[計數] count; counting; tally;
計數能力 numerical ability;
計數器 counter;
~地址計數器 address counter;
~加法計數器 adding counter;
~絕對測量計數器 absolute counter;
~累加計數器 accumulating counter;
~氣流計數器 airflow counter;
本底計數 background counting;
符合計數 coincidence counting;
絕對計數 absolute counting;
偶然計數 accidental count;
品種計數 breed count;
氣泡計數 bubble counting;
氣體計數 gas counting;
數位計數 digital count;
細菌計數 bacterial count; cell counting;
血球計數 blood count;
循環計數 cycle count;

[計算] adding; calculate; calculation; compute; computation; computing; computus; count; do a calculation; estimate; make a work out accounts;
計算按鈕 computed pushbutton;
計算產值 calculate the output value;
計算成本 assess the cost;
計算尺 slide rule;
計算方法 calculating method;
計算機 calculator; computer
~計算機安全 computer security;
~計算機保密 computer privacy;
~計算機編程 computer programming;
計算機編程員 computer programmer;
~計算機病毒 computer virus;
~計算機操作 computer operation;
計算機操作員 computer operator;
~計算機測時儀 computer-chronograph;
~計算機程序 computer programme;
計算機程序開發 computer programme development;
計算機程序設計 computer programming;
~計算機動畫 computer animation;
~計算機犯罪 computer crime;
~計算機輔助 computer-aided;
計算機輔助操作系統 computer-aided operating system;
計算機輔助測試 computer-assisted testing;
計算機輔助動畫 computer-assisted animation;
計算機輔助翻譯 computer-aided translation;
計算機輔助工程 computer-aided engineering;
計算機輔助檢索 computer-assisted retrieval;
計算機輔助教學 computer-aided instruction;
計算機輔助教育 computer-aided education;
計算機輔助軟件工程 computer-aided software engineering;
計算機輔助設計 computer-aided design;
計算機輔助審計 computer-aided audit;
計算機輔助實驗 computer-aided experiment;
計算機輔助系統 computer-aided system;
計算機輔助系統設計 computer-aided system design;
計算機輔助診斷 computer-aided diagnosis;
計算機輔助製造 computer-aided manufacturing;
~計算機管理 computer management;
計算機管理教學 computer-managed instruction;
~計算機化 computerization;
計算機化教育 computerized education;
計算機化流通系統 computer-based circulation system;
計算機化用戶交換網 computerized branch exchange;

J

數據傳輸的計算機化 computerization of data transmission;
~計算機技術 computer technology;
~計算機監控網 computer monitoring network;
~計算機結構語言 computer structure language;
~計算機科學 computer science;
~計算機控制 computer control;
~計算機倫理學 ethics of computer;
~計算機迷 computernik;
~計算機模擬 computer simulation;
~計算機排版 computer typesetting;
~計算機設計語言 computer design language;
~計算機視覺 computer vision;
~計算機數控 computer numerical control;
~計算機思維 computer thinking;
~計算機體系結構 computational architecture;
~計算機通信 computer communication;
~計算機圖形 computer graph;
計算機圖形學 computer graphics;
~計算機外圍設備 computer peripheral;
~計算機網絡設備 computer network facilities;
~計算機文化 computer culture;
~計算機系列 computer series;
~計算機系統 computer system;
~計算機應用 computer application;
~計算機語言 computer language; computerese;
計算機語言翻譯程序 computer language translation process;
~計算機指揮 computer command;
計算機指揮通信 computer directed communication;
計算機指揮網絡 computer command network;
計算機指揮系統 computer command system;
~計算機指令系統 computer instruction system;
~計算機製圖 computer graphing;
~計算機終端機 computer terminal;
~計算機自動測試 computer automatic testing;
計算機自動測試系統 computer automatic testing system;
~計算機自動化 computer automation;
~計算機組織 computer organization;
~報警計算機 alarm computer;
~超大型計算機 super computer;
~超導計算機 superconducting computer;
~超小型計算機 super small computer;
~超越計算機 meta computer;
~代數計算機 algebraic computer;
~單片計算機 single-chip computer;
~電子計算機 computer; electronic computer;
電子計算機主義 computerism;
~對數計算機 logarithmic calculator;
~防空計算機 air defense computer;
~飛機計算機 aircraft computer;
~公式計算機 formula calculator;
~函數計算機 function calculator;
~航天計算機 aerospace computer;
~機載計算機 airborne computer;
~巨型計算機 super huge computer;
~絕對值計算機 absolute value computer;
~空速計算機 air speed computer;
~快速計算機 high-speed calculator;
~領航計算機 air navigation computer;
~模擬計算機 analog calculator;
~全光系計算機 all-optical computer;
~全晶體管計算機 all-transistor computer;
~商用計算機 business computer;
~數字計算機 digital calculator;
~台式計算機 desk calculator;
~通用計算機 all-purpose computer; general purpose calculator;
~網絡計算機 network calculator;
~一台計算機 a computer;
~智能計算機 intelligent computer;
~中型計算機 midicomputer;
~自動數字計算機 automatic digital calculator;
計算精確 calculate to a nicety;
計算狂 arithmomania;
計算癖 arithmomania;
計算器 calculator;
~比例計算器 proportion calculator; ratio calculator;
~便攜計算器 pocket calculator;
~表式計算器 tabular calculator;
~波形計算器 wave form calculator;
~風速計算器 flight calculator; wind calculator;
~盤式計算器 disk calculator;
~聲音回答計算器 audio response calculator;
~濕度計算器 psychrometric calculator;

~手搖計算器 hand calculator;
~速度計算器 speed calculator;
~台式電子計算器 electronic desk calculator;
~旋轉計算器 rotary calculator;
~遠程計算器 remote calculator;
計算人數 count the number of people;
計算失誤 compute faultily;
計算時間 count time;
計算數據 compute data;
計算有誤 there are errors in computation;
計算語言學 computational linguistics;
計算賬目 calculatge items of an account;
計算中心 computation centre;
暗地裏計算 inwardly calculate;
不善計算 not good at consideration;
不屑計算 disdain to make a good consideration of...;
殘數計算 residue calculus;
粗略的計算 rough calculation;
地址計算 address calculation; address computation;
蝶式計算 butterfly computation;
浮動計算 buoyancy calculation;
化學計算 chemical calculation;
簡單的計算 simple calculation;
交叉計算 cross calculation;
交互計算 interactive computing;
校正計算 correction computation; correction computing;
近似計算 approximate computation;
進行計算 perform a calculation; work out the calculation;
精於計算 adept in planning;
可計算 [的] calculable;
模擬計算 analog calculation; analog computation;
平差計算 compensating computation;
平衡計算 balance computation;
氣象計算 meteorological calculus;
燃燒計算 combustion calculation;
容錯計算 fault-tolerant computing;
容積計算 capacity calculation;
色譜圖計算 chromatogram calculation;
設計計算 design calculation;
數學計算 mathematical calculation;
數值計算 numerical calculus;
數字計算 digital calculations;
無法計算 defy calculation;
演繹計算 a priori computation;
業務計算 business calculation;
遠程成批計算 remote batch computing;
自動計算 automatic calculation;
阻力計算 drag calculation;

[計無所出] at a loss what to do; at one's wits' end; unable to think of a way;

[計議] consult; deliberate; talk over;

[計值] evaluation;

氨量計 ammoniometer;
暗計 (1) calculate in one's heart; (2) artful dodge; conspiracy; secret design; secret plot; trick;
比濁計 turbidimeter;
不計 disregard; irrespective of; not take into account;
測力計 dynamometer;
測微計 micrometer;
磁強計 magnetometer;
大計 matter of fundamental importance;
得計 succeed in one's scheme;
電壓計 voltmeter;
定計 devise a stratetum; work out a scheme;
毒計 deadly trap; insidious scheme; venomous pilot;
反間計 stratagem of sowing distrust among one's enemies;
風速計 anemograph;
風向計 registering weather vane;
感光計 sensitometer;
共計 add up to; amount to;
估計 assess; estimate; reckon;
詭計 crafty plot; cunning scheme; trick;
合計 amount to;
核計 assess; calculate; estimate;
加速計 accelerometer;
家計 family livelihood;
奸計 evil plot; wicked scheme;
狡計 crafty trick;
決計 certainly; definitely; have decided;
空城計 empty-city stratagem;
會計 (1) accounting; (2) accountant; bookkeeper;
累計 accumulative total; add up; grand total;
美人計 honey trap; sex trap;
妙計 brilliant scheme; excellent plan;
氣壓計 barometer;
設計 design; draw up a plan; plan; project;
審計 audit;
生計 means of livelihood;
失計 inexpedient; miscalculate; misjudge; unwise;
施計 play tricks;
濕度計 humidometer;
時計 chronometer;

J

授計 tell sb the plan of action;
速度計 speedometer;
體溫計 thermometer;
統計 (1) statistics; (2) add up; count;
溫度計 thermograph;
獻計 make suggestions; offer advice;
心計 calculation; scheming;
血壓計 sphygmomanometer;
壓力計 manometer; pressure gauage;
雨量計 rain gauge;
預計 calculate in advance; estimate;
約計 come roughly to; count roughly;
張力計 tensionmeter;
中計 be taken in; fall into a trap;
綜計 sum up;
總計 add up to amount to; total;

ji

【記】 (1) bear in mind; commit to memory; remember; (2) record; take down; write down; (3) note; record; (4) mark; peronal signet; sign; (5) birthmark;

[記仇] bear grudges; harbour bitter resentment;

[記得] call back to mind; keep in memory; recall; remember; within sb's recollection;
記得快，忘得快 soon learnt, soon forgotten;
清楚地記得 remember clearly;
仍然記得 still remember;
完全記得 remember perfectly;
依稀記得 remember vaguely;

[記分] (1) keep the score; record the points; (2) register a student's marks; (3) record workpoints;
記分單 scoresheet;
記分牌 score board; score indicator;
~電動記分牌 electric scoreboard;
記分員 marker; scorekeeper;
負責記分 keep the score;

[記功] cite sb for meritorious service; record a merit;
不給記功 record no merit;

[記掛] be concerned about; keep thinking about; miss;
記掛海外游子 be concerned about the man residing abroad;

[記過] (1) record a demerit; (2) remember sb's faults;
記過處分 be given a demerit;
記人之過，忘人之恩 remember every fault sb may have and forget even a great mercy done by him;

[記號] designation; mark; marking; sign; tick;
記號筆 marker pen;
標上記號 put signs on;
擦掉記號 erase the marks;
特徵記號 tag marking;
裝配記號 auxiliary aiming mark;
做個記號 make a sign; mark out;

[記恨] bear grudges;

[記錄] get sth down; jot down; keep an account of; make a note of; note down; put down; put in black and white; stick sth down; take a note of; take down; write down;
記錄保持者 record-holder;
記錄標誌 record marker;
記錄片 documentary; documentary film;
~記錄片攝製者 documentarist;
~大型記錄片 full-length documentary;
~藝術紀錄片 artistic documentary;
記錄器 recorder;
~比重記錄器 density recorder;
~點線記錄器 chopper-bar recorder;
~圖表記錄器 chart recorder;
記錄在案 a matter of record; put on record;
安全記錄 safety records;
保持…記錄 hold... record;
~保持不敗記錄 hold an unbeaten record;
~保持世界記錄 hold the world record;
保持記錄 hold a record; keep a record;
創造記錄 break a record; create a record; set a record;
打破記錄 beat a record; break a record; cut a record; set a new record;
~試圖打破記錄 attempt to break a record;
官方記錄 official records;
國家記錄 national record;
精確記錄 accurate record;
歷史記錄 historical records;
平記錄 equalize a record;
少年記錄 junior record;
世界記錄 world record;
~世界記錄保持者 world record holder;
~保持世界記錄 hold the world record;
~平世界記錄 equal the world record;
書面記錄 written record;

刷新記錄 better a record; rewrite the record;
未作記錄 unrecorded;
新記錄 new record;
修正記錄 amendment record;
擇要記錄 note down the essential points;

[記名] put down one's name; sign;
記名投票 disclosed ballot;

[記起] recall; recollect;
記不起 outside sb's recollection;

[記取] bear in mind; remember;
記取教訓 remember the lesson;

[記時] time-keeping;
記時等溫線 chronoisotherm;
記時器 chronograph;
~磁記時器 magnetic chronograph;
~單曆記時器 simple chronograph;
~電動記時器 electronic chronograph;
~紙帶記時器 fillet chronograph;
記時儀 chronograph;
記時員 time-keeper;

[記實] documentary;
記實片 docudrama;
記實戲劇 docudrama;
記實小説 document novel;

[記事] (1) keep a record of events; make a memorandum; (2) account;
記事本 organizer;
~電子記事本 electronic organizer;
記事簿 datebook;
簡短記事 jottings;
歷代記事 chronology of past dynasties;

[記述] give an account of; record and narrate;

[記誦] commit to memory and be able to recite; learn by heart;
記誦公式 tell a formula from one's memory;

[記下] keep a record of; make a minute of; make a note of; minute down; take notes of;

[記性] memory;
記性差 have a poor memory; have a short memory;
記性好 have a good memory; have a long memory;

[記敍] narrate;
記敍文 narrative text;
記敍性話語 narrative discourse;

[記憶] (1) recall; remember; (2) memory;
記憶廣度 span of memory;
記憶卡 memory card;
記憶力 memory; the faculty of memory;
~記憶力不錯 have a decent memory;
~記憶力很差 have a memory like a sieve;
~記憶力強 have a strong memory;
~記憶力弱 have a weak memory;
~記憶力在衰退 one's memory is declining; one's memory is failing;
~鍛煉記憶力 exercise one's memory;
~過目不忘的記憶力 photographic memory;
~失去記憶力 lose one's memory;
~損害記憶力 impair one's memory;
~有健全的記憶力 have a sound memory;
~有驚人的記憶力 have a prodigious memory;
~增加記憶力 improve one's memory;
記憶棒 memory stick;
記憶缺損 retention defect;
記憶喪失 loss of memory; memory loss;
記憶所及 anything that one can remember; as far as one can recollect; as far as one can remember; to the best of one's recollection;
記憶體 memory;
~主記憶體 random access memory (RAM);
記憶猶新 as fresh in one's memory; be very much alive in one's memory; be still fresh in one's memory; be still green in one's memory; be still very much alive in one's memory; remain fresh in one's memories; stick in sb's mind; the memory is still fresh;
記憶增強 hypermnesia;
記憶障礙 dysmnesia;
插曲式記憶 episodic memory;
長期記憶 long-term memory;
短期記憶 short-term memory;
恢復記憶 regain one's memory;
強化記憶 enforce one's memory;
喪失記憶 lose one's memory;
失去記憶 lose the memory of;

[記載] (1) put down in writing; record; (2) account; record;

[記賬] chalk it up; keep accounts;
記賬付款 pay by putting it to one's account;
記賬購物 buy sth on credit;
記賬卡 charge card;

[記者] correspondent; journalist; newsman;

pressman; reporter;
記者團 press corps;
記者席 press box; press gallery;
記者站 correspondent station;
記者招待會 news conference; press conference;
~舉行記者招待會 hold a press conference;
記者證 press card;
採訪記者 reporter;
常駐記者 resident correspondent;
初出茅廬的記者 cub reporter;
電視記者 TV reporter;
高級記者 senior reporter;
流動記者 roving reporter;
攝影記者 news photographer; press photographer;
隨軍記者 embed;
特派記者 special correspondent;
特約記者 stringer;
體育新聞記者 sports reporter; sportswriter;
通訊記者 correspondent;
新聞記者 journo; newspaper reporter;
~女新聞記者 newspaperwoman;
巡迴記者 roving reporter;
一群記者 a group of journalists; a group of reporters;
一屋子的記者 a roomful of reporters;
戰地記者 war correspondent;
助理記者 assistant reporter;
駐國外記者 foreign correspondent;

[記住] at the back of one's mind; bear in mind; carry sth in mind; commit to memory; fix in one's mind; get sth by heart; hold in one's head; impress on one's memory; keep at the back of one's mind; keep in mind; know sth by heart; learn by heart; make a mental note of; memorize; remember; say sth by heart;

諳記 learn by heart;
暗記 (1) secret mark; (2) memorize;
裨記 books of anecdotes;
碑記 record of events inscribed on a tablet;
筆記 notes;
表記 token;
簿記 (1) bookkeeping; (2) account book;
側記 sidelights;
戳記 seal; stamp;
登記 enter one's name; register;
惦記 keep thinking about;
後記 postscript;
牢記 always remember; keep firmly in mind;
銘記 always bear in mind; engrave on one's mind;
切記 be sure to keep in mind;
日記 diary;
散記 random notes; sidelights;
失記 forget;
手記 manuscript;
熟記 learn by heart; memorize;
速記 shorthand; stenography;
胎記 birthmark;
圖記 seal; stamp;
忘記 forget;
遊記 travel notes;
雜記 (1) jottings; notes; (2) miscellanies;
札記 reading notes;
摘記 take notes;
傳記 biography;
追記 postscript;

ji

【既】 (1) already; (2) as; now that; since; (3) as well as; both...and;

[既定] established; fixed; set;
既定方案 existing plan;
既定方針 set policy;
既定目標 fixed goal; set objective;

[既而] later; soon afterwards; subsequently;

[既來之，則安之] let's cross the bridge when we come to it; since we are here, we may as well stay and make the best of it; since we have come, let us stay and enjoy it; since you have come, take your ease;

[既然] as; after; at all; if; inasmuch as; now; now that; once; seeing; seeing that; since; such being the case; well then; what; when, where;
既然如此 in the circumstances; since it is so; such being the case; that being so; under these circumstances; well, then;

[既是] as; now that; since;

[既往] the past;
既往不咎 forgive somebody's past misdeeds; it is needless to blame things that are past; let bygones by bygones; let the past be forgotten; let the dead bury their dead; wipe the slate clean;

既往症 anamnesis;
不咎既往 forgive sb's past misdeeds; let begones be begones; not censure sb for his past misdeeds; overlook sb's past mistakes;

ji

【寄】 (1) mail; post; send; (2) deposit; entrust; park; place; (3) attach oneself to; depend on;

［寄泊港］ port of call;

［寄存］ check; deposit; leave with;
寄存處 checkroom;
~ 衣帽寄存處 cloakroom;
寄存器 register;
~ 地址寄存器 address register;
~ 計數寄存器 counter register;
~ 加數寄存器 addend register;
~ 累加寄存器 accumulator register;
寄存行李 check one's luggage;

［寄放］ leave in the care of; leave with;

［寄件人］ consignor; sender;
退回寄件人 return to sender;

［寄居］ live away from home;
寄居他鄉 live in an alien place;
寄居蟹 hermit crab; soldier crab;
寄召異國 reside in a foreign country;

［寄賣］ consign for sale on commission; put up for sale in a secondhand shop;
寄賣品 consignment merchandise;
寄賣商店 commission store;

［寄情］ confine one's feeling to;
寄情山林 lodge in the mountains and woods — secluded and free from care;
寄情山水 abandon oneself to nature;
寄情詩酒 confine one's feeling to poetry and wine — a sort of pessimistic, negative attitude of intellectuals;

［寄人籬下］ find shelter under sb's roof; live as a parasite on sb; live under another's roof; live under sb's thumb; live under subjugation; under sb else's roof — depend on other people for a living;

［寄生］ parasitic; parasitism;
寄生變形蟲 parasitic amoeba;
寄生蟲 animal parasites; parasites;
~ 寄生蟲病 parasitic disease;
~ 寄生蟲毒性 parasite virulence;
~ 寄生蟲學 parasitology;
~ 人體寄生蟲學 human parasitology;
~ 獸醫寄生蟲學 veterinary parasitology;
~ 醫學寄生蟲學 medical parasitology;
~ 多宿主寄生蟲 pleophagous parasite worm;
~ 人體寄生蟲 parasite of humans;
~ 社會寄生蟲 parasite on the community;
~ 體內寄生蟲 endoparasite;
寄生動物 parasitic animal;
寄生根 parasitic roots;
寄生階級 parasitic class;
寄生菌 parasite;
~ 細胞內寄生菌 intracellular parasite;
寄生生活方式 parasitic mode of life;
寄生物 parasite;
~ 寄生物形態學 morphology of parasites;
~ 寄生物學 parasitology;
~ 植物寄生物學 phytoparasitology;
~ 半寄生物 hemiparasite;
~ 定主寄生物 specific parasite;
~ 不定主寄生物 incidental parasite;
~ 動物寄生物 animal parasite;
~ 糞便寄生物 coprozoic parasite;
~ 固有寄生物 autistic parasite;
~ 兼性寄生物 facultative parasite;
~ 體腔寄生物 celozoic parasite;
~ 外寄生物 ectoparasite;
~ 細胞寄生物 cytozoic parasite;
~ 相互寄生物 reciprocal parasite;
~ 血內寄生物 blood parasite;
~ 專性寄生物 obligate parasite;
寄生細菌 parasitic bacteria; parasitic bacterium;
寄生纖宅蟲 parasitic ciliate;
寄生現象 parasitism;
~ 轉主寄生現象 heteroecism;
寄生政府 parasitic government;
寄生植物 parasitic plants;
間歇寄生 intermittent parasitism;
交互寄生 reciprocal parasitism;
偶然寄生 occasional parasitism;
外寄生 ectoparasitism;
遺傳寄生 genetic parasitism;

［寄售］ consign for sale; on consignment; sale on consignment;
寄售店 consignment shop;
寄售貿易 consignment trade;

［寄宿］ (1) lodge; put up; (2) boarding;
寄宿處 lodging;
寄宿生 boarder;
寄宿學校 boarding school;
寄宿在朋友家 put up at a friend's house;
寄宿者 boarder; lodger;

J

［寄托］ (1) entrust to the care of sb; leave with sb; (2) find sustenance in; place hope on; repose;
寄托哀思 give expression to one's grief;
精神有所寄托 have spiritual sustenance;
情感有所寄托 have emotional sustenance;
［寄望於］ build one's hopes upon; fasten one's hopes on; lay one's hopes on; pin one's hopes on; place one's hopes on; rest one's hope on;
［寄銷］ consignment sale;
［寄信］ mail a letter; post a letter; send a letter;
寄信人 sender;
［寄養］ ask sb to bring up one's child; entrust one's child to the care of sb;
［寄予］ (1) place ...on; (2) express; give; show;
寄予厚望 cherish high hopes;
寄予期望 lay hopes on; pin hopes on; place one's hope on; put hopes on;
寄予深切關懷 give heartfelt sympathy to sb;
寄予無限同情 show infinite sympathy for sb;
［寄語］ send a message; send word;
［寄主］ host;
寄主免疫 host immunity;
寄主植物 host plant;
寄主專一性 host specificity;
動物寄主 animal host;
過渡寄主 bridge host;
輪換寄主 alternate host;
偶見寄主 accidental host;
暫時寄主 temporary host;

匯寄 remit;
另寄 post separately; post under separate cover;
投寄 send a letter to;
郵寄 post; send by post;
轉寄 forward;

ji
【悸】 (1) palpitation of the heart; (2) fear;

惊悸 palpitate with fear;
心悸 palpitation;
餘悸 lingering fear;

ji
【祭】 (1) hold a memorial ceremony for; (2) offer a sacrifice to; (3) wield;
［祭奠］ hold a memorial ceremony for;
［祭禮］ (1) sacrificial rites; (2) memorial ceremony; (3) sacrificial offerings;
行祭禮 perform at the altar;
［祭品］ oblation; sacrificial offerings;
［祭器］ sacrificial utensil;
［祭祀］ offer sacrifices to gods or ancestors;
［祭台］ altar;
祭台助手 altar boy;
［祭壇］ altar; sacrificial altar;
［祭堂］ altar;
家庭祭堂 family altar;
［祭天］ offer sacrifices to heaven;
祭天祈年 offer sacrifices to the gods and pray for rich harvests;
祭天祀祖 a solemn ceremonial thanksgiving sacrifice is offered to heaven and to the ancestors;
［祭文］ elegiac address; funeral oration;
［祭獻］ sacrifice;

公祭 hold a public memorial ceremony; public memorial ceremony;
路祭 offer sacrifices on the route of a funeral procession;
陪祭 accompany the person in charge of offering the sacrifice or holding a memorial ceremony; officiate at funeral or sacrificial rites;
社祭 sacrifice to the god of land;

ji
【跡】 (1) mark; trace; (2) remains; ruins; vestige; (3) indication; sign;
［跡象］ indication; sign; straw in the wind; token;

筆跡 a person's handwriting;
屏跡 avoid; stay away from;
殘跡 vestige;
陳跡 a thing of the past;
發跡 gain fame and fortune; rise;
軌跡 (1) locus; (2) orbit;
痕跡 mark; trace; track;
混跡 unworthily occupy a place among;
穢跡 abominable behavior;
寄跡 sojourn temporarily;
腳跡 footprint;
徑跡 track;
絕跡 be stamped out; disappear;
浪跡 lead a wandering life;
斂跡 go into hiding;

J

劣跡 evil doing; misdeed;
滅跡 destroy the evidence of one's evildoing;
墨跡 (1) ink marks; (2) sb's writing or painting;
匿跡 disappear from the scene; go into hiding;
人跡 human footmarks; traces of human presence;
勝跡 famous historical site;
污跡 smear; stain;
心跡 one's true feelings;
行跡 trace; track;
形跡 a person's movements and expression;
血跡 bloodstain;
遺跡 historical remains; vestige;
油跡 grease spots; oil stains;
真跡 authentic work;
字跡 handwriting; writing;
踪跡 trace; track;
足跡 footmark; footprint; track;

ji
【暨】 (1) and; (2) attain; reach; (3) a surname;

ji
【際】 (1) border; boundary; edge; (2) among; between; inter; (3) inside; (4) occasion; time;
［際遇］ favourable or unfavourable turns in life; spells of good or bad fortune;

邊際 bound; boundary; limit;
國際 international;
空際 in the air; in the sky;
腦際 brain; mind;
實際 practice; reality; practical; realistic;
水際 water margin; waterside;
天際 horizon;
無際 boundless; limitless; vast;
星際 interplanetary; interstellar;
遭際 circumstances; lot;
洲際 intercontinental;

ji
【漈】 bank of a river; shore; waterside;

ji
【跽】 (1) kneel for a long time; (2) kneel; (3) afraid of;

ji
【稷】 panicled millet;
［稷邱］ a surname;

社稷 country; god of the land and the god of grains; state;

ji
【冀】 (1) hope; (2) a name for Hebei Province; (3) a surname;
［冀求］ hope to get;
［冀望］ hope; long for; look forward to;

希冀 hope for; wish for;

ji
【劑】 (1) dose; (2) prepared medicines or drugs; (3) prepare medicines and drugs;
［劑量］ dosage; dose;
劑量測定法 dosimetry;
~幅射劑量測定法 radiation dosimetry;
~照相劑量測定法 photographic dosimetry;
劑量計 dosimeter;
~比色劑量計 colorimetric dosimeter;
~化學劑量計 chemical dosimeter;
~計數率劑量計 counting-rate dosimeter;
~空氣電離劑量計 air ionization dosimeter;
~臨牀劑量計 clinical dosimeter;
劑量學 dosimetry;
~生化劑量學 biochemical dosimetry;
~中子劑量學 neutron dosimetry;
大劑量 high dosage;
減少劑量 reduce the dosage;
累積劑量 accumulated dose;
每日劑量 daily dosage;
全身劑量 body dose;
容許劑量 acceptable dose;
吸收劑量 absorbed dose;
小劑量 low dosage;
增加劑量 increase the dosage;
致死劑量 lethal amount;
［劑貌］ a surname;
［劑型］ form of a drug;

補劑 tonic;
沖劑 medicine to be taken after being mixed with boiled water;
滴劑 drops;
毒劑 toxic; toxicant;
方劑 prescription; recipe;
粉劑 (1) powder; (2) dust;
膏劑 electuary; medicinal extract;
焊劑 soldering flux; welding flux;
合劑 mixture;

J

片劑 tablet;
溶劑 solvent;
熔劑 flux; melting agent;
乳劑 emulsion;
散劑 powder; pulvis;
湯劑 decoction;
調劑 adjust; regulate;
洗劑 lotion;
藥劑 drug; medicament;
針劑 injection;
製劑 preparation;

ji

【髻】 coiffure with a topknot;

ji

【穄】 same as 稷 , pinched millet;

ji

【濟】 (1) cross a river; (2) aid; help; relieve; (3) benefit; of help;

[濟扶] help and relieve;
濟弱扶傾 champion the cause of the underdog; help the weak and relieve those in distress;
濟危扶困 assist people in distress; champion the cause of the underdog; help people with money and rescue people from danger; help the endangered and relieve the less privileged; relieve the less privileged and help the endangered;
濟危扶傾 aid the distressed and support the tottering;

[濟河焚舟] cross the river and burn the ship — show one's determination to fight to the last; draw the sword and throw away the scabbard;

[濟急] give urgent relief;
濟人所急 relieve sb in need;
濟人之急 help a lame dog over a stile; relieve sb in need;

[濟困] help the distressed;
濟困扶危 assist people in distress; help the distressed and succour those in peril; help those in distress and succour those in danger; relieve the less privileged and help the endangered;
濟人之困 save people from their difficulties;

[濟貧] give help to the poor; help the people in distress; help the poor; relieve the people in distress; relieve the poor;
濟貧拔苦 relieve the poor and comfort the afflicted;
濟貧扶困 give help to the poor, to those who are in need;
濟貧扶傾 aid the poor and downtrodden;
濟貧賑苦 help the poor and destitute;

[濟世] assist one benefit mankind; do good to society;
濟世安民 assist one's generation and bring comfort to the common people; benefit the aged and pacify the masses;
濟世拯道 save the society from becoming degraded;
濟世拯民 benefit the world and save the people;
濟世之才 a person endowed with the talent to govern and to serve;

[濟事] of help;
不濟事 no good; not of any help; of no use;
無濟於事 a damp squib; a grain of wheat in a bushel of chaff; a pill to cure an earthquake; avail to nothing; go a very little way; inadequate; it does not help the matter; not enough by a long shot; not to help matters; of no avail; serve no purpose; to no avail; to no effect; to no purpose; useless; without avail; won't help the matter;
~ 一切努力都無濟於事 all one's efforts avail to nothing;

不濟 not good; of no use;
共濟 mutual aid;
經濟 (1) economical; economy; (2) financial condition;
救濟 relieve; succour;
賑濟 aid; provide relief; relieve;
周濟 help out the needy; relieve;
賙濟 relieve the needy;

ji

【薊】 (1) circium, a family of thorny plants; (2) a surname;

[薊苦素] cnicin;
[薊馬] thrip; thripid;

刺薊 field thistle;
大薊 setose thistle;
小薊 field thistle;

J

ji

【覬】 covet; desire for sth belonging to others;

［覬覦］ cast greedy eyes on; cast one's covetous eyes on; covet;

邪目覬覦 cast a covetous eye on; one's shifty eyes squint right and left;

賊眼覬覦 one's shifty eyes squinted right and left;

ji

【罽】 a kind of wooden fabric;

ji

【薺】 capsella bursa-pastoris, a kind of vegetable; shepherd's purse;

［薺菜］ shepherd's purse;

［薺薴］ Chinese mosla;

ji

【騎】 (1) a pronunciation of 騎; (2) a surname;

ji

【鯽】 crucian carp; golden carp;

［鯽魚］ crucian carp; sharksucker;

海鯽 Japanese sea-perch;

銀鯽 pond carp; Prussian carp;

ji

【繫】 bind; tie;

［繫泊］ moor; moor a boat;

［繫繩］ stakerope; tether;

ji

【繼】 (1) continue; follow; succeed; (2) afterwards; then;

［繼承］ carry forward; carry on; come in for; come into; inherit; inherit from; receive...by inheritance; step into...by inheritance; succeed in; succeed to;

繼承父業 carry on the work of one's father;

繼承權 right of inheritance; right of succession;

繼承人 distributee; heir; inheritor; successor; successor;

~合法繼承人 legal successor;

~女繼承人 heiress;

~全財產繼承人 universal successor;

~王位繼承人 heir to the throne;

~唯一繼承人 sole heir;

繼承王位 succeed to the throne;

繼承性 succession;

繼承衣缽 as successor to sb's mantle; inherit the legacy; inherit the mantle of; step into the shoes of; take over the mantle of;

繼承遺志 carry out sb's behests; carry on the unfinished lifework of the father;

批判地繼承 inheriting in a critical way;

［繼而］ afterwards; then;

［繼父］ stepfather;

［繼母］ instant mum; stepmother;

惡毒的繼母 wicked stepmother;

［繼配］ second wife;

［繼任］ (1) succeed; succeed sb in a post; (2) successor;

繼任人 heir;

［繼嗣］ (1) adopt sb as one's son; be adopted; (2) adopted son;

［繼位］ accede; accession to the throne; succeed to the throne;

［繼續］ carry on; continue; continue to; continue up; continue with; get on with; go ahead with; go on; keep at; keep on doing sth; keep on with; last; proceed to; proceed with;

繼續不斷 go on without a break;

繼續革命 continue the revolution;

繼續工作 continue working;

繼續教育 continuous education;

繼續深造 continue to engage in advanced studies;

繼續形象教育 continuing image education;

承繼 (1) be adopted as heir to one's uncle; (2) adopt one's brother's son;

出繼 be legally adopted as son;

過繼 (1) adopt a young relative; (2) have one's child adopted by a relative;

後繼 carry on; succeed;

嗣繼 inherit; succeed;

相繼 in succession; one after another;

中繼 relay;

ji

【】 (1) clear up; stop raining; (2) stop being angry;

晴霽 (of weather) fair and clear;

色霽 calm down after being angry;

雪霽 it's stopped snowing and is clearing up;

J

雨霽 the rain is over;

ji

【驥】 (1) very fast horse; (2) great man; man of outstanding ability;

jia¹

jia

【加】 (1) add; plus; (2) augment; increase; (3) append; put in;

[加班] work an extra shift; work extra hours; work overtime;
加班費 overtime pay;
加班加點 on overtime; put in extra hours; work overtime; work shifts;

[加保] additional insurance;

[加倍] (1) double; twice as much; (2) double; doubling; redouble; (3) doubling germination;
加倍地 doubly;
加倍呵護 redouble one's care;
加倍警惕 redouble one's vigilance;
加倍努力 redouble one's efforts;
加倍小心 doubly cautious; twice as careful;
減數分裂加倍 meiotic doubling;
順次加倍 successive doubling;

[加長] lengthen;

[加法] addition;
加法表 addition table;
加法器 adding machine;
加法運算 addition operation;
二進制加法 binary addition;
幾何加法 geometric addition;
校驗加法 check addition;
邏輯加法 logical addition;

[加工] fabricate; finishing; handle; machining; process; treat;
加工能力 working ability;
加工食品 process food;
加工業 processing industry;
電蝕加工 electro-erosion machining;
仿形加工 contour machining;
放電加工 electric spark machining;
精加工 fine finishing;
精密加工 precision finishing;
影片加工 film adaptation;

[加固] strengthening;
邊緣加固 edge strengthening;
線路加固 track strengthening;

[加官晉爵] advance in rank and position; be advanced in rank and make a higher official; be promoted to a higher office and rank; offer sb a higher official post; rise in the official world;

[加害] do harm to; injure;
加害於人 do harm to sb; do sb an injury;
受到加害 come to harm;

[加號] plus sign;

[加價] hike the price; mark up the price; price mark-up; raise the price;

[加減] add and subtract;
加減乘除 addition, subtraction, multiplication and division; the four operations;

[加緊] intensify; speed up; step up;tighten up;
加緊學習 intensify one's study;
加緊訓練 intensify the training;
加緊準備 speed up preparation;

[加勁] brace; make a greater effort; put more energy into;
加勁工作 work hard;
加把勁 make a push at; make a push for; make a push on; make a push to do sth; make an effort; put one's back into it;
~ 暗中加把勁 make a great effort secretly;
~ 加一把勁 make push to;

[加劇] aggravate; exacerbate; intensify;
加劇病情 aggravate one's illness;
加劇疼痛 aggravate the pain;

[加快] accelerate; acceleration; pick up speed; quicken; speed up;
加快步伐 move ahead faster;
加快生活的節奏 force the pace of life;
加快速度 speed up;
加快一點 hurry things up a little;

[加寬] broaden; widen; widening;
道牀加寬 widening of roadbed;
軌距加寬 gauge widening;
路基加寬 widening of track;

[加料] (1) charge; charging; feed in raw material; (2) reinforce;
加料機 feeder;
~ 包料式加料機 batch feeder;
~ 夾鉗加料機 tong feeder;
~ 螺旋加料機 screw feeder;
~ 旋轉加料機 swivel feeder;
~ 振動加料機 oscillating feeder;
薄層加料 blanket feeding;
側部加料 side charging;

衝天爐加料 cupola charging;
機械化加料 mechanized charging;
間斷加料 intermittent charging;
人工加料 feed in raw material by manual labour;

[加碼] (1) overcharge; raise the price of commodities; (2) raise the stakes in gambling; (3) raise the quota;

[加煤機] stoker;
鏈式加煤機 chain stoker;
批量加煤機 batch stoker;
自動加煤機 automatic stoker;

[加盟] join; participate; take part in;

[加密] encipherment; encrypt; encryption;
加密保護 encryption;
加密狗 dongle;
線路加密 link to link encipherment;

[加冕] coronation; crowning;
加冕典禮 coronation;
加冕為女王 be crowned queen;

[加強] augment; beef up; energize; enhance; intensify; reinforce; reinforcement; strengthen;
加強防禦 strengthen the defense; tighten up the defense;
加強管理 tighten up the management;
加強戰鬥力 strengthen the fighting capacity;
耐磨損加強 abrasion-resistant reinforcement;
凸緣加強 bead reinforcement;

[加權] weighted;
加權平均法 weighted average unit price method;
加權平均價 weighted average price;
加權系統 weighting system;
~ 詞加權系統 term weighting system;
~ 詞頻加權系統 term frequency weighting system;
加權樣品 weighted sample;

[加熱] heat; heat up; warm;
加熱器 heater; heating appliance;
~ 對流加熱器 convector;
~ 防潮加熱器 anti-condensation heater;
~ 攪動加熱器 agitating heater;
~ 進氣道加熱器 airscoop heater;
~ 空間加熱器 air space heater;
把奶加熱 heat up the milk;
補償加熱 additional heating;
電弧加熱 arch heating;
氣動力加熱 aerodynamic heating;

[加入] (1) add; mix; put in; (2) accede to; join;
加入工會 join the trade union;

[加塞兒] jump a queue; push into a queue;

[加深] deepen;
加深理解 deep understanding; get a deeper understanding;
加深裂痕 widen the rift;

[加時賽] extra time;

[加數] addend;
被加數 summand;

[加速] accelerate; acceleration; boost; expedite; quicken; shift up; speed up; turn of speed;
加速度 acceleration;
~ 加速度計 accelerometer;
~ 加速度記錄儀 accelerograph;
~ 半徑加速度 radius acceleration;
~ 背向加速度 front-to-back acceleration;
~ 變加速度 variable acceleration;
~ 側向加速度 sideward acceleration;
~ 長時間加速度 chronic acceleration;
~ 超音速加速度 supersonic acceleration;
~ 赤道加速度 equatorial acceleration;
~ 初始加速度 initial acceleration;
~ 垂直加速度 vertical acceleration;
~ 大加速度 high acceleration;
~ 導彈加速度 missile acceleration;
~ 等加速度 constant acceleration;
~ 定時加速度 timed acceleration;
~ 負加速度 negative acceleration;
~ 高超音速加速度 hypersonic acceleration;
~ 跟蹤加速度 tracking acceleration;
~ 軌道加速度 orbital acceleration;
~ 航道加速度 flight-path acceleration;
~ 合成線加速度 resultant linear acceleration;
~ 橫向加速度 lateral acceleration; transverse acceleration;
~ 後向加速度 rearward acceleration;
~ 淨加速度 net acceleration;
~ 局部加速度 local acceleration;
~ 距離加速度 range acceleration;
~ 跨音速加速度 transonic acceleration;
~ 累積加速度 cumulative acceleration;
~ 離心加速度 centrifugal acceleration;
~ 脈衝式加速度 impulsive acceleration;
~ 目標加速度 target acceleration;
~ 平飛加速度 level-flight acceleration;
~ 平均加速度 average acceleration;
~ 起動加速度 starting acceleration;

J

~ 前向加速度 forward acceleration;
~ 切向加速度 tangential acceleration;
~ 擾動加速度 perturbing acceleration;
~ 上昇加速度 climb acceleration;
~ 瞬間加速度 lightning acceleration;
~ 瞬時加决度 instantaneous acceleration;
~ 頭向加速度 headward acceleration;
~ 凸輪加速度 cam acceleration;
~ 下滑加速度 gliding acceleration;
~ 向首加速度 cephalad acceleration;
~ 向尾加速度 caudad acceleration;
~ 向心加速度 centripetal acceleration;
~ 胸到背加速度 chest-to-back acceleration;
~ 旋轉加速度 rotary acceleration;
~ 亞音速加决度 subsonic acceleration;
~ 移動加速度 translational acceleration;
~ 圓周加速度 circular acceleration;
~ 振幅加速度 amplitude acceleration;
~ 震動加速度 vibrational acceleration;
~ 直接傳動加速度 direc-drive acceleration;
~ 直線加速度 linear acceleration;
~ 重力加速度 gravitational acceleration;
~ 軸向加速度 axial acceleration;
~ 撞擊加速度 impact acceleration;
~ 足向加速度 footward acceleration;
~ 總加速度 gross acceleration;
~ 縱向加速度 longitudinal acceleration;
~ 最大加速度 maximum acceleration; peak acceleration;
~ 最大總加速度 maximum total acceleration;
~ 最高齒加速度 top gear acceleration;
~ 左向加速度 leftward acceleration;
~ 座艙加速度 cockpit acceleration;
加速階段 boost period;
加速進展 expedite the progress;
加速率 acceleration;
~ 直通式加速率 straight-through acceleration;
加速器 accelerator;
~ 電子束加速器 electron-beam accelerator;
~ 電子線性加速器 electron linear accelerator;
~ 線性加速器 linear accelerator;
~ 原子加速器 atomic accelerator;
加速生產 speed up production;
加速行駛 speed up;
加速裝置 accelerator;
電子感應加速 betatron acceleration;
發動機加速 engine acceleration;
光點加速 spot acceleration;
後加速 post acceleration;
急劇加速 slam acceleration; violent acceleration;
絕熱加速 adiabatic acceleration;
突然加速 abrupt acceleration;
穩定加速 firm acceleration;
戰鬥加速 combat acceleration;

[加添] additive; charge up;
加添副詞 additive adverb;
加添介詞 addition preposition;
加添語言 additional language;

[加溫] intensify;

[加細] refine; refinement;
星形加細 star refinement;
重心加細 barycentric refinement;

[加以] in addition; moreover;

[加意] with close attention; with special care;

[加油] (1) come on; get a move on; get going; play up; speed it up; stick it; (2) gas up; pump gas; (3) go; hip, hip, hooray; up;
加油機 tanker;
~ 空中加油機 aerial tanker;
加油器 oiler;
~ 離心加油器 centrifugal oiler;
~ 液壓加油器 hydrostatic oiler;
加油添醋 add highly coloured details to a story; add inflammatory details to a story; exaggerate embellishment to a story;
加油站 filling station; gas station; petrol station;
火上加油 pour oil on the flame;
我隊加油 up our team;

[加元] buck; Canadian dollar;

[加枝添葉] fabricate the details of a story;

[加重] (1) become heavier; increase the weight of; make heavier; (2) aggravate; become more serious; make more serious;
加重危機 aggravate the crisis;
加重語氣 say sth with emphasis;
加重罪過 aggravate an offense;

[加注] fill; refuel;

[加磚添瓦] contribute one bit to; make contributions to; put up bricks and tiles for;

[加罪於人] cast the blame on sb; put the blame on; shift the blame to others;

倍加 doubly; increase by one fold;
参加 (1) join; take part in; (2) give;
堆加 accumulation;
附加 add; additional; appended; attach;
更加 all the more; even more; more;
橫加 flagrantly; violently;
交加 (of two things) accompany each other; occur simultaneously;
累加 summation;
施加 bring to bear on; impose;
外加 add...to;
相加 add together;
愈加 all the more; even more;
再加 besides; in addition;
增加 increase; raise;
追加 add to (the original amount);

jia

【夾】 (1) pinch; place in between; press from both sides; (2) intersperse; mingle; mix; (3) clamp; clip; folder;

[夾襖] lined jacket;

[夾層板] sandwich panel;
蜂窩夾層板 honeycomb sandwich panel;

[夾道] (1) narrow lane; passageway; (2) line both sides of the street;
夾道歡迎 a grand roadside welcome; line the streets to give sb a welcome; line the streets to welcome; stream out to welcome sb along the roadside;
松柏夾道 be lined with the pine and cypress on both sides;

[夾攻] attack from both sides; converging attack; pincer attack; two-way attack;

[夾環] clip;
偏心夾環 eccentric clip;

[夾緊] clamp; tuck tightly;
夾緊尾巴做人 behave oneself by tucking one's tail between one's legs;
夾緊裝置 clamping;

[夾具] clamp; fixture;
鏜孔夾具 boring fixture;
黏合夾具 bonding fixture;
彎曲夾具 bending fixture;

[夾克] jacket;
帶帽夾克 hoodie;
燈芯絨夾克 corduroy jacket;
短夾克 jacket;
~緊腰短夾克 bomber jacket;
軍用夾克 combat jacket;
太大的夾克 oversized jacket;

[夾盤] chuck;

[夾鉗] clamp;

[夾槍帶棒] lash out in all directions; with a string in one's words;

[夾生] half-baked; half-cooked; parboiled;

[夾雜] be cluttered up with; be mingled with; be mixed up with; with;
夾雜物 inclusion;
~大塊夾雜物 bulk inclusion;
~外來夾雜物 foreign inclusion;

[夾竹桃] oleander;

[夾注] interlinear notes;

[夾子] clamp; clip; tongs;
接地夾子 earth clip;

保險夾 safety clip;
報夾 newspapers holder;
長尾夾 binder clip;
瓷夾 porcelain clip;
彈夾 charger; clip;
彈藥夾 cartridge clip;
髮夾 bobby pin; hairpin;
軌夾 rail clip;
睫毛夾 eyelash curler;
書夾 bookends;
索夾 cord clip;
炭精夾 carbon clip;
紙夾 paper clip;

jia

【伽】 character that is not used alone;

[伽藍] Buddhist deity; Buddhist temple;

[伽羅] aloeswood; eagle wood;

[伽瑪] gamma;
伽瑪射線 gamma rays;

jia

【迦】 character used in transliterating foreign sounds;

[迦藍] second name of a Buddhist temple;

jia

【佳】 beautiful; fine; good;

[佳話] deed praised far and wide; a much told tale; a stroy on everybody's lips;

[佳節] festival; happy festival time;
互賀佳節 exchange the compliments of the season;
人逢佳節倍思親 at festivals everyone thinks all the more of his loved ones; when festival time comes round, we think all the more of our dear ones;

J

欣逢佳節 on the happy occasion of the festival;

[佳境] the most enjoyable stages;

漸入佳境 be getting better; be improving; from bad to good conditions; grow better; turn out for the best;

[佳句] beautiful lines in a poem; well-turned phrases;

錦囊佳句 beautiful verses in an embroidered purse — good poems;

[佳麗] (1) beautiful; good; (2) beautiful woman; beauty;

[佳釀] good wine;

佳釀美餚 good wine and delicacies; vintage wine and choice food;

香醪佳釀 carnation sauce and sweet fermented spirits;

[佳偶] a happily married couple;

佳偶天成 a good match as if made in heaven; a happy couple united by heaven; the match is ordained by fate;

天成佳偶 a good match as if made in heaven;

[佳期] (1) nuptial day; wedding day; (2) lover's rendezvous;

[佳人] beautiful woman;

[佳味備醇] chavibetol;

[佳餚] delicacies;

佳餚美酒 excellent wine and delicious dishes; good food and excellent wine;

[佳譯] good translation;

[佳音] favourable reply; good tidings; welcome news;

報佳音 carol;

靜候佳音 I am awaiting the news of your success;

[佳作] excellent work; fine piece of writing; masterpiece;

堪稱佳作 may be rated as a fine piece of work; may be rated as a good piece of writing;

欠佳 not good enough;

尚佳 not too bad; passable;

稍佳 a little better; slightly better;

jia

【枷】 (1) cangue; (2) frame; scaffold;

[枷鎖] chains; fetters; shackles; yoke;

擺脱…的枷鎖 rid oneself of the shackles of sb/sth;

~擺脱非正義統治的枷鎖 cast off the chains of unjust rule;

傳統的枷鎖 yoke of tradition;

披枷帶鎖 carry a prisoner's collar with lock attached to it;

掙脱枷鎖 throw off the shackles;

連枷 flail;

jia

【珈】 a kind of jewelry;

jia

【家】 (1) family; household; (2) one's home; (3) person or family engaged in a certain trade; (4) expert; specialist in a certain field; (5) domestic; tame;

[家財] family fortune;

家財萬貫 a mountain of money;

[家產] family property;

揮霍家產 squander one's family property;

[家常] domestic trivia; the daily life of a family;

家常便飯 (1) common meal; potluck; simple meal; cheese and bread; homely food; plain home cooking; (2) all in the day's work; common occurrence; common practice; daily fare; daily lot; routine; usual practice;

扯家常 chat about everyday family affairs; chitchat; engage in small talk;

談家常 chitchat; engage in small talk; talk about everyday matters;

[家醜] family scandal; the skeleton in the cupboard;

家醜不外揚 conceal the family shame; do not wash your dirty linen in public; domestic foibles should not be exposed; domestic shame should not be published; it is an ill bird that fouls its own nest; wash one's dirty linen at home;

家醜外揚 befoul one's own nest; bring the family skeleton out of the cupboard; drag the family skeleton out into the light of day; exhibit the family skeleton; wash one's dirty linen in public;

[家畜] cattle; domestic animal; farm livestock; livestock;

飼養家畜 raise domestic animals;

屠宰家畜 slaughter domestic animals;

[家傳] be handed down from the older generations of the family;

家傳戶誦 be sung in every family and chanted in every house; become a household word;

家傳秘方 a secret recipe handed down in the family;

[家當] family belongings; property;

[家道] family financial situation;

家道復興 the fortune of the family is revived;

家道艱難 suffer in one's estate;

家道匱乏 live in poverty;

家道衰微 decline in family financial situation;

家道小康 well-to-do family;

家道中落 one's family fortunes decline; one's family has come down in the world; the family is in straitened circumstances; the means of the family are declining;

[家底] family property accumulated over a long time; resources;

家底薄 not financially solid;

家底厚 financially sound;

[家電] household electrical appliances;

白色家電 white goods;

[家蹲] stay idle at home;

[家法] (1) domestic discipline exercised by the head of a feudal household; (2) a rod for punishing children or servants in a feudal household;

[家訪] house visit;

[家國] the family and the nation;

[家和] harmony in the family;

家和百事興 if the family lives in harmony, all affairs will prosper; if there is peace in the home, everything will prosper;

[家戶] door;

家家戶戶 all families without exception; all households; each and every family; from house to house; in every home;

家喻戶曉 be known by one and all; be known to all; be known to each and every family; be known to every household; be widely known; household name; household word; make known to every family; every barber knows that; every family knows it;

千家萬戶 huge numbers of families; hundreds of millions of households; thousands of households; thousands upon thousands of families;

[家雞野雉] a domestic fowl and wild ducks—wife and mistress; a man given to extramarital relations in one's family and outside;

[家給] each family is provided for;

家給戶足 each family is provided for; every household is well provided for;

家給人足 all live in plenty; each and every family live in plenty; each family is provided for and every person is well-fed and well-clothed; every household is well provided for; houses have adequate supplies and people live in contentment; well-to-do homes and well-fed people;

[家計] family livelihood;

[家家] families;

家家有本難唸的經 every family has a skeleton in the cupboard; each family has its own problems;

[家教] domestic discipline; family education; upbringing;

家教雖嚴，醜事難免 accidents will happen even in the best regulated families;

[家境] family circumstances; family financial situation;

家境好 come from a well-to-do family;

家境困難 with one's family in straitened circumstances;

家境貧寒 come from a poor family; in straitened circumstances;

家境清寒 come from an impoverished family;

家境清貧 person of scanty means;

家境優裕 live high off the hog;

[家眷] (1) one's family; one's wife and children; (2) one's wife;

[家口] members of a family; the number of people in a family;

拉家帶口 be burdened with a family; bear family burdens; have heavy; family burden;

[家懶外頭勤] a loafer at home and a hustler outside;

J

[家累] family burden; family cares;
擺脱家累 be free from encumbrances;
[家裏] in the family;
家裏事，家裏了 what happens in the family can be settled in the house;
呆在家裏 stay in;
待在家裏 stay at home; stay home;
住在自己家裏 abide in one's house;
[家門] family clan; family of a high-ranking official; door of a house;
敗辱家門 disgrace one's family;
被趕出家門 be kicked out of one's home; be turfed out of one's home;
忝辱家門 disgrace one's family;
[家奴] domestic servant; family slave;
[家貧如洗] as poor as a church-mouse; penniless; one's family is reduced to absolute destitution; utterly destitute;
[家譜] family tree; genealogy;
家譜圖 family tree;
[家禽] domestic fowl; poultry;
[家史] family history;
整理家史 compile one's family history;
追溯家史 trace sb's family history;
[家世] social standing of one's family;
家世寒微 of plebeian origin;
家世顯赫 of outstanding family background;
[家事] domestic affairs; family affairs;
處理家事 deal with domestic affairs;
[家室] (1) family; (2) wife; (3) residence;
靡室靡家 having no family because of foreign aggression;
宜室宜家 live harmoniously; make a harmonious and orderly home;
已有家室 have a wife;
有家室的人 man of family;
[家書] (1) a letter home; (2) letter from home;
[家塾] family school;
[家屬] dependent; family member;
安置家屬 find a place for one's family members;
[家庭] family; home; household;
家庭暴力 domestic violence; family violence;
家庭背景 family background;
~複雜的家庭背景 complicated family background;
家庭成員 family member; member of a family;
家庭出身 family background;
家庭單位 family unit;
家庭道德 morality of family;
家庭電器化 household electrification;
家庭度假 family holiday; family vacation;
家庭構成 family composition;
家庭關係 family relationships;
家庭和諧 family harmony;
家庭環境 family environment;
家庭計劃 family planning;
家庭價值觀 family values;
家庭間 family room;
家庭教師 home teacher; private tutor;
家庭教育 family education;
家庭結構 family structure;
家庭解體 family disintegration;
家庭經濟 family economy;
家庭糾紛 domestic discord; domestic dispute; family quarrel;
家庭樂趣 amenities of home life;
家庭倫理學 family ethics;
家庭美育 aesthetic education to family;
家庭破裂 family breakdown;
家庭企業 family business; household industry;
家庭圈子 family circle;
家庭社會學 family sociology;
家庭生活 domestic life; domesticity; family life; home life;
~幸福家庭生活 happy domesticity;
~重視家庭生活 value family life;
家庭投資 family investment;
家庭文化 family culture;
家庭問題 family problems;
家庭學校 family school;
家庭醫生 family doctor; family practitioner;
家庭用車 family car;
家庭用品 household articles;
家庭用語 familial language;
家庭職能 family function;
家庭作業 homework;
大家庭 extended family; large family;
單親家庭 one-parent family; single-parent family;
第一家庭 first family;
多人口家庭 multiperson family;
核心家庭 nuclear family; small family;
建立家庭 found a family; set up house;
貧窮的家庭 destitute family;
小家庭 nuclear family; small family;
中等家庭 middle-class famiy;

[家徒壁立] a family with only bare walls; a house empty all around; a house empty on all sides; be utterly destitute; only the walls of the household standing—extreme poverty;

[家無] a family cannot;
家無儋石 not even a picul of rice in the house — living from hand to mouth;
家無二主 a house can't have two masters;
家無隔宿之糧 live from hand to mouth; not to know where the next meal comes from;

[家務] domestic service; household chores; household duties; housework;
家務累贅 be burdened with onerous household chores; family cares;
家務所纏 be tied up with the care of one's family;
操持家務 attend to household duties; manage household affairs;
處理家務 manage one's household;
料理家務 keep house;
做家務 do housework; do the chores; keep house;
~幫人做家務 assist with one's home chores;

[家鄉] homeland; homeplace; hometown; native place;
家鄉風味 local flavour; the pleasing taste of the cooking of one's native place;

[家信] a letter to or from one's family;

[家學] knowledge passed on from generation to generation in a family; knowledge transmitted from father to son;
家學淵源 erudite through paternal teaching and influence; foundation of profound learning inherited by the family; have the deep influence of a scholarly family;

[家宴] family feast;

[家業] family property; property;
家大業大 a big household; lots of work;

[家傭] maid;
家傭房 maid's room;

[家用] (1) domestic; household; (2) domestic money; family expenses; housekeeping money; (3) home application;
家用電器 domestic electrical appliances; home electric appliances; household appliances;
家用信息系統 home information system;
家用醫療器械 household medical instrument;

[家園] hearth and home; home; homeland; homestead;

[家賊] thief in the family;
家賊難防 a thief in the family is difficult to detect; it's most difficult to forestall a thief within the home;
~野賊好捉，家賊難防 a thief from outside is not as dangerous as a thief from within;

[家宅] home; homestead;
浮家泛宅 dwell on boat; a floating family and a drifting abode; boat dwellers; those who make their homes on boats;
家翻宅亂 the house is upside-down — there is no peace in the house;

[家長] (1) head of a family; paterfamilias; patriarch; (2) parents; the parent of a child;
女家長 matriarch;

[家政學] domestic science; home economics; household arts;
家政學校 home-economics school;

[家族] clan; family;
家族史 family history;
家族性 familial;

挨家 from door to door; from family to family; from house to house; from one house to another; house-to-house;

安家 establish residence; insure the welfare of one's family; make one's home in a place; set up a home; settle; settle down; take up one's abode; take up residence;

俺家 I;

百家 (1) various families; (2) various schools of thinkers;

敗家 dissipate the family fortune; squander the family fortune;

搬家 change one's residence; make a move; move; move house; pull up stakes; up sticks;

邦家 one's fatherland; one's nation; one's state;

本家 member of the same clan;

兵家 (1) military strategist in ancient China; (2) military commander; soldier;

病家 patient and his family;

抄家 search sb's house and confiscate his property;

成家 (1) (of a man) get married; (2) become an expert;
持家 run one's house;
仇家 enemy; foe;
出家 become a monk or nun;
船家 boatman;
傳家 hand down from generation to generation in a family;
慈善家 philanthropist;
大家 (1) all; everybody; (2) authority; great master; (3) rich and influential family;
當家 manage household affairs;
到家 be excellent; be perfect; reach a very high level;
道家 Daoist School;
第二個家 second home;
店家 shop owner;
雕刻家 carver; engraver;
雕塑家 sculptor;
東家 hoss;
發明家 inventor;
方家 person who is well versed in certain skill, art,etc.;
分家 divide up family property and live apart;
富家 rich family;
鋼琴家 pianist;
歌唱家 singer; vocalist;
革命家 revolutionary;
公家 organization; public; state;
官家 (1) feudal official; (2) emperor; king;
管家 (1) butler; steward; (2) house-keeper; manager;
歸家 return home;
國家 country; nation; state;
漢學家 Sinologist;
行家 connoisseur; expert;
航海家 banker;
畫家 artist; painter;
皇家 imperial family;
活動家 activist;
鑒賞家 appreciator;
教育家 educationist; educator;
金融家 financier;
酒家 restaurant; wine-shop;
居家 be at home;
舉家 whole family;
劇作家 dramatist;
看家 (1) look after the house; (2) outstanding; special;
老家 native place; old home;
老人家 (1) respectful form of address for an old person; (2) parent;
理論家 theoretician; theorist;
歷史家 historian;
良家 good and decent family;
漫畫家 caricaturist; cartoonist;
冒險家 adventurer;
美術家 artist;
名家 (1) famous expert; master; (2) Logicians;
魔術家 conjurer; magician;
墨家 Mohists;
男家 bridegroom's family;
娘家 parents' home of a married woman;
農家 (1) peasant family; (2) the Agriculturists;
農業家 agriculturist;
女家 bride's family;
批評家 critic;
評論家 critic; reviewer;
婆家 husband's family;
企業家 entrepreneur;
起家 build up; grow and thrive; make one's fortune, name etc.;
親家 (1) parents of one's daughter-in-law or son-in-law; (2) relatives by marriage;
人家 (1) household; (2) family;
儒家 Confucianism;
散文家 essayist;
攝影家 photographer;
身家 (1) one and one's family; (2) family origin;
生物學家 biologist;
聲樂家 vocalist;
時評家 commentator on current affairs;
實業家 industrialist;
史學家 historian; historiographer;
收藏家 collector;
書法家 calligrapher;
書評家 reviewer;
數學家 mathematician;
思想家 thinker;
俗家 parents' home of a monk;
探險家 explorer;
外交家 diplomat;
文學家 man of letters; writer;
舞蹈家 dancer;
戲劇家 dramatist;
小説家 novelist;
心理學家 psychologist;
演説家 orator;
野心家 careerist;
藝術家 artist;
音樂家 musician;
陰謀家 conspirator; intriguer; schemer;
銀行家 banker;
預言家 prophet;

冤家 enemy
岳家 family of one's wife's parents;
雜家 Eclectics;
戰術家 tactician;
哲學家 philosopher;
政論家 political commentator; political writer;
政治家 statesman;
住家 residence;
專家 expert; specialist;
莊家 banker (in a gambling game);
縱橫家 the Political Strategists;
作家 writer;
作曲家 composer; melodist;

jia

【痂】 crust; scab over a sore;
［痂病］ scab;
［痂皮］ crust;

瘡痂 scab;
焦痂 eschar;
結痂 form a scab;

jia

【袈】 the cassock or robe of a Buddhist monk;
［袈裟］ cassock; patchwork outer vestment worn by a Buddhist monk;

jia

【笳】 reed leaf whistle;

胡笳 reed instrument used by the northern tribes in ancient China;

jia

【傢】 furniture; tool;
［傢伙］ (1) tool; utensil; weapon; (2) bloke; bod; chappy; fella; fellow; guy;
笨傢伙 clumsy fellow; fool; simpleton;
蠢傢伙 schmuck; schnook;
古怪的傢伙 queer bird;
好傢伙 good god; good gracious; good heavens; good lord;
壞傢伙 bad apple; baddie; bastard; rogue; rotten apple; scoundrel;
可笑的傢伙 funny chap;
懶惰又邋遢的傢伙 lazy slob;
老傢伙 codger; old bloke; old chap; old man; oldster;
~ 你這老傢伙 you old son of a gun;
討厭的傢伙 a real piece of work;
小傢伙 mite;

［傢具］ furniture; gear; house furnishings;
傢具店 furniture store;
傢具木工 cabinet-maker;
傢具雜物 goods and chattels;
辦公室傢具 office furniture;
鋼製傢具 steel furniture;
舊傢具 used furniture;
木製傢具 wood furniture;
塑料傢具 plastic furniture;
藤製傢具 cane furniture; rattan furniture;
一件傢具 a piece of furniture;
一批傢具 a load of furniture;
一堂傢具 a set of furniture;
一套傢具 a set of furniture; a suite of furniture;
竹製傢具 bamboo furniture;
組合傢具 combination furniture; modular furniture;
［傢什］ furniture; utensils;

jia

【葭】 (1) bulrush; reed; (2) flute;
［葭莩之親］ be distantly related to sb; one's distant relatives;

jia

【嘉】 (1) fine; good; (2) commend; praise;
［嘉獎］ cite; commend;
嘉獎令 order of commendation;
~ 頒發嘉獎令 issue an order of commendation;
明令嘉獎 issue a commendation;
值得嘉獎 deserve commendation;
［嘉禮］ marriage ceremony; wedding ceremony;
［嘉勉］ praise and encourage; urge sb to greater efforts with words of encouragement;
有則改之，無則嘉勉 correct the mistakes, if any; and keep the good record if no mistakes have been committed; correct mistakes if you have committed them and avoid them if you have not; correct mistakes if you have made any and guard against them if you have not; if there is any error, correct it; if not, then avoid it;
［嘉名］ good name; reputation;
［嘉年華會］ carnival;
［嘉釀］ vintage wine;
［嘉歲］ year of bumper harvest;
［嘉許］ approve; praise;
［嘉餚］ choice food; dainty dishes;

J

可嘉 deserving the citation; worth the compliment;

jia
【豭】 boar; male pig;

jia
【鎵】 gallium;

jia²

jia
【夾】 (1) be sandwiched; be wedged between; insert between; (2) press; squeeze; (3) hold sth with pincers or chopsticks; pick up; (4) of two or more layers; (5) folder to keep sheets of paper; (6) carry secretly; (7) contaminate; mix;
[夾攻] attack from both sides;

jia
【恝】 carefree; indifferent; unworried;
[恝置] neglect; take things coolly; treat with indifference;

jia
【郟】 (1) the name of various places in China; (2) side chambers; (3) a surname;
[郟敖] a surname;

jia
【戞】 knock gently; tap;
[戞戞] (1) difficult; hard going; (2) original;
戞戞獨造 have great originality;
[戞然] (1) long; (2) abrupt;
戞然長鳴 long and loud cries;
戞然而止 cease abruptly; come to an abrupt end;

jia
【莢】 pod;
[莢果] pod;

豆莢 pod;
精莢 spermatophore;
榆莢 the fruit of elm;
皂莢 Chinese honey locust;

jia
【袷】 garments with lining;
[袷襖] lined jacket;

jia
【蛺】 butterfly;
[蛺蝶] a kind of butterfly harmful to crop plants;

jia
【裌】 same as 袷, a lined garment or dress;

jia
【筴】 tongs;

jia
【跲】 stumble;

jia
【頡】 deduct; omit;

jia
【鋏】 (1) pincers; tongs; (2) sword; (3) hilt;
[鋏肢] chelophora;

jia
【頰】 cheek; mala;
[頰輔] flesh on the cheeks;
[頰骨] cheekbone;
[頰上添毫] make a portrait come alive by adding some hair on the cheeks — add the punch line;

緩頰 intercede for sb; put in a good word for sb;
面頰 cheek;
批頰 slap one in the face;
腮頰 cheek;

jia³

jia
【甲】 (1) the first; (2) shell; (3) nail; (4) armour;
[甲板] deck; deck armour;
甲板船 decker;
~凹甲板船 well decker;
~單甲板船 one decker;
~平甲板船 flush decker;
~輕甲板船 spar decker;
~遮陽甲板船 awning decker;
船樓甲板 erection deck;
船尾甲板 fantail deck;
後甲板 afterdeck; quarter deck;
駕駛甲板 navigation deck;
露天甲板 exposed deck;
前甲板 foredeck;
輕甲板 spar deck;
散步甲板 promenade deck;
上層甲板 promenade deck;
上甲板 upper deck;
尾樓甲板 poop deck;
下甲板 lower deck;
~最下甲板 orlop deck;
中甲板 middle deck;

主甲板 main deck;
裝甲甲板 ballistic deck;

[甲蟲] beetle;
南瓜甲蟲 pumpkin beetle;
煙草甲蟲 cigarette beetle;

[甲醇] carbinol; methanol; methyl;
戊基甲醇 amyl carbinol;
烯丙基甲醇 allyl carbinol;

[甲骨] oracle bone;
甲骨卜兆 omen read from the cracks on tortoise shells;
甲骨文 oracle bone inscriptions;
卜用甲骨 oracle bone;

[甲乙] A and B;
拉甲打乙 win over A against B;

[甲魚] fresh-water turtoise;

[甲狀腺] thyroid gland;
甲狀腺癌 thyroid carcinoma;
~ 濾泡性甲狀腺癌 follicular thyroid carcinoma;
甲狀腺毒症 thyrotoxicosis;
甲狀腺機能不全 thyropenia;
甲狀腺切除 thyroidectomy;
甲狀腺素 thyroxine;
甲狀腺炎 thyroiditis;
~ 產後甲狀腺炎 postpartum thyroiditis;
~ 慢性甲狀腺炎 chronic thyroiditis;
~ 肉芽腫性甲狀腺炎 granulomatous thyroiditis;
~ 萎縮性甲狀腺炎 atrophic thyroiditis;
~ 硬化性甲狀腺炎 sclerosing thyroiditis;
甲狀腺腫 goitre;
~ 地方性甲狀腺腫 endemic goiter;
~ 結節性甲狀腺腫 nodular goitre;
~ 濾泡性甲狀腺腫 follicular goiter;
~ 彌漫性甲狀腺腫 diffuse goiter;
~ 囊性甲狀腺腫 cystic goiter;
~ 實質性甲狀腺腫 parenchymatous goiter;
~ 突眼性甲狀腺腫 exophthalmic goitre;
~ 中毒性甲狀腺腫 toxic goitre;
副甲狀腺 parathyroid;

[甲子] a cycle of sixty years;

鼻甲 turbinate;
鱉甲 turtle shell;
龜甲 tortoise shell;
花甲 cycle of sixty years;
馬甲 sleeveless garment;
披甲 put on a suit of armour;
鐵甲 armour;
指甲 nail;
趾甲 toenail;
裝甲 plate armour;

jia

【岬】 cape; headland; point; promontory;

[岬角] cape; headland; nook; nore;

jia

【胛】 shoulder; shoulder blades;

[胛骨] shoulder blades;

肩胛 shoulder;

jia

【夏】

[夏楚] ferule; rod for punishing pupils;

jia

【假】 (1) artificial; cod; fake; false; phoney; sham; (2) avail oneself of; borrow; (3) if; suppose;

[假案] feigned case; frame-up; trumped-up case;

[假扮] camouflage; disguise oneself as; dress up as; make sb pass for; masquerade; personate; play the part of; pretend;

[假幣] counterfeit money;

[假鈔] funny money;

[假痴不癲] feign madness without being insane;

[假充] pose as; pretend to be;
假充好漢 pretend to be brave;
假充內行 pass oneself off as an expert; pose as an expert; pretend to be an expert;
假充英雄 pose as a hero;
假充正經 pretend to be honest;

[假道] by way of; via;

[假定] assume; grant; on the supposition of; presume; suppose;
淺度假定 shallowness hypothesis;
提出假定 put forward a hypothesis;
推翻假定 repudiate the hypothesis;
相似假定 similarity hypothesis;

[假髮] switch; toupee; wig;
戴假髮 (1) be bewigged; wear a wig; wiggery; (2) periwig;
~ 不戴假髮 wear one's own hair;
小假髮 hairpiece;

[假花] artificial flower;

[假話] falsehood; lie;

[假活兒] con man; swindler;

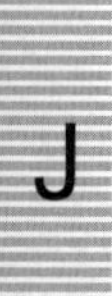

[假貨] fake goods;

[假借] (1) make use of; (2) phonetic loan characters; (3) forgive; tolerate;

假借名義 masquerade under an assumed name; in the name of; under false pretence; under the guise of; under the pretense of; under the pretext of;

假借外力 make use of outside forces;

假借義 figurative sense;

[假口於人] put words into sb's mouth;

[假劣] counterfeit and inferior goods;

[假冒] bogus counterfeit; palm off; pass oneself off as;

假冒產品 bogus product; counterfeit product;

假冒的 bogus; false;

假冒商標 counterfeit trademark;

假冒商品 fake commodity; shoddy goods;

假冒為善 feign kindheartedness; hypocrite; play the hypocrite; under the cloak of virtue;

謹防假冒 beware of bogus imitation; beware of fakes; beware of imitations;

[假名] (1) pseudonym; (2) kana;

假名托姓 pass sb's name as one's own;

[假如] assume; assuming; but for; even if; grant; granted that; if; if only; in case; let; on condition that; on the supposition that; presume; suppose; supposing; unless; what if;

[假若] if; in case; supposing;

[假嗓] falsetto;

[假山] rockery; rockwork;

[假設] assume; grant; hypothesis; hypothesizing; postulate; presume; suppose;

假設成分 dummy element;

假設從句 hypothetical clause;

假設條件 hypothetical condition;

點陣假設 lattice postulate;

反對稱性假設 antisymmetry postulate;

附加假設 additive postulate;

合理的假設 reasonable assumption; valid assumption;

基本的假設 basic assumption; fundamental assumption; underlying assumption;

作出假設 make an assumption;

[假聲] falsetto;

[假使] if; in case; in the event that;

[假釋] conditional release; free a prisoner on probation; release on parole;

[假手] (1) do sth through sb else; make a cat's paw of sb; (2) artificial hand; hand prosthesis;

假手於人 make a cat's paw of sb; make sb else do the work; put into another's hand; use the hand of;

[假説] hypothesis; presumption; presupposition;

構象假説 conformational hypothesis;

容許假説 admissible hypothesis;

[假死] (1) suspended animation; (2) feign death; mimic death; play dead; play possum;

[假托] (1) on the pretext of; pretend; (2) under sb else's name;

假托有病 on the pretext of illness;

[假想] (1) hypothesis; imagination; make-believe; phantom; supposition; (2) fictitious; hypothetical; imaginary;

假想敵 an imaginary enemy;

[假象] (1) false appearance; false impression; (2) false form; false image;

識破假象 see through a false appearance;

造成一種假象 create a deceitful impression;

製造假象 create a false impression; put up a false front;

[假牙] artificial tooth; dentures; false tooth; store teeth;

一副假牙 a set of dentures;

一套假牙 a set of false teeth;

[假意] (1) hypocrisy; insincerity; unction; (2) pretend; put on;

假意奉承 cheap flattery;

假意謙虛 put on an air of modesty;

假意推辭 pretend to decline;

假心假意 pretend to...;

虛情假意 pure hypocrisy; put up a phoney show;

[假造] (1) counterfeit; forge; (2) fabricate; invent;

假造公文 forge official papers;

假造理由 invent an excuse;

假造賬目 falsify accounts;

假造證件 forge a certificate;

假造證據 fabricate evidences;

假造罪名 cook up a false charge against; fabricate an accusation; trump up

charges;

[假賬] false accounts;
查假賬 audit false accounts;
造假賬 cook the accounts; doctor the accounts; draw up false accounts;
做假賬 cook the books; draw up false accounts; falsify accounts;

[假裝] assume; fake sth; feign; have an affectation; let on; look through one's fingers at; make as if; make a pretence of...; make believe; pretend; put on; simulate;
假裝悲痛 put on a show of grief;
假裝不見 look through one's fingers at;
假裝不知 affect ignorance; feign ignorance;
假裝多情 make a pretense of affection;
假裝糊塗 pretend to be ignorant;
假裝積極 pretend to be active;
假裝難過 make a sorry show;
假裝虔誠 pretend to be pious;
假裝熱心 simulate enthusiasm;
假裝正經 assume an air of modesty; assume the guise of a man of integrity; feign a correct posture; pose as a person of high morals; pretend to be a gentleman; pretend to be a saint; put on the appearance of honesty;

[假醉佯狂] pretend to be very drunk and act like a lunatic;

摻假 adulterate;
攙假 adulterate;
超假 overstay one's leave;
打假 anti-fake;
寬假 forgive; pardon;
虛假 false; sham;
裝假 feign; pretend;
作假 (1) counterfeit; falsify; (2) cheat; play tricks; (3) behave affectedly;

jia
【斝】 jade wine cup;

jia
【賈】 (1) a surname; (2) merchant;

大幅賈 potbellied merchant; rich merchant;

jia
【鉀】 potassium;

硫酸鉀 potassium sulphate;
氯化鉀 potassium chloride;
氯酸鉀 potassium chlorate;
硝酸鉀 potassium nitrate;

jia
【檟】 (1) ancient version of 茶, tea; (2) small evergreen shrub;

jia⁴
jia
【架】 (1) frame; rack; shell; stand; (2) erect; put up; (3) fend off; ward off; withstand; (4) help; prop; support; (5) carry sb away forcibly; kidnap; (6) fight; quarrel;

[架橋] throw a bridge;
架橋工人 bridgeman;

[架設] erect; set up;

[架勢] manner; posture; stance;

[架子] (1) frame; rack; shelf; stand; (2) framework; outline; skeleton; (3) haughty manner; posture; stance; airs;
架子大 assume an air of importance;
架子十足 on one's high horse; overbearing; put on airs of greatness;
擺架子 act the lord; arrogant; assume airs; assume great airs; attitudinize; chuck one's weight about; come the heavy over sb; do the grand; get on one's high horse; give oneself airs; go about with one's head in the air; have airs; make a display; make a great show; mount the high horse; put on airs; put on side; put on style; put on the dog; ride the high horse; snobbish; strike an attitude; try it on;
~擺出上級的架子 assume the air of a superior;
~總擺架子 always give oneself airs;
臭架子 high and mighty airs; nauseating airs; the ugly mantle of pretentiousness;
~擺臭架子 put on nauseating airs;
~放下臭架子 drop pretentious airs; shed the ugly mantle of pretentiousness;
搭架子 build a framework; get sth roughly into shape; make an outline of;
放下架子 come off one's high horse; come off one's perch; discard one's haughty airs; pocket one's dignity;
官架子 bureaucratic airs; the airs of an official;

~擺官架子 put on bureaucratic airs; reck of the airs of an official;
~放下官架子 discard bureaucratic airs; drop the bureaucratic airs;
花架子 false and nice appearance; mere form;
空架子 bare outline; mere skeleton;
~擺空架子 affect superiority; be stuck up; make an empty show — put on a showy air; pose for effect; put up airs;
沒架子 unassuming;
拿架子 put on airs; throw one's weight about;
~從不拿架子 never assume great airs;
~處處拿架子 throw one's weight around wherever one is present;

綁架 kidnap;
報架 newspaper file; newspaper rod;
筆架 rack stack for holding Chinese brushes;
吵架 have a row; quarrel;
車架 frame;
牀架 bedstead;
打架 come to blows; fight;
擔架 litter; stretcher;
刀架 tool carriage; tool carrier;
底架 chassis;
吊架 hanger;
功架 an actor's or actress' movements and gestures on the stage;
骨架 framework; skeleton;
畫架 easel;
棚架 canopy frame; shed frame;
瓶架 bottle-holder;
譜架 music stand;
起落架 alighting gear; landing gear; undercarriage;
勸架 try to reconcile parties to a quarrel;
書架 bookshelf;
托架 bracket;
屋架 roof truss;
行李架 baggage rack;
岩架 ledge;
衣架 (1) clothes-rack; coat hanger; (2) clothes stand;
鷹架 scaffold;
樂譜架 music stand;
招架 hold one's own; withstand;
支架 stand; support;
燭架 candlestand; candlestick;

jia

【假】 holiday; leave;

[假期] holiday; leave; vacation;
假期季節 holiday reason;
公共假期 public holidays;
公眾假期 public holiday;
積存假期 accrued leave;
無薪假期 no-pay leave;
有薪假期 paid leave;

[假日] holiday;
法定假日 legal holiday;
港口假日 port holiday;
公共假日 public holiday;
國定假日 national holiday;
照常工作的假日 busman's holiday;

[假條] sick leave certificate;

病假 sick leave;
補假 compensation leave;
產假 maternity leave;
長假 take long leave;
超假 overstay one's leave;
度假 spend one's holidays;
放假 have a day off; have a holiday; have a vacation;
告假 ask for leave;
公假 leave on official business;
寒假 winter vacation;
例假 official holiday;
滿假 (of leave) expire;
年假 (1) New Year holidays; (2) winter vacation;
請假 ask for leave;
事假 leave of absence;
暑假 summer vacation;
銷假 report back after leave of absence;
休假 take a holiday;
續假 extend one's leave of absence;

jia

【嫁】 (1) marry; (2) shift; transfer;

[嫁接] graft; grafting;
科間嫁接 interfamilial graft;
同類嫁接 congenial graft;
同源嫁接 isogeneic graft;
同質體嫁接 homoplastic graft;
遠源嫁接 distant grafting;
種間嫁接 heteroplastic graft;
種胚嫁接 embryo grafting;
自然嫁接 natural grafting;

[嫁娶] marriage;

[嫁妝] dowry; trousseau;

逼嫁 force a woman to marry;
出嫁 (of a woman) get married; marry;

改嫁 (of a woman) remarry;
婚嫁 marriage; wed;
陪嫁 dowry;
再嫁 (of a woman) remarry;

jia

【價】 (1) price; (2) value;

[價格] price; tariff;

價格昂貴 of great price; pricey; pricy; the price is high;
價格暴跌 price nose-diving; price slumping;
價格暴漲 the price jumped;
價格標準 price standard;
價格波動 price fluctuation;
價格補貼 subsidized price;
價格單 price list;
價格凍結 price freeze;
價格動態 prive movements;
價格多少 how much; how much do you charge me; how much do you want; how much does it cost; what is the price; what is the price of sth;
價格方面 price-wise;
價格飛漲 prices shoot up; prices soar;
價格改革 price reform;
價格更改將不予事先通知 prices are subject to change without prior notice;
價格公道 the price is reasonable;
價格構成 price component;
價格管制 price control;
價格規律 law of value;
價格合理 prices are fair;
價格回漲 rebound in prices;
價格極限 price limit;
價格監督 price control;
價格理論 price theory;
價格猛漲 price soaring;
價格歧視 price discrimination;
價格趨平 price leveling off;
價格日疲 price sagging;
價格上漲 a rise in prices;
價格雙軌制 dual-track price system;
價格體系 price system;
價格調整 price adjustment;
價格貼現 discount for price;
價格下跌 drop in prices; fall in prices;
價格下降 price declining;
價格增長率 price increase rate;
價格戰 price war;
價格政策 price policy;
~ 統一價格政策 unified price policy;
價格指數 price index;
價格制 price system;
~ 單一價格制 single price system;
~ 兩重價格制 two-tiered price system;
價格制訂 price setting;
飽和價格 satiety price;
變動價格 make price alterations;
標簽價格 sticker price;
不變價格 constant price;
部頒價格 ministry authorized price;
參考價格 reference price;
產地價格 price in production area;
成本價格 cost price;
成交價格 concluded price;
出口價格 export price;
處理價格 bargain price; sales price;
到岸價格 cost, insurance, and freight;
發票價格 invoice price;
封面價格 cover price;
浮動價格 floating price;
附加價格 extra price;
干預價格 intervention price;
公平價格 fair price; just price;
公議價格 convention price;
供應價格 supplier's price;
估計價格 estimated price;
固定價格 fixed price; set price;
廣告價格 advertised price;
規定價格 stipulated price;
過高的價格 exorbitant price; prohibitive price;
含佣價格 common included price;
行市價格 market price;
合理價格 reasonable price;
~ 不合理價格 unreasonable price;
合同價格 contract price;
核算價格 calculate the price;
黑市價格 black market price;
哄抬價格 whoop up the price;
滑動價格 sliding-scale price;
計算價格 calculate a price;
季節性價格 seasonal price;
記帳付款價格 credit price;
加高價格 mark up a price;
減低價格 mark down a price;
降低價格 cut a price; lower the prices; reduce a price;
交割價格 delivery price;
進口價格 import price;
競爭價格 competitive price;
開盤價格 opening price;
刊物價格 published price;

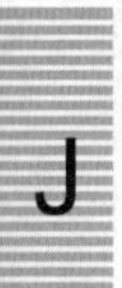

離岸價格 free on board;
糧食價格 grain prices;
~ 放開糧食價格 lift the control over the grain prices;
零售價格 retail price;
壟斷價格 monopolistic price;
略減價格 shade a price;
內定價格 administered price;
拍賣價格 auction price;
批發價格 wholesale price;
票面價格 call price; face value; par value;
期貨價格 forward price;
歧視價格 discriminatory price;
傾銷價格 dumping price;
讓步價格 concessional price;
食品價格 food prices;
市場價格 market price;
~ 國際市場價格 international market price;
~ 國內市場價格 domestic market price;
收盤價格 closing price;
抬高價格 increase a price; put up a price; raise a price;
特別價格 exceptional price;
提高價格 raise prices;
調整價格 adjust a price; price adjustment;
統一價格 unified price;
投標價格 price bidded; price tendered;
推算價格 constructed price;
外匯價格 rate of exchange;
~ 操縱外匯價格 manipulate the rates of exchange;
維持價格 support price;
穩定價格 stabilize prices;
限定價格 limit price;
現貨價格 spot price;
現金付款價格 cash price;
現行價格 current price; market price; prevailing price;
~ 按現行價格 at current price;
消費價格 consumer price;
協定價格 agreement price; coordinated price;
協商價格 negotiated price;
需求價格 demand price;
削低價格 undercut prices;
以極低的價格 for a song;
影子價格 shadow price;
優惠價格 favourable price;
約定價格 strike price;
暫定價格 provisional price;
帳面價格 book value;
正常價格 normal price;
中間價格 intermediate price;
轉售價格 resale price;
自由價格 free price;
最低價格 floor price; minimum price; rock-bottom price;
最高價格 ceiling price; maximum price;
最後價格 final price; last price;

[價廉] cheap; low-priced;
價廉物美 a small price for a good article; cheap and at the same time very good; cheap but good; filling at the price; fine wares at low prices; good and cheap; goods of high quality and low priced; inexpensive and of good quality; inexpensive but elegant; low prices and fine quality; well-made goods at competitive prices;
物美價廉 attractive in price and quality; cheap and of good quality; excellent in quality and cheap in price; excellent quality and reasonable price;
質優價廉 super quality and competitive price;

[價目] marked price; price;
價目表 price list;

[價牌] price tag;

[價錢] price;
價錢多少 how much; what is the damage; what is the money;
價錢合理 the price is fair;
講價錢 bargain;
説個價錢 name a price;
詢問一下價錢 enquire about the price;

[價值] (1) value; (2) cost; worth; (3) value; worth;
價值表現 value expression;
價值衝突 conflicting values;
價值翻倍 double in value;
價值分析 value analysis;
價值工程 value engineering;
價值觀 values;
~ 價值觀念 values;
~ 傳統價值觀 traditional values;
~ 道德價值觀 moral values;
~ 培養價值觀 cultivate values;
~ 宗教價值觀 religious values;
價值規律 law of value;
價值連城 priceless; worth a fortune;
價值論 on value;
價值千金 worth a thousand pieces of

gold;
價值取向 value orientation;
價值形態 value form;
輔助價值 sustaining values;
構置價值 acquisition value;
毫無價值 not worth a straw; of no worth; valueless;
核心價值 core values;
普世價值 universal values;
~培養普世價值 foster universal values;
清算價值 abandonment value;
剩餘價值 surplus value;
實際價值 actual value;
使用價值 use value;

半價 half price;
保價 support value;
綳價 haggle;
貶價 reduce the price;
變價 appraise at the current rate;
標價 marked price;
駁價 haggle prices;
不二價 uniform price;
打價 bargain; haggle over the price;
代價 (1) price; (2) cost;
單價 (1) unit price; (2) univalent;
等價 equal in value; of equal value;
跌價 (of price) go down;
定價 fixed price; list price;
共價 covalence;
估價 appraise; appraised price; evaluate; evaluate the price of commodities;
官價 official price;
還價 counter-offer;
滙價 exchange rate;
貨價 commodity price; price of goods;
基價 base price;
減價 mark down; reduce the price;
講價 drive a bargain over the price; haggle;
廉價 cheap; low-priced;
落價 fall in price;
買價 buying price;
賣價 selling price;
牌價 (1) list price; (2) market quotation;
票價 the price of a ticket;
平價 (1) parity; (2) normal, rational price; (3) currency;
評價 appraisal; appraise; assess; evaluate; evaluation;
起步價 starting price;
人各有其價 everyone has their price;
殺價 (of price) go down;
聲價 reputation;
時價 current price;
實價 actual price;
市價 market price;
售價 selling price;
抬價 raise the commodity prices;
討價 ask a price; name a price;
特價 bargain price; special price;
提價 raise the price;
物價 price;
現價 current price;
虛價 nominal price;
削價 cut prices; lower the price;
壓價 demand a lower price; force prices down;
要價 ask a price; charge;
議價 negotiate a price;
造價 cost;
漲價 rise in price;
折價 evaluate in terms of money;
重價 high price;
總價 total price;
租價 rent;
最低價 rock-bottom price; starting price;
作價 evaluate; fix a price for sth;

jia

【稼】 (1) cultivate; farm; plant; sow; (2) grain;

［稼穡］ farm work; farming; sowing and reaping;

耕稼 do farm work; plough and sow;
莊稼 crops;

jia

【駕】 (1) draw; harness; (2) drive; pilot; sail;

［駕車］ drive (a vehicle);
駕車代步 take a car instead of walking;
駕車回去 drive back in a car;
駕車楫舟 drive a car and pilot a ship;
駕車賽馬 harness race;
駕車者 driver;
~莽撞駕車者 road hog;
酒後駕車 drunk driving;

［駕輕就熟］ able to deal with the situation with ease; be versed in; in one's element; on one's own ground; well qualified for a post;

［駕駛］ drive; pilot; sail;
駕駛艙 cockpit; flight deck;
駕駛飛機 pilot a plane;

J

駕駛考試 driving test;
駕駛盤 steering wheel;
駕駛汽車 drive a car;
駕駛室 wheelhouse;
駕駛學校 driving school;
駕駛儀 pilot;
~ 自動駕駛儀 autopilot;
比例式自動駕駛儀 proportionate autopilot;
定翼機自動駕駛儀 fixed-wing autopilot;
多套自動駕駛儀 multiplicated autopilot;
多餘度自動駕駛儀 multiplex autopilot;
飛機自動駕駛儀 aircraft autopilot;
俯仰自動駕駛儀 pitch autopilot;
關斷自動駕駛儀 disengage autopilot;
慣性自動駕駛儀 inertial autopilot;
機動飛行自動駕駛儀 maneuvering autopilot;
積分式自動駕駛儀 integrating autopilot;
接通自動駕駛儀 engage the autopilot;
軍用自動駕駛儀 military autopilot;
商用自動駕駛儀 commercial autopilot;
雙軸自動駕駛儀 two-axis autopilot;
巡航自動駕駛儀 cruise relief autopilot;
液式自動駕駛儀 fluidic autopilot;
預定程序自動駕駛儀 pre-programmed autopilot;
着陸自動駕駛儀 automatic landing autopilot;
自監控式自動駕駛儀 self-monitored autopilot;
自調式自動駕駛儀 adaptive autopilot;
駕駛員 driver; pilot;
~ 副駕駛員 co-pilot;
~ 後座駕駛員 back seat driver;
駕駛執照 driver's license; driving license;
~ 吊銷駕駛執照 revoke a driving license;
駕駛座 cockpit; driver's seat;
安全駕駛 safe driving;
超速駕駛 speeding;
酒後駕駛 drive under the influence of alcohol; drive when intoxicated;
魯莽駕駛 reckless driving;
危險駕駛 dangerous driving;
無牌駕駛 drive without a license;
左側駕駛 left-hand drive;

[駕馭] (1) drive; (2) control; dominate; master;
駕馭馬車 drive a cart;
駕馭時間 the master of one's time;
駕馭形勢 have the situation well in hand;
駕馭自然 tame nature;

[駕雲而去] be borne thither on a cloud;

保駕 escort the emperor;
車駕 emperor's carriage;
擋駕 decline to receive a guest;
勞駕 excuse me;
凌駕 override; place oneself above;
屈駕 condescend to make the journey;
勸駕 help persuade sb to accept an invitation or post;
枉駕 I'm honoured by your visit;
晏駕 (of a ruler) pass away;
御駕 (1) imperial carriage; (2) emperor;
尊駕 you;

jian¹
jian

【奸】 (1) crafty; evil; treacherous; wicked; (2) traitor; (3) self-seeking and wily; selfish; (4) illicit sexual relations;

[奸臣] traitor minister; treacherous court official;
奸臣當道 the evil governors rule the state;
奸臣逆子 disloyal ministers and unfilial sons;

[奸夫] adulterer;

[奸婦] adulteress;

[奸宄] evildoer; malefactor;
庇匿奸宄 shelter a criminal;

[奸滑] crafty; deceitful; treacherous;
老奸巨滑 as cunning as a fox; as slippery as an eel; crafty old scoundrel; old file; old hand at trickery and deception; past master of machination and manoeuvre; wily old fox; wise old bird;

[奸謀] sinister design;
腹藏奸謀 harbour a sinister design;

[奸佞] (1) crafty and fawning; (2) crafty sycophant;

[奸商] commercial racketeer; dishonest trader; profiteer; unscrupulous merchant;

[奸細] enemy agent; spy;
安插奸細 plant an enemy agent;

[奸險] malicious; treacherous; wicked and crafty;

[奸笑] sinister smile;

[奸邪] (1) crafty and evil; treacherous; (2) crafty and evil person;

[奸心] cunning mind;

[奸雄] arch-careerist; master of political intrigues;

奸雄得勢 an able scoundrel gains power;

[奸賊] conspirator; traitor;

[奸詐] crafty; deceitful; fraudulent; on the crook; treacherous;

奸詐的人 a man of deceit; shyster;

奸詐行徑 duplicity;

奸詐陰險 deceitful and designing;

奸惡狡詐 malicious and cunning;

藏奸 harbour malice;

鋤奸 eliminate traitors; ferret out spies;

漢奸 traitor (to China);

雞奸 buggery; sodomy;

輪奸 rape by turns;

內奸 hidden traitor;

強奸 rape; violate;

耍奸 act in a slick way;

通奸 commit adultery;

誘奸 debauch; seduce;

謫奸 punish the wicked;

誅奸 punish the traitorous;

捉奸 cath adultery in the act;

jian

【尖】 (1) point; tip; top; (2) pointed; tapering; (3) piercing; shrill; (4) acute; sharp; (5) best of its kind; cream of the crop; pick of the bunch;

[尖兵] point man;

[尖脆] (of voice) high and clear;

[尖端] (1) acme; external centre; peak; tip; (2) apex; frontier; leading edge; the most advanced; the sophisticated;

尖端產業 sophisticated industry;

尖端感覺 acmesthesia;

尖端工業 sophisticated industry;

尖端技術 sophisticated technology; the most advanced techniques;

尖端科學 the frontiers of science; the most advanced branches of science;

尖端武器 sophisticated weapons;

[尖角] closed angle;

[尖叫] scream;

不停地尖叫 scream one's head off;

大聲尖叫 give a loud scream;

發出尖叫 utter a scream;

發出一聲尖叫 let out a scream;

高聲尖叫 scream blue murder;

聽到尖叫 hear a scream;

痛得尖叫 scream with pain;

嚇得尖叫 scream with fright; shriek with terror;

一聲尖叫 a scream;

~發出一聲尖叫 let out a scream;

[尖利] (1) cutting; keen; sharp; (2) piercing; shrill;

筆鋒尖利 wield a pointed pen; write in an incisive style;

眼光尖利 have keen eyes;

[尖溜溜] pointed; sharp;

[尖鋭] incisive; keen; penetrating; sharp; sharp-pointed;

尖鋭的 incisive;

尖鋭對立 be diametrically opposed to each other;

尖鋭複雜 acute and complicated;

眼光尖鋭 have sharp eyes; sharp-eyed;

[尖聲] in a shrill voice;

尖聲大叫 scream;

尖聲大笑 screech with laughter;

尖聲呼救 scream for help;

尖聲歡笑 scream with laughter;

尖聲尖氣 in a shrill voice;

尖聲警告 shriek out a warning;

尖聲狂笑 shriek with laughter;

尖聲説話 speak in a high voice;

[尖酸] acrid; acrimonious; tart;

尖酸刻薄 bitterly sarcastic; pungent; sharp and stinging; stingingly; tart and mean;

~尖酸刻薄的 catty;

[尖牙] fang;

上尖牙 eye tooth;

[尖嘴] have a caustic tongue;

尖嘴薄舌 have a caustic and flippant tongue;

尖嘴猴腮 one's mouth sticks and one has a chin like an ape's;

尖嘴嚼舌 fond of gossip; have a sharp tongue;

拔尖 (1) tiptop; top-notch; (2) push oneself to the front;

鼻尖 the tip of the nose;

筆尖 (1) nib; pen point; (2) the tip of a writing brush;

頂尖 (1) tip; (2) centre;

腳尖 the tip of a toe; tiptoe;

舌尖 the tip of the tongue;

眼尖 sharp-eyed;

指尖 the tip of a finger;

J

jian

【肩】 shoulder;

［肩膀］ shoulder;

肩膀結實 strong shoulders;
肩膀寬 have broad shoulders;
拱起肩膀 hunch one's shoulders;
寬厚的肩膀 broad shoulders;
露出肩膀 bare one's shoulder;
輕拍［ ］肩膀 tap sb on the shoulder;

［肩背］ shoulders and the back;

［肩垂病］ drop shoulder;

［肩帶］ shoulder strap;

［肩分離］ shoulder separation;

［肩負］ bear; shoulder; take on; undertake;

肩負重擔 shoulder heavy responsibilities;
肩負重荷 bear a heavy burden; should heavy loads;
肩負重任 bear heavy responsibilities; hold an important position; sustain great responsibilities; take up the heavy responsibility;

［肩關節炎］ inflammation of the shoulder joint; omarthritis;

［肩荷］ carry on the shoulder; shoulder;

［肩胛］ shoulder;

肩胛骨 shoulder blade;

［肩摩］ rub the shoulder;

肩摩轂擊 be overcrowded with people and traffic; go in a jostling crowd; shoulders rubbing and carriages knocking at each other — busy traffic;
肩摩踵接 crowded; rub the shoulder and follow the steps;

［肩上］ on sb's shoulders;

騎在肩上 ride on sb's shoulders;

［肩痛］ omalgia; pain in the shoulder; shoulder pain;

肩痛風 gout in the shoulder; omagra;

［肩頭］ shoulders;

比肩 shoulder to shoulder;
并肩 shoulder to shoulder; side by side;
墊肩 shoulder pad;
披肩 (1) cape; (2) shawl;
敲落肩 knocked-down shoulder;
縮肩 stooped shoulders;
雙肩 hump up one's shoulders; shrug one's shoulders;
聳肩 hump up one's shoulders; shrug one's shoulders;
脱肩 relinquish one's responsibility; shirk one's responsibility;
息肩 be relieved of a responsibility; put down one's burden;
歇肩 remove the load from one's shoulder for a rest;
脅肩 shrug the shoulders;
卸肩 lay down responsibilities;
削肩 sloping shoulders;
一肩 shoulder;
仔肩 bear the burden;

jian

【戔】 little; small; tiny;

［戔戔］ fragmentary; small; tiny;

戔戔之數 insignificant amount of money;

jian

【姦】 (1) adultery; debauchery; licentiousness; (2) attack a woman sexually; debauch; ravish; (3) crook;

［姦夫］ adulterer; intrigant; paramour;

［姦婦］ adulteress; paramour;

［姦情］ adulterous affair;

［姦污］ debauchery; rape; seduce;

姦污婦女 rape a woman;

［姦淫］ (1) adultery; illicit sexual relations; (2) rape; seduce;

姦淫擄掠 rape and loot;
姦淫燒殺 commit rape, arson and murder; engage in rape, arson and murder; rape, burn and kill;

jian

【兼】 (1) double; twice; (2) concurrently; simultaneously;

［兼備］ have both...and...;

才德兼備 have both talent and virtue;
才色兼備 endowed with both good looks and real talent; have both wit and beauty;
德才兼備 combine ability with political integrity; equal stress on integrity and ability; graced with many virtues and talents; have both ability and principles; have both political integrity and ability; possess political integrity and professional competence;
智德兼備 have both wisdom and virtue — consummation of wisdom and virtue;

［兼併］ annex; merge;

兼併鄰國 annex neighbouring countries;
土地兼併 annexation of land;

[兼程] travel at double speed;
兼程而行 travel by long stages;
兼程前進 advance at the double; devour the way;
風雨兼程 press forward regardless of the weather;
日夜兼程 travel day and night;
[兼而有之] have both at the same time;
[兼顧] give consideration to two or more things;
勢難兼顧 the situation is such that one cannot look after both sides at the same time;
[兼課] (1) do some teaching in addition to one's main occupation; (2) part-time teaching; (3) hold two or more teaching jobs concurrently;
[兼權熟計] give mature consideration to all aspects of a question; take the responsibility altogether and plan thoroughly — scheme the whole thing;
[兼任] (1) hold a concurrent post; (2) part-time;
[兼容] compatible;
兼容并包 absorb anything and everything; all-inclusive;
兼容性 compatibility;
~兼容性測試 compatibility test;
~全兼容性 full compatibility;
~軟件兼容性 software compatibility;
~設備兼容性 equipment compatibility;
[兼弱攻昧] annex and absorb the weak countries; annex the weak and attack the dull;
[兼施] by both measures;
攻補兼施 tonification and purgation;
剿撫兼施 quash revolts both by force and pacification measures;
[兼收并蓄] absorb anything and everything; accept and keep anything and everything whether good or bad; incorporate things of diverse nature; swallow anything and everything; take in everything;
[兼職] concurrent job; moonlight; moonlighting; part-time job; side job;
兼職工作 part-time job;
兼職教師 part-time teacher;
兼職老師 part-time teacher;
兼職熱 the popularity of concurrent-post holding;
辭去兼職 resign one's concurrent job;
擔任兼職 hold a concurrent post;
放棄兼職 abandon a concurrent post;
兼司他職 also in charge of other duties;
一份兼職 a part-time job;

jian

【堅】 (1) firm; hard; solid; strong; (2) fortification; stronghold; (3) firmly; resolutely; steadfastly;
[堅不可摧] be so strongly built as to be unbreakable; firm and unyielding; impregnable; indestructible; indomitable; secure against assault; unbreakable;
[堅不吐實] not to breathe a word about the truth; not to tell the truth in any way; obstinately refuse to speak up; persist in telling lies;
[堅持] abide by; adhere to; adherence; assert oneself; be wedded to one's opinion; cling to; face it out; hew to; hold on; hold one's ground; hold out; hold to; insist on; keep to; keep up; maintain; persevere at; persevere in; persevere with; persist in; stand fast; stand firm; stand pat; stand to one's guns; stand up for; stick to; stick to one's guns; uphold;
堅持不懈 adhere to sth unremittingly; hold on consistently and persistently;
~堅持不懈的 indefatigable;
~堅持不懈地工作 peg away;
堅持不渝 firm and unchanging; hang on; persist in one's purpose; persistently; unremitting;
堅持嘗試 persist in an attempt;
堅持到底 carry through firmly to the end; hold on straight to the end; hold on to the last; hold on to the very end; stand fast; stand firm; stay the course; stand to one's guns; stay the course; stick it; stick it out; stick to one's guns;
堅持己見 cling to one's own view; firm in one's view; hold on to one's own views; hold one's course; stand to one's assertion;
堅持立場 (Amer, colloq) dig one's toes in; hold one's ground; sit tight; stand

one's ground; stand to one's colours; stick to one's colours;
堅持努力 persevere in one's efforts;
堅持下去 struggle on;
堅持原則 adhere to principle; stick to principle;
堅持真理 hold firmly to the truth;
堅持自己的立場 keep one's stand; maintain one's ground;
堅持自力更生 insist on self-reliance;

[堅定] determined; firm; pertinacious; resolute; staunch; steadfast;
堅定不移 as steady as a rock; carry a stiff upper lip; firm and steadfast; firm and unshakable; firmly; first, last, and all the time; have a stiff upper lip; immovable; inflexible; invariable; keep a stiff upper lip; resolute and firm; rock-firm; stand fast; stand firm; undeviating; unshakable; unswerving;
~ 堅定不移的 adamant;
堅定沉著 firm and steadfast; steadfast and calm;
堅定的 ;
堅定立場 strengthen one's stand;
堅定信念 strengthen one's conviction;
堅定意志 harden one's purpose;
不堅定 lack of resolution; not firm enough;
從容堅定 stand firm and keep coolheaded;
立場堅定 firm in one's stand;
意志堅定 firm in purpose;

[堅固] firm; solid; strong; sturdy;
堅固不拔 firm and indestructible; firm and unshakable;
堅固耐用 sturdy and durable;

[堅甲利兵] equipped with strong armour and sharp weapons; strong armour and sharp weapons — armed might;

[堅決] determined; firm; resolute; resolved;
堅決反對 put one's foot down; set one's face against; set oneself against;
堅決要求 hold out for;
態度堅決 maintain a firm attitude;
意志堅決 resolute in one's determination;

[堅苦卓絕] endure hardship heroically; extremely hard and bitter; most arduous; showing the utmost fortitude; staunch through trials and tribulations;

[堅牢] fast;
堅牢度 fastness;
~ 耐酸堅牢度 acid fastness;
~ 漂白堅牢度 bleaching fastness;
~ 顏色堅牢度 colour fastness;

[堅強] (1) firm; staunch; strong; (2) strengthen;
堅強不屈 firm and inflexible; keep a stiff upper lip; refuse to yield; unyielding and firm;
意志堅強 strong-willed;

[堅忍] steadfast and persevering in face of difficulties;
堅忍不拔 firm and indomitable; stubborn and unyielding;

[堅韌] firm and tenacious; tough and tensile;
堅韌不拔 firm and indomitable; indomitable; inflexible; intrepid; persistent and dauntless; stubbornly and unyielding;

[堅銳] tough and sharp;
披堅執銳 be fully prepared for battle; in full armour with spike in hand; warrior-like; wear armour and hold weapons;

[堅實] (1) solid; substantial; (2) staunch; strong;
身體堅實 of solid build;

[堅守] hold fast to; stand fast; stick to;
堅守崗位 hold the fort; keep to work post; stand fast at one's post; stand to one's guns; stay at one's fighting post; stick to one's post;
堅守諾言 stand to one's word;
堅守契約 stick to one's agreement;
堅守陣地 hold fast to one's position; hold the field; keep the field; maintain the field; stand one's ground;

[堅挺] firm; strong;

[堅穩] firm; steady;

[堅信] be firmly convinced; confident of; firmly believe;
堅信不疑 firmly believe; have infinite faith in; not to have the slightest doubt;
堅信不渝 keep one's faith inviolate;

[堅毅] firm and persistent; with inflexible will; with unswerving determination;
堅毅頑強 firm and indomitable;

[堅硬] flintiness; hard; rigid; stiff; solid;
非常堅硬 as hard as a bone;

[堅貞] constant; faithful;

J

堅貞不阿 faithful to; stick to one's colours;
堅貞不屈 firm and unyielding; remain faithful and unyielding; stand firm and unyielding;
堅貞不渝 loyal through thick and thin;

[堅執] firm; resolute;

攻堅 assault fortified positions;
中堅 backbone; hard nucleus;

jian

【湔】 wash;
[湔雪] redress a grievance; right a wrong;

jian

【菅】 (1) coarse grass; themeda triandra, (2) a surname;

jian

【間】 (1) among; between; (2) during; in; within a definite time or space; (3) room;
[間不容髮] not a hair's breath in between — the situation is extremely critical;
[間不容息] in a split second;
[間距] interval; space length; spacing;
角間距 angular spacing;
梁間距 beam spacing;
軸向間距 axial spacing;
[間皮] mesothelium;
[間奏曲] entracte; intermezzo;

暗間 inner room;
車間 shop; workshop;
此間 around here; here;
坊間 in the bookshops; on the street stalls;
房間 room;
行間 (1) in army service; (2) between the lines;
居間 mediate between two parties;
空間 space;
裏間 inner room;
民間 (1) among the people; popular; (2) nongovernmental; people-to-people;
年間 during a certain era or age;
期間 course; period; time;
其間 between; during; with a period of time;
人間 man's world; the world;
日間 day time; during the day;
霎時間 in a jiffy; in a split second; in a twinkling;
時間 (1) (the concept of) time; (2) (the duration of) time; (3) (a point in) time;
世間 in society; the world;
瞬間 in the twinkling of an eye;
套間 (1) inner room; (2) apartment; flat;
田間 farm; field;
外間 (1) outer room; (2) outside circles;
晚間 at night; in the evening;
鄉間 country; village;
陽間 this world;
夜間 at night; during the night;
陰間 the nether world;
中間 (1) among; between; (2) centre; (3) middle;

jian

【閒】 (1) calm; placid; quiet; tranquil; (2) leisure; spare time;

jian

【揀】 pick up (with chopsticks);

jian

【煎】 (1) fry in fat or oil; (2) decoct;
[煎熬] suffering; torment; torture;
煎湯熬藥 brew a liquid preparation with medicinal herbs;
[煎炸] frying;

熬煎 suffer; torment;

jian

【椷】 (1) goblet; (2) same as 緘 ;

jian

【犍】 castrated bull; ox;
[犍牛] bullock;

老犍 bullock;

jian

【漸】 (1) permeate; soak; (2) dye;
[漸染] be gradually influenced; be imperceptibly influenced;
[漸潤] saturate with water;

jian

【監】 (1) inspect; supervise; watch; (2) jail; prison;
[監測] monitor; survey;
[監察] control; monitor; supervise;
[監督] (1) control; monitor; supervise; supervision; (2) supervisor;
監督不力 lacking in supervision;
監督成本 monitoring cost;
監督電話 supervision telephone number;
監督管理 supervisory management;
監督人 overseer; supervisor;

監督作用 supervisory role;
財務監督 financial control;
放鬆監督 relax supervision;
接受人民監督 subject oneself to supervision by the masses;
進行監督 exercise supervision;
會計監督 accounting supervision;
受監督 be subjected to supervision;
自動監督 automatic supervision;

［監工］ (1) oversee; supervise work; (2) foreman; overlooker; overseer; supervisor; task master;
副監工 charge hand;

［監管］ oversee;

［監護］ guardianship; tutelage;
監護人 chaplain; custodian; guarder; guardian;
~ 監護人身分 guardianship;
~ 當監護人 chaperone;
~ 法定監護人 legal guardian;

［監禁］ imprison; incarcerate; incarceration; put in jail; take into custody;
被監禁 be imprisoned; go to prison;
單獨監禁 solitary confinement;
非法監禁 false imprisonment;
屢遭監禁 repeatedly suffer imprisonment;
終身監禁 life sentence;

［監考］ (1) invigilate; monitor examinations; (2) invigilation;
監考員 invigilator;

［監控］ control; monitor; monitor and control; monitoring; supervisory control;
監控程序 monitor programme;
監控名單 watch list;
環境空氣監控 ambient air monitoring;
聲監控 acoustic monitoring;

［監牢］ jail; prison;

［監理］ supervisor;
監理工程師 supervising engineer;

［監事會］ supervisory committee;
監事會主席 chairman of the supervisory committee;

［監視］ guard; keep a lookout over; keep watch on; monitor; surveillance;
監視敵人 keep on the watch for the enemy;
監視器 monitor;
~ 波形監視器 wave form monitor;
~ 空氣監視器 air monitor;
~ 線路監視器 actual monitor;
暗中監視 keep one's watch in secret;
大氣監視 atmospheric surveillance;
電子監視 electronic surveillance;
空中監視 aerial surveillance;
埋伏監視 stakeout;
受到監視 come under observation;

［監守］ guard; have custody of; take care of;
監守自盜 embezzle; defalcate; steal goods for which one is responsible; steal money in one's trust; steal what is entrusted to one's care;

［監聽］ monitor;

［監獄］ bucket and pail; clink; cooler; hard site; jail; penitentiary; pokey; poky; prison; slammer;
監獄暴動 prison riot;
~ 發生監獄暴動 a prison riot breaks out;
監獄長 prison governor;
低度設防監獄 minimum security prison;
開放式監獄 open prison;
看守監獄 in charge of a prison;
逃出監獄 escape from prison;

警監 commissioner;
舍監 house master; warden;
學監 educational inspector;
總監 chief inspector;

jian
【箋】 (1) commentary; note; (2) fancy note paper; letter paper; stationary; (3) correspondence; letters;

［箋注］ notes and commentaries on ancient texts;

便箋 memo; notepaper;
信箋 letter paper;

jian
【蒹】 a kind of reed with a pithy stem;

jian
【緘】 (1) close; seal; (2) letter;

［緘藏］ bear in silence; keep silent;

［緘口］ hold one's tongue; keep one's mouth shut; say nothing;
緘口不答 keep silent; seal one's lips and say nothing;
金人緘口 careful in speech; keep one's mouth shut;
三緘其口 a tightly fastened-down mouth; hold one's peace; hold oneself back from saying a word; keep one's peace;

reluctant to voice one's opinions; remain silent; very reluctant to make comments; with one's lips sealed;

[緘默] keep silent; reticent;

緘默不語 keep silent about sth or sb;

緘默寡言 silent and speak little;

保持緘默 button up one's mouth; hold one's tongue; keep a still tongue in one's head; keep one's mouth closed; keep one's mouth shut; keep one's peace; keep silent; remain silent;

被緘默 be muzzled;

打破緘默 break the silence;

恢復緘默 relapse into silence;

jian

【縑】 a kind of fine silk;

jian

【艱】 difficult; hard;

[艱巨] arduous; daunting; enormity; formidable; onerous;

艱巨任務 arduous task; daunting task;

[艱苦] arduous; difficult; hard; hardship; tough;

艱苦跋涉 trek;

艱苦備嘗 experience all kinds of hardship;

艱苦創業 start an undertaking with painstaking efforts;

艱苦奮斗 arduous struggle; brave hard and bitter struggles; fight strenuously; live plainly and work hard; plain living and hard struggle; work diligently in spite of difficulties; work hard and perseveringly;

艱苦樸素 hard work and lead a plain life; live in plain and hardworking way; plain in one's style of living;

艱苦曲折 arduous and tortuous;

艱苦歲月 in times of trials and tribulation;

艱苦與共 go through sufferings and hardships together;

艱苦卓絕 arduous and bitter; extremely hard and bitter;

[艱難] difficult; hard;

艱難竭蹶 lead a hard life; live in extreme poverty;

艱難困苦 difficulties and hardships; hardship and suffering; hardships and deprivations;

艱難曲折 arduous and tortuous; difficulties and setbacks;

艱難時世 hard times;

艱難險阻 difficulties and dangers; difficulties and obstacles; hardships, hazard and obstructions;

步履艱難 walk with difficulty; walk with infirm steps;

共渡艱難 stick together through thick and thin;

國步艱難 the nation is beset by difficulties;

歷盡艱難 go through untold hardships;

[艱澀] intricate and obscure; involved and abstruse;

[艱深] abstruse; difficult to understand;

艱深晦澀 abstract and obscure; hard to understand;

[艱危] difficulties and dangers;

[艱險] hardships and dangers; perilous;

不避艱險 brave hardships and dangers; flinch from no difficulty or danger; make light of difficulties and dangers; shrink from no difficulty or danger;

不怕任何艱險 dare all hardships and perils;

不畏艱險 fearless of danger and difficulty; not to shrink from hardships and crisis;

歷盡艱險 be fraught with peril; experience all kinds of hardships and perils;

冒艱犯險 brave all sacrifices and hardships; carry one's life in one's hands; run risks to do sth;

忍受種種艱險 endure hardships and dangers;

[艱辛] hardships;

備嚐艱辛 drain the cup of sorrow to the dregs; suffer many privations; suffer untold hardships; undergo hardships;

嚐盡艱辛 have experienced all the hardships;

歷盡艱辛 go through all kinds of hardships;

忍受艱辛 bear hardships;

丁艱 be in mourning for parent's death;

維艱 very difficult; very hard;

jian

【韃】 (1) quiver on a horse; (2) keep and collect; store;

jian

【殲】 annihilate; destroy; exterminate;

J

[殲敵] wipe out the enemy;
[殲滅] annihilate; destroy; wipe out;
殲滅戰 war of annihilation;
遭到殲滅 suffer annihilation;

攻殲 attack and destroy; wipe out;
聚殲 round up and annihilate;
圍殲 surround and annihilate;

jian
【鰜】 big-mouthed flounder; sole;

jian
【鶼】 a fabulous bird having only one wing so that a pair must unite in order to fly;
[鶼鶼] pair of lovebirds;

jian
【鰹】 bonito;
[鰹鳥] boody; gannet; sula;
[鰹魚] striped tuna;

jian
【韉】 saddle cloth;

jian3

jian
【柬】 (1) invitation; letter; visiting card; (2) pick; select;
[柬帖] note; short letter;
[柬邀] send a written invitation;

請柬 invitation card;
書柬 letters;

jian
【剪】 (1) clippers; scissors; shears; (2) clip; cut; trim;
[剪報] clipping; newspaper clippings; newspaper cuttings; scraps;
[剪裁] (1) cut out a garment; tailor; (2) cut out unwanted material from a piece of writing; prune;
[剪彩] cut the ribbon at an opening ceremony;
剪彩儀式 ribbon-cutting ceremony;
[剪除] annihilate; exterminate; wipe out;
[剪刀] scissors; shears;
大剪刀 shears;
鋸齒剪刀 pinking scissors; pinking shears;
一把剪刀 a pair of scissors;
[剪斷] cut off; nip off; shear off; snip;
[剪髮] cut one's hair; hairdressing; have a haircut;
[剪輯] (1) cutting; film editing; montage; (2) editing and rearrangement;
剪輯車間 film-editing department;
剪輯導演 montage director;
剪輯機 editor;
~聲畫剪輯機 picture and sound editor editing machine; picture and sound editor;
剪輯員 film-cutter; film-editor;
[剪接] cutting; edit a film; film editing; montage;
[剪具] clipper;
[剪切] shear; shearing;
剪切機 shear;
~電動剪切機 power-driven shear;
~厚板剪切機 heavy-plate shears;
單邊剪切 one-way shear;
交變剪切 alternating shear;
熱剪切 hot shearing;
振盪剪切 oscillatory shear;
[剪貼] (1) clip and paste; (2) cutting out;
剪貼板 clipboard;
剪貼簿 scrapbook;
剪貼圖片集 clip art;
[剪影] (1) paper-cut silhouette; (2) sketch; outline; (3) cucoloris;
[剪紙] paper-cut; scissor-cut;
[剪子] clippers; scissors; shears;
小剪子 small scissors;

裁剪 cut out;
刀剪 cutlery;
夾剪 scissor-shaped clamping tool;
刃剪 snip;
疏剪 thin out (leaves);
修剪 clip; cut; prune; trim;
燕剪 swallow's tail in the shape of scissors;

jian
【趼】 blisters on hands or feet; callous skin; shingles;
[趼子] shingles;

jian
【揀】 (1) choose; pick; select; (2) pick up;
[揀選] choose; pick out; select; sort;

jian
【減】 (1) subtract; (2) cut; decrease; reduce;
[減產] drop in production; reduction of output;

[減低] bring down; cut; lower; reduce;
減低財產損失 reduce property loss;
減低成本 cut the cost; reduce the cost;
減低關稅 reduce the tariff;
減低開支 cut down expenses;
減低速度 ease down; lower speed; slacken speed; slow down;
減低物價 bring down prices; reduce prices;
減低音量 lower the volume;
減低運費 get a reduction in freight;

[減法] subtraction;
減法器 subtractor;
~ 半減法器 half subtractor;
~ 十進制減法器 decade subtractor;
~ 數字減法器 digital subtractor;
二進制減法 binary subtraction;
向量減法 subtraction of vectors;
直接減法 direct subtraction;

[減肥] dieting; lose fat; reduce weight; slim;
減肥村 fat farm;
減肥霜 slimming cream;
減肥丸 diet pill;
減肥者 dieter;
減肥中心 fat farm;
反覆性減肥 yo-yo dieting;
速效減肥 crash diet;

[減幅] range of discount; range of reduction;

[減光] dim the light;
減光器 dimmer;
~ 玻璃減光器 glass dimmer;
~ 前燈減光器 headlight dimmer;
~ 液體減光器 liquid dimmer;

[減緩] retard; slow down;

[減價] cut down prices; mark down; on sale; price breaks; price out; reduce the price;
大減價 grand sale; great reduction in price;
~ 清貨大減價 big clearance price;

[減虧] reduce losses;

[減免] (1) annul a punishment; mitigate a punishment; (2) exempt and reduce;
減免房租 reduce rents;

[減輕] abate; alleviate; ease; lighten; mitigate;
減輕體重 lose weight;
減輕疼痛 ease the pain;
減輕痛苦 palliate the agonizing sufferings;
減輕刑罰 mitigate punishment;

[減熱] desuperheat;
減熱器 desuperheater;
~ 氣冷式減熱器 air-cooled desuperheater;

[減弱] abate; attenuate; damp; fade; trip-out; weaken;
減弱風勢 abate the force of wind; break the force of wind;
減弱火勢 damp down a fire;
減弱疼痛 abate pain;
減弱語 downtoner;
逐漸減弱 wane;

[減色] detract from the merit of; impair the excellence of; lose lustre;

[減少] abate; cut; cut back; cut down; decrease; deplete; diminish; downsize; drop; dwindle; extenuation; fall off; give a reduction; go down; lessen; make a reduction; on the decrease; reduce; sink;
減少存貨 reduce stock;
減少犯罪 diminish crime;
減少伙食 cut down one's diet;
減少開支 cut down expenses;
減少浪費 reduce waste;
減少人口 deplete population;
減少事故 reduce accidents;
減少損失 reduce a loss;
減少運動量 reduce exercise;
急劇減少 reduce sharply;
人口減少 diminish in population;
逐漸減少 dwindle; peter out;

[減聲] noise abatement; noise reduction;

[減數] subtrahend;
被減數 minuend;

[減稅] abate a tax; tax abatement; tax reduction;
減稅期 tax holiday;
減稅優惠 tax break;

[減速] decelerate; deceleration; moderate; reduce the speed; retard; run out of steam; shift down; slow down; slow up;
減速劑 moderator;
減速器 retarder;
~ 自動減速器 automatically operated retarder;

[減縮] cut down; decrease; foreshortening; reduce; reduce and compress;

[減退] abate; decelerate; decline; decrease; drop; fall off; go down;
熱度減退 abatement of the fever;

J

[減刑] abatement from penalty; abatement of penalty; commutation; commute a sentence; mitigate a sentence; reduce a penalty;

[減削] reduce and amend;

[減壓] decompress; pressure reduction; reduce pressue; relax the pressure;
減壓病 decompression sickness;
減壓假 duvet day;

[減員] reduce the number of workers;
自然減員 natural wastage;

[減災] disaster alleviation; disaster reduction; reducing natural disaster;

[減震] shock absorption;
減震墊 shock absorber;
~ 着陸減震墊 landing shock absorber;
減震能力 cushioning ability;
減震器 bumper; bumper absorber; damper; oscillation absorber; shock absorber; vibration absorber;
~ 爆炸減震器 blast damper;
~ 波前減震器 front shock absorber;
~ 動力減震器 dynamic vibration absorber;
~ 後懸掛減震器 rear suspension shock absorber;
~ 滑橇減震器 skid shock absorber;
~ 活塞式減震器 piston-type shock absorber;
~ 可調減震器 adjustable damper;
~ 空氣減震器 air bumper; air damper;
~ 空氣式減震器 pneumatic shock absorber;
~ 磨擦減震器 friction shock absorber;
~ 平衡減震器 balancing bumper;
~ 起落架減震器 landing shock absorber; undercarriage shock absorber;
~ 氣墊減震器 air cushion shock absorber; pneumatic cushion shock absorber;
~ 氣壓減震器 pneumatic bumper;
~ 曲軸減震器 crankshaft vibration damper;
~ 雙動減震器 double-acting damper;
~ 水力減震器 hydraulic shock absorber;
~ 彈簧減震器 spring shock absorber;
~ 套筒減震器 direct-acting shock absorber;
~ 心軸減震器 spindle shock absorber;
~ 液體式減震器 liquid shock absorber;
~ 液壓減震器 hydraulic bumper;
~ 油壓減震器 oil shock absorber;
~ 油壓氣動式減震器 oil-pneumatic shock absorber;
~ 自動調整減震器 self-adjustable shock absorber;
減震筒 damper cylinder;
減震作用 shock absorption
~ 油減震作用 oil shock absorption;
彈簧減震 spring shock absorption;
橡皮減震 rubber shock absorption;
壓縮減震 compression shock absorption;

[減重] abatement of weight;

倍減 demultiply;
裁減 cut down; reduce;
遞減 decrease by degrees;
核減 reduce after verification;
加減 add and subtract;
清減 become thin; lose weight;
衰減 attenuate;
縮減 cut; reduce;
削減 cut down; reduce;
增減 increases and decreases;
酌減 cut down according to circumstances; make considered reductions;

jian

【筧】 bamboo water pipe;

jian

【戩】 (1) exterminate; (2) blessing;

jian

【碱】 alkali; (2) soda;

[碱地] alkaline land;

[碱化] alkalize;

[碱土] alkali soil;

[碱性] alkaline; basicity;
碱性電池 alkaline battery;
碱性反應 alkaline reaction;

[碱中毒] alkalosis;
高空碱中毒 altitude alkalosis;
呼吸性碱中毒 espiratory alkalosis;

屍碱 cadaveric alkaloid;
罌粟碱 opium alkaloids;
植物碱 plant alkaloid;

jian

【儉】 (1) economical; frugal; thrifty; (2) meagre; (3) poor harvest;

[儉樸] economical; thrifty and simple;

[儉省] economical; thrifty;

[儉以防匱] guard against deficiency; waste not, want not;

J

[儉以養廉] frugality makes honesty; thrift nourishes modesty;
[儉約] economical; frugal; sparing; thrifty;
[儉則不缺] waste not, want not;

節儉 frugal; thrifty;
勤儉 diligent and frugal;
省儉 frugal; thrifty;

jian
【翦】 same as 剪 , trim, cut with scissors;

jian
【撿】 collect; gather; pick up;
[撿到] pick up;
撿到便宜 get sth at a bargain;

jian
【檢】 (1) check up; examine; inspect; (2) careful in one's conduct; restrain oneself;
[檢波] detection; rectification;
檢波器 detector;
~ 彩色信號檢波器 chrominance detector;
~ 同步檢波器 commutator detector;
~ 音頻檢波器 aural detector;
非線性檢波 nonlinear detection;
幅度檢波 amplitude detection;
簡單檢波 simple rectification;
柵流檢波 grid current detection;
圖像檢波 image detection;
外差檢波 heterodyne detection;
正交檢測 orthogonal detection;
[檢測] check; detect; examine; test;
檢測器 detector;
~ 聲納檢測器 aural detector;
~ 通用檢測器 all-purpose detector;
~ 原子吸收檢測器 atomic absorption detector;
地址檢測 address detection;
空氣檢測 aerial detection;
生物檢測 biological detection;
雙擇檢測 binary detection;
自動檢測 automatic detection;
自動誤差檢測 automatic error detection;
[檢查] check on; check out; check over; check-up; check up on; examine; go over; go through; inspect; inspection; look at; take a view of ;
檢查工作 check up on work;
檢查身體 have a check-up;
檢查視力 test sb's eyesight;
檢查員 inspector;
~ 海事檢查員 marine inspector;
~ 外勤檢查員 travelling inspector;
檢查站 checkpoint;
~ 邊防檢查站 border checkpoint;
檢查賬目 examine the accounts;
產後檢查 post-natal check-up;
產前檢查 pre-natal check-up;
常規檢查 routine examination;
廠內檢查 factory inspection;
徹底檢查 going-over;
抽樣檢查 curtailed inspection;
定期檢查 periodic check-up;
對應檢查 counter check;
健康檢查 medical check-up;
交叉檢查 cross-check;
教育質量檢查 check-up for educational quality;
接受檢查 undergo an examination;
經受檢查 experience an inspection;
臨時檢查 extraordinary inspection;
受到檢查 be subjected to an examination;
數據檢查 data check;
透視檢查 examine by fluoroscopy;
外觀檢查 exterior inspection;
衛生檢查 health inspection;
嚴格檢查 close check;
驗收檢查 acceptance check; access inspection;
舟艇檢查 boat inspection;
自動檢查 automatic check;
[檢察] procuratorial work;
檢察官 attorney; prosecutor; public prosecutor;
~ 地方檢察官 district attorney;
~ 特別檢察官 special prosecutor;
~ 州檢察官 state attorney;
檢察機關 prosecution organization;
檢察員 procurator;
~ 助理檢察員 assistant procurator;
檢察院 procuratorate;
~ 高級人民檢察院 higher people's procuratorate;
~ 最高人民檢察院 supreme people's procuratorte;
檢察長 procurator-general;
~ 副檢察長 deputy procurator-general; solicitor general;
[檢出] checkout;
自動檢出 automatic checkout;
[檢錯] error detection;
[檢點] (1) check; examine; (2) cautious about

what one says or does;
檢點行李 have one's luggage examined;
行為不檢點 indiscreet in one's conduct;

[檢定] appraise; verify;
生物檢定 bioassay;

[檢舉] accuse; impeach; inform against; report on the guilt of others; report to the authorities;
檢舉箱 accusation letter box;

[檢控] prosecute;
檢控程序 prosecution procedures;

[檢票員] ticket-taker;

[檢視] check up; examine; view;

[檢索] look-up; retrieval; search; searching;
檢索機制 retrieval mechanism;
檢索碼 retrieval code;
檢索命令語言 retrieval command language;
檢索語言 retrieval language;
檢索中心 retrieval centre;
檢索字 search word;
詞素檢索 morpheme index;
地址檢索 address search;
光學檢索 optical search;
內容檢索 content retrieval;
手工檢索 manual searching;
中斷檢索 interrupt search;
資料檢索 data retrieval;

[檢討] (1) review; (2) self-criticism;
全面檢討 comprehensive review;

[檢修] examine and repair; overhaul; overhauling; recondition; service;
檢修房屋 overhaul the building;
徹底檢修 thorough overhaul;
大檢修 overhaul;
定期檢修 regular overhauling;
年度檢修 annual overhaul;

[檢驗] checkout; check-up; examine; inspect; inspection; survey; test; verify;
檢驗器 checker; proofer;
~電容檢驗器 condenser checker;
~管芯檢驗器 stem checker;
~奇偶檢驗器 parity checker;
~懸式檢驗器 overhead proofer;
~自動檢驗器 automatic checker;
檢驗師 assayer;
檢驗台 proofer;
~櫥櫃式檢驗台 cupboard proofer;
~中間檢驗台 intermediate proofer;
~最終檢驗台 final proofer;
經受時間的檢驗 pass the test of time;
預測檢驗 prognosis;
最終檢驗 final inspection;

[檢疫] quarantine;
檢疫管制 quarantine restrictions;
檢疫所 quarantine station;
~動物檢疫所 animal quarantine station;
~植物檢疫所 plant quarantine station;

[檢閱] inspect; review troops;

[檢字] word indexing;
檢字表 index of Chinese characters;
檢字法 indexing system for Chinese characters;

安檢 security check;
抽檢 spot-check;
翻檢 glance through and check;
體檢 have a general check-up;

jian

【裥】 pleats of a skirt;

jian

【謇】 (1) stammer; stutter; (2) speak out boldly;

[謇謇] faithful; loyal;
謇謇直言 outspoken in speech;

[謇諤] candid; frank; outspoken;

jian

【蹇】 (1) crippled; lame; (2) slow; (3) feeble; weak; (4) difficult; hard; (5) haughty; (6) a surname;

jian

【瞼】 eyelid;

[瞼板] tarsus;
瞼板膜 tarsal membrane;
瞼板軟化 tarsomalacia;

[瞼肥厚] blepharopachynsis;

[瞼粉瘤] blepharoatheroma;

[瞼角炎] blepharitis angularis;

[瞼痙攣] blepharism;
症狀性瞼痙攣 symptomatic blepharospasm;
自發性瞼痙攣 essential blepharospasm;

[瞼內翻] entropion;
痙攣性瞼內翻 spastic entropion;

[瞼軟骨] ciliary cartilages;

[瞼水腫] hydroblepharon;

[瞼外翻] ectropion;
老年性瞼外翻 senile ectropion;
麻痺性瞼外翻 paralytic ectropion;

[瞼腺炎] sty;

[瞼炎] palpebritis;
[瞼緣炎] blepharitis;
脂溢性瞼緣炎 seborrheic blepharitis;

巨瞼 macroblepharia;
眼瞼 eyelid;

jian

【簡】 (1) brief; simple; simplified; (2) bamboo slips; (3) letter; (4) choose; select;
[簡報] brief report; briefing; bulletin;
年度簡報 annual bulletin;
[簡本] abridged edition; concise edition;
[簡編] (1) concise edition; (2) short course;
[簡便] abridged edition; handy; simple and convenient;
簡便的方法 handy way;
簡便易行 simple and easy to do;
[簡併] degenerate; degeneration;
簡併度 degeneracy;
~ 波模簡併度 mode degeneracy;
~ 二重簡併度 twofold degeneracy;
~ 二重空間簡併度 twofold spatial degeneracy;
~ 空間簡併度 spatial degeneracy;
~ 任意簡併度 arbitrary degeneracy;
~ 三重簡併度 three-fold degeneracy;
~ 自旋簡併度 spin degeneracy;
二度簡併 doubly degenerate;
三度簡併 triply degenerate;
[簡稱] (1) abbreviated form of a name; abbreviation; shorter form; (2) be called sth for short;
[簡單] (1) plain; simple; uncomplicated; (2) commonplace; ordinary; (3) casual; oversimplified;
簡單並列連詞 simple coordinating conjunction;
簡單不定式 simple infinitive;
簡單詞 simple word;
~ 簡單詞幹
簡單從屬連詞 simple subordinator;
簡單粗暴 do things in a crude, over-simplified way; over-simplification and crudeness; over-simplified and crude; simple and crude;
簡單動詞 simple verb;
簡單過去式 simple past;
簡單化 simplify; simplify matters;
簡單介詞 simple preposition;
簡單句 simple sentence;
簡單明瞭 brief and clear; concise and explicit; in words of one syllable; simple and clear; terse and perspicuous;
簡單淺顯 simple and plain;
簡單數詞 simple numeral;
簡單形式 simple form;
簡單易行 simple and easy to do; simple and practicable;
不簡單 (1) not simple; rather complicated; (2) marvelous; remarkable;
~ 很不簡單 it's by no means simple;
情節簡單 have a simple plot;
頭腦簡單 simple-minded;
[簡短] brief; short;
簡短的 laconic;
簡短扼要 brief and to the point; short and sweet; short and to the point; short but sweet;
簡短乾脆 short and snappy;
簡短鏗鏘 short and snappy;
簡短有力 brief and forceful; punchy;
[簡化] simplification; simplify;
簡化工序 simplify working processes;
簡化漢字 (1) simplify Chinese characters; (2) simplified Chinese characters;
簡化手續 simplify the process;
電路簡化 circuit simplification;
力求簡化 strive for simplification;
人工簡化 artificial simplification;
生物簡化 biotic simplification;
[簡捷] simple and direct; forthright;
[簡潔] brevity; concise; pithy; succinct; terse;
簡潔生動 terse and lively;
簡潔易懂 concise and easy to understand;
説話簡潔 concise in speech;
文筆簡潔 write in a concise style;
文體簡潔 write with pregnant brevity;
言貴簡潔 brevity is the soul of wit;
~ 言貴簡潔，文貴精練 brevity is the soul of wit;
[簡介] blurb; brief introduction; summarized account; synopsis;
[簡括] brief but comprehensive; compendious;
[簡歷] curriculum vitae;
一份簡歷 a curriculum vitae;
[簡練] brevity; pithy; punchy; succinct; terse;
簡練揣摩 select and examine thoroughly;
[簡陋] simple and crude;
設備簡陋 be simply equipped;

因陋就簡 adapt oneself to the available conditions; do things in a simple and thrifty way; do things simply and thriftily; make do with whatever is available; make use of what is available; make use of the available conditions on grounds of frugality;

[簡略] brief; simple; sketchy;

[簡慢] brusque; negligent; short;

簡慢的 brusque;

~簡慢的態度 brusque manner;

[簡明] concise; simple and clear;

簡明扼要 clear and concise; concise and to the point; in a nutshell; short and sweet; terse and concise;

簡明易懂 clear and easy to understand;

[簡樸] plain; simple and unadorned;

生活簡樸 live a simple and frugal life;

文筆簡樸 have a plain style of writing;

語言簡樸 plain in language;

[簡譜] numbered musical notation;

[簡釋] brief explanation;

[簡述] resume; sketch;

[簡體字] simplified Chinese characters;

[簡圖] abbreviated drawing; diagram; sketch;

[簡訊] news in brief;

[簡要] brief; concise and to the point;

[簡易] (1) simple and easy; (2) simply equipped;

[簡約] brief; concise; sketchy;

[簡章] general regulations;

[簡政] streamline administration;

簡政放權 streamline administration and delegate more powers to the lower levels;

[簡直] actually; all right; almost; almost exactly; at all; borders on; complete; downright; enough; fairly; hardly; literally; little short of; might as well; nothing but; nothing less than; nothing short of; scarcely; sheer; simply; so...as to; so much so that; so...that; such...as to; such...that; to the point of; veritable;

簡直不可思議 it is virtually unimaginable;

簡直難以想像 it is hardly conceivable;

簡直太不像話 it is so unreasonable;

從簡 conform to the principle of simplicity;

繁簡 the complicated and the simple;

苟簡 simple and careless;

精簡 retrench; simplify;

木簡 inscribed wooden slip;

手簡 informal personal note to a friend;

書簡 letters;

竹簡 bamboo slip;

jian

【繭】 (1) chrysalis; cocoon; (2) callus;

[繭綢] pongee; tussah silk;

[繭質] cocoon quality;

jian

【鐧】 a kind of ancient weapon; mace;

jian

【鹻】 alkali;

jian

【譾】 mentally shallow; superficial;

jian

【鹼】 alkali; lye;

[鹼量計] alkalimeter;

[鹼土] alkaline earth;

生物鹼 alkaloid;

jian⁴

jian

【件】 a piece of;

[件號] part number; piece number;

[件件俱全] all are complete;

案件 case; law case; legal case;

擺件 display pieces;

部件 assembly; components; parts;

抄件 copy; duplicate;

附件 (1) annex; appendix; (2) enclosure; (3) accessories; attachment;

稿件 contribution; manuscript;

工件 work; work piece;

構件 (1) component; member; (2) component part;

固件 firmware;

函件 correspondence; letters;

機件 parts; works;

急件 urgent document;

扣件 fastener; fastening;

來件 parcel received;

零件 spare parts;

密件 classified document; confidential paper;

配件 (1) parts; (2) replacement;

器件 parts of an apparatus; parts of an appliance;

軟件 software;

事件 event; incident;

條件 (1) condition; factor; (2) qualification; requirement; (3) condition; situation; state;
文件 documents; papers;
物件 article; thing;
信件 letters; mail;
要件 (1) important document; (2) important condition;
硬件 hardware;
郵件 mail; postal matter;
元件 component; element;
軋件 rolled steel strip;
證件 certificate; credentials;
製件 part;
鑄件 cast; casting;
組件 module;
作件 work; workpiece;

jian

【見】 (1) catch sight of; see; (2) appear to be; show evidence of; (3) refer to; see; vide; (4) call on; meet; see; (5) opinion; view;

[見報] appear in the newspaper; be reported in the newspaper;

[見背] die; pass away;

[見財起意] at the sight of money evil ideas rise in one's head; think of stealing on seeing sb's money;

[見長] expert in; good at;

[見得] appear; know; seem;

[見底] bottom out;
一瓢見底 come to the bottom of a bowl with one spoon;

[見地] insight; judgement;
有見地 have a good head on one's shoulders; know enough to come in out of the rain;

[見風使舵] find out how the wind blows; jump on the bandwagon; sail with every shift of wind; see how the wind blows; see which way the cat jumps; trim one's sails; wait for the cat to jump;
見風使舵的人 chameleon;

[見怪] mind; take offence; take sth amiss;
見怪不怪—其怪自敗 become inured to the unusual; facing the fearful without fear — its fearfulness disappears; what once seemed bewildering will no longer be so;
別見怪 don't be offended;
多見不怪 use lessens marvel;
幸勿見怪 I hope that you will not be offended; kindly forgive me; kindly forgive my lack of respect;

[見鬼] absurd; bugger; fantastic; hell; preposterous;
見鬼了 hell's bells; hell's teeth;
見鬼去吧 cram it; go to Halifax; go to hell; see sb blowed before; see sb damed before; see sb dead before; see sb hanged before; see sb in hell before; see sb somewhere before; shove it;
活見鬼 it's sheer fantasy; sheer nonsense; simply absurd; the deuce; utterly impossible; you're imagining things;
見他的鬼 the devil takes him;
真見鬼 son of a bitch; sun of a gun;

[見好] get better; mend;

[見後] see below;

[見機] according to circumstances; as befits the occasion; as the opportunity arises;
見機而作 take advantage of an opportunity that comes one's way;
見機行事 act according to circumstances; act as circumstances dictate; act as the occasion demands; act on seeing an opportunity; adapt oneself to circumstances; do as one sees fit; play sth by ear; play to the score; profit by the occasion; see one's chance and act; use one's own judgment and do what one deemed best;

[見教] favour me with your advice; instruct me;

[見解] idea; opinion; thesis; understanding; view;
見解獨特 have a peculiar view;
見解通達 hold sensible views; show good sense;
持不同見解 hold a different view;

[見景] what one sees;
見景傷情 become beset with memories in one's old haunts and fall into one's melancholy condition again;
見景生情 be moved by what one sees; memories revive at the sight of familiar places; the circumstances excite one's feelings; the scene evokes memories of the past;

[見利] at the sight of profit;

見利棄義 sell one's birthright for a mess of pottage;
見利思義 think of righteousness on seeing gain;
見利妄為 lose sight of everything else in view of a present advantage; stop at nothing to gain profit;
見利忘義 disregard moral principles in pursuit of profit; forget all moral principles at the sight of profits; forget friendship for profit; forget honour at the prospect of profits;

[見諒] excuse me; forgive me;

[見獵心喜] at seeing the hunters one feels delighted; anxious to display one's skill; thrill to see one's favourite sport and itch to have a go;

[見面] (1) meet; meet sb in the face; see; (2) contact; link;
見面分一半 get half of it on seeing it;
見面會 meet-and-greet;
見面禮 a gift presented to sb at the first meeting; a gift such as is usually given to sb on first meeting him;
按約定時間見面 meet at the agreed time;
避不見面 avoid meeting sb;

[見票即付] payable at sight; payable on demand; payable to bearer;

[見前] see above;

[見錢眼開] be moved at the sight of money; be tempted by money; care for nothing but money; open the eyes wide at the sight of money－greedy of money; one's eyes grow round with delight at the sight of money;

[見俏] in great demand;

[見人] see others;
見人之失，知己之失 do not ask for whom the bells toll, they may toll for you;
沒臉見人 too ashamed to face anyone;
無臉見人 feel too ashamed to face people; fly from the face of men; have no face to show to any man;
~ 羞得沒臉見人 hide one's face in shame;
羞面見人 feel ashamed to see others;

[見仁見智] different people, different views; different people have different views; each according to his lights; opinions differ;

[見識] (1) enrich one's experience; widen one's knowledge; (2) experience; knowledge; sensibleness;
見識短 ill-informed;
~ 見識短淺 lacking knowledge and experience; shallow;
見識廣 knowledgeable; well-informed;
~ 見識廣博 have extensive experience; wide in experience;
廣見博識 a wide scope of knowledge; have a rich experience and extensive knowledge;
見多識廣 be richly equipped with general knowledge; experienced and knowledgeable; have a wide range of experience; have great experience; have wide experience and extensive knowledge; know a thing or two; know one's way round; up to a thing or two; with wide experience;
陋見淺識 scratch the surface; understand very little about sth;
沒見識 inexperienced and ignorant;
有見識 farsighted; have an analytical mind; of rich experience;
長見識 broaden one's horizon; gain experience; increase one's knowledge; widen one's knowledge;

[見事生風] arouse trouble with very little cause; create disturbance under a slight excuse; stir up trouble with very little cause;

[見勢不妙] find the situation unfavourable; realize the situation is going against; see bad weather ahead; see that matters are in a bad way;

[見誰學誰] act the ape;

[見死] seeing sb in mortal danger;
見死不救 bear to see sb die without trying to save him; do nothing to save sb from dying; do nothing to save sb from ruin; fold one's arms and see sb die; fold one's hands and see sb die; leave one to sink; leave one to swim; leave sb in the lurch; not to help a dying man; not to rescue those in mortal danger; refuse to help sb in real trouble; see sb in mortal danger without lifting a finger to save him; shut one's eyes to people who are dying; stand by when sb is in peril;

stand calmly by while another is drowning;
見死不懼 fearless in face of death; not be dismayed at the prospect of death;

[見兔顧犬] it is not too late to snatch the opportunity at once; take instant advantage of an opportunity that comes only once in a long while; turn to order a dog to pursue and capture the hare after having seen it;

[見外] regard sb as an outsider;
幸勿見外 don't treat me as a stranger please;

[見旺] doing brisk business; sell well;

[見微知著] a straw shows which way the wind blows; from one small clue one can see what is to come; from the first small beginnings one can see how things will develop; one may see day at a little hole; recognize the world through observation of the part;

[見聞] information; knowledge; what one sees and hears;
見聞不廣 have only limited knowledge;
見聞廣 well-informed;
見聞廣博 have extensive knowledge; well-informed;
大長見聞 a great eye-opener to sb;
多見博聞 have extensive knowledge; have seen and heard much; widely experienced;
寡見少聞 have limited knowledge; have seen few and heard little; ignorant and ill-informed;
廣見博聞 widely experienced;
擴大見聞 broaden one's horizons;
親見親聞 see with one's own eyes and hear with one's own ears;
囿於見聞 be handicapped by lack of knowledge and experience;
增長見聞 broaden one's knowledge;

[見物] see things;
見物不見人 ignore the human factor and see only the material factor; see things but not people — see only material factors to the neglect of human ones;
見物傷情 grief-stricken at the sight of things; the sight of familiar objects fill one with infinite melancholy;
見物思人 seeing the thing, one thinks of the person — the thing reminds one of its owner;

[見習] learn on the job; on probation;
見習期 novitiate; probationary period;
見習生 apprentice;
~ 司法見習生 judicial apprentice;

[見笑] (1) incur ridicule; (2) laugh at;
見笑大方 be laughed at by experts; become a laughingstock of the learned people; expose oneself to ridicule; give an expert cause for laughter; incur the ridicule of experts; make a laughingstock of oneself before experts;
見笑於人 a laughingstock; be laughed at;

[見效] become effective; produce the desired result;
迄未見效 so far there hasn't been any result;

[見性] see the Buddha-like nature;
指心見性 behold the Buddha-like nature within oneself;

[見異思遷] a rolling stone; change about; change one's mind the moment one sees sth new; fickle; inconstant; vagaries of the mind; whimsical;
見異思遷，一事無成 a rolling stone gathers no moss;

[見義勇為] act bravely for a just cause; do boldly what is righteous; help a lame dog over a stile; never hesitate where good is to be done; ready to take up the cudgels for a just cause;

[見宥] excuse; forgive;
尚希見宥 please accept my apologies;

[見於] refer to; see;

[見證] testimony; witness;

拜見 (1) pay a formal visit; (2) meet one's senior or superior;
鄙見 my humble opinion;
陛見 have an audience with the emperor;
不見 (1) not meet; not see; (2) be missing; disappear;
參見 (1) see also; (2) pay one's respects to...;
常見 common;
朝見 have an audience with;
陳見 outmoded ideas;
成見 preconceived idea; prejudice;
創見 original idea;
定見 definite opinion; set view;

J

洞見 see very clearly;
短見 (1) short-sighted view; (2) suicide;
高見 your brilliant idea;
管見 my humble opinion; my limited understanding;
罕見 rare; rarely seen;
回見 see you later;
會見 meet sb;
己見 one's own views; personal opinions;
接見 grant an interview to; receive sb;
僅見 rarely seen;
晉見 have an audience with;
進見 have an audience with;
覲見 present oneself before a sovereign; visit a sacred place;
看見 cath sight of; see;
可見 it is clear that;
窺見 cath a glimpse of;
夢見 dream about; see in a dream;
謬見 absurdity; erroneous views;
目見 see for oneself;
碰見 meet unexpectedly; run into;
偏見 bias; prejudice;
瞥見 catch sight of; get a glimpse of;
起見 for the purpose of; in order to;
淺見 humble opinion; superficial view;
瞧見 catch sight of; see;
請見 beg for an audience; request an interview;
求見 ask for an interview; request an audience;
日見 day by day; with each passing day;
少見 rarely seen;
識見 knowledge and experience;
私見 (1) personal prejudice; (2) personal views;
聽見 hear;
推見 imagine; infer;
習見 commonly seen;
鮮見 be rarely seen;
顯見 clearly show;
相見 imagine; reckon;
謁見 call on; have an audience with;
意見 (1) idea; opinion; suggestion; (2) differing opinion; objection;
臆見 subjective view;
引見 introduce; present;
預見 foresee; predict;
遇見 come across; meet;
遠見 foresight; vision;
再見 good-bye; see you again;
召見 call in;
政見 political view;
主見 ideas of one's own; set view;
撞見 meet by chance; run across;
拙見 my humble opinion;
灼見 profound view;
卓見 brilliant idea; excellent opinion;
足見 it serves to show;

jian

【建】 (1) build; construct; erect; (2) establish; found; set up;

［建材］ building materials;

［建功］ do a deed of merit;
累建奇功 score signal successes again and again;
屢建功勞 distinguish oneself many times;
屢建奇功 establish unusual merits repeatedly; score signal successes again and again;
屢建戰功 win many victories;

［建國］ (1) establish a state; found a state; (2) build up a country;

［建好］ finish building;

［建交］ establish diplomatic relations;

［建立］ build; establish; found; set up;
建立邦交 establish diplomatic relations;
建立信用 build one's credit;
建立友誼 establish friendship;

［建設］ build; construct; develop;
建設單位 organization of construction;
建設公債 construction bond;
建設規模 the scale of contruction;
建設基金 construction fund;
建設經濟學 economics of construction;
建設項目 construction project;
建設型公關 constructive type of public relations;
建設性意見 constructive suggestion;
建設資金 construction fund;
基本建設 capital construction;
硬體建設 physical infrastructure;

［建樹］ attainment; contribute; make a contribution; score an achievement;
毫無建樹 have nothing to show for;
有所建樹 have sth to show for;

［建議］ advise; proposal; propose; proposition; recommend; suggest; suggestion;
採納建議 adopt a proposal;
反建議 counterproposal;
供選擇的建議 alternative proposition;
極力建議 strongly recommend;
接受建議 accede to a proposal; accept a proposal;
提出建議 make a recommendation; make

suggestions; offer a proposal; put up a proposal;
一點建議 a suggestion; a piece of advice;
一個建議 a piece of advice; a word of advice;
一項建議 a suggestion;

[建造] (1) formation; (2) build; construct; form; make;
建造費用 cost of construction;
建造者 builder;

[建制] organizational system;

[建築] (1) build; construct; erect; (2) building; edifice; structure;
建築承包商 building contractor;
建築工 builder;
建築工程 building engineering;
建築工地 building site;
建築工人 builder; construction worker;
建築公司 constructor;
建築環境 building environment; built environment;
建築技術經濟 technological economy of architecture;
建築節能技術 energy saving buildings technology;
建築節能經濟 economy of architectural energy;
建築經濟 economics of architecture;
建築樓房 construct a building;
建築美學 aesthetics in architecture;
建築面積 built-up area;
建築企業 architectural enterprise;
建築橋樑 build a bridge;
建築群 architectural complex;
~古建築群 ancient architectural complex;
建築商 builder; contractor;
建築師 architect;
~一個建築師 an architect;
~總建築師 chief architect;
建築鐵路 build a railway;
建築物 building; edifice; shelter; structure;
~拆除建築物 knock down a building; pull down a building; tear down a building;
~拆毀建築物 demolish a building; destroy a building;
~低矮的建築物 low building;
~附屬建築物 annex;
~蓋建築物 erect a building; put up a building;
~個別建築物 individual building;
~尖角形的建築物 angular building;
~一排建築物 a block of buildings; a line of buildings; a row of buildings;
~一群建築物 a clump of buildings; a complex of buildings;
建築學 architecture science;
建築業 construction industry;
單層建築 one-story building; single-storey building;
多層建築 multi-tier building;
房屋建築 house building;
附屬建築 outbuilding;
高層建築 highprise;
工業化建築 industrialized building;
公共建築 public building;
古建築 ancient architecture; ancient monument; historic building;
宏偉的建築 stately buildings;
抗震建築 antiseismic structure;
臨時建築 temporary building;
上層建築 superstructure; top-out;
水上建築 water dwelling;
土木建築 civil construction;
學校建築 school building;
圓形建築 rotunda;

承建 contract to build;
重建 rebuild; reestablish;
籌建 prepare to construct or establish sth;
創建 establish; found;
封建 feudal; feudalism;
改建 rebuild; reconstruct;
基建 capital construction;
擴建 extend; extension;
興建 build; construct;
營建 build; construct;

jian

【健】 (1) healthy; strong; (2) strengthen; toughen;

[健步] walk with vigorous strides;
健步如飛 at a good bat; fleet of foot; swift of foot; walk as if on wings; walk fast and vigorously; walk with much bounce; walk with springy steps; windfooted; with flying feet;

[健兒] (1) valiant fighter; (2) good athlete; skilled athlete;

[健將] ace; master sportsman; top-notch player;
足球健將 football ace;

J

[健康] as fit as a fiddle; enjoy good health; have good health; healthy; in a good condition; in a state of good health; in condition; in good fettle; in good health; in good looks; in good nick; in good shape; in the pink; wellness;
健康產業 health industry;
健康長壽 enjoy good health and live long; stay healthy and live long;
健康成長 grow up healthy and sound;
健康發展 develop healthily;
健康風險 health risk;
健康檢查 a check-up; a health examination; a physical examination;
健康人格 healthy personality;
健康素質 physical fitness levels;
健康危害 health hazard;
健康威脅 health threat;
健康問題 health problem;
健康證明 medical certificate;
健康忠告 health warning;
保持健康 keep fit; keep health; maintain health;
保護健康 protect the health of...;
公共健康 public health;
恢復健康 recover one's health; regain one's health;
獲得健康 secure good health;
身體健康 in fine health; in good health; one's health;
~注意身體健康 guard one's health;
身心健康 sound in mind and body;
失去健康 lose one's health;
思想健康 sound in mind;
損害健康 damage one's health; impair one's health;
危害健康 endanger one's health;
影響健康 affect one's health;
有礙健康 be harmful to health;
有損健康 compromise one's health;
有益健康 benefit one's health; favour health; good for health;
增進健康 improve health; promote health;
祝你健康 cheers; wish you good health;

[健美] strong and handsome; vigorous and graceful;
健美操 body-building exercise; calisthenics;
健美體操 calisthenics;
健美運動 body building;
健美者 body builder;

[健全] (1) able-bodied; perfect; sane; sound; (2) integrity; perfect; regular; (3) improve; perfect; strengthen;
不健全 defective; imperfect; not well organized; unsound;
身心健全 sound in mind and body;
體制健全 perfect in system;
頭腦健全 in right mind; of sound mind;
制度健全 have regular system;

[健身] body-building;
健身操 body building exercise; calisthenics; daily dozen;
~有氧健身操 aerobics;
健身單車 exercise bike;
健身房 gym; gymnasium;
~去健身房 go to the gym;
健身教練 trainer;
~私人健身教練 personal trainer;
健身俱樂部 health club;
健身狂 gym bunny;
健身器 body-building apparatus; trainer;
~多功能健身器 cross-trainer;
健身球 health ball;
健身運動 body-building exercise;
~有氧健身運動 aerobics;
健身者 body builder;

[健談] good talker; loquacity;
健談的 loquacious;
~健談的人 talkative person;

[健忘] forgetful; have a bad memory; have a memory like a sieve; have a poor memory; have a short memory;
健忘症 amnesia;
~得了健忘症 suffer from amnesia;
~聽覺性健忘症 acousmatamnesia;

[健旺] healthy and vigorous;

[健在] alive; alive and kicking; still living and in good health;
堂上健在 both parents are healthily living; parents are still living and in good health;

[健壯] hale and hearty; healthy and strong;
健壯的 hefty; lusty;
健壯如牛 as strong as a horse;
體格健壯 of a vigorous and healthy constitution; sturdy;

保健 health care; health protection;
剛健 robust; strong and energetic;
矯健 strong and vigorous;
康健 healthy; in good health;

強健 make strong and healthy; stout; strong and healthy;
遒健 strong; vigorous;
穩健 firm; steady;
雄健 energetic; robust; vigorous;
壯健 strong and healthy; sturdy;

jian

【間】 (1) opening; space in between; (2) separate; (3) sow discord; (4) thin out;
[間不容髮] by a hairbreadth; by a hair's breadth; within a hair of; with an ace of; within an inch of;
[間不容息] in a split second;
[間諜] agent; secret agent; spook; spy;
間諜活動 espionage; espionage activities; spying;
~反間諜活動 counterespionage;
間諜軟件 spyware;
間諜首腦 spy-master;
反間諜 counterspy;
空中間諜 spy-in-the-sky;
雙重間諜 double agent;
[間斷] be disconnected; be interrupted; hiatus; interval;
間斷性 discontinuity;
~磁間斷性 magnetic discontinuity;
~簡單間斷性 simple discontinuity;
~無窮間斷性 infinite discontinuity;
[間格] compartment;
[間隔] gap; distance; intermission; interval; region; space;
間隔重覆 epanalepsis;
間隔號 separation dot;
黑間隔 black interval;
擴增間隔 augmental interval;
頻道間隔 channel interval;
實用間隔 practical layout;
位間隔 bit interval;
[間或] now and then; occasionally; once in a while; sometimes;
[間架] ledge;
[間接] indirect; secondhand;
間接賓語 indirect object;
間接陳述句 indirect statement;
間接翻譯 indirect translation;
間接格 oblique case;
間接祈使句 indirect imperative sentence;
間接性施為 indirect illocution;
間接選擇疑問句 indirect alternative interrogation;
間接言語行為 indirect speech act;
間接疑問句 indirect question;
間接引語 indirect quotation;
[間離] alienate; alienation;
間離效果 alienation effect;
[間隙] (1) intermit; intermission; (2) clearance; (3) interstice;
安全間隙 safe clearance; safety clearance;
八面體間隙 octahedral interstice;
充分間隙 ample clearance;
次性間隙 secondary interstices;
頂部間隙 crest clearance;
角形間隙 angular clearance;
接點間隙 contact clearance;
徑向間隙 diametral clearance;
可調間隙 adjustable clearance;
拉延間隙 drawing clearance;
兩面間隙 bilateral clearance;
氣缸間隙 cylinder clearance;
切屑間隙 chip clearance;
容許間隙 allow clearance;
四面體間隙 tetrahedral interstice;
圓周間隙 circumferential clearance;
震動間隙 bumping clearance;
[間歇] blank; dwell; intermission;
間歇地 at bits and starts; at fits and starts;
間歇泉 geyser;
補償間歇 compensatory pause;
脈衝序列間歇 impulse-train pause;

當間 in the centre; in the middle;
反間 sow distrust among one's enemies;
離間 come between; drive a wedge between; sow seeds of discord;
無間 (1) very close to each other; (2) continuously; without interruption; (3) not distinguish;
相間 alternate with;

jian

【閒】 same as 間;

jian

【毽】 shuttlecock;
[毽子] shuttlecock;

jian

【腱】 tendon;
[腱斷裂] disinsertion;
[腱反射] tendon jerk; tendon reflex;
[腱反應] tendon reaction;
[腱鞘] tendon sheath;
腱鞘囊腫 ganglion; ganglia;

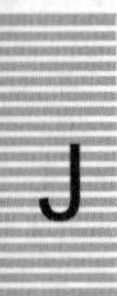

彌漫性腱鞘囊腫 diffuse ganglion;
原發性腱鞘囊腫 primary ganglion;
腱鞘炎 tenosynovitis; tenovaginitis;
~傳染性腱鞘炎 infectious tenosynovitis;
肥厚性腱鞘炎 tenosynovitis hypertrophica;
~化膿性腱鞘炎 purulent tenovaginitis;
結節性腱鞘炎 nodular tenosynovitis;
淋病性腱鞘炎 gonorrheal tenosynovitis;
淋球菌性腱鞘炎 gonococcal tenosynovitis;
肉芽性腱鞘炎 tenosynovitis granulosa;

[腱鞘腫] thecal cyst;
[腱軟骨] tendon cartilage;
[腱炎] tendinitis;

jian

【僭】 assume; usurp;
[僭建物] illegal structure;
[僭越] overstep one's authority;

jian

【漸】 by degrees; gradually; little by little; step by step;
[漸變] gradation; gradual change;
漸變群 cline; continuum;
[漸層法] climax;
[漸漸] a bit at a time; be grown to; begin to; bit by bit; by degrees; by inches; fall to; get to; gradually; inch by inch; little by little; piece by piece; step by step; step-by-step;
[漸降法] anticlimax;
[漸近線] asymptote;
垂直漸近線 vertical asymptote;
拐漸近線 inflectional asymptote;
回環漸近線 loop asymptote;
拋物漸近線 parabolic asymptote;
上漸近線 upper asymptote;
水平漸近線 horizontal asymptote;
增益漸近線 gain asymptote;
[漸進] advance gradually; progress step by step;

杜漸 destroy sth before it becomes apparent;
日漸 day by day; with each passing day;
逐漸 gradually; little by little;

jian

【監】 (1) official position in former times; (2) government establishment; (3) eunuch;

太監 eunuch;

jian

【劍】 sword;
[劍拔弩張] at daggers drawn; at sword's points; dagger's drawing; fingers on the triggers; in a blustering and aggressive manner; rattle one's sabres; ready for a showdown; ready to jump at each other's throat; sabre-rattling; with swords drawn and bows bent;
[劍齒] sabre-toothed;
劍齒虎 sabre-toothed tiger;
劍齒象 stegodon;
[劍膽琴心] the courage of a warrior and the soul of a musician;
[劍花] beancaper;
[劍及履及] perform a task with full vigour and urgency;
[劍戟森森] harbour numerous intentions;
[劍客] fencer; swordsman;
[劍蘭] gladiolus;
[劍龍] stegosaur;
[劍氣珠光] the vigour of a sword and the brightness of a pearl — said of talents;
[劍鞘] sheath;
納劍入鞘 sheathe the sword;
[劍術] fencing; swordsmanship;
花劍劍術 foil fencing;
佩劍劍術 sabre fencing;
[劍俠] knight-errant; swordsman who champions the cause of the downtrodden;

按劍 grasp one's sword;
拔劍 draw a sword; whip out a sword;
寶劍 double-edged sword; treasured sword;
短劍 dagger;
花劍 foil;
擊劍 fence;
蒲劍 calamus leaves;
雙刃劍 rapier; two-edged sword;

jian

【澗】 mountain stream;
[澗流] gill; ravine stream;

山澗 mountain creek; mountain stream;
溪澗 mountain brook;
谿澗 mountain brook;

jian

【箭】 arrow;

[箭靶] target;

[箭不虛發] not a single arrow misses its target;

箭無虛發 no arrow is shot in vain; none of the arrows misses its mark; not a single arrow misses its target;

[箭步] a sudden big stride forward;

側弓箭步 lateral lunge, sideways lunge;

[箭如] arrows come like;

箭如飛蝗 arrows come like flights of locusts; the arrows flow like locusts on the wing;

箭如急雨 arrows fall like pelting rain;

箭如流星 the arrow flows forth like a comet across the sky;

箭如雨下 a shower of arrows; arrows descend like a shower; arrows fall like drops of rain; arrows rain down; the arrows drop down like rainfall; the arrows fall like rain; the arrows fly thick as rain;

箭如驟雨 arrows fall thick as rain; the arrows flow forth in a sudden fierce shower;

[箭頭] arrowhead; arrow point; arrow tip;

綠燈箭頭 green arrow;

閃光指示箭頭 flashing arrow;

雙箭頭 double-head arrow;

危險箭頭 danger arrow;

行車箭頭 direction arrow;

一個箭頭 an arrow;

[箭弦] arrows and bowstrings;

箭在弦上 like an arrow on the bowstring; there can be no turning back;

~箭在弦上，不得不發 be poised to strike; the arrow is on the bowstring;

如箭離弦 like an arrow released from the bowstring; streak off like an arrow from the string of a bow;

如箭在弦 as an arrow on the straining cord — ready to start; in a point of no return; like an arrow in on the bow — poised to strike;

~如箭在絃，一觸即發 like an arrow in the bow, that can be unleashed at any time;

似箭離弦 fly like an arrow from the bow;

暗箭 a sneak attack; an arrow shot from hiding;

毒箭 poisoned arrow;

弓箭 bow and arrow;

火箭 fire arrow; rocket;

寬頭箭 broad arrow;

冷箭 a sneak attack; an arrow shot from hiding;

射箭 archery;

響箭 whistling arrow;

一把箭 a sheaf of arrows;

一箭 an arrow;

一束箭 a sheaf of arrows;

一支箭 an arrow;

折箭 break an arrow;

jian

【賤】 (1) cheap; inexpensive; low-priced; (2) humble; lowly; (3) base; despicable; low-down;

[賤狗] pariah dog;

[賤民] people of a lower social status than the common people;

[賤如土苴] as cheap as dirt; dirt cheap;

卑賤 (1) lowly; (2) mean and low;

低賤 humble; low and degrading;

貧賤 poor and lowly;

輕賤 despise; mean and worthless; underestimate;

微賤 humble; lowly;

猥賤 base; humble; lowly;

下賤 base; low; mean;

jian

【踐】 (1) trample; tread upon; (2) carry out; fulfil; perform;

[踐踏] make havoc of; trample on; trample underfoot; tread on;

自相踐踏 trample each other down; trample on each other;

[踐約] keep a promise; keep an appointment;

蹂踐 stamp down; trample down;

實踐 carry out; practise; put into practice;

jian

【諫】 admonish; remonstrate;

[諫諍] criticize sb's faults frankly;

進諫 remonstrate with the monarch;

諍諫 admonish; criticize sb's faults frankly;

jian

【餞】 (1) farewell dinner; farewell lunch; (2) send off; (3) present as gift;

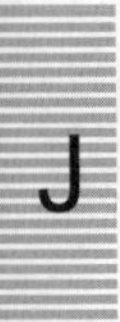

［餞別］ give a farewell dinner;
治酒餞別 prepare a farewell banquet;
［餞行］ give a farewell dinner;

蜜餞 candied fruit; preserved fruit;

jian
【鍵】 key;
［鍵控］ keying;
鍵控器 keyer;
～頻移鍵控器 frequency keyer;
～自動點鍵控器 automatic dot keyer;
差動鍵控 differential keying;
幅移鍵控 amplitude shift keying;
［鍵聯］ binding;
分子鍵聯 molecular binding;
化學鍵聯 chemical binding;
極性鍵聯 polar binding;
晶體鍵聯 crystal binding;
弱鍵聯 low binding;
異極鍵聯 heteropolar binding;
原子鍵聯 atomic binding;
［鍵盤］ fingerboard; keyboard;
鍵盤操作員 keyboarder;
鍵盤式計算機 keyboard computer;
鍵盤手 keyboardist;
鍵盤輸入 keyboard entry;
～鍵盤輸入系統 key entry system;
鍵盤鎖定 keyboard lockout;
鍵盤樂器 keyboard instruments;
電腦鍵盤 computer keyboard;
分類鍵盤 classification keyboard;
輔助鍵盤 companion keyboard; keypad;
小鍵盤 keypad;
字符鍵盤 figure keyboard;
字母收字鍵盤 alphanumeric keyboard;

單鍵 single key;
電鍵 button; telegraph key;
關鍵 hinge; key;
花鍵 spline;
換擋鍵 shift key;
琴鍵 key;
閃跳鍵 flash button;

jian
【檻】 door-sill; threshold;

jian
【濺】 spill; splash; spray; sprinkle;
［濺落］ splash down;
［濺射］ sputtering;
二極管濺射 diode sputtering;
陰極濺射 cathode sputtering;
直流濺射 direct current sputtering;
重離子濺射 heavy ion sputtering;
［濺污］ spatter;

飛濺 splash;
噴濺 splash;

jian
【薦】 (1) offer; present; recommend; (2) fodder for animals; grass; (3) mat; straw-mat; (4) food and dishes; (5) again and again; repeatedly;
［薦舉］ propose sb for an office; recommend;
薦賢舉能 recommend the capable and deserving;

拔薦 recommend for a post;
保薦 recommend;
稿薦 mat;
舉薦 recommend;
推薦 recommend;
引薦 recommend;
追薦 pray for the dead;

jian
【鐧】 protective metal on the axis of a wheel;

jian
【艦】 man-of-war; naval vessel; warship;
［艦船］ ships and warships;
［艦隊］ armada; fleet; naval force; squadron;
常備艦隊 active fleet;
核動力艦隊 atomic fleet;
作戰艦隊 battle fleet;
［艦砲］ chase gun; naval gun; shipboard artillery;
［艦艇］ naval craft; naval ships and boats; naval vessels;
［艦長］ captain of a warship;

兵艦 warship;
登陸艦 landing ship;
巨艦 ammunition ship;
軍艦 man-of-war; naval vessel; warship;
僚艦 consort;
砲艦 gunboat;
旗艦 flagship;
驅逐艦 destroyer;
水雷艦 mine vessel;
巡洋艦 cruiser;
戰艦 man-of-war; warship;

J

jian
【轞】 (1) the noise of wheels; (2) sealed carts for transporting criminals;

jian
【鑑】 (1) mirror; (2) mirror; reflect; shine; (3) scrutinize; study or examine; (4) censure; exhort; instruct; (5) an example serving as a rule or warning;
[鑑於] inasmuch as;

jian
【鑒】 (1) ancient bronze mirror; (2) mirror; reflect; (3) object lesson; warning; (4) examine; inspect; scrutinize;
[鑒別] differentiate; discern; discriminate; discrimination; distinguish; identify;
鑒別碼 authenticating code;
鑒別器 discriminator;
~伴音鑒別器 audio discriminator;
~電子鑒別器 electronic discriminator;
~儀錶鑒別器 instrument discriminator;
鑒別身份 discriminate one's identification;
鑒別是非 discern between right and wrong;
鑒別優劣 differentiate between good and evil; discern good from bad;
鑒別真偽 discern between the true and the falso; discriminate the false from the genuine;
角鑒別 angular discrimination;
振幅鑒別 amplitude discrimination;
軸向鑒別 axial discrimination;
[鑒定] appraise; appraisal; assessment; evaluate; identification;
鑒定成本 appraisal cost;
鑒定會 appraisal meeting;
鑒定人 connoisseur; judge; referee;
鑒定委員會 certifying commission;
工地鑒定 field identification;
光譜鑒定 spectrographical identification;
化學鑒定 chemical identification;
可靠性鑒定 reliability assessment;
[鑒戒] object lesson;
可資鑒戒 can serve as means of warning example;
引為鑒戒 draw a lesson from; learn a lesson from; take warning from;
[鑒賞] appreciate;
鑒賞家 cognoscenti; connoisseur;
[鑒於] as; because of; by reason of; considering; for; for as much as; inasmuch as; in consideration of; in the light of; in view of; now that; on account of; owing to; seeing that; since; take into account; with a view to;
龜鑒 a past event serving as an example or warning to future generations;
借鑒 draw lessons from; lesson; reference; use for reference;
年鑒 almanac; yearbook;
賞鑒 appreciate;
台鑒 your perusal;
圖鑒 illustrated handbook;
印鑒 a specimen seal impression for checking when making payment;

jiang1
jiang
【江】 (1) river; (2) Changjiang River;
[江岸] river bank;
[江潮] tidal bore;
[江海] rivers and seas;
江海不拒細流 rivers need a spring; the sea is never full; the sea refuses no river;
倒海翻江 turn over the sea and river;
翻江倒海 brew storms on rivers and seas; hold back rivers and overturning seas; overturn rivers and seas;
[江河] river;
江河奔瀉 flow like a turbulent river;
江河橫溢 turbulent waters overflowing their banks;
江河湖海 rivers, lakes and the sea;
江河日下 decline steadily; deteriorate day by day; fall away; fast declining; fast deteriorating; general depression; go from bad to worse; on the decline; to the decline;
[江湖] (1) rivers and lakes; (2) all corners of the country;
江湖郎中 quack doctor;
江湖騙子 charlatan; mountebank; swindler;
江湖醫生 mountebank; quack; quack doctor;
江湖藝人 itinerant entertainer; wandering performer;
江湖義氣 code of the brotherhood;
江湖義士 believer in brotherhood;

J

闖江湖 make a living wandering from place to place;
老江湖 man of long experience; old traveller;
流落江湖 live a vagrant life;
落魄江湖 roam about the rivers and lakes – disheartened person; vagrant,
邁蹤江湖 begin life as an adventurer; begin to live a vagabond life;
跑江湖 wander about; wander around without settling down anywhere;
走江湖 become a vagrant; wander from place to place and earn a living by juggling;

[江米] glutinous rice;
江米糰子 glutinous rice ball;

[江平如練] the river lies as smooth as silk;

[江山] (1) landscape; rivers and mountains; (2) country; state power; territories;
江山不老 mountains and rivers remained as they were before;
江山如畫 a beautiful scenery; a picturesque landscape; the land is picturesque; the scenery is like a picture;
江山依舊 the country remains the same;
江山易改，本性難移 a fox may grow gray but never good; a leopard cannot change its spots; a sow, when washed, returns to the muck; clipping a tiger's claws never makes him lose his taste for blood; it is easier to move a mountain than change a man's character; it is easy to move rivers and mountains, but difficult to change a person's nature; the wolf may lose its teeth, but never his nature; what is bred in the bone will come out of the blesh; you can change mountains and rivers but not a person's nature; you cannot make a crab walk straight;
打江山 fight to win state power; seize political power by force;
守江山 defend a country;
鐵打江山 impregnable state; unshakable state power;
指點江山 put the world to rights; set the world to rights;
坐江山 rule the country;

[江水] river water;

[江天一色] the river and the great sky are of the same hue;

[江心] the middle of a river;
江心補漏 mend a leaking boat in midstream – too late;
船到江心補漏遲 it's too late to plug the leak when the boat is in midstream;

春江 spring river;
大江 (1) great river; (2) the Yangzi River;
領江 navigate a ship on a river;
下江 lower reaches of the Changjiang River;
沿江 along the river;

jiang
【姜】 a surname;

[姜太公釣魚，願者上鈎] a willing victim, letting oneself be caught;

jiang
【豇】 cowpea;

[豇豆] cowpea;

jiang
【將】 (1) about to; be going to; shall; will; (2) challenge; incite sb to action; (3) by; by means of; with;

[將錯就錯] leave a mistake uncorrected and make the best of it; make the best of a bad bargain; make the best of a mistake; muddle through; take the wrong and make the best of it;

[將計就計] beat sb at his own game; counterplot; make a counterplot; make use of sb's plot to defeat him; meet another's scheme with one's own; meet one ruse with another; meet one's scheme for another; meet trick with trick; turn sb's trick against him; turn sb's trick to one's own use;

[將近] almost; approximate to; be approaching; be getting on for; be nearing; be pushing; close on; close to; nearly; on the verge of; toward;
將近 50 歲 be approaching fifty;

[將就] make do with; make the best of; put up with;
天將地就 all that could be desired;

[將軍] (1) admiral; general; (2) check; (3) challenge; embarrass; put sb on the spot; (4) a surname;
飛將軍 parachutist;

J

[將來] before long; for the future; from now on; in days to come; in future; in future; in time; in time to come; in the future; in years to come;
將來才會知道 in the womb of time;
將來進行時 future continuous tense;
將來時 future tense;
將來完成進行時 future perfect continuous tense;
將來完成式 future perfect tense;
在不久的將來 in the near future;
[將勤補拙] make up for lack of natural talent through hard work; make up for lack of skill by industry;
[將要] about to; be going to; shall; will;

必將 surely will; will certainly;
即將 be about to; be on the point of;
行將 about to; on the verge of;

jiang
【僵】 (1) numb; stiff; (2) deadlocked;
[僵持] be stalemated; in a stalemate; refuse to budge; refuse to give in;
僵持不下 end in a deadlock; in a stalemate;
[僵化] become rigid; ossify; petrify;
思想僵化 have a rigid way of thinking;
[僵局] deadlock; gridlock; impasse; stalemate;
避免僵局 avoid an impasse;
處於僵局 at a deadlock; at a stalemate;
打開僵局 break the ice; break the deadlock; break the impasse; bring the deadlock to the end; find a way out of a stalemate; find solution for a problem; resolve the deadlock;
打破僵局 break the deadlock; break the stalemate;
結束僵局 bring a deadlock to an end;
陷入僵局 come to a deadlock; reach a deadlock; reach an impasse;
造成僵局 produce a stalemate;
[僵硬] ankylosis;
[僵直] rigidity; stiff;

凍僵 frozen stiff; numb with cold;

jiang
【漿】 starch; thick fluid;

草漿 straw pulp;
打漿 beating;
豆漿 soya-bean milk;
痘漿 vaccine;
翻漿 frost boil; frost heave;
灰漿 (1) whitewash; (2) mortar;
酒漿 alcoholic drink; spirits; wine;
礦漿 ore pulp;
木漿 wood pulp;
腦漿 brains;
泥漿 mud; slurry;
噴漿 whitewash;
肉漿 meat pulp; minced pulp;
瓊漿 good wine;
糖漿 syrup;
調漿 size mixing;
王漿 royal jelly;
橡漿 latex;
血漿 blood plasma;
岩漿 magma;
紙漿 paper pulp; pulp;

jiang
【薑】 ginger;
[薑餅] gingerbread; gingersnap;
人形薑餅 gingerbread man;
[薑草油] ginger grass oil;
[薑花] garland-flower;
[薑泥] ginger paste;
[薑是老的辣] ginger is hottest when it is old; the older the ginger, the more pungent its flavour;
[薑湯] ginger decoction; ginger tea;
[薑味] ginger;
薑味糕點 gingerbread;
薑汁啤酒 ginger beer;

老薑 old ginger;
嫩薑 new ginger;
生薑 ginger;
糖薑 sugared ginger;
五味薑 flavoured ginger;
鮮薑 fresh ginger;
雜錦薑 mixed ginger;
紫薑 red ginger;

jiang
【殭】 dead and stiff;
[殭屍] corpse;
[殭死] dead; ossified;
[殭臥] lie stiff and motionless;

jiang
【螿】 a kind of cicada;

jiang
【繮】 bridle; halter; reins;
[繮繩] bridle; halter; reins;

脱繮 get uncontrollable; run wild;

jiang
【彊】 border; boundary; frontier;
[彊場] battlefield;
彊場捐軀 die on the battlefield;
彊場埋骨 die on the battlefield;
馳騁彊場 gallop across the battlefield;
戰死彊場 die on the battlefield;
[彊界] borders; boundaries; frontiers;
[彊吏] frontier official;
[彊土] territory;
廣闊彊土 vast territory;
[彊域] domain; territory;

邊彊 border area; frontier region;
海彊 coastal areas and territorial seas;
無彊 boundless; limitless;

jiang
【韁】 reins;
[韁繩] halter; jerk line; rein;
放鬆韁繩 let go one's rein; loosen one's rein;
拉緊韁繩 pull up the rein;
勒緊韁繩 gather up one's reins;
握住韁繩 hold the reins;

jiang³
jiang
【槳】 oar;
[槳板] paddle board;
[槳手] boatman;
[槳葉] paddle;

一根槳 an oar;

jiang
【獎】 (1) reward; (2) award; prize; reward;
[獎杯] cup; plate; trophy;
奪得獎杯 win the cup;
[獎懲] bonus-penalty; rewards and disciplinary sanctions; rewards and penalties; rewards and punishments;
[獎罰] rewards or punishments;
獎罰分明 fair in meting out rewards or punishments; keep strictly the rules for reward and punishment;
獎勤罰懶 encourage industry and punish idleness;
獎優罰劣 reward the excellent and punish the inferior; reward the good and punish the bad;
[獎金] bonus; bounty; money award; premium; reward; testimonial; prize-money;
獎金税 tax on bonus;
頒發獎金 award a prize;
長期服務獎金 long-service bonus;
出口獎金 export bonus;
加班獎金 attendance bonus;
濫發獎金 distribute bonuses improperly; issue bonus recklessly;
年終獎金 year-end bonus;
團體獎金 group bonus;
應計獎金 accrued bonus;
[獎勵] award; encourage and reward; reward;
獎勵津貼 incentive grant;
獎勵制度 awards scheme; incentive system;
~設立獎勵制度 introduce an awards scheme;
得到獎勵 receive awards;
受到獎勵 receive praise and honour;
贏得獎勵 win awards;
[獎牌] medal;
獎牌得主 medalist;
獎牌獲得者 medal winner;
獲得獎牌 get a medal; receive a medal;
贏得獎牌 win a medal;
[獎品] award; prize; testimonial; trophy;
獲得獎品 gain an award; win a prize;
提供獎品 furnish prizes;
展出獎品 display trophies;
爭奪獎品 compete for a prize; contest a prize;
[獎券] gift coupon; lottery ticket;
[獎賞] award; reward;
[獎許] acclaim; praise;
[獎學金] fellowship; scholarship;
榮譽獎學金 honorary scholarship;
書院獎學金 college scholarship;
[獎掖] encourage by promoting and rewarding; reward and promote;
獎掖後進 exhort and promote a newcomer;
[獎章] decoration; medal;
頒發獎章 award a medal;
鑄造獎章 cast medals; found medals;

[獎狀] certificate of award; certificate of merit; citation; diploma; honourary credential; testimonial;

褒獎 commend and award; praise and honour;
得獎 win a prize;
發獎 award prizes;
翻譯獎 translation prize;
過獎 make an undeserved compliment; overpraise;
獲獎 win a prize;
嘉獎 commend; praise;
誇獎 commend; praise;
謬獎 make an undeserved compliment; overpraise;
評獎 decide on awards through discussion;
受獎 be rewarded;
授獎 award a prize;
頭獎 first prize;
中獎 win a prize in a lottery;

jiang
【蔣】 a surname;

jiang
【講】 (1) say; speak; talk about; tell; (2) explain; interpret; make clear;

[講道] give sermons; preach;
講道理 give sermons; preach;
講道台 ambo;
講道者 preacher;
對佛講道 preach scripture to a Buddha; teach fish to swim;

[講法] (1) formulation; a way of stating ideas or facts; wording; (2) argument; version;

[講稿] (1) draft or text of a speech; (2) lecture notes;
起草講稿 draft out an speech;
修改講稿 revise the draft of a speech;
準備講稿 prepare a speech;

[講和] make peace; negotiate; settle a dispute;

[講話] (1) address; speak; talk; (2) speech; talk;
講話風趣 speak interestingly;
講話片斷 sound bite;
不和人講話 speak to nobody;
不許講話 no talking;
大聲講話 speak aloud; talk in a loud voice;
低聲講話 speak in a low voice; speak under one's breath;
東拉西扯的講話 ramblings;
模棱兩可的講話 doublespeak; double-talk;
喜歡講話 talkative;

[講價] bargain; haggle over the price;

[講解] explain; expound; interpret;

[講究] particular about; pay attention to;
講究不如將就 it is better to be casual than to be a perfectionist; there is no need to be such a perfectionist;
講究穿着 be particular about clothes;
講究美感 strive for sense of beauty;
講究實效 pay attention to tangible results;
講究外表 particular about appearance;
講究完美 strive for perfection;
講究衛生 pay attention to hygiene;
愛講究 pernickety;

[講課] give a lesson; give a lecture; lecture; teach;

[講理] (1) argue things out; reason with sb; (3) amenable to reason; appeal to reason; listen to reason; reasonable; sensible;
蠻不講理 act arrogantly; high-handed in one's behaviour; impervious to reason; not appealing to reason; persist in being unreasonable; refuse to listen to reason; savage and absurd; unreasonable;
~ 蠻不講理的人 a wilful person;
~ 辦事蠻不講理 act arrogantly;
~ 説話蠻不講理 rough in speech;

[講明] explain; make clear; state explicitly;

[講評] comment on and appraise;

[講情] ask for leniency for sb else; intercede; plead for sb;

[講求] elaborate; particular about; pay attention to; stress; strive for;
講求實效 stress practical results; strive for actual effect;

[講師] lecturer;
大學講師 university lecturer;
高級講師 senior lecturer;
首席講師 principal lecturer;
助理講師 assistant lecturer;

[講授] give a lecture; instruct; lecture; teach;

[講述] give an account of; narrate; recount; relate; tell about;
講述者 narrator;

[講台] dais; lectern; platform; rostrum;

[講壇] (1) platform; pulpit; rostrum; (2)

J

forum; place for public speech;

[講堂] lecture room;
大講堂 auditorium; lecture room; lecture theatre;

[講習] lecture and study;

[講學] discourse on an academic subject; give lectures;

[講演] give a lecture; lecture; make a speech;
公開講演 public lecture;
特約講演 invited lecture;
學校講演 school lecture;

[講義] handout; lecture notes; teaching materials;

[講座] lecture; series of lectures;
出席講座 attend a lecture; go to a lecture;
聽講座 listen to a lecture;
一次講座 a talk;
一系列講座 a course of lectures; a series of lectures;
做講座 do a lecture;

播講 broadcast a talk;
不該講而講 speak out of turn;
從某種意義上來講 in a sense; in one sense; in some senses;
開講 begin lecturing;
聽講 attend a lecture; listen to a talk;
宣講 explain and publicise;
演講 give a lecture; make a speech;
主講 keynote speaker;

jiang⁴
jiang

【匠】 artisan; craftsman;

[匠氣] triteness in artistic work;

[匠人] artisan; craftsman;

[匠心] craftsmanship; ingenuity; inventiveness; originality;
匠心獨具 have great originality;
匠心獨運 exercise one's inventive mind; show one's own ingenuity;
匠心經營 original thought in creation;
獨具匠心 have an inventive mind; have great originality; show ingenuity;

鞍匠 saddler;
補鍋匠 tinker;
工匠 artisan; craftsman;
花匠 floriculturist; gardener;
畫匠 (1) artisan-painter; (2) inferior painter;
金匠 goldsmith;
巨匠 consummate artisan; great master;
木匠 carpenter;
皮匠 (1) cobbler; (2) tanner;
漆匠 (1) lacquerware worker; (2) lacquer man; painter;
巧匠 skilled workman;
石匠 stonemason;
鎖匠 locksmith;
陶匠 potter;
鐵匠 blacksmith; ironsmith;
銅匠 coppersmith;
瓦匠 bricklayer; plasterer; tiler;
錫匠 tinsmith;
鞋匠 shoemaker;
修錶匠 watchmaker;
修傘匠 umbrella renovator;
意匠 artistic conception;
銀匠 silversmith;
珠寶匠 jeweler;

jiang

【降】 drop; fall; lower;

[降等] degradation;

[降低] abate; cut down, debase; drop; lessen; lower; reduce;
降低標準 lower the standard;
降低成本 cost down; cost reduction; cut the cost; lower production costs; reduce cost;
降低關税 lower tariff duties;
降低價格 abate a price;
降低能耗 cut down the consumption of energy;
降低人格 lower one's dignity; lower oneself;
降低生活水準 lower the living standard;
降低物價 cut down the price; level down the price; lower the price;
降低要求 lower the requirement for;
降低語調 lower one's voice;

[降格] lower one's status;
降格以求 accept a second best; fall back on sth inferior to what one originally wanted; look for sth without insisting on the best; set one's aim lower than usual;
詞義降格 degradation of meaning;

[降級] (1) reduce in rank; reduce to a lower rank; sink in the scale; (2) send a student to a lower grade;
降級留用 degrade in rank but retain in

office;

[降價] deflation; price abatement; reduced price;
大降價 bargain sale;

[降解] degradation; degrade;
化學降解 chemical degradation;
可控降解 controlled degradation;
生物降解 biological degradation;
酸降解 acid degradation;
銅降解 copper degradation;
細菌性降解 bacterial degradation;

[降臨] arrive; befall; come; come down;
好運降臨 the arrival of good luck;
夜幕降臨 the night fell;

[降落] (1) descend; drop-down; fall alight; tumble; (2) land; touch down;
降落場 landing field;
~臨時降落場 airstrip;
降落傘 parachute;
~打開降落傘 release a parachute;
降落在機場 land on the airport; touch down at the airport;
垂直降落 make a vertical landing;
飛機無法降落 the plane cannot land;
緊急降落 make an emergency landing;
強迫降落 make a forced landing;

[降旗] lower a flag;

[降傘] parachute;
降傘事故 parachute accident;

[降溫] (1) lower the temperature; (2) a drop in temperature; cool down;

[降心相從] subject one's own will to the dictate of others; submit to others against one's will;

[降雨] rain;
人工降雨 artificial rain;

[降志辱身] give up one's aspiration and live in contempt; lower one's aspiration and denigrate oneself;

沉降 subside;
遞降 be reduced by degrees; go down progressively;
空降 airborne;
昇降 go up and down;
下降 (1) descend; go or come down; (2) decline; drop;

jiang

【洚】 flood;

[洚水] flood; inundation;

jiang

【將】 (1) general; (2) commander-in-chief; (3) command; lead;

[將才] talent as a field commander;

[將官] general;

[將領] high-ranking military officer;

[將門] a line of generals;
將門虎子 a capable young man from a distinguished family;
將門有將 in the family of a general there are more generals — like produces like;
將門之子 come from a line of generals;

[將士] officers and men;

[將相] generals and ministers of state; military and political leaders;
將相本無種，男兒當自強 man is not born to greatness, he achieves it by his own efforts;
出將入相 as good a general as a minister;

[將遇良才] find one's match; a Roland for an Oliver;

[將佐] high-ranking military officers;

敗將 defeated general;
兵將 soldiers and the general;
部將 military officers under one's command;
闖將 daring general; pathbreaker;
大將 (1) senior general; (2) high-ranking officer;
幹將 capable person;
虎將 brave general;
健將 master sportsman; top-notch player;
老將 old-timer; veteran;
麻將 mahjong;
猛將 valiant general;
名將 famous general;
儒將 a general who is an equally accomplished man of letters;
上將 admiral; air chief marshal;
少將 rear admiral;
神將 subordinate general;
宿將 veteran general;
驍將 valiant general;
小將 young general; young pathbreaker;
勇將 fearless general;
賊將 general of the enemy troops; rebel general;
斬將 behead enemy generals;
中將 air marshal; lieutenant general; vice admiral;
主將 chief commander; commending general;
准將 air commodore; brigadier; brigadier

J

general; commodore;

jiang
【強】 inflexible; obstinate; stubborn;
［強嘴］ answer back; reply defiantly; talk back;

倔強 obstinate; stubborn; unyielding;

jiang
【絳】 (1) deep red colour; red; (2) a surname;
［絳脂］ rouge;
［絳紫］ dark reddish purple;

jiang
【糨】 paste; paste together; starch; starched;
［糨糊］ paste; starch paste;

jiang
【醬】 (1) soy; soybean sauce; (2) food in the form of paste;
［醬菜］ pickles; vegetables pickled in soy sauce;
醬菜店 store for selling pickles;
［醬瓜］ soy sauced cucumbers;
［醬芥］ pickled rutabaga;
［醬色］ dark reddish brown;
［醬油］ sauce; soy sauce;
醬油壺 a soy-sauce pot;
醬油煮雞蛋—混蛋 eggs boiled in soy sauce – (lit) muddy eggs; (coll) blackguard; son of a bitch;
淡醬油 light soy sauce;
濃醬油 dark soy sauce;
蘸醬油 dip sth into soy sauce;
［醬紫］ dark reddish purple;

豆瓣兒醬 thick broad-bean sauce;
番茄醬 tomato ketchup;
果醬 jam;
果子醬 jam;
花生醬 peanut butter;
黃醬 salted and fermented soya paste;
蒟醬 (1) betel pepper; (2) thick paste made from betel pepper;
辣醬 thick chilli paste;
麻醬 sesame paste;
甜麵醬 sweet sauce made of fermented flours;
蝦醬 shrimp paste;
蝦子醬 shrimp roe paste;
魚子醬 caviar;
炸醬 fried soya paste;
芝麻醬 sesame paste;

jiao¹
jiao
【交】 (1) deliver; give up; hand in; hand over; (2) join; meet; (3) cross; (4) associate with; (5) bargain; business transaction; deal; (6) acquaintance; friends; friendship; relations; relationship; (7) fall;
［交班］ hand over to the next shift; pass work on to the next shift; turn over one's duty;
［交杯酒］ cross-cupped wine;
［交臂］ (1) cross one's arms; (2) rub shoulders;
兩手交臂 have one's arms folded;
失之交臂 fail to meet sb by a narrow chance; have missed a good chance; have missed sth very desirable; lose sth close at hand; miss at very close range; miss the boat; miss the bus; miss the person; miss the opportunity; slip through sb's fingers;
［交兵］ at war; wage war;
［交叉］ (1) chiasma; crisscross; cross; cross connection; crossing; intersect; intersection; scissors; (2) overlap; (3) alternate; stagger;
交叉點 crossing; intersection; junction;
~平面交叉點 level crossing;
交叉而行 move crosswise;
交叉火力 cross fire;
交叉計算 cross adding;
交叉進攻 alternating attack;
交叉進行 do alternately;
交叉口 intersection;
交叉路 crossroad;
交叉訓練 cross-training;
補償交叉 compensating chiasma;
不全交叉 imperfect chiasma;
側交叉 lateral chiasma;
承重索交叉 carrier cable crossing;
反交叉 back scissors; reverse scissors;
複交叉 multiple chiasma;
互補交叉 complementary chiasma;
立體交叉 flyover crossing;
兩臂交叉 arm crossing;
末端交叉 terminal chiasma;
內交叉 internal chiasma;
平面交叉 at-grade intersection;

曲線交叉 curved intersection;
染色體交叉 chiasmatypy;
銳角交叉 acute angle intersection;
視交叉 optic chiasma;
雙交叉 dual crossing;
外交叉 external chiasma;
~神經外交叉 outer chiasma;
完全交叉 complete intersection;
遠側交叉 distal chiasma;
正交叉 forward scissors; front scissors;
中間交叉 interstitial chiasma;

[交差] report to the leadership after accomplishing a task;

[交出] hand over; surrender;

[交錯] crisscross; entwine; interlace; interlock; intersect;
交錯配列 chiasmus;
杯觥交錯 the cups go gaily round;
觥籌交錯 the cups go gaily round; toast each other;
履舄交錯 mixed shoes and soles of shoes — a number of male and female guests gathered; shoes lie about in disorder;

[交代] (1) account for; brief; explain; justify oneself; make clear; tell; (2) hand over; transfer; turn over;
交代不過去 unable to justify an action;
交代工作 brief one's successor on handling over work; hand over work to one's successor;
交代任務 assign and explain a task; brief sb on his task;
交代問題 account for a problem;
交代政策 explain policy;
交代罪行 confess a crime;
交代作用 metasomatosis;
拒不交代 refuse to give an accounting; refuse to own up;

[交道] contact; dealings;
打交道 come into contact with; deal with; have contact with; have dealings with; make contact with; negotiate with; team up with;
~難打交道 difficult to get along with; hard to deal with;

[交點] node;
交點線 line of nodes;
交點月 draconic month; nodical month;

[交鋒] cross swords with; engage each other; engage in a battle or contest; fight with; struggle with;
與敵人交鋒 engage the enemy in battle; fight a battle with the enemy;
正面交鋒 head-to-head;
~避免正面交鋒 avoid direct confrontation;

[交付] (1) pay; (2) consign; deliver; delivery; hand over; turn over;
交付表決 put to the vote;
交付定金 down payment;
交付房租 pay rent;
交付審查 hand over for investigation;
交付審判 submit to trial;
交付宣判 render a verdict;
交付學費 pay tuition fee;
部份交付 partial delivery;
當場交付 spot delivery;
工地交付 job-site delivery;
快速交付 accelerated delivery;
限期交付 pay within a definite time;
用現金交付 pay in cash;

[交割] complete a business transaction; deliver;

[交媾] coitus; copulate; copulation; screw; sexual intercourse;
交媾困難 dyspareunia;
交媾中斷 onanism;

[交好] friendly with; on friendly terms;

[交互] (1) each other; mutual; (2) alternately; in turn; interactive;
交互技術 interaction technique;
交互式網絡 internet;
交互作用 interaction;
~地月交互作用 earth-moon interaction;

[交還] give back; return;

[交換] exchange; interchange; permutation; swap; swapping;
交換場地 exchange courts;
交換俘虜 make a prisoner exchange;
交換禮物 exchange gifts;
交換器 exchanger;
~混合式熱交換器 direct-contact heat exchanger;
~氣油熱交換器 air oil heat exchanger;
~套管熱交換器 double-pipe exchanger;
交換生 exchange student;
交換吸附 exchange adsorption;
交換消息 exchange messages;
交換意見 compare notes; exchange ideas; give and take; put heads together;
交換語言 interaction language;
交換戰俘 have an exchange of prisoner of

J

war;
程序交換 programme swap;
公平交換 fair swap;
離子交換 ion interchange;
氣體交換 air exchange; gaseous interchange;
熱交換 heat interchange;
數據交換 data interchange;
物物交換 barter one thing for another; exchange article by article;
信息交換 information interchange;
信用交換 credit interchange;
陰離子交換 anion exchange;
有利交換 advantageous exchange;
字節交換 byte swap;

[交火] fight; fire fight;

[交貨] consignment; deliver goods; delivery;
按期交貨 deliver goods on schedule;
遲延交貨 deferred delivery;
船邊交貨 alongside delivery;
當場交貨 spot delivery;
當月交貨 delivery;
合同交貨 contractual delivery;
即時交貨 immediate delivery; prompt delivery;
見單交貨 deliver goods against surrender of the document;
實際交貨 actual delivery;
推定交貨 constructive delivery;
象徵交貨 symbolic delivery;
迅速交貨 early delivery;
延期交貨 delayed delivery; late delivery;
遠期交貨 forward deliver; future delivery;

[交集] be mixed; occur simultaneously;
百感交集 a hundred emotions crowd into the heart; a multitude of feelings surge up; a multitude of feelings welling up; a whirlwind of emotions; all sorts of feelings well up in one's heart; be moved by a mixture of feelings; be overwhelmed with a flood of emotions; conflicting emotions; crowd upon one's mind; fill one's mind with a myriad of thoughts; have mixed feelings; mixed emotions; run the gamut of emotions; with mingled feelings; with mixed emotions;
悲憤交集 with mixed feelings of grief and indignation;
悲喜交集 have mixed feelings of grief and joy;
感愧交集 be moved and ashamed simultaneously; both grateful and shameful; feel grateful and uneasy at the same time;
驚喜交集 have mixed feelings of surprise and joy;
雷雨交集 the thunder was accompanied with a rush of rain;
羞恨交集 shame and resentment mingled;
羞悔交集 be overcome with shame and remorse;

[交際] communication; contact; social intercourse;
交際策略 communication strategy;
交際法 communicative approach;
交際翻譯 communicative translation;
交際負荷 communication load;
交際干擾 communicative interference;
交際功能 communicative function;
交際很廣 have a large circle of acquaintances;
交際花 bell of society; courtesan; social butterfly; society beauty;
交際論 communication theory;
交際能力 communicative competence;
交際甚廣 be widely acquainted; mix much in society;
交際網絡 communicative network;
交際舞 ballroom dancing; social dance; social dancing;
交際性公關 communicative public relations;
交際意義 communicative meaning;
交際語 vernacular;
~交際語法 communicative grammar;
~交際語境 communicative context;
~共同交際語 contact vernacular;
交際者 communicator;
不喜交際 be conserved; not good at getting along with people;
好交際的 clubbable; clubby;
很少交際 mingle very little in society;
忙於交際 busy with social activities;
面對面交際 face-to-face communication;
群體間交際 intergroup communication;
喜於交際 a good mixer; good at getting along with people; sociable;
厭惡交際 dislike society;

[交加] accompany each other; occur simultaneously;
讒口交加 beset by slanders;

風雪交加 a snowstorm is raging;
風雨交加 the wind howls and the rain beats down;
鋒鏑交加 heavy fighting; swords and spears crossed — in close combat;
悔恨交加 have mixed feelings of remorse and shame;
饑病交加 suffer from hunger and disease;
雷電交加 the lightning was accompanied with thunder;
貧病交加 be plagued by both poverty and illness;
拳腳交加 beat up with fists and kicks; violent beating;
拳足交加 give sb both punches and kicks; hit sb by kicks and blows of fists;
雨雹交加 raindrops mix with hail stones come pelting down;
雨雪交加 rain and snow falling mixedly; rain and snow mingle; rainfall and snowfall combine; snow with a mingling of rain;

[交界] border on; have a common boundary; have a common border; juncture of;

[交卷] (1) hand in an examination paper; (2) carry out an assignment; finish up one's job; fulfil one's task;

[交款] make a payment;
交款人 payer;

[交流] exchange; interchange; interflow;
交流電 alternating current;
交流經驗 draw on each other's experience; exchange experience;
交流聲 alternating current hum; hum;
~基極交流聲 base hum;
~柵極交流聲 grid hum;
~絲極交流聲 heater hum;
交流輸入插孔 alternating current input jack;
交流輸入插座 alternating current socket;
交流信息網 information net of communication;
交流者 communicator;
對外交流 foreign exchange;
國際交流 international exchanges;
擴大交流 extend interchange with...;
兩淚交流 with two streams of tears running down one's face;
目光交流 eye contact;
涕淚交流 cry with a flood of tears; shed streams of tears and to snivel; tears and snivel fall down at the same time;
涕泗交流 tears and snivel fall down at the same time;

[交配] copulate; copulation; mating;
不正常交配 illegitimate mating;
更替交配 alternative copulation;
近親交配 consanguineous mating;
配囊交配 gametangial copulation;
配子交配 gametic copulation;
~異形配子交配 heterogamic copulation;
隨機交配 random mating;
兄妹交配 brother-sister mating;
選型交配 assortative mating;
遠親交配 outbreeding;

[交錢] pay;

[交情] friendly relation; friendship;
交情篤厚 our friendship is sincere and deep;
交情深 have deep friendship with;
掰交情 break off friendship; sever relations;
夠交情 in the good graces of sb; on enough good terms;
講交情 do things for the sake of friendship;
拉交情 try to seek friendship of influential persons;
老交情 long-standing friendship; old friend;
賣個交情 do sb a special favour;
念在老交情 for old times' sake;

[交融] blend; mingle;

[交涉] make representations; negotiate; take up with;
辦交涉 carry on negotiations with; take up a matter with;

[交蝕] eclipse;
交食預測 prediction of eclipses;

[交手] be engaged in a hand-to-hand fight; come to grips; fight hand to hand;

[交談] chat; converse; have a conversation; hobnob; talk with each other; touch base with sb;
電話交談 telephone conversation;
簡短交談 short conversation;
傾心交談 have a heart-to-heart chat; have a heart-to-heart talk;
一次交談 a talk;

[交替] (1) replace; supersede; (2) alternate; alternately; in turn; take place by turn;
交替臂 alternate arm;

J

交替地 by turns;
交替格式 alternative pattern;
交替規則 alternation rule;
交替形式 alternative form;
世代交替 alternation of generations;
新老交替 the new replaces the old;
晝夜交替 day alternates with night; day and night alternate;

[交通] (1) unobstructed; (2) communication; traffic; transportation;
交通安全 safe traffic; traffic safety;
~交通安全法規 traffic safety code;
~交通安全員 lollipop lady; lollipop man;
交通便利 have transport facilities;
交通不便 have poor transport facilities; not be conveniently located;
交通部 ministry of transportation;
交通標誌 traffic sign;
交通場所 place of communication;
交通島 police stand;
交通調查 traffic study;
交通堵塞 gridlock; traffic jam;
交通繁忙 heavy traffic;
交通方便 have a good transport service;
交通幹線 the main communication lines;
交通高峰時間 rush-hour traffic;
交通工具 means of communication; transport facilities;
交通規則 traffic law; traffic regulations;
交通黑點 accident black spot;
交通經濟學 traffic economics;
交通警察 traffic policeman;
交通容量 traffic capacity;
交通社會學 traffic sociology;
交通事故 traffic accident;
~一起交通事故 a traffic accident;
交通樞紐 key position of communication;
交通順暢 the traffic is smooth;
交通停頓 hold up the traffic;
交通艇 patrol boat;
交通圖 communications map; route map;
交通現象 traffic behavior;
交通線 communication line;
交通信號燈 traffic lights;
交通巡邏隊 traffic patrol;
交通要道 important line of communications; vital communication line;
交通擁擠 have congested traffic; have dense traffic; have heavy traffic;
交通員 traffic warden;
交通運輸佈局 allocation of communication and transportation;
交通噪音 traffic noise;
交通指揮台 podium;
交通秩序 traffic order;
交通阻塞 a block in traffic; the traffic is held up; the traffic is stacked up; there is a traffic jam; traffic block; traffic jam;
交通錐 traffic cone;
安全交通 traffic safety;
城市交通 urban traffic;
封鎖交通 barring traffic;
公共交通 public communication; public transport; public transportation;
公路交通 highway traffic;
空中交通 air traffic;
路面交通 road traffic;
擾亂交通 disrupt the traffic;
水上交通 waterway traffic;

[交投] trading;
交投暢旺 heavy trading;
交投疏落 light trading;

[交頭接耳] bill and coo; exchange confidential whispers; head to head; heads together and ears stretched out; secret conversations; speak in each other's ears; talk confidentially; talk mouth to ear; whisper into each other's ears; whisper to each other; whispering;

[交往] associate with; contact; rub elbows with;
交往甚密 have an intimate association with; have close contact with; hobnob;

[交響] symphonic;
交響曲 symphony;
交響詩 symphonic poem; tone poem;
交響樂 symphony;
~交響樂隊 symphony orchestra;

[交心] lay one's heart bare; open hearts to each other; open one's heart to;

[交易] business; deal trade; dealing; transaction;
交易成本經濟學 transaction cost economics;
交易額 turnover; volume of business;
~年交易額 annual turnover;
交易費 transaction cost; transaction fee;
交易風險 transaction exposure;
交易會 trade fair; trade show;

交易理論 bargaining theory;
交易圈 pit;
交易日 transaction date;
交易失敗 a deal falls through;
交易市場 market;
~場外交易市場 off-board market; over-the-counter market;
交易稅 transaction tax;
交易所 exchange; house;
交易賬戶 transaction account;
骯髒的交易 dirty deal;
不正常交易 crooked dealings; queasy transaction;
場外交易 over-the-counter trading;
達成交易 strike a bargain;
定期交易 time bargains;
毒品交易 drug trafficking;
非法交易 illegal transaction;
非正當交易 shady deal;
公平交易 even bargain;
合算交易 real bargain;
黑市交易 clandestine dealing;
籠斷交易 ring trading;
買賣交易 bargaining transaction;
秘密交易 clandestine dealings;
內幕交易 insider trading;
內線交易 insider trading;
權錢交易 trading power for money;
套匯交易 arbitrage transaction;
委托交易 agency transaction;
限額交易 rationed exchange;
現貨交易 spot deal;
現金交易 cash business; dealing for money;
一筆交易 a deal;
一次性交易 one-off deal;
一攬子交易 package deal;
一項交易 a deal; a transaction;
易貨交易 barter transaction;
遠期交易 dealing in future;

[交誼] friendly relations; friendship;
交誼舞 ballroom dancing;

[交用] turn over for use;

[交遊] keep company; make friends;
交游廣闊 have a large circle of friends; have a wide acquaintance; have a wide circle of acquaintances;
交遊很廣的人 person of wide acquaintance;

[交戰] at war; engagement; fight; wage war;
明槍交戰 attack by overt means;

[交織] interlace; intertwine; interweave; mingle;
愛恨交織 be overwhelmed by mixed love-hate feelings;
愁慮交織 intense sorrow and concern are mixed in one's heart;
黑白交織 interweave black with white;
悔愧交織 be torn by self-recrimination and repentance;

邦交 diplomatic relations;
撥交 appropriate; issue to;
成交 clench a bargain; clinch a deal; close a bargain; conclude a bargain; conclude a transaction; settle a bargain; strike a bargain;
初交 new acquaintance;
單交 single cross;
遞交 hand over; present;
締交 (1) form a friendship; (2) establish diplomatic relations;
點交 hand over item by item;
跌交 (1) fall; stumble and fall; (2) make a mistake; meet with a setback;
頂交 topcross;
訂交 become friends; form a friendship;
斷交 (1) break off a friendship; (2) sever diplomatic relations;
復交 reestablish diplomatic relations;
故交 old friend;
國交 diplomatic relations between countries;
回交 backcross;
建交 establish diplomatic relations;
結交 associate with; make friends with;
舊交 old acquaintance;
絕交 sever relations;
開交 end; solve;
上交 hand in; turn over to the higher authorities;
社交 social contact; social intercourse;
深交 close friend; profound friendship;
神交 be spiritually attracted to sb one has not met;
世交 (1) friendship spanning two or more generations; (2) old family friends;
摔交 wrestling;
私交 personal friendship;
送交 deliver; hand over;
提交 submit to;
外交 diplomacy; foreign affairs;
相交 (1) intersect; (2) associate with; make friends with;
新交 new acquaintance; new friend;

性交 sexual intercourse;
移交 (1) transfer; turn over; (2) hand over one's job to a successor;
雜交 hybridize;
擇交 choose friends;
知交 bosom friend;
至交 bosom friend;
轉交 pass on; transmit;

jiao
【姣】 (1) good-looking; handsome; pretty; (2) coquettish;
［姣好］ handsome; pretty;

jiao
【郊】 (1) suburbs of a city; (2) ceremony for offering sacrifice to the Heaven and Earth;
［郊狼］ coyote;
郊狼嚎叫 coyotes howl;
［郊區］ burbs; outskirts; suburban district; subsurbs;
郊區居民 suburbanite;
郊區人 suburbanite;
擴展郊區 suburban sprawl;
［郊外］ countryside; outskirts; suburb;
［郊遊］ excursion; go for an outing;
去郊遊 go for an outing; have an outing;

城郊 outskirts of a town; suburban;
禘郊 imperial sacrifice held in the countryside;
荒郊 desolate place outside a town; wilderness;
市郊 outskirts; suburb;
四郊 outskirts; suburbs;
遠郊 outer suburbs;

jiao
【茭】 zizania latifolia, a kind of edible aquatic grass;
［茭白］ wild rice stem;
［茭瓜］ wild rice stem;
［茭筍］ wild rice stem;

jiao
【教】 instruct; teach;
［教書］ teach; teach school;
教書匠 teacher;
教書育人 impart knowledge and educate people;

jiao
【椒】 (1) pepper; other spices; (2) mountain -top;
［椒鹽］ spiced salt;

番椒 chilli; hot pepper;
胡椒 pepper;
花椒 Chinese prickly ash;
辣椒 chilli; hot pepper;
青椒 green pepper;
柿子椒 sweet pepper;
甜椒 green pepper; sweet pepper;
西紅椒 tomato;

jiao
【焦】 (1) burn; charred; scorched; (2) coke; (3) anxious; worried;
［焦點］ (1) focal point; focus; (2) central issue; centre;
焦點副詞 focusing adverb;
焦點附加語 focusing adjunct;
焦點團體 focus group;
焦點小組 focus group
共軛焦點 conjugate focus;
光化焦點 actinic focus;
忽略問題的焦點 neglect the heart of the matter;
化學焦點 chemical focus;
環形焦點 annular focus;
實焦點 real focus;
事情的焦點 the nub of the matter;
問題的焦點 the nub of the problem;
虛焦點 apparent focus;
圓形焦點 circular focus;
爭論的焦點 the nub of the argument;
主焦點 principal focus;
［焦度］ focal power;
［焦化］ coke; coking;
焦化器 coker;
~成漆板焦化器 panel coker;
~流化焦化器 fluid coker;
焦化設備 coker;
催化焦化 catalytic coking;
接觸焦化 contact coking;
瀝青焦化 pitch coking;
連續焦化 continuous coking;
流化焦化 fluid coking;
延遲焦化 delayed coke;
［焦黃］ brown; dry and yellowish; sallow;
［焦急］ anxious; on one's toes; worried;
焦急不安 flutter; in a swivet; on the anxious seat;
焦急萬狀 one's anxiety is at its height; restless with anxiety;
萬分焦急 desperately anxious;

J

一陣焦急 a stab of anxiety;

[焦距] focal distance; focal length;
焦距比 focal ratio;
超焦距 hyperfocal distance;

[焦慮] feel anxious; extremely anxious; have worries and misgivings; inquietude;
焦慮不安 be racked with anxiety; fret and fume; in a flutter of excitement; in a way; on the rack; on tenderhooks; on thorns; toss about;
~焦慮不安的 tizzy;
焦慮的 jittery;
焦慮感 collywobbles;
感到焦慮 experience anxiety; feel anxious;
滿懷焦慮 be filled with misgivings;
神色焦慮 wear an expression of great anxiety;
異常焦慮 be all agitation;

[焦煤] coke;

[焦深] depth of focus;

[焦糖] caramel;
焦糖奶糖 caramel;
變成焦糖 caramelize;

[焦炭] coke;
鍛造焦炭 forge coke;
高爐焦炭 blast-furnace coke;
過濾用焦炭 filter coke;
家用焦炭 domestic coke;
碎焦炭 crushed coke;
冶金焦炭 furnace coke;

[焦土] scorched earth;
一片焦土 with everything burned down and lying in ruins;

[焦心] feel terribly worried;
焦心苦慮 deeply anxious; in deep anxiety;

[焦油] coke tar; tar;
樺木焦油 birch tar;
瀝青焦油 asphalt tar;
煤焦油 coat tar;
酸焦油 acid tar;

[焦躁] impatient; restless with anxiety;
焦躁不安 feel restless and ill-tempered;

[焦灼] deeply worried; very anxious;

底焦 bed coke;
烘焦 get partially burned because of overheating near fire;
結焦 coke; coking;
聚焦 focus;
煉焦 coke;
天然焦 cokeite; mineral coke;
小塊焦 nut coke;
心焦 anxious; worried;
針焦 needlelike coke;
鑄造焦 cupola coke;

jiao

【蛟】 flood dragon;

[蛟龍] flood dragon
蛟龍出洞，猛虎離山 dragons come forth from their lair and tigers leap from the mountain den;
蛟龍得水 happy like a dragon in water — in the most congenial surroundings; the recumbent dragon gets to the water — a bold man gets an opportunity to show his prowess;
蛟龍離水遭蛇戲 a dragon out of water furnishes amusement for the snakes;
蛟龍鎖柱 the rampant dragon is chained to an iron pillar;
蛟龍戲水 a huge dragon winding through the waves;
蛟龍之志 person of great ambitions;

jiao

【跤】 fall; stumble;

jiao

【嶕】 high; unpleasant;

[嶕嶢] high; unpleasant;

jiao

【嬌】 (1) charming; lovely; tender; (2) delicate; fragile; frail;

[嬌波流慧] have beautiful eyes with a very intelligent expression in them;

[嬌滴滴] affectedly sweet; delicately pretty; very beautiful and fascinating;
嬌嬌滴滴 charming; delicate; delicate and helpless;

[嬌慣] coddle; pamper; spoil;

[嬌憨] young and ignorant;

[嬌黃] delicate yellow;

[嬌媚] (1) coquettish; (2) sweet and charming;
千嬌百媚 a face to launch a thousand ships; a thousand charms; beautiful and charming; the beauty of beauties; the pinnacle of beauty and charms;

[嬌嫩] delicate; fragile; tender and lovely;
皮膚嬌嫩 have a pretty, delicate skin;
身子嬌嫩 in delicate health; in frail health;

[嬌氣] finicky; soft; squeamish;

J

［嬌嬈］ enchantingly beautiful;
［嬌生慣養］ be born in the lap of luxury; be brought up in easy circumstances by doting parents; be brought up in clover; be nursed in luxury; be pampered; be spoiled; used to a bed of roses;
［嬌聲］ sweet voice;
嬌聲嬌氣 in a flirtatious tone; speak in a seductive tone; with a sweet girlish voice;
嬌聲嫩語 in a sweet voice;
［嬌艷］ delicate and charming; tender and beautiful;
嬌艷絕倫 delicate and charming beyond compare; so gay as to excel all;
嬌艷無比 gay to excel all;
嬌艷欲滴 look tender and beautiful;
［嬌養］ cosset; pamper;
［嬌縱］ indulge a child; pamper; spoil;

撒嬌 act in a pettishly charming manner; act like a spoiled child; coddle;

jiao

【澆】 (1) pour liquid on; sprinkle; (2) irrigate; water;
［澆薄］ thoughtlessly treacherous;
澆薄之世 the age of demoralization;
［澆愁］ wash away one's sorrow;
借酒澆愁 cry in one's beer; dispel melancholy by drinks; drink down sorrow; drive sb to drink; drown one's sorrows in wine; take to drinking to forget one's sorrows;
以酒澆愁 drown care; drown one's sorrow; drown one's troubles; take to drinking to forget one's sorrows;
［澆花］ water flowers;
雨後澆花 water one's flowers after a good rain — do sth unnecessary;
［澆水］ water a plant;
給植物澆水 water a plant;
［澆注］ pouring;
拔塞澆注 stopper pouring;
補澆注 back pouring;
低溫澆注 cold pouring;

jiao

【膠】 (1) glue; gum; (2) resin; sap; (3) adhere; stick on; stick together; (4) obstinate; stubborn; (5) a surname;

［膠帶］ tape;
雙面膠帶 double-sided tape;
［膠管］ hose; rubber tube;
風水膠管 air and water hose;
耐酸膠管 acid resisting hose;
排酸膠管 acid discharge hose;
［膠合］ glue together;
膠合板 plywood;
~ 波紋膠合板 corrugated plywood;
~ 航空膠合板 aircraft plywood;
~ 三層膠合板 three-ply wood;
~ 斜紋膠合板 diagonal plywood;
［膠捲］ film; film strip; roll film;
縮微膠捲 microfilm;
一個膠捲 a roll of film;
一卷膠捲 a reel of film;
［膠料］ size;
褐色膠料 brown size;
酸性膠料 acid size;
中性膠料 neutral size;
［膠囊］ capsule;
膠囊衣櫥 capsule wardrobe;
［膠片］ film;
膠片捲 film roll;
~ 膠片捲軸 film spool;
安全膠片 safety film;
縮微膠片 microfiche;
［膠漆］ glue and vanish;
情同膠漆 cling together in affection like glue and varnish; close friendship and intimate relations;
如膠似漆 be closely bound together; be deeply attached to each other; cleave together as firmly and inseparably as glue and lacquer; cling to sb like glue; have an affection like glue and varnish; inseparable; like glue and lacquer — very much in love; love each other dearly; remain glued to each other; stick like glue to; stick to each other like glue or lacquer; stick together like glue and varnish;
似膠如漆 like glue and varnish — mutual love and attraction;
［膠乳］ endosperm; latex;
鹼性膠乳 alkali latex;
平均膠乳 average latex;
人造膠乳 artificial latex;
酸性膠乳 acid latex;
［膠束］ micell;
盤狀膠束 disc-shaped micell;

纓狀膠束 fringed micell;
圓柱形膠束 cylindrical micell;

［膠體］ colloid;
膠體顆粒 colloidal particle;
膠體溶液 colloidal solution;

［膠原］ collagen;

［膠着］ agglutinative; reach a deadlock;
膠着語 agglutinative language;
膠着狀態 in a stalemate;

氨草膠 ammoniac;
蟲膠 shellac;
阿膠 donkey-hide gelatin;
割膠 rubber tapping;
骨膠 bone glue; lime glue;
硅膠 silica gel;
栲膠 tannin extract;
鋁膠 alumina gel;
明膠 gelatin;
黏膠 viscose;
凝膠 gel;
皮膠 hide glue;
溶膠 sol;
乳膠 emulsion; latex;
樹膠 gum; resin;
塑膠 plastic cement; plastics;
桃膠 peach gum;
橡膠 rubber;
懸膠 suspensoid;
魚膠 fish glue; isinglass;
炸膠 blasting gelatin;
紫膠 lac; shellac;

jiao

【憍】 arrogant; self-conceited;

jiao

【蕉】 (1) banana; (2) plantain;

芭蕉 bajiao banana;
甘蕉 banana;
美人蕉 canna; Indian shot;
香蕉 banana;

jiao

【燋】 (1) scald; scorch; (2) torch; (3) same as 焦; (4) same as 憔;

jiao

【礁】 reef; shoal;

［礁壁］ reef wall;

［礁石］ reef; rock;

暗礁 submerged reef;
觸礁 on rocks; strike a reef;
環礁 atoll;
裾礁 fringing reef;
珊瑚礁 coral reef;
堤礁 barrier reef;

jiao

【鮫】 shark;

jiao

【鵁】 mycticorax prasinosceles, a kind of water bird;

［鵁鶄］ a kind of aquatic bird mentioned in ancient books;

jiao

【驕】 arrogant; conceited; proud;

［驕傲］ arrogant; big-headed; cock-a-hoop; cock-sure; cocky; conceited; get uppish; get too big for one's breeches; have a big head; pride oneself on; proud; snooty; stuck up; take pride in; too big for one's shoes; uppish; uppity; vain of;
驕傲必敗 pride will cause a fall;
驕傲矜誇 haughty and boastful;
驕傲自大 be bloated with pride; be puffed up; be swollen with pride; conceited and arrogant; cocky; feel high and mighty; have a swelled head; get a swelled head; give oneself airs; self-important; stuck-up;
驕傲自滿 arrogent and complacent; be inflated with pride; big with pride; conceit and self-complacency; conceited;
驕傲自恃 over-confidence and conceit;
過於驕傲 have far too much pride;
我為你感到驕傲 I'm proud of you;
心驕氣傲 arrogant at heart and haughty in manner;

［驕兵］ proud troops;
驕兵必敗 an army puffed up with pride is bound to lose; an army which is cocksure about its invincibility is doomed to defeat; pride goes before a fall; proud troops will certainly be beaten; the self-conceited troops are destined to failure;
驕兵悍將 unruly commander and soldiers;

［驕橫］ arrogant and imperious; insufferably arrogant; overbearing;

[驕橫] ...
驕橫跋扈 arrogant and overbearing; throw one's weight around;
驕橫不法 presumptuous and unlawful;
驕橫一世 overbearing for a time;

[驕矜] haughty; proud; self-important;
驕矜自負 proud and conceited;
驕矜自恃 assume a superior air;
驕矜作態 assume an air of superiority;

[驕慢] arrogant; haughty;

[驕氣] arrogance; conceit; overbearing airs;

[驕奢] arrogance and extravagance;
驕奢淫逸 be rolling luxury; extravagance and dissipation; luxury and debauchery; voluptuous;
淫佚驕奢 lewd and indolent, proud and luxurious;

[驕陽] blazing sun;
驕陽似火 a scorching sun beats down; the sun blazing like a ball of fire; the sun is a ball of fire in the clear sky; the sun is scorching hot; the sun is shining fiercely;

[驕子] privileged person;
天之驕子 a specially privileged person; an unusually blessed person; God's chosen one; the apple of God's eye;

[驕縱] arrogant and wilful; proud and ungovernable;
驕縱放恣 overbearing and debauchery;

天驕 proud son of heaven;
虛驕 superficial and arrogant;

jiao

【鷦】 wren;

[鷦鷯] kitty wren; wren;

[鷦鶥] wren babbler;

[鷦鶯] wren warbler;

jiao²
jiao

【嚼】 chew; masticate; munch;

[嚼臘] chew wax;
味同嚼臘 as dry as dust; it tastes no better than tallow;

[嚼舌] chatter; gossip; wag one's tongue;

[嚼煙] chewing tobacco;

jiao³
jiao

【角】 (1) horn; (2) bugle; horn; (3) cape; headland; promontory; (4) corner; (5) angle;

[角度] (1) angle; degree of an angle; (2) point of view;
從不同角度 at a different angle;
從各種不同角度 from various angles;
從宏觀角度 from a macro perspective;
從全球的角度 from a global perspective;

[角櫃] corner cabinet;

[角距] angular separation;
角距離 angular distance;

[角樓] corner tower;

[角落] corner; nook;
每個角落 every nook and cranny;

[角膜] cornea;
角膜白斑 keratoleukoma;
黏連性角膜白斑 adherent leukoma;
角膜斑 epicauma;
角膜病 keratonosus;
~ 角膜病變 keratopathy;
角膜頂 vertex corneae;
角膜反射 corneal reflex;
角膜乾燥症 xerosis corneae;
角膜鞏膜炎 keratoscleritis;
角膜虹膜炎 corneoiritis;
角膜結膜炎 keratoconjunctivitis;
~ 流行性角膜結膜炎 epidemic keratoconjunctivitis;
角膜潰瘍 corneal ulcer;
角膜擴張 keratoectasia;
角膜癆 phthisis corneas;
角膜裂 corneal cleft;
角膜瘻 corneal fistula;
角膜疱疹 herpes corneae;
角膜軟化 keratomalacia;
角膜痛 keratalgia;
角膜炎 keratitis;
~ 過敏性角膜炎 corneal anaphylaxis;
繼發性角膜炎 secondary keratitis;
~ 潰瘍性角膜炎 ulcerative keratitis;
~ 盤狀角膜炎 disciform keratitis;
~ 泡性角膜炎 phlyctenular keratitis;
~ 深層角膜炎 deep keratitis;
~ 實質性角膜炎 parenchymatous keratitis;
~ 硬化性角膜炎 selerosing keratitis;
巨角膜 macrocornea;
硬化性角膜 sclerocornea;

[角形式] (of hairstyle) angular style;

八角 (1) anise; star anise; (2) aniseed;
倍角 double angle;
鬢角 hair on the temples;

補角 auxiliary angle; supplementary angle;
觸角 antenna; feeler;
藏角 hidden corner;
錯角 alternate angle;
等角 equiangular; isogonal;
底角 base angle;
頂角 vertex angle;
鈍角 obtuse angle;
額角 frontal eminence;
俯角 angle of depression;
拐角 corner; turning;
海角 cape; promontory;
號角 bugle; horn;
犄角 corner; edge;
夾角 angle formed by two lines;
岬角 cape; promontory;
交角 angle between two elements;
口角 (1) corner of the mouth; (2) quarrel;
藍角 blue corner;
稜角 (1) edges and corners; (2) edge; pointedness;
鄰角 adjacent angles;
落角 angle of fall;
內角 interior angle; internal angle;
牛角 ox horn;
平角 straight angle;
牆角 corner formed by two walls;
傾角 (1) dip; (2) inclination; (3) dip angle;
銳角 acute angle;
三角 (1) triangle; (3) trigonometry;
射角 angle of fire;
時角 hour angle;
視角 angle of view; visual angle;
死角 blind angle; dead angle; dead corner;
頭角 brilliance; talent;
凸角 convex corner;
外角 exterior angle; external angle;
犀角 rhinoceros horn;
相角 photo corner;
斜角 (1) oblique angle; (2) bevel angle; (3) beveled corner;
眼角 canthus; the corner of the eye;
羊角 sheep horn;
仰角 angle of elevation;
圓角 filleted corner;
直角 perpendicular angle; right angle;
轉角 corner; outer corner; street corner;
嘴角 corners of the mouth;

jiao

【佼】 (1) attractive; beautiful; charming; handsome; outstanding; (2) a surname;

［佼佼］ above average; outstanding;

jiao

【狡】 crafty; cunning; foxy;

［狡辯］ indulge in sophistry; quibble; resort to sophistry;

［狡狐］ crafty fox;

狡若城狐 as crafty as a fox; as cunning as a fox; as sly as a fox; foxy;

如狐之狡 as crafty as a fox;

［狡猾］ crafty; cunning; slippery; sly; tricky; wilily;

狡猾的對手 cunning opponent;

狡猾的人 cunning person;

像狐狸一樣狡猾 as cunning as a fox;

［狡賴］ deny;

［狡兔］ wily hare;

狡兔三窟 a wily hare has three burrows — a crafty person has more than one hideout; it is a poor mouse that has one hole; the cunning hare secures safety with three openings to its burrow — have many provisions for cunning escape only; the mouse does not trust to one hole only; the mouse that has but one hole is quickly taken;

狡兔死，走狗烹 after the cunning hare is killed, the bound is boiled;

［狡黠］ crafty; cunning; sly;

［狡詐］ crafty; cunning; deceitful;

狡詐奸滑 cunning and knavish;

jiao

【皎】 clear and bright;

［皎皎］ clear and bright; glistening white;

皎皎者易污 the immaculate is easily sullied; the immaculate stains easily;

［皎潔］ bright and clear;

玉心皎潔 a pure heart is unsullied;

jiao

【絞】 (1) entangle; twist; wring; (2) wind; (3) hang by the neck; (4) reaming; (5) skein;

［絞纏］ kink;

［絞車］ winch;

風動絞車 air winch;

欄木絞車 gate winch;

起重絞車 crab winch;

天線絞車 antenna winch;

［絞結］ complicated; entangled;

［絞盤］ capstan;

J

操縱絞盤 control capstan;
動力絞盤 power capstan;
電力絞盤 electric capstan;
捲纜絞盤 warping capstan;
可逆絞盤 reversible capstan;
起錨絞盤 anchor capstan;
牽引絞盤 towing capstan;
手搖絞盤 hand capstan;
水力絞盤 hydraulic capstan;
推桿絞盤 bar capstan;
蒸氣絞盤 steam capstan;

[絞肉機] meat grinder; mincer;

[絞碎機] hasher;
凍肉絞碎機 frozen meat hasher;
肥肉絞碎機 fat hasher; lard hasher;
香腸肉脂絞碎機 sausage meat and fat hasher;

[絞痛] colic;
便秘絞痛 stercoral colic;
腸絞痛 intestinal angina; tormina;
膽絞痛 billary colic;
腹絞痛 angina abdominis; cramps;
闌尾絞痛 appendicular colic;
蠕蟲性絞痛 verminous colic;
銅絞痛 copper colic;
胃絞痛 gastric colic;
消化不良性絞痛 dyspeptic colic;
心絞痛 angina pectoris;
子宮絞痛 uterine colic;
足絞痛 angina cruris;

jiao

【湫】 (1) a river in Gansu Province; (2) small pond;

[湫隘] narrow and low-lying;

jiao

【筊】 (1) a rope made of bamboo strips; (2) a kind of bamboo device used in divination;

jiao

【剿】 destroy; exterminate; put down; stamp out;

[剿盡殺絕] exterminate once and for all;

[剿滅] exterminate; wipe out;

清剿 clean up; suppress;
圍剿 encircle; suppress;
追剿 pursue and wipe out;

jiao

【腳】 (1) foot; (2) base; foot;

[腳板] the sole of the foot;

[腳背] instep;

[腳本] acting copy; acting script; scenario; script;

[腳病] pedopathy;
運動員腳病 athlete's foot;

[腳步] footstep; pace; step; tread;
腳步沉重 have heavy feet; have leaden feet;
腳步大 have big steps;
腳步犯規 foot fault;
腳步快 have a quick step;
腳步踉蹌 dotty; staggering; with unsteady steps;
腳步輕快 have a light foot; light of foot;
腳步聲 footfall; footstep;
放慢腳步 break one's stride; slacken one's pace;
放輕腳步 lighten one's feet; walk softly;
加快腳步 quicken one's steps;
聽到腳步 hear footsteps;
停下腳步 break one's stride;

[腳燈] footlight;

[腳櫈] footrest; footstool;

[腳底] sole;
腳底板兒 sole of the foot;
腳底下 under the feet;

[腳夫] porter;

[腳跟] heel;

[腳踝] ankle;
脆弱的腳踝 delicate ankle;
扭傷的腳踝 sprained ankle;
扭傷腳踝 sprain one's ankle; strain one's ankle; twist one's ankle; wrench one's ankle;
傷了腳踝 hurt one's ankle;
腫脹的腳踝 swollen ankle;

[腳跡] footmarks; footprints;

[腳尖] tip of a toe; tiptoe;
繃直腳尖 point one's toes;

[腳力] (1) strength of one's legs; (2) porter; (3) payment to a porter;
腳力勁健 get strong legs;

[腳鐐] leg irons;
腳鐐手銬 fetters and handcuffs; shackles and manacles;

[腳面] back of a foot; instep;

[腳泡] blisters on the feet;

[腳氣] (1) beriberi; (2) athlete's foot;
腳氣病 (1) beriberi; (2) athlete's foot;

~麻痺性腳氣病 paralytic beriberi;
~濕性腳氣病 wet beriberi;
~萎縮性腳氣病 atrophic beriberi;

[腳手架] scaffold;
挑出式腳手架 bracket scaffold;
懸掛式腳手架 boat scaffold;
竹桿腳手架 bamboo-pole scaffold;
磚工腳手架 bricklayer's scaffold;

[腳踏] pedal;
腳踏車 bicycle;
~腳踏車車道 cycleway;
~腳踏車運動 cycling;
腳踏車運動短褲 cycling shorts;
~腳踏車專用道 cycle lane; cycle path;
~機動腳踏車 motor-mounted bicycle;
~騎腳踏車 cycling; ride a bicycle;
騎腳踏車者 cyclist;
~山地腳踏車 mountain bike;
腳踏船 pedalo;
腳踏兩條船 a fence-sitter; face both ways; fall between two stools; serve two masters; sit on the fence; stand in two boats;
腳踏兩頭便落空 between two stools a person falls to the ground;
腳踏樓梯一步步高 stepping up the stairs – each step is higher;
腳踏實地 do solid work; down to earth; earnest and down to earth; have one's feet firmly planted on solid ground; on firm ground; stand on solid ground; work without bluster and ostentation;
腳踏遊艇 pedalo;

[腳腕子] ankle;

[腳下] under one's feet;
跪倒腳下 throw oneself at sb's feet;

[腳癬] athlete's foot; ringworm of the foot;

[腳心] arch of the foot;

[腳印] footmark; footprint; footstep; step; track;
一串腳印 a trail of footprints;

[腳掌] sole of the foot;

[腳正] straight food;
腳正不怕鞋歪 a clear conscience is a sure card; a straight foot is not afraid of a crooked shoe;
腳正不怕鞋歪，身正不怕影斜 a clear conscience laughs at false accusations; a clean hand wants no washing; a good conscience is a continual feast;

[腳指] toe;
腳指縫 space between two toes;
腳指甲 toe nail;

[腳趾] toe; tootsies;
腳趾頭 toe;
大腳趾 big toe;
~大腳趾頭 big toe;
扭動腳趾 wiggle one's toes;

[腳爪] paw;

[腳鐲] anklet;

拔腳 (1) make a step; take a step; (2) extricate oneself; get away; get free;
蹩腳 inferior; shoddy;
插腳 step inside; take part in;
赤腳 barefoot;
臭腳 smelly feet;
踮腳 stand on tiptoe;
跺腳 stamp one's foot;
跟腳 fitting perfectly;
裹腳 bind the feet;
後腳 (1) rear foot in a step; (2) immediately after;
褲腳 bottom of a trouser leg;
落腳 stay for a time; stop over;
前腳 the forward foot in a step;
牆腳 (1) foot of a wall; (2) foundation;
拳腳 Chinese boxing;
山腳 foot of a hill;
捎腳 give sb a lift;
伸出腳 put one's foot out;
失腳 lose one's footing; slip;
手腳 motion; movement of hands or feet;
順腳 on the way;
跳腳 stamp one's foot;
腿腳 ability to walk; legs and feet;
下腳 get a foothold; plant one's foot;
香港腳 Hong Kong foot;
小腳 bound feet;
歇腳 stop on the way for a rest;
行腳 travel far and wide;
修腳 pedicure;
鴨腳 duck's feet;
頁腳 footer;
一腳 (1) a kick; (2) take part in sth;
一隻腳 a foot;
韻腳 rhyme;
陣腳 (1) front lince; (2) circumstances; position; situation;
注腳 annotation; footnote;
註腳 footnote;

jiao

【僥】 luck; lucky;

［僥倖］ by a fluke; by luck; chance; luckily;
僥倖成功 have the luck to succeed;
僥倖得免 escape by good fortune;
僥倖取勝 gain victory through sheer good luck;
僥倖心情 take a chance with the weather;
心存僥倖 leave things to chance; trust in luck;

jiao

【鉸】 (1) scissors; shears; (2) hinge; (3) shear;

［鉸刀］ reamer;
刀片可調鉸刀 adjustable blade reamer;
對準鉸刀 align reamer;
斜角鉸刀 angular reamer;

［鉸鏈］ hinge;
暗鉸鏈 blind hinge;
蝶形鉸鏈 butterfly hinge;
平接鉸鏈 butt hinge;
雙向鉸鏈 bilateral hinge;

jiao

【餃】 stuffed dumpling ravioli;

［餃子］ dumpling;
餃子皮 dumpling wrapper;
包餃子 make dumplings;
一鍋餃子 a pan of dumplings;

水餃 Chinese dumpling boiled in water;
蒸餃 steamed dumplings;

jiao

【撟】 put right; set right;

jiao

【徼】 fortunate; lucky;

jiao

【矯】 (1) correct; rectify; straighten out; (2) brave; strong; (3) dissemble; feign; pretend;

［矯健］ robust; strong and vigorous;
矯健步伐 vigorous strides;
矯健敏捷 sturdy and nimble;

［矯捷］ agile; brisk; vigorous and nimble;
矯捷如免 as spry as a cat; swift of foot like a hare;

［矯平］ flattening; levelling; roll flattening;

［矯情］ (1) affectedly unconventional; (2) resort to sophistry; use lame arguments; wilfully make trouble;
矯情十足的人 a man of a thousand affectations;
矯情飾詐 deceive by covering up one's real purpose;
矯情鎮物 pretend to be calm;

［矯揉造作］ affected; affection; airs and graces; behave in an affected way; chew up the scenery; contrivance; the affectedness of one's manner; try to deceive by covering up one's real purpose; unnatural and affected;
矯揉造作的 contrived;

［矯飾］ dissemble; feign in order to conceal sth;
矯飾的 pretentious;

［矯形］ orthopedic;
矯形牀 orthopedic bed;
矯形鞋 orthopedic shoe;
矯形醫院 orthopedic hospital;
矯形椅 orthopedic chair;

［矯正］ correct; put right; rectify; straightening;
矯正錯誤 correct a mistake;
矯正發音 correct sb's pronunciation mistakes;
矯正方向 make correction for direction;
矯正口吃 correct a stammer;
矯正偏差 correct a deviation;
矯正視力 correct defects of vision;
矯正手術 corrective surgery;
矯正坐姿 correct faulty sitting posture;
矯枉過正 exceed proper limits; excessive measures; go beyond the proper limits in righting a wrong; overcorrect; overdo in rectifying behaviour; overshoot the mark; straighten the crooked to excess;
熱矯正 hot straightening;

夭矯 curly and majestic;

jiao

【繳】 (1) hand in; hand over; pay; (2) capture;

［繳費］ payment;
稅務繳費 tax payment;

［繳獲］ capture; seize;

［繳款］ pay a bill;
繳款通知 payment notice;
網上繳款 online bill payment;

［繳納］ pay;

［繳稅］ pay taxes;

[繳械] (1) disarm; (2) lay down one's arms; surrender one's weapons;
繳械投降 hand over one's arms and surrender; lay down one's arms and surrender;

上繳 turn in sth to a higher level; turn over sth to the higher authorities;
收繳 capture; take over;

jiao
【蹻】 (1) same as 蹺 ; (2) sandal; shoe;

jiao
【攪】 (1) mix; stir; (2) annoy; disturb;
[攪拌] agitate; agitation; blend; mix; mixing; stir; whip;
攪拌桿 agitator arm;
攪拌機 blender;
~ 單錐鼓式攪拌機 cone blender;
~ 離心式攪拌機 centrifugal blender;
攪拌器 agitator; beater; stirrer;
~ 電動攪拌器 electric agitator;
~ 凍糖攪拌器 icing beater;
~ 風動攪拌器 air-driven agitator;
~ 槳式攪拌器 blade stirrer;
~ 離心攪拌器 centrifugal stirrer;
~ 錨式攪拌器 anchor agitator;
~ 逆轉式攪拌器 contra-rotating;
~ 雙動攪拌器 double motion agitator;
~ 調整攪拌器 correction agitator;
攪拌碗 mixing bowl;
超聲攪拌 ultrasonic agitation;
回流攪拌 flow agitation;
逆流攪拌 countercurrent agitation;
人工攪拌 hand mixing;
液力攪拌 hydraulic agitation;
易於攪拌 stir easily;
[攪打機] beater;
奶油攪打機 cream beater;
糖霜攪打機 cream beater;
[攪動] agitate; agitation; mix; rouse; stir;
充氣攪動 air agitation;
溶池攪動 agitation of bath;
熱攪動 thermal agitation;
聲頻攪動 acoustic agitation;
[攪和] (1) blend; mingle; mix; mix evenly by stirring; stir; (2) mess up; spoil;
[攪亂] arse up; befuddle; confuse; cock up; fuck up; mess up; piss up; screw up; spoil; throw into disorder;
[攪擾] annoy; cause trouble; disturb; harass; stir up; upset;
[攪碎機] masher;
腳踏式攪碎機 foot masher;

打攪 disturb; interrupt; trouble;
胡攪 (1) pester sb with unreasonable demands; (2) argue tediously and vexatiously;

jiao4
jiao
【叫】 (1) cry; shout; (2) call; great; (3) hire; order; (4) call; name; (5) ask; order;
[叫板] ask for trouble; challenge; pick a quarrel;
[叫彩兒] appeal to; be warmly welcomed; welcome; win the applause of;
[叫喊] cry; howl; shout; vociferate; yell;
大喊大叫 cheer and shout; cry and scream; raise a great hue and cry; shout and bellow loudly; shout at the top of one's voice;
怪喊怪叫 bawl and squall;
[叫好] applaud; shout "bravo";
叫好打氣 cheer blatantly;
暗暗叫好 applaud in one's heart; be secretly amazed;
叫倒好 hoot;
拍手叫好 applaud with hand clap; clap one's hands and applaud;
[叫化子] beggar;
[叫喚] call out; cry out;
瞎叫喚 clamour;
[叫回] recall;
[叫勁兒] (1) challenge; have a competition; (2) dispute; oppose;
[叫苦] complain of hardship; complain of suffering; moan and groan;
叫苦不迭 complain incessantly; complain of hard life over and over again; constantly complain; cry bitterness without cease; keep complaining; pour endless grievances;
叫苦叫累 complain of hardship or fatigue;
叫苦哭窮 make a mouth;
叫苦連聲 howl in the bitterness of one's distress;
叫苦連天 complain bitterly; complain to high heaven; cry to heaven; keep on pouring out one's hard lot; pour out endless grievances; showl out in pain; suffer a great deal;

J

暗暗叫苦 groan inwardly;
不叫苦 keep a stiff upper lip;

[叫罵] shout curses;
[叫賣] cry one's goods for sale; cry one's wares; hawk; hawk one's wares; peddle;
[叫門] call at the door to be let in; knock at the door;
沒做虧心事，不怕鬼叫門 if you do nothing wrong, no ghost will knock at your door;
[叫屈] complain of being wronged; protest against an injustice;
[叫嚷] clamour; howl; hue and cry; shout; vociferate;
[叫人] cry for sb;
[叫天天不應，入地地無門] nowhere to turn for help;
[叫囂] clamour; raise a hue and cry;
[叫醒] wake up;
[叫針兒] (1) argue; wrangle; (2) conscientious and meticulous; finicky; inflexible;
[叫座] appeal to the audience; draw a large audience; draw well;
[叫做] be called; be known as;

慘叫 give out sad, shrill cries;
大叫 (1) yell; (2) ululate;
狗叫 yelp;
喊叫 cry out; shout;
號叫 howl; yell;
吼叫 bellow;
呼叫 (1) call out; shout; (2) call;
回叫 call back;
尖叫 scream;
驚叫 cry in fear; scream;
狼叫 a wolf growls; a wolf howls;
驢叫 bray;
名叫 answer to the name of; be called; be known as; be named; by name; by the name of; in the person of; of the name of; rejoice in the name of;
嚷叫 bellow; howl; make an uproar; shout; yell;
嘶叫 neigh; whinny;
啼叫 scream; screech; wail;
鴨叫 quacks of the duck;
羊叫 bas; bleating of a sheep;
豬叫 a pig grunts; a pig squeals; grunting of hogs;

jiao

【校】 check; collate; proofread;
[校訂] check against the authoritative text; emend; revise;
校訂功能 revising function;
校訂譯稿 revise a translated manuscript;
校訂者 reviser;
[校讀] proofreading;
[校對] (1) check; collate; proofread; revise; (2) check against a standard;
校對臂 checking arm;
二級校對 second-grade proofreader;
三級校對 third-grade proofreader;
一級校對 first-grade proofreader;
[校改] alteration; read and correct proofs;
[校核] check;
[校勘] collate; emendate;
[校驗] check; proof; test; verify;
校驗加法 check addition;
校驗器 checker;
~零位校驗器 zero checker;
~數據輸出校驗器 data logger checker;
比色校驗 colour check;
邊緣校驗 bias check;
電碼校驗 code check;
控制校驗 control check;
會計校驗 accounting check;
平衡校驗 balance check;
一致性校驗 consistency check;
自動校驗 built-in check;
[校樣] proof;
長條校樣 galley proof; slip proof;
初校樣 first proof;
讀校樣 correct the proofs;
[校閱] read and revise;
[校正] adjust; check; correct; equalizing; proofread and correct; rectify; revise;
校正錯字 correct misprints;
校正器 corrector;
~高度校正器 altimeter corrector;
~孔徑校正器 aperture corrector;
~瞄準儀校正器 aim corrector;
~色場校正器 colour field corrector;
~象散校正器 astigmatism corrector;
~振幅校正器 amplitude corrector;
重放校正 playback equalizing;
動作校正 action correction;
附加校正 additive correction;
高度校正 altitude correction;
孔徑校正 aperture correction;

象散校正 astigmatic correction;
餘輝校正 after glow correction;
枕形畸變校正 pillow distortion equalizing;

[校準] calibrate; calibration;
校準器 calibrator;
~方位校準器 azimuth calibrator;
~高度錶校準器 altimeter calibrator;
~機內校準器 built-in calibrator;
~加速計校準器 accelerometer calibrator;
~晶體校準器 crystal calibrator;
~距離校準器 range calibrator;
~聲級校準器 sound level calibrator;
比較校準 comparison calibration;
場校準 field calibration;
初始校準 initial calibration;
磁道校準 track calibrate;
電橋校準 bridge calibration;
動態校準 dynamic calibration;
方位校準 azimuth calibration; bearing calibration;
飛行校準 flight calibration;
輻射計校準 radiometer calibration;
互易校準 reciprocity calibration;
計量器校準 meter calibration;
靜力校準 static calibration;
絕對校準 absolute calibration;
亮度校準 brightness calibration;
靈敏度校準 sensitivity calibration;
頻率校準 frequency calibration;
熱校準 thermal calibration;
聲場校準 sound field calibration;
聲壓校準 sound pressure calibration;
時間校準 time calibration;
瞬時校準 transient calibration;
天平校準 balance calibration;
外部校準 external calibration;
壓力校準 pressure calibration;
用水校準 calibration by water;
自動校準 automatic calibration;

参校 proofread;

jiao

【教】 (1) instruct; teach; (2) religion;

[教案] lesson plan; teaching plan; teaching notes;

[教本] textbook;

[教鞭] teacher's pointer;

[教材] instructional material; instructional resources; teaching material;
活教材 live teaching materials; vivid examples for education;
油印活頁教材 mimeographed sheets of teaching materials;

[教程] course of study;

[教導] enlighten; give guidance; instruct; instruction; teach; under the tutelage;
教導活動 instructional activity;
教導有方 skillful in teaching and able to provide guidance;
聽從父母的教導 be receptive to parents' advice;

[教父] godfather; godparent;
教父教母 godparents;

[教給] impart knowledge on sb;

[教官] drillmaster; instructor;

[教壞] lead astray; misguide;

[教皇] pontiff; pope;
教皇的 pontifical;

[教會] church;
教會分裂 schism;
教會會議 synod;
教會教育 ecclesiastical education;
教會學 ecclesiology;
教會學校 church school; missionary school;
教會醫院 missionary hospital;
教會中心主義 ecclesiasticism;

[教誨] edify; teaching; instruction;
教誨的 edifying;

[教具] teaching aid;
立體教具 three-dimensional aid;

[教科書] coursebook; textbook;
標準教科書 standard textbook;
大學教科書 university textbook;
規定教科書 prescribed textbook;
國定教科書 national textbook;
簡明教科書 brief textbook;
審定教科書 authorized textbook;
一本教科書 a textbook;
中小學教科書 elementary and high school textbook; school textbook;
專業教科書 specialized textbook;

[教練] (1) coach; drill; practise; train; (2) coach; instructor; trainer;
教練員 trainer;
高級教練 senior coach;
主教練 head coach;
助理教練 assistant coach;
總教練 chief coach;

[教齡] years of teaching;
[教名] Christian name;
[教母] godmother; godparent;
[教女] goddaughter;
[教派] denomination; religious sect;
[教區] diocese; parish;
教區記事錄 parish register;
教區教堂 parish church;
教區居民 parishioner;
教區學校 parochial school;
教區執事 parish clerk;
[教猱昇木] give boldness to an evildoer; make an evildoer bold; teach a monkey to climb a tree—stir up bad people to evil;
[教師] chalkie; mentor; schoolteacher; teacher;
教師公會 teachers' union;
教師節 Teacher's Day;
教師職業 the teaching profession;
班級教師 class teacher;
大學教師 don; university teacher;
代課教師 emergency teacher; substitute teacher; supply teacher;
二級教師 second-grade teacher;
~小學二級教師 primary school second-grade teacher;
~中學二級教師 seconday school second-grade teacher;
翻譯教師 translation teacher;
高級教師 senior teacher;
~小學高級教師 senior teacher;
~中學高級教師 senior teacher;
家庭教師 home tutor; private teacher;
兼職教師 part-time teacher;
臨時教師 provisional teacher;
男教師 schoolmaster;
女教師 mistress; schoolmistress;
~家庭女教師 governess;
三級教師 third-grade teacher;
~小學三級教師 primary school third-grade teacher;
~中學三級教師 seconday school third-grade teacher;
實習教師 student teacher; trainee teacher;
實習指導教師 instructor;
~高級實習指導教師 senior instructor;
~二級實習指導教師 second-grade instructor;
~三級實習指導教師 third-grade instructor;
~一級實習指導教師 first-grade instructor;
特級教師 teacher of special grade;
外籍教師 foreign teacher;
小學教師 elementary teacher;
一級教師 first-grade teacher;
~小學一級教師 primary school first-grade teacher;
~中學一級教師 secondary school first-grade teacher;
一名教師 a teacher;
中學教師 high school teacher; secondary school teacher;
住校教師 resident tutor;
專職教師 full-time teacher;
[教士] Christian missionary; clergy; clergyman; priest;
教士的 clerical;
教區教士 secular clergy;
女教士 clergywoman; priestess;
寺院教士 regular clergy;
[教室] classroom; school room;
教室參觀 class visitation;
活動教室 mobile classroom;
通用教室 general purpose classroom;
一間教室 a classroom;
在三樓有四間教室 there are four classrooms on the second floor;
專用教室 private classroom; special classroom;
自動化教室 automated classroom;
[教授] (1) instruct; lecture on; teach; (2) professor;
教授得法 have tact in teaching;
教授有方 teach well;
大學教授 university professor;
擔任教授 hold a professorship;
訪問教授 visiting professor;
副教授 associate professor;
互換教授 exchange professors;
兼任教授 adjunct professor;
講座教授 chair professor;
交換教授 exchange professor;
客座教授 guest professor; visiting professor;
名譽教授 honorary professor;
榮譽退休教授 emeritus professor; professor emeritus;
一位教授 a professor;
助理教授 assistant professor;
專任教授 full-time professor;
[教唆] abet; abetment; incite; instigate; put sb up to sth;

教唆犯 abetter;
教唆犯罪 abet a crime;
教唆者 abettor; instigator;
教唆作惡 instigate sb to do evil; urge sb on to evildoing;

[教堂] cathedral; chapel; church;
教堂長椅 pew;
教堂尖塔 steeple;
教堂墓地 churchyard;
教堂執事 churchwarden;
大教堂 cathedral;
~一座大教堂 a cathedral;
婚禮教堂 wedding chapel;
小教堂 antechapel; chantry; chapel;
猶太教堂 synagogue;

[教條] creed; doctrine; dogma;
教條主義 doctrinairism; dogmatism;
~教條主義者 doctrinaire;

[教廷] the Holy See; the Vatican;

[教頭] coach;

[教徒] believer of a religion;

[教務] educational administration;
教務長 registrar;

[教學] (1) education; teaching; (2) teaching and studying; (3) teacher and student;
教學大綱 syllabus; teaching syllabus;
教學督導 instructional supervision;
教學法 didactics; pedagogy; teaching method;
~詞本位教學法 word method;
~翻譯教學法 translation pedagogy;
~各科教學法 special didactics;
~口頭教學法 oral approach;
~普通教學法 general didactics;
~情景教學法 situation method;
教學翻譯 pedagogical translation;
教學反饋 teaching-learning feedback;
教學方法 teaching method;
教學方針 principles of teaching;
教學風格 teaching style;
教學改革 reform in education;
教學工作 teaching;
教學活動 teaching activities;
教學機 teaching machine;
教學技巧 scholastic skills;
教學計劃 teaching plan;
教學理論研究 educology;
教學領導能力 instructional leadership;
教學樓 classroom building; teaching building;
教學模式 teaching model;
教學內容 content of courses;
教學片 educational film;
教學品質 quality of teaching;
~提高教學品質 improve the quality of teaching;
教學評價 teaching evaluation;
教學人員 faculty; teaching staff;
教學設計 teaching design;
教學實習 do practice teaching; student teaching;
~教學實習生 student teacher;
教學水準 level of teaching;
~提高教學水準 raising the level of teaching;
教學團隊 teaching team;
教學相長 both teachers and students make progress by learning from each other; teaching benefits teacher and student alike; teaching benefits teachers as well as students; teaching improves study and study improves teaching; teaching others teaches yourself; to teach is to learn; to the benefit of both teachers and students;
教學效果 teaching results;
教學用圖 picture for teaching;
教學語法 pedagogical grammar;
教學語言學 educational linguistics;
教學原則 teaching principles;
教學質量 quality of instruction;
教學中心 learning centre;
教學助理 teaching assistant;
暗示教學 teaching by allusion;
班級教學 class teaching;
單元教學 composite teaching;
電化教學 electrification instruction; audio-visual education;
翻譯教學 translation teaching;
互教互學 teach and learn from each other;
活動教學 activity teaching;
家中教學 homeschool;
矯正教學 corrective teaching;
實物教學 object teaching;
示範教學 demonstration teaching; teaching by demonstration;
填鴨式教學 the cramming method of teaching; the duck-stuffing type of teaching;
現場教學 on-the-spot teaching;
巡迴教學 circuit teaching;
遙距教學 distance learning;
遠程教學 distance learning;

遠距離教學 long-distance education;
自動化教學 automated teaching;

[教訓] (1) lesson; moral; (2) chide; educate; give sb a talking; lecture sb; teach sb a lesson;
教訓一頓 read sb a lesson;
得到教訓 learn one's lesson;
給人一個教訓 teach sb a lesion;
吸取教訓 draw a lesson from sth; take warning from sth;
一個教訓 a lesson;

[教養] (1) bring up; educate; train; (2) breeding; culture; education; upbringing;
教養院 borstal;
沒有教養 ill bred;
缺乏教養 lack breeding;
養而不教 bear children without educating them; feed only and do not teach;
有教養 cultured; educated; well bred;
~有教養的人 a man of culture;

[教益] benefit from advise; benefit gained from sb's wisdom; enlightenment;
面聆教益 benefit by your advice;

[教義] credo;

[教友] coreligionist;

[教育] inculcate; educate; education; schooling; teach;
教育背景 educational background;
教育部 ministry of education;
教育當局 education authority;
教育電視 educational television;
~教育電視節目 educational television programme;
~教育電視台 educational television station;
~教育電視衛星 satellite instructional television;
教育法 educational law;
教育方針 educational policy;
~貫徹教育方針 carry out the educational policy; implement the educational policy;
~全面貫徹教育方針 carry out the educational policy; implement the educational policy;
教育附加稅 additional tax of education;
教育改革 educational reform;
~進行教育改革 carry on educational reforms; make educational reforms; make reforms in education;
教育工作者 educator;
教育觀 outlook of education;
教育管理 educational management;
教育規劃 educational planning;
教育國際化 education internationalization;
教育過程 educative process;
教育化 educationalize;
教育機構 educational establishment;
教育家 educationalist; educationist;
教育界 educational circles;
~高等教育界 academia;
教育結構 educational structure;
教育經濟學 educational economics;
教育藍圖 education blueprint;
教育倫理學 ethics of education;
教育媒體 educational media;
教育目標 educational objectives;
教育評價 educational evaluation;
教育人口 educational population;
教育設施 educational institution;
教育生態 educational ecology;
教育事業 educational undertaking;
教育體制 educational structure;
教育危機 educational crisis;
教育系統工程 educational system engineering;
教育現代化 modernization of education;
教育心理學 educational psychology;
教育學 pedagogy;
~教育學家 educationist;
~教育學院 college of education;
~比較教育學 comparative education;
~記述教育學 descriptive pedagogy;
~社會教育學 social pedagogy;
~特殊教育學 special pedagogy;
~應用教育學 applied pedagogy;
~幼兒教育學 preschool pedagogy;
教育語言 educational language;
~教育語言學 educational linguistics;
教育預測 educational forecasting;
教育園 educational park;
教育質量 quality of education;
~提高教育質量 improve the quality of education;
教育制度 educational system;
教育組織 educational organization;
安全教育 safety education;
博才教育 versatile education;
補償教育 compensational education; compensatory education;
超前教育 superior education;

成人教育 adult education;
初等教育 elementary education; primary education;
大學教育 college education; university education;
分配性教育 distributive education;
高等教育 advanced education; higher education;
~成人高等教育 adult higher education;
公立教育 public education; state education;
公民教育 civic education;
國民教育 national education;
航空航天教育 aerospace education;
回歸教育 recurrent education;
活教育 living education;
獲得教育 acquire an education;
基礎教育 basic education;
~成人基礎教育 adult basic education;
教會教育 ecclesiastical education;
接受教育 get an education; have an education; receive an education; receive one's instruction; take one's instruction;
進修教育 continuing education; further education;
考察教育 make an inspection on education;
理想教育 ideal education;
良好教育 good education;
男女同校教育 co-education;
普及教育 popularize education; universal education;
普通教育 general education;
青少年教育 adolescent education;
情感教育 affective education;
輕視教育 despise education;
全面教育 all-round education;
全日制教育 full-time education; full-time schooling;
世俗教育 lay education;
受教育 gain an education; get an education; obtain an education; receive an education;
雙語教育 bilingual education;
素質教育 quality-based education;
私立教育 private education;
特殊教育 special education;
提供教育 give an education; provide an education;
推廣教育 spread education;
獻身教育 devote oneself to education;
學齡前教育 preschool education;
學前教育 preschool education;
學校教育 schooling;
義務教育 compulsory education; compulsory schooling; free education;
應試教育 examination-oriented education;
再教育 re-education;
正規教育 formal education;
職業教育 vocational education;
中等教育 secondary education;
~普及中等教育 making secondary education universal;
中學教育 high school education; secondary education;
重視教育 take education seriously;
終身教育 lifelong education;
綜合教育 all-round education; comprehensive education;
主體性教育 principal education;

[教員] instructor; teacher;

[教正] give comments and suggestions;
尚請教正 please advise and correct;

[教主] founder of a religion;

[教子] godchild; godson;
教子有方 bring up one's children properly;

[教宗] pontiff;
教宗的 pontifical;

罷教 teachers' strike;
拜物教 fetishism;
幫教 give guidance; help and educate; help and teach;
保教 assure an education to students; guarantee education and support to children;
弼教 assist in education;
懲教 correction;
傳教 do missionary work; preach one's religion;
賜教 condescend to teach; grant instruction;
道教 (1) Daoist; (2) Daoism;
佛教 Buddhism;
國教 state religion;
候教 await one's instruction;
回教 Islam;
基督教 Christian religion; Christianity;
家教 family education; upbringing;
見教 favour sb with one's advice;
景教 Nestorianism;
喇嘛教 Lamaism;
請教 ask for advice; consult;
求教 ask for advice;

儒教 teachings of Confucius;
身教 teach others by one's own example; teaching with deeds;
説教 deliver a sermon; preach;
叨教 many thanks for your advice;
討教 ask for advice;
天主教 Catholicism;
調教 (1) guide; teach; (2) look after and tame livestock;
文教 culture and education;
邪教 heresy;
新教 Protestantism;
信教 be religious;
宣教 propaganda and education;
雅教 your honoured advice;
言教 give verbal directions; teach by precept; teach by words;
耶穌教 Protestantism;
一神教 monotheism;
伊斯蘭教 Islam; Islamism;
遺教 advice, teaching left by the deceased;
異教 heathenism; paganism;
印度教 Hinduism;
猶太教 Judaism;
在教 be a believer;
正教 Orthodox Church;
政教 the state and the church;
指教 give advice; instruct;
執教 teacher;
主教 bishop;
助教 teaching assistant; tutor;
宗教 religion;

jiao
【窖】 (1) cellar; vault; (2) store things in a cellar;
[窖藏] cellar; depot;
[窖穴] storage pit;
圓形窖穴 round storage pit;

冰窖 icehouse;
菜窖 vegetable cellar;
地窖 cellar;
酒窖 wine cellar;

jiao
【較】 (1) as compare with; compare; in comparison with; (2) comparatively; fairly; quite; rather; relatively; (3) clear; conspicuous; glaring; marked; obvious; (4) compete; dispute; (5) earlier or later; in a greater or lesser degree; more or less;
[較比] comparatively; quite; relatively;
[較炳] clear; conspicuous; obvious;
[較差] relatively poor;
[較大] more;
[較勁兒] (1) have a trial of strength; (2) become worse; get worse;
[較量] (1) have a contest; have a test of strength; (2) argue; dispute;
[較略] generally speaking; in general;
[較然] clear; explicit; marked; obvious;
[較小] less;
[較議] dispute; refute;
[較真兒] earnest; earnestly; seriously;
[較著] conspicuous; obvious;

比較 compare; contrast;
計較 (1) calculate and compare; (2) argue; dispute; (3) consider; plan;

jiao
【斠】 leveling stick;

jiao
【噍】 chew; munch; nibble;
[噍類] living people;

jiao
【嶠】 high-pointed mountain;

jiao
【撟】 raise;

jiao
【徼】 (1) boundary; frontier; (2) take an inspection trip;

jiao
【轎】 (1) palankeen; palanquin; (2) sedan chair;
[轎車] (1) carriage; (2) bus; car; limousine;
大型豪華轎車 limo; limousine;
雙門小轎車 coupe;
一輛轎車 a limousine;

彩轎 bridal sedan chair;
花轎 bridal sedan chair;
山轎 mountain chair;

jiao
【醮】 (1) religious service; (2) marriage; wedding;

打醮 say Mass for the departed souls;

jiao

【覺】 nap; sleep;

補個覺 catch up on some sleep;
睡個好覺 sleep tight;
睡覺 sleep;
午覺 afternoon nap; noontime snooze;

jie¹

jie

【皆】 all; each and every;

jie

【偕】 (1) accompany; (2) together;

jie

【接】 (1) come close to; come into contact with; (2) connect; join; put together; (3) catch; take hold of; (4) receive; take; (5) meet; welcome; (6) take over;

[接班] carry on; succeed; take one's turn on duty; take over from;
接班人 heir; successor;
~ 熱門接班人 heir apparent;
~ 預計接班人 heir apparent;

[接觸] (1) come into contact with; get in touch with; (2) engage; (3) contact; touch;
接觸不良 have poor contact;
接觸傳染 contagion;
接觸從句 contact clause;
接觸恐怖 aphephobia;
接觸器 contactor;
~ 閉塞接觸器 blocking contactor;
~ 輔助接觸器 auxiliary contactor;
~ 加速接觸器 accelerating contactor;
~ 交流接觸器 alternating current contactor;
~ 離心接觸器 centrifuge contactor;
~ 連續接觸器 continuous contactor;
~ 氣閘接觸器 air-break contactor;
接觸物 contactant;
接觸性運動 contact sport;
接觸語言 contact language;
當面接觸 personal contact;
空氣接觸 air contact;
目光接觸 eye contact;
親身接觸 personal contact;
異常接觸 abnormal contact;

[接達點] access point;

[接待] admit; receive;
接待客人 receive guests; take in guests;
接待室 antechamber;
熱情接待 a warm reception; an enthusiastic reception;
~ 給予熱情接待 accord an enthusiastic reception; give a warm reception;
~ 受到熱情接待 be given a warm reception;

[接地] earthing;
板接地 plate earthing;
保護接地 protective earthing;
表面接地 surface earthing;
多點接地 multipoint earthing;
聯鎖接地 interlocked earthing;
外殼接地 earthing of casing;
有效接地 useful earthing;
中點接地 neutral earthing;

[接點] contact;
按鈕接點 button contact;
不良接點 bad contact;
電池接點 battery contact;
電弧接點 arc contact;
滅弧接點 blowout contact;

[接風] welcome visitors;
接風洗塵 give a welcome dinner; treat sb to a dinner on arriving;
把酒接風 pour out the wine of welcome;
擺酒接風 give a banquet to welcome visitors from afar;
治席接風 give a feast in honour of the newly arrived;

[接縫] seam;
緊密接縫 impervious seam;
鍋爐接縫 boiler seam;

[接管] take over; take over control;
接管工作 takeover;

[接軌] (1) connect the rails; (2) integrate;
與國際接軌 be brought in line with international practice; be geared to international standards;

[接合] (1) bonding; copulation; (2) joint; jointing; juncture; (3) zygosis;
接合孢子 zygosperm;
接合嵴 zygon;
接合菌 zygomycete;
接合器 adaptor; bonder; maker;
~ 剪刀接合器 scissors adaptor;
~ 密封接合器 packing adaptor;
~ 球形接合器 ball adaptor;
~ 熱壓接合器 thermocompression bonder;
~ 聲波接合器 sonic bonder;

J

~手工接合器 manual bonder;
~天線接合器 antenna adaptor;
~引線接合器 wire bonder;
接合染色體 zygosome;
接合絲 zygomite;
接合細胞 zygoneure;
接合向性 zygotaxis;
接合性 zygosity;
接合植物 zygophyte;
接合子梗 zygophore;
八字形接合 splayed jointing;
片接合 chip bonding;
輥壓接合 roll bonding;
壓力接合 compression bonding;
正常接合 normal bonding;
~不正常接合 abnormal bonding;

[接濟] give financial help to; give material assistance to; offer pecuniary aid to;

[接見] give access to; grant an interview to; receive sb;
接見代表團 give an audience to a delegation;

[接近] approach; close to; draw near; near;
接近死期 near to death;

[接口] interface;
接口處理機 interface processor;
接口分析 interface analysis;
接口卡 interface card;
基本接口 basic interface;
兼容性接口 compatible interface;
通道接口 channel interface;

[接力] relay;
接力區 change-over area
~接力區標誌 change-over mark
接力棒 relay baton
接力賽 relay race;
接力賽跑 relay race;

[接連] in a row; in succession; on end; running;
接連不斷 continuously; in rapid succession; incessantly;

[接納] accept; admit; adopt; take in;
自我接納 self-acceptance;

[接片] collage;
接片機 splicer; splicing machine;

[接洽] arrange with; consult with; take up a matter with;

[接球] catch a ball; return a ball;
接球方 receiving side;
接球技術好 return well;
接球前衛 fly half; stand-off half;
接球失誤 muff a ball;
接球手 catcher;

[接任] accede; succeed; take over; take over from sb;
接任主席職務 take over the chairmanship;

[接生] deliver; deliver a child; practise midwifery;
接生員 midwife;

[接收] (1) accept; receive; (2) expropriate; take over; (3) admit;
接收機 radio; receiver;
~分集接收機 diversity receiver;
~三用接收機 three-way radio;
~遠距離接收機 distant receiver;
~直接接收機 direct-view receiver;
~自差式接收機 auto dyne receiver;
接收天線 receiver antenna;
接收站 receiving station;
接收制式 receiving system;
定向接收 beam reception; directional reception;
聲頻接收 audible reception;
聽覺接收 aural reception;

[接手] take over; take up matters;

[接受] accept; acceptance; embrace; take;
接受賄賂 accept bribes; on the take;
接受力 acceptability;
接受率 take-up;
接受性 acceptability;
接受者 on the receiving end; recipient;
~接受者介詞 preposition of recipient;
~接受者語言 receptor language;
接受主語 recipient subject;
和盤接受 accept sth in its entirety; accept the entire fact; accept the whole truth;
拒不接受 refuse to accept;
可接受[的] acceptable;
樂於接受 accept with pleasure; take sth like a shot;
臨時接受 provisional acceptance;
難以接受 difficult to accept; stick in sb's craw; stick in sb's throat;
無法接受 beyond the pale;
無奈地接受 lump it;
無條件接受 unconditionally accept;
喜不喜歡都得接受 like it or lump it;

[接送] pick up and send off;
上下學接送 school run;

[接替] replace; succeed; take over; take the place of;

[接通] (1) connect; get through; put through;

(2) contact; get in touch with; meet; (3) have knowledge of; know about;
接通電話 one's call has been put through;
[接頭] joint; splice;
對縫接頭 butt splice;
附着接頭 adhesive joint;
毗連接頭 abutting joint;
斜坡接頭 bevel splice;
[接吻] kiss;
[接線] wiring;
接線板 switchboard;
[接着] (1) catch; (2) carry on; follow; go on; proceed;
[接踵] follow on sb's heels;
接踵而來 arrive in quick succession; arrive one after another in rapid succession; come in quick succession; come one after another; come one on the heels of the other; follow close on another; in the train of;
接踵而起 arise after another; follow on the heels of;
接踵而行 follow at sb's heels;
[接種] inoculate; inoculation; vaccination;
加強接種 booster inoculation;
尿囊接種 allantoic inoculation;
人工接種 artificial inoculation;

暗接 secret joint;
承接 (1) hold out a vessel to have liquid poured into it; (2) continue;
鍛接 forge welding;
焊接 solder; weld;
嫁接 graft;
剪接 video editing;
間接 (1) indirect; (2) second-hand;
交接 (1) connect; join; (2) hand over; (3) associate with;
鉸接 articulate; join with a hinge;
連接 join; link;
聯接 (1) join; link; (2) mate;
鄰接 adjoin; border on;
鉚接 rivet;
內接 inscribe;
銜接 join; link up;
相接 connect with; meet;
芽接 bud grafting;
延接 receive guests;
迎接 greet; meet;
應接 receive;
枝接 scion grafting;
直接 direct; immediate;
肘接 toggle joint;

jie

【揭】 (1) take off; tear off; (2) lift; uncover; (3) bring to light; expose; show up;
[揭暗私] reveal sb's secrets;
[揭擺] bring to light;
[揭背車] hatchback;
[揭不開鍋] go hungry; have nothing in the pot; have nothing to eat; short of food;
[揭醜] reveal; unmask;
[揭穿] debunk; expose; lay sth bare; show up;
揭穿謊言 expose a lie;
揭穿欺詐行為 show up a fraud;
揭穿陰謀 show up an evil plot;
揭穿真面目 cut sb down to size;
[揭底] lay bare the inside story; reveal the inside story;
[揭短] catch sb on the raw; find out sb's weaknesses; rake up sb's faults;
揭人之短 bring up sb's failures; expose sb's defects; expose sb's weaknesses; tread on sb's corns;
[揭發] bring to light; disclose; expose; ferret sth out; give the lie to; lay sth bare; lay open; reveal; show up; uncover; unmask;
揭發間諜 expose a spy;
揭發陰謀 disclose a dark scheme; expose a secret plot;
揭發陰私 expose sb's secrets;
揭發罪行 bring a crime to light;
[揭竿] raise bamboo poles;
揭竿而起 raise a rebellion; rise in a rebellion; rise in resistance; rise up in arms; rise up in revolt; start an uprising;
揭竿舉義 rise in revolt with sharpened sticks;
[揭鍋] bare; reveal;
[揭開] disclose; open; reveal; uncover;
揭開面具 lift the mask — uncover the truth;
[揭露] bring to light; disclose; expose; ferret sth out; lay sth bare; show sth up; uncover;
[揭密] reveal;
[揭幕] inaugurate; unveil a monument;
揭幕賽 opener; opening match;

[揭示] announce; proclaim; promulgate; yield up;
公開揭示 publicly proclaim;
[揭曉] announce; announce the results; make known; publish;

jie

【結】 bear; form; produce;
[結巴] (1) stammer; stumble; stutter; (2) stammerer; stutterer;
結結巴巴 hesitate in speaking; stammer; stammer out; stumble over; stutter;
[結腸] colon;
結腸癌 colon cancer;
結腸病 colonopathy; disease of the colon;
結腸出血 bleeding from the colon; colonorrhagia;
結腸炎 colitis;
~出血性結腸炎 haemorrhagic colitis;
~傳染性結腸炎 infectious colitis;
~節段性結腸炎 segmental colitis;
~局限性結腸炎 regional colitis;
~潰瘍性結腸炎 ulcerative colitis;
~膜性結腸炎 membranous colitis;
~尿毒症結腸炎 uraemic colitis;
~全結腸炎 pancolitis;
~缺血性結腸炎 ischaemic colitis;
~肉芽腫性結腸炎 granulomatous colitis;
~息肉狀結腸炎 colitis polyposa;
痙攣性結腸 spastic colon;
巨結腸 giant colon;
鉛管狀結腸 lead-pipe colon;
右結腸 right colon;
長結腸 dolichocolon;
[結關] clearance;
結關費 customs clearing fee;
結關港 port of clearance;
出口結關 customs clearance;
[結果] (1) bear fruit; fruit; (2) result; upshot; (3) effected; resultative;
結果賓語 resultant object;
結果補語 resultative complement;
結果從屬連詞 subordinator of result;
結果都一樣 amount to the same thing; come to the same thing;
結果格 result case;
結果間接賓語 resultative indirect object;
結果連詞 resultative conjunction;
結果連繫動詞 result linking verb;
結果體 effective aspect;
結果狀語 adverbial of result;
~結果狀語從句 adverbial clause of result;
比較結果 comparative result;
比擬結果 analogue result;
必然結果 corollary; inevitable outcome;
~預言必然結果 forecast the inevitable outcome;
毫無結果 for nothing;
計算結果 computed result;
檢驗結果 check result;
沒有結果 come to nothing;
有偏結果 biased result;
最終結果 end result;
[結核] consumption; TB; tuberculosis;
結核病 TB; tuberculosis;
~初期結核病 pretuberculosis;
結核瘤 tuberculoma;
播散性結核 disseminated tuberculosis;
非典型結核 atypical tuberculosis;
肺結核 consumption; pulmonary tuberculosis; TB; tuberculosis;
肺門結核 hilus tuberculosis;
骨結核 bone tuberculosis;
硅肺結核 silicotuberculosis;
繼發性結核 secondary tuberculosis;
開放性結核 open tuberculosis;
膀胱結核 bladder tuberculosis;
滲出性結核 exudative tuberculosis;
矽肺結核 silicotuberculosis;
原發型結核 primary tuberculous complex;
原發性結核 primary tuberculosis;
增生性結核 productive tuberculosis;
結核性肺炎 tuberculous pneumonia;
[結喉] Adam's apple;
[結痂] encrustation; form a crust;
結痂性疥瘡 crusted scabies;
結痂性濕疹 eczema crustosum;
[結節] tuber;
結節病 nodule disease;
結節性紅斑 erythema nodosum;
麻瘋結節 leproma;
梅毒結節 syphilitic node;
梅毒性結節 tophus syphiliticus;
痛風結節 gouty node;
痛性結節 tuberculum dolorosum;
[結晶] (1) crystal; (2) crystallization; (3) crystalize;
結晶構造學 crystallolography;
結晶器 crystallizer;
~分級結晶器 classifying crystallizer;
~分批結晶器 batch crystallizer;
~攪拌結晶器 agitated crystallizer;

~ 攪動結晶器 agigated batch crystallizer;
~ 密閉結晶器 closed crystallizer;
結晶學 crystallography;
~ 構造結晶學 structural crystallography;
~ 化學結晶學 chemical crystallography;
~ 幾何結晶學 geometrical crystallography;
~ 描述結晶學 descriptive crystallography;
~ 衍射結晶學 diffraction crystallography;
~ 中子結晶學 neutron crystallography;
大量結晶 bulk crystallization;
分批結晶 batch crystallization;
共晶結晶 eutectic crystallization;
假結晶 crystalloid;
聚集結晶 accumulative crystallization;
退火結晶 annealing crystallization;

[結膜] conjunctiva;
結膜反射 conjunctival reflex;
結膜乾燥 xeroma;
結膜黃斑 pinguecula;
結膜結石 lithiasis conjunctivae;
結膜炎 conjunctivitis;
單純性結膜炎 simple conjunctivitis;
~ 過敏性結膜炎 anaphylactic conjunctivitis;
~ 角膜結膜炎 keratoconjunctivitis;
~ 結節性結膜炎 nodular conjunctivitis;
~ 結石性結膜炎 calcareous conjunctivitis;
~ 顆粒性結膜炎 granular conjunctivitis;
~ 淋病性結膜炎 gonorrhoeal conjunctivitis;
~ 淋球菌性結膜炎 gonococcal conjunctivitis;
~ 流行性結膜炎 epidemic conjunctivitis;
~ 濾泡性結膜炎 follicular conjunctivitis;
~ 牛痘性結膜炎 vaccinial conjunctivitis;
~ 膿溢性結膜炎 blennorrheal conjunctivitis;
~ 泡性結膜炎 phlyctenular conjunctivitis;
~ 皮膚結膜炎 dermatoconjunctivitis;
~ 濕疹性結膜炎 eczematous conjunctivitis;
~ 特應性結膜炎 atopic conjunctivitis;
~ 嬰兒膜性結膜炎 infantile purulent conjunctivitis;
~ 游泳池結膜炎 swimming pool conjunctivitis;

[結石] calculus; stone;
結石病 calculosis;
~ 尿酸結石病 uric acid lithiasis;
~ 膀胱結石病 cystolithiasis;
尿路結石 urinary calculi;
尿酸結石 urate calculus;
膀胱結石 bladder stone; vesical calculus;
皮膚結石 skin stone;

[結實] durable; solid; sturdy;

[結轉] carry-over;
結轉金額 carry-over;

[結帳] make out the bill;
結帳離開 check out;
分單結帳 separate bills;
合單結帳 one bill for all;

[結子] seed;

巴結 all over sb; bootlick; brown-nose; buddy up; butter up sb; cotton up to; cozy up to; curry favour with sb; fawn on; flatter; get in with sb; lay on the butter; lay the butter on; lick sb's boots; lick sb's shoes; make up to; play up to; polish the apple; soak sb down; stand in with sb; suck up to; toady to sb; try hard to please;
辦結 deal with and finish; hand and wind up a legal case; take up and complete;
閉結 constipation;
編結 knit; weave;
綵結 woman's hair decoration;
腸扭結 volvulus;
打活結 tie a fast knot;
締結 conclude; establish;
凍結 freeze; freezing;
勾結 collaborate with; collude; collude with; collusion; gang up with; hand and glove with; in league with; join in a plot; play footsie with;
歸結 (1) put in a nutshell; sum up; (2) end of a story;
喉結 Adam's apple; laryngeal protuberance;
糾結 be entangled with; be intertwined with;
連結 cohesive;
聯結 bind; concatenated; join; tie;
了結 bring to an end; finish; settle; wind up;
領結 tie;
黏結 agglutination; bond; cement; cohere;
凝結 coagulate; coagulation; condense; congeal; curdling;
集結 build up; concentrate; mass;
絞結 complicated; entangled;
燒結 sintering;
雙環結 double knot;
死結 fast knot; problem that defies solution; encased knot;
團結 cohesion; draw together; rally; unite; unity;
完結 bring to a conclusion; come to an end; end; finish; over;

J

枉結 condescend to befriend;
小結 (1) brief summary; interim summary; (2) summarize briefly;
惱結 depressed; melancholy;
蟻結 band together;
硬結 callus;
鬱結 suffer from pent-up feelings;
怨結 pent-up hatred;
蘊結 pent-up; restrained;
癥結 (1) basic problem; bottleneck; crucial reason; crux; difficult point; (2) obstruction of the bowels;
終結 conclusion; end; finality; termination;
終結體 terminate aspect;
總結 (1) sum up; summarize; (2) conclusion;

jie

【街】 (1) street; (2) country fair; market;

［街道］ (1) road; street; way; (2) curbside; neighbourhood; residential district;
街道空間 street space;
街道圖 street map;
橫穿街道 cross the street;
僻靜的街道 quiet street;
主要街道 arterial street; main drag;

［街坊］ homeboy; homegirl; homey; neighbour;
街坊活動中心 neighbourhood centre;
街坊鄰里 all the neighbours on the street; all the neighbourhood; neighbourly relations; one's neighbours;
街里街坊 neighbourly relations;
老街坊 old neighbour;

［街市］ (1) downtown streets; (2) market;
六街三市 busy shopping centre in the town; busy streets; down-town area; in every street and marketplace;

［街頭］ street; street corner;
街頭打鬥 street fight;
街頭流鶯 prostitute; streetwalker;
街頭賣唱 roam the streets as a wandering minstrel; sing as a minstrel in the streets;
街頭賣藝 perform in the streets;
街頭乞討 beg for food in the streets;
街頭小店 corner shop;
街頭巷尾 every street and alley; street corners and alleys; streets and lanes;
流浪街頭 run the street;
湧上街頭 pour into the streets;
醉臥街頭 lie drunk in the street;

［街巷］ streets and alleys;
背街小巷 by-lane;
穿大街，走小巷 through a maze of streets and crooked lanes;
穿街過巷 go through streets and alleys;
串街走巷 wander through streets and lanes;
街談巷議 gossip; street gossip; town talk; the gossip of the streets; the talk of the town;
窮街陋巷 shabby street;
三街六巷 the whole town;
填街塞巷 fill up the streets and block the lanes — a great multitude of people;
小街陋巷 little streets and ugly alleys;
小街狹巷 small streets and narrow alleys;

大街 main street;
當街 face the street; near the street;
罵街 insult people on the street;
上街 (1) go into the street; (2) go shopping;
十字街 criss-cross streets;
沿街 along the street;
小街 side street;
一趟街 a street;
一條街 a street;
游街 parade sb through the street;

jie

【階】 (1) stairs; steps; (2) rank;

［階層］ rank; section; stratum;
白領階層 white-collar workers;
各階層的人 great and small; high and low;
灰領階層 gray-collar worker;
上等階層 upper class;
社會階層 social strata; walks of life;

［階乘］ factorial;
反階乘 inverse factorial;
廣義階乘 generalized factorial;
向量階乘 factorial of a vector;

［階地］ terrace;
海岸階地 coastal terrace;
海濱階地 shore terrace;
堆積階地 accumulation terrace;

［階段］ (1) gradation; (2) period; phase; stage;
階段制動 graduated application;
成年階段 adult phase;
發展階段 stage of development;
匯編階段 assembling phase;
競爭階段 competitive stage;
認知階段 awareness stage;

上昇階段 ascent stage;
同化階段 assimilative phase;
學習階段 learning stage;
驗收階段 acceptance phase;
在初期階段 at an early stage;
在後期階段 at a later stage;
在關鍵階段 at the critical period;
在某個階段 at one stage; at some stage;
在那個階段 at that stage;
在稍後階段 at a later stage;
在這個階段 at this stage;
最後階段 death throes;

[階級] (1) class; social class; (2) step; (3) stage;
階級本能 class instinct;
階級隊伍 class ranks;
階級鬥爭 class struggle;
階級分析 class analysis;
階級界限 barrier between classes; class distinction;
階級立場 class standpoint;
階級路線 class line;
階級內容 class content;
階級意識 class consciousness;
階級陣線 class alignment;
階級政策 class policy;
不分階級 classless;
第四階級 fourth estate;
地主階級 landlord class;
工人階級 proletarian class; working class;
農民階級 peasant class;
無產階級 proletariat;
~工業無產階級 industrial proletariat;
~農村無產階級 rural proletariat;
~遊民無產階級 lumpen proletariat;
無階級 classless;
小資階級 petty bourgeoisie;
資產階級 bourgeoisie;
~大資產階級 big bourgeoisie;
~工業資產階級 industrial bourgeoisie;
~壟斷資產階級 monopoly bourgeoisie;
~買辦資產階級 comprador bourgeoisie;
~民族資產階級 national bourgeoisie;
~商業資產階級 merchant capitalist;
~小資產階級 petty bourgeoisie;
中產階級 middle bourgeoisie;

[階梯] flight of stairs; ladder; staircase; steps;
階梯制 ladder system;
當心階梯 mind the steps;
登上階梯 ascend steps;
社會階梯 social ladder;
走下階梯 descend steps;

官階 official rank;
軍階 military rank;
台階 (1) flight of steps; (2) chance to extricate oneself from an awkward position;
音階 scale;

jie
【喈】 harmonious sounds;

jie
【稭】 stalk of corn, hemp, etc.;
[稭稈] straw;
稭稈肥 compost made of stalks;

jie
【嗟】 lament; sigh;
[嗟悔無及] lamentations are of no avail; regret will not mend matters; too late for regrets and lamentations;

jie
【癤】 gnarl; furunculus;
[癤病] furunculosis;

熱癤 heat spots;

jie²

jie
【孑】 all alone; lonely;
[孑孓] mosquito larvae;
[孑然] alone; lonely; in solitude; solitary;
孑然一身 all alone in the world; all by oneself; be all on one's own; be left alone; be left desolate;

jie
【劫】 (1) plunder; raid; rob; (2) coerce; compel; (3) calamity; disaster; misfortune;
[劫車] (1) carjack; (2) carjacking;
[劫持] abduct; abduction; hijack; hold under duress; kidnap;
劫持一架飛機 hijack a plane; skyjack;
劫持者 abductor; captor;
[劫奪] seize by force;
[劫機] air piracy; hijack a plane; hijack an aircraft; skyjack;
劫機事件 hijack;
[劫掠] loot; pillage; plunder; ravage; sack;
劫掠為生 live by plunder;
劫掠一空 make a clean sweep;
[劫難] calamity;
經難歷劫 have gone through the harshest trials; scarred and ravaged;

[劫數] predestined fate;
劫數難逃 it is impossible to escape fate; there is no escape from fate;
劫數已定 one's doom is sealed;
[劫獄] break into a prison and rescue a prisoner; jail delivery;
破牢劫獄 forcible liberation of prisoners from jail;

被劫 be robbed;
打劫 loot; plunder; rob;
盜劫 raid; rob;
浩劫 catastrophe; great calamity;
攔劫 intercept and rob;
搶劫 plunder; rob;
洗劫 loot; sack;
行劫 commit robbery; rob;

jie
【杰】 same as 傑 ;

jie
【玠】 large jade tablet;

jie
【拮】 labour hard;
[拮据] be pushed for money; hard up; in straitened circumstances; short of money;
生活拮据 live from hand to mouth;
手頭拮据 at low-water mark; feel the draught; hard-pressed; in hard need of money; in low water; low in pocket; out of cash; out of pocket; pinched for money; pushed for money; short of funds;

jie
【桔】 orange; tangerine;
[桔梗] (1) platycodon grandiflorus; (2) root of balloon flower;

jie
【桀】 the name of a tyrant;
[桀驁不馴] arrogant and unyielding; intractable and unyielding; obstinate and untamed; stubborn and untamed;

jie
【訐】 (1) expose sb's secret; (2) pry into sb's secret; (3) accuse; charge;

jie
【捷】 (1) nimble; prompt; quick; (2) triumph; victory;
[捷報] news of victory; report of a success;
捷報頻傳 news of victory keeps pouring in; reports of new successes keep pouring in; reports of victory come in showers; steady flow of news of victory; tidings of victory are spreading;
[捷徑] beeline; shortcut;
學無捷徑 there is no shortcut to knowledge;
終南捷徑 golden key to success; high road to fame; high road to success; royal road to fame; shortcut to high office; shortcut to success; snap course to officialdom;
走捷徑 take a shortcut;
[捷足] nimble-footed;
捷足先得 it's the early bird that catches the worm; the early bird catches the worm; the nimble foot gets first;
捷足先登 the early bird catches the worm; the fastest person wins the race;

報捷 announce a victory; report a success;
便捷 (1) easy and convenient; (2) agile; nimble;
大捷 great victory;
告捷 (1) win a victory; (2) report a victory;
簡捷 forthright; simple and direct;
矯捷 brisk; vigorous and agile;
敏捷 agile; prompt; quick;
蹺捷 able to move quickly and easily;
迅捷 prompt; quick;
祝捷 celebrate a victory;
奏捷 win a battle; score a success;

jie
【偈】 (1) brave; (2) hasty; scudding;

jie
【婕】 (1) official title for women in the Han Dynasty; (2) handsome;

jie
【傑】 (1) distinguished; outstanding; prominent; (2) hero; outstanding person;
[傑出] (1) outstanding; prominent; remarkable; (2) set the world on fire;
傑出人物 outstanding personality; prominent figure;
傑出作家 distinguished writer;
[傑作] masterpiece; masterwork;
精心傑作 masterpiece;

怪傑 geek;
俊傑 person of outstanding talent;
人傑 distinguished person;
英傑 hero; outstanding figure;

jie

【結】 (1) knit; weave; (2) knot; tie; (3) congeal; form; (4) conclude; settle; (5) affidavit; written guarantee; (6) junction; (7) node; (8) knot;

[結案] close a case; settle a lawsuit; wind up a case;

[結拜] become sworn brothers or sisters;

[結伴] go with; travel together with;
結伴而行 go in a group; travel in a group;
結伴制 buddy system;

[結冰] freeze; frozen; ice over; ice up;

[結彩] adorn with festoons; decorate with festoons;
懸燈結彩 adorn with lanterns and coloured streamers; celebrate an occasion by hanging lanterns and festoons; hang up lamps and drape festoons; hang up lanterns and coloured bunting;

[結草銜環] express gratitude to one's benefactor; repay sb for his favours even after his death;

[結成] enter into; form;

[結仇] become enemies;
以愛結仇 turn love into hate;

[結存] (1) balance; cash on hand; (2) goods on hand; inventory;
期初結存 opening balance;
英鎊結存 sterling balance;

[結締組織] connective tissue; sheath; syndesm;

[結構] (1) composition; constitution; construction; formation; organization; structure; texture; (2) architecture; construction; structure;
結構變化 structural change;
結構詞 structure word;
結構分析 structural analysis;
結構工程師 structural engineer;
結構工資制 structural wage system;
結構功能主義 structural functionalism;
結構化 structured;
~結構化程序 structured programme;
結構化程序設計 structured programming;
~結構化匯編程序 structured assembler;
~結構化系統分析 structured system analysis;
~結構化語言 structured language;
結構緊縮 structural compression;
結構精巧 exquisite structure;
結構描寫 structural description;
結構破壞 structural damage;
結構歧義 structural ambiguity;
結構式 structural formula;
結構現實主義 structure realism;
結構性翻譯 constructional translation;
結構性就業 structural employment;
結構性失業 structured unemployment;
結構性通貨膨漲 structural inflation;
結構謹嚴 tightly-knit structure;
結構意義 structural meaning;
結構語法 structural grammar;
結構語言學 structural linguistics;
結構語義學 structural semantics;
結構主義 structuralism;
~結構主義語法 structural grammar;
~結構主義語言學派 structuralistic linguistic school;
結構轉移 structural transfer;
比較結構 comparative construction;
表層結構 surface structure;
並列結構 coordinate construction;
成分結構 constituent structure;
處置式結構 disposal construction;
粗結構 coarse texture;
低層結構 underlying structure;
動賓結構 verb-object construction;
獨立結構 absolute construction;
對立結構 absolute construction;
多義結構 polysemous structure;
反常結構 abnormal structure;
方位結構 direction compound;
管形結構 tubular structure;
核心結構 core texture;
宏觀結構 macrostructure;
話語結構 discourse structure;
環形結構 atoll texture;
會話結構 conversational structure;
架空結構 aerial construction;
交梁結構 beam and girder construction;
句法結構 syntactic structure;
句子結構 sentence structure;
名詞結構 nominal construction;
內向結構 endocentric construction;
陪形結構 bathtub construction;
聲學結構 acoustic construction;
土坯結構 adobe construction;

J

賬戶結構 account structure;

[結果] (1) outcome; result; (2) finish off; kill;
結果令人滿意 the result was satisfying;
毫無結果 without any result;

[結合] (1) cohere; combine; integrate; link; unite; (2) be married; be tied in wedlock; be united in marriage;
結合力 cohesion;
~金屬結合力 metallic cohesion;
~粒間結合力 interparticle cohesion;
三結合 three-in-one combination;
學用結合 integrate study and application; integrate what is learnt with practice;
元結合 member aggregate;
音畫結合 audiovisual counterpoint;

[結婚] be married to sb; become one flesh; get hitched; get spliced; get married; have sb to be one's spouse; lead sb to the altar; marry; marry with; take sb to be one's spouse; tie the knot; wed;
結婚蛋糕 wedding cake;
結婚典禮 marriage ceremony; wedding ceremony;
結婚紀念日 wedding anniversary;
結婚介紹所 marriage bureau;
結婚日期 date for one's wedding;
~選定結婚日期 name the date; name the day;
結婚誓約 marriage vow;
結婚晚 marry late;
結婚許可證 marriage certificate;
結婚早 marry early;
結婚照 wedding photo;
結婚證書 marriage certificate;
包辦結婚 be forced into an arranged marriage;
承諾結婚 plight;
假結婚 bogus marriage; sham marriage;
秘密結婚 clandestine marriage;

[結伙] gang up;
拉幫結伙 form cliques; gang up together;

[結集] (1) concentrate; mass; (2) collect articles into a volume;

[結交] associate with; fraternize; make friends with;

[結局] ending; final result; finale; outcome; upshot;
結局悲慘 it'll end in tears;
大結局 grand finale;

[結論] (1) conclusion; (2) verdict;
得出結論 arrive at a conclusion;
遽下結論 pass judgement hastily;

[結盟] align; ally; form an alliance;
結盟修好 enter into an alliance with;

[結親] (1) get married; marry; (2) the families become related by marriage;
兩家結親 unite two families by marriage;

[結清] settle; square up;
結清債務 clear a debt; clear off debts; pay off one's debts; pay up one's debts;
結清賬目 settle one's account;

[結舌] tongue-tied;
結舌禁聲 control one's tongue and keep silent;
瞠目結舌 be struck dumb; be wide-eyed and unable to speak; gape in astonishment; stare dumbfounded;

[結社] form an association;

[結石] calculus; stone;
結石病 lithiasis;
排出結石 discharge stones; pass stones;

[結識] get acquainted with sb; get to know sb; make an acquaintance of;
剛剛結識 recent acquaintances;
偶然結識 pick up an acquaintance with; strike up an acquaintance with;

[結束] abolish; at the conclusion of; bring to a close; bring sth to a conclusion; bring sth to an end; cease; close; come to a close; come to a conclusion; come to a period; come to a termination; come to an end; completion; conclude; draw to a close; draw to an end; end; end in; end off; end on; end up; end with; finish; finish off; in conclusion; jack in; knit up; make an end of sth; over; over and done with; put a period to; put a stop to; put a termination to sth; put an end to; put paid to; round off; see the last of sth; terminate; wind up;
結束階段 end game;
結束談話 wind up a talk;
結束語 peroration;
結束戰爭 end a war; finish a war;
工作即將結束 the work is nearly finished;
即將結束 draw near a close;
全部結束 all over;

[結算] balance accounts; close an account; settle one's accounts; settlement of payments; wind up an account;

結算單據 documents of settlements;
結算日 account day;
結算賬戶 clearance account;
結算中心 clearing house;
多邊結算 multilateral settlement;
國際結算 international settlement of payments;
記帳結算 settlement on account;
經濟結算 economic balance;
雙邊結算 bilateral clearing; bilateral settlement;
現金結算 cash settlement;

[結尾] (1) end; winding-up stage; (2) coda;
小結尾 codetta;

[結業] complete a course; wind up one's studies;
結業證書 graduation certificate;

[結餘] balance;
歸屬結餘 vested balances;
年終結餘 annual balance;
上期結餘 old balance;
現金結餘 liquid balance;
資本賬戶結餘 balance of capital account;

[結緣] become attached to; form ties; take a fancy to sb;

[結怨] become enemies; incur hatred;

[結賬] balance the books; close accounts; close the book; settle accounts;

案結 conclusion of a legal case;
編結 make by weaving; weave;
打結 tie a knot;
締結 conclude; establish;
凍結 congeal; freeze;
乾結 dry and hard;
甘結 pledged undertaking;
勾結 collude with; conspire with;
固結 become solidified; solidify;
歸結 put in a nutshell; sum up;
喉結 Adam's apple;
活結 slip knot;
集結 concentrate; mass;
膠結 cement; glue;
糾結 get entangled; intertwine;
具結 sign an undertaking;
聯結 join; tie;
了結 settle; wind up;
領結 bow tie;
黏結 cohere;
凝結 (1) coagulate; (2) condense; (3) congeal;
扭結 tangle; twist together;
盤結 coil; wind;
燒結 coalesce; sinter;
死結 fast knot;
團結 rally; unite;
完結 be over; finish;
小結 brief summary;
硬結 harden; indurate;
鬱結 pent-up;
症結 crucial reason; crux;
終結 end; finish;
總結 sum up; summarize;

jie
【嵑】 lofty mountain;

jie
【絜】 clean;

jie
【袷】 (1) collar; (2) lapel;

jie
【睫】 eyelash;

[睫毛] eyelash; lash;
睫毛膏 mascara;
睫毛夾 eyelash curler;
睫毛刷 mascara brush;
睫毛油 mascara;
眨動睫毛 flutter one's eyelashes;
假睫毛 false eyelashes;

倒睫 trichiasis;
眉睫 eyebrows and eyelashes;

jie
【箑】 fan;

jie
【節】 (1) joint; knot; node; (2) division; part; (3) length; section; (4) festival; holiday; red-letter day; (5) abridge; (6) economize; save; (7) item; (8) moral integrity;

[節哀] restrain one's grief;
節哀順變 control one's grief and accept the inevitable changes;

[節本] abbreviated version; abridged edition;

[節儉] economical; frugal; thrifty;
節儉的 frugal; thrifty;
~極度節儉的 parsimonious;
躬行節儉 personally practise thriftiness;
鼓勵節儉 encourage thrift;
提倡節儉 encourage frugality;

[節節] steadily; successively;
節節敗退 be steadily losing ground; keep

J

on retreating; make one retreat after another; retreat in defeat again and again; retreat one step after another; suffer one defeat after another;

節節抵禦 fight the enemy at every step; point-by-point defense;

節節潰退 retreat again and again;

節節上昇 rise steadily;

節節勝利 go forward from victory to victory; march forward from victory to victory; push forward from victory to victory; score one victory after another; win a fresh series of victories; win continuous new victories; win many victories in succession; win victory after victory;

[節理] jointing;

[節令] climate and other natural phenomena of a season;

節令不等人 don't miss the right season in farming; time and tide wait for no man;

[節流] reduce expenditure;

節流開源 broaden one's sources of income and reduce the expenditure; regulate the flow and dig a new well;

開源節流 broaden one's sources of income and reduce the expenditures; develop resources and be economical; increase the income and cut down the expenses; increase the income and decrease the expenses; increase the income and reduce the expenditure; open up the source and regulate the flow; tap new resources and economize on expenditures; tap new sources of supply and reduce consumption;

[節錄] excerpt; extract;

[節律] rhythm;

活動節律 activity rhythm;

機體節律 body rhythm;

生物節律 biological rhythm;

[節目] programme;

節目傳輸 programme transmission;

節目存儲器 programme memory;

節目單 programme;

節目選擇 programme selection;

~節目選擇器 programme selector;

節目制作 programme production;

~節目制作技術 programme production technique;

~節目制作人 producer;

節目主持人 anchorperson; compere; emcee; master of ceremonies; MC;

節目主控室 master programme control room;

常備節目 repertoire;

廣播節目 broadcasting programme;

現場採訪節目 live talk show;

娛樂節目 entertainment programme;

~資訊娛樂節目 infotainment;

[節能] energy conservation;

節能量 amount of energy saving;

節能設備 energy-efficent equipment;

節能型 energy-saving;

~節能型產品 energy-saving product;

~節能型經濟結構 energy-saving economic structure;

[節拍] beat; clock; meter;

節拍器 metronome;

打節拍 beat time; keep time;

[節氣] solar term;

二十四節氣 24 solar terms;

[節慶] holiday and festival;

節慶場合 festive occasion;

節慶活動 festival events;

[節日] festival; holiday; red-letter day;

節日快樂 season's greetings;

節日祝賀 compliments of the season;

[節省] cut down; economize; save; use sparingly;

節省不必要的開支 save unnecessary expenses;

節省金錢 save money;

節省精力 sparing of one's energy;

節省開支 cut down the expenses; economize;

節省時間 save time;

[節食] diet; moderate in eating; on a diet;

節食者 dieter;

饑餓節食 starvation diet;

開始節食 go on a diet;

在節食 on a diet;

[節用] economize;

節用裕民 reduce expenditures to enrich the people;

強本節用 enhance agricultural production and reduce the expenses;

[節育] birth control; contraception;

[節約] economize; practise thrift; save;

節約成風 thrift has become the prevailing

practice;
節約糧食 thrifty with grain;
節約燃料 economize on fuel;
節約時間 save time;
多方節約 practise various frugalities;
鼓勵節約 encourage frugality;
盡量節約 practise frugality as much as possible;

[節制] (1) abstinence; abstinency; chasten; check; control; moderate in; (2) command; control;
節制生育 birth control;
節制飲食 control one's diet; moderate in eating and drinking; practise temperance in eating and drinking;
節制慾念 restrain one's desires;
缺乏節制 lack of moderation;
無節制 [的] immoderate;
有節制 [的] abstemious;

[節奏] rhythm;
能夠適應緊張的節奏 able to stand the pace;
生活節奏 pace of life;

拜節 extend holiday greetings; pay a visit on holidays;
半節 half a section;
臂節 elbow;
春節 Spring Festival;
大節 matter of principle; political integrity;
燈節 Lantern Festival;
冬節 Winter Solstice;
兒童節 Children's Day;
復活節 Easter;
符節 tally;
骨節 joint;
關節 (1) joint; (2) key;
過節 celebrate a festival;
環節 (1) link; (2) segment;
擊節 beat time;
季節 season;
佳節 festival; happy festival time;
結節 node; tubercle;
勞動節 Labour Day;
禮節 ceremony; courtesy;
名節 reputation and integrity;
末節 details; non-essentials;
年節 Spring Festival holidays;
品節 conduct and morals; integrity;
氣節 integrity; moral courage;
清明節 Tomb Sweeping Day;
情節 circumstances; plot;
屈節 forfeit one's integrity;
縟節 over-elaborate formalities;
刪節 abbreviate; abridge;
聖誕節 Christmas;
失節 (1) be disloyal; forfeit one's honour; (2) lose one's chastity;
時節 (1) season; (2) time;
使節 diplomatic envoy; envoy;
守節 preserve chastity after the death of one's husband;
體節 body segment;
調節 adjust; regulate;
脱節 be disjointed; be out of line with; come apart;
晚節 integrity in one's later years;
細節 details; particulars;
小節 (1) small matter; trifle; (2) bar; measure;
音節 syllable;
元宵節 Lantern Festival;
章節 chapters and sections;
貞節 chastity;
枝節 (1) minor matters; (2) complication; unexpected difficulty;
中秋節 Mid-Autumn Festival;
肘節 toggle;
竹節 bamboo joint;
撙節 practise austerity;

jie

【詰】 interrogate; question closely;
[詰難] censure; reproach;
[詰問] cross-examine; interrogate; question closely;
[詰責] censure; rebuke; reproach;

駁詰 refute and question;
究詰 ask for an explanation;
盤詰 cross-examine; question;

jie

【楬】 signpost;

jie

【蛚】 (1) cricket; (2) centipede; (3) dragon-fly;

jie

【截】 (1) cut; sever; (2) check; intercept; stem; stop; (3) chunk; length; section; (4) by; up to;
[截掉] amputate;
[截短] shorten; truncate;
[截獲] intercept and capture;

J

[截擊] (1) intercept; (2) interception;
海岸截擊 coastal interception;
盲目截擊 blind interception;
全天候截擊 all-weather interception;

[截流] block the flow of funds;

[截煤機] coal cutter;
長壁截煤機 longwall coal cutter;
沖擊式截煤機 percussive coal cutter;
防爆截煤機 permissible coal cutter;
履帶式截煤機 crawler coal cutter;
萬能截煤機 longwall-shortwall coal cutter;

[截面] cross section;
俘獲截面 capture cross section;
激活截面 activation cross section;
磨角截面 angle-lapped cross section;
特徵截面 characteristic cross section;
吸收截面 absorption cross section;
湮沒截面 annihilation cross section;
圓形截面 circular cross section;

[截盤] jib;
鏈式截盤 chain jib;
彎曲截盤 curved jib;
圓截盤 circular jib;

[截取] intercept;
截取構詞法 clipping;

[截然] completely; entirely; sharply;
截然不同 as different as chalk and cheese; as different as day and night; completely different; distinct from; entirely different; like chalk and cheese; poles apart;

[截圖] dump; shot;
屏幕截圖 screen dump; screenshot;

[截肢] (1) amputate; (2) amputation;
截肢手術 amputation;
被截肢 be amputated;
~被截肢者 amputee;

[截止] close; end;
截止期 cut-off date; deadline;
~錯過截止期 miss the deadline;
截止區 cut-off;
~長波截止區 long wave length cut-off;
截止日期 closing date; deadline;
板流截止 plate-current cut-off;
電子管截止 tube cut-off;
銳截止 sharp cut-off;
圖象截止 visual cut-off;
遙截止 remote cut-off;

[截趾適履] cut one's toes to fit the shoes — a foolish measure;

[截至] by; up to;

矮半截 inferior to others;
攔截 intercept;
阻截 block and intercept; intercept;

jie

【碣】 stone monument; stone tablet;

碑碣 stele;
墓碣 tombstone;

jie

【竭】 (1) deplete; exhaust; (2) exert;

[竭誠] heart and soul; wholeheartedly; with all one's heart;
竭誠服務 serve sincerely;
竭誠歡迎 give a hearty welcome to sb; give sb a cordial welcome; welcome sb heartily; welcome sb most warmly; welcome with open arms;
竭誠款待 entertain with utmost sincerity;
竭誠擁護 give one's wholehearted support;

[竭盡] do all one can; do one's best; do one's utmost; spare no effort;
竭盡棉力 do one's best;
竭盡能事 do one's utmost;
竭盡全力 do all at one's command; do all in one's full strength; do everyting in one's power; do everything one can; do one's level best; do one's utmost to; do sth with all one's ability and with all one's might; exert all one's energy; exert one's full strength; exert one's utmost; go all lengths; go to any lengths; make all possible efforts; make every effort to; pool one's efforts; pull all the stops out; pull out all the stops; put every ounce of strength into the effort; shoot the works; spare no efforts; spare no efforts with might and main; strain every nerve; strain one's efforts; strain oneself to the limit; strive tooth and nail to; strive to the utmost of one's strength; strive with all one's might; take all measures in one's power; to the best of one's ability; with all one's might; with might and main; work to the best of one's ability;
竭盡所能 make every effort;

竭盡心力 exert one's heart and strength to the utmost; exhaust one's mental abilities; put one's body and soul into a task; with all one's mind and energy; work to the best of one's ability;

[竭蹶] destitute; impoverished;

竭蹶而趨 go in haste; stumble when running too quickly;

[竭力] do one's utmost; pull out all the stops; spare no efforts; try by every possible means; try one's best; use every ounce of one's energy;

竭力圖報 do one's utmost to show one's gratitude;

竭力想 endeavour;

竭力做好 do one's best;

盡心竭力 do one's best; do one's level best; exert one's heart and strength to the utmost; go to great lengths; heart and soul; put one's heart and soul into; strain every nerve; use one's best efforts; with all one's heart and might;

傾心竭力 exert oneself to the utmost; exhaust every effort;

用心竭力 attentively and diligently; exhaust one's brain and energy;

[竭澤而漁] catch the fish by draining the pool; drain the pond to catch the fish; fish out by pumping off the water; kill the goose that lays the golden eggs;

耗竭 exhaust; use up;

枯竭 be dried up; be exhausted; drain;

疲竭 be completely exhausted; be tired out;

窮竭 exhaust; use up;

衰竭 tend to end because of decline;

血竭 dragon's blood;

jie

【潔】 clean;

[潔白] pure white; spotless white;

潔白如玉 as white as polished jade;

潔白無瑕 immaculately clean; spotless and flawless; spotlessly white; whiter than white;

[潔淨] clean; spotless;

[潔面] facial cleansing;

潔面劑 cleanser;

深層潔面 deep cleansing facial;

純潔 clean and honest; pure;

高潔 noble and pure; noble and unsullied;

光潔 bright and clean;

簡潔 succinct; terse;

皎潔 bright and clear;

廉潔 honest;

清潔 clean;

聖潔 holy and immaculate; holy and pure;

貞潔 chaste and undefiled;

整潔 clean and tidy; neat;

jie

【羯】 (1) castrated ram; (2) an ancient barbarian people;

[羯羊] wether;

jie

【頡】 deduct; omit;

jie

【櫛】 (1) comb; (2) comb one's hair; cut one's hair; (3) dress up; (4) delete; eliminate; weed out;

jie

【擷】 collect; gather; pick;

jie

【癤】 pimple; small sore;

jie³

jie

【姐】 (1) elder sister; (2) sister; (3) general term for young women;

[姐儿] sister;

窰姐儿 prostitute;

[姐夫] brother-in-law; elder sister's husband;

[姐姐] (1) elder sister; (2) sister;

異父姐姐 elder stepsister;

異母姐姐 elder stepsister;

[姐妹] sisters;

姐妹篇 companion volume;

姐妹城 twin town;

姐妹情誼 sisterhood;

表姐妹 cousins;

~ 親房表姐妹 first cousins;

~ 遠房表姐妹 second cousins;

堂姐妹 cousins;

~ 親房堂姐妹 first cousins;

~ 遠房堂姐妹 second cousins;

異父母姐妹 half-sister;

胞姐 blood elder sisters;

表姐 elder female cousin;

大姐 (1) eldest sister; (2) elder sister;

空姐 air hostess;

堂姐 elder female cousin;

J

小姐 (1) Miss; (2) young lady;

jie

【姊】 elder sister or sisters;

jie

【解】 (1) divide; separate; (2) undo; untie; (3) allay; alleviate; dispel; relieve; (4) explain; interpret; solve; (5) comprehend; understand;

[解嘲] try to explain things away when one is ridiculed; try to get out of a scrape when one is ridiculed;
聊以解嘲 make a feeble attempt to explain things away when one is ridiculed;

[解愁] free oneself from worries; relieve depression;
解愁排難 help people overcome their difficulties;
解愁釋悶 end all care; put an end to care;
分憂解愁 relieve sb of the daily worries; share and lessen worry;
酒不解真愁 liquor cannot dispel real sorrow;

[解除] get rid of; release; relieve; remove; secure;
解除顧慮 free one's mind of apprehensions;
解除合同 annul a contract;
解除婚約 break off one's engagement; dissolve a marriage contract;
解除武裝 disarm;
解除協議 annul an agreement;

[解答] answer; explain;

[解凍] defrost; thaw; thawing; unfreeze;
解凍物價 unfreeze the prices;
解凍資產 thaw out the frozen assets;
紅外線輻射解凍 infrared radiation thawing;
空氣解凍 air thawing;
溫水融化解凍 warm water thawing;

[解毒] antidotal; detox; detoxification;
解毒劑 antidote;
解毒作用 antidotal action;

[解讀] decode;

[解餓] allay one's hunger; satisfy one's hunger; stay one's stomach;

[解乏] recover from fatigue; refresh oneself;

[解放] emancipate; liberate;
解放區 liberated area;
解放思想 emancipate the mind; free oneself from old ideas;

[解僱] boot sb out; cast out; discharge; dismiss; fire; fire out; get one's mittimus; get the bag; get the mitten; give sb the air; give sb the axe; give sb the bag; give sb the boot; give sb the bounce; give sb the chop; give sb the chuck; give sb the mitten; give sb the push; give sb the sack; give the bag to sb; give the bounce; give walking papers to sb; kick out sb; lay off; let out; pay off; sack; send off; stand off; throw sb out of employment; turn away; turn off;
解僱費 dismissal pay;
解僱通知書 notice of dismissal;
被解僱 be given one's marching orders; be sacked; catch it in the neck; get it in the neck; get the air; get the bounce; get the hook; get one's marching orders; get the push; get the sack; give sb the push; knock off; take it in the neck;
大量解僱 mass dismissal;
非法解僱 wrongful dismissal;
臨時解僱 lay-off;

[解恨] vent one's hatred;

[解禁] lift a ban;

[解酒] relieve the effects of alcoholic drinks;
以酒解酒 take a hair of the dog that bit you;

[解救] deliver; rescue; save;

[解決] deal with; dispose of; iron out; make up; patch up; resolve; settle; settle with; solve; sort out; straighten out; tackle; thrast out;
解決辦法 solution;
~好的解決辦法 good solution;
~可行的解決辦法 practical solution; workable solution;
~快捷的解決辦法 quick solution; speedy solution;
~理想的解決辦法 ideal solution;
~令人滿意的解決辦法 satisfactory solution;
~提出解決辦法 put forward a solution; suggest a solution;
~提供解決辦法 offer a solution; provide a solution;
~完美的解決辦法 perfect solution;

~ 唯一的解決辦法 the only solution;
~ 尋求解決辦法 look for a solution; seek a solution;
~ 有效的解決辦法 effective solution;
~ 找到解決辦法 come up with a solution; find a solution;
~ 最好的解決辦法 the best solution;
解決糾紛 resolve a dispute;
解決困難 overcome a difficulty; solve a problem;
解決賠償 settle a claim;
解決問題 crack it; solve a problem; work out a solution;
解決意見 proposal for settlement;
解決爭端 settle the claim; settlement of disputes;
公正解決 equitable settlement; just settlement;
立即解決 immediate settlement;
協商解決 settlement through negotiation;
友好解決 amicable settlement;
圓滿解決 bring matter to a happy close;

[解開] undo; unfasten; unlash; unlatch; unlock; unmake; untie;
解開領帶 loosen a tie; undo a tie; unfasten a tie; untie a tie;
解開疙瘩 fix the misunderstanding;
解開上衣 unbutton a jacket;
解開繩子 undo a string; untie a rope;
解開鞋帶 untie one's shoelaces;

[解渴] quench one's thirst;
解渴消勞 relieve thirst and fatigue;
水能解渴 water appeases thirst;

[解困] help the people to overcome their difficulties;
解困基金 anti-poverty funds;

[解鈴還需繫鈴人] it is better for the doer to undo what he has done; let the one who tied the bell to the tiger take it off—whoever started the trouble should end it; one's fault should be amended by oneself;

[解碼] decode;
解碼器 decoder;
~ 視頻解碼器 video decoder;
~ 音調解碼器 audio tone decoder;
~ 有源解碼器 active decoder;
~ 載波解碼器 carrier decoder;
概率解碼 probabilistic decoding;
混合解碼 hybrid decoding;
可變解碼 modifiable decoding;
排列解碼 permutation decoding;
自適應解碼 adaptive decoding;

[解悶] divert oneself from boredom;
散心解悶 divert one's mind from boredom;

[解難] overcome a difficulty;
解難方法 method for overcoming difficulties;
為民解難 help the people to overcome difficulties;

[解難] remove a calamity;
解難排憂 help people to overcome their difficulties;
消災解難 get rid of calamities and dangers;

[解聘] dismiss an employee; non-reappointment;

[解剖] anatomy; dissect;
解剖刀 scalpel;
解剖學 anatomy;
~ 解剖學家 anatomist;
~ 解剖學知識 anatomical knowledge;
~ 比較解剖學 comparative anatomy;
~ 表面解剖學 surface anatomy;
~ 病理解剖學 pathological anatomy;
~ 部位解剖學 regional anatomy;
~ 大體解剖學 gross anatomy;
~ 動物解剖學 zootomy;
~ 發育解剖學 developmental anatomy;
~ 分層解剖學 clastic anatomy;
~ 動物解剖學 animal anatomy;
~ 模型解剖學 artificial anatomy; plastic anatomy;
~ 人體解剖學 human anatomy;
~ 獸醫解剖學 veterinary anatomy;
~ 系統解剖學 systematic anatomy;
~ 顯微解剖學 microscopical anatomy;
~ 牙體解剖學 dental anatomy;
~ 醫用解剖學 medical anatomy;
~ 藝術解剖學 artistic anatomy;
~ 應用解剖學 applied anatomy;
~ 植物解剖學 phytotomy; plant anatomy;
~ 組織解剖學 histological anatomy;

[解散] (1) dismiss; disband; dissolve; (2) dissolution;
解散議會 dissolve a parliament;

[解釋] elucidate; explain; explicate; expound; give an account of;
解釋程序 interpretation;
解釋法律 interpret laws;
給出解釋 give an explanation;

J

合理的解釋 rational explanation;
進行解釋 make an explanation;
口頭解釋 oral explanantion;
有解釋 offer an explanation;
冗長的解釋 wordy explanation;
作出解釋 offer an explanation; provide an explanation.

[解手] go to the toilet; relieve oneself;

[解綬] return the office seal;
解綬而去 return the office seal and resign;

[解説] comment; explain orally; narrate; narration;
解説詞 commentary;
解説員 announcer; commentator; commentor; narrator;
~體育解説員 sports commentator;
口頭解説 commentary;
書面解説 caption;
新聞解説 news explanation;
作解説 commentate;

[解題] settle a problem; solve a problem;

[解體] break up; disintegrate; dismantle; dismount;

[解脱] (1) extricate oneself; free oneself from; get rid of; (2) absolve; exonerate;
解脱精神負擔 get rid of a mental burden;

[解圍] (1) come to the rescue of the besieged; rescue sb from a siege; (2) ease sb's embarrassment; help sb out of a predicament; save sb from embarrassment;

[解析] analytic;
解析閉曲線 analytic closed curve;
解析概率模型 analytic probability model;

[解疑] disambiguation;

[解憂] assuage sb's sorrow;
解憂消愁 allay sb's grief; allay sb's sorrow; dissipate sb's sorrow; relieve sb from anxiety;
聊以解憂 a crumb of comfort;

[解約] break off an engagement; cancel a contract; rescind a contract; terminate an agreement;

[解脂作用] lipolysis;

[解職] discharge; dismiss from office; relieve sb of his post;

辯解 provide an explanation; try to defend oneself;

大解 have a bowel movement;

電解 electrolysis;

費解 hard to understand; obscure;

分解 (1) break down; decompose; resolve; (2) mediate; reconcile; (3) disintegrate; divide and demoralize; (4) disclose; recount;

和解 become reconciled;

見解 understanding; view;

講解 explain;

開解 straighten out one's life and ease one's anxiety;

寬解 ease sb's troubles; help sb to get over his/her troubles;

離解 dissociate;

理解 comprehend; understand;

諒解 forgive; make allowances for;

了解 (1) comprehend; understand; (2) acquaint oneself with; find out;

裂解 decompose; split;

排解 (1) arbitrate; mediate; (2) divert oneself from loneliness or boredom;

剖解 analyse; dissect;

曲解 misinterpret; twist;

勸解 ease sb's anxiety; help sb to get over their worries;

溶解 dissolve; fuse;

融解 melt; thaw;

水解 hydrolysis;

通解 be proficient in; thoroughly understand;

圖解 explain through diagrams;

瓦解 collapse; disintegrate;

誤解 misread; misunderstand;

詳解 explain in detail;

消解 clear up; dispel;

小解 pass water; urinate;

支解 dismember;

註解 annotate;

jie4
jie

【介】 (1) be situated between; interpose; (2) mind; take seriously; take to heart;

[介詞] preposition;
介詞賓語 object of preposition;
介詞補語 prepositional complement;
介詞動詞 prepositional verb;
介詞短語 prepositional phrase;
~介詞短語狀語 prepositional adverbial;
介詞性副詞 prepositional adverb;
介詞狀語 prepositional adverbial;
伴隨介詞 preposition of accompaniment;
材料介詞 preposition of material;
成分介詞 preposition of ingredient;

刺激介詞 preposition of stimulus;
地點介詞 preposition of place;
短語介詞 phrasal preposition;
二重介詞 double preposition;
反應介詞 preposition of reaction;
方法介詞 preposition of means;
方式介詞 preposition of manner;
分詞介詞 participial preposition;
複合介詞 compound preposition;
合成介詞 complex preposition;
後置介詞 postposed preposition;
話題介詞 preposition of subject matter;
加添介詞 addition preposition;
簡單介詞 simple preposition;
目的地介詞 preposition of destination;
目的介詞 preposition of purpose;
排除介詞 preposition of exception;
條件介詞 preposition of condition;
~否定條件介詞 preposition of negative condition;
雙重介詞 double preposition;

[介入] get involved; interpose; intervene; step in; wade in;
介入訴訟 get involved in lawsuits;
介入戰爭 get involved in the war; intervene in the war;
介入爭端 get involved in a dispute; interfere with a dispute; intervene in a dispute;

[介紹] brief; introduce; lead-in; present; recommend;
介紹情況 brief sb on the situation; fill sb in; put sb in the picture;
介紹人 (1) introducer; sponsor; (2) matchmaker; (3) referee;
介紹信 (1) letter of introduction; (2) letter of recommendation; reference;

[介體] amboceptor;
介體原 amboceptorgen;
免疫介體 immune amboceptor;
溶菌介體 bacteriolyte amboceptor;
溶血介體 haemolytic amboceptor;
天然介體 natural amboceptor;

[介意] get annoyed; mind; take offence;
毫不介意 not care a farthing; not care a fig; not care a straw; not care at all; not mind; pay no attention to; take no notice of;

[介於] between;
介於兩難 hold a wolf by the ears;
介於生死之間 lie between life and death;

[介質] medium;
工作介質 actuating medium;
環境介質 ambient medium;
研磨介質 abrasive medium;

[介子] meson;
標量介子 scalar meson;
帶電介子 charged meson;
橫介子 transverse meson;
輕介子 light meson;
重介子 heavy meson;
縱介子 longitudinal meson;

耿介 honest; upright;
簡介 brief introduction;
狷介 incorruptible;
媒介 intermediary; medium;
評介 review;
中介 intermediary; medium;

jie

【戒】 (1) avoid; guard against; (2) admonish; exhort; warn; (3) drop; give up; stop; (4) Buddhist monastic discipline; (5) ring;

[戒備] exercise vigilance; guard; keep a sharp eye; on the alert; take precautions;
戒備森嚴 be heavily guarded;
加強戒備 enforce vigilance;
解除戒備 lower one's guard;

[戒除] drop; give up; stop; withdraw from;
戒除惡習 give up a bad habit; relinquish a pernicious habit;
戒除嗜好 kick the habit;

[戒毒] come off drugs; detox; get off drugs;

[戒驕戒躁] avoid conceit and impetuosity; guard against conceit and impatience; guard against pride and haste;

[戒酒] abstain from wine; flee from the bottle; refrain from drinking;
戒了酒 off the booze;

[戒律] commandment; precept; religious discipline;

[戒色] avoid the temptation of sex;
戒之在色 avoid the temptation of sex;

[戒心] alertness; vigilance; wariness;
放鬆戒心 ease vigilance over;
懷有戒心 keep a sharp eye;

[戒煙] abstain from smoking; break off smoking; drop smoking; dry out; give up smoking; hold off from smoking;

J

keep away from smoking; keep away from tobacco; lay aside the habit of smoking; lay off smoking; refrain from smoking; stay off cigarettes; stop smoking; through with smoking; wean oneself from smoking;
戒煙戒酒 abstain from tobacco and alcohol; give up smoking and refrain from drinking; give up the habit of smoking and drinking;

［戒嚴］ (1) be placed under martial law; (2) cordon off an area; (3) impose a curfew;
戒嚴令 martial law;

［戒指］ ring;
結婚戒指 wedding bands; wedding ring;
永恒戒指 eternity ring;
摘下戒指 take off one's ring;

懲戒 discipline sb as a warning;
傳戒 initiate sb into monkhood or nunhood;
犯戒 break into a forbidden ground;
鑒戒 object lesson; warning;
警戒 (1) admonish; warn; (2) be on the alert against; guard against;
開戒 break an abstinence;
力戒 do everything possible to avoid;
破戒 (1) break a religious precept; (2) break one's vow of abstinence;
勸戒 admonish; expostulate;
受戒 be initiated into monkhood or nunhood;
訓戒 admonish; advise; rebuke; reprimand;
齋戒 abstain from meat, wine, etc.; fast;
鑽戒 diamond ring;

jie

【屆】 (1) fall due; (2) session;

［屆滿］ at the end of tenure; at the expiration of one's term of office;

［屆期］ on the appointed date; when the day comes;

［屆時］ on the appointed time; on the occasion; when the time comes;

本屆 current; this year;
歷屆 all previous;
上屆 last term; previous term;
下屆 following term; next term;
應屆 current; this year;

jie

【玠】 large jade tablet;

jie

【芥】 (1) mustard plant; (2) tiny;

［芥菜］ Indian mustard; leaf mustard;
芥藍菜 leaf mustard;

［芥蒂］ grudge; ill feeling; unpleasantness;
不存芥蒂 bear no grudge
心存芥蒂 bear sb a grudge; have a grudge against; nurse a grievance;
幸勿芥蒂 don't take it amiss;
胸無芥蒂 no enmity; no grudge in one's mind;

［芥末］ mustard;
芥末杯 mustard bowl;
芥末醬 mustard paste;

［芥子］ mustard;
芥子氣 mustard gas;

草芥 mere nothing; trifle;
醬芥 pickled rutabaga;
荊芥 Nepeta;

jie

【界】 (1) border; boundary; (2) bounds; extent; scope; (3) circles; the world of; (4) kingdom; (5) primary division;

［界別］ constituency;
功能界別 functional constituency;

［界定］ delimit;

［界面］ interface;
界面活性 interfacial activity;
大氣界面 atmosphere interface;
帶電界面 charged interface;
計算機界面 computer interface;
用戶界面 user interface;
~圖形用戶界面 graphic user interface;

［界內］ area within bounds;
在界內 inbounds;

［界説］ definition;

［界外］ area out of bounds;
界外球 line-out;

［界限］ (1) ambit; boundary; demarcation line; dividing line; (2) end; limit;
超出界限 break bounds;
詞素界限 morpheme boundary;
抖振界限 buffet boundary;
假設界限 fictitious boundary;
句界限 sentence boundary;
空泡界限 cavity boundary;
模糊界限 fuzzy boundary;
確定界限 fix limit;
射速界限 beam boundary;

位移界限 displacement boundary;
細胞界限 cell boundary;
字節界限 byte boundary;

[界線] (1) boundary line; (2) dividing line; threshold;

報界 journalistic circles; the press;
邊界 border; boundary;
出版界 publishing circles;
出界 out of bounds; outside;
地界 boundary of a piece of land;
分界 demarcation line; dividing line;
工商界 industrial and commercial circles;
國界 national boundaries;
疆界 border; boundary;
交界 have a common boundary;
教育界 educational circles;
境界 (1) boundary; (2) realm; state;
軍界 military circles;
勘界 survey the boundary;
科學界 scientific circles; scientific world;
商界 business circles; commercial circles;
上界 heaven;
射界 firing area;
省界 provincial boundaries;
史學界 historian circles;
世界 earth; world;
視界 field of vision; visual field;
司法界 judicial circles;
外交界 diplomatic circles;
外界 outside; the outside world;
文化界 cultural circles;
文教界 cultural and educational circles;
文學界 literary circles;
文藝界 literary and art circles;
戲劇界 theatrical circles;
學界 educational circles;
學術界 academic circles;
眼界 (1) field of vision; (2) outlook;
藝術界 art circles;
輿論界 press circles; the media;
政界 government circles; political circles;
自然界 natural world; nature;
宗教界 religious circles;

jie

【疥】 scabies;

[疥蟲] itch mite;

[疥瘡] scabies;

癬疥 ringworm; tinea;

jie

【借】 (1) borrow; (2) lend; (3) make use of; take advantage of; (4) use as a pretext;

[借詞] borrowed word; loanword;

[借貸] (1) borrow or lend money; (2) debit and credit sides;
借貸利率 lending rate;
借貸無門 have no means to borrow money;
國際借貸 international borrowing;
期中借貸 interim borrowing;

[借調] lend personnel; on loan; reassign on loan; second; transfer temporarily;

[借端] find a pretext; make up an excuse; use as a pretext;
借端生事 make up excuses in order to provocate;

[借方] (1) debtor; (2) debit side;
借方賬目 debtor account;

[借古] use the past;
借古謗今 write about the past to criticze the present;
借古誹今 use the past to condemn the present;
借古諷今 deride the contemporary by quoting from history; make use of history to satirize the present; talk about the past to criticize the present; use ancient history to criticize modern times; use ancient things to satirize the present; use the past to disparage the present;
借古諭今 allude to the present by narrating past anecdotes; use the past to allude to the present; use past anecdotes to allude to the present;

[借故] find an excuse;
借故推托 find an excuse to refuse;
借故尋釁 find a pretext to quarrel; pick a quarrel on some flimsy pretext;

[借光] ask for help; excuse one;

[借花獻佛] make a present at another person's expense; make presents provided by sb else; offer sb favours at the expense of another person;

[借還] borrow and return;
東借西還 borrow from one to pay another; rob Peter to pay Paul;
好借好還 make it a point to return

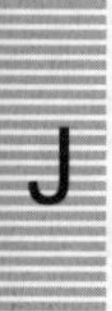

everything one has borrowed;
借而不還 borrow but not return;

[借火] ask for a light;

[借鑒] draw lessons from; draw on the experience of; have successful experiences of others to go by; object lesson; use as a reference;

[借鏡] draw lessons from; draw on the experience of; object lesson; use as a reference;
因人借鏡 learn from other people;
足資借鏡 object lesson;

[借據] receipt for a loan;

[借口] on the excuse of; on the plea of; on the pretext of; under the plea of; under the pretext of;
以…為借口 under the cloak of;
一個借口 a pretext;
用濫了的借口 well-worn excuse;
找借口 find a pretext; make up pretenses;
製造借口 cook up an excuse; make up a pretext; make up excuses;

[借款] (1) ask for a loan; borrow money; borrowing; (2) lend money; offer a loan; (3) loan;
借款權 borrowing power;
借款者 borrower;
地方當局借款 local authority borrowing;
公開借款 public borrowing;
臨時借款 temporary borrowing;

[借錢] ask sb for a loan;
向人借錢 borrow money from sb;

[借入] borrow;

[借屍還魂] find reincarnation in sb's corpse—resurrect in a new guise;

[借勢] rely on one's power;
借勢乘權 rely on sb's power and misuse his/her great influence;
借勢舞權 exercise power by assuming sb's authority;

[借手除敵] kill one's rival by another's hand;

[借書] borrow books;
借書台 lending counter;
借書證 borrower card; library card;

[借宿] put up for the night; stay overnight at sb else's place;

[借條] receipt for a loan;

[借…為名] under the colour of;

[借問] may I ask;

[借以] by way of; for the purpose of; so as to;

[借譯] loan translation;

[借用] (1) borrow; take out a loan; (2) use sth for a different purpose;
發音借用 pronunciation borrowing;
方言借用 dialect borrowing;
文化借用 cultural borrowing;
語言借用 linguistic borrowing;
直接借用 direct borrowing;

[借債] borrow money; raise a loan; take out a loan;
借債度日 live by borrowing; live on loans; pass one's day by borrowing;

[借者] borrower;
借者登記 borrower's register;

[借支] obtain an advance on one's salary;

[借重] count on sb for support; enlist sb's help; rely on sb for support;

[借助] be backed by; by help of; by the aid of; draw support from; have the aid of; on the strength of; through sb's help; with the aid of; with the assistance of; with the help of;
借助詞典 with the help of a dictionary;

[借箸代籌] make plans for sb else;

出借 lend; loan;
典借 mortgage;
假借 (1) make use of; (2) be lenient; be tolerant;
挪借 get a short-term loan;
憑借 depend on; rely on;
求借 beg to borrow;
暫借 borrow for a short time;
摘借 ask for a loan;
租借 hire; lease; rent;

jie

【械】 (1) weapon; (2) implement; (3) fetter; shackle; (4) arrest and put in prison;

jie

【解】 escort from one place to another; forward;

[解送] send under guard;

[解元] the scholar who won the first place in provincial imperial examinations;

遞解 escort a criminal from one place to another;
起解 send a criminal under escort;
押解 send a criminal under escort;

jie

【誡】 admonish; warn;

告誡 admonish; enjoin; warn;
申誡 reprimand;

jie

【藉】 (1) cushion of grass or straw; mat; pad; (2) avail oneself of; by means of; lean on; on the strength of; rely on; (3) on the excuse of; on the pretext of;

[藉故] find an excuse;

[藉口] excuse;
編造藉口 invent an excuse; make up an excuse;
慣常的藉口 usual excuse;
好藉口 good excuse;
極好的藉口 perfect excuse;
現成的藉口 convenient excuse;
找藉口 look for an excuse;

狼藉 (1) in disorder; (2) notorious;
蘊藉 reserved; restrained;
枕藉 lying in disorder; lying on top of each other;

jin[1]

jin

【巾】 piece of cloth;

[巾幗] (1) ancient woman's headdress; (2) woman;
巾幗英雄 female hero; heroine;
巾幗鬚眉 women who act and talk like men;

餐巾 table napkin;
茶巾 tea cloth; tea towel;
綸巾 black silk ribbon scarf;
毛巾 towel;
沙巾 gauze headscarf;
紗巾 gauze kerchief;
頭巾 kerchief; headscarf;
圍巾 muffler; scarf;
浴巾 bath towel;
枕巾 towel used to cover a pillow;

jin

【今】 (1) modern; now; nowadays; present-day; (2) today; (3) of this year; this year;

[今後] along the road; down the road; from now on; henceforth; hereafter; in future; in the days to come;

[今年] this year;

[今人] contemporary people; people of the present era;

[今日] (1) today; (2) now; present;
今日事今日畢 never leave for tomorrow what can be done today; never put off till tomorrow what you can do today;
既有今日，何必當初 if you know the consequences, why should you do it in the first place;
時至今日 at the present time; at this late hour; even now; even to this day; up to now; up to this day;
早知今日，何必當初 given the outcome, it is a pity to think about the way it was at the beginning;
早知今日，悔不當初 if I had known what was going to happen, I would never act as I did;

[今生] this life;
今生今世 this present life;
不昧今生 can still remember what's happened in this life;

[今世] (1) this life; (2) the contemporary age; this age;

[今天] (1) today; (2) now; present;
今天幾號 what date is today; what is the date today;
今天晚上 tonight;
今天星期幾 what day is today;
今天早上 this morning;

[今昔] the present and the past; today and yesterday;
今昔對比 compare the present with the past;
撫今追昔 contemplate the present and recall the past with emotion; evoke memories of the past while living in the present; recall the past and compare it to the present; reflect on the past in the light of the present;
今不如昔 the present is not as good as the past; worse off than before;
今非昔比 no comparison between the past and the present; no longer what it was before; the present cannot be compared to the past; times change; today we are no longer as we have been;
今勝於昔 the present is better than the past;

[今夜] this evening; tonight;

J

［今朝］ (1) today; (2) now; the present;
今朝有酒今朝醉 don't worry today about what you're going to eat tomorrow; enjoy the pleasures of drinking wine here and now; enjoy while one can;
今朝有酒今朝醉，明日愁來明日憂 enjoy the present moment and don't worry about tomorrow;

當今 (1) at present; now; (2) emperor on the throne;
而今 at the present time; now;
目今 nowadays; these days;
迄今 to this day; up to now;
如今 nowadays; these days;
現今 nowadays; these days;
於今 now; nowadays; today;
至今 so far; to this day; up to now;

jin
【斤】 Chinese measure of weight;
［斤斤］ fuss about; haggle over;
斤斤計較 calculating; calculating and unwilling to make the smallest sacrifice; excessively mean in one's dealings; haggle over every ounce; mindful of narrow personal gains and losses; palter with a person about sth; particular about; reckon up every iota; split hairs; split straws; stand on little points; skin a flint; weigh and balance at every detail;
斤斤其明 pay close attention to every detail;
［斤兩］ weight;
搬斤播兩 haggle over every ounce;
半斤八兩 as broad as it is long; as long as it is broad; fifty-fifty; half a pound of one and eight ounces of the other; much of a muchness; not much to choose between the two; nothing to choose between the two; six of one and half a dozen of the other; tweedledum and tweedledee;
半斤對五兩——回事 six of one and half a dozen of the other;
短斤久兩 short weight;
分斤掰兩 count pennies; niggle over personal gain; pinch and scrape; pinch pennies; stingy;
論斤估兩 argue about little details;
沒斤兩 (1) commonplace; (2) worthless;
缺斤少兩 short measure; short weight;

公斤 kilogram;
千斤 very heavy;
市斤 unit of weight;

jin
【金】 (1) metals; (2) money; (3) gold; (4) golden;
［金碧］ gold and green;
金碧輝煌 resplendent and magnificent; shine with gold and jade;
金碧山水 gold-and-green landscape;
［金幣］ gold coin;
［金邊］ gold-rimmed;
金邊的 gold-edged;
金邊眼鏡 gold-rimmed glasses;
［金箔］ gold foil; gold leaf; rolled gold;
［金不換］ cannot be exchanged even for gold; invaluable; more valuable than gold; priceless;
［金蟬脱殼］ escape by cunning manoeuvring; escape like a cicada casting off its skin; make one's escape by artifice; slip away by taking off one's cloak; slip out of a predicament like a cicada sloughing its skin; stratagem for slinking off;
［金城］ strongly guarded city;
金城湯池 impregnable city; strong, well-guarded city; strongly fortified city;
金城鐵壁 tower of strength;
［金額］ amount of money; sum of money;
金額不符 words and figures differ;
金額不足 insufficient fund;
保險金額 insurance amount;
實際金額 actual amount;
拖欠金額 amount in arrear;
總金額 aggregate amount;
［金髮］ blonde hair;
金髮美人 beautiful blonde; blonde bombshell;
金髮女子 blonde;
一頭金髮 with blonde hair;
［金粉］ gold dust;
［金風］ autumn wind;
金風稻草 the fragrance of the paddy is wafted by the autumn breeze;
金風麥浪 a field of wheat undulating in the autumn wind; ripening wheat ripples in the breeze like a golden

wave; the golden wheat ripples in the autumn breeze;
金風去暑，玉露生涼 the golden winds drive away the hot winds of summer and the white dews of autumn bring coolness;
金風颯颯 chilly autumn wind; cool breeze of autumn;
金風送爽 be refreshed by the cool autumn breeze;
金風送香 the autumn wind brings the fragrance of flowers;
金風乍起 the autumn wind starts to blow;
金風驟起 the autumn wind blows violently;

[金剛] Buddha's warrior attendant;
金剛砂 emery;
金剛鐵漢 man of great physical strength; very powerfully built man;
四大金剛 statues of the four guardian gods at the entrance of a temple;

[金光] golden light;
金光大道 bright broad highway; golden road;
金光菊 coneflower;
金光閃閃 glistening; glittering;
萬道金光 myriad golden rays; myriads of golden rays;

[金黃] golden; golden yellow;

[金婚] golden wedding;
金婚紀念 golden anniversary;

[金雞] golden pheasant;
金雞獨立 posing as a pheasant standing on one foot — in praise of one who bears the responsibility alone;

[金獎] gold award; gold medal;

[金匠] goldsmith;

[金桔] kumquat;

[金卡] gold card;

[金庫] chest; exchequer; coffers; national treasury; vault;
中央金庫 central treasury;

[金塊] bullion; gold bullion;

[金礦] gold ore;

[金迷紙醉] be given to sensual pleasures; live an extravagant life;

[金牌] gold medal;
金牌得主 gold medalist;
金牌獎 gold medal prize;
一塊金牌 a gold medal;
一枚金牌 a gold medal;
贏得金牌 win the gold medal;

[金器] gold articles; gold objects;

[金錢] (1) mammon; (2) money;
金錢報酬 money reward;
~計較金錢報酬 care about money rewards;
金錢不足 be pushed for money;
金錢萬能 money is everything; money talks;
愛惜金錢 use money sparingly;
大量金錢 pots of money;

[金槍魚] albacore; bluefin tuna; tuna;
澳大利亞金槍魚 Southern Bluefin tuna;
長鰭金槍魚 albacore; long-finned albacore; long-finned tuna;
大西洋金槍魚 Atlantic tuna;
大眼擬金槍魚 bigeye tuna;
黃鰭金槍魚 Pacific yellowfin albacore; Pacific yellowfin tuna;
一罐金槍魚 a can of tuna; a tin of tuna;

[金球] golden goal;

[金曲] golden oldie;
懷舊金曲 golden oldie;

[金融] banking; finance;
金融的 dollars-and-cents; financial;
金融動態 financial trends;
金融服務 financial service;
金融改革 banking reform;
金融寡頭 financial oligarchy;
金融管理 monetary management;
金融機構 financial institution;
金融家 moneyman;
金融市場 financial market; money market;
金融調控 financial control;
金融危機 financial crisis;
金融政策 monetary policy;
金融資本 financial capital;
金融資產 financial assets;
金融指數 financial index;
金融制度 monetary system;
金融中心 financial centre;
~國際金融中心 international financial centre;
金融自由化 financial liberalization;
國際金融 international finance;
貿易金融 trade finance;
農業金融 agricultural finance;
市場金融 market finance;
微型金融 microfinance;

[金色] gold; golden;

鍍金色 deaurate;

[金石] (1) metal and stone — symbols of hardness and strength; (2) inscriptions on ancient bronzes and stone tablets;

金石絲竹 all kinds of music; various musical instruments;
金石同盟 alliance of perpetuity;
金石為開 sincerity can make metal and stone crack;
金石學 studies of metal and stone;
金石之交 close and intimate friendship;
情同金石 adamantine ties;
言如金石 one's words are as firm as gold and precious stones;

[金絲雀] canary;

[金屬] metal;

金屬盒 tin;
金屬化 metallisation;
~等電位金屬化 equipotential metallisation;
~多層金屬化 multiple-layer metallisation;
~陶瓷金屬化 ceramic metallisation;
金屬疲勞 metal fatigue;
金屬生物化學 metallobiochemistry;
金屬製品 metalwork;
超金屬 supermetal;
非金屬 non-metal;
複合金屬 composite metal;
貴金屬 noble metal; precious metal;
活潑金屬 active metal;
鹹金屬 alkali metal;
鹹土金屬 alkaline earth metal;
賤金屬 base metal;
耐酸金屬 acid metal;
輕金屬 light metal;
添加金屬 additive metal;
一種金屬 a type of metal;
重金屬 heavy metal;

[金條] bullion; gold bar; gold bullion;

[金童] golden boy;

金童玉女 golden boy and jade girl; handsome youths and fine maidens; simple-hearted boys and unsophisticated girls;

[金文] bronze inscriptions;

[金烏玉兔] crow of gold and hare of jade — the sun and moon;

[金屋] love nest;

金屋藏嬌 keep a mistress in a love nest; live with one's lover in a plush apartment; take a concubine;
藏嬌金屋 keep a mistress; take a concubine;

[金無足赤，人無完人] each of us has many imperfections; no person is infallible; there are spots even on the sun;

[金線] gold thread;

[金相學] metallography;

金相學 metallography;
~電子金相學 electron metallography;
~粉末金相學 powder metallography;
~離子透射金相學 ion transmission metallography;

[金星] stars; Venus;

眼冒金星 (1) one's eyes flame with fury; (2) see stars; stars dance before one's eyes;

[金銀] gold and silver;

金銀器 gold and silver ware;
金銀珠寶 gold, silver, and jewllery;

[金魚] goldfish;

金魚缸 goldfish bowl;
一盆金魚 a bowl of goldfish;

[金玉] gold and jade; precious stones and metals; treasures;

金玉良言 golden sayings; good counsels; invaluable advice; pearls of wisdom; precious teaching; profitable advice;
金玉滿堂 gold and jade fill the hall — abundant wealth; have one's house filled with riches;
金玉其外 have a gaudy but deceitful appearance;
金玉其外，敗絮其中 an embroidered pillowcase stuffed with straw; fair without, false within; fair in appearance but rotten to the core; rubbish coated in gold and jade;
金玉之言 precious words; valuable advice;
炊金饌玉 eat luxurious food;
堆金積玉 accumulate wealth; amass a fortune; heap up gold and gems; heap up treasures;
渾金璞玉 unrefined gold and unpolished jade;
積玉堆金 store up gems and pile up gold;
金科玉律 a golden rule and precious precept;
金口玉言 excellent advice; precious words; valuable instructions;

金鑲玉嵌 inlaid with gold and jade;
金聲玉振 good music;
良金美玉 good quality gold and precious stones;
鏤金雕玉 cut gold and carve jade — a fine piece of writing;
如金似玉 like gold and jade;

[金元] American dollar;
金元帝國 dollar empire;

[金磚] gold brick;

[金字塔] pyramid;
能量金字塔 energy pyramid;
數字金字塔 pyramid of numbers;

[金子] gold;
金子終得金子換 true gold will find its price;
一塊金子 a lump of gold;

白金 platinum;
包金 cover with gold leaf; gild;
本金 capital; principal;
彩金 mine for gold;
赤金 pure gold; solid gold;
酬金 commission; emolument; monetary reward; remuneration; reward; service fees;
儲金 savings;
純金 pure gold; solid gold;
錯金 inlaying gold;
代金 cash paid for a material object;
鍍金 (1) plate with gold; (2) get gilded;
罰金 (1) fine; (2) forfeit;
股金 money paid for shares;
合金 alloy;
黃金 gold;
基金 fund;
獎金 money award;
禮金 cash money as a gift;
美金 U.S. dollar;
描金 trace a design in gold;
千金 (1) a thousand pieces of gold; (2) daughter;
沙金 alluvial gold; placer gold;
賞金 money reward; pecuniary reward;
贖金 ransom money;
燙金 (1) bronze; (2) gild;
淘金 gold pan;
五金 (1) the five metals (gold, silver, copper, iron, and tin); (2) hardware; metals;
現金 (1) ready cash; ready money; (2) cash reserve in a bank;
祥金 ancient sacrificial bronze ware;
薪金 pay; salary;
卹金 pension for a disabled person;
冶金 metallurgy;
佣金 commission;
資金 (1) funds; (2) capital;
子金 interest;
租金 rent; rental;
足金 pure gold; solid gold;

jin

【津】 (1) ferry crossing; ford; (2) saliva; (3) sweat; (4) damp; moist; (5) short for Tianjin;

[津津] (1) interesting; tasty; (2) (of water or sweat) overflow;
津津樂道 delight in talking about; prattle to one's heart's content; talk with great relish;
~對自己的成就津津樂道 relish talking about one's achievements;
津津有味 relish; with good appetite; with great interest; with gusto; with keen interest; with much unction; with relish; with zest;
~吃得津津有味 eat sth with keen relish;
汗津津 moist with sweat; sweaty;
甜津津 (1) pleasantly sweet; (2) happy; pleased;
鹹津津 slightly salty;

[津貼] allowance; subsidy;
出差津貼 mission allowance; travel subsistence allowance;
房屋津貼 housing allowance;
航海津貼 sea allowance;
伙食津貼 food allowance;
每日津貼 per diem allowance;
日津貼 per diem;
膳宿津貼 accommodation allowance;
生活費用津貼 cost-of-living allowance;
生活津貼 living allowance;
特別職位津貼 special post allowance;
物價津貼 dearness allowance;
職務津貼 duty allowance;

迷津 labyrinth; maze;
生津 promote the secretion of saliva;
問津 make inquiries;
要津 key post; powerful and influential position;
知津 know the ford; know the way;

jin

【矜】 (1) pity; sympathize with; (2) conceited; self-important; (3) reserved; restrained;

J

［矜才］ rely on one's ability;
矜才使氣 rely on one's ability and act on impulse; self-conceited and insolent on account of one's ability;
［矜持］ reserved; restrained;
舉止矜持 conduct oneself with circumspection;
態度矜持 have a reserved manner;
［矜而不爭］ a dignified person does not argue;
［矜己］ self-conceited;
恃才矜己 self-conceited and proud of one's own talents;
［矜糾收繚］ arrogant and irascible;
［矜誇］ conceited and boastful;
驕傲矜誇 haughty and boastful;

哀矜 feel compassion for; pity;
驕矜 arrogant; haughty; self-important;

jin
【觔】 (1) same as 筋 ; (2) same as 斤 ;

jin
【荊】 (1) thorn; (2) cane for punishment used in ancient China; (3) one's wife; (4) one of the nine political regions in ancient China; (5) a surname;

jin
【衿】 (1) front of a Chinese gown; (2) lapel of a Chinese dress;

青衿 student's dress in ancient times;

jin
【筋】 (1) muscle; (2) sinew; tendon; (3) veins that stand out; (4) anything resembling a tendon or vein;
［筋斗］ somersault;
側身筋斗 cartwheels;
翻筋斗 somersault; turn a somersault;
［筋骨］ muscles and bones; physique;
勞其筋骨 exercise one's sinews and bones with toil;
挑筋剮骨 draw the sinews and cut the bones to pieces — an ancient form of punishment;
［筋節］ muscles and joints;
［筋膜］ aponeurosis;
筋膜炎 fascitis;
［筋疲力盡］ all in; all tuckered out; beaten out; dead on one's feet; dead-beat; dog-tired; exhausted; extremely fatigued; fagged out; give out; knocked out; over-spent; tired out; used up; utterly exhausted; worn out;
筋疲力盡的 bushed;
感到筋疲力盡 feel worn out;

抽筋 (1) pull out a tendon; (2) cramp;
猴皮筋 rubber band;
腦筋 (1) brains; head; mind; (2) ideas; way of thinking;
青筋 blue veins;
蹄筋 tendons of beef, mutton, or pork;
鐵筋 reinforcing bar;
轉筋 twitch;

jin
【祲】 (1) ominous; (2) vigorous;

jin
【禁】 (1) bear; endure; stand; (2) contain oneself; restrain oneself;
［禁不起］ unable to stand trials;
禁不起困苦 unable to stand hardships;
禁不起誘惑 fail to withstand the temptation;
［禁不住］ unable to bear; unable to endure;
禁不住大笑起來 burst out laughing;
禁不住啞然失笑 break into laughter; unable to stifle a laugh;
［禁得起］ able to stand;
禁得起嚴厲的考驗 able to stand severe tests;
［禁得住］ able to bear; able to endure;
禁得住各種誘惑 proof against all temptation;
［禁受］ bear; endure; stand;
［禁煙］ non-smoking;
禁煙的餐廳 non-smoking restaurant;

jin
【噤】 (1) keep silent; keep the mouth shut; shut; (2) shiver;
［噤若寒蟬］ as mute as a fish; as mute as a maggot; as quiet as a lamb; as quiet as a mouse; as quiet as the cicadas in late autumn — be afraid of voicing out one's opinion; as silent as a cicada in cold weather — keep quiet out of fear; become silent as an autumn cicada; keep mum about; maintain a discreet silence;

jin

【襟】 (1) front of a garment; (2) sister's husband;

［襟懷］ (1) bosom; (2) breadth of mind;
襟懷高曠 full of noble thoughts;
襟懷坦白 have largeness of mind; honest and straightforward; open as the day; open hearted and aboveboard; unselfish and magnanimous;

後襟 the back of a Chinese garment;
連襟 brother-in-law;
前襟 front part of a Chinese garment;
胸襟 breadth of mind;
衣襟 the one or two pieces making up the front of a Chinese garment;

jin³

jin

【巹】 nuptial wine cup;

jin

【堇】 viola verecunda; violet;

［堇菜］ violet;

［堇色］ violet;

三色堇 pansy;
紫堇 corydalis;

jin

【僅】 barely; just; merely; only; simply; solely;

［僅僅］ barely; merely; no more than; nothing but; only;
僅僅數秒 a matter of seconds;
僅僅數週 a matter of weeks;

［僅識其貌］ know sb by sight;

［僅以身免］ be saved only the the skin of one's teeth; escape by a hair's breadth; escape with one's bare body; escape with the skin of one's teeth; have a hairbreadth escape; have a narrow escape; narrowly escape with one's life;

不僅 (1) not the only one; (2) not only;

jin

【緊】 (1) close; tight; (2) fast; firm; (3) pressing; tense; urgent; (4) hard up; short of money;

［緊巴巴］ (1) taut; tight; (2) hard up;

［緊繃繃］ (1) taut; tight; (2) stiffened; strained; sullen;

［緊逼］ close in one; press hard;

［緊湊］ compact; terse; tight; well-knit;
情節緊湊 a well-knit plot;

［緊跟］ follow closely; keep in step with; keep up with; tread on the heels of;
緊跟時代 keep abreast of the times;
~緊跟時代的步伐 keep in step with the times;
緊跟形勢 keep abreast of the situation;
緊跟最新潮流 keep up with the latest fashions;

［緊化］ compactification; compacting;
單點緊化 one-point compactification;
等值緊化 equivalent compactification;

［緊急］ critical; emergent; pressing; urgent;
緊急措施 emergency measures;
緊急法令 emergency act;
緊急會議 emergency meeting; urgent meeting;
緊急情況 emergency; urgent situation;
緊急任務 urgent task;
緊急信號 emergency signal;
緊急制動 emergency application;
緊急狀態 state of emergency;
情況緊急 the situation is critical;

［緊緊］ closely; firmly; tightly;

［緊靠］ adjoin;

［緊鄰］ adjoining neighbour; close neighbour; next-door neighbour;

［緊密］ (1) close together; inseparable; (2) rapid and intense; thick and fast;
緊密合作 work in close cooperation;

［緊迫］ imminent; pressing; urgent;
緊迫感 a sense of urgency;
財政緊迫 financial stringency;

［緊俏］ in short supply and high demand; scarce;
緊俏商品 high-demand goods;

［緊缺］ in short supply; scarce;
緊缺商品 commodities in short supply;

［緊身］ close-fitting;
緊身的 close-fitting;
緊身褲 drainpipe trousers;
緊身衣 bodysuit;
~連褲緊身衣 body stocking;

［緊縮］ cut down; reduce; tighten;
緊縮並合句 compressed composite sentence;

J

緊縮複合句 compressed compound sentence;
緊縮開支 reduce expenditure; tighten the purse-strings;
緊縮銀根政策 tight money policy;
結構緊縮 structural compression;

[緊握] clench; grasp; grip; hold;

[緊咬] clench;

[緊要] critical; crucial; important; vital;
緊要關頭 at a pinch; at the critical juncture; at the critical moment; at the last minute; critical point; in a pinch; moment of truth; on a pinch;
無關緊要 it makes no odds;
至關緊要 of utmost importance;

[緊張] be a bundle of nerves; be keyed up; be strung up; be tensed up; nervous; strained; tense; tension; tonus;
緊張病 nervousness;
緊張不安 fluster; jitters; nervous; set sb's nerves on edge;
~ 緊張不安的 edgy; jumpy;
緊張的 flustered; tense;
~ 緊張的氣氛 tense atmosphere;
~ 令人緊張的 creepy;
緊張反射 tonic reflex;
緊張感 collywobbles;
緊張過度 overstressed;
緊張時刻 tense moment;
緊張症 catatonia;
~ 緊張症患者 catatonic;
別緊張 hang loose; stay loose;
非常緊張 be strung-up; break into a sweat; break out in a sweat;
感到緊張 feel nervous;
供貨緊張 short of supply;
渾身緊張 all in a flutter;
令人緊張 nerve-racking; nerve-wracking;
人手緊張 hard up; pressed for money; short of money;
日常生活的壓力和緊張 stresses and strains of everyday life;
資金緊張 short of funds;

[緊追] hot pursuit;
緊追不捨 hot on sb's trail; in hot pursuit;

扒緊 hold firmly;
綁緊 bind tight; fasten tight;
抱緊 hold tightly in one's arms; hug;
吃緊 be critical; be hard pressed;
打緊 critical; serious;
趕緊 hasten; lose no time;
加緊 intensify; speed up;
口緊 close-lipped; close-mouthed;
鬆緊 (1) degree of tightness; (2) elasticity;
嚴緊 close; tight;
要緊 (1) essential; important; (2) critical; serious;
抓緊 grasp firmly;

jin

【廑】 (1) cottage; hut; (2) eager;

jin

【瑾】 fine jade;

jin

【槿】 hibiscus;

[槿麻] gombo hemp;

jin

【殣】 (1) starve to death; (2) bury;

jin

【儘】 (1) to the greatest extent; (2) no more than; within the limits of; (3) first; give priority to; (4) at the furthest end of;

[儘管] although; as; despite; despite of; despite the fact; even if; even though; for all; in spite of; notwithstanding; though; with all;
儘管如此 all the same; at that; at the same time; be that as it may; even now; even so; for all that; for all this; still and all;

[儘快] as early as possible; as quickly as possible; as soon as possible;

[儘量] as far as possible; to the best of one's ability;
儘量多 as many as possible; as much as possible;
儘量快 as quickly as possible; as soon as possible;
儘量早 as early as possible;

[儘先] give first priority to;

jin

【錦】 (1) brocade; (2) bright and beautiful;

[錦標] prize; title; trophy;
錦標賽 tournament; tourney;
~ 網球錦標賽 tennis tournament;
~ 羽毛球錦標賽 badminton tournament;

[錦葵] mallow;
歐洲錦葵 vervain mallow;
小花錦葵 little mallow;

圓葉錦葵 running mallow;

［錦旗］ silk banner;

［錦上添花］ add brilliance to one's present splendour; add flowers to a piece of brocade; add lustre to; be blessed with a double portion of good fortune; make sth even better; make what is good still better; paint the lily; try to improve sth already beautiful;

［錦繡］ as beautiful as brocade; beautiful; splendid;

錦繡大地 land of splendours;

錦繡河山 beautiful land; beautiful rivers and mountains; land of charm and beauty;

錦繡前程 bright prospect; glorious future; very bright future;

錦繡文章 embroidered piece of literature;

錦心繡口 elegant thoughts and flowery speech — the pure spirit of poetry in one's breast and the most delicate, silken phrases on one's lips;

［錦衣］ embroidered dress;

錦衣狐裘 an embroidered dress and a fox-skin robe — a beautiful, costly dress;

錦衣玉食 beautiful dresses and nice food; elegantly dressed and feasting on delicacies; live an extravagant life; live on the fat of the land; swim in luxury;

錦衣朱履 dressed in an embroidered coat with red shoes;

八段錦 eight trigram boxing;

集錦 a collection of choice specimens;

庫錦 brocade with woven patterns in gold and silver threads and coloured floss;

什錦 assorted; mixed;

蜀錦 Sichuan brocade;

雲錦 cloud brocade;

織錦 brocade;

壯錦 Zhuang brocade;

jin

【覲】 have an audience with the head of a state;

jin

【謹】 (1) careful; cautious; circumspect; (2) sincerely; solemnly;

［謹防］ alert to; beware of; cautious of; guard against;

謹防暗箭 guard against a hidden arrow — take precautions against a covert attack;

謹防出錯 take every caution against error;

謹防傳染 guard against infection;

謹防感冒 guard against catching a cold;

謹防疾病 guard against disease;

謹防假冒 beware of imitations;

謹防爬手 beware of pickpockets;

謹防危險 guard against dangers;

謹防小偷 beware of pickpockets;

［謹上］ sincerely yours;

［謹慎］ careful; cautious; circumspect; prudent;

謹慎從事 act cautiously; act with caution; steer a cautious course;

謹慎的 cautious; chary;

~不謹慎的 incautious;

謹慎態度 cautious attitude;

~保持謹慎態度 preserve a cautious attitude;

謹慎小心 look ahead; look round the corner;

謹慎行事 play for safety; take heed in dealing with a matter; watch one's step;

不謹慎 indiscretion;

謙虛謹慎 humble and cautious; modest and prudent;

小心謹慎 careful; cautious; circumspect; discreet; discretion; easy does it; gingerly; prudent; with great care;

［謹嚴］ careful and precise;

［謹以奉聞］ I beg to inform you;

［謹贈］ with the compliments of;

［謹之於始］ be careful of the beginnings;

恭謹 respectful and cautious;

拘謹 cautious; reserved;

嚴謹 (1) rigorous; strict; (2) compact; well-knit;

jin

【饉】 famine; hunger;

饑饉 crop failure; famine;

jin⁴

jin

【近】 (1) close; immediate; near; (2) approaching; approximately; close to; (3) closely related; intimate; (4) easy to understand;

［近岸］ inshore; nearshore;

近岸水域 inshore waters;

[近便] close and convenient; close at hand;

[近代] modern times;

近代詩 modern poetry;

近代史 modern history;

近代英語 modern English;

[近地] terrestrial;

近地點 perigee;

近地空間 terrestrial space;

[近點月] anomalistic month;

[近乎] (1) almost; close to; little short of; near; (2) friendly; intimate;

近乎粗魯 border on rudeness;

近乎瘋狂 border on madness;

近乎荒謬 border on absurdity;

近乎尾聲 almost finished;

[近景] bust;

[近況] how things stand; recent developments;

[近來] lately; of late; recently;

[近鄰] close neighbour; near neighbour; neighbour;

[近路] shortcut;

抄近路 cut a corner; cut corners; take a shortcut;

[近廟欺神] familiarity breeds contempt; one who is near the temple may insult the gods; proximity breeds disrespect; those near the temple make fun of the gods;

[近旁] at one's elbow; near; nearby;

[近期] in the near future; recent; short term;

[近親] close relatives; flesh and blood; immediate family; near relations; proximity of blood;

近親繁殖 inbreeding;

近親家屬 immediate family;

近親交配 inbreeding;

[近日] (1) in the past few days; recently; (2) within the next few days;

近日點 perihelion;

[近世] modern times;

[近視] myopia; nearsighted; nearsightedness; short-sight; short-sighted; short-sightedness

近視反射 myopic reflex;

近視散光 myopic astigmatism;

~ 單純近視散光 simple myopic astigmatism;

單純性近視 primary myopia; simple myopia;

惡性近視 malignant myopia; pernicious myopia;

假性近視 pseudomyopia;

進行性近視 progressive myopia;

老年近視 gerontopia;

曲度性近視 curvature myopia;

[近水樓台] terrace and pavilion near the water — convenient access; waterside pavilion — favourable position;

近水樓台先得月 a person in a favourable position has special advantages; a waterfront pavilion gets the moonlight first — first come, first served; those on the waterfront are the first to see the rising moon — enjoy the benefits of a favourable position;

[近水知魚性，近山識鳥音] those who live near the water know the habits of fish, those who live in the mountains can tell the notes of the birds — the environment in which we live and work influences us in much of what we do;

[近似] approximate; roughly; similar;

近似計算 approximate calculation;

差分近似 difference approximation;

聲學近似 acoustic approximation;

數值近似 numerical approximation;

線性近似 linear approximation;

形式近似 formal approximation;

整體近似 global approximation;

指數近似 exponential approximation;

最優近似 best fit approximation;

[近因] immediate cause;

[近於] bordering on; little short of;

近於荒唐 bordering on the absurd; little short of preposterous;

[近朱者赤] the person who gets in contact with vermilion will become red;

近朱者赤，近墨者黑 evil communications corrupt good manners; those who live with cripples learn how to limp; he that sleeps with dogs must rise with fleas; he that touches pitch shall be defiled therewith; he who keeps company with the wolf will learn to howl; if you lie down with dogs, you get up with fleas; if you live with a lame person you will learn to limp;

near vermilion, one gets stained pink; near ink, one gets stained black; one takes the attributes of one's company;

挨近 be near to; get close to;
傍近 close to ; near;
濱近 close to; near;
湊近 approach; lean close to;
附近 around the corner; nearby;
很近 close to; within easy reach of;
將近 be almost; be close to;
接近 be close to; draw near;
就近 nearby; in the neighbourhood;
靠近 (1) close to; near; (2) approach; draw near;
鄰近 adjacent to; near;
臨近 be close to;
迫近 approach; draw near;
淺近 easy to understand; simple;
切近 (1) be close to; near; (2) be similar;
親近 be on intimate terms with; close to;
貼近 lean close to; press close to;
晚近 during the past few years; in recent years;
偎近 lean close to; nestle up against;
相近 (1) close; near; (2) close to; similar to;
新近 in recent times; lately; recently;
以近 up to;
遠近 (1) distance; (2) far and near;
最近 (1) lately; of late; recently; (2) in the near future; soon;
左近 in the neighbourhood; in the vicinity; nearby;

jin

【勁】 (1) energy; strength; (2) drive; spirit; vigour; zeal; (3) air; expression; manner; (4) gusto; interest; relish;

[勁兒] strength;
一個勁兒 continuously; full of zest; persistently;

[勁頭] energy; spirit; strength; vigour;
勁頭不大 not show much spirit;
勁頭十足 with great zeal;
工作有勁頭 full of drive in one's work;

蒼勁 (1) old and strong; (2) bold; vigorous;
差勁 disappointing; no good;
吃勁 be a strain; entail much effort;
衝勁 enthusiasm; impulse; zeal;
闖勁 pioneering spirit;
帶勁 (1) vigorous; with great energy and efforts; (2) exciting; interesting;
得勁 (1) feel well; (2) fit for use;
對勁 (1) be to one's liking; suit one; (2) get along with;
費勁 be strenuous; entail great effort;
幹勁 drive; enthusiasm;
後勁 (1) after-effect; delayed effect; (2) reserve one's strength;
虎勁 dash; dauntless drive;
犟勁 unyielding will;
賣勁 exert all one's strength; make strenuous efforts;
牛勁 (1) great strength; tremendous effort; (2) obstinacy; stubbornness;
起勁 enthusiastically; vigorously; with gusto;
使勁 exert one's strength; put in one's energy;
鬆勁 relax one's efforts; slacken;
洩勁 feel discouraged; lose heart;
要勁 make strenuous efforts;
一股勁 a burst of energy;
用勁 exert one's strength;
有勁 (1) potent; strong; (2) amusing; interesting; (3) full of gusto;
作勁 help; offer assistance to;

jin

【晉】 (1) advance; enter; (2) promote; (3) the Jin Dynasty; (4) another name for Shanxi Province;

[晉級] advance in rank; be promoted; rise in rank;

[晉見] call on; have an audience with;
晉見主席 call on the chairman;

[晉昇] be promoted to; be given a promotion; elevation; gain promotion; get promoted to; get a promotion; obtain a promotion; receive promotion; win promotion;
得到晉昇 get a promotion; obtain a promotion; receive a promotion;

[晉謁] call on; have an audience with;

jin

【浸】 immerse; soak; steep;

[浸出] leaching;
常壓浸出 atmospheric pressure leaching;
分批浸出 batch leaching;
加速浸出 accelerated leaching;

[浸劑] infusion;
瓊脂肉浸劑 agar meat infusion;
新鮮浸劑 fresh infusions;

[浸禮] baptism; immersion;

[浸泡] bath; immerse; soak; steep;

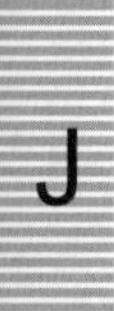

[浸入] immersion;
浸入式 immersion;
~浸入式熱水器 immersion heater;
解析浸入 analytic immersion;
微分浸入 differentiable immersion;
組合浸入 combinatorial immersion;

[浸透] impregnate; saturate; steep; soak; infuse;

[浸液] infusion;
枯草浸液 hay infusion;
腦心浸液 brain heart infusion;

jin

【進】 (1) advance; move ahead; move forward; (2) come into; enter; get into; go into; (3) receive; (4) drink; eat; take;

[進逼] advance on; close in on; press on towards;
步步進逼 press on at every stage;

[進兵] order troops to march forward;

[進步] (1) advance; improve; make advances; make progress; progress; (2) progressive;
進步份子 progressives;
進步人士 progressive personages;
進步勢力 progressive forces;
進步思想 progressive ideas;
進步團體 progressive organizations;
大有進步 advance with rapid strides; have improved greatly; make great strides;
技術進步 technical progress;
經濟進步 economic progress;
渴望進步 eager to progress;
取得進步 achieve progress; make progress;
日有進步 progress constantly; show progress day by day;

[進餐] dine; have a meal;
進餐時間 mealtime;

[進場] march into the arena;

[進城] (1) go into town; (2) enter a big city;

[進程] progress;

[進出] (1) get in and out; pass in and out; (2) receipts and payments;
進出口 (1) imports and exports; (2) exits and entrances;
~進出口經營權 the power to engage in import and export trade;
~進出口貿易 imports and exports;
出出進進 coming and going;
進進出出 come in and out; in and out; shuttle in and out;
跑進跑出 bustle in and out; pop in and out;
時進時出 in and out; now in and now out;
雙進雙出 go with each other all the time;

[進度] (1) rate of advance; rate of progress; (2) planned speed; schedule;
進度報告 progress report;
進度管理 schedule control;

[進而] and then; proceed to the next step;

[進發] set out; start;

[進犯] intrude into; invade;

[進攻] assault; attack; offensive;
進攻計劃 plan of attack;
進攻性武器 attack armature;
交叉進攻 alternating attack;

[進貢] pay tribute;

[進化] evolution;
進化論 theory of evolution;
~進化論者 evolutionist;
~創造進化論 creative evolution;
進化樹 evolution tree;
緩速進化 bradytelic evolution;
機遇性進化 accidental evolution;
人為進化 artificial evolution;
適應進化 adaptive evolution;
微進化 microevolution;
植物群進化 floral evolution;
種內進化 intraspecific evolution;

[進軍] advance; march; move;

[進口] (1) enter a port; sail into a port; (2) import; (3) inlet;
進口代理商 import agent;
進口附加税 import surtaxes;
進口國 importing country;
進口貨 imported goods;
進口汽車 imported car;
進口取代產品 import substitute;
進口商 importer;
進口商品結構 importing goods' structure;
進口税 import taxes;
進口替代產品 import substitutional products;
進口限額 import quota;
進口許可證制度 import licence system;
單邊進口 unilateral import;
復進口 re-import;
鼓風進口 blast inlet;
淨進口 net import;
間接進口 indirect import;

煤氣進口 gas inlet;
排氣進口 exhaust steam inlet;
燃料進口 fuel inlet;
停止進口 import suspension;
無形進口 invisible import;
預計進口 anticipatory import;
暫時進口 temporary import;
直接進口 direct import;
總進口 general import;
專門進口 special import;

[進來] come in; enter; get in;
從後門進來 come in by the back door;
溜進來 slip into; sneak in;

[進路] route;
發車進路 departure route;
關閉進路 closed route;
轉向進路 diverted route;

[進氣] air admission;
進氣口 inlet;
~高超音速進氣口 hypersonic inlet;
~埋入式進氣口 submerged inlet;
~通風進氣口 fan inlet;
嗡鳴進氣 buzz;

[進取] eager to make progress; enterprising; keep forging ahead; up-and-coming;
進取心 aggressiveness; desire to get ahead; enterprising spirit;
不求進取 not strive to make progress; unwilling to keep forging ahead;

[進去] enter; get in; go in;
開進去 drive in;

[進入] enter; get into;
進入角色 enter into the role of a character; play a role;
進入夢鄉 fall asleep; go off to dreamland; go to one's dreams;
進入權 entrée; right of access; right of entry;
強行進入 forced entry;
易進入 accessible;
再進入 re-entry;

[進食] feed; have one's meal; take food;

[進士] a successful candidate in the highest imperial examinations;
不櫛進士 gifted woman; learned girl; talented woman;

[進退] (1) advance and retreat; (2) sense of propriety;
進退兩難 between the devil and the deep blue sea; between two fires; find it difficult both to advance and to retreat; have a wolf by the ears; hold a wolf by the ears; in a cleft stick; in a dilemma; in a fix; in a quandary; in an awkward predicament; in chancery; on the horns of a dilemma; place sb in a dilemma; put sb into a dilemma; up a stump; up a tree;
進退失據 difficult either to advance or to retreat; in a cleft stick; in a fix;
進退維谷 be on the horns of a dilemma; be stuck between a rock and a hard place; between the devil and the deep sea; find oneself in an awkward predicament; in a dilemma; in a fix; up a gum tree; up a tree;
進退無門 fall between two stools; in straits;
進退自如 free to advance or retreat; free to proceed or step back; have room for manoeuvre;
不進則退 move forward, or you'll fall behind; not to advance is to go back;
可進可退 can either advance or retreat at will; free to go forward or back out;
旅進旅退 always follow the steps of others, forward or backward – have no definite views of one's own;
能進能退 able to advance and retire;
以進為退 pretend to move ahead in order to hide the intention to retreat;
以退為進 make concessions in order to gain advantages; retreat for the sake of advancing; retreat in order to advance;
有進無退 burn one's bridges behind one; only advance, never retreat;
有進有退 roll back and forth;
有退無進 only retreat, never advance;

[進位] carry;
並行進位 parallel carry;
部份進位 partial carry;
單位進位 single carry;
二進制進位 binary carry;
反向進位 negative carry;
分組進位 group carry;
累加進位 accumulative carry;
鏈鎖進位 chain carry;
前視進位 look-ahead carry;
前位進位 previous carry;
順序進位 sequential carry;
同時進位 simultaneous carry;
完全進位 complete carry;
延遲進位 delayed carry;

直通進位 standing carry;
錐形進位 pyramid carry;
自動進位 automatic carry; self-instructed carry;

[進行] carry on; go on; in progress; underway;
進行到底 carry sth through to the end; follow sth through to the end; follow through;
進行曲 march;
進行時 continuous tense; progressive tense;
進行體 progressive;
~進行體不定式 progress infinitive;
~進行體助動詞 progressive auxiliary;
按計劃進行 go according to plan;
加緊進行 press ahead with;
順利進行 go like clockwork; progress smoothly; run like clockwork;
照常進行 go ahead;

[進修] engage in advanced studies; further one's education; further one's learning; further one's studies; take a refresher course;
進修教育 continuing education; further education;
進修課程 refresher course;
進修學校 continuation school;
高級進修 advance studies;

[進展] evolve; make headway; make progress; march;
進展不大 make little headway;
進展遲緩 make slow progress; proceed sluggishly;
進展很大 make great advances;
進展很快 progress rapidly;
進展情況 state of play;
進展神速 advance at a miraculous pace; make progress with amazing speed;
進展穩定 make steady progress; progress steadily;
長足進展 quantum leap;
工業進展 industrial progress;
艱難地進展 limp along;
巨大的進展 great progress;
噴氣技術進展 jet progress;
取得進展 (1) get off the ground; (2) make headway;
有進展 be getting somewhere;
周期進展 cycle progress;

[進駐] enter and be stationed in; enter and garrison; march into a place and station there;

凹進 concave; depressed; hollow; indented;
八進 octal; octonary;
搬進 move in;
並進 do two things at the same time;
插進 dip; interject; let in; stick in; thrust into; work in;
衝進 plunge into;
闖進 burst in; inbreak;
促進 accelerate; advance; boost; encourage; facilitate; gear up; promote;
奮進 advance bravely;
改進 improve; make better;
跟進 follow-up;
後進 be less advanced; lag behind;
躋進 enter;
激進 radical;
急進 radical;
繼進 continue to advance;
漸進 advance gradually; progress step by step;
掘進 (1) drive; (2) tunnel;
亢進 hyperfunction;
累進 progress;
邁進 forge ahead; march forward;
冒進 advance rashly;
猛進 advance by leaps and bounds;
前進 advance; forge ahead; make progress; strive forward;
勸進 make a formal appeal to sb to mount the throne;
上進 advance; make progress;
仕進 become an official in order to be prosperous;
挺進 boldly drive on; forge ahead; march forward;
突進 march forward; press onward;
推進 (1) carry forward; push on; (2) drive on; move forward; press onward;
先進 advanced;
行進 advance; march forward;
幸進 be promoted fortunately;
演進 evolve; progress gradually;
引進 (1) recommend; (2) introduce from elsewhere;
躍進 advance with big strides; leap forward;
增進 enhance; promote;
長進 progress;

jin

【禁】 (1) ban; forbid; prohibit; (2) detain; imprison;

［禁閉］ confinement;
禁閉室 confinement cell;
［禁地］ forbidden area; out-of-bounds area; restricted area;
［禁賭］ ban gambling; prohibit gambling; suppress gambling;
［禁錮］ (1) debar from holding office; (2) imprison; keep in custody; put in jail; (3) confine; shackle;
［禁果］ forbidden fruit; illicit sex between unmarried people;
［禁忌］ (1) taboo; (2) abstain from; avoid; (3) contraindication;
禁忌葷腥 abstain from flesh and fish;
禁忌煙酒 abstain from smoking and drinking;
禁忌語 taboo;
百無禁忌 anything goes; no restrictions of any kind; no taboos; nothing forbidden;
言無禁忌 say without taboo;
［禁戒區］ exclusion area;
［禁酒］ prohibition against alcoholic drinks;
［禁絕］ completely ban;
［禁例］ prohibitions; prohibitory regulations;
［禁獵期］ close season;
［禁令］ ban; injunction; interdict; prohibition;
撤消禁令 withdraw a ban;
出口禁令 export ban;
發出禁令 grant an injunction;
廢除禁令 rescind a ban;
廣告禁令 advertising ban;
國際禁令 international ban;
解除禁令 lift a ban;
進口禁令 import ban;
取消禁令 lift a prohibition; rescind a ban;
全球禁令 global ban; worldwide ban;
［禁區］ (1) exclusion zone; forbidden zone; out-of-bounds area; restricted area; restricted zone; (2) preserve; reserve; (3) penalty area;
軍事禁區 military exclusion zone;
［禁聲令］ gag order;
［禁食］ fasting;
禁食日 fast day;
［禁書］ banned book; officially banned book;
［禁用］ forbidden;
［禁漁期］ close season;
［禁慾］ sexual abstinence; suppress sexual urges;
禁慾的 celibate;
禁慾宣言 vow of celibacy;
禁慾主義 asceticism;
~禁慾主義者 ascetic;
［禁運］ embargo;
禁運品 contraband;
［禁止］ ban; bar; clamp down on; debar; forbid; impose an embargo on; lay ban on; place a check on; place sth under a ban; prohibit; proscribe; put sth under ban;
禁止超車 no overtaking;
禁止拍照 no cameras;
禁止入內 no admittance;
禁止停車 no parking;
禁止吸煙 no smoking;
禁止招貼 post no bills;
徹底禁止 complete ban; total ban;
全面禁止 blanket ban;
完全禁止 outright ban;
終身禁止 lifetime ban;
［禁制品］ banned products;

邦禁 prohibitions of a nation;
不禁 can't help but; can't help doing sth; can't refrain from; in spite of;
查禁 ban; prohibit;
弛禁 lift a ban; relax a restriction; rescind a ban;
犯禁 violate a ban;
海禁 ban on maritime trade;
監禁 imprison; put in jail;
解禁 lift a ban;
拘禁 take into custody;
開禁 lift a ban;
門禁 entrance guard;
囚禁 imprison; put in jail;
軟禁 put sb under house arrest;
失禁 become incontinent; suffer from incontinence;
違禁 violate a ban;
宵禁 curfew;
嚴禁 forbid strictly;
謁禁 ban on visitors;
幽禁 imprison; put under house arrest;

jin
【搢】 (1) stick into; (2) shake;

jin
【靳】 (1) ornamental trappings under the neck of a horse; (2) stingy; (3) a surname;

J

jin

【瑨】 a fine piece of jade;

jin

【盡】 (1) exhausted; finished; (2) to the limit; to the utmost; (3) exhaust; use up; (4) put to the best use; try one's best; (5) all; exhaustive;

[盡瘁而死] fag oneself to death;

[盡歡而散] leave only after each one has enjoyed to the utmost;

[盡力] all one's knows; as best as one can; as far as possible; at full stretch; at pains to do sth; break one's neck; do all in one's power; do all one can; do everything in one's power; do one's best do one's level best; do one's utmost; do sth with all one's might; exert oneself; lay oneself out; leave no stones unturned; make an all-out effort; make every effort; make great efforts; make the most of one's chance; move heaven and earth; put one's back into sth; spare no efforts; spare no pains; take great pains in doing sth; to the best of one's ability; to the full; try every means; try one's best; try one's hardest to do sth; with all one's energy; with all one's might;

盡力而為 contribute according to one's ability; do everything in one's power; do everything one can; do one's best; do one's utmost; do sth to the best of one's capacities; do whatever lies in one's power; exert one's utmost; make the best of one's way; shoot one's best;

各盡其力 every person does his/her best;

[盡量] as far as possible; as fully as one can; as much as; do one's best; make the best of; to the best of one's ability; to the full; to the utmost extent;

[盡情] as much as one likes; to one's heart's content; to the full;

盡情發揮 bring into full play;

盡情放縱 have a fling;

盡情歌唱 sing to one's heart's content;

盡情歡樂 make merry to one's heart's content;

盡情款待 treat with the utmost kindness;

盡情流露 give free vent to;

盡情痛哭 cry one's eyes out; cry one's heart out;

盡情吐露 free one's heart; wear one's heart upon one's sleeve;

盡情玩耍 play to one's heart's content;

[盡人皆知] be a proverb for; be known to all; be universally known; common knowledge; it is particularly notorious that; it is widely known that; well-known;

盡人皆知的哲人 well-known philosopher;

[盡是] all; full of; without exception;

[盡頭] (1) the end; (2) the end of a road;

[盡心] do sth with all one's heart; put one's heart and soul into; with all one's heart;

盡心報國 devote one's energies entirely to the service of the state; do one's best for the country;

盡心竭力 do one's best; do one's level best; go to great lengths; heart and soul; put one's heart and soul into; strain every nerve; use one's best efforts; with all one's might;

[盡信書不如無書] books should be read with reservation; it is better not to read the book of history rather than to believe it entirely;

[盡興] enjoy oneself to the full; to one's heart's content;

盡興而歸 return after having enjoyed oneself;

[盡意] express all one intends to express;

言不盡意 I should like to say more; words cannot express all one intends to say;

[盡責] discharge one's duties;

各盡其責 each one does his duty;

[盡職] discharge one's duty; fulfil one's duty;

各盡其職 pull one's own weight;

[盡忠] (1) loyal to; (2) lay down one's life for; sacrifice one's life for;

盡忠報國 be devoted to one's country; dedicate oneself to the service of one's country; defend one's country with heart and soul; devote one's life to the country; do one's best for the country; allegiance to one's country;

盡忠效勞 serve faithfully;

[盡醉方休] drink on until one is drunk; stop drinking only when one is nearly drunk;

耗盡 exhaust; use up;
竭盡 exhaust; use up;
淨盡 completely; utterly;
罄盡 all used up; with nothing left;
窮盡 end; limit;
詳盡 detailed; thorough;
自盡 commit suicide; take one's own life;

jin
【縉】 red silk;

jin
【噤】 keep silent; keep one's mouth shut;
[噤若寒蟬] as silent as a winter cicada — say nothing;

寒噤 shiver in cold or fear;

jin
【覲】 have an audience with a chief of state;
[覲見] have an audience with a chief of state;
[覲禮] rituals performed during an audience;

朝覲 (1) have an audience with an emperor; (2) go on a pilgrimage;

jin
【燼】 embers;

灰燼 ashes;
餘燼 ashes; embers;

jin
【藎】 (1) arthraxon ciliare, a kind of weed whose stalk is used as a yellow dye; (2) faithfulness; great loyalty and love;
[藎草] arthraxon hispidus;

jin
【贐】 farewell present; parting gifts;

jing[1]
jing
【京】 (1) capital of a country; (2) Beijing;
[京城] capital of a country;
[京胡] Beijing opera fiddle;
[京畿] capital city and its environs;
[京劇] Beijing opera;
京劇唱腔 rhyme scheme of Beijing opera;
京劇團 Beijing opera troupe;
傳統京劇 traditional Beijing opera;
現代京劇 modern Beijing opera;
一場京劇 a performance of Beijing opera;
[京師] capital of a country;
[京戲] Beijing opera;
一場京戲 a performance of Beijing opera;

北京 Beijing;

jing
【秔】 non-glutinous rice;
[秔稻] non-glutinous rice which ripens a little late;
[秔米] non-glutinous rice;

jing
【荊】 (1) a kind of bramble; thorn; (2) cane for punishment used in ancient China; (3) my wife; (4) a surname;
[荊布] be simply adorned; in coarse clothing;
[荊釵布裙] thorns for hairpins and cotton cloth for skirts — clothing of a poor woman;
[荊柴] destitute household; poor family;
[荊婦] one's wife;
[荊璞] unpolished precious jade;
[荊蠻] (1) collective name of four ancient counties in Hunan Province; (2) rough and primitive places;
[荊桃] cherry;
[荊條] stems of a bramble made into baskets;
[荊棘] (1) thorns; thorny; (2) difficult situation;
荊棘之冠 thorny crown;
荊棘載途 a path overgrown with brambles — be beset with difficulty;
滿途荊棘 there are brambles all along the road — a path beset with difficulty;
披荊斬棘 blaze a new trail through brambles; blaze a trail through all manner of obstacles; break open a way through bramble and thistle; cut one's way through brambles; force one's way through a thorny path; overcome great difficulties;
銅駝荊棘 the brass camel covered by thorns — great confusion in the land occupied by the enemy;
[荊室] one's wife;

黃荊 five-leaved chaste tree;
識荊 have the honour of making your acquaintance;

J

拙荊 one's wife;
紫荊 Chinese redbud;

jing
【涇】 a river in Shaanxi;
［涇渭］ good and evil;
涇渭不分 fail to distinguish between the good and the bad; make no distinction between clean and muddy — make no distinction between good and evil; no distinction is made between right and wrong;
涇渭分明 as different as the water of the Jinghe and the Weihe — entirely different; be well defined;
不分涇渭 make no distinction between good and evil;
涇清渭濁 as different as night and day;

jing
【耕】 a pronunciation of 耕;

jing
【旌】 (1) banner; flag; (2) cite; make manifest;
［旌旗］ banners and flags;
旌旗蔽日 fluttering banners hide the sun;
旌旗遍野 the banners fill the horizon;
旌旗招展 banners and pennants are flaunting in the wind;

jing
【莖】 stalk; stem;
［莖稿］ straw;
［莖肌］ pedical muscle;

抽莖 put forth;
根莖 rhizome;
花莖 floral axis;
塊莖 stem tuber;
鱗莖 bulb;
球莖 corm;
陰莖 penis;

jing
【睛】 (1) eyeball; (2) pupil of the eye;

定睛 fix one's eyes upon;
眼睛 eye;

jing
【晶】 (1) crystal; (2) bright; brilliant; clear; radiant;
［晶粒］ crystal particle; grain crystal;
［晶片］ chip; crystal plate;
［晶石］ spar;
冰晶石 ice spar;
尖晶石 spinel;
~紅寶石尖晶石 ruby spinel;
~紅尖晶石 almandine spinel;
~鐵尖晶石 iron spinel;
重晶石 heavy spar;
［晶體］ crystal;
晶體測量學 crystallometry;
晶體發生 crystallogenesis;
~晶體發生學 crystallogeny;
晶體管 transistor;
~單極晶體管 unipolar transistor;
~二極晶體管 diode transistor;
~合金晶體管 alloyed transistor;
~合金型晶體管 alloy type transistor;
~類比晶體管 analogue transistor;
~漂移晶體管 drift transistor;
~三極晶體管 triode transistor;
~四極晶體管 tetrode transistor;
晶體檢波器 crystal detector;
晶體生長 crystal growth;
晶體物理 crystallography;
晶體學 crystallography; crystallology;
晶體衍射圖 crystallogram;
晶體熒光 crystallofluorescence;
反鐵電晶體 antiferroelectric crystal;
人造石英晶體 artificial quartz crystal;
三斜晶體 anorthic crystal;
聲光晶體 acousto-optic crystal;
針狀晶體 crystal;
［晶瑩］ sparkling and crystal-clear;

冰晶 ice crystal;
茶晶 citrine; yellow quartz;
單晶 single crystal;
複晶 compound crystal;
結晶 (1) crystal; (2) crystallize; crystallization;
孿晶 twin crystal;
墨晶 smoky quartz;
球晶 spherocrystal;
水晶 crystal; rock crystal;
雪晶 snow crystals;
煙晶 smoky quartz; smoky topaz;
液晶 liquid crystal;
籽晶 seed crystal;

jing
【菁】 (1) flower of the leek; (2) rape; turnip; (3) flowery; ornamental; (4) cream; essence;

[菁華] cream; essence; quintessence;
[菁菁] lush; luxuriant;

蔓菁 turnip;
田菁 sesbania;

jing
【粳】 same as 梗 ;
[粳稻] round-grained non-glutinous rice;

jing
【經】 (1) longitude; (2) deal in; engage in; manage; (3) by way of; pass through; undergo; via; (4) canon; classic; scripture; (5) bear; endure; stand;
[經閉] amenorrhea;
[經常] (1) always; constantly; every now and again; every now and then; every once in a while; every so often; frequent; frequently; from time to time; half the time; many's the time; more often than not; now and again; now and then; often; oftentimes; regularly; time after time; used to; (2) daily; day-to-day; everyday;
經常化 become a regular practice;
不經常 infrequent; not often;
[經遲] delayed menstrual cycle;
[經典] (1) classics; (2) scriptures; (3) classical;
經典文獻 classical documents;
經典著作 classical works;
經典作家 authors of classics;
奉為經典 regard sth as canons;
論經數典 discuss the arts and the classics;
引經據典 (1) quote authoritative works; quote chapter and verse; quote the classics; (2) pedantic;
[經度] longitude;
大地經度 geodetic longitude;
假想經度 fictitious longitude;
天文經度 astronomical longitude;
[經費] funds; outlay;
[經管] in charge of;
[經過] go through; pass; pass through; undergo;
事非經過不知難 a person does not know how difficult sth is unless he / she does it personally; one cannot appreciate the difficulty except through personal experience; one does not realize the difficulty of an undertaking unless he has experienced it before; one never knows how hard a task is until one has done it oneself; you never know till you try;
[經濟] (1) economy; (2) economic;
經濟案件 economic case;
經濟案例 economic case;
經濟報酬 economic returns; financial reward;
經濟保障 economic security;
經濟崩潰 economic collapse;
經濟變革 economic transformation;
經濟波動 economic fluctuation;
經濟佈局 economic layout;
經濟艙 economy class;
~ 經濟艙綜合症 economy class syndrome;
經濟成分 economic component;
~ 多種經濟成分 multiple economic components;
經濟措施 economic measure;
經濟單位 economic unit;
經濟的 dollars-and-cents; economic;
經濟地理 economic geography;
~ 經濟地理位置 economic-geographic situation;
經濟地位 economic status;
經濟法 economic law;
~ 經濟法規 economic laws and regulations;
~ 經濟法庭 economic court; economic tribunal;
~ 經濟法學 economic jurisprudence;
經濟發達 economically developed;
~ 經濟發達地區 economically developed region;
~ 經濟發達國家 economically developed country;
經濟發展 economic development;
~ 經濟發展目標 objective of economic development;
~ 經濟發展戰略 strategy of economic development;
經濟犯罪 economic crime;
經濟放緩 the economy slows down;
經濟封鎖 economic blockade;
經濟負擔 financial burden;
經濟復甦 economic recovery;
經濟復蘇 economic resurgence;
經濟改革 economic reforms;
經濟杠桿 economic lever;
經濟公開 accounts open to the public;

經濟顧問 economic adviser;
~ 首席經濟顧問 chief economic adviser;
經濟管理 economic management;
經濟過熱 overheating of the economy;
~ 防止經濟過熱 present an overheated economy;
經濟合同 economic contract;
~ 經濟合同法 economic contract law;
經濟合作 economic cooperation;
~ 多國經濟合作 multi-economic cooperation;
經濟和社會發展 economic and social development;
~ 促進經濟和社會發展 promote economic and social development;
經濟核算 budgetary accounting; economic accounting; economic reckoning;
經濟核心區 economic key zone;
經濟環境 economic environment;
~ 改善經濟環境 improve the economic environment;
經濟恢復 the economy recovers;
經濟活動 economic activity;
經濟活力 economic vitality;
經濟機制 economic mechanism;
經濟基礎 economic foundation;
經濟技術 economic and technological;
~ 經濟技術合作 economic and technological cooperation;
~ 經濟技術交流 economic and technological exchange;
~ 經濟技術開發區 economic and technological development zone for new and high-level technology industries;
~ 經濟技術系統 techno-economic system;
~ 經濟技術指標 techno-economic indices;
經濟計量學 econometrics;
經濟監督 economic supervision;
經濟結構 economic structure;
~ 優化經濟結構 optimize the economic structure;
經濟界 economic circles;
經濟緊縮政策 economic retrenchment policies;
經濟決策 economic decision;
經濟空間 economic space;
經濟恐慌 economic depression;
經濟寬裕 well-to-do;
經濟擴張 economic expansion;
經濟困難 economic difficulties;
經濟立法 legislative economy;
經濟民主 economic democracy;
經濟命脈 economic arteries;
經濟模式 economic model;
經濟批量 economic lot size;
經濟平衡 economic equilibrium;
經濟破產 economic bankruptcy;
經濟起飛 economic take-off;
經濟區 economic region;
經濟圈 economic ring;
經濟群體 economic group;
經濟滲透 economic infiltration;
經濟審計 financial audit;
經濟師 economist;
~ 高級經濟師 senior economist;
~ 助理經濟師 assistant economist;
經濟失調 economic ailment; dislocation of the economy;
經濟市場化 marketization of the economy;
經濟實惠 economical and practical;
經濟實力 economic strength;
經濟實體 economic entity;
~ 辦經濟實體 run economic entities;
經濟勢頭 economic drive;
經濟手段 economic means;
經濟衰退 recession;
經濟損失 economic loss;
~ 間接經濟損失 indirect economic loss;
經濟私有化 privatization of the economy;
經濟態勢 economic situation;
經濟特區 special economic zone;
經濟騰飛 economic take-off;
經濟體 economy;
~ 小型經濟體 small economy;
經濟體制 economic system;
~ 經濟體制改革 economic structural reform;
~ 新經濟體制 new economic system;
經濟調節 economic regulation;
~ 經濟調節手段 economic means of regulation;
經濟調控 economic control and adjustment;
~ 經濟調控體系 economic regulation system;
~ 宏觀經濟調控 macroeconomic control and adjustment;
經濟網絡 economic network;
經濟危機 economic crisis;
經濟萎縮 economic depression; economic recession; economic slump;

經濟文化類群 economic-cultural group;
經濟穩定 economic stability;
經濟系統 economic system;
~經濟系統分析 economic system analysis;
經濟蕭條 economic depression;
經濟效益 economic benefits; economic effects;
~經濟效益指標 projected economic returns;
經濟協作區 economical coordination area;
經濟心理學 economic psychology;
經濟信息 economic information;
經濟興旺 economic boom;
經濟形式 economical form;
經濟學 economics;
~經濟學家 economist;
古典派經濟學家 classical school economist;
商業經濟學家 business economist;
~安全經濟學 economy of safety;
~比較經濟學 comparative economics;
~部門經濟學 departmental economics;
~供應經濟學 supply-side economics;
~古典經濟學 classical economics;
~宏觀經濟學 macroeconomics;
~開發經濟學 development economics;
~農業經濟學 agricultural economics;
~企業經濟學 business economics;
~實用經濟學 applied economics;
~時間經濟學 time economics;
~投入產出經濟學 input-output economics;
~圖書館經濟學 library economics;
~土地經濟學 land economics;
~微觀經濟學 microeconomics;
~萎縮經濟學 depression economics;
~衛生經濟學 economics of health;
~鄉鎮企業經濟學 economics of town and village enterprises;
~消費經濟學 economics of consumption;
~信息經濟學 information economics;
~災害經濟學 economics of catastrophe;
~戰爭經濟學 economics of war;
~政治經濟學 political economics;
~總合經濟學 aggregative economics;
~總量經濟學 aggregate economics;
經濟循環 economic circulation;
經濟一體化 economic integration;
經濟應用 economic application;
經濟優勢 economic superiority;
經濟預測 economic forecast;
~經濟預測方法 economic forecasting;
經濟援助 economic aid; economic assistance;
經濟運行體制 economic operation mechanism;
經濟增長 economic growth; the economy expands; the economy grows;
~經濟增長率 economic growth rate;
~經濟增長論 economic growth theory;
~經濟增長因素 economic growth factors;
~粗放型經濟增長 extensive economic growth;
經濟政策 economic policy;
經濟制裁 economic sanction;
經濟秩序 economic order;
~整頓經濟秩序 rectify the economic order;
經濟中心 economic centre;
經濟仲裁 economic arbitration;
經濟周期 economic cycle;
經濟轉軌 economic transformation;
經濟資源 economic resources;
經濟作物 cash crop;
病態經濟 ailing economy;
常規經濟 normal economy;
~非常規經濟 non-normal economy;
粗放型經濟 extensive economy;
摧毀經濟 destroy the economy;
大經濟 mega-economy;
單一型經濟 single-product economy;
多種經濟 diversified economy;
發達經濟 developed economy;
~不發達經濟 underdeveloped economy;
封閉型經濟 closed economy;
服務型經濟 service economy;
工業經濟 industrial economy;
公營經濟 public economy;
個體經濟 individual economy;
規模經濟 economy of scale;
管理經濟 handle the economy; manage the economy;
國家經濟 state economy;
~振興國家經濟 invigorate the state economy;
國家資本主義經濟 state-capitalist economy;
國民經濟 national economy;
國營經濟 state economy; state-owned economy;
宏觀經濟 macroeconomy;
環球經濟 world economy;

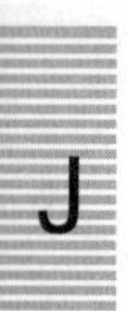

混合經濟 mixed economy;
集體經濟 collective economy;
計劃經濟 planned economy;
農村經濟 rural economy;
農牧經濟 agro-pastoral economy;
農業經濟 agricultural economy; rural economy;
泡沫經濟 bubble economy;
~ 防止泡沫經濟 avoid a bubble economy;
平衡經濟 balanced economy;
貧血經濟 anaemic economy;
破壞經濟 damage the economy;
裙帶經濟 crony economy;
商品經濟 commodity economy;
私營經濟 private economy;
市場經濟 market economy;
~ 自由市場經濟 free-market economy;
損害經濟 harm the economy;
外向型經濟 export-oriented economy;
微觀經濟 microeconomy;
物物交換經濟 barter economy;
鄉鎮經濟 village and town economy;
小農經濟 small peasant economy;
影子經濟 shadow economy;
整體經濟 overall economy;
知識經濟 knowledge economy;
中觀經濟 medium economy;
中央計劃經濟 centrally planned economy;
轉讓經濟 alienation economy;
自由市場經濟 free market;

[經紀] (1) manage a business; (2) broker; manager;
經紀費 brokerage;
經紀服務 broker's service;
經紀人 agent; broker; middleman;
~ 經紀人市場 broker's market;
~ 經紀人事務所 broker office; brokerage house;
~ 經紀人手續費 brokerage commission;
~ 保險經紀人 insurance broker;
~ 獨立經紀人 independent broker;
~ 股票經紀人 stock broker;
~ 核準經紀人 authorized broker;
~ 票據經紀人 bill broker;
~ 商品經紀人 commodity broker; merchandise broker;
~ 投資經紀人 investment broker;
經紀業 brokerage; broking;

[經建] economic construction;

[經久] (1) prolonged; (2) durable;
經久不衰 imperishable; unfading; unfailing;
經久不息 last for a long time; prolonged;
經久耐用 able to stand wear and tear; durable; durable service;

[經絕期] menopause;

[經理] (1) handle; manage; (2) director; manager;
經理負責制 manager responsibility system;
地區經理 regional manager;
分店經理 branch manager;
副經理 assistant manager;
公關部經理 public relations manager;
廣告宣傳部經理 advertising and publicity manager;
旅館經理 hotel manager;
女經理 manageress;
銷售部經理 sales manager;
業務經理 office manager;
營業部經理 business manager;
總經理 general manager; managing director;
~ 董事總經理 managing director;
~ 副總經理 assistant general manager;

[經歷] experience; go through; live through; undergo;
經歷艱苦的時期 have a rough passage;
經歷許多困難 undergo many difficulties;
令人難忘的經歷 unforgettable experience;
親身經歷 first-hand experience; personal experience;
學習經歷 learning experiences;
愉快的經歷 pleasurable experience;

[經綸] statecraft;
經綸天下 regulate the affairs of the state;
大展經綸 put one's statecraft to full use;

[經貿] economics and trade;

[經期] flag day; hell week; menstrual period; menstruation time; time of the month;

[經前] premenstrual;
經前緊張 premenstrual tension;
經前綜合徵 premenstrual syndrome;

[經商] engage in business deals; engage in trade; go into business; in business;
經商本領 one's business capacity;
不再經商 no longer in business;
開始經商 take to business;
棄學經商 discontinue one's studies and go into business; forsake studies for business;

[經史] Confucian classics and histoy;
經史子集 Confucian classics, history, philosophy, and literature;
枕經籍史 excessively fond of ancient books;
[經世] govern a country;
經世濟民 govern and benefit the people;
[經手] deal with; handle;
[經售] distribute; sell; sell on commission;
[經受] (1) experience; (2) stand; undergo; weather; withstand;
經受時間考驗 stand the test of time;
[經書] Confucian classics;
[經緯] (1) main points; (2) meridian and parallel lines;
經緯儀 theodolite;
~方向經緯儀 direction theodolite;
~光學經緯儀 optical theodolite;
~聲經緯儀 acoustic theodolite;
~天文經緯儀 astronomical theodolite;
~懸式經緯儀 hanging theodolite;
經天緯地 an ability to rule the country;
[經文] texts from Confucian classics or Buddhist scriptures;
背誦經文 recite a Buddhist sutra;
[經銷] distribute; sell; sell on commission;
經銷成本 distributive costs;
經銷代理 selling agency;
~獨家經銷代理 exclusive selling agency;
經銷商 distributor;
[經心] careful; conscientious; mindful;
[經學] study of Confucian classics;
[經驗] (1) experience; (2) experience; go through;
經驗不足 lack of experience; not well-experienced;
經驗豐富 have rich experience; well-experienced;
經驗之談 remarks made by a person who has experience; wise remarks of an experienced person;
寶貴的經驗 valuable experience;
~得到寶貴的經驗 gain valuable experience; get valuable experience;
寶貴經驗 valuable experience;
工作經驗 work experience; working experience;
~缺乏工作經驗 lack of working experience;
獲得經驗 gain experience;
積累經驗 accumulate experience;
間接經驗 indirect experience;
交流經驗 exchange experience;
介紹經驗 pass on one's experience;
擴大經驗 widen one's experience;
臨場經驗 game experience;
切身經驗 personal experience;
親身經驗 first-hand experience;
缺乏經驗 lack of experience;
認知經驗 cognitive experience;
吸取經驗 extract experience from;
有經驗 experienced;
增加經驗 enlarge one's experience;
直接經驗 immediate experience;
總結經驗 sum up experience;
[經意] careful; mindful;
不經意 by accident; carelessly;
[經營] deal in; be engaged in trade; engage in trade; go into business; go into trade; manage; operate; run; trade in;
經營分析 operations analysis;
經營範圍 scope of a business;
經營管理 business management;
~經營管理不善 poor planning and faulty operation and management;
~經營管理水平 managerial skills;
~經營管理信息 management information;
~經營管理職權 management's power;
經營規模 scale of business;
經營合理化 business rationalization;
經營活動 operating activities;
經營機制 operative mechanism;
經營決策 management decision-making;
~經營決策系統 management decision system;
經營目標 business goal;
經營能力 business capacity;
經營企業 manage an enterprise;
經營權 power of operation; right of management;
~轉讓經營權 transfer of the right of management;
經營審計 operational audit;
經營無方 mismanagement;
經營系統 management system;
經營信息 management information;
~經營信息系統 management information system;
經營性租賃 operating lease;
經營一體化 management integration;

J

經營預算 operational budget;
經營戰略 management strategy;
經營租賃 operating lease;
粗放經營 extensive management;
大力經營 devote great efforts to the development of;
單一經營 monoculture;
獨家經營 engaged in a line of business without competition;
獨自經營 manage with individual effort;
非法經營 illegal operation;
個人經營 one-man business;
個體經營 individual business;
合資經營 joint operation;
繼續經營 stay in business;
匠心經營 take great pains to create;
苦心經營 take great pains to build up sth;
煞費經營 require much effort to manage;
小本經營 start one's business on a shoestring;
專門經營 deal exclusively in;
自主經營 autonomy in operation;

[經由] by way of; via;

[經援] economic aid;

[經傳] (1) Confucian classics and commentaries on them; Confucian canons; (2) classical works; classics;
名不見經傳 a mere nobody; little known; not well known;

閉經 amenorrhoea;
財經 finance and economics;
曾經 at one time or another;
赤經 right ascension;
傳經 pass on the fruits of experience;
東經 east longitude;
佛經 Buddhist scripture; Buddhist sutra;
絕經 menopause;
羅經 compass;
唸經 chant Buddhist scriptures; recite Buddhist scriptures;
取經 (1) go on a pilgrimage for Buddhist scriptures; (2) learn from sb else's experience;
神經 nerve;
聖經 Bible; Holy Bible;
調經 regulate the menstrual function;
停經 amenorrhoea;
痛經 dysmenorrhoea;
途經 by way of; via;
行經 (1) go by; (2) menstruate;
一經 as soon as; once;
已經 already;
月經 menses; menstruation; period;
自經 commit suicide by hanging oneself;

jing

【兢】 apprehensive; cautious; dread; fear;

[兢兢業業] assiduous; attentive to one's business; careful and conscientious; cautious and attentive; conscientious and do one's best; conscientious and earnest; constantly on one's guard; do things in a careful manner; extremely watchful; with assiduity;

jing

【精】 (1) choice; picked; refined; (2) fine; precise; meticulous; (3) conversant; proficient; skilled; (4) essence; extract; (5) clever; sharp; shrewd;

[精兵] crack troops; elite troops;
精兵簡政 discharge inefficient officers and reduce administrative work; fewer and better troops and simpler administration;
精兵猛將 good soldiers and vigorous leaders; veteran soldiers and able captains; veteran soldiers and bold officers;

[精彩] brilliant; splendid; wonderful;
精彩紛呈 hundreds of high ligths; unusually brilliant — with high lights;
精彩絕倫 superlative;
搞得精彩 go with a swing;
沒精打彩 a cup too low; disheartened; dispirited and discouraged; have a fit of blues; in low spirits; in the blues; in the dumps; lackadaisical; listless; out of humour; out of sorts; out of spirits; seedy; spiritless; with little enthusiasm; with the wind taken out of one's sails;
無精打彩 a cup too low; apathetic and listless; crestfallen; dejected; despondent; disappointed; discouraged; disheartened; dispirited and discouraged; downcast; fall in the blues; flat; get the blues; have a fit of the blues; have the blues; he has left half of his guts behind him; in low spirits; in the blues; in the doldrums; indifferent; lackadaisical; languid; lassitude; lethargic; lethargy; listless;

low-spirited; not interested; out of heart; out of sorts; with no energy; with one's spirit quenched;
~無精打彩的 lethargic; low-spirited;
~無精打彩地工作 work sluggishly;
~感到無精打彩 feel out of spirits;

[精誠] absolute sincerity;
精誠所至，金石為開 absolute sincerity can affect even metal and stone; absolute sincereity will move a heart of stone; faith can move mountains; faith will move mountains; no difficulty is insurmountable if one sets one's mind on it;

[精粗] the fine and the dross;
棄粗取精 discard the dross and keep the finer part; discard the dross and select the essential; reject the dross and assimilate the fine essence;
去粗取精 discard the dross and keep the finer part; discard the dross and select the essential; reject the dross and assimilate the fine essence;

[精萃] cream; pick;

[精粹] pithy; succinct; terse;

[精當] precise and appropriate;

[精讀] intensive reading; perusal;

[精度] accuracy; degree of accuracy; precision; trueness;
測量精度 measurement precision;
尺寸精度 dimensional precision;
多倍精度 multiple precision;
加工精度 machining precision;
數值精度 numerical precision;
運算精度 operational precision;

[精幹] (1) crack; small in number but highly trained; (2) keen-witted and capable;

[精光] (1) with nothing left; (2) bright; shiny;
剝得精光 be stripped off all belongings; be stripped to the skin; strip bare; strip sb to the skin;
赤條精光 completely naked; stark naked; without a shred of clothing on; unclothed;
輸得精光 lose all one's money at gambling; lose one's shirt;
脫得精光 completely nude; stark naked; strip naked;

[精悍] (1) capable and vigorous; (2) pitiful and poignant;

[精華] choice; cream; essence; elite; quintessence;
取得精華 skim the cream off the milk;
取其精華 absorb the quintessence; absorb what is best; skim the cream off;
~取其精華，棄其糟粕 absorb the essence and reject the dross; absorb what is good and reject what is bad; extract sth's essence, leaving out its dregs; extract the essence and discard the dross;
擷取精華 pick the best;

[精簡] cut; reduce; retrench; simplify;
精簡編制 reduce the staff;
精簡的 punchy;
精簡翻譯法 diction-simplification translation;
精簡機構 streamline the government organization;
精簡節約 retrench and economize; retrenchment in expenditure; simplify the administration and practise economy;
精簡課程 cut down the curriculum;
精簡行政 simplify the administration;
精簡冗員 streamline the staff;

[精講多練] teach only the essential and ensure plenty of practice;

[精警] incisive; penetrating;

[精力] energy; oomph; vigour;
精力充沛 be going strong; full of beans; full of go; full of vigour; full of vitality; glow with energy; mettlesome; perky; very energetic;
~精力充沛的人 live wire;
精力過人 full of exceptional vitality;
精力缺乏 anergy;
白費精力 one's efforts fail entirely;
保存精力 conserve one's energy; reserve one's energy;
畢生精力 energy throughout one's life; the energies of a lifetime;
恢復精力 regain one's energy;
徒費精力 flog a dead horse;
旺盛不衰的精力 unflagging energy;
消磨精力 fritter away one's energy;

[精煉] refining;
粗銅精煉 blister refining;
連續精煉 continuous refining;
銅精煉 copper refining;

[精練] (1) refine; (2) concise; succinct; terse;
無比精練 amazingly polished;

J

[精良] excellent; of the best quality; superior;

[精靈] (1) demon; spirit; (2) clever; intelligent; smart;
人精心靈 quick on the uptake;
小精靈 fairy;

[精美] elegant; exquisite; fineness; refineness;
精美絕倫 exquisite beyond compare;

[精密] accurate; precise;

[精明] astute; gumption; sagacious; shrewd;
精明的 canny;
精明幹練 astute and experienced; capable and well-experienced; keen and wise;
精明鬼碰上精明鬼 diamond cut diamond; the shrewd meets the shrewd;
精明過頭 too clever by half;
精明老練 know one's onions; know the score; know what is what; sagacious and seasoned;
精明能幹 competent; shrewd;
精明強幹 able and efficient; clever and capable; intelligent and capable; on the ball; shrewed and capable; skilful and capable; up-and-coming;
處事精明 clever and smart in attending to business;
為人精明 be no fool; be nobody's fool;

[精囊] gonecystis; seminal vesicle;
精囊化膿 gonecystopyosis;
精囊積膿 pyovesiculosis;
精囊石 gonecystolith;
精囊炎 spermatocystitis;
~ 輸精管精囊炎 vasovesiculitis;
精囊周炎 perivesiculitis;
精神性陽痿 psychic impotence;

[精疲力竭] be all in; be pooped out; dead tired; dog-tired; drained; exhausted; fagged out; flake out; flat out; overspent; overtired; tired out; used up; whacked; worn out;
精疲力竭的 very tired; whacked;
~ 使人精疲力竭 wipe sb out;
力盡精疲 strength exhausted;

[精品] choicest goods;
精品店 boutique;
精品酒店 boutique hotel;
精工妙品 beautiful item made with exquisite workmanship;

[精巧] exquisite; ingenious;
精巧的 nifty;

[精確] accurate; exact; exactitude; precise; precision;
精確地 to a nicety;
精確度 precision;
~ 分析精確度 analytic precision;
~ 跟踪精確度 tracking precision;
回答精確 answer precisely; precise in one's answer;

[精鋭] crack; picked;
養精蓄鋭 build up one's energy; build up one's strength; conserve strength; reserve one's strength;
養精蓄鋭，以逸待勞 conserve one's strength and wait for the fatigued enemy;

[精深] profound;

[精神] (1) consciousness; mind; spirit; (2) essence; gist; spirit; substance;
精神安慰 spiritual comfort;
~ 給予精神安慰 administer spiritual comfort;
~ 是個精神安慰 serve as a spiritual consolation;
精神飽滿 as fit as a fiddle; energetic; full of spirit and energy; full of vigour; full of vitality; in good feather; in great feather; in high feather; spirited;
精神崩潰 nervous breakdown;
精神變態 psychosis;
精神病 lunacy; mental disease; mental disorder; mental illness; psychosis;
~ 精神病患者 psychotic patient;
~ 精神病人 lunatic; mental patient;
危險的精神病人 dangerous lunatic;
~ 精神病學 psychiatry;
~ 精神病院 asylum; booby hatch; booby hutch; funny farm; loony bin; lunatic asylum; mental hospital; mental institution; nuthatch; nuthouse; nuttery; psychiatric hospital;
~ 產後精神病 post-partum psychosis;
~ 兒童精神病 child psychosis;
~ 更年期精神病 involutional psychosis;
~ 功能性精神病 functional psychosis;
~ 監獄精神病 prison psychosis;
~ 酒毒性精神病 alcoholic psychosis;
~ 老年期精神病 senile psychosis;
~ 老年性精神病 senile psychosis;
~ 器質性精神病 organic psychosis;
~ 情感性精神病 affective psychosis;
~ 妄想性精神病 delusional psychosis;
~ 原發精神病 primary mental disorder;

~ 中毒性精神病 toxic psychosis;
精神不死 one's spirit will always remain; one's spirit will not vanish;
精神錯亂 (1) be out of one's mind; delirious; insane; mentally deranged; (2) abalienation; amentia; insanity; mental aberration; obfuscation;
精神抖擻 full of beans; full of energy; full of vitality; in fine fettle; in fine fig; in good fettle; in high spirits; vigorous and energetic;
精神發泄 abreaction; catharsis;
~ 運動性精神發泄 motor abreaction;
精神發育 psychogenesis;
精神反常 lose one's mental balance;
精神分裂症 schizophrenia; schizophrenosis;
~ 邊緣性精神分裂症 borderline schizophrenia;
~ 殘留型精神分裂症 residual schizophrenia;
~ 殘留性精神分裂症 residual schizophrenia;
~ 單純型精神分裂症 simple schizophrenia;
~ 反應性精神分裂症 reactive schizophrenia;
~ 緊張性精神分裂症 catatonic schizophrenia; catatonic disorder;
~ 進行性精神分裂症 process schizophrenia;
~ 青春期精神分裂症 hebephrenia;
~ 隱性精神分裂症 latent schizophrenia;
精神分析 psychoanalysis;
~ 精神分析理論 psychoanalytic theory;
~ 精神分析專家 psychoanalyst;
精神負擔 load of care; load on one's mind; mental burden; a weight on the mind;
精神貫注 concentrate one's attention on;
精神煥發 a new lease of life; brim with energy; fresh with energy; in a buoyant mood; in great form; in high spirits; one's spirits rise;
精神恍惚 absent-minded; fall into a trance; in a trance; lose one's wits; one's mind is wandering; out of one's mind;
精神疾病 psychotic illness;
精神疾患 mental disorder; mental illness;
精神寄托 sb's meat and drink;
精神枷鎖 mental fetter; mental yoke; spiritual shackles;
精神健全 compos mentis; sanity;
精神緊張 tension;
精神沮喪 depressed; dispirited; downhearted; in low spirits;
精神矍鑠 hale and hearty; have a green old spirit; live to a green old age; vigorous;
精神科醫生 psychiatrist;
精神可嘉 praiseworthy spirit; splendid spirit;
精神空虛 spiritually barren;
精神狂亂 phrenetic;
精神面貌 mental attitude; mental outlook; spiritual outlook;
精神缺陷 mental deficiency;
精神神經病 psychoneurosis;
精神生活 moral life; spiritual life;
精神失常 be distraught; mental disorder; not to be in one's right mind; out of one's mind;
精神失常 insane; lunacy; psychosis;
精神失調 psychataxia;
精神食糧 food for thought; mental food; nourishment for the mind; spiritual food;
精神衰弱 psychasthenia;
精神萎靡 one's spirits are drooping;
精神文明 spiritual civilization;
~ 精神文明建設 cultural and ethical progress;
~ 加強精神文明 promote spiritual civilization;
精神紊亂 (1) insane; (2) insanity;
精神宣泄 catharsis;
精神奕奕 one's spirit is grand — have a great spirit;
精神障礙 mental aberration;
~ 器質性精神障礙 organic mental aberration;
~ 妄想性精神障礙 delusional disorder;
精神正常 in one's right mind; in sound mind;
精神振奮 in high spirits;
精神支持 moral support;
精神支柱 bulwark;
精神治療 psychotherapy;
精神狀態 mental condition;
超前精神 surpassing spirit;
承擔精神 commitment;
重振精神 get one's second wind;
挫傷精神 damp one's energy;
打起精神 brace up energy; buck up

J

energy; cheer up; keep up one's spirit; pluck up one's spirits; raise one's spirit;
抖擻精神 hyped-up; in high spirits; pull oneself together;
奉獻精神 dedication;
剛毅精神 fortitude;
共融精神 spirit of inclusion;
好問精神 questioning mind;
恢復精神 blow the cobwebs away; clear the cobswebs away; recover one's spirit;
集體精神 collective spirit;
聚精會神 all attention; all eyes and ears; concentrate one's attention; gather one's wits; shake oneself together; in a world by oneself; in a world of one's own; with avid attention; with breathless interest; with great concentration;
磊落精神 open and upright spirit;
龍馬精神 full of vigour; full of vitality;
沒有精神 listless; out of sorts;
求實精神 realistic approach;
時代精神 the spirit of the times;
提不起精神 fell tired and spiritless; unable to pull oneself together;
振奮精神 brace one's energy;
振作精神 boost one's spirits; brace up one's spirits; keep up one's spirits; stir up one's spirits;

[精算] actuarial science;
精算師 actuary;

[精髓] heart; marrow; pith; quintessence;

[精通] a dab at sth; a dab hand at; a master of; A1 at; accomplished in; acquainted with; acquire proficiency in; adept at sth; adept in sth; an expert in; an old hand at; at home in; at one's best in; attain proficiency in; clever at; conversant with; deeply read in; expert at; expert in; excel in; familiar with; gain a mastery of; get a thorough knowledge of; good at; great at; handy at; handy with; have a good command of; have a mastery of; have a thorough knowledge of; have an intimate acquaintance with; have an intimate knowledge of; have the knack of; have sth at one's fingertips; have sth at one's fingerends; hot in; hot on; know from A to Z; know sth from the groundup; know sth very well; learned in; make oneself master of; master; perfect in; perfect oneself in; post oneself up in; practised in; proficient in; skilful at; skilful in; skilled in; steep in; well up on; well versed in;
精通繪畫 skilled in painting;
精通駕駛 proficient in driving;
精通世故 well versed in the ways of the world; worldly-wise;
精通熟練 proficient in sth;
精通外語 proficient at a foreign language;
精通業務 have a good command of one's profession; proficient in one's work;
精通音樂 conversant with music;

[精細] careful; fine; meticulous;
精細耕作 intensive agriculture;

[精心] elaborately; meticulously; painstakingly;
精心策劃 carefully calculated; carefully planned; deliberately designed; elaborately planned; painstakingly engineered;
精心管理 manage with delicacy;
精心護理 nurse with the best of care;
精心傑作 masterpiece;
精心砲製 be carefully dished up; be done with meticulous care; rack one's brains to make sth;
精心培育 take meticulous care of;
精心調理 nurse sb with the best care;
精心研究 study intensively;
精心照料 take precious good care of;
精心製作 elaboration;
精心治療 give meticulous treatment;

[精選] carefully choose; cherrypick; pick out the best; select carefully;

[精雅] elegant;

[精鹽] refined salt; table salt;

[精液] come; cum; semen; sperm;
精液病 spermatopathia;
精液過多 polyspermia;
精液漿 seminal plasma;
精液粒 seminal granules;
精液瘻 spermatic fistula;
精液缺乏 aspermia;
精液生成 gonepoiesis;
精液異常 dysspermia;

膿性精液 pyospermia;

[精益求精] constantly perfect one's skill; constantly strive for perfection; keep on improving; never satisfied with one's achievements; seek for greater perfection; strive constantly for improvement;

[精英] (1) cream; essence; quintessence; (2) elite; person of an outstanding ability;
精英大學 elite universities;
精英論 elite theory;

[精於此道] proficient in the knowledge of;

[精湛] consummate; exquisite;

[精緻] delicate; exquisite; fine;
精緻雅麗 beautifully fine and gracefully delicate;

[精製] make with extra care; purify; refine;

[精裝] clothbound; hardback; hardcover;
精裝本 deluxe edition; hardback; hardcover;
精裝書 hardcover;

[精壯] able-bodied; strong;

[精子] sperm;
精子包囊 spermatophore;
精子發生 spermatogenesis;
精子放出 spermiation;
精子過少 spermacrasia;
精子減少 oligozoospermatism;
精子庫 sperm bank;
精子囊腫 spermatocyst;
精子排放 spermiation;
精子破壞 spermatolysis;
精子缺乏 spermacrasia;
精子溶解 spermatolysis;
精子生成 spermatogenesis;
精子形成 spermateliosis;
精子異常 dysspermia;
精子銀行 sperm bank;
游動精子 zoosperm;

不精 not specialized in;
醋精 vinegar concentrate;
糊精 artificial gum; dextrin;
滑精 involuntary emission;
酒精 alcohol; ethyl alcohol;
麥精 malt extract;
煤精 black amber;
木精 methanol;
受精 be fertilized;
炭精 carbon;
糖精 glucide;
味精 monosodium glutamate;
香精 essence;
妖精 (1) demon; evil spirit; (2) alluring woman;
遺精 seminal emission;

jing

【鯨】 whale;

[鯨魚] whale;
一群鯨魚 a school of whale; a shoal of whale;

白鯨 white whale;
藍鯨 balaenoptera musculus; blue whale;
抹香鯨 sperm whale;
鰮鯨 minke whale;
座頭鯨 hump-back whale;

jing

【鶄】 mycticorax prasinosceles, a kind of water bird;

jing

【驚】 (1) be frightened; (2) alarm; shock; surprise;

[驚詫] amazed; astonished; surprised;

[驚呆] be stricken dumb with amazement; stupefaction;

[驚動] alarm; alert; disturb; shock; startle;
驚師動眾 alert many people;

[驚愕] consternation; stunned; stupefied;

[驚駭] frightened; panic-stricken;
驚駭失色 turn pale with surprise;

[驚鴻] (1) startled wild goose; (2) beautiful woman;
翩若驚鴻 graceful movements of a woman;

[驚呼] cry out in alarm;

[驚慌] alarmed; panic-stricken; scared;
驚慌不安 jittery; nervy; panic-stricken;
驚慌失色 lose countenance;
一時驚慌 in a moment of panic;
一陣驚慌 a dart of panic;

[驚惶] trepidation;
驚惶失措 be freaked out; be frightened out of one's senses; be frightened out of one's wits; be lost in astonishment; be nonplussed; be seized with panic; be struck all of a heap; be struck with dismay; be terrified and flustered; be thrown into a panic; be thrown into panic and dismay; become alarmed and confused; hit the panic button;

J

in a state of panic; lose one's cool; lose one's presence of mind; panic-stricken; push the panic button; thunderstruck;
驚惶失措，手忙腳亂 be thrown into a state of panic and utter confusion;
驚惶失色 stand aghast;

[驚魂] state of being frightened;
驚魂不定 put sb on tenterhooks;
驚魂奪魄 be frightened out of one's wits; be shocked;
驚魂方定 recover from fear and confusion; recover from one's surprise;
驚魂甫定 have hardly recovered from a recent shock; have just recovered from fear and confusion;
驚魂未定 be still badly shaken; be still suffering from the shock;

[驚悸] dread; palpitate with fear;

[驚叫] cry in fear; scream;

[驚厥] faint from fear;

[驚恐] alarmed and panicky; be seized with terror; panic-stricken; terrified;
驚恐而逃 flee in a panic; flee in fright;
驚恐失措 be seized with panic;
驚恐失色 pale with fear;
驚恐萬狀 be convulsed with fear; be filled with mortal fear; be paralyzed with fear; be terrified to the nth degree; in a funk; in a great panic; in a mortal funk;
大為驚恐 be seized with terror; be struck with panic; in a funk;
引起驚恐 cause alarm; excite alarm;

[驚慄] thrilling;
驚慄小說 thriller;

[驚奇] amazed; surprised; wonder;
感到驚奇 be utterly astounded;

[驚擾] agitate; alarm;

[驚人] alarming; amazing; astonishing;
驚人的 startling;
~驚人的效果 startling effect;
驚人駭世 spring a surprise on people;
驚人消息 alarming information; appalling news; shocking news;
驚人之筆 extraordinary forceful phrase;
驚人之舉 shocking action;
驚人之作 amazing work;
貌不驚人 look mediocre; one's looks are not attractive; ordinary appearance;
~人不壓眾，貌不驚人 he is neither an outstanding figure nor a man of attractive features;
一鳴驚人 achieve enormous success at the very first try; become famous overnight; gain worldwide fame and success; have spectacular and sudden success; make one's mark at the first shot; set the world on fire; startle the world;
語不驚人，貌不壓眾 as a speaker he is just so-so, about his face there is nothing to atttract attention; for all his glib tongue, he can lay no claim to eloquence, his looks are ordinary with no marked features to speak of; in speech he has no remarkable address, in looks he has nothing that outstrips other men; nothing striking about the way he speaks, nor does he surpass others in looks;

[驚蛇入草] write cursive characters in a vigorous and nimble style;

[驚視] agaze with surprise;

[驚歎] exclaim with admiration; marvel at; wonder at;

[驚悉] be shocked to learn sth;

[驚喜] be pleasantly surprised;
驚喜參半 half frightened and half pleased;
驚喜交集 have mixed feelings of surprise and joy; joy mingled with surprise;
且驚且喜 be amazed and overjoyed; be both surprised and pleased; be surprised and glad; have a pleasant surprise;
又驚又喜 be pleasantly surprised; surprised and delighted;

[驚嚇] frighten; scare; shock;

[驚險] alarmingly dangerous; breathtaking; thrilling;
驚險不安 be troubled about an imminent danger;
驚險片 adventure film;
非常驚險 hair-raising;
有驚無險 be more scared than hurt; threatening but not dangerous;

[驚心] heart-stirring;
驚心掉膽 be frightened out of one's wits;
驚心動魄 soul-stirring and breath taking;
驚心破膽 be extremely frightened;
怵目驚心 be shocked at the sight of; strike the eye and rouse the mind;

觸目驚心 horrid; shocking; startling; strike the eye and rouse the mind

[驚醒] (1) wake up with a start; (2) awaken; cause to wake up; rouse suddenly from sleep;

[驚訝] raise one's eyebrows;

驚訝極了 surprised is not the word for it;

驚訝無策 strike sb helpless;

故作驚訝 feign surprise; put on a show of surprise;

[驚疑] surprised and bewildered;

驚疑不定 anxious and doubtful;

[驚異] amazed; astonished; astounded; surprised;

眼露驚異 there is a startled look in one's eyes;

吃驚 alarmed; amazed; astonished; astound; be filled with wonder; be taken aback; freeze; give a start; in astonishment; in surprise; marvel at; marvel over; strike with wonder; suprised; take alarm at; take sb by surprise; to one's astonishment; with astonishment; with surprise;

可驚 startling; surprising;

夢驚 night-startlings; night-terror;

受驚 be frightened; be startled;

心驚 palpitated;

虛驚 false alarm;

壓驚 help sb to get over a shock;

震驚 (1) astonish; shock; (2) be shocked;

jing³

jing

【井】 (1) well; (2) sth in the shape of a well; (3) neat; orderly;

[井號] pound key; pound sign;

[井然] methodical; neat and tidy; orderly;

井然有序 in good order; methodical; orderly;

[井水] well water;

井水不犯河水 the well water does not interfere with the river water — I'll mind my own business, you mind yours; well water does not intrude into river water — each one minds his own business;

暗井 blind shaft;

測井 logging;

沉井 open caisson;

初探淺井 trial pit;

電測井 electrical logging;

風井 air shaft; ventilating shaft;

副井 auxiliary shaft;

固井 well cementation;

管井 tube well;

火井 gas well;

枯井 dry well;

礦井 mine; pit;

氣井 gas well;

市井 (1) marketplace; (2) town;

水井 well;

天井 (1) courtyard; small yard; (2) raise;

洗井 flushing;

一口井 a well;

一眼井 a well;

油井 oil well;

主井 main shaft;

鑽井 well drilling;

jing

【阱】 snare; trap;

[阱中之虎] a tiger in the pit;

陷阱 pitfall; trap;

jing

【剄】 cut the throat;

自剄 cut one's own throat;

jing

【景】 (1) scene; scenery; view; (2) condition; situation;

[景點] attraction; beauty spot; scenic spot;

旅遊景點 tourist attraction;

主要景點 main attraction;

[景觀] (1) landscape; (2) enjoy the scenery; view the scenery;

景觀美學 aesthetics of landscape;

景觀生態學 landscape ecology;

地理景觀 geographic landscape;

都市景觀 urban landscape;

複合景觀 composite landscape;

工業景觀 industrial landscape;

培植景觀 cultivated landscape;

鄉村景觀 rural landscape;

植物景觀 vegetable landscape;

[景教] Nestorianism;

[景況] circumstances; situation;

景況不佳 circumstances are not good;

[景氣] boom; prosperity;

不景氣 depression; hard times; recession; slump;
~不景氣綜合症 depression syndrome;
~長期不景氣 chronic depression;

[景色] landscape; outlook; picture; scene; setting; sight; view; vista;
景色淒清 the landscape is bleak; the scene is lonely and sad;
景色如畫 picturesque landscape; the scene is quite a study;
景色似錦 the whole scene is like a huge coloured tapestry;
景色宜人 the beautiful scenery is pleasing; the landscape is extremely beautiful; the landscape is lovely; the scenery is enchanting;
海岸景色 scenery along the shore;
美麗的景色 beautiful view;
田園景色 idyllic scenery; rural scenes;
宜人的景色 pleasant scenery; pleasant view;

[景深] depth of field;
景深表 depth-of-focus scale;

[景泰藍] cloisonne enamel;

[景物] scenery;

[景象] picture; scene; sight;
光亮景象 highlight scene;
室外景象 outdoor scene;
數字景象 digital scene;

[景仰] hold in deep respect; respect and admire;

[景遇] circumstances; one's lot;

[景緻] scene; scenery; view;

背景 (1) background; (2) backdrop;
佈景 scenery for stage;
場景 situation;
觸景 behold a view;
春景 spring scenery;
吊景 drop scenery;
風景 landscape; scenery;
光景 (1) scene; (2) circumstance; condition; (2) quite likely; (4) about; around;
海景 seascape;
後景 background;
幻景 illusion; mirage;
即景 be inspired by what one sees and write a poem;
佳景 fine landscape; lovely scene;
近景 close shot;
絕景 incomparable scene;
美景 beautiful scenery;
內景 indoor scene; indoor setting;
年景 (1) the year's harvest; (2) holiday atmosphere of the Spring Festival;
盆景 miniature trees and rockery; potted landscape;
奇景 extraordinary sight; wonderful view;
前景 (1) foreground; (2) future; prospect; vista;
情景 circumstances; scene; sight;
秋景 (1) autumn scenery; (2) autumn harvest;
取景 find a view;
全景 full view; panorama;
蜃景 mirage;
圖景 prospect; view;
外景 outdoor scene;
晚景 (1) evening scene; (2) one's circumstances in old age;
雪景 snow-covered landscape;
夜景 night scene;
應景 do sth for the occasion;
遠景 (1) distant view; long-range perspective; (2) long shot;
中景 medium shot;

jing

【憬】 awake; come to understand; realize;

[憬悟] come to see the truth; wake up to reality;

憧憬 long for; look forward to;

jing

【儆】 (1) get ready; on guard; (2) caution; warn;

jing

【璟】 lustre of jade;

jing

【頸】 neck; throat;

[頸背] nape;

[頸臂痛] cervicobrachialgia;

[頸部] cervix;
頸部白斑病 leukoderma colli;
頸部按摩 neck massage;
頸部短粗的 bullnecked;
頸部囊腫 cervical cyst;
頸部膿腫 cervical abscess;
頸部膨大 cervical enlargement;

[頸動脈] carotid artery;

[頸反射] neck reflex;
緊張性頸反射 tonic neck reflex;

[頸肌] cervical muscle;

頸肌痛 myalgia cervicalis;
[頸僵硬] stiff neck;
[頸鏈] choker; necklace;
鑽石頸鏈 diamond choker;
[頸內靜脈] internal jugular vein;
[頸肉] chuck;
[頸外靜脈] external jugular vein;
[頸項] nape of the neck; neck; scruff of the neck;
[頸椎] cervical vertebrae;
第二頸椎 epistropheus;
頸椎病 cervical spondylosis;

短頸 brevicollis;
交頸 fondle each other;
膀胱頸 cervix vesicae; bladder neck;
軸頸 axle-neck;

jing

【警】 (1) alert; vigilant; (2) alarm; warn; (3) alarm; (4) police;
[警報] alarm; alert; warning;
警報器 alarm;
~ 警報器按鈕 alarm button;
~ 觸動警報器 set off the alarm; trigger the alarm;
~ 防盜警報器 burglar alarm;
~ 關閉警報器 switch off the alarm; turn off the alarm;
~ 煙霧警報器 smoke alarm;
警報系統 alarm system;
警報裝置 alarm apparatus;
發警報 call an alert; give the alarm; raise the alarm; sound the alarm;
假警報 false alarm;
解除警報 lift the alert; release the alert; white alert;
緊急警報 red alert;
空襲警報 air-raid alert; blue alert;
預備警報 yellow alert;
戰鬥警報 battle alert;
[警備] garrison; guard;
[警察] bluebottle; bobby; clodhopper; constable; cop; copper; cozzer; cozzpot; crusher; jack; jailer; johndarm; law enforcement agent; police; police officer; policeman; boys in blue;
警察部隊 constabulary;
警察部門 police department; police force;
警察局 cop shop; police station;
~ 警察局局長 chief constable;
警察總督察 chief inspector;
便衣警察 plain clothes; plain-clothes cop;
告訴警察 inform the police; tell the police;
賄賂警察 corrupt a policeman with money;
緝毒警察 narc;
老練的警察 hard-bitten cop;
秘密警察 secret police;
男警察 policeman;
女警察 policewoman;
特種警察 special constable;
新手警察 rookie cop;
一隊警察 a platoon of police;
一名警察 a cop; a policeman;
一群警察 a posse of policemen;
一位警察 a cop; a policeman;
[警車] cop car; jam sandwich; Paddy's taxi; police car;
一輛警車 a police car;
[警督] supervisor;
一級警督 first-class supervisor;
[警服] police uniform;
一套警服 a police uniform;
[警告] admonish; caution; warn; warning;
警告性標誌 warning mark;
導航警告 navigational warning;
發出警告 give a warning;
~ 正式發出警告 issue a warning;
忽視警告 ignore a warning;
緊急警告 urgent warning;
事前警告 advance warning;
聽取警告 heed a warning;
嚴重警告 serious warning; stern warning;
一個警告 a warning;
預先警告 advance warning; forewarn; prewarn; warn in advance;
轉相警告 warn each other;
[警官] sergeant;
[警棍] billyclub; nightstick; policeman's baton;
[警戒] (1) admonish; warn; (2) guard against;
警戒孔 cordonnier;
警戒線 cordon; cordon of police;
~ 佈設警戒線 place a cordon; post a cordon;
警戒狀態 state of alert;
~ 處於警戒狀態 in a state of alert; on alert;
擔任警戒 keep guard;
加強警戒 enforce vigilance;

J

嚴密警戒 keep a close watch on;

[警監] commissioner;
二級警監 second-class commissioner;
三級警監 third-class commissioner;
一級警監 first-class commissioner;
總警監 commissioner general;
~副總警監 deputy commissioner general;

[警句] aphorism; epigram;

[警覺] (1) armed (2) vigilance; (3) awaken;
保持警覺 constantly on the alert; have one's wits about one;

[警力] armed police force; police strength;

[警犬] patrol dog; police dog;

[警世] admonish the world;
警世故事 cautionary tale;

[警司] superintendent;
一級警司 first-class superintendent;
總警司 chief superintendent;

[警探] detective;

[警惕] on guard against; vigilant; watch out for;
警惕騙子 watch out for a fraud;
保持警惕 have one's wits about one; keep one's eyes open; maintain a vigilant watch; maintain viligance; on the alert; remain watchful for;
放鬆警惕 ease one's vigilance;
喪失警戒 drop one's guard; lower one's guard;
提高警惕 heighten one's vigilance; raise one's vigilance;

[警衛] guard; security guard;
警衛犬 guard dog;
警衛室 guardroom;

[警務] police affairs; police service; policing;
警務處處長 police commissioner;
警務工作 policing;
警務長 chief superintendent;

[警醒] light sleeper;

[警員] police constable; policeman; police officer;
二級警員 second-class police constable;
一級警員 first-class police constable;

[警鐘] alarm bell;
敲起警鐘 give a warning; raise an alarm; sound the alarm;

報警 (1) call the police; report an emergency to the police; (2) give an alarm;
法警 judicial policeman;
告警 report an emergency;
火警 fire alarm;
機警 alert and resourceful; sharp-witted;
精警 incise; penetrating;
路警 railway police;
門警 police guard at the entrance;
民警 people's police;
示警 give a warning;
違警 violate police regulations;
巡警 policeman;
獄警 prison police;

jing4

jing

【勁】 strong; tough;

[勁敵] formidable adversary; strong opponent; well-matched adversary;
遇到勁敵 have a strong opponent;

[勁風] blast; gale;

[勁旅] crack force; strong contingent;

[勁挺] strong and forceful;

蒼勁 (1) old and strong; (2) (of calligraphy or painting) bold; vigorous;
剛勁 bold and vigorous; sturdy;
強勁 powerful; strong and forceful;
遒勁 powerful; vigorous;
雄勁 majestic and powerful;

jing

【徑】 (1) footpath; path; track; (2) means; way;

[徑流] run-off;
年徑流 annual run-off;
農田徑流 agricultural run-off;

[徑路] route;
代替徑路 alternate route;
計費徑路 toll road;
迂迴徑路 circuitous route;

[徑情直遂] follow a straight line; smoothly achieve what one wishes;

[徑庭] very unlike;
大相徑庭 be as different as day and night; entirely different; make a world of difference; poles apart; quite different; widely divergent;

[徑直] directly; straight; straightaway;
徑直走進屋 go straight into the room;

[徑自] without consulting anyone; without leave;

半徑 radius;

J

捷徑 shortcut;
口徑 (1) bore; calibre; (2) line of action; (3) requirements;
路徑 (1) route; way; (2) method; ways and means;
門徑 access; key; way;
內徑 inner diameter; inside diameter;
球徑 sphere diameter;
田徑 track and field;
途徑 channel; way;
外徑 external diameter; outside diameter;
蹊徑 path; way;
行徑 act; action; move;
直徑 diameter;

jing
【倞】 strong;

jing
【凊】 chilly; cold; cool;

jing
【淨】 (1) clean; (2) completely; (3) merely; nothing but; only; (4) net;

[淨化] clarification; clarify; cleaning; purification; purify;
淨化程度 degree of purification;
淨化器 clarifier; purifier;
~ 管式淨化器 tubular clarifier;
~ 離心淨化器 centrifugal clarifier; centrifugal purifier;
~ 排氣淨化器 exhaust purifier;
淨化物 purifier;
淨化心靈 purify one's soul;
淨化語言 purify the language;
淨化作用 catharsis;
催化淨化 catalytic purification;
機械淨化 mechanical clarification;
酒精淨化 alcohol purification;
空氣淨化 air purification;
離心淨化 centrifugal clarification; centrifugal purification;
生理淨化 biological cleaning;
自動淨化 auto-purification;

[淨空] clearance;
安全淨空 safe clearance;

[淨利] net profit;

[淨土] Paradise of the West; Pure Land;
一抔淨土 a handful of pure earth;

[淨賺] net earnings;

擦淨 clean; erase; wipe; wipe up;
澄淨 clear; pure;
純淨 clean; pure;
乾淨 (1) clean; neat and tidy; (2) completely; totally;
潔淨 clean; spotless;
明淨 clear and bright;
清淨 peaceful and quiet;
心淨 at ease; (of mind) cleared of worries;
自淨 self-purification;

jing
【逕】 (1) path; (2) direct;

jing
【竟】 (1) complete; finish; (2) throughout; whole; (3) eventually; in the end; (4) actually; unexpectedly; (5) go as far as to; go to the length of; have the effrontery to; have the impudence to;

[竟敢] dare; have the audacity; have the impertinence;

[竟然] actually; and; as...as; at all; been and; contrary to expectation; go so far as to; go to the length of; have the effrontery to; have the insolence to; have the prudence to; if you please; no less than; only to find; not a; not once; not one; should; so...as; strangely enough; strange to say; that; to one's surprise; to think of; to think that; unexpectedly; wonder;

畢竟 after all; in the final analysis;
究竟 (1) outcome; (2) what actually happened; (3) actually; exactly; (4) after all; in the end;

jing
【脛】 calf; the part of the leg between the knee and the ankle;

[脛骨] shin bone;

jing
【痙】 convulsion; spasm;

[痙攣] convulsion; cramp; spasm;
痙攣性氣喘 spasmodic asthma;
腸痙攣 enterospasm;
混合性痙攣 mixed spasm;
肌肉痙攣 muscle spasm;
局部痙攣 idiospasm;
面肌痙攣 mimetic convulsion;
面痙攣 facial spasm;
偏側痙攣 hemispasm;

J

強直性痙攣 tonic spasm;
神經性痙攣 neurospasm;
手肌痙攣 cheirospasm;
手痙攣 cheirospasm;
手足痙攣 carpopedal spasm;
書寫痙攣 chirospasm; writer's cramp;
瞳孔痙攣 pupillary athetosis;
痛性痙攣 algospasm; cramp; crick;
習慣性痙攣 habit spasm;
陰道痙攣 colpospasm;
嬰兒痙攣 infantile spasm;
陣發痙攣 clonospasm;
直腸痙攣 proctospasm;
指痙攣 dactylospasm;
趾痙攣 dactylospasm;
中毒性痙攣 toxic spasm;
中暑性痙攣 heat cramp;
子宮痙攣 hysterospasm;

jing

【敬】 (1) honour; respect; (2) respectfully;

[敬愛] esteem and love; respect and love;
互敬互愛 mutual love and deep respect; mutual respect and love;
相敬相愛 be deeply attached to each other; love and respect each other; love each other deeply; mutual respect and affection;

[敬茶] serve tea;
客來敬茶 present the visitors with a cup of hot tea as soon as they step into the house;

[敬辭] polite expression; term of respect;
敬辭花圈 no flowers;

[敬而遠之] courteously keep aloof from sb; courteously stand aloof from sb; give sb a wide berth; keep away from sb as much as possible; keep sb at a distance; keep sb at an arm's length; stay at a respectful distance from sb; steer clear of sb with good grace;
敬鬼神而遠之 reverence ghosts and gods but keep them at a distance;

[敬奉] (1) worship picously; (2) offer respectfully; present politely;

[敬賀] propose a toast; toast;

[敬酒不吃吃罰酒] be constrained to do what one at first refused to; choose to do things the hard way instead of the easy way;

[敬老] respect the old;
敬老慈幼 respect the old and love the young; show respect for the elderly and take good care of the young;
敬老撫幼 respect the elderly people and protect the young; show respect for the elderly and have compassion for the poor;
敬老尊賢 respect the elderly and the wise;

[敬禮] (1) give a salute; salute; (2) extend one's greetings; (3) with best wishes;
此致敬禮 respectfully, with best wishes; with high respect;

[敬慕] worship;
引起世人的敬慕 earn the respect of the world;

[敬佩] admire; esteem; have a great esteem for;
令人敬佩 command sb's esteem;

[敬人者，人恒敬之] he who respects others will be respected; respect a man, he will do the more;

[敬挽] deep condolences from sb;

[敬畏] hold in awe and veneration; revere;

[敬獻] offer respectfully; present politely;

[敬仰] admire; look up to; revere; venerate;

[敬業樂群] study diligently and benefit by the company of friends;

[敬意] esteem; regard; respect; salute; tribute;
表示敬意 props to sb; show respect;
代致敬意 please give him my best regards; plase give my respects to him; remember me kindly to him;
以表敬意 as a mark of respect; as a token of respect;

[敬語] (1) honorifics; (2) respectful speech;
敬語協和 honorifics concord;
環境敬語 setting honorifics;
局外人敬語 bystander honorifics;
所述對象敬語 addressee honorifics;

[敬贈] respectfully presented by;

[敬重] esteem highly; look up to sb with great respect;
博得敬重 earn sb's respect;
深受敬重 be held in high esteem; be highly esteemed;

崇敬 esteem; revere; respect;
恭敬 respectful; with great respect;
回敬 do or give sth in return; return a compliment;

J

可敬 respected; worthy of respect;
虔敬 reverent;
欽敬 admire and respect;
申敬 show respect for;
孝敬 present gifts to one's elders or superiors;
欣敬 pay homage to;
致敬 pay one's respects to; salute;
尊敬 respect; revere; venerate;

jing
【靖】 (1) peaceful; quiet; safe; still; tranquil; (2) pacify; quell; (3) defend; safeguard; (4) a surname;

安靖 (1) peaceful and stable; (2) bring peace and stability;
寧靖 (of social order) orderly and tranquil; peaceful;
平靖 suppress;
綏靖 appease; pacify;

jing
【境】 (1) border; boundary; (2) area; place; territory; (3) circumstances; condition; situation;

[境地] circumstances; conditions;
[境界] (1) boundary; (2) realm; state; (3) the extent reached;
[境況] circumstances; conditions;
境況不濟 be in reduced circumstances;
境況十分富裕 in very comfortable circumstances;
境況越來越糟 on the skids; the situation is getting worse;
[境遇] circumstances; one's lot;
境遇不佳 in narrow circumstances;
境遇尚可 in tolerable circumstances;

邊境 border; frontier;
慘境 miserable condition; tragic circumstances;
出境 exit; leave the country;
處境 plight; situation;
國境 territory;
過境 pass through the territory of a country;
化境 perfection; sublimity;
畫境 picturesque scene;
環境 (1) environment; surroundings; (2) circumstances;
幻境 dreamland; fairyland;
佳境 the most favourable stage;
家境 family conditions; family financial situation;
接境 border on;
窘境 awkward situation; straits;
絕境 blind alley; hopeless situation;
困境 difficult position; plight;
離境 leave a country; leave a place;
夢境 dream; dreamworld;
逆境 adverse circumstances;
情境 circumstances; situation;
入境 enter a country;
仙境 fairyland; paradise; wonderland;
心境 mental state; state of mind;
壓境 press on to the border;
意境 artistic conception;
越境 go beyond the boundary illegally;
止境 end; limit; terminal point;

jing
【靚】 (1) doll up; ornament; (2) quiet; still; tranquil;

jing
【靜】 (1) calm; motionless; still; (2) quiet; silent;

[靜電] electrostatic;
靜電干擾 statics;
~強靜電干擾 heavy statics;
~人為靜電干擾 man-made statics;
~陰雨靜電干擾 precipitation statics;
靜電感應 electrostatic induction;
靜電計 electrometer;
~衝擊靜電計 ballistic electrometer;
~絕對靜電計 absolute electrometer;
~雙極靜電計 binary electrometer;
~雙線靜電計 bifilar electrometer;
靜電印刷 electrostatic printing;
[靜極思動] when one remains idle for too long, one thinks of taking an active role in life;
[靜力學] statics;
解析靜力學 analytical statics;
進化靜力學 evolutionary statics;
流體靜力學 fluid statics;
森林靜力學 forest statics;
圖解靜力學 graphical statics;
應用靜力學 applied statics;
[靜脈] veins;
靜脈瓣 venous valve;
靜脈病 inflammation of a vein; phlebitis;
靜脈波圖 venogram;
靜脈搏 venous pulse;
靜脈充血 venous congestion;
靜脈出血 venous haemorrhage;

J

靜脈發育不良 hypovenosity;
靜脈發育不全 hypovenosity;
靜脈反射 venous reflux;
靜脈切開 venesection;
靜脈曲張病 varicosis;
靜脈炎 inflammation of a vein; phlebitis;
~ 藍色靜脈炎 blue phlebitis;
~ 黏連性靜脈炎 adhesive phlebitis;
~ 膿毒性靜脈炎 septic phlebitis;
~ 血栓性靜脈炎 thrombophlebitis;
~ 增生性靜脈炎 proliferative phlebitis;
靜脈周炎 periphlebitis;
~ 硬化性靜脈周炎 sclerosing periphlebitis;
出球靜脈 revehent veins;
大隱靜脈 great saphenous vein;
膽囊靜脈 cystic vein;
骼內靜脈 internal iliac vein;
股靜脈 femoral vein;
門靜脈 portal vein;
迷路靜脈 labyrinthine vein;
面靜脈 facial vein; frontal vein;
顳靜脈 temporal vein;
膀胱靜脈 vesical veins;
脾靜脈 vena splenica;
前庭靜脈 vestibular veins;
橈靜脈 radial vein;
上腔靜脈 superior vena cava;
腎靜脈 renal vein;
頭靜脈 cephalic vein;
臀上靜脈 superior gluteal veins;
臀下靜脈 inferior gluteal veins;
膝靜脈 genicular vein;
下唇靜脈 inferior labial vein;
下腔靜脈 inferior vena cava;
腋靜脈 axillary vein;
陰部內靜脈 internal pudendal vein;

[靜謐] quiet; still; tranquil;

[靜默] (1) become silent; (2) mourn in silence; observe silence;
靜默致哀 in silent tribute; observe a silence in memory of sb;

[靜穆] solemn and quiet;

[靜悄悄] very quiet;

[靜如死潭] as calm as a pond of dead water; as quiet as a stagnant pool;

[靜水] still water;
靜水流深 smooth water runs deep; still waters run deep;

[靜態] static;
靜態存儲器 static storage;
靜態打印 static printing;
靜態動詞 static verb;
靜態結構明喻 static-structural simile;
靜態美 static beauty;

[靜養] convalesce; have a good rest to recuperate; have a rest cure; rest quietly to recuperate;

[靜音] mute;
靜音鍵 mute button;

[靜止] at a standstill; motionless; static;
靜止鋒 stationary front;
靜止期 resting stage;
靜止狀態 static condition;

[靜坐] (1) sit still as a form of therapy; (2) sit-in strike;
靜坐罷工 sit-in strike;
靜坐不能 akathisia;
靜坐恐怖 kathisophobia;

安靜 calm; hush; peaceful; peaceful and serene; placid; quiescent; quiet; restful; resting; still; tranquil;
背靜 quiet and secluded;
避靜 retreat;
沉靜 calm; quiet;
澄靜 bright eyes; clear and calm;
動靜 activity; movement;
寂靜 quiet; silent;
冷靜 calm; sober;
寧靜 peaceful; quiet; tranquil;
僻靜 lonely; secluded;
平靜 calm; quiet;
清靜 quiet;
肅靜 silence; solemn;
恬靜 peaceful; quiet; tranquil;
文靜 gentle and quiet;
嫻靜 gentle and refined;
心靜 calm;
養靜 flee from the a busy and noisy place to cultivate mental calm;
夜靜 the dead of night; the still of the night;
幽靜 peaceful; quiet and secluded;
湛靜 profound quiet;
鎮靜 calm; composed; cool;

jing

【鏡】 (1) looking glass; mirror; (2) glasses; lens;

[鏡花水月] a mare's nest; a moonshine in the water; an illusion; castles in the air; flowers in a mirror or the moon in the water;

鏡中花，水中月 flowers reflected in the mirror, the moon reflected in the water — all are empty;

[鏡框] (1) picture frame; (2) spectacles frame;

[鏡面] surface of a mirror;
鏡面反射 reflection from a mirror;

[鏡片] plate;
改正鏡片 correcting plate;

[鏡破釵分] separation of husband and wife;

[鏡頭] (1) camera lens; lens; (2) scene; shot;
鏡頭拆卸鈕 lens-change button;
鏡頭剪輯 montage;
暴力鏡頭 carnography;
變焦鏡頭 zoom lens;
標準鏡頭 normal lens;
憋鏡頭 (1) bad camera; (2) a shot gone wrong; (3) ugly or unphotogenic;
長焦距鏡頭 telephoto lens;
擋鏡頭 (1) in view of the camera; (2) in the limelight; show off;
對稱式鏡頭 symmetric lens;
~ 非對稱式鏡頭 asymmetric lens;
附加鏡頭 supplementary lens;
廣角鏡頭 wide-angle lens;
可變焦距鏡頭 zoom lens;
可換鏡頭 interchangeable lens;
拉近鏡頭 zoom in;
慢鏡頭 slow motion;
模型鏡頭 model shot;
拍照鏡頭 picture-taking lens;
搶鏡頭 (1) outshine others; steal the limelight; steal the scene; steal the show; steal the spotlight; (2) fight for a vantage point in taking photographs;
取景鏡頭 viewing lens;
全景鏡頭 follow shot;
三合鏡頭 triplet lens;
上鏡頭 (1) photogenic; (2) appear in a film;
特寫鏡頭 close-up;
~ 大特寫鏡頭 big close shot;
推遠鏡頭 zoom out;
望遠鏡頭 telescopic lens;
外景鏡頭 exterior shot;
魚眼鏡頭 fisheye lens;
遠攝鏡頭 long shot; telephoto lens;
正光鏡頭 anastigmat;
~ 雙正光鏡頭 double anastigmat
中景鏡頭 medium shot;
中遠景鏡頭 medium-long shot;

[鏡子] looking glass; mirror;
鏡子恐怖 catoptrophobia;
把兒鏡子 a mirror with a handle;
一面鏡子 a mirror;
照鏡子 see oneself in the mirror;

凹鏡 concave mirror;
鼻鏡 rhinoscope;
側視鏡 side-view mirror; wing mirror;
導星鏡 guiding telescope;
耳鏡 otoscope;
反光鏡 reflector;
放大鏡 magnifying glass;
風鏡 goggles;
廣角 wide-angle lens;
哈哈鏡 distorting mirror;
喉鏡 laryngoscope;
後視鏡 wing mirror;
花鏡 presbyopic glasses;
火鏡 convex lens;
借鏡 draw lessons from; lesson; reference; use for reference;
近視鏡 spectacles for short-sighted persons;
老花鏡 presbyopic glasses;
稜鏡 prism;
明鏡 bright mirror;
墨鏡 sunglasses;
目鏡 eyepiece; ocular;
內窺鏡 endoscope;
平面鏡 flat mirror; plane mirror;
拋物面鏡 parabolic mirror;
球面鏡 spherical mirror;
三稜鏡 prism;
太陽鏡 sunglasses;
銅鏡 bronze mirror;
透鏡 lens;
凸鏡 convex mirror;
望遠鏡 telescope;
胃鏡 gastroscope;
西洋鏡 (1) peep show; (2) hanky-panky; trickery;
尋星鏡 finder;
眼鏡 glasses; spectacles;

jing

【競】 compete; contest;

[競渡] (1) boat race; (2) swimming race;

[競技] athletics; sports;
競技場 arena; stadium;

[競賽] competition; contest; race;
安全競賽 safety contest;
體育競賽 athletic meet;
選美競賽 beauty contest;
一次競賽 a heat;

J

[競銷] compete for the market;
競銷力 competently marketing ability;

[競選] a candidate for; campaign for; enter into an election contest; put up for; run against sb for; run for; stand for; start for; throw one's hat into the ring; toss one's hat into the ring;
競選承諾 election pledge;
競選活動 election campaign; electioneering;
競選夥伴 running mate;
競選集會 election rally;
競選諾言 election promise;
競選期間 election time;
競選日 election day;
參加競選 run for election; stand for election;
退出競選 stand down;

[競爭] compete; compete against; compete for; compete in; compete with; contend for; contend with sb for; vie for; vie with sb for;
競爭活動 competitive activities;
~ 非法競爭活動 illegal competitive activities;
競爭機制 competitive mechanism;
~ 引進競爭機制 introduce a competitive mechanism;
競爭力 competitive abilities; competitiveness;
~ 市場競爭力 the competitive abilities of the enterprises in the market;
增強市場競爭力 enhance one's market competitiveness;
~ 增強競爭力 increase competitiveness;
競爭能力 ability to compete;
競爭型公關 competitive public relations;
競爭型決策 competitive decision-making;
競爭意識 sense of competition;
競爭戰略 competition strategy;
競爭者 competitor; contestant;
不完全競爭 imperfect competition;
不正當競爭 unfair competition;
刺激競爭 stimulate competition;
導致競爭 constitute a competition; result in a competition;
公平競爭 fair competition; level playing field;
~ 公平競爭法 competition law;
~ 使公平競爭 level the playing field;
鼓勵競爭 encourage competition;
國內競爭 domestic competition;
激烈競爭 keen competition; stiff competition;
~ 面臨激烈競爭 face stiff competition;
盲目競爭 blind competition;
商業競爭 commercial competition;
生存競爭 struggle for existence;
完全競爭 perfect competition;
細胞競爭 cell competition;
相互競爭 competing;
~ 相互競爭的產品 competing products;
遭遇競爭 encounter a competition;
爭長競短 squabble over trifles;
種間競爭 interspecific competition;
種內競爭 intraspecific competition;

jiong[1]

jiong
【扃】 bolt;

jiong[3]

jiong
【冏】 discerning; discriminating; perceiving;
[冏冏] discerning; discriminating; perceiving;

jiong
【泂】 (1) clear and deep (said of water); (2) far and wide;

jiong
【炯】 bright; brightness; clear; shining;
[炯炯] bright; shining;
炯炯發光 one's eyes shoot fire;
炯炯雙目 radiant eyes;
炯炯有神 bright and piercing; sparkling and penetrating;
目光炯炯 one's eyes flashed like a lightning;

jiong
【迥】 (1) far away; (2) widely different;
[迥然] far apart; widely different;
迥然不同 as different as chalk and cheese; as like as chalk and cheese; by no means alike; utterly different;
迥然相異 widely different;

jiong
【逈】 distant; far;

jiong
【絅】 overall with no lining; dust coat;

jiong
【窘】 (1) hard up; in financial straits; in

straitened circumstances; poorly off; (2) awkward; embarrassed; ill at ease; (3) disconcert; embarrass;

[窘不能言] at a loss as to what to say; just too embarrassed to say anything;

[窘境] awkward situation; plight; predicament;

擺脱窘境 extricate oneself from an embarrassing situation;

[窘迫] poverty-stricken;

處境窘迫 in a sorry plight;

大為窘迫 be terribly embarrassed;

經濟窘迫 be embarrassed financially;

深感窘迫 be deeply embarrassed;

生活窘迫 live in poverty;

一陣窘迫 a twinge of embarrassment;

[窘態] embarrassed look;

發窘 become embarrassed; ill at ease;

桔窘 dried up;

困窘 awkward; in a difficult position; in straitened circumstances;

受窘 be embarrassed;

jiu¹

jiu

【究】 (1) dig into; examine; investigate; study; (2) after all; finally; in the end; (3) the very end; the very source;

[究辦] investigate and deal with;

[究詰] try to get to the bottom of a matter;

究根詰底 get to the bottom of sth;

[究竟] after all; actually; at all; exactly; in creation; in heaven; in hell; in nature; in the heck; in the world; in time; nevertheless; on earth; the deuce; the hell; under heaven; under the sun;

究竟在哪裏 where in the world; where on earth;

查究 investigate and ascertain;

根究 get to the very bottom of sth; make a thorough investigation of;

講究 (1) be particular about; careful; pay attention to; stress; (2) exquisite; tasteful;

考究 (1) investigate; observe and study; (2) be particular about; exquisite; fine;

盤究 cross-examine and investigate;

窮究 go seriously into sth; make a thorough inquiry;

深究 get to the bottom of a matter; make a thorough investigation of a matter;

探究 investigate thoroughly; make an inquiry and probe into;

推究 examine; study;

學究 pedant;

研究 (1) research; study; (2) consider; discuss;

終究 after all; eventually; in the end;

追究 investigate thoroughly; probe into;

jiu

【糾】 (1) entangle; (2) gather together; (3) correct; put right; rectify;

[糾察] (1) maintain order at a public gathering; (2) picket;

[糾纏] (1) be entangled; in a tangle; (2) get involved;

糾纏不清 become entangled in; in a tangle; keep on nagging; pester sb eternally; too tangled up to unravel;

糾纏不休 stick to sb like a leech; stick to sb like a limpet;

[糾錯] amend an error; error correction; error recovery;

有錯必糾 mistakes must be corrected as soon as they are discovered;

[糾紛] dispute; issue;

出現糾紛 come into conflict;

發生糾紛 a dispute arises;

婚姻糾紛 matrimonial dispute;

解決糾紛 bring a dispute to a close; decide a dispute;

捲入糾紛 be involved in a dispute; get into a dispute; get involved in a dispute;

民事糾紛 civil disputes;

挑起糾紛 stir up a trouble;

調解糾紛 mediate in an issue;

調停糾紛 solve a dispute;

[糾葛] complication; dispute; entanglement;

[糾集] draw together; get together; muster;

[糾結] be entangled with; be intertwined with;

[糾偏] correct an error; rectify a deviation;

糾偏救弊 rectify deviations and remedy defects; remedy deviations and abuses;

[糾正] correct; put right; redress;

糾正錯誤 amend one's mistake; correct a mistake;

糾正發音 correct one's pronunciation;

糾正陋習 remedy an abuse;

糾正偏差 correct an error; rectify a deviation; right a wrong;

J

糾正物 corrective;
糾正冤案 correct a wrong; redress a wrong;
我錯了的話請糾正 correct me if I'm wrong;

jiu
【赳】 gallant; valiant;
[赳赳] gallant; stalwart; valiant;
雄赳赳 gallantly; valiantly;

jiu
【啾】 (1) the chirping of birds; the chirping of insects; (2) the wailing of infants;
[啾啾] chirp;
啁啾 (of birds) chirp; twitter; warble;

jiu
【揪】 (1) hold tight; seize; (2) drag; pull; tug;
[揪出] discover; ferret out; uncover;
[揪心] anxious; worried;
胃痛得揪心 have a gnawing pain in one's stomach;
[揪住] grab tightly;
揪住不放 grab tightly; hold in a tight grip; tie up in knots;

jiu
【湫】 (1) a river in Gansu Province; (2) small pond;

jiu
【鳩】 (1) pigeon; (2) assemble; collect;
[鳩雛] dovelet;
[鳩尾榫] dovetail;
抽屜鳩尾榫 drawer-front dovetail;
互搭鳩尾榫 lap dovetail;
普通鳩尾榫 common dovetail;
[鳩形鵠面] appearance of poor, starved people; emaciated; haggard;
斑鳩 turtle dove;
海鳩 guillemot;
雉鳩 turtle dove;

jiu
【摎】 entwined like the branches of a tree;

jiu
【樛】 (1) drooping branches; (2) distorted; twisted;

jiu
【噍】 chirping;
[噍噍] chirping;

jiu
【轇】 (1) dispute; (2) disorder;

jiu
【鬮】 lots to be drawn;

jiu³

jiu
【九】 (1) nine; (2) ninth;
[九層之台起於累土] a nine-storey terrace must be constructed from its very base;
[九番] (of mahjong) nine times;
[九九] multiplication;
九九表 multiplication table; nine-times table; Pythagorean table;
九九歌 multiplication table; nine-times table; Pythagorean table;
九九歸一 after all; all things considered; in the last analysis; when all is said and done;
九九歸原 go back to the original place; return to when it started;
[九流三教] all walks of life; people in various trades; people of all sorts;
[九牛] strength;
九牛二虎之力 every ounce of one's strength; spend an immense amount of effort; tremendous effort;
~費盡九牛二虎之力 (1) make herculean efforts; spend a tremendous amount of labour; strain oneself to the limit; with all one's might and main; (2) work overtime;
九牛一毛 a drop in the bucket; a drop in the ocean; a hair off a bull's back;
[九品] nine grades of rank in the feudal regimes;
[九曲十八彎] complicated; difficult; hard; strenuous; twists and turns;
[九泉] grave; netherworld;
九泉之下 after death; in the nether regions; in the lower world; in the netherworld; in the next world; in the realm of shades; under the clod; under the sod;
瞑目九泉 may sb's soul rest in peace;
[九十] ninety;
[九天攬月] clasp the moon in the Ninth Heaven; pluck the moon out of the sky;
[九霄] the highest heavens;

九霄雲外 beyond the highest heavens — far, far away; beyond the ninth heaven — a place too distant to be reached; cast to the winds;
~ 拋到九霄雲外 cast to the wind; forget completely; sink into oblivion; throw overboard;
魂飛九霄 one's spirit flows to heaven — be frightened to death; one's spiritual soul floats away into the ninth sphere of heaven;
魄散九霄 one's spirit flees to the ninth heaven;

重九 Double Ninth Festival;
數九 nine periods following the Winter Solstice;

jiu
【久】 (1) for a long time; (2) of a specified duration;
[久旱無雨] suffer from a severe drought;
[久候不至] do not turn up after a long waiting;
[久假不歸] approriate sth borrowed; fail to return sth after having borrowed it for a long time; keep putting off returning sth that one has borrowed;
[久諫成仇] accumulation of hostilty; become enemies due to constant reproof;
[久久] for a long, long time;
久久不散的 lingering;
~ 久久不散的香味 lingering aroma;
久而久之 as time passes; at long last; eventually; in the course of time; in the long run; in time; with the lapse of time;
[久居別家招人嫌] the fish smells best before it is three days old; to stay in other's home too long is undesirable;
[久居人下] remain in a subordinate position for a long period; remain long in a lowly position;
[久留惹人嫌] a constant guest is never welcome;
[久違] how long it is since we last met;
[久仰] I'm pleased to meet you;
[久遠] ages ago; far back; remote;
望長久遠 for a very long time; plan for a permanent future;
[久蟄思動] after resting for a long time one finally thinks of making a move;
[久住令人厭，勤來親也疏] a constant guest is never welcome; never outstay one's welcome; never overstay one's welcome; never wear out one's welcome;
[久坐不去] burn the planks;

不久 (1) before long; soon; (2) not long after; soon after;
長久 for a long time; permanently;
常久 for a long while;
持久 enduring; lasting; protracted;
多久 how long;
好久 for a long time; long;
很久 for a long time; for years; for yonks; yonks ago;
積久 accumulate in the course of time;
經久 (1) prolonged; (2) durable;
良久 a good while; a long time;
耐久 durable; long lasting;
許久 for a long time; for ages;
永久 everlasting; forever; permanent;
悠久 long; longstanding;
終久 after all; eventually; in the end;

jiu
【糺】 band together; collaborate;

jiu
【灸】 moxa cautery;

針灸 acupuncture;

jiu
【玖】 (1) black jade-stone; (2) elaborate form of 九, nine;

jiu
【糾】 a pronunciation of 糾;

jiu
【赳】 gallant; valiant;

jiu
【韭】 Chinese chives; leeks; scallions;

jiu
【韮】 same as 韭, leeks or scallions;
[韮菜] Chinese chives;
韮菜薹 a bolt of chives;
[韮黃] hotbed chives;

jiu
【酒】 alcoholic drink; anti-freeze; anti-tox; balm; booze; cough medicine;

J

fuel; giddy water; joy juice; juice; laughing soup; liquid fuel; liquid joy; liquor; medication; medicine; mouthwash; oil of joy; pain-killer; prescription; refreshment; sauce; the sauce of life; serum; soothing spirits; syrup; wine;

[酒吧] bar; bar-room; cocktail bar; lounge; pub; watering hole;
酒吧常客 barfly;
酒吧工作站 bar station;
酒吧間 bar-room; cocktail lounge;
酒吧男侍應 barman;
酒吧男招待 barman;
酒吧女侍應 barmaid; cocktail waitress;
酒吧女招待 barmaid;
酒吧侍應生 bartender;
酒吧枱球 bar billiards;
酒吧招待 bartender;
大眾酒吧 public bar;
鋼琴酒吧 piano bar;
公眾酒吧 public bar;
雞尾酒酒吧 cocktail lounge;
葡萄酒酒吧 wine bar;
無上裝酒吧 topless bar;
雅座酒吧 lounge bar;
一個酒吧 a bar;
一家酒吧 a bar;
自由酒吧 free house;

[酒保] bartender;

[酒杯] goblet; wine cup; wine glass;
高腳酒杯 goblet; wine glass;
葡萄酒杯 wine glass;

[酒菜] food and drink; food to go with wine;

[酒廠] brewery; distillery; winery;
伏特加酒廠 vodka distillery;
黑麥酒廠 rye distillery;
藥酒廠 tincture; distillery;

[酒陳味醇，人老識深] wine and judgement mature with age;

[酒店] (1) grogshop; public house; tavern; wineshop; (2) hotel; inn;
二星級酒店 two-star hotel;
豪華酒店 posh hotel; swanky hotel;
三星級酒店 three-star hotel;
四星級酒店 four-star hotel;
五星級酒店 five-star hotel;
一家酒店 a hotel;

[酒館] alehouse; bistro; drunkery; public house; tavern;
小酒館 bistro;
自由酒館 free house;

[酒鬼] alcoholic; alkie; alky; bar fly; booze-artist; caner; drinker; drunk; drunkard; gargler; old soak; piss artist; pisshead; sot; tippler; toper; wine bibber;

[酒過三巡] after three rounds of drinks;

[酒酣] mellow with wine;
酒酣耳熱 succumb to the influence of many cups; mellow with drink;
酒酣飯飽 be fully satisfied with drinks and food; have had enough of both wine and food;

[酒櫃] drinks cabinet;

[酒後] after drinking; under the influence of wine;
酒後茶餘 after meal hours or in leisure time; over a cup of tea or a few glasses of wine;
酒後出醜 disgrace oneself by drinking too much;
酒後胡言 when the wine is in, the wit is out;
酒後駕車 drunk driving;
酒後駕駛 drunk driving;
酒後見真情 in wine there is truth; when the wine is in, the wit is out;
酒後鬧事的年輕人 lager lout;
酒後失德 liquor talks mighty loud when it gets loose from the jug;
酒後失態 act ludicrously when drunk; forget oneself in one's cups; misbehave after drinking; run riot after a bout of drinking;
酒後失言 make an indiscreet remark under the influence of alcohol; say sth wrong when drunk; talk at random after drinking;
酒後失儀 loss of manner after drinking;
酒後思睡 feel drowsy after drinking;
酒後吐真言 in wine there is truth; what soberness conceals, drunkenness reveals; when wine is in, truth is out; wine in, truth out;
酒後無德 misbehave after getting drunk;
酒後餘勇 brave after a few drinks;
酒後滋事 provoke incidents after getting drunk;
~酒後滋事罪 being drunk and disorderly;

[酒壺] decanter; wine pot;

[酒會] cocktail party; drinks party; reception;

wine party;
花園酒會 lawn party;
雞尾酒會 cocktail party;

[酒家] restaurant; wineshop;

[酒窖] cellar; wine cellar;
陳釀酒窖 aging cellar;
香檳酒窖 brut cellar;
裝瓶酒窖 bottling cellar;

[酒精] alcohol; spirit;
酒精比重計 alcoholometer;
酒精燈 alcohol lamp; spirit lamp;
酒精含量 alcoholic content;
酒精療法 alcohologherapy;
酒精氣味 alcoholic odour;
酒精溫度計 alcohol thermometer;
酒精抑鬱症 alcoholic depression;
酒精飲料 alcoholic drinks;
酒精中毒 alcoholism;
純酒精 absolute alcohol;
無水酒精 absolute alcohol;
一點兒酒精 a dollop of alcohol;

[酒具] cocktail set;

[酒來話開] wine looses one's tongue;

[酒闌人散] the wine is running out and the guests are departing;

[酒量] capacity for liquor; one's drinking capacity;
酒量很大的人 deep drinker;

[酒令] drinkers' wager game;

[酒囊飯袋] good-for-nothing person; person who can do nothing but eat and drink; useless person is only good for feasting and drinking;

[酒癖] alcoholic propensities; potomania;

[酒瓶] decanter; wine bottle;
扁酒瓶 hip flask;
水晶酒瓶 crystal decanter;

[酒器] drinking vessel;

[酒氣熏人] a strong smell of liquor in one's breath;

[酒錢] beer money;

[酒肉] wine and meat;
酒肉賓朋，柴米夫妻 friends come together to enjoy good wine and food, man and woman come together to form a family;
酒肉朋友 fair-weather friend;
酒池肉林 an extravagant orgy; Lucullian banquets; steeped in wine and surrounded by women — unprecedented luxury;
肉林酒池 be steeped in wine and surrounded by women; woods of flesh and ponds of wine — live in the world of wine and women;

[酒入舌出] when wine sinks, words swim;

[酒色] wine and women – sexual pursuits;
酒色財氣 wine, women, avarice and pride — the four cardinal vices;
酒色過度 be dissipated in wine and sex;
酒色傷財 wine and wenches empty men's purses;
酒色逸樂 an idle life of pleasure; lead a dissipated life; lead a loose life;
酒色之徒 a debauched man; a philanderer; a voluptuous fellow;
沉湎酒色 abandon oneself to wine and women; indulge in sensual pursuits;
溺於酒色 indulge in wine and women;
貪圖酒色 be addicted to wine and women;

[酒徒] bar fly; bibber; tippler; wine bibber;

[酒窩] dimple;
淺淺的酒窩 slight dimples;

[酒席] banquet; feast;
擺酒席 give a banquet;
辦酒席 prepare a banquet; prepare a feast;
一桌酒席 a table of meal;

[酒心糖] liquor-filled candies;

[酒意] tipsy feeling;
酒意半酣 comfortably drunk; half drunk;

[酒癮] addiction to alcohol;
酒癮大的人 chronic alcoholic;
戒除酒癮 overcome one's addiction to alcohol;

[酒友] drinking companion;

[酒至半酣] in the middle of the feast, when all are well-warmed with wine; when all become mellow with wine;

[酒足飯飽] as full as a tick; pleasantly full; wine and dine to satiety;

[酒醉] a drop too much; about gone; at rest; awash; balmy; barmy; be fired up; be given to drink; be illuminated; be lit up; be lit up like a Christmas tree; be shot; blitzed; boiled; chipper; cooked; corked; corned; crapulous; creamed; crocked; decks awash; drink without limits; drown one's sorrows; drunk; elevated; embalmed; faced; feel good; feel no pain; fish-eyed; flustered; fly

high; fricasseed; fuddle one's nose; gassed; gay; geared-up; get a bag on; get plastered; get smashed; gifted; glowing; glued; greased; groggy; half-seas over; half-under hammered; hang one on; happy; have a bag on; have a bun on; have a buzz on; have a glow on; have a nose to light candles at; have a turkey on one's back; have one over the eight; have the sun in one's eyes; high; high as a kite; in bed with one's boots on; in drink; in one's altitude; in one's cups; in the bag; in the gun; inebriated; inked; intemperate; intoxicated; jolly; jugged; juiced; juiced up; laid-out; loaded; looped; lubricated; maudlin; mellow; merry; oiled; on the grog; ossified; owl-eyed; pass-out; petrified; pickled; pie-eyed; pigeon-eyed; plastered; polluted; potted; preserved; ripped; roostered; salted; saturated; sauced; schizzed out; scottish; see double; sheliacked; shickered; shined; skunked; smashed; soaked; soak it up; squashed; steamed; stewed; stiff; stoned; stretched; tangle-footed; tangled; tanked; tie a bag on; the worse for liquor; tie one on; tight; tipsy; tired; tuned; twisted; under the affluence of incohol; under the influence of alcohol; under the table; under the weather; unsteady on one's feet; vulcanized; walking on rocky socks; wall-eyed; wasted; watch the ant races; well-bottled; with a glow on; wrecked; zonked;

酒醉飯飽 eat and drink to the limit of one's capacity; dine and wine to satiety;

酒醉醺醺 as drunk as a fiddler; dead drunk; in a state of happy intoxication;

酒醉智昏 when wine is in, wit is out;

倚酒三分醉 behave wildly as if one were dead drunk;

把酒 (1) raise one's wine cup; (2) fill a wine up for sb;

白酒 spirit; white spirit;

陳酒 mellow wine; old wine;

淡酒 light wine;

碘酒 tincture of iodine;

店酒 house wine;

罰酒 be made to drink as a forfeit;

桂花陳酒 old wine fermented with osmanthus flowers;

果酒 fruit wine;

黃酒 yellow rice wine;

火酒 (1) alcohol; (2) surgical spirit; spirit;

雞尾酒 cocktail;

假酒 adulterated wine; adulterine alcohol;

金酒 gin;

廉價酒 plonk;

料酒 cooking wine;

烈性酒 stiff drink;

露酒 alcoholic drink mixed with fruit juice;

茅台酒 Maotai;

美酒 good wine;

米酒 rice wine;

釀酒 brewing; make wine;

啤酒 beer;

品酒 wine tasting;

葡萄酒 wine made from grapes;

汽酒 light sparkling wine;

清酒 pure rice wine;

勸酒 urge sb to drink;

人參酒 ginseng liquor;

山杏酒 apricot wine;

山楂酒 hawthorn wine;

燒酒 spirit; white spirit;

水酒 watery wine;

素酒 wine served at a vegetarian feast;

甜酒 sweet wine;

喜酒 (1) wine drunk at wedding feast; (2) wedding feast;

下酒 (1) go with wine; (2) go well with wine;

行酒 serve wine to guests;

醒酒 dispel the effects of alcohol; sober up;

雪利酒 sherry;

藥酒 medicinal liquor;

一杯酒 a cup of wine; a glass of wine;

一口酒 a drink of wine; a mouthful of wine; a suck of wine;

一瓶酒 a bottle of booze; a bottle of wine;

一桶酒 a cask of wine;

一小口酒 a sip of wine;

一小桶酒 a keg of wine;

一壜子酒 a jar of wine;

一桶酒 a barrel of wine; a cask of wine;

一席酒 a banquet; a feast;

一巡酒 a round of wine;

飲酒 drink wine; hit the booze;

酗酒 drink excessively;
祝酒 drink a toast;
縱酒 be on the booze; drink to excess;
最後一杯酒 one for the road;

jiu⁴

jiu

【臼】 (1) mortar for unhusking rice; (2) socket at a bone joint;

［臼齒］ back teeth; molar; molar teeth;
小臼齒 molar;
永久臼齒 permanent molar;

窠臼 set pattern;
石臼 stone mortar;
脱臼 dislocation;

jiu

【究】 (1) dig into; examine; investigate; study; (2) after all; finally; in the end; (3) very end; very source;

jiu

【疚】 (1) prolonged illness; (2) mental discomfort;

負疚 feel apologetic; have a guilty conscience;
愧疚 be ashamed and uneasy;
內疚 compunction; guilty conscience;
歉疚 apology; regret;

jiu

【咎】 (1) blame; fault; (2) blame; censure; punish;

［咎無可辭］ cannot evade responsibility; the responsibility cannot be shirked;

歸咎 attribute a mistake to; put the blame on;
引咎 hold oneself responsible for a serious mistake; take the blame;
自咎 blame oneself; rebuke oneself;

jiu

【桕】 tallow tree;

烏桕 Chinese tallow tree;

jiu

【柩】 coffin with a corpse in it;

［柩車］ hearse;
［柩衣］ pall;

棺柩 coffin with a corpse in it;
靈柩 coffin with a corpse in it;

jiu

【救】 (1) rescue; salvage; save; (2) help; relieve; succour;

［救兵］ reinforcements; relief troops;
搬救兵 ask for help; call in reinforcements;
內無糧草，外無救兵 within there is no fodder, without, no relief troops;

［救國］ save the nation;
救國救民 save the country and people from impending danger; save the country and the people;

［救護］ give first-aid to; relieve a sick or injured person; rescue;
救護車 ambulance;
~流動救護車 ambulet;
救護飛機 ambulance aeroplane;
救護機 aerial ambulance; airbourne ambulance;
救護站 aid station;
救護直昇機 ambulance helicopter;

［救荒］ famine relief;

［救活］ bring sb back to life;

［救火］ fight a fire; fire fighting;
救火車 fire truck;
救火員 a fireman;
抱薪救火 add fuel to the fire; carry faggots to put out a fire; do sth counterproductive;
負薪救火 carrying firewood to put out a fire – make things go from bad to worse;
潑油救火 like trying to extinguish a fire with oil;
以火救火 aggravate the situation; encourage an evil doer; fight the conflagration with fire; pour oil in the fire;

［救急］ help meet an urgent need; help sb to cope with an emergency;
以救眉急 answer urgent needs;

［救濟］ relieve; succour;
救濟貸款 relief loan;
救濟難民 provide relief for refugees;
救濟品 alms; handout;
救濟項目 relief project;
救濟院 almshouse;
緊急救濟 emergency relief;
需要救濟 in need of relief;

［救命］ (1) save sb's life; (2) help;

救命恩人 saviour;
救命稻草 life-saving straw; straw to clutch at;
喊救命 cry for help;

[救貧濟老] help the poor and the old;

[救球] retrieve a ball; save a ball;
救險球 retrieve an impossible shot; save a ball; save an impossible ball;

[救人] save a person;
救人救徹 in saving a person, you must save him/her totally;
救人救到底，送人送到家 if you want to help, go the whole hog and if you see sb off, see him home;
救人一命，勝造七級浮屠 better save one life than build a seven-storey pagoda; better save one man's life than build a pagoda of seven stories; to rescue one person from death is better than to build a seven-storey pagoda for the god;

[救生] lifesaving;
救生包 survival kit;
救生筏 life raft;
救生工具 life preserver; survival kit;
救生圈 life-buoy;
救生術 life-saving;
救生艇 lifeboat;
救生箱 survival kit;
救生衣 life jacket; life vest;

[救世] save the world;
救世軍 Salvation Army;
救世主 Redeemer; Saviour;

[救亡] save the nation from extinction;
救亡圖存 save one's country so that it may survive; save the nation from doom and ensure its survival;
救亡運動 national salvation movement;

[救星] emancipator; liberator; saviour; white knight;

[救援] come to sb's help; rescue;
救援人員 aid worker;

[救災] provide disaster relief; send relief to a disaster area;
救災車 disaster rescue car;
救災指揮車 disaster rescue command car;

[救治] bring a patient out of danger; treat and cure;

[救助] help sb in danger; succour;
救助器材車 rescue appliances truck;
救助資金 relief funds;

補救 rectify; redress; remedy; repair;
搭救 rescue;
得救 be saved;
呼救 call for help;
獲救 be rescued;
急救 first aid; give emergency treatment;
解救 deliver; rescue; save;
匡救 remedy; save;
搶救 rescue; salvage;
求救 ask sb to come to the rescue; cry for help;
贖救 redeem;
挽救 rescue; save;
營救 rescue; succor;
遇救 be rescued; be saved;
援救 rescue; save;
拯救 rescue; save;
自救 save oneself;

jiu

【就】 (1) come near; move towards; (2) engage in; enter upon; go to; take up; undertake; (3) accomplish; make; (4) go with; (5) as far as; concerning; on; in the light of; with regard to; (6) just; merely; only; (7) exactly; precisely; (8) even; even if;

[就伴] accompany sb on a journey; travel together;

[就便] at sb's conveninece; while you're at it;

[就此] at this point; here and now; thus;

[就地] locally; on the spot;
就地待命 stand by for orders; stay where one is, pending further orders;
就地分贓 divide the spoils on the spot; share the loot on the spot;
就地解決 solve a problem right on the spot;
就地開除 fire sb on the spot;
就地免職 remove sb from office on the spot;
就地槍決 shoot sb on the spot;
就地取材 draw on local resources; engage local men for office; gather the material on the spot; get raw materials from local resources; make use of local materials; obtain raw materials locally; obtain raw materials on the spot; use indigenous raw materials; use local materials;
就地正法 carry out a death sentence on the spot; execute a criminal on the spot;

[就…而論] as far as…be concerned; as far as sth goes; as matters stand; as the case stands; as the matter stands; as things are; as things stand; in point of; in respect of; in so far as...be concerned; in terms of; in the case of; so far as...be concerned; so far as...go;

[就範] give in; submit;
不肯就範 refuse to give in; refuse to submit to control;
俯首就範 bend one's head and submit to control; bow the head and conform to the rule — meekly submitting;

[就教] consult; seek advice;
移樽就教 ask for advice on one's own initiative; call personally on sb for advice; take one's wine up and go to sb's table to ask his advice — go to sb for advice;

[就近] in the neighbourhood; nearby;

[就寢] go to bed; retire for the night;

[就讓] let;

[就任] assume one's post; take office; take up one's post;
就任要職 assume a position of great importance;

[就事論事] consider the case as it stands; consider the matter in isolation; consider the matter out of context; deal with a matter on its merits; judge a thing in its own context; take the matter on its merits; talk about a matter to the exclusion of other things;

[就是] (1) exactly; precisely; (2) even; even if;
就是說 in other words; namely; or; that is to say; to wit; viz.;

[就手] while you're at it;

[就算] even if; granted that;

[就位] take one's place;
大家就位 take your places;
各就各位 get ready; man your posts; on your mark; ready; ready all; take your places;

[就緒] in order; ready;

[就要] about to; around the corner; at hand; by way of; close at hand; come on; draw near; get on for; in sight; in view; near at hand; on the brink of; on the point of; on the verge of; on the way;
就要開始 about to begin;
就要離開 about to leave;

[就業] get a job; obtain employment; take up an occupation;
就業安排 job placement; placement;
就業保障 employment security;
~給予保業保障 give employment security;
就業服務中心 job centre;
就業顧問 employment consultancy;
就業機會 employment opportunity; job creation;
就業考試 placement examination;
就業率 employment rate;
就業門路 job opportunities;
就業前景 employment prospects;
就業人口 working population;
~就業人口構成 working population structure;
就業壓力 pressure on employment;
就業指導 occupational guidance;
不穩定就業 unstable employment;
公平就業 fair employment;
合作就業 cooperative employment;
全面就業 full employment;
社會就業 social employment;
隱形就業 unregistered employment;

[就醫] go to a doctor; seek medical advice;

[就義] be executed for championing a just cause; die a martyr;
從容就義 die a martyr to one's principle; go to one's death unflinchingly; meet one's death like a hero; tread the path of virtue calmly;
光榮就義 die a heroic death; prefer death to disgrace; sacrifice one's life for the sake of righteousness;
慷慨就義 die a martyr's death;

[就正] solicit comments;

[就職] accede to an office; assume office; come into office; enter upon office; get into office; go into office; take office;
就職就職 inauguration ceremony;
宣誓就職 make an oath; swear an oath; take an oath;

[就座] be seated; take one's seat;
匆匆就座 seat oneself in haste; take a seat in haste; take one's place with a rush;
招人就座 motion a person to a seat;

成就 accomplish; accomplishment; achieve;

J

achievement; success;

俯就 (1) condescend to take the post; deign to accept a post; (2) make do with; put up with;
高就 be promoted to a higher post;
遷就 accommodate oneself to; yield to;
牽就 (1) accommodate oneself to; yield to; (2) draw a farfetched analogy; give a strained interpretation;
屈就 condescend to take a post offered; deign to accept a position;
生就 be born with; be gifted with;
也就 and then;
早就 long since;
造就 (1) bring up; educate; train; (2) achievements; attainments;
作就 get sth done successfully;

jiu

【廄】 stable;
[廄肥] animal manure;
[廄舍] mew; stall;

jiu

【舅】 (1) maternal uncle; (2) brother-in-law; (3) woman's father-in-law; (4) man's father-in-law;
[舅父] mother's brother; uncle;
[舅舅] mother's brother; uncle;
[舅媽] aunt; wife of mother's brother;
[舅母] aunt; wife of mother's brother;
[舅子] brother-in-law; wife's brother;
大舅子 elder brother of one's mother;
小舅子 uncle;

阿舅 maternal uncle;
姑舅 (1) husband's parents; (2) cousin;
國舅 the prince's maternal uncle;
郎舅 a man and his wife's brother;
妻舅 wife's brother;
外舅 father-in-law; wife's father;
諸舅 all the maternal uncles;

jiu

【僦】 hire; rent;

jiu

【舊】 (1) bygone; old; past; (2) old; second-hand; used; worn; (3) former; one-time;
[舊案] (1) court case of long standing; (2) former practice;
舊案重提 bring up an old case; rake up old matters;
[舊車] old car; second-hand car; used car;
[舊地重遊] revisit a once familiar place;
[舊調重彈] beat over the old ground; dwell repeatedly on the same subject in speaking; harp on the same old tune; harp on the same string; sing the same old tune;
[舊惡] old grievances; old wrongs;
不念舊惡 forgive and forget;
[舊觀] the former appearance; the old look;
迥非舊觀 entirely different from what is used to be;
[舊恨] one's old grudge;
舊恨復燃 one's old grudge flares up anew;
舊恨新愁 all the old and recent sorrows; an old grudge and a new grief – add gloomy and anxious thoughts to the old grudge; heart-breaking regrets and sad memories;
舊恨新仇 all the old and recent hatreds; fresh hatred; new hatred piled on the old; the old and new hatred;
[舊貨] junk; second-hand goods;
舊貨出售 boot sale; car boot sale;
舊貨店 second-hand shop;
舊貨鋪子 junk shop;
舊貨商店 junk shop;
陳廢舊貨 dead stock; dead storage;
收舊貨的人 junk dealer;
[舊交] old acquaintance;
[舊居] former residence; old home;
[舊框框] conventions;
[舊曆] the lunar calendar;
舊曆年 the Lunar New Year;
[舊夢] past experience;
舊夢重溫 renew a sweet experience of bygone days;
重溫舊夢 indulge again in one's pipe-dream; recall the past sweet experience; recapture the dtreams one has lost; relive an old experience; renew one's old romance; renew the ecstasies of sensual delight; revive an old dream; seek once more what one experienced in a dream;
[舊情] friendship of bygone days;
重溫舊情 renew an old friendship; revive the old affection;
共敘舊情 have a talk over old times;

exchange sentiments of friendship with sb;

［舊日］ former days; old days;

［舊詩］ classical poetry; old-style poetry;

［舊時］ old days; old times;

［舊式］ of an old type; old type;

［舊事］ old matter;

舊事重提 bring up the same old matter; rake up the past; recall past events; retell old stories;

舊事休提 let bygones be bygones; not to mention bygones;

［舊書］ (1) old book; second-hand book; used book; (2) books by ancient writers;

［舊歲］ old year; pervious year;

鳴鐘辭別舊歲 ring out the old year;

［舊態復萌］ revent to one's former state; slip back to one's old ways;

［舊物］ used things;

舊物出售 garage sale;

舊物集市 boot sale; car boot sale; flea market;

［舊約］ the Old Testament;

［舊賬］ outstanding debt;

翻舊賬 rake up the past; repetition of the old tale;

算舊賬 have an account to settle with sb; settle old scores;

［舊址］ former site;

陳舊 old-fashioned; outmoded;

除舊 get rid of the old;

穿舊 wear out;

復舊 return to the past;

古舊 antiquated; archaic;

故舊 old friends and acquaintances;

話舊 reminisce; talk about the old days;

懷舊 nostalgic; recollect the good old days or old acquaintances;

念舊 (1) keep old friendship in mind; (2) for old time's sake;

破舊 old and shabby; worn-out;

仍舊 (1) as before; remain the same; (2) still; yet;

守舊 conservative; sticking to old ways;

忘舊 forget old friends and relatives;

敍舊 talk over the old times with old friends;

依舊 as before; still;

照舊 as before; as of old; as usual;

折舊 depreciation;

jiu

【鷲】 eagle;

禿鷲 cinereous vulture;

兀鷲 griffon vulture;

ju¹

ju

【車】 the name of a chessman in Chinese chess game;

ju

【居】 (1) dwell; live; reside; (2) house; residence; (3) in a certain position; occupy a place; (4) assert; claim; (5) lay by; store up; (6) at a standstill; put; stay; (7) a surname;

［居多］ in the majority;

［居高臨下］ have a commanding view from a good vantage point; look down from a height; occupy a commanding position;

［居功］ claim credit for oneself;

居功自傲 claim credit and put on airs; claim credit for oneself and become arrogant; pride oneself on one's merits; style oneself hero; take credit for one's services and be haughty;

居功自矜 be puffed up with pride because of one's services to the country; claim credit and brag about sth one has done; claim credit for oneself and become arrogant; make a merit of sth; pride oneself on one's merits; presume upon one's services and be haughty and imperious; style oneself a hero;

居功自滿 feel smug with one's past achievements;

居為己功 take credit to oneself;

［居間］ between two parties;

居間調停 act as mediator; mediate between two parties;

居間稽古 live in the present and search their ways of the past;

［居留］ inhabite; reside;

居留地 place of residence;

居留國外 reside abroad;

居留權 right of abode; right of permanent residence;

居留證 residence permit;

永久居留 permanent residence;

［居民］ inhabitant; resident;

J

居民身份證 residential identity card;
居民質量 inhabitant's quality;
當地居民 local residents;
島上居民 islander;
固定居民 permanent residents;
郊區居民 suburbanite;
原有居民 original resident;

［居然］ go so far as to; to one's surprise; unexpectedly;
居然有臉 have the face to do sth; have the face to say sth;

［居仁由義］ dwell in benevolence and righteousness; tread the straight and narrow path; walk in the path of virtue;

［居士］ lay Buddhist;

［居所］ home;
第二居所 second home;
居無定所 of no fixed abode; with no fixed abode; without definite residence;
～居無定所的人 dosser;

［居心］ harbour evil intentions;
居心不良 harbour evil intentions; harbour hostile designs; have some dirty trick up one's sleeve; with bad intentions;
居心不善 his heart is bent on evils; ill-disposed;
居心何在 what is sb up to; what is sb's intention; what is the motive behind all this;
居心叵測 harbour evil intention towards; have evil designs; with concealed intentions; with hidden intent; with ulterior motives;
居心險惡 of a malicious disposition; vicious in one's motives;
居心陰險 of a malicious disposition;
暴露居心 reveal one's intentions;
是何居心 what evil intention is this;

［居中］ (1) be placed in the middle; in the middle; (2) mediate between parties;
居中調停 act as peacemaker; mediate between two parties; offer one's good offices between two parties;
居中斡旋 mediate between disputants;

［居住］ dwell; live; make one's abode; reside; take up one's abode;
居住面積 residential area;
居住區 residential district; settlement;
居住條件 housing condition;
居住用地 residential land;
開始居住 take up residence;

安居 settle down;
屏居 live in retirement; out of public life;
卜居 choose a place for one's home;
巢居 (of people) live on trees;
鶉居 without a fixed home;
定居 settle down;
分居 live apart;
共居 live together;
故居 former residence;
寄居 live away from home;
家居 stay at home idle without being employed in any job;
舊居 former residence;
聚居 inhabit a region; live in a compact community;
鄰居 neighbour;
旅居 reside abroad; stay abroad;
姘居 cohabit; live illicitly as husband and wife;
起居 daily life;
遷居 change one's living place; move house;
僑居 live abroad;
群居 live in groups;
散居 live scattered;
孀居 live in widowhood;
同居 (1) live together; (2) cohabit;
蝸居 humble abode;
徙居 move house;
閒居 stay idly at home;
新居 new home; new residence;
宴居 lead a leisurely life;
燕居 live at ease; live at leisure;
穴居 live in caves;
移居 migrate; move one's residence;
逸居 comfortably lodged; live in idleness; live in retirement;
隱居 hermit; live in seclusion; retire from public life; withdraw from society and live in solitude;
幽居 live in seclusion;
寓居 make one's home in;
雜居 live together;
蟄居 live in seclusion;
謫居 live in exile;
住居 dwell; live; reside;
自居 consider oneself as;

ju

【拘】 (1) arrest; detain; (2) limit; restrain; restrict;

［拘捕］ arrest; capture;
被拘捕 be arrested; put under arrest; under arrest;

非法拘捕 false arrest;

[拘謹] overcautious; reserved;

[拘禁] put under arrest; take into custody;
非法拘禁 unlawful incarceration;
受到拘禁 be held in custody; be held in restraint;

[拘禮] punctilious; stand on ceremony;
老不拘禮 the old need not observe the conventions;
熟不拘禮 initimate friends need not cling to ceremony; too familiar with each other to stand on ceremony;
恕不拘禮 pardon me for not standing on ceremony;

[拘留] detain; detention; hold in custody;
拘留室 detention room;
拘留所 detention home; house of detention; remand centre;
~臨時拘留所 lock-up;
拘留中心 detention centre; remand centre;
保護性拘留 protective custody;
~受到保護性拘留 be taken into protective custody;
被拘留 be taken into custody;
~被拘留者 detainee;
防範性拘留 preventive detention;
非法拘留 false arrest;
預防性拘留 preventive detention;

[拘泥] adhere to rigidly; stick to;
拘泥不通 bigoted and impenetrable to reason; opinionated; slow-witted; stubborn and stupid;
拘泥小節 be tied down by trifles; stand on trifles;
拘泥於規則 adhere closely to the regulation;
拘泥於形式 adhere to the form; observe the formality;

[拘束] ill at ease; restrain; restrict;
感到拘束 feel constrained; feel ill at ease;
毫不拘束 not constrained at all;
無拘束 unconfined; unconstrained; uncontrolled; unrestrained;
~毫無拘束 free and easy; free from restraint; unconstrained; without restraint;
無拘無束 as free as the birds; carefree; completely without restraints; free and easy; free as a bird; make oneself at home; unconstrained; uncontrolled; unfettered; unrestrained; without a worry in the world; without any restraint; without hindrance;
~無拘無束的 free and easy;
顯得拘束 look ill at ease;

[拘文牽義] adhere to the written word and principles rigidly; be bigoted by words and dragged to principles;

[拘押] take into custody;

不拘 not confine oneself to; not stick to;

ju
【沮】 (1) a river in Shandong Province; (2) a surname;

ju
【狙】 (1) ape; monkey; (2) lie in ambush;

[狙擊] snipe;
狙擊手 sniper;

ju
【苴】 (1) package; parcel; (2) female plant of the common hemp;

補苴 fill; make up for; supply;

ju
【俱】 (1) all; altogether; (2) accompany; accompanying;

ju
【疽】 ulcer;

鼻疽 glanders;
壞疽 gangrene;
乳疽 intramammary abscess;
炭疽 anthrax;
癰疽 ulcer;

ju
【痀】 humpback; hunchback;

ju
【罝】 net for catching rabbits or hares;

ju
【崌】 (1) Mount Ju in Sichuan; (2) Julai Mountain in Sichuan;

ju
【据】 (1) same as 據; (2) same as 倨; (3) used in 拮据, financial stringency;

拮据 in straits; short of money;

ju
【琚】 jade ornament;

J

ju
【菹】 (1) salted or pickled vegetables; (2) pond with a lot of weeds; (3) mince human flesh and bone;

ju
【趄】 falter;

趑趄 (1) walk with difficulty; (2) hesitate to advance;

ju
【蒩】 same as 菹 ;

ju
【雎】 (1) kind of waterfowl; (2) hesitate;
［雎鳩］ fish hawk; osprey;

ju
【裾】 overlap of a robe;

ju
【駒】 (1) foal; young and fleet-footed horse; (2) the sun;
［駒子］ foaling;

產駒 foaling;
馬駒 foal;

ju
【鋦】 (1) kind of nail for mending crockery; (2) curium;

ju
【鋸】 (1) saw; (2) sawing;
［鋸木］ tree cutting;
鋸木廠 lumbermill; sawmill;
鋸木頭 saw logs;
［鋸子］ saw;

ju²

ju
【臼】 hold or take in both hands; reveal;

ju
【局】 (1) bureau; office; (2) game; innings; set; (3) situation; state of affairs;
［局部］ part; partial;
局部錯誤 local error;
局部地區 parts of an area;
局部利益 partial and local interests;
局部麻醉 local anesthesia;
局部數據庫 local database;
局部同化 partial assimilation;
局部網絡 local area network;
~局部網絡技術 local area network technology;
局部異化 partial dissimilation;
［局促］ (1) cramped; narrow; (2) short; (3) constrain;
局促不安 be abashed; feel abashed; feel constraint; ill at ease; like a cat on hot bricks; out of countenance; queasy; sheepish; stand abashed; strained and uneasy; uncomfortable and uneasy;
局促感 feelings of constraint;
~擺脱局促感 throw off feelings of constraint;
局促一隅 be cramped in a corner – confined in a small place;
［局面］ aspect; phase; prospect; situation;
局面煥然一新 take on an entirely new aspect;
必輸局面 no-win situation;
處理困難局面 handle a difficult situation;
分析局面 analyse a situation; review a situation;
改變局面 alter the situation;
改善局面 improve the situation;
化解局面 defuse the situation;
混亂局面 melee;
控制局面 control the situation;
扭轉局面 save the day;
評判局面 assess a situation;
收拾局面 settle a situation;
雙贏局面 win-win situation;
新局面 new dimension; new situation;
應付局面 deal with a situation;
造成局面 create a situation;
整頓局面 straighten out a situation;
［局內人］ insider;
［局勢］ situation;
調查局勢 investigate a situation;
分析局勢 analyze a situation;
觀察局勢 observe the situation;
國際局勢 international situation;
緊張局勢 tense situation; tension in the area;
控制局勢 command the situation; control the situation;
了解局勢 learn about the situation;
埋怨局勢 grumble over the situation;
扭轉局勢 reverse the situation; tip the balance; turn the balance;
研究局勢 study a situation;
掌握局勢 have the situation under control; have the situation well in hand;

［局外人］ bystander; outsider;
局外人敬語 bystander honorifics;
［局限］ confine; limit; localization;
局限與挑戰 constraints and challenges;
［局長］ director-general;
副局長 deputy director-general;
［局中人］ player;
［局子］ cop shop; police station;

敗局 losing battle;
佈局 (1) layout; overall arrangement; (2) arrangement; composition; (3) position;
財政局 bureau of finance;
城市規劃建設局 urban planning and construction bureau;
出局 out;
儲備物資管理局 bureau of material reserve; reserve goods administration;
大局 general prospect; overall situation;
當局 authorities;
檔案局 archives bureau;
地方稅務局 local tax bureau;
地質勘查局 bureau of geological exploration;
地質礦產局 bureau of geology and mineral resources;
電報局 telegraph office;
電話局 telephone office;
電信局 telecommunication office;
定局 make a final decision;
賭局 gambling party;
對局 play a game of chess;
飯局 dinner party;
格局 pattern; structure;
供電局 bureau of power supply;
國家安全局 national security bureau; state security bureau;
國家測繪局 state bureau of surveying and mapping;
國家檔案局 state archives bureau;
國家地震局 state bureau of seismology;
國家稅務局 state tax bureau;
國家外國專家局 state foreign experts bureau;
國家文物局 state bureau of cultural relices;
國稅局 national tax bureau;
和局 draw; tie;
環境保護局 environmental protection bureau;
技術監督局 technical supervision bureau;
僵局 deadlock; stalemate;
攪局 make a mess of sth;
結局 ending; final result;
決勝局 deciding game;
科技幹部局 bureau of technical cadres;
老幹部局 veteran officials bureau;
糧食局 cereals bureau;
旅遊局 tourism bureau;
農墾局 land reclamation bureau;
騙局 fraud; hoax; swindle;
平局 draw; tie;
棋局 chess game;
氣象局 meteorological bureau;
全局 overall situation; situation as a whole;
蜷局 coil; curl; twist;
審計局 auditing bureau;
時局 current political situation;
世局 world situation;
書局 bookstore; publishing house;
水產局 aquatic products bureau;
危局 critical situation; dangerous situation;
無線通信局 wireless communication office;
物價局 price bureau;
現局 present situation;
新聞出版局 press and publication administration;
信訪局 bureau for letters and calls;
畜牧局 animal husbandry bureau;
煙草專賣局 bureau of tobacco monopoly;
郵電局 posts and communications office;
郵局 post office;
郵政局 post office;
郵政速遞局 postal courier service;
戰局 war situation;
政局 political scene; political situation;
政治局 political bureau;
宗教事務局 religious affairs bureau;
終局 end; outcome;

ju
【侷】 confined; cramped; narrow;
［侷促］ (1) cramped; narrow; (2) short;
侷促不安 feel awkward and ill at ease;

ju
【桔】 orange; tangerine;

ju
【挶】 receptacle for earth;

ju
【掬】 hold in both hands;

ju
【菊】 chrysanthemum;
［菊花］ chrysanthemum;
菊花茶 chrysanthemum tea;
野菊花 wild chrysanthemum;
［菊苣］ chicory;
菊苣根 chicory root;

J

［菊展］ chrysanthemum show;

雛菊 bellis perennis;
翠菊 China aster;

ju
【鉏】 (1) hoe; (2) hoe; (3) eliminate; uproot; (4) a surname;

ju
【跼】 bent; confined; contracted; cramped;

ju
【橘】 Mandarin orange; orange; tangerine;
［橘子］ tangerine;
橘子瓣 segment of a tangerine;
橘子皮 tangerine peel;
橘子水 orange drink; orangeade;
橘子汁 orange juice;
一瓣橘子 a slice of orange;

柑橘 oranges and tangerines;
枸橘 trifoliate orange;
金橘 kumquat;
蜜橘 tangerine;
越橘 cowberry;

ju
【鞠】 (1) bring up; rear; (2) a surname;
［鞠躬盡瘁］ be entirely worn out in performing one's duties; bend oneself to a task and exert oneself to the utmost; devote oneself entirely to; give oneself entirely to public duties; keep pounding away at one's work; spare no effort in the performance of one's duty; tire oneself out in official duties; work with utter devotion;
~ 鞠躬盡瘁，死而後已 bend one's backs to the task until one's dying day; bend oneself to the task unto death; devote every ounce of one's energy and even one's life to; devote one's life to; give one's best, give one's all, till one's heart ceases to beat; loyal and devoted to the end; work with devotion and selflessly dedicate one's entire life to;

ju
【鞫】 interrogate; question criminals;

ju³
ju
【咀】 chew; masticate;
［咀嚼］ (1) chew; masticate; (2) chew the cud; mull over; ruminate;
咀嚼文意 chew the meaning of the phrase;

ju
【沮】 (1) stop; (2) be defeated; lose; (3) damage; destroy; injure; spoil;
［沮喪］ dejected; depressed; disheartened; dispirited;
沮喪的 crestfallen; downcast;
沮喪地 drearily;
沮喪失望的 cast down;
心喪氣沮 the heart mourns and the spirit spoils;
意氣沮喪 crestfallen; dejected; depressed; disheartened; dispirited; in a dejected state; in low spirits;

ju
【柜】 (1) tree of the willow family; (2) same as 櫸;

ju
【矩】 (1) carpenter's square; (2) pattern; regulation; rule; (3) carve;
［矩尺］ carpenter's square;
［矩陣］ matrix;
矩陣化 matrixing;
矩陣胚 matroid;
~ 循環矩陣胚 cycle matroid;
伴隨矩陣 adjoint matrix;
導納矩陣 admittance matrix;
會計矩陣 accounting matrix;
鄰接矩陣 adjacency matrix;
微矩陣 micromatrix;

磁矩 magnetic moment;
力矩 moment of force;
轉矩 rotative moment;

ju
【枸】
［枸櫞］ citron;
枸櫞酸 citric acid;

ju
【莒】 (1) kind of herb; (2) name of an ancient state; (3) name of a county in Shandong;

ju
【筥】 bamboo basket for holding rice;

ju
【踽】 walk alone;

J

[踽踽] walk alone;
踽踽獨行 walk alone; walk in solitude;

ju

【舉】 (1) lift; hold up; (2) act; deed; move; (3) cite; enumerate; give; take; (4) entire; whole; (5) choose; elect;

[舉哀] go into mourning; wail in mourning;
舉哀一天 go into a one-day mourning;

[舉辦] conduct; hold; organize; run;
舉辦畫展 put on a painting exhibition;
舉辦義賣 organize a charity bazaar;
舉辦義演 give a charity performance;
舉辦展覽 give an exhibition; put on an exhibition;

[舉報] report; report on; tip; tip-off;
舉報電話 reporting call;
舉報人 informer;
舉報信 letter reporting on illegal activities;
舉報中心 report centre;

[舉杯] raise one's cup;
舉杯祝觴 drink a toast; raise one's glass to; raise the cup and give a toast; toast;

[舉兵] raise an army to fight;

[舉步] step forward; stride forward;

[舉出] cite; enumerate; itemize;

[舉措] act; behave; move;
舉措失當 act at haphazard; act in an inappropriate manner; make an ill-advised move; make false moves; take improper measures;
補救舉措 remedial measures;
採取舉措 take steps;
臨時舉措 interim measures;
實施舉措 carry out measures; put measures into practice;
新舉措 new measures;
政治舉措 political measures;

[舉鼎絕臏] do a thing beyond one's ability; overestimate one's strength;

[舉動] act; activity; move; movement;
下流舉動 obscenity;
幼稚的舉動 childish act;

[舉凡] all...such as...; range from...to...;

[舉國] entire nation; throughout the nation; whole country; whole nation;
舉國哀悼 the entire country mourns over sb's death; the whole country goes into mourning;
舉國哀慟 the entire country is overwhelmed by sorrow;
舉國悲痛 the whole country is griefstricken; the whole nation is heartbroken with grief;
舉國歡騰 a jubilant atmosphere prevails in the whole country; the nation is astir and the people are filled with joy; the whole nation is in jubilation; the whole nation is jubilant;
舉國若狂 the whole nation is in ecstasy;
舉國上下 everyone in the country; from the leaders of the nation to all the people; the whole nation; the whole nation from the leadership to the masses; throughout the nation;
舉國無雙 have no parallel in the whole country; unparalleled;

[舉火] (1) light a fire; (2) light a kitchen fire; light a stove;

[舉薦] recommend a person;

[舉例] a classic example of this is; as an example; as an illustration; for example; for instance; for one thing; just as an example; to give you an idea; to illustrate my point; take for example; take sth as an example;
舉例說明 cite an example by way of explanation; illustrate with examples;

[舉帽] raise one's hat;
舉帽示敬 raise one's hat in token of respect;

[舉目] look; raise the eyes;
舉目皆是 be found everywhere; can be seen everywhere; meet the eye everywhere;
舉目四望 look around;
舉目無親 a stranger in a strange land; be left alone, with no relative nearby; be stranded far away from one's folks; cannot find anybody whom one knows; find no kin to turn to; find oneself alone and kinless; have neither friend and relation; have no one to turn to;
舉目遠眺 look into the distance;

[舉起] hoist; lift; raise;

[舉觴] take a glass of wine;
舉觴共飲 take a glass of wine with sb;
舉觴祝壽 toast sb and wish him a long life;

[舉世] all over the world; the world over;

throughout the world; universally;
舉世稱快 to the satisfaction of the world;
舉世風從 the whole world follows the example;
舉世公認 be accepted by the whole world; be universally acknowledged;
舉世共知 all the world knows...; be widely known;
舉世皆知 all the world knows; be known to all; it is well known that;
舉世太平 the whole world is in peace;
舉世未聞 be never known before in the whole world;
舉世聞名 be known to all the world; be known to the whole world; of world renown; world-famous; world-renowned;
舉世無敵 matchless in the world; without a match in the world;
舉世無雙 absolutely unrivalled; matchless in the world; unmatched in the world; unrivalled; with no match in the world; without a rival; without parallel in the world;
~舉世無雙的人 world-beater;
舉世遭難 the whole world suffers;
舉世震驚 be shocked all over the world;
舉世矚目 attract the attention of the world; attract worldwide attention; become the focus of world attention; draw the attention of the world; world spotlight;

[舉事] rise in insurrection; stage an uprising;

[舉手] put one's hand up; put up one's hand; raise one's hand;
舉手表決 take a vote by a show of hands; vote by a show of hands; vote by raising hands;
舉手打人 raise one's hand to beat others;
舉手發誓 hold up one's hand and pledge;
舉手可得 within one's grasp;
舉手投降 raise one's arms in surrender;
舉手宣誓 hold up one's hand and take a solemn oath;
舉手贊成 approve sth with a show of hands;
舉手之勞 lift a finger;

[舉賢] promote men of ability;
舉賢黜絀 promote men of ability and dismiss men who are incapable;
舉賢讓能 recommend the worthy and give way to the able;
舉賢援能 promote able men; recommend properly qualified persons for service; use the wise and employ the capable;

[舉行] come off; conduct; give; go off; hold; pass off; stage; take place;
舉行罷工 go on strike; stage a strike;
舉行閉幕式 hold the closing ceremony;
舉行辯論 hold a debate;
舉行大選 hold a general election;
舉行奠基典禮 have a cornerstone-laying ceremony;
舉行國宴 hold a state banquet;
舉行會談 hold talks;
舉行會議 hold a meeting;
舉行結婚典禮 hold a marriage ceremony;
舉行開幕式 hold an opening ceremony;
舉行談判 hold negotiations;
舉行宴會 give a banquet; give a dinner;

[舉隅] take an example;

[舉債] borrow money; raise a loan;
舉債能力 borrowing powers;
消費者舉債 consumer borrowing;

[舉證] adduce; put to the proof;

[舉直錯枉] appoint upright officials and remove the crooked ones; replace the bad officials by good ones;

[舉止] bearing; demeanour; front; habit; manner; mien;
舉止安詳 behave with composure;
舉止沉穩 bear oneself calmly and steadily;
舉止粗野 agrestic behavior; have a coarse manner;
舉止大方 bear oneself well; carry oneself with ease and confidence; comport oneself decently; conduct oneself nobly; have a dignified air; have an easy manner; have poise;
舉止得體 behave in a becoming manner; behave oneself well; behave with decorum;
舉止典雅 elegant in manner;
舉止端詳 behave with serene dignity;
舉止風雅 have refined manners;
舉止古怪 strange behavior;
~舉止古怪的人 oddball;
舉止怪異 go off the rails;
舉止矜持 have a reserved manner;
舉止闊綽 generosity of behaviour;
舉止禮貌 have a polite manner;

舉止恰當 have a proper deportment;
舉止輕佻 behave frivolously; skittish behaviour;
舉止失常 act oddly; act strangely;
舉止斯文 have a cultured manner;
舉止文靜 behave quietly;
舉止文雅 refined in manner;
舉止嫻雅 agreeable in manner; deport oneself gracefully;
舉止言談 one's behaviour and conversation; one's deportment and speech;
舉止優雅 deport oneself gracefully;
舉止異常 aberrant behaviour;
舉止有點失常 out to lunch;
舉止迂腐 have a pedantic air;
舉止莊重 behave with dignity; carry oneself with dignity; deport oneself in a dignified manner; respectfulness of deportment;
~舉止莊重的人 a man of dignified bearing;
不得體的舉止 impropriety;
粗暴的舉止 abrasive manner;
粗魯的舉止 rude actions;
粗野的舉止 agrestic behavior;

[舉趾露踵] at the end of one's means; down at heels; have worn out one's soles;
[舉踵延頸] raise the heels and extend the neck — eager to see;
[舉重] weight lifting;
舉重運動員 strength athlete;

包舉 sum up;
保舉 recommend sb for a post with personal guarantee;
暴舉 act of violence;
並舉 develop simultaneously;
創舉 pioneering work;
大舉 carry out sth on a large scale;
高舉 hold aloft; hold high;
豪舉 (1) bold move; (2) munificent act;
檢舉 report an offence to the authorities;
荐舉 propose sb for an office;
列舉 enumerate; list;
善舉 philanthropic act;
盛舉 grand occasion;
挺舉 clean and jerk;
推舉 nominate;
選舉 elect;
義舉 a magnanimous act;
應舉 take imperial examinations;
抓舉 snatch;
壯舉 heroic undertaking; magnificent feat;

ju
【齟】 irregular teeth;
[齟齬] contretemps; discord; the upper and lower teeth not meeting properly — disagreement;

ju
【櫸】 a kind of elm, with fine-grained wood;

ju⁴
ju
【句】 sentence;
[句柄] handle;
[句層] sentence level;
[句長] sentence length;
[句讀] sentences and phrases; the period and the comma;
[句法] (1) sentence structure; (2) syntax;
句法詞序 syntactic order;
句法對立 syntactic oppositions;
句法範疇 syntactic category;
句法分析 parsing; syntactic analysis;
句法基礎 syntactic base;
句法結構 syntactic structure;
~句法結構標記 syntactic marking;
句法歧義 syntactic ambiguity;
句法實相 syntactic truth;
句法上下文 syntactical co-text;
句法同義重覆 syntactic tautology;
句法限定 syntactic specification;
句法增補 syntactic expansion;
句法轉換 anacoluthon;
[句號] full point; full stop; period;
[句尾重覆] epiphora;
[句型] sentence pattern;
句型轉換 transformation of sentences;
基本句型 basic sentence pattern;
強調句型 emphatic sentence pattern;
[句子] sentence;
句子成份 sentence element;
句子詞 sentence word;
句子分析 parsing;
句子副詞 sentential adverb;
句子結構 sentence structure;
句子連詞 sentence connective;
句子意義 sentence meaning;
句子狀語 sentence adverbial;
拼句子 sentence combining;

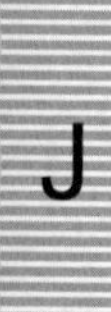

含意不清的句子 ambiguous sentence;

半句 half the utterance;
包孕句 composite sentence;
併列句 compound sentence;
插入句 insertion;
長句 long sentence;
陳述句 declarative sentence;
稱謂句 nominal sentence;
詞句 expressions; words and phrases;
從句 subordinate clause;
從屬句 subordinate clause;
存在句 existential sentence;
單部句 one-member sentence;
單句 simple sentence;
倒裝句 inverted sentence;
疊句 reiterative sentence;
斷句 make pauses in reading unpunctuated ancient writings;
反問句 echo question; rhetorical question;
範句 model sentence;
分句 clause;
分裂句 cleft sentence;
否定句 negative sentence;
複合句 complex sentence; compound sentence;
複句 a sentence of two or more clauses;
副句 clause;
概念句 conceptual sentence;
感歎句 exclamatory sentence;
感歎疑問句 exclamatory question;
合成句 complex sentence;
核心句 kernel sentence;
呼應句 adjacency pairs;
基本句 basic sentence;
集句 a poem made up of lines from various poets;
兼語句 pivotal sentence;
簡單句 simple sentence;
警句 aphorism; epigram;
肯定句 affirmative sentence;
例句 example sentence; illustrative sentence;
連寫句 run-on sentence;
煉句 polish and repolish a sentence;
領句 superordinate clause;
名詞句 nominal sentence;
命令句 imperative sentence;
平衡句 balanced sentence;
破句 pause at the wrong place of a sentence;
祈使句 imperative sentence;
嵌入句 embedded sentence;
省略句 elliptical sentence;
詩句 line; verse;
無主句 sentence with no subject;
先行句 antecedent clause;
敘述句 declarative sentence;
疑問句 interrogative sentence;
語句 sentence;
樂句 phrase;
造句 make sentences;
主句 main clause;
主謂句 subject-predicate sentence;
字句 words and expressions;

ju

【巨】 gigantic; huge; tremendous;

［巨變］ great change; mutation; radical change;

［巨大］ enormous; gigantic; huge; immense; of gigantic proportions; tremendous;
巨大的 colossal; gargantuan; humongous;

［巨額］ big amount; huge sum;

［巨匠］ consummate craftsman; great master;

［巨款］ vast sums;
一筆巨款 a large sum; a large sum of money;

［巨浪］ breaker; huge wave;
海濱巨浪 beachcomber;

［巨人］ giant;
巨人症 gigantism;
~無睪丸性巨人症 eunuchoid gigantism;
泥足巨人 a colossus with feet of clay; a person or a thing strong outside but weak inside;
女巨人 giantess;

［巨石］ boulder;

［巨頭］ baron; magnate; tycoon;
報業巨頭 press baron;

［巨細］ big and small;
巨細無遺 without omitting a single detail;
不分巨細 regardless of size;
事無巨細 all kinds of work, no matter how big or trivial; all matters, big and small; all matters, whether important or trivial;

［巨響］ loud crash;
一聲巨響 a loud crash;

［巨星］ giant; giant star; megastar;
超級巨星 superstar;
超巨星 supergiant;
~紅超巨星 red supergiant;
紅巨星 red giant;
天王巨星 (1) movie icon; (2) musical icon;
亞巨星 subgiant;

[巨型] colossal; giant; heavy; huge; large;
[巨著] great work; monumental work;
皇皇巨著 great brilliant work;

艱巨 arduous; formidable;

ju
【足】 overly humble; overly modest;

ju
【具】 (1) appliance; utensil; (2) capability; talent; (3) equipment; (4) all; complete; the whole; (5) draw up; prepare; write out; (6) a surname;
[具備] be equipped with; be provided with; have; possess;
[具體] concrete; particular; specific;
具體而微 have everything in miniature; similar in shape but smaller in proportions; small but complete;
具體化 concretize;
具體項目 specification item;
具體形象思維 concrete imaginal thinking;
具體行政行為 concrete administrative action;
具體疑問句 specific question;
具體主義 concretism;
[具文] dead letter; mere formality;
一紙具文 a mere scrap of paper; a piece of worthless paper;
[具有] be provided with; have; possess;

鞍具 pommel saddlery;
別具 have a distinctive…; have a special…;
薄具 coarse food;
才具 ability; gift; talent;
餐具 cutlery; dinner set; tableware;
茶具 tea service; tea set;
炊具 cooking utensils;
刀具 knife set;
道具 stage property;
燈具 lamps and lanterns;
釣具 fishing tackle;
賭具 gambling set;
耕具 tillage implements;
工具 implement; instrument; means; tool;
供具 sacrificial vessel;
畫具 painter's paraphernalia;
火具 fuses and detonators;
機具 machines and tools;
夾具 clamping apparatus; fixture; jig;
教具 teaching aid;
量具 measuring tool;
獵具 hunting equipment;
面具 mask;
農具 farm implements; farm tools;
器具 appliance; implement; utensil;
寢具 bedding;
刃具 cutter; cutting tool;
食具 tableware;
索具 rigging;
胎具 model; mould; pattern;
完具 complete; perfect;
玩具 toy;
挽具 harness;
文具 stationery; writing materials;
卧具 beddings;
刑具 instruments of torture;
煙具 smoking set;
用具 apparatus; appliance; utensil;
漁具 fishing tackle;
雨具 rain gear;
戰具 weapon;
鑽具 drilling tool;
坐具 seat;

ju
【沮】 damp; low-lying land; marshy;
[沮洳] damp; low-lying land
[沮澤] marsh; swamps;

ju
【拒】 (1) repel; resist; (2) refuse; reject;
[拒捕] resist arrest;
恃強拒捕 refuse to be arrested with one's strength;
[拒斥] reject;
[拒付] dishonour; refuse payment;
[拒貴納微] reject the worthy and accept the worthless;
[拒諫飾非] reject criticism and whitewash mistakes; reject good advice and gloss over faults; reject representations and gloss over errors; the rejection of criticisms and the whitewashing of one's mistakes;
[拒絕] decline; decline doing sth; decline to do sth; refuse refusal; reject; repulse; throw down; throw over; turn down;
拒絕幫助 refuse sb's help;
拒絕認錯 refuse to make an apology;
拒絕受賄 refuse sb's bribe;
拒絕往來 refuse to interact;

斷然拒絕 adamant refusal; flat refusal; flatly reject; peremptorily dismiss; rebuff; refuse point-blank; shoot down;

抗拒 defy; resist;

ju
【炬】 a torch;

ju
【苣】 lettuce;

苦苣 hare's-lettuce;
萵苣 lettuce;

ju
【倨】 (1) haughty; rude; (2) slightly bent;

ju
【俱】 all; complete;

［俱樂部］ club;
俱樂部會所 clubhouse;
保齡球俱樂部 bowling club;
成立俱樂部 form a club;
高爾夫球俱樂部 golf club;
青年俱樂部 youth club;
人防俱樂部 civil air defence club;
體育俱樂部 sports club;
足球俱樂部 football club;

［俱全］ complete in all varieties;
色色俱全 all kinds are available;
色香味俱全 pleasant to the eye and taste;
樣樣俱全 everything necessary is available;
一應俱全 available in all varieties;

ju
【秬】 black millet;

ju
【据】 (1) according to; base on; (2) arrogant; haughty;

ju
【距】 (1) bird's spur; (2) distance;

［距骨］ ankle-bone; at close range;

［距離］ (1) distance; gap; range; space; (2) apart from; at a distance from; away from;
距離狀語 adverbial of distance;
~ 距離狀語從句 adverbial clause of distance;
安全距離 safe clearance; safe distance;
保持距離 give sb or sth a wide berth; keep a distance; keep sb at arm's length; keep sb at one's length;
~ 小心地保持距離 at a discreet distance;
測量距離 take the distance;
長距離 long distance;
~ 長距離飛行 long-distance flight;
~ 長距離賽跑 long-distance race;
~ 長距離散步 long walk
~ 長距離游泳 swim a long distance;
幾步路的距離 within walking distance;
角距離 angular distance;
近距離 at close range; close range; short distance;
可調距離 adjustable distance;
實際距離 actual distance; actual range;
縮短距離 shorten the distance;
顯示距離 visibility range;
一段距離 a distance; some distance;
有些距離 some distance;
中距離 middle-distance;
~ 中距離賽跑 middle-distance race;
準確距離 accurate distance;

糟距 slot pitch;
測距 find the range of; measure the distance;
差距 (1) disparity; gap; (2) difference;
等距 equidistance;
軌距 track gauge;
行距 row spacing;
焦距 focal distance;
相距 at a distance of; away from;
軸距 wheelbase;
株距 spacing in the rows;

ju
【詎】 an interjection indicating surprise;

ju
【鉅】 (1) great; (2) steel;

ju
【聚】 assemble; gather; get together;

［聚寶盆］ cornucopia; treasure bowl－a place rich in natural resources;

［聚變］ fusion;
催化聚變 catalytic fusion;
核聚變 nuclear fusion;
冷聚變 cold fusion;
原子聚變 atomic fusion;

［聚光］ spotlight;
聚光燈 focus lamp; spotlight;
~ 小聚光燈 downlighter;
聚光光學 light-gathering optics;
聚光鏡 condensing lens;
聚光力 light-gathering ability;

聚光器 condenser;
~暗視野聚光器 dark-field condenser;
~消色差聚光器 achromatic condenser;
~顯微鏡聚光器 microscope condenser;
聚光圈 bezel;
聚光透鏡 collector lens;
聚光纖維 light focusing fibre;

[聚合] (1) get together; (2) polymerization;
聚合體 paradigm;
~複雜聚合體 complex paradigm;
~簡單聚合體 simple paradigm;
聚合物 polymer;
~醛聚合物 aldehyde polymer;
~稀丙醇聚合物 allyl alcohol polymer;
~酰化聚合物 acrylate polymer;
聚合作用 polymerization;
~電子束聚合作用 electron-beam polymerization;
甲性聚合 alkaline polymerization;
間斷聚合 batch polymerization;
離子聚合 ionic polymerization;
整體聚合 bulk polymerization;

[聚會] (1) get together; meet; (2) assembly; beanfeast; bunfight; gathering; meeting;
聚會場所 meeting place;
聚會所 meeting-house;
家庭聚會 family gathering;
節日聚會 festival gathering;
社交聚會 social gathering;
書院聚會 college assembly;
睡衣聚會 pyjama party; slumber party;
政治聚會 political gathering;

[聚積] accumulate; build up; collect;
聚積財富 amass riches;

[聚集] aggregation; assemble; collect; gather;
聚集兵力 assemble forces;
聚集複合詞 aggregative compound;
聚集起來 gather together;
聚集態 state of aggregation;
城市聚集 urban aggregation;
聚才集賢 collect and keep men of talent; gather worthies and collect men of ability;
鏈聚集 chain aggregation;

[聚焦] focusing;
不對稱聚焦 asymmetric focusing;
角聚焦 angular focusing;
偏轉後聚焦 after-deflection focusing;
軟聚焦 soft focus;

[聚居] inhabit a region; live in a compact community;
聚居型式 settlement pattern;

[聚散] meet and depart;
聚散無常 meeting and departing are irregular; the meetings and separations are not constant;
獸聚鳥散 get together and disperse like animals and birds;

[聚沙] pile up grains of sand;
聚沙成塔 every little helps; many a little makes a mickle; many grains of sand pile up will make a pagoda – from increments comes abundance; many small make a great;
聚沙之年 childhood;

[聚束] beaming; bunch; bunching;
聚束作用 bunching action;
電子聚束 electron bunching;
動態聚束 kinematic bunching;
反射聚束 reflex bunching;
級聯聚束 cascade bunching;
理想聚束 ideal bunching;
諧波聚束 harmonic bunching;
最佳聚束 optimal bunching;

[聚蚊成雷] a swarm of mosquitoes; makes a noise like thunder–rumours can cause much disturbance;

[聚星] multiple star;

[聚眾] gather a crowd;
聚眾賭博 come together for gambling; gather together to gamble;
聚眾結社 gather a crowd to form an association;
聚眾鬧事 gather a mob to make trouble;
聚眾毆斗 assemble crowds for beating; come together for engaging in fisticuffs;
聚眾商議 get people together for discussion;
聚眾滋事 assemble a crowd to engage in an affray; collect crowds to stir up trouble; gather a crowd and make disturbances;

重聚 be united;
簇聚 cluster together; crowd together;
攢聚 crowd together; gather closely together; huddle together;
蜂聚 gather in swarms; swarm together;
共聚 copolymerization;
歡聚 have a happy get-together;

J

滙聚 assemble; flock together;
會聚 assemble; flock together;
積聚 accumulate; build up;
集聚 assemble; gather;
凝聚 condense;
縮聚 condense; polymerize;
團聚 (1) reunite; (2) rally; unite;
屯聚 assemble;
嘯聚 band together; gang up;

ju
【虡】 (1) support in the framework for a bell; (2) small table with long legs placed beside a bed;

ju
【劇】 (1) drama; play; opera; (2) acute; intense; severe;
[劇本] drama; play; script;
編寫電影劇本 write a movie script;
寫劇本 write a play;
[劇變] upheaval;
政治劇變 political upheaval;
[劇場] theatre;
兒童劇場 children's theatre;
歌劇場 opera house;
露天劇場 amphitheatre; open-air theatre;
木偶劇場 puppet show theatre;
實驗劇場 experimental theatre;
舞劇場 ballet theatre;
圓形劇場 amphitheatre;
組裝劇場 modular theatre;
[劇咳] acute coughing;
一陣劇咳 a bout of bad coughing; a violent fit of coughing;
一陣陣劇咳 bad coughing bouts;
[劇烈] acute; fierce; severe; violent;
劇烈運動 strenuous exercise;
[劇情] plot of a play;
劇情發展 development of the plot;
劇情梗概 synopsis of the play;
劇情簡介 synopsis;
[劇詩] dramatic poetry;
[劇痛] acute pain; sharp pain;
一陣劇痛 a fit of acute pain;
[劇團] theatrical company; troupe;
兒童劇團 children's theatre; children's dramatic troupe;
京劇團 Peking opera troupe;
實驗劇團 experimental theatre;
舞劇團 dance drama troupe;
業餘劇團 amateur dramatic troup;
[劇院] theatre;
兒童劇院 children's theatre;
歌劇院 opera house;
藝術劇院 art theatre;
[劇照] stage photo; still;
[劇作家] dramatist; playwright;
業餘劇作家 amateur playwright;
專業劇作家 professional playwright;

悲劇 tragedy;
悲喜劇 tragicomedy;
編劇 playwright; screenwriter;
慘劇 tragedy;
醜劇 farce;
獨幕劇 one-act play;
多幕劇 full-length drama; many-act play;
惡作劇 mischief; practical joke;
翻譯劇 translated play;
歌劇 opera;
歌舞劇 musical; song and dance drama;
廣播劇 radio play;
話劇 drama; play;
急劇 rapid; sharp; sudden;
加劇 aggravate; exacerbate; intensify;
街頭劇 street performance;
歷史劇 historical play;
鬧劇 farce;
清歌劇 oratorio;
情節劇 melodrama;
趣劇 farce;
詩劇 poetic drama;
喜劇 comedy;
戲劇 (1) drama; play; (2) script;
笑劇 farce;
啞劇 dumb show; pantomime;
粵劇 Cantonese opera;
樂劇 music drama;
雜劇 comedy; farce; variety show;

ju
【踞】 (1) crouch; squat; (2) occupy;
[踞高臨下] look down from a height;

高踞 set oneself above; stand above;
箕踞 sit with one's legs stretched;
盤踞 illegally or forcibly occupy;

ju
【據】 (1) lay hold of; occupy; seize; take possession of; (2) depend on; rely on; (3) according to; on the grounds of; (4) evidence; grounds; proof;

[據報] it is reported;
 據實而報 give a matter-of-fact account;
[據此] accordingly; in view of the above; on these grounds;
[據點] fortified point; stronghold; strongpoint;
 拔掉敵人據點 capture the enemy's strongholds;
[據實] be based on the fact;
 據實而言 call a pikestaff a pikestaff; call a spade a spade; call things by their proper names; speak the truth;
 據實相告 give sb a factual report; tell according to facts;
 據實招供 confess according to fact; confess the truth at court; confess truthfully; tell the facts in court;
 據實直言 call a spade a spade; call things by their proper names; speak the truth; tell the truth;
[據守] be entrenched in; guard;
[據說] a story is going around that; as the story goes; allegedly; by all accounts; I hear that; it is said; people say that; the story goes that; the story runs that; they say;
[據為己有] appropriate to oneself; have all to oneself; make sth his own; pocket; seize sth for oneself; take forcible possession of sth for oneself;
[據悉] by report; it is reported;
[據險固守] take advantage of a natural barrier to put up a strong defence;

筆據 written note;
單據 bill; invoice; receipt; voucher;
割據 set up a separatist regime by force of arms;
根據 according as; according to; in accordance with; in line with; in the light of; on the basis of;
借據 receipt for a loan;
考據 (1) textual criticism; (2) textual research;
論據 ground of argument;
判據 criterion;
票據 (1) bill; note; (2) receipt; voucher;
憑據 evidence; proof;
契據 contract; deed; receipt;
竊據 usurp;
實據 substantial evidence; substantial proof;
收據 receipt;
數據 data;
信據 evidence; proof;
依據 according to; basis; foundation; in the light of;
約據 written agreement;
佔據 hold; occupy;
證據 evidence; proof; testimony;
字據 written pledge;

ju
【鋸】 (1) saw; (2) amputate;
[鋸開] saw apart;
[鋸末] sawdust;
[鋸子] saw;

齒形鋸 saw;
帶鋸 band saw;
刀鋸 knives and saws;
電鋸 electric saw;
鋼鋸 hacksaw;
弓鋸 bow saw;
拉鋸 be locked in a seesaw struggle;
鏈鋸 chain saw;
手鋸 handsaw;
一把鋸 a saw;
圓鋸 circular saw;

ju
【窶】 destitute; impoverished;

貧窶 impoverished; poor;

ju
【屨】 sandal; shoes made of coarse material;
[屨霜踐冰] alert; take precautions;

ju
【遽】 (1) hastily; hurriedly; (2) alarmed; frightened;
[遽然變色] change one's countenance suddenly;

匆遽 hastily; hurriedly;
惶遽 frightened; scared;
急遽 rapid; sharp; sudden;

ju
【颶】 cyclone; gale; hurricane;
[颶風] hurricane; storm; typhoon;

ju
【瞿】 a surname;

ju

【簴】 pillars beside the crossbeam for hanging bells or drums;

ju

【醵】 pool money;

ju

【懼】 afraid of; dread; fear;

[懼內] henpecked;

[懼怕] dread; fear;

[懼色] look of fear;

了無懼色 look completely undaunted; not to show a trace of fear;

面無懼色 look undaunted; not to look at all afraid; show no fear;

[懼外] xenophobic;

懼外心理 xenophobia;

恐懼 dread; fear;

危懼 worry and fear;

畏懼 dread; fear;

疑懼 apprehend; misgive; suspicious and fearful;

憂懼 be worried and apprehensive;

震懼 in trepidation; terrified;

惴懼 anxious and worried; in fear and trembling;

juan¹

juan

【身】 as in 身毒, an ancient name of India;

juan

【娟】 attractive; good-looking; graceful; pretty;

[娟秀] beautiful; graceful;

風姿娟秀 her deportment and air are refined and attractive — said of a beautiful woman;

嬋娟 (1) graceful; (2) moon; (3) woman;

juan

【捐】 (1) abandon; relinquish; (2) contribute; donate; subscribe; (3) tax;

[捐款] (1) contribute money; donate a sum; gift; (2) contribution; donation; subscription;

公眾捐款 public donation;

慷慨捐款 generous donation;

援助捐款 assistance contribution;

自願捐款 voluntary donation;

[捐棄] abandon; relinquish;

捐棄前嫌 bury the hatchet; forget past grievances; forget previous ill will; let bygones be bygones; throw away the past resentment;

[捐軀] lay down one's life; sacrifice one's life;

捐軀赴義 die for the cause of justice and righteousness; prefer death to disgrace; sacrifice one's life for the sake of righteousness;

為國捐軀 sacrifice one's life for the motherland;

[捐稅] taxes and levies;

抗捐抗稅 refuse to pay levies and taxes;

苛捐雜稅 exaction; exorbitant tax levies; exorbitant taxes and harsh levies; exorbitant taxes and miscellaneous levies; miscellaneous levies and exorbitant surtaxes; multifarious taxes;

[捐獻] contribute; donate; present;

[捐血] donate blood;

捐血者 blood donor;

[捐贈] contribute as a gift; donate; present;

捐贈物 donation;

不具名的捐贈 anonymous donation;

答應捐贈 promise a donation;

[捐助] contribute; donate; offer;

[捐資] make donations;

捐資助學 make donations to help develop education;

房捐 property tax;

募捐 collection donations; solicit contributions;

稅捐 taxes and levies;

賑捐 contribute to relief funds;

juan

【涓】 tiny stream;

[涓埃] insignificant; negligible;

盡涓埃之力 do one's bit; make what little contribution one can;

[涓滴] dribble; driblet; tiny drop;

涓滴不飲 never touch wine; not a single drop of wine passes one's lips; not to drink a drop of wine; not to touch a drop of wine;

涓滴歸公 every bit goes to the public treasury; every cent goes into the public account; turn in every cent of public money;

[涓涓] trickling flow;

涓涓不壅，終為江河 a small leak will sink a great ship; if small leaks are not plugged up in time, they will become

streams;
涓涓細流 tricklet;
[涓流] purling; trickle;

juan
【悁】 angry; indignant;

juan
【圈】 confine; encircle;

juan
【鵑】 (1) cuckoo; (2) azalea;
[鵑鳩] kirombo;

杜鵑 (1) cuckoo; (2) azalea;
噪鵑 Chinese koel;

juan
【鐫】 (1) carve; engrave; (2) be demoted;
[鐫刻] engrave;

雕鐫 carve; engrave;

juan
【蠲】 (1) millipede; (2) bright; clean; pure; (3) clean; cleanse; wash; (4) remit; remove;
[蠲除] relieve of excessive burden; relieve of oppressive measures;
[蠲免] exempt from tax payment;

juan3
juan
【卷】 curl; curly;
[卷曲] curl; curl over;

春卷 spring roll;

juan
【捲】 (1) roll up; (2) carry along;
[捲尺] band tape; measuring tape;
[捲髮] curly hair;
捲髮夾 curler;
[捲積] convolution;
捲積器 convolver;
廣義捲積 generalized convolution;
空間捲積 spatial convolution;
快速捲積 fast convolution;
離散捲積 discrete convolution;
循環捲積 cyclic convolution;
圓周捲積 circular convolution;
[捲角] dog-eared;
[捲簾] blind; roller blind; shade;
[捲毛] curled;
[捲曲] curl;
捲曲的 curly;
[捲取機] coiler;
輥式捲取機 rolling coiler;
三輥式捲取機 three-roll coiler;
雙鉗口捲取機 dual-slot mandrel coiler;
筒式捲取機 drum coiler;
[捲入] be drawn into; be involved in;
使捲入 embroil;
[捲縮] snarl;
[捲逃] abscond;
[捲心菜] cabbage;
一棵捲心菜 a head of cabbage;
[捲煙紙] cigarette paper;
[捲紙] roll;
衛生捲紙 toilet roll;

juan4
juan
【卷】 (1) reel; roll; scroll; (2) reel; roll; spool;
[卷軸] scroll;

案卷 archives; files; records;
白卷 blank examination paper;
彩卷 colour film;
答卷 answer sheet;
考卷 examination paper;
課卷 written exercises;
試卷 examination paper; test paper;
手卷 hand scroll;
壓卷 masterpiece;

juan
【倦】 tired; weary;
[倦得] tired;
倦得發暈 faint with fatigue;
倦得要命 dead tired; dead to the world;
[倦容] tired look;
面有倦容 look tired;
[倦怠] ennui;
[倦意] sleepiness; tiredness; weariness;
[倦游] weary of wondering and sight-seeing;

憊倦 exhausted; weary;
不倦 indefatigable; tireless;
困倦 sleepy;
疲倦 tired; weary;
厭倦 be tired of; be weary of;

juan
【狷】 (1) narrow-minded; quick-tempered;

rash; (2) honest and straightforward;
［狷急］ impetuous; of impatient disposition;
［狷羚］ bubalis;

juan
【悁】 impatient; impetuous; irritable;

juan
【圈】 enclosure for keeping livestock;
［圈養］ rear livestock in pens;

墊圈 bed down the livestock;
籃圈 hoop;
馬圈 stable;
棚圈 covered pen;
起圈 remove manure from a pigsty etc;
羊圈 sheep pen; sheepfold;
中圈 centre circle;

juan
【眷】 (1) family dependant; (2) have tender feeling for;
［眷眷］ bear in mind constantly;
［眷戀］ sentimentally attached to a person or a place;
［眷念］ feel nostalgic about; think fondly of;
眷念不捨 have an unceasing affection for sb;
眷念舊情 remember the old friendship;
［眷屬］ family dependants;
有情人終成眷屬 the lovers finally got married;
~願天下有情人終成眷屬 may all lovers unite in marriage; wish that all lovers in the world could be united in wedlock;
［眷注］ show loving care for; show solicitude for;

寶眷 your family;
家眷 (1) one's family; wife and children; (2) wife;
女眷 womenfolk of a family;
僑眷 relatives of overseas Chinese;
親眷 (1) one's relatives; (2) family dependants;

juan
【鄄】 a county in Shandong Province;

juan
【絹】 silk;
［絹本］ silk scroll;
［絹花］ silk flower;
［絹畫］ classical Chinese painting on silk; silk painting;
［絹人］ silk figurine;
［絹扇］ silk fan;

畫絹 drawing silk;
手絹 handkerchief;

juan
【雋】 (1) fat meat; (2) a surname;

juan
【睠】 same as 眷, care for;

jue¹

jue
【撅】 (1) stick up; (2) snap; (3) pout;
［撅嘴］ pout one's lips;
撅嘴扳臉 have a fit of the pouts;

jue²

jue
【孓】 larvae of mosquitoes;

孑孓 wiggler; wriggler;

jue
【抉】 (1) choose; pick; select; (2) dig; gouge;
［抉擇］ choose;
做出抉擇 make one's choice;

jue
【決】 (1) decide; determine; (2) certainly; definitely;
［決不］ ne'er; not for all the world; not for the world; not for worlds; over my dead body;
決不寬貸 no mercy will be shown; no pardon will be given; on no account will leniency be shown;
決不食言 never to break one's promise; never to go back on one's word; never to retract one's words;
決不退讓 never yield; will under no circumstances give in;
決不向困難低頭 never bow to difficulties;
［決策］ (1) decide a policy; make a strategic decision; make policy; (2) decision-making; policy-making;
決策部門 decision-making department;
決策程序 decision-making procedure;
決策方案 decision alternative;
決策方式 decision-making model;
決策分析 decision analysis;

決策概率 decision probability;
決策管理 decision-making management;
~ 決策管理環境 environment of decision-making management;;
~ 決策管理理論 theory of decision-making management;
決策機構 decision-making body; decision-making organization;
決策機制 decision-making mechanism;
決策技術 technique of decision-making;
決策監督 supervision of decision-making;
決策結構 decision-making structure;
決策科學化 scientification of decision-making;
決策類型 types of decision-making;
決策理論 decision theory;
決策論 decision theory;
~ 描述決策論 descriptive decision theory;
決策民主化 democratization of decision-making;
決策模型 decision-making model;
決策能力 decision-making skills;
決策權 decision-making power;
決策人物 decision-maker;
決策軟技術 soft techniques for decision-making;
決策樹 decision-making tree;
決策體制 decision-making system;
決策系統 decision-making system;
決策效果 decision-making effect;
決策心理 decision-making psychology;
決策行為 decision-making behaviour;
決策硬技術 hard techniques for decision-making;
決策原則 principles of decision-making;
決策者 decision-maker;
決策支持系統 decision support system;
決策職能 decision-making function;
決策中心 decision centre;
決策準則 decision rule;
決策組織 decision-making organization;
程序性決策 programmed decision-making;
~ 非程序性決策 non-programmed decision-making;
規範性決策 standardization decision;
~ 非規範性決策 non-standardization decision;

[決定] decide; decide on; decide upon; make up one's mind; resolve;
決定不做 stop short of doing sth;
決定論 determinism;
~ 環境決定論 environmental determinism;
~ 教育決定論 educational determinism;
~ 精神決定論 psychic determinism;
~ 經濟決定論 economic determinism;
~ 生物決定論 biological determinism;
~ 文化決定論 cultural determinism;
決定權 decision-making power; power to make decisions;
決定性因素 determinant;
不受歡迎的決定 unpopular decision;
草率的決定 casual decision;
倉促的決定 hasty decision;
猝然決定 make a sudden decision;
錯誤的決定 wrong decision;
改變決定 change a decision; reverse a decision;
好的決定 good decision;
~ 不好的決定 bad decision;
堅持自己的決定 stick to one's decision;
快速的決定 quick decision; snap decision;
困難的決定 difficult decision; hard decision; tough decision;
聯合決定 joint decision;
貿然決定 rash decision;
明確的決定 clear decision;
深思熟慮的決定 deliberate decision;
慎重的決定 deliberate decision;
生產決定 output decision;
推遲作出決定 adjourn a decision;
推翻決定 overturn a decision;
行政決定 administrative decision;
業務決定 business decision;
一項決定 a decision;
有爭議的決定 controversial decision;
正確的決定 right decision;
重大決定 big decision; critical decision; crucial decision; major decision;
重要決定 important decision;
最終決定 final decision;
作出決定 arrive at a decision; come to a decision; make a decision; make up one's mind; reach a conclusion; reach a decision; take a decision;

[決鬥] (1) duel; (2) decisive struggle;

[決斷] (1) make a decision; (2) decisiveness; resolve;
決斷力 determination;
~ 有決斷力 have determination;
有決斷力的人 person of determination;
作出決斷 make a final decision;

[決裂] break apart;
[決然] (1) determinedly; firmly; resolutely; (2) definitely; undoubtedly; unquestionably;
[決賽] cup final; final; the finals;
決賽隊 finalist;
決賽選手 finalist;
半決賽 semi-final;
~進入半決賽 reach the semi-final;
半準決賽 quarterfinal;
進入決賽 reach the final; through to the final;
[決勝] decide the issue of the battle; determine the victory;
決勝分 match point;
決勝局 decider;
決勝千里 gain a decisive victory a thousand miles away — a good plan;
決勝賽 decider;
決勝時刻 match point;
[決死] life-and-death;
[決算] (1) closing of accounts; (2) final accounts;
決算表 final statement;
決算審計 audit of returns;
決算書 final report;
決算賬戶 final account;
半年決算 half-yearly closing of accounts;
國家決算 final state accounts;
年終決算 final accounts at the end of the year;
[決心] all set; bent on; bent upon; bound; decide; determination; determine; determined; from a resolution; make a resolution; make up one's mind; out to; pass a resolution; resolve; resolved; set on; set oneself to; set one's heart on; set one's mind on; take a resolution;
決心反對 decide against;
決心復仇 resolve on having one's revenge;
抱定決心 determined; hold on to one's determination;
表明決心 declare one's determination;
下決心 be determined to; brace up; come to a determination; decide; determine; have one's mind made up; make a firm devision; make a resolution; make up one's mind; resolute; resolve;
~下定決心 come to a resolution; make a firm resolve to do sth; make up one's mind;
[決意] determined; have one's mind made up;
[決議] resolution;
決議草案 draft resolution;
議而不決 discuss sth without reaching a decision;
議而不決，決而不行 no decision after deliberation, no action even with a decision;
[決戰] decisive battle; decisive engagement;
決戰決勝 determine to fight and win; determination to fight and win; firm resolve to fight and win;
速戰速決 bring battles to a quick decision; fight a quick battle to force a quick decision; fight and win battles of quick decision; make short work of; prompt action and quick decision;

表決 decide by vote; vote;
裁決 adjudicate; rule;
齒決 bite off with the teeth;
處決 (1) execute; put to death; (2) handle and decide;
否決 veto; vote down;
果決 firm and resolute;
堅決 determined; firm; resolute;
解決 (1) resolve; settle; (2) dispose of; finish off;
潰決 burst; flood overflowing;
判決 bring in a court verdict; court decision; judgment;
槍決 execute by shooting;
取決 be decided by; depend on;
速決 decide quickly;
未決 outstanding; unsettled;
議決 pass a resolution;
自決 decide by oneself; self-determine;

jue

【角】 (1) compete; wrestle; (2) corner;
[角斗] wrestle;
[角力] have a trial of strength; wrestle;
[角色] character; part; role;
角色扮演 role-play;
角色倒轉 role reversal;
角色關係 role relationship;
角色模式 role model;
角色缺陷 role defect;
角色行為 role behavior;
傳統角色 traditional role;
調動角色 role change;

扮演角色 play a character; play a part; play a role;
次要角色 supporting role;
反面角色 negative character;
分派角色 casting;
小角色 bit part;
正面角色 positive character;

[角逐] compete; contend; enter into rivalry; juggle for; tussle;
参加角逐 enter a competition; enter a contest;
重新角逐 compete again; renew competition;

丑角 (1) buffoon; clown; (2) inglorious person;
旦角 female character in Chinese operas;
紅角 popular actor or actress;
口角 bicker; quarrel; wrangle;
坤角 actress;
男角 actor;
女角 actress;
配角 (1) minor role; supporting role; (2) one who does auxiliary work; (3) costar;
生角 male character in Chinese operas;
替角 understudy;
主角 leading role;

jue

【玦】 jade ring with a small segment cut off;

jue

【倔】 hard; intransigent; tough;

[倔強] obstinate; stubborn; unbending; unyielding;
倔強的 headstrong; stiff-necked;

[倔小子] surly dog;

jue

【崛】 rise abruptly;

[崛起] (1) rise abruptly; rise sharply; suddenly appear on the horizon; (2) rise; spring up;

奇崛 peculiar; queer; singular;

jue

【掘】 dig; excavate; make a cave; make a hole;

[掘井] dig a well;
掘井灌溉 drive a well to irrigate the land;
掘井抗旱 sink wells to fight a drought;
臨渴掘井 act too late; lock the stable after the horse is stolen; not to make timely preparations;

採掘 excavate;
發掘 excavate; unearth;
開掘 dig;
挖掘 excavate; unearth;

jue

【桷】 (1) enormous; great; huge; (2) straightforward; upright;

[桷德] great virtue;

[桷直] frank; straightforward;

jue

【訣】 (1) part; separate; (2) sorcery;

[訣別] bid farewell; part;

[訣竅] knack; secret of success; the ropes; tricks of the trade;
美容訣竅 beauty care tips;
烹飪訣竅 cooking tips;
掌握訣竅 master the secrets of success;

口訣 slogan;
秘訣 key to success;
妙訣 knack;
要訣 key to success in doing sth;
永訣 be separated by death;

jue

【桷】 (1) rafter; (2) malus toringo;

jue

【觖】 discontented; dissatisfied; not satisfactory;

jue

【厥】 (1) faint; (2) that; this; the; (3) personal pronoun;

[厥詞] wild talk;
大放厥詞 engage in a wild talk; hold forth; let out a torrent of abuse; loose one's tongue; spout a stream of empty rhetoric; talk a lot of drivel; talk a lot of nonsense; talk drivel; talk wildly;

[厥職] one's duties;
克盡厥職 perform fully the functions and duties of an office;

昏厥 faint; swoon;
驚厥 faint from fear;
痰厥 coma due to blocking of the respiratory system;
暈厥 faint; syncope;

J

jue

【絕】 (1) cut off; sever; (2) exhausted; finished; used up; (3) refuse; reject; turn down; (4) heartless; merciless; (5) desperate; hopeless; (6) excellent; matchless; superb; unique; (7) extremely; most; (8) absolutely; by any means; in the least; on any account; (9) definitive; leaving no leeway; making no allowance; uncompromising;

[絕版] out of print;

[絕筆] (1) last words written before one's death; (2) last work of an author or artist;

[絕壁] crag; precipice;

絕壁懸崖 an inaccessible precipice and a hanging cliff;

[絕不] absolutely not; by no means; definitely not; for anything; in no circumstances; never; never in a million years; not in a million years; not in the least;

絕不相干 have no concern whatever;

[絕唱] peak of poetic perfection;

[絕處逢生] alive in desperation; be snatched from the jaws of death; be unexpectedly rescued from a desperate situation;

[絕代] peerless; unique among one's contemporaries;

絕代風華 an unsurpassed beauty of a generation;

絕代佳人 a belle of rare charm; a lady of remarkable beauty; a marvel of beauty; a peerless beauty; a strikingly beautiful woman; an incomparable beauty; an unrivalled beauty; the most beautiful lady ever seen; the most beautiful maiden of the age; the reigning beauty;

容華絕代 be endowed with a rare and radiant beauty; of unsurpassed beauty;

[絕倒] roar with laughter; shake one's sides;

[絕頂] extremely; utterly;

絕頂聰明 extremely intelligent;

[絕對] (1) absolutely; by a long chalk; definitely; entirely; on no account; (2) the Absolute;

絕對比較 absolute comparative;

絕對不可能 absolutely impossible;

絕對成分 absolute element;

絕對程序 absolute programme;

~絕對程序設計 absolute programming;

絕對從句 absolute clause;

絕對代碼 absolute code;

絕對服從 obey without questioning;

絕對過剩人口 absolute overpopulation;

絕對化 absolutization; absolutize;

絕對活度 absolute activity;

絕對機密 top secret;

絕對肯定式 affirmative apodictic;

絕對論 absolutism;

~絕對論者 absolutist;

絕對收視率 absolute rate of reception;

絕對同義詞 absolute synonym;

絕對誤差 absolute error;

絕對形式 absolute form;

絕對語言 absolute language;

絕對真理 absolute truth;

絕對值 absolute value;

絕對主義 absolutism;

絕對最高級 absolute superlative;

[絕後] (1) without issue; without offspring; (2) very rare;

[絕戶] (1) without issue; without offspring; (2) childless person;

[絕活] special skill; unique ability;

[絕跡] be stamped out; disappear; vanish;

[絕技] consummate skill; unique skill;

絕技異能 extraordinary skill and wonderful ability;

身懷絕技 have the singularly extraordinary skill;

[絕交] break off relations; break with; end a relationship; sever relations with; split chums;

絕交信 Dear John letter;

割席絕交 break off a friendship with sb; break off intercourse; break off with one's friend; break up an old friendship; cut off friendly relations; end the friendship with sb; sever friendship; sever one's connections with sb;

[絕境] blind alley; cul-de-sac; hopeless situation; an impasse;

逼至絕境 drive sb to the wall; push sb to the wall;

身陷絕境 in a hopeless situation; in an impasse;

陷入絕境 come to a dead end; in helpless situation;

[絕句] five-character or seven-character poem;

[絕口] (1) stop talking; (2) keep one's mouth shut;

絕口不談 absolutely silent about; keep one's mouth shut and say nothing; keep one's mouth tight shut about; keep silent and say nothing; never to have a single word to say about; never to say a single word about; not to say a word about; refuse to say anything about; seal one's lips and say nothing;

絕口不提 avoid all mention of; avoid mentioning; make no mention whatsoever of; never to say a single word about;

罵不絕口 curse unceasingly; heap endless abuse upon; let off a string of invectives; pour out torrents of abuse; pour out unceasing abuse; rail incessantly; revile without ceasing;

贊不絕口 heap praises on; praise profusely;

讚不絕口 admire incessantly; full of praise; heap praise upon praise; praise again and again; praise profusely; profuse in praise; rain praise on; repeatedly speak in favour of; unstinting in one's praise;

[絕路] blind alley; deadlock; impasse; road to ruin;

絕路逢生 a narrow escape of one's life; alive in desperation; find a way out in the most critical moment; find rescue in desperate circumstances;

被逼上絕路 be driven into a corner; be driven to desperation;

自尋絕路 bring ruin upon oneself; court destruction; work one's own undoing; wilfully take the road to one's doom;

自走絕路 cut one's own throat; go down the road of destruction; take the road to ruin; work one's own undoing;

走上絕路 come to a dead end; head for one's doom; head toward disaster;

[絕倫] matchless; peerless; unequalled; unsurpassed;

絕倫超群 excel all others; surpass all;

超群絕倫 far above the ordinary; far surpassing one's fellows; outshine all others;

荒謬絕倫 absurd in the extreme;

[絕密] most confidential; strictly confidential; top-secret;

[絕妙] excellent; extremely clever; ingenious; perfect;

[絕滅] die out;

絕滅人性 cannibalistic; inhuman; most barbarous;

[絕命] die;

絕命書 (1) a suicide note; (2) a note written on the eve of one's execution;

命不該絕 be fated not to die;

[絕熱] (1) heat insulation; (2) adiabatic;

絕熱變化 adiabatic change;

絕熱過程 adiabatic process;

[絕色] exceedingly beautiful; of unrivalled beauty;

絕色佳麗 a beauty of beauties; a woman of unsurpassed beauty; an exceedingly beautiful young lady;

[絕食] fast; go on a hunger strike;

絕食抗議 hunger strike;

[絕望] despair; give up all hope; hopeless; lose all hope of;

感到絕望 be filled with despair;

[絕無此意] have absolutely no such intentions;

[絕無] absolutely not;

絕無僅有 one and the only one; the only one of its kind; unique;

絕無其事 nothing of the kind;

[絕藝] consummate art;

[絕育] sterilization;

[絕緣] insulation; isolation;

絕緣基體 insulating base;

絕緣能力 insulating ability;

絕緣器 insulator;

~拉牢式絕緣器 anchorage insulator;

~陶瓷絕緣器 ceramic insulator;

~振鈴形絕緣器 bell shaped insulator;

絕緣體 insulator;

~電池絕緣體 battery insulator;

~電絕緣體 electrical insulator;

絕緣子 insulator;

~蓄電池絕緣子 accumulator insulator;

~飛機絕緣子 aeroplane insulator;

~天線絕緣子 aerial insulator;

電纜絕緣 cable insulation;

電樞絕緣 armature insulation;

熱絕緣 thermal insulation;
石綿絕緣 asbestos insulation;
細麻布絕緣 cambric insulation;

[絕招] (1) masterstroke; unique skill; (2) unexpected tricky move;
拿出絕招 play one's best card; play one's trump card; show one's speciality;

[絕症] fatal illness; incurable disease; terminal disease;

[絕種] become extinct; die out;

弊絕 free from corruption;
屏絕 stop having contact or intercourse with;
摒絕 cut loose entirely;
不絕 ceaselessly;
超絕 superb; unique;
杜絕 completely eradicate; wipe out;
斷絕 cut off; sever;
告絕 be stamped out; disappear; vanish;
隔絕 be isolated; completely cut off;
根絕 completely eradicate; exterminate; uproot;
回絕 decline; refuse;
禁絕 completely ban; totally prohibit;
拒絕 (1) refuse; (2) decline; reject; turn down;
決絕 break off; cut off; sever;
滅絕 become extinct;
氣絕 breathe one's last;
棄絕 abandon; cast aside;
謝絕 decline; refuse;
卓絕 extreme; unsurpassed;
自絕 alienate oneself; destroy oneself;

jue

【腳】 (1) feet; (2) leg of sth;

jue

【駃】 hybrid horse;

jue

【玃】 lawless and wild; unruly;

猖玃 furious; wild;

jue

【鴃】 butcherbird; shrike;

jue

【噱】 loud laughter;

jue

【蕨】 bracken;

[蕨菜] fiddlehead;

[蕨類學] pteridology

jue

【蕝】 as in 茅蕝, to designate assigned position in practising court ceremony;

jue

【爵】 (1) title of nobility; peerage; rank of a peer; (2) ancient wine pitcher;

[爵杯] wine cup;

[爵弁] kind of ceremonial cap in the Zhou Dynasty;

[爵服] degree and costume of nobility;

[爵祿] degree and emolument of nobility;
高爵豐祿 a high position and a privileged treatment; a prominent position and a high salary;

[爵高者憂深] the greater one's care will be, the higher one's position is;

[爵士] Sir;
爵士封號 knighthood;
爵士音樂 jazz; jazz music;
爵士樂 jazz;
~爵士樂隊 jazz band;
~爵士樂迷 jazz buff;
~爵士樂俱樂部 jazz club;
~靈魂爵士樂 soul jazz;

[爵土] land conferred along with a degree of nobility;

[爵位] degree of nobility;
高爵顯位 high nobles in conspicuous positions;
貪爵慕位 covet high position; covet rank and admire position;

[爵章] badges of nobility;

[爵主] heir apparent to a title of nobility;

伯爵 count; earl;
公爵 duke;
官爵 official position and rank of nobility;
侯爵 marquis;
男爵 baron;
襲爵 succeed a hereditary title;
勛爵 (1) feudal title of nobility conferred for meritorious service; (2) lord;
子爵 viscount;

jue

【譎】 (1) cheat; deceive; (2) artful; crafty; wily; (3) hint; imply;

[譎而不正] crafty and far from upright;

[譎詐] crafty; cunning;

jue

【蹶】 (1) tread; (2) stumble and fall; (3) daunt; frustrate;

竭蹶 destitute; impoverished;

jue
【嚼】 chew; masticate;

jue
【覺】 (1) feel; sense; (2) awake; wake; (3) become awakened; become aware;
［覺察］ become aware; detect; perceive;
覺察錯誤 perceive an error;
［覺得］ aware; feel; sense;
覺得餓 feel hungry;
覺得高興 feel happy;
覺得冷 feel cold;
覺得幸運 feel lucky;
老覺得 always feel;
［覺悟］ (1) awareness; consciousness; understanding; (2) become aware of; come to understand;
覺悟過來 come to one's senses;
階級覺悟 class consciousness;
政治覺悟 political consciousness;
［覺醒］ (1) awake; awaken; awakening; (2) waking state;
不覺 unconsciously; without one's knowing;
察覺 become aware of; perceive;
觸覺 sense of touch;
錯覺 illusion; wrong impression;
發覺 detect; discover; find;
感覺 (1) feel; feeling; perceive; sense perception; (2) think;
乖覺 alert; quick;
幻覺 hallucination;
警覺 alertness; vigilance;
冷覺 sense of cold;
色覺 sense of colour;
視覺 sense of sight;
聽覺 sense of hearing;
痛覺 sense of pain;
味覺 sense of taste;
溫覺 sense of heat;
嗅覺 sense of smell;
知覺 (1) consciousness; (2) perception;
直覺 intuition;
自覺 aware; conscious;

jue
【矍】 (1) scared; watch in fright; (2) old but healthy;
［矍鑠］ hale and hearty;

jue
【爝】 torch;
［爝火］ torch fire;

jue
【攫】 seize; snatch; take hold of;
［攫取］ grab; seize;

jue
【鱖】 mandarin fish;
［鱖鯞］ bitterling;

jue
【愯】 awe-struck; respectful;

jue
【蠼】 black insect with six legs;

jue³

jue
【蹶】 kick backward;

jue⁴

jue
【倔】 gruff; rude in manner or speech;

jun¹

jun
【君】 (1) monarch; sovereign; supreme ruler; (2) gentleman;
［君臣］ the king and ministers;
君君，臣臣，父父，子子 let the king be a king, the minister a minister, the father a father and the son a son;
君辱臣死 when the emperor is put to shame, the minister dies;
［君民］ the ruler and the people;
民貴君輕 the people are more important than the ruler;
［君權］ monarchical power;
［君王］ king; lord;
［君主］ crowned head; monarch; sovereign;
君主立憲 constitutional monarchy;
~君主立憲制度 constitutional monarchy;
君主政體 monarchy;
君主專制制度 autocratic monarchy;
封建君主 overlord;
［君子］ gentleman;
君子不念舊惡 a gentleman does not bear grudges;
君子動口不動手 a gentleman uses his tongue but not his fists; a man of honour reasons things out and does not resort to force;
君子好逑 a gentleman's good mate;
君子動口，小人動手 a gentleman uses his tongue, a bastard, his fists;

君子慎交 a gentleman chooses his friends carefully;
君子慎言 a gentleman must be cautious in his speech;
君子協定 a gentleman's agreement;
君子一言，快馬一鞭 a gentleman never goes back on his word; a word spoken can never be taken back; a word spoken is past recalling;
君子之交淡如水 a gentleman's friendship is simple; a hedge between keeps friendship green; friends agree best at a distance;
君子自重 a gentleman takes care of himself; decency forbids;
彬彬君子 refined gentleman;
觀棋不語真君子 a true gentleman should keep silence while watching a chess game; he is truly a princely man who watches in silence a game of chess;
樑上君子 a gentleman on the beam — burglar;
謙謙君子 hypocritically modest person; modest, cautious gentleman;
淑善君子 gentleman; good man; virtuous man;
偽君子 hypocrite;
隱君子 (1) hermit; recluse; (2) opium addict;
癮君子 druggie; drugster;
正人君子 a gentleman; a just and upright man; a man of complete virtue; a man of honour; a man of integrity; a man of moral integrity; a man of strict morals;

暴君 despot; tyrant;
抱節君 bamboo;
郎君 my husband;
人君 king; sovereign;

jun
【均】 (1) equal; even; (2) all; without exception;
[均等] equal; fair; impartial;
技巧均等 equal in skill;
利益均等 equal in benefits;
力量均等 equal in strength;
數量均等 equal in number;
[均分] divide equally; share out equally;
三人均分 three-way split;
四人均分 four-way split;
[均衡] balanced; equalization; even; proportionate;
均衡發展 balanced development;
均衡化 equalization;
~ 延遲均衡化 delay equalization;
~ 直方圖均衡化 histogram equalization;
均衡價格 equilibrium price;
~ 均衡價格論 theory of equilibrium price;
均衡器 equalizer;
~ 孔徑均衡器 aperture equalizer;
~ 衰耗均衡器 attenuation equalizer;
~ 微分均衡器 differential equalizer;
均衡增長論 theory of balanced growth;
保持均衡 equipoise; keep in balance;
不均衡 disproportion;
~ 不均衡的 disproportionate;
延遲均衡 delay equalization;
自動均衡 automatic equalization;
[均勢] balance of power; equilibrium; equilibrium of forces; parity;
[均攤] share equally;
按比例均攤 pro rata average
[均一] even; honogeneous; uniform;
[均勻] even; well-distributed;
均勻的呼吸 constant breathing;
均勻的節拍 constant tempo;
均勻性 homogeneity; uniformity;
~ 不均勻性 heterogeneity;
表面不均勻性 surface heterogeneity;
點陣不均勻性 lattice heterogeneity;
光學不均勻性 optical heterogeneity;
誘發不均勻性 induced heterogeneity;
~ 背景均勻性 background uniformity;
~ 彩色均勻性 colour uniformity;
~ 彈道均勻性 ballistic uniformity;
~ 幅度均勻性 amplitude uniformity;
~ 光學均勻性 optical homogeneity;
~ 化學均勻性 chemical homogeneity;
分得均勻 evenly divided;

秉均 in power; rule a nation;
平均 (1) average; mean; (2) equally; share and share alike; (3) average; averaging; mean; mean value;
人均 per capita;
淑均 fine and fair;

jun
【囷】 granary;

jun
【軍】 (1) armed forces; army; troops; (2) corps; (3) military;

[軍備] armament; arms;
軍備競賽 arms race;
軍備控制 arms control;
擴充軍備 increase armaments;

[軍車] military vehicle;

[軍隊] armed forces; army; troops;
軍隊編制 army organization;
軍隊幹部 military cadre;
軍隊建設 army build-up; army construction;
軍隊建制 military organization;
調動軍隊 put forces in motion;
集結軍隊 mass troops;
一支軍隊 a contingent of troops;
徵集軍隊 raise military forces;
整編軍隊 reorganize an army;
裝備軍隊 equip an army;

[軍閥] warlord;

[軍法] military criminal code; military law;
軍法審判 ourt-martial;
家有家規，軍有軍法 a family has family rules, and an army has army rules;

[軍費] military expenditure;

[軍服] military uniform; uniform;

[軍官] commissioned officer; military officer;
高級軍官 high-ranking officer;
空軍軍官 air officer;
中級軍官 middle-ranking officer;

[軍國] the militia and the nation;
軍國大事 affairs of national defense and administration;
軍國主義 militarism;
~反軍國主義 antimilitarism;

[軍號] bugle;

[軍火] arms and ammunition; munitions;
軍火商 arms dealer;
購買軍火 peddle munitions;
私運軍火 gun-running;
~私運軍火的 arms-trafficking;

[軍紀] military discipline;

[軍艦] naval vessel; warcraft; warship;
一艘軍艦 a warship;

[軍界] military circles; the military;

[軍禮] military salute;

[軍力] military strength;

[軍糧] army provisions;

[軍令] military orders;
軍令如山 military orders are like a mountain; military orders cannot be disobeyed;

[軍旅] army; troops;
軍旅生涯 army life; soldiering;
軍旅之事 military affairs;

[軍馬] charger;
軍馬未動，糧草先行 an army, like a serpent, goes on its belly; an army marches on its stomach;
千軍萬馬 a grand army; a large number of mounted and foot soldiers; a large military force; a large unit; a mighty force; a powerful army with thousands of horses; a powerful army with thousands upon thousand of horses and soldiers; a vast host of infantry and cavaltry; an army of thousands; millions of troops;
~千軍萬馬過獨木橋 thousands upon thousands of men and horses go through a single-log-bridge;
~千軍萬馬，銳不可當 like the charge of a powerful army which no force can stop;

[軍民] military and civilian; soldiers and civilians; the army and the people;
軍民共建 joint construction between the army and the people;
軍民結合 combination of military and civil industries;

[軍旗] army flag;

[軍情] military situation; war situation;
刺探軍情 gather military intelligence; pry about military intelligence; spy on the military movements; spy out military secrets;
謊報軍情 give false information on the military situation;

[軍區] area command; military district; military region;
省軍區 provincial military district;

[軍人] armyman; serviceman; soldier;
軍人價值觀 armymen's value;
軍人倫理學 soldier's ethics;
軍人情感 armyman feeling;
軍人心理素質 armyman's mental quality;
軍人心理訓練 armyman psychological training;
軍人心理狀態 psychological state of soldiers;
軍人性格 soldier's character;
軍人自我意識 soldier's self-consciousness;

殘廢軍人 disabled soldier;
復員軍人 demobilized soldier;
退伍軍人 ex-serviceman;
~退伍軍人症 legionnaire's disease;
女軍人 servicewoman;
現役軍人 person in active service;

[軍容嚴整] the troops are in a gallant array;

[軍師] army advisor; military counsellor;
狗頭軍師 a person who offers bad advice; good-for-nothing adviser; inept adviser; villainous adviser;

[軍士] petty officer; sergeant;
軍士長 sergeant major;
專業軍士 (1) technical petty officer; (2) technical sergeant;

[軍事] military affairs;
軍事部署 military deployment;
軍事衝突 military conflict;
軍事對抗 military confrontation;
軍事法 military law;
~軍事法典 military code;
~軍事法庭 court martial; military court of justice;
~軍事法學 science of military law;
~軍事法院 military court;
軍事工程 military engineering;
軍事顧問團 military advisory group;
軍事管制 military control;
軍事海洋學 military oceanography;
軍事航天技術 military space technology;
軍事基地 military base;
軍事機關 military establishment;
軍事檢察院 military procuratorate;
軍事經濟學 military economics;
軍事擴張 military expansion;
~不搞軍事擴張 not seek for military expansion;
軍事立法 military legislation;
軍事片 military film; war film;
軍事設施 military installation;
軍事社會學 military sociology;
軍事事務 military affairs;
軍事挑衅 military provocation;
軍事心理學 military psychology;
軍事行動 military operation;
軍事學院 military academy;
軍事優勢 military advantage;
軍事援助 military assistance;
軍事長 (1) chief petty officer; (2) master sergeant;
非軍事 nonmilitary;
~非軍事區 demilitarized zone;
~非軍事人員 civilian personnel;

[軍務] military affairs; military tasks;

[軍銜] military rank;

[軍校] military academy; military school;

[軍械] armament; arms; ordnance;
軍械庫 armoury;
軍械士 armourer;
爆炸軍械 explosive ordnance;
海軍軍械 naval ordnance;
航空軍械 airborne armature; aircraft armature;

[軍心] morale of the troops; soldiers' morale;
軍心大振 the morale of the troops has been greatly raised;
軍心動搖 the morale of the troops begins to slump;
動搖軍心 demoralize the army; shake the army's morale;

[軍需] military supplies;
軍需部 commissariat;
軍需官 commissary;
軍需商店 commissary;

[軍訓] military training;

[軍醫] medical officer; military surgeon;
軍醫大學 military medical university;

[軍營] barracks; cantonment; military camps;

[軍用] for military use;
軍用包裝 military package;
軍用標準化 military standardization;
軍用電子學 military electronics;
軍用航空器 military spacecraft;
軍用機場 military airfield;
軍用衛星 military satellite;

[軍樂] military music;
軍樂大號 sousaphone;
軍樂隊 military band;

[軍長] army commander;

[軍政] military-political;

[軍裝] army uniform; military uniform;

邊防軍 frontier force;
裁軍 disarmament;
參軍 join the army;
常備軍 standing army;
充軍 banish;
從軍 join the army;
大軍 (1) huge army; main force; (2) large contingent;
地方軍 (1) local forces; regional troops;
敵軍 enemy troops; hostile forces; the enemy;

督軍 provincial military governor;
孤軍 an isolated force;
冠軍 champion;
國防軍 national defence forces;
海軍 navy;
後備軍 (1) reserves; (2) reserve force;
季軍 second runner-up; the third place;
建軍 establish an army;
將軍 (1) general; (2) high ranking officers;
進軍 advance; march;
禁軍 imperial guard;
空軍 air force;
擴軍 military expansion;
聯軍 allied forces; united army;
陸軍 army; ground force;
盟軍 allied forces;
叛軍 insurgent troops; rebel army;
生力軍 (1) fresh troops; (2) new force;
守軍 defenders; defending troops;
童子軍 boy scout;
行軍 (of troops) march;
亞軍 first runner-up; the second place;
友軍 friendly forces;
御林軍 palace guard;
援軍 reinforcements; relief troops;
正規軍 regular army;
治軍 direct military affairs; direct troops;
駐軍 garrison;

jun
【鈞】 (1) unit of weight; (2) you; your;

jun
【皸】 a chap from dryness; a crack from cold;
［皸裂］ chap;

jun
【龜】 tortoise; turtle;
［龜裂］ (1) full of cracks; (2) chap;
大氣龜裂 atmospheric cracking;

jun
【頵】 large-headed; top-heavy;

jun
【麕】 a species of roe;
［麕集］ flock together; gather; herd together;

jun⁴
jun
【俊】 (1) handsome; pretty; (2) a person of outstanding talent;
［俊傑］ hero; person of outstanding talent;
［俊美］ handsome; pretty;
［俊俏］ pretty and charming;
幽秀俊俏 elegant and graceful;
［俊秀］ handsome; of delicate beauty; pretty;

英俊 handsome; smart;

jun
【峻】 (1) high; lofty; steep; (2) harsh; rigorous; severe; stern; uncompromising;
［峻峭］ high and steep;

陡峻 high and precipitious;
高峻 high and steep;
冷峻 cold; frostly;
陰峻 dangerously steep; precipitous;
嚴峻 severe; stern;

jun
【浚】 dredge;
［浚泥船］ dredger;

疏浚 dredge;
修浚 repair and dredge;

jun
【郡】 county; prefecture;
［郡法院］ county court;
［郡首府］ county town;
［郡縣制］ the system of prefectures and counties;

jun
【捃】 collect; gather; pick up;

jun
【竣】 complete; finish;
［竣工］ complete; finish;
即將竣工 near completion;
提前竣工 be completed ahead of schedule;
己經竣工 have been brought to completion;

告竣 announce the completion of;
完竣 (of a project etc.) be completed;

jun
【菌】 (1) fungi; mushroom; (2) bacteria;
［菌根］ mycorrhiza;
［菌幕］ veil;
邊緣菌幕 marginal veil;
內菌幕 inner veil;
雙層菌幕 double veil;
［菌絲］ hypha;
菌絲體 mycelium;

J

單倍菌絲 haploid hypha;
過渡菌絲 bridging hypha;
結實菌絲 fertile hypha;
氣生菌絲 aerial hypha;

[菌種] type culture;
菌種保藏 type culture collection;

[菌株] strain;
聯合菌株 associate strain;
生態菌株 ecological strain;
有效菌株 effective strain;

[菌子] mushroom;

病菌 pathogenic bacteria;
殺菌 disinfect; sterilize;
細菌 bacterium;
真菌 fungus;

jun

【畯】 (1) official in charge of farmlands in ancient times; (2) crude; rustic;

jun

【雋】 (1) good-looking; (2) extraordinary; outstanding; talented;

jun

【濬】 (1) dig or wash a well; dredge a waterway; (2) deep; profound;

jun

【駿】 (1) fine horse; swift horse; (2) great; outstanding; (3) speedy; swift; (4) rigorous; stringent;

[駿馬] fine horse; gallant horse; steed;
駿馬常有，伯樂難求 horses able to gallop one thousand li are common, but a Bo Le is rare; much water runs by the mill that the miller knows not of;

ka¹
ka

【咖】 form used in transliteration;

［咖啡］ caffy; coffee;

咖啡杯 coffee cup;
咖啡店 coffee shop;
咖啡碟 saucer;
咖啡豆 coffee bean;
~咖啡豆研磨機 coffee grinder; coffee mill;
咖啡館 café; caff' coffee bar; coffee house;
~海濱咖啡館 seafront café;
~一家咖啡館 a café;
咖啡壺 cafetiere; coffee pot;
~大咖啡壺 coffee urn;
咖啡機 coffee machine; coffee maker;
~一台咖啡機 a coffee machine;
咖啡鹼 caffeine;
咖啡精 coffee extract;
咖啡具 coffee set;
咖啡拉花 latte-art;
咖啡片 coffee flake;
咖啡色 coffee; coffee colour;
咖啡師 barista;
咖啡室 coffee room;
咖啡酸 caffeic acid;
咖啡糖 coffee candies;
咖啡廳 coffee shop;
咖啡碗 coffee cup;
咖啡香油 caffeol;
咖啡因 caffeine;
~不含咖啡因［的］ decaffeined;
咖啡渣 coffee grounds;
咖啡種植園 cafetal; coffee farm;
咖啡桌 coffee table;
冰涷咖啡 iced coffee;
冰鎮咖啡 iced coffee;
沖咖啡 make coffee;
喝咖啡 drink coffee;
喝杯咖啡 have a cup of coffee;
即溶咖啡 instant coffee;
淨咖啡 black coffee;
摩卡咖啡 mocha;
牛奶咖啡 milky coffee; white coffee;
濃咖啡 black coffee; strong coffee;
濃縮咖啡 expresso;
泡沫咖啡 cappuccino; frothy coffee;
拋光咖啡 glazed coffee;
清咖啡 black coffee;
熱奶沫咖啡 caffe latte;
熱一下咖啡 warm up some coffee;
生咖啡 green coffee;
速溶咖啡 instant coffee;
淡咖啡 mild coffee; weak coffee;
一杯咖啡 a cup of coffee;
一大杯咖啡 a mug of coffee;
一罐咖啡 a jar of coffee;
煮好的咖啡 brewed coffee;
煮咖啡 make coffee;

［咖啡因］ caffeine;

脱咖啡因的 decaf; decaffeinated;

ka

【喀】 character used for transliterating;

ka

【擖】 scrape off with a knife;

［擖哧］ (1) scrape off with a knife;
(2) discharge sb from office; dismiss; fire; replace;

［擖油］ abuse a previlege; profit at sb's expense; take advantage of sb;

ka³
ka

【卡】 (1) card; cardboard; (2) an abbreviated form for calorie; (3) guardhouse; (4) check point; customs barrier; roadblock; (5) block; check;

［卡車］ autotruck; lorry; truck;

翻斗卡車 skip lorry;
後卸式卡車 rear dump lorry;
攪拌機卡車 agitator truck;
絕熱卡車 insulated lorry;
軍用卡車 army lorry; military motor lorry;
履帶卡車 crawler truck;
平板卡車 flat bed lorry;
傾卸卡車 tipping lorry;
拖運卡車 haul truck;
運輸卡車 haulage truck;
一隊卡車 a fleet of trucks;
一輛卡車 a lorry;

［卡嗒聲］ click;

［卡片］ card; fiche;

卡片目錄 card catalogue; card index;
~卡片目錄櫃 card catalogue cabinet;
卡片索引 card index;
超級卡片 hypercard;
檢查卡片 check card;
控制卡片 control card;
文摘卡片 abstracts card;
一疊卡片 a pile of cards;

一張卡片 a card;
組合卡片 composite card;
作業卡片 assignment card;

[卡盤] chuck;

[卡鉗] calipers;
測管厚卡鉗 pipe calipers;
彈簧接合卡鉗 spring-joint calipers;
彈簧卡鉗 spring calipers;
彈簧內卡鉗 inside spring calipers;
彈簧外卡鉗 outside spring calipers;
內卡鉗 internal calipers;
內外卡鉗 combination calipers; hermaphrodite calipers;
通用卡鉗 leg calipers;
外卡鉗 outside calipers;
彎腳卡鉗 compass calipers;
移動內卡鉗 inside transfer calipers;

[卡通] cartoon;

[卡紙] cardboard;

[卡住] get stuck; seize;

大卡 kilocalorie; large calorie;
吊卡 elevator;
毫卡 millicalorie;
克卡 gram calorie;
千卡 kilocalorie;

ka

【咳】 cough up;

[咳血] cough up blood;

ka4

ka

【喀】 character used for transliterating;

[喀嚓] crack; snap;

kai1

kai

【揩】 clean; dust; rub; scrub; wipe;

[揩布] file;

[揩乾] wipe up;

[揩油] (1) find pickings; get petty advantages at the expense of other people; get what one wants by taking it without permission or by trickery; make some outside gains; scrounge; (2) take advantage of a woman;

kai

【開】 (1) on; open; turn on; (2) make an opening; open up; reclaim; (3) drive; operate; pilot; run; start; (4) move; set out; (5) run; set up; (6) begin; start; (7) hold; (8) draw; make out; write out; (9) boil; (10) percentage; proportion;

[開辦] establish; found; open; set up; start;
開辦費 organization cost;
開辦一家企業 launch a new enterprise;
開辦一所學校 set up a school; start a school;

[開本] book size; format;
八開本 octavo;
對開本 quarto;
六開本 sexto;
六十四開本 64-mo; sixty-fourmo;
三十二開本 32-mo; thirty-twomo;
十八開本 18-mo; octodecimo;
十六開本 16-mo; sextodecimo;
四開本 quarto;

[開閉] open and close;
眼開眼閉 close one's eyes to; pretend not to see; purposely overlook; turn a blind eye to;

[開標] open bids;

[開採] extract; exploit; mine; mining; recover;
開採法 mining;
~多水平開採法 horizon mining;
~選擇性開採法 selective mining;
開採煤炭 cut coal; mine coal;
開採石油 recover petroleum;
開採天然氣 extract natural gas; tap natural gas;
乾法開採 dry mining;
河牀開採 river mining;
自動化開採 automated mining;

[開場] begin; open; opening of a show; start;
開場白 gambit; introductory remarks; lead-in; opening remarks; opening speech; preliminary remarks;

[開車] drive a car;
開車飛馳 speed off;
開車回來 drive back;
開車離開 drive away;
開車去上班 go to work by car;
開車送人回家 drive sb home; give sb a lift;
學開車 learn how to drive;

[開誠] come into the open;
開誠布公 as open as the day; come into the open; frank and sincere; heart to heart; open one's heart to; open out; open-breasted; open-hearted; perfectly

frank; unbosom oneself; utter one's thoughts in sincerity and without reserve; wear one's heart upon one's sleeve; with an open heart;
開誠相見 deal with sb in all sincerity; frank and open; frank with sb; meet sb in sincerity; treat sb open-hearted; unbosom oneself to sb;

[開出] draw out;

[開除] boot out; cast out; dismiss; discharge; drum out; expel; fire; fire out; give sb the axe; give sb the boot; hoot out; kick out; sack; send away; send down; send off; standoff; strike off the rolls; turn out;
開除公職 discharge sb from public employment; take sb's name off the books;
開除學籍 expel sb from the school;
被開除 be dismissed; be expelled from; be sacked; get the push; get the sack;

[開船] sail; set sail;

[開創] inception; found; initiate; open; pioneer; set up;
開創新紀元 open a new epoch;
開創新局面 create a new situation; open up a new prospect;
開創性的 ground-breaking; seminal;
開創一個新時代 create a new era;

[開大] turn up;
把電視開大 turn up the TV;
把暖氣開大 turn up the heating;
把音樂開大 turn up the music;

[開刀] (1) have an operation; operate on; perform an operation; (2) make sb the first target of attack; punish;
給病人開刀 operate on a patient;

[開導] educate and enlighten; enlighten; explain and make sb understand; give guidance to; help sb to see what is right or sensible; help sb to straighten out his wrong or muddled thinking;

[開燈] turn on the light;

[開動] (1) bring into action; bring into operation; call into action; set in motion; start; (2) march; move; on the move;
開動機器 set the machine in motion;
開動腦筋 set one's wits to work; sharpen one's wits; use one's brains; use one's head;
開動宣傳機器 set the propaganda machine in motion;
開動一下腦筋 use your brain;

[開端] beginning; commence; commencement; inception; open end; start;
取得良好的開端 get off to a flying start;
一個吉祥的開端 an auspicious beginning;

[開恩] bestow favours; have mercy on; grant special favour to; show mercy;
哀求開恩 beseech sb for mercy;

[開發] develop; exploit; open up;
開發機構 development institution;
開發機制 build engine;
開發礦山 open out the mine;
開發區 development zone;
~經濟技術開發區 an economic and technological development zone;
~經濟開發區 economic development zone;
開發軟件 develop software;
開發山區 develop mountain areas;
開發系統 development system;
開發銀行 development bank;
開發自然資源 exploit natural resources;
開發智力 tap intellectual resources;
等待開發 await development;
水力開發 water power development;
土地開發 land development;

[開飯] serve a meal;
開飯了 the meal is ready;

[開放] (1) come into bloom; (2) lift a ban; lift a restriction; open to the outside world; open to public use; open to the public; open to traffic;
開放城市 open city;
開放詞類 open word-class;
開放港口 open port;
開放合作環境 open a collaboration environment;
開放經濟理論 open economy theory;
開放類詞 open-class word;
開放日 open day; open house;
開放式計算站 open computing station;
開放時間 opening hours;
開放數據庫 open database;
開放思想 open up one's mind;
開放系統 open system;
~開放系統互連 open systems interconnection;
~開放系統經濟論 theory of open system

economy;
~開放系統經濟學 open system economics;
~開放系統體系結構 open system architecture;
~開放系統組織理論 theory of open-system organization;
開放型 open;
~開放型大學 open university;
~開放型經濟區 open-door economic zone;
~開放型企業 open enterprises;
開放性搭配 open collocation;
不開放 not open;
~圖書館星期天不開放 the library does not open on Sundays;
對外開放 open to the outside world;
~全方位對外開放 open to the outside world in all directions;
改革開放 reform and opening-up;
加快開放 speed up the pace of opening-up;
擴大開放 open China wider to the outside world;
向公眾開放 open to the public;
性格開放 of a liberal disposition;
照常開放 open as usual;

[開赴] march to;
開赴前線 march to the front;

[開關] (1) switch; (2) switch (for an electric lamp);
開關鍵 on-off switch;
安全開關 safety switch;
變換開關 alter switch;
撥動開關 toggle switch;
電燈開關 lamp switch; light switch;
定時開關 time switch;
進入開關 access switch;
空氣開關 air-break switch;
天線開關 aerial switch;
主控開關 master switch;
自動開關 auto-switch;
總開關 master switch;

[開罐器] can opener;

[開工] (1) go into operation; put into operation; start operation; (2) begin construction; start;
開工不足 be operating under capacity;
開工率 rate of operation;

[開國] found a state;
開國大典 ceremony to proclaim the founding of a state; founding ceremony of a state;
開國元勛 founder of the state; founding father of a country;

[開戶] establish an account; open an account;
在銀行開戶 open an account with the bank; start an account at a bank;

[開花] (1) bloom; blossom; come into flower; flower; in bloom; in flower; (2) explode;
開花結果 bloom and bear fruit; blossom and yield fruit — yield positive results;
遍地開花 a mass of flowers; blossom everywhere; flowers are blossoming everywhere; spring up all over the place;
墻裏開花墻外香 one's accomplishments are easily known outside his own unit;

[開化] become civilized; civilized;
半開化 semicivilized;

[開懷] joyful; jubilant; to one's heart's content;
開懷暢談 have a great delightful talk together; have a pleasant conversation;
開懷暢飲 drink freely with great joviality; drink heartily; drink to one's heart's content; go on a drinking spree; have a hearty drink;
開懷大笑 belly-laugh; gales of laughter
開懷歡飲 drink hob nob; hobnob together;

[開荒] cultivate virgin land; open up wasteland; reclaim wasteland;
開荒墾植 open up wasteland for farming; reclaim wasteland and plough new soil;

[開會] attend a conference; attend a meeting; call a meeting; convene a meeting; go to a meeting; have a meeting; hold a meeting; meet;
開會時間 time for a meeting;
~約定開會時間 appoint a time for the meeting;
正在開會 at the meeting;

[開火] engage in battle; fire; open fire;

[開豁] (1) open and clear; (2) with one's mental outlook broadened;

[開價] bid price; make a price; make a quotation; state a price;

[開獎] draw the winning numbers of a lottery; run a lottery;

[開解] straighten one out and ease out his anxiety;

[開禁] lift a ban; rescind a prohibition;

[開卷] begin to read a book; open a book;
開卷考試 an open-book examination;
開卷有益 it is advantageous to open a book to read; reading enriches the mind; reading gives advantages; reading is always profitable; there are always advantages in reading books; there is profit in reading books;

[開課] (1) school begins; start class at the beginning of a new semester; (2) deliver a course; give a course; teach a subject;

[開墾] break ground; bring under cultivation; cultivate; open up wasteland for farming; reclaim wasteland;

[開口] begin to speak; open one's mouth; start to talk;
開口閉口 every time when one opens one's mouth; whenever one speaks;
開口罵人 break into abuse; use abusive language;
開口傷人 offend by rude remarks; use bad language to insult people;
開口説話 lift up one's voice; loosen sb's tongue;
開口笑 deep-fried dough cake;
難以開口 be too embarrassed to say sth; have a bone in the throat;

[開闊] broad open; wide;
開闊的廣場 open square;
開闊的街道 broad street;
開闊的原野 wild open fields;
開闊路面 widen a road;
開闊思路 expand one's mind;
開闊心胸 broaden one's mind;
開闊眼界 broaden one's outlook; broaden one's horizons; widen one's field of vision;

[開朗] (1) clear up; open and clear; (2) optimistic; sanguine;
心情開朗 cheerful;
性格活潑開朗 have a cheerful temperament;
性格開朗 of a sanguine disposition;

[開例] create a precedent;

[開練] (1) start working; (2) come to blows; fight; scuffle;

[開列] draw up a list; list; make a list;
開列名單 make a list of names;
開列清單 draw up a list; make an inventory;
開列如下 as listed below;

[開路] blaze a trail; break a fresh path; open a new road; open a way;
開路人 trailblazer;
開路先鋒 pathbreaker; pathfinder; pioneer; trailblazer; trailbreaker;
逢山開路，遇水搭橋 cut paths through the mountains and build bridges across the rivers;

[開鑼] begin performance;

[開門] answer the door; open the door; push plate;
開門辦學 carry out open-door education; conduct open-door schooling; run classes in an open-door way;
開門紅 get off to a flying start; get off to a good start; let the beginning of the year be crowned with achievements; make a flying start; make a good beginning; start the season off with a bang;
開門見山 come to the point; cut the cackle and come to the horses; declare one's intentions immediately; no beating about the bush; put it bluntly; say point-blank; straight out; without preamble;
開門揖盜 invite disaster by letting in evil-doers; invite trouble upon oneself by letting in evil persons; lay one's house open to theft; open the door and invite the robber in; open the door to robbers; set the wolf to keep the sheep; that's like putting the cat near the goldfish bowl; throw the door open for the robbers;
你們幾點開門 what time do you open;

[開明] enlightened; liberal; liberality; open-minded;
開明的思想 liberal ideas;
開明人士 enlightened person; liberal;
見解開明 liberal in views;
思想開明 liberal in thought;

[開幕] (1) begin the performance; the curtain rises; (2) inaugurate; open;
開幕典禮 founding ceremony; inauguration ceremony; opening

ceremony;
開幕式 opening ceremony;
[開拍] camera;
[開闢] (1) break; hew out; (2) develop; open up;
開闢航線 open an air route;
開闢專欄 start a special column;
[開瓶] open the bottle;
開瓶費 corkage;
~收取開瓶費 charge the corkage;
開瓶器 bottle opener;
[開啟] open; usher in;
開啟新時代 usher in a new era;
[開槍] fire; fire with a rifle; shoot;
[開腔] begin to speak; open one's mouth;
[開竅] be enlightened; begin to understand; have one's ideas straightened out;
[開球] kick off; open ball; open sphere; start the game; tee off;
[開山] cut into the mountain;
開山鼻祖 the earliest founder; the first person to do sth; the originator;
開山祖師 the founder of a religious sect;
[開設] establish; found; open; set up;
開設一門新課程 introduce a new course into the curriculum; offer a new course;
開設醫院 establish a hospital;
[開審] sit at session; start the trial;
[開始] at the outset; be set on foot; be the beginning of; begin; commence; commencement; enter on; enter upon; fall to; get one's feet wet; get started; in the outset; initial; lead off; set about; set in; set on foot; set one's hands to; set out; set sth on foot; start; start in; strike up; take to; take up;
開始辦公 start work;
開始出名 come into repute;
開始從政 enter into politics;
開始的時候 at first; at the start;
開始經商 enter into business;
開始流行 come into vogue;
開始生效 come into effect;
開始體 ingressive aspect;
開始新生活 start a new life;
從零開始 start from scratch; start from the very beginning; start from zero;
從甚麼時候開始 since when...;
從一開始 at the beginning; at the outset; at the start; from the beginning; from the first; from the ground up; from the outset; from the very beginning; from the very first; in the beginning;
重頭開始 start from scratch;
重新開始 begin afresh; make a new start; start afresh; start anew; start over;
剛一開始 right from the start;
好的開始是成功的一半 a good beginning is half the battle; a good beginning makes a good ending; good to begin well, better to end well; the first blow is half done; well begun is half done; well begun is half the battle;
立即開始 start at once;
現在開始 starting from now; starting now;
一開始 to start with;
有一個良好的開始 get off to a good start;
[開市] (1) open the market; (2) first transaction of a day's business;
[開涮] make a fool of; make fun of;
[開水] (1) boiling water; (2) boiled water;
開水淋臭蟲─不死也夠受 a bedbug under a shower of fresh boiling water – unbearably painful;
白開水 plain boiled water;
涼開水 cold boiled water;
燒開水 boil water;
溫開水 lukewarm boiled water;
[開司米] cashmere;
[開庭] hold a court; open a court session;
[開通] broad-minded; enlightened; liberal; open-minded;
[開頭] at the beginning; begin; make a start; start;
開頭萬事難 the first step is always difficult;
[開脫] absolve; exculpate; exonerate; vindicate;
[開拓] continuation; open; prolongation; reclaim;
開拓海外市場 open the overseas market;
開拓荒地 reclaim wasteland;
開拓精神 pioneering spirit;
開拓進取 forge ahead;
開拓前進 advance in a pioneering spirit;
開拓沙漠 reclaim desert;
開拓者 pathfinder; pioneer;
解析開拓 analytic continuation; analytic prolongation;
調和開拓 harmonic continuation;

唯一開拓 unique continuation;

[開挖] excavate; excavation;
乾開挖 dry excavation;
橋基開挖 bridge excavation;
人工開挖 hand excavation;

[開外] above; more than; over;

[開往] be bound for; leave for;

[開胃] appetizing; piquant; stimulate one's appetite; whet the appetite;
開胃菜 entrée;
開胃的食品 appetizing food;
開胃酒 aperitif;
開胃小吃 appetizer; starter;

[開箱] open sb's boxes;
開箱倒柜 open sb's boxes and trunks and turn out the contents;
開箱倒籠 a thorough search; open one's boxes and cases and turn everything inside out; turn the boxes and cases upside down;

[開銷] expenditure; expense; pay expenses;
日常開銷 daily expenses; running expenses;
支付開銷 meet an expense;

[開小差] abscond; absence without leave; absent-minded; decamp; desert; desertion; go over the hill; jump the track; malinger; skulk away; slink away; sneak off; woolgathering;
思想開小差 absent-minded; woolgathering;

[開心] feel happy; full of glee; get a kick; in high glee; make joy; rejoice; take joy;
開心見誠 expose one's feelings; talk from the heart, with nothing concealed; wear one's heart upon one's sleeve;
不開心 (1) displeased; in low spirits; out of humour; unhappy; (2) feel under the weather; indisposed; out of sorts;
非常開心 be tickled pink; chuffed; overjoyed; very happy;
~玩得非常開心 have the time of one's life;
很開心 have a barrel of fun; very happy;
拿別人開心 amuse oneself at other people's expense; make fun of sb;
窮開心 enjoy moments of happiness even in poverty; enjoy oneself despite poverty; extremely happy; try to be happy amidst sorrow;
玩得開心 enjoy oneself; have a good time; have a great time; have a nice time;
尋開心 amuse oneself at sb's expense; joke; make fun of sb;

[開學] school opens; term begins;
開學禮 inauguration ceremony;
~本科生開學禮 inauguration ceremony for undergraduates;

[開顏] beam; smile;
開顏暢飲 smile and drink heartily;
喜笑顏開 a face lit up with pleasure; a face wreathed in smiles; all smiles; an ear-to-ear grin; beaming with smiles; cheerful;
喜逐顏開 a joyful countenance; be wreathed in smiles; beam with smiles; light up with pleasure;

[開眼] add to one's experience; broaden one's mind; broaden one's view; enrich one's experience; open one's eyes; open one's mental horizon; see new things; see the world; widen one's horizons; widen one's view;
開眼界 enrich one's experience; see the world; widen one's horizon; widen one's vision;

[開演] start a performance;

[開洋葷] enjoy a foreign lifestyle; enjoy foreign food;

[開業] (1) go into operation; open for business; set up shop; start business; (2) open a private practice;
獨立開業 private practice;
聯合開業 group practice;
明天開業 will open for business tomorrow;
私人開業 private practice;

[開雲見日] the clouds disperse and the sun appears;

[開展] (1) carry out; develop; launch; promote; unfold; (2) open-minded; politically progressive;
開展…運動 carry on...campaign; launch...movement;
~開展群眾運動 launch a mass movement;

[開戰] (1) make war; open hostilities; (2) battle;

[開張] (1) begin doing business; open a business; (2) first transaction of a day's business; (3) wide and magnificent;

開張大吉 an auspicious beginning of a new enterprise; let great prosperity attend the opening of a shop;
開張營業 open for business;

[開診] begin to treat patients;

[開支] (1) expenditure; expenses; pay expenses; spend; spending; (2) get the pay; pay wages;
開支賬目 expenditure account;
不合法開支 backdoor spending;
家庭開支 household expenses;
節省開支 save expenses;
軍備開支 expenditure on armaments;
軍費開支 military spending;
縮減開支 keep down the expenditure;
消費性開支 consumer spending;
削減開支 curtail expenses; cut down expenses; reduce expenses;
壓縮開支 pinch one's expenditure;
營運開支 operating expenses;
應計開支 accrued expenditure;
政府開支 government spending; public spending;

[開宗明義] come straight to the point; make clear at the outset; make clear the purpose and main theme from the very beginning;

避開 keep away;
叉開 change;
岔開 (1) branch off; diverge; (2) diverge to (another topic); (3) stagger;
拆開 break up; decollate; disconnect; dismantle; open; separate; take apart; unpack;
常開 normally open;
敞開 open wide;
撐開 open; prop up;
吃不開 not in the current demand; unpopular; will not succeed; won't work;
除開 except;
傳開 get air;
吹開 set sth agape;
對開 (1) run from opposite directions; (2) divide into halves; (3) folio;
放開 let go; set free;
分開 (1) part; separate; (2) come out into the open; make known to the public; open; public;
拋開 cast aside; throw off;
撇開 bypass; leave aside;
盛開 be in full bloom;
展開 spread out; unfold;
張開 open;
召開 convene; convoke;

kai3

kai
【豈】 delighted; happy; harmonious; jubilant;

kai
【嘅】 sound of sighing;

kai
【凱】 (1) triumphant strains; (2) triumphant; victorious;

[凱歌] song of triumph; song of victory;
凱歌歸來 return with songs of triumph;
凱歌行雲 songs of victory soar to the skies;
凱歌陣陣 songs of triumph are heard all round;
一曲凱歌 a song of triumph;

[凱旋] return in triumph; with flying colours;
凱旋歸來 come back victorious; return in triump; return with drums beating and banners flying; return with flying colours; triumphant return;

奏凱 be victorious; triumphant;

kai
【剴】 sharpen a knife;

[剴切] (1) true and pertinent; (2) earnest and sincere;
剴切教導 teach earnestly;
剴切詳明 true and clear in every detail;
剴切曉諭 let all clearly understand this;

kai
【慨】 (1) indignant; (2) deeply touched; (3) generous;

[慨然] (1) with deep feeling; with emotion; (2) generously; without stint;
慨然長歎 heave a sigh of regret;
慨然相贈 give generously;

[慨歎] deplore with sighs; lament with sighs; sigh with regret;

[慨允] generously permit; generously promise;

敵慨 hatred towards the enemy;
感慨 sigh with emotion;
慷慨 (1) fervent; vehement; (2) generous; liberal;

kai
【愷】 contented; gentle; good; joyful; kind;

［愷愷君子］ delighted worthy;

kai

【楷】 (1) regular; standard; (2) model; norm; (3) the standard script;

［楷模］ good example; model; pattern;
奉為楷模 hold up as a model; look upon sth as a pattern; regard sth as an example;

［楷書］ regular script;

［楷體］ (1) regular script; (2) block letter;

大楷 (1) regular script in big characters; (2) block letters;
工楷 neat regular script;
小楷 (1) regular script in small characters; (2) lowercase;
正楷 regular script;

kai

【鍇】 refined iron;

kai

【鎧】 armour worn by a warrior;

［鎧甲］ armour; bard;

［鎧裝］ armouring;
鎧裝電纜 armoured cable;
鎧裝線夾 armour clamp;
電纜鎧裝 cable armouring;
封閉式鎧裝 closed armouring;
金屬鎧裝 metal armouring;
開式鎧裝 open armouring;
鐵絲鎧裝 iron-wire armouring;
重鎧裝 heavy armouring;

kai

【闓】 (1) open; (2) happy; harmonious; peaceful;

kai⁴

kai

【欬】 asthma and coughing;

謦欬 (1) cough; (2) talk;

kai

【愒】 idle away;

kai

【愾】 anger; enmity; hatred; wrath;

kan¹

kan

【刊】 (1) print; publish; (2) periodical; publication;

［刊碑立石］ carve and set up stone tablets;

［刊本］ edition of a book;

［刊佈］ announce through printed matter;

［刊登］ carry; publish;

［刊物］ journal; periodical; publication;
定期刊物 periodical;
~不定期刊物 non-periodical;
非法刊物 illegal publication;
內部刊物 restricted publication;
主要刊物 leading publications;

［刊行］ print and publish;

［刊載］ carry; publish;

報刊 newspapers and periodicals;
創刊 start publication;
叢刊 collection; series of books;
發刊 start the publication of a periodical;
復刊 resume publication;
副刊 supplement;
合刊 combined issue;
會刊 (1) proceedings of a conference; (2) journal of an associations;
集刊 collected papers;
季刊 quarterly;
期刊 periodical;
書刊 books and periodicals;
特刊 special issue;
停刊 stop publication;
校刊 college journal; school magazine;
旬刊 a publication appearing once every ten days;
月刊 monthly; monthly magazine;
增刊 supplement; supplementary issue;
周刊 weekly;
週刊 weekly periodical;
專刊 (1) special issue; (2) monograph;

kan

【看】 (1) look after; take care of; (2) keep under surveillance; watch closely;

［看管］ (1) attend to; look after; (2) guard; watch;
看管犯人 guard prisoners;
看管房間 look after one's room;
看管人 caretaker;

［看護］ (1) attend on; look after; nurse; take care of; tend; (2) hospital nurse; nurse;
看護病人 nurse the sick; watch a patient;
看護人 care worker;
看護者 caregiver;

［看家］ (1) look after the house; mind the

house; (2) outstanding ability; special skill;
看家本领 one's speciality;
看家狗 house dog; watch dog;

［看門］ (1) act as a doorkeeper; guard the entrance; (2) look after the house;
看門人 commissionaire; doorkeeper; doorman; gatekeeper; janitor; watchman;

［看人］ judge people;
狗眼看人 judge people by wealth and power; treat people with snobbish attitude;
~狗眼看人低 act like a snob; judge sb by wealth and power; look down on sb; snobbish;

［看守］ (1) guard; watch; (2) goaler; guard; jailor; keeper; turnkey; warder;
看守倉庫 guard a storehouse;
看守犯人 guard prisoners;
看守人 keeper;
~公園看守人 park keeper;
看守員 watcher;
~道口看守員 crossing watcher;
擺脱看守 break away from one's guards;
派人看守 set a watch on;
嚴密看守 closely guard;

［看台］ stand;
大看台 grandstand;
露天看台 bleachers;

［看頭］ sth worth seeing;
沒看頭 nothing interesting to see;

［看押］ detain; keep under detention; take into custody;

［看中］ settle on; take a fancy;

［看住］ watch closely;

［看作］ be considered as; be regarded as; be thought of as; be viewed as; consider...as; look on...as; regard...as; take...as; think of...as; view...as;

飽看 feast one's eyes on; read to one's heart's content;
別看 despite; in spite of;
不管你怎麼看 say what you like;
參看 (1) cf.; see also; (2) consult; (3) read for reference;
查看 check; examine; have a look; look about; look at; look into; look over; look up; make sure; see; see about;
察看 look carefully at; observe; watch;
呆呆地看 gawk;
翻看 leaf through;
觀看 view; watch;
好看 (1) good-looking; handsome; nice; (2) interesting; (3) be honoured; do credit to; (4) deliberately embarrass sb; in a fix; in an embarrassing situation; on the spot;
快來看 roll up;
來看 see from;
難看 as ugly as a scarecrow; as ugly as a toad; bad-looking; ugly; ugly-looking;
竊看 look at sth stealthily; peep;
試看 try and see;
收看 watch;
偷看 act Peeping Tom; peep; steal a glance; steal a look;
望看 respect;
細看 examine in detail; look at carefully;
相看 (1) look at each other; (2) appraise each other;
向前看 look ahead;
小看 belittle; distain; look down on; make light of; slight; think little of; treat lightly;
眼看 (1) imminent; in a moment; soon; (2) see sth happening; (3) look on passively; watch helplessly;
驗看 examine; take a close look;
一看 at a glance;
依我看 for my money;
照看 attend to; keep an eye on; look after;
照看 attend to; keep an eye on; look after;

kan

【勘】 (1) collate; read and correct the text of; (2) investigate; survey;

［勘測］ survey;

［勘查］ prospecting;

［勘察］ (1) survey; (2) prospecting;

［勘探］ prospect; prospecting;
勘探者 prospector;
地質勘探 geological prospecting;
電磁勘探 electromagnetic prospecting;
電法勘探 electrical prospecting;

［勘誤］ corrigendum;

［勘驗］ inquest;

［勘正］ proofread and correct;

查勘 prospect; survey;
校勘 collate;
踏勘 make an on-the-spot survey;
探勘 explore;

kan

【堪】 (1) can; may; (2) bear; endure;
［堪輿］ geomancy;
堪輿師 geomancer;
堪輿先生 geomancer;

不堪 cannot bear; cannot stand;
難堪 (1) embarrassed; (2) hard to endure; intolerable;

kan

【戡】 (1) put down; subdue; suppress; (2) kill; slay;
［戡亂］ put down a rebellion; suppress a rebellion;
戡亂平反 put down a rebellion;
［戡平］ succeed in suppressing a rebellion;

kan

【龕】 niche for an idol; shrine;
［龕室］ ciborium;

壁龕 niche;
佛龕 niche for a statue of the Buddha;
神龕 shrine for ancestral tablets;

kan³

kan

【坎】 (1) bank; ridge; (2) hole; pit;
［坎兒］ (1) barrier; obstacle; (2) code; enigmatic language;
［坎坷］ bumpy; rough;
坎坷不平 rough and bumpy;
坎坷一生 a lifetime of frustrations;
一生坎坷 a lifetime of frustrations; have hard luck all one's life;

門坎 threshold;
石坎 (1) flood control stone ridge; (2) steps cut on a rocky mountain;
心坎 (1) bottom of one's heart; (2) innermost being;

kan

【侃】 (1) chat; (2) boast; (3) bold; frank; straightforward; (4) amiable; pleasant; (5) with confidence and composure; (6) smooth talk;
［侃大山］ chat;
［侃價］ bargain; haggle with a peddler;
［侃侃］ (speak) with fervour and assurance;
侃侃而談 speak freely and frankly; speak with fervour and assurance; talk with ease and fluency;
［侃星］ (1) chatterbox; (2) great boaster;
［侃爺］ big talker;

調侃 mock up sb; ridicule;

kan

【砍】 (1) chop; cut; fell; hack; (2) throw at;
［砍柴］ chop firewood;
砍柴打草 chop firewood; cut firewood;
［砍刀］ chopper;
大砍刀 broadsword;
［砍倒］ fell;
［砍斷］ break apart by chopping; cut in two;
［砍伐］ fell trees;
［砍價］ beat down the price; cut down the price;
大幅砍價 slash a price;
［砍肉］ cut up meat;
砍肉刀 cleaver;
［砍鐵如泥］ the sword would but clean through iron as though it were mud;
［砍頭］ behead; chop off the head; decapitate;
［砍削］ chop back;

kan

【欿】 (1) discontented with oneself; (2) sad and gloomy;

kan

【檻】 door-sill; threshold;
［檻梁］ sill beam;

門檻 threshold;

kan

【闞】 (1) peep; spy; steal a glance; watch secretly; (2) a surname;

kan

【轗】 (of vehicles) proceed with difficulty;

kan⁴

kan

【看】 (1) look at; see; watch; (2) read; (3) consider; think; (4) call on visit; go to see; (5) treat; (6) look after; (7) depend on;
［看病］ consult a doctor; go to see a doctor; see a doctor;
去醫院看病 go to hospital; go to the hospital;

K

K

[看不慣] cannot bear the sight of; detest; disdain; frown on; hate to see;

[看不起] despise; hold in contempt; look down on; scorn;
看不起窮人 look down on the poor;
看不起人 look down on people;
看得起 have a good opinion of; think highly of; think much of;

[看出] aware of; find out; make out; perceive; see;
看出苗頭 feel the pulse; find out which way the wind blows; get the scent of sth; smell a rat;
看不出 unable to detect;

[看穿] penetrate; see through;
看穿別人的把戲 see through sb's little game;
看穿別人的詭計 see through sb's tricks;
一眼看穿 see through at a glance; see through with a discerning eye;

[看待] look upon; regard; treat;
不要把我當小孩看待 don't' treat me like a child;
另眼看待 devote special attention to; give sb a special treatment; keep an eye on; treat sb with special respect;

[看到] (1) catch sight of; see; (2) aware of; note; notice;

[看法] perspective; view; way of looking at a thing;
看法問題 a matter of opinion;
看法一樣 share sb's view;
看法一致 see eye to eye;
持相同的看法 hold the same view;
發表看法 ventilate one's views;
那是你的看法 that's what you think;
一種看法 an idea; an opinion;

[看風駛舵] adapt oneself to circumstances; change course for convenience; climb on the bandwagon; cut the rudder to the wind; jump on the bandwagon; see how the cat jumps; see how the gander hops; see which way the wind blows; serve the time; steer according to the wind; test which way the wind blows; trim one's sails; veer with the wind; wait for the cat to jump;

[看風轉舵] change course for convenience; cut the rudder to the wind;

[看慣] accustomed to seeing; used to seeing;

[看好] have a bright future; have good prospects; stand a good chance of success;

[看花] look at flowers;
看花容易栽花難 flowers are pleasant to look at but difficult to grow;
霧裏看花 have a blurred vision; look at flowers in a fog; see flowers through a mist — see indistinctly;

[看見] at the sight of; catch glimpse of; catch sight of; clap eyes on; come in sight of; get glimpse of; get sight of; have sight of; lay eyes on;
看得見 noticeable; tangible; visible;
親眼看見 see with one's own eyes; witness;

[看看] (1) take a look at; watch; (2) call on; (3) wait;
看看再說 let's wait and see;
好好看看 take a good look at;
親眼看看 see for oneself;
下去看看 go down to have a look;
再看看 take another look at;

[看來] from all appearances; it appears; it looks as if; it looks like; it seems; most probably;
看來要下雨 it looks like raining;
從外表看來 judging by one's appearance;
從已知的情況看來 judging by what is know;
依我看來 in my judgement; in my view; to me;
在我看來 the way I see it; to my way of thinking;

[看破] see through;
看破紅塵 be disillusioned with this human world; see through the emptiness of the material world; see through the vanity of life; see through the vanity of the world; understand and despise worldly affairs; world-weary;

[看齊] (1) dress; (2) emulate; follow the example of; keep abreast with; keep up with; measure up to;

[看輕] look down upon; underestimate;

[看清] (1) see clearly; (2) realize;
看清形勢 make a correct appraisal of the situation; realize the situation;

[看上] like; settle on; take a fancy to;
看上去 have the look of;

[看書] read a book;
愛看書 be fond of reading;
[看透] (1) gain an insight into; understand thoroughly; (2) be resigned to what is inevitable; know clearly; see through;
看透心事 see though what sb has in mind;
[看頭] sth worth seeing;
[看望] call on; look-in; see; visit;
看望傷病者 visit the wounded and sick;
[看戲] see a movie;
[看相] practice physiognomy;
[看着吧] just wait and see;
[看中] be interested in; feel satisfied with; prefer; settle on; take a fancy to;
一眼看中 become infatuated with sb at first sight;
[看重] regard as important; set store by; think highly of; value;
[看朱成碧] take red for green—be dazzled; cannot distinguish colours due to a confused mind;
[看作] look upon as; regard as; take as;
看作洪水猛獸 see sth as dangerous as a deluge or wild beasts;

別看 despite; in spite of;
參看 (1) see; (2) consult; (3) read sth for reference;
查看 examine; look over;
察看 observe; watch;
觀看 view; watch;
好看 (1) good-looking; (2) interesting; (3) in an embarrassing situation; on the spot;
難看 (1) ugly; unsightly; (2) embarrassing; shameful;
試看 try and see;
收看 watch;
踏看 go to the spot to make an investigation;
偷看 peep; steal a glance at;
小看 belittle; look down upon;
眼看 look on passively; watch helplessly;
中看 be pleasant to the eye;

kan

【勘】 (1) check; examine; explore; investigate; (2) collate; compare critically;
[勘測] survey;
[勘察] examine; inspect; investigate;
[勘合] stamp the edges of two separate documents with a seal for being identified;
[勘量] measure; survey;
[勘探] exploration; prospecting;
勘探地震學 exploration seismology;
[勘誤] collate; correct errors;
勘誤表 corrigenda; errata;
[勘驗] check; examine;
[勘災] inspect a disaster area;

kan

【瞰】 (1) spy; watch; (2) overlook;

俯瞰 look down at; overlook;
鳥瞰 get a bird's-eye view;

kan

【闞】 (1) peep; spy; steal a glance; (2) growl; roar; (3) brave; (4) a surname;

kan

【矙】 (1) spy; watch; (2) look downward; overlook;

kang[1]
kang

【康】 (1) health; well-being; (2) a surname;
[康復] convalesce; get well; on the mend; recover; restored to health;
康復工程 rehabilitation engineering;
康復計劃 recovery programme;
康復期 (1) convalescence; (2) recovery period;
~康復期病人 convalescent;
康復器械 recovering apparatus and instruments;
康復醫學 recovery medicine;
康復醫院 convalescent home; convalescent hospital; nursing home;
康復中心 rehabilitation centre;
~殘疾人康復中心 rehabilitation centre for the disabled;
祝你早日康復 get well soon;
[康健] healthy; in good health;
[康樂] (1) healthy and happy; (2) recreational;
[康乃馨] carnation;
[康寧] healthy and undisturbed;
[康泰] in good health;

安康 in good health;
健康 health; healthy; in good shape; sound;
小康 comparatively well-off;

kang

【慷】
[慷慨] generous; liberal; magnanimous;

unselfish;
慷慨悲憤 be impassioned by lamentation and indignation;
慷慨悲歌 chant in a heroic but mournful tone;
慷慨陳詞 give it mouth; present one's views vehemently; speak in excitement;
慷慨成仁 die heroically in battle; sacrifice one's life heroically for justice;
慷慨大方 generous; very generous and hospitable;
慷慨好施 liberal in giving;
慷慨激昂 express with deep feelings and enthusiasm; full of noble sentiments; gallantly and wrathfully; impassioned; in lofty and energetic spirits; in powerful tones; out of the fullness of one's heart; vehement; with strong emotion;
~慷慨激昂的 declamatory;
慷慨解囊 give alms liberally; give generously of one's money; help sb generously with money; liberal of one's money; loosen one's purse strings; loosen up; make generous contributions; put one's hand in one's pocket;
~慷慨解囊的人 bountiful giver;
慷慨就義 die a hero; die a martyr's death; go to one's death fearlessly; go to one's death like a hero; sacrifice one's life heroically for a cause;
慷慨捐輸 generously contribute funds;
慷慨樂助 volunteer to contribute money;
慷慨輸將 make liberal contributions;
慷慨仗義 act in a just and generous manner; just and generous;
慷他人之慨 cut a large thong of another man's leather; cut thongs of other man's hides; free with other's money; generous at the expense of others; rob Peter to pay Paul;

kang
【糠】 (1) husks of rice; rice bran or chaff; (2) empty inside; not sturdy; of inferior quality; things of no value;

秕糠 (1) chaff; (2) worthless stuff;
稻糠 rice chaff;
礱糠 rice chaff;
米糠 rice bran;
篩糠 shiver;
糟糠 distillers' grains; foodstuffs for the poor;

kang²
kang
【扛】 (1) lift; (2) bear; endure; stand; tolerate; (3) cope with; deal with; handle; (4) carry; (5) carry sth on the shoulder;
[扛夫] porter;
[扛活] work as a farm labourer;

kang³
kang
【軛】 a pronunciation of 慷;

kang⁴
kang
【亢】 (1) proud; (2) indomitable; (3) excessive;
[亢奮] extremely excited;
一陣亢奮 an adrenaline rush;

高亢 (1) loud and sonorous; resounding; (2) (of land) high; (3) arrogant; haughty;

kang
【伉】 spouse;
[伉儷] husband and wife; married couple;
伉儷情篤 they are so happily married;
伉儷情深 a married couple very much in love;

kang
【抗】 (1) combat; fight; resist; (2) defy; refuse; (3) a match for; contend with;
[抗癌] anticancer; repel cancer;
抗癌劑 anticarcinogen;
抗癌物 anticarcinogen;
[抗辯] (1) contradict; refute; speak out in one's own defense; (2) counterargument;
妨訴抗辯 plea in abatement;
[抗塵走俗] busy oneself in hankering after personal fame and gain; on constant run for worldly pursuits; wander about among political circles, seeking for a post;
[抗丁抗糧] resist
[抗敵] against the enemy;
奮起抗敵 rise against the enemy;
[抗毒] antitoxic;
抗毒素 antitoxin;

抗毒血清 antitoxic serum;

[抗旱] combat drought; fight a drought; fight against drought;

抗旱救災 combat the drought and carry out relief work;

[抗衡] act as a counterweight to; be evenly matched with; compete; contend with; match; rival;

抗衡的 countervailing;

抗衡力量論 theory of countervailing powers;

[抗洪] combat a flood; fight a flood;

[抗擊] beat back; resist; withstand;

[抗節不附] uphold one's high principles without submitting to threat;

[抗拒] defy; oppose; resist; withstand;

抗拒逮捕 resist arrest;

[抗菌] anti-bacterial; antibiotic;

抗菌處理 anti-bacterial treatment;

抗菌術 antisepsis;

抗菌素 antibiotic;

~揮發抗菌素 volatile antibiotic;

~家用抗菌素 agricultural antibiotic;

~窄譜抗菌素 narrow-spectrum antibiotic;

抗菌作用 antibacterial action;

[抗禮] equal; treat each other as equals without regard to etiquette;

[抗霉素] antimycin;

[抗生菌] antagonistic microorganism;

[抗生素] antibiotic;

廣譜抗生素 broad-spectrum antibiotic;

[抗稅] tax resistance;

[抗訴] counter appeal; counter charge; oppose an action;

[抗酸劑] antacid;

[抗體] antibody;

抗體生成 antibody formation;

保護性抗體 protective antibody;

單價抗體 univalent antibody;

多價抗體 multivalent antibody; polyvalent antibody;

反應抗體 reaginic antibody;

放射性抗體 radioactive antibody;

分泌抗體 secretory antibody;

聯胞抗體 cellbound antibody;

體液抗體 humoral antibody;

兔型抗體 rabbit type antibody;

完全抗體 complete antibody;

~不完全抗體 incomplete antibody;

血清抗體 serum antibody;

循環抗體 circulating antibody;

抑制性抗體 inhibiting antibody;

異帶抗體 heteroligating antibody;

異種抗體 herologous antibody;

熒光抗體 fluorescent antibody;

增強性抗體 enhancing antibody;

[抗炎] anti-inflammatory;

抗炎作用 anti-inflammatory action;

[抗議] object; protest; remonstrate;

抗議集會 protest rally;

抗議加稅 enter a protest against increased taxation;

抗議突然爆發 protests erupt;

抗議團體 protest group;

抗議遊行 protest march;

抗議運動 protest movement;

導致抗議 lead to protests;

發表抗議 voice a protest;

公眾抗議 popular protests;

和平抗議 peaceful protest;

激烈抗議 strongly protest;

街頭抗議 street protest;

舉行抗議 hold a protest; mount a protest; stage a protest;

絕食抗議 go on a hunger strike;

強烈抗議 hue and cry; violent protest;

學生抗議 student portest;

引發抗議 spark off protests;

政治抗議 political protests;

[抗禦] resist and defend;

[抗原] antigen;

抗原分析 antigenic analysis;

抗原性 antigenicity;

抗原血症 antigenemia;

花粉抗原 pollen antigen;

交叉反應抗原 cross reacting antigen;

結合抗原 conjugated antigen;

菌體抗原 somatic antigen;

可溶性抗原 soluble antigen;

釋放抗原 released antigen;

移植抗原 transplanatation antigen;

隱蔽抗原 sequestered antigen;

增強抗原 enhancement antigen;

腫瘤抗原 tumour antigen;

自體抗原 self antigen;

[抗戰] war of resistance against aggression;

[抗震] earthquake-resistant;

抗震建築 earthquake-proof construction; earthquake-resistant structure;

抗震救災 carry out antiquake struggle and relief work; combat the earthquake

and do relief work; combat the quake and carry out relief work;

[抗爭] contend; make a stand against; resist;

抵抗 oppose; resist;
電抗 reactance;
對抗 (1) antagonize; counter; (2) oppose; resist;
反抗 resist; revolt;
感抗 inductive reactance;
頑抗 stubbornly resist;
違抗 defy; disobey;
阻抗 impedance;

K

kang

【炕】 (1) dry; to dry; (2) hot; (3) a brick bed warmed by a fire underneath;

火炕 heated brick bed;
土炕 heatable adobe sleeping platform;

kang

【鈧】 scandium;

[鈧石] befanamite;

kao[1]

kao

【尻】 sacrum;

kao[3]

kao

【考】 (1) give or take an examination; test or quiz; (2) check; inspect; (3) investigate; study; verify;

[考妣] deceased parents;
如喪考妣 wear a funeral face as if newly bereft of both parents;

[考查] check; examine; research; test;

[考察] make an on-the-spot investigation;
考察團 commission; investigation group;

[考場] examination hall;

[考訂] do textual research; examine and correct;

[考古] archaeology;
考古測量 archaeological survey;
考古調查 archaeological investigation;
考古發掘 archaeological excavation;
考古發現 archaeological discovery;
考古工作 archaeological work;
考古學 archaeology;
~考古學家 archaeologist;
田野考古 field archaeology;

[考官] examiner;

[考核] appraise; assess; check; examine;
考核指標 assessment of performance according to fixed norms;

[考究] (1) examine closely; investigate; observe and study; (2) care about; fastidious; particular;
選料考究 choice material;

[考據] textual criticism; textual research;

[考卷] examination paper;
分發考卷 distribute examination papers;
交考卷 hand in examination papers;

[考慮] allow for; conceive of; consider; dwell on; give a thought to; give consideration to; give sth some thoughts; have sth in view; lay sth to heart; look at sth; make allowance for; ponder over; pore on; put into consideration; put on one's thinking cap; reflect on; see about; take account of; take into account; take into consideration; take to heart; think about; think of; think on; think over; turn about; under consideration;
考慮問題 consider a problem;
考慮周詳 give careful consideration to;
不予考慮 leave sb out of account; leave sth out of account;
不值得再考慮 be dead and buried;
從長遠考慮 take the long view of sth;
重新考慮 reconsider;
積極考慮 positively consider;
拒絕考慮 dismiss;
欠考慮 without due consideration;
認真考慮 consider seriously;
慎重考慮 thoughtful consideration;
~經過慎重考慮 upon a fair balance;
預先考慮 prededitation;
在考慮中 on the fire; under consideration;
整夜考慮 take counsel of one's pillow;
仔細考慮 cogitate; cogitation; take counsel with oneself;

[考前] pre-examination;
考前練習 exam practice;
考前溫習 exam revision;

[考勤] check on work attendance;
考勤簿 attendance record;
考勤單 time sheet;
考勤卡 time card;
考勤員 time keeper;
考勤鐘 time clock;

[考取] be admitted into a college after an examination; pass an entrance examination;

[考生] candidate; examinee;

[考試] examination;

考試不及格 be plucked in the examination; bomb; come a cropper; fail in an examination; fall down on; flunk in an examination;

考試成績 exam results;

考試及格 get a pass; get through an examination; go through an examination; pass an examination; scrape through; succeed in an examination;

考試技巧 exam technique;

考試考得不好 do badly in an examination;

考試考得好 do well in an examination;

考試制度 examination system;

考試作弊 cheat in examination;

標準化考試 standardized examination;

參加考試 do an examination; sit for an exam; take an examination;

高中考試 high school examinations;

公務員考試 civil service examination;

駕駛考試 driving test;

開卷考試 open-book examination;

離校考試 school-leaving examination;

模擬考試 mock; mock examination; sham examination;

期末考試 end-of-term examination;

期中考試 mid-term examination;

期終考試 end-of-term examination; final examination; term examination; terminal examination;

入學考試 admission examination; entrance examination;

書面考試 written examination;

順利通過考試 sail through the examination;

通過考試 pass an exam;

~勉強通過考試 scrape through an examination;

~順利通過考試 sail through an examination;

~未能通過考試 fail an exam;

學期考試 end-of-term examination;

學年考試 year-end examination;

學業考試 academic examination;

一次考試 an examination;

應付考試 go up for one's examination;

專業考試 professional exam;

自學考試 examination for self-taught students;

[考題] examination paper; examination question;

出考題 set an examination paper; set examination questions; set the paper;

[考問] examine orally; question;

[考驗] ordeal; test; trial;

久經考驗 long-tested; old and tried; seasoned; well-stelled;

受到考驗 meet a test; put to the test;

一次考驗 a test;

[考證] (1) textual criticism; textual research; (2) engage in textual research;

報考 enter oneself for an examination;

備考 for reference;

補考 take a make-up examination;

參考 (1) consult; refer to; (2) read sth for reference;

查考 examine; try to ascertain;

大考 end-of-term examination; final examination;

待考 remain to be verified;

高考 university entrance examination;

監考 invigilate; invigilator;

期考 end-of-term examination; terminal examination;

思考 deliberate; ponder over; think deeply;

投考 apply for entrance; sign up for an examination;

小考 mid-term examination; quiz;

應考 take an examination;

主考 be in charge of an examination; chief examiner;

kao

【拷】 beat; flog; torture;

[拷貝] copy; replica;

標準拷貝 standard copy;

傳真拷貝 facsimile copy;

靜電拷貝 xerographic copy;

軟拷貝 soft copy;

硬拷貝 hard copy;

[拷打] beat; flog; torture;

[拷問] interrogate with torture; torture sb during interrogation;

kao

【烤】 (1) bake; broil; grill; roast; toast; (2) warm by a fire;

［烤餅］ baked cake;
薄烤餅 griddle-cake;
小圓烤餅 crumpet;
［烤鵝］ roast goose;
［烤火］ warm oneself by a fire;
烤火取暖 warm oneself by the fire;
［烤雞］ roast chicken;
［烤架］ broiler; gridiron;
［烤爐］ brazier; grill; oven; roaster;
閉式烤爐 blind roaster;
電器烤爐 electric grill;
分批烤爐 batch roaster;
人工烤爐 hand-raked roaster;
［烤盤］ baking tray; hotplate;
餅乾烤盤 baking tray; cookie sheet;
烘烤盤 baking sheet;
［烤肉］ grill; roast meat; toast;
烤肉餐館 carvery;
烤肉串 kebab;
［烤箱］ oven;
對流烤箱 convection oven;
多功能烤箱 combination oven;
［烤鴨］ roast duck;

烘烤 bake; toast;

kao
【栲】 mangrove;

kao⁴
kao
【犒】 reward;
［犒勞］ give food and drink for meritorious service; reward with food and drink;
［犒賞］ reward a victorious army with bounties;
犒賞三軍 reward the soldiers for the victory; reward the troops;

kao
【銬】 handcuffs; manacles;

鐐銬 fetters and handcuffs; shackles;

kao
【靠】 (1) lean against; lean on; rest against; (2) come up to; get near; keep to; (3) near; (4) depend on; rely on; (5) trust;
［靠岸］ draw alongside; pull in shore;
［靠背］ back of a chair; backrest;
靠背椅 straight-backed chair;
［靠邊］ keep to the side;
靠邊站 get out of the way; mind your backs; stand aside; step aside;
［靠得住］ dependable; reliable; trustworthy;
講話靠得住 true in word; true to one's word;
靠不住 undependable; unreliable; untrustworthy;
［靠墊］ back cushion;
［靠近］ (1) by; close to; near; (2) approach; draw near;
別靠近 keep away;
~別靠近火 keep away from the fire;
［靠攏］ close up; draw close;
［靠山］ backer; backing; patron;
靠山傍水 fronting water and with a hill on the back; leaning against the hill and facing the river; with the hill at the back and overlooking the river;
靠山吃山，靠水吃水 if you live near the hills, you must get your living from the hill; if near water, from water – very one must look on his own calling for a living; in the mountains, one lives on mountain products; along the coast, on sea products – make a living in one's given circumstances; on the mountain one lives by mountain products, near the water one lives by the products of the sea; those living on a mountain get their living from the mountain; those near the water, from the water; those living on a mountain live off the mountain, those living near the water live off the water – make use of local resources;
靠山臨水 fronting water and with a hill on the back;
有靠山 have an influential supporter; have backing;
~背後有靠山 be well looked after by others; have sb to rely on;
［靠手］ armrest; handrest;
［靠椅］ armchair;
［靠枕］ back cushion;

挨靠 (1) depend on; dependent on; lean on; rest on; rest with; rely on; (2) at the threshold of; close to; near to; next door to;
背靠 back;
可靠 dependable; reliable; trustworthy;
停靠 stop;

投靠 go and seek refuge with sb;
妥靠 reliable; trustworthy;
依靠 depend on; rely on; sth to fall back on; support;
指靠 count on; depend on;

ke¹

ke

【刻】 carve; engrave;

ke

【柯】 (1) pasania cuspidata, a tall evergreen tree; (2) handle of an ax; (3) branch; stalk; (4) a surname;

古柯 coca;
枝柯 branch; twig;

ke

【科】 (1) branch of academic study; (2) department; section; (3) family; (4) pass a sentence;

[科班] (1) old-type opera school; (2) regular professional training;
科班出身 a professional by training; have received professional training for what one is doing;

[科場] place where imperial examinations were held;

[科幻] science;
科幻故事 science fiction story;
科幻小說 science fiction;

[科技] science and technology;
科技報告 scientific and technological reports;
科技潮 sci-tech waves;
科技成果 scientific and technological achievements;
科技詞 technical word;
科技法學 scientific and technological jurisprudence;
科技翻譯 scientific and technological translation;
~科技翻譯員 schientific and technological translator;
科技管理模式 models of scientific and technological management;
科技規範 legal norms concerning sci-tech;
科技規劃 programme for science and technology;
科技合作 sci-tech cooperation;
~科技合作協定 agreement for sci-tech cooperation;
科技激勵制度 encouragement system for science and technology;
科技獎勵 science and technology awards;
科技節 science and technology festival;
科技界 scientific and technological circles
科技進步 advances in science and technology;
科技開發 science and technology development;
~科技開發潛力 scientific and technological development potential;
科技領先 technological lead;
科技培訓 scientific and technical training;
科技評價 science and technology appraisal;
科技人才 scientific and technological talents;
~科技人才庫 database of scientific and technological talents;
~科技人才群體結構 group structure of scientific and technological talents;
科技人員 boffin;
科技示範工程 science and technology demonstration engineering;
科技術語 scientific and technological term;
科技文獻 scientific and technological text;
科技信息 sci-tech information;
~科技信息體制 sci-tech information system;
科技興國 employ science and technology to develop the country;
科技意義 scientific and technological meaning;
科技英語 English for Science and Technology
科技戰略 scientific and technological strategy;
科技咨詢 scientific and technological consulting service;
創新科技 innovative technology;
複雜科技 complex technology;
高科技 high technology; high-tech;
~高科技產業 high-tech industries;
~高科技園 high-tech park;
核科技 nuclear technology;
前沿科技 leading-edge technology;
軟件科技 software technology;
時新科技 white-hot technology;
通訊科技 communication technology;

先進科技 advanced technology;
新興科技 emerging technology;
信息科技 information technology;
引進科技 introduce technology;
引進先進科技 introduce advanced science and technology;
應用科技 apply technology;
最先進的科技 state-of-the-art technology;
最新科技 up-to-date technology;

[科間研究] interdisciplinary research;

[科教] science and education;
科教片 scientific and educational film;
科教興農 develop agriculture through science and eduction;

[科舉] civil service examination;

[科目] (1) course; subject; (2) account;
科目規劃 course planning; subject planning;
必修科目 compulsory course; compulsory subject; obligatory course; obligatory subject; required course; required subject;
翻譯科目 translation course;
基本科目 fundamental subject;
會計科目 accounting subject;
文化科目 cultural subjects;
選修科目 elective; elective course; elective subject; optional subject;
正式科目 formal subject;

[科普] popular science;
科普讀物 popular science readings;
科普片 popular science film;

[科學] science; scientific knowledge;
科學愛好者 a fan for science;
科學昌明 science is flourishing;
科學的 scientific;
~不科學的 unscientific;
科學翻譯 scientific translation;
~科學翻譯工作者 scientific translator;
科學方法論 scientific methodology;
科學工作 scientific work;
~科學工作者 scientific worker;
科學工業園區 science-based industrial zone;
科學共同體 scientific community;
科學顧問 science advisor; science consultant;
科學觀 outook on science;
~大科學觀 outlook on mega-science;
科學館 planetarium; science building;
科學技術 science and technology;
~科學技術大學 university of science and technology;
~科學技術革命 revolution for sci-tech;
~科學技術教育 scientific and technical education;
~科學技術史 history of science and technology;
科學家 boffin; scientist;
科學交流 scientific exchange;
科學界 scientific community;
科學決策 scientific decision;
科學倫理學 scientific ethics;
科學論點 scientific proposition;
科學論斷 scientific thesis;
科學論文 scientific thesis;
科學論證 scientific evidence;
科學美學 science aesthetics;
科學普及讀物 popular science literature;
科學群體意識 group consciousness of science;
科學實驗 scientific experiment;
科學試驗 scientific experiment;
科學術語 scientific term;
科學文化 science culture;
~大科學文化 mega-science culture;
科學文獻 scientific literature; scientific text;
科學心理學 psychology of science;
科學研究 scientific research;
科學儀器 scientific apparatus;
科學園 science park;
科學院 academy of sciences;
科學專欄 science column;
邊緣科學 borderline science;
超科學 super science;
促進科學 promote science;
翻譯科學 science of translation;
核子科學 nuclear science;
後科學 post-science;
環境科學 environmental science;
計算機科學 computer science;
尖端科學 advanced science;
空間科學 space science;
理論科學 abstract science;
潛科學 embryonic sciences; potential science; unestablished sciences;
軟科學 soft science;
行為科學 behavioural science;
研究科學 study science;
一門科學 a branch of knowledge; a science;
自然科學 natural science;

準科學 pre-science;
[科研] sceintific research;
科研成果 achievements in scientific research;
科研機關 scientific research institution;
科研機制 scientific research mechanism;
科研津貼 research assistantship;
科研經費 research funds;
科研開發 science and technology research development;
~ 科研開發能力 capacity for conducting research in science and technology;
科研人員 scientific research personnel;
科研項目 scientific research project;
科研院所 research institutions;
重視科研 put emphasis on scientific research;
[科員] staff member;
[科長] section chief;
副科長 deputy section chief;

本科 undergraduate course;
鼻科 nose department;
產科 maternity department; obstetrical department;
登科 pass civil examinations; receive government degrees;
兒科 department of pediatrics;
耳鼻喉科 ear-nose-throat department;
婦科 department of gynaecology;
工科 engineering course;
骨科 department of orthopaedics;
理科 science course;
泌尿科 urological department;
內科 department of internal medicine;
皮膚科 dermatological department; dermatology;
皮科 dermatological department;
傷科 department of traumatology;
神經科 department of neurology;
外科 surgical department;
文科 liberal arts;
選修科 elective;
牙科 department of dentistry;
眼科 department of ophthalmology;
醫科 medical courses;
預科 preparatory course;
專科 professional training;

ke
【苛】 exacting; severe;
[苛待] treat harshly;
[苛刻] harsh; severe;
[苛求] make excessive demands; overcritical;
苛求無厭 make excessive demands; make excuses without satiety; overcritical;
[苛責] castigate; criticize severely; denounce strongly; excoriate;
[苛政] harsh government; oppressive government; tyrannical government; tyranny;
苛政猛於虎 a bad government is more fearful than a tiger; oppressive administration is fiercer than a tiger; tyranny is even more to be dreaded than tigers; tyranny is fiercer than a tiger;

ke
【泂】 mooring stake;

ke
【珂】 stone-resembling jade;

ke
【疴】 a pronunciation of 痾 ;

ke
【棵】 numerary adjunct for trees;

ke
【軻】 (1) kind of axle; (2) the name of Mencius; (3) a surname;

ke
【稞】 grains ready for grinding; healthy grains;
[稞麥] highland barley;

ke
【窠】 (1) burrow; den; (2) nest; (3) hole; (4) dwelling for people;
[窠臼] set pattern;
不落窠臼 break away from convention; depart from the beaten track; have an original style; not follow the beaten track; not to fall into old ruts; not to get into a rut; off the beaten track; unconventional;

ke
【鈳】 columbium;

ke
【頦】 a pronunciation of 頦;

ke
【瞌】 tired and doze off;
[瞌睡] doze; drowsy; sleepy; somnolence;
瞌睡沉沉 dozing;
瞌睡蟲 drowsy person; sleepyhead;

K

瞌睡重重 heavy with sleep; nodding drowsily;
打瞌睡 doze; doze away; doze off; doze over; drop off; fall into a doze; get a wink of sleep; go off; go off into a doze; have a nap; nod; take a nap;
~想打瞌睡 feel sleepy;

K

ke

【磕】 (1) knock; (2) rap; (3) go all out; risk one's life to fight for sth;
［磕巴］ stammer; stutter;
［磕打］ knock out;
［磕磕絆絆］ bumpy; limping; stumble; walk with difficulty;
［磕磕撞撞］ reel; stumble along; walk unsteadily;
［磕蜜］ chase after girls; look for a girlfriend;
［磕碰］ bump against; collide with; knock against;
［磕頭］ kowtow;
磕頭禮拜 make obeisance and perform the rites of courtesy;
磕頭賠罪 give sb a grand kowtow and apologize;
磕頭碰腦 bump against things on every side; push and bump against one another;
磕頭作揖 kowtow and bow;

ke

【蝌】 tadpole;
［蝌蚪］ todpole;

ke

【顆】 drop; droplet; grain; pill;
［顆粒］ anything small and roundish; dust; bead; pellet;
顆粒不進 not a grain of rice can enter his throat; one can eat nothing;
顆粒歸倉 bring in every single grain; every grain should be sent to the granary; every grain to the granary;
固着顆粒 anchor granule;
奶油顆粒 butter granule;
退化顆粒 degeneration granule;
致密顆粒 dense granule;

ke

【髁】 (1) condyle; hipbone; innominate bone; (2) kneecap; kneepan;

後髁 lateral condyle;
內髁 medial condyle;
前髁 dorsal condyle;
枕髁 occipital condyle;

ke²

ke

【咳】 cough;
［咳寧］ bechisan;
［咳嗽］ cough; have a cough;
咳嗽反射 cough reflex;
咳嗽片 cough lozenge;
咳嗽糖 cough drop;
咳嗽有痰 bring up phlegm when coughing;
持續性咳嗽 persistent cough;
得了咳嗽 catch a cough; get a cough;
逗咳嗽 at each other's throats; find fault; pick a fight; quarrel with someone on account of a person; grudge;
劇烈咳嗽 nasty cough; violent cough;
輕微咳嗽 slight cough;
嚴重的咳嗽 bad cough;
一陣咳嗽 a fit of coughing; a spasm of coughing; a spell of coughing;
一陣陣咳嗽 fits of coughing;
［咳唾成珠］ cough and spit and both the phlegm and saliva become pearl—words uttered by a talent become famous sentences;
［咳血］ cough up blood;

百日咳 whooping cough;
乾咳 dry cough; tussiculation;
劇咳 bad cough;
輕咳 tussicula;
痰咳 loose cough;
陣咳 paroxysmal cough;
止咳 relieve a cough;

ke

【欬】 (1) cough; (2) sound of laughing;

ke

【殼】 covering; husk; shell;
［殼層］ shell;
［殼膜］ shell membrane;
［殼狀物］ hoose; husk;

貝殼 shell;
錶殼 cover of watch; watch-case;
船殼 hull;
彈殼 (1) cartridge case; (2) shell case;
蛋殼 eggshell;

稻殼 rice husk;
谷殼 husk;
腦殼 head;
卡殼 jamming of cartridge; (2) get stuck;
外殼 covering; outer shell;

ke³
ke

【可】 (1) approve; (2) can; may; (3) need; worth; (4) fit; suit; (5) but; yet;

［可愛］ likable; lovable; lovely;
可愛的 adorable; cuddly;

［可悲］ lamentable; pitiable;
可悲可笑 both pitiable and ridiculous;
可悲可咒 pitiable and execrable;

［可比］ comparable;
可比較 comparability;

［可鄙］ contemptible; despicable; mean;
可鄙的事情 despiteful action;

［可編程序］ programmable;
可編程序控制器 programmable controller;
可編程序自動化 programmable automation;
可編程序字處理設備 word-processing equipment with changeable programme;
可編程序邏輯控制器 programmable logic controller;

［可變］ changeable; variable;
可變符號 variable symbol;
可變名詞 variable noun;

［可…不可］ can…but cannot;
可殺不可辱 would rather die than be disgraced;
可望而不可即 beyond reach; inaccessible; may see at a distance but may not approach; unattainable; within sight but beyond reach; within sight but not within reach;
可遇不可求 may come by chance but not by diligent search;
可暫不可長 it may do for the time being, but not long; it will only do temporarily, not permanently;

［可怖］ terrifying;
猙惡可怖 fierce and terrifying;

［可乘］ can be exploited;
可乘之機 an opportunity that can be exploited; window of opportunity;
可乘之隙 Achilles heel; an opportunity that can be utilized; openings to exploit;
無隙可乘 have no loophole to exploit; have no vulnerability to exploit; have no weakness to exploit; have not yet found openings to exploit; no chink in one's armour; no crack to get in by; no loophole to exploit; no weakness to take advantage of; unable to find any chink in sb's armour; watertight;

［可恥］ disgraceful; ignominious; shameful;
可恥下場 end in ignominious fiascos;

［可達性］ accessibility;
發動機可達性 engine accessibility;
目標可達性 accessibility of target;
修理可達性 accessibility for repair;

［可懂度］ intelligibility;
單詞可懂度 discrete word intelligibility;
單句可懂度 discrete sentence intelligibility; sentence intelligibility;
言語可懂度 speech intelligibility;

［可讀］ readable;
可讀性 readability;

［可否］ maybe and may-not-be;
可否之間 between a maybe and a may-not-be;
不加可否 refuse to comment;
不置可否 avoiding saying yes or no; decline to comment; give no opinion whether or not it will do; hedge; indicate neither consent or dissent; noncommittal; not express an opinion; not to express any opinion; not to say ye or no; prevaricate; refuse to comment; say neither buff nor stye; show neither approval nor disapproval; without giving an affirmative or negative answer; yea and nay;

［可觀］ considerable; impressive; sizable;
可觀的收入 a handsome income;
楚楚可觀 being clear and distinct, it is worth seeing;
大有可觀 quite impressive; worthwhile seeing;

［可貴］ admirable; commendable; precious; praiseworthy; valuable;
難能可貴 deserving praise for one's excellent preformance; exceptionally commendable; rare and commendable; unusual and praiseworthy;

［可好］ as luck would have it; just in time; just

right;

[可加] addable;
可加性 additivity;
~完全可加性 complete additivity;
~信息可加性 information additivity;
~有限可加性 finite additivity;

[可見] (1) it is clear that; it is obvious that; (2) visible; (3) judge by;
可見一斑 able to see a sample in its entirety;
由此可見 thus it can be seen;

[可敬] respected; worthy of respect;
可敬可嘉 worthy of respect and praise;

[可卡因] cocaine; coke;

[可靠] dependable; reliable; trustworthy;
可靠的 credible; reliable;
~可靠的情報 reliable information;
~可靠的證據 reliable evidence;
~完全可靠的 copper-bottomed;
可靠性 credibility; dependability; reliability;
~可靠性理論 theory of reliability;
~可靠性研究 reliability study;
~結構可靠性 built-in reliability;
~實際可靠性 achieved reliability;
~線路可靠性 circuit reliability;
可靠賬戶 reliable account;
不可靠 unreliable;
~不可靠的 unreliable;
誠實可靠 honest and reliable;

[可可] cocoa;
可可豆 cacao; cocoa bean;
可可粉 drinking chocolate;
可可油 cocoa butter;
一杯可可 a cup of cocoa;

[可…可…] can...can...;
可歌可泣 heroic and moving; inspiring; move one to song and tears; touching and deserving a song;
可進可守 can take either the offensive or the defensive;

[可口] dainty; delectable; delicious; good to eat; luscious; palatable; savoury; tasty;
濃香可口 aromatic and tasty;
香濃可口 aromatic and tasty;

[可樂] cola;
一罐可樂 a can of cola;

[可憐] pathetic; pitiable; pitiful; poor;
可憐蟲 pathetic creature; poor devil; poor thing; wretch;
楚楚可憐 delicate and touching; miserable;
怪可憐的 how pitiful; pitiful;
其情可憐 sb's situation deserves one's sympathy;
窮得可憐 shocking poor;
形景可憐 in a pitiable condition;
樣子真可憐 look so pitiful;

[可能] can; may; on the cards; possible; probable;
可能性 likelihood; possibility;
~可能性微乎其微 a chance in a million;
~極小的可能性 fat chance; long odds;
並非沒有可能 not beyond the realms of possibility;
不可能 impossible; not likely;
~殆不可能 almost impossible;
~幾乎是不可能 next to impossible; well-nigh impossible;
~近乎不可能 near impossible;
~絕不可能 absolutely impossible; nelly; never in a million years; not in a million years;
很可能 as like as not; high probability; in all probability; it's odds-on that; like enough; strong probability;
儘可能 as far as possible; to the best of one's ability;
有可能 be on the cards;

[可逆性] reversibility;
動態可逆性 dynamic reversibility;
機械可逆性 mechanical reversibility;
微觀可逆性 microscopic reversibility;

[可怕] dreadful; fearful; frightening; frightful; horrible; terrible; terrifying;
可怕的 dreadful; gruesome;

[可欺] (1) browbeaten; can be bullied; easily cowed; (2) easily duped; gullible;

[可氣] annoying; exasperating; irritating;

[可巧] as luck would have it; by a happy coincidence; it so happened that;

[可親] affable;
可親可敬 affable and respectful;
藹然可親 affable; affable and friendly; amiable; friendly; kind and gentle; kindly;

[可取] advisable; desirable; recommendable;
可取之處 point to recommend it; recommendation; saving grace;

[可人] (1) lovely person; (2) satisfactory;

[可是] but; however; yet;

[可視] visual;
可視化 visualization;
~可視化工作平台 visual workbench;
可視特徵 visual aspects;
可視圖文 videotext;
[可數的] countable;
[可謂] it may be called; it may be said that; one may well say;
[可惡] abominable; detestable; hateful; loathesome;
[可惜] it's a pity; it's to be regretted; unfortunately;
棄之可惜 hesitate to discard sth; it is a waste to discard it; unwilling to throw away;
[可喜] gratifying; heartening;
可喜可賀 be congratulated; joy be with you; you are to be congratulated;
[可想而知] can be imagined; have a fair knowledge of; need not go into detail; one can imagine;
[可笑] funny; laughable; ludicrous; ridiculous;
可笑不自量 cut a ridiculous figure because of lack of self-knowledge; make oneself ridiculous by overestimating one's ability; ridiculously overate oneself;
可笑之至 ridiculous in the extreme;
非常可笑 screamingly funny;
荒唐可笑 absurdly ridiculous;
舉止可笑 behave ridiculously;
聽起來可笑 sound ridiculous;
樣子可笑 look funny;
[可心] likeable; satisfying; to the liking of; to the satisfaction of;
可心如意 congenial; find sth satisfactory; things that are after one's heart; to one's heart's content;
[可信] credible; dependable;
可信的 credible;
可信度 credibility;
可信功能 trusted function;
可信路徑 trusted path;
可信任數據庫 trusted database;
[可行] doable; feasible; practicable; workable;
可行性 feasibility;
~可行性研究 feasibility study;
不可行的 unworkable;
[可疑] doubtful; dubious; questionable; suspicious;
可疑的 fishy;
可疑分子 a suspicious character;
[可以] (1) can; may; (2) passable; pretty good; (3) awful;
可以斷言 it can be asserted that; it can be stated definitely; one may predict that;
可以嗎 can you; is it all right to;
~請你…可以嗎 I wonder if you would mind; would you mind;
可以為鑒 exemplary; may be taken as a warning;
可以意會，不可言傳 can be understood but cannot be described; can grasp the meaning but cannot pass on in words;
不知我是否可以 I was wondering if I could; I was wondering if it might be possible for me to;
還可以 not bad; passable;
[可譯] translatable;
可譯性 translatability;
[可用] available; usable;

不可 be forbidden; cannot; must not; not allowed; should not;
兩可 both will do; either will do;
猛可 abruptly; suddenly;
寧可 would rather;
認可 approve; assent to;
未可 cannot;
許可 allow; permit;

ke

【坷】 bad luck; rugged; uneven; unfortunate;

坎坷 (1) bumpy; rough; (2) full of frustration;

ke

【渴】 (1) thirsty; (2) eagerly; thirstily; yearningly;
[渴驥奔泉] a thirsty steed dashing to the spring—run swiftly;
[渴慕] admire; think of sb with respect; yearn after; yearn for;
[渴求] eager about; eager after; eager for; hanker after; hanker for;
[渴望] ache for; anxious for sth; anxious to do sth; aspire; crave; craving; eager about; eager after; eager for; eager to do sth; fall over oneself; hanker for; have a thirst for; hunger after sth; hunger

for sth; hungry for; long after; long for; long to do sth; on tiptoe; pine for; starve for sth; thirst after; thirst for; thirsty for; yearn for;
渴望成名 long for fame; thirsty for fame;
渴望獨立 thirst for independence;
渴望甘露 long for a seasonable rain — said of farmers;
渴望和平 long for peace;
渴望見面 have a yearning desire to see sb;
渴望冒險 have a thirst for adventure;
渴望休息 yearn for rest;
渴望已久 have longed for;
渴望自由 long for freedom; yearn for liberty;

[渴想] earnestly hope; long for;

乾渴 dry and thirsty;
饑渴 (1) hunger and thirst; (2) irresistible desire or longing;
焦渴 parched; terribly thirsty;
解渴 quench one's thirst; slake one's thirst;
口渴 thirsty;
食得鹹魚抵得渴 if you can't stand the heat, get out of the kitchen;
止喝 quench one's thirst;

ke4

ke

【可】

[可汗] Khan;

ke

【克】 (1) able to; can; (2) restrain; (3) capture; overcome; subdue; (4) gram;

[克昌厥後] competent to flourish posterity;

[克服] conquer; overcome; surmount;
克服困難 overcome difficulties;
克服缺陷 overcome one's shortcomings;

[克復] recapture; recover; retake;

[克己] (1) restrain one's selfishness; strict with oneself; (2) claim that the goods are selling at low prices; (3) economic; frugal;
克己待人 treat others with self-denial;
克己奉公 be devoted to public duty; work selflessly for the common good; wholehearted devotion to public duty;
克己復禮為仁 to return to the observance of the rites through overcoming the self constitutes benevolence;
克己利人 benefit others at personal expense;
克己助人 do everything possible to help others;

[克扣] embezzle part of what should be issued;

[克紹箕裘] be a worthy son to an able father; can carry on family tradition; capable of continuing the occupation of one's father;

[克制] exercise restraint; restrain;
克制感情 restrain one's passion;
加以克制 apply restraint;
自我克制 self-abnegation; self-control;

不克 cannot; unable to;
攻克 capture; take;
毫克 milligram;
忽克 centimilligram;
忌克 be jealous and malicious; be jealous and mean;
茄克 jacket;
甲克 jacket;
馬克 (1) mark; (2) markka;
千克 kilogram;
坦克 tank;
休克 shock;

ke

【刻】 (1) carve; cut; engrave; (2) quarter of an hour; (3) moment;

[刻板] (1) cut blocks for printing; (2) inflexible; mechanical; stiff;

[刻本] block-printed edition; carving copy;

[刻薄] acerbity; harsh; mean; unkind;
刻薄成家理無久享 it is certain that the house established by meanness is not longlived;
刻薄寡恩 treat harshly and rarely give generosity;

[刻不容緩] admit of no delay; brook no delay; cannot be delayed even a moment; demand immediate attention; must not lose a minute; no time to lose; not a moment to be lost; of great urgency; permit of no delay; there is no time to be lost; there is no time to lose; there is not a moment to be lost; urgent;
此事刻不容緩 the matter admits of no delay;

[刻毒] acrid; malignant; spiteful; venomous;
刻毒咒罵 malevolent denigration;

malicious denunciation; spiteful curse; venomous abuse;

[刻度] graduation;
刻度器 graduator;
同一刻度 identical graduation;
線性刻度 linear graduation;
游標刻度 venier graduation;

[刻骨] bone-deep; deep-rooted; deeply ingrained;
刻骨仇恨 bear a deep malice towards; bitter hatred; deep hatred; harbour a deep-seated hatred for; implacable hatred; nourish a deep malice towards;
刻骨相思 carve on the bones and think of each other; deep love and remembrance of lovers;
鏤心刻骨 inscribe a debt of gratitude on one's mind;
銘心刻骨 always remember; be imprinted on one's bones and in one's heart — bear in mind forever; engrave on the heart;

[刻鵠類鶩] in carving a snow goose, one produces a duck — the imitation does not quite resemble reality but it is not far away; try to carve a swan and at least you'll get a duck — aim reasonably high and you won't fall far short;

[刻畫] depict; describe; portray;
刻畫入微 describe even to the trifling point; realistic portrayal of character; vivid portrayal of details;

[刻肌刻骨] be deeply touched; be profoundly impressed; will always remember in one's heart;

[刻苦] (1) assiduous; hardworking; painstaking; (2) simple and frugal;
刻苦攻讀 study assiduously; study hard; work hard at studies;
刻苦耐勞 industriousness and stamina; suffer hardship and persevere in toil; willing to go through hardships; work hard without complaint;
刻苦學習 study hard;
刻苦鑽研 lucubrate; study assiduously;
生活刻苦 lead a simple and frugal life;

[刻意] painstakingly; sedulously;
刻意求工 do one's very best to achieve perfection; make every effort to achieve perfection; sedulously strive for perfection;
刻意求精 do one's very best to achieve perfection; perfect one's sill assiduously;
刻意求名 aim at winning a name;

[刻舟求劍] cut a mark on the gunwale of one's moving boat to indicate the place where one's sword has dropped into the river — take measures without regard to changes in circumstances; mark the boat to locate the sword — foolish undertaking; nick the boat to seek the sword — be so pig-headed as to refuse to suit one's action to changed circumstances; seek a sword from a notch on a boat — ridiculous stupidity;

[刻字] carve characters on a seal;
刻字工 carver; punch cutter;

版刻 carving; engraving;
碑刻 inscriptions on tablet;
此刻 at present; now; this moment;
雕刻 carve; carving; engraving; sculpture;
骨刻 bone sculpture;
光刻 photo etching;
即刻 at once; immediately;
忌刻 be jealous and malicious; be jealous and mean;
尖刻 acrimonious; relentless;
鐫刻 engrave;
刊刻 cut blocks; inscribe;
苛克 harsh;
立刻 at once; immediately; right away;
鏤刻 carve; engrave;
漏刻 clepsydra; hourglass; water clock;
銘刻 always remember; engrave on one's mind;
摹刻 carve a reproduction of an inscription;
木刻 wood engraving; woodcut;
頃刻 in a moment; in an instant; instantly;
缺刻 incised;
片刻 a moment; a short while; an instant;
少刻 a moment later; after a little while;
深刻 deep; profound;
石刻 (1) carved stone; (2) stone inscription;
時刻 (1) always; constantly; (2) hour; moment; time;
蝕刻 etching;
谿刻 acrimonious; biting; cutting;
竹刻 bamboo carving; bamboo engraving;

篆刻 seal cutting;

ke

【剋】 limit; overcome;

[剋期] by the end of the time limit; set a time limit;

[剋星] jinx-hex; one's natural enemy;

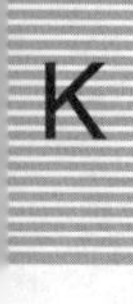

ke

【客】 (1) caller; guest; visitor; (2) passenger; traveller; (3) settle in a strange place; stranger

[客艙] cabin; main cabin; passenger cabin;

[客場] opponent's field;
客場比賽 away game;

[客車] bus; coach;
包房客車 compartment coach;
便餐客車 café coach;
空氣調節客車 air-conditioned coach;
雙層客車 double-deck coach;
通用客車 general-purpose coach;

[客串] guest; guest performer; play a part in a professional performance;
客串演出 cameo;

[客隊] guest team; visiting team;

[客房] guestroom;
客房管理 guestroom management;

[客觀] objective;
客觀的 objective;
客觀分析 objective analysis;
客觀規律 objective law;
客觀世界 the objective world;
客觀性 objectivity;
客觀真理 objective truth;

[客戶] client; customer;
客戶服務熱線 customer services hotline;
忠實客戶 loyal customer;

[客貨輪] passenger-cargo ship;

[客機] aerobus; air bus; airliner; passenger plane;
大型客機 airliner;
珍寶客機 jumbo jet;

[客家] Hakka;

[客居] live abroad;
客居異地 live in a strange land; take up temporary residence in a foreign country;

[客輪] liner; passenger liner;
遠洋客輪 ocean liner;

[客滿] full house; full up; house full;

[客票] passenger ticket;

[客氣] (1) civility; courteous; polite; (2) modest;
客氣話 pleasantry; polite remarks;
別客氣 it's my pleasure; my pleasure; you're welcome;
不客氣 (1) blunt; impolite; rude; (2) don't mention it; not at all; you are welcome;
~不客氣對待 handle without mittens;
請不要客氣 please don't stand on ceremony; you're welcome;

[客人] (1) guest; visitor; (2) guest; passenger; (3) travelling merchant;
客人登記簿 guest book;
怠慢客人 neglect a guest; slight a guest;
接待客人 receive visitors;
款待客人 entertain guests;
一批客人 a batch of visitors; a party of visitors;
一位客人 a guest;
一桌客人 a table of guests;

[客舍] guest house; hotel; inn;

[客歲] last year;

[客套] civilities; polite formula;
客套話 conventional remark;
~客套話而已 one's being polite;
客套一番 make a few polite remarks;

[客廳] drawing room; living room; sitting room;
客廳語言 anteroom language;

[客似雲來] guests are arriving like clouds;

[客棧] hostel;
廉價客棧 doss house; flophouse;

拜客 call on; pay a visit;
賓客 guest; visitor;
播客 podcast;
博客 blog;
逋客 (1) recluse ; (2) fugitive;
常客 frequent caller;
乘客 passenger;
刺客 assassin;
房客 lodger; tenant;
顧客 client; customer; shopper;
過客 passing traveler; transient guest;
豪客 bandit; robber;
好客 be hospitable; keep open house;
賀客 friends who come to congratulate;
會客 receive a visitor;
來客 guest; visitor;
旅客 hotel guest; passenger; traveler;

門客 hanger-on of an aristocrat;
墨客 literati; scholar;
掮客 broker;
請客 entertain guests; give a dinner party; invite sb to dinner;
騷客 poet;
上客 most honoured guest;
生客 stranger;
食客 advisor depending on an aristocrat in ancient times;
熟客 frequent visitor;
説客 (1) persuasive talker; (2) person sent to win sb over;
堂客 (1) women; (2) wife;
外客 guest who is not a relative;
稀客 rare visitor;
香客 pilgrim;
謝客 express thanks to guests;
遊客 sightseer; tourist; visitor;
遠客 guest from afar;
政客 politician;
作客 sojourn;
做客 be a guest;

ke

【恪】 respect; respectful; reverent;

［恪守］ firmly abide by; honour; observe; scrupulously abide by; strictly observe;
恪守本分 scrupulously abide by one's duty;
恪守不逾 adhere faithfully to; strictly abide by; submissively obey;

ke

【嗑】 bite; chew; eat;

ke

【溘】 abrupt; sudden; unexpected;

［溘然長逝］ die suddenly; die without a struggle; one's death is painless as if one has fallen asleep; pass away all of a sudden; pass away suddenly;

ke

【緙】 (1) style of Chinese silk tapestry; (2) weft; woof;

ke

【課】 (1) course; subject; (2) class; (3) lesson; (4) levy;

［課本］ coursebook; textbook;
入門課本 primer;
一套課本 a set of textbooks;
自學課本 self-learning book;

［課程］ course; curriculum; lesson; programme;
課程表 curriculum schedule; school timetable; timetable;
課程發展 curriculum development;
課程改革 curriculum reform;
課程綱要 course syllabus;
課程規劃 curriculum planning;
課程架構 curriculum framework;
課程開發 course development;
~課程開發程序 course development programme;
~課程開發系統 course development system;
課程模式 curriculum model;
課程軟件 courseware;
課程設計 curriculum design;
課程指引 curriculum guide;
課程資料 course material;
課程宗旨 curriculum aims;
安排課程 arrange the curriculum;
報讀課程 apply for a course;
參加課程 attend a course; go on a course;
初級課程 elementary course;
短期課程 short course;
翻譯課程 translation programme;
複修課程 refresher course;
高級課程 advanced course;
函授課程 correspondence course;
核心課程 core course; core curriculum;
活動課程 activity curriculum;
基礎課程 foundation course;
減少課程 cut down the curriculum;
進修課程 extension course;
經驗課程 experience curriculum;
兼讀課程 part-time course; part-time study programme;
開設課程 run a course;
快班課程 accelerated programme;
兩年期課程 two-year course;
培訓課程 training course;
全日制課程 full-time course; full-time programme;
融入課程 be integrated into the school curriculum;
入門課程 introductory course;
生本課程 student-centred curriculum;
雙學位課程 joint honours;
速成課程 crash course;
現有課程 existing course;
小學課程 primary school curriculum;
校本課程 school-based curriculum;
修畢課程 pass through a course;

修讀課程 do a course; take a course;
學分課程 credit course;
學術課程 academic curriculum;
學校課程 school curriculum;
一門課程 a course;
~教一門課程 teach a course;
一年期課程 one-year course;
正規課程 formal curriculum;
~非正規課程 informal curriculum;
正式課程 formal curriculum;
中級課程 intermediate course;
專業課程 professional curriculum;

[課節] class period;
固定課節 fixed period;

[課時] charge du class hour; class period; class time; lesson period; lesson time; period;
課時安排 lesson time arrangement;

[課税] charge duty; duty assessment; levy duty;

[課堂] classroom;
課堂筆記 lecture notes;
課堂討論 classroom discussion;
課堂學習 classroom learning;
課堂作業 class assignment; classwork;

[課題] (1) question for study; (2) problem; task; (3) project; subject; topic;
課題成本核算 project cost accounting;
課題計劃 project planning;
課題經費 project funds;

[課外] after school; extracurricular; outside class;
課外輔導 after-class consultation;
課外活動 extracurricular activities;
課外閱讀 after-class reading;
課外作業 homework;

[課文] text;
背課文 learn a lesson by rote; recite a text;
背誦課文 repeat one's text from memory;
電傳課文 teletext;

[課業] lesson; schoolwork;

[課餘] after class; after school;

[課桌] classroom desk;
活動課桌 adjustable desk;

罷課 class boycott; students' strike;
備課 prepare lessons;
必修課 compulsory course; required course;
補課 (1) make up a missed class; (2) make up for;
操課 (1) military drill; (2) lecture as part of military training;
代課 serve as a substitute teacher;
復課 resume classes;
功課 homework; schoolwork;
基礎課 basic course;
講課 lecture; teach;
開課 (1) school begins; (2) give a course;
曠課 be absent from school without leave;
普通課 general knowledge course;
缺課 miss a class;
上課 (1) attend class; go to class; (2) give a class;
授課 give lessons;
逃課 cut class; play truant;
聽課 attend a lecture; sit in on a class; visit a class;
停課 suspend classes;
下課 come off from class; finish class;
選修課 elective; elective course; optional course;
夜課 night classes;
一節課 a class; a lesson; a period;
一門課 a course; a subject;
一堂課 a class; a lecture; a lesson; a period;
占課 divine by tossing coins; the art of divination;
主課 major course;
專業課 specialized course;

ken³
ken

【肯】 (1) agree; consent; (2) ready to; willing to;

[肯定] absolute; affirm; approve; as sure as death; as sure as eggs is eggs; as sure as fate; as sure as hell; as sure as I'm standing here; as sure as you live; ascertain; certain; confident; confirm; definite; for sure; guarantee; in the affirmative; make sure; positive; sure; swear; with absolute certainty;
肯定成績 affirm the achievements;
肯定反應 affirmative response;
肯定句 affirmative sentence;
肯定是 certainly; it must be so; surely;
值得肯定 laudable;
自我肯定 self affirmation;

[肯肯舞] cancan;

寧肯 would rather;
首肯 nod approval;
中肯 relevant; to the point;

ken
【啃】 (1) bite; gnaw; nib; (2) kiss;
［啃骨動物］ browser;

ken
【墾】 open new land for farming; reclaim land;
［墾荒］ bring wasteland under cultivation; land reclamation; open up virgin soil; reclaim wasteland;
［墾殖］ reclaim and cultivate wasteland; reclaim land and live on it; reclaim wasteland and go in for production;

開墾 bring under cultivation; open up wasteland;
林墾 forestry and land reclamation;
屯墾 station troops to open up wasteland;
圍墾 reclaim land from marshes;

ken
【懇】 (1) earnestly; sincerely; (2) beseech; entreat; request;
［懇切］ earnest; sincere;
懇切陳詞 make a statement earnestly;
懇切希望 earnestly hope; sincerely hope;
［懇請］ cordially invite; earnestly request;
［懇求］ beseech; entreat; entreaty; implore;
懇求體卹 implore for sympathy;
懇求支持 solicit sb's support;
［懇摯］ earnest; sincere;

誠懇 sincere;
勤懇 diligent and conscientious;

ken⁴
ken
【裉】 seams below the sleeves in a garment;

keng¹
keng
【坑】 (1) crater; gully; hole; pit; (2) bury alive; (3) entrap; harm; injure;
［坑害］ entrap; lead into a trap; scheme to do harm;
坑害百姓 bring misfortune to people;
坑害國家 cause great harm to the country;
坑害朋友 ensnare and harm a friend;
［坑坑窪窪］ bumpy; full of bumps and hollows; rough;
［坑人］ cheat; entrap; trap;
［坑洼］ cavity; hollow;
［坑桌］ heated-bed-shaped table;

打坑 dig a hole;
彈坑 shell crater;
糞坑 manure pit;
灰坑 ash can;
火坑 fiery pit; pit of hell;
基坑 foundation;
礦坑 pit;
爐坑 stove;
茅坑 latrine;
泥坑 mud pit;
沙坑 jumping pit;
滲坑 seepage pit;
水坑 water hole;
陷坑 pit; pitfall;
窨坑 pit;
鑄坑 casting pit;

keng
【阬】 same as 坑；

keng
【傾】
［傾人］ frame a person; implicate a person;

keng
【硜】 sound of pebbles rubbing together;
［硜硜］ shallow and stubborn;
硜硜自守 maintain one's position firmly and carefully;

keng
【鏗】 clang; clatter;
［鏗鏘］ ring; clang; jingle;
鏗鏘聲 clangour;
鏗鏘有力 sonorous and forceful;
［鏗然］ loud and clear;

keng³
keng
【肯】 a pronunciation of 肯；

kong¹
kong
【空】 (1) empty; hollow; void; (2) air; the sky; (3) for nothing; in vain;
［空腸］ empty intestine;
空腸潰瘍 jejunal ulcer;
空腸炎 jejunitis;
［空城計］ a stratagem to present a bold front to conceal unpreparedness; empty-city stratagem—bewilder and keep away the enemy by opening the gate of a city

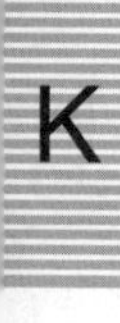

actually left unguarded; the stratagem of the empty city—presenting a bold front to conceal a weak defence;

[空檔] open side; opening;
空檔年 gap year;

[空蕩蕩] deserted; empty;

[空地] open space;
小塊空地 clearing;
一塊空地 an open space;

[空洞] (1) cavity; void; (2) devoid of content; empty; hollow; vague and general; (3) hollow;
空洞浮誇 empty and bombastic; windy verbiage;
空洞無力 washy;
空洞無物 all empty; devoid of content; emptiness; have nothing to show; null and void; shallow understanding; utter lack of content; utter lack of substance; with nothing in it;
內容空洞 devoid of content;

[空對空] air-to-air;
空對空的 air-to-air;

[空翻] somersault;
空翻跳遠 somersault long jump;
阿拉伯空翻 Arab somersault;
側空翻 side somersault;
杠下空翻 under somersault;
後空翻 backward somersault;
~後空翻離杠 backward somersault from the bar;
前空翻 forward somersault in the air;
索上空翻 somersault on the tight rope;
直體空翻 stretched somersault;

[空泛] not specific; vague and general;

[空腹高心] poor in talent but very ambitious;

[空格] (1) blank space; (2) space;
行首空格 indentation;

[空谷] deserted valley;
空谷傳聲 resound in the deep ravines;
空谷足音 sound of footsteps in a deserted valley — a rare and welcome appearance;

[空鍋冷灶] empty pots and cold stove;

[空話] all talk and no cider; empty talk; empty words; flummery; hollow words; hot air; humbug; idle talk;
空話連篇 empty phrases on a scrap of paper; long-winded and devoid of substance; pages and pages of empty verbiage; talk endlessly with no substance at all;
空話騙人 cheat others with an empty promise; mock sb with empty promises;
空話無用 empty boasts are useless;
多做實事，少說空話 more cider and less talk;
光說空話 all talk;
說空話 have empty talk; indulge in idle talk;
一句空話 a meaningless term; a mere phrase; an empty phrase; nothing but empty talk; only a hollow term;
衹說空話 all talk;

[空幻] fanciful; illusive; illusory; imaginary; visionary;

[空際] in the air; in the sky;

[空間] blank; enclosure; interspace; room; space;
空間法 space law;
空間飛行環境 space flight environment;
空間分析 spatial analysis;
空間觀 space concept;
~大空間觀 outlook on mega-space;
空間結構 spatial structure;
空間科學 space science;
空間模式 spatial model;
空間探測 space exploration;
空間通信 space communication;
空間武器 space weapon;
空間醫學 aerospace medicine;
空間語法 space grammar;
空間站 space station;
空間中心 space centre;
抽象空間 abstract space;
第四度空間 fourth dimension;
地月間空間 cislunar space;
個人空間 personal space;
恒星際空間 interstellar space;
加法空間 additive space;
加速空間 accelerating space;
近地空間 terrestrial space;
絕對空間 absolute space;
三度空間 three-dimensional space;
三維空間 three-dimensional space;
四維空間 four-dimensional space;
外層空間 outer space;
星系際空間 intergalactic space;
行為空間 action space;
行星際空間 interplanetary space;

行星外空間 extraplanetary space;
宇宙空間 space;
佔空間 take up space;
子空間 subspace;
~ 補子空間 complementary subspace;
~ 仿射子空間 affine subspace;
~ 循環子空間 cyclic subspace;
最大空間 the maximum space;

[空姐] stewardess;

[空軍] air force; airman; air service;
空軍部隊 air force unit;
空軍顧問 air force adviser;
空軍後勤站 logistics department;
空軍基地 airbase;
空軍列兵 airman basic;
空中女兵 airwoman;
空軍女士兵 aircraftwoman;
空軍前進基地 airhead;
空軍上將 air chief marshal;
空軍少將 air vice-marshal;
空軍實力 airpower;
空軍士兵 aircraftman;
空軍一等兵 airman first class;
空軍准將 air commodore;

[空空] empty; nothing;
空空洞洞 empty; have nothing substantial; hollow; vague and general; with nothing in it;

[空口] speak without acting;
空口白舌 pure bunk; with mere words of mouth;
空口難憑 oral promise is not enough;
空口無憑 words of mouth are no guarantee;
空口説白話 a mere high-sounding talk; all talk and no cider; an empty promise; an empty promise without substance; brag; make empty promises; speak without acting; talk big;

[空曠] emptiness; open; spacious; void; wide;
空曠的草原 open grassland;
空曠的原野 open countryside;

[空廓] open; spacious;
四望空廓 spacious and open on all sides;

[空闊] open; spacious;

[空論] empty talk;

[空門] Buddhism;
遁跡空門 become a monk; conceal oneself in the holy door — become a monk; retire into a cloister; take the monastic vow;
遁入空門 become a Buddhist monk; take the monastic vow;

[空濛] hazy; misty;

[空名] empty name;
不務空名 not to seek empty fame;
空有其名 only nominally;

[空難] air disaster;

[空瓶] empty bottle;
空瓶回收箱 bottle bank;

[空氣] air; atmosphere;
空氣保護 air conservation;
空氣不足的 airless;
空氣動力學 aerodynamics; aerormechanics;
空氣過濾器 air filter;
空氣冷卻 air-cooling;
空氣療法 aerotherapeutics; aerotherapy;
空氣流 airflow;
~ 空氣流動 air movement;
空氣密度 air density;
空氣密封 aeroseal; air seal;
空氣清新劑 air freshener;
空氣熱力學 aerothermodynamiucs;
空氣生物學 aerobiology;
~ 室內空氣生物學 intramural aerobiology;
~ 室外空氣生物學 extramural aerobiology;
空氣調節 air-conditioning;
~ 空氣調節裝置 air conditioning apparatus;
空氣污染 air pollution;
空氣洗滌 air washing;
~ 空氣洗滌裝置 air washing apparatus;
空氣質量 air quality;
飽和空氣 saturated air;
補充空氣 make-up air; supplemental air;
導電空氣 conducting air;
地面空氣 surface air;
顛簸空氣 bumpy air;
放空氣 put out feelers; send out trial balloons;
腐蝕性空氣 corrosive atmosphere;
高層空氣 superior air;
固定空氣 fixed air;
含塵空氣 dust-laden air;
呼吸空氣 draw in air;
~ 大口大口地呼吸空氣 draw in hug gulps of air;
冷空氣 cold air; freezing air;
冷卻空氣 cooling air;

濕空氣 humid air;
輸出空氣 delivery air;
無塵空氣 dust-free air;
無菌空氣 sterile air;
吸入空氣 breathe in the air; draw in air; inhale air;
稀釋空氣 diluent air;
新鮮空氣 fresh air;
~呼吸新鮮空氣 take the air;
~一股新鮮空氣 a breath of fresh air;
~一口新鮮空氣 a mouthful of fresh air;
壓縮空氣 compressed air;
一大口空氣 a gulp of air; a lungful of air;
一點空氣 a whiff of air;
一口空氣 a breath of air;
游離空氣 dissociated air;
助燃空氣 combustion air;

[空前] unparalleled; unprecedented;
空前的 all-time;
空前浩劫 unheard-of calamity;
空前絕後 be unparalleled to this day and also in days to come; surpass the past and future; never known before and never to occur again; unique; unprecedented and unrepeatable; without both precedent and following up; without either precedent or sequel; without peer before their time and after;
空前未有 exist unprecedentedly; it has never been known before; unparalleled; unprecedented; without parallel; without precedent;

[空勤] air duty;
空勤人員 aircrew;
空勤組 aircrew;

[空拳] bare-handed; hold nothing in the hand;
空拳赤手 a hollow fist and bare hands — relying on no one; bare-handed;

[空室] empty room;
靜如空室 as still as an empty room;

[空手] empty-handed;
空手成家 build up one's fortune from scratch;
空手道 karate;
空手而歸 come back empty-handed; return empty;
空手起家 make a fortune starting from nothing;

[空速] airspeed;
空速錶 airspeed indicator;
空速管 airspeed head;
飛行空速 flight airspeed;
基準空速 datum airspeed;
零空速 zero airspeed;
密度空速 density airspeed;
目標空速 target airspeed;
起飛空速 take off airspeed;
下滑空速 glide airspeed;
巡航空速 cruising airspeed;
真空速 true airspeed;
最大空速 full airspeed;

[空談] (1) indulge in empty talk; (2) all talk; empty talk; idle talk; prattle;
空談無益 it is no use just talking; it will not do if one merely pays lip service to;
空談誤國 empty talks jeopardize national interests;
空談虛論 empty talk and high-flown discussions;

[空調] air-conditioning;
空調機 air conditioner;
空調器 air conditioner;
空調設備 air-conditioner;
~安設空調設備 install an air-conditioner;
空調系統 air conditioning;
打開空調 turn on the air conditioning;
中央空調 central air conditioning;

[空投] airdrop;
空投魚雷 aerial torpedo;
物資空投 cargo assault;

[空頭] (1) bear; (2) nominal; (3) vain;
空頭集團 bear clique;
空頭人情 an empty show of sympathy; offer lip-service;
空頭市場 bear market;
空頭賬戶 bear account;
空頭政治 armchair politics;
空頭支票 (1) bad cheque; bounced cheque; dishonoured cheque; dud cheque; empty promise; false cheque; kiting cheque; protest cheque; rubber cheque; unhonoured cheque; (2) a pie in the sky; hot air; lip service;
做空頭 bear; shortsell;

[空文] ineffective law;
一紙空文 a bit of waste paper; a mere scrap of paper; empty phrases on a scrap of waste paper;

[空吻] air kiss;

[空襲] aerial attack; air attack; air raid; make

an air raid; launch an air attack;
空襲警報 air-raid alarm; air-raid warning system;
大規模空襲 air attack in force; heavy air attack;
低空空襲 on-the-deck air attack;
~超低空空襲 treetop attack;
分散空襲 dispersed air attack;
化學空襲 air chemical action;
模擬空襲 simulated air attack;
牽制性空襲 holding air attack;
全天候空襲 all –weather air attack;
燃燒彈空襲 incendiary attack;
撒毒空襲 air spray attack;
突然空襲 surprise air attack;
無人機空襲 drone attack;
迂迴空襲 circuitous air attack;
洲際空襲 intercontinental air attack;

[空喜] windy joy;
一場空喜 a windy joy; one's joy comes to naught;

[空想] daydream; fancy; fantasy; hope in vain; idle dream;
空想的 blue-sky;
空想家 dreamer;
空想社會主義 utopian socialism;

[空心] hollow inside;
空心菜 water spinach;
空心大老倌 fellow of vain pretentions;
空心大樹—不成材 a huge tree with a hollow trunk — not good building material; person of little talent;
空心老大 pretentious and empty person;
空心墻 cavity wall;
空心球 clean shot; open shot;
空心磚 air brick;

[空虛] aeriality; emptiness; hollow; inanity; void;
空虛受益 emptiness is benefited by addition; one is benefited by being humble;

[空穴來風] an empty hole invites the wind — weakness lends wings to rumours; wind comes from the hollow cave — being not a groundless rumour;

[空壓機] air compressor;
空壓機手 air compressor operator;

[空言] empty talk; impractical words;
空言搪塞 put off with words;
空言無補 empty talk is of no avail; mere words will not fill a bushel;
空言無益 empty talk is useless; words pay no debts;
徒托空言 boast; empty talk without deeds; make a lame excuse in vain; make empty promises; render lip service;
託之空言 give empty promises; pay lip service;

[空域] airspace;
垂直空域 vertical airspace;
上層空域 upper airspace;
水平空域 horizontal airspace;
搜索空域 scout the airspace;
通航空域 navigable airspace;
下層空域 low airspace;

[空運] air transport; airlift;
空運公司 air transport company; airshipper;
空運機 air carrier;
空運集裝箱 air container;
大規模空運 airlift;

[空戰] air action; air battle; air-to-air battle; air-to-air combat;
空戰武器 air-to-air armature;

[空中] aerial; air;
空中巴士 airbus;
空中爆炸 air blast; air explosion;
空中測量 aerial survey;
空中導航 aeronavigation;
空中電話 skyphone;
空中飛人 aerialist;
空中服務員 flight attendant;
空中觀測術 aeroscopy;
空中貨運 airfreight;
空中技巧 aerial;
空中加油機 aerial tanker;
空中交通 air traffic;
~空中交通管制 air traffic control;
空中交通管制員 air controlman; air traffic controller;
空中救護車 air ambulance;
空中瞰圖 airscape;
空中客車 airbus;
空中樓閣 aerial-castle; air-castle; cloud-castle; fool's paradise; ivory-tower; castles in Spain; castles in the air; Spanish castle;
空中鬧事 air rage;
空中牽引 aerotow;
空中攝影 aerial photography;
空中索道 aerial rope;
空中鐵路 aerial railway;

空中位置 air-position;
空中小姐 air hostess; stewardess;
~ 一位空中小姐 an air hostess;
半空中 in midair; in the air;
昇入空中 sail up into the clouds;

[空子] hole;
鑽空子 avail oneself of loopholes; exploit an advantage; seize every opportunity to stir up trouble; trick; use means of evasion; work the system;
~ 鑽制度的空子 play the system;

碧空 blue sky;
長空 vast sky;
趁空 avail oneself of leisure time; use one's spare time;
抽空 manage to find time;
當空 high above in the sky;
低空 low altitude; low level;
防空 antiaircraft; air defence;
放空 drive unloaded;
高空 high altitude; upper air;
航空 aviation;
凌空 be high up in the air; soar aloft; tower aloft;
輪空 bye;
落空 come to nothing; fall through;
平空 groundlessly; without foundation;
憑空 groundlessly; without foundation;
撲空 come away empty-handed; fail to meet sb one intends to meet;
晴空 bright sky; clear sky; cloudless sky;
上空 in the sky; overhead;
深空 deep space;
太空 outer space; the firmament;
探空 sound;
騰空 rise high into the air; soar;
天空 the heavens; the sky;
星空 starlit sky; starry sky;
虛空 hollow; void;
懸空 hang in the air; suspend in midair;
夜空 night sky;
一場空 all in vain; come to naught; come to nothing; futile;
真空 vacuum;

kong
【悾】 candid; sincere;
[悾悾] earnest; sincere;

kong
【箜】 kind of ancient musical instrument;

kong³
kong
【孔】 (1) aperture; hole; opening; (2) a surname;

[孔雀] peacock;
孔雀開屏 a peaker flaunting its tail; a peacock in its pride;
孔雀魚 guppy;

[孔隙] hole; pore; small opening;
孔隙度 porosity;
~ 充氣孔隙度 air-filled porosity;
~ 晶體孔隙度 crystalline porosity;
~ 空間孔隙度 air space porosity;

[孔眼] eyelet;

[孔子] Confucius;
孔子放屁—文氣衝天 Confucius being flatulent – literary airs fill the heavens;

鼻後孔 choana;
鼻孔 nostril;
插孔 jack; socket;
腸穿孔 enterobrosis; intestinal perforation;
穿孔 (1) bore a hole; (2) perforation;
打孔 drill; punch a hole;
定位孔 aligning hole;
耳孔 earhole;
放氣孔 air-bleed hole;
汗孔 pore;
基孔 basic bore;
檢查孔 access hole;
毛孔 pore;
面孔 face;
排氣孔 air exit hole;
氣孔 (1) stoma; (2) spiracle; stigma; (3) gas hole; (4) air hole;
人孔 manhole;
搪孔 bore a hole;
通風孔 air hole;
瞳孔 pupil;
中心孔 centre bore;

kong
【恐】 (1) dread; fear; (2) I'm afraid;

[恐怖] dreadful; horrible; terrifying;
恐怖電影 chiller;
恐怖分子 terrorist;
~ 一幫恐怖分子 a group of terrorists;
恐怖感 a feeling of terror;
恐怖故事 horror story;
恐怖活動 terrorist activity;

恐怖片 scary movie;
恐怖失色 pale with fear;
恐怖團體 terrorist group;
恐怖影片 horror movie;
恐怖症 phobia;
~ 昆蟲恐怖症 acarophobia;
~ 螨恐怖症 acarophobia;
恐怖主義 terrorism;
~ 打擊恐怖主義 combat terrorism;
~ 反恐怖主義 counter-terrorism;
~ 生態恐怖主義 ecoterrorism;
恐怖組織 terrorist organization;
癌恐怖 cancerphobia;
白色恐怖 white terror;
擺脫恐怖 cast off fear;
高空恐怖 aerophobia;
居高恐怖 hypsophobia;
曠野恐怖 agoraphobia;
冷恐怖 cheimaphobia;
令人恐怖 horrendous; horrific;
一片恐怖 an atmosphere of terror prevails;
引起恐怖 cause terror;
增加恐怖 add to one's terrors;

[恐嚇] cow; frighten; intimidate; menace; threaten;
恐嚇戰術 scare tactics;

[恐慌] fright; frightened; panic; scared; terrified;
恐慌病 panic disorder;
恐慌萬狀 exceedingly panicky; extremely panicky; panic-stricken;
防止恐慌 avert panic;
健康恐慌 health scare;
引起恐慌 create a panic;
造成恐慌 generate a panic; produce a panic;
製造恐慌 scaremongering;

[恐懼] afraid of; dread; fear; frightened; terrified;
恐懼不安 frightened and restless;
恐懼症 phobia;
~ 城市恐懼症 urbiphobia;
無所恐懼 feel no fear;
消除恐懼 allay fears;
一片恐懼 a flood of terror;

[恐龍] dinosaur;
總食肉恐龍 saurischian dinosaur;

[恐怕] I'm afraid; might as well; perhaps;

[恐…症] phobia;
恐觸症 hapephobia;
恐毒症 fear of poison;
恐飛症 aviophobia; flight phobia;
恐高症 acrophobia;
恐紅症 erythrophobia;
恐火症 pyrophobia;
恐曠症 agoraphobia;
恐冷症 cheimaphobia;
恐馬症 equinophobia;
恐螨症 acarophobia;
恐猫症 ailurophobia;
恐犬症 cynophobia;
恐色症 chromophobia;
恐聲症 acousticophobia;
恐時症 chronophobia;
恐水症 aquaphobia;
恐死症 thanatophobia;
恐縮症 koro;
恐痛症 algophobia;
恐血症 hemophobia;

惶恐 terrified;
驚恐 alarmed and panicky; terrified;
生恐 for fear that;
惟恐 for fear that;

kong4
kong

【空】 (1) leave blank; leave empty; vacate; (2) blank; unoccupied; vacant; (3) empty space; room; (4) free time; leisure; spare time;

[空白] blank space; gap; margin;
空白背書 blank endorsed; endorsed in blank;
空白帶 blank tape;
空白頁 fly leaf;
留出空白 leave a space;
填補空白 fill a void; fill in the gaps;

[空當兒] (1) break; interval; (2) gap;
[空當子] break; gap;
[空額] vacancy;
[空話] hokum;
[空缺] vacant position;
補空缺 fill up a vacancy;
~ 填補空缺 plug the gap;
[空位] vacant seat;
[空隙] (1) interval; (2) gap; space;
詞匯空隙 lexical gap;
[空暇] free time; leisure; spare time;
[空閒] (1) free; idle; (2) free time; leisure; spare time;
空閒時間 one's idle hours;

［空心］ on an empty stomach;

搬空 evacuate;
碧空 azure sky; clear blue sky;
長空 vast sky;
趁空 use one's spare time;
抽空 manage to find time;
得空 be free; have leisure;
填空 (1) fill a vacancy; fill a vacant position; (2) fill in the blanks;
偷空 take time off;
閒空 free time; spare time;

K

kong
【控】 (1) accuse; charge; (2) control; dominate; (3) turn upside down to let the liquid trickle out;

［控告］ accuse; bring a charge against sb; bring a suit against sb; bring an action against sb; call an action against sb; charge; complain; enter a suit against sb; file a suit against sb; have the law of sb; ; institute a suit against sb; lodge a complaint; make a charge against sb; make a complaint; take an action against sb; take the law of sb;
撤消控告 drop a lawsuit; withdraw a charge; withdraw an accusation;
集體控告 class action;
提出控告 lodge an accusation;

［控股］ control stocks; holding;
控股公司 holding company;
控股合併 mergence of controlling interest;

［控訴］ accuse; denounce; make a complaint against;

［控制］ be brought under control; bridle; bring under control; command; contain; containment; control; curb; dominate; gain control of; get command of; get under control; govern; have command over; have control of; have control over; have under control; in control of; in the hands of; keep one's hands on; keep under control; lead sb by the nose; reign; take control of; under sb's thumb; under the control of;
控制變量 control varieties;
控制程序 control programme;
控制仿生學 control bionics;
控制幅度 space of control;
控制鍵 control key;
控制局面 have the situation under control;
控制理論 control theory;
控制領域 fiefdom;
控制論 cybernetics;
～控制論程序 cybernetics programme;
～控制論系統 cybernetics system;
控制器 control unit; controller;
～加速度控制器 acceleration controller;
～可調控制器 adjustable controller;
～模擬控制器 analog controller;
～自動音量控制器 automatic volume controller;
控制群 control group;
控制設備 control appliance;
控制生育 birth control;
控制室 control room;
控制數據系統 control data system;
控制塔 control tower;
控制台 console; control console;
～備用控制台 alternate console;
～編輯控制台 editor console;
～導演控制台 director's console;
～交替控制台 alternate console;
～攝像機控制台 camera control console;
～數字式控制台 digital console;
～顯示控制台 display console;
～小型控制台 consolette;
～中央控制台 control console;
～桌式控制台 desk console;
控制污染 pollution control;
控制系統 control system;
控制險要 command a strategic position;
控制慾極強的人 control freak;
控制站 control station;
控制者 controller;
控制職能 control function;
控制指令 control instruction;
控制終端 control terminal;
控制總線 control bus;
安全控制 emergency control; safety control;
暗中控制 pull the strings;
不受控制 out of control;
超前控制 advanced control;
詞匯控制 vocabulary control;
放鬆控制 loosen one's grip; loosen one's hold;
活化控制 activation control;
可控制的 controllable;
黏着控制 adhesion control;

順序控制 sequence programme control;
酸度控制 acidity control;
提前控制 advance control;
完全控制 stranglehold;
吸收控制 absorption control;
自組控制 self-organization control;

測控 observe and control;
程控 computerized; programmable; programme-controlled;
聲控 audio-controlled;
失控 be out of control;
受控 controlled;
調控 regulate and control;
遙控 remote control;
指控 accuse; charge;
主控 master control;
自控 self-control;

kou¹
kou

【摳】 (1) raise; (2) feel for; (3) inquire into; (4) dig; dig with fingers; (5) stingy; (6) throw at;

［摳門兒］ closefisted; mean; miserly; stingy;

［摳搜］ (1) dig; scratch; (2) miserly; stingy; (3) dawdle; move slowly;

kou³
kou

【口】 (1) cake-hole; fag-hole; mouth; pecker; (2) mouth; rim; (3) entrance; exit; inlet; opening; outlet; (4) cut a hole; (5) a breath of; a drain of; a draught of; a drink of; a gulp of; a morsel of; a mouthful of; a pull of; a sip of; a suck of; a swallow of;

［口岸］ entry port; exit port; port; river port; seaport;

［口碑］ public praise;
口碑載道 be praised everywhere; be warmly praised by one and all; enjoy great popularity among the people; one's praises ring far and wide; win popular praise;

［口…筆…］ the mouth...the brush;
口是風，筆是蹤 words fly, writing remains; words spoken are like the wind; the tracing of the pencil remains;
口誅筆伐 condemn both by word of mouth and in writing; condemn both in speech and in writing; lash out at both by word of mouth and in writing;

［口才］ eloquence; gift of the gab;
口才無雙 unrivalled in eloquence;
有口才 be endowed with rare eloquence; eloquent;

［口吃］ battarism; stammer; stutter;

［口齒］ (1) enunciation; (2) ability to speak;
口齒不清 a twist in one's tongue; speak with a lisp; swallow one's words;
口齒伶俐 a good talker; a ready tongue; clever and fluent; fluent of speech; have a ready tongue; one's tongue is very swift answer; quick of wit and eloquent;
～口齒伶俐的 adroit;
口齒留香 the exquisite verses have left a lingering fragrance in one's mouth;
口齒清楚 have clear enunciation; talk distinctly;
口伶齒俐 gifted with a quick tongue; have a numble tongue;

［口臭］ bad breath; bromopnea; fetid oris; foul breath; halitosis; kakostomia;
口臭症 halitosis; ozostomia;
肝病口臭 liver breath;
肝病性口臭 fetor hepaticus;
鉛中毒口臭 lead breath;

［口出］ what comes out from one's mouth;
口出不遜 make impertinent remarks; talk harshly; use unparliamentary language;
口出大言 boast; brag; utter bold words;
口出狂言 cheek up; talk nonsense; talk wildly;
口出怨言 be discontented and speak resentfully;
禍從口出 a ready tongue is an evil; all one's troubles are caused by his tongue; careless talk leads to trouble; out of the mouth comes evil; disaster emanates from careless talk; evil originates in the mouth; improper language brings sb ruin; misfortunes come from the mouth; out of the mouth comes evil; the tongue talks at the head's cost;

［口傳］ by word of mouth; from mouth to mouth;
口傳心授 an oral teaching that inspires

true understanding within;
口口相傳 from mouth to mouth; pass from mouth to mouth;

[口瘡] aphtha;
口瘡病 aphthosis;
口瘡熱 aphthous fever;
口瘡性口炎 stomatitis aphthosa;
口瘡性潰瘍 aphthous ulcer;
長口瘡 have a thrush;

[口唇] lips;
口燥唇乾 lips are dry and mouth is parched; talk one's tongue dry;

[口袋] pocket;
後口袋 hip pocket;
胸前口袋 breast-pocket;

[口德] propriety in one's remarks;

[口耳] mouth and ears;
口耳相傳 teach orally;
口不捷耳不聽 slow of speech and hard of hearing;

[口發育不良] atelostomia;

[口發育不全] atelostomia;

[口伐] attack verbally;

[口風] one's intention as revealed in what one says;
不露口風 not to breathe a word about;

[口服] (1) profess to be convinced; (2) take orally;
口服心不服 pretend to be convinced;
口服心服 be convinced of; be sincerely convinced;

[口福] gourmet's luck; luck in having nice food; the luck to get sth nice to eat;
口福不淺 it is fortunate to eat such delicious things; luck of having good food; luck of the mouth is not shallow;

[口腹] (1) food; (2) one's mouth and heart;
口腹之欲 bodily desires; the bodily wants of food and drink; the desire for good food;
口蜜腹劍 a cruel heart under the cover of sugar-coated words; a honey tongue, a heart of gall; a Judas kiss; a mouth that praises and a hand that kills; fair without, foul within; give sb sweet talk when there's hatred in the heart; have honey on one's lips and murder in one's heart; have sweet talk, but evil intentions; honey in mouth, dagger in heart; honey on one's lips and murder in one's heart; honey-mouthed and dagger-hearted; hypocrtical and malignant; one's honeyed words hide daggers; play a double game; velvet pas hide sharp claws; with an iron hand in a velvet glove; with peace on one's tongue and guns in one's pocket;

[口乾] dry; thirst;
口乾舌燥 mouth parched and tongue scorched;

[口缸] tooth glass;

[口供] confession; deposition; testimony;
留口供 take deposition;

[口號] shibboleth; slogan; watchword;

[口喝] have a cobweb in the throat; thirsty;
口喝了打井一來不及了 digging a well when one is thirsty — too late;

[口紅] lip rouge; lipstick;
口紅筆 lip liner;

[口惠] empty service; lip service;
口惠而實不至 make a promise and not keep it; pay lip service; great promise with small performance; leaves without figs; promises given in words but not fulfilled;

[口技] ventriloquism; ventriloquy; vocal imitation;
口技表演者 ventriloquist;

[口交] blow job; blow sb; French; French sb; gam; gam sb; give head; gobble sb; gob job; head job; lip service; mouth music; oral sex; plate sb; skull job;

[口角] (1) corner of the mouth; (2) altercation; bicker; quarrel; spat; wrangle;
口角春風 give verbal praise; lavish praise on others by word of mouth; pay compliments to; praise by word of mouth; speak in praise of;
口角唇炎 angular cheilitis;
口角乾裂 angular cheilosis;
口角流津 saliva drops from the corners of one's mouth;
口角炎 angular stomatitis; aphatha;
~傳染性口角炎 angulus infectiosus;

[口緊] closemouth; tight-lipped;
口緊不招禍 a closed mouth catches no flies;
口緊的 close-mouthed;

[口徑] (1) statement about sth; (2) bore; caliber; (3) requirements;

specifications;
口徑不合 what people say does not agree with one another;

[口角] bicker; quarrel; spat; wrangle;
發生口角 a quarrel arises;
與人口角 bandy words with sb;

[口渴] thirsty; with one's tongue hanging out;

[口口聲聲] avow time and again; go on prating about; keep on proclaiming; keep prating about; keep saying all the time; make noisy professions about; pay lip service to; say again and again; talk glibly about;

[口快] speak rashly;
口快心直 blunt, outspoken, but honest; free from affectation and hesitation; open-hearted; wear one's heart on one's sleeve; what the heart thinks, the tongue speaks;

[口令] (1) command; word of command; (2) password; shibboleth; watchword;

[口氣] (1) note; tone; (2) implication; what is actually meant; (3) manner of speaking;
口氣傲慢 take a high tone;
出口氣 vent one's anger; vent one's spleen; work off one's feeling;
改變口氣 change one's tone;
探口氣 ascertain sb's opinions; kite-flying; sound out one's intentions;
歇口氣 catch one's breath; come up for air; get one's wind; stop for a breather; take a breather;
~停下來歇口氣 pause for breath;

[口腔] cavity of the mouth;
口腔疾病 disease in the oral cavity;
口腔痛 stomalgia;
~義齒性口腔痛 denture sore mouth;
口腔外科醫生 oral surgeon;
口腔炎 stomatitis;
膿性口腔炎 pyostomatitis;

[口琴] harmonica; mouth organ;
玻璃口琴 armonica;

[口若懸河] a great talker made a torrent of words; eloquent; eloquent in speech; gift of the gab; glib; great talker; have a great flow of speech; have eloquence on tap; let loose a flood of eloquence; nimble of speech; one's mouth is like tumbling river—talk rapidly; one's words pour forth like a rushing river; pour forth; speak incessantly like a stream; talk glibly; talk in a flood of eloquence; utter a torrent of words; voluble; with an easy flow of language;

[口哨] whistling sound;
吹口哨 whistle; whistle at sb; whistle to sb;
挑逗口哨 wolf whistle;
一聲口哨 a whistle;
~吹一聲口哨 blow a whistle;

[口舌] (1) dispute; exchange of words; quarrel; (2) talk; talk round;
口舌是非 dispute; wagging of tongues;
口舌之爭 contention of mouth and tongue;
白費口舌 speak to the wind; waste one's breath; waste one's words;
~不要白費口舌 keep one's breath to cool one's porridge;
搬口弄舌 make mischief; tell tales;
笨口拙舌 awkward in speech; clumsy of speech; inarticulate; slow of speech;
赤口白舌 tawdry squabble over nothing;
赤口毒舌 slander venomously; speak bitingly;
金口木舌 a bell with a wooden clapper — education;
口笨舌拙 awkward in speech;
輕口薄舌 flippant; like to say nasty things about people; loosetongued; speak impolitely; speak rudely;
妄口巴舌 blasphemous talks; wild talks;

[口實] a cause for gossip; handle;
授人口實 give people a basis for gossip; leave a subject for ridicule;
貽人口實 a source of ridicule; give a handle to; give cause for talk; give occasion for gossip; give sth ground for gossip; give people grounds for ridicule; leave people sth to talk about; provide one's critics with a handle;
予人口實 give cause for gossip; give sb a handle;

[口試] oral examination; oral quiz; oral test;

[口…手…] the mouth...the hands;
口巧手拙 glib in tongue and clumsy in hands; those who are good at making excuses will be good at nothing else;
口問手寫 ask questions and take notes;

[口授] (1) oral instruction; pass on through oral instruction; (2) dictate;

口授筆錄 dictate; one gives verbal instructions and the other records with a pen; talk down from dictation;

[口述] dictate; nuncupate; oral account;
口述歷史 oral history;

[口水] dribble; slaiva; slobber;
流口水 drool; make one's mouth water; run at the mouth;
~使人饞得流口水 make one's mouth water;
淌口水 drooling;

[口說] what is said;
口說不如身臨 to hear it told is not equal to experience;
口說無憑 a verbal arrangement should not furnish a substantial proof; oral expressions cannot be taken as evidence; oral promise is not enough; verbal promise is rather dubious; verbal statements are no guarantee; words alone are no proof; words don't carry conviction;

[口頭] (1) oral; verbal; (2) by word of mouth; in speech; in words; on one's lips; verbal;
口頭禪 byword; catchword; common saying; commonplace saying; pet expression; pet phrase; shibboleth; stock phrase; conventional expressions; parrotcry;
口頭教學法 oral approach;
口頭解釋 oral explanation;
口頭通知 inform orally; notify orally;
口頭文化 oral culture;
口頭文學 oral literature;
口頭協議 verbal agreement;
口頭英語 spoken English;
口頭之交 a friendship which is outward and of the mouth;

[口吐] what is vomited;
口吐毒焰 speak daggers to;
口吐狂言 cheek up; talk nonsense; talk wildly;
口吐蓮華 have the gift of the gab – good at speaking;

[口味] (1) flavour of food; (2) one's taste;
不合口味 not to one's taste;
合口味 suit one's taste;
滿足各種口味 meet all tastes;

[口吻] (1) muzzle; snout; (2) note; tone;
以堅定的口吻 in a firm tone; in a firm voice;

[口誤] a slip of the tongue; an error in speaking;

[口香糖] chewing gum; gum;
夾心口香糖 filled chewing gum;
泡泡口香糖 bubble chewing gum;
球形口香糖 gumball;
一團口香糖 a gob of gum;

[口心] the mouth and the mind;
口心如一 one means what one says; what one says is indeed what one thinks;
佛口蛇心 a Buddha's mouth but a viper's heart – a villainous hypocrite; words of the Buddha and heart of a serpent – honeyed words but evil intent;
口不應心 carry fire in one hand and water in the other; not to have the courage of one's opinion; profess one thing, but mean another; words not agreeing with th heart;
口誦心惟 read sth while pondering its meaning;
口兇心軟 his bark is worse than his bite;

[口信] message; oral message; word;

[口血未乾] the blood in the mouth is not yet dried;

[口炎] stomatitis;
變應性口炎 allergic stomatitis;
傳染性口炎 infectious stomatitis;
汞毒性口炎 mercurial stomatitis;
壞疽性口炎 noma;
壞死性口炎 necrotic stomatitis;
壞血病口炎 stomatitis scorbutica;
接觸性口炎 contact stomatitis;
口瘡性口炎 stomatitis aphthosa;
潰瘍性口炎 ulcerative stomatitis;
淋病性口炎 gonorrheal stomatitis;
淋球菌性口炎 gonococcal stomatitis;
濾泡性口炎 stomatitis follicularis;
梅毒性口炎 syphilitic stomatitis;
霉菌性口炎 mycotic stomatitis;
膜性口炎 membranous stomatitis;
尿毒症口炎 uremic stomatitis;
膿性口炎 pyostomatitis;
鉛毒性口炎 lead stomatitis;
熱帶性口炎 tropical stomatitis;
猩紅熱性口炎 stomatitis scarlatina;
義齒性口炎 denture stomatitis;
中毒性口炎 stomatitis venenata;

[口譯] oral interpretation; interpret;
口譯員 interpreter;

～會議口譯員 conference interpreter;
連續口譯 consecutive interpretation;
聯絡口譯 liaison interpretation;

［口音］ (1) voice; (2) accent;
本地口音 local accent;
～操本地口音 speak with a local accent;
有口音 have an accent;

［口語］ colloquial language; spoken language; vernacular language;
口語詞 colloquial word;
口語的 colloquial;
口語翻譯 speech translation; voice translation;
～口語翻譯系統 voice translation system;
口語能力 articulacy;test of spoken
口語體 colloquial speech;
口語意義 colloquial meaning;
口語英語 colloquial English;
口語用詞 colloquialism;
口語用語 colloquialism;
口語語段 colloquial txt; spoken text;

［口罩］ breathing mask; gauze mask; mask;
外科手術口罩 surgical mask;

隘口 mountain pass;
礙口 be too embarrassing to mention;
凹口 notch;
拗口 hard to pronounce;
版口 type page;
幫口 clan; clique;
艙口 hatch;
槽口 notch;
插口 jack; socket;
岔口 fork;
出口 (1) exit; (2) export;
創口 cut; wound;
瘡口 open part of a sore;
窗口 window;
刀口 (1) edge of a knife; (2) crucial point; right spot;
洞口 entrance to a cave;
渡口 ferry;
封口 (1) seal; (2) heal;
斧口 axe edge;
改口 correct oneself;
港口 harbour; port;
關口 (1) strategic pass; (2) juncture;
海口 seaport;
河口 river mouth; stream outlet;
糊口 eke out one's livelihood; make both ends meet;
虎口 tiger's mouth;
戶口 (1) number of households and total population; (2) registered permanent residence;
還口 answer back; retort;
豁口 breach; break; opening;
火口 crater;
忌口 avoid certain food;
家口 members of a family; the number of people in a family;
緘口 hold one's tongue; say nothing;
借口 use as an excuse;
進口 (1) entrance; (2) inlet;
決口 be breached; burst;
絕口 keep one's mouth shut;
開不了口 have a bone in one's throat;
開口 (1) open one's mouth; start to talk; (2) put the first edge on a knife;
可口 good to eat; tasty;
苦口 (1) admonish in earnest; (2) bitter to the taste;
誇口 boast; brag; talk big;
裂口 (1) breach; gap; split; (2) vent;
路口 crossing; intersection;
門口 doorway; entrance;
滅口 do away with a witness;
槍口 muzzle;
親口 personally;
缺口 breach; gap; notch;
人口 (1) population; (2) number of people in a family;
入口 entrance;
傷口 cut; wound;
失口 make a slip of the tongue;
矢口 swear; vow;
收口 (1) close up; heal; (2) bind off;
漱口 rinse the mouth;
爽口 tasty and refreshing;
順口 smoothly;
鬆口 (1) relax one's bite and release what is held; (2) be less intransigent;
隨口 speaking thoughtlessly;
胃口 appetite; liking;
心口 pit of the stomach;
胸口 pit of the stomach;
住口 shut up; stop talking;
轉口 transit;

kou⁴
kou

【叩】 (1) knock; (2) kowtow;
［叩拜］ kowtow;

[叩門] knock at the door;
叩門求見 knock at the door and ask for an interview;
[叩首] kowtow;
[叩頭] kowtow;
叩頭禮拜 kneel down in prayer;
叩頭賠罪 give sb a grand kowtow and apologize;
叩頭求饒 beat one's forehead on the ground and whine for mercy;
叩頭如泥 repeatedly kowtow by touching the ground with one's forehead;
叩頭如儀 knock one's head on the floor as ceremony; kowtow as custom required;
叩頭謝罪 hit one's forehead on the ground and acknowledge one's guilt;
叩頭作揖 kowtow and bow with a great show of respect;
[叩問] make inquiries;
叩問緣由 make inquiries for the causes;

kou
【扣】 (1) buckle; button up; fasten; (2) cover with an inverted cup; place a cup upside down; (3) arrest; detain; take into custody; (4) deduct; discount; take off; (5) buckle; button; knot; (6) press; pull; (7) smash;
[扣除] deduct; deduction; take off;
工資扣除 wage deduction;
缺陷扣除 defect deduction;
[扣吊] smashes and drop shots;
扣吊結合 combine smashes with drop shots;
[扣釘] fastener;
紙張扣釘 paper fastener;
[扣件] fastener; fastening;
分開式扣件 independent rail fastening;
可調鋼軌扣件 adjustable rail fastener;
直接扣件 direct fastening;
[扣籃] dunk; over-the-rim shot;
[扣留] arrest; detain; hold in custody; seize;
[扣牌] (of mahjong) hold up a tile;
[扣球] smash the ball;
超手扣球 spike over the block;
大掄臂扣球 windmill attack;
反拍扣球 backhand smash;
頭頂扣球 overhead smash;
斜線扣球 cross spike; cross-court smash;
用腕扣球 snap down with the wrist;
正拍扣球 forehard smash;
[扣殺] smash;
大力扣殺 hard smash; powerful smash;
二次扣殺 one-pass attack; two-count spike;
反手扣殺 backhand volley;
高球扣殺 overhead smash;
躍起扣殺 jump smash;
一次扣殺 direct spike;
[扣腕] cock one's wrist;
扣腕動作 cocking wrist action;
[扣押] (1) detain; hold in custody; seize; (2) detention;
[扣壓] pigeonhole; withhold;
[扣眼] buttonhole;
[扣子] buckle; button;
解開一個扣子 undo a button;
扣上扣子 do up a button;

查扣 seize and hold in custody;
搭扣 hasp;
吊扣 suspend;
鈎眼扣 hook and eye;
回扣 sales commission;
快扣 quick spike;
鞋扣 shoe buckle;
一扣 (1) ninety-percent discount; (2) button up;
折扣 discount; rebate;

kou
【寇】 (1) bandit; enemy; (2) invade; pillage; plunder; (3) a surname;
[寇仇] enemy; foe;

草寇 bandit;
敵寇 enemy; foe;
流寇 (1) roving bandits; (2) roving rebel bands;
窮寇 hard pressed enemy; tottering foe;
入寇 invade;
外寇 invading armed forces;
蟻寇 petty robber;
禦寇 guard against bandits; guard against the insults of foreign powers; take precautions against invaders;
賊寇 bandits; rebels;
追窮寇 pursue the tottering foe;

kou
【釦】 button;

kou
【蔻】 cardamon seed;
[蔻蔻] cocoa;

荳蔻 round cardamom;

kou

【轂】 fledgling;

ku¹

ku

【刳】 (1) carve apart; cut apart; (2) gouge; hollow; scoop;

ku

【枯】 (1) withered; (2) dried up; (3) dull; uninteresting;

[枯草] withered grass;

[枯腸] impoverished mind;

[枯槁] (1) withered; (2) haggard; wizened;

憔悴枯槁 haggard from anxiety and dried like a stalk;

[枯骨] the dead;

澤及枯骨 benefit even the dead;

[枯黃] withered and yellow;

[枯寂] dull and lonely;

[枯焦] scorched; withered;

[枯竭] drained; dried up; exhausted;

財源枯竭 the financial resources were exhausted;

水源枯竭 the source has dried up;

[枯井] dry well;

枯井不波 a dried-up well does not have ripples;

枯井打水 make futile efforts; pump a dry well; work to no avail;

[枯窘] dried up;

[枯木] withered tree;

枯木逢春 a withered tree comes to life again – good fortune that comes after a long spell of bad luck; good fortune that comes after a long spell of bad luck; spring comes to the withered tree – get a new lease of life;

枯木死灰 a living corpse; as the withered tree and the dying ambers; dead-alive; lifeless;

枯木朽株 deadwood; withered trees and rotten stumps;

身如枯木，心如死灰 with one's body like a withered tree and one's spirit like dying embers – without warm feelings;

[枯澀] dull and heavy;

[枯樹生花] a dried up tree comes to life again; a withered tree brings forth flowers – rejuvenation;

[枯水] low water;

[枯萎] droop; withered;

[枯楊生稊] get a child at an advanced age; marry a lady much younger than oneself; the old man married a young lady;

[枯燥] dull and dry; monotonous; uninteresting;

枯燥無味 as dry as a chip; as dull as ditch water; barren of interest; cut and dried; drab and dull; dry and tasteless; dry as dust; dull and boring; dull and dry; insipid; sound flat; very dull;

~枯燥無味的書 turgid book;

[枯坐呆等] sit idly without anything to do or wait interminably;

摧枯 crush dry weeds;

乾枯 dried up; withered;

焦枯 dried up; withered;

ku

【哭】 cry; sob; wail; weep;

[哭喊] cry and shout;

[哭哭説説] cry between the words;

[哭哭啼啼] weep and wail; weeping and wailing; whine with plaintive broken sounds;

[哭了] cry;

快要哭了 close to tears;

[哭鬧] cry and scream;

哭哭鬧鬧 make a tearful scene;

又哭又鬧 boohoo; make a tearful scene;

[哭泣] cry; sob; weep;

[哭窮] complain of being short of money;

[哭喪] wail at funeral;

哭喪著臉 a woe-begone look; disconsolately; draw a long face; go around with a long face; make a long face; one looks mournful as if in bereavement; one's face is glum; put on a lon face; wear a long face;

[哭聲] cries;

哭聲哀悽 plaintive cries; sad cries;

哭聲遍野 long-drawn-out howls of misery are heard on every side; the air is rent for miles around with cries of weeping and lamentation;

哭聲載道 cries of misery are heard the whole length of the way;
哭聲震天 a wail of sorrow arises to the very sky; the cries of lamentation rise to the skies; the noise of grief rises to Heaven;
哭不成聲 break down entirely; sob too much to speak; weep too bitterly to speak; unable to speak for weeping;

[哭訴] complain tearfully;
哭訴苦惱 sob out one's grievances;
哭訴原因 blubber the reasons out;

[哭天抹淚] cry piteously; wail and whine;

[哭笑] cry and laugh;
哭笑無常 cry and laugh by turns, without any apparent reason; now he laughs, then he cries; weeping and laughing hysterically;
哭哭笑笑 cry one moment and laugh the next;
又哭又笑 cry and laugh at the same time;
轉哭為笑 smile through one's tears;

哀哭 wail; weep in sorrow; whine;
愛哭 a child who cries frequently;
號哭 cry loudly; wail;
啼哭 cry; wail;
痛哭 cry bitterly; wail;
慟哭 cry one's heart out; wail;
想哭 want to cry;

ku

【窟】 (1) cave; hole; pit; (2) dig the ground and build underground living quarters; (3) den for wild animals;

[窟窿] (1) cave; cavity; hole; (2) debt; deficit;

[窟宅] den; lair;

賭窟 gambling den;
匪窟 bandits' lair;
魔窟 den of monsters;
石窟 grotto; rock cave;

ku

【骷】 human skeleton;

[骷髏] (1) human skeleton; (2) human skull; the death's head;
骷髏頭 death's head;

ku³

ku

【苦】 (1) bitter; (2) bitterness; hardship; pain; suffering; (3) cause sb suffering; give sb a hard time;

[苦艾] absinthe; muggwort;
苦艾酒 absinthe;
苦艾腦 absinthol;
苦艾素 absinthin;

[苦差] hard and unprofitable job;
苦差事 grind;
~幹苦差事 hold the baby;

[苦楚] distress; misery; suffering;
苦楚悲痛 miserable and mournful;
苦楚難言 suffer untold misery;

[苦處] (1) hardships; sufferings; (2) difficulty;

[苦讀] study hard;
苦讀寒窗 persevere in one's studies in spite of hardships;
寒窗苦讀 perserve in one's studies in spite of hardships; studying at a cold window — the life of a poor scholar;

[苦幹] at it; bang away at; plod along; plod on; work hard;
苦學苦幹 study and work hard; study hard and work hard;
埋頭苦幹 bring one's nose to the grindstone; busy oneself in hard work; complete absorption in arduous work; engage oneself in unostentatious hard work; have one's shoulder to the collar; hold one's nose to the grindstone; immerse oneself in hard work; keep one's nose to the grindstone; put one's nose to the grindstone; quietly immerse oneself in hard work; quietly put one's shoulder to the wheel; work doggedly in silence; work very energetically; work with quiet hard application;

[苦工] hard labour; hard work; manual work; moil;
做苦工 break stones;

[苦功] hard work; painstaking effort;
下苦功 take pains;

[苦瓜] bitter gourd;
一根藤上的苦瓜 bitter gourds from the same vine — people with a similar bitter past;

[苦海] abyss of misery; sea of bitterness; sea of woes;
苦海深淵 abyss of misery;
苦海無邊 bitterness without end;

boundless sea of hardship; the bitter sea of life has no bounds; the endless sea of tribulations;

渡過苦海 rescue from life of pains and misery and reach the other shore of salvation;

[苦寒] bitter cold;

[苦活] grunt work;

[苦口] (1) admonish in earnest; (2) bitter to the taste;

苦口利於病 bitter to the taste but good for the disease;

苦口良言 earnest admonition; good advice; it's the bitter truth;

苦口良藥 a good medicine tastes bitter; though bitter-tasting, it is still the best medicine for sb;

苦口婆心 a tender remonstrance; advise in earnest words and with good intention; earnestly and maternally; urge sb time and again with good intentions; with kind and compassionate persuasion;

[苦摳苦攢] work hard and live mean;

[苦苦] hard; strenuously;

苦苦哀告 beg piteously;

苦苦哀求 beg piteously; beg sb in a hundred ways; beg very hard; beseech sb bitterly; entreat piteously; implore bitterly; make an earnest request of sb; press one's suit; press one's suit on one's knees;

苦苦相逼 press hard; run hard;

苦苦相勸 remonstrate earnestly; try one's best to persuade;

苦苦追求 try hard to gain;

[苦樂] misery and happiness;

苦樂不勻 misery and happiness are unequally apportioned; unbalance of grief and joy — there is more distress than happiness;

苦樂共嘗 taste joys and hardships together;

苦樂與共 partake in each other's joys and sorrows; share the rough and smooth with sb; share with sb both prosperity and adversity; take "for better for worse";

苦與樂 joy and woes; pleasure and woes;

苦中作樂 enjoy in adversity; enjoy oneself despite poverty; find happiness in suffering; find pleasure during bitter; seek pleasure in sorrow; sweeten the bitterness of destiny; try to be happy amidst adverse circumstances; try to enjoy oneself despite one's suffering;

先苦後樂 the first to bear hardships, the last to enjoy comforts;

以苦為樂，以苦為榮 feel it a joy and an honour to work under hard conditions;

[苦力] coolie; cooly;

[苦臉] wry face;

做苦臉 make a wry face;

[苦練] drill diligently; practise hard;

[苦悶] dejected; depressed; feeling low; gloomy;

精神苦悶 be depressed in mind;

[苦難] distress; misery; suffering; tribulation;

苦難深淵 abyss of bitterness;

苦難深重 in deep distress; in the depth of misery; long suffering; untold suffering;

救苦救難 bring sb out of the pit of misery; help people in distress; help the needy and relieve the distressed; life sb out of the abyss of darkness; relieve sb's misery; save sb from bitterness and from distress; save sb from the abyss of misery; save those in calamity;

千苦萬難 numerous hardships and difficulties;

忍受苦難 bear up under affliction;

深受苦難 suffer profoundly;

説苦道難 tell all one's woes;

[苦惱] distressed; in vexation; tormented; troubled; vexation; vexed; worried;

苦惱不安 be in agony;

非常苦惱 sorely distressed;

~令人非常苦惱 exteemly vexing;

傾訴苦惱 pour out one's trouble;

[苦肉計] deceive the enemy by torturing one's own man; the ruse of self-injury;

[苦澀] (1) acerbity; bitter and astringent; hard to the taste; (2) agonized; anguished; pained;

[苦水] (1) bitter water; brackish water; (2) gastric secretion; (3) suffering; (4) bitterness; misery; suffering;

倒苦水 grumble; pour out one's grievances;

滿腔苦水 full of grievances;

[苦思] cudgel one's brains; languish for; think

hard;
苦思竭慮 cudgel one's brains;
苦思苦想 cudgel one's brains; make violent mental efforts; ransack one's memory; think hard;
苦思冥想 beat one's brains; puzzle over; think long and hard;

K

[苦甜] the bitter and the sweet;
吃青果—先苦後甜 eating Chinese olives – first bitter, then sweet; (fig) first hardship, then happiness;
[苦痛] pain; suffering;
經歷苦痛 experience the pain;
[苦頭] bitter taste; hardship; suffering;
嚐到苦頭 count the cost; suffer some hardships;
嚐盡苦頭 have a hard time of it;
吃苦頭 burn one's fingers; cost sb dear; cost sb dearly; get the works; run the gauntlet; suffer; to one's cost;
~吃盡苦頭 have a rough time; have had it;
~肯吃苦頭 have the mind favourably inclined to endure hardship;
[苦味] bitter taste;
[苦笑] bitter smile; forced smile; produce a forced smile; wry smile;
[苦心] pains; take trouble to;
苦心孤詣 make extraordinarily painstaking efforts; take great pains;
苦心經營 elaborative in the undertaking; manage painstakingly; mastermind with painstaking effort; take great pains to build up an enterprise; work out with unspaqring efforts;
苦心拼湊 painstakingly piece together; take great pains to rig up;
苦心思索 puzzle over;
苦心致志 by faithful devotion and constancy of purpose;
苦心鑽研 do painstaking research;
苦攖其心 press hard on the mind; weigh on one's mind;
煞費苦心 assiduous; at great pains; at the pains of; cudgel one's brains; from Dan to Beersheba; go through a lot of trouble; go to great pains; labourious; rack one's brains; take pains;
[苦行] ascetic practices; life of self-denial and mortification;
苦行僧 a person who lives a life of self-denial and mortification;
[苦藥] acrid drug;
[苦役] hard labour; penal servitude;
熬過苦役 endure the hard labour;
[苦於] (1) suffer from; (2) more bitter than;
苦於奔命 be hardpressed by duties;
[苦雨] continuous rain;
苦雨淒風 bitter rain and biting wind; distressing rain and depressing winds;
[苦戰] struggle hard; wage an arduous struggle;
[苦衷] difficulties that one is reluctant to discuss;
[苦主] family of the victim in a murder case;
悲苦 grieved and sorrowful; sad;
慘苦 miserable;
吃苦 bear hardships;
愁苦 depressed; worried;
甘苦 (1) sweetness and bitterness; weal and woe; (2) hardships and difficulties experienced in work;
孤苦 friendless and wretched; orphaned and helpless;
寒苦 destitute; poverty-stricken;
何苦 is it worth the trouble; why bother;
疾苦 hardships; sufferings;
堅苦 arduous; extremely hard and bitter;
艱苦 arduous; difficult; hard; tough;
叫苦 complain of hardship; moan and groan;
刻苦 (1) assiduous; hardworking; industrious; (2) simple and frugal;
困苦 in privation;
勞苦 hard work; toil;
貧苦 impoverished; poor;
勤苦 diligent; hardworking; industrious;
清苦 poor;
窮苦 poor; poverty-sticken;
茹苦 put up with hardships;
受苦 have a rough time; suffer;
訴苦 pour out one's woes; vent one's grievances;
痛苦 painful; sad;
挖苦 speak ironically; speak sarcastically;
辛苦 hard; toilsome;
憶苦 recall one's suffering in the old society;

ku

【楛】 crude and easy to break;

ku⁴

ku

【矻】 (1) diligent and industrious; (2) very tired;

ku

【庫】 storehouse; warehouse;

［庫藏］ have a storage of; have in storage; have in store;
庫藏股票 treasury stock;

［庫存］ inventory; repertory; reserve; stock;
庫存分析 analysis of stock;
庫存統計 statistics of stock;
安全庫存 safety stock;
儲備庫存 reserve stock;
商品庫存 merchandise inventory;
最低庫存 minimum inventory;

［庫房］ storehouse; storeroom;

寶庫 treasure-house;
倉庫 depository; storehouse; warehouse;
車庫 garage;
公庫 public treasury;
國庫 national treasury; state treasury;
金庫 state treasure;
冷庫 cold storage;
糧庫 grain depot;
省庫 provincial treasury;
書庫 stack room;
水庫 reservoir;
司庫 treasurer;
血庫 blood bank;
油庫 oil depot; tank farm;

ku

【絝】 breeches; drawers; panties; pants; trousers;

［絝叉兒］ pants or trousers reaching just above the knees; short pants; shorts;

［絝襠］ crotch of trousers;

［絝腳］ part of trousers near or around the ankles;

［絝腿］ legs of trousers;

［絝腰］ waist of trousers;
絝腰帶 waist belt or rope for fastening the trousers;

［絝子］ breeches; pants; trousers;

ku

【酷】 (1) brutal; cruel; oppressive; (2) exceedingly; extremely; very;

［酷愛］ ardently love; very fond of;
酷愛和平 one is ardently devoted to peace; peace-loving;

［酷寒］ bitter cold;

［酷烈］ (1) cruel; fierce; (2) heavy; strong;

［酷氣］ stuffy air;
酷氣蒸人 stuffy air; the air is stifling by the heat;

［酷熱］ extremely hot;
酷熱期 heat wave;

［酷暑］ intense heat of summer;
酷暑寒冬 the dog days of summer and the dead of winter;
酷暑嚴寒 extremely hot or severely cold; in scorching summer and freezing winter;
祁寒酷暑 severe cold and intense heat;

［酷似］ bear a strong resemblance to; exactly like; the very image of;
酷似的人 dead ringer;

［酷刑］ brutal corporal punishment; cruel torture; savage torture;

殘酷 brutal; cruel; ruthless;
冷酷 callous; cold-blooded; heartless; unfeeling;
嚴酷 cruel; ruthless;

ku

【褲】 pants; trousers;

［褲帶］ trouser belt;
勒緊褲帶 tighten one's belt;

［褲襠］ crotch of trousers;

［褲管］ trouser legs;
捲起褲管 roll one's trousers up;

［褲裝］ trouser suit;
紅色褲裝 red trouser suit;
一套褲裝 a trouser suit;

［褲子］ britches; pants; trousers;
穿褲子 wear the trousers;
脱下褲子 take off one's pants;
一條褲子 a pair of trousers;

長褲 pants; slacks; trousers;
襯褲 pants; underpants;
短褲 shorts;
多袋褲 combats;
連衫褲 jumpsuit;
連衣褲 union suit;
棉褲 cotton-padded trousers;

kua¹

kua

【夸】 boast;

［夸夸其談］ a big screed full of bombast; big talk; fustian; gassiness; gassy; indulge bla-bla in the air; bombastic; bombastic twaddle; bragging; gas and gaiters;

hot air; in exaggerations; on stilts; rant windbaggary; run off at the mouth; shoot off; shoot off one's mouth; sound off; spread oneself; stilted conversation; talk a lot of hot air; vaporous; windy; windy talk;

K

kua

【刳】 gouge; hollow; scoop;

kua

【姱】 elegant; fascinating; good-looking; pretty;

kua

【誇】 (1) blow up; boast; exaggerate; overstate; (2) praise;

［誇大］ aggrandize; exaggerate; magnify; overstate;

誇大困難 exaggerate the difficulties;

誇大其詞 a lot of hot air; blow up; draw the long bow; exaggerate; make an overstatement; put it on; represent beyond the bounds of truth; speak in superlatives; stick it on;

誇大缺點 exaggerate the shortcomings;

被大肆誇大 be much exaggerated;

故意誇大 exaggerate purposely;

［誇獎］ commend; compliment sb on; praise;

得到誇獎 get a compliment; receive a compliment;

接受誇獎 accept a compliment;

一種誇獎 a compliment;

［誇口］ boast; brag; talk big;

［誇誇其談］ indulge in verbiage;

誇誇其談的人 gasbag;

［誇耀］ boast of; brag about; flaunt; show off;

誇耀自己 brag about oneself;

［誇張］ (1) exaggerate; overstate; (2) hyperbole;

誇張的語言 inflation of language;

誇張法 hyperbole;

過於誇張的 over-the-top;

［誇嘴］ boast; talk big;

浮誇 boastful; fuddy-duddy;

矜誇 conceited and boastful;

虛誇 boastful; exaggerative;

自誇 boast; sing one's own praise;

kua[3]

kua

【垮】 (1) collapse; topple; (2) wear down; (3) put to rout; (4) fall out of power;

［垮臺］ collapse; fall of a government;

kua[4]

kua

【胯】 groin; space between the legs;

［胯部］ crotch; crutch;

kua

【跨】 (1) step; stride; (2) bestride; ride astride; straddle;

［跨步］ stride;

跨步上籃 stride lay-up;

跨步跳 step;

［跨導］ transconductance;

變頻跨導 conversion transconductance;

初始跨導 initial transconductance;

動跨導 dynamic transconductance;

高跨導 high transconductance;

［跨度］ span;

部份跨度 subspan;

時間跨度 time span;

子跨度 subspan;

［跨國］ transnational;

跨國公司 multinational; transnational corporation;

跨國所得 international income;

跨國政治 transnational politics;

［跨過］ stride;

一跨而過 take in one's stride;

［跨鶴］ ride the crane－become an immortal;

跨鶴西去 ride a crane towards the west－the death of a lady;

［跨境］ cross-border;

跨境貿易 cross-border trade;

跨境業務 cross-border business;

［跨科課程］ interdisciplinary course;

［跨洋過海］ cross the ocean and sea－go abroad;

［跨越］ cut across; hurdle; leap over; stride across;

衝跨 burst; shatter;

多跨 multispan;

橫跨 stretch over or across;

kua

【骻】 waist bone;

kuai[3]

kuai

【舀】 a pronunciation of 舀, ladle;

kuai

【蒯】 (1) scirpus cyperinus var, concolor, a rush, from which many things are weaved; (2) a surname;

[蒯草] wool grass;

kuai

【擓】 (1) scratch; (2) carry on the arm;

kuai⁴

kuai

【快】 (1) fast; quick; rapid; (2) speed; (3) hurry up; make haste; (4) about; before long; on the point of; soon; (5) ingenious; quick-witted; (6) sharp; (7) forthright; plainspoken; straightforward; (8) gratified; happy; pleased;

[快板] allegro;
小快板 allegretto;

[快報] bulletin; newsflash; stop-press news; wall bulletin;

[快步] trot;
快步舞 quickstep;
快步舞曲 quickstep;
快步走 hoof;
慢快步 collected trot;
平穩快步 square trot;
縮短快步 slow trot;

[快餐] fast food; fast meal; quick meal; snack; fast food;
快餐店 fast-food restaurant;
~ 連鎖快餐店 fast-food chain;
快餐食品 fast food;
吃快餐 take fast food;

[快車] express bus; express train; fast train;
快車道 fast lane;
開快車 hurry through one's work; make short work of a job; open the throttle; speed up the work; step on the gas;
一趟快車 an express train;

[快當] prompt; quick;
快快當當 quickly;

[快刀斬亂麻] a swift and ruthless action; cut the Gordian knot; cut a tangled skein of jute with a sharp knife; make lightning decisions; slice through a knot with a sharp knife; take resolute and effective measures to solve a complicated problem in an instant;

[快遞] express delivery; fast mail;
快遞公司 courier;
快遞員 courier;
航空快遞 air express;

[快點] be quick; bustle up; chop-chop; hurry up;
叫他快點 tell him to bustle up;

[快感] delight; pleasant sensation;

[快攻] fast break; quick attack;
快攻球 wide-cat spring attack;
近台快攻 fast attack over the table;

[快好] fast and good;
又快又好 efficient; fast with excellent results;

[快活] cheerful; happy; joyful; merry;
非常快活 happy as a clam;
日子過得很快活 live a happy life;
祝你玩得快活 enjoy yourself; have a good time;

[快進] fast forward;
快進鍵 forward key;

[快來] coming soon;
快來了 coming soon;
快來呀 roll up;

[快樂] cheerful; happiness; happy; joyful; merry;
不快樂 unhappy;
~ 非常不快樂 desperately unhappy;
短暫的快樂 fleeting pleasure;
非常快樂 be on top of the world; be very happy;
感同身受的快樂 vicarious pleasure;
假期快樂 have a great holiday; have a great vacation;
一陣快樂 a stab of joy;
周末快樂 have a good weekend;

[快馬] fast horse;
快馬不用鞭催，響鼓不用重錘 a good horse should be seldom spurred; a willing horse must not be whipped;
快馬加鞭 accelerate the speed; burn up the road on one's way; do a fast job; posthaste; ride whip and spur; spur the flying horse at high speed; whip one's horse up to a swift trot; with whip and spur;

[快門] shutter;
快門速度 shutter speed;
~ 快門速度表 shutter speed scale;
電子快門 electronic shutter;
焦面快門 focal plane shutter;
鏡間快門 between-lens shutter;
鏡中快門 between-the-lens shutter;

中心快門 central shutter; lens shutter;
[快跑] scoot;
多裝快跑 haul more and run faster;
[快人] person who is frank by nature; straightforward man;
快人快事 a fast job done by a straightforward person; a heroic deed performed by a straightforward man;
快人快語 a person of straightforward disposition is outspoken; a straight talk from an honest man; a straightforward talk from a straightforward person; an outspoken man speaking his mind;
快人一言 an intelligent man only needs a hint;
[快手] deft hand; nimble-handed person; quick worker;
快手快腳 agile; do things quickly; do things with celerity; nimble; nimble of hands and fast of feet;
[快速] fast; high-speed; quick; rapid; speedy;
快速充電 quick charging;
快速倒片 quick rewind;
快速地面部隊 mobile ground forces;
快速應用開發 rapid application development;
[快艇] high speed boat; motor boat; speedboat;
快艇比賽 speedboat race;
[快慰] delighted and pleased; glad; pleased;
[快信] express letter;
一封快信 an express letter;
[快修] quick service;
[快要] about to; almost; be going to; in no time; in the twinkling of an eye; like wildfire; nearly; on the verge of;
[快意] comfortable; elated; joyful; pleased satisfied;
[快郵] express mail; special delivery;
[快運] express;
航空快運 air express;
[快嘴] quick-tongued;
快嘴快舌 prone to talk rashly;

不快 (1) be displeased; be unhappy; (2) be indisposed; feel unwell;
暢快 carefree; free from inhibitions;
稱快 express one's gratification;
飛快 at lightning speed; very fast;
趕快 at once; quickly;
很快 any minute now; in a fiffy; in no time; it will not be long;
歡快 cheerful and light-hearted; in a merry mood;
加快 accelerate; quicken; speed up;
盡快 as soon as possible;
涼快 cool off; pleasantly cool;
明快 (1) lucid and lively; (2) straightforward;
勤快 diligent; hardworking;
輕快 (1) brisk; spry; (2) lighthearted; lively;
爽快 (1) comfortable; refreshed; (2) frank; straightforward; (3) readily; with alacrity;
特快 express; express train;
痛快 (1) delighted; very happy; (2) to one's great satisfaction; to one's heart's content;
外快 extra income;
愉快 cheerful; delighted; happy; pleased;
嘴快 have a loose tongue; incapable of keeping secrets; rash in speech;

kuai

【塊】 (1) a bar of; a bit of; a block of; a brick of; a cake of; a chop of; a chunk of; a clot of; a cob of; a cube of; a cut of; a dollop of; a fragment of; a gob of; a gobbet of; a junk of; a knobble of; a loaf of; a lump of; a morsel of; a pane of; a piece of; a round of; a sheet of; a slab of; a slice of; a sod of; a square of; a stick of; a wedge of; (2) dollar;
[塊兒大] large; massive;
[塊頭] hulky; large;
大塊頭 hefty person; hulk; tall person; tall and strong person;

板塊 plate;
冰塊 ice cake;
金塊 gold bullion;
泥塊 lumps of clay;
鉛塊 lead;
石塊 rock; stone;
鐵塊 iron plate;
瓦塊 broken tiles;
血塊 coagulated blood clot;
岩塊 rock;
一大塊 a bulk;
一厚塊 a loaf of;
磚塊 fragment of a brick;

kuai

【會】 add; compute;
[會計] (1) accounting; (2) accountant;

treasurer;
會計部文員 accounts clerk;
會計檔案 accounting dossier;
會計管理 accounting management;
會計規程 accounting regulation;
會計行業 accountancy;
會計年度 financial year;
會計軟件 accounting software;
會計師 accountant; chartered accountant;
~獨立會計師 independent account;
~高級會計師 senior accountant;
~管理會計師 managerial account;
~特許會計師 certified public account;
~主管會計師 accountant in charge;
~助理會計師 assistant accountant;
~註冊會計師 certified public accountant; chartered accountant;
~專業會計師 professional account;
~總會計師 accountant-in-chief; general accountant;
會計事務所 accounting firm;
會計學 accounting;
會計原則 accounting principles;
會計員 bookkeeper; treasurer;
會計長 accountant general;
會計制度 accounting system;
保險會計 insurance accounting;
部門會計 segment accounting;
產量會計 throughput accounting;
常規會計 conventional accounting;
成本會計 cost accounting;
單式會計 single entry accounting;
電腦化會計 computerized accounting;
分析會計 analytical accounting;
~分析會計學 analytical accounting;
複式會計 double accounting; double entry account;
公共會計 public accounting;
公司會計 corporate accounting;
國際會計 international accounting;
基金會計 fund accounting;
機關會計 institutional accounting;
零售會計 retail accounting;
內部會計 internal accounting;
商業會計 business accountancy; business accounting; commercial accounting; mercantile accounting;
市政會計 municipal accounting;
税務會計 tax accounting;
外匯會計 foreign exchange accounting;
銷售會計 sales accounting;
一個會計 an accountant;
銀行會計 bank accounting;
預期會計 forward accounting;
預算會計 budgetary unit accounting;
責任會計 responsibility accouting;
折舊會計 depreciation accounting;
職能會計 functional accounting;
助理會計 accounting assistant;
專業會計 professional accounting;
資產會計 assets accounting;

kuai
【筷】 chopsticks;
［筷子］ chopsticks;
筷子架 chopsticks rest;
長筷子 long chopsticks;
木筷子 wooden chopsticks;
漆筷子 lacquer chopsticks;
一把筷子 a bundle of chopsticks; a pair of chopsticks;
一根筷子 a piece of chopstick;
一雙筷子 a pair of chopsticks;
一枝筷子 a chopstick;
竹筷子 bamboo chopsticks;

碗筷 bowls and chopsticks;
牙筷 ivory chapsticks;

kuai
【蒯】 a pronunciation of 蒯;

kuai
【儈】 broker; go-between; middleman;

市儈 philistine; sordid merchant;
文儈 literary prostitute;
牙儈 broker;

kuai
【劊】 amputate; cut off;

kuai
【澮】 (1) ditches on farmland; (2) a river in Shaanxi and Henan provinces;

kuai
【獪】 artful; crafty; cunning;

狡獪 crafty; cunning; deceitful;

kuai
【鄶】 an ancient state in present-day Henan;

kuai
【檜】 Chinese cypress; Chinese juniper;

K

kuai

【膾】 meat chopped into small pieces; minced meat;

［膾炙人口］ be oft-quoted and widely loved; enjoy great popularity; on everybody's lips; pleasant to all tastes; please all tastes; popular; popular and much praised; twice-told; widely quoted; win universal praise;

kuai

【旝】 (1) flag used by a general; (2) silk pennant for hanging;

kuan[1]

kuan

【寬】 (1) broad; wide; (2) breath; width; (3) relax; relieve; (4) extend; (5) generous; leninet; (6) comfortably off; well-off;

［寬敞］ commodious; roomy; spacious;
寬敞的 commodious;
寬敞舒適 capacious and comfortable; commodious and cosy;

［寬暢］ careful; cheerful; free from worry; happy;

［寬綽］ (1) commodious; roomy; spacious; (2) composed; relax; unperturbed;

［寬打窄用］ budget liberally and spend sparingly;

［寬大］ (1) roomy; spacious; wide; (2) lenient; magnanimous; (3) generous;
寬大處理 be magnanimously treated; give quarter; have mercy on; lenient treatment; show mercy to; treat sb with leniency;
寬大的 lenient;
寬大為懷 attitude of clemency; full of forgiveness; large-hearted; lenient; magnanimous; treat sb leniently; with generous nature;
寬大無邊 excessively leniency; generous to a fault;
寬大政策 a policy of leniency;
十分寬大 full of forgiveness;

［寬帶］ broadband; wideband;
寬帶天線 broadband aerial;

［寬待］ treat liberally; treat with leniency;
寬待俘虜 give lenient treatment to prisoners of war; treat prisoners of war leniently;

［寬度］ breadth; width;
半峰寬度 half-peak breadth;
半值寬度 half breadth;
表面寬度 face width;
等效寬度 equivalent;
縫隙寬度 clearance width;
管道寬度 duct width;
角寬度 angular breadth;
截面寬度 cross-sectional width;
譜線寬度 line breadth;
前肩寬度 front porch width;
圖像寬度 image width;
有效寬度 effective breadth;
丈量寬度 tonnage breadth;
自然寬度 natural breadth;
最大寬度 extreme breadth;

［寬廣］ broad; extensive; spacious; vast;
寬廣博大 vast and extensive;

［寬宏］ broad-minded; large-minded;
寬宏大量 a broad mind; a large heart; big-hearted; broad views; broad-minded and generous; generous and kind; most liberal and large-minded;
襟度寬宏 broad-minded;
氣度寬宏 of magnanimous bearing;

［寬厚］ (1) generous; kind; lenient; magnanimous; tolerant and generous; (2) wide and thick;
寬厚憨直 generous and straightforward; good-natured and honest;

［寬曠］ extensive vast;

［寬闊］ broad; liberal; roomy; spacious; wide;
寬闊的道路 road of great width;

［寬猛並濟］ alternate leniency with severity; gentleness tempered by severity; severity tempered with gentleness; the stick and carrot; use hard and soft tactics in turn; use the carrot and stick;

［寬容］ bear with; lenient; tolerant; toleration;
寬容度 latitude;
宗教寬容 religious toleration;

［寬舒］ (1) free from worry; happy; (2) spacious and smooth;

［寬恕］ clemency; excuse; forgive; pardon;
寬恕過錯 forgive an offense;
被寬恕 be absolved;
得到寬恕 receive forgiveness;
乞求寬恕 beg for mercy; beg forgiveness;
請求寬恕 appeal for mercy; ask for forgiveness;

［寬慰］ comfort; console; easy; soothe;
寬慰地舒一口氣 heave a sigh of relief;
［寬狹］ breadth; width;
［寬限］ extend a time limit; grace;
寬限幾天 extend the deadline a few days;
安全寬限 safety allowance;
［寬心］ at ease; feel at rest; feel free from anxiety; feel relieved; find relief; relaxed; set one's mind at ease;
［寬嚴並濟］ temper justice with mercy;
［寬衣］ disrobe; loose garment; take off one's coat;
寬衣解帶 remove the upper coat and loosen the belt; undress oneself; unfasten the girdle and strip off one's dress;
解帶寬衣 unloose the girdle and remove the upper coat;
［寬裕］ comfortably off; well off; well-to-do;
手頭寬裕 in easy circumstances; in the bucks; well off at the moment; with plenty of money to spend;
［寬縱］ indulge;

從寬 handle leniently;
放寬 loosen; relax restrictions;
加寬 broaden; widen;
心寬 not lend oneself to worry and anxiety;
型寬 molded breadth;
一手寬 hand breadth;
總寬 overall breadth;

kuan³
kuan
【款】 (1) sincere; (2) entertain; receive with hospitality; (3) item; paragraph; section; (4) fund; a sum of money; money; (5) rich person; money bags;
［款步］ move slowly; walk in slow steps; with deliberate steps;
［款待］ entertain; entertain with courtesy and warmth; treat cordially;
款待客人 entertain guests;
款待周到 exercise great hospitality;
［款額］ amount of money;
匯出款額 remitted amount;
［款哥］ rich brother; rich man; young big buck;
［款姐］ rich sister; rich woman;
［款留殷殷］ cordially urge a guest to stay; detain with great enthusiasm;
［款曲］ heartfelt feelings;
互通款曲 express feelings of mutual affection;
［款式］ design; fashion; model; pattern; style;
款式多樣 a great variety of models;
款式繁多 with various patterns;
款式新穎 fashionable style;
［款項］ (1) a sum of money; fund; (2) section of an article in a legal document;
巨額款項 a huge amount of money;
［款語移時］ speak about with minute details for a short time;
［款識］ inscriptions;
［款酌慢飲］ pour the wine in small cups and sip it slowly;
［款子］ a sum of money;
借一大筆款子 borrow a large sum of money;
一筆款子 a sum; a sum of money;

撥款 allocate funds; appropriation;
籌款 raise funds;
存款 deposit money;
貸款 credit; loan;
罰款 fine; forfeit; impose a fine;
放款 make loans;
付款 pay a sum of money;
公款 public money;
匯款 remit money;
貨款 payment for good;
借款 loan;
捐款 contribution; donation;
賠款 indemnity; reparations;
稅款 tax payment;
提款 draw money from a bank;
條款 article; clause; provision;
現款 cash ready money;
押款 borrow money on security;
債款 loan;

kuan
【窾】 empty; hollow;

kuang¹
kuang
【匡】 (1) correct; rectify; (2) assist; save; (3) a surname;
［匡救］ remedy; rescue from disaster; save;
［匡算］ calculate roughly;
［匡正］ correct; rectify;
匡正時弊 make right existing evils;

kuang
【恇】 afraid; fearful; timid; timorous;

kuang
【框】 a pronunciation of 框 ;

kuang
【筐】 rectangular chest woven from bamboo strips;
[筐子] crate; small basket;
糞筐 large bamboo basket;
土筐 basket for holding earth;
竹筐 bamboo basket;

kuang
【誆】 cheat; deceive; lie;
[誆騙] deceive; dupe; hoax;
東誆西騙 swindle on all sides;

kuang²

kuang
【狂】 (1) crazy; mad; (2) violent; (3) unrestrained; wild; (4) arrogant; overbearing;
[狂暴] violent; wild;
狂暴不馴 as mad as March hare; wild and untamed;
狂暴殘虐 fierce and cruel;
狂暴西風 Furious fifty;
[狂奔] run about madly; run about wildly;
[狂飆] hurricane; wild whirlwind;
[狂草] excessively free cursive style in Chinese calligraphy;
[狂放] undisciplined; unrestrained; unruly; wild;
[狂吠] bark furiously; howl;
[狂風] (1) whole gale; (2) fierce wind; wild wind;
狂風暴雨 a furious storm; a gale-driven rain; a heady tempest; a howling wind and torrential rain; a rough weather; a violent storm; a violent wind and driving rain; a windy downpour; an inclement;
狂風大作 a gale is blowing;
狂風惡浪 a fierce storm; great hazards; violent winds and fierce waves – grave perils;
狂風呼嘯 a fierce gale is whistling; the wind howls;
狂風巨浪 a violent gale and a heavy sea; a violent storm and roaring waves;
狂風怒號 a violent wind is howling widely; the storm raves;
狂風驟起 a fierce gale springs up; a sudden gale strikes; suddenly a high wind springs up;
一陣狂風 a blast of wind; a gust of wind;
[狂夫] bohemian; one who cares nothing about conventions;
[狂歌] sing with wild joy;
引吭狂歌 sing with wild abandon;
[狂歡] carnival; rejoice with wild excitement; revel;
狂歡宴會 orgy;
狂歡作樂 hold carnival and make merry; paint the town red;
一陣狂歡 a fit of madness;
[狂瀾] raging waves; roaring waves;
力挽狂瀾 do one's best to stem a raging tide; do one's utmost to save a desperate situation; make herculean efforts to save a critical situation; make the best of a bad business; make vigorous efforts to turn the tide; save the critical situation; turn back the powers of darkness;
[狂亂] derangment; frenzied; mad;
[狂怒] be furious with anger; furor; fury; rage;
一陣狂怒 a fit of rage;
[狂氣] arrogant airs and manner of speaking;
[狂犬病] hydrophobia;
[狂熱] fanatical; fanaticism; feverish; namia; rabid;
狂熱者 enthusiast; fan;
航空狂熱 aeromania;
宗教狂熱 religious fanaticism;
[狂人] (1) kook; lunatic; madman; maniac; (2) an extremely arrogant and conceited person;
狂人囈語 ravings of a madman;
[狂士] bohemian scholar; self-conceited scholar;
[狂態] display of wild manners; insolent and conceited manners; scandalous scene;
[狂濤巨瀾] the angry waves; the raging tide;
[狂妄] arrogant; presumptuous;
狂妄悖逆 ill-behaved and perverse; wanton and disloyal;
狂妄不羈 run wild;
狂妄叫囂 arrogantly clamour;
狂妄無知 conceited and ignorant;
狂妄凶暴 arrogant and violent;
狂妄自大 arrogant and conceited; as

proud as Lucifer; false pride; high and mighty; think one is the whole cheese;

[狂喜] be ravished with joy; rejoice with wild excitement; wild with joy;

[狂想曲] fantasia; rhapsody;

[狂笑] laugh boisterously; laugh wildly; roars of laughter; wild laugh;

一陣狂笑 a gust of laughter;

[狂言] boastful talk; bragging; crazy remarks; crazy talk; incoherent talk; nonsense; ravings; wild language;

[狂野] violent and rough;

狂野的 crazed;

[狂飲] binge; on the piss;

狂飲聚會 booze-up;

狂飲縱慾的 bacchanalian;

周末狂飲 week-end binge;

[狂恣] disolute; profligate; unibhibited; unrestrained;

愛花狂 love flowers;

猖狂 furious; savage;

痴狂 crazy about; infatuated with;

癲狂 (1) demented; mad; (2) frivolous;

發狂 go crazy; go mad;

瘋狂 (1) insane; (2) frenzied; unbridled;

輕狂 frivolous;

凶狂 fierce and ruthless;

陽狂 pretend to be mad;

佯狂 pretend to be made;

躁狂 mania;

張狂 flippant and impudent; insolent;

kuang

【誑】 deceive; delude;

[誑語] falsehood; lies;

kuang⁴

kuang

【況】 (1) in addition; moreover; not to mention; (2) comparative; compare; (3) circumstances; situation; (4) call at; visit; (5) a surname;

[況且] besides; furthermore; in addition; moreover;

[況味] circumstances and sentiment;

病況 patient's condition;

概況 general situation;

何況 let alone; much less;

佳況 in an excellent condition;

近況 the current situation;

景況 circumstances; situation;

境況 circumstances; condition;

情況 (1) situation; state of affairs; (2) military situation;

盛況 grand occasion; spectacular event;

實況 what is actually happening;

戰況 situation on the battlefield;

狀況 condition; state; state of affairs;

kuang

【框】 (1) door frame; (2) frame; framework; (3) skeleton of a lantern;

[框架] frame; framework; framing;

框架建築 frame building;

~框架建築結構

框架結構 frame construction; frame building structure;

黃鉛框架 brass framing;

金屬框架 metal framework;

[框形] frame;

框形天線 frame aerial;

[框子] frame;

窗框 window frame;

方框 square frame;

畫框 frame;

鏡框 picture frame;

門框 doorframe;

kuang

【眶】 rim of the eye; socket of the eye;

眼眶 (1) eye socket; orbit; (2) rim of the eye;

kuang

【貺】 (1) bestow; confer; give; (2) be favoured with; (3) a surname;

kuang

【壙】 (1) tomb; vault; (2) field; open space; (3) leave idle; leave vacant;

kuang

【鄺】 a surname;

kuang

【曠】 (1) spacious; vast; (2) free from worries and petty ideas; (3) neglect; waste; (4) loose-fitting;

[曠達] big-hearted; broad-minded; free; open-minded;

曠達之士 profound scholar; scholar with an open mind;

[曠代] matchless among one's contempoarries;
[曠蕩] boundless; endless;
[曠廢] neglect; out of practice;
曠廢學業 neglect one's studies; neglect school work;
[曠費] waste;
曠費時間 waste one's time;
[曠夫] unmarried man of marriageable age;
曠夫怨女 unmarried man and an unmarried woman; bachelors and spinsters;
[曠工] stay away from work without leave or good reason;
經常曠工 frequent absences from work;
[曠古] from time immemorial;
曠古奇聞 unprecedented story;
曠古迄今 from time immemorial;
曠古未聞 never seen in past history;
曠古未有 unprecedented in history;
曠古以來 since ancient days;
[曠久] lasting; long;
曠久未見 have not been seen for a long time;
[曠課] absent from school without leave; cut classes; cut school; play truant; skip school work;
[曠世] incomparable in the contemporary era; outstanding; unequalled by contemporaries; without peer in one's generation;
曠世奇才 a genius without peer in one's generation; a remarkable talent of many ages;
曠世無雙 stand without peer in one's generation;
曠世逸才 a man of brilliance unequalled by contemporaries;
[曠野] open country; open field; wilderness;
曠野荒郊 a deserted countryside; a wild, desert country; wilderness;
曠野恐怖症 agoraphobia;
一片曠野 a stretch of open country;
[曠職] absent from duty without leave or good reason;

空曠 open; spacious;
寬曠 extensive; vast;

kuang
【礦】 (1) mineral; ore deposit; (2) mine; (3) glance; ore;

[礦藏] lode; mineral resources;
礦藏豐富 rich in mineral resources;
[礦層] ore bed;
[礦產] mineral products;
[礦牀] mineral deposit; ore deposit;
表生礦床 superficial deposit;
[礦工] groover; miner; mineworker; pitman;
[礦脈] ledge; lode; vein;
礦脈結構 vein texture;
[礦泉水] mineral water;
一杯礦泉水 a glass of mineral water;
[礦石] ore;
富礦石 fat ore;
巨礫礦石 boulder ore;
貧礦石 lean ore;
深成礦石 hypogene ore;
一塊礦石 a cob of ore; a piece of ore;
原礦石 crude ore;
[礦體] ore body;
[礦物] mineral;
礦物質 mineral substances;
礦物資源 mineral resources;
非晶體礦物 amorphous mineral;
副礦物 accessory mineral;
鎂鐵質礦物 mafic mineral;
黏土礦物 clay mineral;
燃性礦物 mineral fuels;
生物礦物 biogenic mineral;
有機礦物 organic mineral;
長英礦物 felsic mineral;
自生礦物 authigenic mineral;

採礦 mining;
廠礦 factories and mines;
方鉛礦 lead glance;
輝鉍礦 bismuth glance;
輝銻礦 antimony glance;
輝銀礦 silver glance;
金礦 gold mine;
開礦 open up a mine;
煤礦 coal mine; colliery;
砂礦 placer;
鐵礦 (1) iron ore; (2) iron mine;
銅礦 copper mine;
錫礦 tin ore;
鹽礦 salt mine;
銀礦 silver ore;
油礦 (1) oil deposit; (2) oil field;

kuang
【纊】 cotton;

kuang
【鑛】 mine or mineral;
［鑛山］ mine;
［鑛物學］ mineralogy;

kuang
【鐮】 same as 礦;

kui[1]
kui
【悝】 ridicule;

kui
【盔】 (1) helmet; (2) basin; pot;
［盔甲］ brace; corselet; helmet and armour; suit of armour;
頂盔衣甲 wear a helmet and a coat of mail;
丟盔棄甲 fly pellmell; throw aside one's amour and drop one's arms; throw away everything in headlong flight; throw away one's helmet and coat of mail; throw away one's shield and armour;
一套盔甲 suit of armour;
［盔子］ basin-like container;

鋼盔 helmet;
鍋盔 smalle hard flour pancake;
頭盔 helmet;

kui
【窺】 peep; spy;
［窺測］ spy out;
窺測方向 keep an eye on the way the wind blows in order to achieve one's evil ends; spy out the land in order to accomplish one's schemes;
窺測時機 bide one's time;
［窺見］ catch a glimpse of; detect; get a glimpse of;
［窺視］ out of the corner of one's eye; peep; peep at; spy on; take a furtive glance; watch stealthily;
窺視者 peeping Tom;
從室內窺視 peep into the room;
［窺伺］ lie in wait for; on watch for; watch and wait;
［窺探］ poke one's nose into; pry about; pry into; spy upon;
窺探敵情 spy on the enemy situation;
窺探秘密 pry into sb's secret;
窺探形勢 send up a kite;
到處窺探 pry about;

管窺 have a restricted view; look at sth through a bamboo tube;
竊窺 peep; steal a glance; watch stealthily;
覷窺 peep at;
偷窺 peep;

kui
【虧】 (1) have a deficit; lose; (2) deficient; short of; (3) treat unfairly; (4) wane;
［虧本］ at a loss; lose money in business; lose one's capital; suffer a deficit;
虧本出售 sell at a loss; sell below cost; sell one's hen on a rainy day;
虧本生意 a losing proposition; a money-losing business;
［虧待］ maltreat; treat shabbily; treatly unfairly;
［虧得］ fortunately; luckily; thanks to;
［虧負］ deficient; fail; let sb suffer; suffer;
［虧耗］ lose money; loss by a natural process;
［虧空］ (1) can't make both ends meet; deficit; in debt; in the red; (2) debt; deficit; spend more than one makes;
補足虧空 make up the deficit;
出現嚴重虧空 show a heavy deficit;
拉虧空 get into debt;
彌補虧空 cover a defit; make up a deficit;
［虧累］ in debt; show repeated deficits; unable to make both ends meet;
［虧蝕］ (1) eclipse of the moon; eclipse of the sun; (2) deficit; lose money in business;
虧蝕殆盡 suffer loss to the limit;
［虧損］ (1) deficit; loss; (2) general debility;
虧損企業 loss enterprises;
虧損賬戶 deficit account;
導致虧損 result in a loss;
彌補虧損 make up a deficit;
年度虧損 losses in a year;
［虧心］ go against conscience; have a guilty conscience;
虧心事 a deed that weighs on one's conscience; a discreditable affair; a matter of remorse; sth that gives one a guilty conscience; a thing which conscience condemns;

吃虧 (1) come to grief; get a beating; get the worst of it; suffer losses; take a beating; (2) at a disadvantage; in an unfavourable

situation;
初虧 first contact;
多虧 fortunately; owing to; thanks to;
理虧 be in the wrong; have not much ground;
幸虧 fortunately; luckily;
盈虧 (1) waxing and waning of the moon; (2) profits and losses;

K

kui
【巋】 (1) grand and secure; stately and lasting; (2) rows after rows of small hills;
［巋然］ lofty; steadfastly; towering;
巋然不動 remain firm; remain unmoved; steadfastly stand on one's ground;
巋然獨存 standing alone immutably;
巋然高聳 soar high;
巋然屹立 stand towering; tower;

kui
【闚】 (1) same as 窺; (2) flash; flashing; (3) a surname;

kui²
kui
【奎】 (1) between the buttocks; the stride made by a man; (2) one of the 28 constellations which ancient Chinese astrologers believed to control the literary trends of the world; (3) a surname;

kui
【馗】 (1) path; road; (2) a Daoist immortal famous for catching evil spirits;

kui
【揆】 (1) consider; estimate; investigate; survey and weigh; (2) premier; prime minister;
［揆度］ conjecture; estimate; investigate and consider; observe and estimate;
揆情度理 consider all the bearings of a case — weigh the pros and cons;

kui
【逵】 thoroughfare;

kui
【葵】 (1) sunflower; (2) althaea rosea;
［葵花］ sunflower;
［葵扇］ palm-leaf fan;

冬葵 malva verticillata;
海葵 sea anemone;
錦葵 high mallow;
向日葵 sunflower;

kui
【暌】 (1) in opposition; (2) part; separate;
［暌隔］ separate;
［暌離］ apart; be separated;
［暌違］ separate;

kui
【睽】 (1) separated; (2) in opposition; (3) squint; stare at; (4) strange; unusual;
［睽睽］ gaze; stare;
萬目睽睽 all eyes are staring; all eyes centre on; under the glare of the public;
眾目睽睽 in the face of the world; in the full blaze of publicity; in the full glare of publicity; under the public gaze; under the watchful eyes of the people; with a crowd of people watching; with everybody watching;

kui
【魁】 (1) chief; head; (3) of stalwart build;
［魁岸］ stalwart; tall and muscular;
［魁蛤］ big clam;
［魁士］ eminent scholar;
［魁首］ person who is head and shoulders above others; the brightest and best;
［魁偉］ big and tall; stalwart; strong-built; tall and strong;
［魁梧］ big and tall; burly;
魁梧的 burly; strapping;
魁梧奇偉 gigantic and remarkably great in stature; stout and brave; tall and broad-shouldered;

黨魁 party chieftain;
奪魁 contend for championship;
花魁 winter plum;
罪魁 chief criminal;

kui
【蝰】 viper;
［蝰蛇］ adder; viper;

kui
【騤】 (of a horse) lively; strong; vigorous;
［騤騤］ strong;

kui
【夔】 (1) monster; strange monster; (2) a court musician in the reign of Em-

peror Shun (2255 B.C.); (3) a feudal state in the Zhou Dynasty; (4) a surname;

kui³

kui

【傀】 (1) puppet; (2) gigantic; great; wonderful;

［傀儡］ puppet;

傀儡登場 play the puppet;

kui

【跬】 half a pace;

［跬步］ alf a step;

跬步不離 follow sb closely; keep close to; not let sb out of sight; not move even a half step from;

跬步難行 difficult to move even a short step;

跬步千里 even small steps my carry one a thousand miles;

kui

【頍】 raise one's head;

kui⁴

kui

【喟】 sigh;

［喟然］ the manner of sighing;

喟然長歎 draw a long breath and sigh; heave a deep sigh; let out a long breath; sigh deeply;

喟然興歎 give a sigh of disappointment; heave a sigh of regret; with a heavy sigh;

［喟歎］ sigh with deep feeling;

感喟 sigh with emotion;

kui

【愧】 abashed; ashamed; embarrassed; shameful; suffer pains of conscience;

［愧汗］ extremely ashamed; so ashamed that one even sweats;

［愧恨］ ashamed and remorseful; remorseful;

愧恨交集 be ashamed and angry with oneself; overcome with shame and remorse;

［愧疚］ ashamed and uneasy;

［愧色］ ashamed look;

面有愧色 look ashamed;

［愧痛］ so ashamed as to feel painful;

［愧怍］ ashamed;

愧天怍人 feel sahme before Heaven and fellow human beings;

kui

【匱】 (1) lack; (2) cabinet; chest;

［匱乏］ dificient; short of supplies;

kui

【潰】 (1) burst; (2) break through; (3) be defeated; be routed; (4) fester; ulcerate;

［潰敗］ be defeated; be routed;

［潰兵］ routed troops;

［潰不成軍］ be dispersed in disorder; break ran to put to ront; in pellmell flight; utterly routed; the troops flee in great disorder;

［潰堤］ an inrush;

［潰決］ break; burst; flood overflowing;

［潰爛］ ulcerate;

［潰滅］ collapse and perish; crumble and fall;

［潰破］ break up;

［潰散］ be defeated and dispersed; collapse in disorder; scatter;

［潰逃］ break and flee; escape in disorder; flee helter-skelter; fly pell-mell;

［潰退］ beat a precipitate retreat; retreat as a result of defeat; retreat in disorder;

［潰圍］ break through enemy blockade;

［潰瘍］ canker; ulcer;

潰瘍疫病 light canker;

癌性潰瘍 cancerous ulcer; carcinelcosis;

白喉性潰瘍 diphtheritic ulcer;

崩解性潰瘍 perambulating ulcer;

邊緣性潰瘍 marginal ulcer;

腸潰瘍 enterelcosis;

穿孔性潰瘍 diabrosis; perforating ulcer;

穿通性潰瘍 perforating ulcer;

穿透性潰瘍 penetrating ulcer;

單純性潰瘍 simple ulcer;

柑桔潰瘍 citrus canker;

壞疽性潰瘍 cancrum;

角膜潰瘍 corneal ulcer;

空腸潰瘍 jejunal ulcer;

口瘡性潰瘍 aphthous ulcer;

狼瘡樣潰瘍 lupoid ulcer;

濾泡性潰瘍 follicular ulcer;

尿路潰瘍 urelcosis;

疱狀潰瘍 blister canker;

脾潰瘍 splenelcosis;

前列腺潰瘍 prostatelcosis;

熱帶潰瘍 veldt sore;

熱帶性潰瘍 tropical ulcer;
熱潰瘍 heat canker;
乳房潰瘍 masthelcosis;
神經源性潰瘍 neurogenic ulcer;
腎潰瘍 nephrelcosis;
十二指腸潰瘍 duodenal ulcer;
糖尿病性潰瘍 diabetic ulcer;
痛風性潰瘍 gouty ulcer;
外陰潰瘍 cancrum pudendi;
細菌性潰瘍 bacterial canker;
消化性潰瘍 peptic ulcer;
性潰瘍 venereal ulcer;
壓力性潰瘍 pressure ulcer;
陰部潰瘍 pudendal ulcer;
營養不良性潰瘍 trophic ulcer;
營養神經性潰瘍 trophoneurotic ulcer;
應激性潰瘍 stress ulcer;
症狀性潰瘍 symptomatic ulcer;
指間潰瘍 ulcus interdigitale;
趾間潰瘍 interdigital ulcer;
足底潰瘍 plantar ulcer;

崩潰 collapse; fall apart;
擊潰 rout;

kui
【憒】 confused in mind; muddle-headed;

kui
【蕢】 (1) straw basket; (2) vegetable with red stalk; (3) a surname;

kui
【簣】 bamboo basket for carrying earth;

kui
【餽】 (1) offer food to a superior; (2) present as a gift;
[餽送] present a gift;
[餽贈] give as a present; make a present of sth; present a gift;
餽贈禮品 make a present;

kui
【聵】 (1) deaf; (2) stupid and unreasonable;

昏聵 decrepit and muddleheaded;

kui
【闠】 gate of a market;

kui
【饋】 make a present of;
[饋贈] make a present of sth; present a gift;

反饋 feedback;
中饋 (1) cooking; (2) wife;

kun1

kun
【坤】 (1) one of the Eight Diagrams — Earth; (2) compliance; obedience; (3) female; feminine;
[坤角兒] actress;
[坤宅] bride's family;

乾坤 heaven and earth; the universe;

kun
【昆】 (1) elder brother; (2) off spring;
[昆蟲] insect;
昆蟲學 bugology; entomology;
~昆蟲學家 bugologist;
按蚊屬昆蟲 anopheles;
傳病媒介昆蟲 vector;
肉食昆蟲 carnivorous insect;
食蟲昆蟲 entomophagous insect;
食葉昆蟲 defoliating insect;
一隻昆蟲 an insect;
有害昆蟲 injurious insect;
[昆山片玉] outstanding figure;
[昆仲] brothers; elder and younger brothers;

kun
【崑】 (1) Kunlun Mountain; (2) Kunshan, a county and mountain in Jiangsu;

kun
【琨】 fine rocks next to jade in quality;

kun
【髡】 (1) ancient punishment of shaving the head; (2) shear trees; (3) a surname;

kun
【褌】 drawers; short pants; trousers;

kun
【錕】 used in 錕鋙, the name of a precious sword;

kun
【鵾】 a bird resembling the crane;
[鵾雞] (1) a bird resembling the crane; (2) phoenix;

kun
【鯤】 (1) a kind of legendary fish said to be thousands of miles long; (2) roe; spawn;

kun3

kun
【捆】 (1) bind; bundle up; tie; truss; (2) a

bundle of; a sheaf of; a truss of;

[捆綁] bind; tie up; truss up;

捆綁不成夫妻 love cannot be compelled;

[捆縛] bind; bound; lash; tie up;

kun

【悃】 honest; sincere;

[悃誠] sincere;

[悃愊] utterly sincere;

悃愊無華 have one's heart in the right place; honest and simple; in good earnest; sincerely and honestly;

kun

【綑】 (1) bundle; make a bundle; tie up; (2) weave;

kun

【壼】 lane, passageway or corridor in a palace;

kun

【閫】 (1) same as 梱 ; (2) apartment for the ladies; (3) feminine;

閨閫 women's quarters;

kun⁴

kun

【困】 (1) be beset; be distressed; be hard pressed; be stranded; (2) besiege; encircle; hem in; pin down; surround; (3) fatigued; tired; weary;

[困憊] exhausted;

[困處] in a predicament; in a sorry plight; in dire straits; plight; predicament;

[困頓] (1) exhausted; fatigued; tired out; weary; worn-out; (2) hard up; in financial straits; in straitened circumstances; poverty-stricken;

[困厄] difficult situation; dire straits; distress;

[困乏] exhausted; fatigued; lassitude; tired; weary;

春困秋乏 one feels dizziness in spring and fatigue in autumn;

手頭困乏 hard up for money; in great straits; in straitened circumstances; on the rocks;

[困惑] at a loss; bewildered; not knowing what to do; perplexed; puzzled;

困惑不解 feel puzzled; in a fog; put into a sad state of perplexity; tie sb into knots;

困惑的 confused;

使困惑 baffle; confuse;

[困境] difficult position; morass; plight; predicament; straits;

擺脱困境 above water; escape from a predicament; extricate oneself from a predicament; get sb off the hook; out of hot water;

逼入困境 drive sb into a corner; drive sb to the wall; get sb cornered; push sb to the wall;

財政困境 financial predicament;

處於同樣的困境 in the same boat;

經濟困境 economic morass; economic plight;

陷入困境 fall into a difficulty; find oneself in a pickle; in a tight corner; get into a fix;

[困窘] awkward; embarrassed; in a difficult position; in straitened circumstances;

[困倦] drowsy; sleepy;

[困苦] deep distress; deep poverty; hardship; in privation; tribulation;

困苦勞頓 in great distress and weariness;

經歷困苦 experience hardships;

忍受困苦 endure hardship;

[困龍也有上天時] every dog has his day;

[困難] (1) difficulty; hard; (2) financial difficulties; straitened circumstances;

困難重重 be beset with difficulties; bristle with difficulties; great odds; in a fix; in deep waters;

~ 儘管困難重重 against all odds;

困難出現 difficulties arise;

擺脱困難 get out of difficulties;

財政困難 financial difficulty;

操作困難 operational difficulties;

充滿困難 be fraught with difficulties;

重重困難 difficulties;

~ 克服重重困難 beat the odds; defy the odds; overcome the odds;

構成困難 pose difficulties; present difficulties;

呼吸困難 breathe with difficulty;

迴避困難 avoid the difficulty; dodge the difficulty;

解決困難 smooth away the difficulties;

經濟困難 economic difficulty;

克服困難 overcome difficulties;

誇大困難 magnify difficulties;

面臨困難 face difficulties;

難以克服的困難 impossible odds; overwhelming odds;
輕視困難 make light of difficulties;
消除困難 iron out difficulties;
有困難 have difficulties; have trouble;
遭遇困難 encounter difficulties; expierence difficulties; get into difficulties; run into difficulties;
造成困難 cause difficulties; give rise to difficulties; lead to difficulties;
正視困難 face difficulties squarely;

［困窮］ impoverished; under great financial difficulty; very poor;
［困擾］ nag; perplex; persecute; puzzle;
［困守］ defend against a siege; stand a siege;
困守孤城 be entrenched in a beseiged city;
［困心衡慮］ distressed in mind and perplexed in thought; great pains taken in working out a scheme;

被困 be stuck;
濟困 help people in distress;
交困 be in difficulties;
貧困 in straitened circumstances; poverty-stricken;
窮困 impoverished; in straitened circumstances; poor and hard up;
圍困 besiege; pin down;
坐困 be confined; be shut up;

kun

【睏】 drowsy; sleepy;

kuo⁴

kuo

【括】 (1) embrace; include; (2) search for; seek; (3) restrain; tie;
［括號］ brackets; parentheses;
括號法 bracketing;
大括號 braces;
方括號 angular brackets; square brackets;
~雙方括號 double brackets;
花括號 brace;
尖括號 angle brackets;
圓括號 parentheses; round brackets;
［括約肌］ musculus sphincter; sphincter;
賁門括約肌 cardiac sphincter;
肛門括約肌 anal sphincter;
陰道括約肌 vaginal sphincter;
幽門括約肌 pyloric sphincter;

包括 consist of; include;
概括 generalize; summarize;
簡括 brief but comprehensive; compendious;
囊括 embrace; include;
搜括 extort; plunder;
統括 altogether; include;
綜括 sum up;
總括 sum up;

kuo

【廓】 empty; open; wide;
［廓落］ spacious and quiet;
［廓清］ clean up; sweep away;
廓清積弊 sweep away outstanding abuses;
摧陷廓清 defeat and completely wipe out; demolish and sweep away; wipe the floor with sb;

恢廓 generous; large-minded;
空廓 open and wide; spacious;
寥廓 boundless; vast;
輪廓 outline; rough sketch;
胸廓 thorax;

kuo

【闊】 (1) broad; vast; wide; (2) rich; wealthy;
［闊別］ long parted; long separated; separate for a long time;
［闊步］ make great strides; take big strides; walk in big strides;
闊步而行 stride along at a great pace; stride with a dignified gait; walk with big strides;
闊步高論 take big strides and give a high-flown talk;
闊步高視 take big strides and look high — put on airs;
闊步高談 take big strides and give a high-flown talk;
闊步前進 advance with giant strides; march on in big strides; stride ahead; take big strides forward;
高視闊步 carry oneself proudly; prance; stalk; strut like a turkey-cock; with one's head in the air;
［闊綽］ extravagant; liberal with money; luxurious; ostentatious;
出手濶綽 free-handed;
生活濶綽 live high on the hog;
手頭闊綽 free of hand;
［闊佬］ moneybags; rich man; wealthy man;

[闊氣] extravagant; lavish; luxurious;
擺闊氣 make a parade of one's wealth;
逞闊氣 flaunt one's riches;
裝闊氣 keep up appearances;
[闊人] the rich;
[闊少] young master of a rich family;
闊少作風 the style of a rich youth — the practice of a wealthy fop;
[闊葉] broad-leaved;
闊葉林 broad-leaved forest;
~ 常綠闊葉林 evergreen broad-leaved forest;

擺闊 be ostentatious and extravagant; show off one's wealth;
廣闊 broad; vast; wide;
開闊 (1) open; wide; (2) tolerant;
空闊 open; spacious;
寬闊 broad; wide;
遼闊 extensive; vast;
壯闊 grand; magnificent; vast;

kuo
【擴】 enlarge; expand; extend;
[擴充] augment; enlarge; expand; extend; strengthen;
擴充版 expansion board;
擴充軍備 engage in arms expansion;
擴充內存 extend memory;
擴充設施 augment the equipment;
擴充實力 expand forces;
擴充知識 expand knowledge;
軍備擴充 arms expansion;
[擴詞] amplify the diction;
擴詞法 diction-amplification;
[擴大] aggrandizement; amplify; broaden; dilate; enlarge; enlargement; expand; extend; multiply; swell; widening;
擴大會議 enlarged meeting;
擴大就業 job enlargement;
擴大銷路 broaden the market; develop the market;
擴大眼界 broaden one's horizons; widen one's field of vision; widen one's outlook;
擴大戰果 exploit the victory;
詞義擴大 widening of meaning;
次生擴大 secondary enlargement;
資本擴大 capital widening;
[擴建] expand; extend;
擴建碼頭 extend a wharf;
[擴軍] arms expansion; military buildup;
擴軍備戰 expand armaments and prepare for war;
[擴散] diffuse; diffusion; proliferate; proliferation; scatter about; spread
擴散率 diffusivity;
~ 磁擴散率 magnetic diffusivity;
~ 混合擴散率 mixing diffusivity;
~ 熱擴散率 thermal diffusivity;
~ 液體擴散率 liquid diffusivity;
~ 載氣擴散率 carrier gas diffusivity;
擴散器 diffuser;
~ 空氣擴散器 air diffuser;
~ 流量擴散器 flow diffuser;
~ 壓縮式擴散器 compression diffuser;
擴散謠言 spread rumour;
擴散影響 extend influence;
合金擴散 alloy diffusion;
核擴散 nuclear proliferation;
橫向擴散 horizontal proliferation;
化學擴散 chemical diffusion;
介面擴散 boundary diffusion;
經典擴散 classical diffusion;
流行擴散 epidemic spread;
雙極擴散 bipolar diffusion;
箱式擴散 box diffusion;
有效擴散 active diffusion;
載流子擴散 carrier diffusion;
[擴音器] amplifier; loudhailer; loudspeaker;
手提式擴音器 bullhorn;
[擴展] broaden; develop; expand; extend; spread; spreading;
擴展卡槽 expansion slot;
擴展內存 expand memory;
擴展器 expander;
~ 模擬輸入擴展器 analogue input expander;
~ 自動聲量擴展器 automatic volume expander;
城市擴展 urban sprawl;
程序擴展 programme extension;
海底擴展 sea floor spreading;
類推擴展 analogical extension;
門限擴展 threshold extension;
頻帶擴展 band spreading;
區域擴展 zone spreading;
[擴張] dilation; enlarge; expand; extend; extension; spread;
擴張野心 expansionist ambitions;
擴張主義 expansionism;
~ 軍事擴張主義 military expansionism;

腸擴張 enterectasis;
膽管擴張 cholangiectasis;
膽囊擴張 cholecystectasia;
閉擴張 closed extension;
對外擴張 foreign aggrandizement;
複擴張 complex extension;
海外擴張 overseas expansion;
角膜擴張 keratoectasia;
裂紋擴張 crack extension;
淋巴管擴張 lymphangiectasis;
領土擴張 territorial expansion;
膀胱擴張 megabladder;
腎擴張 nephrectasia;
微血管擴張 telangiectasis;
胃擴張 dilatation of stomach;
循環擴張 cyclic extension;
縱向擴張 vertical expansion;

la[1]
la

【拉】 (1) drag; draw; pull; tug; (2) haul; transport by vehicle; (3) canvass; draw in; win over; (4) drag out; draw out; space out; (5) play a bowed instrument;

［拉拔］ help sb advance;

［拉幫套］ (1) help pull in harness; work for others; (2) lovers;

［拉布］ filibuster; filibustering;

［拉長］ drag out; draw out; elongate; prolong; space out;
拉長耳朵 prick up one's ears;
拉長線 leave sth for future decision;

［拉扯］ (1) drag; pull; (2) bring up; (3) drag in; implicate; (4) chat; (5) borrow; drum up; (6) contract for;
東拉西扯 branch out; do patch work in writing; drag in all sort of irrelevant matters; owe debts all around; pull about; pull and haul; ramble; ramble in talk; talk aimlessly; talk at random; talk incoherently; yakety-yak;
~東拉西扯，文不對題 never stick to the point;
拉拉扯扯 (1) exchange flattery and favours; resort to flattery and touting; scratch each other's back; traffic in flattery and favours; traffic in mutual flattery and commendation; tug; (2) drag about; pull and push; pull sb about; (3) ramble;

［拉牀］ pull-out bed;

［拉搭］ chat; converse; talk;

［拉倒］ drop it; forget about it; leave it at that; let it go at that; never mind;

［拉丁］ Latin;
拉丁詞語 Latinism;
拉丁化 Latinize;
拉丁佬 dago;
拉丁美洲 Latin America;
拉丁文 Latin;
拉丁字母 Latin alphabet;

［拉夫］ press-gang;

［拉弓］ draw a bow;
拉硬弓 (1) bow pulling; force sb to do sth;

［拉鉤］ make a promise to do sth;

［拉花］ pour;
徒手拉花 free pour;

［拉話］ chat; jaw; talk;

［拉環］ pull tab;

［拉架］ mediate in street-fight;

［拉近］ draw close; draw near; draw up;
把椅子拉近 draw up a chair;

［拉鋸］ (1) work a two-handled saw; (2) fight a see-saw battle;
拉鋸戰 a seesaw battle; a stalemate;

［拉開］ (1) draw back; (2) pull asunder; pull open; (3) increase the distance between; space out;

［拉客］ solicit patrons forcibly;

［拉空］ (1) run into debt; (2) miss opportunity;

［拉拉隊］ cheering squad; rooters;

［拉力］ broach; pull; pull-type broach; tensile strength;
拉力器 chest developer; chest expander;
車輪拉力 wheel pull;
成形拉力 form broach; profile broach; shape broach;
齒輪拉力 gear broach;
齒圈拉力 ring gear; broach;
反拉力 counter pull;
後拉力 back pull;
跨式拉力 straddle broach;
六角拉力 hexagon broach;
螺旋拉力 spiral broach;
內拉力 inside broach; internal broach;
平面拉力 surface broach;
樞軸拉力 pivot broach;
外拉力 external broach;
穩恒拉力 steady pull;
細齒拉力 serration broach;
圓孔拉力 round broach;
圓拉力 circular broach;
整體拉力 solid broach;
組合拉力 built-up broach; combined broach;

［拉鍊］ zip; zip fastener; zipper;
拉鍊沒有拉上 one's zip is undone;
拉開拉鍊 unzip;
拉上拉鍊 zip up;
一條拉鍊 a zipper;

［拉攏］ cozy up to; draw sb over to one's side; make a friendship with a self-serving motive; rope in;
拉攏腐蝕 rope in sb and corrupt him; win people over to one's side and corrupt them; win sb over and corrupt him;
拉攏收買 woo and buy over sb;

套拉攏 try to win sb's friendship;

[拉麵] noodles made by pulling the dough;

[拉溺] pass water; urinate;

[拉尿] urinate;

[拉皮] have a face-lift;

拉皮條 pimp;

[拉票] canvass votes; solicit votes;

拉票活動 electioneering;

[拉平] bring to the same level; even up;

拉平比分 even the score up;

[拉人] grab sb;

拉人犯規 grabbing;

[拉繩] drawstring;

[拉屎] crap; deposit; go to stool; empty the bowels; have a bowel movement; move one's bowels; shit;

蹲坑不拉屎 squat over a latrine pit without releasing oneself;

[拉手] (1) hold hands; join hands; (2) pull by the hands;

手拉手 hand in hand;

[拉鎖] zipper;

[拉套] (1) drag cart; (2) help others complete a task;

[拉稀] have diarrhea; have loose bowels; suffer from diarrhoea;

[拉下] haul down;

拉下臉 look displeased; not to spare sb's sensibilities; pull a long face; put on a stern expression;

~拉不下臉 cannot do sth for fear of hurting another person's feelings;

拉下水 corrupt sb; drag sb into the mire; make an accomplice of sb;

[拉削] broaching;

內拉削 internal broaching;

平面拉削 surface broaching;

[拉延] expand; pull;

[拉雜] disorganized; ill-organized; rambling;

拉拉雜雜 not well organized and without a central theme; rambling;

扒拉 (1) move; push aside; push lightly; (2) saute;

半拉 half;

撥拉 move; stir;

欻拉 sizzle;

法拉 farad;

里拉 lira;

羅拉 roller;

沙拉 salad;

拖拉 dilatory; procrastinating; slow; sluggish;

la

【垃】

[垃圾] dregs; garbage; litter; raff; refuse; rubbish; sweepings; trash; waste;

垃圾車 dust cart; garbage truck; garbage wagon; rubbish lorry;

垃圾蟲 litterbug;

垃圾處理 garbage disposal; waste disposal;

垃圾袋 dustbin liner;

垃圾堆 garbage heap; refuse dump;

垃圾工 dustman; garbage collector; garbage man; sanitation worker;

垃圾清除 clearance of refuse;

垃圾清潔工 dustbin man; dustman; garbage collection;

垃圾如山 a mountain of rubbish;

垃圾筒 dustbin; garage can;

垃圾桶 dustbin; garbage can; rubbish bin; trash;

~大型輪式垃圾桶 wheelie bin;

~腳踏式垃圾桶 pedal bin;

~扔進垃圾桶 put sth in the trash;

垃圾箱 ash bin; ashcan; dustbin; garbage can; litter basket; litter bin; rubbish bin; trash can; waste basket; waste bin; wastepaper basket;

~街道上的垃圾箱 orderly bin;

城市垃圾 municipal refuse; town refuse;

處理垃圾 dispose of rubbish;

丟垃圾 dump the rubbish;

焚燒垃圾 burn away refuse;

工業垃圾 industrial refuse;

集攏垃圾 gather up barbage;

家庭垃圾 domestic waste; household waste;

街道垃圾 street refuse;

拋棄垃圾 chuck away rubbish;

清除垃圾 clear away garbage; remove rubbish;

傾倒垃圾 dump the rubbish; dump waste;

掃除垃圾 clear up rubbish; sweep away rubbish; sweep off rubbish;

燒掉垃圾 burn rubbish;

生活垃圾 domestic refuse; household refuse;

收垃圾 collect refuse;

~收垃圾者 reuse collector;

一堆垃圾 a heap of rubbish; a load of

rubbish;
有毒工業垃圾 toxic waste;

la
【喇】 character used for its sound;

哇喇 din; hullabaloo; uproar;

la
【邋】
［邋遢］ (1) sloppy; (2) dirty;
邋遢的 grubby;

la²
la
【旯】 dark corner;

la
【拉】 cut; gash;

la
【剌】 slash open;

la³
la
【喇】 (1) bugle; horn; trumpet; (2) Lama; (3) character used in transliteration;
［喇叭］ (1) suona; (2) brass wind instrument; horn; trumpet; (3) hooter; loudspeaker;
喇叭按鈕 horn button;
喇叭花 white-edged morning glory;
喇叭口 the mouth of a wind instrument;
喇叭褲 bell-bottom trousers; bells; flared pants; kickflare trousers;
喇叭裙 flared skrt;
喇叭筒 megaphone;
按喇叭 blow a horn;
吹喇叭 (1) wind a trumpet; (2) boast; praise; puff up;
複合喇叭 compound horn;
簧喇叭 reed horn;
警報喇叭 alarming horn;
同軸喇叭 coaxial horn;
小喇叭 trumpet;
圓喇叭 circular horn;
［喇嘛］ lama;
喇嘛教 Lamaism;
喇嘛廟 lamasery;

la⁴
la
【剌】 contradict; go against;

la
【腊】 abbreviated form of 臘；

la
【落】 (1) leave out; miss; omit; (2) forget and leave sth behind; (3) fall behind; lag behind;

la
【辣】 (1) hot; peppery; pungent; (2) ruthless; vicious;
［辣不可言］ too hot to be told;
［辣菜］ hot pickled vegetables;
［辣乎乎］ hot; peppery; sort of hot;
［辣醬］ thick chilli sauce;
［辣椒］ capsicum; chilli; hot pepper; red pepper;
辣椒粉 red pepper;
辣椒油 chili oil;
粉末辣椒 powdered pepper;
紅辣椒 hot red pepper; red pepper;
青辣椒 green capsicum;
［辣辣］ burning;
火辣辣 burning;
熱辣辣 burning hot;
［辣手］ (1) ruthless; vicious; (2) hard to do; knotty; thorny; troublesome;
［辣絲絲］ hot; peppery;
［辣酥酥］ hot; peppery;
［辣味］ acrid smell; hot taste; peppery taste; pungency;
［辣燥］ hot-tempered and ruthless;
［辣子］ chilli; hot pepper; pepper;

毒辣 malicious; sinister;
老辣 experienced and vicious;
潑辣 (1) fierce and tough; rude and unreasonable; (2) forceful; pungent; (3) bold and vigorous;
辛辣 (1) hot; pungent; (2) bitter; sharp;

la
【瘌】 favus;
［瘌痢］ favus of the scalp;
瘌痢頭 person affected with favus on the head;
瘌痢頭兒子自己疼 every mother's child is handsome;

la
【臘】 (1) solar year-end sacrifice to gods; (2) the twelfth month in a lunar calendar; (3) cured;
［臘腸］ sausage;
臘腸狗 dachshund; sausage dog;

一對臘腸 a pair of sausages;

[臘盡] end of winter;

臘盡春回 the early spring comes on after the end of the last month of the year;

臘盡春臨 dead winter is past and warm spring is at hand;

臘盡春始 the end of winter and the beginning of spring;

臘盡冬殘 end of the year; towards the end of the lunar year;

[臘梅] wintersweet;

[臘肉] bacon; cured meat;

[臘味] cured meat;

[臘月] the twelfth month in a lunar year;

臘月的白菜—動(凍)了心 a mid-winter cabbage — affected in heart;

寒冬臘月 severe winter; the dead of winter; the deep mid-winter; the teeth of winter;

十冬臘月 the cold months of the year; the tenth, eleventh and twelfth months of the lunar year;

la

【鬎】 favus;

[鬎鬁] favus of the scalp;

la

【蠟】 (1) wax; (2) candle; (3) polish; (4) sallow; yellowish;

[蠟版] mimeography stencil; stencil plate;

[蠟筆] colour crayon; wax crayon;

蠟筆畫 crayon painting;

[蠟光紙] glazed paper;

[蠟果] wax fruit;

[蠟黃] wax yellow; waxen; sallow;

[蠟祭] year-end sacrifice;

[蠟炬] candle;

[蠟淚] wax guttering;

[蠟人] waxwork;

[蠟像] wax figure; waxwork;

[蠟蕊] candle wick;

[蠟紙] (1) wax paper; (2) stencil; stencil paper;

[蠟燭] candle;

蠟燭商 chandler;

點蠟燭 burn a candle;

一羅蠟燭 a gross of candles;

一枝蠟燭 a candle;

白蠟 (1) insect wax; white wax; (2) beeswax;

地蠟 earth wax;

髮蠟 pomade;

封蠟 sealing wax;

蜂蠟 beeswax;

蜜蠟 beeswax;

石蠟 paraffin wax;

燙蠟 polish with melted wax;

脱蠟 dewax;

一層蠟 a coat of wax;

la

【鑞】 alloy of tin and lead for welding;

白鑞 solder;

焊鑞 soldering tin; tin solder;

la⁵

la

【啦】 phrase-final particle;

[啦啦隊] cheer squad; cheering team; pep squad;

啦啦隊隊員 cheerleader;

啦啦隊冠軍 the best cheering team;

啦啦隊活動 cheerleading;

啦啦隊長 cheer leader;

lai²

lai

【來】 (1) arrive; come; (2) crop up; take place; (3) coming; future; next; (4) ever since;

[來賓] guest; visitor;

來賓席 seats reserved for guests;

等待來賓 expect visitors;

歡迎來賓 welcome guests;

婚禮來賓 wedding guest;

接待來賓 receive guests;

[來潮] tides rise; waves rise;

[來遲] late;

來遲了 turn up late;

[來到] arrive; come;

先來後到 first come, first served; in the order of arrival;

[來得] (1) competent; equal to; (2) as; come out as; emerge;

來得及 able to do within time; there's still time;

~我想我們還來得及 I think we shall make it;

來得容易去得快 easy come, easy go; light come, light go; soon gotten, soon spent; what one gets easily one parts with easily;

來得早 come ahead of time;

來得早不如來得巧 to arrive early is not so good as to arrive at the most opportune moment; to come early is not as good as to come in time;

[來電] (1) incoming telegram; your message; your telegram; (2) inform by telegram; send a telegram here;
來電待接 call waiting;
來電過濾 call screening;
來電篩選 call screening;
來電顯示 caller display; caller ID;
來電者 caller;

[來犯] come to attack us; invade our territory;

[來訪] come to call; come to visit;

[來附] flock to; submit to;

[來稿] contribution received by the editor;

[來函] (1) incoming letter; (2) your letter;

[來回] (1) go to a place and come back; make a return journey; make a round trip; (2) back and forth; to and fro; (3) cycle;
來回飛翔 hover back and forth;
來回來去 back and forth; over and over again;
來回票 return ticket; round-trip ticket;

[來件] letter or parcel received;

[來勁] (1) become alive; get excited; get pumped up; inspire; (2) find fault with; make trouble;

[來看] see from;
從長遠來看 in the long haul; in the long run; over the long haul;

[來客] guest; visitor;

[來來] try to do sth;
來來回回 toing and froing;
來來往往 come and go; go to and fro; coming and going in great number; to and fro;

[來歷] antecedent; background; origin; past history; source;
來歷不明 of unknown origin; of dubious background; of questionable antecedents;

[來料] materials from clients;
來料加工 process materials from clients;
來料組裝 assemble imported components;

[來臨] advent; arrive; approach; at hand; come; nigh; onset;
春天即將來臨 spring draws nigh;
大難來臨 a great calamity is at hand;
冬天的來臨 onset of winter;
新時代的來臨 the advent of a new era;

[來路] (1) approach; incoming road; (2) origin; source;
來路不明 (1) unidentified; (2) of questionable origin;
來路不正 of dubious background; of questionable origin;
來路貨 imported goods;

[來年] coming year; next year;

[來情] (1) reason; (2) future matter;
來情去意 mutual expressions of affection;

[來去] (1) round trip; (2) distance between two places; (3) friendly contacts;
來去分明 there is no secret about one's movements;
來去無羈 come and go of one's own free will;
來去無蹤 come and go without leaving a trace behind;
來去自如 come and go freely;
來去自由 freedom to come and go; let them go and come of their own will;
擺來擺去 swing to and fro;
搬來搬去 carry hither and thither; shift from one place to another;
蹦來蹦去 leap about;
差來差去 order sb about;
蕩來蕩去 hanging about; hanging around;
顛來倒去 harp on; over and over; ring the changes on;
動來動去 move incessantly;
翻來翻去 turn sth over and over;
飛來飛去 flit about; flit to and fro; flitter; fly hither and thither; fly round and round;
逛來逛去 hang around;
滾來滾去 tumble;
呼之即來，揮之即去 come at one's call and go at one's beck; have sb at one's beck and call; have sb at one's disposal;
擠來擠去 push about;
來龍去脈 background and sequence; cause and effect; the entire process; the ins and outs; the sequence of events; the ways and wherefores of sth; the whence and whither;
來也匆匆，去也沖沖 come in a rush, and go with a flush;
忙來忙去 at it; on the run;
明去暗來 secret going-on;

跑來跑去 kick about; run back and forth; run here and there; run hither and thither; run to and fro;
説來説去 after all is said and done; no matter how you put it; say the same thing over and over again; the long and short of all this; when all is said, the fact remains that...;
絲來線去 tangled and involved endlessly;
挑來挑去 pick and choose;
推來推去 each declines to accept; pass the buck; shove around;
拖來拖去 pull about; pull and haul;
搖來搖去 swing to and fro;
易來易去 easy come easy go;
直去直來 go and return without undue delay;
轉來轉去 hang around; walk back and forth;
走來走去 pace in anxiety; walk back and forth;

[來人] (1) bearer; incoming envoy; messenger; (2) persons coming;

[來日] (1) coming days; days ahead; days to come; time ahead; (2) tomorrow;
來日大難 difficult days are ahead;
來日方長 have a long future before one; many a day will come yet; there will be a time for that; there will be ample time; there will be plenty of time;

[來生] afterlife; next life; next world; the other world; the world to be; the world to come;

[來使] envoy; messenger;

[來世] (1) afterlife; next life; (2) later generation;

[來勢] oncoming force; the force with which sth breaks out;
來勢甚猛 come with tremendous force;
來勢兇兇 bear down menacingly; break in full fury;

[來書] incoming letter;

[來頭] (1) background; backing; connections; (2) cause; motive behind; (3) force with sth breaks out; (4) fun; interest;
來頭不小 have powerful backing; have poerful connections; with powerful backing;
來頭很大 of impressive background;
有來頭 not the ordinary kind; of some special importance;
～大有來頭 have powerful backing; very influential socially;

[來往] (1) come and go; (2) contacts; dealings; social intercourse;
來往奔波 ceaselessly come and go;
來往賬 account;
～銀行來往賬 bank account;
拔來報往 exchange views; have frequent contacts;
常來常往 frequently see each other; keep in constant contact with each other;
獨來獨往 come and go freely; free and alone; have no contact with anytone;
～獨來獨往的人 lone wolf;
獨往獨來 coming and going freely; completely independent; with no restrictions;
來而不往 not to give after receiving; not to pay a return call on sb;
～來而不往非禮也 courtesy on one side only lasts not long; it is discourteous not to give tit for tat; it is impolite not to pay a return call on sb; it is impolite not to reciprocate; one should give as good as one gets; one should return as good as one receives;
密來暗往 secretly communicate with each other; steal away and return without letting anyone know about it;
明來暗往 secret goings-on;
南來北往 always on the move; shuttle to and fro;
頻來頻往 coming and going hastily – hurrying to and fro;
攘往熙來 busy coming and going; coming and going in crowds; hustling and bustling about;
人來人往 an exciting coming and going of people; many people coming and going; people are hurrying to and fro; people come and go;
同來同往 go to...together and come home together;
熙來攘往 bustling with activity; coming and going in crowds; the hustle and bustle of large crowds; with people bustling about;
有來有往 give-and-take; reciprocal;
直來直往 straightforward;

[來文] document received;

[來信] (1) letter received; (2) incoming letter;
頃接來信 I have just received your letter;
[來意] one's purpose in coming;
來意不善 come with ill intent;
[來由] cause; reason;
沒來由 for no reason; without any cause; without rhyme or reason;
[來源] (1) origin; source; (2) originate; stem from;
能量來源 energy source;
其他來源 alternative source;
食物來源 food source;
重要來源 important source;
主要來源 main source; primary source;
[來札] your letter;
[來者] comer; those who come;
來者不拒 all is fish that comes to his net; all are welcome, none will be turned away; all comers are welcome; keep open door; keep open house; no comer is rejected; refuse nobody; refuse nobody's request; whoever comes will be welcome;
來者不善，善者不來 he could not have come with good intentions; he that fears the gallows shall never be a good thief; he who has come, come with ill intent, certainly not on virtue bent; he who has come is surely strong or he'd never come along; the one who is coming surely has bad intentions; with good intent he would not come;
來者可追 the future may yet be saved; there is still time to amend; what is to come can still be overtaken;
[來自] come from; hail from;
來自基層 from the rank and file; from the wrong side of the track;
來自中國 come from China;

本來 at first; from the beginning; in itself; in the first place; it goes without saying; original; originally; properly speaking; should have; used to be;
比來 all along; always; at all times;
別來 (1) since parting; (2) do not;
纔來 have just arrived; have just come;
重來 make a comeback;
出來 come out; emerge;
從來 all along; always; at all times; never;
到來 arrive; be in the offing;
到頭來 finally; in the end;
邇來 recently;
古來 since time immemorial;
後來 afterwards; later;
胡來 (1) fool with sth; mess things up; (2) make trouble; run wild;
將來 future;
近來 lately; of late; recently;
看來 it appears; it looks as if; it seems;
歷來 all through the ages; always; constantly;
亂來 act recklessly;
如來 Tathagata;
生來 born with;
素來 always; usually;
外來 external; foreign; outside;
往來 come and go;
未來 (1) coming; future; (2) future; tomorrow;
下來 (1) come from a higher place; (2) go among the masses;
想來 it may be assumed that; presumably;
向來 all along; always;
夜來 (1) yesterday; (2) at night;
以來 since;
由來 (1) origin; (2) cause;
原來 former; it turns out; original;
自來 from the beginning; originally;

lai
【徠】 ancient version of 來;

招徠 canvass; solicit (business);

lai
【崍】 a mountain in Sichuan;

lai
【淶】 a river in Shandong and Hebei provinces;

lai
【郲】 (1) a place in Henan Province; (2) a surname;

lai
【萊】 (1) a field lying fallow; (2) weed; wild weeds; (3) a surname;

蓬萊 fabled abode of immortals;

lai
【錸】 rhenium;

lai⁴
lai
【睞】 (1) look at; (2) cock-eyed; squint;

lai

【賚】 (1) bestow; confer; (2) a surname;

lai

【賴】 (1) depend; rely; (2) drag out one's stay in a place; hang on in a place; hold on to a place; (3) deny one's error or responsibility; go back on one's word; (4) blame sb wrongly; put the blame on sb else; (5) blame; (6) bad; no good; poor; (7) a surname;

［賴婚］ repudiate marriage engagement;

［賴貨］ shoddy merchandise;

［賴皮］ rascally; shameless; shameless behaviour; unreasonable;

賴皮臉 a shameless person;

耍賴皮 act shamelessly;

［賴事］ shameless acts; vile deeds;

［賴學］ cut class; play traunt;

［賴以］ depend on; rely on;

［賴債］ bilk one's creditors; repudiate a debt;

［賴賬］ (1) repudiate a debt; (2) go back on one's word;

賴賬的人 deadbeat;

［賴着不走］ continue to stay in; hang on and refuse to clear out; linger about and wouldn't go;

不賴 fine; good; not bad;

抵賴 deny; refuse to admit;

好賴 (1) at any rate; anyhow; in any case; (2) anyhow; no matter in what way;

狡賴 deny;

撒賴 act shamelessly; be perverse;

耍賴 act shamelessly; make a scene;

誣賴 falsely incriminate;

無賴 rascal; rascally; scoundrelly;

信賴 have faith in; trust;

仰賴 be dependent on; rely on;

依賴 be dependent on; rely on;

倚賴 be dependent on; rely on;

有賴 depend on; rest on;

lai

【瀨】 (1) water rushing by; (2) water flowing over shallows; (3) a river in Guangxi; (4) a river in Jiangsu;

lai

【癩】 (1) leprosy; (2) favus of the scalp;

［癩狗扶不上墻］ a carrion kite will never make a good hawk; a mangy cur that won't let itself be helped over a wall; one cannot make a falcon of a buzzard;

［癩瓜］ bitter melon;

［癩蛤蟆］ toad;

癩蛤蟆打哈欠一好大的口氣 a toad yawning – how big the breath is; (pun) big talk;

癩蛤蟆想吃天鵝肉 a toad hankering for a taste of swan; a toad lusting after a swan's flesh; an ugly man hopes to marry a pretty girl; aspire after sth one is not worthy of; dreaming of obtaining impossible pleasures;

［癩痢頭］ favus head;

癩痢頭兒子自己疼 every mother's child is handsome;

［癩皮狗］ (1) mangy dog; (2) loathsome creature;

［癩頭］ favus-infected head; scabies on head;

［癩癬］ favus; rignworm;

［癩子］ a person affected with favus on the head; a person with a scabby head;

lai

【籟】 (1) flute; pipe; (2) unspecified sounds;

天籟 sounds of nature;

萬籟 all sounds;

lan²

lan

【婪】 avarice; covetous; greedy;

貪婪 avaricious; greedy;

lan

【嵐】 mist; mountain vapour;

［嵐影湖光］ the hazy atmosphere of the mountain and the shimmering light of the lake;

山嵐 clouds and mists in the mountains;

曉嵐 morning mist;

lan

【闌】 (1) door curtain; door screen; (2) fence; (3) block up; cut off; separate; (4) late in the night; the end of a year; (5) weakened; (6) withered;

［闌入］ (1) encroah upon a place one is not supposed to enter; (2) mingle; mix;

[闌尾] appendix; epityphlon;
闌尾病 appendicopathy;
闌尾積水 hydroappendix;
闌尾絞痛 appendicular colic;
闌尾結石 appendicular lithiasis;
闌尾結石症 appendicolithiasis;
闌尾淋巴結 appendicular lymph nodes;
闌尾內膜炎 endoappendictis;
闌尾膿腫 appendiceal abscess;
闌尾疝 appendicocele;
闌尾石病 appendolithiasis;
闌尾系膜炎 meso-appendicitis;
闌尾炎 appendicitis;
~阿米巴性闌尾炎 amebic appendicitis;
~腸蟲性闌尾炎 helminthic appendicitis; verminous appendictis;
~穿孔性闌尾炎 perforating appendicitis;
~創傷性闌尾炎 traumatic appendicitis;
~壞疽性闌尾炎 gangrenous appendictis;
~急性闌尾炎 acute appendictis;
~假闌尾炎 pseudoappendicitis;
~接觸性闌尾炎 appendicitis by contiguity;
~節段性闌尾炎 segmental appendicitis;
~慢性闌尾炎 chronic appendicitis;
~跳躍性闌尾炎 skip appendicitis;
闌尾炎性消化不良 appendicular dyspepsia;
闌尾周圍炎 periappendicitis;

lan

【藍】 (1) blue; (2) indigo plant; (3) a surname;
[藍本] (1) model for copying; (2) blueprint; (3) chief source; (4) original version;
[藍籌] blue-chip;
藍籌公司 blue-chip company;
藍籌股 blue-chip share;
[藍靛] indigo;
[藍領] blue collar;
藍領工人 blue collar workers;
藍領階層 blue collar people;
[藍莓] blueberry;
[藍青] (1) blue-green; indigo blue; (2) corrupt; nonstandard;
[藍色] blue; blue colour;
藍色盲 acyanoblupsia; amianthinopsy;
冰藍色 ice-blue;
淡藍色 pastel blue; powder blue;
綠藍色 turquoise blue;
靛藍色 indigo;
淺藍色 light blue;
~淺藍色的 bluish;
青藍色 ultramarine;
深藍色 dark blue; midnight blue; navy blue;
天藍色 azure; cerulean; sky blue;
蔚藍色 cerulean;
[藍天] blue sky;
[藍田] superior parents;
藍田生玉 children born of worthy parents; superior parents produce superior offspring;
藍田種玉 give a worthy son to a worthy father; give birth to sons; make pregnant;
[藍圖] (1) blueprint; project outline; (2) plan for construction;

寶藍 sapphire blue;
碧藍 dark blue;
帶點藍[的] bluish;
靛藍 indigo;
發藍 enamel;
甘藍 wild cabbage;
芥藍 cabbage mustard;
毛藍 darkish blue;
品藍 reddish blue;
燒藍 enamel;
天藍 azure; sky blue;
銅藍 covellite; indigo copper;
蔚藍 azure; sky blue;
湛藍 azure blue;

lan

【攔】 bar; block; hold back;
[攔擋] block; obstruct;
[攔劫] intercept and rob;
[攔截] intercept;
[攔路] bar the road; block the way;
攔路虎 a lion in the way; a stumbling block; a tiger blocking the way; an obstacle; hindrance;
攔路搶劫 block the road and rob the passers-by; commit highway robbery; hold sb and rob him; hold up; waylay;
好狗不攔路 good dogs don't get underfoot — good men don't play the part of stumbling block;
[攔網] block;
攔網成功 shut out;
單人攔網 one-man block;
雙人攔網 two-man block;

［攔腰］ by the waist; in the middle; round the middle;
攔腰抱住 clasp sb by the waist; hold sb by the waist; put one's arms round sb's waist; seize sb about the waist; seize sb round the middle;
攔腰切斷 cut through;
［攔阻］ block; hinder; hold back; obstruct;

遮攔 block; hinder; impede;
阻攔 bar the way; block; stop;

lan
【瀾】 great wave; huge billow;

安瀾 (1) calm; (2) peaceful;
波瀾 billows; great waves;
狂瀾 raging waves;
漪瀾 ripple;

lan
【籃】 (1) basket; (2) basketball goal;
［籃板］ backboard;
籃板球 backboard;
~ 搶籃板球 backboard recovery;
［籃球］ basketball;
籃球比賽 basketball game;
~ 一場籃球比賽 a basketball game;
籃球隊 basketball team;
~ 籃球隊員 basketballer;
~ 男子籃球隊 men's basketball team;
~ 女子籃球隊 women's basketball team;
籃球鞋 basketball shoes;
~ 高幫籃球鞋 high-top basketball shoes;
打籃球 play basketball;
［籃圈］ hoop;
［籃子］ basket;
籃子裏挑花，越挑越眼花 a maiden with many wooers often chooses the worst;
菜籃子 vegetable basket;

編籃 make a basket;
灌籃 slam dunk;
花籃 (1) basket of flowers; (2) gaily decorated basket;
扣籃 slam dunk;
筐籃 basket;
投籃 shoot;
搖籃 cradle;

lan
【襤】 clothes without hem; ragged garments; sloppily dressed;
［襤褸］ ragged; shabby;
襤褸衣衫 tattered garments;

lan
【斕】 multicoloured;

斑斕 bright-coloured; gorgeous; mulicoloured;

lan
【欄】 (1) balustrade; fence; railing; (2) pen for domesticated animals;
［欄杆］ balustrade; bannister; railing;
燈草欄杆—不能靠 a rail made of rotten rushes — a broken reed; unrealiable;
［欄柵］ balustrade; barrier; railing;

畜欄 corral;
存欄 amount of livestock on hand;
低欄 low hurdles;
高欄 high hurdles;
跨欄 hurdle race;
牛欄 cattle pen;
憑欄 lean against the railing;
橋欄 bridge railing;
跳欄 hurdle race;
通欄 banner; banner headline;
中欄 intermediate hurdles;
專欄 special column;

lan
【蘭】 orchid;
［蘭艾］ orchid and artemisia;
蘭艾同焚 impose the same destiny upon the noble and the mean alike; orchid and artemisia are hurt together — good men destroyed with the bad;
［蘭桂］ orchid and cassia;
蘭桂齊芳 the fragrance of the orchid and cassia ascends — sons and grandsons become known in the world;
蘭薰桂馥 as fragrant as orchid and cassia — a man's beautiful mral influence; have many children and grandchildren;
［蘭花］ orchid;
米蘭花 Cape jasmine;
［蘭形棘心］ the appearance of an orchid and heart of a thistle — beautiful in appearance but wicked at heart;
［蘭質蕙心］ beautiful and clever; pure heart and spirit;

草蘭 cymbidium; orchid;
春蘭 cymbidium; orchid;

法蘭 flange;
蕙蘭 a species of orchid;
建蘭 sword-leaved cymbidium;
劍蘭 gladidus gandavensis;
鈴蘭 lily of the valley;
木蘭 lily magnolia;
佩蘭 orchid;
玉蘭 yulan magnolia;
芝蘭 irises and orchids;
珠蘭 zhulan tree;

lan
【襴】 one-piece garment;

lan
【讕】 abuse; calumniate; libel; revile; slander;
［讕言］ calumny; slander;

lan³

lan
【懶】 (1) indolent; lazy; slothful; (2) languid; sluggish;
［懶蟲］ lazybones;
［懶怠］ (1) indolent; lazy; (2) not in the mood to;
［懶蛋］ idler;
［懶得］ be disinclined to; not be in the mood to; not feel like;
懶得管 won't bother to heed it;
懶得説話 not in the mood to talk;
［懶惰］ eat one's on flesh; have no get-upand-go, keep banker's hours; lazy; lethargic; lentitudinous; not to strain oneself; pepless; phlegmatic; sluggish; swing the lead;
懶惰成性 be addicted to a lazy life; have laziness as one's second nature;
懶惰的 lazy;
懶惰的人 slacker;
［懶鬼］ deadbeat; lazybones;
［懶漢］ idler; lazy man; lazybone; sluggard;
懶漢儒夫 the sluggard and the coward;
懶漢鞋 loafer;
餓得死懶漢，餓不死窮漢 a lazy man can starve to death, a poor man won't;
一群懶漢 a horde of lazybones;
［懶驢］ lazy sheep;
懶驢上磨屎尿多 idle folks lack no excuses;
懶驢無輕馱，懶人無輕活 a lazy sheep thinks its wool heavy;
［懶人］ bedsteader; do-nothing; faineant; gold brick; gentleman of leisure; lady of leisure; layabout; lazy person; lazybones; lounger; sleepyhead; vale of resters;
無用的懶人 ne'er-do-well;
［懶散］ careless; indolent; lazy; negligent; slack; sluggish;
懶散的 indolent; lackadaisical;
懶散度日 laze;
懶懶散散 indolent and sluggish; lazy and loosened; slack in;
［懶透了］ bone-idle; bone-lazy;
［懶洋洋］ indolent; languid; languor; lethargy; listless;
懶洋洋的 lanquid; lethargic; listless;
［懶腰］ stretch;
伸懶腰 stretch; stretch and yawn;
［懶於］ not enthusiastic about sth; too lazy to do sth;
懶於學習 too lazy to study;

憊懶 tired and indolent;
懲懶 punish loafers on the job;
躲懶 loaf on the job; shirk; shy away from work;
疏懶 careless and lazy; slothful;
樹懶 sloth;
酸懶 aching and tired;
偷懶 be indolent; loaf on the job;
慵懶 languor;
嘴懶 not inclined to talk much; taciturn;

lan
【覽】 (1) inspect; look; perceive; read; (2) listen; (3) a surname;

便覽 brief guide;
博覽 read extensively;
瀏覽 glance over; look through;
披覽 open and read; persue;
涉覽 read widely;
一覽 bird's-eye view; general survey;
游覽 go sigh-seeing; visit;
閱覽 read;
展覽 exhibit; exhibition; put on display;
縱覽 look far and wide; scan;

lan
【攬】 (1) pull sb into one's arms; take into one's arms; (2) fasten with a rope; (3) canvas; take on; take upon oneself;

(4) grasp; monopolize;

［攬鏡自照］ hold up a mirror to look at one's own reflection; look at oneself in the mirror; taje a mirror to look at oneself;

［攬轡澄清］ seize the reins and bring about peace—have a great ambition to bring about peace in the country at one's first appointment;

［攬權］ abuse one's authority;

攬權納賄 abuse one's authority and take bribes;

攬權專政 arrogate power to oneself and exercise dictatorship; grasp at authority and form a despotic government;

把攬 control; monopolize;

包攬 take on everything; undertake the whole thing;

承攬 contract to do a job;

兜攬 (1) find customers for trade; solicit; (2) take upon oneself;

獨攬 monopolize;

收攬 (1) buy over; win over; (2) have within control;

招攬 solicit;

總攬 assume overall responsibility; take on everything;

lan

【欖】 olive;

橄欖 (1) Chinese olive; the fruit of the canary tree; (2) olive;

lan

【纜】 cable; hawser; mooring rope;

［纜車］ cable car; trolley;

纜車吊椅 chairlift;

登山纜車 cable car;

高架纜車 aerial cable car;

［纜索］ cable; cable rope; hawser; pendant; suspension cable;

纜索鐵路 cable railway; funicular;

電纜 cable; electric cable;

lan⁴

lan

【濫】 (1) flood; overflow; (2) excessive; indiscriminate; lavish;

［濫調］ cliche; hackneyed tune; worn-out theme;

［濫伐］ deforestation;

［濫交］ prosmicuous; sow one's wild oats;

濫交的人 swinger;

［濫權］ abuse authority;

弄法濫權 play with the law and misuse of official authority;

［濫觴］ fountainhead; source;

［濫套子］ hackneyed expressions and formulae; platitudes;

［濫言］ talk nonsense;

［濫用］ abuse; misuse; use indiscriminately;

濫用公款 expend public funds irregularly;

濫用權勢 abuse one's authority; exercise wrongly one's power; override one's commission;

濫用人力 misuse manpower resources;

濫用特權 abuse one's privilege;

濫用無度 use sth without limit;

濫用職權 abuse one's authority; abuse one's position; abuse one's power; override one's commission; presume on one's position;

泛濫 be in flood; inundate; overflow;

lan

【瀾】 (1) dripping wet; overflowing; vast expanse of water; (2) thin rice paste;

［瀾漫］ (1) inundating; overflowing; (2) dripping wet; wet through; (3) carefree; sprightly;

［瀾汗］ vast expanse of water;

瀾汗洪濤 rise or roll in billows;

lan

【爛】 (1) mashed; pappy; sodden; (2) decay; become rotten; fester; go bad; rot; spoil; (3) messy; (4) soft; tender; (5) dissolute; (6) brilliant;

［爛飯］ soft rice;

［爛糊］ mushy; overcooked;

［爛貨］ (1) fast woman; slut; (2) worthless goods;

［爛漫］ (1) bright-coloured; brilliant; glittering; (2) ingenuous; naive; natural; unaffected;

山花爛漫 mountain flowers are in full bloom;

天真爛漫 naïve;

[爛泥] mire; mud; slime; slush;
爛泥糊不上壁 of a pig's tail you can never make a good shaft; of evil grain no good seed can come; you cannot make a horn of a pig's tail; you cannot make a silk purse out of a sow's ear;
爛泥坑 muddy pit;
爛泥塘 muddy pond;
一團爛泥 an amorphous mass of clay;
[爛然] brilliant;
[爛熟] (1) thoroughly cooked; (2) know sth thoroughly;
[爛攤子] awful mess; shambles;
留下一個爛攤子 leave sb an awful mess;
收拾這個爛攤子 handle the shambles;
[爛賬] (1) accounts in a mess; (2) bad debt; bad accounts;
一筆爛賬 accounts are in a mess;
[爛醉] dead drunk;
爛醉的 blotto; bombed;
~喝得爛醉的 bladdered;
爛醉如泥 as drunk as a boiled owl; as drunk as a David's sow; as drunk as a Davy's sow; as drunk as a fiddler; as drunk as a fish; as drunk as a jelly-fish; as drunk as a lord; as tight as a drum; beastly drunk; blind drunk; dead drunk; dead to the world; done to the wide; drunk and incapable; drunk as a lord; drunk as a skunk; drunk like a fish; drunk to the world; far gone; thoroughly drunk;
爛醉如泥的 shitfaced;
喝得爛醉 drink oneself silly;

斒爛 (1) gorgeous; resplendent; (2) multicoloured; variegated colour;
燦爛 bright; glorious; magnificent; resplendent; splendid;
腐爛 (1) become decomposed; become putrid; (2) corrupt; rot;
潰爛 fester; ulcerate;
霉爛 mildew and rot;
糜爛 dissipated; rotten to the core;
破爛 junk; ragged; scrap; tattered; worn-out;
稀爛 (1) completely mashed; pulpy; (2) broken to bits; smashed to pieces;
絢爛 gorgeous; splendid;

lan
【纜】 a pronunciation of 纜;

lang²
lang
【莨】 scopolia japonica, a kind of herb;

lang
【郎】 (1) young man; (2) official title in ancient China; (3) my darling; (4) a surname;
[郎當] (1) unfit; (2) dejected; dispirited; (3) good-for-nothing; worthless;
吊兒郎當 bugger about; careless and casual; dillydally; do a milk; dodge the column; dog it; fool around; fuck about; goof off; idle about; on the mike; slovenly; take a devil-may-care attitude; take things easy; undisciplined; untidy; utterly carefree;

[郎舅] one's wife's brother;
[郎君] my husband;
[郎貓] tomcat;
[郎中] (1) doctor; physician trained in herbal medicine; (2) ancient official title;
郎中風 doctor;
慢郎中 slow coach; slowpoke;

伴郎 best man;
法郎 franc;
令郎 your son;
女郎 girl; maiden; young woman;
情郎 lover;
新郎 bridegroom;
漁郎 fisherman;
貲郎 one who purchases a public post;

lang
【狼】 wolf;
[狼狽] in a difficult position; in a tight corner; in an awkward predicament; in dire straits;
狼狽而去 hurry off in confusion;
狼狽而逃 flee helter-skelter; flee in disorder;
狼狽失據 helpless and with nothing to fall back on;
狼狽鼠竄 flee in consternation;
狼狽逃竄 be badly beaten and flee panic-stricken; flee helter-skelter; flee in a panic; flee in confusion;
狼狽投敵 flee in a panic to defect to the enemy;
狼狽萬狀 be placed in an extremely embarrassing situation; in an awkward

position; in dire confusion;
狼狽為奸 act in collusion with; as partners in crime; be banded together as traitors; collaborate with...in evil-doing; collude in doing evil; in cahoots with each other; involve in a conspiracy; join in a conspiracy; join in villainy; one hand washes another; work in collusion with sb for some evil purpose;
狼狽相 a sorry figure; an awkward look;
狼狽周章 be thrown into utter confusion; panic-stricken; terror-stricken;

L

［狼奔豕突］ run like wolves and rush about like pigs — said of a pack of evildoers who behave in a wild and lawless way; run like wolves and rush like boars — infest and harass about; tear about like wild beasts;
［狼瘡］ lupus;
紅斑狼瘡 lupus erythematosis;
深部狼瘡 lupus profundus;
增殖性狼瘡 lupus hypertrophicus;
腫脹性狼瘡 lupus tumidus;
［狼狗］ wolfhound;
［狼顧］ very suspicious;
［狼孩］ wolf child;
［狼虎］ wolves and tigers;
驅狼防虎 drive out the wolf and guard against the tiger;
如狼似虎 as ferocious as wolves and tigers; as savage as tigers and wolves; like cruel beasts of prey;
［狼獾］ carcajou; glutton;
［狼藉］ (1) be scattered about in a mess; in a mess; in disorder; (2) notorious;
杯盤狼藉 cups, dishes in disorder;
落紅狼籍 falling flowers scatter all about;
聲名狼藉 be badly discredited;
一片狼藉 a complete mess;
［狼叫］ a wolf growls; a wolf howls;
［狼戾無親］ without natural affection;
［狼群］ a pack of wolves;
羊入狼群 a sheep in a pack of wolves — in a perilous position;
［狼貪］ avaricious; greedy;
狼貪虎視 avaricious; covetous; insatiably greedy like wolves and tigers;
~對利潤狼貪虎視 insatiable of interests;
［狼煙］ smoke signal;
狼煙四起 smoke signals rising on all sides — war alarms raised everywhere; warning signals of approaching enemy forces are seen on all sides; with alarms raised at all border posts;
［狼易其衣，不改其性］ the wolf changes his coat, not his disposition;

豺狼 jackal and wolf;
虎狼 (1) tiger and wolf; (2) bandit; robber;
一群狼 a pack of wolves;
一條狼 a wolf;
一隻狼 a wolf;
中山狼 perfidious person;

lang
【琅】 (1) a kind of stone resembling pearl; (2) clean and white; pure; spotless; (3) a surname;
［琅嬛］ Heaven's library;
琅嬛福地 a scenically beautiful place;
［琅琅］ the sound of tinkling, reading aloud, etc.;
琅琅上口 easy to pronounce;

珐琅 enamel;
琳琅 beautiful jade; gem;

lang
【廊】 corridor; hallway; portico;
［廊道］ gallery;
［廊檐］ eaves of a veranda;
［廊子］ corridor; veranda;

長廊 covered corridor; gallery;
髮廊 barber shop;
畫廊 (1) painted corridor; (2) gallery;
迴廊 winding corridor;
門廊 porch; portico;
游廊 covered corridor; veranda;
柱廊 colonnade;
走廊 corridor; passage;

lang
【稂】 grass; weeds;
［稂莠］ good-for-nothing;
不稂不莠 good-for-nothing; useless; worthless;
稂不稂，莠不莠 good-for-nothing; neither fish, flesh nor fowl;

lang
【榔】 (1) betel palm; (2) betel nut;

[榔槺] bulky; cumbersome;
[榔頭] hammer;

檳榔 (1) areca; betel palm; (2) betel-nut;
桄榔 hale and hearty;

lang
【瑯】 same as 琅 ;

lang
【蜋】 (1) mantis; (2) cicada;

lang
【踉】 hop about; jump about;

lang
【螂】 same as 蜋 ;

刀螂 mantis;
蛇螂 dung beetle;
蜣螂 dung beetle;
螳螂 mantis;
蟑螂 cockroach;

lang
【鋃】 (1) chains for prisoners; (2) tolling of a bell;

lang
【鎯】 hammer;
[鎯鐺] (1) iron chains; (2) chank; clang;
鎯鐺入獄 be chained and thrown into prison; be put in chains and thrown into prison;

lang³
lang
【朗】 (1) bright; clear; (2) loud and clear; resonant; sonorous;
[朗讀] read aloud;
[朗朗] (1) sound of reading aloud; (2) bright; light;
書聲朗朗 the hyme of study is clearly heard;
[朗誦] declaim; deliver a recitation; read aloud with expression; recite;
用英語朗誦 recite in English;

開朗 (1) open and clear; (2) optimistic; sanguine;
明朗 (1) bright and clear; (2) clear and evident; obvious; (3) bright and cheerful;
清朗 (1) cool and bright; (2) clear and resounding;
晴朗 fine; sunny;
爽朗 (1) bright and clear; (2) frank and open; hearty;
稀朗 scattered but bright;
硬朗 hale and hearty;

lang
【烺】 (said of fire) bright;

lang
【閬】 (1) high door; (2) big; high; tall; (3) bright; clear; lucid; (4) open and spacious;
[閬苑瑤池] emerald pools and phantom gardens of Fairyland;

lang⁴
lang
【浪】 (1) breaker; ripple; wave; (2) sth resembling a wave; (3) stroll; wander; (4) dissolute; unrestrained; (5) flighty; frivolous;
[浪潮] bandwagon; tide; wave;
罷工浪潮 the wave of the strikes;
~ 平息罷工浪潮 put down the wave of the strikes; suppress the wave of the strikes;
革命的浪潮 the tide of revolution;
新浪潮 new wave;
一波浪潮 a wave;
[浪闖] beat about pointlessly;
[浪蕩] (1) loaf about; loiter about; (2) dissipated; dissolute;
浪蕩不羈 dissipated and unrestrained;
浪蕩男人 lascivious men;
浪蕩女人 a coquette; a harpy; a tramp;
~ 避開浪蕩女人 keep away from loose women;
閒游浪蕩 dissipated; hang about;
在城裏浪蕩 loaf about the town;
[浪放] uninhibited; unrestrained;
[浪費] dissipate; dwindle; extravagant; squander; wastage; waste;
浪費掉 go to waste
浪費精力 fritter away energy;
浪費青春 waste one's youth;
浪費人力 waste manpower;
浪費食物 food wastage;
浪費時間 waste time;
白白浪費 down the drain;
避免浪費 avoid waste;
杜絕浪費 eliminate waste; put an end to waste;
反對浪費 combat waste;
揮霍浪費 waste prodigally;

減少浪費 reduce waste;
鋪張浪費 extravagance and waste;
~反對鋪張浪費 combat extravagance and waste; oppose extravagance and waste;

［浪花］ (1) spray; (2) a happy event in one's life;
浪花蕩漾 the foam of breaking waves is drifting and swirling;
迸起浪花 spray spindrift;
拍岸浪花 surf;

［浪跡］ roam; wander;
浪跡江湖 wander about;
浪跡萍蹤 drift about without any definite trace like running water or duckweed;
浪跡天涯 roam freely all over the world; rove all over the world;

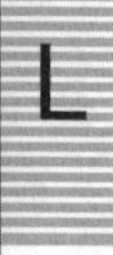

［浪浪］ flowing;

［浪漫］ (1) romantic; (2) frivolous behaviour; not bother about small matters; (3) debauched; dissolute;
浪漫曲 romance;
浪漫詩 romantic poetry;
浪漫主義 romanticism;

［浪孟］ (1) dejected; discouraged; (2) aloud;

［浪人］ (1) vagrant; (2) dismissed courtier; (3) jobless person; unemployed;

［浪士］ debauchee;

［浪濤］ billow; great wave; surge; wave;
浪濤洶湧 bellowiness;
驚濤駭浪 fierce and frightening storm; fierce storms; frightful billows and terrible waves; raging waves; storm and stress; terrifying waves; the waves are wild and the current swift; violent storm;
推濤興浪 egg sb on to do sth;
推濤作浪 do sth to fan the flame — to stir up more trouble instead of being a peace-maker; push and help the waves to sweep on;

［浪頭］ (1) waves; (2) trend;
趕浪頭 climb the bandwagon; get on the bandwagon; jump the bandwagon;

［浪游］ roam for pleasure;

［浪語］ nonsensical joke;

［浪職］ neglect one's duty;

［浪子］ bum; dissipater; loafer; prodigal; rakehell; rounder; wastrel;
浪子回頭 a prodigal son becomes good; return to the fold; the return of the prodigal son;
浪子回頭金不換 a prodial who returns is more precious than gold;

白浪 white horses;
波浪 wave;
放浪 (1) dissolute; (2) unrestrained;
風浪 storm; stormy waves;
海浪 ocean wave; sea wave;
激浪 turbulent waves;
巨浪 billow; breaker; roller;
流浪 lead a vagrant life; roam about;
麥浪 billowing wheat fields; rippling wheat;
孟浪 impetuous; impulsive; rash;
氣浪 blast;
熱浪 heat wave; hot wave;
聲浪 clamour; voice;
涌浪 surge; swell;
濁浪 muddy waves;
縱浪 (1) uninhibited; unrestrained; (2) dissolute; profligate;

lang

【閬】 a pronunciation of 閬；

lao¹
lao

【撈】 (1) drag for; dredge up; fish for; scoop up from the water; (2) gain; get by improper means;

［撈本］ recoup oneself; recover one's losses; win back lost wagers;

［撈錢］ dredge for money; make money; seek money;

［撈取］ fish for; gain;
撈取政治本錢 fish for political capital; seek political advantage;

捕撈 catch; fish for;
打撈 get out of the water; salvage;
漁撈 fishing on a large scale;

lao²
lao

【牢】 (1) fold; pen; (2) sacrifice; (3) jail; prison; (4) durable; fast; firm;

［牢不可破］ adamant; impregnable; indestructible; proof against all assaults; too strong to break; unbreakable;

［牢愁莫遣］ worried not knowing how to drive

away melancholy;

[牢固] fast; firm; secure; solid;

牢固耐用 secure and durable;

[牢記] bear in mind; commit sth to memory; keep firmly in mind; learn by heart; remember well;

牢記不忘 bear in one's mind; embedded in one's memory;

[牢靠] (1) firm; strong; sturdy; (2) dependable; reliable;

[牢牢] firmly; safely;

牢牢記住 firmly bear in mind; keep firmly in mind;

牢牢印在記憶中 be embedded in one's memory; be embedded in one's recollection;

[牢籠] (1) cage; (2) bonds; (3) draw sb over to one's side; (4) snare; trap; (5) bind up; fetter; tie;

牢籠人心 try to win popular support;

[牢騷] complain; grieve; grumble; grumbling;

牢騷滿腹 bear a grudge against; full of complaints; full of grievances; querulous;

發牢騷 beef; beef about; blow off steam; chew the rag; complain; grouch; grouse; grumble; grumble about; grumble at; grumble over; let off steam; make a sour remark; murmur; natter; say devil's paternoster; whine about; work off steam;

~ 不要發牢騷 don't grumble;

~ 大發牢騷 dissipate one's grief extensively; make bitter complaint; pour out a stream of complaints;

~ 找理由發牢騷 find cause to complain;

[牢什子] nuisance;

[牢穩] reliable; safe; secure;

[牢獄] jail; prison;

打入牢獄 throw sb into prison;

劫牢越獄 force open the prison to free the prisoners;

把牢 dependable; safe and secure; strong;

狴牢 jail; prison;

大牢 jail; prison;

地牢 dungeon;

監牢 jail; prison;

囚牢 jail; prison;

水牢 water dungeon;

土牢 dungeon;

坐牢 be imprisoned; be in jail;

lao

【勞】 (1) labour; work; (2) put sb to the trouble of; (3) fatigue; toil; (4) meritorious deed; service; (5) express one's appreciation reward;

[勞保] labour insurance; labour protection;

勞保條例 labour insurance regulations;

[勞瘁] exhausted from excessive work; worn-out;

勞瘁而卒 die wearied and worn; exhausted from excessive work and die;

神勞形瘁 feel very weary; look extremely haggard and tired;

[勞動] (1) labour; work; (2) manual labour; physical labour;

勞動安全 labour safety;

勞動保險 labour insurance;

勞動報酬 labour reward; payment for labour; reward for labour;

~ 得到勞動報酬 receive the reward of one's labour;

勞動部 ministry of labour;

勞動法 labour law;

勞動分工 dvision of labour;

勞動改造 reform through labour;

勞動合同 labour contract;

勞動節 Labour Day;

勞動教養 labour education; reeducation through labour;

勞動經濟學 labour economics;

勞動局 labour bureau;

勞動力 labour; labour force; manpower; workforce;

~ 勞動力人口 labour force population;

~ 勞動力市場 labour market;

~ 半勞動力 auxiliary man-power;

~ 抽象勞動力 abstract human labour;

~ 輔助勞動力 auxiliary labour;

~ 節省勞動力 save labour;

~ 浪費勞動力 waste labour;

~ 廉價勞動力 cheap labour;

勞動模範 model worker;

勞動密集型 labour-intensive;

~ 勞動密集型產品 labour-intensive products;

~ 勞動密集型經濟 labour-intensive economy;

~ 勞動密集型企業 labour-intensive

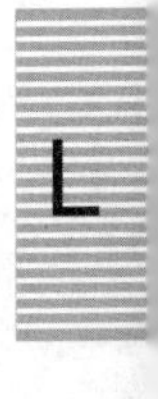

enterprise;
勞動人民 working people;
勞動社會學 sociology of labour;
勞動生產率 productivity of labour;
勞動市場 labour market;
勞動統計學 labour statistics;
勞動者 labourer;
~ 常僱勞動者 confined labourer;
~ 農業勞動者 agricultural labourer;
~ 普通勞動者 ordinary labourer;
勞動爭議 labour disputation;
勞動資源 labour resources;
避免勞動 shun labour;
抽象勞動 abstract labour;
複雜勞動 complicated labour;
僱佣勞動 wage labour;
管制勞動 work under surveillance;
減輕勞動 lighten one's labour;
簡單勞動 simple labour;
腦力勞動 brain work; intellectual work; mental labour;
農業勞動 rural labour;
強迫性勞動 forced labour;
強制勞動 compulsory labour; forced labour;
生產勞動 productive labour;
剩餘勞動 surplus labour;
體力勞動 manual labour; physical labour;
血汗勞動 sweated labour;
義務勞動 volunteer labour;

[勞頓] fatigued; wearied;

[勞乏] overworked; physically exhausted; tired;

[勞工] labourer; worker;
勞工市場 labour market;
勞工行動 industrial action;
流動勞工 itinerant labourer;
契約勞工 contract labour;
血汗勞工 weated labour;
移民勞工 mimmigrant labourer;

[勞獲] pains and gains;
不勞而獲 gain without working; get sth for nothing; make gains without doing any work; obtain without effort; profit by other people's toil; reap without sowing;
不勞無獲 no pains, no gains;

[勞績] merits and accomplishments;

[勞駕] (1) thank you; (2) excuse me; (3) if you please; would you...;
勞駕勞駕 please; thank you so much;

[勞苦] hard work; toil;
勞苦功高 labour hard and achieve much; with toilsome labour and distinctive merits;
勞苦與共 a trouble shared is a trouble halved;
不辭勞苦 does not mind the hardships; make nothing of hardships; put oneself out; spare no pains; take the trouble;

[勞累] exhausted; overworked; run-down; tired;
勞累的 grueling;
~ 勞累的旅途 gueling journey;
勞累過度 burn the candle at both ends; overtired;
避免勞累 avoid exertion;
過度勞累 overwork; undue exertion;
消除勞累 banish fatigue;

[勞力] (1) labour; labour force; (2) able-bodied person;
費心勞力 take a lot of trouble;
節省勞力 labour-saving;

[勞碌] toil;
勞勞碌碌 toil; work hard;

[勞神] a tax on one's mind; bother; trouble;
勞神費力 tax one's mind and strength; weary mind and use strength;

[勞師] (1) take greetings and gifts to army units; (2) tire troops;
勞師動眾 drag in lots of people; mobilize too many troops;
勞師遠征 tire the troops on a long expedition;

[勞什子] hated thing; nuisance;

[勞務] labour service; personal service; physical labour;
勞務報酬 recompense for service; reward for personal services;
勞務出口 export services;
勞務合同 contract for service;
勞務合作 labour service cooperation;
勞務價格 price of labour service;
勞務進口 import of services;
勞務市場 labour market;
勞務收入 income from services;
~ 勞務收入淨額 net return from services;
勞務輸出 export of labour services;
~ 海外勞務輸出 labour services export;

[勞心] work with one's mind;
勞心勞力 labour and toil with mind and body;

勞心者治人 those who labour with minds govern others; those who work with their brains will rule;

勞心者治人，勞力者治於人 those who do mental labour rule and those who do manual labour are ruled; those who toil with their minds make others work for them while those who toil with their hands work for others and serve those who use their minds; those who work with their brains rule and those who work with their brawn are ruled;

［勞燕分飛］ go in different ways; like birds flying in different directions; part; part from each other; separate;

［勞役］ corvee; forced labour; hard labour; penal servitude;

服勞役 receive hard labour;

獄中勞役 prison labour;

［勞逸］ labour and rest;

勞逸不勻 unequal distribution of work; uneven allocation of work;

勞逸兼顧 interchange labour and repose;

勞逸結合 strike a proper balance between work and rest;

好逸惡勞 despise labour and love ease; dislike work and love ease; indulge in easy and comfort and dislike labour; like ease and do not like work; love ease and dislike work;

捨逸就勞 relinquish an elephant for a life of toil;

以逸待勞 conserve strength while the enemy tires himeself through a long march; meet worn-out troop in ease; wait at one's ease for the exhausted enemy; wait in comfort for an exhausted enemy;

［勞資］ labour and capital;

勞資對抗 antagonism between labour and capital;

勞資關係 industrial relations; labour relations; labour-capital relations;

~勞資關係審裁處 industrial tribunal;

勞資合同 labour contract;

勞資合作 labour-management cooperation;

勞資糾紛 dispute between labour and management; industrial dispute; labour dispute;

按勞 according to one's labour;

操勞 (1) work hard; (2) look after; take care;

酬勞 recompense; reward;

代勞 (1) ask sb to do sth for oneself; (2) do sth for sb;

道勞 express one's thanks;

煩勞 trouble;

告勞 tell about one's hard work and toil;

功勞 credit; contribution;

積勞 endure constant overwork;

疲勞 fatigued; tired; weary;

勤勞 diligent; hardworking; industrious;

劬勞 fatigued; overworked;

徒勞 fruitless labour; futile effort;

慰勞 appreciate sb's services and present gifts;

賢勞 work industriously;

効勞 serve; work in the service of;

辛勞 pains; toil;

勛勞 meritorious service;

有勞 sorry to have caused you so much trouble;

lao

【嘮】 chat; have a gab; talk;

［嘮叨］ burble; chatter; clack; garrulous; maunder; prattle away; prattle on;

嘮叨不休 burble; talk a dog's hind leg off; talk a donkey's hind leg off; talk a horse's hind leg off; talk the hind leg off a dog; talk the hind leg off a donkey; talk the hind leg off a horse;

嘮叨個沒完沒了 talk the hind leg off a donkey;

嘮嘮叨叨 babble on and on; burble; go on about; nag; repeat over and over again; say over and over again; talk nineteen to the dozen;

~別總是嘮嘮叨叨 don't be such a nag;

［嘮嗑］ burble; chat; talk;

lao

【撈】 a pronunciation of 撈；

lao

【癆】 consumption; tuberculosis;

［癆病］ tuberculosis;

肺癆 tuberculosis;

骨癆 tuberculosis of bones and joints;

虛癆 consumptive disease;

lao

【醪】 unstrained wine or liquor;

［醪糟］ fermented glutinous rice;

lao³
lao

【老】 (1) aged; old; (2) old people; (3) of long standing; old; (4) outdated; (5) overdone; tough; (6) overgrown; (7) always; constantly; (8) dark;

［老八板兒］ (1) old fogy; (2) inflexible; rigid; stick to old ways;

［老爸］ dad; father;

［老板］ boss; proprietor; shopkeeper;
- 老板娘 (1) shopkeeper's wife; (2) proprietress;
- 巴結老板 crawl to one's boss; fawn on one's boss;
- 大老板 (1) big boss; (2) big shot;
- 飯店老板 restaurant proprietor;
- 服裝店老板 clothes shopkeeper;
- 公司老板 proprietor of an establishment;
- 後台老板 backstage boss;
- 花店老板 florist;
- 客棧老板 keeper of an inn;
- 商店老板 business proprietor;
- 鞋鋪老板 shoemaker;

［老闆］［same as 老板］ boss; guvnor; head; honcho; proprietor;
- 老闆娘 same as 老板娘.
- 後台老闆 paymaster;
- 臨時老闆 caretaker boss;
- 女老闆 proprietress;

［老伴］ one's old man; one's old woman;

［老幫子］ old devil; old fart; old fogy; old person; old rascal;

［老蚌生珠］ a son born in one's old age; an old woman giving birth to a child; have a son in one's old age;

［老鴇］ procuress; woman running a brothel;

［老輩］ old folks; one's elders;

［老本］ (1) capital; original capital; principal; (2) past experience;
- 吃老本 live off one's past gains; live on one's own fat; rest on one's laurels; rest on past achievements;
- 虧了老本 suffer great losses;
- 撈回老本 redeem one's capital;
- 賠了老本 suffer great losses;
- 輸掉老本 lose all one's principal; lose one's last stakes;

［老表］ (1) cousin; (2) buddies; old pals;

［老兵］ old soldier; veteran;

［老病］ old ailment; old and ailing; old and sick;
- 老病侵尋 aging and ailing;

［老伯］ uncle;
- 老伯伯 granddad;

［老財］ landlord; moneybags;

［老巢］ den; lair; nest;

［老成］ experienced; steady;
- 老成持重 an old head on young shoulders; experienced and prudent;
- 老成凋謝 the passing away of worthy old people;
- 老成練達 experienced and versed in one's work; know all the moves on the board; know one's onions; know one's way about;
- 過於老成 too sophisticated;
- 少年老成 young but steady;

［老粗］ rough and ready chap; uncouth person; uneducated person;
- 大老粗 illiterate; rough and ready fellow; rustic; uncouth fellow; uneducated person;

［老大］ (1) old; (2) eldest child; (3) master of a sailing vessel; (4) greatly; very; (5) don; leader of a triad society;
- 老大不小 come of age; grow up;
- 老大哥 elder brother;
- 老大姐 elder sister;
- 老大難 most difficult issue;
- 老大娘 (1) aunty; (2) granny;
- 老大爺 grandpa; uncle;

［老當益壯］ green old age; gain vigour with age; hale and hearty; have a green old age; old but vigorous;

［老到］ experienced; reliable; sophisticated;

［老底］ (1) one's past; (2) family background;
- 兜翻老底 dig up old personal stories to discredit sb; disclose the whole inside story; reveal all the details of sb's disreputable background;
- 揭老底 dig up sb's old stories in order to discredit him; disclose sb's villainous life; drag the skeleton out of sb's closet; dredge up some embarrassing facts about sb's past; expose sb's fault; rake up sb's past faults; reveal sb's unsavoury past; reveal to the world sb's evil character; show sb up;
- 漏了老底 leak out one's personal secrets;

［老弟］ my boy; young fellow; young man;

[老調] hackneyed theme; platitude;
老調重彈 harp on the same string; harp on the shop-worn theme; play the same old tune; sing the same song; strike up a hackneyed tune;
八十歲學吹笙—老調 an eighty-year-old person learning to play a pipe — old tunes (the same old stuff);
唱老調 harp on the same string; sing the same old song;
重彈老調 harp on the same string; sing the same old tune; strike up an old tune;

[老而彌堅] become more firm as one grows old;

[老兒] father;
乾老兒 one's foster father;

[老夫] an old fellow like me;

[老趕] (1) amateur; layman; nonprofessional person; (2) benighted; ignorant;

[老公] hubby; husband; old man;
老公公 (1) grandpa; (2) one's father-in-law; one's husband's father;

[老鴰] crow;
老鴰窩裏出鳳凰 a phoenix grows out from a crow's nest; mediocre parents give birth to extraordinary offsprings;

[老漢] (1) old man; (2) old fellow like me;

[老虎] tiger;
老虎拉輾子—不聽那一套 a tiger drawing a stone roller — not to listen to such an idle talk;
老虎唸經—假裝正經 a tiger chanting scriptures — pretending to be respectable;
老虎屁股摸不得 like a tiger whose backside no one dares to touch — not to be provoked;
老虎頭上拍蒼蠅 beat a fly on the head of a tiger — undaunted and reckless;
老虎頭上搔癢 scratch the tiger's head — dangerous;
老虎頭上捉虱子—不怕死 trying to catch lice on a tiger's head — unafraid of death;
老虎推磨—不吃這一套 a tiger can draw a stone roller but he won't accept the harness;
老虎也有打盹時 even Homer sometimes nods; there are times when ever the tiger sleeps;
老虎摘月亮—夢想 a tiger wanting to pluck down the moon — a pipe dream;
老虎嘴裏拔牙—冒險 pulling teeth from a tiger's mouth — risky;
老虎嘴裏送食 stick one's head into the tiger's mouth — court death;
吃角子老虎 slot machine;
~吃角子老虎機 fruit machine; slot machine;
雌老虎 tigress;
秋老虎 a spell of hot weather in autumn; after summer; afterheat; old wives's summer; scorching heat in early autumn; summery days in early autumn;
山中無老虎，猴子稱大王 among the blind the one-eyed man is king; in the country of the blind, the one-eyed man is king; in the kingdom of blind men, the one-eyed is king; the monkey reigns in the mountains when the tiger is not there; when the cat's away, the mice will play; when the tiger is away from the mountain, the monkey proclaims himself king;
小老虎 tiger cub;
一隻老虎 a tiger;
紙老虎 paper tiger;

[老花] presbyopia;
老花鏡 presbyopic glasses;
老花眼 presbyopia;

[老化] ageing; burn-in;
老化性能良好 good ageing;
老化作用 ageing action;
潮濕老化 humidity ageing;
大氣老化 atmospheric ageing;
功率老化 power ageing;
光熱老化 light-heat ageing;
加壓老化 pressure ageing;
界面老化 interfacial ageing;
頻率老化 frequency ageing;
熱老化 heating ageing;
人工老化 artificial ageing;
人口老化 aging population;
知識老化 ageing of knowledge;
自然老化 atmospheric ageing;

[老話] (1) adage; old saying; saying; (2) remarks about the old days;

[老皇曆] last year's calendar; obsolete practice; old history;

[老驥伏櫪] able men tie down to a routine post; the fine old horse lying in the stable;

[老家] one's native place; one's old home;
回老家 (1) dead; die; go to one's last home; (2) go to hometown; return home;

[老將] old-timer; veteran; veteran player; veteran sportsman;

[老摳兒] miser; scrooge;

[老框框] old ways of doing things; out-moded conventions;

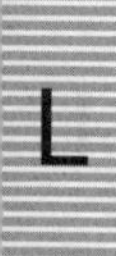

[老辣] experienced and vicious;

[老來俏] become prettier as one gets old; mutton dressed as lamb;

[老例] old practice; old precedent;

[老臉] (1) face; prestige; (2) thick-skinned person;
老臉皮 brazen-faced; thick-skinned;

[老練] experienced; gumption; hard-bitten; know one's way about; practised; seasoned; tactful;
辦事老練 be experienced and work with a sure hand; dispatch one's business with dexterity;
開車老練 expert at driving a car;
目光老練 have an experienced eye;
在外交上老練 be experienced in diplomacy;

[老齡] old age;
老齡化 ageing;
~老齡化國家 ageing nation;
~老齡化社會 ageing society;
老齡經濟學 economics of ageing;
老齡問題 senile problem;

[老路] beaten track; old road;
走老路 follow the old routine; stick to the old path;

[老馬] plug;
老馬失蹄 a good horse stumbles;
老馬識途 a man of long experience knows the ropes; an old hand is a good guide; an old horse knows the way; being very experienced; know the ropes; old stalwarts know best the twists and turns of the way; the devil knows many things because he is old; the experienced knows all the moves of the board; the experienced knows the way;
識途老馬 a man of experience; a person of rich experience; a wise old bird; a worldly-wise man; an experienced person; an old horse which knows the way; an old stager;

[老邁] aged; decrepit; elderly; senile;
老邁昏庸 old and muddleheaded; senile and fatuous;
年高老邁 advanced in age; reach venerable age;

[老命] one's old age;
豁出老命 fight in spite of one's old age;
拼老命 do one's best in spite of one's age; risk one's old bones;

[老衲] old monk;

[老年] advanced in age; anecdotage; caducity; elderly; feel one's age; in the dry tree; mature; old age; senium; sunset years; third age;
老年保健 geriatrics;
老年病學 geriatrics;
老年痴呆 senile dementia;
~老年痴呆症 Alzheimer's disease;
老年大學 senile university;
老年多言期 anecdotage;
老年河 old river;
老年教育 senile education;
老年歧視 ageism;
老年人 old people; senior citizen; the aged;
~老年人問題 aged population's problems;
~老年人協會 association of aged people;
老年型社會 society of the aged;
老年性反射 senile reflex;
老年性萎縮 senile atrophy;
老年性消瘦 geromarasmus;
老年學 gerontology;
老年醫學 gerontology;

[老娘] (1) midwife; (2) grandmother; old mother; (3) old lady;

[老牛] old cow; old ox;
老牛不飲水，不能強按頭 a man may lead a horse to the water, but he cannot make him drink; you can't force an ox to bend its head to drink;
老牛吃嫩草 rob the cradle;
老牛拉破車 drag along at a snail's pace; like an old bullock pulling a broken cart — creep slowly along;
老牛破車 an old ox pulling a rickety cart — making slow progress; the old bullock pulling a broken cart — slow

in action;

老牛舐犢 the old cow licks her calf – old folks dote on their children;

老牛鑽窗眼—騙人 like trying to drive an ox through a window hole – impossible;

[老牌] old brand;

[老婆] wife;

老婆婆 (1) granny; (2) one's husband's mother; one's mother-in-law;

老婆子 my old woman;

怕老婆 be intimidated by one's wife; be scared of one's wife; browbeaten; henpecked;

小老婆 concubine;

[老氣] (1) old mannish; (2) dark and old-fashioned;

老氣橫秋 act as an older; arrogant on account of one's seniority; lacking in youthful vigour;

[老千] deceiver; swindler;

[老拳] fists;

飽以老拳 dust sb's jacket; give sb a proper pummelling; give sb a sound beating; give sb a taste of one's fist – give sb a punch; give sb bellyfuls of fisticuffs; hit sb full in the face; strike sb hard with the fist; whale away at sb with both fists;

餉以老拳 give sb a taste of one's fist – give sb a punch;

[老人] crinkly; crumblie; dusty; golden ager; senile person; senior citizen; well-reserved man; the longer living;

老人家 the elderly;

老人如同風前燭 an old man is like a candle before the wind;

老人政治 gerontocracy;

八旬老人 octogenarian;

發福的老人 portly old man;

頭髮花白的老人 grizzled old man;

[老弱] the old and weak;

老弱病殘 the old, weak, sick and disabled; those who are old, weak, ill or disabled;

老弱殘兵 motley troops unfit for combat duty – incompetent persons for a given job; remnants of a rabble army;

老弱婦幼 old and weak people, women and children;

老弱無能 become so old and weak that one has lost his capacity to do any useful work;

扶助老弱 help the old and the weak;

[老少] the old and the young;

老少良伴 good companies for children as well as adults;

老少無欺 cheat neither the old nor the young; no imposition on the old or young;

老少咸宜 suitable for both young and old;

老老少少 old and young; young and old;

學無老少 in scholarship there is no difference of age; never too old to learn;

有老有少 there are people young and old;

[老師] schoolmaster; teacher;

老師傅 experienced worker; master craftsman;

巴結老師 crawl to one's teacher;

拜老師 become a pupil to a master in a ceremony;

不受歡迎的老師 unpopular teacher;

一位老師 a teacher;

[老實] (1) frank; honest; (2) good; well-behaved;

老實對你說 to be frank with you;

老實話 speak the truth; tell the truth;

~說老實話 call a spade a spade; frankly speaking; speak the truth; tell the truth; to be candid with you; to be frank with you;

老實講 to be frank;

老實交待 make a clean breast of everything come clean; own up;

老實可靠 on the up-and-up;

老實人 straight shooter;

老實認輸 make an honest admission of one's failure;

老實說 frankly;

老實相告 tell the truth;

老實行事 practise honestly;

不老實 dishonest; dishonesty;

過分老實 honest to a fault;

老老實實 behave oneself; conscientiously; honest; honestly and sincerely; in earnest; play no tricks; with sincerity and candour;

手不老實 have sticky fingers;

[老是] always;

[老手] old hand; old stager; past master; veteran;

老手也有失算時　even an expert sometimes makes a mistake;
談判老手　a veteran negotiator;
斲輪老手　experienced man; expert wheelwright; old hand; past master; person of rich experience;

[老鼠] mouse; rat;
老鼠吃貓—自不量力　a mouse wanting to eat a cat — overrating one's own abilities;
老鼠過街，人人喊打　a rat crossing the street is chased by all; the object of universal condemnation;
老鼠嘰吱　mice squeak;
老鼠見貓　a mouse fronting a cat;
老鼠抬轎子—擔當不起　a mouse trying to lift a sedan chair — can't beat it; cannot bear the responsibility;
老鼠咬烏龜，沒法下手　a rat trying to bite a tortoise does not know where to start;
過街老鼠—人人喊打　a rat crossing a street — everyone yells and beats it;
貓哭老鼠　shed crocodile tears;
~ 貓哭老鼠假慈悲　carrion crows bewail the dead sheep, and then eat them; the cat weeps over the mouse; the crow bewails the sheep and then eats it; pretend sympathy and grief; shed crocodile tears;
轉基因老鼠　transgenic mice;

[老態] old; senile;
老態龍鍾　be weighed down with age; come apart at the seams; in one's dotage; look old and clumsy; old and shaky; senile;
顯出老態　show one's age;

[老天] heaven;
老天撥地　too old to move about with ease;
老天不負有心人　heaven rewards the faithul;
老天爺　god; heavens;
~ 老天爺呀　horror of horrors;
老天有眼　there is divine justice after all;

[老頭] (1) old chap; old man; (2) father; (3) husband;
老頭兒　(1) old chap; old man; (2) father; (3) husband;
老頭子　(1) old codger; old fogey; (2) husband; old man;
白鬍子老頭　polar beaver; white-beared old man;
花老頭　dirty old man;
脾氣暴躁的老頭　crusty old man;
脾氣壞的老頭　crtchety old man;

[老撾] Laos;

[老外] (1) layman; raw hand; (2) foreigner;

[老翁] graybeard; old man;

[老鄉] fellow townsman; fellow villager;

[老相] old for one's age;

[老小] grown-ups and children; one's family;
連老帶小　old and young;
上有老，下有小　there are old and young at home;

[老兄] brother; man; mate; old chap; old cock; pardner;

[老羞成怒] be shamed into anger; fly into a rage out of shame; get angry to cover up one's shames; lose one's temper from embarrassment; turn shame into anger;

[老朽] decrepit and behind the times; old and useless;
老朽昏庸　old, worthless, dull and mean;

[老爺] grandfather; grandpa;
老爺車　banger;
~ 一輛老爺車　an old banger;
老爺爺　(1) great grandfather; (2) grandpa;
老爺子　(1) dad; father; (2) old chap; old man;
官老爺　jack-in-office;

[老鷹] eagle;
老鷹放屁—臭氣熏天　an eagle passing wind — stinking to high heaven;

[老幼] young and old;
老幼咸宜　good for both young and old; suitable for people of all ages;
扶老攜幼　bring along the old and the young; carry the babes and support the old folk; help the aged and the young; help the elderly people and children; help the old and guide the young;
全家老幼　the inmates;

[老嫗] old woman;
老嫗能解　intelligible even to a senile woman;

[老帳] old scores;
翻老帳　bring up old scores again; rack up old scores; rekindle old grievances; reopen old scores; thumb through the

records of;

[老者] old man;

[老子] (1) Laozi, a Daoist philosopher; (2) oneself; (3) father;

老子打洞一兒子受用 the father earns, the son spends;

老子天下第一 regard oneself as the number one authority under heaven; think oneself the most important person in the world; think oneself the wisest person in the world;

老子英雄兒好漢 like father, like son; the son of a hero must be a stout fellow too;

乾老子 one's foster father;

艾老 over fifty years old;

卜老 choose a place for retirement;

蒼老 (1) aged; old; (2) forceful; vigorous;

垂老 approaching old age; getting on in years;

父老 elders;

告老 retire on account of age;

活到老學到老 live and learn;

古老 age-old; ancient;

闊老 rich man;

賣老 flaunt one's old age;

耆老 old people;

衰老 decrepit; old and feeble; senile;

偕老 grow old together;

養老 (1) provide for the aged; (2) live out one's life in retirement;

遺老 (1) surviving adherent of a former dynasty; (2) old people who have witnessed big social changes;

元老 senior statesman;

月老 matchmaker;

長老 (1) elder; (2) elder of a Buddhist monastery;

lao

【佬】 (1) fellow; (2) hill-billy; vulgar person;

闊佬 rich guy;

鄉巴佬 country bumpkin;

lao

【姥】 (1) maternal grandmother; (2) midwife; (3) old woman;

[姥姥] (maternal) grandma; (maternal) grandmother;

[姥爺] (maternal) grandpa; (maternal) grandfather;

lao

【銠】 rhodium;

lao

【潦】 (1) disappointed; disheartened; (2) without care;

lao⁴

lao

【烙】 brand; burn; iron;

[烙餅] baked pancake;

[烙印] brand; sear; stigma;

lao

【絡】 net; web;

[絡子] string bag;

lao

【勞】 comfort the tired; entertain the tired;

[勞軍] cheer troops; entertain troops;

[勞來] encourage sb and lead him on;

[勞民] conciliate the people;

lao

【落】 (1) drop; fall; (2) land; perch; (3) get; (4) net income; surplus; (5) place;

[落色] discolour; fade;

[落枕] (1) have a stiff neck; (2) one's head touching the pillow;

lao

【酪】 (1) alcoholic drinks; (2) animal milk; (3) fruit jam; fruit juice;

[酪蛋白] casein; caseinum;

酪蛋白汞 casein-mercury;

酪蛋白酶 caseinase;

酪蛋白素 caseidin;

碘化酪蛋白 iodinated casein;

酸酪蛋白 acid casein;

植物酪蛋白 vegetable casein;

[酪乳] buttermilk;

濃縮酪乳 condensed buttermilk; semi-solid buttermilk;

酸酪乳 sour buttermilk;

酸性酪乳 cultured buttermilk;

甜性酪乳 sweet buttermilk;

乾酪 cheese;

奶酪 cheese;

乳酪 cheese;

lao

【憦】 feel remorse; regret;

lao

【潦】 flood;

lao

【澇】 (1) rot in the field due to flood; (2) flood; torrent;
［澇害］ damage caused by waterlogging;
［澇災］ crop failure caused by waterlogging;

旱澇 drought and flood;
瀝澇 waterlog;
內澇 waterlogging;
排澇 drain flooded fields;

L

le¹

le

【褦】 untidily dressed;

le⁴

le

【仂】 fraction of a number;
［仂語］ phrase;

le

【肋】 rib; side;

le

【泐】 (1) rocks splitting; (2) write letters; (3) carve; (4) coagulate; condense;

le

【扐】 gather in the fingers; pluck;

le

【勒】 (1) rein in; (2) coerce; force; (3) carve; engrave; (4) tighten;
［勒逼］ coerce; force;
［勒交］ force sb to hand sth over;
［勒緊］ tighten;
勒緊褲帶 tighten one's belt;
［勒令］ compel; order;
勒令服從 coerce sb into submission;
勒令聽命 compel obedience from sb;
勒令停業 be closed down by an order;
勒令停職 be suspended from one's office; suspend sb from his post;
勒令退學 order to quit school;
［勒馬］ rein in the horse;
臨崖勒馬 hold in one's horse near a precipice; make a timely turn;
［勒派］ impose; levy on sb;
［勒石］ carve on a stone;
［勒索］ blackmail; extort;
勒索錢財 extort money from sb;
逼債勒索 press for the repayment of debts and practise extortion;
進行敲詐勒索 practise extortion;
［勒抑］ extort and suppress; force sb to reduce the price;

逼勒 blackmail; force;
勾勒 (1) draw the outline of; sketch the contours of; (2) give a brief account of; outline;
彌勒 Maitreya;
轡勒 reins and bit;

le

【樂】 (1) cheerful; happy; joyful; (2) enjoy; find pleasure in; glad to; take pleasure in; (3) amused; laugh;
［樂不可言］ extreme pleasure; unspeakably happy;
［樂不可支］ as pleased as Punch; be overjoyed; be overwhelmed with joy; be thrilled with joy; be thrown into raptures; beside oneself with happiness; can hardly contain oneself for joy; extremely happy; in raptures over; one's joy knows no bounds;
［樂不思蜀］ indulge in pleasure and forget home and duty; have such a good time that one forgets to go home; too happy to think of one's own home;
［樂此不疲］ always enjoy it; never feel bored with it;
［樂道］ only too glad to talk about sth; take delight in talking about sth;
［樂得］ happy to have the chance to; only too glad to; readily take the opportunity to;
［樂而不淫］ pleasant but not obscene;
［樂而忘返］ a slave of pleasure; enjoy oneself and forget all about going home; enjoy oneself so much that one doesn't want to come back; have much enjoyment and forget to return home;
［樂觀］ hope for the best; hopeful; optimistic; sanguine;
樂觀的 upbeat;
樂觀主義 optimism;
抱樂觀 feel optimistic; optimistic;
過分樂觀 overoptimistic;
盲目的樂觀 blind optimism;
［樂極生悲］ after joy comes sorrow; after you fling, watch for the sting; drunken days have all their tomorrows; extreme joy begets sorrow; extreme joy gives

rise to sorrow; great happiness would culminate in sorrow; joy at its height engenders sorrow; pleasure has its sting in its tail; sorrow is laughter's daughter; too great pleasure will bring about sadness; when the highest degree of joy is reached, sorrow will come;
樂極生悲，悲盡樂來 sadness and gladness succeed each other;
樂極生悲，否極泰來 extreme pleasure is followed by sorrow; extreme sorrow must be followed by sth better; when joy reaches its height, it is sorrow's turn; when ill luck reaches its limit, good luck comes in;

[樂趣] delight; pleasure;
家庭樂趣 homely pleasure;
減低樂趣 reduce the pleasure;
社交樂趣 social joy;
增加樂趣 heighten the enjoyment;

[樂如枝鵲] as merry as a cricket;

[樂善好施] act as a good Samaritan; always glad to give to charities; always ready to help in a worthy cause; happy in doing good; love to do philanthropic work; philanthropic-minded;

[樂事] bit of jam; delight; happy event; pleasure;

[樂陶陶] cheerful; happy; joyful;

[樂天] carefree; happy-go-lucky;
樂天派 a good-time Charlie;
樂天知命 be easily contented; content with what one is; contented completely with one's lot; rest content; rest satisfied with one's life; submit to the will of Heaven and be content with one's lot;

[樂土] land of happiness; land of promise; paradise; promised land;

[樂一樂] just for fun;

[樂意] happy; pleased; ready to; willing to;
不樂意 unwilling;
表示樂意 express one's willingness;
甘心樂意 of one's free will; perfectly happy;

[樂於] happy to; take delight in;
樂於幫忙 glad to help; willing to give a hand;
樂於從命 most happy to obey;
樂於效勞 glad to do sth for sb; glad to offer one's services;
樂於助人 eager to help people; only too pleased to help sb; ready to help others; take pleasure in helping others;

[樂園] amusement park; den; paradise;

[樂滋滋] contented; pleased;

[樂子] (1) delight; pleasure; sth one enjoys; (2) joke; laughing stock; poke fun at; sth that makes one laugh;

哀樂 grief and joy;
安樂 peaceful and happy;
和樂 harmonious and happy;
歡樂 gay; happy; joyous;
康樂 peaceful and happy;
快樂 cheerful; happy; joyful;
取樂 amuse oneself; enjoy oneself; seek pleasure;
享樂 indulge in creature comforts;
行樂 indulge in pleasure; seek pleasure;
尋樂 look for distractions; seek amusement;
游樂 amuse oneself; play;
娛樂 amuse; amusement; recreation;
作樂 anuse oneself; make merry;

le⁵
le

【了】 (1) concluded; finished; (2) intelligent; (3) entirely; wholly; (4) complete; finish; understand;

除了 (1) except; (2) besides; in addition to; (3) either…or…;
為了 for; in order to;

lei²
lei

【累】 nuisance;

[累贅] (1) burdensome; troublesome; (2) burden; nuisance;
累贅的 cumbersome;
累累贅贅 burdensome; clumsy;

lei

【雷】 (1) thunder; (2) mine; (3) calamity; catastrophe; disaster;

[雷暴] lightning storm; thunderstorm;

[雷池] bounds;
雷池之限 the utmost limit one can go;
越雷池一步 transgress the bounds;

[雷達] radar;
雷達學 radiolocation;

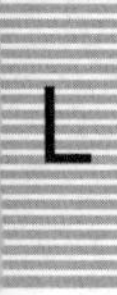

飛機電達 aircraft radar;
防空電達 air search radar;
聲雷達 acoustic radar;

［雷電］ thunder lightning;
雷電交作 lightning accompanied by peals of thunder; lightning and thunder clove the air; the lightning is accompanied with thunder; there is thunder and lightning; thunder and lightning follow one another;
雷轟電閃 anything that vanishes in a flash;

［雷動］ thunderous;
掌聲雷動 a round of applause; a storm of applause set the rafters ringing; applaud to the echo; burst into thunderous applause; the applause is deafening; the applause raises the roof; thunderous applause;

［雷公］ God of Thunder;
雷公打豆腐，揀軟的欺 the God of Thunder strikes the beancurd — bullies pick on the soft and weak;
雷公臉 a face like thunder;

［雷管］ detonator; primer;
高電壓雷管 high-tension detonator;
瞬發雷管 instantaneous detonator;
無煙遲發雷管 gasless delay detonator;
延遲動作雷管 delay-action detonator;

［雷擊］ be struck by lightning; thunderstrike;

［雷鳴］ thunderous; thundery;
雷鳴電閃 thunder rumbles and lightning flashes;
一陣雷鳴 a clap of thunder;

［雷區］ minefield;

［雷聲］ thunder; thunderclap;
雷聲大，雨點小 all gas and gaiters; all mouth and trousers; all piss and wind; make an empty show of strength; much said but little done; much bruit, little fruit; much cry and little wool; much talk, little action; much talk with little result;
雷聲隆隆 the rumble of thunder;
一陣雷聲 a burst of thunder;
一陣隆隆的雷聲 a peal of thunder;
衹聞雷聲，不見雨點 all empty thunder and no rain; full of sound and fury but without action; great cry and little wool;

［雷霆］ (1) thunderbolt; thunderclap; (2) wrath;
雷霆萬鈞 a crushing blow; a devastating punch; an irresistible force; as powerful as a thunderbolt;
~雷霆萬鈞之力 the force of a thunderbolt; the momentum of a thunderbolt; the power of a thunderbolt;
大發雷霆 all on end; bawl at sb angrily; become very angry; blow a fuse; blow one's lid; blow one's lid off; blow one's stack; blow one's top at sb; break into a rage; flare up; flip one's lid; flip one's wig; fly into a passion; fly into a rage; fly off the handle; foam at the mouth; furious; go into a rage; go through the roof; have a fit; in a fit; hit the roof; in a flare of anger; in a flare of temper; in a towering passion; in a towering rage; on the warpath; raise the roof; show one's teeth; throw a fit; throw a huge tantrum; thunder against;

［雷同］ duplicate; identical;
雷同的 cookie cutter;

［雷雨］ thunderstorm;
雷雨大作 the storm bursts with a tremendous peal of thunder and a rush of rain;
雷雨交加 a storm accompanied by peals of thunder;
雷大雨小 big beginning with a small ending; great thunder brings small rain; one's bark is worse than one's bite;
一陣雷雨 a thunderstorm;

暴雷 sudden clap of thunder;
奔雷 thunderbolts;
避雷 light protection;
佈雷 lay mines; mine;
春雷 spring thunder;
打雷 thunder;
地雷 mine;
吊雷 hanging mine;
風雷 (1) tempest; wind and thunder; (2) tempest;
浮雷 floating mine;
詭雷 booby mine; booby trap;
滾雷 rolling mine;
焦雷 clap of thunder; loud thunder;
落雷 thunderbolt; thunderclap;
錨雷 mooring thunder;
悶雷 (1) muffled thunder; (2) shock; unpleasant surprise;

排雷 remove mines;
霹雷 thunderbolt; thunderclap;
起雷 dredgte a mine;
掃雷 clear mines; sweep mines;
手雷 antitank grenade;
水雷 submarine mine;
探雷 detect mines;
跳雷 bounding mine;
魚雷 torpedo;
蟄雷 the first spring thunder;
作雷 bring about one's own rain;

lei
【擂】 (1) grind; (2) beat;

lei
【縲】 black rope;
［縲絏］ rope for trussing up prisoner;

lei
【羸】 (1) emaciated; lean; (2) feeble; weak;
［羸頓］ thin and exhausted;
［羸弱］ frail; thin and weak;

lei
【鐳】 (1) radium; (2) jar; pot;
［鐳射］ laser;
鐳射照射 laser illumination;

lei
【纍】 (1) strung together; (2) a heavy rope; (3) bind; tie; wind round;

負債纍纍 deeply in debt; get into debt; heavily in debt; head over ears in debt; in the red; over head and ears in debt; run in debt; up to one's eyes in debt; up to one's neck in debt; own lots of debts;

lei
【罍】 earthenware wine jar;

lei
【虆】 (1) entwine; wind around; (2) basket for carrying earth;

lei³

lei
【耒】 wooden handle of a plough;

lei
【累】 (1) accumulate; pile up; (2) continuous; repeated; running; (3) involve;
［累次］ again and again; repeatedly;
［累犯］ recidivist;
［累積］ accumulate;
累積股份 accumulated stock;
累積股利 accumulated dividends;
累積經驗 accumulate experience;
累積收益 accumulated income;
累積資料 accumulate data;
累積作用 accumulative action;
［累及］ drag in; implicate; involve;
累及無辜 compromise the guiltless; involve the innocent; make the innocent suffer; the trouble involves innocent people;
［累計］ (1) accumulative total; grand total; (2) add up;
［累加］ accumulation; cumulation; summation;
［累進］ progresion;
累進税 progressive tax;
~超額累進税 progressive tax of income from wages and salaries in exfess of specific amounts;
［累累］ clusters of; heaps of;
累累犯法 break the laws repeatedly; violate the laws countless times;
累累建功 score successes again and again;
累累若喪家之犬 like a homeless dog with its tail between its legs; look dejected like a lost dog; wretched as a stray dog;
累累誤會 a succession of misunderstandings;
結實累累 fruits hanging heavy; fruits growing in clusters;
傷痕累累 scars of wounds strungtogether like beads;
罪行累累 commit countless crimes; have a long criminal record;
［累卵］ precarious situation;
累卵之危 an extremely precarious situation; pressing danger;
勢如累卵 in a very perilous position;
［累年］ for years in succession; year after year;
［累日］ day after day; for days;
［累世］ for many generations; generation after generation;
［累月］ month after month;
累月經年 a long-drawn-out period; for months and years on end; for years; year in, year out;

背累 burden;
儽累 exhausted; tired; weary;
波累 involve in a trouble;

帶累 implicate; involve;
掛累 implicate; involve sb in trouble;
積累 accumulate;
家累 family burden;
虧累 show repeated deficits;
連累 get sb into trouble; implicate;
賠累 sustain losses in business and run into debt;
牽累 (1) tie down; (2) implicate; involve in trouble;
受累 get involved on account of sb else;
拖累 (1) encumber; (2) implicate; involve;
貽累 implicate another;
滯累 the burden of the temporal world;

lei

【誄】 (1) speech in praise of the dead; writings eulogizing a dead person; (2) confer a posthumous title; (3) pray for the dead;

lei

【磊】 (1) heap of stones; (2) great; massive;

［磊落］ open and upright;

磊落不群 superior to the general run;
磊落奇才 of markedly superior talent;
光明磊落 aboveboard; completely open; frank and forthright; on the up-and-up; open and aboveboard; open and upright; plain dealing; plainly and squarely;
嶔崎磊落 honest and upright;
胸懷磊落 frank; honest;

lei

【儡】 (1) puppet; (2) sickly and thin; (3) dilapidated;

傀儡 puppet;

lei

【蕾】 flower-bud;

［蕾鈴］ cotton buds and bolls;

蓓蕾 flower bud;
花蕾 flower bud;
味蕾 taste bud;

lei

【壘】 (1) military wall; rampart; (2) pile; pile up; repeat; repeatedly; (3) base; (4) a surname;

［壘球］ (1) softball game; (2) softball;

［壘手］ baseman;

二壘手 second baseman;
三壘手 third baseman;
一壘手 first baseman;

堡壘 fort; fortress; stronghold;
本壘 home base;
壁壘 barrier; rampart;
地壘 horst;
對壘 be encamped face to face; confront each oether, ready for battle;
街壘 street barricade;
塊壘 (1) indignation; (2) depression; gloom;
偷壘 steal a base;
營壘 (1) barracks and the enclosing walls; (2) camp;

lei

【藟】 (1) variety of climbing plant; (2) entwine; wind; (3) same as 蕾, a flower-bud;

lei⁴

lei

【肋】 a pronunciation of 肋, ribs;

［肋骨］ costa; ribs;

肋骨疼痛 costalgia;
壯筋骨 strengthen the bone, tendon and muscle;

［肋軟骨］ cartilage ribs;

［肋條］ (1) rib; (2) pork ribs;

浮肋 floating ribs;
假肋 false ribs;
真肋 sterual ribs;

lei

【淚】 tears; teardrops;

［淚乾］ one's tears dry up;

淚乾聲竭 one's tears dry up and one's voice fails one;
氣噎淚乾 one's hoarse throat cannot utter another sound and one's eyes cannot shed another tear;

［淚骨］ lachrymal bone;

［淚管］ dacryosyrinx;

淚管閉塞 dacryagogatresia;
淚管瘻 dacryosyrinx;
淚管狹窄 dacryostenosis;
淚管炎 dacryosolenitis;

［淚光］ glistening teardrops;

［淚痕］ tear stains;

淚痕斑斑 be bathed in tears; cover with

grease spots; tear-stained; wet with tears;
~淚痕斑斑的臉 tear-stained face;
淚痕滿面 the face is covered with traces of tears; with a tear-stained face;
淚痕未乾 tears are not yet dry;

[淚花] tears in one's eye;
淚花晶瑩 one's eyes sparkle with tears;
眼含淚花 tears sparkle in one's eyes; have swimming eyes; one's eyes dim with tears;

[淚流] tears stream down;
淚流滿面 one's face is covered with tears; tears cover one's face; tears stream down one's face;
淚流如注 one's eyes are streaming with tears;
淚流雙頰 tears curse down one's cheeks; tears trickle down one's cheeks; the tears run down the cheeks;
老淚橫流 fears flowing from the aged eyes;

[淚人] person who cries; person who is all tears;
淚人兒般 a person melting into tears;
哭成淚人 be dissolved in tears; be drenched in tears; one is all tears;

[淚水] tears; teardrops;
擦去淚水 brush the tears away; dash away sb's tears;
滿眼淚水 an eyeful of tears;
忍住淚水 choke down the tears; keep back sb's tears; restrain sb's tears;
喜悅的淚水 tears of joy;
一陣淚水 a torrent of tears;

[淚涕] tears and snivel;
淚涕交流 one's eyes and nose are flooded; tears and snivel run down the face;
彈淚索涕 sniff and blink away one's tears;

[淚汪汪] eyes brimming with tears; tearful; with watery eyes;
淚汪汪的 tearful;
淚汪汪地 tearfully;

[淚腺] lacriminal gland;
淚腺動脈 lacrimal artery;
淚腺痛 dacryoadenalgia;
淚腺炎 dacryoadenitis;

[淚小管] lacrimal canal;
淚小管炎 canaliculitis;

[淚眼] tearful eyes;
淚眼晶瑩 tears dim one's eyes and sparkle on one's eyelashes; with a brilliant sparkle in one's eyes;
淚眼迷濛 one's eyes are dim with tears; one's eyes become dim by tears; one's eyes are blurred with tears;
淚眼模糊 eyes blurred by tears;

[淚液] tears;

[淚珠] beads of sorrow; teardrops;
淚珠滾滾 tears as big as peas rain down one's checks; tears course down one's cheeks; tears run down one's cheeks like pearls from a broken thread; tears trickled down one's face; the pearly tears roll down the cheeks;
淚珠簌簌 tears trickle down from one's eyes;

迸淚 tears pouring out;
垂淚 shed tears; weep;
含淚 with tears in one's eyes;
揮淚 wipe away tears; wipe one's eyes;
落淚 shed tears; weep;
灑淚 shed tears;
血淚 tears of blood;
眼淚 tears;
燭淚 guttering of a candle;

lei

【累】 (1) implicate; involve; trouble; (2) in debt; owe; (3) tired; weary; (4) family burden;

[累垮] run off one's legs;

勞累 overworked; tired;
受累 be put to much trouble;

lei

【擂】

[擂台] arena; platform for contests in martial arts; ring;
擺擂台 arouse an emulation; give an open challenge; invite an emulation; make challenges to a contest; make open challenges to fights;
打擂臺 rise to the challenge; take up the challenge;

吹擂 boast; brag;

lei

【酹】 make a libation;

lei

【類】 (1) category; class; kind; type; (2) resemble; similar to;

[類比] analogy;
類比推理 reasoning from analogy;

[類別] category; classification; family; genre; tier;
類別詞 classifier; generic term;
類別單位 generic unit;
類別翻譯 generic translation;
類別生格 classifyinbg generic;
職業類別 job classificatrion;

[類詞] class word;
開放類詞 open class word;

[類典] special dictionary;

[類似] analogy; likeness; propinquity; similar;
類似處 analogy;
類似關係 affinity;
類似事件 similar incidents;
互相類似 analogous to each other;
外貌類似 alike in appearance;
性格類似 alike in character;

[類推] analogize; reason by analogy;
類推變化 analogic change;
依此類推 and so on and so forth; the rest may be deduced by analogy; the rest may be inferred;
餘可類推 the rest may be inferred by analogy;
照此類推 on the analogy of this;

[類型] cut; form; mold; type;
類型差異 typological difference;
類型相似 typological similarity;

敗類 degenerate; scum of a community;
貝類 molluscs; shellfish;
編類 arrange systematically;
蟲類 insects; worms;
醜類 evil person; vile creature; villain;
畜類 domestic animals;
詞類 parts of speech;
等足類 isopod;
豆類 beans;
分類 classify;
穀類 cereal crops; grain;
瓜類 goud; melon;
歸類 classify; sort out;
鳥類 birds;
品類 category; class;
人類 humanity; mankind;
十足類 decapod;
同類 of the same kind, class or species;
異類 different kinds of animals and plants;
魚類 fish;
種類 kind; type; variety;

lei

【纇】 (1) knot on a thread; (2) flaw;

leng²

leng

【楞】 Ceylon (used in Buddhist books);

leng

【棱】 (1) edge (2) corrugation; ridge;

[棱柱] prism;
斜棱往 oblique prism;
正棱柱 regular prism;
直棱柱 right prism;

[棱錐] pyramid;

側棱 lateral edge;

leng

【稜】 (1) angle; corner; edge; (2) square piece of wood; (3) awe-inspiring air;

[稜鏡] prism;
近光稜鏡 close-up prism;
立方稜鏡 block prism;
消色差稜鏡 achromatic prism;

leng

【蔆】 old name for spinach;

leng³

leng

【冷】 (1) cold; (2) cold in manner; frosty; (3) cool; (4) deserted; unfrequented;

[冷冰冰] ice old; icy; frosty;
冷冰冰的人 cold fish;
冷冰冰的態度 icy manners;

[冷不防] all of a sudden; by surprise; off one's balance; suddenly; unexpectedly; with one's pants down;

[冷藏] cold storage;
冷藏庫 cold storage; cold store; freezer;
冷藏箱 fridge; ice-box; refrigerator;

[冷淡] (1) give the cold shoulder to; leave sb out in the cold; slight; treat coldly; turn the cold shoulder to sb; (2) cheerless; desolate; slack; (3) cold; coldness; frigid; indifferent;
冷淡待人 make a stranger of sb;
冷淡寡情 cold and unfeeling;
冷淡無情 athymia;
對陌生人很冷淡 be aloof with strangers;

假裝冷淡 feign indifference;
態度冷淡 cold in manner;

[冷凍] freeze;
冷凍格 freezer compartment;
冷凍櫃 freezer;
冷凍室 freezer; freezer compartment;

[冷飯] the same old stuff;
炒冷飯 beat a dead horse; dish up the same old stuff; do the same old thing; flog a dead horse; mount on a dead horse; rehash; say the same old thing;

[冷風] cold air blast; cold wind; cold-blast air;
冷風砭骨 the cold wind cuts one to the marrow;
吹冷風 blow a cold wind over; throw cold water on;
一股冷風 a rush of cold wind;
一陣冷風 a blast of cold wind; a cold wind;

[冷鋒] cold front;

[冷膏] cold cream;

[冷汗] cold sweat;
冷汗遍身 a cold sweat breaks out all over one's body;
冷汗如雨 a cold sweat drips from one's body like rain;
冷汗一身 wet with cold sweat;
捏一把冷汗 break into a cold sweat; hold in one's palm a handful of perspiration; in a cold sweat of anxiety;

[冷箭] arrow shot from hiding; sniper's shot;
冷箭黑槍 stab in the back;
放冷箭 injure insidiously; injure others secretly; make sarcastic remarks; resort to underhand means; stab in the back;

[冷靜] calm; chillax; composed; composure; in cold blood; keep ne's shirt on; phlegm; sober;
冷靜的 phlegmatic;
冷靜明智 level-headed;
冷靜期 cooling-off period;
保持冷靜 cool-headed; keep a cool head; keep calm; keep cool; keep one's head; maintain calm; remain cool;

[冷酷] callous; cold-hearted; grim; unfeeling;
冷酷的心 a bloodless heart;
冷酷無情 a heart of stone; as cold as ice; as cold as nails; as hard as flint; as hard as marble; as hard as nails; be made of stone; cold and unfeeling; cold-blooded; cold-hearted; grim; harden sb's heart; harden the heart of sb; have a heart of stone; have no heart; heart of flint; heartless; merciless; obdurate; steel sb's heart; stony heart; stony-hearted; unfeeling;
~冷酷無情的 cold-hearted;
表情冷酷 look grim;
生性冷酷 cold by nature;
心情冷酷 be hardened in heart;
性情冷酷 cold in disposition;

[冷落] (1) deserted; desolate; unfrequented; (2) cold-shoulder; give sb the cold shoulder; leave out in the cold; snub; treat coldly;
冷落某人 give sb the cold shoulder; leave sb out in the cold;
受冷落 feel left out; out in the cold;
遭到冷落 be left out in the cold;

[冷門] (1) not in vogue; (2) dark horse; unexpected winner;
報冷門 (1) produce unexpected results; (2) choose a profession, trade or subject which gets little attention;
爆冷門 upset;
出冷門 an unexpected winner;
~爆出冷門 produce an unexpected winner; score an upset;
走冷門 choose the less popular course;

[冷面] stony face;
冷面幽默 deadpan humour;

[冷漠] cold and detached; coldness; downbeat; indifferent; unconcerned;
冷漠的 callous;
~冷漠的態度 callous attitude;
冷漠地 coldly;
冷漠寡情 cold and unfeeling; sternly cool and unmoved;
冷漠無情 sternly cool and unmoved; unsympathetic;

[冷凝] condense; condensing;
冷凝濾器 condensifilter;
冷凝器 condenser;
~輔助冷凝器 auxiliary condenser;
~化學冷凝器 chemical condenser;
~聚積冷凝器 accumulating condenser;
~空氣冷凝器 aerial condenser;
~吸氣式冷凝器 aspiration condenser;
~磚製冷凝器 brick condenser;
冷凝液 condensate; liquor condensate;

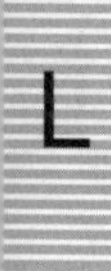

~ 過冷凝液 subcooling condensate;

[冷暖] changes in temperature;

冷暖自知 know by oneself whether it is cold or warm;

時暖時冷 sometimes warm and at other times cold; sometimes warm and sometimes cold;

[冷僻] (1) deserted; out-of-the-way; (2) rare; unfamiliar;

[冷氣] air conditioning; cool air;

一股冷氣 a gust of cold air;

一口冷氣 a cold breath;

~ 倒抽一口冷氣 draw a cold breath; give a gasp of astonishment; hold one's breath; in disappointment; in fear;

[冷槍] (1) sniper's shot; (2) sporadic spots;

打冷槍 fire a sniper's shot; stab in the back;

[冷峭] (1) severely cold; (2) harsh and biting; stern;

[冷清] cold and gloomy;

冷冷清清 cold and aloof; cold and cheerless; cold and dreary; cold and lonely; cold and reserved; coolly and quietly; deserted and quiet; desolate; dull and colourless; in a relatively lukewarm state; in quiet isolation; inactivity; lonely; quiet and still;

[冷卻] become cool; chill; chilling; cool;

冷卻劑 coolant;

~ 化學冷卻劑 chemical coolant;

~ 氣體冷卻劑 gaseous coolant;

~ 有機液體冷卻劑 organic liquid coolant;

冷卻期 cooling-off period;

冷卻器 chillator; cooler; desuperheater;

~ 氨氣冷卻器 ammonia cooler;

~ 爐氣冷卻器 burner-gas cooler;

~ 噴液冷卻器 baudelot cooler;

~ 汽封蒸氣冷卻器 gland steam desuperheater; sealing steam desuperheater;

~ 汽化冷卻器 blister cooler;

~ 酸冷卻器 acid cooler;

~ 吸收冷卻器 absorption cooler;

冷卻室 cooling room;

冷卻水套 cooling-jacket;

冷卻塔 cooling tower;

冷卻系統 colling system;

冷卻液 coolant; liquid coolant;

~ 發動機冷卻液 engine coolant;

~ 切削冷卻液 cutting coolant;

~ 乳化冷卻液 oil-in-water type coolant;

充氣冷卻 charge air cooling;

初冷卻 initial chilling;

輻射冷卻 radiation cooling;

靜止冷卻 non-shock chilling;

絕熱冷卻 adiabatic cooling;

空氣噴射冷卻 air-blast cooling;

人工冷卻 artificial cooling;

燒蝕冷卻 ablation cooling;

鹽水冷卻 brine cooling;

葉片冷卻 blades cooling;

[冷熱] cold or hot;

不冷不熱 neither hot nor cold; neither hostile nor friendly; take a lukewarm attitude;

忽冷忽熱 by fits and starts; cold one minute and hot the next; fever alternates with chills; now hot, now cold; sudden changes of temperature;

時冷時熱 by fits and starts; now hot now cool;

頭要冷，心要熱 cool in the head but warm at heart;

乍冷乍熱 abruptyly change from cold to hot; by fits and starts; change abruptly; now cold, now hot; sometimes hot and sometimes cold;

[冷杉] fir;

冷杉木 fir;

冷杉球果 fir apple; fir ball; fir cone;

冷杉樹 fir;

冷杉針葉 firneedle;

大冷杉 giant fir;

美國冷杉 amabilis fir;

紫果冷杉 red fir;

[冷食] cold rinks and snacks;

[冷水] (1) cold water; (2) unboiled water;

冷水澆頭 feel as if a basin of cold water has been poured over one's head; feel as if doused with cold water; like a bucket of cold water thrown over sb;

潑冷水 a dash of cold water; cast a damp over; damp sb's ardour; dampen sb's spirits; dampen the enthusiasm of; discourage; pour cold water on; put a blanket on; put a damper on; strike a damp over; throw a cold douche upon; throw a wet blanket over; throw cold water on;

~ 大潑冷水 damp down enthusiasm; pour cold water on sb; throw a wet blanket on;

[冷絲絲] a bit chilly;
[冷颼颼] chilling; chilly;
[冷霜] cold cream;
[冷笑] grin with dissatisfaction, helplessness, etc.; laugh grimly; sardonic grin; sneer;
[冷血] cold-blooded; cold-bloodedness;
冷血動物 (1) cold-blooded animal; (2) cold-hearted person; unfeeling person;
冷血殺手 cold-blooded killer;
[冷眼] (1) cool detachment; (2) cold-shoulder;
冷眼看人 give sb the eye; look coldly upon sb;
冷眼旁觀 look coldly from the sidelines; look on as a disinterested bystander; look on coldly; look on unconcerned; look on with a cold eye; see it from the side; stand aloof and look on with cold indifference; stay aloof; take a detached point of view; watch indifferently;
冷眼熱心 affected indifference; outward indifference but inward fervency;
冷眼相看 look at coldly; look coldly upon;
[冷飲] cold drink;
冷飲店 cold drink shop;
[冷遇] cold shoulder; get the cold shoulder;
受到冷遇 meet with a cold acceptance;
遭冷遇 be cold-shouldered; be cut dead; be left in the cold; be snubbed; meet with cold reception;
[冷戰] cold war;
冷戰思維 Cold War mentality;
打冷戰 (1) fight a cold war; (2) shudder with cold;

冰冷 ice-cold;
齒冷 hold sb to ridicule; sneer at;
發冷 feel cold;
乾冷 dry and cold;
過冷 super-cooling;
寒冷 cold; frigid;
淒冷 bleak; depressing;
清冷 (1) chilly; (2) deserted; desolate;
弱冷 low cooling;
陰冷 (1) gloomy and cold; (2) glum; somber;
賊冷 terribly cold;

leng⁴
leng
【愣】 (1) agape with horror; blank; distracted; dumbfounded; stupefied; (2) foolhardy; irresponsible; rash; reckless; rude;
[愣幹] do things rashly;
[愣勁兒] dash; pep; vigour;
[愣神兒] in a daze; stare blankly;
[愣説] allege; assert; insist;
[愣頭兒青] hothead; rash fellow;
[愣怔] in a daze; in a trance; stare blankly;
[愣住] be taken aback; become speechless because of astonishment;

發愣 stare blankly;

leng
【楞】 same as 愣;

li¹
li
【哩】 speak indistinctly;
[哩哩啦啦] scattered; sporadic;
[哩哩囉囉] rambling and indistinct; verbose and unclear in speech;

li²
li
【狸】 (1) fox; (2) racoon dog;
[狸貓] leopard cat;

果子狸 masked civet;
海狸 beaver;
河狸 beaver;
狐狸 fox;
香狸 civet;

li
【梨】 pear;
[梨核] core;
[梨花] pear blossom;
梨花帶雨 a pear blossom bathed in the rain — a weeping beauty;
皚白的梨花 white pear blossoms;
[梨樹] pear;
[梨園] operatic circle;
梨園弟子 operatice players;
梨園世家 come from a family of opera artists;
[梨子] pear;
梨子酒 perry;

巴梨 Bartlett pear;
白梨 a kind of pear;

地梨 a kind of wild plant;
鳳梨 pineapple;
京白梨 white pear;
沙梨 sand pear;
棠梨 birch-leaf pear;
雪白梨 snow pear;
鴨兒梨 Chinese pear;
一個梨 a pear;

li
【犁】 (1) plough; till; (2) plough;
[犁鏵] share;
開荒犁鏵 breaker share;
可換犁鏵 alternative share;
[犁庭掃穴] annihilate the enemy thoroughly; conquer an independent country; overthrow an indepedent country; plough up the enemy's court and destroy his hideouts; wipe out;

步犁 walking plough;
電犁 electric plough;
雪犁 snow plough;

li
【蜊】 a kind of bivalve;

蛤蜊 clam;

li
【漓】 (1) dripping wet; (2) thin;
[漓江] the Lijiang River in Guangxi;

澆漓 not simple and sincere;
淋漓 (1) dripping wet; (2) free from inhibition;

li
【貍】 nyctereutus procynoides, a fox-like animal;

li
【嫠】 (1) black ox; (2) yak;
[嫠不卹緯] a poor widow does not care for the weaving — a patriot who cares not for his own enterprise;
[嫠婦] widow;
[嫠牛] yak;

li
【犛】 (1) black ox; (2) yak;
[犛牛] yak;

li
【璃】 glass; glassy substance;

li
【黎】 (1) many; numerous; (2) dark; black; (3) aborigines of Hainan; (4) a surname;
[黎民] common people; multitude;
[黎明] break of day; dawn; daybreak; first light;
黎明時 at dawn;
等待黎明 wait for the dawn;

li
【氂】 (1) horse tail; (2) long hair; thick hair; (3) yak;

li
【漦】 (1) saliva; spittle; (2) flowing downstream;

li
【罹】 (1) grief; sorrow; (2) be stricken by; meet disaster;
[罹難] (1) die in a disaster; die in an accident; (2) be murdered;
[罹網] enmesh;

li
【縭】 (1) bridal veil; (2) bind; tie;

li
【褵】 same as 縭 ;

li
【釐】 (1) unit of linear measure equal to one thousandth of the Chinese foot; (2) unit of weight equal to one thousandth of the tael; (3) administer; arrange; manage; (4) correct; reform; revise;
[釐定] collate and stipulate;
[釐米] centimeter;
釐米波 centimeter-wave;
釐米倒數 reciprocal centimeter;
克釐米 gram centimeter;
立方釐米 cubic centimeter;
平方釐米 square centimeter;

li
【離】 (1) away from; leave; part from; (2) away from; off; (3) without;
[離岸] offshore;
離岸價格 free on board;
[離別] bid farewell; leave; part;
離別故土 part from one's native land;
離愁別恨 grief at parting; parting sorrows;
離情別緒 grief of parting; parting

sorrows; the feeling of separation;
生離死別 be parted in life and separated by death; part forever;

[離合] be separated and reunited; be separated and recombined;
離合悲歡 sorrow and happiness, separations and reunions; the sorrows and joys of partings and meetings;
離合器 clutch;
~安全滑動離合器 safety slip clutch;
~離心式離合器 centrifugal clutch;
~盤形離合器 disc clutch;
~汽車離合器 automobile clutch;
~氣動離合器 air clutch;
~雙向離合器 bidirectional clutch;
~縮帶離合器 contracting band clutch;
~直接離合器 direct clutch;
~爪形離合器 claw clutch;
~錐形離合器 bevel clutch;
離合詩 acrostic;
離合文 acrostic;

[離婚] break a marriage; divorce; get a divorce;
離婚的人 devorcee;
離婚率 divorce rate;
離婚訴訟 divorce proceedings;
離婚證 certificate of divorce;
合法離婚 divorce legally;
協議離婚 divorce by consent;

[離家] away from home;
離家三里遠，別是一鄉風 go three miles from home, and you're in another land;

[離間] come between; drive a wedge between; set one party against another; sow discord;
離間之計 the scheme of sowing dissension;
挑撥離間 drive a wedge between; forment dissension; forment disunity and dissension; incite one against the other; play one off against the other; sow discord;

[離解] dissociation;
離解俘獲 dissociative capture;
離子離解 ionic dissociation;
氣體離解 aseous dissociation;
水離解 hydrolytic dissociation;

[離經叛道] depart from the right way; deviate from orthodox truth; go astray from the right path; heretical and deviate from the true teachings; wander from the right;

[離境] leave a country or place;

[離久情疏] remoteness begets neglect; salt water and absence wash away love;

[離開] (1) come away; depart from; deviate from; leave; (2) disjunction;
離開房間 leave a room; withdraw from a room;
離開正道 stray from the right path;
離開主題 depart from the main subject; digress from the the main subject;
被迫離開 be obliged to leave;
匆匆離開 beetle off; bundle away; bundle off; bundle out; dash off; get up and dig; get up and dust; hurry away; hurry off; leave in a hurry; leave in haste; make away; pop off;
減數離開 reductional disjunction;
均等離開 equational disjunction;
快速離開 hightail;
離不開 (1) can't do without; (2) too busy to get away;
悄悄離開 slope off;
貼鄰離開 disjunction;
突然離開 shoot off; take one's departure suddenly;
相間離開 alternate disjunction;
迅速離開 decamp;
永遠離開 pack one's bags;

[離譜] far away from what is normal; far off the beam;

[離奇] bizarre; fantastic; odd; weird;
離奇怪誕 eccentric and wild; entirely out of the common;

[離棄] abandon; desert;

[離情] sorrow of parting;

[離去] leave; make tracks; offwards; split;
憤然離去 leave in anger; shake the dust off one's feet; walk off in a huff;
忽忙離去 bundle off; dash off;

[離群] leave society;
離群索居 cut oneself off from society; forsake society and live alone; hole up; hold aloof; isolate oneself; keep oneself to oneself; leave society and live alone; leave the crowd and live alone; live in solitude; live out of the world; live the life of a recluse; live within oneself; plough a lonely furrow; retire into one's shell;

[離任] leave one's post;
離任回國 leave one's post for home;
[離散] dispersed; scattered about; separated from one another;
好離好散 part peacefully from each other;
星離雨散 separate and disperse rapidly;
[離題] deviate from the topic; digress from the subject; get off the track; stray from the point;
離題十萬八千里 completely off the point; go adrift far from the subject; miles away from the subject; there is a far cry to the subject; too far from the mark
離題太遠 go far afield from one's point;
離題萬里 be farther removed from the theme; digress too far afield; get far afield from one's subject; go wide of the mark; it hits a long way from the target; remote from the subject;
別離題 don't get off the track;
話離本題 talk away from the point; wander away from the proper question;
[離鄉] leave one's native place;
離鄉背井，流離失所 be forced to flee one's home as a refugee and be separated from one's family; leave one's native place and wander about;
背井離鄉 away from home; be forced to leave one's hometown; leave one's native place; stay on a strange land;
[離心] centrifugal;
離心法 centrifuging;
離心分離機 centrifuge;
離心機 centrifugal; centrifuge;
~白糖離心機 white sugar centrifugal;
~精制離心機 loaf centrifugal;
~色糖離心機 white centrifugal;
~洗糖離心機 affiniation centrifugal;
~錐鼓離心機 conical drum centrifugal;
離心力 centrifugal force;
離心率 eccentricity;
[離異] bust up; divorce; dissociation; separate;
父母離異 one's parents split up;
[離職] (1) be suspended from office; leave one's job temporarily; (2) leave office;
離職不幹 chuck up one's job; quit office; quit one's job;
[離子] ion;
離子反應 ionic reaction;
離子方程式 ionic equation;
離子化合物 ionic compound;
離子活度 ionic activity;
離子交換法 ion exchange method;
離子交換劑 ion exchanger;
離子運轉 ion revolution;
負離子 negative ion;
激活離子 active ion;
氫離子 hydrogen ion;
~氫離子濃度 hydrogen ion concentration;
~氫離子指數 hydrogen ion exponent;
酸基離子 acid ion;
形成離子 ionize;
陽離子 cation; positive ion;
陰離子 anion; negative ion;
正離子 positive ion;

背離 depart from; deviate from;
別離 leave; take leave of;
剝離 come off; peel off;
撤離 evacuate; leave; withdraw from;
電離 ionization;
分離 (1) separate; sever; (2) leave each other; part;
隔離 isolate; keep apart; segregate;
距離 distance;
暌離 be apart; be separated;
流離 be forced to leave home and wander about;
陸離 weirdly colourful;
亂離 be forced to leave home by war; be separated by war;
迷離 blurred; misted;
叛離 betray; desert;
仳離 (1) (of husband and wife) be separated; (2) divorce one's spouse; forsake one's wife;
偏離 deviate; diverge;
脱離 be divorced from; break away from; separate oneself from;
游離 (1) dissociate; drift away; (2) free;
支離 (1) broken; fragmented; (2) (of writing) incoherent; trivial and jumbled;

li

【醨】 weak wine or liquor;

li

【藜】 pigweed;

li

【黧】 dark yellow;
[黧黑] dark;
黧黑之容 dust complexion;

li

【蠡】 calabash;

[蠡測] measure the sea with an oyster shell — have a shallow understanding of a person;

管窺蠡測 be restricted in vision and shallow in understanding; benighted; look at the sky through a tube and measure the sea with an oyster shell — a metaphor for a man of small experience; view the sky through a bamboo tube and measure the sea with a calabash — be restricted in vision and shallow in understanding;

li

【蘺】 the name of a grass;

li

【籬】 bamboo fence; hedge;

[籬笆] bamboo fence; hedge; hurdle; wattle;

籬笆靠樁，好漢要幫 a fence needs the support of the stakes, an able fellow needs the help of other people;

電籬笆 electric fence;

犬牙形籬笆 virginia fence;

修剪籬笆 clip a hedge;

li

【驪】 (1) black horse; (2) drive a carriage drawn by two horses;

li

【鸝】 oriole;

li³

li

【李】 (1) plum; (2) a surname;

[李代桃僵] bear the blame for another person's mistake; palm off a substitute for the real thing; sacrifice oneself for another person; substitute one thing for another; substitute oneself for another person; substitute this for that;

[李下整冠] adjust one's hat below a plum tree; not avoid suspicion;

李下不整冠 avoid suspicion; don't fix your hat under a plum tree;

[李子] plum;

青李子 greengage;

西洋李子 damson;

桃李 peaches and plums;

行李 baggage; luggage;

檇李 a kind of plum;

li

【里】 (1) neighbourhood; (2) unit of linear measure;

[里程] mileage;

里程碑 milepost; milestone;

~新的里程碑 new milestone;

里程表 mileometer; odometer;

汽油里程 gasoline mileage;

通車里程 traffic mileage;

[里弄] alley; lane;

[里數] mileage;

公里 kilometer;

li

【俚】 (1) rustic; unpolished; vulgar; (2) meaning; purpose; (3) small town or village; tribe;

[俚歌] folk songs;

[俚俗] uncultured; unrefined; vulgar;

[俚語] slang;

同韻俚語 rhyming slang;

學生俚語 schoolboy slang;

li

【悝】 (1) grieved; sad; worried; (2) ridicule;

li

【哩】 mile;

li

【娌】 (1) brother's wife; (2) sister-in-law;

li

【浬】 nautical mile; sea mile;

li

【理】 (1) grain; texture; (2) logic; reason; truth; (3) natural science; (4) manage; run; (5) put in order; tidy up; (6) acknowledge; pay attention to;

[理財] conduct financial transactions; manage money matter;

理財之道 the way of managing financial affairs;

不會理財 not a good financier;

[理睬] heed the presence of; pay attention to; show interest in; take notice of;

不理不睬 give sb the cold shoulder; ignore completely;

不理睬 break with; brush off; close one's ears; cut sb dead; deaf to; fall on deaf ears; get shut of sb; get the go-by;

give a cold shoulder to sb; give no heed to; give sb a brush; give sb the brush; give sb the cut direct; give sb the go-by; give the cold shoulder to sb; hide one's face from; ignore; leave sb alone; leave sb out in the cold; not give sb the time of day; pass by; pay no attention to; pay no heed to; see the back of sb; shut of sb; slam the door in sb's face; stop one's ears; spurn; take no heed of; take no notice of; turn a blind eye to; turn a deaf ear to; turn a cold shoulder to sb; turn one's back on; turn one's blind eye to; turn the cold shoulder to sb; turn up one's nose at;

L

[理當] naturally; of course; should;
理當如此 it's only right and proper; that's just as it should be;

[理短] have no justification; on the wrong side;

[理髮] haircut; have a haircut;
理髮店 barber's shop;
理髮館 barber shop;
理髮鏡 salon mirror;
理髮師 barber; hairdresser;
理髮師帶徒弟—從頭學起 a barber taking on an appretice – (lit) begin with the head; (pun) begin to learn from the very beginning;
理髮椅 charber's chair;
理髮用具 hairdressing tools;

[理會] (1) comprehend; understand; (2) pay attention to; take no notice of;
不理會 inattentive; pay no attention to; unmindful;
無人理會 be not listened to; fall on unresponsive ears; go unheeded;

[理貨] tally;
理貨人 tallyman;

[理解] apprehend; clear up; comprehend; comprehension; cotton on to; get at; get on to; get the hang of; have the hang of; latch on to; make much of; make out; see the hang of; spell out; take in; understand;
理解遲鈍 slow of comprehension;
理解錯誤 interpretive error;
理解方法 comprehension approach;
理解力 comprehension; faculty of understanding; understanding;
理解語義學 interpretive semantics;
不理解 incomprehension; incomprehensive;
~不可理解 beyond one's comprehension;
~不易理解 get sth through one's head;
錯誤理解 misinterpret;
互相不理解 at cross-purposes;
鑑賞性理解 appreciative comprehension;
難以理解 baffle one's understanding; be above comprehension;
批評性理解 evaluative comprehension;
評價性理解 evaluative comprehension;
評批性理解 evaluative comprehension;
突然理解 see the light;
完全理解 fully comprehend;
無法理解 beyond one's comprehension;
易於理解[的] comprehensible;
真正理解 get a real idea of;

[理科] science;
理科學院 college of science;

[理虧] in the wrong;
理虧心怯 in the wrong;
理虧心虛 feel that one is not on solid ground; have a guilty conscience; with one's self-confidence crumbling;
理虧語塞 lose in the argument because one is in the wrong; principle deficient and words blocked;
自知理虧 know that one is in the wrong; realize that justice is not on one's side; realize that one is on the wrong side;

[理論] theory;
理論家 theorist;
~翻譯理論家 translation theorist;
理論上 in principle; in terms of theory; in the abstract; in theory; on the theoretical plane; theoretically;
測試理論 test a theory;
翻譯理論 translation theory;
基礎理論 basic theory;
~基礎理論課 course on basic theory;
解析理論 analytic theory;
會計理論 accounting theory;
聲學理論 acoustic theory;
提出理論 come up with a theory; develop a theory;
證明理論 prove a theory;
支持理論 support a theory
組合理論 combinatorial theory;

[理念] idea; principle;
理念識別系統 mind identity system;

設計理念 design principles;

[理賠] settle a claim;

理賠代理費 claim settling fee;

理賠費 settling feel

[理清] straightened out; straighten up;

理清商務 straighten out one's business affairs;

理清思路 get one's ideas into shape; put one's ideas into shape;

理清賬目 straighten out one's accounts;

[理屈] cannot appeal to good reasoning; find oneself bested in argument;

理屈詞窮 be condemned on one's own showing; be condemned out of one's own mouth; be unable to advance any further arguments to justify oneself; fall silent on finding oneself bested in argument; find oneself devoid of all argument; have nothing left with which to justify oneself; have nothing to say on realizing one's own shay stand; not have a leg to stand on; shut up when defeated in argument; unable to find a word to justify oneself;

[理事] chairman; director; member of a council;

理事長 chairman; director;

~副理事長 deputy chairman; deputy director;

常務理事 managing director;

[理順] rationalize; straighten out;

理順關係 put relations in order; regulate relations; straighten out relationship;

理順經濟秩序 straighten out the economic order;

[理想] ideal;

理想的伴侶 ideal companion;

理想化 idealization; idealize;

理想色彩 ideal colour;

理想選擇 ideal choice;

理想主義 idealism;

~理想主義者 idealist;

崇高的理想 high ideals;

零化理想 annihilating ideal;

奇異理想 ambig ideal;

藝術理想 artistic ideal;

增廣理想 augmentation ideal;

[理性] reason; sense;

理性電影 rational film;

理性觀念 rational idea;

理性社會 rational society;

理性思考 rational consideration;

理性選擇 rational choice;

恢復理性 come to one's senses;

失去理性 lose one's reason; out of one's senses;

違反理性 contrary to reason;

有理性 have reason; have the quality of reason;

[理學] (1) science; (2) idealist school of Confucian philosophy;

理學士 Bachelor of Science;

理學博士 Doctor of Science;

[理應] (1) ought to; should; (2) ought to have; should have;

[理由] account; argument; ground; justification; reason;

擺出理由 put forth reasons;

充分理由 good reason; sufficient cause;

合理理由 valid reason;

接受理由 accept an explanation;

令人信服的理由 compelling reason; convincing reason; credible reason;

雙重理由 double cause;

提出理由 put up a case;

提出種種理由 advance reasons;

唯一的理由 the only reason;

顯而易見的理由 obvious explanation;

想出理由 come up with an explantion; think of an explanation;

有理由 have a reason;

找出理由 find an explanation;

正當理由 legitimate reason; valid reason;

主要理由 major reason;

[理智] intellect; reason;

保持理智 keep one's senses;

恢復理智 recover one's senses;

失去理智 lose one's head;

按理 according to reason;

辦理 conduct; handle;

病理 pathology;

常理 convention; logical thinking;

處理 (1) deal with; handle; (2) sell at reduced prices; (3) treat by a special process;

代理 (1) act for sb; take sb's place; (2) act as an agent; act on behalf of sb in a responsible position;

道理 (1) principle; (2) argument; reason;

地理 (1) geographical features of a place; (2) geography;

定理 theorem;

法理 legal principle; theory of law;
公理 (1) generally acknowledged truth; self-evident truth; (2) axiom;
管理 (1) administer; manage; (2) be in charge of; (3) control; look after;
合理 rational; reasonable;
護理 (1) look after; nurse; (2) tend and protect;
肌理 skin texture;
機理 mechanism;
講理 (1) argue; reason with sb; (2) be reasonable; be sensible; listen to reason;
節理 joint;
經理 director; handle; manage; manager;
料理 arrange; take care of;
倫理 ethics; moral principles;
論理 (1) logic; (2) reason things out;
評理 (1) judge which side is right; (2) have it out; reason things out;
清理 put in order; sort out;
情理 reason; sense;
攝理 hold in an acting capacity;
生理 physiology;
事理 logic; reason; try;
受理 accept and hear a case;
梳理 card;
輸理 be in the wrong;
署理 act as deputy; handle by proxy;
説理 argue; reason things out;
天理 (1) heavenly principles; (2) justice;
條理 orderliness;
調理 (1) nurse one's health; recuperate; (2) look after; take care of;
推理 infer; inference; reason; reasoning;
文理 unity and coherence in writing;
紋理 grain; veins;
無理 unjustifiable; unreasonable;
物理 (1) innate laws of things; (2) physics;
協理 assist in the management of...;
修理 (1) overhaul; repair; (2) prune; trim;
學理 scientific law; scientific principle;
藥理 (1) pharmacodynamics; (2) pharmacology;
醫理 medical knowledge;
義理 argumentation;
引理 lemma;
有理 (1) in the right; reasonable; (2) rational;
原理 principle; tenet;
樂理 music theory;
哲理 philosophical theory;
真理 truth;
整理 put in order; straighten out;
正理 correct principle; the right thing to do;
至理 famous dictum; maxim;
治理 (1) administer; govern; (2) bring under control; harness;
助理 assistant;
自理 take care of oneself;
總理 premier; prime minister;
佐理 assist sb in management;

li

【豊】 a kind of ritual vessel in ancient times;

li

【裏】 (1) lining; inside; (2) inner; (3) in; inside;

[裏邊] inside;

[裏面] inside; interior; inward;
在裏面 be inside;

[裏外] within and without;
裏外夾攻 attack from within and without; be attacked from inside and out; make a front and rear attack;
吃裏爬外 live off one person while secretly helping another — work for the interest of an opposing group at the expense of one's own;
徹裏徹外 downright; in every sense; out and out; through and through;
裏裏外外 indoors and out; indoors and outdoors; ins and outs; inside and out; inside and outside; outs and ins; outside and in;
忙裏忙外 bustle around;

[裏應內合] a concerted attack from within and without; act from inside in coordination with forces attacking from outside; act in concert with the attackers outside; act the part of a Trojan Horse; attack the enemy from within in coordination with operations from without; collaborate from within with forces from without; strike together from without and within; work in collusion, one from without and the other from within; work together, both inside and outside;

li

【鋰】 lithium;

li

【澧】 (1) fountain; spring; (2) a county in Hunan Province;

li

【禮】 (1) ceremony; rite; (2) courtesy; etiquette; manners; (3) gift; present;

[禮拜] (1) ceremonial observances in general; ceremony; rite; (2) week; (3) day of the week; (4) Sunday; (5) weekend;
禮拜二 Tuesday;
禮拜六 Saturday;
禮拜日 Sunday;
禮拜三 Wednesday;
禮拜四 Thursday;
禮拜堂 churh;
~ 禮拜堂關門—不講道理 a church closing down — no preaching; unreasonable;
~ 小禮拜堂 oratory;
禮拜天 Sunday;
禮拜五 Friday;
禮拜一 Monday;
禮拜儀式 liturgy;
頂禮膜拜 bend the knee in worship; bow in worship; make a fetish of; pay homage to; prostrate oneself before; prostrate oneself in worship; show one's devoutest worship;
磕頭禮拜 make obeisance and perform the rites of courtesy;
摩頂禮拜 bend the knee in worship;
屈膝禮拜 bend the knees in worship;
做禮拜 at church; go to church;

[禮單] list of presents;

[禮多] full of courtesy;
禮多必詐 a very polite reason is certainly false; full of courtesy, full of craft; one who is overcourteous is crafty;
禮多人不怪 a man's hat in his hand never did him any harm; all doors open to courtesy; civility costs nothing; no one is offended by too much politeness; one can never be too courteous; one never loses anything by politeness; over-politeness is not a fault;
禮不嫌多 no one is offended by too much politeness;

[禮法] law and discipline rite;

[禮服] ceremonial dress; cocktail dress;
禮服襯衫 dress shirt;
白色禮服 white dress;
軍禮服 dress uniform;
晚禮服 ballgown; evening dress; formal evening dress;
~ 輕薄的晚禮服 airy evening dress;

[禮節] ceremony; courtesy; etiquette; protocol;
禮節附加語 formulaic adjunct;
禮節規定 rules of etiquette;
~ 通常的禮節規定 conventional rules of etiquette;
禮節性拜訪 courtesy call; duty call;
按照禮節 according to protocol;
不拘禮節 unceremonious;
拘於禮節 stand on ceremony;
社交禮節 social etiquette;
外交禮節 amenities of diplomacy; diplomatic propriety;
~ 遵守外交禮節 observe the amenities of diplomacy;
違反禮節 impropriety;
席間禮節 table manners;
正式禮節 formal etiquette;

[禮金] cash gift;

[禮卷] gift token;
購物禮卷 gift certificate; gift token;

[禮帽] homburg;
大禮帽 top hat;
圓禮帽 bowler; round hat;

[禮貌] civility; courtesy; manners; politeness;
禮貌待人 behave civilly toward others;
禮貌舉止 polite manners;
出於禮貌 out of courtesy; out of politeness;
懂禮貌 observe the proprieties;
沒禮貌 have bad manners; have no manners; impolite; wanting in politeness;
有禮貌 courteous; have good manners; have manners; polite;
注重禮貌 put an accent on good manners;

[禮砲] gun salute;
鳴禮砲 fire a salute;

[禮品] gift; present;
禮品包裝 gift package; gift wrap; gift wrapping;
~ 禮品包裝紙 gift wrapping paper;
禮品商店 gift and souvenir shop; gift shop;
紀念禮品 souvenir presents;
結婚禮品 bridal presents; wedding presents;
上等禮品 choice present;
聖誕禮品 Christmas gifts;
謝絕禮品 decline presents;

[禮輕誼重] a small gift given with a sincere

wish; the gift in itself may be insignificant, but the goodwill is deep; the gift itself may not be valuable, but it conveys deep feeling; the thoughtfulness is worth far more than the gift itself;

禮輕人意重 it's nothing much, but it's the thought that counts; the gift is trifling but the feeling is profound;

[禮讓] comity; give precedence to sb out of courtesy;

[禮俗] etiquette and custom;

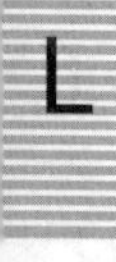

[禮堂] assembly hall;

大禮堂 assembly hall; auditorium; hall;

[禮物] gift; present; pressie; prezzie;

包裝禮物 wrap a present;
打開禮物 open a present; unwrap a present;
訂婚禮物 betrothal presents;
結婚禮物 wedding present;
節日禮物 festive gift;
生日禮物 birthday gift; birthday present;
聖誕禮物 Christmas gift; Christmas present;
收到禮物 get a present; receive a present;
送人禮物 give sb a present;
小禮物 a little something;
~生日小禮物 a little something for one's birthday;
新年禮物 gift for the New Year;
一份禮物 a gift; a present;
一件禮物 a gift; a present;

[禮賢下士] courteous to the wise men and condescending to the scholars; go out of one's way to enlist the services of the talented and learned; treat worthy men with courtesy;

[禮儀] etiquette; protocol; rite;

禮儀大全 book of etiquette;
禮儀的 ceremonial;
禮儀小姐 ritual girl;
禮儀學校 charm school;
禮儀之邦 state of ceremonies;
根據禮儀 according to protocol;
進餐禮儀 table manners;
違反禮儀 against etiquette;
宗教禮儀 ceremonials of religion;

[禮遇] courteous reception;

賓禮 (1) courtesy on the part of a guest; (2) international courtesy;
薄禮 meagre present; modest present; slight gift;
財禮 betrothal gifts;
彩禮 betrothal gifts;
懺禮 ritual for penance;
常禮 regular etiquette;
答禮 return a salute;
典禮 celebration; ceremony;
定禮 bride-price;
非禮 impolite;
割禮 circumcision;
觀禮 attend a celebration;
過禮 present gifts to the bride's family before marriage;
賀禮 gift;
還禮 (1) return a salute; (2) present a gift in return;
回禮 (1) return a salute; (2) present a gift in return;
婚禮 wedding; wedding ceremony;
祭禮 (1) sacrificial rites; (2) memorial ceremony; (3) sacrificial offerings;
見禮 salute upon meeting sb;
浸禮 baptism; immersion;
敬禮 (1) give a salute; salute; (2) extend one's greetings; (3) with high respect;
拘禮 be punctilious; stand on ceremony;
軍禮 military salute;
年禮 New Year gift;
賠禮 apologize; offer an apology;
聘禮 betrothal gifts;
喪禮 funeral; obsequies;
失禮 be impolite; commit a breach of etiquette;
施禮 salute;
受禮 receive a gift;
壽禮 birthday present;
送禮 give sb a present; present a gift to sb;
洗禮 (1) haptism; (2) severe test;
獻禮 present a gift;
行禮 salute;
虛禮 empty forms; mere courtesy;
葬禮 funeral rites;
贈禮 gift; present;

li

【鯉】 (1) carp; (2) epistle; letter;

[鯉庭之訓] instructions from one's father; one's father's advice;

[鯉魚] carp;

鯉魚跳龍門 endeavour to make a success of oneself; get literary advancement; get rapid promotion; succeed in the civil service examination in old times;

鯉魚找鯉魚，鯽魚找鯽魚 birds of a feather flock together; carp goes with carp, and turtle goes with turtle;

鏡鯉 mirror carp;
鯪鯉 pangolin;
裸鯉 naked carp;
無鱗鯉 leather carp;
銀鯉 bleak;

li

【醴】 (1) sweet wine; (2) sweet spring or fountain;

li

【蠡】 (1) wood-boring insect; (2) (of insects) bore or eat wood; (3) worm-eaten;

li

【邐】 continuous and meandering;

li^4

li

【力】 (1) ability; power; strength; (2) force; (3) physical strength;

[力薄] one's ability is frail;
力薄才疏 feeble strength and scanty learning;
力薄能鮮 deficient in strength and ability;
力薄藝疏 one's strength is frail and one's skill is slight;

[力疾從公] attend to one's duties in spite of sickness; attend to one's duties as usual in spite of illness;

[力竭] exhaustion;
力竭而死 die of exhaustion;
力竭聲嘶 exhausted from effort; one's voice becomes hoarse from weariness; with voice hoarse and not an ounce of strength left;
勢窮力竭 in a deplorable plight and powerless;

[力戒] do everything possible to avoid; guard against; strictly avoid;

[力盡神危] be totally exhausted;

[力矩] moment;
抗扭力矩 antitorque moment;
空氣動力力矩 aerodynamic moment;
轉動力矩 angular moment;

[力量] (1) physical strength; (2) ability; clout; force; leverage; power; strength;
力量懸殊 a great disparity in strength;
保全力量 preserve one's strength;
超自然力量 the supernatural;
分散力量 scatter one's forces;
核力量 nuclear forces;
~ 戰略核力量 strategic nuclear forces;
獲得力量 acquire strength;
精神力量 moral strength;
勉盡力量 do one's best;
顯示力量 assert one's power;
一點力量 a bit of strength; an ounce of strength;
知識就是力量 knowledge is power;

[力偶] couple;
慣性力偶 inertia couple;
集中力偶 concentrated couple;
控制力偶 controlled couple;
離心力偶 centrifugal couple;
瞬時力偶 instantaneous couple;

[力氣] effort; physical strength;
費力氣 do one's best;
~ 白費力氣 beat the air; catch at a shadow; fish in the air; plough the air;
花大力氣 exertion;
賣力氣 (1) do one's very best; exert all one's strength; exert oneself to the utmost; spare no effort; strain every nerve; (2) live by the sweat of one's brow; make a living by manual labour;
用力氣 exertion;

[力求] do all one can; do one's best to; make every effort to; strive to; try hard to;
力求上進 strive to make progress; strive vigorously to improve oneself;
力求一逞 make every possible effort to win;

[力圖] strive to; try hard to;
力圖成功 strive to succeed;
力圖否認 strenuously deny; try hard to deny;

[力行] do sth persistently; try hard to practise;
力行不怠 do sth persistently without letup;
躬體力行 attend personally;

[力學] mechanics;
波動力學 wave mechanics;
材料力學 mechanics of materials;
成穴力學 cavitation mechanics;
磁流力學 magnetohydrodynamics
電動力學 electrodynamics;
~ 量子電動力學 quantum electrodynamics;

~相對論電動力學 relativistic electrodynamics;
動力學 dynamics;
~磁氣體動力學 magnetogasdynamics;
~等離子體動力學 plasmadynamics;
磁等離子體動力學 magnetoplasmadynamics;
~空氣動力學 aerodynamics; aeromechanics;
超音速空氣動力學 supersonic aerodynamics;
跨音速空氣動力學 transonics;
亞音速空氣動力學 subsonic aerodynamics;
~流體動力學 hydrodynamics;
~氣體動力學 aerodynamics; gasdynamics;
斷裂力學 fracture mechanics;
分析力學 analytical mechanics;
剛體力學 geostatics;
工程力學 engineering mechanics;
固體力學 solid mechanics;
航空力學 aeromechanics;
滑翔力學 aerodromics;
結構力學 structural mechanics;
建築力學 architecture;
近代力學 modern mechanics;
經典力學 classical mechanics;
靜力學 statics;
~空氣靜力學 aerostatics;
~流體靜力學 hydrostatics;
空氣力學 air mechanics;
理論力學 theoretical mechanics;
量子力學 quantum mechanics;
流體力學 fluid mechanics;
~磁流體力學 magnetofluiddynamics;
~相對論流體力學 relativistic hydromechanics;
牛頓力學 Newtonian mechanics;
氣體力學 aeromechanics; pneumatics;
熱力學 thermodynamics;
~工程熱力學 engineering thermodynamics;
~化學熱力學 chemical thermodynamics;
~空氣熱力學 aerothermodynamics;
~統計熱力學 statistic-thermodynamics;
生物力學 biomechanics;
聲彈性力學 sono-elasticity;
水力學 hydraulics; hydromechanics;
塑性力學 plasticity;
彈性力學 elasticity;
~氣動彈性力學 aeroelasticity;
~熱彈性力學 thermoelasticity;
~熱氣動彈性力學 thermo-aeroelasticity;
~聲彈性力學 sono-elasticity;
天體力學 celestial mechanics;
統計力學 statistical mechanics;
~經典統計力學 classical statistical mechanics;
~量子統計力學 quantum statistical mechanics;
物理力學 physical mechanics;
相對論力學 relativistic mechanics;
岩石力學 rock mechanics;
一般力學 general mechanics;
應用力學 applied mechanics;
原子力學 atomic mechanics;
質點力學 particle mechanics;

[力有未逮] beyond one's power; beyond one's reach;

[力戰] fight hard;

[力爭] (1) do all one can to; work hard for; (2) argue strongly; contend vigorously;
力爭第一 try hard to be in the first place;
力爭精練 strive to be concise;
力爭上游 aim high; endeavour to gain the upper hand; strive for the first place; strive for the best;
力爭勝利 strive hard for victory;
力爭主動 a serious effort to gain the initiative; do all one can to gain the initiative;
力爭最好 strive for the best;
據理力爭 argue on the basis of reason; argue strongly on just grounds; exert one's utmost efforts to fight for one's point of view; try to convince one's opponent with an argument;

[力拙] weak in strength;
力拙才鮮 weak in strength and lacking in ability;
力拙技窮 at the end of one's tether; at the end of one's wits; reach the end of one's power;

爆發力 explosive force;
暴力 force; violence;
爆炸力 explosive force;
筆力 vigour of strokes in calligraphy or drawing;
臂力 arm strength; strength of one's arm;
辨別力 discrimination;
兵力 armed forces; military strength; troops;
不力 not do one's best; not exert oneself;
才力 ability; talent;

財力 financial resources;
側力 side force;
吃力 entail strenuous effort;
持久力 endurance; stamina;
衝力 impulsive force; momentum;
出力 exert oneself; exert one's efforts; make great efforts; put forth one's strength;
創造力 creative power;
磁力 magnetic force;
大力 great strength;
膽力 boldness; bravery; courage;
得力 capable; competent; efficient;
抵抗力 resistance;
電力 electric power;
鼎力 your kind effort;
洞察力 discernment; insight;
動力 (1) motive power; power; (2) impetus; motive force;
獨力 by one's own efforts; on one's own;
法力 supernatural power;
肥力 fertility;
費力 take pains;
分力 component;
奮力 do all one can; spare no effort;
風力 (1) wind-force; (2) wind power;
浮力 buoyancy;
功力 (1) effect; efficacy; (2) craftsmanship; skill;
購買力 purchasing power;
國力 national power;
合力 join forces; pool efforts;
活力 energy; vigour; vitality;
極力 do one's utmost; spare no effort;
記憶力 the faculty of memory;
加力 afterburning; thrust argmentation;
鑒賞力 ability to appreciate;
角力 have a trial of strength; wrestle;
腳力 (1) strength of one's legs; (2) porter; (3) payment to a porter; (4) money reward to a porter for delivery;
接力 relay;
接受力 acceptability;
竭力 do all one can; use every ounce of one's energy;
盡力 do one's utmost; try one's best;
精力 energy; vigour;
酒力 the strength of wine or spirits;
軍力 military strength;
苦力 coolie;
拉力 pulling force;
勞動力 (1) labour force; (2) capacity for physical labour;
勞力 (1) labour; labour force; (2) able-bodied person;
理解力 faculty of understanding;
量力 estimate one's own strength or resources;
馬力 horsepower;
賣力 do one's utmost; exert all one's strength;
魅力 charm; fascination;
猛力 vigorously; with sudden force;
免疫力 immunogenicity;
民力 financial resources of the pople;
魔力 charm; magic; magic power;
目力 eyesight; vision;
耐力 endurance; stamina; staying power;
腦力 intellectual power; mentality;
內力 internal force;
能力 ability; capability; capacity;
凝聚力 cohesion; cohesive force;
扭力 torsional force; twisting force;
努力 exeret oneself; make great efforts; try hard;
判斷力 judgment;
平衡力 equilibrant;
破壞力 destructive power;
魄力 boldness; courage; daring and resolution; vigour;
氣力 effort; energy; strength;
潛力 latent capacity; potential; potentiality;
親和力 affinity;
全力 sparing no effort; with all one's strength;
權力 authority; power;
熱力 heating power;
人力 manpower; manual labour;
殺傷力 antipersonnel force;
神力 extraordinary power; superhuman strength;
生產力 productivity;
生命力 life-force; vitality;
省力 save effort;
實力 actual strength; strength;
視力 sight; vision;
勢力 influence; power;
水力 hydraulic power; water power;
説服力 convincingness;
肆力 do one's best; try all one can;
彈力 elastic force; elasticity; resilience; spring;
體力 physical power; physical strength;
聽力 (1) hearing; (2) aural comprehension;
通力 concerted effort; united effort;
推動力 motive force;
推進力 driving power; propulsive force;
推力 thrust;
外力 external force; outside force;
威力 might; power;
偉力 immense strength; tremendous force;
握力 grip; the power of gripping;

無力 (1) incapable; powerless; unable; (2) feel weak; lack strength;
武力 (1) force; (2) armed strength; force of arms; military force;
物力 material resources;
吸力 attraction;
吸引力 attraction; gravitation;
悉力 go all out; with might and main;
惜力 not do one's best;
想像力 imaginative power;
向心力 centripetal force;
效力 (1) effect; efficacy; (2) render a service to; serve;
協力 join in a common effort; unite efforts;
心力 mental and physical efforts;
學力 educational level;
壓力 (1) pressure; (2) overwhelming force;
壓縮力 compression stress;
眼力 (1) eyesight; vision; (2) judgment;
藥力 efficacy of a drug;
一力 do all one can; do one's best;
毅力 will stamina; willpower;
引力 attraction; gravitational force;
用力 exert oneself; put forth one's strength;
有力 forceful; strong; vigorous;
原動力 motive power;
張力 (1) tension; (2) pulling force;
致力 devote oneself to;
智力 intellect; intelligence;
重力 gravitational force; gravity;
主力 main force; main strength;
注意力 attention;
專力 with concentrated effort;
着力 exert oneself; put forth effort;
資力 financial strength;
阻力 (1) obstruction; resistance; (2) drag; resistance;
坐力 recoil;

li

【立】 (1) stand; (2) erect; set up; (3) erect; upright; vertical; (4) establish; found; set up;

［立案］ (1) put on record; register; (2) place a case on file for investigation and prosecution;

［立場］ position; stand; standpoint;
立場堅定 take a clear-cut stand;
背棄立場 abandon one's original stand;
表達立場 express one's position;
表明立場 define one's position; make one's position known;
達成一致的立場 reach a unified stand;
改變立場 shift one's position;
堅持立場 keep a stand; put one's foot down;
堅守立場 be firm in one's stand; stand by one's guns; stick to one's guns;
階級立場 class standpoint;
喪失立場 depart from the correct stand;
中間立場 middle ground;

［立此存照］ sign the note for investigation;

［立法］ legislate; legislation;
立法機關 legislature;
立法權 legislative power;
立法委員 legislator;
立法選舉 legislative election;
立法者 legislator;
環境立法 environmental legislation;
仲裁立法 arbitration legislation;

［立方］ cube; cubic;
立方根 cubic root;
立方碼 cubic yard;
立方米 cubic metre;
立方體 cube;
~ 半開立方體 half open cube;
~ 測光用立方體 photometric cube;
~ 單位立方體 unit cube;
~ 截角立方體 truncated cube;
~ 面心立方體 ce-centred cube;
~ 置換立方體 permutation cube;
立方英尺 cubic foot;
立方英寸 cubic inch;
測試立方 test cube;
敏化立方 sensitized cube;
奇異立方 singular cube;
完全立方 perfect cube;
原始立方 primitive cube;

［立竿見影］ get quick results; it causes an immediate and obvious consequence; produce an immediate effect;

［立功］ do a deed of merit; make contributions; render meritorious service; win honour;
立功報效 render sb some signal service to prove one's gratitude;
立功受獎 awards will be given to those who perform a meritorious service; be rewarded for a meritorious action; receive awards for having rendered meritorious service; those who have gained merit will be rewarded;
立功贖罪 do good deeds to atone for

one's crimes; make amends for one's crime by good deeds; perform merits to atone for one's crimes;
立功折罪 recognition of good deeds as atonemwnt for crime;
寸功未立 have not made the least contribution;
戴罪立功 atone for one's crimes by doing good deeds; make up for the crime one has committed; redeem oneself by performing a good service;

[立櫃] wardrobe;

[立國] build a nation;
立國之本 fundamental to the building of the country;
以農立國 a nation based on agricultural economy;

[立即] at once; immediately; off hand; promptly;
立即出發 set out; start out;
立即答覆 give an immediate reply; reply immediately;
立即來 come right away;
立即照辦 carry out promptly;

[立刻] as soon as; as quick as a flash; at once; at one stroke; at the drop of a hat; before one could say Jack Johnson; before you found where you are; directly; first thing off the bat; here and now; immediately; in a brace of shakes; in a crack; in a flash; in a jiffy; in a minute; in a moment; in no time; just now; lose no time in...; off hand; on the moment; on the nail; out of hand; promptly; pronto; right away; right now; right off the bat; straight away; straight off; thereupon; this instant; this moment; without a moment's delay; without delay; without hesitation; without loss of time; without thinking much longer;

[立論] (1) present one's argument; set forth one's view; (2) argument; line of reasoning; position;

[立室] take a wife;
立室成家 take a wife and establish a family;
置家立室 marry and set up a home;

[立誓] make a pledge; take an oath;
立誓人 affiant;

[立體] solid; stereoscopic; three-dimensional;
立體角 solid angle;
立體鏡 lens stereoscope; stereoscope;
~測量立體鏡 measuring stereoscope;
~反光立體鏡 mirror stereoscope; reflecting stereoscope;
立體派 cubism;
~立體派畫家 cubist;
~立體派繪畫 cubist painting;
立體聲 stereo;
~立體聲唱機 stereo phonography;
~立體聲唱片 stereo phono;
~單紋槽立體聲 monogroove stereo;
~多聲道立體聲 multichannel stereo;
~環繞立體聲 surrounding sound;
立體音響 stereophony;
立體主義 cubism;

[立憲] constitutionalism; establish the constitutional system;
立憲會議 constituent assembly;

[立言] achieve glory by writing; expound one's ideas in writing;

[立業] start one's career;
掙家立業 establish a home and make achievements;

[立意] (1) be determined; make up one's mind; (2) approach; conception;
立意新穎 in a novel conception; original in conception; show an interesting new approach;

[立正] stand at attention;

[立志] be determined; resolve;
立志復仇 resolve upon having one's revenge;
立志改革 be resolved to carry out reforms;
立志做大事 be determined to do great things;

[立柱] stanchion;
叉式立柱 forked stanchion;
車端立柱 end stanchion;

[立字為憑] give a written pledge;

[立足] (1) find one's niche in; have a foothold somewhere; keep a foothold; (2) base oneself on;
立足點 (1) foothold; footing; (2) stand; standpoint;
立足之地 a footing; a narrow spot for one to stand on; a place for living; a place to put one's feet on — a place to live

in; a place to set one's feet; an inch of land to stand on;

壁立 rise steeply; stand like a wall;
並立 exist side by side; exist simultaneously;
成立 (1) establish; set up; (2) be tenable; hold water;
抽立 lose money;
創立 found; originate;
倒立 stand upside down;
鼎立 confront one another like the three legs of a tripod;
訂立 conclude; make;
陡立 rise steeply;
獨立 (1) stand alone; (2) be independent; be on one's own;
對立 be antagonistic to; counterpose; oppose;
而立 thirty years old;
公立 public;
孤立 isolagted;
國立 state-run;
建立 build; establish; found; set up;
林立 stand in great numbers;
起立 rise to one's feet; stand up;
峭立 rise steeply;
確立 establish;
設立 establish; found; set up;
市立 municipal-run;
豎立 erect; set upright;
樹立 establish; set up;
私立 private;
嗣立 appoint as heir;
聳立 tower aloft;
肅立 stand as a mark of respect;
挺立 stand erect; stand upright;
兀立 stand upright;
屹立 stand erect; stand lofty and firm like a mountain;
直立 stand upright;
峙立 stand lofty and upright; stand towering;
中立 neutrality;
卓立 stand upright;
自立 stand on one's own feet; support oneself;

li

【吏】 civil officer;

官吏 government officials;
墨吏 corrupt official;
胥吏 petty official;
獄吏 pirson officer;

li

【利】 (1) sharp; (2) favourable; (3) advantage; benefit; (4) interest; profit; (5) benefit; do good to;

[利弊] advantages and disadvantages; pros and cons;

利弊得失 advantages and disadvantages, merits and demerits; advantages or disadvantages, and gains or losses;
弊大於利 have more disadvantages than advantages;
弊多利少 more advantages than disadvantages; the disadvantages outweigh the disadvantages;
弊多於利 has more disadvantages than advantages;
弊小於利 do more good than harm;
各有利弊 each has its own advantages and weak points;
互有利弊 cut both ways;
利多弊少 the advantages outweigh the disadvantages;
利少弊多 more harm than good;
有百利而無一弊 have every advantage and no drawback;

[利害] advantages and disadvantages; gains and losses;

利害衝突 clash of interests; conflict of interests;
利害得失 advantages and disadvantages;
利害與共 on shares; share weal and woe;
利害昭然 clearly point to where interest or dangers lie;
變害為利 harm is turned into benefit; turn bane into boon; turn the harm into a benefit;
害多利少 do more harm than good; more disadvantages than advantages; more harm than good;
利己害人 benefit oneself at the expense of others;
密陳利害 send a secret memorial concerning the profit and loss;
曉以利害 warn sb of the possible consequences;
有百害而無一利 bring nothing but harm to; can only do harm to; do only harm and bring no benefit to; have everything to lose and nothing to gain;
有百利而無一害 gain everything and lose nothing; have everything to gain and nothing to lose; have nothing to lose but everything to gain;

喻以利害 explain its advantages and disadvantages; illustrate by explaining advantages and disadvantages;

[利令智昏] avarice blinds the eye of judgment; be blinded by inordinate ambition; be blinded by self-interest; be dizzied by the lust for gain; be obsessed with one's desire for material gains; be thrown off one's balance by the sight of money; bend one's principles to one's interest; desire for money blinds one's mind; gain blinds one's better judgment; money tends to make one do foolish things; profit makes wisdom blind; self is a bad counsellor; self-interest befuddles one's mind; wealth makes wit waver;

[利祿] wealth and position;

利祿熏心 enthusiastic about wealth and emolument;

[利落] (1) agile; dexterous; nimble; (2) neat; orderly;

手腳利落 agile; deft; dexterous; nimble; not to make a hash of;

[利率] interest rate; money rate; rate of interest;

利率大戰 interest rate war;

利率到位 interest rates just to its level;

利率指標 profit index;

利率自由化 liberalization of interest rate;

貸款利率 lending rate;

抵押利率 mortgage rate;

固定利率 fixed interest;

基本利率 base rate;

平均利率 the average rate of profit;

市場利率 market rate of interest;

調整利率 readjust interest rate;

銀行利率 bank rate;

最優惠利率 prime rate;

[利尿] diuresis;

利尿劑 diuretic;

利尿素 diuretin;

利尿藥 diuretic;

[利器] daggers

身藏利器 armed with hidden daggers;

身懷利器 carry a knife with one;

[利錢] interest;

[利權] (1) economic rights; (2) financial power;

[利人] benefit other people;

利人利己 benefit other people as well as oneself;

利己利人 benefit others as well as oneself;

損己利人 help others at one's own expense;

[利刃] sharp knife;

舌如利刃 have a tongue like a razor; one's tongue is as sharp as a sword;

[利潤] profit;

利潤分配 distribution of profits;

利潤幅度 profit margin;

利潤率 rate of profit;

利潤税 profit tax;

~超額利潤税 additional profit tax;

利潤賬戶 profit account;

超額利潤 abnormal profit; excess profit;

超級利潤 superprofit;

純利潤 net profits;

高利潤 high profit;

~高利潤服務 high-profit service;

獲取利潤 gain profit;

巨額利潤 huge profit;

毛利潤 gross margin;

偶然利潤 aleatory;

平均利潤 average profit;

商業利潤 profit from business;

上繳利潤 forward profits to the state;

實際利潤 actual profit;

投資利潤 profit on investment;

銷售利潤 profit on the sale;

一般利潤 normal profit;

應計利潤 accrued profit;

預期利潤 anticipated profit;

總利潤 gross profits;

追求利潤 chase profits;

追逐利潤 chase profits;

最低利潤 minimum profit;

最高利潤 maximum profit;

[利上滾利] at compound interest; with interest compounded;

[利税] profit and tax;

利税分流 pay tax plus a percentage of profits;

[利他主義] altruism;

[利息] interest;

利息回扣 interest rebate;

利息賬戶 interest account;

存款利息 interest on a deposit;

貸款利息 interest on a loan;

法定利息 legal interest;

付利息 pay interest;

供樓利息 mortgage interest;
估算利息 calculated interest;
計算利息 figure interest;
借款利息 interest on borrowing;
累計利息 accumulated interest;
累加利息 cumulative interest;
提供利息 bear interest;
應付利息 interest in red;
應計利息 accrued interest;
應計投資利息 accrued interest on investment;
應收利息 interest in black;
支付利息 interest payment;
追加利息 add-on interest;
資本利息 capital interest;

L

[利益] benefit; gain; interest; profit;
利益集團 interest group;
利益論 theory of interests;
比較利益 comparative advantage;
個人利益 personal interests;
公共利益 public interests;
共同利益 common good;
既得利益 vested interest;
經濟利益 economic benefits;
切身利益 one's immediate interests; one's vital interests;
物質利益 material benefits;
相互利益 mutual advantages; reciprocal benefit;

[利用] avail oneself of; cash in on; exploit; find a use for sth; make the most of; make use of; play on; play up to; play upon; put to use; seize on; seize upon; take advantage of; trade on; trade upon; turn to account; utilize; use; utilization;
利用職權 exploit one's office; take advantage of one's position and power;
被人利用 be used by another person;
~被人利用的人 a cat's paw;
廢酸渣利用 acid waste utilization;
要素利用 factor utilization;
有效利用 effective utilization;
綜合利用 comprehensive utilization;

[利誘] lure by promise of gain;
利誘威逼 beguile with money and oppress with power;
威逼利誘 threaten and bribe;
誘之以利 lure sb by the promise of profit;

[利於] beneficial to; good for;

[利欲熏心] avarice and lust becloud one's heart; be blinded by greed; be lured by profits; be obsessed with the desire for gain; be overcome by covetousness; be possessed by greed for gain; be possessed with a lust for gain; moneygrabbing; on the make; profitdrunk; put profit above conscience; reckless with greed; sordid;

[利嘴] sharp tongue;
利嘴毒舌 a sharp tongue; have a shrewd tongue;
利嘴花牙 have a ready tongue; saponaceous;
利嘴巧舌 have the gift of the gab;

暴利 sudden hug profits;
本利 principal and interest;
便利 (1) convenient; easy; (2) accommodate; facilitate; for the convenience of;
薄利 small profits;
不利 adverse to; bad for; count against; detrimental to; go against; go ill with; harmful to; inimical to; make against; militate against; run against; speak ill for; tell against; turn against; unfavourable for; unfavourable to; weigh against;
創利 create a source of profit; create profit; make a profit;
純利 net profit;
單利 simple interest;
地利 (1) favourable geographical position; (2) land productivity;
鋒利 (1) keen; sharp; (2) incisive; sharp;
福利 welfare; well-being;
複利 compound interest;
高利 high interest;
功利 material gain; utility;
股利 interest on shares;
紅利 (1) extra dividend; (2) bonus;
互利 of mutual benefit;
獲利 make a profit; reap profits;
吉利 lucky; propitious;
尖利 (1) cutting; sharp; (2) piercing; shrill;
淨利 net profit;
流利 fluent; smooth;
毛利 gross profit;
名利 fame and gain; fame and wealth;
牟利 seek profits;
年利 annual interest;
權利 right;

日利 daily interest;
銳利 keen; sharp;
勝利 triumph; win;
失利 suffer a setback;
實利 actual gains; net profit;
爽利 brisk and neat; efficient and able;
水利 (1) water conservancy; (2) irrigation works;
順利 smoothly; successful; without a hitch;
勢利 snobbish;
私利 personal gain; private interests;
犀利 incisive; sharp;
營利 seek profits;
有利 advantageous; favourable;
漁利 ill-gotten gains; profit at other's expense; reap gains by unethical means;
餘利 extra profit; net profit;
月利 monthly interest;
債利 interest on loans; loan interest;
重利 (1) high interest; (2) huge profit;
專利 patent;

li

【例】 (1) example; instance; (2) precedent; (3) regulation; rule; (4) regular; routine;

[例會] regular meeting;
每月例會 monthly meeting;
每周例會 weekly meeting;

[例假] (1) legal holiday; official holiday; (2) menstrual period; period;

[例句] example sentence; illustrative sentence; model sentence;

[例如] for example; for instance; like; such as;

[例題] example;

[例外] exception;
不許有例外 allow no exception;
毫無例外 without any exception;

[例行] routine;
例行公事 a matter of form; a matter of routine; a prescribed course of action; a regular course of official duties; mere formality; perform the routine; regular procedure; routine business; routine work;

[例言] introductory remarks;

[例證] a case in point; example illustration;
提供例證 furnish an example;

[例子] case; example; instance;
例子說明 an example illustrates;
例子顯示 an example shows;
典型例子 classic example; prime example; typical example;
略舉幾個例子 to name but a few; to name but a handful;
明顯的例子 obvious example;
適當的例子 appropriate example;
提供例子 provide an example;
引用了大量例子 an abundance of instances are cited;

按例 according to rules;
比例 (1) proportion; (2) scale;
病例 case;
常例 common practice;
成例 existing model; precedent;
定例 routine; set pattern;
凡例 notes on the use of a book;
範例 example; model;
公例 general rule;
慣例 convention; customary practice; the usual rule;
禁例 prohibitions; prohibitory regulations;
舉例 give an example;
開例 create a precedent;
老例 old practice;
判例 judicial precedent; legal precedent;
破例 break a rule; make an exception;
前例 precedent;
實例 example; living example;
示例 give a demonstration; give a typical example;
事例 example; instance;
俗例 customary rules;
特例 special case;
體例 style; stylistic rules and layout;
條例 ordinances; regulations; rules;
通例 general rule;
圖例 key;
違例 breach of rules; violate the regulations;
先例 precedent;
向例 convention; usual practice;
循例 follow the usual practice;
援例 cite a precedent;
照例 as a rule; as usual; usually;

li

【戾】 (1) abnormal; irregular; perverse; recalcitrant; (2) atrocious; criminal;

暴戾 cruel and fierce; ruthless and tyrannical;
佛戾 go against sb's wishes;
乖戾 disagreeable; perverse;
罪戾 crime; evil; sin;

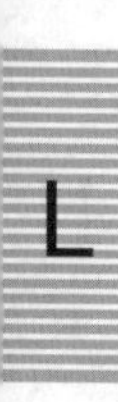

li

【沴】 foul and poisonous; miasma;
［沴氣］ foul air; miasma;

li

【俐】 (1) easy and quick; facile; (2) clever; sharp; (3) in good order; neat; tidy;

伶俐 clever; quick-witted;

li

【苙】 (1) pigpen; pigsty; (2) a kind of medicinal herb;

li

【涖】 (1) arrive; (2) murmur of flowing water;
［涖涖］ murmur of flowing water;
［涖民］ govern the people;
［涖任］ assume office;
［涖政］ administer the government;
［涖止］ arrive; present;
［涖治］ exercise the administration of a government;
［涖阼］ assume the throne;

li

【栗】 (1) chestnut tree; (2) durable; firm; strong and tough; (3) awe-inspiring; fearful; respectful; (4) dignified; majestic; (5) a surname;
［栗苞］ chestnut case;
［栗果］ acorn;
［栗子］ chestnut;
栗子皮 chestnut skin;
栗子樹 chestnut tree;
栗子撻 chestnut tart;
~ 迷你栗子撻 mini chestnut tart;
炒栗子 roast chestnuts;
~ 糖炒栗子 chestnuts roasted with brown sugar;
冷鍋裏撿了個熱栗子 get sth nice unexpectedly;

板栗 Chinese chestnut;
石栗 candlenut tree;

li

【荔】 lichee;
［荔枝］ lichee;
番荔枝 sugar apple;
~ 南美番荔枝 custard apple;
一串荔枝 a bunch of lichees;

薜荔 climbing fig;

li

【鬲】 a kind of caldron;

li

【唳】 the cry of a crane, wild goose, etc.;

li

【笠】 (1) bamboo hat; (2) bamboo shade or covering;
［笠貝］ limpet;

草笠 straw hat;
斗笠 large bamboo rain hat;
箬笠 broad-rimmed hat made of indocalamus splints and leaves;
簑笠 bamboo cape and hat;
竹笠 bamboo hat;

li

【粒】 (1) grain; (2) bead; pill;
［粒狀］ graininess; granular;
粒狀岩 granular rock;
［粒子］ grain; granule; particle;
粒子加速器 particle accelerator;
粒子物理學 particle physics;
反粒子 antiparticle;
反照粒子 albedo particle;
放射性粒子 active particles;
基本粒子 elementary particle; fundamental particle;
加速粒子 accelerated particle;
微觀粒子 microscopic particle;

飯粒 grain of cooked rice;
晶粒 crystalline grain;
顆粒 grain;
米粒 grain of rice;
陶粒 ceramsite;
團粒 granule;
脱粒 (1) thresh; (2) shell;
微粒 (1) particle; (2) corpuscle;
質粒 plasmid;
子粒 bean; grain; kernel; seed;

li

【莅】 arrive; present;
［莅場］ show up on the occasion; present on the occasion;
［莅會］ attend a meeting; present at a meeting;
［莅臨］ arrive; present;

莅臨指導 someone's presence and guidance;

[莅盟] (1) attend a meeting for the conclusion of treaties between countries; (2) keep a rendezvous;

li

【莉】 white jasmine;

茉莉 jasmine;

li

【痢】 diarrhea; dysentery;

[痢疾] dysentery;

阿米巴痢疾 amoebic dysentery;
爆發性痢疾 fulminant dysentery;
病毒性痢疾 viral dysentery;
惡性痢疾 malignant dysentery;
壞血病性痢疾 scorbutic dysentery;
假痢疾 pseudodysentery;
拉痢疾 suffer from dysentery;
流行性痢疾 epidemic dysentery;
日本痢疾 Japanese dysentery;
細菌性痢疾 bacillary dysentery;
原蟲性痢疾 protozoal dysentery;

白痢 (1) dysentery; (2) white diarrhea;
赤痢 dysentery characterized by blood and pus in the stool;

li

【詈】 berate; scold; upbraid; vituperate;

忿詈 scold with anger;

li

【慄】 shudder; tremble;

[慄慄危懼] in fear and trembling; tremble with fear;

li

【溧】 (1) the name of a river flowing through Anhui and Jiangsu; (2) the name of a county in Jiangsu;

li

【蒞】 arrive; present; reach;

[蒞臨] arrive; present;

li

【厲】 (1) rigorous; strict; (2) severe; stern; (3) a surname;

[厲鬼] ferocious ghost;

[厲害] (1) cruel; fierce; severe; sharp; (2) formidable; serious; terrible;

病得厲害 seriously ill;

[厲目而視] look with severe glare;

[厲色] look stern;

厲色正言 speak with stern countenance;
疾言厲色 a hard word and a black look; brusque; harsh words and stern looks; look fierce and talk boisterously; speak gruffly with a stern countenance; sudden outpourings and fierce looks; with a severe countenance and a harsh voice;
盱衡厲色 gaze in stern countenance;
正言厲色 speak with stern countenance;
正顏厲色 a serious manner; in a serious tone and with a solemn look; keep a stern face; keep one's countenance; keep one's face straight; put on a stern countenance; with a severe look; with straight face and in serious tone of voice;

[厲聲] shout angrily; talk harshly;

厲聲斥責 scold with an irritating voice;
厲聲高罵 keep up a stream of furious abuse;

[厲行] make great efforts to carry out; practise; rigorously enforce; strictly carry out; strictly enforce;

厲行改革 make great efforts to carry out reforms;
厲行節約 make a sustained effort to practiseeconomy; practise strict economy; rigorous enforcement of economy;

li

【曆】 calendar;

[曆法] calendar;

[曆日] calendar day;

[曆書] almanac;

曆書時 ephemeris time;

[曆算家] calendarist;

[曆月] calendar month;

[曆鐘] calendar clock;

掛曆 wall calendar;
教會曆 ecclesiastical calendar;
雙月曆 bimonthly calendar;
檯曆 desk calendar;
萬年曆 perpetual calendar;
校曆 academic calendar; school calendar;
陰曆 lunar calendar;
陰陽曆 luni-solar calendar;

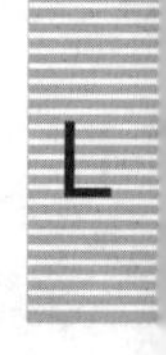

月曆 monthly calendar;

li

【歷】 (1) experience; go through; undergo; (2) covering all; one by one; (3) all previous;

[歷程] (1) course; progress; (2) mechanism;
艱難歷程 odyssey;
人生歷程 life journey; life's journey;
戰鬥歷程 the course of the war;

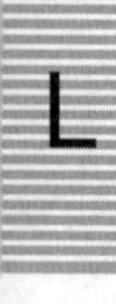

[歷次] all previous occasions; various occasions;
歷次比賽 all past contests;
歷次改革 all previous reforms;
歷次考試 all the past examinations;

[歷代] past dynasties; successive dynasties;

[歷屆] all previous...; successive;
歷屆內閣 successive cabinets;
歷屆政府 successive governments;

[歷經] have experienced;
歷經滄桑 go through all the vicissitudes of life;
歷經甘苦 through thick and thin;
歷經困難 have encountered all kinds of difficulties;
歷經千難萬險 go through hell and high water;
歷經欠收 have seen a series of bad harvests;
歷經危險 have gone through various dangers;

[歷久不衰] long lasting; no slackening of effort with the passage of time;

[歷久彌堅] remain unshakable and become even firmer as time goes by;

[歷來] all long; always; constantly; that is always the case;
歷來認為 have always maintained; have consistently hedl; have held all along; have invariably insisted;
歷來如此 this has always been the case;

[歷歷] clearly; distinctly;
歷歷可見 can be seen distinctly; come clearly into view;
歷歷可考 every detail may be verified;
歷歷可數 can be counted one by one; can be seen distinctly; easy to be counted; every one can be reckoned;
歷歷在目 come clearly into view; leap to the eyes; leap up vividly before one's eyes; present to the mind; remain clear and distinct in one's mind; remain vivid in one's mind's eye; remember clearly to this day; still vivid in one's mind; visible before the eyes;

[歷年] (1) over the years; (2) calendar year; civil year;

[歷任] successively hold the posts of;
歷任經理 successive managers;

[歷時] last; take;
歷時語言學 diachronic linguistics;

[歷史] history; past events; past records;
歷史比較法 historical comparative method;
歷史比較語言學 historical and comparative linguistics;
歷史表明 history shows that;
歷史重演 history repeats itself;
歷史大時代 a great epoch in history;
歷史發展 historical development;
歷史進程 historical course;
歷史名詞 historical term;
~成為歷史名詞 pass into history;
歷史年表 chronological table;
歷史清白 have a clean record;
歷史人物 historical characters;
~評價歷史人物 appraise historical characters;
歷史使命 historic mission;
歷史事件 historic events; historical events;
歷史術語 historical term;
歷史現在時 historical present tense;
歷史新高 historical height;
歷史性現在時態 historic present;
歷史學 historiography;
~歷史學家 historian;
歷史遺留問題 problem left over by history;
歷史悠久 have a long history;
歷史語法 historical grammer;
歷史語言學 historical linguistics;
歷史責任 historical responsibility;
歷史罪人 a person condemned by history;
創造歷史 make history;
當地歷史 local history;
割斷歷史 chop up history;
歪曲歷史 distort history;
一段歷史 a period of history;
早期歷史 early history;

[歷數其罪] enumerate the crimes sb has committed;

li

【勵】 encourage;

［勵精圖治］ brace oneself up and run one's country well; do all one can to make the country prosperous; exert oneself to make the country prosperous; make great efforts to make a good country; make great efforts to build a strong state; rouse oneself for vigorous efforts to make the country prosperous; strengthen the spirit and scheme for governing;

li

【隸】 (1) attach to; belong to; inferior; subordinate to; (2) servant; slave; underling; (3) a type of Chinese calligraphy; (4) learn; practice; (5) a surname;

［隸書］ (in calligraphy) clerical script; official script;

［隸屬］ subordinate to; under the command of; under the jurisdiction of;

奴隸 slave;

li

【髳】 favus;

li

【癘】 (1) ulcer; (2) pestilential vapour;

疫癘 epidemic disease; pestilence;

瘴癘 communicable subtropical diseases;

li

【瀝】 (1) drip; fall down by drops; trickle; (2) remaining drops of wine; (3) strain water or liquids;

［瀝澇］ waterlogging;

［瀝瀝］ (1) rustling; whistling; (2) babbling; (3) dripping;

滴瀝 sound of dripping;

披瀝 (1) open and sincere; (2) loyal and faithful;

淅瀝 (of rain) patter;

餘瀝 heeltap;

［瀝青］ asphalt; bitumen; blacktop; pitch;

瀝青化 asphaltization; bitumination;

瀝青跑道 asphalt-track;

瀝青質 asphaltene;

殘餘瀝青 residual asphalt;

粗瀝青 crude asphalt;

催化瀝青 catalytic asphalt;

脆塊瀝青 bielzite;

帶色瀝青 colour asphalt;

地瀝青 ground pitch;

改良瀝青 modified asphalt;

乾餾瀝青 pyrogenous asphalt;

固體瀝青 solid asphalt; solid bitumen;

合成瀝青 synthetic asphalt;

黑瀝青 abbertite;

湖瀝青 lake asphalt;

加工瀝青 formed asphalt;

加琉瀝青 sulfurized asphalt;

焦油瀝青 tar asphalt;

澆鑄瀝青 poured asphalt;

裂化瀝青 cracked asphalt;

~未裂化瀝青 uncracked asphalt;

氯化瀝青 chlorinated asphalt;

煤焦油瀝青 coal-tar pitch;

泡沫瀝青 foam asphalt;

片狀瀝青 sheet asphalt;

人造地瀝青 artificial asphalt;

乳化瀝青 emulsified asphalt; emulsified bitumen;

軟瀝青 pit asphalt;

滲透用瀝青 penetration asphalt;

石油瀝青 petroleum asphalt;

酸渣瀝青 acid sludge asphalt;

彈性瀝青 elastic bitumen;

天然瀝青 native bitumen; natural asphalt;

無臭瀝青 odourless bitumen;

稀釋瀝青 cutback asphalt;

硝化瀝青 nitrate asphalt;

氧化瀝青 air-blown asphalt; blown asphalt; oxidized asphalt;

液態瀝青 liquid asphalt; liquid bitumen

油瀝青 oil asphalt; oily bitumen;

游離瀝青 free asphalt;

淤渣瀝青 sludge asphalt;

直餾瀝青 straight-run bitumen;

重瀝青 heavy asphalt;

重質瀝青 heavy bitumen;

li

【麗】 (1) beautiful; elegant; fair; fine; magnificent; (2) same as 儷;

［麗人］ beauty;

li

【櫟】 chestnut-leaved oak;

槲櫟 oriental white oak;

麻櫟 oak;

蒙櫟 Mongolian oak;

柞櫟 toothed oak;

li

【礪】 (1) coarse whetstone; (2) sharpen a knife;

淬礪 temper oneself through severe trials;
砥礪 (1) temper; (2) encourage;
磨礪 harden oneself; steel oneself;

li

【礫】 gravel; pebble;
[礫石] gravel; pebble;
礫石石器 pebble tool;
海灘礫石 beach gravel;
含金礫石 auriferous gravel;
原狀礫石 gravel;
[礫岩] conglomerate; conglomerate rock;
白雲石礫岩 dolomitic conglomerate;
冰礫岩 glacial conglomerate;
構造礫岩 tectonic conglomerate;
海退礫岩 regress conglomerate;
火山礫岩 volcanic conglomerate;
煤礫岩 coal conglomerate;
正石英礫岩 orthoquartzitic conglomerate;

漂礫 boulder
沙礫 gravel; grit;
瓦礫 debris; rubble;

li

【櫪】 (1) stable; (2) quercus serrata; (3) wooden device used to torture a criminal by pressing his fingers;

li

【儷】 couple; pair;
[儷影] heart-warming sight of a couple in love;

伉儷 husband and wife; married couple;
駢儷 art of parallelism;

li

【糲】 (1) unpolished rice; (2) coarse; rough;
[糲飯] cooked unpolished rice;
[糲粱] coarse food; simple food;
[糲食] coarse fare;

li

【蠣】 oyster;
[蠣鷸] oyster catcher;

li

【酈】 (1) the ancient name for a part of what is Henan today; (2) a surname;

li

【轢】 (1) (of a wheel) run over; (2) oppress;

淩轢 (1) bully and oppress; (2) push out; squeeze out;

li

【轣】 (1) pulley for drawing water; (2) capstan; windlass;

li

【靂】 thunder; thunderbolt; thunderclap;
霹靂

li⁵

li

【蜊】 clam;

li

【裏】 here; there;

li

【璃】 glass; glassy substance;

lia³

lia

【倆】 (1) two; (2) several; some;

lian²

lian

【帘】 (1) flag sign of a wine-house or tavern; (2) door or window screen;

lian

【怜】 abbreviated form of 憐;

lian

【連】 (1) connect; join; link; (2) in succession; one after another; repeatedly; (3) include; (4) company; (5) even;
[連播] chain broadcast;
[連詞] conjunction; linking word;
並列連詞 coordinating conjunction;
~簡單並列連詞 simple coordinating conjunction;
從屬連詞 subordinating conjunction;
~比例從屬連詞 subordinator of proportion;
~持續從屬連詞 subordinator of duration;
~地點從屬連詞 subordinator of place;
~範圍從屬連詞 subordinator of extent;
~簡單從屬連詞 simple subordinator;
~目的從屬連詞 subordinator of purpose;
~排比從屬連詞 subordinator of exception;

短語連詞 phrasal conjunction;
反意連詞 adversative conjunction;
分詞連詞 participial conjunction;
複合連詞 compound conjunction;
關聯連詞 correlative;
簡單連詞 simple conjunction;
結果連詞 resultative conjunction;
句子連詞 sentence connective;
目的連詞 conjunction of purpose;
相關連詞 correlative conjunction;
原因連詞 causal conjunction;
轉折連詞 disjunctive conjunction;

[連帶] (1) connected; related; (2) joint;
連帶擔保 joint guarantee;
連帶責任 joint responsibility;
連打帶踢 mix kicks with hand blows; kick and hit;
連滾帶爬 roll and crawl;
連哭帶罵 cry and swear; sobs and curses;
連説帶比 gesticulate as one talks; talk and gesticulate;
連説帶笑 laugh and talk;

[連貫] (1) hang together; link up; piece together; (2) coherent; consistent;
連貫性 consistency;

[連鍋端] destroy lock, stock and barrel; get rid of the whole lot;

[連環] series;
連環畫 picture series;
連環計 a series of stratagems; a set of interlocking stratagems; co-ordinate one stratagem with another;
連環漫畫 cartoon;

[連擊] double hit;

[連接] annex; attach; be connected; be joined; clasp; combine; connect; connect with; couple; draw together; fasten; join; link; link up; linkage; put together; unite;
連接詞 conjunction;
~關連連接詞 correlative conjunction;
連接詞素 linking morpheme;
連接代詞 conjunctive pronoun;
連接副詞 conjunctive adberb;
連接功能 connectivity;
連接器 connector;
連接物 connector;
連接性副詞 adverb as conjunct;
連接性能 connectivity;
連接性情態動詞 connective modal;
連接語法 connective grammar;
超連接 hot link;
接插式連接 clickfit;

[連結] cohesive;
連結性 cohesion;
~連結性層次 cohesive level;

[連襟] maternal cousins;

[連累] get sb into trouble; implicate; incriminate; involve;
受連累 be involved in;

[連連] again and again; repeatedly;
連連敗北 suffer one defeat after another;
連連出擊 launch one attack after another;
連連道歉 say "sorry" again and again;
連連道謝 say "thanks" repeatedly;
連連得分 make one score after another; make scores unceasingly;
連連得手 come off repeatedly;
連連點頭 nod again and again; nod repeatedly; nod vigorously;
連連呼救 cry for help unceasingly;
連連獲勝 win one victory after another;
連連舉杯 propose repeated toasts; propose toasts repeatedly;
連連招手 wave one's hands time and again;

[連忙] immediately; in a hurry; instantly; promptly;

[連袂] in pair; together;
連袂成雙 pair off;
連袂而起 rise side by side;
連袂而往 go together to a certain place;

[連綿] continuous; unbroken; uninterrupted;
連綿筆 the ceaseless brush;
連綿不斷 continuous succession; incessant; one after another; unceasing; uninterruptedly; without break; without stopping;
連綿不絕 continuous succession; in an unbroken line; in succession; uninterrupted; without break;
連綿秋雨 the continuous autumn rain;
連綿一片 reach;

[連年] for years on end; for years running; in consecutive years; in successive years;
連年豐收 get good harvests for years running; have good harvests in succession; reap rich harvests for many years running;

[連篇] (1) page after page; throughout a piece of writing; (2) a multitude of articles; one article after another;

連篇累牘 keep on repeating; lengthy and tedious; reiterate again and again; reiterate at great length;

[連任] be reappointed; be reelected; renew one's term of office;
連任主席 be reelected chairman;
謀求連任 seek r-election;

[連日] day after day; for days on end;

[連聲] again and again; repeatedly;
連聲稱讚 full of praise for; rain praises on;
連聲叫苦 one cries out one's bitterness without ceasing;
連聲諾諾 say aye, aye;
連聲認錯 hasten to acknowledge one's error;
諾諾連聲 keep on saying "yes";
唯唯連聲 assent meekly;

[連署] cosign; countersign;
連署國 cosignatory powers;
連署人 cosignatory;

[連鎖] (1) concatenated; (2) chain;
連鎖店 chain store;
連鎖反應 chain reaction; ripple effect;
連鎖經營 chain operation;
連鎖商店 chain store; multiple store;
連鎖信 chain letter;
連鎖裝置 safety interlock;
~安全連鎖裝置 safety interlock;

[連天] (1) reaching the sky; (2) incessantly;
喊殺連天 the air is filled with shourts of "kill! kill!"; the battle cry reached the heavens; the noise of battle filled the sky;

[連同] along with; complete with; together with;

[連續] again and again; at a stretch; consecutive; continual; continuance; continuation; continue; continuously; for...running; in a row; in succession; last; nonstop; on end; one after another; repeated; running; stretch; successively; without a break; without a let-up; without a stop;
連續報導 successive report;
連續不斷 continuous and unbroken; off the reel; right off the reel;
連續出版物 serials;
連續的 consecutive;
~半連續的 demicontinuous;
連續地 on the trot;
連續動作 consecutive action;
連續發問 ask several questions continuously;
連續幾天 for days on end;
連續劇 drama series; serial;
~電視連續劇 television serial;
~十集連續劇 ten-part serial;
連續口譯 consecutive interpretation;
連續適應 homogenic adaptation;
連續體 cline; continuum;
連續統 continuum;
~可分割連續統 cut continuum;
~算術連續統 arithmetic continuum;
~線性連續統 linear continuum;
連續性 continuity;
~連續性部件 continuity-fitting;
~連續性媒體 continuous media;
~不連續性 discontinuity;
幾何不連續性 geometric discontinuity;
吸收不連續性 absorption discontinuity;
有限不連續性 finite discontinuity;
~操作連續性 continuity of operation;
~單向連續性 unilateral continuity;
~分段連續性 piecewise continuity;
~幾何連續性 geometrical continuity;
~經濟連續性 economic continuity;
~局部連續性 local continuity;
~均方連續性 mean square continuity;
~右連續性 right continuity;
連續雨 continuous rain;
連續作戰 fight one battle after another;
近似連續 approximate continuity;
一致連續 uniform continuity;
中數連續 mean continuity;

[連夜] that very night; the same night;
連夜趕回 hurry back that same night;
連夜潛逃 escape in the dark of night; make a moonlight flitting;

[連衣褲] one-piece clothing;
緊身連衣褲 cat suit; leotard;

[連衣裙] frock; one-piece dress;
長袖連衣裙 long-sleeved dress;
短袖連衣裙 short-sleeved dress;
緊身連衣裙 body-hugging dress; close-fitting dress; figure-bugging dress; slinky dress;
寬鬆連衣裙 chemise;

[連音] sandhi
連音形式 sandhi-form;
規則連音 regular sandhi;

強迫連音 compulsory sandhi;
特殊連音 special sandhi;
一般連音 general sandhi;

[連載] publish in instalments; serialize;
連載小説 serial story;

[連戰] successive battles;
連戰皆北 suffer one defeat after another;
連戰皆捷 come out victorious in successive battles;

[連長] company commander;

[連珠] (1) chain of pearls; (2) in rapid succession;
連珠妙語 a sparkling discourse; scintillate witticisms;
連珠砲 continuous firing; drumfire;
~開連珠砲 chatter away like a machine gun; fire away thick and fast; rattle on; shoot off one's mouth;

[連莊] (of mahjong) stay on as the dealer;

[連字號] hyphen;

串連 contact; establish ties;
顛連 (1) difficulty; hardship; trouble; (2) peak upon peak;
接連 in succession; on end;
流連 be reluctant to part; be unwilling to leave a place;
毗連 adjoin; boder on;
牽連 implicate; involve in trouble;
通連 be connected; lead to;
相連 be joined; be linked together;
一連 at a stretch; in a row; in succession on end; running;
株連 implicate; involve in a criminal case;

lian

【廉】 (1) honest and clean; (2) cheap; inexpensive; low-priced;

[廉察] secretly investigate;

[廉恥] sense of honour; sense of shame;
寡廉鮮恥 as bold as brass; be dead to shame; be destitute of shame; be lost to all sense of shame; brazen-faced; have no sense of dishonour and disgrace; have no sense of shame; shameless; unscrupulous and shameless;

[廉得其情] examine and get at the bottom of the thing; find out the real facts;

[廉價] at a low price; cheap; inexpensive; low-priced;
廉價本 cheap edition; low-price edition;
廉價貨物 great bargain; low-priced goods;
廉價品 cheap goods bargain;
廉價市場 flea market;
廉價質劣的 cheapo;
大廉價 bargain sale;

[廉潔] honest; whitehanded; with clean hands;
廉潔奉公 a man of integrity and always works in the public interest; honest in the performance of one's duties; have integrity and public spirit; have integrity and work always in the interest of the public;
廉潔可風 exemplary honesty;
廉潔清正 keep one's hands clean; perform one's duty cleanhanded;
廉潔之士 a gentleman of honesty; a pure official;
廉潔自律 perform one's duty honestly;

[廉明] clean-handed and clearheaded; incorruptible and intelligent;
節義廉明 purity, rectitude and moderateness;

[廉泉讓水] the mellowness of natural condition and social customs of a place;

[廉政] incorrupt government;
廉政建設 build a clean government;
~推進廉政建設 promote a clean government;

低廉 cheap; low;
清廉 free from corruption; honest and upright;

lian

【奩】 dressing case; toilet case;
妝奩 trousseau;

lian

【璉】 vessel used to hold grain offering for the imperial sacrifice;

lian

【漣】 (1) ripple; (2) weeping;

[漣洏] continual flow of tears;

[漣漪] ackers; ripples;
漣漪作用 ripple effect;
起漣漪 ripple;

lian

【憐】 pity; sympathize with;

[憐愛] have tender affection for; love tenderly; show tender care for;
憐近於愛 pity is akin to love; pity is but

one remove from love;
輕憐蜜愛 tender affection between a couple in love;

［憐才］ have sympathy for talented persons;

［憐憫］ commiserate; commiseration; have compassion for; pity; take pity on;
憐憫心 a sense of sympathy;
乞求憐憫 beg for mercy;
無需憐憫 need no pity;
引起憐憫 arouse pity;

［憐貧］ commiserate the poor; pity the poor;

［憐惜］ feel tender and protection toward; have pity for; sympathize with; take pity on;
憐香惜玉 feel compassion for womanhood; have a tender heart for the fair sex; tenderness toward woman;
惜老憐貧 kind to the old and generous to simple people; pity the aged and the poor;
惜香憐玉 tender to the fair sex; tender toward pretty girls;
惜玉憐香 tender to the fair sex; tender toward pretty girls;

哀憐 feel compassion for; pity;
愛憐 show tender affection for;
可憐 (1) pitiful; (2) miserable; (3) have pity on;
乞憐 beg for mercy; beg for pity;
自憐 self-pity;

lian

【蓮】 (1) lotus; water-lily; (2) pureland — Buddhist paradise;

［蓮花］ lotus; lotus flower;
蓮花坐 lotus position;
美如蓮花 as fair as a lily;
舌生蓮花 have the gift of the gab;
雨打蓮花 raindrops are plopping on the lotus;

［蓮藕］ lotus rhizome;

［蓮蓬］ seedpod of the lotus;
蓮蓬頭 (1) sprinkle head; (2) shower nozzle;

［蓮子］ lotus seed;

榴蓮 durian;
睡蓮 water lily;
雪蓮 saussurea involucrate;

lian

【濂】 a river in Hunan Province;

lian

【聯】 (1) ally oneself with; join; unite; (2) antithetical couplet;

［聯辦］ jointly organize;
聯辦單位 joint sponsoring unit;

［聯邦］ commonwealth; federation; union;
聯邦主義 federalism;

［聯播］ broadcast over a radio network; chain broadcasting; network broadcasting; radio hookup; simulcast; simultaneous broadcasting;
聯播節目 joint programme; network show;

［聯防］ joint command of defense forces; joint defense;
區域聯防 zone defence;

［聯冠］ successive winning of the number one title;

［聯號］ chain store;

［聯合］ (1) ally; coalesce; combine; join; unite; (2) combined; joint;
聯合辦學 jointly run a school;
聯合大學 federated university;
聯合國 the United Nations;
聯合會 association; federation; union;
~ 殘疾人聯合會 association for the disabled;
~ 工商業聯合會 industrial and commerce association;
~ 建築業聯合會 construction association;
~ 文學藝術界聯合會 association of literary and artistic circles;
聯合企業 united enterprises;
聯合投標 joint bids;
聯合王國 the United Kingdom;
聯合協作體 combined coordinating system;
聯合信息量 joint information content;
聯合作用 associative action;
政治聯合 political alliance;

［聯歡］ get-together; have a get-together;
聯歡會 get-together; party;

［聯機］ on-line;
聯機幫助 on-line help;
聯機編輯 on-line edit;
聯機編目 on-line cataloguing;
聯機操作 on-line operation;
聯機程序 on-line programme;
聯機處理系統 on-line processing system;
聯機方式 on-line mode;

聯機工作 on-line operation; on-line working;
聯機檢索系統 on-line retrie al system;
聯機交互系統 on-line interactive system;
聯機控制系統 on-line control system;
聯機命令語言 on-line command language;
聯機情報檢索 on-line information retrieval;
聯機設備 on-line equipment;
聯機實時操作 on-line real-time operation;
聯機實時處理 on-line real-time processing;
聯機輸入 on-line input;
聯機數據 on-line data;
~ 聯機數據處理 online data processing;
~ 聯機數據庫 on-line database;
聯機調試 on-line debugging;
聯機通信 on-line communication;
聯機文件 on-line file;
聯機系統 on-line system;
聯機用戶 on-line uscr;
聯機診斷 on-line diagnostics;
聯機終端 on-line terminal;
~ 聯機終端測試 on-line terminal test;
聯機裝置 on-line unit;

[聯加句] conjunct;
列出聯加句 listing conjunct;
列舉聯加句 enumerative conjunct;

[聯加語] conjunct;

[聯結] bind; concatenated; join; tie;

[聯絡] come into contact with; contact; get in touch with; liaise;
聯絡口譯 liaison interpretation;
聯絡人 contact person;
~ 聯絡人姓名 contact name;
保持聯絡 keep in touch; maintain the liaison;
無線電聯絡 radio contact;

[聯袂] side by side jointly;
聯袂出演 perform together;
聯袂而來 come together as a group;
聯袂而往 go together;
聯袂而至 arrive together;

[聯盟] alliance; coalition; confederation; league; union;

[聯綿] continuous; unbroken; uninterrupted;

[聯名] jointly; jointly signed;
聯名請願 send a petition with joint signatures;

[聯翩] in close succession; together;
聯翩而至 arrive one after another; come in close succession;
聯翩思考 brain-storming;

[聯賽] league matches;

[聯鎖] interlock; interlocking;
聯鎖器 interlocker;
~ 換向聯鎖器 reverse interlocker;
~ 台式電聯鎖器 electric table interlocker;
動力制動聯鎖 dynamic interlock;
渡線聯鎖 crossover interlocking;
互相聯鎖 mutual interlock;
繼電聯鎖 all-relay interlocking;
直接聯鎖 dead interlocking;
自動聯鎖 automatic interlock; automatic interlocking;

[聯網] interconnecting network; networking;
聯網運行 interconnected operation;
互聯網 Internet;
~ 互聯網地址 Internet address;
~ 互聯網服務提供商 Internet service provider;
~ 互聯網接入 Internet access;
~ 互聯網連接 Internet connection;
~ 互聯網使用 Internet use;
~ 互聯網用戶 Internet user;
~ 接入互聯網 access the Internet; connect to the Internet;
~ 瀏覽互聯網 surfing;
~ 使用互聯網 use the Internet;
外聯網 extranet;

[聯繫] communicate with; contact; contact with; connection; forge links with; get in touch with; get into touch with; get on to; in touch; keep in contact with; keep in touch with; keep links with; keep touch with; keep up with; maintain links with; mainties with; make contact; make contact with;
聯繫點 point of contact;
聯繫動詞 link verb;
保持聯繫 keep in contact; keep in touch; maintain contact; stay in contact; stay in touch;
~ 與…保持聯繫 keep in touch with...;
避免聯繫 avoid contact;
建立聯繫 establish contact;
緊密聯繫 close-knit links;
經常的聯繫 regular contact;
取得聯繫 get in contact;
失去聯繫 lose contact;
相互聯繫 connectedness;

有聯繫 be offiliated with; relate to;

[聯想] associate; connect in the mind;

聯想詞源學 associative etymology;
聯想記憶 associative memory;
聯想輸入 associative inputting;
聯想思維 associative thinking;
聯想學習 associative learning;
聯想意義 associative menaing;
聯想智力 associative intelligence;
聯想字 association word;
詞群聯想 group association;
詞語聯想 word association;
對比聯想 association by contrast;
感情上的聯想 affective suggestiveness;
自由聯想 free association;

[聯誼] friendship ties;

聯誼會 fellowship;

[聯姻] connections through marriages; unite by marriage;

聯姻締親 unite in wedlock;

[聯營] joint operation;

聯營公司 associated company; joint management company;
聯營合同 contract of association;
聯營體 joint venture;

[聯運] combined transport; through traffic; through transport;

邦聯 confederation;
並聯 parallel connection;
蟬聯 continue to hold a post or title;
串聯 contact; establish ties;
春聯 Spring Festival couplet;
對聯 antithetical couplet;
工聯 trade union;
關聯 be connected; be related;
互聯 interconnect;
綿聯 continuous; unbroken;
上聯 first line of a couplet on a scroll;
通聯 communications and liaison;
挽聯 elegiac couplet;
下聯 second line of a couplet on a scroll;
楹聯 couplet written on scrolls and hung on the pillars of a hall;

lian

【褳】 pouch worn at the girdle;

褡褳 (1) long rectangular bag with an opening in the middle for holding things; (2) jacket;

lian

【謰】 (1) talk endlessly; (2) combination of two closely related characters which form an inseparable thought unit;

lian

【鎌】 same as 鐮;

lian

【簾】 blinds; curtain; window curtain;

窗簾 curtain;
垂簾 hold court from behind a screen;
酒簾 streamer hanging in front of a wine shop;
門簾 door curtain;
眼簾 eye;

lian

【鬑】 hair hanging down the temples;

lian

【鐮】 sickle;

[鐮刀] sickle;

鐮刀菌 fusarium;
一把鐮刀 a sickle;

掛鐮 put away the sickle;
火鐮 steel;
開鐮 start harvesting;
釤鐮 scythe;

lian

【蘞】 a variety of vine;

lian

【鰱】 silver carp;

白鰱 silver carp;
花鰱 spotted silver carp; variegated carp;

lian³

lian

【臉】 (1) countenance; face; (2) front;

[臉兒] appearance;

做臉兒 do sth for the sake of appearance;

[臉紅] (1) blush; blush with shame; (2) flush with anger; get excited; get worked up;

臉紅脖子粗 one's face turns crimson with anger;
臉紅的 flushed;
臉紅耳赤 become red in the face; flush crison up to one's ears; flush up to one's ears;
窘得臉紅 be put to the blush; flush crimson with embarrassment;
臉一陣紅，一陣白 flushing and turning pale alternately; turn white and red

alternately;
臉漲緋紅 flush with embarrassment; turn red as a beetroot;
羞得臉紅 blush from shame; shame flushes one's cheeks;
漲紅了臉 turn red in the face;

[臉頰] cheek; face;
蒼白的臉頰 pallid cheeks;
匆匆的輕吻一下臉頰 give a peck on the cheek;

[臉孔] face;
板起臉孔 as grave as a judge; as grave as an owl; draw a long face; keep a stiff face; keep a straight face; keep one's face straight; look glum; make a long face; put on a solemn face; put on a stern expression; screw one's face up; wear a long face;

[臉面] (1) face; (2) sb's feelings; (3) self-respect;
不顧臉面 have no regard of face;
顧全臉面 save one's face;
為了臉面 for appearance's sake; for decency's sake;

[臉龐] face;
一張臉龐 a face;

[臉盆] washbasin; washbowl;

[臉皮] (1) cheek; face; (2) sense of shame;
臉皮薄 have a thin skin;
臉皮厚 have a thick skin;
臉皮真厚 of all the cheek;
厚臉皮 brazen; cheeky; chutzpah; have a thick skin; shameless; thick-skinned;
~厚臉皮的 cheeky;
老着臉皮 thick-skinned; unabashedly;
臉憨皮厚 have a thick skin; shameless;
沒皮賴臉 brazen-faced; dead to shame; hang on without any sense of shame; shamelessly; thick-skinned and hard to shake off; unshamed;
沒皮沒臉 as bold as brass; have no shame; shameless; thick-skinned and hard to shake off; unshamed; without shame;
撕破臉皮 put aside all considerations of face;
死皮賴臉 as bold as brass; brazen-faced and unreasonable; doggedly and shamelessly; importune shamelessly; shamelessly; thick-skinned and hard to shake off; utterly shameless; with a brazen face;

[臉軟] having too much consideration for sb's feelings;
臉軟心慈 faint-hearted and hesitant; shy and kind;

[臉色] (1) complexion; look; (2) countenance; expression; face; facial expression; puss;
臉色黯黑 have a swarthy complexion;
臉色不佳 don't look very well;
臉色慘白 look deathly pale;
臉色蒼白 pale;
臉色沉鬱 look very sour;
臉色發白 become pale; lose colour; pale about the gills;
臉色發青 blue in the face;
臉色發紫 black in the face; one's face turns purple with anger; with a frightened face;
臉色好轉 improve the complexion;
臉色紅潤 a ruddy complexion; rosy at the gills; rosy cheeks;
臉色焦黃 a sallow face; one's face is sallow;
臉色臘黃 a waxen complexion; one's face is like wax;
臉色青黃 one's face is sallow;
臉色鐵青 one's face is ghastly pale; one's face turns deathly pale; turn livid;
臉色嚴竣 one's face is stern; stern-faced;
臉色一沉 one's face falls;
臉色陰沉 blue about the gills; have a sombre countenance; look glum;
臉色陰鬱 have a face like a fiddle;
臉色莊重 wear a solemn look;
觀人臉色 read a person's face;
臉不改色 keep a straight face; keep one's countenance;
臉無人色 one's face is pale as death;
臉有饑色 hunger seems to be written on one's face;
臉有喜色 a happy expression on one's face;

[臉上] on the face;
臉上發光 a bright countenance; one's face shines;
臉上發燒 have one's ears burn;
臉上抹黑 cast manure on; fling manure on; sling mud at; throw mud at;
臉上貼金 blow one's own trumpet; put feathers in the caps of sb;
臉上無光 lose face; make sb lose face;

臉上寫字，表面文章 writing on one's face – (lit) an essay on the face; (fig) superficial; (coll) no real substance;

[臉膛兒] facial contour;

[臉硬] flinty; ruthless;

[臉子] (1) look; (2) face; (3) displeased appearance;

耍臉子 look at sb angrily;

甩臉子 pull a long face; turn a hostile look;

白臉 white face;

板着臉 keep a straight face; pull a long face; wear a long face;

繃臉 pull a long face;

繃着臉 assume a displeased look; assume a serious look; have a taut face; pull a long face; with a long face; with a straight face;

變臉 suddenly turn hostile;

long face;

isgraced; lose face;

ut; suddenly turn hostile;

face;

ave the face;

1) funny face; grimace; (2) mask used as a toy;

(1) blush; (2) flush with anger; get angry;

blubber one's face;

look good as a result of receiving honour;

pockmarked face;

月臉 moon face;

蒙着臉 cover one's face;

抹臉 suddenly become stern to sb; suddenly turn hostile;

胖圓臉 round bunchy face;

劈臉 right in the face;

破臉 fall out; turn against sb;

撲臉 blow on one's face;

賞臉 do me the favour;

四方臉 square face;

娃娃臉 childish face;

笑臉 smiling face;

鴨蛋臉 oval face;

圓核臉 round face;

長雀斑的臉 freckled face;

爭臉 do credit to;

轉臉 turn one's face;

嘴臉 countenance; feature; look;

lian4

lian

【楝】 melia japonica, a kind of tree;

lian

【煉】 (1) refine; smelt; (2) temper with fire; (3) polish;

[煉丹] make pills of immortality;

[煉鋼] steelmaking;

煉鋼廠 steel mill; steelworks;

煉鋼工人 steelworker;

百煉成鋼 be tempered into steel; steel is only made after it is tempered;

百煉鋼 well-tempered steel;

久煉成鋼 it takes plenty of tempering to produce fine steel; practice makes perfect;

[煉金] alchemy;

煉金術 alchemy;

百煉金 well-tempered gold;

[煉奶] condensed milk;

淡煉奶 evaporated milk;

[煉油] oil refining; rendering

煉油廠 oil refinery; petroleum refinery; refinery;

~地面煉油廠 grass-root refinery;

~化學煉油廠 chemical refinery;

~輕油煉油廠 skimming refinery;

~現代化煉油廠 modern refinery;

低溫煉油 low-temperature rendering;

蒸氣煉油 steam rendering;

吹煉 blow;

錘煉 (1) temper; (2) polish;

鍛煉 (1) steel; temper; (2) have physical training; take exercise;

精煉 concise; purify; refine; succinct;

熔煉 smelt;

塑煉 plasticate;

提煉 extract and purify;

冶煉 smelt;

lian

【練】 (1) white silk; (2) boil and scour raw silk; (3) drill; practise; train;

[練兵] troop training;

[練球] practice a ball game;

練球場 driving range;

[練習] practise;

練習本 exercise book;

練習簿 exercise book;

練習答案 answers to the exercises;

練習打字 practise at typing;

練習曲 etude;

按時練習 practise regularly;

對抗練習 counteracting exercise;
翻譯練習 translation exercise;
飛行練習 flight training;
杠鈴練習 barbell exercise;
經常練習 keep oneself in practice;
刻苦練習 practise assiduously;
課堂練習 classroom practice;
瞄準練習 aiming exercise;
做練習 do exercises;

[練字] practise calligraphy;

諳練 conversant; proficient; skilled;
閒練 familiar with; proficient in;
彩練 coloured ribbon;
操練 drill; practise;
晨練 morning calisthenics;
闖練 be tempered in the world; leave hom to temper oneself;
幹練 capable and experienced;
簡練 concise; succinct; terse;
教練 coach; drill; instructor; train;
精練 concise; pithy; terse;
老練 experienced;
歷練 steel oneself; temper oneself;
凝練 concise; condensed;
排練 rehearse;
熟練 proficient; skilled;
穩練 steady and prudent;
洗練 succinct; terse;
訓練 drill; train;
演練 drill;

lian

【斂】 (1) contract to fold; draw together; (2) collect; gather;

[斂步] hesitate to advance further; hold back from going; slow down one's steps;

[斂財] accumulate wealth by unfair means;

[斂法] tax law;

[斂錢] collect money illegally or immorally;

[斂容] assume a serious expression;

[斂聲屏氣] hold one's breath;

[斂足] hold back; hold one's steps and not go forward; withdraw one's footstep;
斂足不前 hold one's steps and refuse to go further;

聚斂 amass wealth by heavy taxation;
收斂 (1) disappear; weaken; (2) restrain oneself; (3) astringent;

lian

【殮】 prepare a body for the coffin;

[殮埋] shroud and bury;

殯殮 encoffin a corpse and carry it to the grave;
成殮 encoffin;
大殮 encoffin;
入殮 put a corpse into a coffin;
收殮 lay a corpse into a coffin;
裝殮 dress and lay a corpse in a coffin;

lian

【鍊】 forge; refine; smelt; temper;

lian

【歛】 (1) collect; gather; (2) hold together; (3) deduct; substract; (4) ask for sth; desire;

[歛財] accumulate wealth by unfair or illegal means;
詐欺歛財 obtain money under false pretences;

lian

【鏈】 chain;

[鏈接] chaining; link;
超鏈接 hot link; hyperlink;
地址鏈接 address chaining;
反向鏈接 backward chaining;

[鏈扣] cuff link;

[鏈輪] sprocket;
副軸鏈輪 countershaft sprocket;
離合器鏈輪 clutch sprocket;
曲軸鏈輪 crankshaft sprocket;

[鏈狀] chain;
鏈狀分析法 chain analysis;
鏈狀關係 chain relationship;

[鏈子] chain;
一條鏈子 a chain;

錶鏈 watchpchain;
帶鏈 band chain;
吊鏈 chain sling; sling chain;
防滑鏈 antiskid chain;
加速鏈 accelerating chain;
交錯鏈 alternating chain;
鉸鏈 hinge;
拉鏈 zip fastener; zipper;
平衡鏈 balancing chain;
手鏈 bracelet;
鎖鏈 (1) chain; (2) chains; fetters; shackles;
鐵鏈 iron chain; shackles;
項鏈 necklace;

lian

【瀲】 (1) overflowing water; (2) edge of a

large body of water;

lian

【戀】 (1) love; (2) feel attached to; long for;

［戀愛］ in a relationship; in love; love; romance;
戀愛角色 love interest;
戀愛期 courtship;
精神戀愛 platonic love;
三角戀愛 love triangle;
談戀愛 in love;
旋風式的戀愛 whirlwind romance;
在談戀愛 be in love;

［戀歌］ amorous song; love song;
感傷戀歌 torch song;

［戀己癖］ narcissism;
原發性戀己癖 primary narcissism;

［戀舊］ (1) long for the good old days; yearn for the past; (2) yearn for old friends;

［戀母情結］ Oedipus complex;

［戀慕］ have a tender feeling towards;

［戀情］ romance;
夭折的戀情 stillborn romance;
移情別戀 have a new sweetheart; love another person; pass one's affections to another person; transfer one's affections to sb else; turn one's back on one love and go with another;

［戀人］ lover; sweetheart;

［戀上］ fall for;

［戀屍狂］ necromania;

［戀…癖］ philia;
戀屍癖 necrophily;
戀童癖 paedophilia;
~戀童癖者 paedophile;
戀物癖 fetishism;

［戀獸慾］ zoolagnia;

［戀物症］ fetishism;

［戀棧］ unwilling to leave one's official post;

愛戀 be in love with; feel deeply attached to;
暗戀 love secretly;
初戀 first love;
單戀 unrequited love;
懷戀 think fondly of;
眷戀 be sentimentally attached to;
留戀 be reluctant to leave; can't bear to part;
迷戀 be infatuated with;
熱戀 be head over heels in love; be passionately in love;
失戀 be disappointed in a love affair;
貪戀 be unwilling to part with; hate to leave;
依戀 feel regret at parting from;

liang²

liang

【良】 (1) fine; good; (2) good people;

［良材］ (1) good timber; (2) able person;

［良策］ good plan; sound strategy;
終非良策 after all it's not a good plan; it's not a sound strategy after all;

［良辰］ fortunate hour;
良辰吉日 a fortunate hour and a lucky day; a lucky day; an auspicious occasion;
良辰佳日 beautiful day;
良辰美景 a beautiful day in pleasant surroundings; a fine day and a beautiful scene; a pleasant day coupled with a fine landscape;
良辰約會 heavy date;
吉日良辰 a lucky time and day;
美景良辰 a beautiful scene and a fine day; a fine landscape coupled with a pleasant day;

［良方］ (1) effective prescriptions; (2) good plan; sound strategy;

［良港］ good harbour;

［良工］ expert craftsmanship;
良工不尤器 the cunning workman does not quarrel with his tool;
良工苦心 a work embodying one's utmost effort; expert craftsmanship is the result of long practice and hard work;
良工巧匠 clever workmen; experienced artificers; skilled craftsmen; skillful workmen;
良工心苦 a work embodying one's utmost effort; expert craftsmanship; is the result of long practice and hard work;

［良好］ fine; good;
良好的開端，成功的一半 a good beginning is half the battle; well begun is half done;
前景良好 have a bright future; have good prospects;
運轉良好 in good working order;
秩序良好 in good order;
狀態良好 in good order;

［良機］ good opportunity;
良機難再 opportunity knocks but once;
良機勿失 don't let the good chance slip;

錯過良機 balk a fair chance; let a chance slip; let a good chance slip through one's fingers; miss a good opportunity; miss the boat; miss the bus; waste a good opportunity;
錯失良機 miss a golden opportunity;
等待良機 wait for a good chance;
莫失良機 don't let the fair opportunity slip;
失去良機 balk a fair chance; let a chance slip; miss a good opportunity; waste a good opportunity;
提供良機 hold out a fair chance;
痛失良機 let sth slip through one's fingers;
勿失良機 don't miss the boat; don't miss the good opportunity; make hay while the sun shines;
逸失良機 let slip an opportunity;
抓住良機 embrace a good chance;
坐失良機 miss the boat;

[良家] good and decent family;

[良久] a good while; a long time;

[良謀] good stratagem;
腹藏良謀 conceal a good stratagem deep in one's heart; have smart ideas up one's sleeve;

[良田] fertile farmland; good field;
良田美池 rich fields and fine pools;
良田萬頃 thousands of acres of fine land;

[良宵] happy evening;
莫虛良宵 not to miss the opportunity of this lovely evening;

[良心] conscience;
良心不安 have an uneasy conscience;
良心發現 be strung by conscience; one's better nature asserts itself;
良心話 frank words;
~說良心話 to be fair; to be frank;
良心遣責 one's conscience pricks one; pricks of conscience; the strings of conscience;
良心有愧 a guilty conscience; conscience-stricken;
良心責備 have a guilty conscience; have compunctions; one's own conscience rebukes one; prickings of conscience;
壞良心 depraved conscience; heartless;
沒良心 heartless; ungrateful; without conscience;
~沒有良心 consiencelss; have no conscience; get no conscience;
昧良心 disregard one's conscience;
~昧着良心 go aginst sb's conscience; outrage sb's conscience;
滅良心 go against conscience;
抹了良心 blot out all the moral sense; unconscionable;
憑良心 as one's conscience dictates;
喪盡良心 lose conscience; utterly conscienceless;
天理良心 conscience; one's better feelings; the course of nature and one's conscience;
違背良心 against conscience;

[良性] benign;
良性循環 a beneficial spiral; a benign cycle between; a favourable spiral; a sound cycle of economic activities; a virtuous circle;
良性腫瘤 benign tumour;

[良藥] good medicine
良藥苦口 a good medicine tastes bitter; bitter pills have wholesome effects; good advice, like medicine, is hard to take; good medicine is bitter to the taste;
良藥苦口利於病 bitter pills may have blessed effects; good medicine is bitter in the mouth; good medicine tastes bitter to the mouth; the remedy is tough; but it might be salutary;
良藥苦口利於病，忠言逆耳利於行 a bitter medicine cures the disease; although good medicine cures sickness, it is often unpalatable; likewise, sincere advice given for one's well-being, is often resented; faithful words offend the ear but are good for the conduct, good medicine is bitter in the mouth, but good for the disease; honest advice may be unpleasant to hear, but it is best; just as bitter medicine cures sickenss, so unpalatable advice benefits conduct; unpleasant advice, like bitter medicine, has welcome effect;
一劑良藥 a good medicine;

[良醫] good doctor;
久病成良醫 long illness makes the patient a good doctor; prolonged illness makes a doctor of a patient;

[良友] beneficial friend;

[良莠] the good and the bad;

良莠不辨 cannot distinguish weeds from useful plants; not know good from bad;

良莠不齊 rice-shoots and tares are growing together — good and bad people are mixed together; the good and the bad are intermingled;

不分良莠 not discriminate between good and bad;

衛良鋤莠 protecting the good and rooting out the evil;

[良緣] good match for marriage; happy match; harmonious union;

[良知] intuitive knowledge;

良知良能 innate knowledge and natural ability;

不良 bad; harmful; unhealthy;

純良 simple and honest;

從良 (of prostitutes) get married;

改良 (1) improve; (2) reform;

精良 excellent; superior;

善良 good and honest; kind-hearted;

天良 conscience;

溫良 gentle and kind;

賢良 able and virtuous;

馴良 tame and gentle;

優良 fine; good;

liang

【梁】 (1) roof beam; (2) bridge; (3) ridge; (4) the Liang Dynasty (502-557); (5) a surname;

[梁山] Liangshan Mountain; revolt;

逼上梁山 be driven to join the Liangshan Mountain rebels; be driven to revolt; be forced to do sth desperate;

迫上梁山 be driven to revolt; be forced to do sth desperate;

大梁 cross piece;

棟梁 pillar of the state; ridgepole and beam;

橫梁 crossbeam; transverse beam;

津梁 ferry crossing and bridge;

強梁 brutal;

橋梁 bridge;

主梁 girder;

liang

【涼】 (1) cold; cool; (2) disappointed; discouraged;

[涼菜] cold dish;

[涼茶] herbal tea;

[涼粉] bean jelly;

[涼風] cool wind;

涼風拂面 a cool wind soothes one's cheeks;

涼風掠面 a cool breeze brushes one's face; a cool wind sweeps one's cheeks;

涼風輕拂 a cool breeze is gently stirring;

涼風透骨 be chilled to the bones;

涼風習習 a cool breeze is blowing; a fresh light breeze is stirring; the air is soft and cool; the clear breeze blows gently; there is a light breeze blowing;

一股涼風 a cool breeze;

一縷涼風 an icy draught;

[涼快] nice and cool;

涼快極了 very cool indeed;

[涼帽] summer hat;

[涼薯] yam beans;

[涼爽] nice and cool; pleasantly cool;

涼爽清新 cool and sweet-smelling;

涼爽宜人 delightfully cool;

[涼絲絲] a bit cool; chilly; coolish; rather cool;

[涼颼颼] chilly;

[涼台] balcony; veranda;

[涼亭] alcove; kiosk; pavilion; summer house; wayside pavilion;

[涼鞋] foothold; sandal;

布涼鞋 cloth sandal;

露趾涼鞋 open-toed sandals;

皮涼鞋 leather sandal;

塑料涼鞋 plastic sandal;

一雙涼鞋 a pair of sandals;

悲涼 desolate;

冰涼 ice-cold;

蒼涼 bleak; desolate;

乘涼 enjoy the cool in a cool place;

風涼 cool;

荒涼 bleak and desolate; wild;

納涼 enjoy the cool in a cool place;

淒涼 desolate; dreary;

清涼 cool and refreshing;

秋涼 cool autumn days;

受涼 catch cold;

炎涼 change in attitude toward persons; change of temperature;

陰涼 shady and cool;

蔭涼 shady and cool;

着涼 catch a chill; catch cold;

liang

【量】 measure;

［量杯］ measuring cup;

［量度］ measurement;

［量壺］ measuring jug;

［量角器］ angular measure; protractor;

光學量角器 optical protractor;
繪圖量角器 draughtsmen's protractor;
視距量角器 tacheometric protractor;
萬能量角器 universal bevel protractor;

［量熱器］ calorimeter;

爆炸量熱器 bomb calorimeter;
等溫量熱器 isothermal calorimeter;
電氣量熱器 electric calorimeter;
動物量熱器 animal calorimeter;
乾式量熱器 dry calorimeter;
過熱器量熱器 superheater calorimeter;
恒壓量熱器 constant pressure calorimeter;
呼吸量熱器 respiration calorimeter;
激光量熱器 laser calorimeter;
記錄式量熱器 recording calorimeter;
節流量熱器 throttling calorimeter;
金屬絲量熱器 wire calorimeter;
絕熱量熱器 adiabatic calorimeter;
流動量熱器 flow calorimeter;
煤氣量熱器 gas calorimeter;
燃料量熱器 fuel calorimeter;
水流量熱器 water-flow calorimeter;
通用量熱器 universal calorimeter;
氧彈量熱器 oxygen-bomb calorimeter;
蒸氣量熱器 steam calorimeter;

測量 measure; survey;
端量 look sb up and down;
估量 appraise; estimate;
衡量 (1) judge; weigh; (2) consider; think over;
丈量 measure;
酌量 consider; use one's judgment;

liang

【粮】 food; grain; provisions; rations;

liang

【蜋】 dung beetle;

liang

【粱】 grain; sorghum;

liang

【踉】 same as 糧；

liang

【諒】

［諒陰］ (1) imperial mourning; (2) mourning shed;

liang

【輬】 (1) hearse; (2) sleeping carriage;

轀輬 sleeper carriage;

liang

【糧】 (1) food; grain; provisions; (2) grain tax paid in kind;

［糧倉］ barn; grain elevator; grain silo; granary; silo;

港口糧倉 port silo;

［糧草］ army provisions; provisions and fodder; rations and forage;

糧草齊備 provisions for the troops are already prepared; there are plentiful supplies of all kinds;
廣積糧草 accumulate great stores of rations and forage;

［糧店］ grain shop;

［糧盡彈絕］ one's food and ammunition run out; run short of food and ammunition;

［糧票］ food coupon; grain coupon;

［糧食］ cereals; food; grain;

糧食短缺 food shortage;
糧食供應 food supply;
糧食價格 food prices;
糧食恐慌 food scare;
糧食生產 food production;

［糧餉］ provisions and funds for troops;

粗糧 coarse food grain;
存糧 store up grain;
斷糧 run out of grain;
乾糧 solid food;
軍糧 army provisions;
口糧 grain ration;
秋糧 autumn grain crops;
食糧 food; grain;
屯糧 store up grain;
夏糧 summer grain crops;
餘糧 surplus grain;
雜糧 food grains other than wheat and rice;
主糧 staple food grain;

liang³

liang

【兩】 (1) two; (2) twice; (3) both; either; (4) a couple of; couple; (5) a few; some; (6) double (7) unit of weight;

［兩岸］ either side of the river or strait;

兩岸垂楊 on either side of the river there

are drooping willow trees;
兩岸關係 cross-strait relations;

[兩敗俱傷] both sides suffer; cause destruction to both sides; fight like Kilkeey cats; neither side gains;

[兩半] in half; in two; two halves;
分成兩半 halve;
切成兩半 cut sth in half; cut sth into two;
折成兩半 snap sth into half; snap sth into two;

[兩倍] double; twofold; twice as much;

[兩臂] arms;
兩臂側舉 arms sideways;
兩臂前平舉 arms forwards;
兩臂屈伸 arms bending and stretching;
兩臂上舉 arms upwards;

[兩邊] (1) both directions; both places; both sides; (2) both parties; both sides;
兩邊倒 cut both ways; lean now to one side, then to the other; waver;
兩邊得罪 offend both sides;
兩邊跑 go back and forth between two places;
兩邊説情 intercede between two parties;
兩邊討好 carry favour with both sides; ingratiate oneself with both sides; run with the hare and hunt with the hound;
兩邊為難 between two difficulties; in a dilemma;
馬路兩邊 on either side of the road;

[兩便] convenient to both; make things convenient to both; make things easy for both;
兩得其便 to the convenience of both;

[兩遍] twice;
唱兩遍 sing twice over;

[兩鬢] both temples;
兩鬢斑白 gray at the temples; gray temples; with graying temples;
兩鬢蒼蒼 graying at the temples;
兩鬢染霜 one's temples are as white as frost;
兩鬢如霜 one's hair is grayishly white at the temples;

[兩側] ambo-; two flanks; two sides;

[兩重] double; dual; twofold;

[兩次] twice;
兩次三番 again and again; many a time; over and over; repeatedly;

[兩抵] balance each other; cancel each other;

[兩端] both ends; either end; ends;
首鼠兩端 have two minds; hesitating; hesitating what course to adopt; in two minds; procrastinating; undecided in one's course of action; vacillating; waver in determination;
鼠首兩端 hesitate; in two minds; like a rat looking both ways; shilly-shally; unable to decide which to follow; undecided; undecided in course of action;
執其兩端 examine opposing views; hold both ends;

[兩段] two halves; two sections;
兩段攪拌 two-stage agitation;
撅成兩段 snap sth into two;
一刀兩段 a stroke of the sword cut...in two; be clean cut in two; be cut off at a single blow; cut in two; with one blow one cut...in two halves;
一剁兩段 cut into two at a stroke;

[兩耳] ears;
兩耳不聞窗外事 hold aloft from the affairs of the world; not bother about what's happening in the outside world; not care what is going on outside one's window; oblivious of the outside world;
兩耳不聞窗外事，一心祇讀聖賢書 both ears are shut to what goes on outside the window; busy oneself in the clasics and ignore what is going on beyond one's immediate surroundings; pay no attention to what is going on beyond one's study and bury oneself in the classics; the whole mind is concentrated on the sages' books;
兩耳塞豆 close one's ears to anything; shut one's ears to sth; turn a deaf ear to;
兩耳失聰 stone-deaf;
兩耳通紅 one's ears are scarlet;

[兩番] (of mahjong) two times;
翻兩番 double and redouble;

[兩分] dichotomy;

[兩行] two lines;
兩行詩 couplet;

[兩好合一好] friendship cannot stand always on one side;

[兩回事] two different matters; two entirely different things;

[兩極] (1) bipolar; two poles; (2) two opposing extremes;
兩極分化 bipolar differentiation; polarize; produce a polarization of;
兩極形容詞 bipolar adjective;
[兩頰] cheeks;
兩頰緋紅 a blush suffuses one's cheeks; a hot flush spreads over one's face; get red in the face;
兩頰紅潤 with rosy cheeks;
兩頰流淚 the tears fall down one's cheeks;
[兩可] both will do; either will do; it's all right one way or the other;
兩可之間 maybe, maybe not; not knowing which to choose;
[兩口] married couple;
兩口兒 a married couple; husband and wife;
兩口子 a married couple; husband and wife;
[兩肋] both sides of the chest;
兩肋插刀 help at the loss of one's life;
[兩淚] two lines of tears;
兩淚涔涔 two lines of tears keep on rolling down one's cheeks;
兩淚交流 with two streams of tears running down one's face;
兩淚如麻 one's tears are scattered near and far;
兩淚汪汪 eyes brimming with tears;
[兩立] co-exist;
誓不兩立 irreconciliable; resolve not to co-exist with; resolve to destroy sb or die in the attempt; swear not to co-exist with; swear not to exist together under the same heaven; swear that one of the two must be destroyed; vow to fight until the other party falls;
[兩利] benefit both; good for both sides;
[兩臉紫脹] one's face turns purple;
[兩碼事] two entirely different matters;
[兩面] both aspects; both sides; double; dual; two aspects; two sides;
兩面光 try to please both parties;
兩面夾攻 attack from both sides; be caught in a pincer attack; be caught in cross fire; between hammer and anvil; between the hammer and the anvil; between two fires; close in from both sides; make a pincer attack; under crossfire;
兩面進攻 two-pronged attack;
兩面派 double-dealer; double-faced person;
~耍兩面派 be double-faced; play the double game; resort to double-dealing;
兩面三刀 act a double part; double cross; double-dealing; double-faced; double-faced tactics; feign compliance while acting in opposition; have two faces; play a double game; two-faced;
兩面手法 carry fire in one hand and water in the other; double-dealing; double-faced tactics; double game;
兩面受敵 between two fires;
兩面討好 hold with the hare and run with the hounds; keep the favour of both sides; please both sides; run with the hare and hunt with the hounds; trim;
兩面性 dual character;
搞兩面派 an act of duplicity; double-dealing; live a double life;
[兩難] face a difficult choice; in a dilemma;
瘸退兩難 a lame person climbing up a mountain — in a dilemma;
事屬兩難 act either way is difficult;
[兩年] two years;
兩年一次的 biennial;
每兩年 every second year;
[兩旁] both sides; either side;
[兩棲] amphibian; amphibious;
兩棲車輛 amphibious vehicle;
兩棲動物 amphibian;
~兩棲動物學 amphibiology;
兩棲工兵 amphibian engineer;
兩棲攻擊艦 amphibious assault ship;
兩棲類學 amphibiology;
兩棲汽車 amphicar;
兩棲植物 amphibian;
兩棲作戰 amphibious warfare;
[兩全] have regard for both sides; satisfactory to both parites;
兩全其美 complete in both respects; have it both ways; keep the good points of both; make the best of both worlds; perfect in both respects; satisfactory to both sides; satisfy both sides; suit them both; want it both ways;
事難兩全 if you sell the cow, you sell her milk too; the sun does not shine on both sides of the hedge at once; you

cannot have it both ways; you can't eat your cake and have it; you can't seel the cow and drink the milk;

［兩人］ two persons;
兩人成伴，三人不歡 two's company, three's none;
兩人一組 in twos;
～兩人一組排隊 line up in twos;
判若兩人 a ghost of one's former self; a shadow of one's former self;

［兩三］ a couple;
兩三本書 a couple of books;
兩三日內 one of these days;
兩三天 a couple of days;

［兩手］ dual tactics;
兩手叉背 with one's hands behind one's back;
兩手叉腰 akimbo; with arms akimbo; with one's hands on one's hips;
兩手顫抖 one's hands quivering;
兩手空空 be left with nothing whatsoever; empty-handed; nothing is gained;
兩手一攤 spread one's two hands in despair;
兩手準備 have two strings to one's bow; prepare oneself for both eventualities;
～有兩手準備 have two strings to one bow;

［兩條心］ in fundamental disagreement; not of one mind;

［兩頭］ (1) both ends; either end; (2) both parties; both sides;
兩頭吃虧 make the worst of both worlds;
兩頭夾攻 attack from both ends;
兩頭戳舌 carry gossip;
兩頭落空 between two stools; between two stolls one falls to the ground; fall between two stools; if you run after two hares, you will catch neither; if you run after two horses, you will catch none; sit between two stools;
兩頭説情 intercede between two parties;
兩頭討好 hold with the hare and run with the hounds; keep the favour of both sides; please both sides; run with the hare and hunt with the hounds;
兩頭為難 find it difficult to satisfy two conflicting demands; find it hard to please either party;
話分兩頭 tell story from two angles;

［兩位］ two;
兩位數 ouble digits; double figures;

［兩下子］ a few tricks of the trade;
有兩下子 have it in one; have real skill; know a thing or two; know one's stuff;

［兩相］ both parties; both sides;
兩相猜忌 both sides nourish suspicions;
兩相抵消 cry quits;
兩相情願 both are willing; both parties agree of free will; both parties are willing; both sides agree; by mutual consent; with both sides agreeable;

［兩心］ (1) affection for each other; (2) disloyalty;
兩心相許 tact permission to each other;

［兩性］ (1) both sexes; (2) amphoteric;
兩性融合 amphimixis;
兩性色情 amphierotism;
兩性生殖 amphigenesis; amphigony;
兩性體 hermaphrodite;

［兩雄］ two strong forces;
兩雄不并立 a great man cannot brook a rival;
兩雄相遇，其鬥必烈 when Greek meets Greek, then comes the tug of war; when Greeks joined Greeks, then was the tug of war;

［兩眼］ one's eyes;
兩眼發黑 all has turned black before one's eyes; everything turns dark before one's eyes;
兩眼翻白 show the whites of one's eyes;
兩眼冒火 one's eyes flashing;
兩眼望穿 wear out one's eyes watching for sb;
兩眼圓睜 one's eyes nearly start from his head; with wide-open eyes;
兩眼直盯 fix a steady gaze upon; fix one's eyes on; keep one's eyes fixed on; keep one's eyes glued to; rivet one's eyes on;

［兩樣］ different;
兩樣看待 make fish of one and fowl of the other;

［兩用］ dual purpose;
兩用車 dual-purpose vehicle;
～客貨兩用車 station wagon;
～水陸兩用車 amphibious car;

［兩者］ both;
兩者并重 lay equal stress on both; pay equal attention to both;
兩者不可兼得 you can't eat your cake and

have it too;
兩者不可偏廢 neither can be neglected; neither should be overemphasized at the expense of the other;
兩者缺一不可 neither is dispensable;

斤兩 weight;
銀兩 silver;

liang
【倆】 ability; craft;

技倆 intrigue; trick;

liang
【魎】 a kind of monster;

魍魎 demons and monsters;

liang⁴
liang
【亮】 (1) bright; light; (2) enlightened; (3) show;
[亮點] bright spot;
[亮度] brightness; brilliance; luminance;
背景亮度 background brightness; background luminance;
~地面背景亮度 earth background brightness;
邊角亮度 corner brightness;
邊沿亮度 edge luminance;
表面亮度 surface brightness;
彩色亮度 colour brightness;
場亮度 field brightness;
單位亮度 unit brightness;
等效亮度 equivalent luminance;
峰值亮度 peak brightness;
高亮度 high brightness;
光點亮度 point brilliance;
光電亮度 photoelectric brightness;
光度學亮度 photometric brightness;
光亮度 luminance brightness;
光柵亮度 raster brightness;
光學亮度 optical brightness;
恒定亮度 constant luminance;
環境亮度 ambient brightness;
角亮度 angular brightness;
絕對亮度 absolute brightness;
可見亮度 visible brightness;
空間亮度 spatial brightness;
臨界亮度 critical luminance;
平均亮度 average brightness; mean brightness;
屏幕亮度 screen brightness;
青色亮度 cyan brightness;
色調亮度 tonal brightness;
色度亮度 chroma luminance;
聲亮度 acoustic brilliance;
實際亮度 intrinsic brilliance;
適應亮度 adaptation brightness; adaptation luminance;
視覺亮度 visual brightness;
視亮度 apparent luminance;
圖象亮度 image brightness; picture brightness;
相對亮度 relative brightness;
熒光屏亮度 phosphor screen brightness;
真亮度 real brightness;
真實亮度 true brightness;
正射亮度 normal brightness;
主觀亮度 subjective brightness;
總亮度 total brightness;
最大亮度 highlight brightness; maximum brightness;
最小亮度 minimum brightness;
[亮光] light;
亮光光 clean and bright;
一道亮光 a beam of light; a shaft of light;
一點亮光 a pinprick of light;
[亮晶晶] glistening; glittering; sparkling;
[亮堂堂] brilliant; brightly lit; well it;
[亮相] (1) make a stage pose; strike a pose on the stage; (2) declare one's position; state one's views;
[亮錚錚] glittering; shining;

擦亮 polish; rub; shine;
敞亮 light and spacious;
脆亮 clear and melodious;
發亮 shine;
光亮 bright; shiny;
豁亮 (1) roomy and bright; (2) resonant; sonorous;
明亮 (1) bright; light; (2) shining; (3) clear;
漂亮 (1) good-looking; pretty; (2) brilliant; remarkable; smart; splendid;
清亮 clear; crystal;
通亮 brightly lit;
透亮 (1) bright; transparent; (2) perfectly clear;
鮮亮 (of colour) bright; bright and shining;
響亮 loud and clear; resonant;
雪亮 bright as snow; shiny;
油亮 shining; shiny;
月亮 the moon;

liang
【倞】 (1) far; (2) request for;

liang
【晾】 (1) dry in the air; hang in the wind to dry; (2) dry in the sun;

[晾乾] airing; dry by airing; dry in the air; dry out;

[晾曬] air; field; sun-cure;

[晾衣] sun clothes;
晾衣架 clothes hanger; clothes horse;
晾衣繩 clothesline; washing line;

liang
【量】 (1) capacity; (2) amount; quantity; volume; (3) estimate; measure;

[量表] scale;
量表詞 scale word;
難度量表 scale of difficulty;
普遍性量表 scale of generality;

[量才] assess one's ability;
量才度德 estimate one's own moral qualities and ability;
量才錄用 appoint people with talent and ability to their respective positions; assign jobs to people according to their abilities; employ people according to their talents; give sb employment commensurate with his abilities; give sb work suited to his abilities; make appointments to a post according to qualifications;
量才使器 put sb in a position which he is fit for;
量才使用 appointments should be governed by qualifications;
量才選人 select men for their ability;

[量詞] classifier; measure word; quantifier;
不定量詞 indefinite measure word;
空量詞 empty quantifier;
普通量詞 general quantifier;
全稱量詞 generality quantifier;
~無界全稱量詞 unbounded universal quantifier;
有界量詞 bounded quantifier;

[量度] measure;
量度單位詞 measure partitive;
量度生格 genitive of measure;

[量化] quantize;
量化器 quantizer;
~差值量化器 differential quantizer;
~非線性量化器 non-linear quantizer;

[量力] estimate one's own strength or ability;
量力而行 act according to one's capability; act after calculating one's resources; do things according to one's abilities; do what is within one's means; do what one is capable of; do what one's strength allows; estimate one's strength before acting;
不量力 do not consider one's own strength in doing a job; lack of proper estimation of one's strength; not reckon oneself fairly;
不自量力 overplay one's hand; overrate one's ability; overreach oneself;
自不量力 bite off more than one can chew; do sth beyond one's ability; go beyond one's depth; have an incorrect estimation of one's own strength; lack of self-knowledge; not know one's own limitation; not to take a proper measure of oneself; overestimate one's ability; overestimate one's own strength; overestimate oneself; put a quart into a pint pot; unaware of one's own limitation;

[量小] small mind;
量小非君子，無毒不丈夫 a small mind makes not a gentleman, a real man lacks not in venom;
量小力微 small in number and weak in strength;
量小易怒 a little pot is soon hot;

[量子] quantum;
量子場論 quantum field theory;
量子電動力學 quantum electrodynamics;
量子電腦 quantum computer;
量子化 quantization;
~電荷量子化 charge quantization;
~方向量子化 directional quantization;
~幾何量子化 geometric quantization;
~能量量子化 quantization of energy;
~一次量子化 first quantization;
量子理論 quantum theory;
~相對論量子理論 relativistic quantum theory;
量子力學 quantum mechanics;
~相對論量子力學 relativistic quantum mechanics;
量子論 quantum theory;
量子數 quantum number;
量子統計 quantum statistics;

~量子統計力學 quantum statistical mechanics;
量子物理學 quantum physics;
量子學 quantum number;
虛量子 virtual quantum;
振動量子 vibration quantum;
作用量子 quantum of action;

比量 (1) take rough measurement; (2) make a gesture of measuring;
變量 variable;
標量 scalar quantity;
參量 parameter;
測量 gauge; measure; measurement; measuring; survey; surveying;
產量 output; yield;
常量 constant quantity;
充其量 at best; at most;
出產量 annual output; annual yield;
儲存量 storage capacity;
儲量 reserves;
忖量 (1) consider; think over; weigh; (2) conjecture; guess;
大量 (1) a great deal; a great quantity; (2) generous; large-minded; magnanimous;
打量 (1) measure sb with one's eyes; size up; (2) suppose; think;
掂量 estimate; weigh in the hand;
間量 floor space;
膽量 boldness; courage; guts;
等量 equal quantity;
電量 quantity of electricity;
定量 allowance; ration;
動量 momentum;
肚量 magnanimity; tolerance;
度量 magnanimity; tolerance;
發行量 amount of distribution;
飯量 appetite;
分量 weight;
服量 dosage; dose;
工作量 amount of work; work load;
供應量 amount of supply;
慣量 inertia;
過量 excessive;
海量 (1) magnanimity; (2) great capacity for liquor;
含量 content;
耗電量 power consumption;
恒量 constant;
洪量 (1) generosity; magnanimity; (2) great capacity for liquor;
極量 maximum dose;
計量 (1) measure; (2) calculate; estimate;
劑量 dosage; dose;
降雨量 rainfall;
交通量 volume of traffic;
較量 (1) compare in a contest; measure one's strength with; (2) argue; haggle;
盡量 as far as possible; to the best of one's ability;
酒量 capacity for liquor;
力量 (1) physical strength; (2) force; power; strength;
能量 (1) energy; (2) capabilities;
批量 batch; lot;
氣量 (1) ability and insight; (2) tolerance;
器量 tolerance;
熱量 heat capacity; quantity of heat;
容量 capacity;
商量 consult; discuss; talk over;
少量 a few; a little; a small amount;
身量 height of a person; stature;
食量 appetite; capacity for eating;
適量 appropriate amount;
輸電量 volume of power transmission;
數量 amount; quantity;
思量 condier; turn sth over in one's mind; weigh and consider;
吞吐量 the volume of freight handled;
無量 boundless; measureless;
限量 limit the quantity of;
銷售量 sales volume;
小量 a little;
雅量 (1) generosity; magnanimity; (2) great capacity for liquor;
音量 volume of sound;
雨量 rainfall;
質量 (1) quality; (2) mass;
重量 weight;
自量 estimate one's own ability or strength;

liang
【喨】 clear, resonant sound;

liang
【踉】 limp; walk unsteadily;
[踉蹌] stagger;
踉蹌而行 stagger along;
踉踉蹌蹌 press on hurriedly — advance with speed; roll from side to side as a drunken man; stagger about in all directions; stumble along; stumbling and wavering;

蹌踉 stagger;

liang
【諒】 (1) forgive; understand; (2) I expect; I suppose; I think;
［諒必］ most likely; probably;
諒必如此 I think it must be so; presumably it is so;
［諒察］ ask sb to understand and forgive oneself;
［諒解］ make allowance for; understand;
達成諒解 come to an understanding;
互相諒解 make allowance for each other; understand each other;

liang
【輛】 numeral adjunct for vehicles;

liao[1]
liao
【撩】 raise;
［撩起］ raise;
［撩衣］ hold up the lower part of a garment;

liao
【蹽】 (1) stride rapidly; walk swiftly; (2) leave quietly; sneak away;

liao[2]
liao
【聊】 (1) just; merely; (2) a little; slightly; (3) chat;
［聊表微忱］ as a token of good will; as a token of respect; it's merely to express my deference to you; just to show a little of my feeling; merely to show my good will;
［聊堪告慰］ this may be a comfort for you to know;
［聊賴］ sth to live for; sth to rely upon;
百無聊賴 be overcome with boredom; bored; bored stiff; bored to death; feel extremely bored; find time hang heavy on one's hands; idle along; in dreary and cheerless circumstances; suffer from boredom; the day is long to him who knows not how to use it; thoroughly bored; while away one's time aimlessly;
［聊聊］ have a chat;
聊聊數筆 with a few strokes;
［聊且］ for the moment; tentatively;
［聊勝於無］ a little is better than none; better small fish then empty dish; better some of a pudding than one of a pie; half a loaf is better than no bread; it's better than nothing; something is better than nothing; that will be better than one;
［聊天］ bat the breeze; chat; chew the fat; chinwag; chit-chat; fan the breeze; have a chat; have a chin; have a chinwag; have a dish of gossip; shoot bull; shoot the breeze; shoot the bull; swap lies; visit with;
聊天熱線 chat line;
聊天室 chat room;
來聊天 come in for a chat;
［聊以卒歲］ just to tide over the year; one barely makes both ends meet at the end of the year; reach the end of the year without being in debt;

無聊 (1) bored; (2) senseless; silly; stupid;
閒聊 chat;

liao
【尞】 a surname;

liao
【僚】 (1) companion; friend; (2) associate; colleague; subordinate;
［僚屬］ officials under sb in authority; staff; subordinates;
［僚佐］ assistants in a government office;

百僚 all the officials;
官僚 (1) bureaucrat; (2) bureaucratism;
幕僚 advisors;
同僚 colleague; fellow official;

liao
【寥】 (1) few; scanty; (2) deserted; silent;
［寥廓］ boundless; vast;
寥廓天際 the boundless sky;
［寥寥］ very few;
寥寥可數 just a sprinkling; very few;
寥寥數行 just a few lines;
寥寥數語 a few words; with a few mild comments;
寥寥無幾 a pitiably few; only a few; very few;
［寥落］ few and far between; scattered; sparse;

寂寥 lonesome; solitary;

liao
【憀】 (1) depend; rely; (2) disappointed; (3)

clear; easy to understand;

liao

【漻】 deep and clear;

liao

【嘹】 (of voice) resonant;

［嘹亮］ loud and clear; resonant;

嘹亮鸚鵡 vasa parrot;

liao

【寮】 (1) colleague; fellow official; (2) cottage; hut;

［寮棚］ hut; shed;

［寮屋］ squatter structure;

寮屋群 squatter structures;

liao

【獠】 (1) a primitive tribe in Southwest China; (2) fierce; (3) nocturnal hunting; (4) monster; wicked person;

［獠面］ fierce appearance; terrifying looks;

［獠牙］ buckteeth; fangs; long protruding teeth;

青面獠牙 ferocious features of an ogre; fiendish; fiendish monster; green-faced and long-toothed monster; have a fierce look on one's face; have fiendish features; monstrous-looking; terrifying in appearance;

liao

【撩】 (1) excite; provoke; stir up; (2) confused; disorderly;

［撩撥］ (1) banter; tease; (2) incite; provoke;

［撩逗］ entice; provoke;

［撩癢］ tickle;

liao

【潦】 (1) disappointed; disheartened; (2) without care;

［潦草］ (1) hasty and careless; illegible; (2) sloppy; slovenly;

潦草塞責 do a duty perfunctorily; do one's work in a careless and neglectful manner; make a show of doing one's duty; muddle through one's work; perform one's duty in a perfunctory manner;

膚皮潦草 casual; cursory; perfunctory;

［潦倒］ comedown; disappointed; down in luck; unhappy;

潦倒而死 die a dog's death; die like a dog;

潦倒困頓 down and out; in deep water; penniless and frustrated;

落魄潦倒 fall on evil days;

窮愁潦倒 crack up under the strain of poverty and sorrow;

窮困潦倒 down-and-out;

一生潦倒 be a failure all one's life; remain poor all one's life;

liao

【憭】 inclement; severe;

liao

【遼】 (1) distant; far; (2) the Liao River in Manchuria; (3) the Liao Dynasty (915-1125);

［遼闊］ extensive; vast;

［遼落］ open and spacious;

［遼遠］ distant; faraway; remote;

liao

【療】 cure; treat;

［療程］ course of treatment;

重複療程 repeat a treatment;

一個療程 a course of treatment

［療法］ therapy; treatment;

按摩療法 massotherapy;

保守療法 conservative treatment;

超短波療法 ultra-short-wave treatment;

超聲波療法 ultrasonic treatment;

傳統療法 orthodox medical treatment;

催眠療法 hypnotherapy;

電擊療法 electric shock therapy;

對抗療法 allopathy;

放射療法 radiotherapy;

封閉療法 block therapy;

弧形療法 arc therapy;

化學療法 chemotherapy;

抗生素療法 antibiotic therapy;

噴霧療法 aerosol therapy;

日光燈療法 sun-lamp treatment;

日光療法 sun-ray treatment;

熱療法 heat treatment;

溶血療法 hemolytic therapy;

睡眠療法 sleep therapy;

體育療法 physical exercise therapy;

物理療法 physiotherapy;

飲食療法 dietotherapy;

整體療法 holistic healing;

紫外線療法 ultraviolet ray treatment;

綜合療法 composite treatment;

組織療法 tissue therapy;

［療效］ curative effect;

降低療效 weaken the curative effect;

影響療效 affect the treatment;

有療效［的］ curative;
增強療效 improve the effect of a treatment;

［療養］ convalesce; recuperate; recuperation;
療養期 period of recuperation;
療養院 convalescent hospital; nursing home; rest home; sanatorium; vest home;
~工人療養院 worker's sanatorium;
去療養 go for a convalescence;

磁療 magnetism therapy;
電療 electrotherapy;
光療 phototherapy;
化療 chemotherapy;
理療 physiotherapy;
泥療 mud therapy;
水療 hydrotherapy; spa;
醫療 medical treatment;
治療 cure; treat;

liao

【繚】 wind round;
［繚亂］ confused; dazzling; in a confused state of;
眼花繚亂 be dazzled; dazzle one's eyes; in a daze; see things in a blur;
［繚繞］ coil up; curl up;
繚繞耳際 ring in one's ears;

liao

【鐐】 fetters; shackles;
［鐐銬］ fetters; manacles;

liao

【鷯】 wren;
［鷯哥］ grackle; tinkling;
［鷯雀］ wrentit;

鷦鷯 wren;

liao³

liao

【了】 (1) know clearly; understand; (2) end; finish; settle; (3) can;
［了案］ close a case; conclude a case;
［了不起］ amazing; and a half; extraordinary; far from common; proud and overweening; swell with pride; terrific;
了不起的 super-duper;
~了不起的成就 a dazzling achievement;
~了不起的人 phenom;
~沒甚麼了不起 nothing patent;
~那有什麼了不起 what does that matter anyway;
~真了不起 be really something;
［了得］ horrible; terrific;
還了得 this is atrocious;
~這還了得 how awful; how can such a thing be tolerated; how dare; how outrageous; how terrible; that is really going too far; this is simply atrocious; this is the limit; what insolence;
［了斷］ end; finish;
自尋了斷 commit suicide;
［了結］ bring to an end; finish; settle; wind up;
了結塵緣 go to one's account; hand in one's account; pay one's debt to nature; pay the debt of nature;
了結恩怨 dispose of grievance;
了結工作 finish up one's work;
了結一生 end one's life; put an end to one's life;
了結債務 pay off one's debts;
［了解］ comprehend; find out; acquaint oneself with; be tuned in to; understand;
了解客戶需求 be tuned in to customer needs;
了解內情 an insider; in the know;
了解下情 know the condition at the lower levels; know the feelings of the masses; know what is going on at the lower levels;
了解真相 know the facts;
不了解 do not understand; not familiar with;
增進了解 increase mutual understanding;
［了局］ (1) end; (2) a settlement; a solution;
［了了］ (1) know clearly; (2) end; finish; over; settle;
了了分明 perfectly clear;
不甚了了 do not quite understand; not know much about sth;
［了卻］ settle; solve;
［了然］ clear; understand;
了然如畫 as clear as daylight;
一目了然 able to tell its own story; an open book; as clear as the day; as plain as the nose on one's face; carry on its face; clear at a glance; easily comprehensible; he who runs may read; leap to the eye; meet one's eye; see at a glance; see with half an eye; stick out a mile; open-and-shut;

understand fully at a glance;

[了事] dispose of a matter; get sth over;

敷衍了事 attend to a matter negligently; do things carelessly; do things in a perfunctory manner; finish a job carelessly; give a lick and a promise; go through the motions; make a muddle of one's work; muddle through; play at; shuffle through one's work; skimp one's work; slight over; work perfunctorily;

[了無故實] without basis in fact;

[了之] end sth by; evade sth by;

一死了之 end one's troubles by death;

一笑了之 laugh away; laugh out of count;

一走了之 evade the solution of a problem by walking away from it;

臨了 finally; in the end;

明了 be clear about; understand;

末了 finally; in the end;

私了 settle in private;

完了 be over; come to an end;

未了 unfinished;

知了 cicada;

終了 be over; end;

liao

【釕】 ruthenium;

liao

【憭】 clear; intelligible;

liao

【蓼】 (1) smartweed; (2) name of a state in today's Henan province in the Spring and Autumn Period;

水蓼 knotweed;

liao

【燎】 singe;

[燎髮] to singe hair — a thing that can be done very easily;

[燎毛] to singe hair — a thing that can be done very easily;

[燎原] set the prairie ablaze;

勢如燎原 spread like wildfire;

liao

【瞭】 (1) sharp-eyed; (2) clear and bright;

[瞭亮] be clear about; understand;

[瞭然] clear and evident; plain and fully understandable;

liao

【蟟】 a kind of cicada;

liao⁴

liao

【料】 (1) anticipate; expect; (2) material; stuff; (3) feed; (4) makings;

[料到] expect; foresee;

[料理] arrange; manage;

料理後事 make arrangements for a funeral;

料理家務 manage household affairs;

精心料理 manage with delicacy;

日本料理 Japanese dish;

西式料理 western cooking;

[料想] expect; presume; think;

[料子] (1) cloth-making materials; (2) woollen fabric; (3) timber; (4) makings; stuff;

不出所料 as anticipated; as foreseen; as expected; as might have been expected; as predicted; happen just as expected; it does not exceed one's expectations; not at all surprising; not unexpected; things do not turn out beyond one's expectations; think as much; turn out just as expected; within expectation;

不料 to one's surprise; unexpectedly;

布料 cloth;

材料 (1) material; (2) stuff;

草料 fodder; forage;

綢料 silk; silk fabric;

肥料 fertilizer; manure;

廢料 waste; waste material;

敷料 dressing;

工料 labour force and materials;

加料 reinforced;

逆料 anticipate; foresee;

配料 burden;

燃料 fuel;

染料 dye; dyestuff;

史料 historical materials;

飼料 feed; fodder; forage;

塑料 plastics;

碎料 crushed aggregates;

調料 condiment; flavouring; seasoning;

塗料 coating; paint;

香料 perfume; spice;

笑料 joke; laughingstock;

顏料 pigment;

養料 nourishment; nutriment;

衣料 dress material; material for clothing;

意料 anticipate; expect;

飲料 beverage; drink;
原料 raw material;
照料 attend to; take care of;
資料 (1) means; (2) data; material;

liao
【廖】 a surname;

liao
【撂】 lay down; put down;
[撂地] deserted land;
[撂挑子] throw up one's job;
[撂下臉來] suddenly become serious;

liao
【燎】 (1) burn over a wider and wider area; (2) glow; shine;

liao
【瞭】 look down from a higher place;
[瞭望] keep a lookout; look down from a higher place; watch from a distance; watch from a height;
瞭望塔 conning tower; observation tower;
瞭望哨 observation post;

liao
【鐐】 a pronunciation of 鐐;

lie2
lie
【咧】 grin;
[咧咧] (1) gossip; speak carelessly; (2) cry; sob;

lie3
lie
【咧】 stretch the mouth horizontally;
[咧咧] (1) a baby's crying sound; (2) babble;
[咧嘴] grin;
咧嘴傻笑 grin like a Cheshire cat;
咧開嘴笑 one's mouth widens in a smile;
咧着嘴 grin;

lie4
lie
【列】 (1) arrange; line up; (2) enter in a list; list; (3) file; rank; row; (4) each and every; various;
[列車] train;
列車進站 the train is approaching the station;
磁浮列車 magnetic suspension train;
高速列車 high-speed train;
關節列車 articulated train;
貨運列車 freight train; goods train;
救護列車 ambulance train;
客運列車 passenger;
空中列車 aerial train; aerotrain;
氣墊列車 air cushion train;
通勤列車 commuter train;
郵政列車 mail train;
裝甲列車 armoured train;
[列出] enumerate; list;
列出聯加句 listing conjunct;
[列隊] file; line up; rank;
列隊前行 rank off;
列隊入場 march-in;
列隊退場 march-off;
列隊相迎 line up to welcome sb;
[列國] various countries;
遍游列國 travel throughout the world;
[列舉] enumerate; list;
列舉聯加句 enumerative conjunct;
[列聯] contingency;
複列聯 multiple contingency;
淨偏列聯 partial contingency;
均方列聯 mean square contingency;
~樣本均方列聯 sample mean square contingency;
平方列聯 square contingency;
[列強] powers;
[列席] attend a meeting in the capacity of an observer;
列席旁聽 attend the meeting as an observer;
列席作陪 sit at the same table with the guest of honour;
[列陣] array; in battle array;
[列柱] colonnade;
[列傳] collected biographies;

擺列 display in neat rows; place in order;
班列 relative ranks;
編列 arrange systematically; list;
表列 catalogue; list;
並列 be juxtaposed; put...on a par with; put...on an equal footing; put side by side; stand side by side;
陳列 display; exhibit;
出列 leave one's place in the ranks;
隊列 formation;
行列 ranks;
躋列 be ranked among; take one's position among one's equals;
開列 draw up; list;

臚列 enumerate; list;
論列 expound;
羅列 (1) set out; spread out; (2) enumerate;
排列 arrange;
前列 forefront; front rank; front row;
入列 fall in; take one's place in the ranks;
上列 the above; the above-listed;
系列 series; set;
下列 following; listed below;
序列 alignment; array;
一列 a column; a row;
陣列 array;
整列 (1) form neat lines; (2) the whole column; the whole row;

lie

【劣】 bad inferior; of low quality; poor;

[劣等] low-grade; of inferior quality; poor;
劣等貨 goods of inferior quality;

[劣根性] deep-rooted bad habits;

[劣蹟] a misdeed; a notorious record; an evil doing;
劣蹟斑斑 have many dishonorable records;
劣蹟昭彰 notorious; one's bad behaviour is well known; one's misdeeds are very evident to all;

[劣品] poor products;

[劣紳] evil gentry;

[劣勢] inferior position; inferior strength;

[劣質] inferior; of low quality; of poor quality;
劣質工程 shoddy construction;
劣質品 dross;
劣質商品 faulty goods; goods of poor quality; inferior goods;

卑劣 depraved; despicable; mean;
粗劣 cheap; of poor quality; shoddy;
低劣 inferior; low-grade;
惡劣 abominable; despicable;
猥劣 abject; base; mean;
拙劣 clumsy; inferior;

lie

【冽】 crystal-clear;

清冽 chilly; cool;

lie

【洌】 clear and transparent;

lie

【烈】 (1) intense; strong; violent; (2) fiery; staunch; sternic; upright;

[烈度] intensity;
烈度表 intensity scale;

[烈風] strong gale;
烈風淫雨 a strong gale and excessive rains; a strong wind and heavy rain;

[烈火] raging fire; raging flames;
烈火乾柴 a blazing fire and dry wood – from bad to worse;
烈火見真金 a genuine article can stand any test; a man of true worth will come out of a severe test unchanged; an honest person does not fear the light; genuine gold fears no fire; people of worth show their mettle during trials and tribulations; true fears not the flames of slander and injustice; true gold stands the test of fire;
烈火烹油 add strength to what is already strong; pour oil on the flames;
性如烈火 have a fiery disposition; have a very violent temper; one's nature is as a fierce fire;
一陣烈火 a blast of flame; a gust of fire; a gust of flame;

[烈酒] firewater; hard drink; strong drink;

[烈日] burning sun; scorching sun;
烈日當空 the fierce sun is hanging in the sky; the hot sun is high in the sky; with the scorching sun directly overhead;
烈日當頭 the blazing sun is shining right over one's head; the sun beats down; with the scorching sun directly overhead;
烈日似火 like a ball of fire, the sun scorches the earth; the sun blazes like a ball of fire; the sun hangs in the sky like a ball of fire;
烈日炎炎 the sun shines fiercely;
烈日炎炎，遍地似火 the inexhaustible sun seems to enforce his cumulative, innumerable fires upon every inch of ground;
中午烈日 midday sun;

[烈士] martyr;
烈士暮年，壯心不已 a noble-hearted man retains his high aspiration even in old age; the heart of a hero in his old age is as stout as ever;
哀悼死難烈士 mourn for the martyrs;

[烈暑] summer at its hottest;

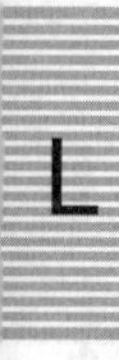

[烈性] (1) spirited; (2) strong; violent;
烈性漢子 a man of character;
烈性子 a fiery disposition;
[烈焰] roaring flame;

暴烈 fierce; violent;
慘烈 desolate; miserable;
熾烈 blazing; burning fiercely; flaming;
剛烈 staunch with moral integrity;
功烈 contribution; merits and achievements;
激烈 acute; intense; sharp;
劇烈 acute; fierce;
酷烈 (1) cruel; fierce; (2) heavy; strong;
猛烈 fierce; vigorous;
強烈 (1) strong; violent; (2) striking;
熱烈 ardent; enthusiastic; warm;
先烈 martyr;
壯烈 brave; heroic;

lie

【捩】 (1) twist with hands; turn; (2) rip apart; tear apart;
[捩傷] sprain;

lie

【裂】 left; crack; rend; rift; split;
[裂變] fission;
二分裂變 double fission;
核裂變 nuclear fission;
原子裂變 atomic fission;
[裂縫] (1) crack; cracking; cranny; crevice; fissure; hiatus; rift; rip; (2) fracture; rupture;
表面裂縫 face crack;
飛翅裂縫 fin crack;
宏觀裂縫 macroscopic cracking;
擠壓裂縫 compression fissure;
冷縮裂縫 cooling fissure;
彌合裂縫 span a rift;
扭曲裂縫 contorted fissure;
疲勞裂縫 fatigue crack; fatigue cracking;
網狀裂縫 chicken cracking;
微觀裂縫 microscopic cracking;
位錯裂縫 dislocation crack;
細裂縫 fine crack;
修補裂縫 mend a split;
一道裂縫 a crack;
[裂痕] crack; fissure; rift;
[裂化] cracking;
牀層裂化 bed cracking;
催化裂化 catalytic cracking;
等分裂化 equal cracking;
加氫裂化 hydrogen cracking;
深度裂化 drastic cracking;
[裂開] come apart; split open; rend;
[裂紋] chine; crack; fissure; flaw; gash;
底部裂紋 basal crack;
風化裂紋 atmospheric crack;
焊縫裂紋 bead crack;
環狀裂紋 annular crack;
時效裂紋 aging crack;
彎曲裂紋 bending crack;
[裂隙] chasm; crack; crevice; fissure; fracture;
[裂殖子] schizozoite;

爆裂 burst; crack;
崩裂 burst apart; crack;
臂裂 abdominal cleft;
迸裂 burst open; split;
拆裂 split open;
唇裂 cleft lip; harelip;
凍裂 frost cleft;
腭裂 cleft palate;
分裂 break up; split;
割裂 cut apart; separate;
決裂 break with; rupture;
皸裂 (of skin) chap;
龜裂 be full of cracks;
面裂 facial cleft;
破裂 burst; split;
氣孔裂 stomatic cleft;
氣門裂 spiracular cleft;
前中裂 antero-median cleft;
舌頜裂 hyomandibular cleft;
生殖裂 genital cleft;
鰓裂 gill cleft; visceral cleft;
咽裂 pharyngeal cleft;
炸裂 blast to pieces; blow up;

lie

【趔】 (1) fall behind; (2) awkward; unskilful;
[趔趄] reel; stagger;

lie

【鴷】 woodpecker;
蟻鴷 nryneck;

lie

【獵】 hunt;
[獵豹] cheetah;
[獵場] hunting ground;
[獵服] safari;
[獵狗] gun dog; hound; hunting dog;
一群獵狗 a pack of hounds;

［獵狐］ fox-hunting; hunting;
獵狐者 huntsman;
~阻止獵狐者 hunt saboteur;
［獵戶］ hunter; huntsman;
［獵獲］ capture in hunting; kill in hunting;
獵獲一隻虎 hunt down a tiger;
［獵鹿］ stalk deer;
獵鹿帽 deerstalker;
獵鹿犬 deerhound;
獵鹿人 deerstalker;
［獵鳥犬］ bird dog;
［獵奇］ hunt for novelty; seek novelty;
［獵槍］ hunting rifle; shotgun; sporting gun;
立式獵槍 over-and-under shotgun; superposed shotgun;
銀樣獵槍頭 a pewterpointed spear; a silvery spearhead made of wax; an impressive-looking but useless person; fine in appearance but of no use in reality;
［獵取］ hunt for; pursue; seek;
獵取功名 after fame; hunt for a good reputation;
獵取榮譽 chase after honours;
［獵犬］ gun dog; hunter; rach; sleuth; sleuth hound;
長耳獵犬 cocker spaniel;
野豬獵犬 boarbound;
一群獵犬 a pack of hounds;
［獵人］ hunter; huntsman;
女獵人 huntress;
［獵涉］ what one reads;
獵涉不精 read widely without intensive studies;
［獵手］ hunter;
［獵頭］ headhunt;
獵頭公司 head-hunting company;
獵頭者 headhunter;
［獵物］ bag; capture; chase; prey;
逼近獵物 gain on the chase;
捕獲獵物 bag the game; bring down the game; capture one's prey;
尋找獵物 hunt for one's prey;
［獵裝］ hunting jacket;

出獵 go hunting;
打獵 go hunting;
射獵 hunt with bow and arrow;
涉獵 do cursory ready;
狩獵 hunt;
田獵 hunt;
行獵 go hunting;
漁獵 fish and hunt;

lie

【躐】 overstep; transgress;
［躐等］ skip over the normal steps;

lie

【鬣】 (1) long beard; long whisker; (2) mane; (3) fin;
［鬣狗］ hyena;
［鬣羚］ serow;
［鬣蜥］ agama;

lin²
lin

【林】 (1) forest; grove; woods; (2) circles; (3) forestry;
［林地］ forest land; timberland; woodland;
［林靜鳥囀］ birds are spilling their song all over the quiet woods;
［林立］ stand in great numbers;
林立的高樓大廈 a forest of tall buildings;
檣帆林立 there are a great number of junks;
［林林總總］ in great abundance; numerous;
［林木］ (1) forest; woods; (2) crop; forest tree; sylva;
林木繁密 densely wooded;
林木森然 be thickly wooded with tall trees;
林木稀疏 the woods are sparse;
見木不見林 not to see the wood for the trees;
［林泉］ forests and streams;
林泉之士 a scholar of the forest and spring — a recluse;
甘歸林泉 willing to grow old among the forests and streams — retire from service;
［林深路隘］ the forest with narrow paths;
［林下］ in the country;
林下風範 a well-behaved and dignified country girl; the refined culture of the hermit;
歸隱林下 retire from official life;
退歸林下 retire from public life;
［林學］ forestry;
［林業］ forestry;
林業工人 forester;
［林蔭］ tree-lined; tree-shaded;
林蔭大道 avenue; boulevard; drive;

林蔭道 avenue; boulevard; drive;
林蔭樹 roadside plants;

矮林 brushwood; coppice;
北部林 boreal forest;
禪林 Buddhist temple;
叢林 (1) forest; jungle; (2) Buddhist monastery;
多層林 polylayer forest;
防風林 windbreak forest;
防護林 shelter-forest;
防沙林 sand-break forest;
防霜林 frost-break forest;
翰林 member of the Imperial Academy;
綠林 forest outlaws;
密林 thick forest;
農林 agriculture and forestry;
森林 forest;
山林 mountain forest; wooded mountain;
樹林 grove; woods;
泰加林 taiga;
椰林 coconut forest;
醫林 medical circles; medical faculty;
藝林 artistic circles;
雨林 rain forest;
原始林 primeval forest; virgin forest,
園林 gardens; park;
造林 afforestation;
竹林 bamboo forest; goves of bamboo;

lin

【淋】 drench; pour;

［淋巴］ lymph;
淋巴癌 lymphoma;
淋巴病 lymphopathia;
~ 性病性淋巴病 lymphopathia venerea;
淋巴發生 lymphogenesis;
淋巴發育不良 alymphoplasia;
淋巴發育不全 alymphoplasia;
淋巴管 lymphatic ducts;
淋巴管擴張 lymphangiectasis;
淋巴管瘤 lymphangioma;
單純性淋巴管瘤 simple lymphangioma;
~ 淋巴管炎 lymphangitis;
潰瘍性淋巴管炎 ulcerative lymphangitis;
淋巴結 lymph node;
~ 膽囊淋巴結 cystic lymph node;
~ 肺門淋巴結 hilar lymph nodes;
~ 闌尾淋巴結 appendicular lymph nodes;
~ 面淋巴結 facial lymph nodes;
~ 脾淋巴結 splenic lymph nodes;
~ 舌淋巴結 nodi lymphoidei linguales;
~ 臀上淋巴結 superior gluteal lymph nodes;
~ 臀下淋巴結 inferior gluteal lymph nodes;
淋巴結病 lymphadenopathy;
~ 皮膚淋巴結病 dermatopathic lymphadenopathy;
淋巴結結核 tuberculosis of lymph nodes;
淋巴結切除 lymphadenectomy;
淋巴結炎 lymphadenitis;
~ 局限性淋巴結炎 regional lymphadenitis;
淋巴結腫大 enlargement of the lymph nodes;
淋巴瘤 lymphoma;
~ 惡性淋巴瘤 malignant tumor;
~ 結節狀淋巴瘤 nodular lymphoma;
~ 濾泡性淋巴瘤 follicular lymphoma;
~ 彌漫性淋巴瘤 diffuse lymphoma;
皮膚淋巴瘤 lymphoma cutis;
淋巴球 lymphocyte;
淋巴肉瘤 lymphosarcoma;
淋巴細胞 lymphocyte;
淋巴腺 lymphatic gland;
~ 淋巴腺癌 cancer of the lymph glands;
~ 淋巴腺結核 lymphadenitis tuberculosis;
~ 淋巴腺炎 lymphadenitis;
淋巴組織 lymphoid tissue;

［淋病］ gonorrhea;

［淋花澆樹］ water flowers and trees;

［淋漓］ (1) dripping wet; (2) free from inhibition;
淋漓盡致 in an unrestrained and through-going way; most incisive; most vividly; scathingly; telling; thoroughly; vividly and incisively;
酣暢淋漓 heartily; to one's heart's content;
鮮血淋漓 drench with blood; drip with blood; fresh blood is streaming out; the blood oozes out;

［淋淋］ dripping;
汗淋淋 wet with sweat;
濕淋淋 drenched; dripping wet;
水淋淋 dripping with water;
血淋淋 (1) dripping with blood; (2) bloodstained; sanguinary;

［淋濕］ be soaked; splashed wet;

［淋雨］ be exposed to the rain; get wet in the rain;

［淋浴］ needle bath; shower; shower bath;
淋浴間 shower stall;

lin

【琳】 beautiful jade;

［琳琅］ beautiful jade; gem;
琳琅滿目 a feast for the eyes; a multitude of beautiful things dazzle the eyes; a superb collection of beautiful things; the eyes are fully filled with the sparkling of gems — resplendent with a multitude of beautiful things;

lin

【痳】 gonorrhea;
［痳病］ gonorrhea;
［痳症］ gonorrhea;

lin

【隣】 (1) neighbor; (2) nearby; neighbouring;

lin

【鄰】 (1) neighbours; (2) adjacent; near; neighbouring;
［鄰國］ neighbouring country;
［鄰接］ adjoin; border on; contiguous to; next to;
彼此鄰接 adjacent to each other;
［鄰近］ (1) adjacent to; close to; near; (2) proximity; vicinity;
鄰近的 adjacent;
鄰近地區 vicinity;
~在鄰近地區 in the neighbourhood; in the vicinity;
鄰近黎明 close to daybreak;
鄰近死期 neafr to death;
鄰近午夜 near midnight;
初等鄰近 elementary proximity;
就在鄰近 near at hand;
平凡鄰近 trivial proximity;
唯一鄰近 unique proximity;
相對鄰近 relative proximity;
［鄰居］ neighbour;
隔壁鄰居 next door neighbours;
［鄰里］ (1) neighbourhood; (2) neighbours; people of the neighbourhood;
鄰里互守 neighbourhood watch;
鄰里鄉黨 one's neighbourhood and associates;
［鄰人］ neighbour;
［鄰舍］ neighbour;
鄰舍街坊 one's neighbours and people in the street;
左鄰右舍 neighbouring families; neighbours on both sides; next door neighbours; one's neighbours;
［鄰域］ neighbourhood;
鄰域半徑 radius of neighbourhood;
鄰域中心 centre of neighbourhood;
基本鄰域 fundamental neighbourhood;
解析鄰域 analytic neighbourhood;
去心鄰域 deleted neighbourhood;
坐標鄰域 coordinate neighbourhood;
逼鄰 neighbouring;
比鄰 (1) neighbour; next-door neighbour; (2) near; next to;
卜鄰 choose neighbours;
地鄰 people whose fields border on each other;
緊鄰 close neighbour;
近鄰 near neighbour;
睦鄰 good-neighbourly;
毗鄰 adjoin; border on;
善鄰 get on well with one's neighbours;
四鄰 one's near neighbours;
相鄰 adjacent; adjoin;
鄉鄰 persons from the same rural neighbourhood;
擇鄰 select neighours;

lin

【嶙】 (of mountains) rugged;
［嶙嶙］ jagged peaks;
［嶙峋］ (1) craggy; jagged; rugged; (2) bony; thin;
怪石嶙峋 jogged rocks of grotesque shapes;
瘦骨嶙峋 a bag of bones; as lean as a rake; as thin as a lath; become as emaciated as a fowl; raw-boned; thin and bony; very skinny;

lin

【燐】 phosphorus;

lin

【璘】 the brilliance of jade;
［璘彬］ lustre of jade in riotous profusion;

lin

【遴】 (1) choose or select carefully; (2) a surname;
［遴選］ choose; select; select sb for a post;
遴選委員會 selection committee;

lin

【霖】 copious rain falling continuously;
［霖雨］ continuous heavy rain;
霖雨為災 continuous heavy rains bring disaster;
甘霖 a good rain after a long drought; timely rainfall;

lin

【麐】 the female of a fabulous animal resembling a deer;

lin

【磷】 (1) same as 燐, phosphorus; (2) water flowing between stones;

［磷細菌］ phosphorous bacterium;

白磷 white phosphorus;
赤磷 red phosphorus;
黑磷 metallic-phosphorus;
紅磷 red phosphorus;
黃磷 yellow phosphorus;
脱磷 dephosphorize;

lin

【臨】 (1) face; overlook; (2) arrive; present; (3) about to; just before; on the point of; (4) copy;

［臨別］ at parting; just before parting;
臨別前夕 on the eve of departure;
臨別一吻 parting kiss;
臨別贈言 a parting advice; a piece of parting advice; give a parting advice; words of advice at parting;

［臨產］ about to give birth;
臨產陣痛 birth pangs; labour pains;

［臨牀］ clinical;
臨牀的 clinical;
臨牀講義 clinical lectures;
臨牀療養 clinotherapy;
臨牀試驗 clinical trilas;
臨牀醫學 clinical medicine;
臨牀診斷 clinical diagnosis;

［臨到］ (1) about to; just before; on the point of; (2) befall; happen to;

［臨風］ to the wind;
臨風觸目，感恨傷懷 the winds and the view seem to press upon one's eyes and move his heart to a deep sadness;
臨風灑淚 sob out one's sorrow to the wind;
臨風招展 streaming in the wind;

［臨河地］ frontage;

［臨機］ as the occasion requires;
臨機處宜 make an emergency decision; rise to the occasion;
臨機處置 one can act properly on the spot; one has to see the thing occur and how it occurs before one knows what to do;
臨機應變 act as circumstances dictate; adapt to changing circumstances; cope with any contingency; decide as situation demands; decide on the spot; trim one's sail;

［臨界］ critical;
臨界安全 criticality safety;
臨界參數 critical constant; critical parameter;
臨界常數 critical constant;
臨界場 critical field;
臨界點 critical point;
臨界故障 critical failure;
臨界角 critical angle;
臨界體積 critical size; critical volume;
臨界溫度 critical temperature;
臨界壓力 critical pressure;
臨界值 critical value;
臨界質量 critical mass;
臨界狀態 critical state;

［臨近］ approach; close by; close on; close to; near; nigh;
臨近黎明 close on daybreak; just before daybreak;
臨近子夜 close upon midnight; just before mid-night;
考試就要臨近 the examination is close at hand;

［臨了］ finally; in the end;

［臨路地］ frontage;

［臨摹］ copy;

［臨難苟免］ shirk at the point of crisis; shrink in face of disaster;

［臨盆］ be giving birth to a child; in labour; parturition;

［臨深履薄］ as if on the brink of a chasm; as if treading on thin ice; as though one stands before a deep pond or walk on thin ice; proceed with extreme caution;

［臨時］ provisional; temporary;
臨時抱佛腳 embrace Buddha's feet in one's hour of need; make a frantic last-minute effort; seek help at the last moment;
臨時詞 nonce word;
臨時湊合 make do for the moment; offhand;
臨時措施 makeshift measures;
臨時的 makeshift;
臨時賠償 interim relief;

臨時演員 extra;
臨時語法 interim grammar;
臨時賬戶 provisional account;
臨時政府 a provisional government;

[臨死] on one's deathbed;
臨死不懼 affront death; fearless in the face of death; meet death with brave composure;

[臨潼斗寶] vie with each other to show off one's wealth;

[臨頭] befall; happen; impend;
大難臨頭 a great calamity is at hand; be faced with imminent disaster;
事到臨頭 at the last moment; now that the critical moment has come; when a thing comes to a critical moment; when the situation becomes critical; when things come to a head;
死到臨頭 be faced with imminent death; death knocks at the door; one's last hour has come;

[臨危] (1) dying; (2) facing death; in the hour of danger;
臨危不顧 leave sb in the lurch;
臨危不懼 betray no fear in an hour of danger; brace in a dangerous situation; face danger fearlessly; face danger without a tremor; fearless in the face of danger; meet danger with assurance; remain fearless before danger; never to turn a hair even in face of danger; undaunted in the face of perils; without fear in face of danger;
臨危不亂 calm in the hour of peril; take a tense situation calmly;
臨危受命 bravely lay down one's life at a crisis; sacrifice for the state in a crisis;
臨危授命 give up one's life in a critical situation; sacrifice for the state in a crisis;
臨危畏縮 quail before dangers;

[臨刑] just before execution;

[臨行] before leaving; on departure;
臨行告別 say goodbye to sb before departure;

[臨淵羨魚] stand on the edge of a pool and idly long for fish;
臨淵羨魚，不如退而結網 dry shoes won't catch fish; it's better to go back and make a net than to stand by the pond and long for fish — one should take practical steps to achieve one's aims;

[臨月] the month when childbirth is due;

[臨陣] before going to a battle;
臨陣觀戰 go out to watch the encounter;
臨陣換將 change horses in midstream; change horses in the middle of a stream; choose a new leader in the middle of an important activity;
臨陣磨刀 do a thing hurriedly at the last moment;
臨陣磨槍 grind the spear just before a battle — without due preparation; rush to make preparations at the last minute; sharpen one's spear only before going into battle;
臨陣退縮 chicken out; get cold feet; skulk when going to battle;
臨陣脱逃 desert on the eve of a battle; run away when going into battle; sneak away at a critical junction; turn tail;

[臨終] approaching one's end; immediately before one's death; on one's deathbed;
臨終聖禮 last rites;
臨終時 at the point of death; in the article of death;
臨終遺言 a deathbed testament; a dying wish; dying words; last words;
臨終囑咐 a deathbed injunction;

賁臨 your illustrious presence;
蹕臨 arrive; visit;
瀕臨 (1) border on; close to; near; (2) on the brink of; on the point of; on the verge of;
俯臨 overlook;
光臨 arrive; be present;
惠臨 arrive; be present;
駕臨 arrive; be present;
降臨 arrive; befall; come;
來臨 approach; arrive;
莅臨 arrive; be present;
面臨 be confronted with; be faced with;
迫臨 approach; get close;
遙臨 approach from afar;
照臨 illuminate; shine on;

lin
【瞵】 (1) look; stare; (2) poor-sighted;

lin
【轔】 (1) the noise of wheels; the rumbling of vehicles; (2) threshold; (3) wheel;

［鱗鱗］ rattle;

lin

【驎】 piebald;

lin

【鱗】 (1) scale; (2) like the scales of a fish;

［鱗次櫛比］ be arranged in close order; be arranged in rows; in orderly rows, like scales on a fish or the teeth of a comb; row upon row;

［鱗爪］ (1) scales and nails; (2) fragments; odd scraps; small bits;

東鱗西爪 bits and pieces; dribs and drabs; fragments; odds and ends;

盾鱗 placoid scale;

魚鱗 fish scale; scale;

lin

【麟】 unicorn;

［麟鳳］ rare treasures;

［麟角］ (1) unicorn horns; (2) rare things;

麟角鳳嘴 unicorn horns and phoenix beaks – something precious and rare;

［麟趾呈祥］ may the hoofs of the unicorn bring you much luck – may you have many good sons;

麒麟 unicorn;

lin³

lin

【凜】 (1) bleak; cold; desolate; (2) apprehensive; shiver with cold or fear; (3) awe-inspiring; imposing;

［凜冽］ biting cold; bitter cold; piercingly cold;

［凜凜］ (1) cold; (2) awe-inspiring; stern;

凜凜如生 it seems alive;

威風凜凜 awe-inspiring;

［凜然］ awe-inspiring; stern;

大義凜然 awe-inspiring righteousness; with a strong sense of righteouness; with stern righteousness;

lin

【懍】 awe-struck; awful; be filled with awe; inspiring awe;

［懍然敬畏］ be struck with awe;

lin

【廩】 (1) granary; (2) supply foodstuff; (3) stockpile;

［廩生］ scholars who live on government grants;

倉廩 granary;

lin

【檩】 the cross-beam in a house;

［檩條］ a purlin;

脊檩 ridgepiece; ridgepole;

lin⁴

lin

【吝】 closefisted; mean; stingy;

［吝嗇］ cheese-paring; mean; miserly; niggardly; skinflint; stingy;

吝嗇的 parsimonious; penny-pinching;

吝嗇鬼 cheapskate; miser; niggard; save-all; saver; skinflint;

吝嗇錢 mean about money;

非常吝嗇 as close as a clam;

［吝惜］ grudge; spare; stint;

吝惜精力 sparing of one's energy;

吝惜錢 stingy about;

鄙吝 (1) vulgar; (2) mean; miserly;

不吝 be generous with; not grudge; not stint;

慳吝 mean; stingy;

lin

【淋】 filter; strain;

［淋酒］ strain wine;

lin

【賃】 (1) hire; rent; (2) hireling;

出賃 let;

租賃 lease; rent;

lin

【磷】 thin;

lin

【藺】 (1) a variety of rush used in making mats; (2) a surname;

［藺因絮果］ the union in marriage of two people is predestined;

lin

【躪】 devastate; lay waste to a place; overrun; trample;

蹂躪 ravage; trample on;

ling¹
ling
【拎】 haul; take;

ling²
ling
【令】 a surname;

ling
【伶】 actor; actress;
[伶仃] be left alone without help; lonely;
孤苦伶仃 alone and friendless; alone and helpless; be left alone; be left in the world without kith and kin; forlorn and alone; friendless and penniless; isolated and wretched; orphaned and helpless; poor and destitute; sad and lonely;
~孤苦令仃，無依無靠 all alone in the world;
瘦骨伶仃 thin and weak; skinny and scrawny;
[伶俐] bright; clever; quick-witted; smart;
伶俐乖巧 clever and tricky;
百伶百俐 very intelligent; very smart;
[伶俜] lonely; solitary;
[伶人] actor; actress;

機伶 intelligent; quick-witted; smart;
優伶 actor; actress;

ling
【怜】 pity; sympathy;

ling
【泠】 (1) a clear sound; (2) mild and comfortable; (3) same as 伶; (4) a surname;
[泠泠] (1) chilly; cool; (2) (of voice) clear;

ling
【囹】 jail; prison;
[囹圄] jail; prison;
身入囹圄 be committed to prison; be sent to goal; be thrown into prison; behind prison bars;
身陷囹圄 be shut up in jail; be thrown into prison;

ling
【岭】 deep in the mountains;

ling
【玲】 tinkling of jade pendants;
[玲琅] tinkling of jades;
[玲玲] tinkling of pieces of jade;
[玲瓏] (1) exquisite; ingeniously and delicately wrought; (2) clever and nimble;
玲瓏剔透 (1) dainty and exquisite; exquisitely carved; (2) bright-minded; quick on the uptake with a ready tongue;
八面玲瓏 a perfect mixer in any company; adept in pleasing everybody; all things to all men; cover all sides beautifully; clever at dealing with people; manage to please everybody; pleasant all round; seek to please all parties; sail with every shift of wind; slick and foxy; slick and sophisticated; smooth and slick; smooth and tactful; smooth-faced; spacious and bright;
~八面玲瓏的人 artful person; good mixer; perfect mixer in any company; smooth article;
嬌小玲瓏 dainty and cute; delicate and exquisite; petite and dainty;
心竅玲瓏 very bright-minded;

ling
【苓】 (1) a variety of fungus; (2) tuckahoe; (3) licorice;

ling
【凌】 (1) approach; cross; pass; traverse; (2) bully; insult; intrude; (3) rise high; tower aloft; (4) ice; (5) a surname;
[凌波] ride the waves; walk over ripples;
凌波而來 come towards sb over the water;
凌波仙子 a fairy walking over ripples;
[凌晨] before dawn; the small hours; the wee hours;
凌晨動身 leave before dawn; set off before dawn; set out before dawn; start off before dawn; start out before dawn;
[凌遲] put to death by dismembering the body;
[凌駕] (1) override; place oneself above; (2) overrunning;
凌駕於他人之上 oppress others to advance oneself;
[凌空] fly high; high up in the air; soar aloft; tower aloft;
凌空飛過 soar through the air;
凌空飛舞 fly in the sky;

凌空飛越 fly across the sky;
凌空俯視 take a bird's-eye view;
凌空盤旋 hover in the sky;
[凌厲] quick and forceful; swift and fierce;
凌厲無前 energetic without precedent;
[凌亂] in a mess; in disorder; messy; untidy;
凌亂無序 confused and disordered; in a litter; in a mess;
[凌虐] maltreat; treat cruelly; tyrannize;
凌虐交加 add insult to injury;
[凌辱] humiliate; insult; maltreat;
凌辱婦女 assault a woman;
凌辱交加 add insult to injury;
備受凌辱 suffer wrongs and contumelies;
甘受凌辱 sit down under insults;
忍受凌辱 pocket an insult; put up with an insult; swallow down an insult;
受到凌辱 be humiliated; suffer humiliation;
[凌夷] decline;
[凌雲] reach the clouds; soar to the skies;
凌雲壯志 high aspirations; lofty aspirations;
壯志凌雲 aim high; cherish lofty aspirations;

冰凌 ice;
防凌 reduce the menace of ice run;
駕凌 place oneself above;
欺凌 bully and humiliate;
侵凌 encroach; infringe;

ling
【菱】 water chestnut;
[菱歌] songs of the water-caltrop pickers;
[菱角] water chestnut;
[菱鎂礦] magnesite;
[菱錳礦] rhodochrosite;
[菱面體] rhombohedron;
[菱形] rhomb; rhombic; rhombus;

ling
【瓴】 (1) concave channels; tilling; (2) bottle with a handle;

ling
【羚】 antelope;
[羚牛] takin;
[羚羊] antelope;
大羚羊 bongo;
一群羚羊 a troop of antelopes;

斑羚 goral;
麋羚 hartebeest;
牛羚 wildebeest;
岩羚 chamois;

ling
【翎】 feather; plume;
[翎毛] (1) feather; plume; (2) birds and animals (in painting);

鵝翎 goose feather;

ling
【聆】 hear; listen;
[聆教] listen to one's instructions;
[聆取] listen to;
[聆聽] listen to;
[聆悉] hear; learn;

ling
【蛉】 (1) dragonfly; (2) a kind of harmful insect;

白蛉 sand fly;
螟蛉 (1) corn earworm; (2) adopted son;

ling
【陵】 (1) high mound; (2) tomb of an emperor;
[陵谷] hills and valleys;
[陵居] live on the highland;
[陵墓] mausoleum; tomb;
[陵寢] mausoleum; emperor's resting place;
[陵替] decay; decline;
[陵夷] decay; decline; deteriorate;
[陵園] cemetery; tombs surrounded by a park;

皇陵 imperial mausoleum;
丘陵 hills; mounds;
山陵 (1) plateau; (2) imperial tomb;

ling
【舲】 a small boat with portholes;

ling
【軨】 (1) the framework on a carriage; (2) the wheels of a carriage;

ling
【鈴】 bell;
[鈴聲] ring tone; ringing sound of a bell; tinkle of bells;
鈴聲震耳 the sound of the bell shakes the ears;

報警鈴 emergency alarm;
閉塞鈴 block bell;
測試鈴 testing bell;
打鈴 striking bell;
單擊電鈴 single-stroke bell;
電鈴 electric bell;
分鈴 extension bell;
風鈴 Aeolian bells; wind chimes;
杠鈴 barbell;
呼叫鈴 call bell;
回答鈴 return bell;
極化鈴 polarized bell;
監視鈴 pilot bell;
警鈴 alarm bell;
門鈴 door bell;
鬧鈴 vibrating;
柵鈴 grid bell;
水下鈴 submarine bell;
信號鈴 annunciator bell;
啞鈴 dumb bell;
預告鈴 advance bell;
指示鈴 indicating bell;

ling

【零】 (1) nought; zero sign; (2) odd; with a little extra; (3) nil; nought; zero; (4) zero; (5) fractional; part; (6) wither and fall; (7) love; nil;

[零鏰兒] coins; small change;

[零點] null; zero;
電零點 electric null;
公共零點 common zeros;
聽覺零點 aural null;
虛零點 false zero;
一般零點 generic zero;

[零度] zero;
零度以下的 sub-zero;
~零度以下的天氣 sub-zero weather;
~零度以下的溫度 sub-zero temperature;
絕對零度 absolute zero;

[零工] (1) odd job; short-term hired labour; (2) casual labourer; odd-job man; part-timer; seasonal worker; temporary worker;

[零花] (1) incidental expenses; (2) pocket money;

[零活兒] chores; odd jobs;

[零件] component; part; spare part;
備用零件 spare parts;
鍍鉻零件 chrome-plated part;
交換零件 change parts;
生產零件 produce parts;
組合零件 assembly parts;

[零亂] all over the place; in a mess; in disorder;

[零落] (1) withered and fallen; (2) decayed; (3) scattered; sporadic;
零零落落 bits here and there; in a piecemeal fashion; scattering;
七零八落 all in a hideous mess; all upside down; at sixes and sevens; chaotic; everything upside down; fall apart into seven or eight pieces; in a state of confusion; in disorder; in great disorder; in ruin; in scattered confusion; scatter about in all directions; scattered here and there; scattering;

[零賣] (1) retail; sell retail; (2) sell by the piece; sell in small quantities;

[零錢] coins; loose change; money of small denominations; small change;
零錢包 change purse;
零錢別找了 keep the change;
小額零錢 small change;
找零錢 give the change;

[零散] scattered;
五零四散 all dispersed;

[零食] between-meal nibbles; snacks;
吃零食 eat a piece; nibble between meals;
喜歡吃零食 fond of snacks; like eating snacks;

[零時] zero hour;

[零售] retail; sell retail;
零售價 retail price;
零售會計 retail accounting;
零售商 retailer dealer;
~網上零售商 e-tailer; electronic retailer;
零售物價 retail price;
~零售物價指數 index of retail price;

[零碎] (1) fragmentary; piecemeal; scrappy; (2) bits and pieces; oddments; odds and ends;
零碎東西 odds and ends;
零碎活兒 odd jobs;
雞零狗碎 bits and pieces of things of little value; fragmentary; in bits and pieces; odds and ends; waifs and strays;
零七八碎 miscellaneous and trifling things; miscellaneous trifles; odds and ends; scattered and disorderly;

零敲碎打 bit by bit; by fits and starts; piecemeal approach;

[零星] (1) fragmentary; odd; piecemeal; (2) a few; a little; a small amount; (3) scattered; sporadic;
零星的證據 fragmentary evidence;
零星片斷 odds and ends;
零星時間 odd moments;
零星小雨 occasional drizzles; scattered showers;
零零星星 fragmentary; odd; piecemeal;

[零用] (1) small incidental expenses; (2) pocket money; spending money;
零用錢 pin money; spending money;
零用現金 petty cash;
~零用現金賬 petty cash account;

[零嘴] nibble between meals;
吃零嘴 nibble between meals; nibble tidbit; take snacks between meals;

[拆零] take apart and sell separately;

凋零 become withered and scatter about;
丁零 jingle; tinkle;
孤零零 all alone; lone; solitary;
飄零 (1) become faded and fallen; (2) drift about alone; lead a wandering life;
拾零 news in brief; sidelights; titbits;
涕零 shed tears;
有零 odd;

ling
【綾】 fine silk cloth;
[綾羅] different kinds of silk;
綾羅綢緞 silk and satin; silks and brocades;
一身綾羅 be dressed in silks and satins;
[綾子] damask silk; thin satin;

ling
【輘】 run over by a vehicle;

ling
【鴒】 wagtail;

ling
【霝】 (1) raindrops; (2) fall;

ling
【鯪】 (1) carp; (2) dace;
[鯪魚] dace;
土鯪魚 mud carp;

ling
【齡】 one's age;

超齡 exceed the age;
椿齡 great age; venerable;
黨齡 Party standing;
高齡 advanced age; venerable age;
工齡 length of service; seniority; working age;
婚齡 marriageable age;
及齡 reach a required age;
妙齡 (of a woman) puberty;
年齡 age;
適齡 of the right age;
髫齡 childhood;
學齡 school age;
役齡 enlistment age;
藝齡 length of sb's artistic career;
育齡 child-bearing age;
稚齡 tender age;

ling
【酃】 (1) a lake in Hunan; (2) a county in Hunan;

ling
【櫺】 (1) carved window-railings; sills; (2) wooden planks which join eaves with a house;

窗櫺 window lattice;

ling
【靈】 (1) clever; quick; sharp; (2) effective; efficacious; (3) intelligence; spirit; (4) elf; fairy; (5) bier;
[靈便] (1) agile; nimble; (2) easy to handle; handy;
腿腳不靈便 walk with difficulty;
腿腳靈便 dexterous of legs and feet; walk without any difficulty;
行動靈便 quick in action;
[靈車] hearse;
[靈丹] miraculous cure; panacea;
靈丹妙藥 cure-all; magic bullet;
靈丹聖藥 elixir; golden remedy; magic drug; miraculous cure; nostrum; panacea;
萬應靈丹 a remedy for all things; a sovereign remedy; an efficacious remedy for all diseases; aun universal panacea; cure-all; elixir vitae; miraculous medicine; panacea; the best medicine in the world;
[靈感] brainwave; inspiration; Promethean fire;

靈感閃現 a sudden flash of inspiration;
靈感思維 inspiration thinking;
靈感源泉 source of inspiration;

[靈光] (1) miraculous brightness; (2) bright light around the head of a god or Buddha in a picture;

[靈魂] soul; spirit; thought;
靈魂骯髒 sinister soul;
靈魂出竅 one's spirit has freed itself from one's body;
靈魂深處 in one's innermost soul; in the depth of one's soul; in the innermost recesses of the heart;
出賣靈魂 sell one's soul;
觸及靈魂 touch sb to his very soul; touch sb to the quick; touch sb to their soul; touch sb's innermost being;
喪失靈魂 lose one's soul;
相信靈魂 believe in spirits;

[靈活] agile; numble; quick;
靈活的 agile;
~不靈活的 clumsy;
靈活多元 flexible and diverse;
靈活反應 flexible response;
~靈活反應戰略 flexible response strategy;
靈活敏捷 active and intelligent; vivacious;
靈活性 flexibility;
~操作靈活性 operational flexibility;
~邏輯靈活性 logical flexibility;
~軟件靈活性 software flexibility;
頭腦靈活 agile mind; have a nimble mind; quick-minded; quick-witted;

[靈機] a brainwave; a sudden inspiration;
靈機一動 a flash of wit; a sudden inspiration; hit on a bright idea; suddenly have a brain wave;
靈機一動，計上心來 one has a brain wave and finds a good solution;

[靈柩] bier; coffin containing a corpse;
靈柩台 catafalque;

[靈媒] spiritual medium;

[靈敏] acute; agile; keen; quick; sensitive;
靈敏度 sensibility; sensitivity;
~單色靈敏度 monochromatic sensibility;
~絕對靈敏度 absolute sensitivity;
~最高靈敏度 ultimate sensitivity;
動作靈敏 active in one's movements;
反應靈敏 quick on the draw;
感覺靈敏 have keen senses;
視覺靈敏 quick-eyed; quick-sighted; keen of sight; quick of sight;
聽覺靈敏 have keen ears; have sharp ears; keen of hearing; quicked-eared;
頭腦靈敏 have a nimble mind; quick-minded; quick-witted;
味覺靈敏 have a sharp of taste;
嗅覺靈敏 have a good nose; have a keen nose; have a sharp sense of smell;

[靈巧] dexterous; ingenious; nimble; skilful;
靈巧的 adroit;
靈巧電話 smart phone;
靈巧敏捷 dexterous and quick; nimbly-bimbly;
身手靈巧 as nimble as a squirrel;
手很靈巧 quick with one's hands;

[靈堂] mourning hall;

[靈通] (1) well-informed; (2) serve the purpose; useful;

[靈犀] tacit comprehension; tacit understanding;
靈犀相通 extremes meet;
靈犀一點通 a meeting of minds;
~心有靈犀一點通 hearts which beat in unison are linked; hearts which have a common beat are linked;

[靈心慧性] intelligent and talented;

[靈性] intelligence;

[靈驗] (1) effective; efficacious; (2) accurate; right;
非常靈驗 work a treat; work like a charm; work like magic;

[靈芝] glossy ganoderma;

百靈 lark;
不靈 ineffective; not work;
辭靈 bow to the coffin before leaving;
魂靈 soul;
機靈 clear; intelligent;
精靈 demon; spirit;
空靈 flexible and elusive;
乞靈 seek help from;
起靈 move sb's coffin to the graveyard;
神靈 deities; divinities; gods;
生靈 the people;
失靈 be out of order;
守靈 keep vigil beside coffin;
停靈 keep a coffin in a temporary shelter before burial;
亡靈 the soul of a deceased person;
顯靈 make the ghost's or spirit's presence or power felt;

心靈 heart; soul; spirit;
性靈 natural disposition and intelligence; spirit;
英靈 spirit of a martyr or esteemed person;
幽靈 ghost; spirit;

ling
【醽】 a kind of wine;

ling³
ling
【領】 (1) neck; (2) collar; neckband; (3) main point; outline; (4) lead; usher; (5) have jurisdiction over; in possession of; (6) draw; get; receive; (7) comprehend; grasp; understand;

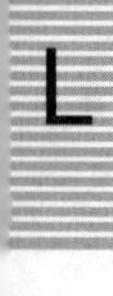

[領班] (1) foreman; gaffer; head waiter; (2) lead;
副領班 charge hand;
女領班 forewoman;
[領兵] (1) lead troops; (2) military officer;
[領唱] (1) lead a chorus; (2) the leading singer;
領唱者 cantor;
[領帶] choker; necktie; tie;
白領帶 white-tie;
打領帶 tie one's tie;
繩領帶 string tie;
一條領帶 a tie;
[領導] (1) lead; (2) leader;
領導層 leadership;
~軍事領導層 military leadership;
領導地位 headship; leadership;
領導風格 style of leadership;
領導機制 leadership mechanism;
領導結構 leadership structure;
領導科學 leadership science;
~領導科學體系 system of leadership science;
領導類型 type of leadership;
領導模式 leadership pattern;
領導目標 objective of leadership;
領導氣質 leadership disposition;
領導權 leadership;
領導人 leader;
~領導人角色 leadership role;
~領導人角逐 leadership contest;
~領導人選舉 leadership election;
~反對派領導人 opposition leader;
~工會領導人 union leader;
~有名無實的領導人 figurehead;
~政黨領導人 party leader;
~政府領導人 government leader;
領導體制 leadership structure;
領導心理學 leadership psychology;
領導行為 leadership behavior;
領導性格 leader's temperament;
領導學 science of leadership;
領導藝術 leadership skills;
領導影響力 leader's impact;
領導有方 exercise able leadership;
領導者 leader; standardbearer;
~市場領導者 market leader;
領導職能 function of leadership;
擔任領導 assume the leadership;
高層領導 top brass
集體領導 collective leadership; group leadership;
集中領導 collective leadership;
教育領導 educational leadership;
名義領導 titular leader;
實行領導 exercise leadership;
校內領導 inner-school leadership;
最高領導 top-ranking leaders;
[領隊] (1) lead a group; (2) group leader;
女領隊 majorette;
[領港] pilot a ship into or out of a harbour; pilotage
領港員 harbour pilot;
[領海] territorial waters;
[領航] (1) navigate; pilot; (2) navigator; pilot;
領航員 aerogator; navigator; pilot;
~二級領航員 second-grade navigator;
~三級領航員 third-grade navigator;
~四級領航員 fourth-grade navigator;
~一級領航員 first-grade navigator;
[領回] get back; take back;
[領會] comprehend; grasp; understand;
領會快 quick on the uptake;
領會慢 slow on the uptake;
容易領會 grasp easily;
深刻領會 acquire a deep understanding of;
未能領會 fail to see into...;
準確領會 understand accurately;
[領教] (1) much obliged; thanks; (2) ask advice; ask for sb's advice; seek sb's advice;
不敢領教 too bad to be accepted;
[領結] tie;
蝶形領結 bow tie;
[領巾] neckerchief; scarf;
[領進] introduce into; lead to; usher into;
[領句] superordinate clause;

[領空] airspace; territorial sky;

[領口] collarbands; neckline;

低領口 low neckline; plunging neckline;

方形領口 square neckline;

[領扣] collar stud;

[領路] lead the way;

領路犬 seeing eye dog;

[領略] appreciate; have a taste of; realize;

[領跑人] pacemaker; pacesetter;

[領情] appreciate the kindess; feel grateful to sb;

[領取] draw; go and get; receive;

[領事] consul;

領事裁判權 consular jurisdiction;

領事代辦 consular agent;

領事館 consulate;

代理領事 acting consul; consular agent; pro-consul;

副領事 vice-consul;

總領事 consul-general;

~ 總領事館 consulate general;

[領受] accept; receive;

[領頭] take the lead; the first to do sth;

領頭鬧事 the first to make trouble;

領頭起舞 lead off a dance;

領頭遊行 head up a parade;

[領土] territory;

領土完整 territorial integrity;

一塊領土 a slice of territory;

[領悟] comprehend; grasp; understand;

領悟得慢 slow on the uptake;

[領洗] be baptised;

[領先] go into the lead; in the lead; lead; take the lead;

領先地位 hold the lead; leadership;

~ 保持領先地位 hold the lead;

~ 處於領先地位 be on top;

~ 恢復領先地位 regain the lead;

~ 失去領先地位 lose the lead;

領先者 front-runner;

上半場領先 take the lead in the first half;

稍稍領先 have a slight lead;

遙遙領先 hold a safe lead;

以微弱優勢領先 have a narrow lead;

[領袖] leader;

公認的領袖 acknowledged leader;

名義上的領袖 figurehead;

[領養] adopt;

[領域] (1) domain; realm; territory; (2) domain; field; realm; sphere; world;

文學藝術領域 the realm of literature and art;

新領域 new frontiers;

一個領域 an area;

在研究領域 in the field of study;

政治領域 the world of politics;

[領子] collar;

揪住領子 grab sb by the collar;

本領 ability; capability; skill;

襯領 collar linging;

襯衫領 shirt collar;

船領 bateau neck collar;

垂領 draped neck collar;

待領 wait to be called for;

帶領 head; lead;

翻領 turndown collar;

方領 square neck collar;

綱領 guiding principle; programme;

高領 turtleneck collar;

海軍領 sailor collar;

雞心領 heart-shaped neck collar;

尖領 V-shaped collar;

將領 high-ranking military officer;

結花領 bow collar;

立領 stand-up collar;

青果領 shawl collar;

認領 claim;

首領 chieftain; head; leader;

率領 command; head; lead;

銅盆領 polo collar;

頭領 headman; leader;

西服領 tailored collar;

蟹鉗領 crabp-claw-shaped collar;

燕子領 wing collar;

要領 (1) essentials; gist; main points; (2) essentials;

衣領 collar;

翼領 wing collar;

引領 eagerly look forward to sth;

佔領 hold; occupy;

招領 announce the finding of lost property;

中立式領 mandarin collar;

ling

【嶺】 mountain; mountain peak; mountain range; the ridge of a mountain;

分水嶺 (1) divide; watershed; (2) line of demarcation; watershed;

海嶺 ridge;

山嶺 mountain ridge;

ling⁴
ling

【令】 (1) command; decree; order; (2) cause; make; (3) season; (4) an ancient official title; (5) excellent; good; (6) your; (7) drinking game; (8) short lyric; song-poem; (9) ream;

［令愛］ your daughter;
［令箭］ an arrow used as a token of authority;
［令郎］ your son;
［令名］ good name; good reputation;
［令親］ your relations;
［令人］ make one;

令人齒冷 arouse sb's scorn; invite contempt;
令人垂涎 make sb's mouth water;
令人惡心 disgusting;
令人發笑 make one laugh; provoke laughter; ridiculous;
令人髮指 get one's hackles up; make one bristle with anger; make one's blood boil; make one's hackles rise; make one's hair stand on end;
令人費解 beyond comprehension; elude understanding; pass comprehension;
令人鼓舞 most encouraging; most heartening;
令人寒心 bitterly disappointing; cast a chill over sb;
令人懷疑 arouse suspicion; open to suspicion;
令人激動 exciting;
令人驚心動魄 make sb stirried to the soul; shake sb to the core;
令人絕倒 have sb's sides shake with laughter; make sb's sides shake with laughter; sidesplitting;
令人落淚 bring tears to one's eyes; make the angels weep;
令人滿意 be all that could be desired; satisfactory;
令人毛骨悚然 bloocurdling; make sb's flesh creep; make sb's hair stand on end; make the flesh creep; send cold shivers down one's spine;
令人膩煩 pall on sb;
令人噴飯 choke with laughter; make sb spurt out his food by laughing; rouse laughter; sidesplitting;
令人捧腹 make one burst out laughing; make sb hold his sides with laughter; set people roaring with laughter; sidesplitting; throw sb into convulsions;
令人起敬 command esteem; command respect;
令人傾心 carry sb off her feet; sweep sb off his feet;
令人肉麻 make sb's flesh creep;
令人深思 call for deep thought; make one ponder; provide food for thought;
令人神往 alluring; attractive; cause one to crave for; cause sb to have a strong desire for; enchanting; fire one's imagination; have a strong appeal for one; look attractive; make one feel that one is in a certain place in spirit;
令人生氣 burn sb up; get on sb's wick; get sb going; get sb's blood up; get sb's dander up; get sb's goat; get sb's back up; get sb's monkey up. put sb's back up; put sb's monkey up;
令人生厭 make one feel disgusted;
令人生疑 be bound to arouse suspicion; liable to raise suspicion;
令人酸鼻 cause sb's heart to ache; make sb want to cry out of pity;
令人歎服 command admiration; compel admiration;
令人歎為觀止 to a miracle;
令人討厭 disgusting;
令人痛心 cut one to the heart;
令人頭痛 cause a headache;
令人惋惜 it is much to be regretted that;
令人望而生畏 awe-inspiring; forbidding;
令人笑死 make sb die of laughter;
令人心服 carry conviction;
令人心寒 cast a chill over one;
令人心酸 cause sb's heart to ache; make sb want to cry out of pity;
令人心碎 break a person's heart; break sb's heartstrings; break the heartstrings of sb; heart-breaking; heartrending;
令人興奮 exciting;
令人啞口無言 strike sb dumb;
令人啞然 strike sb dumb;
令人遺憾 it is to be regretted that...; regrettable;
令人咋舌 make one speechless; take one's breath away;
令人折服 carry conviction; command admiration; compel admiration;
令人振奮的 uplifting;

令人作嘔 disgusting; make one feel disgusted; make one feel like vomiting; make one nauseate; make one sick; make one throw up; make one's gorge rise; makesickish; mawkish; nasty; nauseating; revolting; turn one's stomach;

[令堂] your mother;

[令聞廣譽] a good reputation and an extensive praise;

[令儀令色] of good deportment and of good look;

[令尊] your father;

飭令 order;
傳令 transmit orders;
春令 (1) spring; (2) spring weather;
詞令 language appropriate to the occasion;
辭令 language appropriate to the occasion;
當令 in season;
調令 transfer order;
冬令 (1) winter; (2) climate in winter;
發令 start;
法令 decree; laws and decrees;
功令 decree; laws and decrees;
號令 verbal command;
喝令 shout an order;
即令 even; even if; even though;
將令 order;
節令 climate and phenology of a season;
禁令 ban; prohibition;
酒令 drinker's wager game;
軍令 military orders;
口令 (1) word of command; (2) password; watchword;
勒令 compel;
密令 secretly order;
明令 explicit order; formal decree;
命令 command; order;
秋令 (1) autumn; (2) autumn weather;
申令 order;
時令 season;
司令 commander; commanding officer;
條令 regulations;
通令 general order; issue a general order;
違令 disobey orders;
下令 give orders; order;
夏令 (1) summer; summertime; (2) summer weather;
責令 charge; instruct; order;
政令 government decree;
指令 (1) directive; instructions; order; (2) instruction;
縱令 even if; even though; though;

ling

【另】 another; other; separate;

[另函] (1) separate letter; (2) with another letter;

[另寄] post separately; post under separate cover;

[另外] besides; in addition; into the bargain; moreover;

[另行] at some other time; separately;
另行安排 make other arrangements;

[另議] be discussed separately;

liu¹
liu

【溜】 (1) glide; slide; (2) smooth; (3) slip away; sneak off;

[溜冰] (1) skate; slide on the ice; (2) ice-skate; ice-skating; roller-skating;
溜冰場 ice rink;
溜冰消遣 slide for a pastime;
溜冰鞋 roller skate;
~單排輪溜冰鞋 in-line skate;
溜冰者 blader;
去溜冰 go skating;

[溜槽] chute;

[溜躂] go for a walk; saunter; stroll;
溜躂回來 stroll back;
在林間溜躂 stroll in a wood;
在鄉間溜躂 stroll in the country;

[溜掉] decamp; make oneself scarce; slip away; slope off; vanish;

[溜放] humping;
單溜放 single humping;
雙溜放 double humping;
同時溜放 simultaneous humping;

[溜光] glossy; sleek; smooth;

[溜號] slink off; sneak away;

[溜開] shy off; shy away; slink;

[溜走] leave stealthily; scarper; slink; slip away; slope off;
突然溜走 skip off;

滑溜 sauté with starchy sauce;
順口溜 doggerel; jingle;

liu²
liu

【流】 (1) flow; run; (2) moving from place

to place; (3) circulate; spread; (4) change for the worse; degenerate; (5) a stream of water; (6) class; grade; rate;

[流弊] corrupt practices;
杜絕流弊 put a stop to corrupt practices; put an end to abuses;
以杜流弊 as to put an end to abuses;

[流變] evolution;
流變學 rheology;
~初等流變學 elementary rheology;
~高等流變學 advanced rheology;
~農業流變學 agricultural rheology;
流變儀 rheometer;
~毛細管流變儀 capillary rheometer;
~平衡流變儀 balance rheometer;
~正交流變儀 orthogonal rheometer;

[流槽] launder;
閉式流槽 enclosed launder;
分叉流槽 bifurcated launder;
熱流槽 heated launder;

[流產] (1) abortion; amblosis; (2) fall through; miscarriage; miscarry;
流產感染 septic abortion;
觸染性流產 contagious abortion;
傳染性流產 infectious abortion;
緊迫流產 imminent abortion;
難免流產 inevitable abortion;
膿毒性流產 septic abortion;
人工流產 abortion; artificial abortion; induced abortion;
特發性流產 idiopathic abortion;
完全流產 complete abortion;
晚期流產 late abortion;
習慣性流產 habitual abortion;
先兆流產 threatened abortion;

[流暢] easy and smooth;
文筆流暢 write with ease and grace;
線條流暢 the lines flow smoothly;
寫得很流暢 write fluently; write with fluency;

[流程] flow; flowsheet;
流程圖 flow chart; flow diagram;
~操作流程圖 operational flowchart;
~程序流程圖 programme flowchart;
~數據流程圖 data flowchart;
~系統流程圖 system flowchart;
~詳細流程圖 detail flowchart;
~綜合流程圖 general flowchart;
工作流程 workflow;
混雜流程 hybrid flowsheet;
取樣流程 sampling flowsheet;
熔煉流程 smelter flowsheet;
通用流程 generalized flowsheet;

[流出] effusion; outflow;

[流傳] circulate; hand down; pass current on; spread;
流傳很快 circulate rapidly;
流傳甚廣 spread far and wide;
代代流傳 hand down from generation to generation; transmit from generation to generation;
廣泛流傳 be widely circulated; spread abroad; spread far and wide;
以廣流傳 so that it may spread far and wide;
眾口流傳 spread from mouth to mouth;

[流竄] flee hither and thither;
東流西竄 drift around; fool about; fool around;

[流宕忘返] roam about and forget to return; rove and forget to return; stray and forget to return;

[流蕩] flow; loaf about; roam; rove;

[流動] (1) circulate; flow; run; (2) going from place to place; mobile; on the move; (3) streaming;
流動比率 liquid ratio;
流動的 itinerant;
流動人口 floating population; mobile population;
流動售貨車 vending van;
流動書攤 book mobile;
流動性 fluidity;
~表觀流動性 apparent fluidity;
~過剩流動性 excess liquidity;
~靜止時流動性 fluidity at rest;
~蠕變流動性 creep fluidity;
~現金流動性 cash liquidity;
~最佳流動性 primary liquidity;
流動資產 current assets;
流動資金 circulating capital;
胞質流動 cytoplasmic streaming
緩慢流動 flow sluggishly;
加速流體流動 accelerating fluid flow;
聚集流動 aggregative flow;
向上流動 upwardly mobile;
向下流動 downwardl mobile; flow downward;
血液流動 the flow of the blood;
原生質流動 protoplasmic streaming

[流毒] (1) exert a pernicious influence; (2)

harmful effect; pernicious influence;
流毒甚廣 exert a widespread pernicious influence; exert its poisonous influence widely; spread its poison widely;

[流度] fluidity;
表觀流度 apparent fluidity;
運動流度 kinematic fluidity;

[流芳] leave a good name; leave a reputation;
流芳百世 go down to history; go down to posterity; hand down a good reputation to a hundred future generations; have a niche in the temple of fame; leave a good name to posterity; render one's name immortal; transmit a good name forever; good reputation flowing down for long ages; one's name will perpetually be remembered by posterity; one's name will remain forever a sweet rememberance;

[流放] (1) banish; exile; send into exile; (2) float downstream;

[流風餘韻] remaining influence;

[流感] flu; grippe; influenza;
地方性流感 endemic influenza;
得了流感 caught flu;
甲型流感 influenza A;
禽流感 Avian Flu;
一陣流感 a bout of influenze;

[流光] (1) streamer; (2) time;
流光易逝 time flies; time passes quickly;
導航流光 pilot streamer;
地面流光 ground streamer;
結合流光 junction streamer;

[流過] flow past; traverse;

[流汗] all of a sweat; dripping with sweat; in a sweat; sweat; sweat pour off sb; sweat streaming;
開始流汗 break a sweat; break sweat;

[流會] fail to convene a meeting for lack of a quorum;

[流盡] drain away;

[流寇] roving bandits; roving rebel bands;

[流浪] lead a vagrant life; on the tramp; roam about;
流浪漢 derelict; hobo;
流浪江湖 move about the country without definite employment; roam about all corners of the country;
流浪街頭 roam the streets; run the street; wander about the streets;
流浪貓 alley cat;
流浪者 fugitive; tramp; transient; vagrant;
到處流浪 wander here and there;
在流浪 wander around;

[流淚] all tears; burst into tears; burst out crying; one's eyes filled with tears; tears come to one's eyes; tears filled one's eyes; tears started from one's eyes; weep;
暗中流淚 tears steal down one's cheek;

[流離] be forced to leave home and wander about; become homeless and wander from place to place;
流離顛沛 homeless and wandering from place to place;
流離遷徙 wander about and scatter everywhere;
流離失所 be compelled to leave their homes and roam about for safety; be forced to leave home and wander about; become destitute and homeless; become displaced; constantly on the move; homeless and wandering from place to place; live the life of a refugee; lose one's home; on the rove and out of one's element; wander about homeless;
流離轉徙 migratory and homeless; move from place to place; on the move; wander about;

[流里流氣] rascally;

[流利] (1) fluent; lucid and nice; smooth; (2) fluently; smoothly;
説話流利 speak with fluency;

[流麗] smooth and beautiful;

[流連] delay going; linger around; linger on; linger over; reluctant to part; unwilling to leave;
流連忘返 enjoy oneself so much as to forget to go home; indulge in pleasures without stop; linger on without any thought of leaving;
流連轉徙 wander about and scatter everywhere;

[流量] discharge; flow; flowrate; flux; rate of flow;
流量計 flowmeter;
~截面流量計 area flowmeter;
~膜盒流量計 aneroid flowmeter;
~鋭孔流量計 borehole flowmeter;

~ 轉子流量計 rotameter;
遠距指示轉子流量計 romote indicating rotameter;
錐形蕊柱轉子流量計 tapered centre-column rotameter;
車流量 volume of traffic;
空氣流量 air mass flow;
利益流量 benefit flow;
氯氣流量 chlorine flowrate;
人流量 traffic;
~ 網站人流量 web traffic;
增大流量 augmented flow;

[流露] betray; reveal; show unintentionally;
流露感情 show one's feelings;
流露實情 reveal the truth;
盡情流露 give free vent to;

[流落] lead a wandering life in poverty; strand; wander about destitute;
流落江湖 lead a vagrant life; live a vagabond life;
流落街頭 wander about the streets; live a homeless life;
~ 流落街頭的兒童 street children;
流落他鄉 be stranded in a strange land; become homeless in another country; lead a wretched life far from home; wander destitute far from home;

[流氓] blackguard; blighter; cad; gangster; gaolbird; hoodlum; hooligan; knave; loafer; rascal; rogue; ruffian; scoundrel; villain; wide boy; wrongdoer;
流氓阿飛 gangsters and hooligans; riffraffs; scoundrels and rascals;
流氓行為 roguery;
大流氓 a great rogue;
耍流氓 act indecently; act rudely; behave like a hooligan; behave like a hoodlum; take liberties with women;
小流氓 bovver boy; punk;
一群流氓 a gang of ruffians; a horde of hooligans; a horde of ruffians;
足球流氓 football hooligans;

[流年] (1) a fleeting time; (2) prediction of a person's luck in a given year;
流年不佳 have a year of ill luck;
流年不利 an unlucky year; one's down on one's luck this year; the current year is not favourable to you;
似水流年 time passing swiftly like flowing water; youth slips away like flowing water;

[流派] school; sect;
新流派 new school;

[流入] inflow; influx;
流入俗套 drift into inanities;
超重流入 hyperpycnal inflow;
外資流入 foreign capital inflow;
現金流入 cash inflows;

[流散] wander about and scatter;
大流散 diaspora;

[流沙] shifting sand;

[流失] (1) be washed away; flow away; run off; (2) bleed; wastage;
人才流失 brain drain;
土壤流失 soil loss;
相流失 phase bleetd;
柱流失 column bleed;

[流逝] elapse; glide; pass;
光陰流逝 time flows away;
時光流逝 time moves on;

[流水] (1) running water; stream; (2) turnover in business;
流水不腐 running water never becomes putrid; running water never gets stale;
流水潺潺 gurgling water; streams purl; the murmuring of running water; the stream flows with a rich susurrus;
流水淙淙 a gurgling stream; the murmuring of running water; the stream flows with a rich susurrus;
流水高山 like flowing water and high mountains – bosom; sympathetic appreciation of good music;
流水落花 like fallen flowers carried away by the flowing water; shattered to pieces; sweeping every bit into the dust; utterly routed;
流水人情 human feeling is like running water;
流水賬 current account; day-to-day account; journal account;
~ 流水賬戶 running account;
流水作業 assembly line method; conveyer system; flow process;

[流俗] current custom; prevalent custom;

[流速計] current meter;

[流態] fluid;
流態化 fluidization;
~ 流態化性能 fluidizability;
~ 廣義流態化 generalized fluidization;
~ 經典流態化 classical fluidization;
~ 聚式流態化 aggregative fluidization;

~ 稀相流態化 gas phase fluidization;

[流體] fluid;

流體動力學 fluid dynamics;
航空流體 aerofluid;
加速流體 accelerating fluid;
輸送流體 conveyance fluid;
斜壓流體 baroclinic fluid;

[流通] circulate;

流通貨幣 active money;
流通經濟學 circulation economics;
流通領域 circulation field;
流通渠道 circulation channel;
流通證券 active securities;
保持空氣流通 maintain the circulation of air;
產業流通 industrial circulation;
廣泛流通 circulate extensively;
貨幣流通 currency circulation;
金融流通 financial circulation;
強制流通 compulsory circulation;
商品流通 commodity circulation;
實際流通 active circulation;
信用流通 credit circulation;

[流亡] be forced to leave one's native land; exile; go into exile;

流亡者 displaced person;

[流紋岩] rhyolite;

[流線] streamline;

流線型 streamline;
等熵流線 isentropic streamline;
零級流線 zero-order streamline;
瞬時流線 instantaneous streamline;

[流向] afflux;

[流星] falling star; meteor; shooting star;

流星塵 meteoric dust;
流星軌跡 meteor trajectory;
流星群 meteor stream; meteor swarm; meteoric stream; meteoric swarm;
~ 八月流星群 August meteors;
~ 寶瓶流星群 Aquarids;
~ 金牛流星群 Taurids;
~ 獵戶流星群 Orionids;
~ 麒麟流星群 Monocerids;
~ 獅子流星群 Leonids;
~ 雙子流星群 Geminids;
~ 天秤流星群 Librids;
~ 天龍流星群 Draconids;
~ 天琴流星群 Lyrids;
~ 仙后流星群 Cassiopeids;
~ 仙女流星群 Andromedids;
~ 小熊流星群 Ursids;
~ 英仙流星群 Perseids;
流星餘跡 meteor trail;
流星雨 meteor shower;
~ 流星雨輻射點 meteor shower radiant;
火流星 fireball;
疾似流星 as swift as a shooting star; very quick;
快如流星 as swift as a falling star;
眼如流星 one's eyes are like glittering stars;
一顆流星 a meteor;

[流行] all the fashion; all the go; all the mode; all the rage; all the vogue; become the mode; bring into fashion; catch on; come into fashion; come into style; come into vogue; come into wear; fasionable; in fashion; in general wear; in mode; in style; in the fashion; in the groove; in vogue; popular; prevalent; take on;

流行病 epidemic;
~ 流行病學 epidemiology;
流行病學家 epidemiologist;
~ 水致流行病 water-borne epidemic;
流行的 fashionable; modish; popular;
流行歌曲 popular songs;
流行款式 a style in fashion;
流行起來 come in; come into fashion; come into vogue;
流行式樣 a style in vogue; the prevailing fashions;
流行術語 buzzward;
流行小說 popular fiction;
流行一時 all the rage; in vogue;
流行音樂 pop music;
流行語 catchphrase; in-word;
流行樂 pop music;
~ 流行樂明星 pop star;
不再流行 go out of fashion; no longer in fashion; out of fashion;
十分流行 all the fashion;
越來越流行 become more and more popular;
正在流行 in fashion; in vogue;

[流形] manifold;

代數流形 algebraic manifold;
解析流形 analytic manifold;
特徵流形 characteristic manifold;
有界流形 bounded manifold;

[流血] bleed; shed blood;

流血成河 bloody fighting; massacre;

流血衝突 a sanguinary conflict; bloody conflicts;
流血犧牲 at the cost of one's blood and sacrifices; shed one's blood and lay down one's life;

[流言] floating rumours; gossips; rumours;
流言蜚語 backalley gossips; evil and baseless gossip spread behind one's back; lies and slanders; rumours and gossip; scuttlebutt; slanderous rumours;
~流言蜚語滿天飛 wild rumours are in the air;
流言紛飛 rumours and gossip are everywhere;
流言止於智者 a wise man does not believe in rumours;

[流域] catchment area; drainage basin; watershed;

[流質] fluid; liquid;

[流轉] (1) on the move; roam; wander about; (2) the circulation of sth;

L

暗流 (1) undercurrent; (2) undercurrent of evil social trends or idiological tendencies;
輩流 people of one's generations;
奔流 (1) flow at great speed; pour; pour out; (2) racing current; swift current;
迸流 gush; pour; spit out in all directions; spurt;
表流 surface current; surface flow;
逋流 linger; remain; stay;
側流 effluent;
汊流 tributary of a river;
常流 the average;
潮流 (1) tidal current; tide; (2) trend;
車流 stream of traffic; stream of vehicles;
傳流 circulate; hand down; spread;
導流 diversion;
倒流 flow backwards;
電流 electric current;
對流 confection;
二流 second class; second rate;
風流 (1) distinguished and admirable; (2) talented in letters and unconventional in life style; (3) dissolute; loose;
海流 (1) ocean current; (2) seawater;
寒流 (1) cold current; (2) cold wave;
合流 (1) flow together; (2) collaborate; work hand in glove with sb; (3) merge;
河流 rivers;
洪流 mighty torrent; powerful current;
匯流 converge; flow together;
激流 rapids; torrent; turbulent current;
急流 (1) rapid stream; torrent; (2) jet flow; jet stream;
交流 exchange; interflow;
徑流 runoff;
巨流 mighty current;
輪流 do sth in turn; take turns;
名流 celebrities; distinguished personage;
末流 the later and decadent stage of a school of thought, et;
泥流 mud-rock flow;
逆流 adverse current; countercurrent;
女流 woman;
暖流 warm current;
偏流 direct current flowing on the base of a transistor;
片流 laminar flow;
漂流 (1) be driven by the current; drift about; (2) lead a wandering life;
平流 advection;
氣流 (1) air current; airflow; (2) breath;
遷流 elapse; pass;
潛流 undercurrent; underflow;
清流 clear stream;
曲流 meander;
熱流 (1) thermal current; (2) warm current;
人流 stream of people;
上流 (1) upper reaches of a river; (2) belonging to the upper circles; upper-class;
水流 (1) rivers; streams; waters; (2) current; flow;
水往低處流 the natural flow of water always proceeds from a higher level to a lower one; water finds its own level; water naturally flows downhill;
鐵流 flowing molten iron;
湍流 swift current; torrent;
外流 drain; outflow;
紊流 turbulent flow;
穩流 steady flow;
渦流 (1) the circular movement of a fluid; (2) eddy current;
下流 (1) lower reaches of a river; (2) base; dirty; mean; obscene;
星流 stardrift;
洋流 ocean current;
引流 drainage;
湧流 fow;
源流 source and course of a river;
整流 rectify;
支流 (1) tributary; (2) minor aspects; nonessentials;

中流 mainstream;
主流 (1) main current; main stream; (2) essential aspect; main trend;

liu

【留】 (1) remain; stay; (2) ask sb to stay; keep sb where he is; (3) keep; reserve; save; (4) grow; let grow; wear; (5) accept; take; (6) leave;

[留班] fail to go up to the next grade; stay down;

[留不住錢] burn a hole in sb's pocket;

[留步] don't bother to see me out;

[留出] keep out; set apart; set aside;

[留傳] leave sth to pass on to later generations;

[留存] (1) keep; preserve; (2) extant; remain;
留存收益 retained earnings;

[留待] wait until;

[留底] office copy;

[留話] leave a message; leave word;

[留級] fail to go up to the next grade; repetition; stay down; stay in the same grade;

[留局候領] general delivery;

[留客] ask a guest to stay; detain a guest;

[留戀] (1) can't bear to part; reluctant to leave; (2) recall with nostalgia;
留戀不去 linger about a place;
留戀不捨 unwilling to part with;
留戀過去 yern for the past;
留戀忘返 have much enjoyment and forget to go back home; linger on without any thought of leaving; so enchanted as to forget about home;
留戀一段經歷 recall an experience;

[留門] leave a door unlocked;

[留名] leave behind a good reputation;
留名千古 leave a good reputation for ages;
留名史冊 go down in history;
雁過留聲，人去留名 the wild goose leaves a scream on flying pass; man leaves a reputation after death;

[留難] make things difficult for sb; put obstacles in sb's way;
故意留難 make difficult for sb;

[留念] accept as a souvenir; keep as a souvenir;
合照留念 have a group photo to mark the occasion;
照相留念 take a photo as a memento;
作為留念 as a keepsake;

[留情] show mercy;
毫不留情 act in cold blood; give no quarter; give...no mercy; in spades; not pull any punches; relentlessly; show...no mercy; take off the gloves to; with the gloves off; without gloves;
手下留情 lenient; pull one's punches; show mercy;

[留任] hold over; remain in office; retain a post;

[留神] careful; keep one's eyes on the ball; keep one's eyes peeled; look out for; look sharp; take care;
留神提防 look out for;
過馬路時要留神 be careful when you cross the road;
一不留神 be caught napping;

[留聲機] electric gramophone; gramphone; phonograph;
單速留聲機 one-speed gramophone;
電動留聲機 electric gramophone;
無線電留聲機 radio gramophone;

[留守] stay behind to take care of things;

[留宿] (1) put up a guest for the night; (2) put up for the night; stay over night;

[留下] stay behind; wait behind;
留下過夜 stay for the night;
留下後果 entail consequences;
留下禍根 sow seeds of future trouble;

[留校] (1) stay at school during vacation; (2) retain to work in a college after graduation;

[留心] be careful; take care;
留心腳下 watch your steps;
留心看門 watch the door closely;
留心偷竊 on guard against theft;

[留學] study abroad;
留學生 students studying abroad;
~外國留學生 overseas student;
自費留學 self-funded study abroad;

[留言] leave a message;
留言板 message board;
~網上留言板 message board;
電話留言 phone message; telephone message;
記下留言 take a message;
簡短留言 brief message; short message;

[留洋] study abroad;

[留意] alive to; careful; keep an eye on; keep one's eyes open; look out;
留意細節 pay attention to details;
沒留意 not to notice sb; not to notice sth;
[留影] have a picture taken as a souvenir; take a photo as a memento;
[留用] continue to employ; keep on; remain in employment;
[留職] retain one's post;
留職留薪 paid leave;
留職停薪 no-pay leave; on leave without pay;
[留置權] lien;
代理人留置權 agent's lien;
[留駐] be stationed;
[留字] write down characters;

保留 (1) continue to have; retain; (2) hold back; (3) reserve;
殘留 be left over; remain;
逗留 stop over for a time; tarry;
勾留 break one's journey at; stop over;
稽留 delay; detain;
羈留 (1) stay; stop over; (2) detain; keep in custody;
久留 linger for a long while;
拘留 detain; hold in custody;
居留 reside; stay;
客留 (1) have a capacity of; hold; (2) accommodate; have sb in one's care;
扣留 arrest; detain; hold in custody;
彌留 be dying;
收留 have sb in one's care; take sb in;
停留 remain; stay for a time; stop;
挽留 persuade sb to stay;
淹留 stay over for a long period;
遺留 hand down; leave over;
滯留 be detained; be held up;

liu
【琉】 (1) a glossy and bright stone; (2) glazed; opaque;
[琉璃] azure stone; coloured glaze; glaze;
琉璃貓 a glazed cat — a mean person;

liu
【硫】 sulfur;
[硫化] cure; vulcanization; vulcanize;
硫化機 vulcanizer;
~單人硫化機 individual vulcanizer;
~平壓硫化機 press vulcanizer;
硫化劑 vulcanizator;
硫化膠 vulcanizate;
~化學硫化膠 chemical vulcanizate;
~老化後硫化膠 aged vulcanizate;
~冷硫化膠 cold vulcanizate;
~熱硫化膠 heat vulcanizate;
~填料硫化膠 filled vulcanizate;
無填料硫化膠 filler-free vulcanizate;
超速硫化 flash vulcanization;
等價硫化 equivalent vulcanization;
等效硫化 equivalent cure;
分批硫化 batch cure;
乾蒸汽硫化 dry steam cure;
後硫化 additional vulcanization;
化學硫化 chemical cure;
連續硫化 endless vulcanization;
熱空氣硫化 dry-heat cure;
雙面硫化 bilateral vulcanization;
自動硫化 auto-vulcanization;
[硫酸] sulphuric acid;

棒硫 roll sulphur;
福代硫 Aateck;
脱硫 desulphurize;

liu
【旒】 (1) a silk string used to hold a piece of jade hung on ancient ceremonial caps; (2) a kind of pennant or flag;

liu
【遛】 hang around; linger at a place;

liu
【榴】 pomegranate;
[榴彈] grenade;
榴彈砲 howitzer;
[榴散彈] cluster bomb;
[榴石] garnet;
白榴石 white garnet;
貴榴石 precious garnet;
沙廉榴石 Syrian garnet;
碎石榴石 crushed garnet;
鐵榴石 iron garnet;

石榴 pomegranate;

liu
【劉】 (1) a surname; (2) kill;
[劉海] bangs; fringe;

liu
【瘤】 lump; swelling; tumour;

毒瘤 malignant tumour;

惡性瘤 malignany tumour;
粉瘤 sebaceous cyst;
根瘤 root nodule;
骨瘤 osteoma;
黑瘤 melanoma;
良性瘤 benign tumour;
腦瘤 cerebroma; encephalophyma;
肉瘤 sarcoma;
神經瘤 neuroma;
腺瘤 adenoma;
血管瘤 haemangioma;
脂瘤 lipoma;
腫瘤 tumour;
贅瘤 anything superfluous or useless;
子宮瘤 womb tumour;

liu
【瀏】 (1) clear; limpid; (2) swift;
[瀏覽] browse; dip into; glance over; glance through; look into; look through; pass one's eye over; pass over; run over; skim through; slip over;
瀏覽器 browser;
~ 網頁瀏覽器 web browser;
瀏覽書籍 browse among books;

liu
【鎦】 lutecium;
[鎦金] gold-plating;

liu
【騮】 a legendary fine horse;

liu
【鶹】 owl;

liu³
liu
【柳】 (1) willow; (2) a surname;
[柳暗花明] an enchanting sight in spring time; every cloud has a silver lining;
柳暗花明又一村 every cloud has a silver lining; there is a way out for sb;
[柳眉] arch eyebrows; the eyebrows of a beautiful woman;
柳眉倒豎 her willow-leaf shaped eyebrows rise;
柳眉雙鎖 she knits her beautiful eyebrows;
[柳陌花衢] red-light district;
[柳樹] willow;
柳樹開花—沒結果 a willow tree in bloom – doesn't bear fruit; come to nothing; no result;
[柳條] willow twig;
柳條製品 willow twig products;
[柳絮] catkin;
[柳腰] slender waist of a woman;
杏眼柳腰 apricot-like eyes and soft waistline of a beauty;

檉柳 Chinese tamarisk;
垂柳 weeping willow;
旱柳 dryland willow;
河柳 dryland willow;
紅柳 Chinese tamarisk;
蒲柳 big catkin willow;
杞柳 salix sino-purpurea;
褪色柳 pussy willow;
楊柳 (1) poplar and willow; (2) willow;
一絲柳 a thread of willow;

liu
【綹】 lock; skein; tuft;

liu⁴
liu
【六】 hexa-; six;
[六倍] sextuple; six times; sixfold;
[六邊形] hexagon;
[六畜] the six domestic animals (pig, ox, goat, horse, fowl and dog);
六畜不安 even the domestic animals have no peace; successive family misfortunes;
六畜興旺 the domestic animals are all thriving;
[六合] the six directions: east, west, north, south, heaven and earth; the world or universe;
六合同春 spring comes all over the world;
六合之內 all within the universe;
[六甲] pregnancy;
身懷六甲 be expecting; heavy with child; in a certain condition; in a delicate condition; in a particular condition; in a family way; in an interesting condition; in the family way; pregnant;
[六角] hexagonal;
六角形 hexagon;
[六親] one's kin; the six relations: father, mother, elder brothers, young brothers, wife, children;
六親不和 all one's relatives are not on harmonious terms;

六親不認 disdain to recognize one's kinsmen; disown all one's relatives and friends; leave one's own relative in the lurch; not to recognize one's own closest relatives; refuse to have anything to do with all one's relatives and friends; turn one's back on one's own flesh and blood; unfeeling towards one's kin;
六親同運 all kinsmen share the same fate;
六親無靠 cannot rely on any one of the six relationships – nobody to turn to; have no relatives or friends to depend on;
[六十] sixty;
六十歲學吹打一心有餘力不足 learning how to blow a trumpet and beat a gong at the age of sixty – the spirit is willing, but the flesh is weak;
[六月] (1) the sixth month of the year; (2) June;
六月裏的扇子一家家忙 fans in the sixth lunar month – every household is busy;

禮拜六 Saturday;
十六 sixteen;
星期六 Saturday;

liu
【溜】 (1) rapid; (2) column; row; (3) fluent; skilled;

承溜 eaves gutter;
出溜 slide; slip;
光溜 slippery; smooth;
滑溜 slick; slippery; smooth;
水溜 eaves gutter;
匀溜 (1) even and smooth; (2) of the right consistency;
直溜 perfectly straight;

liu
【遛】 roam; stroll; walk slowly;
[遛達] stroll;
遛達遛達 go for a walk; have a short walk; stretch one's legs; take a walk;
[遛狗] air the dog; walk the dog;
出去遛狗 go out to walk the dog;
[遛遛] take a walk;
遛遛腿 stretch one's legs; take a walk;
[遛馬] take a walk;
[遛彎兒] go for a stroll; out strolling; take a walk;

liu
【霤】 (1) the dripping of water from the eaves; (2) eaves;

liu
【餾】 (1) steam; (2) distilled water;
[餾分] (1) distillate; (2) fraction;
裂化餾分 cracked distillate;
輕油餾分 light oil distillate;
色譜餾分 chromatographic fraction;
窄餾分 close-cut fraction;
中間餾分 intermediate distillate;
重餾分 heavy distillate;
[餾子] finger ring;

lo
lo
【咯】 phrase-final particle;

long²
long
【隆】 (1) grand; (2) prosperous; thriving; (3) deep; intense; (4) bulge; swell;
[隆背] humpback;
[隆冬] midwinter; the depth of winter;
隆冬盛暑 in the deep winter and high summer;
時值隆冬 in the dead of winter; the middle of winter;
[隆隆] rumble;
隆隆聲 rumble; zoom;
[隆胸] breast implant;
[隆重] ceremonious; grand; solemn;
隆重的 ceremonious;
隆重歡迎 roll out the red carpet;
隆重集會 hold a grand rally;
隆重禮儀 impressive ceremony;

咕隆 rattle; roll; rumble;
轟隆 roll; tumble;
穹隆 arched roof; vault;
興隆 flourishing; prosperous; thriving;

long
【龍】 (1) dragon; (2) imperial; (3) huge extinct reptile; (4) a surname;
[龍船] dragon boat;
[龍燈] dragon lantern;
[龍鳳] dragon and phoenix;
龍鳳呈祥 in extremely good fortune;

prosperity brought by the dragon and the phoenix;
鳳肝龍心 rare delicacies;
鳳閣龍樓 imperial palace;
鳳鳴龍吟 the voice of a phoenix and the chant of a dragon;
鳳生鳳，龍生龍，老鼠生的會打洞 as a phoenix little phoenixes begets and a dragon's sons are dragons all, so what is born of rats is capable of boring into a wall;
鳳髓龍肝 rare delicacies;
龍飛鳳舞 beautiful penmanship; elegant handwriting; exquisite calligraphy;
龍樓鳳閣 imperial palace;
龍眉鳳目 have eyebrows like a dragon's and eyes like those of a phoenix; have long eyebrows and long slit eyes;
龍蟠鳳逸 have talent but no opportunity to use it;
龍配龍，鳳配鳳 let beggars match with beggars;
龍生龍，鳳生鳳 eagles do not breed doves; like begets like;
龍生龍，鳳生鳳，老鼠生兒打地洞 a dragon begets a dragon, a phoenix begets a phoenix, and those begotten by rats are good at digging holes;
龍翔鳳舞 the dragon soars and the phoenix dances — dance in a swirling motion;
龍躍鳳鳴 bright in intellect;
龍章鳳姿 great handsome appearance;
描龍綉鳳 do fine needlework;
鳥中之鳳，魚中之龍 a phoenix among birds and a dragon among fish — stand out from one's fellows;
攀龍附鳳 attach oneself to the dragon and the phoenix — put oneself under the patronage of a bigwig; throw oneself under the wing of people of great influence; hurry to the authoritative and hang on to the influential; seek the patronage of a bigwig; worship the rising sun;
砲鳳烹龍 rich and rare dishes; roasted phenonix and boiled dragon;
烹龍砲鳳 boiled dragon and roasted phoenix; cook dainty meats and fine dishes;
偷龍轉鳳 secretly steal male child and substitute female child;

［龍肝豹胎］ great delicacies;
［龍虎］ dragons and tigers;
藏龍臥虎 able men living in hiding; capable people living in solitude;
~藏龍臥虎之地 a lair of dragons and tigers — a place where people of unusual ability are to be found;
毒龍餓虎 rampant dragons and ravening tigers — two evils;
伏虎降龍 tame the tiger and subdue the dragon — overcome powerful adversaries;
虎奮龍驤 eager as tigers and majestic as dragons;
虎踞龍蟠 like a crouching tiger and coiling dragon — a strategic point; like a tiger crouching, a dragon curling — a point of strategic importance;
龍蟠虎踞 like a coiling dragon and crouching tiger — a strategic point; like a dragon curling or a tiger crouching — a place very strategically important;
龍潭虎穴 a dragon's lair and a tiger's cave — a dangerous spot; dragon's watery lair and tiger's den — a hazardous spot; lion's den;
龍騰虎躍 a scene of bustling activity; with vigour and enthusiasm; with vim and vigour;
龍驤虎步 martial gait;
龍驤虎視 person with lofty aspiration and great ideals; walk like a dragon and look like a tiger;
龍行虎步 a majestic gait; one's step is like a dragon's gambol and a tiger's walk;
龍游淺水遭蝦戲，虎落平陽被犬欺 a dragon stranded in shallow water furnishes amusement for the shrimps; and if a tiger goes down to level land, it will be insulted by dogs; hares may pull dead lions by the beard;
龍吟虎嘯 the roar of dragons and tigers; the chants of dragons and the roar of tigers;
龍爭虎斗 a fierce struggle between two evenly-matched opponents; fight like Kilkenny cats; tigers fight with dragons;
盤龍臥虎 talented men still remain in concealment;
擒龍伏虎 capture a dragon and catch a

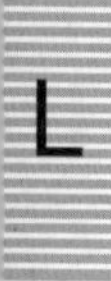

tiger;
擒龍縛虎 hold the dragon and trap the tiger;
生龍活虎 alive and kicking; brimming with energy; bursting with energy; dynamic and vigorous; full of life and energy; full of vigour and vitality; full of vim and vigour;
雲龍風虎 clouds come with the dragon, wind with the tiger; clouds follow the dragon and wind, the tiger — a great leader attracts capable followers; clouds originate with dragon, whereas winds originate with tigers — things of the same kind interact with each other;

［龍井茶］ longjing tea;

［龍捲］ spout;
龍捲風 tornado; twister;
陸龍捲 landspout;
水龍捲 waterspout;

［龍口奪糧］ snatch food from the dragon's mouth — speed up the summer harvesting before the storm breaks;

［龍眉皓髮］ with white hair and white eyebrows;

［龍門］ (1) nobleman's house; (2) Dragon Gate;
龍門陣 chat;
~擺龍門陣 chat; chat together and gossip; engage in chit-chat; talk about anything under the sun; tell a story;
一登龍門，聲價十倍 having once entered the house of a nobleman his fame is ten times greater; once a fish leaps over Dragon Gate its value increases ten-fold;

［龍蛇］ the dragon and the snake;
龍蛇飛動 (1) quick and forceful; (2) swift movement in calligraphy;
龍蛇混雜 good and bad huddled together;
筆走龍蛇 dragons and snakes follow one's writing brush — good penmanship;
強龍難壓地頭蛇 a dragon is no match for a snake in its old haunts; a local villain is hard to subdue; the mighty dragon is no match for the native serpent; even a powerful man cannot crush a local bully;
一龍一蛇 one's actions and manners change when the circumstances change;

［龍潭］ dragon's lake;
龍潭虎穴 dragon's lake and tiger's den;
逃出龍潭，又入虎穴 jump out of the frying pan into the fire;

［龍頭］ (1) cock; tab; (2) dragon's head; (3) leader;
龍頭鳳尾 admirable in all its details; good from beginning to end;
龍頭蛇尾 a brave beginning and a weak ending; begin with vigorous energy but peter out towards the end;
冷熱水混合龍頭 mixer tap;

［龍舞］ dragon dance;

［龍蝦］ lobster;
一隻龍蝦 a lobster;

［龍眼］ longan;

［龍鍾］ decrepit; senile;
龍鍾潦倒 ageing and tottering;

［龍舟］ dragon boat;

蒼龍 most ferocious person;
地龍 earthworm;
飛龍 flying dragon; pterosaur;
海龍 (1) sea otter; (2) pipefish;
合龍 join the two sections of a bridge;
火龍 fiery dragon;
蛟龍 mythical dragon capable of invoking storms and floods;
巨龍 hadrosaurus;
恐龍 dinosaur;
尼龍 nylon;
錢龍 millipede;
禽龍 iguanodon;
虬龍 small dragon with horns;
沙龍 salon;
水龍 fire hose;
小龍 dragonet;
一條龍 a connected sequence; a coordinated process; a long line; one continuous line;
魚龍 ichthyosaur;

long
【窿】 cavity; hole;

long
【癃】 (1) humping of the back in old age; (2) anuria;

疲癃 aged and suffering from various kinds of diseases;

long
【瀧】 (1) raining; rainy; (2) imbued in;

soaked; wet; (3) swiftly; (4) waterfall;

long
【攏】 special fingering in playing the lute;

湊攏 move close to; press near;
歸攏 put together;
合攏 gather up;
聚攏 gather together;
靠攏 close up; draw close;
收攏 draw sth in;
圍攏 crowd around;

long
【嚨】 throat;

喉嚨 throat;

long
【朧】 moon's brightness;

long
【瓏】 (1) clear and crisp; (2) dry; parched; (3) rumbling of a cart; (4) tinkling of metals; (5) dusky;

［瓏璁］ (1) clanking sound of jade or metal; (2) luxuriant and green; verdant;

［瓏玲］ (1) clanking sound of jade or metal; (2) brilliant; bright;

玲瓏 (1) (of things) ingenious and delicate; (2) (of people) clever and nimble;

long
【曨】 (1) dim; vague; (2) bright;

曚曨 dim;
曈曨 becoming bright;

long
【櫳】 (1) the bars across a doorway; (2) cage for animals; pen;

窗櫳 window;

long
【蘢】 a kind of tall grass;

［蘢蔥］ luxuriantly green; verdant;

蔥蘢 luxuriantly green; verdant;

long
【矓】 blurred; hazy;

朦朧 dim; obscure;

long
【礱】 (1) grind; (2) a kind of mill;

long
【籠】 (1) cover; envelop; (2) large box or runk;

［籠絡］ drag in; draw over; rope sb in; win sb over by any means;
籠絡人心 win people's support; win the hearts of the people;

［籠頭］ halter;
沒籠頭的馬 a horse without a halter; uncontrollable person;

［籠形］ cage-shaped;
籠形天線 cage aerial;

［籠罩］ cloak;

［籠中鳥］ caged bird;

［籠子］ (1) cage; (2) basket; container;
小籠子 hutch;

出籠 (1) come out of the streamer; (2) appear; come forth;
樊籠 birdcage;
罐籠 cage;
烘籠 roaster;
回籠 (1) steam again; (2) withdraw from circulation;
牢籠 (1) bonds; cage; (2) snare; trap; (3) draw sb over to one's side; (4) bind up; fetter; tie;
鳥籠 birdcage;
囚籠 prisoner's cage;
紗籠 sarong;
手籠 hand warmer, shaped like a basket;
圓籠 large carrying food basket;
蒸籠 food steamer;

long
【聾】 deaf; hard of hearing;

［聾的］ deaf;
完全聾的 stone deaf;

［聾聵］ deaf;
發聵振聾 awaken the deaf; enlighten the benighted;
發聾振聵 awaken the deaf; enlighten the benighted;
振聾發聵 awaken the deaf; enlighten the benighted; make a deaf man hear and a blind man see; open the ears of the deaf and the eyes of the blind — enlighten another's ignorance; rouse

the deaf and awaken the unhearing;

［聾啞］ deaf and dumb; deaf mute;
聾啞學校 special school for the deaf and dumb;
聾啞症 deaf mutism; partimutism;
天聾地啞 like one deaf and dumb;
推聾作啞 pretend to be deaf and dumb;
又聾又啞 both deaf and dumb; deafmute;
裝聾作啞 pretend ignorance; pretend to be an ignorant; pretend to be deaf and dumb; pretend to hear and know nothing;

［聾症］ deafness;

［聾子］ deaf person;
聾子放砲—散了 a deaf person firing a cannon — no explosion;

傳導性聾 conduction deafness; transmission deafness;
精神性聾 functional deafness;
老年性聾 presbycusis;
迷路性聾 labyrinthine deafness;
皮質性聾 cortical deafness;
偏側聾 hemianacusia;
器質性聾 organic deafness;
全聾 anakusis;
神經性聾 nerve deafness;
中腦性聾 midbrain deafness;
中毒性聾 toxic deafness;

long³

long

【壟】 (1) ridge; (2) raised path between fields;

［壟斷］ (1) monopolize; (2) monopoly;
壟斷石油 oil monopoly;
壟斷市場 corner the market;
壟斷資本 monopoly capital;
差別壟斷 discriminative monopoly;
反壟斷［的］ antitrust;
寡頭壟斷 oligopoly;
國家壟斷 government monopoly;
勞工壟斷 labour monopoly;
外貿壟斷 foreign trade monopoly;
完全壟斷 absolute monopoly;

斷壟 parts of ridges where there are no sprouts;
瓦壟 rows of tiles on a roof;

long

【攏】 (1) collect; gather; (2) lean;

［攏岸］ moor to the shore;

［攏共］ all told; altogether; in all;

［攏子］ fine-toothed comb;

［攏總］ add up; all told; altogether; in all; sum up;

［攏嘴］ close one's mouth;
合不攏嘴 grin from ear to ear;
~笑得合不攏嘴 grin from ear to ear;

併攏 draw close to each other;
歸攏 put together; take in;
靠攏 close up; draw close;
拉攏 cozy up to; make a friendship with a self-serving motive; rope sb in; win sb over to one's side;
收攏 draw sth in;
圍攏 crowd around; draw around; draw round;

long

【隴】 (1) a name of Gansu; (2) same as 壟;

long

【籠】 a pronunciation of 籠;

long⁴

long

【弄】 (1) make fun of; mock; play with; sport with; (2) do; handle; perform;

long

【衖】 lane; alley;

lou¹

lou

【摟】 (1) exact; (2) collect; scrape;

lou²

lou

【婁】 (1) one of the twenty-eight constellations; (2) tether; (3) wear; (4) trail along; (5) a surname;

［婁子］ blunder; trouble;

lou

【僂】 (1) deformed; (2) hunchback; (3) bent; (4) a surname;

佝僂 rickety;

lou

【摟】 drag; drag away; draw; pull;

lou

【嘍】 (1) bandit's lackey or follower; (2) wink;

［嘍羅］ (1) rank and file of a band of outlaws;

(2) lackey; underling;
小嘍囉 flunkey; lackey; underling; unimportant follower;

lou

【樓】 (1) building; (2) floor; storey; (3) superstructure;

［樓房］ building;
蓋樓房 build a building;
買樓房 purchase a flat;
一棟樓房 a building;

［樓閣］ towers;
亭臺樓閣 pavilions and pagodas; pavilions, terraces, and towers;

［樓價］ property price;
樓價高 property prices are high;
樓價回落 correction in property prices;

［樓上］ upstairs;
樓上的窗戶 upstairs windows;
樓上的房間 upstairs room;
看看樓上 see the upstairs;
往樓上 go upstairs;

［樓市］ property market;
樓市發展 property market development
樓市降溫 cool the property market down;

［樓台］ (1) high building; tower; (2) balcony; gallery;

［樓梯］ staircase; stairway; stairs;
樓梯頂 top of the stairs;
樓梯扶手 banister;
樓梯腳 bottom of the stairs;
樓梯井 stairwell;
樓梯平台 landing;
螺旋樓梯 circular stairs; spiral staircase; spiral stairs;
盤旋樓梯 spiral stairs;
跑上樓梯 run up the stairs;
上樓梯 ascend stairs; climb a staircase; come up stairs;
摔下樓梯 fall off the stairs;
未亮燈的樓梯 unlit stairway;
下樓梯 come downstairs; descend stairs;
小心樓梯 mind the steps;
一段樓梯 a flight of stairs;
衹聽樓梯響，不見人下來 all talk and no cider; great pretences and small performances; much cry and little wool; the stair creaks but no one comes down — much talk but no action;

［樓廳］ circle;
樓廳後座 upper circle;
樓廳前座 dress circle;

［樓下］ downstairs;
看看樓下 see the downstairs;

［樓子］ attic;
暗樓子 attic; attic room; garret;

［樓座］ balcony;
頂層樓座 gallery;

彩樓 decorated archway;
綵樓 gaily decorated tower;
岑樓 a mountain-like, lofty and tapering building;
茶樓 teahouse;
城樓 gate tower;
碉樓 watchtower;
吊樓 (1) house projecting over the water; (2) wooden house supported by wooden pillars;
崗樓 watchtower;
閣樓 attic; garret; loft;
更樓 watchtower;
鼓樓 drum tower;
箭樓 watchtower over a city gate;
角樓 corner tower;
砲樓 gun turret;
氣樓 small tower for ventilation on top of a granary;
譙樓 (1) watchtower; (2) drum tower;
青樓 brothel;
望樓 lookout tower; watchtower;
危樓 high tower;
一層樓 a floor; a storey;
鐘樓 (1) bell tower; (2) clock tower;

lou

【蔞】 a kind of artemisia;

［蔞葉］ betel; betel pepper;

lou

【螻】 mole cricket;

［螻蛄］ mole cricket;

蛞螻 mole cricket;

lou

【髏】 human skeleton;

髑髏 skull;
骷髏 (1) human skeleton; (2) death's head; human skull;

lou³

lou

【摟】 embrace; hold in one's arms; hug;

[摟抱] cuddle; embrace; hold in one's arms; hug;
摟摟抱抱 hug;

lou

【簍】 bamboo basket;
[簍子] basket;

笆簍 basket;
背簍 basket that is carried on the back;
字紙簍 wastepaper basket;

lou⁴

lou

【陋】 (1) plain; ugly; (2) humble; mean; (3) corrupt; undesirable; vulgar; (4) limited; scanty; shallow;
[陋規] objectionable practices;
陋規鄙習 corrupt practices and stupid customs;
[陋室] humble room; room totally without decoration;
[陋俗] undesirable customs;
[陋屋] hovel;
[陋習] bad habits; corrupt customs;
狃於陋習 be accustomed to bad habits;
拋棄陋習 renounce one's vicious ways;

鄙陋 shallow; superficial;
醜陋 ugly;
粗陋 coarse and crude;
孤陋 poorly read and ignorant; uncultured;
固陋 ignorant; provincial;
寡陋 ignorant; uninformed;
簡陋 simple and crude;
譾陋 meager; mean; shallow;
僻陋 secluded and desolate;
樸陋 simple and crude;
淺陋 meagre;
猥陋 base; despicable;
愚陋 ignorant and shallow;

lou

【漏】 (1) leak; (2) divulge; (3) leave out; missing;
[漏報] fail to declare; fail to report sth;
[漏掉] drop; leave sth out; miss; omit;
[漏洞] flaw; hole; leak; loophole;
漏洞百出 full of loopholes; riddle with loopholes;
出現漏洞 start a leak;
堵住漏洞 plug up a leak; shut off a leak; stop a leak;
彌補漏洞 patch a leak;
[漏斗] (1) funnel; (2) hopper;
長梗漏斗 thistle tube;
滴液漏斗 drop funnel;
放液漏斗 drainage funnel;
分液漏斗 separatory funnel;
灰箱漏斗 ash pan hopper;
煤漏斗 coal hopper;
受精漏斗 entrance funnel;
斜溝漏斗 chute hopper;
裝料漏斗 charging hopper;
[漏風] (1) air leak; (2) leak out;
[漏盡更殘] the night is waning; the small hours of dawn;
[漏勺] skimmer;
[漏稅] (1) evade payment of a tax; evade taxation; (2) tax dodging;
偷稅漏稅 (1) defraud the revenue; evade a tax; evade the payment of tax; (2) tax evasion;
[漏網] escape from the net; escape unpunished; fall through the net; slip through the cracks; slip through the net;
漏網之魚 a fish out of the net; runaway;
無一漏網 let none slip through the net;
[漏洩] leak;
漏洩春光 give away a secret; send a secret message;
[漏夜] midnight; the dead of night;
[漏子] flaw;
出漏子 blunder; in trouble;
[漏嘴] let slip a remark;
説漏嘴 blurt out;

崩漏 uterine bleeding;
測漏 track down a leak;
磁漏 magnetic leakage;
地漏 floor drain;
撿漏 repair the leaky part of roof;
紕漏 careless mistake; slip;
缺漏 gaps and omissions;
沙漏 (1) sand filter; (2) sand filter used for marking the time;
滲漏 leak; seep;
拾漏 find a chance to pick up some money;
疏漏 careless omission; oversight; slip;
偷漏 evade;
透漏 divulge; leak; reveal;
脱漏 be left out; be missing;

鏬漏 crack; leak;
洩漏 leak; let out;
遺漏 leave out; omit;
痔漏 anal fistula;
走漏 (1) divulge; leak out; (2) smuggle and evade taxes;

lou
【瘻】 (1) goitre; (2) scrofula;
［瘻管］ fistula;

膽囊瘻 amphibolic fistula;
肛瘻 anal fistula;
骨瘻 bone fistula;
淚管瘻 dacryosyrinx;
迷路瘻 labyrinthine fistula;
前庭瘻 vestibular fistula;

lou
【瘺】 (1) goiter; (2) scrofula;

lou
【鏤】 carve; engrave;
［鏤塵吹影］ carve the dust and blow the shadow — impossible; make futile efforts; work in vain;
［鏤刻］ carve; enchase; engrave;

lou
【露】 (1) reveal; show; (2) syrup;
［露白］ show one's belongings; show one's money;
［露齒］ expose one's teeth;
露齒而笑 grin; toothpaste smile;
［露出］ display; reveal; show;
露出才氣 display one's talent; show one's talent;
露出鋒芒 make one's talent felt;
露出馬腳 betray oneself; give the game away; give the show away; let the cat out of the bag; reveal one's true character; spill the beans;
露出笑臉 put on a smile; show a smiling face; wear a smile on one's face;
露出原形 reveal one's true colours; reveal one's true face; show one's real colours;
露出真面目 reveal one's real colours; reveal one's true face; show one's real colours;
［露底］ betray one's confidence; disclose the ins and outs; let out the whole story; reveal the inside story;
［露點］ dew point;
［露富］ show one's riches;
［露臉］ look good as a result of receiving honour or praise; sth that brings honour;
［露面］ (1) appear; appear in public; make an appearance; show one's face; show up; (2) do credit to; win honour for;
避不露面 hide oneself out of the way;
不願意露面 reluctant to show one's face;
匆匆露面 put in a brief appearance;
出頭露面 appear in public; in the limelight; show oneself; show one's head;
短暫露面 put in an appearance;
公開露面 appear in public; make a public appearance; show one's face in public;
及時露面 make a timely appearance; show up in time;
拋頭露面 appear in public; in the limelight; show oneself in public;
~避免拋頭露面 avoid appearing in public;
~喜歡拋頭露面 fond of showing off;
未能露面 fail to put in an appearance;
［露臍裝］ (1) bare midriff; (2) midriff-baring top;
［露怯］ display one's ignorance; make a fool of oneself;
［露台］ patio;
［露頭］ appear; emerge; show one's head;
［露營］ camping;
露營牀 camp bed;
露營活動 camping;
露營者 camper;

草莓露 strawberry syrup;
紅果露 haw syrup;
錮露 plug with molten metal;
果子露 fruit syrup;
山楂露 haw syrup;
洩露 let out; reveal;

lou⁵
lou
【嘍】 phrase-final particle;

lu¹
lu
【嚕】 (1) verbose; wordy; (2) indistinct speech sound;

[嚕蘇] long-winded;
嚕哩嚕蘇 talk endlessly; talk unnecessarily;

咕嚕 murmur; whisper;
胡嚕 (1) rub; (2) scrape together;

lu²

lu

【盧】 (1) cottage; hut; (2) a surname;
[盧比] rupee;
[盧布] rouble;

lu

【廬】 (1) thatched cottage; (2) Mt. Lu in Jiangsi;
[廬舍] farmhouse; house; hut;

茅廬 hut; thatched cottage;

lu

【瀘】 (1) a river in Yunnan; (2) a river in Sichuan;

lu

【爐】 fireplace; furnace; hearth; oven; stove;
[爐邊] fireside;
在爐邊 by the fireside;
[爐火純青] attain perfection; master one's skills to perfection; reach high perfection; the stove fire is pure green — perfection in one's studies;
[爐欄] fireguard; fire screen;
[爐灶] cooking range;
重起爐灶 begin all over again; make a fresh start; start from scratch;
另起爐灶 begin anew; make a fresh start; start all over again; start sth all over again;
[爐渣] (1) clinker; (2) slag;
高鋁爐渣 aluminous slag;
石灰爐渣 calcareous slag;
酸性爐渣 acid slag;
[爐子] stove;
大肚爐子 pot-bellied stove;

壁爐 fireplace;
吹爐 blown converter;
電爐 (1) electric furnace; (2) electric stove; hot plate;
鍛爐 forge;
高爐 blast furnace;
鍋爐 boiler;
火爐 stove;
腳爐 foot stove;
烤爐 oven;
熔爐 (1) smelting furnace; (2) crucible; furnace;
手爐 handwarmer, shaped like a basket;
香爐 incense burner;

lu

【臚】 (1) arrange in order; display; exhibit; (2) belly; (3) skin; (4) convey; forward;
[臚陳] narrate in detail; state;
[臚列] enumerate; list;

lu

【蘆】 (1) reed; rush; (2) gourd;
[蘆薈] aloe; American aloe;

葫蘆 bottle gourd; calabash;

lu

【櫨】 (1) square peck-shaped box half way up a mast; (2) the name of a plant;

欂櫨 a system of brackets inserted between the top of a column and a crossbeam;
黃櫨 smoke tree;

lu

【纑】 (1) thread; (2) soften hemp by boiling;

lu

【罏】 earthen stand for wine jars;

lu

【艫】 bow of a boat;

舳艫 stern of a boat;

lu

【轤】 (1) pulley for drawing water; (2) capstan; windlass;

lu

【鑪】 same as 爐 ;

lu

【顱】 (1) forehead; (2) head; (3) skull;
[顱病] craniopathy;
[顱發育不良] atelocephaly;
[顱發育不全] atelocephaly;
[顱骨] cranium; skull;
顱骨關節 articulationes cranii;
顱骨軟化 craniosclerosis;

[顱骨炎] cranitis;
[顱骨增生] hyperostosis cranii;

扁顱 platycrania;
腦顱 cranium; skull;
頭顱 (1) head; (2) skull;

lu
【鱸】 bass; perch;
[鱸魚] bass; perch;
淡水鱸魚 perch;

lu
【鸕】 cormorant;

lu³
lu
【鹵】 (1) alkaline soil; saline soil; (2) natural salt; (3) rude; unrefined; (4) capture; seize;
[鹵莽] crude and rash; reckless;

茶鹵 strong tea;
斥鹵 impregnated with salt;
勾鹵 add starch to the soup;
鹽鹵 bittern;

lu
【虜】 captive; capture alive; prisoner; take prisoner;
[虜獲] (1) capture; (2) men and arms captured;

俘虜 capture; take prisoner;

lu
【滷】 (1) broth; gravy; sauce; (2) salted; salty;
[滷蛋] spiced corned egg;
[滷雞] pot-stewed chicken;
[滷味] pot-stewed fowl served cold;

lu
【魯】 (1) dull; stupid; (2) rash; rough; rude; (3) a surname;
[魯班門前弄大斧] take the axe from Lu Ban the Great Carpenter — overestimate oneself; teach one's grandmother to suck eggs;
[魯殿靈光] the only living aged statesman; the only prestigious senior who survives; the only survivals;
[魯頓] dull-witted; mentally slow; obtuse; stupid;
[魯莽] crude and rash; rash; reckless;
魯莽陳詞 venture an opinion;
魯莽從事 act impulsively; undertake roughly;
魯莽滅裂 act excitedly and without careful thinking; as gruff as a bear; like a bull in china shop; reckless; rash and careless;
魯莽行事 act rashly; act without thought; take rash action;
魯莽一時，悔之一世 do sth rash will make one repent forever;
魯莽之人 rough fellow;
講話魯莽 careless about one's speech;
滅裂魯莽 careless and casual;
性情魯莽 have a rough manner;
言談魯莽 speak carelessly;

粗魯 rash; rough; rude;
愚魯 foolish; stupid;

lu
【擄】 capture; take captive;
[擄掠] loot; pillage;
姦淫擄掠 rape and loot;

lu
【櫓】 (1) oar; scull; sweep; (2) big shield; (3) long spear; (4) lookout tower on a city wall;

搖櫓 scull;

lu⁴
lu
【六】 six;

lu
【角】
[角里] (1) a place southwest of Suzhou in Jiangsu Province; (2) a surname;

lu
【录】 (1) carved wood; (2) abbreviated form of 祿;

lu
【陸】 (1) land; (2) a surname;
[陸地] dry land; land;
陸地行舟 attempt the impossible; sail a boat on the land;
接近陸地 approach land;
看見陸地 see land;
[陸軍] army; ground force; land force;

陸軍副官 adjutant;
陸軍航空隊 army air forces;

[陸離] weirdly colourful;
光怪陸離 bizarre and motley; grotesque and gaudy;

[陸路] land route; overland route;
經陸路 overland;
一條陸路 an overland route;

[陸橋] land bridge;

[陸上] land; onshore;
陸上生活 life ashore;
陸上石油生產 onshore oil production;
陸上調整 terrestrial adjustment;
陸上線路 landline;

[陸續] in succession; one after another;
陸續倒閉 close down one after another;
陸續到來 arrive one by one; come one by one;

[陸運] land transportation;

大陸 continent; mainland;
登陸 disembark; land;
海陸 sea and land;
內陸 inland; interior; landlocked;
水陸 (1) land and water; (2) delicacies from the land and the sea;
着陸 land; touch down;

lu

【鹿】 deer;

[鹿角] antler;

[鹿皮革] buckskin;

[鹿茸] pilose antler;

[鹿死不擇蔭] a desperate man will resort to anything;

[鹿死誰手] who will win in the struggle;

白唇鹿 white-lipped deer;
公鹿 stag;
馬鹿 red deer;
眉杈鹿 brow-antlered deer;
梅花鹿 spotted deer;
麋鹿 Père David's deer;
母鹿 doe;
水鹿 red deer;
駝鹿 elk; moose;
小鹿 fawn;
馴鹿 reindeer;
一群鹿 a herd of deer;

lu

【淥】 (1) clear water; (2) drip; strain; (3) tributary of the Xing River in Hunan; (4) a surname;

lu

【菉】 green;

[菉竹] green bamboo;

lu

【逯】 (1) go away suddenly for no particular reason; (2) a surname;

lu

【蓼】 high; luxuriant;

[蓼蓼] long and large; luxuriant;

lu

【僇】 (1) kill; massacre; (2) disgrace; shame; (3) collaborate;

lu

【勠】 (1) join; unite; (2) kill; slay;

[勠力] cooperate; join forces; unite efforts;
勠力同心 work together with the same objective in mind;

lu

【碌】 (1) mediocre; (2) busy; occupied; (3) a kind of stone roller;

[碌碌] (1) commonplace; mediocre; (2) busy with miscellaneous work;
碌碌塵寰 busy with miscellaneous work;
碌碌風塵 be exposed to wind and dust;
碌碌無能 a commonplace kind of man with no ability to speak of; a man of common clay with little ability; devoid of ability; have below-the-average capacity for study; incapable of doing things where skill or intellect is needed; incompetent; lacking in ability; mediocre;
碌碌無奇 rough and not wonderful;
碌碌無為 miserable person with no accomplishment of any kind to his credit;
碌碌小人 paltry man; rough and mean fellow;
碌碌庸才 common person of no ability; mediocre man; of inferior and ordinary ability; of most ordinary capacity;
碌碌庸人 rough and commonplace person;

lu

【祿】 (1) happiness; prosperity; (2) emolument; official pay;

[祿蠹] people of the exploiting class who seek

rank and handsome salary;

俸祿 official's salary;
爵祿 the rank of nobility and the emoluments that go with it;

lu

【賂】 bribe; send gift;

賄賂 (1) bribe; (2) bribery;

lu

【路】 (1) path; road; way; (2) distance; journey; (3) way; (4) line; logic; sequence; (5) district; region; (6) route; (7) class; grade; sort;

[路邊] roadside; wayside;
路邊店 drive-in;
在路邊 by the side of the road;

[路標] guidepost; road sign; route marking; route sign;
交通路標 traffic cone;

[路不拾遺] no one picks up what is left by the wayside—honesty previals throughout society;
路不拾遺，夜不閉戶 people are so honest that no one picks up what has been left by the wayside and it is not necessary to lock the doors at night;

[路程] distance travelled; journey;
路程單 waybill;
~資物路程單 freight waybill;
聯運貨物路程單 interline waybill;
回家路程 homeward journey;
縮短路程 shorten one's route;

[路道] (1) approach; way; (2) behaviour;

[路燈] road lamp; street lamp; street light;
路燈柱 lamp post;

[路費] travelling expenses;

[路軌] (1) rail; (2) track;

[路過] pass by; pass through;

[路肩] hard shoulder; shoulder;
軟質路肩 soft shoulder;

[路徑] (1) path; way; (2) method; ways and means;

[路口] crossing; intersection;
環形交叉路口 traffic circle;
十字路口 crossroads; intersection;

[路欄] lane separator;

[路面] pavement; road surface;
路面工 pavement worker;
路面交通 road traffic;
路面下層 subsurface;
重鋪路面 resurfacing;
過水路面 overflow pavement;
混凝土路面 concrete pavement; concrete road surface;
瀝青路面 asphalt surface;
砌塊路面 block pavement;
碎石路面 crazy paving;
條坑路面 qashboard;
無噪音路面 noiseless pavement;

[路牌] street nameplate;

[路旁] roadside; wayside;
路旁餐館 roadhouse;
路旁酒吧 roadhouse;

[路人] (1) passer-by; (2) stranger;

[路上] (1) on the road; (2) en route; on the way;
路上說話，草裏有人 if you talk on the road there will be someone listening in the grass;
正在路上 be on one's way;

[路數] (1) approach; way; (2) a movement in martial arts; (3) exact details; the ins and outs; the inside story;

[路途] (1) path; road; (2) journey; way;
路途遙遠 a long way to go; far away;

[路線] (1) itinerary; route; (2) line;
路線圖 road map;
基本路線 basic line;
貿易路線 trade route;
強硬路線 hard line;
~強硬路線者 hardliner;
群眾路線 mass line;
一條路線 a route;
制定路線 map out a route;
總路線 general line;

[路緣] curb; kerb;

[路遠] great distance;

[路障] roadblock;
設置路障 set up roadblocks;

[路子] (1) approach; means; method; way; (2) connections; influence; pull;
路子野 have a lot of social connections; well connected;
闖出一條新路子 blaze a new path; blaze a path; blaze a trail; blaze a way; blaze new paths; break a new path;
對路子 correct; in line with;
找路子 try to secure help from potential backers;

隘路 narrow passage;
柏油路 asphalt road;
半路 (1) halfway; midway; on the way; (2) in progress;
筆路 (1) technique of calligraphy; (2) style;
閉路 closed circuit;
岔路 branch road; side road;
出路 outlet; way out;
磁路 magnetic circuit;
大路 main road;
帶路 lead the way; serve as a guide;
道路 path; road; way;
電路 electric circuit;
短路 short circuit;
斷路 break the circuit;
對路 (1) satisfy the need; (2) be to one's liking; suit one;
分路 shunt;
趕路 hurry on with one's journey;
公路 highway; road;
管路 pipeline;
過路 pass by one one's way;
海路 sea route; seaway;
旱路 overland route;
航路 (1) air route; (2) sea route;
後路 (1) route to retreat; (2) leeway;
回路 return; return circuit;
活路 (1) means of subsistence; way out; (2) workable method;
近路 shortcut;
絕路 blind alley; impasse;
開路 (1) open a way; (2) lead the way;
來路 (1) incoming road; (2) origin; source;
攔路 block the way;
老路 (1) old road; (2) beaten track;
理路 orderliness;
領路 lead the way;
陸路 land route;
馬路 avenue; road; street;
迷路 get lost; lose one's way;
末路 blind alley; dead end;
陌路 stranger;
旁路 bypass; side road;
歧路 branch road; forked road;
去路 the way along which one is going;
讓路 make way;
山路 mountain road;
商路 trade route;
上路 set off; set out on a journey; start out;
生路 means of livelihood; way out;
熟路 beaten track; familiar road;
水路 water route; waterway;
順路 direct route;
思路 thinking; train of thought;
死路 blind alley; dead end; impasse;
鐵路 railroad; railway;
通路 (1) thoroughfare; (2) passage; passageway;
同路 go the same way;
頭路 first-rate; top quality;
退路 (1) route of retreat; (2) a way of escape;
外路 (of goods) from other cities;
彎路 crooked road;
紋路 lines;
線路 (1) circuit line; (2) line; route;
銷路 market; sale;
小路 minor road; side street;
斜路 evil way; wrong course;
心路 (1) scheme; wit; (2) tolerance; (3) design; intention;
沿路 along the road; on the way;
養路 maintain a road;
一段路 a section of a road;
一條路 a road;
引路 lead the way;
正路 right way;
支路 side road; turn-off;
中路 (of goods) mediocre;
走路 go on foot; walk;

lu

【輅】 (1) heavy carriage; (2) horizontal front bar on a cart or carriage;

lu

【綠】 (1) green; (2) chlorine;
[綠林] forest outlaws;
綠林豪傑 hero of the bush;
綠林好漢 (1) forest outlaws; (2) band of bandits; brigands; highwaymen; robbers;

lu

【漉】 (1) remove sediment by filtering; (2) dripping; wet;

lu

【戮】 join forces; unite forces;
[戮力同心] make concerted efforts; of one mind; pull together and work hard as a team; unite in a concerted effort; work together in a coalition;

lu

【醁】 a kind of green-coloured wine;

lu

【錄】 (1) copy; record; write down; (2) employ; hire; (3) tape-record; (4) collection; record; register;

[錄取] admit; enroll; recruit;
錄取標準 admissions criteria;
錄取分數線 admission line;
錄取名額 admission quota;
錄取入學 matriculation;
錄取手續 admissions procedures;
錄取通知 acceptance notice;
~錄取通知書 admission notice;
錄取學生 enroll students;
錄取原則 admissions policy;
擇優錄取 anyone who makes a good enough scare can be accepted; enroll only those who are outstanding; select the students according to the marks they get;

[錄像] video; videotape;
錄像帶 videocassette; videotape;
~錄像帶盒倉 cassette compartment;
~一盤錄像帶 a videotape;
錄像機 videocassette recorder; video recorder;
~盒式錄像機 videocassette recorder;
錄像教材 video text;
錄像節目 video programme;
錄像設備 recording apparatus; recording equipment;
錄像系統 video recording system;
錄像資料 video data;
關掉錄像 turn off the video;
屏幕錄像 telerecording;
~彩色電視屏幕錄像 colour telerecording;
~直接正片屏幕錄像 direct positive telerecording;
製作錄像 make a video film;

[錄音] film recording; recording; sound recording;
錄音報導 reportage with live recording;
錄音材料 recording material;
錄音車 recording van;
錄音車間 film recording department;
錄音磁帶 magnetic recording;
錄音磁頭 magnetic recording head;
錄音帶 audio tape;
~一盒錄音帶 a casket of magnetic tape;
~一捲錄音帶 a roll of magnetic tape;
錄音導演 sound recording director;
錄音放大器 recording amplifier;
錄音費用 recording fee;
錄音機 recorder;
~唱片式錄音機 dictaphone recorder;
~磁帶錄音機 magnetic recorder;
~單聲道錄音機 monophonic recorder;
錄音技師 sound engineer; sound recordist;
錄音鍵 record button;
錄音設備 recording equipment;
錄音師 sound engineer;
錄音時間 recording time;
錄音速度 recording speed;
錄音效果 recording effect;
錄音指示燈 record indicator;
標準錄音 standard recording;
唱片錄音 sound-on-disc recording;
膠卷錄音 sound-on-film recording;

[錄影機] videocassette recorder;

[錄用] employ; engage; give a post to sb; take on; take sb on the staff;
錄用標準 employment criteria;
錄用人材 employment of talents;
棄瑕錄用 neglect sb's flaws and enlist him — use a capable man in spite of his faults;

備忘錄 memo; memorandum;
筆錄 notes; record; take down;
編錄 excerpt and edit;
簿錄 (1) confiscate property; (2) catalogue of books;
採錄 collect and record;
抄錄 copy; make a copy of;
齒錄 employ;
附錄 appendix;
過錄 copy sth from one notebook to another;
集錄 collect and compile;
輯錄 compile;
記錄 (1) minutes; notes; record; (2) note-taker; (3) keep the minutes; record; take notes;
紀錄 (1) minutes; notes; record; (2) note-taker; (3) keep the minutes; record; take notes;
節錄 abridge;
目錄 (1) catalogue; list; (2) table of contents;
收錄 include;
選錄 select and include;
迻錄 transcribe; write down;
語錄 recorded utterance;
摘錄 excerpt; extract;
著錄 put down in writing; record;

lu

【潞】 several rivers in northern China;

lu

【璐】 fine jade;

lu

【簏】 bamboo trunk;

lu

【轆】 (1) wheel; (2) capstan;

［轆車］ pole dolly;

［轆轆］ rumble;

軲轆 roll; wheel;

lu

【騄】 legendary swift horse;

lu

【麓】 foot of a hill or a mountain;

lu

【露】 (1) dew; (2) beverage distilled from flowers; syrup; (3) reveal; show;

［露背］ backless; sunback;

露背的 backless;

露背上裝 halter top; halter-neck;

［露才揚己］ show off one's knowledge;

［露齒］ expose one's teeth;

露齒而笑 grin; toothpaste smile;

［露出］ reveal; show;

露出狐狸尾巴 betray oneself; give the show away; let the cat out of the bag; show the fox tail;

露出馬腳 betray one's identity; give the show away; give the game away; give the whole show away; let the cat out of the bag; reveal the true state of affairs;

露出破綻 betray one's weak point;

露出喜色 lighten;

露出笑容 reveal a smile;

露出兇相 show one's horns;

露出原形 betray oneself; reveal one's true colours; show oneself in one's true colours;

［露骨］ barefaced; thinly veiled; undisguised;

［露面］ appear in public; make an appearance; show one's face; show one's head;

［露水］ dew;

露水夫妻 illicit lovers;

露水姻緣 casual affair;

露水之歡 temporal joy; worldly pleasures;

［露宿］ sleep in the open;

露宿風餐 brave the wind and dew; hardship of travel; sleep in the open air and eat the wind; the hardships of a traveller; the hardships of travelling;

風餐露宿 brave the wind and dew; go through the rigours of living in the wilderness; stand exposure, deprivation and hunger;

［露臺］ balcony;

［露天］ in the open; in the open air; outdoors;

露天比賽 open-air competition;

露天電影院 open-air cinema; outdoor cinema;

露天舞會 open-air dance party;

露天音樂會 open-air concert; outdoor concert;

白露 White Dew;

敗露 fall through and be exposed;

暴露 expose; lay bare; reveal;

表露 reveal; show;

呈露 reveal; show;

赤露 bare;

惡露 lochia;

發露 appear; become visible; manifest itself;

甘露 Chinese artichoke;

寒露 Cold Dew;

揭露 (1) disclose; expose; (2) ferret out;

流露 reveal; show unintentionally;

裸露 exposed; uncovered;

披露 (1) announce; publish; (2) disclose; reveal; unmask;

曝露 expose sth to the open air;

淺露 explicit; plainly expressed;

袒露 leave uncovered;

透露 disclose; leak; reveal;

吐露 tell;

顯露 appear; manifest itself;

魚露 fish sauce;

雨露 (1) rain and dew; (2) bounty; favour; grace;

玉露 (1) dewdrops; (2) the best green tea;

綻露 reveal a matter;

朝露 morning dew;

lu

【籙】 (1) chart; map; (2) list; memorandum; (3) Daoist amulet or charm;

lu

【鷺】 egret;

白鷺 egret;

蒼鷺 heron;

池鷺 pond heron;

朱鷺 ibis;

lü²

lü

【閭】 (1) a community of 25 families in

ancient China; (2) the gate of a village; (3) gather together; meet; (4) a surname;

[閭里] one's home town; one's native village;
[閭巷] alley; alleyway; lane;
[閭閻] (1) district inhabited by common people; (2) common people;
[閭左] (1) district inhabited by the poor; (2) the poor;

lü

【婁】 trail along; wear;

lü

【廔】 humpback; hunchback;

lü

【瘻】 humpback; hunchback;

lü

【櫚】 palm;
[櫚葉葵] glade mallow;

lü

【驢】 donkey; ass;
[驢車] donkey cart;
[驢叫] bray;
[驢臉] donkey's face; long face;
[驢馬] donkey and horse;
非驢非馬 neither ass nor horse; neither fish, flesh, nor fowl; neither fish, flesh, nor good red herring; neither hay nor grass; nondescript;
驢唇不對馬嘴 a donkey's lips cannot fit into a horse's mouth; an answer that is beside the point; irrelevant answer;
驢年馬月 impossible date; the time will never come;
[驢子] donkey;
一匹驢子 a donkey;

草驢 female donkey;
蠢驢 ass; donkey; idiot;
叫驢 jackass;
毛驢 donkey;
母驢 mare;
野驢 Asiatic wild ass;
一頭驢 a donkey;

lü³

lü

【呂】 (1) a surname; (2) one of the five musical notes in ancient China;
[呂宋] Luzon;

lü

【侶】 (1) companion; mate; (2) associate with;

伴侶 companion; mate; partner;
情侶 lovers; sweethearts;
僧侶 monks and priests;

lü

【旅】 (1) stay away from home; travel; (2) brigade; (3) force; troops;
[旅伴] fellow traveller; travelling companion;
[旅程] journey; itinerary; route;
登上旅程 set off on a journey;
計劃旅程 plan a journey;
縮短旅程 shorten one's journey;
一段旅程 a section of a journey;
[旅店] hostel; inn;
小旅店 coaching inn;
[旅費] travelling expenses;
[旅館] hotel; inn; tavern;
旅館賬單 hotel bill;
蹩腳旅館 crappy hotel;
度假旅館 holiday inn;
經營旅館 keep an inn;
廉價旅館 flophouse;
~骯髒的廉價旅館 fleabag; fleabag hotel;
汽車旅館 motel; motor inn;
小旅館 inn;
~小旅館老闆 innkeeper;
一家旅館 a hotel;
住旅館 lodge at a hotel; put up at an inn;
[旅居] reside abroad; sojourn; stay abroad;
[旅客] (1) hotel guest; (2) passenger; (3) tourist; (4) traveller;
旅客陷阱 tourist trap;
長途旅客 long-distance passengers;
出境旅客 outgoing passenger;
單身旅客 individual passenger;
接待外國旅客 receive foreign travellers;
慢待旅客 neglect a traveler;
內地旅客 mainland visitors; visitors from mainland China;
入境旅客 incoming passenger;
卧鋪旅客 sleeper passenger berth;
一大批的旅客 a large number of tourists;
一群旅客 a party of travellers;
[旅人] traveller;
[旅舍] (1) hostel; (2) hotel;
青年旅舍 youth hostel;
[旅途] journey; trip;
旅途勞頓 fatigued by a journey; the

exertion of travelling; the hardships of a journey; travel-worn;
旅途愉快 a good trip;
~ 祝你旅途愉快 have a good trip;

[旅行] excursion; expedition; go on a trip to; go on an excursion to; have a trip; jaunt; journey to; make a journey to; make a tour of; make a trip to; make an excursion to; on a journey; on a trip to; outing; take a trip to; tour; tour round; travel to; trip; voyage;

旅行安排 travel arrangements;
旅行包 travel bag;
~ 小旅行包 overnight bag;
旅行杯 travel mug;
旅行車 tourist bus;
旅行袋 travelling bag;
~ 大旅行袋 carryall; holdall;
旅行高峰期 peak travel period;
旅行計劃 itinerary;
旅行結婚 wedding tour;
旅行客車 charabanc;
旅行社 tour operator; tourist agency; travel agency;
旅行拖車 camper; camper van; caravan;
旅行者 tourist;
~ 環球旅行者 globetrotter;
旅行支票 traveller's cheque;
旅行鐘 carriage clock; travel clock;
揹包旅行 backpacking;
長途旅行 long journey;
乘船旅行 travel by boat;
獨自旅行 travel alone;
各處旅行 travel around;
火車旅行 train journey; train trip;
繼續旅行 continue one's journey;
結伴旅行 travel together;
經常旅行 do much travelling;
開始旅行 begin a journey; start a journey;
蜜月旅行 honeymoon trip;
去旅行 go on a journey;
徒步旅行 go hiking; go trekking; hike; trek;
一次旅行 a journey;
在外旅行 away on a trip;
正在旅行 on a journey;

[旅遊] (1) tour; (2) tourism;
旅遊錶 travel clock;
旅遊車 touring car; tourist bus;
旅遊城市 tourist city;
旅遊導遊 tourist guide;
旅遊度假區 tourist holiday zone;
旅遊高峰季節 peak tourist season;
旅遊公司 tour operator;
旅遊管理 tourism management;
旅遊環境 tourism environment;
旅遊經濟學 tourism economics;
旅遊景點 places of tourist attraction; scenic spot; tourist attraction; tourist destination;
旅遊科學 tourism science;
旅遊路線 tour route;
旅遊美學 aesthetics of tourism;
旅遊區 tourist area;
~ 旅遊區劃 tourist regionization;
旅遊手冊 guidebook;
旅遊熱 travel boom;
旅遊商品 tourism goods;
旅遊社會學 sociology of tourism;
旅遊勝地 tourist resort; tourist site;
旅遊市場 tourist market;
旅遊團 tourist group;
旅遊旺季 tourist rush season;
旅遊味 touristy;
~ 旅遊味太濃 too touristy;
旅遊吸引力 tourist attraction;
旅遊銷售點 shops at tourist attractions;
旅遊鞋 tourist shoes;
旅遊心理學 psychology of tourism;
旅遊學校 tourism school;
旅遊業 tourism; tourist industry; travel industry;
旅遊中心 tourist centre;
旅遊資源 tourist resources;
~ 旅遊資源開發 developing of tourist resources;
~ 旅遊資源評價 tourist resources evaluation;
~ 旅遊資源信息 tourist resources information;
包辦旅遊 package tour;
包價旅遊 inclusive tour; package tour;
到國外旅遊 travel abroad;
短途旅遊 jaunt;
~ 周末短途旅遊 weekend jaunt;
觀光旅遊 sightseeing tour;
假日旅遊 holiday tour;
神秘旅遊 mystery tour;
生態旅遊 ecotourism;
醫療旅遊 health tourism;

[旅長] brigade commander;

羈旅 live in a strange land;

勁旅 crack force; strong contingent;
逆旅 hotel; inn;
商旅 trade caravan;
行旅 traveller; wayfarer;

lü

【捋】 stroke one's beard;

lü

【梠】 a small beam supporting the rafters at the eaves;

lü

【婁】 tether;

lü

【屢】 repeatedly; time and again;

［屢次］ repeatedly; time and again;
屢次三番 again and again; many times; often; over and over again; repeatedly; time after time;

［屢屢］ again and again; repeatedly; time and again;
屢屢得分 make one score after another;
屢屢得手 succeed time and again;
屢屢失手 fail again and again;
屢屢失算 misjudge repeatedly;
屢屢失誤 slip up again and again;
屢屢作弊 cheat in an examination again and again;
屢試屢躓 fail at each trial;
屢戰屢北 a succession of defeats; be defeated in successive battles; suffer many reverses; suffer repeated defeats;

［屢遭］ suffer again and again;
屢遭暗算 fall prey to a plot over and over again;
屢遭白眼 be treated with disdain repeatedly;
屢遭不測 a succession of misfortunes befall sb;
屢遭不幸 suffer misfortune after misfortune;
屢遭挫折 meet with frequent setbacks; meet with setbacks repeatedly;
屢遭毒打 be beaten up again and again;
屢遭誹謗 be slandered time and again;
屢遭拒絕 be refused again and again;
屢遭冷遇 be treated with chilly disdain;
屢遭慢待 be neglected time and again; be slighted time and again;
屢遭失敗 suffer defeat after defeat;
屢遭誤解 suffer misunderstandings time and again;

lü

【膂】 backbone; spinal column;

［膂力］ brawn; muscular strength; physical strength;
膂力方剛 while one's backbone retains its strength;
膂力過人 possessing extraordinary physical strength;

lü

【履】 (1) shoes; (2) tread on; walk on; (3) footsteps; (4) carry out; fulfil; honour;

［履穿踵決］ both of one's shoes have holes in them; down at heel;

［履及劍及］ perform a task with full vigour and urgency;

［履歷］ biographical data; curriculum vitae; personal details;

［履瓊踩玉］ tread one's way through the snow as though walking through fragments of white jade;

［履險如夷］ go over a dangerous pass as if walking on level ground — cope with a crisis without difficulty; walk over the precipice as if strolling on a highway;

［履新］ take or asume one's new office or post;
履新視事 take up a new appointment and assume office;

［履行］ carry out; fulfil; perform;
履行公民義務 fulfil one's obligations as a citizen;
履行公務 perform one's official duty;
履行合同 carry a contract; comply with an agreement; discharge a contract; fulfil a contract; performance of a contract;
履行諾言 carry out one's promise; fulfil one's promise; hold one's word; keep one's word; live up to one's promise;
履行契約 meet one's obligations;
履行手續 go through the procedures;
履行條約 observe a treaty;
履行義務 carry out one's obligations; comply with one's duty; duty of performance;
履行職責 do one's duty;

［履約］ (1) honour an agreement; (2) keep an appointment;
履約保證 performance bond; performance guarantee;

履約而來 attend an appointment;

步履 walk;
革履 leather shoes;
屐履 shoes;

lü
【鋁】 aluminium;
[鋁鍋] aluminium cooker; aluminium pan; aluminium pot;
[鋁化] aluminization; aluminize;
[鋁勺] aluminium ladle;
[鋁銅] aluminium bronze;

氧化鋁 alumina;

lü
【縷】 (1) thread; (2) lock; strand; wisp; (3) detailed; in detail;
[縷陳] narrate in detail;
[縷解] explain in detail; go into particulars;
[縷縷] continuously;
縷縷陳述 narrate in details;
[縷述] give all the details; go into particulars; state in detail;
[縷析] analyse in detail; make a detailed analysis;
[縷息僅存] hang by a thread;

藍縷 ragged; shabby;
覼縷 narrate in detail;

lü
【褸】 (1) collar of a garment; (2) sloppily; tattered;

襤褸 ragged; shabby;

lü4
lü
【律】 (1) law; regulation; rule; statute; (2) bind by law; control; discipline; keep under control; restrain; (3) a series of standard bamboo tuning pitch-pipes used in ancient music; (4) a form of Chinese poetry — a stanza of eight lines;
[律己] discipline oneself; self-restrain;
律己勸人 exercise self-discipline and try to persuade others to do so;
律己正人 the person who laughs at a hunchback should walk very straight himself; sweep before your own door;
[律例] statutes and precedents;
[律人] treat others;
寬以律人 treat others liberally;
[律師] barrister; lawyer; solicitor;
律師界 legal profession;
律師事務所 law firm; law office;
律師協會 lawyers' association;
辯護律師 counsel; solicitor;
二級律師 second-grade lawyer;
顧問律師 consulting lawyer;
控方律師 prosecutor;
沒有生意的律師 briefless laywer;
女律師 lady lawyer; lawyeress;
聘請律師 hire a lawyer;
三級律師 third-grade lawyer;
四級律師 fourth-grade lawyer;
首席律師 general counsel;
一級律師 first-grade lawyer;
助理律師 assistant lawyer;
做律師 go in for law; practise as a lawyer;

定律 law;
法律 law; statute;
分配律 distributive law;
規律 law; regular pattern;
忽律 alligator; crocodile;
紀律 discipline;
交換律 commutative law;
結合律 associative law;
節律 rhythm and law;
戒律 commandment; religious discipline;
心律 rhythm of the heart;
刑律 criminal law;
旋律 melody;
一律 alike; same; uniform;
音律 temperament;

lü
【率】 (1) lead; (2) act in accordance with; follow; (3) rash and hasty; (4) for the most part; generally; (5) frank; simple and candid; straightforward; to the point; (6) (said of a man) dashing;

百分率 per cent; percentage;
比率 rate; ratio;
表率 example; model; paragon;
粗率 (1) crude and coarse; (2) careless; ill-considered; rash; rough and careless;

概率 probability;
匯率 exchange rate;
機率 probability;
利率 interest rate; rate of interest;
頻率 frequency;
曲率 curvature;
稅率 rate of taxation; tax rate;
速率 rate; speed;
效率 efficiency;
周率 frequency;

lü

【氯】 chlorine;

[氯胺酮] ketamine;

[氯丙酮] chlorinated acetone;

[氯含量] chlorinity;

[氯化] chlorinate;
氯化銨 ammonium chloride;
氯化鋇 barium chloride;
氯化電爐 electric chlorinator;
氯化鈣 calcium chloride;
氯化鉀 potassium chloride;
氯化鎂 magnesium chloride;
氯化鈉 sodium chloride;
氯化器 chlorinator;
氯化氫 hydrogen chloride;
氯化銅 copper chloride;
氯化物 chloride;
氯化鉛 lead chloride;
氯化鋅 zinc chloride;
氯化銀 silver chloride;
氯化作用 chlorination;
鏈上氯化 chain chlorination;
熱氯化 thermal chlorination;

乙酰氯 acetylchloride;

lü

【菉】 (1) a kind of grass; (2) green;

lü

【綠】 green;

[綠草] green grass;
綠草帶 herbaceous border;
綠草如茵 a carpet of green grass; soft green grass carpets the ground; the grass looks like a carpet;

[綠茶] green tea;

[綠燈] (1) (traffic) green light; (2) permission to go ahead with a project;
開綠燈 give free rein; give the go-ahead; give the green light;

[綠豆] green beans; mung beans;
綠豆芽 green bean sprouts; mung bean sprouts;

[綠矾] copperas; green copperas;
葉綠矾 yellow copperas;
針綠矾 while copperas;

[綠化] afforest; make green by planting trees;
綠化城市 green city;
綠化地帶 green belt;
綠化工程 landscape engineering;
綠化區 green area;

[綠色] green; green colour;
綠色的 greenish;
～略帶綠色的 greenish;
綠色革命 green revolution;
綠色經濟 green economy;
綠色能源 green energy sources;
綠色審計 green audit;
綠色食品 green food;
綠色稅 green tax;
綠色運動 green movement;
暗綠色 drab green;
草綠色 grass green;
翠綠色 emerald;
海綠色 sea green;
墨綠色 blackish green;
蘋果綠 apple green;
淺黃綠色 lime green;
青綠色 turquoise;
深綠色 bottle green;
鴨綠色 duck green;
艷黃綠色 viridine green;
一片綠色 a tint of green;

[綠意] green;
一絲綠意 a tint of green;

碧綠 dark green;
草綠 grass green;
常綠 evergreen;
葱綠 (1) pale yellowish green; (2) light green; verdant;
翠綠 emerald green; jade green;
黛綠 dark green;
豆綠 pea green;
墨綠 blackish green;
嫩綠 light green; soft green;
品綠 light green; malachite green;
青綠 dark green;
石綠 mineral green;
水綠 light green;
銅綠 verdigris;
油綠 glossy dark green;

lü

【慮】 (1) consider; take into account; (2) anxious about; worry about;

顧慮 apprehension; be concerned about; misgiving; worry;
掛慮 be anxious about; worry about;
過慮 be overanxious; worry unnecessarily;
焦慮 anxious; worried;
考慮 consider; ponder over;
思慮 consider carefully; deliberate;
疑慮 doubt; misgive; misgivings;
憂慮 be anxious about; worry;
遠慮 foresight; long view;

L

lü

【濾】 filter; strain;

［濾波］ filtering;
多路濾波 multichannel filtering;
匹配濾波 matched filtering;
梳狀濾波 comb filtering;
數字濾波 digital filtering;

［濾光］ light filtering;
濾光片 absorber;
~ 干涉濾光片 interference absorber;
~ 選擇性濾光片 selective absorber;
~ 中性濾光片 non-selective absorber;
濾光器 filter; light filter;
~ 紅外線濾光器 infrared filter;
~ 柔和濾光器 diffuse filter;
~ 紫外線濾光器 ultraviolet filter;

［濾盆］ colander;

［濾器］ colander; strainer;
粗濾器 coarse strainer;
氣管濾器 air pipe strainer;

［濾色］ filter;
濾色鏡 colour filter; filter;
~ 濾色鏡因數 filter factor;
~ 玻璃濾色鏡 glass filter;
~ 補償濾色鏡 compensating filter;

［濾紙］ filter paper;

過濾 filter; filtrate;
滲濾 filtrate; percolate;

luan²

luan

【巒】 pointed hill;

峰巒 ridges and peaks;
岡巒 continuous hills;
山巒 chain of mountains;

luan

【欒】 (1) a small tree with tiny leaves and yellow flowers; (2) the two corners at the mouth of a Chinese bell; (3) a surname;

luan

【臠】 (1) meat chops or cuts; (2) lean; thin;

［臠割］ carve up; slice up;

禁臠 one's exclusive domain;

luan

【灤】 the name of a river in northern China;

luan

【鑾】 bells hung on the imperial chariot or carriage;

luan

【鸞】 a fabulous bird related to the phoenix;

［鸞鳳］ husband and wife;
鸞鳳和鳴 a happily married couple; a happy couple; be blessed with conjugal felicity;
鸞交鳳友 a couple deeply in love;
鸞飄鳳泊 (1) a couple is separated from one another; (2) write with a natural and unrestrained penmanship;
鸞翔鳳集 a galaxy of talent; an assembly of people of ability; gathering of talented people;
鸞翔鳳翥 lively and vigorous movement of penmanship — fine calligraphy;

扶鸞 planchette writing;

luan³

luan

【卵】 (1) egg; (2) ovum; (3) fish roe; (4) testicles;

［卵白］ albumen; egg white;

［卵巢］ oophoron;
卵巢病 oophoropathy;
卵巢管 ovariole;
~ 多滋卵巢管 polytrophic ovariole;
~ 無滋卵巢管 panoistic ovariole;
卵巢瘤 oophoroma;
卵巢體 ovariotestis;
卵巢痛 oophoralgia;
卵巢炎 oophoritis; ovaritis;

~硬化性卵巢炎 sclero-oophoritis;

[卵帶] chalaza;

[卵黃] yolk;
卵黃膜 yolk membrane;
卵黃囊 vitellus capsule;
白卵黃 white yolk;
黃養料卵黃 yellow food yolk;

[卵裂] cleavage;
單性卵裂 parthenogenetic cleavage;
定型卵裂 determinate cleavage;
對角卵裂 diagonal cleavage;
卵黃卵裂 yolk cleavage;
盤形卵裂 discoidal cleavage;
完全卵裂 holoblastic cleavage;
右旋卵裂 dextrotopic cleavage;
中緯卵裂 equatorial cleavage;
左旋卵裂 levotropic cleavage;

[卵囊] egg capsule;

[卵泡] follicle;

[卵石] cobble; pebble; shingle;
內轉卵形線 inrevolvable oval;
平均卵形線 mean oval;

[卵子] egg; ovum;
卵子發生 ovigenesis; ovogenesis;
卵子移植 egg transplantation;

敗育卵 abortive egg;
產卵 lay eggs; spawn;
累卵 a stack of eggs;
排卵 ovulate;
無黃卵 alecithal egg;
營養卵 alimentary egg;
有殼卵 cleidoic egg;
有黃卵 yolky egg;
中黃卵 centrolecithal egg;

luan⁴
luan

【亂】 (1) in a mess; in confusion; in disorder; (2) confused; disturbed; upset; (3) confuse sb; throw sb into chaos; upset sb; (4) arbitrary; indiscriminate; random; (5) promiscuity;

[亂兵] mutinous soldiers; undisciplined troops;

[亂吵吵] vociferous;

[亂竄] run helter-skelter;

[亂紛紛] chaotic; confused; disorderly;

[亂搞] fiddle with; meddle with; mess about; mess with; monkey with; tamper with;

[亂哄洪] in a hubbub; in an uproar; in noisy disorder; tumultuous;
亂亂哄哄 hurly-burly;

[亂畫] doodle;

[亂砍] haggle;
亂砍濫伐 excessive deforestation;

[亂來] act recklessly; unruly;

[亂離] be forced to leave one's home due to war; be rendered homeless by war; be separated by war;

[亂…亂…] haphazardly;
亂打亂刺 tilt in all directions;
亂花亂用 spend money recklessly;
亂抓亂碰 go about one's work blindly and haphazardly;

[亂倫] commit incest; incest;
亂倫的 incestuous;

[亂麻麻] chaotic; confused;

[亂罵] foul abuse; verbal garbage;

[亂蓬蓬] dishevelled; jumbled; tangled;

[亂瓊碎玉] scattered and broken jade—snow;

[亂如絲麻] tanged like silk and hemp;

[亂殺] kill without discrimination;
亂打亂殺 beating and killing without discrimination;

[亂世] troubled times; turbulent days;
亂世出英雄 heroes emerge in troubled times;
亂世生怪事 strange things come to pass in troubled times; strange things happen in times of trouble;
亂世英雄 heroes in a troubled time; heroes in troubled times;

[亂説] blab; gossip; make irresponsible remarks; speak carelessly;
亂説亂動 speak or act in an unruly way; speak or act wildly;
亂説一頓 idle chatter; idle talk; say anything that comes into one's head; talk through one's hat;

[亂套] muddle things up; turn things upside down;

[亂騰騰] confused; upset;

[亂頭粗服] not care about one's appearance; with tangled hair and plain clothes;

[亂塗] doodle;

[亂雲飛渡] clouds scud across the sky;

[亂糟糟] chaotic; confused; in a mess; in a whirl; perturbed;

稀亂八糟 in a pandemonium; in total disorder;

[亂真] (1) look genuine; (2) spurious;

幾可亂真 good enough to pass for genuine;

[亂正] chaos and order;

撥亂反正 bring order out of chaos; restore things to order; set to right what has been thrown into disorder;

[亂子] disorder; disturbance; trouble;

出亂子 get into trouble; go wrong; lead to trouble;

闖亂子 get into trouble; invite trouble;

沒出什麼亂子 no trouble occurred;

鬧亂子 cause trouble;

惹亂子 bring trouble; make mischief; provoke a dispute;

添亂子 aggravate the trouble;

暴亂 revolt; riot;

變亂 social upheaval; turmoil;

兵亂 turmoil caused by war;

錯亂 in disorder; in confusion;

搗亂 (1) create a disturbance; (2) make trouble;

動亂 disturbance; turmoil;

紛亂 chaotic; numerous and disorderly;

胡亂 (1) carelessly; casually; (2) at random;

荒亂 in great disorder; in turmoil;

慌亂 alarmed and bewildered; flurried;

昏亂 befuddled; dazed and confused;

混亂 chaos; confusion;

禍亂 curse; disaster;

惑亂 confuse; puzzle;

霍亂 (1) cholera; (2) acute gastroenteritis;

攪亂 (1) cause trouble; disturb; stir; (2) confuse; throw into disorder;

戡亂 suppress a rebellion;

潰亂 crumble and become confused;

繚亂 confused; in a turmoil;

淩亂 in a mess; in disorder;

零亂 in a mess; in disorder;

忙亂 busy and flurried;

內亂 internal civil strife;

叛亂 armed rebellion; rebel; rise in rebellion;

蓬亂 fluffy and disorderly;

擾亂 create confusion; harass;

喪亂 disturbance; turmoil;

騷亂 chaos; create a disturbance; make trouble; riot;

紊亂 chaotic; disorderly; in confusion;

淆亂 befuddle; confuse;

淫亂 licentious; promiscuous;

有些亂 a bit of a mess;

雜亂 mixed and disorderly; in a jumble;

戰亂 chaos caused by war;

肇亂 cause trouble; create a disturbance;

作亂 stage an armed rebellion;

lüan²
lüan

【孿】 twins;

[孿晶] twin;

互穿孿晶 interpenetration twin;

生長孿晶 growth twin;

[孿生] bear twins; born as twins; twinning;

孿生姐妹 twin sisters;

孿生兄弟 twin brothers;

電孿生 electric twinning;

多合孿生 polysynthetic twinning;

光學孿生 chiral twinning;

形變孿生 deformation twinning;

振盪孿生 oscillatory twinning;

[孿元素] twin elements;

lüan

【攣】 (1) tangled; (2) crooked; (3) contraction;

[攣弱] crooked and weak;

[攣縮] contraction; spasm; twitch;

[攣腰] crooked back;

[攣踠] a sort of arthropathy;

痙攣 convulsion; spasm;

拘攣 cramp;

lüan³
lüan

【孌】 (1) beautiful; handsome; (2) docile; obedient;

[孌美] effeminate;

[孌慕] long after;

[孌童] catamite;

lüe⁴
lüe

【掠】 (1) pillage; plunder; sack; (2) brush past; graze; skim over; sweep past;

[掠奪] pillage; plunder; rob;

掠奪弱小國家 plunder the weaker nations;

掠奪者 booter;

~戰爭掠奪者 freebooter;

[掠過] skim over; sweep past;

掠面而過 flit across one's face;

一掠而過 skim over; sweep past quickly;

[掠美] claim credit due to others;
不敢掠美 not dare to claim credit due to others;
[掠取] grab; plunder; seize;
[掠影] sparkle;
掠影浮光 superficial;
湖光掠影 the lake ripples and sparkles;

焚掠 burn houses and loot;
劫掠 loot; plunder;
擄掠 loot; pillage;
搶掠 loot; plunder;

lüe

【略】 (1) brief; sketchy; (2) a little; slightly; somewhat; (3) brief account; outline; summary; (4) delete; leave out; omit; (5) plan; scheme; strategy; (6) capture; seize;
[略略] briefly; slightly;
[略去] leave out; omit;
略去不提 leave out altogether; make no mention of; omit to mention; omit to say;
略去不談 leave out altogether; make no mention of; pass over;
略去細節 leave out the details;
[略述] describe briefly; give a brief account of; mention briefly; sketch out;
略述大意 give a brief account;
略述梗概 just tell the main points;
略述其要點 sketch out its outline;
略述原委 sketch out the whole story;
略述原因 give a brief account of one's reasons;
[略圖] (1) sketch; (2) sketch map;
[略微] a bit of; a little; a trifle; briefly; slightly; something of; somewhat;
略微說一下 say a few words about;
略微有點感冒 have a slight cold;
略微有點頭痛 have a slight headache;
[略語] abbreviation;
商業略語 commercial abbreviation;

才略 ability and sagacity;
策略 tactics;
從略 be omitted;
粗略 rough; sketchy;
大略 (1) great talent; (2) broad outline; general idea;
膽略 courage and resourcefulness;
方略 general plan;
概略 outline; summary;
忽略 lose sight of; neglect; overlook;
簡略 brief; simple; sketchy;
將略 military strategy and tactics;
節略 memorandum;
經略 manage and scheme;
領略 appreciate; have a taste of; realize;
謀略 strategy;
侵略 invade;
權略 tactics; trickery;
缺略 imperfect; incomplete;
省略 leave out; omit;
史略 brief history;
事略 biographical sketch;
韜略 military strategy;
脫略 unrestrained;
崖略 essential points;
要略 outline; summary;
約略 approximately; roughly;
戰略 strategy;
智略 wisdom and resourcefulness;
傳略 brief biography;

lun¹
lun

【掄】 (1) beat; hit; slap; swing at; (2) brandish; wave; (3) squander; (4) talk nonsense; talk rubbish;
[掄圓了] exert all one's strength; swing one's arms with all one's might;

lun²
lun

【掄】 choose; select;

lun

【倫】 (1) human relations; (2) logic; order; (3) match; peer;
[倫比] equal; rival;
莫與倫比 peerless; there is no rival for it; unequalled; unrivalled;
無與倫比 beyond compare; beyond comparison; defy all comparison; head and shoulders above the rest; incomparable; matchless; out of comparison; past compare; peerless; stand alone; there is no comparison with; there is none to compare to; unbeatable; unequalled; unique; unparalleled; unrivalled; untouched; without compare; without comparison;

without equal; without parallel; without peer; without rival;
~無與倫比的 unequalled; unparalleled;

[倫常] human relations;
[倫理] ethics; moral principles;
倫理教育 ethical education;
倫理模式 ethical model;
倫理學 ethics;

氨倫 spandex;
絕倫 matchless; unsurpassed;
亂倫 commit incest;
人倫 human relations formulated by feudal ethics;
天倫 natural bonds and ethical relationships between members of a family;
同倫 homotopy;
五倫 five human relationships;
彝倫 cardinal human relationships;
軼倫 outstanding; surpass one's contemporaries;

lun
【崙】 Kunlun Mountains;

lun
【淪】 (1) sink; (2) be reduced to; fall;
[淪肌浹髓] be deeply impressed; be greatly affected; extreme gratitude;
[淪落] be reduced to poverty; come down in the world;
淪落風塵 be driven to prostitution; become a prostitute;
淪落街頭 become a beggar;
淪落為騙子 be degraded into cheating;
淪落為乞丐 be degraded into begging;
淪落異鄉 sink in a strange district;
[淪喪] be lost; be ruined; perish;
道德淪喪 sink into moral degradation;
[淪亡] be annexed;
[淪為] be reduced to; become;
淪為妓女 be driven to prostitution; become a prostitute;
淪為流氓 become a tramp;
淪為乞丐 be reduced to beggary; become a beggar;
淪為窮光蛋 fall into poverty;
[淪陷] be occupied by the enemy; fall into enemy hands; flood; submerge;

沉淪 sink into degradation;

lun
【圇】 entire; whole;

lun
【綸】 (1) fishing line; (2) green silk cord;

滌綸 terylene;
經綸 statecraft;
耐綸 nylon;

lun
【論】 (1) a surname; (2) an alternative of 論 in some phrases;

lun
【輪】 (1) wheel; (2) disc; ring; (3) wheel-shaped object; (4) steamboat; steamer; (5) take turns; (6) round;
[輪班] in shifts; on duty by turns;
[輪船] steamer;
輪船代理人 shipping agent;
內河輪船 river steamer;
一艘輪船 a ship;
遠洋輪船 ocean-going vessel;
[輪牀] gurney;
[輪到] it is one's turn to;
輪到你做飯 it's your turn to cook;
[輪渡] ferry;
[輪番] take turns;
[輪換] alternate; rotate; take turns;
[輪迴] (1) coming again and again; (2) transmigration;
[輪姦] gang rape;
[輪廓] contour; line; lineament; outline; profile; rough sketch;
輪廓銳度 contour acuity;
斷面輪廓 profiled outline;
拱圈輪廓 arch profile;
凸輪輪廓 cam profile;
[輪流] alternate; by rotation; by turns; in rotation; in turn; take spells at sth; take turns; turn and turn about;
輪流地 by turn;
輪流工作 work on shifts;
輪流交替 alternation;
~政府的輪流交替 alternation of governments;
輪流開車 take turns driving;
輪流看守 take turns in keeping watch;
輪流值日 on duty by turns;
輪流做飯 take turns to cook;
[輪胎] tyre;
輪胎爆裂 blow-out;
輪胎工 tyreman;

輪胎商 tyreman;
被扎破的輪胎 punctured tyre;
備用輪胎 spare tire; spare tyre;
充氣輪胎 pneumatic tyre;
防滑輪胎 snow tyre;
飛機輪胎 aerotyre; aircraft tyre;
航空輪胎 aerotyre;
後備輪胎 spare wheel;
後輪胎 rear tyre;
抗滑輪胎 adhesion tyre;
空氣輪胎 air tyre;
前輪胎 front tyre;

[輪椅] wheelchair;
[輪種] alternation of crops;
[輪軸] axle;

擺輪 balance wheel;
班輪 regular steamship service;
蟾輪 the moon;
車輪 wheel of a vehicle;
齒輪 gear; gear wheel;
從輪 driving wheel;
導輪 (1) guide pulley; (2) pilot wheel;
動輪 wheel;
渡輪 ferry steamer;
舵輪 steering wheel;
耳輪 helix;
光輪 halo;
後輪 rear wheel;
滑輪 pulley;
江輪 river steamer;
膠輪 rubber tyre;
巨輪 (1) large wheel; (2) large ship;
客輪 passenger ship;
年輪 annual ring; growth ring;
前輪 front wheel;
手輪 handwheel;
拖輪 towboat;
渦輪 turbine;
牙輪 gear; gear wheel;
油輪 oil tanker;
漁輪 fishing vessel;
月輪 full moon;
左輪 revolver;

lun⁴
lun

【論】 (1) discuss; talk about; (2) opinion; statement; view; (3) dissertation; essay; (4) theory; (5) consider; mention; regard; (6) decide on; determine; (7) by; in terms of;

[論辯] debate;
[論處] decide on sb's punishment; punish;
按瀆職論處 be punished for malfeasance;
按違紀論處 be punished for a breach of discipline;
[論敵] opponent in a debate;
[論點] argument; thesis;
持相同的論點 hold the same view;
老一套的論點 stock argument;
提出論點 put forth an argument; put up an argument;
一個論點 an argument;
幼稚的論點 childish arguments;
正確論點 valid argument;
[論調] argument; view;
提出相反的論調 set forth opposite opinions;
[論斷] inference; judgment; thesis;
科學論斷 scientific thesis;
[論功] on the basis of merits;
論功提昇 promotion by merit;
論功行賞 award people according to their contributions; decide on awards on the basis of merit; give people awards according to their contributions; reward sb according to his/her merits;
[論及] touch upon;
[論據] argument; grounds of argument;
論據不足 insufficient grounds;
論據充分 have sufficient grounds;
法律論據 legal argument;
建設性論據 constructive argument;
理論論據 theoretical argument;
[論理] (1) as things should be; normally; (2) logic; (3) have it out; reason things out;
[論列] expound;
[論難] argue against the opponent's viewpoint; debate;
[論述] discuss; expound; relate and analyze;
充分論述 expound adequately;
[論説] (1) comment; expound; (2) as things should be; normally;
論説文 argumentative prose;
[論壇] forum; tribune;
[論文] (1) dissertation; paper; thesis; treatise; (2) discuss literature;
論文答辯 oral defence of one's dissertation;
博士論文 doctoral dissertation;

碩士論文 master's thesis;
學術論文 academic dissertation;
一篇論文 a thesis; an article;
樽酒論文 discuss literature over a glass of wine;

[論戰] argue; controversy; debate; polemic;
[論爭] argument; controversy; debate;
[論證] (1) demonstration; proof; (2) expound and prove; (3) argument;
經濟論證 economic argument;
物理論證 physical argument;
[論著] book; treatise; works;
[論資排輩] arrange in order of seniority; be promoted according to status; give priority to seniority in the selection;
[論罪] determine the nature of the guilt;

罷論 abandoned idea;
本體論 ontology;
辯論 argue; debate;
不論 regardless of;
持論 present an argument;
讜論 unbiased comment;
導論 introduction;
定論 final conclusion; final verdict;
多神論 polytheism;
多元論 pluralism;
二元論 dualism;
泛論 expound generally;
泛神論 pantheism;
方法論 methodology;
概論 introduction; outline;
高論 brilliant views;
公論 public opinion; verdict of the masses;
弘論 informed opinion; intelligent view;
講論 discuss; talk about;
交際論 communication theory;
結論 (1) conclusion; (2) verdict;
進化論 evolutionism;
決定論 determinism;
空論 empty talk;
理論 theory;
立論 present one's arguments; set forth one's views;
量子論 quantum theory;
妙論 witty remark;
謬論 fallacy; falsehood; faulty reasoning;
目的論 teleology;
評論 comment; comment on; commentary; discuss; review;
認識論 epistemology;
社論 (1) editorial; (2) leading article;
史論 history essay;
談論 discuss; talk about;
討論 discuss; talk about;
通論 general survey;
推論 (1) deduce; infer; (2) deduction; inference;
唯物論 materialism;
唯心論 idealism;
無論 no matter what;
無神論 atheism;
先驗論 apriorism;
相對論 relativity; the theory of relativity;
緒論 introduction;
言論 views on politics;
一元論 monism;
議論 comment; discuss; talk;
因果論 theory of causation;
有神論 theism;
輿論 public opinion;
爭論 contention; controversy; debate; dispute;
正論 correct and sensible view;
政論 political comment;
專論 monograph;

luo¹

luo
【捋】 (1) pull; (2) squeeze with one'shand;

luo
【囉】 (1) verbose; wordy; (2) indistinct speech sound;

luo
【囉】 chatter;
[囉嗦] long-winded; wordy;
講話囉嗦 speak wordily;

luo
【攞】 pull; tug;

luo²

luo
【螺】 (1) conch; spiral shell; (2) spiral;
[螺釘] screw;
調節螺釘 adjusting screw;
通氣螺釘 air vent screw;
[螺距] pitch;
表觀螺距 apparent pitch;
葉片螺距 blade pitch;
有效螺距 effective pitch;
[螺菌] spirillum;
[螺母] nut;
球狀螺母 ball nut;
調整螺母 adjust nut;

翼形螺母 wing nut;
止動螺母 arresting nut;

[螺栓] bolt;
緊固螺栓 binding bolt;
聯接螺栓 attachment bolt;
球頭螺栓 ball head bolt;
調整螺栓 adjusting bolt;
繫緊螺栓 anchorage bolt;
軸承螺栓 bearing bolt;
軸螺栓 axle bolt;
裝配螺栓 assembly bolt;

[螺絲] screw;
螺絲刀 screwdriver;
扣緊螺絲 tighten screws;

[螺紋] screw thread; thread;
螺紋梳刀 chaser; screw chaser; thread chaser;
~ 板牙頭螺紋梳刀 die head thread chaser;
~ 叉形螺紋梳刀 double-point thread chaser;
~ 徑向螺紋梳刀 radial thread chaser;
~ 內螺紋梳刀 inside thread chaser;
~ 切向螺紋梳刀 tangential thread chaser;
~ 外螺紋梳刀 outside thread chaser;
~ 圓形螺紋梳刀 circular thread chaser;
粗牙螺紋 coarse thread;
精密螺紋 accurate thread;
鋸齒螺紋 buttress thread;
三角螺紋 angular thread;

[螺線管] solenoid;
合閘螺線管 closing solenoid;
空心螺線管 air core solenoid;

[螺旋] (1) spin; spiral; (2) corkscrew; screw;
螺旋面 helicoid;
~ 管道螺旋面 canal helicoid;
~ 漸開線螺旋面 involute helicoid;
~ 斜螺旋面 oblique helicoid;
~ 右螺旋面 right helicoid;
螺旋槳 airscrew; propeller;
~ 超音速螺旋槳 supersonic airscrew;
~ 定距螺旋槳 constant pitch propeller;
~ 定速螺旋槳 constant speed propeller;
~ 反距螺旋槳 braking propeller;
~ 反時針螺旋槳 anticlockwise propeller;
~ 飛機螺旋槳 aerial propeller; aeroplane propeller; airscrew;
~ 輔助螺旋槳 auxiliary propeller;
~ 高效率螺旋槳 high-performance propeller;
~ 空氣螺旋槳 airscrew;
~ 順時針螺旋槳 clockwise propeller;
~ 調距螺旋槳 adjustable pitch propeller;
~ 右旋螺旋槳 right-hand propeller;
~ 左旋螺旋槳 left-hand propeller;
螺旋菌 spirillum;
~ 螺旋菌狀 spirillum forms;
螺旋式 (of hairstyle) spiral style;
螺旋體 spirochete;
~ 螺旋體病 spirochetosis;
~ 間居性螺旋體 intermediate spirochete;
~ 性比率螺旋體 sex-ratio spirochete;
~ 血內螺旋體 blood spirochete;
螺旋線 helix;
~ 圓柱螺旋線 circular helix;
~ 柱面螺旋線 cylindrical helix;
~ 錐形螺旋線 conical helix;
被控螺旋 controlled spin;
槽紋螺旋 flute spiral;
等角螺旋 equiangular spiral;
共軛螺旋 conjugated spirals;
內螺旋 inside spin;
清理螺旋 cleaning spiral;
雙螺旋 double helix;
水平螺旋 flat spin;
右螺旋 right-hand spin;
左螺旋 left-hand spin;

釘螺 snail;
法螺 (1) triton; (2) conch;
風螺 conch;
海螺 conch;
田螺 river snail;
陀螺 top;
響螺 conch;

luo

【羅】 (1) net for catching birds; (2) collect; gather together; (3) display; (4) sieve; sift; (5) kind of silk gauze; (6) gross; twelve dozen;

[羅綢裹身] dress in silks and satins;

[羅緞] tussore;
穿羅著緞 be dressed in silks and satins;

[羅鍋兒] humpback; humpbacked; hunchback; hunchbacked;
羅鍋兒上山—錢（前）緊 like a humpback climbing a mountain — short of money;

[羅漢] arhat;
羅漢請觀音—客少主人多 Buddhist arhats inviting the goddess Guanyin — more hosts than guests;
八百羅漢 the eight hundred Buddhist

saints;

[羅掘] net and dig;

羅掘俱窮 exhaust all sources of getting money;

羅雀掘鼠 try very hard to scrape money together;

[羅列] enumerate; list out; spell out;

羅列事實 cite facts;

[羅曼蒂克] romantic;

[羅盤] compass;

羅盤儀 box compass;

導航羅盤 course setting compass;

方位羅盤 azimuth compass;

航空羅盤 aircraft compass;

天文羅盤 celestial compass;

星象羅盤 astro compass;

直讀羅盤 direct indicating compass;

[羅網] net; snare; trap;

佈設羅網 bait a trap; lay a snare;

逃脱羅網 escape the net; get out of a trap; slip through the net;

天羅地網 a situation from which there is no escape; nets in the sky and snares on the ground; tight encirclement;

陷入羅網 fall into a trap;

自投羅網 bite the hook; fall into a snare; fall into a trap set for oneself by another; fall into a trap through one's own fault; hurl oneself into the net; involve oneself; put one's feet into the trap; put one's head into a noose; put one's neck in a noose; stumble right into the net; walk into a trap;

[羅帷孤冷] alone and cold in one's bed;

[羅織] frame up;

羅織誣陷 frame sb up;

羅織罪名 cook up charges; frame a case against sb;

[羅致] collect; enlist the services of; gather together; recruit; secure sb in one's employment;

羅致人才 enlist the services of able people; look out for talents and engage their services;

爭相羅致 compete for the service of a capable person;

包羅 cover; embrace; include;

綾羅 different kinds of silk;

綺羅 damask;

紗羅 gauze;

收羅 enlist; gather;

網羅 trap;

閻羅 Yama;

luo

【覼】 speak in a roundabout way;

[覼縷] narrate in detail;

luo

【騾】 mule;

[騾馬] hinny;

[騾子] mule;

一匹騾子 a mule;

驢騾 hinny;

馬騾 mule;

luo

【玀】 a primitive tribe, also known as 猓玀;

luo

【蘿】 (1) a kind of creeping plant; (2) radish; (3) turnip;

[蘿蔔] (1) turnip; (2) radish;

蘿蔔乾 preserved radish;

蘿蔔青菜，各人喜愛 differrent strokes for defferent folks; no dish suits all tastes; tastes differ;

白蘿蔔 white radish;

扁蘿蔔 turnip;

黑蘿蔔 burdock;

紅蘿蔔 (1) carrot; (2) red radish;

胡蘿蔔 carota; carrot;

~ 胡蘿蔔素 carotene;

胡蘿蔔素酶 carotenase;

青蘿蔔 green radish;

糖蘿蔔 sweet beetroot;

小蘿蔔 radish;

菠蘿 pineapple;

蔦蘿 cypress vine;

藤蘿 Chinese wisteria;

luo

【邏】 inspect; patrol;

[邏輯] logic;

邏輯程序 logic programme;

~ 邏輯程序設計 programming in logic;

邏輯分析 logical analysis;

邏輯前提 logical presupposition;

邏輯數據庫 logical database;

邏輯思維 logical thinking;

邏輯謂語 logical predicate;

邏輯形式 logical form;
邏輯學 logic;
~ 邏輯學家 logician;
邏輯運算 logical operation;
邏輯重音 logical stress;
邏輯主語 logical subject;
邏輯作用詞 logical operator;
辯證邏輯 dialectical logic;
電路邏輯 circuit logic;
符合邏輯 logical;
模糊邏輯 fuzzy logic;
偏置邏輯 biasing logic;
數理邏輯 mathematical logic;
微型邏輯 micrologic;
形式邏輯 formal logic;
有源邏輯 active logic;
執行邏輯 actuating logic;
組合邏輯 combinatorial logic;
遵循邏輯 follow logic;

巡邏 go on patrol; patrol;

luo
【籮】 (1) bamboo basket; (2) sieve-like ware with broad edge;
[籮筐] (1) large bamboo basket; (2) large wicker basket;

笸籮 shallow basket;
淘籮 basket for washing rice in;

luo
【鑼】 gong;
[鑼槌] hammer;
[鑼鼓] (1) gongs and drums; (2) traditional percussion instruments;
鑼鼓喧天 a deafening sound of gongs and drums; the sound of gongs and drums echoes to the sky;
緊鑼密鼓 a din of drums and gongs;
密鑼緊鼓 great fanfare; widly beating gongs and drums;

開鑼 begin;
小鑼 small gong;
雲鑼 Chinese gong chimes;

luo³
luo
【虜】 a pronunciation of 虜 ;

luo
【漯】 a river in Shandong;

luo
【裸】 bare; exposed; in a state of nature; in one's birthday suit; in the altogether; in the buff; in the raw; naked;
[裸奔] streak;
裸奔者 streaker;
[裸地] bare area; bare land;
[裸露] exposed; nudity; uncovered;
裸露場面 scenes of nudity;
使裸露 denude;
[裸袒] bare; naked;
[裸體] in a state of nature; in one's birthday suit; in the altogether; in the buff; in the raw; in the rude; naked; nude;
裸體鏡頭 nude scenes;
裸體模特兒 nude model;
裸體沙灘 nude beach;
裸體藝術品 nude;
裸體主義 nudism;
~ 裸體主義者 naturist; nudist;
半裸體 half-naked;
赤身裸體 in the nude; stark naked;
[裸泳] skinny-dipping;
去裸泳 go skinny-dipping;

赤裸 in one's birthday suit; naked; stark naked; without a stitch of clothing;

luo
【攞】 a pronunciation of 攞 ;

luo
【蠃】 solitary wasp;

luo
【臝】 bare; nude;

luo⁴
luo
【咯】 cough;
[咯血] cough up blood;
寄生蟲性咯血 parasitic haemoptysis;
假咯血 pseudohaemoptysis;
心性咯血 cardiac haemoptysis;

吡咯 pyrrole;

luo
【洛】 the name of a river;
[洛陽紙貴] paper is dear in Luoyang – the wide circulation of a popular work;

luo
【烙】 brand; burn; iron;

砲烙 form of cruel punishment in ancient times;

luo
【珞】 jade ornaments for the neck;

瓔珞 necklace of jade and pearls;

luo
【絡】 (1) encompass; wrap around; (2) net; web; (3) cellulose structure in plants or fruits; (4) associate; connect; unite; (5) halter; (6) capillaries; (7) unreel silk; (8) cotton fibre; (9) hemp;

[絡繹] in an endless stream;
絡繹不絕 come and go in a continuous stream; come in a continuous stream; come one after the other; flock in an endless stream; go to and fro in constant streams; in a continuous line; in an endless stream; proceed in a steady stream;

氨絡 ammine;
包絡 envelope;
活絡 adroit in thinking;
橘絡 tangerine pith;
聯絡 (1) come into contact with; get in touch with; (2) contact; liaison;
籠絡 (1) befriend sb with ulterior intentions; (2) win sb over by any means;
脈絡 (1) arteries and veins; (2) sequence of ideas; thread of thought;
網絡 network;

luo
【酪】 a pronunciation of 酪;

luo
【落】 (1) decline; drop; fall; lower; sink; (2) fall behind; lag behind; (3) abandon; leave behind; stay behind; (4) whereabouts; (5) settlement; (6) fall onto; rest with; (7) get; have; receive;

[落筆] put pen to paper; start to write;
[落魄] (1) down and out; in dire straits; (2) abjection; (3) bold and generous; unconstrained;
落魄潦倒 down and out; in dire straits;
[落草] become an outlaw; take to the heather;
落草為寇 go to the greenwood; take to the bush; take to the heather;
[落成] be completed;
[落單] place an order;
[落得] end in; get; result in;
落得如此結局 come to such a pass;
[落地] (1) fall to the ground; (2) be born;
落地大擺鐘 grandfather clock;
落地燈 floor lamp;
落地生根 air plant;
落地扇 a stand fan;
落地式 a floor type;
落地鐘 grandfather clock;
[落第] fail in the imperial examination;
[落髮] shave one's head—become a Buddhist monk;
落髮為尼 shave one's head and become a nun;
落髮為僧 shave one's head and become a Buddhist monk;
[落後] drop behind; fall behind; get behind; in arrear; lag behind; lose ground; take the dust of;
落後分子 backward elements;
落後地區 backward areas; underdeveloped areas;
落後思想 old-fashioned ideas; outdated ideas;
落後狀態 in the slow lane;
鞭策落後 spur those who are backward;
不甘落後 unwilling to be left behind;
技術落後 backward technology;
生產落後 behind in production;
智力落後 mental retardation;
~ 輕度智力落後 mild mental retardation;
自甘落後 be resigned to a state of lagging behind; willing to fall behind;
[落戶] settle;
[落花] flower drop;
落花紛飛 the petals of the flowers are fluttering in the air;
落花流水 beat sb hollow; dropping petals and flowing waters; fallen petals and running waters; utterly routed;
~ 打得落花流水 beat sb into fits; beat sb to sticks; blow into smithereens; break into smithereens; cut to ribbons; dash into smithereens; inflict telling blows; knock into smithereens; knock sb into fits; rout; shatter to pieces; smash to smithereens; smite hip and thigh; wipe the floor with sb;
落花滿徑 a path covered with fallen flowers;

落花如雨 drifting petals fall like rain;
落花生 groundnut; peanut;
落花有意，流水無情 unrequited love;
落花有主 be betrothed to someone; betroth to someone;

[落荒] take to the wild;
落荒而逃 a fugitive from justice; flee into the open country; take to the wilds; turn tail and run;
落荒而走 go off alone into the wilderness; plunge into the wilds and flee;

[落價] drop in price; fall in price;

[落腳] put up; stay; stop over;
落腳點 anchor point;
落腳謀生 settle down and make a living;

[落井下石] do harm to sb when he is already in trouble; drop stones on the person who has fallen into a well; hit a person when he/she is down; pull water on a drowning person; push sb down a well and then drop stones on him;

[落空] come to nothing; fail; fall through;
計劃落空 fail in one's scheme;
兩頭落空 fall between two stools;
努力落空 fail in one's attempt;
談判落空 the negotiations fell through;
希望落空 fail to attain one's hope;

[落淚] shed tears; weep;
暗中落淚 shed a secret tear; weep silent tears;
暗自落淚 shed a private tear;
不見棺材不落淚 not to shed tears until one sees the coffin — refuse to repent until one is faced with complete defeat;
不禁落淚 cannot help shedding tears; cannot help weeping;
差點兒落淚 near tears;
感動得落淚 be melted into tears; be moved to tears; in a melting mood;
見棺落淚 tears start flowing from one's eyes as one sees the coffin;
淚落如豆 tears as big as peas roll down one's cheeks;
令人落淚 bring tears to one's eyes; make the angels weep;
傷心落淚 shed sad tears; weep in grief;

[落落] (1) natural and graceful; (2) aloof; standoffish; unsociable;
落落大方 liberal and dignified; natural and at ease; magnanimous; natural and graceful; poised and dignified;
落落寡合 aloof; eccentric; have few friends; hold oneself unsocially aloof; keep aloof from people; stand-offish; unsociable;
落落寡歡 disheartened and displeased;
落落寡交 keep aloof; keep to oneself;
落落穆穆 cool off toward sb; give sb the cold shoulder; turn a cold shoulder to sb;

[落馬] be brought down;
大批貪官落馬 a large number of corrupt officials have been brought down;
中箭落馬 be hit by an arrow and fall from one's steed;

[落墨] put pen to paper; set ink; start to draw; start to write;
大處落墨 concentrate on the key points; concentrate on the major problems; keep the general goal in view; pay attention to the important points;

[落寞] desolate; lonely;

[落難] in distress; meet with misfortune;
落難兄弟 brothers in misfortune;

[落泊] (1) comedown; down and out; in dire straits; (2) bold and generous; unconstrained;

[落日] setting sun;
落日餘輝 light of the setting sun; the last light of the day; the lingering light of the setting sun;

[落入] fall into;
落入敵手 fall into the hands of the enemy;
落入地獄 drop into perdition;
落入海中 drop into the sea;
落入湖中 fall into the lake;
落入絕境 in a predicament;
落入困境 get into trouble;
落入魔掌 fall into a villain's hands;
落入圈套 be ensnared; be trapped; fall into a trap; fall into sb's snare;
落入水中 fall into the water;
落入陷井 be caught in a pitfall; be ensnared; fall into a trap;

[落實] (1) practicable; workable; (2) ascertain; fix in advance; make sure; (3) carry out; fulfil; implement; put into effect;
落實舉措 put the measures into effect;
落實事實 check out the facts;
落實責任 carry out one's responsibilities; fulfil one's duties;

落實政策 put the policies into practice;

[落水] (1) fall into the water; (2) go astray; degenerate; sink into;

落水狗 bad person who has lost favour or power; drowning dog; like a dog in the water;

~ 打落水狗 beat the dog that has fallen into the water; completely crush a defeated enemy; hit a person who is already down;

~ 救了落水狗，反咬你一口 put a snake in your bosom, and it will sting when it is warm; save a thief from the gallows and he will cut your throat;

落水洞 sink; sinkhole;

拖人落水 drag others down; drag sb into hot water; drag sb into the mire; drag sb into the abyss; get sb into trouble; involve sb in evildoing;

[落湯雞] be drenched and bedraggled; like a bedraggled hen; like a drenched chicken;

如落湯雞 like a drowned rat;

像落湯雞 like a drenched chicken; like a drowned rat;

[落托] (1) down and out; in dire straits; (2) bold and generous; unconstrained;

[落拓] (1) down and out; in dire straits; (2) casual; untrammelled by convention;

落拓不羈 by nature unconventional and straightforward; throw restraint to the wind; unconventional and unrestrained; lively and independent; unconventional and uninhibited;

[落網] be caught; be captured; fall into the net;

不幸落網 unfortunately fall into the net;

[落伍] drop behind; fall behind; straggle;

避免落伍 avoid falling behind the ranks;

不落伍 get with it;

[落霞孤鶩] setting sun and lone ducks;

[落下] fall down;

落下帷幕 drop the curtain;

快速落下 hurtle;

[落選] fail to be chosen; fail to be elected; lose an election;

在選舉中落選 fail to carry an election;

[落葉] (1) fallen leaves; (2) deciduous leaf;

落葉的 deciduous;

落葉歸根 fallen leaves return to the roots — revert to one's origin;

落葉林 deciduous forest;

~ 溫帶落葉林 temperate deciduous forest;

落葉松 dahurian larch; larch;

~ 高山落葉松 alpine larch;

~ 美國落葉松 great western larch;

~ 日本落葉松 Japanese larch;

~ 西伯利亞落葉松 Siberian larch;

風掃落葉 scatter like leaves blown down by the wind;

[落音] come to a pause;

[落英繽紛] fallen flowers scattering around like snow flakes; fallen petals lie in profusion; the ground is full of fallen flowers;

[落雨] rain;

天晴防落雨 always prepare for the worst;

[落座] take one's seat;

敗落 decline (in wealth and position);
碧落 the blue sky;
剝落 peel off;
部落 (1) hamlet; (2) village;
出落 grow;
錯落 scatter and interlock;
低落 downcast; low;
凋落 wither and fall;
跌落 (1) drop down; fall; (2) drop; go down;
段落 (1) paragraph; passage; (2) phase; stage;
墮落 degenerate; go downhill;
發落 deal with;
回落 fall after a rise;
擊落 bring down; shoot down;
濺落 splash down;
降落 descend; land;
角落 corner; hook;
聚落 settlement;
廓落 spacious and quiet;
利落 (1) agile; dexterous; nimble; (2) neat; orderly; (3) finished; settled;
磊落 open and upright;
冷落 desolate; unfrequented;
寥落 few and far between; scattered;
零落 (1) wither and fall; (2) decayed; (3) desolate and scattered;
流落 lead a wandering life in poverty;
淪落 be reduced to poverty; fall low;
沒落 be on the wane;
飄落 land in a floating manner;
破落 be reduced to poverty;
起落 rise and fall; up and down;
群落 community;

灑落 at ease; free from affectation;
撒落 drop; spill;
散落 (1) fall in a scattering way; (2) scatter; (3) be separated and lose touch;
失落 lose;
疏落 scattered; sparse;
數落 scold sb by enumerating his wrongdoings;
衰落 be on the wane; decline;
屯落 village;
脱落 come off; drop; fall off;
奚落 jeer at; scoff at;
下落 (1) drop; fall; (2) whereabouts;
陷落 (1) cave in; sink in; subside; (2) fall into sth; land oneself in; (3) fall into enemy hands;
院落 (1) compound; (2) courtyard; yard;
隕落 fall from the sky;
中落 decline;
墜落 drop; fall;
着落 (1) whereabouts; (2) assured source;
坐落 be located; be situated;

luo
【犖】 (1) spotted ox; (2) of many colours;
［犖犖］ apparent; conspicuous; obvious;
犖犖大端 salient points;

卓犖 extraordinary; outstanding; pre-eminent;

luo
【雒】 (1) a black horse with white mane; (2) brand an animal; (3) the name of a river;

luo
【駱】 (1) a white horse with black mane; (2) camel; (3) a surname;
［駱馬］ llama;
［駱駝］ camel;
駱駝夫 camel driver;
駱駝隊 camel cade camel train; caravan of camels;
駱駝呢 camel hair;
駱駝騎兵 cameleer;
駱駝絨 (1) camel's hair; (2) fabric made of camel's hair;
駱駝刺 camel thorn;
單峯駱駝 dromedary;
一隊駱駝 a caravan of camels;
一群駱駝 a drove of camels;
一頭駱駝 a camel;

luo
【濼】 dock; lay anchor;

luo
【摞】 (1) make a pile; pile; stack up; (2) a pile of; a stack of;

luo5
luo
【咯】 phrase-final particle;

ma¹
ma

【媽】 (1) mother; (2) female servant;

[媽媽] (1) mam; mama; mammy; mater; mother; (2) husband's mother; mother-in-law;
超級媽媽 supermom;
準媽媽 mother-to-be;

[媽咪] (1) mummy; (2) procuress;
性感媽咪 yummy mummy;

阿媽 mom;
大媽 auntie; granny;
乾媽 one's foster mother; one's godmother;
姑媽 father's sister;
後媽 stepmother;
舅媽 aunt; wife of mother's brother;
奶媽 wet nurse;
姨媽 aunt;

M

ma²
ma

【麻】 (1) fibre crops; (2) sesame; (3) coarse; rough; (4) pitted; pocked; pock-marked; (5) have pins and needles; tingle; (6) anaesthesia; (7) a surname;

[麻包] gunny bag; gunny sack; sack;

[麻痺] (1) paralysis; (2) benumb; (3) lower one's guard; slacken one's vigilance;
麻痺大意 drop one's guard; insensitive and negligent; lack of vigilance; lacking vigilance; lower one's guard; off one's guard; slacken in vigilance; unwary;
麻痺發作 ictus paralyticus;
麻痺思想 slacken one's vigilance;
麻痺症 paralysis;
~ 小兒麻痺症 infantile paralysis; polio; poliomyelitis;
白喉性麻痺 diphtheritic paralysis;
表情肌麻痺 mimetic paralysis;
唇麻痺 labial paralysis;
大腦麻痺 cerebral palsy;
大腦性麻痺 cerebral palsy;
感覺麻痺 sensory paralysis;
功能性麻痺 functional paralysis;
喉麻痺 laryngoplegia;
混合性麻痺 mixed paralysis;
假性麻痺 false paralysis;
局部麻痺 local paralysis;
免疫麻痺 immunologic paralysis;
腦部麻痺 cerebral palsy;
偏癱後麻痺 post-hemiplegic paralysis;
鉛毒性麻痺 lead paralysis;
全麻痺 general paralysis;
全身麻痺 have general paralysis;
缺血性麻痺 ischaemic paralysis;
~ 局部缺血性麻痺 ischaemic palsy;
上肢麻痺 brachial palsy;
神經麻痺 neural paralysis;
聲帶麻痺 vocal cord paralysis;
睡眠後麻痺 postdormital paralysis;
睡眠前麻痺 predormital paralysis;
睡眠性麻痺 sleep paralysis;
四肢麻痺 tetraplegia;
消瘦性麻痺 wasting palsy; wasting paralysis;
小兒麻痺 infantile paralysis; pilio; poliomyelitis;
壓迫性麻痺 compression paralysis;
延髓性麻痺 bulbar paralysis;
嬰兒麻痺 infantile paralysis;
震顫麻痺 shaking palsy;
肢麻痺 acroparalysis;
直腸麻痺 proctoparalysis;
終身麻痺 be permanently paralyzed;
周期性麻痺 periodic paralysis;
周圍性麻痺 peripheral paralysis;

[麻布] (1) gunny cloth; sackcloth; (2) linen;
麻布袋 burlap;
粗麻布 burlap; hessian;
幼麻布 gunny cloth; sackcloth;

[麻袋] gunny-bag; gunnysack; jute bag; sack;
麻袋布 hessian; sackcloth;
扛麻袋 carry a gunnysack on one's shoulder;
一條麻袋 a sack;
卸麻袋 lay down a gunnysack;
織麻袋 weave a gunnysack;
裝麻袋 put sth in a gunnysack;

[麻煩] bother sb; cumbrance; give sb trouble; inconvenience sb; lead sb a dance; make trouble for sb; play up on sb; play up sb; play up on sb; put sb to trouble; trouble sb;
麻煩不斷 endless trouble;
麻煩您了 if you don't mind; sorry to trouble you;
麻煩你一下 sorry to trouble you;
麻煩事 a troublesome business; an awful mess; disagreeables;
避開麻煩 shelter from trouble;

避免麻煩 avoid trouble;
不麻煩 no trouble;
帶來麻煩 cause trouble;
極大的麻煩 terrible trouble;
減少麻煩 alleviate trouble;
怕麻煩 dislike trouble;
你不用麻煩 don't trouble yourself;
惹麻煩 ask for trouble; bring a hornet's nest about one's ears; invite trouble; stir up a hornet's nest; stir up a nest of hornets;
小麻煩 pinprick;
一大堆麻煩 a load of trouble;
引起很多麻煩 cause a great deal of trouble;
有麻煩 there is trouble;
找麻煩 (1) ask for trouble; be looking for trouble; (2) find fault; pick on sb; rock the boat;
~ 自找麻煩 be asking for trouble; borrow trouble;
造成麻煩 cause trouble;
真麻煩 what a nuisance;
製造麻煩 cause trouble; make waves;

[麻瘋] leprosy;
麻瘋病 leprosy;
~ 麻瘋病人 leper;
麻瘋反應 lepra reaction;
麻瘋結節 leproma;

[麻將] mahjong;
麻將迷 mahjong enthusiast; mahjong fan;
麻將牌 mahjong tiles;
麻將桌 mahjong table;
搓麻將 play mahjong;
打麻將 play mahjong;
玩麻將 play mahjong;
一場麻將 a game of mahjong;

[麻木] (1) numb; numbness; (1) apathetic; insensitive;
麻木不仁 apathetic; benumbed; dead to all feeling; insensitive; stolid; thick-skinned; unfeeling;
~ 對苦難麻木不仁 be anaesthetized to suffering;
麻木狀態 anaesthetic state;
面麻木 facial anaesthesia;
偏身麻木 unilateral anaesthesia;
四肢麻木 acroanaesthesia;

[麻雀] sparrow;
麻雀唧唧喳喳叫 a sparrow chirps; a sparrow chirrups; a sparrow twitters;
麻雀雖小，五臟俱全 small as it is, the sparrow has all the vital organs; small but complete; the sparrow may be small but it has all the vital organs;
公麻雀 cock sparrow;
養麻雀 raise house sparrows;
一對麻雀 a pair of sparrows;
一群麻雀 a flock of sparrows;
捉麻雀 catch sparrows;

[麻團] deep-fried sesame seed ball;

[麻油] sesame oil;
提煉麻油 extract sesame oil;

[麻疹] measles; rubeola;
出血性麻疹 haemorrhagic measles;
德國麻疹 German measles;
非典型麻疹 atypical measles;
黑麻疹 black measles;

[麻子] (1) pockmark; (2) pockmarked-faced person;

[麻醉] anaesthesia; anaesthetization;
麻醉劑 anaesthetic; anaesthetic agent;
麻醉氣 anaesthetic gas;
麻醉師 anaesthetist;
麻醉效應 anaesthetic effect;
麻醉學 anaesthesiology;
~ 麻醉學專家 anaesthesiologist;
麻醉藥 anaesthetic;
~ 局部麻醉藥 local anaesthetic;
~ 全部麻醉藥 general anaesthetic;
~ 一劑麻醉藥 a whiff of anaesthetic;
表面麻醉 topical anaesthesia;
持續脊髓麻醉 continuous spinal anaesthesia;
傳導麻醉 conduction anaesthesia;
低溫麻醉 hypothermic anaesthesia;
基礎麻醉 basis anaesthesia;
脊尾麻醉 caudal anaesthesia;
脊椎麻醉 spinal anaesthesia;
節段性麻醉 segmental anaesthesia;
浸潤麻醉 infiltration anaesthesia;
靜脈麻醉 intravenous anaesthesia;
局部麻醉 local anaesthesia;
開放式麻醉 open anaesthesia;
冷凍麻醉 refrigeration anaesthesia;
氣管內麻醉 endotracheal anaesthesia;
區域麻醉 field block anaesthesia; regional anaesthesia;
全身麻醉 general anaesthesia;
神經內麻醉 endoneural anaesthesia;
吸入麻醉 inhalational anaesthesia; respiration anaesthesia;

相對性麻醉 relative analgesia;
腰髓麻醉 lumbar anaesthesia;
藥物麻醉 drug anaesthesia;
誘導麻醉 induced anaesthesia;
針刺麻醉 acupuncture anaesthesia;
直腸麻醉 rectal anaesthesia;
中藥麻醉 herbal anaesthesia;
阻滯麻醉 block anaesthesia; inhibition anaesthesia;

蓖麻 castor-oil plant;
大麻 cannabis; hemp; marihuana,marijuana;
發麻 have pins and needles; tingle;
紅麻 blue dogbane;
胡麻 flax;
花麻 male plant of hemp;
黃麻 jute;
劍麻 sisal hemp;
蕉麻 abaca; Manila hemp;
蕁麻 nettle;
青麻 piemarker;
苘麻 piemarker;
肉麻 disgusting; nauseating; sickening;
蛇麻 hop;
酥麻 limp and numb;
酸麻 limp and numb;
天麻 the tuber of elevated gastrodia;
線麻 hemp;
亞麻 flax;
野麻 apocynum venetum;
一縷麻 a strand of hemp;
針麻 acupuncture anaesthesia;
芝麻 sesame;
織麻 weave linen;
主麻 Pjumah;
苧麻 China grass; ramie;

ma
【麼】 particle used in a phrase;

ma
【蔴】 (1) hemp; (2) sesame; sesamum;

ma
【痲】 (1) measles; (2) leprosy; (3) anaesthetize; benumb; paralyze; stupefy; (4) pockmark;

ma
【蟆】 toad;

ma³

ma
【馬】 (1) horse; (2) horse — one of the pieces in Chinese chess; (3) a surname;

［馬背］ horseback;
馬背體操 horseback gymnastics;

［馬車］ cart; horse-drawn cart;
馬車 chariot;
~ 輕型馬車 buggy;
~ 雙輪馬車 chariot;
馬車伕 carter; coachman;
出租馬車 (1) hackney carriage; (2) hansom;
四輪馬車 brougham;

［馬齒］ horse's teeth;
馬齒日增 become older daily; long in the tooth;
馬齒徒增 old and unfit for anything; outgrow one's usefulness;
馬齒已長 advanced in age; old;

［馬達］ motor;

［馬大哈］ careless; careless person; forgetful; scatterbrain;

［馬道］ bridle path;

［馬燈］ barn lantern; lantern;

［馬兒］ horse;
馬兒嘶鳴 horses neigh;

［馬翻人仰］ horses and men all overturned—an utter defeat; horses and men thrown off their feet—utterly routed;
馬仰人翻 be turned upside-down; men and horses thrown off their feet; the rider falls as the horse rears in fright; there is a panic;

［馬夫］ groom; horsekeeper; stableman;

［馬革裹尸］ be killed in battle; be wrapped in a horse's hide after death—die on the battlefield; fall in battle; wrap one's corpse in horse skin;

［馬後砲］ after-thought; belated action; belated advice; belated effort; lock the stable door after the horse has been stolen; too late;
放馬後砲 fire belated shots; criticize sth after it is over; do sth that no longer needs to be done; flog a dead horse; offer belated advice; start firing after the enemy has gone;

［馬虎］ careless; casual; perfunctory;
馬虎從事 discharge business carelessly;
馬虎的 slipshod; sloppy;
馬虎了事 do things in a perfunctory manner; do things in a slipshod manner; get sth done in a slapdash

manner; offhandedly; palter with sth;
馬虎視察 have a perfunctory inspection;
馬馬虎虎 after a sort; in a perfunctory manner; so-so; take no trouble;
做事馬虎 do sth carelessly;

［馬廄］ stable;

［馬腳］ sth that gives the game away;
馬腳套圈 ring boot;
露馬腳 give oneself away; let the cat out of the bag;

［馬褲］ breeches; riding breeches;

［馬拉糕］ Malaysian-style sponge cake;

［馬拉松］ marathon;
馬拉松運動員 marathoner;

［馬力］ horsepower;
大馬力 high-powered;
~大馬力汽車 high-powered vehicle;
計算馬力 calculated horsepower;
開足馬力 at full speed; at full steam; at full throttle; full blast; go at full pelt; go full steam ahead; in the full career; on the top; open the throttle; put into high gear; switch the machine into high gear; with all one's steam on; with full steam on; with the throttle against the stop; with the throttle wide open;
路遙知馬力 distance tests a horse's stamina; judge people after a period of time;
~路遙知馬力，日久見人心 a long journey proves the stamina of a horse and the passage of time tells the true from the false; as distance tests a horse's strength, so time reveals a person's heart;
實際馬力 actual horsepower;
制動馬力 brake horsepower;

［馬鈴薯］ potato; white potato;
馬鈴薯泥 mashed potato;
馬鈴薯片 potato chip;
馬鈴薯條 potato chip;
~炸馬鈴薯條 French fries; fries;
馬鈴薯削皮器 potato peeler;
煎馬鈴薯 fried potato;
烤馬鈴薯 roast potato;
新馬鈴薯 new potato;
一大袋馬鈴薯 a sack of potatoes;
煮馬鈴薯 boiled potato;

［馬路］ avenue; highway; road; street;
馬路邊 roadside; side of the road;
大馬路 main thoroughfare;
穿過馬路 across the road;
過馬路 across a road;
橫穿馬路 run across the street;
跑過馬路 run across the road; run across the street;
跑上馬路 run out into a road;
軋馬路 in love; stroll around the streets;
阻塞馬路 block a road;

［馬毛］ horsehair;

［馬牛襟裾］ a beast in human clothing; a dressed-up horse or ox — lack of etiquette;

［馬屁］ apple-polish; toady;
馬屁精 apple-polisher; arse-licker; ass-kisser; banana oil; boot-licker; brown-noser; creeper; ear banger; flatterer; lickspittle; spaniel; subservient; sycophant; tame spaniel; toady;
馬屁拍在馬腳上 rub sb up the wrong way;
拍老闆的馬屁 suck up to the boss; toady to the boss;

［馬前卒］ cat's paw; foot soldier; pawn; willing servant;

［馬球］ polo;
馬球衫 polo shirt;
打馬球 play polo;

［馬善被人騎，人善被人欺］ make yourself all honey and the flies will devour you;

［馬善逗人騎］ all lay their load on the willing horse;

［馬上］ at any moment; at once; immediately; in a couple of shakes; in no time; in two shakes; pronto; right away; right now; straightaway;
馬上採取行動 take immediate action;
馬上出發 set out right away;
馬上回來 be back in two shakes;
馬上就 immediately; in no time; soon;
馬上不知馬下苦 no one knows the weight of another person's burden;
馬上治天下 rule the world by force;

［馬首是瞻］ dance to sb's tune; look up to sb for direction; take the head of the general's horse as a guide — follow sb's lead;

［馬術］ horsemanship;
馬術比賽 horse show;

［馬蹄］ (1) horse's hoof; (2) Chinese water

chestnut;
馬蹄刀瓢裏切菜—滴水不漏 stingy as cutting vegetables with a hoof-paring knife in a wooden spoon;
馬蹄鐵 (1) horseshoe iron; (2) U-shaped magnet;
馬不停蹄 make a hurried journey without stop; non-stop; push on with one's journey without stop; without a single halt;
馬失前蹄 the horse stumbles; the horse trips;
[馬桶] close-stool; honey bucket; nightstool; stool;
金漆馬桶—外面好看裏面臭 a gold-edged night stool － fine-looking in appearance but stinking inside;
[馬尾] horsetail;
馬尾辮 (of hairstyle) ponytail;
[馬戲] circus;
馬戲表演 circus act;
~馬戲表演場 circus ring;
馬戲團 circus troup;
~流動馬戲團 touring circus; travelling circus;
演馬戲 run a circus;
[馬眼罩] blinders; blinkers;
[馬蠅] horsefly;
[馬賊] mounted bandits;

矮種馬 pony;
備馬 saddle a horse for riding;
鞴馬 ride a horse;
奔馬 a fleeting horse in stampede;
墮馬 fall off from horseback;
駙馬 emperor's son-in-law;
公馬 stallion;
河馬 hippopotamus; river horse;
花毛馬 roan;
軍馬 army horse; charger;
駿馬 fine horse; steed;
老馬 plug;
劣馬 (1) inferior horse; (2) vicious horse;
遛馬 walk a horse;
綿馬 bracken; fern;
母馬 mare;
牛馬 oxen and horses;
駑馬 inferior horse;
拍馬 fawn on; flatter; lick sb's boots;
騎馬 ride horseback;
犬馬 a dog or a horse;
人馬 forces; troops;
戎馬 army horse;
賽馬 horse race;
三趾馬 hipparion;
上馬 (1) mount a horse; (2) start (a project, etc);
駟馬 a team of four horses;
騰馬 stallion;
跳馬 (1) vaulting horse; (2) horse-vaulting;
頭馬 head girsel;
馱馬 pack horse;
擊馬 tie up a horse;
下馬 (1) get down from a horse; (2) discontinue (a project, etc);
響馬 bandits;
搖馬 rocking horse;
一群馬 a herd of horses; a stud of horses;
一匹馬 a horse;
飲馬 water a horse;
雜色馬 roan;
戰馬 battle steed; warhorse;
種馬 stallion; stud;
竹馬 bamboo hobbyhorse;

ma

【嗎】 a character used in transliterating;
[嗎啡] morphine;
嗎啡癮 morphine addiction; morphinism;
乙酸嗎啡 morphine acetate;

ma

【瑪】 agate; cornelian;
[瑪瑙] agate;
瑪瑙軸承 agate bearing;
白瑪瑙 white agate;
帶瑪瑙 banded agate;
蛋白瑪瑙 opal agate;
景色瑪瑙 landscape agate;
藍瑪瑙 blue agate;
血點瑪瑙 blood agate;
雲瑪瑙 clouded agate;

ma

【碼】 (1) yard; (2) code; symbol; (3) pile up;
[碼尺] yard measure;
[碼計] yardage;
[碼頭] (1) dock; pier; quay; wharf; (2) commercial and transportation centre; port city;
碼頭邊 dockside;
碼頭工人 docker; dock worker;
碼頭區 dockland; the docks;
包裝貨碼頭 packed cargo wharf;

駁船碼頭 lighter's wharf;
潮區碼頭 tidal quay;
承受碼頭 sufferance wharf;
渡船碼頭 ferry terminal;
浮動碼頭 landing stage;
浮碼頭 floating pier;
集裝箱碼頭 container wharf;
客運碼頭 passenger pier;
旅客碼頭 passenger pier;
散裝貨碼頭 bulk cargo wharf;
深水碼頭 deep water wharf;
私用碼頭 private landing-place;
停靠碼頭 dock;
突堤碼頭 pier;
卸貨碼頭 discharging dock;
油碼頭 oil terminal;

暗碼 secret code;
補碼 complement;
尺碼 measures; size;
籌碼 chip; counter;
代碼 code;
砝碼 weight;
號碼 number;
加碼 raise the quotation;
密碼 cipher code; secret code;
明碼 (1) plain code; (2) with the price clearly marked;
起碼 (1) at least; (2) elementary; minimum; rudimentary;
數碼 (1) numeral; (2) amount; number;
頁碼 page number;
譯碼 decipher; decode;
源碼 source code;

ma

【螞】

[螞蜂] hornet; wasp;

[螞蟻] ant;
螞蟻搬泰山 ants can move Mount Taishan; the united efforts of the masses can accomplish mighty projects;
螞蟻出洞 ants come out of their holes;
螞蟻啃骨頭 ants gnawing at a bone — a concentration of small machines used on a big job;
螞蟻緣槐 ants climb up and down the locust tree — people inflated with pride;
白螞蟻 termite;
熱鍋上的螞蟻 an awkward state of affairs; ants in a hot frying pan; as restless as ants on a hot pan; full of anxiety; like a cat on hot bricks; like an ant on a hot saucepan;
一隊螞蟻 a column of ants;
一群螞蟻 a colony of ants; a swarm of ants;
一窩螞蟻 a colony of ants; a nest of ants;
一隻螞蟻 an ant;

[螞蚱] grasshopper; locust;

ma

【鎷】 masurium;

ma⁴

ma

【罵】 (1) abuse; call names; curse; swear; (2) condemn; rebuke; reprove; scold;

[罵架] quarrel; wrangle;
參與罵架 take up a quarrel;
引起罵架 cause a quarrel;
在街頭罵架 have a street row;

[罵街] shout abuses in the street;
潑婦罵街 a shrew shouts abuses in the street;

[罵罵咧咧] become abusive; foul-mouthed; intersperse one's talk with curses;

[罵名] bad name; ill name; infamy;

[罵人] abuse; call one names; condemn; curse; give sb a good dressing down; give sb a good wigging; give sb a scolding; give sb a piece of one's mind; give sb the edge of one's tongue; haul sb over the coals; load sb with insults; mutter insults against; rake sb over the coals; reprove; revile; sail into; scold; swear at; take sb to task; tell one off;
罵人的話 imprecation;
罵人話 abuse; abusive language; curse; swear word; word of abuse;
罵人取樂 criticize others as a pastime;
背後罵人 curse sb behind sb's back;
素口罵人 a religious person swears;

嘲罵 jeer and abuse;
斥罵 abuse; reproach; upbraid;
臭罵 curse roundly;
對罵 call each other names; trade insults;
詬罵 abuse; vilify;
叫罵 curse; swear;
亂罵 foul abuse;
怒罵 curse in rage;

數罵 enumerate sb's faults;
唾罵 curse; revile;
笑罵 (1) deride and taunt; mock and insult; (2) deride;
責罵 rebuke; reproach; scold;
詛罵 curse and berate;

ma
【禡】 sacrifice to the local deity performed by marching troops at a camp site;

ma⁵
ma
【嗎】 phrase-final particle used in yes-no questions;

ma
【麼】 same as 嗎;

ma
【蟆】 toad;
蛤蟆 (1) frog; (2) toad;

mai²
mai
【埋】 bury; cover up;
[埋藏] (1) bury; lie hidden in the earth; (2) conceal; hide;
埋藏心頭 nurse in one's bosom;
[埋單] check the bill;
[埋伏] (1) ambush; lie in ambush; (2) hide; lie low; lie in wait;
打埋伏 hide in an ambush; lie in ambush; work in ambush;
中埋伏 fall into an ambush; run into the ambush; walk into an ambush;
[埋進] nuzzle;
[埋名] conceal one's name;
埋名隱蹤 immure oneself;
隱跡埋名 live incognito;
隱姓埋名 conceal one's identity; conceal one's real name; disguise one's name and surname; keep one's identity hidden; live in obscurity; live incognito; live in the shadow; live under an assumed name; sink one's identity;
~隱姓埋名地生活 live in the shadow;
[埋沒] (1) bury; cover up; (2) neglect; stifle;
埋沒人才 stifle real talents;
埋沒英雄 let a hero lie unknown;
[埋首於] be engrossed in; immerse oneself in;
[埋頭] be engrossed in; bury oneself in; immerse oneself in;
埋頭讀書 bury oneself in books;
埋頭幹活 work silently without publicity;
埋頭工作 give oneself over to one's work;
埋頭苦幹 engage oneself in hard work; have one's shoulder to the collar; immerse oneself in hard work; keep one's nose to the grindstone; put one's shoulder to the wheel; work doggedly in silence;
埋頭學問 bury oneself in studies;
埋頭業務 engross oneself in vocational work;
埋頭用功 be buried in study;
[埋葬] bury; entomb;
埋葬地 burial ground;
埋香葬玉 bury a beautiful woman; lay a beauty to rest;
葬玉埋香 (1) bury a beauty; lay a beauty to rest; (2) the untimely death of a beauty;

活埋 bury alive;
殮埋 shroud and bury;
葬埋 inter; bury;

mai
【霾】 (1) cloudy; foggy; misty; (2) dust-storm;
[霾層] fog layer;
[霾滴] mist drop;
[霾因子] haze factor;

北極霾 arctic haze;
冰晶霾 ice-crystal haze;
薄霾 damp haze;
乾霾 dry haze;
陰霾 haze;

mai³
mai
【買】 buy; purchase;
[買辦] comprador;
[買不來] (1) cannot be bought with money; (2) not for sale;
[買不起] beyond sb's purse; not be able to afford;
買不起這輛車 cannot afford to buy this car;
[買菜] buy food;

買菜求益 argue about as if in buying vegetables; calculating and unwilling to make the smallest sacrifice; excessively mean in one's dealings;

[買得過] worth buying;

[買得起] be able to afford sth;

買得起這層樓 can afford to buy this apartment;

[買定] settle a purchase;

[買櫝還珠] (1) buy a box but return the jewels inside — attend to the superficials and neglect the essentials; (2) keep the casket and give back the pearls — make the wrong choice;

[買方] buyer; buying party; purchaser; endee;

買方市場 buyers' market;

[買官鬻爵] buy an office appointment; pay a bribe to obtain an official post;

[買光] clear;

[買好] ingratiate oneself with; play up to; try to win sb's favour;

[買貨學] buyology;

[買價] buying price; purchasing price;

[買進] buy in; buy up;

買進賣出 trade;

[買空] short purchase; buy long;

買空賣空 speculation in securities;

[買賣] (1) business; buying and selling; deals; transactions; (2) shop;

買賣不公 buy and sell at an unreasonable price;

買賣成交 the bargain is closed;

買賣公平 buy and sell at reasonable prices; fair dealings in business; fair in buying and selling; honest in business;

買賣婚姻 mercenary marriage;

買賣精明 smart in one's dealings;

買賣虧本 out of pocket;

買賣人 businessman; merchant; trader;

買賣興隆 do a brisk business; the business is brisk;

倒買倒賣 buy cheap and sell dear;

公買公賣 fair in buying and selling;

賤買貴賣 buy cheap and sell dear;

賤買賤賣 buy and sell at low prices;

拉買賣 solicit business;

攬買賣 solicit trade;

賣刀買犢 abandon evil and do good; mend one's ways;

賣劍買牛 bring a peaceful and industrious life to a lawless area; selling one's swords to purchase oxen for farming — reformation of brigands;

強買強賣 buy and sell under coercion;

小買賣 small business;

一筆買賣 a deal;

一樁買賣 a business transaction;

一號買賣 a business transaction;

做買賣 do business;

[買入] buy;

買入差價 bid spread;

買入價 bid price;

[買通] bribe; buy off;

買通上下 bribe all the officials concerned;

[買帳] acknowledge the superiority of; show respect for;

[買主] buyer; customer; purchaser;

[買醉酒肆] get drunk in a wine house;

炒買 buy at a low price;

導買 attract customers;

收買 (1) buy; purchase; (2) bribe; buy over;

贖買 buy out; redeem;

mai4

mai

【脈】

[脈搏] pulse;

脈搏短絀 pulse deficit;

脈搏過緩 bradysphygmia;

脈搏停止 cessation of pulse;

脈博微弱 acrotism;

脈搏消失 temporary absence of pulse;

[脈衝] pulse; pulsing;

脈衝星 pulsar;

環路脈衝 loop pulse;

寄生脈衝 after pulse;

加法脈衝 add pulse;

確定脈衝 acknowledge pulse;

氣動脈衝 air pulse;

聲脈衝 acoustic pulse;

推進脈衝 advance pulse;

選通脈衝 strobe;

~ 輸出選通脈衝 output strobe;

~ 同步選通脈衝 synchronous strobe;

~ 圓柱選通脈衝 cylinder strobe;

[脈管] angiologia; pulse artery;

脈管痛 vasalgia;

脈管炎 angiitis; vasculitis;

~ 變應性脈管炎 allergic vasculitis;

[脈尖] apex of vein;

[脈弱] weak pulse;
[脈速] rapid pulse;
[脈序] venation;
閉鎖脈序 closed venation;
弧曲脈序 arcuate venation;
假設脈序 hypothetical wing venation;
[脈壓] pulse pressure;

按脈 feel the pulse; take the pulse;
把脈 feel sb's pulse; take sb's pulse;
病脈 abnormal pulse;
代脈 slow and intermittent pulse;
動脈 artery;
二叉脈 dichotomous vein;
肺靜脈 pulmonary;
號脈 feel sb's pulse; take sb's pulse;
橫脈 crossvein; vein;
接脈 feel the pulse;
結脈 slow and intermittent pulse;
靜脈 vein;
命脈 (1) lifeblood; (2) lifeline;
橈脈 radial vien;
偶生脈 adventitious vein;
切脈 feel the pulse;
弱脈 weak pulse;
山脈 mountain chain; mountain range;
實脈 bounding pulse;
虛脈 feeble pulse;
岩脈 rockvein;
掌狀脈 palmate vein;
診脈 feel the pulse;
中肋脈 midrib vein;

mai

【麥】 (1) barley; (2) oat; (3) wheat; (4) a surname;
[麥餅] wheat cake;
[麥克風] microphone; mike;
[麥浪] the billowing wheat fields; the rippling wheat;
[麥粒] grains of wheat;
[麥芒] awn of wheat;
[麥片] oatmeal;
麥片粥 gruel; oatmeal porridge; porridge;
[麥秋] wheat harvest season;
[麥穗] ear of wheat;
[麥田] wheat field; wheatland;
[麥芽] malt;
麥芽粉 crushed malt;
麥芽糖 malt sugar; maltose;
麥芽汁 wort;
~發酵麥芽汁 fermenting wort;
~混和麥芽汁 blending wort;
~啤酒麥芽汁 brewer's wort;
~釀酒麥芽汁 distiller's wort;
大麥芽 barley malt;
乾麥芽 dried malt;
焦化麥芽 caramel malt; crystal malt;
焦黃麥芽 brown malt;
氣乾麥芽 air-dried malt;
[麥子] (1) barley; (2) wheat;
拔麥子 harvest wheat;
一把麥子 a sheaf of wheat;
一捆麥子 a sheaf of wheat;

春麥 spring wheat;
大麥 barley;
冬麥 winter wheat;
黑麥 rye;
稞麥 highland barley;
雀麥 brome;
菽麥 beans and wheat;
小麥 wheat;
燕麥 oat;
一捆麥 a sheaf of wheat;
油麥 naked oats;
莜麥 naked oats;

mai

【賣】 (1) sell; (2) betray; (3) exert to the utmost; not spare; (4) show off;
[賣報] sell newspapers;
賣報人 news vendor;
[賣唱] sing for a living;
[賣出] sell;
賣出差價 offer spread;
賣出價 offer price;
賣不出去 cannot be sold;
[賣得好] sell well;
[賣掉] sell off; sell out;
[賣方] seller; selling party; vendor;
賣方市場 seller's market;
[賣功] parade one's merits; show off what one has done;
[賣瓜] sell melon;
賣瓜説瓜甜，賣花説花香 every cook commends his own sauce; every cook praises his own broth; every peddler praises his own needle;
老王賣瓜，自賣自誇 each priest praises his own relics; every cook praises his own broth; every potter praises his

own pot;

［賣乖］ show off one's cleverness;

討好賣乖 curry favour with; toady to;

［賣關子］ keep sb guessing; keep the listeners in supense; stop a story at a climax to keep the listeners in suspense;

［賣國］ betray one's country;

賣國求榮 betray one's country in exchange for high position; betray one's country in order to get a high position; seek after glory by selling out one's own country; seek power and wealth by betraying one's country; turn traitor for personal gains;

賣國通敵 betray one's country into the hands of the enemy; sell one's country to the enemy;

賣國投降 capitulate and engage in national betrayal;

賣國行為 treasonable act;

賣國賊 traitor to one's country; quisling;

［賣好］ curry favour with; ingratiate oneself with; play up to;

向上司賣好 curry favour with one's superiors;

以微笑賣好 win sb's favour with an ingratiating smile;

［賣價］ selling price;

賣價低 sell sth at a low price;

賣價高 sell sth at a high price;

賣價好 can be sold at a good selling price;

［賣盡當光］ have nothing more to sell or prawn;

［賣勁兒］ exert all one's strength; spare no effort;

唱歌賣勁兒 strain one's voice in singing;

幹活賣勁兒 work hard;

學習賣勁兒 study hard;

［賣空］ short sale;

［賣老］ flaunt one's old age;

倚老賣老 come the old soldier; flaunt one's seniority; presume on one's age; take advantage of one's seniority;

［賣力］ do all one can; do one's very best; exert all one's strength; exert oneself to the utmost; spare no effort; work hard;

賣力氣 (1) do one's very best; exert all one's strength; exert oneself to the utmost; spare no effort; strain every nerve; (2) live by the sweat of one's brow; make a living by manual labour;

更賣力 work even harder;

［賣命］ work oneself to death for sb; work one's fingers to the bone for sb;

賣命工作 work one's fingers to the bone;

賣命效力 work oneself to the bone to render a service to sb;

［賣弄］ parade; show off;

賣弄本事 parade one's abilities;

賣弄筆墨 inkhorn; smell of the inkhorn;

賣弄財富 show off one's wealth;

賣弄風情 (1) coquetry; coquette; (2) coquette with; flirt with; play the coquette; set off one's charm;

~賣弄風情的女人 coquette;

賣弄風騷 flirt around;

賣弄口舌 show off one's glibness in speech;

賣弄玄虛 make a mystery of sth;

賣弄噱頭 play to the gallery; try tricks;

賣弄學問 parade one's knowledge; pedantic; show off one's knowledge;

喜歡賣弄 fond of showing off;

［賣俏］ coquette; flirt; play the coquette;

倚門賣俏 flirt near the door with passers-by;

迎奸賣俏 please a treacherous person sexually;

爭寵賣俏 make the most of one's charms to compete for one's master's favour;

［賣身］ (1) sell oneself; (2) sell one's body; (3) sell one's soul;

賣身求榮 sell one's soul for self-advancement;

賣身投靠 barter away one's honour for sb's patronage; sell oneself for support;

賣臉不賣身 sell one's looks but not one's body;

賣藝不賣身 sell art but not one's body;

［賣文］ sell one's writings;

賣文度日 boil the pot;

賣文為生 depend on one's pen for a living; make a living by one's pen; make a living as a writer; write for a living;

［賣相］ (1) exterior; outward appearance; packaging; (2) appearance; looks;

［賣笑］ be forced to earn a living by prostitution;

賣笑生涯 make a living by prostitution;

倚門賣笑 invite the attention of passers-by; love for sale; show oneself by leaning against a door, as a prostitute;

［賣藝］ make a living as a performer;
街頭賣藝 busk;
~街頭賣藝者 busker;

［賣淫］ accost; cruise; fast life; get the rent; have apartments to let; hustling; Mrs. Warren's profession; on the battle; on the game; on the streets; prostitute oneself; prostitution; see company; sit for company; sit at show windows; social service; street of shame; street of sin; streetwalking; the oldest profession; the social evil; the trade; walk the streets; work for herself;

［賣賬］ buy;
不賣賬 not go for it; not buy it;

［賣主］ seller; vendor;
賣主求榮 betray one's master for the sake of glory; betray one's master to obtain a promotion, honour or power;
邊際賣主 marginal seller;
第一賣主 first seller;

［賣嘴］ self-praise; show off one's skill or kind-heartedness by talking;

［賣座］ attract large numbers of customers; draw large audiences;
賣座率低 not able to draw large andiences;
賣座率高 able to attract large audiences;
不賣座 cannot attract large audiences;
很賣座 attract large audiences;

擺賣 sell from a stand;
標賣 sell by tender;
超賣 oversell;
炒賣 sell at a high profit;
倒賣 resell at a profit;
盜賣 steal and sell public property illegally;
販賣 peddle; sell;
寄賣 consign goods for sale on commission;
叫賣 hawk; peddle;
拍賣 (1) auction; (2) sell off goods at reduced prices;
叛賣 betray; sell;
售賣 sell;
無論多少錢都不賣 not at any price;
義賣 charity bazaar;
折賣 sell one's property;

mai

【邁】 (1) step; stride; (2) advanced in years; old;

［邁步］ make a step; step forward; take a step;
邁步前進 make great strides forward; take step and go forward;
邁不開步 unable to take a step;
邁大步走 a long stride; take long firm steps;
邁方步 take slow, swinging steps; walk slowly;

［邁進］ advance with big strides; forge ahead; stride forward;
邁進新紀元 stride forward into a new epoch;
邁進一步 make a step forward;

［邁向］ march toward;

高邁 advanced in years;
豪邁 great; valiant;
老邁 aged; senile;
年邁 aged; invalidity; old;
衰邁 old and weak; senile;

man²

man

【埋】

［埋怨］ blame; complain; complaint; grumble;
埋怨氣候 complain about the climate;
埋怨社會 blame it on society;
相互埋怨 blame one another;

man

【漫】 (said of water) endless; vast;

man

【蔓】 plants with creeping tendrils or vines;

［蔓草］ grass that creep and spread fast and luxuriantly;
荒煙蔓草 deserted and infested with weed;

［蔓延］ spread; trail;
功能蔓延 feature creep;

［蔓足］ cirrus;

man

【樠】 a kind of tree;

man

【瞞】 hide the truth from;

［瞞哄］ deceive; pull the wool over sb's eyes;

［瞞騙］ bluff;

［瞞稅］ conceal facts to proper taxation;

［瞞心昧己］ act against one's conscience; deceive oneself;
［瞞着］ hold out on;
［瞞住］ close;

蒙瞞 mystify;
隱瞞 conceal; hide;

man
【蹣】 (1) jump over; (2) limp;
［蹣跚］ hobble; limp; walk haltingly;
蹣跚而行 shamble;
步履蹣跚 shambling gait;

man
【謾】 disdain; scorn;

man
【饅】 staffed or unstaffed dumplings; steamed dumplings;
［饅頭］ steamed bread; steamed bun;
斗大的饅頭—吃不下嘴 a big steamed bun — hard to bite;
開花兒饅頭 split-top steamed bun;

man
【鰻】 eel;

白鰻 eel;
海鰻 conger pike;
河鰻 river eel;
盲鰻 hagfish;

man
【顢】 careless; ignorant and stupid;
［顢頇］ muddle-headed and careless; stupid and confused;
顢裏顢頇 casual; muddle-headed; negligent; stupid; thoughtless;

man
【鬘】 fair of hair;

man
【蠻】 (1) fierce; reckless; rough; unreasoning; (2) ancient name for southern nationalities; (3) pretty; quite;
［蠻幹］ act rashly; act recklessly; foolhardy;
蠻幹到底 go on and on regardless of consequences;
［蠻橫］ arbitrary; impervious to reason; peremptory; rude and unreasonable;
蠻橫逼債 press relentlessly for the repayment of loans;
蠻橫逞強 use violence and coercion;
蠻橫無理 audacious; in a truculent and arbitrary way; overbearing and insolent; peremptory; rude and unreasonable; truculent and unreasonable;
蠻橫性格的人 a person with an arbitrary disposition;
蠻橫之極 insolent to the extreme;
服務態度蠻橫 serve people rudely;
説話態度蠻橫 speak with an unreasonable attitude;
［蠻勁］ animal strength;
有一股蠻勁 have sheer animal strength;
［蠻來生作］ do sth by coercion; do sth by force;

粗蠻 rough; unrefined;
刁蠻 obstinate; unruly;

man³
man
【滿】 (1) filled; full; packed; (2) fill; (3) expire; reach the limit; (4) completely; entirely; perfectly; (5) satisfied; (6) complacent; conceited;
［滿杯］ brimmer; bumper; cupful;
請給我斟一滿杯 please give me a bumper;
［滿朝］ in the court;
滿朝公卿 all the officers of the government;
滿朝文武 all the civilian and military officers at court; all the ministers and generals in the imperial court;
［滿當］ brimful; full to the brim;
［滿登登］ be filled with; full of;
［滿額］ fulfil the quota;
生產滿額 reach production quotas;
招生滿額 fulfill the quota of enrolment;
［滿分］ full credit; full marks;
［滿腹］ full of; have one's mind filled with;
滿腹豪情 be filled with pride;
滿腹狐疑 be filled with suspicion; extremely suspicious; full of misgiving; have all sorts of doubts and conjectures in one's mind; very suspicious;
滿腹經綸 full of learning; profoundly learned;
滿腹牢騷 full of complaints; full of

dissatisfaction; full of grievances; have a bellyful of complaints; querulous; have a grudge against everything;
~ 對社會滿腹牢騷 grumble about society;
~ 發洩滿腹牢騷 pour out one's grievances;
~ 宣洩滿腹牢騷 air one's grievances; pour out one's grievances;
滿腹文章 full of learning; profoundly learned;
滿腹辛酸 have a bellyful of bitter sadness;
滿腹疑慮 feel deep misgivings;
滿腹疑團 full of doubts and suspicion;
滿腹憂愁 full of sorrow;
滿腹憂慮 full of sorrow;
滿腹怨氣 full of grievances on account of wrongs; full of hate;
滿腹珠璣 have a well-stored mind; one's mind is full of valuable ideas — extensive knowledge;

[滿貫] slam;
[滿漢全席] full and formal banquet;
[滿懷] be imbued with; have one's heart filled with;
滿懷悲痛 be filled with immense grief;
滿懷必勝信念 fully confident about one's victory;
滿懷仇恨 be imbued with hatred;
滿懷感激之情 full of gratitude to sb;
滿懷豪情 be filled with pride;
滿懷激情 full of emotion;
滿懷夢想 full of dreams;
滿懷熱情 make a warm-hearted effort;
滿懷同情 be imbued with sympathy; overflowing with sympathy;
滿懷希望 fill one's heart with hope; nourish hope in one's heart;
滿懷喜悅 brim with joy; full of joy;
滿懷幸福 be filled with happiness;
滿懷信心 confidently; full of confidence; have full confidence; have one's tail up; with full confidence;
滿懷自信 full of self-confidence;
愁緒滿懷 be distracted with worries; have the weight of the world on one's shoulders;
撞個滿懷 bump into sb; collide with sb; run into sb;
豪情滿懷 be filled with boundless pride; full of pride and enthusiasm; full of spirit;

[滿街] a streetful of;
滿街是人 the street is thronged with people;
[滿口] speak glibly; speak profusely; speak unreservedly;
滿口不絕 simply flow from one's lips;
滿口稱讚 praise profusely;
滿口春風 eloquent in speaking;
滿口答應 consented without any lengthy deliberation; readily promise;
滿口恭維 full of flattery; smarmy;
滿口胡言 full of foolish talk;
滿口謊言 spout lies;
滿口誑讕 tell a pack of lies;
滿口應承 make profuse promises; promise readily; promise with great readiness;
滿口餘香 leave a lingering fragrance in one's mouth;
滿口怨言 one's mouth is full of resentful talk;
滿口髒話的 potty-mouthed;
[滿臉] all over the face;
滿臉堆笑 a benign smile spreads over one's face; one's face is all smiles;
滿臉緋紅 as red as a beetroot; blush like a rose;
滿臉風塵 one's face is full of travelling dust; the whole face covered with dust; weather-beaten countenance;
滿臉汗水 one's face is bathed in sweat;
滿臉橫肉 cross-grained features; ugly, pugnacious looks;
滿臉晦氣 have an ill-omened look; look very depressed;
滿臉驕氣 swell with pride;
滿臉淚痕 one's cheeks are tear-stained; one's face is covered with tracces of tears; one's face is wet with tears;
滿臉殺氣 look like one in a murderous mood;
滿臉生花 smiling all over;
滿臉失望之色 a cloud of disappointment over one's face;
滿臉是淚 one's face is tear-stained;
滿臉鐵青 one's face is darkening;
滿臉通紅 one's face reddens all over;
滿臉笑容 all smiles;
滿臉油污 one's face is black with oil and dust;
滿臉皺紋 full of wrinkles; have a wrinkly face;

滿臉紫脹 one's face becomes deep crimson;

[滿滿] full to the brim; to the full capacity;

滿滿當當 brimming; crowded to the full capacity; full to the brim; pile high;

滿滿一桶水 a bucket full of water;

滿滿一桶雨水 a bucket full of rain;

[滿門] the whole family;

滿門抄斬 exterminate all members of the family;

滿門桃李 a lot of pupils; many disciples;

[滿面] have one's face covered with;

滿面愁容 have one's face covered with lines of worry; look extremely worried;

滿面春風 be all smiles; beam with satisfaction; look like a million dollars; one's face is full of joy; shine with happiness; smile from ear to ear;

滿面春光 have a face like springtime;

滿面紅光 glow with health; have a fine colour in one's cheeks;

滿面歡容 beam with delight;

滿面淚痕 one's face is covered with tear stains; one's face is stained with tears;

滿面怒容 a face contorted with anger; one's face is ablaze with anger; red with anger;

滿面傷痕 one's face is cut and bruised;

滿面通紅 a blush overspreads one's face; flush red all over;

滿面喜色 all smiles; grin from ear to ear; one's face is wreathed in smiles;

滿面笑容 a smile lights up one's face; all smiles; grin from ear to ear; one's face is wreathed in smiles;

滿面羞慚 be overwhelmed with shame; blush with shame; extremely ashamed of oneself; flush crimson; shamefaced;

滿面羞恨 one's face is filled with shame and remorse;

滿面憂容 full of sorrow on one's face;

紅光滿面 healthy and hearty look; be aglow with health; glowing ruddy cheeks; have a healthy colour in one's cheeks; have a high colour; in the pink; one's face is glowing with health;

淚痕滿面 have a tear-stained face; one's face is tear-stained;

淚流滿面 tears stream down one's cheeks;

[滿目] meet the eye on every side;

滿目瘡痍 be covered all over with wounds and scars; distress and suffering can be seen everywhere; see evidence of people's distress everywhere; the country is full of suffering and distress; wherever one looks, there is devastation;

滿目含淚 one's eyes are filled with tears; one's eyes are full of tears;

滿目荒涼 a scene of desolation meets the eye on every side — the sight of a war-worn area;

滿目淒涼 all one can see is grief; desolation is all round; desolation spreads as far as the eyes can reach;

滿目青山夕照明 verdant sunset-bathed hills can be seen everywhere;

滿目蕭索 a melancholy and solitary aspect as far as the eyes can see;

滿目兇光 meet the eye on every side;

琳琅滿目 a feast for the eyes; a multitude of beautiful things dazzle the eyes; a superb collection of beautiful things; resplendent with a multitude of beautiful things;

[滿盤] a dishful of;

[滿期] come to deadline; expire;

[滿腔] have one's bosom filled with;

滿腔悲憤 unutterable sadness fills one's heart;

滿腔愁悶 full of care;

滿腔仇恨 be filled with hatred; burn with hatred; seethe with hatred;

滿腔激情 one's breast is filled with emotion;

滿腔苦水 full of grievances;

滿腔怒火 anger flames in one's heart; be filled with boiling anger; be filled with fury;

滿腔熱忱 be filled with ardour and sincerity; full of enthusiasm; full of zealous feelings; in the fullness of one's heart; with great enthusiasm; with warmth and enthusiasm; with zeal;

滿腔熱情 ardently; enthusiastically; fervently; full of enthusiasm; full of warmth; show earnest concern; warm-heartedly; with wholehearted enthusiasm;

M

滿腔熱血 full of patriotic fervour; full of sympathetic feelings; full of zeal; in the fullness of one's heart; one's heart is filled with enthusiasm;
滿腔羞恨 be filled with hatred and shame;
滿腔怨氣 be full of hate;
眼淚滿眶 the tears are filling one's eyes;

[滿身] be covered all over with; have one's body covered with;
滿身大汗 all of a sweat; in a muck sweat; perspire profusely; sweat all over; sweat like a pig;
滿身流汗 perspire profusely;
滿身是債 up to one's neck in debt;
滿身銅臭 filthy rich; stinking with money;
滿身香味 have perfume all over one;
滿身油膩 cover all over with grime;

[滿師] finish serving one's time; serve out one's apprenticeship;

[滿是] all; cover;

[滿室] room;
滿室生香 the room is fragrant with a delicious perfume; the scent fills the room with fragrance;
滿室幽香 the room is filled with a faint fragrance;

[滿堂] hall; house;
滿堂春風 the hall is filled with an air of cheerfulness;
滿堂喝彩 a round of applause bursts out; universal applause;
滿堂紅 all-round success; success in every field;
滿堂歡笑 the whole hall is filled with joy and laughter;

[滿天] all over the sky;
滿天繁星 the sky is studded with twinkling stars;
滿天飛 be all over the place; exist everywhere;
滿天飛雪 the snow is falling thick;
滿天黃沙 the sky is full of sand and dust;
滿天火光 the sky is reddened with the flames;
滿天叫嚷 the air is filled with cries;
滿天通紅 a red glow hangs in the sky;
滿天烏雲 the entire sky is overspread with dark clouds; the sky is overcast with dark clouds;
滿天星 baby's breath;
滿天星斗 a star-studded sky; bright stars stud the sky; the sky is full of stars;
紅光滿天 a red light shines all over the sky;

[滿頭] have one's head covered with;
滿頭大汗 all of a sweat; be covered with sweat; one's face is bathed in sweat; sweat drips from one's face; sweat streams down one's face; sweat trickles down one's face; with sweat all over one's face;
滿頭汗珠 have beads of perspiration on one's forehead;

[滿心] have one's heart filled with sth;
滿心憤怒 in a towering rage;
滿心歡喜 delighted; full of joy; very pleased; with heartfelt delight;
滿心憂慮 one's heart is full of grief;

[滿眼] (1) have one's eyes filled with; (2) meet the eyes on every side;
滿眼紅絲 with bloodshot eyes;
滿眼兇光 there is a murderous look in one's eyes;

[滿意] pleased; satisfied;
滿意的工作 satisfactory job;
滿意的結果 satisfactory results;
滿意的消息 satisfactory news;
滿意度 level of satisfaction;
~病人滿意度 patient satisfaction;
~工作滿意度 job satisfaction;
~顧客滿意度 customer satisfaction;
~選民滿意度 voter satisfaction;
包你滿意 satisfaction guaranteed; you'll like it, I assure you;
表示滿意 express satisfaction;
對工作滿意 be pleased with one's work;
完全滿意 complete satisfaction;
衷心滿意 be sincerely satisfied with;

[滿溢] spill over;
滿而不溢 full but not overflowing; have talent but not display it; have wealth but not squander it;

[滿園] a garden full of;
滿園春色 a garden full of the beauty of spring; the garden is filled with the brightness of spring; the whole garden is full of sights of spring;
滿園雜草 the garden is overgrown with weeds;

[滿月] full moon;
弓如滿月 one's bow arches like a full moon;

拉弓滿月 pull the bow and stretch it to the utmost;
一輪滿月 a full moon;

[滿載] be laden with; be loaded to full capacity; full load;
滿載而歸 return from a rewarding journey; return with a full load of honours;
滿載貨物 be loaded with cargo;
滿載希望 be laden with promise;

[滿紙] the paper is full of;
滿紙荒唐 the paper is full of nonsense;
滿紙空言 empty phrases on a scrap of paper;
滿紙塗鴉 scrawl all over the paper;

[滿桌] a table full of;
滿桌佳饌 a table full of dainties;
滿桌碗碟 the table is piled with dishes;

[滿足] (1) content; satisfied; (2) fulfil; meet; satisfy;
滿足感 a sense of satisfaction;
滿足現狀 rest content with the existing affairs;
得到滿足 obtain satisfaction;
感到滿足 feel satisfaction;
極大的滿足 real satisfaction;
一點點滿足 a crumb of satisfaction;
易於滿足 content with very little;

[滿座] capacity audience; full house;
滿座風生 extraordinary guests;
滿座高朋 the whole audience is full of men of wisdom;
滿座皆驚 all stand amazed;
滿座生春 one's clever stories kept the whole table amused;
場場滿座 have audiences to capacity;
高朋滿座 a great gathering of distinguished guests; a party of many distinguished friends; all seats are occupied by eminent guests;
天天滿座 have a full house every day;

挨滿 be crowded together;
爆滿 be filled to capacity; be packed; have a full house; sell out;
佈滿 be covered with;
充滿 (1) abound in ; be filled with; (2) be permeated with;
豐滿 (1) plentiful; (2) full and round; plump; (3) full-grown; fully-developed;
屆滿 at the expiration of one's term of office;
美滿 perfectly satisfactory;
期滿 come to an end; expire; run out;
填滿 feed to the full; fill to the full;
完滿 satisfactory; successful;
盈滿 full;
斟滿 fill a cup to the brim;

man

【螨】 acarid; mite;

[螨病] acariasis;

[螨巢] acarodomatium;

[螨蟲] acarid; mite;
螨蟲學 acarology;

[螨恐怖症] acarophobia;

[螨性皮炎] acarodermatitis;

man⁴

man

【曼】 (1) delicately beautiful; graceful; (2) long; vast;

[曼妙] lithe and graceful;

[曼聲] sing or recite in lengthened sounds;
曼聲低語 murmur slowly;
曼聲而歌 prolong sounds when singing;
曼聲吟誦 recite in slow measured sounds;

man

【幔】 curtain; screen; tent;

[幔帳] canopy; curtain; screen;

地幔 mantle;
帷幔 heavy curtain;
孝幔 curtain hung in front of a coffin;

man

【慢】 (1) slow; (2) defer; postpone; (3) rude; supercilious;

[慢班] adjustment class;

[慢藏誨盜] a wealthy traveller is a beacon to the violent; an open door may tempt a saint; at open doors dogs come in;

[慢車] milk train; slow train; stopping train;
慢車道 crawler lane;

[慢待] give sb the cold shoulder; treat sb rudely or discourteously;

[慢工] slow work;
慢工出細貨 a slow artisan produces skilled work; fine products come from slow work; soft fire makes sweet malt;

[慢火] gentle heat; slow fire;

[慢慢] by and by; gradually; leisurely; slowly; step by step;
慢慢地 a bit at a time; by degrees; slowly;

慢慢來 have all the hours God gives us; have all the time in the world;
[慢跑] canter;
[慢説] let alone; to say nothing of;
[慢騰騰] at a leisurely pace; sluggishly; unhurriedly; very slowly;
[慢條斯理] at a slack pace; at a snail's gallop; in a leisurely manner; leisurely; slowly and unperturbed; unhurriedly;
説話慢條斯理 speak slowly;
做事慢條斯理 act unhurriedly;
[慢吞吞] exasperatingly slow; irritatingly slow; jogtrot; languid; poky;
[慢行] go slow;
[慢性] chronic;
慢性病 chronic disease;
慢性子 (1) phlegmatic temperament; (2) slowcoach; slowpoke;
[慢悠悠] unhurriedly; without haste;
[慢着] hold one's horses; wait a minute;
[慢走] don't go yet; goodbye; stay; take care; wait a minute;
走得慢 go slowly; walk slowly;

傲慢 arrogant; haughty; overbearing;
逋慢 headless of orders;
放慢 delay; slow;
高慢 arrogant; haughty; overbearing;
緩慢 slow;
簡慢 negligent;
驕慢 arrogant; haughty;
快慢 speed;
輕慢 without proper respect;
懈慢 neglectful; negligent;

man

【漫】 (1) brim over; flood; inundate; overflow; (2) all over the place; everywhere; (3) casual; free; unrestrained;
[漫筆] informal essay; literary notes; ramblings;
[漫不經心] absent-minded; in a careless way; inadvertent; inattentive; indifferently; let slide; negligent; pay no heed to; remiss; totally unconcerned; wanting in care;
漫不經心地回答 reply indifferently;
對工作漫不經心 negligent in one's work;
對未來漫不經心 careless about the future;
做事漫不經心 do sth carelessly;
[漫步] amble; loiter; pad; perambulation; ramble; roam; stroll; wander;
漫步沙灘 stroll on the beach;
漫步思考 mediate on sth while rambling;
漫步談心 have a heart-to-heart talk when going for a walk;
漫步田野 roam the fields;
漫步校園 take a walk on campus;
漫步巡迴 walk round;
從容漫步 amble;
手挽手漫步 stroll hand in hand;
庭中漫步 stroll in one's garden;
鄉間漫步 ramble;
沿街漫步 roam the streets;
[漫藏誨盜] at open doors dogs come in;
[漫長] endless; very long;
漫長曲折 long and tortuous;
[漫畫] caricature; cartoon;
漫畫家 caricaturist; cartoonist;
漫畫書 comics; manga;
連環漫畫 cartoon strip; comic book; comic strip;
一張漫畫 a cartoon;
政治漫畫 political cartoon;
~政治漫畫作者 political cartoonist;
[漫江碧透] the whole stream is emerald green;
[漫罵] abuse wildly; curse; slander;
[漫漫] boundless;
漫漫白雪 boundless snow;
漫漫長夜 a long night which seems to have no end; all the long, dark night; the night seems to drag on;
路漫漫 the road is endless;
[漫山] the whole mountain;
漫山碧綠 the whole mountain is lined with green trees;
漫山遍野 all over the hills and valleys; over hill and dale;
漫山秋色 the hills are inflamed with autumnal tints;
[漫談] informal discussion; random talk;
漫談人生 discuss life informally;
[漫天] (1) all over the sky; filling the whole sky; (2) boundless; limitless;
漫天徹地 everywhere; fill the sky and the land;
漫天大謊 monstrous lie;
~撒漫天大謊 tell a big lie;
~揭穿漫天大謊 expose a flat lie;
~是漫天大謊 a mounstrous lie;

漫天大霧 a dense fog obscuring the sky;
漫天大雪 snow falls thick and fast; the snow falls in soft flakes;
漫天風雪 wind and snow all over the sky;
漫天討價 ask a sky-high price; set sth at an unreasonably high price;
~漫天討價，就地還錢 the price asked is as high as heaven and that offered as low as the earth; the price is as high as the sky and the offer as low as the earth;
漫天要價 ask a sky-high price; ask an exorbitant price;

[漫游] go on a pleasure trip; knock about; roam; rove; wander; wanderings;
漫遊四方 knock about;
漫遊世界 roam about the world;
徒步漫遊 go on a delightful trip on foot;

[漫譯] free translation;

悖漫 arrogantly impolite; disrespectful; show irreverence;
澶漫 (1) moon away; unrestrained; (2) long and wide;
汗漫 extensive; wide-ranging; widespread;
爛漫 (1) bright-coloured; brilliant; resplendent; (2) naïve; unaffected;
浪漫 (1) romantic; (2) dissipated; dissolute;
彌漫 fill the air; spread all over the place;
散漫 (1) careless and sloppy; undisciplined; (2) scattered; unorganized;

man
【嫚】 affront; despise; insult; slight;

man
【蔓】 plants with creeping tendrils or vines;

[蔓生] overgrow; trail;
[蔓説] windy talk;
[蔓延] (1) creep; extend; sprawl; spread; (2) infest;
旱情蔓延 ravages of a drought spread;
開始蔓延 begin to extend;

延蔓 spread like a vine;
枝蔓 branches and tendrils;

man
【縵】 (1) plain silk; (2) plain; unadorned; (3) slow;

man
【謾】 disrespectful; rude;

[謾罵] abuse; bombard; fling abuses; hurl invectives;
謾罵的 abusive;
謾罵命運 rail against fate;
肆意謾罵 call sb all the names under the sun; heap abuse on sb;
一通謾罵 a tirade of abuse;

man
【鏝】 trowel;

[鏝刀] trowel;
半徑鏝刀 radius trowel;
長方形鏝刀 square nosed trowel;
平鏝刀 flat trowel;
砂漿鏝刀 buttering trowel;
圓鏝刀 round trowel;
磚工鏝刀 bricklayer's trowel;

mang²
mang
【忙】 (1) busy; occupied; (2) hasten; hurry; make haste;

[忙活] bustle about; bustle with; busy;
[忙碌] all go; be engaged in doing sth; be engaged in sth; be occupied with; be swamped with work; bustle; bustle about; busy; get one's hands full; have much to do; have one's hands full; on one's toes; on the go; on the run; one's hands are full; up to one's eyes in work; up to the ears in work;
忙忙碌碌 as busy as a bee; busy going about one's work;
[忙亂] bustle; in a rush and a muddle; tackle a job in a hasty and disorderly manner;
忙忙亂亂 hustle and bustle;
[忙人] busy person;
忙人無智 busy people lack wisdom;
[忙時] busy hour;
[忙於] busy at; busy oneself with;
[忙中有錯] error is always in haste; haste is of the devil; haste makes waste;

不忙 take one's time;
幫忙 do a favour; help; lend a hand;
奔忙 be busy rushing about; bustle about;
匆忙 hastily; in a hurry; in haste;
繁忙 busy;
趕忙 hasten; hurry; make haste;
慌忙 hurried; in a flurry; in a great rush;
急忙 hurriedly; in a hurry; in haste;

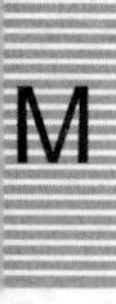

連忙 promptly;
窮忙 (1) be busy making the ends meet; (2) busy for nothing; very busy;
瞎忙 bustle without a plan;
着忙 anxious; panicky;

mang
【邙】 a hill near Luoyang in Henan Province;

mang
【芒】 (1) miscanthus sinensis, a kind of grass; (2) sharp point; (3) beard of wheat; (4) ray of stars;
[芒果] mango;
[芒刺] prickle;
芒刺在背 as a thorn in one's flesh; feel nervous and uneasy; in a most embarrassed and uncomfortable position; like having prickles on one's back;
背若芒刺 feel uncomfortable; like having prickles on one's back;

鋒芒 (1) cutting edge; brilliant spearhead; (2) talent displayed;
麥芒 awn of wheat;

mang
【氓】 rascal; vagabond;

流氓 (1) gangster; hoodlum; rogue; (2) immoral behaviour; indecency;

mang
【盲】 blind;
[盲腸] caecum;
盲腸結腸 caecocolon;
盲腸膨脹 typhlectasis;
盲腸疝 caecal hernia;
盲腸炎 appendicitis; caecitis;
巨盲腸 megacaecum;
[盲從] follow blindly; follow like lambs;
[盲點] blind spot;
[盲動] act blindly; act rashly; skyrocket;
[盲流] job-seeking peasants;
[盲目] blind;
盲目悲觀 blindly pessimistic;
盲目不盲 blind in the eye but not in the mind;
盲目崇拜 blind worship;
盲目發展 blind development;
盲目服從 obey blindly;
盲目競爭 unbridled competition;
盲目樂觀 unrealistically optimistic;
盲目模仿 imitate blindly;
盲目生產 blind production;
盲目搜索 blind search;
盲目投資 blind investment;
盲目行動 act blindly;
盲目行事 follow one's nose;
盲目引進 blind import;
盲目做事 do sth blindly;
[盲人] blind man;
盲人吹喇叭—瞎吹 a blind person blowing a trumpet — talk rubbish;
盲人摸象 blind people trying to size up an elephant — take a part for the whole; people draw a conclusion from incomplete data;
盲人騎瞎馬，夜半臨深池 if the blind leads the blind, both shall fall into the ditch;
盲人瞎馬 like a blind man on a blind horse — rushing headlong to disaster; like the blind leading the blind;
盲人學校 school for the blind;

功能性盲 functional blindness;
精神性盲 psychic blindness;
皮質性盲 cortical blindness;
青盲 glaucoma;
全盲 total blindness;
日蝕盲 eclipse blindness;
日蝕性盲 eclipse blindness;
掃盲 eradicate illiteracy;
色盲 colour blindness;
脱盲 be able to read and write;
文盲 (1) illiteracy; (2) illiterate person;
雪盲 snow blindness;
夜盲 night blindness; nyctalopia;
震蕩性盲 concussion blindness;
晝盲 day blindness;

mang
【庬】 a pronunciation of 庬;

mang
【茫】 (1) boundless and indistinct; (2) ignorant; in the dark;

[茫茫] boundless and indistinct; vast;
茫茫白雪 a boundless expanse of white snow;
茫茫蒼天 vast as the blue sky;
茫茫長夜 it seemed as if the night would never end;

茫茫草原 the boundless grasslands;
茫茫大地，誰主沉浮 who rules over man's destiny on this boundless land;
茫茫大海 boundless ocean; vast sea; wild sea; wildness of waters;
茫茫苦海 endless sea of tribulations;
茫茫泉路 the endless journey to death;
茫茫太空 wildernesses of space;
茫茫天涯 the horizon is unbounded;
白霧茫茫 there is a vast expanse of fog;
草原茫茫 the grassland is boundless;
大海茫茫 there is a vast expanse of sea;
後顧茫茫 the retrospect is uncertain;
沙漠茫茫 there is a vast expanse of desert;
天地茫茫 a limitless, interminable white stretched from the earth to the sky;
一片茫茫 far and wide there is nothing to be seen but the white, empty landscape;
雲海茫茫 there is an immense sea of clouds;

［茫然］ at a loss; blank; ignorant; in the dark; vacant; with an air of abstraction;
茫然不解 at a loss; at sea;
茫然不知 at a loss to understand;
茫然不知所措 at a loss what to do; at one's wits' end; at sea;
茫然若失 all adrift; lose oneself in a reverie;
茫然失措 all adrift; out of one's senses; out of the wits;
茫然無措 all at sea; at one's wits' end; petrified;
茫然無知 in the dark; utterly ignorant;
四顧茫然 see nothing but emptiness all around;

蒼茫 boundless; vast; indistinct; vast;
迷茫 (1) vast and hazy; (2) confused; perplexed;
淼茫 stretch as far as the eye can see;
渺茫 (1) distant and indistinct; vague; (2) not sure; uncertain;
微茫 blurred; hazy; obsure;

mang
【硭】 sodium sulphate;

mang
【鋩】 the point of a knife;

鋒鋩 (1) cutting edge; spearhead; (2) abilities; intelligence; talent displayed;

mang³
mang
【莽】 (1) bushy; weedy; (2) illicium anisatum; (3) impolite; rude; uncultured;
［莽蒼］ (1) open country; (2) (of scenery) blurred; hazy; misty;
［莽漢］ boor; boorish person; ruffian;
［莽莽］ (1) luxuriant; rank; (2) boundless; vast;
［莽原］ wilderness overgrown with grass;
［莽躁］ sudden;
［莽撞］ crude and impetuous;
莽撞行事 crude in one's behaviour;
舉止莽撞 rash in one's manners;
説話莽撞 crude of sb to talk like that;

草莽 (1) rank growth of grass; (2) uncultivated land; wilderness;
粗莽 reckless; rude;
魯莽 crude and rash; reckless;
深莽 land with dense tall grass;

mang
【漭】 expansive; vast;

mang
【檬】 mango;

mang
【蟒】 (1) python; (2) ceremonial robes worn by mandarins;
［蟒蛇］ (1) boa; (2) python;

mao¹
mao
【摸】 a pronunciation of 摸；

mao
【貓】 cat; moggie; moggy;
［貓貓］ cat;
躲貓貓 hide-and-seek;
［貓砂］ cat litter;
［貓鼠同眠］ a cat and a rat sleeping together — officers and thieves are in league; the thieves and the police working together;
［貓頭鷹］ owl;
貓頭鷹唬唬叫 an owl hoots; an owl whoops;
小貓頭鷹 owlet;
一隻貓頭鷹 an owl;
［貓眼石］ chatoyant;

豹貓 leopard cat; ocelot;

雌貓 queen cat;
短尾貓 bobcat;
公貓 tomcat;
郎貓 tomcat;
狸貓 leopard cat;
靈貓 civet;
母貓 mother cat;
豹貓 ocelot;
山貓 leopard cat;
雄貓 tomcat;
熊貓 panda;
野貓 (1) wildcat; (2) alley cat; stray cat;
一隻貓 a cat;

mao²
mao

【毛】 (1) down; (2) hair; (3) feather; (4) wool; (5) mildew; (6) semi-finished; (7) gross; (8) little; small; (9) careless; crude; rash; (10) flurried; panicky; scared; (11) depreciate; no longer worth its face value; (12) a fractional unit of money in China; (13) a surname;

［毛筆］ Chinese brush; writing brush;
一管毛筆 a writing brush;

［毛病］ (1) disease; illness; (2) breakdown; haywire; mishap; trouble; (3) drawback;
毛病多 full of shortcomings; in the wars;
毛病少 there are fewer defects in;
出毛病 go out of order; go pear-shaped; out of order; out of whack;
~ 機器出毛病 the machine is out of order;
老毛病 inveterate disease; old trouble; an old weakness;
挑毛病 find fault; pick holes;
胃有毛病 have stomach trouble;
小毛病 glitch;
有毛病 (1) have rocks in one's head; ill; sick; (2) out of order;

［毛蟲］ caterpillar;
鞭毛蟲 flagellate;
茶毛蟲 Euproctis pesudoconspersa;
胡桃毛蟲 walnut caterpillar;
列隊毛蟲 processionary caterpillar;
毛毛蟲 caterpillar;
鬆毛蟲 pine moth;
纖毛蟲 infusorian;
旋毛蟲 trichina;

［毛豆］ young soya beans;

［毛髮］ hair;
毛髮倒豎 with one's hair standing on end — absolutely terrified;
毛髮悚然 very scary;
毛髮脱落 falling off of hair; hair loss;
毛髮蝟立 one's hair stands on end like the spines of a hedgehog;
毛髮之功 small contributions; tiny deeds;
一叢毛髮 a tuft of hair;

［毛巾］ towel; washcloth; washrag;
毛巾被 cotton blanket;
毛巾杆 towel rail;
毛巾架 towel rail;
一包毛巾 a pack of towels;
一條毛巾 a towel;

［毛坑］ latrine pit;

［毛孔］ sweat pores;

［毛褲］ woolen underpants;
棉毛褲 cotton trousers;

［毛里毛躁］ careless; crude; rash;

［毛利］ gross margin; gross profit;

［毛毛蟲］ (1) carpenterworm; (2) caterpillar;

［毛毛雨］ (1) drizzle; (2) sth unimportant;
下毛毛雨 drizzle;
~ 在下毛毛雨 it's drizzling;

［毛囊］ hair follicle;

［毛皮］ fur; leather;
人造毛皮 imitation fur;
一塊毛皮 a piece of leather;

［毛片］ pornographic movie; porno flick;

［毛錢］ ten-cent coin;

［毛茸茸］ downy; hairy;
毛茸茸的 bushy; fleecy;

［毛毯］ felt; hair felt;
無端毛毯 endless woven felt;
無緯毛毯 knuckle free felt;
吸水毛毯 absorbent felt;
專用毛毯 applying felt;

［毛細］ capillary;
毛細斥力 capillary repulsion;
毛細管 capillary; capillary pipe; capillary tube;
~ 毛細管飽和 capillary saturation;
~ 毛細管比色計 capillator;
~ 毛細管裝置 device for demonstrating capillarity;
~ 玻璃毛細管 glass capillary;
~ 參比毛細管 reference capillary;
~ 膽毛細管 gall capillary;
~ 動脈毛細管 arterial capillary;

~高壓毛細管 high-pressure capillary;
~互聯毛細管 interconnected capillary;
~淋巴毛細管 lymphatic capillary;
毛細活性 capillary activity;
毛細上昇 capillary rise;
毛細下降 capillary depression;
毛細現象 capillarity;
毛細血管 blood capillary;
毛細引力 capillary attraction;
毛細蒸發 capillary evaporation;
毛細作用 capillary action;

[毛線] knitting wool;
毛線衫 sweater;
~高領套頭毛線衫 turtleneck;
一束毛線 a skein of wool; a yarn of wod;
一團毛線 a ball of wool;

[毛衣] wollen sweater;
打毛衣 do knitting work; knit a sweater;
高領毛衣 mock turtleneck;
羔羊毛毛衣 lambswool sweater;
兩件套毛衣 twinset;
套頭毛衣 pullover;
網眼毛衣 holey sweater;
織毛衣 knit a wool sweater;

[毛躁] (1) irritable; short-tempered; (2) rush and careless;

拔毛 pluck out hairs;
鼻毛 nose hair; vibrissae;
鬢毛 hair on the temples;
疵毛 defective wool;
恥毛 (1) woman's pubic hair; (2) one's brush;
次毛 bad; inferior; poor in quality;
大毛 long-haired pelt;
鵝毛 goose feather;
根毛 root hair;
寒毛 fine air on the human body;
汗毛 fine hair on the human body;
毫毛 soft hair on the human body;
鴻毛 goose feather;
雞毛 chicken feather;
睫毛 eyelash; lash;
眉毛 eyebrow;
皮毛 (1) fur; (2) smattering; superficial knowledge;
絨毛 (1) fine hair; (2) nap; pile;
胎毛 foetal hair;
脱毛 lose hair;
細毛 fine soft hair;
纖毛 cilium;
小毛 short-haired pelt;
胸毛 chest hair;
羊毛 sheep's wool;
腋毛 armpit hair; underarm hair;
一撮毛 a tuft of hair;
一根毛 a hair;
陰毛 pubes;
羽毛 (1) feather; (2) plume;
棕毛 palm fibre;

mao

【矛】 lance; pike; spear;

[矛盾] contradiction;
矛盾百出 be riddled with discrepancies; full of contradictions;
矛盾重重 be riddled with contradictions; be torn by contradictions;
矛盾修辭 oxymoron;
辦事矛盾 contradict oneself in what one is doing;
避免矛盾 avoid conflicts;
對抗性矛盾 antagonistic contradiction;
緩解矛盾 alleviate sb's problems;
激化矛盾 intensify contradictions;
階級矛盾 class contradiction;
解決矛盾 solve a problem;
鬧矛盾 in conflict;
內心矛盾 mental conflicts;
説話矛盾 contradict sb's in what he/she is saying;
以子之矛，攻子之盾 beat sb with his own weapon; fight sb with his own weapon; give sb a dose of their own medicine; turn sb's battery against himself;
主要矛盾 principal contradiction;
自相矛盾 contradict oneself; inconsistent; paradoxical; self-contradictory;

[矛頭] bunt; spearhead; spearpoint;
矛頭所向 target of attack;
矛頭向下 direct the spearhead to attack downward;

長矛 lance;
衛矛 winged euonymus;

mao

【茅】 (1) cogon grass; (2) a surname;

[茅草] couch grass; twitch-grass;

[茅房] toilet;

[茅坑] toilet seat;
佔著茅坑不拉屎 a dog in the manger; sit on the toilet seat but not defecate;

[茅廬] thatched cottage;
初出茅廬 beginner; born yesterday;

come out of one's thatched cottage; freshwater sailor; green hand; greenhorn; mere tiro at one's job; new recruit; novice; young and inexperienced;

[茅舍] cottage; thatched cottage;
竹籬茅舍 a thatched cottage with a bamboo fence — a simple dwelling;

[茅廁] latrine; latrine pit;
茅廁裏打哈欠—滿嘴臭氣 yawn in a latrine — use foul language;
茅廁裏的石頭，又臭又硬 like a stone in a privy, hard and stinking;

[茅屋] thatched cottage;

前茅 top of the list;
香茅 lemongrass;

M

mao
【茆】 (1) brasenia schreberi; (2) same as 茅; (3) a surname;

mao
【旄】 (1) a kind of ancient flag, ornamented with animal's hair; (2) same as 髦;

mao
【髦】 (1) children's hairstyle with front hair covering the forehead; (2) mane; (3) talent;

時髦 fashionable; in vogue; stylish;

mao
【氂】 a pronunciation of 氂;

mao
【蝥】 a kind of noxious insect that feeds on the roots of rice plants;

斑蝥 Chinese blister beetle;

mao
【錨】 anchor;
[錨門] anchor bolt;

拔錨 haul in an anchor;
起錨 weigh anchor;

mao
【蟊】 insects that are injurious to crops;
[蟊賊] (1) person who is harmful to the country; (2) pest;

mao³
mao
【卯】 (1) fourth of the twelve Terrestrial Branches; (2) the period from five to seven a.m.; (3) roll call;

點卯 call the roll in the morning;
應卯 answer a roll call;

mao
【泖】 (1) still waters; (2) a river in Jiangsu Province;

mao
【昴】 one of the twenty-eight constellations;

mao⁴
mao
【芼】 (1) choose; select; (2) green vegetables; greens;

mao
【冒】 (1) emit; give off; send out; (2) brave; bold; daring; (3) rashly; (4) inexperienced; (5) falsely; fraudulently; (6) a surname;

[冒充] pass sb off as; pretend to be;
冒充記者 pass oneself off as a journalist;
冒充警察 pretend to be a policeman;
冒充內行 pose as an expert; pretend to be an expert;
冒充學者 pose as a scholar;
頂名冒充 take the name of another;

[冒瀆] annoy a superior; bother a superior;

[冒犯] affront; give offence; offend;
冒犯禁令 violate a prohibition;
冒犯語說法 parrhesia;
避免冒犯 keep off the grass;

[冒汗] perspire; sweat;
急得渾身冒汗 so worried that sweat kept running through one's body;
熱得冒汗 perspiring because of the heat;
曬得直冒汗 keep sweating under the scorching sun;

[冒號] colon;

[冒火] burn with anger; flare up; get angry;
兩眼冒火 one's eyes flashing;

[冒進] advance rashly; premature advance; rash advance;
急躁冒進 impetuous and rash; rush things through;

[冒領] falsely claim as one's own;
冒領他人工資 take another's salary as one's own;

[冒昧] take the liberty; venture;

冒昧陳辭 make bold to express one's views; venture an opinion;
冒昧良心 against one's conscience;
冒昧提出要求 venture to make a request;
冒昧行事 take the liberty of doing sth;
冒昧之舉 rash act;
不揣冒昧 presume; take the liberty of; venture to;
恕我冒昧 with all due respect; with the greatest of respect;

［冒名］ assume another's name; go under sb else's name;
冒名頂替 assume the identity of another person; impersonate; masquerade under a false name; pass sb's name as one's own; pass under a false name;
～冒名頂替者 impostor;
冒名頂姓 use sb's name;

［冒牌］ fake; imitation;
冒牌產品 counterfeit goods; fake goods;
冒牌貨 counterfeit goods; fake goods; pirated goods;
冒牌商標 imitation trademark;
冒牌醫生 quack doctor;

［冒泡］ (1) have a business; have a deal; (2) bubble;
冒泡的水 fizzy water;
冒泡聲 hubble-bubble;

［冒起］ emerge;

［冒失］ abrupt; harum-scarum; rash;
冒失鬼 blunderer; cool character; cool hand; harumscarum; offensive person; rash fellow; sad sack;
冒失行事 handle affairs without consideration;
冒冒失失 heedlessly and unceremoniously; impetuously; rashly; recklessly and abruptly; without due consideration;
說話冒失 speak recklessly;

［冒死］ risk one's life;
冒死進言 appeal at the risk of death;
冒死救人 risk one's life to save sb;
冒死勸進 risk one's life to plead for one's accession;
冒死血戰 risk one's life in battle;
冒死直言 speak frankly risking one's life;

［冒頭］ begin to crop up;

［冒險］ risk; risk one's life; risk one's neck; run risks; take a chance; take a risk; take chances; take the risk of; venture; venture on;
冒險犯難 run risks to overcome obstacles; take the bull by the horns;
冒險家 adventurer;
冒險舉動 leap in the dark;
冒險克艱 run risks to overcome obstacles;
冒險樂園 adventure playground;
冒險生活 life of adventure;
～過冒險生活 live a life of adventure;
冒險行動 a leap in the dark;
冒險一試 chance one's arm;
冒險意識 sense of adventure;
冒險者 adventurer;
冒險主義 adventurism;
～冒險主義者 adventurist;
冒險做事 run the risk of doing sth;
不願冒險［的］ chary;
海上冒險 adventure on sea;

［冒雨］ brave the rain; in spite of the rain;
冒雨而來 come notwithstanding the rain;
冒雨而行 walk in the rain;
冒雨工作 work in the rain;
冒雨回家 return home in the rain;
冒雨前進 advance braving the rain;
冒雨搶修 repair sth in spite of the rain;
冒雨散步 take a walk in spite of the rain;
冒雨上班 go to work in the rain;
冒雨施工 carry out construction braving the rain;
冒雨外出 go out in the rain;
冒雨迎接 meet sb in the rain;

［冒撞］ intrude;
恕我冒撞 pardon me for intruding;

干冒 offend intentionally;
仿冒 counterfeit; fabricate;

mao

【旄】 old;
［旄倪］ old and young;
［旄期］ reach the age of eighty or ninety;

mao

【耄】 (1) in an extremely old age; (2) confused;
［耄年猶勤］ aged yet industrious;

mao

【茂】 (1) exuberant; flourishing; healthy; lush; luxuriant; strong; vigorous; (2) excellent; fair; fine;
［茂密］ dense; thick;
草木茂密 the trees and grass are thick;

森林茂密 the forest is dense;
松樹茂密 the pine trees are thick;
[茂年] vigorous years; youth;
[茂盛] exuberant; flourishing; luxuriant;
植物生產茂盛 the plants are flourishing;

繁茂 lush; luxuriant;
豐茂 lush; luxuriant; profuse;
樸茂 honest; sincere;
蔚茂 lush; luxuriant;
滋茂 luxuriant; teeming;

mao
【眊】 dim-sighted; one's eyes do not see very clearly;

mao
【袤】 length;

廣袤 length and breadth of land;

mao
【帽】 (1) cap; hat; headgear; (2) cap-like cover for sth;
[帽帶] hatband;
[帽頂] crown of a hat;
[帽鈎] hatrack;
[帽徽] cockade; insignia on a cap;
[帽商] hatter;
[帽舌] peak of a cap; visor;
[帽身] body of a hat;
[帽檐] brim of a hat;
[帽針] hatpin;
[帽子] (1) cap; hat; headgear; (2) brand; label; tag;
帽子破了邊—頂好 a hat with a broken brim – tip-top;
帽子戲法 hat trick;
戴高帽子 (1) flatter; lay it on thick; (2) wear a tall paper hat;
戴綠帽子 a husband whose wife has an affair with other men; cuckhold;
~給戴綠帽子 cuckoo;
戴帽子 (1) put on one's hat; wear one's hat; (2) be branded as; be labelled; pin the label of...on sb; put labels on sb;
高帽子 (1) flattery; (2) tall paper hat;
扣帽子 be branded as; give sb a label; pin a label on sb; put a label on sb; stick a label on; stigmatize sb as; tag sb with the label of;
~亂扣帽子 label sb at will; pin labels on people;
一頂帽子 a cap; a hat;
一批帽子 a batch of caps; a lot of hats;
摘帽子 take off one's hat;
~摘下帽子 take off one's hat;

安全帽 hard hat; safety cap;
包頭軟帽 bonnet;
貝雷帽 beret;
筆帽 cap of a pen; cap of a writing brush;
便帽 cap;
冰帽 icecap;
布帽 cloth cap;
草帽 straw hat;
常禮帽 bowler hat; derby;
風帽 weather cap;
高頂禮帽 top hat;
瓜皮帽 skullcap;
火帽 percussion cap;
軍禮帽 dress cap;
軍帽 army cap; service cap;
禮帽 hat that goes with a formal dress;
棉帽 cotton-padded cap;
墨西哥闊邊帽 sombrero;
牛仔帽 cowboy hat;
皮帽 fur hat;
絨球帽 bobble hat;
絨線帽 woolen hat;
三用帽 three-purpose hat;
睡帽 nightcap;
太陽帽 visor; topee;
通風帽 deflector cap;
頭帽 header hat;
脱帽 take off one's hat;
學位帽 mortar board;
有簷帽 peaked cap;
雨帽 rain cap;
圓頂帽 peaked cap with a high crown;
雲帽 cloud cap;
氈帽 felt hat;
遮陽帽 sun hat;
制帽 uniform cap;
鐘帽 bell cap;

mao
【貿】 trade;
[貿然] hastily; rashly; without careful consideration;
貿然拜訪 visit sb without prior appointment;
貿然從事 act rashly;
貿然答應 promise sth without careful

consideration;
貿然前往 go rashly;
貿然下結論 jump to a conclusion;
貿然行事 act rashly; leap in the dark;
貿然許諾 promise sth without careful consideration sth;
貿然選擇 make a hasty choice;
貿然做出決定 make a hasty decision;

［貿易］ trade; trading;
貿易保護 trade protection;
~貿易保護主義 trade protectionism;
貿易不平衡 trade imbalance;
貿易差額 balance of trade;
貿易赤字 trade deficit;
貿易出超 trade surplus;
貿易代表團 trade delegation;
~政府貿易代表團 government trade delegation;
貿易代理人 trade procurator;
貿易額 trade volume;
~雙邊貿易額 bilateral trade volume;
貿易方式 mode of trade;
貿易訪問團 trade mission;
貿易公司 trading company;
貿易關係 trade relationship;
~正常貿易關係 normal trade relations;
貿易管制 trade control;
貿易合同 trade agreement;
貿易匯率 commercial rate;
貿易伙伴 trading partner;
貿易互惠 reciprocity in trade;
貿易量 trade volume;
貿易摩擦 trade conflicts;
貿易逆差 trade deficit;
貿易平衡 balance of trade;
貿易歧視 trade discrimination;
貿易渠道 trade channel;
貿易入超 trade deficit;
貿易市場 trade market;
~鄉村貿易市場 rural trade market;
~自由貿易市場 free trade market;
貿易順差 trade surplus;
貿易談判 trade negotiation;
~多邊貿易談判 multilateral trade negotiation;
~雙邊貿易談判 bilateral trade negotiation;
貿易調解 trade mediation;
貿易條件 trading conditions; trade terms;
貿易統計 foreign trade statistics;
貿易途徑 channel of trade;
貿易團體 trade group;
貿易協定 trade agreement;
貿易盈餘 trade surplus;
貿易戰 trade warfare;
貿易爭端 trade dispute;
貿易政策 trade policy;
~抵償貿易政策 compensation trade policy;
~共同體貿易政策 community trade policy;
~協定貿易政策 agreement trade policy;
貿易指南 trade guide;
貿易制裁 trade sanction;
~單邊貿易制裁 unilateral trade sanctions;
貿易中心 trade centre;
貿易仲裁 trade arbitration;
貿易自由化 trade liberalization;
~世界貿易自由化 world trade liberalization;
貿易組織 trade organization;
保護貿易 protection of trade and commerce; protectionist trade;
~保護貿易政策 protectionist policy;
~保護貿易主義 protectionism;
保護性貿易 protectionist trade;
邊際貿易 marginal trading;
邊境貿易 border trade;
不正常貿易 illicit trade;
補償貿易 compensation trade;
等價貿易 trade of equal value;
~不等價貿易 trade of unequal value;
對外貿易 foreign trade;
~對外貿易慣例 custom of foreign trade;
~對外貿易總額 total volume of foreign trade;
多邊貿易 multilateral trade;
公平貿易 fair trade;
管制貿易 controlled trade;
國際貿易 international trade;
~國際貿易活動 international trade activity;
~國際貿易量 quantum of international trade;
~國際貿易紐帶 nexus of international trade;
~國際貿易值 value of international trade;
國內貿易 internal trade;
過境貿易 transit trade;
~間接過境貿易 indirect transit trade;
~直接過境貿易 direct transit trade;
海外貿易 overseas trade;
互抵貿易 mutual-compensating trade;

間接貿易 indirect trade;
進行貿易 carry on trade in...;
開展貿易 develop trade;
空運貿易 air-borne trade;
擴大貿易 extend trade;
農業貿易 agricultural trade;
洽談貿易 hold trade talks;
三角貿易 triangular trade;
商品貿易 commodity trade;
~商品貿易結餘 balance from commodity trade;
雙邊貿易 bilateral trade; two-way trade;
水平貿易 horizontal trade;
無形貿易 intangible trade; invisible trade;
~無形貿易項目 invisible trade items;
沿海貿易 coastal trade;
易貨貿易 barter; bartering;
影響貿易 affect trade;
有形貿易 tangible trade; visible trade;
直接貿易 direct trade;
中繼貿易 entrepot trade;
中介貿易 intermediate trade;
主動貿易 active trade;
專門貿易 special trade;
轉口貿易 entrepot trade;
自由貿易 free trade;
總貿易 general trade;

財貿 finance and trade;
經貿 economics and trade;
外貿 external trade; foreign trade;

mao
【瑁】 precious piece of jade worn by ancient emperors to match tablets worn by the nobles;

玳瑁 hawksbill turtle;

mao
【楙】 (1) (said of vegetation) lush; luxuriant; (2) the name of a plant;

mao
【貌】 appearance; looks;
[貌合] seemingly in harmony;
貌合神離 appear united outwardly but be divided at heart; seemingly in harmony but actually at variance;
貌合心離 a relationship that seems to be close but in fact is not;
[貌似] in appearance; seemingly;
貌似公允 pretend to be impartial; pretend to be just and fair;
貌似公正 a veneer of fair-mindedness; pretend to play fair; seemingly impartial;
貌似強大 appear to be powerful; look quite strong; outwardly strong; powerful in appearance; seemingly powerful; strong in appearance;
貌似實非 like chalk and cheese;
貌似天仙，心如魔鬼 bear the semblance of an angel but have the heart of a devil;
貌似鮮花，心如蛇蝎 a serpent's heart under an angel face;
貌似有理 apparently reasonable; seem plausible;
貌似忠厚 appear to be honest;

才貌 talent and beauty;
地貌 land form;
風貌 (1) style and features; (2) graceful bearing and handsome appearance; (3) scene; view;
概貌 general picture;
禮貌 courtesy; politeness;
美貌 beautiful; good looks;
面貌 (1) face; features; (2) appearance; looks;
年貌 age and looks;
品貌 (1) appearance; looks; (2) character and looks;
慼貌 appearance of sorrow;
情貌 internal royalty;
體貌 posture and facial features;
外貌 appearance; looks;
相貌 appearance; facial features; looks;
狀貌 appearance; form;

mao
【瞀】 (1) dim-sighted; indistinct vision; near-sighted; (2) feeble-minded; ignorant; (3) confused; confusion; dazzled;

mao
【懋】 (1) grand; great; majestic; (2) trade; (3) encourage;

me⁵
me
【麼】 particle used in the interrogative phrase 甚麼 (what);

多麼 how; what;
那麼 (1) in that way; like that; (2) about; or so;

什麼　what;
要麼　either...or...; or;
怎麼　how; why;
這麼　like this; so; such; this way;

mei²
mei

【沒】 no; not have;
[沒別的] there is nothing else;
[沒錯] (1) I'm quite sure; that's right; you can rest assured; (2) can't go wrong;
說得沒錯　you can say that again;
[沒腳蟹] a crab without legs; in a flurry; supportless person;
[沒勁] (1) boring; uninteresting; (2) good-for-nothing;
沒勁兒　don't have any interest in;
[沒空] have no time; not free;
[沒人] there's nobody;
沒人回答　there's nobody to answer;
[沒命] (1) lose one's life; (2) desperately; for all one's worth; like mad; recklessly;
差點沒命　nearly lose one's life;
險些沒命　on the brink of death;
[沒譜兒] (1) irrelevant; unrealistic; unsettled; unsure; (2) have no idea;
[沒起子] good-for-nothing; hopelessly stupid;
[沒錢] short of money;
[沒趣] feel put out; feel snubbed;
覺得沒趣　feel put out;
討個沒趣　get the cold shoulder;
討沒趣　ask for an insult;
~自討沒趣　bring contempt upon oneself; court a rebuff; invite ridicule; make oneself unwelcome;
[沒事] (1) at a loose end; at leisure; free; have nothing to do; (2) it doesn't matter; it's nothing; never mind; that's all right;
沒事找事　ask for it; ask for trouble; create unnecessary trouble; try hard to find faults;
[沒說的] (1) have nothing to be criticized; really good; unimpeachable; (2) it goes without saying; there's no need to say any more about it;
[沒完] have not finished with sb;
沒完沒了　ceaseless; endless; without end;
吵個沒完　will not stop one's quarrel;
嘮叨個沒完　chatter endlessly;
鬧個沒完　will not stop complaining about sth;
[沒羞] unabashed; unblushing;
沒羞沒臊　brazen-faced; devoid of shame; have no sense of shame; shameless; thick-skinned; unashamed;
[沒學爬就學走] learn to run before one can walk;
[沒有] (1) not have; there is not; without; (2) not so...as; (3) less than;
沒有不散的筵席　the best of friends must part;
沒有不透風的墻　bushes have eyes; fields have eyes, and woods have ears; hedges have eyes and walls have ears;
沒有出路　find oneself in a blind alley; have no way out;
沒有過不去的河　there is no river that cannot be crossed;
沒有好下場　come to no good;
沒有活動餘地　no room to swing a cat; no room to turn in;
沒有經驗的人　a babe in the woods;
沒有理由　unreasonable;
沒有區別　as broad as it is long;
沒有任何機會　not stand the ghost of a chance;
沒有甚麼　nothing wrong with;
沒有甚麼了不起　not enough to; not so great; nothing to be impressed by;
沒有說的　(1) excellent; really good; totally good; (2) it goes without saying; needless to say; there is no need to say more about it; without question;
沒有事做　at a loose end;
沒有頭腦的　dead from the neck up;
沒有王法　in a lawless situation;
沒有興趣　disinterested; have no stomach for;
沒有用　it's usless;
沒有主見的人　a nose of wax;
從來沒有　at no time;
幾乎沒有　next to nothing;
絕對沒有　not by a long shot;
絲毫沒有　not an atom of;
一次都沒有　not once;
[沒轍] have no other way out; have no solution;
[沒治] (1) hopeless; past remedy; (2) excellent; extremely good; first-rate; incredible;
[沒咒唸] can do nothing about it; have no

other way out; have no solution;

［沒主］(1) belong to nobody; (2) unmarried woman;

［沒準兒］(1) maybe; perhaps; (2) have no certainty; have no definite idea;

mei

【枚】 (1) stalk; trunk; (2) numerary auxiliary; (3) gag for troops marching at night when silence means a lot; (4) a surname;

［枚舉］enumerate;

猜枚 guess-the-number game;

mei

【玫】 (1) rose; (2) name for black mica, a sparkling red gem;

［玫瑰］rose;

玫瑰叢 rose bushes;

玫瑰多刺 every rose has its thorns; no rose without a thorn;

玫瑰紅 rose bengal;

玫瑰花 rose;

～一枝玫瑰花 a rose;

玫瑰經 rosary;

玫瑰水 rose water;

一打玫瑰 a dozen roses;

一大束玫瑰 a large bouquet of roses;

一簇玫瑰 a clump of roses;

一束玫瑰 a bouquet of roses;

mei

【眉】 (1) brow; eyebrow; (2) top margin of a page;

［眉筆］eyebrow pencil;

［眉髮］eyebrows and hair;

龐眉皓髮 shaggy eyebrows and hoary head — a healthy, aged person; with white hair and eyebrows;

［眉飛色舞］a look of exultation; beam with joy; brighten up with joy; exultant; one's eyebrows dancing; smack one's lips;

説起他的孩子，他就眉飛色舞 he is enraptured whenever he speaks of his child;

［眉睫］(1) eyebrows and eyelashes; (2) imminent; urgent;

眉睫之禍 imminent disaster;

眉睫之間 in close proximity;

眉睫之利 small immediate interests;

眉睫之內 in close proximity;

迫在眉睫 of the utmost urgency;

火燃眉睫 close at hand; pressing; urgent;

禍在眉睫 in imminent danger;

近在眉睫 before one's eyes; close at hand; in front of one's very eyes;

看人眉睫 subservient;

迫在眉睫 approaching; be hanging over sb's head; extremely urgent; immediate; imminent; likely to happen in no time; pressing; urgent;

失之眉睫 lose sth very soon;

［眉毛］brow; eyebrow;

眉毛鬍子一把抓 try to attend to big and small matters all at once; try to grasp the eyebrows and the beard at the same time;

揚起眉毛 raise one's eyebrows;

一撇眉毛 a brow;

［眉目］(1) features; looks; (2) logic; sequence of ideas; (3) essential;

眉目不清 not well organized in one's writing; the details are not at all clear;

眉目傳情 give sb the eye; make eyes at; send messages of love to sb with one's brows;

眉目含情 her eyes wear an expression of coquetry;

眉目交往 exchange meaningful looks with each other;

眉目清楚 clear and well organized;

眉目清秀 have delicate features; have finely chiselled features;

慈眉善目 benevolent and kind countenance; benignant look;

漸具眉目 grow into a certain, fixed form; take shape gradually;

沒有一點眉目 not have any sign of a positive outcome of the matter;

眉清目秀 beautiful eyes and brow; have beautiful eyes; have delicate features; look clean and pretty;

眉舒目展 feel happy at success; pleased expression; unknit one's eyebrows;

眉語目傳 giving hints with one's eyebrows;

目舒眉展 one's frown fades;

豎眉瞪目 raise one's brows while one's dilated pupils flash with anger; raise one's eyebrows and stare in anger;

有眉目 about to materialize; begin to take

shape;
~有點眉目 get somewhere with the matter;
~有了眉目 begin to take shape;
睜目怒眉 dart fierce looks of hate;

[眉鑷] eyebrow tweezers;
[眉批] notes and commentaries at the top of a page;
[眉如墨畫] one's eyebrows seem as if painted on with Indian ink;
[眉梢] the tip of the brow;
喜上眉梢 look very happy; radiant with joy;
喜溢眉梢 illuminate with joy; light up with joy; one's delight appears on the end of one's eyebrow; sparkle with joy;

[眉梳] eyebrow comb;
[眉頭] one's brows;
眉頭不展 with knitted brows;
眉頭百結 with knitted brows;
眉頭緊鎖 beetle-browed; frown one's brows; knit one's brow; wrinkle one's brows;
眉頭一皺，計上心來 knit the brows and a stratagem comes to mind;
皺眉頭 contract one's brows; frown; knit one's brows; lour;
皺縮的眉頭 contracted brow;

[眉心] between the eyebrows;
[眉眼] (1) amorous glances; (2) appearance; looks;
眉眼傳情 cast amorous glances;
眉眼兒作給瞎子看 waste good acts on sb who will not understand them;
眉眼高低 (1) adopt different attitudes under different circumstances; (2) facial expression;
白眉赤眼 have white eyebrows and red eyes;
粗眉大眼 bushy eyebrows and big eyes; coarse features;
惡眉惡眼 fierce look;
擠眉弄眼 give sb a surreptitious wink now and then; make eyes at sb; wink and cast glances as a signal; wink at each other;
眉高眼低 adopt different attitudes and measures under different circumstances;
眉歡眼笑 all smiles; beam all over one's face; beam with joy; feel happy and smile; grin all over; grin from ear to ear; smile happily; with one's eyebrows arched and laughter in one's eyes;
眉開眼笑 all smiles; be very happy; beam with delight; beam with joy; beaming countenance; feel happy and smile; grin all over; grin from ear to ear; look cheerful; one's eyes sparkle with joy; smile from ear to ear;
眉來眼去 exchange amorous glances; exchange love glances with sb; flirt with each other; leer at sb; make eyes at each other; make sheep's eyes at sb; wink at each other;
擰眉瞪眼 raise one's brows and stare in anger;
濃眉大眼 heavy features; with big eyes and thick eyebrows; with bushy eyebrows and big eyes;
鮮眉亮眼 distinct eyebrows and bright eyes — a good-looking face;
有眉有眼 plausible;
賊眉鼠眼 mean look; have a sneaky look; look like a thief; shifty look;
賊眉賊眼 roguish looks;

[眉宇] forehead;
喜溢眉宇 eyes sparkling with joy; radiant;

愁眉 knitted bows; worried look;
蛾眉 (1) pretty eyebrows; (2) beautiful woman;
橫眉 frown;
劍眉 dashing eyebrows;
柳眉 arch eyebrows;
燃眉 urgently critical;
掃眉 paint eyebrows;
書眉 top margin;
舒眉 relax the brows to show pleasure;

mei

【莓】 berries;

草莓 strawberry;
黑莓 blackberry;
蛇莓 mock strawberry;

mei

【梅】 (1) plum; (2) prune; (3) a surname;
[梅毒] lues; venerea syphilis;
梅毒結節 syphilitic node;
梅毒瘤 gummy tumour;
梅毒疹 syphilid;

初期梅毒 primary syphilis;
地方性梅毒 endemic syphilis;
第二期梅毒 secondary syphilis;
第三期梅毒 tertiary syphilis;
第四期梅毒 quaternary syphilis;
第一期梅毒 primary syphilis;
惡性梅毒 lues maligna;
非性病梅毒 bejel; nonvenereal syphilis;
後期梅毒 late syphilis;
潛伏梅毒 latent syphilis;
實質性梅毒 parenchymatous syphilis;
手掌梅毒 palmar syphilis;
先天性梅毒 congenital syphilis;
遺傳梅毒 heredo lues;
早期梅毒 early syphilis;
早期潛伏梅毒 early latent syphilis;
足底梅毒 plantar syphilid;

[梅花] (1) plum blossom; (2) wintersweet;
梅花傲雪 plum blossom defying frost and snow;
春賞梅花，秋聞桂香 enjoy the plum blossoms in spring and inhale the fragrance of sweet osmanthus flowers in autumn;
一瓣梅花 a petal of plum blossom;
一枝梅花 a branch of plum blossom; a spray of plum blossom;

[梅蘭竹菊] plum blossom, orchid, bamboo, and chrysanthemum;

[梅樹] prune;

[梅雨] plum rain;

[梅子] plum;
青梅子 greengage;

陳皮梅 preserved prune;
寒梅 winter plum;
話梅 plum candy; preserved plum;
黃梅 (1) a folk melody of the Anhui Province; (2) rainy season;
臘梅 wintersweet;
青梅 green plum;
烏梅 dark plum; smoked plum;
楊梅 red bayberry;

mei

【莓】 (1) berry; (2) lichen; moss;

mei

【媒】 (1) go-between; matchmaker; (2) intermediary; intermediate;

[媒介] intermediary; intermediate; medium; vehicle;
媒介關係 media relations;
媒介技術 media technology;
媒介教育 mediated education;
媒介人物 media figure;
媒介社會學 media sociology;
媒介事件 media event;
媒介語 intermediary language;
媒介賬戶 intermediate account;
大媒介 big media;
大眾傳播媒介 mass media;
大眾媒介 mass media;
混合媒介 mixed media;
交換媒介 medium of exchange;
交易媒介 medium of exchange;
利用媒介 utilize the medium;
流通媒介 medium of circulation;
新聞媒介 news media;

[媒孽其短] paint sb black; point out sb's mistakes;

[媒婆] woman matchmaker;

[媒人] go-between; matchmaker;
做媒人 act as a go-between; act as a matchmaker; play cupid;

[媒體] mass media; medium;
媒體研究 media studies;
超媒體 hypermedia;
串流媒體 streaming media;
多媒體 multimedia;
~多媒體電腦 multimedia computer;
~多媒體服務台 multimedia kiosk;
~多媒體個人計算機 multimedia personal computer;
~多媒體軟件 multimedia software;
~多媒體數據庫 multimedia database;
~多媒體信息咨詢系統 multimedia information system;
全國媒體 national media;
新媒體 new media;
新聞媒體 news media;

[媒質] medium;
光密媒質 optically denser medium;
光疏媒質 optically thinner medium;
聲媒質 acoustic medium;
吸收媒質 absorbing medium;

傳媒 disseminate;
觸媒 catalyst;
靈媒 spirit medium;
做媒 be a matchmaker;

mei

【煤】 (1) charcoal; coal; coke; (2) carbon;

(3) soot;

[煤餅] briquette;

[煤倉] coal bunker;

[煤層] coal bed; coal seam;

[煤場] coal yard;

[煤車] coal car;

[煤塵] coal dust;
煤塵爆炸 coal-dust explosion;

[煤船] coaler;

[煤袋] coal sack;

[煤斗] coal scuttle;

[煤毒] carbon monoxide (CO);

[煤窖] coal cellar; coal hole;

[煤耗] coal consumption;

[煤核兒] coal cinder;

[煤黑子] coal miner with a blackened face;

[煤灰] coal ash;

[煤精] black amber; jet;

[煤坑] coal pit;

[煤塊] coal; lump coal;

[煤庫] coalhouse;

[煤礦] (1) coal mine; colliery; (2) coal shaft;
煤礦工人 coal miner;
煤礦井口 pithead;

[煤爐子] coal stove;

[煤末] coal dust;

[煤氣] coal gas; gas used for lighting or heating;
煤氣爆炸 gas explosion;
煤氣錶 gas meter;
煤氣廠 gasworks;
煤氣抄錶員 gasman;
煤氣燈 gas lamp; gas light;
煤氣工 gas fitter;
煤氣公司 gas company;
煤氣管 gas pipe;
煤氣機 coal gas engine;
煤氣庫 gasholder; gasometer;
煤氣爐 gas furnace; gas stove;
煤氣熱水器 gas water heater;
煤氣炭 gas carbon;
煤氣中毒 carbon monoxide poisoning; gas poisoning;
煤氣裝置 gas fittings;
煤氣總管 gas main;

[煤球] briquettes; coal balls made of coal dust and clay;

[煤染劑] mordant;
黑色煤染劑 black mordant;
石油煤染劑 oil mordant;
銅煤染劑 copper mordant;

[煤商] coal dealer; coalman;

[煤水車] tender;

[煤炱] soot;

[煤炭] anthracite; coal; coke; hard coal;
煤炭大王 coal baron;
煤炭店 shop that sells coal;
煤炭商 coal merchant;
煤炭箱 coal bin;

[煤田] coal bed; coalfield;

[煤桶] coal scuttle;

[煤箱] coal hod; coal scuttle;

[煤屑] coal dust;

[煤煙] soot;

[煤油] kerosene;
煤油燈 kerosene lamp;
煤油罐 kerosene container;
煤油爐 kerosene stove;
燈用煤油 burning kerosene;
航空煤油 aviation kerosene;
棕色煤油 brown kerosene;

[煤渣] cinder; clinker; coal cinders; coal slag;
煤渣路 cinder road;
煤渣跑道 cinder track;
煤渣磚 breeze block; cinder block;

[煤磚] briquette;

採煤 mine coal;
儲煤 coal storage;
船用煤 admiralty coal;
肥煤 rich coal;
褐煤 brown coal;
火煤 kindling;
焦煤 coking coal;
塊煤 lump coal;
泥煤 peat;
氣煤 gas coal;
砂煤 sand coal;
篩煤 screen coal;
石煤 bone coal;
瘦煤 lean coal; meager coal;
無煙煤 anthracite coal;
洗煤 coal washing;
煙煤 bituminous coal; soft coal;
一袋煤 a sack of coal;
一塊煤 a lump of coal;
硬煤 hard coal;
原地煤 autochthonous coal;
原煤 raw coal;

mei
【湄】 river bank; shore;

mei
【嵋】 Mount Emei, a Buddhist resort in Sichuan;

mei
【郿】 (1) Mei County in Shaanxi; (2) a town of Lu in the Spring and Autumn Period;

mei
【楣】 lintel;
［楣窗］ fanlight; transom window;

mei
【酶】 enzyme; ferment; zyme;
［酶病］ enzymopathy;
［酶化學］ zymochemistry;
［酶解］ enzymolysis;
酶解作用 zymolysis;
［酶性］ enzymic;
酶性敗壞 enzymic spoilage;
［酶學］ enzymology;

活體酶 organized ferment;
激活酶 activating enzyme;
加成酶 adding enzyme;
凝固酶 coagulative ferment;
凝血酶 ymoplasm;
適應酶 adaptive enzyme;
細菌酶 bacterial enzyme;
消化酶 digestive ferment;
修飾酶 modification enzyme;
需氧酶 aerobic enzyme;
胰酶 zymine;
轉化酶 zymase;

mei
【霉】 damp; mildew; mildewed; mould; musty;
［霉斑］ mildew;
［霉病］ mildew;
葱霜霉病 onion mildew;
黃瓜霉病 cucumber mildew;
［霉臭］ musty smell;
［霉天］ early summer rains;
［霉運］ bad luck;

倒霉 be out of luck; be unlucky; be unlucky;
發霉 become mildewed; go mouldy;
黑霉 mildew; mould;
曲霉 aspergillus;

mei³

mei
【每】 (1) each; every; per; (2) often;
［每次］ at every turn; every time;
每次二粒 two capsules at a time;
［每打］ every dozen;
每打十元 ten dollars a dozen;
［每當］ each time; every time; whenever;
［每到］ (1) everytime; whenever; (2) every place; wherever;
［每逢］ on every occasion; when;
每逢佳節倍思親 each time a festival arrives, one thinks all the more of one's close relatives; on festive occasions more than ever one thinks of one's dear ones far away;
［每隔］ day at certain intervals; every;
每隔一行 every other line; every second line;
每隔兩年 every two years;
每隔一段時期 at set intervals of time;
每隔一天 day about; every other day; every two days;
［每況愈下］ become worse and worse; get increasingly worse; go downhill; go from bad to worse; make bad trouble worse; on the decline; steadily deteriorate; take a bad turn; take a turn for the worse; worse and worse;
情況每況愈下 things take a downward turn;
［每每］ often;
［每年］ every year; per annum;
每年一次 once a year;
［每日］ everyday;
每日每時 daily and hourly; every day and every hour;
每日一次 once a day;
［每天］ a day; daily; day after day; day by day; day in and day out; day in, day out; everyday; from day to day; per day;
每天三餐 three meals a day;
每天晚上 every night;
［每月］ every month; monthly;
［每周］ weekly;

mei
【美】 (1) beautiful; pretty; (2) good; very satisfactory; (3) be pleased with oneself;

[美餐] feast;
[美鈔] dollar; greenback;
[美稱] (1) good name; (2) complimentary; laudatory;
[美德] moral excellence; virtue;
培養美德 cultivate the virtue of sth;
中華美德 Chinese virtues;
[美髮] hairdressing;
美髮產品 haircare products;
美髮師 hairdresser;
[美感] aesthetic feeling; aesthetic sensibility; sense of beauty;
美感層次 level of aesthetic sensibility;
[美工] (1) art designing; (2) art designer;
美工車間 art designing department;
美工刀 craft knife;
美工師 set designer;
[美觀] artistic; beautiful; beautiful to look at; pleasing to the eye;
美觀大方 elegant appearance;
美觀耐用 beautiful and durable;
佈置美觀 be artistically decorated;
[美好] fine; glorious; happy;
美好的 fine;
~ 非常美好的 bootylicious;
美好記憶 happy memories;
美好人生 a life of happiness;
[美化] beautify; embellish; prettify;
美化環境 beautify the environment;
美化物質生活 enrich one's material life;
[美奐美輪] beautiful; magnificent; sumptuous;
美輪美奐 beautiful and sumptuous; magnificent;
[美甲] make one's nails more attractive;
美甲店 nail salon;
美甲沙龍 nail salon;
美甲師 manicurist;
[美景] beautiful scenery; fine view;
飽賞美景 drink in the beauty of a scene;
[美酒] good wine;
美酒佳肴 excellent wine and delicious food; good wine and dainty dishes; vintage wine and choice food;
美酒良肴 good wine and delicious dishes;
美酒珍饌 good wine and choice dishes; good wine and savoury dishes;
[美麗] beautiful;
美麗動人 beautiful and attractive;
美麗富饒 beautiful and rich;
[美滿] happy; perfectly satisfactory;
美滿幸福 full and happy;
美滿姻緣 beautiful and satisfactory marriage; conjugal felicity; happy marriage;
婚姻美滿 enjoy conjugal happiness;
家庭美滿 have a happy family;
結局美滿 end in perfect satisfaction;
生活美滿 lead a happy life;
[美貌] beautiful; good looks;
[美夢] fond dream;
黃粱美夢 daydream; pipe dream;
做美夢 cherish fond hopes; have a sweet dream;
[美妙] beautiful; splendid; wonderful;
歌聲美妙 the singing is beautiful;
行情不美妙 the prices are unfavourable;
前景美妙 the prospects are bright;
青春美妙 youth is wonderful;
情況不美妙 the situation is unfavourable;
舞姿美妙 the dancing is beautiful;
[美名] good name; good reputation;
美名四揚 win popular praise;
美名遠揚 one's good name spreads far and wide; win popular praise;
[美目] beautiful eyes;
美目流盼 the bewitching glance of a beauty;
[美妞] beautiful girl;
[美女] beautiful girl; beautiful woman; beauty; pretty girl;
美女世界 world of beautiful women;
美女簪花 like a beautiful girl wearing flowers in her hair;
一群美女 a bevy of beautiful women;
[美其名曰] call it by the fine-sounding name of; describe it euphemistically as; give it the fine-sounding name of;
[美人] beautiful woman; beauty; looker; queen of hearts;
美人斑 beauty mark;
美人遲暮 a beauty in her old age;
美人芳草 beautiful women and fragrant grass;
美人計 sex trap;
美人魚 mermaid;
美人痣 beauty mark;
紅顏長駐的美人 ageless beauty;
睡美人 sleeping beauty;
[美容] (1) improve one's looks; (2)

cosmetology; (3) beauty treatment;
美容覺 beauty sleep;
美容品 cosmetics;
美容師 beautician;
美容術 beauty art; cosmetology;
美容霜 vanishing cream;
美容院 beauty parlour; beauty salon; beauty shop;
美容中心 beauty centre;
美容專家 beauty specialist; cosmetologist;

[美如] as beautiful as;
美如冠玉 as beautiful as the jade ornament of a cap; handsome man;
美如鮮花 as beautiful as a fresh flower;

[美色] (1) attractive woman; (2) woman's beauty;
惑於美色 be taken by a bewitching face;

[美食] delicious food; delicacy; fine food; good food;
美食甘寢 eat well and sleep well; lead an easy life;
美食家 epicure; foodie; gourmet;
美食酒吧 gastropub;
美食學 astronomy;
品嚐美食 appreciate good food;

[美術] (1) art; fine arts; (2) painting;
美術館 art gallery;
~一個美術館 an art gallery;
美術家 artist;
美術片 cartoon and puppet film;
美術師 artist;
美術學校 art school;
美術學院 academy of fine arts;
美術指導 art director;
美術作品 work of art;
~一部美術作品 a work of art;
工藝美術 decorative arts;
實用美術 applied art;

[美談] story passed on with approval;
傳為美談 a story that is passed on with approval;

[美味] delicacy; delicious food;
美味的 delicious; luscious; toothsome;
~美味的菜餚 toothsome dish;
美味十足 full of flavor;

[美學] aesthetics;
美學功能 aesthetic function;
美學觀點 aesthetic idea;
美學家 aesthete; aesthetician; aestheticist;
美學教育 aesthetic education;
美學理論 aesthetic theory;
美學批評 aesthetical criticism;
美學世界 aesthetic world;
比較美學 comparative aesthetics;
當代美學 contemporary aesthetics;
翻譯美學 translation aesthetics;
語言美學 linguistic aesthetics;

[美言] put in a good word for sb; say a good word for;
我會在經理面前為你美言 I shall manage to say sth on your behalf before the boss;

[美餚佳餐] slapping dinner; slick meal;

[美意] good intentions; kindness;
美意延年 a carefree life insures longevity;

[美育] aesthetic education; art education;

[美譽] good name; good reputation;
享有美譽 enjoy a good reputation;

[美元] American dollar; buck; U.S. dollar;
美元過多 dollar glut;
美元化 dollarization;
美元區 dollar area;
美元危機 dollar crisis;
拋售美元 dollar sale;
歐洲美元 Euro-dollar;

[美制] American system;

[美洲] America;

愛美 (1) love beauty; set great store by one's appearance; (2) be fond of making up; love to make up and wear beautiful clothes;
臭美 (1) beautify; dress up; make up; (2) be stuck on oneself; give oneself airs; swell-headed;
肥美 (1) fertile; rich; (2) fat; luxuriant; plump;
甘美 sweet and refreshing;
華美 gorgeous; magnificent; resplendent;
健美 strong and handsome; vigorous and graceful;
精美 elegant; exquisite;
俊美 handsome; pretty;
孌美 effeminate;
掠美 claim credit due to others; rob sb else's good point; take credit due to sb else;
媲美 be on a par with; compare favourably with; match each other;
審美 appreciate the beauty of;
歎美 praise;
恬美 quiet and nice;
完美 consummate; flawless; perfect;

鮮美 (1) delicious; tasty; (2) fresh and beautiful;
溢美 praise excessively;
幽美 pathetically beautiful;
秀美 elegant; graceful;
優美 exquisite; fine; graceful;
壯美 full of grandeur; magnificent and beautiful;
作美 cooperate; help; make things easy for sb;

mei
【浼】 (1) contaminate; soil; stain; (2) full of water; (3) entrust;
[浼瀆清聽] bother by request;

mei
【鎂】 magnesium;

mei⁴
mei
【妹】 younger sister;
[妹夫] (1) brother-in-law; (2) younger sister's husband;
[妹妹] (1) sister; (2) younger sister;
異父妹妹 younger stepsister;
異母妹妹 younger stepsister;

阿妹 one's little sister;
胞妹 full younger sister;
表妹 younger female cousin;
弟妹 younger brother and sister;
姐妹 (1) sisters; (2) brothers and sisters;
舍妹 one's younger sister;

mei
【沬】 (1) dusk; (2) name of a river; (3) a town in the state of Wei, in today's Henan Province;
[沬血] blood flowing in one's face; a bleeding face;

mei
【昧】 (1) have hazy notions about; ignorant of; (2) conceal; hide;
[昧旦晨興] careladen; hardworking; industrious; rise before dawn;
[昧己瞞心] do evil against one's conscience; play treacherous tricks against one's conscience;
[昧死以聞] appeal to the emperor at the risk of death;
[昧心] against one's conscience;

曖昧 (1) ambiguous; equivocal; (2) dubious; shady;
暗昧 (1) ambiguous; equivocal; (2) dubious; shady; (3) benighted; ignorant;
草昧 primeval; primitive;
茫昧 indistinct; uncertain; vague;
冒昧 make bold; resume; take the liberty;
蒙昧 (1) uncivilized; uncultured; (2) ignorant; unenlightened;
檮昧 benighted; ignorant;
愚昧 benighted; ignorant;

mei
【袂】 sleeves;

把袂 holding sleeves – in loving relationship;
奮袂 make a rigorous start;
聯袂 join sleeves;

mei
【眛】 dim-sighted; poor-visioned;
[眛於] blind to;
眛於世道常情 too ignorant of the ways of the world;
眛於事理 lack common sense;
眛於事實 ignorant of the facts; unaware of the truth;
眛於知識 fail to understand knowledge;

mei
【媚】 (1) favour with; fawn on; toady to; (2) charming; enchanting; fascinating;
[媚骨] obsequiousness;
奴顏媚骨 bowing and scraping; sycophancy and obsequiousness;
[媚人] sugary;
[媚態] coquetry; subservience;
媚態嬌容 seductive appearance and attractive manner;
[媚外] fawn on foreign powers; try to flatter foreigners;
媚外殘民 fawn on the foreigners and persecute one's own people;
媚外崇洋 subservient to foreigners;
媚外非中 toady to the foreign and scorn for the Chinese;
媚外政策 policy of toadying to foreigners;
[媚眼] seductive eyes;
飛媚眼 throw amorous glances at sb;
拋媚眼 make eyes at sb; throw a sultry glance;

諂媚 curry favour with; fawn on; flatter;
狐媚 charm by cajolery; entice by flattery;
嬌媚 (1) coquettish; (2) sweet and charming;

明媚 bright and beautiful; radiant and enchanting;
柔媚 gentle and lovely; graceful and charming;
嫵媚 charming; graceful; lovely;
閒媚 quiet and charming;
獻媚 curry favour with; flatter; try to ingratiate oneself with;
秀媚 elegant and graceful;
姿媚 elegant and graceful manners;

mei
【寐】 deep sleep; doze; drowse; sleep; sound sleep;
［寐而不睡］ lie down but not sleep;

mei
【瑁】 tortoise shell;

mei
【謎】 a pronunciation of 謎 ;

mei
【魅】 (1) elf; goblin; mischievous spirit; (2) charm; mislead;
［魅力］ charisma; charm; enchantment; fascination; glamour; pulling power; spell; winsomeness; witchcraft; witchery;
個人魅力 charisma; mojo;
施展魅力 turn on the charm;
~施展魅力的人 charmer;
藝術魅力 artistic charm;
音樂的魅力 magic of music;
永恒的魅力 unfailing charm;
有超凡魅力［的］ charismatic;
有魅力［的］ attractive; captivating; charming;
增添魅力 add charm to;
展示魅力 display charms;

魑魅 demons and monsters; evil spirits;
鬼魅 forces of evil; ghosts and goblins;

men¹
men
【悶】 (1) close; stuffy; (2) cover tightly; (3) muffled; (4) shut oneself indoors;
［悶氣］ airless; close; stuffy;
悶氣的房間 airless room;
［悶熱］ hot and suffocating; stuffy;
悶熱潮濕 hot and sticky;
悶熱的天氣 sultry weather;
又悶又熱 hot and suffocating; muggy; sultry and stifling;
［悶人］ downer;
［悶燒］ smoulder;
［悶聲］ remain quiet;
悶聲不響 glum silence; remain quiet; remain silent;
悶聲悶氣 in a muffled voice;
［悶死］ bore sb to tears; bore the pants off sb; stiffle; smother; suffocate;
［悶頭兒］ quietly; silently;
悶頭兒幹活 plod away silently;
悶頭兒看書 read doggedly in silence;
悶頭兒寫書 write a book silently;

men
【燜】 a pronunciation of 燜 ;

men²
men
【門】 (1) door; entrance; gate; (2) switch; valve; (3) knack; way to so sth; (4) family; (5) school; sect; (6) branch; field; sphere; (7) a surname;
［門把］ door handle; door knob;
［門窗］ doors and windows;
鎖好門窗 lock up;
［門道］ (1) doorway; knack; way to do sth; (2) contacts; social connections;
門道多 have social connections in;
門道很廣 have numerous contacts with people;
看出門道 get the knack of...;
有門道 get the hang of sth; have the hang of sth; have the knack of doing sth; have the means of sth;
找錯門道 bring one's eggs to a bad market; bring one's hogs to a bad market; bring one's pigs to a bad market; bring one's eggs to the wrong market; come to the wrong shop;
［門第］ family status; pedigree;
門第冷落 one's family is on the decline;
門第之辱 blot on one's escutcheon; disgrace to the family;
詩書門第 family of high academic standing; family that cultivates literature; scholarly family;
~出身於詩書門第 from an intellectual family;
［門兒］ access;
沒門兒 (1) have no access to sth; have no means of doing sth; (2) absolutely impossible; no go; no way; out of the

question; (3) get no clues; not take shape; (4) have no way out; have no idea;

[門房] gatehouse;

[門風] moral standards of a family;

敗門風 disgrace one's family;

[門縫] crack in the door;

門縫裏看人 look at people narrowly, as if through a crack in the door; look down upon sb;

隔著門縫瞧人，把人看扁了 if you peer at a person through a crack, he looks flat; looking at sb through the crack between the door and its frame — looking at people in a narrow way; underestimate people;

[門戶] (1) door; (2) gateway; important passageway; (3) faction; sect; (4) family status;

門戶半開 the door is partly open;

門戶不關緊，聖賢起盜心 an open door may tempt a saint;

門戶洞開 the gate is wide open;

門戶緊閉 the door is tightly shut;

門戶開放 open-door;

~門戶開放政策 open-door policy;

門戶人家 brothel;

門戶相當 families well-matched in social status;

門戶虛掩 the door is off the latch;

門戶之見 factional views; parochial prejudice; sectarian bias; sectarian views; sectarianism;

門戶之爭 sectarian controversies;

傍人門戶 depend on sb's whims and pleasures; live at sb's mercy; rely on sb for a living; under sb's roof;

打開門戶 open the doors;

各立門戶，各自為政 each forms an independent system of his own and goes his own way; set up its own organ and act on its own will;

另立門戶 live in a separate house;

門當戶對 be fairly well matched; in an equal walk of life;

千門萬戶 numerous households; one thousand doors with ten thousand families;

辱門敗戶 bring disgrace and ruin to one's family; bring disgrace on a family; desecrate one's own door; put to shame the name of the house;

小門小戶 a poor, humble family;

踅門瞭戶 loiter and chat at friends' houses;

支應門戶 attend to the door;

[門環] doorknocker; knocker;

[門鉸] hinge;

[門階] doorstep;

正門門階 front doorstep;

[門徑] access; door; gate; key; way;

得窺門徑 just learn the rudiments of the subject;

[門坎兒] threshold;

[門檻] (1) threshold; (2) key to a problem; knack; (3) person who is good at calculation;

老門檻 an expert at th game; an old hand;

[門可羅雀] deserted house; there are few visitors; visitors are few and far between;

[門口] doorway; entrance;

送到門口 accompany sb to the door;

[門類] category; class; kind;

[門聯] gatepost couplet;

[門臉] (1) appearance; (2) shop front;

[門鈴] doorbell; jingle bell;

按門鈴 ring the doorbell;

[門樓] gate tower;

[門路] (1) pull; social connections; (2) channel; knack; know-how; outlet; trick of the trade; way;

發現門路 find the way to do sth;

摸到門路 have learned the ropes; learn the ways of the trade;

熟門熟路 be used to one's ways; familiar with; on good terms with sb;

有門路 have a way out; have powerful connections; know the right places to go to get sth done;

找門路 solicit help from potential backers;

~找到門路 catch the knack of...;

鑽門路 manoeuvre for advantage;

走門路 approach people of influence in seeking an objective;

[門楣] (1) lintel; (2) door header;

敗壞門楣 disgrace one's family;

敗辱門楣 disgrace one's family;

光耀門楣 bring honour to the family name; do honour to one's family; win honour and distinction for one's family;

[門面] (1) facade of a shop; shop front; (2) appearance; facade;

門面大 put on a very prosperous front;

門面小 have a small shop front;

擺門面 keep up appearances; put up a front; put up an impressive front;

撐門面 keep up appearances;

裝門面 adorn for the sake of face; keep up appearances; maintain an outward show; put up a front; window dressing;

~裝門面的 cosmetic;

~裝點門面 keep up appearances; tokenism;

為了裝點門面 for appearance's sake;

壯壯門面 create a good public impression;

[門牌] (1) number plate; (2) house number;

[門票] admission ticket; entrance ticket;

門票很貴 the admission ticket is expensive;

買門票 buy the admission ticket;

免面票 free of entrance ticket charge;

[門墻] one's pupil;

愿拜門墻 I wish to have the honour of becoming your pupil;

[門人] (1) disciple; (2) hanger-on of an aristocrat;

[門神] door-god;

門神老了不捉鬼 when one gets old and tarnished one loses one's value;

反貼門神 the Door-gods are wrongly pasted;

[門生] disciple; pupil;

門生故吏 disciples and old followers; one's intimate part-followers and students;

收門生 take pupils;

[門市] retail sales;

其門如市 have many friends; have many social contacts;

[門廳] hallway;

[門庭] gate and courtyard;

門庭冷落車馬稀 the house is deserted and there are few callers; visitors are few and far between;

門庭若市 many callers; swarming with visitors; thriving business;

門庭衰落 the family had declined in prosperity;

門庭興盛 the family is thriving;

門庭喧鬧 the courtyard is clamorous;

敗壞門庭 disgrace the honour of the family;

光耀門庭 bring honour to the family name; do honour to one's family; win honour and distinction for one's family

[門徒] adherent; disciple; follower;

[門外] outside the door;

門外漢 ignoramus; layman; outsider; philistine; those in the outside;

擯諸門外 lock sb out; shut sb out;

拒之門外 be kept out of the door; close the door on sb; debar sb from entering the house; keep sb outside the door; slam the door in sb's face;

[門衛] bouncer; doorkeeper;

[門無雜賓] never to associate with bad companions;

[門下] (1) hanger-on of an aristocrat; (2) adherent; disciple; follower;

拜在門下 become a pupil to sb;

河汾門下 the well-known scholar has many distinguished students;

依人門下 take shelter under other's door;

[門診] clinic; outpatient service;

門診病人 outpatient;

門診部 clinic; outpatient department;

~門診部主任 head of the outpatient department;

門診時間 consulting hours;

[門柱] doorjamb; doorpost; gatepost;

挨門 door-to-door;

俺門 we;

把門 guard a door; stand watch at a door; watch the door;

拜門 (1) pay thanks by personal visit; (2) become a pupil or apprentice to a master;

閉門 close one's door;

邊門 (1) side door; (2) wicket door;

便門 side door; wicket door;

部門 branch; department;

彩門 decorated gateway;

側門 side door; side entrance;

車門 car door; door;

城門 city gate;

出門 (1) go on a journey; (2) be away from home;

串門 call at sb's home; call on sb; drop around; drop in on sb; look in on sb;

捶門 bang on the door; pound at the door;

大門 entrance door; front door; gate;
登門 call at sb's house;
電門 electric switch;
斗門 sluice gate;
對門 face each other;
耳門 side doors;
糞門 anus;
風門 air door; ventilation door;
佛門 Buddhism;
肛門 anus;
拱門 arched door;
關門 gate of a strategic pass;
國門 (1) gate of the national capital; (2) border; frontier;
寒門 (1) my poor family; (2) humble family;
豪門 rich and powerful family wealthy and influential clan;
後門 (1) backdoor; (2) back influence;
滑門 sliding door;
活門 valve;
家門 (1) door of a house; (2) family clan;
角門 side door;
叫門 call at the door to be let in;
街門 front gate;
開門 (1) open the door; (2) begin business;
空門 Buddhism;
快門 shutter;
冷門 (1) dark horse; (2) profession, trade, or branch of learning that receives little attention;
滿門 whole family;
旁門 side door sidegate;
屏門 screen dorr;
破門 (1) burst open the door; (2) excommunicate;
氣門 (1) valve of a tyre; (2) spiracle; stigma;
前門 front door;
竅門 knack;
球門 goal;
熱門 in great demand; popular;
入門 elementary course;
沙門 Buddhist monk;
紗門 screen door;
上門 (1) call; come or go to see sb; drop in; visit; (2) shut the door for the night;
釋門 Buddhism;
守門 (1) be on duty at the door; (2) keep goal;
送上門 deliver sth to sb's home;
鐵門 (1) iron gate; (2) grille;
同門 pupils of the same master;
推拉門 sliding door;
旋轉柵門 turnstile;
衙門 yamen;
掩門 close the door;
一重門 a door;
一道門 a door;
一門 a branch of;
一扇門 a door;
陰門 vaginal orifice;
應門 be in carge of the opening and closing of the door;
幽門 pylorus;
油門 (1) throttle; (2) accelerator;
遠門 go on a long journey;
正門 front door; main entrance;
轉門 revolving door;

men
【們】 adjunct to a pronoun to indicate plurality;

men
【捫】 (1) feel or touch with hands; hold; (2) search;
[捫櫝估珠] buy a pig in a poke;
[捫心] examine one's conscience; feel one's heart by hand;
捫心無愧 feel no qualms upon self-examination; feel that one has not done anything wrong; have a good conscience; one's heart is in the right place;
捫心自問 an introspection; examine oneself;

men
【糜】 (1) rice variety with red seedlings; (2) congee;

men⁴
men
【悶】 (1) bored; depressed; in low spirits; (2) sealed; tightly closed;
[悶棍] staggering blow;
打悶棍 take advantage of sb's unawareness to strike a heavy blow at him;
[悶倦] bored and listless;
[悶雷] (1) dull thunder; (2) shock; unpleasant surprise;
打悶雷 brood; leave sb in suspense;
[悶瞀] blurring of vision accompanied by restlessness;
[悶悶不樂] broody; depressed in spirits; down in the mouth; feel depressed; get the

hump; glum; have the blues; have the hump; heartsick; in a bad mood; in a very melancholy frame of mind; in a very melancholy spirit; in low spirits; in the doldrums; in the dumps; look blue; mopish; morose; pip; sullen;

［悶氣］ sulks;

懊悶 eat one's heart out;
憋悶 depressed; melancholy;
沉悶 (1) depressing; oppressive; (2) depressed; in low spirits; (3) not frank and open; not outgoing;
愁悶 be depressed; be in low spirits; feel gloomy;
煩悶 be unhappy; be worried;
苦悶 dejected; depressed;
窒悶 close; stuffy;

men
【燜】 braise; stew;
［燜飯］ stewed rice;
［燜燒］ smoldering;

紅燜 stew in soy sauce;

men
【懣】 resentful; sulky; sullen;

憤懣 depressed and discontented; indignant; resentful;

men⁵
men
【們】 a pronunciation of 們；

你們 you (plural);
人們 people; the public;
它們 they;
他們 they;
她們 they;
我們 we;
咱們 we;

meng¹
meng
【矇】 (1) cheat; deceive; swindle; (2) lucky;
［矇哄］ cheat; deceive; hoodwink; swindle;
［矇矇亮］ daybreak; the first glimmer of dawn;
［矇騙］ cheat; deceive; delude; hoodwink;
矇騙百姓 take common people in...;
矇騙父母 delude one's parents;
矇騙公眾 practise deception on the public;
矇騙老師 hoodwink one's teachers;
矇騙上司 deceive one's superiors;
矇騙消費者 cheat consumers;
被外貌矇騙 be cheated by appearance;
連矇帶騙 deceive and swindle sb;

發矇 get confused; get into a muddle;

meng²
meng
【尨】 confused; disorderly;
［尨茸］ fluffy; puffy;

meng
【氓】 people; populace;

群氓 the common herd;
愚氓 fool;

meng
【甿】 the farming population;

meng
【虻】 gadfly;
［虻蟲］ gadfly;

牛虻 gadfly;

meng
【萌】 bud; shoot forth; sprout;
［萌動］ begin an action;
春心萌動 the lustful desire stirs;
春意萌動 the breath of spring stirs;
花蕾萌動 the buds of flowers are blooming;
思潮萌動 a trend of thought is taking shape;
芽在萌動 the buds are shooting forth;
［萌發］ bud; germinate; shoot; sprout;
萌發新葉 germinate new leaves;
萌發新枝 sprout new buds;
［萌生］ conceive; produce;
新觀念萌生 a new concept has come into being;
［萌芽］ germinate; germination; in the bud; in the egg; in the embryonic stage; shoot; sprout;
花粉萌芽 pollen germination;
花在萌芽 the flowers are budding;
假萌芽 false germination;
延期萌芽 delayed germination;
直接萌芽 direct germination;

資本主義萌芽 the seeds of capitalism;

meng

【盟】 (1) ally; covenant; oath; vow; (2) Mongol league;

［盟邦］ allied country; ally;
世代盟邦 hereditary allies;

［盟府］ place for safekeeping records of an alliance; repository of covenants;

［盟國］ allied powers; allies;

［盟機］ allied warplanes;

［盟軍］ allied forces; allied troops;

［盟誓］ make a pledge; oath of mutual devotion; take an oath;
對天盟誓 pledge to Heaven;
海誓山盟 a solemn pledge of eternal love; exchange solemn vows and pledges; make a solemn oath of love; pledge to love forever and a day; pledge undying love; plight one's troth; swear inviolable oaths of mutual love and fidelity; swear unchanging fidelity in oaths high as the mountains and deep as the ocean;
~海誓山盟，永不變心 vow from one's heart to be true to sb one's whole life long;
山盟海誓 a solemn oath made by lovers; a solemn pledge of love; an unalterable oath of marriage; exchange oaths high as the mountains and vows deep as the ocean; lovers' pledge of eternal loyalty; lovers' vows; make a solemn pledge of love; make mutual pledges; marriage vows; pledge of eternal love; pledge to love forever and one day; plight one's faith; swear an aoth of fidelity, vowing never to change unto life's end; swear everlasting fidelity to sb; swear inviolable oaths of mutual love and fidelity; swear to love each other; swear to wait for sb all one's life; swear unchanging fidelity in oaths high as the mountains and deep as the ocean;

［盟首］ leader of an alliance;

［盟心］ swear mutual devotion;

［盟友］ ally;

［盟員］ member of an alliance or a league;

［盟約］ treaty of alliance;
背棄盟約 violate one's treaty of alliance;
廢除盟約 abrogate the oath of alliance;
廢約背盟 annual the treaty and go back on an oath;

［盟長］ the chief of a Mongol league composed of several tribes;

［盟主］ leader of an alliance;

拜盟 be sworn brothers;
敗盟 break a covenant;
背盟 breach of contract; break a promise; break an agreement; violate a treaty;
毀盟 break off an alliance; dissolve an alliance;
會盟 meet to form alliances;
結盟 form an alliance;
聯盟 alliance; coalition; league;
同盟 alliance; league;

meng

【蒙】 (1) cover; (2) meet with; receive; (3) ignorant; illiterate;

［蒙被而睡］ lying in bed with one's head covered by a quilt;

［蒙蔽］ cast a mist before sb's eyes; deceive; hide the truth from; hoodwink; pull the wool over sb's eyes; throw a mist before sb's eyes;
被花言巧語蒙蔽 be deceived by fair words; be fooled by honeyed words;
不再受蒙蔽 no longer be deceived;
一時受了蒙蔽 be hoodwinked for the moment;

［蒙導］ mentor;
根蒙導 root mentor;
花粉蒙導 pollen mentor;
有性蒙導 sexual mentor;
預先蒙導 preliminary mentor;

［蒙混］ deceive or mislead people;
蒙混別人 mislead others;
蒙混公眾 mislead the public;
蒙混過關 bluff one's way out; get by under false pretences; gloss over one's faults; muddle through; slip by; slip through; sneak away in the confusion; steal away;
蒙混自己 deceive oneself;

［蒙瞞］ mystify;

［蒙昧］ barbaric; uncivilized; uncultured;
蒙昧可欺 ignorant and gullible;
蒙昧可笑 be benighted and ridiculous;
蒙昧時代 the age of barbarism;
蒙昧無昧 benighted; childish ignorance;

childishly ignorant; ignorant; illiterate; sluggish and unaware; stupid and ignorant; unenlightened;
蒙昧主義 obscurantism;
擺脱蒙昧 get rid of the state of being uncultured;
[蒙蒙亮] daybreak;
[蒙面] cover one's face;
蒙面襪 stocking mask;
[蒙難] be confronted by danger; fall into the clutches of the enemy;
[蒙騙] bilk;
[蒙上] cover; dim; muffle;
[蒙受] suffer; sustain;
蒙受不白 suffer a wrong through no fault of one's own; unjustly accused;
蒙受不白之寃 be wronged grievously;
蒙受恥辱 be humiliated;
蒙受恩惠 a favour bestowed on sb;
蒙受損失 sustain a loss;
蒙受災難 undergo disaster;
[蒙太奇] montage;
蒙太奇節奏 montage rhythm;
蒙太奇手法 montage;
[蒙頭] cover one's head;
蒙頭大睡 fast asleep with the quilt drawn over one's head; sleep soundly with face covered under sheets; tuck oneself in and sleep like a log;
蒙頭蓋臉 cover one's head and face; with face covered;
[蒙眼] blindfold;
蒙眼布 blindfold;
[蒙在鼓裏] all at sea; be kept in the dark; in the dark; not in the know;

白蒙蒙 hazy; misty; vast expanse of whiteness;
鴻蒙 primordial world, before the universe was formed;
開蒙 teach the children to begin learning to read and write;
欺蒙 deceive and mislead people; dupe; hoodwink;
啟蒙 import rudimentary knowledge to beginners;
渥蒙 be deeply grateful for;
愚蒙 ignorant; unenlightened;
顓蒙 ignorant;

meng
【蝱】 gadfly;

meng
【甍】 rafter;

meng
【瞢】 (1) dim-sighted; poor vision; (2) not bright; obscure; poor visibility; (3) ashamed;

meng
【濛】 drizzly; misty;
[濛濛] drizzly; misty;
濛濛細雨 drizzling rain; fine drizzle; it mizzles;
濛濛煙霧 misty;
塵土濛濛 a rain of ashes; a storm of ashes;
煙雨濛濛 the fine rain is drizzling in the misty weather;

空濛 hazy; misty;
山色空濛 hills shrouded in mist;

meng
【幪】 cover; screen;

meng
【朦】 (1) state of the moon just before setting; (2) dim; hazy; vague;
[朦朧] (1) dim moonlight; hazy moonlight; (2) dim; hazy; obscure;
朦朧詩 misty poetry;
景色朦朧 the view is hazy;
暮色朦朧 it is hazy at dusk;
煙霧朦朧 it is misty;
煙雨朦朧 it is misty and rainy;
月色朦朧 hazy moonlight;

meng
【檬】 (1) kind of locust or acacia; (2) lemon;
[檬鰈] lemon dab;
[檬果] mango;

檸檬 lemon;

meng
【曚】 dim; obscure;
[曚曨] drosy; half asleep; somnolent;

meng
【矇】 blind; ignorant; stupid and obstinate;
[矇矓] drowsy; half asleep; somnolent;
矇矇矓矓 drowsy;

meng
【懵】 ignorant;
[懵懂] muddled; ignorant;

懵懵懂懂 ignorant; muddled;
[懵憒] dull-witted; unaware; uncomprehending;
[懵然] ignorant;

meng
【艨】 ancient warship;

meng³
meng
【猛】 (1) energetic; fierce; vigorous; violent; (2) abruptly; suddenly;
[猛不防] by surprise; suddenly; unaware; unexpectedly;
猛不防冒出一句 make an utterance suddenly;
[猛衝] charge; hurl; hurtle; lunge; make a break; onrush;
猛衝猛打 courageously hit hard at; go at it hammer and tongs; go full blast ahead;
向下猛衝 swoop in;
[猛戳] drove; jab;
[猛攻] attack by storm; attack violently; charge to; fierce attack; onslaught; storm; whale away;
猛攻猛打 storm;
[猛虎離山] like a fierce tiger springing down the mountain; move with a quick and ferocious speed;
[猛虎撲食] like a fierce tiger springing on the prey; with a quick and ferocious speed;
[猛虎下山] a fierce tiger springs down from the top of the mountain; like a tiger dashing down a mountain;
[猛擊] clout; slap; smash;
[猛將] valiant general;
[猛進] push ahead vigorously;
突飛猛進 advance by leaps and bounds; advance swiftly and vigorously; advance very rapidly; advance with seven-league strides; develop rapidly; make a long forward stride; make a spurt of progress; make giant strides; make remarkable progress; phenomenal progress; progress rapidly; rapid development; swift advance;
學業猛進 make a rapid progress in one's studies;
[猛勁兒] (1) put on a spurt; spurt; (2) a spurt of energy; dash;
[猛浪] high sea;
[猛力] jam on; vigorously; with sudden force;
[猛烈] fierce; vigorous; violent;
猛烈攻擊別人 attack others vigorously;
[猛落] pelter;
[猛撲] lunge; swoop down on;
[猛犬] bull dog; fierce dog; vicious dog;
[猛然] abruptly; bam; suddenly;
猛然想起一件事 think of sth suddenly;
猛然省悟 suddenly to wake up;
猛然一動 jerk;
猛然一拉 a jerk; pull with a jerk;
[猛士] brave warrior;
[猛獸] beast of prey;
[猛搖] shake; wrench;
[猛咬] snap;
[猛藥] strong cure;
猛藥起沉痾 desperate diseases must have desperate cures;
[猛漲] break through; leap;
河水猛漲 a river is in spate;
[猛撞] bump; cannon; crash; impingement collision; smash;
[猛追] give a hot pursuit;
[猛揍] tear into;

威猛 domineering;
凶猛 ferocious; violent;
兇猛 ferocious; violent;
迅猛 wsift and violent;
勇猛 bold and powerful; vigorous and valiant;

meng
【艋】 small boat;

舴艋 boat;

meng
【蜢】 grasshopper;

蚱蜢 grasshopper;

meng
【錳】 manganese;

乙酸錳 manganese;

meng
【懵】 ignorant;
[懵懂] ignorant; muddled; muddleheaded;

meng
【蠓】 gnat;

M

meng4

meng

【孟】 (1) first month of season; (2) eldest brother; (3) a surname;

［孟浪］ impetuous; impulsive; rash;
孟浪行事 act rashly;
孟浪之談 reckless talk; rough and wasteful talk;

meng

【夢】 dream;

［夢話］ (1) somniloquy; words uttered in one's sleep; (2) daydream; nonsense;
說夢話 (1) talk in one's dream; talk in sleep; (2) talk nonsense;

［夢幻］ dream; illusion; reverie;
夢幻泡影 a dreamy illusion and an empty bubble; empty bubble; illusion; like a bursting bubble; like a vanishing dream; pipe dream; utterly visionary; vanish like a dream without a trace;
夢幻世界 dream world;
~ 生活在夢幻世界 live in a dream world;
沉溺於夢幻 indulge in reveries;
丟掉夢幻 cast away illusions;
陷入夢幻 fall in a reverie;
消除夢幻 dispel illusions;

［夢見］ dream about; dream of; see in a dream;
夢見故土 dream of one's hometown;

［夢驚］ night-startlings; night-terror;

［夢景］ dreamscape;

［夢境］ dream; dreamland; dreamworld; world of dreams;
進入夢境 go off to dreamland;
如入夢境 as if one landed oneself in a dream; feel as if one were in a dream;
走出夢境 out of dreamland;

［夢寐］ dream; sleep;
夢寐不忘 remember always;
夢寐難忘 remember always, even in sleep; unable to forget sth even in one's dreams;
夢寐以求 crave sth so that one even dreams about it; dream of; eagerly seek; hanker after; hanker for; long for sth day and night; long-cherished; set one's mind all the time on; try one's utmost to achieve what one dreams of; yearn for sth day and night;

［夢魔］ nightmare;

［夢鄉］ dreamland; slumberland;
進入夢鄉 in the arms of Morpheus;
在夢鄉中 in the arms of Morpheus;

［夢想］ (1) dream of; pipe dream; woolgathering; (2) earnest wish; fond dream;
夢想不到 beyond one's imagination;
夢想成真 be a dream come true; realize one's dream;
眠思夢想 think day and night;
祇是個夢想 but a dream;

［夢醒］ awake from a dream;
半夢半醒 half dreaming and half awake;
似夢初醒 as though waking out of a dream;

［夢遺］ nocturnal emission; wet dream;

［夢囈］ balderdash; sleep-talking; somniloquy;

［夢遊］ night-walking; sleepwalking;
夢遊者 somnambulist;
夢遊症 night-walking; sleepwalking;
~ 激動夢遊症 agitated sleepwalking;
~ 平靜夢遊症 calm sleepwalking;

［夢語］ sleep-talking;

［夢兆］ dream omen;

［夢中說夢］ speak of dream in a dream—supernatural; wander in one's speech;

白日夢 pipe dream; walking dream;
春夢 spring dream;
惡夢 horrible dream; nightmare;
酣夢 sweet dream;
好夢 sweet dream;
舊夢 past experience;
美夢 fond dream;
迷夢 fond illusion; pipe dream;
入夢 (1) fall asleep; (2) appear in one's dream;
睡夢 sleep; slumber;
占夢 divine by interpreting dreams;
做夢 (1) have a dream; (2) daydream; have a pipe dream;

mi1

mi

【咪】 (1) meow; (2) smiling;

［咪咪］ (1) mew; miaow; (2) smilingly;
咪咪叫 mew;
笑咪咪 smiling; with a smile on one's face;

mi

【眯】 foreign body getting into the eye;

［眯騰］ have a nap;

mi

【瞇】 (1) close the eyes; (2) narrow the eyes;

[瞇縫] narrow;

mi²

mi

【迷】 (1) be confused; be lost; (2) be fascinated by; crazy about; (3) enthusiast; fan; fiend; (4) confuse; fascinate; perplex;

[迷不知返] go astray not knowing how to return;

[迷彩裝] camouflage uniform;
身穿迷彩裝 wear cambouflage uniforms;

[迷洞] maze cave;

[迷宮] labyrinth; maze;
徑向迷宮 radial labyrinth;
聲迷宮 acoustic labyrinth;

[迷航] drift off course; lose one's course;

[迷糊] (1) blurred; dimmed; misted; (2) confused; dazed; muddled;
辦事迷糊 stupid when dealing with matters;
迷迷糊糊 difficult to make out; in a daze; misty; unclear;

[迷幻藥] hallucinogenic;

[迷魂湯] honeyed words; magic potion; sth intended to turn sb's head;
灌迷魂湯 try to ensnare sb with honeyed words;

[迷魂陣] maze; scheme for consuming sb; scheme to bewitch sb; trap;
擺迷魂陣 lay out a scheme to bewitch sb; muddle sb up; set a trap;

[迷惑] baffle; confuse; in a mist; lead sb up the garden path; perplex; puzzle;
迷惑不解 bewildered; in a puzzle about; perplexed; puzzled; scratch one's head over;
迷惑敵人 confuse the enemy;
迷惑人心 befuddle public opinion; confuse the masses; pull the wool over people's eyes; throw dust in the eyes of the public;
迷惑視聽 confuse the public; hoodwink the public;
迷惑輿論 befuddle public opinion; pull the wool over the eyes of the public; throw dust in the eyes of the public;
令人迷惑 disturb the judgement;

[迷津] maze;
指點迷津 point out the right way to sb when he goes astray; show sb how to get on the right path;
指破迷津 point out where one has gone astray from right path;

[迷離] blurred; misted;
迷離惝恍 blurred; completely bewildered; confused and flurried; indistinct;
迷離撲朔 bewildering; complicated and confusing; confused and unable to distinguish between male and female; confusing; unable to distinguish whether one is a male or a female;
撲朔迷離 complicated and confusing; confusing the eye; throw sb off the scent;

[迷戀] be infatuated with; crush; crush on; madly cling to;
迷戀不捨 head over heels in love with sb;
迷戀骸骨 be infatuated with the old and decayed; stick to the old things;
迷戀酒色 be infatuated with wine and women;
迷戀看書 fond of reading;
迷戀聲色 indulge oneself in sensual pleasures;
迷戀音樂 be carried away by music; immerse oneself in music;

[迷路] cannot find one's way; get lost; go astray; go the wrong way; lose one's bearings; lose one's way; stray; take the wrong road;
迷路炎 labyrinthitis;
~ 細菌性迷路炎 bacterial labyrinthitis;
~ 中毒性迷路炎 toxic labyrinthitis;

[迷漫] hazy; indistinct; vague;
風雪迷漫 the wind and snow reigned everywhere
霧氣迷漫 the fog is heavy;
煙塵迷漫 be covered with smoke and dust;

[迷茫] (1) vast and hazy; (2) confused; dazed; perplexed;
迷茫不知所措 feel dazed and be at one's wits' end;
迷迷茫茫 vast and hazy;

[迷夢] fond illusion; pipe dream;

[迷你裙] mini; miniskirt;

[迷人] alluring; appealing; beautiful;

bewitching; charming; dazzling; delightful; enchanting; fascinating; gorgeous; loving; ravishing; stunning;
迷人的 captivating; charming; dishy; enthralling; ravishing;
迷人身材 delectable body;
迷人眼目 confuse the eyes of the people; fool people; pull the wool over sb's eyes; throw dust in sb's eyes;
風度迷人 have gentle manners;
景色迷人 the scenery is charming;
聲音迷人 have a charming voice;
夜色迷人 the night is charming;
長相迷人 have good looks;

[迷失] lose;
迷失方向 at fault; get lost; lose one's bearings; not to know where one is; off the track; off the trail; on a false scent; on a wrong scent; out of one's bearings; throw off the track;

[迷途] (1) lose one's way; (2) wrong path;
迷途羔羊 the lost sheep;
迷途索途 grope for a way out of the labyrinth;
迷途知返 become aware of one's errors and return from one's wrong path; realize one's errors and mend one's ways; recover one's bearings and return to the fold; return to the correct path;
誤入迷途 take the wrong path by mistake;
走入迷途 go astray;

[迷惘] at a loss; perplexed;

[迷霧] (1) dense fog; (2) anything that misleads people;

[迷信] (1) superstition; (2) have blind faith in;
迷信權威 have blind faith in authority;
打破迷信 destroy superstitions; kill a superstition;
破除迷信 abolish superstition;

[迷住] bewitch; charm; enchant; fascinate;

[迷醉] be fascinated by;

財迷 miser; moneygrubber;
車迷 petrolhead;
沉迷 be deeply enchanted;
痴迷 crazy; infatuated; obsessed;
癡迷 besotted; infatuated;
昏迷 be in a coma; fall into a stupor;
淒迷 (1) desolate and indistinct; (2) distracted; forlorn; sad;
棋迷 chess enthusiast;
球迷 fan;
入迷 be enchanted; become fascinated;
失迷 loswe one's bearings;
舞迷 habitual dancer;
戲迷 theatre fan;
影迷 film fan;
着迷 be captivated; be enchanted; be fascinated;

mi

【彌】 (1) full; overflowing; (2) cover; fill; (3) more;

[彌補] eke out; make good; make up; make up for; remedy;
彌補不足 cover the shortage; make up for the deficiency;
彌補赤字 make up the deficit;
彌補虧損 cover the deficit;
彌補缺點 make good a defect — remedy;
彌補缺陷 remedy a defect;
彌補損失 make good a loss; make up for a loss;
彌補未來 mend one's ways with the future in mind;

[彌縫] cover up mistakes; fill cracks;

[彌勒] Maitreya;

[彌留] dying;
彌留之際 on one's deathbed;

[彌漫] fill the air; pervade; spread all over the place; suffuse;
彌漫着節日氣氛 be permeated by an atmosphere of a jolly holiday;
春意彌漫 spring reigns everywhere;
風雪彌漫 it is a blinding snowstorm;
黃沙彌漫 dust spreads all over the place;
江霧彌漫 a mist hangs over the river;
煙霧彌漫 smoke and fog fill the air;

[彌撒] mass;

[彌天] huge; monstrous;
彌天大謊 a lie out of the whole cloth; a lie that fills the sky; big lie; blatant lie; downright lie; eighteen carat lie; flat lie; glaring lie; monstrous lie; outrageous lie; rank lie; rousing lie; swinging lie; thundering lie; whacking great lie;
彌天大罪 a crime that cries to heaven; extraordinary crime; heinous crime; horrible crime; monstrous crime; towering crime;
彌天亙地 fill the heavens and cover the earth;

彌天討價 open one's mouth too wide;

沙彌 Buddhist novice;

mi

【糜】 (1) congee; porridge; rice gruel; (2) corrupted; mashed; rotten; wasteful;

［糜費］ dissipation; waste;

糜費錢財 waste money on...;

糜費能源 waste energy;

糜費人力 waste manpower;

糜費時間 spend time extravagantly;

糜費資源 waste resources;

防止糜費 avoid waste;

［糜爛］ corrupted; debauched; dissipated; erosion; rotten to the core;

糜爛荒淫 be profligately debauched;

糜爛生活 extravagance;

生活糜爛 lead a dissipated life;

侈糜 extravagant; wasteful;

乳糜 chyle;

mi

【謎】 conundrum; puzzle; riddle;

［謎底］ (1) answer to a riddle; (2) truth;

公開謎底 publish a riddle;

揭開謎底 solve a riddle;

謎語的謎底 answer to the riddle;

尋找謎底 look for truth;

［謎語］ conundrum; riddle;

猜謎 guess a riddle;

燈謎 lantern riddles;

畫謎 picture puzzle;

詩謎 riddle in the form of poem;

mi

【麋】 alces machlis, a kind of deer;

mi

【縻】 connect; fasten; tie;

羈縻 win sb over by any means;

mi

【醚】 ether;

mi

【靡】 (1) extravagant; waste; (2) rot;

［靡費］ spend extravagantly; waste;

風靡 fashionable; popular;

奢靡 extravagant; wasteful;

mi

【禰】 surname;

mi

【瀰】 brimming; overflowing;

［瀰漫］ fill the air; spread all over the place;

mi

【獼】 macaque; monkey;

［獼猴］ macaque;

mi

【蘼】 kind of grass;

荼蘼 roseleaf raspberry;

mi

【醾】 wine brewed for the second time;

mi³

mi

【米】 (1) rice; (2) husked seed; shelled seed; (3) meter; (4) a surname;

［米餅］ rice cake;

［米豆］ black-eyed bean;

［米飯］ cooked rice;

一口米飯 a swallow of cooked rice;

［米粉］ (1) ground rice; rice flour; (2) rice-flour noodles;

炒米粉 fried rice-flour noodles;

［米糕］ rice cake; rice pudding;

［米櫃］ rice cupboard;

［米粒］ grain of rice;

拈起米粒 pick up grains of rice;

［米色］ cream-coloured;

米色的 buff;

［米已成炊］ the damage is done; what is done cannot be undone;

［米制］ metric system;

米制噸 metric ton;

［米珠薪桂］ everything rises in prices, as in famine time; rice is as precious as pearls and firewood as costly as cassia;

白米 white polished rice;

糙米 brown rice; unpolished rice;

炒米 parched rice;

大米 husked rice;

菰米 wild rice;

毫米 millimeter;

紅米 red rice;

黃米 glutinous millet;

江米 polished glutinous rice;

粳米 polished round-grained rice;

厘米 centimeter;
黏米 glutinous rice;
糯米 polished glutinous rice;
千米 kilometer;
蝦米 dried shelled shrimps;
籼米 polished long-grained rice;
小米 millet;
一把米 a handful of rice;
一包米 a sack of rice;
一袋米 a bag of rice; a sack of rice;
一擔米 a load of rice;
一罐米 a jar of rice;
一粒米 a grain of rice;
玉米 (1) corn; maize; (2) ear of maize;

mi
【芈】 a pronunciation of 羊;

mi
【弭】 get rid of; put down; remove;
消弭 prevent (future trouble); put an end to;

mi
【敉】 pacify; quiet; soothe; stabilize;

mi
【眯】 (1) foreign body getting into the eye; (2) close one's eyes into narrow slits;

mi
【靡】 (1) blown away by the wind; (2) no; not;
［靡麗］ magnificent; resplendent;
［靡靡］ decadent;
靡靡之音 beguiling music; corrupting music; decadent music; demoralizing music; lewd music; obscene songs; voluptuous music;
［靡然］ leaning to one side;
靡然從風 go with the fashion; go with the wind — follow the trend;
［靡日不思］ not a day passes without one's thinking of sth;
［靡顏膩理］ beautiful and fair-skinned; have good looks and a delicate skin;
披靡 (1) be swept by the wind; (2) be routed; flee;
頹靡 dejected; discouraged; downcast;
委靡 dejected; dispirited; listless;

mi⁴
mi
【汨】 a river in Hunan;

mi
【泌】 excrete; secrete; seep out;
［泌尿］ uropoiesis;
泌尿科 urinology;
~泌尿科醫生 urologist;
分泌 secrete;

mi
【宓】 (1) quiet; silent; still; (2) a surname;

mi
【秘】 (1) confidential; secret; (2) hold sth back; keep sth secret;
［秘不可解］ be wrapped in mystery;
［秘而不宣］ hold one's cards close to one's chest; keep one's cards close to one's chest; keep secret; keep sth dark; keep sth under cover; keep sth under wraps; keep the news from getting out; not to let anyone into a secret; wall of secrecy;
［秘方］ secret prescription; secret recipe;
［秘訣］ magic code; secret;
成功秘訣 recipe for success; secret of success;
［秘密］ clandestine; confidential; hugger-mugger; secret;
秘密串聯 make secret contacts with sb;
秘密地 behind closed doors; behind the curtain; behind the scene; by stealth; clandestine; confidential; in camera; in confidence; in a corner; in corners; in private; in secret; on the quiet; on the side; on the sly; on the sneak; secretly; under cover; under one's hat; under the counter; under the rose; under the table; under wraps; with closed doors;
秘密關係 clandestine;
秘密交往 get together secretly;
秘密接觸 get in confidential touch with sb;
半公開的秘密 semi-overt secret;
保守秘密 keep a secret; keep it dark;
大秘密 big secret;
揭開秘密 unlock mysteries; unlock secrets;
商業秘密 trade secret;
守秘密 keep a secret;
~誓守秘密 pledge oneself to keep the secret; under an oath of secrecy;

透露秘密 break a secret;
小秘密 little secret;
洩露秘密 disclose a secret; give away a secret;
嚴守的秘密 well-kept secret;
有秘密 have a secret;
知道秘密 know a secret;

[秘史] inside story; secret history;

[秘書] secretary;
秘書處 secretariat;
秘書長 secretary-general;
~副秘書長 depty secretary-general;
二等秘書 second secretary;
三等秘書 third secretary;
私人秘書 private secretary;
一等秘書 first secretary;

奧秘 profound mystery;
便秘 constipation;
神秘 mysterious; mystical;
隱秘 conceal; hide; secret;

mi

【密】 (1) close; dense; thick; (2) intimate; (3) fine; meticulous; (4) secret;

[密不可分] interwovenness;

[密佈] be densely covered;
黑雲密佈 dark clouds spread over the sky — the coming of a storm;
礁石密佈 thick with reefs;
濃雲密佈 dense clouds gathered; overcast with heavy clouds; the clouds are very dense; thick clouds overcast the whole sky;
陰雲密佈 the sky is overcast;

[密度] density; thickness;
密度法 densimetry;
密度計 densimeter; densitometer;
~彩色掃描密度計 chromoscan densitometer;
~光電密度計 photoelectric densimeter;
~光電式密度計 photoelectric densitometer;
~海水光密度計 seawater densitometer;
~累計球形密度計 integrating-sphere densitometer;
~線性光密度計 linear densitometer;
~線性密度計 linear densimeter;
詞匯密度 lexical density;
低密度 low-density;
電流密度 current density;
反常密度 abnormal density;
高密度 high density;
~高密度人口 high density population;
絕對密度 absolute density;
人口密度 population density;
受主密度 acceptor density;

[密封] seal; seal airtight; seal off; seal up;
密封包裝 sealed package;
密封罐頭 seal up a tin;
密封條 draught excluder;
空氣密封 aeroseal;
鉗壓封 clipper seal;
聲密封 acoustic seal;

[密集] close; crowded; concentrated; dense; intensive;
人口密集 be thickly populated;
人群密集 the crowd is dense;

[密件] classified matter; confidential; confidential letter;

[密碼] cipher; code; cryptogram; password; secret code;
密碼鎖 combination lock;
密碼學 cryptography;
密碼子 codon;
~起始密碼子 initiation codon;
~同義密碼子 synonymous codon;
~無意義密碼子 nonsense codon;
~有意義密碼子 sense codon;
~終止密碼子 stop codon; termination codon; terminator codon;
背密碼 memorize a cipher code;
破譯密碼 break a cipher;
譯密碼 decipher a secret code;
知曉密碼 know the cipher;

[密密層層] dense; packed closely layer upon layer; packed ring upon ring; thick;

[密密麻麻] as thick as huckleberries; as thick as stalks in a field of flax; close and numerous; thickly dotted; very dense;

[密密匝匝] dense; thick;

[密謀] connivance; connive; conspire; plot; scheme;
密謀的 conniving;
密謀奪權 scheme for power;

[密切] (1) close; intimate; (2) carefully; closely intently;
密切合作 hand in glove;
密切相關 be closely related;
密切注視 pay close attention to; watch closely;

[密商] hold private counsel; hold secret talks;

[密使] secret envoy; secret emissary;
[密談] (1) secret talk; talk behind closed doors; (2) have a confidential talk;
[密探] nark; secret agent; spy; spook; stool pigeon; undercover man;
[密友] a cup and can; boon companion; bosom friend; close friend; confidant; crony; fast friend; intimate friend;
[密語] cryptolalia;
密語私情 have a confidential conversation of private feeling;
[密約] secret agreement; secret treaty;
[密雲] cloudy;
密雲不雨 dense clouds but no rain — an affair that is fermented long ago; heavily overcast sky without rain; trouble is brewing;

保密 keep sth secret; maintain secret;
稠密 dense;
繁密 dense;
告密 inform against sb; snitch;
機密 classified; confidential; secret;
加密 encrypt;
揭密 reveal;
緊密 (1) close together; inseparable; (2) rapid and intense;
精密 accurate; precise;
絕密 most confidential; to-secret;
茂密 dense; thick;
秘密 confidential; secret;
綿密 fine and careful; meticulous;
濃密 dense; thick;
親密 close; intimate;
疏密 density; spacing;
細密 (1) close; fine and closely woven; (2) detailed; meticulous;
詳密 elaborate; meticulous;
洩密 leak a secret;
嚴密 close; tight;
縝密 careful; deliberate; meticulous;
致密 fine and close; compact;
周密 careful; thorough;

mi
【覓】 hunt for; look for; seek;
[覓取] hunt for; look for; seek;
覓取寶藏 hunt for treasure;
覓取獵物 seek a prey;
覓取食物 hunt for food;
[覓食場] feeding ground;

mi
【嘧】
[嘧啶] pyrimidine;

mi
【蜜】 (1) honey; (2) nectar; (3) sweet;
[蜜蜂] bee; honeybee;
蜜糖嘴巴刀子心 a honey-mouth and a knife-heart — sweet in the mouth and ruthless in the heart;
一大群蜜蜂 an army of bees;
一群蜜蜂 a cluster of bees; a swarm of bees;
[蜜餞] preserved;
蜜餞的 candied;
[蜜月] honeymoon;
蜜月旅行 honeymoon trip;
[蜜棗] candied date; preserved date;

蜂蜜 honey;
割蜜 cut off the honey comb in order to get honey;
花蜜 nectar;
磕蜜 chase after girls;
釀蜜 make honey;
甜蜜 happy; sweet;
搖蜜 extract honey;
一滴蜜 a blob of honey;

mi
【鼏】 cover of a tripod caldron;

mi
【冪】 (1) cloth thus used; cover with cloth; veil; (2) power (in mathematics);

mi
【謐】 (1) quiet; serene; silent; still; (2) careful; cautious;

mian²
mian
【眠】 (1) sleep; (2) hibernation;
[眠目靜思] close the eyes and meditate;

安眠 sleep peacefully;
不眠 egersis;
長眠 die;
成眠 fall asleep; go to sleep;
催眠 hypnosis; hypnotize; lull to sleep; mesmerize;
冬眠 hibernation; winter sleep;
失眠 suffer from insomnia;
睡眠 sleep;

夏眠 aestivate; aestivation;
休眠 dormancy;

mian

【棉】 cotton;

［棉襖］ cotton-padded jacket; lammy; quilted jacket;
大襟棉襖 cotton-padded jack with buttons on the right;
對襟棉襖 cotton-padded jacket with buttons down the front;

［棉被］ quilt with cotton wadding;

［棉布］ cotton; cotton cloth; percale;
白棉布 white cotton;
~ 細白棉布 cambric;
薄紗棉布 cheesecloth;
粗棉布 denim; fustian;
一層棉布 a thickness of cotton;

［棉花］ cotton;
棉花棒 cotton bud;
棉花糖 candyfloss; cotton candy; marshmallow;
一包棉花 a bale of cotton; a parcel of cotton;
摘棉花 pick cotton;
種棉花 cultivate cotton; grow cotton; raise cotton;

［棉鈴］ cotton bud;

［棉帽］ cotton-padded cap;

［棉紗］ cotton yarn;
一包棉紗 a bale of cotton yarn;
一綹棉紗 a skein of cotton yarn;

［棉桃］ cotton boll;

［棉田］ cotton field;

［棉鞋］ cotton-padded shoes;

［棉衣］ cotton-padded clothes;

［棉籽］ cottonseed;

紅棉 silk cotton;
火棉 guncotton;
礦棉 mineral wool;
木棉 silk cotton;
皮棉 ginned cotton;
石棉 asbestos;
絲光棉 mercerized cotton;
絲棉 silk padding;
絮棉 cotton for wadding;
藥棉 absorbent cotton;
原棉 raw cotton;
子棉 unginned cotton;

mian

【綿】 (1) silk floss; (2) continuous; (3) soft;

［綿薄］ humble effort; meagre strength;
綿薄貢獻 make one's humble contribution to;
綿薄微力 one's small effort;
綿薄之力 widow's mite;
愿盡綿薄 I'll do what little I can;

［綿長］ last a long period of time;

［綿亙］ stretch in an unbroken chain;
綿亙東西 stretch from east to west in an undroken chain;
綿亙南北 lies north and south;

［綿裏藏針］ a needle hidden in silk floss — a ruthless character behind a gentle appearance; an iron hand in a velvet glove; the gentle rigidity of a needle wrapped in cotton wool — a soft appearance but a hard heart;

［綿力］ one's limited power;
綿力薄才 weak in strength and lack of ability;
薄盡綿力 do my humble best; do what little I can; exert my humble efforts; make my humble efforts;

［綿聯］ continuous; unbroken;

［綿密］ detailed; fine and careful; meticulous;

［綿綿］ continuous; unbroken;
綿綿不絕 continuous forever; remain unbroken;
綿綿不息 continuous;
綿綿瓜瓞 may your family grow and prosper like spreading melon-vines;
情思綿綿 one's tender affection is endless;
秋雨綿綿 the autumn rain goes on and on;
軟綿綿 (1) feathery; soft; (2) feeble; weak;
細雨綿綿 the drizzle is continuous;

［綿軟］ (1) soft; (2) weak;
綿軟的毛髮 soft hair;
綿軟的毛衣 soft wool;
綿軟的紙張 soft paper;
覺得渾身綿軟 feel weak all over;
身體綿軟 weak;

［綿延］ continuous; stretch long and unbroken;
綿延不斷 continuous and unbroken; go on continually;
綿延千里 stretch a thousand miles;

［綿羊］ sheep;
綿羊咩咩 sheep baa;

M

數綿羊 count sheep;

纏綿 lingering; moving; touching;
海綿 foam rubber; sponge;
連綿 continuous; unbroken; uninterrupted;
絲綿 silk floss; silk wadding;

mian
【緜】 (1) downy; soft; (2) enduring;

mian³
mian
【丏】 (1) curtain to ward off arrows; (2) hidden;

mian
【免】 (1) dispense with; excuse sb from sth; exempt; (2) avert; avoid; escape; (3) forbidden; not allowed;

[免除] (1) avoid; prevent; (2) excuse; exempt; immunize; relieve; remit;
免除處罰 exempt from criminal punishment;
免除禍患 ward off calamity;
免除手續 dispense with the formalities;
免除隱患 remove a hidden peril;

[免得] in order not to; lest; save; so as not to; so as to avoid;
免得吵架 avert a quarrel;
免得鬧僵 avoid coming to a deadlock;
免得惹麻煩 avoid causing trouble;
免得引起誤會 avoid any misunderstanding;
免得走彎路 avoid taking a roundabout course;

[免費] for free; for love; for nothing; free; free of charge; on the cuff; on the house; without charge;
免費參觀 visit without charge;
免費教育 free education;
免費入場 be admitted gratis;
免費入學 go to school free of charge;
免費軟件 free ware;
免費試銷 free trial sale;
免費物 freebie;
免費醫療 free medicine;

[免票] (1) free pass; free ticket; (2) free of charge;

[免試] be excused from an examination;

[免税] duty-free; exemption from duty; free of duty; remission of tax; tax exemption; tax-free;
免税貨物 duty-free goods;
免税進口 duty-free importation;
免税貿易區 tax free trade zone;
免税區 tax-free zone;
免税商店 duty-free shop;
免税商品 duty-free commodities; duty-free goods;
免税物品 duty-free articles;
特准免税 duty remitted;
准許免税 allow exemption from taxation;

[免燙] easy-care; non-ironing; wash and wear;

[免提] handsfree;
免提電話 handsfree phone;
免提式電話 handsfree telephone set;

[免役] exempt from service;

[免疫] immunity;
免疫反應 immunoreaction;
~正常免疫反應 normal immunoreaction;
不正常免疫反應 abnormal immunoreaction;
免疫工程 immune-engineering;
免疫力 immunity;
免疫療法 immunotherapy;
免疫缺陷 immunodeficiency
免疫適應 immunological adaptation;
免疫調節 immunoregulation;
免疫性 immunity;
~自然免疫性 natural immunity;
免疫學 immunology;
免疫作用 immunity;
~繼承免疫作用 adaptive immunity;
~隱性免疫作用 latent immunity;
保護性免疫 protective immunity;
過繼性免疫 adoptive immunity;
後天免疫 acquired immunity;
適應性免疫 adaptive immunity;
天然免疫性 autarcesis;
天然免疫學 autarcesiology;
自動免疫 active immunity;

[免於] avert; avoid;
免於匱乏 free from want;
免於起訴 exemption from prosecution; immunity from suit;
免於受災 avert a disaster;
免於執行 overslaugh;

[免予] excuse sb from; exempt;
免予處罰 exempt sb from being penalized;
免予處分 exempt sb from punishment;

[免責] relief;

[免戰牌] sign used in ancient times to show refusal to fight;

掛免戰牌 hang up a truce sign — refuse battle;

[免職] relieve sb of his post; remove sb from office;

[免罪] exempt from punishment;

罷免 recall;
避免 avert; avoid; refrain from; stave off;
不免 bound to be; unavoidable;
黜免 dismiss;
豁免 exempt; remit;
減免 (1) mitigate; (2) reduce;
蠲免 exempt;
難免 be booked for; hard to avoid;
乞免 beg for exception;
任免 appoint and dismiss;
袒免 remit; bare one's arm and take off one's cap;
未免 a bit too;
以免 in order to avoid; lest; so as not to;
宥免 remit an offense;

mian
【沔】 (1) flood; overflowing; (2) name of a river;

mian
【勉】 (1) exert oneself; strive; (2) encourage; exhort; urge; (3) strive to do what is beyond one's power;

[勉力] exert oneself; make great efforts; try hard;
勉力從事 act with one's best; keep one's ends up;
勉力而為 do one's best; exert one's utmost; try one's best;
勉力為之 do one's best;
勉力向學 strive in one's studies;

[勉勵] encourage; urge;
勉勵上進 incite one to make progress; urge one to go forward;
勉勵向學 strive in one's studies;

[勉強] (1) do with difficulty; manage with an effort; (2) grudgingly; reluctantly; (3) force sb to do sth; (4) farfetched; inadequate; strained; unconvincing; (5) barely enough;
勉強度日 strive to keep body and soul together;
勉強及格 scrape through;
勉強前往 grudge ahead;
勉強通融 stretch a point;
勉強一笑 force a smile;
勉勉強強 by a narrow margin; only just; with a bad grace; with an ill grace; with half a heart;

[勉為其難] agree to do what one knows is beyond one's ability; agree to do what one knows is beyond one's power; be forced to do a difficult thing; contrive with difficulty; do the best one can in a difficult situation; make the best of a bad job; manage to do what is beyond one's power; undertake to do a difficult job as best one can;

奮勉 exert with determination and effort; make a determined effort;
共勉 mutual encouragement;
黽勉 work hard;
勤勉 assiduous; diligent;
勸勉 advise and encourage;
慰勉 comfort and encourage;
勖勉 encourage;
訓勉 instruct and encourage;

mian
【眄】 look askance; ogle;

mian
【娩】 give birth to a child;

[娩出] be delivered of a child; give birth to;
娩出死胎 abort;

分娩 give birth to a child;

mian
【冕】 (1) ceremonial cap for high ministers in old China; (2) crown;

弁冕 cap worn on ceremonious occasions;
加冕 coronation;
日冕 corona;

mian
【湎】 (1) drunk; (2) unaware; (3) changing;

沉湎 be given to; wallow in;

mian
【愐】 (1) give thought to; remember; (2) shy;

mian
【腼】 (1) bashful; shy; (2) quiet and graceful;

[腼腆] bashful; shy;

M

mian
【緬】 far back; remote;
[緬懷] cherish the memory of; recall; think of;
緬懷前輩 recall the seniors;
緬懷前塵 think of the past affairs;
緬懷往事 muse over past memories; recall past events with deep feelings; redolent of the past;
緬懷先烈 cherish the memory of our martyrs;
[緬想] recall; think of;

mian
【覥】 shy; timid;
[覥覥] bashful; shy;

mian⁴
mian
【面】 (1) face; (2) surface; top; (3) directly; face to face; personally; (4) aspect; side; (5) entire area; (6) extent; range; scale; (7) flour; powder; wheat flour; (8) noodles;
[面不改容] not to change colour; one's countenance betrays nothing; one's face is untroubled; remain calm; undismayed; without batting an eyelid; without changing countenance; without turning a hair;
[面不露色] not to allow one's feelings to be visible in one's face;
[面部] face;
面部按摩 facial massage;
面部表情 countenance; facial expressions;
[面斥人過] point out sb's mistake to his face;
[面從心違] comply in appearance but oppose in heart;
[面帶] wear;
面帶病容 look seedy; one's face assumes a sickly countenance;
面帶愁容 look blue; one's face shows a sad expression; one's face shows signs of worry; wear a worried look; wear an air of sadness; with a sad air;
面帶春色 one's face is like the very bloom of health;
面帶饑色 hunger seems to be written on one's face;
面帶倦容 look tired;
面帶怒色 as black as thunder; wear an angry look;
面帶喜色 a happy expression on one's face; wear a happy expression;
面帶笑容 one's face shows a smiling mood; wear a smile; with a smile on one's face; with a smiling face;
面帶慍色 look disgruntled;
[面對] confront; face;
面對而坐 sit facing each other;
面對面 face each other; face to face; face-to-face;
~ 面對面交際 face-to-face communication;
~ 面對面坐 sit face to face;
面對事實 face up to the facts;
面對現實 face reality; face the facts; let's face it; realistic;
勇敢的面對 face up to; stand up to;
[面額] denomination;
[面垢] dirty complexion;
[面骨] facial bone;
[面海背山] face the sea with the hills for a background;
[面和心不和] only friends on the surface; remain friendly in appearance but estranged at heart;
[面紅] flush red in the face;
面紅耳赤 as red as a turkey-cook; blush to the roots; blush up to the ears; colour up; crimson with rage; flush red in the face; flush to the ears; flush with shame; get red in the face; one's face reddens to the ears; red in the face;
面紅耳熱 with one's face flushed and one's ears hot;
面紅過耳 flush up to one's ears;
[面黃肌瘦] flesh emaciated and face yellow; lean and haggard; pale and emaciated; plae and thin; thin and colourless; thin and sallow;
[面積] acreage; area;
面積速度 areal velocity;
面積儀 planimeter;
播種面積 crop area; cultivation area; sown acreage;
承載面積 bearing area;
大面積 large area; large tract of land;
導納面積 admittance area;
等效面積 equivalent area;
電容面積 capacity area;
發射面積 emitting area;

房屋面積 floor area;
輻射面積 radiating area;
耕地面積 acreage under cultivation; agricultural acreage;
換算面積 transformed area;
活動面積 activie area;
接觸面積 apparent area;
節流面積 throttling area;
開採面積 producing area;
可視面積 visual area;
空氣動力面積 aerodynamic area;
擴散面積 diffusion area;
臨界面積 critical area;
流管面積 stream tube area;
流通面積 circulation area;
綠蔭面積 forested area;
牧場面積 grazing acreage;
排水面積 drainage area;
平衡面積 balanced area;
平面面積 flat area;
實際面積 actual area;
受壓面積 compression area;
數碼面積 digit area;
天線面積 antenna area;
投影面積 projected area;
塗布面積 spreading area;
污染面積 contaminated area;
吸收面積 absorption area;
陽極面積 anode area;
印刷面積 print area;
應力面積 stress area;
圓面積 spherical surface;
展開面積 developed area;
轉動面積 slewing area;
總表面積 total surface area;
阻力面積 drag area;

[面頰] chap; cheek;
面頰漲紅 blood rushes to sb's cheeks;

[面角] face angle; -hedral angle;
多面角 polyhedral angle;
二面角 dihedral angle;
平面角 plane angle;
三面角 trihedral angle;
四面角 tetrahedral angle;

[面具] mask; vizard mask;
防毒面具 antigas mask; gas mask;
呼吸面具 breathing mask;
假面具 false front; mask;

[面孔] the face;
面孔尷尬 one's face is a study;
面孔和藹 put on an amiable face;
面孔嚴肅 put on a stern expression;
擺出一副嚴肅的面孔 put on a serious countenance;
蒼白面孔 waxen face;
熟面孔 familiar face;
仰起的面孔 upturned face;

[面臨] be confronted with; be faced with; up against;
面臨激烈競爭 confront fierce competition;
面臨就業壓力 be confronted with the pressure of obtaining employment;

[面露] one's face shows;
面露不安 an anxious expression comes into one's face;
面露不悅 one's face becomes clouded;
面露殺機 one's face is blazed with murderous hatred;
面露喜色 happiness shines from one's face; one's face is beamed with delight; one's face lights up;

[面貌] (1) face; features; lineament; looks; visage; (2) appearance; aspects; looks;
面貌醜惡 ugly and evil of countenance;
面貌醜陋 have an ugly face;
面貌煥然一新 assume an entirely new aspect;
面貌清秀 delicately modelled features; have delicate looks;
面貌一新 take on a completely new look; take on an entirely new aspect;
精神面貌 mental outlook;
社會面貌 social physiognomy;

[面面] gaze at each in every way; see eye to eye;
面面俱到 attend to each and every aspect of a matter; give mature consideration to all aspects of a question; not to miss a thing; take every aspect into consideration; think of every detail; well considered in every aspect;
面面相覷 gaze at each other in speechless despair; look at each other helplessly; look at each other in astonishment, look at each other in blank dismay; look at each other in surprise; look blankly into each other's faces;

[面膜] face mask; face pack;

[面目] (1) face; features; visage; (2) appearance; aspects; looks; (3) face; honour; self-respect; sense of shame;

面目可怖 terrifying in appearance;
面目可憎 abominable countenance; detestable countenance; hateful countenance; repulsive in appearance; repulsive looks;
面目清秀 have a fair and clear face;
面目全非 be changed beyond recognition; beyond recognition; look entirely different; very different from the original;
~ 變得面目全非 change so much that one loses one's identity;
面目全新 change beyond recognition; complete change;
面目一新 assume a competely new appearance; assume a new aspect; give an entirely new complexion to; impart a new spirit to; put a new face on; take on a new look; take on an entirely new aspect;
~ 變得面目一新 present a completely new appearance after being changed;
面目猙獰 ferocious features; look fierce; sinister in appearance; with grossly offensive features;
本來面目 true colours; true features; true look;
~ 露出本來面目 reveal one's true colours; show one's true colours;
真面目 one's real face; one's true colours; one's true features; one's true self;
~ 暴露真面目 reveal one's true features; show oneself in one's true colours;
~ 廬山真面目 the true face of Mount Lu; the truth of a matter or person;
政治面目 political affiliation;

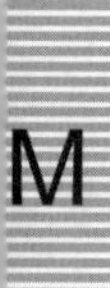

[面嫩] sensitive; timid;
[面龐] contours of the face; face; visage;
[面皮] face;
礙面皮 offend; offend another's face;
[面洽] discuss with sb face to face; take up a matter with sb personally;
面洽事宜 discuss matters with sb face to face;
[面前] before; in face of; in front of;
面前就是佛，何必遠燒香 why ask bishop when the Pope's around;
[面墻而立] ignorant because of not attending to learning; stand facing the wall;
[面容] countenance; face; facial features;
面容消瘦 look emaciated;

[面如] one's face is like...;
面如菜色 pinched look of a hungry person;
面如傅粉 face looks white as if painted; the natural colour of one's cheeks triumphs over the artificial effect of powder and apint;
面如方田 a face presaging good fortune; one's face is as square as the character; square-faced;
面如冠玉 one's complexion is clear as jade;
面如黃臘 one's face is yellow as wax;
面如其心 one's face reveals one's heart;
面如死灰 one's face is as white as a sheet; the face turns the colour of ashes; white and bloodless complexion;
面如桃花 rosy cheeks — said of a beautiful girl;
~ 面如桃花，眉如新月 with a face of peach-blossom loveliness and two brows as finely curved as the sickle of the new moon — said of a beauty;
面如土色 ghastly livid countenance; look ashen; look pale;
[面色] (1) colour of the face; complexion; (2) facial expressions;
面色不好 be off colour;
面色蒼白 look pale;
面色蒼黃 have a sallow complexion;
面色紅潤 have rosy cheeks; ruddy-cheeked;
面色健康 have a healthy complexion;
面色美麗 have a pretty complexion;
面色如臘 ashen-coloured; look sallow;
面色如生 look as if still alive;
面色憂鬱 have a melancholy look; look worried;
白皙面色 fair complexion;
蒼白面色 pale complexion;
紅潤面色 ruddy complexion;
[面紗] veil;
[面善] (1) look familiar; (2) look kind in face;
面善不熟 someone's face looks familiar but one is not acquainted with him;
面善心慈 affable and kind-hearted;
面善心惡 a kind face but a wicked heart; bear the semblance of an angel but have the heart of a devil;
面善心狠 innocent in appearance but a very wolf at heart; the cross on the

breast and the devil in the heart;
面善心詐 a complacent look; wear a happy expression;

[面商] consult personally; discuss with sb face to face; take up a matter with sb personally;

[面神經] facial nerve;
面神經痛 opalgia;

[面生] look unfamiliar;
面生喜色 look happy; wear a happy expression;

[面世] debut;

[面試] audition; interview; oral quiz;
參加面試 attend an interview; go for an interview;
得到面試 get an interview;
第一次面試 first interview;
進行面試 conduct an interview; do an interview;
模擬面試 mock interview;
求職面試 job interview;
一次面試 an interview;
有面試 have an interview;

[面授] face to face teaching; mouth to ear instruction;
面授機宜 brief sb on sth; give a confidential briefing; give confidential instructions in person; give instructions in person as to how to proceed; give personal instructions on an important policy; instruct a policy personally;

[面熟] look familiar;
面熟不詳 that person looks familiar but I can't place him;

[面談] speak to sb face to face; take up a matter with sb personally;

[面體] –hedron;
八面體 octahedron;
~ 正八面體 regular octahedron;
多面體 polyhedron;
~ 凹多面體 concave polyhedron;
~ 凸多面體 convex polyhedron;
~ 正多面體 regular polyhedron;
二十面體 icosahedron;
~ 正二十面體 regular icosahedron;
六面體 hexahedron;
~ 平行六面體 parallelepiped;
斜平行六面體 oblique parallelepiped;
直平行六面體 right parallelepiped;
~ 正六面體 regular hexahedron;
十二面體 dodecahedron;
~ 正十二面體 regular dodecahedron;
四面體 tetrahedron;
~ 正四面體 regular tetrahedron;
五面體 pentahedron;

[面晤] interview; meet;

[面向] (1) face; turn in the direction of; turn one's face to; (2) be geared to the needs of; cater to;
面向對象技術 object-oriented technique;
面向對過程的言 procedure-oriented language;
面向計算機語言 computer-oriented language;
面向群眾 be geared to the needs of the masses; face the masses; identity oneself with the masses;
面向世界 engage oneself globally;
面向消費者 customer orientation;
面向信息的語言 information-oriented language;
面向應用的語言 application-oriented language;
面向用戶的語言 user-oriented language;
面向作業的語言 job-oriented language;

[面謝] thank sb in person;

[面議] discuss personally;

[面罩] mask;
防煙面罩 smoke mask;
供氣面罩 air-supply mask;
氧氣面罩 oxygen mask;

[面值] (1) face value; nominal value; (2) denomination;

[面紙] facial tissue;
布紋面紙 textured paper;
綢紋面紙 silk-finish paper;
光面紙 gloss paper; glossy paper;
~ 半光面紙 semi-gloss paper;
細絨面紙 semi-matte paper;

[面子] (1) face; outer part; outside; (2) face; prestige; reputation;
愛面子 be concerned about face-saving; be concerned about saving face; be concerned about saving reputation; intent on face-saving; keen on face-saving; put a good face on; save face; self-conscious; sensitive about one's reputation;
礙面子 avoid hurting sb's feelings; just to spare sb's feelings;
保全面子 save appearances; save face;

save honour;
撐面子 keep up appearances;
丟面子 lose face;
給面子 do one proud; save sb's face; show due respect for sb's feelings;
~不給面子 not show due respect to sb;
夠面子 gain enough recognition of one's rank; have favourable responses to one's request as a mark of recognition;
顧面子 save face;
~顧全面子 keep up appearances as sth important; mindful of the need for respectability; save appearances; save one's face; spare sb's feelings;
留面子 spare sb's feelings;
~不留面子 injure sb's sensibilities;
賣面子 have regard for sb's face;
沒面子 not prestigious to do sth;
賞面子 accept sth in order to do sb honour; do sb the honour;
失面子 lose face;
耍面子 put a good face on;
撕破面子 cast aside all considerations of face;
死要面子 anxious to keep up appearances; dead determined to save face; try to preserve one's face at all cost;
~死要面子活受罪 keep up appearance to cover up one's predicament; puff oneself up at one's own cost;
為了面子 for countenance;
要面子 anxious to keep up appearances; keen on face-saving;
有面子 enjoy due respect; gain face; have the honour;
找面子 try to save face;
爭面子 try to win for the sake of face;
轉面子 regain lost face;
做面子 do sth for the sake of appearance; put up a pleasant front;

凹面 concave;
八面 all sides;
版面 layout;
北面 north;
背面 back; reverse side;
避面 avoid meeting a person;
表面 (1) face; surface; (2) appearance; outside;
布面 cloth cover;
側面 aspect; flank; side;
層面 aspect;
場面 (1) scene; (2) circumstances; scene; sight; (3) occasion; (4) appearance; façade; front;
出面 act in one's capacity or on behalf of an organization; appear personally;
唇面 labial surface;
單方面 one-sided; unilateral;
當面 face to face; in the face of; to a person's face;
覿面 meet each other;
地面 (1) earth's surface; (2) floor; ground; (3) area; region;
店面 shop front;
東面 east;
斷面 section;
對面 (1) opposite; (2) face to face; right in front;
反面 (1) back; reverse side; wrong side; (2) negative side; opposite;
方面 aspect; field; respect; side;
封面 (1) title page of a thread-bound book; (2) front and back cover of a book; (3) front cover;
鋒面 frontal surface;
浮面 surface;
幅面 width of cloth;
海面 sea level;
後面 (1) at the back; behind; in the rear; (2) later;
護面 mask;
畫面 (1) general appearance of a picture; tableau; (2) frame;
會面 meet;
見面 meet; see;
腳面 instep;
截面 section;
晶面 crystal face;
局面 aspect; phase; situation;
臉面 face; self-respect; sb's feeling;
兩面 (1) both sides; two aspects; two sides; (2) double; dual;
樓面 floor;
露面 appear on public occasions; show one's face;
路面 pavement; road surface;
滿面 have one's face covered with;
謎面 riddle;
謀面 meet;
南面 south;
劈面 right in the face;
片面 (1) unilateral; (2) one-sided;
票面 face value;
平面 plane;
剖面 section;
撲面 blow on one's face;
鋪面 shop front;

前面 (1) ahead; at the head; in front; (2) above; preceding;
橋面 bridge floor;
切面 (1) section; (2) tangent plane;
情面 feelings; sensibilities;
球面 spherical surface;
曲面 curved surface;
全面 all-round; comprehensive; overall;
舌面 the surface of the tongue;
世面 various aspects of society; world;
市面 business; market conditions;
書面 in writing; in written form; written;
雙面 double-faced; two-sided;
水面 surface of the water;
四面 four sides; on all sides;
體面 (1) creditable; honourable; (2) dignity; good-looking; handsome; propriety;
凸面 convex;
橢面 ellipsoid;
外面 (1) outside; (2) exterior; outward appearance; surface;
屋面 roofing;
晤面 interview; meet;
西面 west;
下面 (1) below; under; (2) following; next; (3) lower level; subordinate;
斜面 (1) inclined plane; (2) oblique plane;
鞋面 instep; vamp;
顏面 (1) face; (2) prestige;
一面 (1) one side; (2) one aspect; (3) at the same time; (4) while;
陰暗面 dark side of things;
迎面 face to face; head-on; in one's face;
右面 right side; right-hand side;
正面 (1) front; (2) obverse side; right side; (3) directly; openly; positive;
桌面 tabletop; top of a table;
字面 literal;
左面 left side; left-hand side;

mian

【瞑】 throw into a state of confusion;

［瞑眩］ (1) feel dizzy and upset; (2) dizziness, nausea;

mian

【麪】 (1) flour; (2) dough; (3) noodles;

mian

【麵】 noodle;

［麵包］ bread;

麵包車 baby bus; mini-bus;
麵包店 baker's; bakery; bakehouse;
~一家麵包店 a bakery;
麵包粉 breadcrumbs;
麵包乾 rusk;
~磨牙麵包乾 teething rusk;
麵包果 breadfruit;
麵包盒 bread bin; breadbox;
麵包捲 bap; bread roll;
~乾酪麵包捲 cheese roll;
~火腿麵包捲 ham roll;
麵包籃 bread basket;
麵包皮 crust;
麵包片 slice of bread; sliced bread;
~烤麵包片 toast;
奶酪烤麵包片 cheese toast;
無黃油烤麵包片 dry toast;
麵包圈 bagel; doughnut;
麵包瓤 crumb;
~大氣孔麵包瓤 loose crumb;
麵包師 baker;
麵包箱 bread bin; breadbox;
麵包屑 bread crumbs; crumbly bread; crumbs;
麵包渣 bread crumbs; crumbs;
白麵包 white bread;
不新鮮的麵包 stale bread;
茶點麵包 tea bread;
長棍麵包 baguette;
~脆皮的長棍麵包 crusty baguette;
~法式長棍麵包 baguette;
長麵包 Pullman;
長條麵包 bar bread;
陳麵包 stale bread;
大麵包 loaf;
法國麵包 French bread;
番茄麵包 tomato bread;
乾皮麵包 chippy bread;
光麵包 dry bread;
黑麥麵包 rye bread;
黑麵包 black bread; brown bread; rye bread;
~燕麥黑麵包 brash bread;
黃油麵包 butter bread;
~抹黃油麵包 bread and butter;
~無黃油麵包 dry bread;
加氣麵包 aerated bread;
薑料麵包 ginger bread;
烤麵包 bake bread; toast; toasted bread;
~烤麵包片 toast;
~鯷醬烤麵包 anchovy toast;
口袋麵包 pita bread; pitta bread;
爐火麵包 hearth bread;
裸麥麵包 rye bread;

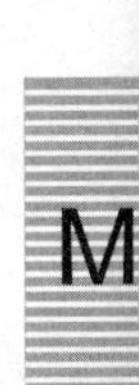

～粗裸麥麵包 pumpernickel;
麻花狀麵包 twist bread;
模烤麵包 box loaf; pan loaf;
模製麵包 tin bread;
奶油麵包 butter bread;
牛角麵包 croissant;
牛奶麵包 milk bread;
農家麵包 cottage bread;
膨鬆麵包 leavened bread;
葡萄乾麵包 currant bread; raisin bread; sultana bread;
切麵包 cut bread; slice bread;
～切麵包板 breadboard;
切片麵包 sliced bread;
全麥麵包 wholemeal bread; wholewheat bread;
散裝麵包 bulk bread;
十字甜麵包 hot-cross bun;
受潮的麵包 soggy bread;
水果麵包 farthing bun;
碎麵包 broken bread;
淡麵包 plain bread;
未烤透的麵包 soggy bread;
小片麵包 canapé;
小圓白麵包 batched bread;
小圓麵包 bread roll; bun;
新烤的麵包 freshly baked bread;
血斑麵包 bleeding bread;
燕麥麵包 oats bread;
羊角麵包 croissant;
一大塊麵包 a chunk of bread;
一大片麵包 a hunk of bread;
一大條麵包 a tommy;
一塊麵包 a chunk of bread; a loaf of bread; a morsel of bread; a piece of bread; a slab of bread; a slice of bread;
一塊磚形麵包 a brick of bread;
一籃麵包 a hamper of bread;
一爐麵包 a batch of bread;
一片麵包 a slab of bread; a slice of bread;
一條麵包 a loaf of bread;
一小塊麵包 a morsel of bread;
一小片麵包 a morsel of bread;
硬皮麵包 crusty bread;
玉米粉麵包 corn bread;
玉米麵包 corn bread; corn pone;
圓頂麵包 round top bread;
主食麵包 bread eaten as a staple food;
做麵包 make bread;

[麵粉] flour; wheat flour;
白麵粉 white flour;
次級麵粉 clear flour;
粗粒麵粉 coarse granular flour;
粗麵粉 break flour;
黑麵粉 brown flour;
普通麵粉 plain flour;
全麥麵粉 wheatmeal;
軟質麵粉 soft flour;
一袋麵粉 a sack of flour;

[麵櫃] flour cupboard;

[麵糊] (1) paste; (2) panada;

[麵湯] water in which noodles have been boiled;

[麵條] noodles;
扁麵條 linguini;
吃麵條 eat noodles;

[麵團] dough;
麵團狀 doughiness;
餅乾麵團 biscuit dough;
發酵麵團 fermenting dough;
硬麵團 hard dough;

白麵 wheat flour;
炒麵 (1) fried noodles; (2) parched flour;
抻麵 hand-stretched noodles;
擔擔麵 Sichuan noodles with peppery sauce;
刀削麵 shaved noodles;
豆麵 bean flour;
方便麵 instant noodles;
掛麵 fine dried noodles; vermicelli;
快熟麵 instant noodles;
涼麵 cold noodles in sauce;
千層麵 lasagna;
切麵 cut noodles; machine-made noodles;
壽麵 birthday noodles;
湯麵 noodles in soup;

miao²
miao

【苗】 (1) seedlings; young plants; (2) the young of some animals; (3) vaccine; (4) sth resembling a young plant; (5) a surname;

[苗而不秀] a flowerless sprout; corn which does not bear fruit; put forth shoots that fail to flower — show great potentialities but to fulfil them;

[苗圃] nursery; nursery garden;
苗圃工人 nurseryman;
播種苗圃 seedling nursery;
固定苗圃 permanent nursery;
林間苗圃 bush nursery;
臨時苗圃 temporary nursery;

批發苗圃 wholesale nursery;
容器育苗圃 container nursery;
森林苗圃 forest nursery;
移動苗圃 shifting nursery; wandering nursery;
移植苗圃 transplant nursery;

[苗條] slender; slim; slim and slender; willowy;
苗條身裁 slender and graceful in stature;
苗條優雅的 lissome;
保持苗條 keep oneself slim;

[苗頭] suggestion of a new development; symptom of a trend;
發現苗頭 notice the suggestion of a new development;
好苗頭 good symptom of a trend;
壞苗頭 bad symptom of a trend;

[苗裔] descendants; progeny; offsprings;

[苗族] Miao nationality;

補苗 fill the gaps with seedlings;
豆苗 bean seedling;
痘苗 vaccine;
扶苗 put a lodged plant upright;
根苗 (1) root and shoot; (2) source; (3) offspring;
花苗 flower seedling;
火苗 tongue of flame;
間苗 thin out seedlings;
菌苗 vaccine;
麥苗 wheat seedling;
禽苗 poultry chicks;
青苗 young crops;
樹苗 sapling;
蒜苗 garlic bolt;
心苗 decisions; intentions;
新苗 young shoots;
疫苗 vaccine;
油苗 oil seepage;
幼苗 seedling;
移苗 transplant seedlings;
魚苗 fish fry; minnow;
植苗 transplant saplings;

miao

【描】 (1) copy; trace; (2) retouch; touch up;

[描畫] depict; describe; draw; paint;
難描難畫 defy description; beyond description;

[描繪] depict; describe; plot; portray;
描繪器 plotter;
~數字描繪器 digital plotter;
~自動描繪器 automatic plotter;
描繪儀 plotter;
~曲線描繪器 curve plotter;
非筆墨能描繪 began description;

[描摹] delineate; depict; portray; trace;

[描述] describe; representation;
描述標題 descriptive title;
描述詞 descriptive word;
描述動詞 descriptive verb;
描述器 describer;
~列車描述器 train describer;
~列車運行圖描述器 train diagram describer;
描述性對等詞 descriptive equivalent;
描述性述謂結構 descriptive predication;
描述語段 descriptive text;
發布描述 issue a description;
簡略描述 thumbnail sketch;
時域描述 time domain description;
提供描述 provide a description;
圖象描述 picture description;
詳細描述 full description;
形狀描述 shape description;
原始描述 original description;
狀態空間描述 state-space description;

[描圖] plot; trace; tracing;
描圖機 plotter;
~坐標描圖機 coordinate plotter;
描圖儀 plotter;
~自動描圖儀 automatic plotter;
描圖紙 tracing paper;

[描寫] depict; describe; portray; represent;
描寫句 descriptive sentence;
描寫功能 descriptive function;
描寫生格 genitive of description;
描寫文 descriptive prose;
描寫性賓格 objective description;
描寫性話語 descriptive discourse;
描寫語法 descriptive grammer;
描寫語言學 descriptive linguistics;
共時描寫 synchronic description;
輕描淡寫 a light sketch and simple writing; be said as if by the way; describe in a light, moderate tone; describe superficially; describe with a delicate touch; dismiss lightly; gloss over; make a short general description of sth; make light of; mention casually; mention in passing; mention sth in a casual manner; mild comments; play down; slough over; slur over; touch

lightly on; touch on sth lightly; water down; write a sketchy account of sth;
~輕描淡寫，文過飾非 make light of sth or gloss over it;
語音描寫 phonetic description;

白描 (1) line drawing in traditional ink and brush style; (2) simple, straightforward style of writing;
回描 retrace;
素描 (1) sketch; (2) literary sketch;
線描 line drawing;

miao
【瞄】 look at attentively; take aim;
［瞄準］ aim; aiming; lay; sight; take aim; train;
瞄準靶心 aim at the bull's-eye;
瞄準器 sight;
~補償瞄準器 compensating sight;
~飛機無線電瞄準器 aircraft radio sight;
~機載炮火瞄準器 airborne gun sight;
方向瞄準 across track aiming;
間接瞄準 indirect aiming;
精確地瞄準 take accurate aim;
雷達瞄準 radar aiming;
練習瞄準 practise aiming;
武器瞄準 weapon aiming;
直接瞄準 direct aiming;
自動瞄準 automatic aiming;

miao³
miao
【杪】 (1) tip of a small branch; twig; (2) end of a period;

歲杪 end of the year;
雲杪 distant and high;

miao
【眇】 (1) fine; small; tiny; unimportant; (2) blind in one eye;
［眇眇忽忽］ elusive; hardly discernible;

幽眇 sophisticated;

miao
【秒】 second;
［秒錶］ chronograph; stopwatch;
［秒針］ second hand of a clock or watch;
［秒制］ second system;
釐米克秒制 centimetre-gram-second system;
米噸秒制 metre-ton-second system;
米公斤秒制 metre-kilogram-second system;

分秒 every minute and second;
毫秒 millisecond;
毫微秒 nanosecond;
閏秒 leap second;
微秒 microsecond;

miao
【渺】 (1) distant and indistinct; vague; vast; (2) insignificant; tiny;
［渺茫］ distant and indistinct; uncertain; vague;
前途渺茫 one's future is left in the air;
［渺然］ boundless; endless; vast;
［渺小］ insignificant; negligible; paltry; tiny;

飄渺 dimly discernible; misty;
杳渺 profound; remote;

miao
【淼】 (of water) extensive or overwhelming;

浩淼 extending into the distance; vast;

miao
【緲】 dim; distant; far;

miao
【藐】 (1) belittle; despise; slight; treat with disdain; (2) insignificant; petite; petty; small;
［藐視］ despise; look down on; treat with contempt;
［藐小］ insignificant; negligible; paltry; tiny;

miao
【邈】 (1) distant; remote; (2) same as 藐；

miao⁴
miao
【妙】 (1) excellent; fine; wonderful; (2) clever; ingenious; subtle;
［妙策］ brilliant scheme; excellent plan;
［妙計］ brilliant scheme; wonderful idea; an excellent plan;
妙計落空 the excellent plan failed;
頓生妙計 an idea occurs to sb suddenly;
錦囊妙計 a secret master plan; ace in the hold; ace up one's sleeve; beautiful scheme; instructions for dealing with an emergency; something up one's sleeve; wise counsel;

使用妙計 make use of a brilliant scheme;
想出妙計 hit upon an excellent idea;

[妙句] quotable quotes;
[妙訣] clever way of doing sth; knack;
[妙齡] young; youthful;
妙齡女郎 budding beauty; young girl;
妙齡少女 young lady;
妙齡正處 at a young age;
正當妙齡 girl in the prime of youth;
[妙論] convincing discourse; extraordinary argument; sparkling discourse;
[妙品] (1) fine quality goods; (2) fine work of art;
[妙手空空] pickpocket;
[妙算] excellent plan;
胸有妙算 have smart ideas up one's sleeve; have some tricks up one's sleeve;
[妙言] witty remark;
妙言俊語 laugh line; punch line;
妙不可言 most intriguing; of indescribable beauty; take the bun; too wonderful for words;
[妙藥] miraculous cure; panacea;
[妙用] magical effect;
[妙語] punchline; witticism; witty remark;
妙語解頤 a clever talk becomes a good joke; wisecracks that really tickle;
妙語驚人 a rapier thrust;
妙語如珠 endless witty remarks; full of witty remarks; pearls of wisdom; scintillating witticisms;
妙語雙關 witty remark with double meanings;

奧妙 mysterious; profound; subtle;
不妙 not too encouraging;
更妙 still better;
絕妙 excellent; extremely marvellous; most wonderful;
曼妙 lithe and graceful;
美妙 splendid; wonderful;
奇妙 marvelous; wonderful;
巧妙 clever; ingenious;
深妙 profound;
神妙 marvelous; wonderful;
宛妙 soft and charming;
玄妙 abstruse; mysterious;

miao
【廟】 shrine; temple;
[廟號] dynastic title;
[廟會] temple fair;
[廟宇] temple;
[廟主] head priest of a temple;
[廟祝] temple attendant in charge of incense and religious service;

拜廟 worship at a temple;
神廟 temple of the gods;
太廟 Imperial Ancestral Temple;
文廟 Confucian temple;
邑廟 district temple;
宗廟 ancestral temple of a ruling house;
祖廟 ancestral temple;

miao
【繆】 a surname;

mie¹
mie
【乜】
[乜斜] glance sideways;

mie
【芈】 bleating of a sheep;

mie
【咩】 baa; bleat; bleating of sheep;

mie⁴
mie
【滅】 (1) go out; (2) beat; convince sb by force; (3) extinguish; put out; turn off; (4) drown; submerge; (5) destroy; exterminate; wipe out;
[滅病] wipe out disease;
除害滅病 wipe out pests and disease;
[滅頂] be drowned;
滅頂之災 be buried beneath the waves; in danger of being swamped; the calamity of being drowned;
[滅火] (1) extinguish a fire; outfire; put out a fire; quell a fire; (2) cut out an engine;
滅火器 extinguisher; fire extinguisher;
~二氧化碳滅火器 carbon dioxide fire extinguisher;
~乾粉滅火器 dry-chemical fire extinguisher;
~酸鹼滅火器 soda-acid extinguisher;
[滅絕] (1) become extinct; (2) completely lose;
滅絕人性 barbarous; beast-like; brutal; cannibalistic; inhuman; most barbarous;

瀕臨滅絕 on the verge of extinction;

[滅門] family termination;

滅門大禍 calamity of exterminating a family;

滅門絕戶 extinction of the whole family;

滅門之禍 calamity of family extermination;

[滅失] loss;

[滅鼠] deratization; rat eradication;

[滅亡] be destroyed; become extinct; die out; perish;

遭到滅亡 meet destruction;

招致滅亡 court destruction;

自趨滅亡 heading for disaster; ride to disaster; run toward disaster;

併滅 destroy;

吹滅 blow out;

覆滅 collapse completely;

幻滅 fall through; vanish into thin air;

毀滅 destroy; exterminate;

殲滅 annihilate; mop up;

剿滅 crumble and fall;

絕滅 die out;

潰滅 crumble and fall;

泯滅 die out; vanish;

磨滅 obliterate; wear away;

破滅 be shattered; evaporate;

撲滅 (1) extinguish; stamp out; (2) exterminate; mop up;

掃滅 exterminate; wipe out;

澌滅 totally disappear; vanish;

死滅 die out;

吞滅 annex (another country);

熄滅 die out; go out;

消滅 (1) die out; perish; (2) abolish; eliminate;

湮滅 annihilate; bury in oblivion;

mie

【蔑】 (1) disdain; slight; (2) none; nothing; (3) smear;

[蔑棄] abandon; despise and cast away; disregard;

[蔑視] despise; scorn; show contempt for;

蔑視法律 despise law;

蔑視婦女 look down on women;

蔑視習俗 show contempt for convention;

遭到蔑視 suffer an affront;

[蔑以復加] cannot be surpassed; reach the limit;

輕蔑 contemptuous; scornful;

污蔑 (1) slander; vilify; (2) defile; sully;

誣蔑 (1) slander; vilify; (2) defile; sully;

侮蔑 despise; scorn;

mie

【篾】 (1) thin and long strip of bamboo for making baskets; (2) a variety of bamboo;

mie

【蠛】 (1) stain with blood; (2) slander; trump up a charge;

[蠛蠓] biting midge; midge;

min²
min

【民】 (1) people; (2) person of a certain occupation; (3) member of a nationality; (4) folk; of the people; (5) civilian;

[民辦] be run by the local people;

民辦大學 university run by the local people;

民辦公助 run by the local people and subsidized by the state;

民辦企業 enterprise run by the local people;

民辦學校 school run by the local people;

[民胞物與] people are my brothers and all things my kinds;

[民變] civil commotion; mass uprising; popular revolt;

[民兵] militiaman; people's militia;

[民法] civil law;

民法通則 general rule of the civil law;

[民防] civil defence;

[民憤] popular indignation; the people's wrath;

民憤極大 incur the great wrath of the masses;

激起民憤 arouse popular indignation;

平息民憤 soothe the people's wrath;

消除民憤 dispel popular indignation;

以平民憤 assuage popular indignation; assuage the people's anger; in order to appease public indignation; put an end to the people's anger;

[民風] folk custom;

民風淳厚 customs are simple and homely; people are honest and warmhearted; people are simple and honest;

民風淳樸 people are simple and honest;

民風澆薄 stingy, selfish character of a locality;
民風日敝 people's customs are declining day by day;

[民歌] folk song;

[民工] civilian worker; labourer working on a public project;

[民國] (1) people's republic; (2) people and the country;
民安國泰 people are at peace and the country is prosperous;

[民航] civil aviation;

[民間] (1) among the people; folk; popular; (2) non-governmental; people-to-people;
民間傳説 folklore; popular legend;
民間歌曲 folk songs;
民間故事 folk tale;
民間疾苦 hardships of the people;
民間交流 people-to-people exchange;
民間經濟團體 non-goernmental economic organization;
民間糾紛 dispute among the people;
民間來往 nongovernmental contacts;
民間貿易 non-governmental trade;
民間團體 non-governmental organization;
民間文學 folk literature;
民間舞 folk dance;
~民間舞蹈 folk dancing;
民間習俗 fold custom;
民間協定 reach non-governmental agreement;
民間信仰 folk beliefs;
民間驗方 fold remedy;
民間藝人 folk artist;
民間藝術 folk art; popular art;
民間音樂 folk music;
民間英雄 folk hero;
民間組織 non-governmental organization;
民間作品 folk literature work;

[民警] people's police; people's policeman;
當民警 serve as people's people;
動員民警 mobilize the people's police;
叫民警 call people'es people;
女民警 people's policewoman;
通知民警 notify the people's police;

[民居] civilian dwelling; private house;
臨河民居 house facing a river;

[民力] financial resources of the people;

[民命] people's life;

[民瘼] sufferings of the people; weal and woe of the people;

[民氣] people's morale; popular morale;

[民強] people are strong;
民強國富 people are strong and the land is fruitful;
民強國固 people are strong and the country is strategically located;
民強國泰 people are strong and the country is prosperous;

[民情] (1) condition of the people; (2) feelings of the people; public feeling;
民情民意 public feelings;
暗訪民情 make secret inquiries into the condition of the people;
俯順民情 defer to popular opinion; in deference to the feelings of the people; kindly favour the public opinion;
了解民情 know public feelings;
體察民情 investigate the condition of the people; size up people's attitude;
體卹民情 understand and sympathize with the feelings of the people;
下順民情 accord with the will of the people;
下與民情 lend one's ear to the appeals of the people; listen carefully to the views of one's subordinates;

[民窮] people are poor;
民窮財盡 complete bankruptcy; means of the people have been used up; people suffer privation and the country has depleted its resources;
民窮財困 people are bled white;
民窮國敝 people suffer privation and the country has depleted its resources;

[民權] civil liberties; civil rights; democratic rights; rights of the people;
民權主義 principle of democracy;
保護民權 safeguard civil rights;
獲得民權 acquire civil rights;
侵犯民權 infringe on democratic rights;
確立民權 establish democratic rights;
喪失民權 forfeit one's civil rights;
維護民權 maintain civil rights;
享有民權 enjoy civil rights;
爭取民權 strive for civil liberties;

[民生] livelihood of the people;
民生凋敝 miserable life of the people; mass impoverishment; people live in destitution;
民生發展 development of livelihood;
民生國計 people's livelihood and national

welfare;
民生日敝 the cost of living is escalating;
民生日蹙 the means of livelihood of the people has become more than ever restricted;
民生日困 people's distress increases daily;
民生涂炭 people are greatly afflicted; plunge the people into misery and suffering;
民生主義 principle of national livelihood;
安定民生 reassure the public;
國計民生 national economy and the people's livelihood; national welfare and the livelihood of the masses;
民不聊生 live on the edge of starvation; make life impossible for the people; the masses live in dire poverty; the people are destitute;
以利民生 for the benefit of people's livelihood;

[民事] civil;
民事案 civil case;
民事案件 civil law case; lawsuit;
民事伴侶關係 civil partner;
民事裁判 civil judgement;
民事法 civil law;
民事法律關係 civil legal relationship;
民事糾紛 civil dispute;
民事權利 civil rights;
~民事權利能力 capacity for civil rights;
民事審判 civil trial;
~民事審判庭 civil court;
民事行為 civil conduct;
~民事行為能力 capacity for civil conduct;
民事責任 civil responsibility;

[民俗] folk custom; folklore; folkways;
民俗文學 folk literature;
民俗學家 folklorist;
化民成俗 influence the people and form moral customs;

[民心] common aspiration of the people; popular feelings; popular sentiments; popular support;
民心所向 common aspiration of the people; where the popular will inclines;
安撫民心 reassure the public;
不得民心 vey unpopular;
洽於民心 in accordance with the will of the people;
深得民心 enjoy the ardent support of the people; well received; win strong popular support;
失民心 lose the support of the people;
順乎民心 meet the wishes of the people;
違背民心 go against the common aspirations of the people;
慰民心 soothe people's feelings;
贏得民心 win popular feelings;

[民選] be elected by people;

[民謠] folk music; folk rhyme; folk songs;

[民以食為天] bread is the staff of life; food is the first necessity of the people;

[民意] popular opinion; popular will; will of the people;
民意測驗 public opinion poll;
民意調查 opinion poll; polling; public opinion poll;
~民意調查者 pollster;
~投票後民意調查 exit poll;
~最新民意調查 latest public opinion poll;
民意所歸 the public sentiment favours;
俯順民意 comply with the people's wishes; comply with the wishes of the people; yield to public opinion;
順從民意 conform with the will of the people; obey the will of the people;

[民營] run by private citizens;
民辦民營 enterprises run by the local people;

[民用] civil; for civil use;
民用補給品 civilian supplies;
民用產品 products for civil use;
民用航空 civil aviation;
民用機場 civil airport;

[民怨] popular discontent;
民怨鼎沸 popular resentment is boiling; public resentment is seething; seething discontent among the masses; seething discontent of the people;
民怨沸騰 popular grievances run high; popular resentment is boiling; public resentment is seething; the people are boiling with resentment;
民怨盈涂 public resentment is seething;

[民樂] folk music;
普及民樂 popularize folk music;
熱愛民樂 love folk music;
宣傳民樂 publicize traditional folk music;

演奏民樂 play folk music;
振興民樂 vitalize folk music;

[民賊] traitor to the people;

[民政] civil administration;

[民眾] common people; masses of the people; populace;
民眾的信心 public confidence;
喚起民眾 arouse the masses of the people;
教育民眾 educate the populace;
利用民眾 make use f the general public;
普通民眾 grass roots;
煽動民眾 agitate the general public;
影響民眾 influence the masses of the people;

[民主] (1) democracy; democratic rights; (2) democratic;
民主黨派 democratic party;
民主改革 democratic reform;
民主革命 democratic revolution;
民主管理 democratic management;
民主化 democratization; democratize;
民主集中制 democratic centralism;
民主監督 democratic supervision;
民主進程 democratic progress;
民主決策 democratic decision-making;
~民主決策機制 democratic decision-making mechanism;
民主渠道 channels for democracy;
民主人士 democrat; democratic personages;
民主協商 democratic consultation;
民主選舉 democratic election;
民主意識 sense of democracy;
民主原則 principles of democracy;
民主主義 democracy;
~民主主義者 democrat;
黨內民主 democracy of the Party;
經濟民主 economic democracy;
社會主義民主 socialist democracy;
無視民主 despise democracy;
走向民主 advance towards democracy;
作風民主 have a democratic work-style;

[民族] nation; nationality;
民族安全 national security;
民族敗類 national outcast; the scum of a nation; national scums;
民族背景 ethnic background;
民族標準語 national standard speech;
民族衝突 ethnic conflicts;
民族大家庭 great family of nationalities;
民族地區 regions of minorities;
民族獨立 national independence;
~維護民族獨立 assert national independence;
民族對立 national antagonism;
民族分裂 separation of nationalities;
民族風格 national style;
民族服裝 national costume;
民族復興 national rejuvenation;
民族感情 national sentiment;
民族歌舞團 nationalities song and dance ensemble;
民族革命 national revolution;
民族關係 ethnic relations;
民族國家 nation state;
民族和解 reconciliation between nations;
民族糾紛 ethnic feuds;
民族救星 savior of the nation;
民族聯盟 national alliance;
民族矛盾 national conflicts;
~挑起民族矛盾 provoke national conflicts;
民族偏見 ethnic prejudice;
民族歧視 ethnic discrimination;
民族區域自治 regional national automnomy;
民族生態 ethnoecology;
民族素質 quality of nation;
民族同化 national assimilation;
民族團結 ethnic harmony; ethnic solidarity; national unity; unity among nations;
~破壞民族團結 undermine the unity of the nationalities;
民族危機 national crisis;
民族性 nationality;
民族學 ethnology;
民族壓迫 national oppression;
民族意識 national consciousness;
民族音樂 national music;
民族英雄 hero of the nation;
民族樂團 national music ensemble; national music orchestra;
民族政策 policy towards nationalities;
民族之林 nations of the world;
民族中心主義 ethnocentrism;
民族主義 nationalism; principle of nationalism;
~民族主義文學 nationalist literature;
~民族主義者 nationalist;
民族自決 national autonomy;
民族自信心 national confidence;
民族自治 national autonomy;

~民族自治權 the right of national self-determination;
民族自尊 national dignity; national self-respect;
~民族自尊心 national pride;
多民族 multinational;
少數民族 ethnic minorities; minority nationalities; national minorities;
兄弟民族 fraternal nationalities;
優等民族 master race;
中華民族 the Chinese nation;

愛民 cherish the people; love the people
安民 give peace to the people; pacify the people; quiet the people; reassure the people; reassure the public;
敖民 idler; lazybones; loafer; lounger; time-waster;
暴民 mobs; mobsters;
邊民 people living on the frontiers;
便民 convenient for the people; provide for the people's convenience;
草民 common people;
臣民 subjects of a kingdom;
船民 boat people;
疍民 boat dwellers;
公民 citizen;
國民 national;
饑民 famine victim;
居民 inhabitant; resident;
黎民 common people;
良民 (1) common people; (2) law-abiding people;
流民 exiled person; refugee;
牧民 herdsman; shepherd;
難民 refugee;
農民 farmer; peasant;
貧民 poor people;
平民 common people;
僑民 alien resident; national of a particular country residing abroad;
全民 all the people; the whole people;
人民 people;
市民 residents of a city; townspeople;
手民 typesetter;
庶民 common people;
順民 abjectly obedient citizens;
選民 elector; voter;
移民 emigrant; immigrant;
逸民 hermit;
游民 vagrant;
漁民 fisherman;
災民 victims of a natural calamity;
殖民 establish a colony;

min
【岷】 (1) Min River in Sichuan; (2) Mount. Min in Sichuan;

min
【忞】 force oneself to do sth;

min
【旻】 autumn;

蒼旻 heavens; sky;

min
【珉】 stone resembling jade;
［珉玉雜淆］ Jadelike stones and genuine jades are mixed together.-scholars of various talents;

min
【閩】 a pronunciation of 閩；

min
【緡】 (1) fish line; (2) cord for stringing up coins;

min³
min
【皿】 shallow container;

器皿 household utensils;

min
【抿】 (1) smooth hair with a wet brush; (2) close lightly; furl; tuck; (3) sip;
［抿嘴］ purse one's lips;
抿嘴而笑 pucker one's face in a smile;
抿嘴忍笑 purse one's lips to suppress laughter;
抿著嘴笑 compress one's lips to smile; one's lips curling in a part smile; smile one's tightlipped smile; smile with closed lips;

min
【泯】 die out; vanish;
［泯滅］ abrogate; die out; disappear; vanish;
泯滅自己的良心 abrogate one's conscience;
［泯泯紛紛］ all in confusion;
［泯沒］ become lost; sink into oblivion; vanish;

消泯 eliminate; exterminate;

min

【敏】 agile; nimble; quick;

［敏度］ acuity;

感色敏度 chromaticity acuity;

色覺敏度 acuity of colour vision;

視敏度 visual acuity;

聽敏度 auditory acuity;

嗅敏度 olfactory acuity;

［敏感］ sensitive; susceptible;

敏感度 sensibility; sensitivity;

~辨色敏感度 hue sensibility;

~回反敏感度 recurrent sensibility;

~撞擊敏感度 impact sensitivity;

敏感菌 sensitized bacterium;

~敏感菌苗 sensitized vaccine;

敏感期 sensitive period;

敏感性 sensibility; sensitivity;

~敏感性分析 sensitivity analysis;

~敏感性問題 sensitivity problems;

~溫度敏感性 temperature sensibility;

敏感作用 sensitization;

~光敏感作用 light sensitization;

對痛苦敏感 susceptible to pain;

過分敏感的 oversensitive;

［敏化］ sensitization; sensitize;

敏化劑 sensitizer;

~熱敏化劑 heat sensitizer;

~照相敏化劑 photographic sensitizer;

化學敏化 chemical sensitization;

染料敏化 dye sensitization;

［敏慧］ clever; keen; sharp-witted;

［敏捷］ acuity; agile; nimble; quick; sharp;

不夠敏捷 not quick enough;

動作敏捷 quick in action; quick in movement;

思維敏捷 mentally quick;

思想敏捷 have an agile mind;

［敏銳］ acuity; acumen; acute; keen; sharp;

敏銳度 acuity;

~亮度敏銳度 brightness acuity;

目光敏銳 quite sharp-eyed;

聽覺敏銳 have sensitive ears;

嗅覺敏銳 have a keen sense of smell;

眼光敏銳 acute eyesight;

［敏事］ earnest in actions;

才吏敏事 able officers are earnest in actions;

不敏 not clever; not intelligent;

過敏 be allergic;

機敏 alert and resourceful;

靈敏 acute; agile; keen; sensitive;

鋭敏 keen; sensitive; sharp-witted;

min

【湣】 confused; mixed;

min

【閔】 (1) commiserate; condole; mourn; pity; sympathetic with; (2) encourage; urge; (3) sorrow; trouble; (4) a surname;

min

【慜】 commiserate; pity;

min

【黽】

［黽勉］ try hard; work hard;

黽勉從事 labour hard;

min

【澠】 (1) a place in Henan; (2) a river and a county in Henan;

min

【閩】 (1) name for Fujian; (2) a river and tribe in today's Fujian Province;

［閩台文化］ culture of Fujian and Taiwan;

min

【憫】 commiserate; feel concerned for; pity;

怜憫 have compassion for; pity;

ming²

ming

【名】 (1) name; title; (2) given name; (3) fame; renown; reputation; (4) celebrated; famous; noted; well-known;

［名不虛傳］ deserve the reputation one enjoys; equal to one's reputation; has a well-deserved reputation; live up to one's name; one's reputation is justified;

［名冊］ register; roll;

保留名冊 retain a register;

花名冊 membership roster; muster roll; register; roster;

立名冊 establish a register;

［名產］ famous product; specialty goods;

［名稱］ appellation; definition; designation; name; nomenclature;

名稱牌 nameplate;

名稱學 onomasiology;

燈頭名稱 lamp base designation;

規定名稱 code designation;
呼叫名稱 call name;
加成名稱 additive name;
目標名稱 target designation;
商標名稱 brand name;
示象名稱 aspect name;
數組名稱 array name;
條件名稱 conditional name;
正確名稱 proper name;

[名城] famous city;
迭克名城 capture one important city after another;

[名馳] one's fame spreads;
名馳遐邇 one's fame spreads far and wide; well-known far and near;
名馳中外 win fame both at home and abroad;

[名垂] leave a name behind; leave a name in;
名垂後世 leave a name behind one; one's name is handed down to future generations;
名垂千古 be crowned with eternal glory; go down in history; have a niche in the temple of fame; have an everlasting name; leave a name in history; on the scroll of fame;
名垂青史 go down in history; go down in the annals of history; make a name in history; one's name will live in history; stamp one's name on the page of history;
名垂史冊 on the scroll of fame; one's name remains forever in history;
名垂竹帛 leave a name in history;

[名詞] (1) noun; (2) phrase; term; (3) name;
名詞詞組 noun group;
名詞從句 noun clause;
名詞短語 nominal phrase;
名詞化 nominalization;
~名詞化形容詞 adjectival noun;
名詞結構 nominal construction;
名詞句 nominal sentence;
名詞派生形容詞 denominal adjective;
名詞性從句 nominal clause;
名詞性關係從句 nominal relative clause;
名詞性物主代詞 nominal possessive pronoun;
名詞修飾語 adnominal;
抽象名詞 abstract noun;
單位名詞 unit noun;
動名詞 gerund;
~動名詞從句 gerundive clause;
~動名詞短語 gerund phrase;
~半動名詞 half-gerund;
~準動名詞 quasi-gerund;
動物名詞 animate noun;
~非動物名詞 inanimate noun;
動作名詞 action noun;
複合名詞 compound noun;
個體名詞 individual noun;
功能名詞 function noun;
活動名詞 event noun;
集合名詞 collective noun;
集體名詞 collective noun;
具體名詞 concrete noun;
可變名詞 variable noun;
可數名詞 count noun; countable noun;
~不可數名詞 uncountable noun;
類名詞 class noun;
歷史名詞 historical term;
普通名詞 common noun;
群體名詞 mass noun;
施動者名詞 agent noun;
物質名詞 material noun;
新名詞 new term;
中心名詞 head noun;
專有名詞 proper noun;

[名次] position in a name list;
名次排列表 ranking list;
排列名次 arrange the names;
爭名次 compete for places;

[名單] name list; roster;
保存名單 keep the name list;
僱員名單 employment list;
黑名單 blacklist;
~被當局列入黑名單 be blacklisted by the authorities;
~被列入黑名單 be put on the blacklist;
~上了黑名單 be written on a black list; on the black list;
會員名單 membership list;
擴充名單 extend the list;
列出名單 compile a name list;
入伍名單 list of recruits;
傷亡名單 the casualty list;
一份名單 a list of names;
一張名單 a list of names;
~列一張名單 make out a list of names;

[名額] number of people assigned or allowed; quota;
名額已滿 the quota has been filled;
名額有限 the number of people allowed is

limited;
代表名額 the number of deputies allowed;
招生名額 planned enrolment figure;

[名分] person's status;

[名貴] famous and precious; rare;
名貴藥材 rare medical herbs;

[名家] (1) famous expert; master; person of academic distinction; (2) School of Logicians;
名家巨擘 celebrated masters;

[名將] famous general; great soldier;

[名叫] answer to the name of; be called; be known as; be named; by name; by the name of; in the person of; of the name of; rejoice in the name of;

[名教] Confucian ethical code;

[名節] reputation and integrity;
名節處死 honour killing;
保全名節 ensure a spotless name and preserve integrity;

[名酒] vintage wine;

[名利] fame and fortune; fame and gain; fame and wealth;
名利雙收 achieve both fame and fortune; gain both fame and wealth; gain both honour and money; win fame and fortune;
名利心 barnal ambition;
不為名，不為利 not work for fame or gain; seek neither fame nor gain;
淡泊名利 indifferent to fame and wealth;
澹泊名利 indifferent towards fame and wealth;
貿名貿利 buy fame and scheme after gain;
名韁利鎖 bondage of reputation and wealth; fetters of fame and wealth;
名引利誘 lure sb by the promise of fame and profit;
求名求利 aim after fame and fortune; pursue fame and fortune; seek fame and wealth; seek name and gain; set one's mind on obtaining fame and wealth;
眩於名利 be dazzled by the prospect of fame and wealth; be obsessed with a desire for fame and wealth;
營名營利 strive for fame and wealth;
爭名奪利 crave for personal fame and gain; spend one's energies in pursuit of fame and fortune; struggle for fame and wealth;
醉心名利 be infatuated with fame and gain;

[名列] be ranked; rank;
名列鰲頭 lead the list; one's name stands first on the list;
名列榜首 rank first;
名列第二 rank second;
名列第三 get the third place; rank third;
名列第一 rank first; take the first place;
名列前茅 at the top of the list; bear away the bell; come out at the top; come out in front; come out on top; come to the fore; lead the list; take the cake; top the list;

[名流] celebrities; distinguished personages;

[名錄] directory;
行名錄 trade directory;
~企業行名錄 business directory;
~書商行名錄 book trade directory;

[名落孫山] come a cropper; fail; fail to pass the examination; take a plough;

[名門] distinguished family; illustrious family;
名門出高人 a remarkable place produces outstanding people;
名門閨秀 daughter of an eminent family;
名門望族 a notable family and great clan — gentility;
名門之後 descendants of an eminent family;
出身名門 come from an illustrious family;
系出名門 come of a noble family;

[名模] famous model; supermodel;
超級名模 supermodel;

[名目] items; names of things;
名目繁多 a host of names; a multitude of names; names of every description;
巧立名目 by various subterfuges; concoct various pretexts; extort taxes under all sorts of names; fabricate various excuses; invent all kinds of pretexts; invent all sorts of names; make a lot of money by various subterfuges; rack one's brains for ingenious devices; under all sorts of names; under all sorts of pretexts;

[名牌] (1) big-name brand; brand name; designation strip; famous brand; name brand prestige; (2) name tag;
名牌產品 brand-name products;

M

名牌大學 prestigious university;
名牌的 branded;
名牌服裝 designer label;
名牌商品 name brand;
名牌香煙 brand-name cigarettes;
名牌衣服 clothes of best brands;
名牌戰略 brand-name strategy;
迷信名牌 have blind faith in famous brands;
主打名牌 premium brand;

[名片] calling card; name card; visiting card;
名片效應 name card effect;
保留名片 keep sb's calling card;
遞上自己的名片 send up one's calling card;
互贈名片 exchange calling cards;
留下名片 leave one's calling card;
印制名片 print calling cards;

[名氣] fame; name; reputation;
名氣很大 of wide fame; very famous;
很有名氣 very famous;
獲得名氣 achieve fame; find fame;
賣名氣 capitalize on one's reputation;
沒有名氣 unknown;
沒有一點名氣 have no fame at all;
小有名氣 popular;
贏得名氣 gain fame; win fame;
有點名氣 enjoy some reputation;

[名曲] masterpiece in music;

[名人] biggie; celebrity; eminent person; famous person; great card; luminary; notable; sleb;
名人廣告 notable advertising;
名人錄 list of celebrities;
名人名言 famous sayings of famous people;
名人世界 the notables' world;
成為名人 become an eminent person;
崇拜名人 worship celebrities;
想做名人 dream of becoming a famous person;

[名山] famous mountains;
名山大剎 famous mountains and magnificent temples;
名山事業 an author's works are destined for posterity;

[名聲] renown; reputation; repute;
名聲不好的 disreputable;
名聲大振 win a wide reputation;
名聲過實 enjoy a higher reputation than justified;
名聲好 enjoy a good reputation;
名聲很壞 be held in ill repute;
名聲掃地 have ruined one's reputation;
名聲遠揚 blaze of fame;
敗壞名聲 defame;
搞壞名聲 disrepute;
損害名聲 blemish one's reputation;
追求名聲 seek fame;

[名勝] beauty spot; scenic spot;
名勝古跡 celebrated historic and cultural sites; famous cultural and historical sites; famous places of interest and relics of olden times; places of historic interest; scenic spots and ancient monuments; scenic spots of historical significance;
名勝區 scenic spots;
保護名勝 preserve scenic spots;
破壞名勝 destry places famous for their historical relics;

[名實] concept and its objective being; name and reality;
名實不符 have an undeserved reputation; reality doesn't correspond to its name; the name falls short of the reality; the reality belies its name; unworthy of the name;
名實相符 reality corresponds to its name; the name matches the reality; worthy of the name;
名不符實 hollow reputation without basis; in reality, it is not what it is said to be; more in name than in reality; not worthy of one's name; the name does not agree with the deeds; the name does not match the reality; the reality belies its name; the title and the reality do not tally; unworthy of the name;
名存實亡 cease to exist except in name; exist in name only; have a mere nominal existence; only a shadow; only an empty title; survive in name only;
名符其實 in every sense of the word; in fact as well as in name; in name and in fact; in reality as well as in name; in the true sense of the terms; live up to the name; true to one's name; veritable; worthy of the name;
名過其實 have an exaggerated reputation; sth more in name than in reality;

名貿實易 the same in appearance but different essentially;
實至名歸 fame follows merit; when one makes a real achievement he becomes known;
循名責實 create the reality that will fit the name; expect the reality to correspond to the name; live up to its name; see that the reality matches the name;
有名無實 a mere name; a poor apology; exist in name only; impressive but worthless; in name but not in reality; in show; it is so in name but not in reality; merely nominal; only a name; remain in name only; symbolic; titular;
有名有實 in name and in fact;
有實無名 in all but name; in everything but name; in name only;

[名士] (1) person with a literary reputation; (2) celebrity with no official post;
名士才媛 famous scholars and gifted ladies;
名士風流 elegance of talents; gaity of renowned scholars; unconventional ways of scholars;
名士派 unconventional and self-indulgent old-style intellectual;
名士淑媛 wit and beauty of the town;
斗方名士 person posed as a literary pursuer;
是真名士自風流 real scholar can afford to be eccentric; true wits make elegant whatever they touch;

[名手] famous artist;

[名堂] (1) achievements; results; (2) reasons; (3) items; variety;
搞不出名堂 cannot achieve anything; cannot produce any significant results;
搞出名堂 achieve sth;
搞甚麼名堂 what gives;
有名堂 show encouraging signs;

[名望] fame and prestige; good reputation; renown;
名望很低 of low standing;
名望很高 of high standing;
保持名望 keep up one's fame and prestige;
失去名望 lose one's good reputation;
享有名望 enjoy fame and prestige;
贏得名望 earn one's spurs; win one's spurs;
有名望 distinguished; famous; noted; prestigious; renowned;

[名位] fame and position;

[名聞] one's name is known;
名聞全國 one's name is known throughout the land;
名聞四海 be renowned throughout the four seas; one's name is known throughout the country;
名聞天下 one is known far and wide; world-famous;
名聞遐邇 be known far and wide; one's name spreads far and wide;
名聞於世 famous all the world over; world-famous;
名聞遠近 be known throughout the world; be renowned far and ear;
名聞中外 be known in China and abroad; be well known both at home and abroad;

[名物] name and description of a thing;

[名下] belonging to sb; related to sb; under sb's name;
名下無虛 have a well-deserved reputation; one's reputation is justified; the reputation is well supported by fact;

[名學] logic;

[名言] celebrated dictum; famous remark; well-known saying;
成為名言 become a famous remark;
傳播名言 spread celebrated dicta;
收集名言 collect well-known sayings;
至理名言 a celebrated dictum; a golden saying; a proverb of lasting value; a quotable quote; a truthful remark; an axiom;

[名醫] famous doctor;
遍訪名醫 consult all famous physicians one can find;

[名義] (1) name; (2) in name;
名義工資 nominal wage;
名義合伙人 nominal partner;
名義上 nominally;
名義上的總統 a titular president;
盜用名義 illegally use the name of; usurp a name;
顧名思義 as its very name implies; as the name indicates; as the name suggests; as the term suggests; just as its name implies; seeing the name of one thing one thinks of its function; the very

name suggests that;
以…名義 in the name of;

[名優] (1) famous actor or actress; (2) famous and of excellent quality;
名優產品 brand-name and quality products;
名優特產品 brand-name, high quality and local products;
名優新產品 brand-name, high quality and new products;

[名譽] (1) fame; reputation; (2) honourary;
名譽擔保 on one's honour;
名譽會員 honorary member;
名譽教授 honorary professor;
名譽掃地 be discredited; be left without a shred of reputation; black eye; come to dishonour; dishonoured reputation; fall into disrepute; lose all standing; one's name is dirt; one's name is mud; out of the window;
名譽攸關 affect one's reputation; one's reputation is at stake;
名譽主席 honorary chairman; honorary president;
敗壞名譽 damage the reputation of; defame; discredit;
保持名譽 retain a reputation;
保全名譽 preserve one's reputation;
不名譽 disgraceful; disreputable;
詆毀名譽 forfeit one's reputation; ruin one's reputation;
沾污自己名譽 blot one's copybook;
干名採譽 seek publicity;
恢復名譽 rehabilitation;
喪失名譽 disrepute;
失名譽 lose a good name;
提高名譽 enhance one's reputation;
追名求譽 chase for fame and honour;
追求名譽 aspire to fame;

[名媛] famous lady;
貴閣名媛 great lady; lady from a noble family;

[名正言順] a correct title and weighty words; come within one's jurisdiction; fitting and proper;
名不正則言不順 if the name is not correct, the words will not ring true;

[名之所在，謗之所歸] when fame is, there will slanders gathered together;

[名著] famous work; masterpiece; masterwork;
瀏覽名著 browse through famous works;
一部名著 a classic;

[名字] (1) first name; forename; given name; moniker; name; (2) title;
報錯名字 give a wrong name;
錯誤的名字 misnomer;
給人取名字 give sb a name;
冒用別人的名字 assume another's name;
起個名字 name sb;
取有名字 have a name;
寫下自己的名字 put one's name down;

敗名 disgrace oneself; tarnish one's reputation;
報名 register for school, etc; sign up;
輩名 generation name;
本名 formal name;
筆名 pen name; pseudonym;
標名 label; title;
別名 alias; another name; second name;
成名 become famous; come to fame; make a name for oneself; make one's name;
馳名 famous; known far and wide; renowned; well-known;
臭名 infamy; notoriety;
出名 famous; make a name for oneself; make one's mark; make one's name; renown; rise to fame; to a proverb; well-known; win a name for oneself;
除名 expunge sb's name from a list; remove sb's name from the rolls; strike one's name off; take sb's name off the books;
大名 (1) formal personal name; (2) your name;
擔名 assume a certain status;
地名 place name;
點名 (1) call the roll; (2) mention sb by name;
定名 choose name for; name;
惡名 bad reputation;
芳名 female's name;
浮名 undeserved reputation;
更名 change one's name;
功名 scholarly honour;
沽名 fish for fame;
掛名 only in name;
戶名 name in account book;
化名 alias; assumed name; use an assumed name;
諢名 nickname;
記名 put down one's name;
假名 (1) pseudonym; (2) kana;
具名 affix one's signature; put one's name to a document, etc.;
聯名 sign jointly;

令名 good name; good reputation;
罵名 bad name; infamy;
美名 good name; good reputation;
命名 name;
奶名 child's pet name; infant name;
匿名 anonymous;
品名 name of an article; name of commodity;
齊名 be equally famous;
簽名 sign one's name;
乳名 child's pet name; infant name;
聲名 reputation;
盛名 great reputation;
書名 title of a book;
署名 put one's signature to; sign;
俗名 local name; popular name;
提名 nominate;
題名 (1) give one's autograph as a memento; (2) title; topic; (3) inscribe one's name;
同名 of the same name or title;
土名 local name;
托名 do sth in sb else's name;
威名 awe-inspiring reputation; prestige;
聞名 famous; well-known;
無名 nameless; unknown;
小名 pet name for a child;
姓名 full name; surname and personal name;
虛名 bubble reputation; undeserved reputation;
學名 (1) scientific name; (2) formal name used at school;
揚名 become famous; become known;
徼名 seek fame;
易名 change one's name;
異名 different name;
隱名 conceal one's name;
有名 celebrated; well-known;
知名 celebrated; famous;
指名 mention by name;
著名 celebrated; famous; noted;
專名 proper noun;
罪名 accusation; charge;

ming

【明】 (1) bright; brilliant; light; (2) clear; distinct; (3) explicit; open; overt; (4) clear-sighted; sharp-eyed; (5) above-board; honest; (6) sight; (7) know; understand; (8) immediately following in time;

[明暗] light and shade;
半明半暗 half-bright and half-shadowy;
忽明忽暗 go in and out; keep flickering;
化暗為明 change dark into light; legalize what is underground traffic;
或明或暗 either overt or covert;
兼聽則明，偏聽則暗 both sides must present their opinions;
兼信則明，偏信則暗 listen to both sides and you will be enlightened, heed only one side and you will be benighted;
明棄暗取 discard openly but take secretly; give away openly and take in secretly — rejecting a thing publicly while taking it secretly;
明灘暗礁 beaches and reefs;
棄暗投明 abandon darkness for light; abandon one's evil ways and follow the path of righteousness; abandon the shade for the sunlight; come over to the side of progress; flee from darkness into the light; forsake darkness and cross over to brightness; forsake darkness for light; give up one's sinful life and live a virtuous life; leave darkness for light; quit the reactionary camp and come over to the side of progress;
棄明投暗 leave the light and plunge into darkness;
若明若暗 a blurred picture of; ambiguous; equivocal; have a hazy notion about; have only a vague idea of; now open now covert; semitransparent; translucent;

[明白] bring home to sb; catch sth; catch the drift of argument; clear; comprehend; dawn on sb; follow; get the drift of; grasp; intelligible; know; make out; make sense of; see; see the drift of; twig; understand;
明白表示 clear expression;
明白了嗎 do you understand;
明白了當 straightforward;
明白人 perceptive person;
~是個明白人 sensible person;
明白如話 as plain as ordinary speech; plain and easy to understand;
明白事理 have good sense; know a thing or two; know one's business; know what is what; reasonable; sensible;
明白易曉 easily understandable; intelligible;
纔明白 understand for the first time;

M

肚裏明白 be clear to oneself; know in one's heart;
講個明白 have a crow to pick with sb; have a crow to pluck with sb; have a crow to pull with sb;
開始明白 cotton on; dawn on;
聽不明白 cannot understand;
突然明白 twig;
終於明白 the penny has dropped;

[明暢] lucid and smooth;
文筆明暢 write in clear and lucid style;
譯文明暢 the translation is clear and lucid;

[明澈] bright and limpid; transparent;
明澈如鏡 as bright and limpid as a mirror;

[明處] (1) where there is light; (2) in public; in the open;
一在明處，一在暗處 one is acting under cover whil eht other is in the open;
有話説在明處 say sth openly;

[明窗淨几] a bright room and clean furniture; a neat desk before a bright window;

[明達] reasonable; showing understanding;
明達公正 sensible and fairminded;
明達賢惠 sensible and virtuous;

[明燈] beacon; bright lamp;
火在遠處是明燈，它在近處燒灼人 the fire which lights up at a distance will burn us when near;

[明矾] alum;
明矾石 alumstone;
銨明矾 ammonium alum;
酸性明矾 acid alum;
鐵明矾 iron alum;
造紙明矾 paper-maker's alum;

[明晃晃] gleaming; shining;

[明慧] wise;

[明火] naked light; open fire;
明火打劫 open robbery; rob with torches and weapons;

[明膠] gelatin;
感光明膠 photographic gelatin;
工業明膠 technical gelatin;
酸法明膠 acid gelatin;
碎粒明膠 kibbled gelatin;
營養明膠 nutrient gelatin;

[明淨] bright and clean; clear and bright;
明淨的天空 the clear and bright sky;

[明鏡] bright mirror;
明鏡高懸 a bright mirror hung high — a just trial by an honest official;

[明快] (1) lucid and lively; sprightly; (2) forthright; straightforward;
辦事明快 handle affairs in a forthright way;
筆調明快 write in a lucid and lively style;
節奏明快 have springtly rhythm;
性格明快 possess a forthright character;

[明朗] (1) bright and clear; (2) clear; obvious; (3) bright and cheerful; forthright;
明朗的秋天 the bright and clear autumn;
明朗的天空 a clear sky;
明朗的月色 bright moonlight;
格調明朗 have a sanguine style;
態度明朗 adopt an unequivocal attitude;
性格明朗 have a cheerful temperament;

[明麗] bright and beautiful;
明麗的秋色 the bright and beautiful autumn scene;

[明亮] (1) bright; light; well-lit; (2) bright; shining; (3) become clear;
明亮的星星 shining stars;
明亮的眼睛 bright eyes;
感到明亮 become clear;

[明了] (1) clear about; clearly understand; (2) clear; intelligibility; plain;

[明令] formal decree; public proclamation;
明令嘉獎 issue a commendation;
明令禁止 prohibit by explicit order;
明令取締 proscribe by formal decree;

[明碼] (1) plain code; (2) with the price clearly marked;
明碼實價 at marked prices; with net prices clearly marked;
明碼售貨 sell at marked prices;

[明媒正娶] formal wedding; marry into sb's house in an open and proper manner; right and legal marriage;

[明媚] bright and beautiful; radiant and enchanting;
明媚的夏日 radiant and enchanting day in summer;
明媚的陽光 bright and beautiful sunshine;
明媚嫺雅，端莊瑩靜 charming yet reserved;
春光明媚 it is a beautiful spring day;
河山明媚 the land is of enchanting beauty;

[明滅] appear and disappear;
忽明忽滅 fitful; suddenly it appears and disappears;

[明明] evidently; it is as plain as daylight that;

it is clear that; plainly; obviously; there can be no doubt that; undoubtedly;
明明白白 as clear as noonday; as clear as the sun at noonday; plain and clear; plain and to the point;
明明赫赫 shine brightly;

[明眸] bright eyes;
明眸皓齒 comely; have bright eyes and white teeth;
明眸善睞 clear eyes with a winning look; shining eyes and attractive looks; the enticing glances of a beauty; the fond gazing of a beauty;
明眸秀眉 clear-eyes with a winning look; enticing glances of a beauty; fond gazing of a beauty;

[明目張膽] before one's very eye; brazen; daringly; fearlessly; in a bare-faced manner; in a flagrant way; openly and wantonly; without caring for any onlookers;
明目張膽做壞事 commit a crime undisguised;

[明年] next year;

[明確] (1) clear and definite; clear-cut; explicit; hard-and-fast; unequivocal; (2) make clear; make definite;
明確表達 refinement;
明確的 clear-cut;
明確說明 offer some clarification on sth;
陳述明確 explicit in one's statement;
答覆明確 give a definite answer;
來意明確 have a distinct intention of coming;
立場明確 take a clear-cut stand;
目的明確 have a clear aim;
指示明確 give explicit directions;

[明人] honest man; person of good sense; wise man;
明人不說暗話 put one's cards on the table;
明人不用細說 a person of good sense sees the game best — needs no explanation;
明人不做暗事 a gentleman must not do anything underhand; a person who is aboveboard does nothing underhand; an honest man does not engage in clandestine dealings; an honest man does nothing underhand; an honest man doesn't do anything underhand;
明人有自知之明 a wise man knows his own limitations;

[明日] (1) tomorrow; (2) near future;
明日黃花 a topic no longer of current interest; overblown blossoms; sth out of fashion; things of the past; things that are past their time;

[明誓] make a pledge; take an oath;

[明說] speak frankly; speak openly;
不便明說 not suitable to speak openly;
不能明說 cannot be stated frankly;

[明太魚] stock fish;

[明天] (1) tomorrow; (2) near future;
明天見 see you tomorrow;
明天晚上 tomorrow evening;
明天早上 tomorrow morning;

[明晚] tomorrow evening;

[明文] proclaimed in writing;
明文規定 clearly stipulated in writing; stipulate explicity; stipulate in explicit terms;
史無明文 there is no historical evidence to that effect;

[明晰] clear; distinct;
表達明晰 express oneself clearly;
講解明晰 explain clearly;
說話明晰 speak distinctly;

[明顯] clear; distinct; evident; obvious; sharp;
效果明顯 the good results are evident;

[明效大驗] have much effect; striking effectiveness;

[明信片] postal card; postcard;
不雅明信片 saucy postcard;
寄明信片 send postcards;
製明信片 make postcards; print postcards;

[明星] celebrity; star;
明星企業 top enterprises;
明星雲集的 star-studded;
超級明星 megastar;
炒明星 create a star through publicity; make a person famous;
崇拜明星 worship stars;
大明星 big star;
電影明星 film star; movie star;
~二流的電影明星 two-bit movie star;
~過氣的電影明星 washed-up movie star;
~性感迷人的電影明星 sultry movie star;
朗月明星 a bright moon and illuminating stars;
目似明星 one's eyes are like lustrous stars;
全明星的 all-star;

戲劇和電影兩棲明星 star of stage and screen;
想當明星 dream of being a movie star;
追逐明星 pursue the stars;
足球明星 football star;

[明刑弼教] integrate punishment with education;

[明眼人] person of good sense; person with a discerning eye; those who have discerning eyes;
明眼人一看便知 anyone with a discerning eye can easily see;
是個明眼人 person of good sense;

[明喻] simile;
靜態結構明喻 static-structural simile;

[明月] bright moon;
明月初上 the bright moon was just emerging;
明月初照 the bright moon begins to shine;
明月當空 a bright moon is shining in the sky;
明月高掛 the moon rides high in the sky; the round, snow-white moon suspends in the sky;
明月寒光 a chilled light seeps from the bright moon;
明月良宵 it is a beautiful warm night with a bright moon;
明月清風 bright moon and gentle breeze;
明月秋空 the silvery bright moon in the clear autumn sky;
明月星空 a bright moon was shining in the starry sky;
明月映湖 the bright moon is calmly reflected in the lake;
明月映雪 the bright moon shines on the heaped snow;
明月載途 the moon is shingly brightly and the path is clearly illuminated;
明月之夜 a moonlit night;
一輪明月 a bright moon; a full bright moon; a full moon; shining white orb of the full moon; the disk of a bright moon;

[明早] tomorrow morning;

[明證] a case in point; clear proof; evidence; token;
出示明證 produce clear proof;
得到明證 get clear proof;
提供明證 supply a clear proof;
需要明證 require clear proof;

[明知] aware; know perfectly well;
明知不對，少說為佳 say as little as possible while knowing perfectly well what is wrong; the less said the better about things that are clearly known to be wrong;
明知故犯 break a law on purpose; commit a crime wilfully; commit an offense on purpose; do sth one knows is wrong; deliberately break a law; knowingly violate the law;
明知故問 ask a question so as to embarrass someone; ask while knowing the answer;
明知山有虎，偏向虎山行 go on undeterred by the dangers ahead;

[明智] sagacious; sensible; wise;
明智的 sensible;
~明智的人 sensible person;
~不明智的 airy fairy;
明智舉措 sagacious measures;
明智之舉 a wise move;

[明珠] bright pearl; jewel;
明珠暗投 a good person fallen among bad company; fling a gleaming pearl into darkness;
明珠美玉 brilliant pearls and beautiful works in jade;
明珠泥埋 fail to bring sb's talent to public notice;
明珠彈雀 gains cannot offset losses; shoot a sparrow with bright pearls — pay too dear for one's whistle; the game is not worth the candle;
掌上明珠 a pearl on the palm — a beloved daughter; one's dear daughter; the apple of one's eye;

報明 state clearly to the higher authorities;
辨明 clear up; make a clear distinction between;
標明 indicate; mark;
表明 indicate; state clearly;
稟明 clarify a matter to a superior; explain to a superior;
不明 (1) not clear; unknown; (2) fail to understand;
查明 find out; prove through investigation;
闡明 clarify; enunciate; expound; shed light on; throw light on;
昌明 flourishing; thriving;
聰明 clever; intelligent;
發明 (1) invent; invention; (2) expound;

分明 clear; clearly; evidently; obvious;
高明 brilliant; master-hand; qualified person; wise;
光明 (1) light; (2) bright; (3) open-hearted;
晦明 dusky or sunny; night and day;
簡明 concise; simple and clear;
精明 bright; smart;
開明 enlightened;
黎明 dawn; daybreak;
流明 lumen;
判明 ascertain; discriminate; distinguish;
平明 daybreak;
齊明 aplanatic;
申明 declare; state;
神明 deities; gods;
聲明 announce; announcement; declaration; declare; statement;
聖明 of keen intelligence and excellent judgment;
失明 go blind; lose one's sight;
説明 (1) explain; illustrate; (2) direction; explanation; show;
通明 brightly lit; well-illustrated;
透明 transparent;
文明 civilization; civilized; culture;
鮮明 (1) (of colour) bright; (2) clear-cut; distinct;
賢明 wise and able;
顯明 distinct; obvious;
詳明 clear and explicit; detailed and clear;
修明 honest and enlightened;
羞明 phtophobia;
宣明 announce; declare;
言明 state clearly;
英明 brilliant; wise;
幽明 the world of the living and that of the dead;
月明 the moon is bright;
載明 record clearly;
彰明 clarify;
注明 give clear indication testify;

ming
【冥】 (1) dark; obscure; (2) deep; profound; (3) dull; stupid; (4) netherworld; underworld;
[冥鈔] nether banknotes;
[冥器] burial object; funerary object;
[冥思] meditate;
冥思出神 in a brown study;
冥思靜坐 transcendental meditation;
冥思苦想 be lost in serious and hard thinking; beat one's brains out; contemplate; cudgel one's brains; in a brown study; puzzle over; rack one's brains; think long and hard;
[冥頑] stupid; thickheaded;
冥頑不靈 callous; dead to all feeling; dull and stupid; impenetrably thickheaded; insensate; silly and clumsy;
[冥想] deep thoughts; meditation; think deeply;
[冥行盲索] fell sth in the dark; walk in the dark and touch blindly;

幽冥 dark; shadowy; the nether world;

ming
【茗】 tea plant; tea;
[茗具] tea set;

ming
【酩】 a pronunciation of 酩;

ming
【溟】 (1) drizzle; (2) boundless; vast; (3) sea;

ming
【暝】 dark; obscure;

晦暝 gloomy; obscure;

ming
【瞑】 night;
[瞑目] close one's eyes in death; die content;
瞑目長眠 rest in peace — said of a dead man;
瞑目長逝 close one's eyes forever;
瞑目而逝 close one's eyes and die;
瞑目九泉 may one's soul rest in peace;
甘心瞑目 die at peace; die content; die without dissatisfaction;
死不瞑目 cannot die in peace; die discontent; die dissatisfied; die with everlasting regret; die with injustice unredressed; die without closing one's eyes; turn in one's grave;

ming
【銘】 (1) inscription; (2) engrave;
[銘感] deeply grateful;
銘感不忘 everlastingly grateful; remember with gratitude always;
銘感肺腑 be borne firmly in mind;
銘感五內 be held in sb's grateful remembrance; engrave on sb's heart;
銘感五中 be held in sb's grateful

M

remembrance; engrave on sb's heart;
銘感終身 remain deeply grateful for the rest of one's life;

[銘饑鏤骨] be engraved on the flesh and bone—everlasting gratitude; feel deep gratitude;

[銘記] always remember; bear firmly in mind; engrave on one's mind;
銘記不忘 be branded on sb's memory; be engraved on the heat and memory; be engraved on the mind; be inscribed on sb's memory; bear in mind; sink into the mind; stick in sb's mind;
銘記國恥 always remember national humiliation;
銘記於心 be engraved on sb's heart; be engraved on the mind; be enshrined in the heart; be implanted in sb's bosom; be impressed on sb's memory; bear in mind; embalm in the memory; enshrine in one's memory; imprint on one's mind; sink into sb's mind; store up in one's heart; treasure up in one's memory;
銘記在心 be engraved on sb's heart; be engraved on the mind; be enshrined in the heart; be implanted in sb's bosom; be impressed on sb's memory; bear in mind; embalm in the memory; enshrine in one's memory; imprint on one's mind; sink into sb's mind; store up in one's heart; treasure up in one's memory;

[銘刻] (1) inscription; (2) engrave; engrave on one's mind;
銘刻於心 be enthroned in the hearts; imprint on one's heart;
銘刻在心 be enthroned in the hearts; imprint on one's heart;

[銘文] (1) epigraph; (2) inscription;

[銘心] always remember; imprint on one's mind;
銘心刻骨 always remember; be imprinted on one's bones and in one's heart — bear in mind forever; engrave on the heart;
刻骨銘心 be engraved on one's bones and heart; be remembered with deep gratitude; eternal gratitude; imprint on the bones and inscribe on the memory — bear in mind forever; remember with gratitude to the end of one's life;
鏤骨銘心 engrave on the bones and imprint on the heart — remember forever with gratitude; wholeheartedly grateful to sb;

碑銘 inscription on a tablet;

ming
【鳴】 (1) cry of birds, animals or insects; (2) ring; sound; (3) air; express; voice;

[鳴笛] blow; whistle;
鳴笛志哀 sound the siren in mourning;
禁止鳴笛 no tooting;

[鳴放] airing of views;

[鳴鼓] beat the drums;
鳴鼓而攻之 attack sb publicly and severely by concerted action; beat the drum and launch the attack — make a scathing indictment; sound the call for attack;
金鼓齊鳴 all the gongs and drums are beating; gongs and drums beat all around; gongs and drums sound; the sound of gongs and drums arise; there is a great noise of drums and gongs;

[鳴號] sound the bugle; trumpet;

[鳴鑼] beat gongs;
鳴鑼擊鼓 beat drums and clang gongs; beat gongs and drums;
鳴鑼聚眾 beat the gongs to collect the people — for a meeting; collect people by beating the gong;
鳴鑼開道 beat the gong and shout to clear the way; clear the way for; open up a road to; prepare the public for a coming event; serve as a huckster for; sound the gongs to clear a way for;
鳴鑼示警 give a warning by beating a gong;

[鳴槍] fire a shot; fire rifles into the air;
鳴槍恫嚇 fire shots to scare sb;
鳴槍示警 fire a warning shot; open fire as a warning;

[鳴響] peal; tingle;

[鳴鐘] toll;
鳴鐘報警 sound the alarm bell;
鳴鐘報時 the clock strikes the hour;
鳴鐘擊鼓 strike the bell and beat the drum;
鳴鐘術 campanology;

哀鳴 wail; whine;
悲鳴 lament; utter sad calls;
喘鳴 stridor;
腹鳴 borborygmus;
共鳴 (1) resonance; (2) sympathetic response;
嗥鳴 howl;
爭鳴 contend;

ming
【螟】 snout moth's larva;
[螟蛉義女] adopted daughter;

大螟 pink rice borer;
蔗螟 sugarcane borer;

ming³
ming
【皿】 a pronunciation of 皿;
ming
【茗】 a pronunciation of 茗;
ming
【酩】 drunk; intoxicated; tipsy;
[酩酊] dead drunk;
酩酊大醉 as drunk as a boiled owl; as drunk as a fiddler; as drunk as a lord; as drunk as a piper; as drunk as a sow; as drunk as an owl; beastly drunk; blind drunk; dead drunk; dead to the wide; drunk and incapable; extremely drunk; full to the gills; go to bed in one's boots; have been in the sun; have the sun in one's eyes; higher than a kite; lose one's legs; out like a light; stew to the gills; stinking drunk; three sheets in the wind; under the table; up to the gills;
ming
【瞑】 a pronunciation of 瞑;
ming⁴
ming
【命】 (1) life; (2) destiny; fate; lot; (3) command; order; (4) assign;
[命案] homicide case;
[命筆] set pen to paper; take up one's pen;
命筆疾書 write down as inspiration dictates;
欣然命筆 happy to start writing;
[命薄] one's life is brief;
命薄如花 one's life as brief as a flower — the short life of a woman;
命薄如紙 one's luck is as thin as paper — the brevity of life;
[命定] be determined by fate; predestined;
[命根子] one's very life; one's very lifeblood;
[命好] lead a charmed life;
[命令] adjure; command; fiat; order;
命令句 command;
命令熄燈 order lights out;
命令虛擬語氣 mandative subjunctive;
命令語言 command language;
頒布命令 issue an order;
撤回命令 withdraw a command;
重述命令 repeat an order;
等待命令 await a command;
發佈命令 issue a command;
發出命令 give orders;
發送命令 dispatch orders;
法庭命令 court order;
服從命令 follow an order; hew the line; hew to the line; obey orders; toe the line; toe the mark; toe the scratch;
接到命令 receive an order;
接受命令 take orders;
拒絕執行命令 refuse to obey orders;
取消命令 countermand one's order;
收到命令 receive orders;
違反命令 violate the command;
無視命令 disobey order; disregard an order; ignore an order;
下命令 give orders; issue an order;
~下達命令 issue orders;
一道命令 an order;
一項命令 an instruction;
直接命令 direct order;
執行命令 carry out an order;
[命脈] lifeblood; lifeline;
國脈民命 the existence as a nation and people;
經濟命脈 economic arteries;
[命名] name; nomenclature; nominate;
命名典禮 naming ceremony;
命名日 name day;
重新命名 rename;
[命若懸絲] one's life hanging by a thread — at death's door; one's life hangs in the balance — at the point of death;
[命數] destiny; fate; lot;
命數已盡 one's hour has come; one's hour has struck;
[命題] (1) assign a topic; set a question; (2) proposition;

M

命題學習 proposition study;
命題意義 propositional meaning;
命題運演 propositional calculus;
存在命題 existential proposition;
等值命題 equivalent propositions;
分析命題 analytic proposition;
基本命題 elementary proposition;
肯定命題 affirmative proposition;
相反命題 contrary propositions;
選言命題 disjunctive proposition;

[命途多舛] adverse fortune; down on one's luck; suffer many a setback during one's life; thorny roads lie ahead;

[命運] destiny; fate; fortune; lot;
命運擺佈 fate ordains one's destiny;
命運不濟 down on one's luck;
命運蹉跎 adverse fate; bad fortune;
命運未卜 uncertain fate;
命運已定 one's destiny is decreed; the lot is cast;
命運注定 fate ordains our destiny;
命運捉弄人 fate always teases people;
擺脱…的命運 escape the fate of…;
~擺脱失敗的命運 save oneself from defeat;
悲慘的命運 sad fate; tragic fate;
殘酷的命運 cruel fate;
可怕的命運 terrible fate;
恐怖的命運 horrible fate;
忍受命運 endure one's lot;
委諸命運 abandon to fate;
相似的命運 similar fate;
相同的命運 same fate;
嚴酷的命運 grim fate;
影響命運 affect the destiny of sth/sb;
掌握自己的命運 master of one's own destiny; master of one's own fate;
支配命運 control the destiny;
最終命運 ultimate fate;

[命中] hit the mark; hit the target; score a hit;
命中靶心 hit the bull's-eye;
命中率高 reach a high percentage of hits;
命中目標 hit the target;
未命中 fail to score the hit;
直接命中 direct hit;

安命 accept one's lot; content with one's lot;
保命 preserve one's life; survive;
奔命 (1) be kept on the run; in a desperate hurry; run for one's life; rush about on errands; (2) do one's best; go all out;
畢命 end one's life;
稟命 at the behest of; by order of;
斃命 meet violent death;
薄命 born under an unlucky star; fate is unkind to; ill-fated; ill-starred;
長命 long life; longevity;
償命 a life for a life; pay with one's life;
成命 order already issued;
從命 obey an order;
催命 keep pressing sb to do sth;
待命 await orders;
抵命 a life for a life; pay with one's life;
度命 make a living;
短命 die young; short-lived;
奉命 act under orders; receive orders;
復命 report on completion of a mission, etc;
革命 make revolution; revolution;
浩命 (1) imperial mandate; (2) woman who was conferred an official title;
活命 (1) earn a bare living; scrape along; (2) save sb's life;
救命 save sb's life;
抗命 defy orders; disobey;
賣命 (1) work oneself to the bone for sb; (2) die for;
沒命 (1) die; lose one's life; (2) desperately; recklessly;
民命 people's life;
拼命 (1) risk one's life; (2) do sth desperately; exert the utmost strength;
請命 plead on sb's behalf;
人命 human life;
任命 appoint;
認命 resign oneself to destiny;
辱命 fail to live up to the expectation of one's superior;
捨命 risk one's life; sacrifice oneself;
生命 life;
使命 mission;
受命 be committed to undertake a task;
授命 (1) give one's life; (2) give orders;
壽命 life; life-span;
死命 death; desperately; doom;
送命 get killed; lose one's life;
算命 tell fortune;
逃命 flee for one's life;
天命 destiny; fate;
聽命 take orders from;
亡命 (1) flee; seek refuge; (2) become desperate;
效命 go all out to serve sb regardless of the consequences;
性命 life;
嚴命 strict order;

要命 (1) drive sb to his death; kill; (2) extremely; terribly; (3) be a nuisance;
遺命 injunctions of a dead person;
詔命 imperial edict;
致命 causing death; fatal;
自命 regard oneself as;
遵命 obey your command;

ming

【瞑】 night;

miu4
miu

【繆】 absurd; erroneous; false; preposterous;

紕繆 error; mistake;
悠繆 absurd;

miu

【謬】 erroneous; false; mistaken; wrong;
[謬采虛聲] believe mistakenly in sb's false reputation;
[謬見] absurd opinion; fallacy; false argument;
持有謬見 hold a wrong view;
發表謬見 publish falsehood;
[謬獎] make an undeserved compliment; overpraise;
[謬論] fallacy; false theory; falsehood;
駁斥謬論 refute a fallacy;
駁倒謬論 crush a fallacy;
散佈謬論 spread absurd theories;
[謬誤] error; fallacy; falsehood; mistake;
謬誤百出 numerous mistakes; there are hundreds of errors;
謬誤形成 a myth grows up;
傳播謬誤 disseminate falsehoods;
戳穿謬誤 explode a myth;
發現謬誤 detect an error;
糾正謬誤 correct the errors;
消除謬誤 get rid of mistakes;
指出謬誤 point out an error;
[謬種] error; fallacy;
謬種流傳 circulation of absurdities; dissemination of fallacy; errors being disseminated;

悖謬 absurd; preposterous;
訛謬 absurdness; error;
乖謬 abnormal; absurd;
荒謬 absurd; preposterous;
刊謬 correct errors;
悠謬 absurd;

mo1
mo

【摸】 (1) feel; stroke; touch; (2) feel for; fumble; grope for; (3) find out; get to know; sound out;
[摸不着邊] unable to touch the gate—cannot understand at all;
[摸彩] draw lot to determine the prize winners in a raffle or lottery;
[摸底] feel out; know the real situation; sound sb out; try to find out the real intention;
摸底細 feel out; sound out; try to find out the real intention or situation;
[摸骨談相] read one's character and tell his fortune by studying his bone structure; tell a person's fortune by feeling his bones;
[摸黑] grope one's way on a dark night;
摸黑前進 grope ahead through the darkness;
[摸門] find the proper approach;
摸門不著 be confused; cannot find the proper approach; not understand at all;
摸門兒 get the hang of sth; learn the ropes;
[摸清] feel out;
摸清敵情 find out about the enemy's situation;
摸清底細 ascertain the actual situation; get to the bottom of the story;
摸清情況 size up the situation;
[摸索] (1) feel about; fumble; grope; (2) try to find out;
摸索而行 grope one's way;
摸索前進 feel one's way into; grope one's way and advance; grope one's way forward;
暗中摸索 feel about in the dark; grope in the dark; grope one's way in the dark; know things only by guessing;
[摸頭] know the real situation; learn the ropes;
摸頭不著 all at sea; unable to find the proper approach or order in the whole thing; unable to make anything out of;
不摸頭 not acquainted with the situation; not up on things;

M

[摸透] get to know clearly; have an insight into;
摸不透 be puzzled; wonder;
[摸着路走] feel one's way; grope one's way;

觸摸 touch;
撈摸 fish for; get by improper means;
掏摸 search and feel;
尋摸 look for; seek;
咂摸 click the tongue;

mo²

mo

【麼】 (1) tiny; (2) special particle found in dramatic dialogues;

mo

【摩】 (1) rub; scrape; touch; (2) mull over; study;
[摩擦] (1) rub; (2) friction; (3) clash;
摩擦層 frictional layer;
摩擦力 friction force;
動摩擦 dynamical friction;
滾動摩擦 rolling friction;
滑動摩擦 break-away friction; sliding friction;
界面摩擦 boundary friction;
靜摩擦 static friction;
輪軸摩擦 axle friction;
聲腔摩擦 cavity friction;
[摩頂放踵] fear no hardships; rub smooth one's whole body from the crown to the heel; sacrifice oneself to save others; wear oneself out from head to foot to help others;
[摩肩] rub the shoulders;
摩肩擦背 go in a jostling crowd;
摩肩擊轂 be crowded with people and carriages; be overcrowded with people and traffic; shoulder to shoulder and hub to hub;
摩肩接踵 be jam-packed with people; jostle each other in a crowd; jostle one another on the way; rubbing the shoulders and following the steps; shoulder to shoulder and closely upon heels;
[摩天] skyscraping;
摩天輪 big wheel;
峻嶺摩天 the high mountains seem to scrape the sky;
[摩托] motor;
摩托車 motor bicycle; motor van; motorbike; motorcycle;
~摩托車後座 pillion;
~摩托車越野賽 motocross;
~低座小摩托車 motor scooter; scooter;
~四輪摩托車 quad bike;
~一輛摩托車 a motorbike;
摩托艇 motorboat;

按摩 massage;
揣摩 try to figure out;
撫摩 stroke;
觀摩 inspect and learn from each other's work; view and emulate;

mo

【摹】 (1) copy; make an exact copy; (2) imitate; model; pattern after;
[摹本] copy; facsimile;
[摹倣] model on; pattern after;
[摹古] model after ancient style;
[摹繪] isography;
[摹刻] (1) carve a reproduction of an inscription or painting; copy by carving; (2) carved reproduction of an inscription or painting;
[摹擬] imitate; mimic; simulate;
[摹拓] take carved impression;
[摹寫] (1) copy; imitate the calligraphy of; (2) depict; describe;
[摹真本] facsimile;

臨摹 copy;
描摹 delineate; depict; portray;

mo

【模】 (1) pattern; standard; (2) imitate; (3) model;
[模本] calligraphy model; painting model;
[模範] exemplary person; fine example; model;
模範僱員 model employee;
模範教師 model teacher;
模範妻子 model wife;
模範學生 model student;
模範作用 exemplary role;
勞動模範 model worker;
樹立模範 set a good example for imitation;
[模仿] copy; imitate; model oneself on;

pattern oneself after;
模仿犯罪 copycat drime;
模仿作品 pastiche;
通過模仿 by imitation;

[模糊] blurred; dim; indistinct; obscure; vague;
模糊不清 blurred and indistinct; go out of focus; indefinable; out of focus;
模糊的 blurred;
模糊關係 fuzzy relation;
模糊集合論 fuzzy set theory;
模糊技術 fuzziness technique;
模糊經濟 fuzzy economy;
模糊決策 fuzzy decision-making;
模糊理論 fuzzy theory;
模糊邏輯 fuzzy logic;
模糊數學 fuzzy mathematics;
模糊思維 fuzzy thinking;
模糊系統 fuzzy system;
模糊效應 fuzzy effect;
模糊意義 fuzzy meaning;
模糊語言 fuzzy language;
淚眼模糊 one's eyes are dim with tears;
模模糊糊 at the back of one's mind; subconsciously; vague;
神志模糊 in a certain state of delirium;
思想模糊 have a vague idea on;
相位模糊 phase ambiguity;
印像模糊 have an indistinct impression of sth;
字跡模糊 the handwriting is blurred;

[模量] modulus;
絕對模量 absolute modulus;
絕熱模量 adiabatic modulus;
抗壓模量 compression modulus;
弦向模量 chord modulus;

[模稜兩可] ambiguous; betwixt and between; cut both ways; dubious; equivocal; in an equivocal way; inconclusive; indecisive; shift and hedge; yea and nay;

[模擬] analogue; analogy; imitate; model; modellation; simulate; simulation;
模擬板 breadboard;
模擬傳輸 analogue transmission;
模擬仿真 analog simulation;
模擬器 simulator;
~核爆炸模擬器 atomic blast simulator;
~離心模擬器 centrifugal simulator;
~信道模擬器 channel simulator;
模擬設計 breadboard design;
模擬事故 simulated accident;
模擬網絡 analog network;
模擬系統 analog pattern;
模擬訓練 simulation training;
模擬作用 modellation;
爆炸模擬 blast analogue;
電機械模擬 electromechanical analogy;
電流模擬 current analogue;
電路模擬 circuit analogue;
電模擬 electrical analogy;
動力模擬 dynamical analogue;
複合模擬 composite analogy;
函數模擬 function analogue;
機械模擬 mechanical analogy;
計算機模擬 computer simulation;
間接模擬 indirect analogue;
可靠模擬 authentic simulation;
可控模擬 controllable simulation;
類比模擬 analog simulation;
力電流模擬 force-current analogy;
氣動模擬 pneumatic analogue;
時分模擬 time division analogue;
數字模擬 digital analogy;
水波模擬 water wave analogy;
水壓模擬 hydraulic analogue;
網絡模擬 network analogy;
顯示模擬 scope analogue;
液壓模擬 hydraulic analogy;

[模式] mode; model; pattern; type;
模式化 modularity;
~操作模式化 functional modularity;
~處理模式化 processing modularity;
模式識別 pattern recognition;
模式選擇 pattern selection;
模式研究 model study;
擺脱…的模式 depart from the pattern of...;
~擺脱通常的模式 depart from the normal pattern;
打破模式 break the mound;
平流模式 advective model;
提供模式 supply a pattern;
學習模式 modes of learning;
~多元化學習模式 diversified moderns of learning;
習得模式 acquisition model;

[模數] modulus;
割線模數 apparent modulus;
壓縮模數 compressibility modulus;
軸向模數 axial modulus;

[模特兒] model;

當模特兒 serve as a model;
攝影模特兒 photographic model;
時裝模特兒 fashion model;

［模型］ (1) model; mock-up; pattern; (2) model set; mould pattern;
模型工 vatman;
模型化 modularity;
~ 獨立程序模型化 programme-independent modularity;
~ 軟件模型化 software modularity;
動力模型 dynamic mock-up;
非循環模型 acyclic model;
核反應堆模型 nuclear mock-up;
建造模型 build a model;
人體模型 manikin;
設計模型 design a model;
實體模型 full-scale mock-up; mock-up;
使用模型 use a model;
提供模型 supply a model;
先進模型 advanced model;

［模子］ mold;

規模 dimensions; scale; scope;
楷模 model; pattern;
名模 supermodel;
指模 fingerprint;
製模 mould;
子模 submodule;

mo

【膜】 any thin membrane that protects internal organs or tissues in the human body;

［膜拜］ prostrate oneself in worship; worship;

瓣膜 value;
表膜 outer pellicle;
薄膜 (1) membrane; (2) film;
耳膜 eardrum;
腹膜 peritonaeum;
骨膜 periosteum;
鼓膜 eardrum;
虹膜 iris;
滑膜 synovium;
角膜 cornea;
結膜 conjunctiva;
肋膜 pleura;
腦膜 meninx;
黏膜 mucous membrane;
胚膜 germinal membrane;
胎膜 foetal membrane;
心內膜 endocardium;
心外膜 epicardium;
胸膜 pleura;

mo

【磨】 (1) rub; wear; (2) grind; polish; (3) wear down; wear out; (4) pester; trouble; worry; (5) dawdle; waste time; (6) die out; obliterate;

［磨擦］ abrade; abrase; rub;
磨擦力 friction force;
磨擦雙手 rub one's hands together;
避免磨擦 avoid friction;
動摩擦 dynamical friction;
滾動摩擦 rolling friction;
滑動摩擦 sliding friction;
減少磨擦 reduce friction;
靜摩擦 static friction;
引起磨擦 cause friction;
製造磨擦 create friction;

［磨蹭］ dally; dawdle; move slowly;
別再磨蹭 get one's finger out; pull one's finger out; take one's finger out;
幹活磨蹭 work slowly;
磨磨蹭蹭 dawdle; dilly-dally; move slowly;

［磨杵成針］ constant dropping wears away a tone; rub a pestle into a needle—perseverance and hard work can assure success; with time and patience the leaf of the mulberry becomes satin;

［磨牀］ grinder;
風動角度磨牀 air angle grinder;
軸頸磨牀 axle journal grinder;
自動校準磨牀 automatic sizing grinder;

［磨刀］ keep one grind a knife; sharpen the knife; sharpen the sword;
磨刀擦槍 keep one's weapon bright against the day of battle; sharpen one's sword and oil one's gun;
磨刀霍霍 busily sharpening one's weapons; sharpen one's weapons to be ready for fighting; sabre-rattling;
磨刀匠 knife sharpener;
磨刀利鈍，困難勵志 stone whets a sword, difficulties strengthen one's willpower;
暗中磨刀 sharpen one's sword on the sly;

［磨叨］ loquacious;

［磨掉］ rub off;

［磨光］ grinding; polish;
磨光的 polished;

磨光機 polisher;
刮垢磨光 scrape the dirt off an object and make it shine — polish and improve;
集中磨光 centralized tool grinding;
砂帶磨光 belt grinding;

[磨耗] abrasion; wear and tear;
均勻磨耗 equalizing abrasion;
切削性磨耗 cutting abrasion;

[磨壞] grind away;

[磨練] hone; put oneself through the mill; steel oneself; temper oneself;
磨練人才 cultivate talents;
磨練意志 steel one's will;

[磨料] abradant; abrasive;
複合磨料 compounded abrasive;
尖角磨料 angular abrasive;
金屬磨料 metal abrasives;
人工磨料 artificial abrasive;
人造磨料 artificial abrasive;
軟質磨料 soft abrasives;
天然磨料 natural abrasive;
微型磨料 micro mold abrasive;
細磨磨料 levigated;

[磨滅] efface; obliterate; wear away;

[磨墨] grind the ink;
磨墨揮毫 grind the ink and flourish the brush to write;
磨墨展紙 grind some ink and spread out a sheet of paper; moisten the ink and rub it on the ink-slab and spread open the paper — ready to write;

[磨難] fire; hardship; slings and arrows; suffering; tribulation;
承受磨難 bear one's tribulation;
忍受磨難 endure hardship;
遭受磨難 go through hardship;
戰勝磨難 overcome hardship;
種種磨難 slings and arrows;
~生活裏的種種磨難 slings and arrows in our life;

[磨破] abrade; wear;
磨破嘴皮 talk oneself hoarse;

[磨石] millstone;

[磨蝕] (1) abrasion; (2) wear sth down;
磨蝕劑 abradant; abrasive;
磨蝕鋭氣 wear down one's spirit;
磨蝕性 abrasiveness;
磨蝕作用 abrasive action;
表面磨蝕 surface abrasion;
冰川磨蝕 glacial abrasion;
河流磨蝕 fluvial abrasion;

[磨損] abrade; abrasion; abrasive wear; wear and tear;
磨損作用 abrasive action;
斷裂磨損 fracture wear;
腐蝕磨損 corrosive wear;
均勻磨損 even wear;
碰撞磨損 gouging abrasion;
容許磨損 allowable wear;

[磨牙] (1) argue endlessly; talk nonsense; (2) idle away time; kill time; (3) crack sth between the teeth; grind one's teeth; grit one's teeth;

[磨洋工] clock watcher; dawdle along; dawdle over one's work; lie down on the job; longer over one's work; loaf on the job; slacking;

挨磨 procrastinate;
熬磨 brave; endure;
耐磨 wear-resisting;
軟磨 use soft tactics;
消磨 (1) wear down; (2) while away;
研磨 (1) grind; pestle; (2) polish;

mo
【糢】 same as 模, blurred; indistinct;

mo
【謨】 (1) course of action; plan; (2) have no; lack; without;

宏謨 grand plan; great project;

mo
【蘑】 a variety of edible mushroom;

[蘑菇] (1) agaric; mushroom; swamm; (2) keep on at; pester; worry;
蘑菇湯 mushroom soup;
蘑菇雲 mushroom cloud;
乾蘑菇 dried mushroom;
泡蘑菇 dawdle; importune; pester; play a game of stalling; play for time; use delaying tactics;
神奇蘑菇 magic mushroom;
鮮蘑菇 fresh mushrooms;
洋蘑菇 meadow mushroom;
野蘑菇 true mushroom;

mo
【魔】 (1) demon; devil; evil spirit; (2) magic; mystic;

[魔棒] magic wand;

[魔法] magic; sorcery; witchcraft; wizardry;

魔法師 enchanter; sorcerer;
~女魔法師 sorceress;
驅除魔法 dispel the charm;
收起魔法 pack up one's sorcery;

[魔怪] demons and monsters; fiends;

[魔鬼] demon; devil; great fisher of souls; monster;
魔鬼列車 ghost train;

[魔劍] magic sword;
一把魔劍 a magic sword;

[魔力] magical powers;

[魔術] a sleigh of hand; magic;
魔術棒 magic wand;
魔術師 conjuror; illusionist; juggler; magician;
~吞火魔術師 fire-eater;
白魔術 white magic;
變魔術 conjure; conjuring; perform sleight of hand;
表演魔術 perform magic;

[魔王] devil;
混世魔王 a devil who creates chaos; a fiend in human shape; an incarnate fiend; devil incarnate; the greatest evildoer;

[魔掌] devil's clutches; evil hands;

[魔杖] magic wand;
揮動魔杖 wave one's magic wand;

[魔障] demon; evil spirit;

[魔咒] magic spell;
解除魔咒 break the spell;

[魔爪] devil's talons;
斬斷魔爪 cut off the tentacles;

癌魔 demon of cancer;
病魔 serious illness;
惡魔 (1) devil; evil spirit; (2) evil person;
夢魔 nightmare;
入魔 be completely bewitched; be infatuated;
睡魔 compulsive desire to sleep;
邪魔 demon; evil spirit;
妖魔 demon; evil spirit;
着魔 be bewitched; be possessed;
中魔 be bewitched; be possessed;

mo

【饃】 steamed dumplings;

[饃饃] steamed dumplings;

mo³
mo

【抹】 (1) apply; plaster; put on; (2) wipe off; (3) blot out; cross out; erase; strike out;

[抹布] rag;

[抹掉] erase; wipe away;

[抹粉] powder;
抹粉擦胭 apply powder and rouge; daub on paint and rub on rouge; paint in glowing colours; powder and paint oneself; powder and rouge;
擦脂抹粉 paint rouge and power;
搽脂抹粉 apply cosmetics; paint and powder one's face; paint and powder oneself; rub on the rouge and daub the paint;

[抹黑] blacken sb's name; bring shame on; defame; discredit; throw mud at;

[抹去] blip; erase; expunge; wipe out;
抹去笑容 wipe the grin off sb's face; wipe the smile off sb's face;

[抹殺] blot out; obliterate; write off;
抹殺成就 obliterate attainment;

[抹藥] apply ointment to the affected area;

塗抹 (1) paint; smear; (2) scrawl; scribble;

mo⁴
mo

【末】 (1) end; tip; (2) minor details; nonessentials; (3) last stage; (4) dust; powder;

[末班車] last bus; last train;

[末代] last generation; last reign of a dynasty;

[末端] end; terminal; termination;
末端核心 end-focus;
樹狀末端 arborescent termination;

[末行] footline; terminal row;

[末後] finally;

[末級] final stage; last stage; upstage;

[末了] finally; in the end; last;

[末路] dead end; impasse;
末路窮途 at bay; be driven into an impasse; desperate; go into the blind alley; reach the end of the rope;
末路之難 the arduousness of the last section of the journey; the nearer to success, the more arduous;
自尋末路 cut one's own thoat;

[末名獎] booby prize;

[末年] last years of;

[末期] final phase; last phase; last stage;

［末日］ (1) doomsday; Judgement Day; (2) doom; end;
末日景象 doomsday scenario;
末日來臨 one's last hour has come;
末日論者 doomsayer; doomster;
末日審判 last judgment;
如臨末日 like one who is approaching the end of his days;
［末梢］ end; ending; termination; tip;
神經末梢 nerve ending;
藤狀末梢 hederiform termination;
爪狀末梢 claw-like termination;
［末世］ last phase;
［末座］ most inferior seat at table;
叨陪末座 be honoured with a seat; sit on the last seat;

本末 (1) whole course of event from beginning to end; (2) fundamental and incidental;
摽末 edge of a sword;
第末 the last one;
顛末 whole process from beginning to end;
粉末 flour; powder;
毫末 (1) tip of hair; (2) extremely small amount;
季末 end of the season;
芥末 mustard;
始末 the whole course from beginning to end;
微末 insignificant; trifling;
月末 end of a month;
周末 weekend;

mo
【沒】 (1) sink; submerge; (2) overflow; rise beyond; (3) disappear; hide; (4) confiscate; take possession of; (5) till the end;
［沒齒］ without teeth;
沒齒不忘 grateful to sb until the last tooth falls out of one's head; never forget as long as one lives; remember for the rest of one's life;
沒齒無怨 without any complaint to the end of one's life;
［沒頂］ be drowned;
［沒落］ decline; wane;
［沒世］ through one's life-time; till the end of one's life;
沒世不忘 remember for life; never forget it till the end of one's life; not to forget it in all one's life;
［沒收］ confiscate; expropriate; forfeit; forfeiture;
沒收財產 expropriate sb's property;

沉沒 sink;
出沒 appear and disappear; haunt;
殂沒 die; perish;
覆沒 (1) capsize and sink; (2) be annihilated; be overwhelmed;
還沒 not yet;
泯沒 become lost; sink into oblivion; vanish;
吞沒 (1) embezzle; misappropriate; (2) engulf; swallow up;
湮沒 be forgotten; be neglected;
隱沒 (1) conceal; hide; (2) disappear gradually;

mo
【抹】 (1) plaster; (2) tight undergarment; (3) turn;
［抹不開］ (1) feel embarrassed; put out; (2) afraid of impairing personal relations; unable to act impartially for fear of offending sb;
［抹不開臉］ unable to act impartially for fear of offending sb;
［抹灰］ apply mortar; plaster a wall;
抹灰工 plasterer;
［抹面］ plaster a wall;
［抹頭］ (1) turn around; (2) head cloth; hood;
［抹月批風］ entertain sb with sliced moon and wind; so poor that one has nothing to entertain one's guests;

mo
【歿】 die;
［歿存均感］ both the living and the dead will be grateful;

mo
【沫】 (1) tiny bubbles on the surface of water; (2) saliva; (3) end; finish;
［沫蟬］ froghopper;
［沫子］ foam; froth;

白沫 frothy saliva;
泡沫 foam; froth; spume;
吐沫 saliva;
唾沫 saliva; spittle;

mo
【茉】 white jasmine;
［茉莉］ jasmine;
白茉莉 Arabic jasmine;

M

mo

【陌】 (1) path between fields; (2) road;

［陌路］ stranger;

陌路相逢 casually meet;

視同陌路 cut sb dead; treat like a stranger;

［陌生］ strange; unfamiliar;

陌生面孔 strange face;

陌生人 stranger;

～你好，陌生人 hello, stranger;

阡陌 criss-cross footpaths between fields;

mo

【秣】 (1) fodder; horse feed; horse grains; (2) feed a horse;

［秣馬厲兵］ groom the horses and drill the troops; keep the army ready for combat; make the army combat-ready; prepare for battle; stay at the ready;

mo

【脈】 (1) arteries; blood vessels; circulation system; veins; (2) pulse; (3) mountain range; (4) things that are related and form a system of some kind; (5) stems of a leaf;

［脈脈］ affectionately; amorously; lovingly;

脈脈含情 amorous; full of affection; full of tender affection; with loving eyes;

mo

【袜】 stomacher;

［袜肚］ (1) waistband; (2) saddle girth;

［袜腹］ stomacher;

［袜胸］ stomacher;

mo

【麥】 a pronunciation of 麥；

mo

【莫】 (1) no; not; (2) don't; (3) a surname;

［莫不］ there's no one who doesn't or isn't;

［莫此為甚］ a more flagrant instance has yet to be found; there is nothing worse than this;

［莫大］ greatest; utmost;

［莫非］ can it be that; could it be; is it possible that;

［莫怪］ no wonder that;

［莫過於］ nothing is more...than;

［莫及］ beyond reach;

鞭長莫及 beyond one's influence; beyond one's reach; beyond the range of one's ability; beyond the reach of one's power; cannot do it much as I would like to; out of range; too far away for one to be able to help;

後悔莫及 cry over split milk; it is too late for regrets; too late to repent;

噬臍莫及 how can one bite one's navel; it is too late to repent; sth impossible;

望塵莫及 a far cry from; be left far behind; be left in the dust; be thrown into the shade; cannot hold a candle to; fall far behind; hopelessly behindhand; lay a long way behind; too far behind to catch up; too inferior to bear comparison; unable to keep pace with; unequal to;

［莫可名狀］ that cannot be described; unable to understand; undescribable; unspeakable;

［莫名］ indescribable; inexpressible;

莫名其妙 absurd; all abroad; all adrift; baffled; cannot make anything of it; difficult to guess what it is all about; in a fog; inexplicable; make neither head nor tail of it; odd; puzzling and inexplicable; queer; rather baffling; seem totally in the dark; unable to guess what it is all about; unable to make head or tail of sth; unable to understand; without rhyme or reason;

莫名所以 find it difficult to explain;

莫名一文 dead block; penniless; not have a bean;

感恩莫名 do not know how to express one's gratitude;

感激莫名 more grateful for this than words can tell; my gratitude beggars description; not to know how to express one's gratitude;

感謝莫名 be deeply grateful;

欣愉莫名 beyond expression; exceedingly pleased;

［莫逆］ intimate; very friendly;

莫逆於心 finding each other congenial; with complete mutual understanding;

莫逆之交 a good and constant friend; an intimate friendship; bosom friends; Damon and Pythias; David and Jonathan; one's intimate friend; the best of friends;

［莫如］ might as well; would be better;

[莫為已甚] do not drive sb into a corner;
[莫須有] concocted; fabricated; fabulous; groundless; phoney; spurious; trumped-up; unwarranted;
[莫之能御] nothing can resist it;
[莫衷一是] fail to come to any agreement; no concensus of opinion; no decision can be reached; no unanimous conclusion can be drawn; unable to agree which is right;

mo
【貉】 (1) a northern barbarian tribe; (2) quiet;

mo
【寞】 lonely; quiet; silent; still;

寂寞 lonely; lonesome;
落寞 lonely; lonesome;

mo
【漠】 (1) desert; (2) indifferent; unconcerned;
[漠漠] (1) foggy; misty; (2) vast and lonely;
[漠然] apathetically; indifferently; with unconcern;
漠然一笑 grin with indifference;
漠然置之 give short shrift; hold loose; look on with unconcern; remain indifferent towards; show no concern for; without any concern for;
[漠視] brush aside; ignore; overlook; pay no attention to; show no concern for; treat with indifference;
漠視勸告 treat sb's advice with indifference;
[漠土] desert soil;

淡漠 (1) apathetic; indifferent; (2) dim; faint; hazy;
廣漠 vast and bare;
荒漠 desert; wilderness;
冷漠 indifferent; unconcerned;
落漠 desolate; lonely;
沙漠 desert;
朔漠 northern deserts;

mo
【膜】 (1) membrane; (2) film; thin coating;
[膜翅目] hymenoptera;
[膜法] membrane method;
[膜片] diaphragm;
[膜外] outside of one's attention, consideration, etc;

表膜 outer pellicle;
薄膜 thin film;
鞏膜 sclera;
結膜 conjunctiva;
視網膜 retina;

mo
【韎】 (1) stockings; (2) Tungusic tribe;

mo
【嘿】 (1) silent; speechless; (2) quiet; still;

mo
【墨】 (1) China ink; ink stick; (2) ink; (3) handwriting or painting; (4) learning; (5) black; dark; (6) a surname;
[墨寶] (1) treasured scrolls of calligraphy or painting; (2) your beautiful painting or calligraphy;
[墨筆] Chinese writing brush;
墨濃筆飽 grind the ink thick and fill the brush with the ink;
[墨斗] carpenter's ink marker;
[墨盒] ink box;
[墨黑] pitch-black;
墨黑的 coal-black;
近墨者黑 he that handles pitch shall foul his fingers; they that touch pitch will be pitched; touch pitch and defiled; touch pitch, and you will be defiled; you can't touch pitch without being defiled;
[墨跡] (1) ink mark; (2) sb's writing or painting;
墨跡未乾 before the ink has dried; before the ink is dry;
[墨鏡] dark glasses; sunglasses;
[墨客] literary men;
風人墨客 poets and literary men;
[墨綠] blackish green;
[墨囊] ink sac;
[墨守] adhere to;
墨守成規 adhere to the old ways; be stuck in a groove; cling conservatively to the old system; devote to conventions; follow a stereotype routine; get into a groove; get into a rut; go round like a horse in a mill; move in a groove;

M

more in a rut; run in a rut; stay in a rut; stick in the mud; stick to accustomed rules; stick to conventions; stick to established practice; stick to outdated ways and regulations; stick to the old ways;
~墨守成規的人 stick-in-the-mud;
墨守舊習 adhere to old customs; stick to old habits;
墨守禮法 stand on ceremony;

[墨水] (1) Chinese ink; (2) writing ink;
墨水池 inkwell;
不褪色的墨水 indelible ink;
磁性墨水 magnetic ink;
喝足墨水 have read a great deal; have read a great many books;
陶瓷墨水 ceramic ink;
無酸墨水 acid-free ink;
隱形墨水 invisible ink;
紙板墨水 carton ink;

[墨刑] tattooing the face as a punishment;

[墨魚] cuttlefish; inkfish; squid;
墨魚肚腸河豚肝—又黑又毒 the intestine of an inkfish and the liver of a globefish — black and venomous;
墨魚乾 dried squid;

[墨汁] Chinese ink; ink;
黑墨汁 Chinese ink;

寶墨 your most valuable handwriting;
褚墨 paper and ink;
淡墨 light ink;
落墨 put pen to paper; start to write;
磨墨 grind the ink;
潑墨 splash-ink;
繩墨 (1) carpenter's line marker; (2) rules and regulations;
石墨 graphite;
貪墨 corrupt;
文墨 writing;
遺墨 letters, manuscripts etc. left behind by the deceased;
油墨 printing ink;
朱墨 ink made of cinnabar;

mo

【磨】 (1) mill; (2) turn around; (3) grind;

[磨坊] mill;
磨坊主 miller;
一座磨坊 a mill;

打磨 burnish; polish;
風磨 air mill; pneumatic mill;
火磨 electric mill;
石磨 stone mill;
水磨 water mill;
折磨 cause physical or mental suffering;

mo

【默】 (1) silent; tacit; (2) write from memory;

[默哀] stand in silent tribute;
默哀一分鐘 observe a one-minute silence;
起立默哀 rise and stand in silent tribute;
為亡靈默哀 pay silent tribute to the dead;

[默禱] pray in silence; say a silent prayer;

[默讀] read silently;

[默劇] dumb show;

[默默] quietly; silently; with mute;
默默而去 go off without a word;
默默而坐 sit mute;
默默落淚 weep in silence;
默默祈禱 pray in silence;
默默忍受 grin and bear it;
默默無聞 be buried in oblivion; in the shade; inglorious; obscurity; of no name; remain in obscurity; unknown to the public; without attracting public attention;
默默無言 keep silent; reticent; remain silent; silently; taciturn; without saying a word;
默默相視 gaze at each other in silence;

[默片] silent film;

[默契] tacit agreement; tacit understanding;
達成默契 reach tacit agreement;
配合默契 cooperate well by tacit agreement;

[默然] silent; speechless;
默然而立 stand mute;
默然而坐 sit speechlessly;
默然哭泣 weep silently;
默然離去 go away without saying a word;
默然無語 fall silent; speechless;

[默認] acquiesce in; give tacit consent to; tacitly approve;
默認現狀 give tact consent to the status quo;

[默示] imply;

[默誦] read silently;

[默想] contemplate; ruminate;
內省默想 introspective meditation;

[默寫] write from memory;

默寫課文 write the text from memory;

［默許］ acquiesce in; tacitly consent to;

默許的 acquiescent;

得到默許 obtain tacit consent;

沉默 (1) reticent; (2) silent;

靜默 (1) become silent; (2) mourn in silence; observe silence;

慎默 cautious and reticent;

玄默 taciturn and meditative;

幽默 humorous;

mo

【瘼】 (1) ailment; disease; illness; (2) hardship; privation; suffering;

民瘼 sufferings of the people; the weal and woe of the people;

mo

【貘】 (1) leopard; (2) panther; (3) tapir;

mo

【驀】 suddenly;

［驀地］ all of a sudden; suddenly; unexpectedly;

驀地站起 leap to one's feet on a sudden; rise to one's feet all of a sudden; stand up suddenly;

［驀然］ suddenly;

驀然想起 suddenly remember;

mo⁵

mo

【麼】 particle;

mou²

mou

【牟】 (1) seek; (2) bellow; (3) a surname;

［牟利］ make profits;

從中牟利 get advantage out of; get some advantage from the delicate position between; have an axe to grind; make a profit for oneself in some deal; make capital out of sth; play both ends against the middle; step in and take the advantage;

［牟取］ bleed; obtain; seek; try to gain;

牟取暴利 make exorbitant profits; profiteer; reap fabulous profits; seek exorbitant profits;

mou

【眸】 pupil of the eye;

［眸子］ eye; pupil of the eye;

凝眸 look with fixed eyes;

mou

【謀】 (1) plan; stratagem; (2) plot; seek; work for; (3) consult;

［謀財］ strive to get money;

謀財害命 kill for money; kill sb and rob him of his money; murder for gain; murder sb for his money; take sb's life and rob him of his money;

以色謀財 use one's looks to get money;

~ 以色謀財的女人 gold digger;

［謀刺］ make an attempt on sb's life; plot to assassinate;

［謀反］ conspire against the state; plot a rebellion; plot treason;

［謀害］ (1) plot to murder; (2) plot a frame-up against; plot against sb;

被謀害 be murdered;

［謀劃］ plan; scheme; try to find a solution;

謀劃許久 have been planning for a long time;

謀劃陰謀 concoct a scheme;

［謀利］ profit; turn sth to profit;

［謀慮］ deliberate;

深謀遠慮 circumspect and farsighted; far-sighted and prudent; foresight; great prudence; think and plan far ahead; think deeply and plan carefully; with great vision and farsightedness;

［謀略］ astuteness and resourcefulness; strategy;

改進謀略 improve one's strategy;

深通謀略 be deeply read in all the rules of strategy;

疏謀少略 lack of schemes and stratagem; not good at planning and plotting;

［謀面］ meet;

素未謀面 never have the pleasure of meeting sb;

［謀求］ in question of; seek; strive for;

謀求出路 look for a way out; seek one's fortune;

［謀取］ obtain; seek; try to gain;

謀取財富 try to gain wealth;

謀取名利 seek fame and gain;

謀取私利 have an eye to the main chance; seek personal gain; seek private interests; trying to obtain profit for oneself; with an eye on the main chance;

M

謀取職位 try to gain a position;

[謀殺] foul play; murder;

謀殺案 murder;

~一起謀殺案 a case of murder;

~一樁謀殺案 a murder;

謀殺犯 murderer;

~女謀殺犯 murderess;

謀殺罪 homicide; murder;

~一級謀殺罪 first-degree murder; murder in the first degree;

殘忍謀殺 brutal murder; cold-blooded murder;

慘遭謀殺 be barbarously murdered;

蓄意謀殺 deliberate murder; wilful murder;

政治謀殺 political murders;

[謀生] earn one's crust; make a living; seek a livelihood;

謀生不易 it is not easy earning a living;

謀生乏術 have no means of getting a livelihood; unable to make a living;

謀生糊口 win one's bread;

糊口謀生 earn one's daily bread; eke out one's livelihood; eke out the barest of living; keep body and soul together; make a living; try to keep the pot boiling;

[謀士] adviser; counsellor;

[謀事] (1) plan matters; (2) look for a job;

謀事在人，成事在天 man proposes, God disposes; man proposes, Heaven disposes; the planning lies with man, the outcome with Heaven;

[謀私] seek personal gains;

以權謀私 abuse one's power for private gain; exploit one's position and power to seek personal gains; take advantage of one's position and power to seek personal gains;

仗權謀私 exploit one's position and power to seek personal gain;

[謀算] (1) plan; scheme; (2) plot; (3) calculate;

老謀深算 canny; circumspect and farsighted; experienced and astute; make every move only after mature deliberation; scheming and calculating;

不謀 without planning;

參謀 (1) staff officer; (2) adviser; give advice;

籌謀 plan and prepare;

共謀 collude;

合謀 (1) conspire; plot together; (2) conspiracy;

機謀 scheme; stratagem;

計謀 scheme; stratagem;

密謀 conspire; plot; scheme;

奇謀 clever strategy;

人謀 strategies made by men;

同謀 accomplice; confederate; conspire;

圖謀 conspire; plot;

陰謀 conspiracy; conspire; plot;

預謀 plan beforehand; premeditate; premeditation;

遠謀 foresight; long view;

惲謀 plan;

智謀 resourcefulness;

主謀 be the chief plotter; chief instigator;

咨謀 take counsel;

鑽謀 curry favour with sb in power for personal gain;

mou

【繆】 precautions; preparations;

mou

【鍪】 (1) a kind of cooking pot; (2) a kind of metal helmet;

mou

【麰】 barley;

mou³

mou

【牡】 a pronunciation of 牡;

mou

【某】 certain; some;

[某處] somewhere;

[某地] somewhere;

[某某] a; a certain; so-and-so; some;

[某人] a certain person;

[某時] sometime;

[某些] a few; certain; some;

mou⁴

mou

【茂】 a pronunciation of 茂;

mou

【袤】 a pronunciation of 袤;

mou

【瞀】 a pronunciation of 瞀;

mu²

mu

【獏】 Mu, a tribe in Hebu, Guangdong

Province;

mu

【模】 matrix; mold; pattern;

［模樣］ appearance; looks;
模樣醜陋 have an ugly look;
模樣漸老 begin to lose one's looks;
模樣平庸 plain;
擺出一副天真的模樣 assume an air of innocence;
笨模樣 dull in appearance;
~ 一副笨模樣 dull in appearance;
大模大樣 high-and-mighty airs; in a showy manner; in an open manner; in an ostentatious manner; look big; pompously; proudly; with a swagger;
惡模惡樣 ferocious appearance; fierce appearance;
怪模怪樣 grotesque; odd-looking; queer in appearance and manners; queer-looking; uncanny;
~ 怪模怪樣的舉動 grotesque antics;
沒模樣了 look haggard;
似模似樣 in a grand manner;
一模一樣 a copy of sb; a splitting image of sb; as like as two peas; copy and apply without any change; cut from the same cloth; exactly alike; exactly the same as; identical; like two peas in a pod; the image of;
~ 長得一模一樣 be a copy of sb;
裝模作樣 act affectedly; act with affected manners; assume a feigned manner; assume great airs; behave in an affected way; feign; give oneself airs; indulge in histrionics; make an appearance of; make a pretense of; put on an act; pretend; pretentious; strike a pose; strike an attitude;
~ 裝模作樣的人 poser;

［模子］ mould; pattern;

鍛模 forging die;
拉模 drawing die;
土模 clay model;
壓模 compression moulding;
硬模 die;
鑄模 casting form;
字模 matrix;

mu³

mu

【母】 (1) mother; (2) female elders; (3) female; (4) origin; parent;

［母愛］ maternal love; mother love;
得到母愛 get mother love;
奉獻母愛 offer maternal love;
失去母愛 lose maternal love;

［母狗］ bitch;

［母雞］ hen;
母雞咯咯叫 a hen cackles; a hen cackles; a hen chucks; a hen chuckles; a hen cluks;
像隻老母雞 like a mother hen;
小母雞 pullet;
一群母雞 a flock of hens;
一隻母雞 a hen;

［母艦］ depot ship; mother ship;

［母馬］ mare;
傳種母馬 brood mare;

［母牛］ cow;
母牛哞哞 cows boos; cows lows; cows moo;
一頭母牛 a cow;

［母女］ mother and daughters;
有其母必有其女 like mother, like daughter; such mother, such daughter;

［母親］ mater; mother;
母親身分 motherhood;
抱住母親 cling to one's mother;
超級母親 supermom;
單身母親 lone mother;
當母親 become a mother;
看望母親 visit one's mother;
兩個孩子的母親 mother of two;
未婚母親 unmarried mother;
在職母親 working mother;

［母權］ mother right;

［母系］ matriarch;
母系社會 matriarchalsociety;

［母線］ bus-bar;
備用母線 auxiliary bus-bar;
負母線 negative bus-bar;
隔相母線 isolated bus-bar;
均壓母線 equalizing bus-bar;
饋路母線 feeder bus-bar;
銅母線 copper bus-bar;
陰極導電母線 cathode bus-bar;

［母校］ alma mater;

［母夜叉］ hag;

［母語］ first language; mother tongue; native language; native tongue;
使用母語 communicate in one's mother

tongue;
說母語 speak one's mother tongue;
~說母語的人 native speaker;
學母語 acquire one's mother tongue;
[母子] mother and son;
母以子貴 the mother's honour increases as her son's position rises;
母子平安 after the birth, mother and child were doing well;
母子之情 love between mother and son;

褓母 baby-sitter; nurse;
鴇母 procuress;
貝母 fritillary;
伯母 aunt; wife of father's elder brother;
慈母 loving mother; mother;
嫡母 address for father's wife by children of concubines;
分母 denominator;
父母 father and mother; parents;
姑母 father's sister;
後母 step-mother;
季母 wife of father's youngest brother;
繼母 step-mother;
教母 godmother;
酵母 yeast;
酒母 distiller's yeast;
舅母 wife of mother's brother;
釀母 yeast;
乳母 wet nurse;
嬸母 wife of father's younger brother;
生母 one's own mother;
聲母 initial consonant;
聖母 (1) female deity; (2) Virgin Mary;
師母 wife of one's teacher or master;
叔母 wife of father's younger brother;
庶母 concubine of one's father;
水母 jellyfish; medusa;
養母 foster mother;
姨母 maternal aunt;
義母 adopted mother;
姻母 aunt by marriage;
岳母 wife's mother;
韻母 simple or compound vowel;
丈母 mother-in-law; wife's mother;
珠母 mother-of-pearl;
字母 letter; letters of an alphabet;
祖母 grandmother;

mu
【牡】 male;
[牡丹] peony; tree peony;
牡丹雖好，也要綠葉扶持 for all its beauty, the peony needs the green leaves to set it off;
[牡蠣] oyster;
牡蠣養殖場 oyster bed; oyster farm;

mu
【姆】 governess; matron; woman tutor;

歐姆 ohm;

mu
【拇】 (1) thumb; (2) big toe;
[拇指] (1) thumb; (2) big toe;
大拇指 thumb;
~豎起大拇指 hold up one's thumb in approval; thumbs up;
~吮大拇指 suck ones thumb;
三拇指 middle finger;
小姆指 one's little finger;
[拇趾] great toe;

mu
【畝】 land measure;
[畝產] yield per unit area;

地畝 fields or farmland;
公畝 acre;
畎畝 farmland; field;
市畝 unit of area;
田畝 fields or farmland;
英畝 acre;

mu
【鉧】 iron;

mu⁴
mu
【木】 (1) tree; (2) timber; wood; (3) made of wood; wooden; (4) coffin; (5) numb; wooden;
[木板] board; plank;
木板牀 plank bed;
木板路 boardwalk;
木板漆畫 wooden screen with lacquer painting;
木板球 wood shot;
一塊木板 a board;
[木版] block;
木版畫 woodblock; woodcut;
[木本] root of a tree;
木本水源 the root of a tree and the source of a stream — the root of a matter;
木本植被 lignose;

木有本，水有源 every tree has its roots and every river has its source;

［木材］ log; lumber; timber; wood;
木材場 lumberyard;
木材廠 lumbermill;
木材商 lumberman; timber merchant;
純淨木材 clean-cut timber;
風乾木材 air dried wood;
農用木材 agricultural timber;
酸性木材 acid wood;
彎曲木材 crooked timber;
細紋木材 close-grained wood;
一段木材 a chunk of wood;
一方木材 a cubic metre of lumber;
油浸木材 creosoted timber;

［木柴］ firewood; wood;
點燃木柴 set the logs ablaze;
一捆木柴 a bundle of firewood;

［木船］ wooden boat;
大木船 big wooden boat;
小木船 small wooden boat;

［木牀］ wooden bed;

［木槌］ wooden hammer;
小木槌 gavel;

［木呆呆］ stonily;

［木雕］ wood carving;
木雕佛像 wood carvings of Buddha;
木雕泥塑 like an idol carved in wood or moulded in clay — as motionless as a statue;
木雕像 wood figurine;
木雕小像 wood figurine;
木雕儀仗俑 wooden entourage figurines;
黃楊木雕 boxwood carving;
檀香木雕 sandal-wood carving;

［木耳］ wood fungus;

［木工］ (1) carpentry; woodwork; (2) carpenter; joiner; woodworker;
木工活 carpentry;
木工手藝 carpentry;
細木工 cabinet-maker;

［木瓜］ (1) Chinese flowering quince; oblonga; (2) papaya; pawpaw;
番木瓜 pawpaw;

［木棍］ stick;
鐵頭木棍 quarterstaff;

［木花］ wood chips;
木花製品 wood chip products;

［木屐］ clogs; wooden sandals;
木屐舞 clog-dance;

［木雞］ wooden chicken;
呆若木雞 as dumb as a piece of wood; as motionless as a wooden image; be insensate like a wooden chicken; be paralyzed with fear; be rooted to the spot; dumb as a wooden chicken; dumb founded; dumbstruck; remain in a state of stupefaction; rivet to the ground; root to the ground; spaced-out; stand like a log; stand like a statue; stand still like a piece of wood; stand transfixed like a back of wood; transfixed with fear;

［木漿］ wood pulp;
褐色磨木漿 brown ground pulp; brown wood pulp;
化學木漿 chemical wood pulp;
磨木漿 groundwood pulp;

［木匠］ carpenter; millman;
木匠帶枷，自作自受 as you make your bed so shall you lie on it; the carpenter in a cangue — selfmade to fit himself;
木匠多了蓋歪房 too many cooks spoil the broth;
學做木匠 learn to be a carpenter;

［木刻］ woodcut; wood engraving;
木刻畫 woodcut;

［木蘭］ lily magnolia; magnolia;

［木立若偶］ stand motionless like a statue;

［木料］ log;
一堆木料 a pile of logs; a stack of wood;

［木馬］ (1) pommelled horse; vaulting horse; (2) hobbyhorse; rocking horse;
旋轉木馬 carousel; merry-go-round;
搖動木馬 rocking horse;

［木乃伊］ mummy;

［木偶］ (1) carved figure; wooden image; (2) puppet;
木偶表演藝術 puppetry;
木偶劇場 marionette theatre; puppet show theatre;
木偶劇團 troupe of puppet show;
木偶片 marionette film; puppet film;
木偶跳舞—幕後操縱 puppets dancing — (lit) strings are pulled by others behind the scenes;
木偶戲 puppet show;
~木偶戲演員 puppeteer;
成為木偶 become a puppet;
掌中木偶 hand puppet; glove puppet;
製作木偶 make a marionette of;

[木器] wood ware;
[木橋] wooden bridge;
雙木橋好走，獨木橋難行 a two-plank bridge is easy to cross, but a single-plank bridge is difficult;
[木琴] xylophone;
[木球] wooden shot;
[木石] wood and stone;
木石為徒 hold oneself aloof from the world; lead a solitary life; with stones as one's companion;
木人石心 a wooden man with a stone heart – unfeeling;
人非木石 man is a sentimental creature;
[木栓] cork;
創傷木栓 wound cork;
疊生木栓 storied cork;
翼狀木栓 winged cork;
[木薯] cassava;
木薯澱粉 cassava;
[木炭] charcoal; vegetable charcoal;
木炭粉 powdered charcoal;
木炭畫 charcoal drawing;
闊葉材木炭 hard-wood charcoal;
粒狀木炭 granular charcoal;
軟材木炭 soft-wood charcoal;
天然木炭 mineral charcoal;
[木俑] wooden figurine;
[木頭] log; timber; wood;
木頭木腦 dull; dull-witted; sit like a bump on a log; stupid; wooden-headed;
木頭人 blockhead; wooden head;
木頭人一推一推動一動 a wooden man never moves without a rush on it;
一大塊木頭 a block of wood;
一根木頭 a log;
一截木頭 a length of log;
一塊木頭 a block of wood; a chunk of wood; a piece of wood;
一塊三角形的木頭 a wedge of wood;
一堆木頭 a pile of logs;
[木紋] wood grain;
[木屋] wooden house;
木屋區 shantytown;
小木屋 cabin; chalet; wooden hut;
[木箱] wooden box;
[木魚] wooden drum;
敲木魚 beat the wooden drum;
[木已成舟] it is already water under the bridge; it is too late to reverse the situation; the dice is cast; what's done is done;

苞木 bamboo;
草木 flora; grass and trees; vegetation;
呆木 dazed and numb;
獨木 single log;
電木 bakelite;
椴木 linden;
伐木 cut; fell; lumber;
棺木 coffin;
灌木 bush; shrub;
橫木 crossbar;
紅木 padauk;
花木 flowers and trees;
樺木 birch;
椄木 graft;
浪木 swing bridge;
林木 (1) forest; woods; (2) forest tree;
麻木 (1) numb; (2) apathetic; insensitive;
苗木 nursery stock;
喬木 arbor; tree;
軟木 cork; softwood;
杉木 China fir;
樹木 trees;
土木 building; construction;
朽木 rotten wood;
硬木 hardwood;
柚木 teak;
樟木 camphor wood;
枕木 sleeper; tie;

mu

【目】 (1) eye; (2) look; regard; (3) item; (4) catalogue; list;
[目標] (1) objective; target; (2) aim; destination; goal;
目標管理 goal management;
~目標管理體系 objective control system;
目標計算機 object computer;
目標控制 target control;
目標評價 target assessment;
目標市場 target market;
目標語言 object language; target language;
暴露目標 give away one's position;
長期目標 long-term goal;
達成目標 achieve one's goal; attain one's goal; reach one's goal;
達到目標 attain one's goal; meet a target; reach one's objective;
~沒有達到目標 miss the mark;
當下目標 immediate goal;

短期目標 short-term goal;
多目標 multi-objective;
~多目標決策 multi-objective decision-making; multi-target decision;
~多目標系統 multi-objective system;
~多目標優化控制 multi-objective optimal control;
發現目標 find the target;
放棄目標 forgo one's aim;
個人目標 personal goal;
共同目標 common goal;
環境目標 environmental objective;
教育目標 educational goal;
漫無目標 aimless; at random;
面積目標 area target;
瞄準目標 train on the target;
模糊目標 blurred target;
人生目標 life goals;
設計目標 design objective;
生活目標 life goal;
實現目標 achieve the objectives; reach a goal; reach a target;
首選目標 prime target;
首要目標 primary goal;
投資目標 investment objective;
習得目標 learned goal;
學習目標 learning objective;
尋找目標 look for the target;
一個目標 a goal; a target; an aim;
制定目標 set one's goal;
主要目標 primary objective;
追求目標 pursue one's goal;
追蹤目標 follow the trail of the objective;
終極目標 ultimate goal;
組織目標 organizational target;

[目不…] one's eyes are without...; one's eyes cannot;
目不及接 too busy for the eyes to see; too many things to be seen;
目不見睫 can't see the lashes in one's own eye — not to know oneself; the eye can't see its lashes — lack self-knowledge;
目不交睫 cannot close one's eyes to sleep; have one's eyes open throughout the night; not a wink of sleep; not to sleep a wink;
目不窺園 never to take a peep into the garden — bury oneself in one's studies; not to cast one's eyes at the garden — absolute concentration on studies;
目不旁顧 without even letting one's eyes wander;
目不忍睹 cannot bear the sight of; one's eyes cannot bear the scene;
目不識丁 battledoor; bull's foot; not to know A from B; not to know a single word; not to know B from a battledore; totally illiterate; unable to recognize a singel written character;
目不暇給 have no time to take in the scene as a whole; have too much to watch; the eye cannot take it all in; there are too many things for the eye to take in; too much for the eye to feast on;
目不斜視 look neither right nor left; not to look sideways; refuse to be distracted;
~目不斜視，耳不旁聽 deaf and blind to everything going on around — concentrate on sth totally;
目不轉睛 all eyes for; fasten one's eyes on; gaze fixedly; gaze with fixed eyes; have one's eyes glued on; keep one's gaze fixed upon; look at intently without winking; look intently at; look with fixed gaze; regard with rapt attention; stare continuously; staringly; watch with the utmost concentration; watch without a blink; not to take one's eyes off; with staring eyes;

[目次] table of contents; contents;

[目瞪口呆] be struck dumb; be dumbfounded; be dumbstruck; gape; gaping; stand aghast; stare in mute amazement; stare openmouthed; stare with astonishment; strike sb dumb; stunned; stupefied;
目瞪口呆，面面相覷 be struck dumb with astonishment, staring at each other in bewilderment;
驚得目瞪口呆 fling one's arms up in horror; stand aghast with surprise;
嚇得目瞪口呆 be paralysed with terror; be scared stiff; strike sb dumb; strike sb speechless;

[目的] aim; goal; objective; purpose;
目的從屬連詞 subordinator of purpose;
目的地 destination;
~目的地介詞 preposition of destination;
~奔向目的地 hasten to the destination; spur forward to one's destination;
~直接目的地 immediate destination;
目的港 port of destination;

目的格 destinative;
目的介詞 preposition of purpose;
目的連詞 conjunction of purpose;
目的聽眾 target audience;
目的語 target language;
~目的語傳統 target language tradition;
~目的語讀者 target language reader;
~目的語對等詞 target language equivalent;
~目的語對應 target language correspondence;
~目的語關係 target language relationship;
~目的語規範 target language norm;
~目的語環境 target language setting;
~目的語文化 target language culture;
~目的語文獻 target language text;
目的在於 with a view of; with a view to; with the purpose of;
目的狀語 adverbial of purpose;
~目的狀語從句 adverbial clause of purpose;
卑鄙的目的 mean intention;
背離目的 deviate from one's purpose;
不可告人的目的 hidden agenda;
達到目的 accomplish an objective; accomplish one's objective; achieve one's end; achieve one's purpose; attain one's goal; gain one's end; home and dry; meet a goal; win one's end;
~沒有達到目的 defeat the purpose;
教學目的 educative purpose;
漫無目的 hit and miss;
明確目的 have a definite purpose;
~沒有明確目的 have no fixed purpose;
無目的的 aimless; at random; without objective;
一個目的 a goal; an aim;
有雙重目的 have a double purpose;
祇問目的，不問手段 choice of the end covers choice of the means; he who wills the end wills the means; the end justifies the means;

[目睹] see with one's own eyes; witness;
親眼目睹 live to see; see with one's own eyes;
眼見目睹 see with one's own eyes;
有目共睹 everyone can see that; it is clear to all that; obvious to all; obvious to everyone; obvious to people; perfectly obvious; plain; plain for everybody to judge for himself; visible to the eye;

[目光] (1) sight; view; vision; (2) gaze; look;
目光呆滯 one's eyesight is restrained; with a dull look in one's eyes; with heavy leaden eyes;
目光短淺 myopic; never to see beyond the end of one's nose; not to see beyond one's nose; shortsighted;
目光炯炯 have eyes with a piercing pleam; eyes bright and shining; one's eyes flash like lightning; with flashing eyes;
目光老練 have an experienced eye;
目光淺近 shortsighted;
目光如電 one's eyes flash like lightning;
目光如豆 as blind as a bat; as blind as a beetle; as blind as a mole; one's circle of vision is as small as a bean － narrow-visioned; shortsighted;
目光如炬 eyes blazing like torches － blazing with anger; farsighted; look ahead with wisdom; with flashing eyes;
目光銳利 eagle-eyed; have an experienced eye; have sharp eyes; have the eye of a sailor; see through a millstone; sharp-eyed; sharp-sighted;
目光貪婪 with a covetous eye on;
目光犀利 look sharply at; one's eyesight is sharp;
目光相接 meet one's eye;
目光遠大 farsighted; have a broad vision; have a great insight; have farsightedness; have large vies; show great foresight; one's eyesight is extensive － farseeing;
目光灼灼 with keen, sparkling eyes;
懷疑的目光 a look of disbelief;
溫柔目光 tender-eyed;

[目擊] see with one's own eyes; witness;
目擊慘案 witness the massacre;
目擊耳聞 fall under one's observation; have seen with one's own eyes and heard with one's own ears; what is seen and heard; what one sees and hears;
目擊其事 witness the event;
目擊者 eyewitness; witness;

[目見] see for oneself;

[目今] nowadays; these days;

[目鏡] eyepiece; ocular;

比較目鏡 comparison eyepiece;
補償目鏡 compensating eyepiece; compensating ocular;
測微目鏡 micrometer ocular;
單心目鏡 monocentric ocular;
複式目鏡 compound eyepiece;
回照目鏡 helioscopic ocular;
立體接目鏡 stereoscopic ocular;
平周目鏡 complanatic eyepiece;
散光目鏡 diverging ocular;
雙目目鏡 binocular eyepiece;
網格目鏡 ocular;
顯微鏡目鏡 microscopic ocular;
消色差目鏡 eyepiece;
引導目鏡 guiding ocular;

[目距] eye distance;

[目力] eyesight; vision;
目力所及 as far as the eye can reach;

[目錄] (1) catalogue; list; contents; (2) table of contents; contents; (3) catalogue; directory; list; repertory; schedule;
目錄室 catalogue room;
目錄學 bibliography;
~目錄學家 bibliographer;
報導目錄 announcement bibliography;
備件目錄 parts catalogue;
補充目錄 additional catalogue;
地區性目錄 regional bibliography;
分類目錄 classified bibliography; classified catalogue;
分析目錄 analytical bibliography;
公開文獻目錄 unclassified bibliography;
累積目錄 cumulative bibliography;
聯合目錄 repertory catalogue;
拍賣目錄 auction catalogue;
書名目錄 title catalogue;
書業目錄 library catalogue; trade bibliography;
文件目錄 file catalogue;
系統目錄 system catalogue;
選題目錄 selected bibliography;
著者目錄 author catalogue;
專書目錄 unit bibliography;
專題目錄 special bibliography;
子目錄 subdirectory;

[目明如鷹] as sharp-sighted as an eagle;

[目前] at present; at the moment; currently; for the moment; just now; right now; up until now;
目前的形勢 actual state of affairs;
到目前為止 as yet; by now; down to date; hitherto; so far; thus far; to date; to this day; until now; up till now; up to now; up to present; up to the present day; up to the present moment;

[目如點漆] one's eyes shine like lacquer;

[目視] visual;
目視無神 dull eyes;

[目送] follow sb with one's eyes; gaze after; watch sb go;
目送睇迎 receive and part with the eyes respectively;
目送手揮 hands and eyes acting in coordination;
手揮目送 shake with the hand and follow with the eye — in bidding farewell;

[目挑心招] seduce sb by attractive looks;

[目無] show no respect to...;
目無法紀 act in utter disregard of law and discipline; bid defiance to the law; defy the law; disregard the law; flout law and discipline; have no regard for laws; lawless; to one's eyes there are no laws and rules; set the law at defiance; show contempt for the law;
~目無法紀的社會 lawless society;
目無光澤 dull eyes; one's eyes are without lustre;
目無下塵 conceited and arrogant; look down on the masses; supercilious;
目無餘子 despise all others;
目無組織 disregard organizational discipline;
目無尊長 show no respect to elders and superiors; with no regard for one's elders and betters;

[目下] at present; now;

[目眩] dazzled; dizzy;
目眩眼花 eyes being dizzy and blurred;
頭昏目眩 feel dizzy;

[目語] communicate with the eyes;

礙目 eyesore; offend the eye; unpleasant to look at; unpleasant to the eye;
案目 usher in the theatre;
閉目 close one's eyes;
蔽目 blindfold; cover the eyes;
編目 catalogue; list; make a catalogue;
弁目 squad leader;
側目 with a side-long glance;
瞋目 glare; stare angrily;
騁目 look into the distance;

觸目 meet the eye;
詞目 headword;
刺目 (1) dazzling; (2) offending to the eye;
奪目 dazzle the eyes;
耳目 (1) what one sees and hears; (2) one who spies for sb else;
反目 fall out;
綱目 detailed outline; outline;
鬼目 Chinese trumpet creeper;
過目 look over so as to check;
極目 look as far as the eye can see;
價目 marked price; price;
節目 item; programme;
舉目 look; raise the eyes;
劇目 list of plays or operas;
科目 (1) course; subject; (2) headings in an account book;
滿目 meet the eye on every side;
盲目 blind;
眉目 (1) features; looks; (2) logic; sequence of ideas;
面目 (1) face; features; (2) appearance; aspect; (3) face; honour; self-respect;
名目 items; names of things;
瞑目 close one's eyes in death; die content;
怒目 fierce stare; glaring eyes;
篇目 (1) title of an article or chapter heading; (2) table of contents;
品目 names of things;
書目 booklist; catalogue;
數目 amount; number;
稅目 tax items;
題目 (1) subject; title; topic; (2) examination questions;
條目 (1) clauses and subclauses; (2) entry (in a dictionary);
頭目 chieftain; head of a gang;
戲目 theatrical programme;
細目 (1) detailed catalogue; (2) detail; specific item;
顯目 conspicuous; showy;
項目 item;
心目 (1) frame of mind; mood; (2) mental view; mind;
醒目 attractive-looking;
序目 preface and table of contents;
亞目 suborder;
眼目 (1) eyes; (2) spy who reports to sb what he sees;
淫目 lascivious looks;
耀目 dazzle;
娛目 please the eye;
張目 (1) open one's eyes wide; (2) boost sb's arrogance;
帳目 items of an account;
眾目 what people see;
注目 fix one's eyes on; gaze at;
子目 specific item; subtitle;
總目 comprehensive table of contents;
縱目 look as far as one's eyes can see;

mu

【沐】 (1) bathe; cleanse; shampoo; wash; (2) holiday; leave; take a leave; (3) enrich; receive favours; steep in; (4) a surname;

[沐猴而冠] a devilish person with imposing attire; a monkey with a hat on — a worthless person in imposing attire; a snobbish social climber; making a monkey show — stupid political figures; wash a monkey and dress it up with a cap;

[沐浴] (1) have a bath; take a bath; (2) bathe; immerse; (3) ablutions; bath;
沐浴更衣 take a bath and put on clean clothes;
沐浴戒齋 bathe one's body and eat only vegetable food; bathe one's body and purify oneself;
沐浴在愛河中 be immersed in love;
戒齋沐浴 fast and bathe oneself;

mu

【牧】 herd; tend;

[牧草] forage grass; herbage;
牧草肥美 the herbage is rich;
牧草茂盛 the forage grass is exuberant;

[牧場] grazing land; green land; pasturage; pasture; pastureland; ranch;
牧場工人 cowhand; rancher;
牧場經營 ranching;
牧場面積 grazing acreage;
牧場主 rancher;
低產牧場 low-yielding pasture;
度假牧場 dude ranch;
灌叢牧場 bush pasture;
季節性牧場 seasonable pasture;
私人牧場 privately held ranch;
天然牧場 natural pasture;
小牧場 paddock;
畜牧場 cattle ranch;
永久牧場 permanent pasture;

[牧畜] animal husbandry; livestock breeding;
[牧地] grazing land; meadowland; pasture;
栽培牧地 cultivated pasture; tame pasture;
[牧歌] pastoral song;
[牧工] hired herdsman;
[牧民] herdsman;
[牧牛] oxherding;
牧牛場 pasture;
牧牛工 cowhand;
牧牛女工 cowgirl;
牧牛人 cowhand;
[牧區] pastural area; pasture areas;
[牧人] herdsman; shepherd;
[牧師] chaplain; churchman; cleric; clergyman; minister; padre; pastor; priest;
牧師的 clerical;
牧師領 dog collar;
牧師住宅 manse;
監獄牧師 prison chaplain;
教區牧師 parson; vicar;
隨軍牧師 padre;
助理牧師 curate;
[牧童] buffalo boy; cow boy; shepherd boy;
牧童放牧 the buffalo boy tends the cattle;
[牧羊] shepherd; tend sheep;
牧羊女 shepherdess;
牧羊犬 sheepdog;
牧羊人 goatherd; shepherd;
如狼牧羊 like a wolf shepherding sheep – rule the people oppressively;

芻牧 graze livestock; pasture livestock;
放牧 graze; put out to pasture;
輪牧 rotation grazing;
畜牧 raise livestock;
游牧 move about in search of pasture; rove around as a nomad;

mu
【苜】 clover;

mu
【莫】 dusk; evening;

mu
【募】 (1) enlist; recruit; (2) raise funds;
[募兵] recruit soldiers;
[募化] collect alms;
[募集] collect; raise;
募集軍餉 collect soldier's pay and provisions;
募集資金 raise a fund;
[募捐] collect donations; pass round the hat; pass the hat round; solicit contributions; whip-round;
募捐長跑 fun run;
募捐糧食 solicit for grain;
募捐盤 collection plate;
募捐箱 collection box;
募捐衣被 collection donations of clothing and quilts;

籌募 collect funds;
勸募 ask for contributions;
宣募 (1) recruit; (2) collect;
招募 enlist; recruit;
徵募 enlist; recruit;

mu
【睦】 harmonious; peaceful;
[睦鄰] good-neighbourliness; remain on friendly terms with the neighbours;
睦鄰關係 good neighbourliness; good-neighbourly relations;
睦鄰相處 get along very well with one's neighours; good neighbours living in harmony; live in amity with one's neighbours; live in friendship;
睦鄰由禮 good relations between neighbours stem from politeness;
睦鄰友好 good neighbourly and friendly relations;
睦鄰政策 good-neighbour policy;
親睦鄰邦 keep on good relations with neighbour countries;

敦睦 promote friendly relations;
悌睦 kind to friends;

mu
【鉬】 molybdenum;

mu
【墓】 grave; mausoleum; tomb;
[墓碑] grave monument; gravestone; headstone; tombstone;
建墓碑 build a gravestone;
立墓碑 set up a tombstone;
[墓地] bone-orchard; bone-yard; burial ground; burial place; cemetery; graveyard;
[墓木已拱] the trees on one's graveyard are already grown tall; deceased long ago; trees around the tomb have grown very

M

large;

[墓石] headstone; tombstone;

[墓室] coffin chamber; vault;

[墓穴] coffin pit; grave; monument; open grave; tomb; vault;

地下墓穴 catacomb;

[墓志] epigraph; inscription on the memorial tablet within a tomb;

拜墓 worship at the grave;

墳墓 grave; tomb;

古墓 ancient tomb;

陵墓 mausoleum; tomb;

丘墓 grave;

掃墓 pay respects to a dead person at his tomb;

省墓 visit one's elder's grave;

mu

【幕】 (1) curtain; screen; (2) act;

[幕後] backroom; backstage; behind the scenes;

幕後操縱 behind-the-scenes manipulation; pull the strings behind the scenes; wirepulling;

~幕後操縱者 paymaster; wirepuller;

幕後策劃 engineer behind the curtain; plot behind the scenes;

幕後活動 backstage manoeuvring;

幕後交易 behind-the scenes deal;

幕後人物 wirepuller;

幕後英雄 backroom boy;

幕後政治活動 backroom politics;

幕後政治交易 backstairs political deals;

幕後指使 direct...from behind the scene; manipulate behind the scene;

在幕後 behind the curtain;

[幕僚] aids and staff; assistant to a ranking official or general in old China;

報幕 announce the items on a programme;

閉幕 (1) lower the curtain; (2) close; conclude;

褚幕 cloth covering a coffin;

毳幕 felt curtain;

黑幕 inside story of a plot;

揭幕 inaugurate; unveil;

結幕 (1) last act; (2) climax; ending; final;

開幕 (1) the curtain rises; (2) inaugurate; open;

內幕 inside story; what goes on behind the screen;

天幕 (1) canopy of the heavens; (2) backgrop (of a stage);

鐵幕 iron curtain;

帷幕 heavy curtain;

謝幕 answer a curtain call;

序幕 prelude; prologue;

煙幕 smoke screen;

夜幕 curtain of night;

銀幕 screen;

雨幕 streaming rain;

氈幕 felt tent;

竹幕 bamboo curtain;

mu

【慕】 admire; yearn for;

[慕名] out of admiration for a famous person;

慕名而來 be attracted to a place by its reputation; come to sb out of admiration of his fame;

慕名求見 have respect for sb's name and ask for an interview;

[慕男狂] nymphomaniac;

愛慕 admire; adore;

景慕 esteem; revere;

敬慕 respect and admire; revere and admire;

渴慕 yearningly admire;

戀慕 have a tender feeling towards;

孌慕 long after;

思慕 admire; think of sb with respect;

羨慕 admire; envy;

向慕 admire; adore;

歆慕 admire; esteem;

仰慕 admire; admire and esteem;

依慕 adore;

蟻慕 long for; yearn for;

永慕 remember forever;

怨慕 be dissatisfied and full of earnest desire;

軫慕 remember with deep emotion;

mu

【暮】 (1) dusk; evening; sunset; (2) late; towards the end;

[暮靄] evening mist;

暮靄沉沉 dusk is falling; evening mist is deepening;

[暮春] end of spring; late spring;

[暮年] declining years; evening of one's life; old age;

暮年淒慘 one leads a miserable life in one's old age;

暮年餘程 remaining journey of one's life;

安度暮年 spend one's declining years with happiness;

將至暮年 approach one's old age;

[暮氣] apathetic airs; apathy;
暮氣沉沉 apathetic; dejected; depressed; desponding; dismal; gloomy; languid; lethargic; lifeless; moody; moping;
暮氣朦朧 the evening light is becoming obscure — in twilight;

[暮色] dusk; gloaming; shadow; twilight;
暮色蒼茫 deepening dusk; spreading shades of dusk; the dusk is gathering; the twilight deepens;
暮色昏沉 the dusk is deepening;
暮色漸濃 twilight is merging into darkness;
暮色深沉 depressing dusk; the dusk is deepening;

[暮雲] evening clouds;
暮雲藹藹 hazy evening clouds;
暮雲春樹 evening clouds and spring trees — think of an absent friend who is far away; longing for friends afar; remembrance of a friend afar;

薄暮 dusk; twilight;
垂暮 dusk; just before sundown;
歲暮 the close of the year;
投暮 dusk;

mu

【穆】 (1) peaceful; sincere; (2) majestic; profound; respectful; reverent; solemn; (3) right side of an ancestral shrine; (4) a surname;

[穆民] name which the Mohammedans call themselves;

[穆清之世] age of peace;

[穆然] (1) peaceful and respectful; (2) meditative;

靜穆 solemn and quiet;
緝穆 at peace with each other;

mu

【繆】 (1) beautiful; (2) harmonious; (3) silent;

na¹
na
【那】 a surname;

na²
na
【南】
[南無] be converted to the dharma;
南無阿彌陀佛 a transliteration of namo amitabha, meaning homage to Amitabha Buddha;

na
【拿】 (1) bring; fetch; get; hold; take; (2) assume great airs; give oneself airs; put on airs; (3) arrest; capture; put under arrest; seize; (4) able to do; sure of; (5) put sb in a difficult position; raise difficulties; (6) with;
[拿把] put on airs; strike a pose in order to enhance one's own importance;
[拿班] assume great airs; put on airs; strike a pose;
拿班做勢 act affectedly; assume airs of importance; assume an appearance; put on airs; with a great show of importance;
[拿辦] arrest and deal with according to law; bring to justice;
[拿不準] be still in the air; be still up in the air;
[拿大] give oneself airs;
[拿大頭] make a fool of sb;
[拿刀動杖] resort to force;
[拿頂] stand on one's head;
[拿放] take or release;
拿得起，放得下 able to advance or retreat; adaptable; flexible;
輕拿輕放 handle gently;
[拿號兒] register;
[拿獲] apprehend; arrest;
拿獲一個扒手 apprehend a pickpocket;
將歹徒拿獲 capture the scoundrel;
[拿喬] strike a pose to impress people;
[拿取] take;
[拿權] in the saddle; wield power;
[拿人] make things difficult for others; put sb in a difficult position; raise difficulties;
拿人出氣 vent one's spleen on sb;
拿人一把 make things difficult for sb;
故意拿人 difficult with sb on purpose;
[拿事] have the power to do sth or to decide what to do;
拿事的人 the person who has the power to do sth;
[拿手] adept; expert; good at;
拿手好戲 a game one is good at; one's favourite game; one's forte; one's speciality; what one excels in;
拿手傑作 one's masterpiece;
拿手招數 one's forte;
[拿糖] give oneself airs; put on airs; strike a pose to impress people;
拿糖作醋 give sb a song and dance about sth; make a statement or explanation interesting in itself but not necessarily true; put on airs purposely; put on an act deliberately;
[拿穩] hold steadily; predict with confidence;
拿不穩 on slippery ground;
[拿走] take sth away;
擅自拿走 waltz off;
[拿住] (1) hold firmly; (2) put under arrest;

捕拿 arrest; catch;
飭拿 give orders for the arrest of;
捉拿 arrest; catch;

na³
na
【那】 (1) that; (2) in that case; then;
[那邊] over there; there;
[那兒] over there;
上那兒去 where are you going;
[那個] that;
那個傢伙 that guy;
那個小子 that chap;
忙了這個又要忙那個 what with one thing and another;
[那還用說] it goes without saying; of course;
[那會儿] at that time;
[那件] that piece;
[那裏] (1) that place; there; (2) where;
[那麼] (1) in that way; like that; (2) about; or so; (3) in that case; such being the case; then;
[那時] at that time; in those days; then;
那時候 at that time;
[那雙] that pair;
[那天] that day; the other day;

［那位］ that; that one;
［那些］ those;
那些天 those days;
［那樣］ in that way; like that; of that kind; so; such;
那樣耐心 so patient;
那樣善良 so kind;
就那樣 that's it; that's that;
［那種］ that kind;

刹那 instant; split second;

na
【哪】 (1) what; which; (2) any;
［哪兒］ where;
哪兒的話 don't mention it;
哪兒知道 who can imagine;
［哪個］ which one;
［哪裏］ (1)where; (2) don't mention it; it's nothing;
哪裏哪裏 don't mention it;
［哪怕］ even; even if; even though; no matter how; though;
［哪些］ which;

na⁴
na
【吶】 (1) cheer; cry out; shout; yell; (2) speak hesitatingly;
［吶喊］ cry out; loud shouts in support; shout loudly; yell;
吶喊抗議 cry out against;
吶喊助威 cheer; shout encouragement; shout loudly to encourage; shout one's support;
播旗吶喊 wave the flag and shout;
搖旗吶喊 acclaim; bang the drum for sb; carry the banner and cheer for; clamour; sound the clarion; voice support for; wave the flag and shout to support one's troops in war;with much shouting and fluttering of flags;

嗩吶 suona born;

na
【那】 that; those;
na
【娜】 tender, slender and graceful; well poised;
na
【納】 (1) admit; receive; (2) accept; take in; (3) bring into; fit into; (4) enjoy; take pleasure in life; (5) give; offer; pay; (6) sew close stitches;
［納財進禮］ give money for gifts;
［納福］ enjoy a life of ease and comfort;
納福迎祥 may you obtain happiness and meet with good luck;
興居納福 may you be well in all circumstances; may you keep in good health and be prosperous;
延祥納福 induce good luck and happiness; receive happiness and blessing;
［納罕］ be surprised; marvel;
［納賄］ (1) offer bribes; (2) take bribes;
納賄枉法 take bribes and break the law;
從不納賄 never take bribes;
經常納賄 often take bribes;
拒絕納賄 turn down bribes;
［納涼］ enjoy the cool;
到海邊納涼 go to the seashore to enjoy the cool;
［納履踵決］ destitute; down at heels; down at the heel; out at the elbows;
［納悶］ feel puzzled; perplexed; wonder;
心中納悶 be perplexed;
［納米］ nanometer;
納米出版 nanopublishing;
納米技術 nanotechnology;
［納入］ bring into; fit into;
納入軌道 bring...into the orbit of; direct...into the orbit of;
納入計劃 bring sth into the plan;
納入正軌 guide into a normal path; lead onto the correct path; put sth on the right course; set sth on the right track;
［納稅］ pay duty; pay tax; tax payment;
納稅程序 procedure of taxation;
納稅年度 tax year;
納稅人 tax bearer; tax payer;
納稅日 tax day;
納稅意識 tax consciousness;
集中納稅 duty to be paid by importer's head office;
口岸納稅 duty to be paid at port of import;
逃避納稅 dodge a tax; evade a tax;
拒絕納稅 refuse to pay taxes;
［納新］ take in the fresh;

採納 accept; adopt;
出納 (1) receive and pay out money; (2) receive

N

and lend books; (3) cashier; teller;

電納 susceptance;

歸納 conclude; induce; sum up;

集納 collect; gather;

繳納 hand in; pay;

接納 accept; admit;

然納 endorse and adopt;

容納 accommodate; have a capacity of; hold;

哂納 kindly accept;

笑納 kindly accept;

延納 employ talents;

na

【衲】 (1) line; mend; patch; sew; (2) monk; (3) robe of a monk;

na

【捺】 (1) press down; press hard with hands; (2) downstroke slanting toward the right in Chinese calligraphy; (3) repress; (4) stitch;

na

【鈉】 natrium; sodium;

na⁵

na

【哪】 phrase-final particle;

nai³

nai

【乃】 (1) to be; (2) so as to; so that; (3) and also; but; however; moreover; (4) that; those; your;

[乃是] (1) but; (2) which is...;

[乃至] (1) leading to; so...as to; so that; (2) consequently; hence;

nai

【奶】 (1) breasts; (2) dairy; milk; (3) breast-feed; suckle;

[奶茶] tea with milk;

[奶場] dairy farm;

奶場工人 dairyman;

奶場女工 dairymaid;

[奶粉] dried milk; milk powder; powdered milk;

固體奶粉 blockmilk;

全脂奶粉 whole milk powder;

壓塊奶粉 blockmilk;

[奶鍋] milk pan;

[奶酪] cheese;

一塊奶酪 a dollop of cheese; a piece of cheese;

[奶媽] wet nurse;

奶媽抱孩子—人家的 the child a wet nurse is holding – sb else's;

[奶名] child's pet name; infant name;

[奶奶] (1) paternal grandma; paternal grandmother; (2) gran; granny; nan; nanna; nanny;

老奶奶 grannie; granny;

~老奶奶結 granny knot;

~老奶奶鞋 granny shoes;

~老奶奶住房 granny flat;

少奶奶 (1) young mistress of the house; (2) daughter-in-law;

姨奶奶 concubine; mistress;

[奶牛] dairy cattle; milch cow;

[奶品] dairy products; milk products;

[奶瓶] (1) feeder; feeding bottle; nursing bottle; (2) milk bottle;

用奶瓶餵 bottle-feed;

[奶水] milk;

[奶糖] toffee;

[奶頭] (1) nipples; teats; (2) nipple of a feeding bottle;

[奶昔] milk shake;

草莓奶昔 strawberry milk shake;

[奶牙] baby teeth; milk tooth;

[奶油] butter; buttercream; cream;

奶油茶點 cream tea;

奶油蛋糕 cream cake;

奶油凍 mousse;

奶油壺 cream-holder;

~小奶油壺 creamer;

奶油膜 cream;

~一層奶油膜 a mantle of milk;

奶油巧克力 milk chocolate;

奶油色的 creamy;

奶油硬糖 butterscotch;

產氣奶油 gassy cream;

春季奶油 spring butter;

粗製稀奶油 creamy cream;

代奶油 creamer;

發酵奶油 fermenting butter;

高脂濃奶油 double cream;

高脂稀奶油 concentrated cream;

攢奶油 whipped cream;

含奶油的 creamy;

濃奶油 heavy cream;

濃縮奶油 clotted cream;

乳清奶油 serum butter;

人造奶油 margarine;

～不加鹽人造奶油 salt-free margarine;
～療效人造奶油 dietetic margarine;
～印模人造奶油 printed margarine;
酸奶油 sour cream;
酸性稀奶油 cultured cream;
甜性奶油 sweet cream butter;
似奶油的 creamy;
鹹奶油 briny butter;
硬質奶油 firm butter;
再製奶油 renovated butter;

［奶罩］ bra;

［奶子］ (1) milk; (2) boobs; breast; knockers; tits;
一對奶子 knockers;

［奶嘴］ nipple of a feeding bottle;

吃奶 suck the breast;
斷奶 wean;
二奶 mistress;
擠奶 milk;
煉奶 condensed milk;
馬奶 mare's milk;
牛奶 milk;
瞎奶 (1) unprotrusive nipple; (2) nipple that gives no milk when sucked;
羊奶 ewe's milk;
漾奶 throw up milk;

nai

【氖】 neon;

［氖燈］ neon lamp;

nai

【艿】 a kind of vegetable;

nai

【迺】 same as 乃;

nai4

nai

【奈】 how; to no avail;

［奈何］ how; to no avail;
沒奈何 have no alternative; have no way out; utterly hopeless;
～刀鈍石來磨，人蠢沒奈何 a blunt knife may be sharpened on a stone; but if a man is stupid there is no help for his stupidity;
如之奈何 what can be done about it; what can we do about it;
徒呼奈何 cry to no avail; regret in vain; utter bootless cries;
徒喚奈何 regret in vain; utter bootless cries; utter unavailing cries of despair;
無可奈何 have no alternative but to...;

豈奈 cannot help but;
無奈 but; cannot help but; have no alternative; however;
怎奈 but; however;

nai

【耐】 able to bear; able to endure;

［耐病性］ disease tolerance;

［耐不住］ unable to bear; unable to stand;

［耐穿］ durable; wear well;
耐穿耐用 stand wear and tear;
很耐穿 very durable clothing;

［耐煩］ have patience; patient; tolerant;
不耐煩 be impatient; champing at the bit;
～等得不耐煩了 champ at the bit;
～活得不耐煩 getting tired of living;

［耐寒］ cold-resistant;
耐寒性 cold endurance; freeze resistance; low-temperature resistance;

［耐旱性］ drought hardiness;

［耐火］ fire-resistant; refractory;
耐火磚 firebrick;

［耐久］ durable;
耐久性 durability;
～表面耐久性 surface durability;
～催化劑耐久性 durability of catalyst;
～木材耐久性 durability of wood;
～室內耐久性 interior durability;

［耐勞］ able to endure hard work;
吃苦耐勞 bear hardships and stand hard work; hardworking and able to bear hardship; inured to hardships; work hard and endure hardship;
刻苦耐勞 work hard without complaint;

［耐力］ endurance;
耐力訓練 endurance training;
耐力運動 endurance sports;
肌肉耐力 muscular endurance;
心血管耐力 cardiovascular endurance;
專項耐力 specific endurance;

［耐磨］ abrasion resistant; wear resistant;
耐磨度 abradability;
耐磨能力 abradability;
耐磨性 abradability; abrasion resistance;
抗熱耐磨 strong resistance to heat and hard wearing;
鑽石耐磨 diamonds are wearproof;

［耐熱］ heat-resisting; heatproof;
耐熱的 ovenproof;
耐熱器皿 ovenware;

N

［耐人尋味］ afford much food for thought; stand careful reading; thought-provoking;
耐人尋味的話 words which provide food for thought;
［耐受］ withstand;
耐受性 tolerance;
［耐心］ patience;
耐心等待 wait patiently;
耐心服務 serve sb patiently;
耐心觀察 observe with patience;
耐心解釋 explain patiently;
耐心傾聽 listen to sb patiently;
耐心細致 in a patient and meticulous way; make patient and painstaking efforts; patient and meticulous;
保持耐心 keep patience;
沒耐心 impatient;
培養耐心 cultivate patience;
失去耐心 lose one's patience; run out of patience with sb;
有耐心 have patience;
~需要有耐心 require patience;
做事耐心 do sth with patience;
［耐性］ endurance; patience;
考驗耐性 try one's patience;
［耐蔭性］ shade tolerance;
［耐用］ durable; withstand wear and tear;
耐用的 hardwearing;
不耐用 cannot withstand wear and tear; not durable;
經久耐用 durable for a long time;
［耐雨性］ rain fastness;
按耐 control; restrain; suppress;
能耐 ability; capability; skill;
叵耐 cannot put up with; cannot tolerate;
忍耐 endure; restrain oneself;

nai
【柰】 (1) apple tree; (2) but; how; (3) then what; (4) no way out of a dilemma; (5) bear; endure;

nai
【鼐】 huge tripod caldron;

nai
【褦】 (1) ignorant; naive; short-witted; stupid; (2) palm-leaf topee;

nan²
nan
【男】 (1) male; man; (2) boy; son;

［男錶］ men's watch;
［男廁］ men's lavatory; the gents;
男廁所 gentlemen; men; men's lavatory; the gents;
［男大當婚］ a grown-up man ought to marry; a man should get married on coming of age; every Jack must have his Jill;
男大當婚，女大當嫁 when men and women are fully grown, they must marry;
［男隊］ men's team;
［男兒］ man;
男兒有淚不輕彈，祇因未到傷心時 a man does not easily shed tears until his heart is broken; men only weep when deeply hurt;
［男方］ the bridegroom's side;
［男服］ menswear;
［男孩］ boy;
男孩文化 lad culture;
男孩樂隊 boy band;
男孩子 boy;
娘娘腔的男孩 cissy boy; sissy boy;
瘦小的男孩 a slip of a boy;
小男孩 little boy;
一群男孩 a group of boys;
［男妓］ gigolo; male prostitute; maud; rent boy; renter; ring-snatcher;
年輕男妓 rent boy;
［男家］ bridegroom's family;
［男爵］ baron;
男爵夫人 baroness;
准男爵 baronet;
［男女］ men and women;
男女不分 ambisextrous; unisex
~男女不分的服裝 unisex clothing;
男女混雜 both sexes mix; men and women mingle together;
男女老少 men and women, old and young; people of all ages and both sexes;
男女老幼 all people regardless of age and sex; people of all ages and both sexes;
男女平等 equal rights for both sexes; equal rights for men and women; equality between men and women;
男女授受不親 it is improper for men and women to touch each other's hand in passing objects;
男女同校 coeducation;

~男女同校的 coed;
男女有別 a distinction should be made between males and females; between the sexes there should be a prudent reserve; males and females should be distinguished;
不男不女 look neither like a man nor a woman;
~男不男，女不女 neither fish, flesh nor fowl;
痴男怨女 amorous youths and languishing maidens; languishing youths and unhappy maidens; perverse lads and plaintive maidens;
曠男怨女 men and women of marriageable age but unmarried;
男盜女娼 behave like thieves and whores; out-and-out scoundrels;
男歡女愛 man and woman in passion of love;
男男女女 men and women;
善男信女 devotees to Buddha; devout men and women; the faithful;
攜男挈女 bring sons and daughters along with one; lead sons and carry daughters;
一男半女 a few children; one or two offsprings;
重男輕女 look up to men and down on women; prefer boys to girls; regard men as superior to women;

[男權運動] masculinist movement;

[男人] (1) dude; man; (2) menfolk; (3) husband;
男人就是這樣 that's men;
男人腔的 butch;
笨男人 knuckle-dragger;
蠢男人 knuckle-dragger;
大男人 macho;
~大男人行為 machismo;
勾引男人 hook man;
老男人 distinguished gentleman; seasoned man;
戀家的男人 family man;
娘娘腔的男人 ponce;
女人氣的男人 ponce;
神秘男人 mystery man;
受男人歡迎的男人 a man's man;
受女人歡迎的男人 a ladies' man;
她的男人 her man;
小男人 little man;
~討厭的小男人 odious little man;
一個名叫…的男人 a man called...;
有個人收入的男人 man of independent means;

[男生] boy student; man student; schoolboy;

[男士] gentleman; man;
男士服裝 menswear;

[男性] (1) male; male sex; (2) man;
男性更年期 viropause;
男性化 masculine;
~男性化的 butch; mannish;
男性疾病學 andrology;
男性學 andrology;
男性雜誌 lad mag;

[男裝] menswear;
男裝部 menswear department;

[男子] male; man;
男子漢 man;
男子氣 masculinity;
男子氣概 machismo; manhood; manliness;
~有男子氣概 manly;
美男子 handsome man; very good-looking man;
女人氣的男子 cissy;
奇男子 a man among men; a remarkable man;
身材好的男子 a fine figure of a man;
同性戀男子 cissy; gay;
未婚男子 bachelor;
一名男子 a man;

大男 unmarried young men;
童男 virgin boy;
舞男 gigolo;
孝男 bereaved son;
宜男 profilic of male children;
長男 eldest son;
鬍男 heavily bearded man;

nan

【南】 south;

[南北] (1) north and south; (2) from north to south;
南北對話 north-south dialogue;
南北向 north-south;
闖南走北 make a living wandering from place to place; make many long journeys; roam all over the country; travel widely;
海北天南 distance from the north sea to the south sky;

面南坐北 facing the south and leaning against the north; facing the south and with the north at one's back;
南販北賈 hurry here and there to make a living;
南糧北調 ship grain from the south to the north; supply grain to the north from the south;
南水北調 divert water from the south to the north;
南轅北轍 go south by driving the chariot north – act in a way that defeats one's purpose; poles apart;
南禦北討 conquer north and south;
天南地北 (1) far apart; from different places; poles apart; separated by vast distances; (2) discursive; rambling;
天南海北 (1) all over the country; (2) discursive; rambling;
走南闖北 journey north and south; roam all over the country; travel everywhere; travel widely; wander up and down the country;
坐北朝南 face south; with a southern exposure;

[南邊] south;
[南風] (1) south wind; (2) westerly wind; (3) (of mahjong) south wind;
南風不競 the opponent is not strong enough;
南風圈 (of mahjong) south wind round;
[南瓜] pumpkin;
[南貨] delicacies from south China;
[南極] Antarctic Pole; South Pole;
南極北斗 a false reputation without reality;

東南 (1) southeast; (2) Southeast; southeast China;
河南 Henan (Province);
西南 (1) southwest; (2) southwest China; (3) Southwest;
指南 guide; guidebook;

nan
【枏】 cedar;

nan
【喃】 murmur;
[喃喃] murmur; mutter;
喃喃不平 express one's discontent by muttering to oneself;
喃喃不休 make endless speeches;
喃喃自語 mumble to oneself; mutter under one's breath; utter one's thoughts unconciously;

呋喃 furan;
呢喃 twittering;

nan
【楠】 cedar;

石楠 Chinese photinia;

nan
【蝻】 nymph;

蝗蝻 nymph of a locust;
跳蝻 nymph of a locust;

nan
【諵】 chatter; gabble;

nan
【難】 (1) difficult; hard; troublesome; (2) put sb into a difficult position; (3) hardly possible; (4) bad; unpleasant;
[難辦] difficult to manage; hard to deal with; tough;
難辦的事 sticky business;
[難保] cannot say for sure; difficult to ensure;
難保性命 one's life is in danger;
旦夕難保 danger is imminent; in imminent peril;
身家難保 live in great danger;
[難辨] hard to distinguish;
贗真難辨 it is hard to distinguish the false from the true;
[難產] (1) difficult labour; (2) slow in coming;
[難處] hard to get along with;
難處的 cantankerous;
遇到難處 meet with trouble;
[難處] difficulty; trouble;
難處的人 a difficult person to get along with;
不難處 easy-going;
相當難處 quite difficult to get along;
[難辭其咎] can hardly absolve oneself of the blame;
[難倒] baffle; beat; daunt;
難倒了 it beats me; that beats me;
不被難倒 not be daunted;
[難道] could it be said that;
[難得] (1) hard to come by; rare; (2) rarely;

seldomly;

難得糊塗 where ignorance is bliss, folly is wise;

難得見面 seldom meet;

難得要命 fun and games;

機遇難得 rare opportunity;

年景難得 the year's harvest is quite rare;

[難點] difficult point; difficulty;

難點不多 there are not many difficult points in sth;

對付難點 tackle a hard nut;

解出難點 work out a difficult point;

是個難點 a hard nut to crack;

找出難點 find out the difficulty;

[難懂] dark; difficult to comprehend; hard to understand;

[難度] degree of difficulty; difficulty;

難度大 very difficult;

難度量表 scale of difficulty;

難度小 less difficult;

高難度 high degree of difficulty;

沒難度 attain no degree of difficulty;

評分難度 graded difficulty;

試題難度 item difficulty;

學習難度 learning difficulty;

有一定難度 acquire a certain degree of difficulty;

有難度 have degrees of difficulty;

[難逢] happen rarely;

千載難逢 extremely rare; extremely rare opportunity; golden opportunity; it happens only once in a thousand years; not likely to occur once in a thousand years; once in a blue moon; only once in a lifetime; opportunity which comes once in a thousand years; such an opportunity would not offer itself in a thousand years; very rare;

[難怪] (1) no wonder; (2) pardonable; understandable;

[難關] barrier; crisis; difficulty; tight squeeze;

難關重重 a bundle of difficulties; a lot of obstacles;

安渡難關 pull through; tide over a crisis; tide over the difficulties;

熬過難關 pull through hard times; tide over difficulties; tide sb over;

擺脱難關 get rid of crisis;

幫助渡難關 give sb a leg up;

重重難關 alps on alps;

渡過難關 go through a difficult pass; go through a difficult period; pull through; tide over a difficulty; tough it out; turn the corner;

共渡難關 tide over the difficulties; weather the hard times;

戰勝難關 clear away all difficulties;

[難管] difficult to govern; hard to rule;

[難過] (1) have a hard time; (2) be saddened by; feel bad; feel sorry; grieved;

感到難過 feel sad; feel sorry for;

日子難過 lead a hard life;

[難解難分] be locked together in a struggle; be sentimentally attached to each other; cannot bear to part; inextricably involved; unable to tear oneself away from sb;

[難堪] (1) intolerable; unbearable; (2) embarrassed;

困苦難堪 suffer unbearable hardships;

[難看] as ugly as a scarecrow; as ugly as a toad; bad-looking; ugly; ugly-looking;

長相難看 look ugly;

臉色難看 look pale;

[難開] hard to open;

羞口難開 too embarrassed to say it; too embarrassed to speak out; too shy to speak;

[難免] be booked for; hard to avoid;

難免發脾氣 can hardly hold oneself back from being angry;

難免受罰 in for it;

難免走彎路 can't avoid taking a roundabout course;

[難人] (1) delicate; difficult; ticklish; (2) person handling a delicate matter;

[難色] appear to be reluctant or embarrassed;

滿臉難色 be completely reluctant;

面帶難色 put on an embarrassed expression;

面有難色 appear to be reluctant; show signs of reluctance; with a look of disinclination;

顯出難色 have a reluctant expression;

[難上難] doubly difficult; extremely difficult;

趕鴨子上樹—難上難 driving a duck up a tree — extremely difficult;

[難捨] loathe to part from each other; reluctant to separate;

難捨難分 be sentimentally attached to each other; cannot bear to part from

each other;
難分難捨 cannot bear to part from each other; find it difficult to tear apart;

[難事] a hard nut to crack; difficulty;

[難受] feel awful; feel bad; feel ill; feel unhappy; feel unwell; suffer pain;
感到非常難受 feel awful;
很難受 feel very bad;
渾身難受 ache all over;

[難説] it is hard to say; you never can tell;
很難説 how long is a piece of string;
有苦難説 find it hard to tell about one's suffering;

[難題] a hard nut to crack; conundrum; facer; headache; hot potato; poser; problem; stinker; teaser; ticklish business;
出難題 pose a difficult problem; set difficult questions; set sb a very difficult task;
解決難題 solve the difficult problem; solve the difficulty;
那真是個難題 that's a real poser;
遇到難題 encounter a difficulty;
找出難題 find out where the problem is;

[難聽] (1) unpleasant to hear; (2) coarse; offensive;
唱得難聽 not good at singing;

[難忘] be fixed in the mind; memorable; never to be erased from the mind; never to be forgotten; unforgettable;
美好歲月難忘 the sweet memories are unforgettable;
沒齒難忘 grateful to sb until the last tooth falls out of one's head; never forget as long as one lives; remember as long as one lives; remember for the rest of one's life;
歲月難忘 the days are memorable;

[難為久計] hard to stand for long;

[難為情] abashed; ashamed; disconcerting; embarrassed; ill at ease; shy;
感到難為情 be abashed at...;

[難聞] smell bad; smell unpleasant; unpleasant to smell;

[難行] difficult to move;
滯礙難行 obstructed and difficult;

[難言] feel embarrassed to mention;
難言之隱 a painful topic; a sore subject; sth embarrassing to mention; sth which ails one's mind and hard to state;

[難以] difficult to; hard to;
難以成交 it is hard to conclude a deal;
難以出口 be too embarrassed to say it;
難以糾正 hard to correct;
難以接受 uneasy to accept;
難以控制 beyond control;
難以理喻 it is hard to convince sb with reason;
難以立足 difficult to keep a foothold;
難以買進 it is hard to buy;
難以賣出 it is hard to push the sales;
難以名狀 beyond description;
難以逆料 beyond one's powers to foresee; it is difficult to conjecture; it is hard to forecast; more than can be expected; there is no telling;
難以啟齒 hard to speak out; have a bone in the throat; stick in sb's throat; too embarrassed to mention sth; too shy to speak out;
難以忍受 hard to bear;
難以容忍 beyond endurance;
難以入睡 have difficulty in going to sleep;
難以實現 difficult of accomplishment;
難以收拾 out of hand;
難以推銷 it is hard to sell;
難以挽回 it is hard to retrieve;
難以忘懷 unforgettable;
難以為繼 difficult to continue; difficult to move ahead; hard to keep up;
難以溫飽 can hardly keep oneself from hunger and cold;
難以相與 hard to get along with;
難以想像 hard to imagine; hard to visualize; unimaginable;
難以形容 baffle description; beyond description; cannot be described by words; difficult to put in words; have no words to express;
難以言喻 beyond expression;
難以抑制 difficult to control; hard to restrain;
難以預料 beyond one's powers to foresee;
難以證明 difficult of proof;
難以置信 beyond belief; hardly worthy of belief; rather hard to swallow; unthinkable;

[難易] the difficult and the ease;
捨難就易 choose the easier task; choose the lighter way;
説易行難 easier said than done;
先難後易 things are difficult at first and

quite easy afterwards; well begun is half done;
由易到難 from the easier to the more advanced;

[難於] difficult to; hard to;
難於控制 get out of hand; out of control;
難於理解 beyond one's depth; out of one's depth;
難於立足 difficult to keep a foothold;
難於啟齒 difficult to speak out one's mind; have a bone in the throat;
難於奏效 hard to get results;

凝難 find it difficult (to do sth) for certain reasons;
煩難 complicated and difficult; difficult to deal with;
繁難 complicated and difficult to deal with; hard to tackle;
費難 give or take a lot of trouble;
艱難 difficult; hard;
兩難 be in a dilemma; be in an awkward position; face a difficult choice;
萬難 all difficulties; extremely difficult; utterly impossible;
為難 (1) feel awkward; feel embarrassed; (2) make things difficult for sb;
畏難 be afraid of difficulty;
作難 (1) feel awkward; feel embarrassed; (2) in a difficult position;

nan³
nan
【赧】 blush; turn red from shame or embarrassment;

[赧紅] rubedo;
[赧然] blushing;
[赧顏] blush; shamefaced;
赧顏抱慚 ashamed; put to the blush;
赧顏赤頸 blush down to one's neck;
赧顏汗下 extremely ashamed; so ashamed that one flushes and sweats;

羞赧 blushed because of shyness;

nan
【腩】 brisket;

nan⁴
nan
【難】 (1) calamity; catastrophe; disaster; (2) blame; reproach;

[難民] displaced person; refugee;
難民潮 refugee wave;
難民營 refugee camp;
~臨時難民營 transit camp;
淪為難民 be reduced to refugees;
遣返難民 repatriate refugees;

[難友] fellow sufferer;
成為難友 become fellow sufferers;

被難 be killed in a disaster etc;
避難 seek asylum; take refuge;
辯難 debate; retort with challenging questions;
駁難 refute and blame; retort and blame;
大難 catastrophe; disaster;
刁難 deliberately put obstacles in sb's way; purposely make things difficult for;
發難 launch an attack; rise in revolt;
非難 blame; censure; reproach;
赴難 help saving the country from danger;
國難 national calamity;
海難 perils of the sea;
患難 adversity; distress; suffering; trials and tribulations;
及難 encounter disaster;
急難 grave danger; misfortune;
劫難 fateful calamity;
苦難 distress; misery; suffering;
困難 difficult; financial difficulties; straitened circumstances;
罹難 (1) die in a disaster or an accident; (2) be murdered;
留難 deliberate set up obstruction for; purposely make things difficult for sb;
論難 argue against the opponent's viewpoint; debate;
落難 encounter difficulty, adversity, etc; meet with misfortune;
蒙難 be confronted by danger; be in distress; fall into the clutches of the enemy;
磨難 hardship; suffering; tribulation;
受難 be in distress; suffer calamities or disasters;
死難 die in an accident or a political incident;
逃難 be a refugee; flee from a calamity;
危難 calamity; danger and disaster;
問難 question and argue repeatedly;
殉難 die for a just cause for one's country;
疑難 difficult; knotty;
遇難 (1) die or be killed in an accident; (2) be murdered;
災難 calamity; catastrophe; disaster;
遭難 meet with catastrophe;
責難 blame; censure;

阻難 obstruct; thwart;

nang²
nang

【囊】 (1) bag; pocket; (2) bag-shaped object; (3) capsule;

[囊空] empty purse;

囊空膽壯，人窮志堅 an empty purse causes a full heart;

囊空如洗 be cleaned out; dead broke; hard up; not a shot in the locker; not to have a bean; one's pocket is empty; penniless; with empty pockets; without a penny in one's purse;

[囊括] embrace; include; sweep up;

囊括四海 bring the whole country under imperial rule;

囊括四海，併吞八方 seize the whole globe;

囊括一空 bag everything; sweep everything into one's net;

囊括一切 all embracing; sweep up everything;

[囊胚] blastula;

囊胚基質 blastostroma;

囊胚形成 blastostroma;

[囊中] in the bag;

囊中物 sth certain of attainment; sth which is in the bag;

~已是囊中物 sth that is certain of attainment;

囊中之錐 a man that will make his mark in the world;

錐處囊中 like an awl in a bag – real talent will be discovered;

[囊腫] cyst;

出血性囊腫 bemorrhagic cyst;

假性囊腫 pseudocyst;

膿氣囊腫 pyopneumocyst;

膿性囊腫 pyocyst;

真性囊腫 true cyst;

支氣管囊腫 bronchocele;

鞍囊 saddle bag;

背囊 knapsack;

抽血囊 blood capsule;

膽囊 gallbladder;

革囊 leather case;

弓囊 bow case;

關節囊 articular capsule; joint capsule;

黑囊 ink sac;

極囊 polar capsule;

頰囊 cheek pouch;

膠囊 capsule;

精囊 seminal vesicle;

口囊 mouth capsule;

卵囊 egg capsule;

毛囊 hair follicle;

內囊 internal capsule;

皮囊 (1) leather bag; (2) man's body;

氣囊 (1) sair sac; (2) gasbag;

軟骨囊 cartilage capsule;

砂囊 gizzard;

腎囊 renal capsule;

腎小球囊 glomerular capsule;

聲囊 vocal sac;

視囊 optic capsule;

私囊 private purse;

嗉囊 crop;

聽囊 auditory capsule;

圖囊 map bag;

外囊 external capsule;

窩囊 (1) vexed; (2) good-for-nothing; hopelessly stupid;

香囊 perfume satchel;

行囊 travelling bag;

陰囊 scrotum;

育囊 brood capsule;

脂囊 adipose capsule; fatty capsule;

智囊 brain truster;

中央囊 central capsule;

子囊 ascus;

nang³
nang

【曩】 former; past;

[曩時] in former times; in the past;

[曩者] in former times; in the past;

nang

【攮】 stab; thrust;

[攮子] bodkin; dagger;

nao²
nao

【怓】 confused; confusion; wild;

nao

【猱】 (1) yellow-haired monkey; (2) scratch;

[猱犬] red dog;

[猱昇] monkey climbing up a tree;

[猱雜] comical and restless; noisily and cynically;

［猱兒］ prostitutes;

nao

【撓】 (1) bend; daunt; force; subjugate; (2) rub; scratch;

［撓頭］ difficult to deal with; difficult to tackle;
撓頭的事 sth difficult to tackle;
感到撓頭 find it difficult to tackle;

［撓癢］ scratch an itchy part;

［撓折］ force to yield;

曲撓 unjust accusation;
阻撓 frustrate; obstruct; thwart;

nao

【橈】 (1) bent wood; (2) devitalize; enfeeble; sap; weaken; (3) disperse; scatter; (4) be wronged; wrong;

［橈敗］ defeated as troops;

［橈動脈］ radial artery;

［橈類］ copelata;

［橈骨］ radius of the forearm;
橈骨神經 radial nerve;

［橈鰭］ telson;

［橈足］ pleopod, swimmeret;
橈足類 copepoda;

［橈萬物］ scatter things here and there;

nao

【譊】 argue;

［譊譊］ arguing voices;

nao

【鐃】 (1) bell used in the army in ancient times; (2) cymbals;

nao³

nao

【惱】 (1) angry; annoyed; furious; indignant; irritated; vexed; (2) hate; resent; (3) unhappy; worried;

［惱恨］ hate; resent;
惱恨別人的成就 resent other people's achievements;

［惱火］ annoy; irritate; vex;
惱火的 irritated; narked;
感到惱火 be irritated by; get narked;

［惱怒］ angry; furious; indignant; irritation;
使惱怒 irk;

［惱人］ annoying; irritating;
惱人春色 suffering from love in spring;
春色惱人 spring's hues are teasing;
頑症惱人 the chronic and stubborn disease is annoying;
真是惱人 really irritating;

［惱羞成怒］ become angry and red-faced; become angry from embarrassment; become angry from shame; fly into a rage with shame; fly into a shameful rage; lose one's temper from embarrassment;

熬惱 unhappy and dejected;
懊惱 be chagrined; chagrin; feel annoyed; feel remorseful and angry; upset; vexed;
煩惱 fret over; worried;
苦惱 distressed; vexed; worried;
羞惱 humiliated and indignant;

nao

【瑙】 agate; conrnelian;

瑪瑙 agate;

nao

【腦】 brain; think box; think tank; topstorey; upper storey; upstairs;

［腦癌］ cancer of the brain; cerebral cancer;

［腦病］ cerebral disease; cerebrosis;
白質腦病 leukoencephalopathy;
大腦病 cerebrosis;
肝性腦病 hepatic encephalopathy;
尿毒症腦病 uremic encephalopathy;
鉛毒性腦病 lead encephalopathy;
外傷性腦病 traumatic encephalopathy;

［腦部］ brain;

［腦充血］ cerebral congestion; encephalemia;

［腦出血］ cerebral hemorrhage;

［腦袋］ bonce; head;
腦袋大了 addle one's head;
腦袋發木 one's mind refuses to work;
腦袋發熱 turn one's head;
腦袋發暈 one's brain begins to reel;
腦袋瓜笨 have a thick skull;
保住腦袋 save one's neck;
耷拉着腦袋 droop one's head; hang one's head;
掉腦袋 lose one's head;

［腦電波］ brainwave;

［腦發育不良］ atelencephalia;

［腦發育不全］ atelencephalia;

［腦反射］ cranial reflex;

［腦肥大］ encephalauxe;

N

［腦蓋］ top of the skull;
腦蓋骨 cranium;
［腦幹］ brain stem;
腦幹反射 brain stem reflex;
［腦瓜頂兒］ top of the head;
［腦瓜兒］ head;
［腦過小］ micrencephalon;
［腦海］ brain; mind;
腦海深處 at the back of sb's mind; in the back of sb's mind;
腦海空虛 spiritually barren;
腦海一片空白 have a blank mind;
［腦後］ disregard;
丟在腦後 completely ignore; let sth pass out of one's mind;
擱置腦後 off one's mind; put out of mind; throw to the winds;
置之腦後 banish from one's mind; cast behind one's back; consign to oblivion; disregard it; forget it; ignore and forget; place in the back of one's mind; put behind one; put...clean out of one's mind; put out of mind; off one's mind;

［腦脊髓膜炎］ cerebrospinal meningitis;
流行性腦脊髓膜炎 cerebrospinal meningitis;
［腦脊髓神經］ cerebrovascular diseases;
［腦脊髓炎］ encephalomyelitis;
病毒性腦脊髓炎 viral encephalomyelitis;
［腦脊液］ cerebrospinal fluid;
［腦積水］ hydrocephalus;
繼發性腦積水 secondary hydrocephalus;
原發性腦積水 primary hydrocephalus;
張力性腦積水 tension hydrocephalus;
中耳炎性腦積水 otitic hydrocephalus;
［腦漿］ brains;
腦漿迸裂 have one's brains dashed out;
腦漿四濺 one's brains are scattered in all directions;
［腦筋］ (1) brains; head; mind; (2) ideas;
腦筋遲鈍 have a slow wit; have slow wits; slow-witted;
腦筋簡單 simple-minded;
腦筋靈活 have a quick wit; have a supple mind; have quick wits; keen and sharp in thinking; quick-witted;
腦筋靈敏 keen and sharp in thinking;
大傷腦筋 cudgel one's brains; puzzle one's brains; put a great strain on sb's nerves; rack one's brains;
動腦筋 cudgel one's brains; deliberate; rack one's brains; ransack one's brains; set one's brains to work; take trouble over; think hard; use one's brains; use one's head; use one's wits;
～動腦筋，想辦法 beat one's brains to find a way out; cudgel one's brains to find a way out; puzzle one's brains to find a way out; rack one's wits to find a solution; rack one's brains to find ways and means; use one's head to think of a way;
動動腦筋 use one's brains; use one's noddle;
動足腦筋 rack one's brains;
費盡腦筋 beat one's brains out;
費腦筋 tax one's brains;
老腦筋 stubborn old brain; old fashioned; old ways of thinking;
傷腦筋 a nuisance; beat one's brains; bothersome; cause sb enough headache; have a hard nut to crack; knotty; task sb's mind; troublesome; trying to the nerves;
～傷透腦筋 cause sb enough headache; give sb a headache;
死腦筋 one-track mind;
［腦科學］ brain science; encephalic;
［腦力］ brains; mental;
腦力勞動 brain work; mental work;
［腦滿腸肥］ heavy-jowled and pot-bellied—said of the idle rich; with a fair round belly and a swelled head; with fat cheeks and a big belly;
［腦膜］ meninges;
腦膜腦炎 meningoencephalitis;
～肉芽腫性腦膜腦炎 granulomatous meningoencephalitis;
腦膜炎 meningitis;
癌性腦膜炎 meningitis carcinomatosa;
病毒性腦膜炎 viral meningitis;
感染性腦膜炎 infectious meningitis;
基底部腦膜炎 basilar meningitis;
～假性腦膜炎 meningism;
結核性腦膜炎 meningitis tuberculosis; tubercular meningitis;
鏈球菌性腦膜炎 streptococcal meningitis;
流行性腦膜炎 epidemic cerebrospinal meningitis; influenza meningitis;
流行性乙型腦炎 epidemic encephalitis B;
慢性腦膜炎 chronic meningitis;

梅毒性腦膜炎 syphilitic meningitis;
鼠疫性腦膜炎 plague meningitis;
細菌性腦膜炎 bacterial meningitis;
隱球菌腦膜炎 cryptococcal meningitis;
腫瘤性腦膜炎 neoplastic meningitis;
[腦膿腫] brain abscess;
[腦瓢兒] top of the head;
[腦貧血] cerebral anemia;
[腦橋] pons;
[腦軟化] softening of the brain;
[腦勺子] back of the head;
[腦神經] cranial nerve;
第二腦神經 second cranial nerve;
第九腦神經 ninth cranial nerve;
第六腦神經 sixth cranial nerve;
第七腦神經 seventh cranial nerve;
第三腦神經 third cranial nerve;
第十二腦神經 twelfth cranial nerve;
第十腦神經 seventh cranial nerve;
第十一腦神經 eleventh cranial nerve;
第四腦神經 fourth cranial nerve;
第五腦神經 fifth cranial nerve;
第一腦神經 first cranial nerve;
[腦室] ventricle;
[腦栓塞] cerebral embolism; cerebromalacia;
[腦損傷] brain damage;
[腦死亡] brain death; cerebral death;
[腦髓] brain;
[腦痛] cerebralgia;
[腦突出] cephalocele;
假性腦突出 pseudocephalocele;
黏連性腦突出 synencephalocele;
[腦外傷] brain surgery;
[腦萎縮] cerebral atrophy;
局限性腦萎縮 circumscribed cerebral atrophy;
[腦下垂體] pituitary gland;
[腦血栓形成] cerebral thrombosis;
[腦炎] brain fever; encephalitis;
白質腦炎 leukoencephalitis;
邊緣性腦炎 limbic encephalitis;
出血性腦炎 hemorrhagic encephalitis;
春季腦炎 vernal encephalitis;
流行性腦炎 epidemic encephalitis;
麻疹腦炎 measles encephalitis;
疱疹性腦炎 herpetic encephalitis;
鉛毒性腦炎 lead encephalitis;
全腦炎 panencephalitis;
日本腦炎 Japanese encephalitis;
細菌性腦炎 bacterial encephalitis;
夏季腦炎 summer encephalitis;
中耳性腦炎 otoencephalitis;
[腦溢血] cerebral apoplexy; cerebral hemorrhage;
[腦硬化] cerebrosclerosis;
彌漫性腦硬化 diffuse cerebral sclerosis;
[腦脹] heavy feeling in the brain;
[腦震蕩] cerebral concussion; concussion; concussion of the brain;
[腦汁] brains;
腦汁絞盡 cudgel one's brains;
腦汁塗地 willing to repay a favour with extreme sacrifice;
絞盡腦汁 beat one's brains; beat one's brains out; busy one's brains; cudgel one's brains; drag one's brains; puzzle one's brains; rack one's brains; ransack one's brains;
[腦腫瘤] brain tumour; encephaloma;
[腦中風] stroke;
[腦子] (1) brains; gray matter; (2) brains; head; intelligence; mental power; mind;
腦子不正常 have a cog loose;
腦子活 clever;
腦子靈活 alert and active; have a quick wit; keen and sharp in thinking;
滿腦子 have one's mind stuffed with;
~滿腦子荒唐念頭 full of nonsense;
~滿腦子名利思想 have one's head filled with thoughts of personal fame and gain;

大腦 brain; cerebrum;
電腦 computer;
後腦 hindbrain;
間腦 tween brain;
前腦 forebrain;
丘腦 thalamus;
人工腦 artificial brain; mechanical brain;
人腦 human brain;
首腦 head;
頭腦 (1) brains; mind; (2) clue; main threads; (3) head; leader;
洗腦 brainwash;
小腦 cerebellum;
醒腦 restore consciousness;
乙腦 epidemic encephalitis B;
中腦 midbrain;
主腦 (1) control centre; (2) chief; leader;

nao⁴
nao
【淖】 mud; slush;

泥淖 bog; mire; morass;

nao

【鬧】 (1) noisy; (2) make a noise; stir up trouble; (3) give vent; (4) be troubled by; suffer from; (5) do; go in for; make;

[鬧病] fall ill; ill;
鬧病在家 stay home for being ill;
愛鬧病 weak and sickly;
很少鬧病 seldom fall ill;

[鬧得] cause; create; raise;
鬧得不可開交 get into a hot dispute;
鬧得雞犬不寧 cause such utter confusion as to make everybody nervous;
鬧得滿城風雨 cause a big scandal; create a sensation; raise an uproar;
鬧得天翻地覆 turn the whole world upside down;
鬧得頭昏腦脹 drive sb crazy;
鬧得烏煙瘴氣 create a foul atmosphere; foul up;
鬧得一塌糊塗 create havoc; make a mess of;

[鬧翻] fall out with sb;
和老板鬧翻 fall out with one's boss;

[鬧鬼] (1) be haunted; (2) play tricks behind sb's back; use underhand means;

[鬧哄哄] boisterous; clamorous; full of noise and clamour; noisy;

[鬧劇] farce;

[鬧嚷嚷] noisy;

[鬧事] affray; create a disturbance; make trouble;
不要鬧事 make no disturbance;
沒事鬧事 make trouble for nothing;
上街鬧事 take to the streets and make trouble;
尋衅鬧事 cause an affray;

[鬧市] busy shopping centre; busy streets; downtown area;
貧居鬧市無人問 a poor man has no friends; poverty parts fellowship; poverty parts friends;
~貧居鬧市無人問，富在深山有遠親 in time of properity, friends will be plenty; in time of adversity, not one amongst twenty;

[鬧騰] (1) a hive of activity; create a disturbance; make a loud noise; noisy; (2) make a joke; make merry;

[鬧心] be agitated; irritate; restless; upset;
家庭不和鬧心 unhappy about being at odds with one's husband;
熱得鬧心 feel unbearable with the scorching heat;
曬得鬧心 feel uneasy under the burning sun;

[鬧着玩兒] joke; horse around;

[鬧中取靜] keep quiet in a noisy neighbourhood;

[鬧鐘] alarm clock;
開鬧鐘 wind up an alarm clock;
上鬧鐘 set the alarm clock;
收音機鬧鐘 clock-radio;

吵鬧 (1) kick up a row; wrangle; (2) make a noise;
胡鬧 act senselessly; run wild;
熱鬧 jolly; lively; scene of bustle and excitement; thrilling sight;
瞎鬧 act senselessly; be mischievous; run wild;
喧鬧 bustling with noise and excitement;

ne⁴
ne

【訥】 slow of speech; slow-tongued; stammer;

[訥吃] spasmophemia;

[訥口少言] not communicative; tight-lipped;

[訥訥] (of speech) slow;

木訥 sincere and honest but slow of speech;

ne⁵
ne

【呢】 interrogative or emphatic particle used after a sentence;

着呢 (of degree) deeply; greatly; very;

nei³
nei

【那】 interrogative particle;

[那個] which one;

[那年] what year; which year;

nei

【餒】 (1) hungry; starve; (2) decay or decomposition of fish; (3) lacking in confidence, courage, etc.;

N

凍餒 cold and hungry;
氣餒 crestfallen; discouraged; disheartened;
自餒 lose confidence; lose heart;

nei4
nei

【內】 (1) inner; inside; within; (2) one's wife or her relatives;

[內包] inclusive;
內包搭配 inclusive collocation;
內包代詞 inclusive pronoun;
內包關係 inclusion;
內包時間 inclusive time;

[內部] bowel; depth; indoor; interior; internal; inward; viscera;
內部的 in-house; interior; internal;
內部紛爭 internal dissension;
內部會計 internal accounting;
內部刊物 restricted publication;
內部聯繫 internal relations;
內部矛盾 interior contradictions;
內部施工 interior construction;
內部消息 inside information;
內部整頓 interior rectification;
內部裝修 interior decorations;

[內成作用] endogenic process;

[內地] hinterland; inland; interior;
內地城市 inland city;
產於內地 be produced in hinterland;
銷往內地 be sold inland;
運往內地 be transported to hinterland;

[內定] cut and dried; decide at the higher level but not officially announced;
內定候選人 designate sb for candidacy;

[內耳] inner ear; internal ear;
內耳道 internal auditory meatus;
~骨性內耳道 bony internal auditory meatus;
內耳霉症 otomycosis;
內耳門 internal acoustic pore;
內耳炎 inner ear infection; labyrinthitis; otitis interna;

[內分] internal division;

[內閣] cabinet;
內閣成員 member of the Cabinet;
內閣會議 cabinet meeting;
參加內閣 go into the cabinet;
更迭內閣 change the cabinet;
核心內閣 inner cabinet;
解散內閣 disband the cabinet;
聯合內閣 coalition cabinet;
影子內閣 shadow cabinet;
組織內閣 form a cabinet;

[內行] (1) an old hand at sth; expert; one who knows how; past master; people who know the ropes; professional; specialist; (2) adept; expert in;
內行的 adept;
充內行 pose as an expert; pretend to be an expert;
假內行 charlatan;

[內訌] internal conflict; internal dissension; internal strife;
內訌四起 be torn by internal strife; civil strife coming up one after another;
避免內訌 avoid internal strife;
促成內訌 precipitate internal conflict;
解決內訌 settle internal conflict;
排除內訌 settle internal conflict;
挑起內訌 stir up internal strife;
引起內訌 cause internal dissension;
製造內訌 sow internal dissension;

[內涵] connotative;
內涵伸延 connotative extension;
內涵意義 connotative meaning;

[內患] internal troubles;
內患外侮 internal troubles and foreign aggression;

[內奸] hidden traitor; quisling;

[內景] indoor scene; scenes shot indoors;
內景攝影 indoor shooting;

[內疚] compunction; guilty conscience; have qualms of conscience; prickings of conscience; self-reproach; the worm of conscience;
內疚良深 suffer from a twinge of remorse;
感到內疚 feel rotten;
~使人感到內疚 guilt-trip;
一陣內疚 a dart of guilt;

[內聚] cohesive;
內聚力 cohesion; cohesive force;

[內科] internal medicine;
內科病房 medical ward;
內科部 medical department;
~內科部主任 head of the medical department;
內科學 internal medicine;
內科醫生 physician;
看內科 see a physician;

[內褲] briefs; knickers; panties; underpants; undershorts;

長內褲 long johns;
短內褲 briefs;
~平腳短內褲 boxer shorts;
~貼身短內褲 briefs;
寬鬆內褲 bloomer;
男裝內褲 undershorts;
女用內褲 drawers; knickers;
一條內褲 an underwear;

[內窺鏡] endoscope;

[內聯網] intranet;

[內陸] inland; interior; landlocked;
內陸開放城市 opened inland cities;
內陸口岸 inland port;
內陸省份 inland provinces;

[內亂] civil strife; internal disorder;
發生內亂 an internal disorder breaks out;
結束內亂 end civil strife;
平息內亂 put down internal disorder;
引起內亂 beget civil strife;

[內幕] inside story; what goes on behind the scenes;
內幕消息 inside information;
內幕新聞 inside dope; inside story;
公開內幕 make the inside story known to the public;
關心內幕 be concerned with inside story;

[內胚層] endoderm;

[內皮] endothelium;
內皮癌 endothelial cancer;
內皮瘤 endothelioma;
~內皮瘤病 endotheliomatosis;
內皮炎 endothelitis;
內皮增生 endotheliosis;

[內切酶] endonucleases;
核酸內切酶 endonucleases;
限制性內切酶 restriction enzyme;

[內情] inside information;

[內燃] internal combustion;
內燃機 internal combustion engine;

[內容] contents; materials; substance;
內容從句 content clause;
內容豐富 rich in content;
內容枯燥 dull in content;
內容空洞 lack content in...;
內容外加語 content disjunct;
內容項目 content item;
學習內容 learning materials;

[內傷] internal injury;

[內生] endogenous;
內生變化 endogenous change;

[內外] domestic and foreign; inside and outside;
內外勾結 collusion between the enemies within and without;
內外夾玫 a crossfire; a simultaneous attack from within and without; attack from both inside and outside; be attacked both from within and without; be attacked from inside and outside;
內外交困 beset with difficulties both at home and abroad; beset with internal and external troubles; beset with troubles internally and externally; in dire straits at home and abroad; on the horns of a dilemma;
內外有別 keep information from outsiders or foreigners;
安內攘外 maintain internal security and repel foreign invasion;
國內外 at home and abroad;
海內外 the country and beyond the seas;
~遍及海內外 extend throughout the country and beyond the seas;
內不避親，外不避仇 shun neither one's relatives nor one's enemies;
攘外安內 resist foreign aggression and pacify the interior;
外柔內剛 an iron fist in a velvet glove; gentle in manner, resolute in deed; outwardly soft and inwardly hard;
外善內奸 fair without, false within; friendly attitude with concealed viciousness;
一個月內外 about one month;

[內務] home affairs; internal affairs;

[內線] back door; inner line;
走內線 curry favour with the wife of one's boss; go through private channels; go through the back door; take the inner line; use private influence to achieve one's end; through backstairs influence;

[內向] introvert; introversion;
內向傳播 intrapersonal communication;
內向的人 introvert;
內向結構 endocentric construction;
內向型人格 introversive personality;
性格內向 be introverted by nature;

[內心] (1) heart; innermost being; (2) incentre;
內心衝突 cognitive dissonance; intrapsychic conflict;

內心獨白 soliloquy; internal monologue;
內心翻騰 one's heart is in a tumult;
內心叫苦 groan inwardly;
內心深處 at the bottom of one's heart; cockles of the heart; in one's heart of hearts; in the depth of one's heart; in the privacy of one's thoughts; the cockles of the heart;
內心世界 one's inner world; the inner world of the heart;
內心無愧 have a clear conscience;
內心有愧 have a guilty conscience;
發自內心 from the bottom of one's heart; of one's own will;

[內省] heart-searching; introspection; self-examination;
內省不疚 find no fault in examining one's heart;

[內銷] domestic sale; sell in the home market;
內銷包裝 domestic package;

[內兄] one's brother-in-law; one's wife's elder brother;

[內需] domestic demand;
刺激內需 stimulate domestic demand;

[內衣] undergarment; underclothes; underdress; underlinen; underwaist; underwear; undies; unmentionables;
內衣褲 underclothes;
~女式內衣褲 lingerie;
短內衣 camisole;
寬鬆內衣 chemise;
連褲緊身內衣 camiknickers;
連身內衣 body suit;
沒穿內衣 go commando;
性感內衣 sexy underwear;

[內因] internal cause;
事物的內因 the internal causes of things;

[內應] planted agent;
做內應 act as a planted agent;

[內在] inbuilt; inherent; inner; internal; intrinsic;
內在的價值 intrinsic value;
內在的魅力 inner charm;
內在關係 internal relations;
內在規律 inherent law;
內在經濟 internal economy;
內在聯繫 inner link;
內在矛盾 inherent contradictions;
內在美 inner beauty;
內在特性 intrinsic properties;
內在性語言 internalized language;
內在性質 inherent quality;
內在意義 intrinsic meaning;
內在因素 internal factor;

[內臟] entrails; innards; internal organs; viscus;
內臟反射 viceral reflex;
內臟肥大 visceromegaly;
內臟過小 splanchnomicria;
內臟疾病 splanchnopathy;
內臟囊 visceral sac;
內臟石 splanchnolith;
內臟痛風 visceral gout;
內臟炎 celitis;
內臟硬化 splanchnosclerosis;
內臟增大 visceromegaly;
內臟正常 eusplanchnia;

[內障] cataract;
老年內障 senile cataract;
外傷性內障 traumatic cataract;
先天性內障 congenital cataract;

[內戰] civil war;
打內戰 be engaged in a civil war; fight a civil war;
發動內戰 unleash civil war;
防止內戰 avert civil war;
結束內戰 end civil war;
譴責內戰 denounce the civil war;
挑起內戰 foment civil war;
引起內戰 bring on civil war;

[內爭] internal strife;

[內政] internal affairs;
內政外交 domestic and foreign affairs; internal affairs and foreign relations;
內政問題 internal affairs;
互不干涉內政 not interfere in each other's internal affairs;
自行處理內政 deal with home affairs by oneself;

[內侄] nephew; the son of one's wife's brother;
內侄女 niece; the daughter of one's wife's brother;

[內置] built-in; `

[內助] one's wife;
賢內助 good wife; the better half;

[內子] my wife;

大內 imperial palace;
對內 domestic; home; internal;
分內 one's duty;
宮內 intrauterine;

國內 domestic; home; internal;
海內 throughout the country; within the four seas;
戶內 indoor;
界內 area within bounds;
懼內 be henpecked;
圈內 within a circle;
入內 be allowed into;
五內 viscera;
以內 less than; within;

nei

【那】 combined form of 那一, often used to indicate emphasis or contempt;
[那天] that day;

nen⁴
nen

【嫩】 (1) delicate; tender; (2) light; (3) inexperienced; unskilled; young;
[嫩綠] green; verdancy;
[嫩芽] burgeon; peel; tender shoot;
[嫩葉] tender leaves;
[嫩枝] spray; twig; epicormic branch; spray; twig;

白嫩 delicate; fair and clear;
面嫩 sensitive; timid;
細嫩 delicate; tender;
鮮嫩 fresh and tender;

neng²
neng

【能】 (1) ability; capability; skills; (2) energy; (3) able; capable; (4) able to; can; capable of;
[能動] active; dynamic; vigorous;
能動性 activism;
~主觀能動性 subjective activity;
能動主義 activism;
[能幹] able; capable; competent; have a lot on the ball;
能幹的女孩子 capable girl;
能幹耐勞 talented and capable of enduring fatigue;
[能夠] able to; can; capable of;
能夠自理 can take care of oneself;
[能級] energy levl;
~能級圖 energy level diagram;
[能見度] visibility;
不良能見度 bad visibility;
飛行能見度 flight visibility;
顯示能見度 display visibility;
優良能見度 excellent visibility;
[能力] ability; caliber; capability; capacity; power;
能力測試 ability test;
能力差異 ability range;
能力工資 ability wage;
能力開發 ability development;
能力水平 ability level;
能力一般的人 men of average ability;
貶低能力 belittle one's capability;
辨色能力 chromatic discrimination power;
表達能力 ability of expression;
測量能力 measurement capability;
超出你的能力 out of your league;
成膜能力 film forming ability;
承載能力 bearing capacity; bearing power; carrying ability;
處理能力 handling ability;
存儲能力 memory capability;
代碼能力 codability;
代謝能力 metabolic capability;
道德判斷能力 ability to make moral judgements;
導向能力 guidance capability;
低等能力 low ability;
低溫起動能力 cold-starting ability;
抵抗能力 resistance capability;
讀寫能力 literacy;
發酵能力 fermentation ability;
發泡能力 foaming ability;
發熱能力 heat-producing capability;
發射能力 emissing ability;
~紅外發射能力 infrared emissing ability;
發芽能力 germination ability;
反射能力 reflecting ability;
分辨能力 resolving ability;
高等能力 high ability;
工作能力 operational capability; working ability;
共通能力 generic skills;
溝通能力 communication skills;
話語能力 discourse competence;
還原能力 reducing ability;
混合能力 mixed ability;
機械能力 machine capability;
計數能力 numerical ability;
計算能力 computing power;
加工能力 working ability;
檢定能力 detection capacity;

減震能力 cushioning ability;
交際能力 communication skills; communicative competence;
競爭能力 ability to compete; competitive power;
決策能力 decision-making skills;
絕緣能力 insulating ability;
口語能力 articulacy;
內在能力 intrinsic competence;
能量吸收能力 energy absorption capability;
黏附能力 adhesive ability;
培養能力 cultivate one's ability;
疲勞能力 fatigue capability;
起動能力 start-up capability;
起重能力 weight-lifting ability;
氣體生成能力 gassing ability;
切削能力 cutting ability;
清洗能力 cleansing power;
人際交往能力 interpersonal skills;
潤滑能力 lubricating ability;
潤濕能力 wetting ability;
散熱能力 heat-sinking capability;
上昇能力 ascending ability;
燒結能力 caking power;
社交能力 social skills;
設計能力 design capability;
輸出能力 fanout capability;
思考能力 thinking skills;
思維能力 ability of thinking;
收益能力 profit ability;
投資能力 ability to invest;
突防能力 defense penetration ability;
推進能力 propulsion capability;
脫水能力 water separation capability;
維修能力 service ability;
無能力 incapable; incapacity;
吸收能力 absorbing ability;
消磁能力 erasing ability;
協作能力 collaboration skills;
心理能力 mental ability;
心算能力 ability of mental arithmetic;
信息提取能力 information extraction ability;
循跡能力 tracking ability;
業務能力 professional ability;
抑制能力 inhibiting ability;
議價能力 ability to bargain;
語言能力 language skills; linguistic ability;
運動能力 athletic ability;
運轉能力 running ability;
展示能力 demonstrate one's ability; go through one's paces; show one's pace;
振動能力 vibration ability;
中等能力 average ability;
裝填能力 filling capability;
自淨能力 self-purification ability;

[能量] energy;
表觀能量 apparent energy;
大量的能量 a quantity of energy;
帶隙能量 band-gap energy;
平均能量 average energy;
天線能量 antenna energy;
正能量 positive energy;

[能貓不叫，叫貓不能] a mewing cat is never a good mouser;

[能耐] ability; capability; skills; talent;
沒能耐 have no skill in sth;
有能耐 have the capability of doing sth;

[能屈能伸] able to adapt to circumstances; can either stoop or stand; flexible; know when to eat humble pie and when to hold one's head high; know when to yield and when not; take the rough with the smooth;

[能人] able man; able person; capable brains;
能人背後有能人 diamond cut diamond; for every able person there is always one still abler; no one can boast of being superior to all others; there are always plenty of able men;
能人才子 a man of ability; a talented person;
能人力士 men of ability;
能人面前莫逞能 not too bold with your betters;

[能忍自安] patience makes peace;

[能事] ability; what one is particularly good at;
極盡能事 do everything possible; spare no efforts;

[能手] capable hand; crackajack; dab; expert; proficient;
持家能手 a dab who is good at running one's home;
網球能手 a dab at tennis;

[能說會道] a glib talker; a good talker; a smart talker; an eloquent speaker; good at talking; have a facile tongue; have a glib tongue; have a nimble tongue; have a ready and eloquent tongue;

have the gift of gab; one's gift of the gab; voluble; with a ready tongue;

[能寫善畫] can write and paint;

[能言善辯] a shrewd tongue; a silver tongue; gift of the gab; have a shrewd tongue; skilled in debate;

[能育性] fertility;

自體能育性 self-fertility;

[能源] energy; energy resources; sources of energy;

能源儲量 energy reserves;
能源地理 energy geography;
能源短缺 energy shortage;
能源發展 energy development;
能源革命 energy revolution;
能源工業 energy industry;
能源公司 energy company;
能源供應 energy supply;
能源技術 energy technology;
~能源技術經濟 energy technology economy;
能源價格 energy prices;
能源經濟 economy of energy;
能源利用 energy resources utilization;
能源生產 energy production;
能源市場 energy market;
能源危機 energy crisis;
能源系統 energy system;
能源消耗 energy consumption; energy use;
能源需求 demand for energy; energy demand; energy needs; energy requirements;
能源政策 energy policy;
能源資源 energy resources;
愛護能源 treasure energy resources;
代用能源 alternate sources of energy;
耗盡能源 sap energy resources;
開發能源 develop the sources of energy;
可再生能源 renewable energy; renewable sources of energy;
~不可再生能源 non-renewable energy; non-renewable sources of energy;
利用能源 utilize energy;
浪費能源 waste energy;
清潔能源 clean energy;
生產能源 generate energy; produce energy;
提供能源 provide energy; supply energy;
替代能源 alternative energy;
新能源 new energy;
一次能源 primary energy;

[能者多勞] all lay loads on the willing horse; an able man has many burdens; an able man is always busy; the abler a man, the busier he gets; the capable ones are always busy;

[能者為師] let those who can serve as teachers;

[能中有能，強中有強] for every able person there is always one still abler;

本能 born ability; instinct;
褊能 of little ability;
不能 cannot; must not; should not;
才能 ability; talent;
逞能 display one's ability; show off one's skill or ability;
磁能 magnetic energy;
低能 incompetent;
電能 electrical energy;
動能 kinetic energy;
高能 high-energy;
功能 function;
官能 function; sense;
核能 nuclear energy;
機能 function;
技能 skill; technical ability; technique;
節能 energy conservation;
可能 can; possible; probable;
良能 intuitive ability;
論能 show off one's skills;
豈能 how could;
全能 all-round;
勢能 potential energy;
太陽能 solar energy;
位能 potential energy;
無能 incapable; incompetent;
賢能 able and virtuous personage;
效能 efficacy; usefulness;
性能 function; performance; property;
原子能 atomic energy;
職能 function;
智能 intellect; intelligence; wit;

neng4
neng

【濘】 pasty; soft and mashy;

[濘泥] mire; mud;

ng2
ng

【嗯】 (expressing doubts) well; what;

ng³
ng
【嗯】 (expressing surprise) hey; what;

ng⁴
ng
【嗯】 (expressing agreement or promise) all right; h'm; that's right; yes;

ni²
ni
【尼】 nun;
[尼庵] Buddhist nunery;
[尼姑] Buddhist nun;
[尼古丁] nicotine;
尼古丁替代療法 nicotine replacement therapy;
尼古丁貼片 nicotine patch;
[尼龍] nylon;

僧尼 Buddhist monks and nuns;
仲尼 another name of Confucius;

ni
【呢】 (1) woolen fabric; (2) murmur;
[呢喃] twittering;
睡中呢喃 muttering in sleep;
[呢絨] wollen goods; wool fabric;
[呢子] wollen cloth;

花呢 fancy suiting;
線呢 cotton suiting;

ni
【怩】 blush; look embarrassed; shy and bashful; socially timid;

忸怩 bashful; blushing;

ni
【泥】 (1) mire; mud; (2) mashed vegetable or fruit;
[泥巴] mire; mud;
[泥地] mud ground; muddy ground;
[泥多佛大] abundant clay makes a large Buddha—through the help of many supports, one's success becomes great; the more the clay, the bigger the statue of Buddha;
[泥工] bricklayer;
[泥垢] dirt; grime;
[泥灰] musky coal; marl; peat;
泥灰岩 marl;
~ 茶綠泥灰岩 tea-green marl;
~ 紅泥灰岩 red marls;
~ 灰質泥灰岩 calcareous marl;
~ 泥質泥灰岩 argillaceous marl;
~ 黏土泥灰岩 clay marl;
~ 砂質泥灰岩 sandy marl;
硅質泥灰 silicious marl;
[泥漿] mud; slurry;
含水泥漿 aqueous slurry;
焦泥漿 coke slurry;
黏土泥漿 clay slurry;
[泥路] dirt road; dirt track;
[泥濘] muddy; miry; sloppy; slushy;
泥濘的 boggy;
[泥牛入海] be gone forever; he that is fallen cannot help him that is down;
[泥菩薩] clay idol;
泥菩薩過江，自身難保 like a bunch of clay idols crossing a river — each one is looking out for his own survival; like a clay idol fording a river, hardly able to save oneself;
[泥鰍] loach; mud fish;
[泥人] clay figurine;
[泥沙俱下] mud and sand are carried along — there is a mingling of good and bad; water flows down with sand and mud together—the good and the bad are mixed up;
泥沙俱下，魚龍混雜 the waters are mudded, the bad becomes mixed with the good; water flows down with sand and mud together;
[泥石流] debris flow;
[泥水匠] bricklayer; plasterer; tiler;
[泥塑] clay figure modeling; clay sculpture;
[泥炭] peat;
無定形泥炭 amorphous peat;
[泥土] clay; earth;
黃泥土 clay;
~ 一層黃泥土 a bed of yellow clay;
一把泥土 a handful of earth; a handful of soil;
一層泥土 a bed of clay; a layer of clay; a layer of earth;
一塊泥土 a cake of clay; a lump of earth;
[泥像] clay statuette;
[泥岩] mudstone;
礫質泥岩 conglomeratic mudstone;

N

卵石泥岩 pebbly mudstone;
［泥俑］ earthern figurine;
［泥足深陷］ get into real trouble;
［泥磚］ adobe;
擋泥 mudguard;
封泥 lute;
垢泥 dirt on the face;
河泥 river silt;
湖泥 lake mud;
灰泥 plaster;
膠泥 (1) clay; (2) daub;
礦泥 slime; sludge; slurry;
爛泥 mud; slush;
軟泥 ooze;
水泥 cement;
蒜泥 mashed garlic;
塘泥 pond silt; pond sludge;
污泥 mire; mud;
印泥 red ink paste used for seals;
油泥 grease; greasy filth;
雲泥 clouds and mud;
滯泥 adhere too closely;

N

ni
【妮】 (1) maid; (2) little darling; little girl;
［妮子］ girl; lass;
小妮子 (1) girl; (2) housemaid;

ni
【倪】 (1) young and weak; (2) division; (3) beginning; (4) bound; limit; (5) a surname;
端倪 clue; inkling;

ni
【猊】 (1) lion; (2) wild beast or wild horse;
狻猊 legendary fierce animal;

ni
【蜺】 reflection of a rainbow;

ni
【輗】 crossbar at the ends of a carriage poles;

ni
【霓】 coloured cloud; rainbow;
［霓虹］ neon;
霓虹燈 neon lamp; neon light; neon tube;
霓虹廣告 neon sign;

ni
【麑】 fawn; young deer;

ni
【臡】 (1) pickled meat; (2) minced meat;

ni³

ni
【你】 you (the masculine gender);
［你不對］ it's your error; it's your fault; the fault is yours; you are at fault; your are erroneous; you are incorrect; you are mistaken; you are wrong; you have got it wrong;
［你稱我心，我合你意］ you scratch my back and I'll scratch yours;
［你好］ hello; hi; how are you; how do you do;
你好嗎 hello; how are things going; how are you; how are you doing; how do you do; how goes it; how's tricks;
［你近來好嗎］ how are you; how are you getting on; how do you do; what is up;
［你敬我一尺，我還你一丈］ kindness is always returned tenfold;
［你們］ you;
你們的 your;
［你我］ you and I;
不分你我 make no distinction between you and I;
你騙不了我 I'm from Missouri; you can't cheat me; you can't do me in; you can't fool me; you can't pull wool over my eyes;
我中有你，你中有我 you are among us and we are among you;
有你沒我 you and I cannot coexist;

ni
【妳】 you(the feminine gender);

ni
【旎】 (1) charming; romantic; tender; (2) the fluttering of the flag;
旖旎 charming and gentle;

ni
【擬】 (1) draft; draw up; (2) intend; plan; (3) imitate;
［擬訂］ draft; draw up; make a draft; map out; work out;
擬訂政策 draw up general policies;
［擬人］ personification;
擬人法 personification;
［擬聲］ onomatopoeia;

擬聲詞 onomatopoeia;
~ 基本擬聲詞 primary onomatopoeia;
擬聲法 onomatopoeia; onomatopoeic method;
擬聲理據 onomatopoeic motivation;
次要擬聲 secondary onomatopoeia;

[擬態] mimicry;
保護性擬態 protective mimicry;
攻擊擬態 aggressive mimicry;

[擬題員] item writer;

比擬 analogy; compare; comparison; draw a parallel; metaphor;
草擬 draft; draw up;
摹擬 imitate; mimic; simulate;
摸擬 imitate; simulate;
虛擬 fabricate; invented; make up; suppositional;
懸擬 conjecture; imagine;

ni

【禰】 the shrine where one's father's sacred tablet is kept;

ni⁴

ni

【泥】 (1) be tied down by conventions, old practices; very conservative; (2) compel;

[泥古] have bigoted belief in the ancients; obstinately follow ancient ways;
泥古不化 stick stubbornly to old rules;

拘泥 rigidly adhering to;

ni

【逆】 (1) contrary; counter; (2) defy; disobey; go against; (3) traitor; (4) converse; inverse;

[逆差] adverse balance; deficit;
貿易逆差 adverse trade balance; passive trade balance; trade deficit; trade gap;
~ 長期貿易逆差 chronic trade deficit;
~ 對外貿易逆差 foreign trade deficit;
暫時逆差 temporary deficit;
總逆差 overall deficit;

[逆成法] back-formation;

[逆耳] grate on the ear; offend the ear; unpleasant to the ear;
逆耳的話 say sth that grates on the ear;
逆耳利行 faithful words offend the ear but are good for improving one's conduct; honest advice, though unpleasant to the ear, benefit conduct;
忠言逆耳 good advice is always unpleasant to the ear;

[逆反] adverse; rebellious;
逆反心理 adverse psychology;

[逆風] (1) against the wind; in the teeth of the wind; (2) adverse wind; contrary wind; head wind;
逆風而駛 sail close to the wind; stream against the wind;
逆風逆水 go against the wind and the current;
逆風駛舟 sail against the wind;

[逆光] backlighting;

[逆境] adverse circumstances; adversity;
逆境善處 behave well in spite of one's misfortune;
逆境知友誼，烈火見真金 fire is the test of gold; adversity of friendship;
擺脱逆境 get out of adversity;
頂住逆境 stand against adversity;
陷入逆境 in adverse circumstances;

[逆料] anticipate; foresee;
逆料到困難 anticipate difficulties;
逆料到麻煩 anticipate troubles;
尚難逆料 still difficult to predict; still hard to say;

[逆流] back current; contraflow; go against the current;
逆流而動 move against the tide;
逆流而上 go against the current; go upstream; run counter to the current of the times; sail against the current;
逆流而行 go against the stream; stem the current;

[逆旅] hotel; inn;

[逆生詞] back-formation word;

[逆時] inverse time;

[逆水] against the current;
逆水而上 go upstream;
逆水行舟 row against the current; sail against the current; sail in the head tide;
~ 逆水行舟，不進則退 a boat sailing against the current must forge aheard or it will be driven back; he that looks not before finds himself behind;

[逆順] the rough and the smooth;
逆來順受 grin and bear it; kiss the rod; make the best of a bad bargain; meekly accept humiliations; resign oneself

to adversity; smile at one's troubles; submissive and patient in adversity; take insults philosophically; take the rough with the smooth; what cannot be cured must be endured;
~拒絕逆來順受 refuse to resign oneself to adversity;
~衹能逆來順受 have to meekly submit to oppression;
逆取順守 keep by the right method what is first acquired wrongly; retain political power by fair means after capturing it by foul;

［逆天］ against nature;
逆天行道 in defiance of nature;
逆天行事 do godless things;

［逆溫］ temperature inversion;
逆溫層 inversion layer;

［逆紋］ cross-grain;
逆紋的 cross-grained;

［逆向］ backward; reverse;
逆向思維 reverse thinking;
~逆向思維法 contrary thinking method;
逆向形態 reversion;

［逆序］ inversion;
逆序法 hysteron proteron;
逆序翻譯法 inversion method;

［逆轉］ become worse; deteriorate; kick back; reverse; set-back; take a turn for the worse;
敗局無可逆轉 the lost battle cannot be reversed;

［逆子］ unfilial son;
逆子讒臣 unfilial sons and disloyal and traitorous statesmen;

悖逆 disloyal;
橫逆 insult;
叛逆 rebel; rebel against; revolt against;
氣逆 circulation of vital energy in the wrong direction;
親逆 greet personally;
忤逆 disobedient to parents;
迕逆 go against one's superiors;

ni

【衵】 woman's underwear;

ni

【匿】 conceal; hide; keep in secret; secretive;

［匿伏］ in hiding; lurk;

［匿跡］ go into hiding; stay in concealment;
匿跡海外 lie low abroad;
匿跡天涯海角 stay in concealment in the remotest corners of the earth;
匿跡銷聲 in complete hiding;

［匿名］ anonymous;
匿名電話 anonymous phone call;
匿名舉報 report an offender anonymously;
匿名揭發 expose sb anonymously;
匿名投票 vote anonymously;
匿名投書 write an anonymous letter;
匿名信 anonymous letter;
~惡意匿名信 poison-pen letter;
~一封匿名信 an anonymous letter; an anonymous missive;
匿名者 anonym;

［匿情］ conceal facts before the law;

［匿喪不報］ keep sb's death a secret;

［匿影］ blanking;
匿影藏形 conceal one's identity; conceal one's own real appearance; hide from public notice; lie low; live obscurely so as to conceal one's true colours;

［匿怨］ entertain secret grudge;

蔽匿 conceal; hide;
避匿 hide away;
晦匿 retire into obscurity;
逃匿 escape and hide; go into hiding;
隱匿 conceal; hide; lie low;

ni

【惄】 pensive; sad; worried;

ni

【溺】 (1) drown; (2) be addicted to;

［溺愛］ coddle; dote on; dote upon; dote on a child; spoil a child;
溺愛寵物 dote on one's pets;
溺愛子女 spoil one's children;

［溺死］ be drowned;

［溺嬰］ infanticide; the drowning of infants;

［溺於］ be addicted to;
溺於酒色 be addicted to drink and sex; be given to wine and women; be sunk in vice and pleasure;
溺於利慾 hanker after money and women; indulge in profits and lust;
溺於名利 bury oneself in the thoughts of fame and gain;
溺於聲色 be addicted to sexuality; lead a

life of dissipation;

[溺職] dereliction; neglect of duty;

溺職受處分 be given disciplinary warning for neglect of duty;

溺職殃民 fail to discharge one's duties and cause hardship to the people;

沉溺 indulge; wallow;

ni

【睨】 look askance;

睥睨 cast sidelong glances at sb; look at sb disdainfully out of the corner of one's eye;

ni

【暱】 close; intimate;

ni

【膩】 (1) fatty; greasy; oily; (2) smooth; (3) dirty; (4) bored; tired; weary; (5) intimate;

[膩煩] (1) be bored; be fed up; (2) hate; loathe;

膩煩刻薄之人 loathe unkind people;

令人膩煩的 cloying;

[膩味] hate; loathe;

膩味應酬 hate social engagements;

叫人膩味 be fed up with;

深感膩味 hate sth bitterly;

[膩子] putty;

快乾膩子 size putty;

乳液膩子 emulsion putty;

油性膩子 oil putty;

肥膩 greasy; rich;

垢膩 dirt; stain;

煩膩 (1) bored; (2) abhor;

稔膩 plump and smooth-skinned;

細膩 greasy; greasy food; oily; oily food;

有點膩 a bit greasy; be too oily;

nian¹

nian

【拈】 pick up; take;

[拈弓] take one's bow;

拈弓搭箭 fit an arrow to the string; seize one's bow and fit an arrow to it; take one's bow and adjust an arrow;

拈弓取箭 quickly one's hands seek one's bow and an arrow is on the string;

nian

【蔫】 (1) fading or withering; (2) ennui; spiritless; (3) calm and quiet; expressionless;

[蔫不唧兒] droopy; listless; sluggish;

[蔫呼呼的] mashed; pulpy;

[蔫壞] treacherous;

萎蔫 wilt;

nian²

nian

【年】 (1) year; (2) annual; yearly; (3) age; year; (4) period of time; (5) harvest; (6) New Year;

[年報] (1) annual report; (2) annal;

[年輩] age and seniority;

[年表] chronological table; chronology;

歷史年表 chronological table;

[年齒] a person's age;

[年初] at the beginning of the year;

[年代] (1) age; time; years; (2) a decade of a century;

年代不詳 without a date;

年代久遠 age-old; of the remote past; time-honoured;

年代學 chronology;

八十年代 the eighties;

代遠年湮 too long ago to be ascertained;

地質年代 geological ages;

過去的年代 bygone era;

和平年代 the time of peace'

進步年代 progressive age;

絕對年代 absolute date;

少不更事的年代 salad days;

相對年代 relative date;

戰爭年代 the war years;

[年底] end of the year; year-end;

在年底 at year's end;

[年度] of the year; year;

年度報告 annual report;

年度計劃 annual plan;

年度經費 annual funds;

年度預算 annual budget;

年度最佳運動員 athlete of the year;

半年度 semi-annual;

財政年度 financial year; fiscal year;

基期年度 basic year;

會計年度 account year; fiscal year;

上年度 previous year;

審計年度 audit year;

下年度 the following year;

[年費] annual fee;
[年分] fraction of the year;
[年份] (1) a particular year; (2) age; time;
[年豐] good crops;
政修年豐 the country enjoys a good government and bumper crops; the people enjoy good government and good crops;
[年富力強] in the full vigour of life; in the heyday of youth; in the prime; in the prime of one's life; young and strong;
[年糕] Chinese New Year cake; Spring Festival cake;
[年高] advanced in years;
年高德劭 advanced in years and virtue; aged and greatly honoured for one's virtues; of advanced years and known integrity; of venerable age and respectable character; of venerable age and eminent virtue; old and virtuous; venerable;
年高望重 aged and celebrated; aged and in high standing; full of years and honour;
[年庚] date of birth; time of a person's birth;
年庚八字 the hour, date, month and year of one's birth;
[年關] end of the year;
年關難熬 it is hard to bear the end of the year;
年關難過 it is not easy to spend the end of the year;
[年光] passage of time;
年光荏苒 the quick passing of time;
[年號] reign title;
[年華] time; years;
年華花信 in the bloom of her youth;
年華無悔 make full use of one's time; spend one's time without regret;
年華似水 time passes like water;
年華虛度 have wasted the best years of one's life; spend vainly the best of one's days; waste one's life; youth passes away;
年華正好 in the prime of one's years;
豆蔻年華 blooming girl; budding beauty; marriageable age;
花信年華 the time when the spring breezes bring the news of the flowers – twenty-four years of age;
逝水年華 the light and moonlight follow each other like flowing water; time passes like flowing water;
似水年華 time passes like flowing water; time passes swiftly as the running of water;
[年畫] New Year pictures; Spring Festival pictures;
[年會] annual conference; annual meeting; annual symposium;
[年貨] goods for use during the Spring Festival;
辦年貨 do New Year shopping; do shopping for the Spring Festival; do Spring Festival shopping;
送年貨 send Spring Festival purchases;
推銷年貨 sell Spring Festival goods;
贈年貨 present Spring Festival goods to sb;
[年級] form; grade; year;
年級老師 form teacher;
低年級 the junior grade;
高年級 the senior grade;
[年紀] age;
年紀大 old;
年紀輕 young;
超過…年紀 be the wrong side of (numeral);
上了年紀 advanced in years; getting on in years; over the hill;
上年紀 be getting along in years; be getting on in years;
一把年紀 advanced in age; advanced in years; be getting on in years;
[年假] (1) annual leave; (2) winter vacation; (3) New Year holidays;
[年間] during the period of; during the time of;
[年鑒] almanac; yearbook;
[年將] one's age is nearing;
年將半百 well along toward fifty;
年將不惑 one is near forty;
年將就木 have one foot in the grave;
[年節] Spring Festival holidays;
[年金] annuity;
年金折扣 depreciation annuity;
年金契約 annuity contract;
標準年金 standard annuity;
長期年金 long-term annuity;
償還年金 redemption annuity;

遞減年金 decreasing annuity;
定額年金 level annuity;
定期年金 limited annuity;
撫卹年金 death annuity;
國民年金 national annuity;
即期年金 immediate annuity;
累進年金 increasing annuity;
連續年金 continuous annuity;
聯合年金 joint annuity;
臨時年金 contingent annuity;
普通年金 ordinary annuity;
確定年金 certain annuity;
世襲年金 hereditary annuity;
退休年金 retirement annuity;
延期年金 deferred annuity;
永續年金 perpetual annuity;
有期年金 terminable annuity;
預付年金 prepaid annuity;
終身年金 annuity for life; life annuity;

[年近] (1) one's age is approaching...; (2) the year is coming to...;
年近半百 about fifty years of age; approaching fifty; getting on for fifty; in the neighbourhood of fifty;
年近古稀 getting on for seventy;
年近花甲 close on sixty years of age;
年近歲迫 coming to the end of the year; the new year is fast approaching; toward the end of the year;

[年景] (1) the year's harvest; (2) the holiday atmosphere of the Spring Festival;

[年刊] annal; year book;
半年刊 biannual;
雙年刊 biennial;

[年老] aged; old;
年老背曲 be bent with age; one's shoulders bow with age;
年老多病 be troubled by sickness and old age; outlive one's age;
年老的 aged;
年老額皺 one's forehead is wrinkled with age;
年老昏憒 become thoughtless with age; in one's dotage; lose one's wits with age;
年老目衰 be getting on in years and one's eyes are failing;
年老色衰 lose one's charm with years;
年老體弱 advanced in age and poor in health; get old and infirm;
年老體衰 be worn with age; be worn out with age;
年老退休 retire due to old age; retire on account of old age;
年老無力 old and powerless;
年老無用 old and losing one's powers; old and useless;
年老血衰 get old and decrepit;
年老腰彎 be bent with age;

[年禮] New Year gift;

[年利] annual interest;

[年力就衰] the physical power is on the decline;

[年齡] be aged...; come into the age of...; one's age is...; ...years old; ...years of age;
年齡不饒人 age will tell;
年齡大 old;
年齡段 age range;
年齡構成 age composition;
年齡歧視 age discrimination; ageism;
年齡群 age bracket; age group;
年齡限制 age limit;
年齡相仿 about the same age;
年齡小 young;
年齡形容詞 age adjective;
年齡壓力 age pressure;
年齡組 age bracket; age group;
成年年齡 age of majority;
成熟年齡 age of maturity;
法定年齡 age of majority; lawful age; legal age;
~達到法定年齡 come of age;
感情成熟年齡 emotional age;
教育年齡 educational age;
結婚年齡 marriageable age;
絕對年齡 absolute age;
平均年齡 average age;
入學年齡 age of admittance;
生態年齡 ecological age;
生殖年齡 reproductive age;
退休年齡 retirement age;
心理年齡 mental age;
學前年齡 pre-school age;
責任年齡 age of discretion;

[年率] annual rate; rate per annum;

[年邁] aged; invalidity; old;
年邁花甲 over sixty years of age;
年邁力衰 aged and feeble; old and infirm; senile;
年邁龍鐘 advanced in age;
年邁者 invalid;

[年貌] age and looks;

[年年] every year; year after year; year by

year; year in year out;
年年如此 year in and year out;
年年如意 New Year greetings;
年復一年 from one year to another; from year to year; one year runs into the next; year after year; year by year; year in and year out; year in, year out;

[年譜] chronicle of sb's life; chronological biography;

[年期] annual period;
半年期 (1) half-yearly period; (2) semi-annual period;
~半年期股利 half-yearly dividend;

[年青] young;
年青氣盛 young and spirited;
年青喪偶 be widowed while still young;
年青志大 young and ambitious;

[年輕] young;
年輕放蕩 sow one's wild oats;
年輕果敢 young and resolute;
年輕化 make sb younger; youthization;
年輕力壯 young and vigorous;
年輕貌美 young and pretty;
年輕氣盛 young and aggressive; young and impetuous;
年輕人 a man young in age; kid; kiddo; young people; youngster;
~好學的年輕人 studious young man;
~説話尖刻的年輕人 sharp-tongued young man;
~一班年輕人 a group of young people;
~英俊的年輕人 handsome young man;
年輕時 in one's younger days; when one was young;
年輕一代 the younger generation;
年輕有為 young and promising;
年輕幼稚的 callow;
不再年輕 no longer young; over the hill;

[年日] days and years;
年長日久 last a very long time;
年陳日久 in the course of time; old and antique; out of date;
年深日久 after a long lapse of time; as the years go by; over a long period of time;

[年少] young of age;
年少氣盛 a young man full of spirit; be young and spirited; young and impetuous;

[年事] person's age;
年事漸長 cut one's eye-teeth; have one's eye-teeth cut;
年事已高 be advanced in years; senile; well on in life;

[年歲] (1) age; (2) years;
年歲不饒人 decay and age are inexorable laws;
年歲久遠 it happened so many years ago;
年歲流逝 the years flowed away;
年歲已高 advanced in years;
年杪歲卒 at the end of the year;
年尾歲杪 late in the year;
上了年歲 be getting on in years;
歲歲年年 every year; from year to year;
增長年歲 put on years;

[年頭] (1) year; (2) long time; years; (3) days; times; (4) harvest;
年頭歲尾 the beginning and end of a year;
年頭月尾 the beginning of a year and the end of a month;
挨年頭 drag out a miserable existence;
熬年頭 go through years in order to wait for an opportunity; suffer and endure through the years;

[年息] annual interest; interest per annum;
半年年息 semi-annual interest;

[年限] age limit; fixed number of years;
工作年限 the number of years set for work;
學習年限 the number of years set for a course of study;

[年薪] yearly salary;

[年夜] eve of the lunar New Year;
年夜糍粑 glutinous rice cakes on the lunar New Year's eve;

[年幼] young;
年幼無知 young and ignorant; young and inexperienced;

[年月] days; years;
何年何月 what year and what day;
艱難年月 hard times;
經年累月 a series of years; for months and years; for months and years on end; for years; month after month and year after year; year in year out;
屢月經年 month after month and year after year — for a long time;
年災月厄 have misfortunes this year; the year destined to bring sb misfortune;
窮年累月 for a very long time; for an interminable period; for years and years without end; for years on end;

from year to year; spend months and years; through the years; year after year;
生卒年月 dates of birth and death;
太平年月 peaceful times;
以往的年月 bygone times;
戰爭年月 war times;
[年長] older in age;
[年中] mid-year; middle of the year;
年中審查 midyear review;
[年終] end of the year; year-end;
年終報告 annual report; year-end report;
年終大掃除 general cleaning at the end of the year;
年終結賬 year-end settlement of accounts;
年終獎 year end bonus;
年終歲暮 at the end of the year; toward the year's end;
年終歲增 everyone considers himself a year older with the ending of the year;
年終總結 the summarization at the end of the year;
[年祝] years of jubilation;
[年尊] advanced in years; old;
[按年] annually; by the year; yearly;

百年 (1) a century; a hundred years; (2) lifetime;
拜年 pay a New Year call; wish sb a Happy New Year;
半年 half a year;
本年 current year; present year; this year;
比年 (1) recent years; (2) every year;
編年 compile annals; prepare a chronological record;
殘年 (1) last days of the year; (2) declining years; the evening of life;
長年 all the year round; long life; longevity;
常年 (1) perennial; throughout the year; (2) year in year out;
陳年 of many years' standing;
成年 coming of age; grown-up; year after year;
當年 that very year; the same year;
豐年 bumper harvest year; good year;
過年 (1) celebrate the New Year; (2) after the New Year;
光年 light-year;
旱年 year of drought;
賀年 extend New Year greetings or pay a New Year call;
後年 the year after next;
荒年 famine year;
幾百年 hundreds of years;
幾千年 thousands of years;
積年 for many years;
今年 this year;
經年 (1) throughout the year; (2) for many years;
近年 in recent years;
來年 next year; the coming year;
老年 old age;
累年 for years in succession; year after year;
歷年 (1) over the years; (2) calendar year;
連年 in consecutive years; in successive years;
明年 next year;
末年 last years of a dynasty or reign;
暮年 declining years; old age;
平年 (1) common year; non-leap year; (2) average year;
前年 the year before last;
前些年 in the previous years;
歉年 lean year;
青年 young people; youth;
去年 last year;
全年 annual; yearly;
閏年 leap year;
上年 last year;
少年 (1) early youth; (2) boy or girl of the age from ten to sixteen;
熟年 a year of good harvest; bumper year;
天年 natural span of life; one's allotted span;
髫年 childhood; young age;
通年 all the year round; throughout the year;
同年 of the same age; the same year;
童年 childhood;
頭年 (1) first year; (2) previous year;
晚年 in old age; one's later years;
往年 in former years;
昔年 in fomer years;
享年 die at the age of;
新年 New Year;
學年 school year;
一年 a year; one year;
翌年 next year;
英年 years of youthful vigour;
幼年 childhood; infancy;
餘年 one's remaining years;
元年 th first year of an era of the reign of an emperor;
早年 one's early year;
整年 all the year round;
中年 middle age;
終年 (1) all the year round; throughout the year;
周年 anniversary;
逐年 year after year; year by year;
轉年 (1) following year; (2) next year;

壯年 (of age) between thirty and forty;

nian
【拈】 (1) hold with fingers; pick up; take with fingers; (2) draw lots;
［拈筆］ pick up a pen to write; take a pen; write;
［拈掇］ point out; refer to;
［拈題］ select a topic for a piece of writing;
［拈弄］ finger and play; fondle;
［拈鬮］ draw lots;
［拈香］ burn joss sticks; offer incense;
［拈鬚］ finger one's beard; stroke one's beard;
［拈酸］ jealous;

nian
【粘】 same as 黏；

nian
【黏】 (1) glutinous; sticky; (2) adhere; bind;
［黏附］ adhere; adhesion; bind; stick;
黏附詞素 bound morpheme;
黏附能力 adhesive ability;
［黏合］ adhere; bind;
黏合劑 adhesive; amorphous binder; binder;
~防水黏合劑 waterproof adhesive;
~固體黏合劑 solid binder;
~聚合物黏合劑 polymer binder;
~樹脂黏合劑 resin binder;
~刷毛黏合劑 brush binder;
~水玻璃黏合劑 sodium silicate binder;
~塑料黏合劑 plastic binder;
~陶瓷黏合劑 ceramic binder;
~透明黏合劑 clear binder;
~推進劑黏合劑 propellant binder;
~型砂黏合劑 sand binder;
~陰離子黏合劑 cationic binder;
［黏糊］ lanquid; slow-moving;
黏糊糊 glutinous; sticky;
［黏結］ agglutination; bond; cement; cohere;
黏結作用 cementing action;
［黏膜］ mucous membrane, mucosa;
［黏土］ clay;
沖積黏土 alluvial clay;
風成黏土 aeolian clay;
風乾黏土 air-dried clay;
風積黏土 air-deposited clay;
活化黏土 activated clay;
球黏土 ball clay;
砂質黏土 arenaceous clay;
酸化黏土 acid-treated clay;
酸性黏土 acid clay;
一塊黏土 a clot of clay;
［黏液］ mucus;
［黏着］ mucus; adhere; adhesion; agglutination; bond; stick together;
黏着力 adhesion force;
黏着能力 tackifying ability;
黏着強度 adhesion strength;
黏着物 adhesive;
~塑性黏着物 plastic adhesive;
黏着性 adhesiveness; cohesiveness;
黏着語 agglutinative language;

nian
【鯰】 catfish;
［鯰魚］ catfish;

nian³

nian
【捻】 (1) nip with fingers; (2) Nian Bandits; (3) twist; (4) follow up;

復捻 second twist;
火捻 (1) kindling; (2) fuse;

nian
【撚】 toy with; twist with fingers;

nian
【碾】 (1) stone roller; (2) roll;

水碾 water-powered roller;

nian
【輦】 (1) handcart; (2) imperial carriage; king's carriage;

nian
【輾】 same as 碾；

nian
【攆】 (1) drive out; expel; oust; show sb the door; (2) catch up;
［攆走］ oust; send sb about his business; send sb packing; send sb to the right-about; show sb the door;

nian⁴

nian
【廿】 twenty;

nian
【念】 (1) miss; think of; (2) idea; thought; (3) attend school; study;
［念叨］ (1) always talk about; talk about

again and again in recollection or anticipation; (2) discuss; talk over;
有事跟大家念叨 have sth to talk over with everybody;

[念舊] (1) keep old friendships in mind; (2) for old time's sake;
從不念舊 never keep old friendships in mind;
時常念舊 often remember old friends;

[念念不置] think of sb without ceasing;

[念頭] idea; intention; thought;
放棄…念頭 give up the idea of;
歪念頭 crooked ideas; depraved thoughts; evil ideas;
怪念頭 whim notion;
一個念頭 an idea;
一閃而過的念頭 a passing thought;
有荒唐的念頭 get an absurd idea into one's head;

抱念 remember; think of;
叨念 chatter incessantly; talk about again and again in recollection or anticipation;
悼念 grieve over; mourn;
惦念 be anxious about; keep thinking about;
惡念 evil intentions;
概念 concept; conception; idea; notion;
感念 recall with deep emotion; remember sb in gratitude;
顧念 remember with concern;
掛念 miss; worry about sb who is absent;
觀念 concept; idea; sense;
懷念 cherish the memory of; think of;
紀念 (1) commemorate; mark; (2) keep sth as a souvenir; keepsake; souvenir;
眷念 feel nostalgic about; think fondly of;
理念 idea; principle;
留念 accept or keep as a souvenir;
牽念 be concerned about sb who is elsewhere; miss; worry about sb who is absent;
閃念 an idea that suddenly comes to mind;
私念 selfish motives;
思念 miss; remember with longing; think of;
體念 give sympathetic consideration to;
妄念 wild fancy;
繫念 be anxious about; worry about;
想念 miss; remember fondly; think of;
邪念 evil thought; wicked idea;
信念 belief; conviction; faith;
蓄念 harbour an idea;
懸念 worry about sb who is absent;
意念 idea; thought;
憶念 recollection;
慾念 craving; desire;
淫念 lust;
瞻念 look to; think of;
軫念 think anxiously about;

nian

【唸】 chant; read; recite;

[唸法] pronunciation;

[唸佛] chant the name of Buddha; pray to Buddha;
敲經唸佛 beat time and chant scriptures;

[唸經] chant scriptures; recite scriptures;
唸經問卜 cast a horoscope and recite the sutra;
唸完經趕和尚 expel the monks when sutra-chanting is over; kick down the ladder;

[唸唸有詞] chant; mumble about; mumble some words;

[唸書] attend school; read; study;

[唸誦] read aloud; recite;

[唸咒] intone a chant; mutter a incantation;

niang²
niang

【娘】 (1) ma; mama; mother; mum; (2) form of address for an elderly married woman; (3) young woman;

[娘家] parents' home of a married woman;
娘家姓 maiden name; nee;
回娘家 visit the parental home;

[娘娘] (1) empress; (2) imperial concubine; (3) goddess;
娘娘腔的 camp; cissy; poncy; sissy; womanish;
~娘娘腔的男子 cissy;

[娘親] relatives on the maternal side;

[娘胎] mother's womb;

[娘姨] maidservant;

[娘子] my wife;
小娘子 young girl;

媼娘 old maid;
伴娘 bridesmaid;
姑娘 (1) girl; (2) daughter;
紅娘 go-between; matchmaker;
後娘 step-mother;

師娘 wife of one's teacher;
喜娘 woman attendant serving as bride's counsel;
新娘 bride;
姨娘 aunt;

niang⁴
niang

【釀】 (1) brew beer; make wine; (2) make honey; (3) lead to; result in; (4) wine;

[釀成] breed; brew mischief; bring on; form gradually; lead to; result in;
釀成悲劇 breed a tragedy;
釀成大錯 breed big mistakes;
釀成大患 bring down a great calamity; cause serious trouble; occasion danger of fatal issue to;
釀成大禍 breed disaster; lead to disaster;
釀成禍患 cause serious trouble;
釀成糾紛 breed disputes;
釀成事故 lead to a disaster;

[釀禍] create troubel ferment disturbances; lead to disaster;

[釀酒] brew beer; make wine;
釀酒工 brewer;
釀酒公司 distiller;
釀酒廠 brewery; distillery;
~微型釀酒廠 microbrewery;
釀酒者 distiller;
釀酒專家 brewmaster;

[釀酶] zymase;

[釀蜜] make honey;

[釀母] yeast;

[釀造] brew beer; make wine;
釀造法 zymotechnics; zymotechnique;
釀造葡萄酒 make grape wine;
釀造所 zythepsary;
釀造學 zymurgy;
啤酒釀造 beer brewing;

佳釀 vintage wine;
酒釀 fermented glutinous rice;
醞釀 (1) brew; ferment; (2) deliberate on; have a preliminary informal discussion;

niao³
niao

【鳥】 bird;

[鳥巢] bird nest; bird's nest;
摸鳥巢 bird's-nesting;
鳥愛其巢，人愛其家 every bird likes its own nest, everyone likes his own home;

[鳥槍] birding piece; shotgun;
鳥槍獨彈 shotgun-slugs;
雙筒鳥槍 double barrel;
自動式鳥槍 automatic shotgun;

[鳥兒] bird;
愛叫的鳥兒—不做窩 a bird that loves to sing does not make a nest; all talk and no action;

[鳥盡弓藏] cast aside the bow once the birds are gone; cast sb aside when he has served his purpose;

[鳥瞰] get a bird's-eye view; look down from above;
鳥瞰全城 get a bird's-eye view of the city;
古代史鳥瞰 a general survey of ancient history;

[鳥類] birds;
鳥類生活 birds' life;
鳥類學 ornithology;

[鳥籠] birdcage;
大鳥籠 birdhouse;
如鳥出籠 like a bird set free from its cage; like a caged bird newly set free;

[鳥鳴] birds sing;
鳥鳴靜林 birds are spilling their songs over the quiet woods;
鳥鳴雀噪 the birds are tuning their songs;
鳥鳴山靜 birds sing while mountains remain silent;
鳥鳴枝梢 the brids were singing on the ends of the branches;

[鳥獸] birds and animals;
鳥飛獸散 scatter like birds and animals – flee helter-skelter;
如鳥獸散 disperse like birds and wild beasts; flee helter-skelter; scatter and flee like birds and beasts – be utterly routed;
絨鳥獸 velvet birds and. animals;
作鳥獸散 flee helter-skelter; flee in every direction; scatter like birds and beasts; stampede;

[鳥為食亡，人為財死] birds die in pursuit of food and human beings die in pursuit of wealth;

[鳥無頭不飛，蛇無頭不行] a bird without a head cannot fly and a snake without a head cannot crawl;

[鳥語] bird call;
鳥語花香 birds sing and flowers give forth their fragrance; songs of birds of scent of flowers;
[鳥嘴] bird's beak;
鳥嘴花 bird's-beak;

比翼鳥 a pair of lovebirds;
布穀鳥 cuckoo;
捕食鳥 predatory bird;
草原鳥 prairie bird;
翠鳥 kingfisher;
對趾鳥 zygodactyle;
蜂鳥 humming bird;
害鳥 pernicious bird;
候鳥 migratory bird;
黃鳥 oriole;
雷鳥 ptarmigan;
留鳥 resident bird;
籠鳥 cage bird;
旅鳥 travelling bird;
母鳥 mother bird;
潛鳥 diving bird;
琴鳥 lyrebird;
水鳥 aquatic bird; water bird;
鐵鳥 aeroplane;
鴕鳥 ostrich;
玩鳥 birding;
溫度計鳥 thermometer bird;
文鳥 manikin;
相思鳥 re-billed leiothrix;
一對鳥 a brace of birds;
一群鳥 a flock of birds;
一隻鳥 a bird;
益鳥 beneficial bird; useful bird;
知更鳥 redbreast; robin;
啄木鳥 woodpecker;

niao
【裊】 (1) curl up as smoke; waver gently; (2) all around, as sound of music;
[裊裊] (1) curling up; (2) continuous sound of music;
裊裊婷婷 curvaceous and soft;
春枝裊裊 the spring sprouts wave in the breeze;
[裊娜] (1) soft and slender; (2) the charming and graceful figure of a woman;

niao
【蔦】 ribes ambiguum, a kind of creeping plant;
[蔦與女蘿] brothers, sisters, and other relatives interrelated and dependent upon one another;

niao
【嬝】 delicate; graceful;
[嬝嬝] (1) curling upward; (2) wave in the wind; (3) slender;
嬝嬝上昇 roll up;
嬝嬝素女 delicate and graceful as a fairy;
嬝嬝婷婷 curvaceous and soft; delicate and graceful; lissome and graceful;
[嬝娜] slender and graceful; willowy;
嬝嬝娜娜 delicate and graceful; slender;
[嬝繞] curling upwards;

niao
【嬲】 dally with; flirt with;

niao4
niao
【尿】 (1) urine; (2) make water; pass water; urinate;
[尿崩症] diabetes insipidus;
垂體性尿崩症 pituitary diabetes insipidus;
腎性尿崩症 nephrogenic diabetes insipidus;
[尿崩停] posterior pituitary insufflation;
[尿閉] anuria; ischuria; suppression of urine;
痙攣性尿閉 ischuria spastica;
矛盾尿閉 ischuria paradoxa;
[尿布] diaper; napkin; nappy;
尿布疹 diaper rash;
尿布桌 changing table;
換尿布 change a diaper;
[尿沉澱] urinary sediment;
[尿牀] wet the bed;
[尿道] urethra;
尿道出血 hemorrhage of the urethra; urethrorrhagia;
尿道膀胱炎 urethrocystitis;
尿道切開 urethrotomy;
尿道痛 urethrodynia;
尿道性血尿 urethral hematuria;
尿道炎 urethritis;
~ 單純性尿道炎 simple urethritis;
淋病性尿道炎 gonorrheal urethritis;
~ 淋菌性尿道炎 gonococcal urethritis;
~ 囊性尿道炎 urethritis cystica;
~ 膀胱尿道炎 cystourethritis;
~ 前尿道炎 preurethritis;
~ 肉芽性尿道炎 urethritis granulosa;

~特異性尿道炎 specific urethritis;
~痛風性尿道炎 gouty urethritis;
~腺性尿道炎 urethritis glandularis;
~性病尿道炎 urethritis venerea;
~預防性尿道炎 prophylactic urethritis;
尿道液溢 urethrorrhea;
尿道溢 medorrhea;
後尿道 posterior urethra;
男尿道 urethra masculina;
女尿道 urethra feminina;
前列腺尿道 prostatic urethra;
前尿道 anterior urethra;

[尿毒症] uremia;
尿毒症性假糖尿病 uremic psuedodiabetes mellitus;
假尿毒症 pseudouremia;

[尿過濃] oligohydruria;

[尿過少] uropenia;

[尿汗] uridrosia;
尿汗症 uridrosis;

[尿壺] chamber pot;

[尿渾濁] cloudy urine;

[尿急] urgent urination;
尿急感 stangury;

[尿結石病] lithiasis;

[尿浸潤] urecchysis;

[尿褲子] wet the bed;

[尿量] urine volume;
尿量不等 anisuria;
尿量減少 hypourocrinia;
尿量增多 hydrouria;

[尿瘻] urinary fistula;

[尿路] urinary tract;
尿路病 urosis;
~阻塞性尿路病 obstructive uropathy;
尿路病變 uropathy;
尿路結石 lithangiuria;
尿路潰瘍 urelcosis;
尿路上皮 urothelium;

[尿囊] allantois;
尿囊膜 allantois;

[尿尿] wee-wee;

[尿頻] frequent micturition; frequent urination; pollakiuria; sychnuria;

[尿少症] oliguria;

[尿失禁] incontinence;
反常性尿失禁 paradoxical incontinence;
間歇性尿失禁 intermittent incontinence;
緊迫性尿失禁 urgency incontinence;
溢流性尿失禁 overflow incontinence;
應激性尿失禁 stress incontinence;

[尿石] urolith;
尿石症 urinary calculus; urolithiasis;

[尿素] carbamide; urea;
尿素酶 urase; urease;

[尿酸] uric acid;
尿酸梗死 uric acid infarct;
尿酸結石 urate calculus;
尿酸結石病 uric acid lithiasis;
尿酸尿 uricaciduria;
~低尿酸尿 hypouricuria;
高尿酸尿 hyperlithuria;
~正常尿酸尿 normouricuria;

[尿糖過多] hyperglycosuria;

[尿蓄積] retention of urine;

[尿血] blood in the urine; hematuria;

[尿液] chamber lye; tea; urina; urine;

把尿 help a small child pass water by holding his legs apart;
憋尿 hold up one's urine;
丙酮尿 acetonuria;
蛋白尿 albuminuria;
導尿 catheterize;
溺尿 make water; urinate;
濃尿 pyuria;
膿尿 pyuria;
排尿 micturate; urinate;
頻尿 pollakiuria;
撒尿 pee; piss;
血尿 blood in the urine; haematuria;
一泡尿 pass water;
遺尿 bedwetting; enuresis;

niao

【脲】 carbamide; urea;

[脲酶] urase; urease;

[脲醛] urea-formaldehyde;
脲醛樹脂 urea-formaldehyde resin;
脲醛塑料 urea-formaldehyde plastics;

二苯脲 acadite;

niao

【溺】 urinate;

便溺 urinate and defecate;

nie¹

nie

【捏】 (1) hold between the fingers; pinch; (2) knead with the fingers; mould; (3)

concoct; cook sth up; fabricate; fake; make up; trump up;

［揑估］ (1) bully; take advantage of; (2) malign sb; scheme against sb; speak ill of sb; (3) act as a go-between;

［揑合］ (1) act as go-between; mediate; (2) fabricate; make up;

［揑碎］ crumb;

［揑造］ concoct; cook sth up; fabricate; fake; trump up;

揑造借口 cook up a pretext; cook up an excuse; feign an excuse;

揑造情節 trump up a story;

揑造是非 circulate a fabricated tale; spread false information; spread rumours;

揑造事實 invent a story; make up a story;

揑造數字 conjure up figures;

揑造誣告 make up stories and fabricate charges;

揑造證據 fabricate evidence;

揑造罪名 trump up charges;

扭揑 affectedly bashful;

nie

【揑】 same as 揑;

nie

【捻】 pinch;

nie²

nie

【苶】 tired; weary;

nie⁴

nie

【乜】 a surname;

nie

【涅】 (1) blacken; dye black; tattoo; (2) block up;

［涅白］ opaque white;

［涅而不緇］ be soaked in a dark liquid without becoming black;

［涅槃］ nirvana;

一佛出世，二佛涅槃 beat sb till he is half dead;

nie

【臬】 (1) institution; law; rule; (2) door-post;

［臬兀］ unstable; unsteady;

圭臬 criterion; standard;

兀臬 intranquil; uneasy; unstable;

nie

【隉】 dangerous; precarious;

nie

【鯢】 jittery; jumpy; worried;

［鯢卼］ uneasy; unhappy; vexed;

nie

【闑】 wood bars on both sides of the central door;

nie

【聶】 (1) whisper into another's ear; (2) a surname;

nie

【鎳】 nickel;

乙酸鎳 nickelous acetate;

nie

【孽】 sin; evil;

［孽根禍胎］ a truly incorrigible son; one's dreadful son; the bane of one's life;

［孽海情天］ the sea of degradation and sentiments; the tumultuous sea of love between man and woman;

［孽因］ sinful cause;

［孽障］ vile spawn; evil creature;

［孽子］ son of a concubine;

孤臣孽子 a minister without support at court and a prince born of a concubine fallen from grace; a solitary minister and a perverse son; a supporter of a lost dynasty; surviving courtiers;

妖孽 (1) person or event associated with evil or misfortune; (2) evildoer;

餘孽 leftover evil; remaining evil element;

造孽 do evil things;

罪孽 evil; sin;

作孽 commit a sin; do evil;

nie

【櫱】 leaves sprouting from the stump of a tree;

nie

【囁】 falter in speech; move the mouth;

［囁嚅］ speak haltingly;

囁嚅不言 move the mouth, but refrain from speaking;

nie

【蘖】 yeast for making liquors;

分蘖 tiller;

nie

【齧】 bite; gnaw;

nie

【躡】 (1) lighten one's step; walk on tiptoe; (2) step on; walk with;

［躡步而入］ enter noiselessly; enter with careful steps;

［躡登］ go up;

［躡蹀］ walking with mincing steps;

［躡屩擔簦］ make a long journey; take a long journey; undertake a long journey;

［躡蹤］ follow along behind sb; track;

［躡足］ (1) walk with light steps; (2) join; participate in;

躡足不前 not to move a step forward;

躡足附耳 press the foot and whisper in the ear – tell a secret;

躡足其間 associate with a certain type of people; follow a trade; join a profession;

躡足潛蹤 walk stealthily;

躡足上流社會 associate with people of upper class;

躡足向前 go forward softly;

躡足政界 participate in political circles;

nie

【鑷】 forceps; pincers; tweezers; (2) nip; pull out;

［鑷子］ tweezer;

防磁鑷子 antimagnetic type tweezer;

金剛石鑷子 diamond tweezers;

細尖鑷子 fine-point tweezer;

游絲鑷子 hairspring tweezer;

眉鑷 eyebrow tweezers;

nie

【顳】 temporal bone;

nin²

nin

【您】 you;

ning²

ning

【甯】 same as 寧;

ning

【寧】 (1) better to...than...; prefer...to; rather; should like to; would rather; would sooner...than do sth; (2) calm; peaceful; quiet; still; tranquil;

［寧靜］ calm; peaceful; quiet; still; tranquil;

寧靜的夜晚 a tranquil night;

寧靜致遠 accomplish sth lasting by leading a quiet life;

暴風雨來臨前的寧靜 the lull before the storm;

打破寧靜 shatter the peace;

［寧可］ better; prefer...to...; prefer to; prefer to ... rather than to...; should like to; would rather; would rather...than; would sooner...than do sth;

寧可人負我，不可我負人 better be the victim of ingratitude than be ungrateful; better suffer ill than do ill; better suffer wrong than do wrong;

寧可信其有，不可信其無 better to believe the worst, and be pleasantly surprised, than to be optimistic and learn the worst; it is better to believe that it exists than it does not;

寧可站著死，不願跪著生 better a glorious death than a shameful life; better die standing than live kneeling; one would rather die on one's feet than live on one's knees;

［寧謐］ peaceful; quiet; tranquil;

［寧缺毋濫］ better to accept fewer than to make up a number by lowering the standard; it is better to leave a deficiency uncovered than to have it covered without discretion; rather go without than have sth shoddy – put quality before quantity; would rather go without than make do with anything not up to the mark; would rather leave the pst vacant than it filled by anybody unqualified for it;

寧少毋濫 put quality before quantity; fewer but better; less but better; rather go without than have sth shoddy;

［寧人息事］ gloss things over to stay on good terms; pacify people and settle matters; palliate the matter; pour oil on the troubled waters; smooth down the

cracks and conciliate the people;
息事寧人 (1) patch up a quarrel and reconcile the parties concerned; (2) give up to avoid trouble; gloss things over to stay on good terms; make concessions to avoid trouble; pour oil on troubled waters;

[寧日] peaceful days;
國無寧日 there is no peace in the country;
永無寧日 never will there be days of peace;

[寧食開眉粥，莫食愁眉飯] it is better to take congee with pleasant feelings than rice that produces sorrow;

[寧死] would rather die;
寧死不屈 prefer death to surrender; true to the last of one's blood; would rather die than surrender; rather die than surrender; would see oneself shot before yielding;
寧死不活 rather be dead than alive;
寧死不講 rather die than speak;
寧死不降 die before yielding; prefer death to surrender; rather die than surrender;
寧死不辱 prefer death to dishonor;
寧死不招 would die before one would confess;
寧死不做 would rather die than do such a thing;
寧死刀下 would rather perish beneath the sword than submit;
寧死勿辱 better to die than be humiliated; choose death before disgrace; prefer death to dishonour;

[寧為雞口，無為牛後] better be a bird's beak than a cow's rump; better be first in a village than second at Rome; better be the head of a dog than the tail of a lion; better be the head of a lizard than the tail of a dragon; better be the head of an ass than the tail of a horse; better be the head of the yeomanry than the tail of the gentry; better to reign in hell than serve in heaven; would rather be leader anywhere than follower;

[寧為玉碎，不為瓦全] better a glorious death than a shameful life; it is better to be a martyr than a confessor; rather be a broken piece of jade than a whole tile — rather die with honour than survive with dishonour; rather be a jade broken than a tile intact — better to die for a noble cause than continue to live a shameful life; rather be a shattered vessel of jade than an unbroken piece of pottery — better to die in glory than live in dishonour; rather fall to pieces like broken jade than remain intact as a worthless tile;

[寧心定氣] quiet the mind and still the passion nature;

[寧作太平犬，莫作離亂人] better be a dog in times of general peace than a man in the midst of civil wars;

安寧 (1) peaceful; peaceful and orderly; quiet; repose; tranquil; (2) calm; composed; free from worry;
歸寧 return to one's paternal home for a visit;

ning

【凝】 (1) coagulate; cohere; condense; congeal; congeal into; curdle; solidify; (2) with fixed attention;

[凝成] congeal into;

[凝固] coagulation; congeal; solidify;
凝固點 freezing point;
分級凝固 fractional coagulation;
間歇凝固 periodic coagulation;
膠水凝固 the glue solidifies;
潛伏凝固 dormant coagulation;
水泥凝固 the cement solidifies;
酸性凝固 acid coagulation;
延緩凝固 delayed coagulation;
早期凝固 premature coagulation;
自凝固 spontaneous coagulation;

[凝灰岩] tuff;
爆發凝灰岩 explosion tuff;
灰質凝灰岩 calcareous tuff;
水生凝灰岩 aquagene tuff;

[凝集] (1) gather; (2) agglomerate; agglutinate; agglutination;
凝集反應器 agglutometer;
凝集素 agglutinin;
~寒冷凝集素 cold agglutinin;
~免疫凝集素 immune agglutinin;
~細胞凝集素 cell agglutinin;
~細菌凝集素 bacterial agglutinin;
~植物凝集素 plant agglutinin;
凝集原 agglutinogen;

間接凝集 mediate agglutination;
鏡檢凝集 microscopic agglutination;
直接凝集 immediate agglutination;
自發凝集 spontaneous agglutination;

[凝膠] gel;
大孔凝膠 large pore gel;
膠態凝膠 colloidal gel;
離子凝膠 ionic gel;
彈性凝膠 elastic gel;
炭黑凝膠 carbon gel;

[凝結] coagulate; coagulation; condense; congeal; curdling;
凝結成冰 congeal into ice;
凝結成塊 clot;
凝集反應 agglutination reaction;
~無凝集反應 having no agglutination reaction;
~有凝集反應 having agglutination reaction;
使凝結 curdle;
酸性凝結 sour curdling;

[凝聚] coagulate; cohere; condense;
凝聚層 sheaf;
~代數凝聚層 algebraic coherent sheaf;
~解析凝聚層 analytic coherent sheaf;
凝聚力 cohesive force;

[凝塊] clot;
血凝塊 blood clot;

[凝眸] focus one's eyes upon;
凝眸而視 behold with a fixed gaze — stare at;

[凝乳] curd;
凝乳計 curdmeter;
家庭自製凝乳 country-style curd;

[凝神] with fixed attention;
凝神諦聽 listen with rapt attention;
凝神屏息 with fixed gaze and bated breath;
凝神傾聽 hang on every word of; listen attentively; listen with rapt attention;
凝神思索 deep in thought; gaze fixedly and ponder; think hard;
凝神細視 look hard;
凝神遠視 look into the distance with fixed gaze;
凝神注視 watch attentively;

[凝視] gaze fixedly; stare;
瞪目凝視 stare with wide eyes;
久久地凝視 stare at sth for a long time;

[凝思] be buried in thought; be lost in thought; deep in thought;
凝思默想 meditate profoundly;
停筆凝思 stop writing to think;

[凝重] dignified; imposing;
氣氛凝重 the atmosphere is solemn;
神情凝重 look dignified;
聲音凝重 in deep forceful voice;
烏雲凝重 the sky is covered with thick black clouds;

凍凝 congeal;
冷凝 condense;

ning
【嚀】 enjoin; instruct;

叮嚀 give repeated exhortations; urge again and again;

ning
【擰】 (1) pull together; twist; wring; (2) pinch; tweak; (3) pigheaded; stubborn;

[擰乾] wring out the water;
[擰緊] screw firmly;
把螺絲擰緊 tighten the screws firmly;
[擰開] unscrew;

ning
【獰】 awe-inspiring look; fierce appearance;

[獰笑] grim smile; grin hideously;

猙獰 ferocious; hideous; savage;

ning
【檸】 lemon;

[檸檬] lemon;
檸檬草 lemon grass;
檸檬茶 lemon tea;
檸檬蛋糕 lemon cake;
檸檬黃 lemon yellow;
檸檬菌素 citromycentin;
檸檬酪 lemon curd;
檸檬汽水 lemonade;
~一杯檸檬汽水 a glass of lemonade;
檸檬醛 citral;
檸檬水 lemonade;
檸檬酸 citric acid;
檸檬形 citriform;
檸檬飲料 lemon drink;
檸檬榨汁器 lemon squeezer;
粗皮檸檬 rough lemon;
甜檸檬 sweet citron;

野檸檬 wild lemon;
一片檸檬 a slice of lemon;

ning^{3}
ning
【擰】 (1) screw; twist; (2) mistaken; wrong; (3) at cross-purposes; differ; disagree;

ning^{4}
ning
【佞】 (1) be gifted with a glib tongue; eloquent; persuasive; (2) fawning; obsequious; (3) believe in superstition;
不佞 I; yours truly;
奸佞 crafty and evil person; crafty and fawning;

ning
【甯】 a surname;

ning
【擰】 wrench;
[擰開] wrench apart;
[擰了] fail;

ning
【濘】 miry; muddy;
泥濘 mire; miry; mud; muddy;

niu^{1}
niu
【妞】 girl; little girl;
[妞兒] girl;
柴禾妞兒 country girl;
胖妞兒 fat girl;
俏妞兒 attractive young woman; cutie; cutie-pie; dish; good-looking girl; lush bint; peach; popsie; popsy; rumpo; tabby;
傻妞兒 silly girl;
小妞兒 small girl; young girl;
[妞妞] little girl;

niu^{2}
niu
【牛】 (1) cattle; ox; (2) a surname;
[牛車] bullock-cart; ox cart;
[牛刀] butcher's knife;
牛刀割雞 break a butterfly on the wheel; crush a fly upon the wheel; employ a steam-hammer to crack nuts; swat a fly with a cannot; use a sledge-hammer on a gnat;
牛刀小試 a master hand's first small display; display only a small part of one's talent; give a little inkling of what one is capable of; show sth of one's ability;
割雞焉用牛刀 why break a butterfly on the wheel; why use an oxcleaver to kill a chicken;
[牛痘] (1) cowpox; (2) smallpox pustule;
壞疽性牛痘 vaccinia gangrenosa;
假牛痘 pseudocowpox;
[牛犢] calf;
[牛肚] ox tripe;
[牛耳] ears of an ox;
執牛耳 in a dominant position; occupy a leading position; play the leading role; rule the roost; take the head; take the lead; the head of the covenant;
[牛糞] cowpat;
[牛驥同皂] horses and oxen kept in the same stable—make no distinction between the wise and the foolish;
[牛肩] chuck;
牛肩肉排 chuck steak;
[牛角] ox horn;
牛角畫 ox horn mosaics;
[牛筋] beef tendons;
紅油牛筋 deep-fried beef tendons with chili oil;
[牛頸] cow's neck;
牛頸鈴 cowbell;
[牛勁] (1) great strength; tremendous effort; (2) obstinacy; strong-willed; stubbornness; tenacity;
[牛郎] cowboy;
[牛馬] beasts of burden; oxen and horses;
牛馬不如 live worse than beasts of burden; more pitiful than cows and horses;
牛馬生活 a dog's life; a life of drudgery; a subhuman standard of life; live like beasts of burden;
當牛做馬 serve sb like a horse; slave for sb; toil like beasts of burden; work like horses and toil like oxen;
耕牛戰馬 ploughing cattle and chargers;
歸馬放牛 desist from military operations and cultivate literary skill; leave military pursuits and promote culture; stop warfare;

呼牛呼馬 let people call me what they will — disregard hostile opinion;
童牛角馬 a hornless ox and a horse with horns — unfounded hearsay;
做牛做馬 slave for sb; toil like beasts of burden; work like a horse;

[牛毛] ox hair;
多如牛毛 as many as the hairs on an ox; countless; innumerable; too numerous to enumerate;

[牛奶] milk;
牛奶場 dairy; dairy farm;
~牛奶場男工 dairyman;
~牛奶場女工 dairy maid;
~牛奶場主 dairyman;
牛奶公司 dairy;
牛奶壺 milk jug;
牛奶糖 milk candy;
~脆心牛奶糖 milk brittle;
含脂牛奶 creamy milk;
生牛奶 raw milk;
脱脂牛奶 fat-free milk; skim milk; skimmed milk;
~半脱脂牛奶 semi-skimmed milk; two-percent milk;
一杯牛奶 a glass of milk; a tumbler of milk;
一大桶牛奶 a large pail of milk;
一點牛奶 a speck of milk;
一罐牛奶 a jug of milk;
一盒牛奶 a carton of milk;
一桶牛奶 a bucket of milk;

[牛腩] brisket;

[牛排] beefsteak;
大塊牛排 chump steak;
多汁美味的牛排 succulent steak;
嫩牛排 tender steak;
生牛排 raw steak;
一塊牛排 a steak;
炸牛排 chicken-fried steak; fried steak;

[牛棚] byre; cowshed;

[牛皮] (1) cattlehide; cow leather; cowhide; (2) brag;
牛皮菜 chard;
牛皮大王 a person given to gross exaggeration; braggart;
牛皮革 cowhide;
牛皮燈籠一點不透 an ox-hide lantern is never bright — a slow-witted person; thick-headed;
牛皮糖 (1) sticky candy; (2) slow-doer;
牛皮癬 psora; psoriasis; serpedo;
~類牛皮癬 parapsoriasis;
~脂溢性牛皮癬 seborrhiasis;
牛皮紙 kraft paper;
吹牛皮 act the braggadocio; boast; brag; draw the long bow; shoot aline; shoot crap; shoot the bull; shoot the shit; stick it on; talk big; talk horse; talk in high language; talk through one's hat; tell large stories;
~大吹牛皮 pitch it strong; talk big;

[牛氣] arrogant; self-important;

[牛肉] beef;
牛肉乾 dried beef;
牛肉塊 beef clod;
牛肉麵 beef noodle;
牛肉末 ground beef;
牛肉湯 beef soup;
牛肉汁 beef gravy;
薄片牛肉 chipped beef;
帶骨牛肉 bone-in beef;
炖牛肉 braised beef;
罐裝牛肉 corned beef;
厚厚一塊牛肉 a slab of beef;
醬牛肉 spiced beef;
絞細牛肉 ground beef;
烤牛肉 broiled beef; roast beef;
熟牛肉 cooked beef;
五花牛肉 marbled beef;
五香牛肉 spicy beef;
鹹牛肉 corned beef;
醃牛肉 corned beef;
一大片牛肉 a joint of beef;

[牛乳] cow's milk;

[牛舍] cowshed;

[牛市] bull market;
牛市場 cattle market;
牛市的 bullish;

[牛頭] cow's head;
牛頭不對馬嘴 contradict each other; far from the mark; farfetched; irrelevant; it lacks a proper connection and relationship; quite a different pair of shoes; things that don't agree; wide of the mark;
牛頭馬面 cruel devils; devils in animal forms; malignant persons;

[牛蛙] bullfrog;

[牛尾] oxtail;

[牛胃] ox tripes;

[牛瘟] cattle plague;

［牛羊］ oxen and sheep;
殺牛宰羊 kill oxen and sheep;
亡羊得牛 lose a sheep and get an ox — the gain is greater than the loss;
［牛衣對泣］ a couple living in extreme poverty;
［牛油］ beef tallow; butter;
牛油果 avocado;
［牛雜碎］ ox giblets;
［牛仔］ buckaroo; cowboy;
牛仔服 cowboy suit;
牛仔褲 blue jeans; jeans;
~緊身牛仔褲 skinny jeans; snug jeans; tight jeans;
~一條牛仔褲 a pair of jeans;
~預先縮過水的牛仔褲 pre-shrunk jeans;
牛仔帽 cowboy hat;
女牛仔 cowgirl;

笨牛 fool; stupid ox;
菜牛 beef cattle;
吹牛 baloney; blast; blow one's own horn; blow one's own trumpet; boast; brag; draw a long bow; eyewash; hot air; plume oneself; shoot the breeze; swing the lead; talk big; talk in high language;
椎牛 butcher oxen; kill an ox;
純種牛 pedigree cattle;
耕牛 farm cattle;
公牛 bull;
供屠牛 slaughter cattle;
牯牛 bull;
海牛 manatee; sea cow;
黃牛 cattle; ox;
活牛 live bovine cattle;
犍牛 bullock; castrated bull;
羚牛 takin;
瘤牛 bos indicus;
牦牛 yak;
母牛 cow;
牡牛 bull;
奶牛 dairy cattle; milch cow; milk cow;
牝牛 cow;
肉用牛 beef cattle; butcher cow;
乳牛 milk cow;
食用牛 stocker cattle;
麝牛 musk-ox;
瘦牛 lean cow;
水牛 buffalo;
天牛 long-horned beetle; longicorn;
鐵牛 tractor;
土牛 mound on a dike or dam;
蝸牛 snail;
犀牛 rhinoceros;
野牛 wild ox;
一大群牛 a mob of cattle;
一群牛 a drove of oxen; a herd of cattle; a herd of cows;
一條牛 a cow;
一頭牛 a cow;
正在吃草的牛 the cattle at browse;
種牛 bull kept for covering;

niu³

niu

【忸】

［忸怩］ bashful; blushing; coy;
忸怩不安 blush with shame and uncomfortable;
忸怩作態 affectedly shy; behave coyly; behave in an affected way; camp it up; campy; strike a pose;
忸忸怩怩 coquette; in an embarrassed manner; shillyshally; turn coy and shy;

niu

【扭】 (1) reverse; turn from...to...; turn into; turn round; (2) confound; confuse; distort; twist; wrench; (3) sprain; wrench; (4) roll; swing; (5) grapple with; seize;

［扭臂舞］ bump 'n' grind;
［扭打］ grapple; wrestle;
扭打成一團 grapple with each other;
扭打格鬥 wrestle and fight;
［扭動］ wiggle;
［扭矩］ torque;
加速扭矩 accelerating torque;
交變扭矩 alternate torque;
控制扭矩 control torque;
［扭力］ torque force;
［扭捏］ behave coyly;
東扭西捏 be affected and unnatural;
扭扭捏捏 affectedly bashful; affectedly shy; niminy-piminy; take mincing steps;
［扭曲］ contort; contortion;
扭曲作直 confound the right and wrong; distort facts; give a false account of the true facts; stand facts on their heads;
面部扭曲 facial contortions;
［扭傷］ sprain; wrench;

N

扭傷脖子 wrench one's neck;
扭傷肩部 sprain one's shoulder;
扭傷手腕 sprain one's wrist;
扭傷足踝 give a wrench to one's ankle;

［扭轉］ reverse; turn back; turn round;
扭轉局面 bring about changes in the situation; turn the tables;
扭轉局勢 reverse a trend; turn the tide;
扭轉看法 reverse oneself about sth;
扭轉乾坤 bring about a radical change in the situation; retrieve a hopeless situation; reverse the course of events; save a country from disaster;

別扭 (1) awkward; difficult; uncomfortable; (2) awkward; unnatural; (3) cannot see eye to eye;

niu
【狃】 (1) covet; (2) be accustomed; be bound by; stick to;

niu
【紐】 (1) handle; knob; (2) button; (3) bond; link; tie;
［紐帶］ bond; link; tie;
［紐子］ button;

秤紐 the lifting cord of a steelyard;
電紐 power switch button;
樞紐 axis; hub; key position; pivot;
弦紐 tuning peg;
旋紐 knob;

niu
【鈕】 (1) button; (2) a surname;
［鈕扣］ button;
一顆鈕扣 a button;
一粒鈕扣 a button;
一套鈕扣 a set of buttons;
［鈕孔］ buttonhole;
［鈕子］ button;

電鈕 button;

niu⁴
niu
【拗】 a pronunciation of 拗;

執拗 obstinate; stubborn; wilful;

niu
【衄】 a pronunciation of 衄;

niu
【謬】 a pronunciation of 謬;

nong²
nong
【農】 (1) agriculture; farming; (2) farmer; peasant; (3) rural;
［農產品］ agricultural products; farm product;
農產品價格 farm products price;
農產品流通體制 circulation pattern of farm products;
農產品貿易 farm products trade;
農產品市場 farm products market;
［農場］ farm;
農場工人 farmhand;
農場雇工 hired hand;
農場住宅 farmhouse;
公司農場 corporation farm;
合作農場 cooperative farm;
經濟農場 commercial farm;
［農村］ village; countryside; the rural area;
農村改革 rural reform;
農村集市 rural fair;
農村經濟 rural economy;
~ 農村經濟政策 rural economic policy;
農村生育率 fertility of countryside;
農村土地使用權 right to use land in the rural area;
住在農村 live in the countryside;
［農地］ agricultural land;
可用農地 agricultural land;
［農夫］ farmer; husbandman; tiller;
農夫市場 farmers' market;
［農工］ (1) peasants and workers; (2) agro-industrial;
農工聯合公司 joint farm-industry corporation;
農工企業 agro-industrail complex;
［農家］ peasant family;
農家宅院 farmyard;
［農曆］ lunar calendar;
［農林］ argiculture and forestry;
農林業 agroforestry;
［農民］ agrarian; farmer; peasant; peasantry;
農民黨 agrarian party;
農民合作社 agrarian co-op;
農民經濟 peasant agriculture;
富裕農民 well-to-do farmer;
個體農民 peasant farmer;
［農商］ farming and business;
棄農經商 give up farm production and

engage in trading; leave farm work behind to engage in trade;

[農事] farm work; farming;

[農田] cropland; cultivated land; farmland;
農田類型 agrotype;
農田水利 irrigation and water conservancy;

[農藥] pesticide;
農藥過敏 pesticide allergy;
農藥污染 pesticide pollution;
低殘留農藥 less-persistent pesticide;
低毒性農藥 low-toxic pesticide;
粒狀農藥 granular pesticide;
噴灑農藥 crop-dusting; crop-spraying;

[農業] agricultural industry; agriculture; farming;
農業佈局 distribution of agriculture;
農業地質學 agrogeology;
農業工程學 agriculture engineering;
農業化學 agricultural chemistry; agrochemistry;
農業環境 agricultural environment;
~農業環境污染 agricultural environment pollution;
農業機械化 agriculturalmechanization;
農業技術 agricultural technology;
~農業技術交流 agrotechnical exchange;
~農業技術經濟 economics of agricultural technique;
~農業技術推廣站 station for popularizing agricultural technique;
~農業技術員 agricultural technician; agrotechnician;
農業家 agriculturist;
農業經濟 agricultural economy;
~農業經濟法 agro-economic law;
~農業經濟結構 agricultural economic structure;
~農業經濟師 agricultural economist;
高級農業經濟師 senior agricultural economist;
農業景觀 agricultural landscape;
農業氣象學 agroclimatology; agrometeorology;
農業情報服務 rural information service;
農業區域環境 agricultural region environment;
農業生產 agricultural production;
~農業生產成本 agricultural production cost;
~商業性農業生產 commercial agriculture;
農業生態 agricultural ecology;
~農業生態環境 agricultural ecological environment;
~農業生態經濟 agricultural ecological economy;
~農業生態系統 agroecosystem;
~農業生態學 agroecology;
農業生物 agrobiological;
~農業生物工程 agrobiological engineering;
~農業生物環境 agrobiological environment;
~農業生物學 agrobiology;
農業水文學 agrohydrology;
農業稅 agricultural tax;
農業土壤學 agrology;
農業微生物學 agromicrobiology;
農業污染源 agricultural pollution sources;
農業污染源 agricultural pollution sources;
農業系統工程 agricultural system engineering;
農業系統科學 agricultural system science;
農業現代化 agricultural modernization;
農業信息系統 agricultural information system;
農業銀行 agricultural bank;
農業用地 agricultural land;
農業政策 agricultural policy;
農業自然資源 natural resources of agriculture;
白色農業 white agriculture;
辦農業 develop the farming industry;
大農業 mega-agriculture;
高效率農業 efficient agriculture;
工業農業 industrial agriculture;
~超工業農業 super-industrial agriculture;
航空農業 aerial farming;
合同農業 contract farming;
合作農業 cooperative agriculture;
混合農業 mixed farming;
計劃性農業 planned agriculture;
立體農業 stereoscopic agriculture;
歐洲農業 continental agriculture;
世界農業 world agriculture;
移動農業 shifting agriculture;
自由農業 free agriculture;

[農藝] agronomy;
農藝師 agronomist;
~高級農藝師 senior agronomist;
~助理農藝師 assistant agronomist;
農藝性狀 agronomical characters;

農藝學 agronomy;
[農用] agricultural use;
農用工業 agroindustry;
農用化學製品 agrichemical;
農用噴霧機 agrosprayer;
農用噴霧器 agroatomizer;
農用汽車 agrimotor;
農用塑料 agriplast;
[農莊] farmstead;
集體農莊 collective farm;
[農作物] agricultural products; crops;

菜農 vegetable grower;
蠶農 sericulturist; silkworm raiser;
茶農 tea grower;
佃農 tenant farmer; tenant peasant;
工農 workers and peasants;
僱農 farm labourer; farmhand;
果農 fruit grower;
花農 flower grower;
林農 forestry farmer;
棉農 cotton grower;
貧農 poor peasant;
神農 legendary ruler in ancient China;
小農 small farmer;
煙農 tobacco grower;
藥農 herbalist;
蔗農 sugarcane grower;
中農 middle peasant;

nong
【儂】 (1) (in old usage) I; me; (2) (in Shanghai dialect) you; (3) (in Ningbo dialect) he; she; (4) a surname;

nong
【濃】 (1) dense; great; heavy; thick; (2) pronounced; strong;
[濃度] concentration; strength;
百分濃度 percentage concentration;
~ 體積百分濃度 volume percentage concentration;
~ 重量百分濃度 weight percentage concentration;
當量濃度 normality;
放射性濃度 radioactivity concentration;
廢酸濃度 acid-spending strength;
酒精濃度 alcohol strength;
克分子濃度 molarity; molar concentration;
~ 重量克分子濃度 weight molar concentration; weight-molarity,
容許濃度 acceptable concentration; admissible concentration;
酸液濃度 acid strength;
添加劑濃度 additive concentration;
[濃髮] shock of hair;
一頭濃髮 a shock of hair;
[濃厚] dense; strong; thick;
黑煙濃厚 be permeated with thick black smoke;
火藥味濃厚 smell strongly of gunpower;
興趣濃厚 be strongly interested in sth; take a keen interest in sth;
雲層濃厚 there are heavy clouds in the sky;
[濃密] dense; thick;
[濃縮] concentrate;
濃縮器 concentrator;
~ 酸濃縮器 acid concentrator;
~ 塔式濃縮器 tower concentrator;
濃縮物 concentrate; condensate;
~ 高蛋白質濃縮物 high protein concentrate;
~ 啤酒花濃縮物 hop concentrate;
~ 魚蛋白濃縮物 fish protein concentrate;
[濃湯] thick soup;
[濃霧] dense fog; smog; smoke;
濃霧迷漫 the air is covered with a heavy mist;
一層濃霧 a blanket of mist;
[濃煙] dense smoke; smoke smudge;
濃煙滾滾 billowing smoke rises; dark smoke billows;
一陣濃煙 a gust of smoke;
[濃艷] bright-coloured; rich and gaudy;
[濃蔭蔽空] the thick branches and leaves seem to blot out the sky;
[濃重] dense; strong; thick;
霧氣濃重 the fog is thick;
顏色濃重 the shade of colour is too deep;
[濃妝] heavy makeup;
濃妝艷服 make up one's face heavily and dress gaudily;

nong
【膿】 purulent matter; pus;
[膿皰] pimple; pustule;
膿皰病 impetigo;
~ 觸染性膿皰病 impetigo contagiosa;
膿皰瘡 impetigo;
膿皰性痤瘡 acne pustulosa;
膿皰性濕疹 eczema pustulosum;

[膿皮病] pyoderma;
增殖性膿皮病 pyoderma vegetans;
[膿癬] kerion;
[膿性水疱] vesicopustule;
[膿胸] empyema; pyothorax;
搏動性膿胸 pulsating empyema;
鏈球菌性膿胸 streptococcal empyema;
潛伏性膿胸 latent empyema;
[膿腫] abscess;
扁桃體周圍膿腫 peritonsillar abscess;
膽道膿腫 biliary abscess;
耳原性腦膿腫 otogenic brain abscess;
肺膿腫 lung abscess; suppuration of the lung;
肝膿腫 liver abscess;
喉膿腫 laryngeal abscess;
頸部膿腫 cervical abscess; neck abscess;
闌尾膿腫 appendiceal abscess;
慢性膿腫 chronic abscess;
梅毒性膿腫 syphilitic abscess;
彌漫性膿腫 diffuse abscess;
腦膿腫 brain abscess; cerebral abscess;
脾膿腫 splenic abscess;
蠕蟲性膿腫 verminous abscess;
腎膿腫 kidney abscess;
無痛膿腫 indolent abscess;
牙槽膿腫 alveolar abscess;
咽後膿腫 retropharyngeal abscess;
齦膿腫 parulis;
游走性膿腫 wandering abscess;
轉移性膿腫 metastatic abscess;

化膿 fester; suppurate;

nong
【穠】 luxuriant growth of plants;
[穠纖得中] right proportions;

nong
【醲】 (1) rich wine; strong wine; (2) same as 濃;

nong
【齈】 a kind of nasal ailment characterized by abundance of snivel;

nong⁴
nong
【弄】 (1) fool with; play with; (2) bring to; create; do; make; (3) fetch; get; (4) distort; play; (5) dally with woman; have sexual relations with women;
[弄筆] distort facts; exaggerate in writing;
[弄潮兒] beach swimmer; seaman;
[弄錯] make a mistake; mistake; mistaken; misunderstand;
弄錯地點 mistake the place;
弄錯時間 mistake the time;
弄錯數字 make mistakes about figures;
弄錯意思 misunderstand sth;
[弄懂弄通] get a clear and thorough grasp of; strive for a good grasp and thorough understanding;
[弄飯] cook; prepare a meal;
[弄鬼掉猴] create trouble; do mischief; make trouble;
[弄好] get sth done;
弄好手頭工作 finish one's piece of work on hand;
把事情弄好 do a good job;
[弄壞] make a mess of; put out of order; ruin;
把事情弄壞 make a mess of things;
[弄僵] bring to a deadlock; deadlock;
[弄巧] try to be clever;
弄巧成拙 cunning outwits itself; get into trouble through clever means; in trying to be smart, one makes oneself look foolish; make a fool of oneself in trying to be smart; outsmart oneself; overreach oneself; overshoot oneself; overshoot the mark; suffer from being too smart; try to be clever but end in being a fool; try to be clever but end up a fool; try to be clever but turn out the contrary; try to be clever only to end up with a blunder; turn out to the clumsy sleight of hand;
使乖弄巧 use skill and play tricks; use tricks;
[弄清] button down; clarify; gain a clear idea of; make clear; understand fully;
弄清事實 ascertain facts;
弄清事實真相 clarify the truth of the matter;
弄清是非 clarify right and wrong; clarify what is right from what is wrong; distinguish right from wrong; thrust out the rights and wrongs;
弄清問題所在 get to the heart of the problem;
[弄權] manipulate power for personal ends;
弄權勒索 abuse one's powers to extort money;

鈎黨弄權 form a clique and abuse power;
專國弄權 having seized all real authority, one acts arbitrarily and despotically;

［弄死］ kill; put to death;
弄死動物 kill animals;

［弄文舞墨］ write in a showy style;

［弄性尚氣］ act on impulse; be swayed by personal feelings; indulge in fits of temper;

［弄糟］ ball sth up; bungle; make a mess of; mar; mess up; spoil;
弄糟一筆買賣 mess up a business;

［弄皺］ ruck; ruffle;

擺弄 (1) fiddle with; move back and forth; (2) manipulate; order about;
搬弄 (1) fiddle with; move sth about; (2) display; show off;
撥弄 (1) fiddle with; move to and fro; (2) manipulate; order about; (3) stir up;
播弄 (1) order about; (2) stir up;
嘲弄 mock; poke fun at;
攛弄 egg on; urge;
搓弄 rub with the hands;
撮弄 (1) dupe; make fun of; play a trick on; (2) abet; incite; instigate;
逗弄 make fun of; tease;
掇弄 (1) put in order; tidy; (2) get things ready; pack; (3) order sb about; (4) stir up;
撫弄 fondle; stroke;
賣弄 flaunt; show off;
盤弄 fiddle; fondle; play with;
侍弄 raise or look after domestic animals, etc. carefully;
耍弄 make fun of; play a trick on;
調弄 (1) make fun of; tease; (2) adjust; arrange; (3) instigate; stir up;
玩弄 (1) juggle with; play with; (2) employ; resort to; (3) dally with;
舞弄 brandish; wave;
戲弄 dupe; hoodwink; make fun of;
愚弄 hoodwink; make a fool of; play a trick on;
捉弄 dupe; play a trick on; tease;
作弄 dupe; make a fool of; play a trick on;

nou⁴
nou

【耨】 (1) hoe; (2) weed;

［耨鋤］ draw hoe;

nu²
nu

【奴】 (1) bondservant; slave; (2) enslave; (3) flunkey; lackey;

［奴婢］ slaves and maid-servants;
奴顏婢膝 abject submission; bend one's knees before; bow and scrape like slaves to; bow low and humiliate oneself; bow low and sweep the ground with one's cap; lick sb's boots; make a great show of obedience and courtesy;

［奴才］ flunkey; lackey;
奴才思想 slavish thinking;
奴才長相 bear oneself with servility;

［奴化］ enslave;
奴化教育 education that aims at enslavement;
奴化政策 a policy of enslavement;

［奴隸］ slave;
奴隸販子 slaver;
奴隸制 slavery;
~廢除奴隸制 abolish slavery;
販賣奴隸 trade in salves; traffic in slaves;
工資奴隸 wage slave;
家庭奴隸 domestic slave;
解放奴隸 emancipate slaves; liberate slaves;

［奴僕］ lackey; servant;

［奴性］ servility; slavishness;
鄙視奴性 disdain servility;
擯棄奴性 cast away slavishness;

［奴役］ enslave; keep in bondage; slavery;
奴役勞動人民 keep the working people in slavery;
奴役制度 chattel slavery;
經濟奴役 economic slavery;

家奴 family slave;
農奴 serf;
洋奴 slave of a foreign master;

nu

【孥】 one's children;

妻孥 wife and children;

nu

【笯】 bird cage;

nu

【駑】 (1) hack; jaded horse; old, worn-out horse; (2) dull; good for nothing; incompetent; stupid;

［駑鈍］ dull; stupid;

[駑馬] inferior horse; jade; screw;
駑馬戀棧 a jaded horse hankering after its stall – an incompetent man clinging to a good position; the old horse always hankers after the old stable and manger;
駑馬千里，功在不捨 if a jade travels a thousand miles, it is only through perseverance;

[駑駘] old and inferior horse;
駑駘竭力 one will do one's best; though but a jade, I'll do my best;
駑駘下駟 a stupid person; a worn-out, old and inferior horse;
駑駘之才，無志騰驤 an old jade like myself has no energy for prancing;

nu3

nu

【努】 (1) do all one can; do one's utmost; exert oneself; make great efforts; put forth; try hard; (2) bulge; protrude; (3) injure oneself through overexertion;

[努力] endeavor; exert oneself; make great efforts; pull one's socks up; try hard;
努力不倦 strive without cease;
努力工作 lay one's shoulder to the wheel; put one's shoulder to the wheel; set one's shoulder to the wheel; work hard;
努力向前 strive for the future;
努力學習 make great efforts in one's study;
不惜一切的努力 an all-in effort;
重新努力 renew one's efforts;
放棄努力 abandon efforts;
放鬆努力 relax one's efforts;
加倍努力 amplify one's efforts; redouble one's efforts;
加緊努力 put one's socks up;
枉費努力 waste one's efforts;
最大努力 do one's utmost;
~盡最大努力 do all one can to do sth; do everything in one's power to do sth; do everything one can to do sth; do one's best to do sth; do one's utmost to do sth; exert oneself to the utmost to do sth; make every effort to do sth; make heaven and earth to do sth; spare no efforts to do sth; take pains to do sth; to the best of one's ability; try in every way to do sth; try one's best to do sth; try one's hardest to do sth; try one's utmost to do sth;
最後一次努力 last hurrah;
作出努力 put forth efforts;

nu

【弩】 bow; crossbow;

[弩弓] crossbow;

[弩箭] bolt;
弩箭離弦 as fast as the arrow flies off the string;

[弩槍] captive bolt;

nu

【砮】 flint arrowhead;

nu4

nu

【怒】 (1) anger; angry; furious; rage; (2) burst; in profusion;

[怒不可遏] angry beyond all control; at boiling point; be angered beyond all control; be hopping mad; beside oneself with anger; beside oneself with rage; boil with rage; in a rage; in great passion; one's rage knows no bounds; too furious to hold back; unable to contain one's anger;

[怒潮] (1) angry tide; raging tide; (2) tidal bore;
怒潮澎湃 roaring torrents;

[怒斥] angrily rebuke; indignantly denounce;
怒斥不道德行為 denounce immoral conduct;

[怒沖沖] furiously; in a rage;

[怒從膽生] one's anger rises out of the depths of one's belly to one's lips;

[怒髮] blow one's hair stands on end;
怒髮衝冠 blow one's top; boil over; bristle with anger; in a towering rage; make one's blood boil; one's hairs stand on end with anger; so angry that one's hair lifts one's cap;
怒髮倒豎 one's hair stands on end with anger;

[怒放] in full bloom;
蓮荷怒放 the water lilies and lotuses unfold their beauty;

[怒海扁舟] a small boat on an angry sea;

[怒號] howl; roar;

北風怒號 the north wind was howling;

[怒吼] howl; roar;

大海怒吼 the sea roars;

[怒火] flames of fury; fury;

怒火沖天 a surge of great fury; one's flames of rage reach the sky; one's fury flames to the sky;

怒火滿腔 anger flames in one's heart; be filled with fury;

怒火如焚 all burn up; very angry;

怒火填膺 be filled with fury; be swollen with indignation;

怒火萬丈 a fit of violent anger; a towering rage; fly into a towering passion; set one's temper in a flame;

怒火直冒 boil over with rage;

發泄怒火 blow off steam; let off steam;

滿腔怒火 anger flames in one's heart; be filled with anger; be filled with boiling anger; be filled with fury; boil with fury; full of anger;

難以遏制的怒火 ungovernable rage;

強忍怒火 contain one's anger; control one's anger;

強壓怒火 swallow one's anger;

眼冒怒火 one's eyes flash with rage;

一陣怒火 a rush of anger;

抑制怒火 check one's anger; restrain one's fury;

[怒罵] curse in rage;

怒罵不休 curse angrily without stopping;

[怒目] fierce stare; glaring eyes;

怒目諦視 look angrily at;

怒目而視 glare at; glare furiously; look daggers at; look with fierce piercing eyes; scowl at; shoot angry glances at; stare angrily;

怒目橫眉 face others with frowning brows and angry eyes;

怒目相視 eyeball to eyeball;

怒目相向 flash fire; gaze upon with animosity; glare at; glower at; look daggers at; stare angrily;

怒目圓睜 stare sb with glaring eyes;

橫眉怒目 dart fierce looks of hate; face others with frowning brows and angry eyes; raise one's eyebrows and stare in anger; straighten the eyebrows and raise the eyes – angry looks;

[怒氣] anger; fury; rage;

怒氣沖沖 ablaze with anger; black with rage; be filled with spleen; boil with indignation; burst with anger; fire up; flare up; fly into a rage; in a fit of spleen; in a fume; in a great rage; in a huff; in hot blood with one's hackles rising up; wrathful; wrathy; wroth;

怒氣衝天 give way to unbridled fury; in a towering passion; in a towering rage;

怒氣全消 one's anger subsided completely;

怒氣填膺 anger fills one's breast; big with rage;

怒氣未消 be still nursing one's anger;

按捺怒氣 refrain one's anger; hold back one's anger;

發泄怒氣 vent one's anger;

平息怒氣 allay one's anger; appease one's anger;

氣平怒息 calm down and cease to be angry; forget one's anger and come round; with one's rage cooled down;

一股怒氣 a flash of anger;

一陣怒氣 a blaze of anger; a fit of anger;

[怒容] angry look; scowl;

怒容滿面 a face contorted with anger; look very angry; one's face darkens; one's face is clouded with anger; the face flashes with rage;

怒容相報 return sb an angry look;

面呈怒容 black in the face;

[怒色] angry look;

怒形於色 betray one's anger; go black in the face; look angry; show signs of anger;

[怒視] glare at; glower at; scowl at;

瞪眼怒視 scowl down; stare and scowl at;

[怒濤] mountainous sea; precipitous sea; furious billows;

怒濤奔騰 angry waves are raging;

怒濤連天 angry sea waves rise to meet the sky at the horizon;

怒濤澎湃 billows raging with great fury;

怒濤洶湧 surge in angry waves;

拗怒 suppress anger;

暴怒 be furious; be in a violent rage; flare up;

勃怒 break into a rage;

嗔怒 get angry;

觸怒 enrage; infuriate; make angry;

大怒 anger;

動怒 fly into a rage; lose one's temper;

發怒 flare up; infuriate;

含怒 be in anger;
激怒 enrage; exasperate; infuriate;
戢怒 restrain one's anger;
惱怒 be angry; be furious;
遷怒 take it out on sb; vent one's anger on sb who's not to blame;
盛怒 furious; in a violent rage;
息怒 calm one's anger; cease to be angry;
易怒 prone to anger;
震怒 be enraged; be furious;
眾怒 anger of the masses; public wrath;

nü3

nü

【女】 (1) female; maiden; woman; (2) cuddle and kiss; daughter; girl;

[女伴] female companion;

[女錶] women's watch;

[女儐] bridesmaid;

[女廁] ladies' room; the ladies; women; women's lavatory;
女廁所 ladies' room; the ladies; women; women's lavatory;

[女大] grown daughter;
女大不中留 a grown daughter cannot be kept unmarried for long;
女大當嫁 a girl of age should be married; a girl should get married on coming of age; a girl should get married upon reaching womanhood; grown-up daughters have to marry; when a girl grows up she should be married;

[女隊] women's team;

[女兒] daughter; girl; one's bottle of water;
女兒般的 daughterly;
女兒家 you girls;
乾女兒 one's adopted daughter;
嫁出女兒潑出的水 a daughter married is like water split;
一個女兒 a daughter;

[女工] female worker; woman worker;
打雜女工 charlady; charwoman;

[女孩] gal; girl; lass;
女孩似的 girlish;
留着劉海的女孩 a girl with a fringe;
排行中間的女孩 middle daughter;
漂亮的女孩 beautiful girl;
傻女孩 silly girl;
生了個女孩 gave birth to a girl;
瘦小的女孩 a slip of a girl;
小女孩 little girl;
一群女孩 a group of girls;
這才是好女孩 that's a good girl;

[女紅] needlework;

[女家] the bride's side; the wife's family;

[女郎] girl; maiden; young woman;
漂亮女郎 dolly bird;
銀白色頭髮的女郎 platinum blonde;

[女流] the weaker sex;

[女帽] bonnet; lady's cap;
鐘形女帽 cloche;

[女僕] housemaid; maidservant;

[女權] girl power; woman's rights;
女權運動 feminist movement;
女權主義 feminism;
~女權主義者 feminist;

[女人] (1) biddy; woman; (2) womenfolk; (3) wife;
女人氣的 poncy; sissy;
矮胖的女人 dumpy woman;
超級女人 superowman;
脆弱啊！你的名字就是女人 frailty, thy name is woman;
非常肥壯的女人 a woman of much avoirdupois;
瘋女人 madwoman;
勾引男子的女人 seductress;
老女人 crowie; matron;
迷信的女人 superstitious woman;
胖女人 fat woman;
神秘女人 mystery woman;
騷女人 woman of loose morals; erotic woman;
天使般的女人 angelic woman;
玩女人 dally with women; flirt with women;
心腸軟的女人 soft-hearted woman;
洋女人 foreign woman;
一個名叫…的女人 a woman called...;
一個女人 a woman;
有個人收入的女人 woman of independent means;
憎恨女人 hate women;
~憎恨女人者 misogynist;

[女色] woman's charms;

[女神] goddess;

[女聲] female voice;

[女生] girl; girl student; schoolgirl; woman student;
走讀女生 day girl;

[女士] lady; madam;
一位女士 a lady;

［女王］ empress; queen;
［女為悦己者容］a girl will doll herself up for him who loves her; the blind man's wife needs no painting;
［女巫］ sorceress; witch;
［女性］ (1) fair sex; fairer sex; female; female sex; weaker sex; (2) woman;
女性電影 chick flick;
女性更年期 menopause;
女性化 feminize;
女性聚會 hen party;
女性文學 feminine literature;
思想開放的女性 liberated woman;
［女婿］ (1) one's son-in-law; (2) one's husband;
上門女婿 live-in son-in-law;
招女婿 have the groom move into one's house after the marriage; take in a son-in-law to bear bride's family name;
［女鞋］ woman's shoe;
露跟女鞋 slingback;
樸素女鞋 court shoes;
拖鞋式女鞋 mules;
細高跟女鞋 stilettos;
［女陰］ cunnus; vulva;
女陰狼瘡 esthiomene;
女陰裂 vulval cleft;
女陰瘙癢 pruritus vulvae;
［女友］ (1) girl friend; (2) female friend;
同居女友 missis; missus;
［女子］ female; woman;
女子氣質 femininity;
女子無才便是德 a girl without ability is virtuous;
獨身女子 spinster;
風塵女子 a lady of easy virtue; a lady of pleasure; a lady of the evening; a sporting lady; a street girl; a woman amidst winds and dust; a woman of pleasure; a woman of the street; a woman of the town; bachelor's wife; courtesan; cousin Betty; fancy girl; fancy lady; fancy woman; prostitute;
勾引人的女子 temptress;
美貌絕倫的女子 a woman of unmatched beauty;
美若天仙的女子 an angel of a woman;
年輕性感的女子 nubile;
奇女子 remarkable woman;
身材好的女子 a fine figure of a woman;
水性楊花的女子 a woman of loose morals;
未婚女子 maiden;

愛女 beloved daughter;
吧女 bar girl; barmaid;
才女 talented woman;
醜女 minger;
兒女 (1) children; sons and daughters; (2) young man and woman;
婦女 woman;
妓女 prostitute;
季女 youngest daughter;
繼女 adopted daughter;
美女 beautiful woman;
男女 men and women;
弱女 young girl;
少女 young girl;
神女 goddess;
甥女 niece; sister's daughter;
石女 woman with a hypoplastic vagina;
士女 (1) young men and women; (2) traditional Chinese painting of beautiful women;
仕女 traditional Chinese painting of beautiful women;
侍女 maid; maid-servant;
室女 unmarried girl;
淑女 gentle and kindhearted girl;
孫女 grand-daughter;
舞女 dance-hostess;
仙女 female celestial;
信女 female believer;
燕女 delight in women;
養女 foster daughter;
妖女 fairy enchantress;
義女 adopted daughter;
侄女 brother's daughter; niece;

nü

【釹】 neodymium;

nü⁴

nü

【忸】 a pronunciation of 忸;

nü

【恧】 ashamed;

nü

【衄】 (1) bleeding nose; nose-bleeding; (2) be defeated; be given a bloody nose;
［衄血］ bleed from five sense organs;

敗衄 be defeated in battle; lose a battle;
鼻衄 epistaxis; nosebleed;

nuan[3]

nuan

【暖】 (1) warm; (2) warm up;
［暖房］ greenhouse;
［暖風］ warm wind;
一陣暖風 a warm wind;
［暖鋒］ warm front;
［暖烘烘］ nice and warm; warm and comfortable;
［暖和］ (1) nice and warm; warm; (2) warm up;
天氣很暖和 it's mild; the weather's mild;
［暖流］ warm current;
暖流湧上心頭 one's heart surges with warm feelings;
一陣暖流 a warm spell;
［暖瓶］ thermosflask;
［暖氣］ warm air;
暖氣鍋爐 heating boiler;
~ 中央暖氣鍋爐 central heating boiler;
暖氣片 radiator;
暖氣設備 heater;
暖氣團 warm air mass;
暖氣系統 heating;
~ 中央暖氣系統 central heating;
［暖水］ warm water;
暖水瓶 thermos bottle; thermos flask;

保暖 keep warm;
飽暖 dressing warmly and eating one's fill;
春暖 warmth of spring;
供暖 heating;
和暖 genial; pleasantly warm;
烘暖 warm by the fire;
冷暖 changes in temperature;
取暖 warm oneself;
溫暖 warm;

nuan

【煖】 genial; warm;

nüe[4]

nüe

【虐】 cruel; maltreat; tyrannical;
［虐待］ abuse; ill-treat; maltreat; tyrannize;
虐待動物 maltreat animals;
虐待兒童 abuse of child; tyrannize over children;
虐待俘虜 maltreat prisoners;
虐待狂 sadist;
虐待配偶 abuse of spouse;
虐待長者 abuse of the elderly;
備受虐待 subject to every kind of maltreatment;
［虐殺］ cause sb's death by maltreating him; kill sb with maltreatment;
虐殺動物 cause the death of animals by maltreating them;
［虐政］ tyrannical government;

暴虐 brutal; ruthless; tyrannical;
凌虐 treat cruelly; tyrannize over;
肆虐 indulge in wanton massacre or persecution;
兇虐 cruel; fierce and brutal;

nüe

【瘧】 malaria;
［瘧疾］ malaria; malarial fever;

寒瘧 a kind of malaria;
暑瘧 malaria in summer;
溫瘧 a kind of malaria;

nüe

【謔】 (1) jest; joke; (2) ridicule; satirize;

nuo[2]

nuo

【挼】 (1) fondle; rub; stroke; (2) crumple;
［挼挲］ fondle; rub; stroke;
［挼搓］ crumple;

nuo

【娜】 slender and graceful; tender; well poised;

婀娜 graceful;

nuo

【挪】 move; shift;
［挪動］ move; shift;
挪動幾步 move a few steps;
挪動傢具 shift the furniture about;
緩慢向前挪動 inch forward;
［挪借］ borrow money for a short time; get a short-term loan;
東挪西借 borrow all around;
［挪開］ move away;
［挪用］ embezzle; misappropriate;
挪用公款 appropriate public funds for personal use; embezzle public funds; illegally draw upon public funds; misappropriation of public funds;

騰挪 transfer (funds, etc) to other uses;

nuo³

nuo

【娜】 tender, slender and graceful;

nuo⁴

nuo

【喏】 address of respect when meeting a superior;

nuo

【搦】 (1) hold; seize; (2) challenge; (3) incite; (4) suppress;

nuo

【諾】 (1) assent; nod; promise; (2) yep; yes;

［諾言］ promise;

背棄諾言 go back from one's word; go back on one's word;

靠不住的諾言 brittle promise;

履行諾言 act up to one's promise; keep a promise;

違背諾言 break a promise; go back on a promise; violate one's promise;

違反諾言 break a promise;

信守諾言 fulfil a promise; keep a promise;

遵守諾言 abide by one's promise; keep respect; stand to one's promise;

作出諾言 hold out a promise;

承諾 undertake to do sth;

輕諾 make easy;

然諾 pledge; promise;

夙諾 previous promise;

宿諾 previous promise;

許諾 make a promise; promise;

應諾 agree to do sth; undertake to do sth;

允諾 consent; promise;

nuo

【懦】 cowardly; dull; timid; weak;

［懦鈍］ weak and dull;

［懦夫］ coward; craven; weakling;

懦夫懶漢 the coward and the sluggard;

可鄙的懦夫 abject coward;

［懦怯］ cowardly;

［懦弱］ cowardly; weak;

懦弱膽怯 timid and weak;

懦弱的 craven; lily-livered;

懦弱可欺 weak and can be bullied;

懦弱無能 weak and useless;

懦弱無用的人 wimp;

怯懦 cowardly; timid and overcautious;

闒懦 weak and incompetent;

愚懦 stupid and cowardly;

nuo

【糯】 glutinous rice;

［糯稻］ glutinous rice;

［糯米］ polished glutinous rice;

香糯米 fragrant glutinuous rice;

o¹

o

【喔】 (expressing sudden realization) ah; dear me; my; my dear; my word; oh; oh, my;

［喔嚄］ oho;

［喔喔啼］ coo-coo-ri-coo; cock-a-doodle-do;

［喔呀］ my god; my goodness; oh, my;

［喔唷］ (1) (expressing surprise) my; my goodness; oh; (2) (expressing pain) oh; ouch;

o²

o

【哦】 (expressing surprise, satisfaction or admiration) ah; oh;

［哦呵］ (expressing surprise, satisfaction, or admiration) aha;

［哦呀］ (expressing surprise) my goodness; oh, my;

［哦唷］ (expressing surprise, sometimes mockingly) oh, my;

o³

o

【呵】 particle used after a phrase to express surprise;

ou¹

ou

【漚】 bubbles; foam; froth;

ou

【歐】 (1) Europe; European; (2) vomit; (3) beat; (4) sing; (5) Ohm; (6) a surname;

［歐風美雨］ the influences of Western culture and civilization;

［歐化］ Europeanize; Westernize;

［歐姆］ ohm;

歐姆表 ohmer;
歐姆電阻 ohmage;
歐姆計 ohmmeter;
~ 數字伏特歐姆計 digital volt ohmmeter;
~ 數字式歐姆計 digital ohmmeter;
歐姆銅合金 ohmal;
比聲歐姆 specific acoustical ohm;
標準歐姆 standard ohm;
倒歐姆 reciprocal ohm;
國際歐姆 international ohm;

毫歐 milliohm;
姆歐 mho;
兆歐 megohm;

ou

【毆】 beat; hit;

［毆斃］ beat to death;

被對手毆斃 be beaten to death by one's opponent;

［毆打］ beat up; hit;

互相毆打 beat each other;

［毆鬥］ box; have a fist fight;

互相毆鬥 box with each other;

［毆殺］ beat to death;

［毆傷］ injure by beating;

被敵人毆傷 be beaten by one's enemy and got injured;

鬥毆 exchange blows;
兇毆 beat up cruelly;

ou

【敺】 assault physically; beat;

ou

【甌】 (1) small tray; (2) cup;

ou

【謳】 chant; sing;

［謳歌］ celebrate in song; eulogize; sing the praises of;

謳歌頌德 praise one's merit;
謳歌英雄 celebrate the heroes in song;
熱情謳歌 sing the praises of;

ou

【鷗】 gull;

［鷗鳥］ hagdon;

海鷗 gull; sea gull;
沙鷗 sea gull;
銀鷗 herring gull;

ou³

ou

【偶】 (1) idol; image; (2) even; in pairs; (3) mate; spouse;

［偶爾］ every so often; occasionally; once in a while; from time to time;

［偶發］ accidental; chance; fortuitous;

［偶極子］ dipole; doublet;

半波偶極子 half-wave dipole;
電偶極子 electric doublet;
反相偶極子 antiphase dipole;
激勵偶極子 excited doublet;

籠形偶極子 cage dipole;
全波偶極子 full-wave dipole;
雙偶極子 double dipole;
有源偶極子 active dipole;
圓孤形偶極子 circular dipole;

[偶句] couplet;
英雄偶句 heroic couplet;

[偶見種] rare species;

[偶然] (1) accidental; by accident; by chance; by coincidence; chance; fortuitous; happen; have a chance; it is by sheer accident that; it so happened that; occasional; (2) at intervals; at times; at whiles; between times; ever and again; every now and again; every now and then; every so often; from time to time; now and then; occasionally; off and on; on occasion; once and a while; once in a while; once or twice; sometimes; whiles;
偶然的 adventitious;
偶然論 accidentalism;
偶然現象 fortuitous phenomena;
偶然相遇 have a chance meeting;
偶然性 circumstantiality;
偶然狀語從句 adverbial clause of contingency;
純屬偶然 it is only by chance that; the long arm of coincidence;
決非偶然 by no accident; it is no accident that;
絕非偶然 by no means fortuitous;
事非偶然 it is no accident that;
事或偶然 as chance would have it;

[偶數] even number;

[偶蹄] cloven hoof;

[偶像] heartthrob; idol; image;
偶像崇拜 idolatry;
拜偶像 idol-worshipping;
崇拜偶像 worship idols;
大眾偶像 popular idol;
流行樂偶像 pop idol;
政治偶像 political idol;

[偶一為之] do sth accidentally; do sth by chance; do sth by way of exception; do sth in the spirit of the occasion; do sth once in a blue moon; do sth once in a while;

電偶 electric coupling;
對偶 (1) antithesis; (2) duality;
奇偶 odd-even;
佳偶 happy couple;
力偶 couple;
配偶 spouse;
求偶 court; woo;
喪偶 bereft of one's spouse, esp. one's wife;
怨偶 unhappy couple;

ou

【嘔】 throw up; vomit;

[嘔吐] anabole; barf; chunder; puke; retch; shoot the cat; throw up; vomit;
嘔吐不止 keep vomiting;
嘔吐袋 sickbag;
嘔吐感 nausea;
嘔吐物 puke;
妊娠嘔吐 vomiting of pregnancy;
一陣嘔吐 a vomiting fit;
引起嘔吐 cause vomiting;
周期性嘔吐 periodic vomiting;
自發性嘔吐 autemesia;

[嘔心] exert one's utmost effort; take great pains;
嘔心瀝血 exhaust one's lifeblood; make painstaking efforts; shed one's heart's blood; spare no pains; strain one's heart and mind; take infinite pains; through painstaking effort; throw all one's energy into; with one's heart-blood; work one's heart out;
嘔心之作 a work embodying one's utmost effort;

乾嘔 retch;
作嘔 feel sick; nausea;

ou

【耦】 (1) plough side by side; (2) couple; (3) spouse;

[耦合] coupling;
耦合劑 coupler;
耦合器 coupler;
~聲音耦合器 acoustic coupler;
~雙向耦合器 bidirectional coupler;
~天線耦合器 antenna coupler;
~自動進場耦合器 automatic approach coupler;
~自動耦合器 automatic coupler;
附加耦合 additional coupling;
交流耦合 alternating-current coupling;
空氣耦合 air coupling;

聲耦合 acoustic coupling;
天線耦合 aerial coupling; antenna coupling;

ou

【藕】 lotus roots;
［藕斷絲連］ even when the lotus-root breaks, the fibres still hold together;
［藕粉］ lotus root starch;
一袋藕粉 a bag of lotus root starch;
一碗藕粉 a bowl of lotus root paste;

ou⁴

ou

【嘔】 annoy on purpose;
［嘔氣］ angry but refrain from showing it; feel annoyed; feel enraged; feel irritated;

ou

【慪】 (1) exasperate; irritate; (2) same as 謳;
［慪氣］ difficult and sulky;

ou

【漚】 soak;
［漚麻］ ret hemp;

pa¹

pa

【趴】 (1) lie face downwards; lie on one's face; lie prone; prostrate oneself; (2) bend over;

［趴架］ collapse; fall down;

［趴下］ lie down;

矮趴趴 short; squat; very low;

馬趴 fall flat on one's face;

pa

【葩】 (1) blossoms in full bloom; flowers; (2) magnificent;

pa²

pa

【扒】 (1) gather up; rake up; scoop up; (2) pick; pilfer; steal; (3) scratch; (4) braise; stew;

［扒糕］ buckwheat cake;

［扒灰］ scoop up ashes—commit incest with a daughter-in-law;

［扒竊］ pick sb's pocket; purse-cutting; steal;

［扒手］ pickpocket; shoplifter;

當心扒手 beware of pickpockets;

謹防扒手 be on the alert for pickpockets; beware of pickpockets;

pa

【爬】 (1) crawl; creep; (2) ascend; clamber; climb; get up; scale; scramble;

［爬蟲］ reptile;

爬蟲學 herpetology;

［爬得快，跌得快］ a sudden rising has a sudden fall; hasty climbers have sudden falls;

［爬高］ climb high; climb up; gain; mount;

飛機很快地爬高 the plane climbed up quickly;

爬得高跌得重 the higher one climbs, the harder one falls;

爬得高，摔得重 the bigger they are, the harder they fall; the higher one climbs, the heavier one falls; the higher one climbs, the heavier one's fall; the higher one goes, the heavier the fall; the higher up, the greater the fall;

［爬杆］ climb the pole;

［爬秤］ pole climbing;

［爬山］ climb a mountain; mountain climbing;

爬山虎 Boston ivy; Japanese creeper;

爬山涉水 climb hills and ford streams; climb mountains and cross rivers; climb up the mountains and cross the streams; traverse mountains and wade through rivers — the hardship in the journey;

爬山越嶺 climb mountains and cross ranges; scramble up the hills; over hills and mountains — the hardship in the journey;

［爬上］ climb; get up; scale; scramble up;

爬上爬下 climb up and down;

爬上懸崖 scramble up a cliff;

［爬繩］ rope climbing;

［爬昇］ climbout;

［爬下］ scramble down; climb down

爬下樹 scramble down a tree;

［爬行］ crawl; creep;

爬行動物 reptile;

［爬泳］ crawl;

練爬泳 practice the crawl;

［爬越］ ascend;

向山上爬 uphill climb;

pa

【耙】 drag; harrow; rabble; rake;

［耙平］ rake;

［耙子］ rabble; rake;

電耙 electric rake; scraper;

釘耙 harrow; spike-tooth rake;

糞耙 dung fork;

木耙 wooden rake;

pa

【琶】 four-stringed guitar or balloon-guitar;

琵琶 pipa, a plucked string instrument;

pa⁴

pa

【帕】 (1) handkerchief; (2) turban; veil; (3) wrap and bind; wrapper;

手帕 handkerchief;

pa

【怕】 (1) afraid of; be frightened; be

scared; fear; (2) fear lest; for fear; worry;

[怕光] fear of light; photophobia;

[怕苦] fear hardship;

怕苦怕累 fear both hardship and fatigue; fear hardships and fatigue;

一不怕苦，二不怕死 defy hardships and death; disregard of hardship and danger; fear neither hardship nor death; fearlessness in the face of trails or death;

[怕人] (1) shy; timid; (2) awful; frightening; horrible; terrifying;

[怕生] shy in the presence of strangers; shy with strangers;

這個孩子怕生 this child is shy in the presence of strangers;

[怕事] afraid of getting into trouble; afraid of getting involved; take no initiative; timid;

膽小怕事 timid and overcautious;

很怕事 be afraid of getting into trouble;

[怕水] water funk;

[怕死] be afraid of death; fear death;

很多人都怕死 many people fear death;

[怕羞] bashful; blushing; coy; shy;

很怕羞 be bashful;

不怕 not afraid of; not fear;

害怕 afraid for sth; afraid of; be frightened; be overcome by fear; be overcome with fear; be scared of; can't say boo to a goose; dread; dreadful; fear; fearful; fly the white feather; for fear of; frighten; frightful; get cold feet; have a dread of; have cold feet; in dread of sb; in dread of sth; in fear of; make one's blood run cold; make one's hair stand on end; mount the white feather; quail; shake in one's boots; show the white feather; strike fear into; tremble in one's shoes;

不怕 not afraid of; not fear;

害怕 afraid for sth; afraid of; be frightened; be overcome by fear; be overcome with fear; be scared of; can't say boo to a goose; dread; dreadful; fear; fearful; fly the white feather; for fear of; frighten; frightful; get cold feet; have a dread of; have cold feet; in dread of sb; in dread of sth; in fear of; make one's blood run cold; make one's hair stand on end; mount the white feather; quail; shake in one's boots; show the white feather; strike fear into; tremble in one's shoes;

後怕 fear after the event;

懼怕 dread; fear;

可怕 dreadful; fearful; frightening; frightful; horrible; terrible; terrifying;

恐怕 (1) I'm afraid; (2) I think; perhaps;

哪怕 even; even if; even though; no matter how; though;

生怕 for fear that; lest; so as not to;

畏怕 dread; fear; stand in awe of;

嫌怕 afraid of;

只怕 afraid of only one thing;

衹怕 afraid of only one thing;

最怕 fear most;

pa^5

pa

【杷】 loquat;

枇杷 loquat;

pa

【琶】 a pronunciation of 琶;

pai^1

pai

【拍】 (1) bang; beat; clap; flutter; pat; pound; slap; strike; (2) bat; racket; (3) baton; beat; beat time; (4) photograph; shoot; take; (5) send; (6) butter sb up; curry favour; fawn on; flatter; ingratiate oneself with sb; lick sb's boots; play up to; toady;

[拍案] bang the table; strike the table;

拍案稱快 slap the table and applaud;

拍案打凳 bang one's fist on the table;

拍案大叫 bang the table and shout and roar;

拍案大怒 slap the table in great anger; strike the table in anger;

拍案而起 pound the table and jump to one's feet; pound the table and stand up; rise to one's full height and smite the table; smite the table and rise to one's feet; stand up pounding the table – very angry;

拍案叫絕 bang the table and exclaim with admiration; express admiration by thumping the table; slap the table and shout "bravo";

拍案驚奇 strike the table in surprise;
捶胸拍案 beat the breast and pound the table;

[拍板] (1) clappers; (2) beat time with clappers; (3) rap the gravel; (4) give the final verdict; have the final say;
拍板成交 clinch a deal; conclude a deal; close a deal; strike a bargain;

[拍打] beat; flutter; pat; slap;
拍桌打凳 bang on the table and kick over the stool; bang the table and kick the benches; swat table and stool;

[拍動] beat;
拍動翅膀 beat the wings;

[拍發] send a telegram;

[拍擊] beat; flap; give a flap;
拍擊聲 beat;

[拍馬] fawn on; flatter; lick sb's boots;
拍馬奉承 blarney; flatter; lick sb's boots;
拍馬屁 adulate; brown-nose; butter sb up; crawl to; curry favour; curry favour with sb; eat sb's toads; fawn on; flatter; give sb the soft-soap; ingratiate oneself with; kiss sb's ass; lay it on thick; lay it on with a trowel; lick sb's boots; lick sb's shoes; lick sb's spittle; obsequious; play up to; polish the apple; soft-soap; suck up to; sycophancy;
~拍人馬屁 ingratiate oneself into sb's favour; ingratiate oneself with sb;
拍馬舞刀 whip up one's horse and circle one's sword; whip up one's steed and ride forth with sword; whirl round one's sword and ride forward;
溜須拍馬 bow and scrape; fawn on; lick sb's boots; shamelessly flatter; suck up to; toady to;

[拍賣] (1) auction; come under the hammer; sell sth at auction; (2) sale;
拍賣出售 sale by auction;
拍賣行 auction company; auction house; auction shop;
拍賣目錄 auction catalogue;
拍賣人 auctioneer;
拍賣商品 auction goods;
拍賣市場 auction market;
被拍賣 bring to the hammer; come under the hammer; go to the hammer; go under the hammer; put up to the hammer; send to the hammer; under the hammer;
公開拍賣 public auction;
國際拍賣 international auction;
假拍賣 mock auction;
減價拍賣 Dutch auction;
競爭性拍賣 competitive auction;
零星拍賣 piecemeal auction;
強制拍賣 forced auction; forced sale;
外滙拍賣 exchange auctions;
網上拍賣 online auction;

[拍攝] photograph; shoot; take a picture;
拍攝程序 shooting procedure;
拍攝電影 shoot a film;
拍攝計劃 shooting plan;
拍攝時間 shooting time;

[拍手] applaud; clap hands; clap one's hands;
拍手稱快 clap and cheer; clap in high glee; clap one's hands in joy; clap one's hands with satisfaction; hail gleefully;
拍手大笑 clap one's hands and laugh aloud; clap one's hands and roar with laughter;
拍手和歌 clap one's hands and join in the chorus;
拍手叫好 applaud; clap one's hands;
拍手贊成 clap one's hands in approval;

[拍膝而歌] sing, beating time on one's knees;

[拍掌] applaud; clap one's hands;
拍掌稱快 clap one's hands in applause; clap one's hands with satisfaction;

[拍照] take a photo;
拍照片 have a photographs taken; photograph; take a photo;
拍照時間 photocall;
不得拍照 no photographs; photo taking is not allowed;

[拍紙簿] pad; scratch pad; writing pad;

[拍子] (1) bat; racket; (2) baton; beat; rhythm; time;
不合拍子 off beat;
打拍子 beat time;
~用腳打拍子 beat time with one's foot;
二拍子 duple time;
三拍子 triple time;
四拍子 quadruple time;

差拍 beat;
掛拍 give up an athlete's life; hang up one's racket; retire from professional athletics;
海綿拍 sponge bat;

合拍 in harmony; in step; in time;
節拍 beat; clock; meter; tempo;
開拍 camera;
木製拍 wooden bat;
強拍 accent; accented beat; strong beat;
球拍 bat; racket;
弱拍 anti-accent; unaccented beat; weak beat;
蠅拍 flyflap; flyswatter;
實拍拍 actually; really;
偷拍 take a photo without permission;
握拍 grip;
蠅拍 flyflap; flyswatter;
正拍 forehand;
執拍 hold the racket;

pai²

pai

【俳】 (1) farce; variety show; vaudeville; (2) comic; satiric; (3) insincere; not serious; (4) walk to and fro;

[俳歌] comic songs;

[俳諧] comic; satiric;

[俳優] comedian;

pai

【徘】 (1) hesitating; indecisive; irresolute; (2) hesitate; hover; waver; (3) linger about; move around; pace up and down; walk to and fro;

[徘徊] (1) linger about; pace up and down; tramp; (2) hesitate; hover; waver;
徘徊不定 in a dilemma; tear;
徘徊不前 hesitate to go forward; pace up and down;
徘徊觀望 see but cannot make up one's mind; take aimless step and stare vacantly around;
徘徊街頭 on the prowl around the streets; roam the streets; wander about the streets; wander up and down the streets;
徘徊歧路 hesitate at the crossroads;

pai

【排】 (1) arrange; arrange in order; put in order; sequence; (2) line; rank; row; (3) a clip of; a line of; a rank of; a row of; (4) platoon; (5) rehearse; (6) raft; (7) blow down; blow off; discharge; drain off; (8) discriminate against; eject; exclude; get rid of; reject; repel; shut out;

[排班] (1) fall by rank; fall in line; (2) arrange turns of work; shift work;

[排版] compose; set; typeset;
排版工 compositor; typesetter;
電腦排版 be set by computers; computerised typesetting;

[排輩] according to seniority;
論資排輩 be promoted according to status; go according to seniority;

[排比] (1) rhetorical use of parallel constructions; (2) arrange in order; (3) parallelism;
排比從屬連詞 subordinator of exception;
排比句 parallel sentences;

[排筆] broad brush; grouped brush for painting; whitewash brush;

[排便] defecate; defecation; void excrement;
排便反射 defecation reflex;
排便節制 fecal continence;
排便恐怖 coprophobia;
排便失禁 acathexia;

[排場] display of splendour; ostentation and extravagance; parade one's wealth; pomp show;
排場大 cocky; in a splendid and extravagant way;
講排場 go in for ostentation and extravagance; go in for pomp; love ostentation;
裝排場 act lord; make the scene to be splendid

[排斥] discriminate against; eject; exclude; exclusion; reject; repel; repulsion; shut out;
排斥異己 discriminate against dissenters; exclude outsiders; get rid of those who disagree with sb; remove those who disagree with sb;
等位排斥 allelic exclusion;
基因組排斥 genomic exclusion;
交換排斥 exchange repulsion;
靜電排斥 electrostatic repulsion;
競爭排斥 competitive exclusion;
離子排斥 ion exclusion;
遭到排斥 be excluded;

[排除] dispel; eliminate; elimination; exclude; get rid of; remove; surmount;
排除副詞 adverb of exception;
排除故障 fix a breakdown; trouble shoot;
排除介詞 preposition of exception;

排除器 eliminator;
~草籽排除器 weed-seed eliminator;
排除萬難 clear away all obstacles; conquer all obstacles; knock over every difficulty; overcome all difficulties; push aside all obstacles and difficulties; surmount every difficulty;
排除危險 eliminate danger;
排除異己 discriminate against those who hold different views; exclude outsiders; get rid of those who disagree with one; push aside the people who disagree with one; remove those who disagree with one; renounce people who do not agree with one; renounce people of different views;
排除飲食 elimination diet;
排除障礙 remove the obstacles;
排除狀語從句 adverbial clause of exception;
免疫排除 immune elimination;
水解排除 hydrolytic elimination;

[排出] discharge; eject; exhaust; pump; squeeze; transpire; vent;

[排擋] gear;

[排掉] drain away;
把水排掉 drain away the water;

[排毒] detox; detoxification;

[排隊] (1) line up; queue; queue up; stand in line; (2) classify and list;
排隊等待 queue up for; stand in a queue;
排隊論 queuing theory;
排隊買票 queue up for tickets; stand in a queue to buy tickets;
按序排隊 line up one after another; sequential queue;
成批排隊 batch queue;
串聯排隊 tandem queue;
錯誤排隊 error queue;
排大隊 stand in a long queue;
信息排隊 message queue;
循環排隊 cyclic queue;
優先排隊 priority queue;

[排筏] raft;

[排放] blow down; blow off; discharge; drain off; emit;
排放交易 emissions trading;
排放物 emission;
~點源排放物 point source emission;
熱量排放 heat discharge;
人為排放 anthropogenic discharge;
有效排放 effective discharge;

[排風扇] exhaust fan;

[排骨] pork ribs; ribs; spare ribs;
大塊排骨 chump chop;

[排灌] drain and irrigate;

[排汗] perspire;

[排行] rank; seniority among brothers and sisters;
排行榜 ranking list;

[排擠] crowd out sb; edge out; elbow out; exclude; oust sb; push aside; push out; squeeze out;
互相排擠 each tries to squeeze the other out; squeeze out each other;

[排架] bent;
雙跨排架 double bent;

[排解] (1) arbitrate; intervene; make peace; mediate; reconcile; resolve; (2) dispel; divert oneself from; find diversion from boredom;
排解糾紛 reconcile a quarrel;
排解爭論 mediate a dispute;
排難解紛 clear up misunderstandings; mediate a dispute; pour oil on troubled waters; settle difficulties; settle disputes; smooth the path and untangle difficulties;
排憂解難 get rid of worries and overcome difficulties;

[排澇] drain flooded fields;
排澇補種 plant again after the water recedes from the flooded fields;

[排雷] demining; remove mines;

[排練] dry run; dummy run; rehearse; run-through;
最後排練 final run-through;

[排列] (1) arrange in order; place; put in order; rank; (2) array; permutation;
排列成行 arrange in a line;
排列方式 ordering; permutation;
排列整齊 arrange in good order; well arranged;
按大小順序排列 arrange according to size;
按時序排列 in chronological order;
按字母順序排列 arrange alphabetically; arrange in alphabetical order;
保碼排列 code preserving permutation;
根據年代排列 arrange in chronological

order;
交錯排列 alternate permutation;
無效排列 invalid array;
線性排列 line array; linear permutation;
循環排列 circular permutation; cyclic permutation;

[排卵] ovulate; ovulation;
排卵過少 oligo-ovulation;
排卵期 period of ovulation;

[排滿] be fully occupied; have one's hands full;
訂貨己排滿 be fully occupied with orders;

[排名] rank; ranking;
排名表 league table; ranking list;
排名最低 at the bottom of the league; lowest ranking;
排名最高 at the top of the league; highest ranking;

[排難而進] go through thick and thin; make one's way through thick and thin;

[排尿] micturate; micturition; pass water; urinate;
排尿反射 micturition reflex;
排尿過緩 bradyuria;
排尿寒戰 urethral chill;
排尿減少 hypouresis;
排尿困難 difficult urination; dysuria;
~痙攣性排尿困難 spastic dysuria;
排尿痛 urodynia;
~排尿痛感 painful urination;
排尿無力 acraturesis;
排尿徐緩 bradyuria;
排尿異常 paruria;
排尿正常 normosthenuria;
排尿中樞 micturition centre;
急迫排尿 precipitant urination; precipitate micturition;
間歇性排尿 stuttering urination;
痛性排尿 alginuresis;

[排偶] parallelism and antithesis;

[排砲] cannonade; salvo;

[排氣] (1) vent; (2) air exhaust; exhaust;
排氣管 exhaust pipe;
排氣機 exhauster;
~電動排氣機 motor-driven exhauster;
~離心排氣機 centrifugal exhauster;
~正壓排氣機 positive-pressure exhauster;
排氣扇 extractor;
凝結排氣 condensation exhaust;
汽車排氣 automobile exhaust;
鐘罩排氣 bell-jar exhaust;

[排遣] dispel; distract one's mind from; divert oneself from; find diversion from loneliness;
排遣煩悶 divert oneself from boredom;
排遣孤獨 divert oneself from loneliness;
排遣無聊 relieve the tedium;
排遣心中的憂慮 dispel one's anxiety;

[排球] (1) volleyball; (2) volleyball game;
排球場 volleyball court;
排球隊 volleyball team;
~男子排球隊 men's volleyball team;
~女子排球隊 women's volleyball team;
打排球 play volleyball;

[排沙簡金] choose the best among a host of things; obtain gold by washing it from sand and gravel; pan gravel for gold; pick gold out of sand; sift sand for gold;

[排山] topple the mountain;
排山倒海 great in momentum; great power and influence; irresistible; overturn a mountain and upset the sea; overwhelming; pound away with the momentum of a torrential tide; topple the mountains and overturn the seas; with the force of an avalanche;
~排山倒海之勢 with the force of a landslide and the power of a tidal wave; with the might of an avalanche;
排山壓卵 topple the mountains to crash the egg — cause a disaster to come;

[排水] drain; drain away water; drain off water; drainage; draining;
排水工 drainer;
排水溝 drain; gutter;
~地下排水溝 blind drain;
~河堤排水溝 counter drain;
~橫向排水溝 cross drain;
~人字形排水溝 chevron drain;
排水管 downspout; drain; drainpipe; waste pipe;
~屋頂排水管 downspout;
~洗水機排水管 washing machine waste pipe;
排水口 outfall;
排水孔 drain; plughole;
排水量 (1) displacement of ships; (2) discharge capacity;
排水能力 drainability;
排水器 drainer;

排水渠 culvert;
排水設備 pumping appliance;
排水系統 drainage;
排水裝置 water-freeing arrangement;
開溝排水 dig trenches to drain the water away;
農田排水 agricultural drain; agricultural drainage;
人工排水 artificial drainage;
斜坡排水 batter drainage;

[排他] exclusive;
排他代詞 exclusive pronoun;
排他的 clannish;
排他性 exclusiveness;
排他語 exclusive;

[排闥] push;
排闥而入 break into a room unceremoniously; enter by pushing open the door discourteously; push a door open unceremoniously and enter; push open the door and enter; push the door open and rush into the room;

[排頭] the file leader; the first person in a row; the procession leader;

[排外] antiforeign; exclusive; oppose everything foreign; clubby;
排外的 clubby;
排外思想 exclusive thinking;
排外運動 antiforeign movment;
排外主義 antiforeignism; exclusivism; xenophobia;

[排尾] the last person in a row;

[排污] dispose of pollutants;
排污口 outfall;

[排屋] row house; townhouse;
精緻排屋 exquisite townhouse;
時尚排屋 modern townhouse;

[排戲] rehearse a performance; rehearse a play;

[排險] remove danger;
排險搶修 eliminate danger and do rush repairs;

[排洩] (1) drain; (2) excrete; let off;
排洩不能 acatharsia;
排洩管 excretory duct;
排洩器官 excretory organ;
排洩物 excrement; ordure;
~動物排洩物 animal excrement;
~腐敗排洩物 decaying excrement;
~人類排洩物 human excrement;
排洩系統 excretory system;
排洩細胞 excretory cells;

[排序] ordering;
合併排序 ordering by merging;
互異排序 distinctly different ordering;

[排煙] discharge smoke;
排煙車 fume exhauster truck;

[排演] rehearse; rehearsal; rehearsing;

[排印] typeset and print; typography;
排印錯誤 typo; typographical errors;

[排長] platoon leader;

[排障] fault-removing;
排障器 cowcatcher;

[排置] put in good order;

[排鐘] chimes;

[排字] compose; typeset; typesetting; typewrite;
排字工 compositor; typesetter;
排字工人 compositor; typesetter;
排字機 composing machine; compositor; typesetter; typesetting machine;
~攝影排字機 photographic typesetter;
~一台排字機 a typesetting machine;
排字架 composing frame;
排字盤 composing stick;
電腦排字 computerized typesetting;

挨排 arrange; make arrangements for;
安排 arrange; arrange for; arrangements; cuddle up; find a place for sth; fix; fix sth; fix up; lay on sth; lay out; make arrangements for; manage; plan; tee up;
編排 arrange; lay out; make up sth;
冰排 ice floe; ice raft;
並排 in a row; in the same row; side by side;
彩排 dress rehearsal;
重排 rearrange; rearrangement;
觝排 get rid of; reject;
發排 send a manuscript to the compositor;
放排 raft;
付排 send to the compositor;
後排 back row;
木排 raft;
牛排 beefsteak;
鋪排 (1) arrange; put in order; (2) extravagant;
前排 front row;
肉排 rib; steak;
縮排 indent;
外排 exclusive;
羊排 lamb chop; mutton chop;
一排 a block of; a line of; a range of; a rank of; a row of; a screen of; an array of;

裁排 make arrangements for;
站排 line up;
照排 phototype setting;
豬排 pork chop;
竹排 bamboo raft;

pai

【牌】 (1) bulletin board; (2) card; inscribed tablet; label; plate; signboard; tablet; tag; (3) archway; gateway; (3) brand; mark; trademark; (4) cards; dominoes; mahjong pieces; playing cards;

［牌匾］ horizontal inscribed tablet; plaque;
［牌賭］ gambling;
［牌坊］ honorific arch; memorial archway; memorial gateway;
［牌號］ (1) mark; shop sign; (2) make; trademark; (3) name of a product;
［牌價］ (1) list price; (2) market price; market quotation;
股票牌價 share quotation;
間接牌價 indirect quotation;
直接牌價 direct quotation;
［牌樓］ (1) decorated archway; (2) temporary ceremonial arch;
三層牌樓 three-storey arch; three tiers of arch;
［牌位］ memorial tablet;
列祖列宗的牌位 ancestral memorial tablet;
［牌照］ license; license plate; license tag;
牌照號碼 registration number;
牌照稅 licence tax;
申請牌照 apply for a license tag;
轉讓牌照 transfer the possession of a license tag;
［牌桌］ card table;
［牌子］ (1) plate; sign; sign post; (2) brand; make; trademark;
老牌子 old brand;
汽車牌子 make of a car;
新牌子 new brand;
~一個新牌子 a new brand;

百搭牌 wild card;
榜牌 bulletin board;
標牌 label; sign;
標語牌 placard;
車牌 license plate; number plate; registration plate;
打牌 (1) play cards; (2) play mahjong;
大牌 (1) celebrity; (2) famous;
擋箭牌 (1) shield; (2) excuse; pretext;
倒牌 lose prestige;
底牌 cards in one's hand;
盾牌 (1) shield; (2) excuse; pretext;
跟牌 (of mahjong) following suit;
骨牌 dominoes;
掛牌 (1) hang out one's shingle; (2) put up a tag;
廣告牌 billboard;
紅牌 red card;
花牌 court card;
記分牌 scoreboard;
價牌 price tag;
獎牌 medal;
金牌 gold medal;
扣牌 (of mahjong) hold up a tile;
老牌 old brand;
亮牌 have a showdown; lay one's cards on the table;
靈牌 spirit tablet;
路牌 street name-plate;
冒牌 fake; imitation;
門牌 (1) number plate; (2) house number;
免戰牌 sign used in ancient times to show refusal to fight;
名牌 (1) big-name brand; brand name; designation strip; famous brand; name brand prestige; (2) name tag;
踫牌 (of mahjong) draw a tile to make three tiles of a kind;
品牌 brand; name brand;
撲克牌 playing cards; poker;
橋牌 bridge;
水牌 lacquered board in shops for erasable writing;
盾牌 (1) shield; (2) excuse; pretext;
攤牌 have a showdown; lay one's cards on the table; show one's hand; showdown;
藤牌 cane shield; ratten shield;
銅牌 bronze medal; copper medal;
王牌 trump card;
胸牌 name tag;
一局牌 a round of cards;
銀牌 silver medal;
雜牌 less known and inferior brand;
招牌 shop sign; signboard;
紙牌 playing cards;

pai

【簰】 bamboo raft;

pai4
pai

【派】 (1) clique; faction; group; school; sect; (2) manner and air; style; (3) appoint; assign; dispatch; send;

［派別］ category; clique; faction; group; school; sect;
派別鬥爭 factional strife;
一個派別 a sect;
宗教派別 religious sect;

［派兵］ dispatch troops; send troops;
派兵遣將 dispatch troops and send generals;
派兵入侵 send one's troops to invade;
派兵佔領 send troops to occupy; send troops to invade and occupy;
派兵駐防 garrison;

［派差］ send sb on errand;

［派出］ send;
派出所 police station;

［派對］ gathering; party;
派對遊戲 party game;
生日派對 birthday party;

［派活］ assign a task;

［派遣］ dispatch; send sb on mission;
派遣部隊 dispatch troops;
派遣代表團 send a delegation;

［派生］ derivative; derive from;
派生詞 derivative;
~ 派生詞幹 derivative stem;
派生反義詞 derivative antonym;
派生構詞法 derivation;
派生數詞 derivation numeral;
派生意義 derivative meaning;
零派生 zero derivation;

［派勢］ manner; style;

［派糖］ dish out sweeteners;

［派頭］ air; manner; panache; style;
派頭不小 put on a lot of airs;
派頭挺足 put on quite a show;

［派系］ clique; faction; grouping;
派系的 cliquey; cliquish;
派系鬥爭 factionalism;
學術小派系 academic clique;

［派性］ cliquism; factionalism; ripper; tribalism;

［派駐］ accredit; dispatch sb to stay at; garrison;

幫派 clique; faction;

保守派 conservatives;

編派 libel; vilify;

抽象派 abstractionism; abstractionist school;

當權派 people in authority; person in power;

黨派 factions; party groupings; political parties and groups;

嫡派 (1) direct line of descent; legal or official branch of a family tree; (2) disciples taught by the master himself;

調派 assign; dispatch; send; send out;

反對派 opposition faction;

反派 negative character; villain;

分派 assign; distribute; dole sth out; hand out;

風派 fence-sitter; time-server; people who see the way the wind blows;

改良派 reformists;

革新派 innovators;

鴿派 dove; dove faction;

觀潮派 person who takes a wait-and-see attitude; bystander; onlooker;

海派 (1) Shanghai style; (2) people who put up a big front;

激進派 radicals;

急進派 radicals;

教派 denomination; religious sect;

勒派 impose; levy on sb;

樂天派 carefree person; happy-go-lucky person; optimist;

兩面派 double-dealer;

流派 school; sect;

名士派 unconventional and self-indulgent old-style intellectual;

騎牆派 fence-sitter;

氣派 airs; bearing; dignified air; fine; impressive; impressive manner; impressive style; manner; style; stylish;

少壯派 younger stalwart faction in a political party;

伸手派 person who has the habit of asking others for help;

實力派 those who actually have strength and hold power;

守舊派 old fogy; old liners;

死硬派 diehards;

攤派 allot; apportion;

特派 commission specially; specially appointed;

頑固派 diehards;

維新派 reformers;

委派 appoint; commission; delegate; designate; send sb in charge of;

溫和派 moderate wing; moderates;

穩健派 moderates;

新派 modern school; new school;

形象派 imagism;
選派 designate; nominate; select;
學派 school; school of thought;
壓派 ride roughshod over;
一派 (1) a faction; a group; a school; (2) a pack of;
鷹派 hawks;
印象派 impressionist; impressionist school;
右派 (1) Right Wing; (2) Rightist;
正派 decency; decent; honest; upright; virtuous;
正統派 orthodox party or school;
政派 political faction; political group;
支派 (1) branch; offshoot; sect; (2) dispatch; order about; send;
指派 appoint; assign; designate; name;
中和派 moderates;
中間派 intermediate forces; middle-of-roaders;
中派 intermediate sections; middle elements; middle-of-the-roaders;
宗派 faction; sect;
左派 (1) Left Wing; (2) Leftist;
做派 (of an opera) acting;

pai

【湃】 billowy; turbulent;

滂湃 (of water) roaring and rushing;
澎湃 surging;

pai

【鎃】 protactinium;

pan[1]

pan

【番】 a county in Guangdong;

pan

【潘】 (1) water in which rice has been washed; (2) a surname;

pan

【攀】 (1) clamber up; climb up; scale; (2) attach oneself to sb powerful; play up to; seek connections in high places; (3) drag into; implicate; involve;

[攀比] compare unrealistically; compare with the higher; make invidious comparisons; vie with each other;
攀比風 craze to vie with each other;

[攀纏] (1) intertwine; (2) wind around;

[攀扯] drag into an affair; implicate sb; involve;

[攀登] clamber; clamber up; climb up; scale; scramble up;
攀登高峰 scale the heights;
攀登架 jungle gym;
攀登峭壁 climb up a cliff;

[攀附] attach oneself to sb powerful; play up to;
攀附權貴 attach oneself to people in power; play up to people of power and influence;

[攀高] (1) climb up; (2) attach oneself to bigwigs;
攀高門親 marry above one's station;
攀高枝兒 (1) attach oneself to bigwigs; (2) seek greener pastures;

[攀供] implicate others in one's confession;

[攀交] attach oneself to bigwigs;

[攀爬] climb;
攀爬架 climbing frame; jungle gym;

[攀配] marry up to higher social level;

[攀親] (1) seek a match; (2) claim kinship; claim relationship;
攀親道故 claim ties of blood or friendship;

[攀談] accost; chat with; chitchat; drag another into conversation; engage in small talk with; have a free and easy talk; hobnob; strike up a conversation;
與朋友攀談 have a chat with a friend;

[攀岩] climbing;

[攀緣] (1) clamber up; climb up; (2) climb up the social ladder through pull;
攀緣而上 climb up;
攀緣植物 climber; creeper;

[攀越] clamber over;

[攀摘] pick from trees;

[攀折] break branches; pick; pluck; pull down and break off;
攀折花木 pick the flowers;

登攀 climb; scale;
高攀 (1) climb; scale; (2) try to form a kind of relationship with sb holding a high position;

pan[2]

pan

【胖】 corpulent; fat; obese;

pan

【般】 (1) linger; (2) comfort; (3) leather bag;

［般樂］ have fun without being conscious of time; pleasure;

［般遊］ play without being conscious of time;

pan

【槃】 (1) wooden tray; (2) great;

涅槃 nirvana;

pan

【盤】 (1) dish; plate; tray; (2) plate-shaped object; (3) coil; twine; twist; wind; wind round; (4) build; (5) check; cross-examine; examine; interrogate; make an inventory; (6) transfer; (7) game; set; (8) a surname;

［盤剝］ exploit; practise usury;
盤剝工人 exploit workers;
盤剝取利 Shylock;

［盤查］ cross-examine; examine thoroughly; interrogate and examine; question;
盤查賬目 check accounts;

［盤纏］ coil; twine; twist; wind round;
用光了盤纏 use up all the money for the journey;

［盤存］ inventory; take inventory;
調整盤存 adjusting inventory;
賬面盤存 book inventory;

［盤點］ check; draw up an inventory; inventory; make an inventory; stocktaking; take stock;

［盤費］ travelling expenses;

［盤根］ get to the bottom of a matter;
盤根錯節 a complicated situation difficult to deal with; a difficult and confused affair; complicated and difficult; deep-rooted;
盤根究底 ask about sth in great detail; close questioning; get to the bottom of things; inquire deeply into sth; try to get to the hearts of a matter;
盤根問底 get to the bottom of an affair; inquire deeply into sth; try to get to the heart of a matter;

［盤桓］ linger; stay; stroll about;
盤桓片刻 spend a little idle time;
盤桓數日 stay for a few days; take relaxation for a few days;
盤桓終日 linger about all day long;

［盤貨］ make an inventory of stock on hand; take inventory; take stock;

［盤詰］ cross-examine; question;
盤詰奸宄 cross-examine bad elements;

［盤究］ cross-examine and investigate;

［盤踞］ be entrenched; occupy illegally or forcibly; settle in;
盤踞要津 hold a place of importance; hold a strategic post; occupy a key post illegally;

［盤坡轉徑］ round the cliffs and follow the narrow path;

［盤繞］ coil; twine; weave; wind round; wreathe;

［盤石］ huge circular stone; rock;
盤石之固 firm as bedrock; sth resting on a solid foundation;
安如磐石 absolute tranquility; as firm as a rock; as firm as Mount Taishan; as secure as Mount Taishan; as solid as a rock; as stable as Mount Taishan; as steady as Mountain Taishan; rock-firm; safe as houses;

［盤算］ calculate; consider and weigh; deliberate; figure; plan; premeditate;
暗中盤算 calculate in one's mind; figure on the sly;
暗自盤算 calculate secretly;
精心盤算 plan carefully;
心中盤算 debate in one's mind; debate with oneself;
左盤右算 calculate carefully; turn over everything in one's mind;

［盤腿］ cross one's legs;

［盤問］ cross-examine; cross-question; inquisition; interrogate;
盤問者 inquisitor;

［盤膝而坐］ sit cross-legged; sit tailor-fashion; sit with one's legs crossed;

［盤旋］ (1) circle around; hover; wheel; (2) linger; stay; tarry;
盤旋而上 spiral up; twist up;
盤旋下降 spiral down;
飛機在空中盤旋 the plan is circling about in the sky;

［盤帳］ audit accounts; check accounts; examine accounts;

［盤桌］ tray table; tray-top table;

［盤子］ dish; plate; salver; saucer; tray;
端盤子 wait tables;
耍盤子 disc-spinning; plate-spinning;
洗盤子 do the dishes; wash dishes;

暗盤 under-the-counter price or terms;
報盤 make a price; make a quotation; make an offer; offer; quote a price; work out the orders;
杯盤 cups and dishes;
錶盤 face of a watch;
撥號盤 dial;
菜盤 serving plate;
茶盤 tea tray; teaboard;
唱盤 turntable;
秤盤 pan of a steedlyard;
稱盤 pan of a steelyard;
磁光盤 magneto-optic disc;
磁盤 disc; magnetic disc;
大盤 platter;
彈盤 cartridge drum;
導盤 godet;
底盤 (1) chassis; (2) base; pedestal;
地盤 domain; sphere of action; turf;
發盤 offer; offering;
發文盤 out tray;
方向盤 steering wheel;
放盤 sale at reduced prices;
光盤 CD; compact disc; optical disc;
果盤 fruit basket; fruit tray;
紅盤 price charged when business begins after the Spring Festival;
花盤 (1) flower disc; (2) disc chuck; faceplate;
還盤 counter-offer; make a counter-offer;
夾盤 chuck;
駕駛盤 steering wheel;
鍵盤 fingerboard; keyboard;
絞盤 capstan;
截盤 jib;
卡盤 chuck;
開盤 opening quotation;
烤盤 baking tray; hotplate;
冷盤 cold dish;
臉盤 cast of one's face;
羅盤 compass;
滿盤 a dishful of;
碾盤 millstone; roller;
胚盤 blastodisc; germinal disc;
片盤 bobbin; film spool;
拼盤 assorted cold dishes; hors d'oeuvres;
平盤 flat plate;
棋盤 checkerboard; chessboard;
卡盤 chuck;
全盤 comprehensive; overall; wholesale;
沙盤 sand table;
深菜盤 deep plate;
收件盤 in tray;
算盤 abacus;
胎盤 placenta;
陶盤 pottery pot;
通盤 all-round; comprehensive; entire; overall;
托盤 pallet; serving tray; tray;
圍盤 repeater;
吸盤 sucker; sucking disc;
小算盤 selfish calculations;
星盤 astrolabe;
虛盤 offer without engagement;
一滿盤 trayful;
一盤 a coil of; a dish of; a game of; a plate of; a reel of;
銀盤 (1) silver dish; (2) moon; (3) galactic disc;
營盤 military camp; barracks;
硬盤 hard disc;
油盤 lacquer tray;
油漆盤 paint tray;
魚盤 fish plate;
育曲盤 seed tray;
圓盤 disc;
早餐盤 breakfast tray;
製冰盤 ice cube tray;
轉盤 (1) turntable; (2) giant stride; (3) disc-spinning; (4) rotary table;
字盤 case

pan

【磐】 huge rock; massive rock;

［磐石］ huge rock; massive rock;

磐石之固 rock-like firmness; the firmness of a rock;

堅如磐石 as solid as a rock;

守如磐石 as steady as a rock;

硬磐 hardpan;

pan

【蟠】 (1) coil; (2) curl up; twisted; (3) occupy;

［蟠龍］ curled-up dragon;

［蟠木］ twisted tree;

［蟠桃］ (1) flat peach; saucer peach; (2) peach of immortality in Chinese mythology;

pan

【蹣】

［蹣跚］ blunder; falter; flounder; hobble; joll dodder; limp; lurch; stagger; stumble; stump; titubate; totter; walk haltingly;

蹣跚而行 drag one's feet slowly along; hobble along; lurch along; walk

lamely;

pan

【鞶】 large belt;

pan⁴

pan

【判】 (1) differentiate; discriminate; distinguish; (2) obviously; (3) appraise; give a mark; (4) decide; determine; judge; (5) condemn; pass a sentence; sentence;

[判別] differentiate; discriminate; distinguish;
判別式 discriminant;
~非線性判別式 non-linear discriminant;
~基本判別式 fundamental discriminant;
~相對判別式 relative discriminant;
判別真僞 distinguish the true from the false;
很難判別 have trouble in distinguishing sth from sth;
紋理判別 texture discrimination;

[判處] condemn; sentence;

[判詞] court verdict;

[判定] decide; determine; judge; predicate; vote;

[判讀] interpretation;
地質判讀 geological interpretation;
航攝像片判讀 aerial photo interpretation;
照片判讀 photo interpretation;

[判斷] assess; decide; determine; judge; size up;
判斷錯誤 misjudge;
判斷距離 judge distances;
判斷力 judgement;
~沒有判斷力 have little judgement;
~失去判斷力 lose one's judgement;
判斷能力 skills of making judgements;
判斷是非 judge between right and wrong;
錯誤判斷 misread;
道德判斷 ethical judgement; moral judgement;
~道德判斷能力 ability to make moral judgements;
獨立判斷 independent judgement;
價值判斷 value judgement;
全稱判斷 universal judgement;
速度判斷 pace judgement;
下判斷 give judgement on; pass judgement on; render judgement on;
正確地判斷 judge rightly;
綜合判斷 synthetic judgement;

[判罰] penalize;

[判給] award;

[判決] decision;
推翻判決 overrule a decision;

[判例法] case law;

[判明] ascertain; discriminate; distinguish; draw a clear distinction;
判明是非 distinguish between right and wrong;
判明真相 ascertain the facts;

[判然] clearly; obviously;

[判若] be as far apart as; the difference is like;
判若黑白 the difference is as between black and white;
判若鴻溝 completely different;
判若兩人 have become quite a different person;
~前後判若兩人 a different person from what one was;
判若水火 completely different;
判若天淵 as far apart as sky and sea; as far apart as the sky and the abyss; the difference is as between high heaven and the deep sea;
判若雲泥 as far removed as heaven is from earth; as great a distance as between the sky and the earth; poles apart; there is a world of difference;

[判刑] pass a sentence; sentence;

[判罪] convict; declare guilty;

裁判 (1) judgment; (2) judge; referee; umpire; (3) act as referee; (4) verdict;
改判 amend a judgment; change the original sentence; commute;
公判 (1) openly pronounce a judgment or verdict; (2) (of the public) judge;
批判 (1) criticize; (2) critique;
評判 judge; pass judgment on;
審判 bring to trial; try;
談判 hold negotiations; talk;
宣判 announce the verdict; pronounce judgement;
嚴判 severe judgment;

pan

【拚】 (1) go all-out for; (2) at the risk of; disregard; give up; (3) reject;

[拚棄] cast; give up;

pan

【拌】 abandon; throw away;

[拌命] risk one's life;
[拌棄] abandon;
[拌石] throw a stone;

pan
【泮】 (1) (in old China) an institution of higher learning; (2) (now rare) dissolve; melt;

pan
【叛】 betray; defect; rebel against; turn a traitor;
[叛變] betray one's country; defect; mutiny; turn a renegade; turn a traitor;
叛變投敵 sell out to the enemy; turn traitor and go over to the enemy;
叛變者 mutineer;
[叛黨] betray the party; turn a traitor to the party;
叛黨叛國 betray the party and country;
叛黨者 turncoat;
[叛敵] treachery;
[叛匪] bandit rebels; rebel bandits;
[叛國] betray one's country; commit treason; turn traitor to one's country;
叛國求榮 betray one's country for high position and great wealth;
叛國篡權 betray the nation and usurp power;
叛國投敵 betray one's fatherland and flee to defect to the enemy; betray the country and go over to the enemy;
叛國罪 high treason;
附敵叛國 betray one's country and attach oneself to the enemy;
[叛教] apostasy;
叛教者 apostate;
[叛軍] insurgent troops; rebel army; rebel forces;
[叛離] betray; desert;
眾叛親離 be opposed by the people and deserted by one's followers; with the masses rising in rebellion and one's friends deserting;
[叛亂] armed rebellion; insurrection; mutiny; rebel; revolt; rise in rebellion;
爆發叛亂 a rebellion broke out;
反叛亂 counterinsurgency;
平息叛亂 quash a rebellion;
掀起叛亂 raise a rebellion;
鎮壓叛亂 suppress a rebellion;
[叛賣] betray; sell;
[叛逆] (1) rebel against; revolt against; (2) rebel;
叛逆家庭 rebel against one's family;
叛逆罪 high treason;
[叛逃] defect;
[叛徒] defector; rat; rebel; renegade; traitor; turncoat;

背叛 apostatize; betray; defect; rebel;
悖叛 rebel; revolt;
反叛 mutiny; rebel; revolt;

pan
【盼】 (1) hope for; long for; look forward to; (2) look;
[盼即示復] hoping for your immediate reply;
[盼望] hope for; long for; look forward to;
盼望佳音 long for good news;
盼望已久 long for;
不再盼望 lose one's hope;
熱切地盼望 earnestly hope for;
日盼夜望 long day and night for; look for sb day and night;

顧盼 look around;

pan
【畔】 (1) boundary between fields; (2) beside; waterside; (3) same as 叛 ;

pan
【襻】 (1) loop for a button; (2) fasten with a rope;

紐襻 button loop;
鞋襻 shoe strap;

pang¹
pang
【乓】 (of a sound) pang;
乒乓 rattle;

pang
【滂】 overwhelming; pouring; streaming; surging; torrential;
[滂湃] roaring and rushing;
[滂沱] pouring; streaming; torrential;
滂沱大雨 downpour; heavy rainfall; heavy shower; pouring rain; torrential rain;
涕泗滂沱 flood of tears; be drenched with tears and snivel tears and mucus run abundantly down one's face;

pang

【磅】 stone-crashing noise;

［磅礴］ boundless; extensive; filling all space; majestic;

大氣磅礴 grand and magnificent; great vitality; have power and range; of great momentum; powerful;

pang

【霶】 rain cats and dogs;

［霶霈］ heavy rain; rain cats and dogs; rain hard; rain heavily;

pang²

pang

【彷】 hesitating; unsettled;

［彷徨］ hesitate; hesitate about which way to go; not know which way to go; walk back and forth;

彷徨歧途 hesitate at the crossroads;

pang

【尨】 (1) shaggy-haired dog; (2) blended; variegated;

pang

【厖】 (1) bulky; mammoth; thick and large; (2) confused; disorderly;

pang

【旁】 (1) side; (2) else; other;

［旁白］ aside; narration; speak aside; voice-over;

旁白者 narrator;

低聲旁白 stage whisper;

［旁邊］ near by position; right by; side;

站在窗戶旁邊 stand by the window;

坐在我旁邊 sit beside me;

［旁觀］ look on; observe from the sidelines; onlooker;

旁觀者 bystander; onlooker; spectator;

~一群旁觀者 a crowd of spectators;

旁觀者清 a bystander is always clear-minded; a spectator sees clearly; an onlooker sees clearly; bystanders see more than players; lookers-on see more than players; lookers-on see most of the game; the onlooker sees most of the game; the onlooker sees the game best; the outsider sees the best of the game; the spectator sees most clearly; the spectator sees most of the sport;

冷眼旁觀 stay aloof;

縮手旁觀 watch from the sideline without interferring;

袖手旁觀 fold one's arms; fold one's arms and look on; hold the ring; look on and do nothing; look on indifferently; look on with folded arms; praise the sea but stay on land; put one's hands in one's sleeves and look on; remain an indifferent spectator; sit around with folded arms; sit out; stand aside; stand by; stand by with folded arms; stand idle; stand idly by; watch indifferently wihout lending a hand; watch with folded arms;

［旁及］ take up;

［旁門］ side door; sidegate;

旁門左道 heresy; all sorts of back doors; unorthodox ways;

左道旁門 (1) heresy; heretical sect; heterodoxy; (2) evil ways; unlawful and tricky ways;

［旁人］ other people; others;

［旁聽］ audit; visitor at a meeting;

旁聽生 associate student; auditing student;

［旁通］ bypass;

［旁騖］ be preoccupied;

馳心旁騖 in an absent-minded sort of way; one's mind keeps wandering off;

心無旁騖 single-minded; without distraction;

心有旁騖 have sth else to go after; preoccupied;

［旁心］ ex-centre;

［旁證］ circumstantial evidence; collateral evidence; side witness;

［旁支］ collateral branch;

［旁族］ collateral family;

近旁 at one's elbow; near; nearby;

兩旁 both sides; either side;

路旁 roadside; wayside;

四旁 all around; back and front; left and right;

一旁 by the side of; on the sideline; one side;

pang

【逄】 a surname;

pang

【傍】 beside; by the side of;

［傍邊］ beside;

［傍聽］ audit a class;

傍聽生 auditing student;

［傍觀］ watch on the sideline;

P

[傍徨] vacillating;
[傍晚] early evening;
傍晚茶 high tea;
[傍系] indirect blood relatives;
[傍人] other people;

pang
【徬】 agitated and indecisive; anxious;

pang
【雱】 snow heavily;

pang
【膀】 bladder;
[膀胱] urinary bladder;
膀胱癌 bladder cancer;
膀胱襞 fold;
~ 直腸膀胱襞 rectovesical fold;
膀胱閉鎖 atretocystia;
膀胱出血 cystorrhagia;
膀胱反射 bladder reflex;
膀胱隔 septum;
~ 直腸膀胱隔 rectovesical septum;
膀胱過度活躍綜合症 overactive bladder;
膀胱過敏 cysterethism;
膀胱積膿 pyocystis;
膀胱積血 haematocyst;
膀胱結核 cystophthisis;
膀胱結石 vesical calculus; bladder stone;
~ 膀胱結石病 cystolithiasis;
膀胱口 opening of bladder;
膀胱潰瘍 cystelcosis;
~ 單純性膀胱潰瘍 ulcus simplex vesicae;
膀胱擴張 megabladder;
膀胱尿道口 vesicourethral orifice;
膀胱尿道炎 cystourethritis;
膀胱疝 vesical hernia;
膀胱滲血 cystostaxis;
膀胱石 vesical calculus; bladder stone;
膀胱痛 cystalgia;
膀胱萎縮 cystatrophia;
膀胱炎 cystitis;
~ 白喉性膀胱炎 diphtheritic cystitis;
~ 變應性膀胱炎 allergic cystitis;
~ 剝脱性膀胱炎 exfoliative cystitis;
~ 出血性膀胱炎 haemorrhagic cystitis;
~ 機械性膀胱炎 mechanical cystitis;
~ 結痂性膀胱炎 incrusted cystitis;
~ 濾泡性膀胱炎 cyrstitis follicularis;
~ 蜜月膀胱炎 honeymoon cystitis;
~ 囊腫性膀胱炎 cystic cystitis;
~ 尿道膀胱炎 urethrocystitis;
~ 氣腫性膀胱炎 cystitis emphysematosa;
~ 前列腺膀胱炎 prostatocystitis;
~ 全膀胱炎 pancystitis;
~ 腎膀胱炎 nephrocystitis;
~ 腎盂膀胱炎 pyelocystitis;
~ 細菌性膀胱炎 bacterial cystitis;
~ 腺性膀胱炎 cystitis glandularis;
~ 陰道膀胱炎 colpocystitis;
刺激性膀胱 irritable bladder;
反射性膀胱 reflex bladder;
高張性膀胱 hypertonic bladder;
痙攣性膀胱 spastic bladder;
巨膀胱 megabladder;
麻痺性膀胱 paralytic bladder;
神經性膀胱 nervous bladder;
神經源性膀胱 neurogenic bladder;
雙膀胱 double bladder;

pang
【螃】 crab;
[螃蟹] crab;
海螃蟹 sea crab;
河螃蟹 freshwater crab;
一隻螃蟹 a crab;

pang
【龐】 (1) big; colossal; enormous; giant; gigantic; huge; massive; (2) innumerable and disordered; (3) face; (4) a surname;
[龐大] ample; big; colossal; enormous; gigantic; huge; mammoth; massive;
龐大的 hulking; humongous;
[龐然] huge;
龐然大物 biggie; formidable giant; huge creature; huge monster; hulk; jumbo; leviathan; mammoth; monstrous creature; thumper; whopper;
[龐雜] in a cumbersome jumble; multifarious and disorderly; numerous and jumbled;
議論龐雜 numerous and jumbled views;

臉龐 cast of one's face;
面龐 (1) contour of one's face; (2) face;

pang⁴
pang
【胖】 chubby; fat; plump;
[胖墩墩] plump; stout;
胖墩墩的身材 ample figure;
[胖乎乎] chubby; plump; pudgy; strutty;
胖乎乎的臉 chubby face;
長得胖乎乎 plump;

[胖胖的] fat;
[胖子] butterball; fat man; fat person; fatso; fatty; stout;
打腫臉充胖子 a jackdaw in peacock feathers; an impudent attempt to represent the defeat as a victory; having one's face slapped until it is swollen to pretend that one has gotten fatter; keep up appearances; keep up with the Jones; put a bold face on the matter; put on a bold front; shabby gentility;
胖小子 fat boy;
小胖子 fatty boy;

矮胖 dumpy; humpty-dumpty; roly-poly; short and fat; short and stout; squat; tubby;
發胖 get fat; put on weight;
虛胖 puffiness;
長胖 become fat; flesh out; flesh up; gain flesh; gain weight; get fat; get flesh; make flesh; pick up flesh; put on flesh; put on weight;

pang
【膀】 make passes at;

pao¹
pao
【泡】 (1) loose and soft; spongy; (2) an amount of excrement or urine;
[泡妞] pick up chicks;
[泡泡] bubble;
泡泡糖 bubble gum;
泡泡浴 bubble bath;
~泡泡浴液 bubble bath;
[泡軟] macerate;
[泡桐] paulownia;
[泡子] small lake;

眼泡 upper eyelid;

pao
【抛】 (1) cast; fling; throw; toss; (2) cast aside; forsake; leave behind; throw away; throw overboard;
[抛光] brightening; buffing; finish; finishing; polishing;
抛光輪 buffer;
電抛光 electrolytic brightening;
乾法抛光 dry polishing;
化學抛光 chemical brightening; chemical polishing;
火抛光 fire finishing;
機械抛光 mechanical buffing;
金剛砂抛光 diamond polishing;
木炭抛光 charcoal finishing;
陽極電抛光 anode brightening; anodized finish;
[抛空] short;
抛空賬戶 short account;
[抛離] quit;
[抛錨] anchor; anchorage; break down;
抛錨停泊 at anchor; cast anchor; come to anchor; drop anchor;
準備抛錨 stand by for the anchor; stand by the anchor;
[抛棄] abandon; cast aside; cast away; chuck out; chuck up; desert; discard; forsake; run out on sb; throw away;
抛棄偏見 cast off prejudices;
抛棄妻兒 abandon one's wife and children;
被抛棄 get the air;
[抛球] throw the ball;
[抛砂機] sandslinger;
單軌式抛砂機 bracket-type sandslinger;
移動式抛砂機 mobile sandslinger;
[抛售] dump; sell sth at low prices; sell sth in big quantities; undersell; unload;
[抛物面] paraboloid;
共焦抛物面 confocal paraboloids;
截抛物面 cut paraboloid;
[抛物線] parabola;
共焦抛物線 confocal parabolas;
收斂抛物線 convergence parabolas;
退化抛物線 degenerate parabola;
[抛擲] throw;
抛擲表演 throwing act;
[抛磚引玉] a modest spur to induce others to come forward with more valuable opinions; cast away a brick and attract a jadestone; throw out a minnow to catch a whale;

pao
【脬】 bladder;

pao²
pao
【刨】 (1) dig; excavate; (2) excluding; not counting;
[刨冰] water ice;
[刨除] reduce;

[刨牀] planer;
仿形刨牀 copying planer;
龍門刨牀 closed planer;
手刨牀 hand planer;
[刨地] dig the ground;
[刨根] get to the root of the matter;
刨根問底 bombard sb with questions; dig out the bottom truth; get to the bottom of things; inquire into the root of the matter;
[刨子] plane;

pao
【咆】 bluster; rage; roar;
[咆哮] bluster; rage; roar;
咆哮如雷 in a thundering rage; roar like thunder; roar with rage;

pao
【庖】 cuisine; kitchen;
[庖廚] kitchen;
[庖丁解牛] dismember an ox as skilfully as a butcher; skilled and magical craftsmanship;

代庖 act in sb's place; do what is sb else's job;

pao
【砲】 refine medicinal herbs;
[砲姜] baked ginger;

pao
【匏】 (1) bottle gourd; calabash; gourd; (2) a kind of wind instrument originally made of a gourd;
[匏瓜] calabash; gourd;
[匏舌] sublingual cyst;

pao
【袍】 gown; robe;
[袍澤] fellow officers;
袍澤同僚 fellow officers; fellow soldiers;
[袍罩兒] long gown worn over a robe;
[袍子] gown; robe;

長袍 long gown; robe;
道袍 Daoist priest's robe;
罩袍 dust-gown; dust-robe; overall;

pao
【麃】 till the land;

pao
【麅】 a species of roe;

pao³
pao
【跑】 (1) run; (2) escape; run away; (3) bustle about; go around; on the go; run about doing sth; run errands; (4) evaporate; (5) away; off;
[跑遍] go around; travel all over;
[跑步] march at the double; run;
跑步過去 run over;
跑步機 treadmill;
跑步前進 advance at the double;
[跑車] racing car; sports car;
低車身跑車 low-slung sports car;
[跑船] make a living as a sailor;
[跑道] (1) landing strip; runway; (2) lane; track;
飛機跑道 aircraft runway; landing strip;
~臨時飛機跑道 airstrip;
簡單跑道 landing strip;
內圈跑道 inside track;
全天候跑道 all-weather track;
塑膠跑道 synthetic surface track;
[跑電] leakage of electricity;
[跑掉] flee;
[跑龍套] general handyman; utility man; play a bit role;
[跑跑顛顛] bustle about; on the go; rush about;
[跑堂] waiter
[跑跳] run and skip;
連跑帶跳 skip and run; by leaps and bounds;
跑跑跳跳 bounce; run and jump;
[跑腿] courier; footman; do legwork; go on errands; run errands;
跑腿活 legwork;
[跑外] go shopping;

奔跑 run; run in great hurry;
長跑 long-distance race; long-distance running;
打跑 beat away;
短跑 dash; short-distance running; sprint;
飛跑 bolt off; dask; race; run very fast; tear;
滑跑 skating;
快跑 scoot;
慢跑 canter;
起跑 start; starting;
搶跑 take away by force;
賽跑 dash; hold a race; race; sprint;
逃跑 abscond; betake oneself to flight; break

away; buzz off; copa heel; cut and run; cut away; cut loose; cut one's stick; decamp; duck; escape; flee; get away; get out; give leg bail; make good one's escape; make off; make one's escape; make one's getaway; move off; run away; run off; scarper; show a clean pair of heels; show legs; show one's heels; slip away; take leg bail; take to flight; take to one's heels; take to one's legs;

偷跑 escape; run away;
嚇跑 scare away; scare off;
小跑 jog; trot;
助跑 approach; run-up;

pao⁴

pao

【泡】 (1) bubble; (2) sth shaped like a bubble; (3) soak; steep; (4) dawdle; dillydally;

［泡菜］ kimchi; pickled vegetable; pickle;
泡菜壜 pickle jar;
朝鮮泡菜 kimchi;
雜錦泡菜 assorted pickles;

［泡茶］ make tea;

［泡飯］ (1) soaked cooked rice in soup or water; (2) cooked rice reheated in boiling water;

［泡沫］ foam; froth; lather; micro-foam; spume; yeast;
泡沫經濟 foam economy; frothy economy;
泡沫體 foam;
~ 多孔狀泡沫體 cellular foam;
~ 酚醛泡沫體 phenolic foam;
~ 瀝青泡沫體 bituminous froth;
~ 耐磨泡沫體 abrasive foam;
泡沫危機 bubble crisis;
泡沫消防車 foam-gun fire engine;
泡沫效應 bubble effect;
泡沫製品 foam article;
肥皂泡沫 soap lather;
礦化泡沫 mineralized froth;
樓市泡沫 property bubble;

［泡湯］ hope dashed to pieces;

［泡影］ bubble; visionary hope;
泡影夢幻 dreams and bubbles; like a vanishing dream;
成了泡影 come to nothing;
化為泡影 come to nothing; end up in smoke; fail to come true; go up in smoke; melt into thin air; vanish into smoke; vanish like soap bubbles;
終成泡影 come to naught; come to nothing; come to nought; come to smoke; end up in smoke; go up in smoke; vanish like a bubble;

打泡 get blisters on one's palm, foot, etc.;
燈泡 bulb; light bulb;
電燈泡 electric bulb;
肥皂泡 soap bubble;
肺泡 lung alveolus;
腳泡 blisters on the feet;
浸泡 bath; immerse; soak; steep;
空泡 cavity bubble;
燎泡 blister raised by a burn or scald;
卵泡 follicle;
冒泡 (1) have a deal; have business; (2) bubble;
胚泡 germinal vesicle;
起泡 (1) blister; bubble; get blisters; (2) bead; foam; form bubbles;
汽泡 bubbles;
氣泡 air bubbles; bubble; gas bubbles;
水泡 (1) bubble; (2) blister;
脱泡 deaerate;
血泡 bleeding blister;
醃泡 marinate;
眼泡 upper eyelid;
液泡 vacuole;

pao

【砲】 (1) big gun; cannon; (2) bombard; gunfire;

［砲兵］ artillery; artillerymen;
導彈砲兵 missile artillery;
高射砲兵 flak artillery;
海岸砲兵 coastal artillery; seacoast artillery;
流動砲兵 roving artillery;
空降砲兵 airborne artillery;
摩托化砲兵 motorized artillery;
汽車牽引砲兵 truck-drawn artillery;
輕砲兵 light artillery;
統帥部砲兵 general reserve artillery;
要塞砲兵 garrison artillery;
支援砲兵 supporting artillery;
~ 直接支援砲兵 direct supporting artillery;
重砲兵 heavy artillery;

［砲彈］ artillery shell; bullet; cannonball; cartridge; shell;
一發砲彈 a shell;

[砲隊] artillery;
高射砲隊 anti-aircraft artillery;
核砲隊 nuclear artillery;
[砲轟] bombard; bombardment; bombing; shell;
[砲灰] cannon fodder;
[砲火] artillery fire; gunfire;
砲火連天 gunfire licks the heavens;
砲火聲 gunfire;
避開砲火 stand clear of the gunfire;
一陣砲火 a burst of gunfire;
[砲擊] bombard; cannonry; shell;
[砲架] gun carriage;
[砲聲] roar of guns; sound of artillery; thunder of guns;
砲聲隆隆 boom of guns; rumble of gunfire;
一陣隆隆的砲聲 a peal of artillery;
[砲手] artilleryman; cannoneer; gun crew; gunner;
[砲台] gun emplacement;
[砲銅] gun metal;
[砲位] emplacement;
[砲戰] gunfight;
[砲仗] firecracker;
沒藥性的砲仗—中看不中用 a fire-cracker without powder — good only for show;
[砲製] (1) cook up; (2) methods of preparing medical herbs;
如法砲製 act after the same fashion; be modelled on; do sth according to a set pattern; do sth exactly as others have done; follow suit; follow the same formula; imitate what is done by others; make sth according to a set pattern; prepare herbal medicine by the prescribed method — follow a set pattern; take a leaf out of sb's book;

岸砲 coastal artillery;
鞭砲 (1) firecrackers; (2) a string of small firecrackers;
打砲 fire a cannon;
大砲 (1) artillery; cannon; (2) boastful person;
發砲 shoot a cannon;
放空砲 boast; brag; empty talk; fire blank shots; indulge in idle boasting; make an empty threat; spout hot air; talk big;
放砲 (1) fire a gun; (2) let off firecrackers; (3) explode; (4) blow out; (5) shoot off one's mouth;
高射砲 ack-ack; anti-aircraft gun;
摜砲 torpedo;
花砲 fireworks and firecrackers;
火箭砲 rocket gun;
火砲 armament; artillery; cannon; gun;
機關砲 machine cannon;
艦砲 chase gun; naval gun; shipboard artillery;
開砲 (1) fire; open fire with artillery; (2) fire criticism at sb;
冷砲 sniper's shot;
禮砲 gun salute;
連珠砲 continuous firing;
馬後砲 after-thought; belated action; belated advice; belated effort; lock the stable door when the horse has been stolen; too late;
排砲 cannonade; salvo; volley of guns;
槍砲 arms; firearms; guns;
山砲 mountain artillery; mountain gun;
水砲 water cannon;
速射砲 quick-fire artillery;
萬砲 ten thousand cannons;
一門砲 a piece of artillery;
中型砲 medium artillery;
重砲 heavy artillery; heavy guns;
主砲 main artillery;

pao

【疱】 acne;
[疱疹] (1) bleb; (2) herpes;
疱疹病 vesicular exanthema;
疱疹熱 herpetic fever;
疱疹性濕疹 eczema herpeticum;
疱疹樣皮炎 dermatitis herpetiformis;
創傷性疱疹 traumatic herpes;
唇疱疹 cold sore;
帶狀疱疹 herpes zoster;
單純疱疹 herpes simplex;
發熱性疱疹 herpes febrilis;
角膜疱疹 herpes corneae;
熱病性疱疹 fever blister;
妊娠疱疹 herpes gestationis;
生殖器疱疹 genital herpes;
水疱疹 tetter;
外傷性疱疹 traumatic herpes;
嘴邊疱疹 cold sore;

膿疱 pustule;
水疱 blister;

pao

【𤿎】 pimple;

pao

【砲】 simplified form of 礮；

pao

【礮】 (1) catapult; (2) artillery piece; cannon; gun;

［礮兵］ (1) artilleryman; gunner; (2) artillery;
礮兵部隊 artillery units;
礮兵連 battery;
礮兵陣地 artillery position;

［礮車］ gun carriage;

［礮彈］ cannon ball; cannon shot; shell;

［礮塔］ barbette; gunhouse; turret;

［礮臺］ battery; fort; gun emplacement;

［礮膛］ bore of a gun;

［礮艇］ gunboat;

［礮筒］ barrel of a gun
礮筒子 a person who shoots off his mouth;

［礮樓］ blockhouse;

［礮口］ gun muzzle;
礮口焰 muzzle flash;

［礮火］ artillery fire; gunfire;
礮火支援 artillery support;
礮火掩護 fire cover;

［礮灰］ cannon fodder;

［礮轟］ (1) bombard with artillery fire; cannonade; (2) concentrated verbal attacks;

［礮擊］ bombard with artillery fire; bombardment; cannonade; shell;

［礮架］ gun carriage; gun mount;

［礮艦］ gunboat;
礮艦政策 gunboat policy;
礮艦外交 gunboat diplomacy;

［礮戰］ artillery action;

［礮仗］ firecracker;

［礮手］ artilleryman; cannoneer; gunner;

［礮身］ gun barrel;

［礮聲］ roaring of artillery pieces; thunder of cannonade;

［礮栓］ breechblock;

［礮座］ barbette; gun platform;

［礮衣］ canvas covering of an artillery piece; gun cover;

［礮眼］ (1) embrasure; (2) borehole; dynamite hole;

［礮尾］ gun breech;

［礮位］ artillery park; gun pit;

pei¹

pei

【呸】 bah; pah; pooh;

pei

【披】 a pronunciation of 披；

pei

【胚】 (1) fetus; (2) embryo; (3) tender sprouts of plants;

［胚層］ blastoderm;
內胚層 entoderm;
外胚層 ectoderm;
中胚層 medoderm;

［胚根］ radicle;

［胚膜］ embryonic membrane;

［胚泡］ germinal vesicle;

［胚乳］ endosperm;
胚乳細胞 endosperm cell;

［胚胎］ embryo; embryon;
胚胎病 embryopathy;
胚胎發生 embryogeny;
胚胎發育 embryonic development;
胚胎學 embryology;
~ 比較胚胎學 comparative embryology;
~ 動物胚胎學 animal embryology;
~ 化學胚胎學 chemical embryology;
~ 進化胚胎學 evolutionary embryology;
~ 描述胚胎學 descriptive embryology;
~ 內向極胚胎學 endoscopic embryology;
~ 生態胚胎學 ecological embryology;
~ 實驗胚胎學 experimental embryology;
~ 外向胚胎學 exoscopic embryology;
~ 系統胚胎學 systemic embryology;
~ 植物胚胎學 plant embryology;
異位胚胎 adventitious embryo;

［胚乳］ albumen; endosperm;

［胚形成］ embryogeny;

［胚珠］ ovule;
橫生胚珠 amphitropous ovule;
直生胚珠 antitropal ovule;

不定胚 adventive embryo;
反足胚 antipodal embryo;
囊胚 blastula;
雙層胚 didermic embryo;
同胚 homemorphism;
直立胚 erect embryo;
侏儒胚 dwarf embryo;

pei

【醅】 unstrained wine;

pei²

pei

【邳】 (1) jubilant; joyful; (2) an ancient place in today's Shandong; (3) a surname;

pei

【培】 (1) bank up with earth; earth up; (2) breed; cultivate; develop; foster; nurture; raise; rear; train;

[培修] repair;

[培訓] cultivate; train;

培訓班 training class;
培訓手冊 training manual;
培訓中心 training centre;
就業前培訓 pre-employment training;
在職培訓 in-service training; on-the-job training;
職業培訓 vocational training;

[培養] breed; cultivate; cultivation; culture; develop; educate; foster; train;

培養費 training cost;
培養感情 develop friendship;
培養基 culture medium;
~ 發酵培養基 fermentation medium;
培養接班人 train successors;
培養良好的習慣 cultivate good habits;
花藥培養 anther culture;
無菌培養 axenic culture;
需氧培養 aerobic culture;
厭氧培養 anaerobic culture;
藝術培養 artistic culture;
藻類培養 algal culture;

[培育] breed; cultivate; foster; nurture; raise; rear;

培育人才 cherish people of ability;
精心培育 take meticulous care of;

[培植] cultivate; culture; educate; foster; raise; train;

培植果樹 cultivate fruit trees;

安培 ampere;
代培 train on behalf of another organization;
栽培 (1) plant and cultivate; tend; (2) educate; foster; train; (3) give special favour; receive special favour;

pei

【陪】 accompany; keep sb company;

[陪伴] accompany; keep sb company;

[陪襯] (1) serve as a contrast or foil; (2) foil; set-off;

[陪嫁] dowry;

[陪祭] accompany the person in charge in offering the sacrifice or holding a memorial ceremony;

[陪練] ladder player; partner training;

[陪審] act as an assessor; serve as an assessor; serve on a jury;

陪審法官 associate judge;
陪審團 jury;
~ 陪審團成員 juror; members of the jury;
~ 陪審團席 jury box;
~ 大陪審團 grand jury;
陪審員 juror; jury;
~ 擔任陪審員 jury service; serve on a jury; sit on a jury;

[陪送] (1) give a dowry to a daughter; (2) dowry;

[陪同] accompany; escort; in the company of; keep company with;

[陪葬] be buried with the dead;

奉陪 keep sb company;
少陪 if you'll excuse me; I'm afraid I must be going now;
失陪 excuse me, but I must be leaving now;
相陪 be accompanied by; in the company of;
追陪 follow and keep company of an elder;
作陪 accompany; be invited along with the chief guest; escort; help entertain the guest of honour;

pei

【裴】 (1) look of a flowing gown; (2) a surname;

pei

【賠】 (1) compensate; make compensation; pay for; (2) lose; stand a loss; sustain losses;

[賠本] lose one's capital; run a business at a loss; sustain loses in business;

賠本生意 losing business;

[賠償] compensate for; make compensation; pay for;

賠償額 amount of claim;
賠償範圍 extent of compensation;
賠償名譽 indemnity for defamation – compensate for damage sustained;
賠償損失 compensate for loss; indemnify sb for the loss incurred; indemnity for

damage; make amends to;
賠償限度 measure of indemnity;
賠償限額 limits of indemnity;
賠償責任 liability for damages;
部份賠償 partial compensation;
殘損賠償 indemnity for damage;
得到賠償 obtain an indemnity;
風險賠償 indemnity for risk;
全部賠償 full compensation;
雙倍賠償 double indemnity;
違約賠償 compensation consequent on violation of contract;
自動賠償 voluntary indemnity;

[賠墊] advance money for another in making payment;

[賠話] apologize;

[賠款] (1) pay an indemnity; pay reparations; (2) cash indemnity; indemnity; reparations;
保險賠款 insurance indemnity;
戰爭賠款 war indemnity;
自動賠款 voluntary indemnity;

[賠禮] apologize; offer an apology;
賠禮道歉 apologize to sb; make an apology to sb; offer sb an apology;

[賠錢] compensate; sustain losses in business;
賠錢貨 (1) money-losing proposition; (2) daughter; girl;

[賠笑] smile obsequiously or apologetically;
賠笑臉 meet rudeness with a flattering smile;

[賠帳] pay for the loss of cash or goods entrusted to one;

[賠罪] apologize; make an apology;
磕頭賠罪 give sb a grand kowtow and apologize;

包賠 guarantee to pay compensation;
理賠 settle a claim;
索賠 demand compensation;
退賠 return what one has unlawfully taken or pay compensation for it;

pei4

pei

【沛】 (1) abundant; copious; (2) quickly; rapidly; suddenly; (3) fall prostrate; (4) reserve water for irrigation; (5) great; high; tall;

[沛然] copious;
沛然雨下 there is a heavy downpour;

充沛 abundant; full of; plentiful;
顛沛 be in destitution; suffer setbacks;
豐沛 plentiful;

pei

【佩】 (1) put on; wear; (2) admire; have a high opinion of; have admiration for; look up to; think highly of;

[佩帶] put on; wear;

[佩服] admire; have a high opinion of; have admiration for;
佩服得五體投地 be struck with admiration;

敬佩 admire; esteem;
欽佩 admire; esteem; respect;
玉佩 jade pendant;
擇佩 choose a spouse;

pei

【帔】 cap worn by women;

pei

【珮】 jade pendant;

pei

【配】 (1) join in marriage; match sb with sb; (2) mate animals; (3) compound; mix; (4) allocate; apportion; distribute according to plan; fit out; ration; (5) coordinate; fit out; (6) make a pair; match; pair; (7) be worthy of; deserve;

[配備] (1) allocate; fit out; provide; (2) deploy; dispose; (3) equipment; outfit;

[配菜] fixings; jardiniere; side dish;

[配錯] mismatch;

[配詞] set words;
為曲調配詞 setting words to a tune;

[配搭] accompany; match; supplement;

[配得上] be worthy of; deserve;

[配對] (1) make a pair; pair; (2) association; mate; pairing; (3) matched pairs;
觸離配對 touch-and-go pairing;
隔場配對 pairing of interlaced field;
染色體配對 chromosome pairing;

[配額] quota;
配額制 quota system;
分配配額 allocated quota;
共同配額 common quota;
絕對配額 absolute quota;
雙邊配額 bilateral quota;

[配方] formula;
天然配方 natural formula;

[配合] (1) concert; cooperate; coordinate; (2) match; fit;
配合默契 cooperate harmoniously;
配合行動 take concerted action;
粗配合 coarse fit;
互相配合 coordinate with each other;
間隙配合 clearance fit;
緊動配合 close running fit;
鬆轉配合 coarse clearance fit;

[配給] allocate; ration; rationing;
配給物 allocation;
石油配給 oil rationing;
信用配給 credit rationing;

[配件] (1) accessory part; (2) replacement;
附加配件 bolt-on component; bolt-on part;

[配角] (1) co-star; (2) bit part; second banana; straight man; supporting actor;
男配角 male supporting role; supporting actor;
~ 最佳男配角 best supporting actor;
女配角 supporting actress;
~ 最佳女配角 best supporting actress;
飾演配角 play a supporting role;
無聲配角 supernumerary;

[配料] ingredient;
一種配料 an ingredient;

[配偶] consort; mate; partner; spouse;
正交配偶 orthogonal mate;

[配套] assort; complement; form a complete set;
配套包裝 set package;
配套成龍 fill in the gaps to complete a set; serialize;
配套措施 support measures;
配套服務 necessary service;
~ 配套服務項目 projects of supplementary service;
配套改革 coordinated reforms;
~ 配套改革措施 measures of supplementary reforms;
整體配套 whole system;

[配位] complexing; coordination;
配位滴定法 complexometry;
配位基 ligand;
~ 單配位基 unidentated ligand;
~ 聚合配位基 polymeric ligand;
配位體 ligand;
~ 交聯配位體 crosslinking ligand;
~ 質子化配位體 protonated ligand;
配位酮 complexon;
次最優配位 suboptimal coordination;
反饋配位 back coordination;
概念配位 conceptual coordination;
三配位 three-fold coordination;
實時配位 real-time coordination;
數字配位 digital coordination;
組織配位 structural coordination;

[配藥] dispense a prescription;
配藥處 dispensary;

[配音] dubbing;
配音導演 dubbing director;
配音機 dubbing machine;
配音片 dubbed film;
配音室 dubbing studio;
配音員 mixer;
~ 混合配音員 dubbing mixer;
後期配音 post dubbing;
華語配音 dubbing in Chinese;
攝製後配音 post-synchronization;

[配樂] dub in background music; incidental music; underscore;
配樂法 orchestration;

[配置] allocate; configuration; configure; deploy; dispose;
優化配置 optimize resource allocation;

[配子] gamete;
配子囊 gametangium;
配子生殖 gametogony;
配子體 gametophyte;
配子細胞 gametid;
配子形成 gamete formation; gametogenesis;
雌配子 female gamete;
雄配子 male gamete;
游動配子 zoogamete;

般配 be well matched; match each other;
搬配 unequally matched in marriage;
比配 match each other;
不配 (1) not qualified to; unworthy of; (2) mismatch;
搭配 (1) assort in pairs; arrange in groups; co-ordinate; combine; (2) collocation;
調配 allocate; deploy;
分配 allot; allotment; apportion; apportionment; assign; assignment; distribute; distribution;
婚配 marry; wed;
繼配 second wife;
交配 copulate; copulation; mating;

攀配 marry up to higher social level;
匹配 (1) marry; mate; (2) match; matching;
失配 mismatch;
調配 blend; mix;
相配 match up; match well; mesh with;
修配 make repairs; supply replacements;
許配 affiance; be affianced to; be betrothed to; betroth one's daughter to;
元配 first wife;
原配 first wife;
支配 (1) allocate; budget; (2) control; dominate;
裝配 assemble; fit together;

pei
【旆】 (1) banner; flag; streamer; (2) pennon with edge of another colour;

pei
【霈】 (1) rain; torrential rain; (2) favour; good grace;

pei
【轡】 bridle; rein;
［轡勒］ reins and bit;
［轡頭］ bridle;

pen¹
pen
【噴】 (1) blow; gush; spout; spurt; (2) splash; spray; sprinkle;
［噴薄］ gush; in a hushing manner; spurt;
噴薄欲出 (of the sun) emerging in all its splendour;
［噴出］ blowout; expulsion;
［噴燈］ blowlamp; blowtorch;
［噴發］ eruption;
高源噴發 plateau eruptions;
裂縫噴發 fissure eruption;
區域噴發 areal eruption;
［噴髮膠］ hairspray;
［噴飯］ laugh so hard as to spew one's food; split one's sides with laughter;
［噴粉］ dust; dusting;
噴粉機 duster; sprayer;
~畜力噴粉機 animal duster;
~飛機噴粉機 airplane duster;
~鼓風式噴粉機 blower duster;
~噴霧噴粉機 spray duster;
作物噴粉 crop dusting;
［噴管］ nozzle;
旋轉噴管 spin nozzle;
［噴焊器］ blowpipe;
低壓噴焊器 injector blowpipe;
電弧噴焊器 electric blowpipe;
［噴灌］ sprinkle;
噴灌機 sprinkler;
~環形噴灌機 circular sprinkler;
~遠射程噴灌機 long-range sprinkler;
噴灌器 sprinkler;
~旋轉式噴灌器 rotating sprinkler;
~搖臂式噴灌器 swing arm sprinkler;
［噴壺］ sprinkling can;
［噴火器］ flame thrower;
［噴淋］ spray;
噴淋洗滌 washing spray;
冷噴淋 cold water spray;
冷卻噴淋 chilling spray;
［噴流］ jet;
環形噴流 annular jet;
空氣噴流 air jet;
［噴碼機］ inkjet printer;
［噴氣］ blow; air injection;
噴氣發動機 jet engine;
噴氣飛機 jet aircraft;
~螺旋槳噴氣飛機 jet-propelled aeroplane;
噴氣推動 jet propulsion;
［噴槍］ airbrush;
［噴灑］ splash; spray; sprinkle;
噴灑設備 spray appliance;
［噴射］ (1) atomization; (2) inject; injection; (3) spray; squirt;
噴射機 jet;
~垂直起降噴射機 jump jet;
噴射劑 propellant;
~氣溶膠噴射劑 aerosol propellant;
噴射器 atomizer; injector; sprayer;
~艙底噴射器 bilge injector;
~火炬噴射器 torch atomizer;
~火焰噴射器 flame sprayer;
~排氣噴射器 exhaust steam injector;
~氣流噴射器 steam jet atomizer;
定壓噴射 constant pressure injection;
空氣噴射 air injection;
離心噴射 centrifugal atomization;
燃油噴射 fuel injection;
無氣噴射 airless injection;
［噴水］ dabble; spray; water spray;
噴水池 fountain;
噴水器 hydraulic spray; perforated water spray;
~上噴水器 top water sprays;
地下噴水 groundwater discharge;
［噴嚏］ sneeze;

打噴嚏 sneeze;
[噴頭] shower head;
手噴頭 portable shower head;
[噴塗] spray; spraying;
噴塗法 spraying;
~火焰噴塗法 blast flame spraying;
空氣噴塗 air spray;
熱噴塗 hot spraying;
自動噴塗 automatic spraying;
[噴吐] gush; spurt;
[噴霧] atomization; mist spray; spray;
噴霧機 atomizer; sprayer;
~帶狀噴霧機 band sprayer;
~動力噴霧機 motor atomizer;
~鼓風噴霧機 air-blast sprayer;
~航空噴霧機 aerial sprayer;
~桶式噴霧機 barrel sprayer;
~旋轉式噴霧機 rotary atomizer;
噴霧劑 spray;
~辣椒噴霧劑 pepper spray;
噴霧器 atomizer; sprayer;
~高壓空氣噴霧器 high-pressure air atomizer;
~肩掛式噴霧器 sprayer knapsack;
~間歇式噴霧器 sprayer-intermittent;
~離心噴霧器 centrifugal atomizer;
~氣流噴霧器 gas stream atomizer;
~氣壓噴霧器 air-blast atomizer;
~農用噴霧器 agroatomizer;
~扇式噴霧器 fan atomizer;
~雙聯式噴霧器 duplex-type atomizer;
~套式噴霧器 sleeve atomizer;
~小型噴霧器 aerosol;
~針形噴霧器 pintle atomizer;
~轉環霧化器 rotary cup atomizer;
點滴噴霧 dripping-drop atomization;
化學噴霧 chemical spray;
加壓噴霧 pressurized spray;
氣壓噴霧 air-blast atomizing;
燃料噴霧 fuel spray;
[噴嘴] (1) atomizer; (2) jet; nozzle; spray head; spray nozzle;
斷火噴嘴 blow-off nozzle;
環形噴嘴 annular nozzle;
加速噴嘴 accelerating jet; acceleration nozzle;
可調噴嘴 adjustable jet;
鹽水噴嘴 brine-spray nozzle;
軸針式噴嘴 pintle-type atomizer;

敞噴 open flow;
井噴 blowout;
氣噴 (of gas) blow out;
嚏噴 sneeze;
香噴噴 (1) sweet-smelling; (2) appetizing; savoury;

pen

【歕】 blow; puff out; snort; spurt;

pen[2]

pen

【盆】 (1) basin; pot; tub; (2) a basin of; a plate of; a pot of; a tub of;
[盆地] basin; bowl; saucer;
谷盆地 valley basin;
鍋狀盆地 cauldron basin;
集水盆地 catchment basin;
山間盆地 intermontane basin;
[盆花] potted flower;
[盆景] bonsai; potted landscape;
[盆栽] pot culture;
盆栽植物 pot plant; potted plant;
[盆子] basin; pot;

便盆 bedpan;
缸盆 blazed earthen basin;
骨盆 pelvis;
海盆 sea basin;
花盆 flowerpot;
火盆 brazier; fire basket; fire pan; fired devil;
聚寶盆 cornucopia; treasure bowl — a place rich in natural resources;
臉盆 washbasin; washbowl;
臨盆 be giving birth to a child; be in labour; parturition;
濾盆 colander;
木盆 wooden basin;
尿盆 chamber pot; urinal;
傾盆 cloudburst; heavy downpour; torrential rain pour down in torrents;
炭盆 brazier; charcoal brazier;
洗衣盆 washtub;
一個盆 a basin;
一盆 (1) a basin; a bowl; a plate; a pot; a tray; a tub; (2) a basin of; a bowl of; a plate of; a pot of; a tray of; a tub of;
浴盆 bath; bathtub;
澡盆 bathtub;

pen

【湓】 (1) gush forth; (2) a river in Jiangxi;
[湓溢] overflow;
[湓湧] gush; surge;

peng[1]

peng

【抨】 (1) censure; impeach; (2) assail verbally; attack; attack verbally; lash out at;

［抨擊］ assail verbally; attack verbally; flay; lash out at;

猛烈抨擊 inveigh against; lash out; stinging attack;

［抨彈］ attack;

peng

【怦】 anxious; eager; impulsive;

［怦怦］ (1) anxious to do sth; eager to do sth; (2) become excited;

［怦然］ with a sudden shock;

怦然心動 eager with excitement; palpitate with excitement;

peng

【砰】 (1) sound of crashing stones; (2) bang; loud, deafening sound; pow;

［砰擊］ bang; thump; thunder; zap;

［砰砰聲］ bang; crack; phut;

peng

【烹】 (1) boil; cook; (2) fry quickly; in hot oil and stir in sauce;

［烹飪］ cooking; culinary art;

烹飪法 cookery;

烹飪技術 culinary skills;

烹飪課程 cookery course;

烹飪設備 cooking equipment; cooking facilities;

烹飪術 cookery;

烹飪書 cookbook; cookery book; recipe book;

烹飪藝術 culinary art;

烹飪油 cooking oil;

烹飪用的 cooking;

烹飪用具 cookware;

高級烹飪 haute cuisine;

素食烹飪 vegetarian cuisine;

［烹調］ cook dishes;

烹調鍋 cooking pot;

peng

【硼】 (1) boracium; (2) sound of splashing;

［硼砰］ sound of water splashing or sloshing;

［硼磕］ (1) loud and clear voice; (2) sound of crashing stones;

［硼化］ boration;

［硼砂］ borax;

［硼酸］ (1) borate; (2) boric acid;

硼酸胺 ammonium borate;

硼酸鋇 barium borate;

硼酸丁酯 butyl borate;

硼酸鈣 calcium borate;

硼酸汞 mercury borate;

硼酸鎂 magnesium borate;

硼酸鈉 sodium borate;

硼酸鉛 lead borate;

硼酸軟膏 boracic ointment;

硼酸水 boracic solution;

硼酸鍶 strontium borate;

硼酸戊酯 amyl borate;

硼酸鋅 zinc borate;

硼酸乙脂 ethyl borate;

摻硼 boron doping;

金剛硼 adamantine boron;

三丙硼 tripropyl boron;

氮化硼 borazon; boron;

peng

【澎】 breaker; spatter; splash; the roaring of colliding billows;

［澎湃］ surge; upsurge;

peng[2]

peng

【芃】 growing luxuriantly; lush;

peng

【朋】 friend;

［朋輩］ friends;

朋輩壓力 peer pressure;

［朋比為奸］ act in collusion with; claw me and I will claw thee; claw me, claw thee; collude in doing evil; conspire for illegal ends; gang up for evil purposes; join in plotting reason; play booty; scratch me and I'll scratch you; scratch my back and I'll scratch yours; work hand in glove with sb for evil doings;

［朋黨］ clique; faction; gang;

朋黨熾結 political cliques spread about;

［朋友］ buddy; chum; friend;

朋友的朋友 a friend of a friend;

朋友千個少，仇人一個多 one foe is too many and a hundred friends too few;

朋友圈 circle of friends;

背叛朋友 betray one's friend; forsake a friend;

背棄朋友 abandon one's friend; go back

on one's friend;
成為朋友 become friends;
出賣朋友 sell sb down the river; sell the pass;
搭話朋友 speaking acquaintance;
點頭朋友 nodding acquaintance;
共同的朋友 mutual friend;
夠朋友 deserve to be called a true friend;
好朋友 bosom buddy; chum; firm friend; good friend;
狐朋狗友 bad friends; barratrous companions; disreputable gangs; evil associates;
壞朋友 vicious companion;
家庭朋友 family friend;
假朋友 false friend;
交朋友 associate with; be in with sb; buddy up to sb; chum around with sb; cosort with sb; get off with; keep company with; keep terms with; make friends with; pat up with; take up with;
結交朋友 make new friends;
酒肉朋友 convivial companions; mercenary friend; fair-weather friend; wine-and-meat friend;
老朋友 buddy; crony; old egg; old friend; old guy; old pal;
良朋密友 bosom friends; great friendship; virtuous companions and intimate friends;
良朋益友 virtuous companions and worthy friends;
男朋友 boyfriend; old man;
~關係固定的男朋友 steady boyfriend;
男性朋友 male friend;
你的朋友 a friend of yours; your friend;
女朋友 girlfriend; lady friend;
~關係固定的女朋友 steady girlfriend;
女性朋友 female friend;
拋棄朋友 abandon one's friend;
人類最好的朋友 man's best friend;
辱罵朋友 abuse a friend;
我的朋友 a friend of mine; my friend;
小朋友 (1) children; (2) child; little boy; little girl;
一群朋友 a circle of friends; a posse of friends;
一位朋友 a friend;
一直是朋友 remain friends;
淫朋狎友 debauching company;
有朋友 have a friend;
知心朋友 bosom friend; intimate friend;
最好的朋友 ace buddy; best friend;

賓朋 guests and friends;
無朋 incomparable; matchless; peerless;
友朋 companions; friends;
醉朋 alcoholic; drunkard;

peng
【彭】 (1) a surname; (2) big; (3) longevity; (4) proud;

peng
【棚】 awning; mat awning; shed; tent;
［棚車］ boxcar;
［棚架］ arbour; canopy frame; shed frame;
［棚屋］ cabana; hut;
［棚子］ shack; shed;

芭棚 screen of straw for barring wind;
彩棚 decorated tent;
綵棚 gaily decorated wooden framework;
草棚 straw shed; thatched shack;
搭棚 (1) put up a shed; (2) build a scalfold;
頂棚 ceiling;
鴿棚 dove house; dove shed;
工棚 (1) builders' temporary shed; (2) work shed;
花棚 flower stand;
涼棚 arbour; mat awning; mat shelter; pergola
寮棚 hut; shed;
陸棚 continental shelf;
馬棚 stable;
牛棚 byre; cowshed;
天棚 (1) ceiling; (2) awning;
席棚 (1) mat shed; (2) mat hoarding;
畜棚 arn;
雨棚 canopy;
罩棚 awning over a gateway or a courtyard;

peng
【硼】 borax;

peng
【澎】 Pescadores;

peng
【蓬】 (1) bitter fleabane; (2) dishevelled; fluffy; rough; rumple; straggle; unkempt; (3) humble; (4) exuberant; flourishing; full of vitality; on the rise; rise up luxuriantly; spring up vigorously; surge forward;
［蓬蓽］ one's humble house;
蓬蓽生輝 my humble house is honoured

P

by your presence; your gracious presence adds glitters to my humble house;
蓬門篳戶 a raspberry door and a bamboo house — house of a poor man;

［蓬勃］ exuberant; flourishing; full of vitality; going full steam ahead;
蓬勃發展 develop tempestuously; forge ahead vigorously; go full speed ahead; grow apace; surge forward full of vigour; surge vigorously forward;
蓬勃高漲 in full swing; on the rise; vigorous growth;
蓬勃興起 rise up luxuriantly; spring up vigorously; surge forward;

［蓬戶瓮牖］ humble cottage; houses of the destitute; miserable living; with weaved fleabane as a door and broken urns as a window;

［蓬累而行］ wander about with bag and baggage;

［蓬亂］ dishevelled; rough; rumple; straggle; unkempt;
頭髮蓬亂 with one's hair tousled;

［蓬蓬］ thick and disorderly;
蓬蓬勃勃 full of vitality; luxuriant and flourishing; rapidly develop; with tremendous momentum; with vigour;

［蓬飄萍轉］ be gone with the raspberry and turned with the duck weed — drift from place to place;

［蓬生麻中］ a raspberry grows among the hemp — the influence of good friends;

［蓬首垢面］ a filthy appearance; unkempt; with dishevelled hair and grimy face; with unkempt hair and a dirty face;

［蓬鬆］ fluffy; puffy;

［蓬頭］ dishevelled hair;
蓬頭垢面 dishevelled hair and dirty face; unkempt appearance; with uncombed hair and dirty face; with dishevelled hair and a dirty face;
蓬頭散髮 shock-head; shockheaded; with dishevelled hair;

飛蓬 bitter fleabane;
蓮蓬 seedpod of the lotus;
亂蓬蓬 dishevelled; jumbled; tangled;
一蓬 a clump of;
轉蓬 float about in a shiftless way, like a leaf blown about;

peng

【膨】 bulge; dilate; expand; inflate; swell;

［膨大］ expand; inflate;

［膨脹］ bulge; dilatation; dilate; dilation; expand; inflate; swell; expansion;
膨脹測定法 dilatometry;
膨脹計 dilatometer;
～示差熱膨脹計 differential dilatometer;
～真空膨脹計 vacuum dilatometer;
膨脹系數 coefficient of expansion;
膨脹儀 dilatometer;
～干涉膨脹儀 interference dilatometer;
～熱膨脹儀 thermal dilatometer;
方體膨脹 cubic dilation;
絕熱膨脹 adiabatic expansion;
熱膨脹 thermal dilation; thermal expansion;
熔化膨脹 melting dilation;
時間膨脹 time dilation;
體積膨脹 cubical dilatation; volume dilatation; volume dilation;
限制膨脹 confined expansion;
線性膨脹 linear dilatation; linear expansion;
需求膨脹 demand inflation;

peng

【篷】 (1) awning; canvass; covering; (2) boat; sail;

［篷帆］ sail;
一套篷帆 a suit of sails;

［篷頂］ top of a tent;
防雨篷頂 flysheet;

［篷帳］ canvass;

車篷 awning of a cart;
船篷 (1) mat or wooden roof of a boat; (2) sail;
帳篷 tent;

peng

【鵬】 roc;

［鵬程萬里］ have a bright future; rise to great heights;

鯤鵬 roc;

peng³

peng

【捧】 (1) hold or carry in both hands; (2) boost; exault;

［捧場］ boost sb in the show; sing the praises of;

P

捧場的人 claqueur;
吹噓捧場 laud; lavish and sing and the praises on others;

［捧腹］ split one's sides with laughter;
捧腹大笑 be convulsed with laughter; burst one's sides with laughter; burst with laughing; crack up; knock in the aisles; lay in the aisles; rock in the aisles; roll in the aisles; shake one's sides with laughter; split one's sides;
捧腹絕倒 fold up; in convulsions of laughter; split one's sides with laughter;
令人捧腹 make one burst into laughter;

吹捧 boast and flatter; laud to the skies;
瞎捧 heap praises on sb blindly;
一捧 a double handful of;

peng⁴

peng

【碰】 (1) bump; touch; (2) meet; run into; (3) take one's chance;

［碰杯］ clink glasses; have a drink;
碰杯祝酒 clink glasses and drink a toast;

［碰壁］ be rebuffed; run into a brick wall; run up against a stone wall;
到處碰壁 from pillar to post; from post to pillar; get into trouble hither and thither; run into snags everywhere; run one's head against stone walls everywhere;
四處碰壁 run into snags everywhere;

［碰不得的人］ a forbidden game;

［碰倒］ upset;

［碰到］ meet with; run into;

［碰見］ alight on; alight upon; bump into; chance upon; come across; come on; come upon; cross sb's path; cross the path of sb; encounter; fall across; fall among; fall in with; light on; light upon; meet unexpectedly; meet with; run across; run into;

［碰牌］ (mahjong) draw a tile to make three tiles of a kind;

［碰碰車］ bumper car; dodgem; dodgem car; Scooter car;
碰碰車遊戲 dodgems;

［碰巧］ as it happened; as luck would have it; by chance; by coincidence; it just so happened that;

［碰傷］ be injured or damaged after being hit by sth;

［碰頭］ (1) meet and discuss; meet up; put heads together; (2) see each other; (3) crash; collide; conflict;
碰頭會 working meeting;

［碰撞］ (1) collide; collision; crash; knock against; run foul of; run into; (2) cannon; hit; impact;
碰撞爆破 collision;
碰撞聲 clunk;
互相碰撞 run foul of each other;

磕碰 (1) collide with; knock against; (2) clash; squabble;
正碰 direct impact;

pi¹

pi

【匹】 a bolt of; a roll of; numerary particle for horses;

pi

【丕】 (1) distinguished; great; vast; (2) in observance of;

pi

【批】 (1) slap sb; (2) criticize; rebut; refute; repudiate; subject to criticism; (3) write comments on; written instructions; (4) wholesale; (5) a batch; a crop; a group; a load; a number; a platoon; a stock; a trove; (6) a batch of; a crop of; a group of; a line of; a load of; a lot of; a number of; a platoon of; a provision of; a rush of; a shipment of; a spate of; a stick of; a stock of; a trove of;

［批駁］ (1) criticize; refute; repel; repute; (2) veto an opinion or a request from a subordinate body;
嚴加批駁 sternly refute;

［批點］ punctuate and annotate;

［批斗］ criticize and denounce sb; criticize and struggle;

［批發］ (1) wholesale; (2) be authorized for dispatch;
批發價 wholesale price;
批發商 wholesaler;
~百貨批發商 general line wholesaler;

～分配批發商 carlot wholesaler;
～全國性批發商 national wholesaler;
～郵購批發商 mail order wholesaler;
～雜貨批發商 general merchandise wholesaler;
～正規批發商 regular wholesaler;
批發市場 wholesale market;
批發中心 wholesale centre;
總批發 wholesale distribution;

[批覆] give an official, written reply to a subordinate body;

[批改] correct;
批改作業 correct students' assignments;

[批亢搗虛] attack the enemy at his weak spots; attack the vital position and unguarded places of the enemy; strike the important position and make a surprise attack on the weak defence of the enemy;

[批號] batch number;

[批頰] slap sb in the face;

[批量] batch; lot;
批量到達 batch arrival;
批量生產 mass production; produce in batches; produce in quantity;

[批判] (1) criticize; debunk; repudiate; (2) critique;

[批評] brickbat; criticize; point out faults;
批評標準 criterion of criticism;
批評浪潮 storm of criticism;
挨批評 be criticized;
點名批評 name and shame;
鑒賞批評 appreciative criticism;
教學批評 teaching criticism;
接受批評 accept criticisms;
口頭批評 oral criticism;
猛烈批評 lambast;
受到批評 get it in the neck;
受到新聞界的批評 be given a bad press; get a bad press;
瞎批評 criticize blindly;
辛辣的批評 biting remark;
嚴厲批評 censure; criticize severely; hit out at; scarify; tear sb to pieces; tear sth to pieces; tear sth to shreds; trash;
藝術批評 art criticism;
有待批評 be open to criticism;
直言不諱的批評 a bit of one's mind;
自我批評 self-criticism;

[批示] (1) written instructions; (2) write an official comment;

[批語] (1) remarks on a piece of writing; (2) comments and instructions;

[批閱] read and amend; read over; read over and give comments;

[批註] (1) annotate on; comment on; (2) annotations; commentaries; marginalia;

[批准] accede; admit of; allow; approve; authorize; clearance; concede; endorse; give a license to; give permission; give sanction to; grant one's request; grant sb permission to; let; license; permit; ratify; sanction;
批准建議 give sanction to the proposals;
得到批准 be given the ratification;
等待批准 wait for ratification;
正式批准 official approval;
自動批准 automatic approval;

挨批 be criticized; be denounced; be subjected to criticism;
報批 request authorization; submit sth for approval;
成批 group by group; in batches;
催批 press for instructions from superiors;
大批 a smart of; large quantities of;
躉批 wholesale;
分批 in batches; in turn;
核批 examine and give comment and instruction;
眉批 notes and commentaries at the top of a page;
評批 evaluative;
簽批 sign and authorize;
肉批 meat pie;
審批 examine and approve;
一大批 a host of; a rush of; an army of;
一批 (1) a batch; a shipment; an array; (2) a batch of; a body of; a consort of; a crop of; a galaxy of; a group of; a muster of; a number of; a party of; a set of; a stock of; a supply of; an array of; an assortment of;
御批 comments made by the emperor;
整批 batch;
朱批 comments or remarks written in red with a brush;
硃批 imperial rescript;

pi

【坯】 unfired bricks, pieces of pottery, etc.;

[坯布] unbleached and undyed cloth;

[坯塊] compact;

精壓坯塊 coining compact;
曲面坯塊 curved-face compact;
雙金屬坯塊 bimetal compact;
柱狀坯塊 cylindrical compact;

pi

【披】 (1) drape over; put on; spread; throw on; wrap around; (2) lay bare; lay open; open; spread out; unbosom; unroll; (3) blaze; break open; crack; cut through; force through; split open;

[披髮] dishevelled hair;
披髮跣足 with dishevelled hair and bare feet;
披髮佯狂 have shaggy hair and to feign madness;

[披風] cape; cloak; mantle; poncho;

[披掛] in military attire; put on one's armour;
披掛上陣 put on one's armour and go into battle;

[披紅戴花] have red silk draped over one's shoulders and flowers pinned on one's breast; wear red silk ribbons and red plowers pinned on one's dress;

[披甲] put on an armour;

[披肩] cape; pashmina; shawl; wraps;
一件披肩 a shawl;

[披巾] shawl;

[披覽] open and read; peruse;

[披瀝] (1) open and sincere; (2) loyal and faithful;
披瀝赤忱 proclaim one's heartfelt devotion to;
披瀝肝膽 open up one's heart; open-hearted;

[披露] announce; make public; publish;
披露肝膽 open up one's heart;
披露心腹 disclose a secret; tell one's innermost thoughts;
披露心曲 disburden one's conscience; disclose one's pent-up feelings; lay bare one's heart; open one's mind; tell one's innermost thoughts; unburden one's mind;
被披露 be brought to light; come to light;

[披麻] wear a sackcloth gown;
披麻帶孝 dress in the coarse hempen cloth of mourning; in deep mourning; put on mourning apparel; wear a sackcloth gown as a sign of mourning;
披麻救火 bring trouble to oneself;

[披靡] (1) be blown away by the wind; be swept by the wind; (2) be routed; flee; put to rout;
所向披靡 advance victoriously everywhere; carry all before one; carry the world before one; mow down all resistance; victorious wherever it goes;

[披散] hang down loosely; stray;

[披頭] disheveled hair;
披頭散髮 dishevelled; have one's hair hanging loose; tousled; unkempt;
披頭跣足 her hair is down and she is barefooted;

[披衣] throw on gown;
披衣而起 throw on gown and rise;

[披閱] open and read; peruse;
披閱群書 peruse books of all sorts; read widely;

紛披 spreading disorderly;

pi

【被】 same as 披;

pi

【砒】 arsenic;

[砒霜] arsenic; white arsenic;
甲之熊掌，乙之砒霜 one person's meat is another person's poison;

[砒酸] arsenic acid;

白砒 white arsenic;

pi

【紕】 blunder; error; mistake; slip;

[紕漏] careless mistake; slip; small accident;

[紕繆] error; mistake;

pi

【劈】 (1) chop; cleave; cut through; level off; rive; split up; (2) right against; (3) strike;

[劈開] rive; split;

[劈理] cleavage;

[劈臉] direct in the face; right in the face;

[劈啪] crack;
劈啪聲 crackling;
~發劈啪聲 crackle;
劈里啪啦 crackle; splutter;

[劈山] blast cliffs; cut through hills; level off hilltops;

劈山改河 cut through a hill to change the course of a river;
劈山引水 cleave hills and lead in water; cut through mountains to bring in water; split up a hill to let the water through; tunnel through mountains to conduct water from one place to another;
劈山造田 level hilltops to enlarge farmland; level off hilltops and turn them into flat fields;

[劈手] make a sudden snatch;

[劈頭] (1) right in the face; straight on the head; (2) at the very start; right at the beginning;
劈頭蓋臉 a vicious assault on a person; direct to one's head and face; right in the face; scold sb to his face;

叉劈 divergent;

pi

【霹】 thunder;

[霹雷] thunderbolt; thunderclap;

[霹靂] thunderbolt; thunderclap;
霹靂舞 break dance; break dancing;
一聲霹靂 a clap of thunder;

pi²

pi

【皮】 (1) skin; (2) hide; leather; (3) fur; (4) cover; wrapper; (5) surface; (6) broad, flat peice; sheet; (7) become soft and soggy; (8) naughty; (9) casehardened; (10) rubber; (11) a surname;

[皮襖] fur-lined jacket;

[皮包] briefcase; leather handbag;
皮包公司 briefcase company;

[皮層] cortex;
皮層形成 cortification;
大腦皮層 brain cortex; cerebral cortex;
木栓皮層 cork cortex;
聽覺皮層 auditory cortex;
胃皮層 gastral cortex;
腦皮層 cortex;
小腦皮層 cerebellar cortex;

[皮帶] (1) leather belt; (2) belt;
皮帶輪 pulley;
~車軸皮帶輪 axle pulley;
~回行皮帶輪 backing pulley;
~離合皮帶輪 clutch pulley;
~鑄鐵皮帶輪 cast-iron belt pulley;
一條皮帶 a belt;

[皮袋] (1) skin; (2) budget;
滿皮袋 skinful;

[皮蛋] preserved egg;
一隻皮蛋 a preserved egg;

[皮膚] skin;
皮膚癌 cancer of the skin; cutaneous carinoma; skin cancer;
皮膚白 fair skin; pale skin; white skin;
皮膚白喉 cutaneous diphtheria;
皮膚變黃 xanthoderma;
皮膚變色 dyschromia;
皮膚病 dermatosis; dermatopathy; skin ailment; skin complaint; skin condition; skin disease;
~皮膚病學 dermatology;
皮膚病學者 dermatologist;
~皮膚病醫生 dermatologist;
~皮膚病預防 dermatophylaxis;
~癌前皮膚病 precancerous dermatosis;
~癌前期皮膚病 precancerous dermatosis;
~工業職業性皮膚病 industrial occupational dermatoses;
~化膿皮膚病 pyoderma;
~結核皮膚病 tuberculosis cutis;
~潰瘍性皮膚病 ulcerative dermatosis;
~菱形皮膚病 diamond skin disease;
~農業職業性皮膚病 agricultural occupational dermatoses;
~糖尿病性皮膚病 diabetic dermopathy;
職業性皮膚病 industrial dermatosis; occupational dermatosis; professional dermatosis;
皮膚病變 dermopathy;
~糖尿病皮膚病變 diabetic dermopathy;
皮膚病藥 dermics;
皮膚搽劑 liniment;
皮膚刺激 skin irritation;
皮膚充血 dermahemia; dermohemia;
皮膚出血 dermatorrhagia;
~寄生性皮膚出血 dermatorrhagia parasitica;
皮膚發育不良 dermatodysplasia;
皮膚發育不全 adermogenesis;
皮膚反射 skin reflex;
皮膚反應 dermoreaction;
皮膚肥厚 dermatauxe;
皮膚乾燥病 xeroderma;
皮膚乾燥症 xerosis cutis;

皮膚骨化 osteodermia;
~皮膚骨化病 osteosis cutis;
皮膚骨瘤 osteoma cutis;
皮膚紅斑狼瘡 cutaneous lupus erythematosus;
皮膚過敏 skin allergy;
皮膚呼吸 skin respiration;
皮膚節 dermatomere;
皮膚結核 dermal tuberculosis; tuberculosis of skin;
~皮膚結核病 dermal tuberculosis; tuberculosis of skin;
~硬化性皮膚結核 tuberculosis cutis indurativa;
皮膚結膜炎 dermatoconjunctivitis;
皮膚結石 skin stone;
皮膚淋巴結病 dermatopathic lymphadenopathy;
皮膚淋巴瘤 lymphoma cutis;
皮膚毛細管破裂 dermatorrhexis;
皮膚霉菌病 dermatophytosis;
皮膚膿腫 dermapostasis;
皮膚青紫 cyanosis;
皮膚軟化 dermalaxia;
皮膚色調 skin tone;
皮膚鬆弛 dermatolysis; one's skin sags;
~皮膚鬆弛症 cutis laxa;
皮膚鬆垂 anetoderma;
皮膚損害 efflorescence;
皮膚萎縮 atrophoderma;
~皮膚萎縮症 atrophodermatosis;
蠕蟲樣皮膚萎縮 atrophoderma vermiculata;
~神經性皮膚萎縮 atrophoderma neuriticum;
皮膚無反應 dermoanergy;
皮膚血管炎 angiodermatitis;
皮膚學 dermatology;
皮膚炎 dermatitis;
皮膚移植 epidermization;
皮膚有光澤 one's skin glows; one's skin shines;
皮膚疣 thymian;
皮膚真菌 dermatophyte;
~皮膚真菌病 dermatomycosis;
皮膚腫塊 phyma;
白嫩的皮膚 fair skin;
白皙的皮膚 lily-white skin;
保護皮膚 protect one's skin;
刺激皮膚 irritate one's skin;
乾性皮膚 dry skin;
敏感性皮膚 sensitive skin;
曬傷皮膚 burn one's skin;
舒緩皮膚 soothe one's skin;
油性皮膚 oily skin;
長雀斑的皮膚 freckled skin;

[皮革] hide; leather;
人造皮革 imitation leather; pleather;

[皮骨] skin and bones;
僅存皮骨 be a skin and bones; lean person;
皮包骨 a bag of bones; a rack of bones; a stack of bones; skin and bones; skinny;
~皮包骨的 scrawny;

[皮殼] leather case;

[皮貨] leather goods;
皮貨店 furrier;

[皮甲] leather armour;

[皮筋儿] rubber band;

[皮裏陽秋] criticism kept to oneself; refrain from outspoken attack; well-covered remarks;

[皮毛] (1) coat; fur; skin and hair; (2) a smattering of; a superficial knowledge of;
皮毛畫 fur patchwork;
皮毛之見 skin-deep views; superficial opinions;
得其皮毛 have superficial knowledge;
僅識皮毛 have superficial knowledge; have scrappy knowledge; only acquainted with skin and hair;
略知皮毛 have only superficial understanding of sth;
皮之不存，毛將焉附 if the skin does not exist, to what could the hair attach;

[皮帽] fur hat;

[皮面] leather binding;

[皮球] ball; rubber ball;
皮球性子—一拍就跳 a rubber ball temper — you pat it and it will jump up; hot-tempered;
踢皮球 kick a ball;
~擅於踢皮球 good at escaping responsibilities;

[皮肉] flesh;
皮肉傷 flesh wound;
皮開肉綻 a mass of bruises; badly bruised; the skin is torn and the flesh gapes open; with skin cut open and flesh torn;

~打得皮開肉綻 be beaten till one's flesh is laid bare; be bruised and lacerated;
皮笑肉不笑 cold smile; false smile; skin-deep smile; put on a false smile; smile hypocritically; twist one's lips into a faint grimace of a smile;
寢其皮而食其肉 hate sb to the extreme; sleep on a person's skin and eat his flesh; sleep on a person's hide and eat his flesh;

[皮實] (1) sturdy; (2) durable;

[皮下] hypodermic; subcutaneous;
皮下血腫 ecchymosis;
皮下組織 subcutaneous tissue;
皮下注射 hypodermic injection;

[皮箱] leather suitcase; leather trunk;

[皮相] skin-deep; superficial;
皮相之談 superficial talk;

[皮鞋] leather shoes;
漆皮皮鞋 patent leather shoes;

[皮炎] dermatitis;
變應性皮炎 allergic dermatitis;
剝脫性皮炎 exfoliative dermatitis;
草地皮炎 meadow dermatitis;
刺激性皮炎 irritant dermatitis;
光化皮炎 erythema solare;
過敏性皮炎 allergic dermatitis; neurodermatitis;
壞疽性皮炎 gangrenous dermatitis;
壞死性皮炎 necrotic dermatitis;
灰色皮炎 ashy dermatitis;
急性皮炎 acute dermatitis;
接觸性皮炎 contact dermatitis;
蟎性皮炎 acarodermatitis;
尿布皮炎 diaper dermatitis;
疱疹樣皮炎 dermatitis herpetiformis;
皮脂溢性皮炎 seborrheic dermatitis;
青斑狀皮炎 livedoid dermatitis;
熱激性皮炎 dermatitis calorica;
日光性皮炎 photodermatitis;
蠕蟲性皮炎 verminous dermatitis;
神經性皮炎 neurodermatitis;
濕疹性皮炎 eczematous dermatitis;
水稻田皮炎 rice field dermatitis;
特應性皮炎 atopic dermatitis;
血吸蟲皮炎 schistosome dermatitis;
藥物性皮炎 dermatitis medicamentosa;
疣性皮炎 verrucous dermatitis;
疣狀皮炎 verrucous dermatitis;
游泳者皮炎 cercarialdermatitis; swimmer'sitch;
增生性皮炎 proliferative dermatitis;
增殖性皮炎 dermatitis vegetans;
脂溢性皮炎 seborrheic dermatitis;
職業性皮炎 occupational dermatitis;
指間皮炎 interdigital dermatitis;
趾間皮炎 interdigital dermatitis;
足皮炎 pododermatitis;

[皮衣] (1) fur garment; (2) leather coat; leather garment;
皮衣製造者 furrier;

[皮影戲] leather-silhouette show; shadow play; shadow show;

[皮質] cortex;

[皮重] tare;
法定皮重 legal tare;
估計皮重 estimated tare;
淨皮重 net tare;
平均皮重 average tare;
實際皮重 actual tare;

[皮子] (1) hide; leather; (2) fur;

扒皮 peel off the skin;
板皮 slab;
包皮 (1) wrapper; wrapping; (2) foreskin; prepuce;
剝皮 strip off the skin;
表皮 (1) epidermis; (2) cuticle;
草皮 sod; turf;
車皮 railway wagon;
扯皮 argue back and forth; dispute over trifles; wrangle;
陳皮 dried tangerine or orange peel;
地皮 (1) land for building; (2) ground;
貂皮 mink; sable; sable skin;
肚皮 belly;
粉皮 sheet jelly made from bean or sweet potato starch;
麩皮 wheat bran;
羔皮 budge; lambskin; kidskin;
刮皮 beam;
桂皮 cassia bark; Chinese cinnamon;
果皮 peel; pill; rind; skin; skin of fruit;
虎皮 tiger skin;
狐皮 fox fur;
畫皮 disguise of an evildoer; mask of an evildoer;
雞皮 chicken's skin;
麂皮 chamois leather;
痂皮 crust;
間皮 mesothelium;
拉皮 have a face-lift;

賴皮 rascally; shameless; shameless behaviour; unreasonable;
臉皮 (1) cheek; face; (2) sense of shame;
毛皮 flick; fur; leather;
面皮 face;
奶皮 skin on boiled milk;
內皮 endothelium;
牛皮 (1) cattlehide; cow leather; cowhide; (2) brag;
潑皮 rascal; rogue;
漆皮 (1) coat of paint; (2) shellac;
俏皮 (1) good-looking; handsome; lively and delightful; nice-looking; smart; winsome; (2) full of charming wits; humourous; sarcastic; witty;
去皮 peel; peeling; remove the skin; skin;
韌皮 bast of a tree;
肉皮 pork skin;
軟皮 soft leather;
桑皮 mulberry bark;
砂皮 emery cloth; emery paper;
上皮 (1) epidermium; (2) outer bark of trees;
蛇皮 snake's skin;
獸皮 animal skin; hide;
書皮 book cover; dust jacket;
樹皮 bark;
栓皮 cork;
蜕皮 exuviate; slough;
桃皮 skin of a peach;
調皮 (1) mischievous; naughty; (2) cunning; tricky; unruly; (3) play tricks;
鐵皮 iron sheet;
頭皮 (1) scalp; (2) dandruff; scurf;
蜕皮 cast off a skin; exuviate;
脱皮 peel;
頑皮 mischievous; naughty; playful;
胃皮 gastrodermis;
嬉皮 grinning;
蝦皮 dried small shrimps;
鮮皮 fresh hide; greenhide;
橡皮 (1) rubber; (2) eraser; rubber;
心皮 carpel; carpellum;
信皮 envelope;
熊皮 bearskin;
妍皮 beautiful skin;
眼皮 eyelid;
羊皮 sheepskin;
一層皮 a layer of skin;
一塊皮 an area of skin;
硬皮 callus;
柚皮 shaddock ped;
真皮 derma;
植皮 skin grafting;
種皮 seed coat;
豬皮 hogskin; pigskin;

pi

【枇】 loquat;

［枇杷］ loquat;

pi

【陂】 (1) reservoir; water pond; (2) hillside;

pi

【毗】 (1) assist; (2) adjacent to; adjoin; border on;

［毗連］ adjacent to; adjoin; border on;

［毗鄰］ adjacent to; adjoin; border on; contiguous to;

pi

【疲】 exhausted; tired; weary; worn out;

［疲憊］ become fagged; exhausted; tired out; weary; worn out;

［疲頓］ be exhausted; be tired out;

［疲乏］ weary;
疲乏不堪 be tired out; be washed out;
感到疲乏 feel weary;

［疲竭］ breakdown; exhaust;

［疲倦］ all in; all tuckered out; burn oneself out; dead beat; dead tired; do sb up; dog tired; done up; exhaust; exhausted; fatigued; feel exhausted; feel run down; feel tired; get run down; jigger; knocked out; knocked up; look run down; look tired; look worn out; look zonked; more dead than alive; overdo; run down; run sb ragged; strained; tire out; tired; tired to death; used up; walk off one's feet; wasted; weary; wiped out; work oneself to the bone; work until one drops; worn out;
感覺疲倦 feel tired;

［疲勞］ (1) fagged; fatigued; tired; weary; (2) fatigue; tiredness;
疲勞過度 excessive fatigue; overfatigue;
疲勞轟炸 air raids aimed at exhausting patience;
疲勞熱 fatigue fever;
疲勞症 apokamnosis;
疲勞沮喪 be reduced to a tired and demoralized state; tire and demoralize sb;
擺脱疲勞 relieve one's fatigue;

刺激性疲勞 stimulation fatigue;
電子疲勞 e-fatigue;
過度疲勞 excessive fatigue; overtax;
航空疲勞 astroasthenia;
極度疲勞 on the ragged edge;
減輕疲勞 lessen fatigue;
慢性疲勞 chronic fatigue;
聲帶疲勞 vocal fatigue;
聽覺疲勞 auditory fatigue;
眼疲勞 copiopia; eye strain;
援助疲勞 aid fatigue;

[疲軟] (1) fatigued and weak; (2) slump; weak;

[疲弱] tired and weak;
經濟疲弱 weakness in the economy;

[疲塌] negligent; slack;

pi

【紕】 hem ornaments;

pi

【蚍】 large ant;

[蚍蜉] ant;
蚍蜉撼大樹 ants trying to topple a giant tree — a person overrating his own strength;

pi

【郫】 (1) a town in the Spring and Autumn Period, in today's Henan Province; (2) a county in Sichuan;

[郫筒] liquor container;

pi

【啤】 character used in transliteration;

[啤酒] ale; beer;
啤酒杯 beer mug; stein;
~ 啤酒杯墊 beer mat;
啤酒泵 beerpull;
啤酒廠 brewery;
啤酒店 beerhouse;
啤酒公司 brewer; brewery;
啤酒館 ale house;
啤酒罐 beer can;
啤酒花 hop;
啤酒節 beer fest; beer festival;
啤酒沫 beer froth;
啤酒泡沫 beer froth;
啤酒瓶 beer bottle;
啤酒商 brewer;
啤酒桶 beer barrel;
餐用啤酒 table beer;
充氣啤酒 carbonized beer;
傳統啤酒 real ale;
大米啤酒 rice beer;
淡啤酒 lager; light ale; mild beer; near beer; pale ale;
淡色啤酒 ale; pale beer;
罐裝啤酒 canned beer;
黑啤酒 black beer; dark beer;
家釀啤酒 home brew;
薑汁啤酒 ginger ale; ginger beer;
浸出啤酒 infusion beer;
苦啤酒 bitter;
烈性啤酒 bock beer; stout beer;
麥芽啤酒 malt liquor;
濃味啤酒 bock beer;
瓶裝啤酒 bottled beer;
輕淡啤酒 light beer;
生啤酒 draught beer; green beer;
桶裝啤酒 keg beer;
外銷啤酒 shipping beer;
鮮啤酒 draught beer;
新啤酒 new beer; young beer;
新鮮啤酒 young beer;
一杯啤酒 a glass of beer;
一大杯啤酒 a mug of beer; a tankard of beer;
一大桶啤酒 a hogshead of beer; a vat of beer;
一罐啤酒 a can of beer;
一口啤酒 a drain of beer;
一品脱啤酒 a pint of beer;
一瓶啤哂 a bottle of beer;
一桶啤酒 a cask of beer;
一箱啤酒 a crate of beer;
一小桶啤酒 a keg of beer;
營養啤酒 nutrient beer;
走氣啤酒 stale beer;

pi

【埤】 (1) low wall; parapet; (2) add to; increase; (3) low-lying;

pi

【陴】 parapet on a city wall;

pi

【琵】 Chinese lute;

[琵琶] Chinese lute;
琵琶別抱 remarried woman; turn the back on one lover and go with another one; widow who marries a second time;
琵琶魚 (1) anglerfish; (2) frogfish;

pi

【脾】 spleen;

[脾病] lienopathy;

[脾充血] splenemphraxis;
[脾出血] splenorrhagia;
[脾大] splenomegaly;
充血性脾大 congestive splenomegaly;
熱帶脾大 tropical splenomegaly;
溶血性脾大 haemolytic splenomegaly;
[脾肺] spleen and lung;
健脾益肺 strengthening spleen and tonifying lung;
脾弱肺虛 asthenia of the spleen and lung;
清脾沁肺 coolness sinks into the heart;
[脾過大] enlarged spleen; splenoparectasis;
[脾過小] microsplenia;
[脾潰瘍] splenelcosis;
[脾氣] temper; temperament;
脾氣暴躁 have a bad temper; have a fierce disposition; have a hot temper; short-tempered; surly;
~脾氣暴躁的人 roughneck;
~脾氣暴躁的少年 surly teenager;
脾氣不太好 a bit crabby;
脾氣很壞 bad-tempered; grumpy; irritable; stroppy;
脾氣壞的 bad-tempered; crabby; grouchy;
~脾氣壞的老頭 crabby old man;
~脾氣壞的人 curmudgeon;
脾氣隨和 good-tempered; have an amiable disposition;
暴脾氣 hot temper;
發脾氣 blow a fuse; blow a gasket; blow one's fuse; blow one's lid off; blow one's top; blow up; cut up rough; flare up; flay into a rage; fly into a temper; get angry; get one's hackles up; have sb's hackles up; hit the ceiling; let oneself go; lose one's temper; make sb's hackles rise; out of temper; vent one's spleen; with one's hackles rising; with one's hackles up;
~愛發脾氣 apt to lose one's temper; combustible; fiery; hot-tempered; hotheaded; short-tempered;
~不發脾氣 keep one's shirt on;
~大發脾氣 blow one's top; blow up; do one's fruit; do one's nuts; flare up; fly into one's tantrums; get into a temper; go off the top; grab for altitude; have a tantrum; lose one's shirt; lose one's temper; throw a tantrum;
~動不動就發脾氣 fire up at least thing;
~亂發脾氣 give loose rein to one's temper;
~為一點小事大發脾氣 fly into a rage at the slightest provocation;
~無端端發脾氣 lose one's temper for nothing;
犯脾氣 get one's dander up; lose one's temper;
改脾氣 change one's disposition;
怪脾氣 oddity; techy; tetchy;
好脾氣 good-tempered;
鬧脾氣 lose one's temper; show ill temper; vent one's spleen;
牛脾氣 bull-headed; dogged; obstinate; pertinacious; pigheaded; stubborn;
少爺脾氣 do whatever one pleases;
使脾氣 get one's dander up; lose one's temper;
耍脾氣 get angry; get into a huff; have a hissy fit; hissy fit; lose one's temper; put on a show of bad temper; throw a hissy fit;
一頓脾氣 a fit of temper;
直脾氣 frank; outspoken;
左脾氣 stubbornly peevish temper;
[脾切除] removal of the spleen; splenectomy;
[脾頭] head of spleen;
[脾尾] tail of spleen;
[脾胃] spleen and stomach;
脾胃不和 incoordination between spleen and stomach;
脾胃不佳 antipathetic; have a poor appetite; lack appetite;
脾胃濕熱 wetness-heat accumulated in the spleen and stomach;
脾胃相投 have similar likes and dislikes; have similar tastes;
調理脾胃 regulate the function of the spleen and stomach;
醒人脾胃 refresh one's mind;
[脾下垂] splenoptosis;
[脾性] disposition; temperament;
溫良的脾性 one's amenity of temper;
[脾虛] asthenia of the spleen; spleen-asthenia;
[脾炎] inflammation of the spleen; lienitis;
[脾硬化] splenokeratosis;
[脾脹大] enlargement of spleen;
[脾腫大] enlargement of the spleen; splenomegalia; splenomegaly;
[脾腫瘤] splenoma;

無脾 asplenia; congenital absence of the spleen;

醒脾 (1) refresh one's mind; (2) make fun of;
運脾 activate the spleen-energy;

pi
【鈹】 beryllium;

pi
【裨】 aid; benefit; supplement;
［裨益］ benefit;

pi
【罷】 exhausted; tired; weary;

pi
【貔】 fierce animal of the panther family;

pi
【羆】 a kind of bear;

pi
【鼙】 small drum used in the army in ancient China;

pi³

pi
【匹】 a match for; equal in force; equal to;
［匹敵］ equal in force; equal to; well matched;
無所匹敵 have no match; second to none;
無與匹敵 peerless; unique; without a rival;
［匹夫］ (1) ordinary person; (2) ignorant person;
匹夫匹婦 common man and woman;
匹夫有責 each and everyone should hold himself responsible for his country's welfare;
匹夫之勇 mere bravado; mere physical courage; personal prowess; reckless courage; sheer deviltry; bravery of a common person; courage of a mean person;
［匹馬］ single horse;
匹馬單槍 a single mounted warrior with a spike;
單槍匹馬 all by oneself; alone; go it alone; play a lone hand; plough a lonely furrow; single-handed;
［匹配］ (1) marry; mate; (2) match; matching;
匹配封裝 envelope match;
不匹配 mismatch;
共軛匹配 conjugate match;
鏡象匹配 image match;
聲匹配 acoustic matching;
雙向匹配 bilateral matching;
天線匹配 aerial matching;
一致匹配 consistent match;
［匹頭］ drapery; dry goods; piece goods; soft goods;
布匹 cloth; piece goods;
一匹 a bolt of; a roll of;

pi
【疋】 bolt; roll;

pi
【庀】 prepare;

pi
【仳】 part company;
［仳離］ divorce;

pi
【否】 (1) bad; wicked; (2) ensure;
［否極泰來］ after a storm comes a calm; after black clouds, clear weather; after extreme bad luck, comes good luck; after rain comes fair weather; every cloud has a silver lining; extremes meet; extremes would find their own mean; out of the depth of misfortune comes bliss; the darkest hour is just before the dawn; things at the worst will mend; when ill luck reaches its limit, good luck comes in; when the world is at the worst it will mend; when the worse comes to the worst, it is likely that events would take a new turn; when things are at the worst they will mend;

pi
【苤】 (1) a kind of plant; (2) luxuriant vegetation;

pi
【痞】 (1) dyspepsia; spleen infection; (2) ruffian; scoundrel;
兵痞 army ruffian;
地痞 local ruffian;
文痞 literary prostitute;

pi
【劈】 (1) cleave; rend; rive; split; (2) wedge;
［劈一字腿］ do the splits;

pi
【癖】 a fondness for; a weakness for; an addiction;

[癖好] a fondness for; a special hobby; favourite hobby; take special liking to sth;
[癖嗜] addiction;
[癖性] habitual tendency; natural inclination; proclivity; propensity;

惡癖 bad habit;
痼癖 inveterate weakness;
乖癖 eccentric; odd;
酒癖 addiction to drinking;
書癖 bookaholic;

pi4

pi

【屁】 fart; wind;
[屁股] backside; behind; boff; bottom; bum; buttocks; cheeks; chuff; duff; fanny; hip; keister;
屁股不幹淨 guilty;
屁股蛋 buttocks;
擦屁股 clear up the mess left by sb else; patch up sth others have not done well;
打屁股 get a slap on the buttocks; get a spanking; get punished; receive punishment; spank;
狗顛屁股 obsequious;
光屁股 in the nude; stark-naked;
~光屁股的 bare-assed;
雞屁股 chicken's buttocks;
摸老虎屁股 beard the lion in its den; run risks; take risks;
[屁滾尿流] be frightened out of one's wits; piss in one's pants; scare the shit out of sb; wet one's pants in terror;
嚇得屁滾尿流 be frightened out of one's wits; frighten the piss out of; scare the shit out of; wet one's pants in terror;
[屁話] horseshit; nonsense; rubbish; shit;
[屁事] your business;
干你屁事 none of your business;
[屁眼] anus; arsehole; butthole;

懂得個屁 not know one's arse from one's elbow;
放屁 (1) backfire; beef-hearts; break wind; break wind backwards; break wind downwards; breezer; cut one's finger; drop a rose; fart; have gas; lay fart; let one fly; make a noise; pass air; pass wind; raspberry tart; rip off a fart; set a fart; gunpowder; shoot rabbits; sneeze; there's a smell of touch bone and whistle; (2) nonsense; talk nonsense; what a crap;
狗屁 horseshit; nonsense; rubbish;
馬屁 apple-polish; toady;

pi

【辟】 same as 僻;

pi

【睥】 (1) look askance; scornful look; (2) battlements atop city walls;
[睥睨] look askance;

pi

【僻】 (1) biased; low; mean; (2) not easily accessible; out of the way; secluded; (3) ambiguous; nebulous; (4) not common; not ordinary;
[僻靜] lonely; secluded;
[僻陋] secluded and desolate;
[僻壤] backwater; little known region; out-of-the-way place;
荒村僻壤 desert;
[僻巷] side-lane;

孤僻 unsociable and queer; unsocial;
乖僻 eccentric; queer;
怪僻 eccentric; kink;
荒僻 (1) desolate and out-of-the-way; (2) rare; unfamiliar;
冷僻 (1) deserted; out-of-the-way; (2) rare; unfamiliar;
偏僻 far-off; out-of-the-way; remote;
邪僻 heterodox;

pi

【擗】 beat the breast;

pi

【澼】 launder; wash;

pi

【甓】 brick;

pi

【譬】 analogy; example;
[譬如] for example; for instance; such as; take for example;
[譬喻] analogy; figure of speech; metaphor; simile;
罕譬而喻 explain clearly with few illustrations;

pi

【闢】 (1) develop; open up; (2) deny; do away with; refute; rid;

[闢謠] deny a rumour; refute a rumour; refute slanders;
精闢 incisive;
透闢 incisive; penetrating; thorough;

pian[1]

pian

【片】 (1) photograph; (2) phonograph record;
[片長] running time;

唱片 gramophone record;
相片 photo; photograph;
影片 film; movie;
照片 photograph; picture;

pian

【扁】 small;
[扁舟] skiff; small boat;

pian

【偏】 (1) be inclined to one side; slanting; (2) favour; partial; prejudiced;
[偏愛] affect; favour; go overboard; have a predilection for; have a preference for; have partiality for sth; love one more than another; partial to; play favourites; predilection; show favouritism to sb; take sides;
[偏安] content to retain sovereignty over a part of the country;
偏安一隅 content to exercise sovereignty over a part of the country;
[偏差] departure; deviation; divergence; drift; offset; variance;
偏差器 deviator;
代數偏差 algebraic deviation;
地轉偏差 geostrophic departure;
絕對偏差 absolute deviation;
絕對瞬態偏差 absolute transient deviation;
絕對系統偏差 absolute system deviation;
均方偏差 mean squared deviation;
載頻偏差 carrier-frequency offset;
總偏差 total departure;
[偏飯] preferential treatment;
吃偏飯 get a special help; receive a particular treatment;
[偏房] (1) wing-room; (2) concubine;
[偏廢] do one thing and neglect another; emphasize one thing at the expense of another;
二者不可偏廢 neither...nor...is overemphasized to the neglect of the other; neither should be overemphasized at the expense of the other;
[偏航] yaw;
偏航阻尼器 yaw damper;
[偏好] predilection;
[偏護] partial to and side with; show partiality for; take sides with;
[偏激] extreme; go to extremes;
意見偏激 hold extreme views;
[偏見] bias; partial opinion; preconception; prejudice; slant; warp;
不抱偏見 have no bias against; hold no prejudice;
產生偏見 create prejudice;
陳腐的偏見 time-worn prejudices;
打破偏見 eradicate prejudice;
毫無偏見 free from bias;
激起偏見 stir up prejudice;
世俗偏見 bias in common views;
消除偏見 eradicate prejudice;
引起偏見 arouse prejudice;
助長偏見 feed prejudice;
[偏角] declination;
磁偏角 magnetic declination;
磁針偏角 declination of magnetic needle;
格網偏角 grid declination;
太陽偏角 declination of the sun;
[偏口魚] flatfish;
[偏勞] please;
[偏離] deflect; departure; diverge; deviate; skew;
偏離常軌 aberrance;
偏離正路 aberrance;
偏離正道 diverge from the right path;
偏離正題 digress from the main subject;
相對偏離 relative departure;
[偏盲] blind in one eye; hemianopia;
偏盲性瞳孔反應 hemiopic pupillary reaction;
同側偏盲 homonymous hemianopia;
完全偏盲 absolute hemianopia;
相對性偏盲 relative hemianopia;
象限偏盲 quadrant hemianopia;
[偏僻] far-off; out-of-the-way; remote;
[偏偏] deliberately; just; only;
偏偏不巧 as ill luck will have it; as luck would have it;

P

偏偏湊巧 as luck would have it; coincidentally;

[偏頗] biased;

無偏無頗 impartial; unbiased; very just;

[偏巧] as luck would have it; by chance; fortunately; it so happened that;

[偏食] dietary bias;

[偏蝕] partial eclipse;

偏食始 beginning of partial eclipse; first contact;

偏食終 end of partial eclipse; last contact;

日偏食 partial solar eclipse;

月偏食 partial lunar eclipse;

[偏袒] bias for; discriminate in favour of; favour; partial to; partial to and side with; take sides with; weigh;

偏袒有錢人 partial towards the rich people;

偏袒一方 biased towards one side; inclined to one side;

[偏疼] partial to sb; show favouritism to sb;

[偏題] catch question; tricky question;

[偏向角] angle of deviation;

[偏斜] deviation;

偏斜眼 deviating eye;

原發性偏斜 primary deviation;

[偏心] (1) bias; partial; partiality; (2) eccentric;

偏心律 eccentricity;

偏心率 eccentricity;

~電機偏心率 motor eccentricity;

~軌跡偏心率 track eccentricity;

偏心輪 eccentric;

~從動偏心輪 follower eccentric;

~固定偏心輪 fixed eccentric;

~可調偏心輪 adjustable eccentric;

~控制偏心輪 control eccentric;

~制動偏心輪 brake eccentric;

偏心器 eccentric;

~游動偏心器 loose eccentric;

偏心距 eccentricity;

~轉動偏心距 eccentricity of rotation;

偏心軸 eccentric;

~開關偏心軸 variable eccentric;

~離心器偏心軸 clutch pivoting eccentric;

大偏心 large eccentricity;

狗不吃屎，人不偏心 when dogs do not eat shit, then people no longer practise favouritism;

[偏壓] bias;

熔絲偏壓 heater bias;

發射極偏壓 emitter bias;

負偏壓 minus bias; negative bias;

基極偏壓 base bias;

可變偏壓 variable bias;

零始偏壓 zero-initial bias;

臨界偏壓 critical bias;

漏偏壓 drain bias;

柵偏壓 gate bias;

延遲偏壓 delay bias;

陰極偏壓 cathode bias;

正偏壓 positive bias;

正向偏壓 forward bias;

自動偏壓 automatic grid;

[偏要] insist on; persist in; would;

[偏遠] faraway; remote;

偏遠地區 remote area;

偏遠山區 backcountry;

偏遠鄉間 backcountry;

偏遠之地 remote place;

~在偏遠之地 in the middle of nowhere;

[偏置] offset;

晶體偏置 crystal offset;

精確偏置 precision offset;

頻率偏置 frequency offset;

載波偏置 carrier offset;

[偏重] be inclined to; emphasize; have a bias towards; lay particular stress on; tend to;

[偏轉] deflection;

偏轉器 deflector;

~聲光束偏轉器 acousto-optic beam deflector;

偏轉散焦 deflection defocussing;

電磁偏轉 electromagnetic deflection;

對稱偏轉 balanced deflection; symmetrical deflection;

~不對稱偏轉 asymmetrical deflection;

角偏轉 angular deflection;

射束偏轉 beam deflection;

糾偏 correct an error; rectify a deviation;

pian

【萹】 a variety of weed or grass with narrow thick blades;

pian

【篇】 (1) piece of writing; (2) sheet of paper;

[篇牘] writings;

累牘連篇 floods of ink; in a prolix style; lengthy and tedious; long and tedious writings; one article after another;

page upon page and volume upon volume;
盈篇累牘 voluminous;

[篇幅] length; space;
[篇目] chapter heading; contents; list of articles; table of contents;
[篇章] canto; literary piece; sections and chapters;

長篇 lengthy essay;
連篇 (1) page after page; throughout a piece of writing; (2) a multitude of articles; one article after another;
詩篇 (1) poem; (2) inspiring story;
一篇 (1) a chapter; a literary article; (2) a piece of; a sheet of;
遺篇 writings left by a deceased author;
終篇 finish writing an article;

pian
【翩】 fly swiftly;
[翩翩] (1) dance lightly; gracefully moving; (2) elegant; smart;
翩翩風度 like an Apollo;
翩翩起舞 dance trippingly; rise and dance in a happy mood;
翩翩少年 beau; dandy; fop; young man of dress; young spark; elegant young man;
翩翩巍巍 stately and imposing — as a palace;
翩翩濯濯 graceful and clean;
[翩然] lightly; trippingly;
翩然而至 come graciously; come tripping down;
翩然莅至 come graciously;
[翩躚] lightly; trippingly;
翩躚起舞 dance trippingly; dance with quick, light steps;

聯翩 in close succession; together;

pian²
pian
【便】 (1) quiet and comfortable; (2) a surname;
[便便] big-bellied; corpulent; fat; pot-bellied;
[便宜] (1) act on one's initiative; (2) cheap; inexpensive; (3) to one's advantage;
便宜貨 cheap article; cheapie; cheapo; twofer;
便宜無好貨 cheapest is the dearest; good cheap is dear;
便宜無好貨，好貨不便宜 cheap goods always prove expensive; dear is cheap — cheap is dear;
揀到便宜 get the better of a bargain;
討便宜 seek undue advantage;
討人便宜 look for advantage of another;
又便宜又好 cheap and good;

pian
【胼】 calluses;
[胼手胝足] toil and moil; with hand and feet becoming callous;

pian
【楩】 a kind of tree;

pian
【駢】 (1) pair of horses; (2) lie side by side; stand; (3) same as 騈, 駢;
[駢體翻譯法] antithesis method;

pian
【諞】 quibble; show off;
[諞能] show off one's skills;

pian
【蹁】 limping; walking unsteadily;
[蹁躚] whirling about in dancing;

pian³
pian
【楩】 a kind of tree;

pian
【諞】 boast; brag; show off;

pian⁴
pian
【片】 (1) flat, thin piece; flat slice; (2) part of a place; (3) cut into slices; (4) brief; fragmentary; incomplete; partial;
[片段] bit; extract; fragment; part; passage; section; segment;
[片甲] fragment of armour;
片甲不存 have not even a fragment of armour remaining; not a single armoured warrior remains — the army is completely wiped out;
片甲不留 have not even a fragment of armour remaining — be completely routed;
[片刻] bit; instant; moment; little while; minute; short while;

稍待片刻 half a moment; just a minute; one moment; stay a minute; wait a jiffy; wait a minute; wait half a jiffy;
稍等片刻 half a moment; just a second; wait a jiff; wait a minute;
少留片刻 please remain for a little while;
少憩片刻 rest a while;
休息片刻 rest a bit; rest for a spell;

[片麻岩] gneiss;
複片麻岩 composite gneiss;
條帶片麻岩 banded gneiss;
眼球狀片麻岩 augen gneiss;

[片面] (1) one-sided; single-faceted; unilateral; (2) lopsided; one-sided;
片面之詞 a one-sided statement; an account given by one party only; one person's word against another's;

[片片] in fragment; in pieces;

[片時] moment; short time; short while;

[片瓦] single tile;
片瓦無存 not a single tile remains — be razed to the ground;
上無片瓦，下無插針之地 have neither a tile over one's head nor a speck of land under one's feet — be poverty-stricken;
上無片瓦，下無寸土 have neither a tile above one's head nor an inch of land beneath one's feet — be utterly destitute; not to own a single brick or an inch of land; own no land and no roof over one's head;

[片言] a few words; a phrase or two; just a few words;
片言半語 half a word; just a few broken words;
片言九鼎 a word has the weight of nine tripods — a word from you carries great weight;
片言可決 can be settled in a few words;
片言折獄 convict a person on hearsay evidence; settle a case with just a few words;
片言只語 a few isolated words and phrases; a phrase or two; half a word; only a few words;
片言只字 just a few words; just a short note;

[片岩] schist;
基性片岩 basic schist;
結晶片岩 crystalline schist;
鈣質片岩 calcareous schist;

[片語] phrase;
口語片語 spoken phrase;

阿片 opium;
苞片 bract;
冰片 borneol;
箔片 chaff; paillon;
薄片 sheet; thin section; thin slice;
草片 grass;
唱片 gramophone record; record;
大片 sheet;
刀片 (1) blade; (2) razor blade;
底片 (1) negative; (2) film;
墊片 shim;
動畫片 cartoon;
動作片 actioner;
短片 short film; short videos;
斷片 fragment; part; passage;
萼片 sepal;
負片 negative;
鈣片 calcium tablet;
畫片 picture postcard; printed picture;
幻燈片 slide;
簧片 reed;
記錄片 documentary;
膠片 film;
接片 collage;
晶片 chip; crystal plate; wafer;
鏡片 lens; plate;
卡片 card; fiche;
麥片 oatmeal;
毛片 pornographic movie; porno flick;
名片 calling card; name card; visiting card;
明信片 postal card; postcard;
膜片 diaphragm;
默片 silent film;
木片 wood chip;
漆片 colour chips;
切片 cut into pieces; section;
肉片 sliced meat;
軟片 film;
鰓片 gill;
上片 start showing a movie;
薯片 crisps; potato chips;
碎片 chip; debris; fragment; patch; segment; shred;
拓片 rubbing;
糖片 lozenge;
圖片 photograph; picture;
西部片 cowboy film; Wild West movie;
蝦片 prawn slices; shrimp cracker;

香片 (1) scented tea; (2) jasmine tea;
相片 photo; photograph; photoprint; pix; print;
像片 photograph;
消炎片 sulphanilamide tablet;
芯片 microchip;
信片 postcard;
新聞片 newsfilm; newsreel;
雪片 snowflake;
鴉片 opium; opium plant;
藥片 pill; tablet;
葉片 (1) blade; leaf blade; (2) vane;
謁片 calling card; visiting card;
一大片 a sheet;
一片 (1) a petal; (2) a blanket of; a blaze of; a body of; a flood of; a mass of; a scene of; a sea of; a sheet of; a slice of; a stretch of; a tract of; an area of; an expanse of;
印片 film printing; printing;
影片 film; movie; picture;
魚片 fish fillet; slices of fish meat;
雲片 cloud sheet;
照片 photo; photograph; pic; picture; print; snapshot;
正片 feature film; positive;
紙片 scraps of paper;
製片 produce a film; producer;
竹片 split bamboos;

pian
【遍】 a pronunciation of 遍 ;

pian
【徧】 a pronunciation of 徧 ;

pian
【騙】 (1) be made a fool of; be taken in by; deceive; fall into a trap; fool; (2) cheat; pull the wool over sb's eyes; swindle;

[騙過] out-trick;
[騙局] fraud; hoax; put-up job; shell game; swindle;
拆除騙局 expose a fraud;
巧妙的騙局 clever fraud;
一場騙局 a sham;
[騙取] cheat sb out of sth; defraud; gain sth by fraud; swindle;
騙取別人的信任 worm oneself into others' confidence;
騙取金錢 diddle;
[騙人] deceive sb;
狗不吃屎—騙人 a dog that does not eat shit − playing false;
[騙術] deceitful trick; hoax; ruse;
騙術高明 one's art of fraud is skillful;
施行騙術 practise fraud;
[騙子] blackleg; blagger; charlatan; cheater; con artist; conman; crook; double crosser; faker; fiddler; flimflammer; humbug; hustler; imposter; phony; swindler; trickster;
騙子失手 a cheat losing control of his hand − be discovered;
江湖騙子 snake oil salesman;
女騙子 conwoman;
小騙子 small-time crook; small-time gangster; small-timer;
虛偽圓滑的騙子 two-faced liar;
一群騙子 a horde of cheaters; a mob of liars;

被騙 be fooled; be swindled;
繃騙 cheat;
串騙 gang up and swindle sb;
盜騙 steal and cheat;
詐騙 blackmail and swindling;
拐騙 (1) abduct; (2) swindle;
哄騙 bamboozle; blandish; cajole; coax; humbug; wheedle;
局騙 swindle; trap; trick;
誆騙 deceive; dupe; hoax;
瞞騙 bluff;
矇騙 cheat; deceive; delude; hoodwink;
蒙騙 deceive; hoodwink;
欺騙 bamboozle; be done in by; beguile; cajole; cheat; chicanery; come around; come round; come over sb; cozen; cross sb up; deceit; deceive; deception; defraud; delude; diddle; do sb down; do the dirty on sb; draw the wool over sb's eyes; dupe; fool; get over sb; give a flap with a foxtail; gum; have sb on; have sb over sth; hocus-pocus; hoodwink; impose on sb; jiggery-pokery; lead sb up the garden path; make a fool of; play a trick on sb; play sb false; play the old soldier over sb; play upon; pluck; practise on sb; pull a fast one over; pull the wool over sb's eyes; put it across on sb; put on sb; put upon sb; rope along sb; see sb coming; sell sb down the river; set one's cap; string along sb; swindle; take advantage of; take in; take sb for a ride; trick; throw dust in the eyes of; throw mud into the eyes of; throw sb a curve; wheedle;
受騙 be cheated; be deceived; be fooled; be

P

swindled; be taken in; be tricked;
行騙 cheat; deceive; practise deception; practice fraud; swindle;
誘騙 beguile; cajole; induce by deceit; inveigle; trap; trick;
詐騙 chicanery; con trick; defraud; jiggery-pokery; swindle;
撞騙 cheat; look about for a chance to swindle; swindle;

piao1

piao

【漂】 drift; float; vagrant; wander;
[漂白] bleach; whiten;
漂白劑 bleach;
[漂泊] drift aimlessly; lead a wandering life;
漂泊不定 drift about; vagrant;
漂泊街頭的人 street people; the homeless;
漂泊無依 a wanderer having no one to depend upon;
漂泊異鄉 wander aimlessly in a strange land;
漂泊者 drifter;
[漂蕩] drift about; wander;
[漂浮] (1) float; (2) showy; superficial;
漂浮法 floatation; floating method;
[漂流] be driven by the current; drift; drift about;
漂流木 driftwood;
漂流作用 driftage;
黑水漂流 black-water rafting;
季風漂流 monsoon drift;
西風漂流 west wind drift;
[漂萍] duckweed;
[漂行] float;
[漂移] be driven by the current; drift; drift about; wander;
漂移度 driftance;
漂移物 drifter;
大陸漂移 continental drift;
電子漂移 electron drift;
基線漂移 baseline drift; baseline wander;
零點漂移 zero wander;
頻率漂移 frequency drift;
視漂移 apparent wander;
增益漂移 gain drift;
[漂游] float; wander;

浮漂 flighty; superficial;
魚漂 float;

piao

【飄】 float; wave to and fro;
[飄泊] drift aimlessly; lead a wandering life;
飄泊無定 drift from place to place; here today and gone tomorrow;
[飄出] blow out;
[飄蕩] drift; flutter; wave;
一生飄蕩 go hither and thither all one's life;
[飄動] float; flutter;
[飄浮] (1) float; (2) showy; superficial;
[飄過] drift; sail;
[飄忽] (1) fleet; move swiftly; (2) float; mobile; uncertain; wave to and fro;
飄忽不定 drift from place to place; wanton;
行蹤飄忽 have no fixed whereabouts;
[飄來] waft;
[飄零] (1) become faded and fallen; (2) drift about alone; lead a wandering life; wandering;
飄零一身 lonely wanderer;
琴劍飄零 the lute and the sword are abandoned as a scholar wanders from place to place;
[飄流] (1) float; (2) drift aimlessly;
飄流四方 knock about the world;
[飄落] drift down; float; land in a floating manner;
[飄飄] tread on air;
飄飄然 be carried away with one's own importance; be puffed up with pride; complacent; light-headed; self-satisfied; smug; tread on air; walk on air;
~ 感到飄飄然 be walking on air;
飄飄若仙 as graceful as a fairy; with ethereal lightness;
飄飄欲仙 on wings; with ethereal lightness;
[飄然] floating in the air;
飄然而去 go off with a swagger;
飄然若仙 move with the calm serenity of a god;
[飄灑] drift; float;
花粉隨風飄灑 aerial drift of pollen;
[飄送] waft;
[飄舞] dance in the wind;
[飄揚] flutter; fly; wave;
彩旗飄揚 coloured flags were fluttering in

the wind;

［飄搖］ drift about in the wind; shake; sway; totter;

［飄逸］ elegant; graceful; possessing natural grace;

［飄溢］ float and brim with;

［飄悠］ drift slowly; float slowly;

［飄轉］ trail;

輕飄 buoyant; light;

piao²

piao

【嫖】 go whoring; visit prostitutes;

［嫖妓］ (1) wench; (2) whoredom; whoring; (3) patronize a prostitute;

［嫖客］ John; whoremaster; whoremonger;

piao

【瓢】 ladle;

［瓢蟲］ ladybird; ladybug;

［瓢瓜］ lagenaria siserariae;

［瓢潑］ heavy downpour; torrential rain;

水瓢 water ladle;

piao³

piao

【殍】 (1) starve to death; (2) person who died from starvation;

piao

【莩】 corpse of a person who was starved to death;

piao

【漂】 (1) bleach; decolourize; (2) potch; rinse;

［漂白］ bleach; bleaching; decolourize;

漂白場 bleach field;
漂白廠 bleachery;
漂白粉 bleaching-powder;
漂白劑 bleach;
~ 過氧化物漂白劑 peroxide bleaches;
漂白率 bleachability;
漂白器 bleacher;
~ 高密度漂白器 high density bleacher;
漂白作用 bleaching action;
電解漂白 electrolytic bleaching;
高濃漂白 high density bleaching;
鉻漂白 chrome bleaching;
還原漂白 reduction bleaching;
棉漂白 cotton bleaching;
熱漂白 thermal bleaching;
酸性漂白 acid bleaching;
氧氣漂白 oxygen bleaching;
油漂白 oil bleaching;

［漂染］ bleach and dye; convert;

［漂洗］ rinse;

piao

【摽】 (1) fall; falling; (2) razor of a sword; (3) high; lofty;

piao

【瞟】 glance; look askance;

piao

【縹】 (1) light-blue silk; (2) light blue; (3) dim; indistinct; misty;

［縹緲］ dimly discernible; misty;

piao⁴

piao

【票】 (1) ticket; ballot; (2) banknote; bill; (3) hostage;

［票房］ booking office; box office;

票房欠佳 box office failure;

［票根］ counterfoil; stub;

［票價］ admission fee; entrance fee; fare; price of a ticket;

飛機票價 airfare;
來回票價 double fare;
聯運票價 combined fare;
旅遊票價 excursion fare;
降低票價 lower the fares;
提高票價 raise the price of a ticket;

［票據］ (1) bill; negotiable instrument; note; (2) receipt; voucher;

票據承兑 acceptance;
票據交換 clearance;
~ 票據交換所 clearing house;
~ 票據交換銀行 clearing bank;
票據貼現 discounted note;
票據賬目 bills account;
不完全票據 incomplete bill;
承兑票據 accept a note;
借款票據 loan bill;
可貼現票據 bankable bill;
拒付票據 dishonoured draft;
商業票據 mercantile bill;
通融票據 accommodation bill;
已背書票據 endorsed bill;
銀行票據 banker's bill;
應付票據 bill payable;

應收票據 bill receivable;
遠期票據 long-dated bill;
執票人票據 bearer bill;

[票面] face value; nominal value; par value;
票面價值 face value; par value;
票面利率 nominal rate;

[票務] ticketing;
電子票務 electronic ticketing;

[票箱] ballot box;

[票子] banknote; bill; paper money;

半票 half fare; half-price ticket;
綁票 hold a person for ransom; kidnap;
包票 certificate of guarantee;
保票 certificate of guarantee;
奔票 strive for a ticket;
本票 bank check; cashier's order; promissory note;
捕票 arrest warrant; warrant for arrest;
補票 buy one's ticket after the normal time;
彩票 lottery ticket; raffle ticket;
查票 check tickets; examine tickets;
鈔票 banknote; paper money;
車票 bus ticket; train ticket;
持票 bearer; hold;
出票 draw;
船票 steamer ticket;
傳票 (1) (of court) summons; (2) voucher;
大票 large bill;
當票 pawn ticket;
訂票 book tickets;
發票 bill; receipt;
反對票 dissenting vote; negative vote;
飯票 meal ticket;
廢票 (1) invalid ticket; (2) invalid ballot;
分票 dispatch tickets;
購票 buy a ticket;
股票 capital stock; equity security; share; share certificate; stock; stock certificate;
滙票 bank draft; bill; bill of exchange; draft; money order; order; remittance;
機票 airplane ticket;
季票 season ticket;
監票 scrutinize balloting;
剪票 punch a ticket;
拘票 arrest warrant; warrant;
開票 (1) open the ballot box and count the ballots; (2) make out an invoice;
客票 passenger ticket;
拉票 canvass votes; solicit votes;
糧票 food coupon; grain coupon;
門票 admission ticket; entrance ticket;
免票 (1) free pass; free ticket; (2) free of charge;
期票 bill of exchange; promissory note; term bill; time draft;
錢票 (1) paper money; (2) vouchers used in canteens in place of cash;
肉票 hostage;
收票 collect tickets;
售票 sell tickets;
撕票 kill a hostage;
跳票 bounced check;
通票 through ticket;
投票 cast a vote; vote;
退票 (1) get a refund for a ticket; return a ticket; (2) dishonoured cheque;
席票 food ticket;
戲票 theatre ticket; ticket for a play;
選票 ballot; vote;
一張票 a ticket;
銀票 bank note;
郵票 postage stamp; stamp;
月季票 season ticket;
月票 (1) monthly pass; (2) monthly ticket;
贈票 free ticket;
站票 ticket for standing room;
支票 cheque;
種票 vote-rigging;

piao
【剽】 (1) plunder; rob; steal; (2) agile;

piao
【嘌】 passing swiftly;

[嘌呤] purine;

piao
【漂】 beautiful; good-looking; nice; pretty; sleek;

[漂亮] beautiful; good-looking; nice-looking; pretty;
漂亮的 lush; nice-looking;
~漂亮的人 beautiful creature;
~非常漂亮的 bootylicious;
漂亮姑娘 beautiful girl;
漂亮話 lip-service;
~說漂亮話 offer lip-service;
漂亮女子 pretty girl;
~一個漂亮女子 a pretty girl;
愛漂亮 like to look pretty;
不只臉蛋漂亮 not just a pretty face;
漂漂亮亮 beautifully;
~打扮得漂漂亮亮 gussy;

piao
【驃】 (1) horse with a yellowish white co-

lour; (2) valiant; (3) galloping;

pie¹

pie

【撇】 (1) cast; throw; (2) left-falling stroke;

［撇開］ bypass; cast aside; ignore; leave aside; neglect; put aside; throw overboard;

［撇棄］ (1) abandon; desert; (2) cast away;

［撇去］ skim;

［撇油］ skim;

撇油器 oil skimmer; skimmer;

浮式撇油器 floating skimmer;

海面撇油器 open-sea skimmer;

轉鼓撇油器 drum skimmer;

pie

【瞥】 dart a look at; shoot a glance at;

［瞥見］ catch sight of; get a glimpse of;

一瞥 (1) quick glance; (2) brief survey; glimpse;

pie³

pie

【苤】 (1) a kind of plant; (2) luxuriant vegetation;

pie

【撇】 (1) (of calligraphy) a stroke made in the lower left direction; (2) purse the mouth;

［撇號］ accent; accent sign;

［撇嘴］ curl one's lip; make a lip; make a mouth; make a wry mouth; make mouths; make up a lip; shoot out the lips; twitch one's mouth;

撇齒拉嘴 wear a contemptuous expression;

pin¹

pin

【姘】 have illicit relations with;

［姘夫］ adulterer; paramour;

［姘婦］ adulteress; mistress;

［姘居］ live illicitly as husband and wife;

［姘識］ get acquainted and have illicit sexual relations with;

［姘頭］ mistress; paramour;

pin

【拼】 (1) piece together; put together; (2) go all out in work; ready to risk one's life;

［拼搏］ combat against; combat with; go all out in work;

拼搏精神 combatant spirit;

最後一次拼搏 last hurrah;

［拼成］ piece together; put together;

［拼湊］ confect; knock together; piece together; rig up; scrape together;

東拼西湊 do patchwork; pitch up from bits; put together from different sources; scrape together; scratchy;

七拼八湊 a patchwork without pattern or order; cobble together; compile from many sources a book; conjoin multifarious elements to form a whole as a patch-quilt; improvise desperately; knock together; piece together; piece together odds and ends; raise money from different sources; rig up; scrape together; scrape together odd amounts to form a sum for a definite purpose;

~七拼八湊的貨色 pieced-together work;

~七拼八湊，雜亂無章 a patchwork without pattern or order; in disorder;

［拼法］ spelling;

舊式拼法 old spelling;

［拼縫］ piece;

［拼合］ piece together; splice;

［拼命］ defy death; fight desperately; go all out; go all out regardless of danger to one's life;

拼命幹活 be hard driven; plug away at sth;

拼命三郎 workaholic;

拼命厮打 fight tooth and nail;

［拼盤］ assorted cold dishes; hors d'oeuvres;

冷拼盤 assorted cold dishes;

涼拼盤 assorted cold dishes;

［拼殺］ grapple;

［拼死］ defy death; fight desperately; risk one's life;

拼死吃河豚—不要命了 like eating a globefish – risk one's life;

拼死拼活 sweat one's guts out; work one's fingers to the bone; work one's tail off; work oneself to death; work oneself to the bone for sth;

拼死掙扎 wage a desperate struggle;

［拼貼］ collage;

拼貼畫 collage picture;

拼貼藝術 collage;

［拼圖］ jigsaw;

[拼寫] spell; transliterate;
拼寫錯誤 spelling error;
[拼一拼] risk one's life;
[拼音] phonetic transcription;
拼音化 alphabetize;
~漢語拼音化 alphabetization of Chinese;
拼音文字 alphabetic script;
~拼音文字學 alphabetology;
羅馬拼音 Romanization;
[拼爭] struggle for;

pin²
pin

【貧】 (1) poor; (2) deficient in; poor in; (3) garrulous;
[貧病] sick and poor;
貧病交集 sick and in straits;
貧病交迫 be beset with poverty and illness; be dogged by poverty and illness at one and the same time; be weighed down by poverty and illness; suffer from both poverty and illness;
貧病相連 poverty and sickness are closely connected;
[貧不足恥] being poor is not disgraceful; poverty is no disgrace;
[貧不擇妻] the poor cannot choose wives;
[貧蛋] prater;
[貧而無諂] poor but not flattering;
[貧乏] meagre; lacking; poor; short of;
[貧富] poverty and affluence; the haves and the have-nots; the rich and the poor;
貧富不均 too much difference between rich and poor; uneven distribution of wealth;
貧富差距 poor-rich disparities; the gap between the rich and the poor;
貧富分化 polarization between the rich and the poor;
貧富共仰 be adored by rich and poor alike; be looked up to by the rich and the poor;
貧富鴻溝 gap between the rich and the poor;
貧富懸殊 extreme disparity between the rich and the poor; there is a wide gap between the rich and the poor; wealth gap;
安富卹貧 stabilize the wealthy and help the poor;
辭富居貧 decline riches and prefer poverty;
富從昇合起，貧因不算來 riches accumulate from small beginnings but poverty from miscalculation; riches spring from small beginning, poverty is the result of extravagance;
劫富濟貧 rob the rich to feed the poor;
嫌貧愛富 despise the poor and curry favour with the rich;
以富欺貧 the rich bully the poor;
以富壓貧 act in the way of the rich oppressing the poor; the rich oppress the poor;
由貧致富 from rags to riches;
[貧寒] poor; poverty-stricken;
[貧瘠] barren; infertile; poor;
貧瘠的 hardscrabble;
地瘠民貧 the soil is sterile and the people poor;
地貧土瘠 sterile land; thin, poor soil;
[貧賤] in straitened and humble circumstances; poor and lowly;
貧賤不移 neither poverty nor lowly condition can make him sever from principle; poor but with lofty ideal;
貧賤夫妻 bread and cheese marriage;
貧賤夫妻百事哀 everything that life brings to the poor and lowly couples is sad;
貧賤驕人 proud of one's poverty;
貧賤之交 friends in the days when hard up;
[貧寠] impoverished; poor;
[貧苦] badly off; poor; poverty-stricken;
訪貧問苦 go to see the poor and ask about their past bitterness; visit poor families to hear their problems; visit the poor and the suffering;
[貧困] impoverished; in straitened circumstances; poor; poverty-stricken;
貧困地區 area of poverty; poor region;
貧困戶 poverty household;
貧困潦倒 broke and out of a job; broke to the wide; on the beach; on the breadline; penniless and frustrated;
貧困線 breadline;
貧困縣 impoverished county;
貧困線 poverty line;
擺脫貧困 emerge from poverty; get rid of poverty; shake off poverty;
長期貧困 unremitting poverty;

城市貧困 urban poverty;
緩解貧困 alleviate poverty;
極度貧困 abject poverty;

［貧民］ pauper; poor people;
貧民窟 back slum; slum;
貧民所 almshouse;

［貧農］ poor peasant;

［貧氣］ (1) mean; miserly; stingy; (2) garrulous; loquacious;

［貧窮］ lean purse; light purse; short purse; slender purse; poor;
貧窮恐怖 peniaphobia;
貧窮落後 impoverished and backward; poor and backward; poverty-stricken and backward;

［貧弱］ miserable; poor and weak;

［貧血］ anaemia;
貧血病狀 anaemic symptoms;
貧血症 anaemia;
病狀性貧血 symptomatic anaemia;
出血性貧血 haemorrhagic anaemia;
地中海貧血 Mediterranean anaemia;
惡性貧血 pernicious anaemia;
高色性貧血 hyperchromic anaemia;
鉤蟲性貧血 hookworm anaemia;
壞血病性貧血 scorbutic anaemia;
難治性貧血 refractory anaemia;
脾貧血 splenic anaemia;
缺鐵性貧血 iron deficiency anaemia;
溶血性貧血 hemolytic anaemia;
生理性貧血 physiologic anaemia;
遺傳性貧血 genetic anaemia;
營養缺乏性貧血 deficiency anaemia;
營養性貧血 nutritional anaemia;
原發性貧血 essential anaemia;
中毒性貧血 toxanaemia;

［貧嘴］ garrulous; loquacious;
貧嘴薄舌 be addicted to senseless talks; garrulous and sharp-tongued; have a caustic and flippant tongue; light and airy utterance; wag one's tongue too freely;
貧嘴賤舌 be addicted to senseless talk; disgustingly talkative; make vulgar jokes; scurrilous;
貧嘴爛舌 be given to nasty talk; have a caustic and flippant tongue; like to say nasty things about people; love to gossip;
耍貧嘴 (1) garrulous; (2) joke a great deal;

安貧 contentment in poverty;
幫貧 help poor rural households;
赤貧 abject poverty; destitute; dire poverty;
次貧 less destitute;
扶貧 help the poor; support the poor;
濟貧 give help to the poor; help the people in distress; help the poor; relieve the people in distress; relieve the poor;
憐貧 commiserate the poor; pity the poor;
清貧 poor;
素貧 in a chronic state of poverty;
脱貧 be lifted out of poverty and backwardness; cast off the label of the poorest; extricate oneself from poverty; get rid of poverty; overcome poverty; shake off poverty; throw off poverty;
卹貧 give relief to the poor;
賑貧 relieve the poor;
嘴貧 chatty; talkative;

pin

【頻】 (1) frequently; repeatedly; (2) frequency;

［頻傳］ keep pouring in;

［頻帶］ band;
寬頻帶 broadband;

［頻道］ channel;
頻道搜索 channel search;
頻道選擇 channel selection;
～頻道選擇器 channel selector;
頻道預選 channel preselection;
公共頻道 public access channel;
換頻道 change channels;
商業頻道 commercial channel;

［頻度］ frequency;
頻度副詞 adverb of frequency;
頻度規則 frequency rule;
頻度狀語 adverbial of frequency;
詞匯頻度 word frequency;

［頻繁］ frequently; often;

［頻率］ frequency; rate;
頻率變化 frequency change;
交叉頻率 across frequency;
吸收頻率 absorption frequency;
指配頻率 allocated frequency;

［頻頻］ again and again; over and over again; repeatedly; time and time again;
頻頻點頭 nod again and again;

［頻仍］ frequent; repeated;

［頻閃儀］ stroboscope;
超聲波頻閃儀 ultrasonic stroboscope;

P

盤式頻閃儀 disc stroboscope;
閃光管頻閃儀 flash tube stroboscope;

變頻 frequency conversion;
差頻 beat frequency;
詞頻 word frequency;
低頻 low frequency;
高頻 high frequency;
行頻 line frequency;
尿頻 frequent micturition; frequent urination; pollakiuria; sychnuria;
射頻 radio frequency;
聲頻 acoustic frequency;
視頻 video frequency;
雙頻 dual band;
調頻 frequency modulation;
音頻 audio frequency;
載頻 carrier frequency;
中頻 intermediate frequency;

pin
【嬪】 (1) court lady; (2) be married to;
妃嬪 (1) imperial concubine; (2) wife of a prince; (3) imperial woman attendant;

pin
【蘋】 duckweed;

pin
【顰】 frown; knit one's brows;
[顰蹙] knit the brows;
顰眉蹙額 knit the brows; make a wry face;
[顰笑] frown or smile;
顰笑不苟 not frown or smile to order; natural;
一顰一笑 (1) every facial expression; (2) affected coquetry of a prostitute;

pin³
pin
【品】 (1) article; product; (2) class; grade; rank; (3) character; quality; (4) sample; savour; taste sth with discrimination;
[品嚐] sample; savour; taste;
[品德] moral character;
品德教育 character education;
建立品德 develop one's personal qualities;
良好品德 desirable moral qualities;
培養品德 develop moral qualities;
學生品德 students' moral qualities;
[品第] (1) evaluate; pass judgment on; (2) grade; position; rank;
[品格] (1) character of a person; one's character and morals; (2) quality and style;
品格高尚 noble-hearted;
品格端方 polished in one's manners;
[品紅] magenta;
品紅色影像 magenta image;
[品節] conduct and morals; integrity;
[品類] category; class;
[品貌] (1) appearance; looks; (2) character and looks; conduct and appearance;
品貌不揚 one's personal appearance is not outstanding;
品貌超群 one's character and appearance surpass others';
品貌端正 a well-shaped figure and decorous appearance; have regular features and correct in behaviour;
[品名] name of a part; name of an article;
[品目] items; names of things;
品目繁多 names and descriptions of articles are numerous;
[品牌] brand; name brand;
品牌策略 brand policy;
品牌打造 branding;
品牌潛力 brand potential;
品牌設計 branding;
非品牌 no-name;
國際品牌 international brand;
[品評] comment on; judge;
品頭評足 carping; find fault with sb; find fault with sth; make frivolous remarks; overcritical;
品月評花 enjoy the moon and the flowers;
[品題] appraise a person;
[品脫] pint;
[品味] savour; taste;
品味細嚼 chew sth slowly to savour it;
[品行] behaviour; conduct;
品行不端 bad conduct; dishonourable behaviour; misconduct;
品行端正 correct in behaviour; good conduct; well-behaved;
品行方正 have an upright character;
[品性] moral character;
善良的品性 good nature;
[品學] character and education;

P

品端學優 morally upright and highly educated;
品學兼優 a good student of good character; excellent both in conduct and learning; of good character and fine education;

[品質] (1) character; quality; (2) quality of commodities;
品質敗壞 morally degenerate;
品質控制經理 quality control manager;
品質意識 sense of quality;
品質優良 excellent quality; of good quality; of the best quality;
標準品質 standard quality;
大路貨品質 fair average quality;
到貨品質 landed quality;
低品質 low quality;
高品質 high quality;
好品質 good quality;
合銷品質 good merchantable quality;
劣品質 bad quality; poor quality;
上等品質 top quality;
頭等品質 first class quality; first-rate quality;
下等品質 inferior quality;
一般品質 common quality;
優等品質 superior quality;
裝船品質 shipped quality;

[品種] (1) breed; cultivated varieties; (2) assortment; variety;
品種齊全 a great variety of goods; complete range of articles; have a good assortment of goods;
多系品種 composite variety;
改良品種 improved variety;
高產品種 high-yield variety;
商業品種 commercial variety;
新品種 new variety;
雜交品種 crossbreed; hybrid variety;

備品 spare parts;
必需品 necessaries; necessities;
舶來品 foreign goods; imported goods;
補品 foods of highly nutritious value; tonic;
殘品 damaged articles; defective goods;
藏品 object;
草織品 straw articles;
產品 produce; product;
陳列品 exhibit;
成品 end product; finished product;
出品 make; manufacture; produce; product;
次品 defective goods; substandard goods; substandard products;
疵品 bad work;
代用品 substitute;
蛋品 egg product;
抵押品 pledge; security;
毒品 narcotic drugs; narcotics;
非賣品 (of articles) not for sale;
廢品 (1) waste product; (2) scrap; waste;
副品 substandard goods;
革製品 leather goods;
供品 offerings;
貢品 articles of tribute;
果品 fruit;
化妝品 cosmetics;
貨品 kinds of goods; quality of product;
極品 best quality; highest grade;
紀念品 keepsake; memento; souvenir;
祭品 sacrificial offerings;
獎品 award; prize; trophy;
禁制品 banned product;
精品 choicest goods;
九品 nine grades of rank in the feudal regimes;
軍需品 military stores; military supplies;
禮品 gift; present;
劣品 poor products;
妙品 (1) fine quality goods; (2) fine work of art;
奶品 dairy product; milk product;
農產品 agricultural products; farm produce;
陪葬品 funeral objects;
棋品 character of a chess player; one's demeanour while playing chess;
人品 (1) character; moral quality; moral standing; (2) bearing; looks;
日用品 articles of daily use; daily necessities;
乳品 dairy products;
乳制品 dairy product;
色品 chroma; chromaticity;
商品 commodity; goods; merchandise;
上品 highest grade; top grade;
奢侈品 luxury goods;
神品 sublime works of art; works of genius;
食品 food; foodstuff; provisions;
試驗品 experimental articles;
試用品 trial product;
收藏品 collection;
輸入品 import;
藤製品 rattan work;
甜品 dessert; sweetmeats;
調味品 condiment; flavouring; seasoning;
託賣品 consignment goods;
完品 (1) perfect piece; (2) perfect quality;
違禁品 contraband goods;

物品 articles; goods;
犧牲品 prey; victim;
下品 (1) inferior; low-grade; (2) short creation;
消費品 consumer goods;
小品 (1) inferior; low-grade; (2) short creation;
宣傳品 propaganda material;
藝術品 arts and crafts; works of art;
贗品 counterfeit; fake; sham;
樣品 exponent; prototype; sample; specimen;
藥品 drugs; medicine and chemical reagents; pharmaceutical products;
一品 the highest rank in officialdom in ancient China;
逸品 superior piece of artistic work;
印刷品 printed matter;
用品 articles for use;
雜品 groceries; sundry goods;
贓品 booty; loot; plunder; stolen goods;
贈品 complimentary gift; gift; giveaway; present;
展覽品 exhibit; item on display;
展品 exhibit; item on display;
戰利品 booty; captured equipment; loot; spoils of war; war trophies;
珍品 curio; delicacies; gem; precious objects; treasures; valuables;
真品 genuine article;
正品 certified goods; certified products; quality goods;
織品 fabrics;
製品 goods; products;
專利品 patent; patented article;
專賣品 monopoly;
裝飾品 ornament;
作品 works;

pin⁴

pin

【牝】 female animal;

［牝雞司晨］ the hen cackles in the morning — a woman usurping man's power;

［牝馬］ female horse; mare;
小牝馬 colt; filly; foal;

［牝牡驪黃］ one's real worth is more valuable than his looks; material aspects of things;

［牝牛］ cow;

pin

【聘】 (1) engage; (2) betroth; (3) be married off; get married; (4) employ;

［聘金］ fee;

［聘禮］ betrothal presents;

［聘請］ call in; hire; recruit;

［聘任］ appoint to a position; engage;
聘任制 appointing system;
短期聘任 sessional appointment;

［聘書］ contract; letter of appointment;

［聘問］ visit a friendly nation on behalf of one's own country;

［聘選］ engage and select;

［聘用］ hire under contract; employ; engage;
聘用和解雇的權力 the power to hire and fire;
聘用制 system of employment under contract;
重金聘用 employ with a high pay; engage an employment at a high salary;

［聘約］ engagement;

報聘 pay a return visit to a friendly country on behalf of one's own government;
辭聘 discharge an appointment; refuse a job offer;
敦聘 sincerely invite sb to undertake a post;
回聘 re-employment;
解聘 dismiss an employee; non-reappointment;
禮聘 invite or engage sb in a polite, respectful way;
受聘 accept a job offer;
下聘 present betrothal gifts;
延聘 employ; engage; invite the service of;
應聘 accept an offer of employment;
招聘 advertise for vacancies; give public notice of a vacancy to be filled; invite applications for a job; recruit; recruit and employ;
徵聘 give public notice of vacancies to be filled; invite applications for jobs;

ping¹

ping

【乒】 (of sound) ping;

［乒乓］ (1) rattle; (2) table tennis;
乒乓球 (1) ping-pong; table tennis; (2) ping-pong ball; table tennis ball;
~打乒乓球 play table tennis;

［乒壇］ table tennis circles;

ping

【娉】 charming; elegant; good-looking; graceful;

［娉婷］ have a graceful demeanour;
娉婷玉貌 slender, beautiful figure;

ping²
ping

【平】 (1) even; flat; level; plain; smooth; (2) bring to the same level; equal; on a level with; on a par; on the same level; (3) level; (4) make the same score; tie; (5) equal; fair; (6) calm; peaceful; quiet; safe; (7) put down; suppress; (8) average; common; (9) a surname;

［平安］ peaceful; safe; safe and sound; well; without mishap;

平安到達 arrive safe and sound; arrive safely;

平安度日 lead a life of peace;

平安回家 arrive home safe and sound;

平安歸來 return without mishap;

平安康泰 peaceful and well-being;

平安脱險 get off with a whole skin; keep a whole skin;

平安無事 all is well; in a whole skin; in peace; safe and sound; tranquillity and peace; with a whole skin; without accident;

平安無恙 in one piece; without scathe; scatheless;

袋袋平安 a pocketful of goodies;

一路平安 have a safe journey;

竹報平安 a family letter reporting all is well;

［平白］ for no reason at all; gratuitously;

平白無故 for no apparent reason; for no reason at all; gratuitously; groundless; without any reason; without provocation; without rhyme or reason;

［平板］ dull; flat; flatbed; monotonous;

平板卡車 flatbed truck;

平板掃描機 flatbed scanner;

平板推車 hand trolley;

［平輩］ of the same generation;

［平常］ (1) ordinary; common; (2) as a rule; as usual; generally; normally; ordinarily; ordinary times; usually; (3) average; mediocre;

平常的 bog-standard;

［平川］ flat plain;

平川廣野 boundless plain;

一馬平川 a boundless expanse of flat land; a great stretch of land; a stretch of open country; a vast expanse of flat land; a wide expanse of flat land; a wide stretch of flat country; the boundless plain; the flat country;

［平淡］ dull; flat; insipid; pedestrian; prosaic; savourless; uninteresting;

平淡無奇 appear trite and insignificant; commonplace; dull; insipid; lack distinction; matter-of-fact; nothing exciting; nothing to write home about; ordinary; pedestrian; plain and inconspicuous; prosaic;

平淡無味 insipid;

［平等］ equal; equality; on an equal footing;

平等待人 treat all on an equal footing; treat others as equals; treat sb like one's equal;

平等待遇 equal treatment;

平等互惠 equality and mutual benefit; equality and reciprocity;

平等互利 equality and mutual benefit; on an equal footing with mutual benefit; reciprocity based on equality;

平等伙伴關係 equal partnership;

平等競爭 fair competition;

平等相待 treat...on equal footing;

平等協商 consultation on the basis of equality;

平等主義 egalitarianism;

使平等 equalize;

［平底］ flat-bottomed;

平底船 flat-bottomed boat; flatboat;

平底鍋 flat-bottomed pan; frying pan;

平底鞋 flat shoes;

［平地］ (1) level the land; rake the ground; (2) flat ground; level ground;

平地車 grader;

平地春雷 a peal of spring thunder roars over the horizon — an unexpected happy event; a sudden clap of spring thunder — a sudden big change;

平地登天 a sudden rise to fame; spring to heaven from the level;

平地而起 rise from the level ground;

平地風波 a storm out of nowhere; a sudden storm on a calm sea; a sudden, unexpected turn of events; an unexpected occurrence; an unforeseen trouble;

平地樓台 like a high building going up from the ground; start from scratch;

平地一聲雷 a peal of spring thunder roars

over the horizon; a sudden big change; a sudden clap of thunder; a sudden rise in fame and position; an unexpected happy event; suddenly comes a clap of thunder; zip across the horizon;
平地再起 start from scratch all over again;
如履平地 as easily as walking on a level road;
夷為平地 level to the ground; raze; reduce the city to a shambles;

[平碟] plate;

[平定] calm down; pacify; put down; quell; suppress;
平定風波 pour oil on troubled waters;
平定叛亂 suppress a rebellion; suppress a riot;

[平凡] common; commonplace; ordinary; undistinguished;
平凡的 corny;

[平反] redress a wronged case; rehabilitate;
平反冤獄 reverse an unjust verdict;
平反昭雪 redress fabricated cases and rehabilitate those who have been wronged; rehabilitate those who have been wrongfully accused;

[平方] (of mathematics) square;
平方根 square root;
平方公里 square kilometre;
平方釐米 square centimetre;
平方米 square metre;
平方器 squarer;
平方英尺 square foot;
平方英寸 square inch;
平方英里 square mile;
加法平方 addition squares;
完全平方 perfect square;
正合平方 exact square;

[平房] bungalow; one-storey house;

[平分] divide equally; go cahoots; go halves; go in cahoots; go in cahoots; to the halves;
平分秋色 divide equally; go fifty-fifty; go halves; go share and share alike; go shares; leg and leg; share equally;
平分天下 divide the country between...and...;

[平憤] redress one's grievances;
為民平憤 redress the grievances of the people;

[平復] (1) be pacified; calm down; subside; (2) be cured; be healed;

[平和] (1) equanimity; gentle; mild; moderate; placid; (2) (of mahjong) a win without points;
平和的 equable;
性情平和 have a calm temper;

[平衡] balance; balanced; balancing; equilibrium;
平衡錘 compensating counterweight; counterbalance; counterweight;
~臂板平衡錘 semaphore counterbalance; semaphore counterweight;
信號臂板平衡錘 semaphore counterbalance;
~接軸平衡錘 spindle counterweight;
~可調平衡錘 adjustable counterweight;
~聯鎖機平衡錘 interlocking frame counterweight;
~料鐘平衡錘 bell counterweight;
~尾桿平衡錘 tail lever counterweight;
平衡動作 movement of balance
平衡分析法 method of balance analysis;
平衡感 sense of balance;
平衡句 balanced sentence;
平衡架 gimbal;
平衡木 balance beam;
平衡器 balance; balancer; counterbalance;
~交流平衡器 alternating-current balancer;
~交流聲平衡器 hum balancer;
~可調平衡器 adjustable counter balance;
~相位平衡器 phase balancer;
~載漏平衡器 carrier leak balancer;
~直流平衡器 direct current balancer;
~指針平衡器 pointer counterbalance;
~轉矩平衡器 torque balancer;
~自動張力平衡器 automatic tension balancer;
平衡物 balancer;
平衡吸附 equilibrium adsorption;
平衡增長 balanced growth;
平衡作用 balancing action;
半微量平衡 semi-micro-analytical balance;
保持…平衡 keep...balance;
~保持心理平衡 keep one's mental balance;
~保持心態理平衡 keep the ecological balance;
保持平衡 balance; hold the balance; keep balance; keep the balance; maintain the balance;

補償平衡 compensation balance;
不平衡 disequilibrium; imbalance;
~長期不平衡 secular disequilibrium;
~周期性不平衡 cyclical disequilibrium;
彩色平衡 colour balance;
產銷平衡 co-ordination of production and marketing;
磁道平衡 track balance;
粗平衡 coarse balance;
達至平衡 strike a balance;
代謝平衡 metabolic balance;
單段平衡 single-section balance;
等效平衡 active balance;
電感平衡 induction balance;
電橋平衡 bridge balance;
電容平衡 capacity balance;
電子平衡 dynetric balancing;
動態平衡 dynamic balancing; dynamic equilibrium;
多基固平衡 polygenic balance;
二元平衡 binary equilibrium;
幅度平衡 amplitude balance;
負載平衡 load balance; load balancing;
~自動負載平衡 automatic load balancing;
輔助平衡 auxiliary balance;
改變平衡 alter the balance; change the balance; shift the balance;
鈣平衡 calcium balance;
供銷平衡 co-ordination of supply and marketing;
供需平衡 co-ordination of supply and demand;
慣性平衡 inertia balance;
橫向平衡 lateral balance;
恢復平衡 redress the balance; regain the balance; restore the balance;
集總平衡 lumped balance;
季節平衡 seasonal balance;
交叉平衡 transposition balance;
競爭平衡 competitive equilibrium;
靜力平衡 standing balance;
靜平衡 static balancing;
流阻平衡 drag balance;
貿易平衡 balance of trade; trade balance;
破壞平衡 destroy the balance; upset the balance;
取得平衡 achieve a balance;
熱平衡 calorific balance; thermal equilibrium;
~鍋爐熱平衡 boiler heat balance;
溶劑平衡 solvent balance;
掃描平衡 sweep balance;
生態平衡 ecological balance;
生物平衡 biological balance;
失去平衡 be off balance; be out of balance; lose one's balance;
~身體失去平衡 be off balance; be out of balance; throw sb off sb's balance;
適當的平衡 correct balance; proper balance; right balance;
使平衡 counterbalance;
數據平衡 data balancing;
酸碱平衡 acid-base balance;
酸鹼平衡 acid-alkaline equilibrium;
隨意平衡 indifferent equilibrium;
隨遇平衡 neutral balance;
碳平衡 carbon balance;
調制平衡 modulation balance;
舵平衡 rudder balance;
穩定平衡 stable equilibrium;
~不穩定平衡 unstable equilibrium;
細緻平衡 detailed balance;
相平衡 phase equilibrium;
延時平衡 delay balance;
營養物平衡 nutrient balance;
載波平衡 carrier balance;
~副載波平衡 subcarrier balance;
找到平衡 find a balance;
振幅平衡 amplitude equilibrium;
正確平衡 correct balance;
矢量平衡 vector balancing;
種群平衡 population balance;
重錘式平衡 counterweight balance;
裝配線平衡 assembly line balancing;
自動平衡 automatic balance;
自動載波平衡 automatic carrier balance;
自然平衡 natural balance;

[平滑] level and smooth; smooth;

[平價] (1) reasonable price; (2) par; parity;
平價供應 under unified state distribution at fixed prices;
平價匯率 par of exchange; par rate of exchange;
平價銷售 reasonable price;
波動平價 fluctuating par;
成本構成平價 cost structure parity;
對換平價 conversion parity;
黃金平價 gold par;
假定平價 hypothetical par;
絕對平價 absolute par;
美元平價 dollar par;
商業平價 commercial par;
鑄幣平價 mint par;

[平靜] calm; quiet; tranquil;
平靜如鏡 glassy calm;

[平靖] (1) suppress a rebellion and stabilize the situation; (2) stable;

[平局] draw; tie;
扳成平局 equalize the score;
打成平局 break even; come out even; draw; draw a game; end in a draw; fight to a standoff; play even; tie it up; tie the score;

[平均] (1) average; mean; (2) equally; share and share alike; (3) average; averaging; mean; mean value;
平均成本 average cost;
~平均成本法 average cost method;
平均服務速率 average service rate;
平均故障間隔時間 mean time between failures;
平均故障時間 average service rate;
平均故障修理時間 mean time to restore;
平均積分點 grade point average;
平均利潤 average profit;
~平均利潤率 average profit rate;
平均毛額 gross average;
平均數 average;
~幾何平均數 geometric mean;
~假定平均數 arbitrary average; assumed average; assumed mean;
~每日平均數 average of daily figures;
~年平均數 annual average;
~普通平均數 common average;
~算術平均數 arithmetic mean;
~調和平均數 harmonic mean;
~週整平均數 adjusted mean;
~序時平均數 chronological average;
~移動平均數 moving average;
~指數平均數 exponential average;
~綜合平均數 compound average;
平均算 strike an average;
平均維修時間 meantime maintenance time;
平均信息速率 average information rate;
平均值 average;
~輔助平均值 auxiliary means;
~匯集平均值 assembly average;
~加權平均值 weighted average;
~漸近平均值 asymptotic mean;
~經驗平均值 empirical mean;
~信號平均值 signal averaging;
平均主義 egalitarianism; equalitarianism;
~絕對平均主義 absolute equalitarianism;
多重平均 multiple averaging;
過程平均 process average;
幾何平均 geometric mean;
累加平均 progressive average;
鄰域平均 neighbourhood averaging;
年平均 annual mean;
群上平均 group averaging;
收入平均 income averaging;
算術平均 arithmetic mean;
相平均 phase average;
移動平均 rolling average;
有效平均 actual mean;
總平均 grand average; overall average;

[平臉] down-faced;

[平列] place on a par with each other; place side by side;

[平流] advection;
平流變化 advective change;
平流層 stratosphere;
平流霧 advection fog;
冷平流 cold advection;
熱平流 thermal advection;

[平面] flat surface; plane; two dimensions;
平面波 plane wave;
平面幾何 plane geometry;
平面圖 planimetric map;
超平面 hyperplane;
~特徵超平面 characteristic hyperplane;
~一般超平面 general hyperplane;
~坐標超平面 coordinate hyperplane;
海平面 sea level;
焦平面 focal plane;

[平民] civilian; common people; populace;
平民百姓 little people;
平民主義 populism;
~平民主義運動 populist movement;
~平民主義者 populist;
平民裝 civilian clothes;
下層平民 pleb; plebeian;

[平年] (1) common year; non-leap year; (2) average year;

[平盤] flat plate;

[平平] average; indifferent; mediocre;
平平當當 smooth-going;
平平凡凡 average and not outstanding; make no figure; mediocre; nothing remarkable;
平平靜靜 in quiet;
平平穩穩 on an even keel; sure and steady;

[平鋪直敘] a monotonous portraying; a

straightfoward narration; narrate in a simple direct way; speak in a dull, flat style; state plainly; tell in a dull, flat way; tell in a simple, straight-forward way;

[平權] equal rights;

[平人] common people; ordinary person;

[平日] (1) ordinary days; (2) every day; week day;

[平山填溝] level hilltops and fill in gullies;

[平生] all one's life; during one's lifetime; one's lifetime; one's whole life;

平生不做虧生事，夜半敲門心不驚 a clear conscience laughs at false accusations; a good conscience is a soft pillow; a quiet conscience sleeps in thunder;

平生大事 the biggest event in all one's life;

平生之願 a lifelong aspiration; a lifelong wish;

得慰平生 fulfil the hope of one's life; fulfil the hopes of a lifetime; gratify the desire of one's whole life; the desire of one's life is satisfied;

素昧平生 strangers to each other; have never made sb's acquaintance; have never met before; have never seen each other before; know nothing about each other; not to know each other before;

[平聲] level tone in Chinese;

[平時] at ordinary times; in normal times; ordinarily;

平時不燒香，急來抱佛腳 do nothing until the last minute; fair weather atheists turn to God in a pinch; neglect one's prayers in times of peace, then embrace the Buddha's feet in a crisis; never burn joss sticks at ordinary times, but embracing the feet of the Buddha in time of need; never burn incense when all is well but clasp Buddha's feet when in distress; when there is urgent business you clasp the feet of Buddha, but when nothing happens you do not even burn incense;

[平實] natural; simple and unadorned;

[平手] draw;

[平順] plain sailing; smooth-going;

[平素] always; customarily; in normal times; ordinarily; usually;

[平台] flat; platform; terrace;

平台集裝箱 platform container;

機艙平台 engine-room flat;

羅經平台 compass flat;

[平坦] even; flat; level; smooth;

[平頭] (of hairstyle) buzz cut; close crop; crew cut; flat-top;

平頭百姓 common people;

平頭正臉 neat appearance; well-featured;

剃平頭 have a crew cut;

[平胃] settle the stomach;

[平穩] even; smooth and steady; stable; steady;

平穩點 stationary point;

平穩過渡 smooth transition;

飛行不太平穩 the flight was not very smooth;

七平八穩 balanced and stable; firm; rigid; solid as a rock; stable;

四平八穩 calm and steady; completely stable and safe; dependable; lacking in initiative and overcautious; on the safe side; play it safe; steady and sure; well-balanced;

[平昔] in the past;

[平息] (1) calm down; come to an end; quiet down; subside; (2) put down; stamp out; suppress;

平息風波 pour oil on the waters; pour oil on troubled waters;

[平心] calmly;

平心而論 do sb justice; frankly; give sb one's due; give the devil his due; honest; in all fairness; to be just and fair;

平心靜氣 calmly; cool-headed; dispassionate; in one's sober senses; unflustered; with a calm mind;

蕩意平心 allay the thought and quiet the mind;

[平信] ordinary mail; surface mail;

[平行] (1) of equal rank; of the same level; on an equal footing; (2) simultaneous; (3) parallel;

平行格 parallelism;

平行四邊形 parallelogram;

平行線 parallel lines;

平行研究 parallel study;

平行作業 parallel operations; simultaneous production;

[平胸] flat chest;
平胸的 flat-chested;

[平易] (1) amiable; unassuming; (2) easy; plain;
平易近人 amiable; amiable and approachable; amiable and easy of approach; easily approachable; easy to approach; easy to get along with; have the common touch; popular among one's colleagues; simple and easy to approach; unassuming and approachable;
~平易近人的品質 common touch;
~平易近人的人 person of easy access;

[平庸] commonplace; indifferent; mediocre; ordinary;
平庸的 banal; mediocre;
平庸無奇 commonplace; nothing out of the ordinary;

[平魚] common pomfret;

[平原] flat country; flatland; plain;
岸灘平原 beach plain;
冰水沉積平原 outwash plain; outwash apron;
剝蝕平原 plain of denudation;
衝積平原 alluvial plain;
泛濫平原 floodplain;
海岸平原 coastal plain;
湖成平原 lacustrine plain;
黃土平原 loess plain;
火山灰平原 ash plain;
盆地平原 basin plain;
沙垻平原 bar plain;
一片平原 a stretch of plain;
準平原 peneplain;

[平允] fair opinion;
持論平允 pass a fair opinion;

[平仄] level and oblique tones;

[平展] open and flat;

[平整] flatten; level;
平整土地 level the land;

[平正] even and straight; neat and smooth;

[平直形式] (of hairstyle) smooth style;

[平裝] paperback;
平裝本 paperback edition;
平裝書 paperback;

[平足] flatfoot;

耙平 rake smooth;
擺平 treat fairly;
扳平 equalize the score;
扁平 flat;
不平 (1) not level; not smooth; uneven; (2) injustice; unfairness; wrong; (3) complaint; grievance; indignant; resentful;
剷平 level; level to the ground;
扯平 even make sb; make even;
承平 peaceful;
持平 fair; impartial; unbiased;
打平 draw a tie;
蕩平 clear away; quell rebellion; sweep off;
地平 ground level; horizon; horizontal plane; terrestrial horizon
墊平 level up;
放平 (1) put sth flat on the ground; (2) knock somebody down;
公平 equitable; equity; fair; fairness; impartial; just;
和平 calm; mild; peace;
矯平 flattening; levelling; roll flattening;
勘平 succeed in suppressing (a rebellion);
拉平 bring to the same level; even up;
敉平 put down; suppress;
清平 peace and tranquility;
掃平 crush; put down; quell an uprising; suppress;
昇平 peaceful;
生平 (1) all one's life; in the course of one's life; one's life-time; (2) biographical sketch;
水平 (1) horizontal; level; (2) level; standard;
太平 peaceful and tranquil;
討平 send armed forces to put down a rebellion;
天平 balance; scales;
填平 fill and level up; fill up and make even;
透平 turbine;
楔平 wedge even;
削平 (1) pare; smooth; (2) conquer; put down; suppress;
壓平 crush; even; flatten; smash;
陽平 the second tone;
熨平 iron;
找平 level up or down; make level;
治平 govern the nation and bring peace to the world;
追平 draw level;

ping

【坪】 flat piece of land; level ground; level piece of ground;

草坪 lawn;
曬坪 sunning ground;

停機坪 tarmac;

ping
【屏】 (1) screen; (2) a set of scrolls; (3) guard; screen; shield sb or sth;
［屏蔽］ screen; shield; shielding;
飛機屏蔽 aircraft shielding;
介質屏蔽 dielectric shielding;
整體屏蔽 bulk shielding;
［屏藩］ (1) screen and fence; (2) protect and safeguard;
［屏風］ screen;
［屏門］ screen door;
［屏幕］ screen;
屏幕構造系統 screen builder system;
屏幕上 onscreen;
屏幕顯示 screen display;
大屏幕 big screen; large screen;
~大屏幕彩色投影機 large screen projector;
~大屏幕彩色投影儀 large screen projector;
~大屏幕投影 large screen projection;
~大屏幕顯示 large screen display;
~超大屏幕 very large screen;
電視屏幕 TV screen;
手寫屏幕 scratchpad;
［屏障］ parclose; protective screen;
物種屏障 species barrier;

插屏 table plague;
耳屏 tragus;
藩屏 line of defence; protective barrier;
掛屏 set of hanging scrolls;
畫屏 painted screen;
開屏 display its fine tail feathers;
壽屏 birthday scrolls inscribed with poems or messages wishing sb a long life;
網屏 screen;
圍屏 folding screen;

ping
【枰】 (1) chessboard; (2) chess game;

ping
【洴】 (1) sound of silk floating in the wind; (2) bleach; wash;
［洴澼］ (1) rinse; (2) sound of water;

ping
【苹】 (1) a kind of herb; (2) same as 萍;

ping
【秤】 balance; steelyard; weighing scale;

ping
【瓶】 bottle; flask; jar; vase;
［瓶膽］ glass liner;
［瓶兒］ bottle;
［瓶蓋］ cap;
［瓶頸］ bottleneck;
瓶頸路段 bottleneck;
［瓶塞］ bottle plug; bottle stopper; cork;
瓶塞鑽 corkscrew;
［瓶裝］ bottled; in bottles;
瓶裝水 bottled water;
［瓶子］ bottle;
空瓶子 empties; empty bottle;
~一批空瓶子 a platoon of empty bottles;
一簍瓶子 a crate of bottles;
一羅瓶子 a gross of bottles;

保溫瓶 thermos bottle; vacuum bottle;
比重瓶 gravity bottle; specific gravity bottle;
標本瓶 specimen bottle;
冰瓶 ice bucket;
瓷瓶 (1) china bottle; (2) insulator; (3) china bowl;
醋瓶 (1) bottle of vinegar; (2) extremely jealous spouse;
膽瓶 vase with a slender neck and a bulging belly;
電瓶 storage battery;
對瓶 twin vases;
海流瓶 current bottle;
花瓶 flower vase; vase;
離心瓶 centrifuge bottle;
量瓶 measuring flask;
奶瓶 feeding bottle; nursing bottle;
暖瓶 thermos bottle; thermos flask;
暖水瓶 thermos bottle; vacuum bottle;
培養瓶 culture bottle;
啤酒瓶 beer bottle;
葡萄酒瓶 burgundy bottle;
氣瓶 air bottle;
取樣瓶 sampling bottle;
熱水瓶 thermos bottle; vacuum bottle;
燒瓶 flask;
雙層瓶 double bottle;
水瓶 water bottle;
稀釋瓶 dilution bottle;
吸氣瓶 aspirator bottle;
吸收瓶 absorption bottle;
洗氣瓶 gas washing bottle;
小鹽瓶 salt shaker;
壓縮空氣瓶 compressed air bottle;

鹽瓶 shaker;
藥瓶 medicine bottle;
飲料瓶 beverage bottle;

ping

【萍】 duckweed;

［萍散蓬飄］ like floating duckweed and falling raspberry—have no fixed abode;

［萍蹤］ tracks of a wanderer;
萍蹤浪跡 a restless fellow like a drifting water plant; come and go without trace; have no fixed abode because of constant travelling;
萍蹤天涯 roam freely all over the world;
萍蹤無定 go hither and thither like a floating weed; one's whereabouts are uncertain; roam about; wander aimlessly;

浮萍 duckweed;
水萍 duckweed;
紫萍 duckweed;

ping

【評】 (1) comment; criticize; review; (2) appraise; judge;

［評比］ appraise through comparison; compare and assess;

［評定］ appraisal; appraise; assess; assessment; evaluate; evaluation; pass judgment on; rate;
故障評定 fault assessment;
教育評定 educational evaluation;
學業成績評定 academic achievement evaluation;

［評斷］ arbitrate; judge;

［評分］ (1) give marks; give points; grade; mark a script; score; (2) decide on work points;
評分標準 standards of grading;
評分法 score;

［評工］ evaluate works;

［評功］ appraise sb's merits; evaluate achievements;
評功擺好 enumerate sb's merits; set forth the merits of sb; speak of sb in glowing terms;
評功記分 calculate work points on the basis of work done; evaluate work and allot workpoints; evaluation of work and allotment of workpoints;

［評估］ appraise; appraisal; assess; assessment; estimate; estimation; evaluate; evaluation;
評估策略 assessment strategies;
評估方向 assessment direction;
評估團 evaluation group;
評估系統 evaluation system;
評估原則 assessment principles;
評估中心 evaluation centre;
持續評估 continuous assessment;
重新評估 reappraise;
多元化的評估 diversified assessment;
全面的評估 holistic assessment;
職務評估 job evaluation;

［評級］ grade; rate;

［評價］ appraise; assess; estimate; evaluate; evaluation; rating;
評價報告分析 analysis for evaluation report;
評價分析 evaluation analysis;
評價過高的 overrated;
評價系統 evaluation system;
評價性理解 evaluative comprehension;
重新評價 reappraise;
界面評價 interface rating;
性能評價 rating of merit;
再評價 revaluation;
主觀評價 subjective assessment;
~主觀評價法 subjective approach;

［評獎］ decide on a prize-winner;

［評介］ review;

［評理］ (1) decide which side is right; judge between right and wrong; (2) have it out; reason things out;

［評論］ comment; comment on; criticize; critique; discuss; make comments on; review;
評論從句 comment clause;
評論家 critic; reviewer;
評論文章 leading article;
評論員 commentator;
負面的評論 negative comment;
歡迎評論 welcome comments;
獲得評論 receive comments;
簡短的評論 brief comment; quick comment;
正面的評論 positive comment;
作出評論 make a comment; pass judgement on;

［評判］ decide; judge; pass judgment on;

評判優劣 judge which is superior;

[評批] evaluative;

評批性理解 evaluative comprehension;

[評審] adjudication; judge;

評審委員會 review and adjudication board;

評審制度 judging system;

[評書] storytelling;

[評述] commentary;

[評説] comment on; evaluate;

[評選] appraise and elect; choose through public appraisal; discuss and elect;

[評議] appraise sth through discussion; deliberate;

[評語] comment; remark;

[評閱] read and appraise;

[評讚] estimate and praise;

[評註] (1) make commentary and annotation; (2) notes and commentary;

[評傳] critical biography;

定評 accepted opinion; critical recognition; public acknowledgement;

短評 brief comment; short commentary;

估評 evaluation;

好評 favourable comments; good review; high opinion of;

講評 comment on and appraise;

劇評 dramatic criticism;

批評 (1) criticism; (2) criticize;

品評 comment on; judge;

社評 editorial;

時評 newspaper commentary on current affairs;

史評 books or writings on history or historic records;

書評 book review;

述評 commentary; review;

瞎批評 criticize blindly;

譯評 translation criticism;

雜評 short commentary;

總評 general comment; overall appraisal;

ping

【馮】 (1) by dint of; on the strength of; (2) gallop;

[馮怒] greatly infuriated; rage; wrath;

[馮河] cross a river without a boat; reckless;

[馮閎] boundless; expansive; vast;

[馮虛御風] a feat attributed to immortals; tread thin air and sail by wind;

[馮資] be based on; depend on; rely upon;

ping

【缾】 bottle;

ping

【軿】 curtained carriage;

ping

【憑】 (1) lean against; lean on; lean over; (2) depend on; rely on; (3) certification; evidence; proof; (4) base on; go by; (5) no matter;

[憑單] bill; certificate; voucher;

[憑借] (1) depend on; rely on; resort to; (2) by means of; on the basis of; on the strength of;

憑借暴力 rely on violence;

憑借個人努力 rely on one's own efforts;

憑借經驗 by virtue of experience;

憑借想像力 draw on one's imagination;

[憑據] evidence; proof;

有憑有據 fully substantiated; furnish with proof and evidence; there is abundant evidence; well-documented; well-founded;

真憑實據 conclusive proof; concrete proff and genuine evidence; genuine evidence; indisputable proof;

[憑空] baseless; groundless; out of the void; out of thin air; without basis; without foundation; without ground;

憑空杜撰 draw on one's imagination; make up out of nothing;

憑空捏造 a sheer fabrication; create out of nothing; dream up; fabricate out of nothing; make out of whole cloth; make up a story; out of the whole cloth; trump up;

憑空起事 make trouble out of nothing;

憑空設想 figment of the imagination;

憑空造謠 create a rumour without basis; fabricate lies out of thin air;

[憑欄] lean against the railing; lean upon a balustrade;

憑欄觀望 lean over the rail looking at;

憑欄遠眺 lean on a balcony and look at the distance; lean on a railing and gaze into the distance;

[憑眺] enjoy a distant view from a height; have a commanding view of; look into the distance from a high place; survey

from a height;
［憑信］ believe; trust;
［憑依］ base oneself on; have sth to go by; rely on;
無所憑依 have nothing to go by;
［憑仗］ depend on; rely on;
［憑照］ certificate; licence; permit;
［憑證］ certificate; evidence; proof; voucher;

任憑 (1) at one's convenience; (2) no matter;
聽憑 allow; let;
文憑 diploma;
依憑 depend on; rely on;

ping
【蘋】 apple;
［蘋果］ apple;
蘋果乾 apple slices;
蘋果核 apple core;
蘋果醬 apple butter; apple jam; apple sauce;
蘋果酒 cider;
~ 乾蘋果酒 dry cider;
~ 烈性蘋果酒 hard cider; scrumpy;
~ 新釀蘋果酒 new cider;
~ 一桶蘋果酒 a cask of cider;
蘋果綠 apple green;
蘋果蜜餞 candied apple;
蘋果脯 preserved apple;
蘋果蓉 apple paste;
蘋果樹 apple tree;
蘋果園 apple orchard;
蘋果汁 apple juice;
焦糖蘋果 candy apple;
烤蘋果 baked apple;
青蘋果 green apple;
酸蘋果 crab apple;
~ 酸蘋果樹 crab apple;
太妃蘋果 andy apple;
一個蘋果 an apple;
一筐蘋果 a basket of apples;
一箱蘋果 a crate of apples;

ping⁴
ping
【聘】 give away a daughter in marriage; marry;

po¹
po
【坡】 bank; hillside; slope;
［坡地］ hillside fields; sloping fields;
［坡頂］ brow of a hill;
［坡度］ gradient; slope; degree of steepness of a slope;
［坡路］ sloping road;
走上坡路 go uphill; make steady progress; on the up-and-up; upgrade;
走下坡路 go downhill; go off the boil; hit the skids; on the decline; on the downgrade; over the hill;

陡坡 steep slope;
護坡 slope protection;
滑坡 (1) landslide; (2) go steadily downhill; slide downhill;
緩坡 gentle slope;
開始走下坡 the rot sets in;
慢坡 gentle slope;
山坡 hillside; mountain slope;
上坡 climb a slope; upslope;
退坡 backslide; fall off;
脱坡 wash away dike slopes;
斜坡 inclination; incline; slope; steep incline;

po
【波】 a pronunciation of 波;

po
【陂】 steep and craggy;
［陂陀］ with ups and downs;
陂陀不平 slanting and uneven;

po
【頗】 (1) rather; somewhat; (2) fairly; quite; very; (3) be inclined to one side; (4) a surname;
［頗為］ rather;
頗為費解 rather difficult to understand;

偏頗 biased; partial;

po
【潑】 (1) splash; sprinkle; (2) rude and unreasonable; shrewish;
［潑婦］ fishwife; harridan; harpy; shrew; shrewish woman; vixen;
潑婦罵街 like a shrew swearing in the street;
［潑辣］ (1) bold and forceful; (2) rude and unreasonable; shrewish;
潑辣貨 ferocious woman; scoundrel;
［潑墨］ splash-ink technique;
潑墨山水 splash-ink landscape;
［潑水難收］ it is no use crying over spilt milk;

P

things done cannot be undone;

活潑 (1) lively; vivid; (2) reactive;

飄潑 (of rain) heavy; torrential;

撒潑 be unreasonable and make a scene;

po²

po

【婆】 (1) old woman; (2) a woman in a certain occupation; (3) one's husband's mother; one's mother-in-law;

[婆家] one's husband's family;

[婆娘] (1) young married woman; (2) one's wife;

懶婆娘的裹腳，又長又臭 foot-bindings of a slattern, long as well as smelly;

[婆婆] (1) one's husband's mother; one's mother-in-law; (2) grandmother;

婆婆媽媽 behave like an old woman; fussy; garrulous; make a fuss of sb; nameby-pamby; shilly-shally about like an old woman; womanishly fussy;

婆婆嘴 gossipy;

婆婆嘴，豆腐心 one's bark is worse than one's bite;

[婆娑] dancing; spiralling; whirling;

婆娑起舞 start dancing; throw oneself into a dance;

[婆心] kind heart;

苦口婆心 admonish earnestly;

一片婆心 exhort kindheartedly; kind heart; motherly feeling;

阿婆 (1) one's grandma; one's granma; one's granmamma; one's granny; (2) one's mother-in-law; (3) old granny;

媼婆 female examiner of corpses;

產婆 midwife;

惡婆 harridan;

公婆 parents-in-law;

姑婆 (1) one's husband's paternal aunt; (2) one's grandfather's sister;

黃臉婆 yellow-faced woman – one's wife;

老婆 wife;

媒婆 woman matchmaker;

虔婆 (1) low woman; (2) madam; procuress;

梢婆 boatwoman;

艄婆 boatwoman;

蛇婆 sea serpent;

神婆 sorceress; witch;

嬸婆 wife of husband's uncle who is younger than his father;

師婆 sorceress; witch;

叔婆 wife of one's grandfather's younger brother;

太婆 one's great-grandmother;

外婆 gran; granny; one's grandmother;

穩婆 midwife;

巫婆 sorceress; witch;

牙婆 procuress;

姨婆 grandaunt;

po

【鄱】 Poyang, the name of a county in Jiangxi;

po

【緐】 a surname;

po

【皤】 white;

[皤皤] hoary; white;

[皤然] white;

po³

po

【叵】 impossible;

[叵測] unfathomable; unpredictable;

居心叵測 harbour evil intention towards; have evil designs; with concealed intentions; with hidden intent; with ulterior motives;

人心叵測 harbour an evil heart; man's heart is incomprehensible; one's heart is past finding out; the heart of man is past finding out;

心懷叵測 cherish evil designs; entertain rebellious schemes; harbour dark designs; harbour evil intentions; have an ax to grind; have an evil intent towards; have some dirty tricks up one's sleeve; nurse evil intentions;

[叵耐] cannot put up with; cannot tolerate;

po

【笸】

[笸籮] shallow basket;

針線笸籮 sewing basket;

po

【頗】 (1) rather; somewhat; (2) fairly; quite; very; (3) inclined to one side; (4) a surname;

po⁴

po

【朴】 saltpeter;

po
【拍】 a pronunciation of 拍 ;

po
【泊】 a pronunciation of 泊 ;

po
【珀】 amber;

琥珀 amber;

po
【迫】 (1) compel; force; (2) pressing; urgent; (3) approach; go towards;

[迫不得已] be compelled by circumstances; be compelled by necessity; be compelled to; be driven to; be forced to; bow to necessity; cannot help; do sth against one's will; have no alternative but to; under the pressure of circumstances; very pressing;

[迫不及待] brook no delay; can wait no longer; hasten to; in haste; lose no time; no sooner...than; too impatient to wait; unable to hold oneself back; unable to wait any longer; with unusual haste;

[迫害] oppress cruelly; persecute;
受迫害 suffer persecution;
~受迫害妄想症 persecution complex;
遭受迫害 suffer persecution;

[迫降] make a forced landing; make an emergency landing;

[迫近] approach; draw near; get close to; imminent;
迫近年關 get close to the end of the year;

[迫臨] approach; get close to;

[迫切] imperative; pressing; urgent;
迫切陳詞 state one's views with a keen sense of urgency;

[迫使] compel; force;
迫使就範 compel sb to submit;

被迫 be compelled; be constrained; be forced;
逼迫 coerce; compel; constrain; force;
急迫 imperative; pressing; urgent;
交迫 (of pressure) come from all sides;
緊迫 imminent; pressing; urgent;
窘迫 (1) poverty-stricken; very poor; (2) hard pressed; in a predicament; in an awkward position;
強迫 coerce; compel; force;
驅迫 order about; urge;
日迫 get closer day by day; time is running out;
威迫 intimidate;
脅迫 coerce; coercion; threaten with force;
壓迫 force; oppress; press hard; repress; ride on sb's back;

po
【破】 (1) broken; damaged; torn; worn-out; (2) break; cleave; cut; damage; split; (3) break with; destroy; get rid of; (4) defeat; capture; (5) expose the truth of; lay bare; (6) lousy; paltry;

[破案] clear up a case; crack a criminal case; solve a case; track down the criminal;

[破敗] dilapidated; ruined; tumbledown;
破敗失修 fall into disrepair;
破牆敗瓦 broken walls and tiles;

[破壁飛去] become wealthy and influencial all of a sudden;

[破冰船] icebreaker;

[破財] lose money;
破財消災 give money in the hope of being freed from trouble; suffer unexpected personal fanancial losses to remove misfortune;
財破災消 free oneself from troubles by giving money;

[破產] (1) bankrupt; become impoverished; become insolvent; go bankrupt; go broke; go into bankruptcy; go to the wall; (2) come to naught; fall through; wrecked;
破產程序 bankruptcy procedure;
破產的 bankrupt;
破產法 bankruptcy law;
破產管理人 bankruptcy administrator;
破產連鎖反應 chain-reaction bankruptcies;
破產資本 bankruptcy cost;
過失破產 negligent bankruptcy;
假破產 fraudulent bankruptcy;
瀕臨破產 on the verge of bankruptcy;
宣告破產 declare bankruptcy;
自願申請破產 voluntary bankruptcy;

[破除] abolish; break with; do away with; eradicate; get rid of;
破除陳規 break away from the conventions;
破除積習 eliminate a longstanding practice — remove a habit;

破除舊習俗 do away with old customs;
破除迷信 abolish blind faith; abolish superstitions; break down fetishes and superstitions; destroy the blind faith in; destroy the myths; do away with fetishes and superstitions; do away with myths; free one's mind of restrictive ideas; get rid of superstition; shatter blind faith; topple old idols;
破除情面 dispense with face-saving; not to spare anybody's feelings;

[破費] go to some expense; spend lots of money;

[破格] break a rule; make an exception; poetic licence;
破格錄用 break a rule to engage sb;
破格使用 make use of sb in defiance of the rules;
破格提昇 break a rule to promote sb; unconventionally promote;

[破罐破摔] write oneself off as hopeless and act recklessly, and make no attempt to mend one's ways;

[破鍋有爛灶，李哥有張嫂] every Jack has his Jill;

[破壞] damage; decompose; destroy; do damage to; failure; wreck;
破壞別人的計劃 crab sb's game; spoil sb's game;
破壞搗亂 carry out sabotage and make trouble;
破壞公共財物 damage public property;
破壞生產 sabotage production;
破壞他人名譽 damage other's reputation;
破壞者 destroyer;
暗中破壞 bore from within;
脆性破壞 brittle failure;
複合破壞 combined failure;
故意破壞 vandalize;
黏合破壞 adhesion failure;
四處破壞 marauding;
蓄意破壞 sabotage;
~蓄意破壞者 saboteur;

[破獲] ferret out; uncover; unearth;
破獲走私集團 unearth a smuggling ring;

[破鏡重圓] retie a loose marriage knot; reunion of a couple after separation;

[破舊] dilapidated; old and shabby; outdated; worn-out;
破舊立新 abolish the old and build up the new; destroy the old and establish the new; discard the old and create sth new; disrupt the old roder and establish a new one; eradicate the old and foster the new; the destruction of the old and the establishing of the new;

[破口] (1) cut; (2) get a cut;
破口大罵 abuse roundly; bawl abuse; curse freely; give vent to a torrent of abuse; heap abuse on; hurl all kinds of abuse against; let loose a flood of abuse; pour out a whole ocean of abuse over; pour out torrents of abuse; raise hail Columbia; rave widely against; shout abuse; swear home; swear like a trooper; swear one's way through swear one's way through a stone wall; swear through a two-inch board; vociferate oaths;
破口而出 belch;

[破爛] (1) dilapidated; ragged; tattered; worn-out; (2) junk; scrap;
破爛貨 dreck;
撿破爛 search in garbage for odds and ends;
收破爛 collect scrap;
~收破爛的人 ragman;
揀破爛的人 bag lady;

[破立] make or break;
不破不立 there's no making without breaking;
善破善立 good at destroying the old and establishing the new;
先破後立 destruction before construction;
有破有立 overthrow certain things and establish others; there are both destruction and construction;

[破例] break a rule; make an exception; stretch a point; stretch the rules; waive a rule;
破例通融 make an exception; strain a point; stretch a point;

[破臉] fall out; turn against sb;

[破裂] break; breakup; burst; bust-up; crack; fracture; rupture; split;
破裂帶 fracture zone;
感情破裂 fall out;
瀕臨破裂 on the rocks;
談判破裂 the negotiations broke down;

[破落] be reduced to poverty; come down in

the world; decline; fall into reduced circumstances;
破落戶 a family that has gone down in the world; an impoverished family;

[破門] (1) burst open the door; (2) excommunication;
破門而出 break through the door and dash out;
破門而入 break in; break into; burst the door in; force open a door;

[破滅] be disillusioned; be shattered; evaporate; fall through;
幻想破滅 be disillusioned;

[破碎] (1) broken; tattered; (2) break into pieces; crush; smash sth into pieces; tear into shreds;
破碎設備 crushing appliance;
破碎支離 be reduced to fragments; fallen apart; torn to pieces;

[破損] breakage; damage;

[破題] first part of an eight-legged essay;
破題兒第一遭 for the very first time; the first time ever; the first time one ever does sth; without precedent in history;

[破涕] stop crying;
破涕為笑 a sudden change from crying into smiles; laugh through one's tears; one's tears give way to laughter; turn tears into smiles;

[破天荒] occur for the first time; take the extraordinary step; unheard of; unprecedented;

[破土而出] break through the soil—said of a young bamboo shoot, etc.;

[破相] face marked by a scar;

[破曉] dawn; daybreak; first light;
破曉時分 at dawn; at the crack of dawn; at the peep of day;

[破鞋] loose woman; wanton;

[破顏] break into a smile;
破顏一笑 break into a smile; break one's stern countenance and smile; crack a smile;

[破衣] duds;

[破甑生塵] in extreme poverty; with the cooking pot covered with dust;

[破綻] (1) burst seam; (2) flaw; weak point;
破綻百出 full of flaws; full of holes; full of loopholes; ragged; rags and tatters;
賣個破綻 feint in combat to attract a thrust by one's opponent; make a feint; pretend to have met a mischance; purposely to give one's opponent an opening; spot sb's weak point;
找破綻 find a flaw;

[破折號] dash;

[破竹] irresistible force;
破竹之勢 an irresistible force; an overwhelming force; easy to attain success;
勢如破竹 advance with irresistible force; carry all before one; carry everything before one; carry the world before one; like a hot knife cutting through butter; like splitting a bamboo; meet with no resistance; push forward from victory to victory; push onward with overwhelming momentum; with irresistible force; without a hitch;
~勢如破竹，所向披靡 brave dauntlessly all difficulties and be ever victorious; smash all enemy resistance and advance victoriously everywhere;

爆破 blast; blow up; demolish; dynamite;
殘破 (1) broken; damaged; dilapidated; spoiled; (2) deficient; incomplete;
查破 break a criminal case; investigate and unearth;
撦破 tear open;
衝破 breach; break through;
戳破 break;
打破 (1) break; smash; (2) break away from;
膽破 be frightened to death; be scared to death;
道破 lay bare; point out frankly; reveal;
點破 bring sth out into the open; lay bare; point out;
攻破 breach; make a breakthrough;
劃破 lacerate;
擊破 break up; destroy; smash;
看破 see through;
潰破 break up;
磨破 abrade; wear;
敲破 shatter; smash;
揭破 bring to light; disclose; expose;
識破 penetrate; see through;
摔破 (1) suffer bruses; (2) break sth by dashing it on the ground;
説破 disclose; lay bare; reveal;
撕破 rip; tear;
突破 break through; make a breakthrough;
稀破 ruptured; tattered; torn;

楔破 cleave with a wedge;
壓破 broken by high pressure;
咬破 (1) bite through; break by the teeth; (2) make a thorough remark about sth;
偵破 bust a crime; clear up a case; crack a criminal case; solve a case;
抓破 injure skin by scratching;
撞破 (1) hurt by bumping; (2) surprise sb in an illegal act or awkward situation;

po
【粕】 dregs; lees; refuse; sediment of liquor;

po
【魄】 (1) soul; (2) boldness; courage; daring and resolution; spirit; vigour;
［魄力］ boldness; daring and resolution;

魂魄 soul;
落魄 (1) down and out; in dire straits; (2) objection; (3) bold and generous;
氣魄 breadth of spirit; imposing manner;
體魄 build; physique;
心魄 heart; soul; spirit;

po
【醱】 brew for the second time;

pou¹
pou
【剖】 (1) cut; cut open; dissect; rip open; (2) analyse; examine;
［剖白］ explain oneself; vindicate oneself;
剖白心跡 lay bare one's true feelings; lay one's heart bare;
［剖斗折衡］ break the measure and destroy the scales – settle a struggle by getting rid of the thing that causes trouble; destroy weights and measures;
［剖腹］ cut open the stomach; make an abdominal incision;
剖腹產子 caesarean;
剖腹藏珠 cut open one's stomach to hide the pearl – sacrifice one's own life to conceal one's treasured possession;
剖腹探查 abdominal laparotomy;
剖腹明心 bare one's heart in all sincerity; disclose one's real feelings; make a clean breast of; slit one's belly to show loyalty – lay open one's heart; tear the heart out of one's breast and show it to sb;
剖腹生產 caesarean birth;
剖腹術 laparotomy;
剖腹剜心 cut open sb's side and dig out his heart; disembowel sb and have his heart torn out;
［剖開］ cut open;
［剖面］ profile; section;
剖面圖 cross-section drawing; profile; sectional diagram;
~標準剖面圖 master profile;
~磁剖面圖 magnetic profile;
~速度剖面圖 velocity profile;
航空剖面 airborne profile;
葉片剖面 blade profile;
翼剖面 airfoil profile;
［剖視圖］ cutaway view;
［剖析］ analyse; decompose; dissect; parse;
剖析事理 analyse the whys and wherefores;
剖析思想 analyse one's thought;
剖析問題 analyse a problem;
剖析原因 analyse the root cause of; get to the bottom of;

解剖 anatomy; dissect;

pou²
pou
【抔】 scoop up with both hands;
［抔水而飲］ drink from cupped hands;

pou
【掊】 break; cut; strike;

pou
【裒】 collect; gather; scrape together;
［裒輯］ collect and edit; compile;

pou³
pou
【剖】 (1) cut; rip open; tear open; (2) analyze; explain;

pou
【掊】 collect; exact;
［掊克］ exact high taxes from people;

pou
【瓿】 jar; pot;

pu¹
pu
【仆】 fall; prostrate;

pu
【扑】 beat; strike;

[扑罰] flogging as a punishment; scourge; whipping as a punishment;
[扑撻] flog; lash; whip;
[扑擊] hit; strike;
[扑作教刑] use a rod to teach and punish;

pu
【痡】 ailment; disease;

pu
【撲】 (1) pounce; pounce on; throw oneself on; (2) devote; (3) attack; rush at; slap at; strike downwards; (4) flap; flutter;
[撲鼻] assail the nostrils;
稻香撲鼻 be greeted by the all-pervasive fragrance of ripening rice;
[撲哧] (1) cloop; fizz; splash; (2) snigger; titter;
撲哧一聲 with a fizz;
撲哧一笑 break into laughter; burst into a laugh; chuckle to oneself; snigger; titter;
[撲打] (1) swat; (2) beat; pat;
[撲粉] (1) face powder; (2) talcum powder; (3) apply powder; put on powder;
[撲救] put out a fire to save life and property;
[撲克] (1) playing cards; (2) poker;
撲克牌戲 poker;
打撲克 (1) play poker; (2) play cards;
[撲空] come away empty-handed; fail to get or achieve what one wants; fail to meet sb one intends to meet;
[撲滿] earthern money box; piggy bank;
[撲面] blow against one's face; blow on one's face;
撲面粉 face powder;
[撲滅] exterminate; extinguish; put out; stamp out;
撲滅火災 stamp out a fire;
撲滅森林大火 put out a forest fire;
[撲簌] tears trickling down;
撲簌淚下 one's tears pour down;
[撲騰] thud; thump;
[撲通] flop; pit-a-pat; plop; splash; thud; thump;
撲通一聲 with a splash;

反撲 launch a counter-offensive to retrieve lost ground; pounce on sb again after being beaten off;

pu
【鋪】 (1) extend; spread; (2) lay; pave;
[鋪陳] describe at great length; elaborate; narrate in detail;
鋪陳華麗 arrange beautifully; decorate attractively;
[鋪牀] make the bed;
鋪牀疊被 make a bed; make the bed; tidy sb's bed and fold up the quilts;
[鋪蓋] bedroll; bedding;
打鋪蓋 set up a bed;
鋪天蓋地 blot out the sky and cover up the earth; blot out the sky and the land;
捲鋪蓋 get one's leave; get one's walking orders; get one's walking ticket; get one's walking-papers; get the air; get the axe; get the bag; get the bird; get the boot; get the bounce; get the chuck; get the gate;
[鋪路] pave the way;
鋪路材料 paving;
鋪路機 paver;
~ 混凝土鋪路機 concrete paver;
~ 瀝青鋪路機 bituminous paver; blacktop paver;
鋪路磚材 brick paving;
搭橋鋪路 facilitate; pave the way for; remove obstacles;
[鋪面] pavement;
護坡鋪面 storm pavement;
人造石鋪面 granolithic pavement;
[鋪排] (1) arrange; put in order; (2) extravagant;
[鋪砌] pave; paving;
大塊石鋪砌 boulder paving;
斜角鋪砌 diagonal paving;
側磚鋪砌 brick-on-edge paving;
[鋪設] build; lay; spread out;
[鋪敘] elaborate; narrate in detail;
[鋪展] sprawl; spread out;
[鋪張] extravagant;
鋪張浪費 extravagance and waste; extravagant and wasteful; profligacy;
鋪張門面 keep up appearances;
鋪張揚厲 in an ostentatious manner; indulge in extravagance and ostentation; praise extravagantly;
大事鋪張 make much of a little; present with a great fanfare;

pu²

pu

【朴】 (1) a kind of oak; (2) plain; simple;

［朴茂］ honest; sincere;

［朴刀］ sword with a long blade and a short hilt;

［朴鈍］ blunt;

［朴陋］ things in their original state;

［朴忠］ faithful; honest; loyal;

［朴樹］ hackberry;

pu

【匍】 crawl; creep; lie prostrate;

［匍匐］ (1) crawl; creep; (2) lie on one's face; lie prone; prostrate oneself;

匍匐哀求 beg piteously; fall prostrate and beg sorrowfully; implore heart-rendingly;

匍匐前進 advance on all fours; crawl forward; creep forward;

pu

【鈈】 polonium;

pu

【脯】 flesh of meat in the general area of chest or breast;

［脯子］ breast meat;

pu

【莆】 county in Fujian;

pu

【菩】 (1) fragrant herb; (2) sacred tree of the Buddhists;

［菩薩］ (1) Bodhisattva; (2) Buddha;

菩薩低眉 kind-looking; with a kind expression on one's face;

菩薩心腸 a great kind heart; have a heart of gold; kind-hearted and merciful;

［菩提］ bodhi;

菩提樹 pipal;

pu

【葡】 (1) grape; vine; (2) short for Portugal;

［葡萄］ grape;

葡萄乾 dried-to-raisin grapes; raisin;

~ 風乾葡萄乾 cured raisin;

~ 天然葡萄乾 natural raisin;

葡萄醬 beshmet;

葡萄酒 wine; wine made from grapes;

~ 葡萄酒商 wine merchant;

~ 葡萄酒專家 wine buff;

~ 白葡萄酒 white wine;

乾白葡萄酒 dry white wine;

~ 陳釀葡萄酒 aged wine; ageing wine;

~ 充氣葡萄酒 aerated wine;

~ 紅葡萄酒 claret; red wine;

~ 加度葡萄酒 fortified wine;

~ 加香葡萄酒 aromatized wine;

~ 開胃葡萄酒 appetizer wine;

~ 熱葡萄酒 mulled wine;

~ 桶裝葡萄酒 bulk wine;

~ 一杯葡萄酒 a glass of wine;

~ 一瓶葡萄酒 a bottle of wine;

葡萄糖 dextrose; glucose;

~ 葡萄糖粉 powdered glucose;

~ 葡萄糖酸 gluconic acid;

~ 葡萄糖糖精 dextrosaccharin;

~ 氨基葡萄糖 glucosamine;

~ 粗製葡萄糖 crude dextrose;

~ 結晶葡萄糖 crystalline dextrose;

~ 精製葡萄糖 refined dextrose;

~ 散裝葡萄糖 bulk handling dextrose;

~ 無水葡萄糖 anhydrous dextrose;

葡萄柚 grapefruit;

葡萄栽培 culture of grapes;

葡萄汁 grape juice;

刺葡萄 brier grape;

狐臭葡萄 fox grape;

毛葡萄 downy grape;

鳥葡萄 bird grape;

去梗葡萄 stemmed grape;

麝香葡萄 muscat grape;

酸葡萄 sour grapes;

無核葡萄 raisin grape;

一串葡萄 a bunch of grapes; a cluster of grapes;

圓葉葡萄 muscadine grape;

紫葡萄 dark-skinned grape;

pu

【僕】 servant; attendant;

［僕從］ footman; hanger-on; henchman; retainer; servant;

［僕婦］ elderly woman servant;

［僕僕］ travel-stained; travel-worn and weary;

僕僕道途 after an arduous journey;

僕僕風塵 endure the hardships of a long journey; endure the hardships of travel; travel-soiled; travel-stained;

［僕人］ domestic servant; servant;

順從的僕人 amenable servant;

［僕役］ domestic servant;

僕役長 butler;

P

公僕 public servant;
男僕 houseboy;
奴僕 lackey; servant;
女僕 handmaiden; maidservant;
童僕 house boys;
義僕 faithful servant;
主僕 master and servant;

pu
【蒲】 (1) vines of the rushes; (2) a surname;

菖蒲 calamus;
摴蒲 dice;
香蒲 cattail;

pu
【捕】 ancient dice game;

pu
【酺】 drink in company;

pu
【幞】 headdress; scarf; turban;
［幞頭］ headdress; scarf; turban;

pu
【樸】 (1) plain; simple; (2) substance of things; things in the rough; (3) honest; loyal; simple; sincere; (4) aphananthe aspera;
［樸厚］ plain, honest and kind; simple and loyal;
［樸陋］ simple and crude; without any artificial decoration;
［樸茂］ simple, honest and kind; sincere and honest;
［樸實］ (1) plain; simple; (2) down-to-earth; guileless; sincere and honest;
樸實無華 simple and unadorned;
［樸素］ plain; simple;
樸素大方 plain and dignified; simple and tasteful;
［樸學］ down-to-earth learning;
［樸直］ honest and straightforward; simple and honest;
［樸質］ natural; simple and unadorned;

誠樸 honest; sincere and simple;
純樸 honest; simple; unsophisticated;
淳樸 honest; simple; unsophisticated;
古樸 of primitive simplicity; simple and ancient-styled;
渾樸 simple and honest;
儉樸 economical; thrifty and simple;
簡樸 simple and unadorned;
勤樸 industrious and frugal;
素樸 (1) simple and unadorned; (2) rudimentary;
質樸 simple and unadorned; unaffected;

pu
【璞】 uncut jade;
［璞玉渾金］ uncarved jade and unrefined gold — unadorned beauty;

pu
【濮】 (1) an ancient river in today's Henan; (2) an ancient barbarian tribe; (3) a surname;

pu
【蹼】 webs on the feet of water fowls;

pu
【醭】 white specks of mildew;

pu³
pu
【圃】 (1) orchard; plantation; vegetable garden; (2) planter;

菜圃 vegetable farm; vegetable garden;
花圃 flower nursery;
苗圃 nursery (of young plants);
蔬圃 vegetable garden;
園圃 garden;

pu
【埔】 (1) arena; plain; (2) mart; port;

pu
【浦】 (1) beach; shore; (2) a surname;

幫浦 pump;

pu
【普】 common; general; universal;
［普遍］ common; general; universal; widespread;
普遍化 generalization;
~詞義普遍化 generalization of meaning;
普遍性量表 scale of generality;
普遍優惠制 general system of preference;
［普查］ general investigation; general survey;
家庭普查 family census;
全面普查 general census;
人口普查 national census; population census;
一體化普查 integrated census;
［普惠］ general preferential;
普惠稅 general preferential duties;

普惠制 generalized system of preferences;

［普及］ (1) disseminate; popularize; spread; (2) popular; universal;

普及本 popular edition;

普及教育 universal education;

普及義務教育 popularization of compulsory education;

［普通］ average; common; general; ordinary;

普通艙 the economy cabin;

普通的 bog-standard;

普通副詞 ordinary adverb;

普通股 common stock;

普通話 colloquial;

普通名詞 common noun;

普通人 average person; ordinary person; the man in the street;

普通數量詞 universal quantifier;

普通稅 general tax;

普通型號 standard model;

普通許可合同 simple licence;

普通語言學 general linguistics;

普通語義學 general semantics;

［普選］ general election; universal suffrage;

普選法 general election law;

［普照］ illuminate all things;

普照大地 illuminate every corner of the land; illuminate the earth; shine over the good earth;

科普 popular science;

pu

【溥】 (1) great; vast; wide; (2) universal;

pu

【譜】 (1) list; record; register; table; (2) musical score; (3) compose a song; (4) general idea; rough picture; (5) collection of examples for reference purpose;

［譜號］ clef;

高音譜號 treble clef;

［譜曲］ set a poem;

為詩詞譜曲 set a poem to music;

［譜子］ music score; music;

擺譜 go in for extravagance; keep up appearance; show off one's wealth; take pains to show off; try to appear rich and elegant;

波譜 spectrum;

菜譜 recipe;

詞譜 collection of tunes of ci poems;

歌譜 music of a song; music score of a song;

光譜 spectrum;

畫譜 (1) book of model paintings or drawings; (2) book on the art of drawing or painting;

極譜 polarogram;

家譜 family tree; genealogical tree; genealogy;

簡譜 numbered musical notation;

離譜 be out of place; go beyond what is proper;

臉譜 types of facial makeup in operas;

年譜 chronicle of sb's life;

棋譜 chess manual;

曲譜 (1) music score of Chinese operas; (2) a collection of tunes of qu;

聲譜 sound spectrum;

食譜 cookbook; recipe;

圖譜 collection of illustrative plates;

姓譜 genealogy;

樂譜 music; music score;

總譜 score;

族譜 genealogical table of a clan;

pu

【鐠】 praseodymium;

pu⁴

pu

【暴】 expose;

［暴露］ be exposed; expose; exposure;

［暴面］ appear; make appearance;

pu

【鋪】 (1) shop; store; (2) plank bed;

［鋪子］ shop; store;

查鋪 bed check; go the rounds of the beds at night;

成衣鋪 tailor's shop;

牀鋪 bed;

當鋪 pawnbroker's shop; pawnshop; pop shop;

地鋪 bed space on the floor; makeshift bed; shakedown;

店鋪 shop; store;

吊鋪 hammock; hanging bed;

飯鋪 eating house; restaurant;

酒鋪 wine shop;

錢鋪 banking house;

犬鋪 doghouse; kennel;

肉鋪 butcher's shop;

山貨鋪 shop selling rustic articles of wood, bamboo, clay, etc.;

上鋪 upper berth;

書鋪 bookstore;

通鋪 wide bed for a number of people;

桶鋪 coopery;
窩鋪 shack; shed;
卧鋪 sleeping berth;
下鋪 lower berth;
鞋鋪 shoeshop;
藥鋪 dispensary; druggist's store; herbal medicine shop;
雜貨鋪 grocery;
中藥鋪 shop of traditional Chinese medicines;

pu

【舖】 same as 鋪 ;

pu

【瀑】 cascade; cataract; waterfall;

［瀑布］ waterfall; falls;
瀑布飛泉 waterfall and flying stream;
小瀑布 cascade;

［瀑流］ cascade; cataract; waterfall;

飛瀑 waterfall;

pu

【曝】 expose to the sun;

［曝光］ exposure;
曝光錶 exposure meter;
曝光表 actinometer; light meter;
曝光不足 underexposure;
曝光過度 overexposure;
曝光計 actinometer;
對數曝光 logarithmic exposure;
二次曝光 double exposure; reversal exposure;
過度曝光 overexpose; overexposure;
適度曝光 correct exposure;
雙掩膜曝光 double resist exposure;
自動曝光 automatic exposure;

［曝露］ be exposed to the open air;
日曝夜露 be exposed to the sun and the dew;

［曝曬］ solarization;

qi¹
qi

【七】 hept-; hepta-; sept-; septenary; septi-; septimal; septuple; seven;

［七八］ seven or eight;

七八成 (1) seventy or eighty per cent; (2) extremely likely; possibly; probably;

七八月的南瓜一皮老心不老 pumpkings in the seventh or eighth month of the lunar calendar — the skin is old but the heart is young; old in age but young at heart;

夾七夾八 at random; cluttered; confused; incoherent; talk incoherently;

亂七八糟 a fine kettle of fish; a glorious mess; a nice kettle of fish; a pretty kettle of fish; all in a tumble; at sixes and sevens; chaotic; higgledy-piggledy; in a clutter; in a littler; in a mess; in a muddle; in a pickle; in a state; in an awful mess; in complete confusion; in wild disorder; jumbly; looking-glass; make a mess of sth; make hay of; rough-and-tumble; topsy-turvy; upside down;

~亂七八糟的 higgledy-piggledy;

~亂七八糟説一通 make a chaos of utterances; talk senselessly;

~房間亂七八糟 one's room is a dump; one's room is in a mess; one's room is topsy-turvy;

~搞得亂七八糟 make a mess;

~將計劃搞得亂七八糟 mess up one's plans; throw one's plans into confusion;

~心裏亂七八糟 feel all hot and bothered; feel very perturbed;

七洞八穿 air-conditioned; full of holes; ragged; riddled with bullets;

七孔八洞 tattered; threadbare; well worn; worn into many holes;

七老八十 advanced in life; aged; at an advanced age; in one's seventies and eighties; very old;

七楞八瓣 of uneven size and formation;

七撓八裂 hinder sb from doing sth; make trouble;

七扭八歪 crooked; disorderly; in a state of great disorder; in disorder; irregular; rig up; uneven;

七溝八梁 full of gullies and ridges; seven gullies and eight ridges;

烏七八糟 dirty; filthy; foul; in a horrible mess; in great disorder; in total confusion; in total disarray; in total disorder; obscene; rubbish;

瞎七搭八 all in confusion; topsy-turvy;

雜七雜八 motley; assorted; farraginous; miscellaneous; mixed;

［七倍體］ heptaploid;

［七邊形］ heptagon; septangle; septilateral;

［七步］ seven steps;

七步成詩 compose a poem within the time required for taking seven steps; make a verse while taking seven steps;

［七次］ seven times; seventh;

［七對］ (of mahjong) seven pairs;

［七番］ (of mahjong) seven times;

［七國］ the seven states in the Warring States Period (403-221 B.C.) — Qin秦, Chu 楚, Yan 燕, Zhao 趙, Han 韓, Wei 魏, and Qi 齊;

［七行詩］ heptastich;

［七級風］ force 7 wind;

［七絕］ four-line seven-character poem;

［七律］ eight-line seven-character poem;

［七面體］ heptahedron;

［七巧板］ seven-piece puzzle; tangram;

［七竅］ the seven orifices in the human head;

七竅流血 bleed from all the seven openings of one's head; bleed from one's nose, eyes, mouth and ears; blood is flowing from the seven openings in one's head;

七竅生煙 angry; blow a fuse; blow a gasket; blow one's lid; blow one's stack; blow one's top; bluster oneself into anger; burnt up; foam with rage; fume with anger; fumigate with anger; in a fume; indignant; livid with rage; one's face sparks with fury; one's eyes smoulder; seethe with anger;

~氣得七竅生煙 boil with anger;

七竅心靈 the heart of the wise;

［七情］ seven human emotions: joy, anger, sorrow, fear, love, hate, and desire;

七情六慾 the seven emotions and six sensory pleasures;

［七日來復］ period of seven days;

［七色］ seven colours of the spectrum;

七色板 Newton's disk;

［七聲］ seven notes of the musical scale;
［七十］ seventy;
七十二變 countless changes of tactics; seventy-two metamorphoses;
七十二行 all sorts of callings; all sorts of occupations; all sorts of professions; all sorts of trades; all the professions and avocations; all walks of life; in every conceivable line of work;
～七十二行，行行出狀元 there are seventy-two professions, and every profession produces its own leading authority;
七十分之一 seventieth;
七十風前燭，八十瓦上霜 a man of seventy is like a candle exposed to the wind; a man of eighty is like the hoarfrost on tiles;
［七夕］ seventh evening of the seventh month;
［七絃琴］ seven-stringed horizontal harp; heptachord; lyre;
［七星瓢蟲］ seven-spot ladybird;
［七葉樹］ horse chestnut;
［七言詩］ poem with seven characters to a line;
［七曜］ seven days of the week;
［七藝］ seven liberal arts: arithmetic, geometry, astronomy, music, grammar, rhetoric, and logic;
［七月］ (1) seventh month of the lunar year; (2) July;

三七 pseudo-ginseng;
十七 seventeen;
田七 pseudo-ginseng;

qi

【沏】 (1) infuse; pour hot water over; (2) raging; rapid; storming; turbulent;
［沏茶］ infuse tea; make tea;
涼水沏茶—沒味兒 making tea with cold water － tasteless;

qi

【妻】 one's ball and chain; one's better half; one's carving knife; one's fork and knife; one's formal wife; one's homework; one's legal wife; one's mother of pearl; one's old Dutch; one's wife;
［妻黨］ one's wife's kinsfolk;
［妻兒］ one's parents, wife and children; the whole family; wife and children;
妻兒老小 one's parents, wife and children; a married man's entire family; wife and family;
遺妻拋兒 forsake one's wife and children;
［妻管嚴］ henpecked;
［妻舅］ one's brother-in-law; one's wife's brother;
［妻女］ wife and daughters;
淫人妻女 violate another's wife and daughters;
［妻孥］ one's wife and children;
罪及妻孥 one's wife and children are punished for one's crimes;
［妻妾］ wife and concubine;
妻不如妾，妾不如偷 a wife is not as good as a concubine, and a concubine is not as good as a mistress;
［妻室］ one's legal wife; one's wife;
［妻小］ one's wife and children;
［妻子］ (1) one's ball and chain; one's better half; one's carving knife; one's fork and knife; one's homework; one's mother of pearl; one's old Dutch; one's wife; (2) one's wife and children;
妻子是別人的好，文章是自己的好 The wife of another person is always better, but one's articles are always superior to others';
背叛妻子 forsake one's wife;
花瓶妻子 trophy wife;
虐待妻子 abuse one's wife;
拋妻棄子 abandon one's wife and children;
妻離子散 a scattered family; be separated from one's family; be separated from one's wife and children; break up a family; families are broken up, with wives separated from their husbands and children separated from their parents; have one's family scattered over different places; one's family is broken up; parents are separated from children, husbands tear themselves away from their wives; the breaking up of a family; the scattering of a family; the wife leaves and the children scatter; with one's family scattered;
～妻離子散，家破人亡 cause the break-up by death or separation of countless

families;
妻賢夫省事，子孝父心寬 a good wife saves her husband a lot of trouble, and a filial son makes his father satisfied;
托妻寄子 entrust one's wife and children to sb;
未來的妻子 future wife;
一味抱怨的妻子 nagging wife;
遺棄妻子 put away one's wife;

愛妻 one's beloved wife;
罷妻 divorce a wife;
髮妻 first wife;
夫妻 husband and wife; man and wife;
後妻 second wife;
換妻 wife-swapping;
棄妻 (1) woman divorced by her husband; (2) divorce one's wife;
前妻 (1) one's ex-wife; one's former wife; (2) one's late wife;
喪妻 be deprived of one's wife;
殺妻 kill one's own wife;
山妻 my wife;
首妻 one's first wife; one's legal wife;
霜妻 widow;
頭妻 (1) one's legal wife; (2) one's former wife;
外妻 concubine;
未婚妻 fiancée;
小妻 concubine;
賢妻 (1) good wife; (2) my dear wife;
筱妻 concubine;
休妻 divorce one's wife;
御妻 control one's wife;
正妻 one's legal wife;

qi
【柒】 seven;

qi
【栖】 (1) (of birds) perch; roost; (2) live; settle; stay;
[栖遲] take a rest;
[栖遑] uneasy and anxious;
栖栖遑遑 rushing about; vexed;
[栖栖然] bustling and excited;

qi
【崎】 jagged; rough; rugged; uneven;
[崎嶇] rugged; uneven terrain;
崎嶇不平 rugged; uneven terrain;
~崎嶇不平的道路 uneven road;
~這條路崎嶇不平 the road is rough;
崎嶇的山脈 rugged mountain range;

qi
【悽】 (1) afflicted; grieved; rueful; sorrowful; suffering; woeful; (2) grievous; pathetic; pitiful; tragic;
[悽慘] hard up; heart-rending; miserable; sad; tragic; wretched;
悽慘的景象 heart-rending scene;
處境極為悽慘 in abject misery;
生活悽慘 lead a miserable life;
[悽惻] grieved; rueful; sad; sorrowful;
[悽楚] grievous; miserable; pathetic; pitiful; saddening; wretched;
[悽愴] (1) cold; desolate; dreary; (2) grievous; miserable; pathetic; pitiful; wretched;
[悽惶] (1) sorrowful and apprehensive; (2) hasty; in a hurry; in haste;
[悽苦] suffering tragically;
[悽戾] grievous; lamentable; sorrowful;
[悽涼] desolate; dreary; melancholy; miserable;
滿目悽涼 desolation all round;
晚景悽涼 lead a miserable and dreary life in old age;
[悽悽] grievous; pathetic; pitiful; sad; sorrowful;
悽悽惶惶 hastily; hurriedly;
[悽戚] sad; sorrowful; woeful;
[悽切] grievous; pathetic; pitiful; saddening; sorrowful;
[悽然] pitiful; sad; sorrowful;
悽然淚落 shed tears in sorrow; shed tears of sadness;
[悽傷] pitiful; sad; sorrowful;
[悽婉] pathetic; pitiful; plaintive; sad; sorrowful;
[悽惘] despondent; disheartened; sad and dejected;

惋悽 pathetic;

qi
【戚】 (1) relations; relatives by marriage; (2) grievous; mournful; pitiful; sad; sorrowful; woeful; worried; (3) battle-axe; (4) a surname;
[戚舊] relatives and old friends;
[戚戚] (1) sorrowful; worried; (2) affected; moved; touched;
戚戚不歡 sorrowful and unhappy;

戚戚自傷 feel sorry for oneself;

[戚然] dejected; depressed; distressed; melancholy;

戚然動容 change countenance when distressed;

[戚施] humpbacked; humped; hunchbacked;

[戚誼] ties between relatives;

哀戚 sad; sorrowful;

悲戚 sad; sorrowful;

親戚 relative;

外戚 relatives of a king or emperor on the side of his mother or wife;

休戚 joys and sorrows;

憂戚 distressed; weighed down with sorrow;

qi

【淒】 (1) chilly; cold; cold and chilly; frigid; (2) bleak weather; cloudy and rainy; weather-beaten; (3) desolate; miserable; sad; sorrowful; unfrequented; wretched;

[淒哀] sad and dreary;

[淒慘] hard up; heartbreaking; heart-rending; miserable; sad; sad and miserable; tragic; wretched;

淒慘景象 tragic scene;

[淒惻] grieved; sad; sorrowful;

[淒楚] heartbreaking; heart-rending; miserable; sad and sorrowful; wretched;

[淒愴] heartbreak; heart rending; miserable; wretched;

[淒風] bitter winds; bleak blasts; bleak winds; chilly winds; cold winds; wailing winds;

淒風苦雨 bitter winds and miserable rains; bleak blasts and dreary rain; bleak winds and wretched rains; chilly winds and cold rains; miserable circumstances; miserable conditions; the wind moans and the rain beats down; wailing winds and saddening rains; wailing winds and weeping rains; wretched circumstances;

淒風切切 the chilly wind sobs;

[淒寒] cold and dreary;

[淒惶] very anxious about;

[淒緊] blowing of the harsh chilly winds;

[淒淚] bitterly cold;

[淒冷] bleak; depressing; desolate;

[淒浰] fast; prompt; quick;

[淒厲] biting; bleak and harsh; forlorn and bitter; sad and sorrowful; shrill and mournful; shrilling; woeful and shrill;

[淒涼] bleak; desolate; desolate and sorrowful; dreary; forlorn; gloomy and forlorn; lonely; lonesome; miserable;

淒涼的景象 desolate scene;

淒涼的生活 desolate life;

淒涼零落 desolate; gloomy and forlorn; miserable;

滿目淒涼 all one can see is grief – full of grief everywhere; desolation all round; desolation spreads as far as the eyes can reach;

身世淒涼 lead a miserable and dreary life; sad life;

[淒迷] (1) cheerless; desolate and indistinct; dreary; (2) depressed; distracted; forlorn; sad;

[淒淒] (1) frigid; windy and rainy; (2) rise of clouds; (3) flowing of tears;

淒淒慘慘 desolating; distressing; heartbreaking;

淒淒惶惶 rushing about in distress;

淒淒切切 mournful; pathetically touching; plaintive;

淒淒涼涼 desolate; forlorn; lonely; miserable;

[淒其] cold and chilly;

[淒切] bitter and sorrowful; mournful; plaintive;

淒切動人 ineffably moving; move one's heart to the point of sadness; sadly moving; so sad and complaisant that it moves people's heart;

寒蟬淒切 it was cold and the cicadas were chirping plaintively;

[淒然] dreary; in sadness; mournful; sad; very sorrowful;

淒然淚下 shed tears in sadness; shed tears of sadness;

淒然一笑 force a wane smile;

[淒傷] grievous; lamentable; mournful; sad; sorrowful;

[淒婉] sad and mild; sadly moving;

淒婉的歌聲 plaintive singing;

[淒艷] (of stories) sad and beautiful;

[淒咽] (of voice) low and sad; sob while

speaking;

qi

【郪】 a river in Sichuan;

qi

【棲】 (1) perch; rest; settle; sit on; stay; (2) dwell; live; stay;

[棲遲] sojourn; travel and rest;

[棲處] (1) stay; dwell; (2) resting place; abode;

[棲遁] in retreat; in seclusion; live in seclusion;

[棲遑] hasty; in a hurry;

[棲居] dwell; live; reside; stay;

[棲苴] grass floating in the water;

[棲流所] refuge for the homeless;

[棲木] dropping board; perch; roost;

[棲泊] come to anchor; sojourn; stay temporarily;

[棲棲] agitated; anxious; jittery; jumpy; nervous; twitchy;

棲棲遑遑 agitated; anxious; jittery; jumpy; nervous; twitchy;

[棲身] dwell; live; live under sb's roof; take shelter; sojourn; stay; stay temporarily;

棲身國外 make one's home abroad;

棲身虎穴 take shelter in a place of danger;

棲身之處 a mere place of shelter; a refuge for the night; a roof over one's head;

棲身之所 a roof over one's head;

[棲神] cultivate one's mind; discipline one's mind;

[棲宿] put up for the night; stay for the night;

[棲息] perch; rest; roost; stay;

棲息地 habitat; sojourn;

去棲息 go to roost;

在樹上棲息 perch on a tree;

[棲止] dwell; settle at a place; sojourn; stay;

共棲 messmatism;

兩棲 amphibian; amphibious;

雙棲 live together as man and wife;

qi

【欺】 (1) bamboozle; cheat; con; deceive; impose; swindle; (2) bully; insult; take advantage of; (3) disregard the dictates of one's own conscience;

[欺誕] cheat by exaggerating;

[欺負] bluff; bluster; browbeat; bulldoze; bully; coerce; insult; intimidate; oppress; overbear; push around; ride roughshod over sb; ridicule; treat sb high-handedly; treat sb rough;

欺負老實人 take advantage of a nice person;

欺負人 (1) bully; (2) bluff;

欺負小國 bully small nations;

軟的欺負硬的怕 bully the weak and fear the strong;

[欺行霸市] boss the marketplace; dominate the market;

[欺哄] beguile; cheat; con; deceive; diddle; dupe; fool; hoax; hoodwink; swindle; take in;

[欺君罔上] deceive the emperor and ignore everybody else; deceive the emperor and those who are above one; deceive the lord and fool the superiors; oppress the prince and deceive one's superiors;

[欺凌] browbeat; bully; bully and humiliate; humiliate; insult; mistreat; ride roughshod over;

備受欺凌 be pretty badly knocked around;

反欺凌 anti-bullying;

~反欺凌活動 anti-bullying campaign;

欺小淩弱 bully the small and the weak;

任人欺凌 allow oneself to be trodden upon;

受盡欺凌 be subjected to endless bullying and humiliation;

[欺瞞] cheat; cover up the truth to cheat; deceive and mislead people; dupe; fool; hoodwink; pull wool over sb's eyes;

[欺矇] befool; cheat; deceive and mislead people; defraud; dupe; fool; hide the truth from sb; hoodwink; pull wool over sb's eyes;

[欺騙] bamboozle; be done in by; beguile; cajoke; cheat; chicanery; come around; come round; come over sb; cozen; cross sb up; deceit; deceive; deception; defraud; delude; diddle; do sb down; do the dirty on sb; draw the wool over sb's eyes; dupe; fool; get over sb; give a flap with a foxtail; gum; have sb on; have sb over sth; hocus-pocus; hoodwink; impose on sb; jiggery-pockery; lead sb up the garden path; make a fool of; play a trick on sb; play sb false; play the old soldier over sb; play upon; pluck; practise on sb; pull a fast one over; pull the wool over sb's eyes; put it across on sb; put on sb; put upon sb; rope along sb; see sb coming; sell sb down the river; set one's cap; string along sb; swindle; take advantage of; take in; take sb for a ride; trick; throw dust in the eyes of; throw mud into the eyes of; throw sb a curve; wheedle;

欺騙的 deceitful;

欺騙顧客 tip the customers;

欺騙技倆 fraudulent methods; tricks of deception;

欺騙蒙混 deceive sb by distorting the truth; dupe and hoodwink sb; pull the wool over sb's eyes;

欺騙群眾 cheat the masses; delude the masses; hoodwink the people;

欺騙色彩 put up a false front;

欺騙手段 cunning means; deceitful manuoeuvres; demagogic trick; subterfuge;

欺騙為生 live by cheating; live by one's wits; live by practising deception;

欺騙小孩 circumvent the children;

欺騙行為 duplicity;

不受人欺騙 nobody's fool;

[欺人] deceive sb;

欺人是禍，饒人是福 bullying people will bring disasters and forgiving people is a blessing;

欺人太甚 a terrible bully; bully others to the extreme; bully others too much; bully sb outrageously; go to extreme lengths; go too far in bullying others; insult a person to excess; it's really too much; take advantage of others beyond the mark; that's going too far; this is really colossal bumbug (coll)

欺人之談 a deceitful lie; deceitful talk; deceptive talk; a forked tongue; a hectoring speech; a lie; a sheer hoax; an eyewash; browbeating words; deceitful words; demagogic stunt; nothing but a hoax; sheer deception;

欺人自欺 be hooked by one's own lies; cheat oneself and others; fool others as well as oneself; try to deceive others only to end up deceiving oneself;

仗勢欺人 bully people on the strength of one's powerful position;

自欺欺人 deceive oneself as well as others;

[欺辱] bully and insult; humiliate;

[欺神滅道] blasphemous and destroy religion;

[欺生] (1) bully newcomers; bully strangers; cheat newcomers; cheat strangers; (2) intractable by strangers; uncontrollable by strangers; ungovernable by strangers; unmanageable by strangers;

鞅罔欺生 worthless person taking advantage of a stranger;

[欺世] deceive the public;

欺世盜名 angle for undeserved fame; deceive the public so as to build up a reputation; deceive the public to win credit for oneself; gain a reputation by deception; gain fame by deceiving the public; gain fame by dishonest means; gain reputation to which one is not entitled by cheating the public; make a name by deceptive means; net fame and hoodwink the public; obtain a good reputation under false pretences; sail under false colours; unsound scholarship; win fame by cheap means; win fame by cheating the world; win popularity by deception; win popularity by dishonest means;

欺世惑眾 deceive people; pull the wool over people's eyes;

欺世亂俗 deceive the people and violate the customs;

釣名欺世 gain a reputation by deception;

[欺罔] beguile; cheat; con; deceive; hoax; hoodwink; pull the wool over;

[欺侮] browbeat; bully; humiliate; insult; play the bully; ridicule; treat sb high-handedly;

受盡欺侮 swallow an insult;

受欺侮 be bullied; be maltreated;

[欺心] disregard the dictates of one's own conscience;

[欺壓] bully and oppress; cheat and oppress; high-handed behaviour; push around; ride roughshod over;

欺壓人民 oppress the people; ride roughshod over the people;

雪壓霜欺 be slighted and insulted by

others;

[欺詐] cheat; deceive; hoodwink; swindle;
欺詐旅客 swindle travelers;
欺詐錢財 defraud sb of money; swindle;
欺詐取勝 delude; gain advantage by deception;

可欺 (1) easily duped; gullible; (2) easily cowed or bullied;

qi

【萋】 (1) dense growth of grass; thick frondage; leafage; luxuriant foliage; (2) cramped; crowded; many;

[萋萋] (1) abundant; luxuriant; (2) clusters of clouds;

qi

【攲】 incline; lean; lean to one side; lurch; slant; tilt;

[攲側] incline; lean; lurch; slant; tilt;
[攲倒] slant and fall;
[攲傾] incline; slant;
[攲危] tottering;
[攲臥] lie in a reclined position;
[攲斜] incline; lurch; slant;

qi

【溪】 a pronunciation of 溪 ;

qi

【漆】 (1) lacquer; paint; (2) apply lacquer; apply paint; coat with lacquer; paint; varnish; (3) lacquer tree; varnish; (4) a surname;

[漆包] enamel cover;
漆包線 enamel-covered wire; enamel-insulated wire;

[漆布] cerecloth; dermateen; leather cloth; varnished cloth;
[漆雕] carved lacquerware;
[漆革] enameled leather; patent leather;
[漆工] (1) lacquering; painting; (2) lacquer man; lacquerer; painter;
[漆黑] complete darkness; jet-black; pitch-black; pitch-dark;
漆黑一團 (1) as black as pitch; complete darkness; in utter darkness; paint in dark colours; pitch-dark; total darkness; totally dark without a glimmer of light; utter darkness; (2) completely ignorant; completely in the dark about sth; entirely ignorant of; in the dark; have no knowledge of sth; in a fog; utterly hopeless;
四周漆黑 pitch-dark all round;
眼前一片漆黑 be left in the dark;
[漆畫] lacquer painting;
[漆匠] lacquer man; lacquerware worker; lacquerer; painter;
[漆皮] (1) coat of paint; patent leather; (2) shellac;
漆皮皮鞋 patent leather shoes;
[漆片] colour chips;
[漆器] lacquerware; lacquerwork;
[漆身吞炭] smear one's body to disguise oneself and eat charcoal to change one's voice — change form and seek vengeance;
[漆書] write in varnish on bamboo tablets;
[漆樹] lacquer tree; varnish tree;

磁漆 enamel;
瓷漆 enamel; enamel paint;
底漆 primer; priming paint;
第一層漆 first coat;
雕漆 carved lacquerware;
堆漆 embossed lacquer;
烘漆 baking finish; stoving finish;
厚漆 paste paint;
火漆 sealing wax;
假漆 varnish;
金漆 gold lacquer;
噴漆 spray lacquer;
清漆 varnish;
乳膠漆 emulsion paint; latex paint;
生漆 raw lacquer;
一道漆 a coat of paint;
油漆 cover with paint; paint;
真漆 lacquer;
中層漆 floating coat;
朱漆 red lacquer; red paint;
最後一層漆 final coat; setting coat;

qi

【慼】 (1) mournful; woeful; (2) ashamed;

[慼貌] sorrowful appearance;
[慼慼] rueful; sad; sorrowful;
[慼容] sad look; sorrowful expression;
[慼憂] sad and depressed;

qi

【緝】 make small stitches; sew in close and

straight stitches;

qi

【諆】 cheat;

qi²

qi

【岐】 (1) the name of a mountain; (2) branch; diverge; fork; (3) deviating; different; divergent;

［岐黃之術］ Chinese herbal medical science;

［岐嶷］ bright;

qi

【其】 (1) her; his; its; their; (2) he, it, she, they; (3) such; that; the; this; (4) interrogative;

［其表］ appearance of sth;

徒有其表 have a good appearance only; keep up appearances — outward show; reduce to pure form;

虛有其表 a penny plain and twopence coloured; appear better than it is; deceptively handsome; good in appearance; good looks without substantial ability; impressive only in appearance; look impressive but lack real worth; many a fine dish has nothing on it; merely ornamental without solidity; one's qualifications are superficial;

［其次］ (1) besides; next; secondly; the next in order; then; (2) next in importance; of minor importance; secondary;

退而求其次 be left with nothing better than the second choice; have no alternative but to give up one's preference; have to be content with the second best; seek what is less attractive than one's original objective; the next best thing;

［其各凜遵］ let all obey the order carefully;

［其間］ among; among them; among which; among whom; between; between them; between which; between whom; during; in; in between; within; within a period of time;

插手其間 have a hand in; meddle in; place oneself in;

置身其間 put oneself in the midst of — be involved;

［其來有自］ it did not happen by accident;

［其樂融融］ very cheerful; with happiness knowing no bounds;

［其貌不揚］ far from beautiful; far from handsome; far from pretty; hard-feathered; hard-visaged; ill-favoured; ill-looking; ill-shaped; not to be much to look at; of undistinguished appearance; one's appearance is ungainly; one's face is ugly; physically unattractive; ugly in appearance;

［其名］ in name;

徒有其名 in name only; nominal;

［其實］ actually; as a matter of fact; in fact; in reality; in truth; really;

其實不然 actually this is not so; in fact that is not the case; it is really not so;

文過其實 beautiful in words but poor in contents;

［其人］ person;

文如其人 a book is no better or worse than its author; like author, like book; the house shows the owner; the style is the man; the writing mirrors the writer; the writing reflects the writer;

［其勢凶凶］ arrogant; bluster; furious in attitude; furiously; give indications of a severe attack as scarlet fever or other ailments; give signs of a spirited attack on the part of the enemy; look formidable; look threatening; put up quite a show;

［其他］ else; other; others; the rest;

其他地方 some other place;

其他費用 other expenses;

其他事情 other things;

［其外］ extra; outside;

［其心可誅］ condemnable in intention; devious in intention; evil-minded; malicious in motive;

［其一］ first; firstly;

二者必居其一 either one or the other;

［其餘］ the others; the remainder; the remaining; the rest;

［其志可嘉］ has a laudable ambition;

［其中］ among; in; among them; among which; among whom; in; in it; in the midst; in which; of them; of those; of which; therein; within;

樂在其中 find pleasure in it;

寢饋其中 completely absorbed in;

更其 even more; more;
何其 how; what;
極其 exceedingly; extremely; most;
卡其 khaki;
淒其 cold and chilly;
如其 (1) if; in case; (2) as for; as to;
惟其 just because;
尤其 above all; especially; in particular; particularly;
與其 rather than;

qi

【奇】 (1) occult; odd; queer; rare; remarkable; special; strange; uncanny; uncommon; unusual; (2) feel strange about; hard to understand; out of nowhere; out of the blue; unexpected; unpredictable; (3) astonishing; surprising; wonderful; (4) exceedingly; extremely;

[奇兵] ambush; an army out of nowhere; attack by surprise; surprise attack; surprise raiders;

[奇才] genius; prodigy; talent; wonder; unusual talent;
奇才異能 a person of rare talent and exceptional ability; a prodigy; extraordinary talents and abilities;
數學奇才 a whiz at mathematics;

[奇點] singularity;
變態奇點 abnormal singularity;
代數奇點 algebraic singularity;
偶然奇點 accidental singularity;

[奇功] distinguished service; meritorious service; outstanding service; remarkable achievements;

[奇怪] (1) curious; funny; odd; queer; strange; surprising; unusual; (2) beyond comprehension; hard to understand; puzzling; strange; unexpected; (3) kaleidoscopic; wonders;
奇怪的 cranky;
~奇怪的是 funnily enough; oddly enough;
感到有點奇怪 feel a bit peculiar;
千奇百怪 a great variety of fantasies; a multitude of wonders; all kinds of strange things; all sorts of strange things; an infinite variety of fantastic phenomena; exceedingly strange; grotesque shapes; numerous strange forms; weird shapes;
說也奇怪 for a wonder; oddly enough; strange to say;
聽起來很奇怪 sound queer;
這事很奇怪 there's sth funny about this;

[奇觀] impressive sight; marvellous spectacle; spectacular sight; wonderful phenomenon; wonderful sight; wonders;
世界七大奇觀 the seven wonders of the world;
蔚為奇觀 be a luxuriant and wonderful spectacle; be a splendid sight; make an impressive sight;

[奇幻] bizarre; fantastic; illusory; queer; singularly varied; strange; visionary;
奇幻莫測 fantastic and unpredictable; mysterious and hard to guess; strange and beyond prediction;

[奇貨可居] a rare commodity worth hoarding; corner the market; hoard as a rare commodity; keep rare commodities for a better price; make a profit by cornering the market; rare and precious goods; rare commodities which can be hoarded for better prices; rare commodity worth hoarding against a later higher price; wait to sell sth valuable at a high price;

[奇禍] unexpected disaster;

[奇蹟] marvels; miracles; strange happenings; strange things; wonders; wonderful achievements;
創造奇蹟 move mountains; work miracles; work marvels;
科學奇蹟 the marvels of science;
歎為奇蹟 admire and praise sth as a wonderful achievement;
完成奇蹟 achieve a miracle;
小奇蹟 minor miracle; small miracle;

[奇技] some rare skill; special feat; special skill; stunt; uncanny feat;
奇技淫巧 clever contrivance and specious skills; diabolic tricks and wicked craft;

[奇計] surprising move; surprising stratagem; uncommon stratagem;

[奇景] extraordinary sight; unusual sight; wonderful scene; wonderful view;

[奇絕] exceedingly enchanting;
[奇崛] outstanding; peculiar; queer; singular; unusual;
[奇麗] beautiful; gorgeous; lovely;
[奇門] Daoist art of becoming invisible;
奇門遁甲 Daoist art of becoming invisible;
[奇妙] intriguing; marvellous; rare; too good to be true; wonderful;
奇妙莫測 mysterious and hard to guess; mysterious and inscrutable;
[奇謀] clever strategy; clever trick; uncanny scheme;
[奇巧] clever; exquisite; ingenious; skillful;
[奇缺] almost nil; critical shortage of; very scarce;
[奇人] (1) queer person; strange person; (2) person of unusual ability;
[奇辱] burning disgrace; crying shame; deep disgrace;
[奇士] remarkable man; unusual person;
[奇事] inexplicable occurrence; strange affair; strange incident; strange matter; strange things; unusual phenomenon;
[奇談] absurd argument; fantastic story; far-fetched tale; strange story; strange tale; unusual story;
奇談怪論 absurdities; absurd arguments; fantastic stories and theories; nonsensical and preposterous arguments; ridiculous charges; strange and monstrous; strange and preposterous ideas; strange tales and absurd arguments; weird contentions;
今古奇談 modern and ancient strange talks;
[奇特] fancy; outstanding; peculiar; queer; singular; strange; striking; unique; unusual;
奇特的景象 exotic scene; strange phenomenon;
舉止奇特 behave queerly;
設計奇特 curious in design;
[奇偉] great and wonderful; singularly spectacular;
[奇文] (1) remarkable piece of writing; (2) preposterous piece of writing; queer writing;
奇文共賞 a remarkable work should be enjoyed together;
[奇聞] fantastic story; sth unheard of; strange story; thrilling tale;
[奇襲] launch a surprise attack on; raid; surprise attack
奇襲敵人 surprise the enemy;
發起奇襲 make a surprise attack;
[奇效] with miraculous efficacy;
[奇秀] wonderfully beautiful;
[奇勛] marvellous feat; outstanding contribution; outstanding service;
[奇驗] (1) unusual efficacy; (2) uncanny accuracy;
[奇異] (1) bizarre; odd; queer; strange; (2) amazed; amazing; curious; surprising;
奇異果 Chinese gooseberries; kiwi fruit;
[奇遇] (1) chance encounter; fortuitous meeting; happy encounter; unexpected encounter; unexpected meeting; (2) adventure;
經歷種種奇遇 go through strange adventures;
[奇緣] unexpected relationship;
[奇珍] curio; rare treasure; rarity;
奇珍異寶 a Jew's eye; all sorts of rare treasures; priceless treasure; rare and valuable objects; rare objects of art; rare treasure; valuable curios;
[奇志] high aspiration; lofty ideal; noble ambition;

稱奇 express one's surprise; express one's wonder;
出奇 extraordinarily; unusually;
傳奇 (1) legend; (2) verse drama;
瓌奇 rare and precious things;
好奇 curious; full of curiosity;
驚奇 amazed; surprised; wonder;
離奇 bizarre; fantastic; odd; weird;
獵奇 hunt for novelty; seek novelty;
蒙太奇 montage;
清奇 novel and wonderful;
曲奇 cookie;
屈奇 odd; strange; unusual;
神奇 magical; miraculous;
瑋奇 peculiar;
希奇 (1) rare; strange; uncommon; (2) appreciate; attach importance to; value;
稀奇 curious; rare; strange;
新奇 new; newfangled; novel; strange;

珍奇 rare and precious;

qi

【歧】 (1) branch; branch road; crossroads; fork in a road; forked road; (2) different; dissimilar; divergent; forked; strayed; (3) anything that goes astray; evil; wrong;

［歧出］ conflicting; confusing; incoherent; inconsistent;

［歧點］ bifurcation point;

［歧管］ manifold;
多歧管 branch manifold;
空氣歧管 air manifold;
汽化器歧管 carburetor manifold;

［歧路］ branch road; crossroads; fork in a road; forked road; wrong road;
歧路徘徊 hesitate at the crossroads;
歧路徬徨 be depressed at the crossroads; hesitant at a road junction; not certain which road to take and remain at the crossroads hesitating; hesitant at the cross-roads as to which way one should go;
歧路亡羊 a lamb goes astray on forked road; a lamb goes astray at a fork in the road — go astray in a complex situation; a straggling sheep; the highway leads a sheep astray with its numerous turnings;

［歧念］ evil ideas; evil thoughts;

［歧視］ discriminate against;
歧視性措施 take discriminatory measures;
就業歧視 discrimination in employment;
身高歧視 heightism;
性別歧視 sexual discrimination;
種族歧視 racial discrimination;

［歧途］ aberration; wrong path; wrong road; wrong track;
歧途徬徨 depressed at the crossroads; hesitant at a road junction;
歧途亡羊 a lamb goes astray on a forked road; a lost sheep on a crooked path;
錯入歧途 err from the right path; fall into wrong path;
誤入歧途 be misguided; be misled; be misled into the wrong path; devious; fall by the wayside; fall into a wrong path; go astray; off the track; take the wrong road by mistake;
走入歧途 deviate from the right path; go astray; go off at a tangent; jump the track; take the wrong turning;

［歧義］ ambiguity; ambiguous words; different interpretations; different meanings; equivocal; sth open to interpretations; various interpretations;
詞匯歧義 lexical ambiguity;
結構歧義 structural ambiguity;
句法歧義 syntactic ambiguity;

［歧異］ different; dissimilar; divergent;

分歧 difference; different; divergence; divergent;
兩歧 different;

qi

【祁】 (1) large; thriving; vigorous; (2) a surname;

［祁紅］ a kind of black tea; black tea produced in Qimen;

［祁劇］ Hunanese opera;

［祁祁］ (1) leisurely; slowly; (2) in crowds; numerous;

qi

【祈】 (1) at one's prayer; pray; say one's prayers; (2) appeal for; beg; beseech; entreat; hope for; request respectfully; supplicate;

［祈報］ rite of offering sacrifices;

［祈賜玉音］ kindly favour me with a reply; please reply;

［祈禱］ at one's prayer; give one's prayers; offer a prayer; pray; say one's prayers;
祈禱會 pray meeting;
祈禱書 prayer book;
祈禱文 prayer;
祈禱者 prayer;
暗暗祈禱 pray in one's heart;
跪下祈禱 kneel down in prayer;
向上帝祈禱 pray to heaven;
在教堂裏祈禱 pray in a church;
做祈禱 give one's prayers; say one's prayers;

［祈福］ pray for blessings;

［祈年］ pray for a bumper crop; pray for a good harvest;

［祈祈］ slowly;

［祈請］ beg; beseech; entreat;

［祈求］ appeal for; appeal to; ask humbly for; call on; cry for; earnestly hope; earnestly request; entreat earnestly;

pray for; supplicate for; supplication;
祈求豐年 pray for a year of abundance;
祈求和平 pray for peace;
祈求寬恕 plead for mercy;
祈求上帝 pray to God;
祈求原諒 beg forgiveness; beg pardon;
祈求援助 entreat assistance; implore assistance;
低頭祈求 bow one's head in supplication;
[祈禳] pray for protection against calamities;
[祈賽] religious rite to thank the gods for their help;
[祈使] imperative;
祈使句 imperative sentence;
~否定祈使句 negative imperative sentence;
~間接祈使句 indirect imperative sentence;
~勸説祈使句 persuasive imperative;
~準祈使句 quasi-imperative;
祈使語氣 imperative mood;
[祈望] hope; look forward to; wish;
[祈雨] pray for rain;

qi
【祇】 (1) god of the earth; (2) at rest; calm; peace; quiet; restful; serene; (3) great;
[祇悔] deep remorse; great regret;
神祇 deities; gods;

qi
【耆】 aged; elderly; in one's sixties; old;
[耆艾] the aged; elderly people; the old people;
耆艾之年 in the years of sixty and fifty respectively;
[耆舊] (1) old friend of similar age; (2) respected old person;
[耆老] golden-ager; aged and respectable person; old-timer; elderly people; old people; senior citizen;
惠恤耆老 kind and sympathetic towards the aged;
[耆儒] aged scholar;
[耆紳] a gentleman advanced in years; an old gentleman;
[耆碩] respected old person;
耆年碩德 advanced in years and noble in character; aged and virtuous;
[耆宿] venerated old people;
紳耆 gentry and elders with prestige;

qi
【旂】 banner; flag;

qi
【崎】 banks of a winding river;

qi
【淇】 a river in Henan;

qi
【畦】 a pronunciation of 畦;

qi
【跂】 (1) extra toe; (2) (of insects) crawling;
[跂跂] crawling; creeping;
[跂蹻] wood sandal and dried-grass sandal;
[跂行] (1) go on foot; walk; (2) creep; move;

qi
【期】 (1) period of time; phase; stage; (2) designated time; predetermined time; scheduled time; time limit; (3) issue; number; term; (4) appointed date; appointed time; make an appointment; (5) expect; hope; look forward to; wait;
[期報] dated newspaper;
[期初] beginning of a period;
期初盈餘 surplus at the beginning of the period;
[期待] anticipate; await; expect; hope; in expectation of; look forward to; wait in hope;
期待成功 aspire to success; expect success;
熱切地期待 look eagerly for;
[期會] meet at a time fixed in advance;
[期貨] forward; futures;
期貨合同 forward contract; futures contract;
期貨價格 forward price;
期貨交易 forward transaction; futures trading; futures transactions;
期貨貿易 futures trade;
期貨市場 forward market; futures market; option market;
~期貨市場管理 management of the option market;
出售期貨 sell for forward delivery;

［期間］ course; duration; during a certain period of time; period; term; time;
撥款有效期間 appropriation period;
查賬期間 audit period;
進氣期間 admission period;
任職期間 during one's term of office;
有效期間 time of effect;

［期刊］ journal; periodical;
期刊登記卡 periodical record card;
期刊閱覽室 periodical reading room;
續訂期刊 renew the subscription to a journal;

［期考］ end-of-term examination;

［期滿］ at the expiration of; come to an end; expire; run out;
服刑期滿 serve out one's sentence;
契約期滿 take up one's indentures;

［期末］ end of term; terminal;
期末存貨 final inventory;
期末考試 end-of-term examination; final examination; terminal examination;
期末盤存 ending inventory;

［期盼］ expect; hope;

［期票］ bill of exchange; promissory note; term bill; time draft;
期票貼現 discounting of bills of exchange;

［期期］ stammering;
期期艾艾 stammer out; stutter out sth; tongue-shy; tongue-tied;

［期求］ crave; crave for; expect; hope to achieve; long for;
期求幫助 count on others' help; expect others' support; hope to receive help;
期求支援 expect support; hope to receive support;

［期權］ options;
期權費 premium;

［期望］ anticipate; count on; count upon; expect; expectation; hope; hope for; hope for and expect; in expectation; in prospect; look forward to; look out for; wish;
期望成功 aspire to succeed; hope for success; hope to succeed;
期望過高 expect too much;
期望和平 hope for peace; yearn for peace;
期望落空 be disappointed in one's expectations;
期望甚殷 cherish high hopes; earnestly look forward; place high hopes;
期望壽命 life expectancy;
期望值 expected values;
不辜負 ... 期望 answer one's expectations; answer the expectations of sb; come up to one's expectations; come up to the expectations of sb; fulfil one's expectations; fulfil the expectations of sb; live up to one's expectations; live up to the expectations of sb; meet one's expectations; meet the expectations of sb; not come short of one's expectations; not come short of the expectations of sb; not disappoint one's expectations; not disappoint the expectations of sb; not let sb down;
不切實際的期望 unrealistic expectations;

［期限］ allotted time; deadline; due time; time limit;
期限已到 the time is up;
期限已過 a deadline passes;
保修期限 term of service;
超過期限 go beyond the time limit;
固定期限 fixed term;
確定期限 set the deadline;
生命期限 the natural duration of life;
延長期限 extend a deadline; extend the time limit;
最後期限 drop-dead date;
遵守期限 meet the deadline;

［期許］ be expected to; expect to;

［期頤］ centenarian; one-hundred-year-old person;
期頤之壽 centenarian; one-hundred-years-old person;

［期於］ expect; hope; look forward to; wish;

［期約］ agree on a time for the delivery of a bribe;

［期中］ interim; midsemester; midterm;
期中報告 interim report;
期中假 half-term;
期中考試 midterm examination;

按期 according to schedule; according to the dates specified; on schedule; on time;
班期 schedule;
本期 (1) this current season; this term; (2) the present class;
冰期 glacial epoch; glacial period; Ice Age;
長期 long-term; over a long period of time;
超期 exceed the time limit;

初期 early days; initial stage;
船期 sailing date;
定期 (1) fix a date; set a date; (2) at regular intervals; periodical; regular;
短期 short period; short-term;
分期 by instalments; by stages;
改期 change the date;
更年期 change of life; climacteric; climacterium; menopause;
工期 time limit for a project;
瓜期 term of service;
歸期 date of return;
過期 exceed the time limit; expire; overdue;
後期 later period; later stage;
花期 florescence;
緩期 postpone a deadline; suspend;
會期 (1) the time or date fixed for a conference or meeting; (2) the duration of a meeting;
婚期 wedding day;
活期 current;
基期 base period;
吉期 wedding day;
即期 immediate; on demand; spot;
佳期 (1) wedding day; (2) rendezvous between lovers;
假期 (1) vacation; (2) period of leave;
交貨期 date of delivery;
屆期 on the appointed date; when the day comes;
近期 in the near future; recent; short term;
禁獵期 close season;
禁漁期 close season;
經絕期 menopause;
經期 flag day; hell week; menstrual period; menstruation time; that time of the month;
剋期 by the end of the time limit; set a time limit;
滿期 come to deadline; expire;
旄期 reached the age of eighty or ninety;
苗期 seedling stage;
末期 final phase; last phase; last stage;
年期 annual period;
愆期 behind time; delay; do sth later than expected; fail to do sth at the appointed time; fail to meet a deadline; fall behind schedule; pass the appointed time;
前期 early days; earlier stage;
潛伏期 incubation period;
青春期 puberty;
窮期 conclusion; end; termination;
任期 incumbency; tenure; tenure of office; term of office; term of service;
日期 date;
如期 as scheduled; at the appointed time; by the scheduled time; in time; on schedule; on time; punctually;
閏期 intercalation;
喪期 mourning period;
時期 period;
始期 (1) beginning of a period; (2) (of law) effective date;
試用期 probation period;
首期 first-phase;
暑期 summer vacation time;
霜期 frost season;
死期 hour of doom; time of death;
同期 corresponding period; same term;
脱期 fail to come out on time;
晚期 late stage; later period;
旺期 most productive period;
危險期 (1) on the verge of death; (2) critical days;
為期 by a definite date;
無期 no definite term; with no end in sight;
誤期 behind schedule; fail to meet the deadline;
先期 before the appointed time; beforehand; earlier on; in advance;
限期 (1) set a time limit; within a definite time; (2) deadline; time limit;
現期 current;
星期 (1) week; (2) weekday;
刑期 prison term; term of imprisonment; term of penalty;
行期 date of departure;
學期 school term; semester; term; term-time;
汛期 flood season;
延期 (1) be postponed; defer; delay; lay over; postpone; put off; put over; (2) extend;
一期 a class of; a period of; a phase of; a term of; an issue of;
幽期 (1) contemplated time for retirement; (2) appointment for a secret meeting;
有效期 term or period of validity; time of efficacy;
逾期 be overdue; exceed the time limit;
預產期 estimated date of childbirth;
預抵期 estimated time of arrival;
預期 anticipate; estimate; expect;
遠期 at a specified future date; forward;
約期 (1) date of appointment; (2) time limit of a contract;
越期 pass the deadline; pass the time limit;
孕期 gestation; pregnancy;
早期 early phase; early stage;
擇期 select a good day;
齋期 fast days;
展期 (1) exhibition period; (2) extend a time

limit; postpone;
中期 medium term; middle period; mid-term;
周期 (1) period; (2) cycle;
週期 cycle; period;
準期 punctually;
租期 lease term; tenancy;

qi
【棋】 (1) board game; game of chess; chess; (2) chessman;
[棋布] spread out in great numbers like chessmen on a chessboard;
棋布星羅 spread all over the place; spread out and scatter about like stars in the sky or chessman on the chessboard;
[棋盒兒] stone box;
[棋局] (1) game of chess; (2) chessboard with the pieces arranged;
[棋類] chess;
棋類比賽 chess competition;
[棋路] chess tactics;
[棋迷] chess enthusiast; chess fan;
[棋盤] checkerboard; chessboard;
棋盤花 zygadene;
~ 棋盤花碱 zygadenine;
棋盤裏的卒子—只能進，不能退 like a pawn on a chessboard – can only move ahead, and there is no turning back;
[棋品] character of a chess player; one's demeanour while playing chess;
[棋譜] chess manual;
[棋聖] (1) chess master; chess sage; champion chess player; wise man at chess; (2) go master;
[棋士] professional chess player;
[棋手] chess player; high-graded chess player;
[棋壇] chess circles; the world of chess;
棋壇新秀 new chess star;
[棋王] chess champion;
[棋星] chess star;
[棋藝] one's skill in playing chess;
[棋友] chess friend; fellow chess player;
[棋戰] chess battle; game of chess; fight it out in chess;
[棋子] a piece in a board game; chess pieces; chessman; counters;
擺好棋子 arrange the chess pieces;

臭棋 hard tactics;
和棋 a draw in chess or other board games;
回棋 retract a false move in a chess game;
悔棋 retract a false move in a chess game;
平棋 a draw in chess or other board games;
死棋 a dead piece in a game of chess; a hopeless case; a stupid move;
跳棋 Chinese checkers; halma;
圍棋 go;
下棋 have a game of chess; play chess;
象棋 Chinese chess;
一步棋 a move in chess;
一局棋 a game of chess;
一盤棋 a board of chess; a game of chess;
弈棋 "go" game;
着棋 play chess;

qi
【琪】 (1) piece of jade; (2) white gem; (3) jade-like precious stone;
[琪樹] (1) jade tree in myth; (2) berry-bearing willow;

qi
【琦】 (1) a kind of jade; (2) same as 奇; (3) admirable; distinguished; extraordinary; outstanding;
[琦瑋] (1) fine jade; (2) distinguished;
[琦行] admirable conduct;

qi
【萁】 beanstalk;

qi
【祺】 (1) auspicious; fortunate; lucky; propitious; (2) calm; peaceful; serene;
[祺然] calmly; peacefully; serene;
[祺祥] auspicious; fortunate; lucky; propitious;

qi
【頎】 large physique; tall; tall stature;
[頎長] tall; tall in physique;
[頎然] tall;

秀頎 beautiful and tall;

qi
【碁】 (1) board game; chess; game of chess; (2) chess player;

qi
【旗】 (1) banner; flag; pennant; standard; (2) emblem; insignia; sign; (3) the Manchus;
[旗桿] flag post; flagpole; flagstaff;
旗桿上掛燈籠—高明 a lantern hanging on

a flagpole — high and bright;
豎立旗桿 erect a flagpole;

[旗鼓] flags and drums;
旗鼓相當 a matched rival; a Roland for an Oliver; closely matched in power; cry quits; diamond cut diamond; equal in contest; equal in match; equal in strength; equal to each other; horse and horse; keen rivalry; neck and neck; of equal strength; the opposing forces match each other in strength; to a good cat, a good rat; well-matched in strength; worthy of one's steel;
旗鼓相當，勝負難分 the two sides are so well-matched that neither can gain the upper hand;
大張旗鼓 by great publicity; flags and drums in array; give wide publicity to; in a big way; on a grand scale; put up a pageantry; with a big display of flags and drums; with a flourish; with a great fanfare; with colours flying and the band playing;
偃旗息鼓 cease all activities; cover the flag and stop beating the drum — on a secret expedition; furl all the banners and silence all the drums; halt the noisy show; lower one's banners and muffle one's drums; roll up the flags and silence the drums; stop all activities and lie low; stop the fanfare;
掩旗息鼓 keep silent; stay quiet; stop clamouring;

[旗號] army signal; banner; flag; standard;

[旗籍] membership among the Manchu bannermen;

[旗艦] flagship;
旗艦產品 flagship product;
旗艦店 flagship store;
~一家旗艦店 a flagship store;

[旗門杆] gate pole;

[旗靡轍亂] the flags droop and the wheels mix up — (fig) a total defeat;

[旗袍] cheongsam;
旗袍裙 close-fitting skirt;

[旗手] (1) flag-holder; flagman; (2) standard-bearer;

[旗魚] sailfish;

[旗語] flag signal;

[旗幟] (1) banner; flag; (2) colours; stand; (3) good example; model; pace-setter; (4) theory; thought;
旗幟如林 with a forest of flags;
旗幟鮮明 a clear banner; a clearcut stand; in a clear-cut way; take a clear-cut stand; unfurl a radiant banner;
拔旗易幟 get off at pull down one's flag and plant another one – shift one's allegiance;
舉起旗幟 lift a flag;

[旗子] banner; flag; pennant; standard;
一面旗子 a flag;

八旗 Eight Banners;
白旗 white flag;
半旗 half-mast; half-staff;
摽旗 signal with a flag;
彩旗 bunting; coloured flag;
黨旗 party flag;
隊旗 team pennant;
國旗 national flag;
降旗 lower a flag;
錦旗 silk banner;
旌旗 banners and flags;
軍旗 army flag;
區旗 regional flag;
昇旗 hoist a flag;
手旗 handflag; semaphore flag;
授旗 present sb with a flag;
帥旗 flag of the commander-in-chief;
團旗 regiment flag;
獻旗 present a banner;
降旗 flag of surrender;
校旗 school flag;
懸旗 hang a flag; hoist a flag;
揚旗 semaphore;
一杆旗 a flag;
一面旗 a flag;
義旗 banner of justice; flag of the troops of justice;
自治旗 autonomous banner;

qi

【齊】 (1) even; in good order; neat; set in order; tidy; uniform; well arranged; (2) equal; flush with; on a level with; on the same plane with; (3) alike; of one; similar; (4) at the same time; simultaneously; together; (5) all present; all ready; complete; (6) along; (7) state of Qi (ca. 11th century B.C. —

221 B.C.); (8) Qi Dynasty (479-502); (9) a surname;

［齊備］ all complete; all ready; complete; everything complete; everything ready;

［齊步］ in step; march; uniform steps;
齊步走 march in step; quick march;

［齊茬儿］ of uniform length;

［齊唱］ sing in chorus; sing in unison;

［齊齒］ of the same age;

［齊楚］ neat and smart;

［齊大非偶］ not to aspire to an alliance with one's betters; too rich to be a good match; unsuitable as partner due to one's superiority;

［齊東野語］ cock-and-bull story; popular report; unreliable talk; vulgarism; what folks say;

［齊集］ assemble; collect; come together; gather;

［齊給］ well-arranged; well-provided;

［齊家］ govern one's family; regulate the family;
齊家治國 regulate the family and govern the state;

［齊截］ neat; well-formed;

［齊理］ arrange in order;

［齊眉］ respect between husband and wife;
舉案齊眉 husband and wife treating each other with courtesy; love and respect each other for life;

［齊盟］ enter into alliance with; make an alliance;

［齊民］ the common people; the masses; the multitude; the ordinary people;

［齊名］ enjoy equal popularity; enjoy equal prestige; equal in fame; equally famous; equally well-known; share a reputation;

［齊年］ of the same age;

［齊驅］ advance abreast — to be equal in ability;

［齊全］ all in readiness; complete; everything complete; nothing missing;
百色齊全 complete range of colours;
尺碼齊全 have a complete range of sizes;
冠帶齊全 in full dress;
貨物齊全 satisfactory variety of goods;
設備齊全 the equipment is complete;
裝備齊全 be fully equipped;

［齊聲］ in chorus; in unison;
齊聲附和 second with one voice;
齊聲高呼 hail with one voice;
齊聲歌唱 sing in chorus; sing in unison;
齊聲喝彩 applaud in unison; cheer in chorus; cheer with one accord; praise in chorus;
齊聲歡呼 cheer in unison;
齊聲回答 answer in chorus; answer in one voice;
齊聲叫喊 cry out in chorus;
齊聲抗議 protest in chorus;
齊聲狂笑 the wild chorus of laughter;
齊聲朗讀 red in chorus;
齊聲讚揚 give a chorus of praise;

［齊心］ of one heart; of one mind;
齊心協力 all of one mind; bend their efforts in a single direction; hang together; join forces in an effort; join hands; make concerted efforts; of one heart; of one mind; pull all together; pull together; put forth a united effort; rally round; shoulder to shoulder; with one heart; with one mind and one heart; with united effort; work as one man; work in concert; work in full cooperation and with unity of purpose; work in harmony; work together as one man;
齊心一致 uniform and one-hearted;

［齊一］ equal; uniform;

［齊整］ neat; orderly; tidy; trim; uniform;
齊齊整整 in good order; neat; tidy;

［齊奏］ play in unison;

擺齊 place in neat order;
保不齊 hard to avoid; may well; not sure;
看齊 (1) dress; (2) emulate; follow the example of; keep abreast with; keep up with; measure up to;
取齊 (1) even up; make even; (2) assemble; meet each other;
如數到齊 all present and accounted for; all present and correct;
説不齊 cannot say for sure;
思齊 want to emulate; wish to equal;
一齊 at the same time; in unison; simultaneously; together;
找齊 (1) even up; make uniform; (2) make up a deficiency;
整齊 (1) in good order; neat; orderly; shipshape; snug; taut; tidy; well-arranged; (2) even;

regular; well-balanced;

qi

【綦】 (1) exceedingly; greatly; hugely; very; (2) dark gray; (3) a shoelace;

[綦嚴] very severe; very stringent;

[綦重] very heavy;

qi

【畿】 a pronunciation of 畿 ;

qi

【錡】 (1) tripod; (2) a kind of chisel;

qi

【臍】 (1) navel; umbilicus; (2) belly flap of a crab; underside of a crab;

[臍橙] sweet oranges;

[臍帶] umbilical cord;

肚臍 belly button; navel;

尖臍 (1) abdomen of a male crab; (2) male crab;

團臍 (1) abdomen of a female crab; (2) female crab;

qi

【薺】 (1) caltrop; (2) water chestnut;

qi

【騎】 (1) ride; sit on the back of; (2) horse rider; (3) cavalryman;

[騎兵] cavalry; cavalryman; mounted troops;

輕騎兵 hussar; light cavalry;

[騎車] ride a bicycle;

騎車帶人 carry a person on one's bicycle; carry a pillion passenger;

[騎從] servants on horseback;

[騎寇] mounted bandits;

[騎虎] ride on a tiger's back;

騎虎難下 between two fires; find it hard to get off a tiger's back, once you are on it; get into a position from which there is no retiring; have a tiger by the tail; have a wolf by the ears; have no way to back down; he who rides a tiger finds it difficult to dismount; he who rides a tiger is afraid to dismount; he who rides on a tiger can never get off; hold a wolf by the ears; in a dilemma; in a fix; in a situation from which there is no easy way out; in an awkward predicament; in chancery; in for it; now you are in for it, you must carry on the best way you can; once one's on a tiger's back, it's hard to get off; one can't dismount from the tiger one is riding; ride a tiger and find it hard to get off; start sth that proves more than one can carry through without danger; unable to extricate oneself from a difficulty; unable to get off the tiger one is riding;

騎虎之勢 in an awkward position from which there is no retreat; in an awkward predicament; the horns of a dilemma;

騎上虎背—欲罷不能 riding on a tiger's back – can't get off from it;

勢成騎虎 a situation from which there is no retreat;

[騎軍] cavalry;

[騎樓] arcade;

[騎驢] (1) ride a donkey; (2) intermediary exploitation;

騎驢逛燈會—走著瞧 riding a donkey to watch a lantern show – ride and watch; wait and see;

騎驢覓驢 forget what one already has; look for a donkey while sitting on one – forgetful; look for sth already in one's hands; look for sth right under one's nose;

騎驢拿拐杖—多此一舉 riding a donkey and holding a cane – an unnecessary action;

騎驢找馬 hold a temporary position while seeking a better job; look for a horse while riding on a donkey; maintain a job while looking for a better one; ride on a donkey while looking for a horse;

[騎馬] horse-riding; on horseback; ride a horse; ride horseback;

騎馬乘轎 come on horseback or on sedan-chairs; on horseback or in chairs;

騎馬釘 staple; saddle stitching;

騎馬逗鹿 go on horseback and watch the deer;

騎馬隊 cavalcade;

騎馬找馬 forget what one already has; hold on to one job while seeking a better one; look for a horse while sitting on one; look for sth far and wide when it is on one's person; ride a horse to look out for a better one; riding a horse while looking for it;

stay on one's job while hunting for a better one;
騎馬者 houseman; rider;
～女騎馬者 horsewoman;
騎兩頭馬 be headed in both directions;
騎瞎馬 do sth aimlessly;
善於騎馬 sit one's horse well;

[騎牛] ride on oxback;
騎牛覓牛 look for an ox while sitting on one – hold on to one job while seeking another;
騎牛追馬—趕不上 riding on oxback to chasing a horse – never able to catch up;

[騎槍] carbine;

[騎牆] sit on the fence; straddle; take no sides; trim; uncommitted between two opposing forces;
騎牆觀望 sit on the fence and take a wait-and-see attitude;
騎牆派 fence-sitter; opportunist; time-server;

[騎射] horsemanship and archery;
能騎善射 a good horseman as well as a crack shot; expert at horseback riding and shooting; talented in riding and shooting;
善騎能射 have skill in riding and shooting;
擅騎善射 be skilled in riding and shooting; excel in horsemanship and marksmanship;

[騎師] equestrian; hardboot; horsebacker; horseman; jockey; rider;

[騎士] (1) cavalier; knight; (2) horseback rider;
騎士的 knightly;
騎士精神 chivalry; knighthood;
遊俠騎士 knight errant;

[騎手] horsebacker; horseman; rider;
女騎手 horsewoman;

[騎術] equestrian skill; equitation; horsemanship;
騎術學校 riding school;

[騎在頭上] lord it over; ride on the backs of; ride roughshod over; sit on the backs of;
騎在頭上，拉屎拉尿 ride on the back of the people and piss and shit on them;
騎在頭上，作威作福 ride roughshod on the back of;

[騎者] rider;
騎者善墮 a skilful rider often falls; even the best make mistakes; the best riders get the most falls; the best riders take a tumble;

驃騎 title of generals in ancient times;
輕騎 light cavalry;
鐵騎 cavalry;
驍騎 brave and fierce cavalry;
驛騎 posthorse;

qi

【騏】 (1) black horse; (2) fine horse; (3) dark blue;

[騏驥] fine horse; steed;
人中騏驥 very clever child;

qi

【麒】 Chinese unicorn;

[麒麟] Chinese unicorn;
麒麟菜 eucheuma;
麒麟兒 infant prodigy; wonder child;

qi

【蘄】 (1) ligusticum; (2) same as 祈, beg; seek;

[蘄艾] Chinese muggwort;

[蘄求] earnestly hope; pray for;

[蘄蛇] long-noded pit viper;

qi

【蠐】 grub;

[蠐螬] grub;

qi

【鬐】 (1) mane; (2) fins;

qi

【鰭】 fins;

[鰭刺] base of fish fins;

[鰭棘] prickly points of fins;

[鰭腳] clasper;
鰭腳動物 pinniped animal;

背鰭 dorsal fin;
腹鰭 pelvic fin; ventral fin;
橈鰭 telson;
肉鰭 fin;
臀鰭 anal fin;
尾鰭 caudal fin; tail fin;
胸鰭 pectoral fin;

qi³

qi

【乞】 ask for alms; beg; entreat; implore;

pray humbly; supplicate;
[乞貸] beg for a loan;
[乞兒] beggar; pauper;
向火乞兒 a facing-fire beggar — a hangeron of glory; a follower of the rich and powerful; the man currying favaour with the powerful;
[乞丐] beggar; pauper;
淪為乞丐 be reduced to beggary;
[乞和] beg for peace; sue for peace;
[乞假] ask for a leave of absence;
[乞漿得酒] ask for water and get wine; get more than one has asked for; get more than what is asked for;
[乞憐] beg for mercy; beg for pity and charity; piteously beg for help;
乞憐於人 appeal to sb for pity;
[乞鄰] beg from a neighbour;
[乞靈] by raising the spectre of; reliance on; resort to; seek help from; turn to sth for help;
[乞盟] (1) beg for peace; sue for peace; (2) pray before the deity;
[乞免] beg for exception; beg to be excused; sue for pardon;
[乞命] beg for life; beg for mercy; plead for one's life;
跪地乞命 lie in the dust pleading for one's life;
[乞巧] festival of the seventh day of the seventh lunar month;
[乞求] beg; beg for; implore; beg sb to do sth; beseech sb to do sth; go down on one's knees; entreat earnestly; entreat sb to do sth; fall on one's knees; go begging; go down on one's knees; implore; make a petition; pass the hat round; pray sb to do sth; solicit sb for sth; solicitation; supplicate sb to do sth; throw oneself at the feet of;
乞求和平 beg for peace; sue for peace;
乞求寬恕 beg for mercy; beg for pardon; implore for pardon; sue for pardon;
乞求憐憫 supplicate for mercy;
[乞饒] ask for pardon;
乞饒求恕 crave mercy; crave pardon;
乞饒於人 beg for mercy; crave pardon;
跪地乞饒 prostrate oneself before sb and beg for mercy and forgiveness; throw oneself on the ground and plead for mercy;
[乞師] ask for military help;
[乞食] beg for food;
乞食度生 beg one's bread;
[乞討] beg; beg for sth; go begging;
乞討食物 beg for food;
[乞降] beg to surrender;
[乞援] ask for assistance; ask for help; beg for aid; turn to sb for help;

容乞 ask permission for;
討乞 beg; beg alms;
行乞 beg; beg one's bread;

qi

【企】 (1) stand on tiptoe; (2) anxiously expect sth; expect; hope; long; look forward to;
[企鵝] penguin;
一隻企鵝 a penguin;
[企管] business management;
[企劃] design; lay out; make a scheme for; plan;
[企立] stand on tiptoe;
[企慕] admire; admire greatly; look up to;
[企盼] expect with eagerness; hope with eagerness;
[企求] desire; desire to gain; hanker after; hanker for; long for; seek after; seek for;
[企圖] (1) attempt; attempt to; contrive; design to; have a go at; in an attempt to; in order to; scheme; seek; try; with intent to; (2) intention; plan; scheme;
企圖僥幸 attempt just to muddle through;
企圖逃路 attempt to escape;
企圖逃税 scheme to evade tax;
企圖逃走 attempt an escape;
企圖心 aggressiveness; enterprising spirit;
企圖行兇 offer violence;
企圖自殺 make an attempt upon one's life;
挫敗企圖 defeat an attempt;
放棄企圖 abandon an attempt;
另有企圖 have an axe to grind; have other intentions;
[企望] hope for; look forward to; yearn for;
企望回音 look for a reply;
[企業] business; enterprise; establishment;

undertaking;
企業標準 company standard;
~企業標準化 enterprise standardization;
企業財務 business finance;
企業成本 business cost; cost in business;
企業承包 contracting for enterprise;
~企業承包人 contractor for enterprise;
企業倒閉 business failure;
企業法人 enterprise legal person;
~企業法人財產權 legal person's property;
~企業法人制度 legal entity system;
企業工資 business wage;
企業公關 enterprise's public relations;
企業管理 enterprise management;
~企業管理學 management science of enterprises;
~企業管理自動化 automation of enterprise management;
企業廣告 business advertisement;
企業合併 business combination;
企業環境 business environment;
企業活力 enterprise vitality;
企業機能 enterprise function;
企業集團 business group; enterprise group;
~緊密型企業集團 tightly organized business group;
企業技術 technology in enterprises;
~企業技術改造 technological renovation in enterprises;
~企業技術進步 technological progress in enterprises;
企業計劃 business plan;
企業家 businessman; enterpreneur;
~企業家精神 spirit of enterpreneurship;
~內部企業家 intrapreneur;
~女企業家 businesswoman;
企業兼併 annexation of enterprises;
企業界 business circles;
企業經濟 enterprise's economy;
~企業經濟管理 management of enterprise's economy;
~企業經濟信息 economic information of enterprises;
~企業經濟行為 economic behaviour of enterprises;
~企業經濟學 enterprise economics;
企業經營 enterprise business;
~企業經營管理 business management economy;
~企業經營決策 business management policy-making;
企業競爭 business competition;
企業虧損 loss incurred in an enterprise;
企業內聚力 cohesive force in enterprise;
企業能量平衡 enterprise energy balance;
企業破產制 enterprise bankruptcy system;
企業設備 enterprise equipment;
~企業設備改造 equipment renovation of enterprises;
~企業設備管理 enterprise equipment management;
企業識別系統 corporate identity system;
企業税收 enterprise tax;
~企業税收政策 policy of enterprise tax;
企業素質 business quality; quality of an enterprise;
企業所得税 enterprise income tax;
企業網絡 enterprise network;
企業文化 enterprise culture;
~企業文化建設 enterprise cultural construction;
~企業文化結構 structure of enterprise culture;
~企業文化理論 enterprise culture theory;
企業下放 place an enterprise under a lower level of administration;
企業行為 business action; enterprise behaviour;
~企業行為理論 theory of enterprise behaviour;
企業信息 enterprise information;
~企業信息工作 enterprise information work;
企業形象 corporate image;
企業債務 enterprise debt;
企業資本 enterprise capital;
企業自有資金 funds at the disposal of enterprises;
企業自主權 decision-making right of enterprises;
企業組織 enterprise organization;
~企業組織形式 forms of business organization;
超級企業 megacorporation;
承包企業 contracting enterprise;
創辦一個企業 build an enterprise;
村辦企業 village-run enterprise;
大企業 big business; large enterprise;
大型企業 sizable enterprise;
單個企業 individual enterprise;
獨資企業 wholly foreign-owned enterprise;

發展企業 develop a business;
附屬企業 subsidiary enterprise;
搞活企業 enliven enterprises; invigorate enterprises;
公共事業企業 public service enterprise;
公私合營企業 state-private enterprise;
公營企業 public corporation;
公用事業企業 utility enterprise;
骨幹企業 backbone enterprise; key enterprise;
寡頭企業 oligopoly;
國營企業 state-owned enterprise;
～半國營企業 para-state enterprise;
國有企業 state enterprise; state-owned enterprise;
合辦企業 joint enterprise;
合併企業 merger;
合資企業 joint venture;
合作企業 co-op; cooperative; cooperative enterprise;
家族企業 family business;
建立企業 build up a business;
接管企業 take over a business;
緊密型企業 tightly organized enterprises;
經營企業 run a business;
虧損企業 loss-making enterprise; money-losing enterprise;
聯合企業 joint business; joint enterprise;
聯營企業 associated enterprise;
壟斷企業 monopoly enterprise;
賣掉企業 sell out one's business;
農業企業 agricultural undertaking;
商業企業 commercial enterprises; commercial undertaking; merchandising business;
試點企業 pilot enterprise;
私人企業 private enterprise; private venture;
私營企業 private undertaking;
外商融資企業 solely foreign-funded enterprise;
外資企業 foreign-funded enterprise;
鄉鎮企業 township enterprise;
小企業 small business; small enterprise;
～搞活小企業 invigorate small enterprises;
校辦企業 school-run enterprise;
信托企業 trust business;
一家企業 an enterprise;
盈利企業 income-producing enterprise;
擁有企業 have a business; own a business;
中小企業 minor enterprise;
自由企業 free enterprise;
自主企業 autonomous enterprise;

[企踵] stand on tiptoe;
企踵延頸 stand on tiptoe and crane the neck — on the very tiptop of expectation;

[企足] stand on tiptoe;
企足而待 expect with eagerness; wait on tiptoe;
企足而望 look forward to on tiptoe; stand on tiptoe to see;
企足以待 wait on tiptoe;

翹企 raise one's head and stand on tiptoe;

qi

【屺】 bare mountain;

qi

【杞】 (1) a species of willow; (2) medlar tree; (3) state of Qi in the Spring and Autumn Period; (4) a surname;

[杞憂] groundless anxieties; groundless fears;
杞人憂天 baseless anxiety; baseless worry; borrow trouble; cherish imaginary fears; entertain groundless fear; entertain imaginary fear; entertain pessimistic fear; groundless fear; have ground fears; meet trouble halfway; excessive anxiety; make a fuss about; overcare; unnecessary worry;

[杞梓] good timber;

枸杞 Chinese wolfberry;

qi

【豈】 how; what;

[豈不] doesn't that; hasn't that; isn't that; won't that; wouldn't it be; wouldn't it result in; wouldn't that;

[豈但] not only;

[豈非] isn't it...; wouldn't it...;

[豈敢] I don't deserve such praise; you flatter me;

[豈可] how can;

[豈奈] cannot help but; have no alternative; have no choice;

[豈能] how could; how is it possible;
豈能容忍 can't brook; how could one tolerate it;

[豈有此理] absurd; arrant nonsense indeed;

by ginger; can anything be more absurd; damn it; dod burn; for crying out loud; hang it all; how absurd; how can there be such a principle; how can this be right; how could such a thing be possible; how absurd it is; how unreasonable; how unreasonable all this is; impertinence; is there such a principle; outrageous; sheer effrontery; that is a ridiculous idea; there is no such a rule; this is arrant nonsense; this is outrageous; this is sheer effornterey; what a thing to say; what nonsense;

[豈止] much more than; not at all limited to;

qi

【起】 (1) get up; go up; rise; rise up; stand up; (2) draw out; extract; pull; remove; uncover; unfold; (3) appear; raise; (4) dispatch; (5) grow; rise; (6) compose; draft; make a draft of an article; prepare a draft; work out; (7) build; establish; found; institute; set up; (8) begin; commence; set out; start; (9) batch; case; group; instance; (10) measure word for accidents;

[起岸] bring cargo ashore; unload a ship; unship a cargo;

[起爆] detonate; ignition; inflammation;

[起筆] (1) first stroke of a Chinese character; (2) the way to start each stroke in writing a Chinese character;

[起兵] dispatch troops; rise in arms; start a military action;
起兵發難 revolt; rise in rebellion;

[起搏] pace making;
起搏器 pacemaker;
~ 核起搏器 nuclear pacemaker;
~ 雙峰起搏器 bimodal pacemaker;
~ 心臟起搏器 cardiac pacemaker;

[起步] (1) break the ice; start; (2) get moving; get off the mark; get started; get underway;
起步晚的人 late starter;
起步早 start young;

[起草] compose; draft; draft out; draw up; make a draft of; map out; prepare a draft; sketch; write out;
起草人 drafter; draftsman;
起草條約 make a draft of a treaty;
起草委員會 drafting committee;
起草文件 draft a document; draw up a document;
起草憲法 draft a constitution;
起草一份計劃 draft out a plan;

[起場] gather in threshed grain on a threshing ground;

[起程] leave; set out; start on a journey;

[起初] at first; at the outset; in the beginning; originally;

[起牀] get off; get out of bed; get up; hit the deck; rise; roll out; show a leg; stir; turn out;
趕快起牀 rise and shine;

[起點] origin; point of departure; starting point; zero;
起點站 departure station;
新起點 new departure;
以…為起點 take...as a starting point;

[起動] get in motion; start; start going; start moving; start running; start working; starting;
起動按鈕 activate button;
起動機 starter;
~ 全壓起動機 across-the-line starter;
~ 調速起動機 adjustable starter;
~ 乙炔起動機 acetylene starter;
起動器 starter;
~ 起動器具 actuating appliance;
~ 彈藥起動器 cartridge starter;
~ 電容起動器 capacitor starter;
~ 汽車起動器 car starter;
起動事故 start-up accident;
電容起動 capacitor start;
冷起動 cold starting;
試起動 experimental starting;
先起動 head start;
延遲起動 delayed start;
再起動 restart;
~ 多次再起動 multiple restart;
~ 遠程再起動 remote restart;
自動起動 automatic start;

[起端] beginning; genesis; origin;

[起飛] get off; get off the ground; hop off; launch; lift off; take off;
起飛事故 take-off accident;
起飛順利 make a good take-off;
起飛性能 take-off ability;
側風起飛 cross wind take-off;

經濟起飛 economic take-off;
全天候起飛 all weather departure;
無滑行起飛 non-run take-off;
助推器起飛 assisted take-off;
準時起飛 take off on time;

[起風] get windy;
起風疙瘩 nettle rash;

[起鳳騰蛟] like the soaring phoenix and the rising dragon;

[起伏] fluctuate; heave rolling; rise and fall; undulate; ups and downs;
起伏地帶 wavy terrain;
起伏跌宕 rise and fall unceasingly;
此起彼伏 as one falls, another rises; break out one after another; follow one after another; here rising, there falling; rise in succession; rise one after another; rising here and subsiding there; up here down there;
幾起幾伏 have a chequered career;
山巒起伏 the mountain ranges rise and fall;
時起時伏 have ups and downs; now rise, now fall; rise and fall in a wave-like manner; vary in intensity from time to time;
心潮起伏 one's heart seemed to rise and fall like the waves;

[起稿] draft; make a draft; prepare a draft; work out a draft;

[起根兒] at first; in the beginning;

[起工] start work;

[起旱] take an overland route;

[起航] begin a voyage; set sail;

[起鬨] (1) gather together to create a disturbance; gather together to stir up trouble; kick up a fuss; stir up trouble; (2) boo and hoot; jeer;
瞎起鬨 boo and hoot;

[起火] (1) catch fire; fire breaking out; on fire; outbreak of a fire; (2) cook meals; do cooking; prepare meals; (3) flare up; get angry; lose one's temper;

[起貨] take delivery; landing; take goods from a warehouse; unload;
起貨單 landing permit;

[起獲] discover and seize;

[起急] get impatient; lose one's patience;

[起家] (1) early background of a successful person; (2) build up a fortune; build up a name; get on in the world; grow and thrive; make one's fortune; make one's way; rise in the world; start an enterprise; start off;
空手起家 from rags to riches; make a fortune starting from nothing;
徒手起家 become rich bare-handed; make a fortune starting from scratch;

[起價] raise the price; mark up the price;

[起見] for the purpose of; for the sake of; in order to; in view of; with a view to; with the view of;
為安全起見 be on the safe side; for reasons of safety; for safety sake;
為方便起見 for convenience's sake;
為簡單起見 for the sake of simplicity;
為穩妥起見 be on the safe side;

[起降] take off and land;

[起轎] set out in a sedan chair;

[起解] pack off; transfer a prisoner under escort;

[起勁] active; eager; energetically; enthusiastically; in high spirits; showing much zeal; vigorously; vociferous; with gusto; with zest and vigour; work frantically;

[起敬] show respect;

[起居] daily life; everyday life at home;
起居室 drawing room; front room; living room; sitting room;
~一間起居室 a sitting room;
起居無時 lead an irregular life;
起居無恙 in good health; live in health;
起居有恒 keep regular hours; lead a regular life; with regular habits; keep bankers hours;
起居注 (1) official in charge of the emperor's daily life; (2) record of the emperor's daily activities;

[起句] opening line of a poem;

[起課] divine;

[起來] (1) rise; rise to one's feet; sit up; stand up; (2) get out of bed; get up; (3) come forward; (4) arise; revolt; rise;
起來革命 rise in revolution;
起來一轟 burst into an uproar;
綁起來 tie up;
大哭起來 burst into tears;
合起來 put together;
加起來 add;

捲起來 roll sth up;
看起來 have the look of; look like;
~看起來不太好 not look too good; not look very well;
~乍看起來 at first appearance; at first glance; at first sight; on the face of it; on the first face;
起不來 unable to get up; unable to rise; unable to stand up;
算起來 all told; in all; in the aggregate; in total;
鎖起來 lock up;
提不起來 (1) unable to lift; (2) have sunk too deep for rescue;
聽起來 ring; sound;
突然哭起來 burst into tears;
突然嗚咽起來 burst into sobs;
突然笑起來 burst into laughter; burst out laughing;
先富起來 get well-off first;
攢起來 save up;
站起來 get to one's feet; get up; rise; stand up;
~站起來關燈 get up and turn off the light;
~慢慢站起來 get slowly to one's feet;
~站不起來 unable to stand up;
腫起來 swell up;
抓不起來 incapable of taking;
坐起來 sit up;

[起立] rise; rise to one's feet; stand up;
起立表決 vote by sitting and standing;
起立發言 take the floor;
起立歡迎 rise to welcome;
起立離桌 rise from the table;

[起利] start bearing interest;

[起靈] move sb's coffin or ashes to the graveyard;

[起落] rise and fall; rising and falling; ups and downs;
起落架 landing gear; undercarriage;
~多輪式起落架 bogie undercarriage;
~伸縮起落架 retractable undercarriage;
~十字軸式起落架 cross-axle undercarriage;
~尾部起落架 tail undercarriage;
起落裝置 landing gear;
大起大落 a big rise and fall; a roller-coaster economy; change radically; major rises and falls in a short period; marked ups and downs; sharp fluctuations;
忽起忽落 a sudden rise and sudden fall;
幾起幾落 several ups and downs;
起起落落 highs and lows; ups and downs;
~一生中的起起落落 the highs and lows of one's life;
時起時落 now rising, now falling;
手起刀落 cut down; raise one's sword and make a cut;

[起碼] (1) elementary; rudimentary; (2) at least; minimum;
起碼常識 elementary knowledge; the ABC of sth;
起碼的公平 a modicum of fairness;
起碼要求 elementary demands; minimum requirements;
起碼知識 elementary knowledge;
起碼資格 minimum qualifications;

[起錨] weigh anchor;
起錨機 capstan;

[起名] be called; be known as; be named; give a name to; go by the name of; name;
起名字 be called; be known as; be named; give a name; name;

[起跑] start; starting;
起跑犯規 false start;
起跑器 starting block;
起跑線 starting line;
起跑信號 pistol shot; starting signal;
起跑閘 starting gate;
急速起跑 fast starting;
集體起跑 mass start;
拉長式起跑 elongated start;
練起跑 practise starts;

[起泡] (1) blister; bubble; get blisters; (2) bead; foam; form bubbles;
腳上起泡 get blisters on one's feet;

[起訖] the beginning and the end;

[起色] a change for the better; improvement; pickup; recuperate; signs of recovery; signs of improvement;
無起色 weak;
有起色 show signs of a rise; show signs of improvement;
~日有起色 improving with each passing day; turning for the better steadily;

[起身] (1) get out of bed; get up; get up in the morning; rise; (2) get off; leave; set out; start; start a journey; start on a journey;
起身告辭 rise and take one's leave; stand

up to say goodbye;
起身迎客 rise to greet one's guests;

[起始] beginning; germ; initiation; origin; parentage; start;
起始點 initial point;
起始動詞 inchoative verb;
起始符 start character;
起始狀態 initial state;

[起事] rise in arms; rise in rebellion; rise in revolt; start armed struggle;
平空起事 make trouble out of nothing;

[起誓] make an oath; swear; swear an oath; take an oath; vow;

[起手] start an action;

[起首] at first; in the beginning; originally;

[起訴] bring a suit against sb; bring an action against sb; charge; file a complaint against sb; file a formal indictment; file a lawsuit; indict; institute legal proceedings; prosecute; start a criminal prosecution against sb; sue; sue sb in a law court;
起訴人 prosecutor;
起訴書 indictment papers; statement of charges;
起訴資格 standing to sue;
被起訴 be prosecuted;
面臨起訴 face prosecution;
提出起訴 bring a prosecution against sb;
正式起訴 begin a prosecution in form;

[起算] start counting from a given point;

[起跳] take off;
起跳板 take-off board;

[起頭] (1) initiate; make a start; originate; start; take the lead; the beginning; the origin; (2) at first; in the beginning; originally;
起頭容易結梢難 it is easier to start sth than to conclude it satisfactorily;

[起土] harvest;

[起臥] get up and sleep;
起臥室 bed-sit; a studio apartment;

[起舞] (1) rise and dance; (2) be excited with joy;
聞雞起舞 rise up upon hearing the crow of a roster and practise with the sword;

[起席] leave a dinner party;

[起息] (1) get up in the morning and retire in the night; (2) start bearing interest;

[起先] at first; in the beginning;

[起釁] provoke a fight; start a feud;

[起行] set out; start on a journey;

[起眼] attract attention; striking;
不起眼 not eye-catching; trivial; inconspicuous; unremarkable;
~ 不起眼的女人 a plain Jane;

[起夜] get up in the night to urinate; take a leak in the middle of the night;

[起疑] become suspicious; begin to suspect; smell a rat; suspect;

[起義] insurrection; launch uprisings; revolt; revolt and come over; rise in revolt; stage an uprising; uprising;
起義軍 insurgent forces;
爆發起義 an uprising breaks out;
舉行起義 rise in revolt;
農民起義 peasant uprising;
武裝起義 armed uprising;
鎮壓起義 put down an uprising;
制止起義 check uprisings;

[起意] conceive a design; conceive an evil idea; harbour an evil design; harbour an evil intention;

[起因] as a result of; causation; cause; origin;
起因不明 start from some unknown cause;
起因可疑 of suspicious origin;
問題的起因 culprit;

[起營拔寨] decamp;

[起用] (1) raise up; (2) reinstate a dismissed official; reinstate a retired official;
起用新秀 put younger people into leadership positions; raise up new talent into office;

[起源] (1) beginning; derivation; genesis; origin; rise in; source; (2) come from; originate from; originate in; stem from; take sth as a starting point;
起源不明 of unknown origin;
起源學 genesis;
~ 人類起源學 anthropogenesis;

[起運] start shipment;

[起贓] recover stolen articles; scrumming; track down and recover stolen goods;

[起早] rise early;
起早摸黑 early to rise and late to bed; from morning till night; rise early and retire late; start work early and knock off late; start work early at dawn and stop late at dusk; work from an early

hour in the morning till late at night; work from dawn till dusk; work very hard all day long;
起早睡晚 get up early and go to bed late; rise early and retire late;
起早貪黑 start work early and knock off late; work from dawn to dusk;

[起止] beginning and end; start-stop;

[起重] jack-up;
起重車 derrick car;
起重機 crane; derrick; hoist; lifter; truck crane;
~安全起重機 safety hoist;
~吊桿起重機 boom crane;
~風動起重機 air motor hoist;
~浮式起重機 barge crane;
~輔助起重機 auxiliary hoist;
~鋼錠起重機 block crane;
~施工起重機 construction hoist;
~應急起重機 breakdown crane;
起重能力 weight-lifting ability;
起重器 jack;
~車輛起重器 carriage jack;
~帶爪起重器 claw jack;
~固定起重器 built-in jack;

[起皺] cockle; crease; crumple; ruck up; wrinkle;
起皺的 corrugated;
外套起皺 one's coat is rucked up;

[起住] the beginning and the end;

[起坐] rise from one's seat as a form of respect;
平起平坐 equal in position; equal in power; hank and hank; on an equal footing; sit as equals at the same table; upsides with;

拔起 uproot;
勃起 boner; erection; hard-on; have an erection; stiffy;
不起 not able to;
藏起 (1) conceal; hide; (2) hide; put out of sight; (3) superinduce over;
攙起 help sb stand up by giving him a hand;
稱得起 deserve to be called; worthy of the name of;
遞起 happen frequently; occur repeatedly;
迭起 happen frequently; occur repeatedly;
對不起 (1) allow me; excuse me; I am sorry; I beg your pardon; if I dare say so; if you don't mind; if you please; pardon; pardon me; sorry; will you forgive me; (2) let sb down; unfair to; unworthy of;
對得起 not let sb down; treat sb fairly; worthy of;
發起 (1) initiate; sponsor; (2) launch; start;
奮起 make a vigorous start; rise; rise up with ardour; risewith force and spirit;
蜂起 rise in swarms;
鼓起 bag; balloon; blowup; call up; gather; muster up; pluck up; puff; rally; swell; take heart;
後起 among the rising generation;
喚起 (1) arouse; summon up; (2) call; recall; (3) evocation;
激起 arouse; evoke; set fire to; set sth on fire; stir up;
記起 recall; recollect;
禁不起 unable to stand trials;
禁得起 able to stand;
舉起 hoist; lift; raise;
崛起 (1) rise abruptly; rise sharply; suddenly appear on the horizon; (2) rise; spring up;
看不起 despise; hold in contempt; look down on; scorn;
撩起 raise;
了不起 amazing; and a half; extraordinary; far from common; proud and overweening; swell with pride; terrific;
隆起 bulge; swell;
買不起 beyond sb's purse; cannot afford;
買得起 able to afford it; swing;
冒起 emerge;
群起 rally together;
瞧得起 esteem; have a high regard for; hold in high esteem; look up to; respect; see much in; think much of; think well of; value;
擎起 lift up;
鵲起 rise at an opportune time;
惹不起 (1) dare not offend; dare not provoke; (2) too powerful to be offended;
惹起 incite; incur; provoke;
舌隆起 lingual swelling;
拾起 pick up;
收起 cut out; pack up; stop;
輸不起 cannot afford to lose;
豎起 erect; hoist; hold up;
説起 as for; begin talking about; bring up; with regard to;
四起 rise everywhere; rise from all directions;
談起 mention; speak of;
騰起 rise; spring;
提起 (1) mention; speak of; (2) arouse; brace up; lift up; raise;

挑起 instigate; provoke; stir up;
突起 (1) break out; suddenly appear; (2) rise high; tower;
挽起 roll up;
晚起 get up late; rise late;
蔚起 flourish; prosper; thrive;
掀起 (1) lift; raise; (2) cause to surge; surge; (3) set off; start;
想起 call to mind; occur; recall; remember; think of;
興起 (1) rise; spring up; (2) be moved and rise;
興起 aroused; excited;
晏起 get up late;
揚起 elevate; kick up;
仰起 fling;
躍起 jump up; leap up;
一起 (1) all together; in company; in the same place; together; (2) a case of;
憶起 call to mind; recall; remember;
引起 arise from; arise out of; arouse; bring about; bring down the house; bring on; bring to; call forth; cause; create; engender; evoke; give rise to; induce; kick up; lead to; lead up to; produce; set off; stir up; touch off; trigger;
緣起 (1) genesis; origin; (2) an account of the founding of an institution or the beginning of a project; (3) foreword; preface;
躍起 jump up; leap up;
再起 (1) recur; revive; rise again; stage a comeback; (2) assume public office again;
早起 (1) early to rise; get up early; (2) early in the morning;
振起 get aroused; rise and meet a challenge; stir up;

qi

【啟】 (1) bring up; open; (2) begin; initiate; set off; set out; start; (3) awaken; enlighten; explain; inspire; prompt; (4) inform; state; (5) activate; boot;

[啟報] report to one's superior and ask for instructions;

[啟閉] on and off; open and close; start and stop;
以時啟閉 open and close according to schedule;

[啟程] set off on a journey; set out; start on a journey;
啟程赴任 set out for the journey and take up the duties of an office;
啟程回家 take off for home;

[啟齒] bring up; mention; open one's mouth to say sth; start to talk about sth;
難於啟齒 difficult to speak out one's mind; have a bone in the throat;
破羞啟齒 come out of one's shell;
赧於啟齒 feel shy to speak;
羞於啟齒 not able to talk because of shyness; the cat gets one's tongue; too embarrassing to say it; too shy to speak out one's mind;

[啟處] take a rest;

[啟迪] awaken; inspire; to open and enlighten;
啟迪後人 inspire and enlighten the future generation;

[啟動] boot; activate; start; start-up; switch on;
啟動程序 boot programme; operating programme;
啟動點 firing point;
啟動碟 startup disk;
啟動費用 start-up costs;
啟動工具包 starter pack;
啟動紀錄 boot record; operating log;
啟動鍵 initiate key; operating key; start key;
啟動器 starter motor;
啟動區 boot sector;
啟動作用 activation;
重新啟動 reboot; reset;

[啟發] arouse; encourage criticism and discussion; enlighten; illuminate; inspire; instruct; prompt mental development; teach;
啟發法 heuristics;
啟發功能 heuristic function;
啟發教學法 elicitation method; heuristic method;
啟發潛能教育 invitational education;
啟發式 method of elicitation;
啟發思維 develop the mind;
得到啟發 gain enlightenment;

[啟封] (1) break the seal; remove the seal; unseal; (2) open a letter; open a wrapper; open an envelope;

[啟航] cast off; set sail; weigh anchor;
啟航出海 put out to sea;

[啟開] open;

[啟口] open one's mouth;
啟口欲言 move one's lips in an attempt to speak;

[啟蒙] (1) impart rudimentary knowledge to beginners; initiate elementary knowledge to beginner; (2) enlighten; free sb from prejudice or superstition; (3) primer;
啟蒙讀物 enlightened reading material; primer;
啟蒙教育 elementary education;
啟蒙老師 child's first tutor; abecedarian;
啟蒙時代 Age of Enlightenment;
啟蒙時期 period of enlightenment;
啟蒙運動 Enlightenment; enlightenment movement;
啟蒙作用 enlightening role;

[啟市] resume business;
初三啟市 reopen on the third day of the first lunar month;

[啟示] enlightenment; important teaching; inspiration; revelation; teaching;

[啟事] announcement; notice;
結婚啟事 announcement of marriage;
張貼啟事 put up a notice;
尋人啟事 notice in a missing person column;

[啟釁] pick a quarrel; provoke a dispute; provoke discord; start a quarrel;

[啟行] set out; start on a journey;

[啟用] start using;

[啟運] start shipment;
啟運港 port of departure;

開啟 open; usher in;
親啟 be opened personally; confidential;

qi

【棨】 a tally in ancient China;

qi

【綺】 (1) figured woven silk material; twilled silk cloth; (2) beautiful; elegant; fair; fine; gorgeous; magnificent; ornate; resplendent;

[綺井] the ceiling of a house;

[綺麗] beautiful; elegant; fair; gorgeous; magnificent;

[綺羅] (1) beautiful silk fabrics; damask; figured woven silk material; (2) person in a beautiful silk dress;

[綺夢] pleasant and romantic dream;

[綺靡] (1) extravagantly beautiful; (2) ornate style;

[綺陌] splendid streets;

[綺年] youthful;
綺年玉貌 a pretty young girl; young and pretty;

[綺情] tender feelings;

[綺室] gorgeous room; magnificent room;

[綺思] beautiful thoughts;

[綺筵] magnificent feast;

[綺語] (1) sexual talk; (2) literary pieces concerning love and sex;

qi

【綮】 sheath for a lancehead;

qi

【稽】 bow to the ground; kowtow;

[稽顙] kowtow with one's forehead touching the ground;

[稽首] kowtow;

qi⁴

qi

【汽】 gas; steam; vapour;

[汽表] steam gauge;

[汽車] automobile; car; motor car; motor vehicle;
汽車保單 cover note;
汽車保險 automobile insurance;
汽車保養 car maintenance;
汽車比賽 motor racing;
汽車餐館 drive-in;
汽車廠 automobile factory;
~汽車廠工人 autoworker;
汽車的 automotive;
汽車電影院 drive-in theatre;
汽車翻轉 car overturned;
汽車防盜警報器 car alarm;
汽車工業 auto industry;
汽車荷載量 carload;
汽車後座 back seat;
汽車技術 automotive technology;
汽車駕駛員 motorist;
汽車警報器 car alarm;
汽車俱樂部 car club;
汽車拉力賽 long-distance endurance test for cars; rally;
汽車旅館 motel;
汽車輪渡 car ferry;
汽車棚 carport;
汽車票 bus ticket;
汽車司機 chauffeur; driver;
~女汽車司機 chauffeurette;

汽車污染 vehicle pollution;
汽車無鉛化 use unleaded fuel;
汽車運輸車 car transporter;
汽車炸彈 car bomb;
汽車站 bus stop;
~ 長途汽車站 coach station;
汽車製造廠 car-builder;
汽車製造業 automotive industry; motor industry;
汽車撞毀 car smashed up;
汽車座位 car seat;
汽車座椅 car seat;
~ 幼兒汽車座椅 car seat;
柴油汽車 crude oil automobile;
出租汽車 cab; taxi;
~ 出租汽車乘客 cab-getter;
~ 出租汽車駕駛人 cabman;
~ 出租汽車停車處 cabstand;
~ 出租汽車站 taxi rank; taxi stand;
~ 坐出租汽車 take a taxi;
電池汽車 battery car;
電動汽車 electric automobile;
乘坐汽車 ride in a car;
防彈汽車 bulletproof car;
趕上汽車 catch a bus;
~ 沒趕上汽車 miss a bus;
高油耗汽車 gas-guzzler;
公共汽車 auto bus; bus; motor bus;
~ 公共汽車乘車證 bus pass;
~ 公共汽車費 bus fare;
~ 公共汽車服務 bus service;
~ 公共汽車候車亭 bus shelter;
~ 公共汽車駕駛員 busman;
~ 公共汽車路線 bus route;
~ 公共汽車票 bus ticket;
~ 公共汽車載客量 busload;
~ 公共汽車站 bus stop;
~ 公共汽車專用車道 bus lane;
~ 公共汽車總站 bus station;
~ 長途公共汽車 coach; long-distance bus;
~ 長途公共汽車總站 coash station;
~ 乘公共汽車 catch a bus; get a bus; ride a bus; take the bus;
~ 單層公共汽車 single-decker;
~ 等公共汽車 wait for a bus;
~ 空中公共汽車 aerobus;
~ 雙層空中公共汽車 double-deck aerobus;
~ 上公共汽車 get on a bus;
~ 雙層公共汽車 double-decker;
~ 下公共汽車 get off a bus;
~ 小公共汽車 minibus;
~ 小型公共汽車 minibus;
~ 一班公共汽車 one scheduled run of a bus;
~ 遊覽公共汽車 excursion bus;
~ 坐公共汽車 take the bus;
豪華汽車 luxury car;
混合動力汽車 hybrid car;
駕駛汽車 work a motor car;
開汽車 motoring;
旅行汽車 dormouse;
農用汽車 agricultural automobile; agrimotor;
氣墊汽車 aeromobile;
氣油汽車 gasoline automobile;
三輪汽車 three-wheeled car;
雙座汽車 two-seater;
水陸兩用汽車 amphibian automobile; amphibious car;
四輪驅動汽車 four-by-four; four-wheel drive car;
停放汽車 park a car;
小汽車 automobile; car; motorcar;
~ 出租小汽車 taxi;
~ 輕便小汽車 runabout;
~ 三輪小汽車 bubble car;
~ 雙座小汽車 coupe;
~ 一輛小汽車 a small car;
~ 硬頂小汽車 hard-top car;
~ 折篷小汽車 convertible car;
小型汽車 compact; compact car; mini-car;
~ 超小型汽車 supercompact car;
一部汽車 a car;
一長串汽車 a string of cars;
一輛汽車 a car;
迎面駛來的汽車 oncoming car;
載重汽車 automotive truck;
摺篷式汽車 cabriolet; convertible;
蒸汽汽車 steam automobile;
重型汽車 heavy-duty car;
裝甲汽車 armoured automobile; armoured car;
坐汽車 ride on a car;

[汽船] steamboat; steamer; steamship;

[汽燈] gas lamp; vapour lamp;

[汽笛] air whistle; hooter; siren; steam whistle; whistle;
汽笛長鳴 the siren hoots;
諧音汽笛 chime whistle;
自動汽笛 automatic whistle;

[汽缸] cylinder;

[汽管] steam pipe;

[汽化] carburize vapourize;

汽化器 carburettor;
~單嘴汽化器 single jet carburettor;
~倒置汽化器 inverted carburettor; reversing carburettor;
~多嘴汽化器 multiple jet carburettor;
~複式汽化器 double carburettor;
~隔膜汽化器 diaphragm carburettor;
~機力汽化器 mechanical carburettor;
~簡單化汽化器 elementary carburettor;
~噴射式汽化器 injection carburettor; spray carburettor;
~噴霧式汽化器 atomizing carburettor;
~起動汽化器 priming carburettor;
~省油汽化器 economy-type carburettor;
~溢流汽化器 flooded carburettor;
~蒸發汽化器 evaporating carburettor;
~自動汽化器 automatic carburettor;
汽化熱 heat of vaporization;

[汽機] steam engine;

[汽酒] alcopop; light sparkling wine; spritzer;

[汽力] steam power;

[汽輪機] steam turbine; turbine;
背壓式汽輪機 back-pressure turbine;
航空燃汽輪機 aero-gas turbine; aircraft gas turbine;
推進汽輪機 ahead turbine;
軸流式汽輪機 axial flow steam turbine;

[汽門] steam valve;

[汽泡] bubbles;

[汽槍] air gun;
玩具汽槍 pop-gun;

[汽水] (1) aerated water; carbonated drink; mineral waters; soda water; soft drinks; (2) steamwater; vapour-water;
薑味汽水 ginger ale;

[汽艇] motor launch; motorboat; powerboat; steam launch;

[汽壓] steam pressure; vapour pressure;
飽和水汽壓 saturation vapour pressure;

[汽油] gas; gasoline; petrol;
汽油彈 petrol bomb;
汽油發動機 petrol engine;
汽油機 internal combustion engine;
汽油桶 petrol canister;
車用汽油 motor petrol;
防凍汽油 anti-icing gasoline;
含鉛汽油 leaded gasoline;
航空汽油 aviation gasoline; aviation petrol;
抗爆汽油 anti-knock petrol;
凝固汽油 napalm;
平衡汽油 balanced gasoline;
四星汽油 four-star;
烷化汽油 alkylation gasoline;
無鉛汽油 lead-free gasoline; unleaded petrol;
吸附汽油 adsorption gasoline;
一桶汽油 a bucket of gasoline; a drum of gasoline;
乙醇汽油 gasohol;
重汽油 heavy petrol;

[汽輾] steamroller;

水汽 moisture; vapour;
蒸汽 steam;

qi

【迄】 (1) till; up to; (2) all along; so far;

[迄今] as yet; by now; hitherto; so far; till now; to date; to this date; to this day; until now; up to; up to now; up to the present day; up to this point;
迄今為止 hitherto; so far; thus far; to this day; up to now;
以迄於今 so far; to date; to this day; up to now;

qi

【妻】 marry a girl; marry off a daughter;

qi

【泣】 (1) come to tears; burst into tears; give way to tears; shed tears; sob; weep; (2) cause to weep; (3) come to tears without crying; tears;

[泣別] part in tears;

[泣不成聲] be choked with tears; choke with sobs; cry one's heart out; cry one's voice out; cry till one's tears dry; weep one's heart out; weep till one's tears dry;

[泣諫] counsel in tears;

[泣叩] a concluding expression in a mourning notice;

[泣訴] accuse while weeping; blubber out one's bitter experiences; sob out one's grievances; tell one's sorrows;
如泣如訴 pathetic and touching; plaintive; plangent;

[泣涕] come to tears for sorrow; weep;
泣涕漣漣 weep profusely;

[泣下] one's tars fall;
泣下如雨 one's tears fall down like rain;

shed tears like rain; weep copious tears;
泣下數行 tears coursing down the cheeks;
[泣血] weep blood;
泣血稽顙 weep blood and knock one's head on the ground;
椎心泣血 deep sorrow; excruciating pains; extreme grief;
[泣杖] cry over the stick;
[泣罪] weep for a criminal's evil-doing;

暗泣 weep behind others' backs;
哀泣 cry sorrowfully;
悲泣 weep with grief;
抽泣 sob;
啜泣 sob;
哭泣 cry; sob; weep;

qi
【契】 (1) agreement; bond; contract; receipt; (2) agree; compatible; harmonious; (3) adopt; (4) carve; cut; notch; (5) a surname;
[契父] adoptive father;
[契合] accord with; agree with; compatible; conform to; correspond to; harmonious; in agreement; tally with;
契合金蘭 on intimate terms;
[契機] (1) moment; (2) critical point of time; juncture; turning point;
[契據] contract; deed; receipt; agreement;
[契母] adoptive mother;
[契女] adoptive daughter;
[契契] pitiful; sad; sorrowful;
[契稅] tax on landownership registration;
[契友] bosom friend; close friend; intimate friend;
[契約] agreement; charter; contract; covenant; deed;
契約當事人 contracting party;
契約關係 contractual relationship;
契約臨時工 contract casual labour;
契約期滿 take up one's indentures;
契約社會 contract society;
契約條款 contract terms;
解除契約 termkinate a contract;
口頭契約 oral contract;
年金契約 annuity agreement; annuity contract;
起草契約 draw up a contract;
簽訂契約 sign a contract;
取消契約 cancel a contract;
撕毀契約 tear up a contract;
投標契約 bidding contract;
退出契約 contract oneself out of;
違反契約 violate one's contract;
修訂契約 amend a contract;
延期契約 extension agreement;
運輸契約 freight agreement;
運送契約 carriage contract;
追加契約 add-on contract;
遵守契約 abide by the contract;
[契紙] contract; deed;
[契舟求劍] carve on a gunwale of a moving boat;
[契子] adoptive son;

白契 unregistered deed or contract;
地契 title deed for land;
佃契 tenancy contract;
房契 title deed for a house;
官契 deeds officially registered with the authorities;
紅契 registered deed or contract;
默契 tacit agreement; tacit understanding;
書契 certificate; deed;
稅契 title deed;
死契 irrevocable title deed;
投契 agreeable; congenial; get along well; meeting of minds;
文契 contract; deed;

qi
【砌】 (1) build; build by laying bricks; lay; pave; raise in layers; (2) stone step;
[砌詞揑控] fabricate charges; frame; trump up charges;
[砌路] build a road; pave a road;
[砌牆] build a wall;
[砌磚] brickwork; lay bricks;
砌磚工 brickmason;
砌磚工人 bricklayer;

雕砌 write in a labored and ornate style;
堆砌 (1) pile up; (2) pile up phrases and sentences;
鋪砌 pave; paving;
鑲砌 inlay; mount;

qi
【氣】 (1) air; gas; respiration; vapour; (2) air; fresh air; (3) aspiration; breath; vitality; (4) atmosphere; weather; (5)

flavour; odour; smell; (6) courage; mettle; morale; spirit; (7) influence; (8) airs; bearing; forbearance; manner; style; tolerance; (9) angry; bitter; furious; hateful; indignant; peeved; resentful; ruffled; sulky; sullen; (10) be enraged; get angry; get annoyed; make angry; provoke to goad; (11) bully; insult; maltreatment;

[氣昂昂] elated; full of courage; full of dash; full of mettle; high morale; high spirit; in high spirits; with high morale;

[氣瓣] air valve;

[氣胞] air cell; respiratory hollow;

[氣泵] air pump;

[氣層] atmosphere;

[氣沖沖] angrily; angry; beside oneself with rage; enraged; fly into a rage; furious; get huffy; in a fit of spleen; in a great temper; in a rage;

[氣沖牛斗] furious; in a towering rage; the vapour rises up to the sky－fly into a great rage;

[氣喘] (1) asthma; (2) gasp; pant; out of breath; short of breath; tracheitis;

氣喘病 heaves;

氣喘如牛 gasp for breath; have bellows to mend; pant like a bull; pant like an ox;

氣喘吁吁 breathe heavily; pant; out of puff; puff and blow; puff and pant; puff hard;

丙酮性氣喘 acetonasthma;

氣不喘，臉不紅 not be out of breath or even faintly flushed;

[氣窗] fanlight; transom;

[氣促] panting; shortness of breath;

[氣袋] airbag;

[氣道] air passage; airway;

[氣得] with anger;

氣得跺腳 stamp one's feet with anger;

氣得發抖 be shaking with anger; shake with anger; tremble with rage;

氣得發火 hot with rage;

氣得臉發黃 yellow with rage;

氣得嘔血 one is so incensed that one literally coughs up blood;

氣得説不出話 choke with anger;

氣得要命 mad as a wet hen;

氣得直喘 gasp with rage;

氣得直哭 weep through anger;

[氣燈] gas lamp;

[氣笛] air whistle;

[氣墊] air cushion; air mattress;

氣墊車 air-brake car;

氣墊船 hovercraft;

氣墊汽車 aeromobile;

[氣動] pneumatic;

氣動機器人 pneumatic robot;

[氣度] (1) air; bearing; manner; spirit; (2) capacity for tolerance; forbearance; tolerance; tolerant spirit;

氣度不凡 in a laudably tolerant spirit;

氣度非凡 impressive appearance; impressive in bearing; uncommon tolerance;

[氣短] (1) be short of breath; breathe hard; pant; (2) dejected; disappointed; discouraged; lose heart;

氣短神昏 choke for breath and lose consciousness; short of breath and in a state of delirium;

[氣氛] air; ambience; atmosphere; mood; political climate;

保護氣氛 protective atmosphere;

電弧氣氛 arc atmosphere;

惰性氣氛 inert atmosphere;

工業氣氛 industrial atmosphere;

混合氣體氣氛 mixed gas atmosphere;

爐內氣氛 furnace inside atmosphere;

破壞氣氛 trouble the air;

氫氣氛 hydrogen atmosphere;

熱處理氣氛 heat-treating atmosphere;

碳質氣氛 carbonaceous atmosphere;

脱碳氣氛 decarburizing atmosphere;

無氧氣氛 oxygen-free atmosphere;

中性氣氛 neutral atmosphere;

[氣忿忿] angry; enraged; furious; mad; wrathful;

[氣憤] angry; be enraged; furious; in anger; indignant; with anger;

感到氣憤 be filled with indignation;

使氣憤 irk;

[氣腹] aeroperitoneum;

氣腹炎 pneumoperitonitis;

[氣慨] air; bearing; heroic manner; heroic spirit; lofty quality; mettle; spirit;

氣慨昂然 full of valour;

豪邁氣慨 heroic spirit; unrestrained spirit;

男子氣慨 virility;

~無男子氣慨 unmanly;
丈夫氣慨 manliness;

[氣缸] air cylinder;

[氣格] character; personality;

[氣哽] choking;

[氣功] breathing exercise; qigong;
氣功療法 treatment method based on breathing therapy;
氣功培訓班 breathing exercise training class;

[氣骨] one's natural character;

[氣管] trachea; windpipe;
氣管病 tracheopathy;
氣管出血 tracheorrhagia;
氣管炎 tracheitis;
~鼻氣管炎 bovine rhinotracheitis;
~喉氣管炎 laryngotracheitis;
~細菌性氣管炎 bacterial tracheitis;
傳導氣管 conducting airway;
腹氣管 ventral trachea;
橫基氣管 transverse basal trachea;
擴散氣管 diffusion trachea;
毛細氣管 capillary trachea;
氣門氣管 spiracular trachea;
生殖氣管 genital trachea;

[氣貫長虹] as lofty in spirit as the rainbow spanning the sky; be filled with a spirit as lofty as the rainbow spanning the sky; be imbued with a lofty spirit; full of noble aspiration and daring;

[氣鍋] ceramic steamer;

[氣恨] angry; bitter; hateful; resentful;

[氣哼哼] angry; enraged; furious; mad;

[氣候] (1) climate; weather; (2) situation;
氣候變化 climate change; climatic change;
氣候測年學 climatochronology;
氣候環境 climatone;
~氣候環境病理學 climatopathology;
氣候療法 climatotherapy;
氣候生成 climatogenesis;
氣候生理學 climatophysiology;
氣候圖 climate map; climatic map;
~氣候圖表 climagraph; climatograph; climograph;
~氣候圖解 climatograph; climogram;
~二維氣候圖 two-dimensional climograph;
氣候型 climatotype;
氣候序列 climosequence;
氣候學 climatology;
~氣候學家 climatologist;
~動力氣候學 dynamic climatology;
~工業氣候學 industrial climatology;
~古氣候學 palaeoclimatology;
~航空氣候學 aero-nautical climatology;
~建築氣候學 building climatology;
~景觀氣候學 landscape climatology;
~雷達氣候學 radar climatology;
~描述性氣候學 descriptive climatology;
~農業氣候學 agricultural climatology;
~氣團氣候學 air-mass climatology;
~生活氣候學 domestic climatology;
~生理氣候學 physiological climatology;
~生態氣候學 ecological climatology;
~生物氣候學 bioclimatology;
~天氣氣候學 synoptic climatology;
~無線電氣候學 radio climatology;
~物理氣候學 physical climatology;
~應用氣候學 applied climatology;
~綜合氣候學 complex climatology;
氣候循環 climatic cycles;
氣候要素 climatic elements;
氣候宜人 delightful weather; pleasant weather;
氣候異常 climatic anomaly;
氣候因素 climatic factor;
氣候因子 climatic factor;
氣候預報 meteorological forecasts; weather forecasts;
北極氣候 arctic climate;
冰蓋氣候 ice-cap climate;
冰原氣候 frost climate; tundra climate;
冰緣氣候 periglacial climate;
草原氣候 steppe climate;
常濕氣候 wet climate;
潮濕氣候 humid climate; wet climate;
成氣候 become popular; gain the upper hand; make good; in power;
~成不了氣候 will not get anywhere;
赤道氣候 equatorial climate;
大陸氣候 continental climate; mainland climate;
大氣候 macroclimate;
島嶼氣候 insular climate;
地質氣候 geologic climate;
地中海氣候 Mediterranean climate;
多雨氣候 rainy climate;
~熱帶多雨氣候 tropical rainy climate;
~溫帶多雨氣候 temperate rainy climate;
副極帶氣候 subarctic climate;
乾燥氣候 arid climate; dry climate;

高山氣候 alpine climate;
高溫氣候 megathermal climate;
高原氣候 highland climate; plateau climate;
光照氣候 illumination climate;
過濕氣候 perhumid climate;
海岸氣候 coastal climate;
海濱氣候 littoral climate;
海洋氣候 marine climate; maritime climate; sea climate;
寒冷氣候 hiemal climate;
環境氣候 environmental climate;
極地氣候 polar climate;
季風氣候 monsoon climate;
~ 熱帶季風氣候 tropical monsoon climate;
經濟氣候 economic climate;
棉帶氣候 cotton-belt climate;
牧場氣候 grassland climate; prairie climate;
平原氣候 plain climate;
區域性氣候 regional climate;
熱帶氣候 tropical climate;
熱型氣候 thermal climate;
人工氣候 artificial climate;
森林氣候 forest climate;
沙漠氣候 desert climate;
山地氣候 mountain climate;
山岳氣候 mouintain climate;
濕潤氣候 humid climate; moist climate;
數理氣候 mathematical climate;
樹木氣候 tree climate;
投資氣候 investment climate;
微生態氣候 ecidio climate;
溫帶氣候 temperate climate;
溫和氣候 benign climate; mild climate;
~ 海洋性溫和氣候 oceanic moderate climate;
西岸氣候 west coast climate;
小氣候 microclimate;
雪林氣候 snow forest climate;
嚴寒氣候 harsh climate;
雨林氣候 rain forest climate;
正常氣候 normal climate;
政治氣候 political climate;
植物氣候 plant climate;
中氣候 mesoclimate;
作物氣候 crop climate;

[氣呼呼] angrily; gasp out; in a huff; panting with rage; spluttering with rage;

[氣化] evaporate; gasify; vaporize;

[氣壞] beside oneself with rage;

[氣輝] airglow;

[氣昏了] be driven mad by anger;

[氣急] flustered and exasperated;

氣急敗壞 breathe hard; come panting and exhausted; desperate and low-spirited; exasperated; flustered and exasperated; get exasperated; in exasperation; panting and dismayed; splutter; utterly discomfitted; with a great spluttering; wrought-up;
~ 挨了棒的狗—氣急敗壞 a dog beaten with a club — flustered and exasperated; utterly discomfited and angry;

[氣節] (1) fine quality; integrity; lofty moral integrity; moral courage; moral principle; righteousness; (2) season; (3) twenty-four solar periods of the year;

[氣盡] run out of vitality;

[氣沮] depressed; dispirited;

心喪氣沮 the heart mourns and spirit spoils;

[氣絕] at one's last gasp; breathe one's last;

氣絕身亡 breathe one's last breath; breathe out one's life; slip one's wind;

[氣孔] blowhole; pore; stoma; vent;

氣孔運動 stomatal movement; stomatic movement;
表面氣孔 surface blowhole;
排氣孔 exhaust vent;
皮下氣孔 subcutaneous blowhole;
一次氣孔 primary blowhole;

[氣口] vent;

排氣口 blow vent;

[氣塊] air parcel;

[氣力] effort; energy; strength;

白費氣力 a fool for one's pains; a waste of breath; a waste of efforts a wild-goose chase; beat the air; beat the wind; bite a file; bite on granite; blow at cold coal; cast water into the Thames; catch a shadow; catch at shadows; draw a blank; draw water in a sieve; fish in the air; flog a dead horse; force an open door; futile; gnaw a file; go on a wild-goose chase; in vain; knock at an open door; labour in vain; labour lost; lash the waves; lose one's labour; lose one's pains; plough the air; plough

Q

the sands; pour water into a sieve; run one's head against into a brick wall; shoe a goose; sow beans in the wind; wash a blackamoor white; wash an ass's ears; wash an ass's head; waste effort on; waste one's breath; waste one's energy; waste one's words;
~ 白費氣力的事 a bad job;
花氣力 make the effort;

[氣量] (1) forbearance; one's breadth of mind; tolerance; (2) ability and insight;
氣量大 broad-minded; generous; large-hearted; magnanimous; tolerant;
氣量狹小 narrow-minded;
氣量小 narrow-minded; petty;

[氣流] (1) air current; airflow; air stream; (2) breath;
超音速氣流 supersonic airstream;
垂直氣流 vertical airstream;
反氣流 counterblast;
風洞氣流 tunnel airstream;
相對氣流 relative airstream;
亞音速氣流 subsonic airstream;

[氣貌軒昂] straight and impressive looking;

[氣煤] gas coal;

[氣門] spiracle;
氣門線 spiracle-line;
鼓膜氣門 tympanic spiracle;
前胸氣門 prothpracic spiracle;
雙室氣門 biforous spiracle;

[氣悶] oppressive; stifling; sultry;

[氣囊] (1) airbag; (2) (of birds) air bladder; air sac;
安全氣囊 airbag; air cushion;
外氣囊 extra air sac;

[氣惱] get angry; get annoyed; peeved; resentful; ruffled; sulky; sullen; take offence;
一陣氣惱 a moment of anger;

[氣餒] become dejected; become down-hearted; crestfallen; dejected; despondent; discouraged; disheartened; down-hearted; lose heart;
毫不氣餒 without flagging;

[氣派] airs; bearing; dignified air; fine; impressive; impressive manner; impressive style; manner; style; stylish;

[氣泡] air bubbles;
氣泡襯墊包裝 bubble pack; bubble wrap;
氣泡酒 bubbly;
~ 一杯氣泡酒 a glass of bubbly;
氣泡破裂 a bubble bursts;
刺破氣泡 prick a bubble;

[氣噴] gas blowout;

[氣魄] (1) boldness of vision; breadth of spirit; broadness of mind; courage; daring; moral strength; spirit; (2) imposing manner;

[氣腔] air chamber;

[氣槍] airgun; air rifle;

[氣球] (1) airballoon; balloon; (2) hot-air balloon;
定高氣球 constant-level balloon;
防空氣球 antiaircraft balloon;
熱氣球 hot-air balloon;
~ 乘熱氣球 ballooning;
乘熱氣球者 balloonist;
小氣球 tiny balloons;
一個氣球 a balloon;
阻塞氣球 barrage ballooon;

[氣人] annoying;
真氣人 it's really annoying;

[氣塞] airlock;

[氣色] colour; complexion; tint;
氣色不好 off colour;
氣色不佳 look blue about the gills; look green about the gills; look white about the gills; look yellow about the gills; look pale; not to look oneself; off colour;
氣色好 look rosy about the gills;
氣色挺好 get a splendid colour;

[氣盛] arrogant; overbearing;

[氣勢] grandeur; imposing manner; majesty; momentum;
氣勢昂昂 forceful; vigorous;
氣勢磅礴 enterprising in spirit; full of power and grandeur; great and momentous; imposing; impressive; magnificent; majestic and momentous; of great momentum; overflowing with energy; powerful; resolute in action; turbulent; with a tremendous momentum; with great momentum;
氣勢十足 full of momentum;
氣勢洶洶 a truculent attitude; an aggressive posture; an overbearing attitude; arrogantly; bluffingly; bluster and swagger; blustering and truculent; ferociously; fiercely; full of bluff;

furiously; get up on one's hind legs; hammer and tongs; have a chip on one's shoulder; have a defiant air as if expecting to fight; have a defiant air as if ready to accept a challenge; in a rush of anger; in a threatening manner; insolently; on the muscle; overbearing; put up quite a show; truculently; violently; with an aggressive posture; with overweening arrogance;
氣勢洶洶，不可一世 bluster and swagger like a conquering hero; overweeningly arrogant as if nobody on earth could beat one;
氣勢雄偉 imposing;

[氣數] destiny; fate; fortune;
氣數已盡 one's days are numbered; one's spell of good fortune has run out;

[氣死] really infuriating;
氣死牛 headstrong person; strong-willed;
氣死人 exasperating; infuriating; maddening;
人比人，氣死人 comparisons are odious; invidious comparisons can only end in chagrin;

[氣態] gaseous state;

[氣體] gas; gaseous body; gaseous fluid; vapour;
氣體常數 gas constant;
氣體打火機 gas lighter;
氣體動力學 aerodynamics;
氣體反應定律 law of gas reaction;
氣體分折 gas analysis
氣體燃料 gaseous fuel;
氣體生成能力 gassing ability;
氣體吸附 gas adsorption;
理想氣體 ideal gas; perfect gas;
~非理想氣體 imperfect gas;
排出氣體 discharge gas;
人造氣體 artificial gas;
實際氣體 actual gas; real gas;
酸性氣體 acidic gas;
完全氣體 ideal gas; perfect gas;
溫室氣體 greenhouse gas;
吸附氣體 adsorbed gas;
吸收氣體 absorbing gas;
陽極氣體 anodic gas;
易燃氣體 combustible gas;
永久氣體 permanent gas;
周圍氣體 ambient gas;

[氣筒] bicycle pump; air pump; inflator;

[氣痛] gas pain;

[氣頭上] in a fit of anger; in a fit of temper; right in the middle of one's fit of rage;

[氣團] air mass;
大陸氣團 continental air mass;
海洋氣團 maritime air mass;
冷氣團 cold air mass;
暖氣團 warm air mass;

[氣味] (1) flavour; odour; smell; (2) likes and dislikes; smack; taste;
氣味相投 birds of a feather; congenial to each other; cut from the same cloth; have the same likes and dislikes; have the same lousy taste; have the same tastes and temperament; like attracts like; like draws like; people who have similar vulgar tastes come together; sharing the same views and preferences; similar in inclinations; two of a kind;
刺鼻氣味 pungent smell; sharp aroma;
發出氣味 give off a smell;
芬芳的氣味 sweet smell;
令人作嘔的氣味 nauseous smell;
硫磺氣味 sulfur-containing aroma;
散發出氣味 emit an odour;
聞到氣味 detect a smell; notice a smell; smell a smell;
一種氣味 a smell;

[氣溫] air temperature; atmospheric temperature;

[氣窩] airlock;

[氣息] (1) breath; (2) flavour; odour; smell;
氣息芬芳 her breath is like the sweet odour of perfumes;
氣息奄奄 at one's last gasp; at the end of their resources; at the point of death; breathe feebly; dying; dying by inches; expiring; fainting; gasping; gasping for breath; moribund; on the point of dying; sinking fast; the breath is dying out; totter on the brink of the grave; with one foot in the grave;
一絲氣息 a small faint breath;

[氣象] (1) climate; meteorological phenomenon; weather; (2) atmosphere; scene; the prevailing spirit;
氣象報告 weathercast;
~氣象報告員 weathercaster;
男氣象報告員 weatherman;
女氣象報告員 weather girl;

氣象觀測 meteorological observation;
氣象火箭 meteorological rocket;
氣象局 weather bureau;
氣象雷達 meteorological radar; weather radar;
氣象區 meteorological region;
氣象哨 meteorological post;
氣象台 climatological station; meteorological observatory; observatory; weather port; weather station;
~氣象臺站網 meteorological network;
氣象圖 meteorological map; weather chart;
氣象萬千 a wonderful and mighty panorama; in all its majesty; magnificent and varied sights; majestic and grand; majestic in all its variety; nature abounds in changes; spectacular; there opens before you extensive views of nature in all its wild grandeur with its ever-changing aspects; things change in a myriad of ways;
氣象衛星 meteosat; meteorological satellite; weather satellite;
~同步氣象衛星 synchronous meteorological satellite;
氣象學 climatology; meteorology;
~動力氣象學 dynamic meteorology;
~高空氣象學 aerology;
~空氣污染氣象學 air pollution meteorology;
~農業氣象學 agroclimatology; agrometeorology;
~生物氣象學 biometeorology;
~應用氣象學 applied meteorology;
氣象要素 meteorological element;
氣象一新 take on a new look; have a make-over;
氣象預報 weather forecast;
氣象站 meteorological station; weather station;
氣象資料 meteorological data;
觀測氣象 make weather observations;
新氣象 pervasive new spirit; prevailing new atmosphere;

[氣性] disposition; temperament;

[氣胸] collapsed lung; pneumothorax;
創傷性氣胸 traumatic pneumothorax;
開放性氣胸 open pneumothorax;
人工氣胸 artificial pneumothorax;
外傷性氣胸 traumatic pneumothorax;
壓力性氣胸 pressure pneumothorax;
月經性氣胸 catamenial pneumothorax;
張力性氣胸 tension pneumothorax;
診斷性氣胸 diagnostic pneumotrorax;

[氣吁吁] gasp for breath; pant;

[氣旋] cyclone;
氣旋風 cyclone wind;
反氣旋 anticyclone;
~北極反氣旋 arctic anticyclone;
~冰原反氣旋 glacial anticyclone;
~高空反氣旋 high level anticyclone; upper-level anticyclone;
~海洋性反氣旋 oceanic anticyclone;
~緩性反氣旋 warm anticyclone;
~極地反氣旋 polar anticyclone;
~南極反氣旋 antarctic anticyclone;
~暖心反氣旋 warm-core anticyclone;
~亞熱帶反氣旋 subtropical anticyclone;
~移動性反氣旋 migratory anticyclone;
~阻塞反氣旋 blocking anticyclone;
焚風氣旋 foehn cyclone;
鋒面氣旋 frontal cyclone;
高空氣旋 high-level cyclone;
環極氣旋 circumpolar cyclone;
冷性氣旋 cold-core cyclone;
熱帶氣旋 tropical cyclone;
溫帶氣旋 extratropical cyclone;

[氣穴] airlock;

[氣壓] air pressure; atmospheric pressure; barometric pressure; pressure;
氣壓表 barometer;
~固體氣壓表 holosteric barometer;
~航空氣壓表 aviation barometer;
~空盒氣壓表 dial barometer;
氣壓測定法 barometry;
氣壓測驗器 baroscope;
氣壓層 barosphere;
氣壓電阻 baroresistor;
氣壓動力學 barodynamics;
氣壓疾病 baropathy;
氣壓計 barometer; air gauge;
~標準氣壓計 normal barometer;
~槽式氣壓計 cistern barometer;
~測量站氣壓計 station barometer;
~稱重氣壓計 weight barometer;
~船用氣壓計 marine barometer;
~虹吸氣壓計 syphon barometer;
~膜盒氣壓計 aneroid barometer;
~球管氣壓計 buld barometer; vessel barometer;

~水銀氣壓計 mercurial barometer;
~彎管氣壓計 siphon barometer;
~無液氣壓計 aneroid barometer;
~自動氣壓計 recording barometer;
氣壓梯度 press graqdient;
~氣壓梯度力 pressure force;
氣壓調節器 barostat;
氣壓圖 barogram; pressure chart;
氣壓溫度記錄器 barothermograph;
氣壓溫度濕度計 barothermohydrograph;
氣壓溫度濕度圖 barothermohygrogram;
氣壓性創傷 barotrauma;
氣壓性耳火 barotitis;
氣壓轉換開關 baroswitch;
氣壓自動記錄器 barometrograph;
飽和汽壓 saturated vapour pressure;
大氣壓 barometric pressure;
~標準大氣壓 standard atmospheric pressure;
低氣壓 barometric low; low pressure;
高氣壓 high pressure;
公制氣壓 metric atmosphere;
海平面氣壓 sea level pressure;
最低氣壓 barometric minimum;
最高氣壓 barometric maximum;

[氣焰] arrogance; bluster; hauteur; overweening arrogance;
氣焰更盛 more domineering than...;
氣焰迫人 act snooty; behave with unbearable insolence; insufferably haughty;
氣焰萬丈 become overweeningly arrogant; extreme arrogance;
氣焰囂張 be puffed up with pride; be swollen with arrogance; become cocky and loud mouthed; behave with unbearable insolence; blustering; ferocious; frantic; frenzied; grow unbridled; make a blatant display of one's power; one's arrogance reaches a peak; overbearing; savage; swollen with overweening arrogance; wild;
氣焰囂張，不可一世 inordinate arrogance; swaggering like conquering heroes;
氣焰熏天 one's arrogance stinks to heaven;
挫其氣焰 humble sb's pride;

[氣油] gas; gasoline; petrol;
氣油彈 petrol bomb;

[氣宇] bearing; dignified and inspiring looks; the manner of a person's carriage; tolerance;
氣宇昂藏 tall and strong;
氣宇非凡 person with unusually dignified looks;
氣宇軒昂 dignified; exalted; have a straight and impressive look; have an imposing appearance; have an impressive bearing; inspiring looks; manly; straight and impressive looking;
軒昂氣宇 dignified; exalted;

[氣韻] tone of a work;
氣韻生動 rhythmic vitality;

[氣脹] flatulence; gas; wind;
氣脹病 bloat;
氣脹痛 gas pains;

[氣質] (1) disposition; mould; temperament; (2) makings; qualities;
氣質特性 characteristics of temperament;
氣質相同 of the same kidney; of the same temperament;
變化氣質 change one's temperament;

[氣腫] emphysema;
創傷性氣腫 traumatic emphysema;
肺氣腫 emphysema; pneumonectasis; pulmonary emphysema;
假性氣腫 false emphysema;
器質性氣腫 anatomic emphysema;
外傷性氣腫 traumatic emphysema;
支氣管性氣腫 bronchial emphysema;

[氣壯] the spirit is strong;
氣壯如牛 appear to be as strong as an ox; as tough as a bull; as fierce as a bull; as strong as an ox; have the constitution of an ox;
~氣壯如牛，膽小如鼠 outwardly fierce as a bull but inwardly timid as a mouse; stout as a bull but timid as a mouse;
氣壯山河 as magnificent as high mountains and surging rivers; full of power and grandeur; magnificent; stirring and inspiring; sublime and heroic; the spirit is so vigorous that it affects even the mountains and rivers;
理直氣壯 bold and straightforward; courageous with sufficient reasons; fully justified; in the right and self-confident; justly and forcefully; strong reasons make strong actions; walk tall;

with full justification and without fear; with perfect assurance;

［氣嘴］ valve;

噯氣 belch; eructation;
氨氣 ammonia;
傲氣 air of arrogance; haughtiness;
霸氣 hegemony;
背過氣 gasp for breath; out of breath; stop breathing;
背氣 faint; fall unconscious;
閉氣 (1) lose consciousness; (2) stop breathing voluntarily;
憋氣 silently resentful;
憋氣 (1) feel suffocated; (2) feel injured and resentful;
屏氣 bate one's breath; hold one's breath;
補氣 invigorate the vital energy;
才氣 literary talent;
財氣 luck in making big money;
岔氣 feel a pain in the chest when breathing;
潮氣 damp; moisture in the air;
沉住氣 hold one's horses; keep calm; keep cool; steady;
充氣 inflate;
臭氣 bad smell; stink;
出氣 blow off steam; give vent to one's anger; let off steam; vent one's spleen;
除氣 deaerate; degassing;
喘氣 (1) breathe; gasp; pant; (2) take a breather;
串氣 collude with; gang up;
打氣 (1) inflate; pump up; (2) bolster up the morale; boost the morale; cheer up; encourage;
大氣 (1) air; atmosphere; (2) heavy breathing;
膽氣 bravery; courage;
氮氣 nitrogen; nitrogen gas;
電氣 electric;
動氣 become angry; get angry; lose one's temper; take offense;
鬥氣 quarrel or compete just for emotional reason;
毒氣 poison gas; poisonous gas;
賭氣 cut off one's own nose to spite one's face; feel wronged and act rashly; get in a rage; in a fit of pique;
短氣 dispirited; downhearted;
斷氣 breathe one's last; die;
廢氣 exhaust fumes; exhaust smoke;
風氣 atmosphere; common practice; ethos; fashion; general mood;
服氣 be convinced;
福氣 good fortune; happy lot;
負氣 do sth in a fit of pique;
肝氣 liver-energy;
供氣 air feed;
骨氣 backbone; moral integrity; strength of character;
官氣 bureaucratic airs;
光氣 phosgene;
孩子氣 childishness;
豪氣 heroic spirit;
浩氣 vigorous atmosphere;
和氣 amiableness; gentle; kind;
緩氣 get a breathing space; take a breather;
換氣 (in swimming) take a breath;
晦氣 unlucky;
活氣 vigorous atmosphere;
火氣 (1) internal heat; (2) anger; temper;
嬌氣 delicate; finicky airs; fragile; squeamishness;
驕氣 arrogance; overbearing airs;
腳氣 (1) beriberi; (2) athlete's foot;
接氣 be coherent;
解氣 vent one's spleen; work off one's anger;
景氣 boom; prosperity;
酒氣 smell of wine;
可氣 annoying; exasperating;
客氣 (1) courteous; polite; (2) modest; speak or behave politely;
吭氣 utter a sound or a word;
空氣 (1) air; (2) atmosphere;
口氣 (1) note; tone; (2) manner of speaking; (3) what is actually meant;
狂氣 arrogtant airs and manner of speaking;
闊氣 extravagant; lavish;
老氣 (1) old mannish; (2) (of clothes) dark and old-fashioned;
冷氣 (1) air-conditioning; (2) air-conditioning installations;
力氣 effort; physical strength;
流氣 hooliganism; rascally behaviour;
漏氣 air leak;
氯氣 chlorine;
煤氣 coal gas; gas;
霉氣 damp;
悶氣 stuffy;
民氣 popular morale; the people's morale;
名氣 name; reputation;
暮氣 lethargy;
男子氣 manliness;
牛脾氣 obstinacy; pigheadedness; stubbornness;
牛氣 arrogant; self-important;
怒氣 anger; fury;

暖氣 central heating;
慪氣 be difficult and sulky;
排氣 exhaust;
脾氣 (1) disposition; temperament; (2) bad temper;
貧氣 (1) miserly; (2) garrulous; wordy;
惹氣 get angry;
熱氣 heat; steam;
瑞氣 celestial phenomena portending peace and prosperity;
銳氣 dash; dauntless courage;
喪氣 feel disheartened; lose heart;
臊氣 foul odour;
殺氣 murderous look; vent one's ill feeling;
傻氣 foolish; stupid;
煞氣 leak slowly;
疝氣 hernia;
傷氣 (1) feel disheartened; (2) undermine one's constitution;
神氣 (1) expression; look; (2) spirited; vigorous; (3) cocky; imposing;
生氣 (1) get angry; take offence; (2) vigorous spirit; vitality;
聲氣 information;
濕氣 (1) dampness; moisture; (2) eczema; fungus infection of hand or foot;
石油氣 oil gas; petroleum gas;
士氣 morale;
手氣 luck at gambling;
受氣 be bullied; suffer wrong;
書卷氣 scholar's style;
暑氣 summer heat;
水蒸氣 steam; water vapour;
鬆氣 relax one's efforts;
送氣 aspirate;
俗氣 in poort taste; vulgar;
歎氣 heave a sigh; sigh;
淘氣 mischievous; naughty;
天氣 weather;
天然氣 natural gas;
通氣 (1) ventilate; (2) keep each other informed;
透氣 (1) ventilate; (2) breathe freely;
土氣 rustic; uncouth;
吐氣 (1) aspirate; (2) feel elated after unburdening oneself of resentment; give vent to pent-up feelings;
尾氣 tail gas;
文氣 manner of writing; style of writing;
霧氣 fog; mist; vapour;
習氣 bad habit; bad practice;
喜氣 happy expression or atmosphere;
閒氣 anger about trifles;
香氣 aroma; fragrance; sweet smell;
消氣 be mollified; cool down;
小氣 mean; stingy;
笑氣 laughing gas; nitrous oxide;
歇氣 stop for a breather or a rest;
邪氣 evil influence; perverse trend;
洩氣 (1) disappointing; frustrating; (2) feel discouraged; lose heart;
懈氣 slacken one's efforts;
性氣 disposition; personality; temperament;
兇氣 ferocious look;
秀氣 (1) delicate; elegant; fine; (2) refined; urbane; (3) delicate and well-made;
學究氣 pedantry;
血氣 (1) animal spirits; vigour; (2) bravery; courage and uprightness;
壓氣 calm sb's anger;
咽氣 breathe one's last; die;
洋氣 (1) Western style; (2) outlandish ways;
氧氣 oxygen;
養氣 nourish the spirit;
一肚子氣 a stomachful of grudge; full of complaints; full of grievances;
一口氣 (1) at one go; in one breath; (2) a spark of life;
一氣 (1) at a stretch; at one go; without a break; (2) hand in glove; of the same gang; (3) a fit; a spell;
一絲氣 a breath of life;
意氣 (1) will and spirit; (2) temperament; (3) personal feelings;
義氣 coe of brotherhood;
英氣 heroic spirit;
勇氣 courage; nerve;
油氣 oil-gas;
語氣 (1) manner of speaking; tone; (2) mood;
元氣 vigour; vitality;
怨氣 complaint; grievance;
雲氣 thin, floating clouds;
運氣 fortunate; fortune; luck; lucky;
瘴氣 miasma;
朝氣 vigour; vitality; youthful spirit;
沼氣 firedamp; marsh gas; methane;
爭氣 try to bring credit to; try to make a good showing; try to win credit for;
蒸氣 vapour;
正氣 (1) healthy atmosphere; (2) vital energy;
脂粉氣 (of a man) sissy;
志氣 ambition; aspiration;
稚氣 childishness;

qi

【訖】 (1) cleared; come to an end; completed; conclude; end; settled; (2) same as 迄, until; up to;

［訖了］ come to a conclusion; conclude; end;

查訖 checked;
付訖 (of a bill) paid;
兩訖 the goods are delivered and the bill is cleared;
起訖 the beginning and the end;
收訖 paid; payment received;

qi

【棄】 (1) cast aside; cast away; discard; discontinue; fall out of; throw aside; throw away; (2) abandon; desert; drop; eliminate; forsake; give up; quit; reject; renounce; sacrifice; turn the back on; (3) forget; (4) renounce the world; throw away one's own life;

［棄背］ suffer loss of one's parents; the death of one's parents;

［棄兵局］ gambit;
吃棄兵局 accepted gambit;
王翼棄兵局 kings gambit;
中心棄兵局 centre gambit;

［棄城］ abandon the city;
棄城而遁 abandon the city and flee;
棄城而逃 abandon the city and flee;

［棄兒］ abandoned child; foundling;

［棄婦］ deserted wife; divorced woman;

［棄觚］ stop writing;

［棄官］ abandon official life; give up one's office;
棄官歸田 give up office and retire into the country;

［棄過圖新］ forsake the old for the new; turn over a new leaf;

［棄甲］ drop one's arms;
棄甲丟盔 drop one's arms and throw aside one's armour; throw off all one's gear;
棄甲拋戈 cast aside one's breastplate and throw away one's arms;
棄甲曳兵 be totally defeated; flee pellmell; flee pell-mell; routed; run for one's life; the soldiers throw away their armour and trail their weapons behind them; throw off the armour and trail the weapons behind;

［棄井］ stop the digging of a well before water is reached;

［棄捐］ abandon; be neglected; cast aside; fall out of favour; reject;

［棄絕］ abandon; cast aside;
棄絕塵世 renounce the world;
棄絕人世 abandon the worldly life;

［棄妻］ (1) a woman divorced by her husband; (2) divorce one's wife;
棄妻拋兒 forsake one's wife and children;

［棄取］ be accepted or rejected; take or reject;
人棄我取 I take what others throw away — my opinion is different from an ordinary one; I will take whatever others don't want;

［棄權］ (1) abstain from voting; abstention; (2) abandonment of a right; abdication; forfeit; waive the right to play;
棄權不投票 abstain from voting;
棄權者 abdicator;
自動棄權 spontaneous abandonment of a right;

［棄人］ abandon sb; desert sb;

［棄世］ (1) die; pass away; (2) abandon worldly life; lift one's head above ordinary things; look far and high;

［棄市］ be executed; public execution;

［棄物］ discarded useless things; trash;

［棄嫌言好］ make a new start with past enmities forgotten;

［棄械而逃］ drop one's weapons and flee;

［棄信］ discard faith;
棄信背義 discard faith and reject righteousness — faithless;
背盟棄信 violate a treaty;

［棄言］ (1) break one's word; unable to keep one's promise; (2) words which have become obsolete and no longer in circulation;

［棄養］ the death of one's parents;

［棄嬰］ abandoned infant; foundling;

［棄置］ cast aside; discard; throw aside;
棄置不顧 lay aside as unworthy of attention; throw up in the wind;
棄置不用 be discarded; discard; lay aside sth; lie idle; shelve sth;

暴棄 be abandoned; despair;
背棄 betray; break faith with; renounce; turn one's back on;

悖棄 turn away from sth in revolt;
鄙棄 disdain; loathe and reject;
擯棄 abandon; cast away; desert; discard; set aside;
摒棄 abandon; discard;
播棄 abandon; cast away; discard; throw away;
丟棄 discard; give up;
放棄 abandon; give up; renounce;
廢棄 abandon; cast aside; discard;
毀棄 annul; ennui; scrap;
見棄 be discarded; be rejected;
捐棄 abandon; relinquish;
離棄 (1) leave; (2) abandon; desert;
蔑棄 abandon; discard;
拚棄 abandon;
拋棄 abandon; throw away;
撇棄 abandon; cast away; desert;
捨棄 discard; give up;
唾棄 disdain and reject; spurn;
嫌棄 cold-shoulder; dislike and avoid;
厭棄 detest and reject; loathe and give up;
揚棄 (1) develop what is useful or healthy and discard what is not; (2) sublate;
遺棄 abandon; forsake;

qi

【跂】 stand on tiptoe; tiptoe;

［跂望］ earnestly wait for; look forward with eagerness; wait on tiptoe;
跂望援助 earnestly wait for help; stand on tiptoe longing for assistance;

［跂想］ eagerly hope; expect anxiously;

［跂踵］ look forward anxiously; wait expectantly;
跂踵而望 look forward to anxiously; look forward to on tiptoe;
跂踵候駕 stand on tiptoe longing for your presence;

［跂訾］ biased; partial; self-opinionated;

［跂足以待］ wait; wait for; stand on tiptoe in wait for;

［跂坐］ sit with legs hanging above the ground;

qi

【詰】 (1) ask; cross-question; enquire; interrogate; question; (2) prohibit; punish; restrain;

qi

【葺】 (1) fix; have sth put in repair; mend; put right; repair; (lit) restore to working order; (2) cover; thatch; (3) bank up; heap together; pile up; stack up;

［葺補］ repair and mend;

［葺覆］ cover;

［葺牆］ repair a wall;

［葺屋］ thatched house;

修葺 renovate; repair;

qi

【器】 (1) apparatus; implement; instrument; tool; utensils; ware; (2) organ; (3) container; vessel; (4) ability; capacity; talent; (5) appearance; bearing; deportment; (6) forbearance; magnanimity; tolerance; (7) have a high opinion of; regard highly; think highly of; think much of;

［器材］ equipment; equipment and materials; supplies;

［器官］ apparatus; organ;
器官移植 organ transplantation;
平衡器官 balancing organ;
人造器官 artificial organ;
生殖器官 reproductive organs;
聽覺器官 auditory organ;
同功器官 analogous organ;
嗅覺器官 organ of the sense of smell;

［器件］ parts of an apparatus;

［器局］ one's intellectual and moral capacity;

［器具］ appliance; implement; utensil; ware;
測量器具 measuring appliance;
電熱器具 electric heating appliance;
起動器具 actuating appliance;
一件器具 an appliance;

［器量］ capacity to forbear; capacity to tolerate; forbearance; the capacity for magnanimity; tolerance;

［器皿］ container; food container; household utensil; kitchen-ware;
空心器皿 terracotta ware;
石英器皿 quartz ware; silica ware;
搪瓷器皿 enameled ware;

［器識］ one's magnanimity and intellectual outlook;

［器使］ employ according to one's talent;

［器小］ small vessel;
器小易怒 a little pot is soon hot;
器小易盈 a small vessel is easily filled;

［器械］ (1) appliance; instrument; apparatus; machinery; (2) military weapons;

Q

weaponry;
器械操 apparatus work; gymnastics;
一件器械 an instrument;
醫療器械 medical appliance;

[器宇] appearance; bearing; deportment;
器宇不凡 with unusual deportment;
器宇軒昂 of dignified bearing;

[器樂] instrumental music;
器樂曲 compositions for instruments;

[器重] have a high opinion of; regard highly; think highly of; think much of;
受器重 be regarded highly;

氨轉化器 ammonia convertor;
暗器 concealed weapons; hidden weapon;
報時器 chronopher;
倍壓器 doubler;
便器 urinal;
變壓器 transformer;
變阻器 rheostat;
兵器 arms; weapons;
捕集器 catcher;
測謊器 lie detector; polygraph;
測微器 micrometer;
測雲器 nephoscope;
測醉器 drunkometer; intoximeter;
成器 grow up to be a useful person;
盛器 receptacle; vessel;
傳感器 pickup; sensor;
瓷器 chinaware; porcelain;
存儲器 memory; storage;
大器 one of outstanding talents;
電器 electrical appliances;
放大器 amplifier;
緩衝器 buffer; bumper;
機器 apparatus; machine; machinery;
加熱器 heaing appliance;
金器 gold vessel;
酒器 drinking vessel;
擴音器 audio amplifier;
禮器 sacrificial vessel;
利器 (1) sharp weapon; (2) efficient instrument; good tool;
濾器 filter;
冥器 burial objects; funderal objects;
木器 wooden articles; wooden furniture;
漆器 lacquerware; lacquerwork;
起釘器 staple remover;
起動器 starter;
容器 container; vessel;
石器 (1) stone artifact; stone implement; (2) stone vessel; stoneware;
陶器 earthenware; pottery;
鐵器 ironware;
銅器 bronze, brass or copper ware;
投影器 projector;
武器 arms; weapons;
兇器 lethal weapon; tool or weapon for criminal purposes;
儀器 apparatus; instrument;
銀器 silver ware;
玉器 jade article; jadeware;
樂器 musical instrument;
指示器 indicator;
竹器 articles made of bamboo;

qi

【憩】 pause for rest; repose; rest; take a rest;

[憩息] have a rest; pause for rest; rest; take a rest;

休憩 have a rest; rest;
游憩 stroll about or have a rest;

qi

【磧】 (1) gravel and sand; (2) desert;

qia1

qia

【掐】 (1) dig the nail into; (2) break; break off; cut off; cut with fingernails; do away with; nip; leave out; nip off; pinch; pluck; remove; (3) clutch; grasp; grip; hold; seize; (4) calculate; count; reckon;

[掐把] (1) hold fast; (2) treat harshly;

[掐斷] break; cut off; nip off;
掐斷電源 disconnect the mains;
掐斷退路 cut off one's retreat;

[掐尖兒] (1) cut off branches of plants so as to hasten growth; prune; (2) practise irregularities in a deal in order to gain benefit;

[掐死] choke to death by strangling with hands;

[掐算] count sth on one's fingers; reckon sth on one's fingers;
掐指一算 calculate; count;

[掐住] grasp; hold; seize;

qia2

qia

【卡】 (1) be sandwiched; be squeezed

in between; be stuffed; become wedged; get stuck; jammed; wedge; (2) bind; clip; fastener;

[卡子] (1) customs office; toll-collecting station; (2) tool for gripping things;

qia³
qia

【卡】 be choked; choke; hold back;

[卡借] stop lending;

[卡盤] chuck;

卡盤車牀 chucker;
拋光輪卡盤 buff chuck;
氣動卡盤 air chuck;
三爪卡盤 cam-ring chuck;
箱形卡盤 box chuck;
心軸卡盤 arbour chuck;
鐘形卡盤 bell chuck;
自動卡盤 automatic chuck;

[卡住不給] deter; hold back;

[卡子] checkpost; clip; fastener;

邊卡 border checkpoint;
磁卡 magnetic card;
打卡 clock; punch a card;
髮卡 hairpin;
關卡 censorship; checkpoint; customs pass; screening;
賀卡 greeting card;
金卡 gold card;
音效卡 sound card;

qia⁴
qia

【恰】 (1) apposite; appropriate; apt; balanced; fitting; proper; right; suitable; (2) exactly; just; (3) just at the time of; just now; just on the point of; then; (4) as luck would have it; by coincidence;

[恰纔] just now; then;

[恰待] just on the point of doing sth;

[恰當] apposite; appropriate; apt; fitting; fitting and proper; proper; suitable;

恰當性 appropriateness;
不恰當 inappropriate; inapt; inaptness;
用詞恰當 use proper words;

[恰好] (1) as luck would have it; by coincidence; (2) exactly; exactly right; just; just right;

恰好趕到 arrive in the nick of time;
恰好趕上 only just in time;
恰好外出 chance to be out;
恰好吻合 fit like a glove;
來得恰好 come in clipping time;

[恰恰] (1) by coincidence; (2) exactly; just; precisely; sharp;

恰恰相反 exactly the reverse; just the opposite; just the other way; on the contrary; over the left; quite the contrary; the very reverse;

[恰巧] as chance would have it; as luck would have it; by chance; by coincidence; chance to; fortunately; happen to;

[恰如] just as if; just as though; just like;

恰如其分 an excellent fit; appropriate; apt; balanced; highly appropriate; modest; no more and no less; suit one down to the ground; in appropriate measure; in proportion; just right; just suited to one's important; neither more nor less than; proper; this epithet fits him like a glove; to a proper extent; well chosen; well measured;
恰如所料 as was expected;

[恰似] like; seem;

[恰遇] chance upon;

[恰正] just when;

[恰值] just at the time of;

qia

【洽】 (1) agree; in accordance with; in harmony; on friendly terms; (2) arrange with; consult with; make arrangements for;

[洽購] arrange a purchase; make arrangements for buying; purchase after talks; talk over conditions of purchase;

[洽商] arrange by discussion; make arrangements with; negotiate; talk over with;

[洽談] make arrangements with; talk over with;

洽談會 discussing meeting;
洽談業務 discuss business;

接洽 arrange with; take up a matter with;
款洽 cordial and harmonious;
面洽 discuss with sb face to face; take up a matter with sb personally;
融洽 harmonious; on friendly terms;
商洽 arrange with sb; consult a matter with sb;

qian[1]
qian

【千】 (1) thousand; (2) a great amount of; a great number of; all kinds of; all sorts of; infinite; many; numerous; (3) again and again; over and over again; repeatedly; (4) a surname;

［千百］ hundreds and thousands;

百孔千瘡 afflicted with all ills; full of errors; full of ills and troubles; in a disastrous state; in a state of ruin or extreme distress; in a very bad shape; riddled with a thousand gaping wounds; scarred and battered;

百縱千隨 yield to all the wishes;

千方百計 a thousand schemes; all sorts of schemes; by a thousand ways and a hundred devices; by all kinds of methods; by all means at one's command; by all sorts of means; by all ways and means; by diverse means; by every conceivable means; by every means imaginable; by every possible means; by fair means or foul; by hook or by crook; by one means or another; contrive in every possible way; cut and contrive; do all in one's power; do all one can; do everything one can do; do everything possible; do one's utmost; employ all available means; every possible means; explore every avenue; go to all lengths; go to any length; go to great lengths; in a hundred and one ways; in a thousand and one ways; in all manner of ways; in countless ways; in every possible ways; inexhaustible in devices and schemes; leave no avenue unexplored; leave no means untried; leave no stone unturned; make every attempt; make every endeavour; make every effort; make every possible effort; move heaven and earth; pull all the stops out; pull out all the stops; resort to every trick; scheme a thousand and one ways; stop at nothing; take every means; try a thousand and one ways; try all means; try by all means; try by hook or by crook; try desperately; try every means; try every method; try every possible way; try in a thousand and one ways; try in a thousand ways; try in every possible way; try in every way; try one's utmost; try to...in all sorts of ways; use all one's ingenuity; use all sorts of wiles and methods; use all sorts of wits and methods; use all ways and means; use every means; use every method; use every possible means; use every stratagem; worry out ways;

~千方百計地 by hook or by crook;

百計千方 all sorts of tricks and stratagems;

千瘡百孔 in the disastrous state of having one thousand boils and a hundred holes;

~千瘡百孔的爛攤子 a hopeless mess;

千錘百煉 be hammered and tempered into steel; be polished again and again; be repeatedly tempered; be revised and polished over and over again; be revised and rewritten many times; be steeled and tempered for a hundred times;; be thoroughly steeled and tempered; be thoroughly tempered; be tried and tested; go through fire and water; steel and temper oneself over and over again; stringent coaching; under severe training and hammering; well-experienced; well-seasoned;

千刀萬剮 cut sb into pieces; give sb a thousand cuts; hack sb to pieces; slice sb into little bits;

千迴百轉 full of twists and turns; innumerable twists and turns; revolve continually;

千迴百轉，善言相勸 seek in a hundred ways to console sb;

千了百當 all in order; everything has been arranged; everything is ready;

盈千累百 hundreds and thousands;

［千層］ multi-layer;

千層餅 abaisse; multi-layer steamed bread;

千層底 strong cloth soles;

千層糕 layer cake;

［千夫］ numerous people; the public;

千夫所指 be condemned by the public; be pointed at by one thousand accusing fingers; be universally condemned; face a thousand accusing fingers; in the dock; up for general castigation

with a thousand accusing fingers levelled against one;

千夫所指，無疾而死 a thousand pointing fingers accse, and a man dies even without a sickness; when a thousand people point accusing fingers at a man he will die even though he is in perfect health – (fig) it is dangerous to incur public wrath;

[千伏] kilovolt;

[千古] (1) a long long time; eternal; for all time; through all ages; through the ages; (2) eternal repose; in eternity;

千古不刊之論 a statement that holds true for all ages;

千古傳誦 this work has been read through all ages;

千古絕唱 a poetic masterpiece through the ages;

千古絕作 a masterpiece throughout the ages;

千古留名 one's name will remain immortal;

千古名言 reputed words for myriad years;

千古奇談 strange stories of the ages;

千古奇聞 a fantastic story; a fantastic tale; a strange tale; an unheard-of fantastic story;

千古奇冤 a wrong as great as history has ever known;

千古唾罵 earn oneself eternal infamy;

千古貽笑 a laughingstock through the ages;

千古遺恨 eternal regret;

千古卓絕 unmatched past or present;

千古罪人 a traitor through the ages; one who stands condemned through the ages;

留芳千古 glorious memory;

一朝千古 die suddenly;

[千斤] (1) a thousand catties; very heavy; weighty; (2) hoisting jack; jack;

千斤頂 jack;

~扁千斤頂 flat jack;

~車庫用大型千斤頂 garage jack;

~頂軸箱用千斤頂 journal box jack;

~風動液壓千斤頂 air-driven hydraulic jack;

~火炮千斤頂 gun jack;

~空心千斤頂 hollow jack;

~理貨千斤頂 cargo jack;

~氣動千斤頂 compressed air jack;

~調節千斤頂 adjustment jack;

~主牽引梁千斤頂 draw-bar jack;

千斤重擔 as exceptionally heavy responsibility;

[千金] (1) a thousand pieces of gold; (2) daughter; (3) extremely precious;

千金難買一口氣 life is the dearest; life is the most precious commodity; there isn't enough gold to buy one breath of life;

千金難買一笑 a fair lady's smile is most precious; a thousand pieces of gold won't purchase a smile; a thousand taels can hardly purchase a smile;

千金市骨 very eager and sincere in recruiting talented men;

千金小姐 a young lady of a wealthy family;

千金一諾 a promise is worth a thousand pieces of gold;

千金一笑 a beauty's smile is very valuable; a million-dollar smile; a smile of a beautiful lady is worth a thousand pieces of gold;

千金一擲 a thousand pieces at a throw of dice; bet thousands on a single throw; gamble at high stakes; lay down as much as some thousand pieces of silver for a single stake; spend money extravagantly; spend money in a big way;

千金易得，知心難覓 it is easier to obtain a thousand pieces of gold than a bosom friend; ten thousand pieces of gold are easier to come by than an understanding heart;

寸地千金 an inch of land is worth a thousand pieces of gold;

一飯千金 grateful to sb and bestow upon the former benefactor a thousand taels of silver; pay back a debt of gratitude with rich reward; repay sb for kindness with rich reward; requite an obligation generously; reward a benefactor handsomely for the favour or help one has received from him;

一諾千金 a promise is as good as a thousand taels of gold; a promise is weightier than one thousand bars of gold; a promise that will be kept; a solemn promise; as good as one's word; one promise is worth a thousand ounces of gold; true to one's words;

一擲千金 make the money fly; play ducks and drakes with one's money; spend money like water; spend money recklessly; throw away money like dirt;

[千軍易得，一將難求] an army of stags led by a lion would be more formidable than one of lions leading a stag; it is easy to have a thousand soldiers, but hard to find a good general; one general is harder to come by than a thousand soldiers;

[千鈞] hundredweight;

千鈞棒 massive cudgel;

千均一髮 a close thing; a hundred weight hanging by a hair; a near thing; at a crucial moment; by a hairbreadth; by the skin of one's teeth; extremely delicate and dangerous situation; hang by a hair; hang by a single thread; hang on by the eyelids; in a most dangerous situation; in an extremely critical situation; in grave danger; very critical situation;

千鈞重負 a crushing burden; a heavy responsibility; a very heavy burden;

一髮千鈞 a hundredweight hanging by a hair — in imminent peril; a thousand piculs suspended by a single hair — in a most precarious state; an impending disaster; hang by a thread; hang by the eyelids; hang on a hair; the sword of Damocles;

[千卡] kilocalorie;

[千克] kilo; kilogram;

[千里] a long distance; a thousand miles;

千里跋涉 trek hundreds of miles; trudge over thousands of miles;

千里冰封，萬里雪飄 a hundred leagues locked in ice; a thousand leagues of whirling snow;

千里搭長棚，沒有不散的筵席 even the longest feast must break up at last;

千里鵝毛 a light gift from afar conveys deep feelings; a present though trifling is accompanied with sincere wishes;

千里光 ragwort;

千里鏡 telescope;

千里馬 a horse that covers a thousand miles a day; a thorough-bred horse; a-thousand-miles-a day horse; a winged steed;

千里馬還需千里人 it takes an appreciative patron of influence and position to turn talent and ability to full account; it takes very good horsemanship to make the most of a pedigreed horse;

千里送鵝毛 (fig) a goose feather sent from a thousand miles away; a small gift sent from afar with deep affection; an insignificant gift sent from afar with good-will;

千里送鵝毛，禮輕情意重 sending a goose feather to sb a thousand miles away — (fig) the gift is light, but the sentiment is weighty; the gift itself may be light as a goose feather; but sent from afar, it conveys deep feeling;

千里迢迢 a long distance; a thousand miles off; far far away; from a long way off; from afar; over a great distance; over a long distance; set out on the long trek to a far distance; thousands of miles away; travel hundreds of miles;

千里眼 (1) farsighted person; (2) farsightedness; (3) telescope;

千里姻緣一線牽 a thousand miles can't keep apart a couple that's fated to wed; marriages are made in heaven; marriage comes by destiny; marriage is destiny; people a thousand miles apart may be linked by marriage; wedding is destiny;

千里之堤，潰於蟻穴 a little thing left unattended may cause a disaster; a small leak will sink a great ship; a solid dyke can collapse because of an ant-hole in it; an ant-hole may cause the collapse of a thousand-mile dyke; one ant-hole may cause the collapse of a thousand-mile dyke; slight negligence may lead to great disaster;

千里之行，始於足下 a journey of a thousand miles must begin with a single step; a thousand-mile journey is started by taking the first step; a thousand-mile journey begins with the first step; everything must have a beginning; he who would climb the ladder must begin at the bottom; in

all things one does, there must be a beginning;

尺幅千里 a good artist can paint mountains and rivers on a foot of paper;

赤地千里 a thousand miles of barren land;

稻香千里 the fragrance of ripening rice spreading a thousand miles;

狗走千里吃屎，狼走千里吃人 the wolf may lose his teeth, but never his nature;

拒之千里 keep a good distance from;

~拒人於千里之外 keep a good distance from sb; keep at arm's length; put sb beyond the pale; wish sb at the end of the earth;

狼走千里吃肉，狗走千里吃屎 the leopard can't change its spots; wolves never lose their taste for meat nor dogs their taste for filth;

平疇千里 a vast expanse of cultivated land;

日行千里 cover a thousand miles in a single day;

一瀉千里 bold and flowing; flows a thousand miles at one plunge; roar on and on for thousands of li; roll thunderously on for a thousand li; rush down a thousand li — flow down vigorously;

志在千里 cherish a great ambition; one aims for the far-off future;

[千慮] a thousand thoughts;

千慮一得 a fool may give a wise man counsel; a fool may sometimes speak to the purpose; a fool's bolt may sometimes hit the mark; a modest way of offering opinion; contain a grain of truth for sb; even a fool may sometimes have a good idea; even a fool occasionally hits on a good idea; even fools sometimes speak to the purpose; one always gets sth by thinking constantly; out of a thousand reflections made by a poor intellect, there may yet be one worth sth;

千慮一失 despite careful planning, there will be a slip here and there; even a wise man sometimes makes a mistake; even the wise are not always free from error; the wise man, in a thousand schemes, must make at least one mistake;

[千米] kilometre;

[千年] a thousand years;

千年萬載 a long long time; many years; thousands of years; throughout the ages;

洞中方七日，世上已千年 only seven days one has been in the cave, while outside millennia have passed;

[千千] thousands;

千部一腔，千人一面 a thousand are written to a single pattern; all pitched on the same note and their different characters undistinguishable except by name; stereotyped;

[千秋] (1) a thousand years; centuries; (2) birthday congratulations;

千秋萬代 everlasting; for all generations; for all the ages to come; for many generations to come; for thousands of years; forever; forever and ever; from generation to generation; generation after generation; in all the generations to come; on a long-term basis; one generation after another to the end of time; remain forever; the ages to come; through the ages; throughout the ages;

千秋萬歲 a long long time; for centuries; throughout the ages;

千秋之後 after death;

各有千秋 each has his own merits; each has his strong points; each has sth special; each has th. to recommend him; each in his own way has sth to be long remembered; each is good in its degree;

[千人] a thousand people;

千人所指 be subjected to the censure of everybody; be subjected to universal condemnation;

千人一面 all alike; all is stereotyped; one face for a thousand people; the faceless masses;

~千人一面，萬口一腔 one face for a thousand people and one mouth for ten thousand people; stereotyped;

[千歲] (1) a thousand years; (2) Your Highness;

[千瓦] kilowatt;

千瓦時 kilowatt hour;

[千萬] (1) a huge amount; ten million; (2) do; it is imperative that; must; sure;
千萬別忘 be sure not to forget;
千萬不要 under no circumstances should we...;
千萬不要忘記 never forget;
千萬年 aeons;
千萬億 quadrillion;
千萬珍重 do take care of yourself;
成千上萬 by the thousands; thousands and tens of thousands;
千遍萬遍 thousands of times;
千難萬難 extremely difficult;
千難萬險 full of difficulties and dangers; myriad hardships and hazards; numerous dangers and hazards; numerous difficulties and dangers; risks and hardships; untold hardships; untold hardships and risks;
千千萬萬 hundreds and thousands; myriads of; tens of thousands; thousands and tens of thousands; thousands and thousands; thousands upon thousands;
千山萬壑 innumerable mountains and valleys;
千思萬愁 abandon oneself to the thousand unknown plaints and grievances;
千絲萬縷 a thousand and one links; a thousand and one ties; be connected by a thousand and one links; be interrelated in a hundred and one ways; be interrelated in innumerable ways; be united by countless ties; countless ties; have all kinds of connections with; innumerable links; maintain manifold links with;
千算萬算，不及天算 whatever human minds intend, it's Heaven that decides the end;
千謝萬謝 a thousand thanks; many, many thanks; profuse thanks; thank sb a thousand times;
千岩萬壑 a thousand cliffs and ten thousand deep ditches; innumerable mountains and valleys; mountains upon mountains;
上千上萬 run to thousands and tens of thousands;
説千道萬 speak again and again;
萬縷千絲 be linked in a hundred and one ways; countless ties; innumerable links;
盈千累萬 in hundreds and thousands; thousands and tens of thousands; thousands upon thousands;

[千周] kilocycle;

[千足蟲] millipede;

老千 deceiver; swindler;
秋千 swing;
萬千 multifarious; myriad;
一千 a thousand; chiliad;

qian
【仟】 (1) leader of one thousand men; (2) a thousand;

qian
【阡】 footpath between fields; path running from north to south;

[阡表] grave stone; tomb tablet;

[阡陌] (1) crisscross footpaths between fields; crisscross paths in the field; (2) path leading to a grave;
阡陌交通 crisscross of paths in fields; highways of traffic running in all directions;
阡陌相連 rice fields follow one after another;
阡陌縱橫 numerous footpaths in the field; the paths crisscross in the fields;
連阡累陌 in every direction;
田連阡陌 fields connected by ditches;

qian
【扦】 (1) penetrate; pick; pierce; (2) pick; sharp-pointed stick;

[扦插] cuttage; cutting;

[扦腳] pedicure; trim toenails;

花扦 broken-off branch with flowers;
蠟扦 candlestick;

qian
【芊】 (1) (of grass) exuberant; lush; verdant; (2) dark green; emerald green; green; (3) a surname;

[芊綿] exuberant; lush;

[芊芊] (1) lush; (2) dark green; emerald green; verdant;

qian
【牽】 (1) drag; drag in; drag into; haul; lead; lead along; pull; take; tug; (2)

affect; be linked up with; be swayed; influence; (3) get involved in; implicate; incriminate; involve; tie up with; (4) control; restrain; (5) far-fetched; forced; strained; unnatural;

[牽纏] implicate; involve;

[牽扯] (1) drag in; drag into; (2) implicate; involve;

[牽動] affect; be swayed; influence;

牽動大局 upset the general situation;

牽動全局 affect the situation as a whole;

牽動人心 affect sb's feeling;

[牽掛] be concerned for; care; feel anxious about; worry; worry about; worry over;

沒有牽掛 free from care;

牽腸掛肚 be kept in painful suspense; cause deep personal concern; deeply concerned; feel constant anxiety about sth; full of anxiety and worry; in an agony of anxiety; in deep distress and feel anxiety; in great anxiety; in great suspense; infinite longing; miss a great deal; on tenterhooks; very worried about sth; wait in great suspense; with deep concern;

牽心掛腸 very worried;

死無牽掛 can die content; rest contented in the grave;

無牽無掛 free from anxiety; free from care; have no cares; without a tie in the world;

~無牽無掛的 carefree;

一無牽掛 have no ties at all;

[牽合] (1) couple by force; match by force; (2) act as go-between; make a match;

[牽累] (1) be tied down by; drag into trouble; fetter; tie down; (2) implicate; involve in; tie up with;

牽累父母 involve parents;

受家庭牽累 be tied down by one's family;

無兒女牽累 without encumbrance;

[牽連] become involved in; drag in; drag into trouble; entanglement; have connections with; implicate; involve; involve in trouble; tie up with;

牽連面很廣 involve a great number of people;

牽連受罪 be involved in a crime and punished;

[牽蘿補屋] in financial straits; mend a leaky roof with vines;

[牽念] be concerned for; miss; worry about sb who is absent;

[牽牛] lead an ox;

牽牛鼻子 lead an ox by the halter; lead the nose of an ox;

~牽牛要牽牛鼻子 an ox must be led by the halter; every herring must hang by its own gill;

牽牛過獨木橋—難過 leading an ox to cross over a single-plank bridge — difficult to get across;

牽牛花 morning glory;

牽牛星 Altair;

[牽強] far-fetched; forced; strained; unnatural;

牽強附會 bring in by head and shoulders; distort the meaning; drag in head and shoulders; draw a forced analogy; far-fetched; force an analogy; forced analogy; give a forced interpretation; give a strained interpretation; make a farfetched comparison; make a strained interpretation; strain the sense; strained; strained explanation; strained interpretation; stretch a point beyond the proper limits; stretch the sense; wrest the sense;

[牽涉] affect; be linked up with; concern; drag in; implicate; incriminate; involve;

牽涉面廣 involve many areas;

[牽手] (1) lead by the hand; (2) one's wife;

[牽挺] formerly; the pedal in a loom;

[牽頭] (1) at the head of; lead off; pull people together; take the lead; the first to do sth; (2) coordinate; (3) coordinator; intermediary;

[牽挽] drag; pull; tug;

[牽線] (1) control from behind the scenes; pull strings; pull wires; use indirect influence to gain one's ends; (2) act as go-between;

牽線搭橋 act as a go-between; bring both sides together; bring one person into contact with another; pull strings and build bridges;

搭橋牽線 bring both sides together; build bridges; mediate;

[牽引] (1) drag; haul; involve; pulling; tow; (2) draw; traction;

牽引車 breakdown lorry; breakdown

truck;
牽引機 tractor;
牽引力 traction; traction force; tractive ability; tractive effort;
~持續牽引力 continuous tractive effort;
~計算牽引力 calculated tractive effort;
~黏着牽引力 adhesion tractive effort;
~有效牽引力 effective tractive effort;
波模牽引 mode pulling;
交流牽引 alternating current traction;
空中牽引 aerotow;
纜索牽引 cable traction;
黏附牽引 adhesion traction;
頻率牽引 frequency pulling;
蓄電池牽引 accumulator traction;

[牽制] check; contain; curb; hold at bay; manacle; pin down; restrain; tie down; tie up;
牽制行動 diversionary move;
牽制於人 be held in check;
互相牽制 hold each other up;
進行牽制 create a diversion;

掛牽 miss; worry about sb who is absent;
拘牽 constrain; put limitations on;

qian

【釺】 borer; drill rock;

[釺銲] brazing;
沉浸釺銲 dip brazing;
電弧釺銲 arc brazing;
高頻釺銲 induction brazing;
化學浸液釺銲 chemical dip brazing;
火焰釺銲 gas brazing;
接觸釺銲 resonance brazing;
金屬浴釺銲 metal dip brazing;
塊釺銲 block brazing;
擴散硬釺銲 diffucsion brazing;
氣焰釺銲 gas-flame brazing;
碳弧硬釺銲 carbon arc brazing;
硬釺銲 solder brazing;

[釺子] hammer drill; rock drill;

qian

【嵌】 bed in; inlay; set in;

[嵌工] craftsmanship displayed in a piece of jewelry inlaid with gold;

[嵌合] chimerism;
嵌合體 chimaera; chimera; chimerism;
~單層嵌合體 haplochlamydeous chimaera;
~多成分嵌合體 polychlinal chimaera;
~二層周緣嵌合體 dichlamydeous chimaera; dipericlinal chimera;
~輻射嵌合體 radiation chimaera;
~輻射性嵌合體 urradiation chimera;
~複層嵌合體 polychlamydeous chimaera;
~嫁接嵌合體 graft chimaera;
~區分周緣嵌合體 sectorial-periclinal chimaera;
~染色體嵌合體 chromosomal chimaera;
~扇形嵌合體 sectorial chimera;
~雙被嵌合體 diplochlamydeous chimaera;
~四親嵌合體 tetraparental chimera;
~血細胞嵌合體 blood chimerism;
~血型嵌合體 blood group chimera;
~異源嵌合體 allogeneic chimaera;
~周緣嵌合體 periclinal chimera;
三層周緣嵌合體 tripericlinal chimera;
~周緣區分嵌合體 mericlinal chimaera;
嵌合現象 chimerism;

[嵌金] inlay with gold;

[嵌入] embedding; insertion; inset;
嵌入句 embedded sentence;
胞腔式嵌入 cellular embedding;
詞匯嵌入 lexical insertion;
解析嵌入 analytical embedding;
微分嵌入 differentiable embedding;
組合嵌入 combinatorial embedding;

[嵌石] inlay with precious stones;

[嵌鎖] deadbolt;

[嵌鑲] inlay;
玉嵌金鑲 inlaid with gold and jade;

qian

【掔】 (1) firm; substantial; thick; (2) be led by; drag along; pull; (3) lead;

qian

【愆】 (1) commiserate; pity; (2) fault; misdemeanour; mistake; transgression; (3) be separated; lose; (4) malignant disease;

[愆伏] unseasonable, especially in weather;

[愆過] fault; mistake;

[愆面] be separated;

[愆期] behind time; delay; do sth later than expected; fail to do sth at the appointed time; fail to meet a deadline; fall behind schedule; pass the appointed time;

[愆序] unseasonable heat or cold;

［愆尤］ fault; mistake; offense;

前愆 past faults;
罪愆 offence; sin;

qian
【鉛】 (1) lead; (2) black lead; graphite stick; pencil lead;
［鉛版］ printing plate; stereotype;
［鉛筆］ lead pencil; pencil;
鉛筆刨 pencil sharpener;
鉛筆袋 pencil case;
鉛筆刀 pencil sharpener;
鉛筆畫 pencil drawing; pencil sketch;
活動鉛筆 mechanical pencil; propelling pencil;
緊握鉛筆 clasp a pencil;
削鉛筆 sharpen a pencil;
一羅鉛筆 a gross of pencils;
自動鉛筆 mechanical pencil; propelling pencil;
［鉛黛］ cosmetics; face powder and eyebrow paint;
［鉛彈］ lead bullet;
［鉛刀］ blunt knife;
鉛刀一割 a man of no ability can also achieve an undertaking sometimes; blunt but may be useful; when a blunt knife is used appropriately by chance, it can also cut things;
［鉛毒］ lead poisoning;
［鉛鈍］ dull;
［鉛粉］ (1) white lead; (2) face powder;
［鉛封］ lead seal;
鉛封完好 seal on;
拆開鉛封 break a lead sealant;
［鉛華］ cosmetics; face powder;
［鉛礦］ lead ore;
［鉛球］ (1) shot; (2) shot-put;
鉛球投擲圈 putting circle;
鉛球運動員 shot putter;
推鉛球 put the weight; shot put;
［鉛印］ letterpress printing; printing by lead plates; relief printing; stereotype;
［鉛中毒］ lead poisoning;
［鉛字］ lead type; letter; printing type; type;
鉛字盤 type cast;
鑄鉛字 cast type;

筆鉛 lead in a pencil;
蒼鉛 bismuth;
乙酸鉛 lead acetate;

qian
【僉】 all; the whole;

qian
【搴】 draw; pluck up; pull;
［搴旗斬將］ pull up the enemy flag and kill the opposing general;

qian
【慳】 (1) close; miserly; niggardly; parsimonious; stingy; (2) deficient;
［慳煩］ avoid making trouble;
［慳儉］ economical; frugal; miserly; stingy; thrifty;
知慳識儉 know how to be economical;
［慳簡］ curtail expenses; cut down expenses;
［慳力］ sparing of one's strength;
［慳吝］ miserly; niggardly; stingy;
［慳囊］ miser; money bag; niggard;
［慳貪］ stingy and greedy;

qian
【遷】 (1) move; move to another place; remove; (2) change; (3) get transferred; (4) be banished;
［遷除］ be appointed;
［遷次］ (1) change of lodgings on a journey; (2) promotion to higher rank; (3) change of season;
［遷地為良］ a change of place is advisable; it's better to move to another place;
［遷調］ get transferred to another post;
［遷鼎］ transport the sacrificial tripod—the change of dynasty;
［遷都］ move the capital to another place;
［遷換］ change;
［遷就］ accommodate oneself to; appease; complaisance; compromise; give in to; meet halfway; unprincipled accommodation; yield to;
遷就姑息 excessively accommodating; overlenient;
遷就態度 an all accommodating attitude;
遷就妥協 make concessions by way of compromise; meet one's disputants more than halfway in order to reach a compromise; waive certain claims;
遷就主義 appeasement; excessive accommodation;
促使遷就 encourage accommodation to;

互相遷就 give a little to each other;
[遷居] change one's residence; move house; move into a new residence; move into another house;
[遷客] an official banished to a minor post;
[遷流] elapse; pass;
[遷怒] blame a person for one's own blunder; take one's resentment out on sb; take one's spleen; out on sb; transfer one's anger on others; vent one's anger on sb who's not to blame; work off one's anger on sb;
遷怒於人 transfer one's anger to others; vent one's anger on others; work off one's rage and resentment on others;
[遷染] be corrupted by evil surroundings;
[遷入] ecdemic;
遷入種 ecdemic species;
[遷善] reform one's ways;
遷善改過 change one's evil ways and reform; reform and become good;
[遷徙] change one's residence; migrate; move; remove;
遷徙流離 homeless and wandering from place to place;
遷徙區 zone of migration;
遷徙自由 freedom of residence; freedom to change one's residence;
反常遷徙 abmigration;
向內地遷移 migrate inland;
[遷延] defer; delay; procrastinate;
遷延時日 become long-drawn-out; cause a long delay; delay for a long time; delay in doing sth to gain time; procrastinate from day to day;
[遷移] migrate; migration; move; remove; shift; transport;
遷移率 mobility;
~電導遷移率 conductivity mobility;
~漂移遷移率 drift mobility;
~微分遷移率 differential mobility;
側向遷移 lateral migration;
反遷移 back migration;
毛管水遷移 capillary migration;
時移情遷 the times are changed and conditions are changed as well;
細胞遷移 cell migration;
原子遷移 atomic migration;
[遷葬] move sb's grave to another place;
搬遷 make a removal; move; move out; move to a new location; relocate;
變遷 changes; vicissitudes;
拆遷 move a building to a new site; pull down and move to another place; relocate after demolition;
超遷 promote sb more than one grade at a time;
喬遷 move a better place or have a promotion;
昇遷 be transferred and promoted;
躍遷 transition;
左遷 be demoted; demote;

qian

【褰】 (1) lift; lift up; raise; (2) drawers; pants; trousers; (3) shrink;
[褰裳] lift up skirts;

qian

【謙】 humble; modest; retiring; self-effacing; unassuming;
[謙卑] modest; humble; self-depreciating;
謙卑遜順 humble and retiring;
[謙沖] modest; unassuming;
[謙辭] (1) humble expression; modest speech; self-depreciatory expression; (2) decline out of humbleness;
[謙恭] civility; humility; modest and courteous; modest and polite; respectful; unassuming;
謙恭的 courteous;
謙恭好學 modest and willing to learn;
謙恭有禮 modest and polite;
表示謙恭 humble oneself;
學會謙恭 learn to be humble;
言詞謙恭 courteous in wording;
[謙光] shining modesty;
[謙和] modest and amiable; modest and gentle; modest and good-natured;
[謙克] humble and self-controlled;
[謙謙] modest;
謙謙君子 a hypocritically modest person; a modest, cautious gentleman;
謙謙有容 modest and tolerable;
[謙讓] modestly decline; modestly yield precedence to others; yield from modesty;
互謙互讓 mutually making a compromise;
[謙受益，滿招損] benefit goes to the humble, while failure awaits the arrogant; modesty brings benefit while pride leads to loss; one gains by modesty

and loss by pride; the modest receive benefit, while the conceited reap failure;

[謙退] modest and retiring; reserved;

[謙虛] (1) humble; modest; self-effacing; unassuming; (2) make modest remarks;

謙虛謹慎 humble and cautious; modest and prudent; modesty and prudence;

~保持謙虛謹慎 remain modest and prudent;

假裝謙虛 counterfeit modesty;

[謙遜] humble; humble and unpresumptuous; humility; lowly; modest; unassuming;

假裝謙遜 affect modesty;

態度謙遜 modest in behavior;

過謙 be too modest;

自謙 be modest; be self-effacing;

qian

【簽】 (1) autograph; put down one's signature; sign; sign one's name; subscribe; (2) make brief comments on a document; (3) bamboo slips used for divination or drawing lots; (4) label; marker; sticker; (5) slender pointed piece of bamboo or wood; (6) tack;

[簽到] register one's attendance; sign in;

簽到簿 attendance book;

簽到處 registration desk; sign-in desk;

[簽訂] conclude; conclude and sign; sign;

簽訂合同 sign a contract;

簽訂條約 sign a treaty;

[簽發] sign and issue;

簽發護照 issue a passport;

簽發文件 sign and dispatch a document;

[簽名] affix one's signature to; attach one's signature to; autograph; put a signature to; put down one's signature; put one's name to; put one's signature to; set one's hand to; set one's name to; sign; sign on the dotted line; sign one's name to; signature;

簽名簿 guest book;

簽名蓋章 put one's signature and seal on; seal and signature; set one's hand and seal to; sign and affix one's seal; sign and put one's personal seal on; sign and seal;

簽名留念 give one's autograph as a memento;

~簽名留念簿 autograph album;

簽名人 the undersigned;

簽名同意 consent by signature;

簽名運動 signature collection campaign; signature campaign; signature drive;

電子簽名 electronic signature;

數字簽名 digital signature;

偽造簽名 forge a signature;

[簽批] sign and authorize;

[簽收] sign after receiving sth; sign for; sign to acknowledge the receipt of sth;

[簽署] sign;

簽署法案 subscribe an act;

簽署國 signatory;

簽署人 the undersigned;

簽署文件 endorse a document with a signature;

簽署協議 subscribe to the agreement;

簽署意見 write comments and sign one's name on a document;

簽署議案 sign the bill;

數碼簽署 digital signature;

無須簽署 no signature is required;

有權力簽署 have power to sign;

[簽條] (1) label; (2) memo; note;

[簽押] put a seal on an official document; sign one's name;

[簽印] put a seal on; sign;

[簽約] sign a contract; sign a treaty;

[簽賬] spending;

簽賬獎賞 spending reward;

簽賬卡 charge card;

[簽證] visa;

辦理簽證 apply for a visa;

出境簽證 exit visa;

吊銷簽證 cancel a visa already issued;

發給簽證 issue a visa;

過境簽證 transit visa;

檢查簽證 examine a visa;

旅遊簽證 tourist visa;

取得簽證 obtain a visa;

入境簽證 entry visa;

商務簽證 business visa;

[簽注] write comments on a document;

[簽字] affix one's signature; initial; put one's name to; put one's signature on; sign; sign on the dotted line; sign one's name; signature;

簽字方 signatory party;

簽字蓋章 sign and seal;
簽字國 signatory; signatory powers; signatory states;
簽字權 power to sign; signing authority;
簽字樣本 specimen signature;
簽字儀式 signing ceremony;
拒絕簽字 withhold one's signature;
親筆簽字 handwritten signature;
偽造簽字 forged signature;

標簽 label; tag;
草簽 initial;
抽簽 ballot; by lot; cast lots; draw cuts; draw lots;
浮簽 pasted marginal note which can be easily removed;
路簽 train-staff;
求簽 pray and draw divination sticks at a temple;
書簽 bookmark;
署簽 inscribe a title-label on a book;
牙簽 toothpick;
藥簽 swab;
印簽 signature;
中簽 be the lucky number in drawing lots, etc.;

qian

【騫】 (1) fly; go up; raise high; rise; soar; soar high; uplift; (2) pull up; (3) frightened;

[騫舉] fly; rise; soar;
[騫騫] (1) flapping; (2) wilful and disrespectful;
[騫騰] go up; soar high;
[騫污] have deficit and be defamed;

qian

【籤】 (1) label; lot; (2) small sharp-pointed stick;

[籤餅] fortune cookie;

qian

【韆】 swing;

qian²

qian

【拑】 (1) grasp; hold; (2) pull out;

[拑口] hold the tongue; keep mum; keep one's mouth shut;

qian

【前】 (1) before; front; in front; (2) ahead; forward; the future; (3) ago; before; (4) ex-; former; formerly; previous; (5) first; front; (6) advance; proceed;

[前輩] elder; forerunners; one's senior; predecessor; the older generation; the last generation; the past generation;
老前輩 old timer; one's elder; one's senior;
[前臂] forearm;
[前邊] (1) ahead; before; in front; the fore part; the front; the front side; (2) above; preceding;
[前叉] fork;
[前車] previous cart;
前車覆，後車戒 it's good to learn at other people's cost; learn wisdom by the follies of others;
前車可鑒 heed previous examples; keep in mind previous examples; one man's fault is another man's lesson; one should take warning of another's mistake; take warning; take warning from previous examples; the cart that has been upset ought to serve as a warning; this is a lesson that merits attention; we should take warning from previous examples;
前車之覆，不可不鑒 let another's shipwreck be your seamark; the cart behind should take heed from the cart in front that overturned; we have to take warning when the cart in front overturns;
前車之覆，後車之鑒 draw a lesson from a previous failure; it is well to profit by the folly of others; make another's shipwreck one's sea-mark; one should take warning from another's mistake; take warning from the overturned cart ahead; the folly of one man is the fortune of another; the overturned cart ahead is a warning to the ones behind; the overturning of the cart in the front is a lesson for the cart behind; the wrecked coach in front should be a warning; we should take warning from the mistakes of those before us;
前車之鑒 a lesson drawn from others' mistakes; a lesson to learn from; a lesson to remember; an example to take warning from; heed previous examples; learn a lession from another's failure; learn from sb else's mistakes; make the overturning of

the chariot in front a warning for the chariot behind; profit by the folly of others; take warning from an accident; take warning from another's mistakes; the overturned cart in front serves as a warning to the carts behind; the wrecked car on the road ahead should serve as a warning to all drivers;

[前塵] (1) (in Buddhism) previous impure conditions; (2) what has happened in the past;
回首前塵 look back upon the past; recall past events;

[前程] (1) future; prospect; (2) career; future career;
前程似錦 have a bright future; have a glorious future; have a rosy future; have an infinitely bright future; have brilliant prospects; have splendid prospects; have the world at one's feet; splendid prospects; one's future is as beautiful as brocade;
前程萬里 bright prospects; have a fine future; have a great career; have one's life before oneself; have the prospect of a very successful career; one's future career will be great;
前程遠大 have a bright future; have brilliant prospects;
各奔前程 each goes his own way; each pursues his own way;
錦繡前程 have a bright future;
有美好前程 have good prospects;

[前仇] past grudge;

[前此] before that; before this; prior to that; prior to this;

[前次] last time; the previous occasion;

[前導] (1) lead the way; march at the head; march in front; precede; (2) guide; person who leads the way; pioneer;

[前燈] headlight;

[前敵] front line;

[前定] decided beforehand; predestined;

[前度劉郎] person who returns to a place he once abandoned;

[前額] forehead;

[前番] last time;

[前方] (1) place ahead; (2) front; front lines;

[前鋒] (1) vanguard; (2) forward; striker;

[前夫] (1) one's ex-husband; one's former husband; (2) one's late husband;

[前功盡棄] all efforts go down the drain; all former achievements are nullified; all labour's lost; all one's earlier achievements are in vain; all one's labour is thrown away; all one's merits count for nothing; all one's previous efforts are wasted; all one's work is wasted; all that has been achieved is spoiled; all the work one has done is wasted; back where one started; forfeit all one's former achievements; have one's previous efforts wasted; labour lost; nullify all the advantages of a series of victories; nullify all the advantages of a series of victories; nullify all the previous efforts; one's previous efforts have proved to be useless; turn all the previous labour to nothing; waste all the previous efforts; waste the efforts already made;

[前滾翻] forward roll;

[前和] front part of a coffin;

[前後] (1) about; altogether; around; around the time of; one time or another; or so; round about; (2) altogether; from beginning to end; from start to finish; (3) before and after; in front and behind; the front and the rear;
前後不一 contradictory; incoherent; inconsistent;
前後顛倒 put the cart before the horse;
前後夾攻 attack...both from the front and in the rear; attack...both in front and in rear;
前後矛盾 antilogy; contradictory; inconsecutive; inconsistent;
前後受敵 be attacked by the enemy both front and back; be caught between two fires; between two fires;
前後搖晃 reel to and fro;
前後一致 hang together;
前後左右 all around; in every direction; on all sides;
跋前疐後 between the devil and the deep blue sea; between the horns of a dilemma; difficult either to advance tor to retreat; find oneself in a dilemma; in a dilemma;

懲前毖後 learn from past mistakes to avoid future ones; learn lessons from the past and keep an eye on the future; take a lesson from the past and avoid future mistakes;

趕前不趕後 it's better to hurry at the beginning than to do things in a rush at the last moment;

顧前顧後 care before and behind; examine what is coming and the possible consequences;

~顧前不顧後 consider only the present and forget about the future; drive ahead without considering the consequences; regard the present moment instead of the future;

顧前忘後 careful at the beginning, but in the end there is a serious oversight;

光前裕後 glorify one's forefathers and enrich one's posterity; glorify the before and enrich the behind; reflect lustre on one's ancestors and enrich one's posterity; win praises for one's ancestors and enrich one's posterity;

忽前忽後 backwards and forwards; go seesaw;

怕前怕後 timid and apprehensive of everything;

前不巴村，後不著店 in an out-of-the-way place; with no village ahead and no inn behind — stranded in an uninhabited area;

前顛後偃 stumble forward and backward;

前堵後追 block the route of advance and pursue from the rear;

前赴後繼 advance and fill the breach left by those fallen; advance wave upon wave; as one falls, others step into the breach; as those in front fall, those behind take up their positions; take up the positions of the fallen and rise to fight one after another; the moment one falls, others step into the breach; those in front advance, those behind come after;

前呼後擁 be accompanied by a large retinue; have a retinue before and behind; those who go before call out and those behind crowd up; with a guard in front and rear; with a large retinue; with a long train of equipage; with escorts in front and behind; with many attendants crowding round;

前街後巷 everywhere; front streets and back lanes;

前倨後恭 change from arrogance to humility; change one's attitude snobbishly; change one's tune; first supercilious and then deferential; haughty before and polite afterward; one's haughtiness has given place to humility; proud at first but humble afterwards; sing a different tune;

前拉後推 with sb pulling in front and others pushing behind;

前仆後繼 as those in front fall, those behind take up their positions; behind the fallen is an endless column of successors; carry forward the cause of the fallen; no sooner has one fallen than others step into the breach; one steps into the breach as another falls; step into the breach as another falls; take up the positions of the fallen and rise to fight one after another; when one in front falls others behind fight on; while those in the front line drop dead, those behind step forward to take their places;

前前後後 back and belly; back and forth; backwards and forwards; from front to rear; full detail of; the entire process; the ins and outs; the whole story; up and down;

前仰後合 be convulsed with laughter; double up; rock backwards and forwards; rock with laughter; shake forwards and backwards; shake one's sides with laughter; split one's sides; stagger forward and backward; sway to and fro;

前有車，後有轍 as one advances, one invariably leaves sth behind for others to follow; the wheels of the cart leave their tracks behind;

褪後趨前 rush forward and backward to show anxiety to serve;

裕後光前 enrich one's posterity and honour one's ancestors;

[前回] (1) last time; (2) last chapter of a novel;

[前記] foreword; preface;

[前腳] (1) the forward foot in a step; (2) hardly...when...; no sooner...than...; the

moment;

[前進] advance; forge ahead; go forward; make progress; march forward; proceed; progress; stride ahead;
前進心 enterprising spirit;
前進一步 take a step forward;
穿梭前進 weave one's way;
大踏步前進 make big strides;
奮勇前進 advance bravely; fight one's way; forge ahead courageously; forge valiantly ahead; march forward;
緩步前進 inch one's way;
謹慎前進 pick one's way;
摸索前進 grope one's way;
破浪前進 breast waves; cleave through the water; cleave through the waves; cut a feather; cut through the waves; plough through the waves;
全速前進 go forward at full speed;
穩步前進 advance slowly but steadily;
循此前進 proceed along this line;

[前景] (1) future; outlook; perspective; prospect; the future as seen in one's imagination; vista; (2) foreground;
前景暗淡 bleak prospect;
前景光明 bright prospect;
前景樂觀 the prospect is cheerful;
短期前景 short-run outlook;
經濟前景 economic outlook;

[前科] criminal record; pedigree;
有前科 person with past convictions; previous conviction;

[前饋] feedforword;
補償前饋 compensating feedforward;
複合前饋 compoundin feedforward;
校正前饋 correcting feedforward;

[前例] precedent;
打破前例 depart from precedents;
史無前例 unheard-of; unprecedented; unprecedented in history; without parallel in history; without precedent in history;

[前列] forefront; front rank; front row; van;
前列腺 prostate; prostate gland;
~ 前列腺癌 cancer of the prostate gland;
~ 前列腺竇 prostatic sinus;
前列腺肥大 prostatic hypertrophy;
良性前列腺肥大 benign prostatic hypertrophy;
~ 前列腺潰瘍 prostatelcosis;
~ 前列腺囊 prostatic vesicle;
~ 前列腺尿道 prostatic urethra;
前列腺膀胱炎 prostatocystitis;
前列腺切除 Prostatectomy; removal of the prostate;
~ 前列腺素 prostaglandin;
~ 前列腺炎 prostatitis;
變應性前列腺炎 allergic prostatitis;
前列腺增生 prostatic hyperplasia;
囊性前列腺增生 cystic prostatic hyperplasia;
最前列 forefront;

[前輪] front wheel;

[前茅] (1) patrol; (2) top of the list;

[前門] front door; front gate;
前門拒虎，後門進狼 drive a tiger out of the front door while a wolf come in the back — one woe goes and another comes; drive a wolf away from the front door only to find a tiger muscle in by the back; drive the tiger from the front door and let a wolf in at the back — fend off one danger only to fall a prey to another; leap out of the frying-pan into the fire; ward off one menace only to fall a prey to another;
前門拒狼，後門防虎 guard against the tiger at the back door while repelling the wolf at the front gate;
前門拒狼，後門進虎 let the tiger in through the back door while repelling the wolf through the front gate;
前門驅狼，後門防虎 rebuff the tiger at the back door while repelling the wolf at the front gate;
前門驅狼，後門拒虎 drive the wolf out of the front gate and prevent the tiger from entering through the back door;
前門走狼，後門進虎 the wolf has left by the front door, but the tiger has entered through the back door;

[前面] (1) ahead; at the head; in front; (2) above; forepart; preceding;
前面的 anterior;
站在前面 keep oneself in the foreground;

[前母] one's father's former wife;

[前腦] forebrain;

[前年] the year before last;

[前排] front row;
前排座位 front-row seats;

[前妻] (1) one's ex-wife; one's former wife; (2) one's late wife;

[前期] earlier stage; early days; prophase;
[前愆] past faults;
[前牆] front wall;
[前情] (1) former affection; relevant past event; past affairs; (2) past relevant cause;
[前驅] forerunner; harbinger; pioneer; precursor; prelude; progenitor; van; vanguard;
[前人] forefathers; people of former times; people of the past; predecessors;
前人開路後人走 one generation opens the road upon which another generation travels;
前人種樹，後人乘涼 ancestors plant trees while descendants enjoy the cool under the tree shade — enjoy the fruits of one's predecessors' efforts; one generation plants the trees under whose cool shade another generation rests; one sows and another reaps; plant trees for the benefit of posterity; profit by the labour of one's forefathers; what we are enjoying now is the fruits of labour expended by our forefathers;
[前任] precursor; predecessor; ex-; former;
[前日] the day before yesterday;
[前晌] forenoon; morning;
[前哨] advance guard; outpost;
前哨戰 skirmish;
[前身] (1) ancestor; predecessor; (2) forerunner; precursor;
[前生] former life; prelife; previous incarnation;
[前世] (1) previous existence; previous life; (2) previous generation;
前世不修今世苦 the lack of self-cultivation in morals in one's pre-existence is responsible for one's present sufferings in this mundane world;
前世姻緣 a match made in heaven; be connected in a former existence; fated marriage;
前世冤家 enemies in their pre-existence;
[前室] antechamber;
[前事不忘 後事之師] if we don't forget the past, we can draw lessons from it; lessons are there to learn from our experience of the past; lessons learned from the past can guide one in the future; past experience, if not forgotten, is a guide for the future; past experience kept in mind is a guide for the future; the past not forgotten is a guide for the future; the remembrance of the deeds of past ages is our best guide in the future; to remember past errors insures one against repetition of the same errors; today is the scholar of yesterday; today is yesterday's pupil;
[前手] predecessor;
[前所] have never before;
前所未見 have never seen before;
前所未聞 have never heard of before; sth hitherto unheard of; unheard; unheard-of;
前所未有 hitherto unknown; sth never existed before; sth never known before; such as never previously existed; unknown before; unprecedented;
[前台] (1) front office; front of house; on the stage; proscenium; the stage; (2) foreground;
前台經理 front-of-house manager;
固定前台 permanent foreground;
~非固定前台 nonpermanent foreground;
~永久固定前台 permanent resident foreground;
[前枱] front desk;
[前提] (1) premise; (2) precondition; prerequisite; presupposition; primary consideration;
大前提 major premise;
邏輯前提 logical presupposition;
潛在前提 potential presupposition;
小前提 minor premise;
[前天] the day before yesterday;
[前廳] antechamber;
[前庭] vestibule;
前庭反射 vestibular reflex;
前庭感覺 vestibular sense;
前庭後院 the front or back yards;
前庭炎 vestibulitis;
[前頭] (1) ahead; in front; take their place in the van; (2) before;
前頭虎，後頭狼—進退兩難 be faced with tigers ahead and wolves behind — in a

dilemma;

前頭烏龜爬上路，後背烏龜趁路爬 as the tortoise in front has climbed up the path, the tortoise behind will follow suit — pattern after others;

[前途] future; promise; prospect;

前途暗淡 bleak prospect; the future is filled with gloom;

前途不可限量 boundless prospects;

前途光明 bright prospect; glorious prospect; rosy prospect; splendid future lies ahead; have the world before one;

前途教育 prospect education;

前途茫茫 have a bleak future; have gloomy prospects; one's future is indefinite;

前途渺茫 have a bleak future; have an uncertain future; have gloomy prospects; one's future seems to be in a haze; one's prospects are bleak;

前途未卜 ambiguous future; hang in the balance; the future remains problematic; the prospects remain undecided;

前途無量 boundless future; have boundless prospects; have unlimited possibilities; of great promise; one's future is boundless;

前途無望 the future is hopeless; unpromising;

有前途 have a future;

~大有前途 bear watching;

~沒有前途 have no future;

[前腿] foreleg;

[前晚] the evening before last;

[前往] go to; leave for; proceed to; proceed toward; start for; visit;

[前衛] (1) advance guard; vanguard; (2) forward; (3) half-back; (4) avant-garde; vanguard;

[前夕] eve; on the eve of; run-up;

選舉前夕 in the run-up to the election;

[前賢] people of virtue of the older generations; the wise men of the past;

前賢先哲 sages of the past; the wise men of the past;

[前嫌] past grudge;

前嫌冰釋 former grievances have melted like ice; it clears the air between them;

前嫌盡釋 agree to bury the hatchet; all previous ills will be removed;

不計前嫌 wipe the slate clean;

盡捐前嫌 forget all the past enmity; let bygones be bygones;

盡釋前隙 forget entirely old grudges;

消釋前嫌 mend one's fences;

[前線] front; frontline;

奔赴前線 start for the front;

上前線 go to the front;

在前線 at the front;

在最前線 in the front line;

[前項] antecedent; preceding article;

[前言] (1) foreword; introduction; preamble; preface; (2) previous remarks; (3) words of past thinkers;

前言不搭後語 babble disconnected phrases; contradict oneself in words; disjointed; incoherent; make contradictory remarks; mumble disconnected phrases; self-contradictory; speak incoherently; talk incoherently; the parts do not hang together; utter words that do not hang together; what one says does not hang together;

[前頁] front matter;

[前夜] eve; the night before last;

[前因] antecedent; cause;

前因後果 antecedents and consequences; cause and effect; ins and outs; the immediate causes and the consequences; the sequence of events; the whole circumstances; the whole story; the whys and wherefores of sth;

[前緣] predestination; predestined ties;

前緣未了 the predestined lot is not yet severed;

了悟前緣 understand fate caused by previous incarnation;

[前院] front courtyard;

[前月] last month; ultimo;

[前兆] forerunner; forewarning; harbinger; omen; premonition;

[前者] former;

[前震] foreshock;

[前肢] forelimb; foreleg;

[前知] foretell the future;

[前指] anaphoric;

前指詞 anaphoric word;

前指替代 anaphoric substitute;

[前置] prepose;
前置詞 preposition;
前置修飾詞 premodifier;
[前綴] prefix;
標號前綴 label prefix;
動詞前綴 verbal prefix;
更替前綴 alternate prefix;
可分前綴 separable prefix;
條件前綴 condition prefix;
[前奏] prelude;
前奏曲 prelude;
[前足] forefoot;
[前座] front bench;
前座議員 front-bencher;
樓廳前座 dress circle; first balcony;

癌前 precancerous;
逼前 press forward;
餐前 pre-meal;
產前 antenatal; post-natal;
超前 lead; outstrip;
從前 a long time ago; as of old; before; "ex-"; former; formerly; in former times; in the old days; in the past; long long ago; many years ago; old; once; once upon a time; some time ago; thousands of years ago; used to be;
當前 (1) before one; facing one; (2) current; present;
跟前 close to; in front of;
婚前 before marriage; premarital;
空前 unprecedented;
面前 before; in face of; in front of;
目前 at present; at the moment; currently; for the moment; just now; right now; up until now;
人前 before sb;
日前 a few days ago; recently; the other day;
賽前 pre-match;
上前 come forward;
生前 before one's death; during one's life-time;
食前 before meal;
史前 prehistoric;
事前 beforehand; in advance;
售前 before-sale;
死前 before death; before one dies;
提前 advance; advance to an earlier date; ahead of schedule; ahead of time; ahead of the game; beforehand; before one's time; in advance; in anticipation; in good time; the date has been moved up; shift to an earlier date;
往前 forward;
無前 invincible; unmatched; unprecedented;
午前 before noon; morning;
先前 before; previously;
向前 ahead; forward; go forward; onward;
學前 pre-primary; pre-school;
簷前 front of the eaves;
眼前 (1) before one's eyes; (2) at present; at the moment; now;
以前 ago; before; "ex-"; former; formerly; in the past; old; once; previous; prior to; since; used to be;
譯前 pre-translation;
御前 in the presence of the emperor;
在前 ahead; before; beforehand; in front;
戰前 before the war; prewar;
朝前 face forward;
陣前 on the battlefield;
之前 ago; before; before this; prior to;
直前 go straightforward;

qian
【虔】 devoted; devout; pious; respectful; reverent;
[虔誠] devoted; devout; pious;
合十虔誠 put one's hands together in prayer;
[虔敬] devotional; respectful; reverent;
[虔恪] respectful; reverent;
[虔婆] (1) low woman; (2) madam; procuress;
[虔虔] reverent; worshipful;
[虔心] piety; sincere reverence;
虔心祈禱 wrestle;
[虔信] piety;

qian
【乾】 (1) first of the Eight Diagrams; (2) father; heaven; male; sovereign;
[乾道] natural law; the ways of heaven;
[乾綱] (1) emperorship; (2) authority of a husband to his wife;
乾綱不振 henpecked;
[乾坤] (1) heaven and earth; universe; (2) male and female;
顛倒乾坤 reverse heaven and earth;
[乾乾] diligent; strive ceaselessly;
[乾象] celestial phenomena;
[乾曜] sun;
[乾元] beginning of heaven's creation;
[乾宅] the bridegroom's home called during a wedding;

qian
【掮】 bear a load on the shoulder;

[掮客] broker;
權力掮客 power broker;
政治掮客 political fixer;

qian
【鈐】 (1) latch; lock; (2) chop; seal; stamp;
[鈐記] chop; official seal;
[鈐鍵] crucial point; key;
[鈐鎖] door lock;
[鈐印] put a stamp on;
[鈐章] (1) put a stamp on; (2) official stamp;

qian
【鉗】 (1) clamps; forcets; pincers; pliers; tongs; tweezers; (2) clamp; grip; hold with tongs; (3) chains put around a prisoner's neck;
[鉗工] (1) bench worker; (2) fitter;
[鉗忌] jealous and unfriendly;
[鉗噤] keep one's mouth shut; keep quiet;
[鉗口] (1) keep one's mouth shut; keep silent; (2) prevent from talking;
鉗口不言 keep mum; keep one's mouth shut;
鉗口結舌 be forced to keep silence; keep mum; keep one's mouth shut; tongue-tied;
[鉗徒] pilloried prisoner;
[鉗制] contain; hold fast; hold tight; immobilize; keep under control with force; pin down; tie down;
鉗制敵人 pin down the enemy;
鉗制行動 containing action;
鉗制輿論 force public opinion to submission; muzzle public opinion;
[鉗子] forceps; pincers; pliers; tongs; tweezers;
一把鉗子 a pair of pliers; a pair of tongs;

大鉗 tongs;
焊鉗 forcepts;
虎鉗 jaw rice;
火鉗 fire tongs;
卡鉗 calipers;
夾鉗 clamp;
老虎鉗 (1) vice; (2) pincer pliers;
手鉗 hand vice; pliers;
台鉗 bench clamp;
鐵絲鉗 wire cutters;
銅絲鉗 wire cutters;

qian
【箝】 (1) pincers; tongs; tweezers; (2) tweezer;
[箝緊] clasp tightly;
[箝口] (1) keep one's mouth shut; keep silent; (2) force to keep silent; gag; prevent from talking;
箝口結舌 (1) keep silent; (2) be forced to keep silent;
箝口無言 button up; shut up;
[箝位] clamping;
反向箝位 back clamping;
負向箝位 negative clamping;
黑電平箝位 black-level clamping;
水平箝位 horizontal clamping;
同步箝位 synchronized clamping;
逐行箝位 line-by-line clamping;
[箝語] restrict freedom of speech;
[箝制] force; pin down; use pressure upon;
[箝子] pincers; tongs; tweezers;

qian
【潛】 (1) conceal; go under; hide; hidden; latent; lie hidden; (2) on the sly; secretly; stealthily; (3) dive;
[潛藏] go into hiding; hide; hide away; in hiding;
潛藏隱伏 lie hidden;
[潛存] exist in hiding; have a submerged existence;
[潛德] hidden virtues; unnoticed virtues;
[潛遁] escape secretly; slip away;
[潛伏] conceal; fly low; hide; incubate; lie hidden; lie low; live in hiding; lurk;
潛伏的疾病 an insidious disease;
潛伏的危機 latent crisis;
潛伏多年 dormant for many years;
潛伏感染 a latent infection;
潛伏期 incubation; incubation period; latent period;
潛伏效果 sleeper effect;
潛伏性 latency;
潛伏以待 lie for;
[潛航] submerge;
潛航速度 submerged speed;
[潛居] live in a hiding place; live in seclusion;
[潛力] hidden force; latent capacity; latent force; latent power; potential; potentiality; unused strength;
繁殖潛力 breeding potential;
工業潛力 industrial potential;
破壞潛力 damage potential;

投資潛力 investment potential;
挖掘潛力 exploit potentialities; tap potentials;
學術潛力 academic potential;
遺傳潛力 genetic potential;
營養潛力 nutritive potential;
致癌潛力 carcinogenic potential;

[潛流] undercurrent; underflow;

[潛龍] hidden dragon; unrecognized sage;
潛龍無用 talent is useless when hidden;

[潛能] potential energy; potentiality;
發揮潛能 develop one's potential;

[潛匿] go into hiding; hide oneself;

[潛熱] latent heat;

[潛入] (1) enter secretly; slip in; slip into; sneak into; steal in; (2) dive into; go under water;

[潛師] move troops secretly;

[潛水] dive; diving; go under water;
潛水器 diver;
~碟形潛水器 diving saucer;
~深海潛水器 bathyscaphe;
球形深海潛水器 bathysphere;
潛水艇 submarine; submersible;
~潛氷艇支援船 support vessel for submersible;
~小型潛水艇 small submersible;
潛水衣 diving suit;
潛水用具 diving appliances;
潛水員 diver;
潛水者 diver;
潛水鐘 diving bell;
常規潛水 conventional diving;
空氣潛水 air diving;
~壓縮空氣潛水 compressed-air diving;
屏氣潛水 breath-hold diving;
去潛水 go diving;
深潛水 deep diving;
徒手潛水 snorkeling;
巡迴潛水 excursion diving;

[潛逃] abscond; desert; flee secretly; slink; slip away;
潛逃人 abscondee; absconder;
潛逃無蹤 abscond without a trace;
非法潛逃 abscond illegally;
拐款潛逃 absquatulate with the funds;
捲款潛逃 make off with money; run away with public money;
棄保潛逃 jump bail;
棄職潛逃 desert one's post and take flight;
畏罪潛逃 abscond to avoid punishment;
攜款潛逃 abscond with funds; abscond with the money; run off with money;

[潛艇] submarine;
潛艇水手 submariner;
核潛艇 nuclear submarine;

[潛望鏡] periscope;
多用途潛望鏡 multi-purpose periscope;
潛艇潛望鏡 submarine periscope;
昇降潛望鏡 elevator periscope;

[潛心] devote oneself to sth; do sth with great concentration; have a quiet concentrated mind;
潛心經史 inquire deeply into classics and history;
潛心研究 study diligently with a quiet mind;

[潛行] go secretly;

[潛修] cultivate oneself in quiet privacy;

[潛虛] live in seclusion;

[潛移默化] a silent transforming influence; an imperceptible influence; be unconsciously influenced by; change and influence unobtrusively and imperceptibly; changes of a person's thinking is a very subtle process; exert a subtle influence on; imperceptibly and gradually influence and change; subtle influence; the quiet and natural influence;

[潛泳] underwater swimming;
水肺式潛泳 scuba diving;

[潛在] latent; lurking; potential;
潛在敵意 latent hostility;
潛在對等 potential equivalence;
潛在功能 latent function; potential function;
潛在能力 potentiality;
潛在前提 potential presupposition;
潛在失業 latent unemployment;
潛在市場 potential market; earning potential;
潛在危害 potential danger; potential risk; potential threat;
潛在意識 subconsciousness;
潛在用戶 potential user;

[潛蹤] tail a person;

qian

【錢】 (1) cash; coins; (2) bugs bunny; dosh; dough; filthy lucre; money; moneys; monies; riches; wealth; (3) fund;

sum; (4) unit of weight; (5) a surname;
[錢包] handbag; moneybag; purse; wallet;
零錢包 change purse; coin purse;
拿出錢包 take out one's purse;
[錢幣] (1) coins; (2) currency; money;
錢幣收藏家 coin collector; numismatist;
錢幣收集 numismatics;
錢幣學 numismatics;
~錢幣學家 numismatist;
[錢財] money; riches; wealth;
錢財身外物 money is not an inherent part of the human being;
得人錢財，與人消災 if one gives me money, I will avert the disaster for him;
訛詐錢財 extort money under false pretences;
揮霍錢財 squander wealth;
巨額錢財 an amplitude of money;
浪費錢財 muddle away one's fortune; waste money;
勒索錢財 extort money from sb;
擁有錢財 possess wealth;
詐騙錢財 obtain money under false pretences;
掌管錢財 control the purse string; hold the purse strings;
[錢鈔] banknotes; money;
[錢出急門家] most of the money comes from households anxious to have the desired thing done quickly; where the demand is urgent, the consumer pays readily even fancy prices;
[錢袋] bag; moneybag; money purse; wallet;
[錢穀] taxes on farmland;
[錢櫃] cashbox; chest; coffer;
[錢滾錢] money begets money;
[錢荒] scarcity of money; short of money;
[錢可使鬼] money can make the devil work for you;
[錢款] money;
一次付清的錢款 lump sum;
[錢糧] taxes on farmland;
[錢癖] inveterate love of money;
[錢票] (1) banknotes; paper money; (2) cash coupons;
[錢鋪] banking house;
[錢生錢，利生利] money begets money;
[錢數] amount of money;

[錢箱] cash box;
[錢債] debt;
[錢莊] banking house; money house; private bank;

幫錢 help with money;
本錢 capital;
簸錢 game of casting coins;
茶錢 (1) payment for tea; (2) tip;
車錢 fare;
趁錢 have lots of money;
出錢 open one's purse;
儲錢 save money;
湊錢 pool money; raise a fund; whip-round;
船錢 charge for the boat service;
存錢 deposit money in a bank; save;
大錢 big money;
賭錢 gamble;
費錢 be costly; cost a lot;
工錢 (1) money paid for odd jobs; (2) charge for a service;
黑錢 bribery; underhand payment;
很多錢 oodles of money;
花不完的錢 money to burn;
花大錢 go to great expense; pay through the nose;
花一大筆錢 cost sb an arm and a leg;
換錢 change money;
價錢 price;
金錢 money;
僅剩的錢 one's last penny;
酒錢 tips;
來得容易的錢 easy money;
利錢 interest;
斂錢 collect money for expenditure;
零錢 (1) small change; (2) pocket money; (3) loose coin;
賠錢 (1) lose money; sustain losses in business; (2) compensate;
熱錢 hot money;
容易賺的錢 money for old rope;
賞錢 money reward; tip;
省錢 be economical; save money;
銅錢 copper cash;
我沒有那麼多錢 I'm not made of money;
洗黑錢 money laundering;
喜錢 tip given to sb on a happy occasion;
閒錢 spare cash;
現錢 cash; ready money;
小錢 (1) copper coins; (2) small sum of bribe;
要多少錢 what's the damage;
一把錢 a sheaf of money;
一筆錢 a sum of money; an amount of money;

一大筆錢 a chunk of change; a large sum; a large sum of money; a pile of money; a tidy sum;
一點錢 a bit of money; a trifling sum of money;
一塊錢 one dollar;
一毛錢 ten cents;
一小筆錢 a small amount of money;
洋錢 silver coins;
銀錢 money;
佣錢 brokerage; commission;
有錢 rich; wealthy;
月錢 monthly payment;
找錢 give change;
掙錢 earn money;
值錢 costly; valuable;
賺錢 make a profit; make money;
租錢 rent; rental;

qian

【黔】 (1) black; (2) another name for Guizhou Province;
[黔劇] ancient Guizhou opera;
[黔黎] common people;
[黔驢] cheap tricks;
黔驢之技 cheap tricks; clumsy tricks; the cheap tricks of the donkey in Guizhou; tricks not to be feared;
[黔首] common people; masses; multitude; people;
黔首黎民 black heads and black-haired people; the people of China;

qian³
qian

【淺】 (1) plain; shallow; simple; superficial; (2) easy to comprehend; simple to understand; (3) not close; not intimate; (4) light; pale; (5) not long in time;
[淺白] plain; simple;
淺白言之 talk in a simple way;
[淺薄] limited; meagre; shallow; superficial; thin;
淺薄的體會 limited experience;
為人淺薄 of a shallow character;
[淺測] superficial conjecture;
[淺嚐輒止] be satisfied with a smattering of knowledge; do not study further; have a tiny sip of; just have a tiny sip of; make a superficial study of sth; not to go into the subject in depth; put away the cup after taking a tiny sip; scratch the surface of; stop after getting a little knowledge of sth; stop after getting a little knowledge of a subject; stop after scratching the surface;
[淺而易見] be easily understood; easy to understand; obvious;
[淺耕] shallow ploughing;
淺耕粗作 shallow ploughing and careless cultivation;
[淺海] epeiric sea; shallow sea;
淺海魚 shallow sea fish;
[淺紅] light red;
[淺見] (1) humble opinion; shallow view; superficial view; (2) one's shallow view;
[淺交] not on intimate terms;
[淺近] easy to understand; fundamental; plain; simple; simple and easy to understand;
淺近的道理 plain and simple reasoning;
目光淺近 shortsighted;
[淺陋] crude; meagre; mean; shallow; vulgar;
淺陋不堪 very shallow and detestable;
[淺明] easy and clear;
[淺色] light colour;
[淺釋] simple explanation;
[淺水] shallow water;
淺水池 shallow end of a swimming pool; shallow pool;
淺水區 shallows;
[淺睡] dogsleep; nap; catnap; have forty winks;
[淺說] elementary introduction;
[淺灘] shallows; shoal;
[淺鮮] insignificant; slight;
[淺顯] apparent; easily understandable; easy to read and understand; obvious; plain;
淺顯道理 a plain truth;
淺顯易懂 clear and easy to understand;
淺顯易明 so shallow and clear that it is easy to understand;
[淺笑] (1) smile imperceptibly; (2) smile;
[淺信] weak faith;
[淺學] shallow learning; superficial learning;
淺學之士 superficial scholar;
[淺易] plain; simple and easy to understand;
淺易讀物 easy reading material; easy readings;
[淺斟] sip wine slowly;
淺斟低唱 sip wine slowly and hum a tune;

淺斟細嚼 sip one's drink and chew the food slowly;

闇淺 shallow, ignorant and stupid;
褊淺 narrow-minded and shallow;
觸淺 (of ships) be stranded; reach a deadlock; run aground;
粗淺 basic; coarse and shallow; shallow; simple; superficial;
短淺 narrow and shallow;
膚淺 shallow; superficial;
浮淺 shallow; superficial;
擱淺 (1) aground; be grounded; be stranded; beach; go aground; ground; run aground; run ashore; (2) a deadlock; at a deadlock; be held up; be suspended; come to a deadlock; reach a deadlock;
深淺 (1) deep or shallow; depth; (2) proper limits; sense of propriety; (3) dark or light;

qian

【遣】 (1) designate; dispatch; send; send away; (2) disband; dispel; drive away; escape from; expel; forget; kill time; (3) banish; deport; drive away; repatriate; send back; (4) release;

[遣詞] choice of words;
遣詞造句 choice of words and building of sentences; diction; rhetorical skill; wording and phrasing;
[遣發] send sb on an errand;
[遣返] deport; repatriate; send back; send home;
遣返戰俘 repatriate prisoners of war;
[遣俘] repatriate prisoners of war;
[遣歸] repatriate; send a prisoner home;
[遣懷] dispel one's sorrow in writing on the spur of the moment;
[遣將] send generals to a battle;
[遣悶] drive away melancholy; kill time;
[遣散] disband; dismiss; send away;
遣散費 golden handshake; redundancy pay; severance pay; termination pay;
[遣送] repatriate; send away; send back; send sb away forcibly;
遣送出境 deport;
遣送回國 repatriate;
[遣興] dispel one's sad thoughts in writing on the spur of the moment;

編遣 reorganize and discharge surplus personnel;
差遣 assign; dispatch; send sb on a mission;
調遣 assign; dispatch;
排遣 divert oneself from loneliness or boredom;
派遣 dispatch; send;
驅遣 (1) drive away; expel; (2) order about;
先遣 be sent in advance;
消遣 (1) pastime; (2) divert oneself;
自遣 amuse oneself; cheer oneself up; divert oneself from melancholy, etc;

qian

【繾】 attached; entangled; inseparable;

[繾綣] (1) deeply attached to each other; make tender love; (2) entangled; inextricably inseparable; (3) parasite;
繾綣情意 entangled relations between lovers;
繾綣之情 deep attachment; sentimental attachment;
兩情繾綣 be deeply attached to each other; deeply in love with each other; the beautiful relations between lovers; the two are cemented by love; they are head over heels in love;

qian

【譴】 (1) castigate; condemn; denounce; disparage; reprimand; reproach; scold; upbraid; (2) punishment;

[譴訶] reproach; scold;
[譴怒] reproof and anger;
[譴責] animadvert; brickbat; castigate; censure; condemn; condemnation; denounce; denunciation; disparage; flay; haul over the coals; repudiate; take to task;
公然譴責 issue a denunciation;
良心譴責 one's conscience pricks one; pricks of conscience; the strings of conscience;
社會譴責 social condemnation;
值得譴責 reprehensible;

qian4

qian

【欠】 (1) behind with; owe; owe money; (2) deficient; insufficient; lacking in; not enough; short of; wanting; (3) raise slightly; (4) yawn;

[欠安] not at ease at heart; not feeling well physically; not very well in health; unwell;

[欠不] almost;
[欠產] production shortfall; shortfall in output;
[欠單] accommodation note;
[欠戶] debtor;
[欠佳] below the average; not good enough; not up to the mark; not very appropriate;
[欠腳] slightly raise one's heels;
[欠款] arrears; balance due; debt; money that is owing; owe money;
還清欠款 pay off one's debt;
收回欠款 recover a debt;
[欠錢] owe sb a debt;
欠人家錢 owe sb a debt;
[欠情] favours not repaid; favours not returned; owe favours;
[欠缺] (1) deficient in; lack; lack in; short of; (2) deficiency; shortcoming;
[欠伸] snap; snapper; stretch oneself and yawn; yawn;
[欠身] bend forward a bit; get ready to stand up as a gesture of courtesy; half rise from one's seat; lean forward a bit; make a gesture of rising; raise oneself slightly;
欠身傾聽 bend one's body slightly forward to listen;
[欠稅] tax arrears;
[欠條] IOU;
[欠妥] amiss; improper; indecorous; not appropriate; not proper; not satisfactory; not very appropriate; out of place;
措辭欠妥 not properly worded;
[欠息] debit interest;
[欠薪] back pay; overdue wages;
[欠譯] under-translation;
[欠債] behind with; fall into debt; get into debt; in debt; in debt to; in deficit; in hock; in hock to sb; in the hole; in sb's debt; in the red; into sb; owe a debt; owe sb money for; run into debt; run into debt to sb;
欠債容易還債難 it's a lot easier to get in the hole than to get out again; it's easier to get in debt than to get out of it;
欠債要清，許願要還 promise a debt; promise is debt;
不欠債 in the clear; keep one's head above water; out of the hole;
付清欠債 settle a debt;
還清欠債 clear a debt incurred;
[欠帳] (1) outstanding accounts; overdue bills; (2) buy on credit; owe money;
[欠資] postage due;
欠資郵件 postage-due mail;

打哈欠 yawn;
掛欠 buy or sell on credit;
哈欠 yawn;
呵欠 yawn;
積欠 arrears; have one's debts piling up; outstanding debts;
清欠 repay all one's debts;
缺欠 be short of; defect; lack; shortcoming;
賒欠 buy on credit;
伸欠 stretch and yawn;
數欠 frequent yawning;
下欠 a sum still owing; still owe;

qian
【芡】 chicken-head;
[芡粉] cooking starch;
[芡實] chicken-head;

粉芡 starch in the form of plaster used in cooking;
勾芡 add thickening to soup, dish, etc.;

qian
【倩】 (1) attractive; beautiful; handsome; pretty; (2) ask sb to do sth; on behalf of oneself; (3) pretty dimples of a smiling woman; (4) son-in-law;
[倩冰委禽] proper formalities are observed in marriage;
[倩代] ask sb else to do sth; on behalf of oneself;
[倩女離魂] a young girl dies of love; a young lady dies for love;
[倩倩] attractive; pleasing;
[倩影] beautiful image of a woman;

qian
【茜】 madder;
[茜草] madder;
[茜素] alizarin;

qian
【慊】 grudge; have hard feelings about; resent;

[慊慊] resentful and discontented; grudging and dissatisfied;

qian

【塹】 (1) chasm; moat; trench; (2) a cavity in the ground; a hole in the ground; a pit;

[塹壕] entrenchment works; moat; trench;
塹壕工事 entrenchment works;
塹壕戰 trench warfare;

地塹 graben;
路塹 cutting;
天塹 natural chasm; natural moat;

qian

【歉】 (1) deficient; insufficient; lean; (2) bad harvest; poor crop; poor harvest; (3) apologize; feel sorry; regret; sorry;

[歉年] lean year;
[歉然] feel sorry; regret;
[歉收] bad harvest; crop failure; have a poor harvest; have bad crops; poor harvest;
[歉歲] a bad year for the crops; a lean year; a year of poor harvest;
[歉意] apology; regret; sorry;
致歉意 tender one's apologies;
~ 謹致歉意 please accept my apologies;
[歉仄] regrettable; very sorry;

抱歉 be sorry; regret;
道個歉 say sorry;
道歉 apologize; make an apology;
荒歉 crop failure; famine;
致歉 make an apology;

Q

qian

【蒨】 (1) luxuriant growth of grass; (2) crimson; red;

[蒨蒨] (1) bright and clear; (2) luxuriant growth;

qian

【槧】 (1) wooden tablet for writing; (2) edition of a book; (3) letter;

[槧本] book printed by engraving;

qian

【縴】 towline; towrope;

[縴板] tracking yoke;
[縴夫] boat tower;
[縴戶] boat tower;
[縴馬] lead a horse;
[縴繩] towline; towrope;
[縴手] (1) go-between; (2) boat tower;

qiang[1]

qiang

【羌】 an ancient tribe in West China;

[羌笛] shepherd's flute;
[羌蠻] ancient barbarian people in West China;
[羌無故實] without basis in fact;

qiang

【羫】 same as 羌;

qiang

【腔】 (1) cavity; (2) speech; (3) melody; pitch; tune; (4) accent; intonation;

[腔腸動物] coelenterate;
[腔調] (1) melody; tune; (2) accent; intonation;
腔調一模一樣 sing exactly the same tune as;
陳腔濫調 platitudes; same old tune; shopworn tune; the tune the old cow died of; worn-out tune;
怪腔怪調 queer tune; speak in a queer way;
京劇腔調 tunes of Beijing Opera;
老腔老調 old tunes and melodies;
南腔北調 mixed accent; mixture of accents;
洋腔洋調 exoticism;
油腔滑調 frivolous and insincere in speech; full of guile and cunning; glib tongue; mealy-mouthed; shifty argument;
轉腔換調 change of tone and pitch;
[腔兒] (1) cavity; (2) tune;

幫腔 echo sb; chime in with sb; give verbal support to a person; speak in support of sb;
鼻腔 nasal cavity;
唱腔 music for voices in a Chinese opera;
齒腔 dental cavity; gum of the tooth; pulp cavity of tooth;
吹腔 type of local opera with flute accompaniment;
答腔 answer; respond;
搭腔 (1) answer; respond; (2) talk to each other;
打官腔 speak in a bureaucratic tone;
腹腔 abdominal cavity;
高腔 kind of rhyme scheme of Chinese opera;
官腔 bureaucratic tone; official jargon;

喉腔 cavitas laryngis;
花腔 (1) florid ornamentation in Chinese opera singing; (2) guileful talk;
京腔 Beijing dialect;
開腔 begin to speak; open one's mouth;
口腔 oral cavity;
顱腔 cranial cavity;
滿腔 have one's bosom filled with;
盆腔 pelvic cavity;
氣腔 air chamber;
聲腔 common systematic tunes of many varieties of Chinese operas;
耍花槍 speak guilefully;
體腔 coelom;
胸腔 thoracic cavity;
裝腔 affect certain airs; behave affectedly;

qiang

【嗆】 (1) peck; (2) foolish; stupid;
[嗆哼] foolish; stupid;

qiang

【搶】 (1) adverse; head winds; (2) hit; knock; strike;
[搶風] head winds;

qiang

【槍】 (1) gun; pistol; rifle; (2) spear;
[槍把] pistol grip;
[槍靶] mark; target;
[槍斃] (1) execute by shooting; kill; shoot to death; (2) reject; shoot down; turn down;
[槍不離肩，馬不離鞍] in constant battle array; one should always be prepared; rifles seldom leave the men's shoulders, and the horses are never unsaddled;
[槍刺] bayonet;
[槍帶] sling;
[槍彈] bullet; cartridge; shell;
彈雨槍林 bullets like rain and spears like a forest — on battle grounds;
荷槍實彈 be armed with loaded guns; carry a loaded rifle; carry rifles loaded with bullets; fully armed;
槍林彈雨 a fierce battle; a forest of guns and a hail of bullets; a hail of bullets; a rain of bullets; a storm of shots and shells; amidst gunfire; bullets shower down like rain; heavy gunfire; in the midst of heavy gunfire; intensive fighting in the battlefield; pikes as dense as trees in a forest; roaring guns and flying bullets; storm of shots and shells; under fire;
真槍實彈 live ammunition; real guns and bullets; steel rifles and bullets;
[槍刀] guns and swords;
槍刀劍戟 arms; weapons;
槍對槍來刀對刀 arm-to-arm combat; it is spear against spear, sword against sword;
[槍法] (1) marksmanship; (2) art of using spears;
[槍桿子] barrel of a gun; shaft of a spear;
槍桿子出政權 political power grows out of the barrel of a gun;
[槍管] barrel of a gun;
[槍機] trigger;
[槍尖] spearhead;
[槍劍] guns and swords;
筆劍唇槍 the pen is as sharp as the sword and the tongue as the spear;
耍槍舞劍 play with the sword and spear;
[槍決] execute by shooting; execute by firing squard;
[槍口] muzzle of a rifle;
[槍砲] arms; firearms; guns;
槍砲匠 gunsmith;
槍砲射擊 gunshot;
槍砲聲 gunshot;
[槍殺] gun killing; kill by shooting; shoot dead;
[槍傷] bullet wound; gunshot wound;
[槍聲] crack of a gun; report of a gun;
槍聲大作 heavy firing breaks out;
[槍手] (1) gunner; marksman; rifleman; (2) ghost writer; (3) hired examinee;
僱用的槍手 hired gunman ghostwriter;
神槍手 crack shot; dead shot; expert marksman; marksman; sharpshooter;
熟練的槍手 gunslinger;
[槍栓] bolt of a rifle;
扳槍栓 pull back the bolt of a rifle;
搬弄槍栓 fiddle with the rifle bolt;
[槍膛] bore of a gun;
[槍替] sit for an examination in place of another person;
[槍頭兒] spearhead;
[槍托] gun stock; rifle butt;

[槍械] firearms; weapons;
槍械走私 gun-running;
[槍眼] (1) embrasure; (2) bullet hole;
[槍魚] marlin;
[槍戰] exchange of fire; fire fight; gun battle; gunfight; shootout;
[槍枝] rifle;
槍枝彈藥 firearms and ammunition;
槍枝管制法 gun control;
攜帶槍枝 pack a gun;

標槍 javelin;
步槍 rifle;
長槍 (1) spear; (2) long-barrelled gun;
持槍 (1) hold a gun; (2) port arms;
衝鋒槍 sub-machine gun; tommy gun;
打槍 fire with a rifle, pistol, etc.; shoot;
大槍 gun; rifle;
刀槍 swords and spears; weapons;
倒槍 reverse arms;
短槍 handgun; short arm;
焊槍 welding blowpipe; welding torch;
花槍 (1) short spear used in ancient times; (2) trickery;
回馬槍 give sb a back thrust;
火槍 firelock;
機關槍 machine gun;
機槍 machine gun;
輕機槍 light machine gun;
重機槍 heavy machine gun;
架槍 pile arms; stack arms;
舉槍 present arms;
開槍 fire with a rifle, pistol, etc; shoot;
來福槍 rifle;
冷槍 sniper's shot;
獵槍 hunting rifle; shotgun;
馬槍 carbine;
鳥槍 (1) fowling piece; (2) air gun;
排槍 volley of rifle fire;
噴漆槍 paint gun;
噴槍 spray gun;
氣槍 air gun; pneumatic gun;
射釘槍 nail gun;
射豆槍 peashooter;
手槍 pistol;
水槍 hydraulic monitor;
托槍 slope arms;
煙槍 opium pipe;
一把槍 a gun;
一杆槍 a rifle;
油槍 oil gun;

qiang
【瑲】 tinkling of jade pendants;
[瑲瑲] chiming of bells; jingling of bells;

qiang
【蜣】 dung beetle;
[蜣螂] dung beetle;

qiang
【蹌】 bustle about; gallop; walk rapidly;
[蹌捍] gallop; walk rapidly;
[蹌蹌] walk in rhythm;
蹌蹌顛顛 bustle about; on the go;

qiang
【鎗】 same as 槍;

qiang
【蹡】 in motion; walking;
[蹡蹡] walking;

qiang
【鏘】 clang; gong; tinkle;
[鏘鏘] (1) clang; tinkle; (2) high; lofty;

鏗鏘 clang; ring;

qiang
【鏹】 corrosive;
[鏹水] corrosive acid; strong acid;

qiang²

qiang
【戕】 (1) butcher; destroy; do violence to; injure; kill; slay; (2) injurious;
[戕害] kill; slay;
戕害無辜 butcher the innocents; commit genocide;
[戕殺] butcher; kill;
戕殺生民 butcher the people;
[戕賊] destroy; do violence to; injure; ruin; undermine;

qiang
【強】 (1) formidable; mighty; powerful; strong; vigorous; (2) enhance; strengthen; (3) brutal; by force; coercive; violent; (4) better; (5) plus; slightly more than;
[強半] (1) over half; (2) the greater half;
[強暴] (1) brutal; coercive; violent; (2) adversary; ferocious;
強暴對待 do violence to;
強暴行為 violent behaviour;
強暴兇悍 ruthless and violent;

鏟除強暴 eradicate fiendish adversary;

[強逼] compel; force;

[強大] big and powerful; formidable; mighty; powerful; powerful and strong;
強大的因素 powerful factor;
強大生命力 great vitality;
勢力強大 powerful in influence;
越來越強大 go from strength to strength;

[強盜] bandit; highwayman; pirate; robber;
強盜扮聖賢 a gangster pretends to be a saint;
強盜發善心—不可能 a bandit showing mercy — it's impossible;
強盜飛機 pirate plane;
強盜邏輯 gangster logic; gun law; law of the jungle;
強盜碰着賊爺爺—黑吃黑 a robber being robbed by a thief — the black swallowing up the black; one bad person taking advantage of another;
強盜侵略行徑 piratical acts of aggression;
強盜收心做好人 the robber who has a change of heart begins to turn over a new leaf;
強盜頭子 chieftain of gangsters; gang boss; gangster boss; godfather; pirate chief; ringleader;
強盜性質 predatory nature;
強盜戰爭 predatory war;
強盜照相—賊頭賊腦 a robber taking his own photo — reflecting a thief's head and brain; stealthy;
一把子強盜 a bunch of bandits; a gang of robbers;
一幫強盜 a band of robbers;
一伙強盜 a band of robbers;
一群強盜 a band of robbers;

[強敵] formidable enemy; formidable foe; powerful enemy; powerful foe;
迭挫強敵 inflict repeated reverses on a formidable enemy;

[強調] bear down on sth; drum in; drum sth; emphasize; hammer away at; hammer in; insist on; lay emphasis on; lay great stress on; lay stress on; make a point of sth; make much of; place emphasis on; place stress on; point up; put emphasis on; put stress on; stress; underline; underscore;
強調詞 emphasizer;
強調德行 emphasize virtues;
強調句型 emphasized pattern;
強調語 emphasizer;
強調指出 point out emphatically;
片面強調 undue emphasis on;
需要強調 require emphasis;

[強度] intensity; strength; tenacity;
電流強度 current intensity;
斷裂強度 breaking tenacity;
乾燥強度 dry tenacity;
絕對強度 absolute intensity; absolute strength;
勞動強度 intensity of labour;
譜帶強度 band intensity;
射束強度 beam intensity;
濕強度 wet tenacity;
吸收強度 absorption strength;
增加強度 additional strength;

[強渡] fight one's way across a river;

[強奪] grab; rob; snatch;

[強風] fresh gale; stiff breeze; stiff wind; strong breeze;

[強幹] able; capable; competent;

[強梗] obstruct like a bully;

[強攻] capture by assault; storm; take by storm;
與其強攻，何其智取 it would be better to use strategy than to attack by force;

[強固] solid; strong;

[強光] strong light;
一陣強光 a flood of light;

[強國] great powers; powerful nations;
強國富民 the nation is powerful and the people are rich;
經濟強國 powerful economy;

[強悍] doughty; fierce; intrepid; valiant;

[強橫] brutal and unreasonable; despotic; dictatorial; high-handed; insolent; overbearing; tyrannical;

[強化] consolidate; intensification; intensify; reinforcement; strengthen; tighten;
強化玻璃 reinforced glass;
強化肌肉 tone up the muscles;
強化機制 strengthening mechanism;
強化理論 theory of intensification;
強化食品 condensed foods; enriched foods;
強化效果 heighten the intensity;
強化形容詞 intensifying adjective;
強化訓練課程 immersion programme;
強化語 intensifier;

負向強化 negative reinforcement;
圖像強化 image intensification;
西向強化 westward intensification;

[強擊] assault;
強擊火砲 assault artillery;

[強記] strong in memory;
博聞強記 have encyclopaedic knowledge; have extensive knowledge and a powerful memory; have wide learning and a good memory; have wide learning and a retentive memory; with a wide range of knowledge and a long memory;

[強加] force on; impose upon;
強加於人 bend others to one's will; force one's views upon others; force sth on sb; impose one's will on others; intrude one's opinions upon others; lay one's will on others; thrust sth upon others;

[強姦] assault sexually; attack sexually; rape; violate;
強姦犯 raptist;
強姦民意 defile public opinion — said of reactionary rulers who force their views on the people and assert their arbitrary actions as wishes of the people;
約會強姦 date rape;

[強健] stout; strong and healthy; sturdy;

[強諫] admonish vigorously;

[強勁] forceful; powerful; strong;

[強勞] compulsory labour; forced labour;

[強力] brute force;
強力膠 glue;
強有力的 brawny; forceful; hardy; mighty; muscular; potent; powerful; strong; sturdy; vigorous;
~強有力的行動 vigorous action;
~強有力的一擊 a forceful strike;

[強梁] bully; ruffian;
強梁霸道 overbearing and violent;

[強烈] (1) intense; severe; strong; violent; (2) intensely; strongly; vigorously;
強烈的反感 violent repugnance;

[強蠻] brutal and unreasonable; fierce;

[強拍] accented beat; strong beat;

[強迫] compel; compulsion; force;
強迫的 compulsory;
強迫接受 cram down sb's throat; force down sb's throat; ram down sb's throat; shove down sb's throat; thrust down sb's throat;
強迫進食 force-feed;
強迫命令 coercion and commandism;
強迫性的 compulsive;
強迫症 obsessive compulsive disorder;
~強迫症患者 obsessive;
~強迫症行為 obsessive-compulsive behaviour;

[強權] brute force; might; power;
強權即公理 might is right; might makes right
強權外交 power diplomacy;
強權政治 power politics;

[強人] (1) capable person; (2) bandit; highwayman; robber; (3) physically strong person; strong man; stout person;
強人政治 government under a powerful ruler;
女強人 able woman; successful career woman;

[強韌] enduring; indomitable; resilient; strong; tenacious; tough;

[強弱] the strong and the weak;
強弱現象 balance of forces;
強弱懸殊 a wide disparity in strength; the strong and the weak differ greatly;
避強打弱 evade the strong and attack the weak;
避強擊弱 avoid the strong and attack the weak;
鋤強扶弱 eradicate those who are despotic and help those who are weak; extirpate evildoers and support the weak people; fight for the weak against the strong; oppose the strong and assist the weak; suppress the strong and aid the weak;
敵強我弱 with one's weak forces facing the enemy's strong forces;
扶弱抑強 assist the weak and curb the violent; fight for the weak against the strong; help the weak and curb the strong; help the weak and restrain the powerful; uphold the weak against the strong;
抗強憫弱 despise the strong, but be gentle with the weak;
能弱能強 able to show oneself weak or strong;

欺弱諂強 tyrannize over the weak but cringe at the sight of the strong;
欺弱怕強 afraid of the mighty and bully the weak; fear the strong and bully the weak; overbear the weak and quail before the strong; scare the weak but fear the strong;
弱肉強食 jungle justice; the big fish eat up the small ones; the law of the jungle; the stronger preying upon the weaker; the weak are the prey to the strong;
恃強凌弱 play the bully; use one's strength to bully the weak;
汰弱留強 weed out the weak and retain the strong;
畏強凌弱 quail before the strong and be overbearing with the weak;
以強凌弱 act in the way of the strong domineering over the weak; oppress the weak by sheer strength;
以弱勝強 defeat a powerful enemy with a weak force; defeat a strong and superior force with a weak and backward force;
抑強扶弱 curb the violent and assist the weak; restrain the powerful and help the weak; restrain the strong and help the weak;
由弱變強 become a strong one; go from weakness to strength;
由弱到強 grow from weak to strong; grow strong from being weak;
助弱抑強 assist the weak and curb the violent; fight for the weak against the strong;
轉弱為強 become strong; transform from weak to strong;

[強身] conducive to health; strengthen the body;
強身藥 analeptic medicine;

[強盛] powerful and prosperous;

[強式] strong form;
強式動詞 strong verb;

[強勢] strong;
強勢代詞 emphatic pronoun;
強勢貨幣 strong currency;

[強手] strong hand;
連挫強手 defeat strong opponents one after another;

[強死] die from violence;

[強似] better than; superior to;

[強酸] strong acid;

[強挺] indomitable; unyielding;

[強襲] attack the enemy by means of an artillery barrage;

[強項] forte; strong; unyielding;
強項不屈 firm in principle and never yield to one's opponent; stiff-necked and unbendable;

[強心劑] heart stimulant;

[強心針] heart stimulant;
打強心針 stimulate;

[強行] break; by force; force; jam;
強行闖入 force one's way in;
強行登陸 forced landing;
強行合併 shotgun merger;
強行進入 force one's way in;
強行通過 force through a document; ram through;
強行突破 force one's way through the barrier;

[強壓] oppress and crush;

[強硬] (1) flinty; hard; stiff; strong; tough; (2) defiant; truculent; unyielding;
強硬手段 with a high hand;
強硬態度 intransigent attitude;
強硬姿態 hard-line stance;
措辭強硬 strongly worded;

[強佔] forcibly occupy; occupy by force; seize;

[強者] strongman;
強者為王 the strongest becomes the king;

[強震] microseism; strong shock;

[強制] coerce; coercion; compel; compulsory; force;
強制辦法 coercive measures;
強制保險 mandatory insurance;
強制兵役 forced conscription;
強制的 coercive;
強制機關 institutions of law enforcement;
強制勞動 compulsory labour;
強制推行 force through;
強制執行 carry out under coercion;

[強壯] energetic; robust; strong; sturdy; vigorous; virile;
強壯的體格 powerful physique;
強壯劑 invigorant; tonic;
兵強馬壯 strong soldiers and sturdy horses;
身強力壯 be possessed of health; hale and strong; in fine feather; physically

strong; sturdy; tough;
相當強壯 fairly strong;
[強宗] powerful clan;

拗強 obstinate and pigheaded; recalcitrant;
逞強 cocky; flaunt one's superiority; throw one's weight round;
富強 prosperous and strong;
剛強 firm; staunch; unyielding;
高強 outstanding; superior;
豪強 despotic; local despot; tyrannical;
好強 aspiring; eager to do well in everything;
加強 beef up; reinforce; strengthen;
堅強 staunch; strengthen; strong;
倔強 obstinate;
民強 the people are strong;
頑強 indomitable; staunch;
壓強 intensity of pressure; pressure;
要強 be eager to surpass others; strive to excel;
嘴強 inclined to argue;
自強 self-improvement;

qiang
【嬙】 court lady;
[嬙媛] ladies-in-waiting;

qiang
【檣】 mast of a ship;

桅檣 mast;

qiang
【牆】 fence; wall;
[牆報] wall newspaper;
[牆壁] wall;
粉刷牆壁 whitewash a wall;
鐵壁銅牆 iron walls and brass partitions; stronghold;
[牆倒眾人推] everybody hits the man when he is down; everybody kicks the man who is down; everyone gives a shove to a falling wall; everyone hits a person who is down; if a wall starts tottering, everyone gives it a shove; lick sb when he is down; make things worse for others who are already in difficulties; the wall tottering, the crowd contributes to its collapse by pushing it; when a man is going down-hill, everyone will give him a push; when a wall is about to collapse, everybody gives it a push;

牆倒眾人推，鼓破眾人捶 he that is down, down with him; once a man falls, all will tread on him;
[牆頂] top of a wall;
扒牆頂 climb up to the top of a wall;
[牆根] the foot of a wall;
[牆畫] mural painting; wall painting;
[牆角] corner between two walls; corner of a wall;
[牆腳] (1) foot of a wall; (2) cornerstone; foundation;
拆牆腳 pull away a prop; undermine;
挖牆腳 cut the ground from under sb's feet; sap a wall; subvert; undermine a wall; undermine the foundation;
[牆上] wall;
牆上畫餅—中看不中吃 drawing a cake on the wall – nice to look at it, but cannot be eaten;
牆上蘆葦，頭重腳輕根底淺 the reed growing on the wall – the head is heavy, the stem thin, and the roots shallow;
牆上一株草，隨風兩邊倒 a tuft of grass on the top of a wall sways left and right in the wind – a fence-sitter;
靠在牆上 lean against the wall;
撞在牆上 bump against the wall;
[牆頭] the crest of a fence; the top of a wall;
牆頭草 fence-rider; man without opinions of his own; opportunist; one who bends with the wind;
牆頭草，隨風倒 the grass on the top of a wall sways with the blowing of the wind;
牆頭上種菜—難交 growing vegetables on top of a wall – watering them is difficult;
[牆頭詩] wall poems;
[牆外漢] amateur; outsider;
[牆有縫，壁有耳] walls have ears; we may be under close watch;
[牆垣] fence; wall;
牆垣有耳 walls have ears;
[牆紙] wallpaper;

城牆 city wall;
擋土牆 retaining wall;
防火牆 fire wall;
粉牆 whitewashed wall;
風火牆 fire wall;

隔火牆 fire division wall;
隔牆 partition;
花牆 lattice wall;
火牆 (1) wall with flues for space heating; (2) network of fire;
女牆 parapet wall;
騎牆 sit on the fence;
山牆 gable;
圍牆 enclosing wall; enclosure;
胸牆 breast work; parapet;
一道牆 a wall;
一堵牆 a wall;

qiang
【薔】 rose;
［薔薇］ rose;
薔薇露 (1) rose water; (2) a kind of wine;
野薔薇 wild rose;

qiang³
qiang
【強】 (1) forced; reluctant; unwilling; (2) compel; enforce; force; impel; make an effort; make by force; strive;
［強逼］ compel; force; make by coercion; make by force;
［強辯］ defend oneself by sophistry;
強辯飾非 argue illogically in glossing over faults; cover up faults with flowery words;
［強辭奪理］ arbitrary arguments; argue irrationally; argue to be impertinent enough; chop logic to defend oneself; distort reason and talk speciously; distort the right and talk speciously; do violence to the meaning and intent of a statement by twisting the meaning of words to suit one's purpose; force an interpretation; force the words in order to extract a meaning; reason fallaciously; resort to sophistry; snatch a victory in arguments; sophisticate; strain the meaning of a statement to the utmost so as to destroy its intent; stretch the meaning of words to the point of unreason; swear black is white; torture the words to suit one's purpose and, by false reasoning, pervert the truth; try to defend an untenable position by recourse to specious arguments; use lame arguments and pervert logic;
［強記］ cram sth into one's memory; cram the memory with sth; force oneself to memorize; strain to memorize sth;
［強借］ borrow forcibly;
［強扭的瓜不甜］ nothing forcibly done is going to be agreeable;
［強迫］ compel; enforce; force; impel;
強迫降落 forced landing;
強迫教育 compulsory education; mandatory education;
強迫命令 categorical order; force one's orders on; force sb to do sth; pull rank on; resort to coercion and commandism;
強迫遷移 forced migration;
強迫推銷 importune sale;
［強求］ demand; exact; extort; forcibly demand; impose; insist on;
強求一律 unify by force;
強求硬索 importune sb for sth;
［強取］ take by force;
［強使］ compel; force;
［強索硬討］ insist on getting sth;
［強笑］ forced smile;
［強顏］ (1) force a smile; (2) shameless;
強顏歡笑 assume a joyous mood reluctantly; force a smile; force oneself to smile; put on an air of cheerfulness; try to look happy when one is sad;
［強佔］ occupy forcibly; take sb by force;
［強制］ compel; compulsory; force; forcible;
強制保險 compulsory insurance;
強制處分 subject to a forcible measure;
強制投票 compulsory voting;
強制執行 execute forcibly; forcible execution;

勉強 (1) do with difficulty; (2) reluctantly; (3) force sb to do sth; (4) inadequate; unconvincing; (5) barely enough; unnatural;
牽強 farfetched; forced; strained;

qiang
【搶】 (1) loot; plunder; rob; steal; (2) grab; seize; seize by force; snatch; take by force; wrest; (3) scramble for; try to beat others in a performance; vie for; vie with each other to be the first; walk

off with; (4) do sth in haste; rush; (5) scrape; scratch;

[搶案] case of robbery;

[搶白] rebuke sb openly; refute sb to his face; reprimand sb to his face; ridicule sb to his face; satirize sb to his face;

[搶答] compete for the chance to answer;
搶答器 buzzer;

[搶渡] cross a river speedily; cross a river with all possible speed;

[搶奪] grab; plunder; rob; seize; seize by force; snatch; wrest;

[搶購] make a rush-purchase of; panic buying; rush to buy; rush to purchase;
搶購潮 wave of panic buying;
搶購風 buying spree; purchasing spree;
~搶購風潮 panic purchasing;

[搶光] take away by force everything that is movable;

[搶婚] carry away a woman and marry her by force;

[搶劫] loot; pillage; plunder; raid; rob; take by force;
搶劫一空 loot to the last pin; rob to the last pin; rob sb lock, stock and barrel;
搶劫銀行 knock over a bank;
搶劫者 raider;
攔路搶劫 highway robbery;
武裝搶劫 armed robbery;
行兇搶劫 mug; mugging; robbery with violence;
~行兇搶劫者 mugger;
砸櫥窗搶劫 smash-and-grab;

[搶救] make an emergency rescue; rescue; rush to rescue; rush to save; salvage; save; take urgent steps to save sth or sb from destruction;
搶救病人 give emergency treatment to a patient;
搶救無效 all rescue measures prove ineffectual;

[搶掠] loot; plunder;
燒殺搶掠 burn, kill and loot;

[搶拍] seize the opportunity to take a photograph;

[搶跑] take away by force;

[搶親] take a woman for marriage by force;

[搶市] rush to market; strive to get one's goods on sale first;

[搶收] get the harvest in quickly; rush in the harvest;

[搶手] find a good market; in great demand; sell well;
搶手貨 a commodity in great demand; goods in great demand; grabbed items; hot consumer goods; shopping-rush goods; very popular item;
非常搶手 go like hot cakes; sell like hot cakes;

[搶灘] make a beach landing in face of enemy resistance;

[搶先] beat sb to it; compete to be the first; do sth before others have a chance to; rush ahead; try to be the first to do sth; try to beat others in performing sth;
搶先得到 grab off;
搶先獲得 nab;
趁機搶先 pull a fast one;

[搶險] go to the rescue hurriedly; rush to deal with an emergency; rush to meet an emergency;
搶險救災 do rescue and relief work;

[搶修] do rush repairs; make urgent repairs on; race against time in making a repair job; rush to repair; rush-repair;

[搶運] race against time in sending out materials; rush delivery of goods;

[搶摘] seize the fruits;

[搶佔] grab; race to control; rush to seize; seize;

[搶走] loot; rap;

[搶嘴] (1) try to beat others in being the first to talk; (2) argumentative; assertive;

qiang

【襁】 carrying band for an infant;

[襁褓] (1) carrying band for an infant; (2) infancy; (3) swaddling clothes;

[襁抱] infancy;

[襁負] (1) infancy; (2) carrying band for an infant;

qiang

【鏹】 corrosive;

[鏹水] corrosive acid;
白鏹 silver;

qiang⁴

qiang

【嗆】 choke; cough;

够嗆 terrible; unbearable;

qiang

【戧】 prop up; shore up; support;

[戧金] gold jewelry; sprinkle gold;

[戧銀] silver jewelry;

[戧柱] side support;

够戧 terrible; unbearable;

qiang

【熗】 (1) quick-fry; (2) same as 嗆 ;

[熗鍋] quick-fry;

qiang

【蹌】 limp; stagger; walk unsteadily;

[蹌踉] stagger;

踉蹌 stagger;

qiang

【蹡】 limp;

踉蹡 stagger;

qiao[1]

qiao

【敲】 (1) beat; knock; pound out; rap; strike; tap; tap out; (2) blackmail; extort; overcharge;

[敲梆] beat the watches; sound night watch with a clapper;

[敲出] pound out; tap out;

[敲打] (1) beat; knock; percuss; rap; strike; tap; (2) say sth to irritate sb;

敲敲打打 beat drums continually;

[敲點] prod;

[敲定] bang the hammer to decide; come to an agreement; fix; get down to a decision; make a final decision;

[敲骨吸髓] beat sb's bones flat for the marrow inside; bleed sb white; bloodsucking exploitation; break the bones and suck the marrow; enforce the most relentless oppression and exploitation; exploit cruelly; milk sb dry; ruthless economic exploitation; suck the lifeblood; wring every ounce of sweat and blood out of sb;

[敲鼓] beat drums;

敲邊鼓 act to assist sb; act to support sb; back sb up; beat the drum on the side; speak a good word indirectly for sb; speak for sb from the sideline; speak for sb in order to help him; speak on behalf of sb; speak to assist sb;

[敲擊] beat; knock; slap;

敲擊樂器 a percussion instrument;

旁敲側擊 attack by innuendo; beat about the bush; devious questioning; fool round the stump; in a roundabout way; make oblique references; make thrusts; make veiled attack;

~ 打半邊鼓—旁敲側擊 beat only one side of a drum – a flank attack;

[敲鑼] beat a gong;

敲鑼打鼓 beat drums and strike gongs; beat gongs and sound drums; to the beat of gongs and drums; with drums beating, cymbals clashing;

敲鑼賣糖—各幹一行 beat gongs or selling sweets – each has his own line of business;

[敲門] bang at the door; bang on the door; knock at a door; knock on the door; rap at the door; rap on the door; tap at the door; tap on the door;

敲門磚 a means to find favour with an influential person; a stepping stone to one's purpose;

用力敲門 hammer at the door;

有人在敲門 there is a knock on the door;

[敲破] shatter; smash;

[敲人] swindle a person;

[敲詩] riddle in verse form;

[敲碎] beat to pieces; knock to pieces;

[敲詐] blackmail; extort; practise their extortions; racketeer;

敲詐勒索 blackmail and impose exactions on; extort and racketeer; extort by false pretenses; extort money from sb; practise blackmail; practise extortion; racketeer; shake down; swindle and squeeze;

[敲鐘] toll a bell;

[敲竹杠] charge an exorbitant price; extort money; fleece; make advantage of sb's being in a weak position to overcharge him; make an exorbitant charge for services rendered; make sb pay through the nose; make sb squeal; overcharge; put the lug on; soak; sponge a person; sponge on sb; squeeze a person for

money; sting; that is as good as blackmail; that is highway robbery;

推敲 weigh;

qiao

【撬】 lift; raise;

［撬杠］ level;

qiao

【橇】 sledge for transportation over mud or snow;

冰橇 sled; sledge;

雪橇 sled; sledge;

qiao

【鍬】 shovel; spade;

鐵鍬 shovel; spade;

qiao

【磽】 hard barren land; poor in soil;

［磽薄］ barren; hard and infertile;

［磽瘠］ hard and barren; hard and infertile;

［磽確］ barren; hard and infertile;

qiao

【蹺】 (1) raise the feet; (2) on tiptoe; (3) stilt;

［蹺板］ seesaw; teeterboard;

［蹺家］ run away from home;

［蹺捷］ able to move quickly and easily; agile;

［蹺課］ avoid attending classes; play hooky;

［蹺蹊］ dubious; extraordinary; fishy; queer; strange;

蹺蹺板 seesaw; teeterboard; teetertotter;

［蹺足以待］ curl up one's leg and wait at ease;

踹高蹺 walk on stilts;

蹊蹺 queer; strange;

qiao

【蹻】 (1) same as 蹺, raise feet; (2) sandals; shoes; (3) stilts;

［蹻工］ art of walking in high-soled boots;

［蹻然不固］ fluid; not firmly fixed; unstable; unsteady;

［蹻足］ (1) raise a foot; (2) very brief period;

蹻足以待 sit down cozily and wait at ease;

qiao²

qiao

【喬】 (1) high; lofty; tall; (2) crafty; disguise; pretend; tricky; (3) a surname;

［喬才］ (1) bad egg; bad fellow; (2) crafty; tricky;

［喬林］ high forest;

［喬木］ arbour; large tree; tall tree; tree;

［喬遷］ move into a new house; move to a new place;

喬遷之喜 best wishes for your new home; celebration of moving into a new house; congratulations on moving into a new building; congratulations on your new home; congratulations on your removal to a new house;

［喬松］ lofty pine;

［喬文假醋］ assuming the airs of a scholar; have a scholarly air;

［喬梓］ father and son;

［喬裝］ disguise oneself; dress up;

喬裝打扮 deck oneself out; disguise oneself; dress oneself up; go about in disguise;

喬裝旅行 travel in disguise;

拿喬 put on airs; strike a pose to enhance one's own importance;

qiao

【僑】 (1) live abroad; overseas; (2) person living abroad; (3) sojourn;

［僑胞］ one's fellow countrymen residing abroad; overseas Chinese;

國外僑胞 Chinese nationals residing in foreign countries;

海外僑胞 Chinese nationals residing abroad;

［僑匯］ overseas remittance;

匯出僑匯 immigrant remittance;

匯入僑匯 emigrant remittance;

［僑居］ live abroad;

僑居國外 reside abroad; sojourn in a foreign land;

［僑眷］ dependents of overseas Chinese;

［僑領］ leaders of overseas Chinese;

［僑民］ alien resident; foreign national;

僑民登記 registration of aliens;

僑民區 alien territory;

［僑務］ affairs concerning nationals living abroad;

［僑資］ overseas Chinese capital;

歸僑 returned overseas Chinese;

華僑 overseas Chinese national;

外僑 foreign national;

qiao

【憔】 emaciated; haggard; thin; wan; withered; worn;

［憔悴］ (1) haggard; thin and pallid; wan and sallow; (2) withered;

憔悴的 haggard;

憔悴枯槁 haggard from anxiety and dried like a stalk;

面容憔悴 weary-looking;

［憔慮］ impatient and anxious;

qiao

【橋】 (1) bridge; bridge-like structure; (2) beams of a structure; (3) elevated; high; tall; (4) a surname;

［橋洞］ bridge opening; the arches of a bridge;

［橋墩］ bridge pier; pier; buttress of a bridge;

聯結式橋墩 braced pier;

筒形橋墩 barrel pier;

斜面式橋墩 batter;

［橋拱］ bridge arch;

［橋孔］ bridge opening;

［橋欄］ bridge railings;

［橋樑］ bridge;

橋樑作用 play the role of a bridge; serve as a link with;

［橋牌］ bridge;

打橋牌 play a bridge game; play bridge;

定約橋牌 contract bridge;

玩橋牌 play bridge;

［橋上］ on the bridge;

［橋塔］ bridge tower;

［橋台］ abutment;

［橋頭］ bridgehead; either end of a bridge;

橋頭堡 (1) bridgehead; (2) bridge tower;

佔領橋頭堡 capture the bridgehead;

橋頭陣地 bridgehead;

船到橋頭自然直 in the end things will mend; things at the worst will mend; when the boat comes to the bridge underpass, it will go through straight; when things at at the worst they will mend; you will cross the bridge when you get to it;

［橋下］ below the bridge;

鞍橋 saddle;

便橋 accommodation bridge; temporary bridge;

船橋 bridge;

搭橋 build a bridge;

吊橋 (1) suspension bridge; (2) drawbridge;

浮橋 bateau bridge; floating bridge; pontoon bridge;

輔助橋 auxiliary bridge;

拱橋 arched bridge;

浪橋 swing-bridge;

鏈橋 chain bridge;

梁式橋 beam bridge;

門橋 boat raft; raft of pontoons;

腦橋 pons;

聲橋 acoustic bridge;

天橋 platform bridge;

旋橋 swing bridge;

一座橋 a bridge;

引橋 approach bridge; bridge approach;

原子橋 atomic bridge;

棧橋 landing stage; loading bridge;

正橋 bridge proper;

自動電橋 automatic bridge;

qiao

【樵】 (1) firewood; fuel; (2) gather firewood; gather fuel; (3) woodcutter; woodman; (4) burn; (5) lookout; tower;

［樵夫］ woodcutter; woodman;

［樵斧］ axe;

［樵歌晚唱］ sing a woodcutter's song at night;

［樵客］ woodcutter; woodman;

［樵女］ female fuel gatherer;

［樵叟］ old woodcutter; old woodman;

［樵薪］ gather firewood; gather fuel;

［樵隱］ recluse who leads a woodcutter's life;

［樵子］ woodcutter; woodman;

qiao

【燋】 emaciated; haggard; worn;

qiao

【蕎】 (1) buckwheat; (2) a kind of medicinal herb;

［蕎巴］ buckwheat cake;

［蕎麥］ buckwheat; straw;

蕎麥粉 buckwheat flour;

qiao

【瞧】 (1) glance at; look; see; (2) glance quickly; steal a glance;

［瞧病］ (1) consult a doctor; see a doctor; (2) examine a patient; see a patient;

［瞧不慣］ not used to seeing cruel scenes;

[瞧不過] not hard-hearted enough to see sth to its brutal end;
[瞧不上眼] be held cheap; beneath notice; consider beneath one's notice; not at all appealing to the eye; not up to one's taste; not worth so much a look at; turn one's nose up at; turn up one's nose at;
[瞧得起] esteem; have a high regard for; hold in high esteem; look up to; respect; see much in; think much of; think well of; value;
瞧不起 have no regard for; hold in contempt; hold in low esteem; look down on; look down one's nose at; look down upon; turn up one's nose at sb;
[瞧得透] see through; understand thoroughly;
瞧不透 not able to understand; unable to see through;
[瞧見] catch sight of; see;
[瞧你的] let's see what you can do;
[瞧熱鬧兒] (1) go and see where the fanfare is; (2) bystander in fights;
[瞧上] set eyes on sth and wish to have it;
瞧得上 good enough to suit one's taste;
[瞧我的] you just watch how I do it;
[瞧一瞧] take a look;
[瞧着] (1) while looking; (2) let's see;
瞧着辦 let's wait and see what happens and plan our strategy then;

qiao

【翹】 (1) long tail feathers; (2) raise one's head; (3) become warped; (4) outstanding;
[翹材] person of outstanding ability;
[翹楚] outstanding person; person of outstanding ability;
人中翹楚 outstanding person;
[翹盼] await eagerly; long eagerly;
[翹企] eagerly look forward to; raise one's head and stand on tiptoe;
[翹翹] (1) tall; (2) swing dangerously; (3) distinguished; talented;
翹翹人才 distinguished and talented person;
[翹曲] warping;
邊緣翹曲 edge warping;
溫差翹曲 temperature warping;
縱向翹曲 longitudinal warping;

[翹首] raise one's head and look;
翹首而望 lift up one's head in expectation; on the tiptoe of expectation; raise one's head and look; raise the head and stand on tiptoe expecting; raise one's head in hope;
翹首抗足 raise one's head and stand on tiptoe in admiration;
翹首企足 crane one's neck and stand on tiptoe in pleasurable expectation; raise one's head and stand on tiptoe to look eargerly ahead;
翹首星空 lift up one's eyes to the starry sky; look up at the starry sky;
翹首以待 on the tiptoe of expectation; raise one's head and look forward to;
[翹望] long eagerly;
[翹足以待] stand on tiptoe;
翹足以待 stand on tiptoe in expectation; wait on tiptoe;
翹足引領 eagerly look forward to; long eagerly; raise one's head and crane one's neck;
[翹嘴] pout one's mouth;
翹嘴撅唇 pout one's lips in displeasure; pout one's mouth in anger;
翹嘴塌鼻 protruding lips and a snub nose;

連翹 capsule of weeping forsythia;

qiao

【譙】 (1) tower; (2) a surname;
[譙樓] (1) watchtower; (2) drum tower;
[譙門] watchtower over the city gate;
[譙譙] frayed and injured;

qiao

【顦】 haggard;

qiao³

qiao

【巧】 (1) clever; ingenious; intelligent; skilful; (2) artful; cunning; deceitful; (3) as it happens; as luck would have it; by a happy chance; coincidentally; fortuitous; opportunely; (4) cute; pretty;
[巧辯] ingenious argument; plausible argument;
巧辯性話語 repartee discourse;
[巧不可階] nothing superior to it; skilful handiwork cannot be rivalled;

unmatched in ingenuity;

[巧當兒] (1) at the opportune moment; (2) coincidence;

[巧得很] as luck would have it; fortunately; quite by coincidence;

[巧發奇中] clever and penetrating remark; skilful in foretelling;

[巧婦] clever woman;

巧婦難為無米之炊 even a clever woman cannot cook a meal without rice; even the cleverest housewife can't cook a meal without rice; if you have no hand you can't make a fist; one cannot make a silk purse out of a sow's ear; one cannot realize a certain purpose without the necessary means; one can't make bricks without straw; the French would be the best cooks in Europe if they had got any butcher's meat; you cannot make an omelette without breaking eggs; you can't make sth out of nothing;

巧婦鳥 wren;

[巧幹] do sth in a clever way; work in a clever way; work ingeniously;

[巧故] artful deceit; artful falsehood;

[巧合] by chance; by coincidence; coincidence; happenstance;

巧合的 coincidental;

意外的巧合 curious coincidence;

[巧極了] extremely coincidental; extremely fortunate; quite by coincidence;

[巧計] artful scheme; artifice; capital plan; clever device; clever strategy; ingenious plan; ingenious scheme; very clever device;

巧計良謀 a clever plan and an outstanding scheme;

[巧匠] clever artisan; craftsman; skilled workman;

[巧捷] skilful and fast;

[巧勁兒] (1) great skill; (2) unexpected event;

[巧克力] choc; chocolate;

巧克力冰淇淋 choc-ice;

巧克力餅乾 chocolate biscuit;

巧克力蛋糕 brownie; chocolate cake; devil's food cake;

巧克力粉 drinking chocolate;

巧克力糖 choccy;

~一盒巧克力糖 a box of chocolates;

巧克力味道 chocolate taste;

純巧克力 plain chocolate;

核桃仁巧克力 walnut chocolate;

黑巧克力 dark chocolate; plain chocolate;

奶油巧克力 milk chocolate;

牛奶果仁巧克力 milk and nuts chocolate;

牛奶巧克力 milk chocolate;

熱巧克力 hot chocolate;

素巧克力 plain chocolate;

一杯巧克力 one chocolate;

一盒巧克力 a box of chocolates;

一塊巧克力 a bar of chocolate;

雜錦巧克力 assorted chocolate;

[巧令詞色] artful speech and flashy manners;

[巧妙] clever; ingenious; skilful; smart; wonderful;

巧妙手段 a clear move; an ingenious move; stratagems;

構思巧妙 be skillfully constructed;

回答巧妙 clever in reply;

[巧譬善導] skilful in illustrating profound truths;

[巧妻常伴拙夫眠] smart girls usually have dumb men for husbands;

[巧取] angle for;

巧取豪奪 by coercion and cajolery; extort by trick or by force; get by cheating or take away by force; grab and keep; grab through deceit or by force; obtain by force or deception; rap and rend; rob by force or by trick; rob by trick or by force; secure by force or by trickery; swindle and rob; take away by artful deceit or by force; take things from others by deceptive means; take way by force or trickery; through deceit or by force;

[巧舌] false words; insincere words;

巧舌如簧 glib-tongued; have a glib tongue; glib-tongued; have a ready tongue; have a reed-like, have a slick tongue; have a silver tongue; have a smooth tongue; have a voluble tongue; have an oily; mealy-mouthed; plausible tongue; smooth-tongued; talk glibly; very plausible tongue;

巧舌頭 articulate person; smart talker;

[巧事] coincidence;

[巧手] dab hand; expert; skilful person;

［巧夕］ seventh day of the seventh lunar month;
［巧笑］ artful smile; smile artfully;
［巧言］ smooth words;
巧言令色 say smooth words to sb and wear a fair face before him; sweet words and insinuating manners;
巧言聳聽 a clever talk that excites one to listen;
［巧於］ a good hand at; an expert at;
巧於運籌 play one's cards well;
巧於周旋 tackle sb with flexibility;
［巧遇］ bump into; casual meeting; chance encounter; run into;
［巧詐］ artful; ingenious fraud; tricky;
［巧者］ the able;
巧者多勞拙者閒 the able always do more work while the clumsy stay idle;
［巧宗兒］ opportunity; piece of good luck; rare chance;

不巧 as luck would have it; unfortunately;
湊巧 as luck would have it; fortunately; luckily;
趕巧 it so happened that; happen to;
剛巧 it so happened that; happen to;
工巧 exquisite; fine;
乖巧 (1) clear; ingenious; (2) cute; lovely;
技巧 skill; technique; workmanship;
精巧 exquisite; ingenious;
可巧 as luck would have it; by coincidence;
靈巧 dexterous; ingenious; nimble;
踫巧 by chance; by coincidence;
偏巧 as luck would have it; it so happened that;
恰巧 by chance; fortunately;
輕巧 (1) light and handy; (2) deft; dexterous;
取巧 resort to trickery to serve oneself;
手巧 dexterous;
討巧 choose the easy way out; try to gain advantage with little effort;
佻巧 (1) skittish and undependable; (2) (of diction) sophisticated but not serious;
細巧 exquisite; fine and delicate;
纖巧 dainty; delicate;
小巧 small and exquisite;
淫巧 lewdly sauve;
真巧 what a coincidence;
智巧 brains and tact;

qiao
【悄】 (1) in a clandestine way; quietly; secretly; (2) sadly; sorrowfully;
［悄悄］ in a clandestine way; quietly; secretly; stealthily;
悄悄到來 come quietly;
悄悄離開 slip away;
［悄然］ (1) sadly; sorrowfully; (2) quietly; softly;
悄然淚下 shed silent tears;
悄然離去 leave quietly;
悄然落淚 shed sad tears; shed silent tears; shed tears in sorrow;
悄然無聲 a perfect silence prevails;
［悄聲］ in a low voice; quietly; talk in a low voice; whisper;
［悄無人蹤］ with not a soul in sight;
［悄語］ speak softly; talk in a low voice; whisper;
悄語低言 speak in whisper;

qiao
【雀】 (1) collective name for small birds; (2) freckled;
［雀子］ freckle;

qiao
【愀】 (1) anxious-looking; doleful; sorrowful; (2) show a sudden change of expression;
［愀慘］ sorrowful;
［愀愴］ doleful; rueful; sad; sorrowful;
［愀然］ (1) sorrowful-looking; (2) grave-looking; stern;

qiao⁴
qiao
【俏】 (1) beautiful; chic; cute; elegant; good-looking; handsome; nice-looking pretty; pretty and cute; smart; winsome; (2) like; resemble; similar; (3) hot; in great demand; sell well;
［俏貨］ goods in great demand; hot commodities; in great demand; sell well;
［俏麗］ beautiful; good-looking; handsome; pretty;
［俏皮］ (1) good-looking; handsome; lively and delightful; nice-looking; smart; winsome; (2) full of charming wits; humorous; make sarcastic remarks; sarcastic; witty;
俏皮話 a clever retort; make sarcastic remarks about; quip; sarcastic

comments; sarcastic remarks; wisecrack; witticism; witty and sarcastic remarks; witty remarks;
~ 説俏皮話 jest; make witty remarks; wisecrack;
八十歲的奶奶搽粉—老俏皮 an eighty-year-old granny applying powder to her face — inappropriate behaviour;
[俏似] like; resemble;
[俏銷] in great demand; sell well;

俊俏 pretty and charming;
賣俏 flirt; play the coquette;

qiao
【峭】 (1) precipitous; sheer; steep; (2) harsh; severe; sharp; stern; strict; unkind;
[峭拔] (1) precipitous; sheer; steep; (2) (said of calligraphy) vigorous;
[峭壁] cliff; crag; sheer cliff; steep precipice;
萬丈峭壁 abysmal precipice;
[峭薄] relentless; strict; unkind;
[峭急] impatient; quick-tempered;
[峭絕] precipitous; very steep;
[峭刻] stern and exacting;
[峭立] rise steeply;
[峭厲] harsh; sharp;
[峭麗] forceful and luxuriant;
[峭直] stern; strict;

陡峭 cliffy; precipitous; steep;
高峭 high and steep;
寒峭 piercingly cold;
峻峭 high and steep;
冷峭 (1) severely cold; (2) stern; unkind and biting;
料峭 chilly;

qiao
【殼】 covering; husk; shell;

貝殼 seashell;
蛋殼 eggshell;
耳殼 auricle;
軀殼 body;
外殼 shell;

qiao
【誚】 blame; censure; reproach;
[誚呵] blame; censure; reproach;
[誚讓] blame; censure; reproach;

譏誚 deride; sneer at;

qiao
【撬】 prize out force with a level; prize up force with a level; pry; pry up;
[撬不動] incapable of prying;
[撬槓] crowbar;
[撬開] open by prying; prize open; pry open;
撬不開 incapable of prying open;
[撬孔] make a hole by prying;
[撬門] pry a door open;

qiao
【鞘】 scabbard; sheath;
[鞘翅] wing cover;
[鞘膜] tunica vaginalis;

翅鞘 elytrum;
刀鞘 scabbard; sheath;
劍鞘 scabbard;
腱鞘 tendon sheath;
神經鞘 neurilemma;
葉鞘 leaf sheath;

qiao
【竅】 (1) aperture; (2) cavity; hole; (3) key points; key to sth; knack; tricks;
[竅門] key to sth; key to success; knack; know-how; secret of success; tricks of the trade;
懂得竅門 know the ropes;
簡單竅門 simple tip;
找竅門 find better techniques; find out the secret to success; find the key to a problem; get the knack of doing sth; try to find the key to a problem;

訣竅 knack; tricks of the trade;
開竅 be enlightened;
七竅 seven apertures in the human head;
通竅 be sensible or reasonable; understand things;
心竅 capacity for clear thinking;

qiao
【翹】 hold up; project upward; stick up; turn upward;
[翹翹板] seesaw;

qiao
【譙】 blame; scold;

qie¹
qie

【切】 (1) carve; chop; cut; mince; sever; slice; (2) tangent;

[切變] shear;

[切布機] rag chopper; rag cutter;

[切菜] cut vegetables;

切菜板 chopping board;

[切除] abscission; cut off; excise; resection; sever;

切除腦瘤 remove a brain tumour;

肺切除 pneumonectomy;

甲狀腺切除 thyroidectomy;

局部切除 local excision;

闌尾切除 appendectomy;

脾切除 splenectomy;

乳房切除 mastectomy;

胃切除 gastrectomy;

子宮切除 hysterectomy; uterectomy;

[切磋] compare notes; learn from each other by exchanging views; learn from each other through discussion;

切磋技術 exchange technology;

切磋琢磨 as knife and file make smooth the bone, so jade is wrought by chisel and stone; compare notes; cut, carve, grind, as one does a piece of jade or ivory; cut and polish until it is worthy; earnest remonstrance produces good result; learn from each other by exchanging views; lucubration; study and learn by mutual discussion; study carefully and learn by mutual discussion; weigh and consider;

磋切求善 correct, seeking for perfection;

如切如磋 learn from each other;

~ 如切如磋，如琢如磨 as knife and file make smooth the bone, so jade is wrought by chisel and stone – help each other in study;

[切點] point of contact; point of tangency; tangency point;

[切丁] cut into cubes; cut into dice;

[切斷] break; cut; cut asunder; cut off; disconnect; key off; key out; sever; shut off; switch off; turn out;

切斷電流 turn off the current;

切斷交通 sever communication lines;

切斷援助 pull the plug;

間歇切斷 intermittent disconnection;

自動切斷 automatic disconnection;

[切割] cut; cutting;

橫向切割 across cutting;

砂輪切割 abrasive cutting;

碳弧切割 carbon arc cutting;

斜邊切割 bevel cutting;

氧熔切割 chemical flux cutting;

[切角] angle of contact; tangential angel;

[切距] length of tangent;

~ 次切距 subtangent

[切開] (1) cut apart; cut open; (2) incision;

膿腫切開 incision of abscess;

尿道切開 urethrotomy;

[切塊] chop into slices; cut into pieces;

[切面] (1) section; (2) tangent plane;

[切麵] cut noodles;

[切片] (1) cut into slices; slice; (2) section;

切片機 slicer;

~ 麵包切片機 bread slicer;

~ 牛肉乾切片機 dried beef slicer;

~ 圓盤切片機 disc slicer;

[切肉] cut the meat;

切肉叉 carving fork;

切肉刀 carving knife; cleaver; meat knife;

冷切肉 cold cuts;

[切入] cut in;

切入點 entry point;

切入籃 lay-up shot;

[切身] one's own;

切身利益 one's immediate interests;

[切絲] cut into shreds; shred;

切絲機 shredder;

~ 捲心菜切絲機 cabbage shredder;

~ 蔬菜切絲機 shredder;

[切碎] cut up;

切碎機 shredder;

~ 塊根切碎機 root shredder;

~ 盤式切碎機 disc shredder;

~ 青飼切碎機 forage shredder;

~ 藤蔓切碎機 vine shredder;

把肉切碎 cut up the meat;

[切線] tangent; tangent line;

二重切線 double tangent;

公切線 common tangent;

拐切線 inflectional tangent;

[切向力] tangential force;

[切削] cutting;

切削能力 cutting ability;

[切絃] chord of contact;

[切圓] tangent circles;

［切紙］ paper-cutting;
切紙刀 paper-cutting knife;
切紙機 paper-cutting machine;

割切 cut off; sever;
剪切 shear; shearing;
懇切 earnest; sincere;
密切 (1) close; intimate; (2) carefully; closely intently;
內切 inscribe;
外切 circumscribe;
餘切 cotangent;
正切 tangent;

qie²
qie
【伽】
［伽藍］ (1) Buddhist temple; (2) Buddhist deity;
［伽羅］ eagle wood;

qie
【茄】 aubergine; eggplant;
［茄袋］ eggplant-plant-shaped bag;
［茄汁］ tomato juice;
［茄子］ aubergine; bringal; eggplant;
茄子開黃花—縱（種）壞了 an eggplant budding with yellow flowers – spoiled;

顛茄 belladonna;
番茄 tomato;

qie³
qie
【且】 (1) further; moreover; still; (2) for the time being; just; (3) for a long time to come; (4) even; (5) as well as; both...and;
［且不］ not for the time being; not going to;
［且慢］ hold it; wait a moment;
［且…且…］ as; while;
且戰且退 carry on the fight while beating a retreat; fight and retire alternately; fight while falling back; fly and fight by turns; retire, fighting at intervals; retreat, stopping at intervals to fight;
［且說］ let us now talk about;
且不說 let alone; not to mention; to say nothing of;
且走且說 chat while walking;
［且住］ hold it; stop it;

並且 and; not only...but also;
而且 (1) and; (2) what is more ;
苟且 (1) drill along; (2) carelessly; (3) illicit; perfunctorily;
姑且 for the moment; might as well;
況且 besides; in addition; moreover;
權且 for the mean time;
尚且 even;
暫且 for the moment; for the time being;

qie⁴
qie
【切】 (1) close to; correspond to; (2) anxious; eager; (3) be sure to; (4) gnash; grind;
［切齒］ gnash one's teeth; grind the teeth in anger; grit one's teeth;
切齒腐心 gnash one's teeth in hatred; hate with all one's soul; in deep hatred and anger;
切齒忍受 grin and bear it;
切齒痛恨 gnash one's teeth in hatred; grind one's teeth in a spurt of hatred; hate bitterly; hate with gnashing teeth; hate with particular venom; have a bitter hatred for; strong indignation;
切齒之仇 bitter hatred that makes one gnash the teeth;
切齒之恨 extreme hatred; grinding hatred;
切齒咒罵 curse with clenched teeth; grind one's teeth and heap curses on;
怒目切齒 intense hatred;
痛心切齒 gnash one's teeth with anger; make sb burn with anger;
［切當］ apposite; appropriate; apt; fitting; proper; suitable; to the point;
［切膚］ keenly felt; very close to oneself;
切膚之痛 acute pain; bitter experience; deep sorrow; keenly felt pain; piercing sorrow; sharp pain; sorrow which cuts to the quick; the pain which one has personally experienced;
［切骨］ bitter; deep; in bitter hatred of; intense; strongly felt;
切骨痛恨 hate like poison; hate with particular venom;
切骨之仇 hate to the very marrow of one's bones;
［切合］ correspond with; fit in with; suit;

切合情況 suit the circumstances;
切合實際 accurately reflect actual conditions;
切合需要 fit in with the needs;

[切忌] avoid by all means; forbid; must guard against; sure to avoid;
切忌生冷 cold and raw food strictly forbidden;

切記] always remember; be sure to keep in mind; be sure to remember; bear in mind; must always remember;

[切近] close; close to; closely related; near; similar;

[切口] (1) incision; (2) cant; professional jargon;

[切脈] feel a patient's pulse;

[切莫] by no means; not on any account; on no account;
切莫見怪 do not take it ill;

[切切] (1) absolutely sure to; important; urgent; (2) pathetic; pathetic sounds; (3) soft sounds;
切切不可等閒視之 it is most important that this struggle should not be taken lightly;
切切此令 this order is to be strictly observed;
切切實實 (1) conscientiously; down-to-earth; earnest; (2) certain; real; sure; (3) strictly; thoroughly;
切切私語 private talk in low voice; talk in whispers;
切切絮語 engage in a low-keyed continuous talk;

[切身] (1) directly affect a person; of immediate concern to oneself; (2) first-hand; one's own; personal;
切身感受 personal impressions and experience;
切身利益 one's immediate interests; one's vital interests;
切身體會 direct experience; first-hand experience; have intimate experience of; intimate experience; intimate knowledge; keenly aware of; one's own experience; personal understanding;
切身之痛 sorrow which hits close at home; the pain of cutting one's body;

[切實] (1) feasible; practical; realistic; (2) conscientiously; earnest;
切實可行 effective; feasible; perfectly feasible; practicable; practical; realistic; workable;
切實有力 effective;
切實有效 down-to-earth and effective; practical and effective;
不切實 not sound feasible;

[切題] keep to the point; pertinent to the subject; relevant to the subject; stick to the topic; to the point;
不切題 beside the mark; irrelevant to the subject; off the point;

[切望] on tiptoe;

[切勿] be sure not to; do not by any means;
切勿倒置 don't turn over;
切勿兒戲 do not childishly make sport of it;
切勿擠壓 don't crush;
切勿見怪 don't take it ill; you must not take it ill;
切勿受潮 keep dry;

[切要] essential; indispensable; of vital importance; very important;

[切中] hit the mark;
切中時弊 cut into the presentday evils;
切中要害 hit home; hit the mark; hit the nail on the head; strike home;

哀切 sad and wretched;
悲切 mournful;
操切 hasty; rash;
關切 be deeply concerned; show one's concern over;
激切 impassioned; vehement;
急切 (1) eager; impatient; (2) in a hurry; in haste;
剴切 (1) true and pertinent; (2) earnest and sincere;
懇切 earnest; sincere;
密切 (1) close; intimate; (2) build close ties, relations, etc.; carefully; intently;
迫切 pressing; urgent;
悽切 grievous; sorrowful;
淒切 mournful; plaintive;
親切 cordial; feel attached to; kind;
清切 (1) sad; sorrowful; (2) rigorous; strict;
確切 definite; precise;
熱切 ardent; fervent; warm and cordial;
深切 deep; profound;
貼切 (of words) apt; proper;
痛切 most sorrowfully; with intense sorrow;

心切 anxious; eager;
一切 all; every; everything;
殷切 ardent; eager;
真切 clear; distinct; vivid;
診切 examine one's pulse;
諄切 sincerely and warmly;

qie
【妾】 (1) concubine; hetaera; lover; mistress; (2) polite term used by a wife when referring herself to her husband;
［妾婦］ (1) a concubine referring to herself; (2) common person; inferior person;

愛妾 one's beloved concubine;

qie
【怯】 (1) coward; lacking in courage; (2) afraid; fear; fright; nervous; timid;
［怯場］ have stage fright; stage fright;
一陣怯場 an attack of stage fright;
［怯夫］ coward;
［怯官］ official fright;
［怯懼］ fear; nervous out of fear;
［怯口］ rustic accent;
［怯懦］ cowardly; timid; timid and overcautious;
［怯弱］ timid and cowardly; timid and weak-willed;
［怯上］ superior fright;
［怯生］ shy with strangers;
［怯疑］ timid and vacillating;
怯而多疑 timid and suspicious;
［怯陣］ (1) battle-shy; (2) stage fright;
［怯症］ (1) impotent; (2) fear and nervousness caused by poor health;

脆怯 cowardly; timid; weak;
膽怯 cowardly; have cold feet; timid;
露怯 display one's ignorance;
羞怯 shy; timid;

qie
【契】 (1) carve; (2) be separated from;
［契闊］ be separated from one another;
契闊之情 remembrance during the time when friends are separated from each other;

qie
【挈】 (1) assist; guide; help; lead; (2) raise; rise above;
［挈帶］ (1) carry; take along; (2) guide; lead;
［挈眷］ travel with one's dependents;
［挈領］ make a summary; make a synopsis; present the main points;
［挈挈］ urgent;

帶挈 take along;
提挈 (1) lead; take along; (2) guide and support;

qie
【愜】 cheerful; contented; gratified; pleased; satisfied;
［愜當］ appropriate; proper;
［愜懷］ contented; satisfied;
［愜心］ contented; pleased; satisfied; satisfactory;
［愜意］ contented; gratified; pleased; satisfied;

qie
【慊】 contented; gratified; pleased; satisfied;

qie
【朅】 depart; go; leave;

qie
【篋】 box; chest; trunk;
［篋篋］ long and thin; slender;
［篋衍］ bamboo box;

藤篋 wicker suitcase;
行篋 travelling suitcase;

qie
【踥】 in motion; walk;
［踥蹀］ in motion; walking;
［踥踥］ moving back and forth;

qie
【鍥】 carve; engrave;
［鍥薄］ merciless; pitiless; unsympathetic;

qie
【竊】 (1) burglarize; pilfer; steal; (2) robber; thief; (3) furtively; secretly; (4) usurp; (5) I;
［竊案］ burglary; theft case;
一起竊案 a burglary;
［竊柄］ usurp the power of the state;
［竊盜］ theft;
竊盜狂 kleptomania;
竊盜罪 larceny; theft;
［竊犯］ burglar; thief;

Q

[竊鉤者誅，竊國者侯] he who steals a hook is killed as a crook; he who steals another's kindom is made a duke; little thieves are hanged, but great ones escape;
[竊國] usurp state power;
竊國大盜 arch usurper of state power;
[竊號] usurp the name of the emperor;
竊號僭稱 usurp imperial titles and arrogate to oneself another rank;
[竊據] be entrenched in; entrench; seize; unjustly occupy; usurp;
竊據要津 craftily seize key posts; usurp important posts;
[竊看] look at sth stealthily; peep;
[竊窺] peep; steal a glance; watch stealthily;
[竊竊] (1) in a low voice; under one's breath; (2) assume busily and brightly;
竊竊暗笑 chuckle to oneself; laugh in one's sleeve;
竊竊交談 converse in whispers;
竊竊私議 comment on sth in whispers; confidential conversation; discuss sth in secret; discuss the matter privately in low tones; exchange views in private; exchange whispered comments; in a subdued voice; in a whisper; murmur secretly; mutter to each other; talk about sth in private;
竊竊私語 murmurous; speak to another in private in a whisper; talk in a low voice secretly; talk in whispers; talk stealthily; the muffled sounds of a conversation; whisper;
[竊取] grab; steal; take sth which does not lawfully belong to one; usurp;
竊取情報 steal information;
竊取人心 steal away sb's heart;
竊取榮譽 take credit where none is due;
竊取要職 usurp a key post;
公然竊取 take a sheet off a hedge;
[竊視] peep;
[竊思] my personal view is that;
[竊聽] bug; eavesdrop; intercept; tap; wiretap;
竊聽電話 tap a telephone wire;
竊聽器 bug device; listening device; listening-in device; tapping device; wire-tapping device;
~ 拆除竊聽器 debug;
搭線竊聽 wiretapping;
電話竊聽 wiretapping;
[竊位] occupy a powerful position without the required talent;
竊位素餐 hold a high position but do nothing for public interest;
[竊謂] I should say that;
[竊嫌] suspected burglar;
[竊笑] chuckle; laugh behind sb's back; laugh secretly; laugh up one's sleeve; snicker; titter;
[竊玉偷香] have an affair with a girl;
[竊賊] burglar; pilferer; thief;
逮捕竊賊 arrest the burglar;
汽車竊賊 car thief;
痛打竊賊 hail blows upon the thief;
珠寶竊賊 jewel thief;
追趕竊賊 take after the burglars;

盜竊 steal;
慣竊 hardened thief;
攘竊 filch; pilfer; steal;
失竊 have things stolen; suffer loss by theft;
偷竊 pilfer; steal;

qin¹
qin

【侵】 (1) aggress; attack; commit aggression against; intrude into; invade; raid; trespass; (2) encroach; in violation of; infringe upon; intrude; use force stealthily; violate; (3) approach; proceed gradually; (4) bad year; poor year; year of disaster;
[侵晨] approaching daybreak; early morning; towards dawn;
[侵奪] seize by force;
[侵犯] encroach upon; in violation of; infringe upon; intrude; molestation; violate;
侵犯版權 infringe a copyright;
侵犯國家主權 encroach upon a country's sovereignty;
侵犯領空 air aggression;
侵犯民權 infringe on civil rights;
侵犯人權 infringe upon human rights;
侵犯主權 violate the sovereignty of;
侵犯著作權 infringement of copyrights;
互不侵犯 mutual nonaggression;
突然侵犯 incursion;
[侵害] encroach on; infringe on; injure; make inroads on; violate;

[侵陵] intimidate; raid and humiliate;
[侵略] aggression; attack; commit aggression against; encroach on; invade; invasion;
侵略成性 aggressive by nature;
侵略軍 invader;
侵略戰爭 aggressive war; war of aggression;
侵略者 aggressor; invader;
侵略陣營 the aggression camp;
侵略政策 policy of aggression;
侵略主義 jingoism;
發動侵略 launch an invasion;
擊退侵略 repel an invasion;
進行侵略 commit aggression against;
經濟侵略 economic aggression; economic invasion;
局部侵略 local aggression;
商業侵略 commercial aggression;
外來侵略 external aggression;
文化侵略 cultural aggression; cultural invasion;
宗教侵略 religion invasion;
[侵權] infringement of right;
侵權人 infringer;
侵權行為 infringement of right;
[侵擾] harass; invade and harass; raid; trespass and cause disorder;
侵擾邊境 harass the frontiers;
[侵入] intrude into; invade; make incursions into; sneak in;
侵入領空 intrude into a country's territorial air space;
非法侵入 unwarranted intrusion;
武裝侵入 armed intrusions;
[侵蝕] corrode; eat into gradually; erode; erosion; weather;
侵蝕公款 embezzle public funds; help themselves to public money;
侵蝕作用 abration;
乾旱侵蝕 arid erosion;
河岸侵蝕 bank erosion;
加速侵蝕 accelerated erosion;
同時侵蝕 contemporaneous erosion;
[侵吞] (1) embezzle; misappropriate; speculate; take by illegal means; (2) annex; swallow;
侵吞公款 embezzle public funds;
侵吞稅款 embezzle tax funds;
[侵襲] hit; invade and attack; make a sneak attack on; make an intrusive attack on; make inroads on; smite;
侵襲城市 invade the city;
[侵曉] dawn; daybreak; early morning;
[侵尋] gradually; little by little;
[侵淫] gradually;
[侵越] encroach; trespass;
[侵早] early morning;
[侵佔] encroach upon; invade and occupy; occupy illegally; seize;
侵佔他人的土地 encroach upon another person's land;
非法侵佔 unlawful infringement;
逐步侵佔 encroach;

入侵 intrude; invade; make inroads;

qin
【衾】 (1) large coverlet; quilt; sheets; (2) dress for the deceased;
[衾單] (1) clothes for the deceased; (2) sheets;
[衾影無慚] a clear conscience in the still hours of the night; conscious innocence; no shame left under the shadow of the coverlet;
[衾枕] quilts and pillows;
衾冷枕寒 a cold pillow and chilly coverlet; loneliness in bed; no bedfellows; loneliness in bed;

qin
【欽】 (1) admire; adore; esteem; look up to; respect; think highly of; revere; venerate; (2) by the emperor himself; (3) a surname;
[欽差] imperial commissioner; imperial envoy;
欽差大臣 imperial commissioner; imperial envoy;
[欽遲] admire; look up to;
[欽崇] admire; adore;
[欽賜] be bestowed by the emperor; be granted by an emperor;
[欽點] be designated by the emperor;
[欽定] be authorized by an emperor;
[欽敬] admire and respect;
欽敬之忱 great admiration and respect;
[欽命] (1) by imperial orders; (2) imperial emissary;
[欽慕] admire; look up to;
[欽佩] admiration; admire; agree wholeheartedly; esteem; respect; think

highly of;
表示欽佩 show one's admiration;
令人欽佩的 admirable;
滿懷欽佩 be filled with admiration; full of admiration;
[欽仰] admire and respect; esteem; look up to; revere; venerate;

qin
【嶔】 lofty (said of mountains);
[嶔崟] precipitous;

qin
【親】 (1) parent; (2) blood relation; next of kin; (3) kinsfolk; relative; (4) marriage; match; (5) bride; (6) affectionate; beloved; close; dear; intimate; love; loving; near to; (7) in person; oneself; personally; (8) kiss;
[親愛] affectionate; beloved; dear; love; loving;
親愛的 dear; dearie; deary; lovey; luv; luvvie; my darling; my dear; my love;
~最親愛的 dearest;
親愛溫柔 affection and tenderness;
[親筆] (1) in one's own handwriting; (2) one's own handwriting;
親筆簽名 autograph; one's own signature; sign manual;
親筆題詞 write an inscription for sb;
親筆信 a letter in one's own handwriting; autograph letter;
[親兵] bodyguard;
[親裁] decide personally;
[親仇] one's friends and foes;
澤及親仇 one's charity takes in both friend and foe;
[親代] the parental generation;
[親等] degree; degree of kinship; degree of relationship;
[親丁] blood relation; close relatives;
[親夫] one's own husband;
[親父] one's own father;
[親供] confess in person; personal confession;
[親故] relatives and old friends;
[親和性] compatibility;
不親和性 incompatibility;
~單倍不親和性 haploid incompatibility;
~核質不親和性 nucleo-cytoplasmic incompatibility;
~配子不親和性 gametic incompatibility;
~染色體不親和性 chromosome incompatibility;
~細胞質不親和性 cytoplasmic incompatibility;
[親家] in-laws;
親家公 one's child's father-in-law;
親家母 one's child's mother-in-law;
[親見] have seen in person; see with one's own eyes;
[親交] (1) deliver personally; (2) intimate friendship;
[親近] close to; intimate; near and dear; near to; on intimate terms with;
親近上司 make advances towards one's superior;
[親眷] family members; one's relatives;
失親少眷 have no folk of one's own;
無親無眷 have neither kin nor relatives;
[親口] from sb's own lips; in person; personally; right from one's own mouth; say sth personally; state personally;
親口答應 make a promise personally;
[親歷] experience personally;
親歷其境 experience personally; go through the whole thing personally; on the scene in person; on the spot in person;
[親力親為] do it yourself;
[親臨] arrive personally;
親臨道賀 tender one's congratulations in person;
親臨吊唁 attend the funeral in person;
親臨督戰 come to...in personal command of military operations;
親臨其事 attend to the matter in person;
親臨指導 come personally to give guidance;
[親密] close; intimate;
親密文體 intimate level of speech;
親密無間 amicable; amity; as close as sock and boot; as thick as thieves; close; closely united; hand and glove; intimate; near and dear; on intimate terms; on very intimate terms with each other; the two are on the most intimate terms with nothing standing between them; warm mutual affection;
親密語 intimate speech;
~親密語言 intimate language;
親密戰友 a close comrade-in-arms;

過份親密 backslapping;

[親母] one's own mother;

[親迎] greet personally; welcome personally;

[親暱] affectionate; in great intimacy; intimate; very intimate;

[親娘] one's own mother;

[親朋] relatives and friends;

[親戚] kinsfolk; kinsmen; kinswomen; relatives;

親戚關係 kinship;

親戚朋友 friends and relations; kinsfolk and friends; kith and kin; relatives and friends;

皇親國戚 a kinsman of the emperor; members of the imperial house; princes and princesses of the royal family; relatives of an emperor;

男性親戚 kinsman;

女性親戚 kinswoman;

[親啟] be opened personally; confidential;

[親切] close; cordial; dear to; feel at home; feel attached to; heartily; intimate; kind; sincere; warm;

親切關懷 kind attention; kind concern; loving care;

親切見面 meet cordially;

親切交談 have a cordial talk with sb;

親切慰問 express one's sincere sympathy to sb;

親切友好 cosy; in a cordial and friendly atmosphere;

待人親切 cordial to sb;

極為親切 pretty close to home;

[親熱] affectionate; cordial; intimate; warm and affectionate; warmhearted;

表示親熱 make a display of one's affection;

[親人] (1) kinsfolk; kinsmen; one's family members; one's parents, spouse, children, etc.; relatives; (2) dear ones; sb's nearest and dearest; those dear to one;

逝去的親人 the dear departed;

[親任] one's confidants;

[親如] as close as; as dear to;

親如骨肉 as one's own flesh and blood;

親如手足 as close as brothers; as dear to each other as brothers; cozy;

親如手足，休戚相關 kindred like brothers, with our joys and sorrows interconnected;

親如兄弟 as close as brothers; dear to each other like brothers;

親如兄弟，打得火熱 treat... as dearly beloved brothers; warmly fraternize with;

親如一家 as dear to each other as members of one family; like one big family;

親如魚水 as inseparable as fish and water;

[親善] friendship; goodwill;

[親上加親] cement old ties by marriage; be doubly related; marry a person who is already one's relative; marry within the clan;

[親身] firsthand; in person; personal;

親身拜訪 a personal visit;

親身出馬 personal participation;

親身經歷 firsthand experience; personal experience;

親身體驗 firsthand experience;

[親生] one's own;

親生兒子 one's own son;

親生父母 birth parent; one's own parents;

親生父親 birth father;

親生骨肉 one's own children; one's own flesh and blood;

親生母親 birth mother;

親生子女 children of one's loins; one's own children;

[親事] (1) marriage; (2) attend to personally;

[親手] oneself; personally; with one's own hands;

親手交付 deliver sth personally;

[親疏] close or distant;

背親向疏 turn from a relative and go to a mere acquaintance;

不分親疏 regardless of relationship;

親不間疏，後不僭先 close relations come before distant ones, and old friendships before new ones; distant relatives can't come between close ones, and new friends can't take the place of old;

親一派，疏一派 warm to one grouping and cold to the other;

日遠日疏，日近日親 remoteness begets neglect, nearness bring about intimacy;

疏不間親 a merest acquaintance should not say anything to estrange sb from one who is dear to him; an

acquaintance may not sow discord among intimate friends; relatives are favoured over outsiders;
由親及疏 from close relations to mere acquaintances;

[親屬] clans; family members; kinsfolk; relatives;
親屬稱謂 kinship terminology;
親屬方言 related dialect;
親屬關係 kinship;
親屬聯繫 the kinship bond;
親屬術語 kinship term;
親屬體系 the kinship system;
親屬語言 related language;
旁系親屬 collateral relative;
直系親屬 directly-related members of one's family;
最近的親屬 next of kin;

[親嗣關係] kinship;

[親隨] aides; entourages;

[親王] prince;

[親吻] kiss;
親吻愛撫 petting;

[親狎] close and intimate;

[親賢遠小] near to worthies and keep away from mean fellows;

[親信] right-hand man; trusted associate; trusted follower; trusted supporter; close associates; confidants; cronies; intimate; one's own men; protege;
安插親信 assign faithful followers to important posts; hand out jobs to one's close associates; place henchmen in important posts; place one's supporters in key positions; place one's trusted followers in key positions; put in one's own men; put one's trusted followers in key positions;
~ 安插親信，排除異己 put in one's own men and kick out all the others; put one's trusted followers in key positions and kick out dissidents;
任用親信 cronyism;

[親眼] personally; see with one's own eyes;
親眼看見 see with one's own eyes; witness;
親眼目睹 live to see; see with one's own eyes;

[親英者] Anglophile;

[親迎] receive personally; welcome personally;

[親友] kith and kin; relatives and friends;

[親魚] parent fish;

[親緣] affinity; relationship;
親緣語義學 kinship semantics;

[親展] (1) meet in person; (2) to be opened by the addressee only;

[親長] one's elderly relatives;

[親征] lead an army personally to war;

[親政] take over the administration from a regent upon coming of age;

[親知] with real personal knowledge;

[親炙] study under sb's direct guidance;

[親子] one's own son;
親子關係 parent-child relationship;

[親自] by oneself; in person; personally;
親自拜訪 make a personal visit;
親自參加 personal participation; take part in person;
親自出馬 attend to the matter personally; come forward oneself; come out in person; come out oneself; come to the fore oneself; confront personally; go out and take care of sth in person; look into the matter personally; personal appearance; personally go to; take personal charge of the matter; take the field oneself; take up the matter oneself; troop forth in person;
親自到場 appear in person;
親自動手 act personally; do the job oneself; personally take a hand in the work; personally take an active part;
親自掛帥 take command; take the command personally;
親自過問 look into the matter personally;
親自檢查 inspect at first hand;
親自看到 see for oneself;
親自申請 apply in person;
親自指揮 take personal charge of operations;
親自致候 pay one's respects in person;

[親族] members of the same clan; one's kinsmen;

[親嘴] a smack on the lips; kiss;

表親 (1) cousin; (2) cousinship;
成親 get married;
單親 lone parent; single parent;
嫡親 blood relations; close paternal relations;
定親 become engaged;

Q

父親 father; old man; pater;
乾親 nominal kinship;
躬親 attend to personally;
和親 make peace with rulers of minority nationalities in the border areas by marriage;
結親 (1) get married; marry; (2) become related by marriage;
近親 close relatives; flesh and blood; immediate family; near relations; proximity of blood;
可親 affable;
老親 (1) old parents; (2) old relatives;
令親 your relations;
六親 one's kin; the six relations: father, mother, elder brothers, young brothers, wife, children;
母親 mater; mother;
娘親 relatives on the maternal side;
內親 relative on one's wife's side; in-law;
攀親 claim kinsehip; profess to be sb else's relation;
搶親 kidnap a woman and marry her;
求親 seek a marriage alliance;
娶親 get married; take a wife; tie the knot; wive;
認親 acknowledge relationship;
舍親 my relative;
事親 treat one's parents;
雙親 father and mother; parents;
説親 act as match-maker;
思親 think of one's relatives, especially parents;
送親 accompany bride to bridgegroom's family on wedding day;
探親 go home to visit one's family or go to visit one's relatives;
討親 take a wife;
提親 bring up proposal of marriage; matchmaking; propose a marriage;
投親 go and live with relatives; seek refuge with relatives;
退親 break off an engagement;
顯親 (1) glorify one's parents; (2) powerful relatives;
相親 size up a perspective spouse;
鄉親 (1) fellow villager or townsman; (2) local people; villagers;
省親 pay a visit to one's parents or elders;
血親 blood relation; blood relatives; consanguinity;
嚴親 father;
養親 support and serve parents;
議親 negotiate a marriage;
懿親 close relatives;
姻親 relation by marriage;
迎親 go to the bride's home to escort her back to wedding;
娛親 please one's parents;
冤親 one's enemies and relatives;
遠親 distant relative; remote kinsfolk;
擇親 make marriage arrangements for one's children;
長親 elder relatives;
招親 (1) have the bridegroom move into one's house after the marriage; (2) marry into and live with one's bride's family;
至親 one's close kin; one's close kinsman; one's very close relative;
周親 closest relatives;
宗親 (1) clan relatives; members of the same clan; (2) brothers by the same mother;
尊親 elders; relatives of a senior generation;
做親 become relatives by marriage;

qin

【駸】 galloping; speeding;
［駸駸］ (1) at full gallop; (2) fast; swiftly;

qin²

qin

【芹】 celery;
［芹菜］ celery;
根芹菜 celeriac;
西芹菜 parsley;
一根芹菜 a stick of celery;

qin

【芩】 phragmites japonica, a kind of medicinal herb;

黃芩 root of large-flowered skullcap;

qin

【秦】 (1) state of Qin (879-221 B.C.); (2) Qin Dynasty (221-207 B.C.); (3) a name for Shaanxi; (4) ancient name of China; (5) a surname;
［秦椒］ pepper;
［秦晉］ alliance between two families by marriage;
秦晉之好 a lifelong alliance by marriage; an alliance between the two families by marriage;
~結秦晉之好 marriage between two families; united in matrimony;
永結秦晉 ensure perpetual alliance between two families by a marriage;

［秦鏡］ judge;
秦鏡高懸 perspicacious decisions in deciding criminal cases;
明如秦鏡 sober as a judge;
［秦樓楚館］ brothels; disreputable quarters of the city; public houses of joy;

qin
【琴】 (1) lute; lyre; (2) musical instrument; (3) a surname;
［琴凳］ music stool;
［琴鍵］ keys of a musical instrument;
［琴鳥］ lyrebird;
［琴譜］ musical score;
［琴棋書畫］ lyre-playing, chess, calligraphy and painting;
［琴瑟］ married couple;
琴瑟不調 a marriage on the rocks; discord between husband and wife;
琴瑟和鳴 conjugal bliss; conjugal felicity; marital harmony;
琴瑟失調 discord between husband and wife; family jars; marital discord;
琴瑟調和 a happy married life; conjugal harmony;
［琴師］ accompanist; music master;
［琴手］ player of a stringed instrument;
［琴絃］ string;
［琴心］ emotional appeal through lute playing;
琴心劍膽 have the soul of a musician and the courage of a warrior;
［琴竹］ mallet;

八弦琴 octachord;
風鳴琴 aeolian harp; aeolian lyre; wind harp;
風琴 organ;
鋼琴 piano;
古琴 guqin, a seven-stringed plucked instrument;
管風琴 organ; pipe organ;
口琴 harmonica;
木琴 xylophone;
手風琴 accordion;
豎琴 harp;
提琴 violin family;
揚琴 dulcimer;
鐘琴 carillon;

qin
【覃】 a surname;

qin
【勤】 (1) assiduous; diligent; hardworking; industrious; sedulous; (2) constant; frequently; often; regularly; (3) attendance; duty;
［勤備］ assiduous; diligent; hardworking; industrious;
［勤惰］ activity and inactivity; diligence and negligence;
［勤奮］ assiduous; diligent; hardworking; industrious;
勤奮苦讀 plod at one's books;
勤奮為成功之母 diligence is the parent of success;
勤奮研究 diligent in one's studies;
工作勤奮 diligent in one's work;
學習勤奮 diligent in one's studies; show application in one's studies;
［勤工］ work hard;
勤工儉學 part-work and part-study system; work-study programme;
勤工助學 hard work to support study; take a part-time job while studying at college;
［勤儉］ diligent and frugal; hardworking and thrifty; industrious and thrifty;
勤儉持家 diligent and frugal in managing a household; diligent and thrifty in running the household; industrious and thrifty in running one's home; industry and thrifty in managing households; manage the household industriously and thriftily; run one's household with industry and frugality;
勤儉建國 build the country industriously and thriftly; build the country through diligence and thrift; build the country with industry and frugality; carry on national construction through hard work and thrift; establish a country through thrift and hardwork;
勤儉節約 diligent and thrifty; industrious and economical;
勤儉耐勞 diligent, frugal and able to endure hardship;
勤儉樸素 industry, thrift and frugality;
勤儉起家 build up a family by hard work and thrift; build up the family's fortune with might and main; grow rich by dint of industry and thrifty; grow rich out of diligence and frugality; rise up through industry and frugality;
崇尚勤儉 advocate industry and thrift;

uphold hardworking and thrift;
克勤克儉 both industrious and thrifty; diligent and economical; hardworking and thrifty; industrious and frugal; practise economy and diligence; save and be economical;

[勤謹] diligent and prudent; dutiful and industrious;

[勤懇] diligent and conscientious; earnestly and assiduously; industrious and honest; painstakingly;
勤懇工作 painstaking with one's work;
勤勤懇懇 diligent and conscientious; diligently and conscientiously; earnest and assiduous; help the local cadres wholeheartedly painstakingly; painstakingly; zealously and earnestly;
~ 勤勤懇懇，埋頭苦幹 diligent and hardworking;
~ 勤勤懇懇，一絲不苟 work diligently and conscientiously and with the greatest care;

[勤苦] work sedulously in defiance of hardships;

[勤快] diligent; diligent and efficient; eager beaver; hardworking; industrious;

[勤懶] hardworking and lazy;
勤吃懶做 eat one's head off but be lazy at work;

[勤勞] diligent; hardworking; industrious; labour sedulously; toil sedulously;
勤勞不虞匱乏 if one is industrious, one will not be short of supplies; industry will keep you from want; poverty is a stranger to industry;
勤勞度日 live by the sweat of one's brow;
勤勞勇敢 diligent and courageous; industrious and brave; industry and courage; valiant and industrious;
勤勞致富 achieve prosperity through hard work; become better off through diligent work; prosper through hard labour;

[勤力] diligent; hardworking; industrious;

[勤勉] assiduous; diligent; earnest and diligent; hardworking; industrious; sedulous;
勤勉好學 diligent and eager to learn;

[勤民] attend to pople's welfare diligently;

[勤能補拙] diligence is the means by which one makes up for one's dullness; make up by diligence for one's want of intelligence; make up for lack of natural talent by hardwork; stupidity can be remedied by diligence; through hard work one can make up for lack of natural talent;

[勤樸] hardworking and thrifty; industrious and frugal;

[勤王] dutiful to the throne;

[勤務] (1) duty; service; (2) fatigue duty;
勤務表 rota;
勤務兵 batman; orderly;
勤務員 orderly; servant;

[勤學] study diligently;
勤學成材 diligent in study and become a man of ability;
勤學苦練 diligent study and practice; study and practise hard; study diligently and train oneself the hard way; study hard and practise painstakingly;

[勤以補拙] make up by diligence for one's want of ability; make up for lack of natural talent by hard work; make up for lack of skill with industry;

[勤於不匱] if one is industrious, one will not be short of supplies;

[勤雜] odd job;
勤雜工 cleaner; dogsbody; gofer; odd-jobber; orderly; service worker;
勤雜活 odd job;
勤雜員 odd-job man; orderly;

[勤政] assiduous in government affairs;

出勤 (1) turn out for work; (2) out on duty;
地勤 ground service;
後勤 logistics; rear service;
考勤 check on work attendance;
空勤 air duty;
內勤 (1) internal or office work; (2) office staff;
缺勤 absent from duty;
手勤 diligent;
外勤 (1) work done outside the office or in the field; (2) field personnel;
辛勤 hardworking; industrious;
夜勤 night duty;
殷勤 eagerly attentive; solicitous;
戰勤 civilian war service;
值勤 be on duty;
執勤 be on duty;

qin

【禽】 birds; fowls; poultry;

［禽場］ poultry farm;

［禽荒］ obsessed with hunting;

［禽獵］ hunt;

［禽類］ bird;

岸禽類 shore bird;

步禽類 walking bird;

走禽類 cursorial birds;

［禽流感］ bird flu;

［禽苗］ poultry chicks;

［禽鳥］ birds; fowls;

［禽獸］ birds and beasts;

禽獸不如 worse than a beast;

禽獸行為 bestial acts; beastliness; brutish acts;

禽有禽言，獸有獸語 birds have bird language and animals have animal talk;

行同禽獸 act like beasts;

衣冠禽獸 a beast in human clothing;

飛禽 aerial creatures; birds;

活禽 live fowl;

家禽 domestic bird; domestic fowl; poultry;

猛禽 bird of prey; raptorial bird;

鳴禽 singing bird; song bird; warbler;

涉禽 wader; wading bird;

水禽 aquatic bird; water bird; waterfowl;

仙禽 crane;

游禽 natatorial bird; swimming bird;

珍禽 rare bird;

走禽 cursorial bird; running bird;

qin

【擒】 arrest; capture; catch; seize;

［擒捕］ arrest; capture; catch; seize;

［擒獲］ arrest; capture;

［擒奸］ capture evildoers;

擒奸討暴 capture troublemakers and fight evil-forces;

擒奸擿伏 arrest and expose evildoers;

［擒拿］ arrest; capture; catch; seize;

擒拿術 arrest technique;

［擒賊］ catch a thief;

擒賊擒王 capturing the ringleader first in order;

~ 擒賊擒王，群龍無首 the rebels will be helpless after their chief is captured;

~ 擒賊先擒王 capture the ringleader first in order to capture all his followers; in capturing thieves, the first thing to do is to capture their chief; stop the trouble at its source; to battle against rebels one must first seize their leader; to catch a gang, first catch its leader; to round up bandits, catch their ringleader first; when capturing bandits, first catch the leader;

以賊擒賊 set a thief to catch a thief;

［擒斬］ capture and behead;

［擒住］ succeed in capturing;

［擒捉］ arrest; capture; catch;

［擒縱］ arresting and releasing;

擒縱自如 arrest and release at will — in perfect control of a situation;

就擒 be caught;

生擒 capture alive;

qin

【蠓】 a kind of small cicada;

［蠓首蛾眉］ a cicada's head and a moth's eyebrows — the look of a pretty lady;

qin

【懃】 cordial; hearty;

［懃懃懇懇］ cordial and sincere;

qin

【檎】 small red apple;

林檎 Chinese pear-leaved crabapple;

qin³

qin

【寢】 (1) sleep; (2) bedroom; (3) coffin chamber; tomb; (4) end; stop;

［寢兵］ stop fighting; stop wars;

［寢車］ sleeper; sleeping carriage;

［寢戈］ use weapons as pillows;

［寢宮］ emperor's resting place; imperial burial place; masoleum;

［寢疾］ be confined to bed by illness;

［寢具］ bedding;

［寢陋］ ugly;

［寢寐］ sleep;

寢寐不安 lie awake with sth on one's mind and worried;

寢寐難安 restless sleep;

［寢門］ the back door to sleeping quarters;

［寢廟］ a temple to the deceased;

［寢食］ sleeping and eating;

寢食不安 be worried by things on one's mind; feel uneasy even when eating and sleeping; have no peace of mind day and night; restless due to deep worries; unable to sleep and eat in peace; unable to sleep or eat quietly; uneasy when eating and sleeping;
寢食俱廢 neglect one's sleep and meal; not care to sleep and eat; skip meals and sleep; wanting neither food nor sleep because of deep worries;
寢食難忘 constantly in one's mind;
不思寢食 have no desire to eat or sleep;

[寢室] bedroom; chamber; dormitory;
[寢衣] bedclothes; sleeping gown;

安寢 be asleep;
就寢 go to bed; retire for the night;
陵寢 emperor's or king's resting place; mausoleum;
晝寢 take a nap;

qin[4]

qin

【沁】 exude; ooze; percolate; permeate; seep; seep into; soak; soak into; soak through;

[沁人心脾] affect people deeply; exhilarating; gladden people's hearts; gladdening the heart and refreshing the mind; gratifying; mentally refreshing; refreshing the mind; touch one's heart;
[沁入] permeate; soak into; soak through;
沁入肺腑 refreshing;
[沁透] infiltrate; penetrate; percolate; permeate; seep in;

qin

【撳】 press down; press with the hand; push; push down;

[撳扣] snap; stud;
[撳鈴] push a bell;
[撳壓] press down; push down;

qing[1]

qing

【青】 (1) blue; green; (2) black; (3) green grass; (4) young crops; not ripe; (5) young; youthful; (6) skin of bamboo; (7) bruise; (8) a surname;

[青幫] secret society in Qing China;
[青不曦的] (1) blue; (2) green;
[青菜] (1) green vegetables; greens; (2) Chinese cabbage;
[青草] grass; green grass;
[青出於藍] indigo comes from the indigo plant yet excels it in colour; surpass one's master in learning; surpass one's teacher in learning; the pupil learns from and excels his teacher; the pupil outdoes his teacher; the pupil outshines the teacher; the pupil surpasses the master;
青出於藍而勝於藍 green comes from blue but it excels blue; have excelled one's masters; know better than one's teacher; progress beyond the ability of one's teacher; successors excel the predecessor; the black dye succeeds the blue and is superior to it; the indigo blue is extracted from the indigo plant, but is bluer than the plant it comes from; the pupil learns from and outdoes his teacher; the scholar may be better than the master; the younger generation outdoes the older generation;

[青春] (1) young adulthood; youth; youthfulness; (2) age;
青春不再 gather roses while ye may; one will never be young again; one's youth never returns;
青春痘 acne;
青春煥發 full of vigour; bursting with youthful energy;
青春活力 vitality; young blood; youthful vigour;
~保持青春活力 retain youthful vitality;
青春年少 in one's very first youth;
青春期 adolescence; puberty; teens; the mark of mouth;
~青春期年齡 age of puberty;
~青春期心理 psychology of the adolescent;
青春期心理衛生 psychological hygience of the adolescent;
~到達青春期 reach the age of adolescence;
青春腺 reproductive glands;
青春虛度 waste the springtide of one's life;
青春一族 teen species;

青春依舊 keep one's youth;
青春之歌 the song of youth;
保持青春 keep one's youth;
浪費青春 waste one's youth;
虛度的青春 misspent youth;
永保青春 always keep one's spirit young; always retain one's youthful vitality; keep alive the fervour of youth; remain youthful forever; retain one's youthful vigour;
珍惜青春 retain youth;

[青瓷] celadon ware;

[青蔥] dark green; fresh green; green and thick; verdant;

[青翠] fresh and green; verdant; verdurous;
青翠欲滴 green and luxuriant;

[青燈] oil lamp;
青燈古佛 an oil lamp before the statue of Buddha;
青燈黃卷 green light and yellow volume — study at night;

[青豆] green bean; green pea; green soya bean;
青豆色 pea green;

[青娥] young girls;

[青梗菜] Chinese greens;

[青光眼] glaucoma;
青光眼斑 glaukomflecken;
青光眼盲 glaucosis;
青光眼評估 glaucoma assessment;
青光眼性白內障 glaucomatous cataract;
青光眼暈 glaucomatous halo;
充血性青光眼 congestive glaucoma;
出血性青光眼 hemorrhagic glaucoma;
創傷性青光眼 traumatic glaucoma;
單純性青光眼 simple glaucoma;
惡性青光眼 malignant glaucoma;
繼發性青光眼 secondary glaucoma;
慢性青光眼 chronic glaucoma;
囊性青光眼 capsular glaucoma;
青少年型青光眼 juvenile glaucoma;
溶血性青光眼 hemolytic glaucoma;
外傷性青光眼 traumatic glaucoma;
炎性青光眼 inflammatory glaucoma;
嬰兒性青光眼 infantile glaucoma;
原發性青光眼 primary glaucoma;
甾體性青光眼 steroid glaucoma;
卒中性青光眼 apoplectic glaucoma;
阻塞性青光眼 obstructive glaucoma;

[青果] (1) Chinese olive; (2) fresh fruits;

[青紅] blue and red;
青紅不分，皂白莫辨 confound right and wrong; without distinguishing blue from red or black from white; without thinking or waiting to distinguish black and white;
青紅皂白 distinction between black and white, right and wrong;
~不分青紅皂白 indiscriminately; make no distinction between black and white; not to distinguish right and wrong;

[青花瓷] blue and white porcelain;

[青黃] the green and the yellow;
青黃不接 a temporary shortage of one thing or another; an interim period of shortage of grain between harvests; at the end of spring and the beginning of summer; before the green corn grows and after the white crop is consumed; gap; gap in succession; in temporary financial difficulty; resources are lacking to tide over the difficult times; shortage of food before the new harvest; temporary shortage; the gap between two harvests; the granary is nearly empty but the new crop is not yet ripe; the shortage of successors; the transition from one to another; when the crop is still in the blade and the old stock is consumed;
臉一陣青，一陣黃 one's face becomes the colour of a green pumpkin, and then turns yellow;

[青灰] bluish gray;

[青簡] book;

[青椒] green pepper;

[青筋] blue veins;

[青酒紅人面，財帛動人心] good wine reddens one's face, while riches stir one's heart;

[青稞] highland barley;

[青睞] favours; good graces; high regard; preferences;

[青欖] olive;

[青驪] black horse; dark horse;

[青蓮色] lavender; pale purple;

[青料] green fodder;

[青鱗魚] herring;

[青樓] (1) brothel; (2) abode of a beauty;

[青綠] dark green;
青綠色 blue green;

青綠山水 blue-and-green landscape painting;

[青梅] green plums; unripened plums;

青梅竹馬 childhood sweethearts; innocent playmates riding on a bamboo stick for a horse; the childhood of a boy and a girl grown up together;

[青霉素] penicillin;

[青苗] rice seedlings;

[青囊] medical practice;

[青年] young man; young people; young person; youth; youthful people;

青年才俊 boy wonder;

青年隊 youth team;

青年節 Youth Day;

青年男女 youth of both sexes;

青年期 adolescence; puberty;

青年人 young people;

青年社會學 youth sociology;

青年心理學 psychology of adolescence;

青年學 study of youth;

青年一代 younger generation;

大齡青年 adult single; unmarried youth above the normal age for marriage;

[青女素娥] green maid and white beauty — frost and moon;

[青萍] green duckweeds;

[青錢] copper coin;

青錢萬選 a remarkable talent; like a copper coin selected out of ten thousand — a piece of beautiful writing;

[青青] blue; green;

[青色] blue;

藏青色 navy blue;

[青山] green hills;

青山碧湖 the clear lake at the foot of the green mountain;

青山不老，綠水長存 the green mountains never grow old and the blue waters flow on forever;

青山疊嶂 green hills roll on in undulating waves;

青山綠水 blue hills and green streams; green hills and blue waters; green mountains and rivers;

青山夕照 the green mountains bathed in sunset glory;

青山煙雨 the green hills are enshrouded in mist and rain;

留得青山在，不愁沒柴燒 as long as the green hills last, there'll always be wood to burn; as long as the green mountains are there, one need not worry about firewood; better the fruit lose than the tree; while there is life there is hope;

眉似青山 her eyebrows are curved like the graceful contours of distant hills; one's brows are arched like lines of distant hills;

[青史] annals of history;

青史留名 be crowned with eternal glory; go down in history; have a niche in history; leave a name in history; leave one's name to posterity;

功標青史 cause one's fame to glow in the pages of history;

名標青史 make a name in history; one's name is handed down in history; stamp one's name on the page of history; vindicate oneself a permanent place in history;

永垂青史 go down in the annals of history;

[青絲] black hair;

[青松] pine;

青松傲雪 the evergreen pine stands straight and unbending in high wind and heavy snow;

青松翠竹 green pines and bamboos of tender green; green pines and verdant bamboos; tall pines of a dark bluish-green contrasting with the light halcyon green of bamboo;

[青苔] green moss; moss;

一層青苔 a cushion of moss;

[青天] (1) the blue sky; (2) incorruptible and wise judge; just judge; upright official;

青天白日 blue sky and bright sun; broad daylight; fine day;

青天霹靂 a bolt from the blue; a thunder clap from a blue sky; an unexpected and sudden change; as a thunderbolt from the unclouded sky;

碧海青天 a blue ocean under a blue sky;

[青銅] bronze;

青銅奔馬 bronze galloping horse;

青銅器 bronzeware;

~青銅器時代 Bronze Age;

超級青銅 super bronze;

齒輪青銅 gear bronze;

低鉛錫青銅 leaded tin bronze;
雕像青銅 statuary bronze;
鋼青銅 steel bronze;
高鉛青銅 high-lead bronze;
高錫青銅 high-tin bronze;
鎘青銅 cadmium bronze;
海軍青銅 naval bronze;
貨幣青銅 coinage bronze;
機用青銅 machinery bronze;
減摩青銅 journal bronze;
金青銅 gold bronze;
抗酸青銅 antiacid bronze;
鋰青銅 lithium bronze;
磷青銅 phosphor bronze;
耐蝕青銅 Hercules bronze;
炮管青銅 gun bronze;
鈹青銅 beryllium bronze; glucinfum bronze;
熱壓青銅 hot-pressed bronze;
軟青銅 soft bronze;
石墨青銅 graphite bronze;
鈦青銅 titan bronze;
鉭鋁青銅 tantalum bronze;
碳青銅 carbon bronze;
鐵青銅 iron bronze;
鎢青銅 tungsten bronzes;
鑲飾青銅 sheathing bronze;
硬青銅 hard bronze;
針青銅 needle bronze;
蒸氣閥青銅 steam valve bronze;
鐘青銅 bell bronze;
鑄造青銅 cast bronze;
裝飾青銅 jewelry bronze;

[青蛙] common pond frog; frog;
青蛙呱呱 frogs croak;
青蛙説話一嘴呱呱 frogs talking — croaking mouths; empty talk;
一隻青蛙 a frog;

[青瓦] gray tile;

[青蝦] freshwater shrimp;

[青霄] azure sky; blue sky;

[青杏] green apricot;

[青煙] light smoke;
一縷青煙 a cloud of blue vapour; a curl of smoke; a light smoke;

[青眼] favours; good graces; high regard; looks of favour; preferences;

[青陽] springtime;

[青魚] black carp; mackerel;

[青雲] (1) high official position; (2) retirement; (3) sky;
青雲之志 great ambitions; have high ambitions; high and noble ambitions; the ambition of soaring up to the blue sky;
青雲直上 a meteoric rise; be promoted quickly in an official career; be promoted to higher and higher posts; come up in the world; fly high; have a meteoric rise; rapid advancement in one's career; rapid promotion of one's position; rapidly go up in the world; rise to fame swiftly; shoot up into eminence; skyrocket into eminence; soar higher and higher in one's career;
平步青雲 get promoted very ast; go up in the world; have a meteoric rise; have a sudden rise in social status; rapidly go up in the world; rise to fame suddenly;
直上青雲 hit the highest literary honours; meteoric rise; rapid advancement in one's career;
志在青雲 cloudward;

[青腫] bruised and swollen;
臉青鼻腫 one's face has grown purple and one's nose is swollen;

[青州從事] fine wine; good liquor; top-grade spirit;

菜青 dark grayish green;
茶青 tea-green colour;
常青 evergreen;
垂青 look up sb with favour; show appreciation for sb;
丹青 red and green; painting;
蛋青 pale blue;
淡青 light greenish blue;
靛青 indigo;
冬青 Chinese ilex;
豆青 pea green;
紺青 dark purple; prune purple;
汗青 (1) sweeting green bamboo strips; (2) annals; chronicles; historical records;
紅青 dark purple; prune purple;
看青 keep watch over the ripening crops;
藍青 (1) blue-green; indigo blue; (2) corrupt; nonstandard;
瀝青 asphalt; bitumen; blacktop; pitch;
年青 young;
群青 ultramarine;
殺青 be completed;
踏青 go for a walk in the country in spring; go

hiking on a spring day; have an outing in spring; spring outing;
貪青 reaming green when it is due to become yellow and ripe;
天青 reddish black;
鐵青 ashen; ghastly pale; livid;
蟹青 greenish-gray;
玄青 deep black;
雪青 lilac;
壓青 green manuring;
鴉青 reddish blue;
瘀青 bruise;
元青 deep black;
藏青 dark blue;
知青 school graduates;
竹根青 bamboo green colour;
竹青 bamboo bark;
竹葉青 (1) green bamboo snake; (2) bamboo-leaf-green liquor;

qing

【卿】 (1) high official in ancient times; (2) emperor's form of address for a minister; (3) term of endearment formerly used between husband and wife or among close friends;

[卿卿我我] lovers' talk; very much in love; whispers of love;

[卿雲] propitious clouds bringing well-being to all;

客卿 person from one feudal state serving in the court of another;

qing

【氫】 hydrogen;

[氫彈] fusion bomb; hydrogen bomb;
氫彈爆炸 H-bomb blast;

[氫化] hydrogenation;
催化氫化 catalytic hydrogenation;
芳香氫化 aromatic hydrogenation;
脂環氫化 alicyclic hydrogenation;

[氫氯酸] hydrochloric acid;

[氫氣] hydrogen;
氫氣球 hydrogen balloon;

[氫氧] oxyhydrogen;
氫氧化物 hydroxide;

脫氫 dehydrogenate;
重氫 heavy hydrogen;

qing

【清】 (1) clean; clear; innocent; pure; stainless; unmixed; unsoiled; unspotted; (2) brief; scarce; (3) honest; innocent; virtuous; (4) quiet; (5) clear; clarified; crystal-clear; distinct; limpid; (6) arrange; place in order; (7) completely; conclude; terminate; thoroughly; with nothing left; (8) clean up; clear up; repay debts; settle; (9) clean up; eliminate; mop up; purge; suppress; wipe out; (10) count;

[清拔] distinguished;

[清白] clean; innocent; pure; stainless; unblemished; unimpeachable; unsoiled; unsullied;
清白的 blameless; in the clear;
清白度日 lead a clean life;
清白歷史 clean slate;
清白人家 decent family;
清白世家 law-abiding family background;
清白無辜 come out with clean hands; innocent;
清白無過 have clean hands;
清白無瑕 unspotted; untainted;
清白無罪 innocent of the crime; with clean hands;
來清去白 one's coming and going are aboveboard;
身家清白 come of a decent family; of respectable descent;
一清二白 completely innocent of the accusation; perfectly clean; spotless; unimpeachable;

[清標] (1) pure and austere look; (2) bright moon;
清標照人寒 the bright moon casts its cool light;

[清倉] make an inventory of the stock in the storehouse;
清倉查庫 make an inventory of warehouses;
清倉大減價 clearance price;
清倉大賤賣 clearance sale;
清倉核資 make an inventory of warehouses;
清倉挖潛 take inventory and dig out buried goods;

[清操] virtuous disposition and behaviour;

[清冊] detailed list; inventory;

[清查] (1) check; check up; examine; inquire

into; investigate; (2) comb out; detect; ferret out; uncover; unearth;
清查戶口 make a residence-check;
清查帳目 examine the accounts;

[清茶] (1) green tea; (2) tea served without refreshments;
清茶淡飯 live in poverty; homely fare; weak tea and simple food;

[清償] clear off; discharge; pay off;
清償債務 clear off debts; discharge liabilities; liquidation of the debt; pay off debts;

[清唱劇] oratorio;

[清徹] clear; crystal-clear; limpid;
清澈見底 so clear that one can see to th bottom;
清澈透明 as clear as crystal; crystalline;

[清晨] dawn; early in the morning; early morning;

[清澄] clear;

[清除] clean up; clear; clear away; clear out; clear-out; discard; dump; eliminate; erase; expel; get rid of; purge; reset; sweep away; weed out;
清除腐敗 eliminate corruption; stamp out corruption;
清除乾淨 make a clean sweep of; sweep clean;
清除垃圾 sweep away rubbish;
清除流毒 eliminate the pernicious influence;
清除影響 eradicate the influence;
清除障礙 clear away obstacles; remove obstacles;

[清楚] (1) clear; distinct; without ambiguity; (2) clear; lucid; (3) bring home to; clear about; know thoroughly; understand;
清楚明白 loud and clear;
清楚明確 lucid and definite; the clearest and most precise;
不清楚 not clear;
~ 隔著雲霧看山頭一不清楚 looking at the top of a hill through clouds and mist — unclear;
搞清楚 cipher out; clarify; get a clear understanding of sth; make clear;
~ 搞不清楚 ball up;
看清楚 make out; open sb's eyes; see clearly;
來歷清楚 have a clear record;
說明清楚 give a clear explanation;
一清二楚 as clear as day; as clear as daylight; as clear as noon; as clear as noonday; as clear as the sun at noonday; as plain as daylight; as plain as a pikestaff; as plain as noonday; as plain as the nose in your face; crystal clear; get down to a spot; patently; perfectly clear; transparently clear;

[清醇] refresh and mellow;

[清脆] clear; clear and melodious; ringing; silvery;

[清單] detailed account; detailed list; inventory; repertoire;
購物清單 shopping list;
價格清單 price list;
結欠清單 account rendred;
開列清單 draw up a list; draw up an inventory; make up a list; write a list;
列出清單 compile a list;
確定清單 account stated;
物品清單 list of articles;
一份清單 a list;

[清淡] (1) delicate; light; mild; weak; (2) light; not greasy or strongly flavoured; (3) dull; slack;
清淡時期 slack spells;

[清黨] purge within a political party;

[清道] (1) clean the street; (2) clear the way for the monarch or official;
清道夫 scavenger;

[清點] check; make an inventory; sort and count; take inventory;
清點貨物 take stock;
清點名單 check the list;
清點資財 make an inventory of the assets of a company;

[清炖] stew in clear soup;

[清芬] (1) soothing aroma; (2) virtues;

[清風] cool breeze; refreshing breeze;
清風勁節 a clear breeze and bright principles;
清風兩袖 live plainly and simply; remain uncorrupted; with only fine breezes in both sleeves — a poor but honest person;
清風亮節 a clear breeze and bright principles — as of one's deportment;
清風明月 a gentle breeze and bright moon — hermits and recluses;

清風撲面 the gentle breeze brushes against one's face;
清風徐來 a cool breeze blows gently; a refreshing breeze is blowing gently; a sweet breeze comes whiffling in; fresh breezes come in slowly;
兩袖清風 have clean hands; remain uncorrupted; with nothing but wind in both sleeves — very poor;

[清福] easy and carefree life;
享清福 live off the fat of the land; live on the fat of the land;
~安享清福 be unoccupied and enjoy happiness;

[清高] aloof from politics and material pursuits; loftiness and aloofness; morally lofty; morally upright; pure and lofty;
清高超拔 lofty and surpassing;
清高絕俗 extremely aloof from mundane affairs;
自鳴清高 claim to be immaculate; consider oneself morally superior to others; imagine oneself to be superior to others; look down on others as vulgar or dishonest; profess to be above politics and worldly considerations;

[清稿] clean copy; fair copy;

[清官] honest and upright official; incorrupt official;
清官難斷家務事 even an honest official can't judge domestic cases; even an upright official finds it hard to settle a family quarrel; even Daniel would find it difficult to form a judgement on disputes within a family; not even good officials can settle family troubles;

[清規] (1) monastic rules for Buddhists; (2) restrictions and fetters;
清規戒律 dos and don'ts; interdictions and taboos; outmoded restrictions; outmoded rules and conventions; restrictions and fetters; taboos and commandments; taboos and prohibitions; tedious and outmoded rules and regulations; the erection of countless taboos; the sacred rules of the religious order;

[清貴] pure and valuable;

[清鍋冷灶] live alone;

[清寒] (1) in straitened circumstances; needy; of limited means; poor; (2) clear and chilly; cold and clear;

[清和] period of tranquility; time of peace;

[清華] (1) outstanding and beautiful; (2) eminent and honest gentlemen; (3) moonlight; (4) enchanting views;

[清還] pay off;
按期清還 repay according to schedule;

[清減] get thin; lose weight;

[清醬] soya sauce;

[清剿] clean up; eliminate; mop up; suppress; wipe out;
清剿殘匪 clean up remnant bandits; round up the bandits;

[清教徒] puritan;

[清節] honest; incorrupt;

[清潔] clean; cleanliness; neat; sanitary; tidy;
清潔度 cleanliness;
清潔工 dustman; sweeper;
~清潔工人 cleaner; cleanser; sanitation worker; street cleaner;
清潔劑 cleaning agent; cleanser;
清潔女工 char; charlady; charwoman;
清潔器 cleaner;
~催化清潔器 catalytic cleaner;
~接點清潔器 contact cleaner;
~自動清潔器 automatic cleaner;
清潔運動 clean-up campaign; sanitation campaign;
保持清潔 keep clean;
冰清玉潔 incorruptible;
使清潔 cleanse;

[清淨] clean and pure; free from annoyance; peaceful and quiet;
清淨無為 discard all desires and worries from one's mind;
六根清淨 the six roots of sensations are pure and clean — free from human desires and passions;

[清靜] quiet; secluded; tranquil;
耳根清靜 hear no more about; free from noise and dirt; peace to one's ears; there will be no more complaints; there will be peace to one's ears;

[清君側] rid the emperor of evil ministers;

[清俊] pretty;

[清苦] in straitened circumstances; plain; poor; poor but clean and honest;

[清臘] paraffin removal;
[清朗] (1) clear and bright; (2) clear; clear and resounding; ringing;
[清冷] (1) chilly; cool; (2) deserted; desolate;
[清理] (1) check up; clean; cleaning; clean up; clear; disentangle; investigate; sort out; (2) liquidate;
清理債務 clear the debt; get out of debts; liquidation of debts;
清理整頓 screen and reorganize;
滾筒清理 barrel cleaning;
噴拋清理 blast cleaning;
噴砂清理 abrasive cleaning;
全部清理 complete liquidation;
停業清理 go into liquidation;
自動清理 voluntary liquidation;
[清麗] clear and attractive style;
[清廉] free from corruption; honest and upright;
[清涼] cool and refreshing;
清涼劑 dose for cooling effect; dose for sobering effect;
[清亮] clear; clear and bright; crystal; limpid;
[清寥] clear and open;
[清洌] chilly; cool;
[清淩淩] clear with light ripples;
[清流] (1) clear stream; (2) virtuous scholar;
[清門] poor family;
[清夢] disturb one's sweet dream;
[清名] unimpeachable reputation; unsoiled name;
[清明] (1) clear and bright; (2) sober and calm; (3) Qingming Festival;
清明節 Qingming Festival; Tomb-sweeping Day;
[清盤] liquidate; liquidation;
清盤人 liquidator;
停業清盤 liquidation;
[清貧] poor; poor and virtuous;
清貧常樂 poverty unmixed with other evils is conducive to abiding happiness;
甘守清貧 glory in honest poverty;
[清平] peace and tranquility;
清平世界 a peaceful and orderly world; peace in the country; this is a time of peace and order;
清平世界，朗朗乾坤 the world is quiet and at peace; times of peace on earth;
[清漆] slick; varnish;
耐碱清漆 alkali-proof varnish;
黏合清漆 adhesive varnish;
氣乾清漆 air drying varnish;
[清奇] novel and wonderful;
[清綺] beautiful; elegant;
清綺絕世 unexcelled elegance;
[清欠] clear up defaults; repay all one's debts;
[清切] (1) sad; sorrowful; (2) rigorous; strict;
[清清] cool;
清清白白 have clean hands; honest; keep one's hands clean; lead a clean life; pure in mind and body; with clean hands;
清清楚楚 absolutely clear; crystal celar; in order; in so many words;
[清泉] crystal-clear fountain;
[清掃] clean; clear; clear-up;
[清尚] high-class; high-society;
[清士] man of honesty and unimpeachable integrity;
[清瘦] lean; spare; thin; thin and lean;
[清疏] clean and dredge;
[清爽] (1) brisk; cool and refreshing; fresh and cool; refreshing; (2) easy; light; quiet and comfortable; relaxed; relieved;
[清水] branch water; clear water;
清水碧波 ripples of crystal clear water;
[清算] (1) audit; clear accounts; clear off an account; examine and repudiate; repudiate; square; (2) settle accounts with; settle scores;
清算老帳 settle old accounts;
清算所 clearing house;
清算銀行 clearing bank;
清算帳目 (1) settle accounts; (2) expose and criticize;
[清泰] calm; peace;
[清談] empty talk; idle talk; impractical discussion; indulge in idle talk;
清談節目 talk show;
~清談節目主持 talk-show host;
清談俱樂部 talking shop;
清談誤國 the country has suffered enough from too much empty talk;
烹茗清談 brew a pot tea and sit together chatting; brew tea and chat;
[清湯] clear soup; light soup;
清湯寡水 dishwater; sth insipid; watery and tasteless; watery soup;
[清天] (1) clear sky; (2) virtuous official;

[清恬] pure and quiet; tranquil and comfortable;
[清甜] fresh and sweet; smooth and sweet;
[清聽] your kind listening;
[清通] clear and smooth style; clearly understandable;
[清退] clear up and return; renounce; return; withdraw;
[清玩] (1) curios; elegant; refined things for people to enjoy; small decorative articles; (2) delight in;
[清望] fine prestige; untarnished reputation;
[清晰] (1) clear; crystal clear; distinct; limpid; vivid; (2) loud and clear;
清晰度 clarity; high definition;
~ 聲音清晰度 sound clarity;
不清晰 blurring;
口齒清晰 clear utterance;
[清洗] (1) clean; cleaning; rinse; wash; wash clean; (2) comb out; eliminate; get rid of; purge; weed out;
清洗機 washer;
~ 高壓清洗機 pressure washer;
清洗癖 ablutomania;
清洗傷口 clean a wound;
清洗行動 purge;
超聲波自動清洗 automatic ultrasonic cleaning;
電化學清洗 electrochemical cleaning;
電解清洗 cathodic cleaning;
定期清洗 periodic cleaning;
鍋爐清洗 boiler cleaning;
就地清洗 in-place cleaning;
陽極清洗 anodic cleaning;
[清閒] at leisure; have all the time one needs; have plenty of leisure; idle;
清閒錢難買 leisure is not sth that money can easily buy;
清閒自在 have a good time oneself;
[清顯] honoured official positions;
[清香] delicate and fresh fragrance; delicate fragrance; faint scent; mild fragrance; pleasant smell; refreshing fragrance;
清香撲鼻 a perfume particularly pleasant to the sense of smell; a sweet scent assails the nostrils; be met by a waft of fragrance;
清香爽口 pleasant to the palate;
[清曉] dawn; daybreak;
[清心] (1) carefree; (2) free one's mind of worries;
清心寡欲 a pure heart and few desires; cleanse one's bosom of perilous stuff; cleanse one's heart and limit one's desires; purge one's mind of desires and ambitions; purify one's heart and diminish one's passions; remove worries an control one's desires;
清心修身 cleanse one's heart and temper one's behaviour;
清心養性 purify one's heart and cultivate one's moral character;
寡欲清心 have few desires and cleanse the heart;
[清馨] delicate fragrance; faint scent;
[清新] crisp; delightfully fresh; fresh; pure and fresh; refreshing;
[清醒] (1) clear-headed; sane; sober; (2) come round; come to; come to one's senses; recover consciousness; regain consciousness;
清醒點 wise up;
清醒劑 a dose of sobriety;
清醒頭腦 a clear head; a clear-minded head;
清醒一下 blow away the cobwebs from one's brain; sober;
十分清醒 wide awake;
[清興] pleasure;
[清修] lead a life of few wants and ambitions;
[清秀] delicate and pretty; delicate-looking; good-looking; well-shaped; with clear-cut features;
[清虛] high and mild; refined and nonaggressive;
[清雅] elegant; graceful; neat and refined; refined;
清雅絕塵 clean and elegant;
[清言入妙] the feast of reason and the flow of soul;
[清樣] final proof; foundry proof;
[清野] clear the fields;
堅壁清野 conceal everything the enemy can eat or use; fortify the defence work and leave nothing usable to the invading enemy; strengthen the bulwarks and leave no provisions outside; strengthen the defence works and clear the fields;
[清夜] in the stillness of the night;

清夜捫心 examine one's conscience in the stillness of the night; examine one's own conscience during a quiet night; make self-examination in the still of the night; place one's hand over one's heart in the stillness of the night;

[清一色] (1) all of one colour; all of the same colour; (2) homogeneous; identical; one and the same; uniform; (3) (of mahjong) all of the same suit; a flush;

[清議] political criticism by scholars;

[清音] voiceless sound;

[清幽] quiet and beautiful; quiet and secluded; secluded and charming;

清幽茂綠 green and quiet;

清幽雅致 elegant; quiet and beautiful; secluded and refined;

[清越] clear and melodious;

[清運] clean up and take away;

[清早] dawn; early in the morning; early morning;

大清早 bright and early; early in the morning; the crack of dawn;

一清早 early in the morning;

[清帳] balance the book; clear an account; pay off all one's debts; settle an account; square an account;

[清真] Islamic; Muslim;

清真寺 mosque;

[清蒸] steam in clear soup;

[清正] clean, honest and just;

為官清正 incorrupt official; pure and upright officer;

[清濁] (1) clear and turbid; (2) honest and dishonest;

清濁不分 unable to distinguish between the clear and the muddy;

辨別清濁 make the pure and the impure distinguishable;

激濁揚清 cast out the wicked and cherish the virtuous; drain away the mud and bring in fresh water — drive out evil and usher in good; eliminate the impure from the pure; eliminate vice and exalt virtue; get rid of the evil and hail the virtuous; remove the wicked and promote the virtuous;

行濁言清 stainless in words but foul in deeds;

揚清激濁 advance the pure to get rid of the evil; bring in fresh water and drain away the mud; publicize the good deeds of good people in the hope that others will emulate them;

載清載濁 sometimes clear, sometimes muddy;

[清酌] wine offered to gods in worship;

查清 check up on; make a thorough investigation of;

償清 clear up;

澄清 (1) eliminate or exterminate; (2) clarify; clean; clear up; make clear; transparent;

蛋清 egg white;

分清 distinguish; draw a clear distinction between; draw a clear line of demarcation between;

風清 the breeze is light;

付清 pay in full; pay off;

河清 the river is clear;

劃清 distinguish; draw a clear line of demarcation;

還清 meet; pay off; wipe off;

結清 settle; square up;

看清 (1) see clearly; (2) realize;

廓清 clean up; sweep away;

冷清 cold and cheerless; deserted;

理清 straightened out; straighten up;

摸清 feel out;

弄清 button down; clarify; gain a clear idea of; make clear; understand fully;

淒清 (1) coldish; (2) sad;

認清 recognize; see clearly;

收清 receive in full;

肅清 eliminate; root out;

謄清 make a fair copy of;

天清 the sky is clear;

聽清 make out;

洗清 redress; wash away;

血清 (blood) serum;

qing

【傾】 (1) bend; incline; lean; lurch; slant; tilt; (2) deviation; tendency; (3) collapse; fall flat; subvert; upset; (4) empty; overturn and pour out; pour out; (5) do all one can; exert oneself to do sth; use up all one's resources; (6) admire; be fascinated; be intrigued;

[傾側] lurch; tilt; vert;

[傾巢] sally forth; swarm out in full strength; turn out in full force;

傾巢而出 come swarming from; get out in a body; go all out for an attack; sally forth in full strength to; swarm out; turn out in full force for an attack; turn out in full force to invade; turn out in full strength;

傾巢來犯 invade in full force;

傾巢援救 sally forth in full force to rescue;

[傾城傾國] exceptionally beautiful woman; so beautiful as to overrun cities and ruin states;

傾國傾城 exceedingly beautiful; of bewitching beauty; of enchanting beauty; so beautiful that she can cause the fall of a city or a state;

[傾倒] (1) collapse; topple and fall; topple down; topple over; (2) decant; empty; pour out; turn out; (3) be infaturated with a woman; be overwhelmed with admiration for; fall for; greatly admire;

傾倒一時 (1) affect the times overwhelmingly; (2) have convulsive effects on one's mind;

為之傾倒 be infatuated with sb; be overwhelmed with admiration for sb; show extreme admiration for;

[傾翻] tipover;

[傾覆] capsize; overturn; topple down; topple over; tumble; turn turtle; upset;

小船傾覆 the small boat turned turtle;

[傾家蕩產] bankrupt and ruined; be completely ruined financially; be reduced to poverty and ruin; become bankrupt; become homeless and bankrupt; bring the family to ruin; bring to ruin; broke; dissipate one's fortune; go bankrupt; lose a family fortune; lose all one's property; lose one's entire fortune; one's estate is totally lost; ruin one's family and dissipate one's fortune; run through one's family fortune; spend one's entire fortune; use up one's family fortune;

[傾角] inclination;

磁傾角 magnetic inclination;

電刷傾角 brush inclination;

氣流傾角 flow inclination;

[傾力而為] bend;

[傾慕] admire ardently; admire deeply; adore; have a strong admiration for;

[傾佩] admire deeply; respect greatly;

[傾盆] cloudburst; heavy downpour; torrential rain pour down in torrents;

傾盆大雨 a flood of rain; a downpour; a heavy downpair; a pouring rain; a torrent of rain; a torrential downpour; cascade; it is raining cats and dogs; pelting rain; pour down; pouring rain; rain buckets; rain cats and dogs; rain hard; rain in torrents; rain pitchforks; rain like billy-o; rain to beat the band; the rain comes down in buckets; the rain pours down;

[傾圮] collapse; in dilapidated condition;

[傾世] die; leave the world; pass away;

[傾訴] make a clean breast of; pour forth; pour out; unbosom oneself; unburden oneself;

傾訴安慰 pour forth comfort;

傾訴苦情 give full vent to one's feelings; pour out one's grievances; the outpouring of the heart; unburden one's heart; unburden oneself of sorrows;

傾訴心曲 lay bare one's pent-up feelings; lay one's heart bare; pour out one's secret concern;

傾訴心中的煩惱 pour out one's trouble;

傾訴衷腸 pour out one's heart; reveal one's innermost feelings;

傾訴衷情 give full vent to one's feelings; open one's heart to sb; pour out one's innermost feelings; reveal all one's innermost feelings; reveal one's heartfelt emotion; say what there is on one's mind without reservation; unbosom every bit of oneself; unburden one's heart; unburden oneself to;

[傾談] get into intimate conversation with; have a good, heart-to-heart talk; have a good talk;

[傾聽] all ears for; hear out; hearken; incline one's ear to; lend an ear to; listen attentively to; listen carefully; pick up

the ears;
傾聽意見 listen attentively to different opinions;
側耳傾聽 crane one's neck to listen; devour every word; harken to; incline one's ear and listen attentively; incline the ear to listen; incline the head and listen attentively; prick up one's ears; strain one's ears;
樂於傾聽 turn a willing ear to;
欠身傾聽 bend one's body slightly forward to listen;
傾耳而聽 hang on sb's lips; lend an attentive ear to; listen attentively; listen with all one's ears;
豎耳傾聽 keep one's ears flapping; prick one's ear;
聳耳傾聽 prick up one's ears;
專心傾聽 be all ears; listen attentively; listen intently;
仔細傾聽 prick up one's ears;

[傾吐] pour out one's heart; reveal one's sorrows; say what is on one's mind without reservation; speak freely of one's thoughts;
傾吐肺腑 have a confidential talk; lay one's heart bare; unbosom oneself to; unbutton one's soul;
傾吐苦水 unburden oneself of one's grievances;
傾吐衷情 pour out one's heart to sb; unbosom oneself;
傾吐衷曲 open one's heart to sb; pour out one's heart to sb; pour out one's thoughts; speak one's bosom; talk to each other to their hearts' content;

[傾危] (1) crooked; mean; (2) highly dangerous; precarious;

[傾箱倒篋] overturn trunks and upset boxes; ransack a house;

[傾向] be inclined to support one side rather than the other; deviation; inclination; leaning; proclivity; proneness; propensity; tend to; tendency; trend;
傾向性詞 biased word;
傾向性疑問句 conducive question;
暴力傾向 aggressive tendencies;
不良傾向 unhealthy tendency;
~制止不良傾向 check the unhealthy tendency;
二值傾向 two-valued orientation;
反傾向 countertendency;
犯罪傾向 criminal tendency;
科學性傾向 scientific aptitude;
平均消費傾向 average propensity to consume;
氣壓傾向 barometric tendency;
投資傾向 propensity to invest;
習得傾向 acquired tendency;
先天傾向 congenital tendencies;
消費傾向 propensity to spend;
學術性傾向 scholastic aptitude;
有傾向 have a propensity;
政治傾向 political leanings
自殺傾向 suicidal tendency;
總的傾向 general temper;

[傾銷] cutthroat sale; dump; dumping;
傾銷市場 a market for dumping goods; dumping grounds;
持久性傾銷 persistent dumping;
出口傾銷 export dumping;
反傾銷 anti-dumping;
偶發性傾銷 sporadic dumping;
社會傾銷 social dumping;
外匯傾銷 currency dumping; exchange dumping;

[傾斜] dip; incline; lean; slant; slope; tilt; tilting;
傾斜度 inclination;
~空中基線傾斜度 air base inclination;
~主軸傾斜度 spindle inclination;
傾斜計 clinometer;
~擺式傾斜計 pendulum clinometer;
~感應傾斜計 induction clinometer;
~橫向傾斜計 lateral clinometer;
~回轉傾斜計 gyroscopic clinometer;
~前後傾斜計 fore-and-aft clinometer;
~球形傾斜計 ball clinometer;
~萬向傾斜計 universal clinometer;
~相對傾斜計 relative clinometer;
傾斜器 clinometer;
~懸式傾斜器 hanging clinometer;
傾斜身體 lean;
傾斜儀 clinometer;
~擺式傾斜儀 pendulum clinometer;
~光學傾斜儀 optical clinometer;
~陀螺式傾斜儀 gyroscopic clinometer;
~側向傾斜儀 lateral clinometer;
~縱向傾斜儀 longitudinal clinometer;
層積傾斜 depositional dip;
場傾斜 field tilt;
車體傾斜 tilting of car body;

後肩傾斜 back porch tilt;
局部傾斜 local dip;
視傾斜 apparent dip;
水平傾斜 horizontal tilt;
吸收傾斜 absorption dip;
向心傾斜 centroclinal dip;

[傾卸] dump;

[傾洩] fall in torrents;

[傾瀉] come down in torrents; flood; flow out; pour down; rush down;
傾瀉而下 pour down; rush down;

[傾心] (1) admire; fall for; fall in love with; lose one's heart to; (2) cordial; heart-to-heart; intimate and candid; warm and sincere;
傾心交談 have a heart-to-heart talk; heart-to-heart chat;
傾心竭力 exert oneself to the uttermost; exhaust every effort to;
傾心吐膽 lay bare one's heart; make a clean breast of; open one's heart wide and lay bare one's thoughts; open one's mind; pour out one's heart; speak one's mind; speak out everything that is in one's heart; tell all that is in one's heart; unbosom oneself; unburden one's mind;
傾心於 fix one's affections on; set one's affections upon;
傾心折服 submit cordially; submit with admiration;
令人傾心 carry sb off her feet; sweep sb off his feet;
吐膽傾心 open one's heart wide and lay bare one's thoughts; pour out one's heart; speak out everything that is in one's heart; unbosom oneself;
一見傾心 fall in love at first sight; love at first sight;

[傾軋] engage in factional strife; engage in internal strife; fight for power; in-fighting; jostle against one another; jostle with one another;
傾軋排擠 subvert and dispose;
內部傾軋 factionalism;

[傾注] (1) empty into; pour into; stream down into; (2) concentrate on; devote; direct to; throw into;
傾注全力 go heart and soul into; put upon the full stretch; strain every nerve;

攲傾 incline; slant;
右傾 right deviation;
左傾 left-leaning; progressive;

qing
【蜻】 dragonfly;

[蜻蜓] dragonfly; flying adder; odonate; skimmer;
蜻蜓點水 a delicate touch; like a dragonfly skimming over the surface of the water; scratch the surface; skim over one's work; touch on sth without going into it deeply; touch superficially; without going into it deeply;
蜻蜓掠水 the dragonflies skim over the water;
蜻蜓搖石柱—妄想 a dragonfly hoping to shake down a stone pillar — sheer fantasy;

qing
【輕】 (1) light; light in weight; (2) degree; not serious; slight; small in number; (3) base; lowly; mean; not important; (4) light; gentle; relaxed; (5) gently; low; softly; (6) rashly; (7) belittle; ignore; make light of; neglect; slight; underestimate;

[輕便] convenient; easy and convenient; handy; light; portable;
輕便鐵路 light railway;

[輕薄] frivolous; given to philandering; philandering;
輕薄兒 fickle and callous fellow; frivolous youth;
輕薄少年 cox-comb; frivolous youngster;

[輕財] make light of wealth;
輕財好義 generous and philanthropic;
輕財重義 make light of money and lay store on justice; make light of wealth and love to be righteous; prize righteousness and benevolence above wealth; regard money lightly and enthusiastic over righteousness;

[輕車] (1) light, swift chariot; (2) light cart;
輕車簡從 as facile as traveling along a familiar road in a light carriage; travel light with light luggage and few attendants;
輕車熟路 a light carriage on a familiar road; a man on his own ground would

find the work light and easy; a scholar working in his own field would be in his proper element; a smooth and easy course; do sth one knows well and can manage with ease; drive in a light carriage on a familiar road; manage with ease by one who knows the ropes; sth one knows well; work with ease from accumulated experience;

[輕脆] flimsy; frail; light and fragile;

[輕淡] light; mild; thin;

[輕敵] belittle the enemy; take the enemy lightly; underestimate the enemy;

[輕度] mild;

[輕紡] light industry and textile industry;

[輕放] put down gently;

[輕風] breeze; light breeze;

輕風拂面 the gentle breeze brushes against one's face;

[輕諷] mock; touch;

[輕拂] flick;

[輕浮] flighty; flippant; frivolous; levity; light; light-headed; playful;

表現輕浮 show levity;

舉止輕浮 behave frivolously;

態度輕浮 have a frivolous manner;

[輕寒] cold; cool; mildly;

[輕忽] ignore; make light of; neglect; slight;

[輕活] cushy job; easy job; soft job;

[輕賤] base; contemptible; mean; mean and worthless;

自輕自賤 belittle oneself; lack self-confidence; lack self-respect; underestimate oneself;

[輕捷] agile; nimble; spry;

[輕舉] do with ease;

輕舉妄動 a leap in the dark; act on impulse without much thought and care; act rashly; act rashly and blindly; act recklessly; act rushly; act without due deliberation and caution; an ill-considered action; an impetuous and imprudent act; do sth foolish; do sth rash; fly in the face of discretion; frivolous and rash in conduct; go heels over head; go it blind; go off at half-cock; go off half-cocked; go off the deep end; impetuosity; imprudent; quarrel with Providence; rash measures; take a reckless action; take action without due deliberation and caution; take rash action; take reckless action; tempt Providence; venture to make overtures;

輕而易舉 a light and easy job; able to do sth hands down; an easy job to do; as easy as ABC; as easy as damn it; as easy as falling off a log; as easy as lying; as easy as pie; as easy as rolling a log; can be done with great ease; come easy to one; come natural to sb; easily; easy; easy to accomplish; easy to do; easy to handle; easy to undertake; effortless; have an easy time; in a walk; like a hot knife through butter; on one's head; so light as to be capable of being lifted up with ease; sth that can be done with very little effort; standing on one's head; very easy to do; with no difficulties;

輕而易舉地 like a hot knife through butter;

[輕快] (1) agile; brisk; light-footed; sprightly; (2) light-hearted; lively; relaxed;

輕快的樂曲 light-hearted melody;

腳步輕快 light on one's feet;

[輕狂] extremely frivolous;

[輕利] (1) think little of material gain; (2) light and sharp;

輕利重名 despite wealth and value reputation;

[輕量] light weight;

輕量級 lightweight;

[輕靈] agile; nimble;

[輕慢] disrespectful; irreverent; neglect; slight; treat sb without proper respect;

輕慢的 cavalier;

輕慢海盜 opportunity makes the thief;

[輕蔑] cock snooks at; contemptuous; despising; disdainful; scornful;

[輕諾] make easy promises;

輕諾寡信 a long tongue has a short hand; a long tongue is a sign of a short hand; a promise, lightly made, is lightly broken; give a promise easily and break it easily; give one's words easily but seldom keep them faithfully; he that promises too much means nothing; airy promise; lavish promise is followed by poor performance; make promises easily but seldom keep

them; many promises lessen faith; many promises weaken faith; promise lightly and seldom live up to one's words; those who are quick to promise are generally slow to perform; too ready compliance is not to be trusted;
~ 這個人總是輕諾寡信 this person is full of airy promises;

[輕飄] buoyant; light;
輕飄飄 (1) light; light as a feather; (2) frivolous;

[輕騎] light cavalry;
輕騎兵 light cavalry;

[輕巧] (1) delicate and well-made; handy; light and efficient; light and handy; light and portable; (2) agile; deft; dexterous; (3) easy; light;

[輕輕] gently; lightly; softly;
輕輕地說 speak softly;

[輕裘] soft furs;
輕裘肥馬 soft furs and well-fed horses — live in luxury;
輕裘緩帶 soft furs and loose girdles — a cosy living;

[輕取] beat easily; carry off easily; gain an easy victory; win hands down;

[輕柔] gentle; pliable; soft;

[輕銳] light and sharp;

[輕傷] flesh wound; minor wound; slight injury; slight wound;

[輕身] (1) make light of one's life; (2) unmarried; without a burden;

[輕生] commit suicide; make light of one's life;
暴殄輕生 commit suicide; make light of one's life;

[輕聲] (1) hushed; in a soft voice; softly; (2) light tone;
輕聲低語 speak softly; whisper;
輕聲吵啞的 husky;

[輕事重報] exaggerate the importance in report; make strong reports about trifles;

[輕視] belittle; bridle at sth; cock a snoot at; cock one's nose; condemn; contemptuous; curl one's lip; despise; disdain; disdainful; disregard; feel contempt for; give sb the go-by; give sth the go-by; hold in contempt; hold in scorn; in contempt of; look down on; look down upon; make light of sb; make little account of; make little of; mocking; pooh-pooh; regard lightly; scorn; scornful of; set light by sb; set little of; set little store by sb; set little store by sth; set no store by sb; set no store by sth; set not much store by; show scorn; slight; snap one's fingers at; sneeze at; take lightly; take no account of; think light of; think little of; think nothing of; think scorn of; treat with contempt; trifle with; turn one's nose up at sb; underestimate; underrate;
輕視傲慢 contempt and pride; despise and be haughty;
輕視敵人 scorn enemies;
輕視困難 make light of difficulties;
輕視體力勞動 look down on manual work;
輕視知識 think little of knowledge;
受人輕視 be slighted;

[輕率] hasty; heedless; indiscreet; levity; make light of; neglect; rash; slight;
輕率從事 handle an affair rashly;
輕率的 imprudent;
輕率魯莽 act recklessly; heedless and reckless;
輕率下判斷 make hasty generalizations;
輕率易變 rash and changeable;
輕率燥急 careless and quick-tempered;

[輕爽] comfortable; easy; relaxed;

[輕鬆] (1) light; light-hearted; relaxed; (2) comfortable; easy; light;
輕鬆的工作 cushy job; light work; soft job;
輕鬆地 airily;
輕鬆心情 in a relaxed mood;
輕鬆愉快 at one's ease; happy and relaxed; happy go-lucky; light and entertaining; light of heart; light-hearted; like a cork; vivacious; with a light heart;
輕鬆自如 free and relaxed;
輕鬆自在 comfortable; happy and unrestrained;
感到輕鬆 feel relief;

[輕佻] capricious; coquettish; flippant; frivolous; giddy; playful; skittish;

sportive;
輕佻浮躁 unstable and fickle-minded;
輕佻儇薄 light and fragile;
[輕脫] frivolous; playful;
[輕微] insignificant; light; little; slight; to a small extent; trifling; trivial; unimportant;
輕微警告 a slap on the wrist;
輕微傷風 catch a slight flu;
[輕侮] insult; contempt; scorn;
[輕閒] at leisure;
[輕瀉劑] laxative;
[輕心] negligent;
掉以輕心 let down one's guard; lower one's guard; take a casual attitude; take sth lightly;
~不可掉以輕心 must not take it lightly;
~不能掉以輕心 not to be lightly valued;
[輕信] believe easily; credulity; easily place trust in; gullible; lightly believe; lightly put faith in; readily believe; readily place trust in; take for granted;
輕信的 credulous; gullible;
輕信謠言 give credence to rumours; listen indiscriminately to rumours;
輕信易惑 it is likely to be perplexed if one believes a thing easily;
過份輕信 over credulous;
[輕刑] light punishment;
[輕型] light; light-duty;
輕型武器 light-duty weapon;
[輕煙] smoke;
一縷輕煙 a plume of smoke;
一柱輕煙 a column of smoke;
[輕言] speak lightly; speak without thinking;
輕言輕語 express oneself with a ready, shallow pertness; flippant; talk jestingly in regard to sth demanding more serious treatment;
輕言細語 say sth under one's breath; speak in a mild tone; speak softly; talk in a soft voice;
輕言招怨 cause hatred by reckless words;
薄唇輕言 garrulous and sharp-tongued; thin lips speak freely;
[輕易] (1) easily; facile; effortless; lightly; readily; (2) rashly; reckless;
輕易丟棄 fribble away; lightly abandon;
輕易放棄 lightly abandon;
輕易放走 let off lightly;
輕易開除 be summarily removed from one's job;
輕易取勝 field day; home free; walk away with; walk off with; win hands down; win in a walk;
輕易喪失 be lightly given up;
輕易之舉 light and easy undertaking;
[輕盈] lissom; lithe; nimble and shapely; slim and graceful;
[輕油] light oil;
[輕雲飄飄] fleecy clouds float past;
[輕重] (1) light and heavy; weight; (2) degree of seriousness; relative importance; (3) propriety;
輕重不分 fail to distinguish the trivial from the important;
輕重倒置 lack a sense of priority; lack a sense of proportion; put the trivial above the important; reverse the order of importance; stress trifles and overlook matters of moment; treat sth important as unimportant and vice versa;
輕重緩急 in the order of importance and emergency; in the order of importance and urgency; in the order of priority; relative importance and urgency;
~不分輕重緩急 without regard to the relative importance or urgency;
~分清楚事情的輕重緩急 get one's priorities right;
輕重量級 light heavyweight;
本輕利重 the capital is small, but the profit remarkable; the costs are low, but the profit is great;
避重就輕 avoid the important and dwell on the trivial; avoiding the main point; ride off on a side issue; shirk a difficult work and take an easy one; take the easier way out; take up minor issues to evade the major ones;
畸輕畸重 attach too much weight to this and too little weight to that; lopsided; unbalanced;
舉足輕重 carry a big weight in; carry weight; hold the balance; occupy a decisive position; of great moment; pivotal; play a decisive role; prove decisive; tip the beam; tip the scales; turn the scales;
~舉足輕重的人 person of consequence;

沒輕沒重 no idea how to behave; rash and rude; tactlessly; without manners;
拈輕怕重 prefer the light and shirk the heavy; prefer the light to the heavy — pick easy jobs and shirk hard ones;
~不要拈輕怕重 don't pick easy jobs and shirk hard ones;
權其輕重 weigh up one thing against another; weigh up the matter carefully;
無足輕重 carry no weight; count for nothing; cut no figure; dinky; fiddling; footy; go for nothing; hole and corner; insignificant; kick the beam; not of great importance; not to amount to a hill of beans; not to amount to a row of beans; not to matter a farthing; not to matter a hoot; not to matter a rap; not to matter a sixpence; not to matter a straw; of little consequence; of little importance; of little moment; of little significance; of no account; of no consequence; pimping; strike the beam;
~無足輕重的人 also-ran; cog in the machine; lightweight; pipsqueak;
做事不知輕重 not know the proper way to act;

[輕舟] light boat; small boat;

[輕妝淡抹] have a simple makeup;

[輕裝] light; light and simple luggage; light fitted; light pack;
輕裝就道 travel light;
輕裝旅行 travel light;
輕裝前進 go forward with one's burdens discarded; march with light packs;
輕裝上陣 come to the battlefront without any mental burdens; go forward with one's burdens discarded; go into battle with a light pack; join battle with a light pack; join the struggle without any burdens; take a load off one's mind; take part in a political movement with nothing on one's conscience; take part in the struggle free of care;

[輕貲] disregard wealth;
輕貲好義 disregard wealth and be devoted to justice; generous and philanthropic; make light of money and love righteousness;
輕貲重義 regard money lightly and be enthusiastic over a public cause;

[輕罪] minor crime; minor offense; misdemeanour;
輕罪重罰 break a fly upon the wheel; deal with a minor offense as if it were a major one; overpunishment;

從輕 settle case on the lenient side;
減輕 abate; ease; lighten;
見輕 get better;
看輕 belittle; underestimate;
口輕 (1) be fond of food that is not salty; (2) young;
年輕 young;

qing

【鯖】 mackerel;

qing²

qing

【情】 (1) affection; emotion; feeling; sentiment; (2) circumstance; condition; detail; fact; situation; (3) nature; reason; (4) affection; love; passion;

[情愛] affection; love;

[情報] inform; information; intelligence;
情報機構 intelligence agency;
情報檢索 information retrieval;
情報局 information bureau;
情報人員 an intelligence agent;
情報搜集 collect information;
情報網 intelligence network;
情報學 informatics;
情報員 secret agent; intelligence agent;
查找情報 seek information;
錯誤情報 misinform;
動態情報 current intelligence;
航攝情報 airphoto intelligence;
互通情報 exchange information; exchange of information; keep each other informed;
即時情報 up-to-the minute information;
假情報 disinformation;
交換情報 exchange information; interchange information;
經濟情報 economic intelligence;
商業情報 commercial intelligence;
搜集情報 collect intelligence;
竊取情報 steal information;
洩露情報 divulge information;

[情弊] dishonest practices; irregularities;

[情不自禁] aptness; be driven by an impulse;

be overcome by one's feelings; be overcome willy-nilly by; be seized with a sudden impulse; be seized with an impulse; be tempted to; beside oneself; cannot contain one's feelings; cannot control oneself; cannot help doing sth; cannot help oneself; cannot hold back one's joy; cannot refrain from; desirous; feel an irresistible impulse; inclined; in spite of oneself; let oneself go; love a person in spite of oneself; spontaneously; unable to hold in check one's desires; unable to curb one's passions; unable to repress one's emotions; unable to restrain oneself; unable to restrain the emotions; unable to suppress one's emotions;

[情不可卻] can hardly decline sb's kind offer;

[情操] (1) sentiment; (2) noble thoughts and feelings;

[情長] lasting affection for one;
情長紙短 much in little; the paper is too short to describe one's deep feeling;

[情場] arena of love;
情場老手 skirt chaser; woman chaser;
情場失意 be disappointed in love; be frustrated in love; be jilted; unlucky in love;

[情腸] loving heart;

[情淡嫌來] faults are thick where love is thin;

[情敵] rival in a love affair;

[情調] affective tone; ambience; emotional appeal; flavour; mood; sentiment;
浪漫情調

[情竇] love;
情竇初開 begin to understand love; reach puberty; the dawn of love; the first awakening of love; the first dawning of love;
情竇未開 before puberty; fancy-free; heart-whole;

[情分] (1) friendship; good feeling; mutual affection; (2) good intentions; good will; solicitude;

[情夫] backdoor man; fancy man; lover; paramour;

[情婦] a bit of jam; fancy woman; housekeeper; inamorata; mistress; illicit girlfriend; one's bit of nonsense; shack job; the other woman;
被包養的情婦 kept woman;

[情甘] voluntary; willing;

[情感] affection; emotion; feeling; frame of mind; friendship between two persons; sentiment;
情感意義 affective meaning;
情感語言 affective language;
情感約制 emotional control;
情感障礙 affective disturbance;
表達情感 show emotion;
訴諸情感 appeal to an emotion;
隱瞞情感 mask one's feelings;

[情歌] love song;

[情海] deep love; the vast, tumultuous sea of love between men and women;
情比海深 one's concern is deeper than the sea;

[情話] lover's chat; lover's honeyed words; lover's prattle; lover's talk; sweetnothings; whispers of love;
情話綿綿 endless whispers of love;
情話喁喁 occupied with endless whispers of love;

[情懷] feelings; mood; passion;
孕育情懷 cultivate passion;

[情火] flames of love;

[情急] in a moment of desperation;
情急智生 an excellent idea occurs to one's mind at the crucial moment; emergency fillips one's wits; good ideas come at times of crisis; have a wily thought in the exigency of the moment; have quick wits in an emergency; hit on a good idea in a moment of desperation; hit on a plan in one's desperation; in the hour of danger, one rises to the occasion; one proves to be most resourceful in an emergency; one's wits fly fast when in great peril; show resourcefulness in an emergency; strike a wise idea in a desperate moment; the idea just comes to one on the spur of the moment; wit comes when one is in a critical moment;

[情姦] adultery from mutual attraction;

[情見乎辭] find true feeling in one's expressions; the feeling is alive in the words; the writer's sincerity shines through his words;

[情節] (1) plot; story; (2) circumstances; details of a case;

情節緊湊 tightknit plot;
情節劇 melodrama;
情節曲折 intricate;
情節嚴重 of a serious nature;
次要情節 subplot;
從屬情節 subplot;
一段情節 an episode;

[情景] scene; sight; circumstances;

情景交融 feelings and the setting are happily blended;
情景教學法 situation method;
情景式反語 situational irony;
情景意義 situational meaning;

[情境] circumstance; context; situation;

情境會話 circumstance talk;
情境效應 circumstance effect;
情境學習 contextual learning;
學習情境 learning context;

[情況] circumstances; condition; how the world goes; situation; state of affairs;

情況報告 information report;
情況逼人 the matter is pressing;
情況變了 the situation has changed;
情況不佳 out of condition;
情況不妙 the prospects are not too encouraging; the state of affairs is far from good; things are in a bad way;
情況不明 ignorance of the situation; the situation is not clear;
情況大概就是這樣 that's about the size of it;
情況惡化 a situation deteriorates; a situation gets worse; a situation worsens;
情況還不止這樣 that's not the whole story;
情況好轉 a situation improves; the situation has ameliorated;
情況滙報 debrief;
~ 情況滙報會 debriefing session;
情況如何 how do affairs stand;
情況危急 in a critical condition;
情況越來越差 things go from bad to worse;
情況狀語從句 adverbial clause of circumstance;
比賽情況 palying conditions;
調查情況 examine the situation;
非常情況 unusual circumstances;
健康情況 the state of one's health;
經濟情況 economic situation;
看情況 depending on circumstances;
摸清情況 feel out the situation;
偶然情況 accidental circumstance; adventitious circumstances;
任何情況 any circumstances;
~ 在任何情況下 under no circumstances;
實際情況 practical situation;
説明情況 explain the situation;
特殊情況 exceptional circumstances; particular circumstances; special circumstances;
有利的情況 advantageous circumstance;
正常情況 normal circumstances;
~ 按正常情況 normally;
重要情況 lowdown;

[情郎] girl's lover;

[情累] burden of love;

[情理] common sense; reason; sense;

情理難容 absurd; incompatible with the accepted code of human conduct; inexcusable feelings; unacceptable sentiments;
背情悖理 consistent neither with convention nor with reason;
達情達理 sensible; show good sense; stand to reason; understanding and reasonable;
合乎情理 stand to reason;
合情合理 entirely reasonable; fair and resasonable; fair and sensible; in a reasonable manner; in all reason; make sense; perfectly logical and reasonable; reasonable and just; seemly and fitting; understandable;
合情理 fitness;
衡情度理 all things considered;
近情近理 acceptable for reason;
洽情合理 fair and reasonable; in accordance with principles and reasons;
入情入理 fair and reasonable; in reason; in reasonable manner; perfectly logical and reasonable; reasonable and just;
順乎情理 conform to reason; stand to reason;
推情度理 consider the circumstances and measure the reasons;

[情侶] lovers; sweethearts;

情侶鸚鵡 lovebird;
恩愛情侶 lovebird;

[情貌] internal and external reverence or loyalty;

[情面] (1) face; face-saving; feelings; personal consideration; sensibilities; (2) friendship; regard for others;
情面難卻 hard to decline for the sake of friendship; hard to refuse for the sake of friendship; it is difficult to break away from personal esteem for sb; the principle of friendship will not admit of a refusal;
礙於情面 for fear of hurting sb's feelings; just to spare sb's feelings; on sufferance; out of consideration for sb's feelings; spare sb's feelings;
不顧情面 have no consideration for sb's feelings;
不講情面 not to care to save the face of; without sparing anyone's sensibilities;
不留情面 disregard others' feelings;
打破情面 do not attempt to spare anybody's feelings;
留情面 spare one's feelings;
~不留情面 disregard to others' feelings or face;
瞻徇情面 reverence out of respect to;

[情濃] strong affection;
茶淡情濃 the tea is weak but the friendship is strong;

[情趣] (1) temperament and interest; (2) appeal; delight; interest;
情趣盎然 brimming with interest in nature;
情趣橫生 perfect decorum;
情趣橫溢 full of wit;
情趣相投 have similar temperaments and interests; temperamentally compatible;
增添情趣 add spice;

[情人] inamorata; lover; paramour; sweetheart;
情人眼裏出西施 beauty is in the eye of the beholder; beauty is in the eyes of the gazer; beauty lies in the lover's eyes; every lover sees a thousand graces in the beloved object; if Jack's in love, he's no judge of Jill's beauty; in the eye of the lover, his beloved is a beauty; love blinds a man to imperfections; love is blind; love sees no fault;
情人座 love seat;
舊情人 ex-lover; old flame; one's former lover; one's former sweetheart;
己婚男人的情人 another woman; the other woman;

[情殺] murder caused by love entanglement;

[情商] ask for a favour as a friend;

[情深] ardent love; strong affections;
情深不露 a true love conceals love; ardent love does not reveal itself;
情深似海 love is as deep as the sea; one's feeling is as deep as the ocean;
情深誼厚 on very good terms with each other; thick in feeling;
情深意濃 head over heels in love; over head and ears in love; strong affections;
別久情深 absence makes the heart fonder;
故劍情深 deep affection of husband and wife who were betrothed in childhood; remember a former wife with tender feelings;
一往情深 be deeply attached to sb; be passionately devoted; cherish a deep-seated affection for; fall deeply in love with sb; gush over; head over heels in love;

[情詩] amatory poem; amatory verses; love poem; love song;
情詩艷詞 love poems in a flowery style;

[情事] circumstances; conditions; situations;

[情勢] circumstances; situations; state of affairs; trend of events;
情勢不佳 things look black;
情勢所阻 be prevented by force of circumstances;
情勢危急 the situation is critical; the situation is desperate;
靜觀情勢 take sounding;
客觀情勢 objective situations;
順應情勢 be resigned to the situation;
應付情勢 cope with the situation;

[情實] (1) facts of an affair; (2) the crime has been confirmed;

[情史] love story;

[情書] amorous letter; love letter;

[情思幽發] muse over past memories; muse over things remote; muse over memories of the past;

[情絲] ties of affection; ties of love;
情絲不斷 the ties of love remain unbroken;
一把慧劍斬情絲 cut the thread of carnal love with a sword of wisdom;
一縷情絲 a thread of love;

[情死] commit suicide for the sake of love; martyrdom to love;

[情愫] innermost feelings; sincere feeling; sincerity;

[情隨] feelings change according to...;
情隨境遷 it is one's own feelings that make things different;
情隨時遷 times change and men's affections become altered;
情隨事遷 as circumstances change man's affections change; as circumstances change, relations between people also change; as times alter men's affections change; one's feeling changes with the changed circumstance; other circumstances, other affections; other things, other feelings; people's feelings change with the circumstances; the alteration of things makes man's feeling change;

[情態] mood; spirit;
情態動詞 modal verb;
情態意義 modal meaning;
情態助動詞 modal auxiliary;

[情天] vast realm of love;
情天恨海 affection as high as the heaven and hatred as deep as the sea; the deep love or regret between men and women;

[情田] one's heart;

[情網] cobweb of love; snare of love;

[情味] interest; sentiment;

[情文] inspiration and essays;
情文并茂 accomplished both in feeling and composition; excellent in both content and language; rich in feeling and eloquent in expression;

[情物] love token;

[情心] compassion;

[情形] circumstances; condition; general condition; situation; state of affairs;
看情形 depending on circumstances;
可疑情形 suspicious circumstances;

[情緒] (1) feeling; mood; morale; sentiments; spirit; (2) depression; moodiness; sullenness;
情緒昂奮 be full of enthusiasm;
情緒不高 in low spirits;
情緒不好 in a mood;
情緒低落 depressed in mind; down in spirits; get one's tail down; in low spirits; low in spirits; low-spirited;
情緒高昂 get one's tail up; high-spirited; in a black mood; in fine feather; in good feather; in great feather; in high feather; in high spirits;
情緒高漲 feeling runs high; moral is high;
情緒忽高忽低 emotion swells and subsides;
情緒激動 be informed with passion;
悲觀情緒 mood of pessimism; pessimism; pessimistic emotion;
度假情緒 holiday mood;
控制情緒 control the emotions;
樂觀情緒 mood of optimism;
矛盾情緒 conflicting emotions;
鬧情緒 disgruntled; have a fit of the sulks; in a fit of depression; in low spirits; mope oneself;
普遍情緒 general mood; prevailing mood;
煽動情緒 fan the flames;
一絲失望的情緒 a faint of disappointment; a taint of disappointment;

[情意] affection; cordiality; feeling; goodwill; love; love and affection; sentiment; tender regards;
情意纏綿 be bound up with affection for; the beautiful relations between lovers;
情意綢繆 head over heels in love;
情意懇摯 show sincere feeling;
情意脈脈 amorous;
情意綿綿 everlasting love; long-lasting love;
~情意綿綿的電話 lovey-dovey call;
情意繾綣 affectionate;
~情意繾綣的書信 affectionate letter;
紅情綠意 tender affections between a couple in love;
濃情蜜意 great tenderness between lovers;
繾綣情意 entangled relations between lovers;
情溶意蜜 head over heels in love;
情投意合 agree in opinion; agree in tastes and temperament; closely allied

in opinion and feelings; congenial; congenial in feelings and interests; fall in love with each other; find each other congenial; finger and thumb; fit in with each other perfectly; get along together agreeably; get on like a house on fire; hand in glove with; have mutual affection; hit it off perfectly; hold similar ideas about life; in complete agreement with each other; in with sb; mutual affection and agreement; of one mind; on friendly terms with sb; perfectly suited to each other; see eye to eye with each other; suit each other perfectly;

甜情蜜意 sweet feeling and honeyed sentiment — tender affections; tender love between man and woman;

虛情假意 a false display of affection; a hypocritical show of friendship; pure hypocrisy; put up a phoney show; very nice to sb but not sincere;

[情義] faithful tie; faithfulness; ties of comradeship; ties of friendship; true feeling;

情義兩全 love and duty both receive their proper need;

寡情薄義 have no affections and be a man of shallow feelings;

假情假義 pretense of affection and goodness;

情至義盡 the climax of one's affection and friendly feelings; with entire sincerity;

[情誼] affection; friendly feelings; friendly sentiments; friendship;

高情厚誼 great favours; highly esteemed kindness and invaluable friendship;

隆情厚誼 great favours and great kindness; profound sentiments of friendship;

[情殷] with warm regard;

[情由] cause; facts and reasons; reason; the hows and whys;

[情有可原] circumstances which lessen a fault; excusable; extenuating circumstances; mitigating circumstances; pardonable; under extenuating circumstances; understandable;

[情慾] carnal desires; erotic feelings; lust; sexual desire; sexual passion;

縱恣情慾 give rein to lusts;

[情緣] sentimental bond;

霧水情緣 dalliance; fling;

[情願] (1) be willing to; (2) had rather; prefer; would rather;

情願投降 offer to submit;

情願退出 be pleased to withdraw;

不情願 grudging; not willing to;

心甘情願 act entirely of one's own free will; most willing to; perfectly happy to; perfectly willing; willingly; willingly and gladly; with a good grace; with good cheer; without protest;

一廂情願 a unilateral wish; a wish cherished by one side only; a wish expressed by one party only; one's own wishful thinking; one-sided wish; unilateral willingness; we soon believe what we desire; wishful thinking;

[情知] fully aware; know for sure; know perfectly well;

情知不妙 one knows it is an evil omen;

情知故犯 deliberate flouting of the law;

[情致] appeal; temperament and interest;

[情狀] situation; state of affairs;

愛情 affection; love; love between man and woman; romantic love;

案情 details of a case; facts of a case; ins and outs of a crime; record of a case;

表情 express one's feelings; expression; facial expression;

病情 patient's condition; state of an illness;

悖情 against human nature;

薄情 disloyal to one's love; fickle; heartless; unfaithful; ungrateful;

補情 repay a kindness;

才情 imaginative power; literary and artistic talent;

常情 reason; sense;

承情 be much obliged; owe a debt of gratitude;

痴情 blind passion; infatuated; infatuation;

傳情 convey or express one's tender feeling;

春情 longing for love; stirrings of love;

催情 promote the sexual maturity of animals with medicines in a given period of time;

道情 chanting fold takes to the accompaniment of simple percussion instruments;

敵情　the enemy's situation; the state of the enemy;
動情　(1) become excited; (2) become enamoured;
多情　tender and affectionate;
恩情　kindness; love;
發情　(1) oestrus; (2) be in heat;
風情　amorous feelings; flirtatious expressions;
敢情　(1) I say; (2) of course; really;
感情　(1) emotion; feeling; (2) affection; love;
寡情　cold-hearted; unfeeling;
國情　condition of a country;
旱情　damage to crops by drought;
行情　prices; quotations;
豪情　lofty sentiments;
激情　fervor; passion;
交情　friendship;
矯情　be affectedly unconventional;
盡情　as much as one likes; to one's heart's content;
劇情　story of a play or opera;
軍情　military situation;
領情　appreciate the kindness; feel grateful to sb;
留情　show mercy or forgiveness;
民情　(1) condition of the people; (2) public feeling;
內情　inside information;
七情　seven human emotions;
墒情　soil moisture content;
求情　solicit a favour;
群情　feelings of the masses; public sentiment;
熱情　enthusiasm; enthusiastic; fervent; warmth;
人情　(1) human relationship; (2) human feelings; sensibilities; (3) gift; present; (4) favour;
任情　as much as one likes; do as one pleases; let oneself to; to one's heart's content;
容情　show mercy;
柔情　tender feelings; tenderness;
色情　sexual emotion;
商情　market conditions;
深情　deep feeling; deep love;
神情　expression; look;
盛情　boundless hospitality; great kindness;
實情　the actual situation; the true state of affairs; truth;
事情　affair; business; matter;
抒情　convey one's emotion; express one's feelings;
説情　plead for mercy for sb; solicit a favour for sb;
私情　personal relationships;
俗情　common, human feelings;
調情　flirt;
同情　show sympathy for; sympathize with;
偷情　have a love affair stealthily;
忘情　be indifferent; be unmoved;
溫情　tender feeling;
無情　devoid of feelings; heartless; merciless;
下情　conditions at the lower levels; feelings or wishes of the masses;
險情　dangerous situation;
詳情　details; detailed information;
心情　mood; state of mind;
性情　disposition; temperament;
徇情　let personal feelings or consideration influence one's judgment and decision;
殉情　die for love;
豔情　love;
疫情　epidemic situation;
隱情　facts one wishes to hide;
幽情　exquisite feelings;
友情　friendship;
輿情　popular feelings; public sentiment;
雨情　rainfall;
災情　condition of a disaster;
真情　(1) facts; real situation; (2) true feelings;
知情　know the facts of a case or the details of an incident;
衷情　heartfelt emotion; inner feelings;
鍾情　be deeply in love;
酌情　act according to the circumstances; take into consideration the circumstances;
恣情　do as one pleases; give free rein to one's passions;
縱情　as much as one likes; to one's heart's content;

qing

【晴】　(1) bright; clear; fair; fine; (2) when the rain stops;

[晴和]　fine and balmy; warm and fine;
[晴霽]　fair and clear;
[晴空]　bright sky; clear air; clear sky; cloudless sky; serene;
　晴空萬里　a big, clear open sky; a clear and boundless sky; a stretch of cloudless blue skies; a wide expanse of clear, sunlit sky; the vast clear sky; there is not a speck of cloud in the sky;
　晴空雨　serein;
[晴朗]　bright and clear; fine; fine and cloudless; sunny;
[晴爽]　dry and pleasant;

[晴天] cloudless day; fine day; sunny day;
晴天霹靂 a bolt from the blue; a sudden thunder from a clear sky; a thunderbolt out of a clear sky; a thunderclap from a blue sky;
[晴夜] clear night;
[晴雨] rain or shine;
晴雨表 barometer; weatherglass;
晴雨無阻 rain or shine;
晴雨衣 mackintosh;
久雨初晴 begin to clear up after perpetual rain;
霎雨即晴 the weather clears up after a passing shower;
乍晴乍雨 shine one moment and rain the next; sudden change from rain to shine; the sky has just cleared and now it rains again;
乍雨乍晴 April weather; sudden changes from rain to shine;

放晴 clear up;
天晴 the sky clears;

qing
【擎】 lift; prop up; support;
[擎舉] lift;
眾擎易舉 if many people work together, even a hard job becomes easier; many hands make light work; three helping one another bear the burden of six; what is supported by the people is easily accomplished; when there are many people it's easy to lift a load;
[擎起] lift up;
擎起大旗 lift up the big banner;
[擎手] raise one's hands — stop doing sth;
擎天支柱 a pillar of strength; a sky-supporting pillar; a tower of strength;
[擎天柱] mainstay of a family;

引擎 engine;

qing
【黥】 ancient punishment of tattooing the face;
[黥面] ancient punishment of tattooing the face;
黥面刖足 have sb's kneecaps removed and his face tattooed;
黥首刖足 brand sb's face and cut off his feet;

qing³
qing
【頃】 (1) unit of area; (2) in a moment; in a short moment; in a twinkling; in an instant; in next to no time; in no time; instant; instantly; moment; (3) just; just now; (4) incline; lean toward one side;
[頃步] half a step;
[頃久] instant;
[頃刻] in a moment; in a short moment; in an instant; instantly;
頃刻瓦解 collapse instantly;
頃刻消失 instantly disappear; vanish in an instant;
頃刻之間 in a twinkling; in an instant; in next to no time; in no time;
[頃者] a short while ago; just now;

俄頃 in a short moment; very soon;
公頃 hectare;
少頃 after a few moments; after a short while; presently;
市頃 unit of area;
有頃 after a while;

qing
【請】 (1) allow; ask; ask about; ask for; beg; beseech; call in; entertain; entreat; go for; help oneself; pray; request; send for; treat; (2) please; pray; (3) engage; hire; invite; seek the service of;
[請安] inquire after an elder; pay respects to sb; wish sb good health;
請安問好 ask about sb's health; give greetings; give one's best regards; inquire after and send best wishes to sb; present one's compliments;
闔第請安 give my kind regards to all your family;
[請便] as you please; do as you please; do as you wish; do what pleases one; help yourself; please yourself;
[請辭] request permission to resign; tender one's resignation;
[請調] ask for a transfer; request assignment;
[請功] recommend sb for a citation of merit;
[請假] be absent on leave; apply for leave; ask for leave; ask for leave of absence;

leave of absence;
請假待命 ask for leave and await orders;
請假回家 go home on leave;

[請柬] invitation; invitation card;
結婚請柬 wedding invitation;
一份請柬 an invitation;
一封請柬 a letter of invitation;

[請見] ask for an interview; request an audience;
款關請見 knock at a door requesting for an interview;

[請將不如激將] to a warrior a challenge is more effective than an invitation;

[請教] ask for advice; consult; learn from; seek advice;
請教一下 pick sb's brain;
向專家請教 call in the experts;

[請進] please come in;
非請勿進 no entry; no unauthorized entry;

[請君入瓮] answer a fool according to his folly; answer in kind; dose a man with his own physique; give sb a dose of his own medicine; hoist sb with his own petard; kindly step into the vat; make a person suffer from his own scheme; pay a man back in his own coin; pay back in kind; repay in kind; use one's own argument; work woe unto others;

[請客] act as host to sb; entertain guests; give a party; invite guests; pay the piper; play the host; sb's treat; stand sb's hand; stand treat;
請客送禮 feed guests and distribute gifts; give dinners or send gifts; give feats and present gifts; lavish private parties and expensive gifts;
請客作東 act as host to sb; pay the piper; play the host; stand one's hand; stand treat;
我請客 my treat;

[請命] (1) ask for clemency; beg for life; plead on sb's behalf; (2) request for instructions;
袒膊請命 begging for life by baring the shoulder and tying the arms behind;
為民請命 appeal for the people; plead for the people;

[請求] appeal for; appeal to; ask; beg; entreat; make an appeal to; request;
請求避難 beg for shelter;
請求捐助 solicit for contributions;
請求寬恕 ask for forgiveness;
請求延期 ask for a postponement;
請求允許 pray for permission;
請求支援 make a request for help;
符號請求 symbol request;
回應請求 respond to a request;
緊急請求 urgent request;
拒絕請求 refuse a request; reject a request; turn down sb's request;
考慮請求 consider a request;
收到請求 receive a request;
數據請求 data request;
特殊請求 special request;
提出請求 advance a request; put in a request; submit a request;
同意請求 agree to a request; grant sb's request;
無視請求 ignore a request;
相關請求 related request;
正式請求 formal request;

[請神] call up an evil spirit;
請神容易送神難 it is easier to call up an evil spirit than to allay it;

[請示] ask for instructions; ask instructions from; request instructions;
請示機宜 ask for instructions from one's superior;

[請帖] invitation; invitation card;
一份請帖 an invitation;

[請托] commit sth to sb's care; request another's help;

[請託] ask for a favour;

[請問] (1) excuse me; please; (2) may I ask; one may ask; we should like to ask; would you please tell me;

[請降] beg to surrender; desire to surrender;

[請訓] ask the emperor for instructions before taking up an official appointment;

[請業] ask questions concerning lessons;

[請謁] ask for an audience;

[請益] ask for advice; ask for instructions;

[請纓] submit a request to the emperor for a military assignment;
請纓殺敵 request to be sent to the front; volunteer for battle;

[請雨] pray for rain;

[請願] make a petition; petition; present a petition;

請願書 written petition;
請願運動 petition drive;
請願者 petitioner;

[請戰] ask for a battle assignment;
請戰書 written requests for a battle assignment;

[請罪] (1) admit one's error and ask for punishment; (2) apologize; appeal for leniency; humbly apologize;
伏地請罪 throw oneself on the ground acknowledging one's faults;
負荊請罪 be contrite and ask for pardon; bring a rod on one's back and ask for punishment; carry a rod and ask to be spanked;

報請 request for permission to do sth;
呈請 apply;
吃請 (1) be invited to a dinner; (2) treat sb to a meal at public expense;
敦請 earnestly invite; earnestly request;
恭請 cordially invite;
僱請 employ; hire;
回請 give a return banquet; return hospitality;
懇請 cordially invite; earnestly request;
聘請 engage; invite;
申請 apply for;
聲請 apply for; request;
提請 submit sth to;
延請 employ; engage;
宴請 entertain to dinner; invite to dinner;
邀請 invite;
約請 ask; invite;

qing⁴

qing

【綮】 critical points; crucial points; gist;

肯綮 critical or important juncture; crux of the matter; place where the muscle and the bone link;

qing

【慶】 (1) blessing; felicity; festivity; joy; (2) celebrate; commemorate; congratulate; offer congratulations; rejoice over; (3) occasion for celebration; (4) a surname;

[慶典] celebration; ceremony to celebrate; gala;

[慶功] celebration;
慶功會 celebration meeting for achievements gained; victory meeting;
慶功酒 jungle juice;
慶功論賞 confer honours according to merits in service while celebrating victory;
慶功宴 celebration party;

[慶賀] celebrate; congratulate; offer congratulations; rejoice over;
表示慶賀 express one's congratulations;
可慶可賀 worthy of congratulations;
前來慶賀 appear to offer one's congratulations;

[慶賞] celebrate and reward;

[慶生會] birthday party;

[慶壽] celebrate the birthday of an old person;

[慶幸] congratulate oneself; rejoice oneself;
暗自慶幸 congratulate oneself; consider oneself lucky; rejoice in secret; rejoice in secret at a stroke of luck;

[慶雲] auspicious clouds;

[慶祝] celebrate; congratulate;
慶祝會 celebration;
~大的慶祝會 big celebration;
~家庭慶祝會 family celebration;
~小的慶祝會 small celebration;
慶祝活動 celebration;
~參加慶祝活動 join in the celebrations;
~舉辦慶祝活動 hold a celebration;
慶祝節日 observe the day;
慶祝生日 celebrate one's birthday;
慶祝勝利 celebrate a victory;
舉杯慶祝 raise one's glasses;
值得慶祝 deserve celebration;

國慶 National Day;
歡慶 celebrate joyously;
吉慶 auspicious; happy; propitious;
節慶 holiday and festival;

qing

【磬】 (1) musical stone; (2) inverted bell;

[磬竭] emptied; exhausted; used up;

[磬口梅] a kind of plum;

[磬折] humpbacked;

qing

【親】 relationships as a result of marriage; relatives by marriage;

[親家] (1) families related by marriage; relatives by marriage; (2) parents of one's son-in-law or daughter-in-law;

親家兒子 brothers of one's daughter-in-law;
親家公 father of one's son-in-law or daughter-in-law;
親家老爺 male parents of the married couple;
親家母 mother of one's son-in-law or daughter-in-law;
親家女兒 sisters of one's daughter-in-law;

qing
【罄】 be exhausted; be used up; empty; exhaust; run out; use up; with nothing left;
［罄筆難書］ too numerous to be cited;
［罄竭］ be exhausted; be used up;
［罄盡］ all used up; exhausted; with nothing left;
［罄匱］ be exhausted; be used up;
［罄然］ well disciplined;
［罄身］ nakedness; nudity;
［罄竹難書］ one's crimes are beyond description; one's crimes are too numerous to be listed in one book; too many to enumerate; too numerous to be listed in one book; too numerous to be recorded; too numerous to inscribe; too numerous to mention; too numerous to record;

告罄 be exhausted; run out;

qing
【謦】 cough lightly; speak softly;
［謦欬］ talking and laughing;

qiong¹
qiong
【邛】 (1) heights; hill; mount; (2) ailment; disease; illness; ill health; (3) a surname;
［邛杖］ bamboo cane;

qiong
【芎】 cnidium officinale, a kind of herb;

qiong²
qiong
【穹】 (1) high and vast; (2) arched; elevated; lofty; vaulted; (3) deep; empty; spacious; (4) firmament; heavens; sky; vault of heaven;
［穹蒼］ azure vault; dome of the sky; firmament; heavens; sky; vault of heaven;
［穹地］ elevation;
［穹頂］ cupola; dome; vault;
［穹谷］ deep valley; ravine;
［穹靈］ gods high above;
［穹隆］ (1) arched roof; vault; (2) long and winding;
［穹廬］ yurt;
［穹冥］ azure vault; dome of the sky; firmament; heavens; sky; vault of heaven;
［穹形］ arch; arched; dome-shaped; vault; vaulted;

蒼穹 firmament; vault of heaven;
天穹 vault of heaven;

qiong
【笻】 a kind of bamboo;
［笻杖］ bamboo stick;

qiong
【惸】 (1) afflicted; anxious; distressed; troubled; upset; worried; (2) brotherless; childless; friendless;
［惸獨］ brotherless and childless; friendless; helpless and lonely;
［惸惸］ anxious; distressed; troubled; worried;

qiong
【蛩】 (1) locust; (2) cricket;
［蛩唱］ chirps of crickets;
［蛩鳴］ chirps of crickets;
［蛩蛩］ anxious; apprehensive; distressed; troubled; worried;
［蛩吟］ chirps of crickets;
蛩吟蟲鳴 the chirps of crickets and hums of insects;

qiong
【煢】 all alone; companionless; friendless; lonely; solitary; without friends or relatives;
［煢單］ all alone in the whole wide world;
［煢獨］ alone; friendless and childless;
［煢居］ live alone; live in solitude;
［煢煢］ all alone; desolate and alone; lonely; solitary;
煢煢孑立 alone and helpless; be left in the world miserably lonely; so lonely as

to have only one's shadow to comfort oneself; stand alone in desolation;

qiong

【跫】 footsteps; the sound of steps;

［跫然］ descriptive of sound of footsteps;

［跫音］ footsteps; the sound of steps;

qiong

【窮】 (1) badly off; deprived; destitute; down on one's luck; hard up for money; impoverished; in an awkward financial situation; in difficulty; in reduced circumstances; indigent; less well off; low income; poor; underprivileged; (2) end; limit; the extreme; the farthest; (3) exhaustive; thoroughly; trace to the very source; (4) extremely;

［窮棒子］ pauper; destitute people;

［窮北］ extreme north; farthest north;

［窮本極原］ coming to the root of the matter; thorough investigation;

［窮兵黷武］ a warmonger; engage in unjust military ventures; exhaust one's military strength in wars with other states; exhaust the troops and engage in war; follow a policy of expansionism by military means; indulge in aggressive wars with all one's armed strength; love wars and military exploits; militaristic and aggressive; resort to war as a national policy; sabre-rattling; the lust of battle; use all one's armed might to wage wars of aggression; wage sanguinary war; wage war frequently; wantonly engage in military aggression; war-loving; war-mongering; warlike;

［窮不聊生］ be reduced to dire poverty;

［窮不失義］ poor yet not losing one's righteousness;

［窮愁］ dejection caused by poverty and sorrow; hard up and depressed;

窮愁潦倒 crack up under the strain of poverty and sorrow; down and out; out at elbows; penniless and frustrated; unfortunate and miserable;

［窮蹙］ in dire straits; poverty-stricken;

［窮措大］ penniless fellow assuming the air of being rich; poor scholar; poverty-stricken scholar;

［窮達］ obscurity or eminence; remain obscure or become distinguished;

窮達有命 failure or success is decreed beforehand; success and failure are predestined;

［窮大手］ poor but putting on a bold front by spending lavishly;

［窮當益堅］ one should become firmer in poverty; the greater one's adversity is, the stronger his fortitude should be; the more hard-pressed, the more one must become standfast and firm; the more hard-pressed, the more one must fight back; the poorer one is, the firmer must be one's resolves;

［窮到骨］ extremely poor; stark poverty;

［窮滴滴］ destitute; poor;

［窮冬］ deep in winter; depth of winter; midwinter; winter at its coldest;

［窮而不憫］ being poor yet one is not grievous;

［窮而後工］ adversity fosters genius; being disgraced one's writing would be skillful; literary excellence is achieved only after many frustrations; poverty impels a man to work harder; poverty serves to stimulate a man to greater efforts; the more adversity the author has, the better his writing would be;

［窮乏］ destitute; penniless; poverty-stricken; wanting;

［窮富］ the poor and the rich;

窮怕親，富怕賊 the poor fear kinsmen, the rich fear thieves;

窮嫌富不要 the poor shun it because of its high price, and the rich dislike it because of its poor quality; too costly for the poor and not good enough for those who can pay;

窮有窮愁，富有富愁 the poor have the poor's troubles, and the rich have the problems of the rich;

［窮根究底］ get down to the bedrock; get to the bottom of; inquire deeply into; probe to the bottom;

［窮光蛋］ pauper; penniless vagrant; poor wretch; ragamuffin;

［窮逛］ fool around without pending money;

[窮鬼] poor person; poverty-stricken fellow;
[窮漢] penniless man; poor devil; poor man; poor person;
[窮極] (1) extremely; in the extreme; (2) abjectly poor; hard up;
窮極侈華 exceedingly prodigal; extremely extravagant;
窮極思變 one will start thinking about changes when he is in extreme poverty;
窮極無聊 absolutely senseless; barren; contemptible; disgusting; do very foolish things in desperation; extreme boredom; feel flat; fiddle-faddle; find time hanging too heavy on one's hands; in Queer Street indeed; lie on one's hands; poky; senseless; utterly bored; vulgar and revolting; vulgar taste; weariness of mind;
窮極智生 from great extremities springs up wisdom;
[窮家] practise thrifty at home;
窮家富路 practise thrifty at home but be amply provided while travelling;
窮家難離，熱土難捨 no one likes to leave his home and bit of land, however humble they may be;
[窮竭] exhaust; run out of; use up;
[窮盡] come to an end; end; end of resources; exhaust; exhaustion; limit;
[窮經] study classics exhaustively;
[窮究] examine sth; go into sth seriously; make a thorough inquiry;
[窮舉] exhaustion;
[窮坑難滿] the pit of avarice can never be filled;
[窮空] poverty and lack;
[窮寇] hard-pressed enemy; tottering foe;
窮寇勿追 build golden bridges for the flying foe; don't press an enemy at bay; don't press too hard on fleeing enemy troops; don't pursue the tottering foe; for a flying enemy make a golden bridge; not to press an enemy at bay; not to press on a desperate enemy; not to pursue a beaten enemy;
[窮苦] destitute; impoverished; in straitened circumstances; poverty; poverty-stricken;
裝窮叫苦 make a poor mouth;
[窮匱] short of; wanting in;
[窮困] be beset by poverty; destitute; distressed and afflicted; impoverished; in narrow circumstances; in straitened circumstances; narrow means; poverty-stricken;
窮困潦倒 down and out; down on one's uppers; fall into want; fall on evil days; in deep waters; misfortune and misery; on the beach; out at elbows; penniless and frustrated; under water; walk on one's shoestrings;
[窮拉拉] destitute; poor;
[窮老] (1) till one's death; (2) aged and destitute; old and poor;
[窮里] obscure place; out-of-the-way place;
[窮理] probe into the very root of things;
[窮忙] be kept busy making the ends meet; busy for nothing; fully occupied; toil all day long just to make both ends meet; very busy;
[窮民] poor people; the destitute;
[窮目] see as far as one can;
[窮鳥不擇枝] a drowning man will catch at a straw; a poor bird will stay on any branch;
[窮鳥入懷] a person in straits would seek support wherever he can find it; an exhausted bird flows into one's bosom－driven by poverty to seek relief; become sb's protege when one is down in his luck;
[窮期] conclusion; end; termination;
[窮氣] look of poverty;
[窮人] destitute people; have-nots; needy; negative saver; person of modest means; poor; poor people;
窮人額上汗，富人盤中餐 the poor man's sweat gives the rich man rice;
嘲笑窮人 make a fool of poor people;
救濟窮人 relieve the poor;
看不起窮人 look down on the poor;
同情窮人 sympathize the poor;
壓榨窮人 grind the faces of the poor;
照應窮人 minister to the poor;
[窮奢極欲] be lapped in luxury; be swathed in luxury; enjoy the best comforts that money can buy, gratifying every fancy that occurs in one's mind; extremely

extravagant and avaricious; go to the extremes of extravagance; have every luxury; in the lap of luxury; indulge in luxury and extravagance; lead a life of utmost luxury, indulging every whim that idleness breeds; live a life of wanton extravagance and profligacy; live in extreme luxury with gratification of every desire; live on the fat of the land; luxury and extravagance; the world, the flesh, and the devil; wallow in luxury; wanton extravagance;

［窮鼠嚙狸］ a desperate rat will turn back to bite the pursuing cat; a rat at bay bites the leopard cat—not to press a foe too hard; a rat, driven to despair, would snap at a cat; when a person is brought to bay, he would fight; when a person is held down with his back to the wall, he would fight;

［窮酸］ poor and pedantic; poor, jealous and pedantic;

窮酸相 manners of a destitute scholar;

［窮通］ failure or success;

窮通有命 success and failure are destined;

［窮途］ at the end of one's rope; dead end; in straits;

窮途短計 when one is very poor, his ambition is not far-reaching;

窮途末路 at one's last gasp; at the end of one's rope; at the end of one's resources; at the end of one's tether; be driven into an impasse; come to a dead end; come to an impasse; come to the end of one's tether; find oneself in a blind alley; go into a blind alley; go into a cul-de-sac; go to the wall; in a position where there is no way out; in an impasse; on one's beam ends; reach an impasse; reach the end of one's resources; the dead end; to the last extremity; with one's back to the wall;

［窮鄉僻壤］ a back country; a backwater where people live in penury; a district shut off from the outside world; a jumping-off place; a place in obscurity; a poky hold; a poor, out-of-the-way place; a poverty-stricken place; a remote backward place; a remote village; an obscure village; an out-of-the-way place; at the back of beyond; at the back of god-speed; back countries; back districts; backwoods; by-place; falling-place; poor villages; remote areas; remote villages; the back of beyond; the depth of the country; the maize country; the remote hamlet; the remote hinterland; the remote village; the remotest corners of the countryside;

［窮巷］ lane in a slum area;

［窮相］ appearance indicating poverty;

［窮則思變］ one will start thinking about changes when he is in poverty; poor people want change; poverty gives rise to the desire for change; when all means are exhausted, changes become necessary; when people are poor, they think of possible change that would remove their poverty; when people are reduced to poverty, they contemplate changes that would improve matters;

［窮治］ manage a matter by first examining into it thoroughly;

［窮追］ go in hot pursuit; hot on sb's trail; pursue vigorously;

窮追不捨 go in hot pursuit; pursue relentlessly; run down a convict;

窮追緊逼 turn the heat on;

窮追猛打 hotly pursue and fiercely attack; vigorously pursue and fiercely beat;

詞窮 arguments exhausted; nothing more to say;

哭窮 complain of being hard up;

貧窮 impoverished; needy; poor;

受窮 be poor; live in poverty;

無窮 endless; inexhaustible;

qiong
【嬛】 all alone; alone; by oneself; in solitude; lonely; lonesome; solitary;

qiong
【瓊】 (1) beautiful gems; fine jade; jewelled; precious jade; (2) beautiful; elegant; excellent; fabulous; fine; good; graceful; luxurious; magnificent;

rich;
[瓊杯] jade wine-cup;
[瓊閣] jewelled palace;
瓊閨秀閣 the maidens' chambers;
[瓊館瑤臺] beautiful kiosks and graceful pavilions;
[瓊華] beautiful gems; fine jade;
[瓊漿] good wine;
瓊漿玉液 carnation sauce and sweet fermented spirit; nectar; fine and delicious wine; top-quality wine;
[瓊樓金闕] fabulously rich residence; magnificent building; richly decorated jade palace;
[瓊樓玉宇] magnificent building; richly decorated jade palace;
[瓊葩] blossoms as pure and white as jade;
[瓊臺] magnificent terrace of a palace;
[瓊筵] elaborate feast; luxurious dinner; sumptuous banquet;
[瓊瑤] (1) fine jade; precious jade; (2) your letter; (3) gift for others;
[瓊音] clear and crisp sound;
[瓊脂] agal-agal; agar;
瓊脂膠 agaropectin;
淀粉瓊脂 starch agar;
甘油瓊脂 glycerin agar;
普通瓊脂 plain agar;
營養瓊脂 nutrient agar;
[瓊姿] elegant appearance; graceful appearance;

qiong
【藭】 cnidium officinale, a kind of medicinal herb;

芎藭 rhizome of chuanxiong;

qiu¹
qiu
【丘】 (1) hill; hillock; mound; mountain; (2) big; elder; (3) deserted; empty; wasted; (4) name of Confucius; (5) a surname;
[丘壑] hills and ravines;
心中丘壑 obstinate to one's own ideas;
胸中丘壑 a mind's intricate thoughts;
[丘井] dried-up well;
[丘陵] hills; mounds;
丘陵地帶 hilly country;
[丘墓] grave;
[丘山] (1) hills and mountains; (2) wild country;
[丘亭] empty pavilion;
[丘墟] wasteland; empty land;
華屋丘墟 a magnificent house has become a mound of earth — vicissitude; ups and downs;
[丘野] rural country;
[丘園] garden in the hills;
[丘疹] papule;
丘疹病 papulosis;
丘疹性痤瘡 acne papulosa;
丘疹性虹膜炎 iritis papulosa;
丘疹性濕疹 eczema papulosum;

比丘 Buddhist monk;
山丘 (1) hillock; (2) grave;
沙丘 sand dune;
蛇丘 esker;
蟻丘 ant hill;

qiu
【邱】 (1) same as 丘; (2) a surname;

qiu
【秋】 (1) autumn; fall; (2) harvest time; (3) year; (4) period; time; (5) season; (6) beautiful; bewitching; bright; (7) amorous; loving; (8) a surname; (9) (of mahjong) autumn;
[秋波] bewitching eyes of a woman; bright eyes of a beautiful woman;
秋波暗送 send silent and endearing messages with bewitching eyes;
秋波傳情 cast sheep's eyes; give a loving glance; give sb; the glad eye; make eyes at sb; throw amorous glances at sb;
秋波流媚 glance at sb with a soupcon of coquetry;
秋波微轉 a slight turn of the bewitching eyes of a beautiful woman; eloquent eyes that send a silent message;
秋波盈盈 one's sidelong glance has the moist gleam of the autumnal waves;
臨去秋波 a departing favour; cast a bewitching look on departing;
送秋波 cast an amorous glance; make eyes at;
~暗送秋波 cast coquettish glances at; cast sheep's eyes at; flirt; leer at; make

eyes at; make goo-goo eyes at; make secret overtures to; ogle at; secretly cast flirtatious looks at; stealthily give sb the glad eye; stealthily send speechless messages;

~大送秋波 give sb the glad eye; make eyes at; make sheep's eyes at; send speechless messages from the eyes;

~頻送秋波 cast amorous glances again and again;

眼似秋波 bright-eyed; in her eyes lay the gleam of the autumn wave; one's eyes glisten with the shine of autumn waves;

[秋播] autumn sowing; fall sowing;

[秋材] autumn wood;

[秋菜] autumn vegetable;

[秋茶] autumn tea;

[秋蟬] autumn cicada;

[秋成] autumn harvest;

[秋蟲] autumn insects;

秋蟲悲月 the autumn insect chirps to the moon;

秋蟲夜鳴 autumn insects chirping at night;

[秋刀魚] saury;

[秋冬] autumn and winter;

秋冬之交 the time when autumn turns into winter;

秋殘冬初 the end of autumn and the beginning of winter;

秋去冬來 autumn gives way to winter; autumn is followed by winter; autumn turns into winter;

秋行冬令 the weather in autumn is as cold as in winter;

[秋分] autumnal equinox;

秋分點 autumnal equinox;

[秋風] autumn breeze; autumn wind;

秋風過耳 like an autumn breeze passing the ear; like wind whistling past one's ears; of no importance; pay no heed to; turn a deaf ear to; unheeded like a passing autumnal breeze;

秋風秋雨 disconsolate winds and rains; mournful winds and monotonous rains;

秋風颯颯 the autumn wind is soughing in the trees;

秋風掃落葉 autumn wind sweeping away dead leaves; carry everything before me; irresistible force; like a gust of the autumnal wind sweeping away the fallen leaves; like the autumn wind sweeping away the withered leaves; make a clean sweep of sth;

秋風送爽 autumn breezes cool sb;

秋風團扇 like fans being out of use after autumn; woman out of men's favour;

秋風蕭瑟 autumn wind is soughing;

打秋風 get money;

[秋楓] maple tree in autumn;

秋楓似炬 the maple tree stands like a huge torch ablaze in the golden autumn;

秋楓吐火 in autumn the maple leaves turn as crimson red as fire;

[秋高] late autumn

秋高馬肥 in late autumn horses are fat;

秋高氣爽 an invigorating autumn climate; dry, crisp air of autumn; fine autumn weather; in the cool, clear autumn days; the autumn sky is clear and the air crisp; the clear and crisp autumn climate;

[秋耕] autumn ploughing;

[秋毫] autumn hair; newly-grown down; sth so small as to be almost indiscernible;

秋毫無犯 forbid the slightest violation of the people's interests; not to cause the slightest damage to the people; not to commit the slightest offence against the civilians; not to encroach on the interest of the people to the slightest degree; not to inflict the slightest harm on the people; not to injure the people in the least; without committing the slightest offence against the civilians; without inflicting the slightest harm;

秋毫之末 the minutest detail in everything; the minutest thing; almost indiscernible particle;

明察秋毫 able to discover the minutest detail in everything — said of a person with a discerning eye; see through a brick wall;

~明察秋毫的人 clairvoyant;

[秋後] after autumn; after the autumn harvest;

秋後的螞蚱—蹦躂不了幾天 like a grasshopper at the end of autumn — nearing its end; like a locust in late autumn — its days are numbered;

秋後算帳 bide one's time to take revenge;

settle accounts with sb afterwards; square accounts with sb when a political movement is over;

[秋季] autumn; autumn season;
秋季的 autumnal;
秋季作物 autumn crops;

[秋景] (1) autumnal scenery; (2) prospects for the autumn harvest;

[秋菊春桃] everything is good in its season;

[秋糧] autumn grain crops;

[秋涼] chilliness in autumn; cool autumn days;

[秋令] (1) autumn; (2) autumn weather;

[秋末] late autumn; the last days of autumn;
秋末冬初 it is the time of the year when autumn changes into winter;

[秋娘] aged woman;

[秋氣] (1) desolate air of autumn; (2) desolate; dilapidated;

[秋千] swing;
打秋千 get on a swing; have a swing; play on the swing;
盪秋千 swing on a swing;
高秋千 high swing;

[秋熱] old wives' summer;

[秋色] autumn scenery; autumnal tints;
秋色平分 leg and leg; share on a fifty-fifty basis;
秋色如焚 the hills are inflamed with autumnal tints;
秋色宜人 bright and beautiful autumn scene; charming autumn scenery; delightful autumn scenery;

[秋扇] fans in autumn — deserted women;
秋扇見捐 cast aside like fans in autumn; share the fate of an autumn fan;

[秋實] fruits in autumn;

[秋事] autumn harvest;

[秋收] (1) autumn harvest; (2) autumn crops;
秋收冬藏 harvest in autumn and store in winter;
秋收秋種 autumn harvesting and sowing;

[秋霜] (1) autumn frost; (2) snowy hair; (3) severity; sternness;

[秋水] (1) autumn water; (2) clear and beautiful eyes of a girl;
秋水潺湲 gently flow the autumn streams;
秋水仙 autumn crocuses; meadow saffrons;
秋水伊人 thinking of an old acquaintance on seeing a familiar scene;
望穿秋水 aspire earnestly; await with great anxiety; gaze with eager expectation; keep gazing anxiously till one's eyes are strained;
眼如秋水 bright-eyed; one's eyes are like autumn water — as clear as water;
眼若秋水，目如寒星 with a pair of eyes like the autumn water and stars of a wintry night;
一泓秋水 an expanse of limpid water in autumn;
~一泓秋水，光照人寒 an autumn lake that cools sb by its cold splendour;
一灣秋水 an arch of autumnal water;

[秋思] autumn thoughts;

[秋天] autumn; autumn days; fall;
秋天賣涼粉—不識時務 selling cold rice noodles in autumn — show no understanding of the times;
在秋天 in autumn;

[秋顏] fading beauty;

[秋意] chilliness of autumn;

[秋雨] autumn rains;
秋雨綿綿 the autumn rain falls day after day without ceasing; the autumn rain goes on and on;

[秋月] autumn moon;
秋月春風 the autumn moon and spring breeze — a beautiful scene on a bright day;
冰壺秋月 a chaste soul which is as pure as a pot made of ice and as bright as the autumn moon;
春花秋月 seasonal views; the spring flower and autumn moon;
弓似秋月 the bow curves like the harvest moon;
面若秋月 one's face is as bright as the mid-autumn moon;
明若秋月 the light that streams from it is like the light of the harvest moon;

[秋雜] autumn sundries;

[秋裝] autumn clothing;

悲秋 feel sad with the coming of autumn;
初秋 early autumn;
春秋 (1) spring and autumn; year; (2) age; (3) annal; history;
寒秋 late autumn;
立秋 Beginning of Autumn;
千秋 (1) a thousand years; centuries; (2)

birthday;

三秋 (1) three autumn jobs; (2) three years;

芟秋 weed and loosen the soil after the beginning of autumn;

深秋 late autumn;

收秋 harvest autumn crops;

晚秋 late autumn; late in the autumn;

中秋 Mid-autumn Festival;

仲秋 mid-autumn;

qiu

【蚯】 earthworm;

［蚯蜥］ worm lizard;

［蚯蚓］ earthworm;

qiu

【楸】 a kind of hard wood used for making chessboard;

［楸枰］ chessboard;

qiu

【龜】 used in 龜茲；

［龜茲］ a country in Central Asia during the Han Dynasty;

qiu

【鞦】 (1) swing; (2) crupper; (3) traces;

［鞦韆］ swing;

打鞦韆 get on a swing; have a swing; play on the swing;

qiu

【鰍】 loach;

泥鰍 loach;

鯕鰍 dolphinfish; dorado;

qiu

【鶖】 a kind of water bird;

qiu²

qiu

【仇】 (1) a surname; (2) spouse;

［仇偶］ one's spouse;

qiu

【囚】 (1) imprison; keep in captivity; put in jail; put in prison; (2) convict; jail-bird; lag; prisoner;

［囚車］ paddy wagon; prison van; prisoners' van;

［囚犯］ convict; innate; jail-bird; prisoner;

囚犯人數 prison population;

處決囚犯 execute a convict;

形同囚犯 be treated like convicts;

押送囚犯 carry convicts;

一幫囚犯 a gang of prisoners;

［囚房］ cell; a prison; a prison cell;

［囚禁］ imprison; imprisonment; keep in captivity; put in jail; put in prison;

被囚禁 be held in captivity;

［囚牢］ jail; prison;

［囚籠］ prisoner's cage;

［囚室］ prison cell;

［囚首垢面］ untidy appearance with prisoner's unkempt hair and unwashed face; with unkempt hair and dirty face;

［囚徒］ convict; jailbird; lag; prisoner;

［囚衣］ convict's clothes; prisoner's garb;

錮囚 occlusion;

階下囚 captive; prisoner;

死囚 death convict;

繫囚 be imprisoned;

qiu

【求】 (1) ask; ask for; beg; entreat; hope for; implore; plead for; pray for; request; solicit; supplicate; (2) aim; court; pursue; seek; set one's mind on; strive for; try to obtain; (3) demand; (4) covet; desire;

［求愛］ court; pay court to; woo;

求愛期 courtship;

向人求愛 make advances to sb;

［求備］ seek completeness;

［求成］ hope for success;

［求代］ seek a substitute to do a duty;

［求貸］ ask for loan;

［求得］ obtain;

求得苟安 seek momentary ease;

［求告］ (1) petition; solicit; (2) entreat; implore; supplicate;

［求和］ (1) hold out the olive branch; make overtures of reconciliation; seek peace with an enemy; sue for peace; try to end hostilities; (2) try to draw a match; (3) summation;

部份求和 partial summation; summation by parts;

屈膝求和 bow the knees to...and sue for peace;

損耗求和 summation of losses;

以戰求和 achieve peace through military means;

[求歡] seek the consent of a woman for a sexual intercourse;

[求凰] seek a wife;

[求婚] ask a woman's hand in marriage; ask for a lady's hand; ask sb in marriage; lead a woman to the alter; make a proposal of marriage; make an offer of marrige; make suit to sb; marry; offer one's hand; pay one's addresses to a lady; pay one's court to a woman; plead one's suit with a woman; pop the question; propose; propose marriage to; seek a marriage alliance; set one's cap at sb; step up to a girl; sue to; sue for a woman's hand in marriage; wed; woo;
求婚被拒絕 get the push;
主動求婚 take the initiative in courtship;

[求積儀] planimeter;
補正求積儀 compensating planimeter;
定極求積儀 polar planimeter;
平方根求積儀 square-root planimeter;

[求見] ask to see; beg for an audience; request an interview; seek an interview;

[求漿得酒] ask for starch but get wine; gain sth unexpectedly; get more than one has asked for;

[求教] ask for advice; consult; seek advice; seek instruction;
虛心求教
ready to listen to advice; willing to take advice;

[求解] (1) seek help in distress; (2) seek the solution to a mathematical problem;
不求甚解 content with superficial understanding; not seek to understand things thoroughly; satisfied with a smattering of knowledge;

[求借] beg to borrow;

[求救] ask for rescue; ask sb to come to the rescue; cry for help; seek help; seek relief;
求救無門 have no way to obtain rescue from any quarters;

[求偶] courtship; seek a spouse;
求偶本能 mating instinct;

[求乞] beg; beg for food; beg for money;
求乞度日 earn one's living by begging;
沿街求乞 beg for money or food in the street;

[求籤] pray and draw divination sticks at a temple;
求籤問卜 ask the gods for an oracle; divine by drawing lots;

[求親] (1) seek a marriage alliance; (2) ask for help from relatives;
求親靠友 ask favours of relatives and friends;

[求情] appeal to mercy; ask for a favour; beg favours from; beg for leniency; intercede; intercession; plead; plead with sb;
求情告饒 beg for pardon; plead for leniency;

[求全] (1) ask for perfection; demand perfection; (2) seek a satisfactory result; try to bring sth to a satisfactory conclusion; try to round sth off;
求全責備 ask for perfection; demand of others nothing less than perfection; demand perfection; hypercritical and demand perfection; look for perfection; nitpick; overcritical; seek to be perfect;
求全之毀 one tries one's best and still gets criticized for it; try to be perfect only to receive reproaches;
求全之心 the desire for perfection;

[求饒] ask for forgiveness; ask for pardon; beg for mercy; beg for one's life; seek pardon;
抱腿求饒 embrace sb's legs and plead for mercy;
跪下求饒 fall to one's knees, begging for mercy; kneel down begging for pardon;
哭着求饒 whine for mercy;
屈膝求饒 capitulate to...and beg for mercy;

[求人] (1) ask for help; (2) look for talents;
求人不如求己 applying to others for help is not as good as applying to oneself; ask another for help is not as good as to help oneself; better depend on oneself than ask for help from others; better do it than wish it done; better do it yourself than ask help from others; better to seek help from oneself than from sb else; God helps those who help themselves; it is better to aid

oneself than to depend on the aid of others; it is better to ask of one's own folk than of outsiders; near is my shirt, but nearer is my skin; relying on oneself is better than relying on others; self-help is better than help from others; the best answer is to roll up your sleeves and do the job yourself;
求人憐憫 plead with a person for pity;
泣求於人 implore sb with tears;

[求仁得仁] achieve what one wishes; carry one's point; get the desired object; obtain an object sought for; persuade others to act as you wish; seek for virtue and get virtue; want sth and succeed in getting it;

[求容] seek room for oneself; seek space for oneself;

[求榮] strive for honour;
求榮反辱 strive for honour but result in shame;
賣友求榮 betray one's master for the sake of glory; betray one's master in order to get a high position; sell one's master and sue for honours;

[求神] beg the gods;
求神問卜 beg the gods and ask of the diviner; pray and consult an oracle; pray to the gods and seek to ascertain by divination; seek divine advice;

[求生] seek to live on; seek to survive; try to remain alive;
求生不得 can hardly keep alive;
求生不得，求死不能 can neither live nor die – utter misery; though one hopes for life one cannot live and though one prays to die one cannot die;
含辱求生 allow oneself to be insulted in order to remain alive;

[求勝] strive for victory;
求勝心切 anxious to gain victory; itch for victory;

[求實] practical-minded; realistic;
求實精神 down-to-earth attitude; matter-of-fact attitude; realistic approach;

[求售] for sale; seek a buyer;
衒玉求售 brag about one's own talent with a view to getting a job; recommend oneself to a position;

[求恕於人] appeal to sb for mercy;

[求田問舍] busy oneself with business deals and have no higher ambition in life;

[求降] beg to surrender; hoist the white flag;

[求學] (1) attend school; go to college; go to school; receive education; study; (2) pursue one's studies; seek knowledge;
發憤求學 very eager in one's studies;

[求異] difference-seeking;
求異決策 difference-seeking decision-making;
求異思維 thinking for dissimilation;

[求雨] pray for rain;
祈神求雨 offer prayers for rain; pray to the gods for rain;

[求援] ask for aid and support; ask for help; request reinforcements; seek help; seek relief;

[求戰] (1) seek battle with; (2) ask to take part in a battle;

[求證] prove; seek confirmation; seek to confirm; seek to prove; seek verification;

[求知] seek knowledge;
求知心切 eager for knowledge;
求知慾 craving for knowledge; thirst for knowledge;
渴望求知 yearn to seek knowledge;

[求職] seek employment;
求職技巧 job-seeking skills;
求職申請書 application for employment;
求職途徑 job-seeking channels;
求職者 jobseekers;

[求助] resort to; seek aid; seek help; turn to sb for help;
求助窗口 help screen;
求助熱線 helpline;
求助於詭辯 resort to sophistry;
求助於人 appeal to sb for assistance; call upon others for help; crave for others' help;
求助於宗教 have recourse to religion;

[求子] pray for a son;

哀求 appeal pathetically; beg; beg humbly; beg piteously; beg pitifully; beseech; entreat; grovel; implore;
吹求 fastidious; hypercritical;
訪求 search for; seek;
干求 beseech; importune; request;
供求 supply and demand;

冀求 hope to get;
講求 be particular about; strive for;
苛求 be overcritical; make excessive demands;
渴求 eager about;
懇求 beseech; implore;
力求 do all one can; make every effort to;
謀求 seek; strive for;
乞求 beg for; entreat;
企求 hanker after; seek for;
祈求 earnestly hope; pray for;
蘄求 earnestly hope; pray for;
強求 impose; insist on;
請求 ask; request;
奢求 excessive desire;
搜求 seek;
索求 seek;
探求 pursue; seek;
推求 ascertain; inquire into;
妄求 inappropriately request;
需求 demand; requirement;
尋求 explore; seek;
央求 beg; implore;
要求 demand; require;
徵求 ask for; solicit;
追求 (1) pursue; seek; (2) chase; run after;

qiu

【泅】 float; swim; wade;
[泅渡] swim across;
[泅水] swim;
[泅者善溺] a good swimmer often gets drowned;

qiu

【虯】 young dragon;
[虯龍] young dragon;
[虯蟠] be curled up like a dragon;
[虯髯] curly whiskers;

qiu

【酋】 (1) chief of a clan; chieftain; (2) end;
[酋矛] a kind of long spear;
[酋長] (1) chief of a tribe; (2) sheik;
酋長國 emirate;

qiu

【毬】 ball; sphere;
[毬果] cones; strobiles;
[毬蘭] wax plant;

qiu

【球】 (1) globe; sphere; (2) ball; (3) ball game; (4) earth; globe; (5) anything shaped like a ball;
[球板] paddles;
[球棒] bat;
一根球棒 a bat;
[球場] (1) ball park; (2) court; (3) field;
球場暴力 fan violence; spectator violence;
草地球場 grass court;
籃球場 basketball playground;
瀝青球場 asphalt court;
黏土球場 clay court;
排球場 volleyball court;
三合土球場 concrete court;
網球場 tennis court;
硬地球場 fast court; hard court;
羽毛球場 badminton court;
[球帶] spherical zone;
[球膽] ball bladder;
[球隊] team;
球隊隊員 team member;
球隊隊長 team captain;
~當球隊隊長 captain a team;
球隊領隊 team manager;
球隊主教練 team coach;
效力於一支球隊 play for a team;
一支球隊 a team;
支持一支球隊 support a team;
[球兒] ball;
[球冠] spherical crown;
[球菌] coccus;
球菌狀 coccus forms;
鏈球菌 streptococcus;
葡萄球菌 staphylococcus;
[球籃] basket;
[球類] balls;
球類運動 ball games;
[球路] style of play;
直線球路 straight course;
[球門] goal;
球門橫梁 crossbar;
球門口 goalmouth;
球門球 goalkick;
球門區 goalmouth; goal area;
球門網 goal net;
球門線 goal line;
球門柱 goalpost;
[球迷] football fan;
一群球迷 a band of football fans;
[球面] sphere; spherical surface;
球面波 spherical wave;
球面度 spherical degree;
球面角 spherical angle;

球面象差 spherical aberration;
超球面 hypersphere;
~ 測地超球面 geodesic hypersphere;
~ 點超球面 point hypersphere;
~ 極限超球面 limiting hypersphere;
~ 實超球面 real hypersphere;
~ 虛超球面 imaginary hypersphere;
~ 有向超球面 oriented hypersphere;
~ 正常超球面 proper hypersphere;
仿射球面 affine sphere;
異種球面 exotic sphere;
組合球面 combinatorial sphere;

[球拍] bat; racket;
球拍夾 racket press;
球拍套 racket case;
羽毛球球拍 badminton racket;

[球賽] ball game; ball match; game; match;
看球賽 watch a ball game;
一場球賽 a ball game;

[球壇] ball-playing circles; ball-playing world;

[球體] spheroid;

[球僮] ball boy; caddy;
女球僮 ball girl;

[球洞] hole;

[球戲] ball game;

[球鞋] gym shoes; sneakers; tennis shoes;

[球心] centre of a sphere;

[球星] athletic star;

[球形] ball-shaped; globular; spherical;

[球衣] sports shirt; sweat shirt;

[球藝] ball game skills;
切磋球藝 swap pointers;

[球員] ballplayer;
側鋒球員 winger;
防守球員 defender;
明星球員 star player;
替補球員 substitute;
中場球員 midfield player; midfielder;

[球證] referee; umpire;

[球座] tee;

白血球 leucocyte; white blood cell;
板球 cricket;
半球 hemisphere;
棒球 baseball;
保齡球 (1) bowling; (2) bowling ball;
冰球 ice hockey;
擦邊球 edge ball; touch ball;
彩球 colourful ball;
綵球 ball wound up from varicoloured silk;
長球 long shot;
持球 carrying; catching; holding;
抽球 drive;
傳球 pass a ball;
槌球 croquet;
搓球 chop;
打球 play a ball game;
地球 the earth; the globe;
頂球 head a ball;
短球 drop shot; short ball;
發球 serve a ball;
罰球 penalty kick; penalty shot;
橄欖球 rugby;
高爾夫球 golf;
環球 round the world; the earth; the whole world;
寰球 the earth; the whole world;
擊球 bat the ball;
界內球 in; in bounds;
界外球 out; out of bounds;
開球 kick off;
康樂球 caroms;
籃板球 rebound;
籃球 (1) basketball;
壘球 softball;
練球 practise a ball game;
鏈球 hammer;
馬球 polo;
煤球 briquette;
排球 volleyball;
皮球 ball;
乒乓球 pinhg-pong ball;
氣球 balloon;
鉛球 shot;
曲棍球 hockey;
全球 whole world;
讓球 concede points;
賽球 play a ball-game match;
色球 chromosphere;
手球 handball;
水球 water polo;
死球 dead ball;
台球 billiard;
天球 celestial sphere;
跳球 jump ball;
網球 tennis;
星球 celestial body;
繡球 ball made of strips of silk;
雪球 snow ball;
血球 bloodcell;
眼球 eyeball;
羽毛球 badminton;
月球 moon;

運球 dribble;
足球 football; soccer;

qiu
【逑】 (1) marry; match; pair; (2) collect; draw together; (3) mate;

qiu
【裘】 (1) furs; (2) a surname;
［裘弊金盡］ fall into a state of poverty; have exhausted one's means; short of living expenses abroad; with coat tattered and gold exhausted;
［裘葛］ clothes; clothing; dress;
裘葛屢更 many changes from furs to hemp — the lapse of many years;
［裘褐］ dress economically; dress simply;
［裘馬］ furs and horses — the rich;
裘馬輕肥 affluent; in good circumstances; wealthy; well-to-do;

貂裘 marten coat;
狐裘 fox fur coat; fox-fur robe;

qiu
【遒】 (1) forceful; powerful; strong; sturdy; vigorous; (2) close; come to an end; (3) concentrate; gather;
［遒健］ strong; vigorous;
［遒緊］ compact and cautious;
［遒勁］ (1) forceful; vigorous; (2) strong; sturdy;
［遒美］ forceful and graceful;
［遒逸］ forceful and moving;

qiu
【賕】 bribe;
［賕紋］ accept a bribe; take a bribe;

qiu
【蝤】 (1) chrysalis of a kind of beetle; (2) May fly; ephemera;
［蝤蛑］ a kind of crab;

qiu³
qiu
【糗】 dry food; dry ration;

qu¹
qu
【曲】 (1) bent; circuitous; crooked; roundabout; tortuous; twisted; winding; zigzag; (2) bend; crook; digress; distort; twist; (3) curved; curvaceous; curvacious; (4) little known; obscure; secretive; (5) biased; unfair; unjust; unjustifiable; wrong; (6) a surname;
［曲背而行］ stoop in walking;
［曲筆］ (1) distortion of the facts; (2) deliberate digression in writing;
［曲庇］ conceal by distorting facts;
［曲別針］ paper clip;
［曲柄］ crank;
球狀曲柄 ball crank;
銳角曲柄 acute angle crank;
鐘形曲柄 bell crank;
組合式曲柄 built-up crank;
［曲從］ obey reluctantly; yield reluctantly;
曲從其意 let him have his wish;
曲從眾意 bend to the public opinion;
［曲度］ curvature;
［曲肱而枕］ bend the arm for a pillow; crook one's arm for head support during sleep; lie with one's head on one's arm; make use of bended arm as a pillow; use one's bended arm as a pillow;
［曲棍球］ (1) field hockey; hockey; (2) hockey ball;
冰上曲棍球 ice hockey;
［曲解］ distort; misconstrue; misinterpret; misrepresent; twist;
曲解詞義 strain the meaning of a word;
曲解人意 misrepresent sb's meaning; put a false construction on sb's remark;
曲解原文 pervert the text;
曲解原意 distort the meaning;
被嚴重曲解 be grossly misinterpreted;
［曲謹］ fastidious about details;
［曲盡其妙］ bring out in a fine and ingenious way all the subtleties in sth; describe minutely and tactfully; express sb fully in a roundabout and detailed way; express the subtlety tactfully and finely; in a subtle and skilful way; the ability of expression;
［曲徑］ winding path;
曲徑通幽 a winding path leading to a secluded spot;
［曲欄］ winding balustrade;
［曲面］ curved surface;
超曲面 hypersurface;
~代數超曲面 algebraic hypersurface;
~管道超曲面 canal hypersurface;

～特徵超曲面 characteristic hypersurface;
雙曲面 hyperboloid;
～單葉雙曲面 uniparted hyperboloid;
～共焦雙曲面 confocal hyperboloid;
～旋轉雙曲面 rotating hyperboloid;

[曲撓] unfair blame; unjust accusation;

[曲奇] cookie;
幸運曲奇 fortune cookie;

[曲全] suppress one's own feelings for the sake of greater interests;
曲全其意 yield and unable to have one's goal to be achieved;

[曲士] cramped scholar; obscure person;

[曲室] secret chamber;

[曲率] curvature;
仿射曲率 affine curvature;
共曲率 common curvature;
漸近曲率 asymptotic curvature;
絕對曲率 absolute curvature;
聯合平均曲率 allied mean curvature;

[曲説] biased statement;

[曲突徙薪] bend the chimney and remove the fuel to prevent a possible fire; guard against danger; make provisions before troubles occur; rectify blocked chimney and remove firewood; take precautionary measures against a possible danger; who repairs not his gutters repairs his whole house;

[曲線] curve;
曲線美 (1) linear beauty; (2) (said of a woman) curvaceous; curvacious; shapely; (3) polar;
曲線圖 graph;
閉曲線 closed curve;
波狀曲線 wave curve;
超越曲線 transcendental curve;
代數曲線 algebraic curve;
對稱曲線 symmetrical curve;
二次曲線 conic;
～二次曲線規 conicograph;
～二次曲線系 system of conics;
～測地二次曲線 geodesic conic;
～共焦二次曲線 confocal conics;
～絕對二次曲線 absolute conic;
～內極二次曲線 inpolar conic;
～雙切二次曲線 bitangent conics;
～同心二次曲線 concentric conics;
～無心二次曲線 noncentral conic;
～線索二次曲線 line conic;
～中心二次曲線 central conic;
活度曲線 activity curve;
極二次曲線 conic polar;
極三次曲線 cubic polar;
加速度曲線 accelerating curve;
絕熱曲線 adiabatic curve;
累加曲線 accumulation curve;
時距曲線 travel time curve;
雙曲線 hyperbola;
～等軸雙曲線 equilateral hyperbola;
～共軛雙曲線 conjugate hyperbolas
～共焦雙曲線 confocal hyperbola;
～立方雙曲線 cubic hyperbola;
特徵曲線 pattern;
同位曲線 corresponding curves;
同位元曲線 . corresponding curves;
吸收曲線 absorption curve;
餘切曲線 cotangent curve;
餘弦曲線 cosine curve;
圓錐曲線 conic section;
正切曲線 tangent curve;
正弦曲線 sine curve;

[曲學] heretical school;

[曲意] make a special concession to achieve others' goals;
曲意逢迎 curry favour with others by roundabout methods; do everything to please sb; flatter by hook or by crook; flatter sb in a hundred and one ways; go out of one's way to curry favour with sb; gratify sb's every whim; lick sb's boots; ply sb with assiduous flattery; submit obsequiously to sb's will;
曲意奉承 use every means to fawn on; elaborate sweet talk; silken flattery;
曲意俯就 have to come to terms with sb;
曲意求全 make special allowances to save a situation;

[曲藝] balladry; ballad-singing and story-telling; musical arts;
曲藝團 recitation and ballad-singing troupe;

[曲折] (1) circuitous; curving; intricate; tortuous; ups and downs; winding; zigzag; (2) complications; intricacy; not smooth; not straightforward;
曲折有致 delightfully complicated;

[曲直] just and unjust; right and wrong;
曲直不分 fail to discriminate the bent and straight — not to distinguish between right and wrong; right and wrong are

not discriminated;

[曲軸] crank; crankshaft;
分段組裝式曲軸 split-clamp crankshaft;
六拐曲軸 six throw crankshaft;
組合式曲軸 built-up crankshaft;

安魂曲 requiem;
插曲 episode; interlude;
賦格曲 fugue;
歌曲 song;
骨彎曲 cyrtosis;
河曲 bend; meander;
間奏曲 entracte; intermezzo;
金曲 golden oldie;
酒曲 distiller's yeast;
卷曲 curl; curl over;
捲曲 curl;
款曲 heartfelt feelings;
狂想曲 fantasia; rhapsody;
名曲 masterpiece in music;
扭曲 contort; contortion;
盤曲 tortuous; zigzagging;
譜曲 set a poem;
翹曲 warping;
屈曲 crooked; curved; meandering; winding;
拳曲 bending; curling; twisting;
蜷曲 coil; curl; twist;
鬈曲 crimping; crinkling; curling;
三部曲 trilogy;
隨想曲 capriccio;
歪曲 distort; misrepresent; twist;
蜿曲 meander;
彎曲 (1) bent; crooked; meandering; winding; zigzag; (2) bend; bending; flex; flexure;
枉曲 bent; crooked; warped;
委曲 (1) tortuous; winding; (2) twists of events;
骫曲 stoop to compromise;
舞曲 dance music;
嬉游曲 divertisement; play; sport;
戲曲 drama; play; theatrical composition; traditional opera;
鄉曲 a place far from town; an out-of-the-way place; remote and out-of-the-way rural areas;
小曲 ditty; popular tune;
邪曲 crooked; wicked;
協奏曲 concerto;
心曲 (1) heart; innermost being; mind; (2) sth weighing on one's mind;
新曲 new musical composition; new song; new tune;
序曲 introduction; overture; prelude;
夜曲 nocturne;
一曲 a song;
迂曲 circuitous; tortuous;
紆曲 (1) twists and turns; wind; (2) insinuating;
圓舞曲 waltz;
怨曲 blues;
樂曲 musical composition; piece of music;
褶曲 fold;
趾彎曲 clinodactyly;
衷曲 heartfelt emotion; inner feelings; the voice of one's heart; words from the bottom of one's heart;
終曲 finale;
奏鳴曲 sonata;
主題曲 theme song;
作曲 compose; composition; set a song to music; write a song; write music;

qu

【屈】 (1) bend; bow; crook; flex; winding; (2) be disgraced; humble; humiliate; knock under; knuckle under to; subdue; submit to; suffer an insult; surrender; yield to; (3) disgrace; humiliation; mortification; (4) injustice; wrong; (5) in the wrong; (6) inferior status in an inferior position; in an uncomfortable position; (7) condescend; (8) a surname;

[屈臂] url;

[屈才] do work unworthy of one's talents; put sb in a position that does not do him justice; put sb on a job unworthy of his talents;

[屈從] capitultate; knock under; knuckle under to; submit to; yield to;
屈從於暴政 bow one's hed to tyranny;
不屈從的 unyielding;

[屈打成招] admit one's guilt under torture; confess after tortures; be forced to plead to a crime undertorture; confess to false charges under torture; confess under torture to a crime one hasn't committed; extort confessions by torture; obtain a confession by means of torture; obtain a confession by tortures; plead guilty under torture;

[屈服] bow down to; bow to; capitulate; give away; knuckle under; submit to; succumb; surrender; yield to; yielding;

反向屈服 reverse yielding;
分佈屈服 distributed yielding;

[屈肌] flexor; musculus flexor;
莖節屈肌 stipital flexor;
撓側腕屈肌 radial flexor;
指淺屈肌 superficial flexor of fingers;
指深屈肌 deep flexor of fingers;

[屈駕] condescend to make the journey;

[屈節] compromise one's integrity; depart from principle; forfeit one's honour;
屈節求榮 humble one's virtue for honour;

[屈就] accept a job too humble for one's position; condescend to take a post offered;
屈高就下 be compelled to be an underling; condescend oneself to contact with people of humble status;

[屈居人下] accept an inferior status; reluctant to be placed under others;

[屈量] fail to drink contentedly;

[屈撓] surrender; yield;

[屈蟠] twisted and entwining tree trunks;

[屈奇] odd; strange; unusual;

[屈曲] crooked; winding;

[屈辱] disgrace; humiliation; mortification; suffer an insult;
深感屈辱 nurse one's humiliation;

[屈身事仇] be forced to serve the enemy;

[屈死] be persecuted to death; be wronged and driven to death;

[屈腿] bend legs;
屈腿騰越 vaulting over with legs together and bent;

[屈枉] treat unjustly; wrong;

[屈膝] bend one's knees; drop on one's knees; fall on one's knees; give in; go down on one's knees; kneel down; knuckle down; succumb;
屈膝跪拜 genuflection;
屈膝禮拜 bend the knees in worship;
屈膝求和 bow the knees to... and sue for peace;
屈膝求饒 capitulate to...and beg for mercy;
屈膝投降 bend and surrender to; bow and surrender to; fall on one's knees to surrender; give in and surrender to; go down on one's knees in surrender; kneel down in capitulation; knuckle under; submit and surrender to; throw oneself at the feet of;
屈膝下跪 drop to one's knees;
屈膝行禮 bob a courtesy; drop a courtesy;
卑躬屈膝 act servilely; bow and scrape; cap in hand; cringe; eat dirt; eat humble pie; grovel in the dirt; grovel in the dust; hat in hand; humble oneself in serving a master; humiliate oneself in serving; kiss the ground; kowtow to; make a great show of obedience and courtesy; menial; on one's knees;
俯首屈膝 kneel down humbly;

[屈心] have a guilty conscience;

[屈折] flexion; inflection;
屈折詞綴 inflectional affix;
屈折後綴 inflectional suffix;
屈折形式 inflection;
~不規則屈折形式 anomalous inflection;
屈折語 inflectional language;
詞根屈折 radical flexion;
詞形屈折 inflection;
構幹屈折 flexion of hip joint;
內部屈折 internal flexion;
語幹屈折 thematic flexion;

[屈指] count on one's fingers;
屈指可數 be numbered; can be counted on one's fingers; count on one's fingers; few and far between; not very many; one can count them on one's fingers; only a few to count; very few;
屈指一算 reckon on one's fingers;

[屈尊] condescend;
屈尊降貴 condescendingly go to call on sb;
屈尊敬賢 stoop in order to show respect to talent;
屈尊求教 condescend to ask for advice;
屈尊下問 deign to ask sb below oneself;
屈尊以求 stoop to conquer;
感到屈尊 feel cheap;

抱屈 bear a grudge; feel wronged; harbour resentment;
憋屈 aggrieved; nurse a grievance;
不屈 unbending; unyielding;
叫屈 complain of being wronged; protest against an injustice;
理屈 cannot appeal to good reasoning; find oneself bested in argument;
蹺屈 curled up; not stretched;
受屈 be wronged;

枉屈 treat unjustly; wrong persons;
委屈 (1) feel wronged; suffer from injustice; (2) be wrongly judged; put sb to great inconvenience;
冤屈 (1) treat unjustly; wrong; (2) injustice; wrongful treatment;

qu
【胠】 (1) open; (2) cast away; put away; (3) armpit; (4) (in ancient warfare) right flank of an army;
[胠篋] open a chest and steal;
胠篋者流 thieves; those who open a chest and steal;

qu
【祛】 (1) up one's arms; raise the sleeve; sleeve; (2) cuffs; sleeves; (3) dispel; relieve; remove; clear of; drive away; drive out; eliminate; expel; get rid of;
[祛除] dispel; drive away; get rid of; relieve; remove; scatter;
祛除邪魔 drive out evil spirits;
祛除疑慮 clear one's mind of doubt; dispel one's misgivings;
祛風散毒 relieve rheumatic pains and act as an antidote to poison;
[祛祛] healthy and strong; stout;
[祛暑] drive away summer heat;
[祛邪] eliminate evil;
祛邪除災 exorcise evil spirits and ward off disaster;
祛邪去惡 eliminate depravity and remove evil;
[祛疑] dispel doubt;
[祛淤活血] remove blood stasis and promote blood circulation;
[祛災] dispel disasters;

qu
【區】 (1) area; district; region; sector; (2) administrative division; border; (3) domain; local; (4) classify; differ from; differentiate; discern; discriminate; distinguish; distinguish between; make a distinction between; (5) few; insignificant; little; trivial;
[區別] differ from; differ in; differ with; different from; differentiate; differentiate among; differentiate between; discern; discriminate; dissimilar from; dissimilar to; dissimilar with; distinct; distinctive; distinguish; distinguish between; distinguish distinction; distinguish from; distinguishable from; draw a distinction between; make a distinction between; tell the difference;
區別對待 deal with each case on its merits; deal with different things in different ways; treat differently;
區別好壞 distinguish between good and bad;
區別情況，分別對待 differentiate between cases and treat them accordingly; distinguish between light and serious cases and handle them differently;
區別善惡 sort out the good from the evil;
區別性成分 distinctive component;
區別真假 distinguish genuine from fake;
不加區別 not make any distinction between; undiscriminatingly;
大有區別 entirely different; poles apart;
使有區別 individuate;
詳加區別 make exact distinctions;
以示區別 in order to show the distinction; so as to distinguish this from other cases;
[區段] section;
[區分] demarcate; differentiate; differentiate between; discriminate; distinguish; make a distinction between; set apart;
不能區分 cannot tell the difference;
難以區分 indistinguishable;
[區劃] compartment; district division;
[區徽] regional emblem;
[區間] interval;
區間閉塞 section blocking;
區間車 shuttle service;
閉區間 close interval;
開區間 open interval;
子區間 subinterval;
[區塊] sub-area; sub-plot;
[區理] deal with one by one;
[區旗] regional flag;
[區區] poor present; shabby gift; trifling; trivial;
區區小事，何足掛齒 don't mention such small things; such a trifling matter is hardly worth mentioning;

區區之數 a contemptible number; an insignificant amount;

[區熔] zone melting;
區熔均化器 zone-leveler;

[區時] zone time;

[區系] fauna;
區系簡化 fauna simplification;
植物區系 flora;

[區域] area; district; domain; part; range; reach; region; sector; territory;
區域發展規劃 regional development planning;
區域防護 area defense;
區域規劃 regional planning;
區域合作 regional cooperation;
~一體化區域合作 integrated regional cooperation;
區域轟炸 area bombing;
區域化 regionalization; zoning;
~固態區域化 solid zoning;
~品種區域化 variety regionalization;
~液體區域化 liquid zoning;
區域環境 regional environment;
區域假定 regional hypothesis;
區域間合作 interregional cooperation;
區域經濟 regional economy;
~區域經濟合作 regional economic cooperation;
~區域經濟學 regional economics;
~區域經濟一體化 regional economy integration;
區域開發 regional exploration;
區域命名系統 domain name server (DNS);
區域生產綜合體 regional production complex;
區域網絡 local area network (LAN);
區域文化 regional culture;
~區域文化模式 regional culture model;
區域系統工程 regional system engineering;
區域性 of regional nature; regional;
區域語言學 areal linguistics;
區域自治 regional autonomy;
~民族區域自治 regional national autonomy;
安全區域 safe region;
調度區域 dispatcher-controlled territory;
軌道電路區域 track circuit territory;
銷售區域 sales territory;
行政區域 administrative divisions;
子區域 subregion;
~相對非緊子區域 relatively noncompact subregion;
~真子區域 proper subregion;

[區長] administrative chief; district head;

白區 white area;
邊區 border area; border region;
城區 the city proper;
城市工業區 urban industry district;
地區 area; clime; district; region;
堆填區 landfill;
防火區 fire district;
放牧區 grazing district;
分區 partition; zonation; zoning;
工區 work area;
海區 sea area;
紅燈區 red-light district;
後區 back zone;
湖區 lake district;
交接區 cross connection district;
郊區 burbs; outskirts; suburban district; suburbs;
教區 diocese; parish;
解放區 liberated area;
金融區 financial district;
禁戒區 exclusion area;
禁區 (1) exclusion zone; forbidden zone; out-of-bounds area; restricted zone; (2) preserve; reserve; (3) penalty area; (4) restricted area;
軍區 area command; military region;
墾區 reclamation area;
礦區 mining area;
雷區 minefield;
林區 forest area;
牧區 pastural area; pasture areas;
山區 mountain area; mountain district; mountainous area;
商業區 commercial district;
社區 community;
深草區 rough;
生物區 biotic district;
時區 time zone;
市區 city proper; downtown area; urban area; urban district;
市轄區 municipal district;
特區 special zone;
塢區 dockland;
轄區 area under one's jurisdiction;
險區 danger zone;
新區 newly developed area;
選區 constituency; electoral district; electoral ward;

音區 region of articulation;
漁區 fishing area;
雨區 rain area; rain field;
雲區 cloud-land;
災區 disaster area; distress area;
戰區 battle zone; theatre of operations; theatre of war; war zone;
中區 (1) central; central area; (2) midcourt;
專區 prefecture;
自治區 autonomous region;

qu
【蛆】 maggot;

船蛆 shipworm;

qu
【蛐】 cricket;
[蛐蛐兒] cricket;
[蛐蟮] earthworm;

qu
【詘】 (1) bend; crouch; (2) submit; yield; (3) short; (4) a surname;

qu
【嶇】 irregular; rugged; uneven;

qu
【瞿】 a surname;

qu
【敺】 drive away; expel;

qu
【趨】 (1) go quickly; hasten; hurry; hurry along; hurry on; run quickly; (2) be inclined; follow; go after; lean toward; tend to become; tend towards;
[趨拜] hurry on to pay respects to;
[趨承] cater to sb;
趨承附和 curry favour with; ingratiate oneself with; play the sycophant;
[趨風] march fast;
[趨奉] fawn on; hasten to please; toady to; try to please;
[趨附] curry favour with; hang on; ingratiate oneself with;
趨附權貴 hanger-on of ranking officials;
[趨候] to to a place to pay respects to sb;
[趨利] go after material gain;
[趨濕性] hygrotaxis;
[趨時] follow the fashion; follow the trend of the times;
[趨勢] (1) tendency; trend; (2) go after people of power;
趨勢分析法 method of trend analysis;
必然趨勢 inevitable trend;
~ 顯示必然趨勢 show the inexorable trend;
大趨勢 general trend; megatrend;
集中趨勢 centralized tendency;
年趨勢 trend;
起毛趨勢 fluffing tendency;
氣候趨勢 climatic trend;
商行趨勢 business trend;
上升趨勢 upward trend;
收斂趨勢 convergent tendency;
下跌趨勢 downward tendency;
中斷趨勢 broken trend;
[趨庭] receive the teachings of one's father;
[趨同] convergent;
趨同論 convergency theory;
趨同適應 convergent adaptation;
趨同現象 convergence;
~ 趨同現象原理 principle of convergence;
[趨向] (1) direction; tendency; trend; (2) incline to; tend to;
趨向動詞 directional verb;
趨向高潮 work up to a climax;
趨向好轉 take a favourable turn;
趨向合併 tend toward consolidation;
趨向極端 run to extremes;
趨向簡單 tend to simplicity;
趨向完善 tend to reach perfection;
進化趨向 evolutionary trend;
經濟趨向 economic trends;
人格趨向 personality trend;
突變趨向 mutation trend;
[趨炎附勢] a follower of the rich and powerful; a snob who plays up to those in power; approach the bustling place and cleave to the strong; attach oneself as subordinate to those in power; cater to those in power; climb on the bandwagon; creep into the good grace of; curry favour with the powerful; curry favour with those in power; fawn upon the rich and powerful persons; to where there is anything to be got; gravitate to those rising in the world; hail the rising sun; hang on to the sleeves of those in power; hurry to the glorious and hang on to the

influential; jump on the bandwagon; play up to those in power; please and flatter wealthy and influential persons; run round perons in warm comfortable circumstances and flatter to the powerful; serve the time; worship the rising sun;

[趨謁] go and see a senior;

[趨迎] hasten to greet a visitor; hasten to receive a visitor;

[趨於] tend;

趨於惡化 tend to deteriorate;
趨於極端 rush into extremes;
趨於零 go to zero;
趨於明確 become clear;
趨於上昇 tend upwards;
趨於穩定 tend towards stability;
趨於下降 tend downwards;

[趨異論] divergence thesis;

[趨之若鶩] go after in a swarm; go after sth like a flock of ducks; scramble for sth;

[趨走] go in haste; run away;

趨走奉承 go in haste and to flatter; subservient;

日趨 day by day; gradually;

qu

【軀】 (1) body; trunk; (2) child in the womb;

[軀幹] body; trunk;

[軀殼] body; human body; outer form;

[軀體] body; carcass; human body;

動物軀體 animal carcass;

捐軀 lay down one's life; sacrifice one's life;
身軀 body; physical stature; stature;

qu

【驅】 (1) go before others; (2) drive; (3) spur; urge; whip on; (4) disperse; drive out; eliminate; expel; get rid of; repel; ward off; (5) command; order about; (6) run about; run quickly;

[驅策] (1) drive; spur; whip on; urge; (2) order sb about;

[驅車] drive a car; drive a carriage;

驅車出去玩一玩 go for a drive; take a drive;
驅車而過 drive past;
驅車離開 drive away; drive off; drive out;
驅車前來 drive over;
驅車前往 drive to a place;

[驅馳] run about busily for others;

[驅蟲] expel insects;

驅蟲治療 anthelmintic treatment;
驅蟲作用 anthelmintic action;

[驅除] drive out; eliminate; expel; get rid of;

驅除鬼怪 keep off evil spirits;
驅除濕氣 drive off moisture;
驅除憂愁 chase away melancholy;

[驅動] drive;

驅動力 driving force;
驅動器 driver;
~ 地址驅動器 address driver;
~ 時鐘驅動器 clock driver;
~ 總線驅動器 bus driver;
四輪驅動 four-wheel drive;

[驅鬼] exorcise evil spirits;

[驅魔] exorcise; exorcism;

驅魔人 exorcist;
驅魔師 exorcist;

[驅迫] be driven; compel; force; order about; urge;

[驅遣] (1) banish; drive away; expel; send away sb; (2) drive; order about; (3) get rid of;

[驅散] break up; dispel; disperse by force; scatter;

驅散濃霧 dispel the thick fog;
驅散人群 disperse a crowd;
驅散霧氣 dispel a mist;

[驅使] (1) be driven; order about; (2) prompt; spur on; urge;

任人驅使 be ordered about;
願供驅使 at your disposal; offer one's services to;

[驅邪] drive out evil spirits;

驅邪符 amulet;
驅邪祛厄 ward off ill luck and evil;

[驅魚] drive the fish;

為淵驅魚 drive the fish into deep waters and the sparros into the thickets;

[驅雲防雹] disperse clluds to prevent a hailstorm;

[驅逐] banish; chase; deport; drive off; drive out; drive out of; eject; evict; expel; extradite; get rid of; oust;

驅逐出境 deport; drive away; expel; expel sb from a country;
驅逐艦 destroyer;

~ 靶標驅逐艦 target destroyer;
~ 導彈驅逐艦 guided missile destroyer;
~ 反潛驅逐艦 antisubmarine destroyer;
~ 護航驅逐艦 convoy destroyer;
~ 艦隊驅逐艦 fleet destroyer;
~ 雷達哨驅逐艦 radar picket destroyer;
~ 水翼驅逐艦 hydrofoil destroyer;
~ 魚雷快艇驅逐艦 torpedo boat destroyer;
~ 遠洋驅逐艦 ocean-going destroyer;

長驅 make a long drive; push deep;
馳驅 (1) gallop; (2) run errands;
齊驅 advance abreast;
先驅 forerun; forerunner; pioneer;

qu²

qu
【劬】 diligent; labour; labour arduously; labour incessantly; toil;
[劬勞] labour arduously; toil; travail;

qu
【朐】 (1) dried meat strips; (2) far; faraway;

qu
【絇】 ornaments for the frontal part of shoes;

qu
【渠】 (1) channel; ditch; drain; (2) deep; great; (3) he; she; (4) a surname;
[渠道] (1) canal; channel; irrigation canal; irrigation ditch; (2) channel; medium of communication;
了解世界的渠道 a window to the world;
雙方交流渠道 two-way communication channel;
銷售渠道 channel of distribution; marketing channel;
行政渠道 administrative channel;
[渠渠] large and spacious;

暗渠 underground channel;
斗渠 lateral canal;
幹渠 main canal; trunk canal;
溝渠 ditch; channel; kennel; lake; trench; irrigation canals and ditches;
河渠 rivers and canals; waterways;
浚渠 dredge a canal;
農渠 field ditch;
水渠 canal; ditch;
支渠 branch canal;

qu
【蚰】 earthworm;
[蚰蟮] earthworm;

qu
【蕖】 (1) taro; (2) as in 芙蕖 , lotus flower;

芙蕖 lotus;

qu
【鴝】 a species of myna;
歌鴝 luscinia;
歐鴝 red-breast; robin;
鵲鴝 magpie robin;

qu
【璩】 (1) ringed ornament; (2) a surname;

qu
【麴】 ferment for brewing; yeast;
[麴車] wine cart;
[麴院] brewery;

qu
【蘧】 (1) a kind of grass resembling wheat; (2) pleasantly surprised; (3) a surname;
[蘧蘧] (1) solid and unmistakable; (2) high up;

qu
【籧】 bamboo mat;

qu
【癯】 emaciated; lean; thin;

qu
【衢】 highway junction; side street; thoroughfare; crossroads;
[衢道] crossroads; side street;
[衢路] thoroughfare;
[衢肆] store beside a thoroughfare;
[衢塗] crossroads; side street;

通衢 thoroughfare;

qu³

qu
【曲】 (1) verse for singing; (2) melody; song; tune; (3) music of a song;
[曲本] music book;
[曲調] melodies; strains; tunes;
難以忘懷的曲調 haunting melody;
[曲高和寡] caviar to the general; find no opportunity to display one's talents; highbrow music can be appreciated

by only a few people; highbrow songs find few singers; sth too highbrow to be popular; songs of a highbrow type will find very few people to join in the chorus; the song is of too high a key for most people to follow; too high-minded to be popular; too highbrow to be popular; unpopular;

[曲盡其妙] give full expression to feeling through the delicacy of touch one has acquired in one's art;

[曲譜] music score of a Chinese opera;

[曲式] musical form;

[曲終] the music is over;

曲終人散 the end of a happy occasion; the music is over and people are gone; the play comes to an end and the audience disperse;

曲終奏雅 brilliant conclusion;

[曲子] melody; song; tune;

演奏曲子 perform a composition;

一支曲子 a piece of music;

變奏曲 variation;

插曲 (1) interlude; (2) songs in a film or play; (3) episode; interlude;

催眠曲 cradlesong; lullaby;

獨奏曲 solo;

賦格曲 fugue;

歌曲 song;

迴旋曲 rondo;

即興曲 impromptu;

間奏曲 intermezzo;

交響曲 symphony;

進行曲 march;

狂想曲 rhapsody;

前奏曲 prelude;

隨想曲 capriccio;

套曲 divertiment;

舞曲 dance music;

戲曲 (1) traditional opera; (2) singing parts in chuanqi and zaju;

小夜曲 serenade;

協奏曲 concerto;

諧謔曲 scherzo;

心曲 (1) innermost being; mind; (2) sth weighing on one's mind;

序曲 overture;

敍事曲 ballade;

選曲 selected songs;

搖籃曲 lullaby;

夜曲 nocturne;

圓舞曲 waltz;

樂曲 musical composition;

終曲 finale;

組曲 suite;

奏鳴曲 sonata;

作曲 compose; write music;

qu

【取】 (1) achieve; acquire; assume; collect; draw; fetch; gain; get; obtain; reach; receive; take; take hold of; win; wrest; yield; (2) aim at; court; seek; (3) adopt; assume; choose; select; take; (4) marry; take a wife;

[取保] get a guarantor; get sb to go bail for one;

取保釋放 be bailed out; be released on bail;

[取便] (1) do as one pleases without restraint; (2) facilitate; promote;

[取不上] unable to get selected;

[取材] collect material; draw materials; gather materials; obtain raw materials; select material; select talent;

[取長] make the best of sth;

矮中取長 make the best of a bad job;

[取償] be paid back for cost or labour;

[取寵] curry favour;

嘩眾取寵 try to please the public with claptrap;

譁眾取寵 court people's favour by saying sth impressive; curry favour by claptrap; gain notoriety by shocking statements; impress people by claptrap; play to the gallery; seek popularity by doing sth sensational; talk big to impress people; try to please the public with claptrap;

[取出] get out; take out;

[取次] in order; in turn; one by one;

[取代] displace; replace; step into sb's shoes; substitute for; substitution; supersede; supplant; take for;

取代基 substituent;

~環式取代基 cyclic substituent;

~角取代基 angular substituents;

~陽性取代基 positive substituent;

~陰性取代基 negative substituent;

被…取代 be supplanted by;

反常取代 anomalous substitution;
鏈上取代 chain substitution;
取而代之 cut out; facilitate a takeover; fill sb's bonnet; fill sb's shoes; nail drives out nail; place oneself in sb's stead; replace; replace sb; step into sb's shoes; substitute sb; supersede; supplant; take over; take sb's place; take the place of; usurp another's position;
染色體取代 chromosome substitution;

[取道] by way of; come by way of; go by way of; via; take a route;

[取得] achieve; acquire; assume; conquest; gain; get; obtain; win; wrest; yield;
取得進展 make progress;
取得立足點 take a foothold;
取得滿分 achieve a perfect score;
取得信任 win confidence;
取得學位 take one's degree;
取得圓滿成功 be crowned with success;
取得一致意見 obtain a unanimous view; reach complete agreement of views;

[取燈兒] match;

[取締] ban; declare a ban on; clampdown; discipline; forbid; interdict; outlaw; prohibit; punish the violator; suppress;
取締非法交易 outlow illicit trade;
取締非法貿易 stamp out an illegal traffic;
取締非法組織 ban illegal organizations;

[取法] follow the example of; model oneself on; take as one's model;
取法乎上 pattern after the first-rate;
取法乎上，僅得其中 aim high or you'll fall below the average;
取法於人 copy sb as example;

[取給] draw; rely on...for supply;

[取和兒] promote peace among quarreling parties;

[取回] fetch back; get back; take back;

[取火] get fire;
燧木取火 get fire from wood by friction;
鑽木取火 bore wood to get fire; drill wood to make fire;

[取經] (1) go on a pilgrimage for Buddhist scriptures; (2) learn from sb else's experience; seek experience; seek for experience;
取經學道 learn from sb else's experience and study the truth;
取經用弘 select the essential from a large quantity of material; select the finest from a vast quantity; take what is wanted from a collection;

[取精用弘] have every luxury; in luxury; live off the fat of the land;

[取景] find a view;
取景器 viewfinder;
~ 萬能取景器 universal finder;

[取決於] be decided by; depend on; depend upon; dependent on; dependent upon; hang on; hang upon; hinge on; it's up to; lie on; rest with ride on; turn on;
取決於供求關係 depend on the relationship between demand and supply;
取決於天氣 depend on the weather;

[取快] for pleasure; for the fun of sth;
取快一時 get joy of the moment; get temporary pleasure; take pleasure for the moment;

[取款] draw money from a bank; take money;

[取樂] amuse oneself; find amusement; have a good time; make merry; seek pleasure;
開心取樂 about one's amusements;
飲酒取樂 drink and make merry;

[取涼] enjoy the cool air;

[取錄] admission; admit;
擇優取錄 admit the best of the examinees;

[取名] christen; name;
取名不當 misname;

[取鬧] raise hell; unreasonable;

[取暖] warm oneself;

[取錢] withdraw money;

[取巧] manipulate; resort to clever manipulation; resort to trickery to serve oneself; take a snap course; use finesse;
取巧圖便 choose the easy way for convenience;
耍奸取巧 act in a slick way to serve oneself; trick and take advantage of people;

[取容] try to please others;

[取善輔仁] choose the good and support the virtuous;

[取捨] accept or refuse; accept or reject; choose; decide what to adopt and what to discard; make a choice; make one's choice; select;

決定取捨 decide what to use;
明捨暗取 profess to spurn, but secretly take sth;

[取勝] score a success; win a victory;
艱難取勝 pull off a victory;
輕易取勝 romp to a victory; romp to a win; whup; win in a breeze;
以多取勝 win victory through numerical superiority;
以智取勝 outsmart; outwit;
最終取勝 clinch victory;

[取水] get water;
掘地取水 dig for water;

[取下] take down;
取下眼鏡 take off one's spectacles;

[取向] orientation;
變形取向 deformation orientation;
晶體取向 crystal orientation;
偶極取向 dipole orientation;
無序取向 disordered orientation;

[取消] abandon; abolish; abrogate; annul; be cleared of; be edged out by; call off; cancel; cancellation; cross out; deprive sb of; discard; dispense with; do away with; liquidate; negate; nullify; obliterate; off; put an end to; reject; relinquish; remove; renounce; repeal; repudiate; rescind; revoke; scrap; strip of; write off;
取消存儲 storage cancellation;
取消訂單 canel the order;
取消決定 rescind a decision;
取消命令 countermand one's order;
取消債務 debt cancellation;
取消資格 deprive sb of his status; disqualify;
進路取消 route cancellation;
人工取消 manual cancellation;
因雨取消 be cancelled because of the rain;
噪音取消 noise cancellation;
自動取消 automatic cancellation;

[取笑] laugh at; make fun of; poke fun at; pull sb's leg; ridicule;
取笑挖苦 ridicule sarcastically;

[取信] enjoy the trust of;
取信於人 establish credibility among others; win confidence; words be trusted;

[取樣] sample; sampling; take a sample;
取樣法 sampling;
~ 隨機取樣法 accidental sampling;
取樣器 sampler;
~ 多級式取樣器 multistage sampler;
~ 複合取樣器 composite sampler;
槽探取樣 pit sampling;
分析取樣 analytical sampling;
空氣取樣 air sampling;
模擬信號取樣 analog sample;
隨機取樣 random sampling;

[取義] die for the casue of justice and righteousness;

[取悅] ingratiate oneself with sb; please; try to please;
取悅於人 curry popularity; ingratiate oneself into sb's favour; ingratiate oneself with sb; try to please sb;
急於取悅 eager to please;
難於取悅 hard to please;

[取之於民] take from the people;
取之於民，用之於民 what is taken from the people is used in the interests of the people;

[取自] after; be extracted from; be derived from; be taken from; derive from; take from;

拔取 choose; draw off; select;
備取 on the waiting list; put on reserve;
逼取 blackmail; extort; take by forcible means;
博取 contend for; court; try to gain;
採取 adopt; take;
萃取 extract;
存取 access;
盜取 embezzle; steal;
奪取 (1) capture; seize; take by force; wrest; (2) court; strive for;
攻取 attack and seize; storm and capture;
換取 exchange sth for; get in return;
獲取 achieve; acquire; gain; obtain;
汲取 derive; draw;
記取 bear in mind; remember;
截取 cut sth into several sections and take one from them;
進取 be eager to make progress; keep forging ahead;
攫取 grab; seize;
考取 be admitted into a college after an examination; pass an entrance examination;
可取 advisable; desirable; recommendable;
撈取 fish for; gain;

獵取 (1) hunt; (2) hunt for; seek;
聆取 listen to and accept;
領取 draw; receive;
錄取 enroll; recruit;
掠取 plunder; seize;
覓取 hunt for; look for; seek;
牟取 bleed; obtain; seek; try to gain;
謀取 obtain; seek; try to gain;
拿取 take;
騙取 cheat sb out of sth; defraud; gain sth by fraud; obtain by fraud; swindle;
剽取 lift; plagiarize;
棄取 be accepted or rejected; take or reject;
強取 take by force;
巧取 angle for;
竊取 grab; steal; usurp;
輕取 beat easily; win an easy victory; win hands down;
擅取 take without authorization;
攝取 (1) absorb; assimilate; (2) take a photograph of; shoot;
拾取 collect; pick up;
收取 collect; gather;
索取 demand; extort;
討取 ask for sth; cadge; demand;
提取 (1) collect; draw; pick up; (2) abstract; extract; recover;
挑取 choose; pick; select;
聽取 hear opinion; listen to;
吸取 absorb; assimilate; draw; drink in; suck up;
襲取 (1) take by surprise; (2) follow; take over;
選取 choose; select;
弋取 catch;
榨取 (1) exploit; extort; rob; (2) extract; press for juice; squeeze;
摘取 pick; select; take;
爭取 compete for; fight for; strive for; try to get; win over;
正取 officially enroll;
支取 draw money;
摭取 (1) collect; pick up; take; (2) plagiarize;
智取 outwit; take by strategy;
抓取 grab; overshot; take by grasping;
自取 (1) ask for; invite; (2) of one's own doing;

qu

【娶】 marry; take a wife;
［娶親］ get married; take a wife; tie the knot; wive;

嫁娶 marriage;
迎娶 (of a man) marry;

qu

【齲】 tooth decay;
［齲齒］ (1) dental caries; (2) carious tooth; decayed tooth;
原發性齲齒 primary dental caries;
［齲蠹］ rotten teeth;

qu⁴

qu

【去】 (1) depart; go; go away; leave; make sb go; quit; send sth; (2) abandon; cast aside; clear away; discard; do away with; eradicate; exterminate; get rid of; put off; reject; remove; throw out; (3) apart from; (4) of last year; (5) gone; past;
［去不成］ cannot go; unable to go;
［去不去］ are you going or not;
［去讒遠色］ get rid of slander and keep away from women;
［去除］ abstraction; dislodge;
強行去除 dislodge;
熱去除 heat abstraction;
［去處］ (1) place to go; whereabouts; (2) place; site;
［去…從…］ 何去何從 decide on what path to follow; what course to follow; what should one do; which way do you choose;
［去得了］ able to attend; able to go;
［去掉］ abandon; cast; clear away; do away with; eradicate; get rid of; put off; throw out;
去掉不良作風 get rid of a bad style;
［去惡務盡］ do away with evil wholly and completely;
［去垢］ clean; descale;
去垢劑 cleaner; detergent;
~ 酸性去垢劑 acid cleaner;
［去骨］ boned;
去骨的 boneless;
去骨肉 boned meat;
［去國］ leave one's country; leave one's fatherland;
［去火］ relieve inflamation or heat;
［去就］ to quit or to stay;
［去殼］ decanning;
高溫去殼 thermal decanning;
熱法去殼 thermal decanning;
氧化去殼 decanning;

[去留] to go or to stay;
去留未決 dismiss or return is not yet decided;
或去或留 go or stay;

[去路] exit; outlet; the way along which one is going; the way leading to a certain place; the way to advance; the way to go out;
攔住去路 block the way; stand barring the way;

[去毛刺] deburring;
電解去毛刺 electrolytic deburring;
化學去毛刺 chemical deburring;
振動去毛刺 vibrator deburring;

[去你的] get stuffed; go to blazes; go to hell; nonsense; shut up your big mouth; the hell you are; up yours;

[去年] last year;

[去皮] peel; peeling; remove the skin; skin;
去皮機 peeler;
~ 馬鈴薯去皮機 potato peeler;
~ 蘋果去皮機 apple; peeler;
化學去皮 chemical peeling;
磨擦去皮 abrasive peeling;
鹽水去皮 brine peeling;

[去任] leave a post; resign from a post;

[去聲] falling tone;

[去世] die; leave the world; pass away;

[去勢] castrate; castration; emasculate;

[去歲] last year;

[去污] decontaminate; decontamination;
去污粉 cleanser;

[去蕪存菁] eliminate the impure and retain the pure; keep the good and get rid of the bad; separate the wheat from the chaff;

[去向] direction in which sb or sth has gone;
去向不明 one's whereabouts are unknown;
the destination is unknown;
不知去向 disappear without a trace; nowhere to be found;

[去雄] castrate; emasculate; emasculation;

[去職] be removed from office; no longer at one's post; resign from office;

剝去 strip; take off;
擦去 erase; wipe off;
衝去 dash onward;
出去 get out; go out; pass out; pop out; step out;
除去 blot out; eliminate; remove; work off;
吹去 blow away;
辭去 resign;
蹲下去 crouch; squat;
奪去 take away from;
拂去 flick away; flip; whisk;
故去 die; pass away;
過不去 (1) cannot get through; impassable; unable to get by; (2) embarrass; find fault with; hard on; make it difficult for;
過得去 (1) able to pass; can get through; crack a crust; may pass in a crowd; might pass in a crowd; would pass in a crowd; (2) not too bad; passable; so-so; tolerable;
過去 (1) antecedent; formerly; in the past; of the past; once; past; previously; (2) go over; go pass; pass by;
過意不去 feel apologetic; feel sorry;
回去 back; go back; return;
進去 enter; get in; go in;
來去 (1) round trip; (2) distance between two places; (3) friendly contacts;
離去 leave; make tracks; offwards; split;
略去 leave out; omit;
抹去 blip; erase; expunge; wipe out;
撇去 skim;
去不去 are you going or not;
扔過去 hurl over to the other side;
刪去 cross off; delete; dash out;
上不去 (1) cannot go up; (2) cannot move forward;
上去 (1) go up; (2) going from a place nearer to a distant place, etc.; upward;
失去 forfeit; lose; miss;
逝去 be gone; depart; pass;
撕去 tear away; tear off;
汰去 eliminate; remove;
剔出去 eliminate; pick out;
跳下去 jump down; leap down;
褪去 cast off; take off;
脫去 (1) strip; take off; throw off; (2) vindicate;
下不去 cause sb to lose face; go against; harass;
下去 (1) go down; (2) downward; go to a distant place from a place nearer;
相去 differ;
鑲進去 set sth in;
咽下去 gulp down; swallow;
掖進去 stuff sth with;
一去 go; leave;
有去 there is departure;
暈過去 faint; pass out;
轉去 go back; turn and go;

qu

【漆】 coal black; pitch black;

［漆黑］ coal black; pitch black; raven;

漆黑的 inky;

漆黑一團 complete darkness;

一片漆黑 completely dark; dismal night; pitch dark;

qu

【趣】 (1) delight; fun; interest; (2) amusing; fascinating; funny; interesting;

［趣兒］ fun; interest;

［趣話］ amusing story; funny story; joke; wisecrack; witticism; witty remark;

［趣劇］ farce;

［趣事］ amusing incident; interesting episode;

［趣談］ farce;

［趣味］ (1) delightful; interesting; (2) liking; preference; taste;

趣味盎然 appealing; full of interest;

趣味索然 dry as dust; insipid;

趣味無窮 afford the great delight; fascinating; of infinite interest;

趣味相投 congenial to one's tastes;

［趣聞］ amusing story;

［趣向］ aptitude; personal inclination;

打趣 banter; make fun of; tease;

逗趣 amuse; make people laugh by funny remarks, etc;

風趣 humour; wit;

佳趣 high spirits; matters of intense interest;

樂趣 delight; joy; pleasure;

沒趣 awkward; rebuked or reproved;

情趣 (1) temperament and interest; (2) appeal; interest;

生趣 joy of life;

識趣 know how to behave in a delicate situation;

天趣 beauty of natural objects or phenomena;

興趣 interest;

雅趣 elegant taste; refined pleasure;

異趣 difference of tastes and interests;

意趣 interest and charm;

幽趣 delight of a quiet and refined place;

有趣 interesting; fascinating;

知趣 know how to behave in a delicate situation;

旨趣 objective; purport;

志趣 aspiration and interest;

qu

【闃】 quiet; still; without people around;

［闃寂］ quiet; still;

［闃其無人］ all is quiet and not a soul is seen;

［闃然］ quiet;

闃然無聲 absolutely still; silent without a human voice;

qu

【覷】 gaze; gaze at; look; peep at; spy on; watch;

［覷步］ spy on;

［覷窺］ peep at;

［覷著眼］ narrow one's eyes and gaze at sth with great attention;

quan¹

quan

【桊】 bowstring;

quan

【悛】 feel remorse; reform; repent;

［悛改］ reform oneself; repent of one's sin;

［悛容］ look of repentance;

［悛心］ repentant heart;

［悛懌］ reform oneself; repent of one's sin;

quan

【圈】 (1) circle; ring; (2) circle; group; (3) encircle; enclose; (4) mark with a circle;

［圈閉］ shut up;

［圈點］ (1) punctuate; (2) mark words and phrases for special attention with dots or small circles;

［圈禁］ keep within an enclosed place;

［圈梁］ girth;

［圈內］ within a circle;

［圈弄］ frame up sb; trap sb by tricking;

［圈圈］ (1) draw circles; (2) circles; cliques;

［圈套］ snare; springe; trap;

佈設圈套 bait a trap; set a trap;

插圈弄套 trap sb with tricks;

墮入圈套 be caught in a trap;

落入圈套 ensnare;

上圈套 be caught in a net; fall into a trap; swallow the bait;

設下圈套 set a snare;

使圈套 set traps;

中了圈套 be caught in a trap;

自入圈套 put one's neck into a noose;

做圈套 set out to trap sb; set the trap;

［圈外］ outside a circle;

圈外人 outsider;

[圈椅] round-backed chair;
[圈閱] read and circle;
[圈子] (1) circle; ring; scope; (2) in one's own neighbourhood;
打圈子 (1) banter; make fun of; tease; (2) beat about the bush; speak in a roundabout way;
兜圈子 (1) circle; go around in circles; take a joy-ride; (2) beat about the bush;
~說話兜圈子 go around in circles;
繞圈子 (1) beat about the bush; talk in a roundabout way; (2) go round and round; make a detour; take a circuitous route;
小圈子 clique; coterie; in-crowd; in-group; inner circle; little clique; small circle; small circle of people; small clique; small coterie;
~搞小圈子 be involved in a small circle; form a small coterie;
~搞個人小圈子 form a little clique;

兜個圈 go for a ride;
扼流圈 choke;
分度圈 graduated circle;
光圈 diaphragm;
花圈 floral wreath; torse; wreath;
劃圈 draw a circle;
極圈 polar circle;
救生圈 life buoy;
籃圈 hoop;
外圈 outer lane;
線圈 coil;
項捲 necklace; necklet;
煙圈 puff;
眼圈 (1) eye socket; orbit; (2) rim of the eye;
羊圈 sheep pen; sheepcote; sheepfold;
一圈 a circle; a lap; a round; one round;
圓圈 circle; ring;
中圈 centre circle;
豬圈 hogpen; pigpen; pigsty;
轉圈 circle; ring; turn; whirl;

quan

【棬】 crooked wood; wooden bowl;
[棬樞] very poor family;

quan²

quan

【全】 (1) all-round; completely; comprehensive; entirely; general; throughout; totally; (2) all; altogether; any and every; complete; entire; full; in full; overall; total; without exception; whole; (3) keep intact; keep whole; (4) a surname;
[全班] whole class; whole squad;
[全般] all; overall; the entire amount;
[全豹] complete picture; entire thing; overall situation; whole picture;
得窺全豹 able to see a sample of sth in its entirety; able to see the entire thing;
一窺全豹 see the entire thing; see the whole picture;
[全部] all; all of a lump; any and every; by the lump; complete; entire; full; in a lum; in one lump; in the lump; lock, stock, and barrel; the entire shoot; the whole shoot; total; without exception; whole;
全部倒裝 full inversion;
全部費用 the overall cost;
全部否定 sheer negation;
全部付訖 payment in full;
全部結束 be all over;
全部力量 all one's energy;
全部審計 complete audit;
全部時間 all one's time;
全部收入 the total of one's gains;
全部完成 be all done;
[全才] all-round talent; all-rounder; master of all trades; versatile person;
[全場] (1) all those present; the hall; the house; the whole audience; (2) all-court; full-court;
全場沸騰 the place seethes with enthusiasm; the whole place is in ferment;
[全稱] full name; name in full;
[全程] entire journey; whole course; whole journey;
全程搜索系統 global search system;
[全德] perfect character;
[全都] all; altogether; every; everyone;
[全對] it's perfectly correct;
[全份] complete set;
[全副] complete; full; the whole set;
全副精力 devote one's energy to; with all one's energy;
全副精神 with all one's energy;
全副武裝 be armed to the teeth; fully

armed; in full battle array; in full battle rig;

[全功] great success;

全功盡棄 nullify all the advantages;

大獲全功 score a great success;

以竟全功 bring a task to a successful conclusion; bring work to completion;

[全國] countrywide; nation-wide; national; the entire country; throughout the country;

全國規模 country-wide;

全國上下 the whole nation from the leadership to the masses;

全國聞名 well-known throughout the country;

全國性 countrywide; national; nationwide;

全國一盤棋 all-round considerations and arrnagement for the nation as a whole; coordinate all the activities of the nation as in a chess game; take the whole country into account;

傳遍全國 spread throughout the world;

名孚全國 win resounding fame throughout the country;

震撼全國 shock the nation;

[全好了] be fully recovered;

[全會] plenary meeting; plenary session; plenum;

[全集] complete works;

[全家] whole family;

全家福 family photo; photo of the whole family;

全家人 all the family; whole family;

禍延全家 bring disaster on the whole family;

[全殲] wipe out to the last man;

[全景] full view; general view; overall perspective; panorama; panoramic view; whole scene;

全景電影 panorama film;

全景寬銀幕電影 cinepanoramic;

全景照相機 panoramic camera;

[全局] overall situation; the situation as a whole; whole situation;

全局地址 global address;

全局分析 make an overall analysis;

全局觀點 an overall viewpoint; judge the situation as a whole;

控制全局 have the overall situation well in hand;

通觀全局 take a comprehensive view of the situation as a whole; take an overall view of the situation;

縱觀全局 take a panoramic view of the situation;

[全軍] entire army; whole army;

全軍崩潰 the army has been utterly routed;

全軍覆沒 be completely annihilated; one's army is completely wiped out; roll up horse and foot; roll up horse, foot and gun; the total destruction of an army; the whole army is annihilated; the whole army is completely wiped out;

[全力] all one's strength; all-out; do everything in one's power; in full strength; spare no effort; with all one's strength; with wholehearted dedication;

全力馳援 rush in full strength to one's rescue;

全力對付 give all one has in the shop; give the best one has in the shop;

全力拼搏 give the old college try;

全力投入 spare no efforts when engaged in;

全力以赴 at full blast; at full stretch; boots and all; call forth all one's energy; dedicate oneself to; devote every effort to; do all in one's power; do everything in one's power; do one's best; do one's damnedest; do one's level best; do one's utmost; flat out; full sail; full steam ahead; full speed ahead; go all out; go for broke; go nap; go to all lengths; hammer and tongs; horse and foot; hummer and tongs; in full sail; like billy-o; make all-out efforts; make every effort to; muster all one's strength to cope with a given situation; overcome difficulties with one's entire energy; put all one's effort into; pull out all stops; put one's back into; put one's best foot forward; put one's best leg forward; put one's foot forward; put forth every effort; put one's heart into; spare no efforts; straight from the shoulder; strain every nerve; strive with all one's might for; tooth and nail; with both hands; with might and main; with teeth and all; with tooth and nail;

~全力以赴的 all-out;

全力支持 do one's best; give all-out support; move heaven and earth; support with all one's strength; support with might and main; throw in one's whole might;
全力支援 back up sb to the hilt;
竭盡全力 at full strain; at strain; by all one's might and main; by might and main; do all at one's command; do all in one's full strength; do all in one's power to; do everything one can; do one's damnedest; do one's level best; do one's utmost; do sth with all one's ability and with all one's might; exert all one's energy; exert all one's powers; exert every effort; exert one's full strength; exert one's utmost; give a hundred and ten percent; give a hundred percent; give one's all; go all lengths; go all out; go to any lengths; hammer and tongs; make all possible efforts; make every effort to; move heaven and earth; on the strain; pool one's efforts; pull all the stops out; pull out all the stops; put every ounce of strength into the effort; put one's best foot forward; shoot the works; spare no efforts; strain every nerve; strain one's efforts; strain oneself; strain oneself to the limit; strive tooth and nail to; strive to the utmost of one's strength; strive with all one's might; with all one's might and main; take all measures in one's power; to the best of one's ability; try all one knows; with all one's might; with might and main; work full out; work to the best of one's ability;
盡全力 make strenuous efforts;
傾其全力 throw in all their forces;

［全貌］ complete picture; full view; overall perspective;
未窺全貌 fail to see the whole picture;

［全面］ across-the-board; all-round; complete; comprehensive; full; full-scale; general; overall; thorough; total;
全面崩潰 total collapse;
全面的 across the board; well-rounded;
全面地 across the board;
全面發展 develop in an all-round way;
全面反攻 general counter-attack;
全面攻擊 all-out offensive;
全面觀點 keep in view what serves the overall interests; see things from an all-round outlook;
全面合作 all-round cooperation;
全面監理 overall supervision;
全面進攻 massive general offensive; overall offensive;
全面經濟管理 overall economic amangement;
全面落實 all-round implementation; carry out in an all-round way; implement in an all-round way;
全面美化 idealize all aspects;
全面內戰 overall civil war;
全面鋪開 spread in breadth;
全面情況 comprehensive picture;
全面提高 all-round upgrading of the management;
全面戰爭 full-scale war; total war;
全面照顧 comprehensive care;
全面質量管理 total quality control;

［全民］ all the people; entire people; whole people;
全民動員 general mobilization of the people; nationwide mobilization; mobilize the people of the whole country;
全民共決 referendum;
全民教育 education for the entire people;
全民皆兵 all the people are soldiers; an entire nation in arms; every citizen is a soldier; everybody is a soldier; make everybody a soldier; turn all the people into soldiers; turn the entire nation in soldiers; turn the entire population into a military force;
全民企業 state-owned enterprises;
全民所有制 ownership by the whole people;
全民政治 democracy; government by all the people;

［全名］ full name;

［全能］ (1) omnipotence; (2) all-round; (3) general purpose;
全能冠軍 an all-round champion;
全能運動 all-round athletic event; the decathlon; the pentathlon;
~女子七全能運動 heptathlon;

［全年］ all the year round; annual; the whole year; throughout the year; year-round;

yearly;
全年供應 year-round supply;

[全盤] all-out; complete; comprehensive; entire; overall; total; wholesale;
全盤崩潰 total collapse;
全盤否定 complete negation; completely repudiate; total repudiation; totally negate;
全盤改革 comprehensive reform;
全盤計劃 overall programme;
全盤接受 accept sth in its entirety; total and uncritical acceptance;
全盤考慮 overall consideration;
全盤肯定 consider it to be wholly positive; wholesale approval;
全盤托出 make a clean breast;
全盤西化 wholesale Westernization;
全盤招供 come clean;

[全球] around the globe; global; the entire globe; the globe; the whole world;
全球變暖 global warming;
全球定位系統 global positioning system;
全球發展 global development;
全球個人通訊 global personal communication;
全球化 globalization;
~ 反全球化 anti-globalization;
全球環境 global environment;
~ 全球環境問題 problem of global environment;
全球經濟 global economy;
全球配額 global quota;
全球網 world wide web;
全球衛生定位系統 global positioning system;
全球衛星通信系統 global satellite communication system;
全球信息系統 global information system;
全球性危機 global crisis;
全球戰略 global strategy;
~ 全球戰略思想 global strategy thought;
全球戰爭 global warfare;
全球主義 globalism;
全球自由貿易 global free trade;
放眼全球 keep the whole world in view;
譽滿全球 achieve global fame; famed the world over; gain a world reputation; internationally renowned; of world renown; world-famous;

[全權] carte blanche; full authority; full powers; plenary powers; plenipotentiary;
全權處理 give sb a free hand; give sb his head;
全權大使 ambassador plenipotentiary;
全權代表 envoy plenipotentiary; plenipotentiary;
全權公使 minister plenipotentiary;
授以全權 vest sb with full authority;

[全然] completely; entirely; totally;
全然不顧 in utter indifference to;

[全人] perfect person; sage;
全人教育 whole-person education;

[全日] full-time;
全日制教育 full-time schooling;
全日制學校 full-time school;

[全身] all over the body; flesh and fell; to the teeth; whole body;
全身不適 general malaise;
全身發抖 shake all over;
全身發癢 itch all over;
全身檢查 general check-up;
全身麻醉 general anesthesia;
全身濕透 wet from top to toe;
全身水腫 anasarca;
全身疼痛 aching all over; general aching;
全身痛 pantalgia;
全身痛疼 ache all over; general aching;
全身萎縮 panatrophy;
全身像 full-length photo; full-length portrait;
全身性肥胖 adiposis universalis;
全身性過敏反應 generalized anaphylaxis;
全身性疾病 systemic disease;
全身性水腫 anasarca;
全身循環 circulate through the body;
全身營養不良 pantatrophia;
牽一髮而動全身 a slight move in one part may affect the entire situation; domino effect; pull a single hair and the whole body is affected — a slight partial move may affect the overall situation;

[全盛] at the peak of development; flourishing; in full bloom;
全盛時期 acme; heyday; one's palmy days; prime; reach one's zenith; reach the peak of its development; the prime; the zenith;

[全勝] complete victory; total victory;
大獲全勝 sail through with flying colours;
取得全勝 gain a complete victory;

[全蝕] total eclipse;

全蝕始 beginning of totality; second contact;
全蝕帶 belt of totality;
全蝕時間 duration of totality;
全蝕終 end of totality; third contact;
日全蝕 total solar eclipse;
月全蝕 total lunar eclipse

[全受全歸] live a perfect life;

[全數] the sum total; the total number; the whole amount;

[全速] at full speed; in high gear; maximum speed; top speed;
全速前進 advance at full speed;

[全套] complete set; full set; package; whole set;

[全體] all; en bloc; en masse; entire; everybody; head and ears; in a body; the whole body; whole;
全體辭職 resign en bloc; resign en masse;
全體會議 plenary meeting; plenary session;
全體利益 interests of the whole;
局部服從全體 the part is subordinate to the whole;

[全天] all day long; all the day; round the clock; whole day long;

[全文] full text;
全文翻譯 full translation;
全文記錄 verbatim record;
全文宣讀 read out in full;

[全無是處] absolutely without merit;

[全武行] brawl; free-for-all;

[全息] holographic;
全息電影 holographic movie;
全息攝影 holography;
~全息攝影系統 holographic-based system;
全息術 holography;
~彩色全息術 colour holography;
~計算機全息術 computer holography;
~聲全息術 acoustical holography;
全息圖 hologram;
~全息圖再現 reconstruction of hologram;
~多色全息圖 multicolour hologram;
~二元全息圖 binary hologram;
~光全息圖 optical hologram;
非光全息圖 nonoptical hologram;
~人工全息圖 artificial hologram;
~聲全息圖 acoustic hologram;
~吸收全息圖 absorption hologram;
~象全息圖 focused image hologram;
全息照相術 holography;

[全線] all fronts; entire length; the whole line;
全線通車 whole line opened to traffic;

[全向] isotropic; omnidirection;
全向導航 omnidirectional range;
全向天線 isotropic aerial; non-directional aerial; omnidirectional aerial;

[全新] brand new;

[全休] complete rest;

[全音] whole tone;

[全優] all-round excellence;

[全知全能] omniscient and omnipotent;

安全 safe; safety; secure; security;
保全 (1) preserve; save from danger; (2) keep in good repair; maintain;
不全 incomplete; partial;
成全 help sb to accomplish sth;
苟全 manage barely to survive; preserve one's own life at all costs;
顧全 show consideration for and take care to preserve;
健全 (1) able-bodied; perfect; sane; sound; (2) integrity; perfect; regular; (3) improve; perfect; strengthen;
俱全 complete in all varieties;
兩全 be satisfactory to both parties; have regard for both sides;
齊全 all in readiness; complete; everything complete; nothing missing;
求全 (1) ask for perfection; demand perfection; (2) seek a satisfactory result; try to bring sth to a satisfactory conclusion; try to round sth off;
曲全 suppress one's own feelings for the sake of greater interests;
十全 full; perfect; utterly;
雙全 complete in both respects; possessing both;
完全 absolutely; complete; completely; entirely; fully; mere; perfectly; pure; thorough; totally; whole;
萬全 failure-proof; perfectly safe; perfectly sound; surefire;
玉全 help accomplish sth;
圓全 (1) complete; satisfactory; (2) help sb succeed;
責全 demand perfection in others; expect others to do a flawless job;
周全 (1) aid; help; (2) complete with all that is desired; comprehensive; thorough;

quan

【泉】 (1) fountain; spring; (2) ancient term for a coin; (3) a surname;

[泉地] oasis;

[泉林] (1) natural scenery; (2) abode of a recluse;

[泉脈] ground water channels;

[泉水] spring water;

[泉臺] grave; tomb;

[泉下] netherworld; world of the dead;

[泉眼] mouth of a spring;

[泉湧] gush out like a fountain;

蜂起泉湧 like the swarming of bees and the flowing of fountain water;

淚如泉湧 a deluge of tears; a flood of tears; a stream of tears; burst into a flood of tears; tears gush forth in floods; tears gush from one's eyes; tears gush out like a bubbling spring; tears well up in one's eyes; tears well up like a fountain; the tears flow in streams;

思如泉湧 ideas keep coming like a swelling spring;

血如泉湧 blood gushes forth in fountains; blood gushes out like a fountain;

[泉源] (1) fountainhead; springhead; wellspring; (2) source;

知識的泉源 the fountain of knowledge;

[奔泉] gushing spring;

飛泉 Cliffside spring;

沸泉 boiling spring;

濆泉 geyser;

黃泉 the netherworld;

九泉 grave; netherworld;

礦泉 mineral spring;

噴泉 fountain;

清泉 crystal-clear fountain;

山泉 mountain spring;

湯泉 hot spring;

溫泉 hot spring; spa; thermal spring;

鹽泉 brine;

涌泉 bubbling fountain; fountain;

湧泉 fountain; spring;

油泉 oil spring;

淵泉 deep springs;

源泉 fountain; fountainhead; original source; source; wellspring;

自流泉 artesian spring;

quan

【拳】 (1) fist; (2) box; give a punch; punch; strike; (3) art of boxing; boxing; pugilism; (4) strength;

[拳棒] fighting feats;

[拳不離手，曲不離口] boxing cannot dispense with the hand, nor songs the mouth; keep one's eye in; keep one's hand in; no day without a line; one cannot strike without the hand, nor sing without the mouth; practice makes perfect; the boxer's fist must stick to its task, and the singer's mouth no rest must ask;

[拳打] strike with fists;

拳打腳踢 beat and kick; beat up; box and kick; cuff and kick; give sb a good beating; strike and kick;

[拳鬥] fist fight;

[拳擊] boxing; pugilism; strike with fist;

拳擊比賽 boxing match; contest at boxing;

~拳擊比賽場地 boxing ring;

拳擊練習 shadow boxing;

拳擊手 boxer; pugilist;

~次輕量級拳擊手 leatheerweight;

~輕量級拳擊手 light heavyweight;

次最輕量級拳擊手 flyweight;

最輕量級拳擊手 tantamweight;

~羽量級拳擊手 featherweight;

拳擊運動 boxing;

比賽拳擊 box against each other;

健身拳擊 boxercise;

徒手拳擊 box with hands;

有氧拳擊 boxercise;

[拳腳] Chinese boxing;

拳腳交加 a violent beating; beat up with fists and kicks;

拳來腳去 exchange blows; give tit for tat;

三拳兩腳 a few cuffs and kicks;

[拳拳] candid; sincere; reverent;

拳拳服膺 adhere to faithfully; have a sincere belief in; keep firmly in the mind; lay it to heart in all reverence;

拳拳之忱 sincere intentions; sincerity;

[拳賽] boxing match;

[拳師] boxer; boxing coach; boxing master; expert in the art of boxing;

拳師狗 boxer;

[拳手] boxer;

［拳術］ art of boxing; Chinese boxing; manly art; noble art of defence;
［拳頭］ fist;
拳頭產品 key products; toped products;
拳頭打跳蚤 break a butterfly on a wheel; hit a flea with one's fist;
挨一頓拳頭 be punched; get a punch;
揮動拳頭 shake one's fist;
揮舞拳頭 punch the air;
握緊拳頭 clench one's fists;
搯拳頭 clench one's fist;
攥緊拳頭 clench one's fist;
［拳王］ boxing champion;
［拳握］ hold in the fist;

挨一拳 get a punch; have it;
猜拳 finger-guessing drinking game; mora; play mora;
打拳 box; practise boxing; shadow boxing;
猴拳 monkey boxing;
花拳 fancy boxing; flowery boxing;
劃拳 finger-guessing game;
豁拳 finger-guessing game;
空拳 bare-handed; hold nothing in the hand;
老拳 fist;
賽拳 (1) finger-guessing game; (2) boxing bout;
雙拳 two fists;
太極拳 Chinese shadow boxing;
螳螂拳 mantis bowing;
握拳 clench one's fust; make a fist;
一拳 a blow;

quan
【荃】 (1) fragrant herb; (2) fine cloth;
［荃察］ your esteemed consideration;

quan
【牷】 (1) ox of one colour; (2) (of a sacrifice) intact;

quan
【痊】 cured; healed; recovery from an illness;
［痊可］ have been cured; have recovered from illness;
［痊癒］ be cured of a disease; bring through; cure; get well; fully recover from illness; heal; heal up; make a recovery; on the mend; on the mending hand; recover; recover from; recover one's health; rid of;
感冒痊癒 throw off a cold;
霍然痊愈 suddenly one recovers from an illness;
完全痊癒 be completely recovered;
無法痊癒 cannot be restored;
小病痊癒 recover from one's indisposition;

quan
【惓】 candid; sincere;
［惓惓］ candid; sincere;
惓惓於懷 remember sth at heart constantly;

quan
【筌】 bamboo fish trap;

quan
【詮】 (1) explain; expound; illustrate; (2) core of sth; truth of sth; (3) appraise; assess; rate; weigh;
［詮次］ arrange in order;
［詮釋］ annotation; explanatory notes; expound; interpret; interpretation;
詮釋學 hermeneutics;
~存在詮釋學 existential hermeneutics;
詮釋循環 hermeneutic circle;
［詮證］ explain correct meaning of the text point by point;
［詮注］ notes and commentary;

quan
【蜷】 (1) be coiled; be curled up; huddle up; wriggle; (2) twisted; wriggly;
［蜷伏］ curl up; huddle up; lie with the knees drawn up; snuggle;
［蜷局］ curled up;
［蜷曲］ coil; curl; swirl; twist; twisted; wriggly;
［蜷縮］ cower; curl up; huddle up; roll up; twisted; wriggly;
［蜷蜿］ wind round and round;

quan
【銓】 (1) estimate; judge; measure; weigh; (2) evaluate qualifications in selecting officials; (3) a surname;
［銓材］ estimate one's ability;
［銓次］ procedures for selecting officials;
［銓度］ estimate;
［銓衡］ measure and select talents;
［銓量］ judge;
［銓論］ discourse;
［銓敘］ select and appoint officials;
［銓選］ select officials after evaluating

qualifications;
[銓擇] evaluate and select;
[銓註] annotate;

quan
【踡】 coiled; contracted; curled; drawn together; not stretched;
[踡伏] coil up;
[踡跼] contracted; not stretched;
[踡屈] curled up; not stretched;

quan
【醛】 aldehyde;
[醛酸] aldehydic acid;
[醛糖] aldose;
丙醛 propionic aldehyde;
丁醛 butyric;
酚醛 phenolic aldehyde;
甲醛 formaldehyde;
乳醛 lactic aldehyde;
糖醛 furfural;
乙醛 acetic aldehyde;

quan
【鬈】 (1) fine hair; (2) curled hair;
[鬈髮] crimps;
[鬈毛] frizzle;
[鬈曲] crimp; crinkle; curl;
鬈曲羊毛 crimpy wool; crinkled wool;

quan
【權】 (1) right; (2) authority; power; (3) advantageous position; (4) assess; weigh; (5) for the time being; temporarily; tentatively; (6) expedient way; expediency; (7) a surname;
[權變] adaptability in tactics; adaptation to circumstances; adjust oneself to changing situations; tact;
權變多謀 full of ideas; resourceful; with all one's wits about one;
[權柄] authority; power;
[權臣] powerful minister;
權臣欺君 powerful officials insult their king;
[權寵] gain powers through favour from the emperor;
[權大於法] power overshadowing law; power treading law; replacing law by power;
[權代] act in another's place temporarily; substitute for another for the time being;
[權典] provisional law; temporary regulations;
[權度] (1) estimate; (2) laws;
[權貴] bigwigs; dignitary; highly-placed personalities; influential figures; influential officials; the mighty;
阿附權貴 attach oneself to some authority; attach oneself to the powerful and influential persons; cling to the powerful; curry favour with influential officials; curry favour with those in power; toady to and chime in with the influential officials;
趨附權貴 a hanger-on of ranking officials;
[權衡] assess; balance; consider; judge and weigh; weigh; weigh and consider balance;
權衡比較 weigh the pros and cons;
權衡得失 weigh the gains and losses; weigh the pros and cons;
權衡利弊 weigh the advantages and disadvantages; weigh up the pros and cons;
權衡利害 take one thing with another; weigh the advantages and disadvantages; weigh the pros and cons;
權衡輕重 judge the comparative importance; make an estimate of the importance of sth; measure how light or heavy the thing is; weigh the comparative importance; weigh up one thing against another; weigh up the matter carefully;
權衡再三 weigh and balance again and again;
兩害權衡，當取其輕 of two evils choose the lesser one;
重加權衡 redress the balance;
[權力] authority; power; power and authority;
權力鬥爭 power struggle;
權力分配 distribution of powers;
權力基礎 power base;
權力機構 governing body;
權力機關 organs of power;
權力結構 power structure;
權力均衡 balance of power;
權力擴張 empire-building;
權力濫用 abuse of power;
權力平衡 balance of power;
權力所在地 locus of authority;

權力位置 position of power;
權力無上 supreme in authority;
權力下放 delegate power to the lower levels; devolution of administrative powers on to lower levels; shift part of the powers to lower levels; transfer power to a lower level;
權力移交 transfer of power;
權力慾 megalomania;
權力政治 power politics;
權力之爭 struggle for power;
權力裝束 power dressing;
權力走廊 corridors of power;
把持權力 keep power;
把攬大權 keep all power in one's own hands; monopolize all power;
法定權力 legal authority;
獲得權力 gain power; get power;
絕對權力 absolute authority;
濫用權力 abuse one's authority; abuse power; misuse one's authority;
失去權力 lose one's authority;
無上的權力 absolute power;
無限的權力 absolute power;
無限制的權力 unrestrained power;
行使權力 exertion of authority; wield power;
有權力 have authority; have power;
運用權力 exercise one's authority; exert one's authority; use one's power; wield one's authority;
真正的權力 real power;

[權利] interest; right;
權利論 theory of right;
出賣權利 sell the right;
放棄權利 abdicate a right;
附屬權利 ancillary right;
公民權利 civic rights;
公認的權利 unquestioned right;
捍衛自己的權利 stand up for one's rights;
基本權利 basic rights;
既得權利 acquired right;
平等權利 equal rights;
人身權利 right of person;
維護權利 assert one's rights; uphold sb's rights;
新獲得的權利 newly-acquired rights;
行使權利 exercise a right;
有權利 have a right;
爭權奪利 fight for more power and profit for oneself; fight for power and gain; fight for selfish gains; scramble for personal gains; scramble for power and gains; struggle for power and money;

[權量] weigh;
[權略] tactics;
[權門] powerful families; the households of powerful ministers;
[權謀] political tactics; schemes and power; the use of schemes and power; trickery;
權謀多變 resourceful;
[權能] (1) authority; powers and functions; (2) exercise of one's rights;
[權且] as a temporary measure; for the moment; for the time being; in the mean time; interim; temporarily;
[權時] expedient; for the time being; temporary;
[權勢] clout; power and influence;
權勢地位 official position and influence;
權勢人物 curry favour with influential people;
~巴結權勢人物 curry favour with influential people;
權勢欲 lust of power;
傲視權勢 hold power and authority in disdain;
濫用權勢 throw one's weight around;
喪失權勢 forfeit the influence;
政治權勢 political clout;
[權術] plot; political trickery; intrigues; politics;
[權威] (1) authority; dean; person of authority; pundit; (2) authority; power and prestige;
權威關係 authority relation;
權威人士 arbiter; authoritative person; authoritative sources;
權威形象 authority image;
權威性格 authoritarian personality;
權威性文獻 authoritative text;
權威主義 authoritarianism;
公認的權威 acknowledged authority;
建立權威 establish authority;
蔑視權威 defy authority;
時尚權威 fashion guru;
學術權威 academic authority;
有權威 carry weight;
[權位] (1) authority; (2) person in authority; (3) position of authority; (4) seat of power; (5) power and position;

爭權奪位 fight for power and position; strive for power and position;

[權限] authority; jurisdiction within certain limits; limitation of authority; limitation of power; limits of authority; power; within the power of jurisdiction; within the rights of;

保留權限 reserved authority;

確定權限 define the competence;

審批權限 rights and limits of examination and approval;

[權要] (1) big wigs; powerful persons; top dogs; (2) confidential matters;

[權宜] expedient; makeshift;

權宜手段 temporary expedient;

權宜之計 expedient measure; make-shift device; matter of expediency; measure of expediency; palliative; shifting tactics; stopgap measure;

[權益] inviolable rights; legal right; rights and interests;

權益法 equity law;

權益均等 rights and interests equal;

合法權益 lawful right and interest;

控股權益 controlling interest;

[權右] big wigs; highly-placed personalities; top dogs;

[權詐] crafty and dishonest; craftiness; trickery;

[權杖] crosier; crozier; a baton as a symbol of office;

罷免權 right of recall;

霸權 hegemony; supremacy;

版權 copyright;

辯護權 right to defence;

表決權 right to vote;

兵權 military leadership; military power;

財產權 property right;

財權 (1) property ownership; (2) power over financial affairs;

產權 property right;

從權 as a matter of expediency;

篡權 usurp power;

大權 authority;

代表權 representation;

當權 hold power; in power;

地權 land ownership;

佃權 tenant right;

發明權 inventor's patent right;

發言權 right to speak;

法權 right;

放權 release authority;

分權 separation of powers;

否決權 veto power;

夫權 authority of the husband;

公民權 civil rights;

公權 public rights;

購股權 option;

股權 equity; shareholding; stock right;

管理權 jurisdiction;

海洋權 maritime rights;

皇權 imperial authority; imperial power;

豁免權 immunity;

極權 totalitarian;

集權 concentration of power; centralization of state power;

繼承權 right of inheritance;

加權 weighted;

監督權 authority to supervise;

居留權 right of residence;

居住權 right of residence;

決定權 power to make decisions;

君權 monarchical power;

軍權 military leadership; military power;

攬權 abuse one's authority;

濫權 abuse authority;

立法權 legislative power;

利權 (1) economic rights; (2) financial power;

領導權 authority; leadership;

領海權 sovereign right over territorial waters;

領空權 sovereign right over territorial sky;

領土權 sovereign right over territory;

留置權 lien;

民權 civil liberties; civil rights; democratic rights; rights of the people;

母權 mother right;

拿權 in the saddle; wield power;

弄權 manipulate power for personal ends;

女權 girl power; woman's rights;

平權 equal rights;

期權 options;

棄權 (1) abstain from voting; abstention; (2) abandonment of a right; abdication; forfeit; waive the right to play;

強權 brute force; might; power;

侵權 infringement of right;

全權 carte blanche; full authority; full powers; plenary powers; plenipotentiary;

人權 human rigths;

認股權 subscription right;

擅權 monopolize power; usurp power;

神權 (1) religious authority; theocracy; (2) rule

by divine right;
實權 real power;
使用權 right of use;
事權 powers or authority of office;
收權 retake the power;
受權 be authorized;
授權 authorize; empower;
司法權 judicial power;
私有權 right of private ownership;
所有權 proprietary rights;
特權 prerogative; privilege;
統治權 right to rule;
王權 authority of a king;
威權 authority; power and prestige;
握權 hold the reins; in command; in power;
無權 have no right;
選舉權 right to vote;
業權 proprietorship;
有權 entitle;
越權 act beyond one's authority; act without authorization; exceed one's power or authority;
債權 claim; creditor's rights; outstanding claims;
掌權 exercise control; in power; wield power;
政權 political power; political regime; regime; reins of government;
職權 authority of office; function and power; powers of office;
制海權 command of the sea; naval supremacy;
制空權 air domination; air supremacy; control of the air;
治權 power of a government;
質權 pledge;
中權 (1) main army; (2) central administration;
主動權 initiative;
主權 (1) sovereign rights; sovereignty; (2) right of autonomy;
著作權 copyright;
抓權 grab power;
專利權 patent;
專權 dictatorial; grab all the power; in full power;
酌處權 discretion;
自決權 right to self-determination;
自治權 autonomy;
宗主權 suvereignty;
族權 clan authority; clan power;

quan

【顴】 cheekbone;
[顴弓] zygoma;
[顴骨] cheekbone; malar bone; zygoma;
顴骨突起 prominent cheekbones; zygoma;
高顴骨 high cheekbones;
[顴肌] musculus zygomaticus; zygomaticus;
[顴神經] nervus zygomaticus;
[顴小肌] zygolabialis;

quan³
quan

【犬】 canine; dog;
[犬齒] canine; canine teeth;
[犬吠] bark; bark of a dog;
百犬吠聲 a barking dog sets the whole street barking;
桀犬吠堯 an evil man's dog barks at a good man — the underling of an evil man will attack whoever he is told to attack;
狂犬吠日 a mad dog barking at the sun — in the futility;
狂犬吠月 bark at the moon; bay at the moon;
[犬類] canine;
犬類疾病 canine disease;
[犬馬] dogs and horses;
犬馬之勞 at sb's beck and call; at sb's disposal; die dog for sb; faithful service; of service; render one's services; serve faithfully like a dog; serve faithfully like a horse; serve like a dog; serve like a horse; serve one's master faithfully;
良馬俊犬 fleet horses and pedigree hounds;
愿效犬馬 I will render what trifling service I can; I would be at your beck and call; I would serve like a dog or a horse;
[犬鋪] doghouse; kennel;
[犬儒] cynic;
[犬舍] doghouse;
[犬牙] (1) canine teeth; (2) fang;
犬牙交錯 have many defiles and passes; in a jigsaw pattern; indented; indenting; interlocked like dog's teeth; interlocking; jagged and interlocking; jigsaw outline; jigsaw patterns; jigsaw-like; wind in and out like dog's teeth; zigzag;
上犬牙 eye tooth;
[犬子] one's son;
虎父無犬子 a tiger father will not beget

a dog son — there will be no laggard among the children of a brave man; an angle does not hatch a dove; eagles do not breed doves;

愛犬 one's beloved dog;
愛斯基摩犬 husky;
導盲犬 guide dog;
諜犬 setter;
狐犬 fox dog;
雞犬 a dog or a cock;
金毛尋回犬 golden retriever;
警犬 patrol dog; police dog;
柯基犬 corgi;
獵鳥犬 bird dog;
獵犬 gun dog; hunter; rach; sleuth; sleuth hound;
猛犬 bull dog; fierce dog; vicious dog;
牧犬 sheep dog; shepherd dog;
猱犬 red dog;
豚犬 (1) pigs and dogs; (2) one's own sons;
野犬 wild dog;
義犬 faithful dog; loyal dog;
鷹犬 falcons and hounds; hired thugs; lackeys;
幼犬 pup;

quan
【甽】 (1) irrigation ditch; (2) mountain stream; (3) canyon; dale; valley;
[甽畝] farmland; field;
甽畝天才 a man of midiocre ability;

quan
【綣】 make tender love; meet in rendezvous;
繾綣 deeply attached to each other;

quan⁴
quan
【券】 (1) ticket; (2) certificate; (3) bond;
國庫券 national treasury bond;
獎券 lottery ticket;
庫券 national treasury bond;
入場券 admission ticket;
勝券 confidence in victory;
優待券 complimentary ticket;
債券 bond; debenture;
招待券 complimentary ticket;
證券 negotiable securities;
左券 copy of a contract held by the creditor;

quan
【勸】 admonish; advise; counsel; encourage; exhort; persuade; try to persuade; urge;
[勸酬] urge to drink;
[勸導] admonish; advise; exhort; exhort and guide; induce; try to persuade; urge;
[勸服] prevail;
[勸告] admonish; advise; counsel; exhort; remonstrate; urge;
不顧勸告 disregard one's exhortation;
不聽勸告 close one's ears to one's advice; deaf to one's advice; give no ear to one's advice; not follow one's advice; not take one's advice; stop one's ears to one's advice; turn a deaf ear to one's advice;
口頭勸告 verbal advice;
[勸和] mediate; reconcile a dispute; reconcile a quarrel; try to make peace;
[勸化] (1) exhort to conversion; urge sb to do good; (2) beg for alms; collect alms;
[勸誨] advise; exhort;
[勸架] mediate a quarrel; mediate between two quarrelling parties; try to patch up a quarrel; try to stop people from fighting each other;
[勸駕] urge sb to do sth;
[勸諫] plead for rectification; remonstrate;
[勸解] (1) help sb to get over his worries; (2) bring people together; exhort to peace; make peace between; mediate;
[勸戒] admonish; dissuade; expostulate; warn;
[勸進] make a formal appeal to sb to mount the throne;
[勸酒] offer a drink; urge sb to drink;
[勸捐] ask for contributions;
[勸勉] advise and encourage; encourage; exhort to great effort; urge;
[勸募] ask for contributions;
[勸善規過] exhort sb to reform himself and urge him to practise virtue;
[勸説] advise; persuade; talk sb into;
勸説祈使句 persuasive imperative;
勸説無效 persuasion proves unawailing;
百般勸説 try to persuade sb in every possible way;
無需別人勸説 need no persuasion;
[勸退] persuade sb to resign;
[勸慰] console; soothe;
百般勸慰 try every means to soothe sb; try to soothe and coax sb;

[勸降] exhort sb to surrender; induce to capitulate; induce to surrender; urge sb to surrender;
勸降手段 the scheme of inducing...to capitulate;
[勸學] exhortation to study; urge sb to study hard;
[勸誘] induce; prevail upon; talk sb into;
[勸阻] advise against; advise sb not to; discourage sb from; dissuade sb from doing sth; talk sb out of; warn sb against;
勸阻無效 have vainly tried to dissuade sb from doing sth try in vain to talk sb out of doing sth;
受到勸阻 be dissuaded;

哀勸 admonish in a tearful voice;
敦勸 exhort earnestly; urge;
奉勸 admonish; advise; give a piece of advice;
規勸 admonish; advise; exhort; expostulate; remonstrate;
哄勸 persuade or coax into doing sth;
解勸 mollify; soothe;
婉勸 friendly persuasion; persuade gently;
相勸 offer advice; persuade;

que¹
que
【缺】 (1) at a loss for; deficient in; for need of; for want of; hard up for; in want of; insufficient; lack; short of; wanting in; (2) imperfect; incomplete; (3) absent; in the absence of; (4) opening; vacancy;
[缺筆] a stroke missing in a written character;
[缺編] below strength; understaffed;
[缺德] mean; villainous; wicked;
缺德鬼 dirty dog; mean fellow; public nuisance; villain;
[缺點] defect; demerit; disadvantage; drawback; failing; fault; foible; hitch; shortcoming; vice; weak point; weakness;
糾正缺點 remedy shortcomings;
克服缺點 overcome the deficiency;
小缺點 foible;
[缺額] opening; place; vacancy;
[缺乏] at a loss for; deficiency; deficient in; do not have; far too little of; for need of; for want of; hard up for; in the absence of; in want of; lack; lack for; lack in; lack of; push for; short of; wanting in;
缺乏風格 lack style;
缺乏活力 lack cordiality;
缺乏經驗 lack experience;
缺乏了解 short in understanding;
缺乏人才 short of talents;
缺乏勇氣 deficient in courage;
缺乏證據 want of evidence;
維生素缺乏 vitamin deficiency;
營養缺乏 alimentary deficiency;
資料缺乏 paucity of information;
[缺憾] discount; regret;
[缺貨] in short supply; out of stock; run out of stock;
[缺角] knocked-off corner;
[缺課] absent from class; absent from school; miss a class;
從不缺課 miss no days of school;
因病缺課 miss classes on account of illness;
[缺口] (1) breach; gap; loophole; opening; (2) deficiency; insufficiency; shortage;
打開缺口 drive a wedge; make a breach;
填塞缺口 calk an opening;
[缺糧] grain deficit; lack food supplies;
[缺漏] gaps and omissions;
補其缺漏 compensate for the shortage and leakage;
[缺欠] (1) defect; imperfection; shortcoming; (2) lack; short of;
[缺勤] absent from duty; absent from work; absentism;
缺勤率 absence rate;
缺勤者 absentee;
[缺少] absence; deficient in; lack; short of;
缺少人手 lack manpower; short of hands; short-handed;
缺少現金 short of ready money;
缺少訓練 lack in training;
缺少資金 in want of funds;
[缺失] deficiency; deletion; hiatus;
染色體缺失 chromosomal deficiency; chromosomal deletion;
細微缺失 minute deficiency;
中間缺失 intercalary deletion;
[缺損] broken away; defect; missing and damaged;
[缺位] leave a post vacant;

[缺席] absent; absent from a meeting; in absentia;
缺席[的] absent;
缺席審判 trial by default;
缺席投票 absentee ballot;
缺席選票 absentee vote;
缺席者 absentee;
長期缺席 long absence;
擅自缺席 absent without notice;
無故缺席 stay away without good cause;
因事缺席 absent through being other engaged;
[缺陷] blemish; defect; drawback; fault; flaw;
缺陷美 the attraction of some imperfection;
缺陷學 defectology;
出生缺陷 birth defect;
內埋缺陷 buried flaw;
容許缺陷 allowable defect;
身體有缺陷 defective in body;
天生缺陷 birth defect;
外表缺陷 appearance defect;
掩蓋缺陷 cover up the deficiencies;
陽離子缺陷 cation defect;
指出缺陷 point out deficiencies;
鑄件缺陷 casting defect;
鑄造缺陷 casting flaw;
[缺氧] anoxia; oxygen deficit;
[缺頁] missing page;
[缺衣] short of clothes;
缺衣少穿 walk on one's shoestrings;
缺衣少食 go short of food and clothes; have not enough food and very little clothing; have no enough in the belly and on the back;

補缺 fill a vacancy; supply a deficiency;
殘缺 fragmentary;
出缺 fall vacant;
短缺 deficiency; deficit; shortage;
肥缺 fat job; lucrative post; plum;
緊缺 in short supply; scarce;
開缺 become vacant;
空缺 vacant position;
美缺 cushy job;
奇缺 almost nil; critical shortage of; very scarce;
欠缺 (1) deficient in; lack; lack in; short of; (2) deficiency; shortcoming;
衰缺 declining and full of defects;
無缺 intact; undamaged;
稀缺 scarce;
遺缺 vacancy;
盈缺 waxing and waning;
優缺 excellent vacancy;
餘缺 surplus and deficiency;
暫缺 left vacant for the time being; out of stock for the time being;

que

【闕】 (1) errors; faults; mistakes; (2) deficient; lack; wanting;
[闕如] deficient; lacking; wanting;
付諸闕如 relegate to the category of things unknown;
盡付闕如 all are exhausted;
尚付闕如 not yet done; still wanting;
[闕失] error; mistake;
[闕文] hiatus in the text;
[闕疑] leave the question open; unsettled point;

que²
que

【瘸】 (1) cripple; (2) lame;
[瘸腿] crippled; lame;
[瘸子] cripple; lame person;
瘸子擔水——步步來 like a lame person carrying a bucket of water — step by step;
瘸子看人——總是歪的 a lame person looking at another person — always looking at things in a distorted way;
瘸子立正——立場不穩 a lame person standing at attention — not taking a firm stand;

que⁴
que

【卻】 (1) fall back; retreat; step back; withdraw; (2) banish; drive back; repulse; (3) decline; refuse; refuse to accept; (4) but; still; yet;
[卻病] cure a disease; prevent a disease;
卻病延年 banish illness and increase long life; banish illness and prolong one's life; prevent disease and prolong life;
[卻步] flinch from; hang back for fear; hang back from; ink back at the sight of; retreat; shrink back from; step back; step back for fear; withdraw;
望而卻步 direct the eyes upon...and step back; flinch; halt in face of; shrink back at the sight of sth

[卻待] be just waiting to;
[卻敵] drive back the enemy; repulse the enemy;
[卻好] by coincidence; it so happened that; just at the right time;
[卻老] immortality;
[卻立] stand back;
[卻扇] get married;
[卻是] in fact; nevertheless; the fact is;
[卻又] (1) but again; (2) then...later;
[卻之不恭] it is disrespectful to refuse; it would be impolite to decline;
卻之不恭，受之有愧 to decline would be disrespectful, but to accept is embarrassing;
[卻走] run backward; turn away;

冷卻 cool;
了卻 settle; solve;
失卻 lose; miss;
退卻 (1) retreat; withdraw; (2) hang back; shrink back;
推卻 decline; refuse;
忘卻 forget;
謝卻 decline; politely refuse;

que
【雀】 (1) general name of small birds; (2) freckled;
[雀斑] freckles;
[雀巢鳩佔] occupy what belongs to others; usurp another's position;
[雀屏中選] be chosen as sb's son-in-law;
[雀往旺處飛] birds always fly to the light;
[雀息] remain quiet; remain silent;
[雀躍] caper; jump for joy; leap with joy;
歡喜雀躍 skipping and jumping about with joy; tread on air;
[雀戰] play a game of mah-jong;

黃雀 siskin;
灰雀 bullfinch;
金絲雀 canary;
孔雀 peacock;
麻雀 sparrow;
攀雀 penduline tit;
山雀 tit;
雪雀 snow finch;
鴉雀 crow tit;
燕雀 bramble finch;
雲雀 skylark;
朱雀 rosefinch;

que
【殼】 coverings; husks; shells;
[殼果] nut;
[殼物] shellish in general;

que
【确】 (1) hard stone; (2) barren; unproductive;
[确切] accurate; pertinent; sound; valid;

que
【搉】 (1) knock; strike; (2) consult; discuss; negotiate;
[搉商] consult; discuss;

que
【碏】 (of stone) many-coloured;

que
【榷】 (1) monopolize; (2) levy taxes;
[榷茶] levy tea taxes;
[榷利] enjoy monopoly;
[榷鹽] levy salt taxes;
[榷運] tax on transportation;
商榷 deliberate; discuss;
揚榷 expound briefly;

que
【愨】 honest; prudent;

que
【確】 (1) certain; real; reliable; secure; sure; true; valid; (2) firmly;
[確保] ensure; guarantee; insure; make certain that; make sure that; see to it that; sure to;
確保安全 ensure safety;
確保無虞 insure that no impediment shall arise;
確保質量 guarantee quality;
[確當] appropriate; correct and proper;
[確定] ascertain; certitude; confirm; define; determine; establish; fix; set;
確定目標 set up a purpose;
確定任務 set the tasks;
確定時限 fix a time frame;
確定限度 establish the limits;
確定型決策 decision-making with certainty;
確定性系統 deterministic system;
不確定 indeterminate;
~ 不確定的 chancy;

尚未確定 be still in the air; be still up in the air;

[確非] actually not; really not; truly not;

[確立] establish firmly;

確立…決心 be firmly determined to;

確立信譽 establish one's credit;

牢固確立 entrenchment;

[確論] definite view; sound statement;

[確切] (1) definite; exact; precise; (2) reliable; true;

確切地 on the nose;

確切無疑 beyond all doubts – quite certain;

確切知道 know for sure;

不確切 imprecise; imprecision; inexact;

用詞確切 exact in one's choice of words;

[確然] affirm; certify; confirm; identify with certainty;

[確認] acknowledge; affirm; confirm;

確認定貨 book confirmation;

確認書 confirmation;

~成交確認書 sales confirmation;

~訂貨確認書 confirmation of order;

~購貨確認書 purchase confirmation;

~外匯合同確認書 exchange contract confirmation;

有待確認 to be confirmed;

[確實] (1) certain; certainty; real; reliable; true; (2) indeed; really; (3) verify;

確實成效 tangible results;

確實無疑 dead certainty; for a certainty;

確實性 certainty;

確確實實 and no mistake; beyond all doubt; for a certainty; for a fact;

[確守] scrupulously abide by; truly adhere to;

[確信] be convinced; certitude; confident; firmly believe; sure;

[確有] there is indeed;

確有其人 there is indeed such a person;

確有其事 it really happened; it's a fact; there is really such a thing; this is the case;

[確診] diagnose; form a correct diagnosis on a disease; make a definite diagnosis;

[確證] conclusive evidence; confirmation; convincing proof; definite evidence; ironclad proof; solid evidence;

[確知] know for sure;

[確鑿] accurate; authentic; based on truth; beyond doubt; conclusive; iron-clad; irrefutable; precise; reliable; sound;

確鑿不移 authentic; authentic and indisputable; beyond all doubt; conclusive; firmly established; iron-clad; irrefutable; quite certain; really reliable and indisputable; sound; well established and irrefutable;

確鑿無疑 beyond all dispute; beyond all doubt; entirely true and doubtless;

確鑿證據 firmly established evidence;

的確 and no mistake; by no means; indeed; in truth; really;

精確 accurate; exact; exactitude; precise; precision;

明確 (1) clear and definite; clear-cut; explicit; hard-and-fast; unequivocal; (2) make clear; make definite;

磽確 barren; hard and infertile;

真確 (1) real; true; (2) clear; distinct;

正確 accurate; appropriate; correct; proper; right;

準確 accurate; exact; precise;

que

【闋】 (1) close the door; shut the door; (2) rest; retire; take a rest; (3) end of a period of mourning; (4) measure word for songs; (5) blank; empty;

que

【闕】 (1) watch-tower outside the palace gate in ancient China; (2) palace; (3) a surname;

[闕門] palace gate;

que

【鵲】 magpie;

[鵲巢鳩佔] occupy some place belonging to another; one person seizes another's place; take what is not one's own; the dove occupying the magpie's nest; the turtle-dove occupies the magpie's nest;

[鵲鷚] magpie lark;

[鵲起] rise at an opportune time;

[鵲笑鳩舞] great joy among the people;

[鵲雁] magpie goose;

練鵲 long-tailed flaycatcher;

喜鵲 magpie;

qun¹
qun

【逡】 move backward; retire; retreat; withdraw;

[逡退] retire from office when nothing could be accomplished;

[逡行] shrink;

[逡巡] hesitate; shrink back; waver;
逡巡不前 hesitate; reluctant to move ahead; waver;

qun²
qun

【群】 a band of; a bevy of; a body of; a clump of; a cluster of; a congregation of; a crowd of; a drove of; a flock of; a galaxy of; a gang of; a group of; a herd of; a horde of; a host of; a mob of; a multitude of; a pack of; a rabble of; a shoal of; a swarm of; a throng of; a troop of;

[群採] prospecting by the masses;

[群策群力] club ideas and exertions; collective wisdom and efforts; draw upon collective wisdom and strength of the masses as a source of power; lay heads together and work in concert; pool everybody's wisdom and efforts; pool the wisdom and strength of the masses; pool the wisdom and efforts of all the people; put heads together and work in concert; united strength and wisdom; with collective wisdom and efforts; with everybody contributing his ideas and strength; with united wisdom and strength; work and pull together; work as a team;

[群雌粥粥] gathering of women with cackling voices;

[群叢] association;
複合群叢 multiple association;

[群島] archipelago; group of islands;

[群雕] group sculpture; sculpture group;

[群而不黨] sociable but not clannish;

[群芳] (1) a great variety of flowers; all kinds of flowers; beautiful and fragrant flowers; (2) a multitude of beauties;
群芳競艷 (1) all flowers strive for elegance; flowers vie with each other in beauty; the flowers vie with one another in loveliness; (2) a host of beautiful women competing for attention;
群芳譜 botanical treatise;
艷冠群芳 beauty surpassing all flowers;

[群集] crowd; gather in great numbers; swarm;
群集本能 gregarious instinct;

[群架] gang fight; gang quarrel;

[群經] all the classics;

[群居] live as a group;
群居生活 gregarious life; social life;

[群聚] crowd together; gather in large numbers; swarm;

[群龍無首] a group of people without a leader; a host of dragons without a head; a multitude without a leader; an army without a general; many dragons without a head; no leader in a host of dragons; sheep that have no shepherd;

[群論] group theory;

[群落] (1) group; (2) a group of;
群落交錯區 ecotone;
群落學 coenology;
~植物群落學 phytocoenology;
動物群落 zoobiocenose; zoocoenosis; zoocoenosium;
生物群落 biocoenosium;
~大生物群落 macrobiocoenosium;
永久群落 permanent community;
植物群落 botanical colony; phytooenosium; phytocommunity;
植物群落學 phytocoenostics;
~穩定植物群落 stable phytocoenosium;
不穩定植物群落 labile phytocoenosium;
~原生植物群落 primary phytocoenosium;

[群氓] common herd;

[群魔亂舞] a horde of monsters run amuck; a host of demons dancing in riotous revelry; demons and monsters dance in a riotous revelry; evil spirits of all kinds dance in riotous revelry; monsters of all kinds dance with glee; rogues of all kinds running wild; scoundrels of all kinds are engaged in all sorts of criminal activities;

[群毆] gather and have a melee;

[群起而攻之] all join in hitting sb hard; all rise against sb; all rise up and attack; all rise to fight; all turn against; attack in a group; everybody points an accusing finger at him; everybody rallies together to oppose sth; fly out in the common cause against; launch a collective attack on sb; launch a massive attack on sb; rally together and come down strongly on; rally together to attack; rally together to uproot; rise against; rise together and expel sb; rise up in a common struggle against; run up against the opposition of all the people; the crowd rises and attacks sb;

[群輕折軸] a combination of insignificant evil deeds can cause serious trouble; that is the last straw, the straw that breaks the camel's back;

[群情] feelings of the masses; public sentiment;
群情鼎沸 a vast upsurge of public opinion and feeling;
群情激憤 mounting public indignation; public sentiments are enraged;
群情洶洶 public feeling runs high; public opinion is deeply stirred;
群情振奮 everyone is exhilarated;

[群山] hills; mountains; range of mountains;
群山環抱 be surrounded by hills;
群山起伏 the surrounding mountains are like the billows of the sea;
高聳的群山 aerial mountains;

[群體] (1) integral entity; (2) group; population;
群體個性 group individuality;
群體功能 mass function;
群體關係 aggregative relationship;
群體間交際 intergroup communication;
群體建設 team building;
群體結構 group structure;
群體決策 group decision-making;
群體利益 group interest;
群體名詞 mass noun;
群體凝聚力 group cohesiveness;
群體社會 mass society;
群體所有格 group genitive;
群體行為 group behavior;
群體形成 zoorium;
群體意識 group consciousness;
次級群體 secondary group;
基底群體 base population;
密集群體 high population;
細胞群體 cell population;
遺傳群體 gentical population;

[群威群膽] display mass heroism and daring; heroism and audacity of the masses;

[群賢] all the wise men; host of wise men;

[群星] (1) myriads of stars; (2) galaxy of stars;
群星燦爛 a galaxy of brilliant heroes; a galaxy of talents;
群星拱月 all the stars twinkle around the bright moon;

[群雄] group of warlords;
群雄割據 fragmentation of a country by rivalling warlords;
群雄四起 heroes spring up everywhere;
群雄爭長 all the heroes strive for supremacy;
群雄逐鹿 feudal lords vye for the throne; powerful politicians fight for supremacy;

[群言堂] letting everyone have his say; rule by the voice of the many;

[群醫] doctors;
群醫束手 doctors can do nothing to help;

[群蟻附膻] a myriad of ants swarm about a piece of meat that smells — strive for filthy lucre;

[群英] a large number of brilliant minds;
群英畢集 a gathering of talents;
群英會 a gathering of outstanding people; a meeting of heroes;
弁冕群英 cap all talents; exceed all talents;

[群眾] common people; general public; masses;
群眾路線 mass line;
群眾情緒 crowd mood;
群眾心理 emotions of the mob;
群眾性比賽 mass tournament;
群眾運動 mass movement;
發動群眾 arouse the masses to action; mobilize the masses;
驅散群眾 disperse a crowd;
脱離群眾 isolate oneself from the masses;
吸引群眾 draw a crowd;

愛群 (1) congenial; gregarious; love company; sociable; (2) love the multitude;

拔群 outstanding; stand out;

敗群 endanger the whole group;
半群 semigroup;
不群 keep oneself aloof;
超群 head and shoulders above all others; preeminent; surpassing all others;
成群 in groups; in large numbers;
詞群 group;
島群 archipelago;
分群 (of bees) hive off;
蜂群 a cluster of bees; a swarm of bees;
害群 bring disgrace to the group;
合群 (1) get on well with others; (2) gregarious;
集群 colony; en masse; in swarms; schooling;
機群 group of planes;
建築群 building complex; cluster of buildings;
狼群 pack of wolves;
離群 leave society;
人群 crowd of people; drove of people; a multitude of people; throng of people;
社群 association; group;
失群 be lost;
隨群 comply with public opinions; do as others do; follow others;
星群 stars;
鴨群 flock of ducks;
羊群 flock of sheep;
樂群 fond of company and learning from one's friends;
一大群 a crowd of;
一群 a bevy of; a circle of; a clump of; a cluster of; a company of; a congregation of; a crowd of; a drift of; a drove of; a flight of; a flock of; a gaggle of; a galaxy of; a gang of; a group of; a herd of; a horde of; a host of; a huddle of; a mob of; a multitude of; a pack of; a party of; a pride of; a rabble of; a school of; a shoal of; a swarm of; a throng of; a troop of; a troupe of; an array of;
軼群 excel the rest;
逸群 head and shoulders above others; outstanding;
魚群 shoal of fish;
震群 earthquake swarm;
種群 population;
族群 ethnic group;

qun

【裙】 petticoat; skirt;

［裙帶］(1) connected through one's female relatives; (2) girdle;
裙帶風 the rule of women;
裙帶關係 nepotism; apron-string influence; petticoat influence;
裙帶經濟 crony economy;

［裙褲］culottes;

［裙子］skirt;
穿着裙子 in a skirt;
多褶邊的裙子 frilly skirt;
及膝的裙子 knee-length skirt;
脱下裙子 take off one's skirt;
一條裙子 a skirt;

百褶裙 skirt with accordion pleats;
背心裙 pinafore dress;
長裙 long skirt;
襯裙 petticoat; underdress; underskirt;
褶裙 pleated skirt;
短裙 short skirt;
對褶裙 box pleat skirt;
喇叭裙 flared skirt;
連衣裙 frock; one-piece dress;
迷你裙 miniskirt;
拼接裙 gored skirt;
牆裙 dado;
太陽裙 sundress;
圍裙 apron;
西服裙 skirt suit;
腰褶裙 full skirt gathered around the waist;
一條裙子 a skirt;
孕婦裙 maternity dress;
褶裙 pleated skirt;

ran2
ran

【然】 (1) correct; most certainly; right; yes; (2) if so; like that; really; so; (3) be that as it may; but; even though; however; in spite of; nevertheless; nonethelss; on the other hand; still; though; (4) a surname;

[然而] be that as it may; but; even though; however; in spite of; nevertheless; nonetheless; on the other hand; still; though; yet;

[然否] is that correct; yes or no;

[然後] after that; afterwards; be followed by; in turn; later; next; then;

[然納] endorse and adopt;

[然諾] give one's oath; give one's word; pledge; promise; vow;

[然信] pledge to keep a promise;

[然也] definitely; surely;

[然疑] between believing and suspecting;

[然則] but; but then; in that case; then;

藹然 (1) glossy; lustrous; luxuriant; (2) affable; amiable; amicable; friendly; gentle; kind;

安然 (1) safe and sound; safely; (2) at rest; feel at ease; free from worry; peaceful;

岸然 gravely; impressive; in a solemn manner; solemn; solemn and dignified look;

闇然 concealed; hidden; murky; obscure;

黯然 (1) dim; faint; gloomy; (2) dejected; depressed; downcast; low-spirited; sad;

昂然 haughtily; proud and bold; upright and fearless; upright and unafraid;

盎然 abundant; alive; exuberant; full; overflowing; rich;

傲然 iron-willed and unyielding; loftily; proud; unyieldingly;

必然 be bound to be; be doomed to; certain; certainly; have to be; inevitable; inevitably; necessarily; sure;

賁然 bright and brilliant;

炳然 bright;

泊然 calm and at rest;

勃然 (1) abruptly; agitatedly; excitedly; suddenly; (2) prosperously; vigorously;

浡然 excited; rising;

不然 but for; or; or else; otherwise;

慘然 grieved; saddened;

粲然 (1) beaming; bright; (2) marked; striking; (3) smiling broadly;

燦然 brightly; brilliantly; gloriously;

惻然 grieved; sorrowful;

悵然 disappointed; upset;

超然 aloof; detached;

誠然 (1) indeed; true; (2) it is true...(but);

惆然 regretful; wistful;

愴然 sorrowful;

猝然 abruptly; sudden; unexpected;

大自然 nature;

淡然 cool; indifferent;

澹然 cool; indifferent;

當然 (1) as it should be; it goes without saying that; only natural; (2) certainly; of course; sure; sure thing; to be sure; without doubt;

蕩然 all gone; nothing left;

定然 certainly; definitely;

陡然 abruptly; unexpectedly;

斷然 (1) absolutely; categorically; flatly; simply; (2) drastic; resolute;

頓然 at once; immediately;

俄然 suddenly;

愕然 astounded; stunned;

幡然 come to a sudden realization; quickly and completely;

翻然 quickly and completely;

斐然 (1) of literary talent; (2) brilliant; striking;

廢然 dispirited and disappointed;

憤然 angry; indignant;

怫然 abruptly; angrily;

艴然 angry look; look angry;

公然 brazenly; in the face of day; openly;

固然 (1) it is true; no doubt; (2) admittedly; of course;

果然 as expected; if indeed; if really; really;

駭然 gasping with astonishment; struck dumb with amazement;

悍然 brazenly; flagrantly; outrageously;

赫然 (1) impressive; (2) terribly angry;

轟然 with a loud crash;

哄然 boisterous; uproarious;

訇然 with a loud crash;

忽然 all of a sudden; suddenly; unexpectedly;

嘩然 in an uproar; outcry;

渙然 disappear; melt away; scatter; vanish;

煥然 shining;

恍然 suddenly;

渾然 (1) completely; without leaving a trace; (2) integral and indivisible;

或然 probable;

霍然 (1) quickly; rapidly; suddenly; (2) be cured quickly;

豁然 open and clear; suddenly enlightened;
既然 as; after; at all; if; inasmuch as; now; now that; once; seeing; seeing that; since; such being the case; well then; what; when, where;
寂然 silent; still;
恝然 indifferent; unconcerned;
戛然 (of a sound) stopping abruptly;
較然 clear; explicit; marked; obvious;
孑然 alone; lonely; in solitude; solitary;
截然 completely; entirely; sharply;
井然 methodical; neat and tidy; orderly;
竟然 actually; and; as...as; at all; been and; contrary to expectation; fancy; go so far as to; go to the length of; have the effrontery to; have the insolence to; have the prudence to; if you please; little expected; manage; no less than; only to find; not a; not noce; not one; should; so...as; strangely enough; strange to say; that; to one's surprise; to think of; to think that; unexpectedly; wonder;
迥然 far apart; widely different;
居然 (1) to one's surprise; unexpectedly; (2) going so far as to;
遽然 abrupt; sudden;
決然 (1) determinedly; resolutely; (2) definitely; undoubtedly;
慨然 (1) with deep feeling; with emotion; (2) generously;
鏗然 loud and clear;
巋然 loftily; steadfastly;
喟然 the manner of sighing;
栗然 trembling;
悢然 sad; sorrowful;
了然 clear; understand clearly;
瞭然 clear and evident; plain and fully understandable;
凜然 awe-inspiring; stern;
茫然 at a loss; blank; ignorant; in the dark; vacant; with an air of abstraction;
貿然 hastily; rashly; without careful consideration;
猛然 abruptly; suddenly;
懵然 ignorant; muddled;
靡然 leaning to one side;
渺然 boundless; endless; vast;
漠然 apathetically; indifferently; with unconcern;
默然 silent; speechless;
驀然 suddenly;
木然 stupefied;
穆然 (1) peaceful and respectful; (2) meditative;
赧然 blushing;
偶然 (1) accidental; by accident; by chance; by coincidence; chance; fortuitous; happen; have a chance; it is by sheer accident that; it so happened that; occasional; (2) at intervals; at times; at whiles; between times; ever and again; every now and again; every now and then; every so often; from time to time; now and then; occasionally; off and on; on occasion; once and a while; once in a while; once or twice; sometimes; whiles;
判然 clearly; obviously;
龐然 huge;
沛然 copious;
怦然 with a sudden shock;
翩然 light; tripping;
飄飄然 be carried away with one's own importance; complacent; self-satisfied;
飄然 floating in the air;
皤然 (of hair) white;
栖栖然 bustling and excited;
淒然 mournful; sad;
戚然 dejected; depressed; distressed; melancholy;
祺然 calmly; peacefully; serene;
頎然 tall;
歉然 feel sorry; regret;
悄然 (1) sad; sorrowful; (2) quiet; soft;
愀然 sorrowful-looking; stern;
跫然 descriptive of the sound of footsteps;
蘧然 pleasantly surprised;
闃然 absolutely still; very quiet;
全然 completely; entirely;
確然 affirm; certify; confirm; identify with certainty;
仍然 and yet; as...as ever; as before; as usual; continue to be; despite; keep on; none the less; notwithstanding; remain; stay; still; yet;
撒然 abruptly;
灑然 frightened; shocked;
颯然 soughing;
騷然 agitated; disturbed; in commotion; tumultuous;
森然 (1) (of tall trees) dense; thick; (2) awe-inspiring;
潸然 tears falling;
尚然 still; yet;
奭然 in a free manner; in utter freedom;
適然 (1) accidentally; by chance; (2) a matter of

course;
釋然 feeling at ease; feeling relieved;
率然 casually; randomly;
爽然 at a loss;
悚然 horrified; terrified;
竦然 fearful; scared;
聳然 rise in sharp elevation;
肅然 respectful; reverently;
雖然 as one is; after; albeit; although; amid; amidst; and yet; as; because; but then; despise; for; for all; however; if; in spite of; in the midst of; not but that; notwithstanding; still; such as it is; that; though; when; while; with all;
索然 dull; insipid; listless;
嗒然 dejected; depressed; despondent;
泰然 calm; composed; self-possessed; unagitated; unalarmed; unperturbed;
坦然 calm; fully at ease; having no misgivings; self-possessed; unperturbed;
倘然 if; in case; supposing;
惝然 crestfallen; discouraged; disheartened; dispirited;
陶然 cheerful; happy; happy and carefree;
倜然 (1) aloof; (2) far and lofty;
惕然 fearful of;
天然 living; native; natural;
恬然 calm; easygoing; nonchalant; unhurried; unperturbed;
靦然 blush for shame; come to blush with shame;
突然 abruptly; all at once; all of a sudden; by the run; cap the climax; out of the blue; short; suddenly; unexpectedly; with a run; with suddenness; without any warning;
徒然 (1) in vain; to no avail; (2) merely; only;
頹然 dejected; disappointed; pliant; submissive;
退然 amiable; humble and tender;
脫然 free; untrammeled;
酡然 (of one's face) flushed with drinks;
宛然 as if; as though; like;
汪然 profusely; vast;
枉然 futile; in vain; to no purpose; useless;
罔然 at a loss; disconcerted; stupefied;
惘然 at a loss; disappointed; frustrated; in a daze; stupefied;
嵬然 lofty; towering;
未然 before it happens; possible; will be a fact;
蔚然 luxuriantly; magnificently;
巍然 imposing; lofty; majestic; towering;
憮然 disappointed; frustrated;
翕然 entirely harmonious; peace and stability;

uniform;
顯然 apparent; clearly; evidently; it is evident that; obviously; visible;
枵然 big;
蕭然 (1) deserted; desolate; lonely; (2) disorderly; in commotion;
囂然 (1) sad; (2) hungry;
欣然 gladly; with pleasure;
訢然 happy; very pleased;
悻然 angry; resentful;
衄然 astonished; startled;
軒然 (1) delighted; smiling; (2) lofty; towering;
泫然 (of water) falling; trickling;
薰然 amiably; gently; warmly;
啞然 (1) silent; (2) describing of the sound of laughter;
嫣然 beautiful; merrily; sweet;
儼然 (1) dignified; solemn; (2) neatly arranged; (3) just like;
晏然 peaceful and easy; quiet and comfortable;
怏然 discontent; unhappy;
杳然 lonely; quiet and silent;
窅然 sad; touched;
曄然 prosperous; thriving;
依然 as...as ever; as before; as usual; nonetheless; remain the same; still;
宜然 suitable;
怡然 contented; happy; pleasant and contented; satisfied and happy;
已然 that which has already become a fact;
亦然 also; similarly; too;
屹然 majestic; towering;
毅然 courageously; firmly; resolutely; with determination;
攸然 joyfully; leisurely;
悠然 (1) carefree and leisurely; in a leisurely manner; (2) distant; far away; long;
油然 (1) involuntarily; spontaneously; (2) copious; densely; luxuriant; profusely;
猶然 (1) just as; just like; (2) still;
躍然 appear vividly;
雜然 all; unanimously;
乍然 abruptly; unexpectedly;
嶄然 (1) completely changed; (2) high and steep;
湛然 (1) calm; quiet; tranquil; (2) transparent;
昭然 clear and obvious; evident; very clear;
輒然 still;
秩然 neat; orderly;
壯然 dignified-looking; forbidding;
灼然 crystal-clear; obvious;
驟然 abruptly; suddenly;

卓然 brilliant; distinguished; eminent; outstanding; stately;
自然 (1) natural world; nature; (2) in the ordinary course of events; naturally; (3) naturally; of course;
縱然 even if; even though;

ran

【髯】 (1) whiskers; (2) heavily-bearded fellow;
[髯毛] beard; beard hair;
[髯奴] heavily-bearded fellow;
[髯叟] bearded old man; old man;

虬髯 curly whiskers;

ran

【燃】 (1) burn; go up in flames; on fire; (2) flare up; ignite; kindle; set fire to; (3) light; put a match to; touch off;
[燃燈] light a lamp;
日不昇火，夜不燃燈 not to light fires by day or lamps by night;
[燃點] (1) ignite; kindle; light; set fire to; (2) burning point; kindling point; point of ignition;
[燃放] set off; set out;
燃放爆竹 set off firecrackers;
[燃料] fuel;
燃料庫 fuel depot; fuel reservoir;
燃料箱 fuel tank;
標準燃料 standard fuel;
代用燃料 alternate fuel; alternative fuel;
固體燃料 solid fuel;
核燃料 nucleare fuel;
~合金核燃料 alloy nuclear fuel;
節約燃料 save fuel;
抗爆燃料 anti-detonation fuel; antiknock fuel; anti-pinking fuel;
礦物燃料 fossil fuel;
浪費燃料 waste fuel;
民用燃料 domestic fuel;
水果燃料 fruity fuel;
酸渣燃料 acid slude fuel;
一批燃料 a supply of fuel;
[燃眉] urgently critical; very dangerous;
燃眉之急 as pressing as a fire singeing one's eyebrows; as urgent as one's burning eye-brows need attention; burning necessity; imminent danger; impending; it is extremely urgent; matter of utmost urgency; of great urgency; pressing danger; pressing need; sth extremely urgent; sth that brooks not a moment's delay; sth that calls for immediate attention;
急如燃眉 as urgent as if the eyebrows are burning;
以救燃眉 meet a pressing need;
暫濟燃眉 temporarily relieve an emergency;
[燃氣] fuel gas;
[燃燒] burn; combustion; firing; flame; in flames; kindle; set on fire;
燃燒病 adustiosis;
燃燒彈 firebomb; incendiary; incendiary bomb; petrol bomb;
燃燒點 the flammability point; the flare point;
燃燒器 burner;
燃燒熱 heat of combustion;
燃燒室 combustion chamber;
不完全燃燒 incomplete combustion;
換層燃燒 differential firing;
混合燃燒 combined firing;
四角燃燒 corner firing;
[燃素說] phlogiston theory;
[燃油] fuel oil;
燃油表 fuel gauge;
燃油管 fuel pipe; oil pipe;
[燃燭] light a candle;

點燃 kindle; light;
助燃 support combustion;
自燃 spontaneous combustion;

ran³

ran

【冉】 (1) gradually; proceed gradually; (2) tender; weak; (3) outer edge of a turtle's shell; (4) a surname;
[冉冉] gradually; imperceptibly; slowly;
冉冉而上 go up slowly;
冉冉上昇 rise gradually; rise slowly;
[冉弱] drooping;

ran

【染】 (1) dye; (2) catch a disease; get infected; infect; infectious; (3) acquire; (4) pullute; soil; (5) have an affair with;
[染病] be infected with a disease; catch a disease; catch an illness; fall ill; get

infected;
[染布] dye cloth;
[染毒] contaminate;
[染髮] colour one's hair; dye one's hair;
染髮劑 dye; rinse;
~深色染髮劑 lowlights;
[染坊] dyehouse; dyeing mill; dye-works;
[染缸] dye vat; dyeing tub; dyejigger;
[染工] dyer;
[染化] educate; exert good influence on;
[染疾] contract a disease; fall ill;
[染料] colourant; dye; dyestuff; tincture;
苯胺染料 aniline dye;
動物染料 animal dyes;
鹼性染料 basic dyestuff;
脒染料 amidine dyestuffs;
偶氮染料 azo dyestuff;
酸性染料 acid dye;
一大桶染料 a vat of dye;
陰離子染料 anionic dye;
[染惹] pollute; soil; taint;
[染色] colouration; dye; dyeing; staining; tinge;
染色處理 chromating;
染色單體 chromatid;
~環染色單體 loop chromatid;
~環形染色單體 ring chromatid;
~同源染色單體 homologous chromatids; chromatid;
~姊妹染色單體 sister chromatid;
~子染色單體 daughter chromatid;
染色劑 colourant;
染色體 chromosome;
~染色體蛋白 chromosomin;
~染色體工程 chromosome engineering;
~染色體學 chromosomology;
~並連染色體 attached chromosome;
~常染色體 autosome; euchromosome;
~單價染色體 monovalent chromosome;
~多價染色體 multivalent chromosome;
~二價染色體 bivalent chromosome;
~二線染色體 bineme chromosome;
~分枝染色體 branched chromosome;
~副染色體 accessory chromosome;
~環狀染色體 circular chromosome;
~淋巴細胞染色體 chromosome from a lymphocyte;
~雙價染色體 bivalent chromosome;
~細菌染色體 bacterial chromosome;
~性染色體 sex cliromosome;
~異染色體 heterochromosome;
染色桶 dye beck;
染色性 chromaticity;
染色質 chromatin;
~染色質核仁 chromatin nucleolus; karyosome;
~染色質粒 chromatin granule;
~染色質網 chromatin network;
~染色質陽性 chromatin-positive;
~染色質陰性 chromatin-negative;
~惰性染色質 inert chromatin;
~非染色質 achromatin;
~核染色質 nuclear chromatin;
~鹼性染色質 basic chromatin;
~性染色質 sex chromatin;
斑點染色 burl dyeing;
底層染色 bottom dyeing;
活體染色 intravital staining;
鹼性染色 basic dyeing;
木材染色 wood staining;
三重染色 triple staining;
深色染色 deep colour dyeing;
酸性染色 acid dyeing;
載體染色 carrier dyeing;
[染污] contaminate; make dirty; smear; stain;
[染習] contract bad habits;
[染液] dye liquor;
[染印法] dyeing transfer process;
[染於蒼則蒼,染於黃則黃] dyed in blue it becomes blue, dyed in yellow it becomes yellow — one takes on the colour of one's company; he that touches pitch shall be defiled; he who keeps company with the wolf will learn to howl;
[染指] come in for a share; encroach on; have a hand in; take a share of sth one is not entitled to;
染指甲 paint fingernails;
染指他人權力 encroach on other people's rights;
染指擇肥 dip one's finger in the pie and claim the lion's share;

撥染 discharge;
傳染 contagious; infect; infection;
點染 (1) add details to a painting; (2) touch up a piece of writing;
感染 (1) infect; (2) affect; infect; influence;
漸染 be gradually influenced; be imperceptibly influenced;
浸染 be contaminated; be imperceptibly

influenced;
臘染 wax printing;
煤染 mordant dyeing;
匹染 piece dyeing;
漂染 bleach and dye;
遷染 be corrupted by evil surroundings;
濡染 be imbued with; dye; imbue; immerse;
陶染 move, influence and mould people;
污染 contaminate; contamination; pollute; pollution; stain;
誣染 libel; slander;
習染 (1) contract a bad habit; fall into a bad habit; (2) bad habit;
渲染 (1) apply colours to a drawing to intensify the effect; (2) give an exaggerated description; play up;
薰染 be influenced and contaminated by one's surroundings;
燻染 influence;
印染 print and dye;
有染 have an affair with;
沾染 be contaminated by; be infected with; be steeped in; be tainted with; become addicted to;
霑染 (1) get affected by a communicable disease; (2) gain a small advantage;
漬染 dye;

ran

【苒】 (of flower and grass) delicate; lush;
［苒苒］ (1) lush; luxuriant; (2) delicate; pliable; tender; (3) lightly floating; (4) gradually; (5) imperceptibly passing;
［苒荏］ passing imperceptibly; time passing gradually;
［苒弱］ (of flowers) drooping;

荏苒 (of time) elapse gradually; slip by;

rang¹

rang

【嚷】 complain; cry;
［嚷嚷］ (1) bawl; howl; make a noise; make an uproar; roar; shout; yell; (2) bring before the public; give to the world; make public; make widely known;
大聲嚷嚷 yell one's head off;

rang

【纕】 same as 攘 , roll up one's sleeve to show the arm;

rang²

rang

【攘】 (1) take by force; (2) contend with; dispel; eliminate; repel; resist; rid; stand up to; ward off; (3) shake;
［攘臂］ bare one's hands;
攘臂高呼 raise one's hands and shout;
［攘除］ dispel; eliminate; rid;
攘除奸邪 get rid of the wicked;
攘除異己 get rid of dissidents;
攘除罪犯 get rid of criminals;
［攘奪］ take by force;
［攘詬］ cleanse oneself of dishonour; clear oneself of a dishonour;
［攘袂］ push up one's sleeves and bare one's arms;
［攘辟］ make way; stand off;
［攘竊］ filch; pilfer; steal;
［攘善］ appropriate other's credit or honour to be his own;
［攘袖］ roll up one's sleeves;
［攘夷］ repel the barbarians;
尊王攘夷 honour the king and drive off the barbarians;
［攘災］ avoid disaster; ward off calamities;

rang

【瓤】 (1) flesh of a fruit; pulp of a fruit; section of an orange; (2) interior part of a thing; (3) inferior; weak;
［瓤兒］ pulp of a fruit;
［瓤口］ taste;

瓜瓤 pulp of a melon;
沙瓤 mushy watermelon pulp;

rang

【禳】 (1) form of sacrifice performed for exorcism; (2) exorcise;
［禳除］ drive away evil spirits;
禳除癘殃 offer sacrifice to drive away evil spirits;
［禳解］ avert a misfortune by prayers; offer sacrifice to gods to rid of evil spirits;
［禳災］ make efforts to avert calamity by offering sacrifices;

rang

【穰】 (1) crowded; (2) confusing; disturbed; mixed-up; (3) stalks of plants; (4) luxuriant; rich;

R

［穰年］ bumper harvest year;
［穰穰］ (1) in abundant measure; rich; (2) confusing; disturbed; mixed-up; (3) luxuriant;
穰穰滿家 a bumper grain harvest; a rich harvest of food crops;
［穰田］ offer sacrifices to gods for a good harvest;

rang³

rang

【嚷】 bellow; call out loudly; create an uproar; cry; howl; make an uproar; shout; yell;
［嚷叫］ bellow; howl; make an uproar; shout; yell;
［嚷嘴］ bicker; quarrel;

吵嚷 clamour; make a racket;
叫嚷 clamour; howl; shout;
喧嚷 clamour; din;

rang

【壤】 (1) earth; loose soil; (2) area; land; place; region; (3) abundant; rich; (4) a surname;
［壤界］ border; boundary;
［壤土］ loam;
粉砂壤土 silt loam;
黏壤土 clay loam;
砂壤土 sandy loam;

黃壤 yellow earth;
灰壤 podzol;
接壤 be bounded by; border on;
僻壤 backwater; out-of-the-way place;
天壤 heaven and earth;
土壤 ground; soil;
沃壤 rich soil;
霄壤 heaven and earth;
棕壤 brown earth;

rang

【攘】 (1) get rid of; reject; resist; weed out; (2) grab; seize; (3) push up one's sleeves; roll up one's sleeves;
［攘臂］ bare the arms; push up one's sleeves and bare one's arms; roll up one's sleeves and reveal one's arms;
攘臂嗔目 fly into a rage; roll up one's sleeves and stare angrily; see red;
攘臂而起 be excited and ready for action; roll up one's sleeves and spring to one's feet;
［攘除］ get rid of; reject; weed out;
［攘奪］ grab; seize; snatch;
［攘攘］ numerous and disorderly;
［攘災］ drive off evil; ward off calamity;

擾攘 hustle and bustle;

rang⁴

rang

【讓】 (1) back down; back out of; concede; give ground; give in; give up; give way; make a concession; yield; (2) invite; offer; (3) allow; ask; let; make; permit; (4) let sb have sth at a fair price; sell sth at a fair price;
［讓步］ back down; back out of; compromise; give in; give way; make a concession; yield;
讓步從句 concessive clause;
讓步從屬連詞 subordinator of concession;
讓步副詞 adverb of concession; concessive adverb;
讓步聯加詞 concessive conjunct;
讓步狀語 adverbial of concession;
~讓步狀語從句 adverbial clause of concession;
不讓步 hold one's ground; keep one's ground; maintain one's ground; stand one's ground;
~絕不讓步 not budge an inch;
很大的讓步 a great concession;
勉強作出讓步 reluctantly make a concession;
［讓茶］ offer sb tea;
［讓渡］ alienate; cede; transfer the possession of; turn over;
［讓過兒］ give in; make a concession; yield;
［讓價］ agree to reduce the price asked; concessional rate;
［讓酒］ offer sb wine;
［讓開］ get out of the way; make way; step aside;
［讓路］ get out of the way; give way; give sb the right of way; make way for sb; make way for sth; step aside;
他們為我們讓路 they made way for us;
［讓球］ concede points;
［讓人］ concessive; conciliatory; yield to

others; yielding;
拱手讓人 give away sth to sb with both hands; give up sth to others without putting up a fight; hand over sth on a silver platter; hand over with a bow; surrender sth submissively;

[讓王] yield the throne to another;
[讓位] (1) abdicate; abdication; resign sovereign authority; yield the throne; (2) offer one's seat to sb; (3) change into; give way to; yield to;
讓位者 abdicator;
[讓我來] allow me;
[讓賢] relinquish one's post in favour of sb better qualifeid; yelid one's position to a better qualified person;
讓賢與能 retire and give room to better men;
[讓煙] offer sb a cigarette;
[讓一讓] excuse me;
[讓與] cede; surrender;
[讓棗推梨] show brotherly love;
[讓賬] insist on footing the bill; want to pay a bill for another;
[讓座] give up one's seat to sb; offer one's seat to sb; yield a seat;

卑讓 defer; yield with courtesy;
出讓 sell;
辭讓 politely decline;
割讓 cede;
互讓 make mutual accommodation;
就讓 even if;
寬讓 be lenient; be tolerant;
禮讓 give precedence to sb out of courtesy or thoughtfulness;
謙讓 modestly decline;
忍讓 be tolerant; exercise forbearance;
禪讓 abdicate and hand over the crown to another person;
推讓 politely and modestly decline;
退讓 give in; make a concession; yield;
揖讓 bowing with hands clasped and giving precedence to the other, a form of courtesy between guest and host;
轉讓 transfer the possession of;

rao²

rao

【蕘】 faggot; firewoood; grass used for fuel;

rao

【饒】 (1) abundant; affluence; fertile; full of; plentiful; rich; (2) forgive; have mercy on; lenient; let sb off; liberal; pardon; pass over; spare; tolerant; (3) give sth extra; let sb have sth into the bargain; (4) garrulous; loquacious; too talkative; voluble; (5) although; even though; in spite of the fact that; whatever; (6) a surname;

[饒侈] affluence;
[饒富] abundant; affluence; plentiful;
饒富詩意 rich in poetic flavour;
[饒命] spare sb's life;
[饒讓] forgive; lenient; tolerant;
[饒人] (1) forgive another person; (2) give others a way out;
嘴不饒人 fond of making sarcastic remarks;
[饒舌] (1) garrulous; have a big mouth; have too much tongue; long tongue; loquacious; naggish; too talkative; voluble; (2) say more than is proper; shoot off one's mouth;
饒舌的人 long tongue;
饒舌多嘴 engage in loose talk; have a loose tongue; speak evil of others; tell tales;
饒舌婦 chatterbox; nag;
饒舌調唇 garrulous and insidious; gossip and sow dissension;
饒舌者 blabbermouth;
[饒恕] forgive; pardon; pass over;
不能饒恕 allow no mercy;
得到饒恕 receive forgiveness;
乞求饒恕 beg forgiveness;
[饒沃] fertile; rich;
[饒益] surplus; abundance; wealthy;
[饒裕] abundance; affluence;

肥饒 rich;
豐饒 rich and fertile;
富饒 abundant; fertile;
告饒 ask pardon; beg for mercy;
寬饒 forgive; pardon; show mercy;
乞饒 ask pardon;
求饒 ask forgiveness; beg for mercy;
討饒 beg for mercy; pardon;

rao³
rao

【擾】 (1) agitate; cause havoc with; harass; trouble; (2) trespass on sb's hospitality; (3) disorder; disturb; mess up;

[擾動] agitate; disturb; disturbance; perturbation;
變曲型擾動 wriggling perturbation;
大氣擾動 atmospheric disturbance;
電磁擾動 electromagnetic disturbance;
動力擾動 energetic disturbance;
環境擾動 environmental disturbance;
熱帶擾動 tropical disturbance;
線性擾動 linear perturbation;
重心擾動 centre-of-gravity disturbance;
阻力擾動 drag perturbation;

[擾害] harass and injure;

[擾亂] agitate; cause havoc with; create confusion; disrupt; disruption; disturb; harass; mess up; perturb;
擾亂軍心 undermine the morale of an army;
擾亂市場 disrupt the market; disturb the market;
擾亂性的 disruptive;
擾亂治安 break the peace; disturb peace and order; upset public order;

[擾民] harass the people;

[擾攘] hustle and bustle; noisy confusion; tumult;

[擾擾] in a state of disorder;

竄擾 harass; invade and harass;
打擾 disturb; trouble;
煩擾 (1) bother; (2) feel disturbed;
紛擾 confusion; disturbance; turmoil;
干擾 disturb; interfere; trouble;
聒擾 make a din;
驚擾 agitate; alarm;
困擾 perplex; puzzle;
侵擾 invade and harass;
騷擾 cause trouble; harass;
肆擾 harass wantonly;
叨擾 thank you for your hospitality;
襲擾 make a harassing attack;
相擾 bother; disturb;
喧擾 make noise and disturb;

rao⁴
rao

【遶】 around; detour; surround;

rao

【繞】 (1) coil; curl; wind; (2) circle; go round; march round; move round; (3) bypass; go around; go by a roundabout route; go round about; go the long way around; in a roundabout way; make a detour; pass round; take a circuitous route; take a devious route; (4) baffle; confuse;

[繞避] pass round;

[繞道] detour; go by a roundabout route; make a detour;
繞道而行 go in a roundabout way; go round; take a devious route;

[繞過] bypass; pass over in a roundabout manner;

[繞口令] tongue twister;

[繞梁] linger long in the air;
繞梁三日 the song lingers long in the air;
繞梁之音 a voice so beautiful that it remains lingering long in the air;

[繞磨] (1) set a trap for framing sb; (2) grind;

[繞彎兒] take a stroll;

[繞行] (1) detour; (2) orbit; revolve around sth;

[繞組] winding;
地址繞組 address winding;
電樞繞組 armature winding;
放大繞組 ampliator winding;
附加繞組 additional winding;
阻尼繞組 amortisseur winding;

[繞嘴] difficult to articulate;
他的名字很繞嘴 his name is really difficult to articulate;

纏繞 (1) bind; twine; wind; (2) harass; worry;
飛繞 wind high above;
環繞 revolve around; surround;
繚繞 curl up; wind around;
裊繞 curling upwards;
盤繞 coil; twine;
圍繞 (1) move around; revolve round; (2) centre on;
旋繞 curl up; wind around;
縈繞 hover; linger;

re³
re

【喏】 well (to attract attention);

re

【惹】 (1) ask for; bring upon oneself; court;

get oneself into; incur; invite; (2) be offended; offend; provoke; (3) arouse; attract; cause; induce; rouse; stir;

[惹不起] (1) dare not offend; dare not provoke; (2) too powerful to be offended;

[惹得] arouse; provoke;

惹得起 dare nettle; dare to offend;

[惹火] excite; inspire;

惹火燒身 bring trouble on one's own head; bring trouble upon oneself; burn one's own fingers; court disaster; immolate oneself by fire; set afire one's clothes in an attempt to burn oneself to death; stir up a fire only to burn oneself — to ask for trouble;

[惹禍] bring calamity on oneself; bring disaster; bring misfortune; court disaster; incur mischief; introduce calamities; stir up trouble;

惹禍招災 court disaster; stir up trouble;

惹禍滋事 court disaster and get oneself into trouble;

招災惹禍 court disasters; invite troubles;

[惹起] incite; incur; provoke;

[惹氣] get angry; incur wrath; provoke one to anger;

[惹事] create trouble; provoke; stir up trouble;

惹事生非 be drawn into a dispute; get oneself involved in a controversy; incur unnecessary trouble; make mischief; meddlesome; provoke a dispute; provoke mischief; rock the boat; stir up trouble; wake a sleeping dog;

[惹嫌] incur hatred; provoke dislike;

[惹笑] set people laughing;

枉惹人笑 this would make the people laugh at someone;

不好惹 not to be pushed around; not to be trifled with; stand no nonsense;

招惹 (1) court; provoke; (2) tease;

re4
re

【熱】 (1) heat; (2) hot; tropical; (3) heat up; warm up; (4) fever; temperature; (5) ardent; be deeply attached; earnest; enthusiastic; have a passion for; love fervently; passionate; warmhearted; zealous; (6) in great demand; popular; (7) craze; fad; (8) eager; envious; (9) thermal; thermo;

[熱愛] ardently love; deep attachment; have a passion for; have deep affection for; have deep love for; love fervently; love passionately; passionate love;

熱愛工作 love work;

熱愛科學 take a keen interest in science;

熱愛人民 have ardent love for the people;

熱愛生活 love life;

熱愛體育 have a passionate love for sports;

熱愛祖國 have ardent love for the motherland;

[熱病] fever;

[熱腸] ardent; eager; enthusiastic; zealous;

[熱潮] bandwagon; great mass fervour; upsurge;

趕熱潮 climb the bandwagon; get on the bandwagon; jump the bandwagon;

經濟建設熱潮 an upsurge in economic construction;

體育運動熱潮 an upsurge in sports activities;

掀起生產熱潮 set off a great upsurge in production;

[熱忱] ardour; earnest; elan; enthusiasm and devotion; sincerity; warmheartedness; zeal;

滿腔熱忱 be filled with sympathetic feelings; full of enthusiasm; in all eagerness;

[熱誠] cordial; eager devotion; earnestness; enthusiasm and devotion; sincerity; warm and sincere;

熱誠歡迎 cordially welcome;

[熱帶] (1) tropical; (2) torrid zone; tropics;

熱帶草原 savannas;

熱帶叢林 tropical jungles;

熱帶風暴 tropical storm;

熱帶風光 tropical scene;

熱帶服裝 tropical wears;

熱帶區 tropical realm; tropical region;

熱帶雨林 tropical rain forest;

熱帶植物 tropical plants;

熱帶作物 tropical crops;

新熱帶區 neotropical region;

亞熱帶 the subtropical zone;

[熱狗] hot dog;

[熱和] (1) warm; (2) amiable; friendly; gentle; (3) close; intimate;

[熱烘烘] (1) glowing with heat; red-hot; white hot; (2) very warm; (3) stirring; (4) affectionate;

[熱呼呼] (1) cosy; nice and warm; piping hot; warm; (2) affectionate; warm and friendly; warmhearted;

[熱昏] have a fever; have heat-stroke;

[熱火] chum up;
熱火朝天 burning with ardour; bustling with activity; flaming; in full swing; stirring and seething; vigorous;

[熱鍵] hot key;

[熱褲] hot pants;

[熱狂] fanatical; frantic; wild with excitement;

[熱辣辣] burning hot; scorching;

[熱浪] heat wave; hot wave; warm wave;
熱浪期 heatave;
一股熱浪 a heat wave;
一陣熱浪 a heat wave;

[熱淚] warm tears;
熱淚滾滾 warm tears streaming down one's face;
熱淚盈眶 eyes abrim of tears; eyes moistening; hot tears well up in one's eyes; in the melting mood; one's eyes brim with warm tears; one's eyes fill with hot tears; one's eyes are suffused with warm tears; tearful; tears of excitement fill one's eyes and nearly brim over; tears of joy spring to one's eyes; the warm tears gush from one's eyes;
~ 讓人熱淚盈眶 bring tears to sb's eyes;
熱淚縱橫 shed hot tears; weep bitter tears;

[熱力] heat energy; thermal energy;
熱力學 thermodynamics;
~ 工程熱力學 engineering thermodynamics;
~ 固體熱力學 thermodynamics of solids;
~ 海洋熱力學 marine thermodynamics;
~ 化學熱力學 chemical thermodynamics;
~ 空氣熱力學 aerothermodynamiucs;
~ 冶金熱力學 metallurgical thermodynamics;

[熱戀] crush; head over heels in love; passionately in love;
熱戀的對象 a crush;

[熱量] quantity of heat;
熱量平衡 heat balance;
吸收熱量 absorption of heat;

[熱烈] ardent; enthusiastic; fervent; fiery; heartily; rousing; vehement; warm;
熱烈鼓掌 applaud wildly; clad enthusiastically; clap with all one's might;
熱烈歡送 give sb a warm send-off;
熱烈歡迎 a warm welcome to sb;
熱烈爭論 hotly argue;
反映熱烈 respond enthusiastically;
氣氛熱烈 lively atmosphere;

[熱門] craze; hot; in good demand; in great demand; major topic of debate; major topic of discussion; popular; sth everyone is after; sth in fashion; sth in vogue;
熱門股票 fancy stock;
熱門話題 heated topic; hot topic of conversation;
熱門貨 brisk sale; goods in great demand; goods which sell well; popular ware;

[熱鬧] (1) boisterous; bustling; bustling with noise and excitement; hustle and bustle; noisy; populous; thronged; (2) cheerful; cheery; lively; merry; (3) flourishing; lively; prosperous; thriving;
湊湊熱鬧 go along for the ride;
湊熱鬧 (1) go along for the ride; join in the fun; take part in the merry-making; (2) add trouble to;
看熱鬧 watch the excitement; watch the scene of bustle; watch the fun;

[熱能] heat energy; thermal energy;

[熱氣] heat; heatiness; hot air; hot gas; hot vapour; steam;
熱氣球 hot-air balloon;
熱氣騰騰 (1) piping hot; smoking hot; steaming hot; (2) astir with emotion; humming; seething with activity;
一股熱氣 a blast of hot air;
一團熱氣 a mass of hot air;

[熱切] ardent; earnest; fervent; sincerely; warm and cordial;

[熱情] (1) ardent passion; ardour; devotion; enthusiasm; fervour; passion; warmth; zeal; (2) ardent; enthusiastic; fervent;

passionate; warm; warmhearted;
熱情奔放 a gush of enthusiasm; an outburst of enthusiasm; bubbling with enthusiasm; fervid; flamboyant; overflowing with enthusiasm;
熱情接待 warm in reception;
熱情相待 treat sb with the utmost cordiality;
熱情洋溢 abundance of the heart; be aglow with enthusiasim; brimming with warm feeling; ebullient; effusive; flowing with enthusiasm; passionate;
~ 熱情洋溢的人 person aglow with enthusiasm;
愛國熱情 patriotic ardour; patriotic fervor; patriotic zeal;
革命熱情 revolutionary ardour;
教學熱情 ardour in teaching;
滿腔熱情 be filled with ardour and sincerity; full of ardour;
一股熱情 a burst of enthusiasm;
一陣熱情 a burst of energy;
宗教熱情 religious fervor;

[熱熔] hot-melt;
熱熔施工 hot-melt application;

[熱身] warm up;
熱身運動 warm-up;
~ 做熱身運動 limber up

[熱水] hot water;
熱水袋 hot-water bag;
熱水瓶 hot-water bottle; thermos; thermos flask;
熱水器 geyser; water heater;
~ 燃氣熱水器 gas water heater;

[熱燙機] blancher;
間歇式熱燙機 batch-type blancher;
連續熱燙機 continuous blancher;
~ 多帶式連續熱燙機 multibelt continuous blancher;
水熱燙機 water blancher;
蒸氣熱燙機 steam blancher;
轉鼓式熱燙機 rotary blancher;

[熱騰騰] piping hot; steaming hot;

[熱天] dog days; hot weather;
大熱天 scorcher;

[熱望] ardently wish; crave; craving; fervently hope; hope earnestly; wish ardently;

[熱線] (1) heat ray; (2) hotline;
熱線電話 hot line; telephone hotline;
熱線節目 talk radio;
查詢熱線 enquiry hotline;

[熱心] ardent; avid; eager; earnest; enthusiastic; warmhearted;
熱心腸 warm heart; warmheartedness;
熱心的 enthusiastic;
~ 熱心的人 enthusias;
熱心地 enthusiastically; with enthusiasm; with zest;
熱心公益 make earnest efforts to promote public good;
熱心科學 eager to promote science;
熱心人 enthusiast;
熱心於 enthusiastic in; make earnest efforts to;
熱心助人 be warmhearted and always ready to help others;
過分熱心 overzealous;
冷眼熱心 affected indifference; outward indifference but inward fervency;

[熱血] fervent; fiery-spirited; hot-blooded; righteous ardour; warm blood; zealous;
熱血動物 warm-blooded animal;
熱血沸騰 burning with righteous indignation; have a boiling passion; in warm blood; one's blood boils with indignation; one's hot blood is boiling; seethe with fervour; with heart afire;
~ 熱血沸騰的 hot-blooded;
甘洒熱血 ready to shed one's blood;
滿腔熱血 be filled with righteous ardour; full of zeal; full of sympathetic feelings;

[熱飲] hot drinks;

[熱脹冷縮] expand when heated and contract when cooled; expand when hot and shrink when cold; expand with heat and contract with cold; heat makes sth expand and cold makes it contract;

[熱衷] (1) crave; hanker after; hanker for; (2) fond of; keen on;
熱衷名利 pursue fame and wealth with fervour;
熱衷者 enthusiast;

燠熱 very hot;
白熱 glow; white glow; white heat; white-hot;
比熱 specific heat;
潮熱 hectic fever;
赤熱 red heat;
熾熱 (1) blazing; red-hot; (2) passionate;
傳熱 conduct heat; heat diffusion; heat transfer;
導熱 conduct heat;

登革熱 dengue fever;
低熱 low fever; slight fever;
地熱 the heat of the earth's interior;
電熱 heat with electric energy;
耳熱 have a burning sensation in the ears; have burning ears;
發熱 (1) generate heat; give out heat; (2) have a fever;
放熱 exthermal;
沸熱 boiling;
廢熱 waste heat;
分子熱 .molecular heat;
乾熱 dry and hot;
高熱 high fever; high heat;
隔熱 heat insulation; heat-proof;
滾熱 burning hot;
過熱 overheat; superheat; superheating;
寒熱 chills and fever;
很熱 like an oven;
紅熱 red heat;
火熱 (1) burning hot; fervent; fiery; (2) intimate;
加熱 heat; heat up; warm;
減熱 desuperheat;
解熱 allay a fever;
絕熱 (1) heat insulation; (2) adiabatic;
酷熱 extremely hot;
狂熱 fanatical; fanaticism; feverish; namia;
冷熱 cold or hot;
悶熱 hot and suffocating; muggy; sultry;
耐熱 heat-resisting; heatproof;
內熱 internal fever;
潛熱 latent heat;
親熱 affectionate; cordial; intimate; warm and affectionate; warmhearted;
秋熱 old wives' summer;
溽熱 oppressively hot;
散熱 disseminate heat;
傷熱 (of fruit, etc.) be damaged by heat;
濕熱 damp and hot;
受熱 be affected by the heat; be heated;
暑熱 heat of summer; hot summer weather; scorching heat;
疼熱 suffer pain and fever;
退熱 bring down a fever;
胃熱 gastric fever; stomach heat;
吸熱 absorption of heat;
炎熱 blazing; burning hot; scorching; very hot;
眼熱 covet; envious;
餘熱 waste heat;
預熱 preheating;
原子熱 atomic heat;
再熱 reheat;
燥熱 dry and hot;
躁熱 dry and hot;
止熱 abort a fever;
灼熱 broil; scorching hot;

ren²
ren

【人】 (1) human being; man; person; (2) adult; grown-up; (3) person engaged in a particular activity; (4) other people; people (5) character; personality; (6) how one feels; state of one's health; (7) each; everybody; (8) personal; private; (9) hand; manpower;

［人搬三度窮，火搬三度熄］ a rolling stone gathers no moss; three removes are as bad as a fire;

［人保］ personal guarantor;

［人本主義］ humanism;

［人表］ person of exemplary conduct;

［人不犯我，我不犯人］ if others let me alone, I'll let them alone; we will not attack unless we are attacked;

［人不可貌相］ a man's worth cannot be measured by his looks; in sizing up people, one must not go by appearances; men cannot be judged by their looks; never judge people by their appearance; one mustn't judge people by their looks; you cannot judge of a tree by its bark; you can't judge a person by his appearance;

人不可貌相，海水不可斗量 a man cannot be known by his looks, nor can the sea be measured by a bushel; the countenance is the title-page to the human volume and often mislead the observer; you can't judge people by appearance, and measure the ocean with the dou — don't judge by appearances;

［人不虧地，地不虧人］ the land won't fail people as long as people don't fail the land; the master's footsteps fatten the soil;

［人不磨，不成道］ one must subject oneself to rigorous discipline before one can become a devotee of a religion;

［人不如故］ old friends are best;

[人不為己，天誅地滅] every man is for himself, or Heaven and Earth will destroy him; God curses those who do not pursue selfish interests; Heaven destroys men who won't look out for themselves; if a man takes no thought for himself, the gods will destroy him; unless a man looks out for himself, heaven and earth will destroy him; when men stop looking out for themselves that will be the end of the world;

[人才] man of ability; person of ability; qualified personnel; talent; talented person;

人才輩出 able men are coming forth in multitudes; great talents appear successively; large numbers of outstanding people come forward; men of talent come out in succession; people of talent coming forth in large numbers; young talents emerge in abundance;

人才不足 a shortage of trained personnel; lack competent personnel; lack qualified personnel;

人才出眾 a person of exceptional ability; a person of striking appearance;

人才赤字 talented people deficit;

人才儲備 personnel storage; talented people faulty;

人才斷層 talented people faulty;

~人才斷層現象 phenonmenon of lacking talented people;

人才法制 legal system for trained talents;

人才公司 talent agency;

人才管理 talent management;

~人才管理體系 management of talented people;

~人才管理學 talent management science;

人才合理流動 rational flow of trained personnel;

人才薈萃 a galaxy of talent; a large gathering of men of talent;

人才濟濟 a galaxy of talents; an abundance of capable people; an array of talents; there is a wealth of talents;

人才價值 talent value;

人才交流 exchange of human talents; exchange of trained personnel; talent exchange;

~人才交流市場 talents exchange market;

~人才交流數據庫 database for the professional resources exchange;

~人才交流信息 information of talent exchange;

~人才交流中心 personnel exchange centre;

人才結構 talent structure;

人才崛起 rise of talents;

人才開發 manpower development; personnel development; talent exploration; tap intellectual resources;

人才庫 talents bank;

~人才庫建設 talents library construction;

人才鏈 talent chain;

人才流動 flow of talented people; mobility of talented personnel; talent flow;

人才流失 brain drain; outflow of talent; talent loss;

~人才流失現象 phenomenon of talents loss;

人才難得 person of ability is hard to come by;

人才培養 personnel training;

人才市場 personnel market; talents market;

人才外流 brain drain;

人才信息 talent information;

人才學 talentics;

人才研究 talent research;

人才引進 talent introduction;

人才預測 talent forecasting;

人才戰略 talent strategy;

人才資源 resources of talents;

愛惜人才 value men of talent;

被埋沒的人才 wasted talent;

高質量人才 high-quality talent;

羅致人才 enlist the services of the able people;

埋沒人才 stifle real talents;

覓致人才 on the lookout for proper personnel;

難得的人才 person of rare talent;

培養人才 train qualified personnel;

潛人才 potential talent;

物色人才 talent scout; talent-spotting;

一表人才 dashing; fine-looking man; handsome; imposing figure; man of striking appearance; with the appearance of a talent;

尊重人才 respect trained personnel;

[人財] life and money;

人財兩空 double loss; lose both men and money; lose both the woman and wealth;

人財兩失 lose both one's money and life; lose not only the money but one's very life also;

人財兩旺 prosperous both in family and purse;

[人車分道] separation of pedestrians from automobiles;

[人臣] minister;

位極人臣 have reached the highest rank open to a subject; rise to be a very high official;

[人稱] first, second or third person;

人稱不定式 personal infinitive;

人稱詞尾 personal ending;

人稱代詞 personal pronoun;

人稱指示詞 person deixis;

第二人稱 second person;

~第二人稱代詞 second person pronoun;

第三人稱 third person;

第四人稱 fourth person;

第一人稱 first person;

~第一人稱代詞 first person pronoun;

概括人稱 generic person;

[人畜兩旺] both men and livestock are flourishing; both the growth of population and stock breading thrive;

[人存政舉] a man lives with his work;

人存政舉，人亡政息 a man lives and dies with his work;

[人大心大] become gradually more assertive as one grows older; grow in independence of mind;

[人大招物議，樹大惹風吹] detraction pursues the great;

[人道] (1) charity; human sympathy; humanism; humanitarianism; humanity; philanthropy; (2) human; humane; (3) sexual union;

人道主義 humanitarianism;

~人道主義的 humanitarian;

~人道主義倫理學 humanitarian ethics;

~現實人道主義 realistic humanitarianism;

~新人道主義 new humanitarianism;

不人道 inhumane;

慘無人道 barbarous; brutal; brutal and inhuman; cold-blooded; cruel; cruel and inhuman; inhuman cruelty;

[人得其位，位得其人] the right man in the right place;

[人地兩宜] the place is fit for the man; the right man at the right place;

[人地生疏] complete stranger; in an unfamiliar environment; stranger in a new land; stranger in a strange place;

[人丁] (1) adult; family number; (2) population;

人丁興旺 have a flourishing population; have a growing family; members of a family increase in numbers;

[人盯人] man-for-man defence;

[人定勝天] human determination will overcome destiny; human will can overpower natural forces; man can conquer nature; man is the arbiter of his own fate; man will surely conquer nature; man will triumph over nature; man's determination will conquer nature; man's fixed purpose is superior to heaven; man's ill conquers heaven; man's will, not heavn, decides;

[人堆兒] crowd of people;

[人多] large number of people;

人多膽壯 gather courage on the strength of numbers; sheer numbers can pluck up one's courage;

人多地少 a large population with relatively little land; have a big population and little land; there are a lot of people and very little land; there are more people and less land;

人多好辦事 many hands make light work;

人多口雜 a diversity of opinions; a rattling and wagging of tongues; much rattle and tattle;

人多力量大 there is strength in numbers;

人多勢眾 dominate by sheer force of numbers; large and powerful; overwhelm with numerical strength; there is safety in numbers;

人多心雜 many men, many minds; there are as many minds as there are men; too many people to have the same opinion; too many people, too many ideas;

人多眼雜 four eyes see more than two; the more people, the more eyes;
人多智廣 four eyes see more than two; more people mean more ideas; two heads are better than one;
人多嘴雜 a babel of voices; agreement is difficult if there are too many people; divided counsel; so many heads, so many opinions; the more people, the more talk; too many people, too many ideas;
地小人多 have a large population in a small area;

[人兒] (1) person; (2) concubine; (3) human figure;

[人犯] criminal; suspect;
一干人犯 a bunch of criminals;

[人浮於事] have more hands than needed; more men than work; more personnel than work available; overstaffed; overstaffing; there are more job hunters than there are jobs; with superfluous staff;

[人格] (1) character; individuality; personality; (2) moral quality; (3) human dignity; legal entity;
人格次 bad character;
人格擔保 be bound by one's honesty; on one's honour;
人格底 ill-bred;
人格分裂 split personality;
人格高尚 have a noble character; have moral integrity;
人格理論 personality theory;
人格掃地 drag personality to the dust; have no human dignity; stoop very low;
人格特徵 personality characteristics;
人格障礙 personality disorder;
多重人格 multiple personality;
誹謗人格 defamation of character;
分裂人格 split personality;
權威人格 authoritarian personality;
雙重人格 double personality; dual personality; split personality;
提昇人格 enhance personal qualities;

[人各] each one; every person;
人各有偶 every Jack has his Jill; every man has his wife; everyone has his spouse;
人各有癖 everyone has his hobby;
人各有所短 each one has his weakness; every bean has its black; every man has his shortcomings; every man has his weak side;
人各有所好 every man has his hobby-horse; every man to his taste; everyone to his own taste;
人各有心，心各有見 each one has his own mind and each mind has its own view;
人各有責 all men have their respective duties;
人各有志 different people have different aspirations; everyone has his own ambition;

[人工] (1) artificial; man-made; (2) human labour; manual work; work done by hand;
人工操作 manual operation;
人工讀入 manual read;
人工繁殖 artificial propagation;
人工分析 manual analysis;
人工呼吸 artificial respiration;
人工湖 artificial lake; man-made lake;
人工降雨 artificial rain;
人工交換 manual exchange;
~人工交換機 manual exchanger;
人工控制 manual control;
人工模擬 manual simulation;
人工神經網 artificial neural net;paranoid personality;
人工生態環境 artificial ecoenvironment;
人工識別 artificial cognition;
~人工識別系統 artificial perception system;
人工受孕 artificial insemination;
人工授精 artificial insemination;
人工言語 artificial speech;
人工語言 artificial language;
人工智能 artificial intelligence;
人工中心局 manual central office;

[人海] huge crowd of people; huge crowds; sea of faces;
人海浮沉 experience all the vicissitudes of life;
人海戰術 human-wave sweep;

[人豪] hero; the ablest and bravest of men;

[人和] support of the people; unity and coordination within one's own ranks;
政通人和 logical administration and harmonious people; the government

functions well and the people enjoy peace;

[人後] behind others;

不落人後 not to lag behind; yield to none;

[人寰] man's world; the earth; the world;

慘絕人寰 a terrible holocaust; atrocities that the world has never witnessed; extremely tragic; most cruel; most savage and inhuman; tragic beyond compare in this human world; most shocking in the human world; so miserable that it can hardly be found in the human life; unprecedented brutality;

[人機] man-machine;

人機對話 man-computer dialogue; man-machine communication;

~ 人機對話翻譯 interactive translation;

~ 人機對話過程 interactive process;

人機工程 human engineering;

~ 人機工程學 ergonomics;

~ 安全人機工程 safety human engineering;

人機交互 human computer interaction;

人機界面設計 man-machine interface design;

人機聯繫 man-machine interface;

人機模擬 man-machine simulation;

人機通信 man-machine communication;

人機系統 man-machine system;

人機學 human engineering;

[人急] when one is at a critical moment;

人急計生 an excellent idea occurs to one's mind at the crucial moment; good ideas come at times of crisis; hit on a good idea in a moment of desperation; one's wits fly fast when in great peril; strike a wise idea in a desperate moment; wit comes when one is in a critical moment;

人急造反，狗急跳牆 despair gives courage to a coward; desperation drives men to rebel and a dog to jump over a wall; the desperate dog will jump a wall, the desperate man will hazard all;

人急智生 urgent sharpens one's wit;

[人己] others and the self;

立己立人 being able to establish oneself, one should help others to do so;

枉己正人 a crooked trying to set others straight; a dishonest person telling others to behave;

先己後人 put one's own interest above that of others; put oneself before others;

以己度人 judge others by oneself; measure another man's foot by one's own; measure another's corn by one's own bushel; measure others after oneself;

以己律人 correct others' behaviour by setting a personal example;

[人給家足] each family is provided for and each person is well-fed and well-clothed; every household is well-provided for;

[人際] interpersonal;

人際傳播 interpersonal communication;

~ 人際傳播模式 interpersonal communication model;

人際反應特質 fundamental interpersonal relations orientation;

人際功能 interpersonal function;

人際關係 human relationship; interpersonal relations; personal relations;

~ 人際關係學 intersonal relations stdies;

~ 基本人際關係 fundamental interpersonal relations;

[人跡] human footmarks; traces of human presence;

人跡罕至 few people tread; untraversed;

人跡計生 a man becomes wise in a crisis;

渺無人跡 remote and uninhabited;

杳無人跡 all is quiet with no one around;

[人家] (1) home; human abode; human residence; (2) another; other; other people; (3) he; she; they;

人家都這樣説 that is what everybody says;

官宦人家 a family that has produced public officials for several generations;

矇人家 hoodwink sb;

勤儉人家 industrious and frugal family;

一處人家 a homestead;

一戶人家 a family; a household;

正經人家 respectable family;

[人間] man's world; world; world of mortals;

人間滄桑 mutability of human affairs; the shifts and changes of life;

人間春色 the fairest in the world of men;

人間地獄 a hell away from Hell; a hell of a life; a hell on earth; a human hell; a living hell; a living inferno; pandemonium;
人間關係 interpersonal relation;
人間何世 what a world is this;
人間樂園 a holy and beautiful paradise on earth; an earthly paradise; paradise on earth;
人間奇跡 man-made miracle; miracle;
人間天堂 heaven on earth;
人間萬物 all things on earth;
人間萬象 phenomenon on earth;
人間辛酸 bitterness of life; bitters of life;
人間羞事 disgrace; public scandal; shame;
人間正道 man's world; the world;
春到人間 now spring has arrived; spring comes to the world of men; spring is here again;
尚在人間 still alive;

[人傑] distinguished person; hero; outstanding personality;
人傑地靈 a place propitious for giving birth to great men; a remarkable place producing outstanding people; the greatness of a man lends glory to a place; the place becomes glorious with the birth of heroes;

[人盡] everybody does his best;
人盡可夫 a promiscuous women; a woman of loose morals;
人盡其才 give full scope to the talents; make the best possible use of each one's abilities; everybody is let to display his talents fully; let everybody fully display his talent; make full use of all possible talent; no talent is to be wasted; people can put their specialized knowledge to best use; the talent of every individual can be turned to good account;
~人盡其才，物盡其用 make full use of human and material resources; make the best possible use of men and material;
人盡其力 everyone doing his best;
人盡其位，位得其人 place the right man in the right place;
人盡其責 everyone should do his duty; let every man do his duty;

[人靜心深] smooth water runs deep; still waters run deep;

[人君] king; sovereign;

[人均] per capita;
人均國民收入 national income at per capita level;
人均收入 per capita income;
人均水平 per capita level;

[人客] caller; guest; visitor;

[人孔] manhole;
分歧人孔 branch manhole;
木桶人孔 cask manhole;
圓頂人孔 dome manhole;

[人口] (1) population; (2) number of people in a family;
人口爆炸 demographic population explosion; population boom; population explosion;
~人口爆炸理論 population explosion theory;
~控制人口爆炸 contain the population explosion;
人口變動 demographic changes;
人口標準化 population standardization;
人口佈局 population arrangement;
人口城市化 population urbanization;
人口抽樣調查 population sampling investigation;
人口稠密 dense in population; densely populated; thickly inhabited;
人口出生率 human fetility;
人口調查 census; demographic survey; population survey;
人口動態 population trends;
人口發展 population growth;
~人口發展速度 rate of population growth;
~人口發展系統 population evolution system;
人口分佈 population distribution;
人口分析 demographic analysis;
人口負增長 negative population growth;
人口構成 population composition;
人口規律 population law;
人口規模 population size;
人口過多 overpopulation;
人口過密 overpopulation;
人口過剩 overpopulation;
人口環境 population environment;
人口減少 a population declines; a population decreases; a population falls; population decrease;

人口結構 demographic structure;
人口經濟規律 economic law of population;
人口經濟學 economics of population;
人口聚集 aggregation of population;
人口可容量 population potential;
人口控制 population control;
人口勞動構成 working structure of population;
人口老化 aging of the population;
人口零增長 zero population growth;
人口密度 population density;
人口模式 population pattern;
人口平衡 population balance;
人口普查 census; population census;
人口生態系統 population ecosystem;
人口生態學 population ecology;
人口死亡率 human mortality;
人口素質 population quality;
人口統計 demographic statistics; population statistics;
~人口統計圖 demogram;
~人口統計學 demography;
~理論人口統計學 pure demography;
~區域人口統計學 regional demography;
~移民人口統計學 migration demography;
人口投資 investment for population growth;
人口突增 population explosion;
人口問題 population problems;
人口稀少 be sparsely populated; have a sparse population;
人口心理 population psychology;
人口信息收據庫 population information database;
人口學 demography;
~人口學會 population association;
人口循環 population cycle;
人口壓力 population pressure;
人口預測 population forecasting;
人口再生產類型 type of population reproduction;
人口增加 accretion of population; population grows; population increases; population rises;
人口增長 population growth;
人口政策 population policy;
人口質量 population quality;
人口眾多 encompass a large population; have a very large population; have an enormous population; with a large population;
人口自然增長率 natural population growth rate;
白人人口 white population;
本土人口 indigenous population;
常住人口 resident population;
成年人口 adult population;
城市人口 urban population;
城鎮人口 urban population;
大部份人口 general population;
大量人口 large population;
待業人口 population waiting for employment;
當地人口 local population;
都市人口 urban population;
工業人口 industrial population;
黑人人口 black population;
老齡化人口 ageing population;
老年人口 elderly population;
流動人口 transient population;
農村人口 rural population;
農業人口 agricultural population;
全部人口 entire population; total population; whole population;
世界人口 world's population;
現有人口 existing population;
在業人口 working population;
自立人口 active population;
總人口 total population;

[人拉肩扛] do it by hand and carry it on one's shoulder;

[人懶嘴不懶] the tongue of idle persons is ever idle;

[人老] old in age;
人老氣壯 old in age, but buoyant in spirit;
人老識廣 old people are learned because of their age; the devil knows many things because he is old;
人老心不老 man grows old in years, but his heart does not grow old; one is old in years but not old at heart; old in age, but young in mind; though old in age, yet young at heart;
人老珠黃 in old age, one is like a pearl whose lustre has faded;

[人類] human; humanity; man; mankind; the human race;
人類本能 human instinct;
人類崇拜 anthropolatry;
人類福祉 the betterment of mankind;
人類環境 human environment;

人類進化 evolution of man;
人類起源 the origin of mankind;
人類社會學 anthroposociology;
人類生命層 anthroposere;
人類生態 human ecology;
- 人類生態環境 human ecological environment;
- 人類生態系統 human ecological system;
- 人類生態學 human ecology;
人類文化語言學 ethnolinguistics;
人類行為學 anthroponomy;
人類學 anthropology;
~人類學家 anthropologist;
~古人類學 palaeoanthropology;
古人類學家 palaeoanthropologist;
~教育人類學 educational anthropology;
~社會人類學 social anthropology;
~文化人類學 cultural anthropology;
人類語言學 anthropological linguistics;
告誡人類 admonish mankind;
解放人類 liberate mankind;

[人離鄉賤] a man away from his native place is worthless;

[人力] arm of flesh; human efforts; human power; human strength; manpower;
人力車 (1) two-wheeled vehicle drawn by man; (2) rickshaw;
人力管理 force administration;
~人力管理數據系統 force administration data system;
人力耗竭 be drained of manpower;
人力外流 brawn drain;
人力物力 human and material resources; manpower and material resources;
~愛惜人力物力 treasure manpower and material resources; use manpower and materials sparingly;
人力優勢 man advantage;
人力資本 human capital;
人力資產 human asset;
人力資源 human resources;
現有人力 available man-power;

[人流] pedestrian traffic; stream of people;
人流如潮 endless flow of people;
加入人流 join in the stream of people;
疏散人流 evacuate an endless flow of people; evacuate large crowds of people;

[人倫] human relations; principles of human relationships;
人倫大端 main principles of human relationships;

[人馬] (1) forces; troops; (2) staff;
人馬齊備 all vehicles and servants are ready;
人馬未動，糧草先行 army provisions should be transported before the troops start marching;
人喊馬嘶 men shouting and horses neighing;
人歡馬叫 people bustling and horses neighing — a busy, prosperous country scene;
人困馬乏 both men and horses are tired; the man weary, their steeds spent, the entire force is exhausted;
人強馬壯 the men are strong and the horses swift;
人嚷馬嘶 men are shouting and horses neighing; the noise of men shouting and horses neighing — a busy, prosperous country scene;
人仰馬翻 be thrown into confusion; men and horses all overturned — badly battered; men and horses thrown off their feet — utterly routed; suffer a total defeat;
人要練，馬要騎 the best horse needs breaking, and the aptest child needs teaching;
原班人馬 former staff; old cast; same batch of people; same company; same old cast;

[人滿] (1) overcrowded; (2) overpopulated;
人滿為患 the house is crowded in every part; the place is packed;
人滿之患 overcrowdedness; the trouble of overpopulation;

[人們] community; folks; human beings; humanity; men; people; the public;

[人面] human face;
人面禽獸 a man with the soul of a beast;
人面獅身像 sphinx;
人面獸心 a beast in human shape; a brute of a man; a brute under a human mask; a fiend in human shape; a man's face but the heart of a beast; a wolf in sheep's clothing; bear the semblance of a man but have the heart of a beast; gentle in appearance but cruel at heart; have the face of a man but the heart

of a beast; with a human face and the heat of a beast;
人面桃花 (1) a charming face among peach blossoms; (2) memory of an old sweetheart;

[人民] people;
人民幣 renminbi;
人民法院 people's court;
人民公僕 public servant of the people;
人民檢察院 people's procuratorate;
人民群眾 masses;
人民調解 people's mediation;
人民政府 people's government;

[人名] personal name;
人名錄 directory;

[人命] human life;
人命官司 case of manslaughter; case of murder;
人命關天 a case involving human life is one of the supreme importance; a case involving human life is to be treated with the utmost care; a human life is of greater value than everything; human life is of utmost importance; there is nothing more important than human life;
人命危淺 at the point of death; critically ill; death is expected at any moment; dying; in danger of death; one's days are numbered; one's life is not long and one is about to die; the span of life is short with many risks to boot;
草菅人命 act with utter disregard for human life; make light of the lives of the people; treat human life as if it were not worth a straw;
事關人命 a man's life is involved; it is a case involving human life;
一條人命 one life;

[人謀] plans made by men; schemes made by men; strategies made by men;

[人腦] human brain;
人腦模擬 brain simulation;

[人貧志不短] poor but not wanting in enterprise; poor but with lofty ideals;

[人品] (1) character; moral quality; moral standing; personality; (2) bearing; looks;
人品敗壞 have corrupt morals;
人品出眾 with an excellent character;
人品端方 a man of good upright character; behave oneself well;

[人前] before sb;
跪在人前 fall on one's knees before sb; kneel at sb's feet;

[人琴俱亡] both the man and his lute have perished — death of a friend;

[人勤] people are diligent;
人勤地不懶 the master's foot makes the ground fat; the master's footsteps fatten the soil; the people are diligent and the fields are never left idle; there the tiller is tireless the land is fertile;
人勤地豐 where the tiller is tireless the land is fertile;

[人情] (1) human feelings; human sympathy; sensibilities; (2) human relationship;
人情薄如紙 human feelings of sympathy are as thin as paper;
人情假 compassionate leave;
人情冷暖 fickleness of human nature; men's feelings are changeable;
人情練達 experienced in the ways of the world; the skilful manipulation of human relationships; understanding of worldly wisdom;
人情人情，在人情願 a favour should be given according to one's own desire; presents are made when people are on a friendly footing;
人情世故 the traditional code of conduct; the ways of people; the ways of the world; what is inherent in human nature and social life; worldly wisdom;
人情世俗 run of people; the respectabilities of social life;
人情似水 human feeling is like running water — it lacks true feelings;
人情味 a human touch; friendliness; hospitality;
人情債 debt of gratitude;
不近人情 beneath the human touch; inconsiderate; not amenable to reason; thoughtless; unreasonable; without regard for others;
出於人情 out of humanity;
脆薄人情 thin and brittle human feeling;
風義人情 deep respect and friendship;
空頭人情 lip service;
賣人情 do sb a favour for personal consideration; do sth for good will;
求個人情 ask for a favour; beg for

leniency;
人在人情在 one dies with the feelings of his relatives and friends towards him; while a man lives, his favours are remembered;
~人在人情在，人死一筆勾 dead men have no friends; friendless is the dead; the dead have few friends;
順水人情 a favour done at little cost to oneself;
送人情 (1) do favours at no great cost to oneself; (2) make a gift of sth;
天理人情 reasonable;
通達人情 understanding and considerate;
托人情 ask an influential person to help arrange sth; ask sb to use his good offices on one's behalf; gain one's ends through connections; seek the good offices of sb;
做人情 do sb a favour;
~做個人情 do sb a favour; do sb a good turn; do sb a special favour;

[人窮] one is poor;
人窮志不短 poor but ambitious; poor but proud;
人窮志不窮 better be poor than wicked; poor but with lofty ideals; though one is poor, he has lofty aspirations;
人窮志短 poverty and ambition make strange bedfellows; poverty chills ambition; poverty stifles ambition; poverty takes away pith; when a man is poor his ambition is not far-reaching;
人窮志堅 poor but have a will of iron;
人窮智短 poverty stifles wisdom; when a man is poor, he is lacking wisdom;
人窮眾人欺 every one leaps over the dyke where it is lowest; flies haunt lean horses;

[人取我與] I will part with whatever others may want;

[人去樓空] find no one else in the room; in the room there is not a single soul — old sights recall to mind the memory of old friends; the bird has flown; the chamber is empty and not an inch of a shadow is visible; the dear one is gone and the chamber remains deserted; the room is empty and the dear one is no longer there;

[人權] human rights;
人權法 human rights act;
人權宣言 (1) Declaration of the Rights of Man and of the Citizen; (2) Declaration of Human Rights;
保障人權 guarantee human rigths;
捍衛人權 defend human rights;
蔑視人權 defy human rights;
侵犯人權 infringe upon human rights;
維護人權 maintain human rights;
尊重人權 respect human rights;

[人群] crowd of people; drove of people; multitude of people; throng of people;
一簇人群 a group of people;

[人人] all and sundry; each one; each person; every person; everybody; everyone; one and all; the whole world; the world and his wife;
人人哀悼 be lamented by all;
人人皆知 all the world knows; everybody realizes that; it is known to all; it is public knowledge;
人人平等 all men are equal; everyone is equal;
人人生日 everybody's birthday;
人人討厭 obnoxious to everybody;
人人為我，我為人人 all for one and one for all;
人人有責 everybody is responsible; everybody's duty; everyone bears his share of the responsibility for;
人人自危 everyone feels insecure; everyone finds himself in danger;
人見人愛 be loved by all; everybody's darling;
人敬人高 respect encourages one to be worthy of it; show respect for him and he will respect himself;
人山人海 a large crowd; a sea of faces; a sea of people; be aswarm with people; huge crowds of people;
我為人人，人人為我 all for one and one for all;

[人日] seventh day of the first month;

[人肉] human flesh;
人肉市場 houses of ill fame; the sex market;

[人瑞] venerable old man or woman;

[人色] colour of a human face;
面無人色 as pale as a ghost; as pale as ashes; as pale as death; ashen-faced;

look ghastly pale; pale-faced;

[人善被人欺，馬善被人騎] make yourself all honey and the flies will devour you; the better-natured, the sooner undone;

[人蛇] illegal immigrant;

[人身] (1) human body; (2) personal liberty;

人身安全 personal safety; personal security; security of person;

~給予人身安全 furnish personal security;

~缺乏人身安全 lack personal security;

~注意人身安全 thoughtful of one's safety;

人身保護令 habeas corpus;

人身保險 personal insurance;

人身攻擊 assault and battery; attacks concerning personal matters; personal abuse; personal attack;

人身權 personal right;

人身危險 physical danger;

人身意外保險 personal accident insurance;

人身自由 freedom of person; personal freedom; personal liberty;

[人參] ginseng;

[人神] man and God;

人神共憤 be hated by both man and God; incur the greatest popular indignation;

[人生] human life; life;

人生百年，終歸一死 all men are mortal; death is common to all; everyone has to die some time; everyone has to die sooner or later; he that is once born, once must die;

人生沉浮 life is full of ups and downs; the vicissitudes of life;

人生大事 the most important event of one's life;

人生地不熟 a stranger in a strange place; unfamiliar with the place and the people;

人生地疏 a stranger in a stange place; unfamiliar with the people and the place;

人生短暫 life is transient;

人生多舛 life is full of troubles;

人生觀 outlook on life; philosophy of life; view of life;

人生何處不相逢 friends may meet, but mountains never greet; in life, where don't people meet;

人生禍福 the haps and mishaps of life;

人生幾何 how brief life is; life is but a span; man's life is not very long; we have only a short life to live;

~對酒當歌，人生幾何 eat, drink, and be merry, for tomorrow we die; enjoy wine and song while we can, for life is short;

人生苦樂 sweets and bitters of life; sweet and sour of life;

人生樂趣 pleasures of life;

人生目標 life goals;

人生七十 three score and ten is the age of men — the normal length of human life;

人生七十古來稀 a man seldom lives to be seventy years old; in all times, few are those ho reach the age of seventy; the dyas of our years are threescore years and ten;

人生榮枯 shifts and changes of human life;

人生如寄 man living in this world is like a sojourner in a hotel; men's life is like boarding in this world;

人生如夢 life is but a dream;

人生如朝露 human life is of short duration like the morning dew; life is but a span; life is ephemeral; man is a bubble; the life of a man is like the morning dew;

人生若夢 life is but a dream; life is but an empty dream;

人生態度 life attitude;

人生辛酸 trials of life; woes and sorrows of life;

人生一世，草生一秋 man lives just a generation, and grass exists just for a year;

人生哲理 philosophy of life;

人生哲學 philosophy of life;

人生自古誰無死 all that lives must die; he that is once born, once must die; man is mortal; since the beginning of human life, who would not die; we shall lie all alike in our graves;

短暫的人生 brevity of human life;

[人聲] voice;

人聲嘈雜 confused noise of voices; confusion of voices; tremendous hubbub;

人聲鼎沸 babel of voices; hubbub of voices; noise and shouts in great

commotion; the clamour of the people bubble up;

杳無人聲 depressing silence reigns and not a human sound is to be heard;

[人師] paragon of learning;

恥為人師 ashamed to be called a teacher;

好為人師 be given to laying down the law; fond of lecturing people; like to lecture people;

羞為人師 ashamed to be called a teacher;

[人士] personage; public figure;

半官方人士 semi-official sources;

成功人士 high achiever;

各界人士 people from all circles; people from all walks of life; people of all walks of life;

工商界人士 industrialists and businessmen;

官方人士 official quarters;

傑出人士 distinguished individual;

民主人士 democratic personage;

消息靈通人士 informed sources;

知名人士 noted personages; well-known figures;

著名人士 notable;

[人世] (1) human life; life; (2) this world;

人世滄桑 mutability of human affairs; the shifts and changes of life; the vicissitudes of human affairs; tremendous changes in the world; tremendous changes in this world of ours;

不久於人世 sb is not long for this world;

離開人世 department this liufe;

在人世 still alive;

~不在人世 no longer living; not be alive;

~在人世間 on the face of the earth;

[人事] (1) human affairs; occurrences in human life; (2) way of the world; (3) consciousness; (4) personnel matters; (5) what is humanly possible;

人事安排 personnel arrangement;

人事變動 changes in personnel; personnel change;

人事不省 unconsciousness;

人事部 personnel office;

人事滄桑 the ebb and flow of life; the shifting scenes of life; the shifts and changes of life;

人事沉浮 there is a tide in the affairs of men;

人事處 personnel office;

人事更迭 a change of personnel;

人事關係 personal connections;

人事管理 personnel administration;

~人事管理學 science of personnel administration;

~人事管理員 personnel supervisor;

人事心理學 personnel psychology;

人事行政 personnel administration;

不懂人事 not know the ways of the world;

不省人事 become unconscious; dead to the wide; dead to the world; fall into a swoon; fall senseless; in a coma; in a dead faint; in a state of coma; lie like a log; lose consciousness; unconscious;

~喝得不省人事 drank oneself blind;

很懂人事 know the ways of the world very well;

盡人事 do all that is humanly possible; do what one can;

~盡人事而聽天命 do one's level best and leave the rest to God's will;

聊盡人事 just to do what is humanly possible;

妙人妙事 an interesting person and his amusing episodes;

其人其事 biographic sketch; that man and that business; the man and his deeds;

[人是鐵，飯是鋼] bread is the staff of life; it is hard to labour with an empty belly;

[人手] (1) human hand; (2) manpower;

人手不夠 understaffed;

人手不足 short of hands; shorthanded; understaffed;

人手翻譯 human translation;

~人手翻譯員 human translator;

人手輔助翻譯 human-aided translation;

人手一冊 everybody has a copy; in everybody's hand;

湊人手 make up the hands;

缺人手 short of hands; short of manpower; short-handed;

[人壽] one's span of life;

人壽保險 life insurance;

人壽不永 come to a premature end; one's life is cut short;

人壽年豐 the land yields good harvests and the people enjoy good health; the people enjoy longevity and the land yields rich harvests; there have been bumper harvests in succession and the

people live to a great age; there is a series of good harvests and the people all live to a great age;

[人數] number of people;
人數不限 there is no limit on the number of people;
點人數 count noses; head count;
法定人數 quorum;
死亡人數 death toll;

[人死] death of a person;
人死不能復活 a dead man cannot be restored to life;
人死口閉 dead men don't bite; dead men tell no tales;
人死口滅 dead men don't bite; dead men tell no tales;
人死留名 a man leaves a name behind him;
人死留名，雁死留聲 he does not die that can bequeath some influence to the land he knows;
人死求醫，賊去關門 counsel after action is like rain after harvest;
人死萬債休 death pays all debts; death quits all scores; death squares all accounts; he that dies, pays all debts;
人死債爛 death pays all debts;
人之將死，其言也善 a man's words are good when death is near; men speak kindly in the presence of death; one makes pretty speeches when he is on his deathbed; when a man is near death he speaks from his heart;

[人隨] everyone follows;
人隨理走 everyone has to listen to reason;
人隨時老 in time everyone gets old;
人隨王法草隨風 man yield to the laws as the grass does to the wind;

[人所共知] as everybody knows; as is known to all; as is well known; everyone knows that; it is clear to all; it is common knowledge that; it is evident to anyone; it is well known that;

[人體] human body;
人體穿刺 body piercing;
人體解剖學 anthropotomy;
人體模型 dummy; mannequin;
人體生物鐘 body clock;
人體特異功能 extraordinary function of human body;
人體微量元素 body trace element;

[人頭] (1) number of people; (2) character; moral quality; (3) relations with people;
人頭混雜 strange mix of people;
人頭擠擠 huge crowds of people;
人頭落地 be killed; lose one's life; one's head falls to the ground; one's head rolls on the ground;
人頭馬 centaur;
人頭牌 court card;
人頭稅 capitation; poll tax;
人頭攢動 a sea of heads pushing and jostling;

[人亡] a person dies;
人亡物在 the handiwork remains though the maker's gone; the relics of the dead; the things are still here but their owner is no more; the things are there just as before, except the beloved one; things remind one of their owner;
人亡政息 when a man expires his work will stop — when a man dies his administration will be cast away;
家破人亡 family ruined or dead; one's family is ruined and all of its members are dead; one's family is broken up and its members killed; the members of one's family are partly dispersed and partly dead; with one's family broken up, some gone away, some dead; with the family broken up and decimated;
物在人亡 the handiwork remains though the maker's gone;

[人望] popularity; prestige;
人望所歸 enjoy popularity; popular with men;

[人微] person in a low position;
人微權輕 the lowly carries little authority; when a man is in a low position, he has little power;
人微言輕 a poor man's tale cannot be heard; as one is in a low position, one's words are of little effect; in one's humble position, one's words do not carry much weight; poor men's reasons are not heard; the poor man's reasons are of no weight; the reasons of the poor weigh not; the words of the lowly carry little weight; when a man is in a low position, his words carry little weight;

[人為] artificial; man-made;

人為刀俎，我為魚肉 one is like a piece of meat placed on sb's chopping block — one's life is at the mercy of those in power;

人為地貌 anthropogenic landform;

人為干擾 man-made interference;

人為過失 human error;

人為環境異常 anthropogenic environment abnormality;

人為困難 man-made difficulties;

人為失誤 human error;

~人為失誤分類 classification of human errors;

~人為失誤預測法 technique for human error prediction;

人為事故 human error accident;

人為萬物之靈 man is the intelligent part of the universe; man is the lord of creation; the human being is the most intelligent among creatures;

人為污染源 man-ade pollution sources;

人為影嚮 man-made influence;

人為噪聲 man-made noise;

人為障礙 artificially imposed obstacles;

事在人為 human effort can achieve everything; human effort is the decisive factor; it all depends on human effort; it is human effort that tells on the outcome; it is man that decides everything; it is man who disposes; man is the decisive factor; the result depends on the actions of people;

[人位兩宜] the right man for the right job; the right man in the right position;

[人文] (1) humanities; (2) human affairs;

人文地理 human geography;

人文薈萃 the gathering of talents;

人文景觀 human landscape; places of historic figures and cultural heritage;

人文科學 arts and humanities; liberal arts; the humanities;

人文學科 the humanities;

人文主義 humanism;

[人無] a man cannot;

人無二死 a man can die but once;

人無千日好，花無百日紅 a man is never happy for a thousand days and a flower never blooms for a hundred; man cannot be always fortunate; flowers do not last forever; men cannot be good for a thousand days, and flowers cannot bloom for a hundred days; nobody is always happy;

[人物] character; figure; person in literature; personage;

人物畫 figure painting; portrait painting;

人物簡介 profile;

人物漫畫 caricature;

人物描寫 character delineation; character portrayal; characterization;

人物塑造 characterization;

人物特寫 figural feature;

人物突出 striking characters; with characters that stand out;

次要人物 minor character;

大人物 big cheese; big gun; big hitter; big shot; top gun;

典型人物 typical character;

反面人物 negative character; villain;

風流人物 (1) romantic person; (2) original genius; truly great and noble-hearted men; truly great men;

風雲人物 (1) celebrity; influential person; (2) person in the news; person of the moment; person of the hour; person of the day;

傑出人物 eminent personage; luminary; outstanding personage;

劇中人物 dramatis personae;

刻畫人物 portray a character;

歷史人物 historical personage;

神話人物 mythical personage;

頭號人物 big gun; top gun;

頭面人物 big gun; big shot; bigwig; eminent person; important person; key member; leading figure; leading light; principal figure; prominent figure; those in the limelight; those in the upper echelons of...; top gun; top people;

顯要人物 notable;

小人物 small beer; small fry; small potatos;

新聞人物 news-maker;

虛構人物 mythical person;

盱衡人物 open eyes on men and things;

正面人物 hero; positive character;

知名人物 noted personage;

中心人物 central character;

重要人物 big wheel; important figure; important personage; leading light;

主要人物 leading character; main character;
卓越人物 remarkable character;

[人像] figure; portrait; image;
人像攝影 human figures photography;
人像照 portrait;

[人小] small person;
人小耳尖 little pitchers have long ears;
人小鬼大 a boy with a high ambition; a child daring to do great mischief; young but tricky;
人小火氣大 a little pot is soon hot; a small man often has a bad temper;

[人心] human emotion; human feeling; human heart; human will; morale; popular feeling; public peeling; the will of the people;
人心不古 human hearts are not what they were in the old days; men are not what they were in the times of long ago; people are not so honest as their ancestors were; public morality is not what it used to be;
人心不同，各如其面 individual thinking is as varied as individual looks; men's hearts are different just as their faces are; men's hearts differ just as their faces do; several men, several minds; so many heads, so many opinions; so many men, so many minds; the hearts of men differ as much as their faces;
人心不足，得隴望蜀 desire hath no rest; no man is content; who is allowed more liberty than is reasonable, will desire more than is allowed;
人心不足蛇吞象 a man whose heart is not content is like a snake which tries to swallow an elephant — insatiable desire; no man ever thought his on too much; no man is content with his lot;
人心大快 the people are all jubilant; the public sentiment is satisfied;
人心都是肉長的 everybody has the sense of mercy;
人心歸向 the feelings of the people are for...the inclination of the hearts of the people;
人心渙散 divided in public opinion; people being not of one mind;
人心惶惶 everyone is jittery; jittery; panicky; people are agitated;
人心莫測 the human heart is a mystery;
人心叵測 harbour an evil heart; man's heart is incomprehensible; one's heart is past finding out; the heart of man is past finding out;
人心齊，群山移 if we all pull together, we can move the highest mountain; when men are of one heart, they can move mountains;
人心齊，泰山移 when men are of one heart, they can accomplish anything;
人心喪盡 completely forfeit the confidence of the people; lose all popular sympathy;
人心思變 all are hoping for a change; people are longing for change;
人心所向 in terms of popular support; popular feelings; the common aspiration of the people; the desire of the people; the direction of popular sentiment; the feelings of the people; what is unanimously supported by the people;
人心惟危 human hearts are evil; human hearts are unfathomable;
人心向背 the feelings of the people; whether the people are for or against; whether the public attitude for or against; who commands popular sympathy; with whom popular sympathy lies;
人心振奮 the people are filled with enthusiasm;
安定人心 quiet the people's minds; reassure the public; set people's minds at ease; set people's minds at rest;
安撫人心 appease the public; pacify public feeling;
百人百心，百人百性 different people think and behave differently; people differ in mind and in character;
敗壞人心 corrupt people's minds; eprave; perversion of one's mind;
大快人心 cause great rejoicing among the masses of the people; cause popular rejoicing; fill people's hearts with a great happiness; it gladdens people's hearts; this cheers the people greatly; to the satisfaction of the masses;
得人心 be beloved and supported by the people; popular; win the favour of the people;

~不得人心 go against the will of the people;
~大得人心 enjoy great popularity; have high prestige among the people;
動搖人心 sway the mind of men;
鼓舞人心 gladden the people's hearts; heartening; inspiring; set the hearts of the people aflame;
蠱惑人心 agitate people by demagogy; be guile people out of the right way; befog the minds of the people; confuse and poison people's minds; confuse public opinion; hoodwink people with demagogy; instil poisonous suspicions into men's minds; resort to demagogy; spread false doctrines to undermine the people's morale; undermine popular morale by spreading unfounded rumours;
撼動人心 move one's heart; shake people's faith;
患難之中見人心 calamity is man's true touchstone;
激動人心 arouse sb's feelings; soul-stirring;
極盡心力 put one's body and soul into a task; work to the best of one's ability;
籠絡人心 try to win people's support by hook or by crook;
買人心 win people's hearts by statecraft;
~邀買人心 buy popularity; dispense favours in order to win popularity;
~買服人心 win the heart of the masses;
迷惑人心 befuddle public opinion; confuse the masses; pull the wool over people's eyes; throw dust in the eyes of the public;
牽動人心 affect sb's feeling;
竊取人心 steal away sb's heart;
人同此心，心同此理 everybody feels the same about this; on this matter people feel and think alike; the sense of justice and rationality is the same with everybody; this is the general feeling shared by all;
日久見人心 a long task proves the sincerity of a person; it takes time to know a person; time is a revealer of a person's sincerity; time reveals a person's heart; time will tell a true friend from a false one;
煽惑人心 agitate people by demagogy; deceive and stir up people's mind; incite people by demagogy; undermine popular morale by spreading unfounded rumour;
深得人心 enjoy immense popular support; high in sb's favour; win the hearts of all;
深入人心 strike root in the hearts of the people;
失去人心 lose the support of the people;
十人十心 many men, many minds;
世道人心 the ways of the world and the heart of human beings;
事久見人心 a long task proves a person's heart;
收買人心 curry favour with the public;
攖人心 disturb peace of mind; disturb people's hearts;
贏得人心 have the support of the people;
誘惑人心 tempt the hearts of the people;
振奮人心 bring up the morale; soul-stirring;
震動人心 make a great impact on people;
震撼人心 have a great impact on; soul-stirring; stirring; thrilling;

［人行］ pedestrian;
人行道 pavement;
~自動人行道 moving sidewalk;
人行橫道 crosswalk; pedestrian crossing; pedestrian crosswalk;
~自控人行橫道 pelican crossing;
人行橋 footbridge;
人行天橋 pedestrian over crossing;
人行小徑 footpath;

［人性］ (1) human nature; humanity; (2) reason;
人性不可變 human nature cannot be changed;
人性的弱點 human foibles;
人性化 humanize;
失去人性 lose one's reason;

［人選］ candidates; choice of persons; the person selected;
當選人選 victorious candidates;
合格人選 successful candidates;
獲獎人選 candidates for the prize;

［人煙］ household; human habitation; signs of a human settlement;
人煙稠密 crowded; densely inhabited; densely populated; packed; populous; swarming; thickly peopled;

人煙輳集，車馬駢馳 horses and carts are passing along side by side; the streets are crowded and noisy;
人煙罕至 a place that is hard to get to;
人煙絕跡 no trace of man and smoke;
人煙稀少 sparsely populated; thinly peopled; thinly settled; uncouth;
荒無人煙 desolate and uninhabited; no human habitation; with no sign of human habitation;
渺無人煙 remote and uninhabited; wild and uninhabited;
杳無人煙 deserted; remote and desolate; unibhabited;

[人言] (1) human speech; (2) public opinion;
人言不可信 don't believe rumours; gossips are not to be believed; words are but wind;
人言鼎沸 a tremendous bubbub; many people talk together and the noise they make is like the bubbling of water boiling in a cauldron;
人言藉藉 gossips are rife; there is a great deal of gossips;
人言可畏 gossip is a fearful thing; the voice of the people is sth to fear;
人言人殊 the accounts are at variance among themselves;
人言嘖嘖 complaints are whispered in a good-natured way; criticism of the people is evident; there are plenty of criticisms; there is a good deal of unfavourable comments;
浪信人言 unwisely believe in other's words;

[人以群分] people are always divided into factions; people of one mind fall into the same group; people of the same sort are usually attracted to one another; people of the same tastes and habits like to be together;

[人意] one's will;
差強人意 barely satisfactory; fair; just passable;
盡如人意 entirely satisfactory; just as one wishes;
未盡人意 not up to expectations;

[人義水甜] perfect harmony between friends;

[人影] human shadow;
人影憧憧 shadows of people moving about;

[人有千算，天只一算] whatever the human minds intend, it's heaven that decides the end;

[人有失錯，馬有漏蹄] a horse stumbles that has four legs; it is a good horse that never stumbles; man sometimes errs, as a horse sometimes stumbles;

[人慾] desires; passions;
人慾橫流 human desires flowing crosswise; mass indulgence in decadent life; people care for nothing but lust;
放縱人慾 indulge one's passion;
控制人慾 control human desires; control one's passion;
滿足人慾 satisfy one's desire;
壓制人慾 subdue one's desire;

[人員] personnel; staff;
人員不足 understaffed;
人員功能測評 evaluation of employer's function;
人員過多 overmanned; overmanning; overstaffed;
保管人員 custodial staff;
管理人員 administrative personnel; administrative staff; managerial personnel;
技術人員 technical personnel;
減少人員 thin the ranks;
領導人員 directing staff;
情報人員 intelligence personnel;
情務人員 intelligence personnel;
商業人員 commercial staff;
行政人員 administrative personnel; administrative staff;
醫務人員 medical staff;
在編人員 permanent staff; those on the regular payroll;
在職人員 in-service staff;
直屬工作人員 immediate staff;
專職人員 full-time staff;

[人猿] ape; man ape;
類人猿 anthropoid ape, manlike ape;

[人緣] popularity; relations with people;
人緣差 enjoy little popularity; unpopular;
人緣好 enjoy great popularity; very popular;
廣結人緣 get the people to like one;

[人贓俱獲] both the man and the stolen goods have been found; catch sb with the goods;

[人造] artificial; imitation; man-made;
人造寶石 hard mass; imitation jewel; manufactured gem;
人造臂 artificial arm;
人造冰 artificial ice;
人造動脈 artificial artery;
人造耳 artificial ear;
人造肥料 chemical fertilizer;
人造肺 artificial lung;
人造革 imitation leather; leatherette;
人造喉 artificial larynx;
人造棉 staple rayon;
人造皮 leatherette;
人造器官 artificial organ;
人造腎 artificial kidney;
人造絲 artificial silk;
人造腿 artificial leg;
人造衛星 artificial satellite; man-made satellite;
人造細胞 artificial cell;
人造心臟 artificial heart;
人造牙 artificial tooth;
人造眼 visilog;
人造引力 artificial gravity;
人造雨 artificial rain;
人造珠寶飾物 costume jewellery;

[人渣] scumbag;

[人證] (1) witness; (2) testimony of a witness;
人證物證 evidence in persons and things; human testmony and material evidence; witness and material evidence;
傳喚人證 summon a witness;
訊問人證 examine a witness;

[人治] rule by man; rule of man;

[人質] hostage;

[人種] ethnic group; human species; race;
人種論 ethnography;
人種起源學 ethnogeny;
人種學 ethnology;
白色人種 the while race;
黑色人種 the black race;
黃色人種 the yellow race;
蒙古人種 the Mongolian race;

[人主] king; sovereign;

[人自為戰] each man fighting all by himself; everybody fights all by himself;

[人自相殘] people struggle against each other;

[人走茶涼] no sooner has the person gone away than the tea cools down; the superficiality of human relationships; the tea cools down as soon as th person is gone;

阿爾巴尼亞人 Albanian;
阿爾及利亞人 Algerian;
阿富汗人 Afghan;
阿根廷人 Argentine;
阿拉伯人 Arab;
埃及人 Egyptian;
矮人 dandiprat; dwarf; midget; short person;
愛財如命的人 miser; money-grubber; old screw;
愛吵架的人 scrapper;
愛出風頭的人 limelight seeker;
愛管閒事的人 back-seat driver; fleabag; meddler; meddlesome person; snooper; stickybeak; stirrer;
愛人 (1) one's husband; (2) one's wife; (3) darling; lover; sweetheart; (4) fiance or fiancee; (5) love others;
安人 pacify the people;
奧地利人 Austrian;
澳大利亞人 Australian;
巴基斯坦人 Pakistani;
巴拿馬人 Panamanian;
巴西人 Brazilian;
白人 white man or woman; white race;
白種人 white man or woman; white race;
邦人 compatriot; fellow countrymen; people of a nation;
幫人 help sb;
鮑人 tanner;
保護人 guardian;
保加利亞人 Bulgarian;
保人 (1) guarantor; (2) bail;
保證人 (1) guarantor; (2) bail;
報案人 a person who reports a case to the security authorities;
報告人 lecturer; speaker;
報人 journalist;
卑人 mean person;
被告人 defendant; the accused;
被害人 the injured part; the victim;
本人 (1) I; me; myself; (2) in person; in the flesh; oneself;
笨人 dullard; fool; nincompoop; simpleton; stupid person; idiot;
逼人 pressing; threatening;
鄙人 I; my humble self; your humble servant;
嬖人 favourite of the ruler;
璧人 fine-looking person;
便人 sb who happens to be on hand for an errand;

辯護人 defender;
別人 another person; somebody else; (2) other people; others;
冰人 matchmaker;
病人 invalid; patient;
波蘭人 Pole;
才能出眾的人 person of excellent calibre;
才人 (1) talented person; (2) rank of ladies-in-waiting in traditional China;
草人 scarecrow;
讒人 slanderer;
常人 common people; man in the street; ordinary people;
超人 out of the common run; superman;
朝鮮人 Korean;
吵人 disturb others by noise;
成年人 adult; grown-up;
成人 (1) become full-grown; grow up; (1) adult; grown-up;
城裏人 city dwellers; townspeople;
承包人 contractor;
承保人 insurer;
承付人 payer;
承兑人 accepter;
承運人 carrier;
承租人 leaseholder; lesee;
乘人 take advantage of sb;
痴人 idiot;
持卡人 cardholder;
仇人 enemy; foe;
疇人 astrologist;
出家人 Buddhist monk; Buddhist nun;
傳人 pass on a special skill, etc.; person who can inherit and pass on a certain branch of knowledge;
創辦人 founder;
創始人 founder; originator;
倡議人 initiator;
蠢人 bird-brain; blockhead; charlie; fool; goofyball; goon; imbecile; joker; moron; muppet; numpty; oaf; wiener;
粗人 boor; careless person; clod; clod-hopper; person of little education; rough fellow; unrefined person;
打人 hit people; strike people;
大人 adult; grown-up;
呆人 fool;
代理人 agent;
代言人 spokesman;
待人 treat people;
帶路人 guide;
單人 single;
丹麥人 Dane; Danish;
當事人 (1) party; (2) person concerned;
得人 having got the right person for the right job;
德國人 German;
等人 wait for sb;
敵人 enemy; foe;
抵押人 mortgagor;
甸人 ancient official title;
奠基人 founder;
丟人 be disgraced; lose face;
動人 moving; touching;
讀書人 intellectual; scholar;
對人 one's attitude towards others;
訛人 blackmail sb;
惡人 evil person; villain;
恩人 benefactor;
發貨人 consignor; shipper;
發明人 inventor;
發起人 initiator; sponsor;
發信人 addresser;
發行人 publisher;
發言人 spokesman;
法國人 French;
法人 corporation; juridical person; legal body; legal entity; legal person;
凡人 (1) ordinary person; (2) mortal;
煩人 annoying; troubling; vexing;
犯人 convict; criminal; prisoner; the guilty;
非人 (1) not the right person; (2) inhuman;
菲律賓人 Filipino;
廢人 (1) disabled person; (2) good-for-nothing;
芬蘭人 Finlander; Finn;
瘋人 lunatic;
逢人 meet;
夫人 lady; ladyship; ma'am; madam; madame;
服人 convince people; subdue others;
付款人 drawee; payer;
負責人 person in charge;
負債人 debtor;
婦人 married women;
富人 rich people;
感人 moving; touching;
剛果人 Congolese;
高人 (1) person of high quality; (2) very capable person;
哥倫比亞人 Colombian;
各人 each one; everyone;
各種各樣的人 men of all conditions;
個人 (1) individual; personal; (2) I;
給人 by sb; give sb; to sb;
跟車人 patcher;

工人 factory worker; factory-hand; worker; workman;
公訴人 public prosecutor; the prosecution;
公證人 notary; notary public;
古巴人 Cuban;
古人 forefathers; the ancients;
故人 ancients; old friend;
寡人 I, the sovereign;
怪人 aberrant; codger; dweeb; eccentric; loon; odd ball; odd fish; oddity; peculiar person; queer bird; queer fish; quite a character; sphinx; strange fish; varietist monster; wacko; weirdo; whacko;
官人 husband;
觀人 judge a person;
貴人 (1) respectable person; (2) title of a female palace official;
國人 compatriots; countrymen; fellow countrymen;
過來人 person who has had the experience;
過人 remarkable; surpassing others;
害人 victimization;
駭人 appalling; astounding; horrendous; horrifying; shocking; terrifying;
漢人 Han people;
好人 (1) fine person; good person; goodie; goody; (2) healthy person; (3) person who tries to get along with everyone;
荷蘭人 Dutch;
黑人 black man; black person; blackamoor; blackie; coon; darkie; darky; golly; eggs and spoons; the Black people;
黑種人 black race;
恨人 misanthrope; sentimental person;
紅人 a favourite with sb in power; craze; blue-eyed boy; fair-haired boy; favourite person; hotshot;
紅種人 brown race;
後來人 successor;
後人 (1) later generations; (2) descendants; posterity;
候選人 candidate;
唬人 bluff; cheat; deceive; frighten;
華人 Chinese;
換人 substitution of players;
壞人 (1) bad person; evildoer; (2) scoundrel;
黃種人 yellow race;
滙款人 remitter;
渾人 unreasonable fellow;
活人 living person; person who is still alive;
己人 self and others;
機器人 robot;
寄件人 sender;
寄信人 sender;
繼承人 (1) heir; inheritor; (2) successor;
加拿大人 Canadian;
佳人 beautiful woman;
賈人 merchant; trader;
嫁人 (of a girl) get married;
奸人 crafty and evil person;
監護人 guardian;
監考人 invigilator;
監票人 scrutineer;
柬埔寨人 Cambodian;
見人 see others;
見證人 eyewitness;
匠人 artisan; craftsman;
叫人 cry for sb;
介紹人 (1) one who introduces or recommends sb; sponsor; (2) matchmaker;
接班人 successor;
今人 contemporary people; people of the present era;
經辦人 person handling a transaction, particular job, etc.;
經紀人 agent; broker; middleman;
經手人 person handling a transaction, particular job, etc.;
驚人 alarming; amazing; astonishing;
救人 save a person;
居間人 intermediary; mediator;
局內人 insider;
局外人 bystander; outsider;
局中人 player;
巨人 colossus; giant;
絹人 silk figurine;
軍人 armyman; soldier;
喀麥隆人 Cameroonian;
開票人 drawer;
看人 judge people;
可人 satisfactory;
客人 (1) guest; visitor; (2) guest; (3) travelling merchant;
坑人 cheat; entrap; trap;
傾人 frame a person; implicate a person;
控訴人 accuser;
快人 person who is frank by nature; straightforward man;
狂人 (1) kook; lunatic; madman; maniac; (2) extremely arrogant and conceited person;
困人 tiring;
闊人 the rich;
拉人 grab sb;
蠟人 waxwork;

來人 (1) bearer; incoming envoy; messenger; (2) persons coming;
懶人 bedsteader; do-nothing; faineant; gentleman of leisure; gold brick; lady of leisure; layabout; lazy person; lazybones; lounger; sleepyhead; vale of resters;
狼人 werewolf;
浪人 (1) vagrant; (2) dismissed courtier; (3) jobless person; unemployed;
老好人 good person;
老年人 old people; the aged;
老人 crinkly; crumblie; dusty; golden ager; senile person; senior citizen; well-reserved man; the longer living;
淚人 person who cries; person who is all tears;
利人 benefit other people;
麗人 beauty;
儷人 beauty;
戀人 lover; sweetheart;
良人 (1) husband; (2) common people;
兩人 two persons;
兩性人 bisexual person; hermaphrodite;
獵人 hunter; huntsman;
鄰人 neighbour;
伶人 actor; actress;
領導人 leader;
領款人 payee;
領路人 guide;
領跑人 pacemaker; pacesetter;
令人 make one;
聾啞人 deaf-mute;
路人 passerby; stranger;
羅馬尼亞人 Romanian;
旅人 traveller;
律人 treat others;
馬來西亞人 Malaysian;
馬里人 Malian;
罵人 abuse; call one names; condemn; curse; give a bad name to sb; give sb a good dressing down; give sb a good wigging; give sb a scolding; give sb a piece of one's mind; give sb the edge of one's tongue; haul sb over the coals; load sb with insults; mutter insults against; rake sb over the coals; reprove; revile; sail into; scold; swear at; take sb to task; tell one off; walk into a meat-pie;
忙人 busy person;
盲人 blind person;
沒人 there's nobody;
媒人 go-between; matchmaker;
每人 all; each; everybody;
美國人 American;
美人 beautiful woman; beauty; looker; queen of hearts;
媚人 sugary;
門人 (1) disciple; (2) hanger-on of an aristocrat;
悶人 downer;
迷人 alluring; appealing; beautiful; bewitching; charming; dazzling; delightful; enchanting; fascinating; gorgeous; loving; ravishing; stunning;
緬甸人 Burmese;
名人 biggie; celebrity; eminent person; famous person; great card; luminary; notable; sleb;
明人 honest man; person of good sense; wise man;
明眼人 person of good sense; person with a discerning eye; those who discerning eyes;
墨西哥人 Mexican;
某人 certain person;
牧人 herdsman;
拿人 make things difficult for others; put sb in a difficult position; raise difficulties;
男人 (1) dude; man; (2) menfolk; (3) husband;
難人 (1) delicate; difficult; ticklish; (2) person handles a delicate matter;
惱人 annoying; irritating;
內人 my wife;
能人 able man; able person; capable brains;
泥人 clay figurine;
擬人 personification;
年青人 young people;
年輕人 young people;
農人 farmer; peasant;
女人 (1) biddy; woman; (2) womenfolk; (3) wife;
挪威人 Norwegian;
偶人 figures made of wood or clay;
怕人 (1) shy; (2) frightening; terrifying;
旁人 other people;
傍人 other people;
碰不得的人 forbidden game;
騙人 deceive people;
平人 common people; ordinary person;
僕人 servant;
旗人 bannerman;
欺人 deceive sb;
其人 the person;
奇人 (1) queer person; strange person; (2) person of unusual ability;
起訴人 prosecutor; suitor;
氣人 annoying;
棄人 abandon sb; desert sb;

千人 a thousand people;
前人 forefathers; predecessors;
強人 (1) capable person; (2) bandit; highwayman; robber; (3) physically strong person; strong man; stout person;
敲人 swindle a person;
親人 (1) kinsfolk; kinsmen; one's family members; one's parents, spouse, children, etc.; relatives; (2) dear ones; sb's nearest and dearest; those dear to one;
青年人 young people;
情人 inamorata; lover; paramour; sweetheart;
窮人 destitute people; have-nots; man of modest means; needy; negative saver; poor people;
求人 (1) ask for help; (2) look for talents;
全人 perfect person; sage;
讓人 concessive; conciliatory; yield to others; yielding;
饒人 (1) forgive another person; (2) give others a way out;
人盯人 man-for-man defence;
仁人 benevolent person;
壬人 cunning deceiver; artful person;
任人 let people do sth without restriction;
日本人 Japanese;
容人 broad-minded; magnanimous; tolerant towards others;
孺人 scholar's wife; wife;
瑞典人 Swede;
瑞士人 Swiss;
三人 three persons;
散人 idle man;
騷人 men of letters;
僧人 monk;
殺人 kill a person; killing; manslaughter; murder;
嫂夫人 respectful term for a friend's wife;
山人 (1) hermit; recluse; (2) astrologer; fortune-teller;
善人 charitable person; kindhearted and benevolent fellow; philanthropist; well-doer;
商人 businessman; merchant; trader;
傷人 (1) hurt people; (2) inflict physical injury on another; (3) harmful to health;
上等人 upper class;
上訴人 appellant;
瘆人 horrify; make one's flesh creep;
舌人 interpreter;
舍人 palace secretary in the Zhou and some later dynasties;
誰人 who;
神人 gods and people;
生人 stranger;
生意人 businessman;
聖人 sage; wise man;
詩人 poet;
拾人 pick up from sb;
食人 cannibal;
時人 contemporaries; people of the time;
識人 able to appraise a person's ability and character correctly;
使人 make people...;
士人 scholar;
世人 common people; people of the world;
示人 let others have a look at; make known; show others;
室人 wife;
筮人 fortuneteller;
適人 marry sb;
收貨人 consignee;
收件人 addressee; consignee;
收款人 payee;
收信人 addressee;
受保人 insurant;
受款人 payee; remittee;
受票人 drawee;
受賄人 bribee;
受益人 beneficiary;
瘦人 bag of bones; lean person; stack of bones; thin person;
蘇丹人 Sudanese;
蘇聯人 Soviet Citizen;
熟人 acquaintance; friend;
戍人 frontier guard; garrison soldier;
庶人 common people;
樹人 educate the young;
耍人 make a fool of sb; make fun of sb; poke fun at others;
雙人 double; two persons; twin;
碩人 (1) slender and healthy beauty; (2) hermit;
私人 personal private;
死人 (1) dead person; the dead; the defunct; (2) to the utmost degree;
寺人 palace attendant;
送人 (1) give presents; send fits; (2) see a person off; see sb off;
俗人 (1) vulgarian; ordinary person; (2) layman;
損人 (1) make caustic remarks; ridicule others; (2) cause material damage to others;
索馬里人 Somali;
他人 another person; other people; others; somebody else;
擡人 beautify; doll up; make sb look better;

R

泰國人 Thai;
坦桑尼亞人 Tanzanian;
替人 substitute;
天人 celestial being; extraordinary beauty;
調解人 mediator; peacemaker;
調人 mediator; peacemaker;
調停人 mediator;
鐵人 iron man;
鐵石人 cruel person; iron-hearted person; unfeeling person;
通人 person of wide knowledge and sound scholarship;
同輩人 contemporary;
同路人 fellow traveler;
同人 colleagues; people of the same trade or occupation;
銅人 bronze image; bronze statue;
瞳人 pupil of the eye;
頭人 headman; tribal chief;
土耳其人 Turk;
土人 aborigines; natives;
推人 push;
托運人 consignor;
託人 ask sb to do sth for oneself;
蛙人 frogman;
外粗內秀的人 rough diamond;
外人 (1) one who is not a native; (2) outsider; (3) alien; foreign;
完人 paragon of virtue; perfect man;
萬人 ten thousand people;
妄人 ignorant and presumptuous person; incorrigible person; stupid and reckless person;
為人 behave; behavior; conduct; conduct oneself;
委托人 principal;
偉人 great man; great personage;
文化人 cultural worker; intellectual;
文人 literary man; literati; man of letters; scholar;
聞人 celebrity; famous person; well-known figure;
倭人 Japanese;
吾人 we;
無人 (1) unmanned; (2) depopulated; uninhabited; unmanned;
武人 armyman; soldier;
誤人 harm people;
昔人 ancient people;
襲人 (1) copy; (2) assail one's nose;
喜人 gratifying; satisfactory;
下等人 lower class;
下人 servant;
嚇人 frightening; terrifying;
仙人 (1) celestial being; immortal; (2) very beautiful woman;
先人 (1) ancestors; forebears; forefathers; previous generations; (2) one's late father;
纖人 fragile person;
閒人 (1) idlers; persons with nothing to do; unoccupied person; (2) persons not concerned;
賢人 person of virtue; worthy man;
線人 informer; nark; stoolpigeon;
鄉人 (1) villagers; (2) persons from the same village;
鄉下人 village people; villager;
相人 practise physiognomy;
宵人 mean person;
小人 (1) base person; mean person; vile character; villain; (2) person of low position;
曉人 (1) explain; tell; (2) reasonable person;
心上人 sweetheart;
新人 (1) new hands; (2) bride; (3) new love; (4) person with modern thoughts;
新西蘭人 New Zealander;
信得過的人 safe pair of hands;
行人 passer-by; pedestrian;
匈牙利人 Hungarian;
羞人 feel ashamed; feel embarrassed;
選人 choose people;
學人 scholar;
雪人 snowman;
亞洲人 Asian;
壓人 overwhelm others;
閹人 castrated person; eunuch;
眼中人 the loved one; the person after one's heart;
洋人 foreigner;
妖人 evil enchanter; sorcerer;
咬人 bite;
要人 biggie; big gun; big shot; heavyweight; prominent figure; VIP; the man of the moment; very important person (VIP);
野人 barbarian; rustic; savage; wild man;
一班人 members of a squad;
一幫人 a band of men; a gang of men; a group of people;
一撥人 a group of men;
一大群人 a great multitude of people; a horde of people;
一代人 a new generation;
一堆人 a group of men; a group of people;
一個多才多藝的人 a person of many

accomplishments;

一個人 a person;

一伙人 a group of people;

一家人 all of the same family; members of a family;

一類人 a sort of person;

一批人 a body of people; a group of people; a number of people;

一群人 a band of people; a class of of people; a clump of people; a crowd of people; a gang of people; a group of people; a horde of people; a multitude of people; a pack of people; a shoal of people; a stack of people; a swarm of people; a team of people; a throng of people; an army of people;

一人 one man; one person;

一種人 a kind of person; a kind of people;

伊朗人 Iranian;

伊人 that person;

宜人 agreeable; delightful; pleasant;

異人 (1) person of extraordinary talents; unusual person; extraordinary person; idiosyncratic person; (2) stranger;

意大利人 Italian;

意中人 person of one's heart; the person one is in love with;

役於人 serve others;

邑人 people of the same county;

易人 change a person;

義人 righteous man;

藝人 actor; artist; entertainer; performing artist; professional player;

因人 (1) depend on others; (2) vary with each individual;

陰人 woman;

引路人 guide;

引人 induce sb;

印第安人 American Indian;

印度尼西亞人 Indonesian;

印度人 Indian;

英國人 British;

迎人 meet sb with;

庸人 deadhead; dead loss; mediocre person;

傭人 servant;

用人 (1) servant; (2) employ people;

幽人 hermit; recluse;

優人 actor;

尤人 blame others;

游人 tourist; visitor;

友人 friend;

有人 (1) some people; somebody; someone; (2) there is sb there;

有身分的人 a man of condition;

有心人 (1) a person who sets his mind on doing sth useful; (2) an observant and conscientious person;

有毅力的人 a man of backbone;

誘人 attract;

於人 to others;

娛人 make sb happy;

愚人 fool; simpleton;

虞美人 corn poppy;

漁人 fisherman;

與人 with people;

玉人 (1) beautiful woman; (2) lapidary;

語人 tell others;

原告人 plaintiff; prosecutor;

原人 ape-man;

原始人 primitive man;

猿人 ape-man;

悦人 delightful; pleasant; pleasing;

越南人 Vietnamese;

粵人 Cantonese;

在家人 layman;

債權人 creditor;

債務人 debtor;

載人 manned;

責人 blame others;

賊人 corned beef; robber; thief;

譖人 slander others;

掌舵人 helmsman;

丈人 (1) respectful form of address for an old man; (2) father-in-law; one's wife's father;

召集人 convener;

找人 look for sb;

哲人 philosopher; sage;

貞人 person of high moral standing and integrity;

真人 (1) immortal; (2) real person;

枕邊人 wife;

證婚人 chief witness at a wedding ceremony;

證明人 certifier;

證人 witness;

知人 know people;

知心人 bosom friend;

至人 (1) man of virtue; sage; saint; (2) perfect man;

智利人 Chilean;

中國人 Chinese;

中間人 mediator; middleman;

中年人 middle-aged person;

中人 agent; go-between; intermediary; mediator; middleman;

仲裁人 arbitrator;

眾人 all people; everybody; many people; the

multitude;
舟人 boatman;
咒人 curse people;
主持人 host; presider;
主婚人 person who presides over a wedding ceremony;
主講人 speaker;
主人 host; master; owner;
助人 help others;
鑄人 educate and influence people;
抓人 arrest sb;
專人 specially assigned person;
賺人 cheat sb;
撞人 burst into; thrust into;
捉刀人 ghostwriter;
梓人 architect; builder; carpenter; wood engraver;
字人 become engaged;
自己人 one of us; people on our own side;
自然人 natural person;
宗人 people of the same clan;
走人 leave;
揍人 slug a person;
族人 clansman; fellow clansmen;
罪人 (1) guilty person; offender; sinner; (2) blame others;
醉人 get oneself drunk;
作人 (1) get along with other people; (2) behave oneself properly; pleasant in manner;
做人 (1) conduct oneself in society; (2) be a decent person;

ren

【仁】 (1) benevolence; charity; human-heartedness; humanity; kindheartedness; kindness; mercy; (2) sensitive; (3) kernel;

[仁愛] kindheartedness;
仁愛之心 kindness;

[仁慈] benevolent; clemency; kind; merciful;
仁慈的 big-hearted; lenient;
仁慈之心 benevolence;
閑淑仁慈 reserved, modest and gracious;

[仁德] benevolence; charity; humanity; kindness; magnanimity;

[仁弟] my dear friend;

[仁果] a kind of fruit;

[仁厚] benevolent and generous;

[仁人] benevolent person;
仁人君子 a benevolent and perfect man; a kindly man of high character; benevolent gentlemen; men of goodwill;
仁人志士 kind and upright men; men and women with high ideals; people with lofty ideals;

[仁心] charity; kindheartedness; kindness;
仁心仁術 with both a benevolent mind and healing art;
仁心仁聞 a good reputation for kindness;

[仁兄] my dear friend;

[仁言利博] words benefit universal benevolence;

[仁義] kindheartedness and justice;
仁義道德 benevolence, righteousness and virtue; humanity, justice and virtue; justice and morality; kindness and magnanimity; virtue and morality;
~口裏仁義道德，心中另盜女娼 fine words dress ill deeads; the friar preaches against stealing and has a goose in his sleeve;
仁義禮智 the four cardinal virtues; humanity, justice, propriety and wisdom;
仁義之師 army of justice;
假仁假義 a wolf in lamb's skin; a wolf in sheep's clothing; don a pious mask; hypocrisy; pass the bottle of smoke; pretend to be the paragon of virtue; sham benevolence and righteousness; sham kindness and goodness;
仁至義盡 do everything called for by humanity and duty; do what is humanly possible to help; exercise great restraint and do one's very best; show extreme patience and magnanimity; show the utmost tolerance and patience; with the utmost patience and magnanimity;
無仁無義 with neither a sense of humanity nor of right;

[仁者] benevolent person;
仁者見仁，智者見智 each according to his lights; the benevolent see benevolence and the wise see wisdom — different people have different views;
仁者無敵 the benevolent has no enemy; the benevolent is invincible;
仁者樂山，智者樂水 a true man loves the mountains, a wise man loves the sea;

[仁政] benevolent government;

不仁 (1) heartless; (2) numb;
成仁 die for a righteous cause;
果仁 kernel;
核仁 (1) nucleolus; (2) kernel of a fruit-stone;
麻仁 hemp seed;
松仁 (1) peach kernel; (2) shelled walnut; walnut meat;
蝦仁 shelled fresh shrimps; shrimp meat;
杏仁 almond; apricot kernel;
種仁 kernel;

ren

【壬】 (1) Ninth of the Ten Celestial Stems; (2) artful and crafty; (3) great; (4) pregnant;

[壬人] cunning deceiver; artful person;

ren

【任】 a surname;

ren³

ren

【忍】 (1) bear; endure; put up with; stand; suffer; tolerate; (2) hardhearted enough to; have the heart to; merciless; (3) forbear; repress;

[忍悲強笑] master one's emotions and force one's voice to a jocular tone;

[忍垢] live in disgrace; live in shame;

忍垢貪生 allow oneself to be insulted to remain alive;

[忍饑] endure hunger;

忍饑熬渴 endure hunger and thirst; put up with hunger and thirst;
忍饑受寒 tighten one's belt;

[忍俊不禁] cannot avoid laughing at; cannot help chuckling; cannot help laughing; cannot help smiling; cannot hold back a smile; cannot repress one's smile; impossible to keep a straight face; impossible to keep one's face straight; laugh in spite of oneself; make sb laugh up his sleeve; simmer with laughter;

[忍淚] hold back one's tears;

忍淚吞聲 choke down one's tears;

[忍耐] endure; exercise patience; exercise restraint; put up with; restrain oneself; tolerant of;

忍耐到底 endure to the end;
忍耐脅迫 stress tolerance;
無法忍耐 beyond forbearance; out of patience;

[忍氣] restrain one's indignation;

忍氣吞聲 control oneself and suppress one's indignation; eat dirt; eat humble pie; eat one's leek; endure without protest; hold back one's anger and say nothing; keep quiet and swallow the insults; pocket an insult; restrain one's anger and abstain from saying anything; restrain one's anger and keep silence; restrain one's indignation; restrain one's temper and say nothing; submit to humiliation; suffer indignities without a protest; supress one's groans; swallow insult and humiliation silently; swallow one's anger; swallow one's pride and endure in silence; swallow one's resentment and dare say nothing; swallow one's wrath and not dare to speak; swallow the insults in meek submission;
忍得一時氣，免得百日憂 to repress a moment's anger may save you a hundred days of sorrow; retraining momentary anger may save a hundred years of sorrow;

[忍讓] exercise forbearance; forbear; forbearing and conciliatory;

忍讓求全 show oneself forbearing and conciliatory for the sake of the common good;
互相忍讓 have forbearance for each other;

[忍辱] bear disgrace and insults; endure contempt;

忍辱報仇 put up with an insult in order to take revenge;
忍辱負重 bear disgrace and a heavy load; bear responsibility and blame; discharge one's duties conscientiously in spite of slanders; discharge one's important duties conscientiously in spite of insults; endure all disgrace and insults in order to accomplish a task; endure humiliation in order to carry out an important mission; grin and bear it; swallow humiliation and bear a heavy load;
忍辱含垢 bite the dust; eat humble pie;

kiss the dust; passively accept insults and humiliations; pocket an insult; silently endure all the disgrace and humiliations; swallow an insult;

忍辱謀勝 stoop to conquer; stoop to win;

忍辱求全 swallow insults for the sake of the common good;

忍辱貪生 allow oneself to be insulted to remain alive;

忍辱偷生 allow oneself to be insulted to remain alive; live on, bearing one's shame;

含垢忍辱 eat dirt; endure disgrace and humiliation;

[忍受] abide; bear; endure; forbear; live up with; lump; put up with; sit down under; stand; suffer; tolerate; undergo;

忍受悲傷 bear up the grief;

忍受不幸 bear up against misfortune;

忍受侮辱 swallow an insult;

不能忍受 unbearable;

默默地忍受 endure quietly;

耐心地忍受 endure patiently;

難以忍受 insufferable; intolerable;

[忍死] hold on to life and save it for some worthy cause; live when one would rather die;

[忍涕] hold back one's tears;

[忍痛] bear the pain reluctantly; suffer pain with dignity;

忍痛割愛 bear pain to give up sth one cares for very much; endure pains silently to give away what one loves; part reluctantly with what one treasures;

忍痛犧牲 reluctantly give up;

[忍無可忍] at the end of one's forbearance; at the end of one's patience; be driven beyond the limits of forbearance; bear the unbearable; beyond all bearing; beyond endurance; come to the end of one's patience; enough to try the patience of a saint; it would try the patience of a saint; out of patience; pass bearing; pass endurance; unable to bear it any longer;

[忍笑] hold back laughter; stifle a laugh;

[忍心] hardhearted; have the heart to; merciless; steel one's heart; unfeeling;

忍心害理 commit a crime in cold blood; do a cruel thing in cold blood; so malicious as to violate justice; ruthless and devoid of human feelings;

忍心撇開 have the heart to leave sb;

於心何忍 how can one bear it in one's heart; how can one bear to do it; how can one have the heart to do it;

[忍性] forcibly restrain one's temper;

[忍住] restrain;

忍住不說 hold fire;

忍住憤怒 hold back one's anger; fight back one's indignation;

忍住眼淚 hold back one's tears; fight back one's tears;

忍不住 be driven beyond the limits of forbearance; beyond endurance; can't help doing sth; can't put up with sth any longer; cannot bear; cannot stand; cannot tolerate sth any longer; come to the end of one's patience; have enough of; have no time for; not to brook; unable to bear; unable to stand; worn out;

~ 忍不住大笑起來 cannot refrain from laughing;

忍不住笑 cannot refrain from laughing;

忍得住 bearable; endurable; put up with;

安忍 endure patiently;

百忍 great endurance; great forbearance;

不忍 cannot bear to; cannot endure;

殘忍 brutal; brutality; cruel; cruelty; merciless; ruthless;

堅忍 steadfast and preserving;

容忍 put up with; tolerate;

濡忍 be forbearing; be tolerant;

隱忍 bear insults; bear patiently; bottom up one's resentment; forbear;

ren

【荏】 (1) perilla ocimoides, a kind of plant whose seeds are a bird feed; (2) fragile; soft; weak;

[荏苒] elapse quickly; pass imperceptibly in the course of time; slip by;

[荏弱] fragile; soft; weak;

ren

【稔】 (1) harvest; ripening of paddy; (2) familiar with sb; (3) used to;

[稔亂] turmoil brewing for a long time;

[稔膩] plump and smooth-skinned;

[稔色] (1) beauty; charm; (2) have a weakness for women;
[稔熟] ripe; know sb well;
[稔知] familiar; know sb quite well;

豐稔 reap a bump harvest;
熟稔 be very familiar with sb; know sb very well;
素稔 have long been familiar with sb;

ren⁴

ren

【刃】 (1) blade of a knife; edge of a knife; (2) kill with a knife or sword; (3) knife; sword;
[刃銼] edge file;
[刃兒] blade of a knife; edge of a knife;
[刃鋼] shear-steel;
[刃剪] snip;
曲刃剪 hawkbill snips;
歪柄直刃剪 handle side straight blades snips;
彎刃剪 curved blades snips;
[刃具] cutting tool;
[刃口] cutting edge;

白刃 naked blade; naked sword; naked weapon; sharp knife;
刨刃 plane iron;
兵刃 arms;
刀刃 blade;
鋒刃 sharp sword;
劍刃 edges of a sword;
開刃 put the first edge on a knife or a pair of scissors;
利刃 sharp sword;
手刃 kill with one's own hand; stab sb to death;

ren

【仞】 (1) measure of length; (2) measure depth;

ren

【任】 (1) appoint; (2) assume a post; employ; take up a job; (3) official; office; (4) allow; give free rein to; let; (5) no matter;
[任謗任勞] give no thought to slander but shoulder one's burdens manfully;
[任便] as you like; as you see fit;
[任達] unrestrained;
[任何] any, whatever; whichever;
任何人 any man alive;
[任咎] take upon oneself all the blame;
[任課] teach a course;
[任勞任怨] bear all the toil and all the blame; bear any hardship without complaint; do everything without complaint; do sth without complaint despite hardships and criticisms; endure hard work and suffer the complaints of others; fulfil one's duties faithfully and energetically; willingly bear the burden of office; work hard and not be upset by criticism; work hard regardless of criticism; work hard without complaint; hardworking and uncomplaining;
[任免] appoint and dismiss; appoint and remove; employment and discharge; hiring and firing;
任免權 power of appointment and removal;
任免行政人員 appoint and remove administrative personnel;
[任命] appoint; commission; designate; nominate;
任命狀 certificate of appointment;
辭去任命 give up an appointment; throw up an appointment;
放棄任命 forgo one's commission;
接受任命 accept the appointment; agree to the appointment;
取消任命 withdraw an appointment;
謝絕任命 decline an appointment;
一項任命 an assignment;
[任憑] (1) at one's convenience; at one's discretion; (2) despite; no matter what;
任憑風浪起，穩坐釣魚船 never mind the storm, just sit tight in the fishing boat — hold one's ground despite pressure or opposition; sit tight in the fishing boat despite the rising wind and waves — face danger with confidence;
[任期] incumbency; tenure; tenure of office; term of office; term of service;
任期將滿 at the end of one's incumbency;
任期屆滿 complete one's tenure of office; complete one's term of office;
任期目標 goals set for one's term of office;

教師任期 teacher tenure;
教員任期 academic tenure;
結束任期 wind up one's term of service;
終身任期 life tenure;

[任氣] be influenced by emotion;
任氣敢為 act recklessly; give the reins to one's passion;

[任情] as much as one likes; do as one pleases; let oneself go; to one's heart's content;
任情縱欲 give rein to lusts;

[任人] let people do sth without restriction;
任人擺布 allow oneself to be ordered about; at the mercy of others; be left to the tender mercies of others; under sb's thumb;
任人欺凌 allow others to walk all over one;
任人唯親 appoint people by favouritism; appoint people on the basis of favouritism; cronyism; employ only the near and dear; give out post on grounds of personal favour; jobs for the boys; nepotism; only relatives are employed;
任人唯賢 appoint people according to their ability and political integrity; appoint people on their merits; employ only the worthy; select good men for service;
任人宰割 allow oneself to be trampled upon; be partitioned by others at will; be slived up by; be trampled upon at will; place oneself at the mercy of; submit oneself to the tender mercies of;

[任是] even if;

[任率] artless; ingenious; innocent and simple;

[任所欲為] give sb a free hand; let sb do as he pleases;

[任天] leave everything to fate;

[任務] assignment; duties; job; mission; responsibility; task;
任務程序編制 task programming;
任務觀點 get-it-over-and-done-with attitude; look on one's work simply as a task to be done; perfunctory attitude; routinist point of view;
任務管理 task management;
任務欄 taskbar;
多任務 multi-task;
~多任務系統 multi-tasking system;
煩人的任務 wearisome task;
趕任務 rush one's job;
艱難的任務 uphill task;
履行任務 carry out one's duties;
逃避任務 flinch from a task;
同時處理多項任務 multitask; multitasking;
完成任務 bring home the bacon; complete one's mission; finish one's task; fulfill a task; fulfill an assignment;
~超額完成任務 overfulfill a task;
委派任務 delegate duties;
一項任務 a task; an assignment;
原始任務 source task;
中心任務 central task;
主任務 main task;
總任務 general task;

[任俠] generous and chivalrous;
任俠好義 chivalrous and fond of assuming obligations;

[任性] capricious; headstrong; intractable; self-willed; unrestrained; wayward; wilful;
任性妄為 act in an arbitrary and reckless manner; give the reins to one's passion;
任性恣意 indulge in emotions;
做事任性 act from caprice;

[任選] optional;

[任意] arbitrarily, at will; just as one wishes; wantonly, wilfully;
任意擺布 do as one likes; manipulate at will; get sb by the short hairs; have sb under one's thumb; order sb about at will; push sb around as one wishes; rule at will; set sb by the short hairs; take sb by the short hairs; turn sb round one's little finger; twist sb round one's finger; wind sb round one's finger; wrap sb round one's finger;
任意編造 arbitrarily invent;
任意打擊 attack others as one pleases; wilfully attack;
任意捏造事實 indulge in pure fabrication;
任意欺侮 bully others at will;
任意球 free kick;
任意通行 free traffic;
任意歪曲歷史 wilful distortion of history;
任意誣蔑 wantonly vilify;
任意享樂 abandon oneself to pleasures;
任意性 arbitrariness;

~任意性狀語 optional adverbial;
任意漲價 raise prices arbitrarily;
任意仲裁 voluntary arbitration;

［任用］ appoint; assign sb to a post; employ; give one a post; hire;
超格任用 promote sb specially and not by rank of service;
定期任用 fixed-term appointment;

［任職］ hold a post; in office; in sb's employ; in the employ of sb; incumbency;
任職期滿 expiration of one's term of office;
堪任此職 suitable for appointment to a post; worthy to fill a post;
堪任重職 adequate for an important post;

［任重］ the task is heavy;
任重道遠 it is a long-term, arduous task to; it is an arduous task and the road is long; one's task is heavy and one's road long; take a heavy burden and embark on a long road; the task is heavy and the road is long — shoulder heavy responsibilities;
位高任重 privilege entails responsibility; rank imposes obligation;

［任縱］ unrestrained;

常任 permanent; standing;
充任 fill the post of; hold the position of;
出任 take up the post of;
擔任 (1) act as; serve as; (2) assume the office of; hold the post of;
到任 assume a post; assume office; take up an official post;
調任 be transferred to another post;
返任 return to one's post;
放任 let alone; let things drift; not interfere;
復任 return to one's former office; take up a position one held formerly;
赴任 be on the way to one's post; go to one's post;
改任 change to another post;
後任 successor;
候任 designate;
級任 teacher in charge of a grade;
己任 one's duty;
繼任 (1) succeed; succeed sb in a post; (2) successor;
兼任 (1) hold a concurrent post; (2) part-time;
接任 accede; replace; succeed; take over; take over from sb;
就任 assume one's post; take office; take up one's post;
離任 leave one's post;
涖任 assume office;
歷任 have successively held the posts of; successively;
連任 be reappointed; be reelected; renew one's term of office;
留任 hold over; remain in office; retain a post;
聘任 appoint to a position; engage;
前任 ex-; former; precursor; predecessor;
親任 one's confidants;
去任 leave a post; resign from a post;
榮任 have the honour of being appointed to a post;
上任 take up an official post;
勝任 able to do sth; be qualified to do sth; capable of doing sth; competent for sth; equal to sth; feel equal to sth; feel up to sth; fit for sth; qualify for sth; up to sth;
首任 the first to be appointed to an office;
聽任 allow; leave free; let; let sb do whatever he likes;
委任 appoint; nominate;
無任 extremely; immensely;
徙任 be transferred to another post; change to another post;
現任 (1) at present hold the office of; (2) currently in office; incumbent; present;
卸任 be relieved of one's office;
新任 newly appointed; newly sworn-in;
信任 be credited with; believe; believe in; bring sb into one's confidence; confide in; credence; give credit; have confidence in; have faith in; have trust in; trust; trust in;
續任 reappoint; reappointment;
選任 choose and appoint;
一任 (1) allow; (2) term of service; tenure; tour;
膺任 be appointed to an office;
責任 (1) duty; responsibility; (2) responsibility for a fault or wrong;
職任 one's position in an office;
重任 heavy responsibility; important mission; important office; important post; important task;
主任 chairman; director; head;
專任 full-time; regular;
自任 appoint oneself to the key post; assume control personally; take personal command;

ren

【妊】 expecting; heavy with child; pregnant; with child;

[妊婦] expectant woman; pregnant woman;
[妊娠] conception; pregnancy;
妊娠囊 gestation sac;
妊娠嘔吐 vomiting of pregnancy;
妊娠疱疹 herpes gestationis;
任娠期 the gestation period; the pregnancy period;
妊娠試驗 pregnancy test;
妊娠子宮 gravid uterus;
單胎妊娠 monocyesis;
宮角妊娠 cornual pregnancy;
宮頸妊娠 cervical pregnancy;
宮外妊娠 extrauterine pregnancy;
過期妊娠 post-term pregnancy;
幻想妊娠 phantom pregnancy;
假妊娠 pseudogestation;
膜性妊娠 membranous pregnancy;
神經性妊娠 nervous pregnancy;
正常妊娠 encyesis;

ren
【紉】 (1) sew; stitch; (2) tie; wear; (3) twist; (4) rope; (5) massage; (6) feel deeply; (7) thread a needle;
[紉緝] mend; repair;
[紉佩] very grateful;
[紉針] thread a needle;

縫紉 sew; tailor;
感紉 be thankful; feel grateful;

ren
【恁】 (1) that; this; so; such; (2) how; what;
[恁般] to such an extent;
[恁的] (1) in this way; to such an extent; (2) how; why;
[恁時] then; when that happens;
恁時節 at that time; when that time comes;

ren
【衽】 (1) lapel of a garment; (2) sleeves; (3) arrange one's lapel; (4) sleeping mat; (5) bedding; place for sleeping;
[衽席] sleeping mat;

斂衽 curtsy;
襝衽 show one's respect by tidying up one's dress and sleeves;

ren
【軔】 (1) skid; (2) block; check; obstruct; (3) soft; (4) idle; (5) measure of length;
[軔固] firm and strong;

發軔 commence an undertaking; set sth afoot;

ren
【紝】 lay the warp; weave;

ren
【訒】 cautious in speech; difficult to speak out;

ren
【姙】 (1) collars; lapels; (2) sleeves; (3) bedding;

ren
【韌】 elastic; pliable but strong; soft but tough; tenacious;
[韌帶] ligament;
交叉韌帶 cruciate ligament;
全韌帶 amphidetic ligament;
十字韌帶 cruciate ligament;
弦音韌帶 chordotonal ligament;
[韌皮] the bast of a tree;
[韌性] (1) tenacity; (2) ductility; toughness;
[韌硬兼蓄] have both the quality of tenacity and hardness;

堅韌 (1) touch and tensile; (2) firm and tenacious;
柔韌 pliable and tough;

ren
【飪】 cook; prepare food;

烹飪 cook food;

ren
【認】 (1) identify; know; make out; recognize; understand; (2) adopt; enter into a certain relationship with; (3) admit; acknowledge; recognize; (4) accept as unavoidable; resign oneself to; (5) offer to do sth; promise to do sth; subscribe; undertake to do sth;
[認背] resign oneself to one's fate;
[認錯] acknowledge a mistake; admit a fault; admit a mistake; climb-down; make an apology;
抱愧認錯 blush at one's mistake; blush scarlet and apologize;
公開認錯 openly acknowledge one's fault;
死不認錯 stubbornly refuse to admit one's

guilt or mistake;

[認得] know; recognize;

[認定] (1) affirm; conclude; decide; firmly believe; hold; identify with; maintain; (2) set one's mind on;

[認罰] admit that one deserves punishment;

[認付] acceptance;
互相認付 cross acceptance;
局部認付 partial acceptance;
無條件認付 absolute acceptance;

[認購] buy; offer to buy; subscribe;
認購股票 subscribe shares;
認購人 subscriber;
認購債務 subscription register;

[認股權] subscription right;
認股權證 warrant;

[認捐] donate; subscribe;
認捐一筆款 undertake to contribute a sum;

[認可] accept; approve; confirm; countenance; give legal force to; ratify; sanction;
認可翻譯 recognized translation;
得到認可 gain credence;
得到一致認可 gain unanimous acceptance;
經當局認可 with approval of the authorities;
全面認可 blanket approval;

[認狼為犬] mistake a wolf for a dog; take a scoundrel for an honest man; take a wicked person for a good one;

[認領] claim; identify and claim;
認領失物 claim a lost article;

[認明] recognize; see clearly;

[認命] accept one's fate; admit that one's misfortune is predetermined by God; resign oneself to destiny;

[認親] acknowledge relationship;
認乾親 acknowledge the adopted relationship;

[認清] get a clear understanding of; identify clearly; know clearly; recognize; see clearly;
認清是非 make a clear distinction between right and wrong;
認清形勢 get a clear understanding of the situation;
認不清 unable to identify;

[認屍] identify a dead body;

[認識] (1) aware of; comprehend; familiar with; know; recognize; understand; (2) cognition; cognizance; knowledge; understanding;
認識功能 recognizing ability;
認識過程 process of cognition;
認識論 epistemology; theory of knowledge;
認識能力 cognitive ability;
認識水平 level of understanding;
感性認識 perceptual knowledge;
客觀認識 objective understanding;
理性認識 rational knowledge;
深刻的認識 a deep understanding of sth;
主觀認識 subjective understanding;

[認輸] admit defeat; concede defeat; give up; hang out the white flag; haul down one's colours; haul down one's flag; lower one's flag; show the white flag; strike one's flag; throw in the sponge; throw in the towel;
認輸投誠 admit defeat and go over to the other side;
不肯認輸 unwilling to acknowledge defeat;

[認同] identification; identify;
認同危機 crisis of identity; identity crisis;
民族認同 national identity;
社會認同 social identity;
身份認同 identity;
~建立身份認同 identity building;
文化認同 cultural identity;

[認頭] (1) consent with much reluctance; (2) endure passively;

[認為] according to sb; account...as; allow...to be; as far as sb can tell; as far as sb is concerned; as sb sees it; be of the opinion; believe...to be; consider it + adjective; consider...as; consider...to be; count...as; deem it...; fancy; feel; for sb's money; for sb's part; have the idea that; hold ...to be; in sb's book; in sb's estimation; in sb's eye; in sb's opinion; in sb's submit; in sb's view; in the eyes of sb; in the opinion of; in the sight of sb; it appears to sb; it seems to sb that; it strikes sb; look upon...as; of the opinion that; presume...to be; put...down as; rate...as; reckon...as; reckon...as; reckon...to be; regard...as;

repute...to be; sb's submit is that...; see...as; set...down as; speak of...as; take...as; take...for; take...to be; think; think of...as; think that; think...to be; to sb's mind; to sb's thinking; treat...as; view...as;
認為某事對自己沒有好處 find no account in sth;
認為某事對自己有好處 find one's account in sth;
認為⋯重要 set great store by sth;
個人認為 personally hold that;
普遍認為 it is generally believed that;
我們認為 in our view;
[認許] acknowledge; approve;
[認賊] take a thief as...;
認賊為子 treat a thief as a son － mistake vain hope for reality;
認賊作父 adopt a gangster for a father; clasp an enemy to one's bosom; national betrayal; regard the enemy as kith and kin; take a rascal as one's benefactor; take foes for parents; take the foe for one's father; treat a thief as one's father;
[認帳] acknowledge a debt; admit a mistake; admit what one has said or done; confess what one has said or done;
不認帳 go back on one's word;
[認真] (1) earnest; conscientious; serious; (2) take seriously; take to heart;
認真對待 deal seriously with; get one's teeth into; sink one's teeth into; take...seriously;
認真負責 conscientious; intense devotion to duty;
認真工作 earnest about one's work;
認真其事 take the matter in earnest; take trouble with a matter;
認真思考 ponder deeply;
認真學習 earnest about one's study;
認真制止 put a firm check on;
辦事認真 conscientious in one's work;
不認真 not serious;
認認真真 in all seriousness;
[認證] authentication;
安全認證 safety authentication;
[認知] cognition;
認知的 cognitive;
認知法 cognitive approach;
認知範疇 cognitive category;
認知工程 cognitive engineering;
認知結構 cognitive structure;
認知科學 cognitive science;
認知心理學 cognitive psychology;
認知行為 cognitive behavior;
認知性對等 cognitive equivalence;
認知性翻譯 cognitive translation;
認知性功能 cognitive function;
認知意義 cognitive meaning;
[認字] (1) able to read; know how to read; literate; (2) learn to read individual characters;
[認罪] acknowledge one's fault; acknowledge one's guilt; admit one's guilt; plead guilty;
認罪書 statement of confession;
認罪態度 attitude toward admission of guilt;
被迫認罪 be forced to admit one's guilt;
不認罪 plead not guilty;
低頭認罪 hang one's head and admit one's guilt; plead guilty;
拒絕認罪 refuse to acknowledge one's fault;

reng¹
reng

【扔】 (1) hurl; throw; (2) abandon; cast aside; discard; get rid of; put aside; throw away;
[扔掉] cast aside; discard; throw away;
扔掉幻想 cast away illusions;
[扔過去] hurl over to the other side;
[扔開] dismiss from consideration;
扔開疑慮 dismiss doubts from one's mind;
[扔棄] discard; get rid of; throw away;
[扔下] abandon; leave behind; put aside; throw down;
扔下工作去約會 put one's work aside to go to one's date;

reng²
reng

【仍】 (1) as before; as usual; remain; remain the same; (2) and yet; still; yet; (3) again and again; over and over;
[仍舊] (1) as before; continue to be; remain the same; (2) still; yet;
[仍然] and yet; as...as ever; as before; as usual;

continue to be; despite; keep on; none the less; notwithstanding; remain; stay; still; yet;

[仍仍] (1) a great many; (2) dejected;

[仍是] still is;

頻仍 frequent; repeated;

reng

【礽】 blessing; bliss; happiness;

ri⁴

ri

【日】 (1) sun; (2) day; daytime; (3) day; (4) daily; every day; (5) Japan; (6) time;

[日安] good day;

[日班] day shift;

[日斑] sunspot;

[日報] daily; daily newspaper; daily paper;

星期日報 Sunday newspaper;

[日薄西山] approaching one's grave; at ons's last gasp; at the point of death; decline like the setting sun; fast declining; in one's later days; like the sun setting in the western hills — declining rapidly; nearing one's end; old age; on one's last legs; one's days are numbered;

[日晡] dusk; sundown; sunset;

[日不暇給] be fully occupied every day; be pressed for time; have insufficient time to attend to all things; have no time to spare; too many things to do in a day; very busy;

[日常] common; daily; day-to-day; everyday; ordinarily; usual;

日常保養 daily maintenance;

日常費用 current expenses; general expenses; running expenses;

日常工作 daily work; day-to-day work;

日常生活 daily life; everyday life;

日常事件 routine matters;

日常現象 phenomena of everyday life;

日常英語 everyday English;

日常用品 articles for daily use;

日常用語 words and expressions for everyday use;

日常語言 everyday language;

[日場] day show; daytime performance; matinee; matinee show;

[日程] agenda for the day; itinerary; programme; schedule;

[日出] rise; sunrise;

日出東方 the sun comes up in the east;

日出而起 get up at sunrise; rise with the sun;

日出而作 go to work at sunrise; rise with the lark; the sun comes forth and we work;

日出而作，日入而息 get up to work at sunrise and retire at sunset; start work at daybreak and retire at sunset;

日出三竿 late in the morning; the sun is three poles high;

日出星沒 the sun blinds the stars;

[日戳] (1) date stamp; dater; (2) datemark;

[日高霧消] the sun is high and the fog begins to diperse;

[日給] daily wages;

[日工] (1) daywork; (2) day labour; (3) day labourer;

計時日工 measured daywork;

[日光] daylight; sunbeam; sunlight; sunshine; the light of the sun;

日光燈 daylight lamp; fluorescent lamp;

日光房 sun lounge; sun porch;

日光能 solar energy;

日光浴 heliotherapy; sunbath;

人造日光 artificial daylight;

一道日光 sunbeam;

[日晷] dial; horologe; sundial;

日不移晷 for a very short time; in less than no time; on the spur of the moment;

日無暇晷 busy from morning to night; with no time to spare;

[日後] in days to come; in future;

[日暉] rays of the sun;

[日計] calculate by the day;

日計不足，歲計有餘 counting daily it is not much, but counting in a year, it makes quite a lot; time and patience beget success;

[日記] diary;

日記本 diary;

日記賬 journal;

~多欄日記賬 columnar journal;

~多欄式日記賬 calendar journal; split column journal;

~現金日記賬 cash journal;

~現金支出日記賬 cash payment journal;

~銀行存款日記賬 bank deposit journal;
日記作者 diarist;
查賬日記 audit diary;
工作日記 work diary;
記日記 keep a diary;
教師日記 teacher's diary;
教育日記 pedagogical diary;
視頻日記 video diary;
一篇日記 a diary;
一則日記 diary entry;
營業日記 business diary;

[日間] at daytime; during the day; in the daytime;
日間活動營 day camp;
日間遊覽 day excursion;

[日見] day by day; show day after day; with each passing day;

[日漸] day by day; with each passing day;
日漸好轉 get better everyday; improve day by day;
日漸起色 improve with each passing day; turn for the better steadily;
日漸強壯 get stronger and stronger;
日漸衰敗 decline day by day;
日漸衰落 become weaker and weaker day by day;
日漸完善 becoming better and approaching perfection day by day;
日漸壯大 be growing steadily;

[日進] constant improvement; improve with each passing day; increase with each passing day;
日進有功 making unremitting efforts to have some progress every day will result in bigger success;

[日久] in the course of time; with the passage of time;
日久弊生 abuses creep in with time;
日久腐爛 decay by time;
日久見人心 a long task proves the sincerity of a person; it takes time to know a person; time is a revealer of a person's sincerity; time reveals a man's heart; time will tell a true friend from a false one;
日久年深 after a long lapse of time; age-old; time-worn; with the passage of time;
日久情深 the longer they stay together the more passionately attach they become to each other;
日久生情 love will come in time;
日久生厭 as time goes on dislike may arise — incur odium in the course of time; familiarity begets contempt; the length of time will create dislike; time wears out one's interest in things;
日久天長 after a considerable period of time; as the years go by; for a long, long time; for keeps; for many, many years to come; in the course of time;
日久玩生 discipline tends to get lax as time goes by;
日久自明 time will show; time will tell;

[日刊] daily publication;

[日來] in recent days; the last few days;

[日理萬機] attend to hundreds of important matters every day; attend to numerous affairs of state every day; be occupied with a myriad of state affairs; busy with a myriad of state affairs every day; deal with hundreds of important problems every day;

[日裏] at daytime; in the daytime;

[日利] daily interest;

[日曆] calendar;
日曆年 calendar year;
日曆月 calendar month;
案頭日曆 desk calendar;
兒童日曆 children's calendar;
瞬跳日曆 instant-jump calendar;

[日糧] daily ration;

[日輪] solar disk;

[日落] sunset;
日落風清 a gentle breeze comes with the sunset;
日落酒 sundowner;
日落平西 the sun is level with the land in the west; the sun is level with the western horizon;
日落西山 the sun declines westward; the sun falls low in the sky; the sun sets in the west; the sun is setting in the west; the sun sinks behind the mountains; the sun sinks in the west;

[日冕] solar corona;
日冕儀 coronagraph;

[日沒] sunset;
日沒沉西 dusk; sundown; sunset;

[日暮] the day wanes;
日暮途窮 approach the end of one's days;

at one's wits' end; at the end of one's rope; at the end of one's tether; come to the end of one's rope; head for doom; in a desperate position; in one's decline; on one's last legs; reach the end of one's tether; the day is waning and the road is ending — approaching the end of one's days;
日暮途遠 have no one to turn to; in a desperate position;

[日內] in a couple of days; in a day or two; in a few days;

[日平西] dusk; sundown;

[日迫] get closer day by day; time is running out;

[日期] date;
日期戳 date stamp;
出版日期 publication date;
出廠日期 release date;
交貨日期 delivery date;
截止日期 closing date; cut-off date; deadline;
確定日期 fix a date; set a date;
確實日期 exact date; precise date;
實施日期 effective date;
天文日期 astronomical date;
選定日期 decide on a date;
最後日期 drop-dead date;

[日前] a few days ago; recently; the other day;

[日趨] day by day; gradually; with each passing day;
日趨惡劣 get worse day by day;
日趨繁榮 become more prosperous with each passing day;
日趨衰落 decline day by day;
日趨完善 become more consummate day by day;
日趨下流 sink lower and lower with each passing day;
日趨壯大 be growing steadily;

[日日] daily; every day;
日日新 daily renewal; daily renovation;
日復一日 day after day; day in and day out; day succeeds day; from day to day;
日甚一日 constant deterioration; getting more serious day after day; getting worse with each passing day; increase in intensity constantly; with increasing intensity; with growing intensity;

[日入而息] retire at sunset;

[日上三竿] late in the morning; the sun has climbed in the sky; the sun is high in the heavens; the sun is high in the sky; the sun is high up in the sky; the sun is well up;

[日食] what one eats daily;
日食艱難 live a hard life; live a straitened life;
日食三餐，夜眠一榻 eat one's three meals a day and sleep all night;
日食萬錢 live in extreme luxury; spend money lavishly;

[日蝕] eclipse of the sun; solar eclipse;
日全蝕 total solar eclipse;

[日天] one full day;

[日頭] (1) the sun; (2) daytime;

[日托] day care;
日托兒所 day nursery;

[日文] Japanese; the Japanese language;

[日夕] day and night;

[日息] daily interest;

[日下] at present;

[日校] day school;

[日新] daily renewal;
日新月盛 daily and monthly increasing;
日新月異 alter from day to day; bring about new changes day after day; change for the better day by day, and month by month; change rapidly; change with each passing day; continuous improvement; every newer; flourish with each passing day; incessant changes in; never-ending changes and improvements; sth new all the time;

[日薪] day wages;

[日星] the sun and the stars;
昭如日星 as evident and obvious as the sun and the stars;

[日夜] day and night; night and day; round the clock;
日夜不安 have no peace day or night; one's heart is not at ease day and night; suffer without any respite;
日夜不寧 restless by day and sleepless by night;
日夜操勞 exert oneself day and night; labour day and night; work indefatigably day and night; work round the clock;

日夜服務 24-hour service;
日夜兼程 press forward day and night; travel day and night;
日夜苦幹 work double tides;
日夜盼望 look for sb day and night; long day and night for;
日夜商店 day and night shop;
日夜辛勞 labour day and night;
把夜當日 turn night into day;
沒日沒夜 day and night; night and day;
日長夜短 days are long and nights short; the day gains on the night; the days are long and the nights short;
日短夜長 days are short and nights long; the days are short and the nights long; the night gains on the day;
日日夜夜 by day and by night; day and night; morning, noon, and night; night and day;
日以繼夜 continuously; day and night; day in and day out; incessantly; night and day without ceasing; round the clock; stay up till dawn;
夜以繼日 around the clock; day and night; double tides; night and day; night succeeds day; round the clock;
以日當夜 make the day serve as night;

[日益] day by day; increasingly; more and more; with each passing day;
日益猖獗 becoming increasingly rampant;
日益粗暴 be increasingly rude;
日益繁榮 becoming flourishing day by day; more prosperous day by day;
日益高漲 evergrowing; grow to every greater heights; move from peak to peak; on the rise; surge to great heights;
日益尖銳 becoming increasingly acute;
日益艱難 be increasingly difficult;
日益進步 showing improvement or progress day by day;
日益強大 be more powerful day by day;
日益深入人心 gain more and more popularity; sink deeper and deeper into people's hearts;
日益嚴峻 becoming increasingly grave;
日益壯大 get stronger day by day; grow from strength to strength; grow stronger day by day; grow stronger each day; steadily grow in strength;

[日用] (1) daily expenses; (2) of everyday use;
日用電器 domestic electrical appliance;
日用工業品 industrial consumer goods; manufactured goods for daily use;
日用開支 general expenses;
日用品 articles of daily use; articles of everyday use; consumer goods; daily necessities;
日用消費品 goods for everyday consumption;
貼補日用 help out the daily expenses;

[日有所思，夜有所夢] if one is thinking about sth when awake, one will continue thinking about it in one's dreams; one dreams at night what one thinks in the day; what one thinks about in the day, one will dream of it at night; what you think about during the day, you dream about at night;

[日語] Japanese;

[日元] yen;

[日月] (1) the sun and the moon; (2) life; livelihood; living; (3) time; (4) saints and sages; (5) emperors and emperesses;
日月蹉跎 the days and months are slipping by;
日月重光 the sun and the moon shine again — bring it to light again;
日月合璧 high in the sky hang sun and moon;
日月經天 as everlasting as the sun and the moon;
日月經天，江河行地 as immutable as the sun, the moon and the rivers — last for ever; eternally unchanging, like the sun and moon passing through the sky or the river flowing across the land; like the sun and moon that move in the sky, or the rivers that flow on the earth — eternal;
日月麗天 the sun and the moon hang in the firmament;
日月如梭 days and months flash by quickly as a weaver's shuttle; days and months fly like a shuttle; the sun and the moon move back and forth like a shuttle — time flies; time flies like a shuttle; time passes as quickly as a shuttle — time passes quickly;
日月入懷 omen of the birth of a son;
日月同輝 shine forever like the sun and

the moon;
~與日月同輝 shine for ever like the sun and the moon;
日月無光 the sun and the moon are dimmed; the sun gives forth no more of its light;
日月星辰 the heavenly bodies; the host of heaven; the sun, the moon and the stars;
日月永照 shine forever like the sun and the moon;
日月爭光 compete with the sun and the moon in light; equal the sun and the moon in glory;
~與日月爭光 compete with the sun and the moon in light; equal the sun and the moon in glory;
敢叫日月換新天 dare to change the sun and moon into a new face; the sun and moon must do their bidding;
功照日月 one's achievements outshine the sun and moon;
光照日月 shine like the sun and the moon;
日就月將 gradual advances; improve with the day; make steady and continual progress; progress with the day; with steady progress from day to day and from month to month;
日居月儲 the elapsing of time; time runs on; with the passage of time;
日昇月恒 daily increasing in prosperity; ever increasing; ever growing; ever prosperous; ever rising; growing prosperous day by day; the sun is rising and the moon waxing — in the ascendant;
日省月試 subject to constant supervision and testing;
日削月峻 be exploited unceasingly and become more and more impoverished; exploit the people;
日增月益 daily increasing and monthly benefitting;

[日暈] solar halo;
日暈主雨 a solar halo means rain;
[日照] sunshine;
[日支] daily expenditure; daily expenses;
[日誌] daily record; journal;
[日中] high noon; midday; noon;
[日子] (1) date; day; (2) days; duration; time; (3) life; livelihood; living;
日子過得怎樣 how's it going;
日子混不下去 difficult to keep on going;
日子越來越不好過 find life getting tougher every day; find things increasingly difficult for; things keep getting harder and harder;
挨日子 drag out a miserable existence; eke out a living; go through hard times; suffer day after day; through one's days in misery;
熬日子 endure hard days; go through hard times; suffer and endure endless days;
大喜日子 one's red-letter day; one's wedding-day;
過苦日子 have a hard time;
過日子 get along; live;
~靠工資過日子 live on one's salary;
~靠養老金過日子 live on one's pension;
~勤儉過日子 live industriously and frugally;
好日子 (1) auspicious day; (2) wedding day; (3) happy life;
~過好日子 lead a happy life;
混日子 drift along; hack around; loaf away; muddle along;
~糊里糊塗混日子 drift aimlessly through life;
~無所事事地混日子 drift about doing nothing;
緊日子 austere life;
~過緊日子 lead a thrifty life; practise austerity;
前些日子 not too long ago; those days;
窮日子 days of poverty; in reduced circumstances; in straitened circumstances; poverty-stricken days; the miserable life of a poor fellow;
虛度日子 trifle away one's time;
有日子 (1) for days; for quite a few days; (2) have fixed a date;
[日昨] yesterday;
[日坐愁城] in deep worry all day long; in deep worry every day;

按日 daily; every day;
白日 (1) daylight; daytime; (2) the sun;
百日 the hundredth day after one's death;
半日 (1) half a day; (2) half-day;
本日 today;
蔽日 cover the sun from view; dull the sunlight;
不日 in a few days' time; within the next few days;

赤日 red sun;
春日 spring days;
次日 next day;
單日 odd-numbered days;
當日 that very day; the same day;
冬日 winter sun; wintry day;
度日 eke out an existence; make a living; pass the day; spend the day; subsist;
改日 another day; some other day;
工日 workday;
工作日 weekday; workday; working day;
穀日 eighth day of the first month in the lunar calendar;
紅日 red sun
吉日 lucky or auspicious day;
即日 (1) this or that very day; (2) within the next few days;
集日 market day;
計日 count in days; reckon by the day;
忌日 anniversary of the death of a parent, ancestor or anyone else held in esteem;
假日 day off; holiday;
間日 every other day;
結算日 account day;
節日 festival; holiday; red-letter day;
今日 (1) today; (2) now; present;
近日 (1) in the past few days; recently; (2) within the next few days;
竟日 whole day;
舊日 former days; old days;
克日 by a fixed date;
來日 (1) coming days; days ahead; days to come; time ahead; (2) tomorrow;
累日 day after day; for days;
曆日 calendar day;
連日 day after day; for days on end;
烈日 burning sun; scorching sun;
淩日 transit;
落日 setting sun;
每日 everyday;
明日 (1) tomorrow; (2) near future;
末日 (1) Judgment Day; (2) doom; end;
年日 days and years;
寧日 peaceful days;
平日 ordinary days;
前日 the day before yesterday;
全日 full-time;
人日 seventh day of the first month;
如日 like the sun;
閏日 leap day;
三日 three days;
上日 (1) first day of the lunar month; (2) festive day;
生日 birthday;
時日 (1) time and date; (2) long duration of time;
是日 that day; this day;
數日 a few days; several days;
曙日 in the morning;
霜日 frost day;
雙日 even-numbered days;
朔日 first day of a lunar month;
素日 generally; usually;
宿日 former days;
歲日 years and days;
他日 later on; some other day; some other time; some time in the future;
天日 day; light; the sky and the sun;
天文日 astronomical day;
通日 all day long;
往日 in bygone days; in former days; in the olden days; in the past;
望日 fifteenth day of a lunar month;
無日 (1) not a single day; (2) soon;
昔日 former times;
暇日 days of leisure; free days; leisure; spare time;
夏日 (1) summer days; (2) summer sun;
向日 (1) sunward; (2) in former days; in the past;
煦日 (1) warm sun; (2) warm and fine day;
旭日 rising sun;
曛日 setting sun;
旬日 ten days;
一日 one day; such a day;
異日 (1) another day; some other day; (2) bygone days; former days;
翌日 following day; next day; tomorrow;
翼日 next day;
陰日 overcast day;
映日 bright sunlight;
永日 all the day; long day;
逾日 pass a day;
雨日 rainy day;
與日 with time;
浴日 (1) bright sunrise; (2) great distinction; great exploits;
月日 month and day;
越日 following day;
雲日 clouds and light; clouds and the sun;
早日 at an early date; early; soon;
擇日 choose a good day;
朝日 morning sun; rising sun;
鎮日 all day long; whole day;
整日 all day long; whole day;
隻日 odd days of a lunar month;

指日 in a few days; in a matter of days;
值日 on duty for the day; one's turn to be on duty;
至日 winter and the summer solstices;
終日 all day long; from morning till night; throughout the day;
周日 (1) weekday; (2) diurnal;
晝日 day; daytime;
逐日 daily; day after day; day by day; every day;
主日 Sunday;
昨日 yesterday;

rong²

rong

【戎】 (1) fighting; war; (2) arms; the apparatus of war; (3) army; military affairs; (4) barbarians living in the western part of China in ancient times; (5) great; (6) help; (7) a surname;

[戎車] chariot; war vehicle;
[戎服] military dress;
[戎路] chariot; war vehicle;
[戎旅] the army;
[戎馬] army horse;
戎馬倉猝 have a hectic military career; in the urgent moment of fighting; lead a hectic life with war horses;
戎馬倥傯 be burdened with pressing military duties; soldiers and horses are in great haste — busily engaged in warfare; have a hectic military career; lead a hectic life with war horses;
戎馬生涯 a military career; a military life; an army life;
戎馬之間 among war-horses; on the fighting line;
[戎蠻] ancient barbarians;
[戎器] arms; weapons;
[戎士] enlisted men; soldiers;
[戎事] military affairs;
[戎裝] martial attire; military dress; military uniform;
戎裝打扮 clad in uniform; in military dress;

兵戎 arms; weapons;
從戎 enlist; join the army;
元戎 supreme commander;

rong

【肜】 ancient sacrificial ritual lasting two successive days;

rong

【容】 (1) contain; hold; (2) forbear; tolerate; (3) forgive; pardon; (4) allow; permit; (5) countenance; face; facial expression; (6) appearance; looks; (7) a surname;

[容不下] unable to accommodate; unable to contain; unable to hold; unable to take in;
[容待] let's wait a minute;
[容光] facial expression; general appearance;
容光煥發 be aglow with health; glow with health; look like a million dollars; in radiating health; one's face glows with health; radiant;
容光煥發，神采奕奕 brim with health and in excellent spirits; glow with health and in high spirits; in buoyant and high spirits;
[容或] may be; perhaps; possibly;
容或有之 perhaps there is a capacity for such an affair; there may be a grain of truth in it; within the bounds of possibility;
[容積] bulk; dimension; content; dimension; holding capacity; volume;
容積變化 volume change;
容積計 volumeter;
表觀容積 apparent volume;
電荷容積 charge volume;
細胞容積 cell volume;
餘隙容積 clearance volume;
[容接] receive guests;
[容量] capacity; measurement; volume;
容量分析 volumetric analysis;
包裝容量 bale capacity;
計算容量 calculated capacity;
絕對容量 absolute capacity;
卡片容量 card capacity;
毛細管容量 capillary capacity;
熱容量 heat capacity;
設備容量 apparatus capacity;
天線容量 aerial capacity;
通路容量 channel capacity;
有效容量 actual capacity;
總容量 total capacity;
[容貌] appearance; countenance; features; lineament; looks;
容貌醜陋 have an ugly appearance; have

poor features;
容貌出眾 superior in looks;
容貌端正 have proper facial features;
容貌端莊 have regular facial features;
容貌漸老 be losing one's looks;
容貌姣美 have fine features; have nice features;
容貌流盼 have alluring eyes and exquisite features;
容貌迷人 have attractive features; have charming features;
容貌拼圖 composite;
容貌清秀 have delicately-modelled features;
容貌秀麗 charming appearance; pretty;
容貌一般 have an ordinary appearance; have plain features; ordinary in one's appearance;
容貌英俊 have a handsome appearance; have a handsome countenance; have handsome features;
容貌整潔 one's person is neat and trim;
~ 保持容貌整潔 keep one's person neat and trim;
都雅容貌 elegant feature;
改容易貌 change one's looks and appearance; one's face changes its hue;
毀掉容貌 mutilate one's features; mutilate the features of sb;

[容納] (1) accommodate; contain; have a capacity of; hold; (2) take in; tolerate;
容納不同意見 tolerate different opinions;
容納動詞 verb of containing;

[容乞] ask permission for;

[容器] container; holder; pack; receiver; vessel;
低壓容器 low pressure vessel;
電解槽容器 cell container;
電容器 capacitor;
混合容器 blending container;
鋁箔容器 aluminum foil container;
密封容器 airtight container;
蓄電池容器 accumulator container;

[容情] forgiving; pardon; show mercy; spare;
毫不容情 make absolutely no allowance; mercilessly; not to pull any punches; without making any allowance

[容讓] give in; make a concession; yield;

[容人] broad-minded; magnanimous; tolerant towards others;
容人之過 tolerant of other people's faults;

[容忍] bear; brook; condone; endure; forbear; put up with; stand; tolerate;
零容忍 zero tolerance;

[容色] peaceful and happy countenance;
容色自若 keep an easy countenance;

[容身] shelter oneself;
容身無地 no place to set oneself in; no place to stay;
容身之地 a place to stay;
~ 無容身之地 no room for; nowhere to lay one's head; there is no place for one in society; with no place to hide;

[容事] have the capacity for work;

[容受] (1) able to contain; able to hold; (2) bear; endure; put up with;

[容恕] excuse; forgive; pardon;

[容圖後報] one will return another's kindness at a later date;

[容限] allowance; tolerance;

[容許] (1) admit; allow; allow of; brook; permit; tolerate; (2) perhaps; possibly;
法律容許 be allowed by the law;
如時間容許 if time permits;
欣然容許 willingly allow;

[容顏] appearance; facial appearance; looks;
容顏憔悴 a melancholy appearance; a sorrowful look;
容顏如玉 a face as beautiful as a flawless gem;
容顏失色 change of colour because of fear;
容顏衰老 lose one's good looks;

[容易] apt to; as easy as ABC; as easy as taking pennies from a blind man; as easy as taking toffee from a child; as easy as you know how; easily; easy; easy as pie; easy-peasy; likely, liable to;
容易變質 apt to deteriorate;
容易的事情 a piece of cake; child's play; easy job;
容易得罪人 liable to give offense;
容易發火 lose one's temper easily;
容易發怒 easy on the trigger;
容易發脾氣 liable to ifts of temper; prone to anger; subject to anger;
容易接近 easy of access;
容易實現的 easy of accomplishment;
非常容易 easy as one's eye;
好容易 have a hard time doing sth; with

great difficulty;
~好容易才找到這份工作 have a hard time finding the job;
極其容易 as easy as ABC; as easy as falling off a log; as easy as pie; as easy as rolling off a log;
説來容易做來難 easier said than done; saying and doing are two things; saying is one thing and doing another;
説時容易做時難 easier said than done;
談何容易 by no means easy; easier said than done; easy to talk, difficult to achieve; how easy it is to talk about it; it's no easy thing; not as easy as it sounds; not as easy as one thinks it to be;
原來很容易 turn out to be easy;

[容隱] hide; not to reveal; try to cover up;
[容與] (1) at ease with oneself; carefree; (2) act under no constraint; give free rein to;
[容悦] curry favour with; flatter; please;
[容止] appearance and manner; looks and carriage;
[容質俱美] both the looks and the disposition are elegant;
[容重] unit weight;

包容 (1) forgive; pardon; (2) contain; hold;
比容 specific volume;
病容 sickly look;
不容 not allow; not tolerate;
倉容 warehouse capacity;
愁容 anxious expression; worried look;
從容 (1) calm; leisurely; unhurried; (2) plentiful;
等容 constant volume;
電容 electric capacity;
動容 be visibly moved; change countenance;
咕容 wriggle;
涵容 bear with; forgive;
花容 woman's face;
毀容 disfigure;
兼容 compatible;
倦容 tired look;
軍容 soldier's discipline;
庫容 storage capacity;
寬容 bear with; lenient; tolerant; toleration;
斂容 assume a serious expression;
美容 (1) improve one's looks; (2) cosmetology; (3) beauty treatment;
面容 countenance; face; facial features;
內容 contents; materials; substance;
怒容 angry look; scowl;
慼容 sad look; sorrowful expression;
求容 seek room for oneself; seek space for oneself;
取容 try to please others;
悛容 look of repentance;
聲容 voices and appearances;
市容 the appearance of a city;
收容 accept; take in;
殊容 extraordinary beauty; stunningly beautiful face;
衰容 face of an old person;
相容 put up with; tolerate;
笑容 smiling expression;
形容 appearance; countenance; describe;
冶容 (1) seductive looks; (2) seductively made up;
儀容 appearance; looks;
遺容 (1) remains; (2) portrait of the deceased;
音容 (1) voice and countenance; (2) likeness of the decesased;
雍容 natural, graceful and poised;
憂容 sad look; worried look;
優容 treat with leniency; treat with magnanimity;
玉容 beautiful face;
御容 portrait of the emperor;
慍容 angry appearnace; displeased look; face of resentment;
陣容 (1) battle array; battle formation; (2) cast; lineup;
整容 perform face-lifting;
姿容 appearance; looks;
縱容 connive at; cosset; pamper; pass over; wink at;
尊容 your face;

rong

【茸】 (1) down; soft, fine hair; (2) downy; fluffy; soft; (3) confused; disorderly; messy; untidy; (4) lush; luxuriant;

[茸鞭] flimmer;
[茸角] antler;
[茸茸] downy; fine; soft and thick;
[茸尾] flag;

鹿茸 pilose antler;

rong

【毧】 (1) down; fine hair; (2) felt;

[毧帽] felt cap; felt hat;
[毧鞋] felt shoes;

rong

【絨】 (1) down; fine wool; velvet; woolen; (2) any kind of woolen goods or fabric with a felt-like surface; (3) fine; flossy; furry;

[絨布] cotton flannel; flannelette;

[絨花] velvet flowers;

[絨褲] sweat pants;

[絨毛] (1) down; fine hair; (2) nap; pile;
絨毛膜 chorion;
絨毛運動 ciliary movement;

[絨帽] wollen hat;
毛絨帽 bobble hat;
絨球帽 bobble;

[絨毯] falnnelette blanket;

[絨線] wool;
絨線帽 woolen hat;
一團絨線 a ball of wool;

[絨衣] sweat shirt;

艾絨 moxa;
鵝絨 goose down;
貉絨 raccoon dog fur;
火絨 tinder;
棉絨 cotton velvet;
呢絨 wool fabrics; woolen goods;
平絨 velveteen;
蒲絨 cattail wood, used for stuffing pillows;
絲絨 velvet;
天鵝絨 velvet;
條絨 corduroy;
駝絨 (1) camel's hair; (2) camel hair cloth;
鴨絨 duck's down; eiderdown;
植絨 flock;

rong

【羢】 fine wool;

rong

【溶】 (1) dissolve; melt; (2) having much water;

[溶點] melting point;

[溶洞] karst cave;

[溶合] mix by solution;

[溶化] dissolve; melt;
溶化熱 heat of fusion;
容易溶化 dissolve easily;

[溶混性] miscibility;
部份溶混性 partial miscibility;
水溶混性 water miscibility;
極限溶混性 limited miscibility;

[溶劑] dissolvant; resolvent; solvent;
活性溶劑 active solvent;
冷凍溶劑 chilled solvent;
兩性溶劑 amphiprotic solvent;

[溶膠] sol;
酪朊溶膠 casein sol;
親水溶膠 hydrophilic sol;
外來溶膠 extrinsic sol;

[溶解] dissolution; dissolve; melt;
溶解度 solubility;
~ 地層溶解度 formation solubility;
~ 退縮性溶解度 retrograde solubility;
~ 選擇溶解度 preferential solubility;
溶解器 dissolver;
~ 分批溶解器 batch dissolver;
~ 罐式溶解器 pot dissolver;
~ 環形溶解器 annular dissolver;
溶解熱 heat of solution;
溶解於水 dissolve in water;
分批溶解 batch dissolution;
無煙溶解 fumeless dissolution;

[溶菌] lysis;
溶菌素 bacteriolysin;
溶菌作用 bacteriolysis;

[溶開] separate by dissolution;

[溶媒] solvent;

[溶溶] broad; vast;

[溶入] dissolve in;

[溶體] solution;
固溶體 solid solution; sosoloid;

[溶血] hemolysis;
被動溶血 passive hemolysis;
反應性溶血 reactive hemolysis;
間接溶血 indirect;

[溶液] liquor; solution;
飽和溶液 saturated solution;
~ 過飽和溶液 supersaturated solution;
標準溶液 standard solution;
當量溶液 normal solution;
規定溶液 tandard solution;
膠體溶液 colloidal solution;
理想溶液 ideal solution;
實在溶液 actual solution;
酸溶液 acid solution;
吸收劑溶液 absorbent solution;

[溶質] solute;
揮發溶質 volatile;
兩性溶質 amphoteric solute;
相反溶質 opposite-type solute;

rong

【榕】 banyan tree;
［榕樹］ banyan tree;

rong

【榮】 (1) flourish; grow luxuriantly; lush; teeming; (2) glory; honour; (3) a surname;
［榮哀］ be honoured when alive and be lamented when dead;
榮哀錄 a collection of eulogies and commemorative writings in honour of an illustrious figure;
生榮死哀 be honoured when alive and be lamented when dead; lament at the death of a famous man; respected while living and mourned when dead;
［榮恥］ honour and dishonour;
［榮寵］ glorious favour;
［榮典］ honorary reward;
［榮光］ glory; splendour;
［榮歸］ return home in triumph; return in glory;
榮歸故里 return to one's hometown in glory; return to one's native place with honour;
［榮華］ glorious a glory and splendor; honour and glory; honour and splendor;
榮華紛褥 glorious and resplendent;
榮華富貴 glory, splendour, wealth and rank; high position and great wealth; honour and wealth; wealth and honour;
榮華美夢 the inebriation of prosperity;
榮華難永 honour and glory are hard to depend on for long;
［榮獲］ be awarded; get the honour; have the honour to get; win; win the honour;
榮獲冠軍 win the championship;
［榮軍］ disabled soldier;
［榮枯］ (1) flourishing and withering; (2) rise and fall; ups and downs;
榮枯得失 flourishing or decaying, gaining or losing; one's success and failure;
榮枯盛衰 the swing of the pendulum;
榮枯與共 flourishing or decaying, gaining or losing; one's success and failure;
春榮冬枯 grow in spring and wither in winter;
［榮美］ glorious and beautiful;
［榮民］ retired servicemen; veterans;
［榮名］ honour and fame;
［榮命］ have the honour of being appointed to a post;
［榮任］ have the honour of being appointed to a post;
榮任高職 be honourably appointed to a high post;
［榮辱］ honour and disgrace; honour and dishonour;
榮辱得失 honour or disgrace, gain or less;
榮辱盛衰 glory and humiliation; prosperity and decline;
榮辱與共 share weal or woe;
［榮盛］ prosperous;
［榮顯］ honour and high position;
［榮幸］ be honoured; have the honour of;
榮幸之至 with pleasure;
［榮養］ support one's parents;
［榮耀］ glory; honour; splendour;
無上榮耀 crowning glory;
一身榮耀 be loaded with honours;
［榮膺］ have the honour of being appointed to a post;
［榮譽］ credit; glory; honour; reputation;
榮譽稱號 honorary title;
榮譽感 sense of honour;
榮譽獎 honourable mention;
榮譽教授 honorary professor;
榮譽軍人 disabled soldiers;
榮譽市民 honorary citizen;
榮譽問題 point of honour;
榮譽學位 honorary degrees;
出賣榮譽 sell one's honour;
放棄榮譽 disclaim the credit;

哀榮 honour after one's death;

繁榮 (1) make sth prosper; (2) booming; flourishing; prosperous;

光榮 glory; honour; honourable;
殊榮 exceptional honour;
希榮 aspire for the glory of high office;
顯榮 rich, illustrious and influential;
向榮 on the road to prosperity;
虛榮 empty glory; vainglory; vainglorious; vanity;
尊榮 dignity and honour;

rong

【熔】 (1) fuse metals; melt; smelt; weld; (2) die; mould; (3) spear-like weapon;
［熔池］ furnace hearth; molten bath;

[熔點] fusing point; melting point; smelting point;
熔解熱 heat of fusion;
[熔度] fusibility;
[熔法] melt;
滴熔法 drip melt;
[熔合] alloy; fuse; merge; mix together;
[熔化] fuse; fusion; melt; melting;
熔化爐 melting furnace;
熔化器 melter;
~岩石熔化器 rock melter;
低壓熔化 low-pressure melting;
電弧熔化 arc melting;
在火中熔化 melt in fire;
[熔劑] flux;
[熔接] weld;
[熔解] fuse; fusion; melt; melting;
[熔塊] frit;
帶色熔塊 coloured frit;
搪瓷熔塊 enamel frit;
透明熔塊 clear frit;
[熔煉] fusion; melt; smelt; smelting;
冷裝熔煉 cold melt;
區域熔煉 zone-melting;
全熔煉 fine melt;
閃速熔煉 flash smelting;
漩渦熔煉 cyclone smelting;
自熱熔煉 autogenous smelting;
[熔爐] (1) melting; pot; smelting furnace; smelter; (2) crucible; furnace;
大熔爐 melting pot;
回轉熔爐 rotary smelter;
間歇式熔爐 batch smelter;
[熔體] melt;
玻璃熔體 glass melt;
聚合物熔體 polymer melt;
[熔岩] lava; magma; molten rock;
熔岩燈 lava lamp;
熔岩灰 lava ash;
熔岩流 lava-flow;
塊熔岩 aphrolithic lava;
塊狀熔岩 block lava;
泥熔岩 aqueous lava;
酸性熔岩 acidic lava;
[熔鑄] casting; founding;

靜熔 dead melt;
助熔 flux;

rong
【蓉】 hibiscus; (2) another name for Chengdu;

豆蓉 fine bean mash;
芙蓉 (1) cotton-rose; (2) lotus;
椰蓉 shredded coconut stuffing;

rong
【融】 (1) melt; thaw; (2) blend; fuse; in harmony; (3) burning; glowing; very bright; (4) cheerful; happy; joyful; (5) a surname;
[融風] spring breeze;
[融合] amalgamate; blend; coalesce; compromise; fuse; fusion; harmonize; mix together;
融合詞 amalgamating language;
融合教育 inclusive education; integrated education;
款洽融合 cordial and harmonious; courteous and genial;
民族融合 fusion of nationalities;
種族融合 fusion of races;
[融化] fuse; melt; thaw;
融化冰雪 thaw ice and snow;
[融會] blend harmoniously;
融會貫通 be well versed in; digest; gain a thorough understanding of the subject through mastery of all relevant material; have a full and thorough understanding through a comprehensive study of the subject; thoroughly acquainted with;
[融解] dissolve; fuse; melt; thaw;
融解點 melting point;
[融洽] harmonious; on friendly terms;
感情融洽 enjoy emotional harmony; harmonize in feeling;
精神融洽 enjoy spiritual harmony;
[融融] (1) cheerful; happy and harmonious; joyful; (2) mild; warm;
融融其樂 harmonious joy;
[融霜] defrosting;
[融水] melt water;
[融通] bring together and understand thoroughly; comprehend;
融通匯票 accommodation bill;
融通人 accommodator;
融通性租賃 finance lease;
融通業務 accommodation line;
[融雪] snow melt;
融雪風 snow eater;

[融資] financing;
融資租賃 financing lase;
非法融資 illegal financing;
間接融資 indirect financing;
直接融資 direct financing;

交融 blend; mingle;
金融 banking; finance;
熔融 melt;
消融 melt;

rong
【嶸】 lofty; majestic; prominent;

崢嶸 (1) lofty and steep; towering; (2) extraordinary; outstanding;

rong
【蠑】 (1) a kind of mollusk; (2) a kind of reptile;

rong³
rong
【冗】 (1) redundant; superfluous; (2) full of trivial details; (3) busyness;
[冗筆] (1) verbosity in writing; (2) unnecessary strokes in painting;
沒有冗筆 free from verbosity;
[冗兵] superfluous troops;
[冗長] lengthy; long-winded; tediously long;
十分冗長 as long as one's arm;
[冗詞] superfluous words;
冗詞贅句 redundant words and expressions;
冗詞贅語 superfluous words; verbiage;
刪掉冗詞 cut out unnecessary words;
[冗費] unnecessary expenses;
[冗官] (1) redundant; superfluous; (2) verbose; (3) tediously long;
[冗冗] (1) excessive; numerous; (2) multitude;
[冗散] leisurely; relaxed;
[冗談] lerema;
[冗餘] redundance; redundancy;
冗餘規則 redundancy rule;
基因冗餘 gene redundancy;
[冗員] deadwood; redundant personnel;
[冗雜] confused; disorderly; lengthy and jumbled; many and diverse; miscellaneous; mixed up;
[冗贅] diffuse; verbose;

撥冗 find time in the midst of pressing affairs;
煩冗 (1) diverse and complicated; (2) lengthy and tedious;
公冗 official busyness;

rong
【氄】 (1) fine and soft; (2) fine hair;
[氄毛] down; fine hair;

rou²
rou
【柔】 (1) soft; soft and tender; supple; (2) soften; (3) amiable; gentle; pliant; submissive; supple; yielding; (4) charming; lovely; sweet; (5) curry favour; win favour by fawning;
[柔板] adagio;
[柔腸] tender heart;
柔腸百轉 deeply sorrowed over;
柔腸寸斷 broken-hearted; the heart breaks when one thinks of one's love;
[柔道] judo;
[柔光] luminescence; soft light;
一層柔光 a luminescence;
[柔和] amiable; gentle; mild; soft; supple; tender;
柔和婉順 gentle and agreeable;
聲音柔和 gentle in voice;
[柔滑] soft and smooth;
柔滑如脂 soft and smooth as grease;
[柔化] melt; soften; tend to become weak and lax;
[柔惠] gentle and kind;
[柔量] compliance;
玻璃態柔量 glassy compliance;
儲能柔量 storage compliance;
對比柔量 reduced compliance;
複柔量 complex compliance;
緩發柔量 delayed compliance;
極限柔量 limiting compliance;
剪切柔量 shear compliance;
拉伸柔量 compliance in extension;
瞬時柔量 instantaneous compliance;
穩態柔量 steady state compliance;
[柔麻] make hemp soft by immersing it in water;
[柔曼] soft and lustrous;
[柔毛] plumule; soft wool;
[柔媚] amiable; gentle and lovely; pliant and yielding;
[柔嫩] delicate; soft and tender; tender;

[柔情] soft and sentimental; tender affection; tender feelings; tender thoughts; tenderness; the tender feelings of a lover;
柔情繾綣 the two find so much delight in each other;
柔情似水 tender and soft as water;
柔情萬種 infinitely affectionate; the indescribable feelings of one desperately in love;
繾綣柔情 tender affection;
一寸柔情 a thread of tender thought;
[柔韌] pliable and tough; supple;
柔韌的 pliable;
保持身體柔韌 keep oneself supple;
[柔軟] easily bent; flexible; lithe; soft; yielding;
柔軟劑 softener;
~織物柔軟劑 fabric softener;
[柔潤] soft and moist;
[柔若無骨] soft as soap;
[柔弱] delicate; low and gentle; soft and meek; weak;
聲音柔弱 weak voice;
[柔色] mild countenance;
[柔聲] in a sweet and girlish voice; soft voice;
柔聲唱 croon;
柔聲説 croon;
[柔術] jujitsu;
[柔順] gentle and agreeable; gentle and yielding; meek; submissive;
性情柔順 have a gentle spirit;
[柔心弱骨] as mild as a dove by nature; tender conscience;
[柔性] femininity; flexibility; gentleness; pliancy; softness;
柔性製造系統 flexible manufacturing system;
柔性自動化 flexible automation;

低柔 soft and low;
剛柔 hardness and softness;
懷柔 make a show of conciliation in order to bring other nationalities or states under control;
嬌柔 tender and charming;
輕柔 gentle; soft;
溫柔 affectionate; gentle; gentle and soft; meek; pleasingly; sweet-natured; warm and tender;
纖柔 delicate and soft;
優柔 (1) leisurely; (2) gentle; mild; (3) weak in character;

rou

【揉】 (1) knead; rub; (2) crumble by hand; roll into; (3) massage; (4) make peaceful; make smooth; subdue; (5) confused; mixed-up;
[揉巴] crumple; knead; rub;
[揉擦] antriptic;
揉擦劑 anatrophic;
揉擦療法 anatripsis;
[揉出淚來] cause tears to flow by too much rubbing of the eyes;
[揉搓] (1) knead; massage; rub; (2) play jokes on; tease;
[揉兒舖] a shop dealing in second-hand jewelry;
[揉合] blend; combine; incorporate; merge;
[揉輪] bend trees to make wheels;
[揉麵] knead dough;
[揉碎] crumble to pieces;
[揉雜] mixed-up;

rou

【蹂】 (1) trample; trample on; tread upon; (2) tread out grain;
[蹂踐] trample; tread upon;
[蹂躪] crush under one's feet; devastate; make havoc of; ravage; trample on;
蹂躪別國主權 trample upon the sovereignity of other countries;
備受蹂躪 under the hoof;
遭到蹂躪 suffer devastation;
[蹂若] trample; tread on;

rou

【輮】 (1) felly; rim of a wheel; (2) trample;
[輮轢] rut; trace of a wheel;

rou³
rou

【糅】 mix; mixed;
[糅合] form a mixture; mix; mix together;
[糅雜] disorderly; mixed;

雜糅 blend; mingle; mix;

rou⁴
rou

【肉】 (1) flesh; meat; (2) flesh; pulp; (3)

carnal; physical;

[肉餅] meat cake; meat pie;
乾肉餅 pemmican;
牛肉餅 beef patty;
小肉餅 patty;

[肉搏] close quarter fighting; fight hand-to-hand; hand-to-hand combat;
肉搏戰 hand-to-hand combat; hand-to-hand fighting;

[肉彈] buxom beauty; sex bomb;

[肉店] butcher's shop;

[肉丁] diced meat;

[肉凍] jelly; meat jelly;
熬肉凍 boil meat into jelly;

[肉販] butcher;

[肉感] buxom; sensual appeal; sensuality; sexy; voluptuous;

[肉糕] loaf;
乾酪肉糕 cheese and meat loaf;
五花肉糕 marble loaf;

[肉冠] comb;

[肉桂] Chinese cassia tree;
肉桂基 cinnamyl;
肉桂色 cinnamomeous;
肉桂酸 cinnamylate;
肉桂酮 cinnamon;
肉桂酰 cinnhyl;
肉桂油 cinnamon oil;

[肉紅] pinkish red;

[肉漿] meat pulp; minced meat;
砍成肉漿 make mincemeat of;

[肉類] meat;
肉類加工 meat-packing;
~肉類加工業 meat-packing;
~肉類加工者 meat-packer;
白色肉類 white meat;
紅色肉類 red meat;

[肉瘤] fleshy tumour; sarcoma;
肉瘤病 sarcosis;
骨肉瘤 osteosarcoma;
淋巴肉瘤 lymphosarcoma;
黏液肉瘤 myxosarcoma;

[肉麻] disgusting; nauseating; sickening;
肉麻吹捧 fulsome praise; use words of praise that give one the creeps;

[肉末] ground meat; minced meat;

[肉泥爛醬] mutilagted and bloody human body;

[肉牛] beef;

[肉排] rib; steak;

[肉批] meat pie;

[肉皮] pork skin;

[肉片] fillet; sliced meat; slices of meat;

[肉票] hostage;

[肉鋪] butcher's shop;
肉鋪老闆 butcher;

[肉色] flesh colour;

[肉身] human body;

[肉參] hostage;

[肉食] (1) meat; (2) carnivorous;
肉食動物 carnivorous animals; meat-eating animals;
肉食性 carnivorous character;
肉食者鄙 the meat-eaters are vulgar – the noblemen are shortsighted and good-for-nothing;
肉食植物 carnivorous plants; insect-eating plants;

[肉絲] shredded meat;

[肉鬆] dried meat floss;
魚肉鬆 dried fish floss;

[肉湯] broth; porridge;

[肉體] carnal; corporeal clod; flesh; flesh and blood; physical; sensory; the human body;
肉體的 carnal;
肉體美 physical beauty;
出賣肉體 sell one's body;
裸露肉體 bare one's body;

[肉跳] apprehensive; awesome; frightening;
肉跳心驚 be filled with fear; on tenderhook; shudder with fear;

[肉痛] (1) anxiety; apprehension; (2) cannot bear to part with sth one loves;

[肉丸] burger; meatball;
肉丸子 faggot;

[肉刑] corporeal punishment;

[肉眼] naked eye;
肉眼凡胎 shortsighted and good-for-nothing person;
肉眼檢查 visual examination;
肉眼能見 can see sth without the aid of instruments; visible to the naked eye;
肉眼扒 rib eye;
肉眼無珠 blind as a mole;

[肉用] carnal; table;
肉用公牛 beef bull;
肉用雞 fryer;
肉用家畜 butcher's beast; table poultry;
肉用牛 beef cattle;

[肉慾] carnal appetite; carnal desire; sexual desire;
肉慾熾盛 sensuality is blazing;
[肉圓] meatballs;
[肉汁] gravy; meat broth; meat juice;
[肉中刺] a thorn in one's flesh; the most hated person; the most hated thing;
肉中挑刺 pluck out the thorn in one's flesh; pull out the thorn in one's flesh;
如肉中刺 as a thorn in one's flesh;
[肉贅] sycoma; wart;

白肉 plain boiled pork; white meat;
敗肉 spoiled meat;
砲肉 barbecue meat; roasted meat;
赤肉 lean pork;
剁肉 hash meat; mince meat;
耳息肉 aural polyp; otopolyus;
肥肉 fat; fat meat; speck;
骨肉 blood relationship; flesh and blood; kindred;
果肉 flesh of the fruit; pulp;
橫肉 muscles that make the face look ugly and ferocious;
紅肉 red meat;
喉息肉 laryngeal polyp;
肌肉 muscle;
頸肉 chuck;
酒肉 wine and meat;
砍肉 cut up meat;
烤肉 grill; roast meat; toast;
臘肉 bacon; cured meat;
鹿肉 vension;
牛肉 beef;
皮肉 flesh;
切肉 cut the meat;
人肉 human flesh;
上肉 prime meat;
生肉 uncooked meat;
食肉 carnivorous;
瘦肉 lean meat;
熟肉 cooked meat; well-done meat;
煨肉 stew meat;
息肉 polyp; polypus;
鮮肉 fresh meat;
鹹肉 bacon; salted meat;
蟹肉 crab meat;
血肉 (1) flesh and blood; (2) as close as flesh and blood;
燻肉 bacon; smoke meat;
醃肉 salted meat; salted pork;
羊肉 mutton;
椰肉 coconut meat;
一刀肉 a cut of meat;
一碟肉 a plate of meat;
一塊好肉 a nice cut of meat;
一塊肉 a chunk of meat; a piece of meat;
一片肉 a slice of meat;
一小塊肉 a bit of meat;
魚肉 (1) fish and meat; (2) victims of oppression; (3) bully; oppress;
宰肉 chop meat; cut up meat;
蔗肉 flesh of the cane;
豬肉 pork;
煮肉 cook meat;
俎上肉 meat on the chopping – a helpless victim;
胙肉 sacrificial meat;

ru²
ru

【如】 (1) according to; follow one's advice; in compliance with; listen to; (2) as; as if; like; (3) as good as; can compare with; equal to; (4) as; for example; for instance; such as; (5) if; supposing; (6) arrive at; go to; (7) ought to; should;
[如臂使指] as the arm directing the fingers – command with ease as one wishes;
臂之使指 as easy as the arm using the fingers; easily controlled;
[如常] as usual; commonplace; ordinary;
[如初] as always; as it was before;
[如此] (1) in this way; like that; so; such; (2) so-called;
如此等等 and so on and so forth; etc.;
如此而已 and that's that; so much for; so that's that; that's all; that is what it all adds up to; that is what it all amounts to;
如此天降 as though sb has come straight from heaven;
如此云云 and so on and so forth;
如此這般 so and so; such and such; thus and so; thus and thus;
但願如此 I wish;
對…同樣如此 for that matter;
更是如此 all the more so;
固當如此 it is just as it should be;
果能如此 if that is so; if things can really turn out that way;
合當如此 it should be like that; it should

be so;
話雖如此 be that as it may; having said that;
儘管如此 even so; having said that;
命該如此 fate would have it so; it is so ordered; it is predestined;
一寒如此 as poor as Job's turkey; be reduced to poverty; down and out; in straitened circumstances; penniless and frustrated;
早知如此 if it had been known that things would turn out this way;
自古如此 it has been this way since the beginning of time;

[如次] as follows;

[如弟] younger sworn brother;

[如蛾赴火] fly into the flame like moths — court self-destruction; like a moth flying to a candle;

[如飛] like flying; quickly; swiftly;
步履如飛 walk very quickly; walk with flying feet;

[如沸如羹] like the bubbling of soup in a pot;

[如風過耳] in one ear and out the other; regard sb's words with indifference; turn a deaf ear to; take sb's words like wind passing the ear;

[如俯拾芥] as easy as to pick dirt from the floor;

[如岡如陵] resembling the hills and mountains — constant and long-lasting;

[如鯁在喉] as if one has a fishbone in one's throat; give vent to one's pent-up feelings; like a fishbone getting stuck in the throat;

[如骨鯁喉，一吐方快] feel suffocated if one doesn't speak out; have a criticism that one must express;

[如故] (1) as before; as usual; (2) like old friends;
並驅如故 go along like they did just now;
一見如故 become fast friends at the first meeting; become intimate at the first meeting; become old acquaintances at the first meeting; hit if off well right fronm the start; like old friends from the start; strike up a friendship with sb at the first meeting; they hit it off immediately;

[如歸] like going home;
賓至如歸 a home from home; guests feel at home in a hotel; make a visitor feel welcome;
視死如歸 defy death; face death unflinchingly; go to one's death as if one were going home; look death calmly in the face; look on death without flinching; look upon death as nothing; make no more of dying than of going home; regard death as going home; unafraid of death;

[如果] but for; but that; failing; if; in case; in case of; in default of; in the absence of; in the event of; in the event that; on condition that; on the understanding; only that; ...permitting; provided; should; suppose; supposing; unless; wanting; what if; when; where; without;
如果實在需要 at a push;
如果我沒有記錯的話 if my memory serves me right;

[如何] how; what;
如何是好 what should one do;
無論如何 no matter what;

[如虎] like a tiger;
如虎蹲山 like a fierce tiger crouching on a mountain;
如虎負隅 like a tiger at bay;
如虎添翼 a tiger with wings added; be greatly reinforced; be greatly strengthened; like a tiger that has grown wings — with might redoubled; like a tiger which has got wings; like a tiger with wings; like adding wings to a tiger; like tigers taking wing; with added strength;
如虎下山 like a tiger rushing down from the mountain;

[如花] like a flower;
如花似玉 as beautiful as flowers and jades; as pretty as a flower; like a slender flower of jade;
如花之美 as beautiful as flowers; as lovely as a spray of blossoms;

[如火] like a fire;
如火燎原 spread like wild fire; spread very rapidly;
如火如荼 as violently as a raging fire; flaring like fire set to dry tinder; like a

raging fire; like wildfire;
紅得如火 as red as fire;
[如劍懸頂] as if a sword hanging overhead; in imminent peril;
[如今] at present; now; nowadays; these days;
事到如今 things have come to such a pass that;
[如金] like gold;
惜墨如金 sparing of ink; use ink as if it were gold – work with scrupulous care;
[如舊] as it has always been; as usual;
[如來] Buddha;
[如雷] like the roar of thunder;
如雷貫耳 it strikes one's ears like the roar of thunder; like the sound of thunder in one's ears; reverberate like thunder;
暴跳如雷 as savage as a meat axe; blow one's stack; blow one's top; burst into a fit of temper; fall into a rage; fly in a rage; fly off the handle; fume with rage; get into a rage; get into a tantrum; get one's monkey up; get one's rag out; get up in the air; go berserk; go on the rampage; go through the roof; go up in the air; have a fit; have a tantrum; hit the ceiling; hit the roof; in a frenzy; in a thundering rage; in a towering rage; leap up furiously; mad with fury; on the rampage; out of one's gourd; raise the roof; rave with fury; spring up in one's rage; stamp about in a frenzy; stamp frantically in anger; stamp with rage;
[如流] follow sb's advice;
倒背如流 can even recite sth backwards; know sth thoroughly by heart;
從諫如流 able to accept advice from one's inferiors; ready to listen to advice;
納諫如流 be modest enough to take counsel with anyone; condescend to listen to advice from one's subordinates;
剖斷如流 decide cases promptly; quick in deviding lawsuits;
[如麻] like hemp;
繁紊如麻 tangled and involved as a cluster of hemp;
[如夢] dreamlike;
如夢初醒 as if one were waking from a dream – come to know what is all about; as if waking from a dream; awake as if from a dream – begin to see the light; wake up as from a drunken sleep – as if one were coming out of a darkness into the light of day;
如夢的 dreamlike;
如夢方醒 as if one were waking from a dream; feel as if one were coming out of darkness into the light of day;
[如命] as highly as one's life;
愛財如命 regard money as one's very life;
一錢如命 flay a flint; prize one copper as highly as one's life; skin a flint;
[如牛] as an ox;
力大如牛 as powerful as an ox; as strong as a bull; have the strength of a horse; with the strength of a bull;
[如烹小鮮] as if cooking a small fish – do sth with ease;
[如其] (1) if; in case; (2) as for; as to;
如其所好 catch sb's fancy; to one's taste;
[如期] as scheduled; at the appointed time; by the scheduled time; in time; on schedule; on time; punctually;
如期而至 come at the appointed time; roll around;
[如日] like the sun;
如日方昇 rising like the morning sun – have bright and boundless prospects;
如日中天 like the sun at high noon – at the zenith of one's career; like the sun in midsky – at the apex of one's power;
[如若] if;
如若不然 if not; otherwise;
[如山] like a mountain;
恩重如山 a great debt of gratitude; favours weighty as a mountain;
令出如山 every order is as firm as a mountain;
屍積如山 the corpses lie about in heaps; the corpses are heaped up like mountains;
言出如山 a promise is a promise; one's words are as stable as mountains; promises must be kept; the world is said and can't be taken back;
義重如山 love justice as one's life; one's integrity is as firm as the mountains;

with firm rectitude like a mountain;

[如上] as above;

如上所述 as mentioned above; as noted above; as remarked above; as stated above;

[如神] like god;

斷事如神 divide a matter wonderfully;

料事如神 foresee with divine accuracy; foretell like a prophet; foretell things accurately; make exact predictions; one's foresight is godlike; possess a second sight; predict like a prophet; predict with miraculous accuracy;

靈效如神 magically efficacious;

其功如神 as effectively as a fairy does;

效驗如神 act like a charm;

用兵如神 deploy troops with great skill; direct military operations with miraculous skill; more than human in the art of war; superb military commander; use ways of fighting as a god does; work miracles in manoeuvring troops;

[如市] like a market;

臣門如市 the house of the influential official is as crowded as a market-place;

[如實] accurately; as things really are; strictly according to the facts; truthfully;

[如適] contented; peaceful and comfortable;

[如數] exact number;

如數償還 pay back in full; pay back the exact amount;

如數付足 pay in full;

如數還清 all duly repaid;

如數家珍 as if enumerating one's family valuables — very familiar with one's subject; at home in; at home on; at home with; have sth at one's finger-ends; have sth at one's finger-tips; like counting family treasures; like telling off one's family treasures — capable of speaking on a subject with great familiarity;

如數收訖 value received;

[如湯沃雪] as easy as melting snow by pouring hot water on it; as though hot water were poured upon snow; like melting snow with hot water — easily done;

[如同] as; like; similar;

如同草芥 no more than the weeds by the roadside;

如同兒戲 like child's play;

如同身受 would regard it as a personal favour to me;

[如土] like dirt;

揮金如土 lavish with one's money; make the money fly; scatter one's gold around as though it were dust; spend money as though it were dirt; spend money like dirt; spend money like soil; spend money like water; squander money like dust; throw one's money about; throw money about like dirt; waste money;

~揮金如土的人 high roller;

[如下] as below; as follows;

如下所述 as below; as stated below;

理由如下 the reasons are as follows;

內容如下 the contents are as follows;

原文如下 the text is as follows;

[如心] contented; gratified; pleased; satisfied;

[如新] brand as if it were new;

[如兄] elder sworn brother;

如兄如弟 act towards one another like brothers and sisters;

[如須] if you have to;

[如需] if you need to;

[如夷] like level ground;

視險如夷 regard a hazardous location as level ground — no fear of danger and difficulties;

[如蟻附膻] like ants attaching themselves to what is rank and foul — attaching oneself to influential people; like ants clinging on a putrid carcass — where there is profit, all struggle for it; like ants clinging to sth rank — swarming after unwholesome things; like ants seeking sth rank-smelling — referring to a swarm of people running after unwholesome things or leaning on influential people for support;

[如意] (1) according to one's wishes; as one likes; as one wishes; (2) S-shaped ornament which is a symbol of good luck;

如意郎君 husband after her own heart; ideal husband; Mr. Right

如意算盤 Alnaschar's dream; calculations

based on wishful thinking; smug caculations; wishing thinking;
稱心如意 after one's own heart; to one's liking;
可心如意 congenial; find sth satisfactory; things that are after one's heart; to one's heart's content;
萬事如意 everything turns out as one wishes;
玉如意 jade scepter; jade with "as you wish";
諸事如意 all goes as one wishes;

[如鷹攫雞] like a hawk carrying off a chicken; like an eagle swooping down on a chicken;

[如蠅逐臭] run after filth, as flies swarm around garbage; like flies after a stink; like flies sticking to what is rank; like flies swarming about a bit of filth; like flies taking to rottenness;

[如影隨形] as the shadow follows the form; like the shadow following the person — very closely associated with each other;

[如魚] like a fish;
如魚得水 in one's element; like a duck to water; like a fish getting to water — find sth very congenial to one or find oneself in suitable or satisfactory surroundings; like a stranded fish put back to water; like fish in water — in one's elements; like fish let into the water;
如魚離水 like a fish out of water;
如魚戲水 as little fishes merrily splashing in the water; splash about like jolly fish;

[如雨] like rain;
如雨駢集 come in like rain drops in great number;
矢下如雨 the arrows come down like a shower;
揮汗如雨 drip with sweat; perspiration comes down like raindrops; sweat like a trooper; sweat profusely;

[如月] like a moon in shape;
滿弓如月 pull one's bowstring to its full extent until the bow is like a full moon in shape;

[如約] according to appointment;

[如雲] like clouds;
冠蓋如雲 caps and carriages coming like clouds — many officials and dignitaries;
猛將如雲 the army has many brave warriors;
僕從如雲 myriads of servants; one's attendants are numerous;
勝友如雲 a cloud of good friends; a great many good friends;
士女如雲 men and women gather like clouds;

[如針刺背] feel as if needles were being stuck into one's back;

[如豬] like a pig;
肥蠢如豬 fat and stupid as a pig;

[如醉] recov as if one is drunk;
如醉方醒 recover as from a fit of drunkenness; wake up as one from a drunken sleep;
如醉如狂 as if one is drunk and has gone mad; as mad as a hatter; like mad;
如醉如夢 look like a man who is drunk or dreaming;

[如坐針氈] as if sitting on a spiked rug; in an extremely uncomfortable position; on hot coals; on nettles; on tenterhooks; like a cat on hot bricks; sit on pins and needles;

比如 for example; for instance; such as;
賁如 brightly ornamental; richly adorned;
邠如 culturally booming or flourishing;
不如 (1) inferior to; not anywhere near; not as good as; not equal to; nowhere near; (2) it would be better to; not anything like; nothing like;
弗如 not as good as; not equal to; worse than;
何如 how about; wouldn't it be better;
恍如 as if; seem; as though; seem;
假如 assume; assuming; but for; even if; grant; granted that; if; if only; in case; let; on condition that; on the supposition that; presume; suppose; supposing; unless; what if;
箭如 arrows come like;
例如 for example; for instance; such as;
美如 as beautiful as;
面如 one's face is like...;
莫如 might as well; would be better;
譬如 for example; for instance;

恰如 be just like;
親如 as close as; as dear to;
闕如 be wanting;
設如 if; supposing;
視如 consider as; hold sth as; regard as; treat as;
宛如 as if; as it were; literally; just like; like;
穩如 as stable as;
無如 but; however;
相如 resemble each other;
心如 one's heart is like...;
儼如 be just like;
晏如 peaceful and easy;
一如 just like;
易如 as easy as;
繹如 continuous;
猶如 as if; just as; like;
有如 just like; like;
裕如 effortlessly; with ease;
正如 exactly as; just as;
至如 as to; with regard to;
諸如 such as;
自如 freely; smoothly; with facility;

ru

【茹】 (1) eat; mouth; taste; (2) entangled roots; (3) experience; (4) stinking; (5) a surname;
［茹恨］ submit in humiliation;
茹恨飲辱 submit in humiliation; submit to overbearing insult; swallow the insults in meek submission;
銜悲茹恨 harbour sorrow and resentment;
［茹素］ abstain from meat; vegetarian;
［茹痛］ endure; suffer;

ru

【儒】 (1) Confucianism; confucianist; (2) learned man; scholar; the learned;
［儒戶］ scholarly family;
［儒家］ Confucian School;
［儒教］ Confucianism;
［儒林］ (1) circle of Confucians; (2) circle of scholars;
［儒生］ Confucian scholar;
［儒學］ teachings of Confucius;
［儒雅］ elegant; learned and refined; scholarly and refined;
風流儒雅 cultured, talented, and refined;
［儒子可教］ the boy is worth teaching; the young man is worthy to be taught;
大儒 learned man; scholar;
腐儒 stale and pedantic scholar;
鴻儒 learned scholar;
犬儒 cynic;
碩儒 great scholar;
俗儒 scholar of shallow learning;

ru

【嚅】 talk indistinctly and falteringly;
［嚅囁］ falter in one's speech; mumble in a low voice;

ru

【孺】 infant; young child;
［孺齒］ young child;
［孺慕］ adore sb as a child adores its parents;
孺慕之誠 honesty in one's longing affection;
［孺人］ scholar's wife; wife;
［孺子］ boy; child;
孺子可教 that boy is teachable; the young man is promising and worthy to be taught;
黃口孺子 callow; suckling babe; babes and sucklings; immature;
婦孺 women and children;

ru

【濡】 (1) immerse; moisten; wet; (2) linger; procrastinate; (3) glossy; smooth; (4) tolerate; (5) endure; patient;
［濡筆為文］ damp the brush and produce an essay;
［濡淡］ dye;
［濡翰］ moisten the brush;
［濡跡］ linger at a place;
［濡溺］ be immersed in;
［濡染］ be imbued with; dye; immerse;
濡染惡習 dye with evil practice;
［濡潤］ make moist;
［濡濕］ make wet; soak; soak by immersion;
［濡首］ overindulge oneself in wine;
［濡滯］ procrastinate; slow;

ru

【襦】 (1) short coat; short top garment; (2) neck-wears for babies; (3) very fine silk fabric;
［襦襖］ short jacket;
［襦褲］ jacket and trousers;

ru

【鴽】 trunix blakistoni, a kind of quail;

ru³

ru

【汝】 thee; thou; thy; you;

[汝等] you;

ru

【乳】 (1) breast; nipple; (2) milk; (3) any milk-like liquid; (4) give birth to; (5) newborn; sucking; (6) triturate;

[乳癌] breast cancer;

[乳媼] wet nurse;

[乳白] cream colour; milky white;
乳白玻璃 opal glass;

[乳哺] feed with milk;

[乳齒] deciduous teeth; milk teeth;

[乳兒] sucking child;

[乳房] apples; bangles; bazoombas; bazungas; beef curtains; blobs; boobs; bosoms; bouncers; bubbies; bumpers; charlies; chestnuts; dairies; easts and wests; fainting fits; female breasts; funbags; jamboree bags; jugs; knobs; knockers; love blobs; milk-jugs; milk-bars; shock absorbers; stonkers; tits; titties; udders; wammers; whammers;
乳房病 mastopathy;
乳房潮紅 breast flush;
乳房大的 well-endowed;
乳房豐滿的 bosomy;
乳房過小 micromastia;
乳房潰瘍 masthelcosis;
乳房切除 mastectomy;
~乳房切除手術 mastectomy;
乳房痛 mammalgia;
乳房下垂 mastoptosis;
乳房小的 flat-chested;
乳房炎 mastitis;
~急性乳房炎 acute mastitis;
~乳房增大 breast augmentation;
假乳房 ; pseudomamma;
結塊乳房 caked breast;
巨乳房 gigantomastia;
男乳房 mamma masculina;
鬆垂乳房 pendulous breasts;
無乳房 amastia;
一對乳房 jugs;

[乳溝] cleavage;

[乳劑] emulsion;

[乳膠] emulsion; latex;
乳膠手套 latex gloves;
人工合成乳膠 latex;

[乳酒] milk-white wine;

[乳酪] curds; junket;
藍紋乳酪 blue cheese;

[乳梨] large white juicy pear;

[乳糜] chyle;
乳糜胸 chylothorax;
~外傷性乳糜胸 traumatic chylothorax;

[乳名] child's pet name; infant name;

[乳母] foster-nurse; wet nurse;

[乳牛] dairy cattle; milch cow;

[乳品] dairy products;
乳品場 dairy;
乳品公司 dairy;

[乳氣] childish; childishness;

[乳食] take nothing but milk as food;

[乳酸] lactic acid;

[乳糖] lactose; milk sugar;

[乳頭] (1) diddies; nipple; teat; tit; tittie; titty; (2) papilla;
乳頭出血 thelorrhagia;
乳頭瘤 papilloma;
~黏液乳頭瘤 myxopapilloma;
乳頭膨起 thelerethism;
乳頭痛 thelalgia;
乳頭突 mamelon;
乳頭炎 acromastitis; thelitis;
~壞死性乳頭炎 necrotizing papillitis;
~硬化性乳頭炎 sclerosing mastoiditis;
觸覺乳頭 tactile papilla;
腮腺乳頭 parotid papilla;
神經乳頭 neurothele;
無乳頭 athelia;
圓錐乳頭 papillae conicae;

[乳腺] mammary gland;
乳腺病 mastopathy;
乳腺出血 mastorrhagia;
乳腺肥大 hypermastia;
乳腺過小 hypomastia;
乳腺痛 mastalgia;
乳腺萎縮 mastatrophy;
乳腺炎 mastitis;
~實質性乳腺炎 glandular mastitis;

[乳臭未乾] smell of the baby; one's mouth is full of pap; unfledged; very young and inexperienced like a sucking child;

[乳牙] baby tooth; milk tooth;

[乳燕] young swallows;

[乳藥] take poison;

[乳液] emulsion;

瀝青乳液 asphalt emulsion;
油包酸乳液 acid-in-oil emulsion;

[乳媼] wet nurse;

[乳暈] areola mammae;
乳暈炎 areolitis;

[乳罩] bra; brassiere;
背心乳罩 support bra;
定型乳罩 padded bra;
無帶乳罩 strapless bra;

[乳汁] milk;
乳汁過多 hypergalactia;
乳汁減小 hypogalactia;

[乳脂] butter; butterfat;

[乳狀液] emulsion;
多色乳狀液 chromophous emulsion;
二元乳狀液 binary emulsion;

泌乳 lactate; lactation;
哺乳 breastfeed; nurse; suckle;
豆乳 (1) soya milk; (2) fermented bean curd;
斷乳 ablactation; wean a baby;
髮乳 hair cream;
蜂乳 royal jelly;
腐乳 fermented bean curd;
膠乳 endosperm; latex;
酪乳 buttermilk;
凝乳 curd;
牛乳 cow's milk;
胚乳 endosperm;
人乳 human milk;
水乳 water and milk;
吮乳 suck the breast;
義乳 falsies;
鐘乳 stalactite;

ru

【辱】 (1) disgrace; dishonour; insult; (2) disgrace; insult;

[辱愛] receive a favour undeservingly;

[辱承] receive a favour undeservingly;

[辱賜] thanks for your gifts;

[辱國] bring shame upon the fatherland; disgrace the mother country;
辱國喪師 bring disgrace on one's fatherland and casualties on the army;
喪地辱國 surrender territory and bring humiliation to the country;
喪權辱國 betray one's sovereignty and humiliate one's nation; humiliate the country and forfeit its sovereignty; humiliate one's nation and forfeit its sovereignty; surrender a country's sovereign rights under humiliating terms;

[辱教] thanks for your instructions;

[辱臨] condescend to come to such a humble place;

[辱罵] abuse; abuse and insult; call sb names; hurl insults;
辱罵性語言 abusive language;
百般辱罵 assail sb with every possible kind of abuse; call all kinds of names; hurl every sort of insult at sb; indulge in scurrilities; shout all sorts of abuse; yell every form of insult;
互相辱罵 hurl insults back and forth;
一連串的辱罵 a volley of abuse;

[辱命] dishonour one's commission; fail to accomplish a mission; fail to live up to the expectation of one's superior;

[辱沒] bring disgrace to; disgrace; insult; unworthy of;
辱沒門楣 bring disgrace upon one's family; disgrace one's family name;

[辱身] disgrace oneself; submit to taint in one's person;

[辱游] indebted to a friend for one's friendship;

恥辱 disgrace; humiliation; shame;
寵辱 fame and humiliation;
玷辱 a disgrace to; bring disgrace on; dishonour; humiliate;
凌辱 humiliate; insult;
欺辱 humiliate;
奇辱 burning disgrace; crying shame; deep disgrace;
屈辱 humiliate; humiliation; mortification;
忍辱 bear disgrace and insults; endure contempt;
榮辱 honour and disgrace; honour and dishonour;
受辱 be humiliated; be insulted;
撻辱 beat and disgrace;
污辱 (1) humiliate; insult; (2) defile; sully; tarnish; (3) rape;
侮辱 humiliate; humiliation; insult; put sb to shame; subject sb to indignities;
刑辱 cruelly injure or humiliate with punishment or torture;
羞辱 (1) dishonour; humiliation; shame; (2) humiliate; put sb to shame; subject sb to indignities;

淫辱 violate a woman;
有辱 bring dishonor to;
折辱 humiliate; insult;

ru⁴
ru

【入】 (1) come into; enter; (2) be admitted into; come into the company of; join; (3) income; means; (4) agree with; conform to; (5) arrive at; reach; (6) disappear; get out of sight;

［入場］ admission; entrance;
入場費 admission charge; entrance fee;
免費入場 admission free; entrance free;
憑票入場 admission by ticket only;
憑證入場 admission by card only;

［入黨］ become a member of a political party; join a political party;

［入道］ (1) become a monk; (2) become a nun;

［入地］ (1) die; (2) sink below the surface of the earth;
鑽天入地 search for an opening for oneself by all possible means;

［入定］ enter into meditation by tranquilizing the body, mouth and mind;
老僧入定 (said of a monk) very calm and without worldly passions;

［入耳］ (1) hear; (2) pleasing to the ear;
不入耳 not worth listening to; unpleasant to the ear;

［入港］ come at port; come into port;

［入閣］ get inside the imperial cabinet;

［入骨］ deep; to the marrow;
恨之入骨 be consumed with hatred for; bear a bitter hatred for; cherish bitter hatred; harbour an intense hatred; hate sb like poison; hate sth like poison; hate sb to the core; hate sb's guts; hate sb to the marrow; hate with all one's soul; nurse an inveterate hatred for;

［入國］ enter a country;
入國問禁 ask about taboos and bans upon arrival in a foreign country;

［入會］ join a society;

［入伙］ join a mess; join a gang;

［入籍］ be naturalized; naturalize;

［入腳］ begin; start;

［入教］ become a follower of a religion;

［入境］ enter a country;
入境簽證 entry visa;
入境問禁 ask about taboos and bans upon arrival in a foreign country; on entering a country, inquire about its taboos;

［入口］ (1) enter the mouth; (2) entrance; entry;
入口處 entrance;
入口點 access point;
入口通道 entrance gateway;
航道入口 channel entrance;
後門入口 back entrance;
檢查點入口 checkpoint entry;
坑道入口 adit entrance;
擴散器入口 diffusor entry;
正門入口 front entrance;

［入殮］ coffin; put a corpse in a coffin;

［入流］ (1) in fashion; (2) attain a certain level;

［入馬］ make progress in courtship;

［入門］ (1) elementary course; primer; the ABC of; the ABC's of; the alphabet of; (2) get ready for more profound study of a subject; have an elementary knowledge of a subject; initiate into;
入門費 down payment;
入門書 ABC book; abecedarium; primer;
入門問諱 learn about its taboos on going to a friend's;
電學入門 the ABC of electricity;
法學入門 the ABC of law;

［入夢］ (1) fall asleep; (2) appear in one's dream;

［入迷］ be enchanted; be fascinated; be obsessed by;
使入迷 entrance;

［入魔］ (1) captivated; deeply fascinated; infatuated; (2) bedeviled; bewitched; spellbound;

［入內］ be allowed into;
禁止入內 no admittance; no entry;

［入侵］ intrude; invade; make an incursion; make inroads;
大舉入侵 invade in full force;
突然入侵 incursion;

［入射］ incidence;
入射點 point of incidence;
入射角 angle of incidence;
入射線 incident ray;
切線入射 glancing incidence;
無規入射 random incidence;
斜入射 oblique incidence;
正入射 normal incidence;

[入神] captivated; deeply absorbed in; enthralled; entranced; spellbound; with ecstasy;
聽得入神 completely absorbed;
想得入神 be entranced in thought;
[入時] fashionable; trendy;
[入世] go into the society;
[入室] attain profundity in scholastic pursuits; become a real expert;
入室操戈 turn sb's argument against him; use sb's thought to attack his own principle;
入室弟子 one who learns an art directly from a master;
穿堂入室 go anywhere as one pleases;
登堂入室 gain the mastery of; pass through the hall into the inner chamber; reach the hall and enter the chamber;
引狼入室 bring disaster upon oneself; bring in a troublemaker; invite disaster by letting in invaders; invite the wolf to enter the fold; lead a wolf into one's house; let the wolf into the sheepfold; open the door to a dangerous foe; set a fox to keep one's geese; set the wolf to keep the sheep; usher the wolves into the house;
[入手] begin with; get under way; proceed from; put one's hand to; start with; take as the point of departure;
[入睡] fall asleep; go into dreamland; go to sleep;
酣然入睡 fall into a deep sleep;
慢慢入睡 drift off;
[入土] be buried; be interred;
入土為安 be laid to rest;
半截入土 in one's dying years;
[入微] in a subtle way; in every possible way;
[入圍] on the shortlist;
入圍名單 shortlist;
[入闈] enter the imperial examination hall;
[入味] (1) tasty; (2) interesting;
[入伍] become a soldier; enlist in the armed forces; enrol; join the army; join up;
[入席] take one's seat at a table for a meal;
入席就座 take one's seat at the table;
[入息] income;
入息保障 income security;
入息稅 income tax;

[入鄉隨俗] a guest must do as his host does; do at Rome as the Romans do; do in Rome as Rome does; go native; observe the customs of the place; one must howl with the wolves; when in Rome, do as the Romans do; when you are at Rome, do as Rome does;
[入選] be chosen; be selected;
[入學] (1) start school; (2) admission; enrol; enter a school; entrance; register;
入學考試 entrance examination;
入學申請 application for admission;
入學通知書 letter of admission;
入學者 enrollee;
入學資格 admission qualifications;
註冊入學 matriculation;
[入眼] agreeable to look at; pleasing to the eye; to one's liking;
不入眼 unpleasing to the eye;
~ 看不入眼 hold in contempt; not to one's liking;
~ 睇不入眼 look at but what is seen does not please the eyes;
[入夜] at night; at nightfall; in the evening;
[入獄] be imprisoned; be sent to jail; put behind bars; put in prison;
入獄一年 one year's imprisonment;
[入院] be admitted to hospital; be hospitalized;
[入月] (1) period of menstruation; (2) menses;
[入雲] into the clouds;
峻嶺入雲 high mountains pierce into the clouds;
[入帳] enter an item in an account; enter into the account book;
[入職] induction;
入職課程 induction course; induction programme;
[入主] enter as a host;
入主出奴 enter as a host and out as a slave – take a sectarian attitude; sectarian views; think of oneself as having a monopoly of all truths and of others as heretics;
[入贅] marry into and live with one's wife's family; son-in-law by adoption;
[入座] take one's seat;
對號入座 (1) sit in the right seat; take one's seat according to the number on the ticket; take one's seat indicated by a place card; (2) hit the nail on the

head;
憑票入座 admission by ticket only;

並入 amalgamate into; incorporate in; merge in;
併入 incorporate in; merge into;
步入 step into;
插入 break in; dig; implant; infix; inlay; insert; insertion; intercalate; interpose; intervene; plug in; run in;
衝入 plunge into;
出入 (1) come in and go out; go out and come in; (2) discrepancy; divergence;
闖入 break in; burst into; force one's way in; intrude into; rush in;
存入 deposit;
打入 (1) banish to; throw into; (2) infiltrate;
代入 substitution;
淡入 fade in;
倒入 decant; pour into;
調入 call in;
墮入 fall into; land oneself in; sink into;
而入 in;
貫入 injection;
歸入 classify; include;
混入 absorption; acceptance; get into an organization without going through the proper procedures; mix oneself inside a body of people; sneak into; worm one's way into;
擠入 squeeze into;
加入 (1) add; mix; put in; (2) accede to; join;
介入 get involved; interpose; intervene; step in; wade in;
借入 borrow;
浸入 immersion;
進入 enter; get into;
捲入 be drawn into; be involved in;
闌入 (1) encroach upon a place one is not supposed to enter; (2) mingle; mix;
流入 inflow; influx;
落入 fall into;
買入 buy;
納入 bring into; channel into;
嵌入 embedding; insertion; inset;
遷入 ecdemic;
潛入 (1) enter secretly; slip in; slip into; sneak into; steal in; (2) dive into; go under water;
切入 cut in;
侵入 intrude into; invade; make incursions into; sneak in;
沁入 permeate; soak into; soak through;
溶入 dissolve in;
捨入 round off;
深入 deepgoing; go deep into; thorough;
滲入 (1) permeate; seep into; (2) infiltrate; penetrate;
收入 (1) earnings; gross; gainings; income; proceeds; receipts; revenue; takings; (2) include; take in;
輸入 (1) import; (2) input;
肅入 usher in;
算入 count;
歲入 annual income; revenue;
投入 (1) put into; throw into; (2) join; pitch in;
突入 charge into;
吸入 inhale;
先入 (1) first impressions; (2) preconception;
陷入 (1) land oneself in; sink into; (2) be immersed in; be lost in;
寫入 write in;
延入 invite to enter;
譯入 translate into;
引入 call; draw into; introduce; lead into;
映入 map into;
湧入 inflow; inrush; rush in;
擁入 crowd into;
長入 evolve; grow into;
直入 go right in;
注入 empty into; injection; pour into;
轉入 change over to; shift to; switch over to;
撞入 burst into; thrust into;

ru

【洳】 damp; moist; oozy;

沮洳 marsh;

ru

【辱】 (1) disgrace; dishonour; insult; (2) condescend; deign; (3) undeservingly;

ru

【溽】 humid; moist;

［溽氣］ the muggy vapour;
溽氣蒸騰 sweltering;

［溽熱］ oppressively hot; sultry;

［溽暑］ sweltering summer weather;

［溽蒸］ damp and hot;

ru

【銣】 rubidium;

ru

【蓐】 bedmat; matting;

［蓐瘡］ (1) bedsores; (2) infantile boils;

［蓐母］ midwife;
［蓐食］ (1) breakfast in bed; take meals in bed; (2) rich food;

臨蓐 the short spell before giving birth;
坐蓐 be confined in childbirth; confinement;

ru
【褥】 bedding; coverlets; cushions; mattresses; quilts;
［褥瘡］ bedsores;
［褥單］ bed sheet;
［褥套］ ticking;
［褥子］ cotton-padded mattress; puff;

被褥 bedding; bedclothes;

ru
【縟】 (1) rich ornament; (2) excessive ceremony; excessive formality;
［縟節］ excessive formality;
［縟禮］ excessive ceremony;
［縟繡］ gorgeous; magnificent; resplendent;

繁縟 over-elaborate;

ruan³
ruan
【阮】 (1) an ancient state in today's Shaanxi; (2) an ancient musical instrument; (3) a surname;
［阮囊羞澀］ embarrassingly short of money; having an empty pocket; in straitened circumstances; lacking sufficient funds to meet necessary expenses; poor; short of cash;

ruan
【軟】 (1) flexible; plastic; pliable; soft; (2) gentle; mild; soft; tender; (3) cowardly; effeminate; feeble; weak; (4) poor in ability; poor in quality; (5) easily moved or influenced;

［軟半］ less than a half;
［軟材］ softwood;
［軟尺］ measuring tape;
［軟飯］ paste-like rice;
吃軟飯 depend on a woman rather than work for a living;
［軟風］ gentle breeze; light wind;
［軟膏］ ointment;
花香軟膏 flower ointment;
抗朦軟膏 anti-dimming ointment;
檸檬色軟膏 citrine ointment;
石油軟膏 petrol ointment;
［軟骨］ cartilage; gristle;
軟骨病 cartilage;
結節狀軟骨病 chondropathia tuberosa;
軟骨成骨 cartilage bone;
軟骨刺 chondrophyte
軟骨蛋白 cartilagine;
軟骨發生 chondrogenesis;
軟骨發育不良 achondroplasia; chondrodysplasia;
軟骨發育不全 dyschondroplasia; chondrodysplasia;
軟骨骼 cartilaginous skeleton;
軟骨骨瘤 chondrostoma;
軟骨環 cartilaginous annulus;
軟骨肌瘤 chondromyoma;
軟骨瘤 cartilaginous tumour; chondroma
~黏液軟骨瘤 myxoenchondroma;
~真性軟骨瘤 true chondroma;
~脂肪軟骨瘤 lipochondroma;
軟骨顱 chondrocranium;
軟骨膜 cartilage membrane;
軟骨破裂 chondroclasis;
軟骨肉瘤 chondrrosarcoma;
軟骨素 chondroitin;
軟骨特技 contortion;
軟骨頭 coward; spineless person; timid person; weak-kneed person;
軟骨形成 chondrosis;
軟骨學 chondrology;
軟骨營養障礙 chondrodystrophy;
軟骨疣 chondrophyte;
軟骨脂肪瘤 chondrolipoma;
關節軟骨 articular cartilage;
假軟骨 pseudocartilage;
肩胛軟骨 bladebone cartilage;
瞼軟骨 ciliary cartilage;
劍突軟骨 ensiform cartilage;
腱軟骨 tendon cartilage;
角軟骨 cornual cartilage;
眶前軟骨 antorbital cartilage;
肋軟骨 costal cartilage;
黏液軟骨 mucocartilage;
盤狀軟骨 discoid meniscus;
舌基軟骨 basihyoidian cartilage;
實質軟骨 parenchymatous cartilage;
鰓軟骨 branchial cartilage;
聽道軟骨 cartilage of acoustic meatus;
聽管軟骨 cartilage of auditory tube;

外耳道軟骨 cartilago meatus acustici;
小角軟骨 corniculate cartilage;
暫時性軟骨 temporary cartilage;

[軟和] (1) soft; (2) gentle; kind;

[軟化] (1) conciliate; soften; softening; softening up; (2) win over by soft tactics;
軟化劑 softener;
~化學軟化劑 chemical softener;
~水軟化劑 water softener;
布帛軟化 cloth softening;
創傷性骨軟化 malacia traumatica;
創傷性脊髓軟化 spondylomalacia traumatica;
肺軟化 pneumomalacia;
鞏膜軟化 scleromalacia;
骨軟化 halisteresis;
機械軟化 mechanical softening;
脊髓軟化 spondylomalacia;
假骨軟化 pseudo-osteomalacia;
瞼板軟化 tarsomalacia;
角膜軟化 keratomalacia;
腦軟化 softening of the brain;
熱軟化 heat softening;
神經軟化 neuromalacia;
腎軟化 nephromalacia;

[軟件] software;
軟件安全分析 software safety analysis;
軟件包 software package;
軟件保護 software protection;
軟件產業 software industry;
軟件成本 software cost;
軟件仿真 software emulation;
軟件服務站 software house;
軟件工程 software engineering;
~軟件工程學 science of software engineering;
軟件環境 software environment;
軟件開發 software development;
~軟件開發包 software development kit;
~軟件開發過程 software development process;
~軟件開發計劃 software development plan;
~軟件開發庫 software development library;
~軟件開發周期 software development cycle;
軟件科學 software science;
軟件可靠性 software reliability;
軟件靈活性 software flexibility;
軟件潛行分析 software sneak analysis;
軟件設計 software design;
~軟件設計過程 software design procedure;
軟件適應性 software adaptability;
軟件完整性 software integrity;
軟件維護 software maintenance;
軟件文件 software documentation;
軟件支持系統 software support system;
翻譯軟件 translation software;
共享軟件 shareware;
基本軟件 basic software;
計算機軟件 computer software;
免費軟件 freeware;
通信軟件 communication software;
通用軟件 common software; general purpose software;
應用軟件 application software;
臃腫軟件 bloatware;

[軟禁] detain a person; house arrest; house confinement; put sb under house arrest;
被軟禁 under house arrest;

[軟綿綿] (1) feathery; soft; velvety; (2) feeble; weak;

[軟木] cork;
軟木塞 cork;

[軟泥] ooze;
抱球蟲軟泥 globigerina ooze;
放射蟲軟泥 radiolarian ooze;
深海軟泥 abyssal ooze; deep-sea ooze;
矽藻軟泥 diatom ooze;
翼足蟲軟泥 pteropod ooze;
有孔蟲軟泥 foraminiferal ooze;

[軟片] film;
單頁軟片 sheet film;

[軟弱] feeble; flabby; weak;
軟弱可欺 weak and can be bullied; weak and easy to bully; weakness or sth one can take advantage of;
軟弱無力 deficient in militancy; doughy; faint; flaccid; have no sting in it; limply; milk-and-water; puniness; puny;
軟弱無能 effete; feeble and incapable; flabby and impotent; in a weak and helpless position; incompetent and in a weak position; ineffectual; weak and incompetent;
生性軟弱 weak by nature;
一時軟弱 in a moment of weakness;
意志軟弱 as weak as water;

［軟食］ soft diet; pap; soft food;

［軟糖］ confection; fondant; fudge; jelly; jelly drops; soft sweets;
果汁軟糖 fruit jelly;
膠凍軟糖 gelled confection; table jelly;
水晶軟糖 agar fruit jelly;

［軟體］ software;
軟體動物 mollusc;
軟體套膜 mantle;

［軟性］ bland; gentle; light; mild; soft;
軟性磁碟 floppy disk;
軟性新聞 human-interest stories; light news; light stories;

［軟硬］ gentle or harsh; soft or hard;
軟硬不吃 neither listen to reason nor bow to force; yield to neither the carrot nor the club;
軟硬兼施 act tough and talk soft; adopt every possible means, tough and soft; bring both force and reason to bear; carrot and stick; coax and threaten by turns; combine hard tactics with soft; combine harsh and mild measures; couple threat with blandishment; couple threats with promises; mix taught with kid-glove tactics; resort to both the hard and the soft way; temper force with mercy; threaten and entreat by turns; try both tough and soft tactics; use all tactics, both soft and tough; use both coercion and persuasion; use both hard and soft tactics; use both indulgent and callous methods; use both persuasion and force; use the stick and the carrot; wield both the carrot and the stick;
軟硬兩手 the stick and the carrot;
軟硬適中 neither too hard nor too soft;
吃軟不吃硬 can be persuaded by reason but not be cowed by force; open to persuation, but not to coercion;
欺軟怕硬 browbeat the weak but fear the strong; brutal towards the weak but powerless towards the staunch; bully the faint-hearted but fear the stout-hearted; bully the soft and fear the hard; bully the soft and fear the tough; bully the weak and avoid the strong; bully the weak and be scared of the strong; bully the weak and fear the strong; bully the weak and give in to the tough; bully the weak but yield to one who can fight back; cringe before the strong and bully the weak; if you're weak it'll bully you, if you're tough it'll give way; meek towards the brutal and brutal towards the meek; oppress the weak and fear the strong; play the bully; take advantage of those who are kind and fear those who are hard;
軟騙硬詐 bluff and dupe people with tricks;

［軟語］ gentle words;
軟語溫存 cherish with soft words; exchange so many endearments; have many caressing and affectionate words to say to one another; murmur sweet endearments;
軟語溫馨 gentle and sweet words; soft, tender and fine voice;

［軟玉］ (1) nephrite; (2) bean curd;
軟玉溫香 as fair as jade; delicate gem with warm fragrance — the flesh and fragrance of a beauty; her body soft and warm, really enticing;

臉軟 having too much consideration for sb's feelings;
綿軟 (1) soft; (2) weak;
泡軟 macerate;
疲軟 fatigued and weak; slump; weaken;
柔軟 easily bent; flexible; lithe; soft; yielding;
手軟 irresolute when firmness is needed; soft-hearted;
鬆軟 (1) fluffy; soft; (2) feeble;
酥軟 limp; soft; weak;
瘈軟 sore and weak;
酸軟 aching and limp;
癱軟 (of arms, legs, etc.) weak and limp;
細軟 expensive clothing and other valuables; jewellery;
心軟 kind-hearted; softhearted; tenderhearted;

ruan
【蝡】 wriggle;

ruan
【蠕】 squirm; wriggle;

［蠕變］ creep;
表觀蠕變 apparent creep;
化學蠕變 chemical creep;
彎曲蠕變 bending creep;
壓縮蠕變 compression creep;

災變蠕變 catastrophic creep;
綜合蠕變 combined creep;
[蠕蟲] creepy-crawly; helminth; worm;
蠕蟲洞 wormhole;
蠕蟲學 helminthology;
環節蠕蟲 annelid;
[蠕動] creep; squirm; wriggle;
磁蠕動 magnate creep;
軌道蠕動 creep of the rails;
錨頭蠕動 anchorage creep;
[蠕蠕] wriggling;

rui²

rui
【甤】 overladden with fruit;

rui
【緌】 ornamental strings on a hat;

rui
【蕤】 (1) drooping leaves, flowers or fruits; (2) shrub;

葳蕤 (of plants) luxuriant;

rui³

rui
【蕊】 (1) flower-bud; unopened flower; (2) stamens or pistils of a flower;
[蕊心] stamens and pistils;
[蕊汁] viscid juice of plants;
[蕊珠] (1) palace of gods; (2) one of the Daoist scriptures;

燈蕊 lampwick; wick;
發蕊 put forth stamens and pistil;
花蕊 stamen and pistil;
石蕊 (1) reindeer moss; (2) litmus;
雄蕊 stamen;

rui⁴

rui
【汭】 bend in a stream;

rui
【枘】 wooden handle;
[枘鑿] cannot see eye to eye; incompatible;
枘鑿不入 fit a square handle into a round socket; incompatible; mentally conflicting;

鑿枘 a round peg in a square hole; incompatible;

rui
【芮】 (1) small; tiny; (2) name of an ancient state in today's Shanxi; (3) a surname;
[芮芮] (of grass blades) slender;

rui
【蜹】 gnat;
[蜹翼] wings of a gnat — very tiny things;

rui
【瑞】 (1) auspicious; fortunate; lucky; (2) a surname;
[瑞氣] celestial phenomena portending peace and prosperity;
[瑞祥] auspiciousness; good fortune; good luck; good omen;
[瑞雪] auspicious snow; timely snow;
瑞雪繽紛 seasonable snow is falling in flakes of mixed sizes; the snow falls in soft flakes;
瑞雪霏霏 the snow begins to fall;
瑞雪紛飛 a good snow is falling; snow falls thick and fast;
瑞雪兆豐年 a fall of seasonable snow gives promise of a fruitful year; a good winter brings a good summer; a heavy snowfall in winter means a bumper harvest; a snow year, a rich year; a timely snow promises a good harvest; Auspicious snow promises good harvest; the auspicious snow argurs well for the next year's harvest; timely snow foretells a bumper harvest; winter snow signifies a year of crops;
[瑞雲] auspicious clouds;
[瑞兆] propitious portent;

吉瑞 sign of good luck;
人瑞 venerable old man or woman;
祥瑞 auspicious sign; propitious omen;

rui
【銳】 (1) acute; keen; sharp; (2) energetic; fighting spirit; vigour; (3) clever; intelligent; quick-witted;
[銳不可當] cannot be held back; full of fighting spirit as to be irresistible; irresistible; no force can stop;
[銳度] acuity; sharpness;
彩色銳度 colour acuity;
光柵銳度 grating acuity;
輪廓銳度 contour acuity;
色差銳度 colour difference acuity;

視覺銳度 visual acuity;
雙目銳度 binocular acuity;
條紋銳度 fringe acuity;
聽覺銳度 hearing acuity;
最大銳度 maximum acuity;

[銳髮] stray hair before the ear;

[銳化] sharpening;
脈衝銳化 pulse sharpening;
圖像銳化 image sharpening;

[銳減] decline sharply; drop markedly;

[銳角] acute angle;
銳角三角形 acute-angled triangle;

[銳利] keen; pointed; sharp;
目光銳利 eagle-eyed; have an experienced eye; have sharp eyes; have the eye of a sailor; hawk-eyed; see through a millstone; sharp-eyed; sharp-sighted;
眼光銳利 have keen sight;

[銳敏] acute; keen; quick-witted; sharp;
銳敏的才智 incisive wit;
銳敏的洞察力 quick insight;

[銳氣] aggressiveness; dash; mettle; vigour; virility;
保存銳氣 preserve vigour;
避其銳氣 avoid the enemy when they are full of vigour;
挫其銳氣 break sb's spirit; cut sb down to size; deflate sb's arrogance; take down a peg or two; take the edge off sb's spirit;
耗盡銳氣 deplete one's vigour;
缺乏銳氣 lack vigour;
失去銳氣 lose one's spirit;

[銳士] man of energy; man of intelligence;

[銳眼] insight; sharp eyes; vision;

[銳意] determination; eager intention; sharp will;
銳意改革 reform with keen determination;

[銳志] determination; earnest intention; sharp will; spirit of enterprise;

鋒銳 keen; sharp;
尖銳 (1) sharp-pointed; (2) incisive; penetrating; (3) piercing; shrill; (4) acute; intense;
精銳 crack; picked;
敏銳 acute; keen; sharp;

rui

【叡】 (1) understand thoroughly; (2) astute and discreet; wise and clever; (3) divine sagacity of sages;

[叡哲] divinely wise; sagacious;

[叡智] wise and far-sighted;

聰叡 bright and far-sighted;

run2

run

【犉】 (1) ox with yellow hair and a black mouth; (2) ox of seven feet tall;

run4

run

【閏】 (1) with leftover; with surplus; (2) deputy; substitute; usurp; (3) intercalate;

[閏秒] leap second;

[閏年] intercalary year; leap year;

[閏期] intercalation;

[閏日] intercalary day; leap day;

[閏統] illegitimate rule;

[閏月] intercalary month in the lunar calendar; leap month;

run

【潤】 (1) fresh; glossy; moist; smooth; (2) lubricate; moisten; (3) embellish; touch up; (4) benefit; profit;

[潤筆] remuneration for a writer, painter, or calligrapher;

[潤寡] aid the poor;

[潤毫] pay for services rendered;

[潤喉糖] lozenge; pastille; throat tablet;
水果潤喉糖 fruit pastille;

[潤滑] (1) lubricate; lubrication; (2) smooth;
潤滑劑 lubricant; wetting agent;
~動物潤滑劑 animal lubricant;
~防凍潤滑劑 antifreezing lubricant;
潤滑能力 lubricating ability;
潤滑器 lubricator;
~空氣管路潤滑器 air line lubricator;
~自動潤滑器 automatic lubricator;
潤滑油 lubricant; lubrication oil;
~鏈潤滑油 chain lubricant;
~制動缸潤滑油 brake cylinder lubricant;
潤滑脂 grease;
~鈣基潤滑脂 albany grease;
~抗老化潤滑脂 ageing-resistant grease;
~氣閘潤滑脂 air brake grease;
~通用潤滑脂 all-purpose grease;
氣體潤滑 aerodynamic lubrication;
霧化潤滑 atomized lubrication;

[潤膩] fine and smooth;
[潤色] polish;
[潤飾] add colour; embellish a piece of writing; polish a piece of writing;
[潤濕] moist and fresh; wetting;
潤濕能力 wetting ability;
鋪展潤濕 spreading wetting;
浸入潤濕 immersional wetting;
優先潤濕 preferential wetting;
[潤澤] (1) agreeable; glossy; moist; sleek; smooth; (2) enrich by favours; lubricate; moisten;

豐潤 plump and smooth-skinned;
光潤 (of skin) smooth;
紅潤 rosy; ruddy; smooth; tender and rosy;
滑潤 lubricant;smooth; well-lubricated;
漸潤 saturate with water;
浸潤 (1) infiltrate; infiltration; soak; (2) be gradually influenced; (3) adhesion;
利潤 profit;
尿浸潤 urecchysis;
柔潤 soft and moist;
濡潤 make moist;
刪潤 revise and polish;
濕潤 moist;
溫潤 (1) mild and smooth; (2) beautiful and tender;
沃潤 fertile and moist;
細潤 fine and glossy;
淹潤 amiable but timid; intimate but shy;
浥潤 moist; wet;
瑩潤 clear and lustrous; polished and glossy;
圓潤 mellow and full;
沾潤 (1) moisten; wet; (2) harvest benefits from the side;
滋潤 moist; moisten;

ruo²
ruo
【挼】 (1) crumple; (2) rub; stroke;
[挼搓] crumple; knead; rub;
[挼挲] fondle; rub; stroke;

ruo⁴
ruo
【若】 (1) as if; like; seem; similar; (2) assuming; if; provided that; suppose; supposing; (3) you;
[若敖鬼餒] have no progeny; without offspring;
[若輩] you all;
[若非] if not; were it not for; unless;
[若干] a certain amount; a certain number; a few; several; some;
[若果] if; provided that;
[若何] how; what; what now;
[若渴] equal to one's thirst;
愛才若渴 have a passion for talent; one's love of talents is equal to one's thirst for water; very fond of talented people;
求賢若渴 seek for the virtuous as a thirsty person for water; seek talent with eagerness; thirst after talents;
嗜賢若渴 one's love for able men is equal to one's thirst for water;
思賢若渴 desire greatly to win the support of the wise; one's love for able men is equal to one's thirst for water;
[若狂] excited;
憤激若狂 wild with excitement;
[若夢] like a dream;
浮生若夢 life is like a dream; man's life is but a dream;
~浮生若夢，為歡幾何 our floating life is but a dream, how often can we enjoy ourselves?
[若若] long and pendent;
[若使] assuming that; if; supposing that;
[若是] if; supposing;
[若許] like this; thus;
[若要] if one wishes to;
若要好，問三老 if you wish good advice, consult an old man;
若要家不和，娶個小老婆 if you want to banish peace from your household, get yourself a concubine;
若要人不知，除非己莫為 don't do it if you don't want others to know it; if you don't want people to know, don't do it; the best way to hide a misdeed is not to commit it; the day has eyes, the night has ears; the only way to keep people from knowing sth is not to dot it; to keep people from talking you must do nothing; what is done at night appears by day;

不若 no match for;
仿若 as if; as though;
恍若 as if; seem;

即若 even; even if; even though;
假若 if; in case; supposing;
莫若 might as well; would be better;
如若 if; in case; supposing;
設若 if; provided; supposing;
倘若 if; in case; supposing;
儼若 be just like;
自若 composed; self-possessed;

ruo

【弱】 (1) delicate; feeble; fragile; infirm; tender; weak; (2) young; (3) inferior; (4) lose; (5) a little less than;

[弱拍] unaccented beat; weak beat;

[弱不好弄] one does not like playing while in his childhood;

[弱不禁風] so delicate a constitution that one is unable to stand a gust of wind; on the lift; too frail to stand a gust of wind;

[弱弟] young brother;

[弱點] Achilles' heel; failing; vulnerable point; vulnerable spot; weak point; weak spot; weakness;
暴露自己的弱點 reveal one's weakness;

[弱冠] coming of age at twenty; twenty-year-old man; youth;
年及弱冠 attain the age of twenty; come of age;

[弱國] weak nation;

[弱翰] writing brush;

[弱累] the burden of bringing up one's children;

[弱冷] low cooling;

[弱柳] (1) pliant willow tree; (2) prostitute;

[弱女] young girl;

[弱式] weak;
弱式動詞 weak verb;

[弱勢] (1) in a relatively weak position; (2) the disadvantaged;
弱勢群體 disadvantaged group;

[弱視] amblyopia; lazy eye;
弱視矯正法 amblyopiatrics;
弱視性眼震 amblyopic nystagmus;
弱視遺傳 recessive inheritance;
弱視者 amblyope;
創傷性弱視 traumatic amblyopia;
尿毒症性弱視 uremic amblyopia;
偏側弱視 hemiamblyopia;
外傷性弱視 traumatic amblyopia;
夜發性弱視 nocturnal amblyopia;
營養缺乏性弱視 deficiency amblyopia;
中毒性弱視 toxic amblyopia;

[弱歲] youth;

[弱息] my child;

[弱項] weak spot; yielding;

[弱小] small and weak;

[弱顏] bashful;

[弱音器] mute; sordino;

[弱者] the weak; the weak and the timid; underdog;
同情弱者 feel sympathy for the underdog;

[弱震] weak shock;

[弱質] feeble constitution; infirm;

[弱智] weak intelligence;
弱智兒童 retarded child;
弱智教育 education for mentally retarded children;

暗弱 dense; stupid;
闇弱 benighted; ignorant, stupid and cowardly; irresolute;
病弱 sick and weak;
薄弱 frail; weak;
孱弱 (1) frail; (2) weak and incompetent; (3) frail; weak;
脆弱 delicate; fragile; frail; frailty; tender; weak;
單弱 feeble; thin and weak;
淡弱 weak;
減弱 abate; attenuate; damp; fade; trip-out; weaken;
老弱 the old and weak;
羸弱 frail; thin and weak;
攣弱 crooked and weak;
脈弱 weak pulse;
懦弱 coward; weak;
疲弱 tired and weak;
貧弱 (of a country) poor and weak;
怯弱 timid and weak-willed;
冉弱 drooping;
苒弱 (of flowers) drooping;
荏弱 fragile; soft; weak;
柔弱 delicate; weak;
軟弱 feeble; weak;
示弱 give in; give the impression of weakness; show the white feather; show weakness; take sth lying down; yield;
瘦弱 emaciated; emaciated and frail; thin and weak;
衰弱 debilitate; fall into a decline; feeble; not healthy; sickly; weak;

體弱 debility;
微弱 faint; feeble; weak;
文弱 effeminate; gentle and frail-looking;
細弱 slender and weak; slim and fragile; thin and delicate;
孅弱 delicate; frail; weak;
纖弱 delicate; slim and fragile;
虛弱 (1) debilitated; debility; in poor health; weak; (2) feeble; flabby; weak;
削弱 abate; cripple; devitalize; enfeeble; put a brake on; sap; weaken;
幼弱 young and delicate;
稚弱 tender and delicate;

ruo
【偌】 as; such;
[偌大] of such a size; so big;
偌大年紀 so advanced in years; so old;
[偌多] so many; so much;

ruo
【蒻】 (1) water plant; wild arum; (2) rush-mat;
[蒻席] rush mat made of arum;
蒟蒻 amorphophallus rivieri;

ruo
【箬】 (1) bamboo cuticle; (2) a kind of bamboo with broad leaves which are often used to make various coverings;
[箬帽] broad-rimmed bamboo hat;
箬帽芒鞋 bamboo hat and grass shoes;
[箬竹] indocalamus;

ruo
【篛】 same as 箬, a kind of bamboo with broad leaves;

ruo
【爇】 burn; set fire;

sa¹

sa

【仨】 three; trinity; trio;

［仨瓜倆棗］ mere trifles; only a few people; only a few things; three melons and two dates; trivia;

sa

【撒】 (1) cast; disentwine; let go; let go one's hold; let out; loosen; release; set loose; unknot; unleash; untangle; (2) scatter; spread; (3) ease; let oneself go; relax; throw off all restraint; (4) display; exhibit; show;

［撒村］ curse; rap out; swear; talk dirty; use vulgar language;

［撒放］ disentwine; release; unknot; unleash; untangle;

［撒糞］ (1) defecate; empty the bowels; evacuate the bowels; loose bowels; move the bowels; relieve bowels; shit; take a shit; (2) talk nonsense; talk rubbish;

［撒瘋］ (1) behave recklessly; (2) vent one's anger;

撒瘋撒癡 headlong; irrational; reckless;

［撒謊］ lie; make up a story; speak falsely; tell a lie;

故意撒謊 lie intentionally;

撒大謊 draw the longbow; lie; lie in one's teeth; lie in one's throat; lie like a trooper; tell a lie;

一味撒謊 lie like a gasmeter;

［撒姦］ play dirty tricks;

［撒嬌］ act in a pettishly charming manner; act like a spoiled child; play the woman;

撒嬌賣乖 act like a spoiled child and show off one's cleverness;

撒嬌撒痴 act spoiled; pout and try all one's sweet wiles; struggle and gesticulate savagely;

撒嬌裝嗔 act as a spoiled child; act in a pettishly charming manner;

裝嗔撒嬌 act in a pettishly charming manner;

［撒腳］ take to one's heels;

［撒酒瘋］ be drunk and act crazy; behave atrociously;

［撒開］ (1) get away; (2) part; (3) let go; release;

［撒科打諢］ introduce comic remarks in dialogue;

［撒賴］ act shamelessly; behave like a hooligan; behave like a rascal; make a scene; raise hell; show villainy;

［撒馬］ give free rein to a horse;

［撒尿］ have a leak; have a slash; make water; pass urine; pass water; pee; pee-pee; piddle; piss; spend a penny; take a leak; take a slash; urinate; wee-wee;

［撒潑］ act hysterically and refuse to see reason; behave rudely; in a tantrum; shrewish and make a scene; unreasonable and make a scene;

撒潑打滾 fly into a tantrum; roll over and over on the floor while scolding others;

撒潑行凶 make a scene and do violence;

［撒氣］ (1) get a flat; go soft; leak; (2) give vent to one's anger; vent one's anger; vent one's ill temper;

［撒手］ (1) leave hold of; let go; let go one's hold; relax the grasp; relax the hold; relinquish one's hold; (2) abandon; give up; refuse to take any further interest in; wash one's hands off the matter;

撒手不幹 chuck up one's job;

撒手不管 refuse to have anything more to do with the matter; refuse to take any further part in; relinquish one's hold on; take no further interest in; wash one's hands of the business;

撒手塵寰 die; leave this mortal world; pass away;

撒手歸西 die; go to the Western Heaven; go west; pass away; pay one's debt of nature;

撒手鐗 one's best card; one's trump card; one's speciality;

［撒腿］ run; start running; take to one's heels;

撒腿就跑 make off at once; scamper;

［撒網］ cast a net; pay out a net; spread a net;

撒網捕風 cast a net to catch the wind; catch the wind with a net; make a vain effort;

撒網捕魚 cast a net to catch fish;

撒網擒賊 set a trap to catch the thief;

攔河撒網 shoot a fishnet across a river;

［撒線］ let out the string of a kite;

[撒丫子] scamper; sneak off;
[撒野] act boorishly; act wantonly; act wildly; behave atrociously; behave rudely; run wild;
[撒嘴] relax the bite;

決撒 break with; rupture;

sa³

sa

【洒】 (1) I; me; (2) pour; shed; spill; spray; sprinkle;
[洒掃] sprinkle water and sweep away the dirt;
[洒水] sprinkle water;
洒水掃地 sprinkle water and sweep the floor;

揮洒 (1) spray; sprinkle; (2) write or paint freely;
噴洒 spray; sprinkle;

sa

【靸】 child's shoes; slip on slippers;
[靸鞋] (1) slippers; (2) strong cloth shoes;

sa

【撒】 (1) disperse; scatter; spread; sprinkle; (2) drop; spill;
[撒播] (1) broadcast; disseminate; spread; (2) sow;
撒播機 broadcaster; seed broadcaster;
~ 飛機撒播機 aerial broadcaster;
~ 肥料撒播機 fertilizer broadcaster;
~ 牽引式撒播機 trailing broadcaster;
[撒豆成兵] cast beans on grounds which are transformed by magic into soldiers; turn handfuls of peas into armies of warriors; turn sprinkled beans into soldiers;
[撒和] (1) go for a stroll; (2) trot a horse;
[撒漫] spend generously;
[撒然] abruptly;
[撒散] scatter about; spread; sprinkle; strew;
[撒水] spray water; sprinkle water;
[撒種] sow seeds;

彌撒 Mass;

sa

【灑】 (1) spill; splash; spray; sprinkle; (2) wash;
[灑汗] perspire; sweat;
[灑淚] shed tears;
灑淚而別 as one said farewell, the tears run down one's cheeks; bid each other farewell with tears in one's eyes; in tears to bid each other farewell; part in tears; take their leave of each other; shedding tears;
灑淚告別 part in tears; pay one's last respects with tears; take a tearful leave;
[灑落] (1) casual and elegant; (2) desolate; dilapidated; (3) give the cold shoulder to sb; rude to sb;
[灑泣] shed tears;
[灑然] frightened; shocked;
[灑灑] continuously; incessantly; voluminous;
灑灑萬言 a lengthy speech; speak at great length;
[灑掃] sprinkle water and sweep the floor;
[灑水] purling; spill water; sprinkle water; watering;
灑水車 sprinkler; street sprinkler; watering car;
灑水壺 watering can;
灑水器 sprinkler;
[灑湯] bungle; fail;
[灑脱] casual and carefree; free and easy; graceful;

漂瀟 (of a person) natural and unrestrained;
瀟灑 natural and unrestrained;

sa⁴

sa

【卅】 thirtieth day of a month; thirty;

sa

【趿】 pick up with the foot;

sa

【颯】 (1) rustle; sound of the wind; whistling; (2) dilapidated; failing; weakened; (3) elegant; graceful; natural and unrestrained;
[颯沓] (1) abundant; crowded; numerous; (2) fly in a flock;
[颯然] soughing; sound of wind; whistling;
[颯颯] bright and brave;
[颯爽] brave; valiant;
颯爽英姿 bold and brave; bright and brave; mighty in spirit and heroic in

bearing; of valiant and heroic bearing; valiant and heroic in bearing;

衰颯 be on the wane; decline; downhearted;
蕭颯 bleak; desolate;

sa

【薩】 (1) Buddhist gods; (2) a surname;
［薩克斯管］ saxophone;
薩克斯管吹奏者 saxophonist;

菩薩 (1) bodhisattva; (2) Buddha; Buddhist idol; (3) kind-hearted person;

sai¹
sai

【塞】 (1) block up; clog up; stop up; (2) fill; fill in; satiate; squeeze in; squeeze into; stuff; (3) cork; plug; seal; stopper;
［塞擦音］ affricate;
［塞車］ be held up in traffic; traffic jam;
遇上塞車 be stuck in a traffic jam;
［塞滿］ fill up; stuff full;
［塞牙］ food stuck between the teeth;
塞牙縫 sth very little;
［塞子］ cork; plug;
呼叫塞子 calling plug;
酒瓶塞子 wine cork;
蓄電池塞子 battery plug;
應答塞子 answering plug;
澡盆塞子 bath plug;
錐形塞子 tapered cork;

鼻塞 nasal congestion;
閉塞 (1) stop up; (2) out of the way;
耳塞 earphone; earplug;
活塞 piston;
填塞 (1) stuff; (2) fulfill as a matter of form;

sai

【腮】 cheek;
［腮幫子］ cheek;
［腮骨］ cheekbone;
［腮頰］ cheek;
［腮托］ chin rest;
［腮腺］ parotid gland;
腮腺管 parotid duct;
腮腺炎 parotitis;
~ 流行性腮腺炎 epidemic parotitis;
~ 膿性腮腺炎 parotitis phlegmonosa;
~ 術後腮腺炎 postoperative parotitis;

sai

【顋】 same as 腮；

sai

【鰓】 branchia; gills of a fish;
［鰓蓋］ gill cover;
鰓蓋骨 operculum;
［鰓裂］ cleft;
［鰓片］ gill;

瓣胸鰭 lobed pectoral fin;
對鰓 zygobranchiate;
海鰓 sea feather; sea pen;

sai⁴
sai

【塞】 fort; fortress;
［塞外］ beyond the borders; beyond the frontiers; beyond the Great Wall; north of the Great Wall;
塞外風光 northern-frontier scene;
塞外江南 lush southern-type fields north of the Great Wall;
［塞翁失馬］ blessing in disguise; mishap may turn out to be a fortune;
塞翁失馬，安知非福 a blessing in disguise; a loss may turn out to be a gain; a loss sometimes spells a gain; every cloud has a silver lining; misfortune may to be a blessing in disguise;

邊塞 frontier fortress;
關塞 fortress;
萊塞 laser;
要塞 fortification; fortress;

sai

【賽】 (1) competition; contest; game; match; race; tournament; (2) compete; contend for superiority; contest; have a competition; rival; (3) comparable to; surpass; (4) a surname;
［賽車］ (1) automobile race; cycle racing; motorcycle race; race car; (2) racing bicycle; racing vehicle;
賽車運動 motor racing;
短程賽車 drag race;
~ 短程賽車汽車 dragster;
改裝賽車 stock car;
微型賽車 go-cart; go-kart;
小型賽車 kart;

[賽船] run a boat race;
[賽狗] dog race;
[賽過] better than; exceed; overtake; surpass;
[賽會] (1) carnival; (2) display; exhibition; exposition;
祈神賽會 religious thanksgiving festival;
迎神賽會 noisy processions and festivals held in honour of local deities;
[賽馬] horse race; horse racing; race; racehorse; racing; the turf;
賽馬場 race course;
賽馬大會 gymkhana;
賽馬跑道 racecourse; turf;
賽馬會 race meeting;
賽馬騎師 jockey;
負重賽馬 welter race;
平地賽馬 flat racing;
讓步賽馬 allowance race;
越野障礙賽馬 steeplechase;
[賽跑] dash; race; sprint;
賽跑道 course;
100 米賽跑 100-metre sprint;
200 米賽跑 200-metre dash;
長距離賽跑 long-distance race;
環城賽跑 round-the-city race;
接力賽跑 relay race;
跨欄賽跑 hurdle race;
兩二三足賽跑 three-legged race;
馬拉松賽跑 marathon race;
套袋賽跑 sack race;
越野賽跑 cross-country race;
障礙賽跑 obstacle race; steeplechase;
中距離賽跑 middle-distance race;
[賽前] prematch;
賽前練習 knock-up;
[賽球] (1) ball game; (2) play a ball game;
[賽拳] (1) finger-guessing game; (2) boxing bout;
[賽事] competition; game; match;
體育賽事 sports event;
[賽艇] (1) rowing; (2) racing boat; shell;
單人賽艇 scull;
摩托賽艇 powerboat;

安慰賽 consolation match;
比賽 compete in a contest; competition; contest; have a race; match; tournament;
表演賽 exhibition match;
參賽 enter a competition; participate in a competition; participate in a match; take part in match;
出賽 compete; play in a match;
初賽 preliminary contest;
對抗賽 dual meeting;
複賽 intermediary heat; play-off; quarter-final; semi-final;
觀賽 watch a sports contest;
冠軍賽 championships;
吉卜賽 gipsy;
加時賽 extra time;
接力賽 relay; relay race;
錦標賽 championship contest;
徑賽 track;
競賽 compete; contest;
決賽 cup final; final; the finals;
聯賽 league matches;
祈賽 religious rite for thanking the gods for their help;
球賽 ball game; ball match; game; match;
拳賽 boxing match;
淘汰賽 elimination series;
田徑賽 track and field meeting;
田賽 field events;
團體賽 team competition;
選拔賽 selective trials;
循環賽 round robin;
邀請賽 invitional tournament;
義賽 benefit match;
友誼賽 friendly match;
預賽 preliminary contest; preliminary heat;
越野賽 cross-country race;

san[1]
san

【三】 (1) three; (2) many; more than two; several;
[三八] three and eight;
[三百] three hundred;
三百六十病，唯有相思苦 of the three hundred and sixty sicknesses, lovesickness is the most difficult to cure;
三百六十行 all sorts of occupations; all trades and professions; all walks of life;
~ 三百六十行，行行出狀元 there are three hundred and sixty trades, and every trade has its master;
~ 三百六十行，行行有規矩 there are three hundred and sixty trades, and every trade has its rules and regulations;

[三班制] three-shift system;
[三杯] three cups;
三杯和萬事，一醉解千愁 having three cups of wine irons out all differences, and getting drunk frees one of all worries;
[三倍] threefold; triple;
三倍體 triploid;
[三部曲] trilogy;
[三彩] three-colour glazed pottery;
[三餐] three meals;
日圖三餐，夜求一宿 have no other ambitions than food in one's stomach and a roof over one's head; three meals during the day and a sound sleep at night are what one wants to get;
[三尺] three feet;
三尺之冰非一日之寒 Rome was not built in one day; the thick ice is not frozen within a day;
[三重] threefold; treble; triple; tripling;
三重唱 trio; vocal trio;
三重翻譯 triple translation;
三重否定 triple negation;
三重奏 instrumental trio; trio;
[三次] ter-; three times; tri-; triple;
三次方程 cubic equation;
[三寸] three inches;
三寸不爛之舌 eloquent tongue; glib tongue;
三寸丁 dwarf; very short person;
[三代] three generations;
三代同堂 three generations living under the same roof;
[三檔] third gear;
[三等] (1) three grades; (2) third grade;
[三段論] syllogism;
假言三段論 hypothetical syllogism;
直言三段論 categorical syllogism;
[三多] three abundances of blessing, longevity and sons;
[三二] three and two;
[三番] (of mahjong) three times;
三番二次 over and over again; time after time; time and time;
三番四復 over and over again; so many times;
三番五次 again and again; many a time; over and over again; repeatedly; time after time; time and again; time and time again; twice and three times;
幾次三番 often and often; repeatedly; time after time; time and again; time and time again;
[三方] tripartite;
三方會談 tripartite talks;
[三分] three parts;
三分人才，七分打扮 good makeup has a lot to do with one's beautiful looks; three-tenths natural figure and seven-tenths makeup;
三分鼎足 vie for hegemony in a three-way tie;
三分像人，七分像鬼 looking ghostly more than a man; more like a devil than a man; three parts like a man and seven parts like a devil;
三分之二 two-thirds;
怕他三分 fear sb somewhat;
入木三分 incisive writings; written in a forceful hand;
[三伏] three periods of the hot season;
三伏天 dog days;
[三更] at blue o'clock; third watch at night;
三更半夜 at blue o'clock; dead of night; half the night; in the dead of night; late at night; midnight; small hours of the day; wee small hours; witching hour;
[三光] the sun, the moon and the stars;
[三國] Three Kingdoms;
[三合板] three-ply board; plywood;
[三合土] mortar;
[三合會] triad society;
[三極管] triode;
晶體三極管 crystal triode;
盤封三極管 disc-sealed triode;
雙三極管 duplex triode;
同心極三極管 all concentric triode;
振蕩三極管 generator triode;
[三級] three-tier; triple;
三級跳 (1) hop, skip, and jump; triple jump; (2) quick promotion;
三級制 three-tier system;
[三家村] small village;
[三角] (1) triangle; (2) trigonometry; (3) three angles;
三角板 set square;
三角測量 triangulation;
~三角測量員 triangulator;
~弧三角測量 arc triangulation;

S

~ 面積三角測量 area triangulation;
~ 相關三角測量 correlation triangulation;
三角櫈 three-legged stool;
三角函數 trigonometric function;
三角褲 briefs; panties;
三角戀愛 love triangle;
三角貿易 triangular trade;
三角旗 pennant; pennon;
三角琴 balalaika;
三角鐵 angle iron; triangle;
三角灣 estuary;
三角形 triangle;
~ 三角形化 triangularization;
~ 三角形旁切圓 escribed circle of a triangle;
~ 等邊三角形 equilateral triangle;
不等邊三角形 scalene triangle;
~ 等腰三角形 isosceles triangle;
~ 鈍角三角形 obtuse-angled triangle;
~ 極三角形 polar triangle;
~ 解析三角形 analytical triangle;
~ 連帶三角形 associated triangle;
~ 球面三角形 spherical triangle;
象限球面三角形 quadrantal triangle
斜角球面三角形 oblique spherical triangle
~ 全等三角形 congruent triangle;
~ 鋭角三角形 acute triangle; acute-angled triangle;
~ 算術三角形 arithmetical triangle;
~ 天文三角形 astronomical triangle;
~ 通弦三角形 chordal triangle;
~ 外切三角形 circumscribed triangle;
~ 原始三角形 primitive triangle;
~ 圓弧三角形 circular triangle;
~ 直角三角形 right triangle; right-angled triangle;
球面直角三角形 spherical right triangle;
三角學 trigonometry;
~ 分析三角學 analytic trigonometry;
~ 球面三角學 spherical trigonometry;
~ 雙曲三角學 hyperbolic trigonometry;
三角債 triangular debt;
三角洲 delta;
平面三角 plane trigonometry;
球面三角 spherical trigonometry;

[三腳] three-legged;
三腳櫈 three-legged stool; unreliable;
三腳架 tripod;

[三教] three schools of teaching－Confucianims, Daoism, and Buddhism;
三教九流 (1) three three religions and the nine schools of thought; (2) adherents of different religions and sects; men of dubious trades; people from all walks of life; people in various trades; people of all sorts; people of different low professions; people of varying social origins and backgrounds; (3) various religious sects and academic schools; various trades;

[三九] (1) three and nine; (2) bitter winter;
三九的蘿卜，涷(動)了心 the turnip in midwinter － the heart is frozen (be affected in heart);
三九天 coldest days of winter;
三九嚴寒 in the bitter winter;
三跪九叩 prostrating oneself three times, and knocking one's head on the ground thrice at each prostration; three genflections and nine bows with the head; thrice kneeling and ine times bowing;

[三軍] (1) armed forces; (2) three armed services－army, navy and air force;
勇冠三軍 distinguish oneself by peerless valour in battle; matchless in bravery; peerless in valour; the bravest of the brave in the whole army;

[三連冠] triple champion; win the championship three times in succession;

[三兩] twos and threes;
道三不着兩 not see reason; talk irrelevantly;
三局兩勝制 best of three games;
三三兩兩 by ones and twos; by twos and threes; in twos and threes;
三頭兩日 in two or three days;
三瓦兩舍 brothels; cathouses; disreputable quarters of the city; houses of ill-fame; places of amusement;
説三不接兩 talk incoherently;
着三不着兩 erratic; ill-considered; thoughtless; thoughtlessly;

[三稜鏡] prisim; triangular prism;

[三稜體] triangular prism;

[三六] three and six;
三六九等 various grades and ranks;
~ 把工作分為三六九等 regard different kinds of work as indications of rank or grade;

~人有三六九等 there are all kinds of people;
三親六眷 all the kinsmen and kinswomen;
三頭六臂 a resourceful and capable man; an extraordinarily able person; three heads and six arms — superhuman;
三推六問 make several cross-examinations;

[三輪] three-wheeled;
三輪車 pedicab; tricycle;
~踩三輪車 paddle a pedicab;
三輪摩托車 motor tricycle; three-wheeler;
三輪汽車 three-wheeled automobile; three-wheeled motorcar;

[三昧] (1) samadhi; (2) knack; secret;

[三面形] trihedral;
倒三面形 reciprocal trihedral;
活動三面形 moving trihedral;
極三面形 polar trihedral;
右手三面形 right-handed trihedral;
主要三面形 principal trihedral;
左手三面形 left-handed trihedral;
坐標三面形 coordinate trihedral;

[三明] the sun, the moon and stars;

[三明治] butty; sandwich; sarnie;
三明治一代 sandwich generation;
單層三明治 open sandwich;
單片三明治 open-faced sandwich;
公司三明治 club sandwich;
火腿三明治 ham sandwich;
露餡三明治 open sandwich;open-faced sandwich;
明蝦三明治 prawn sandwich;
牛肉醬三明治 sloppy joe;
牛肉三明治 beef sandwich;
潛艇三明治 submarine sandwich;
切去邊皮的三明治 sandwiches with the crusts cut off;
一客三明治 a sandwich;

[三年] three years;
新三年，舊三年，縫縫補補又三年 mend your clothes and you may hold out this year; this suit of mine is six years old, but I can make it last another three years;

[三七開] ratio of 3 to 7;

[三青子] (1) rough fellow; rude person; (2) unreasonable person;

[三秋] (1) autumn harvesting, ploughing and sowing; (2) three autumns; three years; (3) three months of autumn;

[三人] three persons;
三人成虎 a lie, if repeated often enough, will be accepted as truth; a repeated slander makes others believe; three people spreading reports of a tiger makes you believe there is one around;
三人知，天下曉 what is known to three is known to everybody; when three know it, all know it;

[三日] three days;
三日京兆 the ups and downs of an official's career;
三日兩頭 almost every day; every other day;

[三色柱] barber's pole;

[三生] three incarnations—the past, the present and the future;
三生有幸 a stroke of luck; consider oneself most fortunate; the greatest fortune in three incarnations; thrice blessed; very lucky;

[三十] thirty;
三十多歲的人 thirtysomething;
三十而立 at thirty, I take my stand;
三十六行 all trades and professions;
~三十六行，行行出狀元 every profession produces its own leading authority; every trade has its master;
三十六計 all the possible stratagems;
~三十六計，走為上計 better make oneself scarce; decamping is the best of all the strategems; of all strategems, to depart is the best; of all the alternatives, clearing out is the best policy; of the thirty-six stratagems, the best one now is to run away — the best thing to do now is to quit; one pair of heels is often worth two pairs of hands;
三十年代 the thirties;
~三十年代初期 the early thirties;
~三十年代晚期 the late thirties;
~三十年代中期 the mid thirties;
三十年風水輪流轉 three generations from shirt sleeves to shirt sleeves;
三十年河東，三十年河西 a chequered career; capricious in rise and fall; changeable in prosperity and decline; fortune is variant; full of ups and downs;

[三思] think carefully;

S

三思而行 be sure you are right, then go ahead; draw not your bow before your arrow is fixed; look before you leap; measure thrice before you cut once; score tice before you cut once; second thoughts are best; think over and over again before acting; think the matter over carefully before acting; think three times before taking action; think thrice before acting;
遇事要三思 use one's head when confronting sth;

[三四] three and four;
挨三頂四 the crowds surge;
不三不四 (1) dubious; frivolous; shady; (2) neither fish nor fowl; neither one thing nor the other;
~不三不四的人 a riff-raff;
低三下四 (1) degrading; humble; lowly; mean; (2) at sb's beck and call; cringing; servile; take oneself down 3 or 4 pegs;
~低三下四地 in an abject way;
顛三倒四 all in confusion; confused; disorderly; incoherent; put the cart before the horse; turn everything topsy-turvy; turn everything upside down;
丟三落四 always forgetting things; always losing this and forgetting that; forget this, that and the other; forgetful; miss this and that;
隔三跳四 skip over; proceed by irregular steps;
顧三不顧四 in a thoughtless way;
狂三詐四 high-handed;
拉三扯四 digress in speaking;
拿三搬四 disobey instructions; find a pretext for refusal; refuse to do what one is assigned to do; resist orders;
怕三怕四 full of worries; have no end of misgivings; timid and apprehensive of everything;
求三拜四 plead and grovel;
三房四妾 have three chambers and four concubines;
三拳敵不過四手 three fists are no match for four hands – a few cannot fight many;
說三道四 make carping comments on; make irresponsible remarks; make thoughtless comments;
~愛說三道四 fond of making irresponsible remarks;
愛說三道四的人 dirt-disher; disher;
調三窩四 goad others on to stir up trouble; make mischief through tittle-tattle; sow discord through gossip; sow seeds of discord everywhere; stir up enmity by gossip; stir up trouble; tell tales;
挑三窩四 choosey; difficult to please; fastidious; pick and choose;
推三拉四 shirk one's work;
推三阻四 decline with all sorts of excuses; fob sb off with excuses; give the runaround; make excuses and put obstacles in the way;
瞎三話四 reckless talk; talk nonsense;

[三歲] three years old;
三歲孩兒定八十 a person's character is all set by the age of three; as the boy is, so is the man; the child is father of the man;
三歲看到老 the child is father of the man;

[三天] three days;
三天打魚，兩天晒網 being negligent in one's work; by fits and starts; fail to keep on doing sth; go fishing for three days and dry the nets for two – work on and off; goofing-off; spend three days fishing and two days drying nets – lack perseverance;
三天兩頭 almost every day; every other day or so; every two or three days; frequently;

[三通] (1) tee; (2) three-pin plug;
大頭三通 bulkhead tee;
排氣三通 blow-off tee;
旁路三通 bypass tee;

[三頭對案] two parties and witness confront in court;

[三維] three-dimensional;
三維象 three-dimensional image;

[三圍] vital statistics;

[三文魚] salmon;
煙三文魚 smoked salmon;

[三五] three and five;
三五成群 in groups of threes and fives; in knots; in small groups; in threes and fives;
攢三聚五 gather in little knots; gather in threes and fives;
三令五申 give repeated orders and

injunctions; repeated orders and injunctions;
三年五載 for three or five years; in a few years; three to five years;
三三五五 in groups of three or five; in small groups;

[三項] three-term;
三項對立 three-term opposition;

[三陽開泰] opening of nature in spring; spring comes in full form;

[三葉草] clover;
三葉草葉子 cloverleaf;
白三葉草 Dutch clover; white clover;

[三一] three and one;
三合一 three-in-one;
三葷一素 three meat dishes and one vegetable dish;
三位一體 (1) Trinity; (2) three-in-one; trinity;

[三用帽] three-purpose hat;

[三元] top three candidates at the three levels of civil service examinations in imperial China;
連中三元 first on the list for the three degrees in succession;

[三月] (1) March; (2) third month of the lunar year;

[三周] three weeks;
三周刊 triweekly;

第三 third;
禮拜三 Wednesday;
兩三 a couple;
十三 a baker's dozen; thirteen;
星期三 Wednesday;
再三 again and again; over and over again; repeatedly; time and again;

san

【參】 formal form of the Chinese character 三;

san³

san

【傘】 (1) umbrella; (2) parachute;

[傘兵] parachute troop; parachuter; paratrooper;
傘兵部隊 paratroops;

[傘骨] ribs of an umbrella;

[傘投] drop by a parachute;

[傘形] umbrella type;

[傘杖架] umbrella stand;

打傘 hold an umbrella;
燈傘 lampshade;
旱傘 parasol; sunshade;
降傘 parachute;
菌傘 pileus;
跳傘 (1) bale out; parachute; (2) parachute jumping;
陽傘 parasol; sunshade; umbrella;
一把傘 an umbrella;
雨傘 brolly; umbrella;
摺傘 folding umbrella;
紙傘 oilpaper umbrella;

san

【散】 (1) come loose; fall apart; loosen; not hold together; scatter; (2) idle; leisurely; (3) medicinal powder; powdered medicine;

[散兵] (1) skirmisher; (2) straggler;
散兵游勇 persons who have not been organized into a collective and act by themselves; stragglers and disbanded soldiers; straggling troops; stray soldiers after defeat;

[散佈] spread;
電子速度散佈 electron-velocity spread;
最大散佈 extreme spread;

[散淡] lead an idle life; relax;

[散蕩] loaf about; play idly;

[散夫] unskilled worker;

[散工] (1) job-work; odd jobs; (2) odd hand;

[散光] astigmia; astigmatism;
散光鏡 astigmatoscope;
~散光鏡檢查 astigmatoscopy;
散光器 diffuser;
散光眼 astigmatic eyes;
~散光眼鏡 astigmatic glasses; astigmatic lenses;
規則散光 regular astigmatism;
混合散光 mixed astigmatism;
生理性散光 physiological astigmatism;

[散逛] loaf about;

[散話] gossip; idle talk;

[散伙] disband;

[散貨] bulk cargo;

[散記] random notes; sidelights; sketches;

[散居] live in scattered places; live scattered;

[散亂] in disorder;
散亂的頭髮 dishevelled hair;

[散漫] (1) careless and sloppy; lax in discipline; slack; undisciplined; (2) scattered; unorganized;
散漫光 diffuse light;
散漫無紀 desultory without discipline — unrestrained;
[散人] idle man;
[散散落落] scattered about;
[散射] scatter; scattering;
空氣散射 air scattering;
流星散射 meteor scatter;
前向散射 forward scatter;
聲散射 acoustic scattering;
遠距散射 long-distance scatter;
[散體] prose;
[散文] (1) prose; (2) essay; prose;
散文翻譯 prose translation;
散文詩 prose poem;
散文語言 prose language;
詞藻堆砌的散文 purple prose;
抒情散文 lyric prose;
[散逸] carefree and secluded;
[散裝] in bulk; loose; unpacked;
散裝貨物 bulk cargo; bulk freight;

拆散 break a set;
懶散 indolent; sluggish;
零散 scattered;
鬆散 (1) loose; (2) inattentive;
閒散 (1) free and at leisure; (2) idle; unused;
象散 astigmatism;
雜散 stray;

san
【糝】 (1) grain of rice; (2) mixing rice with broth;

san
【繖】 canopy; parasol; umbrella;

san⁴
san
【散】 (1) break up; disperse; scatter; (2) disseminate; distribute; give out; (3) dispel; let out;
[散播] disseminate; dissemination; spread;
散播謠言 spread rumours;
散播種子 disseminate seeds;
彈射散播 catapult dissemination;
[散佈] bruit; diffuse; dispersal; disperse; disseminate; intersperse; scatter;
散佈流言蜚語 give currency to slanderous rumours; spread rumours;
散佈謠言 spread rumours;
群體散佈 population dispersal;
種子散佈 seed dispersal;
[散步] go for a stroll; go for a walk; have a stroll; have a walk; peramubulation; stretch one's legs; stroll; take a ramble; take a walk;
散步的人 stroller;
散步去 walkies;
散步消遣 walk for amusement;
出去散步 away for a stroll;
帶狗去步行 take a dog for a walk; walk a dog;
去散步 go for a walk;
悠閒地散步 take a turn in sth;
在海邊散步 take a walk along the beach;
在林間散步 stroll in the woods;
[散場] empty after the show; people file out after a show;
[散發] (1) diffuse; dispersal; disperse; dispersion; drift out; emit; send forth; send out; (2) distribute; give out; issue;
散發魅力 turn on the charm;
散發着…的香味 drifting out the scent of sth; the scent of sth drifting out;
[散會] break up; over;
[散伙] break up partnership; dissolve partnership;
[散焦] defocusing;
偏轉散焦 deflection defocusing;
調制散焦 modulation defocusing;
相位散焦 phase defocusing;
[散開] diffuse; disperse; scatter; spread apart; spread out;
人群散開 the crowd dispersed;
[散落] fallout;
散落物 fallout;
~放射性散落物 fallout of radioactive material; nuclear fallout;
~乾散落物 dry fallout;
農藥散落 fallout of pesticide;
全球性散落 global fallout;
[散漫] disorganized; incompact; loose;
[散悶] dissipate care; dissipate worries; kill time;
[散熱] heat dissipation; heat radiation;
散熱器 radiator;
~車用散熱器 car radiator;
~熱水散熱器 hot-water radiator;

~陽極散熱器 anode radiator;

[散失] (1) missing; scatter and disappear; (2) be lost; dissipate; evaporate; vaporize;

[散心] carefree; direct oneself from cares for relaxation; drive away one's cares; ease up; enjoy a diversion; let one's mind relax; relieve boredom;
散心解悶 divert the mind from boredom;

癌擴散 proliferation of cancer;
迸散 flee in all directions;
播散 disseminate;
拆散 break up;
衝散 break up; scatter;
吹散 blow away;
打散 break up; scatter; thrashing;
發散 diverge;
放散 diffuse; spread;
飛散 fly upward and spread;
分散 decentralized; scattered; (1) disperse; scatter; (2) distribute;
輻散 diverge;
耗散 dissipation;
渙散 lax; slack;
解散 (1) dismiss; (2) disband; dissolve;
潰散 be defeated and dispersed;
擴散 diffuse; spread;
離散 disperse; scatter about;
流散 wander about and scatter;
披散 hang down loosely;
飄散 float in the air and scatter;
遣散 disband; dismiss;
驅散 dispel; disperse;
色散 chromatic dispersion;
失散 be separated from and lose touch with each other;
舒散 (1) take a stroll to relax oneself; (2) remove the feeling of tiredness or get rid of unpleasantness;
疏散 dispersed; evacuate; scattered;
四散 disperse in all directions; scatter about;
鬆散 relax; take one's ease;
逃散 become separated in flight;
消散 dissipate; scatter and disappear;
星散 scatter about like the stars; scatter far and wide;
雲散 clouds disperse;

sang¹
sang

【桑】 (1) mulberry; mulberry tree; white mulberry; (2) a surname;

[桑蠶] mulberry silkworm;
桑蠶絲 mulberry silk;

[桑間濮上] lovers' rendezvous; place for illicit love-making; secret meeting of lovers;

[桑麻] mulberry leaves and hemp;

[桑皮紙] mulberry bark paper;

[桑樹] mulberry tree;

[桑田] plantation of mulberry trees;

[桑土] mulberry fields; mulberry grounds;

[桑葉] mulberry leaves;

[桑榆] (1) the west; (2) the closing years of one's life;
桑榆暮景 closing years of one's life; evening of one's life; one's circumstances in old age;
失之東隅，收之桑榆 lose at sunrise and gain at sunset; lose at the start and win at the finish; lose in hake but gain in harring; lose in the morning and gain in the evening; make up on the roundabouts what one loses on the swings; suffer a loss in one place but make a gain somewhere else; what is lost in the morning is made up in the evening; what one loses on the swings one gains on the roundabouts;

[桑園] mulberry field;

[桑梓] hometown; native place;
桑梓故里 childhood hometown; native village; place where one was born and brought up;
桑梓之情 friendship of fellow countrymen;

滄桑 time brings great changes to the world;

sang

【喪】 (1) funeral; mourning; (2) mourn; (3) death;

[喪服] mourning apparel; mourning costume; mourning dress; mourning garments;

[喪祭] funeral service;

[喪家] bereaved family;

[喪居] live in mourning;

[喪禮] funeral obsequies; funeral rites; obsequies;

[喪亂] death and disorder; disturbance; turmoil;

[喪門] unlucky thing;

［喪期］ mourning period;
［喪事］ funeral affairs;
辦喪事 arrange funeral matters; handle funeral matters;
［喪葬］ burial; funeral;
喪葬費 funeral expenses;
［喪鐘］ death knell; funeral bell; knell;
敲喪鐘 sound of a death knell;
~ 敲響喪鐘 sound the death knell;

報喪 send an obituary notice;
奔喪 hasten home for funeral of a parent or grandparent;
出喪 hold a funeral procession;
初喪 period immediately after a funeral in the family;
除喪 cease mourning when period is over;
吊喪 pay a condolence call;
發喪 (1) send out the obituary; (2) handle funeral arrangements;
服喪 be in mourning;
號喪 cry at funeral;
居喪 be in bereavement;
守喪 keep vigil beside the coffin;
送喪 take part in a funeral procession;
治喪 make funeral arrangements;

sang³
sang
【嗓】 (1) voice; (2) throat;
［嗓門］ voice;
嗓門兒 one's voice;
嗓門喊破 rave oneself hoarse;
嗓門沙啞 have a thick voice;
大嗓門 have a loud voice;
喊破嗓門兒 rave oneself hoarse;
哭啞嗓門 lose one's voice in tears;
拉高嗓門 raise one's voice;
提高嗓門 raise one's voice;
壓低嗓門 lower one's voice;
［嗓音］ one's voice;
嗓音不好聽 have an unpleasant voice;
嗓音不悦耳 have an unpleasant voice;
嗓音不自然 have a strained voice;
嗓音低沉 have a deep voice;
嗓音柔和 have a golden voice;
嗓音如雷 have a stentorian voice;
嗓音悦耳 have a very musical voice;
低沉憂鬱的嗓音 sepulchral voice;
鍛煉嗓音 cultivate the voice;
洪亮的嗓音 sonorous voice;
［嗓子］ (1) larynx; throat; (2) one's voice;
嗓子不好 in bad voice;
嗓子大 have a loud voice;
嗓子好 have a good voice;
嗓子痛 have a sore throat;
嗓子啞了 lose one's voice;
粗嗓子 husky voice;
吊嗓子 exercise one's voice; train one's voice;
假嗓子 falsetto;
破鑼嗓子 coarse voice;
嗆嗓子 choke over one's food;
清嗓子 clear one's throat;
沙嗓子 coarse voice;
真嗓子 natural voice;

本嗓 natural voice;
倒嗓 (of a singer) have a hoarse voice; lose one's voice;

sang
【顙】 (1) forehead; (2) kowtow;

sang⁴
sang
【喪】 (1) be deprived of; lose; (2) decline; go down; (3) be defeated;
［喪敗］ decline and fall; suffer a downfall;
［喪謗］ revile; slander; speak ill of;
［喪膽］ be frightened out of one's wits; disheartened; lose nerve; panic-stricken; smitten with fear; terror-stricken;
聞風喪膽 become panic-stricken at the news; become terror-stricken at the news; lose courage when one hears about; lose heart upon hearing; tremble with fear on hearing of;
［喪夫］ be deprived of one's husband;
［喪國］ lose one's country to the conqueror;
［喪明］ (1) become blind; (2) mourn the death of one's son;
［喪命］ die; dispirited; downcast; feel disheartened; forfeit one's life; get killed; lose heart; lose one's life; meet one's death; meet one's end;
［喪偶］ bereft of one's spouse;
［喪妻］ be deprived of one's wife;
［喪氣］ dejected; depressed; despondent; discouraged; downcast; feel disheartened; have bad luck; in low

spirits; lose heart; out of luck; unlucky;
喪氣話 demoralizing words; discouraging remarks;
灰心喪氣 despondent; discouraged; lose heart; utterly disheartened; yield to despair;

［喪身］ lose one's life;
［喪師］ be defeated in battle; suffer defeat in battle;
喪師辱國 the army is annihilated and the country disgraced;
［喪失］ be deprived of; be stripped of; forfeit; lose;
喪失記憶力 have a lapse of memory;
喪失警惕 drop one's guard; lower one's guard; off one's guard;
喪失勞動力 unable to work;
喪失立場 depart from the correct stand;
喪失理智 lose one's reason;
喪失領土 lose territory;
喪失時機 let slip the opportunity; miss the chance;
喪失信心 lose confidence;
［喪心病狂］ act as if one were crazy; as mad as a March hare; be seized with crazy ideas; bereft of one's senses; frenzied; frantic; become frenzied; lose all balance of judgement; lose one's senses; out of one's right mind;
［喪志］ destroy the mind; lose one's ambition; lose one's determination;

懊喪 dejected; edpressed; despondent;
沮喪 be disheartened; be dispirited; dejected; depressed;
淪喪 perish;
頹喪 dejected; dispirited; listless;

sao¹

sao

【搔】 (1) annoy; irritate; (2) scratch lightly;
［搔背］ scratch the back;
膝癢搔背 scratch the back while the knee is itching – irrelevant;
［搔動］ become restless; commotion; disturbance;
［搔爬］ scratch lightly;
［搔擾］ annoy; cause disturbances; harass;
［搔首］ scratch one's head;
搔首踟躕 at a loss as to what to do; hesitate; in a dilemma; in perplexity; scratch one's head in great perplexity; scratch one's head in hesitation; undecided;
搔首弄姿 coquet with sb; coquettish; flirt; giggle and flirt; posture and preen oneself; stroke one's hair in coquetry – the seductive act of a woman;
［搔頭］ scratch one's head;
搔頭摸耳 hesitating; undecided;
［搔癢］ scratch an itch; scratch the itching place; titillation;
隔靴搔癢 cannot get at the problem; scratch an itch from outside one's boot – take totally ineffective measures; scratch an itch through one's boot – a useless attempt; scratch an itchy place through the boot – fail to get to the root of the matter;

sao

【艘】 numerary adjunct for ships;

sao

【繅】 draw silk from cocoons;
［繅絲］ reel silk from cocoons;
繅絲廠 filature; reeling mill;
繅絲工人 reeler;
繅絲機 reeling machine;

sao

【臊】 bad odour;
［臊根］ penis;
［臊氣］ bad odour; foul smell; stench; the smell of urine;
［臊聲］ notoriety; scandalous reputation;
［臊腥］ frowzy;

害臊 bashful; feel ashamed;

sao

【繰】 draw silk from cocoons;

sao

【騷】 (1) agitate; disturb; upset; (2) feel concerned; worry; (3) literary writings; (4) ill-smelling; stinking; (5) amorous; coquettish; erotic;
［騷動］ commotion; disturbance; riot; tumult; unrest; upheaval;
發生騷動 make tumult;
平息騷動 pacify a tumult;

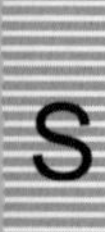

引起騷動 kick up a shindy;
[騷貨] crumpet;
[騷客] bard; poet;
[騷亂] chaos; disturbance; make trouble; riot;
爆發騷亂 trouble flares up;
煽動騷亂 ferment disturbances;
鎮壓騷亂 repress a disturbance; suppress a disturbance;
觸發騷亂 touch off a disturbance;
種族騷亂 race riots;
[騷然] agitated; disturbed; in commotion; tumultuous;
[騷擾] agitate; disturb; harass; harassment; molest;
性騷擾 molest; sexual harassment;
種族騷擾 racial harassment;
[騷人] poet;
騷人墨客 literary men; men of letters; writers and poets;

風騷 (1) literary excellence; (2) flirtatious;
牢騷 complain; discontent; grumble;

sao³
sao

【掃】 (1) clean; clear away; exterminate; sweep; sweep away; sweep with a broom; weed out; wipe out; (2) glance; pass quickly along; sweep; (3) paint; (4) put all together;
[掃除] (1) cleaning; clean up; sweep up; (2) clear away; remove; wipe out;
掃除天下 rid the world of bad elements and bring about universal peace;
掃除文盲 eliminate illiteracy; wipe out illiteracy;
大掃除 give a general cleaning; give a spring-cleaning; give a thorough cleaning;
[掃蕩] make a clean sweep of; mop up; wipe out;
掃蕩摧清 make a clearance and bring about a peaceful condition;
掃蕩殘敵 mop up the remnants of the enemy;
掃蕩海盜 sweep the pirates from the seas;
掃蕩妖氣 get rid of evil influence;
[掃地] (1) sweep the floor; (2) be dragged in the dust; reach an all-time low; reach rock bottom; (3) lose completely; lose entirely;
掃地車 road sweeper;
掃地出門 be swept out like rubbish; drive out sb in dire poverty; drive sb out of his house and deprive him of everything; eject sb from the house; force a family to leave their home without taking anything with them;
掃地以盡 be shattered; be swept away like rubbish; be swept clean; be swept into the dust;
名譽掃地 be thoroughly discredited;
斯文掃地 decadence of the intellectuals;
威風掃地 suffer a drastic fall in one's prestige;
威信掃地 be shorn of one's prestige;
[掃斷] be totally eliminated;
[掃黑] crack down on crime;
[掃黃] crack down pornography; wipe out pornography;
掃黃鬥爭 campaign against pornography;
掃黃運動 anti-pornography campaign;
[掃雷] demining; minesweeping;
掃雷艦 minesweeper
掃雷裝置 minesweeping arrangement;
[掃臉] lose face;
[掃路車] road sweeper;
[掃盲] eliminate illiteracy; wipe out illiteracy;
掃盲運動 campaign to eliminate illiteracy;
計算機掃盲 eliminate computer illiteracy;
[掃眉] paint eyebrows;
掃眉才子 bluestocking; female scholar; gifted maiden; girl poet;
[掃描] interlacing; scan; scanning; sweep;
掃描筆 scanner pen;
掃描器 scanner;
~字幕掃描器 caption scanner;
順序掃描 consecutive scanning;
細密掃描 close scanning;
眼掃描 eye scan;
延時掃描 delayed sweep;
餘弦掃描 cosine sweep;
圓掃描 circular sweep;
[掃墓] sweep a grave; visit a grave to pay respects to the dead;
[掃平] crush; put down; quell an uprising; suppress;
[掃清] clear away;
掃清道路 clear the path; pave the way;

［掃射］ (1) strafe; (2) scan; sweep;
低空掃射 strafe;
［掃搨］ sweep the mat to welcome a visitor;
掃榻以待 sweep the bed against sb's coming; tidy the bedding and await sb's coming;
［掃尾］ round off;
掃尾工作 rounding-off work;
［掃興］ feel disappointed; feel discouraged; have one's spirits dampened; spoil pleasure; throw cold water on;
掃興的人 spoilsport; wet blanket;
掃興而歸 come back disappointed; return disappointed;
令人掃興 spoil one's pleasure; take all the fun out of it;
~令人掃興的人 killjoy;
真掃興 how disappointing;
［掃雪］ sweep away the snow;
［掃帚］ bamboo broom; broom;
長柄掃帚 broomstick;

拜掃 pay respects to a dead person at his tomb;
打掃 clean up; sweep;
橫掃 make a clean sweep of; sweep away;
回掃 flyback;
清掃 general cleaning;
洒掃 sprinkle water and sweep the floor; sweep;

sao
【嫂】 wife of one's elder brother;
［嫂嫂］ elder brother's wife; sister-in-law;
［嫂子］ elder brother's wife; sister-in-law;

表嫂 wife of an elder cousin;
大嫂 (1) eldest brother's wife; sister-in-law; (2) elder sister;
姑嫂 sisters-in-law; woman and her brother's wife;
舅嫂 wife of one's brother-in-law;
兄嫂 elder brother and his wife;

sao⁴
sao
【掃】 broom;
［掃帚］ broom;
掃帚星 (1) comet; (2) jinx;

sao
【臊】 (1) ashamed; bashful; (2) minced meat;
［臊死］ utterly ashamed;

害臊 be bashful; feel ashamed;

se⁴
se
【色】 (1) colour; hue; tinge; tint; (2) countenance; look; (3) kind; sort; (4) scene; scenery; (5) quality; (6) woman's looks; (7) material appearance of things;
［色變］ turn pale;
談虎色變 turn pale even at the mention of the name of; turn pale at the mention of a tiger — become jittery at the mention of sth frightful;
［色彩］ blee; colour; hue; shade; tint;
色彩暗淡 dull colour;
色彩斑爛 bright-coloured; gorgeous; multi-coloured;
色彩變化 colour change;
色彩變幻的 opalescent;
~色彩變幻的天空 opalescent sky;
色彩繽紛 a riot of colour; riotous with colour;
色彩搭配 colour scheme;
色彩畫家 colourist;
色彩療法 colour therapy; therapy of colour;
色彩設計 colour scheme;
色彩鮮明 bright-coloured; in bright colours;
色彩鮮艷 in gay colours;
色彩學 chromatics; chromatology;
色彩絢麗 in dazzling colour;
色彩影嚮 influence of colour;
個人色彩 personal touch;
文學色彩 literary flavour;
一片色彩 a mass of colour;
自然色彩 coloration;
［色差］ (1) chromatism; (2) off colour;
色差通道 colour difference;
［色膽包天］ extremely daring in lewdness;
［色調］ hue; shade of colour; tinge; tone;
淡色調 high key;
對比色調 contrast hue;
互補色調 complementary hue;
深色調 low key;
主色調 dominant hue;
［色淀］ lake;
鹼性色淀 basic lakes;
茜素色淀 alizarine lake;

[色度] chromaticity;
色度飽和 colour saturation;
色度法 chromatometry;
色度計 chromatometer;
色度信號 chromaticity signal;
色度學 chromatometry;
互補色度 complementary chromaticity;
[色鬼] lecher; satyr; sex lupine;
老色鬼 dirty old man; old goat;
[色荒] unrestrained indulgence in lust;
[色覺] chromatic vision;
色覺計 chromatoptometer;
色覺檢查 chromatoptometry;
[色拉] salad;
雞丁色拉 chicken salad;
綠色色拉 green salad;
蘋果色拉 apple salad;
蔬菜色拉 green salad;
水果色拉 fruit salad;
雜錦色拉 mixed salad;
[色狼] lecherous person;
老色狼 old goat;
[色厲內荏] an ass in lion's skin; appear fierce, but weak inside; ferocious in appearance but feeble in essence; fierce in appearance but feeble in essence; fierce in appearance but faint in heart; fierce in appearance but trembling at heart; fierce in appearance but weak within; fierce of mien but faint of heart; have a fierce countenance but a faint heart; looking tough but scared at heart; outwardly fierce but inwardly shaky; outwardly tough but weak inside; the face of an eagle, the heart of a chicken; threatening in manner but cowardly at heart; tough-looking outside but really timid within;
[色盲] chromatodysopia; colour blindness; parachromatoblepsia;
色盲的 colour-blind;
色盲片 colour-blind film;
色盲者 achromat;
部份色盲 chromatopsia;
藍黃色盲 blue-yellow blindness;
藍色盲 blue blindness;
偏側色盲 hemiachromatopsia;
全色盲 complete colour blindness;
遺傳性色盲 amnesic colour blindness;
[色迷] sensualist;
色迷迷的 leer;
老色迷 a fool for women;
[色譜] chromatogram; colour spectrum;
色譜板 chromatographic sheet; chromatoplate; chromatosheet;
色譜棒 chromatopencil;
色譜法 chromatography;
~反沖色譜法 backflush chromatography;
~氣泡柱色譜法 bubble column chromatography;
~親合色譜法 affinity chromatography;
~上行色譜法 ascending chromatography;
色譜分析 chromatographic analysis; chromatography;
色譜管 chromatographic tube; chromatotube;
色譜條 chromatographic strips; chromatostrips;
色譜圖 chromatographic map; chromatomap;
色譜儀 chromatograph; chromatography;
~分析用色譜儀 analytical chromatography;
~流程色譜儀 on-stream chromatography;
~氣相色譜儀 gas chromatography;
自動氣相色譜儀 automatic gas chromatography;
色譜紙束 chromatopack;
不可見色譜 invisible chromatogram;
參比色譜 reference chromatogram;
單向條色譜 one-way strip chromatogram;
燈芯色譜 wick chromatogram;
反沖色譜 backflush chromatogram;
混合色譜 mixed chromatogram;
簡化色譜 summarized chromatogram;
流動色譜 flow chromatogram;
模擬色譜 analogue chromatogram;
平板色譜 flat-bed chromatogram;
液相色譜 liquid chromatogram;
熒光色譜 fluorescence chromatogram;
圓形吸附色譜 circular adsorption chromatogram;
指紋色譜 fingerprint chromatogram;
紙色譜 paper chromatogram;
[色情] carnal desire; lust; lustful; obscene; pronographic; sexual passion; sexy; X-rated;
色情電影 blue movie; erotic film;
色情行當 sex-for-sale activities;
色情狂 (1) erotomaniac; nymphomaniac; sexmaniac; (2) satyriasis;

sexual insanity; (3) erotomania; nymphomania;
~女色情狂 nymphomaniac;
色情旅遊 sex tourism;
色情片 pornographic film;
色情書畫 erotica;
色情思想 voluptuous thoughts;
色情文學 pornography;
色情業 porn industry;
色情作品 erotica; pornography;
~露骨色情作品 hard porn;
兩性色情 amphierotism;

[色散] chromatic dispersion; dispersion;
發熒色散 epipolic dispersion;
反常色散 abnormal dispersion;
介電色散 dielectric dispersion;

[色色] every kind;
色色俱全 all kinds are kept in stock; all kinds of goods are available; complete with all sorts of things;
形形色色 all sorts of things or people;

[色視差] chromatic parallax;

[色視計] chromatoptometer;

[色授魂與] be carried away by bewitching glances between each other; communication between minds without use of words;

[色衰愛馳] affection loses with beauty withering away; lose beauty as well as affection;

[色素] colouring; pigment;
色素體 chromoplast;
色素細胞 chromatophore;
色素質 chromatoplasm;
動物色素 animal pigment;
光敏色素 phytochrome;
內生色素 endogenous pigment;
食物色素 food colouring;

[色味俱佳] pleasant to the eye and taste; with a fine colour and flavour;

[色溫] colour temperature;
色溫計 colour temperature meter;

[色香味美] good in colour, smell and taste; the aroma, colour and taste of the dish are all excellent;

[色樣] kind and quality; variety and style;

[色藝] beauty and accomplishments;
色藝絕倫 unparalleled both in beauty and art;
色藝雙絕 both charm and art are at their height; both charm and art are in their limit; both pretty and talented;

[色慾] lust; sexual desire; sexual passion;

[色澤] colour; colour and lustre; hue; tinge; tint;
色澤鮮明 bright and lustrous; bright-coloured;

[色值] colour value;

[色紙] coloured paper;

[色中餓鬼] satyr; erotomaniac;

曖色 warm colour;
暗色 dark colours; cold colours; deep colours;
白色 white;
憊色 expression of fatigue; tired look;
本色 distinctive character; true qualities;
比色 colorimetric;
辨色 discriminate colours;
變色 (1) change colour; (2) become angry; change countenance;
駁色 parti-coloured; variegated;
補色 complementary colour;
采色 various colours;
彩色 colour; multicolour;
菜色 emacaited look; famished look;
慚色 look ashamed;
茶褐色 dark brown;
茶青色 brownish-green; tea-green colour;
嗔色 angry look; sullen look;
成色 (1) percentage of gold or silver in a coin; relative purity of gold or silver; (2) quality;
橙色 orange;
赤色 brownish-red colour; red;
愁色 worried expression;
出色 outstanding; remarkable; splendid;
春色 (1) spring scenery; (2) cheerful look;
辭色 one's speech and facial expression;
單色 monochromatic; monocolour;
淡色 delicate shade; light colour; tinge;
底色 bottom;
掉色 fade; lose colour;
多色 multi-colour; polychrome;
妃色 light pink;
分色 separation;
風色 (1) how the wind blows; (2) how things stand;
膚色 colour of skin; complexion;
複色 compound colour;
各色 of all kinds; of every description;
國色 national beauty;
寒色 cool colour;
好色 fond of women; lust for women;

褐色 brown; brown colour;
黑色 black; black colour;
紅色 (1) blush; blusher; red; (2) revolutionary;
湖色 light green;
花色 (1) design and colour; (2) variety of designs, sizes, colours, etc.;
黃色 (1) yellow; (2) decadent; erotic; obscene; pornographic;
灰色 (1) ashy; gray; (2) gloomy; pessimistic; (3) ambiguous; obscure;
混一色 (of mahjong) mixed tiles with one suit of characters;
貨色 (1) goods; (2) rubbish; stuff;
基色 primary; primary colours;
減色 detract from the merit of; impair the excellence of; lose lustre;
醬色 dark reddish brown;
戒色 avoid the temptation of sex;
金色 golden;
堇色 violet;
景色 landscape; lookout; picture; scene; setting; sight; view; vista;
酒色 wine and women – sexual pursuits;
懼色 look of fear;
角色 (1) part; role; (2) type of role;
絕色 exceedingly beautiful; of unrivalled beauty;
愧色 look of shame;
藍色 blue; blue colour;
落色 discolour; fade;
冷色 cold colour; cool colour;
厲色 look stern;
栗色 chestnut colour; maroon;
咖啡色 coffee;
臉色 (1) complexion; look; (2) countenance; expression; face; facial expression; puss;
綠色 green; green colour;
濾色 filter;
美色 attractive woman; woman's beauty;
米色 cream-coloured;
蜜色 light yellow;
面色 (1) complexion; look; (2) facial expression;
暮色 dusk; gloaming; shadow; twilight;
難色 embarrassed look; signs of reluctance or unwillingness;
嫩色 light colour; pastel shade; soft colour;
怒色 angry look;
女色 woman's charms;
暖色 warm colour;
藕色 pale pinkish gray;
配色 harmonize colours; match colours;
七色 seven colours of the spectrum;
起色 change for the better; improvement; pickup; recuperate; signs of improvement; signs of recovery;
氣色 colour; complexion; tint;
淺色 light colour;
青蓮色 heliotrope; pale purple;
青色 blue;
清一色 (1) all of one colour; all of the same colour; (2) homogeneous; identical; one and the same; uniform; (3) (of mahjong) all of the same suit; a flush;
秋色 autumn scenery;
全色 panchromatic;
染色 colour; dye;
人色 colour of a human face;
容色 countenance;
柔色 mild countenance;
肉色 yellowish pink;
潤色 polish or embellish;
山色 hills;
上色 best-quality; top-grade;
設色 fill in colours on a sketch; lay paint on;
深色 deep colour;
神色 expression; look;
滲色 bleed;
生色 add colour to; add lustre to; add splendour; give added significance to;
聲色 (1) voice and countenance; (2) women and songs and dances;
失色 (1) turn pale; (2) be eclipsed; be outshone;
殊色 outstanding beauty;
曙色 light of early dawn;
刷色 paint;
雙色 two-tone;
貪色 have a weakness for women;
桃色 (1) peach colour; (2) symbolic of romance; (3) illicit love;
套色 colour process;
特色 characteristics; distinguishing features; special features; unique features;
天色 time of the day as shown by the colour of the sky; weather;
調色 mix colours; mix paints;
土色 ashen; pale;
褪色 fade in colour;
脫色 (1) decolour; decolourize; (2) fade;
晚色 twilight;
五色 five colours (blue, yellow, red, white and black);
物色 choose; look for; scout for; seek out;
喜色 happy expression; joyful look;
緗色 pale yellow;
曉色 scene in the early morning;

猩色 scarlet;
行色 circumstances or style of departure;
秀色 one's beauty;
玄色 dark black;
血色 redness of the skin;
遜色 inferior; that which is inferior;
鴉色 reddish blue;
牙色 ivory colour;
胭脂色 carmine;
言色 words and countenance;
顏色 (1) colour; (2) countenance; facial expression;
眼色 a cue given with the eyes; a hint given with the eyes; expression of one's eyes; meaningful glance; wink;
焰色 flame;
艷色 beauty of a woman;
夜色 dim light of night;
一色 (1) of one colour; of the same colour; (2) of the same type; uniform;
怡色 look cheerful; look pleased; pleasant look;
音色 timbre; tone colour;
淫色 lust;
銀色 silvery;
有色 coloured;
愉色 cheerful expression; pleased look;
漁色 seek carnal pleasure;
玉色 jade green; light bluish green;
原色 beige; primary; primary colours;
怨色 resentful look;
月色 moonlight;
悦色 happy look;
慍色 angry appearance; displeased look; gloomy countenance; irritated look;
雜色 motley; particoloured;
赭色 reddish brown;
正色 (1) pure colours; (2) stern and serious facial expression;
諸色 different kinds;
着色 colour; put colour on;
姿色 beauty; charm; good looks;
紫色 purple; violet;
棕色 brown;
走色 fade; lose colour;
足色 (of gold or silver) of standard purity;
作色 show signs of anger;
怍色 ashamed; blush; colour;

se

【圾】 garbage; refuse; waste;

se

【嗇】 miserly; parsimonious; stingy;

［嗇己奉公］ save money for public welfare by being parsimonious in one's personal spending;

吝嗇 mean; stingy;

se

【塞】 (1) block up; clog; stop up; (2) fill; satiate; squeeze in; stuff; (3) cork; seal; stopper;

［塞擦音］ affricate;
［塞滿］ fill up; stuff full;
［塞音］ plosive;
［塞責］ dabble in one's work; do one's job in a perfunctory manner; do one's job unconscientiously;
聊以塞責 trump up so as to avoid blame;
［塞住］ block up; stop up;
［塞子］ cork; stopper;

鼻塞 have a stuffy nose;
閉塞 (1) close up; stop up; (2) hard to get to; out of the way; (3) unenlightened;
蔽塞 block; blocked;
充塞 cram; fill up;
堵塞 block up; stop up;
梗塞 (1) block; clog; (2) infarction;
栓塞 embolism;
搪塞 do sth perfunctorily or merely as a form; stall sb off;
擁塞 congest; jam;
壅塞 clog up; jam;
淤塞 be choked with silt;
窒塞 block; stop up;
阻塞 block; obstruct;

se

【瑟】 (1) musical instrument; (2) varied and many; (3) elegant and stately; majestic; (4) bright and clear; pure and clean; (5) sometimes used in place of 索, as in 索居;

［瑟瑟］ rustle; sough;
瑟瑟縮縮 soughing of the wind and trembling of the body;
［瑟縮］ cower; curl up with cold; huddle oneself up; shrink with cold; shrink with cower;
瑟縮不安 numbed and uneasy;
［瑟調琴弄］ conjugal harmony; happy married life; harmony between husband and

wife;
如鼓瑟琴 conjugal couple;

蕭瑟 (1) rustle in the air; (2) bleak; desolate;

se
【銫】 caesium;

se
【澀】 (1) harsh; not smooth; rough; uneven; (2) slightly bitter taste that numbs the tongue; (3) difficult; (4) slow of tongue;
[澀度] acerbity;
[澀訥] slow of tongue;
[澀味] astringent taste;

晦澀 hard to understand; obscure;
艱澀 intricate and obscure; involved and abstruse;
枯澀 dull and heavy;
苦澀 (1) bitter and astringent; (2) agonized; anguished; pained;
鹹澀 salty and bitter;
羞澀 bashful; shy;

se
【穡】 (1) gather in the harvest; harvest grains; (2) same as 嗇 ;
[穡夫] farmer;
[穡事] farming; husbandry;

稼穡 farm work; farming; sowing and reaping;

sen¹
sen
【森】 (1) full of trees; luxuriant growth of trees; (2) in multitudes; multitudinous; (3) dark; gloomy; obscure; (4) majestic; serene;
[森藹] flourishing; prosperous; thriving;
[森巴舞] samba;
[森林] forest;
森林保護 forest conservation; forestry preservation;
森林測量 forest surveying;
森林動物學 forest zoology;
森林大火 forest fire; wildfire;
森林工業 timber industry;
森林資源 forest resources;
保護森林 conserve forests; preserve forests;
常綠森林 evergreen woodland;
頂級森林 climax forest;
高山森林 alpine forest;
河源森林 headwater forest;
砍伐森林 deforestation; fell a forest;
濫伐森林 denude forests;
熱帶森林 tropical forest;
危害森林 jeopardize forests;
[森然] (1) dense; thick; (2) awe-inspiring; trembling;
[森森] (1) dense; luxuriant; thick; (2) dark;
[森衛] closely guarded;
[森嚴] awe-inspiring; severe; stern; stern and severe; strict;
森嚴壁壘 closely guarded; strongly fortified;
刁斗森嚴 strict army discipline; the sternness of military orders;
門禁森嚴 the gate is strictly guarded; with the entrances heavily guarded;
[森鬱] dense;

蕭森 bleak; dreary and desolate;
陰森 frightful; gloomy; gruesome;

seng¹
seng
【僧】 (1) Buddhist monk; monk; (2) a surname;
[僧道] Buddhists and Daoists;
不僧不道 neither a priest nor a monk;
[僧侶] clergy; monks and priests;
[僧尼] Buddhist monks and nuns;
[僧人] monk;
[僧寺] Buddhist temple;
[僧俗] monks and laymen;
不僧不俗 neither a monk nor a layman;
[僧徒] Buddhist monk;
[僧院] Buddhist monastery; Buddhist temple;

高僧 eminent monk; monk of high renown;
苦行僧 ascetic monk;

sha¹
sha
【沙】 (1) pebbles; sand; tiny gravel; (2) beach; desert; sandbank; (3) granulated; powdered; sandy; (4) hoarse; husky; (5) a surname;
[沙包] sandbag;

［沙暴］ sandstorm;
［沙場］ battlefield; battleground;
沙場碧血 fall on the battlefield;
沙場埋骨 die on the battlefield; lay down one's life on the battlefield;
［沙塵暴］ dust storm;
［沙蟲］ sandworm;
［沙袋］ sandbag;
［沙丁魚］ sardine;
大西洋沙丁魚 sardine;
油炸沙丁魚 fried sardine;
遠東沙丁魚 Oriental sardine;
［沙堆］ sand dune; sand hill;
［沙俄］ tsarist Russia;
［沙發］ settee; sofa;
沙發牀 sofa bed;
長沙發 chesterfield; couch; divan;
單人沙發 armchair;
三件套沙發 three-piece suite;
雙人沙發 two-seater;
一張沙發 a sofa;
［沙粉］ emery powder;
［沙崗］ sand hill;
［沙鍋］ casserole; earthernware cooking pot; earthenware pot;
沙鍋搗蒜—一捶子買賣 garlic may be pounded in an earthen ware saucepan, but it can be done only once;
沙鍋滾下山—沒好的 earthenware pots after a downhill journey – none is sound;
［沙果］ crab apple;
沙果樹 crab apple;
［沙荒］ sandy wasteland;
［沙皇］ czar; tsar;
［沙坑］ bunker; jumping pit; sandpit; sand trap;
［沙金］ (1) alluvial gold; (2) sand and gold;
披沙揀金 extract the essentials from a large mass of material; pick gold out of sand; sort out the fine gold from the sand; wash gold from gravel;
［沙拉］ salad;
沙拉吧 salad bar;
沙拉醬 salad cream;
拌沙拉 toss a salad;
菠菜沙拉 spinach salad;
馬鈴薯沙拉 potato salad;
水果沙拉 fruit salad;
［沙梨］ sand pear;
［沙礫］ gravel; grit; pebbles;
［沙粒］ grains of sand; sand;
［沙律］ salad;
田園沙律 garden salad;
［沙龍］ salon;
［沙漏］ hourglass;
沙漏身材 hourglass figure;
［沙門］ monk; nun;
［沙彌］ Buddhist novice;
［沙漠］ desert;
沙漠地區 desert area;
沙漠化 desertification;
沙漠之舟 ship of the desert – the camel;
降雨沙漠 rainfall desert;
徑流沙漠 runoff desert;
石質沙漠 stone desert;
一片沙漠 a great tract of sand;
［沙盤］ sand tray;
［沙鷗］ seagull;
［沙丘］ dune; sand dune;
半流動沙丘 semi-mobile dune;
初期沙丘 embryonic dune;
灌叢沙丘 shrub-coppice dune;
［沙沙］ rustle;
沙沙聲 fissle; fistle; rustle;
沙沙雨聲 pattering of the rain;
沙沙作響 rustle;
［沙石］ gravel; sandstone;
飛沙走石 a wind that carries sand and drives stone; dust and stones flying; flying sand and rolling pebbles; sand flows in clouds, pebbles are swept along the ground; throw sand and stones in all directions;
［沙司］ sauce;
辣沙司 hot sauce;
奶油沙司 cream sauce;
蘋果沙司 apple sauce;
［沙灘］ beach; sandbank; sand beach; sandy beach;
沙灘球 beach ball;
沙灘拾荒者 beachcomber;
沙灘椅 beach chair;
沙灘裝 beachwear;
一片沙灘 a beach of sands; a stretch of sandy beach;
［沙糖］ brown sugar; crystal sugar; granular sugar; powdered sugar;
［沙土］ sandy soil;
一層沙土 a layer of sand;
［沙文主義］ chauvinism; jingoism;

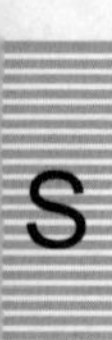

沙文主義者 chauvinist;
民族沙文主義 dominant-nation chauvinism;
[沙蟹] ghost crab; sand crab;
[沙啞] hoarse; husky;
沙啞的耳語 hoarse whisper;
沙啞的嗓音 hoarse voice;
沙啞的呻吟 hoarse groan;
[沙眼] trachoma;
[沙魚] shark;
[沙紙] sandpaper;
[沙洲] cay; sandbank; sandbar; shoal;
[沙錐] snipe;
冬沙錐 common snipe; winter snipe;
針尾沙錐 pintail snipe;
[沙子] (1) sand; (2) pellets;
鐵沙子 iron pellets;
一把沙子 a fistful of sand; a handful of sand;
一粒沙子 a grain of sand;
一勺斗沙子 a bucket of sand;

蚕沙 silkworm excrement;
澄沙 sweetened bean paste;
豆沙 sweetened bean paste;
風沙 sand blown by the wind;
灰沙 dust; sand dust;
流沙 drift sand; quicksand; shifting sand;
泥沙土 (1) silt; (2) mud and sand;

sha
【刹】 check; put on the brakes;
[刹把] brake clank;
[刹車] brake a car;
刹車不靈 ineffective brakes;
刹車燈 brake light;
刹車鼓 brake drum;
急刹車 (1) slam the brakes on; (2) bring to a halt;
[刹那] split second;
一刹那 in a moment; in a split second;

sha
【砂】 (1) coarse sand; gravel; sand; (2) coarse; not smooth; (3) infinitesimal;
[砂布] abrasive cloth; emery cloth;
[砂鍋] marmite;
[砂金] alluvial gold; gold dust;
[砂粒] grit;
金剛砂粒 emery grit; metallic grit;
[砂煤] sand coal;
[砂皮] emery cloth; emery paper;
[砂糖] brown sugar; crude sugar; granulated sugar;
細白砂糖 caster sugar;
[砂田] sandy land;
[砂鐵] magnetic sand;
[砂土] sandy soil;
[砂箱] sandbox;
[砂岩] sandstone;
長石砂岩 arkosic sandstone;
泥質砂岩 argillaceous sandstone;
[砂眼] trachoma;
[砂浴] sand bath;
[砂紙] abrasive paper; emery paper; sandpaper;
[砂磚] sanded brick;

辰砂 cinnabar; vermilion;
丹砂 cinnabar;
毒砂 arsenopyrite; mispickel;
翻砂 cast; found;
鋼砂 (1) corundum; emery; (2) abradant; abrasive;
礦砂 ore sand;
貓砂 cat litter;
硼砂 borax;
鐵砂 (1) iron sand; (2) pellet; shot;
鎢砂 tungsten ore;
型砂 casting sand; moulding sand;
朱砂 cinnabar;
硃砂 cinnabar;

sha
【紗】 (1) yarn; (2) gauze; thin silk;
[紗布] (1) gauze; (2) bandage;
[紗廠] cotton yarn mill;
[紗窗] window screen;
[紗燈] gauze lantern;
[紗羅] gauze;
[紗帽] hat for an official;
摜紗帽 quit office; refuse to do one's duty; resign in a huff; resign in resentment; throw away one's official's hat in a huff;
摘紗帽 dismiss an official;
[紗帳] mosquito net;

臂紗 armband;
抽紗 drawn work;
窗紗 window gauge;
粗紗 low count yarn; rove; roving;

管紗 cop;
黑紗 black armband;
婚紗 wedding dress;
拷紗 gambiered Guangdong gauze;
麻紗 (1) yearn of ramie, flax, etc.; (2) cambric; haircords;
毛紗 wool yarn;
棉紗 cotton yarn;
面紗 veil;
鐵紗 wire cloth; wire gauze;
緯紗 weft; woof;
烏紗 official hat;
一層紗 a layer of veil;
羽紗 camlet;
縐紗 crepe;

sha

【殺】 (1) kill; put to death; slaughter; (2) fight; go into battle; (3) reduce; weaken; (4) extremely; to death;

[殺蟲] kill the insects;
殺蟲劑 insecticide; pesticide;
~化學殺蟲劑 chemical insecticide;
~氯化殺蟲劑 chlorinated insecticide;
~農用殺蟲劑 agricultural insecticide;
殺蟲藥 insecticide; pesticide;

[殺敵] engage in battle; fight the enemy; kill the enemy;

[殺光] kill all;

[殺害] kill; murder;
被殺害 be killed; be murdered; get the works;

[殺機] intention to kill;
暗藏殺機 conceal one's intention of killing;

[殺雞] kill a chicken;
殺雞取卵 eat the calf in the cow's belly; kill the goose that lays the golden eggs; kill the hen for its eggs; kill the hen to get all its eggs — sacrifice future gains to satisfy present needs;
殺雞嚇猴 kill the chicken to frighten the monkey — punish sb as a warning to others; make an example of a few to frighten all the rest;
殺雞焉用牛刀 don't excavate a mountain to catch a rat; why break a butterfly on the wheel; why use a cattle knife for a chicken;
殺雞宰鵝 kill chickens and geese;

[殺價] bargain the price down; cut price down; force down prices; reduce prices; slash prices;

[殺盡斬絕] give no quarter; kill all;

[殺絕] exterminate;

[殺菌] decontaminate; disinfect; kill germs; sterilization; sterilize;
殺菌燈 ultraviolet lamp;
殺菌機 sterilization machine;
殺菌劑 bactericide; disinfectant; germicide;
~氯代芳烴殺菌劑 chloro-aromatic fungicide;
~噴淋殺菌劑 spraying fungicide;
殺菌器 sterilizer;
~回轉式殺菌器 agitating sterilizer;
~間歇殺菌器 discontinuous sterilizer;
~盤管殺菌器 coil sterilizer;
殺菌作用 bactericidal action;
低溫殺菌 cold sterilization;
工業殺菌 commercial sterilization;
間歇殺菌 discontinuous sterilization;

[殺戮] kill; massacre; slaughter; slay;

[殺掠] kill and plunder;

[殺蟎劑] acaricide;

[殺妻] kill one's own wife;

[殺氣] (1) furious look; murderous look; (2) give vent to one's anger; vent one's ill feeling;
殺氣衝天 death is in the air;
殺氣騰騰 full of bellicosity; out to kill; reek of murder; see things bloodshot; sound bellicose;
眼露殺氣 a wicked light shines in one's eyes;

[殺青] be completed;

[殺人] kill a person; killing; manslaughter; murder;
殺人不見血 kill by subtle means; kill without bloodshed; kill without spilling blood; ruin a person by subtle means; ruin a person in a sinister and ruthless way;
殺人不眨眼 cold-blooded; hardhearted; kill a person without batting an eyelid; kill people without winking; kill without batting an eyelid; kill without blinking an eye; murder...in cold blood; slaughter people without blinking; sanguinary;
殺人償命 a murderer must forfeit his life;

one who murders pays the forfeit with his life;
殺人犯 homicide; murder convict; murderer;
~嫌疑殺人犯 alleged murderer;
殺人放火 commit murder and arson; fire and sword; kill people and set places on fire; kill the people and set fire to houses; massacre and arson; murder and burn;
殺人狂 homicidal maniac; homicidomanis;
殺人滅口 do away with a witness; kill all so that there won't be any eyewitness left; kill anyone who might produce evidence against one; kill sb to keep his mouth shut;
殺人魔王 ruthless killer;
殺人如草 massacre people like cutting grass;
殺人如麻 commit innumerable murders; cut men down as one cuts hempen stalks; decimate the population; kill people like flies;
殺人盈城 whole city massacre; slaughter men till a city is filled with bodies;
殺人盈野 slaughter men till the field is filled with bodies;
殺人越貨 kill a person and rob him of his belongings; kill a person and seize his goods; kill and rob; murder for property;
殺人者死 murder is punishable by death;
殺人罪 homicide;
非法殺人 unlawful killing;
過失殺人 manslaughter;
借刀殺人 borrow a knife to kill a man; do harm to sb through the hands of another; harm sb through another's hand; kill one's rival by proxy; kill sb by another's hand; make a third party the instrument of injury; make use of one person to get rid of another; murder a person with a borrowed knife; use a cat's paw to get rid of b.; use another person's power to victimize a third person;
意外殺人 accidental homicide;
正當殺人 justifiable homicide;

[殺傷] inflict casualties; inflict wounds upon; kill and wound;

[殺身] lose one's life;
殺身成仁 die a martyr for a noble cause; die to achieve virtue; die for a just cause; fulfil justice at the cost of one's own life; sacrifice one's life to preserve one's virtue intact;
殺身之禍 fatal disaster; lethal misfortune;
身可殺，志不可奪 true to the last of one's blood;

[殺生] killing;

[殺聲] battle cries;
殺聲連天 air-rending battle cries; the air is filled with shorts of "kill!kill!";
殺聲震天 battle cries reach to the sky;

[殺手] hitman; killer;
兇狠的殺手 vicious killer;
職業殺手 assassin; hitman;

[殺死] account for; bump off; carry off; destroy; dispatch; dispose of; do for; eliminate; erase; execute; finish; finish off; fix; frag; get rid of; give sb the business; kill; knock off; lay low; lay out; make away with; murder; obliterate; off; puff out; put an end to sb; put away; put down; put sb on the spot; put out; put sb out of his misery; put out of way; put sb to silence; put sb to sleep; remove; rub out; send sb up the Green River; send west; silence; slay; snuff out; take; take care of; take sb for a ride; take off; terminate; touch off; waste; wipe out; zap;

[殺頭] behead; decapitate;

[殺退] put to flight; rout;

[殺尾] come to a conclusion;

暗殺 assassinate; assassination; waylay and kill;
搏殺 fight and kill;
捕殺 catch and kill; capture and kill;
殘殺 butchery; carnage; massacre; murder;
慘殺 massacre; murder;
仇殺 kill in revenge;
刺殺 (1) assassinate; (2) bayonet charge;
毒殺 kill with poison;
扼殺 catch by the throat; choke the life out of; have by the throat; hold by the throat; nip; nip in the bud; seize by the throat; smother; strangle; strangle in the cradle; take by the throat; throttle;
故殺 premeditated murder;

減殺 reduce; weaken;
噍殺 high; unpleasant;
絞殺 strangle;
坑殺 bury alive;
扣殺 smash a ball;
亂殺 kill without discrimination;
抹殺 blot out; obliterate;
謀殺 murder;
虐殺 abuse to death; cause sb's death by maltreating him; kill sb with maltreatment;
毆殺 beat to death;
拼殺 grapple;
槍殺 gun killing; kill by shooting; shoot dead;
戕殺 butcher; kill;
情殺 murder caused by love entanglement;
嗜殺 bloodthirsty; fond of killing;
厮殺 fight at close quarters;
肅殺 awe-inspring look;
他殺 homicide;
屠殺 massacre slaughter;
誤殺 (1) unintentional homicide; (2) kill a person by mistake;
兇殺 commit homicide; murder;
掩殺 attack by surprise; make a surprise attack; pounce on;
縊殺 hang; strangle to death;
誘殺 lure to destruction; trap and kill;
宰殺 butcher; slaughter;
椎殺 kill with a mallet;
斫殺 kill with a hatchet;
自殺 be going without a passport; bring about one's own destruction; commit suicide; court destruction; cut one's own throat; die by one's own hand; do a Dutch act; do away with oneself; do oneself harm; do the Dutch act; douse the light; drain the cup of life; drink the waters of Lethe; Dutch act; end it all; end one's days; end one's own life; fall on one's sword; find a way out; go to Lethe; gorge out; happy dispatch; have a fatal accident; kill oneself; lay violent hands on oneself; lover's leap; make the great leap; planned termination; quaff the cup; self-destruction; self-deliverance; self-execution; self-immolation; self-termination; self-violence; solitaire; susanside; take one's own life; take the coward's way out; take the easy way out; take the pipe; take the road of one's doom; top oneself;

sha

【莎】 a kind of insect;

［莎雞］ long-horned grasshopper; spinner;

sha

【抄】 open; widespread;

sha

【痧】 (1) cholera; (2) measles;

［痧子］ measles;

刮痧 popular treatment for sunstroke by scraping the patient's neck, chest or back;
喉痧 scarlet fever;

sha

【剎】 brake; check; stop;

［剎車］ apply the brakes; brake; lash down the load; stop car;

sha

【煞】 (1) brake; bring to a close; bring to an end; end; finish; halt; stop; wind up; (2) bind; fasten; tighten;

［煞車］ apply the brakes; brake; lash down the load; put the brakes on; stop car;

煞車燈 brake light;
煞車油 brake fluid;
煞車指示燈 brake light;
倒輪式煞車 coaster brake;
後煞車 rear brakes;
急煞車 brake hard; brake sharply;
腳煞車 coaster brake;
猛踩煞車 slam on the brakes;
氣動煞車 air brakes;
前煞車 front brakes;
手煞車 emergency brake; handbrake;

［煞氣］ take it out on sb; vent one's anger on an innocent party;

［煞尾］ (1) bring to an end; conclude; finish off; round off; wind up; (2) end; ending; final stage;

［煞賬］ make out a statement;

［煞住］ hold it; stop;

急煞 be worried to death;
抹煞 obliterate; write off;

sha

【裟】 robe of a Buddhist monk;

袈裟 patchwork outer vestment worn by a Buddhist monk;

sha

【鯊】 shark;

［鯊魚］ shark;
鯊魚皮 sharkskin;
鯊魚油 shark oil;
一條鯊魚 a shark;

白斑角鯊 piked dogfish;
扁鯊 angel shark; monkfish;
大星鯊 smooth dogfish;
虎鯊 bullhead shark;
角鯊 spiny dogfish;
貓鯊 lesser spotted dogfish;
星鯊 dogfish; gummy shark;

sha
【鎩】 (1) lance; (2) shed feathers;
［鎩羽］ (1) shed feathers; (2) crestfallen; defeated; discouraged; disheartened;

sha²
sha
【啥】 what; which; who; why;

sha³
sha
【傻】 (1) dumb; foolish; muddle-headed; stupid; (2) naive; (3) act mechanically; tactless; one-track-minded; think mechanically; work mechanically; (4) stunned; stupefied; terrified;
［傻大個兒］ lummox;
［傻蛋］ balmy; blockhead; bloody fool; booby; charley; chuckle head; chump; -clod; clodhopper; clodpoll; clot; cluck; crackpot; cuckoo; daft; dead from the neck up; dense; fat-head; fool; gump; idiot; moon-raker; mug; sawney; schmo; schmuck; silly; simpleton; soft mark; stupid chap;
［傻瓜］ airhead; balmy; beetle-brain; bird brain; blockhead; bloody fool; bonehead; booby; bozo; charley; chowderhead; chuckle head; chump; clod; clodhopper; clodpoll; clot; cluck; crackpot; cuckoo; daft; dead from the neck up; dense; dingaling; dipshit; dope; dork; dumbo; fathead; fool; goofball; goon; gump; halfwit; idiot; jackass; joker; kook; kucklehead; moon-raker; mug; nincompoop; ninny; nit; nitwit; sawney; schmo; schmuck; silly; simpleton; soft mark; stupid chap; wally;
大傻瓜 arrant fool; blinking idiot; comsummate ass;
~十足的大傻瓜 blooming fool;
［傻呵呵］ likable but stupid; not very clever; simple-minded;
［傻乎乎］ cloddish; foolish; silly;
［傻話］ foolish talk; nonsense;
［傻勁］ (1) foolishness; stupidity; (2) childish enthusiasm; foolhardy; with sheer enthusiasm;
一股傻勁 great enthusiasm; single-mindedness;
［傻冒兒］ dodo; fool; stupid person;
［傻氣］ dumb-looking; foolishness; silly manners;
傻裏傻氣 act foolishly; have a screw loose; have a want; muddle-headed; soft in the head; with one's finger in one's mouth;
［傻青兒］ inexperienced;
［傻事］ stupid thing;
做傻事 make an ass of oneself;
［傻笑］ giggle; laugh foolishly; laugh for no conceivable reason; silly smile; smirk;
［傻眼］ be dumbfounded; be stunned;
傻了眼 be stupefied;
［傻子］ blockhead; bloody fool; fool; idiot; imbecile; loon; nincompoop; simpleton;

sha⁴
sha
【廈】 tall building; edifice;

大廈 large building;
後廈 corridor; porch; veranda;

sha
【煞】 (1) evil spirit; fierce god; goblin; malignant deity; (2) much; very; (3) bring to a close; conclude;
［煞白］ deathly pale; ghastly pale; pallid;
［煞腳］ come to a conclusion; halt; stop;
［煞氣］ fierce attitude; ominous look;

回煞 return of the soul of the deceased to one's own home a few days after death;
兇煞 demon; fiend;

sha
【嗄】 (of voice) hoarse;

sha
【歃】 drink blood;
[歃血] smear the blood of a sacrifice on the mouth;
歃血為盟 smear the blood as a sign of the oath;

sha
【箑】 fan;

sha
【翣】 feathers adorning a coffin;

sha
【霎】 (1) instant; in the twinkle of an eye; moment; very short time; (2) drizzle; slight rain;
[霎霎] (1) sound of falling rain; (2) chilly air; cold winds;
[霎眼] wink;

shai1
shai
【篩】 (1) screen; sieve; sifter; strainer; (2) screen; sieve; sift; strain;
[篩出] sift out;
[篩法] sieve method;
[篩煤] screen coal;
[篩米] sieve rice;
[篩選] dressing by screening; screen; sift; sieving;
粗篩選 coarse sizing; preliminary sizing;
連續篩選 step sizing;
[篩子] sieve; sifter;

分子篩 molecular sieve;
過篩 sift out;
平篩 flat sieve;

shai3
shai
【色】 a pronunciation of 色 ;
[色子] dice;
擲色子 cast dice; throw dice;

本色 natural colour;
掉色 fade; lose colour;
落色 discolour; fade;
上色 apply colour;
捎色 (of colour) fade;
套色 chromatography; colour processing;
退色 (of colour) fade;
顏色 dyestuff; pigment;
走色 fade; lose colour;

shai
【骰】 dice;

shai4
shai
【曬】 (1) dry in the sun; expose to sunlight; (2) shine upon;
[曬乾] dry in the sun;
曬乾衣服 give the clothes an airing;
[曬傷] sunburn;
[曬台] flat roof;
[曬圖] make a blueprint;
曬圖設備 blueprinting apparatus;
曬圖紙 blueprint paper;
[曬衣] dry clothes in the sun;
曬衣架 airer; clothes hanger;
曬衣繩 clothes line;
[曬紙] blueprint paper;

沖曬 develop and print;
西曬 (of a room) with a western exposure;

shan1
shan
【山】 (1) hill; mount; mountain; (2) mountain-shaped object; (3) bushes in which silkworms spin cocoons; (4) a surname;
[山隘] mountain pass;
[山岰] col;
[山崩] landfall; landslide; landslip;
山崩地裂 mountains fall and the earth splits;
山崩地陷 the mountain falls and the earth gives way;
[山撥鼠] marmot;
[山坡] hillside; mountain slope; sidehill;
當風的山坡 windy hillside;
滾下山坡 roll down the mountainside;
上坡路 uphill road; upward slope;
[山茶] camellia;
山茶花 camellia;
[山城] city in the mountains;
[山川] mountains and rivers;
山川梗阻 be separated by mountains and rivers; far away from each other;
山川面貌 landscape;
山川修阻 apart by hills and streams; hills and streams separate us far apart;

山川悠遠 hills and streams are far off; mountains and rivers far far away;
山川阻隔 be separated by mountains and rivers;
跋履山川 travel across hills and rivers;
跋涉山川 travel by climbing up hills and ading acrosss rivers;
崇山險川 lofty mountains and turbulent rivers;
積土成山，積水成川 heaped-up earth becomes a mountain, accumulated water becomes a river;
名山大川 famous mountains and great rivers; famous mountains and mighty rivers;
如隔山川 as far apart as if separated by hills and rivers;

[山村] mountain village;

[山倒] collapse of a mountain;
病來如山倒，病去如抽絲 diseases come on horse-back and go away on foot;

[山道] mountain pass;
狹窄蜿蜒的山道 narrow, winding mountain pass;

[山地] (1) hilly area; hilly country; mountainous region; uplands; (2) farmland on a hill; mountain land;
山地健走 hillwalking;
山荒地瘦 barren mountains and sterile land;

[山巔] hilltop; mountaintop; the summit of a mountain;

[山頂] brow of a hill; crest of a hill; hilltop; mountaintop; summit of a mountain; top of a hill; top of a mountain;
山頂洞人 Upper Cave Man;
白雪覆蓋的山頂 snow-capped mountain peaks;
到達山頂 reach the hilltop;
登上山頂 crest a hill;
小山頂 hilltop;

[山洞] cave; cavern; grotto; tunnel;

[山陡路險] the hill is steep and the climb is dangerous;

[山房] mountain lodges;

[山風] mountain breeze;

[山峰] mountain peak; mountain top; peak;

[山岡] hillock; low hill; mountain ridge; ridge;

[山高] high mountains;
山高海深 lofty like mountains and deep like the ocean;
山高皇帝遠 the mountain is high and the emperor far away — it is difficult to get justic;
山高路陡 the mountains are high and the roads are steep;
山高路險 high mountains and precipitous paths;
山高路遠 the distance is far and the mountain is high;
山高水長 as high as mountains and as long as rivers — lasting forever;
山高水低 sth unfortunate; unexpected misfortune;
山高水險 mountains are high, torrents swift;

[山歌] mountaineers' song;

[山溝] gully; ravine; valley;

[山谷] dale; mountain valley; ravine; valley;
翻山越谷 go uphill and down dale; tramp over hill and dale; tramp over mountains and through ravines; travel over mountains and valleys; up hill and down dales;
山鳴谷應 the echo in mountains; the mountain echoes; the valleys echo the sounds of the mountains; with reverberation from hill and valley; yelling in the hill and echoing in the valley;
小山谷 dell;

[山光] pediment;
山光水色 landscape of mountains and lakes or rivers; the beauty of the rivers and mountains;
山光水色，上下一碧 the hills are reflected in the river and even their green colour is clearly shown in the water;

[山海] the mountain and the sea;
背山面海 with hills at the back and the sea in front;
山南海北 (1) all over the country; all over the land; all over the world; beyond mountains and seas; far and wide; far away; in different parts of land and sea; in distant places; south of the mountains and north of the seas — far and wide; up hill and down dale; (2) the remote parts of the world;
文山會海 a mountain of paper work and a

sea of meetings;

[山河] mountains and rivers — the land of a country;
山河大變 a great change in the mountains and rivers;
山河國寶 hills and rivers are national treasures;
山河破碎 the country is disintegrated;
山河似錦 the whole land is as fair as a fine tapestry;
山河依舊 mountains and rivers have remained as they were before; the landscape remains unchanged;
山河易改，本性難移 the leopard cannot change its spots; it is difficult to alter one's character; the leopard can never change its spots; you can change mountains and rivers but not a person's nature;
敢教山河換新裝 dare to rearrange mountains and rivers;
襟山帶河 cloaked by the hills and girded by the river;
氣吞山河 be imbued with a spirit that can conquer mountains and rivers; be filled with the heroic spirit that conquers mountains and rivers; bold; boldness of vision; daring; full of daring; great courage; have the airs of a bold and adventurous man, attempting great things; have the airs of one who can swallow hills and rivers; have the spirit to sweep away mountains and rivers before one; show the spirit of one who is out to conquer the whole world;

[山洪] mountain floods; mountain torrents;
山洪爆發 floodwaters rush down from the mountains; freshets roar down from the mountains; outbreak of mountain torrents; outburst of mountain torrents; the mountain torrents rush down with a terrifying force; torrents of water come rushing down from the mountains; torrents of water rush down the mountain;
山洪泛濫 floodwater rushes down the mountains and spread everywhere;

[山花] pediment;
山花爛漫 bright mountain flowers in full bloom; mountain flowers are growing everywhere; mountain flowers are luxuriantly blooming; the mountain flowers are in riotous bloom; the mountains are overspread with flowers;
山花怒放 the mountain flowers are in full bloom;

[山貨] (1) mountain products; (2) rustic articles;

[山雞] pheasant;
山雞舞鏡 look at one's image in the mirror and pity oneself; self-appreciation;

[山脊] crest; mountain ridge; ridge;
山脊埡口 saddle;

[山肩] shoulder;

[山澗] mountain creeks; mountain streams;

[山腳] base of a mountain; bottom of a hill; foot of a hill;

[山居] lead the life of a hermit;

[山口] mountain pass; pass;

[山嵐] clouds and mists in the mountains;

[山裏] in the mountain;
山裏紅 hill haw;
山裏人 hillbilly; hillman;

[山鏈] mountain chain;

[山梁] flat-topped ridge;

[山林] (1) mountain forest; wooded mountain; (2) the place where a hermit lives;
山林文學 literature of recluses;
山林隱逸 (1) retreat into wooded hill; (2) hermit; recluse;
笑傲山林 wander and live with nature;

[山陵] (1) plateau; (2) imperial tomb;

[山嶺] mountain ridge; ridge;
山嶺連亘 a continuous stretch of mountains;
重山疊嶺 hills piled on hills; hills upon hills;
崇山峻嶺 high mountain ridges; high mountains and lofty hills;
翻山越嶺 cross over mountain after mountain; go over mountains and bound across the peaks; over hills and crests;
光山禿嶺 bare hills and mountains;
鑿山劈嶺 tunnel through mountains and cut across ridges;

[山麓] foot of a mountain;
山麓丘陵 foothills;

山麓沖積平原 mountain apron;
[山路] mountain path; mountain road;
[山巒] chain of mountains; mountain range;
山巒重疊 diversified by hills and mountains; range upon range of mountains; the peaks rising one above the other;
山巒起伏 mountain ranges rising and falling; undulating hills;
綿延起伏的山巒 undulating hills;
[山脈] mountain chain; mountain range; ridge;
[山貓] leopard cat; lynx; wildcat;
[山莓] raspberry;
一碗山莓 a bowl of raspberry;
[山門] Buddhist temple;
[山民] mountaineer;
[山泥] mountain clay;
山泥傾瀉 landslide;
[山砲] mountain cannon;
[山妻] one's wife;
[山丘] (1) hillock; (2) grave;
小山丘 hillock; hummock;
[山區] mountain area;
[山泉] mountain spring;
[山人] hermit; recluse;
[山色] hills;
山色空濛 hills shrouded in misty;
[山神] mountain deity;
[山勢崔巍] mountains stand tall and imposing;
[山水] (1) landscape; natural scenery; scenery with mountains and waters; water from a mountain; (2) mountains and rivers; (3) piece of landscape painting;
山水風光 scenery with mountains and rivers;
山水畫 landscape painting; mountains-and-waters painting;
山水清秀 beautiful landscape;
山水詩 scenic poetry;
山水相逢 meet in th course of one's travels;
山水相連 be connected by mountains and rivers; be linked by common mountains and rivers; have a common boundary;
背山面水 water on the front and hills on the back;
殘山剩水 leftover rivers and remains of mountains — the reduced territories of a nation after aggression by a foreign power;
渡水登山 cross rivers and go up mountains;
翻山涉水 cross rivers and hills;
改山治水 transform mountains and harness rivers;
環山帶水 be surrounded by hills and girdled by water;
寄情山水 abandon oneself to nature;
金碧山水 gold-and-green landscape;
跨山越水 span mountains and rivers;
樂山樂水 love the mountains and love the sea;
千山萬水 a long and arduous journey; a thousand mountains and ten thousand rivers; far off; have come a long way across mountains and rivers; ten thousand crags and torrents; the trials of a long journey; thousands of mountains and rivers;
青綠山水 blue-and-green landscape;
窮山惡水 bare mountains and dangerous rivers; barren hills and unruly waters; barren hills and untamed rivers; barren land; barren mountains and unruly rivers; barren slopes and mountain torrents; poor mountains and torrential rivers; regions where the surface soil is poor and irrigation difficult; rugged hills and turbulent waters;
山環水抱 surrounded by mountains and girdled by a river;
山環水帶 surrounded by hills and giraled by water;
山明水秀 beautiful mountains and rivers; green hills and clear water — picturesque scenery; the mountains are bright and the waters are fair;
山青水淨 clear waters and green hills — the pictorial aspect of a country;
山清水秀 beautiful hills and waters; beautiful mountains and clear waters; the mountains are clear against the sky and the waters very bright — lovely scenery;
山窮水盡 at low water mark; at one's last shift; at the end of one's means; at the end of one's resources; at the end of one's rope; be left high and dry; come to a dead end; come to the end of one's rope; give out; in a desperate situation;

in a hopeless situation; on one's beam-ends; where the mountains and rivers end – be caught in an impasse and can find no way out;
~山窮水盡疑無路，柳暗花明水一村 where hills bend, streams wind and the pathway seems to end, the shady willows and flowers in bloom bring one to yet another village;
山遙水遠 far away; the mountains are high and the water wide;
剩水殘山 the reduced territories of a nation;
水墨山水 ink landscape;
水秀山明 clear waters and green hills – picturesque scenery; the waters are fair and the mountains are bright; the aters are very bright and the mountains are clear against the sky;
一山一水 every hill and every river;
依山傍水 at the foot of a hill and beside a stream; beside a river at the foot of a mountain; by a stream in front and a hill at the back; fronting water and with a hill at the back;
游山玩水 go on trips to different scenic spots; roam in hills and play with water; travel from one beauty spot to another; travel from place to place enjoying the beauties of nature; visit famous mountains and rivers;
遠山近水 beautiful scenery; the faraway mountains and nearby water;
治山治水 transform mountains and harness rivers;
左山右水 with the river on one flank and hills on the other;

[山田] hillside plot;

[山頭] (1) hilltop; top of a mountain; (2) faction; mountain stronghold;
拉山頭 form a faction;
明無山頭暗有礁 hidden factionalism; there are no visible mountains but submerged reefs;

[山頹木壞] a great man passes away; death of a sage;

[山外有山，天外有天] there are mountains beyond mountains and heavens beyond heavens;

[山溪] mountain stream;

[山系] mountain system;

S

[山響] deafening; rattling; thunderous;

[山杏] apricot;
山杏酒 apricot wine;

[山鴉] chough;

[山崖] cliff;
山崖險峻 the cliffs are steep;

[山巖] cliff;

[山羊] goat;
山羊鬍子 goatee;
山羊皮 goatskin;
雌山羊 nanny goat;
公山羊 billy goat; he-goat;
母山羊 she-goat;
石山羊 mountain goat;
小山羊 kid;
野山羊 aegagrus; wild goat;
一群山羊 a flock of goats;

[山陽] sunny side of a mountain;

[山腰] mid-slope of a mountain;
半山腰 halfway of the hillside;
~在半山腰 halfway up the hill;
~坐落在半山腰 be situated on a hillside;

[山藥] Chinese yam;

[山野] mountain villages and the remote wilderness;

[山雨] mountain rain;
山雨欲來風滿樓 coming events cast their shadows before them; strong winds foretell the coming storm; the gale is raging and the storm is about to burst; the rising wind forebodes the coming storm; the turbulent wind precedes the mountain storm; the wind fills the cabin when a mountain rain is about to come; the wind sweeping through the tower heralds a rising storm in the mountains; when wind fills the tower, it heralds a mountain rain;

[山芋] sweet potatoes;
燙手山芋 hot potato;

[山園] (1) villa built in a mountain; (2) mausoleum of an emperor;

[山岳] lofty mountains;
撼山岳，泣鬼神 so moving as to shake the mountains and wring tears from the spirits;
撼搖山岳 it shakes the mountains and hills;
搖山振岳 make the hills tremble and the mountains shake;

[山楂] (1) Chinese hawthorn; (2) haw;
山楂糕 haw jelly;
山楂果 haw apple;
山楂醬 haw jam;
山楂酒 haw wine;
山楂露 haw syrup;
山楂片 haw flake;
[山寨] mountain fortress;
[山莊] country house; mountain villa;
[山嘴] spur;
曲流山嘴 meander spur;
削斷山嘴 truncated spur;
修切山嘴 trimmed spur;

巴山 mountains in Sichuan;
拔山 pull up mountains;
跋山 trek across mountains;
保山 (1) guarantor; (2) go-between;
寶山 source of great wealth;
冰山 (1) iceberg; (2) ice-capped mountain; (3) backer that one can only depend on temporarily;
常山 root of antipyretic dichroa;
朝山 make a pilgrimage to a temple on a famous mountain;
春山 hills in spring;
刀山 mountain of swords;
登山 climb a mountain; climbing; mountain climbing; mountaineering; rock climbing;
斷塊山 fault-block mountain;
封山 close hillside; seal a mountain pass;
高山 high mountain;
隔山 the relationship between siblings of different mothers;
關山 mountains and frontier passes;
海山 seamount;
河山 land; rivers and mountains; territory;
湖山 lakes and mountains;
荒山 barren hills; waste mountains;
火山 volcano;
假山 rockery; rockwork;
江山 (1) rivers and mountains; (2) country; state power;
開山 cut into the mountain;
侃大山 chat;
靠山 backer; backing; patron;
礦山 mine;
煉山 burn the grass and shrubs for afforestation;
梁山 Liangshan Mountain; revolt;
漫山 whole mountain;
名山 famous mountains;
爬山 climb a hill; climb a mountain; mountain climbing;
排山 topple the mountain;
劈山 blast cliffs; cut through hills; level off hilltops;
平頂山 table mountain;
青山 green hill;
丘山 (1) hills and mountains; (2) wild country;
群山 hills; mountains; range of mountains;
如山 like a mountain;
上山 go to the mountains; go up a hill; go up the mountain;
深山 remote mountains;
他山 other hills;
泰山 (1) Mount Tai; (2) father-in-law;
童山 bare hills;
禿山 bare hill; barren hill;
下山 go down a hill; go down a mountain; go downhill;
仙山 mountain inhabited by the immortals;
雪山 snow-capped mountain;
一重山 a mountain;
一山 one mountain;
移山 movement mountains;

shan

【刪】 delete; erase; leave out; take out;
[刪補] revise; rid superfluities and fill inadequacies;
[刪除]
cut off; cut out; cross off; cross out; delete; deletion; leave out; remove; slough off; strike out;
刪除命令 delete command;
刪除文件 delete a file;
刪除無關緊要的空話 slough off unimportant verbiage;
安全刪除 delete safely;
[刪訂] revise;
[刪繁] cut out what is superfluous;
刪繁補缺 cut out what is repetitious and fill in gaps;
刪繁就簡 reduce to bare essentials; simplify by deleting the superfluous; simplify by weeding out superfluities; simplify complicated material; simplify sth by cutting out the superfluous; simplify what is complicated;
[刪改] bowdlerize; delete and change; make corrections and deletions; revise;
[刪節] abbreviate; abridge; chop out;

condense; cut;
刪節本 abbreviated version; abridged edition;
刪節的 abridged;
刪節號 ellipsis;
[刪去] cross off; delete; dash out;
[刪削] cut out; delete; erase; expunge; remove; strike out;
[刪潤] revise and polish;

shan
【杉】 China fir; the various species of fir and pine;
[杉錦] pine of fine quality;
[杉木] fir wood;
[杉樹] cedar;
紅杉 Chinese larch;
冷杉 fir;
水杉 metasequoia;
鐵杉 Chinese hemlock;
雲杉 dragon spruce;
紫杉 Japanese yew;

shan
【姍】 (1) laugh at; ridicule; (2) walk slowly, like a woman;
[姍姍] walk slowly, like a woman;
姍姍而來 come in a stately manner; hear the rustle of one's robe as she approaches;
姍姍來遲 late; slow in coming;
[姍笑] ridicule;

shan
【芟】 (1) cut down; mow; (2) eliminate; (3) scythe;
[芟除] (1) cut down; mow; (2) delete;
[芟穢] weed out causes of harm;
[芟夷] eliminate; exterminate; weed out;

shan
【珊】 (1) coral; (2) tinkling of pendants;
[珊瑚] coral;
珊瑚沉積 coralgal;
珊瑚島 atoll; cay; coral island;
珊瑚礁 coral reef;
珊瑚精 corallin;
珊瑚霉素 coralinomycin;
珊瑚泥 coral mud;
珊瑚色 coral; coralline;
~珊瑚色大理石 corallite;
~珊瑚色陶器 coralline ware;
~土灰珊瑚色 fan coral;
珊瑚藤 corallite;
珊瑚體 corallum;
珊瑚鐘 coralbells;
單帶形珊瑚 single-zoned coral;
蜂窩珊瑚 honeycomb coral;
角珊瑚 horn coral;
腦珊瑚 brain coral;
扇柳珊瑚 fan coral;
石珊瑚 stony coral;
造礁珊瑚 hermatypic coral;
[珊珊] tinkling of jade pendants;
闌珊 come to an end;

shan
【柵】 grid;
[柵極] grid;
柵極電流 grid current;
加速柵極 accelerating grid;
可調柵極 adjustable grid;
諧振腔柵極 cavity grid;

shan
【舢】 sampan;
[舢舨] dinghy; sampan;

shan
【衫】 garment; gown; shirt;
[衫袖] sleeves;
淚沾衫袖 wet one's sleeves with tears;
手長衫袖短，人窮顏色低 poverty makes one feel inferior; when the arm is long, the sleeve seems short; if a man is poor, he can't hold up his head;
彩條衫 colour-streak shirt;
長衫 long gown;
襯衫 blouse; overshirt; shirt;
汗衫 T-shirt; undershirt;
偏衫 a kind of monk's gown;
衣衫 clothes; dress;
罩衫 dustcoat; overall;

shan
【苫】 thatch;
[苫次] in mourning for one's parents;

shan
【扇】 fan; incite; instigate;
[扇出] fan-out;
[扇形] sector;
[扇子] fan;
一把扇子 a fan;
分散扇 dispersion fan;

呼搧 (1) shake; (2) fan;

shan
【釤】 samarium;

shan
【跚】 stagger; walk unsteadily;

盤跚 limp; walk haltingly;
蹣跚 hobble; limp; walk haltingly;

shan
【搧】 (1) fan; (2) incite; stir up; (3) slap on the face;
[搧扇] fan with a fan;

shan
【煽】 (1) fan; (2) fan up; incite; instigate; stir up; (3) boast about; brag about; lavish praise on;
[煽動] blow the coals; fan the flames; incite; inflame and agitate people; stir up trouble;
煽動罷工 incite a strike;
煽動叛工 stir up a rebellion;
煽動行為 demagogy;
煽動性文章 incendiary article;
煽動者 demagogue;
煽動主義 demagogism;
[煽火] fan the fire; fan the flames; stir up trouble;
[煽惑] agitate; deceive; fan suspicions and doubts; incite; rouse with words;
煽惑人心 agitate people by demagogy; deceive and stir up people's mind; incite people by demagogy; undermine popular morale by spreading unfounded rumour;
[煽情] (1) arouse one's enthusiasm; fervour; (2) flirt;

shan
【潸】 tears flowing; weep;
[潸然] tears falling;
潸然淚下 drop a few silent tears; shed silent tears; tears trickling down one's cheeks;
[潸潸] weep continually;
[潸泫] tears flowing; weeping;

shan
【膻】 bad odour of sheep, deer etc.;

shan
【羶】 odour of a sheep or goat;
[羶氣] odour of a goat;
[羶味] odour of a goat;
[羶腥] odour of mutton;

腥羶 smell of fish and mutton;

shan³

shan
【閃】 (1) avoid; dodge; evade; get out of the way; (2) sprain; twist; (3) lightning; (4) flash; sparkle; (5) cast aside; leave behind;
[閃避] dodge; evade; hedge; sidestep;
[閃點] flash point;
[閃電] lightning;
閃電攻擊 lightning attack;
閃電戰 blitz; blitzkrieg; lightning war;
叉狀閃電 forked lightning;
帶狀閃電 fillet lightning; ribbon lightning;
疾如閃電 as quick as lightning;
鋸齒狀閃電 zigzag lightning;
快如閃電 quick as a flash of lightning;
片狀閃電 sheet lightning;
球狀閃電 ball lightning; globe lightning;
星狀閃電 stellar lightning;
迅如閃電 as swift as lightning;
枝狀閃電 streak lightning;
[閃動] flash; flicker; glisten; move fast; play; scintillate; twinkle; waver;
[閃躲] dodge; evade;
[閃發] shoot;
[閃光] (1) blinker light; flare; flash of light; flashing; glare; flashlight; lightning; (2) flame out; flicker; gleam; glint; glisten; glitter; shimmer;
閃光的 coruscating;
閃光燈 blinker; flashlight;
~頻閃閃光燈 strobe light;
閃光器 flasher;
~電子閃光器 electronic flash;
~熱效閃光器 thermal flasher;
~乙炔閃光器 acetylene flasher;
~肘節型閃光器 toggle-type flasher;
刺眼的閃光 discomfort glare;
發出閃光 give a flare;
化學閃光 chemical flash;
外部閃光 external flashing;
直射閃光 direct flash;
一道閃光 a bolt of lightning; a flash of light; a flash of lightning; a shaft of

lightning; a streak of lightning;
直接閃光 direct glare;

［閃過］ flash across; flash past;
一閃而過 as quick as thought; as swift as thought; flash across; flash into; streak past; the slightest flash of;

［閃開］ avoid; dodge; get out of the way; jump aside;

［閃流］ streamer;
回返閃流 return streamer;
先導閃流 leader streamer;

［閃念］ fleeting thought;
一閃之念 fleeting thoughts; thoughts which flash through one's mind;

［閃閃］ flash; flickering; glint; glisten; glitter; scintillating; sparkle;
閃閃發光 dazzle with brilliance; glitter; radiate; scintillating; sparkle; sparkling; twinkling;
寒光閃閃 the swords glitter like frost and snow;
一閃一閃 wink;

［閃身］ (1) dodge; (2) sideways;
閃身進門 walk sideways through the door;

［閃失］ (1) error; mishap; mistake; (2) accident;

［閃爍］ (1) flicker; glimmer; glint; glisten; scintillate; scintillation; twinkle; (2) evasive; noncommittal; vague;
閃爍不定 go in and out; flickering;
閃爍的 coruscating;
閃爍其詞 dodge about; evade issues; hedge; hum and haw; palter; shuffle; speak evasively;
閃爍器 scintillator;
~液體閃爍器 liquid scintillator;
~中子閃爍器 neutron scintillator;
閃爍體 scintillator;
~凝膠閃爍器 gel scintillator;
~液體閃爍器 liquid scintillator;
閃爍耀目 glitz and glamour;
大地閃爍 terrestrial scintillation;
大氣閃爍 atmospheric scintillation;
風燭閃爍 the candle flickers in the wind;
目標閃爍 target scintillation;
天空中繁星閃爍 the sky is ablaze with stars;
天文閃爍 astronomical scintillation;

［閃下］ leave behind;

［閃現］ flash; flicker; flash before one; glint;

［閃耀］ flash; glitter; radiate; shine; sparkle;
星星在空中閃耀 the stars shine in the sky;

打閃 (of lightning) flash;
躲閃 dodge; get out of the way;
忽閃 gleam; glitter;
失閃 mishap; unexpected danger;

shan

【陝】 (1) short for Shaanxi province; (2) a surname;

shan⁴

shan

【汕】 basket for catching fish;

shan

【疝】 hernia;

［疝氣］ hernia;

［疝痛］ abnormal pain caused by spasm colic;

［疝修補術］ hernia repair; herniorrhaphy;

腸節疝 enteromerocele;
腸疝 enterocele;
膀胱疝 vesical hernia;
全疝 complete hernia;
不全疝 incomplete hernia;

shan

【扇】 (1) fan; (2) numerary auxiliary for door or gate leaves;

［扇貝］ fan shell; scallop;
剥開扇貝 shucking scallop;

［扇舞］ fan dance;

［扇形］ (1) fan-shaped; (2) sector;

［扇子］ fan;

衝積扇 alluvial fan;
窗扇 casement;
打扇 fan sb;
電扇 electric fan;
風扇 (1) electric fan; (2) fan;
海扇 fan shell; scallop;
呼扇 (1) shake; (2) fan;
絹扇 silk fan;
葵扇 palm-leaf fan;
門扇 door leaf;
排風扇 exhaust fan;
蒲扇 cattail leaf fan;
秋扇 fans in autumn — deserted women;
郤扇 get married;
搧扇 fan with a fan;
團扇 round fan;

紈扇 round silk fan;
羽扇 feather fan;
折扇 folding fan;
摺扇 folding fan;
紙扇 paper fan;
桌扇 desk fan;

shan
【訕】 (1) laugh at; sneer; (2) abuse; slander; (3) awkward; embarrassed; shamefaced;
[訕謗] backbite; libel; slander;
[訕臉] brazen; shameless;
[訕上] slander one's superiors;
[訕笑] deride; laugh at; mock; ridicule; sneer at;
搭訕 strike up a conversation with sb;

shan
【赸】 try to conceal embarrassment;

shan
【掞】 comfortable; easy; smooth; suave;
[掞藻] smooth, flowery literary style;
[掞張] smooth but untruthful; suave but exaggerating;

shan
【單】 a surname;

shan
【善】 (1) benevolent actions; good; virtuous; (2) good; satisfactory; (3) make a success of; perfect; (4) friendly; kind; (5) relieve; remedy; (6) be skilled in; expert in; good at; (7) properly; (8) apt to;
[善報] reward for good deeds; reward for kindness;
[善本] good edition; reliable text;
善本書 rare book;
[善變] capricious; changeable; fickle;
善變的人 chameleon;
機詐善變 cunning and tactful;
[善待] accord sb good treatment; treat sb well;
[善刀而藏] do not push one's advantage too far;
[善惡] good and evil; virtue and vice;
善惡不分 unable to tell good from evil;
善惡到頭終有報 justice has long arms;
善惡到頭終有報，是非結果自分明 God's mill grinds slowly but sure; the mills of God grind slowly, but they grind exceedingly; the world is a wheel and it will all come round right; wickedness does not go altogether unrequited;
善惡分明 distinguish the good from the bad;
褒善貶惡 glorify virtue and censure vice;
貶惡褒善 censure evil and exalt virtue;
辨別善惡 distinguish between good and evil;
懲惡勸善 punish the wicked in order to exhort others to goodness; punish wickedness and encourage virtue;
遏惡揚善 overlook other people's weaknesses and extol virtues; repress evil and encourage good;
扶善懲惡 support kindness, restrain evil;
改惡從善 abandon evil and do good; change from bad to good; mend one's ways; remove the evil and follow the good; turn from doing evil to good; turn over a new leaf;
好善惡惡 love the good and hate the evil;
庇善罰惡 God blesses the good and punishes the evil;
欺善怕惡 bully the faint-hearted and fear the stouthearted; bully the good people and be scared of the evil ones; bully the meek but cower before a tyrant; bully the weak and kneel and fear the firm; impose on those who are kind and fear those who are severe; oppress the good and timid and fear the wicked;
去惡從善 exterminate the evil and follow the good; reform; shun the evil and follow the good;
棄惡從善 forsake evil and learn to do good; repent and be good; shun evil and do good;
勸善懲惡 poetic justice;
勸善戒惡 exhort sb to be good and guard him against evil; persuade sb to do good and dissuade him from doing evil;
善善惡惡 like the good and hate the bad; love good and shun evil; love goodness and hate vice; love the good and shun evil; use the good and get rid of the bad;
識善辨惡 discern the difference between the good and evil; know right from

wrong; know the difference between right and wrong;
習善滅惡 learn good and forsake evil;
隱惡揚善 conceal the faults of others and praise their good points; conceal sb's wickedness and boast his goodness; conceal the evil and make known the good; conceal what is evil and publicize what is good; cover up another's bad deeds and praise his virtues; hide sb's evil deeds and praise his good ones; hide sb's wrongdoing and praise his good deeds; overlook sb's faults and dwell more on his good points;
~為別人隱惡揚善 conceal the faults of others and praise their good points;
遠惡近善 keep away from the evil and be near to the good;
彰善癉惡 commend the good and condemn the evil; exhibit virtue and denounce vice; praise the good and hate the evil; praise the kind hearted and hate the evil-intended; publicize and encourae the good and detest the evil;

[善賈而沽] sell at a good profit — wait for an opportunity and sell at high price;

[善果] reward of good deeds;

[善後] cope with the aftermath of a disaster;
善後事宜 problems arising from an accident;
以善其後 in order to effect an improvement in the future;

[善舉] benevolent action; good deed; philanthropic act;
共襄善舉 cooperate with this great project;
以襄善舉 in aid of charity;

[善類] good and honest people; good people; people of goodwill;

[善良] gentle; good; good and honest; kindhearted; well-disposed;
善良的 good-natured;
稟性善良 frank by nature; the milk of human kindness;
心地善良 have a kind heart; kind-hearted;

[善美] perfect and beautiful;
盡善盡美 leave nothing to be desired; perfect; perfection itself; perfectly good and beautiful; perfectly satisfactory; reach the acme of perfection; the very perfection of beauty;

[善門] door of virtues;
善門難開 the door of virtues is hard to open — it is difficult to begin to do good;

[善謀] (1) good scheme; (2) good at thinking out schemes;

[善人] charitable person; kindhearted and benevolent fellow; philanthropist; well-doer;
惡蛇不咬善人 a poisonous snake will not bite a charitable man;

[善善從長] capable of learning from others' strong points to offset one's weakness;

[善士] benevolent person; good man; philanthropist;

[善事] benefaction; charitable work; charity; good deeds; philanthropic acts;
善事從家裏做起 charity begins at home;

[善忘] amnesia; forgetful; prone to forget; weak of memory;
善忘的人 absent-minded person;

[善為說辭] put in a good word for sb;

[善小利微] small benefit with tiny profit;

[善心] benevolence; compassionate heart; good intention; kind heart; kind-hearted; kindness; mercy;
大發善心 become so benevolent that;

[善言] well-intentioned advice;
善言相勸 advise with good words; kind advice and persuasion;

[善以為寶] value virtue as a treasure;

[善意] good faith; good intentions; goodwill;
出於善意 good in intention;
真心善意 open and true-hearted; sincerely and with good intentions; with sincerity and good intentions;

[善游者溺] a good swimmer often gets drowned; good swimmers at length are drowned;

[善有善報] a good act will be well rewarded; fortune is the companion of virtue; good will be rewarded with good; goodness will have a good reward; kind deeds pay rich dividends to the doer;
善有善報，惡有惡報 get what's coming

to one; fortune is the good man's price, but the bad man's bane; good has its reward and evil has its recompense; good will be rewarded with good and evil with evil; if you do good, good will be done to you; but if you do ill, the same will be measured back to you;

[善於] be adept in; be adroit at; be good at; be skilled in;
善於辭令 gifted with a silver tongue;
善於計算 good at figures;
善於模倣的人 mimic;
善於應對 good at repartee;
善於用人 know how to choose the right person for the right job; know how to make proper use of personnel;

[善欲人見非為真善，惡恐人知便是大惡] to do good in order that men may see it is not true goodness; to do evil and fear that men may know it is indeed great evil;

[善戰] brave and skilful in fighting;
善戰善勝 good at fighting and winning;

[善終] die a natural death; die in one's bed; hospice care;
善終服務 hospice care;
不得善終 be impossible to acquire a peaceful end; may not die a natural death;
不獲善終 not able to die a natural death;

[善自為謀] able to take good care of oneself; apt at devising a good plan for oneself; capable in planning for one's own interests; give one's full consideration to; good at looking after oneself; know how to look after oneself; know how to take care of oneself;

[善自珍攝] coddle oneself; please take good care of yourself;

不善 (1) a bad hand at; not good at; (2) bad; evil; ill; (3) quite impressive;
慈善 benevolent; charitable; philanthropic;
從善 follow good advice;
改善 ameliorate; better; improve; improvement; mend; modify; perfect;
和善 genial; kind and gentle;
面善 (1) look familiar; (2) look kind in face;
遷善 reform one's ways;
親善 goodwill;
攘善 appropriate other's credit or honour to be his own;
賞善 reward the good;
妥善 appropriate; proper; satisfactory; well arranged;
完善 consummate; faultless; improve and perfect; perfect;
為善 do good;
偽善 hypocritical;
徙善 change for the better; reform;
相善 on friendly terms; on good terms;
心善 kind heart; kind-hearted;
行善 do charitable work; do good deeds; do good works; show mercy;
揚善 spread others' good deeds;
一善 one good deed;
友善 amicable; friendly;
責善 exhort sb to practise good deeds;
至善 the highest level of virtue; the supreme good;
作善 do good turns;

shan

【鄯】 a region in Chinese Turkestan;

shan

【擅】 (1) act on one's own responsibility; arrogate to oneself; do sth on one's own authority; (2) expert in; good at; (3) arbitrary; unauthorized; unilateral; (4) monopolize; take exclusive possession;

[擅便] consult one's own convenience only;

[擅兵] maintain an army without authorization;

[擅長] apt at; be accomplished in; excel in; expert in; good at; skilled in;
擅長計算 good at figures;
不擅長 bad at; poor at;

[擅場] dominate the scene; excel in a certain field; outshine all those present;

[擅改] change without authorization; revise without authorization;

[擅國] usurp the powers of the throne;

[擅利] enjoy monopoly;

[擅美] get all the credit;

[擅命] arrogate power to oneself; defy restrictions;

[擅取] take without authorization;
擅取權力 arrogate power to oneself;

［擅權］ assume dictatorial powers;
［擅違］ disobey; violate;
［擅用］ appropriate; take and use as one's own; use without permission;
擅用私刑 administer justice without legal authority; take the law into one's own hands;
擅用職權 act on one's own authority; usurp powers;
［擅自］ arbitrarily; do sth without authorization; take the liberty;
擅自處理 settle a matter without authorization; take the law into one's own hands; take the liberty to decide matters by oneself;
擅自改動 act presumptuously;
擅自為謀 decide all by oneself; have one's own way of doing things;
擅自行動 act presumptuously; take it upon oneself; take presumptuous actions on one's own;
擅自修改 make unauthorized change; modify without authorization;
擅自作主 make a decision without authorization; take an unauthorized action;

專擅 do sth on one's own authority; usurp authority;

shan
【膳】 food; meals; provisions; viands;
［膳房］ (1) kitchen; (2) imperial kitchen;
［膳費］ board expenses;
［膳食］ diet; food; meal; meat; victuals;
不提供膳食 give no board;
混合膳食 mixed diet;
即席膳食 ready-to-eat meal;
生酮膳食 ketogenic diet;
學校膳食 school meal;
［膳宿］ bed and board; board and lodging; food and lodging;
膳宿生 boarding student;
提供膳宿 provide board and lodging;
［膳廳］ dining hall; mess hall;
［膳饌］ cuisine;

用膳 have one's meals;

shan
【嬗】 be replaced; change;
［嬗變］ (1) evolution; (2) transmutation;
感生嬗變 induced transmutation;
人工嬗變 artificial transmutation;
原子嬗變 atomic transmutation;
自然嬗變 natural transmutation;

shan
【禪】 abdicate;
［禪讓］ abdicate and hand over the crown to another person;
［禪位］ abdicate the throne;

shan
【繕】 (1) mend; repair; (2) copy; transcribe;
［繕補］ mend;
［繕校］ copy and proofread;
［繕就］ copy; finish copying; transcribe;
［繕錄］ transcribe;
［繕清］ make a fair copy;
［繕生］ cultivate life for health;
［繕寫］ copy; write out;
［繕性］ cultivate one's nature;
［繕修］ mend; repair;
［繕正］ copy neatly; write a fair copy;

修繕 renovate; repair;

shan
【蟺】 same as 蟮, earthworm;

shan
【贍】 (1) provide for; supply; support; (2) abundant; adequate; plenty; sufficient;
［贍家］ support a family;
贍家養口 support one's family;
贍家養小 support a family;
［贍卹］ contribute money to charity;
［贍養］ provide for; provide with means of support; support;
贍養費 alimony;
贍養父母 support one's parents;
贍養家屬 providing support for the dependents;
贍養家庭 support of the family;
［贍足］ abundant; plenty;

shan
【鱔】 eel;
［鱔糊］ stewed eels;
［鱔魚］ eel;

白鱔 white eel;

黃鱔 finless eel; ricefield eel;

shang¹ shang

【商】 (1) confer; consult; discuss; exchange views; (2) business; commerce; trade; (3) businessman; dealer; merchant; trader; (4) quotient; (5) a note of the ancient Chinese five-tone scale; (6) Shang Dynasty (c. 16th-11th century B.C.); (7) a surname;

[商標] brand; trademark;
商標代理 agency of trademark registration;
商標法 trademark law;
商標管理 trademark administration;
商標禁忌 trademark taboo;
商標名 brand name;
商標權 ownership of trademark;
商標設計 design of trademarks;
商標使用權 right to use the trademark;
商標訴訟 action for trademark registration;
商標信賴 loyalty to trademark;
商標許可 trademark license;
商標紙 trademark tag;
商標註冊 trademark registration;
商標轉讓 trademark transfer;
馳名商標 well-known trademark;
假商標 fake trademarks;
影射商標 counterfeit trademarks;
註冊商標 registered trademarks;

[商埠] commercial port; trading port;

[商場] bazaar; business world; department store; emporium; market; marketplace; shopping arcade;
商場如戰場 the business area is like a battlefield;
百貨商場 department store;
~大百貨商場 emporium;
自選商場 self-service market; supermarket;

[商船] merchant ship;
商船隊 merchant navy;

[商店] shop; store;
百貨商店 department store;
倉儲式商店 warehouse store;
大商店 emporium;
地下商店 walkdown;
兒童商店 children's shop;
共平商店 fair-price shop;
合作商店 co-op; cooperative;
寄售商店 commission house;
逛商店 browse around the shops; wander around the shops;
廉價商店 discounter;
零售商店 retail shop;
批發商店 wholesale shop;
特產商店 speciality shop;
小商店 corner shop; minimart; store;
信託商店 trust shop;
性用品商店 sex shop;
一家商店 a shop;
折扣商店 discount shop;
自選商店 self-service shop;

[商定] agree; come to an agreement; decide through consultation;

[商法] commercial law; mercantile law;

[商販] pedlar; small retailer; trader;

[商港] commercial port; mercantile port; seaport; trading port;

[商行] commercial firm; commercial house; trading company;

[商號] business entity; business establishment; corporate name; firm; shop; store;

[商會] chamber of commerce;
國際商會 chamber of international commerce;
進出口商會 chamber of commerce for import and export;
中華總商會 Chinese chamber of commerce;

[商機] business opportunity;
一個商機 a business opportunity; a niche;

[商家] business firm;

[商賈] businessmen; merchants;

[商界] business circles; business world; commercial circles; commercial world;
商界人士 business community;
進入商界 go into business;
立足於商界 establish oneself in business;

[商量] confer; consult; discuss; exchange views; exchange opinions; hold a discussion; put heads together; talk over;

[商品] commodities; goods; merchandize; wares;
商品包裝 commodity packaging;
商品差價 price difference of commodities;
商品陳列室 showroom;
商品出口 commodity export;

~商品出口總額 total commodity export;
商品道德 business ethics;
商品房 commodity house;
商品化 commercialization; commodification;
商品技術學 technique for commodities;
商品檢驗 commodity inspection;
商品交換 exchange of commodities;
商品交易會 trade fair;
商品交易所 commodity exchange house;
商品經濟 commodity economy;
商品進口 commodity import;
~商品進口總額 total commodity import;
商品流通 circulation of commodities;
商品貿易 commodity trade;
商品美學 commodity aesthetics;
商品能源 commercial energy;
商品審美 commodity aesthetics;
商品生產 commodity production;
商品信譽 commodity reputation;
商品組合 article mix;
商品作物 cash crop;
殘缺商品 defective goods; flawed goods;
出口商品 export goods;
~再出口商品 re-exported goods;
出租商品 merchandise held for rental;
處理商品 disqualified goods;
大宗商品 bulk commodity;
代購商品 merchandise purchased on behalf of others;
代銷商品 merchandise on consignment;
待運商品 merchandise awaiting transportation;
低檔商品 low-priced goods;
低質商品 shoddy goods;
複製商品 reproduction goods;
高檔商品 expensive goods; high-grade goods;
高質商品 quality goods;
華麗商品 tinsel goods;
積壓商品 dead stock;
季節性商品 seasonal commodity;
滯銷商品 poor seller; slow seller; unmarketable goods;
經濟商品 economic goods;
拒收商品 merchandise delivered but not accepted;
虧損商品 merchandise priced below cost;
流行商品 hot item;
免税商品 duty-free;
耐用商品 durable goods;
內銷商品 goods made for domestic market;
農業商品 agricultural commodity;
奢侈商品 luxury goods;
試產商品 trial-produced goods;
特價商品 bargain-priced goods;
脱銷商品 out-of-stock commodity;
偽劣商品 poor quality commodities;
~假冒偽劣商品 fake poor quality commodities;
五金商品 hardware;
一級商品 first-class goods;
易變商品 perishable goods;
液體商品 liquid goods;
議價商品 negotiated-priced goods;
在途商品 merchandise in transit;
再生商品 recycled product;
主要商品 staple commodity;

[商洽] arrange with sb; discuss together; take up a matter with sb;

[商情] business conditions; market conditions; market information;

[商榷] consult; counsel; deliberate; discuss; discuss and consider;
可商榷 open to dispute;

[商人] businessman; merchant; trader;
大商人 big merchant;
女商人 businesswoman;
小商人 small trader;
中等商人 middle merchant;

[商事] commercial affairs;

[商談] confer; discuss; exchange views; negotiate; talk over;

[商討] deliberate over; discuss;

[商務] business affairs; commercial affairs;
商務艙 business class; club class;
商務代表 commercial representative; trade representative;
商務名片 business card;
商務英語 Business English;
商務中心區 central business district;
電子商務 e-commerce;

[商業] business; commerce; trade;
商業暴利 commercial straggering profits;
商業標準化 commercial standardization;
商業部 ministry of commerce;
商業城市 commercial cities;
商業承兑匯票 trade acceptances;
商業傳播 business communication;
商業道德 business ethics;
商業登記 commercial registration;
商業電視 commercial TV;

~ 商業電視片 TV commercial;
商業電台 commercial radio;
商業電子化 commercial electronicilization;
商業翻譯 commercial translation;
商業風險 business risk;
商業服務 business service;
商業廣告 advertisement; commercial;
商業化 commercialization; commercialize;
商業匯票 commercial bill;
商業活動 business activity;
商業機構 commercial establishment;
商業街 commercial street;
商業界 business community;
商業經濟 commercial economy;
~ 商業經濟區 commercial economic region;
商業區 business park; commercial area; commercial district; downtown;
商業會計 business accountancy;
商業利益 commercial profit;
商業區 business zone; commercial district;
商業數據 business data;
~ 商業數據處理 business data processing;
商業通信網 business communication network;
商業網 commercial network; trade network;
~ 商業網點 point of connection in the commercial network;
~ 商業網體系 commercial network system;
~ 商業心理學 psychology of commerce;
商業文獻 commercial text;
商業信息 business information;
~ 商業信息系統 business information system;
~ 商業信息需求 business information demand;
商業信譽 trade credit;
商業行為 business practices;
~ 限制性商業行為 restrictive business practices;
商業學 business studies;
商業樣品 commercial sample;
商業銀行 commercial bank;
商業用戶 business customer;
商業賬戶 commercial account;
商業終端設備 business terminal;
商業主義 commercialism;
國際商業 international business;
輕視商業 despise trade;
投機商業 speculative business;

[商議] confer; deliberate; discuss; discuss and debate; discuss and deliberate;

[商用] commercial use;
商用計算機 business computer;
商用語言 commercial language;

[商譽] goodwill;

[商約] business contract; commercial treaty;

[商展] trade fair;

[商戰] commercial war; trade war;
商戰風雲 winds of business war;

[商酌] deliberate over; discuss and consider;

布商 draper;
廠商 firm; manufacturer;
承包商 contractor;
籌商 consult; discuss; hold a discussion;
出版商 publisher;
出口商 exporter;
磋商 consult; exchange views;
代理商 agent;
富商 millionaire businessman;
工商 industry and commerce;
共商 discus together; hold joint discussion;
官商 officials and merchants;
罐頭食品商 canned food trader;
行商 itinerant trader;
會商 hold a conference or consultation;
傢具商 furniture dealer;
奸商 commercial racketeer; dishonest trader; profiteer; unscrupulous merchant;
經商 engage in business deals; engage in trade; go into business; in business;
經銷商 distributor;
進口商 importer;
舊貨商 secondhand dealer;
客商 travelling merchant;
零售商 retailer;
帽商 hatter;
煤商 coal dealer; coalman;
密商 hold private counsel; hold secret talks;
面商 consult personally; discuss with sb face to face; take up a matter with sb personally;
麵包商 baker;
農商 farming and business;
拍賣商 auctioneer;
批發商 wholesaler;
皮革商 fellmonger;
皮貨商 fur dealer;

洽商 arrange by discussion; make arrangements with; negotiate; talk over with;
情商 ask for a favour as a friend;
搉商 consult; discuss;
參商 (1) unable to meet each other; (2) on bad terms;
紳商 the gentry and merchant class;
書商 bookman; bookseller;
私商 businessman; merchant;
糖果商 seller of preserved fruits;
通商 commercial intercourse; have trade relations; trade;
外商 foreign businessmen; foreign merchants; foreign tradesmen;
婉商 consult with sb tactfully or politely;
文具商 stationery seller;
五金商 ironmonger;
晤商 discuss in an interview; face-to-face negotiation;
洽商 discuss;
相商 confer; consult; consult with; exchange views; talk over with;
協商 bargaining; consult; consult with each other; discuss; negotiate; negotiation; talk things over;
行商 itinerant merchant; itinerant trader;pedlar; traveling salesman;
藥品商 druggist;
藥商 chemist; drug dealer;
殷商 prosperous merchant;
銀器商 silversmith;
魚商 fishmonger;
雜貨商 grocer;
招商 canvass business; invite outside investment;
智商 intelligence quotient (IQ);
製造商 manufacturer;
中間商 middleman;
珠寶商 jeweller;
諮商 counseling;
坐商 shopkeeper; tradesman;

shang

【湯】 flowing water;

［湯湯］ flowing turbulently;

shang

【傷】 (1) cut; injury; wound; (2) cut; hurt; injure; (3) distressed; grief; grieve; (4) impede; (5) develop an aversion to sth; get sick of sth; (6) harmful to; hinder;

［傷疤］ scar;
揭人傷疤 turn the knife in the wound; twist the knife;

［傷悲］ distress; grief;

［傷兵］ wounded soldier;

［傷病人員］ the sick and wounded;

［傷財］ lose money; waste money;
廢時傷財 cause loss of time and money;
勞民傷財 a sheer waste of energy and money; exhausting and expensive; harass the people and waste money; spend blood and treasure; tire the people and drain the treasury; waste money and manpower;

［傷殘］ invalidity; maim; permanent disability; the wounded and disabled;
傷殘人 physically handicapped person; the disabled;
傷殘者 invalid;

［傷處］ wound;

［傷悼］ mourn or grieve over the deceased;

［傷風］ catch cold; cold; flu; have a cold; head cold; influenza; sniffle;
傷風敗俗 a breach of morality; act immorally; corrupt public morals; demoralizing; harmful to society's morals; indecent; injure public morality; injurious to public morality; offend public decency; pervert manners and customs; shameless;
破傷風 tetanus;

［傷感］ be deeply moved; be deeply touched; distress; distressed; sentimental; sick at heart;
傷感的 bluesy;
~傷感的音樂 bluesy music;
傷感力 pathos;
傷感情 hurt the feelings of; lacerate sb's feelings; step on sb's toes; sting sb to the quick; take it ill; touch sb on the raw; tread on sb's corns; wound sb's sensibilities;
傷時感事 deeply worried about the current situations of the nation;

［傷害］ harm; hurt; impair; injure;
免受傷害 escape injury;
人身傷害 bodily harm;
受到傷害 come to harm;
造成傷害 cause an injury;

［傷寒］ typhoid fever; typhus;
城市傷寒 urban typhus;

副傷寒 paratyphoid;
~ 禽副傷寒 avian paratyphoid;
~ 豬副傷寒 swine paratyphoid;
[傷耗] damage;
[傷痕] bruise; hack; scar;
傷痕纍纍 be badly cut up;
傷痕文學 scar literature; wounded literature;
渾身傷痕 all one's body is covered with bruises;
[傷懷] distressing mood; grief;
感物傷懷 be deeply affected at seeing sth — touch to the heart;
[傷患] the sick and wounded;
傷患問題 injury problems;
[傷口] wound;
包扎傷口 bind up a wound; dress a wound bandaging;
洗傷口 bathe a wound;
治癒傷口 heal a wound;
[傷勞] injury due to overwork;
[傷人] (1) hurt people; (2) inflict physical injury on another; (3) harmful to health;
惡口傷人 say libelous things about sb; use bad language to insult people;
惡語傷人 give sb the rough side of one's tongue; make disparaging remarks about sb; malicious remarks hurt people to the quick; use bad language to insult sb;
~ 惡語傷人恨不消 slander always leaves a slur; slander leaves a scar behind it; the wicked words hurting others cause unperishable hatred;
~ 惡語傷人六月寒 slander is hurtful; vicious slander makes one feel cold even in the hotest time;
憂能傷人 care killed a cat; grief hurts one's health; worry may injure a man;
[傷身] harmful to the health; injurious to health;
氣大傷身 cut off one's nose to spite one's face(coll);
養虎傷身 bring up a tiger to injure oneself;
[傷神] beat one's brains out; nerve-racking; overtax one's nerves;
[傷生] do harm to sb's life;
[傷逝] grieve over the deceased; mourn over the loss of a dear person;
[傷勢] condition of an injury;
傷勢輕微 suffer slight injuries;
[傷損] injury; trauma;
[傷痛] mourn;
[傷亡] casualties; injuries and deaths;
傷亡慘重 suffer heavy casualties;
傷重身亡 died of a mortal wound;
[傷心] break one's heart; broken-hearted; grieved; hurt one's feelings; sad;
傷心慘目 break the heart and distress the eye; pitiful; too ghastly to look at; too horrible to look at; tragic;
傷心落淚 shed sad tears; weep in grief;
傷心事 grief; old sore; painful memory; sore spot;
為人傷心 one's heart bleeds for sb;
無比傷心 devour one's heart; eat one's heart out;
一陣傷心 a spasm of grief;
[傷者] casualty;

哀傷 distressed; dolour; feel grief; feel sorrow; grieve; mourn; mournful; sad; sorrowful;
暗傷 (1) internal injury; invisible injury; (2) indiscernible damage; internal damage;
悲傷 sad; sorrowful;
擦傷 abrasion; chafe; graze; scrape;
慘傷 sorrowful; tragic;
蟲傷 insect bite;
創傷 trauma; wound;
戳傷 stab; stab wound;
刺傷 stab and wound;
挫傷 bruise; contusion; dampen; discourage;
刀傷 knife wound;
跌傷 fall and get hurt; get injured by a fall;
凍傷 frostbite;
負傷 be injured; be wounded;
肝損傷 liver damage;
感傷 feel sad; feel sorrowful;
工傷 injury suffered on the job;
骨傷 bone fracture;
骨損傷 bone injury;
毀傷 damage; injure;
火傷 burn (caused by fire);
擊傷 wound;
勞傷 internal lesion caused by overexertion;
捩傷 sprain;
鱗傷 a mass of bruises;
腦損傷 brain damage;
腦外傷 brain surgery;

內傷 (1) internal injury; (2) disorder of internal organs caused by improper diet, fatigue, emotional strains, sexual excess, etc;
扭傷 sprain; wrench;
毆傷 beat and injure;
踫傷 be injured or damaged after being hit by sth;
悽傷 pitiful; sad; sorrowful;
淒傷 grievous; lamentable; mournful; sad;
槍傷 bullet wound;
輕傷 flesh wound; minor wound; slight injury; slight wound;
殺傷 inflict casualties; inflict wounds upon; kill and wound;
燒傷 burn; fire burn;
神傷 dejected;
受傷 be injured; be wounded; get an injury; get hurt; have an injury; receive an injury; suffer an injury; sustain an injury;
摔傷 get hurt in a fall;
死傷 killed and wounded; war casualties;
損傷 (1) cause loss to; damage; damnification; damnify; harm; hurt; impair; injure; (2) casualties; losses;
探傷 flaw detection;
歎傷 lament;
燙傷 burn; scald;
外傷 external injuries; wound;
惋傷 regret sorrowfully;
無傷 doesn't matter; no harm;
誤傷 accidentally injure; hurt by mistake;
軋傷 run over and injure;
驗傷 examine an injury;
養傷 heal one's wounds; nurse one's injuries;
憂傷 distressed; laden with grief; weighed down with sorrow; worried and grieved;
有傷 destructive to; harmful to;
瘀傷 bruise; contusion;
砸傷 be injured by a crashing object;
炸傷 be injured in bombing;
中傷 cast aspersions on sb; defamation; defame; hurt sb insidiously; malign; slander; vilify;
重傷 serious injury; serious wound;
撞傷 contuse; injure by bumping;
抓傷 scratch;
灼傷 burn;
自傷 (1) inflict injury on oneself; (2) feel sorrow for oneself; pity oneself;

S

shang
【殤】 (1) die young; (2) national mourning;

國殤 national martyr;

shang
【觴】 (1) wine vessels; (2) offer drinks to others;
［觴豆］ wine and food;
［觴詠］ chant poems while drinking;
觴詠之樂 joy of drinking and composing poems;
［觴政嫺習］ quite familiar with all sorts of wine-games;

濫觴 fountainhead; source;

shang³
shang
【上】 rising tone or third tone in Chinese phonetics;

shang
【晌】 (1) high noon; (2) a certain duration or interval of time; (3) a day's work;
［晌飯］ midday meal; lunch;
［晌覺］ afternoon nap;
［晌午］ high noon; midday; noon;

半晌 (1) half of the day; (2) a long time; quite a while;
頭晌 forenoon; morning;
歇晌 take a midday nap or rest;
一晌 a short moment;

shang
【賞】 (1) award; bestow; give to an inferior; grant a reward; reward; (2) award; reward; (3) admire; appreciate; enjoy;
［賞賜］ award; grant a reward;
［賞罰］ rewards and punishments;
賞罰不明 good work is not duly awarded nor bad work punished; neither rewarded nor penalized for going a good or a bad job; no distinction is made between those meriting rewards and those deserving punishments;
賞罰分明 confer reward and inflict punishment impartially; discriminating in one's rewards and punishments; fair in meting out rewards or punishments; keep strictly the rules for reward and punishment; mete out the proper awards and penalties; reward the worthy while giving due punishment

to those who deserve it;
賞罰嚴明 strict and fair in meting out rewards and punishments; give rewards and punishments impartially;
賞功罰罪 give rewards for good service and punishments for faults;
有賞有罰 duly mete out rewards and punishments; mete out punishments or rewards as the case demands; there should be due rewards and punishments;

[賞封] grant a reward; reward to a junior from a senior;
[賞格] amount of cash reward offered;
[賞光] asking sb to come to a party; honour sb with one's presence;
[賞花] enjoy the sight of flowers;
[賞鑒] appreciate;
[賞金] bonus; money reward; pecuniary reward;
[賞臉] do sb a favour; favour sb with the one's presence;
[賞錢] money reward; tips;
給賞錢 give tips;
[賞善] reward the good;
賞善罰惡 bless the good and punish the evil; reward the good and punish the bad; reward the virtuous and punish the wicked;
[賞識] appreciate; recognize the worth of;
[賞玩] admire the beauty of sth; delight in; enjoy; enjoy the sight of;
賞玩古董 delight in antiques;
[賞析] make appreciative comments;
作品賞析 works appreciation;
[賞心] please the heart;
賞心樂事 a happy event that pleases everyone; pleasant things that one enjoys doing;
賞心悅目 a feast for the eye; a perfect delight to the eye; cheerful and pleasing to the eye; find the scenery pleasing to both the eye and the mind; flatter the heart and please the eye; gladden the eyes and heart; gladden the heart and please the eye; let the eye take in the landscape and please the spirit; pleasant to look at; pleasant to the eye;
[賞雪] enjoy snow scenes;
[賞音] appreciate music;
[賞雨] enjoy rainy scenes;
[賞月] admire the full moon; enjoy moonlight; enjoy the glorious full moon;
賞月觀花 appreciate the moon and flowers;
[賞閱] read and appreciate;

稱賞 praise and extol; speak highly of;
導賞 guided tour;
觀賞 enjoy the sight of; view and admire;
擊賞 appreciate;
激賞 greatly admire; highly appreciate;
鑒賞 appreciate;
獎賞 award; reward;
犒賞 reward a victorious army, etc. with bounties;
慶賞 celebrate and reward;
受賞 be rewarded; get a reward;
歎賞 exclaim in appreciation; praise and admire;
玩賞 enjoy; take delight in;
欣賞 appreciate; enjoy;
行賞 reward the meritorious;
懸賞 offer a reward; post a reward;
讚賞 admire; appreciate;

shang⁴
shang

【上】 (1) above; (2) up; upper; upward; (3) better; higher; superior; (4) before; first; preceding; previous; (5) on; summit; top; (6) emperor; (7) ascend; go up; mount; (8) go to; leave for; (9) send in; submit; (10) forge ahead; go ahead; (11) enter the court; go to court; (12) fill; supply; (13) place sth in position; set; (14) apply; paint; (15) be carried in a publication; put on record; (16) screw; wind; (17) be engaged in work at a fixed time; (18) as many as; up to;
[上岸] go ashore; land;
[上班] go on duty; go to office; go to work; on duty; start work;
上班遲到 be late for work;
按時上班 get to work on time; start work on schedule;
步行上班 walk to one's office;
沒來上班 be absent from work;
去上班 go to work;

在上班 on duty;
照常上班 business as usual;
準時上班 report for work on time;

[上報] (1) appear in the newspapers; (2) report to a higher body; report to the leadership;

[上輩] (1) ancestors; (2) one's elders; the elder generation of one's family;

[上邊] (1) upper side; (2) up there;

[上賓] distinguished guest; guest of honour;
待如上賓 be treated as a guest of honour; treat sb as a highly honoured guest; treat sb as the most honoured guest; treat sb like a distinguished guest;
敬如上賓 treat sb as an honoured guest;
延為上賓 secure sb as guest of honour;
尊為上賓 respect above the salt;

[上坡] climb a slope; upslope;
上坡霧 upslope fog;

[上不來] cannot come up;

[上不去] (1) cannot go up; (2) cannot move forward;

[上部] (1) first part; (2) first volume;

[上菜] (1) best dishes; (2) place dishes on the table; serve a dish;

[上蒼] God; Heaven;

[上策] best plan; best policy; best stratagem; best thing to do; best way; best way out; first choice; the optimal policy;

[上層] upper levels;
上層建築 superstructure; top-out;
上層階級 upper class;

[上場] (1) appear on the stage; enter; go on stage; (2) enter the court; enter the field; join in a contest; take part in the competition;

[上朝] go to the imperial court;

[上車] get in the car; get into a car; get into a vehicle; get on a train;

[上秤] put on the scale and weigh;

[上船] board a ship; embark; go aboard;

[上牀] get into bed; go to bed; hit the hay; hit the sack;
上牀睡覺 go to bed;
爬上牀 climb into bed;
跳上牀 jump into bed;

[上次] last time; the previous occasion;

[上達] reach the higher authorities;
上達天聽 present memorials to the emperor directly; send memorials directly to the emperor; submit memorials to the throne;

[上代] former generations; previous generations;

[上當] be caught with chaff; be duped; be fooled; be taken in; be tricked; bite at a bait; play into someone's hands;
上當受騙 be duped and misled; be hoodwinked and misled; be taken in; be tricked; get duped and fall in a trap; swallow a gudgeon; swallow the bait; take the bait;
上當者 dupe;
不易上當的 canny;
別上當 don't walk into that trap;
徹底上當 be completely taken in;
吃虧上當 be fooled and get into trouble; have suffered and have been deceived;
輕易上當 jump at the bait;
上大當，吃大虧 be badly fooled and suffer severely;
上一回當，學一回乖 a burnt child dreads the fire; if you are taken in once, you will be wary next time; once bitten, twice shy;

[上德] highest virtue;

[上燈] light the lamp; light up;

[上等] first class; first-rate; superior; superior quality;
上等兵 (1) seaman first class; (2) private first class;
上等貨 goods of superior quality;

[上帝] God; the Absolute;
見上帝去了 go to see God;
去見上帝 meet your maker;

[上吊] commit suicide by hanging; hang oneself;

[上端] top; upper edge; upper end; upper extreme;

[上顎] roof of the mouth; upper jaw;

[上方] (1) above; the place above; (2) celestial realm;
上方寶劍 the imperial sword — a symbol of high authority, investing the bearer with discretionary powers;

[上訪] visit the capital;

[上墳] visit sb's grave;

[上風] (1) windward; (2) advantage; superior position; upperhand;

搶上風 jockey for an advantageous position;

佔上風 come out on top; come out top dog; gain the upper hand; gain the wind of; get the better end of; get the start of; get the upper hand; get the wind of; have the advantage over; have the upper hand of; have the wind of; on the windward side; prevail over; stand at advantage; take advantageous position; take the wind of; windward;

[上峰] higher-up; upper echelon;

[上告] complain to the higher authorities or appeal to a higher court;

[上工] begin work; go to work; start work;

[上鈎] be tricked into doing sth; fall into a trap; get hooked; rise to the bait; swallow the bait;

[上古] ancient times; prehistoric times; remote ages;

[上官] (1) one's direct superior in office; (2) a surname;

[上光] glazing; polishing;

上光榮榜 on the rolls of fame;

[上好] best-quality; excellent; first-class; superior; the best; tip-top;

[上核] cokernel;

差分上核 difference cokernel;

耦合的上核 cokernel of a couple;

射的上核 cokernel of a morphism;

[上戶] wealthy family;

[上回] last time; on a previous occasion;

[上火] (1) heat; inflamation; (2) suffer from internal heat;

[上級] higher authorities; higher level; higher-ups; in higher position of responsibility; superiors;

巴結上級 make up to one's senior officer;

下級服從上級 the lower level is subordinate to the higher level;

[上計] best plan;

[上家] (of mahjong) opponent on the left;

[上將] (1) general; (2) admiral;

空軍上將 air chief marshal;

四星上將 four-star general;

五星上將 (1) general of the army; (2) general of the air force; (3) five-star admiral; fleet admiral; (4) five star general;

～海軍五星上將 fleet admiral;

[上交] hand in; turn over to the higher authorities;

[上繳] turn in sth to a higher level; turn over to the higher authorities;

[上街] (1) go into the street; go on the street; (2) go shopping;

[上界] heaven;

[上進] advance; go forward; make progress;

上進心 desire to advance; the desire to do better; the urge for improvement;

不求上進 have no desire to make progress; make no effort to seek progress;

[上勁] energetically; with great vigour; with gusto;

[上客] the most honoured guest;

[上課] (1) attend a class; attend class; go to a class; take a class; (2) conduct a class; give a lesson;

按時上課 punctual for class;

不去上課 dodge a lesion; play truant;

[上空] high up in the air; in the sky; midair; overhead;

[上口] (1) able to read aloud fluently; easy to read; easy to speak; (2) make smooth reading;

[上款] name of the recipient;

[上來] come up;

答不上來 at a loss how to answer;

[上梁] main beam;

上梁不正下梁歪 a crooked stick will have a crooked shadow; fish begins to stink at the head; if a leader sets a bad example, it will be followed by his subordinates; if the upper beam is not straight, the lower ones will go aslant — when those above behave unworthily, those below will do the same;

[上列] above; above-listed; above-mentioned;

[上流] (1) upper reaches of a river; (2) upper circles; upper-class;

上流社會 the fashionable world; the great world; the high society; the polite society; the upper class; the world of fashion;

[上樓] go upstairs;

奔上樓 dash upstairs; flay upstairs;

[上路] set out on a journey; start off;

[上馬] (1) mount a horse; (2) to horse; (3) get going; let the ball roll; make a start; start;
扶鞍上馬 get into the saddle; mount a horse;
[上門] (1) call; come to see sb; drop in; visit; (2) bolt the door; shut the door for the night;
上門費 call-out charge;
上門服務 call-out; domiciliary services; make house calls;
上門工作 house call;
上門看病 house call;
[上面] (1) above; on the surface of; on top of; over; top; upper surface; (2) above-mentioned; aforesaid; foregoing; (3) higher authorities; (4) aspect; respect;
最上面 the very top;
[上年] last year;
[上皮] (1) epidermium; (2) outer bark of trees;
上皮癌 epithelioma;
上皮瘤 epithelioma;
~ 彌漫性上皮瘤 diffuse epithelioma;
~ 神經上皮瘤 neuroepithelioma;
上皮組織 epithelial tissue; epithelium;
扁平上皮 pavement epithelium;
分泌上皮 secretory epithelium;
黏液上皮 mucoepidermoid;
神經上皮 neurepithelium;
腎小球上皮 glomerular epithelium;
生殖上皮 germinal epithelium;
[上片] start showing a movie;
[上品] goods of superior quality; highest grade; top grade;
最上品 the prime quality;
[上鋪] the upper berth;
[上氣不接下氣] be short of breath; breathless; gasp for breath; lose one's breath; lose one's wind; out of breath; out of puff; pant for breath;
八十歲的老頭吹喇叭—上氣不接下氣 an eighty-year-old man blowing a trumpet — out of breath;
[上前] come forward;
[上去] go up; upward;
看上去 look like;
~ 看上去很好 look well;
~ 看上去很累 look tired;
~ 看上去很年輕 look young;
[上任] assume office; enter upon office; take up an official post;
[上日] (1) first day of the lunar month; (2) festive day;
[上色] (1) colouration; to colour sth; (2) best-quality; top-grade;
[上山] go to the mountains; go up a hill; go up the mountain;
上山擒虎易，開口告人難 climbing a mountain to capture a tiger is easier than begging alms — there is nothing more difficult than begging; he that goes a-borrowing goes a-sorrowing;
上山下鄉 go and work in the countryside and mountain areas; go to the mountainous and rural areas;
[上上] (1) very best; (2) before last;
上上大吉 very good omen;
上上下下 (1) above and below; from cellar to garret; from garret to kitchen; from top to bottom; up and down; (2) all; the whole;
[上身] (1) upper part of the body; (2) blouse; jacket; shirt; upper outer garment;
[上昇] ascend; go up; rise; soar;
垂直上昇 vertical ascent;
大幅上昇 huge rise; massive rise;
動力上昇 powered ascent;
~ 無動力上昇 power-out ascent; powerless ascent;
急劇上昇 sharp rise; steep rise;
絕對溫度上昇 adiabatic temperature rise;
快速上昇 rapid rise;
陸續上昇 progressive rise;
毛細上昇 capillary ascent; capillary rise;
明顯上昇 significant rise; substantial rise;
穩步上昇 steady rise;
顯著上昇 dramatic rise;
最速上昇 steepest ascent;
最優上昇 synergic ascent;
[上士] (1) petty officer first class; (2) sergeant first class;
空軍上士 flight sergeant;
[上市] go on the market; in season; listed; listing;
上市公司 listed company;
上市證券 listed securities;
[上世] prehistoric times; primeval times;
[上手] begin; start;
[上壽] (1) advanced age; (2) drink a toast for longevity;

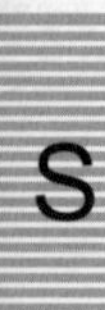

[上書] make a presentation in writing; present a petition; send in a memorial; submit a written statement to a higher authority;

[上述] above-mentioned; aforementioned; as said above;

上述的 above-mentioned;

[上訴] appeal; lodge an appeal;

上訴法院 Appeal Court; appeals court; appellate court; court of appeal;

上訴理由 grounds for an appeal;

上訴權 right of appeal;

上訴人 appellant;

上訴制度 the appeal system;

不服上訴 appeal against;

駁回上訴 dismiss an appeal; reject an appeal; throw out an appeal; turn down an appeal;

等待上訴 pending appeal;

受理上訴 allow an appeal;

提出上訴 bring an appeal; file an appeal; make an appeal; lodge an appeal;

正式上訴 formal appeal;

[上司] boss; superior official;

巴結上司 fawn on one's superiors;

頂頭上司 one's direct superior; one's immediate superior;

[上溯] (1) sail upstream; (2) trace back to;

[上算] (1) economical; profitable deal; (2) deserving; worthwhile;

不上算 bad bargain; not profitable;

[上鎖] lock;

[上臺] (1) appear on the stage; go on the stage; go up onto the platform; (2) assume office; assume power; come to power; in charge; rise to power; take up an official post;

[上檯] make a parade of the bride's trousseau on the streets;

[上堂] (1) go to class; (2) go up the hall;

[上膛] be loaded;

[上套] fall into a trap;

[上體] upper part of the body;

[上天] (1) God; Heaven; Providence; (2) fly sky-high; go up to the sky;

上天入地 leave no stone unturned; spare no efforts; try by hook to look for sth; try every means to seek;

上天無路，入地無門 can neither fly up to the sky nor hide underground – find no way out; cannot find a way to heaven or earth; in desperate straits; there is no path to Heaven one can go, no door to Earth that one can enter – nowhere to turn; there is no road to heaven and no door into the earth – no way of escape; up against the wall;

捧上了天 crack up to the nines; laud to the skies; praise above the moon;

[上頭] (1) above; the top; up; (2) authorities;

[上位] (1) top seat; (2) person occupying a leading position;

[上尉] (1) lieutenant; (2) captain;

海軍上尉 lieutenant;

空軍上尉 flight lieutenant; lieutenant;

[上文] preceding text;

[上午] forenoon; morning;

前天上午 on the morning the day before yesterday;

整個上午 all morning; all the morning;

[上下] (1) high and low; old and young; ruler and subjects; senior and junior; superior and inferior; (2) above and below; from top to bottom; up and down; (3) go up and come down; go up and down; (4) about; more or less;

上下打量 examine sb from head to foot; eye sb from head to toe; look sb from head to foot; look sb over from head to foot; look sb up and down; measure sb from head to foot; scrutinize sb from head to foot; size sb from head to foot; stare at sb up and down;

上下顛倒 turn upside down;

~上下顛倒的 upside down;

上下和睦 the superiors and the inferiors are on good terms;

上下交迫 between the beetle and the block;

上下交困 both the higher and the lower levels find themselves in a predicament;

上下其手 act in collusion with; distort facts to suit one's private ends; get up to tricks; in collusion with sb; league together for some evil end; manoeuvre for some evil end; practise fraud; work hand in glove with sb;

上下四方 in all directions;

上下通氣 full communication between the higher and lower levels;

上下脱節 cause dislocation between

higher and lower organizations;

上下文 co-text; context;

~句法上下文 syntactical co-text;

上下相安 the leadership and the rank and file are on good terms; the superiors and the inferiors live together peacefully;

上下一條心 both the higher and lower levels are united as one; of one heart and mind; the leadership and the rank and file are of one mind;

上下左右 every which way;

傲上卹下 haughty to the proud but kind to the humble;

蔽上蒙下 deceive superiors and hoodwink subordinates;

不分上下 make no distinction of rank; neck and neck; not to know one's place;

不上不下 be suspended in midair; in a dilemma; in a fix; not know what to do;

不相上下 about the same; equally matched; more or less of equal strength; neck and neck; nip and tuck; on a level with; on a par with; without much difference;

諂上傲下 pay too much respect to one's superiors and despise those who are of lower ranks;

諂上欺下 be servile to one's superiors and tyrannical to one's subordinates; fawn on those above and bully those below;

承上啟下 connect with the foregoing and carry forward to a new paragraph; continue from the above and introduce the following; form a connecting link between the preceding and the following;

從上到下 from cellar to garret; from garret to kitchen; from the highest levels down to the grass-roots; from top to bottom;

蹿上跳下 bounce up and down;

忽上忽下 seesaw; up and down;

幾上幾下 go up or step down many times;

拉上補下 even things up;

買上告下 bribe all the officials concerned; bribe both the higher and lower officials;

瞞上不瞞下 deceive only the superiors and not the subordinates;

瞞上欺下 conceal the true state of affairs from above and below; hoodwink those above and bully those below;

~善於瞞上欺下 be inclined to hoodwink one's superiors and bully one's inferiors;

媚上驕下 fawn upon one's superior and insult one's subordinates;

媚上欺下 fawn on and please superiors and trea inferiors high-handedly; fawn upon one's superior and insult one's subordinates;

能上能下 able to work at both higher and lower levels; able to work both at the top and down below; ready to work at any post, high or low; ready to work both at the top or at the grass roots;

捧上壓下 fawn on one's superiors and bully one's subordinates;

七上八下 agitated; all upside down; an unsettled state of mind; at sixes and sevens; in a fidget; in a mental flurry of indecision; in a state of discomposure; in a turmoil; in an unsettled state of mind; in anxiety and nervousness; in confusion; on tenterhooks; like a well in which seven buckets are drawn up and eight dropped down; one's heart is revolting; perturbed; put into a flutter; the nervous palpitation of the heart due to fright or other causes; things are at sixes and sevens; throw into a flutter; very agitated; very perturbed; very upset; with a frightful mind; with misgivings;

欺上凌下 deceive superiors and oppress inferiors;

欺上瞞下 cheat one's superiors and defraud one's subordinates; cheat those below one and hoodwink those above; conceal the true state of affairs from above and below oneself; deceive one's superiors and delude one's subordinates; deceive one's superiors and hide the truth from one's subordinates; decesive one's superiors and subordinates;

欺上壓下 deceive one's superiors and put pressure on one's subordinates;

欺下罔上 cheat one's subordinates and fool one's superiors; oppress the people and hide the truth from higher

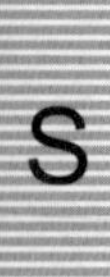

authorities;
上不沾天，下不著地 have nothing to hang on to above and no solid ground to rest one's feet on below; touch neither the sky nor the ground — be suspended in midair;
上諂下驕 fawn upon one's superiors and look down upon those below; flatter those in high position and despite those of lower ranks;
上躥下跳 run around on sinister errands; run clandestine errands up and down the line;
上敬下和 respectful towards his superiors and kindly towards those under him;
上情下達 make what is going on at higher levels known to lower levels; transmit an order from above;
上行下效 if a leader sets a bad example, his subordinates will follow suit; if a leader sets a bad example, it will be followed by his subordinates; subordinates follow the example of their superiors; the doings of superiors are imitated by inferiors; the inferiors imitate the superiors; those below follow the example of those above; those in subordinate positions will follow the example set by their superiors;
跳上跳下 bounce up and down; jump up and down;
由下而上 from below; from the bottom to the top; from the lower level upward;
直上直下 very steep;
自上而下 from above; from above to below; from the top down; from top to bottom;
自下而上 from below; from below to above; from bottom to top; from the bottom up;

[上弦] first quarter of the moon;

[上限] superior limit; top limit; upper limit;
有上限的 capped;

[上香] go to a temple to pray; offer incense;

[上相] come out well in a photograph; photogenic;

[上校] (1) captain; (2) colonel;
上校軍銜 colonel;
空軍上校 group caption;

[上行車] up train;

[上刑] apply the third degree; put sb to torture; torture;

[上旋] topspin;

[上選] choicest;

[上學] at school; attend school; go to school;
不去上學 stay away from school;
回去上學 go back to school;
開始上學 start school;
騎自行車上學 cycle to school;
在大學上學 at college; at university;

[上旬] first ten days of a month;

[上眼] worth looking at;
看不上眼 disdain; hold in contempt; spurn;

[上演] give a public performance; on show; perform; put on the stage; stage;
上演本 stage version;

[上藥] apply ointment to the affected area;

[上衣] blazer; jacket; upper garment;
登山上衣 alpine jacket;
短上衣 jacket;
~緊身短上衣 bomber jacket;
~寬鬆短上衣 loose-fitting jacket;
~露腹短上衣 crop top;
解開上衣 unbutton one's jack; unfasten one's jacket;
射擊上衣 shooting jacket;
脫上衣 strip to the waist;
一件上衣 a top;

[上癮] be addicted to sth; become addicted to a certain drug or habit; get into one's blood; get into the habit of doing sth; habit-forming;
喝酒上癮 addict oneself to drinking;
吸煙上癮 be addicted to smoking;

[上映] on; run; screen; show a film;
上映比率 quota;
上映影片目錄 film repertoire;

[上油] apply lubricant; replenish lubricating oil;

[上游] (1) upper reaches of a river; (2) advanced position;
上游源頭 headwaters;
河的上游 upper reaches of a river;

[上愚] most stupid;

[上諭] imperial edict;

[上元] fifteenth of the first lunar month;

[上苑] royal garden;

[上月] last month;

[上漲] go up; rise;

不斷上漲 rise steadily;
價格上漲 price rise;
租金上漲 rent rise;

[上陣] (1) go into battle; (2) pitch into the work;

[上肢] upper limbs;

[上智] most intelligent; sage; wisest;

[上週] last week;

[上裝] (1) dress up; make up; (2) top;
比基尼上裝 bikini top;

[上足] (1) capable students; (2) superior horses;

[上祖] remote ancestors;

[上座] (1) seat of honour; (2) customers begin to come into a place;
上座率 admissions;
~影院上座率 cinema admissions;

挨不上 beside the point; extraneous; have no relations; impertinent; inapplicable; inconsequent; irrelative; irrelevant; not to the purpose;
岸上 bank; shore;
背上 put on the back for carrying;
北上 go north; proceed northward;
繃上 tack down; tack on;
比不上 inferior to; no peer for; not come near; comparable to; not hold a candle to;
比得上 bear comparison with; can compare with; compare favourably with;
閉上 close; shut;
冰上 ice;
穿上 put on;
船上 on board;
牀上 (1) bedding; (2) on the bed;
春上 in spring;
戴上 don; put on;
地上 on the floor; on the ground;
翻上 swing up;
犯不上 not worth;
犯上 go against one's superiors;
奉上 have the honour to send;
府上 (1) your family; your home; (2) your native place;
趕上 (1) catch up with; get up to; keep pace with; keep up with; overtake; (2) run into; (3) in time for;
跟上 abreast of; catch up sb; catch up with sb; come up with; draw up with; gain on; get up to; hold pace with; keep abreast of; keep pace with; keep up with; overtake; pull up with;
關上 close;
海上 at sea; maritime; on the sea; seaborne;
合上 close; shut;
皇上 His Majesty;
火上 to the fire;
肩上 on sb's shoulders;
謹上 sincerely yours;
看上 like; settle on; take a fancy to;
臉上 on the face;
戀上 fall for;
樓上 upstairs;
陸上 land; onshore;
路上 (1) on the road; (2) en route; on the way;
馬上 at any moment; at once; immediately; in a couple of shakes; in no time; in two shakes; pronto; right away; right now; right off; right off the bat; straight away;
蒙上 cover; dim; muffle;
爬上 climb; get up; scale; scramble up;
配得上 deserve; worthy of;
氣頭上 in a fit of anger; in a fit of temper; right in the middle of one's fit of rage;
牆上 wall;
橋上 on the bridge;
瞧得上 good enough to suit one's taste;
怯上 superior fright;
取不上 unable to get selected;
如上 as above;
訕上 slander one's superiors;
身上 (1) on one's body; (2) have sth on one; with one;
聖上 Your Majesty;
使不上 not usable; unfit to be used;
世上 in the world; on earth;
數不上 not important enough; not qualified;
樹上 above the tree; on the tree;
拴上 fasten;
水上 above the water; on the water; over the water;
說不上 (1) cannot say; cannot tell; (2) do not fit the description; not worth mentioning;
算上 count in; include;
鎖上 lock;
臺上 on the stage;
談不上 far from being; out of the question;
堂上 (1) parents; (2) form of address for magistrates or judges;
天上 the heavens; the sky;
添上 (1) add to; (2) besides; in addition to;
頭上 on the head; on top;
塗上 apply; lay on; smear; spread on;

晚上 at night; in the evening;
網上 internet; online;
往上 upward;
無上 highest; paramount; supreme;
侮上 arrogant to one's superior;
席上 (1) scholars; the learned; (2) on the dining table;
線上 on-line;
向上 (1) up; upward; (2) make progress; strive upward; try to improve oneself;
心上 at heart; in one's heart; in one's mind; in the heart;
形而上 metaphysical; noumenal;
掩上 shut;
以上 (1) above; more than; over; (2) above-mentioned; foregoing;
涌上 rush; stream; upwell;
在上 on high;
長上 (1) elder; senior; (2) boss; superior;
早上 morning;
之上 above; on; over;
直上 rise quickly;
紙上 on paper;
至上 (1) highest; supreme; (2) come first;
追上 draw level;
祖上 ancestors; forebears; forefathers;

shang
【尚】 (1) still; yet; (2) esteem; honour; set great store by; uphold; value; (3) a surname;
[尚德] respect the virtuous;
[尚佳] not too bad; passable;
[尚可] (1) acceptable; passable; (2) still permissible; still possible;
[尚祈] I hope; I pray;
[尚且] (1) even; (2) still; yet;
[尚然] still; yet;
[尚武] militaristic;
尚武精神 encourage a military spirit; martial spirit; militarism;
[尚賢] exaltation of the virtuous;
[尚義] love uprightness;
[尚勇] esteem valour;
[尚猶] still; yet;
[尚自] still; yet;

崇尚 advocate; uphold;
風尚 prevailing practice, custom, habit, etc.;
高尚 lofty; noble;
好尚 love and uphold;
和尚 Buddhist monk;
時尚 fashion;
俗尚 current fashion;
習尚 common practice; custom;

shang⁵
shang
【裳】 clothing; dress; garment; lower garments; skirt;

衣裳 clothes; clothing;

shao¹
shao
【捎】 (1) carry; take along at one's convenience; (2) brush over lightly; (3) wipe out;
[捎帶] carry; take along at one's convenience;
[捎腳] give sb a lift;

shao
【弰】 ends of a bow;

shao
【梢】 (1) tip of a branch; (2) end of sth; (3) rudder; (4) (now rare) sound of wind;
[梢公] boatman;
[梢溝] trench made by running water;
[梢末] extreme end of sth;
[梢婆] boatwoman;
[梢梢] (1) blowing sound of wind; (2) strong and vigorous;
[梢頭] (1) tip of a branch; (2) end of spring; (3) top log;
[梢雲] auspicious clouds;
[梢子] (1) tip of a branch; (2) boatman; (3) short pants;

鞭梢 whiplash;
辮梢 end of a plait;
釘梢 shadow sb; tail sh;
眉梢 tip of the brow;
末梢 end; tip;
樹梢 tip of a tree; treetop;
下梢 (1) end; (2) ending; outcome;

shao
【稍】 (1) a bit; a little; slight; (2) rather; somewhat; (3) bit by bit; gradually;
[稍次] slightly inferior in quality;
[稍淡] a little too weak;
[稍後] a little later; later; shortly afterward;

soon afterward;
稍後再説 talk to you later;
[稍候] wait for a while;
[稍緩] a little slower; not so fast; put off for a while;
[稍加] make some addition; slightly more;
稍加修改 make a few alterations; make slight changes;
[稍佳] a little better; slightly better;
[稍覺] feel slightly;
[稍可] moderately successful; slightly better;
稍可即止 stop after being moderately successful;
[稍濃] a little too thick;
[稍稍] a little; just a little; slightly;
[稍微] a bit; a little; a trifle; rather; slightly;
[稍瑕] have a little leisure;
[稍嫌] slightly more or less than the ideal state;
[稍許] a little;
[稍異] slightly different; somewhat different;
[稍縱即逝] fleeting; transient;

shao
【筲】 basket for washing rice;
[筲箕] basket for washing rice;

斗筲 ancient bamboo container;
水筲 water pail;

shao
【艄】 (1) stern of a boat; (2) helm; rudder;
[艄夫] (1) helmsman; (2) boatman;
[艄公] (1) helmsman; (2) boatman;
[艄婆] boatwoman;

船艄 stern;

shao
【蛸】 a variety of spiders;

蠨蛸 a kind of spider;

shao
【燒】 (1) burn; (2) bake; cook; (3) fry after stewing; stew after frying; (4) roast; stew; (5) have a temperature; run a fever; (6) fever;
[燒杯] beaker;
鋼製燒杯 steel beaker;
微燒杯 micro beaker;
錐形燒杯 conical beaker;
[燒餅] sesame seed cake;
糖燒餅 sesame seed cakes with sugar;
[燒菜] cook; do cooking; prepare a meal;
燒菜做飯 prepare a meal;
[燒茶] boil tea;
[燒飯] cooking;
[燒鍋] container for making liquor;
燒鍋做飯 light the fire to cook dinner; make fire to cook food;
[燒化] cremate; melt down by fire; reduce to ashes;
[燒灰] reduce to ashes;
[燒燬] burn down; burn up; destroy in fire;
燒燬文件 burn up the documents;
被火燒燬 be destroyed by fire;
[燒火] build a fire; light a fire; make a fire; tend the kitchen fire;
採薪燒火 gather sticks for a fire;
[燒活] paper structures burned in a funeral;
[燒焦] burnt; scorch; sear; singe;
燒焦的 charred;
[燒結] sintering;
燒結本領 agglutinating power;
加壓燒結 compression sintering;
連續燒結 continuous sintering;
缺陷燒結 defect sintering;
[燒酒] white spirits;
[燒烤] roast;
露天燒烤 cookout;
~ 露天燒烤餐 cookout;
[燒鳥] roast bird;
[燒瓶] flask;
長頸燒瓶 boiling flask;
三角燒瓶 conical flask;
吸收燒瓶 absorption flask;
[燒傷] burn; fire burn;
二度燒傷 second-degree burn;
三度燒傷 third-degree burn;
四度燒傷 fourth-degree burn;
一度燒傷 first-degree burn;
醫治燒傷 healing of burns;
[燒蝕] ablation;
燒蝕材料 ablatant; ablative; ablator;
~ 低溫燒蝕材料 low-temperature ablator;
~ 碳化燒蝕材料 charring ablator;
燒蝕層 ablator;
表面燒蝕 surface ablation;
大氣燒蝕 atmospheric ablation;
輻射燒蝕 radiation ablation;
高超音速燒蝕 hypersonic ablation;

火焰燒蝕 flame ablation;
氣動熱燒蝕 aerothermal ablation;
氣動燒蝕 aerodynamic ablation;
熱燒蝕 thermal ablation;
熔化燒蝕 melting ablation;
昇華燒蝕 sublimating ablation;
瞬時燒蝕 transient ablation;
穩態燒蝕 steady ablation;
蒸發燒蝕 vaporizing ablation;
駐點燒蝕 stagnation-point ablation;

[燒水] boil water; heat water;
[燒死] burn to death;
[燒香] burn incense; burn joss sticks;
燒香拜佛 burn incense and pray; burn incense and worship the gods;
燒香還願 burn incense and redeem a pledge; burn incense and return thanks; burn incense in fulfillment of a vow; fulfill a vow by burning incense;
燒香許願 burn incense and make a vow to the gods;
揀佛燒香 offer incense to right deity — curry favour from the right person; select a Buddha for whom one will burn the incense — treat people differently;
[燒心] (1) anxious; apprehensive; fretful; uneasy; (2) heartburn;
[燒灼] burn; scorch; singe;

焙燒 bake; roast; roasting;
叉燒 barbecue pork; roast pork;
低燒 low fever;
煅燒 calcine;
發燒 have a fever;
焚燒 burn; set on fire;
高燒 high fever;
紅燒 braise in soy sauce;
火燒 baked wheaten cake;
燃燒 (1) burn; kindle; (2) combustion; inflammation;
退燒 bring down a fever;
延燒 (of fire) spread;

shao²
shao
【勺】 ladle; scoop; spoon;
[勺口兒] cooking skill and style of a cook;
[勺子] dipper; ladle; scoop; spoon;
一把勺子 a ladle;
一個勺子 a ladle;

長柄勺 dipper;
炒勺 round-bottomed frying pan;
漏勺 conlander; strainer;
馬勺 ladle;
湯勺 soup ladle;
掌勺 be the chef;
鑄勺 ladle;

shao
【杓】 container; receptacle;
[杓儿] spoon;
[杓球場] golf course;
[杓子] wooden ladle;

shao
【芍】 peony; paeonia;
[芍藥] Chinese peony;

白芍 the root of herbaceous peony;
赤芍 the root of herbaceous peony;

shao
【韶】 (1) beautiful; excellent; harmonious; splendid; (2) continuous;
[韶刀] flippant; garrulous;
[韶光] (1) beautiful springtime; (2) glorious youth;
韶光易逝 time passes quickly;
[韶華] (1) beautiful springtime; (2) glorious youth;
韶華不再 one cannot regain one's youth; spring time waits for no man; the splendour of youth never returns;
韶華似水 the splendour of youth passes away like water;
韶華虛度 idling one's youth away; pouring one's life in the sand — wasting one's youth;
[韶景] beauties of spring;
[韶韶擺擺] din; nag;
[韶秀] delicate and pretty; good-looking and handsome;

shao³
shao
【少】 (1) few; little; small; (2) absent; lack; lose; missing; short of; wanting; (3) a little while; a moment; (4) quit; stop;
[少安毋躁] be patient; calm oneself and wait patiently; don't be impatient, wait for a while; just keep your hair on; keep calm, don't get excited; please calm

down a little and do not get excited; take it easy, don't make a fuss;
[少吃多餐] have many meals but littl food at each; often and little eating;
[少待] wait for a little while;
少待片刻 please wait a little while;
[少而精] fewer but better; smaller quantity, better quality;
[少管] don't meddle in;
少管閒事 don't meddle in others' affairs; don't put your finger in the pie; mind your own business; none of your business;
[少候] please wait for a little while;
[少見] rare; seldom seen; unique;
少見多怪 a man who has seen little regards many things are strange; comment excitedly on a commonplace thing; consider sth remarkable simply because one has not seen it before; having seen little, one gets excited easily; he who has little experience has many surprises; ignorant people are easily surprised; kick up a fuss; the less a man has seen the more he has to wonder at; things rarely seen are regarded as strange; things seldom seen seem strange; wonder at what one has not seen; wonder is the daughter of ignorance;
[少刻] a moment later; after a little while;
[少來] (1) refrain from coming; (2) sparing in doing sth;
少來這一套 let's have no more of this;
[少勞少得] small pains, small gains;
[少量] a few; a little; a small amount; a sprinkling of;
少量白雪 a sprinkling of snow;
少量的 daub;
~少量的酒 dram;
~少量的油漆 a daub of paint;
少量地 in dribs and drabs;
[少慢差費] achieve less, slower, worse and with less economical results; fewer, slower, poorer and more costly; get few, slow, poor and expensive results; get fewer and poorer results, and progress be slower and costs higher; inefficient and expensive; lead to smaller, slower, poorer and wasteful results;
[少陪] if you'll excuse me; I'm afraid I must be going now;
[少頃] a little while; a short time; a short while; after a few moments; after a short while; presently;
[少時] a moment later; after a little while;
[少數] a few; a small number; minority;
少數黨 minority political party;
~少數黨領袖 minority leader;
少數民族 minority ethnic group; minority nationality;
少數人 a few people; a small number of people; the minority;
~少數人語言 language minority;
少數團體 minority group;
[少說為佳] few words are best; least said, soonest mended; the least said, the soonest mended; the less said about it, the better;
[少停] pause for a little while;
[少微] slightly;
[少問] refrain from asking;
[少校] (1) lieutenant commander; (2) major;
[少許] a few; a little; a modicum;
[少有] exceptional; rare; scarce; seldom;
[少智為福] ignorance is bliss;

頂少 at least;
短少 be deficient; fall short;
多少 amount; more or less; number; somewhat; to some extent;
減少 decrease; reduce;
缺少 be short of; lack;
稀少 rare; scarce;
至少 at least;

shao⁴
shao

【少】 (1) young; youthful; (2) junior; juvenile; son of a rich family; younger master;
[少艾] young beauty;
[少東] son of the master;
[少婦] young married woman; young woman;
漂亮的少婦 nymph;
[少將] (1) rear admiral; (2) major general;
[少年] (1) early youth; young; (2) boy; juvenile; teenager; youth;
少年白頭 young man with white hair;

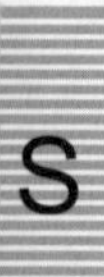

少年不知勤學早，白頭方悔讀書遲 who does not study diligently in his youth will, when old, repent that he puts it off till too late;
少年得志 enjoy success when young;
少年隊 junior team;
少年法庭 juvenile court;
少年犯 juvenile delinquent;
少年犯罪 juvenile delinquency;
少年宮 children's palace;
少年紀錄 junior record;
少年老成 accomplished though young; an old head on young shoulders; young and competent; young but experienced;
少年人 young person; youth;
少年罪犯 juvenile delinquent;
慘綠少年 handsome young man; young people who have refined manners;
青少年 juniors; teenagers; young boys and girls; youngsters;
~青少年犯 juvenile delinquent; juvenile offender;
~青少年犯罪 juvenile delinquency;
~青少年犯罪問題 problems of juvenile delinquency;
青少年犯罪心理學 juvenile delinquency psychology;
青少年犯罪學 juvenile criminology;
青少年犯罪研究 studies of juvenile delinquency;
任性的少年 wayward teenager;
五陵少年 rich and handsome young men;

[少女] damsel; lass; maid; maiden; young girl;
少女時期 girlhood;
美少女 nymph;
時髦少女 teenybopper;
性感少女 nymphet;

[少時] when one is young;

[少尉] (1) ensign; (2) second lieutenant;
海軍少尉 ensign;
候補少尉 midshipman;

[少爺] (1) young master of the house; (2) your son;
大少爺 (1) eldest son of a rich family; (2) eldest son of one's master; (3) spendthrift; spoilt son of a rich family;
~大少爺作風 behaviour typical of the spoiled son of a rich family; extravagant ways;

[少有大智] person of great wisdom when young;

[少壯] young and energetic; young and vigorous;
少壯不努力，老大徒傷悲 a lazy youth, a lousy age; a man who does not work hard in his youth will be grieved when he grows old; an idle youth, a needy age; idle young, needy old; if one does not exert oneself in youth, one will regret it in old age; if you lie upon roses when young, you'll lie upon thrones when old; it will be too late to bewail the time wasted in one's youth; laziness in youth means sorrow in old age; laziness in youth spells regret in old age; one who misspends his youth will grieve in vain in old age; reckless youth makes a rueful age; rejoiced at in youth, repented in age;
少壯派 stalwarts;

[少子] youngest son;

惡少 young ruffian;
闊少 sons of rich families;
老少 old and young;
年少 young;

shao
【劭】 (1) encourage; urge; (2) admirable; beautiful; excellent; graceful; respectable;

shao
【邵】 (1) advanced in age; (2) name of various places in the ages; (3) a surname;

shao
【哨】 (1) whistle; (2) chat; gossip; talk; (3) patrol; (4) guard station; outpost;

[哨兵] guard; sentry;

[哨岡] sentry post;
三步一崗，五步一哨 be heavily sentried; with sentries posted every few yards;
五步一崗，十步一哨 sentries are posted only a few steps from each other;

[哨聲] whistling;

[哨所] post; sentry post;
邊防哨所 frontier guard post;
前沿哨所 forward post; outpost;

[哨探] spy on the movements of the enemy;

[哨子] whistle;
吹哨子 blow a whistle;

布哨 set up security patrols;
步哨 sentinel; sentry;
查哨 go the round or guard posts; inspect the sentries;
吹哨 blow a whistle;
放哨 be on sentry duty; stand guard;
崗哨 (1) lookout post; (2) sentinel; sentry;
呼哨 whistle;
口哨 whistling sound through rounded lips;
前哨 advance guard; outpost;
巡哨 conduct reconnaissance; scout;

shao
【紹】 (1) bring together; connect; join; (2) continue; handdown;
［紹承］ inherit; succeed to;
［紹述］ continue; follow;

shao
【潲】 rain slanted by wind;
［潲雨］ (1) rain slanted by wind; (2) get wet by the slanting rain;

she¹
she
【奢】 (1) extravagant; lavish; luxurious; wasteful; (2) excessive; inordinate; (3) brag; exaggerate;
［奢侈］ extravagant; gay; given to pleasure; luxurious; prodigal; wasteful;
奢侈繁華 extravagant and making a great show; luxurious and busy;
奢侈品 articles of luxury; luxuries; luxury goods; ornaments; unnecessaries;
奢侈税 taxes on luxuries;
避免奢侈 abstain from luxuries;
拋棄奢侈 throw away one's luxury;
窮奢極侈 in the lap of luxury; squander recklessly;
生活奢侈 wallow in luxury;
［奢華］ extravagant; luxurious; luxury; prodigal; showy; sumptuous;
奢華墮落 extravagant and degenerate;
陳設奢華 be luxuriously furnished;
衣著奢華 be extravagant in dress;
［奢儉］ extravagant and frugal;
從儉入奢易，由奢返儉難 it is easy for the frugal to become extravagant, but very difficult to reverse the process;
戒奢尚儉 refrain from luxury and uphold frugality;
奢入儉難 once accustomed to luxury, one is hard to live a frugal life;
由儉入奢易，中奢入儉難 it is easy to go from economy to extravagance but not from extravagance to economy;
［奢靡］ extravagant; lavish; wasteful;
［奢泰］ extravagant;
［奢望］ extravagant hopes; high expectations; wild wishes;
［奢想］ think wishfully;
［奢言］ extravagant talk;
奢易儉難 it is hard for one to live a frugal life;
［奢願］ wild wish; wishful thinking;
［奢遮］ ostentatious; sensational;

she
【畬】 land gained from burning;
［畬族］ She nationality;

she
【賒】 (1) buy on credit; sell on credit; (2) distant; faraway; (3) postpone; put off; slow; (4) extravagant; luxurious;
［賒單］ I.O.U. receipt;
［賒購］ buy sth on credit; get sth on credit; purchase on credit; buy on tally; buy on tick;
賒購商品 purchased merchandise on account;
賒購賬戶 credit account;
拒絕賒購 refuse credit;
允許賒購 give credit; offer credit;
［賒貨］ get goods on credit;
［賒欠］ buy on credit; give credit;
賒欠憑證 credit note; credit voucher;
概不賒欠 no chits; no credit is allowed to anybody; no credit is given;
［賒賣］ credit sales;
［賒米來食］ get rice to eat on credit;
［賒貸］ credit;
賒貸無門 no way of getting a credit or loan;
［賒銷］ charge sales; sell on credit;
［賒賬］ on account; on credit;
賒賬卡 charge card; store card;

she²
she
【什】 (1) miscellaneous; sundry; (2) ten; (3) squad;

she
【舌】 (1) tongue; (2) tongue-shaped object;

[舌癌] tongue cancer;
[舌白斑病] leukoplakia lingualis;
[舌板] lingual plate;
[舌瓣] lingual tongue flap;
[舌背] dorsum of tongue;
[舌本] back of the tongue; root of the tongue;
[舌發育不良] ateloglossia;
[舌發育不全] ateloglossia;
[舌肥大] macroglossia;
偏側舌肥大 hemimacroglossia;
[舌肥厚] pachyglossia;
[舌鋒] eloquence;
[舌根] root of the tongue;
[舌尖] tip of the tongue;
[舌痙攣] glossospasm;
[舌裂] cleft tongue;
[舌隆起] lingual swelling;
[舌麻痺] lingual paralysis;
[舌門] valve;
[舌面] lingual surface;
[舌巧如簧] have a tongue like a reed organ;
[舌人] interpreter;
[舌苔] coating on the tongue; fur on the tongue;
舌苔很厚 tongue heavily coated;
[舌癱] lingual paralysis;
[舌痛] glossalgia;
剝脱性舌痛 glossodynia exfoliativa;
痛風性舌痛 gouty glossalgia;
[舌頭] tongue;
搬舌頭 sow discord;
傳舌頭 gossip; spread rumours; tell tales;
大舌頭 lisp; lisper;
拉舌頭 gossip; slander;
伸出舌頭 put out one's tongue; stick out the tongue;
吐舌頭 stick one's tongue out;
[舌萎縮] lingual atrophy;
偏側舌萎縮 hemilingual atrophy;
[舌繫帶切開] frenotomy;
[舌下垂] glossoptosis;
[舌下神經] hypoglossal nerve;
[舌下腺] sublingual gland;
[舌咽] glossopharygeal;
舌咽神經 glossopharygeal nerve;
[舌炎] glossitis;
偏側舌炎 hemiglossitis;
特發性舌炎 idiopathic glossitis;
萎縮性舌炎 atrophic glossitis;
游走性舌炎 glossitis migrans;
自發性舌炎 idiopathic glossitis
[舌戰] argue heatedly; debate with verbal confrontation; have a verbal battle with;
舌戰群儒 have a heated dispute with a group of scholars;
舌戰智斗 match wits and engage in a battle of words;
一場舌戰 a heated dispute;
[舌中隔] septum of tongue;
[舌腫] glossoncus;
[舌周炎] periglossitis;

冰川舌 glacier tongue;
冰舌 glacier tongue;
長舌 fond of gossip; tongue enough for two sets of teeth;
齒舌 radula;
唇舌 (1) lips and tongue; (2) argument; persuasion; plausible speech; talking round; words;
毒舌 bad tongue; biting tongue; bitter tongue; caustic tongue; dangerous tongue; have a vicious tongue; sharp tongue; sharp-tongued; venomous tongue; wicked tongue;
分葉舌 lobulated tongue;
鼓舌 show off one's volubility and skill in talking, specifically mouth sweet words;
黑舌 black tongue;
喉舌 (1) throat and tongue; (2) mouthpiece;
厚舌 pachyglossia;
厚苔舌 encrusted tongue;
火舌 fireflow; licking flame; tongues of fire;
嚼舌 (1) chatter; gossip; (2) argue meaninglessly;
撟舌 raise the tongue in an effort to speak;
結舌 (1) unable to speak because of fear or groundlessness; (2) tongue-tie;
巨舌 glossocele;
口舌 (1) dispute; quarrel; (2) talking round;
帽舌 peak of a cap; visor;
皰舌 sublingual cyst;
巧舌 false words; insincere words;
饒舌 (1) garrulous; have a big mouth; have too much tongue; loquacious; naggish; too talkative; voluble; (2) say more than is proper; shoot off one's mouth;
吐舌 flash forth the tongue;
小舌 lingula; uvula;
鞋舌 shoe flap; tongue;
學舌 (1) mechanically repeat other people's

words; parrot; (2) gossipy; loose-tongued;
搖舌 talk glibly;
咬舌 have a lisp; lisp; speak imperfectly; speak with a lisp;
葉舌 ligule;
咋舌 be left speechless or breathless;
皺襞舌 lingua plicata;
皺裂舌 wrinkled tongue;
皺縮舌 wrinkled tongue;
豬舌 pig's tongue;
嘴舌 mouth and tongue;

she

【折】 (1) fail in business; lose money; (2) break; snap;

［折本］ get into red; lose money;

［折耗］ damage; lose money; loss;

虧折 lose money in business; lose one's capital;

she

【佘】 surname;

she

【甚】 what;

［甚麼］ what;
甚麼地方 where;
甚麼話 bosh; what nonsense;
甚麼人 (1) who; (2) no matter who; whoever it is;
甚麼時候 when;
甚麼事 (1) what's the matter; (2) no matter what; whatever it is;
甚麼樣 what kind; what sort;
~過得甚麼樣 how's it going; what's happening; what's up;
看甚麼 what are you looking at;
你想要甚麼 what do you want;
你在等甚麼 what are you waiting for;
你在説甚麼 what are you talking about;
算得甚麼 it's nothing; of no special account; trivial;
我們還等甚麼 what are we waiting for;

she

【蛇】 serpent; snake;

［蛇瓜］ snake gourd;

［蛇皮］ snake's skin;

［蛇婆］ sea serpent;

［蛇丘］ esker;

［蛇鼠］ (1) snakes and mice; (2) wicked people
蛇鼠橫行 wicked people run rampant;

［蛇頭］ snake's head;
蛇頭鼠尾 sneaky, crafty look;
蛇頭鼠眼 a snake's head and a rat's eyes; crafty; cunning; wily;
蛇無頭不行 a snake cannot crawl when its head is injured — importance of a leader;

［蛇蝎］ snakes and scorpions — vicious people;
蛇蝎心腸 have a murderous heart;
毒如蛇蝎 as vicious as a viper;
心如蛇蝎 have the heart of a devil; one's heart is as poisonous as any viper or scorpion;

［蛇行］ (1) move like a snake; take a zigzag course; (2) crawl; creep along;

［蛇形］ S-shaped; snake-like;

地頭蛇 local tyrant;
毒蛇 poisonous snake venomous snake; viper;
蝮蛇 Pallas pit viper;
海蛇 sea snake;
環蛇 bungarus; krait;
蝰蛇 viper;
兩頭蛇 amphisbaena;
盲蛇 typhlops braininus;
蟒蛇 boa; python;
蘄蛇 long-nosed pit viper;
水蛇 water snake;
四腳蛇 lizard;
襪帶蛇 garter snake;
眼鏡蛇 cobra;
一條蛇 a snake;
遊蛇 grass snake;

she

【揲】 sort out divining stalks;

she

【闍】 Buddhist high monk;

［闍梨］ Buddhist monk; monk;

she³

she

【舍】 same as 捨；

she

【捨】 (1) abandon; forsake; give up; let go; part with; reject; relinquish; renounce; (2) give alms; give to charity; dispense charity;

［捨得］ not to grudge; willing to part with;

［捨己］ sacrifice oneself;
捨己從人 give up one's own views and follow those of others; sacrifice one's

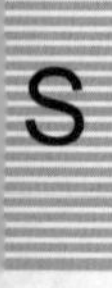

own wishes to those of others;
捨己救人 risk one's life for another; risk one's own life to save others; sacrifice one's life to save others; save others' lives at the risk of one's own;
捨己為公 make personal sacrifices for the public good; sacrifice oneself in the interest of the public;
捨己為人 give up one's own interests for the sake of others; risk one's life for others; risk one's life to save others; sacrifice oneself to protect others; sink oneself;

[捨命] give up one's life; in disregard of one's safety; risk one's life; sacrifice oneself;
[捨棄] abandon; give up; relinquish; renounce;
[捨入] round off;
捨入法 rounding-off method;
捨入數 rounded number; rounding number
[捨身] give up one's life; sacrifice oneself;
捨身報國 die for the sake of the country; the great sacrifice;
捨身成仁 die for a righteous cause; die for the sake of the cause;
捨身救人 give one's life to rescue sb; sacrifice oneself to save others;
[捨生] sacrifice one's life;
捨生取義 die for righteousness; give one's life for the sake of righteousness; prefer justice to life; sacrifice one's life for the sake of righteousness;
[捨我其誰] if I can't do it, who can; who but myself can do it;
[捨象取鼠] relinquish an elephant for a rat — put away a great profit for a small one;
[捨輿登舟] change from a carriage to a boat;

不捨 begrudge;
割捨 give up; part with;
難捨 loathe to part from each other; reluctant to separate;
取捨 accept or reject; make one's choice;
施捨 give alms; give in charity;

she4

she

【舍】 (1) house; (2) inn; (3) halt; rest; stop; (4) self-depreciatory possessive pronoun for the first person singular in formal speech;

[舍弟] my younger brother;
[舍監] house master; warden;
男舍監 housemaster;
女舍監 housemistress;
[舍妹] my younger sister;
[舍匿] hide;
[舍親] my relatives;
[舍人] kind of palace secretary in the Zhou and some later dynasties;
[舍姪] my nephew; my niece;

房舍 house;
廬舍 humble house or hut;
旅舍 hotel;
茅舍 thatched cottage;
禽舍 artificial bird's nest;
寺舍 temple building;
宿舍 dormitory; living quarters;
田舍 farmhouse;
校舍 school building; school-house;
豬舍 pig house;

she

【社】 (1) agency; association; corporation; organization; organized body; (2) community; society; (3) god of land;

[社會] community; society;
社會安定 have the public quiet; have social stability; have social tranquility;
~擾亂社會安定 disturb social tranquility;
社會安寧 peace of society; social tranquility;
~破壞社會安寧 disturb social tranquility;
~擾亂社會安寧 disturb the peace of society;
社會保險 social insurance;
社會保障 social security;
~社會保障模式 model of social security;
~社會保障體制 social security system;
~社會保障制度 social security system;
社會背景 social background;
社會弊病 social evil;
社會弊端 social abuses; social corruption;
~根治社會弊端 cure the ills of society;
~揭露社會弊端 expose social abuses;
社會變革 social changes; social transformation;
~經歷社會變革 undergo social transformation;
社會變遷 social change;
社會參與 social participation;

~社會參與論 theory of social participation;
社會產權 social equity;
社會成本 social cost;
社會衝突 social conflict;
~社會衝突論 theory of social conflict;
社會觸覺 social sense;
社會等級 social rank;
社會地位 social position; social standing; social status;
社會動盪 social unrest;
社會動力 social force;
社會棟梁 pillars of society;
社會發展 social development;
~社會發展史 history of social development;
社會方言 social dialect;
~社會方言變體 social dialectal variation;
社會分化 social differentiation;
社會風氣 social values; standards of social conduct;
~敗壞社會風氣 corrupt social values; debase standards of social conduct;
社會福利 social benefits; social welfare;
~享受社會福利 enjoy social benefits;
社會服務 community services; social services;
社會工程 social engineering;
社會工作 social work;
社會公德 social ethics;
社會公民 citizen;
社會公益事業 undertaking of public welfare;
社會關係 (1) social relations; (2) one's social connections;
社會規範 social norm;
社會和諧 social harmony;
社會化 socialization; socialize;
~社會化言語 socialized speech;
~再社會化 resocialization;
社會環境 social environment;
社會活動 social activities;
社會集資 raise fund from society;
社會技術系統 socio-technical system;
社會監督 social supervision;
社會交換理論 social exchange theory;
社會角色 social role;
社會教育 social education;
社會階層 social class;
社會階級 social class;
社會結構 social structure;
社會接受力 social acceptability;
社會解體 social disintegration;
社會進步 social progress;
社會進化 social evolution;
社會經濟背景 socio-economic background;
社會經濟系統 socio-economic system;
社會距離 social distance;
社會決定論 theory of social determinism;
社會均衡 social equilibrium;
社會科技教育 social sci-tech education;
社會科學 social science;
社會流動 social mobility;
社會民生 people's livelihood;
社會名流 noted public figures; socialites; the elite of society; very important persons; well-known persons;
社會模式 social model;
社會區域環境 socio-regional environment;
社會趨勢分析 analysis of social trends;
社會審計 social audit;
社會生活噪聲 noise of social activities;
社會聲望 social prestige;
社會時間預算 social time budget;
社會事業 social undertakings;
社會雙語現象 societal bilingualism;
社會思維 social thinking;
社會思想 social thought;
社會所有制 social ownership;
社會統籌 combination of socially united planning;
社會網絡 social network;
~社會網絡結構 social network structure;
~社會網絡組織 social network organization;
社會文化 social culture;
~社會文化一體化 socio-cultural integration;
社會問題 social problem;
社會系統 social system;
~社會系統工程 social system engineering;
社會賢達 community leaders; public personages; the worthy of society;
社會現象 social phenomena;
社會效益 social efficiency;
社會心理 social psychology;
社會心理學 social psychology;
社會信息系統 social information system;
社會性方言 sociolinguistic dialect;
社會行動論 social action theory;
社會行政 social administration;

社會學 sociology;
~社會學語言學派 sociolinguistics;
~保健社會學 health sociology;
~比較社會學 comparative sociology;
~城市社會學 urban sociology;
~動物社會學 animal sociology;
~普通社會學 general sociology;
~人類社會學 anthroposociology;
~生態社會學 ecological sociology;
~田園社會學 rural sociology;
~圖書館社會學 sociology of library;
~性社會學 sexual sociology;
~應用社會學 applied sociology;
~災害社會學 sociology of calamity;
~植物社會學 plant sociology;
~職業社會學 occupational sociology;
社會研究 social research;
社會演化 social evolution;
社會養老保險 social old age insurance;
社會意識 social consciousness;
社會意義 social meaning;
社會議題 social issues;
社會語境 social context;
社會語言能力 sociolinguistic competence;
社會語言學 sociolinguistics;
社會語義學 sociosemantics;
社會宇宙觀 social cosmology;
社會預測 social prediction;
社會運動 social movement;
社會贊助 social support;
社會渣滓 dregs of society; riffraff; scum of society;
社會哲學 social philosophy;
社會政策 social policy;
社會指標 social index; social indicator;
社會治安 public security; social security;
~社會治安情況 law and order situation;
社會制裁 social sanction;
社會制度 social system;
社會秩序 public order;
~安定社會秩序 ensure public order; maintain public order;
~安靖社會秩序 ensure law and order;
社會中堅 salt of the earth;
社會主義 socialism;
~社會主義多元論 socialist pluralism;
~社會主義經濟 socialist economy;
~社會主義市場經濟 socialist market economy;
~社會主義社會 socialist society;
~社會主義制度 socialist system;
~國家社會主義 state socialism;
~科學社會主義 scientific socialism;
~空想社會主義 utopian socialism;
~市場社會主義 market socialism;
~藝術社會主義 aesthetic socialism;
~有中國特色的社會主義 socialism with Chinese characteristics;
社會組織 social organization;
社會總需求 social total demand;
安定社會 stabilize society; tranquilize society;
部落社會 tribal society;
產業社會 industrial society;
~超產業社會 super-industrial society;
單面社會 one-dimensional society;
動物社會 animal society;
反社會的 antisocial;
放任的社會 permissive society;
封建社會 feudal society;
豐裕社會 society;
服務社會 service the society; post-service society;
父系社會 patrilineal society;
富裕社會 affluent society;
工業社會 industrial society;
~超工業社會 super-industrial society;
~後工業社會 post-industrial society;
共產主義社會 communist society;
黑社會 criminal syndicate; triad society;
階級社會 class society;
母系社會 matrilineal society;
奴隸社會 slave society; slavery;
人類社會 human community;
融入社會 be integrated in the community;
商品社會 commodity society;
上層社會 upper class; upper crust;
上流社會 upper class; upper crust;
氏族社會 clan society;
他擇性社會 alternative society;
未發展社會 undeveloped society;
污染社會 contaminate society;
營利社會 acquisitive;
原始社會 primitive society;
資本主義社會 capitalist society;

[社稷] country; god of the land and the god of grain — the state;
社稷之臣 important courtier; pillar of the state;
匡扶社稷 help the country;
執干戈，衛社稷 take up arms to defend the state;

[社交] social contact; social intercourse;
社交功能 social function;
社交禮節 social etiquette;
社交能力 social acceptability;
社交生活 social life;
社交網絡 social network;
社交舞 social dancing;
社交指示詞 social deixis;
[社論] editorial; leading article;
社論撰寫人 editorialist;
一篇社論 an editorial;
[社廟] temple to the god of the land;
[社評] editorial;
[社區] community;
社區變遷 community change;
社區參與 community participation;
社區衝突 communal conflict;
社區發展 community development;
社區服務 community service;
社區工作 community work;
社區公益金 community chest;
社區活動 community activities;
~社區活動中心 community centre;
~參與社區活動 participate in community activities;
社區精神 community spirit;
社區警政 community policing;
社區文化 community culture;
社區學校 community college;
社區研究 community studies;
社區資源 community resources;
社區中學 community college;
社區中心 community centre;
次社區 sub-community;
虛擬社區 virtual community;
[社群] association; group;
弱勢社群 underprivileged groups;
~關懷弱勢社群 show concern for the disadvantaged;
學習社群 learning community;
[社團] association; civic organization; corporation; mass organization;
社團法人 corporation aggregate;
社團言語 community speech;
社團語言 community language;
社團賬戶 society account;
參加社團 join a society;
組成社團 form a society;
[社員] member of an association;
[社長] president;
副社長 deputy director; vice president;

報社 newspaper office;
出版社 publishing house;
村社 village community;
翻譯社 translation agent;
合作社 cooperative;
結社 form an association;
旅社 hotel;
旅行社 travel service;
通訊社 news agency; news service;
譯社 translation agency;

she

【拾】 ascend; go up;
[拾級而上] ascend by stairs; go up by a flight of steps; mount up a flight of steps;

she

【射】 (1) fire; shoot; (2) discharge in a jet; (3) send out; (4) allude to sth or sb; insinuate;
[射靶] shoot at the target;
[射程] firing range; range of fire; reach; throw;
[射擊] (1) fire; shoot; (2) shooting;
射擊術 marksmanship;
射擊運動 shooting;
~泥鴿射擊運動 clay pigeon shooting;
飛靶射擊 skeet shooting;
[射箭] (1) discharge an arrow; let fly an arrow; shoot an arrow; (2) archery;
射箭運動 archery;
[射精] ejaculation; ejaculation of semen; gonobolia; spermatization;
射精遲緩 ejaculatio retardata;
射精過緩 bradyspermatism;
射精過早 ejaculatio praecox; premature ejaculation;
射精徐緩 bradyspermatism;
射精障礙 defective ejaculation;
不全射精 ejaculatio deficiens;
[射流] efflux; spray;
射流技術 fluidics;
高壓射流 high-pressure spray;
錐形射流 convergent spray;
[射門] shoot; shoot at the goal; shooting;
射門機會 scoring chance;
單手肩上射門 one-hand shoulder shot;
反彈球射門 drop kick;
高吊射門 high shot;
弧線射門 cured shot;
淩空射門 volley shot;
跳起射門 jump shot;

魚躍射門 diving jump shot;
原地射門 standing shot;
轉身射門 pivot shot; turnaround shot;

[射石飲羽] have the strong willpower that can make an arrow pierce even stone;

[射手] gunner; marksman; shooter;
神射手 marksman;

[射線] ray;
射線發生 actinogenesis;
射線管 ray tube;
~電子射線管 cathode ray tube;
~陰極射線管 cathode ray tube;
射線質 actinogen;
光化射線 actinic ray;
星射線 aster ray;
陽極射線 anode ray;
陽射線 positive ray;
陰極射線 cathode ray;
宇宙射線 cosmic ray;
原子射線 atomic ray;
中心射線 central ray;

[射影] projection; projective;
反向射影 opposite projective;
拋物性射影 parabolic projective;
循環射影 periodic projective;
正射影 orthogonal projection;

暗射 allude to; hint; hint obliquely at; insinuate; make an allusion to; throw out a hint;
簇射 shower;
攢射 gather closely together;
點射 fire in bursts; fixed fire;
發射 (1) discharge; fire; launch; project; shoot; (2) emit; transmit;
反射 reflex; reflection;
放射 radiate;
輻射 irradiation; radiance; radiation;
急射 quick fire;
濺射 sputtering;
鐳射 laser;
漫射 diffusion;
噴射 atomization; inject; injection; spray; squirt;
平射 flat fire;
齊射 salvo; volley;
騎射 horsemanship and archery;
繞射 diffract;
日射 insolation;
入射 incidence;
散射 scatter;
掃射 (1) strafe; (2) scan; sweep;
試射 fire for adjustment;
彈射 (1) launch; shoot off; (2) censure; pick faults and criticize;
投射 (1) cast; throw; (2) cast; project;
透射 (1) homology; (2) transmission;
臥射 prone fire;
斜射 (1) shine obliquely; (2) fire obliquely;
衍射 diffract; diffraction;
艷射 dazzling;
隱射 hint; insinuate;
影射 allude to; hint at; innuendo; insinuate;
映射 (1) cast light upon; shine upon; (2) mapping;
照射 illuminate; shine;
折射 refract; refraction;
直射 collineation;
注射 get a shot; inject;
縱射 enfilade;

she

【涉】 (1) wade; (2) experience; (3) cross; (4) entangle; implicate; involve; (5) a surname;

[涉筆] start to write;
涉筆成趣 make a sparking line as it comes by itself; write freely and well;

[涉及] deal with; involve; refer to; relate to; touch upon;
涉及醜聞 be caught up in the scandal;

[涉覽] read casually; skim;
涉覽群書 read widely;

[涉歷] one's past experience;

[涉獵] browse; dabble in; do desultory reading; read cursorily;
涉獵書籍 dip into books for casual reading; wide and superficial reading;

[涉世] get along in the world; make one's way through the world;
涉世不深 have no experience in life; have scanty experience of life; have scanty knowledge of the world; have seen little of the world; inexperienced in affairs of the world;
涉世未深 inexperienced in affairs of the world;

[涉事] give a narration;

[涉水] wade; wade into the water;
涉水過河 cross a river by wading; ford a stream; splash through the stream; wade across a river;

[涉訟] be involved in a lawsuit;

[涉外] concerning foreign affairs or foreign nationals;

涉外案件 foreign-related case;
涉外法規 laws and regulations concerning foreign affairs;
涉外婚姻 marriages with foreigners;
涉外經濟法 economic laws concerning foreign affairs;
涉外經濟法規 laws and regulations concerning external economic relations;
涉外經濟合同 economic contract concerning foreign affairs;

[涉嫌] be involved in a crime; be suspected of being involved; come under suspicion; inviting suspicion; suspect;
[涉險] adventure; be engaged in an adventure;
[涉想] think about;
[涉於春冰] tread on ice in spring — dangerous;
[涉足] set foot in;
涉足花叢 fool around with women; visit brothels;
涉足其間 set foot there;
涉足仕途 join the civil service; start an official career;

跋涉 trek; trudge;
干涉 (1) interfere; intervene; (2) interference;
關涉 be connected; involve;
交涉 negotiate;
牽涉 drag in; involve;
徒涉 ford; wade through;

she

【設】 (1) establish; found; set up; (2) furnish; provide; (3) arrange; devise; plan; work out; (4) given; if; in case; suppose;

[設備] appliance; devices; equipment; facility; installation; instrumentation; system;
設備保養 maintenance of equipment;
設備處理控制 installation processing control;
設備附件 equipment appurtenance;
設備更新 renewal of equipment;
設備管理 facilities management;
設備控制 device control;
設備使用費 access charge;
設備裝配 furniture and fixture;
設備綜合效率 comprehensive effectiveness of equipment;
安全設備 safety apparatus; safety devices; safety equipment; safety installation
安裝設備 install equipment;
大型能量設備 bulk energy facility;
導航設備 navigation apparatus;
地面儀表設備 ground instrumentation;
房屋設備 building and equipment;
輔助設備 auxiliary facilities;
改進設備 improve equipment;
高性能設備 high performance equipment;
工場設備 plant equipment;
供電設備 electricity system;
供水設備 running water system;
機器設備 machinery equipment;
攪動設備 agitating equipment;
磨料設備 abrasive blasting equipment;
煤氣設備 gas system;
暖氣設備 steam heating system;
破碎設備 crushing appliance;
昇降設備 lifting appliance;
提供設備 supply equipment;
體育設備 athletic facility;
通風設備 ventilation;
通氣設備 aeration equipment;
外部設備 external instrumentation;
一套設備 a set of equipment;
執行設備 actuating equipment;
裝好設備 set up one's apparatus;

[設辭] excuse; pretext; subterfuge;
[設定] set;
初始設定 initialize;
[設餌] bait one's hook;
設餌放釣 bait one's hook and cast one's line;
[設法] devise a way; do what one can; think of a way; think up a method; try;
[設防] fortify; garrison; set up defences;
設防地帶 fortified zone;
一層設防 a line of defence;
[設館] found a private village school;
[設或] in case of; supposing that; what if;
[設計] depict; design; devise; draw; layout; layout work; map out a plan; plan; sketch;
設計單位 design organization;
設計費 charges for design;
設計理念 design principles;
設計評審 design review;
設計容量 design capacity;
設計師 designer;
~佈景設計師 set designer;
~服裝設計師 costume designer;

~建築設計師 architect;
~總設計師 chief designer;
設計圖解 designograph;
設計新穎 modern design;
設計原則 design principles;
設計展 design exhibition;
設計周全 devise with perfection;
設計狀況 design situation;
設計自動化 design automation;
~設計自動化系統 design automation system;
牀身設計 body design;
分類器設計 categorizer design;
輔助設計 aided design;
積本設計 block design;
精心設計的 well-thought-out;
課程設計 curriculum design;
美術設計 art design;
聲學設計 acoustical design;
先進設計 advanced design;
元件設計 cell design;
在設計中 still on the drawing-board;

[設阱] set up a pitfall;
設阱陷害 set up a pitfall for betraying;
設阱自陷 put a halter round one's own neck;

[設局] (1) set up a trap; (2) establish a bureau;

[設立] establish; found; set up;

[設如] if; supposing;

[設若] if; provided; suppose;

[設色] apply colour in painting;
設色柔和 painted in quiet colours;

[設身處地] considerate; place oneself in others' position; put oneself in another's place; put oneself in sb else's position;

[設施] (1) amenities; facility; installation; measure; (2) plan and execute;
設施齊全 full facilities;
安全設施 safety devices; safety equipment; safety installations;
城市設施 urban facilities;
公共設施 communal facilities;
基礎設施 infrastructure;
教學設施 teaching facilities;
旅遊設施 tourist amenities;
排水設施 drainage facility;
配套設施 supporting facilities;
~提供完善配套設施 provide all the necessary supporting facilities;
神施鬼設 as superb as if designed by the supernatural;
完善設施 comprehensive facilities;
文化設施 cultural amenities;

[設使] if; supposing that; what if;

[設想] (1) assume; conceive; envisage; imagine; (2) idea; rough plan; scheme; tentative idea; tentative plan;

[設宴] give a banquet; give a dinner party; throw a banquet;
設宴餞行 a feast is given on the occasion of one's departure; give a banquet in honour of; give a farewell party in honour of;
設宴接風 hold a banquet in honour of sb's safe arrival; prepare a feast to welcome sb home;
設宴款待 entertain by giving a dinner; give a banquet in honour of; give a feast for the entertainment of;
設宴洗塵 give a dinner to sb on his return from travel; prepare a feast of welcome;

[設營] encampment;

[設有] come complete with;
設有二間睡房 come complete with two bedrooms;

[設帳] (1) pitch a tent; (2) set up a school;
設帳授徒 set up a school and instruct students;

[設置] (1) establish; found; put up; set up; (2) fit; install;

安設 install; set up;
擺設 furnish and decorate; furnishings; interior decoration;
常設 permanent; standing;
陳設 display; furnishings; set out;
創設 create; establish; found; set up;
敷設 lay;
附設 have as an attached institution;
公設 postulate;
假設 assume; hypothesis; suppose;
架設 erect;
建設 build; construct; construction;
開設 (1) open or set up; (2) offer;
鋪設 lay; spread out;
特設 ad hoc;
添設 add more furniture, etc.;
虛設 existing in name only; nominal;
專設 ad hoc;
裝設 be equipped with; equip; install;

she

【赦】 amnesty; excuse; forgive; pardon;

[赦過] pardon a fault;

[赦令] decree for pardon;

[赦免] absolve; excuse; pardon; remit a punishment;

赦免令 decree for pardon;

~頒布赦免令 publish a decree for pardon;

赦免戰犯 depurge a war criminal;

請求赦免 ask for pardon;

[赦宥] pardon;

[赦罪] absolve sb from guilt; forgive an offender; pardon sb;

宣佈赦罪 pronounce the absolution;

罪不容赦 one's crimes are too wicked to be pardoned;

大赦 general amnesty;

特赦 special amnesty;

she

【攝】 (1) absorb; assimilate; attract; take into; (2) shoot; take a photograph of; (3) conserve; (4) act for; (5) regulate; (6) represent;

[攝持] take proper care of one's life;

[攝動] perturbation;

解析攝動 analytic perturbations;

周期攝動 periodic perturbation;

阻力攝動 drag perturbation;

[攝魂] summon souls of the dead;

攝魂奪魄 hold spellbound; under the spell;

[攝力] attraction;

[攝譜儀] spectrograph;

恒偏向攝譜儀 constant deviation spectrograph;

天體攝譜儀 astronomical spectrograph;

[攝取] (1) absorb; assimilate; take in; (2) take a photograph of; shoot;

[攝生] keep fit; pay attention to health;

調養攝生 nurse and recuperate oneself;

[攝食] feed; feeding;

攝食活力 feeding activity;

攝食適應 feeding adaptation;

攝食行為 feeding behaviour;

[攝氏度] Celsius degree; centigrade;

[攝像] (1) make a video recording; (2) shoot pictures;

攝像管 tube;

~電視攝像管 camera tube;

攝像機 camcorder; camera; pickup camera;

~攝像機附加器 camera adaptor;

~攝像機機頭 camera head;

~攝像機控制器 camera control unit;

~便攜式電視攝像機 mobile camera;

~便攜式攝像機 camcorder;

~彩色編碼攝像機 colour encoding camera;

~彩色電視攝像機 colour television camera;

~彩色攝像機 colour video camera;

~插入攝像機 inlay camera;

~超聲波攝像機 ultrasonic camera;

~傳真攝像機 facsimile camera;

~低速攝像機 low-speed camera;

~電影電視攝像機 telecine camera;

~高速攝像機 high-speed camera;

~跟蹤攝像機 tracking camera;

~轟炸攝像機 bomb strike camera;

~紅外攝像機 infrared camera;

~機載雷達攝像機 airborne radar camera;

~激光攝像機 laser camera;

~計算機攝像機 computer camera;

~立體攝像機 stereo camera;

~慢速攝像機 slow-motion camera;

~取樣攝像機 sampling camera;

~手提攝像機 hand-held camera;

~數字電視攝像機 digital television camera;

~水下電視攝像機 underwater television camera;

~通用攝像機 all-purpose camera; general-purpose camera;

~微型電視攝像機 miniature television camera;

~位移攝像機 displacement camera;

~無線電攝像機 radio camera;

~析象攝像機 image dissection camera;

~新聞採訪攝像機 newsmaking camera;

~一架攝像機 a camcorder;

~直接攝像機 direct pickup camera;

攝像師 cameraman;

[攝行] act for another;

[攝影] (1) shoot; take a photograph; (2) photography; (3) film; shoot a film;

攝影比賽 photo contest;

攝影測量學 photogrammetry;

攝影車間 cinematographing department;

攝影底片 photographic film;
攝影飛機 camera plane;
攝影機 camera;
~ 攝影機定位 camera position;
~ 攝影迷 shutterbug;
~ 攝影機升降架 camera crane; dolly crane; studio crane;
~ 攝影藝術 art of photography; photography;
~ 單像攝影機 one-shot camera;
~ 電視攝影機 cinematographic camera;
~ 電影攝影機 cine camera; film camera; cinema camera; movie camera;
~ 反射攝影機 mirror camera;
~ 方位攝影機 aspect camera;
~ 隔音攝影機 sound-proof film camera;
~ 航空測量攝影機 air survey camera;
~ 記錄攝影機 recording camera;
~ 靜物攝影機 still camera;
~ 快速攝影機 quick-motion camera;
~ 繪圖航空攝影機 aerial mapping camera;
~ 立體聲攝影機 stereophonic camera;
~ 連續攝影機 chronophotographic camera;
~ 慢速攝影機 slow-motion camera;
~ 全景攝影機 panoramic camera;
~ 掃描攝影機 smear camera;
~ 身歷聲攝影機 stereophonic camera;
~ 聲畫攝影機 motion-picture sound camera;
~ 雙頭攝影機 double-headed camera;
~ 特技攝影機 stunt film camera;
~ 天文攝影機 astrophotocamera;
~ 同步攝影機 synchronous camera;
~ 新聞攝影機 newsreel camera;
~ 一架攝影機 a camera;
~ 自動攝影機 automatic camera;
~ 鑽孔攝影機 borehole camera;
攝影記者 news photographer;
攝影棚 sound stage;
攝影器 camera;
~ 旋轉攝影器 photographic revolver;
攝影槍 photographic gun;
攝影師 camera operator; cameraman; photographer;
~ 錄像攝影師 videographer;
~ 一群攝影師 a posse of photographers;
~ 自由攝影師 freelance photographer;
攝影室 studio;
攝影術 photography;
~ 航空攝影術 aerophotography;
~ 顯微攝影術 photomicrography;
攝影藝術 art of photography; photography;
攝影展覽 photo exhibition;
攝影者 photographer;
攝影主任 director of photography;
攝影助理 assistant operator;
愛好攝影 go in for photography;
彩色攝影 colour photography;
航空彩色攝影 aerial colour photography;
航空攝影 aerial photography;
~ 攝影製圖 aerial photo mapping;
機載攝影 airborne photography;
空中攝影 aerial photography;
立體攝影 stereo photography;
內景攝影 floor work; indoor shooting;
全息攝影 holography;
特技攝影 stunt photography; trick photography;
外景攝影 exterior shooting; location shooting;
顯微電影攝影 microphotography;
移動攝影 travelling photography;

[攝政] act as regent; serve as regent;
攝政期 regency;

[攝製] produce;

拍攝 photograph; shoot; take a picture;
調攝 take good care of oneself (after an illness);
統攝 exercise control over; govern;

she

【麝】 musk deer;

[麝馥] musk;
麝馥蘭香 a breath of musk and the scent of orchids;
麝蘭散馥 sweet perfumes are constantly diffused around;

[麝牛] musk ox;

[麝香] musk;
麝香鹿 musk deer;
麝香貓 musk cat;
麝香薔薇 musk rose;
麝香樹 musk wood;
麝香鼠 musk rat;
麝香酮 muskine;
麝香鴨 musk duck;
大環麝香 macrocyclic musk;
多環麝香 polycyclic musk;
合成麝香 synthetic musk;
天然麝香 natural musk;
有麝自然香，不必當風揚 a man may love

his house well, and yet not ride on the ridge; a man may love his house well without riding on the ridge; good wine needs no bush; musk can be smelt without airing it – talent needs no advertisement;

［膐月］ the moon;

shei²
shei

【誰】 (1) who; whose; (2) anyone; someone;

［誰的］ whose;

［誰敢］ who dares;

［誰家］ (1) whose home; (2) who;

［誰肯］ who is willing;

［誰料］ who could have expected; who could have known;

［誰能］ who can; who could;

［誰人］ who;

誰人背後無人說，哪個人前不說人 who is not talked about by others behind his back, and who does not talk about others behind their backs;

［誰種誰收］ harvest going to the tiller; the crops to the tillers;

shen¹
shen

【申】 (1) explain; explicate; express; set forth; state; (2) the ninth of the twelve Earthly Branches; (3) appeal; plead; (4) expand; extend; (5) a surname;

［申辦］ bid;

［申報］ (1) report to a high body; (2) declare sth;

［申辯］ argue one's case; contend; defend oneself; explain oneself;

［申斥］ rebuke; reprimand;

當眾申斥 criticize sb in public; reprove sb before the public;

［申旦］ from night till morning;

［申告］ file a complaint;

［申解］ explain; state;

［申誡］ rebuke; reprimand;

［申敬］ show respect for;

［申救］ rescue a person from wrongful treatment;

［申理］ redress wrong;

［申令］ decree; order;

［申明］ avow; declare; explain; explicate; expound; state;

申明大義 appeal to a man's sense of right;

公開申明 openly avow;

［申請］ apply for; apply to sb for; ask for; be in for; file for; make a request; make an application for; put in for; request;

申請借款 loan application;

申請離婚 file for a divorce;

申請人 applicant; claimant;

申請書 written request; application form;

~保險申請書 application for insurance;

~空白申請書 blank application form;

~填寫申請書 fill out an application;

~信用證申請書 credit application;

~一大堆申請書 a crop of applications;

撤回申請 withdraw one's application;

地區申請 regional application;

遞交申請 send in one's application;

分案申請 divisional applications;

國際申請 international application;

國家申請 national application;

機密申請 confidential application;

拒絕申請 refuse an application;

書面申請 written application;

同意申請 grant an application;

一份申請 an application;

優先權申請 priority application;

早先申請 previous application;

專利申請 patent application;

最初申請 initial application;

［申述］ explain in detail; state;

申述來意 explain the purpose of one's visit; explain what one has come for;

申述立場 state one's position;

［申訴］ appeal; complain;

申訴權 right of appeal;

［申說］ state reasons;

［申討］ denounce; openly condemn;

［申謝］ acknowledge one's indebtedness; express one's gratitude; extend one's thanks;

［申冤］ redress an injustice; right a wrong;

申冤雪恨 ask for redress of an injustice to wreak revenge; revenge a wrong;

申冤昭雪 redress a grievance and have it setted satisfactorily;

［申奏］ make a petition; report to the throne;

重申 reaffirm; restate;

引申 extend;

shen

【伸】 (1) extend; straighten; stretch; stretching; (2) report;

[伸長] elongate; extend; lengthen; prolongate; elongation;
伸長脖子 crane one's neck to; stretch out one's neck;
伸長計 extensometer;
~ 橫向伸長計 lateral extensometer;
~ 機械伸長計 mechanical extensometer;
~ 簡單伸長計 simple extensometer;
~ 鏡示伸長計 mirror extensometer;
過度伸長 excessive elongation;
恒載伸長 constant load elongation;
裂斷伸長 break elongation;
彈性伸長 elastic stretching;
天線伸長 antenna elongation;
線性伸長 linear stretching;

[伸出] extend; project; overhang; reach; runout;
伸出的 outspread; outstretched;
伸出援手 lend a helping hand;
伸出雙手 reach out one's hands;

[伸開] extend; spread; stretch out;

[伸欠] stretch and yawn;

[伸手] hold out one's hand; reach out one's hand; stretch out one's hand;
伸手不見五指 darkness visible; Egyptian darkness; pitch-dark; so dark that you can't see your hand in front of you;
伸手可及 at arm's length; within reach;
茶來伸手，飯來張口 have a living without doing any work; live off without doing any work;
到處伸手 ask for help at all places; poke one's fingers everywhere; reach out in all directions; reach out one's hand everywhere; stretch one's tentacles everywhere;
向上伸手 reach up;
衣來伸手，飯來張口 lead the life of a parasite; live as a parasite; live on the labour of others;

[伸訴] air a grievance; present a complaint;

[伸縮] (1) expand and contract; lengthen and shorten; stretch out and draw back; (2) adjustable; elastic; flexible;
伸縮性 latitude;
伸縮餘地 latitude; room for adjustment;
伸縮自如 capable of expansion and contraction;

[伸腿] (1) stretch one's legs; (2) step in; (3) die; kick the bucket; turn up one's toes;
伸腿瞪眼 dead;
伸腿空間 legroom;

[伸延] elongate; extend; stretch;
內涵伸延 connotative extension;

[伸腰] staighten one's back; straighten oneself up;

[伸展] extend; spread; spread out; stretch; stretching;
伸展器 stretcher;
~ 臂伸展器 arm stretcher;
垂直伸展 vertical stretching;

[伸張] expand power; promote; uphold;
伸張正氣 champion of justice; promote healthy tendencies;
伸張正義 uphold justice;

[伸直] straighten; stretch out;
把腿伸直 straighten one's leg; straighten out one's leg;

[伸志] have one's ambition fulfilled;

牽伸 draw;
欠伸 stretch oneself and yawn;
延伸 extend; stretch;

shen

【身】 (1) body; trunk; (2) life; (3) one's own person; oneself; personally; (4) one's moral character and conduct; (5) main part of a structure; (6) in person; personally; (7) suit;

[身敗名裂] be utterly discredited; bring disgrace and ruin upon oneself; lose all standing and reputation; lose one's fortune and honour; one's name is mud;
身敗名裂，遺臭萬年 bring ruin and eternal shame on oneself; bring ruin and everlasting infamy upon oneself;

[身邊] (1) at one's side; one's immediate surroundings; one's vicinity; (2) on one; with one;
身邊沒帶錢 have no money on one;
站在父親的身邊 stand at one's father's side;

[身病體羸] ill and weak; physical wreck;

[身不由己] do sth not of one's own free will; helpless; incapable of resistance;

involuntarily; lose control of oneself; unable to contain oneself; one's limbs no longer obey one; unable to act according to one's own will; unable to contain oneself; under compulsion;

[身材] build; figure; physical build; physique; stature;

身材矮小 of small bulk; short and slight in figure; short and slight in stature; short and small in stature; short in stature; small in stature;

身材短小 microsoma;

身材豐滿 fleshy;

身材高大 of great stature;

身材魁梧 of great height and powerful build; of imposing stature; tall and sturdy;

身材苗條 have a slender figure;

身材瘦小 slight of figure; slight of stature;

身材窈窕 have very graceful figure; her stature is gentle and graceful;

身材勻稱 of proportional build;

量身材 take one's measurements;

迷人身材 delectable body;

中等身材 medium in stature; of middle height;

[身殘] broken in body;

身殘志不殘 broken in health but not in spirit;

身殘志堅 broken in body but firm in spirit;

[身長] (1) height; stature; (2) length;

[身穿] attire oneself in; be attired in; be clad in; be clothed in; be dressed in; dress oneself in; have on; wear;

身穿縞素 be dressed entirely in white; be dressed in mourning white;

[身底下] (1) under the body; (2) place where one is living;

[身段] (1) figure; physique; (2) postures;

[身份] capacity; identity; status;

身份不明 of unknown identity; one's legal identity not clarified; one's standing is not clear; unidentified;

身份認同 identity;

身份偷竊 identity theft;

身份危機 crisis of identity; identity crisis;

身份象徵 citizenship card; identity card;

身份證 identity card;

~身份證號碼 identity card number;

~身份證件 identity document;

~身份證明 proof of identity;

~身份證制度 identity card system;

暴露身份 reveal one's identity;

不合身份 incompatible with one's status;

不同的身份 different identity;

符合身份 befit one's position;

公民身份 citizenship status;

降低身份 lower one's dignity;

假身份 false identity;

確定身份 determine one's identity;

新的身份 new identity;

業餘身份 amateur status;

以個人身份 in one's individual capacity;

以官方身份 in the official capacity;

隱瞞身份 conceal one's identity;

有失身份 beneath one's dignity;

真實身份 true identity;

自貶身份 abase oneself;

自降身份 lower oneself;

[身高] a person of...meters; have a height of ...meters; height; ...meters in height; ...meters tall; stand...meters; stature; top...meters;

[身故] die;

[身後] after one's death;

身後名 posthumous fame;

身後事 funeral affairs;

身後無出 die without issue; without progeny after one's death;

身後蕭條 die without leaving progeny behind; without money after one's death; with progeny after one's death;

[身家] ancestry; family background; pedigree;

身家百倍 a meteoric rise in social status; come up in the world; find oneself substantially elevated in fame and status; have a sudden rise in social status; one's position and reputation shoot up hundred-fold; receive a tremendous boost in one's prestige; rise in the world; rise to high note;

身家不清 of mean descent; of mean parentage;

身家難保 live in great danger;

身家清白 come of a decent family; of respectable descent;

身家性命 one's life and family possessions;

[身價] (1) one's social status; (2) selling price of a slave;

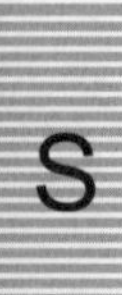

身價十倍 go up in the world; one's value increases tenfold; the marketprice of sth has suddenly shot up tenfold;

[身兼] hold simultaneously;

身兼兩職 wear two hats simultaneously;

身兼數職 hold several posts simultaneously;

[身教] teach by personal example; teach others by one's own example; teaching with deeds;

身教勝於言教 a good example is the best sermon; example is better than precept; examples move more than words; the example of good man is visible philosophy;

身教言傳 instruct sb not only in words, but by deeds; teach by precept and example;

[身歷聲] high fidelity;

[身量] one's height; one's physical dimensions;

[身列戎行] stand in the military ranks—join the army;

[身臨其境] as though one were there in person; being there in person; experience personally; on the spot in person; visit the place in person; watch the scene in person;

[身輕] light body;

身輕如燕 with a body as light as a swallow's;

身輕如葉 one's body is as light as a leaf;

身輕言微 in my humble position, my word does not carry much weight; when one's position is low, one's words carry little weight;

[身軀] one's body; one's bulk; one's person; one's stature;

[身上] (1) on one's body; (2) on one; with one;

身上發光，肚裏發慌 silks and satins put out the fire in the kitchen; silks and satins put out the kitchen-fire;

[身世] experiences in one's lifetime; one's life; one's life experience; one's lot;

身世淒涼 a sad life; lead a miserable and dreary life;

[身勢語] kinesics;

[身手] (1) skills; talent; (2) agility; dexterity;

大展身手 fully display one's skill; give full play to one's talents; show one's capabilities;

顯身手 display one's talent; do one's stuff; exhibit one's skill; reassert oneself; show one's skill; show one's paces; show one's stuff; show one's talent; strut one's stuff;

~大顯身手 bring one's talents into full play; come out strong; cut a dashing figure; display one's skill to the full; distinguish oneself; give a good account of oneself; give full play to one's abilities; play one's prize; show one's best; turn one's talents to full account;

~一顯身手 display one's skill;

一試身手 try one's hand;

[身首] trunk and the head;

身首異處 be beheaded; be dismembered; sever the head from the trunk;

[身受] (1) experience personally; (2) accept personally; receive in person;

身受重創 severely wounded;

感同身受 appreciate it as a personal favour; be deeply affected by ... as if one had experienced it oneself; count it as a personal favour; feel indebted as if it were received in person; I shall count it as a personal favour; I would consider it as a personal favour to me;

[身體] (1) bod; body; (2) health;

身體安康 alive and well; in good health;

身體表面 body surface;

身體不好 in bad health; out of health;

身體不適 off colour; under the weather;

身體不舒服 not feel like anything;

身體差 in poor health; in poor nick;

身體發育不良 aplasia; dysplasia; hypoplasia;

身體發育不全 aplasia; dysplasia; hypoplasia;

身體感覺 boidly sensation;

身體好 have good health;

身體檢查 medical check-up; physical check-up; physical examination;

身體健康 alive and well; in fine health; in good health; sound in body;

身體力行 carry out by actual efforts; earnestly practise what one advocates; practise what one preaches; set an example by personally taking part;

身體強壯 have a strong body; in vigorous

health;
身體損害 physical damage;
身體虛弱 in weak health;
身體搖擺 body rocking;
身體硬朗 be strong;
身體語言 body language;
保養身體 take care of one's health;
保重身體 take care of oneself;
撐起身體 prop oneself up;
摧殘身體 ruin one's health;
鍛鍊身體 exercise the body;
檢查身體 have a check-up;
緊貼身體 cling to the body;
裸露身體 bare the body;
挺直身體 erect one's figure;
彎曲身體 bend the body;
注意身體 look after one's health;
滋補身體 nourish the body;

[身痛] bodily pain; body pain;

[身無] have not one's own;
身無長物 have no personal superfluities; have no valuable things; have nothing; have only bare necessities;
身無己出 have no children of one's own;

[身先士卒] charge at the head of one's subordinates; in the van of one's officers and men; lead the charge;

[身心] body and mind;
身心不健康 in an ill condition of body and mind;
身心不寧 feel uneasy in body and mind; on pins and needles;
身心純潔 pure in mind and body;
身心恍惚 ill at ease and somehow confused;
身心健康 physically and mentally healthy; sound in body and mind;
身心交瘁 be mentally and physically exhausted; in a state of complete bodily and mental prostration;
身心疲勞 weary in body and mind;
身心舒泰 body and mind at ease; there is peace in one's body and mind;
身心一致 body and mind accord; body and soul are in harmony;
身心愉快 feeling well both physically and mentally;
鍛煉身心 exercise the body and the mind;

[身影] a person's silhouette; figure; form;
一個高大的身影 a tall figure;

[身孕] pregnancy;

[身在福中不知福] not to appreciate the happy life one enjoys; take one's good fortune for granted; you don't know when you're well-off;

[身子] (1) body; trunk; (2) pregnancy;
身子不太舒服 not feel well;
身子一軟 one's body goes limp;
帶身子 become pregnant;
光着身子 in a state of undress; naked;
雙身子 pregnant woman;
探身子 bend forward;
~探起身子 get up;
挺直身子 straighten up;
有了身子 pregnant;
重身子 pregnant;
轉過身子 turn around; twist round;

挨身 force one's way;
安身 make one's home in a place; settle; take refuge; take shelter;
拔身 break away from busy schedule; escape; get away;
半身 (1) one side of the body; (2) half of the body;
保身 save one's own skin;
本身 in itself; itself; oneself; personally;
遍身 all over the body;
補身 build up one's health;
藏身 go into hiding; hide oneself;
側身 lean to one side; on one's side; sideways;
插身 (1) edge in; squeeze in; (2) get involved in; take part in;
抄身 frisk; search sb;
車身 automobile body;
稱身 fit;
持身 conduct oneself;
赤身 naked;
敕身 discipline oneself; prudent in conduct;
抽不開身 cannot leave to do sth else;
抽身 get away; leave;
出身 (1) class origin; family background; (2) one's previous experience or occupation;
船身 body of a ship;
牀身 lathe bed;
存身 make one's home; take shelter;
單身 (1) single; unmarried; (2) live alone;
動身 begin a journey; depart; departure; go on a journey; leave for a place; set out on a journey;
獨身 (1) separated from one's family; (2) bachelorhood; single; spinsterhood; unmarried;

發身 puberty;
翻身 (1) turn over; (2) free oneself; stand up;
反身 reflexive;
分身 spare time from one's main work to attend to sth else;
俯身 bend;
孤身 lonely figure;
合身 fit;
河身 river bed;
後身 (1) back of a person; (2) back of a garment;
護身 protective one's body;
化身 embodiment; incarnation;
渾身 all over; from head to foot;
機身 fuselage;
己身 oneself;
緊身 close-fitting;
可身 fit nicely;
老身 old woman (referring to oneself);
爐身 furnace stack;
賣身 (1) sell oneself or a member of one's family; (2) sell one's body; sell one's soul;
滿身 be covered all over with; have one's body covered with;
帽身 body of a hat;
砲身 barrel of a gun;
礮身 gun barrel;
平身 stand up after kowtowing;
棲身 dwell; live; live under sb's roof; obtain shelter; sojourn; stay; stay temporarily;
起身 (1) get out of bed; get up; get up in the morning; rise; (2) get off; leave; set out; start; start a journey; start on a journey;
前身 (1) ancestor; predecessor; (2) forerunner; precursor;
欠身 bend forward a bit; get ready to stand up as a gesture of courtesy; half rise from one's seat; lean forward a bit; make a gesture of rising; raise oneself slightly;
強身 conducive to health; strengthen the body;
切身 (1) directly affect a person; of immediate concern to oneself; (2) first-hand; one's own; personal;
親身 first-hand; in person; personal;
全身 all over the body; flesh and fell; the whole body; to the teeth;
熱身 warm up;
人身 (1) human body; (2) personal liberty;
容身 make one's home; shelter oneself;
肉身 human body;
辱身 disgrace oneself; submit to taint in one's person;
喪身 get killed; lose one's life;
殺身 lose one's life;
閃身 (1) dodge; (2) walk sideways;
傷身 be harmful to the health;
上身 (1) upper part of the body; (2) blouse; jacket; shirt; upper outer garment;
捨身 sacrifice oneself;
屍身 corpse; dead body; remains;
失身 (of a woman) lose one's chastity; lose virginity;
守身 behave oneself correctly;
贖身 redeem oneself;
束身 restrain oneself; self-control;
搜身 body search; frisk; make a body search; search a person;
隨身 carry about; carry sth with one; on one's person; take with one;
替身 (1) double; replacement; stand-in; substitute; understudy; (2) scapegoat;
貼身 (1) next to the skin; (2) personal;
挺身 straighten one's back;
通身 all over the body; whole body;
投身 give oneself to; join; plunge into; throw oneself into;
託身 entrust oneself to; live at a friend's place;
脱身 escape; extricate oneself; get away from; get free; leave; shake off;
委身 (1) become the wife of; (2) consign oneself to sb;
紋身 tattoo;
棲身 dwell; live; stay;
下身 (1) lower part of the body; (2) private parts; (3) trousers;
陷身 land oneself in;
獻身 devote oneself to; give one's life for; offer oneself to a cause;
修身 cultivate one's moral character; cultivate oneself; practise moral culture;
踅身 turn around; turn the body;
養身 keep one's body fit; nourish one's body;
腰身 girth; waist; waist measurement; waistline;
一身 (1) all over the body; whole body; (2) suit; (3) all alone; concerning one person only; single person;
以身 in one's own person; personally;
有身 pregnant;
葬身 be buried;
澡身 take a bath;
正身 one's real person; one's real self;
隻身 all by oneself; alone; by oneself;
致身 dedicate one's life to;
置身 place oneself; stay;
終身 all one's life; lifelong; whole life;

周身 all over the body; whole body;
柱身 shaft;
轉身 face about; turn round; turn the body;
追身 close to the body;
自身 oneself; self;
縱身 jump; leap;

shen
【呻】 drone; groan; moan;
［呻呼］ groan in pain;
［呻喚］ groan in illness;
［呻吟］ groan; moan;

shen
【娠】 pregnant;
妊娠 be pregnant;

shen
【砷】 arsenic;
［砷化物］ arsenical; arsenide;
［砷酸］ arsenate; arsenic acid; arsenicum;
砷酸銨 ammonium arsenate;
砷酸鈣 calcium arsenate;
砷酸鈷 cobaltous arsenate;
砷酸鉀 portassium arsenate;
砷酸鈉 sodium arsenate;
砷酸鉛 lead arsenate;
砷酸鐵 ferric arsenate;
砷酸銅 copper arsenate;
砷酸鋅 zinc arsenate;
砷酸亞鐵 iron arsenate;
砷酸銀 silver arsenate;
［砷中毒］ arsenic poisoning; arsenical poisoning;
慢性砷中毒 arseniasis; arsenicalism

shen
【甡】 (1) many; numerous; (2) crowded;

shen
【參】 (1) name of a star; (2) ginseng;
［參商］ (1) animosity between two brothers; (2) the morning and evening stars;

刺參 a kind of sea cucumber;
丹參 the root of red-rooted salvia;
黨參 dangshen;
海參 sea cucumber; sea slug;
苦參 sophora flavescens;
人參 ginseng;
沙參 root of straight ladybell;

shen
【深】 (1) deep; (2) abstruse; difficult; profound; (3) penetrating; thoroughgoing; (4) close; intimate; (5) dark; deep; (6) late; (7) greatly; very;
［深黯］ dark; dark and obscure;
［深奧］ abstruse; profound; recondite;
深奧的 abstruse;
深奧晦澀 abstruse and hard to understand;
深奧難知 abstruse; beyond understanding; past comprehension;
意義深奧 have a profound significance;
［深閉固拒］ obstinate and perverse;
［深不可測］ abysmal; bottomless; deep and unfathomable; enigma; extremely abstruse; fathomless; have no bottom; immeasurably profound; too deep to be fathomable; too deep to be known; too profound to be measured; unfathomable;
［深菜盤］ deep plate;
［深草區］ rough;
［深藏］ reserved;
深藏不露 keep one's own counsel; real knowledge is not showy;
深藏若虛 modest about one's talent; hide one's light under a bushel; not to be given to boasting; reserved and humble;
［深成作用］ deep-seated process;
［深層］ (1) depth; (2) in-depth;
深層結構 deep structure;
深層意義 deep meaning;
深層語義學 deep semantics;
［深長］ profound;
［深沉］ (1) dark; deep; (2) deep; dull; heavy; (3) conceal one's real feelings;
故作深沉 affected sophistication;
暮色深沉 the dusk is deepening;
［深仇］ deep hatred;
深仇大恨 bear a deep grudge against sb; bitter and deep-seated hatred; deep hatred; deep-seated hatred;
苦大仇深 have been through much bitterness and is thirsting for revenge; suffer bitterly and nurse deep hatred; suffer bitterly in the old society and have a deep hatred;
［深處］ depths; profundity; recesses;
在河流深處 in the depth of the river;
在內心深處 in the depth of one's heart;
在森林深處 in the depths of the forest;

S

[深叢] deep in the woods;

[深度] (1) depth; (2) profundity; (3) sophistication;

深度計 depthometer;

海圖深度 chartered depth;

加工深度 finish depth;

間隙深度 gap depth;

臨界深度 critical depth;

螺紋深度 flight depth;

[深恩] great favours;

[深耕] plough deep;

深耕密植 deep ploughing and close planting;

深耕細作 deep ploughing and careful cultivation;

[深宮] forbidden palace; harem;

[深溝] gully;

[深痼] chronic; deep-rooted;

[深閨] boudoir;

深閨處女 maiden in the innermost chamber;

深閨幽閣 deep, hidden boudoir; the remoteness of the inner apartments;

[深海] deep sea;

深海動物 abyssal fauna;

深海階地 deep-sea terrace;

深海盆地 abyssal basin; deep-sea basin;

深海平原 deep-sea plain;

深海丘陵 abyssal hill;

深海缺口 abyssal gap;

深海探測器 sea probe;

深海魚 abyssal fish;

[深恨] (1) deep hatred; (2) deeply regret;

[深紅] dark red;

深紅大綠 dark red and deep green;

深紅淺紫，鴨綠鵝黃 in different hues of scarlet, purple, blue and yellow;

[深厚] (1) deep; profound; (2) deep-seated; solid;

深厚的基礎 solid foundation;

深厚的友誼 profound friendship;

深仁厚澤 profound benevolence and great favours;

[深化] deepen;

[深交] long and intimate friendship;

[深井] deep well;

[深究] study sth deeply;

不加深究 not get to the bottom of a matter;

[深居簡出] dwell in seclusion rarely coming out; lead a secluded life; live a secluded life; live in seclusion and seldom come out; live with few social contacts; seldom go out;

[深刻] (1) deep; profound; (2) carve deep; (3) incisive; poignant;

寓意深刻 be pregnant with meaning;

[深坑] chasm; deep pit; abyss;

[深藍] dark blue;

[深慮] deep consideration; think deeply;

[深莽] land with dense tall grass;

[深昧] dark; gloomy; obscure;

[深渺] deep and far;

[深妙] abstruse and uncanny; profound;

[深念] think deeply;

[深淺] (1) deep or shallow; depth; (2) proper limits; sense of propriety; (3) dark or light;

黃毛鴨子下水—不知道深淺 a duckling entering the water – not knowing the depths; inexperienced;

交淺言深 have a hearty talk with a slight acquaintance; have a slight acquaintance with sb but talk intimately with him;

沒深沒淺 impudent and thoughtless;

由淺入深 from the easy to the difficult; from the elementary to the profound; from the shallower to the deeper; from the simple to the more complex; from the superficial to the deep; go from the easy to the difficult and complicated;

自淺入深 from easy to difficult; from shallow to deep; from the shallower to the deeper; from the simple to the more complex;

[深切] deep; heartfelt; profound;

深切地理解 understand thoroughly;

深切關懷 be deeply concerned about; show profound concern for;

深切懷念 dearly cherish the memory of;

[深情] deep affection; deep feeling; deep love;

深情厚意 long and close friendship; profound friendship; profound sentiments of friendship;

深情似海 being attached as deep as the sea; with love as deep as the sea;

[深秋] late autumn; late fall;

[深趣] deep interest; enthusiasm;

[深入] (1) go deep into; penetrate into; (2)

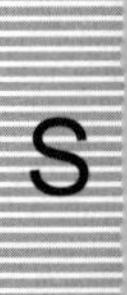

deepgoing; thorough;

深入不毛之地 penetrate deeply into the bare land;

深入的 in-depth;

深入敵後 penetrate far behind enemy lines;

深入腹地 make a deep thrust into; penetrate deeply into;

深入基層 go deep to the grass-roots levels; go down to the basic levels; go into the midst of the basic level; go to the grass-roots units; go to the units at the basic level;

深入淺出 bring out what is difficult to understand in easy language; explain the profound in simple terms; simple and profound; use simple language to explain profound ideas; with profundity and an easy-to-understand approach;

深入群眾 go deep among the masses; go into the midst of the common people; immerse oneself among the masses; take deep root among the masses;

深入人心 be deeply rooted among the people; find its way ever deeper into the hearts of the people; gain popularity; go deep into the hearts of the people; penetrate deeply into the people's mind; sink deep into people's heart; strike a deeper chord in the hearts of the people;

深入生活 plunge into the thick of life;

深入實際 go deep into the realities of life;

深入細緻 deep-going and careful; in a meticulous and deep-going way; thoroughgoing and painstaking;

誘敵深入 lure the enemy in deep;

[深色] deep colour;

[深山] deep in the mountain; remote mountains;

深山大海 mountain ranges and mighty oceans;

深山大澤 high mountains and marshlands;

深山老林 deep mountain forests; remote, thickly forested mountains;

深山密林 deep mountain and thick forests; dense forests in the deep mountains; hilly areas with forests;

深山峽谷 deep mountain valleys;

[深深] deeply; keenly; profoundly; very deeply;

[深室] prison cell;

[深識] farsight; profound understanding;

[深水] deep waters; deepwater;

深水港 deepwater port;

深水碼頭 deepwater wharf;

深水炸彈 deep charge bomb;

[深思] chew over; deep in contemplation; deep thought; ponder deeply over; think deeply about;

深思熟慮 careful consideration; chew the cud; consult with one's pillow; deliberation; give careful consideration to; ponder deeply; think and contemplate thoroughly; think over carefully; turn sth over in one's mind;

[深算] careful deliberation; careful planning;

[深邃] deep and far; profound and abstruse;

寓意深邃 have a profound message;

[深談] intimate talks;

深談細論 discuss in detail;

[深痛] deep grief; lament deeply;

[深為] deeply; greatly; highly;

[深微] deep; profound;

深微奧妙 abstruse and mysterious;

[深文周納] use every means to have an innocent person pronounced guilty;

[深惡痛絕] abhor; cherish an undying hatred for; detest; harbour intense hatred for; hate; hate like poison; have a deep-seated hatred; have a great aversion; hold in abhorrence; hold in abomination; shun like poison;

[深悉] fully aware; know thoroughly;

[深宵] deep in the night;

[深心] deep in one's heart;

[深信] be deeply convinced; believe strongly; deep faith; firmly believe;

深信無疑 be thoroughly convinced; believe firmly; believe without a shadow of doubt; have every confidence in; have no doubts as to the correctness of; have not the slightest doubt; pin one's faith to; put one's faith in;

[深省] make a thorough self-examination;

發人深省 call for deep thought; give sb sth to think about; make sb think;

provide food for thought; prompt sb to deep thought; set people thinking; thought-provoking;
~十分發人深省 give abundant food for speculation;

[深夜] deep in the night; in the small hours of the morning; late at night;
深夜時分抵達 arrive at the deep of night;
工作到深夜 work at all hours; work deep into the night;
談到深夜 talk deep into the night;
在深夜 in the deep of night;

[深意] abstruse meaning; profound meaning;

[深憂] deep worries;

[深淵] abyss; chasm; very dangerous place;
深淵恐怖 bathophobia;
掉進深淵 fall into the abyss;
如臨深淵 as if on the brink of a deep gulf — acting with extreme caution; cautious as though at the brink of a deep abyss; feel like standing upon the edge of a abyss;
推下深淵 push down in the bottomless pit;
墜入深淵 all into an abyss;

[深遠] deep and far; far-reaching; profound and lasting;
影響深遠 have a far-reaching influence;

[深願] would be very glad to;

[深造] pursue advanced studies; take a more advanced course of study; take up advanced studies;
出國深造 pursue advanced studies abroad;

[深湛] profound and thorough;

[深知] know thoroughly; realize fully;
深知世故 know the world well; worldly-wise;

[深重] extremely serious; very grave;

恩深 one's kindness is vast;
高深 advanced; profound; recondite;
根深 be deep rooted;
更深 in the dead of night;
加深 deepen;
艱深 abstruse; difficult to understand;
焦深 depth of focus;
精深 penetrating and profound; profound;
景深 depth of field;
進深 distance from the entrance to the rear;
情深 ardent love; strong affections;
殊深 deeply; extremely; profoundly;
水深 depth of water;
夜深 in the dead of night; late at night;
幽深 deep and quiet; deep and serene;
淵深 erudite; profound;
資深 senior;
縱深 depth;

shen
【紳】 (1) gentleman; gentry; the middle class; (2) girdle; sash; (3) tie;

[紳董] local gentry;

[紳宦] retired government officials;

[紳耆] gentry and elders;

[紳商] gentry and merchant class;

[紳士] gentleman; gentry;
紳士淑女 ladies and gentlemen;
紳士協定 gentleman's agreement;

豪紳 bullying gentry; despotic gentry;
縉紳 gentry; officialdom;
劣紳 evil gentry;
耆紳 gentleman advanced in years;
士紳 gentry;
鄉紳 country gentleman; squire;

shen
【莘】 (1) long; (2) numerous; (3) a kind of plant; (4) a surname;

[莘莘] many; numerous;
莘莘學子 a large number of students;

shen
【蔘】 (1) ginseng; (2) one of the 28 constellations;

shen
【詵】 (1) ask; question; (2) address; speak to; (3) many; numerous;

[詵詵] (1) many; numerous; (2) harmoniously collecting;

shen
【燊】 vigorous;

shen²
shen
【神】 (1) deities; gods; immortals; spiritual beings; (2) magical; marvellous; miraculous; mysterious; mystical; supernatural; wondrous; (3) mind; soul; spirit; (4) airs; appearances; expressions; looks; (5) clever; smart;

[神兵] divine troops;

[神不安啼] cry with irritability;
[神不守舍] absent-minded; delirious; have ants in one's pants; in an absent way; mentally wandering; one's mind is somewhat unhinged; out of one's mind; out of one's wits;
[神采] countenance; expression; look;
神采飛揚 in good feather; in high spirit;
神采煥發 a happy look; brim with energy and vitality; full of spirit and energy; with a joyful face; with sparkling eyes;
神采飄逸 have an elegant bearing;
神采奕奕 as fit as a fiddle; as fresh as a daisy; beaming and buoyant in spirits; brim over with health and spirits; brim with energy and vitality; full of beans; full of spirit and energy; glowing with health and radiating vigour; in buoyant spirits; in fine fettle;
[神馳] allow the thoughts to fly to an adored person;
神馳左右 my spirit is always with you;
心蕩神馳 be transported with; fall head over heels for; lose control of one's mind and will;
心往神馳 let one's thoughts fly to a person; let one's thoughts fly to a place; long for;
[神殿] sanctuary; temple;
[神恩] divine favour;
[神峰] outstanding dignity;
[神鋒] sword;
[神佛] gods and Buddha;
求神拜佛 pray to Buddha for help;
[神父] Catholic father; priest;
[神功] miracle; prodigious feat; supernatural accomplishment;
[神怪] (1) gods and spirits; (2) mysterious; mystical; supernatural;
[神龜] supernatural tortoise;
[神鬼] gods and ghosts;
神鬼莫測 even devils cannot circumvent;
神鬼怕惡人 even a devil is afraid of an ugly mug;
神鬼喪膽 even devils and gods lose their courage;
敬神送鬼 appease the gods and drive away the demons;
瞞神弄鬼 play tricks;
矇神賺鬼 deceive and swindle;
牛鬼蛇神 all sorts of bad characters; bad elements of all kinds; evil people of all descriptions; forces of evil; ghosts and monsters; monsters and demons;
弄神弄鬼 make much ado about the gods; rouse gods and devils;
求神問鬼 divine by drawing lots;
神工鬼斧 divine workmanship; finger of God; prodigious skill; superlative craftsmanship; supernatural skill; the secret workings of nature;
神怒鬼怨 commit so many evil-doings that cause great indignation of gods and grumbles of demons;
神使鬼推 be driven and pushed by evil spirits; the twists and turns of fate;
疑神疑鬼 afraid of one's own shadow; distrustful; full of doubts; have unnecessary suspicions; imagine all sorts of things; suspicious; terribly suspicious;
裝神弄鬼 make faces; make grimaces;
做神做鬼 creep like a ghost; do mischief; play tricks;
[神漢] sorcerer; wizard;
[神乎其技] how marvelous; wonderful is one's art;
[神乎其神] fantastic; miraculous; wonderful;
[神化] be deified; deify; make a god of;
[神話] fairy tale; myth;
神話故事 myth;
神話時代 mythological age;
城市神話 urban myth;
創造神話 create a myth;
類乎神話 sound like a fairy tale;
現代神話 modern myth;
[神魂] (1) mind; state of mind; (2) soul;
神魂不定 be deeply perturbed; be distracted; have the jitters;
神魂顛倒 be carried away with; be clouded and confused in mind; be entranced; be fascinated head over heels; be held spell-bound; be infatuated; be transported; out of one's mind; out of one's wits;
~使人神魂顛倒 sweep sb off their feet;
神魂飛越 go off into ecstasies;
神魂飄蕩 be fascinated; go off into ecstasies;
[神機] (1) God-given chance; (2) divine plan;
神機妙算 ability to divine the unknown;

admirable calculations; crafty plan; divine strategy; marvellous prediction; wonderful foresight; uncanny machinations and subtle calculations;

[神蹟] marvellous event; miracle;
神蹟劇 miracle play;

[神交] be spiritually attached to a friend one has not met;

[神經] nerve;
神經板 nerve plate;
神經崩潰 nervous breakdown;
神經病 (1) mental disorder; nervous disease; neurosis; (2) neurotic;
~ 神經病科專家 neuropathist;
~ 神經病學 neurology;
神經病學家 neurologist;
~ 創傷性神經病 traumatic neuropathy;
~ 精神神經病 psychoneurosis;
~ 酒精性神經病 alcoholic neuropathy;
~ 老年性神經病 senile neuropathy;
~ 鉛毒性神經病 lead neuropathy;
~ 鉛中毒性神經病 lead neuropathy;
~ 缺血性神經病 ischaemic neuropathy;
~ 糖尿病神經病 diabetic neuropathy;
~ 外傷性神經病 traumatic neuropathy;
~ 壓迫性神經病 compression neuropathy;
~ 營養不良性神經病 dystrophoneurosis;
~ 運動性神經病 kinesioneurosis;
~ 中毒性神經病 toxic neuropahty;
~ 周圍神經病 peripheral neuropathy;
~ 軸周性神經病 periaxial neuropathy;
神經不正常 nervous disorder; one's nerves are out of kilter;
神經衝動 nervous impulse;
神經創傷 neurotrauma;
神經錯亂 beside oneself; blow one's top; mental disorder; nervous disorder; take leave of one's senses;
神經電腦 neural computer;
神經幹 nerve trunk;
神經根 nerve root;
~ 神經根病 radiculopathy;
~ 神經根痛 radiculalgia;
神經弓 neural arch;
神經溝 neural groove;
神經官能症 neurosis;
神經管 nerve duct;
神經過敏 have a fit of nerves; heebie-jeebies; jimjams; neurotic; oversensitive; react nervously; thin-skinned; too nervous;
神經漢 madman;
神經機能病 neurosis;
神經脊 nerve ridge;
神經檢查 neurological examination;
神經節 ganglion;
~ 背神經節 dorsal ganglia;
~ 觸角神經節 antennulary ganglion;
~ 大腦神經節 cerebral ganglia;
~ 腹神經節 ventral ganglia;
~ 基底神經節 basal ganglia;
~ 頸動脈神經節 carotid ganglion;
~ 口神經節 buccal ganglion;
~ 腦神經節 cerebral ganglion;
~ 前庭神經節 ganglion vestibulare;
~ 三叉神經節 trigeminal ganglion;
~ 腎上神經節 suprarenal ganglia;
~ 腎神經節 ganglia renalia;
~ 聽神經節 auditory ganglion;
~ 植物性神經節 autonomic ganglion;
神經緊張 be all nerves; nervous; nervous strain; one's nerves are high-strung; one's nerves are on edge;
神經科學 neuroscience;
神經瘤 nerve tumour; neuroma;
~ 殘肢性神經瘤 stump neuroma;
~ 創傷性神經瘤 traumatic neuroma;
~ 聽神經瘤 acoustic nerve neuroma;
~ 真性神經瘤 true neuroma;
神經末梢 nerve endings;
神經胚 nerve embryo;
神經疲勞 nervous exhaustion;
神經纖維網 neuropil;
神經軟化 neuromalacia;
神經失常 have bats in one's belfry; mentally deranged; nervous breakdown;
神經衰弱 neurasthenia;
神經損傷 nerve damage;
神經索 nerve cord;
~ 腹神經索 ventral nerve cord;
神經統禦 nervous control;
神經痛 neuralgia;
~ 殘肢神經痛 stump neuralgia;
~ 關節神經痛 arthroneuralgia;
~ 卵巢神經痛 ovariodysneuria;
~ 膀胱神經痛 cystoneuralgia;
~ 偏頭痛性神經痛 migrainous neuralgia;
~ 特發性神經痛 idiopathic neuralgia;
~ 周圍神經痛 peripheral neuralgia;
~ 足神經痛 pododynia;
神經網絡 neural network;
神經細胞 nerve cells;

神經系統 nervous system;
~不隨意神經系統 involuntary nervous system;
~中樞神經系統 central nervous system;
~周圍神經系統 peripheral nervous system;
神經興奮 nerve impulse;
神經炎 neuritis;
~多發性神經炎 polyneuritis;
~節段性神經炎 segmental neuritis;
~酒精性神經炎 alcoholic neuritis;
~梅毒性神經炎 syphilitic neuritis;
~膿毒性神經炎 septineuritis;
~鉛毒性神經炎 lead neuritis;
~鉛中毒性神經炎 lead neuritis;
~前庭神經炎 vestibular neuritis;
~飲食性神經炎 dietetic neuritis;
~游走性神經炎 migrating neuritis;
~中毒性神經炎 toxic neuritis;
~周圍神經炎 peripheral neuritis;
~軸周性神經炎 periaxial neuritis;
~坐骨神經炎 sciatic neuritis;
神經語言學 neurolinguistics;
神經元 neuron; neurone;
~傳出神經元 efferent neurone;
~傳入神經元 afferent neurone;
~感覺神經元 sensory neurone;
~聯合神經元 association neurone;
~聯絡神經元 internuncial neurone;
~聽覺神經元 auditory neurone;
~抑制性神經元 inhibitory neurone;
~中間神經元 intermediate neurone;
~錐體神經原 pyramidal neurone;
神經戰 psychological warfare; war of nerves;
神經症 neurosis;
~實驗性神經症 experimental neurosis;
~疑病性神經症 hypochondriacal neurosis;
~真性神經症 actual neurosis;
神經質 nervous temperament; nervosity;
~神經質的 nervy;
神經中樞 nerve centre;
臂神經 brachial nerve;
尺神經 ulnar nerve;
刺激神經 irritate one's nerves;
穿皮神經 perforating cutaneous nerve;
傳出神經 efferent nerve;
傳入神經 afferent nerve;
第二神經 second nerve;
第九神經 ninth nerve;
第六神經 sixth nerve;
第七神經 seventh nerve;
第三神經 third nerve;
第十二神經 twelfth nerve;
第十神經 seventh nerve;
第十一神經 eleventh nerve;
第四神經 fourth nerve;
第五神經 fifth nerve;
第一神經 first nerve;
動眼神經 oculomotor nerve;
腓腸神經 sural nerve;
腓神經 peroneal nerve;
腹神經 abdominal nerve;
副交感神經 parasympathetic nerve;
副神經 accessory nerve;
~脊副神經 accessory nerve;
感覺神經 sensory nerve;
股神經 femoral nerve;
關節神經 articular nerve;
滑車神經 trochlear nerve;
脊神經 spinal nerve;
脊髓神經 spinal nerve;
加速神經 accelerator nerve;
交感神經 sympathetic nerve;
頸神經 cervical nerve;
脛神經 tibial nerve;
肋間神經 intercostal nerve;
迷走神經 vegus nerve;
面神經 facial nerve;
腦神經 cranial nerve;
內臟神經 splanchnic nerve;
普通感覺神經 nerve of general sensibility;
前庭神經 vestibular nerve;
橈神經 radial nerve;
三叉神經 trigeminal nerve;
舌下神經 hypoglossal nerve;
舌咽神經 glossopharyngeal nerve;
視覺神經 optic nerve;
視神經 optic nerve;
聽覺神經 auditory nerve;
聽神經 acoustic nerve;
外展神經 abducent nerve; nervus abducens;
味神經 nerve of taste;
向心神經 afferent nerve;
胸神經 thoracic nerve;
嗅覺神經 olfactory nerve;
嗅神經 olfactory nerve;
腋神經 axillary nerve;
陰道神經 vaginal nerve;
營養神經 trophic nerve;
影響神經 affect the nerves;
運動神經 motor nerve;
展神經 abducent nerve;
軸神經 axial nerve;

自主神經 autonomic nerve;
坐骨神經 sciatic nerve;

[神龕] sanctuary; shrine for ancestral tablets;

[神力] divine power; extraordinary power; marvellous ability; superhuman strength;

[神聊] groundless talk; tall tale;

[神靈] (1) deities; divinities; gods; (2) marvelous; prodigious;
神靈附體 spirit possession;
崇拜神靈 adore gods;

[神秘] mysterious; mystical;
神秘莫測 be enveloped in mystery; be shrouded in mystery; be veiled in mystery;
神秘劇 mystery play;
神秘人物 mysterious person; person shrouded in mystery;
神秘色彩 mystique;
神秘性 mystique;
神秘主義 mysticism;
~神秘主義者 mystic;
故作神秘 make a mystery of sth;
神神秘秘 hush-hush;

[神妙] ingenious; marvellous; wonderful; wondrous;
神妙莫測 ingenious; inscrutable; so subtle as to be difficult to guess what comes next;

[神廟] temple of the gods;

[神民] gods and people;
神怒民痛 be abominated even by immortals and mortals;

[神明] deities; divinities; gods; spirits;
神明保佑 have divine help;
奉若神明 deify; laud...as sacrosanct; make a fetish of sth; put sb on a pedestal; regard...as a demigod; revere ... as sacred; sanctify; worship
敬若神明 make a fetish of sth; pay to sth the same respect one would have offered to a god; respect sb as God;

[神謀魔道] as if urged by gods or demons;

[神鳥] phoenix;

[神農] legendary ruler in ancient China;

[神女] (1) goddess; (2) harlot; prostitute;

[神品] sublime works of art; works of genius;

[神婆] sorceress; witch;

[神奇] magical; miraculous; mystical; peculiar; wondrous;
神奇奧妙 mysterious and profound;

[神祇] deities; gods;

[神氣] (1) air; expression; manner; (2) dignified; imposing; (3) spirited; vigorous; (4) cocky; overweening; put on airs;
神氣活現 act in a proud way; as proud as a peacock; give oneself airs; high and mighty; look truculent; on the high ropes; very cocky; walk heavy; with an air of importance;
神氣十足 as proud as a peacock; come the heavy; extremely pompous; grow cocky; lordly; overbearing; put on grand airs; with great show of pomp and circumstance;
~神氣十足的人 stuffed shirt;
八仙吹喇叭—神氣十足 the Eight Taoist Immortals blowing trumpets — full of godlike airs; putting on grand airs;
神安氣定 have a calm and quiet mind; peace of mind;
神喪氣沮 in low spirits and discouraged;
神完氣足 full of spirit and energy;

[神情] air; appearance; expression; facial expression; look;
神情哀切 have a mournful look; have a sad look;
神情恍惚 in a trance;
神情性感 have a sultry look;
神情嚴厲 have a stern look;
神情自若 remain calm; with an easy grace;
擺出冷淡的神情 put on cold airs;
關切的神情 concerned air;
若有所思的神情 thoughtful look;
痛苦的神情 agonized look;

[神權] (1) religious authority; theocracy; (2) rule by divine right;
神權政體 theocracy;
神權政治 theocracy;

[神人] gods and people;
神人共憤 arouse the indignation of immortals and mortals alike; be hated by immortals and mortals alike; incur the wrath of all gods and men;
神人共鑒 may it be taken as evidence both by gods and men;
神人共悅 arouse great joy for all gods and men; sth that gladdens both immortals and mortals;

神人共誅 be punished by both gods and men;
神人相通 communication exists between gods and human beings;

[神色] look; expression;
神色藹然 look amiable;
神色不變 calm in undertaking sth;
神色不定 one's expression is unsettled;
神色不動 calm in undertaking;
神色不對 look queer;
神色不正 looks quite unnatural;
神色慌張 look flurried;
神色惶遽 look scared;
神色稍定 has somewhat overcome one's panic;
神色怡然 look unperturbed;
神色異常 not to be one's usual self;
神色鎮定 calm and collected; show composure and presence of mind;
神色自若 look unperturbed; perfectly calm and collected; show composure and presence of mind;
神動色飛 lively expression on one's face; vivacious look;

[神傷] dejected;
暗自神傷 sick at heart;
黯然神傷 down; down in the mouth; downhearted; feel dejected; feel depressed; feeling low;

[神聖] divine; holiness; holy; sacred;
神聖不可侵犯 holy and inviolable; sacred and inviolable;
神聖文獻 sacred text;
神聖義務 sacred duty; sacred obligations; sanctities;
神聖之地 holy place;

[神示] prophecy;

[神術] marvellous technique; wondrous tricks;

[神思] mental state; state of mind; thoughts;
神思不安 one's heart and mind are disturbed;
神思不定 be distracted;
神思恍惚 a little cracked; absent-minded; be lost in a reverie; be perturbed in spirit; distracted; distraught; grow quite bemused; have a slate loose; have a slate missing; in a disturbed state of mind; in a confused state of mind; in a state of mental confusion; in a trance; muzzy; wool-gathering;
神思昏亂 be greatly disturbed in one's mind;
神思紊亂 one's mind is in a turmoil;

[神似] alike in spirit; an excellent likeness; spiritual resemblance;
形肖神似 achieve a likeness both in shape and in spirit;

[神速] lightning speed; marvellously quick; with amazing speed;
兵貴神速 speed is most valuable in military affairs; speed is precious in war; swift movement is the best tactics;
收效神速 yield marvelously quick results;

[神算] (1) clever plan; (2) miraculous foresight; miraculous prediction;

[神髓] essence; quintessence;

[神態] airs; bearing; facial expressions; manners; mien;
神態昂然 dignified and impressive;
神態倦息 have a weary expression;
神態悠閒 look perfectly relaxed;
神態自若 appear calm and at ease; appear composed; look perfectly calm;

[神通] magical power; remarkable ability; supernatural power;
神通廣大 have great magic power; have sth going for one; infinitely resourceful; possess marvelous abilities; possess unusual powers; very resourceful;
大顯神通 display one's prowess; give full play to one's remarkable skill;
各顯神通 each displays his prowess; each plays his long suit; each shows his special prowess; everyone gives full play to his ability;

[神童] boy of remarkable aptitude; child prodigy; quiz kid; whiz kid; whizzkid; wonder boy;
金融神童 financial whizzkid;

[神往] be carried away; be charmed; rapt; take one's breath away; yearn for at heart;
筆隨神往 go ahead and let the story go wherever one's imagination let one;
為之神往 be captivated; be carried away; be fascinated;

[神威] invincible might; martial prowess;

[神位] memorial tablet; spirit tablet;

[神巫] sorcerer; wizard;

[神武] intelligent and courageous; wise and

powerful;

[神物] (1) phenomenon; prodigy; wonder; (2) deity; immortal; supernatural being;

[神悟] marvelously quick understanding;

[神仙] celestial being; immortal; supernatural being;

神仙下凡 a fairy becomes incarnate; immortals descend to the earth;

神仙魚 angelfish;

神仙中人 the happiest mortal alive;

[神像] (1) image of a dead person; (2) idol; statue of a god;

[神效] magical effect; marvellous effect; miraculous effect; wondrous efficacy;

[神學] theology;

神學家 theologist;

神學院 seminary; theological college;

基督教神學 Christian theology;

解放神學 liberation theology;

神經神學 neurotheology;

[神醫] great doctor; marvellous physician;

[神異] (1) gods and spirits; (2) magical; miraculous; mystical; wondrous;

[神意] divine will; the will of God;

[神勇] extraordinarily brave; superhuman bravery;

[神遊] feel as if one were visiting a place; make a mental travel; tour a place by imagination;

[神佑] divine help;

[神宇] appearance; look;

[神諭] oracle;

[神職人員] churchman; cleric; clergy; clergyman;

神職人員的 clerical;

女性神職人員 churchwoman; clergywoman;

[神志] consciousness; mind; sense; spirits;

神志不清 clouded in mind; delirious; in a confused state of mind; in a state of a coma; not in one's right mind; out of one's senses; unconscious;

神志恍惚 one's mind wanders; wandering in one's mind;

神志昏亂 one's mind is confused; one's mind is wandering;

神志昏迷 delirious; in a state of delirium; lose consciousness;

神志清明 in full possession of one's faculties;

神志清醒 in a clear state of mind; in full possession of one's faculties; in one's right mind; in one's sober senses; remain fully conscious;

[神智] intelligence; mental ability;

神智不清 clouded in the mind; incapable of clear thinking; muddle-headed;

[神主] memorial tablet; spirit tablet;

愛神 Amor; Cupid; Eros; God of Love; Venus;

安神 (1) calm the nerves; (2) relieve uneasiness of body and mind;

媼神 goddess of earth;

拜神 worship gods;

財神 (1) God of Wealth; (2) money-makers;

操神 bother; tax on one's mind; trouble;

出神 abstractedness; abstraction; aphelxia; be lost in thought; in a trance; spellbound;

傳神 lifelike; vivid;

定神 (1) collect oneself; compose oneself; pull oneself together; (2) collect one's thoughts; concentrate one's attention; take a grip on oneself;

費神 (1) may I trouble you to do sth; would you mind doing sth for me; (2) waste of energy;

分神 give some attention to;

丰神 manner;

鬼神 ghosts and gods; spirits; supernatural beings;

海神 Neptune; Poseidon;

火神 god of fire;

精神 (1) consciousness; dauber; gist; mind; spirit; (2) essence; gist; spirit; substance;

勞神 bother; tax on one's mind; trouble;

留神 careful; keep one's eyes on the ball; keep one's eyes peeled; look out for; look sharp; take care;

門神 door god;

凝神 with concentrated attention;

女神 goddess;

棲神 cultivate one's mind; discipline one's mind;

請神 call up an evil spirit;

求神 beg the gods;

人神 man and God;

如神 like god;

入神 captivated; deeply absorbed in; enthralled; entranced; spellbound; with ecstasy;

山神 mountain deity;

傷神 be nerve-racking; overtax one's nerves;

失神 (1) absent-minded; careless; inattentive; (2) in low spirits; out of sorts;

死神 graim monarch; great leveller; great

whipper-in; Grim Reaper; Mr Mose; old floorer; old man Mose; old Mr Grim; pale horse;
祀神 worship gods;
送神 send off the gods after the offering of sacrifices;
淘神 bothersome; trying;
提神 arouse; elate; give oneself a lift; refresh oneself; stimulate;
天神 deity; god;
跳神 sorcerer's dance in a trance;
通神 capable of buying the gods;
瘟神 god of plague;
巫神 sorcerer; wizard;
心神 mind; mood; state of mind;
形神 body and spirit;
醒神 inducing resuscitation;
凶神 demon; evil spirit;
兇神 demon; fiend;
眼神 (1) expression in one's eyes; gleams of the eyes; light; (2) eyesight;
養神 have mental relaxation; repose; rest to attain mental tranquility;
一神 monotheistic;
怡神 inspire peace and harmony in one's mind;
頤神 have a mental relaxation; rest one's mind;
有神 (1) full of spirit; (2) miraculous;
灶神 kitchen god;
走神 absent-minded;

shen³

shen

【沈】 a surname;

shen

【哂】 give a sneering smile;
［哂納］ kindly accept the gift;
尚乞哂納 I beg you to accept this small present; please do me the favour of accepting this present;
［哂笑］ laugh at with contempt;

shen

【矧】 (1) still more; (2) also; (3) gums;

shen

【審】 (1) careful; cautious; judicious; (2) examine; go over; investigate; review; (3) interrogate; try; (4) appreciate; discern; know; (5) indeed; really;
［審查］ censor; censorship; check; examine; investigate;
審查經費 check up on the funds;
審查屬實 the fact is established after investigation;
自我審查 self-censorship;
［審察］ careful observation; study carefully;
［審處］ (1) try and punish; (2) deliberate and decide;
［審諦］ attentive to every detail;
［審定］ authorize; check and decide; examine and approve;
［審訂］ examine and revise;
審訂教材 revise teaching materials;
［審度］ deliberate; consider the pros and cons; study and estimate;
審度情勢 consider all the circumstances; study and weigh conditions;
［審斷］ examine and decide; pass a judgement after an examination;
［審稿］ examine and approve manuscripts;
［審核］ examine and consider; examine and verify;
審核預算 verify a budget;
預算審核 budget auditing;
［審計］ audit;
審計標準 auditing standards;
審計風險 audit risk;
審計跟蹤 audit trails;
審計機關 audit agency;
審計師 auditor;
～高級審計師 senior auditor;
～助理審計師 assistant auditor;
審計手續 audit procedure;
審計員 audit clerk; auditor;
～常駐審計員 resident auditor;
～獨立審計員 independent auditor;
～內部審計員 internal auditor;
～外聘審計員 external auditor;
審計長 chief auditor;
審計制度 auditing system;
審計準則 auditing standards;
財政審計 financial audit;
常任審計 standing audit;
定期審計 periodical audit;
績效審計 performance audit;
內部審計 internal audit;
事後審計 post-audit;
事前審計 pre-audit;
特別審計 special audit;
外部審計 external audit;
系統審計 operational audit;
遵循審計 compliance audit;

S

[審理] hear; try;
審理案件 hear a case; try a case;
雙重審理 double jeopardy;
[審美] appreciate the beautiful; appreciation of the beauty; aesthetic;
審美差異 aesthetic difference;
審美錯覺 aesthetic illusion;
審美幻覺 aesthetic hallucination;
審美家 aesthete;
審美價值 aesthetic value;
審美距離 aesthetic distance;
審美體驗 aesthetic experience;
審美文化 aesthetic culture;
審美享受 aesthetic enjoyment;
審美效應 aesthetic effect;
審美意識 aesthetic consciousness;
~多向型審美意識 multidirectional aesthetic consciousness;
審美意志 aesthetic determination;
審美知覺 aesthetic perception;
審美直覺 aesthetic intuition;
[審判] (1) bring to trial; try; (2) trial;
審判不公 miscarriage of justice;
審判程序 court proceedings;
審判機關 judicial organ;
審判結束 the trial is concluded;
審判權 jurisdiction;
審判室 courtroom;
審判庭 tribunal;
~經濟審判庭 conomic court;
~民事審判庭 civil adjudication tribunal;
~刑事審判庭 criminal adjudication tribunal;
~行政審判庭 administrative court;
審判員 judge;
~助理審判員 assistant judge;
審判長 chief judge;
~副審判長 associate chief judge;
接受審判 stand trial;
無效審判 mistrial;
[審批] examine and approve;
審批手續 procedures of approval;
~辦理審批手續 go through the procedures of approval;
~簡化審批手續 simplify the procedures of approval;
[審慎] careful; cautious; circumspect; prudent;
審慎從事 steer a cautious course;
審慎樂觀 cautious optimism; guarded optimism;
[審時觀變] examine the signs of the times and mark the changes of the affairs;
[審問] examine; hear; interrogate; question; try;
[審悉] find out carefully; get to know;
[審訊] inquest; interrogate; try;
初步審訊 preliminary bearing;
[審議] consider; deliberate; examine;
審議機關 deliberative body;
[審閱] check and approve; examine; review;

編審 copy editor; read and edit;
初審 first trial;
複審 (1) recheck; reexamine; (2) review a case which has been passed by a lower court;
公審 hold a public trial;
候審 await trial;
會審 (1) joint hearing; (2) make a joint checkup;
開審 sit at session; start the trial;
陪審 (1) act as an assessor; (2) serve on a jury;
評審 judge;
受審 be on trial; be tried; stand trial;
提審 (1) bring a prisoner before the court; (2) review;
聽審 be tried; stand trial;
預審 preliminary hearing;
原審 first trial;
再審 (1) review; (2) retrial;
終審 final judgment; last instance;

shen
【諗】 (1) think of; (2) announce; let know; tell; (3) remonstrate; (4) conceal; hide;

shen
【嬸】 (1) aunt; (2) sister-in-law;
[嬸母] aunt; wife of father's younger brother;
[嬸娘] aunt; wife of father's younger brother;
[嬸嬸] aunt; wife of father's younger brother;

表嬸 wife of father's younger cousin;

shen
【瀋】 (1) fluid; juice; liquid; water; (2) short for Shenyang;

shen
【讅】 aware; know;

shen⁴
shen
【甚】 (1) exceedingly; extremely; to a great extent; to a high extent; very; (2)

more than;
[甚多] very many; very much;
[甚好] very good; very well;
[甚或] even; go so far as to;
[甚麼] how;
甚麼匠人出甚麼 like workman, like work; the work shows the workman;
沒甚麼 it doesn't matter; it's nothing; never mind; that's all right;
[甚是] exceedingly; extremely; very;
[甚囂塵上] cause a riotous clamour; cause a temporary clamour; make a great noise; make a lot of noise;
[甚至] as...as; enough; even; far from; go so far as to; if anything; if not more; in fact; indeed; nay; negative + so much as; nor yet; not a; not a single; not once; not one; not to say; or more; reflexive pronoun; so...that; so far from; so much so that; such...that; the comparative; the superlative; very; yews;

過甚 exaggerated; excessive;
幸甚 very hopeful and worth rejoicing;

shen
【脤】 (1) raw meat for sacrifice; (2) bottom; buttocks;

shen
【腎】 (1) kidney; (2) testicle;
[腎病] kidney disease;
腎病變 nephropathy;
~ 滲透性腎病變 osmotic nephrosis;
~ 脂性腎病變 lipoid nephrosis;
腎病腎炎 nephrosonephritis;
~ 出血性腎病腎炎 haemorrhagic nephrosonephritis;
毒性腎病 toxic nephrosis;
返流性腎病 reflux nephropathy;
壞死性腎病 necrotizing nephrosis;
急性腎病 acute nephrosis;
空泡性腎病 vacuolar nephrosis;
空泡樣腎病 hydropic nephrosis;
流行性腎病 epidemic nephrosis;
慢性腎病 chronic nephrosis;
霉菌性腎病 mycotic nephrosis;
膜性腎病 membranous nephropathy;
尿酸腎病 uric acid nephropathy;
輕鏈型腎病 light-chain nephropathy;
缺血性腎病 ischaemic nephropathy;
腎小球腎病 glomerulonephropathy;
腎盂腎病 pyelonephrosis;
糖尿病腎病 diabetic nephropathy;
痛風腎病 gouty nephropathy;
痛風性腎病 gouty nephropathy;
隱性腎病 larval nephrosis;
脂性腎病 lipoid nephrosis;
終末期腎病 end-stage renal disease;
中毒性腎病 toxic nephrosis;
[腎充血] nephrohemia;
[腎出血] nephrorrhagia;
[腎動脈] renal artery;
[腎發育不良] renal dysplasia;
[腎發育不全] renal dysplasia;
[腎肥大] nephromegaly;
[腎功能不全] renal insufficiency;
[腎關閉] renal shutdown;
[腎積水] hydronephrosis;
膿性腎積水 pyohydronephrosis;
[腎結核] renal tuberculosis;
[腎結石] calculus renalis; kidney stone; nephrolith; renal calculus;
腎結石病 lithiasis;
腎結石炎 nephrolithiasis;
繼發性腎結石 secondary renal calculus;
原發性腎結石 primary renal calculus;
[腎孔] nephrostomy;
[腎口] nephrostomy;
[腎虧] asthenia of kidney;
[腎潰瘍] nephrelcosis;
[腎擴張] nephrectasia;
[腎瘤] kidney tumour; nephroma;
[腎門] hilum of kidney;
[腎囊] capsulae renis;
[腎膿腫] kidney abscess;
[腎膀胱炎] nephrocystitis;
[腎破裂] kidney fracture;
[腎切除] nephrectomy;
[腎軟化] nephromalacia;
[腎疝] nephrocele;
[腎上腺] adrenal gland;
腎上腺素 adrenaline;
腎上腺病 adrenopathy;
腎上腺功能病 adrenalism;
腎上腺功能不全 adrenal insufficiency;
繼發性腎上腺功能不全 secondary adrenal insufficiency;
腎上腺功能不足 adrenal insufficiency;

~ 原發性腎上腺功能不足 primary adrenal insufficiency;

[腎神經節] ganglia renalia;

[腎石] kidney stone;

腎石切除 nephrolithotomy;

[腎衰竭] renal failure;

急性腎衰竭 acute renal failure;

慢性腎衰竭 chronic renal failure;

[腎痛] nephralgia;

[腎下垂] nephroptosis;

[腎小囊] renal capsule;

[腎小球] glomerulus;

腎小球病 glomerulopathy;

~ 糖尿病性腎小球病 diabetic glomerulopathy;

~ 萎陷性腎小球病 collapsing glomerulopathy;

腎小球上皮 glomerular epithelium;

腎小球腎病 glomerulonephropathy;

腎小球腎炎 glomerulonephritis;

~ 狼瘡腎小球腎炎 lupus glomerulonephritis;

~ 慢性腎小球腎炎 chronic glomerulonephritis;

~ 腎小球腎炎 membranous glomerulonephritis;

腎小球炎 glomerulitis;

腎小球硬化 glomerulosclerosis;

~ 糖尿病性腎小球硬化 diabetic glomerulosclerosis;

[腎虛陽痿] impotence due to kidney asthenia;

[腎炎] nephritis;

腎炎綜合症 nephritic syndrome;

~ 急性腎炎綜合症 acute nephritic syndrome;

變性腎炎 degenerative nephritis;

出血性腎炎 haemorrhagic nephritis;

急性腎炎 acute nephritis;

結石性腎炎 lithonephritis;

狼瘡腎炎 lupus nephritis;

鏈球菌腎炎 streptoccal nephritis;

梅毒性腎炎 syphilitic nephritis;

囊性腎炎 capsular nephritis;

膿性腎炎 purulent nephritis;

鉛毒性腎炎 saturnine nephritis;

妊娠期腎炎 nephritis of pregnancy;

滲出性腎炎 exudative nephritis;

實質性腎炎 parenchymatous nephritis;

輸血性腎炎 transfusion nephritis;

水腫性腎炎 dropsical nephritis;

痛性腎炎 nephritis dolorosa;

細菌性腎炎 bacterial nephritis;

猩紅熱腎炎 scarlatinal nephritis;

氮血症性腎炎 azotemic nephritis;

硬結性腎炎 indurative nephritis;

增生性腎炎 productive nephritis;

[腎硬化] nephrosclerosis;

惡性腎硬化 malignant nephrosclerosis;

老年性腎硬化 senile nephrosclerosis;

良性腎硬化 benign nephrosclerosis;

小動脈性腎硬化 arteriolar nephrosclerosis;

[腎盂] pelvis of ureter;

腎盂病 pyelopathy;

腎盂積水 nephrohydrosis;

腎盂腎病 pyelonephrosis;

腎盂腎炎 nephropyelitis; pyelonephritis;

~ 急性腎盂腎炎 acute pyelonephritis;

~ 膀胱腎盂腎炎 cystopyelonephritis;

~ 氣性腎盂腎炎 emphysematous pyelonephritis;

~ 妊娠性腎盂腎炎 pyelonephritis of pregnancy;

腎盂炎 pyelitis;

~ 結痂性腎盂炎 encrusted pyelitis;

~ 結石性腎盂炎 calcipyelitis;

~ 囊性腎盂炎 pyelitis cystica;

~ 膀胱腎盂炎 cystopyelitis;

~ 妊娠期腎盂炎 pyelitis gravidarum;

~ 妊娠腎盂炎 encyopyelitis;

~ 肉芽腫性腎盂炎 pyelitis granulosa;

~ 腺性腎盂炎 pyelitis glandularis;

[腎臟] kidneys;

腎臟病 kidney disease;

腎臟結石 kidney stone;

腎臟炎 nephritis;

充血腎 congested kidney;

副腎 adrenal gland;

後期腎 metanephros;

後腎 hind-kidney;

膿腎 pyonephrosis;

盤狀腎 disk kidney;

前期腎 pronephros;

前腎 forekidney;

人造腎 artificial kidney;

外腎 testicle;

洗腎 dialysis;

原腎 nephridia;

shen

【慎】 careful; cautious; prudent; scrupulous;

[慎獨] cautious when one is alone;
[慎密] meticulous;
[慎默] cautious and reticent;
[慎始] careful about the beginning of an endeavour;
慎始敬終 careful in the beginning and respectful in the ending;
[慎思] think carefully;
慎思而後行 look before you leap;
慎思明辨 discriminate with wisdom; think carefully and clearly;
[慎微] careful about minute details;
謹小慎微 circumspect; overcautious;
[慎勿] careful not to;
慎勿告人 be sure not to tell any one; between ourselves; between you and me;
[慎刑] mete out punishments carefully;
[慎言] speak cautiously;
慎言律己 speak cautiously and practise self-discipline;
慎言慎行 exercise caution in speech and conduct;
[慎之又慎] double cautious; make assurance doubly sure; treat sth with extreme prudence;
[慎終追遠] carefully attend to the funeral rites of parents and follow them when gone with due sacrifices; conduct the funeral of one's parents with meticulous care and let not sacrifices to one's remote ancestor be forgotten;
[慎重] careful; cautious; considerate; discreet; prudent;
慎重從事 act cautiously; steer a cautious course;
慎重處理 exercise prudence in dealing with...;
慎重回答 give a careful answer;
慎重將事 handle a matter with care;
慎重其事 careful; do sth in a serious manner; handle with care; prudent; serious and earnest; take careful precautions; very careful;
慎重擇交 choose friends with care;
不慎重 indiscreet;

不慎 careless;
謹慎 careful; cautious; prudent;
審慎 cautious; prudent;
失慎 careless; not cautious;

shen
【蜃】 clams;
[蜃車] hearse;
[蜃景] mirage;
[蜃氣] mirage;

shen
【葚】 mulberry;

shen
【滲】 infiltrate; ooze; percolate; permeate; seep;
[滲出] ooze; seepage; seep out;
氣體滲出 gas seepage;
[滲井] seepage pit;
[滲坑] seepage pit;
[滲漏] ooze out; seepage; seep out;
滲漏暈 leakage halo;
地下水滲漏 ground water seepage;
渠道滲漏 canal seepage;
[滲入] (1) permeate; seep into; (2) infiltrate; penetrate;
滲入地下 permeate the ground; seep into the ground;
滲入作用 infiltration;
[滲碳] carburizing;
滲碳法 carburization;
滲碳劑 carburizer;
~ 固體滲碳劑 solid carburizer;
~ 緩和滲碳劑 mild carburizer;
滲碳燒結 carbusintering;
滲碳體 cementite;
~ 共晶滲碳體 eutectic cementite;
~ 粒狀滲碳體 granular cementite; nodular cementite;
~ 球狀滲碳體 globular cementite; modulous cementite; spherical cementite;
~ 游離滲碳體 free cementite;
~ 珠光體滲碳體 pearlitic cementite;
表面滲碳 surface carburizing;
高溫滲碳 high-temperature carburizing;
固體滲碳 solid carburizing;
過度滲碳 excess carburizing;
緩和滲碳 mild carburizing;
活性滲碳 activated carburizing;
局部滲碳 local carburizing;
氣體滲碳 gas carburizing;
液體滲碳 bath carburizing; liquid carburizing;

[滲透] infiltrate; penetrate; percolate; permeate; infiltration; osmosis; seepage; seep through;
滲透分析 dialysis;
滲透前進 advance by infiltration;
滲透壓 osmotic pressure;
滲透作用 osmosis;
潮溫滲透 moisture seepage;
非法滲透 illegal infiltration;
經濟滲透 economic infiltration;
逆滲透 reverse osmosis;
熱滲透 heat infiltration;
逐步滲透 gradually penetrate;
[滲析] dialysis;
滲析器 dialyser;
滲析液 dialysate;
電滲析 electrodialysis;

光滲 irradiation;
抗滲 impervious;
外滲 exosmosis;

sheng[1]
sheng

【昇】 (1) ascend; go up; raise; rise; (2) advance; promote; (3) hoist; (4) litre; (5) a surname;
[昇班] (1) go up one grade in school; (2) advance to a higher grade; be promoted;
[昇高] heighten; increase; rise;
停止昇高 top out;
血壓昇高 rise in blood pressure;
[昇格] elevate; promote; upgrade;
詞義昇格 elevation of meaning;
外交關係昇格 upgrade diplomatic relations;
[昇官] promote in office;
昇官發財 a good career and easy money; attain high ranks and acquire great wealth; become an official and lead an easy life; climb the official ladder and become wealthy; get power and money; promote in office and become rich; secure office and riches; seek official position or wealth; seek position and wealth; successful in politics and business; win promotion and get rich;
[昇號] sharp;
[昇級] (1) be promoted; escalate; promote; (2) advance to a higher grade;
[昇降] hoist and lower; rise and fall;
昇降機 elevator; lift;
~帶式昇降機 belt elevator;
~高爐昇降機 blast-furnace elevator;
~建築工程昇降機 builder's lift;
~旋臂昇降機 arm conveying elevator;
名昇實降 kick sb upstairs;
明昇暗降 apparent promotion but real demotion; apparently ascend but actually descend — degradation instead of promotion; kick sb upstairs; promote sb in name but demote him in reality;
[昇留級] promote or hold back students;
升留級制度 system of promoting or holding back students;
[昇平] peace and prosperity;
昇平盛世 an age of peace and prosperity;
[昇旗] hoist a flag;
[昇遷] get transferred to a higher position;
[昇堂] (1) appear in court to conduct a trial; (2) ascend to the hall;
昇堂入室 attain mastery;
[昇騰] (1) fly up; leap up; rise; (2) flourish in business; make good progress;
[昇天] ascend to heaven; go up to the heaven;
[昇學] enter a higher school;
[昇運機] elevator;
斗帶式昇運機 belt-trough elevator;
螺旋昇運機 auger elevator;
氣動昇運機 air elevator;
[昇值] appreciate; revaluation;
貨幣昇值 currency revaluation; upward revaluation of currency;

遞昇 rise progressively;
飛昇 fly up to heaven;
高昇 be promoted to a higher position;
公昇 litre;
毫升 millilitre;
回昇 pick up; rise again;
躋昇 go up; mount;
晉昇 gain promotion;
猱昇 monkey climbing up a tree;
榮昇 be promoted in glory;
上昇 ascend; go up; rise;
市升 unit of dry measure for grain;
提昇 (1) promote; (2) elevate; hoist;
擢昇 advance; promote;

sheng

【生】 (1) bear; beget; breed; cause; create; give birth to; give rise to; produce; (2) be born; come into being; come into existence; (3) grow; (4) existence; life; (5) livelihood; (6) living; (7) get have; (8) light a fire; (9) green; unripe; (10) crude; raw; uncooked; unripe; (11) barbarian; savage; uncultured; unprocessed; unrefined; untamed; (12) strange; unaquainted; unfamiliar; unknown; (13) mechanical; stiff; (14) very; (15) disciple; pupil; student; (16) male characters in a Beijing opera; (17) a surname;

[生搬硬套] apply mechanically; copy mechanically and apply indiscriminately; do by rote; mechanical application; rote;

[生病] be ill; be taken bad; be taken ill; be taken sick; fall ill; fall sick; get sick; take ill; take sick;

[生財] make money;
- 生財有道 able to make money; expert in making money; find a way of earning money; have the knack of making money; know how to make money; the way to become wealthy; ways and means to gain profit;
- 和氣生財 amiability attract riches; an even temper brings wealth; friendliness is conducive to business success; harmony brings wealth; peace breeds wealth;

[生菜] (1) lettuce; (2) raw vegetables; salad;
- 一棵生菜 a head of lettuce;

[生產] (1) bring out; come up with; make; manufacture; produce; production; put out; turn out; (2) give birth to;
- 生產佈局 distribution of production;
- 生產部經理 production manager;
- 生產成本 production cost;
- 生產定額 fixed production quota;
- 生產方式 mode of production;
- 生產跟單員 product co-ordinator;
- 生產工具 instruments of production;
- 生產關係 mode of production; relations of production;
- 生產管理 production management;
- ~生產管理系統 management operating system;
- 生產過程 productive process;
- 生產過剩 overproduction;
- 生產國際化 internationalization of production;
- 生產滑坡 drastic decline in the production;
- 生產活動 activity in production;
- 生產技術 technology;
- 生產計劃 production plan;
- 生產集團化 production groupification;
- 生產集約化 production intensification;
- 生產進度 rate of production;
- 生產勞動 productive labour;
- 生產力 productivity;
- ~初級生產力 primary productivity;
- ~次級生產力 secondary productivity;
- ~解放生產力 emancipate productivity; liberate productivity;
- ~資本生產力 capital productivity;
- 生產率 productivity;
- ~遞減生產率 productivity;
- ~計算生產率 calculated productivity;
- ~平均生產率 average productivity;
- ~提高生產率 raise productivity;
- 生產能力 production capacity;
- 生產潛力 productive potentialities;
- 生產設備 production facilities;
- 生產時間 lead time;
- 生產水平 production level;
- 生產稅 production tax;
- 生產體系 production structure;
- ~一條龍生產體系 integrated production structure; through-train production structure;
- 生產投資 production investment;
- 生產文明 production civilization;
- 生產限額 production quota;
- 生產線 production line;
- 生產效率 production efficiency;
- 生產信息 production information;
- ~生產信息控制系統 production information and control system;
- ~生產信息系統 production and operation information system;
- 生產要素 element of production; production factor;
- 生產預算 production budget;
- 生產責任制 system of production responsibility;

生產主義 productivism;
生產資料 capital goods; means of production;
~生產資料所有制 ownership of the means of production;
生產指標 production target;
生產總值 total output value;
~國民生產總值 gross national product;
~國內生產總值 gross domestic product;
安全生產 safety in production;
~安全生產教育 education in safety production methods;
~安全生產責任制 safety responsibility system;
成批生產 batch production; produce by batch;
大量生產 mass production;
單元生產 cellular production;
分批生產 batch production;
副業生產 sideline production;
過量生產 overproduction;
集體生產 collection production;
加速生產 step up production;
軍用生產 defense production;
開始生產 go into production;
民用生產 civilian production;
農業生產 agricultural production;
批量生產 bulk production;
削減生產 curtail production;
小生產 small-scale production;
再生產 reproduction;
增加生產 boost production;
直接生產 direct production;
自動化生產 automated production;

[生成] generative;
生成程序 generating programme;
生成器 generator;
生成熱 heat of formation;
生成物 product;
生成誤差 generated error;
生成語法 generative grammar;
生成語義學 generative semantics;
生成轉換理論 generative transformational theory;
生成轉換語法 generative transformational grammar;

[生辰] birthday;
生不逢辰 be born at a wrong time; be born at an unlucky hour; be born under an unlucky star; live in a bad time; live in the wrong age; luckless; unlucky;

[生吃] eat sth raw; eat sth without cooking;

[生詞] new word;

[生存] exist; live; survival; survive;
生存競爭 struggle for existence;
生存空間 living space;
生存權利 right to life;
生存條件 condition for existence;
生存希望 chance of survival;
適者生存 survival of the fittest;

[生動] lifelike; lively; vivid;
生動逼真 vivid; word picture;
生動感人 lively and touching; vivid and moving;
生動活潑 lively; vigorous and lively; vivid and vigorous;
生動明快 vivid and clear-cut;

[生分] strange; unfamiliar; unfriendly;

[生俘] capture alive;

[生父] one's own father;

[生格] generic; genitive;
生格從句 genitive clause;
後置生格 post-genitive;
類別生格 classifying generic;
量度生格 genitive of measure;
描寫生格 genitive of description;

[生根] root; strike root; take root;
生根開花 take root and blossom;

[生花] flowery;
生花妙筆 beautiful style of writing; brilliant writing; deft in writing; gifted pen;
生花妙語 flowery phrases;
筆底生花 write like an angel;
夢筆生花 dream of being a successful writer; good at writing beautiful poems; imaginative;
妙筆生花 write like an angel;

[生化] biochemistry;
生化形態學 biochemical morphology;
生化學 biochemistry;
~無生化學 abiochemistry;
生化藥劑 biochemical;
生化戰爭 biochemical warfare;

[生還] come back alive; return alive; survive;
生還者 survivor;
無一生還 none survived;

[生活] (1) life; (2) exist; live; (3) livelihood;
生活安定 lead a settled life; live a stable life;
生活安寧 tranquil life;
生活安逸 live well;

生活必需品 necessities of life; subsistence needs;
生活方式 lifestyle; modes of living; way of life;
~ 城市生活方式 urban mode of existence;
~ 非傳統生活方式 alternative lifestyle;
~ 改變生活方式 amend one's way of living; change one's lifestyle;
~ 農村生活方式 rural lifestyle; rural mode of existence;
~ 一種生活方式 a lifestyle;
生活費 cost of living; living expenses;
~ 生活費用 cost of living;
生活豐裕 comfortable off; live in plenty;
生活孤獨 lonely life;
生活規律 law of life;
生活還得繼續 life goes on;
生活環境 living environment;
生活簡樸 lead a simple and frugal life; plain living;
生活教育 informal education;
生活經歷 life experiences;
~ 生活就是這樣 such is life; that's life;
生活考驗 tests of a rigorous life;
生活空間 life space;
生活困難 be badly off; in bad circumstances; in reduced circumstances; in straitened circumstances;
生活力 viability; vigour; vitality;
~ 生活力缺失 abiotrophy;
生活糜爛 lead a fast life;
生活模式 lifestyle;
~ 健康生活模式 healthy lifestyle;
生活貧困 live in reduced circumstances;
生活淒涼 miserable and dreary life;
生活氣息 flavour of life;
生活區 area of life;
生活設施 amenity;
生活實踐 practice in daily life;
生活舒適 in easy circumstances; in good circumstances; in flourishing circumstances;
生活水平 living standards; standard of living;
生活水準 living standards; standard of living;
生活體驗 life experience;
生活條件 living conditions;
~ 改善生活條件 ameliorate living conditions; improve the living conditions;
生活問題 problem of livelihood;
生活無著 have no means of support; unable to eke out a living;
生活習慣 living habits;
~ 良好生活習慣 good living habits;
生活型 life form;
生活小節 matters concerning personal life; trifling personal matters;
生活寫意 lead a comfortable life;
生活型 life form;
生活優裕 live high off the hog; live in affluence; well off;
生活在自己的世界裏 live in a world of one's own;
生活質素 life quality;
生活資料 means of livelihood; means of subsistence;
安定的生活 settled life; stable life;
~ 喜歡安定的生活 prefer a stable life;
安樂生活 bread buttered on both sides;
獨身生活 celibacy; single life;
放蕩的生活 life of debauchery;
非人生活 miserable life;
浮華生活 showy and luxurious life;
過和平的生活 live in peace;
過忙碌的生活 lead a busy life;
過貧困的生活 have a miserable life; live in poverty;
過愜意的生活 lead a contented life;
過幸福的生活 live a happy life;
過正常的生活 live a normal life;
家庭生活 family life;
開始獨立生活 spring one's wings;
坤伶生活 livelihood of an actress;
那就是生活 that's life;
日常生活 daily life; day-to-day life; everyday life;
社交生活 social life;
生不如死的生活 living death;
雙重生活 double life;
~ 過雙重生活 lead a double life; live a double life;
私人生活 personal life;
私生活 one's private life; privacy of an individual;
討生活 drift along aimlessly; make a living; seek living;
維持生活 get sustenance; make a living;
~ 勉強維持生活 scrape a living; scratch a living;
下層社會生活 low life;
現代生活 contemporary living; modern

living;
現實生活 the real world;
學校生活 school life;
夜生活 night life;
早年生活 early life;
找生活 earn a living;
正常生活 normal life;
組織生活 regular activities of the Party organization;

[生火] build a fire; fire up; light a fire; make a fire;
拾柴生火 gather sticks to make a fire;

[生貨] raw materials; unprocessed goods;

[生機] (1) exuberant; full of life; liveliness; overflowing with vigour; vitality; (2) chances of survival;
生機盎然 brimming over with vigour and vitality; brimming over with vitality; exuberant; full of life; overflowing with vigour;
生機勃勃 full of vigour;
一片生機 vigorous signs of life;
一線生機 a fighting chance; a gleam of hope; a last hope of recovery; a slim chance of life; a slim chance of survival;

[生計] bread and butter; livelihood; means of livelihood;
奪人生計 take the bread out of sb's mouth;
另謀生計 try to find some other means of livelihood;
維持生計 earn a living;
自謀生計 make one's own living; shift for oneself; support oneself;

[生薑] green ginger;
生薑老的辣，奸人老的滑 an old fox needs no craft; old foxes want no tutors;

[生境] habitat;
生境變壞 habitat deterioration;
生境退化 habitat deterioration;
生境型 site type;
生境因素 site factor;
複合生境 complex habitat;
河牀生境 channel habitat;
水生生境 aquatic habitat;

[生聚] grow in population and accumulate a fortune;
生聚教訓 lick one's wound;

[生客] new guest; stranger; unfamiliar guest;

[生恐] very apprehensive;

[生來] (1) born with; by birth; inborn; (2) since one's birth;
生來記憶好 born with a good memory;
生來體弱 delicate from birth;

[生冷] uncooked and cold;

[生理] physiology;
生理反應 physiological reaction;
生理年齡 physiological age;
生理時鐘 biological clock; body clock;
生理學 physiology;
~比較生理學 comparative physiology;
~電生理學 electrophysiology;
~動物生理學 animal physiology; zoonomy; zoophysiology;
~解剖生理學 anatomical physiology;
~適應生理學 adaptation physiology;
~細胞生理學 cell physiology; cellular physiology;
~應用生理學 applied physiology;
~植物生理學 plant physiology;
生理要求 physiological requirement;
生理語言學 bio-linguistics;

[生力軍] (1) fresh troops; (2) new force;

[生利] (1) bear interest; (2) make profit;

[生憐] have tender affection for;

[生靈] living beings; the people;
生靈荼毒 plunge the people into the depths of suffering;
生靈荼炭 people in great affliction; plunge the people into misery and suffering; ruin is spelled on the people;

[生路] (1) a way to make a living; a way to survive; means of livelihood; way out; (2) strange road; unfamiliar road;

[生滅] birth and death;
不生不滅 neither created nor destroyed;
自生自滅 abandon sb to his fate; emerge of itself and perish of itself; grow and die without outside interference; run its course;

[生民] people; populace;

[生命] life;
生命安全 safety of life;
~保證生命安全 ensure the safety of human life;
生命本能 life instinct;
生命產生 biophoiesis;
生命層 biosphere;
生命單元 bion;

生命的奧秘 mystery of life;
生命規律學 bionomy;
生命跡象 sign of life;
生命科學 life science;
生命力 bioenergy; breath; life-force; spirit; vitality;
生命圈 lebenskreis;
生命維持系統 life support system;
生命系統 biological system;
生命線 lifeblood; lifeline;
生命悠關 life or death; vital; vitally important;
生命之水 water of life;
生命之虞 at the peril of one's life; in danger of losing one's life;
愛惜生命 value one's life;
寶貴的生命 valuable life;
~浪費寶貴的生命 waste valuable lives;
熱愛生命 have a lust for life;
失去生命 lose one's life;
無生命 lifeless;
~無生命的 inanimate;
虛擲生命 burn one's candle at both ends;
延長生命 prolongation of life;

[生母] one's own mother;

[生怕] for fear that; lest; so as not to;
生怕失敗 for fear of failure;

[生癖] not frequently seen; uncommon; unusual;
生僻的字眼 rarely used words;

[生平] (1) all one's life; in the course of life; life-time; (2) biographical sketch;
生平不作虧心事，夜半敲門不吃驚 a good conscience is a soft pillow; if all your life you have had a clear conscience, you need not fear a knock at the door at midnight;
生平大志 great wish of one's life;
生平故事 life story;
生平事蹟 one's life story;
生平快事 most delightful experience in one's life;
生平素志 one's lifelong wish;
生平心願 ambition of a lifetime;

[生氣] (1) angry; angry about sb; angry at sb; annoyed; be fed up; be fed up to the eyelids; be fed up to the gills; be fed up to the teeth; be filled with fury; be incensed against; be incensed at; be incensed by; be incensed with sb; be offended with sb; become angry; become livid; beside oneself with anger; blow a fuse; blow a gasket; blow off steam; blow one's cool; blow one's top; blow one's stack; bluster oneself into anger; boil over; boil with rage; bridle with anger; bristle with anger; buck up rough; burn; burn with anger; burn with wrath; bust a blood vessel; call sb down; create a scene; cross; cross as two sticks; cross with sb; cut up rough; down on sb; enraged; exasperated; fall into a rage; fire up; flare up; flip one's lid; flip one's raspberry; fly into a fury; fly into a passion; fly into a rage; fly into a temper; fly off the handle; foam at the mouth; fretful; fumed; furious; get a miff; get angry at sb; get angry with sb; get back at; get cross with sb; get hot under the collar; get into a huff; get into a passion; get mad with sb; get on one's nerves; get one's back up; get one's bristles up; get one's dander up; get one's Irish up; get one's monkey up; get one's quills up; get one's rag out; get one's own back; get out of bed on the wrong side; get someone; get someone's goat; get under sb's skin; give provocation; give sb a fit; give someone a piece of one's mind; give someone curry; give someone Larry Dooley; go crook at sb; go off the deep end; go off the handle; go off the top; go to market; grab for altitude; grow hot under the collar; have a fit; have a hemorrhage; have a miff; heat; huff; in a huff; in a passion; in a pet; in a rage with sb; in a stew; in a temper; in a thundering rage; in a tiff; in one of one's furies; in temper; in the sulks; incense; indignant at sth; irritate; kick up a row; kick up a shindy; kick up rough; lay out in lavender; lay someone out; let sb have it; livid; lock horns; look black; lose control; lose one's rag; lose one's temper; mad about; mad with sb; make a scene; make angry; make one's blood boil; miff; one's back is up; out of temper; peevish; pitch into; play sb up; put one's back up; put one's hackles up; put one's Irish up; put sb into a huff; raise Cain; rattle; red in the face; red with anger; rub sb with wrong way; ruffle one's feathers; ruffled; see red; seethe; set one's back up; set one's teeth on edge; show one's wrath on sb; sizzle; slip off the handle; spit nails; spitfire; spleen; stick in sb's crop; take amiss; take umbrage; take a miff; take a pique against sb; take huff; take offence at; take sth amiss; take the pet; take umbrage; tell someone off; throw a scene; thunder at a person; tick off; touch one home; under provocation; vent one's wrath on sb; vexed; white with anger; white with rage; (2) ; liveliness; vitality;

生氣盎然 brim over with life; full of vigour;

生氣勃勃 alive with activity; dynamic; full of animal spirit; full of life; full of vitality; vivid with life; with telling effect;

~生氣勃勃，蒸蒸日上 full of vitality, thriving with each passing day;

生氣的 pissy; steamed-up;

生氣蓬勃 active; dynamic and vigorous; full of life and vigour; lively; vigorous;

生氣極了 angry isn't the word for it;

暗暗生氣 be inwardly angry;

別為這事這麼生氣 don't get so steamed-up about it;

非常生氣 be mortally offended; have a cow; very angry;

虎虎有生氣 full of vim and vigour; vigorous and energetic;

叫人生氣 tee sb off;

惹人生氣 make a person angry;

容易生氣 be easily offended;

使生氣 antagonize;

越發生氣 grow doubly angry;

[生前] before one's death; during one's lifetime; while one was alive;

生前死後 alive or dead; during life and after death;

生前友好 friends of the deceased;

生前注定 predestined in previous incarnation;

[生擒] capture alive; take sb alive;

生擒活捉 capture alive;

[生趣] joy of life; pleasure of life;

了無生趣 lose all interest in life;

[生人] stranger;

辨認生人 distinguish strangers;

[生日] birthday;

生日蛋糕 birthday cake;

生日賀卡 birthday card;

生日快樂 happy birthday; many happy returns;

~祝你生日快樂 happy birthday; many happy returns;

生日禮物 birthday gift; birthday present;

生日派對 birthday party;

生日慶祝活動 birthday celebrations;

百歲生日 one's hundredth birthday;

過生日 keep a birthday; observe a birthday;

慶祝生日 celebrate one's birthday;

做生日 celebrate one's birthday; give a birthday party;

[生肉] uncooked meat;

[生色] add colour to; add lustre to; add splendour; give added significance to;

大為生色 give colour to;

[生澀] choppy; jerky; lacking in fluency; not smooth;

[生殺予奪] have sb completely in one's power; have sb's fate in one's hands; have sb's life and property at one's disposal; hold power over sb's life and property;

[生生] continuous reproduction;

生生不息 continuous reproduction breed in an endless succession; life and growth in nature;

生生不已 the lives of living brings go on without end; the new superseding the old without end;

生生世世 generation after generation;

[生事] create a disturbance; give rise to disturbance; make trouble;

生事作耗 instigate incidents and make trouble;

[生手] beginner; greenhorn; new learner; novice; tyro; inexperienced head; green at; sb new to a job;

[生受] bear; suffer;

[生疏] (1) disacquaintance; not familiar;

unfamiliar; strange; (2) out of practice; rusty; (3) not as close as before; not on intimate terms;

[生絲] raw silk;

[生死] life and death;

生死搏斗 life-and-death struggle; struggle for existence;

生死不明 not knowing whether one is dead or alive;

生死不忘 will never forget as long as one lives;

生死存亡 die or not; life or death;

生死度外 face death with indifference; without any regard for one's own life;

生死關頭 a critical juncture; a life-and-death choice; a life-or-death crisis; a matter of life or death; a moment when one's fate hangs in the balance; an important juncture of life and death; one's fate hangs in the balance;

生死未卜 hard to tell whether the person is alive or not; whether the person will survive is uncertain;

生死相依 stick together with sb in life and death;

生死由命，富貴在天 life and death are all according to destiny, and wealth and title are decreed by heaven; life and death are decreed by fate, rank and riches determined by heaven; life and death are preordained, wealth and honour come from heaven;

生死有命 life and death are decreed by fate; life and death lie in the lap of the gods; the number of one's days is fixed;

生死與共 go through thick and thin together; live or die together; live or die with sb; share a common destiny; stick together in life and death; with a common destiny;

生死之交 a friend until death; a friendship of life and death; be sworn to live or die together; friends who are ready to die for each other;

從生到死 from cradle to grave; from the womb to the tomb;

九死一生 a close call; a close shave; a hairbreadth escape; a narrow escape from death; a near go; a near touch; a ten percent chance to survive; a tight squeeze; escape by a hairbreadth; have a narrow escape; nine chances to die and one chance to live; survive all perils; the chances of survival are very slim;

生不帶來，死不帶去 at birth, we bring nothing, at death we take away nothing; man brings nothing at birth, and at death takes away nothing; one does not bring anything when one comes into the world, nor does one take anything when one leaves it; you can't take it with you;

生寄死歸 life is a temporary residence and death is returning home; to live is like being a lodger in the world, and to die is like returning home;

生老病死 birth, age, illness and death; birth, death, illness and old age;

生拖死拽 drag by force more dead than alive;

誓同生死 pledge ourselves to live and die together;

同生共死 live and die together; live and die with sb; share life and death with sb;

同生死，共患難 share weal and woe;

有其生必有其死 what has life must also die;

自生到死 from birth till death; from cradle to grave; from the cradle to the grave; from the womb to the tomb;

醉生夢死 dream away one's life; fiddle while Rome is burning; go on the batter; lead a befuddled life; live a befuddled life; revel away the time; sleep away one's life;

[生態] ecology;

生態安全 ecological security;

~集體生態安全 collective ecological security;

生態變種選擇 ecotypical selection;

生態表型 ecophenotype;

生態層 ecophere;

生態城 ecotown;

生態村 ecovillage;

生態大災難 ecocatastrophe;

生態地理 ecogeography;

生態發展 eco-development;

生態分布 ecological distribution;

生態幅度 ecological range;

生態革命 ecological revolution;

生態工程 ecological engineering;
生態觀 ecological outlook;
生態環境 ecological condition; ecological environment; ecotope;
~保護生態環境 preserve the ecological environment;
生態活性論 eco-activism;
生態價 ecological value;
生態經濟 eco-economy; ecological economy;
~生態經濟綜合效益 eco-economic comprehensive benefit;
生態滅絕 ecocide;
生態農業 ecological agriculture;
生態平衡 balance of nature; ecological balance;
~保持生態平衡 keep the balance of nature;
生態評價 ecological assessment;
生態氣候 ecoclimate; ecological climate;
~生態氣候學 ecoclimatology;
生態生理學 ecophysiology;
生態同類群 ecodeme;
生態危機 ecological crisis;
生態系列 ecological spectrum;
生態系統 ecosystem;
~淡水生態系統 freshwater ecosystem;
~動態生態系統 dynamic ecosystem;
~農業生態系統 agricultural ecosystem;
~群落生態系統 community ecosystem;
生態小生境 ecological niche;
生態效益 ecological effect;
生態型 ecotype;
~生物生態型 biotic ecotype;
~土壤生態型 edaphic ecotype;
~沼澤生態型 swamp ecotype;
生態休閒 ecofallow;
生態學 ecology;
~生態學家 ecologist;
~生態學者 ecologist;
~草地生態學 grassland ecology;
~地文生態學 physiographic ecology;
~動態生態學 dynamic ecology;
~動物生態學 animal ecology; zooecology;
~淡水生態學 freshwater ecology;
~港灣生態學 estuarine ecology;
~個體生態學 autecology; individual ecology;
~古生態學 palaecology;
~海岸生態學 coast ecology;
~海洋生態學 marine ecology;
~核生態學 nuclear ecology;
~化學生態學 chemical ecology;
~環境生態學 ecology;
~昆蟲生態學 insect ecology;
~理論生態學 theoretical ecology;
~陸地生態學 terrestrial ecology;
~描述生態學 descriptive ecology;
~鳥類生態學 bird ecology;
~全球生態學 global ecology;
~群落生態學 synecology;
~人類生態學 anthropoecology; human ecology;
~森林生態學 forest ecology;
~生理生態學 physiological ecology;
~生態系統生態學 ecosystem ecology;
~生物地球化學生態學 biogeochemical ecology;
~生物生態學 bioecology;
~文藝生態學 ecology of art and literature;
~物理生態學 physical ecology;
~溪流生態學 stream ecology;
~行星生態學 planetary ecology;
~醫用生態學 medical ecology;
~應用生態學 applied ecology;
~幼蟲生態學 larval ecology;
~遠洋深海生態學 abyssopelagic ecology;
~植物生態學 phytoecology; plant ecology;
~作物生態學 crop ecology;
生態意識 ecological awareness;
生態災害類型 types of ecological disaster;
生態災難 ecological disaster;
生態政策 ecopolicy;
生態種 ecospecies;
生態宗 ecological race;

[生徒] pupils; students;

[生吞活剝] force an interpretation of text without understanding; gulp sth down uncritically;
活剝生吞 accept...uncritically; interpret the text crudely without real understanding; skin alive and gulp down; swallow sth raw and whole; transplant indiscriminately;

[生物] (1) animate object; living things; (2) biology; (3) organism;
生物胞素 biocytin;
~生物胞素酶 biocytinase;
生物病 bionosis;

~生物病原 biopathogen;
生物材料 biomaterial;
生物測量 biomeasurement;
生物產業 bioindustry;
生物沉澱作用 bioprecipitation;
生物傳感連接器 bioconnector;
生物艙 biocabin; biopak;
生物層 biostrome;
生物處理 biotreatment;
生物磁學 biomagnetism;
生物催化 biocatalysis;
~生物催化劑 biocatalyst;
生物帶 biozone;
~複合生物帶 composite biozone;
生物地層學 biostratigraphy;
生物地球化學 biogeochemistry;
生物電池 bio-battery; biocell;
~海洋生物電池 marine biocell;
生物電控制 biocontrol;
生物電流 biocurrent;
~腦生物電流 cerebral biocurrent;
生物電路芯片 biochip;
生物電勢 bioelectric potential; biopotential;
生物電 bioelectricity;
~生物電發生 bioelectrogenesis;
~生物電化學 bioelectrochemistry;
~生物電極 bioelectrode;
~生物電療 biogalvanic source;
~生物電流 bioelectric current;
~生物電勢 bioelectric potential; biopotential;
~生物電學 bioelectricity;
~生物電源 biogalvanic source; biopower;
~生物電子學 bioelectronics;
生物動力學 biodynamics;
生物發光 bioluminescence; biophotogenesis;
~生物發光現象 biological luminescence;
生物反饋 biofeedback;
生物反應器 bioreactor;
生物防禦 biophylaxis;
生物仿真 biosimulation;
生物分解 biolysis;
生物分類學 biotaxy;
生物分析 bioanalysis;
生物分子 biomolecule;
生物浮游物 bioseston;
生物沸石 biozeolite;
生物高分子 biological high polymer;
生物隔離 biological isolation;
生物工程 bioengineering;
~生物工程經濟 bioengineering economy;
~生物工程學 bioengineering;
生物工藝學 biotechnology;
生物過濾 biofiltration;
~生物過濾器 biofilter;
生物航行 bionavigation;
生物合成 biosynthesis;
~誘變生物合成 mutational biosynthesis;
生物化學 biochemistry;
~分子生物化學 molecular biochemistry;
~輻射生物化學 radiation biochemistry;
~海洋生物化學 marine biochemistry;
~細胞生物化學 cellular biochemistry;
~有機生物化學 organic biochemistry;
生物活度 biological activity;
生物活性 biological activity;
~生物活性劑 bioactivator;
生物計 biometer;
~生物計劃 bio-programme;
~生物計算機 bio-computer; biological computer;
生物技術 biotechnology;
~生物技術產業 biotechnology industry;
~生物技術企業 biobusiness;
生物劑量學 biodosimetry;
生物監測 biological monitoring;
生物監定 bioassay;
生物降解 biodegradation;
~生物降解能力 biodegradability;
生物礁 bioherm;
生物膠 biogum;
生物結石 biolith;
生物節律 biological rhythm;
生物解剖學 biotomy;
生物晶體學 biocrystallography;
生物淨化 biological purification;
生物靜力學 biostatics;
生物科學 bioscience;
生物控制論 biocybernetics;
生物力學 biomechanics;
生物鏈 biological chain;
生物量 biomass;
~群落生物量 community biomass;
~生理生物量 physiological biomass;
~微生物量 microbial biomass;
生物療法 biotherapy;
生物流變學 biorheology;
生物倫理學 bioethics;
生物論 biognosis;
生物膜 biomembrane;
生物能 bioenergy;
~生物能量學 bioenergy;

S

生物擬態 biomimesis;
生物年代 biochron;
~ 生物年代型 biochronotype;
~ 生物年代學 biochronology;
生物平衡 biobalance;
生物氣候 bioclimate;
~ 生物氣候圖 bioclimatograph;
~ 生物氣候學 bioclimatology;
生物氣體 biogas;
生物氣象學 biometeorology;
生物侵蝕 bioerosion;
生物區 biota;
~ 海洋生物區 marine biota;
生物圈 biosphere;
~ 海洋生物圈 marine biosphere;
生物全息技術 biological hologram technique;
生物群落 biocenose; biocenosis; biome;
~ 生物群落型 biome type; biorealm;
~ 生物群落學 biocenology;
~ 草地生物群落 grassland biome;
~ 凍原生物群落 tundra biome;
~ 亞生物群落 biociation;
生物色素 biochrome;
生物殺滅劑 biocide;
生物社會學 biosociology;
生物生理學 biophysiology;
生物聲納 biosonar;
生物聲學 bioacoustics;
生物實驗室 biological laboratory;
生物適應性 biocompatibility;
生物受感器 biosensor;
生物數學 biomathematics;
生物水平面 biolevel;
生物素 biotin;
生物碎屑 biodetritus;
生物陶瓷 bioceramics;
生物體 biosome;
生物天文物理學 bioastrophysics;
生物條件 biological conditions;
生物通氣 bioaeration;
生物同位素 bioisotope;
生物統計學 biostatistics;
生物透析液 biodialysate;
生物拓樸學 biotopology;
生物危害 biohazard;
生物微型化 biomicrominiaturization;
生物衛星 biosatellite;
生物溫度 biotemperature;
生物穩定劑 biostabilizer;
生物物理學 biophysics;
~ 生物物理學家 biophysicist;
生物霧 biofog;
生物系列 bioseries;
生物系統 biosystem;
~ 生物系統學 biosystematics; biosystematy;
生物系統學家 biosystematist;
生物相 biofacies;
生物心理學 biopsychology;
生物學 biology;
~ 生物學者 biologist;
~ 淡水生物學 freshwater biology;
~ 洞穴生物學 biospeleology;
~ 發生生物學 developmental biology;
~ 放射生物學 bioradiology; radiation biology;
~ 非生物學 abiology;
~ 分子生物學 molecular biology;
~ 古生物學 palaeontology;
~ 光化生物學 actinobiology;
~ 光生物學 photobiology;
~ 海洋生物學 marine biology;
~ 化學生物學 chemical biology;
~ 環境生物學 environmental biology;
~ 教育生物學 educational biology;
~ 精神生物學 psychobiology;
~ 空氣生物學 aerobiology;
~ 量子生物學 quantum biology;
~ 農業生物學 agrobiology;
~ 群體生物學 population biology;
~ 人類生物學 anthropobiology;
~ 生殖生物學 reproductive biology;
~ 室內空氣生物學 intramural aerobiology;
~ 室外空氣生物學 extramural aerobiology;
~ 實驗生物學 experimental biology;
~ 數學生物學 mathematical biology;
~ 水生生物學 aquatic biology;
~ 天體生物學 astrobiology;
~ 外太空生物學 exobiology;
~ 微生物學 microbiology;
~ 無機生物學 abiophysiology;
~ 細胞生物學 cell biology;
~ 心理生物學 psychobiology;
~ 新生物學 neontology;
~ 宇航生物學 space biology;
生物岩 biolith;
~ 生物岩類 biolithite;
~ 非可燃性生物岩 acaustobiolith;
生物遙測器 biopack;
生物遙測術 biotelemetry;
~ 海洋生物遙測術 marine biotelemetry;

生物藥劑學 biomedicine;
生物儀器 bio-instrument;
生物印痕 bioglyph;
生物宇宙航行學 bioastronautics; biocosmonautics;
生物語言學 biolinguistics;
生物元素 bioelement;
生物製劑 biological agent; biologics; biopreparate;
生物製品 biotic preparation;
生物鐘 biochronometer; biological clock;
~生物鐘學 biochronometry;
生物周期 biocycle;
生物主義者 biocrat;
生物轉化 bioconversion; biotransformation;
生物自衛 biophilia;
超級生物 superanimal;
底棲生物 benthos;
~定居底棲生物 sedentary benthos;
~海洋底棲生物 marine benthos;
~游移底棲生物 vagrant benthos;
非生物 inanimate object;
浮游生物 floating organism;
古生物 ancient extinct life;
~古生物化學 fossils of ancient extinct life;
~古生物學 palaeontology;
廣溫性生物 eurythermal organism;
廣鹽性生物 euryhaline organism;
海底生物 benthos;
化能生物 chemoheterotroph;
微生物 microbe; microorganism;
厭氣生物 anaerobic organisms;
游泳生物 swimming organism;
遠洋生物 pelagic organism;

[生息] (1) bear interest; (2) exist; grow; live; multiply; propagate;

[生效] become effective; come into effect; come into force; come into operation; effective; enter into force; go into effect; take effect; valid;
一月一日起生效 effective 1 January;

[生心] disloyal to;

[生性] (1) affinity; by nature; natural disposition; nature; (2) aloof; unfriendly;
生性傲慢 immodest personality; imperious by nature;
生性暴戾 of a violent temper;
生性膽怯 timid of disposition;
生性多疑 prone to suspicion;
生性固執 stubborn by nature;
生性活潑 have a lively disposition;
生活謹慎 of a reserved disposition;
生性懦弱 rather soft and tender-hearted by nature;
生性嗜權 have an affinity for power;

[生鏽] get rusty; rust; rustines;
容易生鏽 get rusty easily;
鐵不磨生鏽，水不流發臭 iron grows rusty without whetting, water becomes stale without running;

[生涯] (1) career; life; profession; (2) livelihood;

[生厭] become bored; become tired of sth;
令人生厭 irksome;

[生養] give birth to and bring up children;
生養死葬 nourish one's relatives while alive and bury them when dead;

[生業] business;
各安生業 follow one's usual pursuits;

[生疑] become suspicious; suspicious;

[生意] (1) life and vitality; tendency to grow; (2) business; business deal; trade;
生意盎然 full of life;
生意不景氣 business is lagging;
生意經 businessmen's talk;
生意清淡 business is dull;
生意人 businessman; business person;
~有錢的生意人 well-heeled businessman;
生意蕭條 business is bad; business is stagnant;
生意興隆 brisk business; booming business; business is booming; prosperous trade; trade is brisk;
生意興隆通四海，財源茂盛達三江 prosperity in business reaches the four seas, financial resources come from the three rivers;
兜生意 solicit trade;
經營生意 operate a business;
拉生意 solicit business; tout for business;
搶生意 compete for business; hustle; undercut;
小生意 small business;
一筆生意 a business deal;
做生意 conduct business; do business; do business transactions;

[生硬] arbitrary; awkward; inflexible; rigid; stiff;

生硬的 gruff;
生拉硬曳 drag sb along against his will; drag sb along kicking and screaming; stretch the meaning;
態度生硬 stiff in manner;

[生有涯而知無涯] art is long, life is short; life is limited, but knowledge is limitless;

[生育] bear; give birth to;
生育力 fecundity; fertility;
~分組生育力 cohort fertility;
~同年代人生育力 generation fertility;
生育率 birth rate; fertility;
~世界生育率 world fertility;
~有效生育率 effective fertility;
生育能力 fertility;
生育藥 fertility drug;
生育子女 bear children;
不能生育 generational sterility;
節制生育 birth control;
計劃生育 family planning;

[生源] biogenic;
生源説 biogenesis;
~無生源説 abiogenesis;
~有生源説 biogenesis;

[生長] develop; grow; grow up; growth;
生長茂密 grow densely;
生長茂盛 grow abundantly;
生長曲線 curve of growth;
生長痛 growing pains;
生長因數 growth factor;
苦裏生，甜裏長 be born in misery but brough up in happiness;
畸型生長 grow abnormally;
生殖生長 reproductive growth;
水溶液生長 aqueous solution growth;
吞併生長 cannibal growth;
土生土長 born and brought up in one's native land; born and brought up in the locality; home-born; native-born;
外加生長 appositional growth;
異常生長 abnormal growth;
營養生長 vegetative growth;

[生殖] engender; generate; procreation; reproduction;
生殖管 gonaduct;
生殖力 fecundity; reproduction;
生殖器 genital organs; genitals; reproductive organs;
~生殖器肥大 edeauxe; genital hypertrophy;
~生殖器發育不全 agenosomia;
~生殖器發育過度 hypergenitalism;
~生殖器發育障礙 dysgenitalism;
~生殖器官 reproductive organ;
~生殖器過小 microgenitalism;
~男性生殖器 male genital organs;
~女生殖器 muliebria;
~無生殖器 agenosomia;
生殖細胞 generative cell; reproductive cell; sex cell;
單親生殖 monogenetic reproduction; monogony; parthenogenesis;
~產雄單親生殖 androgenetic parthenogenesis;
~人工單親生殖 artificial parthenogenesis;
~周性單親生殖 cyclical parthenogenesis;
單性生殖 parthenogenesis; parthenogeny;
~單性生殖世代 parthenogenetic generation;
分裂生殖 schizogamy; schizogenesis;
輔助生殖 assisted reproduction;
兩性生殖 zoogamy;
配子生殖 gametic reproduction;
同配生殖 homogamy;
無性生殖 agamogenesis; asexual reproduction; monogony;
~無性生殖單體 parthenogonidium;
雄性生殖 arrhenotoky;
異配生殖 heterogamy;
有性生殖 sexual reproduction; zoogamy;

[生子] give birth to a child;
私生子 adulterine child; babe of love; child born out of wedlock; illegitimate child; love child; natural child;

[生字] new word; unfamiliar word;

安生 (1) quiet; still; (2) peaceful; restful; (3) live in peace;
白生生 as white as snow; white and delicate;
半生 (1) half a lifetime; (2) half-baked; half-raw; not well cooked;
畢生 all one's life; in one's whole life; lifelong; lifetime; throughout one's lifetime;
畢業生 graduate;
殘生 (1) declining years; one's remaining years; (2) survivor;
蒼生 common people;
插班生 student who joins a class in the middle of the course;
產生 (1) engender; produce; (2) come into being; emerge;
長生 long life; longevity;
超生 excuse from death; spare life;

出生 be born; be sent into the world; come into the world; see the light of day;
初生 (1) primary; nascent; (2) newborn;
畜生 (1) domestic animal; (2) beast; dirty swine;
此生 one's life;
叢生 (1) clump; grow thickly; overgrow; (2) break out;
次生 secondary;
催生 expedite child delivery; hasten parturition;
脆生 (1) crisp; (2) gentleman; mister; sir;
翠生生 fresh and green;
大學生 university student;
誕生 be born; come into being; come into existence; come into the world; emerge;
獨生 the only child born into the family;
對生 opposite;
耳生 strange-sounding; unfamiliar to the ear;
發生 arise; come about; come over; come to pass; come up; fall out; go off; go on; happen; occur; spring up; take place; turn up;
仿生 bionic;
放生 (1) free captive animals; (2) buy captive fish or birds and set them free;
腐生 saprophytism;
復生 become alive again;
高才生 brilliant student;
更生 (1) regenerate; revive; (2) renew;
工讀生 part-time worker student;
公費生 student supported by the state;
共生 (1) intergrowth; paragenesis; (2) symbiosis;
骨發生 osteogenesis; ostosis;
好生 (1) exceedingly; quite; (2) carefully; properly;
橫生 (1) grow wild; (2) be full of; be overflowing with; (3) happen unexpectedly;
後生 have a youthful appearance; lad; young;
互生 intergrowth;
花生 earth chestnut; groundnut; peanut;
化生 metaplasia;
回生 (1) bring back to life; (2) forget through lack of practice; get rusty;
活生生 (1) actual; alive; alive and kicking; in real life; living; real; (2) while still alive;
寄生 (1) (of plants and animals) live on or within another organism; (2) lead a parasitic life;
寄宿生 boarder; resident student;
夾生 half-baked; half-cooked;
降生 (of a founder of a religion, etc.) be born;
接生 deliver; deliver a child; practise midwifery;
接線生 telephone operator;
今生 this life;
救生 lifesaving;
考生 candidate; examinee;
來生 afterlife; next life; next world; the other world; the world to be; the world to come;
練習生 trainee;
廩生 scholars who live on government grants;
留級生 students who fail to go up to the next grade;
留學生 students studying abroad;
孿生 bear twins; born as twins; twinning
落花生 groundnut; peanut;
輪生 verticillate;
蔓生 overgrow; trail;
門生 disciple; pupil;
萌生 germinate; sprout;
面生 look unfamiliar;
民生 people's livelihood;
陌生 strange; unfamiliar;
謀生 make a living; seek a livelihood;
男生 boy student; man student; schoolboy;
囊生 domestic slave of a Tibetan slave-owner;
內生 endogenous;
女生 girl; girl student; schoolgirl; woman student;
怕生 shy in the presence of strangers; shy with strangers;
派生 derivative; derive from;
旁聽生 auditor;
平生 all one's life; always; at all times; one's whole life;
欺生 (1) bully newcomers; bully strangers; cheat newcomers; cheat strangers; (2) intractable by strangers; uncontrollable by strangers; ungovernable by strangers; unmanageable by strangers;
前生 former life; prelife; previous incarnation;
親生 one's own (children, parents);
輕生 commit suicide; make light of one's life;
求生 seek to live on; seek to survive; try to remain alive;
人生 human life; life;
儒生 Confucian scholar;
三生 three incarnations – the past, the present and the future;
喪生 lose one's life;
殺生 kill livestock, fowls, etc.;
繕生 cultivate life for health;
傷生 do harm to sb's life;
捨生 sacrifice one's life;
攝生 keep fit;
師生 teachers and students;
實習生 trainee;

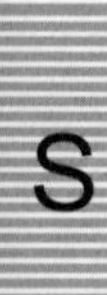

侍應生 attendant; waiter;
收生 practise midwifery;
手生 lack practice and skill; out of practice;
書生 intellectual; scholar;
雙生 twins;
死生 dead or alive;
胎生 viviparity; zoogony;
貪生 care for nothing but saving one's skin; cravenly cling to life;
逃生 escape with one's life; flee for one's life;
天生 be born with; bred in the bone; congenital; inborn; inherent; innate; natural;
偷生 drag out an ignoble existence; have no ambition than just to get by; lead an ignoble existence; live on without meaning; live on without purpose;
頭生 firstborn;
投生 be reborn; be reincarnated in a new body;
為生 make a living;
衛生 health; hygiene; hygienic; sanitation;
寤生 give birth to a baby while asleep;
先生 (1) teacher; (2) gentleman; mister; sir; (3) doctor;
現生 the present incarnation; this present life;
庠生 student of a prefectural county school;
小生 (1) young male actor in Chinese operas; (2) your pupil;
小學生 schoolchild;
寫生 paint from life or nature;
新生 (1) newborn; newly born; (2) new life; rebirth; regeneration; (3) new student;
鬚生 bearded character;
學生 (1) pupil; student; (2) disciple; follower;
牙發生 odontogenesis;
衍生 drive;
眼生 look unfamiliar; unfamiliar by sight;
養生 keep in good condition; keep in good health; nourishing of life; preserve one's health;
野生 uncultivated; undomesticated; wild;
一生 all one's life; from the womb to the tomb; lifetime; throughout one's life;
醫生 doc; doctor; medic; medical doctor; medical practitioner; medico; physician; surgeon;
佾生 boy dancers;
營生 earn a living; make a living;
永生 (1) eternal life; (2) immortal;
優生 eugenics;
有生 birth; in one's remaining years;
餘生 (1) remainder of one's life; (2) survival;
再生 (1) come to life again; (2) regenerate; (3) regenerate; reprocess;
怎生 how;
增生 hyperplasia; multiplicate; proliferate;
招生 enrol new students; recruit students;
治生 make a living;
中學生 middle school student; secondary school student;
終生 all one's life; one's whole life; throughout one's life;
眾生 all living creatures; all sentient beings;
諸生 all the students;
住校生 boarder;
轉生 reincarnate;
孳生 breed; grow and multiply; multiply; propagate;
滋生 (1) breed; multiply; propagate; reproduce in large numbers; (2) cause; create; provoke;
資優生 bright student;
鯫生 (1) contemptible fellow; (2) my humble self;
走讀生 non-resident student;
尊生 respect life;

sheng

【昇】 (1) ascend; (2) peace; (3) a surname;
［昇格］ elevation of status;
［昇華］ sublimation;
［昇級］ advance to a higher class; be promoted; promote;
［昇降］ promotion and demotion;
昇降機 elevator;
昇降設備 lifting appliance;
［昇天］ ascend to heaven;

sheng

【牲】 livestock;
［牲畜］ domestic animals; livestock;
良種牲畜 well-bred beast;
飼養牲畜 breed cattle;
屠宰牲畜 slaughter a beast;
［牲口］ livestock;

三牲 three sacrifices;
犧牲 (1) sacrifice oneself; (2) do sth at the expense of;

sheng

【陞】 (1) same as 昇一 ascend; elevate; hoist; promote; rise; (2) a surname;

sheng

【笙】 reep pipe wind instrument;
［笙歌］ music and songs; playing and singing;

笙歌不夜 fluting and singing are heard all night; music and songs are kept up throughout the night;

[笙管] pipes of a reep pipe wind instrument;
笙簫管笛 flutes and pipes;

[笙簧] reeds of a reep pipe wind instrument;

蘆笙 reed pipe wind instrument;
排笙 reed pipe wind instrument with a keyboard;

sheng

【勝】 competent enough;

[勝冠] at the age of twenty;

[勝任] competence; competent; equal to; qualified;
勝任的 competent;
勝任愉快 adequate for and happy with a job;
才不勝任 an ability inadequate for the position; incompetent; talents not equal to the post;
力不勝任 beyond one's ability; beyond one's capacity; beyond one's competence; beyond one's reach; bite off more than one can chew; out of one's reach; unequal to one's task; without the required ability to undertake a given task;
力能勝任 competent at; strong enough to deal with sth;

sheng

【甥】 (1) nephew; (2) son-in-law;

[甥兒] nephew; sister's son;

[甥女] niece; sister's daughter;

[甥孫] grandnephew; grandniece;

sheng

【聲】 (1) sound; tune; voice; (2) make a sound; (3) music; (4) initial consonant; (5) tone; (6) fame; reputation;

[聲波] acoustic wave; sonic wave; sound wave;
超聲波 supersonic wave; ultrasonic wave;
~超聲波發射器 ultrasound transmitting transducer;
~超聲波發生器 ultrasonic generator;
~超聲波接收器 ultrasonic receiver;
~超聲波探傷器 ultrasonic reflectoscope;
~超聲波洗滌 ultrasonic cleaning;
低聲波 infrasonic wave;

[聲稱] assert; claim; declare; make an allegation; proclaim;
一致聲稱 declare with one accord;

[聲帶] (1) vocal cord; (2) sound tape;
聲帶麻痺 vocal cord paralysis;
聲帶疲勞 vocal fatigue;
聲帶炎 chorditis;
~結節性聲帶炎 chorditis tuberosa;
原聲帶 original sound tape;

[聲調] note; pitch of voice; tone;
聲調低沉 in a low, sad voice;
聲調激昂 in an impassioned tone;
聲調語言 language of tone;

[聲光] (1) reputation; (2) sound and light;
聲光學 acousto-optics;

[聲華] good reputation;

[聲喚] call aloud; shout;

[聲價] fame of a person;
聲價甚高 be held in high esteem; be held in high repute; of great celebrity;
聲價十倍 one's reputation is tenfold higher;

[聲控] audio-controlled;
聲控撥電話 voice dialling;
聲控自動錄音系統 voice activated system;

[聲浪] clamour; voice;

[聲淚俱下] cry while speaking; in a tearful voice; make a pitiful plea;

[聲名] fame; reputation;
聲名大振 one's reputation be greatly boosted;
聲名赫赫 be held in good repute; gain a high reputation; have an awe-inspiring fame; illustrious;
聲名狼籍 bad reputation; be badly discredited; be reported of; be held in ill repute; be ill reputed; be utterly discredited; cloudy reputation; fall into discredit; gain extreme notoriety; have a bad name; in bad odour; in disrepute; infamous; notorious; notorious reputation; raffish; unsavory reputation; tear one's reputation to shreds; with an unsavory reputation;
聲名掃地 be thoroughly discredited; fall into disrepute; one's name is mud;
聲名鵲起 shoot to fame;
聲名洋溢 gain a wide reputation; one's fame spreads everywhere;
聲名遠揚 one's fame spreads far and wide;

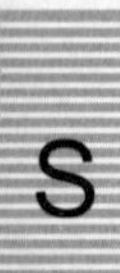

聲名載道 win popular praise;

[聲明] (1) announce; assert; declare; make a statement; state; (2) declaration; statement;

聲明在案 have a statement placed on record;

聲明贊成 declare oneself in favour of;

斷然聲明 declare positively;

發表聲明 issue a statement; make a solemn statement; make a statement;

公開聲明 public statement; state openly;

官方聲明 official statement;

簡短聲明 brief statement; short statement;

事先聲明 declare beforehand;

書面聲明 written statement;

誤導的聲明 misleading statement;

虛假聲明 false statement;

宣讀聲明 read out a statement;

一項聲明 an announcement;

一致聲明 unanimously declare;

鄭重聲明 declare solemnly;

莊嚴聲明 solemnly state;

[聲母] initial;

零聲母 zero initial;

[聲納] sonar;

聲納兵 sonarman;

飛機攜帶聲納 air transportable sonar;

陣列聲納 array sonar;

主動聲納 active sonar;

[聲能學] sonics;

[聲氣] (1) information; (2) tone; voice;

聲氣相求 birds of the same feather flock together; share the same interests and purpose;

聲氣相投 echo answers; have spiritual affinity;

粗聲粗氣 speak in an injured voice; with a deep, gruff voice;

粗聲大氣 a deep, gruff voice;

怪聲怪氣 speak in a strange voice or an affected manner;

好聲好氣 gently; in a gentle voice; in a good-natured way; in a kindly manner;

互通聲氣 exchange information; keep in contact with each other;

老聲老氣 speaking with a steady voice; the sound and look of an old person;

怯聲怯氣 in a timid and unnatural tone; lumpish;

喪聲唉氣 complaining and whining;

聲應氣求 have spiritual affinity;

甕聲甕氣 in a low, muffled voice; low sound as in an enclosure;

妖聲妖氣 speak flirtatiously;

[聲請] make requests with reasons stated;

[聲容] voices and appearances;

聲容并茂 both the rhythm and substance are flourishing in parallel;

聲容笑貌 a person's voice and expression; have a stentorian voice;

[聲如裂帛] a noise like tearing up silks; the sound is like the ripping of silk;

[聲色] (1) voice and countenance; (2) music and women;

聲色俱厲 come down hard on; come down like a ton of bricks; fulminate; severe in voice and countenance; speak in a cross tone and with a severe expression; stern both in voice and in countenance; use a severe voice and show a stern countenance;

聲色犬馬 a dissipated and luxurious life; carnal pleasures; drown oneself in sex and pleasures;

聲色自娛 amuse oneself with sensual pleasures; have one's fling; indulge oneself in song and with women;

聲色縱飲 give oneself over to debauchery and drink;

不動聲色 maintain one's composure; stay calm and collected; not bat an eyelid; not turn a hair;

不露聲色 keep a low profile; keep one's countenance; keep one's counsel; not show one's feelings; not show one's intentions; not to betray one's intentions;

繪聲繪色 hit off; a lively description; lively; vivid;

嚴聲厲色 with stern tones and severe countenance;

[聲勢] fame; impetus; influence; momentum; prestige and power;

聲勢浩大 gigantic in strength and momentum; great in strength and impetus; impressive display of power; influential; large-scale; mammoth; powerful and dynamic;

聲勢淩人 overwhelm the weaker with excessively strong language;

聲勢顯赫 have a powerful influence;

聲勢凶凶 bluster; hammer and tongs;

大張聲勢 great pageantry; put on a big show;
虛張聲勢 a pompous but empty show of power and influence; bluff; bluff and bluster; bluff purposely; bluff with a big show; empty show; flaunt one's authority; flourish one's authority; full of bravado; maintain the appearance of strength; make a deceptive show of power; make a demonstration; make a display; make a false show of strength; make an empty show of strength; make pretenses; outward demonstration; outward show; play a game of bluff; put on a bluff; run a bluff on; swank; swashbuckling; throw a bluff on;

[聲述] explain; present reasons; state reasons; tell;

[聲説] expound; narrate;

[聲嘶] hoarseness;
聲嘶力竭 exhausted from shouting; hoarse and exhausted; shout at the top of one's voice; shout oneself blue in the face; shout oneself hoarse;

[聲速] velocity of sound;

[聲討] attack verbally; condemn; denounce;
聲討會 denunciation meeting;

[聲望] cachet; fame; popularity; prestige; renown; reputation;
聲望低 sb's stock is low;
聲望高 sb' stock is high;
聲望日隆 one's reputation becomes more and more impressive;
人有聲望，其言自重 if one has a reputation, his words carry greater weight;
失去聲望 lose one's reputation;

[聲威] prestige; renown;
聲威大震 gain great fame and high prestige; gain resounding fame;

[聲聞] fame; reputation;
聲聞過情 enjoy a higher reputation than justified; the facts do not quite correspond to one's reputation;
聲聞於天 the voice is heard by heaven;

[聲問] (1) information; (2) fame; reputation;

[聲息] (1) noise; sound; voices; (2) information;
聲息相聯 keep in touch with each other;
聲息相聞 keep in touch with each other;

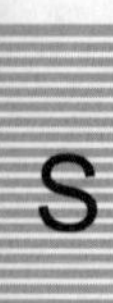

密通聲息 secretly communicate with each other;

[聲先奪人] one's name is enough to strike terror in other's hearts;

[聲響] noise; sound;
不聲不響 make no reply; mute; not making a sound; not utter a word; without saying a word;

[聲像] sound image;
聲像處理 audio-video processing;
~聲像處理系統 audio-video processing system;
~聲像處理中心 audio-video processing centre;

[聲學] acoustics; phonics;
聲學比 acoustic ratio;
聲學家 acoustician;
聲學近似 acoustic approximation;
波動聲學 wave acoustics;
大氣聲學 atmospheric acoustics;
超聲學 ultrasonics;
電聲學 electroacoustics;
非線性聲學 non-linear acoustics;
分子聲學 molecular acoustics;
工程聲學 engineering acoustics;
航空聲學 aeroacoustics; aviation acoustics;
環境聲學 environmental acoustics;
會場聲學 auditorium acoustics;
幾何聲學 geometrical acoustics;
建築聲學 architectural acoustics;
劇場聲學 theatre acoustics;
理論聲學 theoretical acoustics;
生理聲學 physiological acoustics;
生物聲學 bioacoustics;
室內聲學 room acoustics;
室外聲學 acoustics of the open air; free acoustics;
水聲學 hydroacoustics; marine acoustics;
水下聲學 underwater acoustics;
微波聲學 microwave acoustics;
物理聲學 physical acoustics;
心理聲學 psychological acoustics;
音樂聲學 musical acoustics;
音樂廳聲學 concert hall acoustics;

[聲言] announce; claim; declare; profess;

[聲音] sound; voice;
聲音合成設備 acoustic synthesizer;
聲音輕柔溫和 soft and gentle voice;
聲音笑貌 one's voice and expression;
聲音信息處理 acoustic information

processing;
聲音應答設備 audio response unit;
低沉的聲音 deep voice; low voice;
平靜的聲音 level voice;
奇怪的聲音 strange sound;
輕柔圓潤的聲音 soft and velvety voice;
提高聲音 pitch one's voice; raise one's voice;
聽到聲音 hear a sound;
一堆聲音 a babble of voices;
優美的聲音 beautiful voice;
壓低聲音 lower one's voice;

[聲譽] fame; reputation; prestige;
聲譽鵲起 become famous overnight; win one's reputation rapidly;
聲譽掃地 be discredited; blast sb's fame; come to dishonour; fall into discredit; lose all standing;
聲譽提高 grow in stature;
聲譽下降 decline in reputation;
聲譽卓著 be held in high repute; be widely known with a good reputation; enjoy a good reputation; have a good reputation;
保持聲譽 maintain a fame;
保全聲譽 preserve one's prestige;
獲得聲譽 get a reputation;
損害聲譽 damage one's reputation;
享有聲譽 win a high admiration;
贏得聲譽 win one's renown;
影響聲譽 affect one's reputation;

[聲援] express support for; give moral support; support;
聲援信 message of support;

[聲樂] vocal music;
聲樂家 vocalist;

[聲韻學] phonology;
古老聲韻學 archaic phonology;

[聲張] announce; disclose; make public;
別聲張 keep mum; mum's the word;
不得聲張 mum's the word;
不要聲張 don't let it out;

[聲罪致討] denounce the guilty and to chastise;

哀聲 mourning;
安聲 quiet; silent; still;
伴聲 sound accompaniment;
悲聲 plaintive cries; sad voice;
彩聲 acclamation; applause;
豺聲 roar as fiercely as a wild beast;
超聲 ultrasonic;
成聲 lose one's voice;
出聲 make a noise; speak; utter a sound;
傳聲 transmit sound;
次聲 infrasonic sound;
促聲 entering tone;
大聲 in a loud voice; loud;
帶聲 voiced;
得得聲 clip-clop;
低聲 in a low voice; in a whisper; under one's breath; with bated breath;
地聲 earthquake sound;
嘟嘟聲 beep; blare; toot;
發聲 phonation; vocalize;
放聲 in a loud voice;
蜚聲 become famous; make a name;
風聲 (1) sound of the wind; (2) news; rumours; talks;
高聲 sing loudly; speak loudly;
歌聲 singing; sound of singing;
隔聲 sound insulation;
鼓聲 drumbeat; tum;
鼾聲 sound of snoring;
和聲 harmony;
哼聲 hum;
齁聲 snore; sound of snoring;
喊聲 hubbub; yell;
號聲 clarion calls are sounded from all sides;
哼聲 heave ho; hum; yo-heave-ho; yo-ho;
吼聲 roar;
呼聲 cry; voice;
歡聲 cheer;
回聲 bounce back; echo;
惠聲 reputation for kindness;
貨聲 cry of one's ware;
假聲 falsetto;
尖聲 in a shrill voice;
減聲 noise abatement; noise reduction;
嬌聲 in a sweet and girlish voice;
卡嗒聲 click;
吭聲 utter a sound or a word;
哭聲 cries;
雷聲 thunder; thunderclap;
厲聲 shout angrily; talk harshly;
連聲 again and again; repeatedly;
練聲 vocalize;
鈴聲 ring tone; ringing sound of a bell; tinkle of bells;
曼聲 sind or recite in lengthened sounds;
悶聲 remain quiet;
名聲 renown; reputation; repute;
男聲 male voice;

擬聲 imitation; onomatopoeia;
女聲 female voice;
砲聲 roar of guns; sound of artillery; thunder of guns;
礮聲 roaring of artillery pieces; thunder of cannonade;
砰砰聲 bang; crack; phut;
平聲 level tone in Chinese;
七聲 seven notes of the musical scale;
齊聲 in chorus; in unison;
槍聲 the crack of a gun; the report of a gun;
悄聲 in a low voice; quietly;
輕聲 (1) hushed; in a soft voice; softly; (2) light tone;
去聲 falling tone;
人聲 voice;
柔聲 in a sweet and girlish voice;
入聲 falling-rising tone;
柔聲 in a sweet and girlish voice; soft voice;
臊聲 notoriety; scandalous reputation;
殺聲 battle cries;
哨聲 whistling;
身歷聲 high fidelity;
失聲 (1) cry out involuntarily; (2) lose one's voice;
嘶澌聲 fizz;
濤聲 surf; the sound of roaring billows;
同聲 speak at the same time; speak simultaneously;
童聲 child's voice;
吞聲 gulp down one's sobs; swallow one's sobs;
威聲 prestige;
尾聲 (1) epilogue; (2) end; (3) coda;
聞聲 hear the noise;
無聲 noiseless; silent;
吸聲 sound absorption;
細聲 very low voice;
先聲 first signs; harbinger; herald;
象聲 onomatopoeia;
響聲 noise; sound; echo;
相聲 comic dialogue; crosstalk;
消聲 noise elimination;
小聲 in a low voice; under one's breath;
笑聲 laugh; laughter; sound of laughter;
嘯聲 singing; sqeak; squeal; whistle;
心聲 aspirations; heartfelt wishes; intentions; the heart's desire; thinking; thoughts;
虛聲 (1) bluff; make a deceptive show of power; (2) empty reputation; undeserved reputation;
噓聲 breathe out slowly; catcall;
揚聲 (1) raise one's voice; (2) boast prestige;
一聲 say a word; utter a word;
怡聲 pleasing voice that is soft and tender;
逸聲 decadent music;
淫聲 lewd songs;
應聲 at the sound of;
有聲 having sound;
雨聲 sound of rain;
猿聲 gibbon's howls;
怨聲 cries of discontent;
噪聲 buzz; din; noise;
則聲 make a sound; utter a word;
仄聲 oblique tones;
掌聲 applause; clapping; the sound of clapping;
鄭聲 immoral ballads;
鐘聲 sound of tolling a bell; toll of a bell;
囀鳴聲 tweedle; warble;
吱聲 make a sound; utter sth;
縱聲 laugh at the top of one's voice; shout at the top of one's voice;
做聲 break silence; make noise; speak;

sheng
【鼪】 yellow weasel;

sheng²
sheng
【澠】 (1) a place in Henan; (2) a river and a county in Henan;

sheng
【繩】 (1) cord; line; rope; string; (2) restrain; restrict; (3) correct; rectify;
[繩尺] criterion; law; rule; standard;
[繩檢] exercise self-restraint;
[繩鋸木斷] little strokes fell great oaks;
繩鋸木斷，水滴石穿 constant dropping wears away the stone;
[繩墨] (1) marking lines; (2) rules of conduct;
拘守繩墨 stick to the rules;
[繩其祖武] follow in the steps of one's ancestors; imitate one's forebears; tread in the footsteps of one's ancestors; step into the shoes of one's predecessors;
[繩愆糾謬] correct faults and errors; correct mistakes;
[繩橋] suspension bridge;
[繩趨尺步] behave according to decorum; behave in a fit and proper way; strictly upright and correct in one's behaviour;
[繩繩] (1) continuous; unending; (2) cautious; (3) righteous;

[繩索] cord; cordage; rope;
[繩梯] rope ladder;
[繩正] correct; rectify;
[繩之以法] bring sb to justice; keep sb in line by punishments; prosecute according to the law; punish sb according to law; restrain sb by law;
[繩子] cord; line; rope;
解開繩子 cast off a line;
拴繩子 fasten with a rope;
一根繩子 a piece of string; a rope;
一卷繩子 a coil of rope;
一捲繩子 a coil of rope;
一圈繩子 a coil of rope;

草繩 straw rope;
結繩 tie knots;
纜繩 thick rope;
麻繩 rope made of hemp;
擰成一股繩 make joint efforts; pull together; twist into a rope — stick together;
爬繩 climb a rope; rope-climbing;
旗繩 halyard;
軟繩 tightrope;
跳繩 rope skipping;
線繩 cotton rope;
一團繩 a ball of string;
紙繩 paper string;
準繩 criterion; yardstick;
棕繩 coir rope;
走繩 rope-dancing; ropewalking;

sheng³
sheng

【省】 (1) economize; save; (2) abridge; leave out; omit; reduce; (3) province;
[省便] convenient; save energy, trouble etc.;
[省城] provincial capital;
[省吃] eat sparingly;
省吃儉用 eat sparingly and spend frugally; economical in everyday spending; go slow with; live frugally; pinch and scrape; practise austerity; save money on food and expenses; scrape and screw; skimp and save; stint oneself;
[省得] (1) lest; (2) so as to avoid; so as to save;
[省電] save electricity;
[省分] province;
[省會] provincial capital;
[省減] cut; economize; lessen; reduce;
[省儉] frugal; thrifty;
[省界] provincial boundaries;
[省力] economize labour; save effort; save energy; save labour;
[省略] (1) abridge; elide; leave out; omit; (2) abbreviation; ellipsis;
省略句 elliptical sentence;
省略祈使句 elliptical imperative sentence;
省略式 contraction;
省略所有格 elliptic genitive;
[省錢] economical; save money; save one's pocket;
省工省錢 save both labour and money;
[省卻] avoid; save;
[省時] save time; timesaving;
省時省工 save time and work;
[省事] (1) save trouble; simplify matters; (2) easy; it's more convenient;
[省試] provincial examination;
[省下] save money;
[省心] save worries;
[省用] economize; save;
[省長] governor of a province; provincial governor;
副省長 deputy governor; vice-governor;
[省字號] apostrophe;

儉省 economical; thrifty;
節省 economize; use sparingly;
外省 other provinces;

sheng

【眚】 (1) eye ailment; eye disease; film; (2) blunder; error; fault; mistake; (3) corruption; (4) reduce; save; (5) calamity; disaster;
[眚災] faults and misfortune;

sheng⁴
sheng

【乘】 (1) historical records; (2) carriage; (3) division of Buddhist teaching; (4) team of four horses;
[乘客] passenger;
頭等艙乘客 first-class passenger;
[乘馬] team of four horses;

大乘 (1) Great Vehicle; Mahayana; (2) high order;
上乘 (1) Great Vehicle; Mahayana; (2) high

order;
史乘 annals; history;
小乘 (1) Hinayana; Little Vehicle; (2) mediocrity;

sheng
【晟】 light; splendour; the brightness of the sun;

sheng
【盛】 (1) exuberant; flourishing; prosperous; (2) energetic; vigorous; (3) grand; magnificent; (4) abundant; plentiful; rich; (5) common; popular; (6) deeply; greatly; (7) a surname;

[盛產] abound in; teem with;
盛產石油 rich in oil;

[盛傳] be widely known; be widely rumoured;

[盛大] grand; magnificent; majestic; spectacular;
盛大的招待會 grand reception;

[盛典] big ceremony; grand ceremony; grand occasion;

[盛冬] midwinter;

[盛飯] ladle rice into a bowl;

[盛服] ceremonial attire; in full dress; rich dress; splendid attire;

[盛會] distinguished gathering; grand meeting; magnificent assembly;
享有盛名 enjoy a good reputation;

[盛年] prime of one's life;
正當盛年 in the prime of life;

[盛怒] fury; in a violent rage; in great anger; rage; wrath;
盛怒之下 in a blaze of passion;

[盛氣] (1) exploding rage; (2) arrogant; haughty; (3) full of spirit;
盛氣淩人 arrogant; bully others; carry things with a high hand; come out strong; come the quarter-deck over sb; domineering; give cheek; give oneself airs; imperious; lift up one's horn; on one's high horse; overbearing; ride the high horse; treat others rudely through arrogance; up stage; uppish;
盛氣淩人，不可一世 throw one's weight about and become overbearing;

[盛情] boundless hospitality; great kindness; utmost sincerity;
盛情款待 treat sb with the utmost cordiality;
盛情難卻 difficult to decline sb's generous intentions; difficult to deny sb's great hospitality; difficult to refuse such kindness; hard to turn down the warm-hearted offer; it would be ungracious not to accept your kindness;
盛情送別 give sb a good send-off;

[盛食厲兵] have a hearty meal and sharpen one's weapon — get ready for fight;

[盛世] flourishing age; heyday;

[盛事] grand occasion; great event;

[盛暑] sweltering summer heat; the hot days of summer;
盛暑嚴冬 in sultry summer and in freezing winter;

[盛衰] prosperity and decline; rise and fall; ups and downs; wax and wane;
盛衰榮枯 extremes of fortune;
盛衰榮辱 glory and humiliation; prosperity and decline; the vicissitudes of life; ups and downs;
盛衰無常 capricious in rise and fall; changeable in prosperity and decline; have a chequered career;
盛衰興廢 rise and fall; ups and downs; vicissitudes; waning and waxing;
永盛不衰 blossom forever; forever green;

[盛王] ruler of great virtue;

[盛夏] midsummer; the height of summer;

[盛行] current; in vogue; prevail; prevalent;
盛行一時 become current; in vogue; prevail for a time;

[盛顏] one's look in the prime of one's life;

[盛筵] grand banquet; nosh-up; splendid meal; sumptuous dinner;
盛筵必散 even the best party must have an end; even the grandest feast must have an end;
盛筵難再 difficult to have such a grand feast again; grand gatherings do not take place every day; it is very rare for sb to attend such a great banquet;

[盛宴] grand banquet; sumptuous dinner;
盛宴款待 kill the fatted calf for...;
舉行盛宴 give a Lucullan feast; hold a Lucullan;

[盛意] generosity; great kindness; thoughtfulness; warm-heartedness;
盛意難卻 cannot ignore sb's kindness; it is difficult to decline sb's generous

intention;

[盛譽] great fame; high reputation;
滿載盛譽 cover with glory;

[盛讚] highly praise; pay high compliments; praise profusely; speak of sb in glowing terms;

[盛饌] feast; sumptuous dinner;

[盛裝] be dressed in one's best; dress out; dress up; in fine array; in full dress; in rich attire;
盛裝打扮 be dressed in one's best;
盛裝赴會 put on glad rags for the party;
盛裝華服 gorgeously dressed;
盛裝舞步賽 dressage;

[盛妝艷服] elaborate toilet;

昌盛 prosperous;
熾盛 ablaze; flaming;
鼎盛 at the height of power and splendours; in a period of great prosperity;
繁盛 bloom; boom; flourishing; grow; mushroom; prosperous; sprout; thriving;
豐盛 bumper; rich; sumptuous;
極盛 heyday; zenith;
隆盛 grand and solemn;
茂盛 flourishing; luxuriant;
強盛 (of a country) powerful and prosperous;
全盛 flourishing; in full bloom;
旺盛 exuberant; full of vitality; overflowing with life; vigorous;
心盛 enthusiastic; in high spirit;
興盛 flourishing; prosperous; thriving; up in the ascendant; vigorous;
殷盛 abundant; flourishing; prosperous; thriving;
壯盛 healthy; strong and prosperous;

sheng

【剩】 remnant; surplus;

[剩飯] leftover rice; leftovers from a meal;
廚中有剩飯，路上有饑人 there is leftover rice in the kitchen, but there are starving travellers on the way;

[剩貨] leftover goods; leftovers;

[剩錢] have money left;

[剩下] be left over; remain;
只剩下 only remain;

[剩餘] excess; remainder; residue; surplus;
剩餘定理 remainder theorem;
~ 中國剩餘定理 Chinese remainder theorem;
剩餘人員 surplus staff;
~ 剩餘人員安置 placement of surplus staff;
剩餘物 leavings;
略有剩餘 show a small surplus;
稍有剩餘 slight surplus;

過剩 excess; surplus;
下剩 be left;
餘剩 remainder; surplus;

sheng

【勝】 (1) success; victory; (2) excel; get the better of; superior to; surpass; triumph; win; (3) distinctive; excellent; superb; wonderful; (4) can bear; equal to;

[勝敗] success or failure; victory or defeat;
勝敗乃兵家常事 defeats and victories are ordinary things to a general; for a military commander, winning or losing a battle is a common occurrence; victory and defeat are the soldier's lot; victory and failure are common things among soldiers;
勝敗未卜 it is uncertain whether one will succeed or fail;
勝敗未定 victory is not yet decided; victory or defeat is undecided;
反敗為勝 come from behind to turn the score; come from behind to win the game; pull out of the fire; snatch a victory out of defeat; turn defeat into victory; turn the battle's tide; turn the tables; turn the tide;
勝不驕，敗不綏 not made dizzy with success nor discouraged by failure; not puffed up by success, undismayed by failure; not to become cocky with success or downcast over defeat; not to get conceited because of victory or disheartened in case of defeat;
勝者為王，敗者為寇 losers are always in the wrong;
轉敗為勝 change defeat into victory; convert defeat into victory; go from defeat to victory; pull out of the fire; snatch a victory out of defeat; turn a defeat into a victory; turn defeat into victory; turn the tables on sb;

[勝出] come out on top; end up to the better; win;

[勝地] famous scenic spot; place of natural

beauty;

[勝而不驕] without growing conceited with victory;

[勝負] success or failure; victory or defeat;

勝負難測 the issue is in doubt till the last shot; the result is anybody's guess till the final point is won; with the outcome of the game hanging in the balance;

勝負難分 the battle is hung in the balance; the winner or loser cannot be distinguished;

勝負難料 hard to say who will be the victor; the day is doubtful; wide open;

勝負未卜 cannot predict who will be the winner; it is difficult to foretell which side would win;

勝負未定 an open issue; victory hangs in the balance;

勝負已定 the game is set;

不分勝負 a draw; a drawn battle; break even; come out even; draw; end in a draw; end in a tie; end neither in victory nor defeat; tie;

不論勝負 win or lose

決出勝負 slug it out;

攝影定勝負 photo finish;

誰勝誰負 which will win out; who conquers whom; who will defeat whom; who will win; who wins over whom;

孰勝孰負 who wins and who loses;

[勝過] better than; excel; have a pull over; have it all over; outstrip; prevail over; superior to; surpass;

勝過一籌 gain one-upmanship over; one-up;

銷量勝過 outsell;

遠遠勝過 outclass;

在數量上勝過 outnumber;

[勝蹟] historical relics;

[勝景] scenic beauty;

[勝利] (1) triumph; victory; win; (2) successfully; triumphantly;

勝利閉幕 come to a successful close;

勝利沖昏頭腦 be carried away by success; get dizzy with success; victory turns the heads of;

勝利果實 fruits of victory;

勝利前進 march onward victoriously;

勝利遊行 victory parade;

勝利在望 get on the final stretch; see land; victory is in sight;

勝利在握 victory is within grasp;

勝利者 victor; winner;

奔向勝利 march on to the victory;

歌頌勝利 carol the victory;

獲得勝利 achieve victory; score a victory; win a score;

~輕易獲得勝利 walkover;

~最終獲得勝利 win the day; win through in the end;

取得勝利 score a victory; win a victory;

一連串勝利 a series of victories; a string of victories;

重大勝利 important victory;

[勝券] confidence in victory; confident of victory; sure to win;

必操勝券 have the game in one's hands; sure to win;

穩操勝券 be certain to win; have full assurance of success; have the game in one's own hands;

[勝任] able to do sth; be qualified to do sth; capable of doing sth; competent for sth; equal to sth; feel equal to sth; feel up to sth; fit for sth; qualify for sth; up to sth;

勝任工作 competent at a job; prove equal to the task;

勝任愉快 fully competent; prove more than equal to the task; well qualified;

[勝似] better than;

[勝訴] win a lawsuit;

勝訴方 successful party;

勝訴人 winner of a lawsuit;

[勝算] stratagem which ensures success; sure of success;

勝算在握 have the cards in one's hand; have the game in one's hands; hold the cards in one's hand; success is almost within one's grasp;

操勝算 find success within one's grasp; sure of success; sure to win;

~可操勝算 can be sure of success; have the cards in one's hand; hold the cards in one's hand; stand a good chance of victory;

[勝於] better than; outstrip;

勝於他人 throw all the others into the shade;

[勝仗] victorious battle; victory;

打勝仗 win battle;

[勝之不武] it brings no honour to the victor in an unequal contest;

必勝 cannot be defeated; cannot fail; will most certainly win; will win certainly;

不勝 (1) cannot bear; unequal to; (2) extremely; tremendously; (3) cannot help doing sth; too...to;

常勝 ever victorious;

乘勝 exploit a victory; follow up a victory;

打勝 bear off the palm; beat; best; carry off the palm; carry the day; conquer; defeat; down; gain the victory over; get sb down; get the better of sb; have it on sb; have it over sb; have the best of it; have the scale of; one too many for sb; pervail over; put a head on sb; put to rout; route; smash; triump over; win; win the day;

戴勝 hoopoe;

得勝 bear away the bell; bear the bell; bring home the bacon; carry away the bell; carry off the bell; coast home; come through with flying colours; triumph; win; win a victory;

方勝 woman's head-dress with sides sliding up;

好勝 seek to do others down; try to be pre-eminent;

獲勝 come out on top; triumph; victorious; win victory;

決勝 decide the issue of the battle; determine the victory;

名勝 place famous for its scenery or historic relics; scenic spot;

求勝 strive for victory;

取勝 score a success; win a victory;

全勝 complete victory;

殊勝 remarkable and outstanding;

險勝 edge out; narrow victory; nose out; win by a narrow margin; win by a neck; win by a whisker;

形勝 favourable geographical position; topographical advantages;

雄勝 strategic pass;

優勝 superior; winning;

戰勝 defeat; overcome; triumph over;

爭勝 contend for the upper hand; try to win;

制勝 prevail; triumph; victorious; win;

智勝 outflank; outfox; outsmart;

逐勝 pursue enemy troops in retreat;

sheng

【聖】 (1) sage; saint; (2) holy; sacred; (3) emperor;

[聖餐] Lord's Supper;

聖餐杯 chalice;

[聖誕] Christmas;

聖誕歌 Christmas carol;

聖誕節 Christmas; Christmas Day;

聖誕卡 Christmas card;

聖誕快樂 Merry Christmas;

聖誕老人 Father Christmas; Santa Claus;

聖誕禮物 Christimas gift;

聖誕前夜 Christmas Eve;

聖誕樹 Christmas tree;

~ 一棵聖誕樹 a Christmas tree;

白色聖誕 white Christmas;

[聖地] (1) the Holy Land; (2) sacred land; sacred place; shrine;

[聖殿] holy place;

[聖恩] imperial graciousness;

[聖歌] canticle;

[聖潔] holy and immaculate; holy and pure;

聖潔的人 holy person;

[聖經] Holy Writ; the Bible; the Holy Bible;

聖經翻譯 Bible translation;

聖經文學 Biblical literature;

聖經文獻 biblical text;

聖經學 Biblicism;

聖經用語 Biblical language;

[聖廟] Confucian temple;

[聖明] capable and virtuous;

[聖墓] tomb of a sage;

[聖人] sage; wiseman;

聖人也有三分錯 even a wise man makes some mistakes; sages, however wise, are human and can make mistakes;

主保聖人 patron saint;

[聖水] holy water;

一池聖水 a pool of holy water;

[聖壇] altar;

聖壇裝飾畫 altarpiece;

大聖壇 the High Altar;

婚禮聖壇 hymeneal altar; nuptial altar;

家庭聖壇 family altar;

主聖壇 the High Altar;

[聖堂] sanctuary;

[聖徒] apostle; saint;

聖徒節 saint's day;

[聖賢] sages and men of virtue; saints;

人非聖賢，孰能無過 all men but saints are apt to make mistakes; men are not saints, how can they be free from

faults; to err is human;

[聖諭] imperial edict;

[聖樂] sacred music;

[聖戰] holy war; sacred war;

[聖職] holy post;

擔任聖職 take holy orders;

[聖者] sage; saint;

[聖旨] imperial directive; imperial edict; imperial will;

朝聖 pilgrimage;

神聖 holy; sacred;

sheng

【賸】 (1) overplus; surplus; (2) remains; remnants; residues; (3) superfluous;

[賸下] be left over; leave behind;

[賸餘] leave in surplus; remnants;

賸餘價值 surplus value;

賸餘物資 surplus; surplus goods;

shi¹

shi

【尸】 (1) corpse; dead body; skeleton; (2) direct; preside;

[尸毒] cadaverine;

[尸骨] bones of the dead; skeleton;

[尸骸] bones of the dead;

[尸諫] admonish at the cost of one's own life;

[尸居] lazy life;

[尸利] hang on to one's job for profit;

[尸祿] hold a sinecure and act like a personator of the dead;

[尸身] dead body;

[尸體] corpse; dead body;

辨認尸體 identify a corpse;

[尸位] hold a sinecure;

尸位素餐 enjoy the emolument of office without merit; entrench oneself in a position and do no useful work; feast at the public crib; feed at the public trough; get pay without doing any work; hold a sinecure job and eat the bread of idleness; hold an office without doing a stroke of work; hold down a job without doing a stroke of work; hold on to one's post while doing nothing; take pay but neglect the office;

[尸祝代庖] perform a duty on behalf of another without authorization;

古尸 age-old corpse;

僵尸 corpse;

收尸 bury the dead;

死尸 dead body; corpse;

驗尸 autopsy; post-mortem;

shi

【失】 (1) fail; fall through; lose; (2) defeat; failure; (3) let slip; miss; neglect; (4) fail to achieve one's end; (5) defect; defective in; err; have a slip; mishap; mistake; slip; (6) deviate from the normal; (7) break a promise; go back on one's word; neglect; not act according to; violate;

[失敗] a kick in the teeth; come a cropper; come unstuck; defeat; fail; fail to do sth; failure; fall down; fall through; fizzle out; flop; get a cropper; go to the wall; licking; never come to anything; pluck in sth;

失敗率 failure rate;

失敗情緒 defeatist sentiments;

失敗為成功之母 failure is the mother of success; failure is the only high-road to success; failure teachers success;

失敗之作 flop;

失敗主義 defeatism;

~失敗主義者 defeatist;

避免失敗 avert failure; avoid failure;

徹底失敗 total failure; total washout;

承認失敗 acknowledge one's defeat; admit defeat; admit failure; concede defeat; throw in the sponge; throw in the towel;

歸於失敗 prove abortive;

接受失敗 accept defeat; accept failure;

結果失敗 result in a defeat;

突然失敗 crash and burn;

完全失敗 complete failure;

一連串失敗 a series of failures; a string of failures;

遭到失敗 take a beating; take a hammering;

遭遇失敗 meet with failure; suffer a defeat;

着着失敗 fail in every move;

注定失敗 be doomed to failure; be foredoomed;

[失策] bad scheming; inexpedient; miscalculate; misjudge; misstep;

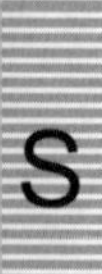

mistake; poor strategy; poor tactic; unwise;

[失察] neglect one's supervisory duties; oversight;
一時失察 an oversight on one's part;

[失常] abnormal; go into a spin; go mad; not normal; odd; off form; perform below one's normal capacity;
失常的 demented;
精神失常 distraught; not be in one's right mind; want two pence in the shilling;
情緒失常 emotional illness;
舉止開始失常 lose one's marbles;
舉止失常 act oddly;

[失寵] fall into disfavour; in disfavour; in disgrace; out of favour;
失寵於人 in bad odour with sb; out of favour with sb;

[失傳] be lost; fail to be handed down from past generations; lose the tradition of;

[失措] lose one's head; lose one's presence of mind;
驚惶失措 be out of countenance; lose one's head from fear; panic;

[失當] improper; impropriety; inappropriate;
處理失當 be not properly handled;
措置失當 not properly handled; mismanage;

[失道寡助] an unjust cause finds meagre support;

[失掉] (1) lose; (2) miss;
失掉機會 miss a chance;
失掉理智 lose one's senses;
失掉聯繫 lose contact with;
失掉民心 lose popular support;
失掉權力 be stripped of power;

[失度] excessive; immoderate;

[失和] at loggerheads; become estranged; fail to keep on good terms; on bad terms;
母子失和 mother-son rift;

[失怙] lose one's father; orphaned;

[失悔] regret; remorseful;

[失魂] be stricken by sorrow; frightened; out of one's wits;
失魂落魄 be driven into distraction; dejection; despondent; listless; lose one's soul; lose one's wits; out of one's wits; panic-stricken; within an inch of one's life;
失魂喪膽 be driven to distraction; be frightened out of one's life; strike awe into one's heart;

[失火] catch fire; fire; on fire;

[失機] miss a chance;
機不可失 a golden opportunity not to be missed; don't let such an opportunity slip; it's now or never; not to miss an opportunity; now for it; opportunity knocks but once; such a chance must not be lost; such a chance must not be missed;
~機不可失，時不我待 we cannot afford to let time slip through our fingers, as time waits for no one;
~機不可失，時不再來 an occasion lost cannot be redeemed; don't lip slip an opportunity, it may never come again; don't lose a golden opportunity; it's now or never; opportunity knocks but once; when an opportunity is neglected, it never comes back t you;

[失計] miscalculation; poor scheming;

[失檢] careless in personal conduct; indiscretion;

[失腳] lose one's footing; slip; slip on the ground;
失腳跌倒 lose one's footing and fall;

[失節] (1) commit a breach of virtue; disloyal; forfeit one's integrity; (2) commit adultery; lose one's chastity;

[失禁] incontinence;
失禁的 incontinent;
大小便失禁 gatism;

[失據] lose one's guidance;

[失覺] fail to perceive; negligent;

[失控] incontrollable; out of control; runaway;
失控的 rampant;
~失控的通貨膨脹 rampant inflation;

[失口] a slip of the tongue; say sth improper;

[失款] (1) lose money; (2) lost money;

[失禮] commit a breach of etiquette; discourtesy; impoliteness; indiscreetness; misbehaviour; rude;

[失利] suffer a defeat; suffer a setback;
軍事失利 military defeat;
票房失利 fail big at the box office;
意外失利 shock defeat;

[失戀] be crossed in love; be jilted; lose one's love;

[失靈] act up; not work; not work properly;

out of order;
開關失靈 the switch is out of order;

[失落] drop; lose;
失落感 sense of loss;

[失迷] get lost; lose one's bearings; lose one's way;

[失密] leak out official secrets due to inadvertence;

[失眠] insomnia; lose sleep; suffer from insomnia;
失眠症 insomnia;
~失眠症患者 insomniac;
失眠之夜 wakeful night; white night;
初期失眠 initial insomnia;
夜晚失眠 have a restless night;
原發性失眠 primary insomnia;
中期失眠 middle insomnia;

[失明] become blind; blind; go blind; lose one's sight;
雙目失明 lose the sight of both eyes;

[失陪] excuse me, but I must be leaving now;

[失配] mismatch;
比色失配 colorimetric mismatch;
反應性失配 reactivity mismatch;
負載失配 load mismatch;
晶格失配 lattice mismatch;
隨機失配 random mismatch;

[失氣] deeply disappointed; frustrated;

[失竊] be visited by a burglar; have things stolen; suffer loss by theft;

[失去] forfeit; lose; miss;
失去控制 at large; get out of control; get out of hand; runaway;
失去理性 lose one's mind;
失去生命 lose one's life;
失去時效 cease to be in force; no longer effective;
失去信心 lose confidence;
失去一切 lose everything;
失去勇氣 lose heart; lose one's nerve;
失去知覺 lose consciousness;
失去自制 lose one's head;

[失卻] lose; miss;

[失群孤雁] solitary wild goose;

[失散] be scattered; be separated from and lose touch with each other; lost and scattered;
失眠症 anhypnosis;

[失色] (1) become pale; lose colour; turn pale; (2) be eclipsed; be outshone;
黯然失色 be cast into the shade; be eclipsed; be outshined; be overshadowed; be thrown into the shade; cut down sb; cut sb out of all feather; dim; dismal; dwarf sb into insignificance; fall into the shade; fall into the shadow; gloomy; pale into insignificance; sober; take shine off sb; take the gilt off the gingerbread;
~使別的…黯然失色 put sb in the shade; put sth in the shade;
大驚失色 be frightened and change colour; be greatly frightened; be pale with fear; gray-faced with fright; grow alarm and turn colour; have a blue fit; turn pale with fright;
驚慌失色 lose countenance;
相顧失色 look at each other in dismay;
相形失色 appear far worse in comparison; be tarnished by comparison; far too inferior by comparison; lose countenance by comparison; show a great difference by comparison; take the shine out of;

[失身] (1) lose one's chastity; lose one's virginity; (2) incur danger;
失身的女子 fallen woman;

[失神] (1) absent-minded; careless; inattentive; (2) in low spirits; out of sorts;

[失慎] (1) careless; not cautious; (2) cause a fire through carelessness;

[失聲] (1) cry out involuntarily; (2) lose one's voice;
失聲大笑 burst out laughing;
失聲喊叫 exclaim outright;
失聲痛哭 be choked with tears; burst out weeping; cry in a sad voice; lose control and cry out loud;
痙攣性失聲 spastic aphonia;
痛哭失聲 choke with tears; cry oneself hoarse;

[失時] let slip the opportunity; miss the opportune moment; miss the right opportunity; miss the season;

[失實] inaccurate; inconsistent with the facts;

[失識症] agnosia; inability to recognize objects by use of the senses;
觸覺失識症 tactile agnosia;

[失事] accident; crash; fatal accident; have an accident; meet with an accident;

[失勢] fall into disgrace; lose one's power and influence;
失勢退隱 fall into disgrace and go into retirement; hide one's diminished head;
[失手] accidentally drop; slip;
[失守] fall;
[失算] miscalculate; miscalculation; misjudge; mistake;
[失所] be displaced; become homeless; homeless;
[失態] conduct oneself ludicrously; forget oneself; misbehave;
[失調] (1) dislocate; disturbance; imbalance; lose balance; (2) ailment; lack of proper care;
比例失調 lack of proportion;
~ 比例嚴重失調 serious disproportion; serious imbalance;
加速失調 acceleration disturbance;
經濟失調 economic ailment;
內心失調 intrapsychic ataxia;
生態失調 ecological disturbance;
生物失調 biological disturbance;
[失望] beyond hope; chagrin; despair; disappointed; discouraged; lose hope;
失望情緒 despair;
~ 一陣失望情緒 a fit of despair;
悲觀失望 abandon oneself to despair; become disheartened; lose faith in;
大為失望 feel very disappointed;
導致失望 be drawn to despair;
感到失望 be chagrined; be disappointed;
令人失望 disappointing;
~ 令人失望的情況 bummer;
[失物] lost articles; lost property;
失物歸主 return the things lost to the owner;
失物招領 advertise for the owner of a lost thing; articles found, owner please contact;
~ 失物招領處 lost-and-found; lost property;
待領失物 lost property;
[失誤] (1) bodge; fault; miss; muff; error; omission; (2) slip up; slip-up;
失誤分析 miscue analysis;
接球失誤 muff a ball;
判斷失誤 a lapse in judgement; a misjudgement; an error in judgement;
一個失誤 a mistake;
[失陷] fall; fall into enemy hands; fall to the enemy;
失地陷城 cities and territory lost;
[失笑] cannot help laughing; laugh in spite of oneself;
[失效] (1) cease to be effective; lose effectiveness; lose efficacy; (2) be no longer in force; become invalid; fall into abeyance; go into abeyance;
失效率 failure rate;
失效商標 invalidated mark;
關鍵失效 critical failure;
日久失效 out of date;
突變失效 catastrophic failure;
退化失效 degradation failure;
自動失效 automatically cease to be in force;
[失寫症] agraphia;
精神性失寫症 mental agraphia;
聽覺性失寫症 acoustic agraphia;
遺忘性失寫症 agraphia amnemonica;
運動性失寫症 motor agraphia;
雜亂性失寫症 jargon agraphia;
[失信] break one's promise; break one's word; go back on one's word;
失信於朋友 cop out on one's friends;
失信於人 break faith with others; go back on one's words;
[失修] disrepair; fall into disrepair; in a dilapidated state; in bad repair; in disrepair; wanting in repair;
年久失修 be worn down by the years without repair; for long years out of repair; in bad repair; long neglected and in disrepair;
[失學] be deprived of education; be obliged to discontinue one's studies; lack formal education; unable to go to school;
[失血] lose blood;
[失言] improper remark; make an indiscreet remark; make improper utterances; put one's foot in one's mouth; say what should not be said; slip of the tongue;
失言招怨 cause hatred by reckless word;
後悔失言 bite off one's tongue; bite one's tongue off;
酒後失言 make an indiscreet remark under the influence of alcohol;
言多必失 he that talks much errs much;

loquacity brings mistakes; loquacity is sure to err; much babbling is not without offence; much talk leads to faults; one is bound to have a slip of the tongue if one talks too much; talkativeness induces error; too much talking leads to error;
言多有失 if you talk too much, you may say the wrong thing;

[失業] at a loose end; at an idle end; at leisure; at loose ends; in dry dock; jobless; on the beach; on the dole; out of a job; out of bread; out of employment; out of work; fall out of employment; go on the dole; have no work; lose one's employment; lose one's job; lose one's work; unemployed; unemployment;
失業保險 unemployment insurance;
失業工人 job-hopping workers;
失業津貼 unemployment benefit;
失業救濟 unemployment compensation; unemployment relief;
失業率 unemployment; unemployment rate;
~失業率上升 increase in unemployment; rise in unemployment;
~失業率水平 level of unemployment;
~失業率下降 a fall in unemployment; a reduction in unemployment;
~減少失業率 bring down unemployment; cut unemployment; reduce unemployment;
失業數字 unemployment figures; unemployment statistics;
失業者 gentleman at large; the jobless; the unemployed;
~一大批失業者 an army of the unemployed;
半失業 (1) partly unemployed; (2) semi-employed; (3) underemployed;
變相失業 disguised unemployment;
長期失業 long-term unemployment;
長期性失業 chronic unemployment;
臨時性失業 casual unemployment;
面臨失業 face redundancy;
潛在失業 disguised unemployment;
輸出失業 exporting unemployment;
造成失業 cause unemployment;
周期性失業 cyclic unemployment;

[失宜] improper; inappropriate;
處置失宜 handle improperly;

[失意] dejected; disappointed; frustrated; not doing well; unlucky;
名場失意 be disappointed in examination for degrees;
情場失意 be frustrated in love;
掩飾失意 hide one's disappointment;

[失義] loss of rectitude;
引喻失義 quote phrases to confound the eternal principles of rectitude;

[失迎] fail to meet a guest;
失迎失迎 excuse me for not meeting you at the gate; I'm sorry I was out when you called;

[失語] aphasia;
失語症 aphasia;
~觸覺性失語症 tactile aphasia;
~傳導性失語症 conduction aphasia;
~發展性失語症 developmental aphasia;
~功能性失語症 functional aphasia;
~混合性失語症 combined aphasia;
~混合型失語症 mixed aphasia;
~聽覺性失語症 acoustic aphasia;
~完全失語症 complete aphasia;
~完全性失語症 total aphasia;
~遺忘性失語症 amnesic aphasia;
~語義性失語症 semantic aphasia;
~運動性失語症 aphemia; logaphasia;
~雜亂性失語症 jargon aphasia;
~真性失語症 true aphasia;
~智能性失語症 intellectual aphasia;
兒童失語 childhood aphasia;
感覺性失語 receptive aphasia; sensory aphasia;
痙攣性失語 aphthongia;
運動性失語 aphemia; motor aphasia;

[失約] break one's promise; fail to keep an appointment; stand sb up;

[失著] make an unwise move; miscalculate; miscalculation;

[失真] (1) distortion; (2) lack fidelity; not true to the original;
編碼失真 code distortion;
不對稱失真 asymmetrical distortion;
黑點失真 black spot distortion;
弧形失真 arc distortion;
特徵失真 characteristic distortion;

[失政] misrule a nation;

[失職] delinquent; dereliction of one's duty; neglect one's duty; negligence of duty; negligent in the performance of duties;

[失重] loss of weight; weightless; weightlessness; zero gravity;
失重適應 weightlessness adaptation;
[失主] owner of lost property;
[失諸正鵠] miss the target;
[失蹤] disappear; missing;
追蹤失蹤 trace missing persons;
失蹤者 missing person;
[失足] (1) lose one's footing; slip; (2) commit a mistake; take a wrong step in life;
失足落水 slip and fall into the water;
失足青年 young boys and girls embarking on the road of degradation and crime;
一失足成千古恨 a false step becomes the regret of a lifetime; a moment's error can bring a lifelong regret; a moment's error will bring about sorrow for a thousand years; a single error can cause incalculable suffering; a single slip may cause lasting sorrow; a wrong step results in eternal regret; do wrong once and you'll never hear the end of it; old sin makes new shame; one false step brings everlasting grief; one pitfall leads to endless misery and regret; the error of a moment becomes the regret of a lifetime;

報失 report the loss of sth to the authorities concerned;
得失 (1) gain and loss; success and failure; (2) advantages and disadvantages;
丟失 lose;
掛失 report the loss of;
過去 (1) fault; slip; (2) offence;
流失 be washed away; run off;
冒失 abrupt; rash;
迷失 lose one's way;
散失 (1) be lost; scatter and disappear; (2) vanish; vaporize;
喪失 forfeit; lose;
閃失 accident; mishap;
疏失 careless mistake; remissness;
損失 lose; loss;
亡失 lose;
消失 disappear; vanish;
遺失 lose;
走失 (1) be lost; wander away; (2) lose the original shape, flavour, etc.;
坐失 let sth slip by;

shi
【虱】 louse;
[虱目魚] milkfish;
[虱子] louse;
除去虱子 delouse;

shi
【屍】 carcass; corpse; dead body;
[屍骨] skeleton of a corpse;
屍骨成堆 corpses are piled up high;
屍骨堂 charnel house;
屍骨未寒 hardly cold in the grave; sb's remains are barely cold yet;
[屍橫] dead bodies lie;
屍橫遍野 a field littered with corpses; be literally strewn with enemy corpses; be littered with enemy corpses; be littered with the bodies of enemy dead; dead bodies scatter over the wilderness; the field is strewn with corpses;
屍橫血染 dead bodies lie in the streets and blood stains the road;
[屍諫] admonish at the cost of one's own life;
[屍居餘氣] a little breath is left in the body — dying; a living corpse; at one's last gasp; at the point of death; critically ill with a weak breath; more dead than alive;
[屍身] corpse; dead body; remains;
[屍體] cadaver; corpse; dead body; remains;
屍體檢驗 post-mortem;
動物屍體 carcass;
掘出屍體 exhume;
一具屍體 a body; a corpse;

shi
【施】 (1) act; bear; bring into effect; carry out; come into force; do; execute; go into effect; put into effect; put into force; (2) bestow; give; give to others; grant; hand out; (3) exert; impose; (4) apply; execute; use; (5) a surname;
[施恩] do favours to others;
[施放] discharge; fire;
施放煙幕 lay a smoke screen;
[施肥] apply fertilizers; fertilize; fertilizer application; spread manure;
施肥量 application rate;
合理施肥 adequate fertilization; rational application of fertilizer;

護養施肥 maintenance application;
機械化施肥 mechanized application;
土壤施肥 fertilization of the soil;

[施粉] apply face powder; powder one's face;
施朱傅粉 paint and powder oneself;

[施工] start building; start construction;
施工單位 unit in charge of construction;
施工管理 construction management;
施工進度 construction progress;
施工現場 construction site;
熱熔施工 hot-melt application;

[施計] play tricks;
計無所施 at a loss about what to do; there is nothing one can do; up the creek;
無計可施 at a loss about what to do; at the end of one's resources; at the end of one's tether; at the end of one's wit; put in a quandary; there is nothing one can do;

[施加] bring to bear on; exert; impose;
施加壓力 bring pressure to bear on sb; put pressure on sb;
施加影響 exert one's influence on sb;

[施教] educate; instruct; teach;

[施救] rescue and resuscitate;

[施勞] boast of one's merit;

[施禮] make a bow; salute;

[施散] scatter;

[施捨] give alms; give to charity;
施捨物 alms; handout;
懇求施捨 solicit alms;
乞求施捨 beg for alms;

[施設] arrange; decorate;

[施施] complacently; leisurely;

[施事] agent; agentive;
施事格 agentive case;
施事名詞 agent noun;
施事實詞 agent substantive;
施事主語 agentive subject;
施事者 agent;
施事作用 agentive role;

[施威] display one's power; exhibit one's power; impress with force; show severity;

[施為] action; behaviour; conduct;
施為性言語行為 illocutionary act;
施為性作用 illocutionary force;
施為意義 illocutionary meaning;
間接性施為 indirect illocution;

[施洗] baptize;

[施行] (1) apply; come into force; execute; go into effect; put in force; (2) act; carry out; enforce; implement; perform; put sth in practice;
施行急救 administer first aid;
開始施行 go into effect;
着即施行 to be enforced immediately;
遵法施行 obey the laws and put into operation;

[施藥] dispense medicine free of charge;

[施醫] give free medical service;

[施用] apply; employ; use;
分期施用 split application;

[施與] bestow; give to charity; give to the poor; grant;

[施展] give full play to; put to good use;
施展本領 give full play to one's talent; put one's ability to good use;
施展雄才 put one's great ability to use;

[施診] give free medical treatment;
施診給藥 treat sb and give him medicine freely;

[施賑] give to the poor;

[施政] administer political administration; administrate; administration; execute government orders; govern;
施政報告 administrative report; policy address;
施政方針 administrative policy;
施政綱領 administrative programme;
惡劣施政 misrule;

[施主] (1) alms giver; benefactor; (2) donor;
施主雜質 donor impurity;

shi

【師】 (1) master; teacher; tutor; (2) example; model; paragon; (3) person skilled in a certain profession; specialist; (4) teach; (5) model after another; pattern after another; (6) one's master; one's teacher; (7) division; (8) army; troops; (9) a surname;

[師表] paragon worthy of emulation; person of exemplary virtue;

[師承] have learned under; the succession of teachings from a master to his disciples;

[師道] (1) succession of teachings from masters to disciples; (2) truth in learning from a master; (3) principles a

master abides by;
師道尊嚴 absolute authority of the teachers; teacher's dignity;
師嚴道尊 a master must be stern in order to teach the students to respect learning;

[師弟] (1) junior fellow apprentice; (2) son of one's master; (3) father's apprentice;

[師法] (1) emulate; imitate; model after; pattern after; (2) knowledge handed down by one's master; methods taught by one's teacher;
師法古人 imitate the ancients; model oneself after the ancients;

[師範] normal;
師範大學 normal university;
師範教育 normal education;
師範學校 normal school;

[師傅] master worker;
千個師傅千個法 a thousand masters, a thousand methods;
認師傅 apprentice oneself to sb;
修鞋師傅 cobbler; shoe mender;

[師父] (1) master; master worker; (2) polite form of address to a monk or nun;
師父領進門，修行在個人 the master initiates the apprentices, but their skill depends on their own efforts; the master teaches the trade, but the prentice's skill is self-made;

[師公] master's master;

[師古] pattern after the ancient;
事不師古 act regardless of the ancients' modes; not follow the conventional ways;

[師老] troops fighting for a long time;
師老兵疲 the troops have been in operation too long and soldiers are extremely tired;
師老無功 troops fighting for a long time without success;

[師門] school founded by a master;

[師母] wife of one's teacher;

[師婆] sorceress; witch;

[師生] teachers and students;
師生員工 teachers, students, administrative personnel and workers;
尊師愛生 respect teachers and love students; show respect for teachers and love for students; the students respect their teachers and the teachers love their students; the teachers cherish the pupils who in turn respect the teachers;

[師事] acknowledge sb as one's master; serve and respect sb as one's teacher;

[師徒] master and apprentice; teacher and pupil;
名師出高徒 an accomplished disciple owes his accomplishment to his great teacher;

[師兄] (1) one's senior fellow apprentice; (2) son of one's master; (3) father's apprentice;
師兄弟 fellow apprentices of one and the same master;

[師訓] teacher education;
職前師訓 initial teacher education;

[師爺] private advisor;

[師友] friend from whom one can seek advice;
半師半友 half teacher, half friend;
良師益友 good teachers and helpful friends;

[師長] (1) teacher; (2) division commander;
敬師尊長 respect one's elders and teachers;

[師丈] husband of one's teacher;

[師直為壯] army fighting for a just cause has high morale; only a righteous army may have a grand morale;

[師資] persons qualified to teach; teachers;
師資不足 the shortage of teachers;
師資培訓 teacher training;

按摩師 massager;
拜師 acknowledge a person as one's master or teacher;
班師 withdraw troops from the front; return after victory;
禪師 honorific title for a Buddhist monk;
出師 (1) finish one's apprenticeship; (2) dispatch troops to fight; send out an army;
廚師 chef; cook;
從師 acknowledge sb as one's master or teacher;
大師 (1) great master; (2) Great Master;
導師 (1) teacher; tutor; (2) guide of a great cause; teacher;
鋼琴師 pianist;
鼓師 drummer;
化妝師 make-up man;
畫師 painter;
揮師 dispatch troops to fight; send out an army

to war;
回師 return to triumph;
會師 effect a junction; join forces;
技師 technician;
講師 lecturer;
教師 teacher;
京師 capital of a country;
軍師 army adviser;
老師 teacher;
理髮師 barber;
錄音師 sound engineer;
律師 lawyer; solicitor;
滿師 finish one's apprenticeship;
美工師 set designer;
美容師 beautician;
魔術師 magician;
牧師 pastor;
琴師 opera fiddler;
拳師 boxing coach;
誓師 take a mass pledge;
塾師 tutor of a private school;
水師 navy;
豎琴師 harpist;
訟師 law practitioner;
天師 Daoist master;
調酒師 barkeeper; barman;
投師 seek instruction from a master;
巫師 sorcerer; wizard;
先師 teacher or master of the older generations;
小提琴師 violinist;
興師 dispatch troops; send an army;
雄師 powerful army;
修腳師 pedicurist;
醫師 doctor;
義師 righteous army;
樂師 accompanist;
照明師 lighting electrician;
宗師 master of great learning and integrity;
尊師 respect the teacher;

shi

【絁】 a kind of coarse silk fabric;

shi

【獅】 lion;
[獅吼] lions roar;
如獅之吼 roar like a lion;
[獅虎] lions and tigers;
獅虎不群居 lions and tigers live by themselves;
[獅身人面像] sphinx;
[獅頭鵝] lion-headed goose;
[獅子] lion;
獅子般強壯的 leonine;
獅子鼻 pug nose; snub nose;
獅子搏兔 like a lion pouncing on a hare — go all out even when tackling a minor problem; not to stint the strength of a lion in wrestling with a rabbit — go all out even when fighting a small enemy; use a lot of strength to perform a small feat;
獅子大開口 ask for a huge sum of money; charge sb an arm and a leg; demand an exorbitant price; open one's mouth wide; too greedy;
獅子狗 Beijingese; peke; Pekinese; Pekingese;
獅子吼叫 a lion roars;
獅子咆哮 lions roar;
獅子頭 stewed meat balls;
獅子舞 lion dance;
獅子座 (1) Leo; (2) the Lion's Seat — the seat for the Buddha;
一群獅子 a pride of lions;
一頭獅子 a lion;

美洲獅 cougar; mountain lion;
母獅 lioness;
幼獅 baby lion;

shi

【詩】 poem; poetry; verse;
[詩伯] great poet; master in poetry;
[詩詞] poetry and rhymed prose;
詩詞歌賦 poetry, rhymed prose, songs and odes;
濃詞艷詩 exquisite poems and verses;
[詩稿] draft poems; scripts of poems;
[詩歌] poems and songs; poetry;
詩歌翻譯 poetry translation;
詩歌功能 poetic function;
詩歌朗誦 poetry readings; recitation of poems;
詩歌語言 poetic language;
[詩格] style of poetry;
[詩虎] riddles in poetry form;
[詩畫] poetry and painting;
工詩善畫 be well versed in painting and poetry; good at painting as well as poetry;
能詩善畫 have superior abilities to write poetry and good in painting;
品詩論畫 discuss poetry or painting;

詩中有畫，畫中有詩 there is painting in one's poetry, and poetry in one's painting;

［詩話］ notes on poetry;
［詩集］ collections of poems; poetry anthology;
［詩箋］ paper for writing poems;
［詩句］ line; verse;
［詩劇］ drama in verse; poetic drama;
［詩謎］ riddle in the form of a poem;
［詩奴］ inferior poets; poetasters;
［詩癖］ deep love for poetry;
［詩篇］ (1) poems; (2) inspiring story;
［詩情］ poetic sentiment;

詩情畫意 a quality suggestive of poetry; idyllic; poetic;

［詩窮而後工］ in poetry one gains depth after suffering;
［詩人］ poet;

挂冠詩人 poet laureate;
成為詩人 become a poet;
女詩人 poetess;

［詩史］ (1) history of poetry; (2) epic;
［詩思］ poetic inspiration; poetical thoughts;
［詩壇］ circle of poets; poetic circles;

詩壇祭酒 foremost of poets;

［詩體］ style of a poem;

詩體學 prosody;

［詩文］ (1) poetic prose; (2) literary works in general;
［詩興］ poetic inspiration; poetic mood; urge for poetic creation;

詩興大發 in an exalted, poetic mood; feel a strong urge to write poetry;

［詩選］ collection of poems; poetry anthology;
［詩學］ poetics;
［詩以言志］ poetry serves as a medium to convey one's aspiration;
［詩意］ poetic flavour; poetic quality; romantic atmosphere;

詩意盎然 rich in poetic flavor;
饒有詩意 rich in poetic flavor; very poetic;

［詩友］ friend in poetry;
［詩韻］ (1) rhyme; (2) rhyme book; rhyming dictionary;
［詩章］ (1) poems; (2) inspiring story;

白話詩 free verse poem;
打油詩 doggerel; ragged verse;
古詩 ancient poetry;
和詩 compose verses to match those by others;
近代詩 modern poetry;
近體詩 modern-style poetry;
舊詩 classical poetry; old-style poetry;
舊體詩 classical verse; verse In classical forms;
劇詩 dramatic poetry;
朦朧詩 misty poetry;
七行詩 heptastich;
七言詩 poem with seven characters to a line;
牆頭詩 wall poems;
敲詩 riddle in verse form;
情詩 amatory poem; amatory verses; love poem; love song;
散文詩 poetry in prose;
史詩 epic;
抒情詩 lyric poetry;
頌詩 eulogistic poem;
誦詩 intone a verse; recite a poem;
題詩 write poems on sth;
歪詩 doggerel;
輓詩 funeral ode; elegy; threnody;
無題詩 titleless poem;
無韻詩 blank verse;
五言詩 poem with five characters to a line;
寫詩 compose a poem;
新詩 new-style poetry;
敘事詩 narrative poem;
艷詩 love poem in a flowery style;
一句詩 a line of poem; a line of verse;
一行詩 a line of verse;
一首詩 a poem;
軼詩 scattered poems;
音詩 tone poem;
吟詩 hum verse; recite poems;
應景詩 occasional verse;
詠詩 chant poems;
韻詩 rhymed poetry;
贊美詩 hymn;
自由詩 free verse;
作詩 write poems;

shi

【蓍】 milfoil;
［蓍草］ milfoil;
［蓍龜］ (1) milfoil and tortoise divination; (2) foresight;

shi

【鳲】 cuckoo;
［鳲鳩］ cuckoo;

shi

【蝨】 louse;

［蝨多不痒，債多不愁］ when you are covered with lice, you don't itch; when you are up to your ears in debt, you stop worrying;

［蝨子］ louse;

壁蝨 (1) tick; (2) bedbug;
飛蝨 plant hopper;
雞蝨 a kind of parasitic insect;
龍蝨 predaceous diving beetle;
牛蝨 ox louse;
水蝨 beach louse;
體蝨 body louse;
頭蝨 head louse;
陰蝨 crab louse;

shi

【濕】 (1) damp; get wet; humid; moist; wet; (2) (in Chinese medicine) ailments caused by high humidity;

［濕答答］ dripping wet;

［濕度］ dampness; humidity;
濕度比 psychrometric ratio;
濕度表 humidometer;
濕度測定 humidity test;
濕度測量術 hygrometry;
濕度低 low humidity;
濕度高 high humidity;
濕度計 hygrometer; psychrometer;
~冷部位濕度計 cold-spot hygrometer;
~吸氣濕度計 aspirated hygrometer; aspiration psychrometer;
~吸收濕度計 absorption hygrometer;
~自計濕度計 recording hygrometer;
濕度記錄器 gygrograph;
濕度調節器 humidity controller; humidity regulator;
濕度圖 hygrogram;
濕度下降 humidity declines;
濕度學 hygrology;
濕度儀 hygronom;
濕度指數 humidity index;
飽和濕度 saturation humidity;
測量濕度 measure humidity;
大氣濕度 atmospheric humidity;
環境濕度 ambient humidity;
絕對濕度 absolute humidity;
空氣濕度 air humidity;
~減少空氣濕度 decrease air humidity;
~增加空氣濕度 increase air humidity;
土壤濕度 soil humidity;
相對濕度 relative humidity;

［濕呼呼］ damp; humid; moist;

［濕津津］ damp and wet; moist with sweat; sweaty;

［濕冷］ damp and chilly;
濕冷的 dank;

［濕淋淋］ drenched; dripping wet;
濕淋淋的衣服 sopping wet clothes;

［濕路］ wet road;
濕路打滑 hydroplane;

［濕漉漉］ drenched; dripping wet;

［濕蒙蒙］ damp; moist;

［濕氣］ dampness; moisture;

［濕熱］ damp and hot;

［濕潤］ damp; humidification; moist;
空氣濕潤 humid air;

［濕水貨］ water-damaged goods;

［濕透］ drench; wet through;
濕透的 drenched; soaked; soaking; soggy;
濕透了 sopping;
渾身濕透 be drenched; be soaked; be soaked to the skin; be wet to the skin; be wet through; get a thorough souse; have not a dry thread on; wet as a drowned rat; wet to the skin;

［濕疣］ condyloma;
扁平濕疣 flat condyloma; condyloma latum;
梅毒濕疣 syphilitic condyloma;
生殖器濕疣 genital wart;
性病濕疣 condyloma acuminata;

［濕疹］ eczema; tetter;
濕疹性皮炎 eczematous dermatitis;
扁平濕疹 moist papule; mucous papule
變應性濕疹 allergic eczema;
擦爛性濕疹 eczema intertrigo;
紅斑性濕疹 eczema erythematosum;
結痂性濕疹 eczema crustosum;
鱗屑性濕疹 eczema squamosum; scaly tetter;
牛痘性濕疹 eczema vaccinatum;
膿疱性濕疹 eczema pustulosum;
疱疹性濕疹 eczema herpeticum;
丘疹性濕疹 eczema papulosum;
濕潤性濕疹 eczema madidans;
水泡性濕疹 eczema vesiculosum;
特應性濕疹 atopic eczema;
嬰兒濕疹 infantile eczema;

幼兒濕疹 infantile eczema;
脂溢性濕疹 seborrheic eczema;
職業性濕疹 occupational eczema;

卑濕 dampness of low-lying land;
比濕 specific humidity;
潮濕 damp; moist;
風濕 rheumatism;
寒濕 cold-dampness;
淋濕 be soaked; splashed wet;
濡濕 make wet; soak; soak by immersion;
潤濕 moist and fresh; wetting;
暑濕 summer-heat and damp;
浥濕 moist; wet;
燥濕 hot and moist;
沾濕 (1) damp; make wet; moisten; wet; (2) imbued with;
蘸濕 dip;

[溗濕] be soaked through;

shi²
shi

【十】 (1) ten; (2) tenth; (3) topmost; (4) complete; perfect;

[十八] eighteen;
十八般武藝 be skilled in wielding the 18 kinds of weapons — be skilled in various types of combat;
十八重地獄 the eighteen hells;
十八羅漢 the eighteen Buddhist saints;
十有八九 as like as not; eight or nine chances out of ten; in all likelihood; in all probability; in eight or nine cases out of ten; most likely; most probably; mostly; ninety-nine times out of a hundred; ten to one; very likely; with every chance to;
十之八九 eight or nine cases out of ten; most likely; nine times out of ten; ninety-nine times out of a hundred;
~ 十之八九他都是對的 nine times out of ten he's right;
女大十八變 a girl changes eighteen times before reaching womanhood; a girl changes fast in physical appearance from childhood to adulthood; a growing girl changes a great deal;

[十百] ten and one hundred;
以十當百 pit ten against a hundred; ten will be worth a hundred;

[十倍] deca-; tenfold;
身價十倍 go up in the world; one's value increases tenfold; the marketprice of sth has suddenly shot up tenfold;

[十邊形] decagon;

[十成] one hundred percent; very sure;

[十惡不赦] guilty beyond forgiveness; guilty of unpardonable evil; too wicked to be pardoned; unpardonable crime;

[十二] twelve;
十二番 (of mahjong) twelve times;
十二碼球 penalty kick;
十二面體 dodecahedron;
~ 五角十二面體 pentagonal dodecahedron;
~ 斜方十二面體 rhombic dodecahedron;
~ 正十二面體 regular dodecahedron;
十二月 (1) December; (2) twelfth month of the lunar year;
十二指腸 duodenum;
~ 十二指腸潰瘍 duodenal ulcer;
~ 十二指腸炎 duodenitis;

[十分] (1) completely; extremely; fully; utterly; very; (2) ten minutes;
十分寶貴 most valuable;
十分高興 be very pleased;
十分在行 know the A to Z of sth;
十分鐘 ten minutes;

[十行俱下] read ten lines at one glance; take in ten lines at a glance;

[十級風] force 10 wind;

[十誡] the Ten Commandments;

[十進] decimal;
十進法 denary scale;
十進位 decimal system;
十進制 decimal system;

[十九] (1) nineteen; (2) nine and ten;
十拿九穩 a sure thing for; almost certain; almost ninetenths certain; as sure as a gun; in the bag; it's dollars to buttons; ninety percent sure; pretty sure; ten to one; very sure of success;
~ 缸裏捉鱉—十拿九穩 catching a turtle in a jar — ninety percent sure;
十室九空 almost all houses are empty; nine houses out of ten are deserted; nine out of ten houses are stripped bare; nine out of ten houses are vacant;
十羊九牧 nine shepherds look after ten sheep — too many government officials;

[十里] ten miles;

十里飄香 the fragrance of flowers is wafted miles away;

[十六] sixteen;

[十面] ten-sided;

十面埋伏 ambush on all sides;

十面體 decahedron;

[十年] decade; decennium;

十年寒窗 bury oneself in books for a long time; persevere ten years in one's studies in spite of hardships;

十年河東，十年河西 capricious in rise and fall; changeable in prosperity and decline; chequered;

十年九不收 the land produces practically nothing nine years out of ten;

十年九不遇 hardly occur once in ten years; not to occur once in ten years; very rare;

十年九旱 be hit by drought nine years out of ten; drought prevails almost every year; have drought nine years out of ten;

十年九荒 corps fail nine years out of ten;

十年樹木，百年樹人 it takes ten years to grow a tree, but a hundred years to bring up a generation of people; it takes ten years to grow trees, but a hundred years to rear people;

[十七] seventeen;

[十全] all complete; full; perfect; utterly;

十全十美 all roses; complete; flawless and perfect; leave nothing to be desired; out of this world; perfect; perfect in every respect; perfect in every way; perfect to the last degree; the acme of perfection; the pink of perfection; up to the knocker;

[十三] baker's dozen; thirteen;

[十四] fourteen;

十四行詩 sonnet;

[十萬] one hundred thousand;

十萬八千里 a distance of one hundred and eight thousand miles; poles apart;

十萬火急 desperately urgent; express; extremely urgent; in a hot haste; in extreme urgency; most urgent; whip and spur;

[十位] tens digit;

[十五] (1) fifteen; (2) ten and five;

十五分鐘 a quarter; fifteen minutes;

十五個吊桶打水，七上八下 in a turmoil;

拔十得五 get fifty percent; get half of what one asks for;

[十一] (1) eleven; (2) ten and one;

十一月 (1) November; (2) eleventh month of the lunar calendar;

十不得一 not one in ten; obtain not even one in ten; unable to get one out of ten;

[十億] milliard;

[十月] (1) October; (2) tenth month of the lunar year;

[十指] fingertips;

十指連心 the nerves of the fingertips are linked with the heart;

十指纖纖 one's delicate bamboo-shoot fingertips;

[十字] cross; cross-shaped;

十字架 cross;

十字街 cross street;

~十字街頭 busy city streets; crisscross streets;

十字路口 (1) the junction of crossroads; (2) a moment or decision;

十字型的 cruciform;

[十足] completely; downright; extremely; one hundred percent; out-and-out; perfect; perfectly; sheer;

十足的謊言 a thoroughgoing lie;

十足地 downright;

風頭十足 one's show is at its height;

幹勁十足 full of drive; full of energy; go all out; go at sth with a will;

合十 put the palms together;

shi

【什】 (1) assorted; miscellaneous; sundry; varied; (2) ten; (3) squad;

[什百] tenfold or hundredfold;

[什錦] assorted; mixed;

素什錦 saute assorted vegetables;

[什器] miscellaneous utensils;

[什物] articles for daily use; odds and ends; sundries; sundry items;

[什襲而藏] store away like treasure; treasure a thing by wrapping it up carefully;

[什一] one tenth;

shi

【石】 (1) rocks; stones; (2) stone inscriptions; stone tablets; (3) an ancient

musical instrument; (4) a surname;
[石斑] grouper;
石斑魚 grouper;
~ 七斑石斑魚 true grouper;
~ 雲紋石斑魚 kelp grouper;
[石板] flagstone; slabstone; slate;
石板畫 lithograph;
石板上甩烏龜—硬碰硬 a tortoise pounding a slabstone — a case of the tough confronting the tough;
鋪路石板 paving stone;
一塊石板 a slab of stone;
[石碑] stele; stone tablet;
[石壁] cliff; precipice;
[石標] cairn;
[石雕] (1) stone carving; stone sculpture; (2) carved stone;
石雕佛像 stone statue of the Buddha;
[石洞] stone cave;
[石堆] cairn;
[石膏] plaster;
石膏板 plasterboard;
石膏像 plaster figure; plaster statue;
石膏柱 column; pillar;
~ 雪花石膏柱 alabaster column;
地板石膏 flooring plaster;
黑石膏 dark plaster;
緩硬石膏 hard finish plaster;
硬石膏 anhydrite;
牙科石膏 dental plaster;
[石工] mason; masonry;
[石拱橋] arched strone bridge;
[石化] petrochemical;
石化產品 petrochemical;
石化工業 petrochemical industry;
[石灰] lime;
石灰乳 milk of lime;
石灰石 limestone;
~ 帶紋石灰石 banded limestone;
~ 高硅質石灰石 cherty limestone;
石灰水 limewater;
~ 一桶石灰水 a bucket of whitewash;
石灰岩 limestone;
~ 長石質石灰岩 arkosic limestone;
~ 加積石灰岩 accretionary limestone;
~ 瀝青石灰岩 asphaltic limestone;
苛性石灰 caustic lime;
氣硬石灰 air-hardening lime;
燒石灰 calcined lime;
有效石灰 active lime;
[石匠] mason; stonemason;
[石階] stone step;
[石刻] stone inscription;
石刻品 stone carvings; stone composition;
[石坑] stone pit;
[石窟] grotto; rock cave;
[石塊] boulder; gobbet; knuckle; pebble; piece of rock; piece of stone;
[石礦場] quarry;
[石蠟] paraffin;
氯化石蠟 chlorinated paraffin;
天然石蠟 native paraffin;
液體石蠟 fluid paraffin; liquid paraffin;
[石榴] carthaginian apple; pomegranate;
石榴紅 garnet;
~ 石榴汁糖漿 grenadine;
石榴裙 (1) red skirt; woman's petticoat; (2) feminine charms;
石榴石 carbuncle;
石榴汁 pomegranate juice;
安石榴 pomegranate;
番石榴 guava;
[石路] gravel road; pebble road; stone-paved road;
[石馬] stone horse;
[石棉] asbestos; cotton asbestos;
石棉板 asbestos board;
石棉布 asbestos cloth;
石棉沉着病 amianthosis;
石棉粉 flake asbestos;
石棉片 sheet asbestos;
石棉繩 asbestos cord;
石棉水泥 asbestos cement;
石棉織品 asbestos fabric;
長絨石棉 long-fibred asbestos;
低級石棉 low-grade asbestos;
短絨石棉 short-fibred asbestos;
高級石棉 amianthus;
鐵石棉 amosa asbestos;
透閃石棉 abkhazite;
[石磨] grindstone; millstone;
[石墨] graphite;
石墨化 graphitization;
~ 固體石墨化 solid-state graphitization;
~ 一次石墨化 primary graphitization;
共晶石墨 eutectic graphite;
塊狀石墨 blocky graphite;
游離石墨 free graphite;
[石腦油] naphtha;
粗石腦油 crude naphtha;

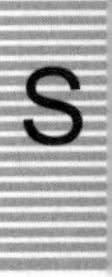

芳族石腦油 aromatic petroleum naphtha;
煤焦油石腦油 coal-tar naphtha;

[石破天驚] earth-shattering and heaven-battering; heaven-shaking; sensational; world-shaking;

[石器] stone artifact; stone implement; stone objects; stone tool; stone vessel; stoneware;
石器時代 Stone Age;
~新石器時代 Neolithic Age;
新石器時代晚期文化 late Neolithic culture;
新石器時代早期文化 early Neolithic culture;
新石器時代中期文化 mid-Neolithic culture;
舊石器 paleolith;
~舊石器時代 Paleolithic Age;
石核石器 core tool;
石片石器 flake tool;
曙石器 eolith;
~曙石器時代 Eolithic Age;
細石器 microlith;
~細石器文化 microlithic culture;
新石器 neolith;
~新石器時代 Neolithic Age;

[石牆] stone wall;

[石橋] stone bridge;

[石蕊] litmus;
石蕊試驗 litmus test;
石蕊試紙 litmus paper;

[石灘] rocky shallows;

[石頭] pebble; stone;
摸着石頭過河 careful; look before you leap; move steadily;
一車石頭 a load of stones;
一堆石頭 a heap of stones;
一方石頭 a cubic metre of stones;
一塊石頭 a cob of stone; a piece of rock; a piece of stone;

[石土] pebble;
卵石土 land pebble;

[石屋] stone house;

[石像] stone statue;

[石印] lithographic printing; lithography;

[石英] quartz;
石英錶 quartz watch;
石英晶體 quartz crystal;
石英鐘 quartz clock;
傳聲石英 acoustic quartz;
多孔石英 cell quartz;
結晶石英 crystal quartz;
碎石石英 crushed quartz;

[石油] black gold; fossil soil; oil; petroleum;
石油車 oil tank truck;
石油大王 oil baron;
石油工人 oilman;
石油工業 petroleum industry;
石油公司 oil company; petroleum company;
~國際石油公司 international oil company;
石油化工 petrochemical engineering;
石油美元 petrodollars;
石油醚 light petroleum;
石油氣 petroleum gas;
石油溶劑 lacquer petroleum;
石油商 oilman;
初級石油 primary petroleum;
高沸點石油 high point petroleum;
合成石油 synthetic petroleum;
瀝青質石油 asphaltic petroleum;
人造石油 artificial petroleum;
皂化石油 saponated petroleum;

[石隕石] meteoric stone; meteorolite;

[石竹] carnation;

[石柱] stone pillar;

[石子] cobble; cobblestone; pebble;
燧石子 flint pebble;

暗石 hidden rock;
絆腳石 obstacle; stumbling block;
寶石 gem; precious stone;
鼻石 rhinolith;
筆石 graptolite;
砭石 stone needle;
窆石 stones used in gliding a coffin down a tunnel;
採石 quarry;
側石 curb; curbstone;
長石 feldspar;
腸石 intestinal calculus;
磁石 (1) magnetic; (2) magnet;
大理石 marble;
大石 rock;
膽結石 cholelithiasis;
膽石 cholelith; gallstone;
奠基石 cornerstone; foundation stone;
電石 calcium carbide;
墊腳石 stepping-stone;
堆石 rockfill;
鵝卵石 cobble; cobblestone;

礬石 alunite;
肺石 pneumolith;
沸石 zeolite;
浮石 pumice;
氟石 fluorfite; fluorspar;
肝石 hepatolith;
矸石 waste rock;
硅石 silica;
花崗石 granite;
滑石 talc; talcum;
化石 fossil;
火石 fire-stone; flint;
基石 anvil; cornerstone; footing stone; foundation stone; rock;
礁石 reef; rock;
結石 calculus; stone;
界石 boundary stone;
金剛石 diamond;
金石 (1) metal and stone; (2) inscriptions on ancient bronzes and stone tablets;
晶石 spar;
菊石 ammonite;
巨石 boulder;
鈧石 befanamite;
礦石 ore;
勒石 carve on a stone;
礫石 gravel;
榴石 garnet;
卵石 cobble; pebble; shingle;
貓眼石 chatoyant;
毛石 rubble;
明石 alum;
磨刀石 whetstone;
磨石 millstone;
木石 wood and stone;
墓石 headstone; tombstone;
尿石 urolith;
盤石 huge circular stone; rock;
磐石 huge rock; monolith;
磐石 huge rock; massive rock;
拌石 throw a stone;
嵌石 inlay with precious stones;
沙石 gravel; sandstone;
閃石 hornblende;
腎結石 calculus renalis; kidney stone; nephrolithus; renal calculus;
腎石 kidney stone;
石隕石 meteoric stone; meteorolite;
矢石 arrows and stones in ancient warfare;
試金石 touchstone;
水磨石 terrazzo;
碎石 chippings; rubble;
燧石 flint;
頑石 coarse rock; insensate stone; unpolished stone;
霰石 aragonite;
硝石 nitre; saltpeter;
楔石 keystone;
信石 arsenic;
牙石 tartar;
岩石 rock;
藥石 (1) medicines and stone needles for acupuncture — remedies; (2) sincere admonitions;
熒石 fluorite;
螢石 fluorite;
油石 oilstone;
玉石 jade;
圓石 cobble; cobblestone;
月石 borax;
鉞石 axe stone;
雲石 marble;
隕石 aerolite; stony meteorite;
殞石 meteorite;
箴石 stone probes;
鐘乳石 stalactite;
柱石 mainstay; pillar;
磚石 masonry;
琢石 ashlar;
鑽石 (1) diamond; (2) jewel;

shi

【拾】 (1) collect; pick up; (2) ten; (3) put away;
［拾得］ find; pick up;
［拾掇］ (1) arrange in order; put in order; tidy up; (2) fix; repair; (3) discipline; punish; settle with;
拾掇房間 make up a room;
［拾荒］ glean and collect scraps;
［拾級而上］ ascend the stairs;
［拾金不昧］ not to pocket the money one picks up; return money found;
［拾零］ news in brief; sidelights; titbits;
［拾起］ pick up;
拾起話頭 take up the thread of a conversation;
［拾取］ collect; pick up;
［拾人］ pick up from sb;
拾人涕唾 plagiarize;
拾人牙慧 offer another's ideas as one's own; pick up phrases from sb and pass them off as one's own; pick up what

others say; plagiarize; steal others' dieas; take up and adopt others' thoughts instead of using one's own;
拾人餘唾 pick up whatever others say; plagiarize;
[拾遺] appropriate lost property;
拾遺補闕 make good omissions and deficiencies; make up for omissions and deficiencies;
路不拾遺 no one picks up what's left by the wayside;

掇拾 (1) tidy up; (2) collect; gather;
揀拾 pick up;
收拾 (1) put in order; tidy; (2) get things ready; pack; (3) mend; repair; (4) punish; settle with;
摭拾 pick up;

shi

【食】 (1) eat; (2) food; meal (3) feed; food for animals; (4) for cooking; edible; (5) same as 蝕, eclipse;
[食不重肉] not to take a second course of meat;
[食不厭精] meticulous about fine food; one does not object to the finest food;
[食單] menu;
[食道] gullet;
食道癌 cancer of the esophagus carcinoma esophagi;
~早期食道癌 early stage of carcinoma esophagi;
食道炎 esophagitis; inflammation of the esophagus;
[食而不化] eat without digesting — read without understanding; suffer from indigestion;
[食古不化] pedantic; swallow ancient learning without digesting it;
[食管] esophagus; gullet;
食管部份切除 esophagectomy; surgical removal of the esophagectomy;
食管痙攣 esophageal spasm;
~彌漫性食管痙攣 diffuse esophageal spasm;
食管狹窄 stenosis of the esophagus;
食管炎 esophagitis; inflammation of the esophagus;
~病毒性食管炎 viral esophagitis;
念珠菌性食管炎 candida esophagitis;
老年性食管 presbyesophagus;
[食街] food street;
[食盡鳥投林] when the food is gone the birds return to the wood;
[食具] dinner service; tableware;
[食客] hanger-on of an aristocrat;
[食糧] food; grain;
[食量] appetite; capacity for eating;
[食料] eatables; edibles; foodstuffs;
[食毛踐土] live on the land and eat what it produces;
[食米] rice;
[食品] eats; food; food items; food products; foodstuffs; provisions;
食品袋 food bag; taker bag;
食品店 bakery; confectionary; food store;
食品加工 food processing;
食品節 food fest; food festival;
食品添加劑 food additives;
食品通貨膨脹 agflation;
食品污染 food pollution;
食品屑 crumb;
食品工業 food industry; food technology;
超級食品 superfood;
寵物食品 pet food;
方便食品 convenience food;
輔助食品 accesary foods;
功能性食品 functional food;
罐頭食品 canned food; tinned food;
國際食品 international food;
加工食品 processed food;
健康食品 health food;
垃圾食品 junk food;
冷藏食品 chilled food;
冷凍食品 frozen food;
美味食品 grourment;
嗜好食品 fancy food;
特選食品 fancy food;
脱水食品 dehydrated food;
外賣食品 take-away;
現成食品 delicatessen;
小孩食品 baby food;
野餐食品 picnic supplies;
嬰兒食品 baby food;
營養食品 health food;
[食譜] collection of recipes; cookbook;
[食前] before meal;
[食人] cannibal;
食人風俗 cannibalism;
食人獸 man-eater;

率獸食人 tyranny of government;

[食肉] carnivorous;

食肉動物 carnivore;

食肉寢皮 eat sb's flesh and sleep on his hide — want to see the person one hates destroyed; have sb's flesh eaten and his hide slept on — bitter hatred for one's enemy;

食肉鳥 bird of prey;

食肉性 carnivority;

[食色性也] desire for food and sex is part of human nature;

[食少事繁] a lot of work and scanty meals; eat little and work much;

[食宿] bed and board; board and lodging;

安排食宿 arrange accommodations for sb;

東食西宿 without a definite place for board or lodging — make full use of the advantages offered;

全食宿 full board;

[食堂] canteen; dining room; lunchroom; mess hall; restaurant;

部隊食堂 mess hall;

[食糖] sugar;

[食物] ailment; eatable; edible; food; foodstuff; provision;

食物類別 food group

食物鏈 food chain;

食物券 food coupon; food stamp;

食物循環 food cycle;

~海洋食物循環 marine food cycle;

食物銀行 food bank;

食物中毒 food poisoning;

安慰食物 comfort food;

超級食物 superfood;

供應食物 virtual;

固體食物 solid food; solids;

沒吃的食物 uneaten food;

一口食物 a mouthful of food;

一小口食物 a morsel of food;

易飽的食物 stodge;

易腐食物 perishable foodstuff;

有機食物 organic food;

油膩食物 fatty foods;

[食言] break one's promise; break one's words; eat one's own words; fink out; go back on one's word;

食言而肥 break faith with sb; break one's promise; fail to make good one's promise;

不食所言 fulfil one's promise; not go back on one's word;

自食其言 break one's promise; go back on one's own words; run away from one's own guns;

[食鹽] salt; table salt;

[食用] (1) be used for food; edible; (2) living expenses;

食用動物 meat animals;

食用色素 food colouring;

食用油 edible oil;

[食油] cooking oil; edible oil;

[食玉炊桂] food as expensive as jade and fuel as expensive as cassia — extremely high cost of living; high prices of rice and fuel;

[食慾] appetite; belly;

食慾不佳 off one's feed; one's appetite is poor;

食慾不振 have a poor appetite; lose one's appetite; loss of appetite;

食慾過盛 bulimia;

食慾好 have a good appetite;

食慾缺乏 anorexia;

~神經性食慾缺乏 anorexia nervosa;

食慾抑制藥 anorexic;

引起食慾 work up an appetite;

[食指] forefinger; index; index finger;

食指浩繁 densely populated; many mouths to feed;

[食租衣税] live on rents and taxes;

白食 free meal;

飽食 eat to one's heart's content; glut;

暴食 eat too much at one meal;

捕食 catch and feed on;

蠶食 nibble;

饞食 greedy and voracious;

茶食 cakes and sweetmeats;

吃食 eatables; edibles; food;

粗食 coarse food;

存食 suffer from indigestion;

打食 (1) hunt for food; seek food; (2) help to digest and excrete; relieve indigestion with a drug;

獨食 domineering; selfish;

耳食 believe all that one hears;

飯食 food;

副食 non-staple food;

旰食 a late meal — too busy; eat late and get up early;

環食 annular eclipse of the sun;

伙食 board; fare; food; meal; mess; table;
即食 ready to eat instantly;
忌食 avoid certain food;
節食 diet; moderate in eating; on diet;
進食 have one's meal; take food;
禁食 fasting;
酒食 food and drink;
絕食 fast; go on a hunger strike;
克食 help one's digestion;
冷食 cold drinks and snacks;
糲食 coarse fare;
糧食 cereals; food; grain;
零食 between –meal nibbles; snacks;
流食 liquid;
美食 delicious food; delicacy; fine food; good food;
麵食 cooked wheaten food;
民食 people's grain or food and drinks;
偏食 (1) partial eclipse; (2) partiality for a particular kind of food;
乞食 beg for food;
寢食 sleeping and eating;
全食 total eclipse;
日食 solar eclipse;
肉食 (1) meat; (2) carnivorous;
乳食 take nothing but milk as food;
蓐食 (1) breakfast in bed; take meals in bed; (2) rich food;
軟食 soft diet; soft food;
膳食 food; meals;
傷食 dyspepsia caused by excessive eating or improper diet;
攝食 hunt for food;
侍食 serve one for dinner;
疏食 coarse meal;
蔬食 (1) vegetarian diet; (2) simple food;
熟食 cooked food; prepared food;
素食 vegetarian diet;
速食 fast food;
甜食 (1) confection; sweet food; sweetmeats; (2) afters; desert;
挑食 faddy;
停食 gastric disorder; indigestion;
退食 retire from a meal;
吞食 devour; swallow;
吸食 suck; take in;
鮮食 (1) fresh food; (2) eat fresh food;
消食 help to digest;
小食 refreshments; snacks;
厭食 apocleisis; lack of appetite;
饜食 eat to repletion;
衣食 food and clothing; what one lives on;
飲食 diet; drink and eat; eatables and drinkables; food and drink;
魚食 fish food;
玉食 dainties; delicacies;
月食 lunar eclipse;
擇食 select one's food;
蒸食 steamed wheaten foods;
終食 the duration of a meal;
豬食 pig feed;
主食 principal food; staple food;
啄食 eat by pecking; peck;
自食 be responsible for one's own action;
坐食 eat without toiling;

shi
【射】 when pronounced as a verb;

shi
【時】 (1) a long period of time; days; time; times; (2) fixed time; (3) hour; o'clock; time of day; (4) season; (5) current; fashionable; present; seasonable; timely; (6) chance; opportunity; (7) proper and adequate; (8) now and then; from time to time; occasionally; (9) now...now...; sometimes...sometimes; (10) tense; (11) a surname;

[時弊] current failings; current malpractice; ills of the time;

[時病] (1) malady of the age; (2) seasonal ailments;

[時不] there is no time;
時不可失 now for it; now or never; there is no time like the present; there is no time to lose;
時不我待 time and tide wait for no man; time stays for no man; time will not wait for us;
時不我與 lost time is never found again; time and tide wait for no one; time is running out;
時不宜遲 there's no time to be lost;
時不再來 lost time is never found again; such a chance will not present itself again; time lost cannot be won again; time lost is gone for good; time lost will return no more; time past cannot be recalled; time will never come again; time will not come back again;

[時差] time difference;

時差反應 jet lag;
[時常] every now and again; frequently; often; oftentimes; usually;
[時辰] one of the twelve two-hour periods;
[時代] age; epoch; era; period; times;
時代潮流 tendency of the day; trend of the times;
時代錯誤 anachronism;
~時代錯誤對等詞 anachronistic equivalent;
時代感 period feel;
時代精神 spirit of the time;
時代聚焦 times focus;
時代思潮 current trend of thoughts;
不同時代 different eras;
電腦時代 computer age;
電子時代 electronic age;
封建時代 feudal times;
工業時代 industrial age;
~超工業時代 superindustrial age;
紅銅時代 copper age;
劃時代 epoch-making;
~劃時代的改革 revolutionary transformation;
煉丹時代 alchemistic period;
啟蒙時代 Age of Enlightenment;
青銅時代 bronze age;
石器時代 anthropolithic age; Stone Age;
~舊石器時代 palaeolithic age;
~新石器時代 neolithic age;
~中石器時代 mesolithic age;
鐵器時代 iron age;
銅器時代 bronze age;
新時代 new era;
畜牧時代 pastoral age;
原子時代 atomic age;
[時段] time interval;
[時而] from time to time; sometimes;
[時分] (1) time division; (2) periods; seasons;
黃昏時分 at dusk; at twilight;
黎明時分 at the crack of dawn;
三更時分 at the third watch;
深夜時分 in the deep of night;
夜深時分 the deep of night;
正午時分 the meridian hour;
[時風] timely winds;
[時光] (1) time; (2) days; times; years;
時光飛逝 as the days whizzed by;
時光流逝 the race of time;
~時光流逝不回頭 time marches on;
時光荏苒 flight of time; time passes gradually; time zips by;
時光易逝 time passes quickly;
快樂時光 happy hour;
虛度時光 fiddle away;
[時過境遷] circumstances change with the passage of time; things have changed with the passage of time; times have passed and circumstances have changed;
時過境遷，滄海桑田 time works great changes;
[時號] time signal;
[時候] (1) time; (2) hour; juncture; moment; time;
趁時候 take advantage of the chance;
大多數時候 most of the time;
到時候 in due time;
開始的時候 at first;
前些時候 not too long ago; those days;
任何時候 any time;
~在任何時候 at any time;
晚些時候 late;
~星期二晚些時候 late on Tuesday;
在適當的時候 in due time;
早些時候 early; some time earlier;
~下午早些時候 early in the afternoon;
~星期五早些時候 early on Friday;
這個時候 at this moment in time;
[時會] (1) good luck; opportunity; (2) meet frequently;
[時機] opportune moment; opportunity;
時機不對 out of turn;
時機不恰當 out of season;
時機成熟 the opportunity is ripe;
時機一到 at the opportune moment; when the opportunity arises;
把握時機 seize the opportunity; seize the right time;
不失時機 let slip no opportunity of; in good time; lose no time; seize the opportune moment;
等待時機 bide one's time; wait for an opportunity;
靜待時機 wait till the clouds roll up;
選擇時機 choose the right moment;
抓住時機 seize the right opportunities;
[時計] chronometer;
[時價] current prices; market prices; ruling prices; running prices;
[時間] duration; hour; time;

時間逼人 time presses;
時間表 schedule; timeline; timetable;
時間不足 be pushed for time;
時間差 time lag;
時間詞 time words;
時間到了 time's up;
時間點 time-when;
~ 時間點從屬連詞 subordinator of time-when;
時間方面 time-wise;
時間附加語 time adjunct;
時間副詞 temporal adverb;
時間關係附加語 time relationship adjunct;
時間過長的 overlong;
時間過渡聯加語 conjunct of temporal transition;
時間機器 time machine;
時間計量 time measurement;
時間價值 time value;
時間緊迫 be pressed for time; be pushed for time; it'll be a push; time is pressing;
時間經濟學 time economics;
時間就是金錢 time is money;
時間控制器 timer;
時間框架 time frame;
時間流逝 as time goes by; with the passage of time;
時間頻度附加語 time frequency adjunct;
時間相依 time dependence;
時間效應 temporal effect;
時間形容詞 temporal adjective;
時間性 the time factor;
時間序列預測 time-series analysis forecasting;
時間延續附加語 time duration adjunct;
時間一分一秒地過去 the minutes tick past; the time is ticking away;
時間指示詞 time deixis;
時間主語 temporal subject;
時間狀語 adverbial of time;
~ 時間狀語從句 adverbial clause of time;
挨時間 dawdle; loiter; play for time; procrastinate; stall; stall for time;
愛惜時間 be economical of one's time; make the best use of one's time;
白費時間 fritter away one's time; kick one's heels; potter away one's time; trifle away one's time; waste one's time;
辦公時間 office hours;
寶貴的時間 precious time;
~ 失去寶貴的時間 lose one's precious time;
~ 贏得寶貴的時間 try to gain time precious to one;
爆炸時間 detonation time;
編譯持續時間 compiling duration;
標準時間 standard time;
長時間 for a long time;
~ 長時間地 till the cows come home;
充裕的時間 plenty of time;
存取時間 access time;
打發時間 piddle the time away; while away one's time;
~ 打發時間的工作 busywork;
大部份時間 most days; most of the time;
到時間了 time's up;
電弧時間 arc duration;
飛行時間 airtime;
趕時間 against time; in a hurry; in a rush;
黃金時間 prime time;
交貨時間 delivery time;
交通擁擠時間 rush hour;
結省時間 save time;
截止時間 closing time;
解碼時間 decode time;
絕對時間 absolute time;
開播時間 airtime;
開放時間 opening hours;
空閒時間 hours of disengagement; leisure time; vacant hours;
~ 在空閒時間 in one's own time;
寬限時間 grace period; time allowance;
浪費時間 dawdle the hours away; waste of time;
留意時間 watch the time;
沒有時間 time is not on our side;
每隔一定時間 at regular intervals;
磨時間 kill time;
內包時間 inclusive time;
搶時間 race against time;
任何時間 any time;
~ 在任何時間 at all hours; at any hour of the day;
霎時間 in a jiffy; in a split second; in a twinkling; in an instant;
上下班時間 commuter time;
所需時間 turnround;
探測時間 detection time;
探望時間 visiting hours;
通話計費時間 chargeable duration;
拖時間 delay; stall for time;

~ 拖延時間 play for time;
夏令時間 summer time;
消磨時間 kill time; pass the time;
一段時間 a period of time; some time;
一霎時間 in a jiffy; in a split second; in a twinkle; in a twinkling; in a wink; in the twinkling of an eye;
有的是時間 time is on our side;
預定時間 planned time;
~ 按預定時間 on schedule;
~ 遲於預定時間 behind schedule;
~ 先於預定時間 ahead of schedule;
佔用了全部時間 absorb all of one's time;
爭取時間 buy time;
裝卸時間 decking time;
作用時間 actuation duration;

[時艱] difficult times;
弘濟時艱 extensive relief of current difficulty;
匡濟時艱 relieve the timely difficulties;

[時節] (1) season; (2) time;
春耕時節 season for spring ploughing;
秋收時節 harvest time;

[時禁] current prohibitions;

[時局] current political situation; world situation;

[時距] time interval;

[時刻] (1) hour; moment; time; (2) always; constantly; continually;
時刻不忘 keep...in mind at all times;
時刻留意 keep one's eyes open;
時刻準備 ready at all times;
關鍵時刻 critical moment; in the nick of time;
每時每刻 all the time; at all times;
特定時刻 juncture;
無時無刻 all the time; always; at all times; at any moment; constantly; every hour and every moment; incessantly;
最黑暗的時刻 darkest hour;
最輝煌的時刻 finest hour; greatest hour;
最糟的時刻 low point;

[時空] space-time;

[時曆] calendar; almanac;

[時令] seasons; time of year;
時令不正 unseasonable weather;

[時碼] time code;
時碼讀出器 time code reader;

[時髦] fashionable; in vogue; modern; stylish; up-to-date; vogue;
時髦詞 vogue word;
時髦的 fashionable; funky; groovy; modist;
~ 穿着時髦的 dressy;
~ 非常時髦的 swanky;
時髦人物 hipster;
時髦用語 buzzword;
時髦自信的 debonair;
穿著時髦 be fashionably dressed;
趕時髦 climb the bandwagon; follow the fashion; get on the bandwagon; get with; jump the bandwagon; switch on; try to be in the swim;
~ 不好趕時髦 not like to be in the swim;
學時髦 follow the fashion;

[時命] (1) one's luck; (2) current government orders;

[時評家] commentator on current affairs;

[時期] (1) age; era; period; times; (2) duration;
巔峰時期 noontide of;
加速時期 accelerating period;
歷史上最光輝的時期 most brilliant chapter in the history;
少壯時期 pride of youth;
一段時期 an episode;
一段走運的時期 a streak of luck;
原始氏族時期 primitive gens period;

[時區] time zone;

[時人] contemporaries; people of the time;
妙絕時人 unparalleledly wonderful in one's time;

[時日] (1) time and date; (2) long duration of time;
假以時日 give sufficient time;
寬限時日 days of grace;
曠延時日 procrastination of time;
每時每日 daily and hourly; every day and every minute;

[時尚] craze; fad; fashion; trend; vogue;
時尚達人 fashionista;
時尚熱潮 craze;

[時時] constantly; continually; frequently; often;
時…時 intermittent; now...now...; off and on; sometimes...sometimes...;
時時處處 always and everywhere; in all matters;
時時刻刻 all the time; always; at every moment; at moments; constantly; continually; every minute; every now and then; hour by hour;
時輟時續 by fits and starts;

時緊時緩 now speed it up, now slow it down;
時作時輟 by fits and starts; on and off; work and stop every now and then; work in jerks;
時做時停 work and stop every now and then; work by fits and starts;

[時世] age; epoch; era; times;
汩沒時世 go with the current of the age;

[時式] modern fashion; modern style; up-to-date style;

[時事] current affairs; current events; current state of affairs;
時事報告 report on current events;
時事即景 passing show;
時事論壇 affairs review;
時事評論 criticisms on current events;
時事述評 current events survey;
時事政治 politics of current events;
時事追蹤 current events tracing;

[時勢] current situation; current trend of events; time and circumstances; trend of the times;
時勢使然 it is the natural outcome of the time and circumstances; trend of the times makes it so;
時勢所趨 trend of the times;
時勢造英雄 a hero is nothing but a product of his time; circumstances create heroes; he is born in a good hour who gets a good name; the times produce their heroes;
趁時及勢 make use of the time and circumstances;
乘時乘勢 catch the time and seize the rigth moment;
審時度勢 judge the hour and size up the situation; make an assessment of the situation; observe the times and judge the occasion; see how the gander hops; see how the land lies;

[時速] speed per hour;

[時態] tense;
時態簡化 tense simplification;
時態序 sequence of tense;
時態一致 concord of tenses;
時態轉移 tense shift;
現在時態 present tense;
~歷史性現在時態 historic present;

[時務] current affairs; trend of the times;
識時務 know how the wind blows; understand the times;
~識時務者為俊傑 a great man knows how to ride the tide of his time; a hero must bow to circumstances; a wise man submits to circumstances; adapt yourself to the times; he is wise who understands the times; one is able and wise who understands the signs of the times; the man who can recognize the facts of a situation is a paragon of men; the superior people are those who understand the times; those who suit their actions to the time of day are wise; those ho suit their actions to the times are wise; time-servers are clever; whosoever understands the times is a great man;
不識時務 do not understand the times;

[時下] at present; at the moment; in these days; nowadays; of the moment;
時下最熱門的話題 hot topics;

[時鮮] (1) in season; (2) seasonable delicacies;

[時賢] contemporary men of ability and integrity; great scholars of the period; social leaders of the time;

[時限] deadline; time limit;
設定時限 set a time limit;

[時效] (1) effectiveness; (2) prescription; (3) ageing;
時效性 limitation;
低溫時效 low-temperature ageing;
高溫時效 high-temperature ageing;
合金時效 alloy ageing;
階段時效 stepped ageing;
金屬時效 ageing of metal;
臨界時效 critical ageing;
取得時效 positive prescription;
熱時效 warm ageing;
消失時效 negative prescription;
雙時效 double ageing;
延緩時效 delayed ageing;

[時新] stylish; trendy;

[時興] all the vogue; faddish; fashionable; in vogue; popular; prevailing;

[時行] fashionable; popular;

[時序] seasons; times;
時序控制 time programme control;
時序易遷 the seasons change;

[時宜] what is appropriate to the occasion; what is proper at the time;

時宜性 appropriateness;
恰合時宜 exactly appropriate to the occasion; exactly in keeping with the times;
正合時宜 seasonable; well timed;

[時移] times change;
時移俗易 customs change with the times; customs vary with the change of ages; other times, other manners; times change, and with them customs and habits too; times have changed, so have the social customs;
時移物換 things change as time flies; tings have changed with the passing of time;

[時疫] epidemic;

[時雨] (1) timely rains; (2) culture and education;
時雨春風 stimulating influence of teachers;

[時遇] one's luck;
時遇不濟 out of luck;

[時譽] esteem; honour; popularity;

[時運] fortune; luck; times;
時運不濟 down on one's luck; fall on evil days; have bad luck; off one's luck; out of luck; under a cloud;
時運亨通 hit the jackpot; lucky; one's luck is in; one's star is on the ascendant;
時運維艱 the times are difficult;

[時針] hour hand of a clock;

[時政] current political affairs;

[時鐘] clock;
時鐘酒店 love hotel;
時鐘速度 clock speed;
時鐘週期 clock cycle;
便攜式時鐘 carriage clock;
重調時鐘 reset a clock;
數字時鐘 digital clock;

[時裝] fashion; fashionable dress;
時裝表演 fashion show;
~時裝表演台 catwalk;
時裝店 boutique; fashion shop;
時裝公司 fashion company; fashion house;
時裝節 fashion festival;
時裝界 fashion world;
時裝模特 fashion model;
時裝拍攝 fashion shoot;
時裝設計 fashion design;
~時裝設計師 fashion designer;
時裝秀 fashion show;
時裝業 fashion industry;
時裝展覽 fashion show;
昂貴的時裝 couture; expensive fashion;

按時 according to a fixed time; according to the scheduled time; according to the time specified; at the right time; duly; in due course; in due time; in good time; in time; on schedule; on scratch; on time; punctually;
報時 give the correct time;
背時 (1) behind the times; (2) out of luck; unlucky;
標準時 standard time;
悖時 behind the times;
比時 at that time; then;
彼時 at that time;
晡時 late afternoon;
餔時 evening; late afternoon; suppertime;
補時 added time;
不時 at times; at whiles; between whiles; ever and again; every now and again; every now and then; from time to time; now and again; now and then; occasionally; on occasion; once in a while;
超時 overrun;
潮時 time of tide;
辰時 period of the day from 7 a.m. to 9 a.m.;
丑時 period of the day from 1 a.m. to 3 a.m.;
此時 at present; for the time being; now; right now; this moment;
待時 wait for the right moment;
當時 at that time; at the moment; at the time; just at that moment; then;
得時 in luck;
登時 at once; immediately; then and there;
定時 at regular time; fixed time; timing;
短時 short time;
頓時 at once; immediately; in a short space;
多時 a long time;
費時 be time-consuming; take time;
複合時 compound tense;
干時 seek to keep up with the times; suit the occasion;
工時 labour time; man-hour; task time; working hours;
共時 synchronic;
過時 (1) behind the times; go out; go out of fashion; obsolete; out of date; out of fashion; out of style; out-dated; (2) past the

appointed time;
亥時 period of the day from 9 p.m. to 11 p.m.;
何時 at what time; when;
及時 at a most opportune moment; at the right time; in due course; in due time; in good season; in good time; in season; in the nick of time; in time; promptly; timely; without delay;
即時 forthwith; immediacy; immediately; real-time; simultaneous;
幾時 what time; when;
計時 reckon by time;
記時 time-keeping;
屆時 on the appointed time; on the occasion; when the time comes;
進行時 continuous tense; progressive tense;
舊時 old days; told times;
課時 class hour; class period; class time; lesson period; lesson time; period;
立時 at once; immediately; right away;
歷時 last; take;
臨時 (1) at the time when sth happens; (2) for a short time; temporary;
零時 zero hour;
忙時 busy hour;
某時 sometime;
那時 at that time; in those days; then;
曩時 in former times; in the past;
逆時 inverse time;
農時 farming season;
片時 a moment; a short time; a short while;
平時 (1) at ordinary times; in normal times; (2) in peacetime;
區時 zone time;
趨時 follow the fashion;
權時 for the time being;
恁時 then; when that happens;
入時 fashionable; stylish; trendy;
霎時 in a jiffy; in a split second; in a twinkling;
少時 a moment later; after a little while; when one is young;
申時 period of the day from 3 p.m. to 5 p.m.;
省時 save time; timesaving;
失時 let slip the opportunity; miss the opportune moment; miss the right opportunity; miss the season;
實時 actual time; real time; true time;
適時 at the right moment; at the right time; in good time; in the nick of time; timely;
守時 punctual; time keeping;
授時 time service;
順時 in luck; on time; up time;
瞬時 instantaneous;
斯時 presently; such a time; this time;
巳時 period of the day from 9 a.m. to 11 a.m.;
四時 four seasons;
隨時 (1) at all times; at any time; (2) as the occasion demands; whenever necessary;
歲時 time of year; times and seasons;
天時 (1) climate; weather; (2) opportunity; timeliness;
同時 all at once; all together; and; at once; at one fell; at one swoop; at one time; at the same time; in the meantime; in the same breath; meanwhile; moreover; simultaneously;
瓦時 watt-hour;
往時 formerly; in the past;
為時 the time is;
未時 period of the day from 1 p.m. to 3 p.m.;
午時 period of the day from 11 a.m. to 1 p.m.;
誤時 behind time;
昔時 in former days; in the olden days;
暇時 at leisure; at one's leisure; in one's leisure time; spare time;
閒時 leisure; spare time;
限時 fix the time; set a deadline; set a time limit; set the time;
現時 at present; now;
興時 fashionable; popular at the moment;
行時 (1) all the rage; fashionable; in vogue; (2) in the ascendent;
小時 hour;
戌時 period of the day from 7 p.m. to 9 p.m.;
學時 class hour; period;
延時 time-delay;
一時 (1) a period of time; (2) for a short while; momentary; temporary; (3) now...now...; one moment..., the next;
移時 a brief period of time; a little while;
異時 past time;
寅時 period of the day from 3 a.m. to 5 a.m.;
應時 (1) in season; seasonable; (2) at once; immediately;
有時 at times; now and then; sometimes;
酉時 period of the day from 5 p.m. to 7 p.m.;
遇時 catch the right opportunity; ride at the crest of one's fortune;
閱時 last a period of time;
早時 in former times;
暫時 at the moment; for the moment; for the present; for the time being; temporary; transient; yet;
戰時 wartime;
準時 at the scheduled time; on schedule; on the

S

button; on the dot; on the minute; on the tick; on time; prompt; punctual; sharp; to the minute; to the tick; to the very moment;
子時 period of the day from 11 p.m. to 1 a.m.;
走時 in a spell of good luck;

shi

【湜】 (of water) transparent;
[湜湜] clear stream;

shi

【實】 (1) concrete; solid; substantial; tangible; (2) actual; real; true; (3) fact; reality; truth; (4) faithful; honest; sincere; (5) fruit; seed;
[實地] (1) on the spot; (2) in real earnest; indeed;
實地調查 on-the-spot investigation;
實地考察 fieldwork; on-the-spot investigation; inspect on the spot;
實地實驗 field experiment;
實地試驗 field test;
[實幹] do solid work; get right on the job; steadfast in one's work; take real action;
實幹的人 doer;
[實話] truth;
實話實說 lay it on the line; not beat about the bush; not to mince words; put it on the line; speak frankly; talk straight; tell the truth;
講實話 speak the truth;
說實話 not mince matters; speak frankly; talk straight; tell the truth;
[實惠] (1) material benefit; real benefit; tangible benefit; (2) solid; substantial;
得到實惠 receive great material benefits;
講實惠 practical-minded;
空談而無實惠 all talk and no cider;
[實績] actual results; tangible achievements;
[實際] (1) practice; reality; (2) practical; realistic; (3) actual; concrete; real;
實際編碼 real coding;
實際工資 real wages;
實際經驗 practical experience;
實際困難 practical difficulties;
實際利益 actual benefits;
實際情況 actual situation; reality;
實際上 actually; as a matter of fact; as good as; as it is; at bottom; at root; in effect; in essence; in fact; in point of fact; in practice; in reality; in truth; indeed; for all practical purposes; morally; practically; properly speaking; really; to all intents and purposes; to all purposes; virtually; when; whereas;
實際生活 real life;
實際收入 real income;
實際收益率 actual income rate;
實際數據庫 real database;
不切實際 impracticable; not to correspond to reality; out of touch with reality; unpractical; unrealistic;
~不切實際的 airy fairy; blue-sky; cock-eyed;
符合實際 correspond to reality;
客觀實際 objective reality;
[實價] actual price; real price;
[實踐] (1) practice; (2) carry out; live up to; put into practice; reduce to practice;
實踐出真知 experience is the mother of wisdom; genuine knowledge comes from practice; practice yields genuine knowledge;
實踐活動 practical activities;
實踐經驗 practical experience;
實踐能力 practical abilities;
實踐諾言 keep one's word; make good one's promise;
實踐哲學 practical philosophy;
實踐自己的主張 put one's ideas into practice;
翻譯實踐 translation practice;
躬行實踐 practise what one preaches;
會計實踐 accounting practice;
農業實踐 agricultural practice;
親身實踐 hands-on;
生活實踐 practice in daily life;
[實距] actual distance;
[實據] substantial evidence; substantial proof;
查無實據 investigations show no evidence; no evidence is found after a thorough investigation;
查有實據 investigation reveals valid evidence;
披露實據 disclose valid evidence;
提供實據 produce factual evidence;
[實況] factual conditions; what is actually happening;
實況錄音 live recording; on-the-spot recording;

實況轉播 field pick up; location broadcasting; outside broadcasting;

[實力] actual strength; strength;

實力相當 close game; match each other in strength; well-matched in strength;

保存實力 conserve one's forces; preserve one's strength;

國防實力 national defence capabilities;

恢復實力 recover one's strength;

軟實力 soft power;

[實利] actual gains; net profit; practical value; tangible benefits;

[實例] case; example; living example;

包含實例 contain an example; include an example;

發現實例 find an example;

舉一個實例 cite an actual example;

引用實例 cite an example;

[實錄] faithful record;

[實拍拍] actually; really;

[實情] actual situation; real picture; real story; true state of affairs; truth;

實情實理 actual situation and the real reason;

實情實事 real facts and real sentiments;

了解實情 know the score;

説明實情 clear up the truth;

委系實情 this is the true story;

[實權] real power;

無實權的 ceremonial;

[實施] become effective; bring into action; bring into effect; bring into force; bring into operation; call into action; carry into effect; carry out; come into effect; come into force; come into operation; go into effect; go into force; go into operation; implement; put into action; put into effect; put into force; put into operation; put into practice; take effect;

實施評價 approaisal on the implementation;

實施條例 enforcement regulations;

~頒布實施條例 issue enforcement regulations;

實施細則 detailed rules and regulations of implementation;

付諸實施 bring into effect; carry into effect; carry into execution; carry into practice; carry out; give teeth; put into action; put into execution; put into effect; put into practice;

見之實施 carry out; put into effect;

[實時] actual time; real time; true time;

實時操作系統 real-time operating system;

實時處理 real-time processing;

~實時處理系統 real-time processing system;

實時監控 real time monitoring;

~實時監控系統 real-time monitor control system;

實時聯機操作 real-time on-line operation;

實時輸入 real-time input;

實時數據處理 real-time data processing;

實時系統 real time system;

實時性研究 study of real-timeliness;

實時專家系統 real-time expert system;

[實事] (1) facts; (2) solid work;

實事求是 act in a practical and businesslike manner; base on facts; be practical and realistic; call a pikestaff a pikestaff; call a spade a spade; come down to earth; do things in a down-to-earth manner; give consideration to facts; have one's feet on the ground; in a matter-of-fact way; in a practical and realistic way; make conscientious efforts to do things; practical; practical and realistic; seek the truth from facts; true to facts; truthful and factual; use a practical approach;

辦實事 do sth concrete;

實有其事 it really happed; it's a fact;

做實事 do solid work; perform real deeds;

[實屬公便] it is fitting and proper; it is for the benefit of all parties concerned; truly just and expedient;

[實數] real number;

[實體] (1) substance; (2) entity;

實體安全 entity security;

實體結構圖 entity structure diagram;

實體經濟 real economy;

保險實體 risk-bearing entity;

單獨實體 separate entity;

獨立實體 separate entity;

法人實體 legal entity;

經濟實體 economic entity;

統一實體 consolidated entity;

[實物] (1) material object; (2) entity; matter;

實物工資 wages in kind;

實物教學 object teaching;

[實習] externship; field trip; fieldwork;

internship; practice;
實習教師 trainee teacher;
實習生 extern; intern; trainee;
實習醫生 intern;
對口實習 doing practice geared to the needs of the job;
教學實習 doing practice teaching;
野外實習 conducting field-work;

[實現] accomplish; achieve; attain; bring about; come true; complete; difficult of accomplishment; easy of accomplishment; enforce; fruition; materialize; realize;
實現改革 bring about a reform;
實現計劃 realize a plan;
自我實現 self-actualization;

[實相] truth;
實相條件 truth-condition;
分析實相 analytic truth;
句法實相 syntactic truth;

[實效] actual effect; effect; real effect; substantial results;
求實效 seek practical results;
~講求實效 strive for substantial results;
確有實效 prove to be really effective;
注重實效 emphasize practical results;

[實心] (1) honest; sincere; (2) in a serious manner; (3) solid;
實心話 words spoken from one's heart;
實心實意 honest and sincere;

[實行] bring into effect; carry into effect; carry out; implement; practise; put into action; put into effect; put into practice;
實行經濟改革 carry out economic reforms;
徹底實行 follow through;
諭令實行 order to put into operation;

[實學] real learning; sound scholarship;
有虛名並無實學 enjoy a reputation unwarranted by real learning;

[實驗] experiment; test; trial run;
實驗報告 laboratory report;
實驗對象 guinea pig;
實驗劇場 experimental theatre;
實驗劇團 experimental theatre;
實驗失敗 fail in an experiment;
實驗師 experimentalist;
~高級實驗師 senior experimentalist;
~助理實驗師 assistant experimentalist;
實驗室 laboratory;
~實驗室試驗 laboratory tests;
~實驗室研究 laboratory studies;
~電化實驗室 electrochemical laboratory;
~活動實驗室 mobile laboratory;
~研究實驗室 research laboratory;
實驗員 laboratory technician;
對比實驗 contrast experiment;
急性實驗 acute experiment;
進行實驗 carry out an experiment; conduct an experiment; do an experiment; perform an experiment;
科學實驗 scientific experiment;
控制性實驗 controlled experiment;
慢性實驗 chronic experiment;
實際實驗 practical experiment;
實驗室實驗 laboratory experiment;
一次實驗 an experiment;
做實驗 conduct an experiment; conduct experiments; do an experiment; make a test;

[實業] industry; industry and commerce;
實業家 businessman; entrepreneur; industrialist;
~女實業家 businesswoman;
實業救國 save the nation by engaging in industry;

[實義] full;
實義詞 full word;
~實義詞素 content morpheme;
實義動詞 full verb;
實義名詞 stock noun;

[實用] (1) practical use; (2) functional; practical; pragmatic; useful;
實用程序 utility programme;
實用翻譯 practical translation;
實用技術 approproiate technology;
~實用技術信息庫 apporpriate technology information database;
實用軟件 utility software;
實用文獻 practical text;
實用系統 utility system;
實用語言學 practical linguistics;
實用指南 practical guide;
實用主義 pragmatism;
不實用 unusefulness;

[實在] certainly; for sure; in fact; in truth; indeed; really; truly;
說話實在 shoot straight;
實實在在 down-to-earth; in the name of goodness; on the level;

[實戰] actual combat;

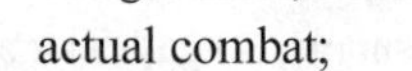

實戰訓練 exercise under battle conditions;
實戰演習 combat exercise with live ammunition;

[實證] authentic proof;
實證論 positivism;
實證主義 positivism;
~實證主義者 positivist;

[實質] essence; substance; texture;
實質性部分 nitty-gritty;
實質性測試 substantive tests;

避實 avert disasters;
跴實 (1) tread; tread down; (2) mat down;
踩實 mat; trample down;
查實 investigate and verify;
沉實 (1) firm; powerful; weighty; (2) solid; steady;
誠實 honest;
充實 enrich; replenish; rich; substantial; substantiate;
瓷實 solid; substantial;
從實 based on the fact; in light of the fact;
粗實 solid;
篤實 (1) honest and sincere; (2) solid; sound;
敦實 solid; stocky;
肥實 (1) fat; stout; (2) fat;
符實 conform to reality; tally with the fact;
故實 historical facts;
果實 (1) fruit; (2) fruits; gains;
頇實 thick and solid;
憨實 (1) stalwart; sturdy; (2) simple-hearted;
核實 check; verify;
厚實 thick;
槲實 acorn;
芰實 water caltrop;
紀實 on-the-spot report; record of actual events;
記實 documentary;
堅實 (1) solid; substantial; (2) staunch; strong;
結實 (1) bear fruit; (2) durable; solid; (3) strong; sturdy; tough;
據實 be based on the fact;
口實 cause for gossip; handle;
老實 (1) frank; honest; (2) well-behaved; (3) easily taken in; simple-minded;
落實 (1) practicable; workable; (2) ascertain; fix in advance; make sure; (3) carry out; fulfill; implement; put into effect;
密實 closely knit; dense;
名實 name and reality;
皮實 (1) sturdy; (2) durable;
平實 natural; simple and unadorned;
樸實 (1) plain; simple; (2) guileless; sincere and honest;
其實 actually; as a matter of fact; in fact; in reality; in truth; really;
芡實 Gorgon fruit;
切實 (1) feasible; practical; (2) conscientiously; earnestly;
情實 (1) facts of an affair; (2) the crime has been confirmed;
秋實 fruits in autumn;
求實 be particular about the matter-of-fact attitude;
確實 (1) certain; certainty; real; reliable; true; (2) indeed; really; (3) verify;
如實 accurately; as things really are; strictly according to the facts; truthfully;
失實 be inconsistent with the facts;
史實 historical facts;
事實 fact; reality; truth;
屬實 be verified; true; turn out to be true;
松實 pine nut;
塌實 (1) dependable; earnest; steadfast; steady and sure; (2) at ease; free from anxiety; having peace of mind;
踏實 practical; realistic;
妥實 proper and reliable; well arranged;
委實 indeed; really;
務實 deal with concrete matters relating to work;
現實 (1) actuality; reality; things as they are; (2) actual; practical; pragmatic; real;
翔實 detailed and accurate; full and accurate;
詳實 full and accurate;
橡實 acorn;
寫實 write or paint realistically;
心實 honest; truthful;
信實 reliable; trustworthy;
杏實 apricot fruit;
虛實 false or true; the actual situation;
敍實 factual;
嚴實 (1) close; tight; (2) safely;
依實 according to fact; confess truthfully;
殷實 substantial; well-off;
勻實 even; neat; uniform;
扎實 (1) strong; sturdy; (2) down-to-earth; solid;
折實 (1) reckon the actual amount after a discount; (2) adjust payment in accordance with the price index of certain commodities;
真實 authentic; factual; real; true;
榛實 hazelnut;
徵實 collect levies in kind;
證實 affirm; authenticate; confirm; confirmation; corroborate; corroboration; demonstrate;

prove; verify;
忠實 faithful; true;
竹實 bamboo seed;
壯實 robust; sturdy;
拙實 big and strong; raw and sturdy; solidly built;
着實 (1) indeed; really; (2) concrete and substantial; dependable;
子實 beans; grains; kernels; seeds;

shi

【碩】 eminent; great;
[碩大無朋] gigantic; mammoth; unequalled in huge size;
[碩輔] virtuous minister;
[碩果] great fruits;
碩果僅存 rare survival;
[碩惠] great indebtedness;
[碩老] learned elder; old venerable scholar;
[碩量] lenient capacity for tolerance;
[碩儒] great Confucian scholar; great scholar;
[碩望] person of great fame; much respected person;
[碩學] erudite scholar;
碩學鴻儒 erudite and wise scholar;
宏才碩學 profound learning and great abilities;
宏儒碩學 profound literati and great learners;
[碩言] boastful talks; grand words;
[碩彥] learned scholar; person of great talent;

shi

【蝕】 (1) lose; (2) corrode; eat up slowly; erode; (3) eclipse;
[蝕本] lose money; lose one's capital;
蝕本生意 business running at a loss; losing business; unprofitable venture;
[蝕財] lose money;
[蝕耗] loss; wear and tear;
[蝕刻] etch; etching;
[蝕年] eclipse year;
[蝕損] suffer losses;
[蝕限] eclipse limit;

冰蝕 ice erosion;
剥蝕 corrode; denude; erode; wear away;
初蝕 first contact;
吹蝕 deflation;
風蝕 wind erosion;
腐蝕 (1) corrode; etch; (2) corrode; corrupt;
光線日蝕 optical eclipse;
海蝕 marine corrosion;
環蝕 annular eclipse;
虧蝕 abrasion;
偏蝕 partial eclipse;
侵蝕 (1) corrode; erode; (2) embezzle; misappropriate;
全環蝕 full annular eclipse;
全蝕 total eclipse;
日蝕 solar eclipse;
溶蝕 corrosion;
水蝕 water erosion;
天文蝕 astronomical eclipse;
微粒蝕 corpuscular eclipse;
銷蝕 corrode; wear out;
月蝕 lunar eclipse;
中心蝕 central eclipse;

shi

【蒔】 (1) cultivate; plant; transplant; (2) anethum graveoleus, a kind of spice;
[蒔花] grow flowers;
[蒔蘿] anethum graveolens, a kind of spice;
[蒔秧] transplant rice seedlings;

shi

【識】 (1) discern; know; recognize; (2) knowledge; (3) opinion; view;
[識拔] appreciate and promote;
[識辨] discern; distinguish;
[識別] discern; distinguish; identification; identify; recognition; spot;
識別好壞 tell the right from the wrong;
識別機 recognizer;
~ 模式識別機 pattern recognizer;
識別力 power of discernment;
識別器 recognizer;
~ 字識別器 word recognizer;
識別真僞 distinguish true from false;
車輪自動識別 automatic car identification;
符號識別 character recognition;
聚合識別 cluster identification;
列車自動識別 automatic train identification;
人工識別 artificial cognition;
數據識別 data recognition;
數字識別 digital recognition;
文獻識別 bibliographic identification;
細胞識別 cell recognition;
[識貨] able to tell good from bad; appreciate; know all about the goods; know what

is what;
[識記] memorize;
[識見] insight; knowledge and experience; understanding;
識多見廣 have a wide range of experience; have extensive knowledge and wide experience; learned and experienced;
[識荊] have the honour of knowing sb in person; have the honour of making sb's acquaintance;
識荊恨晚 regret not to have known you before;
[識破] penetrate; see through;
識破騙局 see through a fraud;
[識趣] have tact; know how to behave in a delicate situation; tactful;
[識人] able to appraise a person's ability and character correctly;
慧眼識人 develop a sharp eye for discovering able people;
[識相] know how to avoid embarrassment; know when to yield with grace; sensible; tactful;
[識者] expert; those in the know;
[識字] able to read; literate;
識字知禮 recognize characters and be acquainted with rules of etiquette;
看圖識字 learn characters through pictures; learn reading by way of pictyures; learn to read with the aid of pictures;

辨識 identification; recognize;
標識 identify;
博識 erudite; learned;
不識 fail to see; ignorant of; not appreciate; not know;
才識 ability and insight;
常識 (1) general knowledge; (2) common sense;
膽識 courage and insight;
見識 enrich one's experience; experience; insight; knowledge; widen one's knowledge;
結識 get acquainted with sb; get to know sb;
姘識 get acquainted and then have illicit sexual relations with;
認識 know; knowledge; recognize; understanding;
賞識 appreciate; recognize the worth of;
熟識 be well acquainted with; know well;
相識 acquaintance; be acquainted with each other;
學識 knowledge; learning;
意識 awake to; be conscious of; consciousness; realize;
知識 (1) knowledge; (2) intellectual; pertaining to learning or culture;
卓識 judicious judgment; superior insight or judgment;

shi
【鰣】 hilsa herring; reeves shad;
[鰣魚] hilsa herring; reeves shad;

shi³
shi
【史】 (1) annals; chronicles; history; (2) official historian in ancient China; (3) a surname;
[史不絕書] history abounds in examples of this; history is full of such instances;
[史冊] annal; book of history;
名留史冊 remain immortal in the annals;
永垂史冊 go down forever in the annals of history;
載入史冊 be written into the annals of history; go down in history;
[史官] historiographer; official historian;
[史觀] concept of history;
唯物史觀 materialist conception of history;
唯心史觀 idealist conception of history;
[史館] national archives;
[史話] historical narrative; historical story;
[史蹟] (1) historical events; (2) historic relics;
[史籍] historical records; history;
[史家] historian;
[史料] historical data; historical materials;
[史略] brief history; outline history;
[史論] critical essay on history;
[史評] historical criticism;
[史前] prehistoric;
史前時代 prehistoric age;
史前史 prehistory;
[史乘] annals; historical works; history;
[史詩] epic;
一首史詩 an epic poem;
[史實] historical facts;
[史書] annal; book of history; historical records; history;

[史無前聞] unheard of in history;
[史學] (1) history; (2) historiography;
史學家 (1) historian; (2) historiographer;
史學研究 historical research;
史學證據 historical evidence;

稗史 historical romance; unofficial history;
病史 medical history;
廠史 history of a factory;
刺史 feudal provincial or prefectural governor;
村史 village history;
典史 government secretary;
國史 (1) history of a nation; (2) court historian;
家史 family history;
經濟史 economic history;
經史 Confucian classics and history;
經營史 business history;
歷史 history; past events; past records;
秘史 inside story; secret history;
農業史 agrarian history;
青史 annals of history;
情史 love story;
生態史 ecological history;
詩史 (1) history of poetry; (2) epic;
太史 court historian;
通史 comprehensive history; general history;
文史 literature and history;
先史 prehistoric;
信史 authentic history; faithful historical account; true history;
艷史 amorous adventures; love affairs; romantic adventures;
野史 privately compiled history; unofficial history;
雜史 unofficial history;
戰史 annals of war; war history;
正史 history books written in biographical style; official history;
專史 specific history;
左史 official historian;

shi

【矢】 (1) arrow; dart; (2) pledge; swear; take an oath; vow; (3) display; (4) straightforward; (5) faeces;
[矢車菊] bachelor's button; bluebottle; centaury; cornflower;
矢車菊苷 centaurin;
海紅矢車菊 large centaury;
小矢車菊 small centaury;
[矢服] quiver for holding arrows;
[矢口] assert positively; insist emphatically; state categorically; swear; vow;
矢口不移 adhere to one's declaration; stick to one's original statement;
矢口成言 words uttered become a saying;
矢口抵賴 deny flatly; refuse pointblank to admit; refuse to admit even unto death;
矢口否認 deny by oath; deny firmly; flatly deny;
矢口狡賴 persistently quibble and deny one's errors; quibble and prevaricate, refusing to admit one's guilt;
[矢量] phasor; vector;
矢量分析 vector analysis;
彩色矢量 colour phasor;
電流矢量 current phasor;
信號矢量 signal phasor;
載波矢量 carrier phasor;
[矢窮紘絕] at one's wits' end; without resources;
[矢石] arrows and stones in ancient warfare;
矢石俱下 shower of arrows and stones; stones and arrows flow about in all directions; stones are rolled down and arrows shot;
矢石如雨 arrows and crossbow bolts begin to fall like rain; arrows and stones come down like a shower; arrows and stones fall like rain; shoot arros and hurl stones like rain;
[矢志] swear that one will never change;
矢志不移 swear to adhere to one's chosen course; one's resolve is unshaken; take an oath not to change one's mind;
矢志力行 make a detremined effort;
矢志靡他 swear that one would stick it out;

飛矢 flying arrow;
嚆矢 (1) arrow with a whistle attached; (2) forerunner; harbinger; precursor;
流矢 flying or stray arrow;
餘矢 coversed sine;
正矢 versine;

shi

【弛】 neglect; relax; unstring;
[弛廢] neglect; negligence;
[弛緩] relax;
[弛禁] lift a restriction; rescind a prohibition;
[弛張] tension and relaxation;

shi

【豕】 hog; pig; swine;
[豕膏] pig's fat;
[豕牢] pigpen; pigsty;
[豕奴] swineherd;
[豕突] run wild;
豕突狼奔 the pigs dash and the wolves rush;
[豕心] avaricious; greedy;

shi

【使】 (1) send; tell sb to do sth; (2) apply; employ; use; (3) cause; enable; make; (4) envoy; messenger; (5) if; provided; supposing;
[使絆子] put a spoke in sb's wheel; try to trip sb up;
[使不慣] not familiar with the use of; not used to;
[使不上] not usable; unfit to be used;
[使出] exert; use;
使出渾身解數 bring all one's skill into play; bring forth all the talent one has; do all that one is capable of; do one's best; exert oneself to the utmost to; use all one's skill;
[使得] (1) can be used; usable; (2) feasible; workable; (3) make; render;
使得上 can be used; employable; usable; useful;
使不得 must not; undesirable;
[使壞] (1) play a dirty trick; up to mischief; (2) destroy;
[使喚] (1) answer the beck and call of; run errands for; (2) order others to do sth;
[使節] diplomatic envoy; envoy; legate;
教皇使節 legate;
外交使節 diplomatic envoy;
文化使節 cultural envoy;
[使勁] apply force; exert effort; strain; use force;
使勁兒 exert all one's strength; put in energy;
使勁幹活 work hard;
[使酒] get drunk and behave irrationally;
[使君有婦] married man; one who has a wife;
[使命] mission;
使命感 calling; sense of calling; sense of mission;
完成使命 accomplish one's mission;

[使女] chambermaid; housemaid; maidservant;
[使氣] be influenced by sentiment in handling things;
[使錢] (1) use money; (2) bribe;
[使人] make people...;
使人發瘋 drive sb crazy; drive sb mad; drive sb round the bend;
使人情緒高昂 set on fire;
使人厭惡 put sb's teeth on edge; set sb's teeth on edge;
使人作嘔 make sb's gorge rise; make sb's stomach rise; turn sb's stomach; turn the stomach of sb;
[使徒] apostles; disciples;
[使役] attendants; servants;
[使用] apply; employ; make use of; resort to; use;
使用額 amount of disbursement;
使用費 user fee;
使用價值 use value;
使用率 rate of utilization;
使用權 right of use;
使用壽命 service life;
不再使用 out of use;
過度使用 overuse;
開始使用 come into use;
[使者] emissary; envoy; messenger;
綠衣使者 mail carrier; mailman;
派遣使者 dispatch an envoy;
天國使者 angelic messengers;
友好使者 ambassador of goodwill; goodwill ambassador;

差使 assign; commission; official post; send;
出使 be sent on a diplomatic mission; serve as an envoy abroad;
促使 impel; lead on to; spur; urge;
大使 ambassador;
公使 envoy; minister;
即使 even; even if; even though; notwithstanding;
假使 if; in case; in the event that;
來使 envoy; messenger;
密使 secret emissary; secret envoy;
迫使 compel; force;
強使 compel; force;
驅使 (1) order about; (2) prompt; spur on;
設使 if; supposing;
唆使 abet; incite;
倘使 if; in case;
特使 special envoy;

天使 angel;
向使 if; in case;
信使 courier; messenger;
行使 exercise; perform;
役使 use; work;
支使 (1) order about; (2) put sb off; send away;
指使 abet; instigate;
致使 cause; result in;
主使 abet; incite; instigate;
專使 special envoy;
縱使 even if; even though;

shi

【始】 (1) beginning; first; start; (2) begin; start; (3) not...until; only then; (4) a surname;

[始創] create; found; initiate; originate;
始創者 founder;
~ 始創者之一 founder member;

[始點] initial point;

[始基] beginning and foundation;

[始末] (1) from beginning to end; (2) ins and outs; whole story;
始末根由 whole story;
敬陳始末 make a respectful statement of the beginning and the end;

[始期] (1) beginning period; (2) (of law) effective date;

[始業] establish a business;

[始願] (1) first wish; very first ambition; (2) only then is one willing to...;

[始終] all along; first, midst, and last; from beginning to end; from start to finish; remain; throughout;
始終不懈 indefatigable; persistent; unremitting from beginning to end; untiring perseverance;
始終不渝 carry the torch; firm and unchanging all along; remain faithful to one's promise; steadfast; unchanged from beginning to end; unswerving;
始終其事 dedicate oneself to a job from first to last; manage sth from beginning to end;
始終如一 always the same from first to last; consistent from beginning to end; first, last, and all the time; stick on from first to last; the same from beginning to end;
從始至終 from beginning to end; from first to last; from start to finish;
貫徹始終 go the distance;
全始全終 all the way; carry a matter through; finish what is started; from the beginning to the very end; it begins well and ends well; see sth through; stick to sth to the very end;
善始善終 begin well and end well; do well from start to finish; good beginning and good ending; good from beginning to end; persevere to the end; see sth through;
始亂終棄 desert a girl after robbing her of her chastity; first he abuses her and in the end he gives her up; have illicit intercourse at the beginning and desert her at the end; love them and leave them;
無始無終 eternity; lacking beginning and end; timeless; without beginning and ending;
一竟始終 stick to sth to the very end;
有始無終 begin well but end badly; begin well but fall off towards the close; do things by halves; give up halfway; have a beginning but no end; leave an undertaking unfinished; start sth but fail to carry it through;
有始有終 carry out an undertaking from start to finish; carry sth through to the end; do sth well from beginning to end; finish what is started; go through with sth from start to finish; have a beginning and an end; in for a penny, in for a pound; prosecute to the end;
自始至終 all the time; all the way; all the way through; all the while; at both the end and the beginning; during the whole period; from A to Z; from beginning to end; from cover to cover; from first to last; from start to finish; from the egg to the apple; from the very beginning; from top to toe; the whole time; the whole way; throughout;

[始祖] (1) earliest ancestor; first ancestor; (2) founder;
始祖馬 hyracothere;
始祖鳥 archaeopteryx;
始祖象 moerithere;

[始作俑者] creator of a bad precedent; first to set a bad example; initiator of evil;

倡始 advocate the creation of sth; invent;

創始 initiate; originate;
更始 begin a new page;
經始 lay out the ground plan of a fortified work;
開始 at the outset; be set on foot; be the beginning of; begin; come on; commence; commencement; enter into; enter on; enter upon; fall to; get one's feet wet; get started; in the outset; initial; lead off; put one's hands to; set about; set in; set on foot; set one's hands to; set out; set sth on foot; set to; start; start in; strike up; take to; take up;
起始 beginning; germ; initiation; origin; parentage; start;
慎始 careful about the beginning of an endeavour;
伊始 beginning;
原始 (1) firsthand; original; (2) origin; source; (3) backward; primitive;
肇始 begin; commence; initiate; start;
終始 from beginning to end;

shi

【屎】 droppings; dung; excrement; faeces; poop; poopoo;
[屎坑] dung pit;
[屎尿] body waste; excrement and urine;
[屎盆子] commode;

鼻屎 bogey; bogie; booger; nasal secretion;
屙屎 move the bowels;
耳屎 earwax;
狗屎 dog dirt; dog dung;
拉屎 crap; deposit; go to stool; empty the bowels; have a bowel movement; move one's bowels; shit;
眼屎 gum in the eyes; secretions of the eyes;

shi

【駛】 (1) drive; run; sail; (2) fast; fleeting; speed;
[駛船] sail a ship;
借風駛船 sail with the wind;
[駛赴] be bound for;
[駛回] go back; return; sail back;
[駛近] approach;
[駛離] bear off; pull away;
[駛行] go; run; sail;

奔駛 run quickly; speed;
疾駛 ride fast;
駕駛 drive; pilot;
行駛 go; travel;

shi4
shi

【士】 (1) gentleman; man of learning; scholar; (2) armyman; soldier; (3) officer; (4) expert; professional; (5) commendable person; (6) bodyguard in Chinese chess; (7) surname;
[士兵] rank-and-file soldiers; soldiers;
訓練士兵 train soldiers;
一名士兵 a soldier;
[士官] non-commissioned officer;
士官學校 school for non-commissioned officers;
[士可殺，不可辱] a scholar prefers death to humiliation;
[士林] intelligentsia; literary circles; scholastic community;
嘉惠士林 benefit young students or scholars;
[士民] (1) people; (2) intellectual; scholar;
[士敏土] cement;
[士農工商] scholars, farmers, artisans and merchants;
[士女] (1) young men and women; (2) traditional Chinese painting of beautiful women;
[士氣] morale;
士氣昂揚 have high morale;
士氣大振 martial spirit has been roused greatly;
士氣低落 morale in the ranks is sinking; morale of the troops is sinking lower; troops are in low morale;
士氣旺盛 have high morale;
動搖士氣 shake the morale;
鼓勵士氣 boost morale;
鼓舞士氣 a shot in the arm; boost morale; enhance troop morale;
恢復士氣 recover the morale;
增強士氣 stiffen the morale;
振作士氣 bring up the morale;
[士人] educated man; scholar;
[士紳] gentry;
[士庶] common people;
[士伍] rank and file of soldiers;
[士子] candidates of the civil service examinations;
[士卒] privates; soldiers;
[士族] gentry;

巴士	bus;
拂士	straightforward adviser; wise counselor;
便士	penny;
辯士	(1) able speaker; gifted debater; (2) sophist;
兵士	foot soldier; soldier;
博士	(1) doctorate; (2) learned scholar;
策士	schemer; tactician;
道士	Daoist priest;
的士	cab; taxi; taxicab;
鬥士	fighter; warrior;
方士	(1) necromancer; (2) alchemist;
寒士	poor scholar;
虎士	brave warrior;
護士	nurse;
技士	junior technician;
將士	officers and men;
教士	Christian missionary; clergy; clergyman; priest;
進士	successful candidate in the highest imperial examinations;
居士	lay Buddhist;
爵士	knight; Sir;
軍士	petty officer; sergeant;
狂士	bohemian scholar; self-conceited scholar;
魁士	eminent scholar;
浪士	debauchee;
烈士	martyr;
猛士	barve warrior;
名士	(1) person with a literary reputation; (2) celebrity with no official post;
謀士	adviser; counselor;
男士	gentleman; man;
女士	lady; madam;
奇士	remarkable man; unusual person;
棋士	professional chess player;
騎士	cavalier; knight;
清士	man of honesty and unimpeachable integrity;
曲士	cramped scholar; obscure person;
人士	personage; public figure;
戎士	enlisted men; soldiers;
鋭士	man of energy; man of intelligence;
善士	benevolent person; good man; philanthropist;
上士	(1) petty officer first-class; (2) sergeant first-class;
紳士	gentleman; gentry;
碩士	Master;
退士	(1) recluse; (2) retired official;
衛士	bodyguard; warrior;
武士	(1) palace guards in ancient times; (2) man of prowess; warrior;
下士	corporal;
賢士	person of high moral standing; distinguished men;
相士	(1) fortune-teller; (2) appraise a person's latent ability;
信士	(1) believer; follower of a religion; (2) honest man;
修士	brother; friar; monk;
衒士	boastful scholar;
學士	(1) scholar; (2) holder of the bachelor's degree;
雅士	person of refined tastes; refined scholar;
彥士	refined and accomplished scholar;
逸士	(1) man of great virtue; (2) scholar retiring from the world;
醫士	practitioner with secondar medical school education;
義士	high-minded or chivalrous person;
隱士	hermit; recluse;
勇士	brave and strong man; warrior;
游士	free-lancing scholar;
院士	academician;
戰士	(1) man; soldier; (2) champion; fighter; warrior;
爪士	lackeys; retainers;
貞士	man of integrity; man of virtue;
芝士	cheese;
志士	honest patriot; man of high ambitions; man of purpose and virtue; persons of ideals and integrity;
智士	intellect; brainpower;
中士	(1) petty officer second-class; (2) sergeant;
助產士	midwife;
爪士	lackeys; retainers;
壯士	brave man; hero; man of stout heart;

shi

【氏】 (1) clan; family; (2) family name; surname; (3) character placed after a married woman's maiden name;

[氏譜] family tree; genealogy; lineage;

[氏族] clan; family;
- 氏族社會 clan society;
- 氏族制度 clan system;

華氏	Fahrenheit;
攝氏	Celsius;
無名氏	anonymous person;
姓氏	surname;

shi

【市】 (1) market; marketplace; (2) city; mu-

nicipality; (3) buy; sell; (4) surname;

[市場] bazaar; market; marketplace;

市場報告 market report;
市場層次 market levels;
市場導向 market oriented;
市場調查 market survey;
市場動態 market trend;
市場動向 market trend;
市場對策 market counter measures;
市場分配模型 market allocation model;
市場分析 market analysis;
市場份額 market share;
市場風險 market risk;
市場封鎖 market blockade;
市場供求關係 relation between market supply and demand;
市場供應 market supplies; supply of commodities;
市場管理 market management;
市場火旺 active market; brisk market; flourishing market;
市場機制 market mechanism;
市場價格 market price;
市場價值 market value;
市場街 market street;
市場經濟 market economy;
~ 市場經濟戰略 market management strategy;
市場力量 market forces;
市場領導者 market leader;
市場疲軟 inactive market; sagging market; slack market; sluggish market;
市場潛力 market potential;
市場情況 market situation;
市場情緒 market sentiment;
市場生態 market ecology;
市場失效 market failure;
市場特點 characteristics of markets;
市場體系 market system;
~ 培育市場體系 foster a market system;
市場調節 market regulation;
~ 市場調節價 market-adjusted price;
市場貼現率 market exchange of discount;
市場蕭條 slack market;
市場心理學 market psychology;
市場信息 market information;
市場需求 market demand;
市場營銷功能 marketing function;
市場預測 market forecasting;
市場佔有率 market share;
市場戰略 market strategy;
白銀市場 silver market;
飽和市場 saturated market;
不活躍市場 heavy market; inactive market; thin market;
不完全市場 imperfect market;
操縱市場 manipulate the market;
超級市場 supermarket;
~ 一家超級市場 a supermarket;
成熟市場 mature market;
承兑市場 acceptance market;
出口市場 export market;
初級市場 basic-level market; primary market;
翻譯市場 translation market;
繁榮市場 flourish the market;
搞活市場 invigorate the market;
國際市場 international market;
~ 打進國際市場 go into the international market; step into the international market;
國內市場 domestic market; home market;
國外市場 foreign market;
海外市場 market abroad;
黃金市場 gold market;
灰色市場 gray market;
匯兑市場 bill market;
活躍市場 active market;
金融市場 financial market; money market;
金銀市場 bullion market;
景氣市場 booming market;
就業市場 job market;
勞務市場 labour market;
買方市場 buyer's market;
賣方市場 seller's market;
拍賣市場 auction market;
商品市場 commodity market;
調節市場 regulate the market;
消費市場 consumer market;
新興市場 emerging market;
爭取市場 capture market;
資本市場 capital market;
資金市場 capital market;
自由市場 open market;
綜合市場 aggregate market;

[市棍] city shark; rascal of a marketplace;

[市徽] emblem of a city;

[市集] (1) fair; market; (2) small town;

[市價] current price of a commodity; market price;

[市郊] city outskirts; outskirts of a city; suburbia;

市郊群集 city-suburban conglomerate;

市郊商店區 shopping centre;

[市斤] catty;

[市井] marketplace; town;

市井無賴 riffraff; scoundrels of the marketplace;

市井細民 average men about town; ordinary townsfolk; small townsfolk;

市井小人 gigmanity; philistine;

市井之流 average man about town; townsman; townspeople;

市井之言 subject of general conversation; talk of the town; town talk;

[市儈] (1) broker; (2) crafty businessman; sordid merchant; tradesman; (3) philistine; vulgar;

市儈氣 vulgar and greedy;

市儈俗物 horrid men at the market; trader who counts only the pennies;

[市樓] wineshop;

[市面] (1) business situations; market conditions; (2) sights and splendours in big cities; world of the rich;

市面繁榮 business is brisk; trade is flourishing;

市面蕭條 business is slack;

[市民] citizens; residents of a city; townspeople;

市民權 freedom of the citizen;

市民收入 citizens' incomes;

市民文化 civic culture;

全體市民 citizenry;

升斗市民 ordinary citizens;

小市民 urban petty bourgeois;

[市內] in the city;

市內電話 local call;

[市區] city proper; downtown area; urban area; urban district;

市區重建 urban renewal;

[市人] townspeople;

[市容] appearance of a city;

參觀市容 go sight-seeing in the city; have a look around the city;

[市肆] shops and stores in a market;

[市隱] hermit in a city;

[市語] business jargon; trader's slang;

[市長] major;

市長夫人 majors;

市長女助手 mayoress;

市長任期 mayoralty;

市長職位 mayoralty;

市長職責 mayoral duties;

副市長 deputy mayor;

競選市長 run for mayor;

[市鎮] market towns; small towns; towns;

[市政] municipal administration;

市政大廈 civic centre;

市政府 city government; municipal government;

市政工程 municipal works;

~市政工程管理 municipal engineering management;

市政會 city council;

市政會計 municipal accounting;

市政設施 municipal infrastructure;

市政廳 city hall; town hall;

~市政廳大樓 city hall;

市政學 civics;

市政中心 civic centre;

[市中心] city centre; downtown; downtown area; town centre;

靠近市中心 near the centre of the town;

罷市 shopkeepers' strike;

白市 legitimate market;

菜市 (1) food market; (2) vegetable market;

超市 supermarket;

城市 city; town;

都市 city; metropolis;

股市 stock market;

海市 mirage;

行市 (1) market; (2) quotation;

黑市 black market;

花市 flower fair; flower market;

灰市 gray market;

集市 country fair; market;

街市 downtown streets;

開市 (1) (of a shop) reopen after a cessation of business; (2) first transaction of a day's business;

利市 profit;

樓市 property market;

門市 retail sales;

鬧市 busy shopping centre; busy streets; downtown area;

牛市 bull market;

啟市 resume business;

棄市 be executed; public execution;

搶市 rush to market; strive to get one's goods on sale first;

如市 like a market;

上市 (1) go on the market; (2) be in season;

撻市 disgrace sb in public;

蛙市 noise of frogs in the evening;
小市 bazaar;
曉市 morning market;
熊市 bear market;
墟市 fair grounds of a village;
夜市 night fair; night market;
應市 be offered for sale; go on the market; put on the market;
魚市 fish market;
早市 morning market; trade in the morning;

shi

【世】 (1) one's life; one's lifetime; (2) from generation to generation; generation; through generations; (3) age; epoch; era; (4) world;

[世變] changes in a situation;
坐觀世變 sit and watch how the wind blows;

[世仇] (1) blood feud; family feud; hereditary enemy; (2) a bitter enemy in a family feud;

[世傳] be handed down through generations; hereditary;

[世代] (1) generation; (2) from generation to generation; for generations; generation after generation; (3) epoch; era;
世代交替 alternation of generations;
世代書香 a family of scholars for generations; one's family has been always one of scholars;
世代相傳 hand down generation after generation; hand down to sb from one generation to another;
世代相沿 be handed down from generation to generation;
後生世代 advanced generation;
世世代代 age after age; for generations; from age to age; from generation to generation; generation after generation; throughout the ages;
無性世代 asexual generation;
雜種世代 hybrid generation;

[世道] manners and morals of the time; way of the world;
世道常情 manners and morals of the time; way of the world;
世道陵夷 practice of the world is declining to a low level;
世道人情 manners and morals of the time; way of the world;
世道人心 ways of the world and the heart of human beings;
世道日衰 public morals and mores are getting worse day by day; social practice is deteriorating day by day;

[世德] traditional morals;

[世法] (1) tradition; traditional practices; (2) common truths;

[世風] common practice of society; general mood of society;
世風不古 public morals and mores are no longer what they were in the good old days; social practices have deteriorated;
世風澆薄 there are scarcely any public morals to speak of these days;
世風澆薄，人心不古 plain dealing is dead, and die without issue;
世風日下 the moral degeneration of the world is getting worse day by day;
世風日下，道德淪亡 the moral degeneration of the world is getting worse every day;

[世故] (1) art of dealing with people; ways of the world; (2) shrewd; worldly; worldly-wise;
飽經世故 be well experienced in ways of the world; have seen the elephant; generation to generation;
不諳世故 ignorant of worldly affairs; unworldly;
洞明世故 have seen the ways of the world;
精於世故 know what o'clock it is;
久經世故 be long-tested; have weathered many storms; well-experienced in the ways of the world;
老於世故 be versed in the ways of the world; have seen much of the world; have worldly wisdom; know all the answers; man of the world; worldly-wise;
深於世故 have seen much of life; sophisticated;
通曉人情世故 know the world;

[世及] passing from generation to generation;

[世紀] century;
世紀之交 turn of the century;
跨世紀 trans-century;
跨世紀工程 trans-century project;

[世家] aristocratic family; old and well-known

family;
世家子弟 youngsters of an aristocratic family;
古老世家 family of ancient lineage;
來自銀行家世家 come from a long line of bankers;
音樂世家 family of musicians;

[世間] in society; on earth; in the world; the earth; the world;

[世交] long-standing friendship between two families; old family friends;

[世界] global; the earth; the world;
世界安全 world security;
世界杯 World Cup;
世界潮流 world trends;
世界大同 universal brotherhood;
世界大戰 global war; world war; the World War;
世界各地 around the world;
世界格局 world structure;
世界公民 global citizen;
世界觀 one's world view;
世界紀錄 world record;
世界末日 doomsday; end of the world;
世界事務 world affairs;
世界水平 international level; world standard;
世界聞名 world-famous; world-renowned;
世界語 Esperanto; universal language; world language;
世界真小 it's a small world;
世界種 world species;
世界主義 cosmopolitanism;
世界著名 world-famous;
~世界著名的 world-famous;
創造世界 create the world;
大千世界 boundless universe;
第三世界 third world;
放眼世界 have the whole world in view; keep the whole world in view; open one's eyes to the whole world
廣濶的世界 big world; wide world;
花花世界 the dazzling human world with its myriad temptations; the gay and material world the varicoloured world; this mortal world; world of self-indulgent luxury; world of sensual pleasures;
環遊世界 take a round-the-world tour; travel round the world;
毀滅世界 destroy the world;
極樂世界 Buddhist Paradise; nirvana;
漫遊世界 knock about the world;
面向世界 engage oneself globally;
內心世界 one's inner world; the inner world of the heart;
全世界 entire world; whole habitable globe; whole world;
統治世界 dominate the world; rule the world;
外面的世界 outside world;
微觀世界 microcosm;
未知世界 the unknown;
物質世界 material world;
震驚世界 astonish the world;
拯救世界 redeem the world;
征服世界 conquer the world;
周遊世界 go around the world; tour around the world; travel the world;

[世局] world situation;

[世路] ways and state of the world;

[世面] society; state of the world; various aspects of society; world;
見世面 get a look at the elephant; see life; see the elephant; see the world;
~見大世面 get a glimpse of the world of the great;
~見過世面 have experienced life; have seen much of life; have seen the world;
見過世面的人 a man of the world;
沒見過世面 green and inexperienced;

[世情] ways of the world;

[世人] common people; people of the world;
世人耳目 public opinion; the eyes and ears of the public;

[世上] in the world; on earth;
世上罕見 be rarely seen in the world;
世上無不散的筵席 even the longest feast must break up at last;
世上無難事，祗怕有心人 all difficulties on earth can be overcome if men but give their minds to it; it is dogged that does it; it's dogged as does it; nothing in the world is difficult for one who sets his mind to it; nothing is difficult for a man who wills; nothing is difficult in the world for anyone who sets his mind on it; nothing is difficult to a man who wills; nothing is difficult to a man with a will; nothing

is impossible to a willing heart; where there's a will there's a way;
世上無雙 best one in the world; have no parallel on earth;
來到這個世上 come into the world;
[世事] affairs of human life; affairs of the world;
世事滄桑 affairs of human life are ever-changing; the world is changing all the time; worldly affair is like the sea and mulberry plantation;
世事洞明皆學問，人情練達即文章 a grasp of mundane affairs is genuine knowledge, understanding of worldly wisdom is true learning;
世事無常 affairs of the world are inconstant;
世事有成必有敗，為人有興必有衰 one must have failures as well as succseses, one must have sorrow as well as joy;
不諳世事 ignorant of worldly affairs; not familiar with the ways of the world;
超然世事 hold aloof from the affairs of human life;
[世俗] (1) common customs; social conventions; (2) secular; worldly;
背世離俗 leave the world and its vulgarities;
世俗常情 manners and morals of the time; the way of the world;
世俗人文主義 secular humanism;
世俗之見 common views; vulgar point of view;
世異俗移 other times and other manners;
沾染世俗 be corrupted by worldly ways;
[世所僅見] have no parallel anywhere;
[世態] ways of the world;
世態人情 ways of the world;
世態炎涼 fickleness of the world; inconstancy of human relationships; snobbishness of human relationships;
[世途] way of the world;
初入世途 start in life;
[世外桃源] heaven cut off from the outside world; secluded paradise;
[世無其匹] unrivalled in the world;
[世務] worldly affairs;
世務纏身 be entangled by worldly affairs;
[世襲] hereditary; inherit;
世襲階級 caste;
世襲制度 hereditary system; patrilinear system of inheritance;
君主世襲 line of monarchs;
[世系] bloodline; family tree; genealogy; pedigree; stock;
[世緣] secular ties and affairs;
[世子] crown prince;
[世族] aristocractic family politically influential for generations;

傲世 look down on the world
百世 period of a hundred generations;
半世 half a lifetime;
辟世 withdraw from the world;
避世 retire from the world;
塵世 this mortal life; this world;
出世 (1) be born; come into the world; (2) come into being; (3) renounce the world; stand aloof from worldly affairs;
處世 conduct oneself in society;
傳世 be handed down from ancient times;
辭世 pass away;
蓋世 matchless; unparalleled;
後世 later ages;
濟世 be a benefactor to society;
家世 family background;
今世 (1) this life; (2) present era; this age;
近世 modern times;
舉世 throughout the world; universally;
來世 next life;
累世 for many generations; generation after generation;
亂世 troubled times; turbulent days;
末世 last phase of an age;
沒世 all one's life;
棄世 die; pass away;
前世 previous existence;
去世 die; pass away;
人世 the world;
入世 go into the society;
身世 one's life experience; one's lot;
盛世 flourishing age; heyday;
時世 age; epoch; era; times;
逝世 die; pass away;
晚世 modern times;
萬世 all ages; generation after generation;
問世 be published; come out;
下世 (1) die; pass away; (2) next life;
先世 ancestors; forefathers;
現世 be disgraced; lose face; this life;
謝世 die; pass away;
厭世 be disgusted with the world; be pessimistic;

永世 forever;
閱世 see the world;
在世 be living;
治世 times of peace and prosperity;
濁世 (1) chaotic times; the corrupted world; (2) mortal world;

shi

【仕】 (1) official; (2) enter government service; fill an office; serve the government; (3) bodyguard in Chinese chess;

[仕進] advance into government service; become an official in order to become prosperous;
不樂仕進 unwilling to enter public life;

[仕路] official career;

[仕女] (1) young men and women; (2) traditional Chinese painting of beautiful women;
仕女圖 portrait of a lady;

[仕途] political career; official career;
仕途捷徑 short cut to officialdom;
仕途偃蹇 be stranded in one's official career; have an unsuccessful official career; unfortunate in one's official career;

出仕 become an official;

shi

【示】 (1) indicate; show; (2) make known; notice; notify; (3) instruct; teach; (4) demonstrate; set an example;

[示愛] show one's feeling to one of the opposite sex;

[示波器] oscillograph;
示波器 oscillograph; oscilloscope;
~ 比較示波器 comparison oscilloscope;
~ 電子示波器 electron oscillograph;
~ 高級示波器 advanced oscilloscope;
~ 機電示波器 electronmechanical oscillograph;
~ 校準示波器 calibrated oscilloscope;
~ 自動示波器 automatic oscillograph;

[示範] demonstrate; demonstration; set an example;
示範教學 teaching by demonstration;
示範者 demonstrator;
視聽示範 audio-visual demonstration;

[示教] teach;

[示警] give a warning;

[示例] give a demonstration; give typical examples;

[示人] let others have a look at; make known; show others;

[示弱] give in; give the impression of weakness; show the white feather; show weakness; take sth lying down; yield;
不甘示弱 hate to show the white feather; refuse to admit being inferior; ill-prepared to have one's weakness shown up; not to be outdone; reluctant to show weakness; unwilling to admit oneself outdone; unwilling to be outshone;
毫不示弱 not giving any impression of weakness; not taking sth lying down;

[示威] (1) demo; demonstrate; hold a demonstration; (2) make a show of force;
示威遊行 demonstration;
示威者 demonstrator;
~ 一大群示威者 a mob of demonstrators;
~ 一群示威者 a troop of demonstrators;
參加示威 go on a demonstration; join a demonstration; participate in a demonstration; take part in a demonstration;
大型示威 large demonstration;
發動示威 stage a demonstration;
發生示威 a demonstration takes place;
和平示威 peaceful demonstration;
激起示威 provoke a demonstration;
靜坐示威 sit-in;
舉行示威 hold a demonstration;
驅散示威 break up a demonstration;
引發示威 spark a demonstration;
政治示威 political demonstration;
組織示威 organize a demonstration;

[示象] aspect;
補充示象 additional aspect;
輔助示象 subsidiary aspect;
接近示象 approach aspect;
~ 預告接近示象 advance approach aspect;
接近限速示象 approach-restricted speed aspect;
接近中速示象 approach medium aspect;
進行示象 proceed aspect;
容許示象 permissive aspect;
退行示象 backup aspect;

拖掛示象 dragging aspect;
位置示象 position aspect;

[示意] drop a hint; give a sign; hint; indicate one's wish; motion; signal;
示意圖 directory;
點頭示意 give a nod as a signal; signal by nodding;
頷首示意 give a nod as a signal;
以目示意 give a hint with the eyes; give sb a meaning look; give sb the wink; make a sign with the eyes; make eyes at; throw the eye at; tip sb the wink;
用手勢示意 make a signal by the motion of the hand;
用眼示意 hint by the eye;

[示知] inform; notify;

[示眾] exhibit to the public; publicly expose; put before the public; show to the public;

暗示 allude to; hint; suggest; suggestion;
榜示 announce by putting up a notice;
標示 indicate; mark;
表示 express; expression; indicate; show;
出示 show or exhibit for inspection;
告示 bulletin; official notice;
揭示 (1) announce; promulgate; (2) bring to light; reveal;
牌示 proclamation put up on a notice board;
批示 write instructions or comments on a report;
啟示 enlighten; enlightenment; inspiration; inspire;
請示 ask for instructions;
提示 point out; prompt;
圖示 be illustrated by charts and diagrams;
顯示 display; show;
曉示 notify; tell explicitly;
宣示 announce; declare;
訓示 instructions to subordinates;
演示 demonstrate;
預示 betoken; presage;
展示 open up before one's eyes; reveal;
昭示 declare publicly; make clear to all;
指示 (1) indicate; point out; (2) directive; instruct; instructions;

[示蹤] tracer;
示蹤元素 tracer element;
示蹤原子 tracer atom;

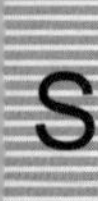

shi

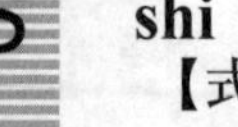

【式】 (1) fashion; style; type; (2) form; model; pattern; (3) ceremony; ritual; (4) equation; formula; (5) mode; mood;

[式微] decline;

[式樣] mode; model; style; type;
式樣美觀 attractive fashion;
式樣新穎 in a novel style; stylish;
各式各樣 all kinds of; all sorts of; every kind of; in every shape and form; of every description; of every hue; of various descriptions;
流行式樣 fashion;

[式子] (1) posture; (2) equation; formula;

鞍式 saddle-type;
八柱式 octastyle;
板式 type of metre for music in Chinese operas;
版式 format;
便攜式 portable;
程式 (1) form; pattern; (2) programme; programming;
單花式 (of hairstyle) wavy;
單式 single entry;
等式 equality; equation;
調式 mode;
法式 method; model; rule;
髮式 hair style; hairdo;
方式 fashion; pattern; way;
分式 rational fraction;
服式 line; style of dress;
複式 double entry;
格式 form; format; layout; mode; style;
根式 radical;
公式 expression; formula;
狗爬式 dog paddle; doggy paddle;
盒式 cassette;
恒等式 identity;
角形式 (of hairstyle) angular style;
舊式 old type; old-style;
款式 design; fashion; model; pattern; style;
坤式 women's style;
老式 old-fashioned; outdated;
立式 upright; vertical;
模式 mode; model; pattern; type;
男式 men's clothing;
女式 women's clothing;
平直形式 (of hairstyle) smooth style;
強式 strong form;
曲式 musical form;
弱式 weak;
時式 up-to-date style;
雙花式 (of hairstyle) symmetric waves;
算式 equation;

胎座式 placentation;
梯式 ladder-shaped;
童花式 (of hairstyle) pageboy style;
圖式 schema;
紋孔式 pitting;
卧式 horizontal;
西式 Western style;
項式 nomial;
新式 latest type; new type; new-style;
形合式 hypotaxis;
形式 form; shape;
樣式 form; model; pattern; style; type;
頁式 page;
一站式 one-stop;
儀式 ceremony; rite;
意合式 parataxis;
因式 factor;
招式 movements in martial art;
針式 pin-type;
整式 integral expression;
正式 formal; official; regular;
制式 regular; regulation;
中式 Chinese style;
準式 criterion; regulation; rule;
子式 minor;
嘴把式 prater;

shi

【事】 (1) affair; matter; thing; (2) accident; trouble; (3) job; occupation; task; (4) duties; functions; (5) involvement; responsibility; (6) attend; serve; wait upon; (7) be engaged in;

[事敗垂成] abortive attempt; fail on the verge of success; fail when success is already in sight;

[事必躬親] attend to everything personally; see to everything oneself; take care of every single thing personally;
事必躬親的負責人 chief cook and bottle washer;

[事必有因] every why has a wherefore;

[事必有兆] common events cast their shadows before them;

[事變] (1) incident; (2) emergency; exigency; (3) course of events;

[事不關己，高高掛起] another's care will not rob you of sleep; let things drift if they do not affect one personally; things of no personal concern are relegated to the background;

[事不過二] lightning never strikes twice;

[事不過三] not do anything more than three times;

[事不宜遲] delays are dangerous; it permits of no delay; one must lose no time in doing sth; the matter brooks no delay; the matter should not be delayed; there is not a moment to lose; there should be no delay; this matter must not be delayed;

[事不由己] things are beyond one's control; things are getting out of hand;

[事出有因] a thing has its cause; everything hath its seed; it is by no means accidental; no smoke without fire; not devoid of truth; there is a reason for it; there is good cause for it; there is no smoke without fire; this happens not without reason; where there's smoke there's fire;

[事典] encyclopaedia;

[事端] dispute; disturbance; incident; trouble;
挑起事端 provoke incidents;
製造事端 create disturbances;
滋生事端 kick up a breeze;

[事發] be exposed; the story is out;
東窗事發 be exposed; come to the light; disclosure of a crime; disclosure of a plot; one's criminal conspiracy was unmasked; the design has taken air; the story is out;

[事非得已] there is no other choice;

[事功] cause and contribution;
事功之學 learning about deeds;
急於事功 desirous of achievement;
事半功倍 achieve double the result with only half the work; achieve maximum results with little effort; get better result with less effort; get twice the result with half the effort; get twofold results with half the effort; half the work with double results;
事倍功半 achieve little result despite herculean effort; get half the results with double the effort; the mountain labours and brings forth a mouse; twice the work with half the results;
特殊事功 remarkable achievements;

［事故］ accident; failure; fault; malfunction; mishap; mistake; trouble; troublesome incident;
事故處理系統 business processing system;
事故調查 accident inquiry; accident investigation;
~事故調查人員 accident investigator;
事故發生率 accident rate;
事故受害人 accident victim;
事故數據處理方式 transaction data processing system;
事故圖形處理 business graphic processing;
事故現場 scene of an accident;
事故終端系統 affairs terminal system;
事故狀態 accident condition;
避免事故 avoid accidents;
出事故 have an accident;
電車事故 tram accident;
發生事故 an accident happens; an accident occurs;
非死亡事故 nonfatal accident;
飛行事故 air accident; aircraft accident; flight accident; flying accident;
輻射事故 radiation accident;
核事故 nuclear accident;
減少事故 reduce accidents;
降傘事故 parachute accident;
捲入事故 be involved in an accident;
模擬事故 simulated accident;
碰擦事故 fender-bender;
起動事故 start-up accident;
起飛事故 takeoff accident;
輕微事故 minor accident;
人為事故 human error accident;
湍流事故 turbulence accident;
脫軌事故 derail accident;
未出事故 without incident;
污染事故 contamination accident;
小事故 mishap;
嚴重事故 bad accident; serious incident;
一場事故 an accident;
一次事故 an accident;
一連串事故 a succession of accidents;
一起事故 an accident;
意外事故 unexpected accident;
~一連串的意外事故 a chapter of accidents;
預防事故 prevent an accident;
遭遇事故 meet with an accident;
造成事故 bring about an accident;
責任事故 accident arising from one's negligence; human element accident;
致命事故 fatal accident;
重大事故 major accident;

［事過境遷］ the affair is over and the situation has changed; the events have passed and the situation has change; the incident is over and the circumstances are different; things change with the passage of time;
人在事在，事過境遷 out of sight is out of mind;

［事過情遷］ people's feelings change with the circumstances;

［事後］ after an event; afterwards; since then;
事後聰明 after-wit; hindsight; wise after the event; wise behind; wise behindhand;
事後的想法 afterthought;
事後回想 hindsight;
事後諸葛亮 second guesser; wise after the event; wise in retrospect;

［事機］ (1) confidential affairs; secret affairs; (2) circumstances; situation; trend of events;
事機已熟 the time is ripe;

［事急］ urgency;
事急膽生 despair gives courage to a coward;
事急無法律，路急無君子 necessity knows no law; urgency makes one neglect discipline and manners;

［事跡］ achievement; deed;
英雄事跡 heroic deeds;

［事假］ leave of absence;

［事件］ event; incident;
事件調查室 incident room;
事件動詞 event verb;
事件發生 an incident happens; an incident occurs;
事件主語 eventive subject;
暴力事件 violent incident;
悲慘事件 tragic incident;
必然事件 certain event;
不同事件 separate incident;
不幸事件 tragic event; unfortunate incident;
處理事件 deal with an incident; handle an incident;

當前事件 current event;
尷尬事件 embarrassing incident;
個別事件 isolated inmcident;
互斥事件 exclusive event;
可怕的事件 terrible affair;
歷史事件 historic events; historical events;
戀愛事件 love affair; romantic affair;
偶發事件 adventitious occurrence;
生活事件 life event;
討論事件 talk the matter over;
相關事件 related incident;
小事件 minor incident; small incident;
一樁事件 an accident;
一個事件 an event;
一連串事件 a chain of events; a train of events;
一系列事件 a series of events; a trains of events;
引發事件 provoke an incident; spark off an incident;
預謀事件 got-up affair;
災變性事件 catastrophic event;
整個事件 whole incident;
重大事件 major incident; momentous event;
重要事件 important event; significant event;
最新事件 latest event;

[事理] logic; reason; way of doing business;
達於事理 understanding and amenable to reason;
剖明事理 analyse the whys and wherefores;
通達事理 understand ways of doing business;

[事例] precedent; example; instance;

[事略] biographical sketch; brief biography;

[事前] before an event; beforehand; in advance;
事前事後 before and after the event;

[事親] treat one's parents;
事親至孝 treat one's parents with great respect and tender affection;

[事情] affair; business; case; event; incident; instance; matter; thing;
事情的發展 course of events;
事情的另一面 opposite side of the coin; other side of the coin;
事情的真相 facts of the case; truth of the matter;
幹危險的事情 play with fire;
很多事情 many things; thousands of things;
極其重大的事情 affair of great importance;
簡單的事情 straightforward matter;
緊急的事情 urgent matter;
決定事情 resolve the matter; settle the matter;
考慮事情 consider the matter;
難以對付的事情 nemesis;
輕而易舉的事情 doddle;
容易決定的事情 open-and-shut case;
手頭的事情 matter at hand; matter in hand;
討論事情 discuss the matter;
提出事情 raise the matter;
一件事情 one thing;
有很多操心的事情 have a lot on one's mind;
重大的事情 weighty matter;

[事權] powers of office;

[事實] fact; reality; truth;
事實層次 factual level;
事實錯誤 factual error;
事實動詞 factive verb;
事實俱在 all the facts are at hand; the facts are all there; these are all accomplished facts;
事實恰恰相反 the facts are just the opposite; the opposite is the case;
事實如此 such are the facts; such is the fact; this is how things stand;
事實上 actually; as a matter of fact; in fact; in reality;
事實勝於雄辯 facts are more eloquent than words; facts are stronger than arguments; facts speak louder than words; the effect speaks, the tongue needs not;
事實昭彰 facts are well borne out;
事實真相 facts of the case; nitty-gritty; truth of the matter;
背離事實 deviate from the truth;
悖離事實 away from the truth; wide of the truth;
不符合事實 wide of the mark;
不顧事實 disregard facts; fly in the face of the facts; have no regard for the truth; ignore the facts
承認事實 admit the truth;
大量的事實 a mass of facts;

顛倒事實 give a false account of the facts; turn things upside down;
犯罪事實 facts related to crimes;
既成事實 accomplished facts; established fact; fait accompli;
講出事實 tell a truth;
面對事實 face facts;
弄清事實 establish relevant facts;
千真萬確的事實 solid facts;
潤飾事實 embellish the true story;
歪曲事實 strain a point;
玩弄事實 play fast and loose with the facts;
誣捏事實 fabricate a false story;
渲染事實 colour the facts;

[事事] everything;
事事拗違 all things conspire against one; everything goes athwart with me;
事事處處 at every turn;
事事帶頭 take the lead in every kind of work;
事事干預 poke one's nose into everything;
事事如意 every success; everything answers; everything comes off satisfactorily; everything falls into one's lap;
事事如願 crown with success; everything is as one wishes;
事事順暢 things are going ahead;
事事挑剔 cavil at everything;
事事小心 careful in everything;
事事周到 everything is fully done;
無所事事 at a loose end; at an idle end; at loose ends; be engaged in nothing; be occupied with nothing; dilly dally; do nothing; eat one's head off; fool about; fool around; goof; goof off; hang about; hang around; have nothing to do; idle about; idle along; idle away one's time; kick one's heels; loaf; lost and bewildered; mess about; mess around; moon about; not to do a hand's turn; not to do a stitch of work; not to lift a hand; play about in a foolish way; saunter; stroll; twiddle one's thumbs; twirl one's thumbs; vegetate;
~呆在家裏無所事事 slop around one's home;
~一整天無所事事 ponce about all day; ponce around all day;

[事勢] general course of events; the trend of things in general;

[事態] situation; state of affairs;
事態曝光 the incident came to light;
事態嚴重 the situation is serious;

[事體] affairs; business; matters; systems of matters;

[事物] articles; objects; things;
無價值的事物 dead duck;

[事務] (1) affairs; routine; work; (2) general affairs;
事務繁忙 have a lot of work to do;
事務羈身 be detained by one's duties;
事務員 clerk;
~輔助事務員 auxiliary clerk;
公共事務 public affairs; public life;
國際事務 international affairs;
教育事務 educational affair;
金融事務 financial affairs;
經濟事務 economic affairs;
了結事務 wind up one's affair;
民政事務 civil affairs;
內部事務 internal affair;
清算事務 liquidation affairs;
世界事務 world affairs;

[事先] beforehand; in advance; prior;
事先安排 cut and dry;
事先知道 foreknowledge;
事先做好準備 get everything ready beforehand;

[事項] item; matter;
待辦事項 things to do;
~待辦事項名單 to-do list;
注意事項 matters needing attention; points for attention;

[事業] (1) cause; undertaking; (2) enterprise; facilities; (3) career;
事業成功 have made a go of the business;
事業單位 state-run institution;
事業順利 have a successful career;
事業心 career ambition;
促進自己的事業 advance one's career;
闖出一番事業 carve out a career for oneself;
發展事業 build up the business;
公共事業 public utilities; utility;
教育事業 educational business; educational undertaking;
商務事業 commercial business;
運輸事業 transport undertaking;
終身事業 lifelong career; one's lifework;
專注於事業 attend to one's business;

[事宜] arrangements; matters concerned;
未盡事宜 unfinished matters; unsettled affairs;

[事由] (1) origin of an incident; (2) main content;

[事與願違] a result cross to the purpose; achieve the opposite of what one has intended; contrary to what one expects; events do not happen as one wishes; get the opposite of what one wants; one does not succeed in carrying out one's intention; reality does not accord with hopes; the reality is just contrary to one's wish; the result is contrary to one's expectations; the result is the reverse of one's wishes; the result runs counters to one's desire; things do not come up to one's expectations; things do not turn out the way one anticipates; thing do not turn out the way one wants it; things go crisscross;

[事主] victim of a crime;

礙事 (1) hindrance; problem; obstacle; in the way; keep under sb's feet; (2) matter; of consequence; serious;
暗事 clandestine action; illicit conduct; secret plot; underhand affair;
白事 funeral;
百事 all sorts of things; everything;
敗事 bungle a matter; spoil a matter;
辦事 handle affairs; work;
本事 (1) original story; source material; (2) ability; capacity; skill; (3) able; capable;
鄙事 mean matters; trifles;
參事 adviser; counselor;
差事 not up to standard; poor;
差事 (1) assignment; errand; (2) commission; official post;
蕆事 be completed; be finished;
常事 common occurrence; ordinary affairs;
塵事 worldly affairs;
成事 accomplish sth;
醜事 abominable affair; disgraceful affair; scandal;
出事 have an accident; meet with a mishap;
處事 deal with affairs;
炊事 cooking; kitchen work;
蠢事 tomfooleries;
從事 about; be bound up in; be engaged in; busy with; be occupied in; be occupied with; devote oneself to; go in for; occupy oneself with; work on; take up;
大事 (1) great event; important matter; major event; major issue; (2) overall situation; (3) in a big way;
抵事 effective; serve the purpose;
頂事 effective; serve the purpose; useful;
董事 director; trustee;
懂事 intelligent; reasonable; sensible;
斷事 divide a matter;
多事 (1) eventful; (2) meddlesome;
惡事 misdeeds;
法事 Buddhist or Daoist mass;
凡事 everything;
犯事 commit a crime or an offence;
房事 sexual intercourse;
費事 give or take a lot of trouble;
僨事 spoil matters;
佛事 Buddhist ceremony; Buddhist service;
幹事 secretary in charge of sth;
更事 experience in practical affairs;
工事 defence works; fortifications;
公事 (1) official business; public affairs; (2) official documents;
共事 fellow workers; work together;
故事 (1) old practice; routine business; (2) story; tale; (3) plot;
怪事 strange thing; supernatural event;
管事 (1) in charge; run affairs; (2) effective; of use; (3) manager; steward;
國事 national affairs;
海事 (1) maritime affairs; (2) accident on the sea;
罕事 rare event; rare thing;
憾事 matter of regret;
好事 (1) good deed; good turn; (2) act of charity; (3) happy event;
好事 meddlesome; officious;
何事 what matter;
恨事 matter for regret;
橫事 sudden misfortune; unexpected calamity;
紅事 happy occasion;
後事 (1) what happened afterwards; (2) funeral affairs;
壞事 (1) bad thing; evil deed; (2) make things worse; ruin sth;
婚事 marriage; wedding;
混事 drift along; muddle along;
禍事 calamity; disaster;
吉事 sacrificial ceremony, wedding ceremony, etc.;

紀事 record events;
記事 (1) (of a child) begin to remember things; (2) keep a record of events; make a memorandum; (3) account; record the events;
濟事 effective; of help;
家事 domestic affairs; family affairs;
接事 take up a post and start work;
就事 take up one's post;
舊事 old matter;
舉事 rise in insurrection; stage an uprising;
軍事 military affairs;
快事 happy event; sth satisfactory and delightful;
賴事 shameless acts; vile deeds;
樂事 bit of jam; delight; happy event; pleasure;
理事 chairman; director; member of a council;
兩回事 two different matters; two entirely different things;
兩碼事 two entirely different matters;
了事 dispose of a matter; get sth over;
領事 consul;
另一回事 a different kettle of fish; another kettle of fish;
錄事 office clerk;
沒那回事 nothing of the sort;
沒事 (1) at a loose end; at leisure; free; have nothing to do; (2) it doesn't matter; it's nothing; never mind; that's all right;
民事 civil; relating to civil law;
敏事 earnest in actions;
謀事 (1) plan matters; (2) look for a job;
拿事 have the power to do sth or decide what to do;
難事 a hard nut to crack; difficulty;
鬧事 affray; create a disturbance; make trouble;
能事 ability; what one is particularly good at;
年事 a person's age;
農事 farm work; farming;
怕事 afraid of getting into trouble; afraid of getting involved; take no initiative; timid;
屁事 your business;
奇事 inexplicable occurrence; strange affair; strange incident; strange matter; strange things; unusual phenomenon;
起事 rise in arms; rise in rebellion; rise in revolt; start armed struggle;
啟事 announcement; notice;
前事 antecedent event;
巧事 coincidence;
親事 (1) marriage; (2) attend to personally;
情事 circumstances; condition; situation;
秋事 autumn harvest;
趣事 amusing incident; interesting episode;
惹事 create trouble; provoke; stir up trouble;
人事 (1) human affairs; occurrences in human life; (2) way of the world; (3) consciousness; (4) personnel matters; (5) what is humanly possible;
戎事 military affairs;
容事 have the capacity for work;
賽事 competition; game; match;
喪事 funeral arrangements;
穡事 farming; husbandry;
傻事 stupid thing;
善事 benefaction; charitable work; charity; good deeds; philanthropic acts;
商事 commercial affairs;
涉事 give a narration;
生事 create a disturbance; give rise to disturbance; make trouble;
省事 save trouble; simplify matters;
盛事 grand occasion; great event;
失事 accident; crash; fatal accident; have an accident; meet with an accident;
施事 agent; doer of the action in a sentence;
師事 acknowledge sb as one's master or teacher;
時事 current affairs; current events; the current state of affairs;
實事 (1) facts; (2) solid work;
世事 affairs of human life; affairs of the world;
視事 assume office; attend to business after assuming office;
受事 object of an action in a sentence;
署事 (1) deal with public affairs; (2) public affairs;
順事 matters that one is happy to talk about;
説事 (1) negotiate; try to come to an agreement; (2) explain an idea; expound a theory; make things clear;
司事 carry out one's duties;
私事 private affairs;
斯事 this matter;
祀事 religious services;
訟事 lawsuit; litigation;
俗事 (1) secularity; (2) daily routine; everyday matters; mundane affairs; worldly affairs;
瑣事 trifles; trivial matters;
他事 other business; other matters;
通事 (1) interpreter; (2) diplomatic affairs; official intercourse between two states;
同事 (1) colleague; fellow worker; (2) work in the same place; work together;
推事 judge;
外事 external affairs; foreign affairs;

完事 come to an end; finish; get through;
萬事 all things; everything;
往事 history; past events; the past; things that have come to past;
問事 attend to work;
無事 nothing;
物事 affair; business;
誤事 bungle matters;
喜事 (1) happy event; joyous occasion; (2) wedding;
細事 matters of little significance; trifles; trifling matters;
閒事 (1) a matter that does not concern one; other people's business; (2) unimportant matter;
小事 minor matter; petty thing; small matter; trifle; trivial matter;
曉事 understanding and experienced;
心事 a load on one's mind; secrets in one's mind; sth weighing on one's mind; worry;
刑事 criminal; penal;
行事 (1) act; handle matters; (2) behaviour; conduct;
省事 clever and understanding; conscious;
幸事 good fortune;
兇事 (1) unlucky matters; (2) violence that involves casualties;
敍事 narrate; recount;
尋事 pick a quarrel; seek a quarrel; stir up trouble;
雅事 refined activities of the intelligentsia;
饜事 busy; plenty to do;
豔事 erotic affairs; romantic adventures;
要事 important matter; urgent business;
一碼事 the same thing;
一事 belong to the same organization;
易事 easy matter;
異事 (1) peculiar affair; (2) different matter; (3) be engaged in different occupations;
遺事 (1) incident of past ages; (2) deeds of those now dead;
軼事 anecdote;
逸事 anecdote;
議事 discuss official business;
用事 (1) act; handle things; manage things; (2) be in power;
有事 (1) be engaged; busy; occupied; (2) if sth happens; get into trouble; meet with an accident; when problems crop up;
御事 manage affairs;
遇事 when anything comes up; when anything crops up;
韻事 (1) literary or artistic pursuits, ofen with pretense to good taste and refinement; (2) romantic affair;
在事 hold a position; in charge of;
戰事 clashes; fighting; hostilities; war;
招事 bring trouble on oneself; invite trouble;
找事 (1) look for a job; seek employment; (2) look for trouble; pick a quarrel;
肇事 cause trouble; create a disturbance; stir up disturbances; stir up trouble;
正事 one's proper business;
政事 government affairs;
知事 magistrate of a county;
執事 (1) attendant; (2) asking sb's attendants to convey what one wants to express;
治事 transact business;
指事 self-explanatory characters;
滋事 cause trouble; create trouble; disturb peace;
最拿手的事 meat and drink to sb;
做該做的事 walk the walk;
做事 (1) act; do a deed; handle affairs; (2) have a job; work;

shi

【侍】 (1) attend upon; serve; wait upon; (2) attendant; servant;

[侍婢] maidservant;
侍臣] courtier;
　女侍臣 lady-in-waiting;
[侍從] acolyte; attendant; retinue; servant;
[侍奉] attend on; serve; wait upon;
　侍奉箕帚 perform one's wifely duties;
　侍奉衽席 become a wife to a man;
[侍候] attend upon; look after; serve; wait upon;
　侍候病人 look after a patient;
[侍姬] concubine;
[侍立] in attendance;
　侍立一旁 stand at sb's side in attendance;
[侍弄] raise or look after domestic animals carefully;
[侍女] maid; maidservant;
[侍妾] concubine;
[侍食] serve one for dinner;
[侍衛] imperial bodyguard; bodyguards;
[侍應生] waiter; attendant;
[侍者] servant; waiter; attendant;

伏侍 attend upon; wait upon;
服侍 attend upon; wait upon;
內侍 royal attendant;

陪侍 (of juniors) stand by the side of and wait upon the senior;
隨侍 attend upon sb;

shi

【使】 (1) emissary; envoy; (2) be appointed as a diplomatic envoy;

［使臣］ envoy; representative of a country abroad;

［使館］ diplomatic mission; embassy;

［使節］ diplomatic envoy; envoy;
使節團 (1) diplomatic mission; (2) diplomatic corps;

［使君］ emissary; envoy;
使君有婦 married man; one who has a wife;

［使領館］ embassies and consulates;

［使者］ messenger; emissary; envoy;

shi

【室】 (1) apartment; chamber; home; room; (2) office; section; (3) one's wife;

［室邇人遐］ grieve over the dead; long for sb afar; the house is nearby but the person is far away;

［室家］ (1) family; home; (2) married couple;
室家之樂 connubial bliss;
室家之累 family burden;

［室內］ indoor; interior;
室內比賽 indoor competition;
室內設計 interior design;
室內天線 indoor antenna; internal antenna;
室內音樂 chamber music;
室內遊戲 indoor games;
室內游泳池 indoor swimming pool;
室內樂 chamber music;
室內運動 indoor sports;
室內照明 interior illumination; interior lighting;
室內裝飾 interior decoration;
在室內 indoors;
~留在室內 stay indoors;

［室怒市色］ being abused at home, one sells his indignity elsewhere;

［室女］ virgin; unmarried girl;

［室人］ wife;

［室外］ outdoor; outside;
室外活動 outdoor activities;
室外天線 exterior aerial; outdoor antenna;

［室溫］ room temperature;
標準室溫 normal room temperature;

暗室 dark house; darkroom;
闇室 dark room;
凹室 alcove; cubicle;
辦公室 office;
保管室 storeroom;
編輯室 editorial section;
別室 (1) concubine; (2) another room;
病室 sickroom; ward;
播音室 broadcasting studio;
餐室 dining room;
艙室 cabin;
側室 concubine;
茶室 tea house; tea room;
陳列室 exhibition room; showroom;
傳達室 reception room;
爨室 kitchen;
待產室 labour room;
地下室 basement; cellar;
調度室 dispatcher's room;
斗室 small room;
放映室 projection room;
宮室 (1) dwelling room; (2) imperial palace;
鼓室 tympanum;
廣播室 broadcasting room;
候車室 waiting room;
候機室 airport lounge; waiting room;
候客室 antechamber; reception room;
候診室 waiting room;
化驗室 laboratory;
化妝室 dressing room;
畫室 studio;
皇室 imperial family; imperial household; royal household;
會客室 reception room;
會議室 conference room;
急診室 emergency ward;
繼室 second wife;
家室 (1) husband and wife; (2) family; family dependents;
教室 classroom; schoolroom;
教研室 teaching and research section;
接待室 reception room;
荊室 my wife;
龕室 cidorium;
空室 empty room;
控制室 controlling room;
立室 take a wife;
陋室 humble room; room totally without decoration;
錄音室 recording room;

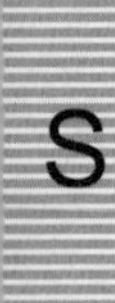

滿室 roomful;
密室 room used for secret purposes;
墓室 coffin chamber; vault;
腦室 ventricles of the brain;
妻室 one's legal wife; one's wife;
綺室 gorgeous room; magnificent room;
前室 antechamber;
寢室 bedroom; chamber; dormitory;
囚室 prison cell;
曲室 secret chamber;
入室 attain profundity in scholastic pursuits; become a real expert;
深室 prison cell;
實驗室 laboratory;
收發室 office for incoming and outgoing mail;
手術室 operating room; operating theatre;
私室 private room;
外室 one's mistress living outside;
王室 (1) royal family; (2) imperial court;
溫室 conservatory; glasshouse; greenhouse; hothouse;
臥室 bedroom;
下室 bedroom;
吸收室 absorption chamber;
吸煙室 smoking room;
先室 my late wife;
心室 ventricle;
休息室 lobby; lounge;
醫務室 clinic;
陰室 (1) one's bedroom; one's private quarter; (2) underground cellar for storage of ice;
窨室 cellar; vault;
浴室 bathroom; shower room;
閱覽室 reading room;
在室 (said of girls) still unmarried;
雜用室 utility room;
展覽室 exhibition room; showroom;
診療室 consulting room;
診室 consulting room;
正室 (1) one's legal wife; (2) one's male heir;
治療室 clinic;
資料室 reference room;
宗室 (1) imperial clan; (2) imperial clansman;

shi

【恃】 (1) depend on; presume upon; rely on; (2) one's mother;

[恃愛] presume on your kindness and affection;

[恃寵] presume on being a favourite of sb powerful;

[恃德者昌] he who relies on virtue will thrive; those who rule by virtue will thrive;
恃德者昌，恃力者亡 those who rely on virtue will thrive and those who rely on force will perish;

[恃功而驕] presume upon one's services and be haughty and imperious;

[恃貴] presume on one's high position;

[恃力] rely on force; rely on one's power;
恃力者亡 he who relies on force will perish; those who rely on force will perish;

[恃勹] rely on crooked ways and violence;

[恃勢] presume on one's position;
恃勢凌人 trust to one's power and insult people; use one's power to bully others;
恃勢倚財 rely on one's position and wealth to do evil;
恃勢專橫 rely on one's position to treat others with injustice;

[恃眾] presume on numbers; take advantage of superiority in numbers;

仗恃 rely on;
自恃 capitalize on; count on; self-assured and arrogant;

shi

【拭】 brush off; clean; dust; wipe; wipe away;

[拭除] brush sth off; wipe sth off;

[拭拂] wipe, dust and clean;

[拭淨] wipe and clean;

[拭淚] wipe tears;

擦拭 clean; cleanse;
拂拭 whisk off; wipe off;
揩拭 clean; wipe off;

shi

【是】 (1) correct; right; yes; (2) that; this; which; (3) be; (4) exist; (5) certainly; really; (6) justify; praise;

[是必] certainly; must be; surely;
是必有故 there must be a reason;

[是的] correct; right; that's it; yes;

[是非] (1) right and wrong; right or wrong; yes and no; yes or no; (2) discord; dispute; quarrel;
是非不分 cannot tell black from white;

confuse right and wrong; confuse truth and falsehood; fail to distinguish good from bad; fail to distinguish right and wrong; make no distinction between right and wrong;

是非不明 have no sense of right or wrong; unable to tell right from wrong;

是非顛倒 confound right and wrong;

是非分明 clear about what is right and what is wrong; the rights and wrongs are perfectly clear;

是非公允 just appraisal of right and wrong;

是非簍子 gossiper;

是非難逃眾人口 it is hard to avoid criticism of one's action by others;

是非曲直 merits and demerits; proper and improper; reasonable and absurd; right and wrong; truth and falsehood;

是非人 one who stirs up strife;

是非題 true-or-false question;

是非問題 a matter of right and wrong;

是非相貿 right and wrong are mixed up;

是非疑問句 yes-no question;

是非允當 just appraisal of right and wrong;

是非之地 a place where one is apt to get into trouble;

是非之心 one's conscience; the instinct to tell right from wrong;

是非之心，人皆有之 every man has a sense of right and wrong;

是非祗為多開口，煩惱皆因強出頭 you get into trouble because you speak too much, you get vexed because you strive to take the lead;

是非自有公論 public opinion is the best judge; public opinion will decide which is right and which is wrong; right or wrong will be left to public discussion; the public will judge the rights and wrongs of the case;

搬弄是非 carry tales; create troubles and dissensions; indulge in tittle-tattle; make mischief; make mischief through tittle-tattle; sow discord though gossip; stir up trouble by gossip; tell tales;

~搬弄是非的 catty;

搬弄是非的人 long tongue; loose tongue; scandalmonger; talebearer;

~愛搬弄是非 tablebearing;

辨別是非 distinguish between right and wrong; know right from wrong;

辨明是非 distinguish between right and wrong;

播弄是非 sow discord; sow dissension; stir things up; stir up trouble; tell tales;

不辨是非 fail to make a distinction between right and wrong;

不分是非 confuse right and wrong; confuse truth and falsehood; fail to distinguish right from wrong;

大是大非 the cardinal issue of right and wrong; the major issues of principles;

顛倒是非 confound right and wrong; confuse truth and falsehood; distort truth; give a false account of the true facts; invert justice; lead people's error; reversal of right and wrong; reverse right and wrong; stand facts on their heads; the perversion of truth; turn right into wrong; turn things upside down; twist the facts;

今是昨非 come to realize how wrong one has been all these years; realize how one has been wrong; wake up to one's past folly after realizing what is right today; things of the present are right and those of the past are wrong;

~覺今是而昨非 realize now that one has been wrong in the past;

口是心非 a hypocrite; affirm with one's lips but deny in one's heart; agree in words but disagree in heart; carry fire in one hand and water in the other; carry two faces under one head; cry with one eye and laugh with the other; double-dealing; double-faced; duplicity; hypocrisy; outwardly agree but inwardly disagree; pay lip service; play a double game; play the hypocrite; right with the mouth but wrong at heart; say one thing and mean another; say yes and mean no; show a false face; the mouth specious and the mind perverse; though one speaks well, one's heart is false;

來是是非人，去是是非者 since one has caused the trouble it's up to him to fix it;

來説是非者，必是是非人 he who chatters to you will chatter of you; the dog that fetches will carry;

明辨是非 clear about what is right and

what is wrong; discern between right and wrong; distinguish between truth and falsehood; distinguish clearly between right and wrong; distinguish right from wrong; know right from wrong;

難辨是非 difficult to discriminate between right and wrong;

扭是為非 confuse truth and falsehood; reverse right and wrong; turn right into wrong;

惹是非 incur unnecessary trouble; provoke a dispute; stir up ill will; stir up trouble;

~莫惹是非 let the sleeping dog lie;

~惹起是非 provoke a dispute; stir up trouble;

是古非今 admire everything ancient and belittle present-day achievements; consider anything old as good and reject everything that is modern; praise antiquity and denounce the present; praise the past to condemn the present;

是是非非 gossips; scandals;

孰是孰非 which is right and which is wrong; who is right and who is wrong;

誰是誰非 who is in the right who is in the wrong; who is right and who is wrong;

似是而非 apparently right but actually wrong; as like as chalk and cheese; look right, but really wrong; seemingly correct but really incorrect;

挑弄是非 stir up one side against the other;

物是人非 the things are still there but men are no more the same ones;

閒是閒非 irrelevant disputes about affairs;

[是否] are you; if; is it; whether; whether or not;

是否有當 if it be deemed proper; whether this is proper;

[是故] therefore;

[是日] that day; this day;

[是問] be held responsible;

惟君是問 I hold you responsible for it;

[是幸] be much obliged;

[是以] therefore; hence;

便是 even if;

別是 can it be that; is it possible that;

不是 not;

才是 only then is...;

纔是 then and only then is...;

但是 but; nevertheless; yet;

當是 mistake sth for another; think that;

多的是 plentiful;

凡是 all; any; every;

光是 alone; merely; solely;

國是 national affairs;

還是 after all; all the same; else; had better; indeed; might as well; more; nevertheless; or; really; still; yet;

橫是 maybe; perhaps; probably;

或是 or;

既是 as; now that; since;

盡是 all; full of; without exception;

就是 (1) exactly; precisely; (2) even; even if;

可是 but; however; yet;

老是 always;

滿是 all; cover;

乃是 (1) but; (2) which is...;

卻是 in fact; nevertheless; the fact is;

任是 even if;

仍是 still is;

若是 if; supposing;

甚是 exceedingly; extremely; very;

算是 at last; finally;

雖是 although; still; though;

若是 if; supposing;

倘是 if; in case; supposing;

惟是 only that;

為的是 for the purpose of; for the sake of;

先是 former; original;

像是 look like; seem;

許是 maybe; perhaps;

要是 if; in case; supposing;

也是 also the same;

因是 because of this;

硬是 (1) actually; really; (2) just; simply;

由是 from this; hence;

又是 (1) again; (2) also; (3) still another; (4) the same as;

於是 as a result; consequently; hence; so; then; thereafter; thereupon; thus;

正是 exactly so; yes;

只是 (1) but; yet; (2) just; merely; only;

祇是 (1) just; merely; only; (2) but then; however; simply;

自是 (1) naturally; of course; (2) from then on; since then;

總是 after all; always; any; as a rule; at last; be bound; be certain; be sure; commonly; constantly; ever; "-ever"; eventually; every;

frequently; generally; have a habit of; however; invariably; keep doing sth; must; never; no matter; one; some; sooner or later; used to; usually; when; where; will; without exception; would;

shi

【柿】 persimmon;
［柿餅］ dried persimmon;
［柿樹］ persimmon tree;
［柿子］ persimmon;
柿子核 stone;
柿子椒 redpepper; sweetbell;

蓋柿 lid persimmon;
磨盤柿 lid persimmon;

shi

【舐】 lick;
［舐犢］ lick the calf;
舐犢情深 deep mother love; love of old parents; very affectionate toward one's children;

shi

【豉】 fermented beans;

shi

【逝】 (1) be gone; depart; pass; (2) die; pass away;
［逝去］ be gone; depart; pass;
［逝世］ die; pass away;
［逝者如斯］ it passes like this;
［逝止］ going and staying;

病逝 die of an illness;
飛逝 fleet away; pass swiftly;
流逝 elapse; glide; pass;
傷逝 grieve over the deceased;
身逝 die;
仙逝 die; pass away;
消逝 die away;

shi

【視】 (1) look at; see; (2) consider; look upon; look upon as; regard; regard as; take it for; (3) inspect; observe; watch; (4) imitate; take as a model;
［視差］ parallax;
視差位移 parallactic displacement;
絕對視差 absolute parallax;
色視差 chromatic parallax;
［視察］ examine; inspect; inspection visit; observe; review; see; visitation;
視察地形 survey the terrain;
視察團 inspection team; study group;
視察現場 take a view of the scene;
視察主任 inspection officer;
［視唱］ sightsinging;
［視朝］ give audience; hold a court;
［視窗］ window;
彈出式視窗 pop-up window;
［視導］ inspection;
視導報告 inspection report;
視導探訪 inspection visit;
［視…而定］ contingent upon
［視感控器］ perceptron;
［視界］ field of view; field of vision; range of vision;
［視距儀］ tachemeter;
［視覺］ point of view; sense of sight; vision; visual sense;
視覺詞匯 sight vocabulary;
視覺焦點 eye-catcher;
視覺空間 visual space;
視覺敏銳 visual acuity;
視覺識別系統 visual identity system;
視覺藝術 visual arts;
視覺印象 visual impression;
視覺中樞 visual centre;
白晝視覺 day vision;
單眼視覺 monocular vision;
過渡視覺 mesopic vision;
間接視覺 indirect vision;
亮度視覺 brightness vision;
明晰視覺 distinct vision;
無色視覺 achromatic vision;
中間視覺 mesoptic vision;
［視力］ eyesight; power of vision; sight; vision;
視力不好 have defective vision;
視力不佳 have poor vision;
視力測試 visual acuity testing;
視力好 have good eyesight;
視力普通 have an average eyesight;
視力衰退 failing eyesight;
愛護視力 take good care of one's eyesight;
保護視力 preserve eyesight;
單眼視力 monocular vision;
檢測視力 give a test of one's eyesight;
［視頻］ video;
視頻編碼參數 video coding parameter;
視頻編碼指令 video coded order;
視頻點播服務 video on demand;

視頻電話 video phone;
視頻電纜 video cable;
視頻放大 video amplification;
視頻高密度系統 video high density;
視頻格式 video format;
視頻後向運動矢量 video backward motion vector;
視頻化社會 video society;
視頻會議 video conference;
視頻卡 videocard;
視頻塊 video block;
視頻密碼 video cipher;
視頻輸出 video out;
視頻數據系統 videotext system;
視頻顯示 video display;
視頻選擇器 video selector;

[視如] consider as; hold sth as; regard as; treat as;
視如敝屣 regard as worn-out shoes — cast aside as worthless; regard as worthless as worn-out shoes — have the greatest contempt for;
視如草芥 hold sth as grass — regard as if no importance; regard as worthless;
視如糞土 consider as beneath contempt; look upon as dirt; look upon as filth and dirt; treat sth as mud; treat sth as the mud beneath one's feet;
視如己出 regard sb almost as one's own child; treat a child as if he were one's own; treat sb as one's own child;
視如寇仇 regard sb as one's enemy;
視如蛇蝎 deem to be snakes and scorpions; have a great aversion to; regard with great detestation;
視如玩物 be treated as playthings;
視如珍寶 care for as precious stones — hold sth in high esteem; regard sb or sth as a jewel of the greatest value;

[視若] consider as; hold sth as; regard sth as; treat as;
視若兒戲 consider it as mere child's play; treat as a trifle; trifle with;
視若禁臠 regard her as an inaccessible woman; regard sth as a forbidden slice of meat;
視若畏途 look upon it as an objectionable pursuit; think of it as a dangerous road;
視若無睹 be undisturbed by what one has seen; ignore; show no concern for; shut one's eyes to; take no notice of what one sees; turn a blind eye to;
視若無物 gaze at it as nothing; regard as nothing;
視若至寶 hold sth in high esteem; regard as priceless;

[視膳問寢] wait on meals and rest of parents; wait on one's parents and attend to their meals and rest;

[視事] assume office; attend to business after assuming office;

[視聽] (1) knowledge and experience; (2) public opinion; (3) audio-visual;
視聽法 audio-visual method;
視聽技術 audiovisual technique;
視聽教材 audio-visual aids;
視聽教具 audio-visual aids;
視聽教學 audio-visual teaching;
視聽教育 audio-visual education;
視聽節目 audio-visual programme;
視聽設備 audo-visual equipment;
視聽手段 audio-visual means;
視聽信息 audio-visual information;
視聽中心 audio-visual centre;
視聽座 visual-listening booth;
混淆視聽 call black white; confuse the people; confuse the public; confuse public opinion; lead the public opinion astray; mislead the people; mislead the public; throw dust in sb's eyes;
聳動視聽 create a sensation;
以正視聽 ensure a correct understanding of the facts; in order to ensure a correct understanding of the facts; so as to clarify matters to the public; so that the public may know the facts;

[視同] consider as; treat as;
視同兒戲 consider as child's play; not to take seriously; regard it as unimportant; take it lightly; treat a serious matter as a trifle; trifle;
視同具文 regard as merely empty words;
視同路人 make a stranger of; regard sb as a stranger; treat as outsiders; treat as strangers; treat sb as a passer-by stranger; treat sb like a stranger;
視同陌路 cut sb dead; give sb the go-by; treat sb as if he were a complete stranger;
視同神明 look upon sb as superhuman;
視同手足 find in sb a friend as

smypathetic as a brother; treat sb as one's own brother;
視同一律 consider all as alike; identify with;
視同一體 accord the same treatment to all; impartial; look as an integral whole; make no distinction;
視同珍寶 hold sth in high esteem; look upon it as a treasure;

[視網膜] retina;
視網膜病 retinitis;
~白血病性視網膜病 leukemic retinophathy;
~出血性視網膜病 hemorrhagic retinopathy;
~腎性視網膜病 renal retinopathy;
~滲出性視網膜病 exudative retinopahty;
~糖尿病視網膜病 diabetic retinopathy;
~糖尿病性視網膜病 diabetic retinopathy;
~早產兒視網膜病 retinopathy of prematurity;
~增生性視網膜病 proliferative retinopathy;
視網膜發育不良 retinal dysplasia;
視網膜發育不全 retinal aplasia;
視網膜脱離 detached retina;
視網膜炎 retinitis;
~白血病性視網膜炎 leukemic retinitis;
單純性視網膜炎 simple retinitis;
梅毒性視網膜炎 syphilitic retinitis;
尿毒症性視網膜炎 uremic retinitis;
盤狀視網膜炎 disciform retinitis;
~妊娠性視網膜炎 gravidic retinitis;
~日光性視網膜炎 solar retinitis;
~日蝕性視網膜炎 solar retinitis;
~腎性視網膜炎 renal retinitis;
~滲出性視網膜炎 exudative retinitis;
~糖尿病性視網膜炎 diabetic retinitis;
~增生性視網膜炎 proliferating retinitis;
轉移性視網膜炎 metastatic retinitis;
卒中性視網膜炎 apoplectic retinitis;
視網膜移植 retina transplant;
緊壓性視網膜 coarctate retina;

[視為] consider as; regard as;
視為當然 take for granted;
視為禁臠 regard as one's exclusive domain; regard sth as a forbidden slice of meat — regard her as an inaccessible woman;
視為具文 consider as a mere form of words; look to as a mere form; regard as mere empty words; regard the law as a dead letter;
視為失敗 write off;
視為畏途 afraid to undertake; look upon it as an objectionable pursuit; regard as a road full of dangers — regard as an undertaking full of difficulties; regard as dangerous; regard it as dangerous road to take;
視為知己 look upon sb as one's best friend; treat sb as a bosom friend;
視為至寶 regard as priceless; set great store by;

[視位] apparent position;

[視線] (1) eyesight; (2) line of sight; (3) line of vision;
擋住視線 obstruct the view;
轉移視線 (1) divert public attention; divert sb's attention; draw attention to some other matter; (2) divert the line of sight; turn the gaze;

[視像] video;
視像點播 video-on-demand;
視像管 vidicon;
~電子感生導電視像管 electron-induced conductivity vidicon;
~硫化銻視像管 antimony trisulphide vidicon;
視像會議 video conferencing;

[視學] educational inspector; inspection;
視學小組 inspection team;
視學制度 inspection system;

[視野] field of vision; horizon; visual field;
視野清晰 get a clear view;
視野狹窄 have tunnel vision;
國際宏觀視野 global perspective;
國際視野 horizons of the world;
進入視野 come into view;
擴闊視野 broaden horizons; broaden the vision;
歷史視野 historical perspective;

[視譯] sight translation;

[視運動] apparent motion;

傲視 despise; regard superciliously; scorn; show disdain for; treat with disdain; turn up one's nose at;
逼視 (1) look at from close-up; watch intently; (2) stare at sternly;
鄙視 despise; look down upon; scorn;
側視 side-looking;
瞠視 stare at;

仇視 regard as an enemy; look upon with hatred;
讎視 hostile to; regard with hostility;
敵視 adopt a hostile attitude towards; antagonistic to; hostile to;
諦視 examine closely; scrutinize;
電視 small screen; teevee; television; TV;
短視 (1) myopia; nearsightedness; (2) lack foresight; shortsighted;
鶚視 look fiercely;
訪視 make a house call;
俯視 look down at; overlook;
複視 diplopia;
後視 back vision;
忽視 blank; disregard; give a cold shoulder; ignore; look down on; neglect; overlook;
環視 look around;
幻視 vision; visual hallucination
監視 guard; keep a lookout over; keep watch on; monitor; surveillance;
檢視 check up; examine; view;
近視 myopia; nearsighted; nearsightedness; shortsighted; shortsightedness;
驚視 agaze with surprise;
敬視 offer congratulations to;
可視 visual;
窺視 out of the corner of one's eye; peep; peep at; spy on; take a furtive glance; watch stealthily;
藐視 despise; look down on; treat with contempt;
蔑視 despise; scorn; show contempt for;
漠視 brush aside; ignore; overlook; pay no attention to; show no concern for; treat with indifference;
睨視 look askance;
目視 visual;
凝視 gaze fixedly; stare;
怒視 glare at; glower at; scowl at;
平視 look at the front horizontally;
歧視 discriminate against;
竊視 peep;
輕視 belittle; bridle at sth; cock a snoot at; cock one's nose; condemn; contemptuous; curl one's lip; despise; disdain; disdainful; disregard; feel contempt for; give sb the go-by; give sth the go-by; hold in contempt; hold in scorn; in contempt of; look down on; look down upon; make light of sb; make little account of; make little of; mocking; pooh-pooh; regard lightly; scorn; scornful of; set light by sb; set little of; set little store by sb; set little store by sth; set no store by sb; set no store by sth; set not much store by; show scorn; slight; snap one's fingers at; sneeze at; take lightly; take no account of; think light of; think little of; think nothing of; think scorn of; treat with contempt; trifle with; turn one's nose up at sb; underestimate; underrate;
弱視 amblyopia; weak sight;
掃視 look around; sweep one's eyes over;
審視 examine; look closely at;
熟視 look carefully and for a long time; scrutinize;
探視 visit; visitation;
透視 (1) penetrate; see though; (2) gain a perspective of; perspective; (3) grasp the essence; (4) to x-ray;
望視 look upwards;
無視 brush aside; consider as unimportant; defy; disregard; have no high opinion of; ignore; pay no attention to;
忤視 look at with a jaundiced eye; look defiantly at;
相視 look at each other;
小視 belittle; despise; feel contempt for sth; look down upon;
斜視 askance; cast a sidelong glance; cockeyed; look awry; look sideways; skew; skew-eyed; slant; slant; squint-eyed; strabismus
省視 (1) call upon; pay a visit to; (2) examine carefully; inspect;
雄視 dominate;
巡視 make an inspection tour;
蟻視 despise;
淫視 come-hither look; lascivious looks;
鷹視 fierce look;
影視 film and television;
遠視 (1) farsightedness; hypermetropia; hyperopia; (2) look from a distance; (3) far-sighted; long-sighted;
瞻視 behold; look; look up to;
珍視 cherish; have a high opinion of; prize; treasure; value;
診視 examine (a patient);
正視 face squarely; face up to; look at sth without bias; look squarely at; look straight in the eye;
直視 look steadily at;
重視 attach importance to; cherish; consider important; make much account of; pay attention to; take account of; take into account; take sth seriously; think highly of; think the world of; value;
注視 focus one's look on; gaze at; look

自視 attentively at; watch;
自視 consider oneself; imagine oneself; think oneself;
坐視 keep hands off; sit by and watch; sit tight and look on; watching without extending a helping hand;

shi

【貰】 (1) lend; lease; loan out; (2) forgive; pardon; (3) buy on credit; sell on credit;
［貰酒］ buy wine on credit;
貰酒款客 get wine on credit in order to entertain friends;
［貰赦］ pardon a criminal offence;
貰赦不究 pardon and not to inquire into;

shi

【勢】 (1) force; influence; power; (2) momentum; tendency; (3) the outward appearance of a natural object; (4) circumstances; situation; state of affairs; (5) gestures; signs; (6) male genitals;
［勢必］ be bound to; certainly will; undoubtedly;
勢必倒霉 in for it;
［勢不可當］ a trend that cannot be halted; advance irresistibly; irresistible; nothing can hold it back; overwhelming;
［勢不兩立］ absolutely antagonistic; at daggers drawn; at enmity; at the opposite pole to; completely incompatible; diametrically opposed to; extremely antagonistic to; implacable hostility; irreconcilable with; swear not to coexist with; unable to coexist;
［勢均力敵］ all square; balance in power; balance of forces; diamond cut diamond; equal in authority and power; equal scale; even scale; evenly matched; in an equilibrium; level; lever-pegging; match each other in strength; neck and neck; nip and tuck; well-matched; well-matched in strength;
雙方勢均力敵 the two sides are evenly matched;
［勢力］ force; influence; power;
勢力範圍 sphere of influence; stamping ground; stomping ground; zone of influence;
惡勢力 forces of evil; vicious power;
潛勢力 latent power;
有深遠的勢力 have a long arm;
壯大勢力 expand one's forces;
［勢利］ snobbish;
勢利成性 snobbish proclivities;
勢利小人 snob;
~鄙視勢利小人 disdain a man for his snobbishness;
勢利眼 (1) snobbish attitude; (2) snob; (3) judge a person by wealth and power;
勢利之交 a friendship based on power and influence;
反向勢利 inverted snobbery;
［勢所必至］ be bound to come;
［勢態］ attitude;
［勢頭］ (1) impetus; momentum; (2) situation; state of affairs; tendency; the look of things;
勢頭不對 the situation is unfavourable;
增長勢頭 momentum of growth;
~保持良好的增長勢頭 maintain the healthy momentum of growth;
［勢焰］ arrogance and power;
［勢要］ the influential and the mighty;
［勢在必行］ essential; imperative; must be enforced; sth has to be enforced; the time has come for action;

把勢 (1) martial art; (2) person skilled in martial art or trade; (3) skill; technique;
筆勢 force of calligraphy;
病勢 degree of seriousness of an illness; patient's condition;
財勢 wealth and power;
趁勢 act when a good chance is available; take advantage of a favourable situation;
乘勢 avail onesef of; strike while the iron is hot;
稱勢 potential;
磁勢 magnetic potential;
大勢 general situation; general trend of events;
得勢 (1) in power; (2) ascent to power; get the upper hand; in the ascendant;
地勢 physical features of a place; terrain; topography of the land;
電勢 electric potential; potential;
風勢 force of wind;
攻勢 offensive;

國勢 (1) national power; (2) national situation at a given moment;
架勢 manner; posture; stance;
借勢 rely on one's power;
就勢 making use of momentum; taking the opportunity;
局勢 situation;
均勢 balance of power; equilibrium; equilibrium of forces; parity;
來勢 oncoming force; the force with which sth breaks out;
劣勢 inferior position; inferior strength;
派勢 manner; style;
氣勢 imposing manner; momentum;
強勢 strong;
情勢 circumstances; situations; state of affairs; trend of events;
趨勢 tendency; trend;
去勢 castrate; castration; emasculate;
權勢 power and influence;
弱勢 (1) in a relatively weak position; (2) the disadvantaged;
傷勢 condition of an injury or wound;
生勢 the way a crop is growing;
聲勢 impetus; momentum;
失勢 fall into disgrace; lose one's power and influence;
時勢 current situation; current trend of events; time and circumstances; trend of the times;
事勢 general course of events; trend of things in general;
恃勢 presume on one's position;
手勢 gesture; sign;
守勢 defensive;
水勢 (1) flow of the water; (2) direction of the flowing water;
順勢 (1) taking advantage of an opportunity; (2) at one's convenience; without taking extra trouble;
態勢 posture; state;
頭勢 (1) situation; state of affairs; (2) tendency;
頹勢 declining trend;
威勢 power and influence; prestige and influence;
位勢 potential;
現勢 current situation; present situation;
挾勢 presume upon one's influence; take advantage of one's power;
形勢 (1) terrain; topographical features; (2) circumstances; situation;
倚勢 rely on one's position; rely on one's power;
音勢 intensity of sound;
優勢 dominant position; goodness; predominance; preponderance; superiority; supremacy; the upper hand; vigour;
造勢 media hype; spin;
長勢 the way a crop is growing;
仗勢 take advantage of one's power or connections with influential people;
陣勢 (1) battle formation; (2) circumstances; condition;
逐勢 strive for power and influence;
肢勢 standing posture;
姿勢 (1) bearing; carriage; deportment; (2) gesture; posture;
作勢 assume a posture; pretend; put on airs;

shi

【嗜】 addict; be addicted to; delight in; fond of; have a liking for; like; relish;

［嗜賭］ addited to gambling;
嗜賭如命 be addicted to gambling;

［嗜好］ addiction; fad; habit; hobby;
深嗜篤好 date on; delight in; enjoy greatly;
習得嗜好 acquired taste;

［嗜酒］ addiction to the bottle; be addicted to drinking; keep to the bottle;
嗜酒成癖 be addicted to drinking; be given to drink;
嗜酒好賭 love wine and gambling to excess;
嗜酒好色 be addicted to drinking and lewdness; crazy about wine and women; fond of drink and women;
嗜酒狂 alcoholomania; dipsomaniac;
嗜酒癖 alcoholophilia;

［嗜癖］ hobby; special liking for sth;
嗜痂成癖 eccentric taste; have an uncommonly low taste;

［嗜殺］ bloodthirsty; fond of killing;
嗜殺成性 bloodthirsty; fond of killing; sanguinary;

［嗜食癖］ addephagia;

［嗜血］ bloodsucking; bloodthirsty;

［嗜慾］ sensual desires;

shi

【弒】 kill one's superior; murder one's senior;

［弒父］ commit patricide; patricide;
弒父弒君 murder one's own father and one's sovereign;

［弒君］ commit regicide; regicide;

弒君者 regicide;

[弒母] commit matricide; matricide;

弒母罪 matricide;

[弒逆者] one who commits patricide or regicide;

[弒兄] commit fratricide; fratricide;

shi

【筮】 divine by means of the stalks of the milfoil;

[筮人] fortune teller;

[筮仕] enter on an official career;

shi

【試】 (1) experiment; test; try; (2) examination; test; trial; (3) put up a trial balloon; sound out; (4) a surname;

[試辦] do sth on an experimental basis; run a pilot scheme;

[試爆] test explosion;

[試場] examination hall; examination place; test ground;

[試穿] fit sth on; try on;

[試管] test tube;

試管架 test-tube stand;

試管嬰兒 test-tube baby;

[試婚] trial marriage;

[試劑] reagent;

分析純試劑 analytical reagent;

活化試劑 activating reagent;

碱性試劑 alkaline reagents;

生物碱試劑 alkaloid reagent;

吸收試劑 absorption reagent;

[試金石] litmus test; touchstone;

[試鏡] screen test;

進行試鏡 undergo a screen test;

[試舉] attempt; trial;

第二次試舉 second attempt;

第三次試舉 third attempt;

第一次試舉 first attempt;

[試卷] examination paper; test paper;

打印試卷 type a test paper;

批改試卷 correct an examination paper;

審閱試卷 look through a test paper;

[試看] try and see;

[試試] have a try; try;

試試看 have a shot at; suck it and see;

開始試試 start in;

試一試 give it a try; give sth a whirl; try; have a whack at sth; take a whack at sth;

[試探] explore; feel out; probe; put up a trial balloon; sound out; test;

試探反應 fly one's kite;

試探民意 sound out public opinion;

試探虛實 try to find out the abstract and the concrete;

[試題] examination question; test question;

試題庫 item bank; question bank;

~ 試題庫建設 question bank built-up;

[試頭水兒] among the first to eat, see or enjoy sth;

[試圖] attempt; try;

試圖逃跑 make an attempt at escaping;

[試問] it may well be asked; let me ask; may we ask; we should like to ask;

[試想] considering that; just think; think it over;

[試銷] place goods on trial sale; trial sale;

試銷產品 trial sale products;

[試行] put into trial use; trial implementation; try out;

[試演] dress rehearsal; preview; trial performance; make a dress rehearsal;

[試驗] experiment; test; testing; trial;

試驗成功 try one's experiment with success;

試驗器 tester;

~ 電容試驗器 condenser tester;

~ 陣列試驗器 array tester;

試驗室 laboratory;

~ 分析試驗室 analytical laboratory;

~ 化學試驗室 chemical laboratory;

倒車試驗 astern trial;

動物試驗 animal experiment;

飛機試驗 aircraft testing;

估價試驗 assessment trial;

進行試驗 make an experiment;

錨設備試驗 anchor trial;

清晰度試驗 articulation testing;

受控試驗 controlled experiment;

酸凝試驗 acid coagulation test;

酸熱試驗 acid heat test;

酸值試驗 acid value test;

一次試驗 a test;

一系列試驗 a series of experiments;

音響試驗 acoustic test;

作為試驗 as a trial;

[試樣] sample; specimen;

疲勞試樣 fatigue testing specimen;

全級試樣 all-level sample;

壓坯試樣 compact specimen;
真實試樣 authentic sample;

[試衣] fitting;
試衣服 fit sth on; try on a dress;
試衣間 fitting room;
試衣鏡 fitting mirror;
試衣室 fitting room;

[試映] give a preview; preview

[試用] on probation; on trial; try out;
試用期 probational period;
試用人員 probationer;

[試紙] test paper;
薑黃試紙 turmeric paper;
石蕊試紙 litmus paper;

比試 (1) have a competition; (2) measure with one's hand or arm;
筆試 written examination; written test;
測試 measure and test;
嘗試 attempt; endeavor; take a hack at sth; try;
初試 (1) first attempt; first try; preliminary test; (2) preliminary examination;
春試 imperial examinations held in spring;
殿試 palace examination;
赴試 go to take part in examinations;
複試 hold or attend a re-examination; reexamine; re-examination;
公開試 public examinations;
會試 metropolitan examination;
考試 examine; examination; test;
口試 oral examination; oral quiz; oral test;
免試 be excused from an examination;
面試 audition; examine face to face; interview; oral quiz;
省試 provincial examination;
探試 try to find out;
調試 debug; debugging;
廷試 imperial examination;
縣試 county examination;
小試 make a casual trial;
應試 sit for an examination; take an examination;
預試 preexamine; preliminary examination;

shi

【軾】 (1) horizontal front bar on a cart; (2) leaning board in a sedan chair;

shi

【飾】 (1) decorations; ornaments; (2) adorn; decorate; dress up; ornament; polish; (3) act the part of; impersonate; play the role of; (4) excuse oneself ona pretext; fake; (5) cover up; deceive;

[飾詞] (1) excuse; pretext; (2) polish a piece of writing;

[飾非] hide and gloss over one's faults;
強辯飾非 argue illogically in glossing over faults; cover up faults with flowery words;
文過飾非 conceal faults and gloss over wrongs; conceal mistakes and complete the undoing; cover up one's errors; explain away one's errors; explain away one's shortcomings and mistakes; gild over one's vices; gloss over one's mistakes; pretend to have done nothing; slur over and excuse one's crimes; smooth over one's faults; varnish errors; whitewash faults;

[飾過] hide and gloss over one's faults; whitewash;

[飾偽] fake; make sth in order to deceive;

[飾物] adornments; decorations; ornaments;
環狀飾物 circlet;

[飾演] act the part of; play; play the role of;

[飾終] funeral rites;

窗飾 window decorations;
粉飾 gloss over; prettify; sugar up; varnish; whitewash;
服飾 biliment; costume; dress; dress and personal adornment; equipage; trappings;
花飾 ornamental design;
諱飾 conceal the truth; make a deceptive display;
矯飾 dissemble; feign in order to conceal sth;
誇飾 describe in an exaggerative way; exaggeratedly embellish;
潤飾 add colour; embellish a piece of writing; polish a piece of writing;
首飾 jewelry; ornaments; trinkets;
頭飾 head ornament;
塗飾 (1) cover with paint, lacquer, etc.; (2) whitewash;
文飾 deceive by an impressive appearance;
胸飾 brooch;
修飾 (1) adorn; decorate; embellish; (2) make up and dress up; (3) polish; (4) modify; qualify;
嚴飾 order strictly;
掩飾 (1) camouflage; cloak; conceal; cover up; cover-up; gloss over; put a good face on; (2) deception;

衣飾 clothes and ornaments;
油飾 paint over with wood oil;
緣飾 embellish with words;
藻飾 (1) embellishments in writing; (2) polish writings;
妝飾 adorn; dress up; woman's personal adornments;
裝飾 (1) adorn; decorate; embellish; ornament; set off; (2) deck; doll up; make up;

shi
【鈰】 cerium;

乙酸鈰 cerous acetate;

shi
【誓】 (1) pledge; swear; vow; (2) oath; vow; (3) take an oath;
[誓詞] pledge; oath;
莊嚴誓詞 solemn vow;
[誓師] (1) rally to pledge resolution before going to war; (2) take a mass pledge;
誓師出征 harangue troops and set out for an expedition;
誓師大會 meeting to pledge mass effort;
[誓死] dare to die; pledge one's life;
誓死不二 pledge to be true to death; remain loyal even unto death;
誓死不屈 swear to die rather than submit – even death won't make one yield;
誓死捍衛 defy death to defend;
[誓同泉穴] vow to be constant even unto the grave;
[誓言] solemn pledge; vow; oath;
交換誓言 exchange vows;
結婚誓言 wedding vows;
禁言誓言 vow of silence;
立下誓言 take a vow;
履行誓言 fulfill a pledge;
違反誓言 break one's oath;
遵守誓言 keep a vow;
[誓愿] pledge; vow;
設誓起愿 swear; take an oath;
[誓約] solemn pledge; vow; oath;
背棄誓約 break a vow;
婚姻誓約 marriage vows; wedding vows;
立下誓約 take a vow;
取消誓約 abrogate one's vow;
神聖誓約 holy vow; sacred vow;

發誓 pledge; swear;
立誓 take an oath; vow;
盟誓 make a pledge; take an oath;
明誓 make a pledge; take an oath;
起誓 swear; take an oath;
宣誓 make a pledge; take an oath;

shi
【奭】 (1) red; (2) angry; (3) a surname;
[奭然] in a free manner; in utter freedom;

shi
【適】 (1) fit; proper; suitable; (2) exactly; just right; opportune; right; (3) accidentally; by chance; (4) at ease with oneself; comfortable; well; (5) follow; go; pursue; (6) arrive at; go; reach; (7) get married; marry;
[適纔] just now;
[適從] follow; head in a direction;
無所適從 at a loss what to do; at a loss which one to follow; be distracted; not to know what course to pursue; not to know what to do; not to know where to turn to; not to know whom to turn to;
[適當] appropriate; fit; proper; suitable;
適當的安排 proper arrangement;
極其適當 singularly appropriate;
[適得其反] accomplish the very opposite; counterproductive; exactly opposite; get exactly the opposite; just the reverse of what is expected; on the contrary; run counter to one's desire; turn out just the opposite of;
[適得其所] well suited with one's place;
[適度] appropriate; appropriate measure; moderate; moderate degree; proper; to a moderate degree; within limits;
適度人口 optimum population;
長短適度 right length;
批評適度 temperate in one's criticism;
需求適度 moderate in one's demands;
[適逢] at the very time when;
適逢其會 come at the right time; happen to be present on the occasion; lucky enough to be there at the time;
[適合] appropriate for; apt for; becoming; calculate for; fit; fit for; fit in with; sit sb like a glove; good for; just the job for; perfect for; proper; right for sb; suit; suitable for;
適合變化 adaptation;

適合動詞 verb of suiting;
勉強適合 barely suitable for sth;

[適間] just a moment ago; just now;

[適可而止] be satisfied with what is proper; bind the sack before it be full; enough is as good as a feast; enough is enough; know how far to go; know when to say when; know when to stop; not overdo sth; stop at the proper moment; stop before going too far; stop where you reach the limit; there is a limit;

[適口] agreeable to the taste; palatable; pleasant to the palate; tasty;

[適來] just now;

[適量] appropriate amount;

[適齡] of the right age;
適齡兒童 children of school age;
適齡青年 young people old enough to do sth;

[適然] (1) accidentally; by chance; (2) a matter of course;

[適人] marry sb;

[適時] at the right moment; at the right time; in good time; in the nick of time; timely;

[適銷對路] readily marketable; ready marketability;

[適宜] appropriate; fit; proper; suitable;
不適宜 inappropriate; inapt; inaptness;
行為適宜 act rightly;

[適意] agreeable; as desired; comfortable; enjoyable;
自適其意 get one's own way;

[適應] accommodate oneself to; accustom oneself to; adapt to; adjust; become seasoned to; come to terms with; fit; make adjustment to; season oneself to; suit; tune in to;
適應方式 mode of adaptation;
適應環境 adapt to circumstances; adaptation to environment; stretch one's legs according to the coverlet;
適應活動 adaptive activity;
適應能力 adaptive capacity;
適應性 adaptability;
~ 適應性反應 adaptability response;
~ 適應性訓練 adaptability training;
~ 適應性政治 politics of adaptation;
~ 特化適應性 specialized adaptation;
~ 相對適應性 relative adaptability;
適應需要 meet the needs of;
多面適應 manifold adaptation;
感覺適應 sensory adaptation;
光適應 light adaptation;
互相適應 coadaptation;
活動性適應 active adaptation;
機能適應 functional adaptation;
連續適應 homogenic adaptation;
免疫適應 immunological adaptation;
能適應的 adaptable;
前發適應 anticipation adaptation;
趨同適應 convergent adaptation;
色適應 chromatic adaptation;
生物適應 biotic adaptation;
失重適應 weightlessness adaptation;
視力適應 visual accommodation;
自適應 adaptive;
~ 自適應結構 adaptive structure;
~ 自適應控制 adaptive control;
~ 自適應系統 adaptive system;

[適用] apply to; suit; suitable for use;
適用程序 utilities;
適用技術 applied technology;
不適用 inapplicable;
普通適用 universally applicable;

[適於] fit; fit for; suit; suitable for;

[適值] coincidentally; happen by coincidence; happen exactly when; just when;

[適中] (1) adequate; appropriate; just right; moderate; (2) be well situated;
大小適中 of moderate size;
地點適中 be conveniently situated;

安適 (1) peaceful and comfortable; quiet and comfortable; (2) snug;
不適 discomfort; indisposed; malaise; out of sorts; trouble; unwell;
酣適 sound sleep;
合適 appropriate; becoming; right; suitable;
如適 contented; peaceful and comfortable;
舒適 comfortable; cosy;
順適 casual; composed; natural;
恬適 quiet and comfortable;
閒適 leisurely and comfortable; quiet and comfortable;

shi

【噬】 bite; gnaw; snap at;

[噬菌作用] fungivorous action;

反噬 trump up a countercharge against one's

accuser;

吞噬 gobble up; swallow;

shi

【澨】 (1) water front; (2) waterside; (3) a river in Hubei;

shi

【諟】 (1) same as 是; (2) consider; examine; judge;

[諟正] examine and correct;

shi

【謚】 posthumous title;

[謚法] regulations for conferring posthumous titles;

[謚號] posthumous title;

shi

【釋】 (1) elucidate; explain; interpret; (2) clear up; dispel; disperse; (3) be relieved of; let go; relieve; (4) pardon; release; set free; (5) Buddhism;

[釋部] Buddhist sutras;

[釋出] disengage;

[釋道] Buddhism and Daoism;

[釋典] Buddhist scriptures; Buddhist sutras;

[釋放] release; set free;

釋放囚犯 release the prisoners;

獲得釋放 get off;

取保釋放 be bailed out; be released on bail;

無罪釋放 go scot-free;

~被無罪釋放 walk free;

刑滿釋放 be released upon completion of a sentence;

有條件釋放 conditional discharge;

[釋教] Buddhism;

[釋卷] put a book aside;

手不釋卷 diligent reader; studious;

[釋悶] disperse melancholy; chase away gloom;

[釋然] (1) at ease; relaxed; (2) have all the misunderstandings cleared up;

[釋手] loosen one's grip; relax the hold;

愛不釋手 can hardly bear to put it down; can hardly tear oneself away from; fond of and unwilling to part with; fondle admiringly; it is hard to put it down; like sth so much that one cannot bear to part with it; love sth so much that one is loathe to part with it; love sth too much to part with; too fond of sth to let go of it; so delighted with it that one could hardly bear to put it down; so fond of sth that one cannot take one's hands off it; unable to tear oneself away from sth; unputdownable; unwilling to let sth out of one's hands;

[釋嫌] (1) dispel suspicion; (2) dispel ill feeling;

[釋疑] clear up doubts; dispel doubts; resolve a doubt; settle uncertainties;

以釋群疑 allay doubt in the public's mind; remove doubt in public's mind;

[釋義] expatiation; explain; interpretation;

重新釋義 reinterpretation;

[釋藏] Buddhist sutra;

保釋 bail; release on bail;

冰釋 be dispelled; disappear without a trace; vanish;

闡釋 explain; expound; interpret;

獲釋 be released; get off; set free;

假釋 conditional release; free a prisoner on probation; release on parole;

簡釋 brief explanation;

解釋 elucidate; explain; explicate; expound; give an account of;

開釋 release;

考釋 make textual criticisms and explanations;

淺釋 simple explanation;

詮釋 annotate; make explanatory notes;

稀釋 dilute; dilution; thinning;

消釋 clear up; dispel;

真釋 true and correct explanation;

注釋 annotate; annotation; explain with notes; explanatory notes;

shi5

shi

【匙】 key;

shou1

shou

【收】 (1) accept; receive; take; (2) put away; retrieve; take back; take in; (3) collect; draw together; gather; (4) contain; have; (5) income; money received; receipts; (6) gather in; harvest; (7) bring to an end; close; come to a close; end; stop; (8) control; re-

strain;
[收報機] radiotelegraphic receiver; telegraphic receiver;
[收編] incorporate into one's own forces;
[收兵] call off a battle; end hostilities; recall troops; withdraw troops;
鳴金收兵 beat the gong and recall the troops — call off a battle; beat the gongs and withdraw the army; beat the retreat; beat upon a brass gong and call back one's men; sound a gong to recall one's troops; sound the retreat;
[收捕] arrest;
[收藏] collect; collect and keep; enshrine; store up;
收藏古董 collect antiques;
收藏古畫 collect old paintings;
收藏家 collector;
收藏無用東西的人 pack rat;
[收操] make an end of drill;
[收場] (1) end up; stop; wind up; (2) conclusion; end; ending;
草草收場 wind up matter hastily;
[收成] crop; harvest;
[收存] receive and keep; receive for custody; receive for keeps;
[收到] achieve; get; obtain; receive;
[收發] (1) receive and dispatch; (2) dispatcher;
易發難收 easy to send forth and yet difficult to receive;
[收放] receive and dispatch;
易放難收 it is easier to indulge in an expensive habit than to get rid of it;
[收費] charge; collect fees;
收費表 tariff;
收費廁所 pay W.C.;
收費處 (of roads) tollgate;
收費電話 charged call;
收費電視 charged TV; pay TV;
~收費電視頻道 pay TV channel;
收費橋 tollbridge;
收費亭 tollbooth;
收費站 tollgate;
按人收費 capitation;
半價收費 be charged at half price;
固定收費 fixed charge;
亂收費 arbitrary imposition of fees; random charges;
少量收費 small charge;
象徵式收費 nominal charge;
最低收費 minimum charge;
[收服] bring under control; subdue;
[收復] recapture; recover; resume; retrieve;
收復河山 recover lost territory;
收復失地 recover lost territory;
[收割] gather in; harvest; reap;
收割機 harvester;
~豆類作物收割機 bean harvester;
~甘蔗收割機 cane harvester;
~聯合收割機 combined harvester;
~玉米收割機 corn harvester;
收割者 harvester;
[收工] call it a day; end the day's work; knock off; pack up; stop work for the day; wrap up;
[收購] buy out; buy up; purchase; takeover;
惡意收購 hostile takeover;
槓桿收購 leveraged buyout;
融資收購 leveraged buyout;
[收回] (1) call in; claw back; recall; recover; regain; resume; retrieve; take back; (2) countermand; retract; withdraw;
收回成命 recall an order; retract an order; revoke a command; swallow one's words; the revocation of an edict; withdraw an order;
收回建議 withdraw a proposal;
收回前言 eat crow; eat one's leek; eat one's words;
收回投資 recoup capital outlay;
收回主權 regain sovereignty;
[收貨] take delivery; take delivery of goods; take over;
收貨代理人 receiving agent;
收貨人 consignee;
收貨員 goods clerk;
[收獲] (1) gather in the crops; harvest; reap; (2) gains; results;
收獲者 harvester;
[收集] collect; gather;
收集標本 make a collection of specimens;
收集垃圾 collect garbage;
收集者 collector;
[收監] commit to jail; imprison; put in prison; take into custody;
[收件] receive a document or letter;
收件盤 in tray;
收件人 consignee; addressee;
收件箱 inbox;
[收繳] capture; take over;

[收緊] take up; tighten up;
收緊器 take-up;
~帶式運輸機收緊器 belt-conveyor take-ups;
~重力式收緊器 gravity take-up;
[收舊利廢] recycling of waste;
[收據] receipt;
承保收據 binding receipt;
發貨人收據 sender's receipt;
一張收據 a receipt;
正式收據 official receipt;
[收看] watch;
繼續收看 stay tuned;
[收口] heal;
[收款] receive money; make collection;
收款處 cash desk; cashier's;
收款窗口 cash window;
收款人 payee;
收款檯 cash desk;
收款員 cashier; deposit teller; receiving teller;
[收攬] (1) buy over; win over; (2) have sth/sb within control;
收攬民心 buy popular support; win over the people's support;
[收淚] stop crying;
[收禮] accept a present;
[收斂] (1) weaken or disappear; (2) restrain oneself; (3) convergence; converging;
收斂管道 converging duct;
收斂性 convergence;
~絕對一致收斂性 absolute uniform convergence;
~偶然收斂性 accidental convergence;
~殆必收斂性 almost sure convergence;
加速收斂 accelerating convergence;
漸近收斂 asymptotic convergence;
近似收斂 approximate convergence;
條件收斂 conditional convergence;
[收殮] lay a body in a coffin;
[收留] give shelter to; have sb in one's care; take sb in;
[收攏] draw sth in;
收攏人心 try to win people's support by every artifice;
[收錄] (1) employ; recruit; take on; (2) include;
[收羅] (1) collect; gather; (2) enlist;
收羅人才 recruit qualified personnel;
[收埋] collect and bury;

[收買] (1) buy in; purchase; (2) bribe; buy over; nobble;
收買人心 buy popular support; buy popularity; try to win popular support;
[收拿] arrest; detain;
[收納] accept; take in;
拒不收納 refuse to take;
[收票] collect tickets;
收票員 lobbyman; ticket collector;
~女收票員 lobbywoman;
[收起] cut out; pack up; stop;
[收訖] (1) paid; payment received; (2) received in full;
[收錢] collect payments;
[收清] received in full;
[收取] collect; gather;
[收權] retake the power;
[收容] accept; accommodate; give shelter to; house; take in;
收容難民 house refugees;
收容所 camp; temporary reception centre;
[收入] (1) earnings; gross; gainings; income; proceeds; receipts; revenue; takings; (2) include; take in;
收入不足 deficit in revenue;
收入等級 income bracket;
收入減少 sb's income falls; sb's income goes down;
收入來源 source of income; source of revenue;
收入水平 income level;
收入税 income tax;
收入損失 loss of income;
收入再分配 redistribution of the revenues;
收入增加 sb's income goes up; sb's income increases; sb's income rises;
收入賬 receiving account;
收入政策 incomes policy;
不正當收入 illegitimate income;
財務收入 financial income;
財政收入 revenue;
充裕的收入 ample income;
出口收入 export proceeds;
純收入 net income; net proceeds;
低收入 low income; small income;
地產收入 estate income;
額外收入 perk; perquisite;
附加收入 additional revenue;
高收入 high income; large income;
個人收入 personal income;

共同收入 joint income;
固定收入 fixed income;
關稅收入 customs revenue;
國家收入 national revenue;
國庫收入 public revenue;
國民收入 national income;
國外收入 income earned abroad;
貨幣收入 proceeds in cash;
集體收入 collective income;
家庭收入 family income; household income;
淨收入 net income; net receipt; net revenue;
絕對收入 absolute income;
可支配收入 disposable income;
累計收入 accumulated income;
利息收入 interest income;
年收入 annual income; yearly income;
農業收入 agricultural income;
平均收入 average income;
人平收入 per capita income;
提供收入 provide an income;
外匯收入 earnings from foreign exchange;
穩定的收入 steady income;
現金收入 cash receipts;
銷售收入 proceeds of sale;
一般收入 general revenue;
一份收入 an income;
應計收入 accrued revenue;
應納稅的收入 taxable income;
營業收入 operating income;
佣金收入 commission income;
有收入 have an income; receive an income;
預算收入 budgetary revenue;
增加收入 increase one's income;
資本收入 capital income;
總收入 aggregate income; gross income; total expenditure;
~ 全年總收入 gross annual income;

[收生] (1) intake; (2) midwifery;
收生額 intake;
收生婆 midwife;

[收拾] (1) clear away; gather up; put in order; tidy; (2) get things ready; pack; (3) mend; repair; (4) punish; settle with; torture;
收拾殘局 clear up a messy situation; clear up the mess; pick up the pieces; settle a disturbed situation;
收拾牀鋪 make the bed;
收拾房間 tidy up the room;
收拾停當 put in good order;
收拾碗筷 clear away the bowls and chopsticks; clear the table;
收拾屋子 tidy up the room;
收拾行李 pack one's luggage;
汗漫不可收拾 broken beyond all bounds; indiscriminate; superficial;

[收束] (1) bring together; collect; (2) bring to a close; (3) pack for a journey;

[收稅] collect taxes;
收稅人 tax collector;
收稅員 tax collector;
依法收稅 levy taxes according to law;

[收縮] (1) contract; contraction; deflate; retractation; shrink; shrinkage; (2) concentrate one's forces; draw back;
收縮核 retract;
~ 弱收縮核 weak retract;
~ 形變收縮核 deformation retract;
收縮力 contractile force;
收縮期 systole;
收縮性 contractibility; contractness;
初等收縮 elementary contraction;
存款收縮 deposit contraction;
二次收縮 double shrinkage;
加壓收縮 compression shrinkage;
絕熱收縮 adiabatic contraction;
空氣收縮 air shrinkage;
離心收縮 eccentric contraction;
雙重收縮 double shrinkage;
向心收縮 concentric contraction;
形變收縮 deformation retraction;

[收條] receipt;

[收聽] listen in; tune in;
收聽新聞 listen in to the news;
~ 收聽新聞廣播 listen to the news broadcast;
收聽者 listener;
繼續收聽 stay tuned;

[收尾] (1) come to a conclusion; wind up; (2) concluding passage;

[收文] incoming dispatches;
收文匣 inbox; in tray;

[收下] accept; receive;

[收效] bear fruit; get the desired result; produce effects; prove effective; yield results;
收效神速 yield marvellously quick results;

收效顯著 bring notable results;

[收心] (1) bring one's mind back from; concentrate on more serious things; get into the frame of mind for work; (2) have a change of heart;

收心歸正 get into the right frame of mind; give up evil ways and return to the rigth path;

[收信] get a letter; receive a letter;

收信人 addressee; consignee;

[收押] detain; take into custody;

[收養] adopt; take in and bring up;

收養孤兒 adopt an orphan;

[收益] earnings; gains; income; proceeds; profits;

收益能力 profit ability;

參股收益 equity earnings;

差額收益 differential earnings;

淨收益 net earning; net yield;

累積收益 accumulated earnings;

企業家收益 entrepreneurial earnings;

無形收益 invisible earnings;

現今收益 cash earnings;

營業收益 business earnings;

[收音機] radio; receiver;

收音機外殼 cabinet;

長波收音機 long-wave radio;

超外差式收音機 superhet radio set;

車廂收音機 seat radio;

打開收音機 switch on the radio; switch the radio on; turn on the radio;

關掉收音機 switch off the radio; turn off the radio;

交流電收音機 mains set;

晶體管收音機 transistor radio;

礦石收音機 crystal radio;

汽車收音機 car radio;

時鐘收音機 clock radio;

調幅收音機 amplitude modulation receiver;

調頻收音機 frequency modulation receiver;

聽收音機 listen to the radio;

小型收音機 personal radio;

新型收音機 late-model radio;

一台收音機 a radio;

直流電收音機 battery set;

鐘控收音機 clock radio;

自差式收音機 auto-dyne radio;

[收銀] collect money;

收銀機 cash register machine;

收銀台 cash desk;

[收葬] bury the dead;

[收債] collect a debt;

收債人 debt collector;

[收支] income and expenses; revenue and expenditure;

收支缺口 gap between revenue and expenditure;

收支逆差 balance of payments deficit;

收支平衡 balanced budget; balance; balance accounts; balance expenditure with income; break even; maintain a balance between receipts and payments; the accounts are balanced;

收支相抵 clear expenses; expenses balance receipts; live within one's income; make buckle and tongue meet; make ends meet; the income balances the expenditure;

增收節支 raise revenues and reduce expenditures;

[收租] collect rentals; collect rents;

採收 gather; harvest;

查收 (1) find sth enclosed; (2) check and accept;

創收 create a source of income; earn income; extra earning; perk;

點收 check and accept;

豐收 bump harvest; have a bumper harvest;

回收 reclaim; recover; recovery; retrieve;

接收 (1) receive; (2) expropriate; take over; (3) admit;

麥收 wheat harvest;

沒收 confiscate; expropriate; forfeit; forfeiture;

簽收 sign after receiving sth; sign to acknowledge the receipt of sth;

歉收 bad harvest; crop failure; have a poor harvest; have bad crops; poor harvest;

搶收 get the harvest in quickly; rush in the harvest;

秋收 autumn crops; get in the autumn harvest;

税收 tax revenue;

歲收 annual income;

托收 collection;

吸收 (1) absorb; assimilate; assimilation; draw; imbibe; soak up; suck up; take up; (2) enlist; recruit;

夏收 (1) get in the summer harvest; (2) summer crops;

驗收 check and accept; check before acceptance; check upon delivery;

應收 receivable;

招收 recruit; take in;
征收 levy and collect taxes;
徵收 collect; impose; levy;

shou²
shou
【熟】 a pronunciation of 熟 ;

shou³
shou
【手】 (1) hand; (2) have in one's hand; hold; (3) convenient; handy; (4) personally; (5) person doing or good at a certain job;

[手背] back of the hand;
[手筆] (1) sb's own handwriting or painting; (2) literary skill;
[手臂] arm;
揮舞手臂 flap one's arms; saw the air; wave one's arms about;
伸展手臂 stretch one's arm;
縮回手臂 haul off;
[手邊] at hand; on hand;
在手邊 handily; handy;
~ 近在手邊 close at hand;
~ 錢在手邊，食在嘴邊—難留住 if you have money in hand or carry your snacks along with you, they are unlikely to be held onto very long; money burns a hole in one's pocket; money in the hand and food in the mouth are difficult to hold onto;
[手錶] watch; wrist watch;
帶鬧手錶 alarm watch;
電池手錶 accumulator watch;
電子手錶 accutron;
鍍金手錶 gold-plated watch;
防磁手錶 antimagnetic watch;
防震手錶 shockproof watch;
看手錶 check one's watch;
盲人手錶 blindman's watch;
石英手錶 crystal-oscillator watch;
修理手錶 mend a watch;
[手冊] directory; handbook; how-to; manual;
翻譯手冊 translation handbook;
會計手冊 account manual;
實施手冊 enforcement manual;
書商手冊 bookman's manual;
[手袋] handbag; purse;
小手袋 vanity case;
[手到病除] illness departs as a touch of the hand; sickness retires at one's touch; the disease is cured as soon as one sets his hand to it;
[手動] by hand; hand-driven;
手動工具 hand tool;
[手段] means; measure; medium; method;
手段附加語 instrumental adjunct;
手段高明 play one's cards well;
手段拙劣 hanky-panky tactics;
卑鄙手段 contemptible means; dirty tricks;
不擇手段 beg, borrow or steal; by fair means or foul; by hook or by crook; resort to all means; stick at nothing; stick at nothing to do sth; stoop to anything; stop at nothing; unscrupulously; use any means to attain one's end; use all kinds of methods;
敷衍手段 slovenly manner of attending to business;
高壓手段 high-handed measures;
耍手段 play games;
玩手段 manipulate; resort to foul means; resort to scheming;
行政手段 administrative means;
[手法] (1) skill; technique; (2) gimmick; trick;
手法高明 play a good game;
卑劣手法 despicable trick; mean trick;
慣用手法 well-trodden ground; well-trodden path; well-trodden road;
兩面手法 dual tactics;
[手稿] manuscript;
一扎手稿 a sheaf of manuscripts;
原始手稿 original manuscript;
[手工] (1) handiwork; (2) by hand; handmade; manual;
手工業 handicraft industry;
~ 家庭手工業 cottage industry;
手工藝 craftsmanship; handicraft; handicraft art;
~ 手工藝工人 artisan; craftsman;
~ 手工藝品 artifact; handicraft;
手工做的 handcrafted; handmade;
[手骨] bones of the human forelimbs;
[手關節] articulations of the hand;
手關節炎 cheirarthritis;
[手機] (1) handset; (2) mobile phone;
手機號碼 mobile phone number;
翻蓋手機 clamshell phone; flip phone;
拍照手機 cameraphone;

[手腳] (1) motion; movement of hands or feet; (2) trick; underhand method;
手腳不乾淨 hands are not too clean; in the habit of stealing; light-fingered; questionable in money matters; seek minor illicit gains; sticky-fingered; sticky-handed; with dirty hands;
手腳不靈活 have one's fingers all thumbs;
手腳利落 agile; deft; deterous; numble; not to make a hash of;
礙手腳 cumbersome; drag; hinder the movement of sb's hand and feet; nuisance; stand in the way;
絆手絆腳 encumber the free movement of one's limbs; in the way;
笨手笨腳 acting clumsily; all fingers and thumbs; all thumbs; awkward; cach-handed; clumsy; have a hand like a foot; have one's fingers all thumbs; heavy-handed; one is awkward with one's hands;
~笨手笨腳的 cack-handed; clumsy;
笨手笨腳的人 klutz;
比手劃腳 make lively gestures;
粗手笨腳 awkward; clumsy; maladroit; with a heavy hand;
大手大腳 spend extravagantly; wasteful;
凍手凍腳 freezing cold;
放開手腳 have one's hands and feet unfettered;
費手腳 take much handwork and footwork; take much physical labour; take much time and energy;
花錢大手大腳 liberal of one's money;
慌了手腳 be greatly alarmed; be seized with a panic; be thrown into a panic; be thrown off one's balance; become panicky;
慌手慌腳 in a great flurry;
捆住手腳 bound hand and foot; hogtie;
亂了手腳 be thrown into chaos; be thrown into a panic; be thrown into confusion; in disarray;
慢手慢腳 slow in doing things;
毛手毛腳 brash and clumsy; careless; clumsily; recklessly; rough-handed;
~做事毛手毛腳 do things recklessly;
捏手捏腳 let one's hand and foot take too great liberties; move around lightly; walk gingerly; walk on tiptoe; walk with light steps; with light steps and soft movements of one's hands;
躡手躡腳 do things stealthily; make one's way noiselessly to; tiptoe; walk gingerly; walk on tiptoe; with light steps and soft movements of one's hands;
七手八腳 all flurry and confusion; all hitching in; all lend a hand to; bustle about; great hurry and bustle; helter-skelter; hurriedly; in a bustle; in great haste; many people doing sth at the same time in a disorganized manner; serve hand and foot; several men engaged in a scuffle; take all together; too many cooks spoil the broth; with everybody lending a hand; with many people taking part; with seven hands and eight feet;
輕手輕腳 cautiously without any noise; do sth gently; gently; light-handed and light-footed; nimble-fingered and light-heeled; on tiptoe; softly;
手忙腳亂 act with confusion; all in a hustle of excitement; be thrown into confusion; frantically busy; helter-skelter; in a flurry; in a frantic rush; in a great bustle; in a great hurry and amid confusion; in a muddle; running around in circles; thrown into confusion;
擡手動腳 manner; personal behaviour;
提手躡腳 walk on tiptoe;
舞手弄腳 play gestures;
小手小腳 lacking boldness; mean; niggling; stingy; timid;
羞手羞腳 dare not move; timid;
指手劃腳 (1) gesticulate; make gestures; wave the hands and throw the feet about; (2) carp and cavil; make indiscreet remarks or criticisms; order people about; point right and left;
窒手窒腳 obstructing hand and foot; troublesome;
做手腳 mess about with; play a trick; tamper with sth;

[手巾] hand towel; handkerchief; towel;

[手絹] hand towel; handkerchief; towel;
一塊手絹 a handkerchief;
一條手絹 a handkerchief;

[手銬] cuffs; handcuffs;
手銬腳鐐 handcuffed and shackled; handcuffs and shackles;

帶上手銬 handcuff;
給…戴手銬 cuff;
金手銬 golden handcuffs;

[手口相應] action and words are in correspondence;

[手快] deft of hand;
眼明手快 clearly discerning, swift-handed; nimble; one's eye is clear and one's hand swift; quick of eye and deft of hand; see things clearly and act speedily; sharp of sight and quick of hand; sharp-eyed and quick-moving;

[手辣] be vicious or unscrupulous;
心毒手辣 callous and cruel; cold-blooded; merciless at heart and in deeds; vicious and ruthless;
心黑手辣 black-hearted and cruel;
心狠手辣 be merciless and vicious;

[手裏] in sb's hands;
在可靠的人手裏 in safe hands;

[手榴彈] grenade; hand grenade;
發煙手榴彈 smoke grenade;
簡易手榴彈 improvised grenade;
進攻性手榴彈 offensive grenade;
燃燒手榴彈 frangible grenade; incendiary hand grenade;

[手輪] handwheel;
操縱手輪 maneuvering handwheel;
閥開關手輪 valve control handwheel;
方向手輪 traversing handwheel;
回令手輪 reply handwheel;
回轉手輪 slewing handwheel;
絞盤手輪 capstan handwheel;
起動手輪 starting handwheel;
調速手輪 speed regulating handwheel;
星形手輪 star handwheel;

[手民] typesetter;
手民之誤 misprint; typographical error;

[手帕] handie; handkerchief; hanky;

[手氣] luck at gambling etc.;
手氣不佳 luck goes against one;
手氣好 have the Midas touch

[手槍] handgun; pistol; shooter;
手槍皮套 holster;
拔出手槍 pull a pistol;
撥出手槍 draw a pistol;
大氣手槍 air pistol;
大威力手槍 high-power pistol;
左輪手槍 revolver;

[手巧] deft; dexterous; skilful with one's hands;

[手勤] diligent; hardworking; industrious;
手勤腳快 keen and quick in one's work;

[手球] handball;
手球犯規 handball;
手球運動 handball;

[手刃] kill with one's own hand; stab sb to death;

[手軟] irresolute when firmness is needed; soft-hearted;

[手生] lack practice and skill; out of practice;

[手勢] gesture; sign;
手勢論 pasimology;
手勢語 gestural language;
打手勢 gesticulate; make a gesture;
下流手勢 obscene gesture;
用手勢 use gesture;
做手勢 gesticulate; gesticulation;

[手書] (1) write in one's own hand; (2) personal letter;

[手術] operation; surgical operation;
手術成功 the surgery is successful;
手術刀 lancet; scalpel;
手術室 operating room; operating theatre;
常規手術 routine operation;
大手術 major operation; major surgery;
接受手術 under the knife; undergo an operation;
緊急手術 emergency operation; emergency surgery;
施手術 carry out an operation; carry out surgery; do an operation; do surgery; perform an operation; perform surgery;
挺過手術 survive an operation;
微創手術 keyhole surgery;
無血手術 bloodless surgery;
小手術 minor operation; minor surgery;
移植手術 transplant operation;
做手術 carry out an operation; have a surgery; perform an operation;

[手套] gloves; mitten;
棒球手套 mitt;
帶指手套 fingered glove;
戴上手套 draw on one's gloves;
獨指手套 mitt; mitten;
帆布手套 canvas mittens;
防毒手套 gas-protective glove;
防震手套 vibration-absorbing mitten;
滑雪防護手套 ski mitts;
擊劍手套 fencing glove;
烤箱防熱手套 oven mitt;
連指手套 mitt; mitten;

練習手套 bag glove;
皮手套 leather glove;
潛水手套 diving mitten;
拳擊手套 boxing gloves;
射擊手套 shooting glove;
石棉手套 asbestos glove;
脱下手套 pull off one's gloves;
一副手套 a pair of gloves;
一雙手套 a pair of gloves;
摘下手套 take off one's gloves;
抓球手套 catching glove;

[手提] mobile; portable;
手提包 handbag;
~男士手提包 manbag;
~女用小手提包 clutch bag;
手提袋 bag;
大手提袋 tote bag;
手提電話 mobile phone;
手提電腦 portable computer;
手提箱 portmanteau; suitcase;
手提儀表 portable appliance;
肩扛手提 carry on one's shoulders or with one's hands;

[手頭] (1) at hand; on hand; right beside one; (2) one's financial condition at the moment;
手頭不便 hard up; have little money to spare; short of cash;
手頭拮据 at low-water mark; feel the draught; hard-pressed; in low water; in hard need of money; low in pocket; out of cash; out of pocket; pinched for money; pushed for money; short of funds; uptight; when the chips are down;
手頭緊 hard up for money; short of money;
手頭寬裕 in easy circumstances; in the bucks; well off at the moment; with plenty of money to spend;
手頭困乏 hard up for money; in great straits; in straitened circumstances; on the rocks;
手頭闊綽 free of hand;

[手推車] barrow; burl; cart; handcart; pushcart; trolley; wheelbarrow;
購物手推車 shopping cart; shopping trolley;
嬰兒手推車 pushchair;
支架式手推車 jib barrow;

[手腕] (1) wrist; (2) artifice; finesse; stratagem; sleight of hand;
手腕動作 wrist work;
手腕子 wrist;
扳手腕 arm wrestle; arm wrestling; do arm wrestling;
扭傷手腕 sprain one's wrist; twist one's wrist;
耍手腕 juggle with; manoeuvre; play tricks;

[手紋] handprint;

[手無] without in one's hands;
手無寸鐵 barehanded; defenceless; unarmed; with no weapon in one's hand; without arms;
手無縛雞之力 cannot play pew; cannot punch one's way out of a paper bag; lack the strength to truss a chicken — physically very weak; not to have strength enough in one's hands to tie a chicken fast;

[手下] (1) under; under the leadership of; (2) at hand; (3) at the hands of sb; (4) lackey;
手下敗將 a warrior vanquishes by one's hand; one who has suffered defeat at one's hands; one's defeated opponent; one's vanquished foe;
手下留情 lenient; pull one's punches; show mercy;

[手相] palmistry;
手相家 chiromancer;
手相術 chiromancy;
看手相 read sb's palm;

[手心] (1) palm; palm of the hand; (2) control; in the hands of sb;

[手續] formalities; procedures; processes; routines;
手續費 commission; handling charge; service charge;
~保兑手續費 confirmation commission;
~通知手續費 advising commission;
~統一手續費 flat commission;
~托收手續費 collection commission;
~延期手續費 extension commission;
~轉讓手續費 transfer commission;
辦手續 go through formalities;
報關手續 customs formality;
出口手續 export formality;
法律手續 legal formalities;
過境手續 transit formality;
履行手續 perform formalities;

行政手續 administrative formalities;

[手眼] (1) trick; (2) hand and eye;

手眼通天 exceptionally adept in trickery;

手眼協調 hand-eye coordination;

手急眼快 act dexterously; deft of hand and quick of eye; neat-handed and sharp-sighted;

[手癢] (1) itchy fingers; one's fingers itch; (2) have an itch to do sth;

[手藝] craftsmanship; handicraft; skill; workmanship;

耍手藝 make a living by some special skill;

一門手藝 a trade;

~學一門手藝 learn a trade;

[手淫] do-it-yourself; fluff one's duff; hand job; jack off; jerk off; masturbation; play with oneself; wank;

行手淫 wank;

[手語] sign language;

[手諭] handwritten directive; one's instructions;

頃奉手諭 I have just received your instructions;

[手札] personal letter;

[手閘] handbrake;

[手掌] palm;

手掌多汗 volar hyperhidrosis;

手掌紅斑 palmar erythema;

[手杖] walking stick;

一根手杖 a stick;

[手指] finger;

手指笨拙 be all fingers and thumbs;

手指縫儿 space between two fingers;

手指骨 bones of digits of hand;

~手指骨體 corpus phalangis manus;

~手指骨頭 caput phalangis manus;

手指關節 articulations of digits of hand;

手指畫 finger drawing; finger painting;

~手指畫顏料 finger-paints;

手指僵木 have one's fingers all thumbs;

手指拼寫 fingerspelling;

刺破手指 prick one's finger;

擠傷手指 squeeze one's fingers;

夾傷手指 jam a finger;

砍掉一個手指 chop off a finger;

燒傷手指 burn one's fingers;

伸出手指 thrust out one's fingers;

搖搖手指 wag one's finger;

一個手指 a finger;

[手紙] toilet paper;

[手中] in the hands of;

落入小人手中 fall into the wrong hands; get into the wrong hands;

[手鐲] bangle; bracelet;

金手鐲 gold bracelet;

一個手鐲 a bracelet;

一隻手鐲 a bracelet;

鑽石手鐲 diamond bracelet;

[手足] (1) brothers; members; (2) hands and feet;

手足發紺 acrocyanosis;

手足過長 acrodolichomelia;

手足痙攣 carpopedal spasm;

手足口病 hand-foot-and-mouth disease;

手足情深 the love between brothers is deep;

手足痛 cheiropodalgia;

手足無措 all in a fluster; at a loss how to act; at a loss what to do; bewildered; disconcerted; feel completely at a loss; lose oneself; panic-stricken; perplexed;

手足相殘 fraternal strifes;

手足之情 brotherhood; brotherly affection; fraternal tie; the yoke of brotherhood;

攣其手足 hands and feet crooked;

親如手足 as close as brothers; as dear to each other as brothers; cozy;

情同手足 affectionate to each other like brothers; be attached to each other like brothers; brotherly friendship; close like brothers; have the same affection for each other as though they were brothers; kindred like brothers; like born brothers; love another as one does one's brothers; regard each other as brothers; with brotherly love for each other;

~情同手足的 brotherly;

如手如足 like brothers;

視同手足 brother sb;

手胼足胝 callosities found both on one's hands and feet — working hard;

手舞足蹈 cut a caper; dance for joy; dance with excitement; dance with joy; flourish; gesticulate merrily; gesticulate with hands and feet; kick up one's heels; shake one's hands and stamp one's feet; wave one's arm and

beat time with one's feet; wave one's arms and stamp one's feet in joy; with vigorous movements of hands and feet;

~快樂得手舞足蹈 dance for joy;

無所措手足 at a loss what to do; find no place to put one's hands and feet; have nowhere to put hand or foot — at a loss to know how to conduct oneself; not to know what to do;

礙手 hindrance; in the way;

把手 (1) grid; handle; handlebar; knob; (2) person;

擺手 swing one's arms; wave one's hand

罷手 discontinue an action; give up; pause; stop;

白手 empty-handed;

扳手 (1) spanner; wrench; (2) lever;

幫手 assistant; helper; helpmate;

搏手 at the end of one's wits; powerless;

擦手 dry one's hands;

叉手 folded arms;

插手 (1) lend a hand; take part; (2) have a hand in; poke one's nose into;

纏手 hard to deal with; troublesome;

出手 (1) dispose of; get off one's hands; sell; (2) skills displayed in making opening moves;

觸手 tentacle;

吹鼓手 (1) bugler; trumpeter; (2) eulogist;

垂手 (1) obtain sth with hands down; within easy reach; (2) let the hands hang by the sides; stand with one's hands hanging by the sides;

揣手 tuck each hand in the opposite sleeve;

湊手 at hand; within easy reach;

搓手 wash one's hands with invisible soap and imperceptible water;

措手 deal with; manage;

搭手 give a hand; help sb; render sb a service;

打手 bully; hatchet man; hired thug; hired roughneck; muscleman;

倒手 change hands;

到手 come to one's hands; in one's hands; in one's possession;

得手 come off; do fine; go smoothly; succeed;

敵手 (1) adversary; antagonist; match; opponent; (2) enemy hands;

丟手 give up; wash one's hands of;

動手 (1) get to work; start work; (2) handle; touch; (3) hit out; raise a hand to strike;

毒手 murderous scheme;

對手 (1) adversary; antagonist; opponent; rival; (2) equal; match;

多手 like to try one's hand at things;

舵手 cox; coxswain; helmsman; steersman;

二手 second-hand;

反手 backhand;

放手 (1) let go; let go one's hold; (2) do or act boldly and freely; give one a free hand to do sth;

分手 be separated; break up; drift apart; part company; say good-bye to; split up with sb;

佛手 (1) fingered citron; (2) Buddha's hand;

扶手 (1) banisters; handrail; rail; (2) armrest;

副手 (1) assistant; helper; (2) deputy;

高手 ace; hotshot; master; master hand;

歌手 singer; songster; vocalist; warbler;

拱手 (1) make an obeisance by cupping one hand in the other before one's chest; (2) submissively;

勾手 stroke with a hook;

鼓手 drummer;

劊子手 (1) executioner; (2) butcher; hatchetman; slaughterman;

國手 grand master; national champion;

過手 handle; receive and distribute; take in and give out;

好手 adept at; capable person; good hand; past master;

號手 bugler; trumpeter;

黑手 evil backstage manipulator; vicious person manipulating sb or sth from behind the scenes;

後手 room for sth;

護手 handguard; nipper;

划手 oarsman;

還手 strike back;

揮手 wave; wave of the hand; wave one's hand;

回手 (1) turn round and stretch out one's hand; (2) hit back; return a blow;

棘手 difficult to handle; knotty; thorny; ticklish; troublesome;

假手 (1) do sth through sb else; make a cat's paw of sb; (2) artificial hand; hand prosthesis;

槳手 boatman;

交手 be engaged in a hand-to-hand fight; fight hand to hand;

接手 take over; take up matters;

解手 go to the toilet; relieve oneself;

經手 deal with; handle;

淨手 (1) wash one's hands; (2) relieve oneself;

就手 while you're at it;

舉手 put one's hand up; put up one's hand; raise

one's hand;
靠手 armrest; handrest;
空手 empty-handed;
快手 deft hand; nimble-handed person; quick worker;
拉手 (1) hold hands; join hands; (2) pull by the hands;
辣手 (1) ruthless; vicious; (2) hard to do; knotty; thorny; troublesome;
老手 old hand; old stager; past master; veteran;
壘手 baseman;
兩手 (1) dual tactics; (2) capability;
獵手 hunter;
名手 famous artist;
拿手 adept; be good at; expert;
能手 capable hand; crackajack; dab; expert; proficient;
扒手 pickpocket; shoplifter;
拍手 applaud; clap hands; clap one's hands;
砲手 artilleryman; cannoneer; gun crew; gunner;
礮手 artilleryman; cannoneer; gun crew; gunner;
劈手 make a sudden snatch; snatch sth suddenly;
平手 draw;
棋手 chess player; high-graded chess player;
旗手 (1) flag-holder; flagman; (2) standard-bearer;
騎手 horsebacker; horseman; rider;
起手 start an action;
牽手 (1) lead by the hand; (2) one's wife;
前手 predecessor;
縴手 (1) go-between; (2) boat tower;
槍手 (1) gunner; marksman; rifleman; (2) ghost writer; (3) hired examinee;
強手 strong hand;
搶手 find a good market; in great demand; sell well;
巧手 dab hand; expert; skilful person;
親手 oneself; personally; with one's own hands;
琴手 player of a stringed instrument;
擎手 raise one's hands — stop doing sth;
窮大手 poor but putting on a bold front by spending lavishly;
拳手 boxer;
人手 hand; manpower;
入手 begin with; get under way; proceed from; put one's hand to; start with; take as the point of departure;
撒手 (1) leave hold of; let go; let go one's hold; relax the grasp; relax the hold; relinguish one's hold; (2) abandon; give up; refuse to take any further interest in; wash one's hands off the matter;
三隻手 pickpocket;
殺手 hit man; killer;
上手 begin; start;
射手 marksman; shooter;
伸出手 put one's hand out;
伸手 (1) hold out one's hand; reach out one's hand; stretch out one's hand; (2) ask for help;
身手 (1) skills; talent; (2) agility; dexterity;
生手 beginner; greenhorn; new learner; novice; tyro; inexperienced head; green at; sb new to a job;
聖手 divine physician;
失手 accidentally drop; slip;
試手 try to do;
釋手 loosen one's grip; relax the hold;
熟手 old hand; practiced hand;
甩手 (1) swing one's arms; (2) refuse to do; wash one's of;
水手 deck hand; mariner; sailor; seaman;
順手 (1) smoothly; without difficulty; (2) conveniently; without extra trouble; (3) doing sth as a natural sequence or simultaneously;
鬆手 let go; loosen one's grip
隨手 without extra trouble;
縮手 draw back one's hand;
燙手 (1) scald one's hand; (2) difficult to manage;
替手 standby; substitute; understudy;
提手 handle;
艇手 launchman;
投手 pitcher;
徒手 bare-handed; empty-handed; freehand; unarmed;
褪手 hide one's hands in sleeves;
脫手 (1) slip out of hand; (2) dishoard; dispose of; get out of one's hand; sell;
挽手 arm in arm; hand in hand; hold hands;
窩起手 cup one's hand;
握手 clasp hands; shake hands;
洗手 (1) wash one's hands; (2) stop doing evil and reform oneself; (3) wash one's hands of sth;
下手 (1) put one's hand to; set about; set to; start; start doing sth; (2) commit a crime; (3) assistant; helper; inferior attendant;
先手 on the offensive;
孅手 delicate hands of a woman;
纖手 delicate hands;
歇手 stop doing sth;
攜手 (1) hand in hand; hold each other's hand; (2)

cooperate;
寫手 hack;
心手 mind and hand;
新手 greenhorn; green hand; greenhorn; new hand; novice; raw recruit;
信手 at random; conveniently; without a previous plan;
凶手 murderer; assassin;
兇手 assassin; killer; murderer;
選手 competitor; contestant; player;
眼手 hands and eyes;
搖手 (1) handle; (2) shake one's handle in admonition or disapproval; wave one's hand;
一把手 chief; first in command; head;
一手 (1) good at; proficiency; skill; (2) move; trick; (3) all alone; all by oneself; single-handed;
一雙手 a pair of hands;
一隻手 a hand;
易手 change hands;
義手 artificial hand;
應手 smoothly; without a hitch;
硬手 able person; good hand;
右手 (1) right hand; (2) right; right-hand side;
馭手 driver of a military pack train; soldier in charge of pack animals;
援手 (1) aid; extend a helping hand; rescue; save; (2) helper;
扎手 (1) prick the hand; (2) difficult to handle; thorny;
張手 open one's hands;
沾手 (1) touch with one's hand; (2) have a hand in;
招手 beckon with the hand; wave one's hand;
正手 forehand;
隻手 single-handed;
執手 hold hands;
主攻手 ace spiker;
住手 cut it out; hands off; stay one's hand; stop; stop it;
助手 aide; assistant; help;
轉手 (1) change hands; fall into another's hands; pass on; sell what one has bought; (2) brief period of time;
着手 put one's hand to; set about; set one's hand to; start doing sth;
左手 (1) left hand; (2) left; left-hand side;

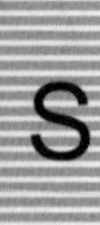

shou

【守】 (1) defend; guard; protect; (2) keep watch; watch; (3) wait; (4) abide by; maintain; observe; stick to; (5) close to; near;

[守備] garrison; on garrison duty; perform garrison duty;
[守財奴] cheapskate; miser; niggard;
[守常] stick to tradition;
守常不變 conservative and opposed to change;
[守車] caboose;
[守臣] king's guardians;
[守成] maintain the achievements of one's predecessors;
守成不變 holding to existing custom; reluctant to accept changes;
[守城] defend a city;
[守法] abide by the law; keep the law; law-abiding; observe the law;
必須守法 must abide by the law;
奉公守法 carry out official duties and observe the laws; conscientious and law-abiding; dutiful and law-abiding; just and respect the law; respect justice and abide by the laws;
居官守法 law-abiding official;
知法守法 know the laws and abide by them; understand and abide by the law;
[守更] keep watch during the night;
[守寡] keep living as a widow; live in widowhood; remain a widow; remain in widowhood;
[守恒] conservation;
守恒定律 conservation law;
~能量守恒定律 law of conservation of energy;
~質量守恒定律 law of conservation of mass;
不守恒 non-conservation;
~能量不守恒 non-conservation of energy;
~宇稱不守恒 non-conservation of parity;
電荷守恒 charge conservation;
動量守恒 momentum conservation;
能量守恒 conservation of energy;
奇異性守恒 strangeness conservation;
輕子守恒 lepton conservation;
熱量守恒 heat conservation;
物質守恒 conservation of matter;
宇稱守恒 parity conservation;
質量守恒 conservation of mass;

[守候] (1) bide one's time; expect; wait for; wait; (2) keep watch;
[守護] defend; guard; protect; ward; watch;
[守節] not remarry; preserve chastity after the death of her husband;
[守舊] adhere to past practices; conservative; resistant to advances; stick to old ways;
[守軍] defending troops;
[守口如瓶] as close as an oyster; as dumb as an oyster; as silent as the grave; as silent as the tomb; be buttoned up; be tight-mouthed; breathe not a word of a secret; button up one's lip; button up one's mouth; hold one's cards close to one's chest; keep a calm sough; keep a still tongue in one's head; keep dumb as an oyster; keep mum; keep one's lips buttoned; keep one's mouth closed; keep one's mouth shut; keep one's mouth tight as a jar; keep one's tongue between one's teeth; keep the mouth closed like a bottle; keep the mouth shut as that of a jar; one's lips are sealed; stay tight-lipped; tight-mouthed;
守口如瓶，防意如城 guard your mouth as though it were a vase and guard your thoughts as if you were a city wall;
守口如瓶旳 close-mouthed;
[守靈] keep vigil beside the coffin; stand as guards at the bier;
[守門] (1) on duty at the door; watch the door against burglars; (2) keep goal;
守門人 doorkeeper;
守門員 goalie; goalkeeper; goaltender;
[守諾] integrity; keep one's promise;
重誠守諾 integrity;
[守喪] keep vigil beside the coffin; remain in mourning for one's parent;
[守身] behave oneself correctly;
守身如玉 keep one's chastity; keep one's integrity; keep oneself as pure as jade — take heed of one's virtue;
[守時] punctual; time keeping;
[守勢] defensive;
採取守勢 assume the defensive; be on the defensive;
[守死善道] hold on even to dead in order to perfect one's virtue;
[守歲] stay up late or all night on New Year's Eve;
[守土] defend the territory of one's country;
守土有責 duty-bound to defend the territory of one's country;
[守望] keep guard; keep watch;
守望臺 watchtower;
守望相助 give mutual help and protection; help one another in defence work; keep watch together in mutual defence; mutuality;
[守衛] defend; guard;
夜間守衛 night watchman;
[守孝] observe mourning for one's parent;
[守夜] keep night watch; keep watch at night; spend the night on watch;
守夜者 watchman;
通宵守夜 keep up a vigil throughout the night;
巡更守夜 outwatch the night;
[守業] maintain what has been achieved by one's forefathers; safeguard one's heritage;
[守義] maintain one's integrity;
[守約] honour a pledge; keep one's promise;
[守則] regulations; rules;
安全守則 safety regulations;
[守正不阿] stick to justice despite pressure; uphold fairness without favouring anyone;
[守職] stick to one's duty;
[守制] remain in mourning for one's parent;
[守株待兔] stand by a stump waiting for more hares to come and dash themselves against it — trust to chance and windfalls;
[守拙] remain free from ambitions;
養心守拙 keep to one's primitive simplicity;

把守 guard;
保守 (1) guard; keep; (2) conservative;
操守 personal integrity;
扼守 guard; hold;
防守 defend; defense; guard; parry;
攻守 offensive and defensive;
固守 be deeply entrenched in; defend resolutely;
堅守 defend resolutely; stick firmly to one's post, etc.;
監守 guard; have custody of;

據守 be entrenched in; guard;
看守 (1) guard; watch; (2) goaler; guard; jailor; keeper; turnkey; warder;
恪守 firmly abide by; honour; observe; scrupulously abide by; strictly observe;
困守 defend against a siege; stand a siege;
留守 stay behind to take care of things;
墨守 adhere to;
確守 truly adhere to; scrupulously abide by;
失守 fall;
戍守 defend; garrison;
廝守 take care of each other; wait upon each other;
死守 (1) defend to the death; defend to the last; make a last-ditch defense; (2) obstinately cling to; rigidly adhere to;
退守 retreat and stand on the defensive;
信守 abide by; stand by;
嚴守 strictly observe or abide by;
有守 adhere to principles; have moral fortitude;
鎮守 garrison; guard;
職守 duty; post;
株守 hold on stubbornly to a silly idea; take no action but wish that sth would come one's way;
駐守 defend; garrison;
自守 self-defence;
遵守 abide; adhere to; observe;
坐守 guard resolutely;

shou

【首】 (1) head; (2) beginning; first; (3) chief; emperor; head; leader; (4) bring charges against sb;

[首倡] initiate; pioneer; start;

[首創] found; initiate; start;

[首次] first; first time; for the first time;
首次公演 first performance; premiere;
首次文摘 primary abstract;

[首當其衝] bear the brunt; suffer the brunt; take the brunt; the first to bear the brunt; stand in the breach;

[首都] capital; capital city;

[首惡] principal criminal; ringleader;

[首犯] principal criminal; ringleader;

[首府] (1) prefecture where the provincial capital is located; (2) capital of a prefecture; (3) captial of a colony;
縣首府 county town;

[首富] richest family of a district;

[首級] human head;

[首屆] first;

[首肯] approve; consent; nod approval; nod assent; nod one's head in approval;
給予首肯 give an affirmative nod;

[首領] chieftain; head; leader;

[首難] first to start an uprising;

[首腦] boss; chief; head; key member; mastermind;
首腦會議 summit conference; summit meeting;
首腦人物 leading figure;
國家首腦 head of state;

[首妻] (1) one's first wife; (2) one's legal wife;

[首期] first-phase;
首期工程 first-phase project;

[首屈一指] bear the palm; come first on the list; come out first; second to none; stand highest in esteem; the best; the best one; the foremost; the top;

[首日封] first-day cover;

[首如飛蓬] dishevelled hair;

[首飾] jewelry; ornaments; trinkets;
首飾盒 casket; jewelry box;

[首途] embark on a journey; set out on a journey; start a journey; start on one's way;

[首推] consider sb first;

[首尾] (1) beginning and end; head and tail; (2) from beginning to end;
首尾重覆法 anadiplosis;
首尾倒置 tail first;
首尾相接 nose to tail;
首尾相應 head and tail corresponding with each other;
藏首納尾 hide one's head and pull in one's tail — play down one's massive image;
神龍見首不見尾 appear and disappear in quick succession; move in and out with wizardly elusiveness; secretive in one's movement and trace;
畏首畏尾 be frightened all over; fear both the head and the tail — be filled with misgivings and fear; full of misgivings; have too many fears; overcautious;

[首位] (1) first place; (2) place of honour;
躍居首位 leap to first place;

[首席] (1) seat of honour; (2) chief; highest-positioned; highest-ranking; senior;

首席代表 chief delegate;
首席小提琴 concertmaster; first violin;

［首先］ above all; above all else; as a starter; at first; at the beginning; beyond all else; beyond all things; come first; first; first and foremost; first of all; first off; for one thing...for another; in the first place; in the first instance; primary; the first thing; the very first; to begin with; to start with;
首先發言 speak first;

［首相］ prime minister;
首相府 residence of a prime minister;
副首相 vice-premier;

［首要］ chief; first; of the first importance;
首要翻譯 primary translation;
首要分子 major culprit; ringleader;
首要任務 most important task;
首要條件 most important requirement;

［首頁］ first page; title page;

［首映］ premiere;
首映之夜 opening night;

［首語重覆］ aphora;

［首長］ chief; senior officer;

昂首 hold up one's head; raise one's head;
白首 hoary head;
榜首 top candidate of an examination;
匕首 dagger;
部首 radicals by which characters are arranged in traditional Chinese dictionaries;
倡首 initiate; propose;
螭首 top of various structures adorned with a representation of the hornless dragon;
出首 (1) report to the authorities; (2) confess one's crime; voluntarily surrender oneself;
垂首 hang one's head;
低首 lower one's head;
頓首 kowtow;
匪首 bandit chieftain;
俯首 bow one's head;
頷首 nod;
皓首 hoary head;
回首 (1) turn one's head; turn round; (2) look back; recollect;
禍首 arch-criminal; chief culprit; chief offender;
稽首 kowtow;
居名單之首 top a list;
聚首 gather; meet;
叩首 kowtow;
魁首 person who surpasses all others; the brightest and the best;
饅首 steamed bread; steamed bun;
盟首 leader of an alliance;
起首 at first; in the beginning; originally;
黔首 common people; masses; multitude; people;
翹首 raise one's head and look;
濡首 overindulge oneself in wine;
戎首 one who starts a war;
搔首 scratch one's head;
身首 the trunk and the head;
授首 be beheaded; get killed;
歲首 beginning of the year;
徒首 bareheaded;
為首 headed by; the leader of; with sb as the leader;
位列名單之首 at the top of a list;
下首 right-hand seat;
懸首 display chopped-off head;
驤首 raise the head proudly;
梟首 decapitate a person and hang his head on a pole;
徇首 show the head of a decapitated offender to warn against repetition of the offense;
搖首 shake one's head in disapproval;
抑首 lower one's head;
鷁首 bow of a boat;
獄首 wardsman;
元首 (1) chief executive; head of a state; ruler; (2) beginning;
斬首 decapitate; behead; guillotine;
姿首 pretty face and beautiful hair;
字首 prefix;
自首 (1) confess one's crime; give oneself up to law; surrender oneself to the authorities; voluntarily surrender oneself; (2) surrender to the enemy;
左首 left; left-hand side;

shou⁴
shou

【受】 (1) accept; get; receive; (2) be subjected to; suffer; (3) endure; stand; suffer; take; tolerate; (4) pleasant;

［受保人］ insurant;

［受病］ catch a disease; fall ill; fall sick;

［受茶］ receive the presents of betrothal;

［受禪］ receive an abdication;

［受寵］ endear oneself to; find favour in the eyes of sb; gain grace; gain upon sb;s heart; gain sb's favour; get in good

with sb; get on the right side of sb; in favour with sb; in good with sb; in sb's favour; in sb's good books; in sb's good graces; in with sb; make time with sb; receive favour from a superior; win sb's favour;
受寵若驚 be overwhelmed by a special favour; be overwhelmed by an unexpected favour; be surprised by the great favour one gets; on a pedestal; receive much more favour than one expected;

[受挫] be baffled; be defeated; be foiled; be frustrated; be thwarted; suffer a setback;

[受凍] suffer from cold;
受凍挨餓 endure cold and hunger; go cold and hungry; suffer from cold and hunger;
挨饑受凍 suffer hunger and cold;
挨冷受凍 suffer from cold;

[受動] affected;
受動賓語 affected object;
受動間接賓語 affected indirect object;

[受罰] be fined; be penalized; be punished;

[受封] be appointed with a title;

[受格] objective case;

[受夠了] enough of it;

[受僱] be employed;
受僱於人 be employed by sb;
終身受僱 life employment;

[受過] bear the blame;
代人受過 be made scapegoat for sb; bear the blame for sb else; carry the can; suffer for the faults of another; take the blame for others; take the can back;
頂人受過 take the blame for others;

[受害] be affected; be afflicted; be damaged; be victimized; fall victim; suffer injury; suffer losses;
受害不淺 badly misguided; ill-advised; suffer a lot; suffer not a little;
受害人 the victim; the victimized party;

[受寒] catch cold; suffer from a cold;

[受惠] be benefited; receive benefit;
受惠不淺 gain much advantage from; profit greatly; receive great benefit;

[受賄] accept bribes; be bribed; on the take; receive bribes; take bribes;
受賄罪 acceptance of bribes;
不敢受賄 dare not take bribes;
堅拒受賄 fight against graft;
棄法受賄 cast aside the laws and accept bribes;

[受獎] (1) be cited; (2) be rewarded; get a prize;
受獎台 victory podium; victory rostrum;

[受教] (1) receive education; (2) be benefited by advice; receive guidance;

[受盡] have one's fill of; suffer all kinds of; suffer enough from;
受盡熬煎 be subjected to all kinds of suppering;
受盡欺淩 suffer all sorts of bullying and humiliation;
受盡折磨 suffer a lot; suffer all kinds of tortures;

[受精] be fertilized; fertilization;
受精卵 amphicytula;
閉花受精 cleistogamy;
反常受精 abnormal fertilization;
皮下受精 cutaneous fertilization;
人工受精 artificial fertilization; artificial insemination;
體內受精 internal fertilization;
體外受精 external fertilization;
異花受精 allogamy; cross fertilization;
異體受精 cross-fertilization;
自體受精 autogamy; self-fertilization;

[受驚] be frightened;

[受窘] be embarrassed;

[受控] controlled;
受控詞 control term;
受控語言 controlled language;

[受苦] have a rough time; suffer hardships;
受苦受難 downtrodden; have a hard time; have a rough time; have one's fill of sufferings; in a difficult and bitter plight; live in misery; suffer hardships;
受苦者 sufferer;

[受款人] payee; remittee;

[受累] be inconvenienced; be involved; be put to much trouble; get involved in a trouble;

[受理] accept and hear a case;
受理控訴 accept a complaint;
受理訴狀 receive a petition;
不受理 refuse to entertain;

[受禮] (1) receive a gift; (2) receive a

salutation;

[受涼] catch a cold; catch cold; get a cold; have a cold; take colds;

[受命] accept an order; on the order of; receive an appointment; receive instructions;

見危受命 be entrusted with one's mission at a critical and difficult moment; receive an appointment in sight of danger;

[受難] in distress; suffer calamities; suffer disasters;

[受騙] be cheated; be deceived; be fooled; be swindled; be taken in; be tricked;

受騙者 dupe;

[受票人] drawee;

[受聘] accept a job offer;

[受氣] be bullied; punching bag; suffer indignities; suffer wrong;

受氣包兒 doormat;

[受屈] be wronged; suffer a grievance; suffer indignity;

[受熱] be heated;

[受辱] be humiliated;

當眾受辱 be insulted before a large company; be insulted in the presence of others;

蒙垢受辱 swallow insults and humiliations;

[受傷] be injured; be wounded; get an injury; get hurt; have an injury; receive an injury; suffer an injury; sustain an injury;

避免受傷 avoid injury; escape injury;

多處受傷 multiple injuries;

容易受傷 prone to injury;

[受賞] be awarded; get a reward;

[受審] be tried; on trials; stand trial;

[受事] recipient;

受事賓語 recipient object;

[受暑] suffer from heat;

[受水] intake;

受水區 intake area

[受胎] be impregnated; conceive;

[受托] be entrusted with;

受托人 consignee; trustee;

~被動受托人 bare trustee;

~債券受托人 bond trustee;

受人之托 be entrusted with sth by sb; be requested by others to do sth;

[受洗] be baptized;

[受降] accept the surrender of the vanquished enemy;

[受刑] be punished; be tortured;

[受訓] receive training;

[受業] (1) learn from a master; (2) your student;

[受益] benefit by; benefit from;

受益格 benefactive case; on benefit basis;

受益基準制

受益良多 benefit a great deal; derive much benefit;

受益人 beneficiary;

~第二受益人 second beneficiary;

~第一受益人 first beneficiary;

~收益受益人 income beneficiary;

~下一代受益人 young-generation beneficiary;

~信托受益人 trust beneficiary;

~原受益人 original beneficiary;

~直接受益人 immediate beneficiary;

~最終受益人 final beneficiary;

受益原則 benefit principle;

滿招損，謙受益 one loses by pride and gains by modesty; pride leads to loss while modesty brings benefit; self-satisfaction will incur losses, modesty will receive benefit;

[受用] (1) enjoy; enjoyable; (2) comfortable; feel good;

受用不盡 benefit from sth all one's life; enjoy a benefit forever;

一生受用 enjoy the benefit all one's life;

終生受用 benefit from sth all one's life;

[受愚] be duped; be fooled; be tricked;

[受援] receive aid;

受援國 recipient country;

[受孕] be impregnated; become pregnant;

人工受孕 artificial insemination;

[受災] be hit by a natural adversity;

受災地區 disaster area; stricken area;

[受知] be appreciated and well-treated by a superior;

[受主] acceptor;

受主中心 acceptor centre;

[受罪] have a bad time; purgatory; suffer hardships;

活受罪 have a hell of life; suffer greatly; suffer terribly;

挨受 suffer;
飽受 suffer to the fullest extent;
筆受 put down in writing what sb else is dictating;
稟受 (1) endure; (2) nature;
承受 (1) bear; endure; (2) inherit;
感受 be affected by; experience; feel;
好受 feel better; feel more comfortable;
接受 accept; acceptance; embrace; take;
禁受 bear; endure; stand;
經受 experience; stand; undergo; weather; withstand;
領受 accept; receive;
蒙受 suffer; sustain;
耐受 withstand;
難受 feel awful; feel bad; feel ill; feel unhappy; feel unwell; suffer pain;
忍受 abide; bear; endure; forbear; live up with; lump; put up with; sit down under; stand; suffer; tolerate; undergo;
容受 (1) be able to contain or hold; (2) endure; put up with;
身受 (1) experience personally; (2) accept personally; receive in person;
授受 give and accept; give and receive; grant and receive;
享受 enjoy;
消受 (1) enjoy; (2) bear; endure;
遭受 be subjected to; suffer;

shou
【狩】 (1) hunting in winter; (2) imperial tour;
[狩獵] hunting; venery;
狩獵場 hunting ground;
狩獵者 huntsman;
~女狩獵者 huntress;

shou
【售】 (1) sell; (2) carry out intrigues; make one's plan work;
[售出] sell; succeed in selling;
[售後] after-sale;
售後服務 after-sale service; post-sale service;
~售後服務站 service station;
售後回租 leaseback;
[售貨] sell goods;
售貨單據 sales slip;
售貨機 vending machine;
~自動售貨機 dispenser;
售貨收據 sales slip;
售貨員 salesclerk; salesgirl; salesman; salesperson; shop assistant; shop clerk;
~男售貨員 salesman;
~女售貨員 salesgirl; saleswoman;
[售價] price; selling price;
售價另議 price upon request;
售價由…起 prices starting from;
[售賣] sell;
售賣機 machine;
~自動售賣機 coffee machine;
~自動飲料售賣機 drinks machine;
[售票] sell tickets;
售票處 booking office; box office; ticket booth; ticket counter; ticket office;
售票機 ticket machine;
售票口 wicket;
售票員 (1) conductor; ticket seller; (2) booking clerk; booking-office clerk; box-office clerk;
~女售票員 conductress;
[售前] before-sale;
售前服務 before-sale service;
[售罄] be completely sold out; sell out;
[售完] be sold out;
出售 auction off sth; close out sth; for sale; offer for sale; on offer; on sale; on the block; on the market; put sth on the market; put sth up for auction; put sth up for sale; sell; sell off sth;
搭售 make a tie-in sale;
代售 be commissioned to sell sth;
兜售 hawk; peddle;
躉售 sell wholesale;
發售 put on sale; sell;
寄售 consign for sale on commission; put up for sale in a secondhand shop;
獎售 encourage to sell products and give reward;
經售 distribute; sell on commission;
零售 retail; sell retail;
拋售 dump; sell sth at low prices; sell sth in big quantities; undersell; unload;
配售 ration;
攤售 spread out goods for sale in booth;
脱售 sell out;
惜售 be reluctant to sell out;
銷售 market; sale; sell; sell goods; selling;
預售 advance booking; open to booking;
轉售 sell what one has bought;
租售 for rent; for sale;

shou
【授】 (1) award; confer; give; hand over

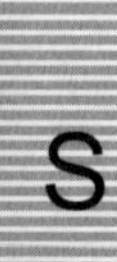

to; vest; (2) instruct; teach; tutor; (3) give up;

[授粉] pollination;
人工授粉 artificial pollination;
異花授粉 allogamy; cross-pollination;
自由授粉 free pollination;

[授給] award; remunerate;

[授官] make sb an official;
因任授官 make sb an official according to his talents;

[授計] tell sb the plan of action;

[授獎] award a prize;
授獎儀式 prize-awarding ceremony; prize-giving ceremony;

[授精] insemination;
人工授精 artificial insemination;

[授課] give instructions; give lessons; teach; teach a class; tutor;

[授名] give a name to a person;

[授命] (1) authorize; give orders; (2) give one's life; lay down one's life;
授命組閣 authorize sb to form a cabinet;

[授旗] present sb with a flag;

[授權] authorize; delegate power; empower; warrant;
授權代表 authorized representative;
授權書 letter of authorization;
授權委托書 letter of attorney;

[授人以柄] give others sth to talk about oneself; offer another a hold on oneself;

[授首] be beheaded; get killed;

[授受] give and accept; give and receive; grant and receive;
授受不親 no physical contact between a man and a woman except between man and wife;
私相授受 give and accept in private; give undercover payments; have underhand secret dealings; make an illicit transfer; make an underhand transaction;

[授徒] teach students;

[授銜] confer sb the title of;

[授勛] award a decoration; confer medals; confer orders;

[授業] teach; tutor;

[授意] suggest; incite sb to do sth; inspire;

[授與] award; confer; endow; give; grant;

[授職] confer a rank; give an official job to;
沿才授職 assignment on merit basis; employ men according to their abilities;

傳授 pass on; teach;
函授 teach by correspondence;
講授 instruct; lecture; teach;
教授 instruct; professor; teach;
口授 (1) oral instruction; (2) dictate;
面授 face-to-face teaching;
天授 endowed by nature; inborn; innate;
追授 be posthumously awarded;

shou

【壽】 (1) long life; longevity; old age; (2) age; life; (3) life span; (4) birthday; (5) for burial; funerary; (6) a surname;

[壽斑] senile plagues;

[壽板] coffin;

[壽比南山] live as long as Mount Nanshan; many, many happy returns of the day;

[壽辰] birthday;

[壽誕] birthday anniversary;

[壽紀] person's age;

[壽考] long life;

[壽禮] birthday presents;

[壽聯] longevity couplets;

[壽麵] birthday noodles;

[壽命] age; life; life-span; lifetime; longevity; the life span of a person;
本體壽命 bulk lifetime;
平均壽命 lifespan;
實際壽命 actual lifetime;
使用壽命 lifespan;
延長壽命 prolong life;
預期壽命 expectation of life;

[壽母] aged mother;

[壽木] coffin;

[壽數] person's destined age;

[壽桃] (1) longevity peaches; (2) (peach-shaped) birthday cake;

[壽同彭祖] as old as Methuselah;

[壽文] congratulations on one's birthday;

[壽穴] graveyard built when one is alive;

[壽衣] dead clothes; graveclothes;

[壽終正寢] dead and buried; die a natural death; die in bed of old age; die of old age; die on one's bed; die peacefully in bed;

拜壽 congratulate an elderly person on his birthday; offer birthday felicitations;
長壽 long life; longevity;
福壽 good fortune and long life;
高壽 (1) long life; longevity; (2) your venerable age;
慶壽 celebrate the birthday of an old person;
人壽 one's span of life;
商壽 long life; longevity;
上壽 (1) advanced age; (2) drink a toast for longevity;
嵩壽 longevity;
損壽 shorten one's life;
夭壽 die young;
益壽 lengthen one's life;
祝壽 celebrate sb's birthday; offer birthday congratulations; wish sb a happy birthday;
作壽 celebrate a birthday;
做壽 celebrate the birthday; hold a birthday party;

shou

【綬】 cordon; silk ribbon attached to a seal;
［綬帶］ cordon;
［綬章］ cordon;

印綬 seal and its silk ribbon;

shou

【瘦】 (1) emaciated; slim; thin; (2) lean; (3) tight; (4) not fertile; poor;
［瘦巴］ lean; skinny;
［瘦長］ lanky; long and thin; skinny and tall; tall and lean; tall and thin;
［瘦骨］ thin and bony;
瘦骨嶙峋 a bag of bones; as lean as a rake; as thin as a lath; become as emaciated as a fowl; thin and bony; very skinny;
瘦骨伶仃 skinny and scrawny; thin and weak;
［瘦猴兒］ dry bones;
［瘦瘠］ (1) emaciated; thin; (2) barren; infertile; poor; unproductive;
［瘦金體］ (in calligraphy) slender gold style;
［瘦馬］ lean horse;
［瘦人］ a bag of bones; a stack of bones; lean person; thin person;
［瘦肉］ lean; lean meat;
［瘦弱］ emaciated; emaciated and frail; thin and weak;
瘦弱的男人 wimp;
身體瘦弱 weal health;
［瘦腿］ thin legs;
瘦腿褲 derainpipe trousers;
［瘦小］ thin and small;
又瘦又小 short and slight;
［瘦削］ angular; gaunt; slim; very thin;
身材瘦削 angular;
［瘦硬］ fine and forceful;
［瘦子］ lean person; living skeleton; thin person;

乾瘦 bony; skinny;
清瘦 lean; thin;
消瘦 become thin;

shou

【獸】 (1) animal; beast; (2) beastly; bestial;
［獸畜］ beast;
豕交獸畜 treat people like beasts;
［獸類］ animals; beasts;
［獸皮］ animal skin; hide;
［獸炭］ animal charcoal;
［獸行］ beastly conduct; brutal act;
［獸性］ barbarity; brutish nature;
獸性大發 give full play to one's animal disposition; raise one's animal disposition;
獸性難改 wild beasts never change their nature;
獸性主義 animalism;
~獸性主義者 animalist;
［獸醫］ vet; veterinarian; veterinary surgeon;
獸醫師 veterinarian;
獸醫藥劑學 zoopharmacy;
獸醫員 veterinarian assistant;
獸醫治療學 zootherapy;
［獸疫］ animal disease;
［獸欲］ animal desire; beastly appetites; beastly pleasure; bestial urge; brutal appetite; carnal desire;

袋獸 marsupial;
害獸 harmful animal;
猛獸 beast of prey;
鳥獸 birds and beasts; fur and feather;
禽獸 birds and beasts;
野獸 wild animal; wild beast;
幼獸 whelp;
走獸 beast; four-footed animal;

shu¹

shu

【殳】 a kind of ancient weapon made of bamboo; halberd;

shu

【抒】 (1) convey; express; give expression to; (2) ease; lighten; relieve; unburden;

[抒發] express; give expression to; voice;
抒發感情 express one's feelings;
抒發己見 declare oneself; express one's opinion;

[抒懷] pour out one's heart; relieve the heart of emotions; unburden one's heart;

[抒難] ease; lighten distress; relieve;

[抒情] express one's emotion; express one's feelings;
抒情愛情詩 lyrical love poetry;
抒情達意 express one's thoughts and feelings;
抒情風格 lyricism;
抒情歌曲 ballad;
抒情散文 lyric prose;
抒情詩 lyric; lyric poem; lyric poetry;
~ 抒情詩人 lyric poet;
抒情性 lyricism;
借景抒情 take advantage of a scene to express one's emotion;

[抒寫] describe; express; write of;
抒寫以詞 express one's feelings by means of words and phrases;

[抒意] express one's ideas;

發抒 express; voice;

shu

【叔】 (1) paternal uncle; younger brothers of one's father; (2) younger brothers of one's husband; (3) general designation for members of one's father's generation who are younger than one's father; (4) decline; (5) a surname;

[叔伯] paternal uncles;
叔伯般的 avuncular;

[叔父] uncle;

[叔公] granduncle;

[叔舅] one's mother's younger brother;

[叔母] wife of one's father's younger brother;

[叔婆] wife of one's grandfather's younger brother;

[叔嬸] aunt; wife of a junior uncle;

[叔叔] (1) uncle (younger brother of one's father); (2) uncle (younger brother of one's husband);

[叔翁] granduncle;

[叔丈] one's wife's uncle;

[叔姪] uncles and nephews;

[叔子] one's husband's younger brother;

[叔祖] granduncle; one's grandfather's younger brother;
叔祖母 grandaunt; wife of one's grandfather's younger brother;

表叔 father's younger male cousin;
堂叔 father's younger male cousin;

shu

【姝】 (1) beautiful girl; pretty lady; (2) beautiful; lovely; pretty;

shu

【洙】 a river in Shandong;

shu

【書】 (1) write; (2) script; style of calligraphy; (3) book; writings; (4) letter; (5) certificate; document;

[書案] writing desk;

[書包] satchel; school bag;
書包帶 book strap;
背書包 carry a school bag on one's back;

[書報] books and newspapers;
書報攤 bookstall; bookstand; newsstand;

[書本] book;
啃書本 pore over one's books;
摳書本 pore over one's books;

[書標] book label; label;

[書不盡言] I cannot write all I have to say; there is more what I want to say but cannot;

[書冊] book;

[書蟲] bookworm;

[書櫥] bookcase;
有腳書櫥 living dictionary; walking dictionary; walking encyclopaedia; walking library;

[書袋] bag for books;
掉書袋 excessive foindness of making literary quotations and historical allusions;

[書單] book list;
一份書單 a list of books;
[書擋] bookend;
[書店] bookshop; bookstore;
[書牘] correspondence; letters; written messages;
[書蠹] bookworm;
[書法] calligraphy; handwriting; penmanship;
書法比賽 handwriting competition;
書法家 calligrapher; calligraphist;
書法秀美 beautiful handwriting;
[書坊] bookshop; bookstore;
[書房] study;
[書肺] book lung;
[書館] bookstore;
[書歸正傳] let us come back to our main story;
[書櫃] bookcase;
[書函] letter; correspondence;
[書翰] letter; correspondence;
[書號] book number; call number;
[書後] postscript;
[書畫] paintings and calligraphy; works of calligraphy and painting;
書畫家 master in calligraphy and painting;
書畫院 calligraphy and painting school;
破書殘畫 old books and broken fragments of painting;
石刻書畫 petroglyph; petrograph;
[書籍] books; literature; works;
書籍恐怖 bibliophobia;
書籍買賣 bibliopoly;
各類書籍 books of all sorts;
收集書籍 collect books;
一批書籍 a batch of books;
[書脊] backbone of a book; spine of a book;
[書記] (1) secretary; (2) clerk;
書記處 secretariat;
~書記處候補書記 alternate member of the secretariat;
~書記處書記 secretary of the secretariat;
書記官 court reporter;
書記員 clerk; secretary;
副書記 vice-secretary;
候補書記 alternate member;
省委書記 secretary of the Provincial Committee of the Communist Party of China;
支部書記 secretary of Party branch;
總書記 General Secretary;
總支書記 secretary of the general branch of the Communist Party of China;
[書家] calligrapher;
[書夾] bookends;
[書賈] book dealer; bookseller;
[書架] bookcase; bookrack; bookshelf;
公開書架 open shelf;
滑動書架 roller shelf; sliding shelf;
旋轉書架 revolving bookcase;
[書價] book prices;
[書簡] letters;
[書局] bookstore; press; publishing house;
[書卷] books and scrolls;
書卷氣 savour of books; scholar's style;
[書卡] book card;
[書刊] books and periodicals;
[書靠] book end;
[書客] bookseller;
[書空咄咄] in great disillusion;
[書庫] stack room;
[書立] book end;
[書林] treasury of books;
[書樓] library;
[書眉] top margin; top of a page;
[書面] in writing; in written form; written;
書面答覆 written reply;
書面交際 written communication;
書面教材 written material;
書面申請 written application;
書面聲明 written statement;
書面通知 written notice;
書面文獻 written text;
書面形式 black and white; in written form;
書面英語 written English;
書面語 written language;
[書名] book title;
書名號 book-title mark;
書名卡 title card;
[書目] bibliography; book catalogue; booklist;
書目提要 bibliography
書目信息服務 information service of bibliography;
評述性書目 pure bibliography;
暫定書目 interim bibliography;
[書皮] book cover; book jacket; cover; dust cover;
[書癖] bibliomania;
[書評] book review;
書評專欄 book review column;

[書鋪] bookstore;
[書契] certificate; deed;
[書簽] bookmark;
[書如其人] like author, like book;
[書商] bookman; bookseller;
[書生] bookish person; intellectual; scholar; student;
書生本色 essential characteristics of a scholar;
書生氣 bookish approach; bookish cast of mind; bookishness;
~書生氣的 donnish;
書生氣十足 behave like a bookish scholar; bookish in the extreme; much too bookish;
書生之見 bookish approach; impractical view of a bookish person; pedantic view;
白面書生 fair-complexioned scholar; gentle scholar; inexperienced youth; pale-faced intellectual;
窮書生 destitute student; poor scholar;
一介書生 nothing but a scholar;
[書聖] calligraphic prodigy;
[書虱] booklice;
[書手] copyist;
[書肆] bookstore;
[書攤] bookstall; bookstand;
[書套] book jacket; slipcase;
[書題] title of a book;
[書體] calligraphic style;
[書亭] book-kiosk; bookstall;
[書筒] envelope;
[書香] having literary or intellectual fame;
書香門第 literary family; scholarly family; intellectual family; family of scholars;
書香人家 family of scholars; literary family;
書香子弟 children from a scholarly family;
[書寫] write; writing;
書寫表達障礙 disorder of written expression;
書寫不能 agraphia;
書寫錯亂 graphorrhea;
書寫倒錯 paragraphia;
書寫痙攣 chirospasm;
書寫困難 dysgraphia;
書寫麻痺 scriveners' palsy;
書寫紙 writing paper;
書寫自如 write with facility;
普通書寫 longhand;
[書信] correspondence; letters; missive; written messages;
書信體 epistolary style;
~書信體小說 epistolary novel;
書信往來 keep on shuttlecocking letters; keep up regular correspondence with sb;
[書頁] page;
[書衣] book jacket;
[書友會] book club;
[書院] academy;
書院導師 college tutor;
[書札] correspondence; letters;
[書賊] biblioklept;
[書齋] study;
[書展] book fair;
[書帙] book jacket;
[書桌] desk; writing desk;

哀的美敦書 ultimatum;
白皮書 official government report; white paper;
百科全書 encyclopaedia;
板書 write on the blackboard; writing on the blackboard;
謗書 defamatory writing;
保證書 guarantee; written pledge;
寶書 treasure book;
報告書 written report;
背書 (1) endorsement; (2) recite a lesson from memory; repeat a lesson;
編書 compile books; edit books;
兵書 book on the art of war;
帛書 book copied on silk;
參考書 reference book;
藏書 collect books; collection of books; library;
草書 cursive hand; cursive script;
辭書 dictionary; lexicographical work;
叢書 anthology; collection; series; series of books; set;
讀書 (1) read; study; (2) attend school; (3) read a book;
法書 (1) model calligraphy; (2) your calligraphy;
工具書 reference book;
古書 ancient books;
故書 (1) ancient books; (2) old books;
官書 government publications;
國書 credentials; letter of credence;
好書 good book;

婚書 marriage certificate;
疾書 write swiftly;
家書 (1) letter home; (2) letter from home;
教書 teach; teach school;
教科書 textbook;
借書 borrow books;
禁書 banned book; officially banned book;
經書 Confucian classics;
舊書 (1) secondhand book; used book; (2) books by ancient writers;
楷書 regular script;
看書 read a book;
來書 incoming letter;
曆書 almanac;
隸書 clerical script; official script;
六書 six categories of Chinese characters;
秘書 secretary;
唸書 (1) read; study; (2) attend school;
聘書 contract; letter of appointment;
評書 storytelling;
漆書 write in varnish on bamboo tablets;
情書 amorous letter; love letter;
請愿書 petition;
上書 make a presentation in writing; present a petition; send in a memorial; submit a written statement to a higher authority;
申請書 application;
史書 annal; book of history; historical records; history;
手書 (1) write in one's on hand; (2) personal letter;
説明書 manual;
説書 storytelling; tell stories;
填色書 colouring book;
通書 almanac; calendar;
偷書 steal a book;
投書 send a letter to;
圖書 books;
委任書 certificate of appointment;
委托書 trust-deed;
文書 (1) documents; official dispatchs; (2) copy clerk;
下書 deliver a letter;
閑書 books for killing time;
閒書 books for killing time; light readings;
寫書 write a book;
新書 (1) new book; (2) newly published book;
行書 running hand;
休書 divorce announcement letter;
修書 (1) compile a book; (2) write a letter;
血書 letter written in one's own blood;
妖書 magical books;
爻書 intertwined scripts;
一抱書 an armful of books;
一本書 a book;
一筆書 one stroke script;
一冊書 a copy of the book;
一堆書 a pile of books;
一課書 a lesson;
一摞書 a pile of books;
一批書 a batch of books;
一套書 a set of books;
一箱書 a box of books;
醫書 medical book;
移書 write a letter to sb;
遺書 (1) posthumous papers; (2) letter left by one immediately before death;
音書 correspondence; information; letters; news;
淫書 obscene books;
有份量的書 able book;
戰書 letter of challenge; written declaration of war;
詔書 imperial edict;
正書 regular script;
證明書 certificate; testimonial;
證書 credentials; certificate;
直書 write straightforwardly;
致書 send a letter;
籀書 majuscul seal script;
著書 author a book;
篆書 seal character; seal script;
字書 dictionary; lexicon; wordbook;
自白書 statement making clear one's position;

shu

【梳】 comb;
［梳篦］ dress up one's hair;
［梳法］ combing;
 禿頭梳法 combover;
［梳理］ combing;
［梳頭］ comb one's hair;
 梳頭髮 comb one's hair;
［梳洗］ clean up; comb one's hair and wash up; wash and dress;
［梳妝］ doll up; dress and make up;
 梳妝打扮 be dressed up; deck oneself out; dress smartly; get slicked up; make one's toilet; make up one's face and dress gaudily; primp; prink oneself up;
 梳妝室 dressing room;
 梳妝台 dressing table; vanity table;
［梳子］ comb;
 一把梳子 a comb;

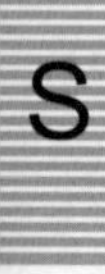

眉梳 eyebrow comb;
木梳 wooden comb;

shu
【淑】 (1) good; pure; refined; virtuous; (2) beautiful; charming; (3) clear;
[淑德] female virtues;
[淑範] paragon of female virtues;
[淑華] fine and outstanding;
[淑景] beautiful scenery;
[淑均] fine and fair;
[淑美] beautiful; beautiful and virtuous;
[淑女] gentlewomen; ladies;
淑女似的 ladylike;
[淑清] clear and bright;
[淑慎] gentle and respectful;
[淑心] pure heart;
[淑行] virtuous conduct;
[淑性] gentle disposition;
[淑儀] rank of court ladies in ancient China;
[淑姿] graceful deportment; graceful manner;

賢淑 virtuous and understanding;
貞淑 pure and chaste;

shu
【殊】 (1) different; (2) special; strange; (3) distinguished; outstanding; remarkable; (4) extremely; really; very much; (5) exceed; over; (6) cut off; sever;
[殊別] different;
[殊不可解] really difficult to understand;
[殊寵] special favour;
[殊等] special class;
[殊功] distinguished services; extraordinary achievements;
[殊技] excellent skill;
[殊績] notable services;
[殊久] very long;
[殊絕] distinguished; rare;
[殊科] different categories;
[殊類] different types;
[殊力] special strength;
[殊能] special skill; unusual ability;
[殊容] stunningly beautiful face; extraordinary beauty;
[殊榮] special honours;
[殊色] outstanding beauty;
[殊深] deeply; extremely; profoundly;
殊深軫念 express deep solicitude for sb; feel deeply concerned;
[殊勝] remarkable and outstanding;
[殊死] desperate; life-and-death;
殊死戰 desperate fight; fight to the last man; life-or-death battle;
~作殊死戰 fight a last-ditch battle; fight to the bitter end; fight with a rope round one's neck; put up a desperate fight; wage a life-and-death struggle;
[殊俗] (1) strange customs; (2) extraordinary;
[殊文] different language; strange language;
[殊效] marked efficacy; special efficacy;
[殊異] extraordinary; special;
勢殊事異 both the conditions and matters are different;
[殊域] strange lands;
[殊遇] special kindness; special treatment;

特殊 particular; special;
懸殊 great disparity; wide gap;

shu
【紓】 (1) mitigate; relax; slacken; slow down; (2) extricate from; free from; remove;
[紓革] get rid of evil;
[紓緩] slacken;
[紓禍] extricate from the grip of misfortune;
[紓困] provide financial relief;
紓民困 relax the people's burden;
[紓難] extricate from straits; extricate from trouble; give relief in times of distress;
毀家紓難 give up one's property to relieve the country from imminent danger; offer all one has to help in charity; sell family properties to relieve the distress of people; spend one's fortune for the country during a crisis;
[紓憂] remove worries;

shu
【菽】 beans; peas;
[菽麥] beans and wheat;
不辨菽麥 cannot tell beans from wheat; have no knowledge of practical matters; incapable of distinguish between beans and wheat; not able to know beans from wheat; not to know chalk from cheese;

[菽粟] beans and grains;

shu

【疏】 (1) dredge; (2) few; sparse; thin; (3) distant relations; (4) not familiar with; unfriendly; (5) careless; neglectful; (6) scanty; (7) disperse; scatter;

[疏布] coarse cloth;

[疏導] channel; dredge; persuasion;
疏導交通 relieve traffic congestion;

[疏防] fail to take precautions; neglectful of necessary precautions;

[疏放] (1) careless; lax; loose; unbridled; wanton; (2) unconventional in style;

[疏忽] blunder; carelessness; clanger; inadvertence; lapse; negligence; oversight; remiss;
疏忽錯誤 missing error;
疏忽大意 carelessness; inattentive and heedless; neglectful and careless;
疏忽招盜賊 negligence invites robbers; opportunity makes the thief;
疏忽職守 asleep at the switch;
共同疏忽 contributory negligence;

[疏開] deploy; disperse; extend;

[疏狂] uninhibited; unrestrained;

[疏闊] (1) careless; not well-conceived; (2) impracticable; unrealistic; (3) part for a long time;

[疏懶] careless and lazy; idle; indolent; lazy; loose; slothful;
疏懶放肆 lazy and careless — indolent and rude;

[疏朗] clear;

[疏理] (1) dredge and improve; (2) put in order;

[疏柳寒煙] a stretch of cold water against some sparse willow trees and a frosty sky;

[疏漏] careless omissions; oversights; slips;
疏漏之處 oversight of one's duties; oversights and omissions;
疏而不漏 loose but never miss;

[疏落] few; scattered; sparse;
疏疏落落 scattered; sparse;

[疏略] neglect inadvertently;
疏略傲慢 negligent and insolent; unconventional and impudent;

[疏慢] neglect inadvertently;

[疏密] (1) looseness and density; (2) neglect and watchfulness;
疏密不勻 of uneven density;

[疏散] (1) dispersed; scattered; sparse; (2) evacauate;

[疏神] careless; in advertent;

[疏失] at fault; careless mistake; negligent; remiss; remissness;

[疏食] coarse meal;
疏食飲水 simple and plain food;

[疏鬆] (1) loose; puff; (2) loosen;
土質疏鬆 the soil is porous;

[疏通] (1) clean; dredge; (2) mediate between two parties;
疏通渠道 dredge the channel;
疏通知遠 real understanding gives one foresight; showing deep understanding and foresight;

[疏外] distant;

[疏懈] idle; lazy; neglectful; negligent;

[疏星] sparse stars;
疏星寥落 only a few solitary stars twinkling in the sky;

[疏野] impolite; rude;

[疏遠] alienate; become estranged; drift apart; estrange; keep at a distance; not close; not in close touch;
互相疏遠 be estranged from each other;
逐漸疏遠 drift apart;

[疏宗] distantly related clan;

粗疏 careless; inattentive;
扶疏 luxuriant and well spaced;
荒疏 be out of practice; get rusty;
空疏 empty; void;
生疏 (1) not familiar; (2) out of practice; (3) aloof; distant;
稀疏 few and scattered; sparse;
蕭疏 (1) bleak; desolate; (2) sparse but graceful;
注疏 notes and commentaries;

shu

【舒】 (1) open; relax; smooth out; spread; stretch; unfold; (2) easy; leisurely; slow; unhurried; (3) a surname;

[舒勃] develop; expand; grow;

[舒暢] (1) comfortable; free from worry; happy; pleasant; (2) leisurely and harmonious;
心情舒暢 feel happy; have ease of mind;

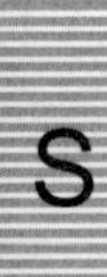

[舒遲] leisurely; slow; unhurried;
[舒發] express one's emotion;
[舒服] (1) comfortable; cosy; (2) well;
不舒服 discomfort; feeling uncomfortable; feeling unwell; uncomfortable; under the weather; unwell;
~ 感到不舒服 feel sick; feel uncomfortable; feel very bad;
舒舒服服 in ease and comfort; nice and cosy; comfortable;
[舒懷] free the mind from tension; set the mind at rest;
[舒緩] leisurely; relax; relaxed;
[舒筋] relax the muscles;
舒筋活絡 stimulate the circulation of the blood and cause the muscles and joints to relax;
舒筋活血 relax the muscles and enliven the blood; relax the muscles and stimulate the blood circulation;
[舒捲] fold and unfold; roll back and forth;
舒捲自如 do as one pleases;
[舒眉] relax the brows to show pleasure;
舒眉展眼 beam with joy; lift one's eyebrows and open one's eyes; relax the brows and stretch the eyes to show pleasure;
[舒散] (1) take a stroll to relax oneself; (2) leisurely; relaxed; remove the feeling of tiredness;
[舒適] comfortable; cosy; snug;
舒適的 comfy;
~ 舒適的天氣 pleasant weather;
~ 舒適的椅子 comfortable chair; comfy chair;
舒適範圍 comfort zone;
手感舒適 comfortable feel;
[舒泰] happy and healthy; well;
[舒坦] at ease; comfortable; happy; in good health;
[舒心] agreeable; pleasant;
工作舒心 have happy work;
[舒徐] leisurely;
[舒腰伸臂] lean back and stretch one's arms;
[舒展] limber up; relax; stretch; unfold;
舒展一下筋骨 limber up one's muscles and joints;
[舒張] relaxation;

shu

【攄】 (1) comfortable; easy; (2) ancient Chinese gambling game roughly resembling today's dice game;

shu

【樞】 (1) centre; hinge; pivot; (2) a kind of tree;
[樞奧] confidential affairs; confidential information;
[樞臣] chief courtier; premier; prime minister;
[樞垣] censorate;
[樞機] vital element;
樞機主教 cardinal of the Catholic Church;
[樞路] key road;
[樞密使] lord chancellor;
[樞密院] Privy Council;
[樞紐] axis; hub; key position; pivot;
商業樞紐 commercial hub;
[樞務] duty of the premier; state affairs;
[樞要] centre of administration;

電樞 armature;
戶樞 door-hinge;
支樞 pivot;
中樞 centre;

shu

【蔬】 (1) greens; vegetables; (2) vegetarian diet;
[蔬菜] green; greenstuff; veg; vegetable; veggie;
蔬菜水果店 greengrocer's;
蔬菜水果商 greengrocer;
蔬菜湯 vegetable soup;
罐頭蔬菜 canned vegetable;
冷藏蔬菜 chilled vegetables;
新鮮蔬菜 fresh vegetables; fresh veggies;
一碟蔬菜 a dish of vegetables;
一份蔬菜 a portion of vegetables;
什錦蔬菜 assorted vegetable;
[蔬飯] vegetables and rice;
[蔬果] vegetables and fruit;
[蔬圃] vegetable garden;
[蔬食] (1) vegetarian diet; (2) simple food;

菜蔬 (1) greens; vegetables; (2) dishes at a meal;

shu

【樗】 ailanthus altissima;
[樗材] good-for-nothing; useless person;
[樗樹] tree of heaven;

shu

【輸】 (1) convey; haul; transport; (2) do-

nate; contribute money; hand in; submit; (3) be beaten; be defeated; lose;

[輸不起] cannot afford to lose;
輸不起的人 bad sport; poor sport; sour loser;
輸得起 can afford to lose;
~ 輸得起的人 good sport;

[輸誠] (1) show sincerity; (2) surrender;

[輸出] (1) export; (2) output;
輸出量 output;
~ 心輸出量 cardiac output;
輸出音量控制 output volume control;
黃金輸出 gold export;
商品輸出 commodity export;
聲功輸出 acoustic power output;
聲輸出 acoustical output;
實際輸出 actual output;
偽裝輸出 camouflaged export;
資本輸出 export of capital;

[輸家] loser;

[輸精管] deferent duct;
輸精管結扎 ligation of spermatic duct;
輸精管精囊炎 vasovesicalitis;

[輸虧] lose at a battle;

[輸理] in the wrong;

[輸卵管] fallopian tube; oviduct;
輸卵管炎 salpingitis;
~ 出血性輸卵管炎 hemorrhagic salpingitis;
~ 肥厚性輸卵管炎 hypertrophic salpingitis;
~ 結節性輸卵管炎 nodular salpingitis;
~ 實質性輸卵管炎 parenchymatous salpingitis;
~ 溢流性輸卵管炎 salpingitis profluens;

[輸尿管] ureter;
輸尿管石切除 ureterolighotomy;
輸尿管炎 ureteritis;
~ 囊性輸尿管炎 ureteritis cystica;
~ 腺性輸尿管炎 ureteritis glandularis;
巨輸尿管 megaloureter;

[輸錢] lose money in gambling;

[輸入] (1) import; (2) input;
輸入程序 input programme;
輸入國 importer;
輸入輸出 input and output;
~ 輸入輸出部件 input-output unit;
~ 輸入輸出管理 input-output management;
~ 輸入輸出控制系統 input and output; control system;
~ 輸入輸出媒體 input-output media;
輸入選擇開關 input selector;
輸入語段 input text;
黃金輸入 gold import;
交流輸入 alternating current input;
競爭輸入 competitive import;
模擬輸入 analog input;
任意輸入 arbitrary input;
聲頻輸入 audio input;
天線輸入 aerial input; antenna input;
條件輸入 condition entry;
先期輸入 anticipated import;
延期輸入 delayed entry;
異步輸入 asynchronous input;
作用輸入 action entry;

[輸送] carry; convey; conveying; transport;
輸送帶 conveyor belt;
輸送機 conveyer;
~ 帶式輸送機 band conveyer;
~ 風動輸送機 air float conveyer;
~ 攪動式輸送機 agitated conveyer;
~ 鱗板輸送機 apron conveyer;
~ 螺旋輸送機 auger conveyer;
~ 皮帶輸送機 belt conveyer;
輸送器 conveyer;
~ 袋輸送器 bagged conveyer;
~ 鏈板式輸送器 chain-and-slat conveyer;
~ 鏈桿式輸送器 chain-web conveyer;
~ 氣流式輸送器 blast conveyer;
輸送裝置 conveying appliance;
固體氣動輸送 pneumatic conveying of solids;
機械輸送 mechanical conveying;

[輸血] (1) blood transfusion; (2) give aid and support;
輸血打氣 give sb a shot in the arm;
輸血反應 transfusion reaction;
輸血過多 overtransfusion;
宮內輸血 intrauterine transfusion;

[輸贏] defeat or victory; losses and gains;

[輸運] transport; transportation;

傳輸 disseminate; transmission;
服輸 acknowledge defeat; admit defeat;
灌輸 (1) irrigate; (2) imbue with; instil into;
捐輸 contribute; donate;
認輸 concede defeat; throw in the towel;
運輸 carriage; convey; transport;

shu

【攄】 (1) express; make known; set forth; vent; (2) gallop;

[攄陳] present a proposal;

[攄誠] frank;

[攄憤] vent one's indignation;
[攄懷] give vent to one's emotion;
[攄意] give expression to one's feelings;

shu²

shu

【秫】 a glutinous variety of millet;
[秫酒] wine made from glutinous rice;
[秫米] husked sorghum;

shu

【孰】 (1) what; (2) which; who; whom;
[孰若] it would be better to; what is better than;
[孰謂] who says that;

shu

【塾】 (1) ante-room; vestibule; (2) family school; village school;
[塾師] (1) private tutor; (2) tutor of a family school;
[塾學] family school;
村塾 village school;
家塾 family school;
私塾 old-style private school;
學塾 old-style private school;
義塾 private school charging no tuition;

shu

【熟】 (1) ripe; ripen; (2) cooked; well done; (3) processed; (4) familiar; well acquainted; (5) deep sleep; (6) expert; experienced; practised; skilled; versed; (7) deeply; thoroughly;
[熟諳] an expert in; familiar with; good at; well experienced; well versed in;
熟諳時事 be acquainted with the current events;
熟諳世事 have a large business experience;
熟諳水性 expert swimmer;
[熟菜] cooked food;
買熟菜 buy cooked food;
[熟道] familiar road;
[熟地] cultivated land;
[熟讀] memorize by rote; read carefully over and over again;
熟讀成誦 learn by heart; read again and again until one knows by heart;
熟讀唐詩三百首，不會作詩也會吟 when one learns the three hundred poems of the Tang Dynasty by heart, one is sure to be able to write poetry;
熟讀詳味 study earnestly and search out the essence;
[熟飯] cooked rice;
生米做成熟飯 the rice is already cooked — what's done can't be undone;
[熟慣] familiar;
[熟貨] finished products;
[熟記] commit to memory; learn by heart; memorize;
[熟精] expert; practised; skilful;
[熟客] frequent visitor; old customer;
[熟練] dexterous; experienced; practised; proficient; skilled;
熟練的 adept; skilled;
~不熟練的 amateurish;
熟練工人 experienced workers; skilled workers;
~半熟練工人 semi-skilled labourer;
半熟練 semi-skilled;
經驗熟練 ripe with experience;
[熟路] familiar route;
[熟慮] consider carefully;
熟慮斷行 think deliberately and execute promptly;
熟慮果斷 deliberate in counsel and prompt in action;
[熟眠] deep sleep;
[熟能生巧] dexterity is the product of long practice; practice makes perfect; skill comes from long experience;
[熟年] bumper year; plentiful year; year of good harvests;
[熟人] old acquaintance;
[熟稔] know sb very well; very familiar with sb;
[熟肉] cooked meat; well-done meat;
[熟食] cooked food; prepared food;
熟食店 deli; delicatessen;
[熟識] know a thing or two; know well; very familiar with;
[熟視] look carefully and for a long time; scrutinize;
熟視無睹 care nothing for; close one's eyes to; fail to notice; ignore; indifferent to; look at but pay no attention to; not to see sth right under one's nose; pay no attention to a familiar sight; regard as of no

consequence; take no notice; turn a blind eye to;

[熟手] experienced hand; old hand; skilled hand;

[熟水] boiled water;

[熟睡] dead to the world; fast asleep; sleep like a log; sleep soundly; sound sleep;

[熟思] consider carefully; deliberate; ponder deeply; think over carefully;

[熟鐵] wrought iron;

[熟銅] wrought copper;

[熟透] (1) well-cooked; (2) thoroughly ripe; (3) very familiar with;

熟透的 well-done;

[熟脱] very familiar with; well versed;

[熟悉] acquaint oneself with; at home in; at home with; be acquainted with; be apprised of; conversant with; familiar to sb; familiar with; familiarize oneself with; get in with; great on; have an intimate knowledge of; have sth at one's fingertips; in with; know sth from A to Z; know sth like a book; know sth like the back of one's hand; know sth or sb well; very familiar with;

熟悉內情 familiar with the workings of the organization; in the know; know the inns and outs of the matter; know the inside story of; know the ropes;

彼此熟悉 familiar with each other;

不熟悉 unacquainted; unfamiliar with;

[熟習] have the knack of; learn by heart; practised in; skilful at; skilled in; well versed in;

熟習業務 well versed in one's field of work;

[熟語] idiom;

[熟知] know intimately; know very well; well acquainted with;

熟知內情 know the ropes; learn the ropes;

[熟字] familiar word;

諳熟 conservant with; proficient in; quite familiar;

半熟 half-cooked;

不熟 (1) not yet done; still raw; (2) unacquainted with; unfamiliar with;

成熟 fluent; practised; skilful; well versed;

純熟 skilful; well versed;

催熟 accelerate the ripening of;

讀熟 learn by heart;

燉熟 stew until it is done;

耳熟 familiar to the ear; sound familiar;

腐熟 become thoroughly decomposed;

爛熟 (1) thoroughly cooked; (2) know sth thoroughly;

面熟 look familiar;

稔熟 ripe; know sb well;

晚熟 late maturing;

習熟 familiar with; understand;

嫻熟 adept in; consummate; expert; skilled in;

性早熟 sexual precocity;

馴熟 (1) obedient; (2) skilled;

眼熟 look familiar; seem to know; seemingly familiar by sight;

圓熟 dexterous; proficient; skilled; skillful;

早熟 (1) ripen early; (2) reach puberty early; (3) precocious;

煮熟 cook thoroughly;

shu

【贖】 (1) buy; ransom; redeem; (2) atone for; expiate;

[贖出] get back from pawn; redeem;

[贖當] redeem sth pawned;

[贖回] ransom; redeem;

[贖價] ransom; ransom price;

[贖金] ransom; ransom money;

[贖救] redeem;

[贖款] ransom;

[贖買] buy out; redeem;

[贖命] save one from death penalty by a payment;

[贖身] buy back one's freedom; redeem oneself;

[贖刑] buy freedom from punishment;

[贖職] dereliction of duty;

[贖罪] atone for one's crime; atonement;

將功贖罪 atone for one's mistakes by meritorious service;

立功贖罪 perform meritorious services to atone for one's crime;

以生命贖罪 atone one's sin with life;

回贖 redeem pawned articles;

自贖 atone for one's crime; redeem oneself;

shu³

shu

【暑】 (1) heat; heat of summer; hot; hot

weather; (2) mid-summer; summer;
[暑病] summer-heat disease;
[暑伏] dog days of summer; hottest spell of summer;
[暑季] heated term; summer time;
[暑假] summer holidays; summer vacation;
[暑瘧] marlaria in summer;
[暑期] (1) summer; (2) summer vacation; summer vacation time;
暑期班 summer class;
暑期學校 summer school;
[暑氣] heat of summer; scorching heat;
暑氣迫人 the summer heat is very oppressive; the summer heat is threatening;
暑氣熏蒸 stifling summer heat;
[暑熱] heat of summer; hot summer weather; scorching heat;
暑熱天 dog days of summer; hot summer days;
一陣暑熱 a spell of summer heat;
[暑濕] summer-heat and damp;
[暑歲] year of heat and drought;
[暑天] hot days; hot summer days; summertime; the dog days of summer;
[暑月] summer months;

避暑 avoid the summer heat; escape the summer heat; go away for summer holidays; go to a summer resort; run away from summer heat; take a summer vacation;
殘暑 lingering heat of late summer;
防暑 heatstroke prevention;
伏暑 dog days; hot season;
感暑 affection by summer heat;
寒暑 cold and hot seasons;
酷暑 intense heat of summer;
烈暑 summer at its hottest;
祛暑 drive away summer heat;
溽暑 humid summer weather;
盛暑 dog days; sweltering summer heat; very hot weather;
受暑 suffer from heatstroke;
消暑 relieve a summer heat; take a summer holiday;
小暑 Slight Heat;
炎暑 dog days of summer; hot summer; summer at its hottest; sweltering summer days;
蒸暑 steaming heat of summer;
中暑 be affected by the heat; heat-stroke; suffer heatstroke or sunstroke; sunstroke

shu

【黍】 millet;
[黍谷生春] a change for the better of a needy life;
[黍離麥秀] grieve for the conquered country; the grains grow luxuriantly among the ruins of the former capital;
[黍米] millet grain;
[黍子] millet;

蜀黍 sorghum
玉蜀黍 corn; maize;

shu

【署】 (1) government office; office; public office; (2) arrange; make arrangements for; (3) act as deputy; handle by proxy; (4) put one's signature to; sign;
[署理] act as deputy; acting; handle by proxy;
[署名] put one's signature to; sign;
署名人 undersigned;
署名文章 signed article;
[署長] administrator;
副署長 deputy administrator;

部署 (1) deploy; dispose; (2) map out;
副署 countersign;
公署 government office;
連署 cosign; countersign;
簽署 sign;
行署 administration office (within a province);
專署 prefectural commissioner's office;

shu

【蜀】 (1) an ancient kingdom in present-day Sichuan; (2) alternative name for Sichuan;
[蜀犬吠日] a dog of Shu barking at the sun — an ignorant person making a fuss about sth that he alone finds strange;
[蜀繡] Sichuan embroidery;

shu

【鼠】 mouse; rat;
[鼠輩] mean creatures; scoundrels;
此等鼠輩 such a good for nothing;
無能鼠輩 useless kind;
[鼠竄] run away like frightened rats; scamper off like a rat; scurry away like frightened rats;

鼠竄而逃 flee like rats — abscond;
鼠竄狼奔 run away in all directions; run hither and thither like rats and wolves;
抱頭鼠竄 be frightened away; cover one's head and creep away; cover the head and scurry away like a rat back to its hole; flee helter-skelter; flee in a panic; flee with arms covering one's head; run away frightened like a rat; run away like rats; run off like a rat; run wildly like cornered rats; scamper off like a rat; scurry away like a frightened rat; throw one's arms over one's head and run away;

[鼠膽] cowardice;
[鼠肚雞腸] extreme pettiness of character; narrow-mindedness; suffer affronts without resentment;
[鼠遁] flee helter-skelter like a rat;
[鼠目] (1) small, protruding eyes; (2) short-sighted;
鼠目寸光 lack of vision and prevision; lack of foresight; not to be able to see beyond one's nose; not to see an inch beyond one's nose; see no further than one's nose; see only what is under one's nose; short-sighted;
獐頭鼠目 facial features suggesting cunning and meanness; rat-eyed and buck-headed; with head like deer, eyes like rats — contemptibly ugly; with the head of a buck and the eyes of a rat — repulsively ugly and sly-looking;

[鼠首僨事] as timid as a rat which peeps out its head and dares to do nothing; excessive timidity and caution spoil affairs;
[鼠思] pensive;
[鼠牙雀角] litigate; litigation over trifles;
[鼠眼] (1) small, protruding eyes; (2) lack of foresight;
蛇頭鼠眼 a snake's head and a rat's eyes; crafty; cunning; wily;
賊眉鼠眼 have a sneaky look; look like a thief; mean look; shifty-eyed; thievish-looking; with furtive eyes and sullen look;

[鼠藥] rat poison;
一盒鼠藥 a box of rat poison;

[鼠疫] pestilence; plague;

[鼠子] mean fellow;

白鼠 white mouse;
豹鼠 chipmunk;
倉鼠 hamster;
巢鼠 harvest mouse;
袋鼠 kangaroo;
飛鼠 flying squirrel;
鼢鼠 myospalax;
負鼠 opossum;
溝鼠 a kind of rat;
海狸鼠 coypu; nutria;
褐家鼠 rat;
黑家鼠 rat;
花鼠 chipmunk; Siberian chipmunk;
滑鼠 mouse;
黃鼠 ground squirrel; suslik;
灰鼠 squirrel;
姬鼠 a kind of rat;
家鼠 mouse; rat;
老鼠 mouse; rat;
旅鼠 lemming;
盲鼠 zoker;
滅鼠 deratization; rat eradication;
沙鼠 gerbil;
山撥鼠 marmot;
蛇鼠 (1) snakes and mice; (2) wicked people;
麝鼠 muskrat;
水鼠 water vole;
松鼠 squirrel;
天竺鼠 cavy; guinea pig;
田鼠 field mouse;
跳鼠 jerboa;
豚鼠 cavy; guinea pig;
蝟鼠 hedgehog;
鼯鼠 flying squirrel;
鼷鼠 house mouse;
黠鼠 (1) cunning rat; (2) cunning person;
鼹鼠 mole;
小鼠 mouse;
銀鼠 snow weasel;
竹鼠 bamboo rat;

shu

【數】 (1) count; enumerate; list; (2) be reckoned as exceptionally good;

[數不過來] countless; innumerable; too many to be counted;
[數不盡的] countless;
[數不清] countless; innumerable;
[數不上] not important enough; not qualified;
[數不着] not count as outstanding;

數得着 be regarded as outstanding; goods quality; outstanding;

[數詞] numeral;
倍數詞 multiplicative numeral;
分配數詞 distributive numeral;
分數數詞 fraction numeral;
序數詞 adjective numeral;

[數錯] miscount;

[數典忘祖] disown one's forefather; forget one's own origin; give all the historical facts except those about one's own ancestors — ignorant of the history of one's own country;

[數黑論黃] garrulous; make unfounded statements; talk wildly; wordy;

[數九] nine periods following the winter solstice;
數九寒天 coldest days of the year; in the depth of winter;

[數落] (1) blame; rebuke; reprove; scold sb by enumerating his wrong-doings; (2) cite one example after another; enumerate;

[數罵] enumerate sb's faults;

[數米而炊] count the grains of rice before cooking them — overcareful;

[數冪] exponent;
分指數冪 fractional exponent;
負指數幕 negative exponent;

[數錢] count money;

[數數兒] count; name numbers;

[數説] (1) accuse; reproach; (2) enumerate;
亞洲數一數二的富豪 the first or second richest man in Asia;

[數字] (1) characters that denote amounts; (2) digit; digital; figure; (3) amount;
數字手錶 digital watch;
數字顯示 digisplay;
數字鐘 digital clock;
數字轉換器 digitizer;
~峰高數字轉換器 peak height digitizer;
~圖像數字轉換器 image digitizer;
~質譜數字轉換器 mass spectrum digitizer;
~軸角模數字轉換器 shaft position digitizer;
~坐標數字轉換器 coordinate digitizer;
阿拉伯數字 Arabic digital; Arabic numerals;
大打數字 long figure;
獨立數字 independent digit;
二進制數字 binary digit; binary numeral;
估計數字 estimative figure;
羅馬數字 Roman numerals;
模擬數字 analog digital;
聲信號數字 sound signal digital;
十二進數字 duodecimal numeral;
十進制數字 decimal digit; decimal numeral;
十六進制數字 hexadecimal digit; hexadecimal numeral;
虛報數字 give inflated figures in a report;
一列數字 a column of figures;
有效數字 effective figure;

按數 according to the number; proportionately;
百分數 percentage;
半數 half; half the number;
報數 count off; number off;
倍數 multiple;
變數 variable; variate;
卜數 art of fortunetelling;
不名數 abstract number;
參數 parameter;
常數 constant;
乘數 multiplier;
超越數 transcendental number;
充數 make up the number; merely to take a part; serve as a stopgap;
重數 multiplicity;
除數 divisor;
次數 frequency; number of times;
湊數 (1) make do; serve as a stopgap; (2) make up the amount; make up the number;
代數 algebra;
單數 odd number;
倒數 (1) count backwards; (2) reciprocal;
導數 derivative;
底數 base;
點數 tally;
讀數 reading;
對數 logarithm;
噸數 tonnage;
多數 majority; most; plural; pluri-;
範數 norm;
分數 (1) grade; mark; score; (2) fraction; fractional number;
負數 negative number;
複名數 compound number
複數 (1) plural number; (2) complex number; plurality;
概數 approximate number;
公倍數 common multiple;

公因數 common factor;
公約數 common divisor;
夠數 enough; sufficient in quantity;
函數 (maths) function;
號數 number;
合數 composite number;
奇數 odd number;
基數 cardinal number;
基數 base number; cardinal number; radix;
級數 array; progression; series;
計數 count; counting; tally;
加數 addend;
減數 subtrahend;
劫數 predestined fate;
里數 mileage;
歷數 count one by one; enumerate;
路數 (1) approach; way; (2) movement in martial arts; (3) exact details; ins and outs; inside story;
名數 denominate number
命數 one's destiny; one's fate; one's lot;
模數 modulus;
偶數 even number;
氣數 destiny; fate; fortune;
錢數 amount of money;
全數 sum total; total number; whole amount;
人數 number of people;
如數 exactly the number;
少數 a few; a small number; minority;
實數 real number;
壽數 person's destined age;
術數 (1) ways of administering a nation; (2) fortune-telling;
雙數 even number;
素數 prime number;
算數 (1) of importance; (2) count; hold; mean what one says; stand;
歲數 age; years;
天數 (1) fatalism; fate; predestination; (2) predestined disaster; predestined tragedy;
為數 amount to; number;
維數 dimension; dimensionality;
無理數 irrational number;
無數 (1) countless; infinity; innumberable; myriad; numerous; uncounted; (2) an unknown number of; not know for certain; uncertain;
悉數 all; enumerate in full detail; every single one; the entire sum;
系數 coefficient;
係數 coefficient;
小數 decimal; decimal fraction;
虛數 imaginary number;
序數 ordinal; ordinal number;
異數 (1) different rank; (2) courteous reception; unusual favour;
因數 factor;
印數 print run;
有理數 rational number
有數 know how things stand;
約數 (1) estimated number; (2) exact divisor;
運數 fate; fortune; luck;
招數 (1) move in chess (2) movement in Chinese martial art; (3) device; scheme; trick;
著數 (1) move in chess; (2) movement in Chinese martial art; (3) device; trick;
整數 integer; integral number; round number; round sum; whole number;
正數 positive number;
指數 exponent; index; index number; indices;
質數 prime number;
自變數 argument; independent variable;
自然數 natural number;
總數 aggregate; amount; total; total amount;
最小公倍數 least common multiple (LCM);
最大公約數 greatest common divisor (GCD);

shu

【薯】 sweet potato; yam;

［薯片］ crisps; potato chips;
一包薯片 a bag of crisps; a bag of potato chips;

［薯條］ chip;
薯條店 chip shop;
炸薯條 chips;
～一袋炸薯條 a bag of potato chips;

［薯蕷］ Chinese yam;

白薯 sweet potato;
豆薯 yam bean;
甘薯 sweet potato;
紅薯 sweet potato;
馬鈴薯 potato;
木薯 cassava;

shu

【藷】 same as 薯 , sweet potato;

shu

【屬】 (1) category; class; kind; (2) genus; (3) subordinate to; under; (4) belong to; subordinate to; (5) dependants; family members; (6) be; (7) be born in the year of one of the twelve animals;

［屬地］ annexed territory; colony; dependent domain;
［屬國］ dependent state; vassal state;
［屬吏］ subordinate officials;
［屬僚］ subordinate;
［屬實］ be verified; true; turn out to be true;
查明屬實 prove to be true after investigation;
［屬下］ subordinates;
［屬性］ attribute; nature; property; quality;
表目屬性 entry attribute;
串屬性 string attribute;
遞歸屬性 recursive attribute;
計數屬性 count attribute;
繼承屬性 inherited attribute;
精度屬性 precision attribute;
空間屬性 space attribute;
類型屬性 type attribute;
列式屬性 alignment attribute;
目標屬性 target attribute;
事件屬性 event attribute;
數量屬性 quantitative attribute;
算術屬性 arithmetic attribute;
維數屬性 dimension attribute;
文件屬性 file attribute;
整數屬性 integer attribute;
字符屬性 character attribute;
綜合屬性 synthesized attribute;
［屬於］ be attached to; be part of; belong to; pertain to; remain with; reside with; subscribe to; vest with;
［屬員］ officials under a superior official;

shu
【鸆】 blackbird;

shu4
shu
【戍】 defend; garrison; guard;
［戍邊］ garrison the frontiers; guard the border; guard the frontier;
［戍樓］ garrison watchtower;
［戍人］ frontier guard; garrison soldier;
［戍守］ defend; garrison;
［戍役］ garrison duty;
［戍卒］ garrison soldier;

衛戍 garrison;

shu
【束】 (1) bind; tie; (2) bod; bunch; bundle; head; sheaf; taft; (3) a beam of; a bouquet of; a bunch of; a bundle of; a cluster of; a hank of; (4) control; restrain; (5) a surname;
［束帶］ drawstring;
［束髮］ reach boyhood;
束髮帶 headband;
［束縛］ bind up; fetter; restrain; tie;
束縛手腳 bind sb hand and foot; hamper the initiative of; tie sb's hands;
擺脱束縛 shake off fetters; shake off the yoke;
解除束縛 liberation from bondage;
［束躬］ control oneself; restrain oneself; self-restrain;
［束緊］ bind up; lace up;
［束身］ restrain oneself; self-control;
束身藏拙 hide one's inadequacy by keeping quiet;
［束手］ have one's hands tied; helpless;
束手待斃 die without a fight; fold one's hands and await destruction; fold one's hands and wait for death; fold one's hands and wait to be slain; resign oneself to extinction; wait for death with hands bound up; wait for death with tied hands; wait helplessly for death;
束手就縛 allow oneself to be seized without putting up a fight; be captured; just to stand still to be bound;
束手就擒 allow oneself to be arrested without offering any resistance; allow oneself to be seized without putting up a fight; resign oneself to being held as a prisoner; submit to arrest with folded arms;
束手受縛 wait calmly to be put into bonds;
束手束腳 be bound hand and foot; be bound hands and feet; overcautiousness; undue caution;
束手無策 at a loss what to do; have one's hands tie; helpless; no way out; up a stump;
［束之高閣］ bundle sth up and place it on the top shelf; cast on the shelf; hang by the wall; in cold storage; lay aside and neglect; perch on the highest shelves; put aside from duty; put it away

unheeded;
[束裝] pack up;
束裝就道 pack up for a journey;

波束 beam;
電子束 electron beam;
管束 check; control; restrain;
光束 light beam;
花束 bouquet; bunch of flowers;
激光束 laser beam;
檢束 examine and restrain (oneself);
結束 close; conclude; end; finish; wind up;
拘束 awkward; constrained; ill at ease; restrain; restrict;
離子束 ion beam;
前束 toein;
聲束 acoustic beam;
收束 (1) bring together; collect (2) bring to a close (3) pack (for a journey)
維管束 vascular bundle;
約束 bind; keep within bounds; restrain;
裝束 attire; dress;

shu
【沭】 a river in Shandong;

shu
【述】 (1) explain; expound; give an account of; relate; state; (2) carry forward; continue;
[述評] commentary; review;
[述説] give an account of; narrate; recount; state; tell;
[述謂結構] predication;
從屬述謂結構 subordinate predication;
描述性述謂結構 descriptive predication;
[述職] report; report on one's work;
回國述職 return to one's country and report;
[述作] compose and create; write;
述而不作 pass on the ancient culture without adding anything new to it;

備述 report completely;
筆述 narrate in writing;
編述 arrange and narrate;
闡述 elaborate; expound; state;
陳述 state;
稱述 narrate; recount; state;
傳述 it is said; they say;
供述 confess; own up;
記述 record and narrate;
講述 narrate; relate; tell about;
口述 give an oral account;
縷述 go into particulars; state in detail;
論述 expound; relate and analyze;
描述 describe;
上述 above-mentioned; aforementioned;
申述 explain in detail; state;
行述 brief biography of a deceased person;
敍述 narrate; relate;
譯述 translate freely;
著述 compile book; write;
轉述 report; relate sth as told by another;
撰述 book; compose; work; write; writing;
追述 tell about the past; recount;
自述 account in one's own words; recount or narrate by oneself;
綜述 summarize; sum up;
祖述 worship and follow the example of forefathers' theory or conduct;

shu
【恕】 (1) excuse; forgive; pardon; (2) beg your pardon; excuse me; (3) consideration for others; forbearance;
[恕道] principle of forgiveness;
[恕過] forgive a fault; pardon the mistake;
[恕宥] excuse; forgive;
[恕罪] forgive a mistake; forgive a sin; pardon an offense;

寬恕 forgive;
饒恕 forgive; pardon;
容恕 forgive; pardon;

shu
【倏】 hastily; suddenly;
[倏爾] abruptly; suddenly;
[倏忽] all of a sudden; quickly; very suddenly;
[倏瞬] brief glimpse;

shu
【庶】 (1) deviant; (2) born of a concubine; (3) multitudinous; numerous; populous; various; (4) common; general; (5) common people; commoners; (6) almost; nearly;
[庶乎] so as to; so that;
[庶黎] common people; commoners; masses; multitude;
[庶民] common people; commoners; multitude;
[庶母] one's father's concubine;

[庶女] commoner's daughter;
[庶人] common people;
禮不下庶人 rites do not extend to the common people;
[庶物] all the things of the universe;
[庶務] (1) business matters; general affairs; (2) person in charge of business matters;
[庶眾] common people; commoners; masses; multitude;
富庶 rich and populous;

shu

【疏】 (1) present point by point; (2) annotate; explicate;

shu

【術】 (1) art; skills; techniques; (2) methods; tactics;
[術科] skills courses;
[術士] (1) one who practises occult arts; (2) scholars;
[術數] (1) ways of administering a nation; (2) fortune-telling;
[術語] jargon; technical terms; term; terminology;
術語標準 terminological standard;
術語規範化 terminology standardization;
術語學 terminology;
國際術語 international term;
化學術語 chemical terminology;
科技術語 scientific and technological term;
科學術語 scientific term;
會記術語 accounting terminology;
歷史術語 historical term;
親屬術語 kinship term;
推廣術語 promotion terminology;
醫學術語 medical terminology;
有機術語 organic terminology;
專門術語 technical term;
[術智] clever and skilful;

催眠術 hypnotism; mesmerism;
法術 magic arts;
復位術 reduction;
詭辯術 sophistry;
棍術 cudgel play;
國術 traditional Chinese boxing and fencing;
航海術 navigation;
滑翔術 gliding;
幻術 magic; conjuring;
惑術 deceitful tricks; guile; ruse;
技術 (1) skill; technique; technology; (2) technical equipment;
駕駛術 driving skill;
劍術 fencing; swordsmanship;
矯正術 orthopedics;
蠟版術 cerography;
煉丹術 art of making pills of immortality (as a Daoist practice);
煉金術 alchemy;
馬術 horsemanship;
美容術 beauty-art;
美術 art; fine arts;
密碼術 cryptography; cryptology;
魔術 magic; sleigh of hand;
木刻術 xylography;
騙術 deceitful trick; hoax; ruse;
騎術 equestrian skill; horsemanship;
切斷術 amputation;
清創術 debridement;
拳術 art of boxing; Chinese boxing; manly art; noble art of defence;
權術 political trickery; scheme and tactics in politics;
柔術 jujitsu;
射擊術 marksmanship;
神術 marvelous technique; wondrous tricks;
手術 operation; surgical operation;
算術 arithmetic;
體現術 stereoscopy;
吻合術 anastomosis;
巫術 black art; black magic; sorcery; witchcraft; witchery;
武術 art of defence; chivalry; martial arts;
舞術 art of dancing;
仙術 magic arts;
顯微術 microscopy;
相手術 palmistry;
相術 physiognomy;
邪術 demonic magic; sorcery; voodooism;
心術 designs; intentions; schemes;
星占術 astrology;
學術 academic; intellectual; learning; science;
妖術 black art; sorcery; witchcraft;
遙測術 telemetry;
醫術 art of healing; leechcraft; medical skills;
移植術 transplantation;
藝術 (1) art; (2) conforming to good taste; craft; skill;
印刷術 art of printing; printing;
詐術 cheating; chicanery; fraud; guile;
占星術 astrology;
戰術 art of war; military tactics;

植皮術 skin grafting;
指紋術 dactylographic;
治術 ways and means of a good government;
智術 stratagem; trickery;

shu

【署】 (1) arrange; make arrangements for; (2) act as deputy; handle by proxy; (3) sign; put one's signature to; (4) put down; write down;

[署辦] act as a deputy;

[署款] put down one's signature; sign one's name;

[署理] acting; deputy;

[署名] affix one's name to; put one's signature to; sign; sign one's name;

[署簽] inscribe a title-label on a book;

[署事] (1) deal with public affairs; (2) public affairs;

[署書] calligraphic style for ornamental tablets;

[署字] sign on a document;

shu

【裋】 cotton clothes of a boy servant;

shu

【墅】 country house; summer place; villa;

shu

【漱】 (1) gargle; rinse the mouth; (2) wash;

[漱滌] rinse; wash;

[漱口] gargle the throat; rinse the mouth;
漱口杯 mug; mug for mouth-rinsing; tooth glass;
漱口水 gargle; mouthwash;
漱口液 gargle;
漱石枕流 clean one's teeth with rocks and pillow one's head on the streams – refers to the nobility and purity of a hermit;

[漱液] gargarism;

shu

【數】 (1) figure; number; (2) amount; number; quantity; sum; (3) a few; several; (4) destiny; fate; (5) art;

[數倍] manifold; several times;

[數詞] numerals;
短語數詞 phrasal numeral;
複合數詞 compound numeral;
基數詞 cardinal numeral;
簡單數詞 simple numeral;
派生數詞 derivation numeral;
序數詞 ordinal numeral;

[數次] a few times; several times;

[數滴] a few drops; several drops;

[數額] amount; number; quota; sum;
超出數額 exceed the number fixed;
相應數額 matching amount;

[數據] data; record; information;
數據安全性 data security;
數據包 data package;
數據保護 data security;
數據標繪器 dataplotter;
數據採集 data acquisition;
~數據採集系統 data acquisition system;
數據採控系統 data acquisition and control system;
數據操縱語言 data manipulation language;
數據操作員 data operator;
數據抽象語言 data abstraction language;
數據處理 data handling; data processing;
~數據處理程序 data processing procedure;
~數據處理機 datatron;
~數據處理器 datatron;
~數據處理實用程序 data-handling system;
~數據處理系統 data processing system;
數據處理系統審計 electronic data processing system audit;
~數據處理站 data processing station;
~數據處理中心 data processing centre;
~自動數據處理 datamation;
數據傳輸 data transmission;
~數據傳輸系統 daa transmission system;
~數據傳輸效率 data transmission utilization measure;
數據窗 data window;
數據存儲 data storage;
~數據存儲公司 data storage company;
數據存取 data access;
~數據存取裝置 data access equipment;
數據發聲器 dataphone;
數據分析 data analysis;
數據管理 data management;
~數據管理程序 data management programme;
數據管理程序系統 data management programme system;
~數據管理系統 data management system;

~ 數據管理員 data administrator;
數據機 modem;
數據記錄 data logging;
數據記述語言 data description language;
數據加密 data encipherment;
~ 數據加密標準 data encryption standard;
~ 數據加密設備 data encipherment equipment;
~ 數據加密算法 data encryption algorithm;
數據檢索 data retrieval;
數據交換 data interchange;
~ 電子數據交換 electronic data interchange;
數據控制員 data control clerk;
數據庫 data bank; data base;
~ 數據庫管理 database management;
數據庫管理軟件 database management software;
數據庫管理系統 database management system;
數據庫管理員 database administrator;
~ 數據庫控制 database control;
數據庫控制系統 database control system;
~ 數據庫實用程序 database utility programme;
~ 初始數據庫 initial database;
~ 關係數據庫 relational database;
~ 中文數據庫 Chinese database;
~ 中央數據庫 centralized database;
~ 主存數據庫 main memory databases;
~ 主動數據庫 active databases;
~ 總體數據庫 global database;
~ 組分數據庫 component database;
數據塊級 block level;
數據遷移 data migration;
數據區 data area;
~ 基本數據區 prime data area;
數據驅動 datadriven;
~ 數據驅動方法 data-driven method;
數據手冊 databook;
數據通信 data communication;
~ 數據通信網 data communication network;
~ 數據通信網絡體系 data communication network system;
~ 數據通信系統 data communication system;
~ 數據通信站 data communication station;
~ 數據通信終端 data communication terminal;
數據挖掘 data mining;
數據網絡 data network;
~ 數據網絡控制 data network control;
~ 數據網絡控制系統 data network control system;
~ 數據網絡控制中心 data network control centre;
數據系統 data system;
數據壓縮 data compression;
數據閱讀器 data reader;
數據站 data station;
數據終端 data terminal;
~ 數據終端設備 data terminal equipment;
數據轉換 data switching;
數據總線 data bus;
安全數據 safety data;
~ 安全數據集 safety data set;
~ 安全數據庫 safety data bank;
安全數據庫系統 safety data bank system;
抽象數據 abstraction data;
風速數據 air speed data;
航空數據 aeronautical data;
近似數據 approximate data;
絕對數據 absolute data;
科學數據 scientific data;
模擬數據 analog data;
輸入數據 data-input;
修正數據 adjusted data;
元數據 metadata;
原始數據 raw data;

[數量] amount; magnitude; number; quantity;
數量詞 quantifier;
~ 存在數量詞 existential quantifier;
~ 普通數量詞 universal quantifier;
充足的數量 liberal quantity;
大的數量 large quantity;
到貨數量 landed quantity;
額外數量 extra quantity;
估計數量 estimagted quantity;
平均數量 average quantity;
同等數量 equal quantity;
有限數量 limited quantity;
中等數量 moderate quantity;
裝船數量 shipped quanityt;
追加數量 additional quantity;
準確數量 exact quantity;
總數量 total quantity;
最低數量 critical mass;

[數列] number sequence; sequence;
遞減數列 decreasing sequence;
遞增數列 increasing sequence;
無界數列 unbounded sequence;

無限數列 infinite sequence;
有界數列 bounded sequence;
有限數列 finite sequence;

[數碼] (1) digit; figure; numeral; numerical code; (2) digital; (3) amount; number;
數碼不符 words and figures differ;
數碼化 digitize;

[數目] amount; number; sum;
數目字 digits; numbers; numerals;
確定數目 ascertain the number;
限制數目 limit the number;

[數年] a few years; several years;

[數日] a few days; several days;

[數天] a few days; several days;

[數位] digital;
數位詞 classifier;
數位電腦 digital computer;
數位電視 digital television;

[數學] mathematics;
數學不好 weak in math;
數學分析 mathematical analysis;
數學化 mathematization;
數學家 mathematician;
初等數學 elementary mathematics;
純粹數學 pure mathematics;
高等數學 higher mathematics;
環境數學 environmental mathematics;
計算數學 computational mathematics;
經典數學 classical mathematics;
離散數學 discrete mathematics;
理論數學 abstract mathematics; pure mathematics;
羅馬數學 Roman mathematics;
模糊數學 fuzzing mathematics;
擅長數學 good at math;
商業數學 business mathematics;
數值數學 numerical mathematics;
應用數學 applied mathematics;
有窮數學 finite mathematics;
運算數學 operational mathematics;
組合數學 combinatorial mathematics;

[數以] the number is counted by...;
數以百計 by hundreds; by the hundreds; count by the hundreds;
數以萬計 by tens of thousands; numbering tens of thousands; numerous;

[數月] a few months; several months;

[數值] figure; magnitude; numerical number; numerical value; value;

[數字] (1) digit; figure; numeral; (2) amount; quantity;
數字磁帶錄音機 digital audio tape;
數字電話網 data telephone network;
數字電視 data television;
數字仿真 digital simulation;
數字光盤 optical digital disk;
數字盒式錄音磁帶 digital compact cassette;
數字化音頻磁帶機 digital audio tape;
數字激光唱機 digital compact disc player;
數字計算機 digital computer;
數字控制 numerical control;
數字命令語言 digital command language;
數字輕便盒式磁帶機 digital audio tape;
數字聲場處理器 digital sound field processor;
數字聲頻唱盤 compact disc digital audio;
數字式磁帶計數器 digital tape computer;
數字視頻交換技術 digital video interactive technology;
數字圖書館 digital library;
數字圖像處理 digital image processing;
數字信號處理器 digital signal processor;
數字音頻 digital audio;
~數字音頻唱片 digital audio disc;
~數字音頻磁帶 digital audio tape;
數字音響 digital sound;
數字用戶信令 digital subscriber signaling;
數字自動跟踪 digital auto tracking;
核對數字 check the figures;
核實數字 verified figures;
生產數字 production figures;
輸出數字 output digit;
天文數字 astronomical figures;
玩弄數字 juggle with figures;

按數 according to the number; proportionately;
百分數 percentage; per cent;
半數 half; half the number;
報數 count off; number off;
倍數 multiple;
被乘數 multiplicand;
被除數 dividend;
被加數 summand;
被減數 minuend;
輩數兒 position in the family hierarchy; seniority in the family or clan;
變數 variable;
卜數 art of fortunetelling;
不名數 abstract number;
參數 parameter;
差數 difference in number;
常數 constant;

成數 (1) round number (2) percentage;
乘數 multiplier;
充數 make up the number; serve as a stopgap;
抽象數 abstract number;
出數兒 (of rice) rise well with cooking;
除數 divisor;
次數 frequency; number of times;
湊數 (1) make up the number or amount (2) server as a stopgap;
答數 answer; solution;
大多數 majority;
代數 algebra;
單數 (1) odd number (2) singular number;
導數 derivative;
倒數 reciprocal;
得數 answer; solution;
底數 (1) base number (2) truth or root of matter;
讀數 reading;
對數 logarithm;
多數 most; majority;
額數 fixed number of amount;
繁分數 complex fraction;
反函數 inverse function;
分數 (1) fraction (2) mark; grade;
份數 number of copies;
負數 negative number;
負指數 negative exponent;
複數 (1) complex number (2) plural number;
概數 approximate number; round number;
根指數 exponent; index;
公倍數 common multiple;
公因數 common factor;
公約數 common divisor;
夠數 enough; sufficient in quantity;
過數 count;
函數 function;
和數 sum of two or more numbers (also shortened as 和);
互質數 relatively prime;
奇函數 odd function;
奇數 odd number;
基數 (1) cardinal number (2) base;
積數 product;
級數 progression; series;
計數 count;
加數 addend;
假分數 improper fraction;
減數 subtrahend;
簡分數 common (or vulgar) fraction;
劫數 inexorable doom; predestined fate;
禮數 courtesy; etiquette;
零數 fractional amount; remainder;
零指數 zero exponent;
路數 (1) approach; way; (2) movement in martial arts; (3) exact details; inside story; ins and outs;
馬赫數 Mach number;
毛數 approximate number;
名數 concrete number;
命數 destiny; fate; lot;
模數 modulus;
逆函數 inverse function
偶數 even number;
平均數 average; mean;
全數 total number; whole amount;
權數 flexibility in tactics; shifts in politics;
如數 exactly the number or amount;
掃數 total sum; whole amount;
商數 quotient;
少數 few; minority; small number;
實數 (1) actual amount or number (2) real number;
數數兒 count; reckon;
壽數 person's destined age;
雙數 even number;
素數 prime number;
算數 count; hold; stand;
歲數 age; years;
套數 (1) cycle of songs in a traditional opera; (2) series of skills and tricks in martial art;
天數 predestination;
同餘數 congruent numbers;
維數 dimension; dimensionality;
為數 amount to; number;
尾數 odd amount in addition to the round number (usually of credit balance);
未知數 unknown number;
無理數 irrational number;
無數 countless; innumerable;
悉數 every single one; all;
係數 coefficient;
相對數 relative index;
小數 decimal;
解數 skill in martial arts;
心數 calculation; planning; scheming;
虛數 (1) unreliable figure (2) imaginary number;
序數 ordinal; ordinal number;
已知數 known number;
因變數 function
因數 factor;
隱函數 implicit function;
有理數 rational number;
有數 (1) a few; not many; only; (2) know exactly how things stand; have a definite idea of

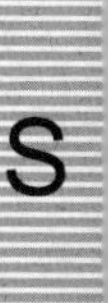

what one's doing;
餘函數 complementary function;
餘數 remainder;
原函數 primary function;
約數 (1) approximate number; (2) divisor;
招數 (1) move in chess; (2) movement in martial art; (3) device; trick;
着數 (1) move in chess; (2) movement in martialart; (3) device; trick;
真分數 proper fraction;
整數 (1) integer; whole number (2) round number (or figure);
整指數 integral exponent;
正數 positive number;
支數 number of yarn;
指數 index; index number;
質量數 mass number;
質數 prime number;
質因數 prime factor;
眾數 (of statistics) mode;
轉數 revolution;
自變數 independent variable;
自然數 natural number;
總數 sum total; total;
最佳數 optimum number;
作數 be valid; count;

shu

【豎】 (1) perpendicular; vertical; upright; (2) erect; set up; set upright; stand; (3) (in calligraphy) vertical stroke; (4) young servant;

[豎夫] coolie; servant;

[豎立] erect; set upright; stand;

[豎毛] hair standing on end;

[豎起] erect; hoist; hold up;
豎起大拇指 hold up one's thumb in approval; thumbs up;
豎起耳朵聽 prick up its ears; prick up one's ears;

[豎琴] harp;
一架豎琴 a harp;

[豎眼] angry looks;
橫眉豎眼 put on a fierce look;

[豎子] (1) boy; youngster; (2) good-for-nothing;
橫豎 in any case; anyway;

shu

【澍】 (1) seasonal rain; timely rain; (2) be saturated with rain-water;

shu

【樹】 (1) tree; (2) cultivate; grow; plant; (3) establish; set up; uphold;

[樹碑] erect a memorial tablet;
樹碑立傳 glorify sb by singing the praises of his life; glorify sb in order to secure him a place in history;

[樹本] (1) root of a tree; (2) build a good foundation for sth;

[樹叢] grove of trees;
矮樹叢 coppice; copse;

[樹大] big tree;
樹大根深 a big tree strikes roots deeply; a big tree with deep roots;
樹大蔭寬 the bigger the tree, the bigger its shade — a powerful man can easily shield his followers;
樹大招風 a person in a high position is liable to be attacked; the higher the tree, the stronger the wind;
~樹大招風，名高招怨 after honour and state, follow envy and hate; destraction pursues the great;

[樹黨] form a clique;

[樹德] establish one's virtues; examplify one's integrity;

[樹敵] antagonize; make an enemy of sb; set others against oneself;
樹敵太多 antagonize too many people; make too many enemies;
樹敵招怨 arouse a nest of hornets; bring a hornet's nest about one's ears; put one's head into a hornet's nest;
到處樹敵 arouse a nest of hornets; bring a hornet's nest about one's ears; make enemies everywhere; pit oneself against the people everywhere; raise a nest of hornets;

[樹巔] highest point of a tree; top of a tree;

[樹頂] top end of a trunk; treetop;

[樹恩] give favours;

[樹蜂] wood wasp;

[樹幹] trunk of a tree;

[樹高] height of tree;
樹高千丈，落葉歸根 a tree may grow a thousand feet high, but its leaves fall back to the roots — a person residing away from home eventually returns to his native soil; no matter how tall a tree grows, its leaves fall down to its roots;

[樹根] root of a tree;
拔樹尋根 go to the very source of sth; trace to the very roots;
樹有根，水有源 every tree has its roots and every river its source — everything has its origin;
[樹膠] gum; resin;
樹膠樹 gum tree;
[樹教] establish a religion;
[樹節] establish one's virtue; preserve one's integrity;
[樹介] icicles on a tree;
[樹籬] brush hurdle; hedge;
灌木樹籬 hedgerow;
一排樹籬 hedgerow;
[樹立] establish; set up;
樹立榜樣 set an example;
[樹林] bush; forest; trees; woods;
樹林線 timberline;
穿過樹林 walk through the woods;
紅樹林 mangrove;
見樹不見林 fail to see the wood for the trees; cannot see the wood for the trees;
小樹林 coppice; copse; grove; spinney;
一片樹林 a forest;
[樹苗] sapling; seedling;
種植樹苗 start seedlings;
[樹木] arbour; trees;
樹木辦 tree management office;
樹木倒塌 falling of trees;
樹木衰老 ageing of trees;
樹木學 dendrology;
保護樹木 protect trees;
砍伐樹木 cut down trees;
修剪樹木 prune a tree;
祇見樹木，不見森林 cannot fail to se the wood for the trees; see the minute details but miss the major issue; unable to see the forest for the trees;
[樹皮] bark;
樹皮鞣料 tanning bark;
毒樹皮 ordeal bark;
更新樹皮 renewed bark;
裂縫狀樹皮 fissured bark;
流蘇樹皮 fringe tree bark;
片狀樹皮 flake bark;
人要臉，樹要皮 face is as important to man as the bark is to the tree;
人有臉，樹有皮 "face" is as important to man as the bark is to tree;
退熱樹皮 fever bark;
[樹人] educate the young;
樹人樹木 nurture men and plant trees;
[樹上] above the tree; on the tree;
[樹蛙] tree frog;
[樹威] establish one's reputation;
[樹下] under the tree;
[樹熊] koala; wallaby;
[樹勳] establish one's name by great accomplishments;
[樹葉] foliage; leaves of a tree;
[樹蔭] bower; shade of a tree;
綠樹成蔭 the trees give welcome shade; the trees make a pleasant shade; trees shade the street;
~ 綠葉成蔭子滿枝 be burdened with children as the tree is with fruit; green leaves make a shade and the boughs are filled with fruit — girl becomes young mother, having many children;
[樹影] shadow of a tree;
[樹欲靜而風不止，子欲養而親不在] the tree wants to remain quiet, but the wind won't stop; the son wants to serve his parents in their old age, but they are no more;
[樹怨] antagonize; make an enemy of; make enemy;
[樹枝] bouch; branch; twig;
扒住樹枝 hold on to a branch;
枯樹涸枝 dried and dead trees;
一根樹枝 a branch; a branch of a tree;
[樹脂] resin;
胺醛樹脂 aldehyde resin;
醇醛樹脂 aldol resin;
鑄模樹脂 casting resin;

矮樹 low tree; bush;
桉樹 eucalyptus tree; gum tree;
白楊樹 poplar;
柏樹 cypress;
貝葉樹 Patra;
材樹 timber tree;
茶樹 tea tree;
檫樹 sassafras;
常綠樹 evergreen tree;
橙樹 orange tree;
大樹 big tree;
稻樹 fontanesia;
登臺樹 large-leaved dogwood;

冬青樹 evergreen; holly;
楓樹 (1) Chinese sweet gum (2) maple;
楓香樹 Chinese sweet gum;
公孫樹 ginkgo;
古樹 ancient tree; old tree;
歸那樹 cinchona;
桂樹 cassia;
果樹 fruiter; fruit tree;
紅樹 mangrove;
樺樹 birch; birch wood;
槐樹 ash-tree; Chinese scholartree; locust; locust tree; pagoda-tree;
黃金樹 eucalyptus;
建樹 attainment; contribute; make a contribution; score an achievement;
空桐樹 dove tree;
苦皮樹 bitter bark;
奎寧樹 cinchona;
闊葉樹 broadleaf tree;
老樹 aged tree;
栗樹 chestnut tree;
楝樹 chinaberry;
梨樹 pear;
柳樹 willow;
落葉樹 deciduous tree;
沒藥樹 myrrh;
梅樹 prune;
母樹 maternal plant;
木棉樹 kapok tree;
菩提樹 botree; pipal;
朴樹 hackberry;
七葉樹 horse chestnut;
漆樹 lacquer tree;
槭樹 maple;
琪樹 (1) jade tree in myth; (2) berry-bearing willow-shaped tree;
榕樹 banyan;
桑樹 mulberry;
杉樹 cedar;
聖誕樹 Christmas tree;
柿樹 persimmon tree;
樗樹 tree of heaven;
松柏樹 coniferous tree;
松樹 pine; pine tree;
娑羅樹 sala;
娑羅雙樹 saltree;
塌樹 toppling tree;
桃樹 peach tree;
鐵樹 cycad;
桐油樹 tung tree;
桐樹 tung tree;
烏飯樹 oriental blueberry;
梧桐樹 phoenix tree;
橡膠樹 rubber tree;
橡皮樹 rubber tree;
橡樹 oak;
小樹 sapling;
行道樹 rows of trees on both sides of the streets;
杏樹 apricot; apricot tree;
楊柳樹 willow;
楊樹 poplar;
腰果樹 rubber tree;
搖錢樹 a legendary tree that sheds coins when shaken — a ready source of money; a milch co; a money tree — a ready source of income; cash cow; money-maker; money-spinner;
椰樹 coco; coconut palm; coconut tree;
一叢樹 a clump of trees;
一棵樹 a tree;
一行樹 a line of trees; a row of trees;
一類樹 a type of tree;
一排樹 a row of trees;
榆樹 elm;
玉樹 (1) young person with talent and good looks; (2) locust tree;
育樹 cultivate trees;
月桂樹 bay tree; laurel;
棗樹 jujube tree;
樟樹 camphor tree;
針葉樹 conifer; coniferous tree;
植樹 plant trees;
種樹 plant trees;
棕櫚樹 palm;
棕樹 palm;
槭樹 maple;
柞樹 oak; oak tree;

shu

【曙】 dawn; daybreak;
［曙風］ morning breezes;
［曙光］ first light of morning; light at dawn;
假曙光 false dawn;
勝利的曙光 dawn of victory;
終於見到曙光 see light at the end of the tunnel;
［曙後星孤］ orphaned girl;
［曙日］ in the morning;
［曙色］ gray of the morning; light at daybreak; light of early dawn;

shua[1]

shua

【刷】 (1) brush; (2) brush; clean with a

brush; scrub; (3) daub with a brush; paste up with a brush; (4) eliminate; remove; (5) rustle; swish;

[刷扮] dress up; make up;
[刷恥] wipe away disgrace;
[刷課] cut class; play hooky; play truant; skip school;
[刷馬] curry a horse;
[刷清] clear of a charge;
[刷色] paint;
[刷洗] brushing; clean; scrub; wash out;
刷洗地板 scrub the floor;
內部刷洗 inside brushing;
瓶內刷洗 internal brushing;
[刷新] (1) freshen; refurbish; renovate; (2) break;
刷新紀錄 better a record; break a record, shatter;
[刷牙] brush the teeth;
[刷夜] spend the night outside with shady characters;
[刷印] print;
[刷子] brush;
鍋刷子 pot brush;
一把刷子 a brush;

板刷 scrubbing brush;
沖刷 (1) scour; wash out (2) erode;
發刷 hairbrush;
粉刷 whitewash;
鍋爐管刷 boiler tube brush;
睫毛刷 mascara brush;
馬刷 body brush;
氣刷 air brush;
石墨刷 black-lead brush;
炭刷 carbon brush;
碳刷 carbon brush;
洗瓶刷 bottlebrush;
洗刷 (1) scrub; wash and brush; (2) clear oneself of (stigma, guilt, etc.);
鞋刷 shoe brush;
牙刷 toothbrush;
印刷 print;
振刷 bestir (or exert) oneself; display vigour;
鬃刷 bristle; brush;

shua³
shua

【耍】 (1) have fun; play; (2) flourish; play with; (3) play tricks;

[耍叉] make trouble;
[耍刀舞棒] wave knives and sticks;
[耍家兒] gambler;
[耍懶] loaf; loiter;
[耍鬧] frolic; sport;
[耍弄] deceive; dupe; make a fool of; make fun of; play a trick on;
耍弄把戲 play a dirty game;
耍弄花招 perform a sleight of hand;
耍弄手段 use strategy;
[耍錢] gamble;
[耍人] make a fool of sb; make fun of sb; poke fun at others;
[耍戲] make a fool of sb;
[耍笑] (1) have fun; joke; pun fun at; (2) make fun of; play a joke on sb;
[耍子] play; sport;

玩耍 amuse oneself; play;
戲耍 make fun of; play tricks on; tease;
雜耍 varity show;

shuai¹
shuai

【衰】 decline; wane;

[衰敗] at a low ebb; at the wane; decline; decline and disintegrate; fall into decay; wane;
衰敗沒落 on the decline;
[衰憊] feeble; weak and tired; weary;
[衰弊] decadent and corrupt;
[衰變] decay; disintegration;
衰變率 decay rate;
~放射性衰變率 radioactive decay rate;
[衰耗] pad control; weaken and deteriorate;
[衰疾] decrepit and beset by illness;
[衰減] attenuation; impairment;
衰減器 attenuator;
~可調衰減器 adjustable attenuator;
~聲頻衰減器 audio attenuator;
~天線衰減器 aerial attenuator;
~吸收式衰減器 absorptive attenuator;
傳導型衰減 conductive impairment;
串音衰減 crosstalk attenuation;
交叉衰減 cross attenuation;
截止衰減 cut-off attenuation;
介質衰減 dielectric attenuation;
臨界衰減 critical attenuation;
聲衰減 acoustic attenuation;
損耗性衰減 dissipative attenuation;

圓柱狀衰減 cylindrical attenuation;
總衰減 complete attenuation;

[衰竭] collapse; exhaustion; failure; prostration; tend to end because of decline;
再衰三竭 be weakened and demoralized; nearing exhaustion; on the verge of exhaustion; virtually exhausted;

[衰倦] enfeebled and tired;

[衰老] decrepit; go out; grow old; old and feeble; senile;
衰老無用 outlive one's usefulness;
未老先衰 become senile before one's age; get old before one's time; prematurely senile;

[衰落] decay; decline; decline and fall of; fading; go downhill; go into oblivion; on the wane;
波導型衰落 duct tttpe fading;
日趨衰落 fall into decay with each passing day;
吸收性衰落 absorption fading;
振幅衰落 amplitude fading;

[衰邁] old and weak;

[衰缺] declining and full of defects;

[衰容] face of an old person;

[衰弱] debilitate; fall into a decline; feeble; not healthy; sickly; weak;
心臟衰弱 have a weak heart;

[衰颯] (1) decline; on the wane; (2) downhearted;

[衰世] age of decline and tumult;
衰世之秋 in the age of decadence;

[衰替] decline; wane;

[衰頹] discouraged and despondent; on the wane; weak and degenerate;

[衰退] decay; decline; downturn; dye out; failing; weakening;
記憶力衰退 be losing one's memory;
引起衰退 bring about its decline;

[衰亡] become feeble and die; the decline and fall; wither away;

[衰微] decline; wane;
衰微破敗 enfeebled; the plight of the declined; the road of decline and destruction;

[衰息] come to a halt;

[衰謝] old and desolate; wither and fall; wither away;

[衰朽] decrepit; feeble and decaying; old and useless;

[衰顏] face of an old person;

[衰止] dye out;

興衰 rise and decline (of a nation); ups and downs;
早衰 early ageing; premature senility;

shuai

【摔】 (1) fall; fall down; lose one's balance; tumble; (2) hurtle down; plunge; (3) break; cause to fall and break; (4) cast; fling; throw; throw to the ground; (5) get rid of; shake off;

[摔打] (1) beat; knock; (2) experience hardship; rough it; temper oneself;

[摔倒] fall; tumble;
摔倒在地上 fall to the ground;

[摔掉] (1) cast off; dash down; throw away; (2) shake off;

[摔斷] fracture;
摔斷了腿 fracture one's leg;

[摔跤] fall down; suffer a fall; trip and fall; tumble;
摔跤選手 wrestling talent;
練習摔跤 practise wrestling;
職業摔跤 professional wrestling;

[摔角] wrestle;

[摔破] (1) suffer bruises; (2) break sth by dashing it on the ground;

[摔傷] get hurt in a fall;

[摔手] swing the arms;

[摔死] be dashed to death; fall to death;

[摔碎] break into pieces after falling; shatter; smash;

shuai³

shuai

【甩】 (1) move backward and forward; swing; (2) fling; throw; toss; (3) leave sb behind; throw off;

[甩掉] cast off; give sb the air; throw away;
甩掉包袱 cast off a burden;
甩不掉 cannot get rid of; cannot shake off;

[甩髮] long, hanging wig;

[甩了] have cast away; have thrown away;

[甩賣] disposal of goods at reduced prices; markdown sale; off a clearance sale;

reduction sale; sale at a reduced price;
大甩賣 grand sale;

[甩手] (1) swing one's arms; (2) ignore; refuse to do; take no heed; wash one's hands of;

shuai⁴

shuai

【帥】 (1) commander-in-chief; (2) commander in Chinese chess; (3) command; lead; (4) comply with instructions; follow instructions; (5) dashing; smart-looking;

[帥領] command;

[帥旗] flag of the commander-in-chief;

[帥印] seal of the commander-in-chief;

大元帥 generalissimo;
掛帥 assume leadership; take command;
將帥 commanding general;
統帥 commander in chief; commander (in ancient times);
元帥 (1) marshal (2) supreme commander (in ancient times);
主帥 commander in chief;

shuai

【率】 (1) command; lead; (2) hasty; rash; (3) frank; simple and candid; straightforward; (4) generally; usually;

[率常] usually;

[率爾] abruptly; at random; casually; hastily; impetuously; rashly;
率爾操觚 write without due consideration
率爾而對 answer thoughtlessly; give a hasty reply; reply without thinking;

[率懷] follow one's bent; follow one's heart's desire;

[率領] command; head; lead;

[率然] casually; randomly;

[率任] dissolute; without self-control;

[率師] lead troops;

[率同] be accompanied by; lead all the others in;

[率悟] quick in understanding; realize quickly;

[率先] take the lead in doing sth; the first to do sth;

[率性] (1) one's natural disposition; (2) act according to the dictates of one's conscience;

[率意] (1) act on the spur of the moment; follow one's inclination; (2) with all one's sincerity;
率意孤行 act solitarily according to one's own will;

[率由] act according to; follow;
率由舊章 act in accordance with established rules; follow precedents; follow the beaten track; follow the established pattern; follow the old practice; observe the old rules;

[率允] promise at random; promise carelessly;

[率真] forthright and sincere;

[率直] blunt; candid; candour; frank; honest; straight; straightforward; unreserved;

[率眾] lead a crowd; lead a large group of people;
率眾而逃 escape with scores of one's men;
率眾前往 go at the head of many people;

表率 example; model;
草率 careless; perfunctory;
粗率 rough and careless; ill-considered;
大率 generally; roughly;
輕率 hasty; rash;
坦率 frank and open; straightforward;
統率 command;
相率 one after another;
真率 sincere; unaffected;
直率 forthright; frank;

shuai

【蟀】 cricket;

蟋蟀 cricket;

shuan¹

shuan

【拴】 (1) fasten; tie up; (2) drive a wedge between two parties;

[拴不住心] (1) unable to hold a man's heart; (2) unable to keep one's mind fixed;

[拴插] look after the food and clothing of a child;

[拴捆] bind; tie up;

[拴馬] tie up a horse;

[拴上] fasten;

[拴束] (1) pack; tie up; (2) restrain;

[拴住] (1) hold; (2) make fast; tie up;

shuan

【栓】 (1) bolt; plug; wooden peg; (2) stopper for a bottle;

[栓皮] cork;

[栓塞] embolism;

[栓子] embolus;

鞍騎形栓子 saddle embolus;

惡性栓子 malignant embolus;

反常栓子 paradoxical embolus;

膿毒性栓子 septic embolus;

脂栓子 fat embolus;

避孕栓 contraceptive suppository;

螺栓 (screw) bolt;

木栓 cork; phellem;

砲栓 breechblock;

槍栓 rifle bolt;

消火栓 fire hydrant;

血栓 thrombus;

shuan

【閂】 bolt of a door; latch of a door;

門閂 door bar; door bolt;

shuan⁴

shuan

【涮】 (1) rinse; (2) boil in a chafing pot; (3) cheat; cheat with lies; deceive; make a fool of; swindle; (4) make fun of;

[涮馬] groom a horse;

[涮洗] rinse;

shuang¹

shuang

【霜】 (1) frost; hoarfrost; (2) white and powdery; (3) coolness; grave; indifference; (4) pure and clean; virtuous;

[霜鬢] hoary hair on the temples;

[霜操] incorruptibility; moral uprightness;

[霜晨] frosty morning;

[霜刀] sharp, shining knife;

[霜涷] frost;

[霜妃] frost;

[霜害] frost injury;

[霜花] frostwork;

[霜妻] widow;

[霜天] bleak sky;

[霜威] awe; gravity and severity;

[霜雪] (1) frost and snow; (2) snowwhite;

[霜葉] leaves turning white;

[霜月] seventh month in the lunar calendar;

巴豆霜 defatted croton seed powder;

白霜 hoarfrost;

鬢霜 temples covered with white hair;

冰霜 (1) moral integrity (2) austerity;

除霜 defrosting;

風霜 hardships of a journey or of one's life;

黑霜 black frost;

金雞納霜 quinine;

抗霜 frost-resistant;

冷霜 cold cream;

砒霜 arsenic; white arsenic;

秋霜 (1) autumn frost; (2) snowy hair; (3) severity; sternness;

融霜 defrosting;

柿霜 powder on the surface of a dried persimmon;

糖霜 beet sugar; glace icing; icing;

晚霜 late frost;

無霜 frostless;

嚴霜 severe frost symbolic of cold temperament;

鹽霜 salt efflorescence;

一層霜 a layer of frost; a sheet of frost;

早霜 early frost;

終霜 latest frost;

shuang

【雙】 (1) both; dual; twin; two; (2) brace; couple; pair; (3) even; (4) double; twice; twofold;

[雙倍] double; twice the amount; twice the number; twofold;

雙倍償還 pay in twice the amount;

[雙臂] arms;

舉起雙臂 raise one's arms;

露出雙臂 bare one's arms;

張開雙臂 open one's arms wide;

[雙邊] bilateral;

雙邊的 bilateral;

雙邊對話 dyad;

雙邊關係 bilateral relations;

雙邊會談 bilateral talks;

雙邊貿易 bilateral trade; two-way trade;

雙邊協定 bilateral agreement; bilateral treaty;

[雙部] binomial;

雙部句 two-part sentence;

[雙層] bilayer; double-deck;

雙層牀 bunk bed;

雙層公共汽車 double-decker;
[雙程] round trip;
[雙重] double; dual; twofold;
雙重標準 double standard;
雙重翻譯 double translation;
雙重否定 double negative;
隻重關係從句 double relative clause;
雙重國籍 dual nationality;
雙重匯率 dual rate;
雙重活度 double activity;
雙重價格制 douvble price system;
雙重領導 dual ledership;
雙重人格 dual personality; split personality;
雙重所有格 double genitive;
[雙打] doubles;
混合雙打 mixed doubles;
[雙對] in pairs;
成雙成對 in couples; in pairs; pair off;
[雙耳鍋] double-lug pot;
[雙方] both sides; the two parties;
雙方同意 mutual consent;
[雙工] duplex;
雙工電報 duplex telegraphy;
半雙工 half duplex;
橋接式雙工 bridge duplex;
雙信道雙工 double-channel duplex;
[雙關] expression with double meaning;
雙關語 double entendre; pun;
一語雙關 double-edged remark; pun; single phrase with a double meaning;
[雙管齊下] do two things at the same time; use a double-barrelled approach;
[雙花式] (of hairstyle) symmetric waves;
[雙簧] (1) oboe; (2) collaboration between two persons;
雙簧管 oboe;
~低音雙簧管 alto oboe;
~中音雙簧管 coranglais;
唱雙簧 collaborate with each other;
演雙簧 collaboration between two persons;
[雙極] dipole;
[雙腳] both feet; the two feet;
拽開雙腳 let free one's steps — walk quickly;
[雙眉] one's brows;
雙眉緊鎖 from deeply; one's brows knit together; one's brows tightly knit;
緊鎖雙眉 contract the eyebrows; knit the eyebrows; one's eyebrows are knit in a frown;
[雙面] double-edged; double-faced; reversible; two-sided;
[雙名] given name consists of two characters; binomial;
[雙目] both eyes;
雙目鏡 binocular;
~紅外雙目鏡 infrared binoculars;
~夜視雙目鏡 night-vision binoculars;
雙目炯炯 one's eyes are piercingly bright;
雙目深陷 the eyes wax hollow;
雙目失明 become blind; blind in both eyes; go blind in both eyes; lose one's eyesight; lose the sight of both eyes;
雙目無神 lacklustre in one's eyes; one's eyes are lustless;
淚湧雙目 tears come into one's eyes; tears start to the eyes;
[雙頻] dual band;
[雙棲] live together as man and wife;
[雙親] one's parents;
[雙全] complete in both respects; possessing both;
父母雙全 both parents are alive;
智勇雙全 possess both wisdom and courage;
[雙拳] two fists;
雙拳難敵四手 not even Hercules could contend against two;
[雙人] double; two persons; twin;
雙人牀 double bed;
雙人房 double room; twin room;
雙人舞 a dance for two persons;
雙人組合 double act;
[雙日] even days;
[雙色] two-tone;
雙色植物 amphichrome;
[雙生] twins;
雙生女 twin sisters;
雙生子 twin brothers;
聯體雙生 conjuncted twins;
相以雙生 concordant twins;
[雙手] both hands; two hands;
雙手奉上 present respectfully with both hands;
雙手拱讓 give away sth to sb with both hands;
雙手合十 put one's palms together devoutly;

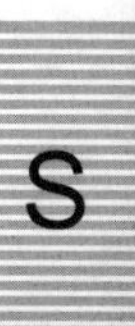

雙手靈巧 have a light hand;
雙手贊成 all for it; raise both hands in approval; support fully;
交叉雙手 fold one's hands;
[雙數] even number;
[雙雙] in pairs;
雙雙對對 in pairs and couples;
雙宿雙飛 keep each other's company; live like man and wife; sleep and move together;
[雙瞳翦水] clear, beautiful eyes of a pretty girl;
[雙腿] legs;
雙腿交叉 with one's legs crossed;
雙腿修長的 leggy;
[雙喜臨門] a double blessing has descended upon the house; two happy events come at the same time;
[雙向] bidirectional; bilateral; double-direction; two-way;
雙向承包制 double-directioncontracting system;
雙向交流 two-way exchanges;
雙向流動 bidrectional flow;
雙向式影像 two-way video;
雙向選擇 bilateral selection;
[雙星] binary star; double star;
分光雙星 spectroscopic binary;
[雙性的] AC/DC; ambisextrous; bisexual;
[雙眼] eyes;
雙眼凹陷 have sunken eyes;
雙眼井 twin-mouthed well;
雙眼皮 double-fold eyelid;
~割雙眼皮 undergo an operation for double-fold eyelids;
望穿雙眼 wear out one's eyes by gazing anxiously;
[雙氧水] hydrogen peroxide;
[雙語] bilingual;
雙語數據庫 bilingual database;
雙語體現象 diglossia;
雙語現象 bilingualism;
~複合雙語現象 compound bilingualism;
雙語知識庫 bilingual knowledge bank;
雙語制 bilingualism;

混雙 mixed doubles;
那雙 that pair;
無雙 matchless; peerless; unique; unparalleled; unrivaled;
一雙 (1) a couple; a pair; braces; dual; twain; (2) a pair of;

shuang
【瀧】 a river in Hunan;

shuang
【孀】 widow;
[孀婦] widow;
[孀居] widow; live in widowhood;

孤孀 widow;
居孀 live as a widow;
遺孀 relict; widow;

shuang³

shuang
【爽】 (1) bright; clear; crisp; (2) frank; openhearted; straightforward; (3) feel well; (4) fail; lose; miss;
[爽脆] (1) brisk; keen and energetic; (2) sharp and clear; (3) frank; outright; straightforward; (4) crisp and tasty;
爽脆的 crunchy;
[爽當] agile; brisk;
[爽德] depart from virtue; lose virtue;
[爽慧] adroit; agile; intelligent;
[爽口] palatable; tasty; tasty and refreshing;
[爽快] brisk and neat; frank; readily; with alacrity;
辦事爽快 work readily and briskly;
不爽快 (1) not frank; (2) out of sorts;
爽爽快快 with a good grace;
為人爽快 frank and straightforward;
心裏爽快 at ease;
[爽朗] candid; frank and open; hearty; straightforward;
爽朗的笑聲 hearty laughter;
純樸爽朗 honest and frank;
天氣爽朗 it is serene;
[爽利] brisk and neat; efficient and able;
[爽然] at a loss; dejected; disappointed; discouraged;
爽然頓失 be banished from one's breast;
爽然若失 at a loss; not to know what to do;
[爽身粉] talc; talcum powder;
[爽神] refreshing;
[爽心] cheerful; gratified; pleased; satisfied;
爽心悅目 entertaining; refreshing to the heart and pleasing to the eye;
[爽信] fail to keep a promise;

[爽性] may just as well;
[爽約] break an appointment; fail to keep an appointment; stand sb up;
[爽直] candid; forthright; frank; outspoken; straightforward;
爽直不羈 by nature a frank and straightforward fellow;
稟性爽直 frank by nature;

不爽 (1) not well; in a bad mood; (2) accurate; without discrepancy;
豪爽 forthright; straightforward;
滑爽 smooth and comfortable;
清爽 (1) fresh and cool; (2) relaxed; relieved;
颯爽 of martial bearing; valiant;
直爽 frank; candid; forthright;

shui²
shui
【誰】 a pronunciation of 誰；

shui³
shui
【水】 (1) Adam's ale; Adam's wine; aqua; didn't oughter; dirty daughter; water; (2) river; (3) general term for rivers, lakes, seas, etc.; water; (4) juice; liquid; (5) flood; (6) a surname;
[水壩] dam;
[水杯] water glass;
[水泵] water pump;
[水筆] (1) water-colour paintbrush; (2) fountain pen;
[水標] water mark;
[水錶] water gauge; water meter;
[水兵] marine; sailor; seaman;
二等水兵 able seaman;
見習水兵 ordinary seaman;
三等水兵 ordinary seaman;
一等水兵 able seaman; leading seaman;
[水波] ripples of water;
[水彩] watercolour;
水彩畫 watercolour painting;
[水草] (1) water and grass; (2) waterweeds;
水草豐美 a place with plenty of water and lush grass; lush pasture;
一根水草 a blade of waterweed;
逐水草而居 live where there is water and grass; migrate to wherever water and grass are available; move from place to place in search of water and grass;
[水產] aquatic products; marine products;
[水程] sea voyage; voyage by water;
[水池] pond; pool; water tank;
[水出有源] all water has sources;
[水到] when water comes;
水到船行 only when there is water can a boat sail;
水到渠成 when conditions are ripe, success will come; where water flows, a channel is formed;
[水道] watercourse; waterway;
通航水道 navigable waterway;
網狀水道 braided channel;
[水稻] paddy; rice;
雜交水稻 hybrid rice;
[水滴] water drops;
水滴集多成大海，經歷集多成學問 water drops collected together form a sea and experience gathered together becomes knowledge;
水滴石穿 a constant drip will wear a hole in a stone; constant dripping will wear the stone; constant effort brings success; dripping water wears through rock; liitle strokes fell great oaks;
[水底] at the bottom of water;
水底撈月 dredge the moon out from the bottom of the water; effort in vain;
水底植物 benthopyte;
[水電] water and electricity;
[水貂] mink;
[水痘] chicken pox;
[水粉畫] qouache;
[水分] water;
水分循環 hydrological cycle;
黏合水分 adhesive moisture;
無效水分 unavailable water;
吸收水分 absorption moisture;
有效水分 available water;
最適水分 optimum moisture;
[水管] waterpipe;
[水國] watery region;
[水果] fruit; slump;
水果蛋糕 fruit cake;
水果店 fruit store;
水果罐頭 canned fruit;
水果軟糖 fruit jelly;
水果商 fruiterer;
水果糖 fruit drops;
多汁水果 rich fruit;

罐頭水果 canned fruit;
燴水果 stewed fruit;
牆栽水果 wall fruit;
熱帶水果 tropical fruit;
軟水果 soft fruit;
酸味水果 acid fruit;
糖水水果 compote;
一籃水果 a basket of fruit;
應時水果 fruit in season;
種植水果 grow fruit;

[水合] hydration;
水合物 hydrate
離子水合 ionic nydration;
直接水合 direct hydration;

[水紅] pink;

[水壺] (1) kettle; (2) water flash;

[水化] hydration;
水化器 hydrator;
水化物 hydrate;

[水患] flood disaster; floods;

[水火] (1) water and fire; (2) incompatible; (3) miseries;
水火不辭 forge ahead unflinchingly even if one has to go through fire and water; shun no difficulty and danger and not to hesitate to lay down one's life;
水火不相容 agree like cats and dogs; agree like pickpockets in a fair; as incompatible as fire and water; diametrically contrary; exclude each other like fire and water; irreconcilable as fire and water; mutual aversion; mutually antagonistic; water and fire do not mix;
水火無情 fire and water have no mercy; floods and fires have no mercy for anybody; water and fire are merciless; water and fire show no sympathy to men;
不辭水火 through thick and thin;
勢如水火 incompatible as fire and water; mutually antagonistic;

[水貨] smuggled goods;
水貨客 parallel trader;

[水解] hydrolysis;
水解產物 hydrolyzate;
水解性敗壞 hydrolytic spoilage;
分段水解 graded hydrolysis;
酸性水解 acidic hydrolysis;
主水解 main hydrolysis;

[水井] well;

[水浸] flooding;
嚴重水浸 serious flooding;

[水盡魚飛] rats desert a sinking ship; when the water fails the fish fly;

[水晶] crystal;
水晶飽 bun containing sweetened pork fat;
水晶宮 crystal palace;
水晶球 crystal ball;
水晶糖 crystal candies;

[水靜流深] smooth water runs deep; still waters run deep;

[水酒] diluted wine;
略備水酒 have prepared some ordinary wine;

[水坑] pool; puddle;

[水庫] reservoir;
一座水庫 a reservoir;

[水來土掩] if water approaches, a dam is made from the earth;
水來土掩，兵來將迎 if water approaches, a dam is made from the earth; if soldiers approach, we will send soldiers to stop them;

[水雷] mine;
沉底水雷 bottom mine;
反潛水雷 antisubmarine mine;
淺江河水雷 amphibious mine;
音響水雷 acoustic mine;

[水冷] water-cooling;

[水裏來，湯裏去] easy come, easy go; light come, light go; lightly come, lightly go;

[水力] hydraulic power; water power;
水力發電站 hydroelectric station; hydropower station;
水力開採 hydraulic mining;
水力學 hydraulics;
~井筒水力學 wellbore hydraulics;
~明渠水力學 hydraulics of open channels;

[水利] (1) water conservancy; (2) irrigation works;
水利工程 irrigation works; water conservation project;
~考察水利工程 water conservation projects;
水利局 water conservancy bureau;
水利設施 water conservancy facilities;
水利資源 water resources;
興修水利 build irrigation works;

[水簾] cascade; waterfall;
[水量] amount of water; water volume;
[水療] spa;
水療項目 spa menu;
熱石水療 hot stone therapy;
[水流] water current; water flow;
水流千轉歸大海 a river with a thousand twists and turns will eventually flow into the sea; follow the river and you'll get to the sea; no matter how far a man goes, he will eventually come back home;
水流湍急 rapid flow; rushing current; the current is swift;
交叉水流 cross-current;
[水龍] fire hose;
水龍捲 waterspout;
水龍頭 cock; faucet; tap; water tap;
~ 廚房水龍頭 kitchen tap;
~ 打開水龍頭 turn on the taps;
~ 冷水龍頭 cold tap;
~ 熱水龍頭 hot tap;
~ 洗面器水龍頭 basin faucet;
~ 浴室水龍頭 bath tap;
[水漏] water clock;
[水路] (1) watercourse; waterway; (2) by water;
水路偷渡者 illegal immigrants via sea route;
國際水路 international waterway;
[水陸] land and water;
水陸畢陳 a feast in which figures every delicacy from land and sea;
水陸兩用 amphibious;
~ 水陸兩用車 amphicar;
水陸雜陳 both land and sea food mixed together;
[水落石出] argue the matter out; come out in the wash; come to light; everything is thrashed out; the time will come to reveal the whole truth; the truth comes out; the truth is out;
查個水落石出 get to the bottom of a matter; investigate sth thoroughly;
[水綠] light green;
[水門] floodgate; sluice; water gate;
水門汀 cement;
[水密] watertight;
[水蜜桃] honey peach;
[水面] water surface;
躥出水面 leap out of water;
浮出水面 float on the surface;
露出水面 rise to the surface of the water;
[水明如鏡] the water is as clear as a mirror;
[水磨石] terrazzo;
[水母] jellyfish;
[水泥] cement;
水泥廠 cement plant;
水泥成品 finished cement;
水泥叢林 concrete jungle;
水泥攪拌機 cement mixer;
高鋁水泥 high alumina cement;
建築水泥 building cement;
攪拌水泥 agitate the cement;
快凝水泥 accelerated cement;
耐火水泥 furnace cement;
耐酸水泥 acid-proof cement;
凝膠水泥 gel cement;
鋪水泥 lay cement;
散裝水泥 bulk cement;
石棉水泥 asbesto cement;
速凝水泥 accelerated cement;
一袋水泥 a bag of cement; a sack of cement;
優質水泥 quality cement;
[水鳥] aquatic birds; water birds; waterfowls;
[水牛] buffalo;
一群水牛 a herd of buffaloes;
[水泡] (1) bubbles; (2) blister;
水泡性濕疹 eczema vesiculosum;
[水疱] blister; bulla;
水疱疹 tetter;
膿性水疱 vesicopustule;
移動性水疱 ambulant blister;
[水砲] water cannon;
高壓水砲 water cannon;
[水瓢] water ladle;
[水平] (1) level; standard; (2) horizontal;
水平測試 proficiency test;
水平考試 proficiency test;
水平如鏡 the surface of the water is as smooth as a mirror;
水平線 horizontal line;
低水平 low level;
基本水平 basic level;
~ 基本水平分類 basic level category;
技術水平 technical level;
能力水平 ability level;
生產水平 production level;
適應水平 adaptation level;
先進水平 advanced standards;

~國際先進水平 advanced international standards;
~超越國際先進水平 surpass advanced international standards;
~達到國際先進水平 reach the advanced international standards;
~趕上國際先進水平 catch up with advanced international standards;
~接近國際先進水平 approach advanced international standards;
~世界先進水平 advanced international standards; the world's advanced levels;
眼光水平 ye-level;
一般水平 average;
~達到一般水平 up to the average;

[水萍] duckweed;

[水瓶] water-bottle;

[水潑不進，針插不進] watertight and impenetrable

[水氣] moisture; steam; water vapour;

[水槍] water gun; water pistol;
玩具水槍 squirt gun; water pistol;

[水芹] cress; water fennel;

[水清] the water is clear;
水清見底 the water in the stream is so clear that one can see down to the bottom;
水清可鑒 the water is so clear that you can see your reflection in it;
水清無魚 there is no fish in clear water;

[水球] (1) water polo; (2) water polo ball;
水球運動 water polo;

[水渠] ditch; trench;

[水溶性] solubility;

[水乳] water and milk;
水乳不分 mix like water and milk;
~如水乳不分 inseparable; mix like water and milk;
水乳交融 hand and glove with each other; in harmony like water and milk; in perfect harmony;

[水上] above the water; on the water; over the water;
水上芭蕾舞 water ballet;
水上城市 aquapolis;
水上飛機 aquaplane;
水上街市 overwater market;
水上旅館 aquatel;
水上人家 boat dwelllers;
水上體操 aquathenics;
水上運動 aquatic sports; water sports;

[水杓] water ladle;

[水蛇] water snake; aquatic snake;

[水深] depth of water;
水深火熱 abyss of suffering; depths of misery; keep in suffering; live in great misery;
水深流急 the water is deep and the current fast;
流靜水深 smooth water runs deep; still waters run deep;

[水勢] (1) flow of the water; (2) direction of the flowing water;

[水手] crewman; deck hand; mariner; sailor; seaman;
水手艙 forecastle;
水手領 crew neck;
水手長 boatswain; bosun;
水手裝 sailor suit;
當水手 work as a sailor;
普通水手 deckhand;
一個水手 a sailor;
有經驗的老水手 old salt;

[水塔] water tower;

[水獺] otter;

[水苔] duckweed;

[水潭] pond; pool;

[水塘] pond; pool;

[水天一色] the sea seems to melt into the sky; the water and the sky are of one hue; the water and the sky merge in one colour;

[水田] paddy field; rice field;

[水聽器] hydrophone;
電容水聽器 capacitor hydrophone;
浮標水聽器 buoyed hydrophone;
全向水聽器 all directional hydrophone;

[水亭] pavilion on the water;

[水桶] bucket; pail;

[水土] (1) water and soil; (2) natural environment and climate;
水土保持 conservation of soil and water;
水土病 acclimation fever;
水土不服 not acclimatized; unable to adjust to a place;
水土流失 soil and water erosion;
保持水土 conserve water and soil;
服水土 acclimation; acclimatization;
~不服水土 not acclimatized;

[水汪汪] bright and attractive eyes of a

woman;
水汪汪的眼睛 watery eyes;
[水位] water level; water mark;
水位線 water mark;
~低水位線 low water mark;
低水位 low water;
地下水位 water table;
高水位 high water;
~高水位期 high water;
~高水位線 high water mark;
[水文] hydrographic;
水文學 hydrology;
水文站 hydrographic station;
[水螅] polyp;
[水系] river system;
[水下] submerged; under water;
水下爆炸 underwater burst;
[水仙] Chinese sacred lily; daffodial; dilly; lily; narcissus;
水仙花 daffodil; dilly; narcissus;
~一棵水仙花 a daffodil;
~一束水仙花 a bunch of daffodils;
紅口水仙 pinkstar lily;
[水鄉] region of rivers and lakes;
水鄉春色 spring in a waterside village; spring time in a waterfront village;
水鄉澤國 land flooded with water;
[水箱] cistern; water tank;
[水向低處流，人往高處走] water always flows from a higher to a lower level, but everybody has an ambition to rise higher up in society;
[水榭亭閣] pavilions, towers and terrace halls on the water;
[水瀉] diarrhea;
[水心] centre of a stream;
[水星] Mercury;
[水性] (1) unpredictable temperament; (2) water condition;
水性楊花 easy to seduce; fickle and lascivious; wanton; woman of easy virtue; woman of loose morals;
[水鴨] teal;
鹹水鴨 salted teal;
[水壓] water pressure;
[水淹] in flood;
[水翼船] hovercraft; hydrofoil craft; hydroplane;
[水翼艇] hydrofoil;
反潛水翼艇 antisubmarine hydrofoil;
雙體水翼艇 twin-hull hydrofoil;
載貨水翼艇 cargo hydrofoil;
[水銀] mercury;
水銀燈 mercury vapour lump;
水銀弧光燈 mercury arc lump;
[水印] watermark;
局部水印 localized watermark;
陰暗水印 shade craft watermark;
[水有源，木為本] a stream has its source; a tree has its root;
[水域] water area;
[水源] (1) waterhead; (2) source of water;
林盡水源 the trees end where the water begins;
[水雲母] hydromica;
[水運] transportation by water;
水運會 swimming gala;
水運碼頭 a port handling river or ocean cargo;
[水災] flood disaster; floods;
水災破壞 flood damage;
[水葬] burial at sea; burial in the sea;
[水閘] floodgate; water gate;
火閘管理員 lock keeper;
[水戰] naval warfare;
[水漲船高] boats go up with the level of the water;
水漲船高，泥多佛大 boats go up with the level of the water; the Buddha becomes big with the amount of clay;
[水至清則無魚] fish do not come when water is too clear; water which is too clean has few fish; when the water is too clear there are no fish — one should not demand absolute purity;
[水蛭] leech;
[水滯生蟲蛆，人懶思淫欲] as worms are bred in a stagnant pool, so are evil thoughts in idleness;
[水質] water quality;
水質保護 water quality conservation;
水質監測 water quality monitoring;
水質檢驗 water quality monitoring;
水質評價 water quality assessment;
[水中撈月] catch the moon in the water; fish in the air; plough the sand; fruitless attempt; pluck the moon from the lake; vain and ineffectual effort;

[水腫] edema;
水腫病 edema disease;
水腫形成 edematization;
水腫性丹毒 edemerysipelas;
惡性水腫 malignant edema;
肺水腫 edema pulmonary; pulmonary edema;
風濕性水腫 rheumatismal edema;
骨膜水腫 periosteodema;
饑餓性水腫 hunger swelling;
假水腫 pseudoedema;
瞼水腫 hydrohlepharon;
局限性水腫 circumscribed edema;
流行性水腫 epidemic dropsy;
黏液水腫 myxedema;
普遍性水腫 hyposarca;
氣性水腫 gaseous edema;
全身水腫 hyposarca;
全身性水腫 anasarca;
腎病性水腫 nephrotic edema;
腎性水腫 renal edema;
實質水腫 solid edema;
胎兒水腫 fetal hydrops;
胎盤水腫 placental edema;
特發性水腫 idiopathic edema;
萎縮性水腫 atrophedema;
心性水腫 cardiac edema;
心源性水腫 cardiac edema;
心臟水腫 cardiac edema;
血管神經性水腫 angioneurotic edema;
壓痕性水腫 pitting edema;
炎性水腫 inflammatory edema;
陰囊水腫 hydrocele;
隱性水腫 invisible edema;
營養不良性水腫 alimentary edema;
暫時性水腫 edema fugax;
脂肪水腫 lipedema;
趾水腫 dactyledema;
終末期水腫 terminal edema;
中毒性水腫 toxic edema;
周期性水腫 periodic edema;
足水腫 podedema;

[水柱] water column;

[水準] level; standard;
水準支撐 horizontal support;
到達水準 up to standard;

[水漬] (1) drench; (2) water stains; watermarks;
水漬貨 goods with water stains;

[水族] aquatic animals;
水族館 aquarium;

氨水 ammonia spirit; ammonia water; aqua ammonia;
白水 (1) plain boiled water; (2) clean water;
背水 with one's back to the river;
碧水 blue waters;
冰水 ice water; icy water;
踋水 tread water;
踩水 tread water;
茶水 tea or boiled water (supplied to walkers, trippers, etc.)
摻水 (1) dilute; (2) fill with half truth;
攙水 water down;
潮水 tidewater;
吃水 (1) drinking water; (2) absorb water;
池水 pond water;
抽水 draw water; pump water;
春水 spring water;
淡水 fresh water;
滴水 drip;
地表水 surface water;
地下水 groundwater;
跌水 drop;
耳積水 hydrotis;
發水 flood;
反水 defect; turn one's coat;
防水 waterproof;
放水 (1) turn on the water (2) (of a reservoir) draw off;
肥水 rich water;
廢水 liquid waste; waste water;
糞水 manure and urine;
風水 fengshui; geomancy;
泭水 swim;
腹水 ascites; ascitic fluid;
泔水 swill; slops; hogwash;
鋼水 molten steel;
供水 water supply;
溝水 ditch-water;
灌水 pour water into sth;
滾水 boiled water; boiling water;
海水 seawater; the sea;
汗水 perspiration; sweat;
喝水 (1) drink water; (2) suffer losses in business;
河水 river water;
洪水 deluge; flood; torrent; waterflood;
紅藥水 mercurochrome;
湖水 lake water;
划水 arm pull;
滑水 water ski;
匯水 remittance fee;
會水 good at swimming;

S

渾水 muddy water;
活水 flowing water; fresh current; running water;
禍水 force compared to flood, causing trouble, disaster, etc.;
積水 hydrops;
汲水 draw water;
擊水 swim;
集水 catchment;
給水 (1) feed water;(2) supply water;
澗水 gully stream;
江水 river water;
洚水 flood; inundation;
澆水 water a plant;
膠水 glue; mucilage;
結晶水 crystal water; water of crystallization;
井水 well water;
靜水 still water;
開水 (1) boiling water; (2) boiled water;
可飲用的水 drinkable water; potable water;
口水 dribble; slaiva; slobber;
枯水 low water;
苦水 (1) bitter water; brackish water; (2) gastric secretion; (3) suffering; (4) bitterness; misery; suffering;
礦泉水 mineral water;
淚水 tear; teardrop;
冷水 (1) cold water; (2) unboiled water;
瀝水 waterlogging caused by excessive rainfall;
涼水 (1) cold water; (2) unboiled water;
兩點水 one of the Chinese character components;
領水 (1) inland waters; (2) territorial waters;
流水 (1) running water; (2) turnover in business;
鹵水 (1) bittern; (2) brine;
露水 dew;
落水 (1) fall into water; (2) go astray; degenerate; sink into;
墨水 (1) book learning; (2) ink; (3) prepared Chinese ink;
奶水 milk;
腦積水 hydrocephalus;
逆水 against the current;
膿水 pus;
暖水 warm water;
怕水 water funk;
排水 drain; drain away water; drain off water; drainage; draining;
噴水 dabble; spray; water spray;
汽水 (1) aerated water; carbonated drink; mineral waters; soda water; soft drinks; (2) steamwater; vapour-water;
潛水 (1) go under water; drive (2) phreatic water;
淺水 shallow water;
鏹水 corrosive acid; strong acid;
清水 branch water; clear water;
秋水 (1) autumn water; (2) clear and beautiful eyes of a girl;
泅水 swim;
取水 get water;
泉水 spring; spring water;
染髮水 hair dye;
熱水 hot water;
融水 melt water;
軟水 soft water;
散水 apron;
三點水 one of the Chinese character components;
洒水 sprinkle water;
撒水 spray water; sprinkle water;
灑水 purling; spill water; sprinkle water; watering;
山水 (1) mountains and rivers; scenery with hills and waters; (2) traditional Chinese painting of mountains and waters; landscape; (3) water from a mountain;
上水 feed water to a steam engine, radiator.; upper reaches; upstream;
燒水 boil water; heat water;
涉水 wade; wade into the water;
深水 deepwater;
生水 unboiled water;
昇水 premium;
腎積水 hydronephrosis;
聖水 holy water; water at some temple, credited with performing cures;
失水 loss of water; (of water) run off; seep into the ground;
十滴水 “10 drops”, a popular medicine for summer ailments;
石灰水 limewash;
受水 intake;
熟水 boiled water;
雙氧水 hydrogen peroxide;
順水 downstream; with the stream;
死水 backwater; dead water; stagnant water; unfree water;
縮水 shrink;
泰水 mother-in-law;
潭水 deep water;
蹚水 tread water; wade water;
糖水 syrup;
天水 sky and water;
甜水 (1) fresh water; (2) sugar water;
挑水 shoulder water with a pole;
跳水 dive; diving; jump into the water;

貼水 agio;
鐵水 molten iron;
停水 cut off the water; cut off the water supply;
透水 pervious to water;
吐水 guttation;
脱水 dehydration; deprivation (or loss) of body fluids; dewatering;
外水 extra income;
王水 aqua regia;
尾水 tail water;
溫水 lukewarm water;
污水 drainage; foul water; polluted water; sewage; waste water;
霧水 dew;
吸水 absorb water;
溪水 brook; stream;
嬉水 paddle;
細水 small stream;
戲水 play in water; play with water;
下水 (1) be launched; enter the water; (2) launch a boat; (3) fall into evil ways; take to evildoing; (4) downriver; downstream;
鹹水 saline water; salt water;
涎水 saliva;
香蕉水 banana oil;
香水 fragrance; perfume; scent; toilet water; wash;
硝鏹水 nitric acid;
小水 urine;
瀉水 drain off water;
薪水 pay; salary; wages;
溴水 bromine water;
鬚後水 aftershave;
蓄水 retain water;
血水 (1) blood; (2) bloodstained water;
鹽水 brine; salt water;
眼積水 hydrophthalmos;
羊水 amnion fluid; amniotic fluid;
揚水 pump up water
藥水 (1) liquid medicine; medicinal liquid; (2) lotion;
一杯水 a cup of water; a glass of water;
一大口水 a gulp of water;
一擔水 a bucket of water;
一滴水 a drop of water;
一點水 some water;
一缸水 a jar of water;
一股水 a jet of water;
一罐水 a jar of water;
一壺水 a jug of water;
一口水 a draught of water; a drink of water; a mouthful of water; a swallow of water;
一滿桶水 a bucketful of water;
一盆水 a basin of water;
一片水 a body of water; a stretch of water;
一瓢水 a ladle of water;
一瓶水 a bottle of water;
一灘水 a pool of water;
一桶水 a barrel of water; a bucket of water; a cask of water; a pail of water; a tub of water;
一汪水 a pool of water; a puddle of water;
一小口水 a sip of water;
一小桶水 a breaker of water;
一舀子水 a ladle of water;
引水 (1) diversion; draw or channel water; (2) pilot a ship into harbour;
飲水 drinking water;
飲用水 drinking water; potable water;
硬水 hard water;
油水 (1) grease; (2) profit;
游水 swim;
魚水 fish and water;
雨水 (1) rain; rainfall; rainwater; (2) Rain Water (2nd solar term);
遠水 distant water;
運水 transport water;
沾水 soak in water;
漲水 swell; swell of a river;
蒸餾水 distilled water;
止水 stagnant water; still water;
治水 prevent floods by water control; regulate rivers and watercourses; river control; tame a river;
重力水 free water; gravitational water;
重水 heavy;
貯水 store water;
注水 water flooding;
逐水 relieve oedema or abdominal distension through diuresis or purgation;
濁水 turbid water;
紫藥水 gentian violet;
自來水 (1) running water; tap water (2) water supply;
走水 be on fire;

shui4

shui

【帨】 handkerchief; kerchief;

shui

【稅】 duties; taxes;
［稅單］ tax form; tax list;
［稅額］ amount of tax to be paid;
［稅法］ tariff law; tax law;

[税後] after tax;
税後淨利 net profit after tax;
税後利潤 after tax profit;
税後收入 after-tax earnings;
[税基] tax base;
[税金] tax due; tax money;
[税捐] duty; tax; tax and levy;
[税課] levy; taxation;
[税款] tax due; tax money; tax payment;
税款專用 earmarking of taxes;
[税吏] tax collector; tax official;
[税利] tax and profit;
税利分流 separating taxes from profits;
[税率] duty rate; tax rate;
比例税率 proportional tax rate;
普通税率 normal rate; normal tariff;
限制税率 limited tax rate;
一般税率 general tariff;
優惠税率 preferential duty rate;
最低税率 minimum rate; minimum tariff;
[税收] tax revenue;
税收參考價格 tax reference price;
税收負擔 tax burden;
税收管理 tax revenue management;
税收管轄權 tax jurisdiction;
税收政策 tax policy;
~加強税收政策 tighten tax collection;
財政税收 fiscal levy;
[税務] affairs pertaining to taxation; tax administration;
税務顧問 tax adviser;
税務機關 tax authority;
税務局 tax bureau; tax office;
税務會計 tax accounting;
税務所 tax collecting station;
税務員 tax collector; tax official;
[税則] customs order; customs tariff; tariff schedule; tax regulations;
[税制] taxation; tax system;

版税 royalty (on books);
保税 keep in bond;
報税 (1) report tax returns; (2) declare dutiable goods;
暴利税 windfall tax;
比例税 proportional tax;
避税 evade duty; evade tax; tax avoidance; tax dodge; tax evasion;
補税 (1) pay a tax one has evade (2) pay an overdue tax;
財税 tax and finance;
查税 tax inspection;
抽税 levy a tax;
出口税 export duty;
從價税 ad valorem duty;
從量税 specific duty;
地產税 landed estate taxes;
丁税 poll tax;
法人税 corporation tax;
房產税 house tax;
附加税 additional tax; supertax; surtax;
賦税 taxes;
港口税 import duty;
個人所得税 individual income tax;
工商税 industrial and commercial taxes;
貢税 tribute and taxes;
關税 customs; customs duties; duty; tariff;
過境税 transit duty;
貨物税 commodity tax;
減税 abate a tax; tax abatement; tax reduction;
間接税 indirect tax;
交税 pay tax;
繳税 pay tax;
進口税 import duty;
捐税 taxes and levies;
抗税 tax resistance;
課税 charge duty; duty assessment; levy duty;
累進税 progressive tax; progressive taxation;
利潤税 profit tax;
利税 profit and tax;
漏税 evade payment of a tax; evade taxation; tax dodging;
瞞税 conceal facts to proper taxation;
免税 duty-free; exemption from duty; free of duty; remission of tax; tax exemption; tax-free;
納税 pay duty; pay tax; tax payment;
農業税 agricultural tax;
契税 tax on landownership registration;
欠税 tax arrears;
人頭税 capitation; poll tax;
商品税 commodity tax;
商業税 commercial tax;
上税 pay taxes;
實物税 tax paid in kind;
收税 collect taxes;
所得税 income tax;
碳税 carbon tax;
逃税 avoid tax payment; evade a tax; tax avoidance; tax evasion;
通過税 transit duties;
通行税 transit duty;
偷税 evade taxes;

屠宰税 tax on slaughtering animals;
土地税 land tax;
退税 tax refund; tax reimbursement;
完税 duty paid; pay taxes;
銷售税 sales tax;
印花税 stamp duty; stamp tax;
營業税 business tax; transactions tax; turnover tax;
雜税 irregular taxes; miscellaneous taxes;
增值税 value-added tax;
徵税 levy tax; tax collection; taxation;
直接税 direct tax;
重税 heavy taxation;
租税 land tax and other levies;

shui

【睡】 sleep;
[睡車] sleeper; sleeping car;
[睡袋] sleeping bag;
[睡得] sleep;
睡得安穩 sleep easy;
睡得正甜 deep sleep; be sleeping a sound sleep; sleep soundly;
[睡過頭] oversleep;
[睡覺] asleep; conk off; conk out; doze; fall asleep; fall into a deep sleep; get to sleep; go bye-bye; go to bed; go to roost; go to sleep; have a nap; have a sleep; heavy with sleep; hit the hay; hit the pad; hit the sack; hit the slats; kip; kip down; put sb to sleep; roll in; sack in; sack out; shut-eye; sleep; sleep a dead sleep; slumber;
睡覺時間 time for bed;
白天睡覺 sleep in the daytime;
不睡覺 stay up;
去睡覺 go bye-bye;
上牀睡覺 hit the sack;
睡大覺 have a long sleep;
睡午覺 take an afternoon nap;
晚點睡覺 have a late sleep;
想睡覺 feel sleepy;
早點睡覺 have an early night;
[睡蓮] pygmy water lily; water lily;
白睡蓮 white pond lily;
[睡帽] nightcap;
[睡夢] in one's dreams; in sleep; sleep; slumber;
[睡眠] brother of death; sleep; slumber; somnus;
睡眠病 sleeping disease; sleeping sickness;
睡眠不足 insufficient sleep; not have enough sleep; want of sleep;
睡眠發生 hypnogenesis;
睡眠反射 hypnic jerks;
睡眠過度 hypersomnolence;
~原發性睡眠過度 primary hypersomnia;
睡眠後麻痺 postdormital paralysis;
睡眠開關 sleep switch;
睡眠前麻痺 predormital paralysis;
睡眠性麻痺 sleep paralysis;
睡眠障礙 dyssomnia; sleep disorder;
慢波睡眠 slow wave sleep;
陣發性睡眠 paroxysmal sleep;
[睡魔] extreme sleepiness;
[睡袍] night-robe; sleeping gown;
女式睡袍 nightdress; nightgown;
[睡下] lie down;
[睡鄉] (1) dreamland; land of Nod; (2) state of being asleep;
[睡醒] wake up from sleep;
[睡眼] sleepy eyes;
睡眼矇朧 blink sleepily; drowsy; eyes heavy with sleep; with eyes still heavy from sleep; sleepy-eyed;
睡眼惺松 have a drowsy look; eyes still heavy with sleep; sleepy with eyes half closed;
[睡衣] bathrobe; nightclothes; nightgown; nighty; sleeping gown; nightclothes; nightwear; pajamas;
睡衣聚會 sleepover;
襯衫式長睡衣 nightshirt;
一件睡衣 a nightdress;
[睡椅] reclining chair;
活動睡椅 chaise longue;
[睡意] drowsiness; sleepiness;
一絲睡意 a wink of sleep;

安睡 sleep peacefully; sleep soundly; sleep undisturbedly; sleep well;
沉睡 be sunk in sleep; fast asleep;
酣睡 dead to the world; fall into a deep sleep; fast asleep; sleep like a log; sleep soundly;
鼾睡 heavy sleep; snore away soundly; sound, snoring sleep;
好睡 good night;
昏睡 sleep lethargically;
瞌睡 drowsy; sleepy; sleepiness;
淺睡 dogsleep; light sleep; nap; catnap; have forty winks;

去睡 go to sleep;
入睡 fall asleep; go to one's dreams; go to sleep;
深睡 deep sleep; sound sleep;
熟睡 dead to the world; fast asleep; sleep like a log; sleep soundly; sound sleep;
甜睡 fast asleep; sound sleep;
晚睡 keep late hours;
午睡 afternoon nap; have a nap after lunch;
小睡 beauty sleep; catnap; catch some Z's; forty winks; lie down; nap;
早睡 sleep early;
裝睡 feign sleep; pretend sleep; pretend to be asleep; sham sleep;

shui

【説】 influence; persuade; try to persuade;
[説服] bring around; bring over; convince; persuade; prevail on;
有説服力 convincing; eloquent; persuasive; reasoned;
[説客] lobbyist;

遊説 go about trying to persuade a monarch into adopting one's political viewpoint (in ancient times);

shun³
shun

【吮】 lick; suck;
[吮痕] suck;
愛的吮痕 love bite;
[吮墨] deep in thought while writing;
[吮奶] suck milk;
[吮乳] suck the breast;
[吮吸] absorb; suck;

吸吮 absorb; suck;

shun

【楯】 (1) horizontal bar of a railing; (2) same as 盾;

shun⁴
shun

【舜】 (1) legendary sage ruler in ancient China; (2) hibiscus;
[舜華] (1) hibiscus; (2) beautiful appearance of a girl;
[舜日堯年] golden age; reign of the legendary emperors Yao and Shun;

shun

【順】 (1) in the same direction as; with; (2) along; (3) arrange; in sequence; put in order; (4) act in submission to; cause to surrender; follow; obedient; obey; submit to; yield to; (5) agree with; agreeable; fall in with; suit; suitable; (6) at one's convenience; conveniently; (7) take the opportunity to; (8) pick up sth on the sly; shoplift; steal; walk off with sth; (9) in sequence; (10) clear and well-written; readable; smooth;
[順把] obedient;
[順便] at one's convenience; conveniently; in passing; while sb is about it; without extra effort; without taking extra trouble;
順便拜訪 stop by;
順便説説 by the way;
順便探訪 stop by;
順便走訪 drop round;
[順差] favourable balance; in the black; surplus;
貿易順差 balance of trade surplus;
[順暢] smooth; unhindered;
[順成] accomplish sth without obstacles;
[順磁性] paramagnetism;
電子順磁性 electronic paramagnetism;
分子順磁性 molecular paramagnetism;
核順磁性 nuclear paramagnetism;
原子順磁性 atomic paramagnetism;
自旋順磁性 spin paramagnetism;
[順次] by turns; in order; in proper sequence; in sucession; in turn;
[順從] comply; fall in with; obedient to; submit to; yield to;
順從的 amenable; compliant;
順從父母 obedient to one's parents;
順從時勢 swim with the current;
不順從的 disobedient;
[順帶一提] by the way; incidentally; mention in passing;
[順當] easy and smooth; without a hitch;
順順當當 by a happy chance; easily; smoothly; win in a canter;
一輩子很順當 have an easy life;
[順道] (1) obey good reasons; (2) do sth on the way to a place;
[順德] docile virtue;
[順耳] pleasant to the ear; pleasing to the ear;
聽起來順耳 music to one's ears;

[順風] (1) favourable wind; tail wind; (2) good luck; (3) bon voyage; (4) move with the wind;
順風扯蓬 sail with the wind — take advantage of;
順風扯旗 start an undertaking at an opportune moment;
順風吹火 do a job made easy by outside help; have a favourable wind to blow the fire;
順風而呼 champion a cause that enjoys popular support; promote a public cause;
順風耳 well-informed person;
順風順水 drift with the wind and the current; sail with the wind;
順風揚帆 with swelling sails before the fair wind;
順風轉舵 steer according to the wind; take one's cue from changing conditions; tack with the wind; trim one's sails;
順風轉向 change to suit the prevailing political climate;
祝你一路順風 bon voyage;

[順服] gladly serve under; obedient; obey; submit;

[順竿兒爬] follow sb's cue and do everything to please him; readily fall in with other people's wishes;

[順和] soothing;
順和人意 go with what people feel or desire;

[順候] regards to; with best regards;

[順懷] follow one's desires;

[順境] in easy circumstances; in favourable circumstances;

[順口] (1) read smoothly; (2) say without thinking; slip out of one's tongue; speak casually; speak without much thought; talk casually;
順口答應 promise casually; promise without hesitation;
順口溜 doggerel; jingle;
不順口 not easy to say;

[順理] logical; reasonable;
順理成章 follow as a matter of course; follow a logical train of thought; follow a rational line; in a clear and ordered pattern; logical; lucid and logical; well-reasoned;

[順利] click well; smoothly; successfully; without a hitch;
出師順利 get off on the right foot; without a hitch in the first encounter;
非常順利 plain sailing;
進行順利 go on smoothly;
順順利利 by a happy chance; without a hitch;
一切順利 everything goes smoothly;
~祝你一切順利 all the best; best;

[順溜] (1) in good order; (2) smoothly; (3) obedient; (4) good looking; look comfortable; nice;
做事很順溜 have easy work;

[順流] (1) go with the current; (2) do things properly;
順流地 downriver;
順流而下 go downstream; go with the current;

[順路] (1) on the way; (2) direct route; regular route;

[順民] abjectly obedient citizens; people who surrender to their new lord;

[順命] (1) obey orders; (2) leave one's fate to heaven;

[順情] show respect for what others feel;
順情順理 in harmony with one's feelings and reason — proper and regular;

[順適] casual; composed; natural;
諸凡順適 everything goes on smoothly;

[順時] in luck; on time; up time;

[順事] matters that one is happy to talk about;

[順勢] (1) take advantage of an opportunity; (2) at one's convenience; without taking extra trouble;
順勢而為 do things by following nature;

[順手] (1) smoothly; without difficulty; (2) conveniently; without extra trouble; (3) do sth as a natural sequence; (4) convenient and easy to use; handy;
順手牽羊 go off with sth near at hand; go on the scamp; lead away the sheep off hand — pick up sth in passing; steal sth in passing; walk away with sth;

[順水] downstream; with the stream;
順水人情 a favour done at little cost to oneself; a favour that costs one nothing; a friendly gesture without extra cost to oneself;
順水推舟 do sth without extra effort;

swim with the current; take advantage of a favourable trend;

[順頌大安] with best wishes for your health;

[順俗] act according to the customs; go with the crowd;

[順遂] easy going; go smoothly; go well; in satisfactory circumstances; without a hitch;

[順藤摸瓜] follow the vine to get the melon— track down sb by following clues;

[順天] follow the mandate of heaven;

順天者昌，逆天者亡 those who obey the mandate of heaven will prosper, while those who defy it will perish;

[順我] follow me;

順我者昌，逆我者亡 boost up those who bow to me and suppress those who oppose me; I shower blessings on those who submit to me and do all I can to subvert those who resist; let those who comply with me thrive and those who resist me perish; those who bow to me would prosper and those who resist would perish;

順我者生，逆我者死 there is life for those who are with me, death for those against — said of the brutal rule of a tyrant;

[順心] gratifying; satisfactory;

不順心 go amiss;

諸事順心 all is well;

[順序] (1) plain sequence; sequence; succession; (2) according to right order; in proper order; in turn;

按照字母順序 in alphabetical order;

[順延] postpone; put off;

順延一天 put off a day accordingly;

[順眼] pleasant to the eye; please the eye; pleasing to the eye;

不順眼 cannot bear the sight of; disagreeable to the eye; eye sore; get tired of; incurring dislike; look odd;

~看不順眼 disgusting; eyesore; not to one's taste; offensive to the eye; repulsive to the eye; to one's dislike;

[順譯法] translation in regular sequence;

[順應] adjust to changes; comply with; conform to;

順應潮流 conform to the historical trend of the time; go with the tide of historical development;

順應環境 accord with one's environment; hang up one's fiddle anywhere;

順應民心 comply with the aspirations of the people;

順應時代 conform to the times;

順應時勢 go with the stream;

順應水平 adjustment level;

順天應人 follow the mandate of heaven and comply with the popular wishes of the people;

[順運] with a lucky chance;

[順着] along; with;

[順職] dutiful; live up to one's duty;

筆順 stroke order;

恭順 respectful and submissive;

歸順 pay allegiance to;

和順 amiable; gentle;

理順 rationalize; straighten out;

逆順 the rough and the smooth;

平順 plain sailing; smooth-going;

柔順 gentle and agreeable; gentle and yielding; meek; submissive;

隨順 accord with obey; yield;

通順 clear and coherent; fluent; smooth;

婉順 complaisantly obliging;

溫順 docile; gentle; good-natured; meek; obedient;

降順 surrender and give allegiance to; yield and pledge allegiance to;

孝順 dutiful; filial; show filial obedience to one's parents;

馴順 tame and docile;

遜順 humble and yielding; respectfully obedient;

一順兒 in the same direction or sequence;

依順 obedient;

忠順 loyal and obedient;

shun

【瞬】 (1) twinkling; wink; (2) in a very short time;

[瞬變] transient;

傳真瞬變 facsimile transient;

灰度瞬變 gray scale transients;

上昇瞬變 building-up transient;

[瞬華] ephemeral;

[瞬間] in a minute; in a wink; in an instant; in the twinkling of an eye;

瞬間動作動詞 momentary event verb;

瞬間壓力 instantaneous pressure;

[瞬目] flash a glance;
[瞬時] instantaneous;
瞬時速度 instantaneous velocity;
[瞬息] in a wink; in the twinkling of an eye;
瞬息千里 in the twinkling of an eye a thousand miles is made;
瞬息榮華 ephemeral grandeur;
瞬息萬變 in a flux; many changes within a short time; undergo a myriad changes in the twinkling of an eye;
瞬息之間 from one minute to the next; in a twinkling; in the course of the twinkling of an eye; in the twinkling of an eye;

一瞬 a flash; an instant; the twinkling of an eye;
轉瞬 in a flash; in a twinkle;

shuo¹
shuo

【説】 (1) say; speak; talk; utter; (2) clarify; explain; (3) description; narration; statement; (4) teaching; theory; (5) scold; talk to;
[説白] spoken parts in an opera;
説白道綠 comment on various things without restraint;
説白了 put in plain language;
[説不開] unable to reach a mutual understanding;
[説不來] (1) cannot get along with sb; (2) unable to speak; unable to utter;
[説不齊] cannot say for sure;
[説不清] cannot be explained clearly;
説不清，道不明 it is not sth that one can explain clearly and make people understand;
[説不上] (1) cannot say; cannot tell; (2) do not fit the description; not worth mentioning;
説不上來 cannot remember it now; cannot tell; not know how to say it; unable to get the words out;
[説曹操，曹操就到] talk of the devil, and he is sure to appear;
[説出] reveal; speak out; take the words out of sb's mouth; utter;
説不出 cannot utter a word; lose one's tongue; one's tongue fails one; words fail one;
~説不出話 cannot utter a word; lose one's tongue; one's tongue fails one; words fail one;
~説不出口 unable to speak out; unspeakable; unutterable;
~説不出名來 cannot put a name to sth.
[説穿] reveal; unravel by some remarks;
[説詞] plea; pretext; excuse;
[説錯] speak incorrectly;
[説到] as to; mention; refer to; speak of;
説到曹操，曹操就到 speak of an angel and you'll hear his wings; speak of the devil; talk of the devil and he is sure to appear; the devil is never nearer than when we are talking of him;
説到底 after all; at bottom; in the final analysis; in the last analysis; in the ultimate analysis;
~説到底，他衹是個凡人 after all he was a mere mortal;
説到做到 as good as one's word; do what one says; fit the action to the word; live up to one's word; match one's deeds to one's words; match one's words with deeds; practise what one preaches; suit the action to the word; the equal of one's word;
[説得] what is said;
説得出，做得到 carry out one's pledge; mean what one says; speak and follow through in action;
説得倒容易 it's easy to talk so;
説得多，做的少 great boast, small roast;
説得過去 acceptable; excusable; pardonable; passable;
説得好 well said;
説得好聽 fine words; make an unpleasant fact sound attractive; says you; talk fine; use fine-sounding phrases;
説得活靈活現 give a vivid description; make it come to life; tone sth up with colour and life;
説得來 able to get along; on good terms;
説得上 deserve mention;
説得天花亂墮 elaborate in high-flown phraseology; give an extravagantly colourful description; talk about sth in superlative terms;
説得下去 passable;
説得一套，做得一套 say one thing but do quite another;

説得有理 reasonable; sound; sound reasonable;

[説定] agree on; settle;

説不定 maybe; perhaps; probably;

[説法] (1) way of reasoning; way of saying a thing; (2) argument; statement; version;

説法不一 have different versions;

冒犯語説法 parrhesia;

現身説法 act as an example to others; advise sb by using one's own experience as an example; explain sth by citing one's own experience; give a demonstration in person; make a personal example as an effective means of convincing others; take oneself as an example; use one's own experience to persuade sb to do sth; warn others by taking oneself as an example;

[説服] bring around; bring round; bring over; convince; gain over; get round; persuade; prevail on; prevail upon; talk around; talk over; talk round;

説服力 authority; convincingness; force; persuasion; point; stringency;

[説幹就幹] a word and a blow; act without delay; let no grass grow under one's feet; non sooner said than done; not to let grass grow under one's feet;

[説鬼鬼就到] talk of the devil and he will appear;

[説好] agree on; come to an agreement;

説好話 put in a good word for sb;

説好説歹 use all means of persuasion;

[説合] (1) bring two parties together; (2) discuss; talk over;

[説和] act as a mediator; compromise a quarrel; mediate; mediate a settlement;

[説話] (1) say; speak; talk; (2) chat; talk; (3) gossip; talk; (4) in a minute; in no time; right away;

説話笨拙 put one's foot in one's mouth;

説話彬彬有禮 keep a civil tongue;

説話不算數 break one's word; fail to keep one's promise; go back on one's word;

説話粗魯 have a rough tongue;

説話得體 say nothing out of the way;

説話頂用 one's words carry weight;

説話兜圈子 beat about the bush;

説話風趣 witty talker; speak in a humorous vein;

説話尖刻 have a sharp tongue;

説話刻薄 have an acid tongue;

説話困難 have a frog in one's throat;

説話冒失 have a big mouth;

説話輕率 one's tongue is too long for one's teeth;

説話算數 as good as one's word; honour one's own words; keep one's word; live up to one's word; one means what one says; true to one's word;

~ 説話算數的人 a man of his word;

説話聽音，鑼鼓聽聲 the words are the mirror of one's mind;

説話小心 watch what you say; watch your language; watch your month; watch your tongue;

説話有趣 have a colour turn of phrase;

説話有條理 talk sense;

説話圓滑 have a smooth tongue;

~ 説話圓滑的人 smooth talker;

説話之間 in a short while; while talking;

説話中肯 hit the nail on the head; speak to the point;

説話走火 go too far in what one says; shoot off one's mouth; talk without careful choice of words and overstep limits;

不説話 keep silent;

~ 半晌不説話 keep silent for a moment;

長話短説 make a long story short; make short of long;

低聲説話 speak in a low voice; speak in whispers;

多做事，少説話 more cider and less talk; work more and talk less;

橫着説話 deliberately contrary;

開口説話 open one's mouth;

看人説話 tailor one's words according to the person addressed;

讓事實説話 let the facts speak for themselves;

説來話長 it's a long story;

説甚麼話 what are you talking about;

用鼻音説話 talk through the nose;

自説自話 say to oneself; talk to oneself;

[説謊] lie; tell a lie; tell wild tales;

説謊者 fibber; holy friar; liar; story-teller;

~ 卑鄙的説謊者 abject liar;

[説教] deliver a sermon; expound sth mechanically; preach; talk rubbish;

説教詩 didactic poetry;

[説開] explain;

[説客] lobbist; persuasive talker; one who undertakes to sell an idea; person often sent to win sb over;

[説口] boast;

[説了算] have the final say;

説了算數 I mean what I say;

説了不算 eat one's words; fail to keep a promise; go back on one's word;

[説理] argue; reason things out; reasonable;

[説媒] act as matchmaker;

[説明] clarify; explain; expound; illustrate; show;

説明句 explicative sentence;

説明來意 make clear what one has come for;

説明理由 give reasons;

説明清楚 make clear;

説明書 instruction book; synopsis; written explanation;

~一本説明書 a book of instructions;

説明文 exposition; expository prose;

説明文字 caption; line note;

説明原委 explain why and how;

説明真相 give the facts;

按照説明 follow the instructions;

把話説明 strike a light;

便於説明 for convenience of illustration;

附有説明 come with instructions;

舉例説明 illustrate by examples;

詳細説明 poop sheet;

閱讀説明 read the instructions;

政策説明 policy statement;

[説破] expose by some remarks; unravel by some remarks;

説破嗓門 talk oneself hoarse;

[説起] as for; begin talking about; bring up; with regard to;

説起來 as a matter of fact; in fact;

[説親] act as a match-maker;

説親道熱 sound very friendly; with mild and affectionate words;

[説情] intercede for sb; plead for mercy for sb; solicit favour on behalf of others;

托人説情 ask sb to put in a good word;

挽人説情 ask sb to put in a nice word;

央人説情 ask sb to put in a word for; ask sb to speak on one's behalf;

[説時遲，那時快] before you can say knife; in less time than it takes to describe it; quicker than words can tell;

[説事] (1) negotiate; try to come to an agreement; (2) explain an idea; expound a theory; make things clear;

[説書] storytelling; tell stories;

説書的 storyteller;

[説要] joke;

[説説而已] just a few casual remarks;

[説死] make it definite;

[説通] succeed in reaching an understanding;

[説妥] come to an agreement;

[説項] ask leniency or special consideration; intercede for sb; put in a good word for sb; try to persuade;

代人説項 intercede for sb; make intercession; put in a good word for sb; speak for sb;

浼人説項 request one to say a good word for sb;

[説笑] chat and laugh; kid; joke; talk and laugh;

説笑打諢 make all manner of quips and jokes;

説笑話 tell jokes;

説笑解悶 be engaged in a lively conversation with sb;

説笑取樂 talk and laugh and seek to enjoy themselves;

説説笑笑 have a pleasant talk together; joke and chat freely; laughing and chatting;

有説有笑 chat in a relaxed way; cheerful; lively; talking and laughing;

[説知] inform; let sb know; notify;

[説準] it's settled;

[説走就走] announce the intention to leave and really mean it;

[説嘴] (1) boast; brag; (2) argue; quarrel;

[説做] what is said and what is done;

光説不做 be all mouth and trousers; just sit and talk;

少説多做 few words and many deeds; work more and talk less;

少説空話，多做實事 less empty talk and more hard work;

衹説不做 all talk and no deed;

做的比説的多 better than one's word;

按説 according to the fact or common sense;

白說 speak in vain;
稗說 novel; story;
別說 let alone;
不說 don't say;
陳說 explain; state;
稱說 name sth; when speaking;
成說 accepted theory or formulation;
傳說 it is said; legend; they say; tradition;
粗略地說 roughly speaking;
大聲點說 speak up;
分說 explain matters;
更不必說 let alone; not to mention; not to speak of; to say nothing of; without mentioning;
關說 ask favour of sb for (e.g. a friend);
好說 I really don't deserve this;
胡說 rubbish; sheer nonsense; talk non-sense;
話說 (the story) says (often in the beginning of a story)
假說 hypothesis; supposition;
解說 explain orally;
界說 definition;
據說 allegedly; it is said; they say;
論說 as things should be; comment; expound; normally;
慢說 let alone; to say nothing of;
漫說 let alone; to say nothing of;
那還用說 you're telling me;
難說 it's hard to say;
你倒好意思說 now you're talking;
評說 comment on; evaluate;
淺說 elementary introduction;
勸說 advise; persuade;
卻說 now the story goes;
申說 state reasons;
數說 (1) enumerate; (2) reproach sb by citing his wrong-doing;
述說 narrate; recount; state;
訴說 narrate; recount; relate; tell;
雖說 although; though;
聽說 be told; hear of;
聽我說 I'll tell you what;
圖說 illustrated handbook; pictorial handbook;
無須多說 suffice it to say;
瞎說 talk at random; talk irresponsibly;
小說 novel;
邪說 fallacy; heresy;
敍說 narrate; tell;
學說 doctrine; theory;
演說 deliver a speech; make an address; speech;
依我說 if you ask me;
臆說 assumptions; hypothesis;
雜說 (1) different versions; (2) fragmentary argumentation;
再說 besides; put off until some time later; what's more;
照說 as a rule; ordinarily;
正如我所說 like I said; like I say;

shuo⁴

shuo

【妁】 go-between; matchmaker;

媒妁 go-between; match-maker;

shuo

【帥】 a pronunciation of 帥;

shuo

【朔】 (1) begin; (2) north; (3) new moon; (4) first day of the month of the lunar calendar;

[朔邊] northern frontier;
[朔方] dreary land in the north; north;
[朔風] biting north wind;
朔風凜冽 the north wind is piercingly cold;
朔風怒號 bitter north wind howls;
[朔馬] horses of northern breeds;
[朔漠] northern deserts;
[朔氣] (1) cold air; (2) twenty-four solar periods of the year;
[朔日] first day of the lunar month;
[朔望] first and the fifteenth day of the lunar month;
朔望月 lunar month;
[朔雪] heavy snow in the north;
[朔月] first day of the lunar month;

晦朔 the last and first day of a lunar month;

shuo

【搠】 (1) stab; thrust at one's enemy; (2) daub; smear;

shuo

【碩】 great; large;

[碩大] very large;
碩大無朋 as fat as a porpoise; big in stature and eminent in virtue without comparison; exceptionally large; gigantic; mammoth; of enormous size; of unparalleled size; unequalled in huge size;
[碩輔] virtuous minister;

[碩果] big and ripe fruits; great achievements; rich fruits;
碩果僅存 one and the only one; the only one who survives;
碩果累累 countless rich fruits; innumerable great achievements;
碩果壓枝 the trees are overburdened with fruit;
[碩惠] great indebtedness;
[碩老] learned elder; old venerable scholar;
[碩量] lenient capacity for tolerance;
[碩人] (1) slender and healthy beauty; (2) hermit;
碩人之寬 a great man is at ease;
[碩儒] great Confucian scholar; great scholar;
[碩士] (1) wise man; (2) holder of the master's degree;
碩士課程 master programme;
碩士學位 master's; master's degree;
教育學碩士 master of Education;
理科碩士 master of science; MSc;
文學碩士 MA; master of arts;
哲學碩士 master of philosophy;
[碩望] man of great fame; much respected man;
[碩彥] learned scholar; man of great talent;
肥碩 (1) (of fruit) big and fleshy (2) (of limbs and body) large and firm-fleshed;
豐碩 rich; plentiful and substantial;

shuo
【槊】 lance; spear;

shuo
【數】 frequently; often; repeatedly;
[數欠] frequent yawning;
[數數] frequently; often;
[數四] over and over again; repeatedly;
頻數 frequent and continuous;

shuo
【蟀】 a pronunciation of 蟀;

shuo
【爍】 (1) bright; glisten; glitter; shining; sparkle; (2) melt;
[爍亮] glistening; glittering; sparkling;
[爍爍] glitter; sparkle;
星光爍爍 glittering stars in the dark sky;

shuo
【鑠】 (1) melt metals with fire or heat; smelt; (2) waste away; weaken; wear off; (3) lustrous; shining; (4) powerful;
[鑠石流金] the sun shines so hot on stones that gold might have melted there;
爍石流金 the sun shines so hot on stones that gold might have melted there;
[鑠鑠] brilliant; glitter; lustrous; sparkle;
矍鑠 (of old people) hale and hearty;
閃爍 (1) be evasive; be vague; (2) glimmer; glisten; twinkle;

si¹
si
【司】 (1) attend to; manage; preside over; take charge of; (2) department; (3) a surname;
[司法] administration of justice; judicature;
司法部 judiciary;
司法部門 judicial departments;
司法獨立 independence of the judiciary;
司法機關 judicial organs;
司法鑑定 judicial testimony;
司法界 judicial circles;
司法權 judicature; jurisdiction;
司法體制 judicial system;
司法系統 judicature; judicial system; judiciary;
[司機] chauffeur; driver;
司機室 cab; driver's cab; engineer's cab; motorman's cab; operating cab;
~機車司機室 locomotive cab; tender cab;
~前置式司機室 forward-type cab;
~折棚司機室 vestibuled cab;
司機座椅 driver's seat;
公車司機 bus driver;
火車司機 engine driver;
貨車司機 truck driver; trucker;
卡車司機 truck driver; trucker;
星期日司機 Sunday driver;
肇事逃逸的司機 hit-and-run driver;
指定司機 designated driver;
[司空見慣] a common enough thing; a common occurrence; a common sight; a matter of common occurrence; a matter of common practice; a matter of repeated occurrence; be accustomed to seeing such things; commonplace; it is quite common for...; order of the day;

[司庫] official treasurer;
[司令] commander; commanding officer;
司令部 command; command post; headquarters;
司令軍 commandant;
司令員 commander;
~ 副司令員 second-in-command;
警備司令 garrison commander;
軍區司令 military area commander;
總司令 commander-in-chief;
~ 總司令部 general headquarters;
[司馬] (1) minister of war in ancient China; (2) a surname;
[司馬昭之心，路人皆知] a plot known to all;
[司事] carry out one's duties;
各司其事 each attends to his own duties;
[司線員] linesman;
[司藥] chemist; duggist; pharmacist;
[司儀] master of ceremonies;
[司長] department chief; director-general; head of a department;
副司長 deputy director-general;
[司職] take up one's duties;
各司其職 each performs its own functions;
[司鑽] driller;

盎司 ounce;
公司 company; corporation; firm; incorporation;
官司 lawsuit;
勒克司 lux; metrecandle;
羅曼司 romance;
派力司 palace;
上司 boss; superior;
土司 (1) such a headman; (2) system of appointing national minority hereditary headmen in the Yuan, Ming and Qing Dynasties;
陰司 netherworld;
有司 officials;
員司 government employees of medium and lower ranks;

si

【私】 (1) personal; private; (2) selfish; (3) clandestine; private; secret; (4) contraband; illegal; illicit; (5) have an affair with; have illicit relations;
[私奔] elope; run away;
[私弊] corrupt practices;
[私產] private property;
[私娼] unlicensed prostitute; unregistered prostitute;
[私仇] personal enmity; personal grudge;
報私仇 satisfy a personal grudge;
公報私仇 use official regulations as pretext to settle a score;
官報私仇 an officer avenges oneself; revenge personal grievances in the name of the public; use one's position to get even with another person for a private grudge;

[私處] genitals; private parts; privates;
[私德] personal morals; personal virtue; private conduct;
[私第] private residence;
角巾私第 lead a hermit's life; live as a recluse in one's hometown;
[私房] (1) private savings; (2) confidential;
私房話 confide one's secrets to sb;
私房錢 private savings;
~ 談私房話 confide one's secrets to sb; exchange confidences;
[私憤] personal spite;
[私話] confidential talks;
[私會] secret rendezvous;
[私貨] contraband goods; smuggled goods;
[私己] (1) privately; (2) one's own benefits;
[私計] selfish plan;
[私家] private;
私家車 private car;
[私見] personal prejudice; personal opinion; bias;
[私交] personal friendship;
私交甚篤 have an amicable personal friendship;
[私立] private; privately run;
私立大學 private college;
私立學校 private school;
[私利] personal gain; private interests;
謀私利 have an eye to the main chance;
~ 不謀私利 seek no personal gain;
圖私利 pursue private ends; seek personal gain;
為私利 on one's own account;
[私了] solve sth privately;
[私囊] private pocket;
飽私囊 fill one's pocket;
~ 飽入私囊 embezzle public funds;
~ 肥飽私囊 line one's pockets;

~圖飽私囊 feather one's own nest; plan to fill one's own pocket — embezzle for private gains; try to enrich oneself; try to line one's pockets;
~以飽私囊 fill one's pocket;
肥私囊 line one's pocket;

[私念] selfish motives;

[私情] personal relationship;
不徇私情 be not swayed by personal considerations;
不循私情 not be swayed by personal considerations;

[私人] personal; private;
私人拜訪 personal call; personal visit;
私人房地產 private housing estates;
私人訪問 private visit;
私人飛機 private aircraft;
私人股份 private shares;
私人公司 private company;
私人關係 personal relations;
私人經濟 private economy;
私人秘書 personal secretary; private secretary;
私人企業 private enterprise;
私人投資 private investment;
私人問題 personal question;
私人醫生 personal doctor;
私人賬戶 private account;
任用私人 fill a post with one's own man;

[私商] smuggler;

[私室] private room;

[私事] personal affairs; private affairs;

[私塾] old-style private school;

[私談] confidential talks; private talks; talk in private;

[私逃] abscond; elope;

[私田] privately owned farmland;

[私通] (1) collaborate with enemy forces; have secret communication with; (2) adultery; fornication; illicit intercourse;
與人私通 commit adultery;

[私吞] misappropriation; privately take possession of;

[私下] in private; in secret; privately; under the rose;
私下裏 on a personal level;
私下商議 discuss a matter in private;
私下説的 off the record;

[私心] selfish motives; selfishness;
私心雜念 selfish consideration; selfish ideas and personal considerations;
私心自用 selfish and self-satisfied;
別具私心 have an axe to grind;

[私刑] illegal punishment;
私刑逼供 put sb to illegal torture to extract confession;
私刑拷打 torture sb by private punishment;

[私營] privately operated; privately run;
私營工商業 privately operated industrial and commercial enterprises;
私營經濟 private economy;
~私營經濟成份 private sector of economy;
私營企業 private-owned enterprise;

[私用] (1) for personal use; (2) illegal use;

[私有] private; privately owned;
私有化 privatization;
私有經濟 private economy;
私有制 system of private ownership;

[私語] (1) whisper; (2) confidence;

[私慾] selfish desires;

[私願] personal wish;

[私運] smuggle;
私運軍火 run arms;

[私章] personal seal; private chop;

[私自] privately; secretly; without permission;
私自做事 do things without asking anyone;

藏私 hide sth illegally;
販私 sell prohibited goods;
公私 public and private;
緝私 arrest smugglers;
家私 family property;
謀私 seek personal gains;
無私 selfless; unselfish;
徇私 act wrongly out of consideration of personal relationship;
陰司 shameful secret;
隱私 one's secrets; private matters one is not willing to disclose or tell others;
營私 seek personal gain;
自私 self-centered; selfish;
走私 smuggle;

si

【思】 (1) contemplate; consider; deliberate; think; (2) long for; recall; remember; think of; (3) thinking; thought; (4) grieve; mourn; (5) admire;

[思辨] (1) speculate; (2) armchair thinking; (3) analyze mentally;
思辨哲學 speculative philosophy;

[思潮] (1) ideological trend; popular ideas; trend of thought; (2) changing tides of one's thoughts; thoughts;
思潮起伏 disquieting thoughts surging in one's mind; flood of ideas now rising now falling;

[思春] pine for the opposite sex;

[思忖] consider; contemplate; ponder; think;
思忖半晌 remain thoughtful for a few moments;

[思凡] think of worldly pleasures;

[思過] feel remorse; ponder upon one's fault; repent; ruminate upon one's faults;
思過半矣 can largely comprehend the rest;
靜居思過 live in reclusion and make self-examination;
明罰思過 discover one's faults and reflect on one's errors;

[思舊] remember old times; think of old friends; think of old times;

[思考] contemplate; ponder over; reflect on; think deeply;
思考力 power to think;
思考能力 thinking skills;
思考問題 ponder a problem;
獨立思考 independent thinking; think independently;
~獨立思考的人 independent thinker;
多角度思考 see things from different angles;
橫向思考 lateral thinking;
理性思考 rational thinking;
跳出框框思考 think outside the box;

[思戀] cherish the memory of; long for sb one loves;

[思量] consider; contemplate; think; turn sth over in one's mind; weigh and consider;
暗自思量 turn over in one's mind;

[思路] one's train of thought;
思路錯誤 on the wrong track;
思路敏捷 think on one's feet;
思路正確 on the right track;
打斷思路 interrupt one's train of thought;

[思慮] consider carefully; contemplate; deliberate; turn over and over in one's mind;
思慮過度 worry beyond measure;
思慮周到 brood over adequately;
澄其思慮 purify one's thoughts;
殫思極慮 rack one's brains;
思前慮後 ponder over the cause and effect of a thing; recall former days and be anxious about the future;
思深慮遠 think deep and consider far; think deep and far ahead;
淫思苦慮 think deeply and consider earnestly;

[思慕] (1) admire; think of sb with respect; (2) remember;
思慕前賢 long and admire for former worthies;

[思念] long for; miss; recall; remember fondly; think of; yearn;
思念戰友 long for one's comrades-in-arms;

[思齊] want to emulate; wish to equal;
見賢思齊 emulate those better than oneself; when one sees another better than oneself, try to equal him;

[思親] think of one's relatives, especially parents;

[思索] ponder; search one's mind for an answer; speculate; think deeply;
不假思索 offhand; readily; without stopping to think; without thinking; without hesitation;
~不假思索地 off the tope of one's head;
費人思索 exhaust one's mind to think;
用心思索 do some hard thinking;

[思維] thinking; thought;
思維定勢 thinking set;
思維方式 way of thinking;
思維模式 mindset;
思維能力 ability of thinking;
創造性思維 creative thinking;
二值思維 two-valued thinking;
概念思維 conceptual thinking;
感性思維 affective thinking;
集體思維 convergent
具體思維 concrete thinking;
聯想思維 associative thinking;
邏輯思維 logical thinking; thinking in terms of logic;
我向思維 autistic thinking;
新思維 think outside the box;
形式思維 thinking in terms of images;

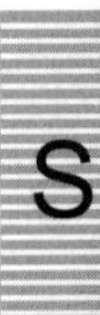

再四思維 think over and over again;

[思鄉] homesick; think of one's home;

思鄉病 homesickness;

思鄉心切 get homesick; long for one's home;

[思想] (1) ideas; ideology; thinking; thought; (2) recall; remember; think of;

思想包袱 a load on one's mind; sth weighing on one's mind;

思想鬥爭 ideological struggle; struggle in mind;

思想方法 method of thinking;

思想改造 ideological remoulding;

思想感情 thinking and feeling;

思想工廠 think factory;

思想家 ideologist; thinker;

思想僵化 ossification of thinking; rigid way of thinking; stagnation of thought;

思想教育 ideological education;

思想覺悟 political awareness; political consciousness;

思想落伍 old-fashioned in thinking; outdated ideas;

思想敏銳 actue thinking;

~思想敏銳的人 acute thinker;

思想認識 ideology and understanding;

思想體系 ideological system;

思想問題 ideological problem;

思想狹隘的 small-minded;

思想性 ideological content;

思想幼稚 childish thinking; naive;

思想戰 ideological warfare;

思想自由 freedom of thought;

~思想自由的人 freethinker;

思想作風 style of thinking; way of thinking;

骯髒的思想 dirty mind;

暴露思想 bare one's thoughts; expose one's thoughts; lay bare one's thoughts;

表達思想 express thoughts;

超越時代的思想 ideas in advance of the time;

敞開思想 open up one's thoughts;

搞通思想 straighten out one's thinking;

胡思亂想 be lost in various fancies and conjectures; be moved by confused, foolish reflections; confuse one's brain by foolish ideas; cranky; engage in fantasy; entertain all sorts of ideas; entertain foolish ideas; flights of fancy; flights of imagination; get ideas into one's head; give free play to one's imagination; go off into wild flights of fancy; go woolgathering; have a bee in one's bonnet; have a bee in one's head; have a maggot in one's brain; have a maggot in one's head; have irresponsible thoughts; indulge in flights of fancy; let one's fancy run wild; let one's imagination run wild; let one's mind wander; one's wits go a wool-gathering; run woolgathering; spoil one's head by thinking nonsense; think confusedly; woolgathering;

~白天做夢—胡思亂想 dreaming in the daytime – going off into wild flights of fancy;

~喜歡胡思亂想 fond of daydreams;

集中思想 collect one's thoughts;

解放思想 emancipate the mind;

軍事思想 military thinking;

狂思亂想 imagine all sorts of ideas; indulge in fantasy;

七思八想 think a lot about; in thought;

千思萬想 a million thoughts; think over and over again;

前思後想 careful deliberation; chew and cud; ideas revolve in one's mind; ponder; ponder and brood upon; think over again and again; turn over sth in one's mind;

日思夜想 have sb daily and nightly in one's thoughts;

儒家思想 Confucian thought;

思前想後 ponder on the past and future; ponder over; think back and forth to oneself; think of the past and future; think over again and again; turn over in one's mind;

新思想 modern thinking; modern thoughts;

一種思想 an idea;

指導思想 guiding thought;

自由思想 freethinking;

~自由思想家 freethinker;

左思右想 crack one's brains over; cudgel one's brains; deep in thought; keep thinking; muse on sth; ponder; rack one's brains; ruminate; think back and forth; think from different angles; think of this and that; think over and over; think over from different angles;

turn sth over in one's mind;

[思緒] (1) one's thinking; train of thought; (2) feeling; mood;
 思緒不寧 feel perturbed;
 思緒紛亂 confused state of mind; confused train of thoughts;
 思緒萬千 a myriad of thoughts crowd into one's mind; fill one's mind with a myriad of thoughts and ideas;
 千思萬緒湧上心頭 all sorts of feelings well up inside sb;

[思憶] think of and remember;

[思議] imaginable; thinkable;

哀思 grief; mourning; mourning for the dead; sad feeling about the deceased; sad memories;
才思 creativeness; imaginative power;
沉思 be buried in thought; be lost in thought; contemplative; deliberating; in a brown study; meditate; meditative; pensive; ponder; reflective;
愁思 deep longing; forlornness; melancholy;
單相思 unrequited love;
諦思 consider carefully; ponder deeply;
反思 introspection; self-examination; self-reflection;
構思 conception; work out the plot of a literary work or the composition of a painting;
苦思 cudgel one's brains; languish for; think hard;
冥思 meditate;
凝思 be buried in thought; be lost in thought; deep in thought;
綺思 beautiful thoughts;
竊思 one's personal view;
情思 affection; thought;
秋思 autumn thoughts;
三思 think carefully;
深思 deliberate; ponder deeply over;
神思 mental state;
慎思 think carefully;
詩思 poetic inspiration; poetical thoughts;
熟思 consider carefully; deliberate; ponder deeply; think over carefully;
鼠思 pensive;
所思 what one thinks;
覃思 deep in thought; deep thought; meditation;
文思 flow of thoughts and ideas in writing; thread of ideas in writing; train of thought in writing;
遐思 wild and fanciful thoughts;
相思 (1) in love with each other; lovesickness; miss each other; pine for each other; yearning between lovers; (2) acacia;
鄉思 homesickness; nostalgia;
孝思 heart of filial piety;
心思 (1) ideas; intelligence; thoughts; (2) thinking; thoughts; (3) mood; state of mind;
尋思 consider; meditate; ponder; reflect; think sth over;
意思 (1) idea; meaning; (2) desire; opinion; wish; (3) token of affection; (4) look like; seem;
夠意思 (1) generous; really kind; (2) really something;
好意思 have the nerve;
小意思 trivial token of kindly feelings (as of a gift);
繹思 think of continuously;
幽思 meditate; ponder; thoughts on things remote;
憂思 pensive;
于思 long and thick beard and mustache;
於思 full of beard; rich in whiskers;
運思 think hard;
追思 think back;

si

【斯】 (1) this; (2) then; thus; (3) a surname;

[斯時] presently; such a time; this time;

[斯世] this worldly life;

[斯事] this matter;

[斯文] (1) culture; (2) gentle; refined; (3) educated class;
 斯文敗類 black sheep of the literary circles; polished scoundrels; refined rascal; ruffians in scholars' gowns;
 斯文掃地 a disgrace to the educated class; bring disgrace on the intellectuals; disgrace one's scholarly dignity; the decadence of the intellectuals;
 貓不吃魚—假斯文 a cat not eating fish – pretending to be refined in manner;
 斯斯文文 cultured; elegant; gentle; refined;

毒瓦斯 poisonous gas;
法西斯 fascist;
如斯 such; like this;
托拉斯 trust;
瓦斯 gas;
螽斯 katydid; long-horned grasshopper;

si

【絲】 (1) silk; (2) threadlike object; (3) a

tiny bit; a trace; (4) a breath of; a flicker of;

[絲綢] silk; silk cloth;
絲綢之路 the Silk Road;
絲綢之鄉 the home of silk;
人造絲綢 imitation silk;

[絲帶] silk braids; silk ribbons;
夾絲絲帶 wired ribbon;

[絲兒] tender and delicate things;

[絲瓜] sponge gourd; towel gourd;

[絲毫] a bit; a particle; a shred; an iota; the least bit; the slightest amount; the slightest degree; the tiniest;
絲毫不差 fit it to a hair; not err by a hair's breadth; just right; tally in every detail; to a hair; to a nicety; to a tee; to an inch; to the letter; to the turn of a hair; without a shade of difference; without the slightest difference;
絲毫不動 won't stir a finger;
絲毫不苟 not in the least carelessness;
絲毫不顧 not to care a bean; not to care a cuss; not to care a dam; not to care a fig; not to care a groat; not to care a hang, not to care a hoot; not to care a pine; not to care a straw; utterly disregarding;
絲毫不含糊 clear-cut; in black and white terms; transparent;
絲毫不減 not to bate a jot of one's demands;
絲毫不爽 perfectly accurate; right in every detail; to a hair's breadth;
絲毫不損 not a hair of one's head shall be touched;
絲毫無誤 not to deviate a hair's breadth;

[絲淚] little teardrops;

[絲蘿] marriage;

[絲棉] silk batting; silk padding; silk wadding;

[絲帕] silk handkerchief;

[絲絲拉拉] endless tangles and involvement;

[絲絲入扣] all threads neatly tied up; ingenious and touching; right on the beat; with meticulous care and flawless artistry;

[絲襪] silk socks; silk stockings;
魚網絲襪 fishnet stockings;

[絲網] gauze; silk screen;
絲網印刷 screen printing;
石棉心鐵絲網 asbestos centre gauze;
鋼絲網 steel wire gauze;

[絲線] silk thread;
一綹絲線 a skein of silk thread;

[絲雨] drizzle; misty rain;

[絲竹] (1) Chinese musical instruments; (2) music;
絲竹之聲 the sound of music;

拔絲 (1) candied floss; (2) wire drawing;
保險絲 fuse; fuse-wire;
玻璃絲 glass silk;
蠶絲 natural silk; silk;
長絲 filament;
廠絲 filature silk;
抽絲 (1) reel off raw silk from cocoons; (2) snag;
刺絲 barbed wire;
寸絲 inch of silk;
單絲 monofilament;
燈絲 filament (in a light bulb or valve);
電熱絲 heating wire;
釣絲 fishing line;
廢絲 waste silk;
粉絲 vermicelli
復絲 multifilament;
鋼絲 steel wire;
花絲 (1) filament (2) filigree;
絹絲 spun silk (yarn);
菌絲 hypha;
刻絲 (1) type of waving done by the tapestry method in fine silks and gold thread; (2) dress materials or articles made in the above-mentioned way;
緙絲 (1) type of waving done by the tapestry method in fine silks and gold thread; (2) dress materials or articles made in the above-mentioned way;
拉絲 wiredrawing;
辣絲絲 hot; peppery;
冷絲絲 a bit chilly;
涼絲絲 a bit cool; coldish; rather cool;
柳絲 wicker;
螺絲 screw;
毛絲 broken filament;
木絲 wood wool;
尼龍絲 nylon yarn;
黏膠絲 viscose;
掐絲 filigree; wire inlay;
鉛絲 (1) galvanized wire; (2) lead wire;
切絲 cut into shreds; shred;
青絲 black hair;
情絲 ties of affection; ties of love;
人造絲 artificial silk; rayon;

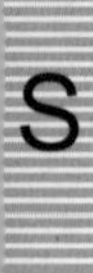

肉絲 shredded meat;
桑蠶絲 mulberry silk;
繅絲 reel silk;
生絲 raw silk;
熟絲 boiled-off silk;
雙宮絲 doupion silk;
碳絲 carbon filament;
甜絲絲 (1) happy; quite pleased; (2) pleasantly sweet;
鐵絲 iron wire;
銅絲 copper wire;
鎢絲 tungsten filament;
細絲 fine thread;
纖絲 fibril;
煙斗絲 pipe tobacco;
煙絲 cut tobacco; pipe tobacco;
一絲 a breath of; a flicker of;
游絲 (1) gossamer; (2) hairspring;
雨絲 drifting rain; fine rain;
蛛絲 cobweb; gossamer; spider's thread; thread of a spider;
竹絲 bamboo splint;

si
【罳】 screen with meshes or holes;

罘罳 (1) screen in ancient times; (2) metal net under the eaves used to keep off birds;

si
【嘶】 (1) neigh; (2) hoarse;
［嘶叫］ neigh; whinny;
馬嘶叫 a horse whinnies;
［嘶澌聲］ fizz;
［嘶啞］ hoarse; hoarse-voiced;
嘶啞的哭聲 hoarse cry;

si
【廝】 (1) male servant; (2) fellow; guy; (3) in company with each other; together; with each other;
［廝吵］ make a fuss together; quarrel with each other;
［廝打］ come to blows; exchange blows; tussle;
揪住廝打 pommel each other with fists;
［廝共］ in company with each other; together;
［廝會］ meet each other;
［廝混］ (1) mingle; mix with each other; (2) fool around together;
［廝見］ see each other;
［廝鬧］ have a spree;
［廝認］ recognize each other;
［廝殺］ fight at close quarters; slaughter one another;
［廝守］ take care of each other; wait upon each other;

小廝 manservant; page;

si
【撕】 rip; tear;
［撕打］ beat up; maul;
［撕掉］ tear off; tear up;
［撕毀］ destroy by tearing; tear to shreds; tear up;
撕毀合同 scrap a contract; tear up a contract;
撕毀手稿 tear up the manuscript;
撕毀協定 tear an agreement to shreds; tear up an agreement;
［撕開］ rip open; tear open;
［撕爛］ rip to pieces; tear to shreds;
［撕票］ kill a hostage;
［撕破］ rip; tear;
撕破畫皮 rip off sb's mask; strip sb of his disguise;
撕破臉 come to an open break in friendship with each other; have no consideration for sb's feelings; offend sb openly; rip open the face; shed all pretences of cordiality;
撕破面子 cast aside all consideration of face; not to spare sb's sensibilities;
［撕去］ tear away; tear off;
［撕碎］ destroy; rip to pieces; rive; tear to pieces;
［撕下］ tear down;
撕下假面具 tear off the mask;
［撕咬］ bait; worry;

si
【澌】 (1) drain completely; drain dry; drain out; exhaust; (2) sound of breaking;
［澌盡］ drain out; exhaust;
［澌滅］ totally disappear; vanish;
［澌澌］ sound of the pouring rain;

si
【緦】 (1) fine jute cloth; (2) spin jute thread or yarn;

si
【螄】 a kind of mollusk with spiral shell;

螺螄 snail; spiral shell;

si
【鍶】 strontium;

si
【鷥】 egret;

鷺鷥 egret;

si³
si
【死】 (1) dead; die; die for; join the angels; (2) to the death; (3) extremely; to death; (4) deadly; implacable; (5) fixed; inflexible; rigid; (6) closed; impassable; (7) adamantly; stubbornly; unyieldingly;

[死板] inflexible; rigid; stiff;
辦事死板 work in a mechanical way;
表情死板 expressionless face;
動作死板 stiff movements;

[死別] be parted by death; part never to see each other again;

[死不] stubbornly refuse to; would rather die than;
死不承認 refuse to admit even unto death;
死不放手 hold on like grim death;
死不改悔 absolutely unrepentant; flatly refuse to mend one's ways;
死不甘心 die with regret;
死不回頭 refuse to mend one's way;
死不悔悟 absolutely unrepentant; incorrigible; never to repent even unto death;
死不開口 shut one's mouth tight;
死不瞑目 cannot die in peace; die discontent; die dissatisfied; die with everlasting regret; die with injustice unredressed; die without closing one's eyes; turn in one's grave;
死不認錯 stubbornly refuse to admit one's mistakes;
死不投降 nail one's colours to the mast;
死不要臉 brazen-faced; dead to all feelings of shame; dead to shame; devoid of shame; extremely shameless; lose all sense of shame; utterly devoid of shame; utterly shameless;
死不足惜 death is not to be regretted;

[死纏] entangle;
死纏不休 persist in arguing endlessly; pursue sb in an annoying manner;
死纏活纏 entangle a person incessantly;
死纏硬要 pester sb for sth

[死擋] resist to death;

[死黨] diehard followers; sworn confederates; sworn followers;

[死得其所] die a worthy death; die in the rigth path;

[死等] wait indefinitely without giving up hope;

[死敵] deadly enemy; mortal enemy; sworn enemy; arch adversary; arch enemy; implacable foe;

[死地] hopeless situation;
置之死地 expose sb to mortal danger; kill sb; put sb to death;
~置之死地而後快 will be content with nothing less than sb's destruction; will be satisfied with nothing less than sb's undoing; will not be happy with anything less than the destruction of; will not be satisfied until sb has been destroyed;
欲置之死地而後快 in an attempt to finish it off for good; would be satisfied with nothing short of sb's destruction;
~置之死地而後生 confront a person with the danger of death and he will fight to live;

[死店活人開] everything depends on how one manages it; man's action and thought determine the success of an endeavour;

[死而不僵] dead but showing no signs of rigour;

[死而有知] if the dead knew;

[死狗] dead dog;

[死鬼] you devil; you hellion;

[死海] dead sea; Dead Sea;

[死後] after death; post-mortem; posthumous; postmortal;
死後無嗣 die without an heir;

[死灰] dying embers;
死灰復燃 come to life again; like dying embers that flare up; make a comeback; rejuvenated; rekindled; rise from the ashes;
死灰槁木 dead ashes and dry sticks;
槁木死灰 dead trees and cold ashes — complete apathy; rotten wood and dead ashes — a living corpse; withered wood or cold ashes — utterly destitute

of passion and desires;
臉如死灰 one's face is like a death mask; one's face is the colour of wood ash; one's face turns ashen; one's face turns pale;
心如死灰 one's heart is like dead ashes — utterly dispirited;

[死活] (1) dead or alive; fate; life or death; (2) in any case; anyway; no matter what; simply;
半死不活 between life and death; half-dead; more dead than alive; neither dead or alive;
不知死活 have no idea of death or danger;
好死不如惡活 a living ass is better than a dead lion;
累死累活 work desperately;
你死我活 grim; I will fight you to the finish; life-and-death; mortal;
~拼個你死我活 fight to the bitter end;
~爭得你死我活 contend for sth fiercely;
七死八活 almost dead; be tortured almost to death; half dead; hovering between life and death; on the verge of death;
死拉活拽 drag and pull with all one's strength;
死求活磨 pester sb beseechingly;
死去活來 come round after fainting; faint and revive; half dead; hover between life and death; in extreme distress; in extreme pain; only half alive; within an inch of one's life;
~打得死去活來 beat sb to a frazzle; beat within an inch of his life;
~哭得死去活來 cry one's heart out; cry oneself dead;
死說活說 persuade by all means;
尋死覓活 seek one's own death; threaten sb with death; threaten to kill oneself; try to commit suicide; want to end one's own life;

[死忌] death anniversaries;

[死記] mechanical memorizing; memorize by rote;
死記硬背 cram up; learn by rote; memorize mechanically; hammer into; rote;

[死寂] deathly stillness;
死寂無聲 as dead as a doornail; deathly stillness;

[死結] fast knot; problem that defies solution; encased knot;

[死井] dried-up well;

[死勁兒] (1) all one's might; all one's strength; (2) for all one's worth; with all one's might; with all one's strength; with might and main;
下死勁 make frantic effort to;

[死絕] be completely annihilated; die out;

[死扛] (1) go all out to support or shoulder responsibilities; (2) refuse to confess; refuse to reveal information;

[死磕] risk one's life;

[死啃] (1) eat without work; (2) persist unduly in request; (3) read a book without thinking;
死啃書本 try to memorize books without thinking;

[死了] at the utmost;
死了張屠夫，不吃渾毛豬 no man is indispensable;
吵死了 boisterous;
撐死了 (1) at the utmost; finally; to the end; (2) stuffed to the gills; too full;
累死了 shagged;

[死力] (1) all one's strength; (2) strive with all one's efforts; with all one's strength; with might and main;
死力抵抗 fight tooth and nail; resist with might and main;

[死靈] souls of the dead;

[死路] (1) blind alley; dead end; impasse; (2) fatal route; no way out; the road to destruction; the road to ruin;
死路一條 a blind alley; doomed; no way out; the road to extinction;
一條死路 a blind alley;
自投死路 fall into a certain destruction; take the road to ruin on one's own accord; throw oneself to ruin;
自尋死路 bring about one's own destruction; sign one's own death warrant; self-sought ruin; invite one's own destruction;

[死馬] dead horse;
死馬當作活馬醫 doctor a dead horse as if it were still alive; make a lost attempt to save an impossible situation; make every possible effort; try as a last resort to save a hopeless situation;

[死滅] die out;

[死命] (1) cause to die; death; doom; (2) desperately; with all the power and strength at one's command;
死命掙扎 struggle desperately;
[死木] dead-wood;
[死難] die a martyr's death; die in an accident;
[死拼] fight to the death;
[死期] hour of doom; time of death;
[死乞白賴] entangle without stop; importunate; lie shamelessly; paster sb endlessly; plead hard; shamelessly nag at;
[死前] before death; before one dies;
[死囚] death convict;
死囚牢房 condemned cell;
死囚區 death row;
[死人] (1) dead person; the dead; the defunct; (2) to the utmost degree;
活死人 dead-alive person; living dead person;
笑死人 ludicrous to the utmost degree; make one laugh to death;
羞死人 feel terribly embarrassed; how embarrassing; simply die of shame;
軋死人 run over and kill;
[死喪] death and burial;
[死傷] casualties; killed and wounded;
死傷慘重 casualties are heavy; take a heavy toll of lives;
扶傷救死 heal the wounded and rescue the dying;
救死扶傷 heal the sick and wounded; heal the wounded and rescue the dying; rescue the dying and heal the wounded;
[死神] dead; graim monarch; great leveller; great whipper-in; Grim Reaper; Mr Mose; old floorer; old man Mose; old Mr Grim; pale horse;
[死生] dead or alive;
死生不渝 unchangeable whether dead or alive;
死生有命 a person's life is governed by fate; it's all a matter of fate how long one is going to live; life and death are foreordained; life and death are predetermined;
~死生有命，富貴在天 death and life are decreed; life and death are determined by fate, rank and riches decreed by heaven; life and death are preordained; riches and honour depend upon Heaven; wealth and honour come from Heaven;
起死回生 bring back to life; bring new hope to a serious situation; bring sb back from death; bring the dead to life; bring the dying back to life; come back to life; effect a miraculous cure; make the dead come back to life; raise from death; raise one from the dead and turn him alive; raise sb from death; recall to life; restore the dead to life again; restore the dying to life; resuscitate; revive the dead; save the dying; snatch a patient from the jaws of death; wrest a patient from the jaws of death;
捨死忘生 disregard one's own safety; forget about one's own safety; heedless of one's own safety; risk death and give up one's life; risk one's lie; without thought of one's life and death;
死則同死，生則同生 if this is your time to die, I will die with you; if to live, then I will live with you;
死中求生 struggle in a desperate situation for survival;
險死還生 close call; narrowly escaped death; near shave;
昨死今生 lead a new life from now on; reform one's ways and be reborn;
[死屍] corpse; dead body;
[死守] (1) defend to the death; defend to the last; make a last-ditch defense; (2) obstinately cling to; rigidly adhere to;
死守陣地 defend the position to the last;
[死水] backwater; dead water; stagnant water; unfree water;
一潭死水 a pool of stagnant water; a pond of stagnant water; dull and inactive; dull and sluggish situation; stagnant water;
[死胎] dead fetus; stillbirth;
[死土] dead soil;
[死亡] all over with sb; all up with sb; among the immortals; an old floorer; answer the final summons; answer the last roll call; answer the last muster; asleep in Jesus; asleep in the Arms of God;

asleep in the valley; at peace; at rest; be all washed up; be blown across the creek; be blown away; be blown creek; be brought to one's last home; be called to one's account; be called to one's long account; be called home; be called to God; be called to the beyond; be called to the Great Beyond; be cast into outer darkness; be cleaned out of the deck; be cut off; be done for; be gathered to one's fathers; be gone; be gone to Davy Jones's locker; be knocked out; be promoted to glory; be removed to the divine bosom; be rocked to sleep; be salted away; be sent to one's account; be shuffled; be taken to paradise; be translated into higher sphere; be trumped; be washed out; be written off; bite the dust; black out; blow sb away; bow off; bow out; breathe one's last; buy a one-way ticket; buy the farm; call it quits; cancel one's account; cash in; cash in one's chips; cease to be; cease to exist; cease to live; check in; check out; close one's career; close one's days; close one's eyes; close one's life; close up one's account; close upon; close upon the world; coil up one's ropes; come to an end; conk out; count daisies; croak; cross over; cross over the Great Divide; cross over the River Jordan; cross the bar; cross the Bar; cross the great divide; cross the River Styx; cut; cut adrift; cut one's cable; cut one's stick; dangle in the sheriff's picture depart; decease; demise; depart; depart from this life; depart from this world; depart to God; depart to the world of shadows; die; die in one's boots; dissolution; do one's bit; down for good; draw one's last breath; drop hooks; drop off the hooks; drop off the twig; drop the cue; drop the curtain; end; end in one's death; expire; fade away; fade out; fall; fall on sleep; final sleep; fire one's last shot; flunk out; fold up; frame; free; give up the breath; give up the ghost; give up the soul; give up the spirit; go beyond; go blooey; go down to the shades; go flooey; go forth; go hence; go home; go home in a box; go off; go off the hooks; go out; go out of the world; go out of this world; go the way of all flesh; go the way of all nature; go to a better world; go to the way of all the earth; go to Davy Jones's locker; go to heaven; go to hell; go to Jordan's banks; go to meet one's maker; go to one's account; go to one's doom; go to one's grass; go to one's last home; go to one's long home; go to one's own place; go to one's resting place; go to one's reward; go to sleep; go to the hereafter; go to the land of heart's desire; go to the last roundup; go to the mansions of rest; go to the races; go up salt river; go west; God rest his soul; grounded for good; hand in one's account; hand in one's dinner pail; hang up one's harness; hang up one's hat; hang up one's tackle; have fallen asleep; have fallen asleep in the Lord; have fallen by the wayside; have found rest; have gone to a better place; have gone to a better land; have gone to a better life; have gone to a better world; have gone to the Great Adventure; have gone to the happy hunting ground; have gone under; have one's name inscribed in the book of life; he is coming home; hide one's name under daisies; hit the rocks; home and free; hop off one's twig; hop the last rattler; hop the twig; in Abraham's bosom; in Davy Jones's locker; in heaven; in one's coffin; in the dust; in the grand secret; in the hereafter; in the undiscovered country; it's taps; join in the immortals; join one's ancestors; join the angelic choirs; join the angels; join the feathered choir; join the heavenly choir; join the invisible choir; join the ever increasing majority; join the Great majority; join the silent

majority; jump the last hurdle; kick in; kick off; kick the bucket; last rest; launch into eternity; lay down life's burden; lay down one's knife and fork; lay down one's life; lay down one's pen; lay down one's shovel and hoe; leave this world; lie asleep; lose one's life; lose the decision; make an end of sb; make away with sb; make one's final exit; make the ultimate sacrifice; meet one's death; meet one's end; meet one's fate; mortal; move off; negative patient care outcome; never-ending sleep; no longer with us; no more; one's eternal rest; one's eyes are closed; one's heavenly rest; one's hard-earned rest; one's last taboo; out of pain; out of the game; out of the running; over the creek; pale horse; pass away; pass in one's alley; pass into stillness; pass on; pass out; pass out of the picture; pass over the Jordan; pass to the other side; pay Charon; pay day; pay one's fee; pay one's harp; pay one's last debt; pay saint Peter a visit; pay the debt of nature; peg out; perish; permit the water of life to run out; pop off; pop off the hooks; pop out; present at the last roll call; present at the last muster; pull the plug; push the clouds around; push up daisies; put sb out of his misery; put sb out of his pain; quit it; quit the scene; rest; rest in Abraham's bosom; rest in peace; return to dust; return to earth; ride into sunset; ring off; ring out; run one's course; run one's race; safe anchorage at last; safe in the arms of Jesus; say hello to Charon; say the last good-bye; see Confucius; settle all scores; settle one's account; shuffle off this mortal coil; shut up shop; sleep; sleep in the grave; sleep one's final sleep; sleep one's last sleep; sleep the big sleep; sleep the eternal sleep; sleep the final sleep; sleep the long sleep; sleep the never-ending sleep; sleep the sleep of death; sleep the sleep that knows no breaking; sleep the sleep that knows no waking; sleep with one's fathers; slip into outer darkness; slip off; slip off the hooks; slip one's cable; slip one's ropes; slip the cable; snuff it; step off; stick one's spoon in the wall; stop living; strike out; succumb to; suffer death; sup with Pluto; surcease; switch out the lights; take a count; take one's departure; take one's last sleep; take one's rest; take one-way ride; take the count; take the big jump; the big jump; the call of God; the curtain call; the end of the ball game; the eternal sleep; the final curtain; the final department; the final kick off; the final summons; the great leveller; the great whipper; the grim reaper; the last bow; the last call; the last getaway; the last great change; the last send-off; the last sleep; the last voyage; the long sleep; the remains; throw up the cards; throw sixes; toss in one's marbles; turn up one's toes to daisies; under the daisies; wink out; with God; with the angels; with their Father; write the last chapter; yield up the breath; yield up the ghost; yield up the soul; yield up the spirit;

死亡集中營 death camp;

死亡恐怖 thanatophobia;

死亡率 death rate; mortality; mortality rate;

~癌死亡率 cancer mortality;

~差別死亡率 differential mortality;

~群組死亡率 cohort mortality;

~生態死亡率 ecological mortality;

死亡人數 body count; death toll;

死亡妄想 necromimesis;

死亡陷阱 death trap;

死亡小分隊 death squad;

死亡約會 rendezvous with death;

死亡證 death certificate;

死亡總數 death toll;

功能性死亡 functional death;

臨牀死亡 clinical death;

瀕於死亡 at death's door; at one's last gasp; have one foot in the grave; nearing one's doom; on one's last legs; on the brink of death; on the verge of

death; totter on the brink of the grace;
身體死亡 somatic death;
生殖死亡 reproductive death;
卧牀死亡 cot death;
遺傳死亡 genetic death;
意外死亡 accidental death;
正常死亡 national death;

[死巷] blind pass; culdesac;

[死心] drop the idea forever; give up the idea forever; give up one's hope for good; have no more illusions about the matter; think no more of sth;
死心塌地 dance obediently; dead set on; head over heels; hell-bent on; unreservedly; wholeheartedly;
死心眼兒 as obstinate as a mule; be bent on one purpose; obstinate and simple-minded; stubborn; too pig-headed;
不死心 not give up hope; unresigned; unwilling to give up;
~還不死心 refuse to give up hope;

[死刑] capital punishment; death penalty; death sentence;
死刑執行 death warrant;
處以死刑 put to death; put to execution;
廢除死刑 abolition of capital punishment;

[死性] having a one-track mind; inflexible; obstinate; stiff; stubborn;

[死訊] news of sb's death;

[死樣] doltish; stupid and dull; wooden;

[死因] cause of death;
死因未定裁決 open verdict;

[死硬] (1) inflexible; rigid; stiff; (2) diehard; obstinate;
死硬派 diehards;

[死有餘辜] death still leaves a margin of his inexpiable guilt; death would not be a sufficient punishment for his crimes; even death cannot atone for his crimes; even death would be too good for him; even death would not expiate all his crimes;

[死於] die as a result of;
死於非命 buy it; catch a packet; come to a bad end; die an unnatural death; meet an untimely end; premature death;
死於橫禍 die a violent death; meet with a sudden death;

[死戰] battle to the last; desperate fight; fight to the death; life-and-death battle;
決一死戰 determine to fight to the death; fight sb to the finish; fight to one's death; fight to the very last; fight with a rope round one's neck; fight with sb to the death; risk all in one desperate battle; wage a life-and-death struggle;

[死者] dead; deceased; departed soul;

[死症] fatal disease; incurable disease;

[死豬] dead pig;
死豬不怕開水燙 a dead mouse feels no cold;

[死罪] capital crime; capital offence; penalty of death;

半死 half-dead;
暴死 die of a sudden disease; die suddenly; die-off; meet sudden death;
逼死 hound sb to death;
必死 will certainly die; will certainly get killed;
濱死 dying; have one foot in the grave; near to death;
瀕死 near death; on the brink of death;
病死 die of an illness;
不死 half dead;
慘死 die a tragic death; die distressingly; meet with a tragic death;
處死 execute; put to death; put to execution;
遄死 die very quickly;
垂死 at the last breath; dying; expiring; fading fast; going; going belly up; going for your tea; have one foot in the grave; knocking on heaven's door; moribund; on one's last legs; receive notice to quit; sinking; slipping;
猝死 die suddenly; drop dead; sudden death;
打死 (1) beat to death; (2) shoot to death; (3) dispatch; (4) kill; (5) stop; (6) smite sb dead;
抵死 defy death; fight desperately;
吊死 hang by the neck; hang oneself;
釘死 (1) nail securely; (2) crucify; nail to death;
凍死 die of frost; freeze and perish; freeze to death;
毒死 kill with poison; poison;
扼死 strangle; throttle;
餓死 starve to death;
該死 (1) damned; dang; (2) deserve to die; ought to die;
肝壞死 hepatic necrosis;
梗死 infarction;
骨壞死 osteonecrosis; recrosis of bone;
橫死 die a violent death; meet with a sudden

death;
壞死 necrosis;
急死 sudden death;
假死 (1) suspended animation; (2) feign death; mimic death; play dead; play possum;
見死 seeing sb in mortal danger;
僵死 dead; ossified;
決死 file-and-death;
客死 die in a place other than one's hometown or in a foreign country;
臨死 on one's deathbed;
冒死 risk one's life;
悶死 bore sb to tears; bore the pants off sb; stiffle; smother; suffocate;
溺死 be drowned;
寧死 would rather die;
弄死 kill; put to death;
怕死 afraid of death; fear death;
拼死 defy death; fight desperately; risk one's life;
氣死 really infuriating;
掐死 choke to death by strangling with hands;
強死 die from violence;
情死 commit suicide for the sake of love; martyrdom to love;
屈死 be persecuted to death; be wronged and driven to death;
人死 death of a person;
忍死 hold on to life and save it for some worthy cause; live when one would rather die;
臊死 utterly ashamed;
殺死 account for; bump off; carry off; destroy; dispatch; dispose of; do for; eliminate; erase; execute; finish; finish off; fix; frag; get rid of; give sb the business; kill; knock off; lay low; lay out; make away with; murder; obliterate; off; puff out; put an end to sb; put away; put down; put sb on the spot; put out; put sb out of his misery; put out of way; put sb to silence; put sb to sleep; remove; rub out; send sb up the Green River; send west; silence; slay; snuff out; take; take care of; take sb for a ride; take off; terminate; touch off; waste; wipe out; zap;
燒死 burn to death
身死 die;
生死 life and death;
誓死 dare to die; pledge one's life;
殊死 desperate; life-and-death;
摔死 be dashed to death; fall to death;
説死 fix definitely; make it definite;

送死 court death; seek one's doom;
速死 die quickly; hasten one's death;
踢死 kick to death;
萬死 die ten thousand deaths; risk any danger to do sth;
枉死 be wronged and driven to death; die through injustice;
畏死 afraid of dying; fear death;
想死 (1) get tired of life; long for death; (2) dying for; long very much for;
傚死 devote oneself to a cause regardless of one's life; render one's service at the risk of losing one's life;
心死 abandoned; heartless; in a state of stupour;
兇死 die by violence; meet a violent end;
尋死 (1) commit suicide; (2) try to commit suicide;
燻死 suffocated to death;
壓死 (1) crush to death; (2) die after being hit by a car;
淹死 be drowned;
佯死 feign death; pretend to be dead;
要死 to death;
縊死 hang oneself;
砸死 be crushed to death;
炸死 kill by bombing;
詐死 fake death; feign death; play dead; pretend to be dead;
戰死 be killed in action; die in a battle;
找死 court death; invite death; seek death;
至死 till death; to the death; to the last; unto death;
致死 cause death; deadly; lethal; result in death;
裝死 death mimicry; feign death; play dead; sham death;
撞死 kill by bumping;
作死 look for trouble; seek one's death; take the road to ruin;

si⁴

si

【巳】 (1) sixth of the twelve Terrestrial Branches; (2) 9 to 11 a.m.; (3) a surname;

［巳時］ period of the day from 9 a.m. to 11 a.m.;

si

【四】 (1) four; (2) fourth; (3) all around;

［四百］ four hundred;

四百週年 quatercentenary;

［四倍］ quattuor;

[四壁] four walls of a room;
四壁蕭條 as poor as a church mouse;
家徒四壁 a family with nothing but for walls; a house empty of all furniture; as poor as a church-mouse; as poor as Job; have nothing but the bare walls in one's house — be utterly destitute; there is not a stick of furniture around;

[四邊] all around; all sides; four sides;
四邊形 quadrangle;
~平行四邊形 parallelogram;

[四表] all directions; beyond limits of the visible world;

[四不像] hoge-podge of sth that resembles nothing; neither fish, flesh, fowl, nor good red herring; neither fish nor fowl; nondescript;

[四次] four times;
我讓你猜四次 I'll give you four guesses;

[四重] quadruple;
四重唱 quartet;
四重奏 quartet;

[四處] all around; everywhere; in all directions;
四處哀告 impore everyone's commiserations;
四處奔走 go hither and thither;
~四處奔走找工作 hit the pavement in search of a job;
四處看 look around;
四處蔓延 run wild;
四處碰壁 be driven from pillar to post; be snubbed at all places; get into trouble on all sides; run into snags at every turn; run one's head into stone walls everywhere;
四處受敵 find oneself hemmed in on every side;
四處尋找 look into every hole and corner; search high and low;
四處張揚 publicize everywhere; spread all over the place;

[四大皆空] all the four elements are absent from the mind;

[四檔] fourth gear;

[四方] (1) all sides; the four directions; (2) square; (3) cubic;
四方八面 every which way; far and near; in all directions;
四方步 walk in a pompous manner;
四方臉 square face;
四方響應 response comes from every quarter;
四四方方 of the shape of a real square;
網開四方 the nets are spread in all directions; the trap has been laid;
志在四方 go far away from one's home and aspire to a great career; ready to realize one's aspiration anywhere all ove the country;

[四顧] look around;
四顧茫然 see nothing but emptiness all around;
四顧無人 look around to find nobody anywhere;
騁目四顧 gaze in four directions; look around;

[四海] (1) four seas; (2) whole country; (3) whole world;
四海風從 the world follows;
四海飄零 drift from one place to another;
四海同悲 the whole nation is grief-stricken; the whole nation is heartbroken with grief;
四海為家 lead a wandering life; make one's home everywhere; make one's home anywhere; make one's home wherever one is; wherever one goes one finds a place as one's home;
~四海為家的人 citizen of the world; cosmopolitan;
四海一家 all people belong to one family; the whole country is united; the whole world is one family;
四海之內皆兄弟 all men between the Four Seas should be brothers; all within the Four Seas are brothers; we are all Adam's children; within the four seas all men are brothers;
遨遊四海 roam about the various parts of the world;
放諸四海而皆準 applicable everywhere; universally applicable;
廣交四海 make friends extensively;
名揚四海 become famous all over the world; enjoy reputation everywhere; well-known in the world;
名震四海 one is well known all over the world;
五洲四海 all over the world; all parts of the world; the Five Continents and

Four Seas;

眼空四海 consider everyone and everything beneath one's notice; look down on everyone else; supercilious;

衍溢四海 overflowing to the four seas;

[四合院] quadrangle;

[四極管] tetrode;

半導體四極管 semiconductor tetrode;

晶體四極管 crystal tetrode;

束射四極管 beam tetrode;

[四季] all the year round; at all seasons; the four seasons;

四季不凋 bloom throughout the year;

四季常青 evergreen; remain green throughout the year;

四季豆 French bean; green bean; kidney beans; spring bean;

四季桔 tangerine;

四季如春 each season seems like spring; it's like spring all the year round;

四季宜人 delightful in all seasons;

[四郊] outskirts; suburbs of a city;

[四腳] hands and legs;

四腳朝天 fall backwards with hands and legs in the air; fall down on one's back with legs pointing up; fall on one's back;

四腳蛇 lizard;

[四開] quarto;

四開本 quarto;

[四兩] four taels;

四兩撥千金 accomplish a great task with little effort by clever maneuvres;

[四鄰] one's near neighbours;

四鄰八舍 all the neighbouring households;

[四馬分屍] draw and quarter;

五馬分屍 dismemberment by five horses — dividing up; sharing out; tear a body limb from limb by five horses — a form of death sentence in ancient times;

[四面] all round; all sides; four sides; on all sides; on four sides;

四面挨打 be pounded on all sides;

四面八方 all around; all directions; all parts; all quarters; all sides; at every hand; every which way; far and near; far and wide; here, there and everywhere; high and low; in all directions; length and breadth; on all hands; on all sides; on every side; right and left; round;

四面出擊 hit out in all directions; make attacks in all directions;

四面楚歌 be assailed on all sides; be besieged; be besieged on all sides; be corned and urged on all sides; be deserted by allies and left alone to face the enemy; be driven to the wall; be surrounded by the enemy on four sides; desperate; in dire straits; land oneself in a tight spot; under attack from all directions; under fire from all quarters;

四面環山 be embosomed in hills; be surrounded by mountains;

四面夾攻 attack on the four sides;

四面玲瓏 tactful with all sorts of people;

四面埋伏 hid in all four directions;

四面受敵 be exposed to enemy attacks on all sides; under attack from all directions;

四面受困 be hemmed in from all sides;

四面體 tetrahedron;

~局部四面體 local tetrahedron;

~連鎖四面體 desmics tetrahedron;

~元四面體 elementary tetrahedron;

~坐標四面體 coordinate tetrahedron;

四面圍困 besiege on all sides;

[四旁] all around; back and front, left and right;

[四起] rise everywhere; rise from all directions;

伏兵四起 the ambushed soldiers leapt out all round;

[四散] disperse everywhere; disperse in all directions; scatter about; scatter in all directions;

四散奔逃 flee helter-skelter; flee in all direction; flee in disorder; stampede;

四散逃竄 be scattered in all directions;

[四十分] (1) forty marks; (2) twenty minutes to a certain clock;

[四時] four seasons;

[四體] arms and legs; four limbs;

四體不勤 parasite whose four limbs do not toil;

四體不勤，五穀不分 can neither do physical work nor distinguish rice from wheat;

[四停八當] have everything in readiness;

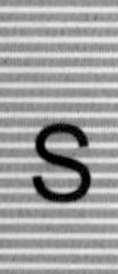

well-disposed indeed;

[四圍] all around;

[四五] four and five;

四分五落 all split up; be scattered in four directions and cast down; scatter to the four directions and five parts;

四捨五入 half adjusting; round to the nearest whole number;

[四向] towards all directions;

[四野] surrounding country; vast expanse of open ground;

[四葉草] four-leaf clover;

[四隅] four corners;

[四月] (1) April; (2) fourth month of the lunar calendar; (3) four months;

[四肢] all fours; arms and legs; four limbs;

四肢百骸 all the limbs and bones;

四肢發達，頭腦簡單 have well-developed limbs but a moronic head;

四肢發育過度 acrometagenesis;

四肢無力 feel weak in one's limbs;

[四周] all around;

四周圍 all around; on all sides; on every side;

環顧四周 look about; look all around; look around;

[四座] all the people present;

語驚四座 one's words electrify his listeners;

封四 back cover;

禮拜四 Thursday;

星期四 Thursday;

si

【寺】 monastery; mosque; shrine; temple;

[寺觀] Buddhist temple; Daoist temple;

[寺廟] house of god; temple;

[寺人] eunuch; palace attendant;

[寺舍] temple building;

[寺院] monastery; temple;

寺院學校 abbey school; monastic school;

[寺主] abbot;

佛寺 Buddhist temple;

喇嘛寺 lamasery;

禮拜寺 mosque;

清真寺 mosque;

石窟寺 Cave Temple;

閹寺 palace eunuch;

si

【汜】 stream that branches and afterwards merges again;

si

【伺】 reconnoiter; spy; watch;

[伺便] wait for a chance convenient for one;

[伺察] investigate; spy; trace secretly;

[伺服] serve; servo;

伺服機構 servo; servomechanism;

~ 反向伺服機構 reverse servo;

~ 方位伺服機構 azimuth servomechanism;

~ 跟蹤伺服機構 tracking servo;

~ 液壓伺服機構 hydraulic servomechanism;

伺服系統 server system; servosystem;

~ 位置伺服系統 positional servosystem;

~ 自適應伺服系統 adaptive servosystem;

[伺機] wait for one's chance;

伺機報復 bide one's time for revenge; find some way to retaliate; seek one's revenge on;

伺機而動 keep secretly ready for the right time; wait for a favourable moment to make a move; wait for an opportunity to take action; watch for the proper moment for action;

伺機反撲 bide one's time for a counterattack; seek opportunities to launch a counterattack; wait for a chance to spring a counterattack; wait for an opportunity to counterattack;

伺機下手 play a waiting game;

伺機再起 wait for an opportunity to stage a comeback;

[伺探] investigate secretly; spy;

狙伺 lie in wait for;

窺伺 be on watch for; watch and wait (for a chance to act);

si

【似】 (1) like; resemble; seem; similar; (2) appear; as if; seem;

[似…非…] it is like..., but it it not...;

似懂非懂 have only a hazy notion; not quite understand;

似夢非夢 it is like a dream and yet it is no dream;

似通非通 plausible;

似笑非笑 there's a faint smile on one's face; with a spurious smile; with an

attempt at a smile;
似醉非醉 in a half-drunken state;
[似乎] as if; as it appears; it appears that; it looks as if; it looks like; it seems; seem; seemingly;
似乎是如此 so it appears;
看起來似乎 it begins to appear that...;

好似 be like; look like; seem;
渾似 almost like; as if; just like;
近似 approximate; roughly; similar;
酷似 be exactly like; the very image of;
類似 analogous; likeness; similar;
貌似 look alike in appearance; seemingly;
恰似 be alike; seem;
強似 be better than; be superior to;
神似 be an excellent likeness;
勝似 be better than; surpass;
相似 alike; similar;
肖似 look very much alike;
形似 be similar in form or appearance;
疑似 suspect to be;

si
【兕】 female rhinoceros;

si
【姒】 (1) wife of one's husband's elder brother; (2) (in ancient China) elder of twins; (3) a surname;

si
【泗】 (1) nasal mucus; snivel; (2) name of a county; (3) name of a river;

si
【祀】 offer sacrifices to; worship;
[祀典] religious rites;
[祀奉] worship;
[祀孔] offer sacrifices to Confucius;
[祀神] worship gods;
[祀事] religious services;
[祀天] offer sacrifices to heaven;
[祀祖] offer sacrifices to one's ancestors; worship ancestors;

奉祀 offer sacrifices to gods or ancestors;
祭祀 offer sacrifices to gods or ancestors;

si
【俟】 (1) await; wait for; (2) as soon as; until;
[俟便] when it is convenient;
[俟候] wait for;
[俟機] wait for an opportunity; watch for one's chance;
[俟即] as soon as; when...then;
[俟駕] (1) wait for the emperor's arrival; (2) wait for your arrival;
[俟命] leave everything to fate;
[俟時] wait for an opportunity;
[俟死] await death;
[俟至] wait until;

si
【食】 feed; give food to;
[食母] wet nurse;

si
【耜】 plough;

si
【笥】 bamboo box; bamboo chest;
[笥匱囊空] all the boxes and bags are empty; extremely poor;

si
【嗣】 (1) inherit; succeed to; (2) continue; follow; (3) descendant;
[嗣產] inherit a fortune;
[嗣承] succeed in line;
[嗣後] after that; afterwards; hereafter; later on; subsequently;
[嗣繼] inherit; succeed;
[嗣立] appoint; be appointed as heir;
[嗣歲] coming year;
[嗣位] succeed to the throne;
[嗣響] succeed to one's forefather's business;
[嗣業] inherit a business; inherit a fortune;
[嗣音] continue one's messages;
[嗣子] (1) heir; (2) adopted son;

後嗣 descendant; offspring;
繼嗣 adopt sb as one's son; heir; inheritor;
絕嗣 heirless; without offspring;
子嗣 male offspring; son;

si
【肆】 (1) behave without restraint; indulge in; let loose; unbridled; wanton; (2) four; (3) marketplace; shop; (4) display; exhibit;
[肆陳] exhibit;
[肆口] talk without much thought;
肆口大罵 abuse sb outrageously and without any restraint;

肆口漫罵 rail and swear at wildly; swear home; swear like a lord; swear one's way through a stone wall; use profane language freely;

［肆力］ do all one can; do one's best; do one's utmost; try one's best;

［肆掠］ indulge in looting without restraint;

［肆目］ stretch one's eyes as far as one can see;

［肆虐］ indulge in wanton massacre or persecution; wreak haoc;

［肆其簧鼓］ make trouble by spreading unreliable reports;

［肆擾］ harass wantonly;

［肆行］ act at the dictate of one's own will without any thought for others; act recklessly; indulge;

肆行無度 live immoderately;

肆行無忌 act disorderly and care for nobody;

［肆言詈辱］ abuse outrageously and without any restraint; swear wildly;

［肆意］ at will; recklessly; wantonly; wilfully; without any restraint;

肆意嘲弄 ridicule unscrupulously;

肆意揮霍 freely squander;

肆意劫掠 indulge in looting;

肆意謾罵 call sb all kinds of names; use scurrility;

肆意生長 grow wild;

肆意歪曲事實 wantonly distort the facts;

肆意污蔑 wantonly slander;

肆意侮謾，語多乖戾 resort to unbridled insults and vilifications and use absurd and offensive language;

［肆飲］ indulge in drinking;

［肆應］ good at dealing with varied matters properly;

［肆志］ be puffed up with pride;

大肆 recklessly; violently;

放肆 unbridled; unscrupulous;

市肆 shop; store;

恣肆 (1) forceful and unrestrained; free and natural; (2) unbridled; unrestrained; willfully;

si

【飼】 (1) feed; raise; (2) feed; fodder; forage;

［飼槽］ feeding trough;

［飼草］ forage grass;

［飼料］ feed; fodder; forage;

飼料玉米 field corn;

飼料作物 fodder crop; forage crop;

發酵飼料 fermented fodder;

菌類飼料 fungus fodder;

顆粒飼料 granulatged feed;

［飼養］ breed; raise;

飼養家禽 raise poultry;

飼養人 breeder;

~牲畜飼養人 stockbreeder;

飼養員 keeper; stockman;

［飼育］ raise; rear;

鼻飼 nasal feedings;

si

【駟】 (1) team of four horses; (2) horses; (3) four; (4) name of a star;

［駟不及舌］ a word lightly spoken goes faster than a team of four horses; even a team of four horses cannot overtake and recover what is already said;

［駟馬］ team of four horses;

駟馬高車 high carriage and four horses – symbol of wealth and nobility;

駟馬難追 even with a team of four horses, it is difficult to overtake carelessly uttered words;

song¹

song

【松】 (1) firs; pines; (2) a surname;

［松柏］ pine and cypress;

松柏長青 as evergreeen as fir and pine; may you live long and remain strong like the evergreen pine and fir tree; remain as evergreen as the pine and cypress;

松柏後凋 everygreens survive winter best; pine and cypress survive winter best; the pine and cedar are everygreen; the pine and the cypress are the last to wither;

松柏節操 fortitude; honest and virtuous conduct; lofty character;

松柏森森 dense pine and cypress trees;

柏節松操 chastity of the cypress and the pine tree – of chaste widowhood;

［松板］ deal board;

［松風水月］ the soughing of pines and the

reflection of moonlight on the water;

[松果] strobile;

松果菊 coneflower;

[松鶴] pines and cranes;

松鶴長春 may you life be as long as the pines and the cranes;

松鶴延齡 live as long as the pine and crane; longevity;

[松花蛋] preserved eggs;

[松篁交翠] pines and bamboos vie with each other in verdure;

[松雞] grouse;

松雞肉 grouse;

一群松雞 a pack of grouse;

[松焦油] pine tar;

[松節油] turpentine; turps;

粗木製松節油 crude wood turpentine;

粗松節油 crude turpentine;

乾鎦松節油 destructive distillation turpentine;

脂化松節油 fat turpentine;

[松林] pinewood; pinery;

[松蘿] pine lichen;

[松毛] pine needles;

松毛蟲 pine moth;

[松明] pine torches;

[松木] pine-wood planks;

[松鼠] squirrel;

一隻松鼠 a squirrel;

[松樹] pine; pine tree;

一棵松樹 a pine tree;

一株松樹 a pine;

[松塔] (1) pine cone; (2) cone of the lacebark pine;

[松濤] soughing of the wind in the pines sounds like roaring waves;

松濤風吟 the sighing sound of the wind in the pines;

[松香] abietyl; colophony; rosin;

松香素 abietine;

松香烯 abietene;

松香脂 abietene;

化合松香 combined rosin;

普通松香 common rosin;

脱氫松香 dehydrogenated rosin;

酯化松香 esterified rosin;

[松針] pine needle;

[松子] pine nut; pine seed;

白果松 ginkgo pine;

白皮松 lacebark pine;

白松 white pine;

保泰松 phenylbutazone;

蒼松 (1) dried meat floss; (2) green pine; (3) loosen; relax; (4) not hard-up; soft; well-off; (5) let go; untie;

赤松 Japanese red pine;

果松 Korean pine;

海松 Korean pine;

紅松 Korean pine;

黃松 yellow pine;

勁松 sturdy pines;

可的松 cortisone;

羅漢松 yew podocarpus;

落葉松 larch;

馬拉松 marathon;

馬尾松 masson pine;

喬松 lofty pine;

強的松 prednisone;

青松 pine;

水松 Chinese cypress;

雪松 cedar;

油松 Chinese pine;

魚松 dried fish floss;

song

【崧】 (1) high mountain; (2) eminent; lofty; outstanding;

song

【淞】 a river in Jiangsu;

song

【嵩】 (1) Songshan in Henan; (2) high; lofty;

[嵩壽] longevity;

song

【鬆】 (1) lax; loose; slack; (2) loosen; relax; slacken; (3) light; soft; (4) release; unfasten; untie;

[鬆綁] (1) undo sth tied; untie sb; (2) relax restrictions;

[鬆餅] muffin;

藍莓鬆餅 blueberry muffin;

英式鬆餅 English muffin;

[鬆弛] (1) flabby; limp; loose; relax; relaxation; slack; (2) lax;

鬆弛句 loose sentence;

鬆弛同位 loose apposition;

表觀鬆弛 apparent relaxation;

反常鬆弛 anomalous relaxation;

信用鬆弛 credit relaxation;

壓縮鬆弛 compression stress relaxation;

［鬆脆］ crisp and soft;

［鬆動］ become flexible;

［鬆泛］ easygoing; relaxed;

［鬆緊］ tension and relaxation;

鬆緊帶 elastic cord;

明鬆暗緊 to all appearances, relaxation; in reality, quite the opposite;

前鬆後緊 slacken at the beginning and have to speed up towards the end;

時緊時鬆 at times tense and at times relaxed; now in an acute and now in a relaxed form;

［鬆勁］ loose strength; slack;

鬆勁情緒 slack mood;

鬆勁洩氣 slackness and despondency;

［鬆開］ let loose; loosen; unclasp; unfix; unlink; unlock;

［鬆口］ (1) relax a bite; (2) show a degree of flexibility in negotiating;

鬆口氣 get a breathing spell; relax for a while;

［鬆快］ (1) less crowded; (2) feel easy; (3) relax;

［鬆氣］ relax one's effort;

［鬆軟］ (1) fluffy; soft; (2) feeble;

鬆軟的 floppy;

［鬆散］ loosely arranged; incompact; not solid;

鬆鬆散散 loose;

［鬆手］ let go the hands; relax the hold;

［鬆鬆垮垮］ behave in a lax way; slack and perfunctory; slacken one's efforts;

鬆鬆垮垮，拖拖拉拉 slacken one's efforts and drag one's heels;

［鬆土］ loosen the soil; scarify the soil;

鬆土鏟 shovel;

~箭形鬆土鏟 arrow-head shovel;

~培土鬆土鏟 covering shovel;

~鑿齒鬆土鏟 chisel-tooth shovel;

［鬆懈］ loosening; lose momentum; relax; relax efforts; slack; slacken;

［鬆心］ carefree;

耙鬆 harrow up;

放鬆 chillax; loosen; relax; slacken; uncage;

乾松 dry and soft;

蓬鬆 fluffy; puffy;

輕鬆 light; relaxed;

肉鬆 dried meat floss;

疏鬆 loose; loosen;

稀鬆 (1) loose; poor; sloppy; (2) trivial; unimportant; (3) indifferent; not interested;

牙鬆 looseness of the tooth;

song³

song

【悚】 fearful; frightened; horrified; terrified;

［悚懼］ frightened; terrified; tremble with fear;

［悚然］ horrified; in terror; terrified; terror-stricken;

悚然而懼 afraid of; fear-stricken;

悚然而立 stand up in terror; stand up terrified;

悚然發立 trembling with hair standing on end;

悚然驚魂 soul trembling with fear;

毛骨悚然 be absolutely terrified; be frightened from the tips of one's hair to the marrow of his very bones; be overcome with horror; bloodcurdling; give sb the creeps; have gooseflesh; make one's blood run cold; make one's flesh creep; send chills up sb's spine; with one's hair standing on end;

［悚悚］ dread; fear; fright; scare;

［悚惕］ fearful;

震悚 astonish; shock;

song

【竦】 (1) respectful; (2) awed; horrified; terrified; (3) lofty; towering;

［竦懼］ frightened; terrified; tremble with fear;

［竦然］ fearful; scared;

song

【慫】 incite; instigate;

［慫動］ incite; instigate;

［慫恿］ abet; edge on sb; egg sb on; goad on sb; goad sb to do sth; goad sb into doing sth; incite; instigate; put sb up to sth; set on; urge sb to do sth urge sb into doing sth;

慫恿支持 with the support and connivance of sb;

song

【聳】 (1) lofty; rise up; towering; (2) alarm; alert; sensational; shock; warn; (3) egg on; urge;

［聳動］ (1) egg on; urge; (2) be alarmed; be

moved;
聳動視聽 create a sensation;
[聳肩] shrug one's shoulders;
聳肩哈腰 shrug one's shoulders and offer an ingratiating smile;
[聳懼] frightened; shocked; terrified;
[聳立] rise up steeply; tower aloft;
[聳然] rise in sharp elevation;
[聳聽] alarm others with sth sensational; stimulate others;
[聳恿] egg on; urge;
高聳 (stand) tall and erect; towering;

song⁴

song

【宋】 (1) Song Dynasty (960-1279); (2) Song Dynasty (420-479), one of the Southern Dynasties; (3) a surname;
[宋版] Song edition;
[宋詞] *ci*-poetry of Song;
[宋瓷] Song porcelain;
[宋體字] Song typeface;

song

【送】 (1) carry; convey; deliver; (2) despatch; send; (3) give; give as a present; present; (4) accompany; see sb off; see sb out; send off;
[送報] deliver newspapers; paper round;
送報男孩 paperboy;
送報女孩 papergirl;
送報生 newsboy;
[送別] give a send-off; see sb off; send-off; wish sb bon voyage;
送別會 farewell party; send-off;
送君千里，終須一別 accompanying sb a thousand miles, and yet there is bound to be a parting at last; although you escort a guest a thousand miles, yet must the parting come at last; although you escort your guest a thousand miles, yet must you part in the end; even if you accompany a guest a thousand miles, you must at last come to the parting place;
[送殯] attend a funeral; take part in a funeral procession;
送殯行列 cortege;
出喪送殯 follow the coffin on foot in the funeral procession;
[送達] deliver to; dispatch to; send to;
[送到] deliver to; send to;
[送飯] bring meals;
[送官] deliver a criminal to the court for punishment;
送官究辦 turn sb over to the court to be dealt with;
[送鬼] eorcise evil spirits;
[送還] give back; return;
[送回] send back; return;
[送貨] deliver goods;
送貨上門 deliver goods to the consumer's home; deliver goods to the doorstep of a customer; home delivery service; sell goods at the customers' doors;
送貨員 delivery man;
[送餞] give a send-off party;
[送交] deliver to; hand over;
[送客] escort a visitor on his way out; see a visitor out;
送客到門口 accompany a guest to the door;
[送老] (1) pass one's later years; (2) prepare the dead for burial;
[送禮] give sb a present; present a gift to sb; send gifts;
給上司送禮 offer gifts to one's superiors;
[送命] bring death upon oneself; get killed; go to one's doom; lose one's life;
[送奶] deliver milk;
送奶車 milk float;
送奶工 milkman;
送奶路線 milk round;
[送氣] aspirate;
送氣音 aspirated sound;
[送情] convey one's feelings;
[送人] (1) give presents; send fits; (2) see a person off; see sb off;
[送喪] attend a funeral; take part in a funeral procession;
[送神] send off the gods after the offering of sacrifices;
[送死] court death; seek one's doom;
[送往事居] nourish the living and bury the dead — do one's duty;
[送信] carry letters; deliver a message; deliver letters; send letters;
送信人 messenger boy;
[送行] (1) say goodbye to sb; see sb off; (2)

give a send-off party;
[送葬] attend a burial ceremony; take part in a funeral procession;
送葬行列 cortege;
[送終] attend upon a dying parent or other senior member of one's family; prepare for the burial of one's parents;

白送 give away; send a gift with nothing in return;
伴送 escort;
保送 recommend sb for admission to school, etc.;
報送 select and send sb;
播送 airing; airplay; beam; broadcast; transmit;
不送 don't bother to see sb out;
抄送 make a copy for; send a duplicate to;
傳送 convey; deliver; transfer; transmit; transport;
遞送 deliver; send;
斷送 forfeit; ruin;
發送 (1) consignment; dispatch; send; sending; (2) transmit by radio;
放送 broadcast; send out;
分送 distribute; send;
奉送 give away free; offer as a gift;
附送 give as a bonus;
后送 evacuation;
護送 convoy; escort;
歡送 see off; send off;
賫送 send sb sth as a present;
接送 pick up and send off;
解送 send under guard;
餽送 present a gift;
目送 follow sb with one's eyes; gaze after; watch sb go;
扭送 seize sb and hand him over to (the public security authorities, etc.)
陪送 dowry; give a dowry to a daughter;
遣送 repatriate; send back;
輸送 carry; convey; transport;
選送 select and recommend;
押送 send a person to prison; send to another place under escort;
迎送 greet and see off;
遠送 see one off far;
運送 consignment; convey; ship; transport;
葬送 bury; ruin; spell an end to;
贈送 give as a present; present as a gift;
致送 give; send;
轉送 (1) make a present of what one has been given; (2) pass on;
資送 (1) send away with money provided; (2) give a dowry to a daughter on her marriage;
祖送 give a farewell luncheon;

song
【訟】 (1) bring a case to court; bring a dispute to court; lawsuit; litigation; (2) argue over the right and wrong of sth; demand justice; dispute; (3) in public; publicly; (4) (now rare) regret; repent;
[訟案] case at law; case in court;
[訟師] law practitioner; lawyer; attorney at law;
惡訟師 ambulance chaser;
[訟事] lawsuit; litigation;
[訟庭] court of law;
[訟言] announce; declare; speak in public;
[訟獄] lawsuit; litigation;

詞訟 legal case; lawsuit;
辭訟 legal case; lawsuit;
涉訟 be involved in a lawsuit;
訴訟 lawsuit; litigation; suit;
聽訟 try a case;
興訟 start a lawsuit;

song
【頌】 (1) acclaim; eulogize; extol; laud; praise; (2) eulogy; hymn; ode; paean; song; (3) express good wishes;
[頌詞] complimentary address; congratulatory speech; eulogy;
[頌歌] carol; hymn; song; ode;
聖誕頌歌 Christmas carols;
[頌美] acclaim; praise the achievements of others;
[頌詩] eulogistic poem;
[頌揚] acclaim; eulogize; extol; laud; praise; sing sb's praises;
頌揚備致 laud...to the skies; praise profusely;
值得頌揚 laudable;
[頌讚] acclaim; praise;

忭頌 be pleased to offer best wishes;
稱頌 eulogize; extol; praise;
傳頌 be widely read;

song
【誦】 (1) chant; intone; read aloud; recite;

(2) poem; song;
[誦讀] chant; intone; read aloud; recite;
[誦經] recite passages from scriptures;
[誦詩] intone a verse; recite a poem;
[誦説] read and explain;
[誦習] learn by recitation;

諳誦 recite from memory;
闇誦 recite in silence;
背誦 recite; repeat from memory;
傳誦 be on everybody's lips; be widely read;
記誦 learn by heart;
朗誦 read aloud with expression;
默誦 read silently;

sou¹

sou

【搜】 (1) look for; search; seek; (2) inquire into; investigate;
[搜捕] hunt for; manhunt; search and arrest; track down and arrest;
搜捕異己 witchhunt;
全國搜捕 national manhunt;
[搜查] ransack; rummage; search;
搜查違禁品 make a search for contraband;
幫助搜查 assist search;
徹底搜查 shakedown;
到處搜查 look up and down;
放棄搜查 abandon a search;
進行搜查 carry out a search;
停止搜查 call off a search;
展開搜查 launch a search; mount a search;
[搜出來] find; recover; search out;
[搜根剔齒] search minutely for sb's smallest fault; very particular about one's choice;
[搜購] collect for purchase;
[搜刮] claw; extort; fleece; expropriate; plunder;
搜刮私人財產 expropriate privately owned assets;
[搜集] collect; gather; seek and gather;
搜集意見 solicit opinions;
[搜緝] hunt down; search for;
[搜檢] search and investigate;
[搜救] search for and rescue;
[搜羅] collect; gather; recruit;
搜羅人才 gather and engage geniuses; hunt up talents; recruit qualified persons; scout for talent;
搜羅證據 collect evidences – proofs;
[搜拿] hunt for a fugitive;
[搜求] find; look for; seek;
[搜身] body search; frisk; make a body search; search a person;
搜身檢查 body search;
[搜索] beat about; ferret about; fossick; hunt for; scout around; search for;
搜索枯腸 beat one's brains; beat one's brains out; cudgel one's brains; rack one's brains; scratch through one's mind for sth; think hard;
搜索前進 advance and reconnoitre;
計數搜索 counter search;
數值搜索 numerical search;
[搜討] scrutinize and investigate; study carefully;
[搜剔] choosy; faultfinding; pick; select; weed out;
[搜尋] look for; search for; seek; seek and find;
搜尋線索 search for clues;
仔細搜尋 comb through;
自我搜尋 egosurf;

摳搜 (1) dawdle; move slowly; (2) dig or dig out with a finger or sth pointed; miserly;

sou

【嗖】 (1) laughing expression; (2) sound one makes to drive away birds; (3) whiz;
[嗖嗖] with laughter;
嗖嗖聲 zing;
~ 子彈的嗖嗖聲 the zing of bullets;

sou

【廋】 (1) conceal; hide; (2) search;
[廋詞] puzzle; riddle; enigma;
[廋疏] search;
[廋索] look for sth hidden;
[廋語] puzzle; riddle; enigma;

sou

【溲】 (1) urinate; (2) drench; immerse; soak;
[溲便] urinate;
[溲溺] urinate;
[溲器] urinal;

sou

【蒐】 (1) collect; gather; (2) hunt for; look

for; search for; (3) retire and live in seclusion;

［蒐集］ collect; gather;

蒐集郵票 collect stamps;

蒐集資料 collect information;

［蒐羅］ search and collect;

［蒐索］ search;

蒐索樹林 search the forest;

sou

【餿】 (1) decayed; rancid; rotten; stale; (2) foul; lousy;

［餿臭］ rotten and smelly;

［餿酸］ stale;

sou

【颼】 (1) blown about by wind; (2) swishing sound of a fast-flying object; whiz;

［颼乾］ make sth dry or cool by wind;

颼颼 sound of wind;

冷颼颼 (of wind) chilling; chilly;

涼颼颼 (of wind) chill; chilly;

sou³

sou

【叟】 elder; old man; old person; old people; senior;

sou

【嗾】 (1) give vocal signals to a dog; whistle to a dog; (2) instigate;

［嗾使］ abet; incite; instigate;

sou

【瞍】 blind; have eyes without eyeballs;

［瞍矇］ blind man;

sou

【擻】 flutter; quake; shake; tremble;

［擻抖抖］ shivering; trembling;

抖擻 be in high spirits; pluck up;

sou⁴

sou

【嗽】 clear the throat; cough;

咳嗽 cough;

su¹

su

【甦】 come back to life; regain consciousness; resurrect; revive; rise from the dead;

［甦醒］ come back to life; come to; revive;

su

【酥】 (1) brittle; fragile; frail; (2) crisp; fresh; (3) lustrous; (4) shortbread;

［酥餅］ crisp biscuit;

［酥脆］ crisp;

酥脆花生 crisp peanuts;

［酥燈］ oil lamp in front of the Buddha;

［酥髮］ lustrous hair;

［酥酪］ kumiss;

［酥麻］ frail and numb;

［酥軟］ feeble; lacking strength;

［酥糖］ (1) crisp candy; crunchy candy; (2) sugar cake;

［酥胸］ soft and smooth skin of a woman's breast;

［酥油］ butter;

酥油茶 buttered tea;

冰花酥 frost shortbread;

蟾酥 dried venom of toads; toad cake;

合子酥 meat shortbread;

辣酥酥 somewhat (but not too) pungent;

麻酥酥 tingle;

千層酥 filo;

桃酥 peach-shaped shortbread;

悉酥 rustle;

杏花兒酥 almond shortbread;

油酥 (1) crisp; (2) flaky; (3) short;

su

【穌】 (1) collect; take; (2) come to; revive; rise again; (3) rest;

su

【蘇】 (1) come back to life; come to; resurrect; revive; (2) Soviet; (3) a surname;

［蘇打］ soda;

蘇打塊 block soda;

蘇打水 club soda;

重蘇打 heavy soda;

植物蘇打 vegetable soda;

［蘇息］ (1) rest; (2) come back to life; revive;

［蘇醒］ awake; come to; come round; regain consciousness; revive;

白蘇 common perilla;

復蘇 (1) come back to life or consciousness; (2)

recover;
嚕蘇 long-winded;
屠蘇 a kind of wine in ancient times;
紫蘇 purple perilla;

su²
su

【俗】 (1) conventions; customs; (2) common; popular; (3) unrefined; vulgar; (4) lay; secular; (5) tasteless; trite;
[俗筆] vulgar style of writing;
[俗不可耐] atrocity; intolerable vulgarity; too vulgar to be endured; unbearably vulgar; vulgar in the extreme;
衣着俗不可耐 one's dress is an atrocity;
[俗不傷雅] commonplace but do not injure elegance;
[俗稱] (1) secular name of a monk; (2) commonly called; commonly known as; common name;
[俗耳] vulgar ears;
[俗好] popular tastes;
不投俗好 not cater to the popular tastes;
[俗化] vulgarize;
[俗話] adage; common sayings; popular sayings; proverb;
[俗家] parents' home of a monk;
[俗見] current prejudices;
囿於俗見 blinded by current prejudices;
[俗累] worldly troubles;
[俗吏] petty official;
[俗例] customary rules;
[俗流] (1) common lot of people; (2) layman;
[俗陋] vulgar;
[俗慮塵懷] all worldly cares;
[俗論] popular opinion;
[俗名] local name; popular name; secular name; trivial name;
[俗念] layman's ideas; worldly thoughts;
[俗氣] (1) in poor taste; vulgar; (2) hackneyed;
俗氣的 gaudy; lurid;
[俗情] common, human feelings;
[俗人] (1) vulgarian; ordinary person; (2) layman;
[俗儒] scholar of shallow learning;
[俗尚] common conventions; current fashions;
[俗世] earthly life;
拋棄俗世 renounce the world;
[俗事] (1) secularity; (2) daily routine; everyday matters; mundane affairs; worldly affairs;
[俗識] common sense;
[俗説] popular version;
[俗隨時變] other times, other manners;
[俗態] vulgar manner;
[俗套] conventions; conventional patterns; social conventions;
不落俗套 conform to no conventional pattern; depart from convention; off the beaten track;
陳詞俗套 conventional phrases;
[俗謂] there is a common saying;
[俗務] chores; everyday matters; worldly cares;
俗務纏身 be restrained with ordinary affairs; be tied down by everyday affairs;
[俗姓] secular surname of a Buddhist monk;
[俗學] secular studies;
[俗諺] common saying;
[俗謠] popular songs;
[俗議] popular opinion;
[俗語] common saying; folk adage; proverb;
[俗欲] worldly thoughts;
[俗緣未了] the time has not yet come for entering the monastery;
[俗拙蠢物] common run of stupid, vulgar creatures;
[俗子] vulgar person;
傖夫俗子 vulgar person;
凡夫俗子 mortals; ordinary people;
[俗字] popular form of a character;

拔俗 free from vulgarity; outstanding and unique; rise far above the common lot;
鄙俗 low; philistine; vulgar;
不俗 not hackneyed; original; uncommon;
傖俗 vulgar;
從俗 conform to conventions; follow local customs; follow traditions;
粗俗 coarse; uncouth; vulgar;
低俗 low in taste; trashy; vulgar;
風俗 customs;
獷俗 barbarian ways; uncivilized customs;
還俗 resume secular life;
俚俗 uncultured; unrefined; vulgar;
禮俗 etiquette and customs;
流俗 current custom; prevalent custom;
陋俗 objectionable customs; undesirable

customs;
民俗 folk custom; folklore; folkways;
僧俗 monks and laymen;
世俗 (1) common custom; social conventions; (2) secular worldly;
釋俗 explain in common words, phrases, etc.;
殊俗 (1) strange customs; (2) extraordinary;
順俗 act according to the customs; go with the crowd;
隨俗 act according to prevailing customs; comply with convention; do as everybody else does; follow local custom;
通俗 common; popular;
脱俗 free from vulgarity; free oneself from worldly ways; not be bound by conventions; otherworldly;
污俗 vulgar custom;
習俗 convention; custom; habitude; practice;
炫俗 flaunt; show off;
尋俗 ordinary;
循俗 follow customs and traditions;
雅俗 the refined and the vulgar; the sophisticated and the simple-minded;
謠俗 folklore;
遺俗 old custom; traditional practices;
易俗 change customs; change practises;
異俗 (1) different custom; (2) bad custom;
庸俗 low; philistine; vulgar;

su4

su

【夙】 (1) early in the morning; (2) long-standing; old; (3) have inborn; inherited;

［夙仇］ old enemy;

［夙慧］ be born intelligent; have inborn intelligence;

［夙駕］ set out early; start a journey early;

［夙諾］ previous promise;

［夙儒］ learned scholar;

［夙世］ previous incarnation;

夙世有緣 two people who were connected in a former existence;

夙世冤家 bitter enemy; enemy in one's former life;

［夙昔］ (1) in the past; past times; (2) day and night;

［夙夜］ day and night; morning and night;

夙夜匪懈 busy morning and night; never to relax morning and night; non-stop from morning to night; work diligently day and night;

夙夜辛勞 toil early and late;

夙夜憂思 grieve over sb day and night;

夙夜在公 be in one's office day and night;

夙興夜寐 early to rise and late to retire; get up early and go to bed late; on one's feet early in the morning and allow oneself no rest until late at night; rise early and retire late; rise early and sleep late; work hard from early morning till late in the evening;

［夙願］ long-cherished wish; old wish;

夙願難償 one's long-cherished hope is hard to realize;

夙願已償 one's long-cherished wish has been fulfilled; one's old desire is gratified; the great wish of one's life is gratified;

得償夙願 have fulfilled one's long-cherished wish; realize one's long-cherished hope;

以償夙願 realize one's long-cherished hope;

［夙怨］ old grudges;

［夙志］ long-cherished ambition;

su

【泝】 same as 溯；

su

【素】 (1) pure white silk; (2) unbleached and undyed; white; (3) plain; quiet; simple; (4) mourning; (5) vegetable food; (6) up to the present; (7) native; (8) basic elements; elements; (9) generally; habitually; usually;

［素愛］ frequent;

［素材］ source materials;

［素菜］ vegetable dishes;

［素餐］ (1) vegetable meal; (2) vegetarian; (3) not work for one's living;

素餐尸位 occupy a high position without doing anything;

［素常］ commonly; habitually; ordinarily; usually;

［素稱］ commonly known as; ordinarily known as; usually called;

［素淡］ quiet colours;

［素髮］ gray hair; white hair;

［素飯］ vegetarian diet;

［素封］ become wealthy without holding a

public office;
[素服] white mourning dress;
[素故] old friend;
[素官] poor government official;
[素懷] long-cherished ambition;
[素檢] simple and disciplined;
[素交] long-known friend; true old friend; old acquaintance;
[素舊] old friendship;
[素淨] plain and neat; quiet colours;
[素來] all along; always; up to the present;
[素練] (1) white silk; (2) cascade; waterfall;
[素履] (1) simple life; (2) common scholar contented with a quiet and simple life;
[素門] poor family;
[素描] (1) draw; sketch; (2) literary sketch;
素描簿 sketchbook;
淡妝素描 have simple make-up;
[素貧] in a chronic state of poverty;
[素樸] (1) simple and unadorned; (2) rudimentary;
[素秋] autumn; fall;
[素稔] have long been familiar with sb;
[素日] commonly; daily; generally; usually;
[素尚] (1) simple and plain; (2) virtues;
[素食] (1) vegetarian diet; (2) vegetarian;
素食餐館 vegetarian restaurant;
素食主義 vegetarianism;
~素食主義者 vegetarian;
[素事] funeral matters;
[素識] have been familiar with; have known;
[素數] prime number;
[素王] the uncrowned king — Confucius;
[素望] one's good reputation and prestige;
[素位] one's current position;
[素聞] have been frequently told; have often heard;
[素昔] ordinarily; regularly; so far; usually;
[素席] vegetarian feast;
[素心] (1) simple and honest; (2) one's conscience;
[素行] one's true disposition;
[素雅] quiet and in good taste; simple but elegant; unadorned and in good taste;
[素仰] have always admired; have always looked up to;
[素養] accomplishment; attainment;
有素養[的] cultivated;
[素業] former profession; former vocation;
[素一] simple and honest;
[素衣] (1) plain clothes; (2) white mourning dress;
[素隱行怪] live as a recluse scholar and behave eccentrically;
[素油] vegetable oil;
[素友] old friend;
[素願] long-cherished ambition;
[素約] old promise;
[素月] chaste moon;
[素知] have known for some time;
[素質] quality;
素質測驗 aptitude test;
高素質 high quality;
國民素質 national qualities;
整體素質 overall quality;
[素志] long-cherished ambition;
[素妝淡描] have a simple makeup;

矮壯素 cycocel;
氨苄青霉素 ampicillin;
胺霉素 amidomycin;
螯酶素 chelocardin;
白霉素 albomycin;
巴龍霉素 paromomycin;
茶素 caffeine;
吃素 abstain from eating meat; vegetarian;
赤霉素 gibberellin;
春雷霉素 kasugarnycin;
詞素 morpheme;
膽紅素 bilirubin;
氮素 nitrogen;
地霉素 terramycin;
毒素 (1) poison; (2) toxin;
乾酪素 casein;
肝素 heparin;
縞素 white mourning dress;
更生霉素 actinomycin D;
鈷胺素 vitamin B12;
胡蘿蔔素 carotene;
寒素 destitute; poor;
合霉素 syntomycin;
核素 nuclein; nuclide;
核黃素 lactoflavin; riboflavin;
黑色素 melanin;
紅霉素 erythromycin;
花青素 anthocyanidin;
黃素 flavin;
灰黃霉素 griseofulvin;
激乳素 prolactin;

S

激素 hormone;
薊苦素 cnicin;
甲狀腺素 thyroxine;
酵素 (1) enzyme; (2) ferment;
結核結素 tuberculin;
結素 tuberculin;
金霉素 aureomycin;
卡那霉素 kanamycin;
抗敵素 a kind of antibiotic;
抗毒素 antitoxin;
抗菌素 antibiotic;
抗霉素 antimycin;
抗生素 antibiotic;
孿元素 twin elements;
酪素 casein;
滷素 halogen;
氯霉素 chloramphenicol; chloromycetin;
類毒素 antitoxin;
鏈霉素 streptomycin;
硫胺素 vitamin B1;
麻黃素 ephedrine;
尿膽素 urobilin;
尿素 carbamide; urea;
內毒素 endotoxin;
檸檬素 citrin; vitamin P;
凝集素 agglutinin;
平素 always; customarily; in normal times; ordinarily; usually;
樸素 plain; simple;
茜素 alizarin;
強力霉素 doxycycline;
青霉素 penicillin;
慶大霉素 gentamicin;
曲古霉素 trichomycin;
溶菌素 bacteriolysin;
溶血素 haemolysin;
茹素 abstain from meat; vegetarian;
色素 colouring; pigment;
腎上腺素 adrenaline;
生長素 growth hormone;
四環素 tetracycline;
宿素 (1) usually; (2) old and experienced;
胎裡素 a born vegetarian;
同位素 isotope;
土霉素 oxytetracycline; terramycin;
吐根素 emetine;
外毒素 exotoxin;
紈素 (1) fine gauze; (2) white silk;
維生素 vitamin;
味素 gourmet powder; monosodium glutamate;
味之素 gourmet powder; monosodium glutamate;
纖維素 cellulose;
香蘭素 vanillin;
像素 pixel;
酵素 enzyme;
新霉素 neomycin;
性激素 sex hormone;
血色素 haemochrome;
雅素 (1) personal background; (2) old friendship; (3) virtue in simplicity;
要素 chief factors; chief ingredients; essentials; essential facts; key elements;
葉紅素 phylloerythrin;
葉黃素 xanthophylls;
葉綠素 chlorophyll;
胰島素 insulin; pancreatin;
義素 sememe;
因素 element; factor;
音素 phoneme;
營養素 nutrient;
有素 have a solid foundation;
語素 morpheme;
元素 element;
原素 element;
正定霉素 daunomycin;
質素 quality;
制黴菌素 nystatin; mycostatin;
重元素 heavy element;
緇素 Buddhist monks and laymen;
字素 grapheme;
自力霉素 mitomycin G;

su

【涑】 a tributary of the Yellow River;

su

【宿】 (1) lodge for the night; lodge; sojourn; stay overnight; (2) long-cherished; long-harboured; long-standing; old; (3) old; veteran; (4) a surname;

[宿弊] long-standing malpractice;
[宿敵] one's ancient antagonist;
[宿根] root of one's present lot;
[宿好] (1) old friend; (2) predilection;
[宿恨] old feud; old grudge; deep-rooted rancour;
[宿慧] innate intelligence;
[宿疾] chronic complaint; old complaint; old trouble;
調治宿疾 attend and cure an old illness;
[宿將] veteran general;
[宿老] old man;
[宿留] stay overnight;

［宿命］ predestination;
宿命論 determinism; fatalism;
［宿日］ former days;
［宿儒］ learned scholar;
［宿膳］ board and lodging;
［宿舍］ dormitory; hall of residence; hostel; living quarters;
宿舍主任 hostel warden;
青年宿舍 youth hostel;
學生宿舍 hall of residence; student hostel;
學校宿舍 school dormitory;
已婚宿舍 married quarters;
［宿世］ former existence;
［宿素］ (1) usually; (2) old and experienced;
［宿頭］ inn to stop at for the night;
［宿昔］ (1) days gone by; the past; (2) long-standing;
［宿歇］ pass the night and rest;
［宿學］ erudite; well-learned;
宿學舊儒 a scholar of profound learning;
宿學之士 a scholar of profound learning;
［宿夜］ morning and night;
［宿業］ karma;
［宿營］ bivouac; camp out;
宿營拖車 camper; camper van;
［宿緣］ predestinate love;
了此宿緣 fulfil a predestinate love;
［宿願］ long-cherished wish;
了此宿願 fulfil a long-cherished wish;
［宿怨］ old grudges; old scores;
宿怨舊恨 old scores;
報宿怨 settle old scores;
藏怒宿怨 have resentment rankling in one's mind; nurse rancour against;
泯棄宿怨 disregard old grievances;
［宿債］ long overdue debt;
［宿志］ long-cherished ambition;
［宿主］ host;
定局宿主 definitive host;
中間宿主 intermediate host;
終宿主 final host;
［宿罪］ sins of a previous existence;

歸宿 a home to return to;
寄宿 (1) lodge; put up; (2) board; boarding;
借宿 put up for the night; stay overnight at sb else's place;
留宿 (1) put up a guest for the night; (2) put up for the night; stay overnight;
露宿 sleep in the open;
棲宿 put up for the night; stay for the night;
耆宿 venerated old people;
膳宿 bed and board; board and lodging; food and lodging;
食宿 bed and board; board and lodging;
投宿 check in for the night; put up for the night; seek temporary lodging;
外宿 stay outside overnight;
棲宿 rest for the night;
歇宿 lodge; make an overnight stop; put up for the night; spend the night; stay for the night;
信宿 stay over for two consecutive nights; two nights;
淹宿 overnight;
一宿 overnight stay; one night;
軫宿 one of the twenty-eight constellations;
住宿 get accommodation; lodge; put up; stop at; stay overnight;

su

【速】 (1) fast; prompt; rapid; speedy; (2) speed; velocity; (3) invite;
［速成］ complete rapidly;
速成班 accelerated class; crash course; express class; intensive course;
速成課程 crash course;
［速凍］ quick-frozen;
速凍包裝 deep-frozen food packaging; quick-frozen food packaging;
［速動比率］ quick ratio;
［速度］ speed; velocity;
速度變化 variation in speed;
速度放慢 the pace slackens; the pace slows;
速度極限 speed limit;
速度計 speedometer;
~磁力式速度計 magnetic-type speedometer;
~鐘式速度計 clock-type speedometer;
速度加快 the pace accelerates; the pace quickens;
速度調整 velocity adjustment;
速度限制 speed limit; speed restriction;
速度性能 speed ability;
保持速度 keep up with the pace;
保持穩定的速度 keep up a steady speed;
法定速度 legal speed limit;
發音速度 rate of articulation;
放慢速度 slacken one's speed; slow down;
分離速度 separation velocity;

高速度 high speed;
~超高速度 ultraspeed;
即時速度 instantaneous velocity;
加快速度 gather speed; increase speed; speed up;
加速度 acceleration;
~法向加速度 normal acceleration;
~角加速度 angular acceleration;
~切向加速度 tangential acceleration;
~線加速度 linear acceleration;
減速度 deceleration;
角加速度 angular acceleration;
角速度 angular velocity;
絕對速度 absolute velocity;
平均速度 average velocity;
瞬時速度 instantaneous velocity;
線加速度 linear acceleration;
線速度 linear velocity;
相對速度 relative velocity;
以極快的速度 at breakneck speed;
以忙亂的速度 at a frantic pace; at a hectic pace;
以蝸牛般的速度 at a snail's pace;
以穩定的速度 at a steady pace;
以最快的速度 with all speed;
勻速度 uniform velocity;

[速記] shorthand; stenography; take sth down in shorthand;
速記法 method of shorthand;
速記能力 stenographic aptitude;
速記學校 shorthand school;

[速決] quick decision;

[速率] rate; speed; tempo;
速率計 speedometer;
~電子速率計 electronic speedometer;
加速速率 accelerated speed;
取數速率 access speed;
實際速率 actual speed;

[速溶] instant; quick to dissolve;
速溶咖啡 instant coffee;

[速食] fast food;
速食店 fast-food restaurant;
速食麵 instant noodles;

[速死] die quickly; hasten one's death;

[速算法] short-cut method of counting;

[速調管] klystron;
放大速調管 amplifying klystron;
寬帶速調管 broadband klystron;

[速效] quick results; speedy relief;

[速寫] (1) sketch; (2) literary sketch;

變速 change speed; gear shift; speed change;
步速 pace;
超速 (1) exceed the speed limit; (2) hypervelocity;
車速 speed of a motor vehicle;
初速 initial velocity;
從速 as soon as possible; without delay;
低速 low speed; low velocity; slow speed;
飛速 at full speed;
風速 wind speed;
高速 express; fast; high rate; high speed; high velocity; swift;
光速 at top speed; post-haste;
急速 at high speed; rapidly; very fast;
加速 accelerate; acceleration; boost; expedite; quicken; shift up; speed up; turn of speed;
減速 decelerate; deceleration; moderate; reduce the speed; retard; run out of steam; shift down; slow down; slow up;
空速 airspeed;
快速 fast; high-speed; quick; rapid; speedy;
流速 (1) velocity of flow; (2) current velocity;
脈速 rapid pulse;
全速 full speed;
射速 firing rate;
神速 marvelously quick; with amazing speed;
聲速 velocity of sound;
失速 stall;
時速 speed per hour;
星速 hurriedly; without delay;
迅速 prompt; rapid; speedy; swift;
音速 speed of sound; velocity of sound;
轉速 rotational speed; tachy;

su

【粟】 (1) grain; (2) millet; (3) goosebumps; gooseflesh; goose pimples; (4) a surname;

[粟帛] grain and cloth;

[粟倉] barn for grain; granary;

[粟飯] coarse staple food;

[粟紅貫朽] (1) in a land of plenty; (2) in times of great prosperity;

[粟米] corn; grain; maize;

[粟子] millet;

菽粟 grain;
罌粟 opium poppy;

su

【肅】 (1) respectful; reverent; (2) majestic; serious; solemn; (3) clean up; elimi-

nate; mop up; (4) a surname;
[肅覆] reply respectfully;
[肅敬] respectful;
[肅靜] solemn silence;
[肅客] receive a guest;
[肅立] stand upright as a mark of respect;
肅立默哀 stand in silent tribute;
肅立致敬 stand in reverence showing respect;
[肅穆] solemn and respectful;
[肅清] clean up; eliminate; mop up; root out; wipe out;
肅清封建勢力 eradicate feudal forces;
肅清流毒 eliminate the pernicious influence;
[肅然] respectful; reverently;
肅然起敬 be filled with deep veneration; call forth in sb a feeling of profound respect; hold sb in awe; hold sb in high respect; register a profound respect; stand respectfully before sb;
肅然生畏 be struck with awe;
[肅入] usher in;
[肅殺] awe-inspring look;
肅殺之氣 awful atmosphere;
[肅肅] (1) respectfully; reverently; (2) in a hurry; swiftly;
[肅坐] sit erect and in silence;

su

【訴】 (1) inform; relate; tell; (2) accuse; charge; complain; file a complaint; (3) appeal to; petition; resort to;
[訴苦] air one's grievance; complain about one's grievances; pour out one's woes; vent one's grievances;
訴苦窮兒 tell others of one's state of poverty;
訴苦訴冤 voice one's grievances and state the wrong;
訴苦訴怨 air one's grievances; pour out one's discontent and grievances;
低聲訴苦 bleat;
[訴説] (1) air grievances; complain; (2) narrate; recount; relate; tell;
訴説苦衷 recount one's worries and difficulties; tell one's troubles;
[訴訟] lawsuit; litigation; suit;
訴訟案件 court case;
訴訟參與人 litigant participant;
訴訟程序 legal procedure; legal proceeding; legal process;
訴訟代理人 agent ad litem; legal representative;
訴訟當事人 litigant;
訴訟費 legal cost;
訴訟費用 court costs;
訴訟權 litigation rights;
訴訟時效 prescription;
訴訟條例 rules of procedure;
訴訟行為 action at law;
法律訴訟 legal proceedings;
放棄訴訟 abandon proceedings; abandonment of action;
集體訴訟 class action;
面臨訴訟 face a lawsuit;
民事訴訟 civil action;
提出訴訟 litigate; press charges;
委托訴訟 proceedings with a reference;
刑事訴訟 criminal prosecution;
支持訴訟 support a lawsuit;
支付訴訟 pay the cost of the lawsuit;
中止訴訟 suspend proceedings in a lawsuit;
[訴冤] complain about grievances; state injustice;
[訴諸] appeal to; resort to;
訴諸法律 go to law;
訴諸公論 appeal to public opinion; appeal to verdict of the masses;
訴諸武力 appeal to arms; appeal to force; betake oneself to arms; have recourse to force; resort to force; resort to the use of force; resort to violence;
[訴狀] petition; plaint; written complaint;

哀訴 unbosom oneself in grief; whine;
敗訴 lose a lawsuit;
陳訴 recite; state;
反訴 countercharge; counterclaim;
告訴 inform; let know; make know; tell;
公訴 public prosecution;
抗訴 counter appeal; countercharge; oppose an action;
控訴 accuse; denounce; make a complaint against;
哭訴 complain tearfully;
起訴 bring a suit against sb; bring an action against sb; charge; file a complaint against sb; file a formal indictment; file a lawsuit; indict; institute legal proceedings; prosecute; start a criminal prosecution against sb; sue; sue sb in a law court;

泣訴 accuse while weeping; blubber out one's bitter experiences; sob out one's grievances; tell one's sorrows;
傾訴 make a clean breast of; pour forth; pour out; unbosom oneself; unburden oneself;
上訴 appeal; lodge an appeal;
申訴 appeal; complain;
伸訴 air a grievance; present a complaint;
勝訴 win a lawsuit;
投訴 complain; write to state or request;
原訴 accusation; charge;
自訴 action initiated by an injured party without the participation of the public prosecutor; private prosecution;

su

【嗉】 crop of a bird;
[嗉子] crop of a bird;

su

【塑】 (1) mould in clay; (2) plastics; (3) figure; model;
[塑膠] plastic cement; plastics;
塑膠布 plastic cloth;
塑膠帶 plastic bags;
塑膠花 plastic flowers;
塑膠皮 plastic leather;
塑膠紙 plastic paper;
塑膠炸彈 plastic bomb;
[塑料] plastic material; plastics;
塑料編織帶 plastic woven sack;
導電塑料 conductive plastics;
低溫塑料 cold plastics;
多孔塑料 aerated plastics;
瀝青塑料 bitumen plastics;
農用塑料 agriplast;
泡沫塑料 aerated plastics;
[塑像] (1) make an idol; (2) plastic figure; statue;
小塑像 figurine;
一座塑像 a statue;
[塑性] plasticity;
後增塑性 inverted plasticity;
理想塑性 ideal plasticity;
熱塑性 hot plasticity;
[塑造] (1) model; mould; (2) portray;

彩塑 colour modelling; painted sculpture;
雕塑 carve and mould; sculpture;
面塑 dough modelling;
泥塑 clay sculpture;
注塑 produce plastic articles by injection moulding;

su

【溯】 (1) go against the stream; go upstream; (2) recall; trace back;
[溯查] inquire into the origin of sb;
[溯洄] go upstream;
[溯江而上] go upstream in a boat;
[溯游] go upstream;
[溯源] trace to the source;
[溯自] ever since;

回溯 look back upon; recall;
上溯 (1) sail upstream; (2) trace back to;
追溯 date from; trace back to;

su

【愫】 honesty; sincerity;

情愫 (1) emotion; feeling; (2) genuine feeling; real intention;

su

【愬】 (1) complain; tell one's prblems; (2) frightened; scared;
[愬愬] afraid; frightened; scared;

su

【膆】 (1) crop of a bird; (2) fat;

su

【觫】 shrink and tremble in fear;

su

【蔌】 vegetables;

su

【簌】 petals fall in great quantities;
[簌簌] (1) rustle; (2) tears stream down;
淚珠簌簌 tears trickle down from one's eyes;
眼淚簌簌 one's tears fall fast; tears stream down;
珠淚簌簌 big tears trickle down from one's eyes; one's tears fall like pearls; tears trickle down one's cheeks; the tears run down one's face like water dropping through a sieve;

簏簌 droop; hang down;
撲簌 (of tears) trickle down;

su

【謖】 (1) closed; folded; (2) raise; rise;
[謖謖] tall and straight;

su

【鷫】 a kind of wild swan;

suan¹

suan

【痠】 (1) ache; (2) muscular pains; (3) tinkle;

［痠懶］ sore and weary;

［痠軟］ sore and weak;

［痠疼］ ache;

suan

【酸】 (1) acid; (2) sour; tart; (3) spoiled; stale; (4) grieved; sad; sick at heart; sorrowful; (5) impractical; pedantic; (6) ache; (7) stingy;

［酸敗］ turn sour;

［酸鼻］ feel like crying; grieve;

［酸菜］ (1) pickled cabbage; (2) pickled vegetables;

［酸醋］ vinegar;
　拈酸吃醋 jealous;

［酸度］ acesence; acidity;
　酸度計 acidimeter;
　表現酸度 apparent acidity;
　過量酸度 excessive acidity;
　活性酸度 active acidity;
　加水酸度 hydrolytic acidity;
　平均酸度 average acidity;
　潛在酸度 potential acidity;
　胃酸度 gastric acidity;

［酸果］ tart fruit;

［酸化］ acidize;
　酸化處理 acidizing;
　分級酸化 stage acidizing;
　選擇性酸化 selective acidizing;

［酸辣］ sour and hot;
　酸辣醬 chutney;
　~ 芒果酸辣醬 mango chutney;
　酸辣湯 sour-and-hot soup;

［酸溜溜］ (1) sour; tart; (2) envious; jealous;

［酸梅］ sour plum;
　酸梅晶 sour plum flavour instant powder;
　酸梅湯 sweet-and-sour plum juice;

［酸奶］ sour milk; yoghurt;
　一罐酸奶 a pot of yoghurt;

［酸軟］ aching and limp;
　腳酸腿軟 one's feet give way and one's legs are without strength;

［酸甜］ sweet and sour;
　酸甜苦辣 all the joys and sorrows of life; all the sweet and bitter experiences of life; the sweets and bitters of life;
　又酸又甜 sweet yet tart;

［酸痛］ ache; pins and needles;
　渾身酸痛 ache all over; the whole body aches;

［酸味］ acidity; sour; tart flavour;

［酸心］ (1) heartbroken; grieved; sad; (2) heartburn;

［酸性］ acidity;
　酸性反應 acid reaction;

［酸雨］ acid rain;

［酸中毒］ acidosis;
　代謝性酸中毒 metabolic acidosis;
　糖尿病性酸中毒 diabetic acidosis;

噯酸 acid eructation; the rising up of acid from the stomach;
胺酸 amino acid;
氨基酸 amino acid;
悲酸 heartbreaking; moved to tears; touching; wanting to cry;
變酸 turn sour;
草酸 oxalic acid;
醇酸 alcohol;
醋酸 acetic acid;
膽酸 cholic acid;
發酸 (1) turn sour; (2) ache slightly;
泛酸 pantothenic acid;
硅酸 silicic acid;
果酸 tartaric acid;
寒酸 miserable and shabby; shabby; sorry; scrubby;
核酸 nucleic acid;
甲酸 formic acid; methanoic acid;
尖酸 acrid; acrimonious; tart;
雷酸 fulminic acid;
磷酸 phosphoric acid;
硫酸 sulphurous acid;
氯酸 chloric acid;
尿酸 uric acid;
硼酸 boric acid;
強酸 strong acid;
氰酸 cyanic acid;
窮酸 poor and pedantic;
醛酸 aldehydic acid;
鞣酸 tannic acid;
乳酸 lactic acid;
弱酸 weak acid;
羧酸 carboxylic acid;
鈦酸 titanic acid;

酞酸 phthalic acid;
鉭酸 tantalic acid;
碳酸 carbonic acid;
銻酸 antimonic acid;
胃酸 hydrochloric acid in gastric juice;
硝酸 nitric acid;
心酸 be grieved; feel sad;
辛酸 bitter; miserable; sad;
煙酸 nicotinic acid;
鹽酸 hydrochloric acid;
葉酸 folic acid;
乙酸 acetic acid;
蟻酸 formic acid;
油酸 oleic acid;

suan⁴

suan

【筭】 (1) ancient device for working with numbers; (2) scheme;

suan

【算】 (1) calculate; compute; count; figure; reckon; (2) plan; scheme; (3) guess; suppose; think; (4) consider; deem; regard as; (5) carry weight; count; (6) at long last; in the end; (7) let it be; let it pass; (8) include; (9) a surname;

[算不清] innumerable; uncountable;

[算尺] slide rule;

[算出] figure out; work out;

[算錯] miscalculate;

[算法] (1) algorithm; (2) arithmetic;
算法語言 algorithmic language;
程序算法 programmed algorithm;
極小化算法 minimization algorithm;
交換算法 exchange algorithm;
模糊算法 fuzzy algorithm;
數組算法 array algorithm;
通用算法 universal algorithm;
統計算法 statistical algorithm;
形式化算法 formalized arithmetic;
最優法算法 optimization algorithm;

[算卦] tell one's fortune;

[算計] (1) consider; plan; (2) scheme against sb; plot against sb;
有算計的 calculating;

[算來] by counting;
算來算去 compute over and over; count over and over;

[算了] call it quits; drop it; forget about it; forget it; leave it at that; let it go at that; that's enough;

[算命] fortune telling; tell one's fortune;
算命先生 fortune teller;

[算盤] abacus;
算盤使用者 abacist;
算盤頭腦 miser;
算盤珠 beads on an abacus;
撥算盤 click the abacus;
扒拉算盤 click the beads of an abacus;
打算盤 operate an abacus; use an abacus;
~ 打錯算盤 make a wrong decision; miscalculate;
如意算盤 wishful thinking;
~ 打如意算盤 expect things to turn out as one wishes; indulge in wishful thinking; reckon without one's host;
小算盤 calculating; selfish calculations;
~ 打小算盤 petty and scheming;

[算清] find out the sum of;

[算入] count;

[算上] count in; include;
全算上 count everything in;

[算式] equation;

[算是] at last; finally;

[算術] arithmetics;
算術化 arithmetization;
算術級數 arithmetical progression;
算術家 arithmetician;
算術平均 arithmetic average;
算術題 arithmetic problem;
~ 一道算術題 an arithmetic problem;
算術運算 arithmetic operation;
遞歸算術 recursive arithmetic;
泛算術 universal arithmetic;
複數算術 complex arithmetic;
化學算術 chemical arithmetic;
加性算術 additive arithmetic;
矯正算術 remedial arithmetic;
三進制算術 ternary arithmetic;
商業算術 business arithmetic;
剩餘算術 residue arithmetic;
做算術 do sums;

[算數] (1) of importance; (2) count; hold; mean what one says; stand;
説話算數 live up to one's word;

[算題] arithmetic problem;

[算我的] charge it to my account;

[算學] mathematics;

[算賬] (1) balance accounts with sb; balance the books; cast accounts; do accounts;

make out bills; work out accounts; (2) pay the bill; (3) get even with sb; settle accounts with sb; square accounts with sb;

[算子] operator;

諳算 calculate mentally;
暗算 attack by treachery; plot; plot against; plot in secret; secret plot; secretly plot against; treachery;
筆算 (1) do a sum in writing; (2) written calculation;
測算 (1) estimate; (2) measure and calculate;
成算 calculated plan;
籌算 count;
粗算 rough estimate;
錯算 miscount;
打算 (1) be going to; intend; have a mind to; mean; plan; think; (2) calculation; consideration;
倒算 seize back confiscated property;
電算 compute;
掂算 calculate; estimate;
概算 budgetary estimate;
估算 calculate roughly; estimate; reckon;
合算 reckon; worthwhile;
核算 adjust accounts; business accounting; check computation;
划算 deserving; worthwhile;
劃算 calculate; consider and weight; paying; to one's profit;
換算 conversion;
計算 adding; calculate; calculation; compute; computation; computing; computus; count; do a calculation; estimate; make a work out accounts;
結算 balance accounts; close an account; settle accounts; settlement of payments; wind up an account;
精算 actuarial science;
就算 even if; granted that;
決算 (1) closing of accounts; (2) final accounts;
口算 chant out the result while doing the sums in one's head;
匡算 calculate roughly;
妙算 excellent plan;
謀算 (1) plan; scheme; (2) plot; (3) calculate;
盤算 calculate; consider and weigh; deliberate; figure; plan; premeditate;
起算 start counting from a given point;
掐算 count sth on one's fingers; reckon sth on one's fingers;
清算 (1) audit; clear accounts; clear off an account; examine and repudiate; repudiate; square; (2) settle accounts with; settle scores;
上算 (1) economical; profitable deal; (2) deserving; worthwhile;
深算 careful deliberation; careful planning;
神算 (1) clever plan; (2) miraculous foresight; miraculous prediction;
勝算 stratagem that ensures success;
失算 miscalculate; miscalculation; misjudge; mistake;
說了算 have the final say;
推算 calculate; reckon;
誤算 miscalculate; miscount;
寫算 write and be good at figures;
心算 do sums in one's head; mental arithmetic;
演算 calculus; calculation; do exercises in mathematics; mathematical exercises;
驗算 check computations;
一算 calculate; count;
預算 budget; calculate in advance; estimate;
運算 arithmetic; operation;
照算 (1) charge accordingly; (2) charge without deduction;
折算 convert; equivalent to;
指算 (1) count by fingers; (2) the use of the abacus;
珠算 calculation with an abacus; operation on the abacus; reckoning by the abacus;
總算 (1) all things considered; in general; on the whole; (2) at last; at long last; finally; in the end; in the long run;

suan

【蒜】 garlic;
[蒜瓣] garlic clove;
[蒜苗] garlic sprouts;
[蒜泥] mashed garlic;
[蒜薹] young garlic shoots;
[蒜頭] bulb of garlic; head of garlic;

大蒜 garlic;
葫蒜 rocambole;
青蒜 young garlic stalk and leaves;
石蒜 short-tube lycoris;
糖蒜 garlic in syrup; sweetened garlic;
一瓣蒜 a clove of garlic;
一掛蒜 a braid of garlic;
一頭蒜 a bulb of garlic;
裝蒜 affected; feign ignorance; make a pretence; pretend not to know; pretentious;

suan

【篹】 bamboo basket; splint basket;

sui¹

sui

【荽】 parsley;

sui

【睢】 (1) raise one's eyes; (2) at random; (3) name of a place; (4) name of a river; (5) a surname;

恣睢 reckless; unbridled;

sui

【綏】 (1) appease; pacify; repose; soothe; tranquilize; (2) retreat; (3) strap to help sb mount a carriage; (4) banner; flag;

［綏撫］ pacify; placate; soothe; tranquilize;

［綏靖］ pacify; resotre peace and order;

sui

【雖】 although; even; even if; though;

［雖然］ as one is; after; albeit; although; amid; amidst; and yet; as; because; but then; despise; for; for all; however; if; in spite of; in the midst of; not but that; notwithstanding; still; such as it is; that; though; when; while; with all;

［雖是］ although; still; though;

［雖説］ although; even though; though;

［雖…猶…］ though...still;

雖敗猶榮 feel proud even in defeat;

雖死猶榮 die a glorious death;

雖死猶生 live on in spirit;

［雖則］ even if; still; though;

sui²

sui

【隋】 (1) Sui Dynasty (581-618); (2) a surname;

［隋候之珠］ precious pearl in an ancient legend; very valuable and precious things;

sui

【綏】 a pronunciation of 綏 :

sui

【隨】 (1) come after; follow; go along with; trace; (2) adapt to; comply with; listen to; submit to; (3) let sb do as he likes; (4) accompany; along with; (5) look like; resemble; (6) a surname;

［隨伴］ accompaniment;

隨伴介詞 accompaniment preposition;

［隨筆］ informal essays; jottings; literary notes; literary rambles; miscellaneous writings;

［隨便］ (1) casual; informal; random; (2) as you like; as you please; as you see fit; make do with anything; make no choice;

隨便的 cavalier;

隨便地 haphazardly;

隨便你 anything you say; whatever you say;

隨便説幾句 make some casual remarks;

隨便挑 choose whatever you like;

隨便找個籍口 cobble up an excuse;

各隨其便 each does exactly as he likes;

講話隨便 free with one's tongue;

隨你的便 do as you like; do as you please; have it your own way;

隨隨便便 careless about things; casually; easy-going; free and easy; in a casual way; let the world lie lightly on one's shoulders; rather casual; take things easy; too easy going;

主隨客便 a host respects the guest's wishes; the host must accord to the guest what he likes; the host must do as the guest wishes;

［隨波逐流］ drift with the current; follow the crowd; follow others blindly; go with the stream; serve the time; swim down the tide; swim the stream;

［隨常］ commonly; usually;

［隨處］ anywhere; everywhere; in all places;

隨處可得 can be obtained anywhere;

隨處可見 can be seen everywhere;

［隨從］ (1) accompany; attend; (2) attendants; entourage; retinue; suite;

隨從人員 entourage;

［隨大流］ follow the crowd; follow the general trend; go with the tide;

［隨地］ any place; anywhere; everywhere;

隨地吐痰 spit anywhere; spit on the floor;

［隨動］ follow-up;

隨動件 follower;

隨動控制 follow-up control;

［隨風］ according with the wind;

隨風倒 bend with the wind – be flexible;

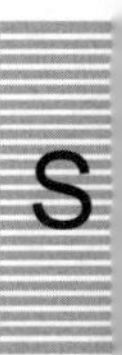

go with the breeze; veer with the wind;
~隨風倒柳 the willow leans with the wind — a person of no principles;
隨風飄舞 whirl about in the wind;
隨風駛舵 change one's course of action according to the wind; dance and sing in all weathers; do things according to the way the wind blows; sail with the wind; steer with the wind; take one's cue from changing conditions;
隨風轉舵 change one's course of action according to the wind; do things according to the way the wind blows; tack with the wind; take one's cue from the changing conditions; trim the sails to the wind;

[隨和] amiable; easy to get along with; easy-going; obliging;
隨和的 good-tempered;
~隨和的人 amiable character;
脾氣隨和 have an amiable disposition;
性情隨和 carefree temper;

[隨後] follow; immediately afterward; in no time at all; right after; right off; soon afterwards;
隨後到達 arrive soon after;
隨後的 ensuing;
~隨後的幾年 ensuing years;

[隨即] forthwith; immediately; instantly; on the instant; on the nail; on the spot; presently;

[隨機] (1) random; unplanned; (2) as the situation allows;
隨機處理 random processing;
隨機存儲 random access;
~隨機存儲分配 random allocation;
~隨機存儲器 random access memory;
隨機存取 stochastic access;
~隨機存取軟件 stochastic-access software;
~隨機存取系統 stochastic-access system;
隨機錯誤 random error;
隨機復原 randomizing;
隨機干擾 random disturbance;
隨機化 stochastic restoration;
隨機檢索 stochastic retrieval;
隨機模型 stochastic model;
隨機文件 random file;
隨機信號 random signal;
隨機應變 act according to the circumstances; act in consonance with the requirements of the occasion; adapt to changing circumstances; adjust to changing circumstances; change with each shift in the situation; do as the changing circumstances demand; do as the circumstances dictate; equal to the occasion; improvise; play it by ear; rise to the occasion; suit one's actions to changing conditions;

[隨口] blurt out whatever comes into one's head; slip out of one's tongue without much thought; speak without thinking;
隨口答應 agree without thinking; promise at once without hesitation;
隨口而出 escape from sb's lips; fall from sb's lips;
隨口之言，有口無心 say whatever enters one's head;

[隨群] comply with public opinions; follow others;

[隨身] carry sth about; carry sth with one; on one's person; take with one;
隨身警報器 personal alarm;
隨身聽 walkman;
隨身武器 side arms;
隨身物品 clobber;
隨身行李 personal luggage;

[隨時] anytime; as the occasion demands; at all times; at any time; whenever;
隨時隨地 always and everywhere; any time and in any place; at all times and places; when and where; whenever and wherever possible;
隨時制宜 change tactics as the situation demands;

[隨手] at hand; conveniently; immediately; readily; without extra trouble;
隨手關門 close the door behind one; shut the door after you;

[隨順] accord with; comply with; obey; yield;

[隨俗] act according to prevailing customs; comply with conventions; do as everybody else does; follow local customs;
隨俗沉浮 drift along with the world;

[隨…隨…] no sooner...than...;
隨傳隨到 be brought up to court when needed;
隨到隨吃 guests are served as they arrive;
隨叫隨到 at call; on call; on hand; within

call;
隨説隨做 no sooner said than done;
[隨同] accompany; follow; in company with; together with;
[隨鄉入鄉] a guest must do as his host does; do in Rome as the Romans do; in a strange land, do as the natives do; other countries, other ways; when in Rome, do as the Romans do;
[隨想曲] capriccio;
[隨行] accompany; go along; go together; in company with;
隨行人員 entourage; party; retinue; suite;
[隨興] on a whim;
[隨學隨忘] no sooner learnt than it is forgotten;
[隨宜] comply with propriety;
[隨意] ad lib; as one pleases; at will; free rein;
隨意的 haphazard;
隨意散播 throw away;
隨意審計 voluntary audit;
隨意歪曲事實 make free with the facts;
隨意文體 casual level of speech;
不隨意 involuntary;
[隨遇而安] able to adapt oneself to different circumstances; adapt easily to any circumstances; at home wherever one is; feel at ease under all circumstances; make the best of it; reconcile oneself to one's situation; take the world as it is; take the world as one finds it; take things as they are; take things as they come;
[隨員] retinue; suite; entourage;
[隨緣樂助] donate according to the situation; give assistance as one can afford;
[隨葬] be buried with the dead;
[隨着] along with; in pace with; in the wake of;
隨着季節變化 change with the seasons;
隨着時間的推移 as time progresses;
[隨之而來] ensuing from; in its wake; in the train of;
[隨踵而至] come one after another in succession;
[隨眾] follow the crowd;
[隨珠彈雀] kill a bird with a precious pearl — gain a trifle at great cost; pay too dear for one's whistle; shoot birds with pearls — gains cannot offset losses;

伴隨 accompany; follow;
長隨 servant;
跟隨 follow; go after;
親隨 aides; entourages; follower;
情隨 feelings change according to...;
人隨 everyone follows;
尾隨 at the tail of; follow at sb's heels; tag along after; tail behind;
相隨 (1) follow; (2) accompany;
依隨 comply with; follow;
追隨 follow;

sui3

sui

【嶲】 an old town in today's Sichuan;

sui

【髓】 essence; marrow; pith;
齒髓 dental pulp; pulp of the tooth;
骨髓 bone marrow; marrow;

脊髓 spinal cord; spinal marrow;
精髓 heart; marrow; pith; quintessence;
腦髓 brain;
神髓 essence; quintessence;
心髓 innermost beings; innermost feelings;
牙髓 dental pulp;
延髓 medulla oblongata;
真髓 essence;

sui4

sui

【祟】 (1) evil spirit; ghost; (2) haunt and plague; (3) evil influence of demons;
[祟惑] be confused by evil influence;

鬼祟 stealthy; tricky;
邪祟 evil-doing; evil thing;
作祟 (1) (of ghosts, spirits, etc.) haunt; (2) cause trouble; make mischief;

sui

【歲】 (1) year; (2) year of age; (3) the year's harvest;
[歲不我與] time and tide wait for no man;
[歲差] (1) equation of equinoxes; (2) precession;
赤經歲差 precession in right ascension;
赤緯歲差 precession in declination;
日月歲差 lunisolar precession;
周年歲差 annual precession;

[歲出] annual expenditures;
[歲除] New Year's Eve; end of a year;
[歲寒] (1) severe winter; (2) the closing years of one's life; (3) times of anarchy;
歲寒而知松柏後凋 only when winter comes do we realize that the pine and the cedar are evergreen;
歲寒三友 three durable plants of winter — pine, bamboo and plum blossom;
歲寒松柏 the pine and the cypress endure the cold winter together;
歲寒知松柏 adversity reveals virtue; only when the year grows cold do we see the qualities of the pine and the cypress;
歲寒知松柏，患難見交情 a friend is never known but in time of need; a friend is never known till a man has need; adversity reveals virtue;
[歲華] (1) procession of the seasons; (2) time of year;
[歲計] annual budget;
[歲盡春歸] an early spring comes on after the year ends;
[歲杪] end of a year;
[歲暮] (1) late season of a year; (2) closing years of one's life;
歲暮年終 end of the year;
歲暮天寒 cold weather sets in as the year draws to its close;
[歲日] years and days;
歲日並進 the years of one's age pass away with the time;
日長如歲 every day seems as long as a year;
日長歲久 for a long time;
[歲入] annual income; annuel revenue;
[歲時] time of the year; times and seasons;
[歲收] annual income;
[歲首] beginning of a year;
[歲數] age; years;
上歲數 get on in years;
[歲尾] end of a year;
歲尾年頭 the tail and head of the year;
[歲夕] New Year's Eve;
[歲夜] New Year's Eve;
[歲月] (1) times and seasons; (2) years;
歲月不待人 time and tide wait for no man; time marches on;
歲月不羈 time marches on;
歲月蹉跎 idle away one's time; let time slip by without accomplishing anything; the years drift by;
歲月既往，不可復追 lost time is never found again;
歲月教人長智慧 years bring wisdom;
歲月流逝 the years run on; the years fly on; time flies;
歲月悄悄催人老 time is a file that wears and makes no noise;
歲月如流 months and years pass by like a stream; time flies;
歲月無情 time and tide wait for no man;
歲月崢嶸 the most uncommon years and months of one's life;
蹉跎歲月 dawdle one's life; dawdle one's time; fool one's time away; fritter one's time away; idle about; idle away one's time; lead an idle life; let time slip by without accomplishing anything; live an idle life; live in idleness; on the racket; profane the precious time; spend one's time in dissipation; spend one's time in frolic; trifle away one's time; waste time; while away one's time;
過去的歲月 bygone days;

百歲 one hundred years old;
敗歲 a year of bad crops;
比…大…歲 elder than sb by...years; one's elder by...years; ...years elder than sb; ...years one's elder; ...years one's senior; ...years senior to sb;
比…小…歲 one's junior by...years; ...years junior to sb; ...years one's junior; ...years one's younger; ...years younger than sb; younger than sb. by ...years;
常歲 every year;
辭歲 bid farewell to the passing year; celebrate the lunar New Year's Eve;
多少歲 how old;
幾歲 how old;
嘉歲 a year of bumper harvest;
舊歲 old year;
客歲 last year;
年歲 (1) age; (2) years;
千歲 (1) a thousand years; (2) term of respect for princes and dukes;;
歉歲 bad year for the crops; lean year; year of poor harvest;
去歲 last year;

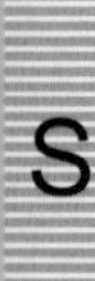

弱歲 youth;
三十來歲 thirty-something;
三歲 three years old;
守歲 stay up late or all night on New Year's Eve;
暑歲 a year of heat and drought;
嗣歲 the coming year;
太歲 (1) ancient name for the planet Jupiter; (2) a legendary God; (3) backstage ruler; overlord; the powerful;
同歲 of the same age;
晚歲 (1) in recent years; lately; (2) late harvest; (3) old age; one's later years;
萬歲 (1) long live; (2) emperor; (3) His Majesty; (4) Your Majesty;
昔歲 last year;
獻歲 beginning of a new year;
新歲 beginning of a new year;
虛歲 nominal age;
旬歲 whole year;
早歲 in one's youth; one's early years;
肇歲 beginning of a new year;
終歲 throughout the year; whole year;
周歲 first anniversary; one full year of life;
週歲 full year;
足歲 actual age; real age;
卒歲 tide over a year;

sui

【碎】 (1) break to pieces; smash; (2) broken; fragmentary; smashed; torn; (3) trifling; trivial; unimportant; (4) gabby; garrulous;

[碎冰船] icebreaker;
[碎布] oddments of cloth;
[碎步兒] short quick steps;
[碎紛紛] broken to pieces;
[碎工] odd jobs;
[碎爛] smashed beyond recognition;
[碎裂] torn to pieces;
[碎密] complicated and disorderly;
[碎片] chip; debris; fragment; patch; segment; shred;
玻璃碎片 splinters of glass;
分子碎片 molecular fragment;
裂成碎片 break in fragments;
撕成碎片 be torn to ribbons; tear to pieces;
原碎片 primary fragment;
原子碎片 atomic fragment;
重碎片 massive fragment;
[碎石] chippings; rubble;
[碎屍萬段] cut sb into pieces and into ten thousand bits; cut sb into ten thousand pieces; cut sb to pieces; cut sb up into ten thousand pieces; hack sb into a thousand pieces; hew a body to pieces; tear sb to shreds; tear sb limb from limb; tear sb into thousands of pieces;
[碎務] chores;
[碎屑] bits; chippings; fragments; parings; scraps;
奶酪碎屑 cheese parings;
削下的碎屑 parings;

拗碎 break in pieces;
掰碎 break sth into pieces with one's fingers;
扯碎 tear asunder;
打碎 batter; break into pieces; pound; smash;
剁碎 hash; mince;
粉碎 (1) crush; shatter; smash; (2) be broken into pieces; shiver; shred;
零碎 bits and pieces; fragmentary; odds and ends; piecemeal; scrappy;
捏碎 crumb;
牛雜碎 ox giblets;
破碎 (1) broken; tattered; (2) break into pieces; crush; smash sth to pieces; tear into shreds;
敲碎 beat to pieces; knock to pieces;
切碎 cut up;
揉碎 crumble to pieces;
摔碎 break into pieces after falling; shatter; smash;
撕碎 destroy; rip to pieces; rive; tear to pieces;
瑣碎 trifling; trivial;
心碎 broken heart; heartbreak; heart-broken;
細碎 in small, broken bits;
壓碎 crush to pieces;
軋碎 break; crush; crush to pieces;
研碎 grind to pieces;
玉碎 broken jade;
砸碎 break into pieces; break to pieces; shatter; smash;
雜碎 chopped cooked entrails of sheep or oxen;
嘴碎 garrulous; loquacious; talkative;

sui

【遂】 (1) fulfil; satisfy; (2) succeed; (3) then; thereupon;

[遂過] help finish a mistake;
[遂即] then; thereupon;
[遂及] and then;
[遂令] lead to; result in;

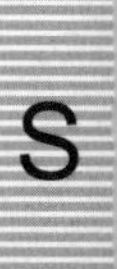

[遂其大望] attain one's ambition;
[遂事] bygones; one thing that has had its course;
遂事不諫 let bygones by bygones; useless to remonstrate about what has passed;
[遂心] do sth after one's own heart; fulfil one's desire; have one's own way; have one's will; to one's liking;
遂心如意 after one's heart; one's wishes are met; perfectly satisfied;
遂心所欲 follow what one's heart desires; have one's will; satisfy one's desire; to one's liking;
[遂意] fulfil one's desire; have everything going one's way; to one's liking;
[遂愿] fulfil one's desire; have one's wish fulfilled;
[遂則] afterwards; and then;
[遂致] consequently; subsequently; thereupon;

不遂 fail to materialize or accomplish;
甘遂 root of a kansui;
順遂 go smoothly; go well;
未遂 (1) not accomplished; not fulfilled; (2) abortive;

sui
【誶】 reproach; scold; upbraid;
[誶罵] reproach; scold; upbraid;

sui
【隧】 (1) tunnel; underground passage; (2) turn; turn back; (3) (in ancient China) tower on the wall to watch fire signals;
[隧道] tunnel;
隧道效應 tunnel effect;
隧道二極體 tunnel diode;
背斜隧道 anticline tunnel;
分岔隧道 branch tunnel;
海底隧道 harbour tunnel;
空調隧道 conditioning tunnel;
冷卻隧道 cooling tunnel;
一孔隧道 a tunnel;
一條隧道 a tunnel;

sui
【燧】 (1) flint; (2) beacon; torch;
[燧石] chert; flint;
燧石化 chertification;
燧石質 cherty;
白燧石 white chert;
骨狀燧石 bone chert;
結核狀燧石 nodular chert;
砂質燧石 sandy chert;
生物燧石 biogenic chert;
無機燧石 inorganic chert;

烽燧 beacon fire;
陽燧 brass speculum;

sui
【穗】 (1) fruits in a cluster grown at the tip of a stem; (2) ear of grain; (3) a name for Guangzhou; (4) candle snuff;
[穗子] fringe; tassel;

稻穗 ear of rice;
谷穗 ear of millet;
果穗 ear of grain;
接穗 scion;
麥穗 ear of wheat;
吐穗 earing; heading;
秀穗 put forth flowers or ears;
孕穗 booting;

sui
【邃】 (1) deep; far; remote; (2) deep; profound;
[邃古] remote past; time immemorial;
[邃戶] abysmal entrance to a large, quiet house;
[邃密] (1) deep; (2) abstruse and full; profound;

精邃 profound;
深邃 (1) deep; (2) abstruse; profound;
幽邃 deep and quiet;

sun¹
sun
【孫】 (1) descendant; grandson; (2) generations below that of the grandchild; (3) second growth of plants; (4) a surname;
[孫女] granddaughter;
孫女婿 granddaughter's husband; grandson-in-law;
外孫女 daughter's daughter; granddaughter;
[孫子] (1) grandchild; grandson; (2) son of a bitch;

重孫 great-grandson;

稻孫 new rice shoot grown from the old stalk;
兒孫 children and grandchildren; descendants;
甥孫 grandnephew; grandniece;
徒孫 disciple's disciple;
外孫 daughter's son; grandson;
王孫 offspring of the nobility; prince's descendants;
文孫 your grandson;
玄孫 great-great-grandson;
曾孫 great-grandson;
長孫 (1) one's son's eldest son; the eldest grandson; (2) a surname;
侄孫 brother's grandson; grandnephew;
姪孫 grandnephew; one's brother's grandson;
子孫 children and grandchildren; descendants; posterity; scion;
從孫 grandsons of one's brothers;
祖孫 ancestors and descendants; one's grandparent and grandchild;

sun

【飧】 (1) cooked food; (2) supper; (3) mix cooked rice with water;

sun

【猻】 monkey;

猢猻 macaque;
兔猻 steppe cat;

sun

【蓀】 a kind of aromatic grass;

sun³

sun

【筍】 bamboo shoots;

[筍乾] air-dried bamboo shoots;
[筍瓜] winter squash;
[筍雞] broiler; young chicken;
[筍尖] tender tips of bamboo shoots;
[筍鴨] duckling; young duck;

春筍 spring bamboo shoot;
冬筍 winter bamboo shoot;
蘆筍 asparagus;
毛筍 shoot of mao bamboo;
石筍 stalagmite;
萵筍 asparagus lettuce;
竹筍 bamboo shoot;

sun

【損】 (1) decrease; lose; (2) damage; harm; (3) caustic; cutting; sarcastic;

[損德] cause damage to one's virtue; injure one's virtue by misdeed;
[損根子] wicked person;
[損公] damage the public interest;
損公肥己 feather one's own nest at the expense of the public interest; line one's own pockets at the expense of the public;
損公肥私 feather one's nest at public expense; injure the public interest to profit the private interest; line one's own pockets at the expense of the public; pursue private interests at the expense of public interests; seek private gain at public expense;
損公利私 benefit oneself at the expense of public interests; damage the interests of the state to benefit one's own units; seek self-interest at the public expense;
[損害] cause damage; cause loss; damages; damnify; harm; impair; injure; losses;
避免損害 avoid damage;
不帶來損害 break no bones;
防止損害 prevent damage;
微小的損害 minor damage;
造成損害 do damage;
[損耗] (1) deterioration; dissipation; loss; waste; wear and tear; (2) spoilage; wastage;
催化劑損耗 catalyst attrition;
飛機損耗 aircraft attrition;
弧降損耗 arc drop loss;
集電極損耗 collector dissipation;
降低損耗 reduce the wastage;
能量損耗 energy dissipation;
聲損耗 acoustic loss;
天線損耗 antenna loss;
吸收損耗 absorption loss;
嚴重損耗 war of attrition;
陽極損耗 anode loss;
[損壞] breakdown; damage; failure;
損壞名聲 damage one's good name;
腐蝕損壞 corrosion damage;
累積損壞 cumulative damage;
臨界損壞 critical damage;
塗層損壞 coating damage;
意外損壞 accidental damage;
隱蔽損壞 concealed damage;
造成損壞 cause damage;
[損年] die young; shorten one's life span;

[損人] (1) make caustic remarks; ridicule others; (2) cause material damage to others;
損人保己 clear oneself at the expense of sb;
損人肥己 enrich oneself at the expense of sb; feather one's own nest at the expense of the public interest; impoverish others in order to enrich oneself; line one's own pockets at the expense of the people;
損人利己 benefit oneself at the expense of others; benefit oneself at the expense of others; gain at others' expense; harm others but benefit oneself; hurt others for the sake of one's own gain; hurt others for the sake of one's own gain; injure others for one's own profit; injure others for the sake of one's own advantage; injure others in order to benefit oneself; profit at another's expense; profit by doing harm to others; profit oneself at the expense of others; seek satisfaction for oneself at the cost of others; seek personal ends at the expense of others;

[損傷] (1) cause loss to; damage; damnification; damnify; harm; hurt; impair; injure; (2) casualties; losses;
損傷兵力 reduce military strength;
損傷元氣 suffer tremendous loss in strength or resources;
避免損傷 keep out of harm's way;
剝皮損傷 butcher damage;
生物損傷 biological damage;
受到損傷 sustain damage;
未受損傷 without damage;
戰鬥損傷 battle damage;

[損失] lose; loss; wastage;
損失不貲 suffer no small amount of damage;
損失分攤 loss apportionment;
損失金錢 lose one's money;
變產損失 loss on realization of assets;
承擔損失 bear a loss;
風壓損失 air loss;
累計損失 aggregate losses;
彌補損失 make up a loss;
年度損失 annual loss;
賠償損失 compensate; make good the damage; pay for a loss;
水災損失 damage from a flood;
造成損失 cause damage;

[損壽] shorten one's life;

[損益] (1) increase and decrease; (2) gains and losses; profit and loss;
損益相抵 the gains offset the losses;
損益賬 profit and loss account;
七損八益 seven impairments and eight supplements;

[損陰壞德] harm by underhand means; indulge in evildoings;

[損友] bad company; injurious friend;

貶損 (1) criticize; (2) belittle; depreciate; derogate; play down;
擦損 be damaged by friction or rubbing;
殘損 damaged; spoiled;
純損 net loss;
估損 appraisal of damage; assessment of loss;
海損 cargo damage; ship damage;
耗損 consume; depletion; lose; waste;
呼損 call loss;
毀損 breakage; damage; impair;
虧損 (1) deficit; loss; (2) general debility;
勞損 strain;
磨損 abrade; abrasion; abrasive wear; wear and tear;
破損 be damaged; be worn;
缺損 broken away; defect; missing and damaged;
傷損 trauma; injury;
蝕損 deteriorate; lose in value;
無損 cannot harm; intact;
消損 (1) grow less and less; wear off; (2) wear and tear;
役損 weaken from fatigue;
抑損 (1) reduce; (2) modest;
有損 hurt; impair;
增損 profits and losses;
折損 damage;
嘴損 cutting in speech; sharp-tongued;

sun

【榫】 tenon and mortise;

[榫頭] tenon and mortise;

[榫牙] tenon;

[榫眼] mortise;

[榫子] tenon and mortise;

卯榫 mortise and tenon;
脱榫 be out of joint;

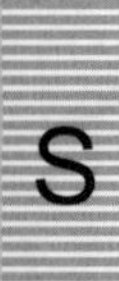

suo¹

suo

【唆】 abet; incite; instigate;

[唆弄] incite; instigate;

唆弄是非 sow discord;

[唆使] abet; incite; instigate;

教唆 abet; instigate;

囉唆 (1) long-winded; wordy; (2) talk at length; troublesome;

調唆 incite; instigate;

挑唆 abet; incite; instigate;

suo

【娑】 dance; frisk; gambol; saunter;

[娑羅樹] sal tree;

[娑娑] (1) loose; (2) flutter; fly;

婆娑 dancing; whirling;

suo

【梭】 (1) weaver's shuttle; (2) move to and fro; (3) swift;

[梭標] spear;

[梭布] native cloth;

[梭巡] move around to watch and guard; patrol to and fro;

[梭魚] mullet;

[梭子] weaver's shuttle;

梭子蟹 swimming crab;

穿梭 shuttle back and forth;

suo

【莎】 cyperus rotundus;

suo

【桫】 (1) horse chestnut; (2) sal tree;

suo

【挲】 rub hands together;

suo

【蓑】 (1) raincoat of straw; (2) (now rare) cover with grass;

[蓑草] sedge;

[蓑笠] bamboo cape and hat;

[蓑衣] coir raincoat;

suo

【簑】 same as 蓑 ;

suo

【縮】 (1) contract; decrease; reduce; shorten; shrink; (2) draw back; recoil; wince; withdraw;

[縮本] (1) abridged edition; (2) pocket size edition;

[縮短] contract; curtail; cut; cut down; reduce in length; shorten; shrink; tuck;

縮短詞 lipped word;

縮短從句 abbreviated clause;

縮短法 shortening;

縮短工作時間 shorten hours;

縮短學制 shorten the period of schooling;

熔期縮短 shortening of the melting period;

[縮格] indent;

[縮合] condensation;

醇醛縮合 aldol condensation;

反縮合 retrograde condensation;

分子間縮合 intermolecular condensation;

分子內縮合 internal condensation; interstitial condensation;

固相縮合 solid phase condensation;

環化縮合 cyclizative condensation;

水解縮合 hydrolytic condensation;

線型縮合 linear condensation;

[縮回] draw back; flinch; recoil; wince;

[縮減] curtail; cut; cut down; decrease; lessen; reduce;

縮減從句 abridged clause;

縮減機構 trim inefficient units and get rid of unnecessary ones;

縮減開支 cut back on expenditure;

縮減食量 cut down on one's intake of rich foods;

[縮略] abbreviate;

縮略詞 abbreviation;

~字母縮略詞 alphabetic abbreviation;

縮略語 abbreviation;

~縮略語詞典 abbreviation dictionary;

[縮排] indent;

[縮手] (1) draw back one's hand; (2) shrink from doing sth;

縮手旁觀 watch from the sideline without interfering;

縮手縮腳 become irresolute and passive; get cold feet; overcautious; shrink from doing sth; shrink with cold; timid and flinching;

縮手無策 fold one's hands helplessly;

[縮水] shrink;

[縮小] contract; lessen; narrow; reduce; shrink;

縮小尺寸 diminish in size;
縮小範圍 reduce the scope;
詞義縮小 narrowing of meaning;

[縮寫] (1) abbreviate; abbreviation; (2) abridge;
縮寫詞 abbreviation;
縮寫者 abbreviator;
設計縮寫 design abbreviation;

[縮印] reprint books in a reduced format;

[縮影] miniature; epitome;

[縮約] contracted;
縮約動詞 contracted verb;
縮約否定詞 contracted negative;
縮約否定形式 contracted negative form;
縮約肯定形式 contracted positive form;
縮約形式 contracted form;

[縮語] abbreviation;
設計縮語 design abbreviation;
業務縮語 service abbreviation;

抽縮 contract; shrink;
搐縮 contract; shrink;
龜縮 shrink back like a turtle drawing in its head and legs;
減縮 cut down; decrease; foreshortening; reduce; reduce and compress;
簡縮 simplify;
緊縮 cut down; reduce; tighten;
捲縮 snarl;
攣縮 contraction; spasm; twitch;
濃縮 concentrate; enrich;
蜷縮 cower; curl up; huddle up; roll up; twisted; wriggly;
瑟縮 cower; curl up with cold; huddle oneself up; shrink with cold; shrink with cower;
伸縮 (1) expand and contract; lengthen and shorten; stretch out and draw back; (2) adjustable; elastic; flexible;
收縮 (1) contract; contraction; deflate; retraction; shrink; shrinkage; (2) concentrate one's forces; draw back;
塌縮 collapse; tumble down;
退縮 backtrack; cower; cringe; flinch; hold back; recoil; shrink;
萎縮 atrophy; dry up and shrink; shrink back; shrivel; wither;
畏縮 cower; cringe; flinch; lose one's nerve; recoil; shrink;
蝟縮 curl up like a hedgehog; recoil; scared; shrink; wince;
壓縮 compaction; compress; compression; condense; cut down; reduce;
展縮 flexible;
漲縮 swelling and shrinking;

suo³
suo

【所】 (1) location; place; position; (2) building; bureau; institute; office; (3) that which;

[所愛] what one likes; what one loves;
另有所愛 have another sweetheart;

[所長] one's forte; one's strength; one's strong point; what one is good at;
寸有所長 an inch has length – every man has his strong point;
非其所長 out of one's domain;
各顯所長 each displays that in which he excels;
各有所長 each has his good points; each has his special talents; each man has his merits; each one has his good points; each one has sth. in which he excels;
各展所長 each gives full play to their strong point;
盡其所長 work to the best of one's ability;
師其所長 learn from sb's good points;
用非所長 put sb in a position that is not suitable for that person;
展其所長 give full play to one's strong point;
正合所長 right down one's alley; right up one's alley;

[所措] what is done;
莫知所措 at a loss; at a loss about what to do; not know what to do; perplexed;
罔無所措 not know what to do;

[所得] (1) income; (2) what one gets; what one receives;
所得税 income tax;

[所動] be swayed;
不為所動 not be attracted; not be swayed;

[所短] one's shortcomings or defects;
補其所短 make up for one's shortcomings or defects;

[所費] the cost incurred;
所費不貲 have spent a fortune; incur a considerable expense; the cost is hard to calculate;

[所歸] object;
時望所歸 object of public esteem;

[所好] one's inclination; one's likes;

從其所好 follow what one desires; in accordance with one's taste; let one have one's way;

阿其所好 pander to sb's whims; play up to sb's whims;

~擅長阿其所好 good at sycophancy;

各隨所好 let each do what they want;

各有所好 each follows his own bent; each has his hobby; each has his likes and dislikes; every man has his hobby-horse; everyone to his own taste; every man to his taste; tastes differ; there is no accounting for tastes;

投其所好 cater to sb's likes; cater to sb's pleasure; cater to sb's tastes; cater to sb's wishes; cater to the needs of sb; give sb exactly what he likes; hit on what sb likes; offer what sb is hankering after; rub sb the right way; suit one's fancy; take a fancy to; take sb's fancy; tickle the ear of sb; to one's liking;

~狗嘴裏拋骨頭—投其所好 throw bones into a dog's mouth — cater to sb's likes;

[所及] within reach;

力所不及 above one's bend; beyond one's ability; beyond one's bend; beyond one's depth; beyond one's grasp; beyond one's power; beyond one's strength;

力所難及 beyond one's power; beyond one's physical strength;

力所能及 as one's capacity allows; as one's forces can reach; in one's power; to the best of one's ability; to the full extent of one's capabilities; to the full extent of one's strength; within one's capacity; within one's reach;

力之所及 to the best of one's power; what lies in one's power to carry out; within one's power;

[所急] what is anxious about;

急人所急 anxious about what others are anxious about; anxious to help those in grave danger; eager to meet the needs of others;

[所見] what one sees;

所見略同 agree mostly; fall in with sb's views on; have similar views; share each other's view to a certain extent;

所見所聞 what is heard and seen; what one sees and hears;

攄所見 set forth one's views;

[所料] expected;

誠非所料 be really unexpected;

出乎所料 beyond expectation; out of one's reckoning;

大出所料 well beyond expectation;

果如所料 as expected; sure enough;

[所謀] what is planned;

所謀不遂 fail in an attempt;

[所難] difficult for sb;

強人所難 compel sb to do sth against his will; constrain sb to do things that are beyond his power; force some work on a person who is not equal to it; force sb to do sth against his will; force sth down sb's throat; impose a difficult task on sb; impose upon a person a task he is incapable of doing; saddle sb with a difficult task; try and force people into doing things they don't want to; try to make sb do what is against his will; try to make sb do what is beyond his power; try to make sb do what he is unable to;

[所能] do the best one can;

各盡所能 each does his best; each does the best he can; work according to his ability;

~各盡所能，按勞分配 from each according to his ability, to each according to his work;

[所求] request to be made;

禮下於人，必有所求 when someone humbles himself before you, he must have some request to make of you;

[所失] what is lost;

若有所失 feel as if bereft of sth; feel as if sth were missing; feel disturbed as if having lost sth; feel the lack of sth; look distracted;

以補所失 repay the loss;

[所屬] subordinate to one; under one's command;

[所述] mention;

如前所述 as mentioned before; as set forth;

[所思] what one thinks;

匪夷所思 sth one could never imagine; unimaginable; unthinkable;

略有所思 have half a mind to;
若有所思 as if absorbed in thought; as if deep in thought; as if thinking of sth; pensive; seem lost in thought; wistful;

[所望] what is expected;
不負所望 answer one's expectation; come up to one's expectation; cut the buck; cut the mustard; deliver the goods; live up to expectations; meet one's expectation; up to the mustard;
大出所望 well beyond one's hopes; well beyond one's expectations;
大失所望 (1) body blow; (2) extremely disappointed; greatly disappointed; (3) lose great popularity;
~令人大失所望 great disappointment;

[所為] what one does;
任其所為 give one a free hand; let one do as one pleases;

[所謂] so-called; what is called;
所謂…者 go under the name of; what is called; what is known as;
無所謂 all the same; cannot be designated as; cannot be called; indifferent; not care; not deserve the name of; not matter;

[所聞] what one sees;
所聞所見 what one sees and hears;
略有所聞 have heard sth about the matter;

[所問] what is asked;
答非所問 an answer wide of the mark; an irrelevant answer; answer beyond the question; answer what is not asked; the answer is beside the question; dodge the question; give an irrelevant answer; give an answer wide off the mark; the answer evades the question;
~所答非所問 give an irrelevant answer;

[所想] think;
想人所想 think what is on others' minds;

[所需] needs; requirements;
各取所需 each takes what he needs; you pay your money and you take your choice;

[所學] what is learned;
用非所學 be engaged in an occupation not related to one's training; one's study is completely divorced from one's work;

[所養] be provided for;
老有所養 the elderly will be looked after properly; provide for the elderly;

[所以] as a result; so; therefore;
所以然 the reason why; they whys and wherefores;
忘乎所以 be carried away by sth; be lost in; forget oneself; get swollen-headed; go to down; have one's head in the clouds; let oneself go; slaphappy;
忘其所以 be carried away; beside oneself with enthusiasm;

[所用] the chosen; what is used;
所用非人 choose the wrong person for a job;

[所有] (1) own; possess; (2) possessions; (3) all;
所有格 genitive;
~所有格代詞 possessive pronoun;
~所有格形容詞 possessive adjective;
~地點所有格 local genitive;
~零所有格 zero genitive;
~群體所有格 group genitive;
所有權 ownership; proprietary rights;
~保留所有權 with retained ownership;
~放棄所有權 relinquish possession;
~改變所有權 change ownership;
~混合所有權 mixed ownership;
~市政所有權 municipal ownership;
~維持所有權 preserve possession;
所有人 all and sundry; all the people;
~所有人都有出席會議 all and sundry attended the meeting;
所有者權益 owner's equity;
所有制 ownership;
~所有制結構 structure of ownership;
~個體所有制 individual ownership;
~公社所有制 communal ownership;
~集體所有制 collective ownership;
~全民所有制 ownership by the entire people;
~三級所有制 three-level ownership;
盡其所有 exhaust all one's resources; give everything one has; give one's all;
罄其所有 empty one's purse; offer all one has; spend all that is available;
屬國家所有 be owned by the state;
為政府所有 in government possession;

[所欲] what one desires;
肆其所欲 do what one wishes without restraint;
隨心所欲 as one pleases; as one sees fit; at one's own discretion; at one's sweet will; at one's will; do anything one's

S

heart dictates; do as one likes; do as one pleases; do whatever one wants; follow one's bent; follow the heart's desire; go sb's way; have an entirely free hand in; have one's way; take one's own course;

~隨心所欲的 freewheeling;

[所餘] leftovers; remnant; what is left; what remains;

[所願] one's wishes;

得遂所願 attain one's end; obtain one's heart's desire;

終遂所願 have one's will; have one's wish;

[所在] (1) location; place; (2) where;

所在地 location; seat; site;

問題所在 the whole point;

義之所在 where justice lies;

[所憎] what the people hate;

憎人所憎 hate what the people hate;

[所長] bureau chief; director; institute;

副所長 deputy director;

[所知] what one knows;

就我所知 for all I know; for what I can tell; so far as I can tell; so far as I know; to the best of my belief;

據…所知 as far as one's knowledge goes; as far as one's knowledge is concerned; as far as sb knows; for all one knows; for what sb can tell; from what sb can tell; to one's knowledge; to the best of one's knowledge;

[所指] reference; signified;

所指層次 referential level;

所指詞 referential word;

所指對等 referential equivalence;

所指對象 referent;

~所指對象敬語 referent honorifics;

所指對應 referential correspondence;

所指架構 frame of reference;

所指介詞 preposition of reference;

所指聯加語 referential conjunction;

所指歧義 referential ambiguity;

所指實相 referential truth;

所指同義詞 referential synonym;

所指意義 referential meaning;

所指準確性 referential accuracy;

後所指 cataphoric reference;

呼應所指 anaphoric reference;

前所指 anaphoric reference;

十手所指 be condemned by all; target of public condemnation; what ten fingers point to — everybody knows;

~十目所視，十手所指 be watched by ten eyes and pointed to by ten fingers;

[所致] as a result of; be caused by; result from; the result of;

興之所致 when one is in high spirits; when the fit is on sb;

[所鍾] love;

情有所鍾 have a lover in one's heart;

避難所 asylum; haven; refuge; sanctuary;

便所 lavatory; pirvy; rest room; toilet;

廁所 amenities; bog; can; cloakroom; cloaks; closet; cludge; comforts room; commode; convenience; crapper; John; lav; lavatory; lavvy; loo; lounge; marble-palace; powder room; toilet; washroom; water closet; W.C.;

場所 arena; place of activity;

暢所 freely;

處所 location; place;

救護所 medical aid station;

居所 home;

拘留所 house of detention; lock-up;

看守所 lock-up for prisoners awaiting trial;

派出所 local police station; police substation;

棲流所 refuge for the homeless;

前所 have never before;

哨所 post; sentry post;

失所 be displaced; become homeless; homeless;

收容所 collecting post;

托兒所 childcare centre; nursery; nursery school;

託兒所 crèche; day care centre; nursery;

無所 all things;

一所 a measure word;

醫療所 clinic; dispensary;

醫務所 clinic;

有所 somewhat; to some extent;

寓所 abode; dwelling; place of residence; residence;

在所 will;

招待所 guest house; hostel;

診療所 clinic;

診所 clinic;

指揮所 command port;

住所 abode; domicile; dwelling place; home; residence;

suo

【索】 (1) cable; large rope; thick rope; (2) inquire into; search; (3) squeeze; tighten; twist; (4) ask; demand; (5)

all alone; all by oneself; (6) dull; insipid; (7) a surname; (8) (of mahjong) bamboo suits;

[索償] claim;
巨額索償 claim a large sum of money;

[索道] (1) cableway; ropeway; (2) tramway;
架空索道 aerial tramway;
空中索道 aerial rope;
雙線索道 bicable tramway;

[索賄] extort bribes;
索賄受賄 solicit and accept bribes;

[索價] demand a price; quote a price; state a price;
索價過高 open one's mouth wide; overcharge;

[索解] search for an explanation;

[索居] go into retreat; live alone;

[索具] cordage;

[索命] demand one's life;

[索寞] crestfallen; despondent; discouraged;

[索賠] claim indemnity; demand compensation;
索賠調查人 claims investigator;
索賠理算人 claim adjuster;
索賠期限 deadline for demanding compensation;
索賠清單 claim sheet;
索賠權 right to claim;
~保留索賠權 reserve the right to claim;
索賠人 claimant;
索賠手續 claims procedure;
索賠通知 notice of claim;
索賠文件 documents for claim;
索賠原因 cause for claim;
殘損索賠 damage claim;
承諾索賠 grant a claim;
放棄索賠 drop a claim; waive a claim;
接受索賠 accept a claim;
考慮索賠 consider a claim;
滿足索賠 meet a claim; satisfy a claim;
品質索賠 quality claim;
清理索賠 clear up a claim;
受理索賠 entertain a claim;
數量索賠 quantity claimed;
提出索賠 lodge a claim;
向保險公司索賠 claim on the insurance;
向賣方索賠 claim agains the sellers;
要求索賠 lodge a claim;

[索求] in search of; seek;

[索取] ask for; demand; exact; extort;
索取報酬 exact payment;
索取賠償 claim indemnity;

[索然] dry; dull; insipid; listless;
索然寡味 flat and insipid;
索然涕下 be depressed and shed tears;
索然無味 cut and dried; frigidity; in bad taste; insipidly; not interesting; spiritlessly; tasteless;

[索書單] book slip;

[索書號] call number;

[索性] might just as well; simply;

[索要] demand; ask for;

[索引] (1) concordance; (2) index;
索引卡 index card;
索引書 index volume;
卡片索引 card index;
編索引 compile an index;
作者索引 author index;

[索隱] expose sth hidden;
索隱行怪 look for the abstruse and behave eccentrically;

[索閱] references upon request;

絆馬索 ropes for tripping the enemy's horses;
逼索 force; obtain by force;
比索 peso;
船索 ship's rigging;
吊索 halyard; sling;
帆索 rigging;
鋼索 steel rope;
戽索 bucket rig;
脊索 notochord;
檢索 look-up; retrieval; search; searching;
絞索 noose;
纜索 cable; cable rope; hawser; pendant; suspension cable;
勒索 blackmail; extort;
利索 (1) agile; nimble; (2) neat; orderly; (3) finished; settled;
麻索 hemp rope;
摸索 (1) feel about; fumble; grope for; (2) try to find out;
繩索 cord; cordage; rope;
思索 ponder; search one's mind for an answer; speculate; think deeply;
搜索 beat about; ferret about; fossick; hunt for; scout around; search for;
廋索 look for sth hidden;
蒐索 search;
探索 explore; find out; look into; probe; search for; seek; study;

套索 lasso; noose;
鐵索 (1) cable; (2) iron chain;
弦索 strings of an instrument;
線索 clue; lead; thread;
蕭索 bleak and chilly; chilly; deserted; desolate; lonely;
須索 (1) blackmail; extort; (2) must;
尋索 explore; seek;
追索 (1) search for; (2) make insistent demands for payment; press for payment;
走索 rope dancing; rope walking;

suo

【嗩】 a trumpet-like wind instrument;
[嗩吶] suona horn;

suo

【瑣】 petty; trivial;
[瑣才] a person of little capability;
[瑣辭] petty talks;
[瑣事] trifles; trivial matters;
瑣事縈身 be preoccupied with trivialities; get bogged down in petty matters;
家庭瑣事 domestic trivialities;
日常瑣事 everyday chores;
[瑣碎] trifling; trivial;
瑣碎物品 odds and ends; odds and sods;
瑣碎之事 trivial matters;
[瑣聞] bits of news; scraps of information;
[瑣務] trifling matters;
[瑣細] (1) frivolous; petty; trifling; (2) troublesome;

煩瑣 many and miscellaneous trifles;
繁瑣 many and miscellaneous trifles;
委瑣 (1) petty; trifling; (2) of wretched appearance;
猥瑣 of wretched appearance;

suo

【鎖】 (1) lock; (2) chains; fetters; (3) confine; lock;
[鎖閉] locking;
活動橋鎖閉 bridge locking;
預先鎖閉 advance locking;
自動鎖閉 automatic locking;
中央鎖閉 central locking;
~ 中央鎖閉系統 central locking;
[鎖邊] stitch edges;
[鎖定] lock; lock in; locking;
鎖定按鈕 locking push button;
鎖定機構 lock-in mechanism;
鎖定同步 locking synchronism;
鎖定裝置 locking device;
[鎖骨] clavicle; collarbone;
[鎖櫃] locker;
[鎖國] close a country to international intercourse;
[鎖簧] spring of a lock;
[鎖匠] locksmith;
[鎖孔] keyhole;
[鎖鏈] chains;
[鎖鐐] fetters; manacles;
[鎖眉] frown; knit one's brows;
[鎖門] lock a door; lock a gate;
[鎖上] lock;
[鎖頭] lock;
[鎖眼] work buttonholes;
愁眉鎖眼 knit one's brows and cast down one's eyes in despair; knit one's brows in despair;
[鎖住] lock up;
鎖不住 cannot be kept in confinement; cannot be locked up;
暗鎖 built-in lock;
插鎖 deadbolt; mortise lock;
耳閉鎖 aural atresia;
封鎖 block; blockade; seal sth off;
掛鎖 padlock;
枷鎖 chains; fetters; shackles; yoke;
連鎖 (1) concatenated; (2) chain;
聯鎖 interlock; interlocking;
碰鎖 spring lock;
嵌鎖 deadbolt;
鈐鎖 door lock;
上鎖 lock;
石鎖 stone dumb-bell in the form of an old-fashioned padlock;
轉字鎖 combination lock;
撞鎖 spring lock;

suo

【鏁】 same as 鎖;

Chan Sin-wai

漢英
順逆序大辭典
A New Comprehensive Chinese-English Dictionary

商務印書館

目錄 Table of Contents

前言 Introduction .... i – xxxviii

辭典正文 The Dictionary

Volume 1 (A-H) .... 1 – 1011

Volume 2 (J-S) .... 1013 – 2227

Volume 3 (T-Z) .... 2229 – 3307

筆劃索引 Stroke Index .... 3309 – 3338

T

ta¹

ta

【他】 (1) he; him; (2) another; other; some other; some-;

[他處] elsewhere;

[他方] (1) other party; (2) other places;

[他就] accept another job;

[他媽的] blast it; bloody hell; damn it; dash it; God damn you; God damned; golly; gosh; hang it all; hell; son of a bitch; sun of a gun; to hell with it;

[他們] they; them;

他們的 their;

他們倆 they both;

[他那號人] people of that sort;

[他年] another year; sometime in the future;

[他人] another person; other people; others; somebody else;

假手他人 do sth by another hand;

累及他人 implicate others; involve others;

延及他人 have effect on others;

尊重他人 respect for others;

[他日] later on; some other day; some other time; some time in the future;

[他山] other hills;

他山攻錯 stones from other hills may serve to polish the jade of this one — advice from others may help one overcome one's shortcomings; other hills' stones may be good for working jade — other people's advice can be of help;

他山之石，可以攻玉 stones from other hills may serve to polish the jade of this one — advice from others may help one overcome one's shortcomings;

[他事] other business; other matters;

[他圖] different scheme; another plot;

另有他圖 find another way out; make another plan; take another line of policy; work out a different scheme;

[他往] go elsewhere;

[他鄉] alien land; other lands; place far away from home;

他鄉遇故知 come upon an old friend in a strange country; meet an old friend away from home; run into an old friend in a distant land;

他鄉作客 live in a strange land;

客死他鄉 die abroad; die in a strange land;

身在他鄉 in a foreign land;

異國他鄉 totally unknown places;

[他心] dishonesty; insincerity; treachery; unfaithfulness;

[他意] another intention;

[他用] another use;

[他志] other ambitions; other ideas;

頓萌他志 have other ideas suddenly;

吉他 guitar;

結他 guitar;

卡他 catarrh;

排他 exclusive;

其他 else; other; others; the rest;

無他 (1) for no other reason than; nothing else; (2) dedicated; loyal; (3) in good health; safe;

ta

【它】 (1) it; (2) that; (3) this;

其它 else; other;

[它們] they;

ta

【她】 she;

[她們] they;

ta

【牠】 it;

ta

【趿】 wear shoes in a casual way;

[趿拉] wear shoes in a casual way;

ta

【塌】 (1) cave in; collapse; fall down; fall in; fall in ruins; (2) droop; sink; (3) at ease; calm down; settle down; (4) little house;

[塌鼻] flat nose; snub nose;

[塌方] (1) cave in; collapse; overbreak; (2) landslide; landslip;

[塌實] (1) dependable; earnest; steadfast; steady and sure; (2) at ease; free from anxiety; have peace of mind;

塌實的人 dependable person;

工作塌實 steadfast in one's work;

睡得很塌實 have a good, sound sleep;

[塌縮] collapse; tumble down;

[塌臺] business failure; collapse; downfall; fall

T

from power;

［塌陷］ cave in; collapse; sink; subside;
天塌地陷 as if the heaven had fallen and the earth collapsed; like giant earthquakes and landslides;

崩塌 collapse; crumble;
衝塌 (of flood water, etc.) cause sth to collapse;
倒塌 cave in; collapse; come down; fall down; topple down;
疲塌 inactive; slack;
坍塌 cave in; collapse;
頹塌 collapse;

ta

【鉈】 thallium;

ta

【褟】 (1) lace of a dress; lace-trimmed hem of a dress; (2) singlet;

ta³

ta

【塔】 (1) pagoda; (2) tall pointed building; (3) lighthouse;

［塔頂］ top of a pagoda;

寶塔 pagoda;
標語塔 slogan pylon;
冰塔 serac;
常壓塔 atmospheric tower;
初餾塔 primary tower;
燈塔 beacon; lighthouse;
電視塔 television tower;
反應塔 reaction tower;
分餾塔 fractional column; fractionating tower;
佛塔 pagoda;
合成塔 synthetic tower;
回收塔 recovery tower;
紀念塔 memorial tower; monument;
金字塔 pyramid;
精餾塔 rectifying (of fractionating) tower;
冷卻塔 cooling tower;
煤塔 coal tar;
砲罩塔 bubble-cap tower
砲塔 gun turret; turret;
礮塔 barbette; gunhouse; turret;
氣提塔 stripping tower;
橋塔 bridge tower;
閃蒸塔 flash tower;
舍利塔 Buddhist shrine; pagoda for Buddhist relics; stupa;
水塔 water tower;
松塔 (1) pine cone; (2) cone of the lacebark pine;
提純塔 purifying column; purifying tower;
提取塔 extraction column; extraction tower;
填充塔 packed column; packed tower;
跳傘塔 parachute tower;
鐵塔 (1) iron pagoda; iron tower; (2) pylon; transmission tower;
吸收塔 absorption column; absorption tower;
洗滌塔 washing column; washing tower;
信號塔 signal box;
氧化塔 oxidizing column; oxidizing tower;
蒸餾塔 distillation column; distillation tower;
貯氣塔 gas storage;
鑽塔 boring tower; derrick;

ta⁴

ta

【拓】 copy characters from an ancient tablet or tomb by rubbing over a paper placed on its surface;

［拓本］ book of rubbings;
［拓片］ rubbing;
［拓撲學］ topology;
［拓印］ (1) monotype; (2) rubbing;

ta

【沓】 (1) reiterated; repeated; (2) connected; crowded together; joined; piled up; (3) lax; (4) talkative;

［沓合］ pile one upon another; superimpose;
［沓沓］ (1) lax; (2) chattering and talkative; (3) run quickly;
沓沓多言 talkative;
沓沓事物 complex things;
［沓雜］ confused; crowded and mixed;
［沓至］ come one after another without stop;

重沓 redundant; repetitious;
拖沓 indecisive and sloppy; sluggish;
雜沓 numerous and disorderly;

ta

【嗒】 dejected; depressed; despondent; in low spirits;

［嗒然］ dejected; depressed; despondent;
嗒然若喪 deeply despondent; downcast; mournful and dejected; of a broken heart;
嗒然若失 disappointed; look blank; look dejected;
［嗒喪］ dejected; depressed; despondent; in low spirits;

T

ta

【搨】 (1) make a rubbing of an inscription on stone; (2) make an exact copy with paper and writing brush;

[搨碑] make a rubbing of an inscription on a stone tablet;

[搨本] rubbing from a stone tablet;

ta

【榻】 bed; crouch;

[榻布] a kind of coarse cloth;

病榻 sickbed;
同榻 share a bed;
臥榻 bed;
下榻 take up abode;

ta

【漯】 a river in Shandong;

ta

【遢】 careless; negligent; slipshod; untidy;

邋遢 sloppy; slovenly;

ta

【踏】 (1) step on; tread on; (2) go to the spot;

[踏板] (1) footboard; (2) pedal; treadle;
車輪踏板 wheel-operated treadle;
車牀踏板 lathe treadle;
電磁式踏板 electromagnetic treadle;
電器踏板 electric treadle;
軌道踏板 rail treadle; track treadle;
衡重踏板 weighing treadle;
加速器踏板 accelerator pedal;
離合器踏板 clutch pedal;
水銀踏板 mercury treadle;
閘踏板 brake treadle;

[踏步] march in place; mark time;
踏步不前 cease to advance; mark time and make no headway;
大踏步 in big strides;

[踏歌] beat time to a song with the feet;

[踏踐] trample upon; tread on;

[踏腳] step;
踏腳板 (1) footboard; (2) foothold; (3) footrest;
踏腳石 stepping stone;

[踏遍] traverse the length and breadth of a place;

[踏青] go for a walk in the country in spring; go hiking on a spring day; have an outing in spring; spring outing;
踏青賞春 go out to enjoy the beautiful scenery in springtime;
踏青賞花 enjoy flowers in a spring outing; go for a walk in the country in spring and enjoy the beauty of the flowers;
到郊外踏青 have a walk in the outskirts;
拾翠踏青 enjoy natural charms; go to scenic spots;

[踏實] practical; realistic;
踏踏實實 conscientious in one's work; fully conscious of one's responsibility and act accordingly and consistently; go about one's work with honesty and sincerity of purpose; honest with oneself and about one's work; true to one's word and one's duties;

[踏雪尋梅] go over the snow in search of plums;

[踏月] walk in the moonlight;

踐踏 trample under foot; tread on;
糟踏 (1) insult; ravage; (2) sexually assault; violate; (3) ruin; waste;

ta

【撻】 chastise; flog; strike; whip;

[撻罰] (1) corporal punishment; flogging; (2) punish;

[撻伐] send troops to punish;
大張撻伐 declare war on a country to punish it for its iniquities;

[撻辱] beat and disgrace;

[撻市] disgrace sb in public;

鞭撻 castigate; lash;
佻撻 frivolous; impudent; skittish;

ta

【獺】 otter;

海獺 sea otter;
旱獺 marmot;
水獺 otter;

ta

【蹋】 (1) tread on; (2) kick;

[蹋地] beat time to a song with the feet;

糟蹋 (1) insult; ravage; (2) violate (a woman); (3) ruin; waste;

T

ta

【鉈】 thallium;

ta

【闒】 (1) door upstairs; (2) sound of bells and drums; (3) bad; mean;

［闒懦］ (1) humble; (2) weak and incompetent;

［闒茸］ contemptible; mean; worthless;

ta

【譗】 sound of bells and drums;

ta

【蹋】 slip; stumble;

［蹋倒］ slip and fall;

［蹋足］ slide;

ta

【闟】 (1) door; (2) wicket gate; (3) fast;

tai[1]

tai

【胎】 (1) embryo; fetus; (2) birth; (3) padding; stuffing; wadding; (4) roughcast; (5) tyre;

［胎動］ fetal movement;

［胎兒］ fetus; embryo; unborn baby;

胎兒病 fetopathy;

胎兒發育 fetation;

胎兒呼吸 fetal respiration;

胎兒水腫 fetal hydrops;

巨頭胎兒 capitones;

［胎糞］ meconium;

胎糞吸入 meconium aspiration;

［胎垢］ smegma embryonum;

［胎記］ birthmark;

［胎教］ antenatal training; foetus education; prenatal education;

［胎毛］ lanugo hair;

［胎膜］ fetal membrane;

［胎盤］ placenta;

胎盤病 placentopathy;

胎盤迴圈 placenta circulation;

胎盤瘤 placentoma;

胎盤水腫 placental oedema;

胎盤形成 placentation;

分散胎盤 diffuse placenta;

兩葉胎盤 duplex placenta;

盤狀胎盤 discoidal placenta; placenta discoidea;

腎形胎盤 placenta reniformis;

胎兒胎盤 fetal placenta;

［胎生］ viviparity; zoogony;

胎生動物 viviparous animals;

卵胎生 ovoviviparity;

［胎死腹中］ death in the womb;

［胎位］ position of a fetus;

［胎座式］ placentation;

頂生胎座式 apical placentation;

基底胎座式 basal placentation;

中軸胎座式 axile placentation;

中柱胎座式 central placentation;

安胎 medicine to prevent miscarriage;

蚌胎 concept of an oyster — a pearl;

胞胎 births;

爆胎 blow-out;

車胎 tyre;

打胎 have an abortion;

墮胎 aborticide; induced abortion; forced abortion; have an induced abortion;

怪胎 reak; genetic freak;

鬼胎 sinister design; ulterior motive;

懷胎 conceive; in the family way; pregnant;

禍胎 cause of the disaster; root of the trouble;

輪胎 tyre;

棉花胎 cotton wadding (for a quilt);

內胎 inner tube of a tyre;

泥胎 (1) unfired pottery; (2) unpainted clay idol;

娘胎 mother's womb;

胚胎 embryo;

葡萄胎 hydatidiform mole; vesicular mole;

受胎 become pregnant; stillbirth;

雙胞胎 twins;

死胎 stillborn fetus; stillbirth;

投胎 be reincarnated in a new body;

頭胎 firstborn;

脱胎 (1) be born out of; (2) process of making bodiless lacquerware;

外胎 tyre (cover);

珠胎 (1) abnormal growth caused by a little grain of sand in an oyster; (2) human embryo in a woman's body;

竹胎 bamboo shoot;

墜胎 abort; abortion;

tai

【苔】 fur on the tongue;

舌苔 coating on the tongue; fur on the tongue;

tai[2]

tai

【台】 (1) raised platform; stage; terrace; (2) stand; support; (3) platform-shaped

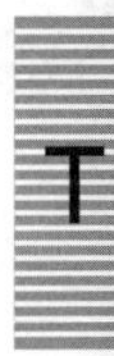

object; (4) desk; table; (5) broadcasting station; (6) special telephone service; (7) measure-word; (8) you; (9) short for Taiwan;

[台本] acting copy; acting script;

[台詞] stage dialogue; actor's lines;

背台詞 say one's part; speak one's lines; speak one's part;

唸台詞 read the lines;

潛台詞 unspoken words;

忘了台詞 forget one's lines;

[台地] terrace;

沖積台地 alluvial terrace;

大陸台地 continental terrace;

梯級台地 graded terrace;

[台端] you;

[台風] stage manners;

[台駕] you;

[台教] your advice;

[台階] (1) flight of steps; (2) chance to extricate oneself from an awkward position;

[台球] billiard;

台球室 billiard room;

台球桌 billiard table;

[台柱] (1) important actor in a troupe; (2) important person in an organization;

壁爐台 mantelpiece;

報時台 (telephone) time inquiry service;

裁判台 referee's platform or stand;

操縱台 control board; control panel;

查號台 directory inquiries; information;

拆台 cut the grass from under sb's feet; cut the ground from under sb's feet; pull away a prop; pull the rug out from under;

長途台 long distance; toll board; truck call service;

出台 (1) appear on the stage; (2) appear publicly;

出納台 (1) (of a bank, etc.) cashier's desk; teller's desk; (2) (of a library, etc.) circulation desk;

船台 (building) berth; slipway;

窗台 windowsill;

打印台 ink pad; stamp pad;

導航台 (1) guidance station; (2) non-directional radio beacon (NDB);

倒台 downfall; fall from power;

登台 go up on the stage; mount a platform;

燈台 lampstand;

敵台 enemy broadcasting station;

地台 platform;

電視台 television station;

電台 (1) broadcasting station; radio station; (2) transceiver; transmitter-receiver;

斷頭台 guillotine;

發射台 launching pad; launching stand;

烽火台 beacon tower;

服務台 information and reception desk; service counter; service desk;

干擾台 jamming station;

工作台 working bench; working table;

觀禮台 reviewing stand; visitors' stand;

觀象台 observatory;

盥洗台 washstand;

歸航台 homer;

櫃台 bar; counter; desk;

鍋台 kitchen range surface; top of a kitchen range;

後台 (1) backstage; (2) backstage supporter; behind-the-scenes backer;

祭台 altar;

駕駛台 bridge (of a ship);

檢閱台 reviewing stand;

講台 dais; lectern; platform; rostrum;

鏡台 dressing table;

開台 begin a theatrical performance;

看台 bleachers; stand;

控制台 controlling console;

垮台 collapse; fall from power;

蠟台 candlestick;

擂台 arena; ring (for martial contests);

稜錐台 frustum of a pyramid;

楞台 frustum of a pyramid;

蓮台 Buddha's seat in the form of a lotus flower;

涼台 balcony; veranda;

瞭望台 lookout tower; watchtower;

樓台 (1) high building tower; (2) balcony;

陸台 table;

露台 balcony; veranda;

砲台 battery; fort;

拼版台 makeup table;

氣象台 meteorological observatory;

平台 platform; terrace;

遷車台 transfer platform;

前台 (1) front office; front of house; on the stage; proscenium; the stage; (2) foreground;

橋台 abutment;

拳擊台 boxing ring;

上台 (1) assume power; come to power; (2) appear on stage; go up onto a platform;

曬台 flat roof;

手術台 operating table;

守望台 watchtower;

梳妝台 dressing table;
跳台 diving platform; diving tower;
塌台 collapse; fall from power;
塔台 control tower;
天文台 astronomical observatory;
舞台 arena; stage;
戲台 stage;
下台 (1) get out of an embarrassing situation; (2) step down from stage;
寫字台 writing desk;
硯台 ink slab; ink stone;
陽台 balcony;
移車台 transfer platform;
印台 ink pad; stamp pad;
與台 person of a low status;
圓台 frustum of a cone;
圓錐台 frustum of a cone;
月台 railway platform;
灶台 top of a kitchen range;
站台 railway platform;
偵聽台 intercept station;
震動台 vibrobench;
指揮台 control tower;
燭台 candlestick;
主席台 platform; rostrum;
轉播台 relay station;
轉台 revolving stage;
裝料台 charging deck;
裝配台 assembly table;
組裝台 assembly table;

tai

【邰】 (1) an ancient state in today's Shaanxi; (2) a surname;

tai

【苔】 lichen; moss;
[苔痕] mossy traces;
[苔蘚] moss and lichen;
苔蘚學 bryology; muscology;
[苔癬] lichen;
[苔衣] moss;

青苔 moss;
紫菜苔 a kind of vegetable;

tai

【臺】 (1) lookout; observatory; tower; (2) elevated platform; stage; stand; terrace; (3) title of respect; (4) short for Taiwan; (5) a surname;
[臺本] playscript with stage directions;
[臺步] stage walk;
[臺詞] one's lines;
[臺階] (1) staircase; steps; (2) category; level; (3) chance to extricate oneself from an awkward position;
[臺曆] desk calendar;
[臺上] on the stage;
[臺下] off the stage;
[臺榭] terraces and pavilions in a garden;

吹臺 fail; fall through;
靈臺 heart; soul; spirit;
燈臺 lampstand;

tai

【颱】 hurricane; typhoon;
[颱風] hurricane; typhoon;
颱風動向 typhoon movement;
颱風路徑 typhoon track;
颱風眼 typhoon eye;
強颱風 violent typhoon;

tai

【駘】 (1) jade; worn-out horse; (2) exhausted; jaded; weary; (3) incompetent;
[駘藉] crush under the feet; trample;

駑駘 (1) inferior horse; (2) mediocre person; stupid, slow-witted person;

tai

【擡】 (1) lift; raise; (2) carry;
[擡不動] incapable of lifting;
[擡槓] argue; bicker; quarrel; wrangle;
愛擡杠 love to dispute for its own sake; love to have a crow to pick with sb; love to have high words with sb;
與別人擡槓 argue with others;
總好擡槓 ready to argue for nothing;
[擡高] raise the price;
擡高票價 raise the ticket price;
擡高身價 advertise oneself; boost one's prestige; build oneself up; climb over the heads of others; put a higher value on oneself; raise one's status; raise oneself in others' esteem;
擡高聲譽 raise one's reputation;
擡高物價 effect a price hike; raise commodity prices;
[擡價] force up commodity prices;
[擡舉] good favour; good turn; do a good turn;
擡舉別人 praise others;

不識擡舉 not worthy of praise;

［擡人］ beautify; doll up; make sb look better;

［擡頭］ (1) raise one's head; (2) upsurge;

擡頭見喜 meet happiness wherever one goes;

擡頭挺胸 be full of confidence; chin up and chest out;

擡起頭 raise one's head;

羞得擡不起頭來 hide one's face;

哄擡 (of prices) drive up;

tai

【檯】 table;

［檯布］ tablecloth;

［檯燈］ desk lamp; table lamp;

一對檯燈 a twin lamp fixture;

［檯曆］ desk calendar;

［檯面］ stakes;

［檯球］ table tennis;

工作檯 workbench;

tai⁴

tai

【太】 (1) greatest; highest; (2) more; most senior; (3) excessively; much; over; too; (4) extremely; very; (5) a surname;

［太半］ greater half;

［太婆］ great-grandmother;

老太婆 old woman;

~老太婆吃黃蓮—苦口婆心 an old woman eating Chinese goldthread — bitter tasting in one's mouth; well-meant advice;

［太初］ beginning of the world;

［太多］ too many; too much;

攬事太多 have too many irons in the fire;

［太妃糖］ toffee;

可可太妃糖 cocoa toffee;

軟質太妃糖 chewing toffee;

香草太妃糖 vanilla-flavoured toffee;

杏仁太妃糖 almond toffee;

［太公］ great-grandfather;

［太古］ prehistorical times; remote antiquity; time immemorial;

［太貴］ too expensive;

［太和］ great harmony;

［太后］ empress dowager;

皇太后 empress dowager;

［太極拳］ Chinese shadow boxing;

［太監］ eunuch;

［太空］ firmament; great void; outer space; space;

太空產業 space industry;

太空艙 space capsule;

太空船 spacecraft; spaceship;

太空飛行 space flight;

太空服 (1) quilted car coat; (2) spacesuit;

太空計劃 space programme;

太空垃圾 space rubbish;

太空漫步 spacewalk;

太空人 astronaut; spaceman;

太空實驗室 space laboratory;

太空時代 space age;

太空探險 space exploration;

太空通訊 space communication;

太空武器 space weapon;

太空行走 spacewalk;

太空移民 space migration;

太空站 space station;

遨遊太空 travel through space;

外太空 outer space;

［太…了］ too...;

太棒了 excellent; great;

太老了 long in the tooth;

［太廟］ ancestral shrine of an emperor;

［太平］ peace and tranquility;

太平間 mortuary;

太平景象 picture of peace and prosperity; atmosphere of peace;

太平龍頭 fire hydrant; fire plug;

太平門 exit; safety door;

太平鳥 waxwing;

太平盛世 halcyon days; reign of peace, order, and prosperity; time of national peace and order; times of peace;

太平梯 fire escape; safety ladder;

太平無事 all in peace; all is well; everything is all right; in perfect tranquillity; peace and tranquillity; security; the world is at peace;

安享太平 enjoy a peaceful age; enjoy times of peace;

永保太平 remain peaceful forever;

［太上皇］ backstage ruler; overlord; supersovereign; supreme ruler;

［太上老君］ the very high lord;

［太甚］ too much;

［太史］ court historian;

[太歲] (1) planet Jupiter; (2) powerful and influential figure in a locality;
太歲頭上動土 beard the lion in its den; defy the mighty; provoke sb far superior in power;
~ 敢在太歲頭上動土 dare to leap on an earth god's head to make trouble; provoke sb far superior in power;
花花太歲 King of Lechers;
鎮山太歲 Lord of the Mountain;

[太太] (1) madame; Mrs.; (2) lady; madam; (3) one's wife;
老太太 (1) old lady; (2) one's mother-in-law; sb's mother;
~老太太吃柿子—揀軟和的捏 an old lady chooses only soft persimmons to bite – bully the weak;
~ 老太太打哈欠—一望無涯 (牙) an old woman yawning – as far as the eye can see; boundless;
~ 老太太的裹腳布—又臭又長 an old woman's foot binds – stinking and long;
~ 老太太哭大妞兒—沒盼兒 an old woman weeping for her dead daughter – a hopeless thing;
姨太太 concubine; mistress;

[太晚] too late;

[太息] heave a deep sigh; lament; sigh;
搖頭太息 shake one's head and heave a deep sigh; shake the head and utter a deep sigh;

[太虛] great void; universe;
魂歸太虛 be removed by death; die; go to one's account;

[太陽] the sun;
太陽潮 solar tide;
太陽出來了 the sun has come out;
太陽燈 artificial sunlight; sunlamp;
太陽底下點燈—多餘 light a lamp in the sunlight – redundant; superfluous;
太陽電池 solar cell;
~ 太陽電池板 solar panel;
太陽風 solar wind;
太陽輻射 solar radiation;
太陽感測器 solar sensor; sun sensor;
太陽光 solar rays; sun rays;
太陽鏡 eyewear; sunglasses;
太陽曆 solar calendar;
太陽帽 sun hat; visor; topee;
太陽能 solar energy;
~ 太陽能電池 solar battery;
~ 太陽能供電器 solar power supply;
~ 太陽能熱水器 solar hot water heater;
太陽年 solar year;
太陽鳥 sunbird;
太陽裙 sundress;
太陽日 solar day;
~ 真太陽日 true solar day;
太陽時 solar time;
~ 平太陽時 mean solar time;
太陽同步軌道 sun-synchronous orbit;
太陽系 Solar System;
~ 太陽系起源 origin of the solar system;
~ 太陽系儀 orrery;
太陽眼鏡 sunglasses;
太陽椅 lounge chair; sun lounger;
太陽魚 sunfish;
太陽圓面 disc of the sun;
半夜太陽 midnight sun;
綠太陽 green sun;
寧靜太陽 quiet sun;
曬曬太陽 catch a few rays; catch some rays;
曬太陽 bask in the sun; be exposed to the sun; sunbathe;
射電太陽 radio sun;
視太陽 apparent sun;
真太陽 true sun;
子夜太陽 midnight sun;

[太爺] great-grandfather;
老太爺 (1) elderly gentleman; (2) one's father-in-law; sb's father;

[太醫] imperial physician;

[太陰] (1) moon; (2) lunar;
太陰潮 lunar tide;
太陰曆 lunar calendar;
太陰年 lunar year;
太陰月 lunar month;
太陰周 lunar cycle;

[太子] crown prince;
皇太子 crown prince;

以太 ether;

tai

【汰】 (1) excessive; (2) eliminate; remove; sift;

[汰揀] wash and polish;

[汰去] eliminate; remove;

裁汰 cut down; reduce;
刪汰 delete; leave out;

淘汰 (1) eliminate through selection or completion; (2) die out;

tai

【泰】 (1) big; great; (2) ease; peaceful; quiet; safe; (3) extreme; most; (4) Thailand; (5) good luck; (6) good health;

[泰半] greater part; majority; more than half;

[泰斗] dean; doyen; leading authority;

[泰而不驕] poised but not arrogant;

[泰然] calm; composed; self-possessed; unagitated; unalarmed; unperturbed;

泰然處之 bear sth with equanimity; behave with composure in the face of a crisis; remain keep one's head; take it easy; remain calm when sth unusual happens; remain cool in the face of danger;

泰然自若 as cool as a cucumber; behave with perfect composure; compose one's countenance; have no nerves; keep a stoic calm; keep cool; keep one's countenance; keep one's head; remain cool and collected; self-possessed; take sth coolly; with a stiff upper lip; with great composure;

~泰然自若地 with aplomb;

處之泰然 bear sth with equanimity; equanimous; face sth with equanimity; impassive; not bat an eyelid; not stir an eyelid; remain unruffled; take it easy; take sth in good part; take things calmly;

[泰山] (1) Mount Tai; (2) father-in-law;

泰山北斗 eminent authority in a learned field; person of high and honourable renown in literature; person of high character and great prestige;

泰山不讓土壤 a learned man never stops his pursuit of knowledge;

泰山鴻毛 sth heavy compared to sth light;

泰山梁木 sage;

泰山壓頂 bear down on one with the the weight of Mount Taishan; with the force of an avalanche;

~泰山壓頂不彎腰 not bend one's head even if Mount Taishan topples on one; not bend one's head even under the weight of Mount Taishan; not give in to any pressure;

泰山壓卵 a great power crushes the weak – the result is certain;

安如泰山 as firm as a rock; as firm as Mount Taishan; as secure as Mount Tai; as solid as a rock; as stable as Mount Taishan; as steady as Mount Taishan; not in the slightest danger;

安若泰山 as firm as a rock; as firm as Mount Taishan; as secure as Mount Tai; as solid as a rock; as stable as Mount Taishan; as steady as Mount Taishan;

挾泰山以超北海 carry Taishan Mountain under one's armpit so as to leap across the North Sea – obviously impossible; jump over the northern sea with Mount Tai under one's arm – a mere fantasy;

有眼不識泰山 entertain an angel unawares; fail to recognize a great person; have eyes but fail to see Mount Taishan;

[泰水] one's mother-in-law;

安泰 healthy; in good health; safe and sound;

康泰 in good health;

清泰 calm; peace;

奢泰 extravagant;

舒泰 happy and healthy; well;

tai

【鈦】 titanium;

tai

【態】 (1) appearance; condition; form; (2) attitude; position; (3) bearing; carriage; department; manner; (4) voice; (5) state of matter;

[態度] (1) bearing; manner; (2) attitude; position;

態度暧昧 assume an ambiguous attitude; be on the hedge;

態度傲慢 adopt an arrogant attitude; get on one's high horse; put on air;

態度大方 have an easy manner;

態度好 courteous; elegant; well-behaved; well-mannered;

態度和藹 amiable; kindly; one's demeanor is dignified and courteous;

態度和平 amicable; friendly; peaceful attitude;

態度壞 discourteous; ill-mannered; impertinent; impolite;

態度明朗 adopt an unequivocal attitude; take a clear-cut position;
態度神秘 air of mystery;
態度生硬 stiff in manner;
態度外加語 attitudinal disjunct;
態度嫻雅 have refined manners;
擺出傲慢的態度 put on an air of assumption;
擺出自命不凡的態度 assume an attitude of superiority;
表明態度 make one's attitude clear;
觀望態度 take a wait-and-see attitude;
堅定態度 firm attitude;
~保持堅定態度 maintain a firm attitude;
冷漠的態度 aloof manner;
理性態度 in a rational manner;
輕鬆愉快的態度 airy manner;
人生態度 attitude;
~積極的人生態度 positive attitude;
耍態度 get into a huff; lose one's temper;
務實態度 in a practical manner;
以友好的態度 in an amicable manner;
正面態度 positive attitudes;

[態勢] (1) situation; state; (2) posture;
態勢不好 in face of unfavourable situation;
軍事態勢 military posture;
戰略態勢 strategic situation;

變態 (1) abnormal behaviour; abnormal conditions; abnormality; (2) metamorphosis;
表態 declare oneself; declare where one stands; make known one's position towards an issue; state one's view on; take one's stand;
病態 abnormal state;
步態 gait; walk;
常態 normal behaviour; normal conditions; normality;
醜態 buffoonery; ugly performance;
動態 (1) cause of action; developments; general trend of affairs; tendencies; trends; (2) dynamic condition; dynamic state;
鈍態 passivity;
峰態 kurtosis;
富態 fat; plump; stout;
固態 solid state;
故態 old manners; one's old way;
憨態 silly appearance;
基態 ground state;
激發態 excited state;
膠態 colloidal state;
靜態 static state;
窘態 signs of embarrassment;
狂態 display of wild manners; insolent and conceited manners; scandalous scene;
老態 old; senile;
臨界態 critical state;
流態 fluid;
媚態 coquetry; subservience;
擬態 imitation; mimicry;
氣態 gaseous state;
情態 mood; spirit;
神態 airs; bearing; facial expressions; manners; mien;
生態 ecology; organisms' habit, modes of life and relation to their environment;
失態 conduct oneself ludicrously; forget oneself; misbehave;
時態 tense;
世態 ways of the world;
事態 situation; state of affairs;
勢態 attitude;
俗態 vulgar manner;
體態 carriage; posture;
同態 homomorphism;
物態 state;
心態 mentality;
形態 (1) form; pattern; shape; (2) morphology;
懸膠態 suspensoid state;
液態 fluid state; liquid state;
儀態 bearing; demeanour; deportment;
異態 strange bearing; strange manner;
意態 air; appearance; bearing; manner;
語態 voice;
稚態 pedomorphism;
主動態 active voice;
狀態 condition; situation; state; state of affairs; status;
姿態 (1) attitude; pose; (2) carriage; posture;
組態 configuration;
醉態 drunkenness; the state of being drunk;
作態 act pretentiously; affect; pose; strike an attitude;

tan¹
tan

【坍】 collapse; fall into ruins; sliding of earth;

[坍方] (1) cave in; collapse; (2) landslide; landslip;
[坍塌] cave in; collapse;
[坍臺] (1) expose one's weakness before the public; (2) let sb know sth;

T

tan

【忲】 a polite version of 他；

tan

【貪】 (1) corrupt; venal; (2) have an insatiable desire for; greedy; (3) covet; hanker for;

［貪杯］ be addicted to the bottle; indulge in drinking; too fond of drinking;

貪杯好賭 love wine and gambling;

貪杯好色 be addicted to wine and women; fond of wine and women; hanker after wine and women; love to drink and be fond of wine and women; love to drink and be fond of women;

［貪財］ cupidity; have an itching palm; moneygrabbing;

貪財害命 commit murder for money; kill for money;

貪財好利 covet wealth and profits;

貪財喪生 perish from love to wealth;

貪財嗜殺 covet riches and shave the desire to kill;

貪財受賄 hanker for money and accept bribes;

天生貪財 be born with an itching hand;

［貪吃］ eat piggishly; gluttonous;

貪吃懶做 greedy for food and lazy in one's work; lazy glutton;

［貪大］ strive for what is big;

貪大求全 strive for grandiose projects;

貪大求洋 crave for big and foreign things; go after what is big and foreign;

［貪多］ grasp too much;

貪多必失 all covet, all lose; covetousness breaks the bag; dogs that put up many hares kill none; grasp all, lose all;

貪多反失 grasp all, lose all;

貪多壞事 grasp all, lose all;

貪多嚼不爛 attempt too much; big mouthfuls often choke; bite off more than one can chew; he that grasps at too much, holds nothing fast; if one covets too much, one can't masticate it thoroughly; spread oneself thin;

貪多求快 place undue emphasis on quantity and speed;

貪多務得 greedy and acquisitive; insatiable covetousness;

［貪高騖遠］ run after a high position or far-off things;

［貪花］ indulge in carnal passion;

貪花戀酒 hanker after wine and women;

［貪賄］ have an itching palm; practise graft; take bribes;

貪賄害民 injure people and squeeze money;

貪賄枉法 embezzle money and break the law; receive a bribe and distort the law; take bribes and pervert the laws;

貪賄無藝 infinitely greedy for gain; inordinately rapacious; know no bounds in graft and bribery; set oneself no bounds to graft and bribery; take bribes insatiably;

［貪婪］ avaricious; covetous; cupidity; green; greedy; rapacious;

貪婪成性 avarice becomes a second nature;

貪婪的 acquisitive; covetous; greedy;

~貪婪的目光 greedy eyes;

貪婪如狼 greedy as a pig; wolfish greed;

貪婪喪生 fall a victim to one's own avarice;

貪婪無厭 avarice knows no bounds; insatiably covetous and gluttonous;

貪婪追求知識 greedy for knowledge;

目光貪婪 with a covetous eye on;

［貪狼］ as greedy as a pig; very greedy person;

［貪利忘身］ perish for being covetous;

［貪戀］ can't bear to part with; cling to; desire; hate to leave; long for; reluctant to leave; unwilling to part with sb one loves;

［貪吝］ avaricious and miserly;

［貪名］ greedy for fame;

貪名釣譽 greedy for both fame and praise;

貪名逐利 greedy for fame and gain;

［貪念］ covetous thoughts;

［貪求］ covet; desire; long for;

［貪色］ have a weakness for women;

［貪生］ care for nothing but saving one's skin; cling to life cravenly;

貪生怕死 afraid to risk one's neck; care for nothing but saving one's skin; cling to life and fear death; cling to life at all costs; cowardly; mortally afraid of death;

含垢貪生 allow oneself to be insulted in oreer to remain alive;

螻蟻貪生 even an ant does not want to

die; even an ant struggles for life;

［貪食症］ bulimia;

［貪睡］ fond of sleep; lazy;

［貪饕］ gluttonous;

［貪頭］ bait; inducement;

［貪圖］ covet; desire; hanker after; hope; long for; seek; wish;

貪圖安逸 hanker after an easy and comfortable life; indulge in an easy and comfortable life; look for a life of ease and security; love comfort; seek an easy life; seek ease and comfort; the desire for an easy life;

貪圖便利 choose the easy way;

貪圖富貴 desire wealth and honour greatly;

貪圖金錢 greedy for money; money-grubber;

貪圖口腹 pamper one's appetite;

貪圖享樂 indulge in a life of pleasure and comfort; love for pleasure;

貪圖享受 seek a life of pleasure;

貪圖小利 covet small advantages; greedy for small gains; hanker after petty gains; seek for trifling advantages;

［貪玩］ fond of fooling around; fond of playing;

［貪污］ corruption; embezzlement;

貪污成風 corruption has become a common practice;

貪污盜竊 take bribes and steal; engage in graft and theft; graft and embezzlement;

貪污瀆職 corrupt and negligent about one's duties;

貪污分子 person guilty of corruption;

貪污腐敗 graft and corruption;

貪污腐化 be given to bribery and corruption; corruption and degeneration; graft and corruption;

貪污受賄 accept bribes; embezzle money and engage in corrupt practices; guilty of corruption and accepting bribes;

~反對貪污受賄 fight against corruption and bribery;

貪污行賄 commit bribery;

變相貪污 commit bribery in disguised form;

［貪小］ greedy for small gains or profits;

貪小便宜 covet little advantages; go after petty advantages; greedy for small advantages; on the fiddle; out for small advantages;

貪小失大 be tempted by small gains and suffer a big loss; covet a little and lose a lot; go for the little things and miss things that are worthwhile; lose the sheep for a ha'porth of tar; penny-wise and pound-foolish; seek small gains but incur big losses; spoil the ship for a halfpennyworth of tar; the desire for a little gain often means a serious loss after all; win battles but lose the war;

［貪心］ avaricious; cupidity; greedy; insatiable; voracious;

貪心不足 covetousness; greedy and dissatisfied; insatiable desire; insatiable greed;

貪心難改 unrepent greediness;

［貪慾］ avarice; greed;

貪慾無饜 avarice and lust without limit; no limit to lust and covetousness;

［貪贓］ accept bribes; practise graft; take bribes;

貪贓枉法 corrupt; pervert justice and accept bribes; take bribes and bend the law; take bribes and break laws; twist the law in order to obtain bribes;

［貪嘴］ gluttonous; greedy; piggish;

狼貪 avaricious; greedy;

慳貪 stingy and greedy;

tan

【攤】 (1) open; spread out; (2) apportion; divide equally; share out; (3) booth; stall; stand; (4) fry batter in a thin layer;

［攤償］ pay back one's debt by instalments;

［攤販］ booth-keeper; stall keeper; street pedlar; vendor;

［攤還］ repay in instalments;

攤還借款 repay one's loan in instalments;

［攤開］ spread out; unfold;

攤開地圖 spread out a map ;

［攤牌］ have a showdown; lay one's cards on the table; show one's hand; showdown;

迫使對方攤牌 force a showdown; force one's opponent to show his hand;

［攤派］ allot; apportion;

硬性攤派 apportion inflexibly; assignment inflexibly;

[攤位] booth; stall;
攤位女郎 booth bunny;
市場攤位 market stall;
[攤子] (1) booth; stall; vendor's stand; (2) set up;
地攤子 open space stall; outdoor stall;
~擺地攤子 operate an open space stall;
亂攤子 hopeless mess;
散攤子 disband;

擺攤 (1) operate a stall; set up a stall along the street; set up a stall in the market; (2) maintain a large staff or organization;
報攤 news stall; news stand;
菜攤 vegetable stall;
地攤 articles displayed on the sidewalk floor;
分攤 divide prorata; share;
公攤 equally shared by all;
貨攤 stall; stand;
舊貨攤 second-hand stall;
均攤 share equally;
練攤 set up a stall;
收攤兒 pack up the stall; wind up the day's business;
書攤 bookstall; bookstand;
小攤 booth; stall; stand;
雜貨攤 grocery stall;

tan

【灘】 (1) beach; (2) sandbank; (3) shoal;
[灘多水急] with many shoals and rapids;
[灘頭] beachhead;
灘頭堡 beachhead;

暗灘 hidden shoal;
濱後灘 back beach;
海灘 beach; coastal beach; sea beach;
河灘 rapids; river;
急灘 rapids;
前灘 foreshore;
淺灘 shallows; shoal;
搶灘 make a beach landing in face of enemy resistance;
沙灘 beach; sandbank; sandbeach; sandy beach;
石灘 rocky shallows;
灣頭灘 bay head beach;
險灘 dangerous shoal; rapids;
消波灘 spending beach;
鹽鹼灘 alkali flat;
鹽灘 saline; salt marsh;
一灘 (1) a puddle of water; a smudge; a stain; (2) a pool of; a puddle of;

tan

【癱】 paralysis;
[癱瘓] at a standstill; be paralysed; break down; paralysis;
癱瘓發作 paralytic stroke;
半癱瘓 semiparalysis;
四肢癱瘓 quadriplegia;
下身癱瘓 paraplegia;
~下身癱瘓者 paraplegic;
血管癱瘓 vasoparesis;
終生癱瘓 be paralyzed for life;
周期性癱瘓 periodic paralysis;
[癱軟] weak and limp;
政治癱軟 weak politics;
[癱子] paralytic;

單癱 monoplegia;
瘋癱 paralysis;
偏癱 hemiplegia; hemiplegic paralysis;
輕癱 paresis;
舌癱 lingual paralysis;

tan²

tan

【郯】 (1) an ancient state in today's Shandong; (2) a surname;

tan

【覃】 (1) involve; spread to; (2) deep and vast; profound;
[覃第] (1) vast residence; (2) one's house;
[覃恩] favour for all;
覃恩隆情 great grace and favour;
[覃思] deep in thought; deep thought; meditation;
覃思而行 think deeply before taking an action;
覃思隆情 great graces and favours;

tan

【痰】 expectoration; phlegm; sputum;
[痰火] phlegm-fire;
[痰飲] phlegm-retention disease;
[痰涎] expectoration; phlegm; spittle;
[痰盂] spittoon;

化痰 disperse phlegm; reduce sputum;
咯痰 cough up phlegm;
咳痰 cough up phlegm;
喀痰 cough up phlegm;
綠色痰 green sputum;

濃痰 purulent sputum;
祛痰 eliminate the phlegm;
五更痰 cough before dawn;
驗痰 sputum test;

tan

【彈】 (1) send forth; shoot; (2) rebound; (3) play an instrument; (4) elastic; (5) accuse; impeach;

[彈唱] sing and play;

[彈冠] flip one's cap;
彈冠相慶 congratulate each other in anticipation of fat jobs; congratulate each other on the prospect of getting good appointments; jubilant over their new appoints and honours;

[彈劾] accuse; impeach;

[彈簧] spring;
彈簧牀 spring bed;
彈簧牀墊 spring mattress;
彈簧門 swing door;
彈簧秤 spring balance;
加速器彈簧 accelerator spring;
減震器彈簧 absorber spring;
空氣彈簧 air spring;
調整彈簧 adjusting spring;

[彈回] rebound;

[彈力] elastic force; elasticity; resilience; spring;
彈力鞋 congress shoes;
失去了彈力 loose elastic force;

[彈琴] play a musical instrument;
對牛彈琴 cast pearls before swine; play one's guitar to an ox; preach to deaf ears; talk of ice to a butterfly; talk over people's heads; thrum the lute before a buffalo; waste good acts on sb who won't understand; waste one's effort; waste one's time;
~ 好像在對牛彈琴 like talking to a brick wall;
亂彈琴 act like a fool; talk like a fool; talk nonsense; talk wet;

[彈球] play marbles;
彈球戲 pinball;

[彈射] catapult;
彈射器 catapult;
~ 機上彈射器 airborne catapult;
~ 氣力彈射器 air catapult;
~ 昇空彈射器 launching catapult;

[彈跳] jumping;
高空彈跳 bungee jump; bungee jumping;
~ 高空彈跳者 bungee jumper;

[彈性] elasticity; flexibility; resilience; spring;
彈性採購戰略 flexible acquisition strategy;
彈性測定法 elastometry;
彈性蛋白腖 elastose;
彈性電阻 elastoresistance;
彈性動力學 elastokinetics;
彈性高聚物 elastopolymer;
彈性工作時間 flexible working hour;
彈性化 elastification;
彈性極限 elastic limit;
彈性計 elastometer;
~ 共振彈性計 resonance elastometer;
彈性經濟 flexible economy;
彈性靜力學 elastostatics;
彈性瀝青 elaterite;
彈性流塑料 elastothiomer;
彈性粘蛋白 elastomucin;
彈性凝膠 elastogel;
彈性時間 flexible time;
彈性塑料 elastoplast;
彈性體 elastomer;
~ 導電彈性體 conductive elastomer;
~ 合成彈性體 synthetic elastomer;
彈性外交 elastic diplomacy;
彈性閹割 elastration;
彈性預算 flexible budget;
彈性原則 flexible principles;
彈性制 flexible system;
構型彈性 configurational elasticity;
價格彈性 price flexibility;
絕熱彈性 adiabatic elasticity;
臨界彈性 critical elasticity;
撓曲彈性 bending elasticity;
收入彈性 revenue flexibility;
體積彈性 bulk elasticity;
無彈性 anelasticity;

[彈指] short moment;
彈指光陰 time zips by;
彈指可待 can be accomplished in a very brief space of time; in a twinkling; in the snap of a finger;
彈指可得 can take sth with a snap of the fingers;
彈指一揮 with a mere snap of the fingers;
彈指之間 at the snap of a finger; in a flash; in a moment; in a short moment; in the twinkling of an eye; in an instant; instantly;

T

[彈奏] play; pluck;

動彈 move; stir;
回彈 resilience;
古調獨彈 one's speech and behaviour not being in keeping with the times; strike up the hackneyed tunes alone;
抨彈 assail; attack (in speech or writing);
評彈 storytelling and ballad singing in Suzhou dialect;

tan

【潭】 (1) deep pool; deep water; (2) deep; profound;
[潭奧] deep; profound;
[潭第] one's residence;
[潭府] one's residence;
[潭水] deep water;
[潭祉] great happiness;

潮水潭 rock pool;
泥潭 morass; quagmire;
水潭 pool; puddle;

tan

【談】 (1) chat; discuss; talk; (2) what is said or talked about; (3) a surname;
[談兵] discuss the military strategy;
虎帳談兵 discuss the strategy in the military camp;
[談柄] butt; joke;
[談不上] far from being; out of the question;
[談到] refer to; speak of; talk about;
[談得來] get along with sb;
[談鋒] eloquence; incisiveness of speech; thread of discourse; volubility;
談鋒甚健 a good talker; have the gift of the gab; loquacious; talk volubly;
談鋒犀利 incisive in conversation;
[談話] (1) chat; colloquy; conversation; talk; (2) say; state;
談話題材 conversational piece;
長時間的談話 talkfest;
發表書面談話 make a written statement;
含糊談話 ambiguous talk;
即興談話 riff;
加入談話 engage in conversation;
一次談話 a talk;
[談客] able talker;
[談空說有] (1) get together and chat; (2) talk about speculative philosophy;
[談論] discuss; speak about; talk about;
談論國事 discuss state affairs;
談論音樂 talk music;
高談闊論 set the world to rights; sound off; talk incessantly; talk with eloquence; very articulate speech;
~好高談潤論 like to reason aloud;
~經常高談潤論 often talk in a lofty strain;
[談判] (1) bargain; (2) negotiate; negotiation; talk;
談判代表 negotiating representative; negotiator;
談判基礎 basis for negotiation;
談判開始 negotiations start;
談判老手 adroit negotiator;
談判破裂 breakdown in negotiations;
談判手段 negotiation tactic;
談判條件 bargaining power;
談判桌 conference table;
談判中斷 the talks break down;
重開談判 resume the talks;
重啟談判 resume negotiations;
對等談判 hold talks on a reciprocal basis;
多邊談判 multilateral negotiations;
工會談判 union negotiations;
關税談判 tariff negotiation;
和平談判 peace negotiations; peace talks;
恢復談判 resume negotiations;
集體談判 collective bargaining;
~勞資自由集體談判 free collective bargaining;
結束談判 conclude negotiations;
進行談判 conduct negotiations;
舉行談判 hold talks;
開始談判 enter into negotiations;
貿易談判 trade negotiations;
~多邊貿易談判 multilateral trade negotiations;
秘密談判 backstage negotiations;
雙邊談判 bilateral negotiations;
一場談判 a round of negotiations;
着手談判 initiate negotiations;
中斷談判 break off negotiations;
主張談判 advocate negotiations;
[談起] mention; speak of;
[談談] have a chat;
談談你的前途 have a talk on one's future;
大談特談 keep on talking about; prate; talk at length;

想和你談談 would like to have a talk with you;

[談天] chat; make conversation;

談天説地 bat the breeze; chat about all sorts of subjects; chat idly; fan the breeze; gossip and chat; shoot the breeze; talk of anything under the sun;

説地談天 (1) talk about everything under the sun; (2) eloquent; skilled in speech;

[談吐] manner of speaking; style of conversation; the way a person talks;

談吐笨拙 not shine in conversation;

談吐不俗 talk in good taste;

談吐風雅 person of pleasing address;

談吐高雅 have a refined style of conversation;

談吐如流 eloquent in talking;

談吐文雅 have a refined style of conversation; one's talk is elegant; talk with a polite and cultivated language;

談吐幽默 talk with a sense of humour;

[談笑] obtain talk and laugh cheerfully;

談笑封侯 obtain a high rank easily; rise in the world with great ease;

談笑風生 charming person with a valuable humorous tongue and winsome blossom-like smiles; joke and chat freely; intersperse a speech with humorous remarks; needle a speech with humour; personable man with his winning smiles and facetious stories; play the conversation in a gay manner; talk and laugh cheerfully; talk cheerfully and humorously; talk in a breezy way; talk in a jovial mood; there is sth charming about the way one talks and smiles;

談笑如前 talk and laugh together as in days gone by;

談笑戲謔 chat and jest;

談笑之中存至理 many a true word is spoken in a jest;

談笑自若 completely at ease; go on talking and laughing as if nothing had happened;

[談心] have a heart-to-heart talk; heart-to-heart; serious and intimate discussion;

促膝談心 heart-to-heart talk;

[談言微中] make one's point through hints; speak tactfully but to the point;

筆談 (1) converse by writing; (2) make a written speech; sketches and notes;

不談 not talk about;

常談 platitude;

暢談 speak glowingly of; talk freely and to one's heart's content;

侈談 prate about; prattle about; talk glibly about;

叢談 essay or book composed of a number of parts that are same or similar in nature;

訪談 interview;

和談 peace negotiations; peace talks;

會談 discuss terms; hold talks; negotiate; talks;

健談 good at talking;

交談 chat; converse; have a conversation; hobnob; talk with each other; touch base with sb;

接談 meet and talk with sb;

空談 empty talk; idle talk; indulge in empty talk;

口談 state orally;

漫談 informal discussion; random talk;

美談 story passed on with approval;

密談 secret or confidential talk; talk behind closed doors;

面談 speak to sb face to face; take up a matter with sb personally;

攀談 accost; chat with; chitchat; drag another into conversation; engage in small talk with; have a free and easy talk; hobnob; strike up a conversation;

奇談 absurd argument; fantastic story; far-fetched tale; strange story; strange tale; unusual story;

洽談 make arrangements with; talk over with;

淺談 elementary introduction;

清談 empty talk; idle talk; impractical discussion; indulge in idle talk;

傾談 have a good, heart-to-heart talk; pour out one's heart;

冗談 lerema;

趣談 interesting tale;

商談 confer; discuss; exchange views; negotiate; talk over;

深談 intimate talks;

手談 play go;

私談 confidential talks; private talks; talk in private;

晤談 converse; have a talk; interview; meet and talk;

細談 talk in detail;

洽談 consult together; discuss together;

閒談 chat; chinwag; chit-chat; confabulate;

engage in chitchat; small talk;
相談 converse; talk together;
鄉談 local dialects; native dialects;
詳談 go into details; talk out;
笑談 comic stories; laughingstock; object of ridicule;
虛談 empty talk; impractical suggestions;
敍談 chat; chit-chat; get together and chat; talk together;
懸談 make a rambling talk;
言談 conversation; the way one speaks; words and speech;
淫談 obscene talks;
游談 (1) canvass; go canvassing; (2) play and talk;
雜談 chat; rambling talk; random talk; tittle-tattle;
麈談 converse leisurely while holding a duster;
縱談 speak freely; talk freely; talk without inhibition;
座談 have an informal discussion;

tan
【壇】 (1) altar; (2) raised plot of land for planting flowers; (3) forum; platform; (4) circles; world; (5) earthern jar; jug;
［壇場］ area of an altar;
［壇子］ earthen jar;

歌壇 circle of singers; song circles;
花壇 flower bed;
祭壇 altar; sacrificial altar;
講壇 (1) platform; pulpit; rostrum; (2) forum; place for public speech;
劇壇 theatrical circles;
論壇 (1) forum; (2) tribune;
排壇 volleyball world;
乒壇 table-tennis circles;
棋壇 chess circles;
球壇 ball-playing circles;
聖壇 altar;
詩壇 circle of poets; poetic circles;
體壇 sports circles; sports world;
文壇 literary arena; literary circles; literary forum; literary world; world of letters;
杏壇 teaching profession;
藝壇 art circles;
吟壇 poetic circles;
影壇 film circles; filmdom;
樂壇 music circles;
政壇 political arena;
築壇 build an altar;
足壇 football circles;

tan
【曇】 cloudy; overcast;
［曇花］ orchid cactus; broad-leaved epiphyllum;
曇花一現 a flash in the pan; bloom for a very short time; last briefly; like the morning dew; short-lived; vanish as soon as it appears;
［曇曇］ cloudy; overcast;

tan
【澹】
［澹臺］ (1) a surname; (2) a lake in Jiangsu;

tan
【檀】 (1) sandalwood; (2) a surname;
［檀林］ Buddhist monastery;
［檀香］ incense made of sandalwood;
檀香木 sandalwood;
檀香扇 sandalwood fan;

青檀 wingceltis;
旃檀 white sandalwood;
紫檀 red sandalwood;

tan
【罈】 same as 罎；

tan
【罎】 earthern jar;
［罎子］ earthern jar;
罎子裏養王八－越養越抽抽 like a tortoise living in a pot － ever diminishing;
耍罎子 jar-balancing; vat juggling;

tan
【譚】 (1) same as 談；(2) a surname;

tan³
tan
【忐】 (1) apprehensive; (2) timid; (3) indecisive; vacillating;
［忐忑］ be mentally disturbed; be perturbed;
忐忑不安 all of a tremble; be overwhelmed with anxiety; feel troubled and uneasy; fidgety; have palpitation of the heart from nervousness; in a flutter; in a tremble; in fear and trembling; in rather a nervous state; nervous and uneasy; on nettles; on the anxious bench; on the anxious seat; on the tremble; restless; uneasy; unsettled and uneasy;

T

tan

【坦】 (1) level; wide and smooth; (2) candid; frank; open; (3) calm; composed; peaceful; self-possessed; (4) son-in-law; (5) a surname;

［坦白］ candid; confess; frank; honest; tell the truth;
坦白從寬 tell the truth and you will receive a lighter sentence; leniency towards those who acknowledge their crimes;
坦白從寬，抗拒從嚴 anyone who comes clean gets treated with leniency; anyone who holds back the truth gets treated harshly; leniency to confessor, but severity to resisters; leniency to those who confess and severity to those who resist;
坦白地 frankly; honestly;
~非常坦白地 in all honesty;
坦白交待 come clean; make a clean breast of one's crimes;
坦白真言 in so many words;
坦白自首 surrender and confess one's crimes;
完全坦白 make a clean breast of sth;
胸懷坦白 frank; open;

［坦誠］ candid;
坦誠的 candid;
不坦誠 uncandid;

［坦蕩］ (1) broad and level; (2) big-hearted; magnanimous;
胸懷坦蕩 open-hearted and aboveboard;

［坦克］ tank;
坦克部隊 cavalry;
反坦克 anti-tank;
~反坦克砲 anti-tank artillery; anti-tank cannon; anti-tank gun;
兩棲作戰坦克 amphibious tank;
小坦克 baby tank; tankette;

［坦露］ bare;
坦胸露腹 bare-chested;
坦胸露脯 bare one's breast;

［坦然］ calm; fully at ease; self-possessed; unperturbed; with no misgivings;
坦然無懼 remain calm and undaunted;
坦然自若 calm and confident; completely at ease; in a state of peaceful repose; in the manner natural to one;
處之坦然 preserve one's equanimity; take sth undisturbedly;

［坦率］ blunt; candid; candour; frank; outspoken; straightforward; upfront;
坦率無私 frank without secrecy;
坦率正直 frank and honest; straightforward and candid;
保持坦率 candid;
不坦率 unfrank;

［坦途］ easy path; highway; level road; smooth ride;
學無坦途 there is no royal road to learning;

［坦直］ straightforward;

平坦 even; level; smooth;
舒坦 at ease; comfortable;

tan

【袒】 (1) bare; leave uncovered; strip; (2) give protection to; protect; shield;

［袒庇］ partial to; screen;

［袒護］ give protection to; partial to; protect; shield; side with;
袒護一方 partial to one side;
公然袒護 shield openly;

［袒露］ bare; expose; leave uncovered;
袒肩露臂 expose one's neck and shoulders;
袒胸露背 expose one's chest and back;
袒胸露臂 bare one's chest and arms; expose one's chest and arms;
袒胸露脯 bare one's breast;

［袒免］ bare one's left arm and take off one's cap — gesture of great sorrow in ancient times;

［袒裼］ bare one's breast and arms; take off one's jacket and expose part of the body;
袒裼裸裎 stand completely naked; with one's arms and body naked;

［袒衣］ dress in a hurry and leave part of the flesh showing;

偏袒 be partial to; side with;
左右袒 be partial to; take sides with;
左袒 be partial to; take sides with;

tan

【毯】 (1) blanket; (2) carpet; rug;

［毯子］ (1) blanket; (2) carpet; rug;
羔羊毛毯子 lambswool blanket;

一牀毯子　a blanket;
一條毯子　a blanket;

安樂毯　security blanket;
壁毯　tapestry (used as a wall hanging);
地毯　carpet; rug;
掛毯　tapestry;
毛毯　wool blanket;
棉毯　cotton blanket;
絨毯　flannel blanket;
線毯　cotton blanket;

tan
【黮】 (1) pitch-black; pitch-dark; (2) confidential; private; secret;

tan⁴
tan
【炭】 (1) charcoal; (2) coal; (3) (in chemistry) carbon;
[炭筆] charcoal pencil;
[炭黑] carbon black; black;
炭黑顏料　charcoal black;
白炭黑　white carbon black;
輥筒炭黑　roller black;
爐法炭黑　furnace-treated black;
石墨化炭黑　graphitized carbon black;
天然性炭黑　gas-produced black;
煙道炭黑　impingement black;
[炭化] carbonize;
炭化作用　carbonization;
[炭畫] charcoal drawing;
[炭灰] ashes;
[炭火] charcoal fire;
[炭疽] anthrax;
[炭烤] charbroil;
[炭爐] charcoal stove;
[炭盆] brazier; charcoal brazier;
[炭酸] carbonic acid;
[炭田] coal field;
[炭油] coal tar;
[炭渣] cinder;

白炭　hard charcoal;
冰炭　as incompatible (or irreconcilable) as ice hot coals;
草炭　peat;
青岡炭　charcoal made of oriental white oak (Quercus aliena);
骨炭　animal charcoal; bone black; bone charcoal;
黑炭　black charcoal;
活性炭　activated charcoal; active charcoal;
焦炭　coke;
煤炭　coal;
木炭　charcoal;
泥炭　peat;
塗炭　misery and suffering; mud and ashes; utter misery;
脱色炭　decolorizing charcoal;
藥用炭　medical charcoal;

tan
【探】 (1) explore; find; locate; search; try to find out; (2) tempt; try; venture; (3) pay a call on; visit; (4) stretch forward; stretch out; (5) scout; spy; watch;
[探本] trace the origins;
[探病] visit the sick;
[探測] detect; search; survey;
探測桿　dowsing rod;
探測器　detector; probe;
~ 海岸探測器　beach detector;
~ 金屬探測器　metal detector;
~ 裂縫探測器　break detector;
~ 氣流探測器　airstream detector;
~ 聲波探測器　acoustical detector;
~ 水聲探測器　detectoscope;
~ 體探測器　bulk detector;
~ 阻抗探測器　impedance probe;
探測水深　take soundings;
探測者　dowser;
高空探測　aerological ascent;
海洋探測　marine exploration;
[探訪] call on; pay a visit to; visit;
探訪親友　visit one's relatives and friends;
上門探訪　domiciliary visits;
[探戈] tango;
探戈舞　tango;
[探究] investigate thoroughly; make a thorough inquiry; probe into;
探究原因　look into the causes;
[探空儀] sonde;
臭氧探空儀　ozone sonde;
雷達探空儀　radar sonde;
[探明] ascertain; find out by inquiry; prove; verify;
探明儲量　proved reserves;
[探囊取物] achieve one's aim easily; as easy as taking sth out of one's pocket; little effort is needed to produce the results;

T

［探親］ go home to visit one's family; look in one's kinsfolk; visit one's relatives;
探親訪友 pay a visit to relatives and friends; visit one's relatives and friends;

［探求］ hunt; look into; pursue; search after; seek; study; try to find out;
探求真理 seek for the truth;

［探傷］ detect a flaw;
探傷法 defectoscopy;
探傷圖 defectogram;
探傷儀 defectoscope;
~ 超聲波探傷儀 ultrasonic defectoscope;

［探試］ try to find sth out;

［探視］ visit; visitation;
探視權 visitation rights;
探視時間 visiting hours;

［探索］ explore; look into; probe; search for; seek; study; try to find out;
探索法 heuristics;
探索性預測 exploratory forecasting;
星際探索 interplanetary exploration;

［探討］ fish for; inquire about; investigate; make an approach to; make inquiries about; nose about for; nose into; poke one's nose into; pry into; spy into; try to find out;

［探聽］ inquire about; investigate secretly; make inquiries; poke one's nose into; prey into; spy; try to find out;
探聽秘密 pry a secret out of sb;
探聽下落 inquire about the whereabouts of sb;
探聽消息 enquire about sb;
探聽虛實 try to ascertain the strength of the enemy; try to find out about an opponent; verify the facts by making inquiries;

［探望］ (1) call on; look in; pay a visit to; visit; (2) look about;

［探問］ inquire after; make cautious inquiries about;

［探悉］ ascertain; find out; learn;

［探險］ explore; make explorations; venture into the unknown;
探險隊 expedition team; exploration party;
探險家 explorer;
北極探險 arctic expedition;

［探信］ make inquiries;

［探詢］ inquire about; make cautious enquiries about; try to sound out;

［探隱］ research into secret facts;

［探幽尋勝］ visit scenic spots;

［探友］ visit friends;

［探賾索隱］ delve into the abstruse; investigate and trace the hidden facts; search for hidden meanings; unravel mysteries;

［探照燈］ searchlight;
防空探照燈 anti-aircraft searchlight;
紅外探照燈 infrared searchlight;
閃動探照燈 flickering searchlight;

［探子］ (1) detective; scout; spy; (2) probe;

暗探 make secret inquiries; pry; secret agent; spy out;
包探 detective;
槽探 trench;
初探 first exploration;
刺探 detect; make roundabout inquiries; make secret inquiries; pry; spy;
打探 ask about; inquire about; investigate; reconnoitre;
敵探 enemy spy;
警探 detective; police-spy;
勘探 explore; prospect;
窺探 poke one's nose into; pry about; pry into; spy upon;
密探 nark; secret agent; spy; spook; stool pigeon; undercover man;
哨探 spy on the movements of the enemy;
試探 explore; feel out; probe; put up a trial balloon; sound out; test;
伺探 investigate secretly; spy;
星探 talent scout in the movie industry;
覘探 peep; spy; watch and investigate stealthily;
偵探 (1) do detective work; gumshoe; investigate; (2) detective; spy;
鑽探 explore; explore by drilling; investigate; prospect;
坐探 enemy agent planted within one's own ranks;

tan

【碳】 carbon;

［碳化］ carbonization; carbonize;
碳化劑 carburetant;
碳化器 carbonizer;
碳化氫 carbureted hydrogen;
碳化砂 carbon sand;
碳化物 carbide; carbonide;

~多孔碳化物 porous carbide;
~活性碳化物 activated carbide;
~金屬碳化物 metallic carbide;
~球狀碳化物 globular carbide; spheroidal carbide;
碳化矽 carborundum;
碳化作用 carbonification; carboniogenesis; carbonization;
電碳化 electrical carbonization;
局部碳化 partial carbonization;
連續碳化 continuous carbonization;
[碳稅] carbon tax;
[碳酸] carbonic acid; carbonate;
碳酸飽和 carbonation;
碳酸鈣 calcium carbonate;
碳酸鋰 lithium carbonate;
碳酸鋁 aluminium carbonate;
碳酸泉 carbureted spring;
碳酸鉈 thallium carbonate;
碳酸血症 carbonemia;
碳酸鹽 carbonate;
碳酸銀 silver carbonate;

二氧化碳 carbon dioxide;
放射性碳 radiocarbon;
活性碳 activated carbon;
滲碳 carburize; cement;
退火碳 annealing carbon;
脱碳 decarbonize;

tan

【歎】 exclaim in admiration;
[歎服] praise and admire;
令人歎服 command admiration;
[歎號] exclamation mark;
[歎嘉] eulogize; extol; glorify; praise;
[歎美] praise;
[歎氣] heave a sigh; sigh;
[歎傷] lament;
[歎賞] exclaim in appreciation; praise and admire;
[歎為觀止] acclaim a work of art as the acme of perfection; be lost in wonder; hold it to be the best; take one's breath away in astonishment; the most magnificent sight of all;
[歎息] (1) lament; moan; wail; (2) exclaim; (3) sigh;
低頭歎息 hang one's head and sigh;

哀歎 bemoan; bewail; lament; sigh in sorrow; sigh woefully;
悲歎 deplore; lament; sigh mournfully; sigh over;
長歎 deep sigh; heave a deep sigh; sigh deeply;
稱歎 acclaim; praises;
感歎 sigh with feeling;
浩歎 sigh deeply;
驚歎 exclaim in surprise or with admiration; wonder at;
慨歎 deplore with sighs; lament with sighs; sigh with regret;
喟歎 sigh with deep feeling;
惋歎 deplore; regret;
羨歎 praise;
興歎 heave a sigh;
詠歎 intone; sing;
怨歎 sigh with bitterness;
贊歎 exclaim in praise; gasp with admiration;
讚歎 gasp in admiration; praise highly;
自歎 pity oneself; regret; sigh to oneself;

tang¹
tang

【湯】 (1) boiling water; hot water; (2) hot springs; (3) broth; soup; (4) a surname;
[湯匙] soup spoon; tablespoon;
湯池金城 a wall of metal and a moat of hot water;
湯池之固 impenetrable defense works;
[湯飯] soup and cooked rice;
殘湯剩飯 a few crumbs; leftovers of a meal; remains of food;
[湯鍋] soup pot;
湯鍋裏煨鴨子—只露一個嘴 a duck in a pot shows only its beak;
[湯火不避] not shirk to go through hot water and fire;
[湯麵] noodles in soup;
來碗湯麵 a bowl of noodles, please;
[湯杓] soup ladle;
[湯碗] soup bowl;
小湯碗 soup bowl;
[湯藥] liquid and medication;
換湯不換藥 change in form but not in content; have a superficial reform; have no real change; make a superficial change; offer the same old stuff but with a different label;
[湯圓] balls of glutinous rice;

熬湯 stew meat for broth;
白湯 clear soup;
菜湯 vegetable soup;
茶湯 gruel of millet flour and sugar;
盛湯 ladle out soup;
池湯 big pool in a bathhouse;
蛋花湯 egg-flower soup;
番茄湯 tomato soup;
高湯 (1) soup stock; (2) thin soup;
羹湯 broth;
灌米湯 bewitch sb by means of flattery; butter sb up; lay it on thick; lay the butter on;
薑湯 ginger decoction; ginger tea;
綠豆湯 mung bean soup;
迷魂湯 magic potion;
米湯 (1) thin rice gruel; (2) water in which rice has been cooked;
麵湯 water in which noodles have been boiled;
牛肉湯 beef broth;
濃湯 thick soup;
泡湯 hope dashed to pieces;
盆湯 bathtub cubicle;
片兒湯 a kind of food made from wheat flour, in the shape of small, thin pieces, boiled in water;
清湯 clear soup; light soup;
人參湯 ginseng decoction;
肉湯 broth; porridge;
灑湯 bungle; fail;
酸辣湯 vinegar-pepper soup;
酸梅湯 sweet-and sour plum juice;
溫湯 (1) hot spring; (2) lukewarm water;
續命湯 a decoction to stimulate a dying person; life-saver;
舀湯 ladle out soup;
一匙湯 a spoon of soup;
一鍋湯 a pot of soup;
一碗湯 a bowl of soup;
魚湯 fish stew;

tang

【蹚】 (1) tread; tread on; wade; (2) walk through mud or water;

［蹚水］ tread water; wade water;
　　蹚水過河 wade a stream;

鏟蹚 weed, loosen the soil, and earth up between rows of plants;

tang

【鏜】 (1) noise of drums and gongs; (2) small gong;

［鏜鏜］ noise of drums;

tang²
tang

【唐】 (1) Tang Dynasty (618-907); (2) a surname;

［唐突］ abrupt; blunt; brusque; impertinent; rude;
　　唐突古人 show disrespect for one's ancestors;
　　唐突無禮 try sth on;
　　唐突西施 impudent to a good person;
　　出言唐突 make a blunt remark;
　　恕我唐突 excuse me if I'm being too blunt; I don't want to pry;

荒唐 (1) absurd; nonsensical; preposterous; (2) dissipated; loose;
頹唐 dejected; downhearted;

tang

【堂】 (1) hall for a specific purpose; (2) main room of a house; (3) relations between cousins; (4) court of law;

［堂奧］ (1) innermost recess of a hall; (2) interior of a country; (3) profundity of thought;
　　堂奧未窺 have not seen the innermost recess of the house;
［堂伯］ paternal uncle who is older than one's father;
［堂弟］ first cousin; younger male cousin;
［堂房］ relationship between cousins of the the same paternal grandfather;
［堂倌］ waiter;
［堂皇］ grand; magnificent; stately;
　　堂皇大方 dignified and liberal;
　　富麗堂皇 beautiful and imposing; gorgeous; grandeur; magnificent; of majestic splendour; palatial; resplendent; splendid and sumptuous; sumptuous;
　　堂而皇之 dignified bearing; in state;
［堂姐］ elder female cousin; first cousin;
［堂妹］ first cousin; younger female cousin;
［堂堂］ (1) dignified; impressive; (2) high aspirations and boldness of vision; (3) awe-inspiring; formidable; imposing;
　　堂堂大國 great, powerful nation;
　　堂堂大丈夫 dignified gentleman;
　　堂堂皇皇 in state; magnificent;

堂堂儀表 dignified in appearance; grand air; imposing appearance; impressive-looking;
堂堂正正 fair and square; honourable and fair; open and aboveboard;
堂堂之陣 awe-inspiring military strength; grave and dignified array of soldiers; imposing array of troops;
相貌堂堂 dignified in appearance;

[堂屋] central room;
堂屋椅子輪流坐，媳婦也有做婆時 the seats in the great hall all come in rotation; the daughter-in-law will some day be a mother-in-law;

[堂兄] elder male cousin; first cousin;
堂兄弟 cousins on the paternal side;

[堂族] members of the same clan;

庵堂 Buddhist convent; nunnery;
菴堂 Buddhist monastery;
坳堂 hollow in the ground;
拜堂 perform formal bows by bride and groom in the old custom in China; perform the formal wedding ceremony;
禪堂 meditation room; room in Buddhist monastery set apart for meditation;
穿堂兒 hallway (connecting two courtyards in an old-style Chinese compound);
祠堂 ancestral hall; ancestral temple; clan hall;
大禮堂 assembly hall; auditorium;
大堂 court of law; great hall; principal hall in a yamen;
嫡堂 cousins of the same grandfather by the direct line;
法堂 court of law;
佛堂 family hall for worshipping Buddha;
高堂 (1) large hall with high ceilings; (2) one's parents;
公堂 (1) ancestral hall; memorial temple; (2) law court; tribunal;
過堂 appear in court to be tried;
哄堂 bring the room down; fill the room with laughter;
會堂 assembly hall; hall;
祭堂 altar;
紀念堂 commemoration hall; memorial hall;
講堂 classroom; lecture room;
教堂 cathedral; church;
課堂 classroom; schoolroom;
禮拜堂 church;
禮堂 assembly hall; auditorium;
亮堂 (1) bright; light; (2) clear; enlightened;
靈堂 mourning hall;
令堂 your mother;
滿堂 roomful;
名堂 (1) achievement; result; (2) item; variety; (3) reason; what lies behind sth;
廟堂 imperial court; royal court;
盆堂 bathtub cubicle;
群言堂 rule by the voice of the many;
上堂 (1) go to class; (2) go up the hall;
昇堂 (of a judge) hold a court trial;
食堂 canteen; dining room; mess hall;
聖堂 sanctuary;
食堂 canteen; dining room; lunchroom; mess hall; restaurant;
提堂 bring to court;
天堂 heaven; paradise;
廳堂 hall;
同堂 (1) of the same paternal grandfather; (2) live under the same roof;
下堂 be divorced by one's husband; leave one's husband;
萱堂 your mother;
學堂 school;
一言堂 one person alone has the say;
印堂 (Chinese physiognomy) top of the nose bridge connecting the eye-brows;
育嬰堂 foundling hospital;
浴堂 bathhouse; public bath;
澡堂 bathhouse; public baths;
齋堂 dining room in a Buddhist temple;
中堂 (1) form of address for a grand secretary in the Ming and Qing Dynasties; (2) central scroll hung in the middle of the wall of the main room;
尊堂 your mother;

tang

【棠】 crab apple; wild apple;

棣棠 kerria;
海棠 Chinese flowering crab apple;
秋海棠 begonia;

tang

【塘】 (1) bank; bund; dike; embankment; (2) pond; square pool; tank;

[塘鵝] pelican;
[塘肥] pond sludge used as manure;
[塘泥] pond silt; pond sludge;
[塘魚] pond fish;

坳塘 small pond;

T

池塘 (1) big pool in a bathhouse; (2) pond; pool;
海塘 sea well;
爛泥塘 muddy pond;
泥塘 bog; mire; morass;
水塘 pond; pool;
葦塘 pond;

tang

【搪】 (1) keep out; ward off; (2) do sth perfunctorily; evade; (3) daub; spread over;

[搪瓷] enamel;
搪瓷鍋 enamel pan;
黑板搪瓷 blackboard enamel;
建築搪瓷 architectural enamel;
耐酸搪瓷 acid-proof enamel;

[搪饑] ward off hunger by eating whatever is available;

[搪塞] do sth perfunctorily; dodge; fob sb off; palter; parry sth; prevaricate; stall sb off;
搪塞差事 perform a duty perfunctorily;
搪塞推諉 dodge about; evade the issue; give some lame apology;

[搪突] abrupt; rude;

[搪賬] evade paying one's debts;

tang

【膛】 (1) breast; chest; (2) cavity; (3) chamber of a firearm;

[膛口] muzzle of a gun;
彈膛 chamber;
爐膛 chamber of a stove of furnace;
砲膛 (of a cannon) bore;
槍膛 (of a gun) bore;
上膛 (of a gun) be loaded; palate;
胸膛 chest;

tang

【糖】 (1) sugar; (2) candy; sweets;

[糖廠] sugar mill; sugar refinery;

[糖醋] sugar and vinegar; sweet and sour;
糖醋魚 sweet-and-sour fish;
糖醋豬肉 sweet-and-sour pork;

[糖錠] lozenge;

[糖粉] icing sugar; powdered sugar;
給蛋糕撒糖粉 frost a cake; ice a cake;

[糖分] sugar content;

[糖膏] massecuite;
低級糖膏 low-grade massecuite;
高級糖膏 high-grade massecuite;
甜菜糖膏 beet massecuite;

[糖罐] sugar bowl;

[糖果] bonbons; candies; confectionery; sweets;
糖果店 candy shop; confectionery;
糖果盒 candy container;
糖果商 confectioner;
充氣糖果 aerated candy;
酸味糖果 acid drop;
一把糖果 a handful of candies;
一包糖果 a packet of sweets;
一袋糖果 a bag of candies;

[糖化醪] mash;
成熟糖化醪 finished yeast mash;
高濃度糖化醪 high-concentration mash;
穀物糖化醪 grain mash;
麥芽糖化醪 malt mash;

[糖漿] molasses; sirup; syrup;
糖漿粉 dried syrup;
桔片糖漿 orange syrup;
加香糖漿 flavoured syrup;
玉米糖漿 corn syrup;
止咳糖漿 cough syrup;

[糖薑] sugared ginger;

[糖精] saccharine;

[糖蜜] (1) molasses; (2) sugar and honey;
赤糖蜜 blackstrap molasses;
純淨糖蜜 clarified molasses;
如糖似蜜 like sugar and honey;
甜菜糖蜜 beet molasses;
稀糖蜜 diluted molasses;

[糖尿] (1) diabetes; (2) glucosuria;
糖尿病 diabetes;
~ 糖尿病人 diabetic;
~ 糖尿病壞疽 diabetic gangrene;
~ 糖尿病性酸中毒 diabetic acidosis;
~ 氨基酸型糖尿病 amino diabetes;
~ 病理性糖尿病 pathologic glycosuria;
~ 成年型糖尿病 adult-onset diabetes mellitus;
~ 成熟型糖尿病 maturity-onset diabetes mellitus;
~ 穿刺性糖尿病 puncture diabetes;
~ 脆性糖尿病 brittle diabetes;
~ 假糖尿病 pseudodiabetes;
~ 青銅色糖尿病 bronze diabetes;
~ 妊娠糖尿病 gestational diabetes;
~ 腎性糖尿病 renal diabetes;
~ 生長期糖尿病 growth-onset diabetes mellitus;
~ 隱性糖尿病 latent diabetes;

~ 幼年型糖尿病 juvenile diabetes mellitus;
~ 甾體性糖尿病 steroid diabetes;
~ 甾體源性糖尿病 steroidogenic diabetes;
糖尿上眼 diabetic eye disease;
阿拉伯糖尿 arabinosuria;
丙酮糖尿 acetonglycosuria;
良性糖尿 benign glycosuria;
情緒性糖尿 emotional glycosuria;
腎性糖尿 renal glycosuria;
消化性糖尿 digestive glycosuria;
飲食性糖尿 alimentary glycosuria;
中毒性糖尿 toxic glycosuria;

[糖片] lozenge;

[糖霜] icing;
撒糖霜 frosting;
一層糖霜 a layer of icing;

[糖業] sugar industry;

[糖衣] sugar-coated; sugar-coating;
糖衣砲彈 sugar-coated bullets;

[糖紙] sweet wrapper;

白糖 powdered sugar; refined white sugar;
半乳糖 galactose;
棒棒糖 candy cane; lollipop; lolly;
棒糖 all-day sucker; candy stick; lollipop; sucker;
冰糖 crystal sugar; rock candy;
薄荷糖 peppermint drops;
冰糖 crystal sugar; rock candy;
粗糖 raw sugar; unrefined sugar;
單糖 monosaccharide; monose;
低血糖 hypoglycemia;
多聚糖 polysaccharide;
多糖 polysaccharide;
方糖 cube sugar; lump sugar; sugar cube;
楓糖 maple sugar;
肝糖 glycogen;
關東糖 a kind of malt candy (originating in the northeast);
果糖 fructose; laevulose;
核糖 ribose;
紅糖 brown sugar;
花生糖 peanut brittle;
黃糖 brown sugar;
夾心糖 sweets;
夾心硬糖 filled hard candy;
薑味糖 ginger candy;
焦糖 caramel;
酒心糖 liquor-filled candy;
咖啡糖 coffee candy;
口香糖 chewing gum; gum confection;
麥芽糖 malt sugar; maltose;
棉花糖 marshmallow;
拿糖 give oneself airs; put on airs; strike a pose to impress people;
奶糖 cream candy; toffee;
奶油糖 cream confection;
檸檬糖 lemon candy;
牛奶糖 toffee;
牛皮糖 sticky candy;
泡泡糖 bubblegum;
派糖 dish out sweeteners;
皮糖 a kind of sweets made from sugar and some starch;
葡萄糖 glucose;
瓊脂糖 agarose;
醛糖 aldose;
乳糖 lactose; milk sugar;
乳脂糖 taffy; toffee;
軟糖 confection; fondant; fudge; jelly; jelly drops; soft sweets;
潤喉糖 lozenge; pastille; throat tablet;
沙糖 brown sugar; crystal sugar; granular sugar; powdered sugar;
砂糖 brown sugar; crude sugar; granulated sugar;
食糖 sugar;
雙糖 disaccharide;
水果糖 fruit confection; fruit drops;
水晶糖 crystal candy;
酥糖 crisp candy; crunchy candy; sugar cake;
太妃糖 toffee; toffee;
甜菜糖 beet sugar;
酮糖 ketose;
脱糖 desugar;
喜糖 sweets presented to friends, relatives, etc. at wedding;
血糖 blood sugar;
藥糖 lozenge;
椰子糖 coconut candy; coconut confection;
一包糖 a package of sweets;
一層糖 a coat of sugar;
一匙糖 a spoonful of sugar;
一點糖 a dash of sugar;
一塊糖 a lump of sugar;
一顆糖 a sweet;
一小塊糖 a knobble of sugar;
飴糖 malt sugar; maltose;
硬糖 hard candy;
榨糖 refined sugar;
蔗糖 (1) cane sugar; (2) sucrose;
製糖 refine sugar;

T

tang
【螗】 small cicada;

tang
【螳】 mantis;
[螳臂擋車] kick against the pricks; throw straws against the wind;
[螳斧] axe-shaped forelegs of a mantis;
[螳螂] mantis; praying mantis;
螳螂捕蟬，黃雀在後 the mantis stalks the cicada, but behind them lurks the oriole – covet gains ahead, unaware of danger behind; the mantis stalks the cicada, unaware of the oriole lurking behind – be so short-sighted as to confine one's attention to immediate interest regardless of aftermath;
螳螂拳 mantis boxing;

tang
【醣】 carbohydrate;
[醣蛋白] glycoprotein;

tang³
tang
【帑】 (1) public funds; public money; (2) treasury;
[帑藏] treasury;
公帑 public money;
國帑 national funds; public funds;

tang
【倘】 if; in the event of; supposing;
[倘或] if; in case;
[倘然] if; in case;
[倘若] if; in case; in the event of; supposing;
[倘使] if; in case; supposing;
[倘是] if; in case; supposing;

tang
【淌】 drip; flow; trickle;
[淌汗] perspire;
黃汗直淌 sweat profusely;
[淌下] shed;
流淌 (of liquids) flow; run;

tang
【惝】 discouraged; disheartened; dispirited;
[惝怳] dejected; despondent; discouraged; disheartened; dispirited;
[惝恍] confused;
惝恍迷離 feel confused; feel lost;
惝恍無定 dispirited and distracted;
[惝然] crestfallen; discouraged; disheartened; dispirited;

tang
【躺】 in a lying position; lie; lie down; recline;
[躺倒] lie down;
躺倒不幹 stay in bed and refuse to shoulder responsibilities any longer;
[躺下] lie down;
[躺椅] chaise longue; deckchair;
草地躺椅 lawn chair;
摺疊躺椅 deckchair;

tang⁴
tang
【趟】 journey; trip;
趕趟 be in time for;
光趟 glossy; sleek; smooth;

tang
【燙】 (1) burn; scald; (2) heat; warm; (3) iron;
[燙髮] give a permanent wave; perm; wave hair;
[燙金] gild; gold stamp;
燙金字 gilt lettering;
[燙酒] heat wine in hot water;
[燙傷] burn; scald;
[燙手] (1) scald one's hand; (2) difficult to manage;
錢多得燙手 have money to burn;
[燙一燙] have sth heated; have sth ironed;
[燙衣] iron clothes;
燙衣服 iron clothes;
燙衣工 press ironer;
燙衣機 ironer; ironing machine;
電燙 perm; permanent hair styling; permanent wave;
滾燙 boiling hot; burning hot;
火燙 have one's hair permed; perm; scalding; very hot;
冷燙 cold wave;
熟燙 (of fruit) damaged; spoiled;

tao¹
tao
【叨】 be favoured with; get the benefit of;
[叨沓] greedy and slack;

［叨光］ much obliged to you;
［叨教］ many thanks for your advice; thank you for your advice;
［叨擾］ thank you for your hospitality;

tao

【掏】 (1) draw out; pull out; take out; (2) dig; scoop out; (3) steal sth from sb's pocket;
［掏溝］ dredge a ditch;
［掏井］ dredge a well;
［掏摸］ (1) search and feel; (2) steal; (3) be given money after begging;
［掏錢］ spend money; take out money;
［掏心］ from the bottom of one's heart;
掏心掏肺 speak from the bottom of one's heart;

tao

【滔】 (1) flood; inundate; (2) fluent;
［滔風］ east wind;
［滔濫］ overflow;
［滔滔］ (1) billowy; surging; torrential; (2) fluent; keep up a constant flow of words;
滔滔不絕 a flood of words; an unceasing flow of words; flow on without stopping; pour out words like a flood; rattle on; shoot off one's mouth; spout eloquent speeches; talk a horse's hind legs off; talk fluently and endlessly; talk incessantly; talk nineteen to the dozen; talk oneself out of breath;
~滔滔不絕的 voluble;
滔滔不絕的話語 flood of words;
滔滔千言 flood of words;
滔滔善辯 eloquent; skilled in debating;
滔滔雄辯 torrent of eloquence;
滔滔言辭 flood of words;
［滔天］ (1) billowy; dash to the skies; (2) heinous; monstrous;
滔天大禍 terrible disaster;
滔天大浪 rolling mountains of waves;
滔天大罪 atrocity; extremely serious offense; heinous crimes; horrible crimes; monstrous crimes; towering crimes; vicious crimes;
滔天罪行 great sin; flagrant crime; monstrous crimes;
波浪滔天 waves running high;
駭浪滔天 dreadful foaming waves;
罪行滔天 monstrous crimes;

tao

【絛】 ribbon; sash; silk band;
［絛蟲］ tapeworm;

tao

【搯】 pull out; take out;

tao

【濤】 big wave; billow; great swelling;
［濤波］ billows; great waves;
［濤聲］ sound of roaring billows; surf;
［濤濤］ (1) surging; torrential; (2) keep up a constant flow of words;
［濤頭］ wave crest;
波濤 billows; great waves;
浪濤 billows; great waves;
林濤 (of a forest, stirred by winds) roar like waves;
怒濤 furious waves;
松濤 soughing of the wind in the pines;

tao

【韜】 (1) bow case; sheath case; (2) conceal; hide; (3) art of war; military strategy; tactics;
［韜筆］ let the pen idle; write no more;
韜筆鉗口 put away the pen and keep the mouth tight;
［韜光］ conceal one's talents;
韜光晦跡 conceal one's ability and bide one's time; hide one's capacities and bide one's time;
韜光養晦 hide one's light under a bushel;
［韜晦］ conceal one's true features or intentions; lie low;
韜晦待時 hide one's capacities and bide one's time;
韜晦隱居 hide one's light under a bushel and live in seclusion;
［韜略］ military strategy;
韜略用詳 a strategy is planned to minute details;

tao

【饕】 ferocious mythical animal;
［饕餮］ (1) ferocious mythical animal; (2) fierce and cruel person; (3) glutton; gourmand; voracious eater;
饕餮之徒 gluttons; greedy people;

tao[2]

tao

【洮】 name of a river in Gansu;

T

tao

【桃】 (1) peach; (2) peach-shaped object; (3) a surname;

［桃符］ (1) Spring Festival couplets; (2) peachwood charm;

桃符換舊 the old scrolls are replaced by new ones — Lunar New Year's Day;

［桃核］ pit; stone;

［桃紅］ light red; pink;

桃紅柳綠 red peach blossoms and green willows; the peach blossoms and the willow turns green; the peach trees are in bloom and the willows are turning green;

硫靛桃紅 thioindigo;

［桃花］ peach blossom;

桃花薄命 miserable beauty;

桃花臉 peach-blossom face of a beauty; rosy cheeks;

桃花心木 mahogany;

桃花魚 minnow;

桃花運 (1) romance; (2) luck in love;

~交桃花運 be successful in romantic affairs;

面若桃花，心如蛇蝎 she has a fair face, but a foul heart;

［桃李］ (1) one's disciples; one's pupils; (2) peaches and plums; (3) beauty of a woman;

桃李不言，下自成蹊 peaches and plums do not have to talk, yet the world beats a path to them; silence is wisdom and gets friends;

桃李滿門 have a great number of students; have many pupils;

桃李滿天下 have former students in all parts of the country; have pupils everywhere; have students all over the country;

桃李滿園 the garden is full of peach and plum trees;

桃李門牆 disciples and students of a master;

桃李年華 in one's young age;

桃李飄香 the fragrance of thousands of peach and plum trees in bloom fills the air;

桃李盛開 the peach and plum trees are in full bloom;

桃李盈門 a whole family of peaches and plums — many disciples;

桃李盈庭 peaches and plums fill up the courtyard — have a great number of students;

桃李爭春 peaches and plums emulate each other in springtime;

桃李爭妍 peach and plum blossoms rival each other in beauty; peach and plum trees vie with one another in the splendour of their blossoms;

桃李爭艷 peach and plum emulate each other in the springtime;

門牆桃李 one's disciples; pears and plums in one's house walls — one's pupils;

色艷桃李 as beautiful as flowers;

桃三李四 peach trees take three years to bear fruits and plum trees four;

投桃報李 exchange gifts; give a plum in return for a peach; return a favour with a favour;

夭桃濃李 beautiful peach and plum blossoms; beautiful young ladies; pretty girls;

以李報桃 exchange gifts; give plums for peaches; reciprocate a favour;

［桃柳］ peach trees and willows;

桃柳相間 intersperse peach trees between the willows;

桃柳爭妍 peach and plum trees vie to be the top attraction of spring;

［桃木］ peachwood;

山核桃木 hickory;

［桃皮］ skin of a peach;

［桃脯］ peaches preserved in honey;

［桃仁］ dried meat of a walnut; peach kernels;

［桃腮］ peach-red cheeks;

桃腮杏眼 peach-red cheeks and almond-shaped eyes; rosy cheeks and almond eyes;

淚灑桃腮 her tears fall like pearls and beans; pearly tears never cease to roll down her peach-like cheeks;

［桃色］ (1) peach colour; (2) symbolic of romance; (3) illicit love;

桃色案件 legal cases involving love and sex;

桃色新聞 news of illicit love; newspaper stories of love and sex;

［桃樹］ peach tree;

山核桃樹 hickory;

［桃月］ third month of the lunar year;

［桃子］ peach;

成熟的桃子 ripe peaches;
一筐桃子 a basket of peaches;

碧桃 flowering peach;
扁桃 (1) almond; (2) flat peach;
核桃 walnut;
胡桃 walnut;
夾竹桃 oleander;
金絲桃 Hypericum chinese;
荊桃 cherry;
毛桃 wild peach;
獼猴桃 carambola;
棉桃 cotton ball;
蟠桃 (1) flat peach; (2) peach of immortality in Chinese mythology;
山核桃 pecan;
山桃 mountain peach;
壽桃 (1) longevity peaches; (2) (peach-shaped) birthday cake;
水蜜桃 honey peach;
仙桃 divine peach;
杏桃 prune and peach trees;
羊桃 carambola;
楊桃 carambola; star fruit;
夭桃 beautiful peach;
櫻桃 cherry;

tao

【逃】 (1) abscond; escape; flee; fly; run away; (2) avoid; dodge; evade; shirk;

[逃奔] flee; run away to;

[逃避] dodge; escape; evade; run away from; shirk;
逃避斗爭 evade struggle;
逃避困難 avoid a difficulty; dodge a difficulty;
逃避逮捕 evade arrest;
逃避死亡 cheat death;
逃避現實 escape reality;
逃避責任 fudge on an issue;

[逃兵] deserter; fugitive soldier; slacker;

[逃竄] disperse and flee; flee in disorder; run away;
東逃西竄 be driven from pillar to post; flee in all directions; scamper from one hole to another;
聞風逃竄 run away upon learning the news;

[逃遁] run away;

[逃反] seek refuge from social unrest;

[逃犯] escaped convict; escaped criminal; outlaw;

[逃歸] escape from a dangerous place and return home;

[逃荒] flee from a famine; get away from a famine-stricken area;
逃荒要飯 flee from one's native village and beg for a living;

[逃婚] escape marriage; run away from wedding;

[逃家] run away from home;

[逃嫁] (1) desert one's husband and remarry; (2) run away when one is reluctant to marry;

[逃軍] (1) desert the troops; (2) deserter;

[逃課] cut class; ditch class; play truant; skip class;

[逃離] escape; flee;
逃離者 escapee;
安然逃離 get off scot-free;

[逃名] avoid fame; shun publicity;
逃名避譽 avoid fame and praise;

[逃命] flee for one's life; run for one's life;
匆匆逃命 run for one's life;

[逃祿] avoid employment;

[逃難] flee from a calamity; seek refuge from calamities;

[逃匿] escape and hide; flee to a hiding place; go into hiding;

[逃跑] abscond; break away; buzz off; copa heel; cut and run; cut away; cut loose; cut one's stick; decamp; duck; escape; flee; get away; get out; give leg bail; make good one's escape; make off; make one's escape; make one's getaway; move off; run away; run off; scarper; show a clean pair of heels; show legs; show one's heels; slip away; take leg bail; take to flight; take to one's heels; take to one's legs;
想要逃跑 feel like running away;

[逃散] become separated in flight; flee in all directions; fly asunder;

[逃生] escape; escape with one's life; flee for one's life;
趕快逃生 take time to escape;
死裏逃生 be saved from death; be snatched from the jaws of death; close call; close shave; escape by a hairbreadth; escape by the skin of

one's teeth; escape death by a narrow margin; escape with one's bare life; hairbreadth escape; have a close bout with death; miss death by a hair's breadth; narrow escape from death; narrow shave; near thing;
無處逃生 nowhere to escape;

[逃世] go into seclusion; run away from the world;
逃世深居 retire from the world and dwell in deep seclusion;

[逃稅] avoid paying tax; evade taxes; tax avoidance; tax evasion;
逃稅手段 tax shelter;
逃稅者 tax dodger;

[逃脱] break away; break free; escape from; free oneself from; get clear of; make good one's escape; succeed in escaping from;
逃脱者 escapee;
逃脱責任 succeed in evading responsibility;
平安逃脱 go scot-free;

[逃亡] abscond; become a fugitive; escape; flee from home; fly; go into exile; run away;
逃亡者 fugitive;

[逃往] flee toward;

[逃席] leave a feast without permission;

[逃刑] escape the sentence;

[逃學] bunk off; cut class; escape school; hooky; play hookey; play hooky; play truant; skip school; skive off; truancy; truant;
逃學者 truant;

[逃逸] break loose and get away; escape; runaway;
逃逸速度 escape velocity;

[逃隱] flee into seclusion;

[逃債] dodge a creditor; run away from a creditor;

[逃之夭夭] decamp; do a bolt; do a bunk; do a guy; fly the pit; get clear away; make a get-away; make a run of it; make bolt for it; shoot the pit; show a clean pair of heels; show one's heels; slip away; take a clean pair of heels; take to one's heels;

[逃走] escape; flee; fly away; make one's escape; run away; take flight; take to one's heels;
逃走的機會 chance to escape;

[逃罪] escape punishment;

奔逃 flee off; run away;
逋逃 flee from justice;
出逃 flee; run away;
竄逃 flee in disorder; scurry off;
捲逃 abscond;
潰逃 break and flee; escape in disorder; flee helter-skelter; fly pell-mell;
叛逃 defect;
潛逃 abscond; desert; flee secretly; slink; slip away;
私逃 abscond; elope;
脱逃 escape; flee; run away;
外逃 (1) flee the country; (2) flee to some other place;
在逃 have escaped;

tao

【淘】 (1) wash in a pan; (2) clean out; dredge; scout; (3) tax; (4) naughty;

[淘換] choose; search for; select;

[淘金] gold washing;
沙裏淘金 have the essential extracted from a huge amount of material; pan gravel for gold; pick the best from a vast quantity; sift gold from sand; sift sand for gold;
淘沙揀金 wash the sand for gold;
洗沙淘金 wash sand for gold;

[淘井] scour a well; wash a well;

[淘漉] (1) dredge; (2) wash;

[淘米] wash rice;
洗菜淘米 wash the vegetables and prepare the rice;

[淘氣] mischievous; naughty;
淘氣包 naughty rascal;
淘氣的 impish; puckish; roguish;
淘氣鬼 little horror; mischievous imp;
淘氣異常 unusually mischievous;
小淘氣 elf; little horror; naughty rascal; tyke; urchin;

[淘汰] elimination; weed out;
淘汰標準 elimination criteria;
淘汰出去 clean it out;
淘汰率 mortality;
淘汰賽 cup tie; elimination series; knockout;

人為淘汰 artificial selection;

[淘淘] (1) water flowing; (2) wash;

[淘寫] pour out one's heart;

tao

【陶】 (1) earthenware; pottery; (2) make pottery; (3) cultivate; mould; (4) contented; happy; joyful; (5) a surname;

[陶場] potter's factory; potter's workshop;

[陶瓷] ceramics; pottery and porcelain;

陶瓷刀具 cutting ceramics;
陶瓷工 ceramist;
陶瓷工藝 ceramics;
陶瓷塑料 ceramoplastic;
陶瓷像 porcelain figure; pottery figure;
陶瓷學 ceramics; ceramography;
陶瓷製品 ceramics;
傳統陶瓷 traditional ceramics;
磁性陶瓷 magnetic ceramics;
電子陶瓷 electronic ceramics;
多孔性陶瓷 porous ceramics;
高壓陶瓷 high-tension ceramics;
工業陶瓷 industrial ceramics;
光學陶瓷 optical ceramics;
極化陶瓷 polarized ceramics;
技術陶瓷 technical ceramics;
建築陶瓷 architectural pottery; structural ceramics;
結晶陶瓷 crystalline ceramics;
金屬陶瓷 metal ceramics;
絕緣陶瓷 insulating ceramics;
美術陶瓷 artistic ceramics;
熱壓陶瓷 hot pressed ceramics;
鐵電陶瓷 ferroelectric ceramics;
細陶瓷 fine ceramics;
藝術陶瓷 art pottery;
英國陶瓷 English pottery;
中國陶瓷 Chinese pottery;

[陶誕] cheat; swindle;

[陶工] potter;

[陶匠] pottery maker;

[陶盤] pottery pot

彩繪陶盤 colour painted pottery dish with short stem;

[陶器] china; crockery; earthenware; pottery;

白雲石陶器 dolomite earthenware;
粗陶器 coarse earthenware; stoneware;
古銅色陶器 bronzed pottery;
衛生陶器 sanitary earthenware;
硬質陶器 ironstone;

[陶情] feel pleased and at ease with the world;

陶情山水 relax one's mind in nature;

[陶然] cheerful; happy; happy and carefree;

陶然自得 in a happy frame of mind;

[陶染] move, influence and mould people;

[陶陶] (1) endlessly; infinitely; (2) mild and warm;

樂陶陶 cheerful; happy; joyful;

[陶土] potter's clay; pottery clay;

[陶瓦] bricks and tiles;

[陶文] inscriptions on pottery;

[陶冶] (1) mould pottery and smelt metals; (2) cultivate; shape;

陶冶情操 cultivatge one's mind;
陶冶性情 mould a person's temperament;

[陶鐘] pottery vessel for wine;

彩繪陶鐘 colour-painted pottery vessel for wine;

[陶鑄] educate and mould people of talent;

[陶醉] be intoxicated with; drink in; revel in;

自我陶醉 have self-complacence; narcissism;

白陶 white pottery;
彩陶 ancient painted pottery; coloured pottery; painted pottery;
彩釉陶 glazed coloured pottery;
赤陶 terracotta;
黑陶 black pottery;
樂陶陶 cheerful; happy; joyful;
熏陶 exert a gradual, uplifting influence on; nurture;

tao

【萄】 grapes;

tao

【檮】 blockhead; ignorant and stupid;

[檮昧] benighted; dull and stupid; ignorant;

[檮杌] (1) fierce legendary beast; (2) ferocious person;

tao

【燾】 illuminate extensively;

[燾育] nurse all the things on earth;

tao³

tao

【討】 (1) send a punitive expedition against; send armed forces to suppress; (2) ask for; beg for; demand; (3) marry; (4) incur; invite; (5) discuss; examine into; research; study;

[討償] ask for a reward;

[討伐] punish by force of arms; quell; send a punitive expedition against; send armed forces to suppress;
討伐叛軍 suppress the rebellion through an expedition;
討伐入侵者 fight against the invaders;

[討飯] (1) beggar; (2) beg for food;
討飯三年懶做官 a beggar for three years is not interested in becoming an official;

[討好] blandish; butter up; cotton up to; curry favour with; fawn on; fawn upon; get in with; ingratiate oneself with; keep sb sweet; make up to; play up to; please; polish the apple; shine up to; suck up to; sweeten up; throw oneself at; throw oneself at sb's head; toady to;
討好賣乖 blandish; curry favour with; fawn over and show off one's cleverness; toady to;
討好上司 curry favour with one's superiors;
討好獻媚 fawn over and curry favour with;
百般討好 shine up to;
出力不討好 do a thankless task;
奉承討好 fawn over sb; flatter; lick the feet of sb; make up to; please; toady;
兩邊討好 please both sides;
兩面討好 run with the hare and hunt with the hounds;
向人討好 ingratiate oneself with a person;

[討還] get sth back;
討還血債 demand payment of a blood debt; make sb pay for his bloody crimes; make sb pay his blood debt;

[討價] ask a price; name a price;
討價還價 bargain; bargain with sb for a supply of sth; chaffer; dicker; drive a bargain; haggle about a price; haggle for a price; haggle over a price; haggle with sb over the price of sth; palter;
瞞天討價，就地還錢 the price is as high as the sky and the offer as low as the earth;

[討賤] ask for insult through lack of self-respect;

[討教] ask for advice; may I ask for your advice;
特來討教 take one's way out for advice;

[討究] study and find the truth;

[討亂] quell an uprising;

[討論] chew over; come into question; debate on; discuss; go into; have a debate with sb about sth; have a discussion about; have a discussion on; moot; talk about; talk over; have a debate with sb on sth;
討論板 talkboard;
討論會 colloquium; discussion meeting; forum; seminar; symposium;
討論區 talkboard;
討論式 method of discussion;
討論事件 talk the matter over;
討論文 discussion text;
參加討論 join in the discussion; participate in the discussion;
課堂討論 class discussion;
口頭討論 oral discussion;
為了方便討論 for the sake of arguing;
詳盡討論 discuss exhaustively;
引起討論 generate a discussion;
自由討論 associative discussion;

[討平] send armed forces to put down a rebellion;
討平叛亂 put down a rebellion;

[討乞] beg; beg alms;

[討錢] ask for money; ask for repayment;

[討巧] act artfully to get what one wants; choose the easy way out; get the best for oneself at the least expense; try to gain advantage with little effort;

[討親] take a wife;

[討情] ask for forgiveness; beg sb off; plead for leniency; plead for sb;
討情告饒 beg for pardon; plead for leniency;

[討求] beg; demand;

[討取] ask for sth; cadge; demand;

[討饒] ask for forgivenness; ask for leniency; beg for mercy; beg for pardon;
討饒乞恕 beg for forgiveness; crave mercy; implore for pardon;

[討嫌] annoying; disagreeable; incur dislike;
千萬不要討嫌 never try to be annoying;

[討厭] abhorrent of; adverse to; allergic to; antipathetic to; averse to; bad news; be annoyed with; be annoyed at; be browned-off with; be disgusted at; be disgusted by; be disgusted with; be fed up with; bore; detest; disagreeable; disgusting; dislike; hate; have a dislike for; have a distaste for; have a horror of; have an aversion to; have no time for; have no use for; hold sth in abomination; indisposed; loathe; nasty; nuisance; pain in the neck; repugnant to; sick of; take a dislike to; tired of; trouble; troublesome;

討厭的人 bad egg; blister; irritating person; wanker;
討厭鬼 bigbore; git; mush; pest;
非常討厭 regard with great detestation;
令人討厭 abominable;
惹人討厭 make a nuisance of oneself; obnoxious;
討人厭 excite disgust; excite dislike; go against the stomach; incur hatred;
真討厭 rats; what a nuisance;

[討債] ask for the payment of a debt; demand the repayment of a loan;
討債鬼 nuisance;
討債人 debt collector;

[討帳] ask for a payment; demand the payment of a debt;

按討 investigate a rebellion and put it down; quell an uprising;
檢討 (1) check up; examine; inspect; (2) make a self-criticism;
乞討 beg; beg for sth; go begging;
商討 deliberate over; discuss;
申討 denounce; openly condemn;
聲討 attack by words; condemn; denounce;
搜討 scrutinize and investigate; study carefully;
探討 fish for; inquire about; investigate; make an approach to; make inquiries about; nose about for; nose into; poke into; pry into; seek out by inquiry; spy into; try to find out;
研討 deliberate; study and discuss;
征討 go on a punitive expedition; quell; subjugate;
追討 (1) dun for; (2) pursue and subdue;

tao⁴
tao

【套】 (1) case; envelope; sheath; wrapper; (2) cover with; slip on; (3) noose; snare; trap; (4) interlink; overlap; (5) bend of a river; (6) curve in a mountain range; (7) trace; (8) harness; hitch up; (9) knot; loop; (10) copy; model on; (11) convention; formula; (12) coax a secret out of sb; pump sb about sth; (13) try to win; (14) (measure-word) a gang of; a nest of; a pack of; a series of; a set of; a suit of; a suite of; a tissue of;

[套版] colour woodblock printing;
[套杯] set of cups;
[套餐] set menu;
四道菜的套餐 four-course set menu;
[套房] ensuite; suite;
小套房 flatlet;
[套購] purchase illegally;
[套管] sleeve; sleeving;
玻璃套管 sleeving;
玻璃套管 glass sleeving;
電纜套管 sleeve;
激活套管 active sleeve;
連接套管 adapter sleeve;
[套話] conventional verbal exchanges; polite formula;
[套匯] arbitrage;
套匯行為 arbitrage;
複合套匯 compound arbitrage;
[套間] flat;
小套間 flatlet;
[套牢] lock up;
[套禮] conventional courtesies;
[套利] arbitrage;
套利公司 arbitrage house;
股票套利 arbitrage of stocks;
商品套利 commodity arbitrage;
雙邊套利 bilateral arbitrage;
[套連] connect up by ties;
[套氣] formality;
[套衫] shirt;
運動套衫 jersey;
[套色] colour process;
[套鞋] overshoes;
橡膠套鞋 overshoe;
[套用] apply mechanically; use indiscriminately;
[套裝] suit;
長褲套裝 pant suit; trouser suit;
女童套裝 girl's suit;
運動套裝 sweatsuite;

T

被套 (1) bedding bag; (2) quilt cover; (3) cotton wadding for a quilt;
筆套 (1) cap of a pen, pencil or writing brush; (2) sheath of a pen;
避孕套 condom;
襯套 bush; bushing;
成套 form a complete set;
耳套 earmuffs;
封套 cover; envelop; jacket;
河套 bend of a river;
活套 flexible; free; unconstrained;
客套 civilities; exchange polite words, greetings, etc.; polite formula;
拉幫套 (1) help pull in harness; work for others; (2) lovers;
拉套 (1) drag cart; (2) help others complete a task;
老套 old stuff;
鏈套 chain case;
龍套 (1) actor playing a walk-on part in Chinese operas; (2) utility man;
亂套 in a mess; muddle things up; turn things upside down;
棉套 cotton-padded covering for keeping sth warm;
跑龍套 general handiman; utility man; play a bit role;
配套 assort; complement; form a complete set;
圈套 snare; springe; trap;
全套 complete set; full set; package; whole set;
褥套 cotton-padded mattress; puff;
散套 a kind of *sanqu*, a type of verse with tonal patterns modeled on tunes drawn from folk music;
上套 fall into a trap;
手槍套 holster;
手套 (1) baseball gloves; (2) gloves; mittens; mitts;
書套 book jacket; slipcase;
俗套 (1) convention; conventional pattern; (2) convention; customary social etiquette;
頭套 actor's headgear;
襪套 ankle socks; socks;
外套 (1) loose coat; outer garment; (2) overcoat;
袖套 detachable sheath covering a sleeve; oversleeve;
枕套 pillowcase; pillowslip;
軸套 axle sleeve;

tao⁵
tao

【萄】 a pronunciation of 萄 , grape;

葡萄 grape;

te⁴
te

【忒】 (1) excessive; too; very; (2) change; (3) err;

奧斯忒 oersted (Oe);

te

【特】 (1) exceptional; extraordinary; particular; peculiar; special; unique; unusual; (2) for a special purpose; specially; (3) secret agent; spy; (4) especially; (5) but; merely; only;

[特別] (1) extraordinary; out of the ordinary; particular; peculiar; special; unusual; (2) especially; particularly; specially;
特別背書 special endorsement;
特別辯護人 special pleader;
特別代理人 special agent;
特別會議 ad hoc meeting; special meeting;
特別獎 special award;
特別節目 special programme;
特別津貼 special allowances;
特別提款權 special drawing rights;
特別委員會 ad hoc committee;
特別行政區 special administrative region;
特別業務 special service;
特別助理 special assistant;

[特產] special local products; specialities;
土特產 local and special products;

[特長] special merits; special skills; specialities; strong points; what one is skilled in;
發揮每個人的特長 give scope to everyone's special skill;
音樂不是他的特長 music is not his strong points;

[特出] distinguished; eminent; extraordinary; outstanding; prominent;

[特此] hereby;
特此奉告 I beg to inform you that;

[特大] (1) especially big; (2) the most;
特大城市 super city;
特大號 extra large size; king-size;
特大型企業 mega corporation;

[特等] crack; of the special class; of the special grade; special class; special grade; top grade;

T

[特地] exclusively; for a special purpose; go out of one's way; make a special effort; on purpose; specially;

[特點] characteristics; distinguishing features; hallmark; peculiarities; special features; traits;
生理特點 physiological characteristics;

[特定] (1) specially appointed; specially designated; (2) given; specific;

[特恩] special favour; special kindness;

[特工] secret service agent; special agent;
特工部門 secret service;
特工處 secret service;
特工人員 secret service agent; special agent;

[特故] intentionally; on purpose;

[特輯] special number of a periodical;

[特急] extra urgent; of special urgency;

[特級] of the special class; of the special grade;
特級廚師 super chef;
特級大師 grandmaster;
特級教師 special-class teacher;
特級質量 superfine quality;

[特技] (1) stunts; tricks; (2) special effects;
特技飛行 aerial acrobatics; fly acrobatics;
特技鏡頭 trick shot;
特技攝影 stunt photography; trick photography;
特技攝影機 stunt film camera;
特技效果 trick effects;
編隊特技 formation acrobatics; synchronized acrobatics;
表演性特技 exhibition acrobatics;
標準特技 classical acrobatics; standard acrobatics;
低空特技 low-altitude acrobatics;

[特價] bargain price; special offer;
特價出售 sell at a bargain price;
特價商店 outlet store;

[特獎] grand prize; special prize;

[特刊] special edition;

[特快] express;
特快專遞 emergent; special delivery;

[特派] commission specially; specially appointed;
特派記者 special correspondent;

[特區] special zone;
特區經濟 special-zone economy;
特區經濟學 special-zone economics;
特區社會 special-zone society;
特區政府 special-zone government;

[特權] prerogative; privilege;
特權階級 privileged class; privilegentsia;
特權思想 special privilege mentality;
財政特權 fiscal privileges;
濫用特權 abuse one's privileges;
享受特權 exercise a privilege;
行政特權 executive privilege;
政治特權 political privilege;
最少特權 least privilege;

[特色] characteristics; distinguishing features; special features; unique features;
共同特色 common denominator;
無特色 characterless;
藝術特色 artistic characteristics;
中國特色 Chinese characteristics;

[特赦] special amnesty; special pardon;
特赦令 decree of special amnesty;
特赦罪犯 under an amnesty;

[特設] ad hoc;

[特使] ambassador; emissary; special envoy;

[特殊] exceptional; particular; peculiar; special; unique;
特殊才能 special talent;
特殊搭配 special collocation;
特殊定式動詞 anomalous finitive verb;
特殊化 become privileged;
搞特殊化 seek personal privileges;
特殊教育 special education;
特殊性程度 degree of specificity;
特殊用途語言 language for special purposes;

[特為] for this particular reason; particular for the sake of;

[特務] secret agent; special agent; spy;
特務活動 espionage;
特務機關 espionage agency; spy agency;
特務組織 spy organization;

[特效] special effects;
特效藥 specific; wonder drug;

[特寫] (1) feature article; feature story; (2) close-up; feature; sketch;
特寫鏡頭 extreme close-up;
特寫作家 feature writer;
大特寫 large close-up;

[特性] character; characteristics; distinctive features; peculiarities; properties; trait;
傳熱特性 heat-transfer character;
金屬特性 metallic character;

客觀特性 objective trait;
疲勞特性 endurance character;
生態特性 ecological character;
適應特性 adaptive trait;
吸收特性 absorption characteristic;
習得特性 acquired characteristic;
先天特性 native trait;
象差特性 aberration characteristic;
遺傳特性 emphytic character;
音響特性 acoustic characteristic;

[特寫] (1) feature story; (2) close-up;
特寫鏡頭 close-up shot;

[特許] chartered; concession; franchise; special permission;
特許會計師 chartered accountant;
特許經營 franchise;
特許經營權 franchise;
特許經營人 franchisee;
特許權 chartered right; franchise; patent;
特許狀 charter;

[特選] carefully chosen; hand-picked;

[特邀] specially invite;

[特意] for a special purpose; intentionally; on purpose; specially;

[特異] peculiar; singular; strange; unusual;
特異功能 extraordinary powers;
特異性 specificity;
絕對特異性 absolute specificity;
抗原特異性 antigenic specificity;
免疫特異性 immunologic specificity;
生化特異性 biochemical specificity;
生物學特異性 biological specificity;

[特優] excellent; extraordinary;

[特有] exclusive; peculiar; special; unique;

[特約] contributing;
特約稿 special contribution;
特約記者 special correspondent;
特約經銷 special sales;
特約經銷處 special sales agency;
特約經銷商 special sales dealer;
特約評論員 special commentator;
特約維修 special repair;
特約維修處 special repair agency;
特約演員 guest actor;
特約撰稿人 special contributor;

[特徵] aspect; characteristic; characterization; distinctive feature; feature; hallmark; trait;
特徵成分 diagnostic component;
特徵描述 characterization;
特徵生格 genitive of characteristics;
地理特徵 geographical features;
合成特徵 composite character;
檢驗特徵 checking feature;
面部特徵 facial characteristics;
年齡特徵 age characteristic; age feature;
聲學特徵 acoustic feature;
屬性特徵 attributive character;
文化特徵 cultural trait;
遺傳特徵 familial trait;
指示特徵 indicative character;
自動特徵 automatic feature;

[特質] characteristics; peculiarities; special qualities;

[特指] refer particularly to; specific reference;
特指程度 degree of specificity;
特指詞 specific term;
特指單位 specific unit;
特指生格 specifying genitive;
特指性 specificity;
特指疑問句 specific interrogation;

[特種] particular kind; of a special kind; special type;
特種部隊 special forces;
特種工藝 special arts and crafts;
特種審計 special audit;

[特准] special permit;

波特 baud;
不特 not only;
敵特 enemy agent; enemy spy;
獨特 distinctive; original; special; unique;
反特 anti-espionage;
防特 guard against enemy agents;
非特 not only;
伏特 volt;
詭特 marvellous; remarkable;
基爾特 guild;
模特兒 model;
普特 pood;
奇特 fancy; outstanding; peculiar; queer; singular; strange; striking; unique; unusual;
喀斯特 karst;
瓦特 watt;

te

【慝】 evil; evil idea; vice;

te

【鋱】 terbium;

teng²

teng

【疼】 (1) ache; hurt; pain; sore; (2) dote on;

fond of; lovely dearly;
[疼愛] be fond of; love dearly;
疼愛自己的孩子 love one's own children;
[疼熱] suffer pain and fever;
[疼痛] ache; pain; soreness;
疼痛產生 algogenesia;
疼痛發生 algogenesia;
疼痛反應 pain reaction;
疼痛加劇 the pain increases;
疼痛恐怖 algophobia;
疼痛再發作 pain recurs;
疼痛障礙 pain disorder;
精神性疼痛障礙 psychogenic pain disorder;
感到疼痛 feel pain; have a pain; in pain;
骨節疼痛 arthralgia;
渾身疼痛 be aching all over; have pains all over;
減輕疼痛 alleviate the pain; relieve the pain;
經歷疼痛 experience pain;
精神性疼痛 psychalgia;
輕微疼痛 aches and pains;
全身上下疼痛 have aches and pains;
忍受疼痛 bear the pain; suffer from pain;
睡發性疼痛 hypnalgia;
一陣疼痛 a pang of pain; a spasm of pain;
感到一陣疼痛 feel a pang of pain;
[疼癢] pains and itches;
不疼不癢 of no real benefit; pointless;
偏疼 be partial to sb; show favourism to sb;
痠疼 ache;
頭疼 have a headache; headache;
胃疼 stomachache; stomach pain;
心疼 (1) be distressed; feel sorry; (2) love dearly;

teng
【滕】 (1) a state during the Spring and Autumn Period; (2) a surname;

teng
【縢】 (1) bind; restrain; restrict; tie; (2) band;
[縢履] shoes for bound feet;

teng
【謄】 copy; transcribe;
[謄本] copy; transcript;
[謄錄] copy out; transcribe;
[謄清] make a clean copy; make a fair copy of;
謄清本 fair copy;
[謄寫] copy out; transcribe;
謄寫員 amanuensis; copyist; scribe;
[謄正] make a clean copy;

teng
【藤】 rattan; vine;
[藤鞭] rattan whip;
[藤壺] barnacle;
[藤黃] gamboge;
[藤蘿] wisteria;
[藤牌] cane shield; rattan shield;
[藤條] cane; rattan;
挨藤條 get the cane;
吃藤條 get the cane;
[藤箱] rattan case;
[藤椅] cane chair; rattan chair;
[藤製品] rattan work;
[藤桌] rattan table;
[藤子] rattan;

teng
【騰】 (1) gallop; jump; (2) clear out; make room; vacate; (3) ascend; fly; go up; rise; soar; (4) surrender; transfer; turn over;
[騰出] clear; empty; make way;
騰出時間 take some free time;
[騰達] prosper; thrive;
飛黃騰達 advancement in one's career;
[騰房] vacate;
[騰飛] rise rapidly; soar; take off;
[騰貴] shoot up; skyrocket; soar;
[騰歡] rejoice; roar with joy;
[騰蛟起鳳] like the soaring phoenix and the rising dragon — one's name in literature is becoming famous;
[騰捷] flit; fly swiftly;
[騰空] fly in the sky; rise high in the air; rise to the sky; soar;
騰空而過 swing through the air;
騰空而起 rise high into the air; rise to the sky; shoot into the sky;
騰空飛越 soar into the sky to jump over;
騰空球 fly ball;
[騰馬] stallion;
[騰挪] (1) transfer funds to other uses; (2) move sth to make room;
[騰起] rise; spring;
[騰遷] empty and remove;
[騰閃] dodge; evade; ward off;
騰身而過 jump over sth;

[腾腾] (1) constantly rising up; seething; soaring; steaming; (2) slowly;
亂騰騰 confused; upset;
慢慢騰騰 sluggishly; unhurriedly;
慢騰騰 slow; sluggishly;
熱騰騰 steaming hot;
[騰驤] leap high; prance;
[騰笑] arouse laughter; seething; steaming;
騰笑海內 be laughed at in the whole country;
騰笑萬方 cause laughter everywhere;
[騰躍] (1) active; lively; (2) skyrocket;
[騰越] jump over; vault;
騰越障礙 jump over obstacles;
背騰越 back vault; rear vault;
側騰越 side vault;
俯騰越 face vault; front vault;
剪絞騰越 scissors vault;
屈腿騰越 vault over with one's legs together and bent;
水平騰越 hecht vault;
側手翻騰越 cartwheel vault;
直角騰越 rear vault;

奔騰 (1) gallop; (2) roll on in waves; surge forward;
倒騰 (1) engage in buying and selling; (2) turn upside down;
搗騰 (1) engage in buying and selling; (2) turn upside down;
翻騰 (1) rise; seethe; (2) tuck dive; (3) turn sth over and over;
飛騰 fly swiftly upward; soar;
沸騰 boil over; boiling; ebullition; seethe with excitement;
歡騰 great rejoicing; jubilation; rejoice;
亂騰 confused; disordered;
亂騰騰 confused; upset;
慢騰騰 at a leisurely pace; sluggishly; unhurriedly; very slowly;
眯騰 have a nap;
鬧騰 (1) chat, laugh and have fun; (2) create confusion; disturb;
撲騰 move up and down; thud; thump;
騫騰 go up; soar high;
熱騰騰 piping hot; steaming hot;
昇騰 (1) fly up; leap up; rise; (2) flourish in business; make good progress;
騰騰 seething; steaming;
剔騰 expose secrets maliciously;
踢騰 (1) kick at random; (2) spend money freely;
圖騰 totem;
驤騰 forge ahead;
興騰 become increasingly prosperous; gain vigour;
喧騰 hubbub; noise and excitement;
暄騰 fluffy; soft;
折騰 (1) cause physical or mental suffering; (2) do sth over and over again; (3) toss about; turn from side to side;
蒸騰 transpiration;

teng

【籐】 same as 藤, rattan;
[籐椅] rattan armchair;
[籐杖] rattan walkingstick;

白藤 cane plant; rattan;
常春藤 Chinese ivy;
葛藤 entangled relationship;
紅藤 Sargent gloryvine;
胡蔓藤 elegant Jessamine;
雞血藤 reticulate millettia;
買麻藤 sweetberry joinfir;
夜交藤 vine of mulitflower knotweed;
魚藤 trifoliate jewelvine;
紫藤 Chinese wisteria;

ti¹

ti

【剔】 (1) clean with a pointed instrument; pick; (2) pick out and throw away; pick out inferior materials; reject; scrape off; (3) scrape meat off bones; take out bones from meat;
[剔出去] eliminate; pick out;
[剔除] eliminate; get rid of; reject;
剔除糟粕，吸其精華 reject the dross and assimilate the essence;
[剔刀] scraping knife;
[剔騰] expose secrets maliciously;
[剔透] (1) well-expressed; (2) keen and perceptive;
[剔牙] pick one's teeth;

挑剔 be fastidious; nitpick;

ti

【梯】 (1) ladder; stairs; steps; (2) sth to depend on; sth to lean on; (3) terraced; (4) intimate; private;
[梯次] phases;
梯次比賽 ladder tournament;

梯次隊形 echelon formation;

[梯隊] echelon; echelon formation;

梯隊結構 orderly system of succession;

[梯航] long, arduous voyages;

[梯級] stairs; steps;

[梯己] (1) intimate; (2) private savings of a family member;

[梯階] (1) steps of a ladder; (2) means to achieve a result;

[梯氣] very intimate;

梯氣話 intimate talk;

[梯式] ladder-shaped;

梯式模型 ladder-shaped model;

[梯田] bench terrace; terrace; terraced fields;

梯田耕作 terrace agriculture;

層層梯田 tiers of terraced fields;

稻米梯田 terraced rice fields;

修梯田 build terraced fields;

一層梯田 a tier of terraced field;

[梯形] trapezoid;

梯形公式 trapezoid formula;

等腰梯形 isosceles trapezoid;

[梯子] ladder; stepladder;

扶穩梯子 steady a ladder;

架起梯子 put up a ladder;

爬上梯子 climb up a ladder;

爬下梯子 climb down a ladder;

小型梯子 small ladder;

安全梯 emergency staircase; fire escape ladder;

避火梯 fire escape;

電梯 electric elevator; electrical lift; elevator; lift; passenger lift;

扶梯 staircase;

滑梯 chute; slide;

晃梯 balancing on an upright ladder;

階梯 (1) flight of stairs; ladder; (2) stepping stone;

樓梯 staircase; stairs;

盤梯 spiral staircase; winding staircase;

軟梯 rope ladder;

昇降梯 elevator; lift;

繩梯 rope ladder;

太平梯 fire escape stairs;

梯恩梯 trinitrotoluene (TNT);

天梯 very long ladder fixed onto tall buildings, etc.;

桅梯 shrouds of a ship;

舷梯 accommodation ladder; gangway ladder;

懸梯 hanging ladder;

魚梯 fish ladder;

雲梯 aerial ladder; scaling ladder;

竹梯 bamboo ladder;

ti

【踢】 (1) kick; (2) play football;

[踢踏舞] tap dancing;

[踢開] (1) kick open; (2) kick sth out of the way;

[踢球] (1) kick a ball; (2) play football;

[踢死] kick to death;

[踢騰] (1) kick at random; (2) spend money freely;

[踢舞] tittup;

ti²

ti

【荑】 sprout;

ti

【啼】 (1) cry; weep aloud; (2) caw; crow;

[啼叫] scream; screech; wail;

[啼哭] cry; wail;

[啼泣] sob; weep;

[啼笑皆非] between tears and laughter; choke sb up; find sth both funny and annoying; one does not know whether to laugh or to cry; unable to cry or laugh;

悲啼 cry mournfully;

哭哭啼啼 endlessly weep and wail;

喔喔啼 coo-coo-ri-coo; cock-a-doodle-do;

夜啼 morbid night crying of babies;

猿啼 gibbon's howling;

ti

【提】 (1) carry in one's hand; (2) lift; lift by hand; raise; (3) bring up; pull up; put forward; (4) draw out; extract; make delivery; obtain; (5) bring forward; mention; propose; refer to; suggest; (6) dipper; (7) rising stroke; (8) a surname;

[提案] draft resolution; motion; proposal;

撤消提案 withdraw a proposal;

支持提案 sponsor a proposal; support a proposal;

[提白] prompt;

提白者 prompter;

[提拔] advance; elevate; give sb a pull; promote;

提拔人才 promote a talent;
破格提拔 promote unconventionally;

[提包] bag; briefcase; handbag;
手提包 handbag;

[提筆] lift one's pen to write;
提筆疾書 take up a pen and write rapidly; write without stopping to reflect;
提筆忘字 forget how to write a character when writing;

[提撥] (1) appropriate; (2) remind;

[提補] (1) select and fill a post; (2) remind;

[提倡] advocate; encourage; promote; recommend;
大力提倡 advocate strongly;

[提出] advance; bring forth; bring forward; bring in; bring up; come up with; lodge; pose; pour; present; propose; put forth; put forward; rain; raise; set forth; set forward; set up; submit; suggest;
提出保釋 post bail;
提出否決 interpose one's veto;
提出建議 broach a proposal;
提出解決方案 propose a solution;
提出警告 sound a warning;
提出控訴 enter a complaint;
提出口號 devise a slogan;
提出威脅 pose a threat;
提出想法 put forth an idea;
提出異議 challenge; raise an objection; take exception;
提出證明 bring forward proof;

[提詞] prompt;
提詞員 prompter;
給演員提詞 prompt an actor;

[提袋] handbag;

[提單] bill of lading;
提單持有人 holder;
空運提單 airway bill;

[提到] mention; refer to;
順便提到 mention in passing;

[提燈] lantern;
提燈會 lantern parade; lantern procession;

[提點] (1) remind; (2) an official post in ancient China;

[提督] provincial commander-in-chief;

[提防] cautious; guard against; on the alert; watchful;

[提綱] outline; syllabus; synopsis;
提綱挈領 bring out the most essential points; concise and to the point; give one a general idea of a subject; give the gist of a matter; give the main points; hit the high spots; mention the main points;
教學提綱 outline for teaching;

[提高] enhance; heighten; improve; increase; lift; put to a higher position; raise;
提高警覺 heighten one's vigilance; keep a watchful eye on; on the ball;
提高警惕 enhance one's vigilance; heighten one's vigilance; sharpen one's vigilance; step up one's vigilance;
提高認識 deepen one's understanding;
提高水位 raise the water level;
提高透明度 increase the transparency;
提高物價 boost the prices;
提高效率 raise the efficiency;
提高勇氣 pluck up one's courage;
技能的提高 upskilling;

[提供] furnish; offer; provide; supply;
提供援助 give aid; provide assistance;
提供貸款 offer a loan;
提供意見 offer an opinion;
提供贊助 provide assistance; provide support;
提供者 purveyor;

[提孩] child;

[提環鍋] loop-handled pot;

[提貨] lading; make delivery of goods;
提貨單 bill of lading;

[提及] get a mention; mention; refer to; retrospect;
沒有提及 fail to mention; make no mention of; neglect to mention; omit to mention;
順口提及 mention in passing;

[提級] upgrading;

[提價] go up; raise the price;
擅自提價 rise price arbitrarily;

[提交] refer to; submit sth to;
提交報告 submit a report to;

[提舉] promote sb;

[提款] draw money; withdraw deposit; withdraw money from a bank;
提款單 withdrawal slip;
提款機 teller machine;
自動提款機 automatic teller machine; cash dispenser; cash machine; hole in the wall;
提款卡 cash card;

自動提款卡 cash card;
提款賬戶 drawing account;

[提籃] handbasket;

[提煉] extract and purify; refine;

[提名] nominate;
提名人 nominator;
公民提名 civic nomination;

[提起] (1) mention; speak of; (2) arouse; brace up; lift up; raise;
提起精神 brace oneself up; cheer up; raise one's spirits;

[提氣] excite; inspire; raise one's morale;

[提前] advance; advance to an earlier date; ahead of schedule; ahead of time; ahead of the game; beforehand; before one's time; in advance; in anticipation; in good time; the date has been moved up; shift to an earlier date;
提前安排 plan ahead;
提前考試 take an examination ahead of schedule;
提前退休 early retirement;
提前召開大會 convene the congress before the due date;
被提前 be advanced to;

[提挈] (1) carry; lead; marshal; take along; take with one; (2) give guidance and help to; guide and support;
左提右挈 (1) give mutual help; help each other; (2) give guidance and help to; guide and support;

[提親] bring up a proposal of marriage; matchmaking; propose a marriage;

[提琴] violin family;
提琴師 brother of the string;
大提琴 cello; violoncello;
大提琴家 cellist;
大提琴演奏家 cellist;
大提琴演奏者 cellist;
拉大提琴 play cello;
一把大提琴 a cello;
低音提琴 contrabass; double bass;
小提琴 fiddle; violin;
小提琴獨奏 violin solo;
小提琴盒 violin case;
小提琴家 violinist;
小提琴老師 violin teacher;
小提琴手 fiddler; violinist;
小提琴演奏家 violinist;
小提琴演奏者 violinist;
第一小提琴 first violin;
拉小提琴 play violin;
四分三小提琴 three-quarter violin;
一把小提琴 a violin;
中提琴 viola;

[提請] submit sth to;
提請大會批准 submit to the congress for approval;

[提取] (1) collect; draw; pick up; (2) abstract; extract;
提取石油 extract oil;
取行行李 collect one's luggage;
提取銀行存款 draw money from a bank;

[提神] arouse; elate; give oneself a lift; refresh oneself; stimulate;
喝杯茶提神 refresh oneself with a cup of tea;

[提審] bring sb before the court; bring sb in custody to trial;

[提昇] (1) advance; promote; (2) elevate; hoist; (3) lift;
提昇機 elevator; hoist;
風動提昇機 air hoist;
罐籠提昇機 cage hoist;
平板提昇機 apron elevator;
平衡提昇機 balanced hoist;
昇帶式提昇機 bucket-belt elevator;
圓筒提昇機 barrel hoist;
提昇銷售量 increase sales;
二級提昇 two-stage hoisting;
平衡提昇 balanced hoisting;
不平衡提昇 unbalanced hoisting;

[提示] (1) tips; (2) cue; hint; point out; prompt;
回聲提示 echoic prompt;
形式提示 formal prompt;
正文提示 textual prompt;

[提堂] bring to court;

[提問] ask a question; pose a question; quiz;
提問者 questioner;
別害怕提問 don't be afraid to ask questions;

[提箱] suitcase;

[提攜] aid; assistance; help;

[提心] have one's heart in one's mouth;
提心吊膽 be filled with anxiety; be haunted with fear; cautious and anxious; have one's heart in one's mouth; in a state of suspense; in great terror; live in constant fear; on tenterhooks; restless and anxious;

scared;
提心吊膽的 jumpy;
提心在口 cautious and anxious; have one's heart in one's mouth;

［提醒］ call attention to; remind; warn;
［提選］ choose; select;
［提訊］ bring sb up for trial;
［提要］ abstract; epitome; summary; synopsis;
論文提要 abstract of a thesis;
［提掖］ (1) lead and support sb; (2) recommend sb for promotion;
提掖後進 advance juniors; lead and support juniors;
［提議］ move; propose; propound; put forth suggestions; suggest;
提議修改法律 propose a change in the law;
反對這項提議 demur at a suggestion;
贊同提議 assent to a proposal;
［提早］ ahead of schedule; in advance; shift to an earlier time;

別提 it's not necessary to say;
重提 bring up again; mention again;
孩提 early childhood; infancy;
免提 handsfree;
菩提 bodhi;
前提 (1) premise; (2) precondition; prerequisite; presupposition; primary consideration;
手提 mobile; portable;
休提 do not mention;

ti

【隄】 dike; embankment; levee;
［隄岸］ dike; embankment; levee;
［隄壩］ dikes and dams;
［隄邊］ by the side of a levee;
［隄堰］ dike; levee; embankment;

ti

【綈】 glossy thick silk fabric;
［綈袍］ robe made of inferior silk;
綈袍之誼 old friendship;
綈袍之意 remembrance of old favour;

ti

【緹】 (1) reddish yellow silk; (2) reddish yellow soil; (3) red; reddish;

ti

【蹄】 hoof;
［蹄插］ shoe;
通電蹄插 hot shoe;

鐵蹄 cruel oppression of the people;

ti

【醍】 (1) cream of the milk; (2) a kind of reddish wine;
［醍醐］ finest cream;
醍醐灌頂 (1) be enlightened; be filled with wisdom; (2) suddenly feel refreshed;
如飲醍醐 be enlightened; suddenly feel refreshed;

ti

【題】 (1) subject; topic; (2) commentaries; notes; (3) inscribe; sign; write; (4) a surname;
［題跋］ colophon; preface and postscript;
［題筆］ write;
［題壁］ write on the wall;
［題材］ subject matter; theme;
題材範圍 range of subjects;
題材新穎 original in the choice of the subject;
［題詞］ (1) write an inscription; (2) dedication; inscription; (3) foreword;
題詞廂 prompter's box;
［題額］ write on a horizontal tablet;
［題畫］ write on a painting;
［題解］ (1) key to exercises; (2) explanatory notes on the title or background of a book;
［題名］ (1) autograph; inscribe one's name; (2) subject; title; topic; (3) entitle; name a work;
題名留念 give one's autograph as a memento;
金榜題名 one's name is put on the published list of successful candidates; pass the examination; succeed in a civil examination;
雁塔題名 have one's name inscribed on the pagoda of the Wild Goose — have attained a doctor's degree;
［題目］ (1) subject; title; topic; (2) examination questions;
考試題目 examination questions;
一道題目 an exercise problem;
作文題目 title for a composition;
［題詩］ write poems on sth;
［題署］ write on scrolls of couplets;
［題外］ beyond the subject being discussed;

［題字］ (1) autograph; (2) inscribe; inscription; write on sth;

本題 main question; main subject; main theme; point at issue; subject under discussion;
標題 caption; header; heading; headline; title;
乘題 the second part of the eight-part essay, further expounding the meaning of implication of the topic;
出題 (1) assign a topic; set a question; set a theme; (2) make out questions;
點題 bring out a topic;
反題 antithesis;
副標題 subheading; subtitle;
副題 subtitle;
合題 synthesis;
話題 subject matter; subject of a talk; topic of a conversation;
解題 settle a problem; solve problems;
考題 examination question;
課題 (1) question for study or discussion; (2) problem; task;
離題 deviate from the topic; digress from the subject; get off the track; stray from the point;
例題 example;
留題 leave one's comments;
論題 proposition;
命題 (1) assign a topic; set a question; (2) proposition;
難題 a hard nut to crack; conundrum; facer; headache; hot potato; poser; problem; stinker; teaser; ticklish business;
拈題 select a topic for a piece of writing;
偏題 catch question; tricky question;
品題 appraise a person;
破題 the first of an eight-part essay, explaining the essence of the title in one of two sentences;
切題 keep to the point; pertinent to the subject; relevant to the subject; stick to the topic; to the point;
試題 examination or test question;
書題 title of a book;
算題 arithmetic problem;
貼題 relevant; to the point;
問答題 question-and-answer drills;
問題 (1) case; issue; matter; point; problem; question; subject; thing; (2) defect; drawback; error; fault; mistake; trouble;
無題 untitled;
習題 exercises;
小標題 subhead; subheading;
選答題 multiple choice;
議題 subject under discussion; topic for discussion;
正題 (1) subject of a talk or essay; (2) thesis;
主題 issue; key subject; main theme; motif; point; problem; proposition; question; subject; theme; thesis; topic; topical subject;
專題 special subject ; special topic;
轉題 change the subject;

ti

【鵜】 pelican;

ti

【鮷】 anchovy;

［鮷梨］ anchovy pear;
鮷梨樹 anchovy pear;

ti

【騠】 hybrid horse produced by mating a donkey with a stallion;

ti³

ti

【體】 (1) part of the body; body; (2) essence; state of a substance; substance; (3) form; shape; style; (4) aspect (of a verb); (5) put oneself in another's position; (6) system;

［體壁］ (animal) body wall;
胚外體壁 extra-embryonic somatopleure;

［體裁］ literary form;

［體操］ exercise; gymnastics;
體操器械 gymnastic apparatus;
體操選手 gymnast;
體操運動員 gymnast;
輔助體操 compensatory gymnastics;
矯正體操 corrective gymnastics; remedial gymnastics;
練習體操 practise gymnastics;
馬背體操 horseback gymnastics;
模仿體操 trench gymnastics;
柔軟體操 calisthenics;
雙人體操 companion exercise; couples exercise;
衛生體操 sanitary gymnastics;
醫療體操 curative gymnastics; medical gymnastics; therapeutic gymnastics;
藝術體操 artistic gymnastics;
自由體操 floor exercise; free exercises;
做體操 perform gymnastics; take exercise;

T

[體察] experience and observe;
體察民情 observe the people's condition;
體察下情 try to understand what is going on at the lower levels;

[體臭] body odour;

[體大思精] broad in conception and meticulous in details; extensive in scope and penetrating in thought;

[體罰] corporal punishment; physical punishment;
變相體罰 impose a corporal punishment in disguised form;

[體範] model; pattern;

[體高] height of a person;

[體格] build; physique;
體格檢查 check-up; physical examination;
體格魁梧 gigantic in stature; of great stature; one's physical form is strong and stout;
體格健全 able-bodied;
體格健壯 strong physique;
體格強壯 of powerful build; of strong physique;
敦實的體格 stocky build;

[體會] comprehend intuitively; know from experience; learn from experience; realize; understand through sth beyond the intellect;
體會言外之意 read between the lines;
切身體會 direct experience; first-hand experience intimate experience; have intimate experience of; intimate knowledge; keenly aware of; one's own experience; personal understanding;
深有體會 have an intimate knowledge of sth;

[體積] bulk; size; volume;
體積計 volumeter;
體積膨漲 volume expansion;
減少體積 reduce the volume;
有效體積 active volume;
原子體積 atomic volume;

[體例] layout; style;

[體力] physical capacity; physical power; physical strength;
體力不夠 not enough strength;
體力充沛 full of physical strength;
體力活動 physical exercise; physical exertion;
體力勞動 physical labour;
鄙視體力勞動 despise manual labour;
恢復體力 regain one's strength;
消耗體力 burn the candle at both ends;

[體例] general form;
體例繁多 regulations are numerous;
印刷體例 style sheet;

[體諒] allow for; be considerate of; make allowances for; show understanding and sympathy; sympathetic toward;

[體貌] (1) figure and face; (2) decorum; propriety;
體貌周全 one's features and manners are refined;

[體面] (1) dignity; face; honour; propriety; (2) creditable; honourable; respectable; (3) good-looking; handsome;
體面掃地 be thoroughly discredited; lose face altogether; suffer a complete loss of face;
不體面 unseemly;
不顧體面 regardless of one's reputation;
不失體面 maintain one's dignity; not lose face;
維持體面 keep up appearances; save appearances;
有失體面 compromising;
有失體面的照片 compromising photo;

[體能] physical strength; stamina;

[體魄] build; physique;
鍛鍊體魄 go in for physical training;
強壯的體魄 strong physique; vigorous health;

[體腔] coelom;
胚外體腔 exocoelom; extraembryonic coelom;

[體認] perceive intuitively;

[體弱] debility;
體弱多病 broken in health;

[體態] carriage; posture;
體態輕盈 graceful carriage; soft, well-rounded figure; supple body;
優美的體態 beautiful posture;

[體壇] sports circle; the sporting world;
體壇捷報 exciting news from the sports world;
體壇新秀 new star in the sports circle;

[體貼] considerable; kind; thoughtful;
體貼病人 show a patient every consideration;

體貼入微 care for sb with great solicitude; extremely considerate towards sb; extremely thoughtful; full of kind attentions; look after sb with meticulous care; show every possible consideration towards sb; take sb to one's bosom; treat sb with great consideration;

[體統] decency; decorum; propriety;
不成體統 do things against the traditions;
大失體統 great loss of face;
有失體統 disgraceful; scandalous;

[體味] (1) body odour; (2) appreciate; savour;

[體溫] body temperature;
體溫表 clinical thermometer;
體溫計 clinical thermometer;
體溫上昇 temperature rise;
體溫下降 temperature drop; temperature fall;
量體溫 take sb's temperature;

[體無完膚] a mass of bruises; be refuted down to the last point; be scathingly criticized; be thoroughly refuted; be torn to pieces; be torn to shreds; have cuts and bruises all over the body;
被打得體無完膚 be beaten black and blue;

[體惜] understand and have pity on sb;

[體系] hierarchy; setup; system;
制定體系 formulate a system;
自成體系 create a system of one's own; establish one's own system;

[體現] embody; give expression to; incarnate; reflect;

[體香劑] body deodorant;

[體行] embody sth in one's own actions;

[體形] body shape; build; physique;
體形苗條 have a good figure;
保持體形苗條 keep one's good figure;

[體型] build; external physical appearance;
體型健美 be in shape;
保持體型健美 get in shape; keep in shape;

[體卹] considerate of and sympathize with; favour; show solicitude for; understand and sympathize with;

[體驗] experience firsthand; firsthand experience; learn through one's personal experience; learn through experience;
體驗創作 experiential creation;
體驗孤獨 experience loneliness;
體驗生活 observe and learn from real life;
親身體驗 first-hand experience;
生活體驗 life experience;

[體要] (1) gist; outline; summary; (2) concise; succinct; terse;

[體育] physical training; sports; sports activities;
體育愛好者 sports enthusiast; sports fan;
體育版 sports section;
體育報 sports newspaper;
體育比賽 sports contest;
體育場 gymnasium;
體育場所 athletic field;
體育鍛鍊 physical conditioning; physical training;
體育館 gymnasium;
體育會 athletic club;
體育活動 sports activities;
體育記者 sportswriter;
體育界 sports world;
體育美學 aesthetics of physical culture;
體育迷 sports fan;
體育名人 sports personality;
體育片 athletic film; sports film;
體育器材 athletic equipment;
體育設施 sports facilities;
體育用品 sports goods;
體育運動 athletic sports; physical culture and sports;
體育中心 sports centre;
體育裝備 sports equipment;
愛好體育 go in for sports;
競技體育 competitive sport;

[體制] setup; structure; system;
體制改革 structural reform;
體制轉軌 system transforming;
管理體制 management system;
國家體制 state system;

[體質] bodily constitution; physical make-up;
體質孱弱 in delicate health; one's bodily constitution is weak;
增強體質 build up health; build up one's body;

[體重] body weight;
體重減輕 lose weight;
體重增加 put on weight;
留意體重 watch your weight;
增加體重 gain weight; put on weight;

[體壯] strong body;
肩寬體壯 have broad shoulders;

白色體 leucoplast;
白體 lean type;
半導體 semiconductor;
半流體 semifluid;
孢子體 sporophyte;
本體 (1) noumenon; thing in itself; (2) main part; principal part;
編年體 annalistic style in historiography;
扁桃體 tonsil;
變形體 plasmodium;
報章體 newspaper style;
筆體 handwriting;
蔽體 cover the body;
遍體 all over the body;
變體 variant; variety;
病原體 pathogen;
玻璃體 vitreous body;
補體 complement;
草體 (1) (in Chinese calligraphy) characters executed swiftly and with strokes flowing together; (2) running hand;
查體 physical examination;
長方體 cuboid; rectangular parallelepiped;
超導體 superconductor;
成體 adult;
船體 body of a ship; hull;
垂體 hypophysis; pituitary body (or gland);
磁流體 magnetic fluid;
磁體 magnetic body; magnet;
大體 (1) cardinal principle; general interest; (2) by and large; for the most part; more or less; on the whole; roughly;
單倍體 haploid; monoploid;
單晶體 monocrystal;
單體 monomer;
導體 conductor;
得體 appropriate; befitting one's position or suited to the occasion; decorum; propriety;
等離子體 plasma;
電晶體 transistor;
胴體 body; carcass; trunk;
多倍體 polyploidy;
多晶體 polycrystal;
多面體 polyhedron;
二倍體 diploid;
發光體 luminary; luminous body;
翻譯體 translationese;
繁體 unsimplified form of Chinese;
反覆體 iterative aspect;
仿宋體 imitation Song-Dynasty style typeface;
非導體 insulator;
非晶體 amorphous body;
非生物體 inorganic matter;
輻射體 radiating body;
富礦體 ore shoot;
復合體 compound;
得體 (of conduct, speech, etc.) proper or appropriate;
感應體 inductor;
剛體 rigid body;
哥特體 gothic;
個體 (1) individuality; personality; thing; (2) individual; particular;
共同體 community;
共生體 symbiont;
古體 old styles;
固體 solid; solid body;
國體 (1) national prestige; (2) state system;
海綿體 sponge;
黑體 (1) black body; (2) boldface;
黃體 corpus luteum;
後體 opisthosoma;
肌體 (1) human body; (2) organism;
機體 (1) airframe; (2) organism;
集合體 aggregate;
集體 (1) collectively; (2) collective ownership; (3) collective; community; group; team;
幾何體 solid;
記敍體 narrative;
紀傳體 history presented in a series of biographies;
膠體 colloid;
角柱體 prism;
角錐體 pyramid;
結果體 effective aspect;
結晶體 crystal;
解體 break up; disintegrate; dismantle; dismount;
介體 amboceptor;
晶體 crystal;
晶狀體 crystalline lens;
進行體 progressive;
具體 concrete; particular; specific;
絕緣體 insulator;
菌絲體 hypha;
開始體 ingressive aspect;
楷體 (1) block letter; (2) regular script;
抗磁體 diamagnet;
抗體 antibody;
可體 be a good fit;
客體 object;
空心體 hollow body;
礦體 ore body;
口語體 colloquial speech;
老宋體 Song typeface, a standard typeface first used in the Ming Dynasty (1368 – 1644),

T

but popularly attributed to the Song Dynasty (960 — 1279);
類星體 quasi-stellar object;
立體 (1) solid; (2) stereoscopic; (3) three-dimensional;
立方體 cube;
連續體 continuum;
良導體 good conductor;
磷光體 phosphor;
菱面體 rhombohedron;
稜柱體 prism;
稜錐體 pyramid;
流體 fluid;
柳體 calligraphy style of Liu Gongquan of the Tang Dynasty;
輪生體 verticil; whorl;
螺旋體 spirochaeta;
裸體 in a state of nature; in one's birthday suit; in the altogether; in the buff; in the raw; in the rude; naked; nude;
落體 falling body;
媒體 mass media; medium;
面體 –hedron;
黏附體 adherend;
腦上體 pineal body;
腦下垂體 hypophysis; pituitary gland;
配子體 gametophyte;
胼胝體 corpus callosum;
駢體 rhythmical prose style, marked by parallelism and ornateness;
拋射體 projectile;
七倍體 heptaploid;
七面體 heptahedron;
氣體 gas;
前體 prosoma;
球體 spheroid;
軀體 body; carcass; human body;
全體 all; en bloc; en masse; entire; everybody; head and ears; in a body; the whole body; whole;
群體 (1) integral entity; (2) group; population;
染色體 chromosome;
熱導體 heat conductor;
熱電體 pyroelectrics;
人體 human body;
溶體 solution;
熔體 melt;
肉體 carnal; corporeal clod; flesh; flesh and blood; physical; sensory; the human body;
軟體 software;
三倍體 triploid;
三稜體 triangular prism;
散體 prose style free from parallelism; simple, direct prose style;
騷體 poetry in the style of Li Sao (a poem by poet and statesman Qu Yuan of the fourth century B.C.);
身體 (1) body; (2) health;
商籟體 sonnet;
上體 upper part of the body;
滲碳體 cementite;
生物體 organism;
屍體 corpse; dead body; remains;
詩體 style of a verse, poem, etc.
實體 substance;
事體 affairs; business; matter; systems of matters;
噬菌體 bacteriophage; phage;
手寫體 hand-written form; script;
瘦金體 (in calligraphy) slender gold style;
書體 calligraphic style;
書信體 epistolary style;
水晶體 crystalline lens;
四倍體 tetraploid;
四疊體 corpora quadrigemina;
四六體 a euphuistic style of parallel constructions known especially for pairs of sentences of four and six characters;
四體 arms and legs; the four limbs;
松果體 pineal body;
宋體 Song typeface;
彈性體 elastomer;
天體 celestial body; heavenly body;
鉄素體 ferrite;
鐵氧體 ferrite;
通體 entire body; the whole;
酮體 acetone; ketone body;
統體 whole body;
統一體 entity; unity;
透明體 transparent body;
突變體 mutant;
團體 group; organization; team;
橢圓體 ellipsoid;
微粒體 microsome;
文體 (1) recreation and sports; (2) literary form; style; type of writing;
五體 the five body constituents — tendon, vessel, muscle, hair and skin, bone;
物體 body; object; subject; substance;
下體 (1) lower part of the body; (2) private parts;
腺垂體 adenohypophysis;
腺體 gland;
斜體 italic (type);
信息體 informosome;

星體 celestial (or heavenly) body;
形體 (1) body; physique; (of a person's body) shape; (2) form and structure;
敍事體 narrative;
懸浮體 suspended substance; suspension;
芽體 bud; sprout;
顏體 calligraphy style of Yan Zhenqing of the Tang Dynasty;
掩體 blindage; bunker;
贋晶體 pseudocrystal;
液體 fluid; liquid;
葉綠體 chloroplast;
一體 (1) all people concerned; (2) organic whole;
遺體 (of the dead) remains;
印刷體 block letter; print hand;
永磁體 permanent magnet;
有機體 organism;
幼體 larva;
玉體 your esteemed health;
圓柱體 cylinder;
圓錐體 cone;
載體 carrier;
章回體 type of traditional Chinese novel with each chapter headed by a couplet giving the gist of its content;
趙體 calligraphy style of Zhao Mengfu of the Yuan Dynasty;
整體 entirely; whole;
正體 (1) block letter; (2) (in Chinese calligraphy) regular script; standardized form of Chinese characters;
政體 system of government;
肢體 (1) limbs; (2) limbs and trunk;
質體 plastid;
中間體 intermediate;
中心體 central body;
主體 (1) main body; main part; principal part; (2) subject;
珠光體 pearlite;
篆體 seal character;
自傳體 autobiographical novel; autobiography;
字體 (1) form of a written or printed character; script; typeface; (2) style of calligraphy;
總體 overall; total;

ti4
ti

【弟】 show brotherly love;

ti

【剃】 shave;
［剃刀］ razor; shaver;
安全剃刀 safety razor;
［剃鬚］ shave;
剃鬚刀 shaver;
~電動剃鬚刀 battery shaver; electric shaver;
剃鬚膏 shaving cream;
［剃頭］ (1) have one's head shaved; shave one's head; (2) have a haircut; have one's hair cut;
剃頭刀擦屁股－懸得乎 clean the buttucks with a barber's knife － dangerous enough;
剃光頭 have a crew cut; shave one's head bald;

ti

【悌】 love and respect one's elder brother; show brotherly love;
［悌睦］ live at peace as brothers;
［悌友］ kind to one's friends; show brotherly love to one's friends;

孝悌 show filial piety and live up to fraternal duty;

ti

【涕】 (1) tears; (2) nasal mucus; snot;
［涕淚］ tears;
涕淚交流 cry with a flood of tears; shed streams of tears and snivel;
涕淚俱下 tears and mucus flow down together;
涕淚縱橫 with tears streaming down one's face;
［涕零］ shed tears;
涕零如雨 tears stream down like rain drops;
感激涕零 be brought to tears of gratitude; be moved to tears of gratitude; shed grateful tears; thank sb with tears in one's eyes; with tearful gratitude;
［涕泣］ cry; weep;
涕泣沾襟 wet the front part of one's garment with tears;
［涕泗］ tears and mucus;
涕泗橫流 tears and mucus flow down rapidly;
涕泗交流 tears and mucus fall down at the same time;
涕泗滂沱 a flood of tears; be drenched with tears; tears and mucus run abundantly down one's face;

[涕洟] tears and mucus;

鼻涕 nasal mucus; snot;
滴滴涕 DDT (dichloro-diphenyl-trichloroethane);
破涕 stop crying;

ti

【俶】 not bound by conventions; unconventional;
[俶儻] free and easy; unconventional;

ti

【倜】 (1) raise high; (2) unoccupied; unrestrained;
[倜然] (1) aloof; (2) far and lofty;
[倜儻] elegant in a casual way; free; unconventional; untrammeled;
倜儻不羈 free; untrammeled and romantic in character;
倜儻不群 handsome dandy;
風流倜儻 casual and elegant bearing;

ti

【屜】 drawer;

抽屜 drawer;
籠屜 bamboo or wooden utensil for steaming food; food steamer;

ti

【惕】 (1) careful; cautious; prudent; (2) afraid; (3) anxious;
[惕厲] on guard; on the alert;
[惕然] fearful of;
[惕勵] exercise caution and discipline; on guard; watch closely;
[惕惕] apprehensive; fearful;
[惕息] pant from fear;

怵惕 feel apprehensive;
警惕 be on guard against; be vigilant; vigilance;

ti

【逖】 distant; far; remote;

ti

【替】 (1) replace; substitute; take the place of; (2) decay; decline; (3) neglect; (4) for; on behalf of;
[替補] alternate;
替補隊員 benchwarmer;
[替代] replace; substitute for; supersede;
替代技術 alternative technique;
替代能源 alternative energy;
替代效應 substitution effect;
替代形式 pro-form;
替代性經濟 alternative economy;
前指替代 anaphoric substitute;
[替工] (1) fill in; work as a substitute; (2) substitute worker; temporary substitute;
[替壞] decay; decline; deteriorate;
[替換] displace; replace; replacement; substitute for; substitution; take the place of;
部份替換 partial substitution;
地址替換 address substitution;
前向替換 forward substitution;
主語替換 subject replacement;
[替角] understudy;
[替人] substitute;
替人幫腔 take up sb's refrain;
替人打算 be considerate of others;
替人説項 intercede for sb; plead on behalf of a person; put in a good word for sb; speak favourably of sb;
替人作保 stand security for sb;
替人作伐 act as a matchmaker for sb; marriage broker for sb;
[替身] (1) (in a film) double; replacement; stand-in; substitute; understudy; (2) scapegoat;
替身演員 body double; stunt man;
特技替身 stunt double;
[替手] standby; substitute; understudy;
[替死鬼] fall guy; person made to suffer for sb's mistake; scapegoat; whipping boy;
[替天行道] carry out heavenly wishes; enforce justice on behalf of heaven; execute heavenly wishes;
[替懈] neglect;
[替罪羊] fall guy; scapegoat; whipping boy;
做替罪羊 scapegoat;

代替 replace; take the place of;
倒替 replace; substitute;
頂替 replace; take sb's place;
更替 replace; substitute;
交替 (1) do sth alternately; take turns; (2) supersede; replace;
接替 replace; take over;
陵替 (1) (of law and order) break down; (2) decline;
槍替 practise fraud by sitting for an examination

in the place of another person;
衰替 decline;
演替 succession;

ti

【殢】 greatly distressed;
［殢酒］ suffer from alcoholism;

ti

【嚔】 sneeze;
［嚔噴］ sneeze;
阿嚔 atishoo;
噴嚔 sneeze;

ti

【薙】 (1) weed; (2) cut one's hair; shave one's hair;
［薙刀］ shaving knife;
［薙髮］ cut hair; haircut; shave hair;

tian¹
tian

【天】 (1) firmament; heavens; sky; vault of heavens; (2) day; (3) overhead; (4) period of time in a day; time; (5) climate; seasons; weather; (6) elements; nature; natural; (7) Heaven; (8) God;
［天啊］ ah; alas; bless me; bless my heart; bless my soul; bless the mark; Cheese and Crust (Jesus Christ); damn; darned (damn); dear; dear me; Gads me (God save me); Gads my life (God save my life); Gee (Jesus), God bless the mark; God save my life; good gracious; gosh; gracious me; heart alive; mercy on us; my; my God; my goodness; oh, dear; save the mark;
［天崩］ the heaven split;
天崩地坼 both heaven and earth are falling to pieces; deafening sounds;
天崩地裂 like giant earthquakes and landslides;
天崩地陷 the heavens split and the earth sinks;
［天邊］ ends of the earth; remotest places;
天邊海角 remote regions; uttermost parts of the earth; world's end;
出現在天邊 appear on the horizon;
遠在天邊，近在眼前 seemingly far away, actually close at hand;
［天兵］ troops from heaven;
天兵天將 divine troops descending from heaven;
［天稟］ endowed by heaven; natural endowments;
［天不負人］ all is for the best; heaven rewards the faithful;
［天不假年］ God doesn't give sb a life long enough to accomplish his task;
［天才］ endowment; flair; genius; natural talent; talent;
天才兒童 child prodigy; gifted child;
天才反被天才誤 geniuses often betray themselves into great errors;
天才論 theory of an innate genius;
音樂天才 ability in music;
有天才 have a flair for;
［天產］ natural products;
［天窗］ skylight; high windows;
開天窗 put in skylight — leave a blank in a publication to show that sth has been censored;
［天賜］ endowed by Heaven; given by Heaven;
天賜的 heaven-sent;
天賜甘霖 godsent rain;
天賜良機 heaven-sent chance; heaven-sent opportunity;
天賜良緣 heaven-sent marriage;
天賜之福 mercy;
天賜之物 godsend; manna;
［天打雷劈］ be struck by a lightning and split in two halves;
［天大］ as large as the heavens; extremely big;
恩比天大 one's kindness and benevolence is as great as heaven;
［天道］ (1) ways of Heaven; (2) weather;
天道不諂 heaven's way isn't uncertain;
天道好還 God's way goes in a cycle;
天道如網 punishment is lame, but it comes; the mills of God grind slowly but sure;
天道無親 the ways of heavens are impartial;
天道無私 the ways of heaven are impartial;
［天敵］ natural enemy;
［天底］ nadir;
天底下 in this world; on earth; under the sun;
［天地］ (1) heaven and earth; (2) universe; world; (3) field of activity; scope of

operation;
天地比壽 may one's age be as that of heaven and earth;
天地不容 heaven and earth do not tolerate; heaven forbid;
天地間 in the universe; in this world;
天地交泰 celestial and terrestrial forces in harmony; peaceful and prosperous times;
天地良心 from the bottom of one's heart; in all fairness; in all justice; in fact; in my soul of souls; speak the truth;
拜天地 bow to heaven and earth as part of wedding ceremony;
冰天雪地 a world of ice and snow; all covered in ice and snow;
撐天柱地 support the heaven and pillar the earth;
頂天立地 dauntless; indomitable;
動天地，泣鬼神 move the universe and cause the gods to weep;
嚎天動地 call upon Heaven and Earth;
轟天震地 the heavens thunder and the earth shakes;
呼天喚地 call to heaven and earth; cry to heaven;
呼天搶地 cry bitterly and loudly in excessive grief; utter cries of anguish;
花天酒地 attend a dinner with sing-song girls; be in the world of wine and women; be on the loose; be on the tiles; be out on the tiles; go on the loose; go on the racket; go on the tiles; guzzle and carouse to one's heart's content; guzzle and have a good time; have one's fling; indulge in fast life and debauchery; lead a decadent and dissolute life; lead a fast life; live in the world of wine and women; sow a large crop of wild oats;
徹夜花天酒地 on the tiles;
昏天黑地 dark rule and social disorder; decadent; dissipated; dizzy; in total darkness; perverted; pitch-dark;
將天比地 it is as though heaven were brought to compare with earth; it would be like comparing heaven with a lump of dirt;
驚天地，泣鬼神 startle the universe and move the gods;
驚天動地 earthshaking; shake heaven and earth; startle the world; surprise the world; titanic; tremendous; worldshaking;
開天闢地 beginning of history; creation of heaven and earth;
哭天哭地 wail bitterly;
欺天罔地 deceitful in the extreme; defy heaven and earth;
搶天呼地 call to heaven and earth;
説天説地 (1) boast; brag; (2) eloquent; skilled in speech;
天不言自高，地不言自厚 good wine needs no bush;
天差地遠 poles apart; there is a vast difference between the two;
天摧地塌 as if the skies were falling and the earth rising;
天覆地載 all under heaven and upon earth; what is under heaven and borne by the earth;
天寒地凍 freezing; severe cold and frozen land; the weather is so cold that the ground is frozen; very cold;
天荒地老 far back; of the remote past;
天經地義 both natural and right; by nature; fundamental truth; God's truth; matter of course; nature's law and earth's way; only natural; perfectly justified; right and proper; stand to reason; universal truth; very reasonable;
天剋地沖 evil person;
天搖地轉 as though earth and sky were spinning violently;
天造地設 created by nature; ideal; natural creation; natural match; naturally constituted;
天知地知，你知我知 between ourselves; between you and me; between you and me and the bedpost; no one knows besides you and I;
無天無地 lawless and godless; reckless;
謝天謝地 God be praised; God be thanked; thank God; thank goodness; thank heavens; thank one's stars; thank the Lord;
怨天怨地 be grieved up to the heights of heaven; blame Heaven and Earth; murmur against heaven and earth;
責天怨地 blame heaven and earth; nag;
戰天鬥地 battle against nature; battle the elements; combat nature; fight against heaven and earth; struggle with nature;

指天畫地 behave without decorum; fling one's arms about; point right and left;

[天頂] zenith;
天頂距 zenith distance;
天頂儀 zenith telescope;
浮動天頂儀 floating zenith telescope;
大地天頂 geodetic zenith;
地心天頂 geocentric zenith;
向天頂 zenithward;

[天定] be fixed by heaven; predestined; predetermined; preordained;

[天蛾] hawk moth; sphinx moth;

[天鵝] swan;
一群天鵝 a game of swans;
一隻天鵝 a swan;
幼天鵝 cygnet;

[天方] Arab countries;

[天分] natural endowment; natural gift; talent;

[天府] region of abundance;
天府之國 God's country;

[天賦] (1) endowed by nature; inborn; innate; (2) endowments; natural gift; talent;
天賦多才 be endowed with talents;
天賦異稟 unusual natural abilities;
天賦之才 innate gift; person of natural endowment;
有天賦 talented;
沒有天賦的 talentless;
有天賦的 talented;

[天蓋] canopy;

[天高] as high as the sky;
天高地厚 as high as the heavens and as deep as the earth – profound;
天高皇帝遠 heaven is high and the emperor is far away – no help can be offered;
天高氣爽 the sky is high and the weather fine;
天高聽卑 heaven is high but listen to the lowliest;
天高雲淡 the sky is high and the clouds are thin;
恩比天高 one's concern is higher than the sky;
心比天高 very ambitious;

[天工] work of nature;
巧奪天工 art beats nature; art improves nature; by application, man has improved on nature's ways; fine workmanship that excels nature; human ingenuity has done things which nature has failed to; ingenuity that rivals the work of God; it rivals nature; man can outmatch nature in skill; so wonderful in workmanship as to excel nature; superb craftsmanship that puts nature to shame; wonderful workmanship; workmanship which excels nature; works of art may surpass nature;

[天公] God; lord in heaven; ruler of heaven;
天公不作美 the gods are against us; the heaven is not cooperative – weather turns foul when some activity requiring fine weather is scheduled to take place; the weather let us down;
天公地道 absolutely fair; exactly as it should be; fair and just; fully justifiable; the most natural and fine arrangements;

[天宮] heavenly palace;

[天鼓] thunder;

[天光] (1) daylight; daytime; (2) sunbeam; sunlight;

[天國] (1) Kingdom of Heaven; (2) paradise;
天國之門 pearly gates;

[天河] the Galaxy; the Milky Way;

[天候] weather;
全天候 all-weather;
全天候溫室 all-weather greenhouse;

[天花] (1) smallpox; (2) ceiling;
天花板 ceiling;
多孔天花板 perforated ceiling;
漫射天花板 diffuser ceiling;
無柵天花板 contact ceiling;
吸聲天花板 acoustic ceiling;
有梁的天花板 beamed ceiling;
天花亂墜 give an extravagantly colourful description; in extravagant terms; in the most glowing terms; talk sb's head off;
~吹得天花亂墜 boast in the most fantastic terms; give an extravagant account of; laud to the skies; make a wild boast about; show off to the nines;
爆發型天花 fulminant smallpox;
扁平天花 flat smallpox;
出血性天花 haemorrhagic smallpox;
惡性天花 malignant smallpox;
假性天花 varioloid;
普通天花 ordinary smallpox;

輕天花 modified smallpox;

[天機] (1) nature's mystery; sth inexplicable; (2) God's design;

天機不可洩漏 don't say a word about it to a soul; God's design must not be revealed to mortal ears; heaven's secrets must not be divulged; the secrets of Providence should not really be told; the will of Heaven must not be disclosed;

天機雲錦 as beautiful and exquisite as a heavenly-woven brocade;

洩漏天機 give away a secret;

一語道破天機 leave bare the secret of sth with one remark;

[天極] celestial pole;

北天極 north celestial pole;

南天極 south celestial pole;

[天際] horizon;

[天界] heaven;

[天井] (1) atrium; courtyard; patio; small yard; (2) skylight;

[天九] game of dominoes;

[天空] blue blanket; firmament; heavens; sky; void;

天空的 celestial;

天空地闊 of boundless capacity; of liberal views;

天空濾色鏡 sky filter;

天空實驗室 skylab;

翱翔天空 roam over the sky;

朝天空 heavenward;

多雲天空 cloudy sky;

灰藍色的天空 steely sky;

凝視天空 turn one's gaze to the sky;

晴朗的天空 clear sky;

乳白天空 white-out sky;

碎亂天空 amorphous sky;

無雲天空 cloudless sky;

仰望天空 look at the sky;

照亮天空 light up the sky;

[天籟] sounds of nature;

[天理] (1) heavenly principles; natural law; (2) justice;

天理不容 heaven and earth will not tolerate; intolerable injustice;

天理良心 one's better feelings; one's conscience;

天理難容 God forbid; heaven forbid;

天理人情 law of nature and feelings of humans – reasonable;

天理人欲 heavenly principles and human desires;

天理循環 the course of nature goes round; the guilty is always punished and the kind-hearted rewarded under the law of heaven;

天理昭彰 evil is always punished; God's justice is manifest; Heaven at last repays a crime; Heavenly principles are clear and transparent; the law of Heaven always prevails;

喪天害理 against reason and nature;

傷天害理 commit crimes; cruel and heartless; do things offensive to God and reason; do things that are against reason and nature; ruthless and devoid of human feelings;

上逆天理，下違父教 disobey the command of heaven above and of one's father on earth;

順乎天理 conform to the course of nature;

順乎天理，合乎人情 conform to the course of nature and the ways of the people;

[天良] one's conscience;

天良泯滅 lose one's conscience;

昧沒天良 blot out one's conscience; darken one's mind; obliterate one's conscience;

喪盡天良 nothing of conscience was left;

[天亮] dawn; daybreak; daytime;

天亮以前趕到 get to a place before daybreak;

守夜到天亮 outwatch the night;

[天倫] natural bonds and ethical relationships between members of a family;

天倫之樂 amenities of home life; family happiness; family love and joy; the happiness of a family union; the joy of family life together;

共敘天倫 enjoy family happiness together;

[天馬] heavenly horse;

天馬行空 a heavenly horse flying in the air – an unrestrained and vigorous style that brims with talent; a heavenly steed soaring across the skies – a powerful and unconstrained style;

[天明] dawn; daybreak;

[天命] (1) divine mandate; heavenly mandate; destiny; fate; God's will; the mandate

of heaven; (2) one's lifespan;
天命不韜 heaven's decrees are beyond doubt;
天命難逃 every bullet has its billet; it is difficult to escape from one's fate;
諟天命 this is heaven's decree;

[天幕] (1) canopy of the heavens; (2) backdrop of a stage;

[天哪] jeez;

[天年] one's allotted span; one's natural span of life;
盡其天年 die a natural death; exhaust one's natural years; live one's full span;
壽滿天年 die a natural death;
以享天年 enjoy one's declining years;
以終天年 complete one's allotted span of life; fulfil one's natural life;
終其天年 complete one's allotted span of life; live one's full span;

[天女] (1) heavenly maids; (2) fairy;
天女散花 the heavenly maids scatter blossoms;
天女下凡 a fairy from Heaven;

[天平] balance; scales;
單盤天平 single-pan balance;
分析天平 analytical balance;
化學天平 chemical balance; chemical scales;
簡式天平 simple balance;
記錄天平 recording balance;
精密天平 precision balance;
空氣動力天平 aerodynamic balance;
空氣阻抑天平 air damping balance;
鏈碼天平 chain balance;
密度天平 density balance;
膜天平 film balance;
扭力天平 torsion balance;
配重天平 counterpoised balance;
色度高頻平衡 chroma radio frequency;
試金天平 assay balance;
托盤天平 counter balance; table balance;
微量天水 microbalance;
超微量天平 ultra microbalance;
電動微量天水 electric microbalance;
記錄式微量天水 recording microbalance;
遙控操作天平 remote operated balance;
藥劑天平 prescription balance;
藥用天平 apothecary scale; pharmacist balance;
游碼式天平 sliding weight balance;
阻尼天平 damped balance;
自重天平 dominant scales;

[天氣] weather;
天氣報告 weather report;
天氣分析 weather analysis;
天氣晴朗 fine weather;
天氣圖 weather map;
傳真天氣圖 facsimile weather map;
地面天氣圖 surface weather map;
天氣型 weather type;
天氣炎熱 it's hot;
天氣諺語 weather lore;
天氣異常 weather anomaly;
天氣預報 weather forecast;
當天天氣預報 short-range forecast;
簡明天氣預報 forecast bulletin;
近期天氣預報 medium-range forecast;
數值天氣預報 numerical forecast;
天氣驟變 sudden change of weather;
抱怨天氣 complain about the weather; grumble about the weather;
~抱怨天氣太熱 complain of the heat;
不利天氣 adverse weather;
多麼好的天氣 what a beautiful day;
惡劣天氣 nasty weather; severe weather;
反常的天氣 abnormal weather; freakish weather;
惡劣的天氣 abominable weather;
寒冷的天氣 arctic weather; cold weather;
一陣寒冷的天氣 a spell of cold weather;
好天氣 fine weather; good weather;
壞天氣 falling weather;
悶熱天氣 oppressive weather;
討厭的天氣 abominable weather;
天和氣朗 the sky is clear and fair and the air is neither hot nor cold;
天朗氣清 the sky is clear and bright; the sky is serene and the air refreshing;
溫暖天氣 warm weather;
一陣溫暖天氣 a spell of warm weather;
炎熱的天氣 hot weather;
宜人的天氣 agreeable weather;

[天譴] God's punishing hands; wrath of heaven;

[天橋] footbridge;
天橋把式—光説不練 practising martial art on a footbridge — speaking without practising;

[天清] the sky is clear;
天清日晏 fine and peaceful day;
天清月明 the sky is clear and the moon

bright;

［天晴］ the sky is clear;

打草趁天晴 make hay while the sun shines;

風轉天晴 the wind turns and the sky clears;

雨過天晴 after a shower the sky clears; after a storm comes a calm; after black clouds, clear weather; after rain comes fair weather; after rain comes sunshine; the rain stops and the sky clears up; the skies clear up after a storm; the storm subsides and the sky clears; the sun shines again after the rain;

［天穹］ firmament; vault; vault of heaven;

［天球］ celestial sphere;

天球赤道 celestial equator;

天球地平 celestial horizon;

天球儀 celestial globe; celestial sphere; cosmosphere;

天球子午圈 celestial meridian;

天球坐標 celestial coordinates;

［天然］ living; native; natural;

天然財富 natural resources;

天然景色 natural scenery;

天然氣 natural gas;

天然資源 natural resources;

［天壤］ heaven and earth;

天壤之別 a whale of a difference; a world of difference; all the difference in the world; as far apart as heaven and earth; great difference as between heaven and earth; poles apart; vast difference; worlds apart;

天壤之隔 as far apart as heaven and earth;

［天人］ celestial being; person of extraordinary beauty;

天人合一 man is an integral part of nature;

天人相應 correspondence between man and the universe; relevant adaptation of the human body to the natural environment;

驚為天人 take sb for a fairy;

誇為天人 praise sb to the very skies as sth more than human;

欺天罔人 deceive heaven and men;

天從人願 by the grace of God; fortune is on one's side; heaven accords with human wishes; heaven has disposed matters according to one's wishes; providence grants what is desired by men;

天怒人怨 the gods are angry and the people resentful; the wrath of God and the resentment of men; widespread indignation and discontent;

應天順人 act according to God's will and the desire of the people; act in accordance with Heaven and fulfill the desire of mankind; follow the mandate of heaven and comply with the popular wishes of the people; obey God's will and act in accordance with people's feelings; obey the will of Heaven and be in harmony with men; obey the will of Heaven and concur with the wishes of mankind; please Heaven and be kind to others; respond to the will of Heaven and the desire of the people;

憂天憫人 worry about the destiny of mankind;

［天日］ day; light; the sky and the sun;

暗無天日 a world of darkness; an abyss of darkness; complete darkness; days of darkness; gross lack of justice under misgovernment; in the dark days; lack of justice; total absence of justice; under the dark rule; utter darkness;

不見天日 in total darkness;

補天浴日 have great exploits; make a great accomplishment; make a peerless achievement; make monumental contributions; mend the sky and wash the sun;

慘無天日 so miserable as if the sun disappeared in the sky;

偷天換日 place a substitute by subterfuge; play a sly trick; substitute the fake for the genuine; try to cheat people by underhand means;

堯天舜 piping days of peace;

移天易日 modify the heaven and change the sun — used figuratively of those who play deceivingly with political power; usurp political power; usurp the throne;

有天無日 devoid of justice; have no scruple at all; reckless and dissipated;

指天誓日 call heaven to witness; swear by the heaven and sun as witness; take an oath under heaven;

[天色] (1) colour of the sky; (2) time of the day; (3) weather;
天色暗淡 overcast sky; the light begins to fall;
天色黯黑 it's dark;
天色突變 the weather has suddenly changed;
天色微明 the sky is faintly light with the dawn;
天色已晚 it's getting dark;
天色陰郁 the weather is gloomy;

[天上] heavens; sky;
天上的 celestial;
天上人間 immeasurably vast difference;
捧到天上 applaud a person to the skies;
向天上 heavenward;
一在天上，一在地下 one is high up in the sky, while the other is down-to-earth;

[天神] celestial being; deity; god;

[天生] be born with; bred in the bone; congenital; inborn; inherent; innate; natural;
天生愛哭的人 natural crier;
天生的 inborn; inbred;
天生國色 be endowed with dazzling beauty;
天生麗質 born beauty; flawless beauty; heavenly beauty; one's native charm;
天生尤物 born siren; sex-kitten;
艷女天生 beautiful woman by nature;

[天師] Daoist master;

[天時] climate; weather;
天時不正 abnormal weather;
天時、地利、人和 favourable climatic, geographical, and human conditions;

[天使] angel;
天使長 archangel;
大天使 archangel;
高級天使 cherub;
守護天使 guardian angel;
小天使 cherub;

[天數] (1) fatalism; fate; predestination; (2) predestined disaster; predestined tragedy;
天數難逃 one can hardly escape one's destiny;

[天水] the sky and water;
天連水，水連天 the sky and the water seem to merge;

[天臺] flat roof;

[天堂] abraham's bosom; heaven; paradise;
天堂地獄 heaven and hell;
天堂樂土 paradise;
天堂鳥 bird of paradise;
上有天堂，下有蘇杭 there is paradise above and Suzhou and Hangzhou below;
在天堂 in Abraham's bosom;

[天體] celestial body; heavenly body;
天體測量學 astrometry;
基礎天體測量學 fundamental astrometry;
照相天體測量學 photographic astrometry;
子午天體測量學 meridian astrometry;
天體磁學 astromagnetism;
天體彈道學 astroballistics;
天體地理學 astrogeography;
天體地質學 astrogeology;
天體動力學 astrodynamics;
天體仿生學 astrobionics;
天體分光計 astrospectrometer;
天體分光儀 astrospectroscope;
天體光度計 astrophotometer;
天體光度學 astrophotometry;
光電天體光度學 photoelectric astrophotometry;
目視天體光度學 visual astrophotometry;
照相天體光度學 photographic astrophotometry;
天體光譜學 astrospectroscopy;
照相天體光譜學 photographic astrospectroscopy;
天體化學 astrochemistry;
天體力學 astromechanics;
天體立體照片 astrostereogram;
天體年代學 astrochronology;
天體氣象學 astrometeorology;
天體氣象學家 astrometeorologist;
天體生理學 astrobiology;
天體生物學 astrobiology;
天體探測 astrosurveillance;
天體物理學 astrophysics;
高能天體物理學 high-energy astrophysics;
理論天體物理學 theoretical astrophysics;
天體演化學 cosmogony;
天體營 nudist camp;
天體照相學 astrography;

[天天] daily; day in, day out; every day;
天天變化 fluctuate from day to day;
天天向上 make progress day by day; make steady progress every day;

[天條] laws of God in heaven;

[天庭] forehead;

天庭飽滿 full forehead; high and full forehead;

[天外] (1) unexpected; (2) far and high;

天外有天 good is good, but better carries it; though good be good, yet better is better;

魂飛天外 one's soul flows beyond the skies; one's spirits rise to the clouds; one's soul seems to leave one's body and fly beyond the confines of heaven;

[天王星] Uranus;

[天網恢恢] God's justice is all-encompassing; the net of heaven stretches everywhere;

天網恢恢，疏而不漏 God comes with leaden feet, but strikes with iron hands; God's mill grinds slow but sure; Heaven's vengeance is slow but sure; Justice has long arms; punishment is lame, but it comes; punishment may be slow, but it comes; the mills of God grind slowly but sure; the mills of God grind slowly, yet they grind exceedingly small; the net of Heaven has large meshes, but it lets nothing through;

[天文] (1) astronomy; (2) heavenly bodies;

天文單位 astronomical unit;

天文彈道學 astroballistics;

天文地理 astronomical geography;

上知天文，下知地理 know astronomy as well as geography; know everything in heaven above and the earth below;

天文電子學 astronics;

天文觀測 astronomical observation;

天文館 planetarium;

天文考古學 archaeoastronomy;

天文曆 almanac;

航海天文曆 nautical almanac;

天文年曆 astronomical yearbook;

天文時 astronomical time;

天文數字 astronomical figure;

天文台 astronomical observatory; observatory;

天文學 astronomy;

天文學家 astronomer; stargazer;

大地天文學 geodetic astronomy;

地面觀測天文學 ground-based astronomy;

電視天文學 television astronomy;

方位天文學 positional astronomy;

觀測天文學 observational astronomy;

航海天文學 nautical astronomy;

恒星天文學 stellar astronomy;

紫外線恒星天文學 stellar ultraviolet astronomy;

紅外天文學 infrared astronomy;

幾何天文學 geometrical astronomy;

空間天文學 space astronomy;

雷達天文學 radar astronomy;

理論天文學 theoretical astronomy;

描述天文學 descriptive astronomy;

球面天文學 spherical astronomy;

射電天文學 radio astronomy;

長波射電天文學 long-wave radio astronomy;

地面射電天文學 ground-based radio astronomy;

空間射電天文學 space-based radio astronomy;

太陽射電天文學 solar radio astronomy;

實用天文學 practical astronomy;

數學天文學 mathematical astronomy;

位置天文學 positional astronomy;

行星際天文學 interplanetary astronomy;

形態天文學 morphological astronomy;

引力天文學 gravitational astronomy;

照相天文學 photographic astronomy;

子午天文學 meridian astronomy;

天文儀 astroscope;

天文鐘 astronomical clock;

[天無二日，國無二主] only one supreme ruler in a country, as there is only one sun in heaven;

[天無絕人之路] every cloud has a silver lining; every day brings its own bread; God never shuts one door but He opens another; God will not close all doors; Heaven never seals off all the exits; there is always a way out; when one door shuts another opens;

[天無三日晴，地無三尺平] there never were three sunny days in a row, or three square feet of level land;

[天物] products of nature;

暴殄天物 reckless waste of the products of nature; spoil things by rough usage; waste and miuse things at one's will; waste gifts of God; waste natural products;

T

［天下］ (1) China; (2) land under heaven; world; (3) domination; rule;

天下安瀾 the country enjoys peace and tranquility;

天下本無事，庸人自擾之 peace reigns throughout the world and only the ignorant people disturb it themselves; though peace reigns over the land, the stupid people create trouble for themselves;

天下大亂 big upheaval throughout the world; great disorder across the land; great disorder on the earth; great disorder under heaven; in perpetual chaos; state of great confusion; the whole country is in chaos; universal great disorder; violent upheavals;

天下大勢 historical trends; momentum of history;

天下大治 great order across the land; well-ordered world;

天下第一 No.1 in the world; peerless; the best in all the land; the first under heaven;

天下鼎沸 all below heaven are boiling like a cauldron;

天下獨步 (1) cut a great figure; (2) unequalled; unmatched; unparalleled in the world;

天下歸心 throughout the empire all hearts turn to one;

天下奇聞 a most fantastic tale; a very strange story; the most absurd thing in the world;

天下攘攘 all the hustle and bustle in the world; the country is in a chaotic condition;

天下擾攘 the state is thrown into confusion;

天下太平 all is at peace; all is quiet in the world; all will be right with the world; peace reigns over the land; peace reigns under heaven; the world is at peace; universal peace;

天下為公 the world belongs to everybody; the world is for all;

天下聞名 all under heaven know one's name;

天下烏鴉一般黑 all crows are equally black; all crows under the sun are black; crows are black all the world over; evil people are bad all over the world; in every country dogs bite; they are all bad;

天下無不散之筵席 all good things must come to an end; even the finest feast comes to an end sometime; even the finest must break up at last; no feast on earth can last forever; there is no permanent feast on earth;

天下無敵 all-conquering; ever-victorious; invincible; invincible throughout the world; there is none to equal one on earth; there is none under Heaven to equal one; with equal in the world;

天下無敵的人 world- beater;

天下無難事，只怕有心人 all difficulties on earth can be overcome if men but give their minds to it; every difficulty on earth can be overcome if men but give their minds to it; it's dogged as that does it; nothing in the world is difficult for anyone who has a strong determination; nothing is difficult in the world for one who sets his mind to it; nothing is impossible to a willing heart; nothing is too difficult for one who has a mind to do it; where there's will, there's a way;

天下無雙 absolutely unrivalled; matchless; none such under heaven; not an equal in the world; unique; unparalleled in the world; without equal;

天下興亡，匹夫有責 every man has a share of responsibility for the fate of his country; everyone is responsible for his country;

天下洶洶 the whole country is in upheaval;

天下一家 all under heaven are of one family;

幫天下 rule of gangs;

包打天下 take on all the responsibilities;

鞭笞天下 flog the world;

遍天下 all over the world;

我們的朋友遍天下 we have friends over all the world;

打天下 (1) seize power by force; struggle to seize state power; (2) build up one's position; establish an enterprise; originate a cause; originate an undertaking; set up an enterprise; start an enterprise;

道行天下 the right way prevails;
甲天下 number one in the world; the finest under heaven;
兼善天下 benefit all the pople in the world;
君臨天下 the sovereign descends the world;
名孚天下 one's fame has filled the world;
名滿天下 gain a world reputation; world-renowned;
名揚天下 one's name is known far and wide; one's name spreads all over the world;
普天之下 all over the world; all the world over; in all corners of the earth; in every part of the world; under the scope of heaven;
一匡天下 restore peace to the country; unite the country; unite the whole empire under one government;
以天下為己任 consider the transformation of the world as one's task; have the weight of the world on one's shoulders;
以謝天下 appease public indignation; appease the wrath of the world;
語妙天下 unequalled in wisecracking;
譽滿天下 enjoy tremendous popularity in the world; one's fame spreads throughout the world;
轍環天下 leave one's footprints all over the country;

[天仙] (1) goddess; (2) beauty;
天仙化人 as beautiful as an angel from heaven; stunning beauty;
天仙下凡 celestial beauty comes down to earth;

[天線] aerial; antenna;
天線插座 antenna socket;
天線發射機 antenna transmitter;
天線放大器 antenna amplifier;
天線系統 antenna system;
全向天線系統 omnidirectional antenna system;
天線陣 antenna array;
閉路天線 closed aerial;
波導式天線 waveguide antenna;
拆疊天線 collapsible aerial; folded antenna;
超短波天線 ultra-shortwave antenna;
成對天線 twin antenna;
船用天線 shipboard antenna;
等效天線 equivalent antenna;
地面天線 buried aerial;
電視發射天線 television transmitting antenna;
蝶型天線 butterfly antenna;
定向天線 beamed antenna; directional antenna; directive aerial; spray antenna;
方位天線 homing antenna;
飛機天線 aeroplane antenna; aircraft antenna;
分集式天線 diversity antenna;
複合天線 double antenna;
公共天線 communal aerial;
紅外天線 infrared antenna;
後部天線 aft antenna;
環視天線 all-round looking antenna;
環形天線 coil aerial; loop aerial;
機翼天線 wing antenna;
假天線 dummy antenna; mock antenna;
簡單天線 plain antenna;
接收天線 pick-up antenna; receiver aerial;
警戒天線 alerting antenna;
抗干擾天線 anti-interference antenna;
寬帶天線 broadband aerial; wideband aerial;
框形天線 frame aerial;
菱形天線 diamond antenna;
偶極天線 dipole antenna;
平頂天線 flat-top antenna;
切口天線 notch antenna;
曲折天線 zigzag antenna;
全息天線 holographic antenna;
全向天線 isotropic aerial; non-directional aerial; omnidirectional aerial;
室內天線 indoor aerial; indoor antenna; internal aerial;
室外天線 exterior aerial; open aerial; outdoor antenna;
水中天線 submerged antenna;
調諧天線 tuning antenna;
微波天線 microwave aerial;
屋頂天線 loft aerial;
遙測天線 telemetering antenna;
有源天線 active antenna;
主天線 master antenna;

[天象] astronomical phenomena; celestial phenomena;
天象館 planetarium;
天像儀 planetarium;

[天性] natural disposition; natural instincts;

T

natural temperaments; nature;
天性聰明 intelligent by nature;
天性乖戾 sullen by nature;
天性忠厚 have a sincere and kindly nature;
第二天性 second nature;
違背天性 against nature;

[天幸] close shave; providential escape;

[天涯] end of the world; remotest corner of the earth;
天涯處處有芳草 there are fragrant flowers in every land – there are able men everywhere;
天涯海角 at the ends of the earth; at the world's end; the back of beyond; the end of the earth; the end of the sky and the corners of the sea; the four corners of the earth; the remotest corners of the earth; the utmost angle of the world; the uttermost parts of the earth; the world's end;
天涯原咫尺，此地又逢君 the world is but a little place, after all;
地角天涯 all four quarters of the land; separated far apart; the ends of the earth and the horizon of the sky; the four corners of the earth;

[天啊] ah; alas; bless my heart; bless my soul; dear; dear me; mercy on us; my; my eye; my foot; my god; my goodness; oh, dear; oh, my; well;

[天演] evolution;

[天衣無縫] a seamless heavenly robe – flawless; devine garments without seams – faultless; leave nothing to be desired; without a trace;

[天意] god's will; the will of heaven;
天意人緣 Heaven's will and human affinity – providence and natural affinity;

[天宇] (1) heavenly regions; sky; (2) whole world; (3) capital of a country;

[天雨] it rains;
天雨連綿 it continues to rain;
天雨路滑 it's raining and the road is slippery;

[天與人歸] both Heaven and the people turn to one; Heaven has complied with the wishes of the people;

[天淵] high heavens and deep seas; poles apart;
天淵相隔 as far apart as the sky and the sea;
天淵之別 a world of difference; as different as heaven and hell; as far apart as sky and sea; vastly different;

[天緣] predestined friendship;
天緣湊巧 lucky coincidence;

[天雲] heaven and clouds;
天低雲暗 dark clouds hang low in the sky;

[天災] natural calamity; natural disaster; act of God;
天災橫禍 unforeseen calamities sent from Heaven;
天災人禍 natural calamities and man-made misfortunes; natural disasters and wars;
遭受天災 suffer natural disaster;

[天真] artless; innocent; naive;
天真爛漫 childlike innocence; innocent and artless; innocent and carefree; like a lamb; naive; simple and unaffected;
天真無邪 innocent and pure; pristine innocence; simple-hearted; unsophisticated;
率性天真 naivete; simple and innocent;

[天職] natural duty;

[天竺] ancient name of India;
天竺葵 geranium;

[天軸] celestial axis;

[天主] God;
天主教 Catholicism;

[天姿] natural beauty;
天姿國色 indescribably beautiful; matchless beauty; possess reigning beauty; rare beauty; surpassing beauty; unequalled in beauty;

[天資] flair; inborn talent; intellectual capacity; natural endowment; natural gift; talent;
天資很好 gifted;
天資穎慧 be by nature endowed with remarkable talents;
有音樂天資 have an aptitude for music;

[天子] emperor; Son of Heaven;
挾天子以令諸侯 control the emperor and command the nobles; have the emperor in one's power and order the nobles about in his name;

[天足] natural feet; unbound feet;

白天 day; daytime;
半邊天 (1) half the sky; (2) women of the new society; womenfolk;
半天 (1) half of the day; (2) a long time; quite a while; (3) period of time in a day; (4) in the air; midair;
變天 (1) change of weather; (2) restoration of reactionary rule; (3) changes of political situations;
賓天 death of an emperor;
參天 reaching to the sky; towering; very tall;
蒼天 (1) blue sky; (2) Heaven;
長天 vast of heaven;
朝天 face the sky;
成天 all day long; all the time;
衝天 soaring; towering;
春天 spring; springtime;
大後天 three days from now;
大前天 three days ago;
當天 that very day; the same day;
登天 climb up to the sky;
頂破天 at most;
冬天 winter;
翻天 overturn the heavens; shake the sky;
伏天 dog days; hot summer days;
改天 another day; some other day;
歸天 die; pass away;
海天 the sea and the sky;
旱天 drought; dry days; dry weather;
航天 space flight;
好天 fine day; lovely weather;
昊天 (1) heaven; (2) parents' great, good kindness; (3) summer;
黑天 night;
後半天 afternoon;
後天 (1) the day after tomorrow; (2) acquired; postnatal;
皇天 heaven;
黃梅天 rainy season;
回天 save a desperate situation;
幾天 a few days;
祭天 offer sacrifices to heaven;
見天 every day;
江天 vast space over a river;
今天 (1) today; (2) now; the present;
景天 red-spotted stonecrop;
九天 highest heaven; Ninth Heaven;
藍天 blue sky;
老天 God; heaven;
樂天 carefree. happy-go-lucky;
禮拜天 Sunday;
連天 (1) reach the sky; (2) incessantly;
連陰天 rainy weather for several days running;
聊天 bat the breeze; chat; chew the fat; chinwag; chit-chat; fan the breeze; have a chat; have a chin; have a chinwag; have a dish of gossip; shoot bull; shoot the breeze; shoot the bull; swap lies; visit with;
露天 in the open; in the open air; outdoors;
滿天 all over the sky; skyful;
漫天 (1) all over the sky; (2) boundless; limitless;
霉天 early summer rains;
每天 a day; daily; day after day; day by day; day in and day out; dayin, day out; everyday; from day to day; per day;
彌天 huge; monstrous;
明後天 day after tomorrow;
明天 tomorrow;
摩天 skyscraping;
那天 that day; the other day;
逆天 against nature;
潑天 extremely big; too many;
前半天 morning;
前天 day before yesterday;
青天 (1) blue sky; (2) incorruptible and wise judge; just judge; upright official;
清天 (1) clear sky; (2) virtuous official;
情天 vast realm of love;
晴天 cloudless day; fine day; sunny day;
秋天 autumn; autumn days; fall;
全天 all day long; all the day; round the clock; whole day long;
熱天 dog days; hot weather;
任天 leave everything to fate;
日天 one full day;
三伏天 dog days;
三九天 coldest days of winter; third nine-day period after the Winter Solstice,
三天 three days;
上半天 forenoon; morning;
上天 (1) God; Heaven; Providence; (2) fly sky-high; go up to the sky;
昇天 go up to the heaven;
暑天 dog days of summer; hot days; hot summer days; summertime;
數天 a few days; several days;
霜天 (1) frosty day; (2) cold and frosty sky;
順天 follow the mandate of heaven;
祀天 offer sacrifices to heaven;
談天 chat; make conversation;
滔天 (1) billowy; dash to the skies; (2) heinous;

T

monstrous;
聽天 submit to the will of Heaven;
通天 (1) direct access to the highest authorities; (2) exceedingly high;
頭天 (1) last day; the day before; the previous day; (2) first day;
晚半天 at dusk;
西天 Western heaven;
下半天 afternoon;
夏天 summer;
霜天 frosty day;
晚半天 (at) dusk; toward evening;
下半天 afternoon;
先天 (1) congenital; inborn; innate; (2) a priori; innate; natural physical endowments;
星期天 Sunday;
許多天 many's the day;
喧天 make a deafening sound;
巡天 tour the heavens;
熏天 becloud the sky;
炎天 dog days; hot day;
豔陽天 bright spring day; bright sunny skies;
仰天 look up to heaven;
一半天 in a day or two;
一天 (1) a day; (2) one day; (3) all day long; from morning till night; the whole day;
陰天 cloudy day; overcast sky;
雨天 rainy day;
籲天 appeal to God;
怨天 blame Heaven;
月黑天 moonless night;
雲天 clouds and sky — high above;
早半天 morning;
早些天 a few days earlier;
這天 on this particular day;
整天 all day; all day long; the whole day;
中天 culmination; meridian passage;
終天 (1) all day long; from morning till night; (2) all one's life; forever;
周天 a complete circle of 360 degrees;
昨天 yesterday;

tian

【添】 (1) add; add to; increase; replenish; (2) have a baby;

［添本］ increase capital;

［添兵］ reinforce;

添兵減灶 bring in reinforcements while reducing cooking stoves;

［添補］ complete what is lacking; get more of sth; make sth complete; replenish;

添補不足 add sth in order to make up a deficiency;

［添財］ become wealthy;

添財添丁 prosper by becoming wealthy and by adding members to the family;

［添菜］ have additional dishes;

［添丁］ beget a son; have a baby boy born into the family;

添丁發財 may your family increase and may you be prosperous;

［添多］ add more; increase;

添多減少 increase or decrease the number of;

［添飯］ replenish rice;

［添附］ add to; additional; enclose; supplement;

［添加］ add to; increase;

添加劑 additive; additive agent;
~ 打漿添加劑 beater additive;
~ 防剝落添加劑 antistripping additive;
~ 防焦添加劑 anticoking additive;
~ 防靜電添加劑 static dissipator additive;
~ 防老化添加劑 age-inhibiting additive;
~ 防磨添加劑 wear preventive additive;
~ 防沫添加劑 antifoam additive;
~ 防污添加劑 antifoulant additive;
~ 滑爽添加劑 slip additive;
~ 聚合添加劑 polymeric additive;
~ 抗爆添加劑 antiknock additive;
~ 抗磨損添加劑 antiwear additive;
~ 抗酸添加劑 antiacid additive;
~ 抗氧添加劑 antioxidant additive;
~ 氯化添加劑 chlorinated additive;
~ 氣油添加劑 gasoline additives;
~ 去垢添加劑 detergent additive;
~ 石油添加劑 petroleum additive;
~ 食品添加劑 food additives;
~ 食物添加劑 food additives;
~ 飼料添加劑 feed additive;
~ 香味添加劑 flavour additive;
~ 阻凍添加劑 antifreeze additive;

添加飾物 doll up sth;

添油加醋 add colour and emphasis; add highly coloured details to a story; add inflammatory details to; embroider; play up; read things into; spice up; with great unction; with much emphasis and many flowery phrases;

添技加葉 add details to a story; embellish a story; embroider; have sth to add to;

添磚加瓦 add bricks and tiles to; contribute one's bit to; do one's bit to help; do what little one can to help;

work together to build;
[添價] raise the price;
[添上] (1) add to; (2) besides; in addition to;
[添設] set up additionally;
[添造] build more; construct; expand;
[添置] acquire; add to one's possessions; purchase additionally; put in extra furniture;

加添 additive; charge up;
增添 add; add to; increase; supplement;

tian²
tian

【田】 (1) farmland; field; (2) a surname;
[田邊地頭] edges of a field;
[田產] real estate;
[田地] (1) agricultural land; farmland; field; (2) plight; wretched situation;
耕種田地 work the fields;
掃田刮地 do manual work; engage in manual labour; toil;
一塊田地 a field;
這步田地 such a deplorable situation; such a pass;
[田賦] taxes on agricultural land;
[田家] farming family; peasant family;
[田間] in the field;
田間勞動 farm work; field labour;
[田徑] track and field;
田徑比賽 track-and-field games;
田徑場 playing field;
田徑隊 track and field team;
田徑服 trackie;
田徑賽 track and field events;
田徑項目 track event;
田徑運動 track and field;
田徑運動員 track-and-field athlete;
[田里] rural area; rural community;
[田廬] farmhouse;
[田螺] mud snail; pond snail;
[田賽] field events;
田賽項目 field events;
[田舍] farmhouse;
[田鼠] field mouse;
[田土] soil and land;
瘦土薄田 poor soil and barren land;
[田野] cultivated land; fields; open country;
田野實驗 field experiment;
廣闊的田野 vast field;
蔥蘢的田野 verdant fields;
[田園] countryside; fields and gardens;
田園風光 rural scenery;
田園荒蕪 fields and gardens turn to a jungle;
田園生活 idyll life;
田園詩 pastoral; pastoral poem;
田園詩人 pastoral poet; idyllist;
田園文學 idyllic literature; pastoral literature;
[田月桑時] farming season;
[田主] landlord;
[田莊] country estate; farmhouse; farmstead;
[田租] farm rent;

耙田 harrow a field;
阪田 (1) hillside farm field; (2) rugged and stony field;
薄田 barren land; unfertile land;
大田 land for growing field crops;
丹田 public region;
稻田 paddy; rice field;
低產田 low-yield field;
豐產田 high-yield plot;
肥田 (1) fertile land; (2) fertilize the soil;
高產田 high-yield field;
耕田 cultivate; till a field;
瓜田 melon patch;
歸田 resign from office and return home;
旱田 (1) dry farmland; (2) dry land;
湖田 land reclaimed from a lake;
瘠田 barren land;
礦田 ore field;
良田 farmland; fertile;
麥田 wheat field;
煤田 coal field;
海綿田 mellow soil field; spongy soil;
棉田 cotton field;
農田 cultivated land; farmland;
坡田 hillside field; sloping field;
畦田 furrowed field; ridged field;
氣田 gas field;
桑田 mulberry field;
沙田 sand flat; tidal land;
砂田 sandy land;
山田 hillside plot;
試驗田 experimental field; experimental plot;
水田 paddy field;
台田 platform fields; raised fields;
蹚田 turn the soil and dig up weeds;
梯田 terrace; terraced field;
屯田 have garrison troops or peasants open up

T

wasteland and farm (in the Han Dynasty);
圩田 low-lying paddy fields surrounded with dikes;
閑田 (1) public land; (2) wasteland;
心田 (1) heart; (2) intention;
鹽田 saline; salt pan;
秧田 rice seedling bed;
樣板田 demonstration field; demonstration plot; model plot;
油田 oil field;
園田 vegetable garden;
造田 turn the land into cultivated fields;
種田 farm; till the land;
種子田 seed-breeding field;

tian

【恬】 (1) calm; quiet; peaceful; (2) not care at all;
[恬波] calm waters;
[恬不] have no sense of;
恬不為怪 take no offense at; take no wonder of it; not be surprised at all;
恬不為意 nonchalant; remain unruffled;
恬不知恥 blush like a black dog; brazen-faced; devoid of any sense of shame; die to shame; have no sense of shame; have no sense of shame at all; not feel ashamed; past all sense of shame; past shame; shameless; totally devoid of sense of shame; unashamed; unblushingly; without any sense of shame; without shame;
~ 恬不知恥的人 person without a sense of shame;
恬不知悔 devoid of any sense of repentance; have no compunction;
[恬淡] indifferent to fame or gain;
恬淡寡欲 contented and indifferent to worldly gain; quiet in mind with few desires;
恬淡自甘 quiet in mind with few desires;
[恬澹] contented; indifferent to worldly gain;
[恬和] quiet and gentle;
[恬靜] peaceful; quiet; tranquil;
[恬瀾] calm;
[恬美] quiet and nice;
[恬謐] peaceful; quiet; tranquil;
[恬漠] indifferent and undisturbed;
恬漠無事 nonchalant and uneventful;
[恬然] calm; easygoing; nonchalant; unhurried; unperturbed;
恬然自若 calm and at ease; nonchalant and composed;
處之恬然 remain unruffled; take sth unperturbedly;
[恬適] quiet and comfortable;
[恬退] contented and reserved; uninterested in wealth and glory;

tian

【畋】 (1) cultivate land; (2) hunt game;
[畋獵] hunting;

tian

【甜】 (1) honeyed; luscious; sweet; (2) sound; (3) agreeable; pleasant;
[甜菜] beet; sugar beet;
甜菜根 beetroot;
甜菜泥 pureed beets;
甜菜尿 beeturia;
甜菜糖 beet sugar;
白甜菜 white beet;
菜用甜菜 garden beet;
低糖甜菜 low-sugar beet;
紅甜菜 red beet;
飼料甜菜 fodder beet;
[甜點] afters; confection; dessert; sweet;
餐後甜點 afters;
分享甜點 split a dessert;
[甜疙瘩] dough drops;
[甜瓜] muskmelon; sweet melon;
[甜醬] pickled in sweet soy sauce;
甜醬八寶瓜 muskmelon pickled in sweet soy sauce;
甜醬甘露 Chinese artichoke pickled in sweet soy sauce;
甜醬黃瓜 cucumber pickled in sweet soy sauce;
[甜津津] (1) pleasantly sweet; very sweet; (2) happy; quite pleased;
[甜酒] sweet wine;
泡泡甜酒 alcopop;
[甜辣] sweet but vicious;
口甜心辣 honey on the lips and viciousness in the heart;
[甜美] (1) luscious; sweet; (2) comfortable; pleasant; refreshing;
味道甜美 have a sweet taste;
[甜蜜] (1) honeyed; sugary; sweet; (2) affectionate; fond; happy;
[甜品] dessert; sweetmeats;
甜品酒 dessert wine;

[甜食] (1) confection; sweet food; sweetmeats; (2) afters; desert;
愛吃甜食 have a sweet tooth;
冷凍甜食 frozen desert;
膩味甜食 loathe sweets;
要不要甜食 any afters;
[甜水] (1) freshwater; (2) sugar water;
[甜睡] fast asleep; sound sleep;
[甜絲絲] (1) pleasantly sweet; (2) gratified; happy;
心裏感到甜絲絲 feel quite pleased;
[甜酸苦辣] sweet, sour, bitter, and peppery—all the sweet and bitter experiences of life;
[甜頭] (1) pleasant flavour; sweet taste; (2) benefit; good; sugar plum;
嚐到甜頭 become aware of the benefits of; come to know the good of; gain some profit from;
[甜味] sweet taste;
甜味劑 sweetener;
人造甜味劑 artificial sweetener;
玉米甜味劑 corn sweetener;
甜味料 sweetener;
天然甜味料 natural sweetener;
營養性甜味料 nutritive sweetener;
[甜香] sweet and fragrant;
[甜心] sweetheart;
[甜滋滋] (1) pleasantly sweet; (2) delighted; gratified; happy; pleased;

奧甜 sweet and luscious;
甘甜 sweet;
苦甜 the bitter and the sweet;
清甜 fresh and sweet; smooth and sweet;
酸甜 sour and sweet;
香甜 (1) fragrant and sweet; (2) sleep soundly;

tian
【湉】 flow placidly;
[湉湉] calm; sluggish; tranquil;

tian
【填】 (1) fill up; stuff; (2) fill in; write;
[填飽] cram; feed to the full;
填飽肚子 be adequately fed; fill the belly;
[填報] fill in a form and submit it to the authority;
[填表] fill in a blank; fill out a form;
[填補] fill; fill up; make up;
填補空白 fill in gaps; stop a gap;
填補虧空 make up a deficit;
填補缺額 fill a vacancy;
填補蛀牙 fill a decayed tooth;
[填充] fill in the blanks; filling;
填充物 infill;
空心填充 hollow filling;
數字填充 digital filling;
柱填充 column filling;
[填詞] fill in words;
填詞法 the method of filling-in words;
合意填詞法 acceptable word method;
[填發] fill in and issue;
[填房] second wife after the first wife's death;
[填海] reclaim; reclamation;
填海拓地 redeem land from the sea;
銜石填海 labour in vain;
[填空] (1) fill a vacancy; (2) fill in the blanks;
填空測驗 cloze test;
[填料] filler; jointing; packing;
電纜填料 cable filler;
規則填料 regular packing;
活性填料 active filler;
麻填料 hemp jointing;
氣密填料 air packing;
石棉填料 asbestos jointing;
疏鬆填料 bulking filler;
[填平] fill and level up; fill up and make even; spackling;
填平補齊 even up; fill up the gaps;
填平鴻溝 close the gap between; fill in the gap;
[填塞] caulk; fill; pack; stuff;
[填色書] colouring book;
[填字游戲] crossword puzzle;

充填 fill in; fill up;
回填 backfill;
裝填 load; ram;

tian
【闐】 (1) fill; fill to the brim; (2) full of;
[闐闐] (1) brimming; flourishing; full; (2) sound of drums;
[闐溢] fill to the brim;

駢闐 enumerative; numerous;
喧闐 bustling and crowded;

tian³
tian
【忝】 (1) disgrace; shame; (2) depreciatory

expression referring to oneself; (3) unworthy of the honour;
[忝列門牆] have the honour to be accepted as sb's student;

tian
【殄】 (1) end; terminate; (2) exterminate; root out; weed out; wipe out; (3) waste;
[殄瘁] misfortune and poverty; ruin;
[殄絕] bring to an end; bring to termination;
[殄滅] exterminate thoroughly; extirpate;
[殄難] eliminate dangers and hardships; exterminate dangers;

tian
【腆】 (1) affluence; prosperous; (2) good; virtuous; (3) protruding; (4) bashful; (5) blush;
[腆默] blush and keep silence;
[腆顏而言] speak with a bashful countenance;
[腆贈] costly presents; expensive gifts;
靦腆 bashful; shy;

tian
【舔】 lap; lick; taste;
[舔犢] lick a calf;
舔犢情深 very affectionate toward one's children;
舔犢之愛 paternal love;
[舔洗] wash by licking;
[舔一舔] taste by licking;

tian
【靦】 ashamed; embarrassed;
[靦臉] brazen it out; shameless;
[靦冒] ashamed; embarrassed;
[靦然] blush from shame;
[靦顏] bashful; shy; timid;

tiao¹
tiao
【挑】 (1) choose; pick; select; (2) find; (3) carry on the shoulder with a pole; shoulder;
[挑撥離間] foment bad relations between two groups;
[挑錯] find fault; pick flaws;
[挑擔] carry a load with a carrying pole;
看人挑擔不吃力 none knows the weight of another's burden; the burden is light on the shoulders of another;
[挑燈夜戰] burn the midnight oil;
[挑逗] tantalize; tease;
[挑夫] bearer; porter;
[挑揀] choose; pick; select;
挑揀飲食 particular about food;
挑吃揀喝 choose one's food;
挑肥揀瘦 fastidious in choosing what one chooses; particular in one's selection; pick the fat or choose the lean – choose whatever is to one's personal advantage;
總想挑肥揀瘦 seek to pick the best;
揀精挑肥 choose whatever is to one's personal advantage; fastidious; pick and choose; very choosy; very particular;
挑毛揀刺 captious; find fault; pick holes;
到處挑毛揀刺 find fault at anything;
挑三揀四 choose; choosy; difficult to please; fastidious; pick and choose; pick this and choose that; quick to find fault;
~ 挑三揀四的人 person who is not easy to please;
挑挑揀揀 choosy; pick and choose;
[挑開] brush aside with a poker;
[挑賣] peddle;
[挑取] choose; pick; select;
[挑食] faddy;
[挑水] shoulder water with a pole;
井邊挑水井邊賣 carry coal to Newcastle; sell water at the well;
[挑剔] carp; fastidious; hypercritical; nitpick; pick fault;
挑剔的 fastidious;
愛挑剔的 fussy;
挑剔責難 find fault with sb;
百般挑剔 nitpick;
無可挑剔 unimpeachable;
[挑選] choose; pick; pick out; select; single out; take one's pick of;
從中挑撰 make a choice among;
精挑細選 hand-picked;
千挑萬選 select;
隨意挑選 pick out at random;
[挑眼] fastidious; overcritical; pick fault;

長挑 tall and slender;
單挑 do sth by oneself; work on one's own;
頭挑 the best choice; the choicest;

tiao
【恌】 (1) worry; (2) frivolous;

tiao
【祧】 (1) ancestral temple; (2) become heir to;

tiao²

tiao
【佻】 (1) frivolous; imprudent; (2) act in a furtive manner; steal; stealthily; (3) eelay; dilatory; slow; (4) provoke;
[佻薄] frivolous; not dignified;
[佻巧] frivolous and tricky;
[佻竊] steal;
[佻佻] (1) walk alone; (2) slight and elegant;
佻佻公子 slight and elegant gentleman;
[佻脫] frivolous; frivolous and careless; undisciplined;

輕佻 frivolous; skittish;

tiao
【迢】 distant; far; remote;
[迢遞] far-off; faraway;
[迢迢] far and remote; far away; remote;
迢迢旅途 remote journey;
迢迢遠行 take a long journey;
[迢遙] distant; far;

tiao
【苕】 plant used for making brooms;
[苕帚] broom;

tiao
【條】 (1) twig; (2) long narrow piece; strip; (3) article; item; (4) in good order;
[條案] long and narrow table;
[條暢] clear and orderly; clear and smooth; smooth and well-organized;
[條陳] (1) present item by item; (2) written presentation;
[條達] (1) logical; orderly; reasonable; (2) bracelet;
[條對] give answers to every question asked;
[條幅] scroll;
[條規] rules and regulations;
[條痕] streak;
濕條痕 wet streak;
樹脂條痕 resin streak;
[條件] clauses; conditions; factors; terms;
條件被動式 conditional in passive form;
條件變量 conditional variable;
條件從句 conditional clause;
條件從屬連詞 subordinator of condition;
條件反射 conditional reflex; conditioned reflex;
條件反應 conditional response;
條件關係 conditional relation;
條件匯編 conditional assembly;
條件進行式 conditional in progressive form;
條件句 conditional clause;
條件時 conditional tense;
條件式 conditional form;
條件完成進行時 conditional in perfect progressive form;
條件性形容詞從句 contingent adjective clause;
條件敍實謂詞 conditional factive predicate;
條件狀語 adverbial of condition;
條件狀語從句 adverbial clause of condition;
不利條件 adverse conditions;
大氣條件 atmospheric condition;
反極條件 antipole condition;
封閉性條件 closed condition;
夠條件 qualified; reach the standard;
假設條件 assumed condition; hypothetical condition;
交替條件 alternation condition;
老化條件 aging condition;
滿足條件 meet a condition;
容許條件 admissible condition;
設定條件 impose a condition;
提出條件 propose conditions;
同意條件 accede to terms;
無條件 unconditional; without preconditions;
無條件答應 make an absolute promise;
無條件投降 unconditional surrender;
因果條件 causality condition;
有條件的 conditional; with conditions attached;
周圍條件 ambient condition;
自然條件 natural conditions;
[條款] article; clause; provision;
罰款條款 penalty clause;
附件條款 accessories clause;
泊位條款 berth clause;
簽證條款 attestation clause;
全險條款 all-risks clause;
商標條款 trademark clause;

修改條款 amending clause;
一項條款 a clause;
仲裁條款 arbitration clause;
轉讓條款 assignment clause;
可轉讓條款 assignability clause;
最後條款 final articles;
最惠國條款 most favoured nation clause;

[條理] (1) logical; reasonable; (2) orderly; methodical; proper arrangement; proper presentation;
條理不清 badly organized; improper arrangement; unmethodical;
條理貫通 go through in regular sequence;
條理井然 in good order and with good reasoning;
毫無條理 out of order;
缺乏條理 lack method;
順條順理 comply; go along; pliant; obedient;
有條理 methodical; structured;
很有條理 well structured;
有條有理 coherent; like a clock; logical; methodical; orderly; properly and logically arranged; systematic; very clear and precise; very systematic; well organized and clearly stated;

[條例] imperative; ordinance; regulation; rule;
公司條例 company ordinance;
勞保條例 labour insurance regulations;
污染防治條例 pollution prevention ordinance;
暫行條例 interim regulations;

[條碼] bar code;
條碼長度 bar code length;
條碼校驗符 bar code check character;
條碼系統 bar code system;
條碼閱讀器 scanner;
條碼字符 bar code character;

[條目] details; particulars;

[條條] in good order; logical; reasonable;
條條大路通羅馬 all rivers run into the sea; every road leads to Rome;
條條框框 conventions; conventions and taboos; regulations and restrictions; restrictions and fetters; rules and regulations;

[條文] clause; article;

[條紋] fringe; streak; striped;
等角條紋 constant-angle fringe;
樹脂條紋 pitch streak;
鐵素體條紋 ferrite streaks;
細條紋 fine streak;
消色差條紋 achromatic fringe;
遠場條紋 far-field fringes;
有條紋[的] @@banded;

[條形碼] bar code;
條形碼技術 bar codes technique;
條形碼開發 development of bar codes;

[條形圖] bar chart; histogram;

[條約] convention; pact; treaty;
訂條約 sign a treaty;
多邊條約 multilateral treaty;
廢除條約 annul a treaty;
國際條約 international treaty;
合作條約 treaty of cooperation;
~友好合作條約 treaty of friendship and cooperation;
貿易條約 commercial treaty;
秘密條約 backdoor treaty;
批准條約 ratify a treaty;
起草條約 draft a treaty;
簽訂條約 sign a treaty;
雙邊條約 bilateral agreement;
違反條約 violate a treaty;
仲裁條約 arbitration treaty;

[條子] memo; note; short letter;
布條子 strip of cloth;
下條子 send notes to one's subordinates;
寫個條子 write out a note;
一張條子 a note; a slip of paper;
紙條子 narrow strip of paper;

板條 lath;
報條 glad tidings; good news; happy event; report of success;
編條 plait;
便條 chit; informal note; memo; note;
病假條 certificate for sick leave;
布條 strip of cloth;
插條 transplant a cutting;
撐條 stay;
齒條 rack;
赤條條 stark-naked; with not a stitch on;
椽條 rafter;
詞條 dictionary entry;
磁條 magstripe;
粗線條 (1) rough-and-ready; slapdash; (2) rough outlines; thick lines;
單條 vertical scroll of painting or calligraphy;
電焊條 welding electrode; welding rod;
發條 (1) clockwork spring; (2) mainspring;
粉條 noodles made from bean or sweet potato

starch;
封條 paper strip seal;
輻條 spoke;
鋼鋸條 hacksaw blade;
焊條 welding rod;
回條 short note acknowledging receipt of sth; receipt;
匯流條 busbar;
假條 (1) application for leave; (2) leave permit;
教條 (1) creed; doctrine; dogma; (2) doctrinarism; dogmatism;
戒條 commandment; religious discipline;
借條 receipt for a load (IOU);
金條 gold bar;
荊條 twigs of the chaste tree;
鋸條 saw blade;
口條 pig's or ox's tongue (as food);
拉條 brace; stay;
鏈條 chain;
柳條 wicker; willow twig;
爐條 fire bars; grate;
路條 pass; travel permit;
棉條 sliver;
麵條兒 noodles;
苗條 (of a woman) slender; slim;
篾條 (1) rind of reed or sorghum; (2) thin bamboo strip;
屏條 set of hanging scrolls (usu. four in a row);
鉛條 (1) lead; slug; (2) lead (for a propelling pencil);
簽條 slip of paper (to a document or inserted in a book) with comments on it;
欠條 bill signed in acknowledgement of debt;
請假條 written request for leave;
收條 receipt;
藤條 rattan;
天條 laws of God in heaven;
通條 (1) cleaning rod; (2) poker;
細線條 hachure;
線條 line;
蕭條 (1) desolate; bleak; (2) (of business) depression; very dull;
信條 article of creed of faith; creed; precept;
壓條 layer;
沿條兒 braid or tape for joining parts of a dress;
銀條 silver bar;
影條 shadow stripes;
油條 deep-fried twisted dough sticks;
枝條 branch; twig;
字條兒 brief note;

tiao

【笤】 straw broom;
［笤把］ long straw broom;
［笤帚］ straw broom;
［笤子］ Chinese trumpet creeper;

tiao

【蜩】 cicada;
［蜩甲］ shell of the cicada;
［蜩螗沸羹］ confusion and disorder of state affairs; hubbub of voices; noisy and in confusion;

tiao

【調】 (1) fit in perfectly; suit well; (2) blend; mix; (3) adjust; regulate; (4) mediate; (5) make fun of; provoke; tease;
［調光器］ dimmer;
［調和］ (1) in harmonious proportion; (2) mediate; reconcile; (3) compromise; make concessions;
調和肝脾 regulate the function of the liver and spleen;
調和一下 compromise;
調和折衷 compromise; split difference; strike a balance;
［調劑］ (1) make a prescription; (2) adjust; make adjustments; regulate;
調劑身心 provide physical and mental relaxation;
調劑生活 enliven one's life;
［調價］ regulate the price;
週價措施 price-regulating measures;
［調節］ accommodation; adjust; condition; governing; measure; monitor; regulate; take care of;
調節器 governor;
~ 背壓調節器 backpressure governor;
~ 補給空氣量調節器 additional air governor;
~ 飛球調節器 ball governor;
~ 輔助調節器 auxiliary governor;
調節室溫 regulate the room temperature;
調節稅 adjustment tax;
財政調節 financial adjustment;
點火調節 ignition governing;
對準調節 alignment adjustment;
幅度調節 amplitude adjustment;
負調節 negative accommodation;
鼓風調節 blast governing;

T

機能性調節 functional accommodation;
積分調節 integral governing;
絕對調節 absolute accommodation;
空氣調節 air conditioning;
旁通調節 by-pass governing;
色溫調節 colour temperature adjusting;
市場調節 market regulation;
雙眼調節 binocular accommodation;
停氣調節 cut-out governing;
相對調節 relative accommodation;
液壓調節 hydraulic governing;
賬務調節 accounting adjustment;
正調節 positive accommodation;
綜合調節 comprehensive regulation;

[調解] adjust; arbitrate; conciliation; demodulation; make peace; mediate; mediation; modulation; patch up;
調解技巧 mediation skills;
調解家庭糾紛 mediate in a family quarrel;
調解器 demodulator;
~ 伴音調解器 audio demodulator;
~ 寬帶調解器 broadband demodulator;
~ 色度調解器 chrominance demodulator;
~ 雙折射調解器 birefringent demodulator;
~ 信道調解器 channel demodulator;
調解人 intermediary; peacemaker;
調解委員會 mediation committee;
調解爭端 arbitrate a case; mediate between two warring countries; peace-maker;
彩色信號調解 colour signal demodulation;
從中調解 act as an intermediary between...and...;
電子調解 electronic countermodulation;
反調解 countermodulation;
平衡彩色調解 balanced colour demodulation;
群調解 group demodulation;
色彩調解 chroma demodulation;
相干調解 coherent demodulation;

[調酒] wine-mixing;
調酒器 shaker;
調酒師 barkeeper; barman; bartender; mixologist;
調酒學 mixology;

[調侃] jeer; joke; make fun of; mock up sb; ridicule a person; scoff; tease;

[調控] regulate and control;
宏觀調控 macro-control;
~ 宏觀調控目標 macro-control target;

[調理] (1) nurse one's health; recuperate; (2) look after; take care of;
化學調理 chemical conditioning;
精心調理 nurse with great care;

[調料] dressing;

[調弄] (1) make fun of; tease; (2) adjust; arrange; (3) instigate; stir up;

[調配] blend; mix;

[調皮] (1) mischievous; naughty; (2) cunning; tricky; unruly; (3) play tricks;
調皮搗蛋 make trouble; mischievous; monkey business; run a rig; run one's rigs; troublesome; ungovernable;
調皮鬼 naughty guy;

[調情] court; flirt; hanky-panky; philander; play at love; romp;
調情作樂 make love for amusement;

[調人] mediator; arbitrator;

[調色] mix colours; mix paints;
調色板 palette;
調色刀 palette knife;

[調試] debug; debugging;
調試程序 debugging programme;
~ 調試程序包 debugging programme package;

[調停] accommodate; heal the breach; intervene; mediate;
調停者 mediator;
暗中調停 fix things behind the scenes;

[調味] flavour; flavouring; sauce; season; season food;
調味醬 dressing;
調味料 condiment; dressing;
~ 沙拉調味料 salad dressing;
~ 液體調味料 liquid condiment;
調味品 condiment; dressing material; flavouring; seasoning; spice;
~ 芳香調味品 aromatic condiment;
~ 人工調味品 artificial flavouring;
~ 辛辣調味品 acrid condiment;

[調息] regulate one's breath;

[調戲] assail with obscenities; flirt with women; indecent assault; molest; play the make on; take liberties with;

[調笑] make fun of; poke fun at; tease;

[調協] (1) harmonious; (2) mediate;

[調諧] (1) harmonious; (2) resonate; syntonize; tune; tuning;
調諧器 tuner;

~ 帶通調諧器 bandpass tuner;
~ 晶體調諧器 crystal tuner;
~ 天線調諧器 antenna tuner;
~ 調頻調諧器 frequency-modulation tuner;
重合調諧 coincidence tuning;
電容調諧 capacitance tuning;
空腔調諧 cavity tuning;
色彩調諧 harmonious in colour;
天線調諧 aerial tuning;
自動調諧 autotune; autotuning;

[調謔] crack a joke; tease;

[調壓] pressure regulation;
調壓裝置 pressure regulation appliance;

[調養] recuperate after an illness; take good care of oneself;
調養攝生 nurse oneself and recuperate;
調養身體 nurse one's body;

[調音] tune;
調音師 tuner;
~ 鋼琴調音師 tuner;

[調整] adjust; adjustment; regulate; setting; trim; tune-up;
調整計劃 revise plan;
調整機構 adjusting the organizational structure;
調整價格 readjust prices;
調整器 corrector;
~ 混合物調整器 mixture corrector;
~ 日曆調整器 date corrector;
~ 雙曆調整器 double corrector;
~ 外部快慢調整器 outer regulator corrector;
~ 周曆調整器 day corrector;
調整賬戶 adjusting account;
重新調整 realignment;
動力調整 power setting;
季節性調整 seasonal adjustment;
可調整 adjustable;
空中調整 aerial adjustment;
零位調整 zero setting;
陸上調整 terrestrial adjustment;
水中調整 aquatic adjustment;
線路調整 circuit conditioning;

[調制] modulation;
調制器 modulator;
~ 平衡調制器 balanced modulator;
~ 色度調制器 chroma modulator;
~ 聲光調制器 acoustooptic modulator;
波幅調制 amplitude modulation;
導納調制 admittance modulation;
光源調制 active light modulation;

[調製] prepare;

空調 air-conditioning;
排調 make fun of; ridicule; tease;
烹調 cook dishes;
失調 (1) detune; maladjust; (2) dislocate; lose balance; (3) lack proper care after an illness;
微調 fine tuning; trimming;
協調 coordinate; harmonize;

tiao

【髫】 (1) children's hair style; (2) child; youngster;

[髫齡] childhood; youth;

[髫年] childhood; young age;

垂髫 early childhood;

tiao

【齠】 shed the milk teeth;

[齠年] childhood;

[齠容] youthful look;

tiao^3

tiao

【挑】 (1) push sth up with a pole or stick; raise; (2) pick; (3) instigate; provoke; stir up; (4) dally; make a pass at; seduce;

[挑撥] arouse; cause disputes; incite; instigate; provoke; sow discord;
挑撥離間 blow the fire; create dissension; drive a wedge between; foment dissension; incite one against the other; make bad blood; make mischief between; pit one against the other; play off one against the other; poison the relations between; provocation and estrangement; set by the ear; set one party against another; sow dissension; sow seeds of discord; stir up bad feelings; stir up ill will;
挑撥是非 cause alienation between; foment discord; foment trouble;

[挑燈] (1) stir the wick; (2) hang lantern;
挑燈撥火 instigate;
挑燈苦讀 raise the wick and study hard;
挑燈夜讀 continue reading by lamplight; trim one's lamp to read;
挑燈夜戰 continue working by lamplight; fight by torchlight;

T

［挑動］ incite; provoke; stir up; tar on;
挑動好奇心 arouse curiosity;
挑動內戰 provoke a civil war;
［挑逗］ arouse amorous desires; provoke; seduce; tantalize; tease;
挑逗尋釁 pick a quarrel with sb;
［挑費］ daily expenses;
［挑工］ leave a job; quit; resign;
［挑弄］ play a joke on; tease;
挑弄是非 arouse ill-will between two parties; stir up one side against the other;
［挑起］ instigate; provoke; stir up;
［挑情］ make amorous advances;
［挑剔］ be captious; be hypercritical; be fastidious; carp about; carp at; carp on; find fault with; get at; get on to; gun for; jump at; nag at; nibble at; nitpick; peck at; pick apart; pick a hole in; pick at; pick holes in; pick on; yap at;
［挑釁］ aggression; defiance; provoke;
挑釁的 aggressive;
挑釁者 aggressor;
蓄意挑釁 premeditated provocation;
［挑戰］ (1) challenge; challenge to battle; throw down the gauntlet; (2) challenge;
挑戰書 cartel; written challenge;
發出挑戰 throw down the gauntlet;
接受挑戰 pick up the gauntlet; take up the gauntlet;
進行挑戰 throw down the gauntlet;
面臨挑戰 face the challenge;
向人挑戰 pick up a fight;
應對挑戰 meet a challenge;

出挑 develop one's skills;
細高挑 (1) tall and slender figure; (2) tall, slender person;
細挑 tall and slender;

tiao
【窕】 (1) slender; (2) charming and attractive; (3) quiet and modest; (4) beautiful; good; wonderful;

窈窕 (1) (of a woman) gentle and graceful; (2) (of a palace, landscape, etc.) secluded;

tiao⁴
tiao
【朓】 end of a lunar month when the moon is setting in the west;

tiao
【眺】 look far away from above; take a look at faraway things;
［眺望］ look far away; look into the distance from a high place; overlook; survey;

憑眺 gaze from a high place into the distance;
遠眺 look far into the distance;

tiao
【跳】 (1) bounce; jump; leap; spring; (2) beat; move up and down; pulsate; throb; (3) make omissions; skip;
［跳班］ skip a grade in school;
［跳板］ access board; drawboard; gang board; gangplank; springboard;
當跳板 serve as a springboard;
起跳板 take-off board;
彈跳板 spring-board;
助跳板 diving board; springboard; take-off board;
［跳槽］ (1) jump the trough; (2) change jobs; get new employment; job-hopping; jump ship;
辭工跳槽 from one job to another; leave one's work and go to another;
［跳出］ jump out; leap out;
跳出樊籠 get out of the cage — freed, liberated;
跳出火坑 escape from a living hell; escape the fiery pit of perdition; escape the pit of fire;
［跳動］ beat; bounce; jitter; move up and down; pulsate; run-out;
端面跳動 ending beats;
行間跳動 line-to-line jitter;
輝度跳動 brightness beats;
徑向跳動 diameter run-out;
亮度跳動 brightness beats;
偏心跳動 eccentricity run-out;
幀跳動 frame-to-frame jitter;
［跳讀］ skip; skip in reading; skip through;
［跳高］ high jump;
跳高架 jump stand;
俯臥式跳高 belly roll jump;
剪式跳高 scissors jump;
［跳過］ jump across; jump over;
［跳河］ jump into the river to drown oneself;
［跳級］ acceleration; skip a grade;

T

學習跳級 academic acceleration;

[跳接線] jump cables; jump leads;

[跳樓] jump to death from a building;
跳樓貨 distress merchandise;

[跳馬] horse-vaulting;
橫跳馬 side horse;
縱跳馬 long horse;

[跳票] bounced check;

[跳棋] halma;
西洋跳棋 checkers; draughts;
中國跳棋 Chinese draughts;

[跳牆] jump down from a wall in desperation; jump over a fence;
狗急跳牆 a cornered beast will do sth desperate; a cornered dog tries to jump over a high wall; a dog will leap over a wall in desperation; be drive to extremities; despair give courage to a coward; desperation drives a dog to jump over a wall; drive a dog into a corner and over a wall; drive a dog into a corner and he'll fight; leap over a wall like a desperate dog; one will take desperate measures if pushed to the wall; the desperate dog will jump a wall; the desperate kick of a cornered beast; when a dog is cornered, it will jump over a wall — when a person finds himself cornered, he would take any risks and make a desperate struggle;

[跳球] jump ball;

[跳傘] parachute;
跳傘運動 skydiving;

[跳繩] jump rope; rope jumping; rope skipping; skipping rope;

[跳水] dive; diving; jump into the water;
跳水板 diving board;
跳水保護員 divekeeper;
跳水表演 diving exhibition;
跳水池 diving pool;
跳水者 diver;
跳水自殺 jump into the water and drown oneself;
抱膝跳水 cannon ball; crouched jump;
臂立跳水 armstand dive; handstand dive;
花式跳水 fancy diving;
滚翻跳水 somersault diving;
立定跳水 standing dive;
跑動跳水 running dive;
跑動轉體跳水 running twist dive;
跳板跳水 springboard diving;
向後跳水 back dive; backward dive;
向前跳水 forward dive; front dive; swallow dive; swan dive;
向前屈體跳水 back-jack-knife dive;
向前直體跳水 forward header dive;
旋轉式跳水 screw dive;
燕式跳水 swallow dive; swan dive;

[跳台] diving platform;

[跳汰機] jig;
離心跳汰機 centrifugal jig;
雙式跳汰機 duplex jig;

[跳跳蹦蹦] cut a caper; skip and jump about;

[跳投] jump shot;
籃下跳投 lay-up;

[跳脱] bracelet;

[跳舞] boogie; dance; shake a leg; toe and heel;
跳舞會 ball; dancing party;
跳舞廳 dancer;
跳舞音樂 dance music;
不跳舞 sit out a dance;
帶頭跳舞 lead the ball; lead the dance; open the ball;

[跳下去] jump down; leap down;

[跳遠] broad jump; long jump;
跳遠運動員 long jumper;
三級跳遠 hop, step, and jump; triple jump;

[跳躍] caper; dance; hop; jump; leap;
跳躍前進 bound forward;
斜線跳躍 oblique jump;
星狀跳躍 star jump;
障礙跳躍 obstacle jump;
中心跳躍 centre jump;

[跳蚤] flea;
跳蚤市場 flea market;
跳蚤項圈 flea collar;
拳頭打跳蚤 break a butterfly on a wheel; hit a flea with one's fist;
撐杆跳 pole jump; pole vault;

[跳閘] tripping;
串聯跳閘 series tripping;
手動跳閘 hand tripping;

迸跳 jump about;
蹦跳 bounce; jump;
單腳跳 hop;
開口跳 a clown who is skilled in martial arts;
兩跳 double bounce;
跑跳 run and skip;

起跳 take off;
肉跳 apprehensive; awesome; frightening;
彈跳 bounce; spring;
心跳 (1) heartbeat; (2) palpitation of the heart caused by fear or anxiety;
轉體跳 turning leap;

tiao

【糶】 sell grain;
［糶糧］ sell grain;
［糶米］ sell rice;

出糶 sell grain;
平糶 (of the government) sell the grain in stock at normal prices in a famine year to ease class contradiction;

tie¹

tie

【帖】 (1) obedient; submissive; (2) proper;
［帖耳］ droop one's ears like a dog; submissive;
［帖服］ submissive and subservient;

tie

【怗】 (1) compliant; observant; submissive; subservient; (2) peaceful; quiet;
［怗服］ compliant; resigned; submissive;
［怗靜］ peaceful and quiet;

tie

【貼】 (1) glue; paste; stick; (2) keep close to; nestle closely to; (3) allowance; subsidy;
［貼本］ below cost; lose money in a business;
貼本生意 losing business;
賠上功夫又貼本 spend time and money doing sth;
［貼補］ help with money; make up a deficiency; subsidize; supplement;
貼補家用 help out with the family expenses;
［貼耳］ ready to listen;
［貼金］ (1) cover with a gold leaf; gild; (2) boast about oneself; brag about oneself; prettify; touch up;
［貼近］ close to; lean close to; nearby; nestle up against; press close to;
［貼錢］ pay out of one's own pocket;
［貼切］ appropriate; apt; felicitous; proper; suitable; to the point;
措詞貼切 aptly worded; well put;
［貼身］ (1) next to the skin; (2) personal;
貼身丫頭 personal maid;
［貼題］ pertinent; relevant; to the point;
［貼現］ discount;
貼現行市 discount market;
貼現經紀人 discount broker;
貼現率 bank rate; discount rate;
銀行貼現 bank discount;
再貼現 rediscounting;
真貼現 true discount;
［貼心］ close; intimate;
貼心話 words spoken in confidence;
貼心貼意 amiable and obliging;
［貼譯］ faithful translation;

幫貼 subsidize;
補貼 allowance; subsidize; subsidy;
餐貼 food allowance;
倒貼 pay for the upkeep of a lover;
房貼 poster for a house to let;
伏貼 (1) fit perfectly; (2) comfortable; cosy; (3) obedient; submissive;
服貼 (1) docile; obedient; submissive; (2) be convinced; (3) fitting; proper; well arranged; well-done;
鍋貼 lightly fried dumpling;
剪貼 clip and paste in a scrapbook or on cards; cutting out (as school-children's activity);
津貼 allowance; subsidize; subsidy;
拼貼 collage;
體貼 give every care to; show consideration for;
妥貼 appropriate; fitting; proper; satisfactorily;
偎貼 lean close to; snuggle up to;
穩貼 proper and secure; safe and sound;
一貼 (1) glue; paste; (2) a piece of;
張貼 paste up; placard; plaster; post; post up; put up;
招貼 bill; placard; poster;

tie³

tie

【帖】 (1) invitation card; (2) document; label; placard; (3) copybook of calligraphy; (4) medical prescription;
［帖子］ (1) invitation card; (2) money order;

安帖 feel at ease;
八字帖 written marriage proposal on which is stated the date of one's birth;
拜帖 visiting card;
碑帖 rubbing from a stone inscription;
服帖 (1) obedient; submissive; (2) proper; well-done;

稟帖 petition;
庚帖 written marriage proposal on which is stated the date of one's birth;
換帖 be sworn brothers by exchange of papers bearing name, year and place of birth, pedigree, etc.;
回帖 money order receipt to be signed and returned to the sender;
柬帖 note; short letter;
寧帖 (of mind) at ease; calm; tranquil;
揭帖 written notice;
請帖 invitation; invitation card;
熨帖 (1) calm; (2) (of word usage) appropriate; proper;
妥帖 appropriate; proper;
下帖 send out an invitation card;
字帖 brief notice;

tie

【鐵】 (1) iron; (2) arms; weapons; (3) hard or strong as iron; (4) indisputable; unalterable; (5) determine; resolve; (6) a surname;

[鐵案] irrevocable case of fact;
鐵案如山 an ironclad case; borne out by ironclad evidence; facts as irrevocable as a mountain; irrefutable conviction;

[鐵板] (1) iron plate; (2) a kind of percussion instrument;
鐵板釘釘 decided;
鐵板釘鋼釘—硬到家 as hard as nails – have no consideration for sb's feelings;
鐵板一塊 monolithic bloc; of one cut;

[鐵棒] iron bar;
一根鐵棒 an iron bar;

[鐵筆] stencil pen;

[鐵餅] discus throw;
擲鐵餅 shot put;

[鐵鏟] shovel;
一把鐵鏟 a shovel;

[鐵窗] (1) window with iron grating; (2) prison; prison bars;
鐵窗風味 life behind bars; life in jail; prison life;
鐵窗之苦 hard life in prison;

[鐵牀] iron bed;

[鐵彈] cannonball;

[鐵道] railroad; railway;
單軌鐵道 monorail;

[鐵釘] iron nail;

[鐵定] definitely; ironclad; not subject to change; unalterable;

[鐵工] blacksmith;

[鐵罐] can; tin;

[鐵軌] rail; track;
單線鐵軌 single line track rail;
雙線鐵軌 double

[鐵棍] iron rod;

[鐵鍋] frying pan; iron pot;

[鐵漢] (1) man of iron; strong fellow; (2) person of firm principle;
鐵漢無情 a person of iron is hard-hearted;

[鐵畫銀鉤] excellent penmanship; vigorous touches and fine strokes in calligraphy;

[鐵甲] steel armour;
鐵甲車 armoured car; armoured vehicle;

[鐵價] fixed price;

[鐵匠] blacksmith; ironsmith;
鐵匠鋪 smithy;

[鐵鏈] iron chain;

[鐵路] rail; railroad; railway;
鐵路服務 rail service;
鐵路公司 railway company;
鐵路工人 railwayman;
鐵路連接 rail links;
鐵路路軌 railroad line; railway line;
鐵路旅客 railway passenger;
鐵路橋 railway bridge;
鐵路事故 rail accident;
鐵路網絡 railway network;
鐵路運輸 railway transportation;
鐵路終點站 railhead;
高架鐵路 elevated railroad; elevated railway;
海岸鐵路 coast railway;
環形鐵路 circular railway;
空中鐵路 aerial railroad;
輕便鐵路 light railway;
一條鐵路 a railway;
窄軌鐵路 narrow gauge railway;

[鐵馬] armoured horses;
金戈鐵馬 shining spears and armoured horses;

[鐵門] metal security door;

[鐵皮] iron sheet;

[鐵騎] cavalry;

[鐵器] ironware;
鐵器時代 Iron Age;

[鐵青] ashen; bluish black; ghastly pale; livid;
鐵青着面 with an ashen face;

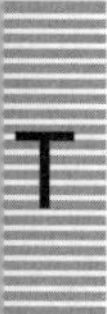

氣得面色鐵青 turn livid with rage;
[鐵鍬] spade;
一把鐵鍬 a spade;
[鐵人] iron man;
[鐵勺] metal ladle;
[鐵石人] cruel person; iron-hearted person; unfeeling person;
[鐵樹] cycad;
鐵樹開花 the iron tree bursts into flowers — sth hardly possible; the iron tree in blossom — sth seldom seen;
[鐵絲] iron wire;
鐵絲網 wire netting;
~細鐵絲網 chicken wire;
[鐵塔] iron tower;
[鐵條] iron rod;
[鐵腕] iron fist; iron hand;
鐵腕人物 despotic person; iron-handed person; tyrannical person;
[鐵鞋] skate;
單邊鐵鞋 single-edged skate;
雙邊鐵鞋 double-edged skate;
踏破鐵鞋 wear out the iron shoes — search painstakingly everywhere;
~踏破鐵鞋無覓處，得來全不費工夫 find sb by chance after a painstaking search; find sth accidentally after tracking miles in vain for it;
[鐵心] have a heart of iron;
鐵心務農 determined farmer;
[鐵鏽] corrosion; rust;
[鐵硯] iron slab;
鐵硯磨穿 grind a hole in an iron slab — study excessively; long years of persistence;
磨穿鐵硯 long years of ardent study; rub through an iron inkstone; study assiduously;
[鐵氧體] ferrite;
鋇鐵氧體 barium ferrite;
鈷鐵氧體 cobalt ferrite;
人造鐵氧體 artificial ferrite;
[鐵衣] (1) armour; (2) iron rust;
[鐵柵欄] iron gate;
[鐵線] wire;
鐵線蓮 clematis;
[鐵砧] anvil;
[鐵證] ironclad proof; irrefutable evidence;
鐵證如山 a mass of ironclad evidence; be confirmed by irrefutable evidences; irrefutable, conclusive evidence; irrefutable proof;
[鐵中錚錚] distinguished among men; outstanding person among mediocre people; the finest of metals;
[鐵柱成針] an iron pestle can be ground down to a needle; constant dripping wears the stone; little strokes fell great oaks; perseverance will prevail;
[鐵嘴] chatterbox; good talker; talkative;

白鐵 galvanized iron;
白口鐵 white iron;
鑌鐵 wrought iron;
波紋鐵 corrugated iron;
槽鐵 channel iron;
場磁鐵 field magnet;
出鐵 tap a blast furnace;
磁鐵 magnet;
電磁鐵 electromagnet;
電烙鐵 (1) electric iron; (2) electric soldering iron;
打鐵 forge iron; work as a blacksmith;
地鐵 subway; tube; underground (railway);
丁字鐵 T-iron;
鍍錫鐵 galvanized iron; tinplate;
鍍鋅鐵 zinc-plate;
鍛鐵 wrought iron;
廢鐵 scrap iron;
鋼鐵 iron and steel; steel;
鉻鐵 ferrochrome;
硅鐵 ferrosilicon;
海綿鐵 sponge iron;
焊鐵 soldering iron;
灰口鐵 gray pig iron;
灰生鐵 gray pig iron;
灰鐵 gray pig iron;
角鐵 angle iron;
烙鐵 (1) flatiron; iron; (2) soldering iron;
煉鐵 iron-smelting;
硫酸亞鐵 ferrous sulphate;
錳鐵 ferromanganese;
馬口鐵 (1) galvanized iron; (2) tinplate;
馬蹄鐵 (1) horseshoe; (2) horseshoe magnet; U-shaped magnet;
鉛鐵 galvanized (sheet) iron;
三角鐵 (1) angle iron; L-iron; (2) triangle;
砂鐵 magnetic sand;
生鐵 pig iron;
熟鐵 wrought iron;
蘇鐵 sago cycas (cycas revolute);
銅鐵 iron and steel;

銜鐵 armature;
銑鐵 cast iron;
氧化鐵 ferric oxide;
亞鐵 ferrous;
一塊鐵 a piece of iron;
乙酸鐵 ferric acetate;
隕鐵 meteorite iron; siderite;
鑄鐵 cast iron;

tie⁴

tie

【帖】 (1) write on silk; (2) engrave characters of famous calligraphers on stone; (3) test papers (in the Tang, Song, and Yuan dynasties);
［帖碼］ register;

碑帖 rubbing from a stone inscription (usually as a model for calligraphy);
法帖 model of calligraphy for practice;
畫帖 book of model paintings or drawings;
習字貼 calligraphy model; copybook;
字帖 copybook for calligraphy;

tie

【飻】 (1) fierce legendary animal; (2) greedy and gluttonous person;

饕飻 (1) fierce and cruel person; (2) taotie, a mythical ferocious animal; (3) glutton; gourmand; voracious eater;

ting¹

ting

【汀】 (1) beach; shore; (2) sandbank;
［汀線］ beach line;
［汀洲］ sand shoal; islet in a stream;

水門汀 cement;

ting

【聽】 (1) hear; listen; (2) follow; heed; obey; (3) allow; let; (4) can; tin;
［聽斑］ acoustic spot;
［聽板］ auditory plate;
［聽不進］ close one's ears;
［聽差］ foot man; gopher;
［聽從］ accept; comply with; heed; listen and follow; listen to; obey;
聽從調遣 accept an assignment;
聽從吩咐 at sb's beck and call; do sb's bidding;
聽從指揮 obey orders;
［聽錯］ hear incorrectly;
［聽到］ hear; listen in; meet the ear; notice;
偶然聽到 overhear;
［聽道］ auditory canal; ear canal;
聽道軟骨 cartilage of acoustic meatus;
［聽懂］ take; understand;
［聽讀不能］ alexia;
［聽而不聞］ hear but pay no attention; hear without understanding; turn a deaf ear to;
［聽反射］ auditory reflex;
［聽管］ auditory canal;
［聽慣］ get used to hearing;
［聽候］ pending; wait for;
聽候差遣 at sb's disposal; await assignment;
聽候處理 pending further instructions;
聽候吩咐 at sb's command; at sb's service;
聽候分配 wait for one's assignment;
［聽話］ (1) obedient; (2) do as sb says;
聽話的 biddable;
聽話聽聲，鑼鼓聽音 the words are the criterion of the man; when you listen to someone talk, listen to their tone; when you listen, listen to speaker's tone of voice;
聽話聽音 listen for the meaning behind sb's words; when you hear people talk, listen to their tone; when you listen, listen to speaker's tone of voice;
不聽話 disobedient; insubordinate;
［聽見］ hear;
聽見風，就是雨 run after a shadow;
聽不見 cannot hear;
［聽講］ attend a lecture; listen to a talk;
［聽覺］ acoustic perception; auditory sense; sense of hearing;
聽覺保護 hearing conservation;
聽覺不良 hearing defect;
聽覺不靈 be dull of hearing;
~聽覺不靈的 hard of hearing;
聽覺遲鈍 amblyacousia; bradyacusia; dullness of hearing;
聽覺反射 acoustic reflex;
聽覺過敏 abnormal acuteness of hearing; hyperacousia;
聽覺減退 hypoacusia; partial loss of hearing;

聽覺缺陷 hearing defect;
聽覺敏鋭 oxycoia;
聽覺神經 acoustic nerve;
聽覺受損的 hearing-impaired;
聽覺調整 auditory adjusting;
~ 聽覺調整裝置 auditory adjusting apparatus;
聽覺語言 auditory language;
單耳聽覺 monaural hearing; unilateral hearing loss;
失聽覺 auditory agnosia;
雙耳聽覺 binaural hearing;
相對聽覺 relative hearing;

[聽課] (1) attend a lecture; sit in on a class; (2) visit a class; visit a classroom;
聽課筆記 lecture notes;

[聽力] (1) sense of hearing; (2) aural comprehension;
聽力計 acumeter;
聽力減退 hypoacusis; partial loss of hearing;
聽力檢查 hearing test;
聽力喪失 hearing loss;
~ 傳導性聽力喪失 conductive hearing loss; transmission hearing loss;
~ 功能性聽力喪失 functional hearing loss;
聽力試驗 audiometric test;
超人的聽力 clairaudience; power to hear sounds beyond ordinary experience;

[聽能] sense of hearing;

[聽你的] you're the doctor;
全聽你的 at your command;

[聽其言而觀其行] hear their words and judge them by their deeds; hear what a man says and see how he acts; judge people by their deeds, not by their words; listen to a man's words and watch his deeds; listen to what a man says and watch what he does;

[聽清] make out;
聽不清 unable to hear distinctly;

[聽取] hear; listen to;
聽取工作報告 listen to a work report;
虛心聽取 listen patiently; listen with an open mind;

[聽審] be tried; stand trial;

[聽説] be said; be told; hear of;
道聽途説 get by hearsay; gossip; listen to gossip; pick up hearsay knowledge; rumour; hearsay;
~ 相信道聽途説 believe the gossip of the streets;
我聽説 a little bird told me;

[聽筒] receiver; telephone receiver;
電話聽筒 handset;
放回聽筒 replace the receiver;
放下聽筒 put down the receiver;
拿起聽筒 lift the receiver; pick up the receiver;
手機聽筒 handset;

[聽聞] (1) hear; (2) what one hears;
動人聽聞 excite one to hear about; exciting to hear;
聳人聽聞 arrest public attention; cause false alarm; electrify; make a sensation; sensational;

[聽寫] dictate;
聽寫員 amanuensis;

[聽信] (1) wait for information; (2) believe; believe what one hears; listen to sth and believe it;
聽信讒言 hear and believe slander; lend a ready ear to slander;
聽信謠言 listen to and believe rumours;
過耳之言，不可聽信 hearsay is not reliable; words overheard are not to be trusted;
偏聽偏信 believe in one-sided story; hear a lop-sided view of the matter and take it to be true; heed and trust only one side; listen to and believe only in certain people's opinions; listen to only one side; listen to sb and be biased towards him; partial to; take sb's word with an inclined ear;

[聽譯] post-listening interpretation;

[聽由尊便] it lies with you;

[聽診] auscultation;
聽診法 stethoscopy;
聽診器 stethoscope;
~ 電子工業聽診器 electronic industrial stethoscope;
~ 電子聽診器 electronic stethoscope;
~ 雙耳聽診器 binaural stethoscope;
產科聽診 obstetric auscultation;
桿聽診 rod auscultation;
間接聽診 mediate auscultation;
口科聽診 oral auscultation;
叩聽診 stroke auscultation;
~ 叩聽診器 auscultoplectrum;

平行聽診 parallel auscultation;
透手聽診 transmanual auscultation;
振動聽診 vibratory auscultation;
直接聽診 direct auscultation;

［聽證會］ hearing; public hearing;

［聽眾］ audience; listeners;
聽眾反應 audience response;
聽眾敬語 audience honorifics;
滿場聽眾 capacity crowds;
目的聽眾 target audience;

不聽 would not listen;
側聽 eavesdrop;
打聽 ask about; find out; get a line on; inquire about;
盜聽 eavesdrop; tap a phone;
諦聽 listen attentively;
動聽 interesting to listen to; moving; persuasive; pleasant to listen to;
好聽 (1) pleasant to hear; pleasant to listen to; pleasing to the ear; (2) high-sounding;
幻聽 phonism;
監聽 monitor;
聆聽 listen respectfully;
留心聽 listen for; listen out;
難聽 (1) coarse; offensive; (2) unpleasant to hear; (3) scandalous;
旁聽 (1) attend a lecture as an associate student; audit at a lecture; (2) be present (at a conference, etc.) as a visitor;
傍聽 audit a class;
竊聽 bug; eavesdrop; intercept; tap; wiretap;
清聽 your kind listening;
傾聽 all ears for; hear out; hearken; incline one's ear to; lend an ear to; listen attentively to; listen carefully; pick up the ears;
視聽 (1) knowledge and experience; (2) public opinion; (3) audio-visual;
收聽 listen in; tune in;
聳聽 alarm others with sth sensational; stimulate others;
探聽 inquire about; investigate secretly; make inquiries; poke in; prey into; spy; try to find out;
聽一聽 have a listen;
偷聽 bug; eavesdrop; tap;
誤聽 mishear;
悉聽 follow one's order;
細聽 listen attentively;
訊聽 make inquiries;
隱聽 eavesdrop; keep quiet and listen;
偵聽 intercept; monitor;
中聽 agreeable to the hearer; pleasant to the ear;
重聽 hard of hearing;

ting

【廳】 (1) central room; hall; (2) government agency;

［廳堂］ hall;

［廳長］ commissioner; director-general (of a department);
副廳長 deputy director-general;

辦公廳 general office;
財政廳 department of finance;
餐廳 (1) dining hall; dining room; (2) restaurant;
大廳 hall;
電子工業廳 electronic industry department;
對外貿易經濟合作廳 foreign trade and economic co-operation department;
飯廳 dining hall; mess hall;
紡織工業廳 textile industry department;
公安廳 public security department;
官廳 government offices;
廣播電視廳 radio broadcasting and television administration;
花廳 drawing room; parlour;
會議廳 hall; meeting room;
機械工業廳 mechanical industry department;
監察廳 supervisory department;
建設廳 construction department;
建築材料工業廳 building materials industry department;
交通廳 communications department;
客廳 drawing room; parlour;
勞動廳 labour department;
林業廳 forestry department;
樓廳 circle;
貿易廳 trade department;
煤炭工業廳 coal industry department;
門廳 entrance hall; hallway; vestibule;
民政廳 department of civil affairs;
農業廳 agriculture department;
前廳 antechamber; vestibule;
輕工業廳 light industry department;
人事廳 personnel department;
膳廳 dining hall; mess hall;
商業廳 department of commerce;
水利廳 water conservancy department;
司法廳 justice department;
文化廳 department of culture;
衛生廳 public health department;
舞廳 ball room; dance hall;
物資廳 goods and materials department;

T

休息廳 lounge;
宴會廳 banquet hall;
冶金工業廳 metallurgical industry department;
音樂廳 concert hall;
正廳 (1) main hall; (2) stall;
重工業廳 heavy industry department;

ting²

ting

【廷】 court; imperial court;
［廷試］ imperial examination;
［廷議］ court discussion; court meeting; discussion at imperial court;
［廷爭］ debate at court in the emperor's presence;

朝廷 (1) royal court; (2) imperial government;
宮廷 (1) palace; (2) royal or imperial court;
教廷 Holy See; Vatican;
內廷 imperial palace;

ting

【亭】 (1) booth; kiosk; pavilion; (2) slim and erect; (3) exactly during;
［亭亭］ (1) erect; (2) gracefully slim;
亭亭如蓋 standing straight and topped with leaves; standing towering with a canopy of leaves;
亭亭聳立 standing alone;
亭亭玉立 slim and graceful; stand gracefully erect; tall and straight;
［亭午］ high noon; midday; noon;
［亭子］ kiosk; pavilion;
打掃亭子 sweep out the pavilion;

報亭 newsstand;
碑亭 pavilion built over a stone tablet;
茶亭 tea booth; tea stall;
崗亭 police box; sentry box;
湖心亭 pavilion in the middle of a lake;
涼亭 alcove; kiosk; pavilion; summer house; wayside pavilion;
售貨亭 stall; stand;
書亭 book-kiosk; bookstall;
水亭 pavilion on the water;
驛亭 courier station; post house;
郵亭 postal kiosk;
竹亭 bamboo pavilion;

ting

【庭】 (1) front courtyard; front yard; hall; yard; (2) imperial court; (3) court of justice; law court;
［庭階石礎］ steps and the stone structures;
［庭決］ hand down a sentence summarily;
［庭舍］ house;
［庭闈］ (1) parents' abode; (2) parents;
［庭午］ (1) noon; (2) bright moon in the sky;
［庭詢］ court hearing;
［庭議］ court meeting;
［庭園］ flower garden; garden;
［庭院］ courtyard; patio;
門前庭院 dooryard;
［庭長］ chief justice; presiding judge;
［庭中］ in the yard;

仲裁庭 arbitration tribunal; court of arbitration;
出庭 appear in court; before the court; enter an appearance;
椿庭 father;
大家庭 big family; community;
法庭 court; court of law; courtroom; law court; tribunal;
合議庭 collegiate bench (of judges, or of a judge and people's assessors);
家庭 family; household;
逕庭 very unlike;
開庭 call a court to order; open a court session;
門庭 gate and courtyard;
前庭 vestibule;
趨庭 receive the teachings of one's father;
訟庭 court of law;
天庭 middle of the forehead;
退庭 retire from the courtroom;
王庭 imperial court;
閑庭 quiet courtyard;
小家庭 small family;
休庭 adjourn;
中庭 atrium;

ting

【停】 (1) cease; halt; park; pause; stop; (2) stay; stop over; (3) be parked; lie at anchor;
［停辦］ close down; discontinue; scrap; stop running; suspend;
［停泊］ anchor; berth; call; dock;
停泊處 anchorage;
［停步］ come to a halt;
停步不前 cease to advance; come to a halt; mark time; stay;
［停產］ stop production;
停產企業 inoperative enterprise;

停產整頓 suspend operation pending consolidation;

[停車] (1) draw up; pull up; stop; (2) park; park a car;
停車場 car park;
~多層停車場 multistorey; parking garage;
~公共停車場 parking garage;
~立體停車場 multistorey car park;
~露天停車場 parking lot;
停車處 parking;
停車罰款通知書 parking ticket;
停車房 garage;
停車計時收費器 parking meter;
停車距離 safe stopping distance;
~安全停車距離 safe stopping distance;
停車棚 carport;
停車位 parking space;
停車信號燈 parking light;
停車制動器 parking brake;
靠邊停車 pull over;

[停當] all set; ready settled;
一切準備停當 everything is ready;

[停電] (1) blackout; power cut; power failure; power outrage; (2) cut off power supply;
停電期 outage;

[停頓] (1) at a standstill; grind to a halt; halt; pause; stagnate; standstill; stop; suspend; (2) pause in speaking;
停頓不前 at a dead end;
交通陷於停頓 the traffic was at a standstill;
內部停頓 internal pause;
陷於停頓 bring sth to a standstill; come to a standstill;
最小停頓 minimum pause;

[停放] park; place;
停放車輛 park cars;

[停飛] suspension of flight;

[停付] stop payment;

[停擱] stop and shelve;

[停工] shut down; stop work; suspend work; time out;
計劃停工 scheduled shutdown;
正常停工 orderly shutdown;

[停航] suspend air service; suspend shipping service;

[停火] cease fire;
停火協議 cease-fire agreement;

[停機] shutdown;
安全停機 safe shutdown;

[停經] menolipsis;
停經期 menopause;

[停刊] stop publication;

[停課] suspend classes;

[停留] remain; stay for a time; stop;
停留時間 retention period;
允許停留 allow stopovers;
中途停留 stop off;

[停水] cut off the water supply;

[停屍架] bier;

[停堆] shutdown;
化學停堆 chemical shutdown;
緊急停堆 emergency shutdown;

[停息] cease; stop;

[停下] shut down; stop;
停下來 come to a stop;
~停下來想一想 stop to think;
忽停忽下 it has been raining off and on;
慢慢停下 come to a halt;

[停歇] (1) close down; stop doing business; (2) cease; stop; (3) rest; stop for a rest;

[停薪] stop payment to an employee;
停薪留職 stop payment of sb's salary but allow him to retain office;

[停學] drop out of school; rusticate; stop going to school; suspend sb from school;
被停學 be suspended from school;

[停訊] stop court proceedings;

[停業] close down; close a business; go out of business; stop doing business; terminate a business; wind up business;

[停雲落月] staying clouds and setting moon — thinking of absent friends or relatives;

[停戰] armistice; break off the action; cessation of hostilities; put up the sword; truce;
停戰談判 armistice;
停戰協定 armistice; truce;

[停職] suspend sb from his duties; suspend sb from office; suspension;
停職反省 be temporarily relieved of one's post for self-examination;

[停止] at a halt; at a standstill; at an end; bring an end to; bring to a halt; bring to a standstill; call a halt; call off; cease; close; come off it; come to a

conclusion; come to a halt; come to a standstill; come to an end; conclusion; cry a halt; desist; end; fall calm; grind to a halt; halt; make an end of; pause; put an end to; stop; suspend; terminate; wind up;
停止罷工 call off a strike;
停止工作 stop working;
停止廣播 go off the air; stop broadcasting;
停止爭吵 cease from quarrelling;
停止裝置 stop;
~ 安全停止裝置 safe stop;
驟然停止 dead stop;
零值停止 zero pause;
延續停止 extended shutdown;
自動停止 automatic shutdown;

[停滯] at a standstill; be held up; bog down; stagnate; stagnation;
停滯不前 at a standstill; bog down; mark time; refuse to make progress; remain stagnant; stagnate;
停滯賬戶 sleeping account;
持續停滯 secular stagnation;
經濟停滯 economic stagnation;

不停 without stop;
居停 live; one's landlord; reside; stay;
尿崩停 posterior pituitary insufflation;
少停 pause for a little while;
調停 act as an intermediary; intervene; mediate;
消停 silent; steady;
暫停 (1) suspend; (2) time-out;

ting
【婷】 attractive; graceful; pretty;
[婷婷] attractive and well poised; graceful;
婷婷玉立 slim and graceful; tall and erect;

裊裊婷婷 lithe; lissome; slim and graceful;
娉婷 (of a woman) have a graceful demeanour;

ting
【渟】 (1) (of water) not flowing; still; (2) (of water) clear;

ting
【蜓】 dragonfly;

蜻蜓 dragonfly;

ting
【霆】 sudden peal of thunder; thunderbolt;
[霆擊] as quickly as lightning;

雷霆 (1) thunder-like power or rage; (2) thunderbolt; thunderclap;

ting³
ting
【町】 boundary between agricultural lands;
[町畦] low bank of earth between fields;

ting
【挺】 (1) erect; straight; (2) deal with; handle; (3) stick out; straighten up; (4) endure; stand; (5) rather; very;
[挺拔] (1) tall and straight; (2) forceful;
挺拔不群 stiff upright and uncommon to all;
筆力挺拔 forceful strokes in handwriting or drawing;
[挺而走險] (1) make a reckless move; risk danger in desperation; (2) be forced to break the law;
[挺好] not half bad; quite good;
[挺節] hold fast to one's principle; virtuous;
[挺進] boldly drive on; press onward; push forward;
挺進敵後 boldly drive into the areas behind the enemy lines;
[挺舉] clean and jerk;
[挺立] stand erect; stand firm; stand up straight; stand upright;
挺立不拔 stand upright and rock-firm;
挺立如松 stand erect and majestic as green pines;
挺立山頭 stand firmly on the hill;
[挺身] straighten one's back;
挺身而出 bell the cat; bolster oneself up; come forward courageously; come out boldly; stand up and volunteer to help; step forth bravely; step forward boldly; step forward bravely; thrust oneself forward to face a challenge;
挺身反抗 stan up and fight; stand up to an enemy;
挺身應付 desperate;
[挺昇] rise steeply;
[挺挺] stiff; straightforward; unbending; unyielding;
[挺胸] square one's shoulders; throw out one's chest; thrust out one's chest;
挺胸突肚 a high breast and big belly; puff up one's chest; stand straight in a gesture of self-confidence; stick

out one's chest; stretch the chest and expand the belly; with one's chest stuck out;
昂然挺胸 throw out one's chest proudly;
擡頭挺胸 chin up and chest out; swell with confidence;

[挺秀] elegant and prominent; tall and graceful;
挺秀超群 eminent above the masses;

[挺嚴] rather stiff; very strict;

[挺硬] stiff and stubborn; unyielding and tough;

[挺直] erect; straight and upright;
挺直身體 draw oneself up; straighten up;
挺直身子 draw oneself up;

筆挺 (1) bolt upright; standing very straight; (2) trim; well-ironed;
倒挺 quite; rather;
堅挺 strong;
勁挺 strong and forceful;
牽挺 formerly; the pedal in a loom;
強挺 indomitable; unyielding;
牙挺 elevator;
英挺 distinguished; outstanding; prominent;
硬挺 (1) endure with all one's will; endure with one's best; hold out with all one's might; put up with all one's might; stick out; (2) rigid; stiff;
直挺挺 bolt upright; straight; stiff;
鑽挺 drill collar;

ting

【梃】 (1) cane; cudgel; club; stick; (2) branch; stalk; stem; (3) straight and strong;

[梃杖] club; stick;

ting

【艇】 long, narrow boat;

[艇手] launchman;

登陸艇 landing boat; landing ship;
飛艇 aeroboat; airship; dirigible;
海防艇 coastal defence boat;
核潛艇 nuclear-powered submarine;
護衛艇 corvette; escort; vessel;
划艇 canoe; pulling-boat; rowboat;
艦艇 naval craft; naval ships and boats; naval vessels;
警戒艇 guard boat;
救生艇 lifeboat;
快艇 high speed boat; motor boat; speedboat;
獵潛艇 submarine chaser;
砲艇 gunboat;
汽艇 motor boat;
潛艇 submarine;
潛水艇 submarine;
賽艇 racing boat; row; run a boat race; shell;
掃雷艇 minesweeper;
橡皮艇 pneumatic boat; rubber dinghy;
巡邏艇 patrol boat;
遊艇 pleasure boat; yacht;
魚雷艇 torpedo boat;

ting

【鋌】 run quickly; rush;

[鋌刺] stick;

[鋌而走險] embark on a reckless adventure; like an animal at bay; make a reckless move; rush into danger;

ting⁴
ting

【聽】 (1) let; (2) comply with; submit to; (3) govern; manage; rule; (4) judge and decide;

[聽便] as one pleases; please yourself;

[聽斷] pass judgment after hearing the case;

[聽命] at sb's command; follow orders; take orders from;
聽命於人 be at someone's service;
俯首聽命 at sb's beck and call; be submission; bend one's neck; bow down to obey submissively; obey sb's order with all due submission; obey with bent head; submissively hear and obey;
唯唯聽命 murmur one's assent;

[聽憑] allow; let;

[聽任] allow; leave free; let; let sb do whatever he likes;
聽任擺布 at sb's disposal; leave free; let alone; submit to any arrangement others have made for oneself; wax in sb's hands;
聽任宰割 place oneself at the mercy of;
聽任自便 consult one's own convenience;
聽之任之 allow...to continue; leave alone; let...go unchecked; let matters drift; let sb have his own way; let things go hang; take a laissez-faire attitude;

[聽使] (1) convenient; suitable for use; (2)

T

await instructions and be ready for errands;

[聽訟] serve as a judge in a lawsuit;

[聽天] submit to the will of Heaven;

聽天安命 accept the situation;

聽天由命 abandon oneself to one's fate; abide by the will of Heaven; abide one's destiny; abide one's fate; accept the situation; at the mercy of nature; bow to the inevitable; leave things to chance; resign oneself to one's fate; submit to the will of Heaven; trust to chance; trust to Providence; turn one's face to the wall;

[聽政] administer; govern; hold court; rule;

tong¹

tong

【恫】 pain;

tong

【通】 (1) open; through; (2) open up; (3) go to; lead to; reach; (4) connect; communicate; (5) notify; tell; (6) know; understand; (7) authority; expert; (8) coherent; logical; (9) common; general; popular; (10) all; general; overall; throughout; whole;

[通報] (1) circulate a notice; (2) circular; (3) bulletin; journal; (4) brief; give information with; share information with;

通報表揚 circulate a notice of commendation;

[通便] facilitate bowel movement; purging; relief of constipation;

通便劑 cathartic; laxative;

[通病] common deficiencies; common failings; common faults; common ills;

[通才] general talent; universal genius; versatile scholar; all-round person;

通才教育 liberal education;

[通常] as a rule; generally; normal; ordinarily; usual;

通常情況下 under normal conditions;

[通暢] (1) easy to read; highly readable; smooth; (2) passing freely;

[通車] (1) open to traffic; (2) have transport service;

[通徹] understand thoroughly;

[通稱] (1) be generally called; be general known as; so called; (2) common name; general term; popular name;

[通達] (1) understand clearly; (2) open to traffic; unobstructed; (3) lead to;

通達距離 distance range;

通達人情 understanding and considerate;

通達世情 be thoroughly acquainted with the worldly affairs; know the world; well acquainted with the ways of the world;

通達事理 understand ways of doing business;

七通八達 reach out in all directions;

四通八達 accessible from all directions; lead in all directions; open on all sides; open out on all sides; very advantageously located;

通權達變 act as the occasion requires; adapt to circumstances; adaptable to changing circumstances; capable of versatility; do as necessity demands; flexible; follow a flexible course of action;

[通帶] passband;

等效通帶 equivalent passband;

電路通帶 circuit passband;

輸入通帶 input passband;

[通道] aisle; avenue; channel; entryway; gallery; pass; passage; passageway; thoroughfare; tunnel;

抽氣通道 bleed-off passage;

地下通道 underpass;

公共通道 public corridor;

廣播通道 broadcast channel;

進入通道 access passage;

秘密通道 secret passage;

模擬通道 analogue channel;

人行道道 walkway;

色度通道 chromatic channel;

雙通道 binary channel;

運彈通道 ammunition passage;

中心通道 central passage;

[通敵] collude with the enemy; fraternize; have illicit relations with the enemy;

[通電] (1) cable all concerned; (2) link with the source of an electric current; supply electricity to;

[通牒] diplomatic note;

最後通牒 last warning;

發通牒 send diplomatic note;

[通都大邑] large city; metropolis; metropolitan city;

[通讀] (1) read through; (2) understand what one reads;

[通風] (1) air; ventilate; ventilation; (2) be well ventilated; (3) divulge information; tip-off;

通風報信 divulge secret information; furnish secret information; pass on information to; provide sb with information; send a secret message; send news secretly; tip sb off;

通風窗 ventilation window;

通風的 airy;

通風管道 ventilation duct;

通風機 ventilator;

~ 輔助通風機 auxiliary ventilator;

~ 離心通風機 centrifugal ventilator;

~ 天棚通風機 ceiling ventilator;

通風降溫 ventilation and cooling;

通風帽 cowl;

通風器 ventilator;

~ 風扇通風器 fan ventilator;

~ 自動通風器 automatic ventilator;

通風筒 ventilator;

~ 朝上通風筒 upcast ventilator;

~ 蘑菇形通風筒 mushroom ventilator;

通風裝置 ventilating arrangement;

車廂通風 car ventilation;

可調通風 adjustable ventilation;

空氣通風 air ventilation;

密不通風 (1) airtight; stuffy room without ventilation; (2) closely surrounded; heavily guarded;

讓房間通風 let the room air out;

人工通風 artificial ventilation;

鐵惢通風 core ventilation;

[通告] (1) announce; give public notice; (2) announcement; circular; circular note; public notice;

通告全國 let the public know;

官方通告 official announcement;

看看通告 read the public notice;

一個通告 an announcement;

一張通告 a notice;

正式通告 formal announcement;

[通功易事] division of labour; have an intercommunication of the production of labour and an interchange of one's services; interchange production and labour; share out the work and cooperate with one another; work in cooperation with a due division of labour;

[通共] altogether; all told; in all;

[通國] whole country; whole nation;

[通過] (1) get past; pass through; traverse; (2) adopt; carry; pass; (3) by; by means of; by way of; through; (4) ask the consent of;

通過稅 transit tax;

通過障礙物 break the barriers;

鼓掌通過 adopt by acclamation; approve by acclamation; take action by acclamation;

[通航] open to air traffic;

通航水域 navigable waters;

開始通航 open up navigation;

[通好] establish friendly relations; have friendly relations;

[通紅] flaming red; red through and through;

臉漲得通紅 blush scarlet; flush scarlet; go scarlet; turn scarlet;

[通話] (1) call; communicate by telephone; message; (2) converse; hold a conversation; talk with sb;

通話電纜 communication cable;

通話時間 call time; talk time;

[通婚] be related by marriage; intermarry;

異族通婚 mixed marriage;

[通貨] currency; current money;

通貨緊縮 deflation; disinflation;

通貨膨脹 currency inflation; inflation;

~ 通貨膨脹率 rate of inflation;

~ 長期通貨膨脹 chronic inflation;

~ 導致通貨膨脹 cause inflation; lead to inflation;

~ 抵制通貨膨脹 combat inflation; fight inflation;

~ 惡性通貨膨脹 boiling inflation;

~ 加劇通貨膨脹 fluel inflation; push up inflation;

~ 絕對通貨膨脹 absolute inflation;

~ 瓶頸式通貨膨脹 bottleneck inflation;

~ 失控的通貨膨脹 runaway inflation;

~ 調整性通貨膨脹 adjustment inflation;

~ 遏制通貨膨脹 check inflation; control inflation; curb inflation; curtail inflation;

本國通貨 domestic currency;

貶值通貨 depreciated currency;
存款通貨 deposit currency;
軟通貨 soft currency; soft money;
收縮通貨 deflation of currency;
信用通貨 credit currency;
硬通貨 hard currency; hard money;
銀行通貨 bank currency;
增值通貨 currency;
資產通貨 assets currency;

[通緝] list as wanted; order the arrest of a criminal at large;
通緝犯 a criminal wanted by the law;
~頭號通緝犯 the most wanted man;
通緝令 wanted circular;
被警察當局通緝 be wanted by the police;
下令通緝 issue a wanted circular;

[通姦] adulteration; adulterate; adultery; commit adultery; fornication; illicit intercourse;
通姦者 adulterator;

[通解] general solution;

[通覽] overall view of a situation;
通覽全局 see the whole aspect of sth;

[通例] common practice; general rules; usual practice;

[通力] concerted effort;
通力合作 act with united strength; cooperate fully; cooperate with a common effort; everybody pitching in for common work; give full cooperation to; make a concerted effort; pool together efforts; pull together; the full cooperation;

[通連] be connected; lead to;

[通聯] communications and connections;

[通亮] brightly lit up; well-illuminated;
火光通亮 the flames lit up brightly;

[通量] flux;
磁通量 magnetic flux;
電通量 electric flux;

[通令] (1) issue a general order; (2) general order;
通令各省 issue a general order to all provinces;
通令嘉奬 issue an order of commendation;

[通路] access; highway; passage; route; thoroughfare;
全天候通路 all-weather access;

[通論] (1) sensible argument; (2) general survey; introduction;

[通名] identify oneself; introduce to each other;

[通明] ablaze; brightly lit; well-illuminated;
燈火通明 ablaze with lights; be brightly lit;
一片通明 in a blaze;
照得通明 be lighted up;

[通謀] conspire;

[通年] all the year round; the whole year; throughout the year;

[通盤] all-round; comprehensive; entire; overall;
通盤安排 comprehensive arrangement;
通盤籌劃 calculate the whole lot at once; draw up an all-round scheme — a complete plan; make a general estimate;
通盤估計 all-round estimate;
通盤合作 over-all collaboration;
通盤計劃 overall plan;
通盤考慮 consider every possible angle; take all things into consideration;

[通氣] exchange information;
互不通氣 not exchange information;

[通情] reasonable; understanding and considerate;
通情達理 common sense; good judgement; gumption; have the grace to; ordinary sense; reasonable; reasonable and fair; sensible; show common sense; show good sense; sound sense; stand to reason; stand to sense; understanding and reasonable; use reason;
淳和通情 agreeable and reasonable;

[通衢] highway; main road; thoroughfare; towngate;

[通人] person of wide knowledge and sound scholarship;
通人達才 erudite and informed people; people of wide reading and great ability; people well versed in ancient and modern;

[通日] all day long;

[通融] (1) get around regulations; make an exception in sb's favour; stretch rules; (2) accommodate sb with a short-term loan;
通融辦理 stretch a point;

[通儒] erudite scholar; person of great

learning and practical sense;

[通商] commercial intercourse; have trade relations; trade;

通商口岸 commercial port; trading port;

通商條約 trade treaty;

[通身] all over the body; on the whole body;

[通神] capable of buying the gods;

財能通神 money can move the gods; ready money is Aladdin's lamp;

錢可通神 if one has money, one may associate with the gods; money can do everything; money can move the gods; money makes the mare go; money talks; money will move the gods; who holds the purse rules the house;

錢能通神 all things are obedient to money; money makes the mare go; money makes the world go round;

[通史] comprehensive history; general history;

[通事] (1) interpreter; (2) diplomatic affairs; official intercourse between two states;

通事達理 understand human affairs; understand the principles which underlie human affairs; understand things; understanding and amenable to reason;

[通書] almanac; calendar;

[通順] clear and coherent; fluent; smooth;

文理通順 coherent writing;

[通俗] common; popular;

通俗的 demotic;

通俗讀物 books for popular consumption;

通俗分類 folk taxonomy;

通俗歌曲 popular song;

通俗化 popularize;

通俗科學 popular science;

通俗上口 easily accepted among the people; easy to sing;

通俗文化 pop culture; popular culture;

通俗文學 popular literature;

通俗小說 popular fiction;

通俗易懂 popular and easy to understand;

[通天] (1) direct access to the highest authorities; (2) exceedingly high;

通天本領 exceptional ability; superhuman skill;

通天人物 people with connections to high-ranking leaders;

手眼通天 exceptionally adept in trickery;

[通通] altogether; completely; entirely; wholly; without exception;

[通同] collude; gang up; in common;

通同舞弊 ally in evil; collude in cheating; join together in practising fraud;

通同作弊 act fraudulently in collusion with sb; collude in cheating; collude in evildoing; gang up to cheat; in collusion over corrupt practices; work together in illegal transactions;

[通統] all; without exception;

[通透] understand thoroughly;

[通途] thoroughfare;

[通脫] open-minded; unconventional;

通脫不羈 free from petty formalisms and unrestrained;

通脫之才 person of unconventional wit;

[通向] lead to;

[通宵] all night; the whole night; throughout the night;

通宵達旦 all night long; all night till dawn; all the night through; all through the night; throughout the night; throughout the night until dawn; till daybreak; work round the clock; work through the night;

通宵工作的人 all-nighter;

通宵沒睡 long night;

通宵值班 on duty all night;

[通曉] familiar with; have a good knowledge; thoroughly understand; understand;

通曉世故 perfectly familiar with the ways of the world;

通曉事理 thoroughly understand the reason;

通曉一行，走遍天下 who hath a good trade through all waters may make;

通曉英文 understand English;

[通心粉] macaroni;

粗通心粉 cannelloni;

乾酪通心粉 macaroni cheese;

[通信] communicate by letter; correspond; telecommunication;

通信鴿 carrier pigeon; homing pigeon;

通信技術 communication technology

~ 通信技術衛星 communication technology satellite;

~ 通信技術現代化 modernization of communication technology;

通信媒體 transmission media;

通信軟件 communications software;

通信設備 communication equipment;

T

~安全通信設備 safety communication equipment;
通信網絡 communication network;
通信衛星 communications satellite;
~通信衛星系統 communications satellite system;
通信信息 communication information;
通信員 (1) correspondent; dispatch rider; messenger; (2) radioman;
~飛行通信員 flight radioman;
二級飛行通信員 second-grade flight radioman;
三級飛行通信員 third-grade flight radioman;
四級飛行通信員 foruth-grade flight radioman;
一級飛行通信員 first-grade flight radioman;
通信中心 communication centre;
通信終端 communication terminal;
單工通信 simplex communication;
多路通信 multiple telecommunication;
航空導航通信 aeronautical telecommunication;
互相通信 write to each other;
有線通信 wired telecommunication;

[通行] (1) go through; pass through; travel through; (2) current; general;
通行車道 through lanes;
通行無阻 accessible to public; go everywhere without obstruction; open thoroughfare;
通行性 generality;
~通行性程度 degree of generality;
~通行性量表 scale of generality;
通行證 pass; safe conduct;
~安全通行證 safe conduct;
~獲得成功的通行證 passport to success;
安全通行 safe conduct; safe passage;
路不通行 no thoroughfare;
停止通行 be closed to traffic;
自由通行 have free passage;

[通性] common characteristics;

[通訊] (1) communication; correspondence; (2) news dispatch; news report; newsletter;
通訊錄 address book;
通訊社 news agency; news service;
通訊手段 means of communication;
即時通訊 instant messaging;
~即時通訊服務 instant messaging services;
無線電通訊 wireless;
無線通訊 wireless communications;

[通夜] all night; the whole night;
通夜不眠 lie awake all night;
通夜思索 consult one's pillow all night;

[通譯] (1) translate; (2) interpret;

[通用] be used universally; current; in common use;
通用操作系統 common operating system;
通用程序 common programme;
通用飛機 general purpose aircraft;
通用匯編程序 general assembly programme;
通用匯編語言 general assembly language;
通用貨幣 current money;
通用集裝箱 general purpose container;
通用計算機 general purpose computer;
通用商品代碼 universal product code;
通用審計 generalized audit;
~通用審計程序 generalized computer audit programme;
~通用審計軟件 generalized audit software;
通用軟件 general purpose software;
通用英語 English for General Purposes;
通用語言 lingua franca; universal language;
通用中文 universal Chinese;
通用終端 general purpose terminal;

[通則] general principle;

[通知] dispatch a notice; give notice; inform of; let one know; make sth known; notify; send a circular; send sb the news;
通知單 advice note; notification slip;
~經紀人通知單 broker's advice;
通知書 advice;
~承兑通知書 accepted bill of advice;
~電話通知書 telephonic advice;
~發貨通知書 shipping advice;
~損失通知書 loss advice;
~修改通知書 amendment advice;
按照通知 as per advice;
到貨通知 advice of arrival;
電報通知 cable advice;
匯款通知 remittance advice; remittance note;
確切通知 definite advice;
行車通知 traffic advice;
一份通知 a notice; an announcement;

一批通知 a batch of circulars;
預先通知 give advance notice;
裝運通知 shipment advice;

百事通 know-all
變通 accommodate sth to circumstances; adapt oneself to circumstances; flexible;
博通 erudite; have a broad knowledge of;
不通 (1) be blocked up; be obstructed; impassable; (2) do not make sense; ungrammatical; illogical;
暢通 unblocked; unimpeded;
串通 collaborate; collude; collude with; collusion; complicity; conspire with; gang up; in collusion with; work hand in glove with;
粗通 know a little about;
打通 break through; open up;
共通 applicable to both or all;
勾通 collaborate; collude with;
溝通 link up;
貫通 (1) be well versed in; have a thorough knowledge of; (2) link up; thread together;
亨通 (1) be prosperous; (2) go smoothly;
紅通通 bright red; glowing;
互通 interflow;
會通 master; understand thoroughly;
交通 (1) communicate; (2) associate with; (1) liaison; (2) liaison man; (3) communications; traffic;
精通 be proficient in; be well versed in;
卡通 (1) animated cartoon; (2) cartoon;
開通 dredge; enlightened; liberal; obstacle from; open-minded; remove;
連通 be connected; lead to;
靈通 well-informed;
流通 (1) circulate; float about; (2) (of money, commodities) circulate;
買通 bribe; buy over;
眠爾通 miltown;
木通 akebi;
撲通 flop; pit-a-pat; splash; thump;
普通 common; ordinary;
清通 (of writings) clear and coherent; smooth;
三通 tee; tee joint;
深通 be proficient in; have a good command of; master;
神通 remarkable ability supernatural power;
疏通 (1) dredge; (2) ease misunderstandings; (3) mediate between two parties;
私通 (1) have illicit intercourse; (2) have secret communication with;
通通 all; completely; entirely;
萬事通 know-all;
相通 be interlinked; communicate with each other;
圓通 accommodating; flexible;
中國通 old China hand; Sinologue;

tong²

tong

【仝】 (1) same as 同 ; (2) a surname;

tong

【同】 (1) alike; equal; identical; in common; same; similar; the same as; (2) together; (3) agree; share; (4) and; with;

［同案］ codefendant;
同案犯 accomplice;

［同班］ (1) in the same class; (2) classmate;
同班同學 classmate;

［同伴］ companion;

［同胞］ (1) compatriot; countryman; fellow countryman; (2) born of the same parents;
同胞手足 born of the same parents;
同胞兄弟 full brothers;
同胞姊妹 full sisters;
港澳同胞 compatriots in Hong Kong and Macao;

［同輩］ fellow; peer; of the same generation; one's equal;

［同病相憐］ adversity makes strange bedfellows; fellow sufferers have mutual sympathy; misery makes strange bedfellows; fellow sufferers have mutual sympathy; fellow sufferers sympathize with each other; misery loves company; people similarly afflicted fall pity for one another; people with the same trouble having sth in common; persons afflicted with a similar ailment sympathize with each other; poverty makes strange bedfellows; similarly afflicted people pity each other; sufferers of the same illness sympathize one another; those who have the same complaint sympathize with each other;

［同步］ synchronization; synchronize;

T

synchronizing; synchronous;
同步傳輸 synchronous transmission;
同步光纜網 synchronous optical network;
同步軌道 geostationary orbit;
同步計算機 synchronous computer;
同步器 synchronizer;
~ 頻道同步器 channel synchronizer;
~ 自動同步器 automatic synchronizer;
同步通信 synchronous communication;
同步網絡 synchronous network;
同步衛星 synchronous satellite;
同步效果 synchronicity;
同步增長 increase simultaneously;
同步轉移 synchronous transfer;
同步裝置 synchronizer;
不同步 asynchronous;
~ 不同步性 asynchronism; asynchronization;
彩色同步 colour synchronization;
垂直同步 vertical hold;
後沿同步 after-edge synchronization;
交變同步 alternate synchronizing;
強制同步 forced synchronizing;
人工同步 manual synchronizing;
水平同步 horizontal hold;
信道同步 channel synchronization;
行同步 line hold;
載頻同步 carrier-frequency synchronization;
自動同步 automatic synchronization;

[同儕] same generation;

[同仇敵慨] a common danger causes common action; be filled with hatred for their common enemy; bound by a common hatred for the enemy; face the common enemy with the same bitter hatred; hate the same enemy; share a bitter hatred of the enemy; treat sb as a common enemy;

[同窗] classmate; schoolmate;
同窗友情 friendship as schoolmate;
同窗之誼 friendship among fellow students;

[同牀] share the same bed;
同牀共枕 share the same bed and the same pillow; sleep on the same couch;
同牀異夢 sleep in the same bed but dream different dreams; strange bedfellows;

[同詞] identical word;
同詞法 word equivalence;
同詞翻譯法 word equivalence;
同詞異譯法 diverse rendering of the identical word;

[同黨] (1) of the same party; (2) member of the same party;

[同道] (1) people engaged in the same pursuit; (2) people with the same ideals;
同道為友 their friendship grows out of common ideals;
同道中人 people of the same line;

[同等] of the same class; of the same rank; of the same status; on an equal footing; parity;
同等對待 put on an equal footing;
同等學歷 on the same education level;
同等重要 of equal importance;
同等組 peer group;

[同隊] of the same team;
同隊隊員 teammate;

[同惡相濟] aid and abet each other in wrongdoings; conspire with sb in illegal acts; evildoer collude with each other; league together for some evil end; take part in a conspiracy with sb; the wicked help the wicked;

[同房] (1) of the same branch of a family; (2) have sexual intercourse; sleep together; (3) share the same room;

[同感] consensus; empathy; sympathy; the same feeling;
深有同感 fully agree; have the same feeling;

[同庚] of the same age;
同庚同時 be born on the same date;

[同根] of the same root;
同根同心 of the same root and of the same mind;

[同工] (1) equal work; (2) equal skill;
同工同酬 equal pay for equal work; get the same pay for the same joy; receive the same pay as others doing the same work;
同工異曲 different tunes render with equal skill;

[同構] isomorphism;
代數同構 algebraic isomorphism;
解析同構 analytic isomorphism;
容許同構 admissible isomorphism;

[同歸] reach the same goal;
同歸於盡 all come to an end; all perish together; end up in common ruin; get

killed at one and the same time; perish together;
殊途同歸 all roads lead to Rome; arrive at the same end by different means; converge with; different roads lead to the same goal; end up in the same way; reach the same destination by different routes; reach the same goal by different means; the different roads all reach the same end;

[同行] (1) in the same line; in the same occupation; in the same trade; (2) people of the same trade or occupation;
同行嫉妒 professional jealousy; two of a trade are always jealous of each other; two of a trade seldom agree;
同行是冤家 the herringman hates the fisherman; two of a trade never agree;
大家是同行 we are in the same trade;

[同好] people with the same hobby;

[同化] assimilate; assimilation;
不易同化 do not readily assimilate;
部份同化 accommodation;
局部同化 partial assimilation;
逆同化 regressive assimilation;
順同化 progressive assimilation;

[同伙] (1) collude with; work in partnership; (2) associate; confederate; partner;

[同夥] cohort;

[同居] cohabit; cohabitation; live together; shack up with;
同居分爨 live in the same house, but eat separately; live under the same roof but have separate kitchens;
同居男朋友 live-in boyfriend;
同居女朋友 live-in girlfriend;
同居情人 live-in lover;
同居試婚制 cohabitation as trial marriage;
同居者 domestic partner;
非法同居 illicit cohabitation;

[同樂] share happiness with others;
與民同樂 enjoy with the people; make merry with the people; rejoice together with the people; share the happiness with the people;
與眾同樂，其樂更樂 joys shared with others are more enjoyed;

[同類] of the same kind; similar;
同類不相殘 crows are smart enough not to peck out each other's eyes; crows will not pick out crows' eyes; dog does not eat dog; hawks will not pick out hawks' eyes;
同類產品 similar products;
同類相殘 kill one's own kind;
同類相知 like knows like;

[同量] of the same amount; of the same quantity;

[同僚] co-worker; colleague;

[同齡] contemporary; peer;
同齡群 peer group;
同齡人 contemporary; peer;
~同齡人壓力 peer pressure;

[同流合污] associate oneself with undesirable elements; associate with an evil person; associate with evil elements; follow the bad example of others; foul one's hands with; go along with sb in his evil deeds; go with the stream; in collusion; join in the courses of the vicious and unite in their bad practices; join with the vicious; soil one's hands with;

[同路] go the same way;
同路人 fellow traveller;

[同倫] homotopy;
胞腔式同倫 cellular homotopy;
代數同倫 algebraic homotopy;
鏈同倫 chain homotopy;
收縮同倫 contracting homotopy;

[同門] fellow disciple;
同門異戶 hold the same views with minor differences;

[同盟] confederacy; confederation; league; alliance;
同盟罷工 joint strike;
同盟國 allied nations;
同盟條約 treaty of alliance;
防務同盟 defensive alliance;
~締結防務同盟 enter into a defensive alliance;
結成同盟 enter into an alliance; form an alliance;
經濟同盟 economical alliance;
軍事同盟 military alliance;
兩國同盟 dual alliance;
三國同盟 triple alliance;
四國同盟 quadruple alliance;

[同名] homonym; namesake; synonym; of the same given name;
同名同姓 of the same surname and given name;

T

同名異姓 with the same first name but with different surnames;

[同命] share the same destiny; under the influence of the same stars;

[同謀] (1) conspire; conspire with sb; (2) accomplice; confederate; conspirator;

[同年] (1) of the same year; (2) of an age; of the same age;
他們都是同年 they are of an age;

[同袍] (1) comrades in arms; (2) share the same robes with;
同袍同澤 comrades in the same army; fellow fighters;

[同胚] homemorphism;
等度連續同胚 equicontinuous homeomorphism;
解析同胚 analytic homeomorphism;
微分同胚 differentiable homeomorphism;
相對同胚 relative homeomorphism;

[同情] bleed for sb; commiserate; commiseration; compassion; empathy; feel pity for; feel sympathetic with; have pity for; have pity on; have sympathy for; have sympathy for; in sympathy with; one's heart bleeds for sb; show compassion for; show sympathy for; sympathetic with; sympathize with; take compassion on; take compassion upon; take pity on;
同情疲勞症 compassion fatigue;
同情心 fellow feeling; sympathy;
表同情 commiserate; express one's sympathy;
~ 表示同情 commiserate; express one's sympathy; offer one's sympathy;
~ 深表同情 express deep sympathy; show deep sympathy for; sympathize with someone from the bottom of one's heart;
博得同情 win sympathy;
博取同情 enlist sb's sympathy; seek sb's sympathy; win sympathy;
出於同情 on compassionate grounds;
感到同情 feel sympathy for sb; have sympathy for sb;
假同情 spurious sympathy;
滿腔同情 brim over with sympathy;
值得同情 deserve sympathy;

[同慶] celebrate together; universal celebration;
普天同慶 the whole nation joins in jubilation; the whole world joins in congratulations; universal celebration; universal joy;

[同仁] colleague; fellow member;

[同日而語] mention at the same time; mention in equal terms; mention in the same breath; name in the same day;

[同聲] (1) speak simultaneously; (2) with the same voice;
同聲傳譯 simultaneous interpretation;
同聲歌頌 praise with the same voice;
同聲相應 act in unison;
~ 同聲相應，同氣相求 like attracts like; like calls to like; like dras to like; like to like; like will to like; similar sounds echo one another, and the same odour merge together — people of an inclination fall into the same group;
同聲一哭 share the same feeling of grief;
齊口同聲 say in unison;
異口同聲 cry out in one voice; in unanimous agreement; in unison; join in the chorus of; sing the same tune in different keys; speak with one voice; unanimously; with one accord; with one voice;

[同時] all at once; all together; and; at once; at one fell; at one swoop; at one time; at the same time; in the meantime; in the same breath; meanwhile; moreover; simultaneously;
同時並進 develop simultaneously; go hand in hand with;
同時並舉 develop…and…; simultaneously; start…at the same time;
同時並重 receive equal and simultaneous emphasis;
同時存在 exist side by side; exist simultaneously;
同時發生 happen at the same time;
與此同時 at the same time; coincident; concurrent; in the meantime; meanwhile; simultaneously;

[同事] colleague; co-worker; fellow worker; mate;
老同事 old colleague;
新同事 new colleague;

[同素異形] allotropy;
同素異形體 allomorph; allotrope;

[同歲] of the same age;
[同榻] share a bed;
[同態] homomorphism;
代數同態 algebra homomorphism;
解析同態 analytic homomorphism;
容許同態 admissible homomorphism; allowed homomorphism;
[同堂] (1) of the same paternal grandfather; (2) live under the same roof;
同堂兄弟 male cousins with the same paternal grandfather;
四世同堂 four generations under one roof;
五代同堂 have five generations of a family living under the same roof;
五世同堂 a family of five generations gathered together in the hall; a family with five generations under the same roof; five generations are alive at the same time;
[同位] apposition;
同位從句 appositive clause;
同位聯加語 conjunct of apposition;
同位生格 appositive genitive;
同位素 isotope;
~同位素標記法 isotope labelling method;
~同位素分離 isotope separation;
~同位素量 isotopic weight;
~同位素學 isotopy;
~放射性同位素 radioisotope;
~濃縮同位素 enriched isotope;
~碳同位素 carbon isotope;
~子同位素 daughter isotope;
同位義項 co-hyponym;
同位音 allophone;
同位語 apposition; appositive;
~同位語從句 appositive clause;
~賓格同位語 objective appositive;
~從屬同位語 subordinate apposition;
同位指示語 indicator of apposition;
緊密同位 close apposition;
[同文同種] of the same language and race;
[同物相醫] like cures like;
[同喜] good luck for us all; thank you for your congratulation;
[同系物] homologue;
低級同系物 lower homologue;
對數同系物 logarithmic homologue;
高級同系物 higher homologue;
核同系物 nuclear homologue;
正同系物 normal homologue;
[同鄉] countryman; fellow provincial; fellow townsman; fellow villager; homeboy; home girl; homey;
[同心] (1) be united at heart; be united in common purpose; with one heart; (2) concentric; homocentric;
同心幹 fight as one man; work with one heart;
同心同德 be dedicated to the same cause; dedicate ourselves heart and soul to the same cause; of one heart and one mind; of one mind; with one heart and one mind;
同心協力 hang together; have one heart to help each other; make a united effort; make concerted efforts; of one mind; pull together; shoulder to shoulder; unite in a concerted effort; unite in spirit and action; with concerted effort; with united strength; work in concert with sb; work in cooperation; work in full cooperation and with unity of purpose; work together with one heart;
同心圓 concentric circles;
合力同心 make a united effort; unite in a concerted effort; with concerted effort; work in full co-operation and with unity of purpose; work together with one will;
戮力同心 all exert themselves as one person; all work with a singleness of purpose and unity of effort; make concerted efforts; of one mind; pull together and work hard as a team; unite in a concerted effort; work together in a coalition;
協力同心 all of one mind; cooperate with one heart; make concerted efforts; of one heart; unite together in a common effort; with one heart; work as one man; work in full cooperation and with unity of purpose;
[同形] homotype;
同形異義詞 homograph;
同形異義語 homonymous expression;
同形異音異義詞 heteronym;
[同性] (1) of the same sex; (2) of the same nature; (3) isomorphism;
同性伴侶 same-sex couple;
同性關係 same-sex relationship;
同性戀 homosex; homosexual; homosexuality;

T

~同性戀關係 homosexual relationship;
~同性戀婚姻 same-sex marriage;
~同性戀女人 lesbian; lipstick lesbian;
搞同性戀女人 dike;
~同性戀群體 gay community;
~同性戀者 gay; homosexual; shirt-lifter;
同性戀者酒吧 gay bar;
男同性戀者 backdoor man; brown hatter; bum boy; bum chum; fag; faggot; fruit; gay; ginger; homo; horse's hoof; inspector of manholes; jeanie-boy; jeer; jessie; King Lear; lavender; limp-wrist; male homosexual; pansy; pillow-biter; pineapple; piss-hole bandit; ponce; poof; pooftah; poofter; poove; pouffe; puff; queer; raging queer; shirt-lifter; sod; tickle-you-fancy; tinkerbelle; turd-burglar; woofter;
女同性戀者 dike; dyke; goose girl; les; lesbian; leso; lezo; lezzie; lizzie;

[同姓] of the same surname;

[同學] classmate; co-disciple; fellow student; school chum; schoolmate;
同學會 alumni association;
老同學 old school chum; old school friend; old schoolmates;

[同樣] (1) as...as; equal; same; similar; (2) in the same way; likewise; similarly;
同樣地 by the same token; likewise;
也同樣 likewise;

[同業] (1) of the same trade or business; (2) people of the same trade;
同業公會 guild; trade union;
同業聯盟 cartel;
同業相軋 one potter envies another; the potter envies the potter; two of a trade are always jealous of each other; two of a trade never agree;

[同一] identical; the same;
同一鼻孔出氣 breathe through the same nostrils; in tune with; talk exactly one like the other;

[同義] synonymous;
同義重覆 tautology;
~句法同義重覆 syntactic tautology;
同義詞 synonym;
~半同義詞 semi-synonym;
~代詞同義詞 pronominal synonym;
~絕對同義詞 absolute synonym;
同義關係 synonymy;

[同異] similarities and differences;
求同存異 put aside differences to seek common ground; seek common ground while accepting the existing differences; seek common ground while reserving differences;

[同意] access; accede to; accession; agree; agreement; agree to; agree with; approve; approve of; assent to; assentation; by agreement; come along; comply with; concur; consent; consent to; cotton to; fall in with; go along with; go with; hold with; in agreement with; in favour of; say amen to; see eye to eye with; see with;
同意書 agreement; letter of agreement;
~不煩擾同意書 nondisturbance agreement;
同意要求 accede to a request;
同意者 assentient;
表示同意 express approval; indicate one's approval;
不同意 disagree; without one's consent;
點頭同意 agree with a nod; nod in agreement; show approval by nodding;
恕不同意 beg to differ;
雙方同意 by mutual consent;
一致同意 by common consent; unanimously agree; with one assent;
~經一致同意 by common consent;

[同音] homophone;
同音同形異義詞 homonym;
同音異義詞 homophone;
同音異義雙關語 paronomasia;
笙磬同音 get on well with each other; in perfect harmony; live in harmony;

[同語雙敍] syllepsis;

[同源] of the same origin;
同源賓語 cognate object;
同源詞 cognate word;
~同源詞並列 paregmenon;
同源的 cognate;
同源關係 affinity;
同源模型 homology model;
同源語言 cognate language;
甲語言與乙語言同源 A language is akin to B language;

[同志] comrade;

[同舟] in the same boat;
同舟共濟 aid each other; hang together;

in fair weather or in foul; in the same boat; people in the same boat help each other; pull together to tide over difficulties; row in the same boat; sail in the same boat; sail on the same tack; two in distress make trouble less;
吳越同舟 even mortal enemies should help each other in the face of common danger;

[同種] of the same race;
同種同文 of a common racial stock and culture;

[同住] live together;
和母親同住 abide with one's mother;

[同宗] (1) clansman; (2) have common ancestry; of the same clan;

[同族] of the same clan;

伴同 accompany;
幫同 assist; help;
不同 different; disparity; distinct; diverse; imparity; not alike;
大同 Great Harmony;
等同 be equal to; equate;
共同 (1) common; (2) jointly; together;
苟同 agree without giving serious thought; readily subscribe to (sb's view);
會同 (handle an affair) jointly with other organizations concerned;
混同 confuse; mix up;
伙同 gang up with sb; in collusion with; in league with; work in collusion with; work in league with;
夥同 gang up with; in league with;
雷同 (1) echo what others have said; (2) identical; same;
連同 along with; together with;
陪同 accompany; keep company;
如同 as; like;
隨同 be in company with;
通同 collude; gang up;
相同 identical; same;
協同 cooperate with; work in coordination with;
偕同 along with; in the company;
一同 at the same time and place; together;
異同 (1) difference and similarities; (2) dissent; objection;
約同 invite sb and go together with him/her;
贊同 agree with; approve of;

tong
【彤】 (1) red; vermilion; (2) name of an ancient state;

[彤弓] crimson bow;

[彤闈] imperial palace;

[彤雲] red clouds;
彤雲密佈 the sky is filled with thick clouds;

tong
【佟】 a surname;

tong
【峒】 (1) a mountain in Gansu; (2) a tribe in Guangxi and Guizhou;

tong
【桐】 (1) paulownia; (2) a surname;

[桐樹] tung tree;

[桐葉] leaves of a paulownia;

[桐油] tung oil;
桐油紙 oilpaper;

珙桐 dove tree;
泡桐 paulownia;
梧桐 Chinese parasol (tree);
油桐 tung oil tree; tung tree;
罌子桐 tung oil tree; tung tree (Aleurites fordii);

tong
【茼】 a kind of green vegetable;

[茼蒿] crown daisy chrysanthemum;

tong
【童】 (1) child; minor; (2) virgin; (3) unmarried; (4) page; page boy; (5) bald; bare; (6) a surname;

[童工] (1) child labourer; (2) child labour;
做童工 as a child labourer;

[童花式] (of hairstyle) pageboy style;

[童話] children's story; fairy tale; juvenile story;
童話片 fairy film; film adapted from a fairy tale;
一則童話 a fairy tale;

[童昏] naive and ignorant; young and ignorant;

[童婚] child marriage;

[童戀] calf love;

[童蒙] (1) childish ignorance; (2) ignorant children;

[童男] virgin boy;
童男童女 young boys and girls;

[童年] childhood; youth;
童年時代 cap and feather days; childhood;

T

童年之交 boyhood chum; childhood friend;
快樂的童年 one's happy childhood;

[童女] maiden; virgin;

[童僕] boy; boy servant;

[童山] bare hills;
童山禿嶺 bare hills and mountains;
童山濯濯 bare and barren hills; hills denuded of vegetation; treeless hills;

[童聲] child's voice;
童聲合唱 children's chorus;

[童叟] children and elderly people;
童叟無欺 no imposition on the young and the old;
黃童白叟 young and old;

[童心] childish heart; childishness; childlike innocence;
童心未泯 retain a childish heart; take no offense at a child's babble;
猶有童心 aged person with a youthful heart; feel oneself young though aged;

[童星] child star; underage film star;

[童言無忌] a child says what he/she thinks; take no offense at child's babble;

[童顏] ruddy complexion and hoary head;
童顏皓首 ruddy complexion and hoary head;
童顏鶴髮 have white hair and a ruddy complexion;

[童養媳] child bride;

[童謠] children's folk rhymes; nursery songs;

[童貞] chastity; virginity;
失去童貞 lose one's virginity;
~使失去童貞 deflower;

[童裝] children's garments;

[童子] boy; child; kid; lad; minor;
童子軍 scout;
~童子軍活動 scouting;
~童子軍領隊 scoutmaster;
~男童子軍 boy scout;
~女童子軍 girl scout;

報童 newsboy; newspaper delivery boy; newsy; paperboy;
兒童 children;
孩童 child;
家童 boy servant;
金童 golden boy;
孌童 catamite;
牧童 buffalo boy; cow boy; shepherd boy;
神童 boy of remarkable aptitude; child prodigy; quiz kid; whiz kid; whizzkid; wonder boy;
書童 boy serving in a scholar's study;
頑童 naughty child; urchin;
仙童 fairy messenger boy;
小童 child;
鞋童 shoeshine boy;
學童 school child; school children;
幼童 young child;

tong
【筩】 (1) bamboo pipe; (2) hook for fishing;

tong
【酮】 ketone;

[酮胺] ketoamine;

[酮醇] ketol;

[酮化] ketonize;

[酮酶] ketolase;

[酮醛] keto-aldehyde;

[酮酸] ketonic acid;

[酮糖] ketose;
阿拉伯酮糖 araboketose; arabulose;

[酮體] acetone; ketone body;

安眠酮 hyminal; methaqualone;
丙酮 acetone;
薄荷酮 menthone;
硅酮 silicone;
黃体酮 progesterone;
甲睾酮 methyl-testosterone;
氯噻酮 chlorthalidone;
魚藤酮 rotenone;

tong
【僮】 (1) boy; (2) servant; (3) a surname;

tong
【銅】 (1) brass; (2) bronze; (3) copper;

[銅板] copper coin;
銅板切豆腐—兩面光 a bean curd knife is sharp on both sides (metaphorically, a fence-sitter);

[銅版] copperplate;
銅版畫 copperplate engraving;

[銅幣] copper coin;

[銅臭] the stench of money; the stink of money;
銅臭熏天 copper smell stinking to high heaven;
滿身銅臭 filthy rich; stinking with money;
一身銅臭 the whole body smells of copper;

［銅佛］ brazen Buddha;
一尊銅佛 a brazen image of Buddha;
［銅鼓］ bronze drum;
［銅管］ (1) steel tube; (2) brass;
銅管椅 steel-tube chair;
銅管樂隊 brass band;
銅管樂器 brass wind; brass-wind instruments;
［銅匠］ coppersmith;
［銅鏡］ copper mirror;
［銅綠］ patina;
［銅牌］ bronze medal; copper medal;
［銅錢］ copper coin;
［銅人］ bronze image; bronze statue;
［銅絲］ copper wire;
［銅鐵］ iron and steel;
銅筋鐵骨 iron constitution; brass muscles and iron bones; strong and solid body; tough and strong as iron and steel; with vigorous sines and bones and strengthened muscles;
銅盔鐵甲 brass helmet and iron armour – uniform of ancient warriors;
銅牆鐵壁 a bastion of iron; a stronghold; a wall of bronze; iron wall; tower of strength;
銅頭鐵額 courageous and cruel;
［銅像］ bronze image; bronze statue;
一座銅像 a bronze statue;
［銅鏽］ patina;
［銅元］ copper coin;

白銅 copper nickel alloy;
冰銅 matte;
沉淀銅 cement copper;
沉積銅 deposited copper;
電解銅 cathode copper; electrolytic copper;
紅銅 (1) red copper; (2) copper-tin-zinc-lead alloy;
黃銅 brass; yellow metal;
聚結銅 coalesced copper;
康銅 constantan;
冷拉銅 cold-drawn copper;
硫酸銅 cupric sulphate;
鋁銅 aluminium bronze;
砲銅 gun metal;
青銅 bronze;
熟銅 wrought copper;
乙酸銅 cupric acetate;
溴化銅 copper bromide;
鑄銅 cast copper;
自然銅 native copper;
紫銅 red copper;

tong
【潼】 (1) high and lofty; (2) tributary of the Yellow River; (3) county in Shanxi;
［潼潼］ lofty appearance; rise very high;

tong
【曈】 twilight before sunrise;
［曈曨］ twilight of daybreak;
［曈曈］ (1) bright; (2) glistening;

tong
【朣】 the rising moon;

tong
【橦】 (1) type of trees in Sichuan with flowers that can be used to produce fabric; (2) flag pole; mast of a ship;

tong
【瞳】 (1) pupil of the eye; (2) ignorant; stupid;
［瞳孔］ the pupil of the eye;
瞳孔閉合 coreclisis;
瞳孔變形 coremorphosis;
瞳孔測量法 coremetry;
瞳孔反射 pupillary reflex;
瞳孔反應 pupil reaction; pupillary reflex;
~偏盲性瞳孔反應 hemiopic pupillary reaction;
瞳孔計 coreometer;
瞳孔痙攣 pupillary athetosis;
瞳孔擴大 mydriasis;
~痙攣性瞳孔擴大 spasmodic mydriansis;
~麻痺性瞳孔擴大 paralytic mydriasis;
瞳孔癆 corephthisis;
瞳孔散大 mydriasis;
瞳孔縮小 miosis;
~刺激性瞳孔縮小 irritative miosis;
~麻痺性瞳孔縮小 paralytic miosis;
瞳孔狹小 stenocoriasis;
瞳孔異常 dyscoria;
瞳孔異位 corectopia;
瞳孔整復 corepraxia;
緊張性瞳孔 tonic pupil;
［瞳矇］ ignorant;
［瞳子］ pupil of the eye;

tong
【艟】 ancient warship;

tong³
tong
【統】 (1) control; govern; rule; (2) interconnected system; (3) all; completely; together; totally; wholly; (4) gather into one; unify; unite; (5) tube-shaped article of clothing;

[統稱] (1) be called by a joint name; known together as; (2) general designation;

[統籌] plan as a whole;
統籌安排 logistics; make overall arrangements;
統籌規劃 overall planning; plan as a whole;
統籌兼顧 make overall plans and take all factors into consideration; overall planning and all-round consideration; unified planning with due consideration for all parties concerned;
統籌全局 take the whole situation into account and plan accordingly;
統籌人 coordinator;

[統共] altogether; in all; total;

[統計] (1) census; statistics; (2) add up; count;
統計方法 statistical method;
統計局 statistics bureau;
~ 中央統計局 central bureau of statistics;
統計力學 statistical mechanics;
統計量 statistic;
~ 輔助統計量 ancillary statistics;
~ 條件統計量 conditional statistic;
~ 完全統計量 complete statistic;
~ 有偏統計量 biased statistic;
統計熱力學 statistic-thermodynamics;
統計師 statistician;
~ 保險統計師 actuary;
~ 高級統計師 senior statistician;
~ 助理統計師 assistant statistician;
統計數字 statistics;
統計物理學 statistical physics;
統計學 statistics;
~ 統計學家 statistician;
~ 目錄統計學 bibliostatistics;
~ 生物統計學 biometrics, biometry; biostatistics;
~ 事故統計學 accident statistics;
統計語言學 statistical linguistics;
統計預測 statistical forecasting;
統計員 statistical clerk;
保險統計 actuarial statistics;
幅度統計 amplitude statistics;
精密統計 accurate statistics;
流產統計 abortion statistics;
量子統計 quantum statistics;
農業統計 agricultural statistics;
應用統計 applied statistics;

[統考] joint examination; unified examination; uniform examination;

[統類] categories; kinds;

[統例] general rules;

[統屬] subordination;

[統帥] (1) commander; commander-in-chief; (2) command;
統帥部 high command;
最高統帥 commander-in-chief;

[統率] command; lead;

[統體] whole body;

[統統] all; completely; entirely; wholly;

[統一] integrate; unify; unite; unity;
統一定價 uniform price;
統一分配 overall assignment;
統一思想 reach a common understanding; seek unity of thinking;
統一體 continuum;
統一天下 unification of the whole country;
統一行動 act in unison; coordinate action; seek unity of action;
統一戰線 the united front;
經濟統一 economic unity;
民族統一 national unity;

[統戰] united front;

[統治] dominate; govern; reign; rule;
統治階級 ruling class;
統治者 ruler;
財閥統治 plutocracy;
加強統治 consolidate rule;
外族統治 alien rule;
王權統治 imperial rule;

傳統 convention; tradition;
道統 Confucian orthodoxy;
法統 legally constituted authority;
高統 high boots;
籠統 ambiguous; general; indistinct;
閏統 illegitimate rule;
體統 decorum;
通統 all; without exception;
統統 all; completely; entirely;
系統 system; systematic;
血統 blood lineage; blood relationship;
一統 unify a country;

正統 (1) legitimism; (2) orthodox;
總統 president of a republic;

tong
【筒】 cylinder; pipe; tube;
[筒管] bobbin;
[筒形] shape of a tube or ball;
捲成筒形 roll up;
[筒子] tube; tube-shaped object;
槍筒子 barrel of a gun;
襪筒子 stocking leg;
竹筒子 bamboo tube;

爆破筒 Bangalore torpedo;
筆筒 brush pot; pen container;
傳聲筒 (1) megaphone; loud hailer; (2) person who parrots another;
打氣筒 bicycle pump; inflator;
電筒 electric torch; flashlight;
浮筒 buoy; float; pontoon;
滾筒 cylinder; roll;
號筒 bugle;
花筒 a kind of fireworks;
話筒 (1) megaphone; (2) microphone; (3) telephone transmitter;
火箭筒 bazooka; rocket launcher;
唧筒 pump;
箭筒 quiver;
井筒 pit shaft;
喇叭筒 megaphone;
量筒 graduated cylinder;
量雨筒 precipitation gauge;
砲筒 barrel of a gun;
氣筒 bicycle pump; inflator;
籤筒 thick bamboo tube used for divination or drawing lots;
手電筒 electric torch; flashlight;
套筒 sleeve; muff;
聽筒 (1) earphone; headphone; (2) telephone receiver; (3) stethoscope;
襪筒 leg of a stocking;
萬花筒 kaleidoscope;
信筒 mailbox; pillar-box; postbox;
袖筒 sleeve;
藥筒 medicinal tube;
郵筒 mailbox; pillar-box;
岩心筒 core barrel;
擲彈筒 grenade discharger; grenade launcher;

tong
【捅】 (1) poke; stab; (2) stir up; (3) disclose; give away;
[捅婁子] make a blunder; make a mess of sth;
總好捅婁子 prone to make silly mistakes;
[捅馬蜂窩] arouse a nest of hornets; arouse hornets' nest;
敢捅馬蜂窩 dare to challenge troublesome people;

tong
【桶】 a barrel of; a breaker of; a bucket of; a bucketful of; a cask of; a drum of; a keg of; a pail of; a pailful of; a pipe of; a tub of; a tubful of; a vat of; a wood of;
[桶匠] cooper;
[桶鋪] coopery;
[桶子] barrel; bucket; keg; pail;

便桶 chamber pot;
冰桶 ice bucket;
吊桶 bucket; well-bucked;
飯桶 (1) big eater; (2) fathead; good-for-nothing; (3) rice bucket;
恭桶 closestool; commode;
火葯桶 powder keg;
淨桶 urinal stool;
馬桶 night stool;
染色桶 dye beck;
水桶 bucket; pail;
痰桶 spittoon;
提桶 pail;
鐵桶 pail;
脱泡桶 deaerator;
油桶 oil drum;

tong⁴
tong
【痛】 (1) ache; pain; (2) poignant; sadness; sorrow; sorrowful; (3) bitterly; deeply; extremely; (4) to one's heart's content;
[痛愛] love deeply; love passionately;
[痛抱喪明] mourn for the death of one's son;
[痛不可忍] the pain is intolerable; unbearably painful;
[痛不欲生] be overwhelmed with sorrow; be so overwhelmed with grief that one hardly wishes to live;
[痛斥] bitterly attack; sharply denounce;
痛斥謬論 sharply denounce a fallacy;
遭到痛斥 get a roasting;
[痛楚] anguish; pain; suffering;
[痛處] sore spot; tender spot;

揭人痛處 expose sb's weaknesses;
擊中痛處 hit sb on a tender place; hit sb squarely in a sore spot; hit sb to the quick;
觸到痛處 cut sb to the quick; hurt sb to the quick; rub it in; sting sb to the quick; touch a sore spot; touch sb on a sore place; touch sb on a tender place; touch sb on the raw; touch sb on the quick; touch sb's sore spot; wound sb to the quick;

[痛打] beat soundly; give a severe thrashing; make hamburger out of sb; skin alive;
痛打落水狗 flog the cur that has fallen into the water; relentlessly beat the dog in the water; merciless with bad people even when they are down;
痛打一頓 give sb a good beating; give sb a sound thrashing;
挨一頓痛打 get a painful beating;
一頓痛打 a sound flogging;

[痛悼] grieve over the death of sb bitterly;

[痛詆] berate; revile; vituperate;

[痛定思痛] bring home the lessons painfully learned; draw a lesson from a bitter experience; recall a painful experience; recall one's sufferings when they are over; recall past pain — as a warning for the future; recall the past with pangs in the heart; take one's painful experience to heart; think out the reason after bitter lesson; think over the reason after a bitter lesson;

[痛風] gout;
痛風病 gout;
~害痛風病 be afflicted with gout;
痛風石性痛風 tophaceous gout;
痛風性關節炎 gouty arthritis;
草酸中毒性痛風 oxalic gout;
典型痛風 regular gout;
~非典型痛風 irregular gout;
關節痛風 articular gout;
繼發性痛風 secondary gout;
假痛風 pseudogout;
假性痛風 pseudogout;
肩痛風 omagra;
內臟痛風 visceral gout;
鉛毒性痛風 saturnine gout;
鉛中毒性痛風 lead gout;
潛伏性痛風 latent gout;
手痛風 cheiragra;
手足痛風 cheiropodagra;
特發性痛風 idiopathic gout;
原發性痛風 primary gout;
肘痛風 anconagra;
足痛風 podagra;

[痛改前非] correct thoroughly one's errors; earnestly repent and correct one's errors; redeem one's past wrongs; reform earnestly one's misdeeds; reform with a keen sense of error; repent past mistakes; sincerely mend one's ways; thoroughly rectify one's errors;

[痛感] feel keenly;
痛感失望 really feel no hope;

[痛恨] abhor; abhorrence; deeply regret; detest; hate deeply; lament;
痛恨在心 habour a bitter hatred in one's mind;

[痛悔] repent bitterly;

[痛擊] attack bitterly; hit bitterly; deal a heavy blow; give a hard blow;

[痛經] dysmenorrhea;
充血性痛經 congestive dysmenorrhea;
繼發性痛經 secondary dysmenorrhea;
痙攣性痛經 spasmodic dysmenorrhnea;
卵巢性痛經 ovarian dysmenorrhea;
膜樣痛經 membranous dysmenorrhea;
炎性痛經 inflammatory dysmenorrhea;
原發性痛經 primary dysmenorrhea;
自發性痛經 essential dysmenorrhea;

[痛覺] algesthesia; pain sense; sense of pain;
痛覺過度 hyperpathia;
痛覺過敏 hyperalgia;
痛覺減退 hypoalgesia;
痛覺缺失 analgesia; analgia;
痛覺異常 paralgesia;

[痛哭] cry bitterly; uncontrolled weeping; wail; weep bitterly;
痛哭流涕 cry and shed bitter tears; cry bitterly; cry one's heart out; set one's eyes at flow; shed tears in bitter sorrow; shed tears of anguish; weep bitter tears; weep bitterly;
痛哭失聲 be choked with tears;
痛哭一場 give free vent to one's sorrow with many tears and loud laments; have a good cry;
痛哭欲絕 cry one's heart out;

抱頭痛哭 cry in each other's arm; embrace one another's head and weep; fall upon one another's shoulders and weep; hang on sb's neck and weep out; throw into each other's arms and cry one's heart out; wail sorrowfully; weep in each other's arm;

椎心痛哭 cry one's heart out;

盡情痛哭 cry one's eyes out; cry one's heart out;

[痛苦] affliction; agony; pain; suffering;

痛苦的爭扎 bitter struggle;

痛苦萬狀 inflict untold suffering on;

飽嘗痛苦 have the black ox tread on one's foot;

感到痛苦 feel miserable;

極度的痛苦 extreme pain;

減輕痛苦 abate one's pain; reduce suffering;

絕望的痛苦 anguish of despair;

失敗的痛苦 gall of defeat;

死亡的痛苦 death throes;

無法忍受的痛苦 unendurable pain;

延長痛苦 prolong one's agony;

一陣痛苦 a spasm of pain;

[痛快] (1) have a wonderful time; have one's fill of; to one's heart's content; (2) frank and straightforward; simply and directly;

痛快地吃 eat heartily;

痛快淋漓 extremely comfortable; impassioned and forceful; satisfying in every respect; with great eloquence; with great nerve and gusto;

痛快一時 have an uproarious time; let oneself go;

喝個痛快 drink one's fill;

哭個痛快 cry one's heart out; weep one's fill;

親痛仇快 grieve one's own people and gladden the enemy; grieve those near and dear to us and gladden the enemy; pain one's friends and please one's enemies; sadden one's friends and gladden one's enemies; sadden one's own folk and gladden the enemy;

親者痛，仇者快 grieve one's own people and gladden the enemy; grieve those near and dear to us and gladden the enemy; sadden one's friends and gladden one's enemies; sadden one's own folk and gladden the enemy;

痛痛快快 forthright; simple and direct; straight forward; straight off;

圖一時痛快 seek momentary gratification;

玩個痛快 get one's jollies; have a wonderful time;

笑得痛快 have a good laugh; laugh outright;

[痛罵] berate; give sb a good dressing down; revile; skin alive;

痛罵一頓 break into a torrent of abuse at sb;

一頓痛罵 a stream of abuses;

[痛毆] beat savagely; give a sounding beating;

[痛切] most sorrowfully; poignant; pungent; with intense sorrow;

痛切陳詞 make a deeply-felt plea;

痛切反省 examine oneself seriously; examine oneself with feelings of deep remorse;

[痛惡] abhor; detest bitterly; hate bitterly;

[痛惜] deplore; regret deeply;

痛惜良機 regret the chance;

痛惜前非 repent deeply one's past;

[痛心] distressed; grieved; heartbroken; very sorry;

痛心疾首 be filled with resentment; deplore greatly; feel bitter about; hate bitterly; hate deeply; resent deeply; with bitter hatred;

痛心切齒 gnash one's teeth with anger; make sb burn with anger;

疾首痛心 with an aching head and a broken heart;

令人痛心 cut one to the heart;

[痛癢] (1) difficulties; (2) sufferings; (3) consequence; (4) importance;

痛癢相關 care for one another's comfort and happiness; pain and itch are closely connected — mutual sympathy; share a common lot; sympathize with each other's trials;

不關痛癢 a matter of no consequence; do not care a bit; insignificant; irrelevant; pointless; show no concern; without any bite;

不痛不癢 perfunctory; scratching the surface; superficial; wishy-washy;

又癢又痛 irritating and painful;

[痛飲] drink one's fill; drink to one's heart's content; piss-up; quaff;

痛飲黃龍 drink heartily a cup of victory;
[痛責] scold severely;
哀痛 deep mourning; deep sorrow; feel the anguish of sorrow; feel the pain of grief; great sorrow; grief; profoundly grieved;
悲痛 deep sorrow; grief; grieved; lamentation; sorrowful;
背痛 back pain; backache; dorsodynia;
臂痛 arm pain;
鼻痛 rhinalgia;
病痛 slight illness;
擦痛 chafe;
慘痛 bitter; deeply grieved; grievous; painful;
腸絞痛 intestinal angina;
腸痛 enterodynia;
沉痛 (1) deeply felt; (2) deep feeling of grief;
持續痛 continuous pain;
齒痛 toothache;
觸痛 tenderness;
戳痛 piercing pain;
創痛 pain from an injury;
刺痛 prickle; sharp pain;
肚痛 collywobbles;
鈍痛 dull pain;
耳痛 earache; have a pain in the ear; otalgia;
放射痛 radiating pain;
腹絞痛 angina abdominis; cramps;
腹痛 abdominal pain; stomach ache;
肝痛 hepatodynia;
骨痛 ostalgia;
喉痛 laryngalgia; sore throat;
肌痛 muscular rheumatism; myalgia; pain in the muscles;
激痛 severe pain;
肩痛 omalgia; pain in the shoulder; shoulder pain;
絞痛 angina; colic;
頸臂痛 cervicobrachialgia;
精神性痛 algopsychalia;
經痛 dysmenorrheal;
痙攣痛 crampy pain;
局部痛 topalgia;
劇痛 acute pain; sharp pain;
苦痛 pain; suffering;
愧痛 be so ashamed as to feel painful;
潰爛痛 sore pain;
烈痛 tearing pain;
腦痛 cerebralgia;
偏頭痛 migraine;
氣痛 gas pain;
輕痛 slight pain;
全身痛 pantalgia;
忍痛 bear the pain reluctantly; suffer pain with dignity;
肉痛 (1) anxiety; apprehension; (2) cannot bear to part with sth one loves;
茹痛 endure; suffer;
疝痛 colic;
傷痛 mourn;
燒痛 burning pain;
舌痛 glossalgia;
身痛 bodily pain;
深痛 deep grief; lament deeply;
神經痛 neuralgia;
腎痛 nephralgia;
酸痛 ache; pins and needles;
疼痛 ache; pain;
頭痛 ache in one's head; cephalalgia; have a headache; headache;
胃絞痛 gastric colic;
胃空痛 gastralgokenosis;
胃痛 gastralgia; stomachache;
頑痛 persistent pain;
心絞痛 angina pectoris;
心痛 cardiac pain; feel the pangs of the heart;
胸痛 have a pain in the chest;
牙神經痛 odontoneuralgia;
牙痛 toothache;
壓痛 pressing pain;
咽痛 pharyngalgia;
眼痛 eye strain;
腰痛 lumbago;
隱痛 secret anguish;
陣痛 labour pains; throes of childbirth;
鎮痛 ease pain;
肢痛 melagra;
止痛 assuage pain; kill pain; relieve pain; stop pain;
腫痛 swollen and inflamed;
灼痛 burning pain;
足痛 pain in the sole of the foot; pododynia;
作痛 ache; cause pain; painful;

tong

【衕】 alley; lane;

tong

【慟】 extreme grief;
[慟哭] wail; weep bitterly;
撫尸慟哭 cry over sb's body; mourn loudly over sb's remains; stroke the corpse and cry bitterly; weep bitterly over sb's corpse; weep over sb's corpse;

tou¹
tou

【偷】 (1) burglarize; filch; pilfer; steal; (2) secretly; stealthily; (3) find time;

［偷安］ live in complacency; seek temporary ease;
偷安逾閒 content with an easy life; seek ease and comfort without high aspirations;
苟且偷安 enjoy ease against one's principles; enjoy ease with a false sense of security;

［偷吃不肥，做賊不富］ no one grows fat or becomes rich by stealing;

［偷盜］ pilfer; steal;

［偷渡］ stow away;
偷渡者 stowaway;

［偷兒］ thief;

［偷風不偷月，偷雨不偷雪］ thieves steal on windy or rainy nights, not on moonlit or snowy nights;

［偷工減料］ cheat in work and cut down on materials; do a sloppy job; do shoddy work and use inferior material; perfunctory in doing sth; scamp work and stint material; use inferior materials and turn out substandard goods;

［偷寒送暖］ do everything to please others; have affectionate concern for others; see the comfort of;

［偷合苟容］ fall in with others' wishes and acquire admittance;

［偷換］ substitute stealthily sth for;

［偷活］ live in disgrace; live without much purpose; while away one's life span aimlessly;

［偷雞不著蝕把米］ go for wool and come back shorn; try to steal a chicken only to end up losing the rice;

［偷雞摸狗］ (1) act on the sly; do things stealthily; engage in under-the-table dealings; on the sly; thief; (2) have illicit relations with women;

［偷看］ peep; steal a glance; steal a look;

［偷空］ snatch a moment; take time off;

［偷窺］ peep;
偷窺表演 peepshow;

［偷懶］ eat one's own flesh; lazy; loaf on the job;
偷懶的人 slacker;
別偷懶 shift one's arse;

［偷梁換柱］ perpetrate a fraud; resort to fraudulence; steal the beams and change the pillars; steal the beams and pillars and replace them with rotten timbers; try by underhand means;

［偷拍］ take a photo without permission;
被偷拍 be papped;
惡意偷拍 pap; paparazzi;

［偷跑］ escape; run away;

［偷搶］ steal or rob;
不偷不搶 not steal anything or rob anyone;
去偷去搶 steal and rob;

［偷巧］ take a shortcut;

［偷竊］ filch; larceny; pilfer; purloin; steal;
偷竊狂 kleptomania; kleptomaniac;
慣於偷竊的 light-fingered;
偷香竊玉 have illicit sexual relations; indulge in secret relations with women; intrigue; pick up loose women;

［偷情］ carry on a clandestine love affair; have a secret love affair; two-time;
偷情的人 two-timer;

［偷生］ drag out an ignoble existence; have no ambition than just to get by; lead an ignoble existence; live on without meaning; live on without purpose;
偷生怕死 cling to life and be scared of death; cowardly; live dishonourably for fear of death;
苟且偷生 drag out an ignominious existence;
含辱偷生 swallow the shame and save one's skin;

［偷書］ steal a book;
偷書狂 bibliokleptomania;
偷書癖 bibliokleptomania;

［偷聽］ bug; eavesdrop; tap;

［偷偷］ covertly; on the sly; secretly; stealthily; without others' knowledge;
偷偷離開 sneak away; sneak out;
偷偷摸摸 behind close doors; by stealth; covertly; do sth stealthily; furtively; hole and corner; in a sneaky way; in corners; like a thief in the night;

on the quiet; on the sly; stealthily; surreptitiously; under the counter;
~偷偷摸摸的 furtive;
[偷襲] attack by surprise; sneak attack; sneak raid; surprise attack;
輕兵偷襲 dispatch light-footed soldiers to spring a surprise attack on;
[偷閒] avail oneself of a leisure moment; snatch a moment of leisure; steal a moment of leisure;
抽空偷閒 spare a few moments from work; take advantage of any free time;
忙裏偷閒 allow oneself a bit of time; at odd hours; at odd moments; at old times; snatch a little leisure from a busy life; snatch leisure from a busy life; steal a little leisure from the rush of business; take a break in the midst of work; take a breathing spell in the midst of pressing affairs;
[偷笑] chuckle;
[偷心] steal sb's heart;
[偷眼] cast a furtive glance; steal a glance; take a furtive glance;
[偷營劫寨] attack a camp by surprise; attack the enemy secretly; launch an attack on a camp by surprise; make a surprise attack on an enemy's camp; night attack on a camp; raid an enemy camp; surprise and plunder a camp;
[偷雨不偷雪，偷風不偷月] thieves would steal on rainy or windy nights, rather than on snowy or moon-lit nights;
[偷運] illegally transport;
[偷走] appropriate; mooch; rob; run off; walk off with;
[偷嘴] steal food; take food on the sly;
慣偷 confirmed thief; habitual thief; hardened thief;
小偷 burglar; petty thief; pilferer; sneak thief; thief;

tou²
tou

【投】 (1) fling; throw; toss; (2) drop; put in; (3) throw oneself into; (4) cast; project; (5) deliver; send; (6) agree with; fit in with; (7) join; submit;

[投案] give oneself up to the police; surrender oneself to the police;
投案自首 give oneself up to the authority; go to the police and confess; surrender oneself to justice; surrender oneself to the police;
[投保] cover; insure; take out an insurance policy;
投保金額 sums insured;
投保人 policyholder;
投保項目 insured items;
[投奔] go to a place for shelter;
投奔親戚 go to one's relatives for help; seek refuge with relatives;
[投筆從戎] cast aside the pen to join the army; give up civilian pursuits for a military career; renounce the pen for the sword; throw aside the writing brush and join the army; throw down the pen and join the army;
[投鞭斷流] if the soldiers throw their whips into the river, it would be enough to stem the current;
[投標] bid; enter a bid; submit a tender; submit public bids in; tender;
投標保證 bid bond; tend bond;
~投標保證金 bid bond; tend bond;
投標程序 bidding procedure;
投標價 tender price;
投標階段 bidding phase;
投標買賣 tender bidding;
投標人 bidder; tenderer;
投標文件 tender documents;
投標有效期 validity of tenders;
投標語言 bid language;
公開投標 competitive tender; public bidding; public tender;
~國際公開投標 competitive international bidding;
國際投標 international bidding;
密封投標 closed biddings; sealed biddings;
[投產] go into operation; put into production;
按時投產 go into operation on schedule;
建成投產 be completed and put into operation;
[投誠] cross over; surrender;
攜械投誠 come over from the enemy's side bringing weapons;
[投彈] (1) drop a bomb; (2) throw a hand

grenade;

[投敵] defect to the enemy; go over to the enemy; surrender to the enemy;

投敵叛變 go over to the enemy and turn traitor;

倒戈投敵 betray to the enemy; turn a traitor; turncoat;

[投遞] deliver;

投遞信件 deliver letters;

[投店] put up at an inn; seek lodging in a tavern;

[投放] (1) throw in; (2) put goods on the market;

[投附] offer one's services to;

[投稿] contribute an article; submit a piece of writing for publication;

投稿人 contributor;

歡迎投稿 contributions are welcome;

[投戈講藝] lay aside weapons for a while so as to pursue learning;

[投合] agree; agree with; cater to; get along; see eye to eye;

投合口味 cater to one's taste; pander to one's palate; pander to one's taste;

投合時好 in the fashion;

投合心意 catch on; suit one's purpose;

[投河] commit suicide by throwing oneself into the river; drown oneself;

投河奔井 commit suicide by drowning oneself in the water; jump into the river or throw oneself into a well;

[投繯] commit suicide by hanging; hang oneself;

投繯自縊 hang oneself;

[投荒] head for distant places;

[投火] commit suicide by jumping into the fire;

[投機] (1) opportunistic; seize a chance to seek private gain; speculate; (2) agreeable; congenial;

投機操縱 speculate and manipulate;

投機倒把 play the market; speculate; speculation and profiteering;

投機分子 opportunist; soldier of fortune; speculator;

投機買賣 engage in speculation; speculative trade;

投機取巧 opportunistic; resort to dubious shifts to further one's interests; seek private gain by dishonest means; seize every chance to gain advantage by trickery; speculate and take advantage of an opportunity; use every trick in shortcuts and finesse; wheel and deal; wheeling and dealing;

~ 投機取巧的人 wheeler-dealer;

投機失敗 fail in speculation;

投機商 adventurer;

~ 女投機商 adventuress;

投機賺錢 make some good speculations;

投機鑽營 serve personal interests through trickery; speculate and secure personal gain;

股票投機 speculation in stocks;

話不投機 cannot see eye to eye with sb; disagreeable conversation; dissidence of opinion in talks; mistime one's remarks; not talk to the point;

~ 話不投機半句多 dissidence of opinions makes it useless to talk; if one argues with a disagreeable man, half a sentence is too much; if there's no common ground, a single word is a waste of breath; in a disagreeable conversation one word more is too many; when the conversation gets disagreeable, to say one word more is a waste of breath;

談得投機 have a very pleasant talk;

~ 談得很投機 have a most agreeable chat;

[投寄] send a letter to;

[投井] drown oneself in a well;

投井下石 attack sb who has already fallen from power; kick sb when he/she is down;

投井自盡 drown oneself in a well; throw oneself into a well;

[投軍] become a serviceman; enlist oneself; join the army;

[投考] go in for an examination; take an entrance examination of a school;

[投靠] (1) go and live as dependent; go and seek refuge with sb; (2) give oneself up to; surrender to;

投靠親友 go and seek refuge with one's relatives and friends;

賣身投靠 barter away one's honour for sb's patronage; hire oneself and throw in one's lot with; hire oneself out to; sell oneself for support;

明靠暗投 attach oneself to sb in the open

and to another one in secret;

[投籃] shoot; try for the basket;
投籃不中 miss the basket;
投籃得分 shoot a basket;
背向球籃轉身投籃 backup shot;
單手投籃 one-hand shot;
高弧度投籃 high arch shot;
勾手投籃 hook shot;
急起投籃 stop shot;
近距離投籃 close-in shot;
練習投籃 shoot baskets; shoot hoops;
面向球籃投籃 facing shot;
跳起投籃 jump up and shoot;
原地投籃 set shot;
運球投籃 drive shot;
轉身投籃 pivot shot;

[投老] retire due to old age;

[投袂而起] burst forth suddenly; throw up one's sleeves and rise; whisk one's sleeves and stand up;

[投矛器] spear thrower;

[投命] die for; give one's life to;

[投暮] dusk; get dark;

[投票] cast a vote; take a vote; vote;
投票表決 decide by voting; vote by ballot;
投票程序 voting procedure;
投票反對 vote against;
投票否決 vote sth down;
投票機 voting machine;
投票間 booth;
投票權 right to vote;
投票人 voter;
~投票人數 polling; turnout;
投票人數多 heavy polling;
投票人數少 light polling;
~猶豫不決的投票人 waverer;
投票日 polling day;
投票時間 polling hours;
投票亭 polling booth; voting booth;
投票通過 vote through;
投票通知卡 poll card;
投票箱 ballot box; polling booth;
投票站 polling station;
~投票站編號 polling station code;
~投票站地址 address of polling station;
~投票站名稱 name of polling station;
~指定投票站 designated polling station;
投票贊成 vote for; vote in favour of;
投票資格 eligibility to vote;
不記名投票 secret ballot;
不信任投票 no-confidence vote; vote of no confidence;
~通過對政府不信任投票 pass a vote of no confidence in the government;
參加投票 go to the polls;
策略性投票 tactical voting;
公民投票 plebiscite;
譴責投票 vote of censure;
全民投票 referendum;
缺席投票 absentee vote;
秘密投票 ballot; secret ballot;
無記名投票 ballot; secret ballot;
自由投票 free vote;

[投契] agreeable; congenial; get along well; meeting of minds;
投契之談 congenial talk; heart-to-heart talk;

[投棄] abandon; give up;

[投親] go and live with one's relatives; seek refuge with one's relatives;
投親訪友 look up relatives and friends;
投親靠友 go and seek refuge with one's relatives and friends; go and stay with relatives or friends as a dependent; go to one's relatives or friends for help; join relatives and friends to find a means of living;

[投球] pitch;
投球犯規 no ball;
投球手 bowler;

[投入] (1) put into; throw into; (2) join; pitch in;
投入產出 input-output;
~投入產出法 input-output method;
~投入產出分析 input-output analysis;
~投入產出經濟學 input-output economics;
~投入產出總承包 total contract of input and output;
投入使用 on stream;

[投射] (1) cast; throw; (2) cast; project; shoot;

[投身] give oneself to; join; plunge into; throw oneself into;
投身革命 join in the revolution; join the revolutionary ranks;

[投師] seek instruction from a master;
投師訪友 learn from a master and call on friends to exchange knowledge;

[投手] pitcher;
投手練習區 bull pen;
旋轉球投手 spinner;

[投書] send a letter to;

T

[投鼠忌器] hesitate to pelt a rat for fear of smashing the dishes beside it; reluctant to act against a lower official for fear of implicating someone more important; spare the rat to serve the dishes — hold back from taking action against an evildoer for fear of involving good people; when you throw stones at a rat, beware of the vase;

[投宿] check in for the night; put up for the night; seek temporary lodging;

[投訴] complain; write to state or request;
投訴程序 complaints procedure;
投訴信 letter of complaint;
處理投訴 deal with a complaint; handle a complaint;
收到投訴 have a complaint; receive a complaint;
提出投訴 file a complaint; lodge a complaint; make a complaint;

[投胎] be reincarnated in a new body;

[投托] place in the care of another;

[投下] (1) drop; throw down; (2) invest in;

[投降] capitulate; give up; make submission to; surrender; yield to;
放下武器投降 lay down one's arms;
舉手投降 raise one's arms in surrender;
棄戈投降 throw aside one's spears and give in;
屈膝投降 bend and surrender to; bow and surrender to; fall on one's knees to surrender; give in and surrender to; go down on one's knees in surrender; kneel down in capitulation; knuckle under; submit and surrender to; throw oneself at the feet of;

[投影] cast a shadow; projection; shadow;
投影電視 projection television;
投影放大器 episcope;
投影規則 projection rules;
投影機 projector;
~光閥投影機 light-valve projector;
投影器 projector;
~彩色圖像投影器 colour image projector;
~弧光投影器 arc light projector;
~傾斜投影器 oblique projector;
投影儀 overhead projector;
不透明投影 opaque projection;
地圖投影 map projection;
等距方位投影 azimuthal equidistant projection;
等距投影 equidistant projection;
等積投影 equal-area projection;
方位投影 azimuthal projection;
球面投影 stereographic projection;
球心投影 gnomonic projection;
全球投影 globular projection;
任意投影 arbitrary projection;
橢圓投影 oval projection;
圓錐投影 conic projection;
~多圓錐投影 polyconic projection;
圓柱投影 cylindrical projection;
正射投影 orthographic projection;
正形投影 conformal projection;

[投郵] mail; send a letter by mail;

[投緣] agreeable; congenial;

[投擲] cast; hurl; throw; throw away;
投擲圈 throwing circle;

[投中] make a basket; shoot the ball in;
投中得分 make a goal;

[投注] bet;
點差投注 spread betting;

[投資] (1) invest; (2) investment;
投資安全 investment safety;
~確保投資安全 secure investment safety;
投資保證 investment guarantee;
投資比例 proportion of investment;
投資場所 outlet for investment;
投資大戰 investment war;
投資多樣化 investment diversification;
投資多元化 investment diversification;
投資額 amount of capital invested;
投資方式 form of investment;
投資方向 investment orientation;
投資公司 investment company;
投資估算 investment estimation;
投資顧問 investment adviser;
投資規模 investment scale;
投資過度 over-investment;
投資合理性 investment rationalization;
投資核算 investment calculation;
投資環境 the environment for investment;
投資回報 return on an investment;
投資回收 returns on investment;
~投資回收期 payback period;
投資活動 investing activities;
投資機會 investment opportunities;
投資基金 investment funds;
投資監理 investment supervision;

T

投資結構 structure of investment;
投資決策 investment decision;
投資利潤額 income on investment;
投資能力 ability to invest;
投資熱點 investment hot spot; popular investment spot;
投資市場 investment market;
投資入伙 admission by investment;
投資收益 investment income;
投資收益率 return on investment;
投資所得 investment income;
投資項目 investment project;
~外商投資項目 foreign-funded project;
投資信託公司 investment trust company;
投資學 science of investment;
投資銀行 investment bank;
~投資銀行家 investment banker;
投資債券 invested capital;
投資者 investor;
~投資者信心 investor confidence;
投資總額 aggregate investment; total amount of investment;
投資總規模 volume of total investment;
長期投資 long-term investment;
刺激投資 stimulate investment;
短期投資 short-term investment;
額外投資 additional investment;
輔助投資 ancillary investment;
股票證券投資 portfolio investment;
鼓勵投資 bid to boost investment; encourage investment;
國外投資 invest abroad;
海外投資 foreign investment; overseas investment;
集體投資 pool;
間接投資 indirect investment;
淨投資 net investment;
私人投資 private investment;
收回投資 disinvestment; recoup one's investment;
停止投資 disinvestment;
外來投資 inward investment;
無效投資 inefficient investment;
吸引投資 attract investment;
一攬子投資 package investment;
直接投資 direct investment;
自籌投資 funds collected by oneself;

交投 trading;
空投 airdrop;
傘投 drop by a parachute;
跳投 jump shot;
相投 agree with each other; compatible; congenial;

tou
【骰】 literary pronunciation of 骰;

tou
【頭】 (1) bonce; chump; crust; head; (2) hair; hair style; (3) ends; top; (4) beginning; first; (5) stub; remnant; (6) boss; chief; head; leader; (7) aspect; side; (8) leading; (9) last; previous;

[頭班車] first bus; first train;

[頭版] (1) front page; (2) first edition;
頭版報導 front-page story;
頭版頭條 headline news in the front-page;
頭版文章 front-page article;
頭版新聞 front-page news;

[頭部] head; top;
頭部按摩 head massage;

[頭寸] (1) cash; (2) money supply;
頭寸寬裕 easy monetary position; money is easy;
頭寸支絀 money is tight; tight monetary position;

[頭道] (1) first time; (2) first;

[頭燈] headlamp; headlight;

[頭等] best quality; first-class; first-rate;
頭等艙 first-class cabin;
頭等大事 cardinal task; major event; matter of paramount importance; task of prime importance; thing of the first importance;
頭等重要 of the first importance;

[頭頂] pate; top of the head;
頭頂空間 headroom;
微禿的頭頂 balding crown of one's head;

[頭額] one's forehead;

[頭兒] (1) head; one's chump; (2) boss; (3) ends; (4) extremes;
有頭兒 begin to show promise of success;

[頭髮] hair; hair on the human head;
頭髮花白 grizzled hair;
頭髮蓬亂 shockheaded; tow-head; tow-headed;
熬白了頭髮 suffer so much that one's hair has turned gray prematurely;
白頭髮 gray hair;
擺弄頭髮 fiddle about with one's hair;
長及肩部的頭髮 shoulder-length hair;
扯頭髮 tear one's hair;

吹動頭髮 blow one's hair;
短頭髮 close haircut;
蓬亂的頭髮 shaggy hair;
紅頭髮 red hair;
~紅頭髮的人 redhead;
剪頭髮 cut one's hair;
留頭髮 allow the hair to grow;
難梳理的頭髮 unruly hair
弄直頭髮 straighten sb's hair;
披着頭髮 in one's hair;
齊肩的頭髮 shoulder-length hair;
染頭髮 dye one's hair;
梳理頭髮 arrange one's hair;
梳頭髮 brush one's hair; comb one's hair;
梳整頭髮 get up one's hair;
豎起的頭髮 spiky hair;
綰起頭髮 coil up one's hair;
烏黑的頭髮 jet-black hair;
洗頭髮 wash one's hair;
雪白的頭髮 snowy hair;
一把頭髮 a wisp of hair;
一縷頭髮 a wisp of hair;
一綹頭髮 a lock of hair; a tuft of hair, a wisp of hair;
一縷頭髮 lick;
棗紅色的頭髮 chestnut hair;
紮起頭髮 tie one's hair up;
捽住頭髮 grasp by the hair;
做頭髮 do one's hair; have one's hair done at a beauty parlour; style one's hair;

[頭蓋] cranium; skull;
頭蓋骨 cranium; skull;

[頭號] (1) leading; number one; principal; size one; (2) first-rate; the best; top quality;
頭號敵人 number one enemy;
頭號新聞 headline news; leading story in a newspaper;

[頭花] headdress flower;

[頭昏] dizzy; giddy;
頭昏目眩 feel dizzy;
~一陣頭昏目眩 a fit of fainting;
頭昏腦脹 feel dizzy and have a headache; feel one's head swimming; get very dizzy and one's head begins to ache; make sb's head swim;
頭昏眼花 dazed; dizzy; feel dizzy and with eyesight dimmed; light-headed; mentally confused; one's head begins to swim and one's eyes were misted; punch-drunk; see stars; slap-happy; with head giddy and eyes dazzled;
嚇昏了頭 be struck dumb; be stunned;

[頭獎] first prize;

[頭角] brilliance; talent;
頭角崢嶸 brilliant; eminent; have a noble brow; outstanding; prominent and dignified manner; showing extraordinary gifts; very promising;
不露頭角 in the shade;
初露頭角 begin one's rise to fame; begin to cut a conspicuous figure; begin to show one's ability; make first appearance;
嶄露頭角 begin to show one's brilliant talents; cut a striking figure; display remarkable ability; go up in the world; make a brilliant figure; make oneself conspicuous; show up prominently; stand out conspicuously;

[頭腳] head and foot;
賣頭賣腳 sell one's head and feet; show one's face in public;
頭輕腳重 head light and feet heavy; with one's mental equilibrium being disturbed by pride;
頭重腳輕 one's head grows heavy and one's feet grow light; top-heavy; weigh down;

[頭巾] coverchief; hijab; headscarf; kerchief; scarf; turban; wimple;
大頭巾 bandanna;
一條頭巾 a kerchief; a turban;

[頭靠] headrest;

[頭盔] helmet;
防護頭盔 crash helmet;

[頭裏] (1) before; earlier; (2) in front;

[頭領] leader;

[頭顱] (1) head; (2) skull;
拋頭顱，洒熱血 shed one's blood and lay down one's life;

[頭路] (1) clue; main thread; (2) one's job; one's occupation;

[頭馬] head girsel;

[頭毛] hair;

[頭面] head and face;
改頭換面 camouflage; change only the appearance; change the outside only; disguise; disguise in a different garb; dish up in a new form; make only superficial changes; in a disguised

form; refurnish; rehash;
三頭二面 cunning; double-faced;
神頭鬼面 monstrosities;

[頭名] the first;
得頭名 come first; come out first; come out on top; come out top; get the first place; head the list; stand first on the list; take the first place; win the first place;

[頭目] chief; chieftain; head of a gang; head of a group; leader; ringleader;

[頭腦] (1) brains; gray matter; mind; noddle; (2) clues; main threads;
頭腦不清 mixed-up; muddle-headed;
頭腦不正常 be a button short; have a button missing; have a few buttons loose; have a few buttons missing; have lost a button; not have all one's button on;
頭腦遲鈍 have a slow wit; have slow wits;
~頭腦遲鈍的 slow-witted;
頭腦冬烘 badly read and extremely bigoted; die hard; ultraconservative; with musty ideas;
頭腦發昏 lose one's head;
頭腦發脹 have a big head; have a swelled head; get a big head;
頭腦簡單 light in the head; see things too simply; simple-minded;
頭腦冷靜 coolheaded; have a cool head; have one's wits about one; level-headed; sober-minded;
~頭腦冷靜的 cool-headed;
~保持頭腦冷靜 keep a cool head; keep one's cool; keep one's head;
頭腦靈活 have a mind like a steel trap; have a quick wit; have an active brain; have quick wits; quick-witted;
頭腦清楚 clearheaded; with an alert mind;
頭腦清醒 clearheaded; keep a cool head; level-headed; sober-minded;
~頭腦清醒的 clear-headed;
~保持頭腦清醒 know if one is coming or going;
~使頭腦清醒 blow the cobwebs away; clear the cobwebs away;
頭腦正常 have all buttons; have all one's button on;
巴頭探腦 peep furtively from behind; stretch one's head in search;
笨頭笨腦 dead from the neck up; have a thick skull; muddle-headed; with a wooden head;
不用頭腦 not use one's head;
痴頭痴腦 crazy; idiotic;
遲鈍的頭腦 torpid mind;
衝昏頭腦 be carried away; be eaten up; be lost in; become dizzy with; beside oneself with; dizzy with; get dizzy with; get swollen-headed; giddy with; go to sb's head; have one's head turned; in heaven; lose one's head in; lose one's mind; off one's head; out of one's mind; turn one's head;
~被感情衝昏頭腦 be carried away by emotion;
~讓勝利衝昏頭腦 dizzy with success;
呆頭呆腦 a bit weak in the head; -; dull-looking; idiotic; idiotic-looking; muddle-headed; pudding-headed; stupid; stupid-looking;
~呆頭呆腦的樣子 look like a dummy; look like a stuffed dummy;
獃頭獃腦 dull-looking;
鬼頭鬼腦 crafty and sinister; furtive; hiding and peeping; peeping and prying; secretive; stealthy; thievish;
憨頭憨腦 doltish; foolish; silly; with a stupid head and a dull brain;
很有頭腦 have plenty of brains;
昏頭昏腦 absent-minded; addle-brained; addleheaded; be infatuated; forgetful; muddleheaded; not know if one is on one's head or one's heels;
渾頭渾腦 muddle-headed;
倔頭倔腦 blunt in manner and gruff of speech;
愣頭愣腦 foolhardy; hothead; impetuous; rash; reckless;
毛頭毛腦 impetuous; rush;
沒甚麼頭腦 not have much up top;
沒頭沒腦 absent-minded; listless; without a clue; without rhyme or reason;
迷糊不清的頭腦 bemist mind;
摸不著頭腦 cannot make head or tail of sth; unable to make head or tail of sth;
怯頭怯腦 nervous and clumsy, timid and unsophisticated;
清晰的頭腦 tidy mind;
清醒頭腦 clear head;
~保持清醒頭腦 screw one's head on tight;
傻頭傻腦 (1) foolish-looking; (2)

cloddish; clumsy and stupid; foolish; muddle-headed; off one's dot; silly;
伸頭探腦 crane one's neck to watch; poke one's head to peek at; stretch the neck in an effort to find out;
壽頭壽腦 stupid-looking;
縮頭縮腦 cower from fear; faint-hearted; hesitant; shrink from fear; shrink from responsibility; timid;
探頭探腦 act stealthily; crane one's neck to peer; peep furtively from behind; poke out one's head to peek at; pop one's head in and look about; probe furtively;
土頭土腦 countrified; hillbilly; hob-nailed; rustic; stupid and uncouth; unsophisticated;
褪頭縮腦 slink away;
瘟頭瘟腦 go about in a daze;
無頭無腦 completely without a clue; disorderly and confused; muddled and mixed-up;
有頭無腦 stupid;
有政治頭腦 be politically minded;
丈二和尚摸不著頭腦 at all sea; in a fog; in a haze; know nothing of the essentials; cannot touch the head of the ten-foot monk — cannot make head or tail of sth;

[頭年] (1) first year; (2) last year; previous year;

[頭皮] (1) scalp; (2) dandruff;
頭皮按摩 scalp massage;
搔頭皮 scratch one's head;
~搔搔頭皮 scratch one's head;
硬着頭皮 brace oneself to do sth; brazen it through; braren it out; force oneself; put a bold face on it; steel oneself; summon up courage; toughen one's scalp;
~硬着頭皮頂住 brace oneself and bear with it; hold out tenaciously;

[頭妻] (1) one's legal wife; (2) one's former wife;

[頭球] header;

[頭人] headman; tribal chief;

[頭上] on the head; on top;
頭上安頭 fit on a head where there is a head — superfluous;
頭上長瘡，腳底流膿 rotten to the core; with boils on the head and feet running with pus — rotten from head to foot;

[頭虱] head louse;

[頭飾] head ornament;
冕狀寶石頭飾 tiara;

[頭勢] (1) situation; state of affairs; (2) tendency;

[頭胎] firstborn;

[頭疼] headache;
頭疼腦熱 headache and slight fever; slight illness;

[頭天] (1) last day; previous day; the day before; (2) first day;

[頭挑] best choice; choicest;

[頭痛] ache in one's head; cephalalgia; have a headache; headache;
頭痛的事 headache;
~最頭痛的事 bugbear;
頭痛發熱 have a headache and fever; have a headache and high temperature;
頭痛腦熱 a headache and slight fever;
頭痛醫頭，腳痛醫腳 a defensive stopgap measure; cure only the symptoms; sporadic and piecemeal steps; take only palliative measures for one's illness; treat the head when the head aches, treat the foot when the foot hurts — treat symptoms but not the disease; treat the head when there's a headache, and the foot when there's a footache — apply palliative remedies;
鼻淵頭痛 headache of nasosinusitis;
充血性頭痛 congestive headache; hyperemic headache;
穿刺性頭痛 puncture headache;
創傷後頭痛 post-traumatic headache;
發熱性頭痛 pyrexial headache;
功能性頭痛 functional headache;
緊張性頭痛 tension headache;
咳嗽性頭痛 cough headache;
兩側頭痛 amphicrania;
偏頭痛 blind headache; migraine; migraine headache; sick headache;
~典型偏頭痛 classic migraine;
~偏癱性偏頭痛 hemiplegic migraine;
~神經性偏頭痛 neurologic migraine;
貧血性頭痛 anaemic headache;
器質性頭痛 organic headache;
外傷後頭痛 post-traumatic headache;
象限頭痛 quadrantal cephalalgia;
症狀性頭痛 symptomatic headache;
中毒性頭痛 toxic headache;

[頭頭是道] clear and logical; closely reasoned and well argued; coherent and cogent; systematic and orderly;

[頭尾] head and tail;

徹頭徹尾 absolute; arrant; complete; completely; double-dyed; down-right; down to the ground; dyed in the wool; entire; every inch; fair; first, midst, and last; from A to Z; from Adam; from beginning to end; from first to last; from head to foot; from start to finish; from the sole of the foot to the crown of the head; from tip to toe; from top to bottom; genuine; head over heels; in every sense; in toto; neither more nor less; of the deepest dye; one-hundred percent; out-and-out; out of the whole cloth; outright; pure; pure and simple; sheer; simple and pure; thorough; thorough-going; throughout; through-and-through; to all intents and purposes; to the back; to the back-bone; to the hilt; to the marrow; to the quick; to the tips of one's fingers; to the world; whole; utter;

見頭知尾 as soon as one perceives the head of sth he knows what the tail is;

掐頭去尾 break off both ends; do away with unnecessary parts at both ends; leave out the beginning and the end; nip off unwanted parts; remove the superfluous part;

缺頭短尾 fragmentary; incomplete;

説頭知尾 if the head were spoken of in a matter, at once he knew the tail also;

無頭無尾 with neither head nor tail; without beginning or end; without head or tail;

有頭無尾 begin sth but never finish it; begin well but fall off towards the close; give up before sth is finished; have a beginning but no end; leave a job incomplete; leave sth half done; start off but never finish; start sth but not finish it;

有頭有尾 complete; do a job from beginning to end; start sth and finish it;

斬頭去尾 make short by omitting the foremost and hindmost parts; quote out of context;

[頭銜] official title of a person;

放棄頭銜 renounce a title;

[頭屑] dandruff;

[頭緒] clues; leads; main threads;

頭緒紛繁 have too many things to take care of; highly complicated;

頭緒萬千 have too many things to attend to; the clue is extremely confused; the issue is perplexing and embarrassing;

毫無頭緒 in a hopeless tangle;

千頭萬緒 a host of problems; a multitude of things; a myriad of intricacies; a thousand and one things to attend to; all issues; be faced with a multitude of problems; be involved in thousands of intricacies; have innumerable things to attend to; many loose ends; many ramifications; thousands of strands and loose ends; too many things to attend to; very complicated; very confused;

~千頭萬緒，日理萬機 deal with a host of miscellaneous problems every day;

~千頭萬緒，湧上心頭 a thousand confused thoughts come to one's mind;

全無頭緒 make neither head nor tail of it;

有頭緒 have found the clue; near solution;

~有了頭緒 on the scent;

[頭癬] favus of the scalp;

[頭暈] dizzy; giddy;

頭暈目眩 be afflicted with vertigo; dizzy; dizzy of head and dim of eyes; have a dizzy spell; light in the head; light-headed; one's eyes swim in one's head; rocky;

頭暈腦脹 feel dizzy and have a headache;

頭暈眼花 dizzy; dizzy head and blurred eyes; dizzy of head and dim of sight; feel dizzy; feel strange; one's head is spinning;

一陣頭暈 a spell of dizziness;

[頭遭] first time;

[頭脹] feel heavy in the head;

[頭足] head and feet;

頭足倒置 turn everything upside down;

科頭跣足 bareheaded and barefooted; without a hat and barefooted;

評頭品足 carping; comment on; excessive criticism; find fault with; make frivolous remarks; overcritical; size up;

T

案頭 desktop; on one's desk; on the desk; tabletop;
昂起頭 lift up one's head;
熬頭 reward for long hardship; reward for long patience;
鰲頭 championship; first place;
把頭 gangmaster; labour contractor;
白頭 (1) gray hair; hoary head; (2) old age;
包工頭 labour contractor;
報頭 masthead; nameplate; newspaper heading;
抱頭 cover one's head with one's hands;
背兒頭 (of hairstyle) all back;
奔頭 prospect; sth to strive for;
筆頭兒 (1) nib; pen point; (2) writing skill;
鼻頭 nose;
篦頭 to comb one's hair with a fine-toothed comb;
鱉縮頭 behave cowardly; hide oneself from danger;
埠頭 port; wharf;
捕頭 head constable;
佈頭 (1) leftover of a bolt of cloth; (2) odd bits of cloth;
彩頭 auspicious sign; good luck; lucky; omen of profit; omen of victory;
蒼頭 (1) lackey; servant; (2) soldier;
糟頭 trough (in a livestock shed);
插頭 plug;
唱頭 pickup;
車頭 locomotive;
城頭 top of the city wall;
鋤頭 hoe;
船頭 bow; prow; stem;
牀頭 bedhead; bedside; head of a bed;
垂頭 hang one's head;
磁頭 head; magnetic recording head;
葱頭 onion;
從頭 (1) from the beginning; from the top; (2) anew; once again;
寸頭 (of hairstyle) crew cut;
搭頭兒 sth minor (to go with the major one);
打頭 (1) take a percentage (or cut) of the winnings in gambling; (2) drive head; take the lead;
大頭 (1) mask; (2) silver dollar; (3) larger (or thicker) end of sth; major part;
帶頭 take the initiative; take the lead;
彈頭 bullet; projectile nose; warhead;
當頭 (1) head on; right on sb's head; right over head; (2) imminent;
倒頭 lie down; touch the pillow;
到頭 at the end; to the end;
燈頭 (1) holder for the wick and chimney of a kerosene lamp; (2) electric light socket; lamp holder;
低頭 (1) hang one's head; (2) submit; yield;
地頭 (1) edge of a field; (2) (of a page) lower margin;
點了點頭 give a nod;
點頭 give a nod; give permission; nod; nod assent; nod one's head;
電唱頭 pickup;
掉頭 change direction; turn about; turn round;
調頭 change direction; turn about;
頂頭 come directly towards one;
渡頭 pier;
斷頭 be beheaded;
對頭 (1) correct; on the right track; true; (2) normal; right; (3) get on well; hit if off; on good terms with sb;
多彈頭 multiple warhead;
多頭 many aspects; many-sided; multiple;
額頭 brow; forehead;
二鍋頭 marry for the second time;
翻跟頭 loop the loop; somersault; turn a somersault;
分頭 (1) separately; several; (2) hair partings; parted hair;
墳頭 grave; mound;
風頭 (1) trends of events; (2) publicity one receives; (3) the way the wind blows;
佛頭 Buddha's head;
幞頭 kind of man's headdress in ancient times;
斧頭 axe; hatchet;
軋頭 dog;
丐頭 leader of beggars;
竿頭 head of a pole;
鎬頭 pick; pickaxe;
個頭兒 height; size;
跟頭 somersault;
工頭 foreman; ganger; headman; overseer; taskmaster;
骨頭 (1) bone; (2) person of a certain character;
寡頭 oligarch;
關頭 critical point; juncture; moment;
罐頭 can; canning; tin;
光頭 bareheaded; shaven head; shaven-head;
龜頭 balmony; glans penis;
過頭 (1) excessive; go too far; undue; (2) go beyond the limit; overdue;
焊頭 welding head;
號頭 number;
和頭 (1) both ends; (2) front end of a coffin;
核彈頭 nuclear warhead;

黑頭 (in Chinese opera) painted face;
紅菜頭 beetroot;
喉頭 larynx; throat;
猴頭 hedgehog hydnum;
後頭 (1) afterwards; (2) at the back; behind; in the rear; (3) later;
虎頭 tiger's head;
戶頭 bank account;
花頭 artifice; fresh ideas; ruses; tricks;
滑頭 shifty; slick; slippery; slippery fellow; sly customer;
話頭 thread of discourse;
喚頭 (of peddlers, etc.) percussion instruments (to attract customers);
回頭 (1) later; (2) turn one's head; turn round; (3) repent;
彗頭 head of comet;
火車頭 (railway) engine; locomotive;
火頭 (1) house where a fire started; (2) anger; (3) duration and degree of heating, cooking, smelting, etc.; (4) flame;
機頭 (of an aircraft) nose;
尖頭 pointed end; sharp end;
肩頭 shoulder;
箭頭 (1) (as a sign) arrow; (2) arrowhead;
接頭 (1) connect; join; joint; (2) contact get in touch with; (3) have knowledge of; know about;
街頭 street; street cornet;
盡頭 end;
勁頭 (1) energy; strength; (2) drive; vigour;
鏡頭 (1) camera lens; (2) scene; shot;
巨頭 magnate; tycoon;
钁頭 pick; pickaxe;
開頭 (1) at the beginning of; beginning period; (2) begin; start; (3) make a start;
刊頭 masthead of a newspaper of magazine; nameplate;
看頭兒 sth worth seeing or reading;
炕頭兒 (1) edge of a *kang*; (2) warmer end of a *kang*;
磕頭 kowtow;
空頭 (on the stock exchange) bear; nominal; phony; short-seller;
口頭 (1) oral; verbal; (2) by word of mouth; in speech; in words; on one's lips; verbal;
叩頭 kowtow;
扣頭 discounted sum;
苦頭 bitter taste; hardship; suffering;
塊頭 hulky; large;
瘌痢頭 (1) person's head affected with favus; (2) person affected with favus on the head;
來頭 (1) background; backing; connections; (2) cause; motive behind; (3) force with sth breaks out; (4) fun; interest;
癩頭 favus-infected head; scabies on head;
榔頭 hammer;
浪頭 (1) waves; (2) trend;
老頭 (1) old chap; old man; (2) one's father; (3) one's husband;
裏頭 inside; interior;
兩頭 (1) both ends; either end; (2) both parties; both sides;
獵頭 headhunt;
臨頭 befall; happen;
零頭 (1) odd; (2) remnant (of cloth);
領頭 be the first to do sth; take the lead;
留頭 let the hair grow long;
龍頭 (1) cock; tab; (2) dragon's head; (3) leader;
籠頭 halter;
露頭 (1) appear; emerge; (2) outcrop; outcropping; show one's head;
馬鍋頭 head of a caravan;
碼頭 (1) dock; hoverport; pier; quay; wharf; (2) commercial and transportation centre; port city;
埋頭 be engrossed in; bury oneself in; drown in; duck; give up to; immerse oneself in;
慢鏡頭 slow motion;
饅頭 steamed bread; steamed bun;
滿頭 have one's head covered with;
矛頭 bunt; spearhead; spearpoint;
冒頭 begin to crop up;
眉頭 brows;
蒙頭 cover one's head;
苗頭 suggestion of a new development; symptom of a trend;
摸頭 know the real situation; learn the ropes;
抹頭 (1) turn around; (2) head cloth; hood;
木頭 log; timber; wood;
拿大頭 make a fool of sb;
奶頭 (1) nipple of a feeding bottle; (2) nipple; teat;
撓頭 difficult to deal with; difficult to tackle;
年頭 (1) days; times; (2) long time; years; (3) year; (4) the year's harvest;
念頭 idea; intention; thought;
排頭 file leader; person at the head of a procession;
派頭 air; style; manner;
轡頭 bridle;
噴絲頭 spinning jet; spinning nozzle;
噴頭 (1) shower nozzle; (2) sprinkler head;
碰頭 meet and discuss; put heads together;

蓬蓬頭 shower nozzle;
辟頭 at the very start; right in the face; straight on the head;
劈頭 at the very start; right in the face; straight on the head;
姘頭 paramour;
平頭 closely cropped hair;
起頭 beginning; originate; start;
前頭 (1) above preceding; (2) ahead; at the head; in front;
牆頭 top of a wall;
橋頭 either end of a bridge;
帩頭 kind of man's headdress in ancient times;
拳頭 fist;
人頭 number of people;
認頭 accept the losses as it is;
乳頭 (1) nipple; teat; (2) papilla;
氫彈頭 H-warhead; hydrogen warhead;
搔頭 scratch one's head;
殺頭 behead; decapitate;
山頭 (1) faction; mountain stronghold; (2) hilltop; top of a mountain;
上頭 (1) above; the top; up; (2) authorities;
梢頭 (1) tip of a branch; (2) end of spring; (3) top log;
少白頭 (1) young person with graying hair; (2) prematurely gray;
舌頭 tongue;
蛇頭 snake's head;
石頭 pebble; rock; stone;
獅子頭 large meatball;
勢頭 (1) impetus; momentum; (2) look of things; tendency;
手頭 (1) at hand; on hand; (2) one's financial condition at the moment;
梳頭 comb one's hair;
水龍頭 faucet; (water) tap;
水頭 (1) head; (2) flood peak; peak of flow;
睡過頭 oversleep;
宿頭 inn to stop at for the night;
蒜頭 bulb of garlic; head of garlic;
榫頭 tenon and mortise;
鎖頭 lock;
擡頭 (1) begin a new line, as a mark of respect when mentioning the addressee in letters, official correspondence, etc.; (2) gain ground; look up; rise; raise one's head; (on receipts, bills, documents, etc.) name of the buyer or payee or space for filling in a name;
貪頭 bait; inducement;
灘頭 beachhead;
湯頭 prescription for a medical decoction;
濤頭 wave crest;
剃頭 (1) have one's hair cut; have a haircut; (2) have one's head shaved;
天地頭 top and bottom margins of a page; upper and lower margins of a page;
天頭 top margin of a page;
甜頭 (1) pleasant flavour; sweet taste; (2) benefit; good; sugar plum;
頭頭 head; leader;
禿頭 bald head; bald; baldheaded;
推頭 (1) cut sb's hair (with clippers); (2) have a haircut;
瓦頭 hanging edge of a dripping tile;
外頭 out; outdoors; outside;
彎頭 bend; elbow;
窩頭 steamed bread of corn, sorghum, etc.;
烏頭 rhizome of Chinese monkshood;
洗頭 have one's hair washed; shampoo; wash one's hair;
下頭 (1) as follows; (2) below; under;
先頭 ahead; before; formerly; in advance; in front; in the past;
線頭 (1) end of a thread; (2) odd piece of thread;
想頭 (1) idea; notion; thought; (2) expectation; hope; (3) thinking;
綃頭 a silk hood for binding the hair;
心頭 (1) heart; intention; mind; (2) heart of an animal;
行頭 (1) actor's costumes and paraphernalia; (2) clothing; costume;
興頭 enthusiasm; keen interest;
虛頭 false statement; lie;
楦頭 (1) hat block; (2) shoe last; shoe tree;
丫頭 (1) girl; (2) slave girl;
壓頭 pressure head;
咽頭 pharynx;
煙頭 cigarette end;
羊頭 sheep's head;
搖頭 shake one's head;
一頭 (1) along with something else; (2) directly; headlong; (3) suddenly; (4) a head; (5) a bulb of; a head of;
癮頭 addiction; strong interest;
迎頭 directly; head-on;
蠅頭 small as the head of a fly; tiny;
由頭 excuse; pretext;
油頭 sleek hair;
魚頭 (1) fish's head; (2) difficult part of a job;
玉搔頭 jade hairpin;
芋頭 (1) taro; (2) sweet potato;
寃大頭 person who spends a large sum of money

in vain;
圓頭 (of hairstyle) round cut;
源頭 fountainhead; source;
月頭 (1) time for monthly payment; (2) beginning of a month;
暈頭 (1) blockhead; (2) feel dizzy;
雲頭 wavy cloud pattern;
韻頭 head vowel, any of the three vowels "i", "u", and "ü" in certain compound vowels, as "i" in "iang".
竈頭 kitchen place;
賊頭 bandit leader; chief robber;
占頭 bad omen;
找頭 change (from money paid);
兆頭 omen; portent; sign;
折根頭 fall head over heels; somersault;
折頭 discount rate;
針頭 syringe needle;
枕頭 pillow;
枝頭 on the branch;
指頭 (1) finger; (2) toe;
鐘頭 hour;
豬頭 pig's head;
柱頭 (1) column cap; column head; (2) stigma;
抓頭 scratch the head;
磚頭 fragment of a brick;
轉頭 turn one's head;
賺頭 profit;
鑽頭 bit (of a drill);
準頭 accuracy; judgement; standard;
斫頭 behead; decapitate;
走到頭 walk to the end of the road;
嘴頭 mouth; tongue;
做頭 advantage to be gained from some activities; expected results;

tou⁴
tou

【透】 (1) pass through; penetrate; (2) let out; let through; (3) complete; thorough;

[透徹] incisive; penetrating; thorough;
講得透徹 drive home;

[透頂] (1) in the extreme; to the utmost; (2) reach the head;
腐敗透頂 decadent in the extreme; rotten to the core; thoroughly corrupt;
荒唐透頂 absolutely ridiculous; cap the climax of absurdity; most illogcial; preposterous to the extreme; utterly absurd;

[透風] (1) let the wind through; (2) blab; divulge a secret; let out a secret; tell a secret;
密不透風 airtight; keep it very secret;

[透骨] chilled to the bone; piercing;

[透過] (1) pass through; penetrate; (2) through the intermediary of;

[透汗] perspire all over;

[透鏡] lens;
透鏡光柵 lenticulation;
透鏡旋轉台 turret;
凹透鏡 concave lens; concave mirror;
凹凸透鏡 meniscus; meniscuslens;
~ 發散凹凸透鏡 divergent meniscus;
~ 校正凹凸透鏡 correction meniscus;
~ 球面凹凸透鏡 spherical meniscus;
大孔徑透鏡 high-aperture lens;
發散透鏡 negative lens;
分光透鏡 beam-splitting lens;
負透鏡 negative lens;
複消色差透鏡 apochromatic lens;
會聚透鏡 positive lens;
加速透鏡 accelerating lens;
可變焦距透鏡 zoom lens;
聲透鏡 acoustic lens;
凸透鏡 convex lens;
~ 雙凸透鏡 lenticular;
複曲面雙凸透鏡 toric lenticular;
球柱面雙凸透鏡 spherocylindrical lenticular;
條式雙凸透鏡 ribbon lenticular;
延伸雙凸透鏡 prolonged lenticular;
吸收透鏡 absorption lens;
消球差透鏡 aspherical lens;
消色差透鏡 achromatic lens;
正透鏡 positive lens;

[透了] very;
乾透了 bone dry;
恨透了 detest; hate to the utmost degree;
懶透了 bone idle;

[透漏] come to light; divulge; let out; reveal;

[透露] disclose; divulge; leak; reveal;
透露風聲 disclose information; leak information;
透露機密 disclose a secret;
半透膜 semipermeable membrane;

[透明] lucent; transparent;
透明包裝 see-through package;
透明度 openness; see-through clarity; transparency; transparency clarity;
~ 大氣透明度 atmospheric transparency;

~ 海水透明度 seawater transparency;
透明片 transparency;
透明性翻譯 transparent translation;
半透明 semitransparent;
不透明 non-transparent; opaque;
~ 不透明性 opacity;

[透膜] permeable membrane;
[透闢] penetrating; revealing;
[透平] turbine;
[透氣] (1) let air through; (2) give vent to a pent-up feeling of discontent; (3) relax from strain;
透氣的 breahable;
透不過氣 smother; suffocate;
~ 透不過氣來 gasp for breath;

[透射] (1) homology; (2) transmission;
透射比 transmittance;
~ 背景透射比 background transmittance;
~ 光透射比 luminous transmittance;
~ 光學透射比 optical transmittance;
~ 環路透射比 loop transmittance;
~ 屏幕透射比 screen transmittance;
雙軸透射 biaxial homology;
中心透射 central homology;
軸性透射 axial homology;

[透視] (1) penetrate; see though; (2) gain a perspective of; perspective; (3) grasp the essence; (4) to x-ray;
等角透視 isometrical perspective;
空間透視 aerial perspective;
熱點透視 penetrate the focus;
散點透視 cavalier perspective;
斜角透視 oblique perspective;

[透心涼] (1) extremely cold; freezing; heartfelt cold; penetrating coolness; (2) utterly disappointing;
[透着] appear; look; seem;
[透支] cash advance; make an overdraft; overdraw; take out an overdraft;
透支額 overdraft;
透支服務 overdraft facility;
現金透支 cash advances;

猜透 guess correctly; make a correct guess; outguess;
參透 understand profundities;
吃透 ascertain thoroughly; have a thorough grasp; understand thoroughly;
穿透 pass through; penetrate; penetration; pierce through;
浸透 impregnate; saturate; steep; soak; infuse;
看透 (1) gain an insight into; understand thoroughly; (2) be resigned to what is inevitable; know clearly; see through;
淋透 be drenched through (with rain);
摸透 get to know clearly; have an insight into;
瞧得透 see through; understand thoroughly;
沁透 infiltrate; penetrate; percolate; permeate; seep in;
深透 penetrating; profound and thorough;
滲透 (1) infiltrate; (2) osmose; (3) permeate; seep;
濕透 be wet through; get drenched;
剔透 (1) well-expressed; (2) keen and perceptive;
通透 understand thoroughly;

tu¹

tu

【凸】 convex; protruding; raised;

[凸版] relief printing plate;
凸版印刷 anastatic printing; letterpress; relief printing;

[凸出] bulge; cripling; embossment; project; protrude;
[凸化] convexification;
[凸鏡] convex mirror;
[凸輪] cam;
凸輪傳動 cam-gearing;
凸輪系統 camming;
凸輪組 cam group;
發碼凸輪 coding cam;
進氣凸輪 admission cam;
離合器凸輪 clutch cam;
三星凸輪 cloverleaf cam;
推動凸輪 actuating cam;
軸向凸輪 axial cam;

[凸面] convex;
[凸性] convexity;
局部一致凸性 local uniform convexity;

[凸緣] flange;
[凸月] gibbous moon;
適配凸緣 adapter flange;
無孔凸緣 blank flange;
閘凸緣 brake flange;

凹凸 concave-convex;
仿凸 convexoid;
廣凸 convexoid;
過凸 excess convexity;

tu

【禿】 (1) bald; bare; (2) bare; (3) blunt;

without a point; (4) incomplete; unsatisfactory;

[禿筆] (1) low skill at composition; poor writing ability; (2) worn-down writing brush;

[禿頂] bald; bald at the top of the head; bald-headed; become bald; slaphead;

[禿髮] alopecia;
禿髮症 alopecia;

[禿驢] bald ass;

[禿山] bare hill; barren hill;

[禿頭] bald head; bald; baldheaded;

[禿子] baldhead; baldy; slaphead;

光禿禿 bald; bare;
漸漸變禿 balding;
兀禿 (1) (of water, etc.) lukewarm; (2) not clear-cut; not straightforward;

tu

【鵚】 kind of water bird;

tu

【突】 (1) charge; dash forward; (2) abrupt; suddenly; (3) projecting;

[突變] (1) abrupt change; change suddenly; sudden change; (2) mutation;
突變型 mutant;
~ 回復突變型 reversible mutant;
~ 可見突變型 visible mutant;
~ 生化突變型 biochemical mutant;
~ 自然突變型 natural mutant;
突變學説 theory of mutation;
突變種 mutant variety;
突變子 muton;
錯義突變 missense mutation;
基因突變 gene mutation;
染色體突變 chromosomal mutation;
人工突變 man-made mutation;
無義突變 nonsense mutation;
隱性突變 recessive mutation;
真點突變 true point mutation;
致死突變 lethal mutation;

[突出] (1) give prominence to; highlight; stress; (2) outstanding; remarkable;
突出重點 give prominence to the key points; make the focal points stand out; stress the main points;
~ 突出重點副詞 focusing adverb;
使突出 acceuate;

[突觸] synapse;

[突擊] (1) assault; attack suddenly; make a sudden and violent attack; make a surprise attack; (2) do a crash job; make a concentrated effort to finish a job quickly;
突擊部隊 shock troops;
突擊隊 commando; shock brigade;
~ 突擊隊員 commando;
突擊任務 rush one's job;
垂直突擊 vertical assault;
轟炸突擊 bomb attack;
火箭突擊 rocket assault;
機降突擊 airmobile assault;
空降突擊 airborne assault;
~ 模擬空降突擊 simulated airborne assault;
空中協同突擊 coordinated aerial assault;
空中直接突擊 direct air assault;
全面突擊 all-out attack;
傘兵突擊 parachute assault;
原子突擊 atomic attack;

[突破] breakthrough; make a breakthrough;
突破點 breakthrough point;
突破防線 break through a defence line;
突破難關 break the back of a tough job;
新的突破 new breakthrough;

[突起] (1) rise up; (2) break out;
奇峰突起 a grotesque peak thrusts itself towards the sky; peaks tower magnificently;
異軍突起 a new faction appears all of a sudden; a new force suddenly coming to the fore;
戰事突起 hostilities broke out;

[突然] abruptly; all at once; all of a sudden; by the run; cap the climax; out of the blue; short; suddenly; unexpectedly; with a run; with suddenness; without any warning;
突然出現 crop out; crop up;
突然大笑 burst out laughing;
突然襲擊 sudden onslaught; surprise attack;
突然想起 flash upon;
突然走開 ;

[突如其來] abruptly; arise suddenly; arrive unexpectedly; come all of a sudden; come suddenly; come unexpectedly; happen suddenly; happen unexpectedly;

T

［突突］ (1) chug; (2) pit-a-pat;
［突圍］ break through enemy encirclement;
突圍而出 break out of an encirclement; break through the encirclement;
［突兀］ (1) lofty; towering; (2) abrupt; sudden; unexpected;
［突襲］ surprise attack;
凌晨突襲 dawn raid;
閃電式突襲 lightning attack;
原子突襲 atomic action;
［突眼］ exophthalmos; protuberant eyes;
搏動性突眼 pulsating exophthalmos;
惡性突眼 malignant exophthalmos;
內分泌突眼 endocrine exophthalmos;

奔突 (1) push one's way by shoving or bumping; (2) run quickly; speed;
鼻突 nasal process;
馳突 dash about;
衝突 clash; conflict;
骨突 apophysis;
喉突 laryngeal protuberance;
鶻突 bewildered; confused; muddled;
膏突 (1) follicle; (2) flower bud;
米突 metre;
豕突 run wild;
唐突 offensive; rude;
搪突 abrupt; rude;
足突 foot process;

tu²

tu

【荼】 (1) bitter edible plant; (2) white flower of reeds; (3) harm; poison;
［荼毒］ afflict with great suffering; cause disaster; cause injury; harm; poison; torment;
荼毒生靈 abuse and oppress the people; cause suffering to the people; cruelly injure the people; plunge the people into the depths of suffering;
荼毒思想 pollute sb's mind;

tu

【屠】 (1) slaughter; (2) butcher; massacre; slaughter; (3) a surname;
［屠城］ kill all the residents of a conquered city; massacre all residents of a conquered city;
［屠刀］ butcher's knife; carnificial knife;
［屠販］ butchers and vendors;
［屠夫］ (1) butcher; slaughterer; slaughterman; sticker; (2) ruthless ruler;
［屠戶］ butcher;
［屠戮］ massacre; slaughter;
［屠門大嚼］ feast oneself in imagination at the butcher's door — vain ambition;
［屠殺］ butcher; butchery; massacre; slaughter;
大屠殺 carnage; massacre;
強制屠殺 forced slaughter;
［屠燒］ kill and burn on a conquered land;
［屠宰］ butcher; slaughter;
屠宰場 abattoir; slaiughterhouse;
～城市屠宰場 municipal abattoir;
～市立屠宰場 municipal abattoir;
屠宰牲畜 slaughter animals;
農家屠宰 home slaughter;
無痛屠宰 humane slaughter;
斷屠 ban butchery of pigs, etc.
浮屠 (1) Buddha; (2) Buddhist; (3) pagoda; stupa;

tu

【徒】 (1) on foot; (2) bare; empty; (3) merely; only; (4) in vain; to no avail; (5) apprentice; disciple; follower; pupil; (6) fellow; person; (7) foot soldiers; infantry; (8) imprisonment;
［徒兵］ foot soldiers; infantry;
［徒搏］ hand-to-hand combat;
［徒步］ go on foot;
徒步跋涉 march;
徒步旅行 hiking; travel on foot;
［徒黨］ band; clique; faction;
［徒弟］ apprentice; disciple; pupil;
收徒弟 take an apprentice;
［徒工］ apprentice;
做徒工 work as an apprentice;
［徒勞］ bad job; bark at the moon; bay at the moon; be a fool for one's pains; be sent on a fool's errand; bite on granite; burn daylight; fight a losing game; fruitless labour; futile effort; go for nothing; go on a fool's errand; hold a candle to the sun; in vain; milk the bull; milk the ram; shoe the goose; sleeveless; to no avail; to no purpose; waste; wild-goose chase; without avail;
徒勞往返 hurry back and forth for nothing; make a futile journey; make a trip in vain; make a vain trip;

T

徒勞無功 an ass for one's pains; beat the air; draw water in a sieve; drop a bucket into an empty well; flag a dead horse; labour in vain; labour to no purpose; make a futile effort; make useless trouble; milk a he-goat; not to succeed after trying hard; plough the waves; plowing the wave; prove futile; sow the sands; use vain efforts; wasted effort; work to no avail; work without achieving anything;

徒勞無益 all to no purpose; come to naught; end in smoke; fish in the air; flog a dead horse; futile; hold a candle to the sun; lash the waves; of no avail; of no purpose; plough the air; plough the sand; shoe a goose; sow beans in the wind; weave a rope of sand; work in vain;

徒勞之舉 beat the air; futile effort; losing game; plough the sands; wild goose chase;

[徒然] for nothing; in vain; ineffectual; meaningless; to no avail; useless;

[徒涉] wade across;

[徒師] foot soldiers; infantry;

[徒手] bare-handed; empty-handed; freehand; unarmed;

徒手搏斗 fight bare-handed;

徒手畫 freehand drawing;

徒手起家 become rich bare-handed; make a fortune starting from scratch;

[徒首] bareheaded;

[徒裼] barefooted and barebreasted;

[徒跣] move on one's bare feet;

[徒刑] imprisonment; sentence;

無期徒刑 life imprisonment; life sentence;

~無期徒刑犯人 lifer;

~服無期徒刑 serve a life sentence;

有期徒刑 fixed-term imprisonment; set term of imprisonment;

[徒行] go on foot; hike; walk;

[徒眾] crowd; gang; croup of followers;

[徒自] in vain; of no avail;

徒自驚擾 become needlessly alarmed; frighten oneself without reason;

[徒坐] sit in leisure; sit without doing anything;

暴徒 ruffian; thug;

歹徒 evildoer; scoundrel;

黨徒 (1) henchman; (2) member of a clique or a reactionary political party;

賭徒 gambler;

惡徒 rascal; scoundrel;

非徒 not only;

匪徒 bandit; gangster;

佛教徒 Buddhist;

回教徒 Islamite;

基督徒 Christian;

奸徒 crafty person; evildoer;

教徒 believer of a religion;

酒徒 wine bibber;

門徒 disciple; follower;

叛徒 renegade; traitor;

清教徒 Puritan;

囚徒 convict; prisoner;

僧徒 Buddhist monks;

聖徒 believer; disciple; devotee;

師徒 teacher and pupil (relationship);

天主教徒 Catholic;

邪教徒 heretic;

新教徒 Protestant;

信徒 believer; devotee; disciple;

兇徒 murderer; villain;

學徒 apprentice; be an apprentice; serve one's apprenticeship; trainee;

異教徒 heathen; pagan;

宗教徒 person with religious faith;

tu

【途】 road; way;

[途程] course; road; way;

[途次] stopover; travellers' lodging;

[途經] go by way of; pass through; via;

[途徑] approach; avenue; channel; pathway; road; way;

不同途徑 various means;

~透過不同途徑 through various means;

關鍵途徑 critical path;

裂解途徑 fragmentation pathway;

能量途徑 energy pathway;

排洩途徑 excretion pathway;

求職途徑 job-seeking skills;

外交途徑 diplomatic channels;

[途窮] at the end of one's resources; come to the end of a road;

[途中] en route; on passage; on the way;

半途 halfway; midway;

長途 long-distance;

短途 short-distance;

歸途 homeward journey; one's way home;

宦途 official career;
路途 (1) journey; one's way home; (2) path; road;
旅途 journey; trip;
迷途 lose one's way; wrong path;
歧途 wrong road;
前途 future; prospect;
窮途 dead end;
仕途 official career;
首途 set out on a journey; start a journey;
坦途 highway; level road;
通途 through-fare;
畏途 dangerous road;
沿途 on the way; throughout a journey;
用途 use;
征途 journey;
中途 halfway; midway;

tu

【稌】 glutinous rice;

tu

【塗】 (1) apply; smear; spread on; (2) scrawl; scribble; (3) blot out; cross out; efface; erase; obliterate; (4) mire; mud; (5) a surname;

［塗層］ coat; coating;
表面塗層 finish coat;
防鏽底塗層 anti-corrosive prime coat;
浸漬塗層 dip coat;
耐酸塗層 anti-acid coat;
屏蔽性塗層 barrier coat;
水泥石棉塗層 cement asbestos coating;
碳氮化物塗層 carbonitride coating;
陶瓷塗層 ceramic coat;

［塗改］ alter; erase and change the wording of an article; obliterate;
塗改文件 tamper with a document;
塗改液 correction fluid;

［塗料］ coating; paint;
發光塗料 luminous paint;
膠黏塗料 bonded coating;
冷鐵塗料 chill coating;
耐酸塗料 anti-acid coating;
屏蔽塗料 barrier coating;
網紋塗料 cobweb coating;

［塗抹］ (1) erase; obliterate; (2) doodle; scribble;
東塗西抹 draw paint everywhere;

［塗上］ apply; lay on; smear; spread on;
［塗飾］ (1) cover with paint; (2) whitewash;
［塗污］ smear;
［塗鴉］ (1) scribble; poor calligraphy; write badly; (2) graffiti;
［塗脂］ apply powder;
脣若塗脂 have rich red lips;

海塗 shallows; shoal;
糊塗 bewildered; confused; fuzzy-wuzzy; muddled;
灘塗 shallows; shoal;
烏塗 (1) (of water, etc.) lukewarm; (2) not clear-cut; not straightforward;

tu

【葖】 turnip;

tu

【圖】 (1) chart; diagram; drawing; map; picture; portrait; (2) attempt; conspire; plan; scheme; (3) pursue; seek; (4) aim; intention; purpose; (5) a surname;

［圖案］ design; pattern;
雕刻圖案 carve a design;
構想圖案 conceive a design;
繪製圖案 draw a design;
修飾圖案 embellish a design;

［圖板］ (1) drawing board; (2) printing plate;
［圖版］ plate;
［圖報］ try to repay sb's kindness;
圖報恩德 hope to repay one's kindness;
感恩圖報 feel grateful for a kind act and plan to repay it; grateful for sb and seek ways to return his kindness; owe a debt of gratitude and hope to requite it;

［圖表］ chart; diagram; figure; graph; pictogram; table;
一張圖表 a diagram;

［圖冊］ atlas; illustrated books;
光譜圖冊 spectral atlas;
氣候圖冊 climatic atlas;
污染圖冊 pollution atlas;

［圖存］ strive for survival;
［圖釘］ drawing pin; thumbtack;
［圖畫］ drawing; painting; picture;
圖畫符號 pictogram;
圖畫文字 pictograph;
圖畫紙 cartridge paper;
連環圖畫 cartoon series;
美如圖畫 as handsome as paint;

［圖解］ diagram; figure; graph; graphic

analysis;
圖解比較 graphical comparison;

[圖廓] map boarder; map margin;
圖廓注記 border information; marginal information;

[圖賴] try to deny what one has said or done;

[圖利] desire to make money; plan to make money;
唯利是圖 be bent solely on profit; be interested only in personal gain; blind to all but one's own interest; care solely for profit; have an eye to the main chance; plan only how to get money; pursue profit as one's only aim; put profit-making first; scheme after nothing but gain; seek nothing but profits; seek only profit; intent on nothing but profit;
惟利是圖 be bent solely on profit; be intent on nothing but profit; interested only in material gain;
無利可圖 no advantage to be gained; no profit will come in; profitless; unprofitable;

[圖名] for the sake of prestige; pursue fame;
圖名圖利 seek fame and wealth;

[圖謀] conspire; plan; plot; scheme;
圖謀不軌 concoct a plot; conspire against the state; engage in illegal activities; harbour evil intentions; hatch a sinister plot; incite sedition; make dishonest schemes; plan a rebellion; plot sth unlawful;
圖謀不遂 fail in one's plot;
圖謀私利 seek personal interests;

[圖片] photograph; picture;
圖片説明 caption;
收集圖片 collect pictures;
塑性圖片 plastigraph;

[圖譜] atlas;
彩色圖譜 colour atlas;

[圖窮匕見] when the map is unrolled, the dagger is revealed;

[圖示法] iconography;

[圖式] schema;
表象圖式 representational schemata;
認知圖式 cognitive schema;

[圖書] book;
圖書出版 bibliogony;
圖書館 library;
~圖書館館長 chief librarian; librarian;
~圖書館集成系統 integrated library system;
~圖書館經濟學 library economics;
~圖書館社會學 sociology of library;
~圖書館系統管理 library system management;
~圖書館現代化 library modernization;
~圖書館學 science of library;
~圖書館員 bibliothecary; librarian;
~圖書館自動化 library automation;
~參考圖書館 reference library;
~儲藏圖書館 depository library;
~大學圖書館 college library; university library;
~多媒體圖書館 multimedia library;
~兒童圖書館 children's library; juvenile library;
~教育圖書館 educational library;
~借閱圖書館 lending library;
~流動圖書館 bibliobus; bookmobile; circulating library;
~少年兒童圖書館 children's library;
~團體圖書館 corporation library;
~學院圖書館 college library;
~中央圖書館 central library;
圖書目錄 library catalogue;
圖書心理學 biliopsychology;
圖書資料 books and reference materials;
咖啡桌圖書 coffee table book;

[圖騰] totem;

[圖文] pictures and texts;
圖文並茂 the picture and its accompanying essay are both excellent;
圖文廣播 teletext;

[圖像] image; imagery; picture;
圖像處理 image processing;
圖像干擾 image interference;
圖像合成 image synthesis;
圖像失真 image distortion;
圖像識別 image recognition;
圖像輸出設備 image output device;
圖像輸入設備 image input device;
圖像數據庫 image database;
圖像鎖定 image lock;
圖像信息 graphic information;
~圖像信息處理 graphic information processing;
~圖像信息系統 graphic information system;
圖像映射原語 bit boundary block transfer;

T

編碼圖像　coded pictures;
大量的圖像　a mass of images;
光圖像　optical image;
黑白圖像　black-and-white image;
模糊圖像　blurred image; blurred picture;
耐酸圖像　acid-resistance image;
掃描圖像　scan imagery;
聲頻圖像　audio image;
消色差圖像　achromatic image;

[圖形] contour; figure; graph; outline; sketch;
圖形處理　graphic processing;
~計算機圖形處理 cornputergraphics;
圖形核心系統　graphical kernel system;
圖形界面　interface;
圖形輸入語言　graphic input language;
圖形數據庫　image database;
圖形顯示　picture display;
圖形用戶界面　graphic user interface;
圖形語言　graphic language;
畫影圖形　draw a portrait;

[圖樣] blueprint; design; drawing; mould; pattern;

[圖章] chop; seal; stamp;
刻圖章　engrave a seal; make a chop by carving;
橡皮圖章　rubber stamp;
一枚圖章　a seal;

百美圖　picture showing a large number of beautiful women;
版圖　domain; territory;
餅分圖　pie chart;
冰圖　ice atlas;
不圖　not seek; to one's surprise; unexpectedly;
佈線圖　wiring diagram;
草圖　draft; outline; preliminary sketch; rough draft; rough sketch; rude drawing; scheme; sketch plan; sketching; thumbnail sketch;
側面圖　side view;
側視圖　side view;
插圖　demonstration; figure; illustration; insert; insert map; inset; plate;
春宮圖　pornographic pictures;
導游圖　tourist map;
底視圖　bottom view;
底圖　base map;
地層圖　stratigraphic map;
地貌圖　geomorphologic map;
地圖　map;
地形圖　relief map; topographic map;
地輿圖　atlas;
地質圖　geologic map;
電路圖　circuit diagram;
頂視圖　vertical view;
讀圖　interpret blueprints; interpret drawings;
斷面圖　section; sectional drawing;
防火圖　fire atlas;
分佈圖　distribution map;
風向圖　wind rose;
附圖　attached map or drawing; figure;
構圖　make the composition;
構造圖　seismic (or earthquake) chart (or map);
掛圖　(1) hanging chart; (2) wallchart; wall map;
海圖　marine chart; nautical chart; sea chart;
弘圖　grand prospect; great plan;
宏圖　great plan; grand prospect;
鴻圖　great plan; grand prospect;
後視圖　back view; rearview;
畫圖　draw designs, maps, etc.; picture;
繪圖　chart; draft; sketch;
簡圖　diagram; sketch; simple illustration;
截圖　dump; shot;
接線圖　connection diagram; wiring diagram;
結構圖　structural drawing;
藍圖　(1) blueprint; project outline; (2) plan for construction;
力圖　strive to; try hard to;
立面圖　elevation (drawing);
立體圖　stereoscopic drawing;
流程圖　flow chart; flow diagram;
略圖　sketch; sketch map;
描圖　plot; trace; tracing;
腦電圖　electroencephalogram (EEG)
鳥瞰圖　bird's-eye view
平面圖　(1) plan; (2) plane figure;
剖面圖　section; sectional drawing;
剖視圖　cutaway view;
拼圖　jigsaw;
剖視圖　cutaway view;
企圖　(1) attempt; attempt to; contrive; design to; have a go at; in an attempt to; in order to; scheme; seek; try; with intent to; (2) intention; plan; scheme;
氣候圖　climatic chart;
前視圖　front view;
曲線圖　diagram (of curves);
全視圖　full view; general view;
曬圖　blueprint; make a blueprint;
上視圖　top view;
設計圖　design drawing;
施工圖　working drawing;
示功圖　indicator card; indicator diagram;
示意圖　(1) schematic diagram; schematic drawing; (2) sketch map;

視圖 view;
試圖 attempt; try;
私圖 personal plan; selfish scheme;
縮尺圖 scale drawing;
他圖 different scheme; another plot;
太極圖 diagram of the universe;
貪圖 covet; hanker after;
天氣圖 synoptic chart; weather map;
條形圖 bar chart; histogram;
投影圖 projection drawings;
透視圖 perspective drawing;
土壤圖 soil map;
妄圖 try in vain; vainly attempt;
希圖 attempt; harbour the intention of;
線路圖 circuit diagram;
詳圖 detailed drawing; detailed map;
斜視圖 oblique drawing;
心電圖 electrocardiogram;
心動圖 cardiogram;
星圖 star atlas; star chart; star map;
雄圖 great ambition; grandiose plan;
瓆圖 nation; state;
徐圖 slowly;
岩相圖 lithofacies map;
要圖 important plan; urgent task;
意圖 intent; intention; purpose;
有向圖 digraph;
右上圖 top right;
輿圖 map;
遠圖 plan far ahead; plan for the future;
雲圖 cloud atlas; cloud chart;
折線圖 broken-line graph;
震波圖 seismogram;
正面圖 front view;
正視圖 elevation; front view;
指示圖 indication view;
製圖 cartograph; make charts; make maps;
狀態圖 state diagram;
壯圖 ambitious attempt; attempt at sth spectacular;
縱視圖 longitudinal view;
左上圖 top left;

tu

【酴】 (1) distiller's grain; distiller's yeast; (2) wine brewed for the second time;

tu

【鵌】 a kind of bird which shares its nest with rats;

tu³

tu

【土】 (1) earth; soil; (2) ground; land; (3) indigenous; local; native; (4) home-made; indigenous; (5) unenlightened; unrefined; (6) opium;

［土壩］ earth dam; earth-filled dam;

［土產］ local products;

［土城］ city wall made of clay;

［土地］ (1) ground; land; soil; (2) territory; (3) dirt; (4) front;
土地登記處 land registry;
土地法 agrarian laws;
土地改革 agrarian reform; land reform;
土地公 God of Earth;
土地管理局 land office; land registry;
土地規劃 land planning;
~土地規劃學 science of land planning;
土地經濟學 land economics;
土地均分論 agrarianism;
~土地均分論者 agrarian;
土地均分運動 agrarianism;
土地利用 land use; land utilization;
~土地利用圖 land-use map;
土地廟 temple of the God of Earth;
土地批租 land lease;
土地評價 land evaluation;
土地神 gnome;
土地使用 land use;
~土地使用權 right to use land;
~土地使用權轉讓 transfer of the right to use land;
土地市場 land market;
土地業權人 title holder of the land;
土地擁有者 land owner;
土地增值 rise in land value;
土地租賃 land lease;
分配土地 apportion land;
豐土沃地 fertile piece of land;
耕種土地 till the land;
灌溉土地 irrigate land;
開拓土地 clear land;
可轉讓的土地 alienable lands;
清除土地 strip a field;
一大片土地 a tract of land;
一方塊土地 a sod of land;
一塊土地 a parcel of land; a piece of land; a plot of land;
一片土地 a stretch of land;
一片狹長的土地 a strip of land;
擁有土地 own land;

［土豆］ (1) peanuts; (2) potatoes; spud;
新土豆 new potato;

［土法］ traditional method;

土法烹調 country cooking;
土法上馬 get on the job with local methods; start with indigenous methods;
土法生產 produce by indigenous methods;
[土番] aborigine; uncivilized native;
[土匪] bandit; brigand;
消滅土匪 sweep away the bandits;
一股土匪 a gang of bandits;
[土風舞] country dancing; folk dance;
[土瓜] yam beans;
[土棍] local bully; local rascal; ruffian;
[土豪] local tyrant;
土豪劣紳 evil and powerful elements in a community; local bullies and evil gentry; local depots and bad gentry; local ruffians and the oppressive gentry; local tyrants and evil gentry;
[土話] colloquial expressions; dialects; local dialects;
[土黃] colour of loess; yellowish brown;
[土貨] local produce; local products; native products;
[土坑] heated bed;
[土牢] dungeon;
[土脈] (1) land; (2) soil in spring;
[土木] (1) civil; (2) earth and wood;
土木工程 civil engineering;
~土木工程師 civil engineer;
[土坯] adobe;
[土氣] rustic; uncouth;
人很土氣 rustic man;
土裏土氣 countrified; hillbilly; rustic; stop a clock; uncouth; unsophisticated;
~土裏土氣的 countrified;
[土壤] ground; soil;
土壤保持 soil conservation;
土壤比熱 specific heat capacity of soil;
土壤比重 specific gravity of soil;
土壤導熱性 heat conductivity of soil;
土壤地帶性 soil zonality;
土壤調查 soil investigation;
土壤發育 soil development;
土壤反應 soil reaction;
土壤肥力 soil fertility;
土壤分類 soil classification;
土壤改良 soil improvement;
土壤概圖 reconnaissance soil map;
土壤固相 soild phase of soil;
土壤鹹度 soil alkalinity;
土壤膠體 soil colloid;
土壤結持度 soil consistence;
土壤結構 soil structure;
土壤空氣 soil air;
土壤力學 soil mechanics;
土壤流失 soil loss;
土壤密度 soil density;
土壤剖面 soil profile;
土壤氣相 gaseous phase of soil;
土壤侵蝕 soil erosion;
~防止土壤侵蝕 soil erosion control;
土壤容重 volume weight of soil;
土壤溶液 soil solution;
土壤三相 three-phase of soil;
土壤生物 soil organism;
土壤施肥 fertilization of the soil;
土壤濕度 soil humidity;
土壤水 soil water;
~土壤水份 soil moisture;
土壤酸度 soil acidity;
土壤通氣性 soil aeration;
土壤團聚體 soil aggregate;
土壤團粒 soil granule;
土壤溫度 soil temperature;
~土壤溫度錶 soil thermometer;
土壤污染 soil pollution;
土壤詳圖 detailed soil map;
土壤亞綱 soil suborder;
土壤亞類 soil sub-group;
土壤液相 liquid phase of soil;
土壤質地 soil texture;
土壤製圖 soil mapping;
土壤組成 soil constitution;
潮濕的土壤 watery soil;
粗質土壤 coarse-textured soil;
肥沃的土壤 fertile soil;
固結土壤 consolidated soil;
結殼土壤 incrusted soil;
可耕土壤 arable oil;
農業土壤 agricultural soil;
貧瘠的土壤 sick soil;
細質土壤 fine-textured soil;
一層土壤 a layer of earth;
自然土壤 natural soil;
[土人] natives;
[土喪] burial in the ground;
[土色] ashen; pale;
[土星] Saturn;
[土音] local accent; local pronunciation;
[土語] local dialects; patois;
[土賊] bandit;

T

[土長] native born;
根生土長 be born and raised in a place; indigenous; native-born; root of a growth;
[土質] condition of the soil;
[土製] crudely manufactured;
[土著] aboriginals; natives;

安土 feel at home wherever one is;
邦土 territory of a country;
本土 (1) one's native country; (2) one's native land; (3) metropolitan territory;
表土 surface soil; topsoil;
塵土 dust;
沖積土 alluvial soil;
出土 (1) be excavated; be unearthed; (2) come up out of the ground;
瓷土 china clay; porcelain clay;
寸土 an inch of land;
撮土 scoop up rubbish with a dustbin;
撢土 brush off the dust; whisk away the dust;
底土 subsoil;
凍土 frozen earth (or ground, soil);
動土 break ground; start a building;
礬土 alumina;
糞土 dung and dirt; muck;
風土 natural conditions and social customs of a place;
浮土 dust collected on furniture, etc.; surface dust;
腐殖土 humus soil;
改土 improve the soil;
故土 native land;
觀音土 kind of white clay;
硅藻土 diatomaceous earth; diatomite;
國土 territory land;
黑鈣土 black earth; chernozem;
黑土 black earth;
紅土 (1) laterite; red soil (or earth); (2) red iron ore powder;
黃土 loess;
灰化土 podsol; podzol;
回填土 backfill;
穢土 dirt; refuse; rubbish;
混凝土 concrete;
瘠土 barren land; poor soil;
疆土 territory;
焦土 scorched earth – ravages of war;
淨土 the Pure Land or Paradise (where the Buddhas and Bodhisattvas live);
客土 (1) earth removed from some other place to improve the local soil; (2) foreign land; strange land;
樂土 land of happiness; paradise;
栗鈣土 chestnut soil;
領土 territory;
泥土 (1) clay; (2) earth; soil;
黏土 clay;
培土 earth up; hill up;
漂礫土 boulder clay;
破土 (1) (in starting a building, project, etc.) break ground; (2) (of a seedling) break through the soil; (3) start spring plough;
壤土 loam;
入土 (of a dead person) be buried;
三合土 construction material made up of lime, sand and clay;
三和土 construction material made up of lime, sand and clay;
沙壤土 sandy loam;
沙土 sandy soil;
砂土 sandy soil;
生土 immature soil;
士敏土 cement;
守土 defend the territory of one's country;
熟土 mellow soil;
水土 (1) natural environment and climate; (2) water and soil;
死土 dead soil;
松土 soft soil;
陶土 potter's clay; pottery clay; kaolin;
鐵礬土 ferrous alumina;
沃土 fertile soil; rich soil;
鄉土 (1) home village; native soil; (2) local; of one's native land;
心土 subsoil;
煙土 crude opium;
鹽堿土 saline-alkali soil;
鹽土 saline soil; solonchak;
鹽漬土 salinized soil;
一把土 a handful of earth;
一層土 a bed of clay;
一堆土 a mound of soil;
一方土 a cubic metre of earth;
一塊土 a clod of earth; a clump of earth; lump of earth;
壅土 hill (up);
髒土 dust and rubbish; refuse;
沼澤土 bog soil;
赭土 ochre;

tu 

【吐】 (1) spit; (2) say; tell; utter;
[吐哺握發] one's eagerness to look for

worthies and virtuous officials; spat out a mouthful in the middle of eating and bound up one's hair in the midst of a bath in order to see visitors;

[吐出] spit out; utter;

[吐露] confess; disclose; reveal; tell;

吐露心事 pour out one's heart;

吐露真情 come out with the truth; tell the truth; unbosom oneself;

吐露真相 come out with the truth; unbosom oneself;

吐露衷曲 come out with the truth; come out with what is in one's heart of hearts; outpour one's heart; unbosom oneself;

盡情吐露 free one's heart; wear one's heart upon one's sleeve;

[吐沫星子] saliva drops;

[吐氣] give vent to pent-up feelings;

慢慢吐氣 let one's breath out;

軒眉吐氣 air of pride and satisfaction;

揚眉吐氣 blow off steam in rejoicing; elated; feel proud; feel proud and elated after one suddenly comes to fame, proud and elated; wealth or good luck; happy and proud; hold one's head high; stand up with head high;

[吐棄] cast aside; reject; spurn;

[吐舌] flash forth the tongue;

如蛇吐舌 flash forth like the tongue of the striking serpent;

縮頭吐舌 shrug and stick out the tongue;

[吐水] guttation;

[吐絲器] spinneret;

[吐痰] spit phlegm; spit;

禁止吐痰 spitting is prohibited

噴吐 gush; spurt;

傾吐 pour out one's heart; say what is on one's mind without reservation;

談吐 style of conversation;

吞吐 swallow and spit; take in and send out in large quantities;

tu

【釷】 thorium;

tu⁴

tu

【吐】 (1) spew; throw up; vomit; (2) disgorge; give up unwillingly;

[吐沫] saliva;

[吐血] spit blood; spit out blood; vomit blood;

[吐瀉] vomiting and diarrhoea; vomiting and purging;

上吐下瀉 suffer from vomiting and diarrhea; vomit and have watery stools; vomiting and purging;

口吐 what is vomited;

嘔吐 anabole; barf; chunder; puke; retch; shoot the cat; throw up; vomit;

噴吐 gush; spurt;

傾吐 pour out one's heart; reveal one's sorrows; say what is on one's mind without reservation; speak freely of one's thoughts;

談吐 manner of speaking; style of conversation; the way a person talks;

吞吐 (1) swallow and spit; (2) take in and send out in large quantities;

想吐 want to throw up;

一吐 get it off one's chest;

tu

【兔】 hare; rabbit;

[兔唇] harelip;

[兔毫] writing brush;

[兔籠] hutch;

[兔起鶻落] bold and agile calligraphy; the moment a hare is flushed out, the falcon swoops down－quick flow of writer's thoughts and imagination;

[兔死狗烹] kill the hounds for food once the hares are bagged－eliminate trusted aids when they have outlived their usefulness; the hounds are killed for food once all the hares are bagged－trusted aides are eliminated when they have outlived their usefulness;

[兔死狐悲] like grieves for like; like mourns the death of like;

兔死狐悲，物傷其類 like mourns over the death of like; when the hare dies the fox mourns, and so animals grieve for their kind;

[兔脱] escape fast;

[兔崽子] bastard; brat;

[兔子] bunny; hare; rabbit;

兔子不吃窩邊草，老鷹不打窩下食 a rabbit doesn't eat the grass near its

own burrow, and a wise fox doesn't rob his neighbour's henroost; foxes prey farthest from their earths;
兔子尾巴—長不了 a hare's tail – can't be long; the tial of a rabbit can't be long – won't last long;
一對兔子 a couple of rabbits; a pair of rabbits;
一群兔子 a flock of rabbits;
一隻兔子 a rabbit;

［兔走烏飛］ movement of the sun and the moon; time flies; time passes swiftly;

白兔 rabbit;
家兔 rabbit;
狡兔 wily hare;
脱兔 escaped hare;
野兔 hare;
玉兔 the Jade Hare – the moon;

tu

【菟】 dodder;

tuan¹
tuan

【湍】 (1) (of a current) rapid; (2) rapid;
［湍動］ turbulence;
［湍激］ rapid;
［湍急］ rapid; swift; torrential;
［湍流］ rapid; swift current; torrent; turbulence;
湍流滾下 torrents of water rolling down;
湍流事故 turbulence accident;
湍流增強器 turbulizer;
空氣湍流 air turbulence;
晴空湍流 clear-air turbulence;

急湍 swift current;

tuan²
tuan

【團】 (1) circular; round; (2) sphere; sth shaped like a ball; (3) a lump of; a mass of; (4) group; mission; organization; party; society; (5) regiment; (6) unite;
［團拜］ mass greetings;
［團隊］ team;
團隊比賽 team game;
團隊合作 team effort; teamwork;
團隊精神 team spirit;
團隊協作 play as a team;
團隊遊戲 team game;
教學團隊 teaching team;
專業團隊 professional team;
~建立專業團隊 build a professional team;
［團粉］ cooking starch;
［團結］ cohesion; draw together; rally; unite; unity;
團結互助 work in unity and close cooperation; work in unity and help one another; unity and mutual aid;
團結就是力量 union is strength; unity is strength;
團結一致 cohere with united action; forge the closest unity; in unity and solidarity; monolithic solidarity; stick together; unite as one;
團結友愛 fraternal unity; solidarity and friendship;
團結自救 get united for one's own salvation;
安定團結 stability and unity;
精誠團結 consolidate with faith and dedication; solidate with dedication and honesty;
內部團結 inner cohesion;
［團聚］ (1) reunite; (2) rally; unite;
親人團聚 reunite with one's family and relatives;
全家團聚 family reunion;
一家團聚 in the bosom of one's family;
［團塊］ soil;
土壤團塊 aggregate of soil;
［團年］ family reunion during the Spring Festival;
團年飯 Lunar New Year Eve dinner;
［團扇］ round fan;
［團體］ body; group; team; organization;
團體操 group calisthenics;
團體傳播網絡 communication network in groups;
團體道德 group morality;
團體冠軍 team title;
團體論 theory of community;
團體票 group ticket;
團體賽 team competition;
團體素質 group quality;
團體壓力 group pressure;
解散團體 dissolve an organization;
新聞團體 the press corps;
學生團體 student body;
［團團轉］ in a confused haste; turn round and

T

round;
急得團團轉 pace up and down in a state of agitation;
忙得團團轉 round round in circles; up to one's ears in work;
團團打轉 run hither and thither;
[團員] member;
[團圓] reunion; union;
團圓飯 a family reunion dinner; a reunion dinner;
大團圓 (1) happy reunion; (2) happy ending;
[團長] regimental commender;
代表團團長 head of a delegation;
[團子] dumpling;
[團坐] sit around in circle;

兵團 (1) army; (2) corps; formation; large (military) unit;
財團 (1) consortium; syndicate; (2) financial group;
參觀團 visiting group;
大兵團 large troop formation;
代表團 delegation; mission;
黨團 (1) parliamentary group of a political party; (2) political parties and other organizations; (3) the Party and the League;
兒童團 Children's Corps;
發色團 chromophore;
歌劇團 opera troupe;
歌舞團 song and dance ensemble (or troupe);
工作團 work team;
共青團 Communist Youth League;
官能團 functional group;
觀光團 sightseeing party; visiting group;
合唱團 chorus;
話劇團 theatrical company;
還鄉團 home-going legion; landlords' restitution corps;
伙食團 mess;
集團 block; circle; clique; group; ring;
檢查團 inspection party;
劇團 theatrical company; troupe;
軍團 army group;
考察團 observation group;
樂團 philharmonic society; philharmonic orchestra;
領事團 consular corps.;
旅行團 touring party;
麻團 deep-fried sesame seed ball;
馬戲團 circus troupe;
麵團 dough;
暖氣團 warm air mass;
蒲團 cattail hassock; rush cushion;
氣團 air mass;
青年團 Communist Youth League;
曲藝團 recitation and ballad-singing troupe;
商團 group or society of businessmen;
社團 mass organizations;
師團 division;
使團 diplomatic corps;
團團 all round; round and round;
外交團 diplomatic corps;
慰問團 group sent to convey greetings and appreciation;
文工團 art troupe; song and dance ensemble;
小集團 clique; faction;
星團 (star) cluster;
星系團 cluster of galaxies;
星雲團 nebulous cluster;
一大團 a glob;
疑團 doubts and suspicions;
藝術團 art ensemble; troupe of musicians and artists;
原子團 atomic group;
雲團 cloud cluster;
雜技團 acrobatic troupe;
智囊團 brain trust;
主席團 presidium;
助色團 auxochrome;

tuan
【摶】 (1) roll round with the hand; (2) rely on; (3) take or follow a trail, etc.;
[摶飯] roll rice balls;

tuan
【糰】 round dumplings made from glutinous rice flour;
[糰子] small dough cake;

麵糰 dough;
麵糰糰 (of face) fat;
湯糰 stuffed dumplings made of glutinous rice flour served in soup;

tuan⁴
tuan
【彖】 (1) chapter in the *Book of Changes*; (2) hedgehog; hog; porcupine;

tui¹
tui
【推】 (1) push; shove; (2) grind; turn a mill or grindstone; (3) cut; pare; (4)

T

move along; promote; push forward; (5) enlarge; extend; (6) deduce; find out; infer; look into; ponder; (7) push away; refuse; shift; shirk; (8) be postponed; defer; delay; hold over; postpone; put off; retard; (9) choose; elect; (10) esteem; have a high opinion of; have a high regard for; hold in esteem; praise highly; recommend; respect; stand in awe of; think highly of;

[推本] go to the source;
推本窮源 look for the causes;
推本溯源 ascertain the cause; detect the reason; go into the source of a matter; scrutinize the root of things; seek the cause; trace the origin;

[推病] excuse oneself on the pretext of illness; feign sickness;

[推測] conjecture; deduce; guess; guesswork; infer; predict; reckon;
推測後果 calculate the effect;
根據推測 by inference;

[推誠] act in sincerity; place confidence in;
推誠相見 deal with sb in good faith; deal with sb in sincerity; open one's heart to sb; talk frankly without hedging about; treat sb with sincerity;

[推遲] be postponed; advance; defer; delay; hold over; postpone; put off; retard;
推遲會議 advance a meeting;

[推崇] esteem; have a high opinion of; have a high regard for; hold in esteem; praise highly; recommend; respect; stand in awe of; think highly of;
推崇備至 admire sb very much; have the greatest esteem for; laud sth to the skies;
備受推崇的 be highly acclaimed;

[推出] (1) push out; (2) present;
推出新產品 put out a new product;
推不出 (1) unable to decline; (2) unable to push out;

[推辭] decline; reject;
推辭之詞 words for declining sth;
萬勿推辭 please do not refuse;

[推戴] support;

[推擋] half volley with push;

[推倒] bulldoze; overturn; push over; topple;
推倒重來 be replaced with a new one; make a new start; scrap it and start all over again; start all over again;

[推定] deduce; infer;

[推動] actuate; drive; give impetus to; goose; lend impetus to; promote; propel; push forward;
推動工作 expedite the work; push the work forward;
推動力 driving force; promoting force;
推動器 driver;
~ 超前同步推動器 advance sync driver;
~ 陽極推動器 anode driver;
推動者 prime mover;

[推斷] deduce; infer; inference;
文法推斷 grammatical inference;
置信推斷 confidence inference;
作出推斷 draw an inference;

[推度] infer;
以理推度 infer from reasoning;

[推翻] (1) overrule; overthrow; overturn; topple; turn over; (2) cancel; repudiate;
推翻假設 explode a hypothesis;
推翻舊案 reverse the old verdict;
推翻決定 overturn a decision;
推翻協議 repudiate an agreement;
推翻政府 overthrow the government;

[推服] admire; consider better than oneself; respect;

[推故] make excuses;

[推廣] extend; popularize; propagate; spread;
推廣期 promotional period;
推廣先進經驗 spread advanced experience;
推而廣之 by a logical extension of this point; by an extension of this logic; give extended application;

[推薦] recommend;
推薦書 letter of recommendation;

[推獎] praise;

[推進] (1) carry forward; push ahead; push on; (2) advance; drive; move ahead; propel; propulsion; push forward;
推進工作 push ahead with one's work;
推進劑 propellant;
~ 推進劑泵 propellant pump;
~ 單組元推進劑 monopropellant;
~ 低溫推進劑 cryogenic propellant;
~ 固體推進劑 solid propellant;
~ 固液體推進劑 hybrid propellant;

~化學推進劑 chemical propellant;
~火箭推進劑 rocket propellant;
~液體推進劑 liquid propellant;
推進力 propulsion;
~風推進力 wind propulsion;
~核能推進力 nuclear propulsion;
~火箭推進力 rocket propulsion;
~噴氣推進力 jet propulsion;
推進器 booster; propeller;
推進裝置 propulsive arrangement;
電磁推進 electromagnetic propulsion;
電熱推進 electrothermal propulsion;
飛機推進 aircraft propulsion;
連續推進 continuous propulsion;

[推襟送抱] bare one's heart to sb; disclose everything to sb; lay one's heart bare to sb; meet in all sincerity; open one's heart to sb; sincere in dealing with others; talk in all sincerity; treat sb with sincerity; unbosom oneself to;

[推究] examine; investigate; reason out; study;
推究事理 study the whys and wherefores of things;

[推舉] (1) choose; elect; (2) clean and press;

[推開] (1) push away; (2) get away from;
推不開 unable to get out of; unable to push away;

[推類] reason by analogy;

[推理] infer; inference; reason; reason out; reasoning;
推理高明 make brilliant deduction;
推理小說 detective stories;
推理性理解 inferential comprehension;
推理性連詞 inferential conjunction;
常識推理 common-sense reasoning;
法律推理 legal reasoning;
歸納推理 inductive inference;
近似推理 approximate reasoning;
科學推理 scientific reasoning;
類比推理 analogical reasoning; reasoning from analogy;
邏輯推理 logical reasoning;
謬誤推理 fallacious inference;
演繹推理 deductive inference;

[推力] thrust;
推力室 thrust chamber;
反推力 backward thrust;
輔助推力 augmented thrust;
拱推力 arc thrust;
軸向推力 axial thrust;

[推論] corollary; deduction; inference;
推論性轉換 discursive transformation;
推論語義學 inferential semantics;
由此推論 by inference;

[推拿] manipulation; massage;

[推敲] deliberate; weigh;
推敲詞句 consider carefully words and phrases; seek the right word; weigh one's words;

[推求] ascertain; inquire into;

[推球] push a ball; shove a ball;

[推卻] decline; refuse;
幸勿推卻 I hope that you will not refuse; pray do not refuse;

[推讓] (1) decline; (2) deferent; yielding;
你推我讓 defer to each other;

[推人] push;
推人犯規 pushing;

[推算] calculate; reckon;

[推土機] bulldozer; dozer;
推土機手 bulldozer operator;
刮鏟推土機 blade dozer;
履帶推土機 crawler-mounted bulldozer;
水下推土機 underwater bulldozer;
坦克推土機 tank dozer;
小型推土機 calf-dozer;
斜角推土機 side dozer;

[推推搡搡] push and shove;

[推托] find a pretext for not doing sth; find an excuse for; make an excuse for; offer as an excuse; plead; shirk;

[推脫] evade; shirk;
推脫責任 shirk one's responsibility and duty;
推脫職責 evade doing a duty;

[推諉] pass the buck; shift responsibility onto others;
推諉搪塞 shift responsibility onto others and use evasive answers;
推諉責任 buck passing; pass the buck to;

[推問] examine and investigate;

[推想] deduce; guess; imagine; infer; reckon;

[推銷] market; merchandise; peddle; promote sales; sales promotion; selling;
推銷人員 sales people;
推銷商品 promote the sale of goods;
~推銷商品的電話 cold call;
推銷員 salesman; salesperson;
~電話推銷員 telemarketer;
~花言巧語的推銷員 smooth-talking salesman;

T

~男推銷員 salesman;
~女推銷員 saleswoman;
~圓滑的推銷員 smooth salesman;
挨戶推銷 door-to-door selling;
層壓式推銷 pyramid selling;
傾力推銷 high pressure selling;
軟推銷 soft sell;
上門推銷 cold call;
直接推銷 direct marketing;
逐戶推銷 house-to-house selling;

[推卸] irresponsible; shirk;
推卸責任 abandon one's obligations; absolute oneself from responsibility; pass the baby; pass the buck; shirk one's responsibility; shift the duty from one's shoulders;
推卸責任，委過於人 shirk one's responsibility and try to impute it to others; shirk responsibility and shift the blame onto others;
上推下御 shift the blame on to the higher-ups or one's subordinates;

[推謝] decline an offer on some pretext or other;

[推行] carry out; implement; implementation; practise; promote; pursue; put into practice;
推行模式 modes of implementation;
推行新政策 pursue new policies;
令出推行 every order is effectively enforced;

[推許] approve; esteem and commend; praise;

[推選] choose; elect;
推選某人為主席 elect sb chairman; elect sb to be chairman;

[推延] delay; postpone; procrastinate; put off;
推延會議 postpone a meeting;

[推移] (1) elapse; pass; (2) develop; evolve;
與世推移 change with the times;

[推重] admire; have a high regard for; hold in esteem;

挨推 delay and shirk one's duty;
公推 recommend by general acclaim;
類推 analogize; reason by analogy;
首推 consider sb first;
助推 boost;

tui²
tui

【隤】 collapse; fall in ruins;

tui

【頹】 (1) collapse; crumble; dilapidated; ruined; (2) decadent; declining; emaciated; weakened; withered; (3) dejected; dispirited; (4) cascade down; descend;

[頹敗] decadent; declining; degenerating; depraved;

[頹惰自甘] lazy and self-indulgent;

[頹放] decadent and dissolute; slovenly;

[頹廢] decadent; dispirited;
頹廢的情緒 decadent sentiments;

[頹風] corrupt practices; degenerate practice; moral degeneracy;
頹風敗俗 decadent customs; degenerate manners and bad customs;

[頹齡] closing years of one's life; the declining years;
頹齡龍鐘 advanced in age; in declining years and the period of senility;

[頹靡] crestfallen; dejected; downcast;

[頹然] dejected; disappointed; pliant; submissive;

[頹喪] beaten; dejected; discouraged; dispirited; down in the mouth; in the dumps; listless; ruined;
頹喪不振 dejected after defeat;

[頹勢] declining tendency;
止住頹勢 stop the rot;

[頹塌] collapse;

[頹唐] dejected; dispirited; downhearted;
頹唐不安 disconsolate and ill at ease;

[頹替] deteriorate; disintegrate; fall apart; ruined;

[頹陽] setting sun;

[頹垣斷壁] crumbling walls and dilapidated houses;

[頹運] declining fortune;

tui³
tui

【腿】 (1) leg; (2) leglike support; (3) ham;

[腿肚子] calf of the leg;

[腿杆子] lower leg; shank;

[腿跟] heel;

[腿骨] leg bone;

[腿腳] capable of walking;
腿腳不俐落 walk with difficulty;
腿腳不靈便 have difficulty walking; walk

with difficulty;
腿腳俐落 walk briskly;

[腿筋] sinews of one's legs;

[腿麻] one's leg has gone numb;

[腿毛] hair on legs;

[腿酸] one's legs are tired;
腿酸腳軟 one's legs are tired from walking for a long time;

[腿子] henchman; hired thug; lackey;

拔腿 (1) extricate oneself; get away; take to one's heels; (2) take a step;
綁腿 leg wrappings; puttee;
跛腿 crippled; lame;
粗腿 thick leg;
大腿 thigh;
二郎腿 with ankle on knee;
飛毛腿 fleet-footed; fleet-footed runner; fleet of foot;
分腿 straddle;
弓形腿 bandy leg; bowleg;
裹腿 puttee;
寒腿 rheumatism in the legs;
後腿 hind leg;
護腿 boothose; gaiter; legging; shin guard;
火腿 gammon; ham;
雞腿 chicken's leg;
假腿 artificial leg; peg leg;
巨腿 macroscelia;
絝腿 legs of trousers;
褲腿 trouser legs;
兩條腿 two legs;
羅圈腿 bandy legs; bowlegs;
盤腿 cross one's legs;
跑腿 courier; foot-man; do legwork; go on errands; run errands;
劈一字腿 do the splits;
前腿 foreleg;
屈腿 bend legs;
瘸腿 lame;
人造腿 artificial leg;
撒腿 run; start running; take to one's heels;
伸伸腿 stetch one's legs;
伸腿 (1) die; kick the bucket; (2) participate in sth. (to gain an advantage); (3) stretch one's legs;
瘦腿 thin legs;
雙腿 legs;
小腿 shank;
歇腿 stop on the way for a rest;
腰腿 nimbleness of one's waist and legs;
右腿 right leg;
豬腿 (1) pig's legs; (2) ham; legmeat of the hog;
左腿 left leg;

tui⁴
tui

【退】 (1) move back; recede; regress; retreat; retrogress; withdraw; (2) bow out; quit; withdraw from; (3) decline; recede; (4) fade; (5) give back; return; send back; (6) cancel;

[退避] keep out of the way; withdraw and avoid; withdraw and keep off;
退避三舍 give one a wide berth; give way to sb to avoid a conflict; keep a good distance from sb; keep at arm's length;
退避賢路 retreat from the path of worthies — yield one's post to a virtuous talent;

[退兵] (1) retreat; withdrawal; (2) force the army to retreat;
退兵之計 plan for repulsing the enemy;

[退步] fall behind; lag behind; retrogress;
留個退步 leave some leeway; leave some room for manoeuvre;

[退場] leave the stage;

[退朝] retire from the court;

[退出] bow out; drop out; quit; renounce; secede; withdraw from;
退出比賽 drop out of a race;
退出會場 walk out of a meeting;
退出歷史舞台 step down from the stage of history;
退出戰鬥 withdraw from acting;
退出組織 withdraw from an organization;
抽身退出 pull up the drawbridge;

[退黨] withdraw from a political party;
威脅退黨 threaten to quit the party;

[退敵] repel the enemy;

[退後] fall backward; move backward;

[退化] become vestigial; degenerate; degeneration; deteriorate;
品種退化 variety degeneration;
社會風氣退化 degrading social morals;
微生物退化 microbiological degeneration;
系統發育退化 phylogenetic degeneration;

[退還] give back; return;

[退換] exchange a purchase;
貨物出門，概不退換 goods sold are not returnable;

[退回] (1) give back; return; send back; (2) go back; retreat;
退回押金 return a deposit;
[退婚] annul engagement for marriage; break off an engagement;
[退火] anneal; annealing;
退火鋼 annealed steel;
退火爐 annealing furnace; lehr;
~連續退火爐 continuous lehr;
~彎板退火爐 bending lehr;
常化退火 normarzing annealing;
成卷退火 coil annealing;
倒逆退火 inverse annealing;
低溫退火 low temperature annealing;
電爐退火 electric furnace annealing;
電熱退火 electric annealing;
分批退火 batch annealing;
高溫退火 high-temperature annealing;
光亮退火 clean annealing;
光焰退火 flame annealing;
精密退火 fine annealing;
局部退火 local annealing;
擴散退火 diffusion annealing;
臨界退火 critical annealing;
爐內退火 furnace annealing;
密閉退火 close annealing;
雙重退火 duplex annealing;
碳化物退火 carbide annealing;
脱碳退火 decarburizing annealing;
脱氧退火 deoxidized annealing;
完工退火 finish annealing;
完全退火 complete annealing; full annealing;
循環退火 cycle annealing;
壓縮退火 compression annealing;
罩式爐退火 cover annealing;
真空退火 vacuum annealing;
中溫退火 medium temperature annealing;
[退伙] cancel an arrangement to eat at a mess;
[退貨] cancel the orders; return of goods;
退貨退錢 return merchandise for a refund;
概不退貨 no refunds for returned goods;
[退居] (1) retreat; withdraw; (2) decline; go down;
退居第二位 drop to second place;
退居二線 without to the second line of duty;
退居幕後 retire backstage; retire from a prominent position and take a less important one;
[退款] reimburse;
全額退款 full refund;
[退路] (1) route of retreat; (2) leeway; manoeuvre; (3) fallback; sth to fall back on;
斷絕退路 burn one's bridges;
留退路 hedge one's bets; leave ground for retreat;
~留個退路 leave some leeway;
自斷退路 burn one's bridges behind one; burn one's boats; burn one's bridge;
[退票] (1) get a refund for a ticket; return a ticket; (2) dishonoured cheque;
[退錢] refund; reimburse;
[退親] break off an engagement;
[退卻] (1) retreat; withdrawal; (2) decline; flinch; hang back; shrink back;
[退然] amiable; humble and tender;
[退讓] climb down; climb-down; give in; make a concession; yield;
退讓賢路 let abler men take one's place; retire and give room to better men; yield one's post to a virtuous talent; yield one's post to better men;
絕不退讓 never yield;
[退熱] bring down a fever;
[退燒] bring down a fever; the temperature has come down; remove fever;
[退食] retire from a meal;
[退士] (1) recluse; (2) retired official;
[退守] retreat and stand on the defensive;
[退稅] tax refund; tax reimbursement;
退稅證明書 debenture;
[退縮] backtrack; cower; cringe; flinch; hold back; recoil; shrink;
退縮不前 withdraw from advancing;
畏葸退縮 recoil from fear;
[退庭] retire from the courtroom;
[退位] abdicate; abdicate the throne; back space; give up the throne;
恭請退位 golden handshake;
[退無可退] be left with no room for retreat; there is no place to retreat to; there is no room for further retreat;
[退席] (1) leave a banquet; (2) leave a meeting; walk out;
[退休] retire;
退休金 pension; retirement pay; retirement pension;
~農業退休金 farm retirement pension;

退休年齡 retirement age;
退休社團 retired social group;
退休心理 psychological state of the retired;
半退休 semi-retired;
提早退休 early retirement;

[退學] discontinue one's schooling; drop out; drop out of school; leave school; withdraw from a school;
退學生 dropout;
退學者 dropout;
勒令退學 order to quit school;
因病退學 leave school owing to bad health;

[退役] be discharged from military service;
退役軍官 retired officer;

[退隱] go into retirement; retire from public life;
退隱林泉 go to grass; go where the woodbine twineth; retire to the woods;

[退約] break off a contract; break off an agreement;

[退職] resign from office; retire;
退職金 golden handshake;
退職年齡 age of retiring;

[退走] retreat; withdraw;

敗退 retreat after defeat; retreat in defeat;
屏退 order sb to retire;
病退 resign one's job because of illness; retire due to illness; withdrawal due to illness;
潮退 the tide goes out;
撤退 pull out; withdraw;
斥退 (1) dismiss sb from his post; expel from a school; (2) shout at sb to go away;
辭退 discharge; dismiss; give sb the air; turn away;
促退 hinder progress;
打退 beat back; beat off; repulse;
倒退 backward motion; go backwards; fall back; retreat; retrospect; review;
告退 (1) ask for leave to withdraw from a meeting, etc.; leave the scene; (2) resign from office;
海退 regression;
後退 back away; backlash; draw back; fall back; recess; retreat; retrograde;
擊退 beat back; repel;
減退 abate; decelerate; decline; decrease; drop; fall off; go down;
進退 (1) advance and retreat; (2) sense of propriety;
潰退 beat a precipitate retreat; retreat as a result of defeat; retreat in disorder;
謙退 modest and retiring; reserved;
清退 clear up and return; renounce; return; withdraw;
勸退 persuade sb to resign;
逡退 retire from office when nothing could be accomplished;
殺退 put to flight; rout;
衰退 decay; decline; downturn; dye out; failing; weakening;
恬退 contented and reserved; uninterested in wealth and glory;
消退 fade away; gradual vanish;
引退 retire from office; resign;
隱退 go and live in seclusion; reclusion; resign; retire; retire from political life;
勇退 withdraw courageously;
早退 leave early; leave earlier than one should;
逐退 drive back; repulse;

tui

【蜕】 (1) exuviate; slough off; (2) slough; exuviae;

[蜕變] (1) undergo transformation; (2) decay; (3) disintegration;
分支蜕變 branch disintegration;
人為蜕變 artificial disintegration;
原子蜕變 atomic disintegration;

[蜕化] (1) exuviate; slough off; (2) degenerate;
蜕化變質 become morally degenerate; degenerate;
墮落蜕化 demoralization and degeneration;
思想蜕化 become ideologically corrupt;

[蜕皮] exuviate; slough;

蟬蜕 cicada slough; extricate oneself; get rid of;
蛇蜕 snake slough;

tun[1]

tun

【吞】 (1) engulf; gulp down; swallow; (2) annex; take possession of;

[吞併] annex; gobble up; swallow up; take possession of another's property;
吞併財物 take others' property;
吞併國土 annex the land of other countries;

[吞掉] gobble up;

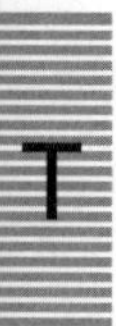

一口吞掉 devour in one gulp; gobble up in one go;

[吞服] take medicine;

[吞滅] conquer and annex;

[吞沒] embezzle; engulf; misappropriate; swallow up;

吞沒巨款 misappropriate a huge sum;

[吞聲] gulp down one's sobs; swallow one's sobs;

吞聲忍淚 choke down one's tears;

吞聲飲泣 gulp down sobs; sob bitterly; swallow the voice and tears;

含泣吞聲 choke down one's tears;

忍淚吞聲 choke down one's tears;

[吞食] devour; swallow;

肥己吞食 grow rich out of others;

[吞噬] devour; engulf; gobble up; swallow;

吞噬作用 phagocytosis;

被大火吞噬 be swallowed up by fire;

[吞吐] (1) swallow and spit; (2) take in and send out in large quantities;

半吞半吐 half concealed and half told; half concealing, half telling; mince matters; partly concealed and partly confessed; tell only half of it;

吞吐量 cargo handling; the volume of freight handled;

吞吞吐吐 hem and haw; hesitate in speech; hum and haw; mince words; mutter and mumble; prunes and prism; say hesitantly; speak in a halting way; speak of things with scruple; speak with reservation; stumble over one's words; tick over;

~吞吞吐吐地說 peep to say;

吞雲吐霧 blow a cloud — smoke tabacco; puff; smoke; smoke opium; smoke tobacco; take puffs;

[吞咽] swallow;

吞咽功能 deglutition;

吞咽困難 dysphagia;

吞咽食物 swallow food;

痙攣性吞咽困難 dysphagia spastica;

狼吞虎咽 a devil to eat; bolt; bolt down; cram; devour ravenously; eat in a terrible hurry; eat like a horse; eat like a wolf; eat like a pig; eat with the appetite of a wolf; engorge; engulf; fill oneself; garbage down; glut oneself; gluttonize; gobble up; gorge; gormandize; guzzle; indulge one's appetite; make a beast of oneself; make a pig of oneself; overeat; pitch in; raven; ravenous; scoff; stuff; tickle one's palate; tuck in; voracious; wade into the meal; walk into; water at the mouth; wire into; wolf down one's food;

麻痺性吞咽困難 dysphagia paralytica;

炎性吞咽困難 dysphagia inflammatoria;

吞佔 take possession of land illegally;

并吞 annex; merge; swallow up;

併吞 annex and absorb; swallow up entirely;

獨吞 pocket profit without sharing with anyone else; take exclusive possession of;

活吞 raw and whole; swallow sth;

慢吞吞 exasperatingly slow; irritatingly slow; jog-trot; languid; poky;

鯨吞 annex (territory); swallow like a whale;

侵吞 (1) embezzle; misappropriate; (2) annex; swallow up;

私吞 possession of; private y take;

tun

【暾】 sunrise;

[暾暾] blazing; bright; glowing;

朝暾 then early morning sun;

tun²

tun

【屯】 (1) collect; stockpile; store up; (2) station; (3) village;

[屯堡] military fortress; military outpost;

[屯兵] station troops;

[屯積] hoard up;

[屯聚] assemble; gather together;

[屯糧] board up grains; stockpile grains;

[屯紮] be stationed; encamp;

駐屯 (of troops) be stationed or quartered;

tun

【囤】 hoard; stockpile; store up;

[囤貨] store up commodities;

[囤積] corner; hoard; speculation;

囤積居奇 corner the market; engross the market; hoard and corner; rig up; store up goods and raise their price; store up goods to make a good bargain;

[囤糧] store up food for the army;

T

tun
【芚】 a kind of vegetable;

tun
【豚】 (1) small pig; (2) a surname;
［豚肩］ pig's shoulder;
［豚犬］ (1) pigs and dogs; (2) one's own sons;
［豚鼠］ guinea pig;

白鰭豚 Lipotes vexillifer;
海豚 dolphin;
河豚 balloonfish; globefish; puffer;
江豚 black finless porpoise;
土豚 earth pig;

tun
【飩】 stuffed dumplings;

餛飩 dumpling soup; won ton;

tun
【臀】 (1) behind; bottom; buttocks; rump; (2) (now rare) bottom of a vessel;
［臀部］ buttocks;

tun⁴
tun
【褪】 (1) slip out of sth; strip; take off one's clothing; (2) fade; fall off; (3) move backward; retreat;
［褪色］ fade in colour;
褪色柳 pussy willow;
［褪手］ hide one's hands in sleeves;
［褪套兒］ break a promise;

tuo¹
tuo
【托】 (1) hold in the palm; lift on the palm; support with the palm; (2) sth serving as a support; (3) serve as a foil; set off; (4) ask; charge; consign; entrust; owe to; rely upon; (5) give as a pretext; plead;
［托臂］ cantilever;
［托病］ on pretext of illness; plead illness; under the pretext of being ill; use sickness as an excuse;
托病辭職 ask for resignation on the pretext of illness; be relieved of one's office on the pretence of ill health; make illness an excuse to resign one's post;
［托詞］ find a pretext; make an excuse;
托詞謝絕 decline on some pretext;
［托墊］ coaster;
［托兒所］ child-care centre; nursery; nursery school;
全托托兒所 boarding nursery; full-time nursery;
日托托兒所 day nursery;
［托福］ thanks to you;
［托付］ commit sth to sb's care; entrust;
［托孤］ entrust an orphan to sb;
［托故］ give a pretext; make an excuse; use an excuse;
托故離開 make an excuse and leave;
托故早退 leave early under some pretext;
［托管］ deposit; mandate; trusteeship;
［托賴］ be indebted to;
［托名］ do sth in sb else's name;
［托盤］ pallet; serving tray; tray;
拆解式托盤 disposable pallet;
易耗托盤 expendable pallet;
裝車托盤 loading pallet;
［托收］ collection;
托收代理人 agent for collection;
跟單托收 documentary collection;
光票托收 clean collection;
票據托收 bill collection;
同城托收 city collection;
息票托收 coupon collection;
異地托收 country collection;
［托牙］ denture;
部分托牙 partial denture;
全口托牙 complete denture; full denture;
［托運］ check; consign for shipment;
托運人 consignor; shipper;

拜托 request sb to do sth;
杯托 saucer;
茶托 saucer;
襯托 provide a contrast; server as a foil;
付托 entrust; put sth in sb's;
烘托 (1) add shading around an object to make it stand out; (2) throw into sharp relief;
花托 receptacle;
賄托 ask sb to do sth for a consideration;
寄托 (1) entrust to the care of sb; leave with sb; (2) find sustenance in; place hope on; repose;
假托 (1) on the pretext of; (2) by means of; through the medium of; under sb else's name;

落托 (1) bold and generous; unconstrained; (2) down and out; in dire straits;
摩托 motor;
槍托 (rifle) butt; buttstock;
請托 commit st to sb's care; request another's help;
全托 put one's child in a boarding nursery;
日托 (of children) day care;
入托 (of children) start going to a nursery;
腮托 (of a violin or viola) chin rest;
受托 be entrusted with;
投托 place in the care of another;
推托 find a pretext for not doing sth; find an excuse for; make an excuse for; offer as an excuse; plead; shirk;
委托 commission; entrust; trust;
僞托 forge ancient literary or art work, or pass off modern works as ancient ones;
相托 entrust;
信托 commission; entrust; trust;
依托 backing; depend on; prop; reply on; support;
倚托 depend on; rely on;
整托 put one's child in a boarding nursery;
重托 great trust;
囑托 entrust;
轉托 ask some one else to do what is asked of one;

tuo

【拖】 (1) drag along; haul; pull; (2) delay; drag out; procrastinate; (3) implicate; involve;

[拖把] mop; swab;
橡膠拖把 squeegee;
用拖把拖地 mop the floor;

[拖板] (1) mop; (2) extension board;

[拖車] trailer;
多軸拖車 multiaxle trailer;
配電拖車 power distribution trailer;
四輪拖車 four-wheel trailer;

[拖船] tug;
救助拖船 rescue tug;
錨作拖船 anchor handling tug;

[拖帶] (1) drag along; (2) implicate; involve;
拖泥帶水 be bedraggled; be dragged through mud and water; beat about the bush; do things sloppily; messy; obscure style; sloppy; slovenly; unclean; untidy;

[拖刀計] feigning defeat in order to kill the enemy;

[拖地] mop;

[拖垮] be weakened; be worn down;
拖不垮，打不爛 indestructible; tough and unbeatable;

[拖拉] (1) dilatory; foot-dragging; (2) put off;
拖拉機 tractor;
~拖拉機拖車 tractor-trailer;
~農用拖拉機 farm tractor;
~通用拖拉機 all-purpose tractor;
~小型拖拉機 baby tractor;
拖拖拉拉 dilatory; drag one's heels; heep on putting off; let the grass grow under one's feet; procrastination; take one's time;

[拖累] (1) burden; drag; encumber; (2) implicate; involve; saddle with;
受家務拖累 be tied down by household chores;

[拖輪] tug; tugboat;

[拖欠] behind in payment; default; in arrears;
拖欠房租 arrears of rent;
拖欠稅款 in arrears with tax payment;

[拖網] trawl;
拖網漁船 trawler;
~遠洋拖網漁船 distant water trawler;
~中層拖網漁船 middle water trawler;
高口拖網 vinge trawl;
桁拖網 beam trawl;
上層拖網 pelagic trawl;
水底拖網 bottom trawl;
網板拖網 otter trawl;
中層拖網 mid-water trawl;

[拖尾] (1) smear; (2) streaking; (3) tailing;
白色長拖尾 long whie smear;
長拖尾 long streaking;
短拖尾 short streaking;
反極性拖尾 reverse polarity smear;
負拖尾 negative streaking;
附帶拖尾 attendant tailing;
黑色拖尾 black smear;
譜帶拖尾 band tailing;
正拖尾 positive streaking;
中頻拖尾 mid-band streaking;

[拖鞋] clogs; slippers;
布拖鞋 cloth slipper;
木拖鞋 wooden clogs; wooden slippers;
人字拖鞋 flip flops;
雙帶式拖鞋 cross-band slipper;
一雙拖鞋 a pair of slippers;
一隻拖鞋 a slipper;

T

[拖行] tow;
空中拖行 aerotow;
[拖延] defer; delay; drag on; postpone; procrastinate; put off; put over; stall for time;
拖延策略 delaying tactic;
拖延的 dilatory;
拖延時間 play for time; stall for time;
故意拖延 drag one's feet; obstructionism;
為爭取時間而拖延 play for time;

tuo

【託】 (1) charge with; commission; entrust to; rely on; (2) ask; request; (3) consign; consignment; (4) use as an excuse; (5) send messages indirectly;
[託辦] do sth entrusted by others; consign;
[託病] use illness as an excuse;
託病謝絕 decline on being ill;
[託辭] make excuses;
託辭謝絕 decline on some pretext;
[託兒所] crèche; day care centre; nursery;
日間託兒所 day nursery;
[託諷] give vent to one's feelings in writing;
[託福] thank you;
[託付] commission; entrust to;
[託孤] entrust an orphan to the care of a guardian;
[託故] find a pretext; make an excuse;
[託管] mandate; trust;
[託交] (1) c/o; deliver sth in care of sb; (2) befriend; make friends with;
[託賣品] consignment goods;
[託名討便] seek advantage by assuming another's name;
[託人] ask sb to do sth for oneself;
[託身] entrust oneself to; live at a friend's place;
[託言] make excuses;
[託運] consign; consign for shipment;
託運人 consignor;

拜託 request sb to do sth;
付託 charge sb with sth; commit sth to sb; consign; entrust; leave sth to sb; leave sth with sb; put sth in sb's charge; refer sth to sb; trust sb with sth; trust sth to sb;
請託 ask for a favour;
信託 confide; entrust; trust;
央託 entrust; request;
寓託 imply;
屬託 ask sb to do sth;
囑託 entrust; request sb to do sth;
轉託 entrust through another person;

tuo

【脱】 (1) strip; take off; undress; (2) peel; shed; (3) abandon; cast off; renounce; (4) escape from; get out of; leave; (5) miss out; omit; (6) if; in case; perhaps;
[脱靶] miss the target in shooting practice;
完全脱靶 entirely miss the market;
[脱班] (1) late for work; (2) behind schedule;
[脱產] be released from production;
脱產進修 mid-carried studies;
脱產學習 be released from one's regular work to study;
半脱產 partial sabbatical from work;
[脱出] come off; take off;
脱出樊籠 get out of the cage; shake off the yoke;
[脱黨] give up party membership; quit a political party;
脱黨者 postate;
[脱掉] take off;
把衣服脱掉 get one's kit off;
[脱髮] alopecia; baldness; falling out of hair; lose one's hair; trichomadesis;
脱髮症 alopecia;
產後脱髮 postpartum alopecia;
創傷性脱髮 traumatic alopecia;
精神性脱髮 psychogenic alopecia;
局限性脱髮 alopecia areata;
梅毒性脱髮 syphilitic alopecia;
男性型脱髮 male pattern alopecia;
普通脱髮 common baldness;
全部脱髮 alopecia totalis;
生長期脱髮 anagen effuvium;
壓迫性脱髮 pressure alopecia;
應激性脱髮 stress alopecia;
早老性脱髮 premature alopecia;
[脱稿] complete a manuscript;
[脱光] strip nude;
[脱軌] be derail;
[脱果現象] abscission of fruit;
脱軌事故 derail accident;
[脱機] off-line;
脱機編輯 off-line editing;
脱機操作 off-line operation;

~脱機操作系統 off-line operating system;
脱機管理 off-line management;
脱機系統 off-line system;

[脱彊] bold; get uncontrollable; run away; run wild;
脱彊之馬 a horse that has slipped its tether; a horse without a bridle; a runaway horse — uncontrollable; like a horse without a bridle; run wild;

[脱節] be disjointed; come apart; out of line with; ungear;

[脱臼] dislocate;

[脱開] escape; extricate; withdraw;
猛地脱開 tear loose;

[脱空] (1) work hard without any success; (2) lie;

[脱口] slip out of the mouth;
脱口成章 slip out of the mouth and become an essay — said of a literary talent; speak beautifully;
脱口而出 being quick with one's tongue; blurt out; bolt; come in pat; escape one's lips; let slip; one's tongue runs before one's wit; pass one's lips; ready tongue; say sth unwittingly; pop out; say the first thing that comes into one's head; slip out of one's lips; speak by impulse;
脱口秀 chat show; talk show;
~脱口秀主持人 talk show host;

[脱蠟] dewax; dewaxing;
丙烷脱蠟 propance dewaxing;
尿素脱蠟 urea dewaxing;
溶劑脱蠟 solvent dewaxing;
壓濾脱蠟 dewaxing;

[脱懶] escape from duty;

[脱離] (1) be divorced from; breakaway; break away from; separate oneself from; (2) away from; not within in; out of;
脱離本題 digress from the subject;
脱離關係 break off relations; cut off from; cut ties; sever connections; sever relations;
脱離苦海 get rid of this troublesome life; get out of the abyss of misery; leave this sea of bitterness; shake off this mortal coil;
脱離群眾 alienate oneself from the masses; be divorced from the masses; cut oneself off from the masses; lose touch with the masses; stay apart from the masses;
脱離危險 out of danger;
脱離現實 be divorced from reality; unrealistic;

[脱硫] desulfate; desulfurize; desulfation; desulphurization; desulphurize devulcanization;
脱硫劑 desulfurizer;
脱硫器 desulfurizer;devulcanizer;
脱硫作用 desulfidation;
加氧脱硫 hydrogenating desulfurization;
接觸脱硫 contact desulfurization;
磷酸鹽脱硫 phosphate desulfurization;
排煙脱硫 stack desulfurization;
抑制劑脱硫 inhibitor desulfurization;
直接脱硫 desulfurization;

[脱漏] be left out; be omitted; lalcuna; missing; omit;
脱漏法網 get out of the clutches of the law;

[脱落] abscission; come off; drop; fall off; let go; peel off;
脱落現象 abscission;
花蕾脱落 flower abscission;
毛髮脱落 lose one's hair;

[脱毛] molt; shed; the falloff of old hair;
脱毛劑 depilatory;
脱毛霜 depilatory cream;

[脱帽] raise one's hat; take off one's hat;
脱帽默哀 bare one's head and mourn in silence;
脱帽致敬 take off one's hat to sb;

[脱貧] be lifted out of poverty and backwardness; cast off the label of the poorest; extricate oneself from poverty; get rid of poverty; overcome poverty; shake off poverty; throw off poverty;
脱貧計劃 anti-poverty plan;
脱貧致富 cast off poverty and become prosperous;

[脱期] fail to come out on time;

[脱去] (1) strip; take off; throw off; (2) vindicate;

[脱然] free; untrammeled;
脱然無累 without a worry in the world;

[脱色] (1) decolour; decolourize; (2) fade;

[脱身] escape; extricate oneself; get away from; get free; leave; shake off;
脱身策略 exit strategy;

脱身離去 go away quietly and quickly;
脱身之計 a plan of escape; a plan that helps one to slip away;
脱不開身 cannot disengage oneself; cannot get away;
~整天忙得脱不開身 be tied up all day;

[脱手] (1) slip out of the hand; (2) dishoard; dispose of; get off one's hands; sell;

[脱售] sell out;

[脱水] abstraction; dehydrate; dehydration; dewater; dewatering;
脱水定時器 spin—dry timer;
脱水機 dehydrator;
~酵母脱水機 yeast dehydrator;
脱水劑 dehydrator;
脱水器 dehydrator; dewaterer;
~離心脱水器 centrifuge dehydrator;
~氣體管道脱水器 gas line dehydrator;
~氣體脱水器 gas dehydrator;
脱水桶 spin-dry tub;
脱水物 anhydride;
脱水作用 moisture abstraction;
超聲脱水 ultrasonic dehydration;
電脱水 electric dehydration;
機械脱水 mechanical dehydration;
加熱脱水 thermal dehydration;
浸漬脱水 submersion dehydration;
空氣脱水 air dehydration;
離心脱水 centrifugal dewatering;
兩面脱水 double side dewatering;
氣體脱水 gas dewatering;
缺鹽性脱水 salt deficient dehydration;
日曬脱水 sun dehydration;
使脱水 dehydrate;

[脱俗] free from vulgarity; free oneself from worldly ways; not be bound by conventions; otherworldly;
脱俗的人 plain people;
很脱俗 free from vulgarity;

[脱胎換骨] cast off one's old self and take on a new self; get rid of one's mutual frame; remould oneself thoroughly; turn over a new leaf; undergo a complete change;

[脱糖] desugar;

[脱逃] escape from; run away; withdraw;

[脱兔] escaped hare;
動如脱兔 as nimble as an escaping hare when going into action;
~靜如處子，動如脱兔 deliberate in counsel, prompt in action;
矯如脱兔 as fast as an escaped hare; swift as an eagle; swift of foot like a hare;
驚猿脱兔 startled monkeys or hare — flee in disorder;
快如脱兔 as fast as a swfit-footed hare;

[脱位] dislocate; dislocation;
半脱位 semi-dislocation;
病理性脱位 pathologic dislocation;
不全脱位 incomplete dislocation;
部份脱位 partial dislocation;
初期脱位 primitive dislocation;
創傷性脱位 traumatic dislocation;
單純脱位 simple dislocation;
宮內脱位 intrauterine dislocation;
關節脱位 abarticulation;
開放性脱位 open dislocation;
外傷性脱位 traumatic dislocation;
完全脱位 complete dislocation;

[脱誤] omissions and errors;

[脱下] drop; shed; take off;

[脱險] bring through; escape danger; out of danger; out of the woods;
安全脱險 escape in a whole skin; escape with life and limb; out of danger;
虎口脱險 a narrow escape;
平安脱險 escape unharmed;

[脱銷] out of stock;

[脱鞋] remove shoes; take off shoes;

[脱氧] desoxydate; desoxidation;
脱氧劑 desoxidant; desoxidizer;
脱氧麻黃鹼 desoxyephedrine;
脱氧皮質酮 desoxycorticosterone;

[脱衣] remove one's clothing; take off one's clothes;
脱衣舞 lap dancing; striptease;
~脱衣舞表演 strip show;
~脱衣舞女 exotic dancer; stripteaser;
~脱衣舞演員 stripper;
~脱衣舞夜總會 strip club;
~表演脱衣舞 do a strip;

[脱穎而出] become eminent; come out into the open; come to the fore; distinguish oneself; fully display one's talents;

[脱脂] defat; degrease; degreasing;
脱脂劑 degreaser;
~非侵蝕性脱脂劑 non-etching degreaser;
~噴霧脱脂劑 spray degreaser;
脱脂奶 skim milk;
脱脂乳 buttermilk;

T

超聲波脱脂 ultrasonic degreasing;
電解脱脂 electrolytic degreasing;
鹼脱脂 alkali degreasing;
煤油脱脂 kerosene degreasing;
溶劑脱脂 solvent degreasing;
乳化脱脂 emulsion degreasing;

[脱罪] exonerate sb from a charge;

擺脱 break away from; break from; break off; break loose; cast off; clear of; clear off; clear sb of sth; cut loose from; do away with; extricate oneself from; find freedom from; free from; free of; free oneself from; free sth of; get rid of; get sth off one's hands; get out; get over; give sb a miss; give sth a miss; give sb the go-by; give sth the go-by; rid; rid of; rid oneself of; see the back of sb; shake off; wash one's hands of;
超脱 be detached; original; transcend worldliness; unconventional;
出脱 (1) absolve sb from guilt or blame; (2) dispose of; grow (prettier, etc.); (3) manage to sell;
訛脱 error and missing character in a text;
活脱兒 remarkably like;
解脱 (1) extricate oneself; free oneself; (2) free oneself from worldly care;
開脱 absolve; exculpate; exonerate; vindicate;
夸脱 quart;
品脱 pint;
輕脱 frivolous; playful;
灑脱 casual and carefree; free and easy; graceful;
熟脱 very familiar with; well versed;
逃脱 break away; break free; escape from; free oneself from; get clear of; make good one's escape; succeed in escaping from;
佻脱 frivolous and careless; undisciplined;
跳脱 bracelet;
通脱 open-minded; unconventional;
兔脱 escape; run away like a hare;
推脱 evade; shirk;
虚脱 collapse; prostrate; prostration;
穎脱 distinguish oneself in performance;
掙脱 get rid of; shake off; struggle to free oneself;
縱脱 uninhibited; unrestrained;

tuo²

tuo

【佗】 (1) load; (2) he; (3) a surname;

tuo

【沱】 (1) rivers; streams; waterways; (2) name of a river; (3) continuous heavy rains;

[沱若] tears flowing down;

滂沱 pouring; torrential;

tuo

【陀】 craggy; rugged terrain;

[陀螺] gyro; whipping top; whirligig;
陀螺操縱 gyrocontrol;
陀螺儀 gyro; gyroscope;
~低溫陀螺儀 cryogenic gyroscope;
~電陀螺儀 electric gyro; electric gyroscope;
~方位陀螺儀 azimuth gyro;
~航向陀螺儀 azimuth gyro;
~雙積分陀螺儀 double-integrating gyroscope;
~位移陀螺儀 displacement gyroscope;
低溫陀螺 cryogenic gyro;
飛行陀螺 flight gyro;

佛陀 Buddha;
盤陀 (1) (of stone surface) uneven; (2) tortuous; zigzagging;
陂陀 uneven;
頭陀 mendicant Buddhist monk;

tuo

【柁】 large tie-beam;

房柁 girder;

tuo

【跎】 (1) miss one's footing; stumble; (2) miss the opportunity; vacillate;

蹉跎 waste time;

tuo

【馱】 carry a load on the back;

[馱鞍] packsaddle;

[馱包] load carried by animals;

[馱馬] packhorse;

tuo

【駝】 (1) camel; (2) hunchbacked; (3) carry on the back;

[駝背] hump; humpback; humpbacked; hunchbacked;
駝背的人 hunchback;
弓腰駝背 bend low; bunchbacked;

[駝峰] hump of a camel;
雙駝峰 double hump; dual hump;

重力駝峰 gravity hump;
自動化駝峰 automatic hump;

［駝鳥］ ostrich;

［駝絨］ camelhair;

［駝子］ humpbacked person; hunchback;

單峰駝 Arabian camel; one-humped camel;
駱駝 camel;
雙峰駝 Bactrian camel; two-humped camel;
橐駝 camel;

tuo

【鴕】 ostrich;

［鴕鳥］ ostrich;
鴕鳥政策 ostrich policy; ostrichism;

鷸鴕 kiwi;

tuo

【橐】 bag; bag without bottom; sack;

tuo

【鼉】 a kind of water lizard;

tuo³

tuo

【妥】 (1) firm; safe; secure; (2) appropriate; proper; (3) ready;

［妥當］ appropriate; proper; well-thought-out;
安排妥當 jack up; make proper arrangements;
準備妥當 make ready;

［妥靠］ reliable; trustworthy;

［妥洽］ (1) come to an agreement; (2) have the same opinion;

［妥善］ appropriate; proper; satisfactory; well arranged;
妥善安排 judicious preparation; make appropriate arrangements; well-thought out arrangements;

［妥實］ proper and reliable; well arranged;

［妥貼］ appropriate; fitting; proper; satisfactorily;
妥貼穩當 everything satisfactorily arranged on a sound basis;
辦事妥貼 handle matters well; manage things properly;

［妥協］ come to terms; compromise;
達成妥協 reach a compromise;
折中妥協 compromise; split the difference;

阿米妥 amytal;
安妥 (1) safe and proper; secure; well placed; (2) antu;
巴比妥 barbitone; barbital;
辦妥 finish doing sth properly;
苯巴比妥 luminal; phenobarbital; phenobarbitone;
不妥 improper; inappropriate; not proper; not the right way;
平妥 smooth and appropriate;
欠妥 amiss; improper; indecorous; not appropriate; not proper; not satisfactory; not very appropriate; out of place;
説妥 come to an agreement;
停妥 well-arranged; well-settled;
穩妥 proper and secure; reliable; safe; safe and dependable; sound;

tuo

【庹】 fathom; length between outstretched arms;

tuo

【橢】 elliptical; oblong; oval;

［橢率］ ellipticity;

［橢球］ ellipsoid;
變形橢球 deformation ellipsoid;
介質橢球 dielectric ellipsoid;
密集橢球 concentration ellipsoid;

［橢圓］ ellipse; oval; oval-shaped;
橢圓光度法 ellipsometry;
橢圓規 ellipsograph;
橢圓形 ellipse; oval;
~橢圓形鏡子 oval mirror;
橢圓性 ellipticity;
~強橢圓性 strong ellipticity;
~一致橢圓性 uniform ellipticity;
~真橢圓性 proper ellipticity;
橢圓狀 ellipticity;
潮流橢圓 current ellipse;
共焦橢圓 confocal ellipses;
絕熱橢圓 adiabatic ellipse;
同心橢圓 concentration ellipse;
退化橢圓 degenerate ellipse;

tuo⁴

tuo

【拓】 develop; open up;

［拓邊］ open up borderlands; open up new frontiers;

［拓地］ expand the territory; territorial expansion;
攔海拓地 reclaim fields from the sea;

圍海拓地 gain land from the sea; reclaim land from the sea;

[拓荒] reclaim wasteland; open up virgin soil;
拓荒者 pathbreaker; pioneer; trailblazer;

[拓寬] broaden;
拓寬馬路 broaden the road;
拓寬視野 widen one's view;

[拓撲] topology;
拓撲學 topology;
~ 分析拓撲學 topology;
~ 化學拓撲學 topology;
代數拓撲 algebraic topology;
典型拓撲 canonical topology;
凝聚拓撲 coherent topology;
容許拓撲 admissible topology;

[拓展] expand; prolongate; prolongation;
直接拓展 direct prolongation;

[拓殖] open up new land for settlement;

開拓 open up; developing; opening;

落拓 (1) bold and generous; unconstrained; (2) down and out; in dire straits;

tuo

【柝】 watchman's rattle;

tuo

【唾】 (1) saliva; spittle; (2) spit;

[唾罵] revile; spit on and curse;

[唾面自乾] drain the cup of humiliation;

[唾棄] cast aside; conspue; disdain and reject; infamy;
唾棄別人 see nothing good in others;
被人唾棄 be looked down upon;

[唾手可得] acquire sth easily; acquire sth with a wet finger; extremely easy to come at; get sth without great effort; get...without lifting a finger;

[唾液] saliva;
唾液過多 hypersalivation;
唾液過少 hyposialosis;
唾液減少 hyposalivation;
唾液缺乏 aptyalism;
唾液試驗 saliva test;
唾液腺 salivary gland;
~ 唾液腺病 salivary gland disease;
唾液腺瘻 salivary fistula;
唾液腺炎 sialadenitis;
唾液腺腫大症 sialosis;
分泌唾液 secrete saliva;
滿口唾液 with one's mouth full of saliva;

tuo

【魄】 dispirited; out of luck;

落魄 (1) bold and generous; unconstrained; (2) down and out; in dire straits;

tuo

【蘀】 fallen leaves and barks; withered leaves;

tuo

【籜】 shell of bamboo shoots;

wa¹

wa

【哇】 (1) sound of vomiting; (2) cry; make a crying sound; sound of crying by a child; (3) ooh;

［哇啦］ din; hullabaloo; uproar;
哇啦哇啦 a hubbub of voices; gabble away; make a hullabaloo; prate;

［哇哇］ cry; make a crying sound;
哇哇大哭 cry very loudly;

wa

【挖】 dig out; excavate; gouge; pick; scoop out;

［挖補］ cut and mend; gouge and mend; mend by replacing the damaged part; patch up; put in repair; replace a damaged part with mending material;

［挖掉］ dig out; dig up; eradicate;

［挖東牆補西牆］ digging the eastern wall to repair the western one; fail to make ends meet; keep up in one place at the expense of others;

［挖洞］ make a cave; make a hole;

［挖改］ cut and make changes;

［挖根］ dig sth up by the roots; uproot;

［挖溝］ ditch up;
挖溝機 ditcher;
~動力臂式挖溝機 power arm ditcher;
~機引挖溝機 tractor ditcher;
~履帶式挖溝機 gopher ditcher;
~錨式挖溝機 anchor ditcher;
~轉臂式挖溝機 jib-type ditcher;

［挖角］ lure away the employees of another company by making attractive offers;

［挖井］ dig a well;

［挖掘］ dig; dig out; excavate; grave; grub; hoe; unearth;
挖掘地點 diggings;
挖掘古物 excavate ancient relics;
挖掘機 digger; excavator; shovel;
~挖掘機手 excavator operator;
~叉式挖掘機 fork-type digger;
~長臂挖掘機 high-front shovel;
~螺旋挖掘機 helical digger;
~排水溝挖掘機 drain digger;
~昇運式挖掘機 hoover digger;
~圓盤挖掘機 dish digger;
挖掘坑道 sap a gallery;
挖掘潛力 exploit potentialities; exploit the potential; tap potentials; tap the latent power; uncover latent potentialities;
挖掘潛能 tap the latent power;

［挖空］ hollow;
挖空心思 cudgel one's brains; rack one's brains; think hard; work one's head to the bone;

［挖苦］ hurt others by sarcastic remarks; ridicule; satirize; speak ironically; speak sarcastically;
挖苦話 ironical remarks; verbal thrusts;
挖苦刻薄 hurt others by sarcastic remarks;
挖苦人 hold sb up to ridicule; pour ridicule on sb;
挖苦人的恭維話 back-handed compliment; left-handed compliment;

［挖泥］ dredge; dredge up mud;
挖泥船 dredge; dredge boat; dredger;
~多斗式挖泥船 bucket ladder dredge;
~吸揚式挖泥船 pump dredge;
~旋槳式挖泥船 cutter dredger;
~懸桿式挖泥船 side-boom dredge;
挖泥機 dredge; dredger;
~絞刀式挖泥機 cutter dredge;
~鏈斗式挖泥機 chain dredger;
~陸地挖泥機 dry dredger;
~昇降式挖泥機 elevator dredge;
~抓斗式挖泥機 grapple dredge;

［挖土］ earth excavation;
挖土工 excavator;
挖土機 excavator; shovel;
~反鏟挖土機 backacting shovel;
~纜索挖土機 dragline cableway excavator;
~履帶式挖土機 caterpillar-mounted excavator;
~蒸汽挖土機 steam shovel;
~抓斗挖土機 clamshell excavator; cramshell shovel;

［挖眼］ gouge out eyes;
割鼻挖眼 cut off the nose and gouge out the eyes;

開挖 excavate;

wa

【媧】 mythical sister and successor of Fu Xi, the legendary emperor;

女媧 goddess in Chinese mythology;

wa

【蛙】 frog;

[蛙吹] croaks of frogs;
[蛙卵] frogspawn;
[蛙鳴] croak; croaks of frogs;
蛙鳴蟬噪 croaks of frogs and chirp of cicadas; meaningless arguments;
[蛙人] frogman;
[蛙市] noise of frogs in the evening;
[蛙泳] breaststroke;
[蛙魚] toadfish;

W

井底之蛙 a frog in a well – a short-sighted person; a frog living at the bottom of a well – a person with a very limited outlook; an ill-informed and uneducated person;
牛蛙 bullfrog;
青蛙 frog;
樹蛙 tree frog;
雨蛙 tree toad;

wa

【窪】 (1) deep; (2) depression; hollow; pit; swamp;
[窪地] depression; low-lying land; marsh land;
[窪田] low-lying field;
[窪陷] low-lying; sunken;

低窪 low-lying;
坑坑窪窪 bumpy; full of bumps and hollows; rough;
水窪 water-logged depression;

wa

【鼃】 frog;

wa²

wa

【娃】 (1) beautiful woman; (2) baby; child; -ling; (3) exquisite; fine;
[娃娃] (1) baby; child; (2) doll; dolly;
娃娃車 baby buggy; baby car;
娃娃牀 cot; crib;
娃娃臉 baby face;
~ 娃娃臉的 baby-faced;
娃娃魚 giant salamander;
抱娃娃 (1) give birth to a child; (2) look after a child;
布娃娃 rag doll;
隔山不聽娃娃哭 out of sight; out of mind;
玩具娃娃 dolly;
小娃娃 (1) moppet; (2) small child;
洋娃娃 doll;
[娃子] (1) baby; child; (2) newborn animal; (3) slave;

放牛娃 child cowherd;
嬌娃 pretty young girl;
胖娃娃 chubby child;

wa³

wa

【瓦】 (1) roofing; tile; (2) earthenware; made of baked clay; pottery; (3) watt; (4) a surname;
[瓦當] eaves tiles;
[瓦房] a house with tiled roof; tile-roofed house; tiled house;
[瓦釜雷鳴] an unworthy man making a sensation and enjoying popularity; earth pots making a lot of noise – bombastic politicians in power while good men are out;
[瓦工] (1) bricklaying; plastering; tiling; (2) bricklayer; tiler;
[瓦罐] clay jar; earthen jar; pottery container;
瓦罐不離井上破 the pitcher goes so often to the well that it leaves its handle or its mouth; the pitcher goes so often to the well that it is broken at last; the pot goes so often to the water that it is broken at last;
[瓦匠] bricklayer; plasterer; tiler;
[瓦解] breakdown; collapse; crumble; disintegrate; disorganized; fall apart; fall into pieces;
瓦解冰銷 disintegrate like tiles and dissolve like ice; melt like ice and break like tiles; vanish from the scene;
瓦解土崩 fall apart; fall to pieces; in great tumult;
[瓦塊] fragments of a tile;
[瓦藍] tile blue;
[瓦楞] (1) corrugated; (2) rows of tiles on the roof;
瓦楞紙 corrugated paper;
[瓦礫] (1) brash; debris; rubble; (2) worthless things;
化為瓦礫 in ruins; reduce to rubble;
一堆瓦礫 a pile of rubble;
[瓦裂] broken like a tile;
[瓦器] crockery; earthenware; pottery;
[瓦時] watt-hour;
瓦時計 watt-hour meter;
[瓦斯] gas;

［瓦特］ watt;
瓦特計 wattmeter;
~氣流瓦特計 airflow wattmeter;
~熱輻射計型瓦特計 bolometer type wattmeter;
~熱量計式瓦特計 calorimetric wattmeter;
~無定向瓦特計 astatic wattmeter;
光瓦特 light watt;
國際瓦特 international watt;
有效瓦特 true watt;
［瓦子］ (1) brick; (2) brothel;
［瓦作］ bricklayer; plasterer;

板瓦 a kind of tile;
碧瓦 green glazed tile;
滴水瓦 a kind of tile with a drooping edge on one end;
缸瓦 earthen ware;
蝴蝶瓦 Chinese style tile;
脊瓦 ridge tile;
琉璃瓦 glazed tile;
弄瓦 give birth to a girl;
千瓦 kilowatt (KW);
石棉瓦 asbestos shingle; asbestos tile;
水泥瓦 cement tile;
陶瓦 earthenware tile;
筒瓦 semicircle shaped tile;
小青瓦 Chinese style tile;
一片瓦 a tile;
閘瓦 brake-block;
兆瓦 megawatt;
軸瓦 axle bush;

wa⁴

wa
【瓦】 cover the roof with tiles; tile;
［瓦刀］ bricklayer's cleaver;

wa
【袜】 simplified form of 襪;

wa
【襪】 hose; socks; stockings;
［襪帶］ garters; suspenders;
［襪底］ sole of a stocking;
［襪套］ ankle socks; socks;
［襪筒］ leg of a stocking;
［襪子］ hoses; socks; stockings;
臭襪子 stinky socks;
毛襪子 wollen socks;
毛線襪子 woolen sock;
一對襪子 a couple of socks;
一雙襪子 a pair of socks;

衩襪 stockings without bands;
長筒襪 stockings;
長襪 knee socks;
短襪 ankle socks; anklets; socks; sox;
連褲襪 pantyhose;
尼龍襪 nylon socks;
絲襪 silk socks; silk stockings;
彈力襪 stretch socks;
線襪 cotton socks;
鞋襪 shoes and socks;
羊毛襪 woolen socks or stockings;
一雙襪子 a pair of socks;
織襪 knit socks; knit stockings;

wa⁵

wa
【哇】 phrase-final particle;

wai¹

wai
【歪】 (1) askew; aslant; awry; crooked; out of the perpendicular; slanting; tilted; (2) depraved; devious; evil; underhand;
［歪才］ unique artistic talent;
有歪才 have a talent of working out crooked ideas;
［歪打正着］ hit the mark by a fluke; score a lucky hit;
［歪道］ underhand ways;
邪門歪道 crooked means; dishonest methods; dishonest practices; immoral or illegal doings; underhand ways;
［歪風］ (1) evil wind; ill wind; (2) unhealthy tendency; unhealthy trend;
歪風邪道 crooked means; dishonest practices;
歪風邪氣 adverse tendencies; evil trends; evil winds and noxious influence; unhealthy signs and trends; unhealthy trends and evil practices;
一股歪風 a gust of evil wind;
［歪貨］ fallen angels; rotten apple; wanton girls;
［歪路］ crooked course;
走上歪路 go off the rails;
［歪扭］ skew;
歪七扭八 askew; aslant; crooked; twist around;
歪歪扭扭 askew; crooked; not straight;

shapeless and twisted; twisted; twisting;

[歪曲] distort; misrepresent; twist;
歪曲別人的話 twist the words of others;
歪曲事實 distort facts; fact-fudging; fudge a fact; twist facts;
不容歪曲 not have one's words twisted;

[歪詩] doggerel;

[歪歪倒倒] cranky;

[歪斜] askew; aslant; crooked;
動態歪斜 dynamic skew;
靜態歪斜 static skew;
字符歪斜 character skew;

[歪心] crooked mind; evil mind; twisted mind;

[歪嘴] wry mouth; wry-mouthed;
笑歪了嘴 laugh one's mouth crooked;

骨歪 displacement of the fractured end of a bone;

wai⁴
wai

【外】 (1) on surface; out; outer; outside; outward; (2) another; other; (3) alien; external; foreign; nonlocal; (4) amateurish; green; inexperienced; lay; raw; unprofessional (5) diplomatic; (6) relatives of one's mother, sisters or daughters; (7) besides; extra; in addition; more; plus; (8) unofficial;

[外辦] outsource;

[外包] contract out; outsource;

[外幣] foreign currency;

[外邊] (1) exterior; out; outside; (2) another place; far-away place;

[外表] exterior; guise; on surface; outside; outward appearance;
外表的 superficial;
外表老實 have an honest appearance;
外表上 outwardly;
講求外表 pay special attention to appearances;

[外賓] foreign guests; foreign visitors;

[外埠] nonlocal ports;

[外部] exterior of anything;
外部傳播 external communication;
外部公眾 outside public;
外部環境 external environment;
外部世界 the outside world;
外部損失成本 external failure cost;

[外財] extra income; illegal gains; windfall;

[外層] outer; outer field;
外層空間 outer space;
外層空間法 law of the outer space;

[外差] heterodyne;
外差法 heterodyne;
~ 等幅外差法 equal heterodyne;
~ 它激外差法 separate heterodyne;

[外成作用] exogenic process;

[外出] go out; out of town;

[外敵] foreign enemy;

[外地] nonlocal; other places;
外地人 nonlocal person;

[外電] dispatches from foreign news agencies;

[外調] transfer to other places;

[外耳] external ear; outer ear;
外耳道 external auditory meatus;
~ 外耳道反射 external auditory meatus reflex;
~ 外耳道癤 furuncle of the external auditory canal;
~ 外耳道異物 foreign body in the external auditory canal;
~ 骨性外耳道 bony external auditory meatus;
~ 軟骨性外耳道 cartilaginous external auditory meatus;
外耳道炎 otitis externa;
~ 惡性外耳道炎 malignant otitis externa;
彌漫性外耳道炎 diffused otitis externa;
外耳孔 external auditory foramen;
外耳門 external acoustic pore; porus acusticus externus;
外耳濕疹 eczema of the external ear;
外耳炎 otitis externa;
~ 壞死性外耳炎 necrotizing otitis externa;
~ 急性外耳炎 acute otitis externa;
癤性外耳炎 furuncular otitis externa;
局限性外耳炎 circumscribed otitis externa;
彌漫性外耳炎 diffuse otitis externa;

[外分] external division;

[外敷] for external application;
外敷內服 for external application or to take it orally;
外敷藥 medicine for external application;

[外港] outer harbour; outport;

[外公] one's maternal grandfather;

[外觀] outward appearance; external looks;

[外國] foreign country; overseas;

外國貨 imported goods;
外國口音 foreign accent;
外國男孩子 foreign boy;
外國女孩子 foreign girl;
外國朋友 foreign friends;
外國人 foreigner;
外國投資 foreign investment;
外國文藝 foreign cultures;
外國語 adventitious language; foreign language; foreign tongue;
~一門外國語 an adventitious language;
外國資金 foreign capital;
裏通外國 have illicit relations with a foreign country; maintain traitorous relations with a foreign country;

[外行] (1) amateurish; inexperienced; lay; unprofessional; (2) greenhorn; layman; nonprofessional; outsider; raw hand;
外行的 amateurish;
外行管內行 nonprofessionals leading professionals;
外行話 lay language; layman's language;
外行人 lay; layperson;
~女外行人 laywoman;

[外號] nickname;

[外話] vulgar speech;

[外患] foreign aggression; foreign intrusion; foreign invasion;
外患內憂 foreign aggression and internal disturbance; foreign invasion and domestic trouble; foreign invasion and internal revolt; trouble coming from without and anxiety arising from within;
外患頻仍 subject to repeated foreign aggression;

[外匯] foreign currency; foreign exchange;
外匯波動 exchange fluctuation;
外匯儲備 foreign currency reserve;
外滙貸款 foreign exchange loan;
外匯短缺 shortage of foreign exchange;
外匯風險 foreign exchange risk;
外匯管理 exchange control;
~外匯管理法令 exchange control regulations;
~外匯管理機構 exchange control authorities;
~外匯管理制度 exchange control system;
外匯管制 foreign exchange control;
外匯行情 exchange quotation;
外匯會計 foreign exchange accounting;
外匯平衡 balance of foreign exchange;
外匯期權 option for foreign currency;
外匯市場 foreign exchange market;
外匯收支 balance of exchange;
外匯條款 exchange clause;
外匯調劑 foreign exchange adjusting;
外匯投機 exchange speculation;
外匯危機 exchange crisis;
外匯限額 foreign exchange allowance;
外匯限制 exchange restriction;
外匯業務 foreign exchange business;
外匯銀行 foreign exchange bank;
申請外匯 application for exchange;

[外活] extra work;

[外籍] foreign nationality;
外籍教師 foreign teacher;
外籍人士 alien; foreigner;

[外加] additional; applied; extra; in addition to; more; plus;
外加語 disjunct;
~風格外加語 style disjunct;
~內容外加語 content disjunct;

[外間] (1) outside; (2) outsiders; people not in the know;

[外交] diplomacy; foreign affairs;
外交病 diplomatic cold;
外交部 Ministry of Foreign Affairs;
外交部長 minister of foreign affairs;
外交辭令 diplomatic language; diplomatic parlance;
外交官 diplomat; diplomatic official; diplomatist;
~老練的外交官 master diplomat;
外交關係 diplomatic relations;
~斷絕外交關係 sever diplomatic relations;
~恢復外交關係 resume diplomatic relations;
~建立外交關係 establish diplomatic relations;
外交慣例 diplomatic practice;
外交活動 foreign activities;
外交豁免權 diplomatic immunity;
外交機關 diplomatic establishment;
外交家 diplomat; diplomatist;
外交能手 adept in diplomacy;
外交僑民 foreign national;
外交人員 diplomatic personnel;
外交勝利 diplomatic triumph;
外交使節 diplomatic envoy;
外交使團 diplomatic corps;

外交事務 foreign affairs;
外交手腕 diplomatic skill;
外交特權 diplomatic immunity; diplomatic privileges;
外交途徑 diplomatic channels;
外交團 the diplomatic corps;
外交文件 diplomatic documents;
外交郵袋 diplomatic bag;
外交語言 diplomatese;
外交原則 diplomatic principle;
外交政策 foreign policy;
穿梭外交 shuttle diplomacy;
公開外交 open diplomacy;
國際外交 international diplomacy;
美元外交 dollar diplomacy;
炮艦外交 gunboat diplomacy;
軟弱外交 weak-kneed diplomacy;

[外界] (1) external world; outside world; (2) outside;
來自外界 come from the outside;

[外借] circulation;
不外借 not for circulation;

[外景] exterior; location; outdoor shots;
外景拍攝 location shooting;
外景攝影 exterior shooting; location shooting; outdoor shooting;

[外科] surgical department; surgery;
外科病房 surgical ward;
外科醫生 surgeon;
~ 神經外科醫生 neurosurgeon;
~ 眼外科醫生 ophthalmic surgeon;
外科主任 head of the surgical department;
創傷外科 traumatology;
矯形外科 orthopedic surgery;
腦外科 cerebral surgery;
普通外科 general surgery;
心臟外科 department of cardiac surgery;
整形外科 plastic surgery;

[外快] additional income; extra income; extra money; side money;
撈外快 get extra income; make extra money;

[外來] external; foreign; outside;
外來表達法 alienism;
外來成分 alienism;
外來詞 alien word;
~ 外來詞匯 lexical borrowing;
外來句 syntactic borrowing;
外來人口 external population;
外來因素 extraneous factor;
外來語 foreign terms; loanword;

[外力] (1) outside force; (2) external force; foreign influence;

[外流] drain; exodus; flow outward; outflow;

[外路] places other than one's own;
外路人 stranger; outsider;

[外露] exposed;
牙腳外露 root exposed;

[外賣] carry-out; take-away;
外賣餐館 carry-out;
外賣食品 carry-out;

[外貿] external trade; foreign trade;
外貿部 ministry of foreign trade;
外貿公司 foreign trade corporation;
外貿局 foreign trade bureau;
外貿商場 stores of imports and exports;
外貿商品 imports and exports;
外貿市場 foreign trade market;
外貿盈餘 foreign trade surplus;
外貿政策 foreign trade policy;
外貿仲裁 foreign trade arbitration;

[外貌] appearance; aspect; exterior; outward appearance; external looks; looks;

[外面] out; outside;
最外面 outermost;

[外排] exclusive;
外排代詞 exclusive pronoun;

[外胚層] ectoderm;

[外婆] gran; granny; one's maternal grandmother;

[外妻] concubine;

[外僑] foreign nationals; foreign residents;

[外切酶] exonucleases;
核酸外切酶 exonucleases;

[外勤] (1) field-work; legwork; work done outside the office or in the field; (2) field personnel; field worker;

[外人] (1) outsiders; strangers; (2) foreigners;
別對外人講 between ourselves; between you and me;
如待外人 treat sb as a stranger;

[外商] foreign businessmen; foreign merchants; foreign tradesmen;
外商獨資企業 foreign-owned enterprise;
外商投資項目 foreign-invested project;

[外傷] external injuries; wound;

[外甥] (1) nephew; (2) daughter's son;
外甥打燈籠—照舅 back in the old rut; the nephew lighting a lantern to give light to his uncle – remain unchanged;
外甥女 niece;

[外省] other provinces; province other than one's own;
外省人 people from other provinces;
[外事] external affairs; foreign affairs;
[外室] one's mistress living outside;
[外宿] stay outside overnight;
[外孫] one's daughter's son; one's grandson;
外孫女 one's daughter's daughter; one's granddaughter;
[外逃] (1) flee to some other place; (2) flee the country;
[外套] blazer; outerwear; overcoat;
便服外套 sport coat; sport jacket; sports coat;
穿上外套 put on one's overcoat;
~幫人穿上外套 help sb into his overcoat;
皮外套 car coat;
無袖外套 jerkin;
一件外套 a jacket;
[外頭] out; outdoors; outside;
[外位] extraposition;
外位成分 extraposition word;
[外文] foreign language;
[外侮] external aggression; foreign aggression;
共禦外侮 unite to resist foreign aggression;
[外物] material comfort;
外物 slave to material comfort;
[外務] (1) matters outside one's job; (2) external affairs; foreign affairs;
[外向] extroversion; outgoing;
外向的人 extrovert;
外向型 export-oriented;
~外向型經濟 export-oriented economy;
~外向型企業 export-oriented enterprise;
外向型企業集團 groups of export-oriented enterprises;
[外相] foreign minister;
[外銷] export sales; export trade; for export;
外銷員 sales representative;
[外心] circumcentre;
[外型] appearance; contour; external form; outline; profile;
[外延] denotation; epitaxy; extension;
外延意義 denotative meaning;
低溫外延 low temperature epitaxy;
硅外延 silicon epitaxy;
汽相外延 vapour phase epitaxy;
異質外延 hetero epitaxy;
真空外延 vacuum epitaxy;
周相外延 solid epitaxy;
[外洋] abroad; overseas;
[外衣] coat; jacket; outer garment; outerwear;
短厚外衣 donkey jacket;
脱下外衣 take off one's coat;
[外逸層] exosphere;
[外因] external cause;
[外陰] vulva;
外陰病 vulvopathy;
外陰白斑症 leukoplakia vulvae;
外陰潰瘍 ulcus vulvae;
~急性外陰潰瘍 ulcus vulvae acutum;
外陰裂 vulval cleft;
外陰瘙癢 pruitus vulvae;
外陰炎 vulvitis;
~潰瘍性外陰炎 ulcerative vulvitis;
~糜爛性外陰炎 erosive vulvitis;
~濕疹型外陰炎 eczematiform vulvitis;
~糖尿病性外陰炎 diabetic vulvitis;
~萎縮性外陰炎 atrophic vulvitis;
外陰陰道炎 vulvovaginitis;
[外用] for external application; for external use;
[外語] foreign language;
外語園地 foreign languages corner;
[外遇] have extramarital affairs; illegal love affairs; paramour;
有外遇 have an extramarital affair;
[外援] external assistance; foreign aid; outside help;
需要外援 need outside help;
[外在] external; extrinsic;
外在經濟 external economy;
外在美 pulchritude;
[外債] external loans; foreign debts;
外債管理 foreign debt management;
舉借外債 borrow large sums of money from foreign powers;
[外展] abducent; abduction;
外展服務 outreach;
外展肌 abducent muscles; abductor;
外展神經 abducents;
[外長] foreign minister;
[外賬] overdue bill;
[外植] external implanatation;
[外指] exophoric reference;
[外質] ectoplasm;
[外資] foreign capital; foreign investment;
外資結構 foreign capital structure;

外資立法 foreign capital legislation;
外資企業 foreign-funded enterprise;
外資銀行 foreign bank;
利用外資 utilization of foreign investment;
吸引外資 absorb foreign capital; attract foreign capital; lure overseas funds;

[外子] reference to one's own husband;

保外 be released on bail;
不外 not beyond the scope of; nothing more than;
出外 leave for another town, city, etc.;
除外 added to; after; among other things; any other...than; apart from; as well as; aside from; bar; barring; besides; beyond; but; else; except; except for; excepting; excluding; exclusive of; in addition to; independent of; independently of; into the bargain; next to; no other than; none but; not; not counting; not including; on top of; other than; otherwise; otherwise than; outside; outside of; over and above; save; save and except; save for; save that; saving; short of; than; to the exclusion of; unless; with the exception of;
窗外 outside the window;
此外 and; and...as well; as well as; besides; furthermore; in addition; in addition to; moreover; what with...and what with;
等外 substandard;
度外 outside one's consideration;
對外 external; foreign;
額外 added; additional; extra;
分外 (1) all the better; all the more; especially; extremely; more than ever; particularly; (2) beyond one's duty; not one's duty; not one's job; outside the scope of one's duty;
格外 (1) additional; extra; (2) all the more; especially;
郭外 beyond the outer city wall; outside the city;
國外 abroad; external; overseas;
海外 abroad; overseas;
號外 (of a newspaper) extra;
紅外 infrared; infrared ray;
戶外 outdoors;
化外 area outside the pale of Chinese civilization;
婚外 extramarital;
見外 regard or treat sb as an outsider;
郊外 countryside; outskirts; suburb;
界外 area out of bounds;
懼外 xenophobic;
局外 not concerned with sth;
開外 above; over;
課外 after school; extracurricular; outside class;
老外 (1) layman; raw hand; (2) foreigner;
裏外 within and without;
例外 be an exception; exception;
另外 another; besides; in addition; moreover; other;
媚外 fawn on foreign powers; try to flatter foreigners;
門外 outside the door;
膜外 outside of one's attention, consideration, etc;
內外 (1) about; around; (2) domestic and foreign; inside and outside;
排外 antiforeign; exclusive; oppose everything foreign; parochial;
跑外 go shopping;
其外 extra; outside;
圈外 outside a circle;
塞外 beyond the borders; beyond the frontiers; beyond the Great Wall; north of the Great Wall;
涉外 concerning foreign affairs or foreign nationals;
室外 outdoor; outside;
疏外 distant;
四外 all around; everywhere;
題外 beyond the subject being discussed;
天外 (1) unexpected; windfall; (2) far and high;
物外 beyond the physical world;
騖外 depart from one's proper role;
向外 (1) turn outward; (2) upwards of;
霄外 beyond the sky;
校外 after school; outside school;
言外 between the lines; beyond the words spoken;
野外 field; open country;
以外 (1) except; in addition; other than; (2) beyond; outside; without;
意外 (1) unforeseen; unexpected; (2) accident; mishap; surprise;
域外 foreign country; beyond the frontier; outside China;
員外 (1) ministry councilor; (2) address for a rich landowner etc., somewhat similar to "esquire";
援外 (1) cite; quote; (2) appoint or recommend one's friends or favourites; (3) foreign aid;
在外 excluding; not including; outside;
之外 besides; beyond; except; in addition;

中外 at home and abroad; China and foreign countries; Chinese and foreign; in China and abroad;
駐外 be stationed abroad;
作外 stand on ceremony;

wan¹

wan

【剜】 carve out; cut out; exhaust; gouge out; scoop out;

［剜刀］ reamer;

［剜空］ gouge hollow;
剜空心思 exhaust one's ingenuity; exhaust one's wits;

wan

【蜿】 creep; meander; wind up; wriggle; zigzag;

［蜿曲］ meander;

［蜿蜒］ (1) wriggle; (2) creeping; meander; snake; wind; zigzag;
蜿蜒而上 wriggle up to;
蜿蜒流過 meander through;
蜿蜒前進 advance tortuously;
道路蜿蜒 a road winds;
河流蜿蜒 a river winds;

wan

【豌】 garden pea; pea;

［豌豆］ garden pea;
碗豆粉 pea flour;
豌豆糕 mashed-pea cake;
豌豆泥 mashed peas;
豌豆湯 pea soup;
寬葉香豌豆 everlasting pea;
青豌豆 green peas;
香豌豆 sweet pea;
野豌豆 wild pea;
一粒豌豆 a pea;
紫花豌豆 field pea;

wan

【彎】 (1) bent; bowed; crooked; curved; snaky; tortuous; (2) bend; (3) bend; curve; turn;

［彎度］ camber;
變彎度 variable camber;
大彎度 heavy camber;
彈簧彎度 spring camber;
葉片彎度 blade camber;
中線彎度 centre-line camber;
最大彎度 maximum camber;

［彎弓］ (1) drawn bow; (2) ready to shoot the arrow; (3) arch;

［彎管］ elbow;
排氣彎管 exhaust elbow;
排水彎管 drain elbow;
直角彎管 square elbow;

［彎路］ (1) crooked road; tortuous path; winding course; (2) circuitous course; detour; roundabout way;
少走彎路 avoid detours;
走彎路 do in a wrong way; follow a zigzag course; make a detour; take a roundabout route; take a tortuous course; take a wrong path; travel a tortuous road;

［彎橋］ curved bridge;

［彎曲］ (1) bent; crooked; meandering; winding; zigzag; (2) bend; bending; flex; flexure;
彎曲的 crooked;
彎曲設備 bending apparatus;
彎曲手指 flex one's fingers;
臂彎曲 brachiocyllosis;
衝擊彎曲 impact bending;
純彎曲 pure bending;
單純彎曲 simple bending;
點陣彎曲 lattice bending;
反彈性彎形彎曲 antielastic bending;
反向彎曲 reversed bending;
厚度彎曲 thickness flexure;
鍵彎曲 bond bending;
抗彎曲 counter bending;
聯合彎曲 combined flexure;
平面彎曲 plane flexure;
曲曲彎彎 full of twists and turns; there are a good many twists and turns all the way;
三點彎曲 three-point bending;
射束彎曲 beam bending;
同面彎曲 uniphanar bending;
同向彎曲 similar flexure;
彎彎曲曲 crooked; having many bends and curves; in and out; in twists and turns; meandering; snaky; tortuous; twist and turn; zigzag;
斜彎曲 skew bending;
預壓痕彎曲 pinch bending;
圓彎曲 circular bending;
直角彎曲 right-angle bending;
直線彎曲 straight-line bending;
縱向彎曲 longitudinal bending;

［彎頭］ bend; elbow;

風口彎頭 eyesight; elbow;
鉸接彎頭 adjustable elbow;
接合彎頭 joint elbow;
軟管彎頭 hose elbow;

[彎腰] bend one's back;
彎腰曲背 crooked; with one's back bent;

[彎子] bend; curve;

W

拗彎 twist;
臂彎 crook of the arm;
拐彎 (1) turn a corner; (2) turn round; pursue a new course;
急彎 (1) sharp turn; (2) turn suddenly; (3) elbow;
曲曲彎彎 tortuous; winding;
繞彎兒 (1) go for a stroll; (2) beat about the bush; talk in a roundabout way;
胃大彎 greater curvature;
胃小彎 lesser curvature of the stomach;
轉彎 make a turn; swerve; take a turn; turn a corner; turn in another direction;

wan

【灣】 (1) bay; cove; gulf; (2) bend of a stream; (3) anchor; moor;

[灣口] mouth of a bay;
[灣流] gulf stream;
[灣子] curve;

港灣 harbour;
海灣 bay; gulf;
河灣 river bend;
峽灣 fiord;

wan²

wan

【丸】 (1) pellet; pill; small ball; (2) egg; (3) bolus; capsule; pill; (4) completeness; completion;

[丸辭] circular argument;
[丸劑] medical pill; pill;
[丸藥] medicine in pill form;
[丸子] (1) ball; fish ball; meat ball; (2) medical pill; pill;
肉丸子 meatball;
炸丸子 fried meat balls;

彈丸 (1) bullet; pellet; shot; (2) small bit of land; tiny area;
定心丸 set one's mind at rest; sth capable of setting one's mind at ease; sth that soothes one's nerves;
睾丸 achers; acres; apples; balls; ballocks; bollocks; clappers; clusters; cobblers; cods; danglers; dusters; family jewels; flowers; gollies; goolie; knackers; marbles; nads; nuts; pills; plums; testicles; testis; wedding kit; wedding tackle;
蠟丸 (of medicine or other things) wax-coated pill;
雷丸 stone-like omphalia (omphalia lapidescens);
開心丸兒 words of comfort;
寬心丸兒 words of comfort; reassuring words;
泥丸 mud ball;
肉丸 meatball;
藥丸 pill of Chinese medicine;
魚丸 fishball;
樟腦丸 camphor ball; mothball;

wan

【刓】 round off; trim;

wan

【完】 (1) complete; entire; flawless; flawless and perfect; in good condition; in good shape; in perfect condition; intact; integrated; undamaged; unharmed; whole; (2) exhaust; run out; use up; (3) be completed; be done for; be finished; bring to a conclusion; come to a close; come to an end; complete; end; finish; get through; over; settle; through with; (4) a surname;

[完備] be adequately furnished; be fully equipped; complete; perfect;
完備化 completion;
~ 測度空間的完備化 completion of a measure space;
~ 賦值的完備化 completion of a variation;
~ 一致空間的完備化 completion of uniform space;
完備性 completeness;
~ 變分完備性 variational completeness;
~ 序列完備性 sequential completeness;
~ 組合完備性 combinatorial completeness;

[完畢] be done; complete; end; finish;
[完璧歸趙] return a thing intact to its owner; return sth to its owner in good condition;
[完成] accomplish; bring to success; complete;

completion; finish with sth; fulfil; fruition;
完成工作 finish the work off;
~迅速完成工作 whip through one's work;
完成計劃 fulfil one's plan;
完成進行時 perfect progressive tense;
完成進行體不定式 perfect progressive infinitive;
完成任務 accomplish one's mission; accomplish the task; fulfil the task; have the task completed;
完成日期 completion date;
完成時 perfect tense;
完成式動名詞 perfect gerund;
完成體不定式 perfect infinitive;
完成體進行式 perfect tense progressive;
完成學業 finish with school;
即將完成 near completion;
盡快完成 complete with all possible haste;
如期完成 meet a deadline;
尚未完成 be not completed yet;
提前完成 be completed ahead of time;
未完成 incomplete;
迅速完成 rattle through;

[完蛋] all over; all up; be busted; be doomed; be done for; be finished; be ruined; busted; collapse;

[完點] fixed point;
完點運算 fixed point operation;

[完稿] complete the manuscript; finish a piece of writing; through with a manuscript;

[完工] complete a project; finish doing sth; get through;
完工在即 near completion; will soon be completed;
峻事完工 complete and finish sth;
克期完工 set a date for completing the work;
走向完工 move towards the completion;

[完好] flaultless; flawless; in good condition; in perfect condition; intact; perfect; whole;
完好無缺 flawless; flawless and perfect; intact; undamaged;
完好無損 excellent without damage; in good condition; in good repair; in good shape; intact; sound and intact;

[完婚] conclusion of marriage; get married; marry;

[完結] bring to a conclusion; come to an end; end; finish; over;

[完聚] get together;

[完卷] finish an examination paper;

[完竣] be completed;

[完了] (1) come to an end; completion of a term; over; that's all; (2) doomed; hopeless;

[完滿] complete; satisfactory; successful;
完滿結束 come to a satisfactory close;

[完美] consummate; flawless; perfect;
完美無缺 as good as gold; faultless; flawless and perfect; in good shape; leave nothing to be desired; perfect in every way; the acme of perfection; the pink of perfect;
完美主義 perfectionism;
不夠完美 lack perfection;
近乎完美 near perfect;
形式完美 perfect in form;

[完品] (1) perfect piece; (2) perfect quality;

[完全] absolutely; complete; completely; entirely; fully; mere; perfectly; pure; thorough; totally; whole;
完全不定式 full infinitive;
完全地 completely;
完全對等 complete equivalence;
完全翻譯 total translation;
完全否定詞 complete negative;
完全合併 be completely integrated;
完全禁食 abstain from food in whole;
完全經濟核算 complete economic accounting;
完全經濟體系 complete economic system;
完全句 syntactic borrowing;
完全康復 return to one's perfect health;
完全實現 realize to the full;
完全同化 total assimilation;
完全同義詞 complete synonym;
不完全 imperfect; incomplete;
完完全全 at all points; every whit; from the sole of the foot to the crown of the head; from top to toe; head and ears; to a miracle; thoroughly;

[完人] paragon of virtue; perfect man;
人無完人 nobody's perfect;
人無完人，金無足赤 no one is without his faults; there are lees to every wine; there are spots even on the sun; there

W

are spots in the sun;

[完善] consummate; faultless; improve and perfect; perfect;
完善地 to perfection;
日臻完善 becoming better and approaching perfection day by day;
臻於完善 approximate perfection; reach perfect;
自我完善 self-improvement;

[完事] come to an end; finish; get things done; get through;

[完稅] duty paid; pay taxes;

[完整] complete; entire; intact; integrated; undamaged; whole;
完整無缺 in good condition; intact; undivided;
完整無損 in good shape; intact; integrated;
完整性 integrity; perfection;
~ 光學完整性 optical perfection;
~ 化學完整性 chemical integrity;
~ 結晶完整性 crystalline perfection;
~ 漆膜完整性 film integrity;
~ 數據完整性 data integrity;
~ 水密封完整性 watertight integrity;
~ 系統完整性 system integrity;
不夠完整 not sufficiently complete;
不完整 bug; imperfect;
~ 不完整性 imperfection;
複式不完整性 complex imperfection;
晶體不完整性 crystal imperfection;
前在不完整性 pre-existing imperfection;
恢復完整 regain one's integrity;
領土完整 territorial integrity;

辦不完 too much for one to finish;
吃不完 can't be eaten out;
沒完 have not finished with sb;
售完 be sold out;
説完 finish speaking;
未完 unfinished;
學不完 have an endless amount to learn;
用不完 cannot be used up; too many or too much for use;

wan
【芄】 metaphlexis stauntoni;

wan
【玩】 (1) amuse oneself with; enjoy; find pleasure in; have fun; (2) juggle with; play; play with; toy with; (3) employ resort to;

[玩兒] play; play with; toy with;

[玩個夠] have a good time;

[玩忽] ignore; neglect; trifle with;
玩忽職守 a dereliction of duty; derelict of duty; ignore one's duty; neglect of duty;
故意玩忽 willfully neglect;

[玩話] joke;

[玩火] play with fire;
玩火者必自焚 all they that take the sword shall perish with the sword; he who plays with fire gets burned; he who plays with fire will get burnt; those who play with fire will get burned in the end; those who play with fire will perish by fire; whoever play with fire will perish by fire;
玩火自焚 be ruined by one's own presumption; burn one's own fingers; fry in one's own grease; get burned by playing with fire; stir up a fire and burn oneself; those who play with fire will be perished by fire;

[玩家] hobby lover;

[玩具] plaything; toy;
玩具店 toy shop;
玩具小屋 doll's house;
玩具製作者 toyman;
吹氣玩具 inflatable toy;
刺繡玩具 embroidered toy;
電子玩具 electronic toy;
毛絨玩具 cuddly toy; soft toy;
泥塑玩具 clay toy;
皮毛玩具 fur toy;
軟玩具 soft toy;
絨毛玩具 plush toy;
絨製玩具 chenille toy;
陶瓷玩具 ceramic toy;
通花玩具 crocheted toy;
玩玩具 play with one's toys;
一袋玩具 a bag of toys;

[玩樂] play;
認真工作，盡情玩樂 work hard, play hard;

[玩弄] (1) dally with; flirt with; (2) juggle with; play with; (3) employ; resort;
玩弄詞句 go in for rhetoric; juggle with words; play the game of words;
玩弄詞藻 play with words;
玩弄婦女 dally with women; flirt with women;

玩弄花招 employ some tricks;
玩弄兩面手法 resort to double-dealing tactics;
玩弄女人 make a toy of a woman;
~玩弄女人的人 philanderer;
玩弄權術 play politics; resort to the expediency of;
玩弄權術的人 skilled political tricker;
玩弄字眼 juggle with words; play with words;
玩弄兩面手法 engage in double-dealing; have two faces; play a double game;

[玩偶] doll; toy figurine;

[玩賞] enjoy; take pleasure in;
玩賞風景 enjoy the scenery;

[玩耍] amuse oneself; enjoy oneself; have fun; play;
在戶外玩耍 play out;

[玩味] contemplate; ponder; ruminate;

[玩物] plaything; toy;
玩物喪志 excessive attention to trivia saps the will; pursuit of petty pleasures thwarts high arms; indulge oneself in pleasures and have no serious ambition; play through life and have no serious ambition; pursuit of pleasures in trivialities weakens a man's will to make progress; sap one's spirit by seeking pleasures; trifle with playthings and lose one's lofty aspirations;

[玩笑] banter; jest; joke; leg-pull;
半開玩笑 half in jest and half in earnest; half jokingly;
開玩笑 crack a joke; cut a joke; in joke; in play; jest; joke; laugh at; make a joke; make fun of; make game of sb; make jests; make sport of sb; play a joke on; pull one's leg; tease;
~開玩笑吧 one's kidding;
~你是在開玩笑吧 you've got to be kidding;
開人玩笑 make a joke about sb; make a mockery of sb; make fun of sb; make merry over a person; play a joke on sb; put the joke on sb;

[玩意] (1) plaything; toy; (2) gadget; stuff; thing;
小玩意 doodah;

把玩 fondle (books, toys, jades, etc.);
古玩 antique; curio;
好玩兒 amusing; funny; interesting;
清玩 delight in; elegant, refined things for people to enjoy;
賞玩 admire the beauty of sth.; appreciate; enjoy;
貪玩 fond of fooling around; fond of playing;
文玩 articles for enjoyment;
褻玩 treat with disrespect because of over-intimacy;
遊玩 (1) amuse oneself; play; (2) go sight-seeing; stroll about;
珍玩 rare curios;

wan

【紈】 fine silk fabrics;

[紈絝] silk trousers;
紈絝不餓死，儒冠多誤身 the rich do not die of hunger, most scholars fail in their career;
紈絝子弟 curled darlings; dandy; fob; gilded youth; good-for-nothing young man from a wealthy family; playboy; profligate son of the rich;
綺襦紈絝 fops from a rich family; young fops of wealthy and noble families;

[紈扇] round silk fan;

[紈素] fine, white silk;

wan

【烷】 (1) alkane; (2) fire;

[烷基] alkyl;
烷基苯 alkylbenzene;
烷基汞 mercury alkyl;
烷基化 alkylate; alkylation;
烷基鈉 sodium alkyl;
烷基硼 boron alkyl;
烷基鉛 lead alkyl;
酯烷基 ester alkyl;

丙烷 propane;
丁烷 butane;
庚烷 heptane;
己烷 hexane;
甲烷 methane;
戊烷 pentane;
辛烷 octane;
乙烷 ethane;

wan

【頑】 (1) dense; dull; foolish; ignorant;

insensate; pigheaded; stupid; thickheaded; (2) headstrong; inveterate; obstinate; stubborn; (3) defiant; mischievous; naughty; recalcitrant; ungovernable; unruly; (4) play; romp about;

［頑敵］ die-hard enemy; inveterate foe; stubborn enemy;

［頑鈍］ (1) dull and obtuse; foolish; obtuse; stupid; thickheaded; (2) shameless person;

頑鈍無恥 dull and shameless;

［頑梗］ dogged; obstinate; perverse; pigheaded;

［頑固］ (1) bullheaded; headstrong; pertinacious; obstinate; stubborn; (2) be bitterly opposed to change; die-hard;

頑固保守 brassbound; incorrigible; irretrievably obstinate; stubborn and conservative; stubborn and intransigent;

頑固不化 incorrigibly obstinate; set in one's way;

頑固分子 die-hard; die-hard element;

頑固派 die-hard;

老頑固 old diehard; old fogey; old stick-in-the-mud;

［頑抗］ put up a desperate resistance; stubbornly resist;

負隅頑抗 fight stubbornly with one's back to the wall; make a final desperate struggle; make a last-ditch fight; put up a desperate struggle; put up a stiff resistance; resist desperately; with their backs to the wall, they fight stubbornly;

［頑劣］ good-for-nothing; stubborn and stupid;

［頑民］ ungovernable people; unruly people;

［頑皮］ mischievous; naughty; playful;

頑皮的 puckish;

天生頑皮 naturally naughty;

［頑強］ indomitable; staunch; tenacious;

頑強地抵抗 offer stubborn resistance;

［頑石］ coarse rock; insensate stone; unpolished stone;

頑石點頭 even a piece of stone would have been moved; even the rocks nod in approval during one's preaching;

［頑耍］ play; romp about;

［頑童］ naughty child; urchin;

［頑癬］ stubborn dermatitis;

［頑症］ chronic and stubborn disease; persistent ailment;

刁頑 cunning and stubborn;

冥頑 stupid; thickheaded;

愚頑 ignorant and stubborn; stupid and obstinate;

wan³

wan

【宛】 (1) crooked; roundabout; tortuous; winding; (2) as if; as though; (3) a surname;

［宛妙］ soft and charming;

［宛然］ as if; as though; like;

宛然如生 it would look like a live one;

［宛如］ as if; as it were; literally; just like; like;

宛若天仙 divinely beautiful; look like a heavenly fairy;

宛若游龍 her bodily movement is as graceful as a swimming dragon; one's swimming is as lithesome as a wandering dragon;

［宛宛］ clinging; twisting;

［宛延］ long and winding; meander;

委宛 mild and roundabout; tactful;

wan

【娩】 agreeable; complaisant;

婉娩 gentle and agreeable; meek;

wan

【挽】 (1) draw; hold back; pull; (2) roll up; (3) lament sb's death; (4) coil up; gather into;

［挽臂而行］ walk arm in arm;

［挽髮成髻］ gather hair into a knot;

［挽弓］ draw a bow;

［挽回］ redeem; retrieve;

挽回敗局 retrieve a defeat;

挽回大局 restore the general situation; save the general situation from worsening;

挽回局面 retrieve the situation;

挽回劣勢 improve one's position;

挽回面子 redeem one's reputation; save face;

挽回損失 retrieve a loss;

挽回危局 retrieve a critical situation;

不可挽回 past remedy;

[挽救] remedy; rescue; save;
非人力所能挽救 beyond all human help;
[挽留] persuade sb to stay; request sb to stay; urge sb to stay;
[挽起] roll up;
挽起褲腳 rull up the bottom of one's trouser legs;
挽起袖子 roll up one's sleeves;
[挽手] arm in arm; hand in hand; hold hands;
[挽引] pull with force;
[挽住] hold back;

敬挽 with deep condolences from sb;
推挽 push-pull;

wan

【婉】 (1) agreeable; amiable; genial; gentle; gracious; pleasant; tactful; (2) beautiful; courteous; elegant; good-looking; graceful; with courtesy;
[婉辭] (1) euphemisms; gentle words; tactful expressions; (2) decline with great courtesy; graciously decline; politely refuse;
[婉麗] beautiful; lovely;
[婉勸] friendly persuasion; persuade gently;
[婉商] negotiate with tact and courtesy;
[婉順] complaisant; obliging;
[婉婉] amiable; graceful;
[婉謝] decline with great gentleness and courtesy; politely decline; refuse with thanks;
[婉言] gentle words; speak tenderly; tactful expressions;
婉言拒絕 decline with entreaties; polite refusal; refuse politely;
婉言釋怨 a soft answer turns away wrath;
婉言相勸 gently persuade; plead tactifully;
婉言謝絕 decline sb with thanks; graciously decline; politely refuse; polite refusal; refuse with thanks;
[婉愉] at ease; harmonious; relaxed;
[婉約] graceful and restrained;
[婉轉] (1) indirectly; persuasively; tactfully; (2) sweet and agreeable;
婉轉取媚 worm oneself into other's good graces;
措辭婉轉 put it tactfully;
歌喉婉轉 have a sweet voice;

哀婉 pathetic; sad and moving; sadly sweet;
和婉 mild;
悽婉 pathetic; pitiful; plaintive; sad; sorrowful;
淒婉 sad and mild; sadly moving;
委婉 euphemistic; ingratiating; mild and roundabout; suave and moving; soft-spoken; tactful;
溫婉 gentle; obedient;
燕婉 friendly; genial;
幽婉 profound and complicated;

wan

【晚】 (1) evening; night; sunset; (2) far on in time; late; (3) junior; younger;
[晚安] good evening; good night; night; night night;
[晚班] night shift;
[晚報] afternooner; evening paper;
[晚輩] one's juniors; the younger generation;
[晚餐] dinner; supper;
晚餐吃得很少 have a light dinner;
晚餐時間 dinner time;
浪漫晚餐 romantic dinner;
四道菜晚餐 four-course dinner;
一頓晚餐 a supper;
燭光晚餐 candle-lit dinner;
[晚場] evening performance; evening show;
[晚車] night train;
[晚禱] compline; evening prayers;
[晚到] arrive late;
[晚點] behind schedule; late;
[晚飯] dinner; evening meal; supper;
吃晚飯 eat dinner; have dinner; have supper;
~出去吃晚飯 dine out; go out for dinner; go out to dinner;
~吃完晚飯 have eaten supper; finish eating dinner; finish eating supper;
供應晚飯 serve dinner;
一頓晚飯 a supper;
做晚飯 cook dinner; make dinner;
[晚福] old age bliss;
[晚會] evening gathering; evening party; night party; party; social evening;
一個晚會 an evening party;
主題晚會 theme party;
[晚婚] late marriage; marry at a mature age; marry late in one's life;
晚婚晚育 later marrig and later child-bearing;

W

［晚間］ at night; in the evening; nocturnal;

［晚節］ one's integrity in one's closing years;
晚節不保 lose one's virtue in old age;
晚節不全 lose one's virtue in old age;
晚節末路 in one's later life; one's closing years; towards the end of one's life;
晚節自保 hold fast to one's integrity in one's old age;
保持晚節 hold fast to one's integrity in one's old age;
寒花晚節 the cold flower in its ending — to preserve one's personality in old age;

［晚近］ during the past few years; in recent years; lately; recently;

［晚進］ junior; newcomer;

［晚景］ (1) evening scene; (2) one's circumstances in old age;
晚景淒涼 a lonely, dreary life in old age; lead a miserable and dreary life in old age; lonely and poor in old age;

［晚來］ come late;

［晚年］ in the gloaming of one's life; late in one's life; old age; one's later years; one's remaining years; sunset; the afternoon of life; the closing years of one's life; the last years of one's life; the latter years of one's life; twilight years;
安度晚年 spend one's remaining years in happiness; spend one's remaining years peacefully;
安享晚年 enjoy a peaceful old age; spend one's old age peacefully; spend one's remaining years in peace and comfort;
步入晚年 in the sunset of one's day;
以娛晚年 amuse oneself in old age; rejoice one's declining years;
在晚年 in later years; in the evening of life;

［晚娘］ stepmother;

［晚期］ late stage; later period;

［晚起］ get up late; rise late;

［晚秋］ late autumn; late in the autumn;

［晚色］ twilight;

［晚上］ at night; evening; in the evening;
晚上工作 work nights;
晚上好 good evening;
晚上九點 at nine o'clock in the evening;
明天晚上 tomorrow evening; tomorrow night;
星期天晚上 Sunday nights;
一個晚上 one night;
有一天晚上 one night;
昨天晚上 last evening; last night; yesterday evening;

［晚世］ modern times; recent years;

［晚霜］ late frost;

［晚歲］ (1) in recent years; lately; (2) late harvest; (3) old age; one's later years;

［晚霞］ evening glow; sunset clouds; sunset glow;
晚霞滿天 the setting sun kindles the sky;
晚霞晴千里 a red sky at night is the shepherd's delight; a red sky in the evening indicates fine weather for a thousand li.
晚霞似火 the glow of sunset is as red as fire;

［晚學］ your pupil;

［晚宴］ dinner party; dinner;
晚宴嘉賓 dinner guest;
晚宴舞會 dinner dance;
正式晚宴 black-tie dinner;

［晚運］ one's lot during old age;

［晚照］ shining of the setting sun;
疏林晚照 the evening sun gleams through the grove;

挨晚 towards evening;
傍晚 at dusk; at nightfall; dusk; late in the afternoon; nightfall; toward evening; twilight;
不言晚 it's never too late;
明晚 tomorrow evening;
前晚 the evening before last;
傍晚 early evening;
太晚 too late;
向晚 toward the evening;
夜晚 dark hours; in the night; night;
早晚 (1) morning and evening; (2) sooner or later; (3) time; (4) some day; some time in the future;
昨晚 last night;

wan

【莞】 smiling;

［莞爾］ smile;
莞爾一笑 give a soft smile; slight smile;

wan

【晥】 (1) an ancient state in present-day

Anhui; (2) alternative name of Anhui;

wan

【琬】 (1) a kind of jade tablet slightly tapering at the top; (2) mature character of a gentleman;

［琬琰］ mature character of a gentleman;

琬琰之章 esteemed letter;

wan

【菀】 (1) exuberant; lush; luxuriant; (2) clogged; stagnant;

紫菀 aster;

wan

【碗】 bowl;

［碗櫥］ cupboard; dresser;

［碗碟］ bowls and dishes;

碗碟櫃 hutch;

［碗櫃］ cupboard; dresser; kitchen dresser;

［碗口］ rim of a bowl;

［碗筷］ bowls and chopsticks;

碗筷狼籍 bowls and chopsticks lie in disarray;

一副碗筷 a set of bowl and chopsticks;

茶碗 teacup;

瓷碗 china bowl;

飯碗 (1) rice bowl; (2) job; means of livelihood;

海碗 big bowl; huge bowl; large bowl;

湯碗 soup bowl;

鐵飯碗 iron rice bowl; secure job;

洗碗 wash the dishes;

一個碗 a bowl;

一套碗 a nest of bowls;

一碗 a bowl of;

粥碗 porringer;

wan

【畹】 measure of land equalling 20 or 30 mou;

wan

【綰】 bind up; coil up; string together;

［綰結印綬］ take office;

［綰起頭髮］ coil up one's hair;

wan

【輓】 (1) draw a cart; pull a cart; (2) mourn; (3) same as 晚 ;

［輓對］ elegiac couplet;

［輓歌］ dirge; funeral hymn; elegy; lament; threnody;

唱輓歌 keen; sing a dirge;

一支輓歌 a lament;

［輓近］ lately; of late; recently;

［輓聯］ elegiac couplet; funeral scrolls;

［輓詩］ funeral ode; elegy; threnody;

wan

【踠】 crooked leg;

wan

【惋】 (1) deplore; lament; regret; (2) be alarmed; be astonished;

［惋愕］ alarmed; astonished;

［惋恨］ animus; enmity;

［惋悽］ pathetic;

［惋傷］ regret sorrowfully;

［惋歎］ deplore; regret;

［惋慟］ deplore; lament;

［惋惜］ feel sorry about sth; feel sorry for sb; have pity for; regret; sympathize with;

令人惋惜 to be regretted;

無須惋惜 entail no regret;

惆惋 regretful; wistful;

wan

【腕】 wrist;

［腕骨］ wrist bones;

［腕鐲］ bracelet;

［腕子］ wrist;

掰腕子 hand wrestling;

扳腕子 arm wrestle; arm wrestling; do arm wrestling;

肐膊腕子 wrist;

扼腕 wring one's wrists in sorrow or excitement;

翻腕 turn over the wrists;

胳膊腕 wrist;

割腕 slit one's wrists;

護腕 bracer; wrister;

扣腕 cock one's wrist; oral arm;

手腕 (1) wrist; (2) artifice; finesse; stratagem; sleight of hand;

鐵腕 iron hand;

懸腕 keep the arm off the desk;

玉腕 the wrist and forearm of a beautiful woman;

wan⁴

wan

【萬】 (1) ten thousand; (2) a large number

of; a very great number; all; all the different kinds; every; in many different ways; numerous; various; multifarious; myriad; (3) absolutely; by all means; incomparably; extremely; utterly; very; very much; (4) a surname; (5) (of mahjong) ten-thousand;

W

[萬安] (1) do not worry; (2) very safe;

[萬般] (1) all; all the different kinds; every; in many different ways; various; (2) extremely; utterly;

萬般皆下品，惟有讀書高 all occupations are base, only book-learning is exalted; learning is the noblest of human pursuits; only the learned rank high, all other trades are low; to be a scholar is to be the top of society;

萬般無奈 as a last resort; have no alternative; there is no alternative;

[萬邦] all nations; nations all over the world; the myriad states;

揉此萬邦 gain domination by war or force; subdue all other states;

[萬寶全書] a master of everything; a person who knows everything;

[萬倍] ten thousandfold;

[萬變不離其宗] change ten thousand times without departing from the original stand; change time and again, yet stay much the same; remain essentially the same despite all apparent changes; remain unchanged in aim despite all apparent changes; while the appearances may vary, the essence remains unchanged;

[萬不能行] should under no circumstances be put through;

[萬代] all ages; eternity;

[萬端] innumerable; multifarious;

感慨萬端 all sorts of feelings well up in one's mind; with great feeling;

[萬惡] absolutely vicious; all the evils; diabolic; extremely wicked; extremely evil; extremely vicious;

萬惡淫為首 lewdness is the worst of all sins;

萬惡之源 the mother of all sin; the root of all evil; the source of all evil;

[萬方] (1) all nations; all places; myriad regions; (2) extremely; incomparably; (3) all and every way;

萬方多難 natural disasters and man-made calamities everywhere;

[萬分] deeply; extremely; very much;

萬分哀痛 immense sorrow;

萬分抱歉 deeply regretful; extremely sorry; very sorry;

萬分悲痛 be overtaken by heartrending grief;

萬分感動 be deeply moved; be deeply touched;

萬分感謝 grateful beyond words; thank you very much indeed; with heartfelt thanks;

萬分高興 be greatly delighted; be highly pleased; extremely happy; very happy; wild with joy;

萬分遺憾 a thousand pities;

懊惱萬分 much to one's annoyance; much to one's chagrin;

悲痛萬分 be deeply grieved; be far gone in grief;

駭愕萬分 amazing to the greatest degree;

驚恐萬分 horror-struck;

[萬夫] ten thousand men;

萬夫不當 any number of men cannot withstand him; can overcome even ten thousand soldiers; have the strength that ten thousand men cannot withstand; invincible; mightier than ten thousand; ten thousand men cannot prevail against him;

萬夫之勇 a host in oneself; brave enough to match ten thousand warriors;

[萬福] wish you all happiness; wish you good luck;

[萬古] eternally; for a long long time; forever; immortal; through the ages;

萬古不變 eternal and immutable; eternally immutable; forever immutable; never-changing; the same for all time; unchangeable; unchanged from time immemorial;

萬古不易 prevailing overtime;

萬古長存 everlasting; immortal; last forever; live forever; remain forever; remain generation after generation; remain immortal;

萬古長青 bloom forever; evergreen; everlasting; flourishing forever;

forever green; go down in history; last forever; live for centuries; live long; remain fresh forever;

萬古流傳 be remembered forever;

萬古流芳 a good name that will last forever; achieve immortal fame; be remembered throughout the ages; go down eternal in history; hand down a good reputation to a hundred future generations; leave a good name that ill live forever; leave a good name to posterity; leave a good reputation for generations; one's name will go down in history and shine forever; one's name will remain forever as fragrant as flowers; render one's name immortal;

萬古千秋 eternally; through all eternities; throughout the ages;

[萬貫] ten million cash; very rich;

萬貫家財 vast wealth; very wealthy;

家有萬貫財，不如一身健 health is better than wealth;

[萬國] all nations; all over the world; countless states; international;

萬國公法 international laws;

[萬戶] ten thousand households;

萬戶更新 all houses take on a new look;

萬戶侯 high position;

萬戶蕭疏 thousands of homes are deserted;

[萬花筒] kaleidoscope;

[萬花爭艷] all kinds of flowers in full bloom;

[萬急] very urgent;

[萬家] ten thousand families;

萬家燈火 a myriad twinkling lights; lamps and candles of a myriad families; myriad lights twinkling in the city;

萬家生佛 a living Buddha to ten thousand families — a benefactor to all;

[萬箭] ten thousand arrows;

萬箭攢心 one's heart aches as if pierced by ten thousand arrows; one's heart has been pierced with a thousand arrows;

萬箭齊發 ten thousand arrows shoot at once;

[萬劫] countless ages; countless generations;

萬劫不復 be doomed eternally; beyond redemption; irretrievable; never to be recovered;

[萬金油] a cure-all ointment—Jack of all trades and master of none;

[萬籟] all sounds;

萬籟俱寂 a profound silence prevails over all; absolute quiet; all is quiet; all is still; all sounds are hushed; all nature is hushed; all sounds are still; silence reigns everywhere; silence reigns supreme;

[萬類] all things on earth;

[萬里] ten thousand miles;

萬里長城 the Great Wall;

萬里長空 the vastness of heaven; vast clear skies;

萬里長征 a long march of ten thousand miles; go on a journey of thousands of miles;

萬里江山 vast territory of the motherland;

萬里鵬程 unlimited future;

萬里晴空 a clear and boundless sky; a sky without a speck of cloud;

萬里迢迢 over a great distance; thousands of miles away; very far away;

萬里無雲 cloudless;

階前萬里 distance is no barrier;

明見萬里 man of far sight;

[萬靈藥] cure-all; panacea; wonder drug;

[萬流赴壑] countless things converging on the same spot;

[萬馬] ten thousand horses;

萬馬奔騰 like ten thousand stampeding horses; like thousands of horses at full gallop; roll on with tremendous vitality; surge onward like ten thousand horses galloping; ten thousand horses gallop forward — all go full steam ahead;

萬馬齊喑 ten thousand horses stand mute — a lifeless atmosphere; ten thousand horses are all muted;

[萬民] all the people;

德澤萬民 bestow universal favour on the people;

師保萬民 act as teacher and guardian of the myriad people;

[萬目睽睽] all eyes are staring; all eyes centre on; under the glare of the public;

[萬難] (1) extremely difficult; well-nigh impossible; (2) all difficulties; every difficulty;

萬難同意 can by no means agree;
萬難照辦 impossible to do as requested;
不辭萬難 not to shirk all hardships; through thick and thin;
排除萬難 battle against the odds; struggle against the odds;

[萬能] (1) all-powerful; omnipotent; (2) all-purpose; multi-purpose; universal;
萬能博士 jack-of-all-trades; Mr. Know-all;
萬能靈藥 cure-all- panacea;

[萬年] all ages; eternity; ten thousand years;
萬年曆 perpetual calendar;
萬年青 Chinese evergreen;

[萬念俱灰] abandon oneself to despair; all hopes are dashed to pieces; all thoughts are blasted; completely discouraged; extremely pessimistic; in the slough of despond; totally devoid of ambition and hope;

[萬弩齊發] all the bows are discharged at once; like all bows discharge at once; myriads of bolts fly through the air;

[萬砲] ten thousand cannons;
萬砲齊轟 bombard...with ten thousand guns; direct the fire of ten thousand guns at; ten thousand cannons booming;
萬砲齊鳴 roar like thousands of guns; thousands of guns roar at the same time;

[萬千] multifarious; myriads;
感慨萬千 be filled with a thousand regrets; be filled with painful recollections;
萬水千山 be separated by a myriad of rivers and thousands of hills; a trying journey of ten thousand crags and torrents;
~萬水千山衹等閒 hold light ten thousand crags and torrents; scorn ten thousand torrents and a thousand crags;
儀態萬千 charming poises and exquisite bearing;

[萬頃] vast space;
萬頃碧波 vast expanse of water;

[萬全] failure-proof; perfectly safe; perfectly sound; surefire;
萬全之策 completely safe plan; perfect scheme; sure card;
萬全之計 absoltely safe measure; completely safe plan; prudential policy; surefire plan;
計出萬全 one's plan is foolproof;

[萬人] ten thousand people;
萬人空巷 all the people of the place have turned out; everyone turns out; the whole town turns out;
萬人莫敵 can fight one's way out and take on any challenger;
萬人唾罵 everyone spats out sb's name with loathing;

[萬世] all ages; generation after generation; myriad generations;
萬世景仰 honoured and respected by all ages;
萬世留芳 be remembered throughout the ages; leave a good name for posterity; one's name will go down in history and shine forever;
萬世師表 an exemplary teacher for all ages; the model teacher of all generations; the teacher for all ages;
澤及萬世 the good grace will be felt for countless generations to come;

[萬事] all things; everything;
萬事從寬 take a lenient attitude toward everything;
萬事大吉 all is well; all is well and propitious; all things go well; all is right; everything goes off without a hitch; everything is in order; everything is just fine; everything is propitious; things are going strong; time and time are favourable; with the sun of fortune smiling;
萬事大吉，天下太平 everything is fine and all is right with the world;
萬事亨通 everything goes off without a hitch; everything goes well; everything is going smoothly;
萬事吉利 all the best; all things are going well;
萬事俱備 complete with everything needed; everything has been arranged; everything is ready;
萬事俱備，衹欠東風 all is ready except for the east wind — all is ready except for the final decisive thing;
萬事莫求全 don't ask for perfection;
萬事起頭難 all beginnings are hard; all things are difficult before they are

easy; beginnings are always hard; everything is difficult at the start; everything is hard in the beginning; it is the first step that costs; it is the first step that is troublesome; nothing is easy in the beginning; the first step is the hardest; the initial step is always difficult;

萬事如意 carry all before one; carry everything before one; everything falls into one's lap; everything goes well; everything is as one wishes; good luck in everything; have all one's wishes; may all go well with you; may all your heart's wishes be fulfilled;

萬事順吉 all things are going well;

萬事通 jack-of-all-trades; know-all;

萬事萬物 all nature; myriads of things;

萬事休 all is lost;

[萬殊] all different; myriads of variations;

[萬死] die ten thousand deaths; risk any danger to do sth;

萬死不辭 be determined to do sth even at the cost of one's own life; not to recoil from death; not to shrink from any sacrifice; shrink from no sacrifice; willing to risk any danger; would risk a myriad deaths;

萬死一生 a very slim chance of keeping oneself alive; only one chance in ten thousand of preserving the life; very risky;

罪該萬死 a thousand deaths will not atone for one's crime; guilty of a crime deserving ten thousand deaths; guilty of a crime for which even death cannot atone; guilty of a crime for which one deserves to die ten thousand deaths; the crime deserves a myriad deaths;

[萬歲] (1) long live; (2) emperor; your majesty;

萬歲千秋 die; live a long life;

自由萬歲 long live freedom;

[萬萬] (1) a great many; (2) absolutely; extremely; wholly; (3) a hundred million;

萬萬不可 absolutely forbidden; absolutely impossible; absolutely no; in no event; not by any means; positively do not; under no circumstances; will never do;

萬萬不行 absolutely out of the question;

萬試萬靈 every time it works; prove successful in every test; though be used ten thousand times, yet it ever does succeed;

[萬無] absolutely not; never; not the least;

萬無一失 absolutely certain; absolutely safe; absolutely sure; as safe as anything; as safe as houses; as safe as the Bank of England; cannot fail under any circumstances; certain to succeed; guarantee complete success; have no danger of going wrong under any circumstances; neck and heels; no risk at all; not a chance of an error; nothing will go wrong; on the safe side; perfectly safe; sure of success; surefire;

~ 萬無一失的 airtight; fail-safe; foolproof; surefire;

[萬物] all things on earth; all things under the sun; everything in the world;

萬物叢生 grow in great variety and profusion;

萬物之靈 lords of creation; the intelligent part of the universe; the paragon of animals; the soul of the universe; the wisest of all creatures — the human beings;

煦育萬物 make all things grow by action of heat; make all things grow by warmth;

[萬象] all manifestations of nature; every phenomenon on earth;

萬象更新 all looks fresh and gay; all things take on a new aspect; everything is fresh again; everything looks new and fresh; everything takes on a new look;

萬象回春 all manifestations of nature return with spring;

萬象森羅 everything under the sun; myriads of things; the phenomena of nature;

森羅萬象 all-embracing; all-inclusive; everything under the sun; majestic and myriad phenomena — various phenomena appear to one's eye; myriads of things;

[萬幸] by sheer luck; fortunately; most lucky; very fortunate; very lucky;

[萬言] ten thousand words;

日試萬言 rapidity in writing;

[萬一] contingency; eventuality; if by any chance; in case; in case of; in the event of; just in case; should it happen that;

防備萬一 ready for all eventualities;

萬不失一 absolutely safe; no danger of anything going wrong; no risk at all; not one lost in ten thousand;

萬裏挑一 not one like...can be found in ten thousand;

以備萬一 provide against contingencies;

以防萬一 just in case; make provision against emergencies; on the safe side; prepare for any contingency; provide against accident; ready for all eventuality;

準備萬一 expect the extremity;

[萬億] billion;

[萬用錶] multi-meter;

電子萬用錶 electronic multi-meter;

數字式萬用錶 digital multi-meter;

[萬有] all creation; all things under the sun;

萬有引力 gravitation;

[萬丈] (1) bottomless; fathomless; (2) lofty towering;

萬丈高樓平地起 a high building, a low foundation; great oaks from little acorns grow; great undertakings have small beginnings; high buildings rise from the ground; lofty towers are all built up from the ground;

萬丈高樓起於累土 a building ten thousand feet high must be constructed from its very base;

萬丈光芒 brilliant radiance; shine in all its splendour; shine with boundless radiance;

萬丈深淵 a bottomless chasm; an abyss;

[萬眾] millions of people; the multitude;

萬眾歡呼 the crowd cheer vociferously;

萬眾歡騰 all the people sing and dance for joy; millions of people rejoice; the people dance for joy; universal rejoicing;

萬眾睢睢 all eyes are staring;

萬眾一心 all for one and one for all; all have one heart; all of one heart; all unite in one purpose; millions of people unite as one man; unite as one; with one heart and one mind;

[萬狀] (1) extremely; in the extreme; (2) all possible shapes and forms; myriad forms;

惶急萬狀 in great urgency;

惶恐萬狀 be frightened out of one's senses; be seized with fear;

憂懼萬狀 extremely anxious and fearful;

百萬 million;

巨萬 (of wealth, etc.) enormous;

千百萬 a great amount of; a great number of; lots and lots of;

千萬 (1) a huge amount; ten million; (2) do; it is imperative that; must; sure;

十萬 one hundred thousand;

一萬 (1) ten thousand; (2) one and ten thousand;

億萬 hundreds of millions; millions upon millions;

wan

【蔓】 creeper; tendril;

瓜蔓 melon;

壓蔓 cover a vine with earth at different lengths;

wan

【翫】 (1) careless or casual due to familiarity; (2) play;

[翫忽] careless; negligent;

[翫愒] trifle away one's time;

[翫物] toys;

wang¹

wang

【汪】 (1) accumulate; collect; soak; (2) pool; puddle; (3) bark; (4) boundless; deep and extensive; vast; (5) a surname;

[汪然] profusely; vast;

汪然出涕 weep profusely;

[汪汪] (1) tearful; tears welling up; (2) bark; bowwow; yap;

淚汪汪 eyes brimming with tears; tearful; with watery eyes;

~兩淚汪汪 eyes brimming with tears;

~眼淚汪汪 one's eyes swim with tears;

水汪汪 (of children's or young women's eyes) bright and intelligent;

油汪汪 (1) dripping with oil; full of grease; (2) glossy; shiny;

汪汪亂叫 yap;

[汪洋] a vast expanse of water; boundless;

vast;

汪洋大海 the boundless sea; the mighty ocean; the vast expanse of the sea;

汪洋一片 a vast expanse of water; boundless seas;

一片汪洋 a broad expanse of water; a flood of water; a sheet of water; a vast expanse of water; a waste of waters; a world of waters;

[汪子] puddle of water;

一汪 a pool of; a puddle of;

wang²
wang

【亡】 (1) flee; refuge; run away; (2) be gone; lose; (3) decease; destroy; die; pass away; perish; (4) dead; deceased; lost; (5) conquer; subjugate; (6) the late;

[亡故] decease; die; pass away;

[亡國] (1) let a state perish; subjugate a nation; the fall of a nation; (2) conquered nation;

亡國滅種 national doom and racial extinction; national subjugation and genocide; ruin the state and destroy the race;

亡國奴 conquered people; subjugated people;

亡國之民 th people of a conquered nation;

亡國之音 decadent music; degenerate music; sentimental music; the tune presaging the fallen state;

[亡化] die; pass away;

[亡魂] ghost; spectre; the soul of a deceased person;

[亡靈] ghost; spectre; the soul of a deceased person;

[亡命] (1) flee; go into exile; refuge; seek refuge; (2) desperate;

亡命他鄉 live in exile;

亡命之徒 badmen; dead rabbits; desperado; fugitive; refugees from justice; ruffian;

[亡羊補牢] better late than never; lock the stable door after the horse has been stolen; mend the fold after losing the sheep; mend the sheepfold after losing the sheep; take precautions after one has suffered loss;

亡羊補牢，猶未為晚 it is never too late to mend the corral even when the sheep are lost; it is not too late the mend the fold even after some of the sheep is lost;

[亡友] deceased friend;

哀悼亡友 mourn a deceased friend;

[亡者] the dead;

敗亡 be defeated and overthrown;

逋亡 abscond; escape; flee;

昌亡 prosper or perish;

出亡 flee; live in exile;

存亡 (1) live or die; (2) survive or perish;

悼亡 deceased wife; mourn deceased wife;

覆亡 demise; fall;

梏亡 be fettered in mind by greed;

救亡 save the nation from extinction;

流亡 be forced to leave one's native land; go into exile;

淪亡 be annexed;

滅亡 be destroyed; become extinct; die out; perish;

人亡 a person dies;

散亡 be lost; (of book, etc.) scatter and disappear;

喪亡 die; perish;

傷亡 be wounded and killed; casualties; injuries and deaths;

身亡 die;

衰亡 become feeble and die; decline and fall; wither away;

死亡 all over with sb; all up with sb; among the immortals; an old floorer; answer the final summons; answer the last roll call; answer the last muster; asleep in Jesus; asleep in the Arms of God; asleep in the valley; at peace; at rest; be all washed up; be blown across the creek; be blown away; be blown creek; be brought to one's last home; be called to one's account; be called to one's long account; be called home; be called to God; be called to the beyond; be called to the Great Beyond; be cast into outer darkness; be cleaned out of the deck; be cut off; be done for; be gathered to one's fathers; be gone; be gone to Davy Jones's locker; be knocked out; be promoted to glory; be removed to the divine bosom; be rocked to sleep; be salted away; be sent to one's account; be shuffled; be taken to paradise; be translated into higher sphere; be trumped; be washed out; be written off; bite the dust; black out; blow sb away; bow off; bow out; breathe one's last; buy a one-way ticket; buy the farm; call it quits; cancel one's account; cash in; cash in one's chips; cease to be; cease to exist; cease to live; check in; check out; close one's career; close one's days; close one's eyes; close one's life; close up one's account; close upon; close upon the world; coil up one's ropes; come to an end; conk out; count daisies; croak; cross over; cross over the Great Divide; cross over the River Jordan; cross the bar; cross the Bar; cross the great divide; cross the River Styx; cut; cut adrift; cut one's cable; cut one's stick; dangle in the sheriff's picture depart; decease; demise; depart; depart from this life; depart from this world; depart to God; depart to the world of shadows; die; die in one's boots; dissolution; do one's bit; down for good; draw one's last breath; drop hooks; drop off the hooks; drop off the twig; drop the cue; drop the curtain; end; end in one's death; expire; fade away; fade out; fall; fall on sleep; final sleep; fire one's last shot; flunk out; fold up; frame; free; give up the breath; give up the ghost; give up the soul; give up the spirit; go beyond; go blooey; go down to the shades; go flooey; go forth; go hence; go home; go home in a box; go off; go off the hooks; go out; go out of the world; go out of this world; go the way of all flesh; go the way of all nature; go to a better world; go to the way of all the earth; go to Davy Jones's locker; go to heaven; go to hell; go to Jordan's banks; go to meet one's maker; go to one's account; go to one's doom; go to one's grass; go to one's last home; go to one's long home; go to one's own place; go to one's resting place; go to one's reward; go to sleep; go to the hereafter; go to the land of heart's desire; go to the last roundup; go to the mansions of rest; go to the races; go up salt river; go west; God rest his soul; grounded for good; hand in one's account; hand in one's dinner pail; hang up one's harness; hang up one's hat; hang up one's tackle; have fallen asleep; have fallen asleep in the Lord; have fallen by the wayside; have found rest; have gone to a better place; have gone to a better land; have gone to a better life; have gone to a better world; have gone to the Great Adventure; have gone to the happy hunting ground; have gone under; have one's name inscribed in the book of life; he is coming home; hide one's name under daisies; hit the rocks; home and free; hop off one's twig; hop the last rattler; hop the twig; in Abraham's bosom; in Davy Jones's locker; in heaven; in one's coffin; in the dust; in the grand secret; in the hereafter; in the undiscovered country; it's taps; join in the immortals; join one's ancesters; join the angelic choirs; join the angels; join the feathered choir; join the heavenly choir; join the invisible choir; join the ever increasing majority; join the Great majority; join the silent majority; jump the last hurdle; kick in; kick off; kick the bucket; last rest; launch into eternity; lay down life's burden; lay down one's knife and forfk; lay down one's life; lay down one's pen; lay down one's shovel and hoe; leave this world; lie asleep; lose one's life; lose the decision; make an end of sb; make away with sb; make one's final exit; make the ultimate sacrifice; meet one's death; meet one's end; meet one's fate; mortal; move off; negative patient care outcome; never-ending sleep; no longer with us; no more; one's eternal rest; one's eyes are closed; one's heavenly rest; one's hard-earned rest; one's last taboo; out of pain; out of the game; out of the running; over the creek; pale horse; pass away; pass in one's alley; pass into stillness; pass on; pass out; pass out of the picture; pass over the Jordan; pass to the other side; pay Charon; pay day; pay one's fee; pay one's harp; pay one's last debt; pay saint Peter a visit; pay the debt of nature; peg out; perish; permit the water of life to run out; pop off; pop off the hooks; pop out; present at the last roll call; present at the last muster; pull the plug; push the clouds around; push up daisies; put sb out of his misery; put sb out of his pain; quit it; quit the scene; rest; rest in Abraham's bosom; rest in peace; return to dust; return to earth; ride into sunset; ring off; ring out; run one's course; run one's race; safe anchorage at last; safe in the arms of Jesus; say hello to Charon; say the last good-bye; see Confucius; settle all scores; settle one's account; shuffle off this mortal coil; shut up shop; sleep; sleep in the grave; sleep one's final sleep; sleep one's last sleep; sleep the big sleep; sleep the eternal sleep; sleep the final sleep; sleep the long sleep; sleep the never-ending sleep; sleep the sleep of death; sleep the sleep that knows no breaking; sleep the sleep that knows no waking; sleep with one's fathers; slip into outer darkness; slip off; slip off the hooks; slip one's cable; slip one's ropes; slip the cable; snuff it; step off; stick one's spoon in the wall; stop living; strike out; succumb to; suffer death; sup with Pluto; surcease; switch out the lights; take a count; take one's departure; take one's last sleep; take one's rest; take one-way ride; take the count; take the big jump; the big jump; the call of God; the curtain call; the end of the ball game; the eternal sleep; the final curtain; the final department; the final kick off; the final summons; the great leveller; the great whipper; the grim reaper; the last bow; the last call; the last getaway; the last great change; the last send-off; the last sleep; the last voyage; the long sleep; the remains; throw up the cards; throw sixes; toss in one's marbles; turn up one's toes to daisies; under the daisies; wink out; with God; with the angels; with their Father; write the last chapter; yield up the breath; yield up the ghost; yield up the soul; yield up the spirit;

逃亡 abscond; become a fugitive; escape; flee from home; fly; go into exile; run away;

危亡 at stake; in danger of elimination; in great danger; in peril;

消亡 (1) demise; die out; extinct; perish; wither; wither away; (2) subduction;

興亡 prosperity and adversity; rise and fall;

夭亡 die young;

陣亡 be killed in action; fall in action; fall in battle;

wang

【王】 (1) king; monarch; royal; ruler; sovereign imperial; (2) nobility; prince; (3) grand; (4) a surname;

［王八］ (1) tortoise; turtle; (2) cuckold; (3) person who works in a brothel;

王八旦 bastard; son of a bitch;

罐裏養王八，成心憋人 punching bag; be tied down hand and foot;

［王霸］ kings and hegemons;

稱王稱霸 act like an overlord; cock of the walk; come it over; declare oneself king or emperor; domineer; king it over; lord it over; queen it over; rule supreme;

［王朝］ (1) imperial court; royal court; (2) dynasty;

［王城］ royal city;

［王儲］ crown prince;

［王道］ benevolent government; kingly way;

［王帝］ king;

稱王稱帝 declare oneself king;

［王法］ law; law of the land;

王法無親 the law has no respecter of persons; the law is irrespective of persons; the law takes no account of relationship;

王法無私 the law has no partiality;

［王妃］ prince's concubine; princess consort;

［王府］ palace of a prince;

［王公］ princes and dukes; princes and nobles; the nobility;

王公大臣 imperial princes and court ministers; princes and ministers; the dukes and high ministers; the princes, dukes and ministers;

王公貴族 kings, princes and aristocrats; the nobility;

［王宮］ royal palace; imperial palace;

［王瓜］ cucumber;

［王冠］ imperial crown; royal crown;

［王國］ (1) kingdom; (2) domain; realm;

必然王國 realm of inevitability;

［王侯］ princes and marquises; the nobility;

王侯將相 princes and earls, generals and minsters;

［王后］ queen; queen consort;

狂歡節王后 carnival queen;

［王命］ royal decrees;

［王牌］ trump card;

手中握有王牌 keep an ace up one's sleeve;

［王權］ authority of a king;

神授王權 divine right;

［王蛇］ python;

[王室] (1) royal family; (2) imperial court;
王室記者 court corrrespondent;
乃心王室 love of one's country; patriotic;
[王孫] (1) descendants of the nobility; (2) monkey; (3) a surname;
王孫公子 aristocrats; blue-blooded young men;
[王庭] imperial court;
[王位] crown; kingship; throne;
承繼王位 accede to the throne; succeed to the throne;
登上王位 ascend the throne;
放棄王位 abdicate; abdicate the throne; give up the throne;
即王位 accede to the throne;
失去王位 lose the throne;
佔據王位 occupy a throne;
[王章] royal institution;
[王者] (1) emperor; king; (2) true royal sovereign;
王者之風 air of a prince;
[王子] king's son; prince;
王子犯法，與庶民同罪 all men are equal in the eyes of the law; anyone, no matter who he is, who violates the law must be dealt with according to the law; if a prince violates the law, he must be punished like an ordinary person;
[王族] imperial kinsmen; members of the royal family; persons of royal lineage; the royal family;

霸王 despot; overlord;
草頭王 king of the bushes; chieftain of outlaws, bandits, etc.;
稱王 declare oneself king;
大王 (1) master in sth; one who is good at sth; (2) king; magnate; (3) bandit chief;
帝王 emperor; monarch;
蜂王 (1) queen bee; (2) queen wasp;
國王 king;
活閻王 devil incarnate; tyrannical ruler;
君王 king; lord;
龍王 the Dragon King (the God of Rain in Chinese mythology);
魔王 (1) despot; tyrant; (2) Prince of the Devils;
女王 queen;
棋王 chess champion;
親王 prince;
勤王 (1) send troops to support the kind when the latter is in trouble; (2) serve the royal house;
拳王 boxing champion;
讓王 yield the throne to another;
攝政王 prince regent;
盛王 ruler of great virtue;
獸王 king of beasts – the lion;
素王 uncrowned king – Confucius;
天王 (1) deity; God; (2) emperor;
先王 (1) late emperor; (2) ancient sage sovereigns;
遜王 abdicated king;
閻王 (1) King of Hell; Yama; (2) extremely cruel and violent person;
蟻王 queen ant;
作王 to be a king;

wang

【忘】 a pronunciation of 忘；

wang³

wang

【往】 (1) bound for; depart; go; go toward; in the direction of; make a trip to; toward; (2) formerly; in former times; in the past; past; previously; used to;
[往常] as one used to do previously; as usual; habitually in the past; make it a rule; used to;
往常不這樣 not like that before;
[往初] formerly;
[往返] arrive and depart; come and go; go there and back; journey to and fro; make a round trip; to and fro;
往返奔波 ceaselessly come and go;
往返票 return ticket;
~一張往返票 a return ticket;
[往復] (1) move back and forth; reciprocate; (2) contact; intercourse;
[往古] in ancient times;
往古來今 from ancient time until now; since time immemorial;
[往後] (1) backward; going back; (2) from now on; hereafter; in the future;
[往還] coming and going; contact; dealings; have social dealings with; intercourse; keep in contact;
[往回走] turn back;
[往來] (1) back and forth; come and go; go and return; to and fro; (2) contact; dealings; intercourse;

往來馳騁 gallop to and fro;
往來透支 overdrafts on a current account
往來無阻 freedom of movements;
往來賬戶 book account;
不相往來 have no dealings with each other;
承往繼來 a follower of past traditions and a trail blazer for future generations;
觀往知來 study the past and foretell the future changes;
晦往明來 as day follows night and night follows day;
繼往開來 a follower of past traditions and a trail blazer for future generations; carry forward the cause pioneered by one's predecessors and forge ahead into the future; carry on the past and open a way for future;
鑒往知來 he that would know what shall me must consider what has been; look into the past so that one can predict future development; predict the future by reviewing the past;
老死不相往來 be completely isolated from each other all their lives; not to visit each other all their lives;
禮尚往來 as the call, so the echo; courtesy demands reciprocity; deal with sb as he deals with you; pay sb back in his own coin; scratch my back and I will scratch yours;
日往月來 days and months pass; time flies; with the passing of days and months;
商業往來 business dealings;
數往知來 deduce what is likely to happen in the future by reviewing what has taken place in the past; in retracing the past, the future can be known;
送往迎來 bid farewell to those departing and greet the arrival of newcomers; escort the parting and welcome the coming; give entertainment to others; greet and say goodbye to the customers; meet and send off visitors; receive and see guests; see off those who depart and welcome those who arrive; speed the parting guests and welcome the new arrivals; welcome visitors and see them off;
因往推來 judge the future from the past;
友好往來 friendly exchanges;
彰往察來 consider the past events and examine the gain or loss in future; evidence the past and scrutinize the future;
中斷往來 discontinue social contacts;

[往年] in bygone years; in former years; in the years past;

[往日] in bygone days; in former days; in the olden days; in the past;
往日艱辛回味甜 that which was bitter to endure may be sweet to remember;

[往聖] ancient sages;

[往時] formerly; in the past;

[往事] history; past events; the past; things that have come to past;
往事不能挽回 we cannot undo the past;
往事感懷 recall past events with deep feeling;
往事緬懷 muse over past memories;
往事如煙 past events have faded like a puff of smoke;
往事休提 let bygones be bygones;
感懷往事 be moved to think of the past affairs; recall past events with deep feeling;
回憶往事 recall the past;
緬懷往事 muse over past memories;
談起往事 talk of the past;
已成往事 be water under the bridge;

[往往] easily; frequently; liable; more often than not; often; prone to; usually;
往往如此 it happens frequently that;
往往有之 as it often happens;

[往昔] in former times; in the past;
往昔的 of yesteryear;

[往哲] ancient saints and sages;

[往者] the past;
往者不可諫 let bygones by bygones; the past is past reproof; things past cannot be recalled;
往者不可追 that which is past is lost and irrecoverable; what is done cannot be undone;
往者已矣 what's gone is gone;

遄往 go quickly;
過往 (1) come and go; (2) associate with; have friendly intercourse with;
既往 the past;
交往 associate; contact; rub elbows with;
開往 be bound for; leave for;

來往 (1) come and go; (2) contacts; dealings; social intercourse;
前往 go to; leave for; proceed to; proceed toward; start for; visit;
神往 be carried away; be charmed; rapt; take one's breath away; yearn for at heart;
他往 go elsewhere;
逃往 flee toward;
無往 wherever one goes;
向往 be attracted toward; look forward to; yearn for;
嚮往 look forward to; yearn for;
已往 before; in the past; previously;
以往 before; formerly; in the past; previously;

wang
【枉】 (1) bent; crooked; twisted; warped; (2) abuse; bend; distort; pervert; twist; (3) do wrong; suffer wrong; treat unjustly; wrong; (4) futile; in vain; to no purpose; useless; vainly; waste;

[枉尺直尋] compromise on minor points so as to gain on the major issue; make only small concession, but gain quite considerably; only one foot is crooked and eight feet are straight;

[枉道事人] distort the truth in order to please others; please a superior by immoral ways;

[枉斷] abuse law by distorting it; decide unfairly;

[枉法] abuse law; pervert the law; twist law to suit one's own purpose;
枉法從私 bend the law to suit private interests;
貪贓枉法 pervert justice for a bride; take bribes and bend the law;
因私枉法 flout the law for private considerations;

[枉費] of no avail; try in vain; waste;
枉費唇舌 a mere waste of breath; waste one's breath;
枉費工夫 spend time and work in vain; waste time and energy;
枉費精力 flog a dead horse;
枉費錢財 throw away good money for nothing;
枉費心機 a fool for one's pains; bay at the moon; bark at the moon; bay the moon; beat the air; beat the wind; flog a dead horse; fruitless efforts; futile; go down the drain; go on a wild goose chase; in vain; make futile efforts; rack one's brains in vain; scheme in vain; scheme without avil; try in vain to; waste one's contrivances; waste one's efforts; waste one's labour; waste one's pains; wreck one's brain without results;

[枉駕] I am honoured by your visit;

[枉結] condescend to befriend;

[枉曲] bent; crooked; warped;

[枉屈] treat unjustly; wrong persons;
受枉屈 be wronged;

[枉然] futile; in vain; to no purpose; useless;

[枉死] be wronged and driven to death; die through injustice;

屈枉 wrong; treat unjustly;
冤枉 (1) not repaying the effort; not worthwhile; (2) treat unjustly; wrong; wrongly accused;

wang
【罔】 (1) deceive; libel; slander; (2) disregard; not; (3) crooked;

[罔顧] despite; disregard; not take into consideration;
罔顧人道 inhuman;

[罔極] (1) infinite; (2) transgress;
罔極之恩 kindness of one's parents;

[罔見] fail to see;

[罔然] at a loss; disconcerted; stupefied;
罔然無知 in ignorance of;

[罔聞] give no heed to;
付之罔聞 give no heed to; turn a deaf ear to;

[罔效] in vain; ineffective; to no avail;

[罔養] hesitate; unable to make a decision;

[罔有] have not;

欺罔 cheat; deceive;

wang
【惘】 dejected; disappointed; discouraged; feel disappointed; feel frustrated; feel lost; in a daze;

[惘然] at a loss; disappointed; frustrated; in a daze; stupefied;
惘然若失 all adrift; feel disturbed as if having lost sth; feel lost; look blank;

look distracted; vacant;
[惘惘無主] irresolute without decision;

悵惘 distractedly; listless;
迷惘 at a loss; perplexed;

wang

【網】 (1) net; (2) network; (3) bring together; collect; (4) catch with a net; net;
[網吧] Internet café;
[網版] printing screen;
[網蟲] webhead;
[網漏吞舟] the meshes of the law are so large that a whale could slip through; the net has such wide meshes that even fishes large enough to gulp a boat can escape from it; the net of justice is so lenient that an important criminal could escape from it;
[網羅] (1) assemble; bring together; collect; (2) net; trap; (3) enlist the services of; recruit;
網羅人材 enlist able men; net talents; recruit talented people;
[網絡] network;
網路安全 internet safety;
網絡病 cybersickness;
網絡佈局 network topology;
網絡操作 network operation;
~ 網絡操作技術 network operating system;
~ 網絡操作員 network operator;
~ 網絡操作中心 network operating centre;
網絡存取控制 network access control;
網絡犯罪 cybercrime;
網絡防毒 network virus protection;
網絡分析 network analysis;
~ 網絡分析員 network analyst;
~ 網絡分析中心 network analysis centre;
網絡服務 network service;
網絡負載分析 network load analysis;
網絡干擾 moiré;
網絡購物 cybershopping;
~ 網絡購物者 cybershopper;
網絡管理 network management;
~ 網絡管理系統 network management system;
網絡規劃 network planning;
網絡技術 network technique;
~ 網絡技術分析 technical analysis of networks;
網絡家庭 network family;
網絡接口機 network interface;
網絡結構 network structure;
網絡空間 cyberia; cyberspace;
網絡控制 network control;
~ 網絡控制程序 network control programme;
~ 網絡控制語言 network control language;
~ 網絡控制站 network control station;
~ 網絡控制中心 network control centre;
網絡理論 network theory;
網絡模擬 network analogy;
網絡目錄服務 netware directory service;
網絡欺凌 cyberbullying;
網絡欺詐 cyberfraud;
網絡企業家 netpreneur;
網絡軟件 network software;
網絡世界 cyberland;
網絡適配器 network adapter;
網絡數據庫 network data base;
網絡體系結構 network architecture;
網絡圖 network diagram;
網絡系統 network system;
網絡虛文件 network virtual file;
網絡學 webology;
網絡研討會 webinar;
網絡一體化 network integration;
網絡應用 network application;
網絡語言 internetese;
網絡運行中心 network operating centre;
網絡終端 network terminal;
道路網絡 road network;
公路網絡 motorway network;
廣泛網絡 extensive network;
廣域網絡 wide area network (WAN);
加法網絡 adding network;
建立網絡 build up a network; establish a network;
箭頭網絡 arrow network;
巨大網絡 large network;
邏輯網路 logical network;
模擬網絡 analog network;
平衡網絡 balance network;
全通網絡 all-pass network;
設置網絡 set up a network;
衰減網絡 attenuation network;
天線網絡 aerial network;
調整網絡 adjustment network;
鐵路網絡 railway network;
通信網絡 communication network;

形成網絡 form a network;
譯碼網路 decoding network
有源網絡 active electric network;

[網民] netizen; webhead;
銀髮網民 silver surfer;

[網膜] retina;

[網前球] drop shot;

[網球] (1) tennis; (2) tennis ball;
網球場 tennis court;
~草地網球場 grass court;
~硬地網球場 hard court;
網球教練 tennis coach;
網球拍 tennis racket;
網球運動 lawn tennis;
愛打網球 keen on tennis;
草地網球 lawn tennis;
傳近網球 close set;
傳遠網球 deep set;
打網球 play tennis;
一場網球 a game of tennis;
硬地網球 court tennis;

[網上] internet; online;
網上衝浪 surf the Internet;
網上購物 online shopping;
網上廣告 online advertising;
網上交易 online trading; online transaction;
網上禮儀 netiquette;
網上流量 Internet traffic;
網上書店 online bookstore;
網上推廣 online promotion;
網上銀行服務 internet banking;
網上營商 online business;
網上語言 internetese;
網上約會 internet dating;
網上招聘 e-recruit;

[網頁] web page; website;
網頁掛存服務 web-hosting service;

[網魚] net fish;

[網站] web;
網站管理員 webmaster;
門戶網站 portal;
入門網站 portal;
色情網站 pornographic website;
微型網站 microsite;

[網誌] blog; weblog;
視頻網誌 video blogging;

[網狀] reticular;
網狀結構 reticular formation; reticular structure;

[網子] net;

安全網 safety netting;
保健網 health care network;
測候網 reseau;
長網 fourdrinier wire;
抄網 dip net;
觸網 touch net;
刺網 gill net;
打網 weave a net;
地網 counterpoise;
電力網 power network;
電視網 television network;
電網 electrified wire netting; live wire entanglement;
定制網 fix net; set net;
吊貨網 cargo net;
法網 arm of the law; net of justice;
髮網 hairnet;
封網 block;
灌溉網 irrigation network;
廣播網 rediffusion (or broadcasting) network;
河網 network of waterways;
匯兌網 remittance network;
火力網 fire net; network of fire;
火網 fire net; network of fire;
交通網 network of communication lines;
勘探網 prospecting network;
攔網 block;
罹網 enmesh;
聯絡網 liaison net;
聯網 interconnecting network; networking;
零售網 retail network;
流網 drift net;
漏網 escape from the net; escape unpunished; slip through the cracks; slip through the net;
漉網 vat-net;
羅網 net; snare; trap;
落網 be captured; be caught; fall into the net;
內聯網 intranet;
排灌網 irrigation and drainage network;
配電網 distribution network;
起網 haul the net;
情網 cobweb of love; snare of love;
球網 net (for all ball games);
撒網 cast a net; pay out a net; spread a net;
商業網 communication network;
上網 go on the Internet;
收音網 radio rediffusion network;
輸電網 gird system; power transmission network;
水網 network of rivers;
絲網 gauze; silk screen;
鐵路網 railway network;

鐵絲網 (1) wire entanglement; (2) wire netting; wire meshes;
通訊網 communication network;
拖網 dragnet; trawlnet;
圍網 purse net; purse seine;
僞裝網 camouflage net; garnished net;
文網 arms of the law;
憲網 arm of law; net of justice;
曳網 seine;
醫療網 medical and health network;
魚網 fishing net; fishnet;
漁網 fishing net; fishnet;
運輸網 transport network;
繒網 lift net;
織網 spin a web;
蜘蛛網 cobweb; spider web;
蛛網 cobweb; spider web;
轉播網 relay network;

wang
【輞】 felloe; felly; rim of a wheel;

輪輞 rim (of a wheel);

wang
【魍】 a kind of monster;
[魍魎] demons and monsters;

wang⁴
wang
【妄】 (1) absurd; false; untrue; (2) ignorant; stupid; (3) ill-considered; rash; reckless; untoward; (4) frantic; frenetic; wild;
[妄動] act rashly; act recklessly; ill-considered actions; rash actions; reckless actions; take rash actions; take reckless actions;
[妄斷] jump to the conclusion;
[妄費] lavish; waste;
[妄加] give recklessly or lightly;
妄加猜測 make wild guesses;
妄加評論 make improper comments;
妄加指責 make rash criticism;
[妄念] improper thoughts; wild fancies;
[妄求] absurd desire; inappropriate request; presumptuous demand;
[妄人] ignorant and presumptuous person; incorrigible person; stupid and reckless person;
[妄圖] try in vain; vainly attempt;
妄圖虛名 run after empty fame;
[妄為] act without principle; reckless acts; untoward behaviour;
逞性妄為 act on impulse; act recklessly; behave unscrupulously;
恣意妄為 act willfully;
姿意妄為 behave unscrupulously; run amuck;
[妄想] absurd pursuit; daydream; delusion; forlorn hope; kink; vain hope; wishful thinking;
妄想痴呆 paraphrenia;
妄想狂 paranoia;
痴心妄想 idle dream;
癡心妄想 daydreaming; silly and fantastic notions;
[妄言] (1) talk nonsense; tell tlies; (2) rant; wild talk;
妄言妄聽 both to speak and hear absurdly; don’t take it too seriously;
[妄庸] very common and somewhat conceited;
[妄語] (1) talk nonsense; tell lies; (2) rant; wild talk;
妄語虛詞 wild talks and vain words;
[妄自] excess presumptuous;
妄自菲薄 excessively humble; have a sense of inferiority; have too low an opinion of oneself; improperly belittle oneself; look down upon oneself; think lightly of oneself; think too lowly of oneself; underestimate oneself; undervalue oneself; unduly humble oneself;
妄自尊大 aggrandize oneself; arrogant and overweening; be eaten up with pride; be given to swaggering; be puffed up with pride; be puffed up with self-importance; be well wadded with conceit; boast wildly of oneself; get too big for one’s boots; get too big for one’s breeches; get too big for one’s shoes; get too big for one’s trousers; give oneself airs; grow too big for one’s boots; have too high an opinion of oneself; indulge in foolish display; overbearing; overweening; put on the ritz; selfconceited; self-glorification; self-important; set oneself up as superior to everyone; swell with pride; think no end of oneself; think no small beer of oneself;
妄自尊大的人 stuffed shirt;

W

[妄作] act wildly and illegally;
妄作主張 make a presumptuous decision;

姑妄 see no harm in sth;
狂妄 extremely conceited; wildly arrogant;
虛妄 invented; unfounded;
愚妄 benighted but conceited; ignorant but self-important;
譫妄 delirium;

wang

【忘】 (1) escape from one's mind; escape one's memory; fail to remember; forget; get sth out of one's head; get sth out of one's mind; go out of one's mind; have sth off one's mind; let slip from one's mind; pass out of one's mind; slip one's memory; slip one's mind; (2) miss; omit; (3) neglect; overlook;

[忘本] (1) bite the hand that feeds one; ungrateful; (2) forget one's class origin; forget one's past suffering;
忘本之人 one who forgets the original source – ungrateful;
戒勿忘本 admonish one of one's duty;

[忘掉] forget; let slip from one's mind;
忘掉煩惱 keep one's mind off one's troubles;

[忘恩] bite the hand that feeds one; devoid of gratitude; ungrateful;
忘恩負義 devoid of gratitude; bite the hand that feeds one; forget sb's kindness and turn one's back upon him in return; forgetful of all favours one has been given; have no sense of gratitude and justice; kick down the ladder; kick over the ladder; show ingratitude for favours received; show no sense of gratitude; turn one's back on righteousness and forget kindness; turn on one's friend; ungrateful; ungrateful and act contrary to justice; ungrateful and leave one's benefactor in the lurch;
~忘恩負義者 ingrate;
~過河打渡子—忘恩負義 beating the ferryman after crossing the river – ungrateful;
施惠不記心，受德莫忘恩 do not remember favours you bestow upon others; do not forget favours others bestow upon you; have no recollection of favours given, do not forget benefits conferred;

[忘懷] dismiss from one's mind; forget; forgetful; unmindful;
忘懷得失 not worried about personal gains or losses;
難以忘懷 indelible; unforgettable;

[忘記] escape from sb's mind; escape sb; escape sb's memory; fail to remember; forget; get sth out of one's head; get sth out of one's mind; go out of sb's mind; have sth off one's mind; pass out of sb's mind; slip sb's memory; slip sb's mind;
忘記開會 forget about the meeting;
被忘記 slip one's memory; slip one's mind;
不忘記 bear in mind; not forget;

[忘舊] forget old friends and relatives; snobbish;

[忘了] forget; oblivious of;

[忘年交] a friendship in which the difference of years is forgotten; friendship between generations; friendship between old and young people; good friends despite great difference in age; the best of friends in spite of the difference of age;

[忘情] (1) be unruffled by emotion; indifferent; unmoved; (2) let oneself go; unable to control oneself;
忘情地唱歌 let oneself go and sing lustily;
不能忘情 be still emotionally attached;

[忘卻] drop from one's mind; fade from one's mind; forget; oblivion;

[忘我] oblivious of oneself; selfless; take no heed of oneself;
忘我精神 altruism;

[忘形] be carried away; beside oneself; get carried away; have one's head turned;
忘形之交 a friendship in which all outward ceremony of physical existence can be ignored; spiritual friendship between a noble and a commoner;
樂而忘形 beside oneself with joy; cannot contain oneself for joy; leap out of

one's skin;

[忘性] absent-mindedness; forgetfulness;

[忘憂] forget cares and worries;

忘憂草 day lily;

樂以忘憂 seek pleasure in order to free oneself from care;

不忘 not forget;

淡忘 fade from one's memory;

健忘 forgetful; have a bad memory; have a memory like a sieve; have a poor memory; have a short memory;

難忘 be fixed in the mind; memorable; never to be erased from the mind; never to be forgotten; unforgettable;

善忘 amnesia; forgetful; prone to forget; weak of memory;

遺忘 forget; neglect;

wang

【往】 to; toward;

[往後] backward; from now on; hereafter; in the future; later on;

往後走 turn back and proceed;

[往前] forward;

往前看 look forward;

一往無前 advance bravely; forge ahead valiantly; go ahead boldly; indomitable; press forward with indomitable courage;

一往直前 go ahead boldly; go ahead bravely without looking back; go right on; go straight onward;

[往上] upward;

往上跑 go uphill; run up;

[往下] downward;

往下説 talk on;

wang

【旺】 flourishing; prolific; prosperous; vigorous;

[旺地] good land; prosperous place;

[旺季] boom season; busy season; high season; peak period;

過弓旺季 out of season;

蘋果旺季 apple season;

[旺期] most productive period;

[旺盛] exuberant; full of vitality; overflowing with life; vigorous;

精力旺盛 very energetic and vigorous;

士氣旺盛 have high morale;

[旺月] busy month; rush month;

[旺運] a spell of good luck; good fortune; good luck;

持旺 continue to sell well;

見旺 doing brisk business; sell well;

健旺 healthy and vigorous;

興旺 flourishing; prosperous;

wang

【望】 (1) gaze into the distance; look far ahead; (2) call on; visit; (3) expect; hope; look forward to; (4) prestige; reputation;

[望八] expecting the eightieth birthday very soon;

[望巴巴] anxious; apprehensive;

[望帝] cuckoo;

[望風] keep watch; on the lookout;

望風捕影 be taken in by rumours; on a false scent; on a wrong scent; on the wrong track; pursue a phantom;

望風而來 come from all directions;

望風而降 everyone surrenders at the mere rumour of sb's coming;

望風而逃 flee at the mere sight of the oncoming force; flee before sb; run away at the rumour of the approach of; turn tail at the mere rustle of a leaf;

望風披靡 flee helter-skelter at the mere sight of the oncoming force; flee pell-mell before sb; melt away at the mere whisper of sb's coming;

望風撲影 give a wild-goose chase; launch a witch hunt; search without any clue;

望風引領 gaze at the wind and stretch out the neck — anxiously expecting sb;

[望衡對宇] in the neighbourhood; live near each other;

[望候] give a greeting;

[望見] see;

望不見 incapable of seeing;

[望看] respect;

[望樓] guardhouse; lookout tower; watchtower;

[望視] look upwards;

[望文生義] interpret without real understanding; take the words too literally;

[望聞問切] look, listen, question and feel the pulse — four ways of diagnosis;

W

[望眼欲穿] aspire earnestly; gaze anxiously till one's eyes are overstrained; have long been looking forward with eager expectancy; look for with impatient expectancy; look on with longing eyes; wear out one's eyes looking for; one's expecting eyes are going to be worn out; one's eyes are worn out watching for sb;

[望洋興歎] gaze at the ocean and complain of its infinitude — feel utterly helpless in face of a task beyond one's capability; lament one's littleness before the vast ocean;

[望遠鏡] telescope;

望遠鏡筒 telescope tube;

對準望遠鏡 alignment telescope;

反射望遠鏡 mirror telescope; reflecting telescope; reflector;

計數器望遠鏡 counter telescope;

伽利略望遠鏡 Galilean telescope;

射電望遠鏡 radio telescope;

雙目望遠鏡 binocular telescope;

~稜鏡雙目望遠鏡 prismatic bicocular telescope;

雙筒望遠鏡 binocular telescope; binoculars;

~一副雙筒望遠鏡 a pair of binoculars;

天文望遠鏡 astronomical telescope;

無線電望遠鏡 radio telescope;

消球差望遠鏡 aplanatic telescope;

消色差望遠鏡 achromatic telescope;

小型望遠鏡 spyglass;

一架望遠鏡 a telescope;

照相望遠鏡 photographic telescope;

折射望遠鏡 refracting telescope;

折軸望遠鏡 coude telescope;

[望月] full moon;

倚欄望月 lean against the rail to look at the moon;

[望族] distinguished family; prominent family; respected and influential clan;

巴望 await anxiously; eager to; expect; hope for anxiously; look forward to;

拜望 call on; call to pay one's respects; visit;

才望 talent and prestige;

承望 expect (usu. used in negative construction);

春望 look from high up in spring;

德望 a person's moral prestige;

觀望 (1) look around; (2) look on (from the sidelines); wait and see;

過望 beyond one's expectations;

渴望 ache for; aspire; be all agog to; be eager about; be eager after; be eager for; hanker after; hanker for; hankering; long for; pine for; thirst for; yearn after; yearn for;

厚望 great expectations;

鵠望 eagerly look forward to; thirst for;

冀望 hope; long for; look forward to;

酒望 a streamer hanging in front of a wine shop;

觖望 complain (out of discontent); have a grudge against sb out of discontent;

絕望 despair; give up all hope; hopeless; lose all hope of;

看望 call on; visit;

渴望 ache for; anxious for sth; anxious to do sth; aspire; crave; craving; eager about; eager after; eager for; eager to do sth; fall over oneself; hanker for; have a thirst for; hunger after sth; hunger for sth; hungry for; long after; long for; long to do sth; on tiptoe; pine for; starve for sth; thirst after; thirst for; thirsty for; yearn for;

了望 keep a lookout; watch from a height or a distance;

瞭望 keep a lookout; look down from a higher place; watch from a distance; watch from a height;

彌望 meet the eye on every side;

名望 fame and prestige; good reputation; renown;

凝望 fix one's gaze on; look with fixed eye;

盼望 look forward to; yearn for;

期望 expect; hope;

祈望 hope; wish;

跂望 look forward with eagerness; wait on the tiptoe;

企望 hope for; yearn for;

熱望 ardently wish; hope fervently;

人望 prestige; popularity;

奢望 extravagant hopes; high expectations; wild wishes;

深望 keenly hope;

聲望 cachet; fame; popularity; prestige; renown; reputation;

失望 beyond hope; chagrin; despair; disappointed; discouraged; lose hope;

碩望 man of great fame; much respected man;

守望 keep guard; keep watch;

朔望 the first and the fifteenth day the lunar month; syzygy;

素望 one's good reputation and prestige;

探望 (1) call on; look in; look up; pay a visit to; visit; (2) look about;
眺望 look far away; look into the distance from a high place; overlook; survey;
威望 cachet; imposing reputation; prestige;
聞望 fame; reputation;
無望 despair of; hopeless; without hope;
物望 object of popular admiration;
希望 care; desire; expect; expectation; have a yen for; hope; look forward to; want; wish;
相望 look at each other;
想望 (1) desire; expect; hope; long for; (2) admire; look up to;
信望 prestige; reputation;
懸望 hope with misgivings; long for anxiously; look forward eagerly;
仰望 (1) look up at; look up to; (2) rely on sb for instructions, support, etc.; respectfully seek guidance or help from;
遙望 look into the distance;
顒望 eager for; hoping anxiously;
有望 hopeful; promising;
慾望 desire; long for; longings; lust;
怨望 grudge; resentment;
願望 aspiration; desire; wish;
月望 the 15th day of a month;
在望 (1) in sight; in view; visible; (2) will soon materialize;
責望 blame and complain when sb fails to accomplish a difficult task;
瞻望 (1) look far ahead; look forward; (2) look up to;
展望 (1) look into the distance; (2) envisage; envision; look ahead; look into the future; outlook;
張望 (1) peep through a crack; (2) look about; look around; look into the distance;
指望 (1) count on; look forward to; look to; (2) hope; prospect;
衆望 people's expectations; popular confidence;
屬望 centre one's hope on; look forward to;
矚望 (1) gaze at; look long and steadily upon; (2) look forward to;
資望 qualification and prestige; seniority and prestige;

wang

【朢】 original form of 望, the fifteenth day of each month of the lunar calendar;

wei¹

wei

【委】 in a carefree manner, as in 委蛇;

［委蛇］ in a carefree manner;

虛與委蛇 deal with sb courteously but without sincerity; feign civility; pretend kindness; pretend politeness and compliance; pretend to have interest and sympathy;

wei

【威】 (1) dignity; majesty; (2) authority; impressive strength; might; power; (3) awe; awe-inspiring; (4) a surname;

［威逼］ browbeat; coerce; intimidate; menace; threaten by force;

威逼利誘 alternate intimidation and bribery; compel by threat or lure by money; corerce and bribe; intimidate by force and beguile with money; persuade and cajole sb with veiled threats; practise intimidation and bribery; resort to all kinds of threats and inducements; resort to both mild and stern measures; threaten and bribe; try to get sb through both force and bribery;

威逼利誘，不為所動 immune to bribery and indomitable before threats;

［威風］ (1) power and prestige; (2) awe-inspiring; imposing; impressive; majestic looking;

威風凜凜 awe-inspiring; have a commanding presence; have an awesome bearing; imposing; majestic-looking; with great dignity;

威風掃地 completely discredited; make a clean sweep of sb's prestige; sweep every bit of sb's prestige into the dust; one's dignity and prestige are swept into the dust; one's reputation is dragged in the dust; suffer a drastic fall in one's prestige; with every shred of one's prestige swept away; with one's dignity in the dust;

威風十足 one's prestige is at its apogee — having an awe-inspiring reputation;

八面威風 aura of awesome might; awe-inspiring reputation extending in every direction; august; awful; bright and bold; commanding; commanding presence; give oneself majestic airs; having an awe-inspiring reputation everywhere; influential in every

quarter; lordly; magisterial; make magnificent appearance; present a magnificent appearance;
擺威風 give oneself airs; put on airs;
逞威風 lord it over; show off one's strength; swagger about;
大施威風 throw one's weight about;
抖威風 throw one's weight about;
滅人威風 run sb down;
耍威風 make a show of authority; overbearing; throw one's weight about;
殺殺威風 deflate the opponent's arrogance; take sb down a peg or two;
顯威風 impress sb with one's authority; show one's prowess;

[威服] coerce; overawe;

[威福] punishment and reward;
威福自恣 assume great airs;
擅作威福 punish or reward according to one's whim;

[威力] force; might; power;
威力無比 extremely powerful;
威力無窮 an invincible force; colossal power; infinitely powerful; the might knows no bounds;
法律的威力 arm of the law;

[威猛] domineering;
威而不猛 awe-inspiring but kind at heart; dignified but not violent; imposing but not fierce; majestic and yet not fierce; stern but not ferocious;

[威名] awe-inspiring reputation; fame based on great strength or military exploits; prestige; renown;
威名遠揚 one's august name is widely known; one's fame spreads far and wide; one's renown reputation spreads extensively;

[威迫] intimidate;
威迫利誘 alterante intimidation and bribery; carrot and stick; coaxing and coercion; coerce and bribe; combine threats with inducements; compel by threat or lure by money; intimidate by force and beguile with money; persuade and cajole sb with veiled threats; practise intimidation and bribery; resort to all kinds of threats and inducements; resort to both mild and stern measures; stick and carrot; threaten and bribe; threats and blandishment;
威迫手段 scare tactics;

[威權] authority; power and prestige;

[威懾] deter; deterrence; submit sb to power and threat; terrorize with military force;
威懾力量 deterrent; deterrent force; deterrent power;
~核威懾力量 nuclear deterrence;
威懾政策 deterrent policy;
積極威懾 active deterrence;

[威聲] prestige;

[威士忌] whisky;
威士忌酒 whisky;
~純威士忌酒 straight whisky;
~高酒度威士忌酒 ignited whisky;
~檸檬威士忌酒 whisky sour;
~辛辣威士忌酒 peppery whisky;
~玉米威士忌酒 corn liquor; corn whiskey;
陳年威士忌 aged whisky;
黑麥威士忌 rye whisky;
糧食威士忌 grain whisky;
烈性威士忌 stiff whisky;
雙保威士忌 double-stamp whisky;

[威勢] power and influence; prestige and influence;

[威望] cachet; imposing reputation; prestige;
威望大震 gain great fame and high prestige;

[威武] (1) force; might; power; (2) mighty; powerful;
威武不能屈，富貴不能淫 not to be subdued by wealth or rank;
威武不屈 defy steadfastly all brute force; no force can bend one; not to be subdued by force; not to bow to pressure; not to submit to force; refused to be daunted by brute force; remain unyielding in face of brutal force; unyielding in the face of force;
威武雄壯 full of power and grandeur; magnificent and mighty;
威武壯麗 powerful and splendid;
威武之師 mighty army;

[威嚇] awe; bully; cow; intimidate; overawe; threaten;
大聲威嚇 bluster out threats;

[威脅] threat; imperil; menace; threaten;
威脅恐嚇 threaten and intimidate;

受到威脅 on the hazard; under threat;
以死威脅 threaten sb with death;

[威信] cachet; popular trust; prestige;
威信掃地 be shorn of one's prestige; be thorougly discredited; sweep every bit of sb's prestige into the dust; with one's dignity in the dust;
威信失去 lose prestige;
威信下降 decline in prestige;
保持威信 keep up one's prestige;
個人威信 personal prestige;
~追求個人威信 seek personal prestige;

[威嚴] (1) awe; awe-inspiring air; dignity; prestige; (2) severity; sternness;
保持威嚴 keep up one's prestige;
具有威嚴 possess dignity;

[威儀] dignity of demeanour; impressive and dignified manner; majesty;

[威震] inspire awe;
威震敵膽 have powerful combat strength that strikes terror into the hearts of the enemy;
威震華夏 become famous and fear-inspiring throughout China;
威震九州 awe the whole land; hold the world in awe;
威震全國 win resounding fame throughout the country;
威震全球 one's power shakes the world; win worldwide renown;
威震四方 known far and wide for one's military prowess;
威震四海 inspire awe throughout the country;
威震天下 inspire awe throughout the country; one's majesty is felt throughout the whole country;
威震一時 the terror of one's age;

[威重] dignified and awe-inspiring;

雌威 tantrum of a shrew;
德威 display one's virtue and dignity;
恩威 kindness and severity;
發威 demonstrate one's courage and power;
國威 national prestige;
虎威 frightful appearance of a tiger;
權威 (1) authority; dean; person of authority; pundit; (2) authority; power and prestige;
神威 invincible might; martial prowess;
聲威 prestige; renown;
施威 display one's power; exhibit one's power; impress with force; show severity;
示威 (1) hold a demonstration; (2) display one's strength; put on a show of force;
樹威 establish one's reputation;
霜威 awe; gravity and severity;
下馬威 severity and power displayed by an official upon taking office;
憲威 official prestige;
雄威 grand and powerful ;
宣威 extend one's power;
炎威 oppressively imposing;
揚威 attain eminence; show one's great authority;
淫威 abuse of power; despotic power;
餘威 remaining prestige or influence;
振威 extend one's imposing prestige; inspire awe;
助威 boost the morale of; cheer for; encourage; goad on;
作威 bossy;

wei

【偎】 (1) cuddle; embrace; (2) lean close to; snuggle up to; (3) intimate;

[偎愛] intimately in love;
[偎傍] stay close together;
[偎抱] cuddle; hug;
[偎近] lean close to; nestle up against;
[偎臉] put cheek and cheek together;
[偎貼] lean close to; snuggle up to;
[偎依] lean close to; snuggle up to;
偎紅倚翠 cuddle to the red and lean towards the purplish blue — have many concubines; frequent brothels;
偎偎依依 hold each other close swaying to and fro with emotion; nestle up to each other; rub one's face against one whom she loves;

依偎 lean close up; snuggle up to;

wei

【崴】 lofty;

[崴嵬] lofty; towering;

wei

【萎】 (1) wilt; wither; (2) ill; sick; (3) decline; fall; weaken;

[萎絕] wither;
[萎落] weaken and decline; wither and fall;
[萎靡] dispirited; listless;
萎靡不振 despondent; lethargic; unable to

pick oneself up;

［萎縮］ atrophy; dry up and shrink; shrink back; shrivel; wither;
萎縮性水腫 atrophedema;
萎縮症 atrophy;
斑狀萎縮 macular atrophy;
變性萎縮 degenerative atrophy;
病理性萎縮 pathologic atrophy;
創傷後骨萎縮 post-traumatic atrophy of bone;
代償性萎縮 compensatory atrophy;
廢用性萎縮 disuse atrophy;
肝萎縮 hepatatrophia;
睾丸萎縮 atrophia testiculi;
骨萎縮 bone atrophy; osteanabrosis;
關節周肌萎縮 arthritic atrophy;
關連性萎縮 correlated atrophy;
紅色萎縮 red atrophy;
灰色萎縮 gray atrophy;
急性黃色萎縮 acute yellow atrophy;
肌病性萎縮 myopathic atrophy;
肌肉萎縮 ischemic muscular atrophy;
肌萎縮 muscular atrophy;
～神經性肌萎縮 neurotic atrophy;
機能性萎縮 functional atrophy;
饑餓性萎縮 inanition atrophy;
間質性萎縮 interstitial atrophy;
老年性萎縮 senile atrophy;
彌漫性萎縮 diffuse atrophy;
面萎縮 facial atrophy;
腦回萎縮 convolutional atrophy;
腦萎縮 cerebral atrophy;
腦葉萎縮 lobar atrophy;
內分泌性萎縮 endocrine atrophy;
偏心性萎縮 eccentric atrophy;
全身萎縮 general atrophy; panatrophy;
軟化性萎縮 halisteretic atrophy;
色素性萎縮 pigmentary atrophy;
生理性萎縮 physiological atrophy;
視神經萎縮 optic atrophy;
衰竭性萎縮 exhaustion atrophy;
特發性肌萎縮 idiopathic muscular atrophy;
胃萎縮 gastric atrophy;
心萎縮 acadiotrophia;
壓迫性萎縮 compression atrophy; pressure atrophy;
牙槽萎縮 alveolar atrophy;
牙髓萎縮 pulp atrophy;
牙周萎縮 periodontal atrophy;
炎性萎縮 inflammatory atrophy;
眼萎縮 ophthalmatrophia;
嬰兒萎縮 infantile atrophy;
營養不良性萎縮 metatrophy;
營養神經性萎縮 trophoneurotic atrophy;
脂肪萎縮 adipose atrophy;
脂性萎縮 fatty atrophy;
中毒性萎縮 toxic atrophy;
子宮萎縮 metratrophia;

［萎謝］ fade; wither;

凋萎 wither; wither and fall;
枯萎 be withered; wither;
氣萎 become dejected; be discouraged; lose heart;

wei

【逶】 curved; tortuous; winding;
［逶迤］ meandering; winding;

wei

【渨】 bend on a river;

wei

【隈】 bay; bend in the hills or river; cover; mountain recess;

山隈 mountain recess;

wei

【微】 a pronunciation of 微；

wei

【煨】 bake; burn in ashes; roast; simmer; stew;
［煨燼］ ashes;
［煨肉］ stew meat;

wei

【椳】 sockets which hold doors in place;

wei

【葳】 (1) flourishing; luxuriant; (2) used for various plants;

紫葳 Chinese trumpet creeper (Campsis grandiflora);

wei²

wei

【危】 (1) danger; dangerous; far from settled; not too encouraging; perilous; precarious; (2) endanger; fear; (3) honest; just; straightforward; (4) high; lofty; (5) a surname;

［危殆］ in a critical condition; in great danger; in jeopardy;

[危篤] critical; dying;
病在危篤 ill and failing fast;

[危害] endanger; harm; hazard; injure; jeopardize;
危害治安 jeopardize public security;
急性危害 acute hazard;
健康危害 health hazard;
沒有危害 safe from harm;
生態危害 environmental hazard;
污染危害 contamination hazard;
造成危害 work the mischief;

[危機] crisis; critical point; crunch; precarious moment;
危機不斷 lurch from crisis to crisis; lurch from one crisis to another;
危機重重 be bogged down in crises; crisis-ridden;
危機四伏 a crisis of danger lurks in four corners; be plagued by crisis; be ridden with crisis; be threatened by growing crisis; crisis-ridden; danger lurks on every side;
危機一發 hang by a hair; hang by a thread; sway in the balance; swing in the balance; the crisis is imminent;
擺脫危機 extricate oneself from a crisis;
出現危機 reach a crisis;
度過危機 pass a crisis;
緩和危機 ease a crisis;
加劇危機 intensify the crises;
克服危機 tide over the crises;
面臨危機 face a crisis;
農業危機 agricultural crisis;
商業危機 commercial crisis;
陷入危機 come to a crisis;
信用危機 credit crisis;
循環危機 cyclic crisis;
一次危機 a crisis;
銀行危機 bank crisis;
引起危機 provoke a crisis;
中年危機 mid-life crisis;

[危及] endanger; imperil; jeopardize;
危及安全 endanger the security of; jeopardize the safety of;
危及生命 endanger one's life;

[危急] hazardous; in a desperate situation; in a state of emergency; pressing; urgent;
危急存亡之秋 a time when national existence hangs in the balance; at the moment of crisis; in critical time; period of national crisis;
存亡危急 at the critical juncture of life and death;

[危局] critical situation; dangerous situation; desperate situation;
解救危局 save the situation;
應付危局 meet the crisis;

[危懼] apprehensive; worry and fear;

[危卵] as precarious as a stack of eggs;
危卵之急 as precarious as a stack of eggs; in jeopardy;
危如累卵 as dangerous as eggs piled one on the other; as hazardous as eggs piled up; as precarious as a pile of eggs; in a terrible dilemma; in an extremely precarious situation; on thin ice;

[危難] calamity; danger and disaster;

[危亡] at stake; in danger of elimination; in great danger; in peril;

[危危欲墜] crumbling; on the verge of collapse; ramshackle;

[危險] dangerous; perilous; risky;
危險重重 full of peril;
危險地帶 dangerous zone;
~避開危險地帶 avoid a dangerous zone;
危險地區 danger area;
危險分子 dangerous elements; undesirable elements;
危險工作 dangerous work;
~危險工作津貼 danger money; danger pay;
危險警告燈 hazard lights;
危險品 dangerous cargo; hazardous article;
~危險品包裝 dangerous articles package;
危險評價 risk evaluation;
危險區域 danger zone;
危險示警燈 hazard lights;
避開危險 avert danger; ward off a danger;
避免危險 avoid danger;
不顧危險 ignore danger;
不畏危險 defy the peril;
充滿危險 be fraught with danger;
杜絕危險 eliminate danger;
防止危險 avert a danger;
感到危險 sense danger;
害怕危險 apprehend danger;
極端危險 grve danger; serious danger;
極其危險 a close shave;
謹防危險 carefully guard against dangers;
冒生命危險 risk one's life; risk one's

neck;
冒着危險 brave dangers;
沒有危險 safe from danger;
面對危險 face danger;
面臨危險 face a danger;
藐視危險 despise danger;
排除危險 obviate a danger;
潛在危險 potential danger;
逃避危險 escape a peril;
提防危險 look out for squalls;
脫離危險 out of danger;
相當危險 great danger;
有生命危險 in peril of one's life;
有危險 in danger;
遭受危險 be exposed to dangers;
致命危險 mortal danger;

[危言] alarmist talk;
危言聳聽 alarmist talk; exaggerate things just to scare people; make an inflammatory statement; raise a false alarm; say frightening things just to raise an alarm;
危言危行 cautious speech and conduct;

[危重] critical; grave;

[危坐] sit rigidly;
正襟危坐 all seriousness; dress well-buttoned; sit bolt upright; sit in great state; sit square;

安危 safety; safety and danger;
濱危 close to death; dying; have a close encounter with great danger;
瀕危 (1) be in imminent danger; (2) be terminally ill;
病危 (1) be at one's last gasp; (2) be in imminent danger;
垂危 approaching death; at one's last gasp; close to death; critically ill; near one's end; terminally ill;
扶危 help those in danger;
艱危 difficulties and dangers;
臨危 (1) be dying (from illness); (2) be in the hour of danger; face death or deadly peril;
攲危 tottering;
傾危 (1) crooked; mean; (2) highly dangerous; precarious;

wei

【微】 (1) diminutive; insignificant; little; micro-; minute; negligible; slight; small; tiny; trifling; (2) humble; inferior; low; mean; (3) obscure; uncertain; unclear; (4) fair; gentle; (5) delicate; profound; subtle; tricky; (6) faint; feeble; weak; (7) decline; (8) a surname;

[微波] microwave;
微波技術 microwave technology;
微波爐 microwave oven;
微波天線 microwave aerial;
微波武器 microwave weapon;

[微薄] little; low; mean; thin; trifling;
收入微薄 have a meager income;

[微不足道] inconsiderable; insignificant; negligible; not enough to speak of; not worth mentioning; so small that it is not worth noticing; stand for cipher; too insignificant to be worthy of mention; too small to be worth mentioning; too trivial to mention; trivial matters hardly worthy of mention;
微不足道的人 lightweight;

[微辭] hint; veiled criticism;

[微分] differential; differentiation;
微分電路 differentiator;
~反饋微分電路 feedback differentiator;
~非線性微分電路 nonlinear differentiator;
微分法 differentiation;
~電微分法 electrical differentiation;
~方向微分法 directional differentiation;
~分數微分法 fractional differentiation;
~高階微分法 higher order differentiation;
~共變微分法 covariant differentiation;
~數字微分法 digital differentiation;
~圖解微分法 graphic differentiation;
微分方程 differential equation;
微分公式 formula of differentiation;
微分學 differential calculus;
二項式微分 binomial differential;
法向微分 normal differentiation;
解析微分 analytic differential;
偏微分 partial differentiation;
全微分 total differentiation;
數字微分 digital differential;
特徵微分 characteristic differentiation;
外微分 exterior differential;
完全微分 complete differential;
遂次微分 successive differentiation;

[微風] breeze; fair wind; gentle breeze;
微風習習 a gentle breeze is blowing;

山谷微風 valley breeze;
夏日微風 summery breeze;
一陣微風 a breeze; a capful of wind; a light breeze; a slight gust of wind;

[微觀] microcosmic;
微觀翻譯 microscomic translation;
微觀分析 micro analysis;
微觀搞活 microeconomic flexibility;
微觀規劃 micro planning;
微觀教育 micro-education;
~微觀教育規劃 micro-educational planning;
~微觀教育系統 micro-educational system;
微觀結構 micro-structure;
微觀經濟 micro-economy;
~微觀經濟決策 microeconomical decision;
~微觀經濟學 microeconomics;
微觀力學 micro-mechanics;
微觀社會學 microsociology;
微觀社會語言學 micro-sociolinguistics;

[微乎其微] an iota; as trifling as it is; extremely minute; extremely trifling; minute; negligible in quantity; next to nothing; very insignificant; very little;
微乎其微的機會 a dog's chance; cat—hell's chance;

[微積分] calculus; differential and integral calculus; fluxionary calculus;
多變量微積分 calculus of several variables; multivariable calculus;
複變微積分 complex calculus;
絕對微積分 absolute calculus;
矢量微積分 ector; calculus;
隨機微積分 stochastic calculus;

[微機] microcomputer;
微機功能 microcomputer function;
微機開發 microcomputer developing;
~微機開發系統 microcomputer developing system;
微機系統 microcomputer system;

[微賤] humble; inferior; low and mean;
出身微賤 a person of obscurity; one's origin is ignoble; rise from humble beginnings; rise from obscurity;

[微粒] particle; particulate;
微粒輻射 corpuscular radiation;
微粒物質 particulate matter;
個別微粒 discrete particle;
空氣中懸浮微粒 air-borne particulate;
磨料微粒 abrasive particle;
氣載微粒 air-borne particle;
懸浮微粒 aerosol;

[微量] microscale;
微量分析 microanalysis;
~半微量分析 semimicroanalysis;
~超微量分析 supermicroanalysis;
微量元素 trace element;

[微茫] obscure; uncertain; unclear;

[微眇] small; trifling;

[微秒] microsecond;

[微妙] delicate; subtle; tricky;

[微末] insignificant; trifling;

[微情] delicate affair; subtle affair;

[微弱] faint; feeble; weak;
微弱的呼吸 faint breath;

[微生蟲] bacteria; germ; microbe;

[微生物] microbe; microorganism;
微生物學 microbiology;
~農業微生物學 agromicrobiology;
固有微生物 autochthonous microorganism;
活性微生物 active microorganism;
土壤微生物 solar microbe;
需氧微生物 aerobic microorganism; aeromicrobe;
厭氧微生物 anaerobic microorganism;
異養微生物 heterotrophic microbe;
暫居微生物 transient microbe;
自養微生物 autotrophic microbe;

[微微] diminutive; minute; small;
微微一笑 give a wee smile;

[微息] weak and feeble;

[微細] minute; tiny; very small;

[微嫌] slight animosity;

[微小] little; small; tiny;
謹小慎微 cautious and meticulous; overcautious in small matters; punctilio; stand on stepping-stones; strain at a gnat; timid and overcautious; timorous and punctilious;

[微笑] smile;
微笑服務 smiling for service;
慈祥的微笑 affable smile;
答以微笑 respond with a smile;
動人的微笑 prepossessing smile;
含淚微笑 smile through one's tears;
頷首微笑 nod smilingly;
會心微笑 smile a smile of understanding; understanding smile;

口帶微笑 a smile plays on one's lips;
滿意的微笑 contented smile;
迷人的微笑 ravishing smile; winning smile; winsome smile;
拈花微笑 gain a thorough understanding of esoteric Buddhist teachings;
讓人寬心的微笑 reassuing smile;
相互微笑 exchange smiles;
一閃即逝的微笑 fleeting smile;

[微型] mini; miniature;
微型唱片 mini disc;
微型化 microminiaturization;
微型教學 microteaching;
微型小說 mini story;

[微恙] slight indisposition;
偶染微恙 fall slightly indisposed;

[微意] token of gratitude;

[微雨] drizzle; light rain;

[微震] microseism; slight shock;
初期微震 preliminary tremor;

[微醉] squiffy;

卑微 humble; inferior; lowly; petty and low;
翠微 shady retreat on a green hill;
低微 humble; lowly;
霏微 heavy with mist or drizzle;
寒微 of humble origin; of low station;
精微 profound and delicate;
略微 a bit of; a little; a trifle; anything of; briefly; slightly; something of; somewhat;
輕微 insignificant; light; little; slight; to a small extent; trifling; trivial; unimportant;
人微 person in a low position;
入微 in every possible way; very thoughtful;
稍微 a bit; a little; a trifle; rather; slightly;
衰微 declining;
少微 slightly;
深微 deep; profound;
慎微 careful about minute details;
式微 the decline of;
衰微 decline; wane;
希微 extremely little; very little;
熹微 (of morning sunlight) dim; pale;
細微 fine; minute; slight; subtle; tiny;
顯微 show the minute points;
些微 a bit; a little; slight;
隱微 (1) invisible; latent; (2) profound;
幽微 (of sound, smell, etc.) faint; weak;

wei

【薇】 (1) osmunda regalis, a kind of fern; (2) used with other characters for a variety of plants;

薔薇 rose;
野薔薇 multiflora rose;
紫薇 crape myrtle;

wei

【巍】 lofty; towering;

[巍峨] lofty; tall and rugged; towering;

[巍然] imposing; lofty; majestic; towering;
巍然不動 firm as a rock; stand firm; stand steadfest;
巍然屹立 as firm as a rock; rise like a mountain; stand as firm as a rock; stand firm; stand lofty and firm; stand majestically like a mountain; stand rock-firm; stand towering like a mountain;

[巍巍] imposing; lofty; majestic; towering;

顫巍巍 faltering; tottering;
崔巍 (of mountains, buildings, etc.) lofty; towering;

wei
wei

【為】 (1) act; do; (2) act as; serve as; (3) administer; exercise; govern; handle; manage; (4) become; (5) be; make; mean;

[為伴] with the companionship of;
與壞人為伴 in bad companions;
與書本為伴 with the companionship of books;

[為禱] that is what I humbly pray for;

[為德不卒] do a good deed not to the finish;

[為惡] do evil;
為惡不悛 insist on doing evil without repentance;

[為非作歹] commit all sorts of evil; commit crimes; commit evil deeds; do evil at will; do evils without scruple; do mischief; evil and wicked; on the cross; perpetrate all kinds of evils; perpetrate outrages;

[為害] cause damage;
為害滋甚 cause greater havoc than ever;

[為患] bring trouble; cause of trouble;

[為力] endeavour; make efforts; strive;

[為難] (1) awkward; distressed; feel awkward; feel embarrassed; in a dilemma; in

a pickle; in difficulties; troubled; (2) make things difficult for;
左右為難 stand at a nonplus;
[為期] by a definite date;
為期不遠 in the near future; soon; the day expected is around the corner; the day is at and; the day is not far off; the day is not too distant;
為期甚遠 the day is far away;
為期一周的 weeklong;
[為人] behave; conduct oneself;
為人不自在，自在不為人 he that will not endure labour in this world, let him not be born;
為人不作虧心事，夜半敲門不吃驚 a clear conscience laughs at false accusations; a good conscience is a soft pillow; a good conscience is not afraid; a man whose conscience is void of offence is not alarmed by a knock at his door in the middle of the night; a quiet conscience sleeps in thunder; a safe conscience makes a sound sleep;
為人處世 one's attitude towards life; the way one conducts oneself;
為人風趣 have a high sense of humour;
為人高尚 conduct oneself nobly;
為人公正 upright in character;
為人明智 conduct oneself wisely;
為人清白 open and honest;
為人師表 a model for others; a model of virtue for others; a paragon of virtue and learning; worthy of the name of a teacher;
為人爽快 frank and straightforward;
為人四海 generous to people;
為人所愚 be fooled by sb;
為人坦率 frank and open;
為人在世 live in this world;
為人正派 a man of decency;
為人正直 upright;
為人之道 the rules of conduct;
[為善] do good;
為善最樂 doing good is the greatest source of happiness; to do good is the happiest thing;
勸人為善 advise people to do good;
[為生] make a living;
無以為生 live on nothing;
以寫作為生 make a livelihood by writing;
[為時] the time is;
為時尚早 it is still too early; the time is not yet ripe;
為時己晚 a day after the fair; it's too late;
[為首] headed by; the leader of; with sb as the leader;
[為數] amount to; number;
為數不多 few in number; have only a small number; in negligible quantity; limited in number; not many;
為數不少 come up to a large number; many; quite a number;
為數甚多 in large quantity; strong in number;
為數有限 limited in number; not many;
[為…所…] by;
為環境所迫 by force of circumstances;
[為所欲為] act as one wishes; act wilfully; do as one pleases; do one's thing; do what one wants to do; do whatever one likes; get away with murder; get one's own way; have one's full swing; have one's way; self-abandoned; take one's own course; unscrupulous; without let or hindrance;
[為伍] associate with; mix with;
不與壞人為伍 keep from bad company;
羞與為伍 ashamed of sb's company; ashamed to be seen in the same company; consider it beneath one to associate with sb; feel ashamed to associate with sb; feel ashamed to be in the same rank with sb;
[為限] not to exceed; serve as a limit; within the limit of;
[為幸] it would be fortunate;
[為學] engage in studies;
[為要] it is important that;
[為業] as a means of livelihood;
[為政] in government administration;
為政不在多言 acts speak louder than words in government administration;
為政之道 the proper governance of a state;
[為證] serve as evidence; serve as proof;
[為止] (1) till; until; up to; (2) no further;
迄今為止 up to now;
[為重] attach most importance to;
以大局為重 put the general interest first;
以友誼為重 value the friendship highly;
[為主] give first place to; give priority to;

mainly; the most important;

wei

【韋】 (1) leather; tanned leather; (2) a surname;

［韋編三絕］ study diligently;

［韋衣］ (1) hunting clothes; (2) simple clothes;

W

wei

【桅】 the mast of a ship;

［桅燈］ (1) mast light; range light; (2) barn lantern;

［桅杆］ mast; mast of a boat;

固定桅杆 fixed mast;

起重桅杆 lifting mast;

移動桅杆 travelling mast;

［桅檣］ mast;

［桅繩］ stay;

［桅梯］ shrouds of a ship;

船桅 mast;

wei

【唯】 alone; only;

［唯獨］ alone; exception; only;

［唯恐］ for fear of; for fear that; lest;

唯恐天下不亂 anxious to stir up trouble; crave nothing short of nationwide chaos; desire to see the world plunged into chaos; desire to stir up trouble; sow discord to serve private ends;

［唯美主義］ aestheticism;

唯美主義者 aesthete;

［唯名論］ nominalism;

［唯我獨尊］ assume air of self-importance; autocratic; be puffed up with pride; bossy; egoistic; exalt only one's own self; overlordship; pride oneself upon one's ability; stand upon one's pantofles;

［唯我論］ solipsism;

唯我論的 solipsistic;

［唯物］ materialist;

唯物辯證法 materialist dialectics;

唯物論 materialism;

~機械唯物論 mechanistic materialism;

唯物主義 materialism;

~辯證唯物主義 dialectical materialism;

~歷史唯物主義 historical materialism;

［唯心］ idealist;

唯心辯證法 idealist dialectics;

唯心論 idealism;

~主觀唯心論 subjective idealism;

唯心主義 idealism;

~歷史唯心主義 historical idealism;

［唯一］ only; sole; the only kind; the only one; unique;

［唯有］ only;

wei

【帷】 curtain; screen; tent;

［帷幔］ cloth partitions; screens;

［帷子］ curtain;

牀帷 bed-curtain;

羅帷 bed-curtain;

wei

【惟】 (1) alone; only; (2) but; however; only that; (3) thinking; thought;

［惟獨］ alone; only;

［惟恐］ for fear that; lest;

惟恐落後 fear that one should lag behind;

惟恐天下不亂 desire to see the world plunged into chaos;

［惟妙惟肖］ remarkably true to life; so skilfully imitated as to be in distinguishable from the original;

［惟其］ just because;

［惟神論］ pantheism;

［惟是］ only that;

［惟我獨尊］ egoistic; extremely conceited; no one is noble but me; overweening;

［惟一］ only; sole; the only one; the only thing of its kind; unique;

惟一無二 the one and only; the only one and be second to none;

［惟有］ only;

不惟 not only;

恭惟 compliment; flatter;

wei

【圍】 (1) encircle; enclose; hem in; surround; (2) all round; around;

［圍捕］ arrest by closing in on the criminal from all sides;

［圍場］ enclosure;

［圍城］ (1) besiege a city; encircle a city; (2) besieged city;

圍城打援 besieze a city to annihilate the enemy relief force; lay siege to a city and hit at enemy reinforcements;

[圍地] enclosure;
[圍堵] beseize;
圍者如堵 the crowd is so thick in the street that one can hardly get through it; the spectators stand round like a wall;
圍追堵截 encircle, pursue, obstruct and intercept;
[圍攻] attack from all sides; beleaguer; beseize;
圍攻城堡 surround a castle for an attack;
圍攻要塞 lay siege to a fortress;
被圍攻 under a siege;
頂住圍攻 stand the siege;
猛烈圍攻 push the siege;
停止圍攻 abandon a siege;
圍而不攻 encircle without attacking;
遭到圍攻 come under attack from all sides;
[圍殲] surround and annihilate;
[圍剿] attack from all sides; encircle and suppress;
[圍巾] muffler; scarf;
厚圍巾 muffler;
圍上圍巾 put a scarf round the neck;
一條圍巾 a scarf;
印花大圍巾 bandanna;
羽毛長圍巾 feather boa;
雜色圍巾 belcher;
摘掉圍巾 take off one's muffler;
[圍困] besiege; hem in; pin down; strand;
[圍欄] pen;
遊戲圍欄 playpen;
[圍獵] hunt by encircling the game;
[圍攏] crowd around; draw around; draw round;
圍攏過來 crowd around;
[圍爐] sit and chat around the fireplace;
[圍屏] folding screen;
[圍棋] go;
[圍牆] fence; enclosing wall; enclosure;
[圍裙] apron;
連胸圍裙 pinny;
[圍繞] (1) around; round; (2) centre on; move round; revolve round;
圍繞四周 lie around;
[圍堰] cofferdam;
半潮圍堰 half-tide cofferdam;
單牆圍堰 single-wall cofferdam;
格孔式圍堰 cellular cofferdam;
上游圍堰 upstream cofferdam;
雙壁圍堰 double wall cofferdam;
下游圍堰 downstream cofferdam;
[圍住] be surrendered;
團團圍住 be surrendered; besiege closely; cluster round; encircle; surround completely; surround in a tight ring;
[圍桌] cloth hanging over the sides of a table;
[圍嘴] bib;

包圍 besiege; encircle; engulf; envelopment; hem around; hem in; hen about; lay siege to; surround;
重圍 tight encirclement;
打圍 encircle and hunt down (animals); hunt;
堤圍 dike; embankment;
範圍 ambit; boundary; confines; extent; limits; range; scope; spectrum;
氛圍 atmosphere;
合圍 (1) (of a tree, etc.) so big that one can just get one's arms around;
解圍 (1) come to the rescue of the besieged; force an enemy to raise a siege; rescue sb from a siege; (2) ease sb's embarrassment; get sb out of a fix; help sb out of a predicament; save sb from embarrassment;
潰圍 break through enemy blockade;
入圍 on the shortlist;
三圍 the vital statistics;
四圍 all around;
四周圍 all around;
突圍 break out of an encirclement;
外圍 periphery;
胸圍 (1) bust; chest measurement; (2) bra;
腰圍 (1) girth; waist; (2) girdle;
周圍 about; around; on every side; round vicinity; surroundings;

wei

【幃】 (1) curtain; (2) perfume-bag; (3) women's apartments;
[幃幕] drapery; drapes;

wei

【違】 (1) break; contrary to; defy; disobey; disregard; go against; infringe on; run counter to; violate; (2) evil; fault; (3) profound; (4) decline;
[違礙] prohibition; taboo;
[違拗] defy; disobey;
[違背] breach; contrary to; disobey; disregard; go against; run counter to; violate;

W

違背傳統 run counter to tradition;
違背禮儀 offend decency;
違背諾言 go back on one's word;
違背條約 violate a treaty;
違背原則 violate a principle;
違背真理 depart from the truth;

[違法] against the law; break the law; illegal; unlawful; violate the law;
違法必究 law breakers will be dealt with; violations of the law must be prosecuted; violators are brought to justice;
違法分子 law-breaker;
違法亂紀 breach of law and discipline; break laws and violate discipline; in contravention of law and discipline; infringe laws and violate discipline; offences against law and discipline; violate the law and discipline; violations of the law and of discipline;
違法失職 transgression of the law and neglect of duty;
違法行為 illegal act; malfeasance; unlawful act;
違法者 law-breaker;

[違反] act against; contradict; disregard; infringe; run counter to; transgress; violate;
違反本意 against one's inclination;
違反常規 out of rule;
違反道德 offensive to morality;
違反合同 in breach of the contract;
違反紀律 breach of discipline;
違反交通規則 violate traffic regulations;
違反禮節 violatge etiquette;
違反歷史潮流 run counter to the trend of history;
違反人性 go against nature;
違反事實 fly in the face of facts; in defiance of facts;
違反條約 act in violation of the stipulations;
違反校規 offend the code of the school;
違反刑法 commit a criminal offense;
違反自然規律 violate the rules of nature;

[違犯] act contrary to; infringe; violate;
違犯法律 violate the law;
違犯規則 infringe rules;

[違規] against regulations;

[違和] ill; indisposed;
貴體違和 your precious health is not all that it might be;
政躬違和 an official is indisposed while on duty;

[違禁] defy a prohibition; violate a ban;
違禁品 forbidden goods and articles;

[違警] breach of police regulations; break a police regulation;

[違抗] defy; defy and oppose; disobey;
違抗法律 disobedient to the law;
違抗命令 act in defiance of orders; disobey orders;
公然違抗 at open defiance with;

[違理] defy good reasoning; unreasonable;

[違禮] disregard proper rules of behaviour; go against accepted etiquette;

[違例] contrary to practices;
嚴重違例 in gross violation of;

[違令] disobey orders;

[違失] errors; faults; misconduct;

[違世] drop out;

[違忤] disobedient and unruly;

[違誤] disobey orders and cause delay;

[違憲] unconstitutional; violation of the constitution;

[違心] against one's will; contrary to one's convictions;
違心服從 comply against one's will;
違心之論 insincere utterances; obviously insincere talk; statement contrary to one's inner belief; utterances which are contrary to right; words uttered against one's conscience;

[違約] (1) breach of contract; break a contract; violate a treaty; (2) breach; break off an engagement; break one's promise; infringement;
違約責任 liability for breach of contract;

[違章] break rules and regulations;
違章操作 operate a machine contrary to its instructions;
違章超速 break the speed limit;
違章駕駛 driving against traffic regulation;
違章建築 buildings erected without a license;
違章行駛 drive against traffic regulations;

久違 how long it is since we last met; I haven't seen you for ages;

睽違 separate;

擅違 disobey; violate;
相違 (1) (in opinion) disagree; (2) part;
依違 hesitate;

wei

【嵬】 (of a mountain) high and uneven;
[嵬峨] lofty;
[嵬然] lofty; towering;
[嵬嵬] lofty; towering;

崔嵬 high; rocky mound; towering;

wei

【維】 (1) hold fast; hold together; secure; tie up; (2) maintain; safeguard; (3) thinking; thought;
[維持] eke out; keep; maintain; preserve;
維持紀律 maintain discipline;
維持生活 support oneself;
維持生命 keep body and soul together;
維持體力 preserve one's strength;
維持體面 keep up appearances;
維持現狀 hold fast to the status quo; let things go on as they are; maintain the present condition; maintain the status quo;
維持性 maintenance;
維持原判 affirm the original judgement; uphold the conviction;
維持治安 maintain public order;
維持秩序 preserve order;
[維和] peace-keeping;
維和部隊 peace-keeping force;
[維護] defend; keep; maintain; preserve; protect; safeguard; uphold; upkeep;
維護傳統 uphold one's heritage;
維護費 sums of maintenance;
維護工程師 service engineer;
維護團結 uphold unity;
維護中心 service centre;
例行維護 routine maintenance;
[維艱] very difficult; very hard;
度日維艱 pass the day hardly; pass the day with difficulty; scratch along;
旅食維艱 the difficulties in lodging and boarding;
[維妙維肖] absolutely lifelike; almost identical with; in facsimile; remarkably true to life; speaking likeness; the very image of; to a hair; to the life; to the turn of a hair; true to life; true to nature; with minute exactitude; with startling reality;
[維生素] vitamin;
維生素原 primary vitamin;
多種維生素 multivitamin;
抗出血維生素 antihemorrhagic vitamin;
抗感染維生素 anti-infective vitamin;
生育維生素 fertility vitamin;
生殖維生素 reproductive vitamin;
水溶性維生素 water-soluble vitamin;
[維數] dimension; dimensionality;
標準維數 canonical dimension;
常維數 constant dimension;
複維數 complex dimension;
覆蓋維數 covering dimension;
漸近維數 asymptotic dimension;
容量維數 capacity dimension;
數組維數 dimensionality of array;
[維他命] vitamin;
[維繫] keep; maintain; make secure and bind together;
維繫型公關 connecting type of public relations;
[維新] make political reform; reform;
[維修] keep in good repair; maintain; maintenance; service; upkeep;
維修房屋 maintain houses and buildings;
維修費 cost of maintenance;
維修顧問 service advisor;
維修良好 in good repair;
維修能力 service ability;
維修汽車 service a car;
維修項目 service item;
大廈維修 upkeep of a building;
故障維修 breakdown maintenance;
接觸維修 contact maintenance;
外勤維修 outcall service;
需要維修 need repairing;
應急維修 emergency maintenance;

恭維 adulation; butter up; compliment; flatter;
三維 three-dimensional;
思維 deliberate; think deeply; thinking; thought;
纖維 fibre; staple;
相維 support each other;
縶維 retain;
枳維 maintain a relationship;

wei

【濰】 a river in Shandong;

wei

【闈】 (1) side doors of a palace; (2) living

quarters of the queen and the imperial concubines; (3) ladies' living quarters; private quarters; (4) hall where the civil service examination of former times took place;

[闈墨] selections from papers of successful candidates at imperial examinations;

春闈 (1) side gate of an imperial palace; (2) imperial examination hall (in ancient times);
宮闈 palace chambers;
秋闈 imperial examinations (in Ming and Qing dynasties) held in autumn;
入闈 enter the imperial examination hall (in feudal China);

wei3
wei

【尾】 (1) rear; tail; (2) end; final; last; (3) remaining; remaining part; remnant;

[尾巴] tail;
尾巴翹上天 very cocky;
尾巴主義 tailism;
夾起尾巴 tuck one's tail;
夾着尾巴 run away with one's tail between one's legs;
翹尾巴 cocky; crow over; get cocky; get one's tail up; get stuck-up; haughty and snooty; on the high ropes; stick one's tail up; wag one's tail in the air; wax fat and kick;
搖尾巴 wag one's tail;

[尾大不掉] leadership rendered ineffectual by recalcitrant subordinates; the tail is too big to way — subordinate growing too powerful to be at one's command; too cumbersome to be effective;

[尾燈] taillight;

[尾端] tail of sth;

[尾骨] coccyx;

[尾聲] coda; end game;

[尾隨] at the tail of; follow at sb's heels; tag along after; tail behind;
尾隨不捨 chase closely and without giving up; follow sb closely; follow up; hot on sb's trail;

擺尾 shopkeepers' strike; flick the tail; wag the tail;
蠆尾 poisonous tail of a scorpion — a harmful thing or person;
赬尾 toils of a gentleman;
船尾 stern;
詞尾 suffix;
斷尾 dock (the tail);
虎尾 tiger's tail;
彗尾 tail of a comet;
機尾 tail (of an aircraft);
交尾 mate; pair;
結尾 (1) ending; winding-up stage; (2) coda;
闌尾 appendix; epityphlon;
馬尾 horsetail;
末尾 (1) end; (2) end; fine;
牛尾 oxtail;
排尾 last person in a file;
砲尾 gun breech;
礮尾 gun breech;
脾尾 tail of spleen;
茸尾 flag;
掃尾 round off; wind up;
殺尾 come to a conclusion;
煞尾 (1) bring to an end; conclude; finish off; round off; wind up; (2) end; ending; final stage;
收尾 (1) come to a conclusion; wind up; (2) concluding passage;
首尾 (1) from beginning to end; (2) beginning and end; head and tail;
歲尾 end of a year;
頭尾 head and tail;
拖尾 (1) smear; (2) streaking; (3) tailing;
巷尾 end of a lane;
押尾 (1) after; last; (2) sign at the end of a document;
燕尾 forked tail; swallow tail;
搖尾 wag the tail;
頁尾 footer;
魚尾 fish tail;
鳶尾 iris;
韻尾 tail vowel,
豬尾 pig's tail;
麈尾 duster;
字尾 suffix;

wei

【委】 (1) appoint; entrust; (2) abandon; cast aside; give up; throw away; (3) shift; (4) indirect; roundabout; (5) end; (6) dejected; listless; (7) committee;

[委頓] broken down; tired down; wearied; worn-out;

[委過] shift blame;
委過於人 impute one's responsibility to others; lay one's faults at other people's door; lay the blame on others; shift the blame on to sb else;

[委積] accumulate; pile up;

[委靡] dejected; dispirited; listless;
委靡不振 dejected and apathetic; dispirited and invert; feel blue; have one's heart in one's boots; in low spirits; listless; low in spirits;

[委命] (1) leave oneself to fate; yield to fate; (2) commission; depute; (3) serve under sb with dedication;

[委派] appoint; commission; delegate; designate; send sb in charge of;

[委棄] abandon; discard; give up; throw away;

[委曲] (1) tortuous; winding; (2) twists of events;
委曲求全 compromise for the sake of the general interest; compromise out of consideration for the general interest; in a spirit of conciliation and compromise; make accommodations for the sake of the overall interest; make concessions to achieve one's aim; quite accommodating and care for overall interests; show oneself forbearing and conciliatory for the sake of the common good;
委曲婉轉 in a roundabout way; mild and roundabout; with soft words;

[委屈] feel wronged; nurse a grievance; suffer from injustice;
受委屈 (1) get a bum deal; suffer a wrong; suffer humiliation; (2) be inconvenienced; be troubled;

[委任] appoint; nominate;
委任權 power of attorney;
委任狀 certificate of appointment;
謝絕委任 decline an appointment;

[委身] (1) become the wife of; (2) consign oneself to sb;

[委實] indeed; really;
委實招供 confess truthfully;

[委瑣] (1) details; petty; trifling; (2) of a wretched appearance; (3) stickler for forms;

[委托] commission; entrust; trust;
委托代理 agency by mandate;
委托合同 contract on commission;
委托加工 processing deal;
委托人 principal;
~外國委托人 foreign principal;
~顯名委托人 named principal;
~隱名委托人 unnamed principal;
擇優委托 award contracts to the best qualified bidders;

[委婉] euphemistic; ingratiating; mild and roundabout; suave and moving; soft-spoken; tactful;
委婉動聽 in a specious manner that moves others to listen;
委婉否定 paradiastole;
委婉曲折 in a specious manner and in a crooked way;
委婉語 euphemism;
~委婉語氣 mild tone;

[委員] (1) commissioner; (2) committee member;
委員會 commission; committee; council;
~委員會成員 committee member;
~委員會會議 committee meeting;
~委員會委員 member of a committee;
檢察委員會委員 member of the procuratorial committee;
審判委員會委員 member of the judicial committee;
~委員會主席 committee chair; committee chairman;
~部門委員會 department committee;
~部長委員會 ministerial committee;
~財務委員會 finance committee;
~常務委員會 standing committee;
~成立委員會 form a committee; set up a committee;
~程序委員會 steering committee;
~村民委員會 villagers' committee;
~督導委員會 steering committee;
~法制委員會 commission for legal affairs;
~翻譯委員會 translation committee;
~管理委員會 management committee;
~規劃委員會 planning committee;
~計劃生育委員會 family planning commission;
~計劃委員會 planning commission;
~加入委員會 join a committee;
~建設委員會 construction commission;
~教育委員會 education commission; education committee;

~經濟體制改革委員會 commission for restructuring economy;
~經濟委員會 economic commission;
~居民委員會 neighbourhood committee;
~科學技術委員會 scientific and technological commission;
~聯合委員會 joint committee;
~民族事務委員會 nationalities affairs commission;
~任命委員會 appoint a committee;
~特別調查委員會 ad hoc commission of inquiry;
~特別委員會 special committee;
~體育運動委員會 physical culture and sports commission;
~無線電管理委員會 radio administration;
~行政委員會 administrative council;
~院務委員會 assembly of fellows;
~政法委員會 law commission;
~政府委員會 government committee;
~執行委員會 executive committee;
~指導委員會 guiding committee; steering committee;
~專責委員會 select committee;
~咨詢委員會 advisory committee;
委員長 chairman;
~副委員長 vice-chairman;
常務委員 member of the standing committee;
代理委員 delegation; deputation;
國務委員 state councilor;
候補委員 alternate member;
~中央候補委員 alternate member of the central committee;
中央委員 member of the central committee;
主任委員 chairman of a committee;
~副主任委員 vice-chairman of a committee;

[委之於地] cast sth upon the ground;

[委罪] put the blame on sb else; shift blame onto sb else;

部委 ministries and commissions;
差委 appoint;
常委 member of a standing committee;
黨委 Party committee;
地委 prefectural committee;
工委 working committee;
加委 carry out the formalities of appointment;
區委 district Party committee;
省委 provincial committee;
市委 municipal committee;
推委 shift responsibility onto others;
縣委 county committee;
原委 all the details; the ins and outs (of a story, case, etc.);
政委 commissar; political commissar;

wei

【洧】 a river in Henan;

wei

【娓】 (1) complying; subservient; (2) attractive; beautiful; pleasant; (3) diligent and tireless;

[娓娓] tirelessly;
娓娓不倦 talk tirelessly;
娓娓動聽 pleasing to the ear; rattle out the most attractive rhetoric; smooth-spoken; speak with absorbing interest; talk in an impressive way;
娓娓而談 talk effusively; talk familiarly on and on; talk volubly;

wei

【偽】 (1) adulterate; counterfeit; fake; false; (2) puppet; (3) artificial; simulated; (4) illegal;

[偽幣] (1) adulerate coin; counterfeit money; (2) money issued by a puppet government;

[偽鈔] counterfeit bank note;

[偽國] illegal state;

[偽軍] puppet army;

[偽善] hypocritical;
偽善的話 cant;

[偽造] counterfeit; fabricate; falsify; forge;
偽造鈔票 counterfeit bills;
偽造公文 make a counterfeit of official papers;
偽造口實 feign an excuse;
偽造歷史 fabricate history;
偽造品 counterfeit articles; forgery;
偽造簽名 forge a signature;
偽造新聞 falsify news;
偽造賬目 falsify accounts;
偽造者 forger;
偽造證件 forge a certificate;

[偽證] perjury;
作偽證 bear false witness;

[偽裝] camouflage; disguise; feign; guise; mask; pretend;

偽裝積極 pretend to work diligently;
偽裝技術 cloaking;
偽裝進步 pretend to be progressive;
偽裝友善 under the guise of friendship;
偽裝中立 feign neutrality;
偽裝專家 camoufleur;
戳穿偽裝 pierce the disguise;
電子偽裝 electronic camouflage;
防雷達偽裝 radar camouflage;
拋開偽裝 throw off one's disguise;

wei

【偉】 (1) big; extraordinary; gigantic; great; (2) a surname;

［偉岸］ tall and robust;
［偉大］ extraordinary; great; mighty;
［偉績］ brilliant achievements; glorious achievements; great achievements; great exploits; great feats;
建立偉績 establish greatness;
［偉力］ immense strength; mighty force; tremendous force;
［偉論］ your great speech;
瑩聽偉論 have a clear hearing of your great speech;
［偉器］ man of great capability;
［偉人］ great man; great personage;
歷史偉人 great historical character;
［偉業］ exploits; great career; great cause; monumental accomplishments;

傀偉 great and imposing;
宏偉 grand; magnificent; splendid;
魁偉 big and tall; stalwart; strong-built; tall and strong;
奇偉 great and wonderful; singularly spectacular;
雄偉 grand; magnificent;
英偉 great;

wei

【唯】 yea; yes;

［唯唯否否］ echo others; have no independent opinion; yes or no;
［唯唯諾諾］ obsequious; servile; subservient; with servility; yes-man;

wei

【痏】 mark on the skin; scar;

wei

【猥】 (1) many; multitudinous; multifarious; numerous; varied; (2) base; lewd and licentious; low; obscene; vulgar; wanton;

［猥鄙］ base; despicable; mean;
［猥詞］ obscene language; salacious words;
［猥獕］ hideous; ugly; unsightly;
［猥妓］ prostitute;
［猥賤］ base; humble; low and vulgar; lowly;
［猥劣］ abject; base; mean;
［猥陋］ base; despicable; mean;
［猥瑣］ low and petty; of dreadful appearance; of wretched appearance;
［猥褻］ indecency; lewd; obscene; salacious;
猥褻的 indecent; lascivious; lubricious;
猥褻露體 indecent exposure;
猥褻侵犯 indecent assault;
猥褻行為 indecent acts;
猥褻言語 aeschrolalia;
［猥雜］ numerous and varied;

卑猥 mean; obscene;
淫猥 obscene;

wei

【痿】 impotent; paralysis;

陽痿 impotence;

wei

【葦】 reed;

［葦席］ reed mat;
［葦杖］ whip of reeds;
［葦子］ reed;

蘆葦 reed;

wei

【煒】 (1) bright; brilliant red; glowing; (2) dark red;

wei

【瑋】 (1) a kind of jade; (2) precious; rare; splendorous;

［瑋寶］ rare treasure;
［瑋奇］ peculiar;
［瑋玉］ rare treasure;

瑰瑋 (1) remarkable; (2) (of language or style) ornate;

wei

【隗】 (1) high; lofty; (2) a surname;

wei

【骩】 bend; twist;

［骩法］ abuse the law; violate the law;

［骫曲］ stoop to compromise;

wei

【緯】 (1) woof; (2) parallels showing latitude on a map; (3) books about charms, omens; etc., circulated as appendices to the classics;

［緯度］ degrees of latitude; latitude;
假定緯度 assumed latitude;
假想緯度 fictitious latitude;
天文緯度 astronomical latitude;

［緯世］ govern a country;
緯世之才 ability to rule the state;

［緯線］ parallel;
標準緯線 standard parallel;
天文緯線 astronomical parallel;

北緯 northern latitude;
讖緯 divination combined with mystical Confucianist' belief (prevalent during the Eastern Han Dynasty 25-220);
赤緯 declination;
黃緯 latitude;
南緯 southern latitude;

wei

【諉】 evade; pass the buck; shirk;

［諉過］ lay the blame on others;
諉過於人 lay one's faults at other people's door; lay the blame at the door of another; put the blame at the door of another; put the blame on sb else; saddle a blame upon a person; shift the blame onto other shoulders; try to impute it to others;

wei

【頠】 quiet; tranquil;

wei

【鮪】 tuna;

wei

【薳】 (1) name of a herb; (2) a surname;

wei

【韙】 proper; propriety; right;

不韙 error; fault;

wei⁴

wei

【未】 (1) have not; not yet; (2) no; not; (3) a surname;

［未必］ may not; not always; not necessarily; not sure;
未必盡然 not always so; not necessarily so;
未必如此 may not necessarily turn out that way; not necessarily so;
未必知道 not necessarily know;

［未便］ find it hard to; improper; inadvisable; not be in a position to; not convenient; not in a position to;

［未曾］ did not; have not; never before;

［未嘗］ (1) have not; (2) might not;
未嘗不可 it's not necessarily impermissible; there is no reason why it should not be;
未嘗不是 can't say that it is wrong;

［未定］ uncertain; undecided; undefined; unfixed;
未定草 preliminary draft;

［未遑］ busy; occupied; too busy to; too occupied to;

［未婚］ single; unmarried;
未婚夫 fiance;
未婚男子 bachelor;
未婚妻 fiancee;

［未及］ not enough time left to do sth; unable to make it in time;

［未幾］ (1) soon afterwards; (2) not many;

［未見］ have not seen; not yet seen;
未見其人，先聞其聲 sb who is not yet here, but his voice has already been heard;
見所未見 see things of which one has hitherto been unaware; see what one has never seen before;
前所未見 have never seen before;

［未經］ have not yet;

［未竟］ unaccomplished; unfinished;
未竟之緒 unfinished task;
~續未竟之緒 carry on an unfinished task; take up where another has left off;
未竟之業 unaccomplished cause; unfinished task;
未竟之志 unaccomplished intention; unfulfilled ambition;

［未決］ outstanding; uncertain; undecided; unsettled;
勝負未決 the outcome is not yet decided;
懸而未決 hang in the wind; in suspense; in the balance; in the scale; leave hanging in the air; leave in the air; not

yet decided; outstanding; pending; remaining; unresolved; unsettled; up in the air;
~事情至今懸而未決 the matter is still in abeyance;

[未可] cannot;
未可厚非 excusable; give little cause for criticism; give no cause for much criticism; justifiable; not altogether inexcusable; not to subject it to much criticism;
未可樂觀 give no cause for optimism; nothing to be optimistic about;
未可逆料 cannot be foretold; problematic;
未可一概而論 must not make sweeping generalizations;
未可預卜 cannot foretell;
未可知 uncertain;

[未來] (1) approaching; coming; future; next; (2) future; in the future; tomorrow;
未來觀 ideas about the future;
未來光明 the future looks bright;
未來教育 future education;
未來美好 the future looks good;
未來派 futurism;
未來人才學 study of future talents;
未來學 futurity; futurology;
未來研究學 science of futuristic study;
未來主義 futurism;
未來資源 future resources;
暗淡的未來 disconsolate future;
籌劃未來 map out one's future;
洞察未來 see deep into the future;
共創未來 build a future together;
關心未來 thoughtful of the future;
計劃未來 plan for the future;
面對未來 face the future;
預測未來 look into the future; see the future;
預見未來 foretell the future;
預言未來 foretell the future; predict the future;
展望未來 look to the future; view the future;

[未了] outstanding; unfinished; unfixed; unsettled;
未了公案 unsettled case;
未了事宜 unfinished business;

[未萌] yet to bud; yet to come into existence; yet to develop;
弭患未萌 nip trouble in the bud;

[未免] a bit too; go too far; too; unavoidably;
未免太過份 go a bit too far;

[未能] cannot; fail to; have not been able to;
未能免俗 cannot but follow conventional practice; have to follow the customs; unable to be exempted from convention; unable to rise above the conventions;
未能奏效 fail of the effect;

[未然] before it happens; possible; will be a fact;
防患未然 crush the source of trouble in the egg; nip in the blossom; make provisions before troubles occur; prevent trouble before it happens; provide against possible troubles; stifle in the cradle; take preventive measures; take precautionary measures;

[未若] cannot be compared with; not as good as;

[未時] period of the day from 1 p.m. to 3 p.m.;

[未遂] abortive; not accomplished; not fulfilled;

[未完] unfinished;
未完待續 to be continued;

[未有] can never be; have never been; have never had;
得未曾有 unprecedented; without precedent;

[未月] sixth month of the lunar calendar;

[未知] unknown;
未知可否 not to know whether sth can be done;
未知鹿死誰手 unable to predict who will be the winner;
未知數 (1) unknown number; (2) uncertain; unknown;
未知信息 unknown information;
全然未知 be utterly unknown;

尚未 cannot yet; not yet;

wei

【位】 (1) location; place; site; (2) position; rank; (3) throne; (4) figure;

[位卑] in humble station;
位卑言高 in humble station with high talk;

[位錯] dislocation;
邊界位錯 boundary dislocation;

締合位錯 associated dislocation;
複合位錯 compound dislocation;
混合型位錯 composite dislocation;
特徵位錯 characteristic dislocation;

[位點] site;
可變位點 mutable site;
突變位點 mutant site;

[位分] one's social status;

[位勢] potential;
有界位勢 bounded potential;
自守位勢 automorphic potential;

[位移] displacement;
角位移 angular displacement;
絕對位移 absolute displacement;
原子位移 atomic displacement;
軸向位移 axial displacement;

[位於] be located; be situated; lie; sit on; stand on;
位於海濱 be situated near the sea;

[位置] (1) location; place; seat; site; (2) place; position;
位置變化 position change;
位置很好 occupy a good place;
脆性位置 fragile sites;
點陣位置 lattice position;
乾燥位置 dry place;
觀察位置 observation place;
恒星位置 star place;
互換位置 change places;
局部位置 narrow place;
絕對位置 absolute location;
空中位置 air position;
鄰接位置 adjoining position;
平均位置 mean place;
束縛位置 binding site;
數位位置 bit location; bit site;
數字位置 digit place;
鎖定位置 latched position;
顯著位置 prominent place; prominent position;
優勢位置 advantage position;
有利位置 vantage point;
原子位置 atom site;
中央位置 central location;
軸向位置 axial location;

[位子] take a seat;
好位子 good seat;
空位子 empty seat; vacant seat;
佔個位子 take a seat;

本位 (1) one's own department or unit; one's own post; (2) standard;
變位 conjugate;
泊位 berth;
部位 place; position;
艙位 (1) cabin seat or berth; (2) shipping space;
車位 car park; parking space;
船位 ship's position;
牀位 bed; berth; bunk;
詞位 lexeme;
篡位 usurp the throne;
單位 entity; unit;
到位 reach the designated place;
地位 (1) place; (2) social position; status;
帝位 throne;
電位 potential;
定位 fixed position; location; orientate; position;
訂位 booking; reservation;
對位 counterpoint;
噸位 tonnage;
二進位 binary system;
二位 two-place;
法位 tagmeme;
方位 (1) bearing; position; (2) direction;
復位 (1) be restored to the throne; (2) replace;
負電位 negative electric potential;
崗位 post; station;
各位 (1) every; (2) everybody (a term of address);
個位 unit;
洪水位 flood level;
換位 (1) change of positions; (2) transposition;
及位 ascend throne; ascend to power; assume position; assume reign;
即位 (1) take one's seat; (2) ascend the throne;
繼位 accede; accession to the throne; succeed to the throne;
金本位 gold standard;
進位 carry (a number, as in adding);
就位 take one's place;
爵位 rank of nobility;
空位 vacant seat;
枯水位 dry season water level;
兩位 two;
靈位 temporary memorial tablet;
密位 mil;
名位 fame and position;
那位 that; that one;
牌位 memorial tablet;
砲位 emplacement;
礮位 artillery park; gun pit;
配位 complexing; coordination;
品位 grade;

鋪位 berth; bunk;
箝位 clamping;
竊位 occupy a powerful position without the required talent;
權位 (1) authority; (2) person in authority; (3) position of authority; (4) seat of power; (5) power and position;
缺位 leave a post vacant;
讓位 (1) abdicate; abdication; resign sovereign authority; yield the throne; (2) offer one's seat to sb; (3) change into; give way to; yield to;
禪位 abdicate and hand over the crown to another person;
上位 (1) top seat; (2) a person occupying a leading position;
神位 memorial tablet; spirit tablet;
尸位 hold a job without doing a stroke of work;
十位 decade;
視位 apparent position;
首位 first place;
數位 digital;
水位 water level; water mark;
嗣位 succeed to the throne;
素位 one's current position;
胎位 position of a foetus;
攤位 booth; stall;
同位 apposition;
退位 abdicate the throne;
脱位 dislocation;
外位 extraposition;
王位 throne;
席位 seat;
限位 spacing;
相位 phase;
穴位 acupoint; acupuncture point;
學位 academic degree; degree;
勳位 rank;
遜位 abdicate;
牙移位 tooth migration;
一位 a; one;
移位 shift;
易位 translocation;
音位 phoneme;
銀本位 silver standard;
油位 oil level;
越位 offside;
在位 in power; in the position; on the throne; reign;
站位 positioning; standing room;
正電位 positive electric potential;
職位 position; post;
中位 (1) median; (2) central;
諸位 all of you; everybody; ladies and gentlemen;
主位 seat of the host;
坐位 (1) place to sit; seat; (2) thing to sit on;
座位 (1) place to sit; seat; (2) thing to sit on;

wei

【味】 (1) flavour; taste; (2) smell; odour; (3) interest; (4) distinguish the flavour of; (5) figure;

[味道] flavour; taste;
一種味道 a taste;
有味道 flavoursome;
~ 沒有味道 have no taste;

[味碟] relish dish;

[味兒] odour; scent; smell;

[味精] gourmet powder; monosodium glutamate;

[味覺] faculty of taste; gustation; gustatory sense; taste sense;
味覺遲鈍 amblygeustia;
味覺倒錯 parageusia;
味覺過敏 hypergeusia;
味覺減退 hypogeusesthesia;
味覺缺失 ageustia;
味覺缺損 taste-blindness;
味覺異常 allotriogeustia;

[味蕾] taste bud;

[味盲] taste blindness;

變味 go stale;
茶味 tea flavour;
臭味 foul smell; stink;
醋味 (1) feeling of jealously; (2) smell of vinegar;
對味 (1) seem all right; (2) to one's taste;
乏味 drab; dull; insipid; lacking in flavour; lackluster; off-flavour; tasteless;
風味 local colour; local flavour; special flavour;
甘味 (1) delicious food; (2) appetite for food;
夠味兒 just the thing; quite satisfactory;
海味 choice seafood; marine food products; seafood;
汗味 stink with perspiration;
糊味 the smell of burnt food;
回味 (1) aftertaste; recollect the pleasant flavour of; (2) call sth to mind and ponder over it; enjoy in retrospect;
火藥味 smell of gunpowder;
嘉味 dainty dishes;

薑味 ginger;
口味 (1) a person's taste; (2) flavour or taste of food;
苦味 bitter taste;
況味 circumstances and sentiment;
辣味 pugent (or peppery) taste;
臘味 cured meat, fish, etc.;
滷味 pot-stewed fowl, meat, etc. served cold;
美味 delicacy; delicious food;
南味 food-stuff from South China;
膩味 hate; loathe;
品味 savour; taste;
氣味 (1) flavour; odour; smell; (2) smack; taste;
情味 interest; sentiment;
趣味 (1) delightful; interesting; (2) one's liking; one's preference; one's taste;
人情味 human interest; human touch;
入味 (1) tasty; (2) very interesting;
澀味 astringent taste;
羶味 odour of a goat;
酸味 acidity; tart flavour;
提味 render palatable (by adding condiments); season;
體味 (1) body odour; (2) appreciate; savour;
甜味 pondering; ruminate;
調味 flavour; flavouring; sauce; season; season food;
玩味 contemplate; ponder; ruminate;
無味 (1) dull insipid; (2) tasteless; unpalatable;
五味 (1) five flavours (sweet, sour, bitter, pungent and salty); (2) all sorts of flavours;
細味 think over carefully;
鮮味 fresh flavour;
鹹味 saline taste; saltiness;
香味 fragrance, sweet smell;
鄉味 homegrown product;
辛味 acrid taste;
腥味 the smell of fish;
興味 interest;
血腥味 smell of blood;
尋味 chew sth over; ruminate; think over;
煙味 smell of smoke;
藥味 (1) herbal medicines in a prescription; (2) flavour of a drug;
野味 game; venison;
一味 (1) blindly; habitually; invariably; (2) ingredient;
異味 (1) rare delicacy; (2) peculiar smell;
意味 (1) implication; meaning; significance; (2) flavour; impression; touch; (3) portend;
繹味 seek out the meaning;
吟味 recite with appreciation; recite with relish;
魚腥味 fishy smell;
餘味 aftertaste; agreeable aftertaste; pleasant impression; remaining taste;
韻味 lasting appeal; lingering charm;
珍味 rare delicacies;
滋味 flavour; taste;
走味 lose flavour;

wei

【為】 (1) for; for the benefit of; in the interest of; (2) for; for the sake of; (3) because; on account of;

［為愛反害］ kill with kindness;

［為此］ because of this; for it; for the purpose; for the reason; for this reason; on this account; to this end;

［為叢驅雀］ drive the sparrows into the woods — drive those forces that can be united to the enemy side;

［為的是］ for the purpose of; for the sake of;

［為公］ for public good;

為公為私 in public and private; on public and private grounds;

［為何］ for what reason; what for; why;

［為虎］ assist the tiger;

為虎傅翼 add wings to a tiger — help a villain do evil; give wings to a tiger — assist an evildoer; lend wings to a tiger — lend support to the evildoers;

為虎作倀 act as a cat's-paw; act as a guide to a tiger; act as the paws of the tiger; assist the evildoer; help a villain do evil; help an evil person do evil; hold a candle to the devil; make common cause with an evildoer; play the jackal to the tiger; serve as the enemy's jackal;

［為己］ for personal interest;

［為了］ by way of; for; for the purpose of; for the sake of; in order to; so as to; to; to the effect that; with a view to; with an eye to; with the aim of; with the intent to; with the object of; with the purpose of; with the view of;

為了…起見 for the purpose of; in order to;

為了安全起見 for reasons of safety; for safety purposes;

［為名］ (1) be famed for; (2) for; in the name of under the name of; under the pretext

of; under the veil of;
為名為利 for fame and for wealth; run after fame and gain; seek fame and wealth;
以宗教為名 in the name of religion;

[為人] for others' interest; for the sake of others;
為人説項 ask leniency for sb; intercede for sb; put in a good word for sb; say a good word for sb; speak well for sb;
為人張目 boost sb's arrogance; serve the schemes of sb;
為人著想 considerate of others; show thought for others;
為人作冰 act as a go-between;
為人作嫁 make bridal clothes for others to wear — put oneself out for others; work on the bridal finery for another;
處己為人 put oneself in the place of others;

[為甚麼] how is it that; what for; why; why is it that; why oh why;
為甚麼不 why not;
為甚麼是我 why me;
不知道為甚麼 not know why;
究竟為甚麼 why ever; why on earth;

[為私] for one's personal interest;

[為着] for; in order to;

不失為 may after all be accepted as;
成為 become; turn into;
大為 greatly; very;
難為 (1) be a tough job to; embarrass; it's kind of you; press;
人為 artificial; be done by man; man-made;
認為 think; reckon;
妄為 take rash action;
無為 inactivity; letting events develop naturally;
行為 action; behaviour; conduct;
以為 consider; think;
因為 because; for; on account of;
有為 promising;
作為 (1) action; conduct; (2) achievement; accomplishment; (3) as; (4) regard as; take for;

wei

【畏】 (1) be afraid of; be scared of; dread; fear; stand in awe of; (2) respect; revere;

[畏避] avoid sth out of fear; evade because of fear; recoil from; flinch from;

[畏憚] have scruples about;

[畏敵] fear the enemy;
畏敵如虎 fear the enemy as if he were a tiger;

[畏法] fear the law;

[畏服] submit from fear; yield from awe;

[畏忌] dread; fear; have scruples;

[畏敬] stand in awe of;

[畏懼] awe; be scared of; dread; fear;
毫不畏懼 dauntless; without a trace of fear;
無所畏懼 bold; daring; dauntless; fearless; have nothing to fear; not afraid of anything; undaunted;

[畏難] afraid of difficulty; fear difficulty;
畏難而退 be awed by the difficulty and retreat; crawfish;
畏難情緒 fear of difficulty; lack of confidence;

[畏怕] dread; fear; stand in awe of;

[畏怯] be scared of; chicken-hearted; cowardly; fear; timid;
畏怯不前 balk; show one's white feather;

[畏死] afraid of dying; fear death;

[畏縮] cower; cringe; flinch; lose one's nerve; recoil; shrink;
畏縮不前 balk; hang back; hesitate to press forward; recoil in fear; start back;
畏畏縮縮 hang back; have the jitters; in a funk;

[畏途] (1) dangerous road; (2) a task shirked by everybody; perilous undertaking;
視為畏途 afraid to undertake; look upon it as an objectionable pursuit; regard as a road full of dangers — regard as an undertaking full of difficulties; regard as dangerous; regard it as a dangerous road to take;

[畏葸] afraid; timid;
畏葸不前 afraid to advance; hang back; too timid to go ahead;
畏葸退縮 recoil from fear;

[畏友] a friend of stern moral integrity; a respectable friend; an esteemed friend;
畏友嚴師 a friend of high moral character and a teacher of stern integrity; an esteemed friend and a severe teacher;

[畏罪] afraid of punishment; dread punishment for one's crime;
畏罪而逃 flee for fear of being punished; flee to escape punishment;
畏罪潛逃 abscond to avoid punishment; escape one's due punishment;
畏罪自殺 commit suicide for fear of punishment; commit suicide to escape punishment; kill oneself from fear of punishment; kill oneself to escape punishment;
情虛畏罪 conscious of guilt and afraid of punishment;

不畏 defy;
怖畏 afraid; dread; scared;
大無畏 dauntless; utterly fearless;
敵敵畏 DDVP; dichlorvos;
敬畏 hold in awe; hold in high esteem; revere;
無畏 dauntless; fearless;

wei

【胃】 stomach;
[胃癌] cancer of the stomach; gastric cancer;
[胃安] centrine;
[胃病] gastric disease; gastropathy; stomach trouble;
周期性胃病 gastroperiodynia;
[胃部] stomach;
胃部不適 stomach ache; stomach upset; upset stomach;
胃部日術 omach operation;
[胃腸] stomach intestine;
胃腸病 gastroenteropathy;
~變應性胃腸病 allergic gastroenteropahty;
胃腸的 gastrointestinal;
胃腸神經官能症 gastro-intestinal neurosis;
胃腸痛 gastroenteralgia;
胃腸炎 gastroenteritis;
~急性胃腸炎 acute gastroenteritis;
[胃出血] bleeding from the stomach; gastrorrhagia;
[胃穿孔] stomach perforation;
[胃大彎] greater curvature;
[胃底] fundus of stomach;
[胃肝炎] gastrohepatitis;
[胃過敏] have a sensitive stomach; irritability of the stomach;
[胃火] stomach fire;
胃火上昇 rising up of stomach fire;
[胃絞痛] gastric colic;
[胃結腸反射] gastrocolic reflex;
[胃鏡] gastroscope;
[胃空痛] gastralgokenosis;
[胃口] (1) appetite; belly; (2) liking;
胃口不好 have a poor appetite; have no desire for food; off one's feed; poor appetite;
胃口不佳 have no appetite;
胃口大 big appetite;
胃口小 small appetite;
倒胃口 (1) feel like vomiting; feel sick; make one nauseous; ruin one's appetite; spoil one's appetite; (2) fed up to the teeth; get fed up; get tired of someone or sth; have no interest in someone or sth;
調胃口 whet one's appetite;
對胃口 (1) appetizing; palatable; (2) to sb's liking; to sb's taste;
好胃口 good appetite;
合胃口 suit one's taste; to one's taste;
沒胃口 have no appetite; not to one's liking;
失去胃口 lose one's appetite;
影響胃口 ruin one's appetite; spoil one's appetite;
有胃口 have an appetite;
[胃潰瘍] gastric ulcer;
惡性胃潰瘍 gastric malignancy;
[胃擴張] dilatation of stomach;
[胃皮] gastrodermis;
[胃破裂] gastrorrhexis;
[胃氣] stomach energy;
胃氣不和 disorder of stomach energy;
[胃氣脹] ruminal tympany;
繼發性胃氣脹 secondary ruminal tympany;
原發性胃氣脹 primary ruminal tympany;
[胃切除] gastrectomy; surgical removal of the stomach;
[胃熱] gastric fever; stomach heat;
胃熱上逆 adverse rising of stomach heat;
[胃軟化] gastromalacia;
[胃神經痛] gastralgia;
[胃十二指腸炎] gastroduodenitis;
[胃石病] gastrolithiasis;
[胃酸] gastric acid; hydrochloric acid in gastric juice;

胃酸過多 gastric hyperacidity;
胃酸過少 gastric hyporacidity;
胃酸缺乏 absence of hydrochloric acid in the gastric secretions of the stomach; achlorhydria;

[胃癱] gastroplegia;
[胃疼] stomachache; stomach pain;
[胃痛] stomachache;
[胃萎縮] gastric atrophy;
[胃狹窄] gastrostenosis;
[胃下垂] gastroptosis;
[胃下口鉗] pylorus clamp;
[胃腺] gastric gland;

胃腺瘤 gastric adenoma;
胃腺炎 gastradenitis;

[胃消化] gastric digestion;

胃消化不良 gastric dyspepsia;

[胃小彎] lesser curvature of the stomach;
[胃炎] gastritis;

剝脫性胃炎 exfoliative gastritis;
出血性胃炎 hemorrhagic gastritis;
肥厚性胃炎 hypertrophic gastritis;
急性胃炎 acute gastritis;
濾泡性胃炎 follicular gastritis;
慢性胃炎 chronic gastritis;
糜爛性胃炎 erosive gastritis;
萎縮性胃炎 atrophic gastritis;
息肉性胃炎 polypous gastritis;
硬化性胃炎 cirrhotic gastritis;
中毒性胃炎 toxic gastritis;

[胃液] gastric juice;
[胃臟] stomach;
[胃汁] gastric juice;

敗胃 spoil one's appetite;
腸胃 belly; intestines and stomach;
重瓣胃 ruminant stomach;
翻胃 feel nausea; nauseating;
反胃 retch; nausea; regurgitation; regurgitation of food;
蜂巢胃 honey-comb stomach; reticulum;
健胃 good for the health of the stomach;
巨胃 enlarged stomach; gastromegaly;
開胃 appetizing; piquant; stimulate one's appetite; whet the appetite;
瘤胃 rumen;
脾胃 spleen and stomach;
牛胃 ox tripes;
平胃 settle the stomach;
前胃 forestomach;
溫胃 warm the stomach;
無胃 agastria; congenital absence of the stomach;
洗胃 gastric lavage;
益胃 reinforcing the stomach; tonifying stomach;
硬化胃 sclerotic stomach;
滯胃 indigestion; lie heavy on sb's stomach; lie heavy on sb's stomach;
皺胃 abomasum;

wei

【偽】 (1) counterfeit; false; (2) artificial; simulated; (3) illegal; not legally constituted;

[偽幣] counterfeit money; spurious coin;
[偽鈔] counterfeit bank note;
[偽善] hypocrisy;
[偽造] counterfeit; fabricate; falsify;
[偽證] perjury;
[偽裝] camouflage; disguise; mask;

敵僞 enemy and the puppet regime (during the War of Resistance Against Japan);
虛僞 hypocritical;
作僞 fake (works of arts, cultural relics, etc.); forge;

wei

【尉】 (1) company-grade military officer; (2) (in former times) a grade of military official;

[尉官] military junior officer;

大尉 captain; senior captain;
上尉 captain; lieutenant; flight lieutenant;
少尉 acting sub-lieutenant; ensign; pilot officer; second lieutenant;
太尉 highest rank of military officers in the Song Dynasty; one of the three heads of the army and government in the Qin and Han Dynasties;
中尉 first lieutenant; flying officer; lieutenant junior grade; lieutenant; sub-lieutenant;
准尉 warrant officer;

wei

【渭】 name of a river;

wei

【慰】 (1) assuage; comfort; console; relieve; soothe; (2) be relieved;

[慰安] comfort; soothe;
[慰存] comfort; show sympathy;

[慰藉] comfort; console; give solace; soothe;
慰藉物 comforter;
尋求慰藉 seek solace;
[慰解] console by relieving one's depression;
[慰勞] appreciate sb's services and present gifts; send one's best wishes to in recognition of services rendered;
[慰留] try to retain sb in office;
[慰情勝無] a little gift for comfort is better than nothing;
[慰問] convey greetings to; express sympathy and solicitude for; extend one's regards to; salute;
慰問函 letter of sympathy;
慰問信 a letter expressing one's sympathy; a letter of condolence; consolation letter; letter of sympathy;
慰問者 comforter;
表示慰問 express one's solicitude;
[慰唁] condole the bereaved;

安慰 comfort; consolatory; console;
撫慰 comfort; console;
告慰 comfort; console;
快慰 delighted and pleased;
寬慰 comfortable; easy;
勸慰 console; soothe;
欣慰 be gratified;
自慰 console oneself;

wei
【蔚】 (1) grand; luxuriant; ornamental and colourful; (2) colourful;
[蔚藍] azure; sky-blue;
蔚藍的 azure;
[蔚茂] lush; luxuriant;
[蔚然] luxuriant; magnificently;
蔚然成風 become a common practice; become the order of the day;

茺蔚 motherwort;

wei
【衛】 (1) defend; guard; protect; (2) bodyguard; guard; keeper; (3) the name of a state in the Zhou Dynasty; (4) a surname;
[衛兵] bodyguard; guard;
衛兵室 guardroom;
[衛道] protect traditional cultural heritage;
衛道之士 bluenose; moralist;
[衛隊] armed escort; bodyguards; squad of bodyguards;
[衛國] defend one's country;
衛國衛民 defend the country and protect the people;
[衛護] guard; protect; safeguard;
衛護者 guardian;
[衛冕] defend a title;
[衛生] cleanliness; health; hygiene; sanitation;
衛生城市 hygienic city; sanitational city;
衛生檢查 health inspection;
衛生巾 curse rag; manhole cover; sanitary napkin; sanitary pad; sanitary towel; rags;
衛生經濟學 economics of health;
衛生棉 sanitary napkin;
衛生面貌 health conditions;
衛生球 camphor ball;
衛生設備 sanitary facilities;
衛生署 Department of Health;
衛生習慣 hygienic habit;
衛生學 hygienics;
~心理衛生學 mental hygienics;
~學校衛生學 school hygienics;
衛生衣 a kind of tight cotton underwear;
衛生員 medical orderly;
衛生知識 hygienic knowledge;
衛生紙 bog roll; tissue paper; toilet paper;
不衛生 unhygienic; insanitary;
個人衛生 personal hygiene;
工廠衛生 plant sanitation;
工業衛生 industrial hygiene;
公共衛生 public health;
公眾衛生 community health;
環境衛生 environmental health; environmental hygiene; environmental sanitation;
家庭衛生 family hygiene;
檢查衛生 inspect the sanitary conditions;
講究衛生 practise hygiene;
講衛生 pay attention to hygiene;
教學衛生 hygiene of teaching;
口腔衛生 dental health; dental hygiene;
勞動衛生 labour health; labour hygiene;
森林衛生 forest hygiene;
生理衛生 physical hygiene;
食品衛生 food hygiene; food sanitation;
[衛士] bodyguard; warrior;
環境衛士 eco-warrior;
生態衛士 eco-warrior;
貼身衛士 bodyguard;

[衛星] (1) satellite; the moon; (2) artificial satellite; man-made satellite;
衛星城 satellite town;
衛星處理機 satellite processor;
衛星導航 satellite navigation;
衛星電視 satellite television;
~衛星電視廣播 satellite television broadcasting;
~衛星電視教育 education by satellite television;
~衛星電視接收機 satellite television receiver;
衛星發射中心 satellite launch centre;
衛星廣播 satellite broadcasting;
~衛星廣播技術 broadcast satellite technique;
衛星加密系統 satellite encryption systems;
衛星教學 satellite instruction
衛星商業系統 satellite business system;
衛星壽命 satellite lifetime;
衛星探測 satellite sounding;
衛星天線系統 aerial system for satellites;
衛星通信 satellite communications;
~衛星通信系統 sitcom;
~衛星通信中心 satellite communication centre;
衛星通訊技術 satellite telecommunications technology;
衛星線路 satellite circuit;
衛星遙感 satellite remote sensing;
衛星中轉站 satellite relay;
衛星轉播站 satellite station;
測繪衛星 cartographic satellite;
地球衛星 earth satellite;
~人造地球衛星 artificial earth satellite;
發射衛星 launch a satellite;
科學研究衛星 scientific research satellite;
氣象衛星 meteorological satellite;weather satellite;
~同步氣象衛星 synchrononous meteorological satellite;
人造衛星 artificial satellite;
商業衛星 commercial satellite;
通訊衛星 communications satellite; comsat;
同步衛星 synchronous satellite;
~地球同步衛星 geostationary satellite;
無源衛星 passive satellite;
一顆衛星 a stellite;
應用技術衛星 applications technology satellite;
有源衛星 active satellite;
載生物衛星 biosatellite;
偵察衛星 reconnaissance satellite;
~高級偵察衛星 advanced reconnaissance satellite;
專用衛星 special satellite;

保衛 defend; safeguard;
陛衛 imperial guard;
側衛 flank guard;
防衛 defend;
輔衛 guard; guide and protect;
拱衛 surround and protect;
捍衛 defend; guard; protext; safeguard; take up the cudgels for; uphold;
後衛 (1) full back; (2) guard; (3) deep defender; rear guard; rear flank defender;
護衛 bodyguard; guard; protect;
火衛 Martian satellite;
警衛 guard; security guard;
門衛 entrance guard;
前衛 (1) advance guard; vanguard; (2) forward; (3) half-back; (4) avant-garde; vanguard;
攝衛 conserve one's health; keep fit;
森衛 closely guarded;
侍衛 guard; imperial bodyguard;
守衛 defend; guard;
土衛 satellite of Saturn; Saturnian satellite;
驍衛 the imperial guards;
右後衛 right back;
右前衛 right half; right halfback;
中衛 central defender; centre halfback; inside defender;
自衛 defend oneself; self-defense;
左後衛 left back;
左前衛 left half; left halfback;

wei

【蝟】 hedgehog;
[蝟集] crowded and complicated;
諸事蝟集 have too many irons in the fire; have too many things to attend to;
[蝟毛而起] rise in rebellion; rise up in numbers;
[蝟鼠] hedgehog;
[蝟縮] curl up like a hedgehog; recoil; scared; shrink; wince;

刺蝟 hedgehog;

wei

【謂】 (1) say; tell; (2) call; designate; name;

(3) meaning; sense; (4) assume; of the opinion; think;

［謂詞］ predicate;

［謂語］ predicate;

謂語從句 predicative clause;
謂語動詞 inflective verb;
謂語附加語 predicative adjunct;
謂語形容詞 predicative adjective;
賓語謂語 objective predicative;
動詞謂語 verb predicate;
複合謂語 compound predicate;
合成謂語 omplex predicate;
簡單謂語 simple predicate;
解析謂語 analytic predicate;
邏輯謂語 logical predicate;
算術謂語 arithmetic predicate;
形容詞謂語 adjective predicate;

不謂 to one's surprise; unexpectedly;
稱謂 appellation; title;
何謂 what is meant by; what is the meaning of;
可謂 it may be said (or called); one may well say;
所謂 so-called; what is called;
無所謂 indifferent; not deserve the name of; not matter;
無謂 meaningless; senseless;

wei

【遺】 (1) send or present as gift; (2) be laid upon; be left to;

［遺書］ send a letter;

wei

【濊】 (1) deep and expansive; (2) dirty; (3) name of a river;

wei

【餧】 same as 餵;

wei

【餵】 feed; raise;

［餵飯］ feed sb with rice;

餵飯餵水 feed and give sb drinks;

［餵奶］ breast-feed; feed a baby with milk; nurse; suckle;

［餵養］ feed; keep; raise; rear;

人工餵養 bottle-feeding;

wei

【魏】 (1) lofty; magnificent; stately; (2) Kingdom of Wei (220 – 265), one of the Three Kingdoms; (3) a surname;

wen¹

wen

【溫】 (1) lukewarm; warm; (2) temperature; (3) heat up; warm up; (4) review; revise; (5) a surname;

［溫飽］ adequate or ample food and clothing; adequately fed and clothed; dress warmly and eat one's fill; have enough to eat and wear;

溫飽水平 subsistence level;
溫飽問題 adequate food and clothing; problem of food and clothing;
~ 解決溫飽問題 provide people with adequate food and clothing;
溫飽型 simply adequate;

［溫標］ thermometric scale;

華氏溫標 Fahrenheit's thermometric scale;
絕對溫標 absolute scale;
開氏溫標 Kelvin's thermometric scale;
蘭金溫標 Rankine thermometric scale;
列氏溫標 Reaumurs thermometric scale;
攝氏溫標 Celcius' thermometric scale;

［溫差］ difference in temperature;

溫差發電器 thermal converter; thermoelectric generator
溫差致冷器 thermoelectric cooler;
平均年溫差 mean annual temperature range;

［溫牀］ breeding ground; hotbed; advantageous conditions;

［溫辭］ gentle words; mild words;

［溫存］ (1) attentive; emotionally attached; (2) affectionate; caressing; gentle; kind; loving; tender;

［溫帶］ temperate zone;

溫帶雨林 temperate rain forest;
北溫帶 north temperate zone;
南溫帶 south frigid zone;

［溫度］ temperature;

溫度變化 temperature variation; variation of temperature;
溫度標 temperature scale;
~ 華氏溫度標 Fahrenheit temperature scale;
~ 絕對溫度標 absolute temperature scale;
~ 攝氏溫度標 Celsius' temperature scale;
溫度表 thermometer;
溫度計 thermometer;
~ 報警溫度計 alarm thermometer;

~電阻溫度計 resistance thermometer;
~輔助溫度計 auxiliary thermometer;
~附裝溫度計 attached thermometer;
~華氏溫度計 Fahrenheit thermometer;
~酒精溫度計 alcohol thermometer;
~絕對溫度計 absolute thermometer;
~空氣溫度計 air thermometer;
~氣體溫度計 gas thermometer;
~曲桿溫度計 angle-stem thermometer;
~攝氏溫度計 Celsius thermometer;
~水銀溫度計 mercurial thermometer;
~通風溫度計 aspiration thermometer;
~遙測溫度計 telethermometer;
溫度記錄器 thermograph;
~電溫度記錄器 electric thermograph;
~雙金屬溫度記錄器 metallic thermograph;
~通風溫度記錄器 aspiration thermograph;
溫度上昇 temperature rise;
溫度調節器 thermoregulator;
溫度下降 the temperature has dropped;
保持溫度 keep the heat;
活化溫度 activation temperature;
絕對溫度 absolute temperature;
絕熱溫度 adiabatic temperature;
平均溫度 mean temperature;
天線溫度 antenna temperature;
退火溫度 annealing temperature;
最低溫度 minimum temperature;
最高溫度 maximum temperature;
最適溫度 optimum temperature;

[溫風] warm brreze;

[溫恭自虛] gentle and modest;

[溫和] (1) mild; moderate; temperate; warm; (2) facile; gentle; mild;
溫和的 balmy; clement;
~溫和的人 accessible person;
溫和派 moderate faction;
~溫和派的 centrist;
恭儉溫和 modest and retiring by nature;
態度溫和 mild of manner;
談吐溫和 moderate in speech;
天性溫和 have a mild nature;
性情溫和 as mild as a lamb; mild disposition;

[溫厚] gentle and sincere;

[溫克] gentle and self-restrained;

[溫良] gentle and kind; good-natured;
溫良柔順 gentle and obedient;

[溫暖] (1) warm; (2) kindness; warmth;
溫暖起來 warm up;
溫暖如春 as warm as spring;
溫暖舒適 warm and comfortable;
感到溫暖 feel the kindness;
享受太陽的溫暖 enjoy the warmth of the sun;

[溫情] (1) kindness; tender feelings; warm feelings; warm-heartedness; (2) too soft-hearted;
溫情緋惻 with tender and romantic sentiments;
溫情脈脈 full of tender affection; sentimental;
充滿溫情 full of tender feelings;

[溫泉] hot spring; spa; thermal spring;
溫泉浴 hot-spring bath;
溫泉浴場 a hot-spring resort;

[溫柔] affectionate; gentle; gentle and soft; meek; pleasingly; sweet-natured; warm and tender;
溫柔敦厚 gentle and kind; tender and gentle;
溫柔鄉 (1) brothel; (2) experience of enjoying female charms in an intimate manner;
百般溫柔 infinitely affectionate;
聲音溫柔 gentle in voice;
性格溫柔 mild in disposition;

[溫潤] (1) mild and smooth; (2) beautiful and tender;
溫潤可親 lovable and approachable;

[溫室] glasshouse; greenhouse; hothouse;
溫室氣體 greenhouse gas;
溫室效應 greenhouse effect;

[溫水] lukewarm water;
溫水浴 hot water bath; warm water bath;

[溫順] docile; gentle; good-natured; meek; obedient;

[溫婉] gentle; obedient;

[溫溫] kindly; mild-mannered;

[溫文] gentle and polite;
溫文爾雅 cultured in manners; debonaire; genial, cultured and elegant; gentle and graceful; gentle and quiet of disposition;

[溫習] review one's lessons; revise;
溫習功課 get up; review one's lessons;

[溫馨] warm and fragrant;

[溫煦] mild and warm;

[溫血] warm-blooded;

溫血動物 warm-blooded animal;

［溫馴］ docile; easily controlled; meek; tame;

［溫雅］ gentle and cultivated; gentle and graceful; refined;

［溫顏］ happy and agreeable look;

［溫足］ well-off; well-to-do;

W

保溫 heat preservation; keep warm; preserve the temperature;

超低溫 ultralow temperature;

超高溫 ultrahigh temperature;

常溫 (1) normal atmosphere; (2) homoiothermy;

重溫 brush up; review;

等溫 isothermal;

低溫 (1) low temperature; (2) microtherm; (3) hypothermia;

地溫 ground temperature;

高溫 high temperature;

恆溫 constant temperature;

加溫 intensify;

降溫 (1) lower the temperature; (2) a drop in temperature; cool down;

爐溫 furnace temperature;

逆溫 temperature inversion;

氣溫 air temperature; atmospheric temperature;

色溫 colour temperature;

室溫 room temperature;

體溫 (body) temperature;

土溫 soil temperature;

虛溫 virtual temperature;

wen

【瘟】 epidemic; pestilence; plague;

［瘟病］ seasonal febrile diseases;

［瘟神］ god of pestilence; god of plague;

［瘟疫］ pest; pestilence; plague;

暴發瘟疫 an epidemic bursts forth;

防止瘟疫 avert pestilence;

染上瘟疫 catch the plague;

春瘟 seasonal febrile diseases in spring;

大頭瘟 erysipelas on the head;

冬瘟 seasonal febrile diseases in winter;

雞瘟 chicken pest;

牛瘟 bovine pest; cattle plague; rinderpest;

暑瘟 febrile disease in summer, including encephalitis B, etc.

豬瘟 hog cholera; swine fever;

wen

【轀】 (1) hearse; (2) sleeping carriage;

［轀輬］ (1) ancient sleeping car; (2) hearse;

wen

【鰛】 sardine;

wen²

wen

【文】 (1) character; piece of writing; script; (2) language; (3) literary composition; writing; (4) literary language; (5) civil; civilian; (6) certain natural phenonmena; (7) cover up; paint over; (8) a surname;

［文案］ clerical; desk;

文案工作 desk job;

［文本］ text; version;

文本編輯 text editing;

文本範例 boilerplate;

文本理論 text theory;

文本語言學 text linguistics;

超文本 hypertext;

庫文本 library text;

權威文本 authorized version;

外部文本 external text;

［文筆］ literary talent; pen; style of writing;

文筆粗俗 write coarsely;

文筆高超 superb writing;

文筆簡潔 write in a concise style;

文筆流暢 one's writing is fluent; write in an easy and fluent style;

文筆流利 write in an easy and fluent style;

文筆明快 bright in style;

文筆樸真 simple and straightforward writing;

文筆生動 write in a lively style;

文筆犀利 trenchant pen;

［文不對題］ beside the mark; beside the point; irrelevant; off the point; the content of the writing is inconsistent with the title; wide of the mark;

［文不加點］ never to blot a line in writing — have a facile pen; the writing is faultless; write well, fast and without need of revision; write with facility;

［文才］ aptitude for writing; literary gift; literary talent;

［文采］ (1) elegant appearances; (2) beautiful colour;

文采風流 elegant in manner, attitude and speech;

文采絢麗 one's writing sparkles;

文采郁郁 displaying literary elegance;

[文昌魚] lancelet;

[文抄公] plagiarist;

[文辭] (1) diction; language; (2) writings;
文辭艱澀 involved and abstruse writing;
文辭優美 elegant language; exquisite diction;

[文檔] file;
壓縮文檔 zip file;

[文德] refining influence of learning and art;

[文斗] verbal struggle;

[文牘] official documents and correspondence;
文牘主義 excessive red tape;

[文法] grammar;
文法替換 enallage;
文法學家 grammarian;
二義性文法 ambiguous grammar;
格文法 case grammar;
屬性形狀文法 attributed shape grammar;
正則文法 canonical grammar;

[文房] library; study;
文房四寶 four treasures in the study — writing brush, ink stick, ink slab and paper;

[文風] (1) literary style; style of writing; (2) popular interest in learning;
文風樸實 simple style of writing;
犀利的文風 astringent style of writing;
整頓文風 rectify the style of writing;

[文稿] draft; manuscript;

[文告] announcement in writing; manifesto; message; proclamation; public notice; statement;

[文官] civil official; civil servant;
文官武將 both civil and military officers;
文官制度 civil service;

[文翰] (1) literary writings; (2) pheasant-like bird;

[文豪] eminent writer; great writer; literary giant; literary lion;

[文虎] lantern riddles;

[文化] (1) civilization; culture; (2) culture; education; literacy;
文化背景 cultural background;
文化變遷論 theory of cultural change;
文化剝奪 cultural deprivation;
文化不可譯性 cultural untranslatability;
文化不利因素 cultural disadvantage;
文化差異 cultural variation;
文化承傳 cultural heritage;
文化衝擊 cultural crash; cultural shock;
文化衝突 cultural conflict;
文化重搭 cultural overlap;
文化詞 cultural word;
~半文化詞 semi-cultural word;
文化叢 cultural complex;
文化大革命 Cultural Revolution;
文化定型 cultural crystallization;
文化對等 cultural equivalent;
文化多元性 cultural pluralism;
文化惰性 cultural inertia;
文化翻譯 cultural translation;
文化反饋 cultural feedback;
文化氛圍 cultural atmosphere;
文化干擾 cultural interference;
文化工業 cultural industry;
文化宮 cultural palace;
文化古蹟 cultural objects and historic relics;
文化規範 cultural norm;
~文化規範論 cultural norm theory;
文化涵義 cultural connotation;
文化核心 cultural core;
文化互化 transculturation;
文化環境 cultural environment;
文化基因 gene of culture;
文化機構 cultural organization;
文化機關 cultural institution;
文化積累 cultural accumulation;
文化交流 cultural exchange;
~文化交流活動 cultural exchange activities;
文化焦點 cultural focus;
文化界 cultural circles;
文化進化理論 theory of cultural evolution;
文化經紀人 cultural broker;
文化經濟學 economics of culture;
文化景觀 cultural landscape;
文化距離 cultural distance;
文化空白 cultural blank;
文化空隙 cultural gap;
文化流 cultural flow;
文化論 culturalism;
~多元文化論 multiculturalism;
文化民族性 cultural nationality;
文化模式 cultural patterns;
文化偏見 cultural bias;
文化企業 cultural enterprise;
文化歧義 cultural ambiguity;
文化潛移 acculturation;
文化圈 cultural ring;

W

文化人 intellectual;
文化人類學 cultural anthropology;
文化沙漠 cultural desert;
文化衫 cultural shirt;
文化滲透 cultural infiltration;
文化市場 cultural market;
文化事業 cultural enterprises;
文化適應 acculturation;
文化術語 cultural term;
文化水平 educational level;
文化所指 cultural reference;
文化突變 cultural mutation;
文化退化 cultural devolution;
文化系統 culture system;
文化相對論 cultural relativism;
文化相對性 cultural relativity;
文化相容性 cultural compatibility;
文化心態 cultural psychology;
文化形貌 cultural configuration;
文化形態 cultural morphology;
~文化形態史觀 historical view of cultural morphology;
文化學 culturology;
文化演變 cultural evolution;
文化搖籃 cradle of culture;
文化移入 acculturation;
文化遺產 cultural heritage;
文化遺存 cultural remains;
~尊重文化異同 respect cultural differences;
文化意義 cultural meaning;
文化異同 cultural differences;
文化隱喻 cultural metaphor;
文化語言 cultural language;
文化增長率 cultural growth rate;
文化戰略 cultural strategy;
文化障礙 cultural barriers;
文化質量 cultural quality;
文化中心 cultural centre;
~體育文化中心 sports and cultural centre;
文化主題 cultural theme;
文化主義 culturalism;
~文化主義者 culturist;
~雙文化主義 biculturalism;
文化資本 cultural capital;
白領文化 white collar culture;
並喻文化 co-figurative culture;
不喜歡文化藝術的人 philistine;
餐館文化 restaurant culture;
茶文化 tea culture;
超文化 super culture;
城市文化 urban culture;
傳播文化 spread culture;
次文化 subculture;
大眾文化 pop culture;
多元文化 multiculturalism;
扼殺文化 stifle culture;
古代文化 ancient culture;
湖湘文化 the culture of Hunan and Hupei;
交叉文化 cross culture;
口頭文化 oral culture;
跨文化 trans-culture;
~跨文化傳播 trans-cultural communication;
流行文化 pop culture;
目的語文化 target language culture;
齊魯文化 the culture of Shandong;
青年文化 youth culture;
輕視文化 despise culture;
人類文化 human culture;
外國文化 alien culture;
亞文化 subculture;
有文化的 cultured;
正統文化 accepted culture;
~反正統文化 counterculture;

[文會] literary society;

[文火] gentle heat; slow fire;

[文集] collected works;

[文籍] book;

[文件] document; file; paper;
文件編排系統 filing system;
文件翻譯 documentary translation;
文件分享 file sharing;
文件櫃 file cabinet; filing cabinet;
文件夾 lder;
文件名 filename;
文件壓縮 file compression;
成串文件 string file;
地址文件 address file;
附帶文件 accompanying document;
附加文件 append file;
基本文件 basic documents;
批文件 make comments on documents; write instructions on documents;
投標文件 bid documents;
一份文件 a document;
一批文件 a batch of documents;
一扎文件 a bundle of papers;
應用文件 application file;
預算文件 budget document;
整理文件 arrange documents;

[文教] culture and education;

［文靜］ gentle and quiet; gracefully quiet;

［文句］ diction; language;

文句艱澀 make difficult reading;

［文具］ stationery; writing materials; writing tools;

文具店 stationer;

文具商 stationer;

［文科］ liberal arts;

文科大學 university of liberal arts;

文科科目 liberal studies;

文科學校 liberal arts school;

文科院校 colleges of liberal arts;

［文庫］ collection of literary works; library;

［文理］ unity and coherence in writing;

文理不通 illogical and ungrammatical; ungrammatical and incoherent; solecism;

文理清通 one's style of writing is clear and easy;

文理通順 coherent writing; have unity and coherence; make smooth reading;

［文例］ illustrative passages;

［文林］ writer's resort;

［文馬］ piebald horses;

［文盲］ illiterate; illiterate person; illiteracy;

半文盲 semiliterate;

掃除文盲 antiilliteracy; wipe out illiteracy;

［文貌］ civility; courtesy; politeness;

［文廟］ Confucian temple;

［文名］ literary fame;

［文明］ (1) civilization; culture; (2) civilized;

文明待客 receive guests honourably;

文明經商 do business with civility;

文明生產 civilized production;

文明水平 level of civilization;

文明學校 civilized school;

不文明 incivility;

城市文明 city civilization;

重建文明 rebuild civilization;

道德文明 moral civilization;

高度文明 high civilization;

精神文明 spiritual civilization;

物質文明 material civilization;

原始文明 primitive civilization;

［文魔］ bookworm;

［文墨］ (1) writing; (2) mental;

掉文舞墨 write in showy style;

［文憑］ diploma;

文憑熱 diploma fad;

獲得文憑 obtain a diploma;

濫發文憑 issue diplomas recklessly;

［文氣］ emotional impact of a writing; manner of writing; style of writing;

［文人］ literary man; literati; man of letters; scholar;

文人方士 scholars and alchemists;

文人畫 painting of man-of-letters;

文人墨客 men of letters; men of literature and writing; writers and poets;

文人相輕 men of letters tend to despise one another; scholars tend to scorn each other; two of a trade never agree; writers like to disparage one another;

文人學士 literati; men of letters; scholars and men of letters;

文人雅士 refined scholars;

［文弱］ effeminate; gentle and frail-looking;

文弱書生 effeminate scholar; frail scholar; the frail intellectual type;

［文史］ literature and history;

［文士］ man of letters;

［文書］ (1) documents; official dispatchs; (2) copy clerk;

文書工作 clerical work;

一通文書 an official document;

［文思］ flow of thoughts and ideas in writing; thread of ideas in writing; train of thought in writing;

文思枯窘 devoid of inspiration; run out of ideas to write about; the source of one's inspiration has dried up;

文思敏捷 have a ready pen;

［文孫］ your grandson;

［文壇］ literary arena; literary circles; literary forum; literary world; world of letters;

文壇健將 great man of literature; hero of the quill;

文壇巨擘 literary mogul; master in literature;

文壇名人 men eminent in literature;

文壇掌故 literary anecdotes;

轟動文壇 make a sensation in the literary world;

震驚文壇 come as a shock to the literary world;

［文體］ (1) literary form; literary style; type of writing; (2) recreation and sports;

文體生動 possess a racy style;

文體適應性 stylistic adaptation;

改善文體 polishy up the style;
親密文體 intimate level of speech;
學究式文體 academese;

[文網] arms of the law;

[文武] civil and military;
文武並用 combine force with non-violence;
文武官員 civil and military officials; officials and officers;
文武兼備 be accomplished with both the pen and sword; well-educated and trained in military exercises;
文武全才 a master of both the pen and the sword; a person of both literary and military capacity; a person versed in both civil and military affairs; able to wield both the pen and the gun; be versed in both civil and military affairs;
文武雙全 adept with both the pen and the sword; be endowed with civil and martial virtues; well versed in both literary and martial arts;
不文不武 incapable;
才兼文武 talented both mentally and physically; having both military and literary talents;
能文能武 able to do mental and manual labour; efficient in both brainy and brawny activities; skilled both in literary talents and military arts;
棄文就武 abandon the pen for the sword; cast aside one's books and take up military life; desert letters to become a soldier; quit civilian life and join the military; the book is laid aside for the gun;
輕文重武 emphasize military training at the expense of the humanities; emphasize physical training at the expense of the humanities; put the sword above the pen;
文經武緯 a man of both literary and military capacity; proficient both in civil and military knowledge; with both civil and military ability;
文來文對，武來武對 civility meets civility; violence meets violence; give sb tit for tat; return blow for blow; stick for stick and carrot for carrot;
文恬武嬉 the civil officials are indolent and the military officers frivolous;
文通武達 proficient both in civil and military knowledge;
興文偃武 promote culture and economy and desist from war;
偃文修武 the book is laid aside for the gun;
偃武修文 beat swords into ploughshares; desist from military activities and encourage culture and education; desist from war and encourage the arts of peace; disband the troops and attend to civilian affairs;
亦文亦武 engage in civilian as well as military affairs;
允文允武 good at wielding both pen and weapon; good both in civil and in military affairs; truly civil and truly military; versed in literary and military arts;
重文輕武 emphasize civil administration at the expense of national defense; put mental pursuits above material arts; put mental training above physical training;
重武輕文 put intellectual pursuits above martial arts; the arts of war are prized above the arts of peace;

[文物] cultural relics; historical relics;
文物保護 preservation of cultural relics; protection of historical relics;
~文物保護區 historic reservation;
文物發掘 excavation of historical relics;
文物古蹟 cultural relics and historic sites;
文物遺趾 historical culture sites;
出土文物 unearthed cultural objects; unearthed relics;
罕見文物 rare relics;
歷史文物 historical relics;
修復文物 restore relics;

[文獻] documents; literature; records;
文獻標引工作 document indexing;
文獻檢索 document retrieval;
文獻交流 document exchange;
文獻情報源 documental source of information;
文獻數據庫 document data bank;
文獻信息 documental information;
文獻中心 document centre;
表情文獻 expressive text;
查文獻 read up the literature;
二手文獻 secondary source;
法律文獻 legal text;

翻譯文獻 translated literature;
科技文獻 scientific and technological text;
目的語文獻 target language text;
權威性文獻 authoritative text;
一次文獻 original document;

[文選] a collection of literary works; literary selections; selected works;

[文學] literature;
文學才華 literary ability;
~文學才華橫溢的人 man of brilliant literary ability;
文學創作 literary creation;
文學詞語 literary word;
文學電視 literature television;
文學翻譯 literary translation;
~文學翻譯者 literary translator;
文學風格 literary style;
文學革命 literary revolution;
文學家 literary man; man of letters; writer;
文學價值 literary value;
文學獎 literary award;
文學節 literary festival;
文學界 literary arena; literary circles; literary world; world of letters;
文學經典 classics of literature;
~不朽的文學經典 abdiding classics of literature;
文學流派 schools of literature;
文學能力 literary competence;
文學批評 literary criticism;
文學批評學 study of literary criticism;
文學評論 literary criticism;
文學士 bachelor of arts;
文學信息反饋 literary information feedback;
文學遺產 legacy of literature; literary heritage;
文學語段 literary text;
文學語言 literary language;
文學院 faculty of arts;
文學作品 literary works; works of literature;
~一部文學作品 a work of literature;
愛好文學 be found of literature;
報告文學 reportage;
暴露文學 literature of exposure;
比較文學 comparative literature;
不懂文學 weak in literature;
純文學 belles-lettres;
兒童文學 children's literature;
翻譯文學 translated literature;
口頭文學 oral literature;
民間文學 folk literature;
民俗文學 folk literature;
軟文學 light literature;
俗文學 popular literature;
通訊文學 reportage;
新文學 new literature;

[文雅] cultured; elegant; gentle; graceful; polished; refined;
文雅清秀 elegant and handsome;
風度文雅 have an air of gentility;
舉止文雅 refined in manner;
談吐文雅 elegant in speech;

[文言] classical Chinese;

[文藝] belles-lettres; literature and art;
文藝傳播 dissemination of arts;
文藝隊伍 ranks of writers and artists;
文藝復興 Renaissance;
文藝革命 revolution in literature and arts;
文藝工作 literary and artistic work;
文藝工作者 literary and art workers; literature and arts workers; workers in the literary and artistic fields; writers and artists;
文藝節 literature and art festival;
文藝界 literary and artistic circles;
文藝批評 literary and arts criticism; literary criticism;
~文藝批評家 literary critic;
文藝群體 art group;
文藝人口 art population;
文藝社會 art society;
~文藝社會管理 management of arts and literature society;
~文藝社會機制 mechanism of literary society;
~文藝社會學 sociology of art;
文藝社區 art community;
文藝生態學 ecology of art and literature;
文藝思潮 the trend of literary thoughts;
文藝消費力 art consumption capability;
文藝消費學 consumption of art and literature;
文藝消費意識 consciousness of art consumption;
文藝學 study of art and literature;
文藝預測 art prediction;

[文義] literary content;

[文娛] cultural recreation; entertainment;

文娛活動 recreational activities;

[文員] clerk; pen pusher;

[文苑] writers' gathering place;

[文責] author's responsibility;

文責自負 the author takes sole responsibility for his views; the writer is responsible for the consequence of his article;

[文摘] digest; abstract;

文摘報 abstracts paper;

文摘工程 abstracts engineering;

文摘價值 evalue of abstracts;

文摘精萃 abstracts of abstracts;

文摘體 abstracts style;

文摘系統 abstracts system;

文摘信息量 volume of abstracts information;

文摘意識 consciousness of abstracts;

分類文摘 classified abstract;

簡易文摘 brief abstract;

科技文摘 science abstract;

書評文摘 book-review digest;

作者文摘 author abstract;

[文章] (1) article; composition; essay; (2) literary works; writings; (3) hidden meanings; implied meanings;

文章巨公 giant of literature;

文章魁首 outstanding writer of the day;

文章是自己的好 each bird is well pleased with his own voice; each bird loves to hear himself sing; every ass loves to hear himself bray; every cook commends his own sauce; every cook praises his own broth;

表面文章 window dressing;

~做表面文章 work for appearance sake;

大有文章 there's more to it than meets the eye; there's much more to it than appears;

大做文章 blow up; kick up a big fuss; kick up a rumpus about; make a big fanfare over; make a big issue of sth; make a fuss; turn out much propaganda;

發表文章 publish an article;

趕寫文章 dash off articles;

官樣文章 dead letter; a mere scrap of official paper; an unpractical routine document; mere formalities; official formality; officialese; red tape;

話裏有文章 that's an insinuating remark; there is an insinuation in that remark;

孔夫子門前賣文章 show off in the presence of an expert; teach fish to swim; teach one's grandmother how to suck eggs;

評論文章 commentary;

潤色文章 polish up an article;

煽動性文章 incendiary article;

署名文章 signed article;

消遣文章 anodyne writing;

修改文章 correct an essay;

學院派文章 academese;

一段文章 a paragraph;

一篇文章 a piece of writing; an article; an essay;

做文章 (1) write an essay; (2) make a fuss about sth; make an issue of;

[文職] civil post;

文職幹部 civilian staff;

文職人員 the civil service;

[文治] civil administration;

文治武功 political achievements and military exploits; political and military achievements;

[文謅謅] genteel; pedantic;

文文謅謅 speak courteously;

[文字] (1) character; script; (2) written language;

文字編輯 edit a text;

文字處理 word processing;

~文字處理系統 word processing system;

文字改革 reform of the written language;

文字交 friendship cemented by literature;

文字枯澀 dull and heavy style;

文字欠通 the writing is not altogether grammatical;

文字清通 lucid writing;

文字通暢 smooth writing;

文字文化 literary culture;

文字學 philology;

~拼音文字學 alphabetology;

文字遊戲 juggle with terms; play with words;

文字獄 literary inquisition; literary prosecution;

文字之交 literary friends; literary friendship;

文字自動翻譯系統 word automatic translation system;

表意文字 idographic writing; phonogram;

拼音文字 alphabetic script;

識文斷字 able to read; literate;

圖畫文字 pictorial writing;
文從字順 clear and idiomatic; clear and smooth in writing; readable and fluent;
象形文字 hieroglyph; hieroglyphic writing; hieroglyphics; pictograph;
咬文嚼字 bookish; chop logic; mince words in speech; over-fastidious about the choice of words; pay excessive attention to wording; pedantic; speak like a book; split hairs; spout phrases out of some book; talk pedantically;

[文宗] one whose writings are modeled after;

案文 text;
八股文 (1) eight-part essay (a literary composition prescribed for the imperial civil service examinations, known for its rigidity of form and poverty of ideas); (2) stereotyped writing;
跋文 postscript;
白話文 writings in the vernacular;
白文 (1) unannotated edition of a book; (2) intagliated characters (on a seal); (3) text of an annotated book;
榜文 message; proclamation; statement;
碑文 inscription on a tablet;
本文 (1) this text, article, etc.; (2) main body of a book;
變文 popular form of narrative literature flourishing in the Tang Dynasty (618-907), with alternate prose and rhymed parts for recitation and singing often on Buddhistic themes;
炳文 luminous style;
成文 existing writings; written;
呈文 official document submitted to a superior petition;
重文 variant form of a Chinese character;
禱文 prayer;
電文 content of a telegram;
牒文 official dispatches;
短文 short essay;
發文 dispatch; outgoing message;
梵文 Sanskrit;
繁文 empty forms;
範文 model essay;
分文 single cent; single penny;
浮文 padding; verbiage;
訃文 obituary;
公文 government documents; official documents;
古文 ancient style prose;
國文 Chinese as the national language;
和文 Japanese;
華文 Chinese;
換文 exchange of notes;
記敍文 narration; narrative text;
祭文 funeral oration; elegiac address;
甲骨文 inscriptions on bones or tortoise shells of the Shang Dynasty (circa 16th-11th century B.C.)
今文 official script, an ancient style of calligraphy current in the Han Dynasty (206 B.C.-A.D.220), simplified from xiaozhuan;
金文 bronze inscriptions;
經文 texts from Confucian classics or Buddist scriptures;
具文 dead letter; mere formality;
拉丁文 Latin (language);
課文 text;
空文 ineffective law;
來文 document received;
論説文 argumentation;
論文 paper; thesis;
賣文 sell one's writings;
盲文 braille;
明文 proclaimed in writing;
銘文 epigraph; inscriptions;
駢文 rhythmical prose style characterized by parallelism and ornateness;
奇文 (1) remarkable piece of writing; (2) preposterous piece of writing; queer writing;
情文 inspiration and essays;
全文 full text;
闕文 hiatus in the text;
人文 (1) humanities; (2) human affairs;
日文 Japanese; Japanese language;
散文 essay; prose;
上文 foregoing paragraphs or chapters; preceding part of the text;
詩文 (1) poetic prose; (2) literary works in general;
石鼓文 inscriptions on drum-shaped stone blocks of the Warring State Period (475-221 B.C.)
時文 eight-part essay (a literary composition prescribed for the imperial civil service examinations, known for its rigidity of form and poverty of ideas);
實用文 practical writings (as in official documents, notices, receipts, etc.);
釋文 annotate the pronunciation and meaning of words; do textual research on ancient script;

收文 incoming dispatches;
壽文 congratulations on one's birthday;
殊文 different language; strange language;
水文 hydrology;
説明文 expository writing; exposition;
斯文 (1) culture; (2) cultured or refined person; gentle; refined; the educated class;
陶文 inscriptions on pottery;
天文 astronomy;
條文 article; clause;
圖文 pictures and texts;
外文 foreign language;
溫文 gentle and polite;
文言文 classical style of writing; writings in classical Chinese;
舞文 fiddle at writing;
檄文 (1) official call to arms; (2) official denunciation of the enemy;
戲文 (1) actor's lines; (2) classical local opera of Wenzhou, Zhejiang Province;
下文 (1) what follows in the passage, article, etc.; (2) later development; outcome;
詳文 official report to the superior;
小品文 essay; familiar essay;
行文 (of a government office) send an official communication to other organizations; style or manner of writing;
雄文 profound and great writing;
修文 develop culture and education;
虛文 (1) empty forms; (2) dead letter; mere formality;
序文 foreword; preface;
敘事文 narrative; narrative prose;
敘文 preface;
衍文 redundancy due to misprinting or miscopying;
諺文 Korean alphabet;
洋文 foreign language;
陽文 characters cut in relief;
一文 single cent;
異文 alternate script;
逸文 ancient writings no longer extant;
藝文 literature and fine arts;
譯文 translated text; translation;
陰文 characters cut in intaglio;
引文 quoted passage; quotation;
英文 English;
應用文 practical writing (as in official documents, notices, receipts, etc.);
語體文 prose written in the vernacular;
語文 (1) language; (2) language and literature;
鬻文 write for pay;
原文 (1) original text; (2) original;
源文 source text;
韻文 literary composition in rhyme; verse;
雜文 essay;
藏文 Tibetan language;
徵文 solicit articles or essays;
正文 main body (of a book, etc.); text;
政論文 political essay;
中文 Chinese;
鐘鼎文 inscriptions on ancient bronze objects;
籀文 style of calligraphy current in the Zhou Dynasty (11th century – 256 B.C.);
朱文 characters on a seal carved in relief;
屬文 compose a piece of prose writing;
祝文 congratulatory message;
主文 main body of a court verdict;
註文 annotation; explanatory note;
轉文 lard one's speech with literary allusions;
撰文 write articles;
綴文 compose an essay; write a composition;
咨文 (1) official communication; (2) report delivered by the head of a government on affairs of state;
諮文 official communication between equals;
作文 composition; write a composition;

wen

【紋】 (1) grains; lines; veins; (2) ripples; (3) prints; (4) wrinkles on the face; (5) tattoo;

[紋孔式] pitting;
管間紋孔式 intervascular pitting;
交叉場紋孔式 cross-field pitting;
切向紋孔式 tangential pitting;
篩狀紋孔式 sieve pitting;
梯狀紋孔式 scalariform pitting;

[紋理] grain; lines; stripes; veins;

[紋身] tattoo;
祝髮紋身 cut off one's hair and tattoo the body;

[紋章] coat of arms; crest;
紋章學 heraldry;

凹紋 intaglio design;
斑紋 streak; stripe;
邊紋 fringe;
緞紋 satin weave;
花紋 decorative pattern; figure;
蓮花紋 lotus design;
裂紋 (1) crackle; (2) crackle-like design;
螺紋 (1) thread (of a screw); (2) whorl (in fingerprint);

羅紋 whorl (in fingerprint);
平紋 plain weave;
手紋 lines on one's palm;
擡頭紋 wrinkles on one's forehead;
條紋 streak; stripe;
笑紋 lines on one's face when smiling;
斜紋 (1) twill; (2) twill (weave);
掌紋 hand lines;
指紋 finger print;
縐紋 creases; wrinkles;

wen
【蚊】 gnat; mosquito;
［蚊蟲］ gnats; mosquitoes;
［蚊雷］ buzz of a swarm of mosquitoes;
［蚊香］ mosquito coil; mosquitorepellent incense;
［蚊帳］ mosquito curtain; mosquito net;
一頂蚊帳 a mosquito net;
［蚊陣］ swarms of mosquitoes;
［蚊子］ gnat; mosquito;
蚊子放屁一小氣 mosquito breaking wind; small wind; stingy;
蚊子叫 mosquitoes buzz; mosquitoes drone; mosquitoes hhum;
無數的蚊子 a zillion mosquitoes;
一群蚊子 a swarm of mosquitoes;

按蚊 anopheles; malarial mosquito;
大蚊 crane fly;
黑斑紋 yellow fever mosquito;
瘧蚊 malarial mosquito;
搖蚊 chironomid; midge;
伊蚊 yellow-fever mosquito;

wen
【雯】 colouring on the clouds;

wen
【聞】 (1) hear; (2) news; stories; (3) famous; well-known; (4) reputation; repute; (5) smell; (6) a surname;
［聞報］ hear it reported; learn of;
［聞風］ on hearing sth;
聞風而動 act without delay upon hearing the news; answer the call with immediate action; go immediately into action; go into action without delay;
聞風而歸 hearing of sb's correct attitude, leave one's home and go to see him;
聞風而起 rise up on hearing the news; take action as soon as one hears about;
聞風而逃 escape on getting wind of the matter; get wind of...and escape; run away upon learning the news;
［聞過］ when one is told of one's errors;
聞過即改 correct one's mistakes as soon as it is pointed out;
聞過則喜 feel happy when told of one's errors; feel thankful when told of one's shortcomings; glad to have one's errors pointed out;
［聞見］ learn by seeing;
［聞名］ (1) distinguished; famous; renowned; well-known; (2) familiar with sb's name; know sb by repute;
聞名不如見面 to know a man by repute is not as good as meeting him face to face; to know a person by repute is not as good as seeing him in the flesh; to know someone by repute is not as good as meeting him face to face;
聞名全國 well-known throughout the country;
聞名全球 well-known throughout the world;
聞名喪膽 be overawed by sb's name; the bare mention of sb's name is enough to scare someone;
聞名四方 become famous throughout the land;
聞名天下 become famlous throughout the land; enjoy tremendous popularity in the world; known far and wide; world-famous;
聞名遐邇 known to all, far and near; one's fame spreads far and near; well-known far and near;
聞名於世 be famed the world over; be known to the world; world-famous; world-renowned;
但聞其名，未見其人 I have only heard of his name but have not met him in person;
世界聞名 achieve world-wide fame;
［聞人］ celebrity; famous man; well-known figure;
［聞聲］ hear the noise;
聞聲而至 hurry in, hearing sb's shout;
聞聲知鳥，聞言知人 a bird is known by its note, and a man by his words;
如聞其聲，如見其人 as if one could hear the voice and see the person;

like seeing the real person as well as hearing his voice;

［聞所未聞］ have never even heard of sth; have never heard of such a thing; hear of sth extremely unusual; unheard of;

［聞訊］ hear the news; learn of the news;

［聞知］ hear; know from others; learn;

聞一知十 hear one point and know the ten sequences; infer the whole matter after hearing but one point;

謗聞 malicious gossip;
不聞 turn a deaf ear to;
醜聞 scandal;
傳聞 hearsay; it is said; rumour; talk; they say;
多聞 have wide experience;
耳聞 hear about; hear of;
緋聞 pink journalism; sexy journalism;
風聞 get wind of; learn through hearsay;
訃聞 obituary;
寡聞 ignorant; not well read; uninformed;
罕聞 rarely or seldom heard of;
好聞 pleasant to smell; smell good;
忽聞 hear suddenly; learn of sth unexpectedly;
穢聞 ill repute (referring to sexual behaviour); reputation for immorality;
見聞 information; what one sees and hears;
舊聞 past events, anecdotes, trivial matters, etc.;
名聞 one's name is known;
難聞 smell bad; smell unpleasant; unpleasant to smell;
奇聞 fantastic story; sth unheard of; strange story; thrilling tale;
趣聞 amusing story;
聲聞 fame; reputation;
素聞 have been frequently told; have often heard;
所聞 what one sees;
瑣聞 bits of news; scraps of information;
聽聞 (1) hear; (2) what one hears;
罔聞 give no heed to;
洽聞 learned; of wide knowledge; widely read;
謏聞 known only to a small circle;
新聞 news;
腥聞 notoriety; scandalous acts;
要聞 front-page story; headlines; important news items;
遺聞 hearsay that was handed down;
逸聞 anecdote;
異聞 (1) strange story; strange tale; unusual news; (2) different report;
軼聞 anecodote;
逸聞 anecdote;
預聞 participate in sth and be in the know;
與聞 have a participant's knowledge of; let into; participate in the affair;
乍聞 suddenly learn for the first time;
珍聞 fillers; news tidbits; valuable information;

wen³

wen

【刎】 cut one's throat;

［刎頸］ cut one's throat;

刎頸之交 a friendship to the death; bosom friends who are willing to die for one another; Damon and Pythias friendship; friends sworn to death; friends that are ready to die for each other;

刎頸自戮 commit suicide by cutting one's throat;

自刎 commit suicide by cutting one's throat;

wen

【吻】 (1) lip; (2) tone of one's speech; (3) kiss;

［吻別］ kiss sb goodbye;

［吻合］ coincide; dovetail; fit; identical; tally; tally with;

意見吻合 have identical views;

與事實吻合 fit the facts;

［吻痕］ hickey;

齒吻 teeth and lips;
鴟吻 ornament on roof ridge, in the shape of a leg-endary animal;
初吻 one's first kiss;
唇吻 (1) eloquence; one's words; what one say; (2) lips;
飛吻 blow a kiss;
告別之吻 farewell kiss;
給人一個飛吻 blow sb a kiss;
鈎吻 elegant Jessamine;
激情一吻 a passionate kiss;
接吻 kiss;
空吻 air kiss;
口吻 (1) muzzle; snout; (2) note; tone;
輕輕一吻 little kiss;
親吻 kiss;
舌吻 deep kiss; tongue kiss;
深情一吻 an affectionate kiss;
偷吻 snatch a kiss; steal a kiss;
晚安之吻 goodnight kiss;

溫柔一吻 a tender kiss;

wen

【脗】 (1) kiss; (2) join together; match; tally; (3) lips;

[脗合] identical; match; tally;

wen

【穩】 (1) firm; stable; steady; (2) certain; sure; (3) secure;

[穩便] reliable and convenient; safe and convenient;

[穩步] steadily; with steady steps;
穩步不前 mark time and make no advance;
穩步前進 advance steadily; make steady progress; proceed by steady steps; progress steadily; steer a steady course;
穩步上昇 go up steadily;
穩步增長 steady-state growth;

[穩當] proper and secure; reliable; safe; safe and sound; secure;
穩當的方法 reliable method;
穩穩當當 safe and secure;

[穩定] (1) stabilization; stabilize; (2) stable; steady;
穩定劑 stabilizer;
~晶體穩定劑 crystal stabilizer;
~燃料油穩定劑 fuel oil stabilizer;
~水分穩定劑 moisture stabilizer;
~碳化物穩定劑 carbide stabilizer;
穩定經濟 stabilize the economy;
穩定器 stabilizer;
~可操縱穩定器 all-movable stabilizer;
~速度穩定器 speed stabilizer;
~振幅穩定器 amplitude stabilizer;
穩定情緒 reassure sb; set sb's mind at rest;
穩定物價 stabilize prices;
穩定性 stability; stabilizing ability;
~儲藏穩定性 can stability;
~老化穩定性 ageing stability;
~臨界穩定性 marginal stability;
~氣流穩定性 airflow stability;
~容積穩定性 bulk stability;
穩定裝置 stabilizer;
保持隱定 keep firm; keep stable;
不穩定 instability; unstable;
~不穩定性 instability;
動態不穩定性 dynamic instability;
空氣動力不穩定性 aerodynamic instability;
燃燒不穩定性 combustion instability;
~對流不穩定 convective instability;
~絕對不穩定 absolute instability;
~斜壓不穩定 baroclinic instability;
長期穩定 long-term stability;
方位穩定 azimuthal stabilization;
基極穩定 base stabilization;
就業穩定 employment stabilization;
體積穩定 dimensional stabilization;
通貨穩定 currency stabilization;
旋轉穩定 spin stabilization;

[穩固] firm; secure; stable; stable and firm; steady;
地位穩固 hold a stable position;
職位穩固 stable in office;

[穩健] firm; firm and steady; moderate; safe; steady;
辦事穩健 go about things steadily;

[穩練] steady and prudent;

[穩婆] midwife;

[穩如] as stable as;
穩如磐石 as stable as a huge rock — firm, solid; as steady as a rock;
穩如平地 as stable as a great rock — firm, solid; as steady as a rock;
穩如泰山 as firm as a rock; like a rock;

[穩貼] proper and secure; safe and sound;

[穩妥] proper and secure; reliable; safe; safe and dependable; sound;
穩妥可靠 as steady as a rock; safe and reliable;

[穩下] calm down;

[穩紮穩打] go about things steadily and surely; go ahead steadily and strike sure blows; play for safety; proceed steadily and step by step; wage steady and sure struggle; slow and steady;

[穩重] dignified; modest; prudent; sedate; staid; steady;
穩重一點 act your age;
十分穩重 extremely steady;
穩穩重重 quiet and serious; sedate; staid; steady;

[穩住] (1) hold back sb from intervening in one's plans; (2) make stable;
穩住陣腳 hold one's ground; secure one's position;

[穩賺] make a profit with certainty; money in the bank;

穩賺項目 cash cow;

安穩 (1) sedate; staid; steady; (2) smooth and steady;

把穩 dependable; firm; hold fast; sure about; trustworthy;

不穩 insecure; unstable; unsteady;

沉穩 (1) deep; profound; (2) sedate; staid; steady;

工穩 (of poetry, prose, etc.) neat and perfect;

牢穩 reliable; safe; secure;

拿穩 hold steadily; predict with confidence;

平穩 smooth; smooth and steady; stable;

站穩 (1) come to a stop; (2) stand firm; take a firm stand;

嘴穩 able to keep a secret; discreet in speech;

wen⁴

wen

【文】 conceal; cover up; gloss over;

［文過］ cover up one's fault;

文過飾非 cover up one's fault by clever use of words in writing;

［文飾］ deceive by an impressive appearance;

wen

【抆】 wipe;

［抆淚］ wipe one's tears away;

［抆拭］ wipe away;

wen

【汶】 a river in Shandong;

wen

【紊】 confused; disorderly; involved; tangled;

［紊亂］ chaos; confusion; disorder;

wen

【問】 (1) ask; (2) ask after; inquire after; (3) examine; interrogate; (4) hold responsible;

［問安］ pay one's respect; send greetings; wish sb good health;

問安視膳 take good care of one's parents;

［問案］ hear a case; hold court; try a case;

［問卜］ consult fortune-tellers; divine; seek guidance from divination;

［問答］ conversation; dialogue; questions and answers;

回答教授法 catechism;

一問一答 ask and answer interchangeably; one asking and the other answering;

有問必答 answer all questions asked;

［問道於盲］ ask a blind man for directions; ask the blind to show the way; the blind leading the blind;

［問鼎］ inquire about the bronze tripod－covert the throne;

問鼎中原 aspire after the throne; find for the tripod in the central plain － attempt to usurp the throne; have an ambition for the throne;

［問短］ make sb unable to answer;

［問卦］ consult oracles;

［問好］ ask after; extend greetings to; say hello to; send one's regards to;

代我向她問好 say hello to her for me;

她向您問好 she sends her regards to you;

相互問好 exchange of amenities;

向你夫人問好 remember me to your wife;

［問號］ (1) interrogation mark; question mark; (2) unknown factor; unsolved problem;

使用問號 use a question market;

［問候］ extend greetings to; send one's regards to;

互致問候 exchange greetings;

謹致問候 best regards; best wishes;

親切的問候 amiable greeting;

［問話］ ask questions;

［問疾］ visit and console a patient;

［問價］ shop around;

［問津］ make inquiries;

不敢問津 not dare to make inquiries;

無人問津 nobody cares to ask about it;

［問卷］ questionnaire;

問卷設計 questionnaire design;

回答問卷 answer a questionnaire;

人格問卷 personality questionnaire;

散發問卷 distribute questionnaires;

設計問卷 draw up a questionnaire;

填寫問卷 fill in questionnaires;

［問路］ ask the way;

投石問路 throw a stone to clear the road;

［問明］ ask for explicit answers; find out the details;

問明底細 find out the details of the case;

問明原委 find out origin of affair;

［問難］ ask difficult questions in a debate; question and argue repeatedly;

［問世］ be published; come out; debut; see the light of day;

［問事］ attend to work;

[問題] (1) case; issue; matter; point; problem; question; subject; thing; (2) defect; drawback; error; fault; mistake; trouble;
問題纏身的 embattled;
問題成堆 a batch of questions; be weighed down with all sorts of problems;
問題的核心 heart of the matter;
問題兒童 problem child;
問題少年 juvenile delinquent; problem youth;
問題是 the thing is;
問題行為 problem behaviour;
把問題解決 bring an issue to a close;
伴隨問題 adjoint problem;
避開問題 avoid a question;
成問題 become a problem; open to question;
~不成問題 beyond doubt; offer no problem; out of the question;
~大成問題 in doubt; very doubtful; very questionable;
~錢不成問題 money is no object;
澄清問題 clear up problems;
出問題 get into trouble;
出現問題 a problem arises; a problem comes up; a problem occurs;
處理問題 address a problem; address an issue; deal with a problem; deal with an issue; handle a question; meet a problem; sort out a problem; tackle a problem;
次要問題 side issue;
翻譯問題 translation problem;
分歧問題 bifurcation problem;
分析問題 analyze the problem;
個人口味的問題 a matter of personal taste;
個人喜好的問題 a matter of personal preference;
個人選擇的問題 a matter of personal choice;
關於那個問題 on that score;
回答問題 answer questions;
迴避問題 avoid an issue; dodge a question; dodge an issue; duck an issue; evade a question; evade an issue;
亟待解決的問題 burning question;
解決問題 decide an issue; resolve a problem; resolve an issue; serve the purpose; settle an issue; solve a problem; tackle an issue;
經濟問題 economic issue;
考查問題 regard a matter;
考慮問題 consider a problem;
跨國問題 transnational problems;
棘手的問題 sticky issue;
歷史遺留問題 questions left over by history;
連珠炮似的問題 a barrage of questions;
沒問題 no muss, no fuss; no sweat; no worries;
面對問題 face a problem; face an issue;
內在問題 built-in problem;
弄清問題 straighten matters out;
社會問題 social issue;
深奧的問題 deep question;
雙重問題 two-sided problem;
説明問題 explain matters;
私人問題 personal question;
討論問題 debate an issue; discuss an issue;
提出問題 bring up an issue; pose a question; raise a problem; raise an issue;
提問題 ask a question; raise a question;
突出問題 highlight an issue;
問清問題 probe into the matter;
問問題 ask a question;
小問題 snag;
~有小問題 have rough edges; rough around the edges;
研究問題 study a question;
掩蓋問題 blanket a question;
一大堆問題 a host of problems; a mountains of problems;
一個問題 a problem; a question;
一類問題 a kind of problem;
一連串問題 a string of questions; a volley of questions;
一系列問題 a series of problems;
一項問題 a question;
有問題 doubtful; go pear-shaped; have a question; questionable; unreliable;
~有問題的 amiss;
誘導性問題 loaded question;
遇到問題 encounter problems; experience a problem;
原則問題 a matter of principle;
~作為原則問題 as a matter of principle;
造成問題 cause a problem; create a problem; pose a problem; present a

problem;
爭論問題 argue issues;
爭論未決的問題 a moot question;
正確看待問題 view the problem in its right perspective;
政治問題 political issue;
重大問題 all-important subject;
總合問題 aggregation problem;

[問訊] ask; enquire; send one's regards to;
[問診] method of interrogation in Chinese medical diagnosis;
[問住] unable to answer a question asked;
[問罪] call a person to account; condemn; denounce; rebuke; reprimand; reprove;
問罪之師 an army for punitive purpose;
~興問罪之師 make a punitive expedition;

逼問 force sb to answer; press for an answer;
不問 (1) disregard; ignore; not consider pay no attention to; (2) let off;
查問 interrogate; question;
讎問 ask difficult questions;
打問 interrogate with torture; torture sb during interrogation;
叮問 make a detailed inquiry; question closely;
釘問 question persistently;
發問 ask a question; fire off; pose a question; put a question; raise a question;
反問 (1) ask a rhetorical questions; (2) ask (a question) in reply;
訪問 (1) call by; call on; interview; pay a call; visit; (2) access;
顧問 adviser; consultant; counselor;
過問 concern oneself with; give one's view on sth; participate in sth;
好問 great curiosity to ask all sorts of questions;
詰問 closely question; cross-examine;
借問 may I ask;
考問 examine orally; questions;
拷問 torture sb during interrogation; interrogate with torture;
叩問 make inquiries;
盤問 cross-examine; interrogate;
聘問 visit a friendly nation on behalf of one's own country;
請問 (1) excuse me; please; (2) may I ask; one may ask; we should like to ask; would you please tell me;
少問 refrain from asking;
審問 examine; hear; interrogate; question; try;
聲問 (1) information; (2) fame; reputation;
是問 be held responsible;
試問 it may well be asked; let me ask; may we ask; we should like to ask;
所問 what is asked;
探問 (1) make cautious inquiries about; try to find out (news, facts, intention, etc.); (2) visit and inquire after;
套問 tactfully sound sb out; trap sb into telling the truth;
提問 put questions to; quiz;
推問 examine and inquire;
慰問 express sympathy and solicitude for;
細問 question in detail;
下問 learn from one's inferior;
省問 ask about; send one's respects to;
學問 (1) branch of study; (2) learning; knowledge;
詢問 ask about; inquire;
訊問 (1) ask about; inquire; (2) interrogate;
疑問 doubt; questions;
音問 mail; message;
責問 blame and demand an explanation; call sb to account;
質問 call to account; interrogate; query; question;
追問 examine minutely; make a detailed inquiry; question closely; question insistently;
自問 (1) ask oneself; examine oneself; (2) reach a conclusion after weighing a matter;

wen

【搵】 (1) wipe off tears; (2) press with fingers;
[搵淚] wipe off tears;

wen

【聞】 reputation;
[聞達] eminent; famous and influential; illustrious;
[聞人] famous person; prominent figure;
[聞望] fame; reputation;

wen

【璺】 crack in jade;

裂璺 crack;

weng¹

weng

【翁】 (1) father; (2) father-in-law; (3) old man; (4) title of respect; (5) a surname;
[翁姑] a woman's parents-in-law;

白頭翁 (1) Chinese bulbul; (2) root of Chinese pulsatilla;
不倒翁 tumbler;
鳧翁 water cock;
富翁 man of wealth; rich man;
老翁 graybeard; old man;
叔翁 granduncle;
信天翁 albatross;
主人翁 (1) hero or heroine; leading character in a novel, etc.; protagonist; (2) master;
醉翁 old drunkard;
尊翁 your father;

weng
【嗡】 hum or buzz of insects;
［嗡嗡］ buzz; drone; hum;
嗡嗡叫 buzz; hum;
嗡嗡狼蛛 purring spider;
嗡嗡聲 boominess; drone; hum; zoom;
嗡嗡響 buzzing;

weng
【鶲】 flycatcher;

長尾鶲 paradise flycatcher;

weng³
weng
【滃】 swelling or rising (said of rivers and clouds);
［滃渤］ rising mist;
［滃鬱］ be filled with vapour;

weng
【蓊】 flourishing; lush; luxuriant growth;
［蓊勃］ lush; luxuriant;
［蓊鬱］ lush; luxuriant;

weng⁴
weng
【甕】 jar; jug; pot; earthen jar; urn;
［甕鼻］ blocked up nose;
［甕闊］ liberal with money;
［甕牖］ small round window like the mouth of a jar;
甕牖繩樞 using broken jars for windows and ropes for door hinge — living in extreme poverty;
［甕中］ in a jar;
甕中之鱉 a rat in a hole — in a place from which escape is impossible; a turtle in a jar — bottled up; dead duck; dead pigeon; trapped;
甕中捉鱉 catch a turtle in a jar — go after an easy prey; sure catch;

菜甕 jar for pickling vegetables;
水甕 water jar;

weng
【罋】 same as 甕 ;

wo¹
wo
【倭】 old name for Japan;
［倭瓜］ cushaw; pumpkin;
倭瓜子 pumpkin seed;
老倭瓜 cushaw; pumpkin;
［倭國］ ancient name for Japan;
［倭寇］ Japanese pirate;
［倭人］ Japanese;

wo
【喔】 (1) (of a cock) crow; (2) (an interjection expressing understanding) oh;
［喔喔］ cock-a doodle-do; coo-coo-ri-coo;
喔喔聲 cocka-doodle-doo;
喔喔啼 cock-a doodle-do; coo-coo-ri-coo;

wo
【渦】 eddy; whirlpool;
［渦流］ eddy;
渦流形成 eddy-making;
空氣渦流 air eddy;
相對渦流 relative eddy;
軸向渦流 axial eddy;
［渦旋］ eddy;
渦旋運動 vortex motion;
湍流渦旋 turbulent eddy;
下風渦旋 less eddies;
中尺度渦旋 mesoscale eddies;

氣渦 gas eddy;
水渦 eddies of water;
旋渦 eddy; whirlpool; vortex;
漩渦 eddy; whirlpool; vortex;

wo
【萵】 lettuce;
［萵苣］ lettuce;
結球萵苣 cabbage lettuce; crisp-head lettuce;
散葉萵苣 leaf lettuce;
腌萵苣 pickled lettuce;
皺葉萵苣 crinkle garden lettuce; curled lettuce;
［萵筍］ lettuce;

W

wo

【窩】 (1) cave; den; nest; (2) apartment; house; living quarters; (3) harbour; hide; (4) block; check; hold in; obstruct;

［窩藏］ harbour; shelter;
窩藏竊賊 screen thieves;
窩藏贓物 harbor stolen goods;
窩藏罪犯 give shelter to a criminal;

［窩火］ have pent-up anger;

［窩囊］ (1) be annoyed; feel vexed; (2) cowardly and timid; good-for-nothing; hopelessly stupid; stupid;
窩囊氣 petty annoyances;
多窩囊 how stupid;

［窩心］ feel irritated; feel vexed;

艾窩窩 steamed cake made of glutinous rice with sweet filling;
安樂窩 cosy net;
抱窩 sit on the nest to hatch eggs;
被窩 folded quilt;
鼻窩 nasal pit;
動窩 make a move;
蜂窩 (1) honeycomb-like thing; (2) honeycomb;
夾肢窩 armpit;
胳肢窩 armpit;
狗窩 doghouse; kennel;
雞窩 chicken coop; henhouse; roost;
酒窩 dimple;
馬蜂窩 hornet's nest;
挪窩 (1) move (house); (2) move to another place;
氣窩 airlock;
山窩 out-of-the-way mountain area;
笑窩 dimple;
心窩兒 pit of the stomach;
眼窩 eye socket;
眼下窩 eye socket;
燕窩 bird's nest; edible bird's nest;
腋窩 armpit;
一窩 (1) a family; a nest; a nestful; (2) a brood of; a litter of;
肘窩 armpit;

wo

【蝸】 snail;

［蝸居］ humble abode;

［蝸牛］ snail;
蝸行牛步 at a snail's space;

耳蝸 acoustic labyrinth; cochlea;

wo³

wo

【我】 (1) I; (2) we; (3) self; (4) my; (5) our;

［我輩］ us; we;

［我的］ my;
我的媽呀 my sainted aunt;

［我們］ us; we;
我們的 our;

［我行我素］ act according to one's will regardless of others' opinions; do things one's own way; follow one's bigoted course; gang one's own gait; go one's own way; in a world by oneself; in a world of one's own; in one's own sweet way; persist in one's old ways; stick to one's old way of doing things; take one's own course;
我行我素的人 individualist;

大我 the collective; the greater self; the spiritual;
敵我 the enemy and ourselves;
故我 my old self;
你我 you and I;
順我 follow me;
忘我 oblivious of oneself; selfless; take no heed of oneself;
小我 individual;
自我 (1) oneself; self; (2) ego;

wo⁴

wo

【沃】 (1) irrigate; (2) (of land) fertile;

［沃壤］ rich soil;

［沃潤］ fertile and moist;

［沃土］ fat soil; fertile land; fertile soil;

［沃沃］ (1) robust; (2) glossiness;

［沃衍］ fertile area;

［沃野］ fertile land;
沃野彌望 boundless horizon;
沃野千里 a vast expanse of fertile land;

［沃洲］ oasis;

肥沃 fertile; rich;
饒沃 (of soil) fertile; rich;

wo

【臥】 (1) lie down; rest; sleep; (2) lay across; lie across; place across;

［臥病］ be confined to bed; be laid up; bedridden on account of illness;

臥病不起 cannot rise from one's sickbed;
臥病在牀 be confined to one's bed by sickness; be laid up with illness; ill in bed; sick abed; stay in bed; take to one's bed;

[臥不安席] be too worried to get into sleep; feel uneasy even in sleep;
[臥車] railway sleeping car;
[臥牀] lie in bed;
臥牀不起 be abed; remain in bed;
~ 因痛風發作而臥牀不起 be abed with gout;
臥牀休息 rest on a bed; repose on a bed;
[臥倒] drop to the ground; lie down; take a prone position;
[臥底] act as a stool pigeon;
[臥房] bedroom;
[臥寐求之] beg for it in sleep; seek for sth even in sleep;
[臥內] bedroom;
[臥室] bedroom;
[臥榻] bed;
[臥薪嘗膽] endure hardships to accomplish some ambition; sleep on the brushwood and taste the gall — nurse vengeance;

被臥 quilt;
俯臥 lie prostrate;
偃臥 lie on one's back; lie supine;
仰臥 lie on the back; lie supine; supination; supine;

wo

【偓】 (1) narrow-mindedness; (2) a surname;
[偓促] dirty; filthy;

wo

【涴】 (1) meander; wind; (2) soil; stain;

wo

【握】 (1) grasp; grip; hold; (2) a handful;
[握筆] hold a brush; hold a pen;
[握臂] grasp the arm;
[握別] part; shake hands at parting;
[握法] grip;
直拍握法 pen-hold grip;
[握翰] hold a pen;
[握緊] grasp firmly; hold fast;
[握卷] hold a book to read;
[握拍] grip;
握拍法 grip;
~ 正拍握拍法 forehand groundstroke;
~ 正手握拍法 forehand grip;
[握拳] clench one's fist; make a fist;
[握權] hold the reins; in command; in power;
[握手] clasp hands; shake hands;
握手成交 give one's hand on a bargain; shake hands on the bargain;
握手告別 shake hands with sb in farewell;
握手為定 shake on it;
握手惜別 grasp a person's hand in farewell;
握手言和 conciliate one's opponents; shake hands to make peace;
握手言歡 bury the hatchet; give us your fist; greet sb with a hearty handshake; hold hands and chat cheerfully; shake hands and make up; shake hands to show affection;
握手有力 have a strong shake;
緊緊握手 shake hands with a grip;
握握手 put it there;
與許多人握手 press the flesh;
[握抓] hold;

把握 (1) grasp; hold; seize; (2) assurance; certainty;
反握 palm up; supinated grip; undergrip;
緊握 clench; grasp; grip; hold;
拳握 hold in the fist;
在握 in one's hands; under one's control; within one's grasp;
掌握 grasp; in one's grasp; know well; master; within one's power;

wo

【渥】 (1) dye; (2) great kindness;
[渥恩] great kindness; profound benefaction;
[渥惠] great kindness; profound benefaction;
[渥蒙] deeply grateful for;
[渥澤] great kindness; profound benefaction;

優渥 favourable; liberal; munificent;

wo

【幄】 big tent;

帷幄 army tent;

wo

【斡】 revolve; rotate; turn;

［斡旋］ (1) mediate; mediation; (2) good offices;
斡旋者 mediator;
從中斡旋 mediate between disputants;

［斡運］ move in a circle;

［斡轉］ revolve; rotate;

W

wo

【齷】 (1) narrow; small; (2) dirty;

［齷齪］ dirty; filthy;
卑鄙齷齪 base; foul; mean; sordid;

wu[1]

wu

【巫】 (1) shaman; witch; wizard; (2) sorcery; witchcraft; (3) a surname;

［巫婆］ witch;
老巫婆 witch; wizard;

［巫神］ sorcerer; wizard;

［巫師］ sorcerer; wizard;

［巫術］ black art; black magic; sorcery; witchcraft; witchery;

［巫醫］ witch doctor;

［巫祝］ witch; wizard;

男巫 warlock;
女巫 sorceress witch;
神巫 sorcerer; wizard;

wu

【污】 (1) dirt; filth; (2) dirty; filthy; (3) corrupt; (4) defile; smear;

［污點］ black mark; blemish; blot; defect; flaw; flick; smear; smirch; smotch; smudge; smut; smutch; spot; stain;
丟掉污點 take the stain out;
去除污點 wipe out a blot;
消除污點 eliminate blemishes;
有污點 have a stain;

［污工］ masonry;
混凝土污工 cement masonry;
石污工 masonry;
~ 成層毛石污工 rubble masonry;
~ 錘琢石污工 hammer-dressed masonry;
磚砌污工 brick masonry;

［污垢］ dirt; filth; impurity; soil;
標記污垢 labeled soil;
模擬污垢 model soil;
天然污垢 natural soil;
一層污垢 a film of dirt;

［污穢］ dirty; filthy; foul;
污穢的語言 filthy language;
污言穢語 bestial words;

［污跡］ smears; stains;

［污吏］ corrupt official;

［污漫］ besmirch; smear;

［污蔑］ (1) calumniate; slander; vilify; (2) defile; sully; tarnish;

［污名］ dishonour; infamy;
清洗污名 clear one's name;

［污泥］ mire; mud;
污泥濁水 filth; filth and mire; mire; muck; sludge and filth;
出污泥而不染 come out of the mud unsoiled; emerge unstained from the filth;
活性污泥 activated sludge;
膨脹污泥 bulking sludge;
厭氧污泥 anaerobic sludge;
沾滿污泥 foul with mud;

［污染］ contaminate; contamination; pollute; pollution; stain;
污染單位 pullter;
污染地區 contaminated area;
污染控制 pollution control;
污染區 polluted area;
污染事故 contamination accident;
污染物 contaminant; contaminator; pollutant;
~ 污染物濃度 concentration of pollutant;
~ 污染物排放標準 emission index;
~ 大氣污染物 atmospheric contaminant; atmospheric pollutant;
~ 腐蝕污染物 corrosion contaminant;
~ 海灘污染物 beach pollutant;
~ 環境污染物 environmental pollutant;
~ 空氣污染物 aerial contaminant; air contaminant;
~ 排氣污染物 exhaust contaminant;
~ 氣載污染物 air-borne contaminant;
~ 人為污染物 artificial contaminant;
~ 細菌污染物 bacterial pollutant;
~ 致癌污染物 carcinogenic contaminant;
污染源 pollution source;
污染指數 pollution index;
大氣污染 air contamination; air pollution; atmospheric pollution;
防污染 decontamination;
~ 防污染系統 decontamination system;
防止污染 avoid contamination;
光污染 light pollution;

化學污染 chemical contamination;
環境污染 environment pollution;
減輕污染 pollution abatement; reduce pollution;
精神污染 cultural pollution;
空氣污染 aerial pollution; air contamination; air pollution;
控制污染 pollution control;
農業污染 cultural pollution;
汽車污染 vehicle pollution;
氣流污染 air stream contamination;
熱污染 thermal pollution;
生物圈污染 biospheric contamination;
聲污染 acoustical pollution;
食品污染 food pollution;
水污染 water pollution;
~ 水污染控制 water pollution control;
水質污染 water pollution;
細胞污染 bacteriological contamination;
噪音污染 noise pollution;
~ 消除噪音污染 abate noise pollution;

［污辱］ (1) humiliate; insult; (2) defile; sully; tarnish; (3) rape;

［污水］ drainage; foul water; polluted water; sewage; waste water;
污水處理廠 sewage plant; sewage plant; sewage treatment plant; sewage works;
污水管 sewer; waste pipe;
~ 側向污水管 lateral sewer;
~ 戶內污水管 private sewer;
~ 生活污水管 sanitary sewer;
污水坑 cesspit;
城市污水 municipal sewage;
處理污水 deal with effluents;
含油污水 oily sewage;
未經處理的污水 untreated sewage;
有機污水 organic sewage;

［污俗］ vulgar custom;

［污物］ ordure;

［污濁］ dirty; filthy; foul; muddy;

［污漬］ blot; stain;
頑固污漬 stubborn stains;

卑污 despicable and filthy; foul;
玷污 smear; stain; sully; tarnish;
垢污 dirt; filth;
奸污 rape or seduce;
貪污 corruptions; graft;
血污 blood stain;
油污 greasy dirt;

wu

【於】 interjection roughly equivalent to alas, bravo, hurrah, etc.; what;

［於菟］ tiger;

wu

【屋】 (1) house; (2) room;
村屋 village house;

［屋場］ hamlet; village;

［屋頂］ housetop; roof; rooftop;
屋頂板 roofing slate;
屋頂窗 dormer;
~ 扁圓頂屋頂窗 surbased dormer;
~ 三角形屋頂窗 gabled dormer;
~ 斜波式屋頂窗 rampant dormer;
屋頂花園 roof garden;
屋頂天線 loft aerial;
屋頂氈 roofing felt;
大屋頂 overhanging roof;
趕牛上屋頂—不可能 driving a cow up onto the roof — impossible;
拱型屋頂 arch roof;
螺旋式小圓屋頂 spiral cupola;
毛屋頂 carcass-roofing;
爬上屋頂 climb onto the roof;
平屋頂 flat roof;
曲線屋頂 curved roof;
人字屋頂 gabled roof;
扇形屋頂 arched roof;
雙坡屋頂 gabled sloping roof;
四坡屋頂 hipped roof;
懸臂屋頂 cantilever roof;
圓屋頂 cupola;
支撐屋頂 support the roof;
鐘形屋頂 bell roof;

［屋脊］ ridge of a roof;

［屋架］ roof truss;

［屋漏］ leak in the roof;
屋漏更遭連夜雨，船破又遇頂頭風 misfortunes never come alone; one misfortune calls up another; one misfortune comes on the neck of another; one misfortune rides upon another's back;
屋漏偏遭連夜雨 it never rains but it pours; misfortunes never come singly; one misfortune comes in the wake of another; one woe doth tread upon another's heels; the heaviest rain falls on the leaky house; the rain falls throughout the night with the roof already leaking — an added misfortune;

［屋面］ roof;

屋面板 roof boarding;
屋面工 roofer;
屋面瓦 roof tile;
玻璃屋面 glass roof;
分隔屋面 compartment roof;
瓦屋面 tile roofing;
組合屋面 built-up roof;

[屋舍] building; cottage; house;

[屋檐] eaves;
屋檐天線 eaves aerial;
居人屋檐下，豈敢不低頭 he must need go whom the devil drives; he must stoop that hath a low door; needs must when the devil drives;
身在屋檐下，怎敢不低頭 being under the eaves, dare one not low one's head;

[屋宇] building; house;

[屋主] owner of a house;

[屋子] house; room;
擠了一屋子 the room is packed;
收拾屋子 put one's house in order;

矮屋 low house;
北屋 north rooms;
草屋 hut;
東屋 east wing;
髮屋 barber shop;
房屋 buildings; house;
金屋 love nest;
寮屋 squatter structure;
裏屋 inner room;
陋屋 hovel;
茅屋 thatched cottage;
木屋 wooden hut; wooden house;
排屋 row house; terraced house;
棚屋 cabana; hut;
葺屋 thatched house;
石屋 stone house;
書屋 study;
堂屋 central room;
外屋 outer room;
西屋 west wing;
小屋 cottage; hut; little house;
整屋 repair a house;

wu

【烏】 (1) crow; (2) black; dark; dark colour; (3) how; what; when; (4) a surname;

[烏豆] black beans;

[烏髮] (1) dark hair; raven hair; (2) dye the hair black;

[烏飛兔走] how time flies; time flies;

[烏龜] (1) tortoise; turtle; (2) cuckold;
烏龜吃巴豆—不知死活 a tortoise eating croton-oil seeds － unaware of the death ahead;
烏龜王八 all kinds of scoundrels; turtles, tortoises and all the scum of the earth;

[烏合之眾] a crowd assembled like crows; a disorganized horse; a disorderly band; a gathering of crowds; a mob; a motley crew; a motley force that knows no discipline; a rabble; an awkward squad; an undisciplined mob; ragtag and bobtail; scratch team; sheep that have no shepherd; sheep without a shepeard; tag, rag and bobtail;

[烏黑] jet-black; pitch-black; raven black;
烏黑的 coal-black;
~烏黑的眼睛 coal-black eyes;

[烏亮] glossy black; jet-black;

[烏溜溜] dark and liquid;

[烏龍] wulong tea;
烏龍茶 wulong tea;
烏龍球 own goal;
擺烏龍 make an error; speak with exaggeration;

[烏木] ebony;

[烏紗] ancient official hat;
烏紗帽 (1) black gauze cup; (2) official post; (3) headgear of an official;
~丟烏紗帽 be dismissed from office;

[烏托邦] utopia;
反面烏托邦 dystopia;

[烏鴉] crow; raven;
烏鴉翅膀遮不住太陽 the wings of a crow cannot blot out the radiance of the sun;
烏鴉黑色 corbeau;
烏鴉叫聲 caw;
烏鴉笑豬黑，自醜不覺得 the pot calls the kettle black; the raven said to the rook; Stand away, black-coat; thou art a bitter birds, said the raven to the starling;
紅嘴烏鴉 chough;

[烏煙瘴氣] foul atmosphere; noisy, filthy and wildly lawless; the atmosphere is so thick that you could cut it with a knife; vicious practices;

[烏有] nothing;
烏有先生 Mr Nothing － a fictitious

character;

化為烏有 bring to naught; come to naught; come to nothing; crumble to dust; disappear into thin air; dissolve into thin air; dwindle away into nothing; go down the drain; go for naught; go glimmering; go out of existence; go up in smoke; melt into thin air; pass into nothingness; vanish into nothingness; vanish into thin air;

[烏雲] black clouds; dark clouds;

烏雲蔽日 murky clouds obscure the sun — bad ministers surrounded the emperor;

烏雲沉沉 black clouds hang low; dark clouds move down;

烏雲滾滾 dark clouds billow;

烏雲籠罩 covered with dark clouds; dark clouds hanging over;

烏雲滿面 with a cloudy countenance;

烏雲密佈 black clouds gather overhead;

烏雲壓城城欲摧 the city might crumble under the mass of dark clouds;

烏雲壓頂 black clouds press down overhead; dark clouds are gathering overhead;

烏雲遮天 black clouds blot out the sky; dark clouds obscure the sky; the sky is covered with dark clouds;

驅散烏雲 dispel the cloud;

[烏賊] cuttlefish; inkfish;

[烏竹] black bamboo;

[烏嘴黑眉] dark in complexion;

草烏 a kind of medicinal herbs;

何首烏 tuber of multiflower knotweed;

金烏 sun;

wu

【惡】 (1) how; where; (2) ah; o; oh;

wu

【嗚】 (1) sob; weep; (2) hoot; toot; zoom;

[嗚呼] (1) alack; alas; (2) die;

嗚呼哀哉 what a tragedy;

嗚呼歸天 breathe out one's life;

[嗚嗚] hoot; purr;

[嗚咽] make mournful sounds; sob; weep; whimper;

wu

【鄔】 (1) names of various places in ancient times; (2) a surname;

wu

【誣】 accuse falsely; bring a false charge against;

[誣謗] libel; slander;

[誣服] plead guilty when one is not;

[誣告] bring a false charge against; lodge a false accusation; trump up a charge against;

誣告好人 falsely accuse an innocent person;

誣告罪 offence of malicious accusation;

[誣害] accuse falsely; calumniate; frame sb up; injure by spreading false reports about;

[誣賴] accuse falsely; falsely incriminate; inculpate;

誣賴好人 incriminate innocent people;

[誣良] charge a good person;

誣良為娼 charge a virtuous woman with prostitution;

誣良為盜 accuse as innocent person of theft; bring a false charge of theft against an upright man; accuse good people as robbers; charge an innocent man with robbery;

[誣衊] caluminiate; libel; slander; smear; vilify;

誣衊不實之詞 slander and libel;

誣衊構陷 calumniate and implicate;

誣衊運動 smear campaign;

大肆誣衊 heap calumny on;

造謠誣衊 calumny and slander;

[誣染] libel; slander;

[誣罔] accuse falsely; bring a false charge against;

[誣陷] frame a case against; frame sb; frame sb up; incriminate falsely; make false charge against sb;

[誣證] perjury; give false testimony;

辯誣 offer an explanation; plead innocence;

wu²

wu

【毋】 (1) no; not; (2) a surname;

[毋寧] rather...than;

[毋忘在莒] don't foreget national humiliation in time of peace and security; remind not to forget the national humiliation

but to recover the lost territory;
[毋為戎首] don't be the first to start a war;
[毋需] do not need;
[毋庸] need not;
毋庸諱言 it is no secret that; needless to cover up; no need for reticence; to be frank; there's no need for reticence;
毋庸遠慮 do not worry about the distant future;
毋庸置疑 beyond all doubt; beyond the shadow of a doubt; it is no question; there is no room for doubt that; true beyond all question; without a doubt; without a shadow of doubt;
毋庸贅述 it is pointless to belabour the obvious; need not enlarge upon it; there is no need to go into details;
毋庸贅言 need not go into the details; no need to repeat it;

wu
【吾】 (1) I; (2) we;
[吾輩] we;
[吾儕] people like us; we;
[吾人] we;
支吾 equivocate; hum and haw;

wu
【吳】 (1) Kingdom of Wu (222 – 280), one of the Three Kingdoms; (2) a surname;
[吳牛喘月] have an excessive fear out of misgivings; the water buffalo panting at the sight of the moon — fear of a thing due to mistaking it for sth else;
[吳下阿蒙] ignorant person;

wu
【浯】 name of a river;

wu
【梧】 (1) firmiana; (2) prop; support; (3) prop up; support; (4) a surname;
[梧桐] Chinese parasol tree; firmiana;
梧桐子 dryandra seeds;
魁梧 big and tall; stalwart;

wu
【無】 (1) destitute of; lack; not have; nothing; wanting; without; (2) negative; no; none; not; (3) no matter whether; regardless of;
[無礙] all right; do not matter; no harm; not in the way;
無礙大局 not to affect the situation as a whole;
[無備] unprepared; without preparation;
[無比] incomparable; matchless; peerless; unparalleled; without peer;
無比憤慨 furiously indignant at..;
無比憤怒 furiously indignant;
無比毅力 tremendous resoluteness;
無比英勇 unrivalled in bravery;
無比勇敢 unparalleled in bravery;
無比憂傷 devour one's heart;
無比優越 unsurpassed in excellence;
無比自豪 infinitely proud of oneself;
力大無比 unparalleled in physical strength; without a match in physical prowess; without equal in strength;
[無裨] of no avail; of no help; useless;
無裨於事 of no help; won't do any good; won't help matters;
[無邊] boundless; brimless; rimless; vast and expansive;
無邊風月 boundless natural charms;
無邊無礙 without restraints of any sort;
無邊無岸 boundless and shoreless;
無邊無際 a vast expanse of; boundless; endless; illimitable; immeasurable; limitless; measureless; shoreless; unbounded; unlimited; unmeasured; vast;
[無病] without an illness;
無病而死 die without a known cause; die without any illness;
無病呻吟 adopt a sentimental pose; groan when there is no physical pain; groan while not really in pain; make a fuss about an imaginary illness; moan and groan without being ill; pine without cause;
無病一身輕 to be healthy is a blessing;
[無不] all; all without exception; invariably;
[無補] of no avail; of no help; useless; won't help;
無補大局 do not help the whole situation; of no great help to the overall situation;
無補於事 do not help matters; of no avail; of no help; not to help matters; will not mend matters;

於事無補 it doesn't help the situation; it does nothing good; it makes no difference to the matter; it would not help matters;

[無猜] childlike innocence; unsuspicious;

兩小無猜 innocent playmates;

[無產] proletariat;

無產階級 the proletariat;

[無常] (1) changeable; variable; (2) impermanence; transiency;

出沒無常 appear at intervals; appear and disappear unexpectedly; come and go unexpectedly

反覆無常 capricious; change about; fickle-minded; whimsical;

聚散無常 meetings and departings are irregular;

冷熱無常 blow hot and cold;

喜怒無常 of variable temper;

作輟無常 at fits and intervals; by fits and starts;

[無恥] brazen; cheeky; impudent; shameless;

無恥勾當 shameless practices;

無恥讕言 brazen lie; impudent and tendentious allegations; shameless babblings; shameless slander;

無恥透頂 be lost to all sense of shame; brazen to the extreme; shamelessness beyond description;

無恥之徒 abandoned character; cool beggar; people who have lost all sense of shame; shameless people; unscrupulous person;

無恥之尤 brazen in the extreme; completely devoid of a sense of shame; devoid of shame altogether; most shameless of all; shameless beyond description; the height of impudence; utterly shameless;

卑鄙無恥 mean and having no sense of shame; mean and vulgar;

厚顏無恥 as bold as brass; be dead to shame; be lost to shame; be past shame; be without shame; brass-visaged; brazen-faced; have a nerve; have no shame; have rubbed one's face with a brass candlestick; have the effrontery to; have the front to do sth; have the gall to do sth; have the hide to do sth; impudent; shameless beyond description; too impudent and shameless;

荒淫無恥 dissipated and unashamed; licentious and decadent; profligate and shameless; shameless dissipation; shamelessly dissipated;

老而無恥 old and shameless;

[無出其右] have no equal; have no match; matchless; never to see anything that goes beyond it; no one can be placed higher than him; no one excels him; nobody can better him; peerless; second to none; unequalled; unexcelled; without equal;

[無處] nowhere;

無處安身 have nowhere to make one's home;

無處藏身 have nowhere to hide oneself; no place to hide;

無處存身 find no shelter; have no place to call one's home; have nowhere to live; have nowhere to seek a shelter;

無處可去 have nowhere to go;

無處棲身 have no place to stay;

無處容身 have no place of refuge; have nowhere to rest;

[無從] can hardly; do not know where to + verb; no way;

無從答覆 in no position to answer;

無從入手 there is no way to begin;

無從説起 not to know where to begin; out of the question;

無從知道 there is no knowing; unable to find out;

無從置喙 impossible to put in a word;

無從著力 fail to see where to direct one's effects;

無從著手 have no way of handling; unable even to get started;

[無措] (1) act strangely; (2) jumpy;

惶恐無措 up a stump;

[無道] injustice; tyrannical; unjust;

荒淫無道 be profligate and devoid of principles;

[無敵] invincible; unconquerable; unmatched;

無敵不克 carry all before one; invincible; make conquests on all sides;

無敵於天下 invincible under heaven; unmatched anywhere in the world; with no peer in the whole world;

所向無敵 all-conquering; break all enemy resistance; ever-victorious; invincible;

matchless wherever one goes; sweep all before one;

[無底洞] bottomless pit;

[無的放矢] aimless and fruitless; discharge one's pistol in the air; let fly at nothing; shoot an arrow at a nonexistent target; shoot an arrow without a target; shoot when there is no target; shoot without a target;

[無地自容] can find no place to hide oneself for shame; feel too ashamed to show one's face; have no place to hide oneself;

[無動於衷] aloof and indifferent; completely indifferent; dead to all feeling; flinty-hearted; remain completely unmoved; unconcerned; unmoved; untouched;

聽到消息無動於衷 hear the news with nonchalance;

[無獨有偶] curious coincidence; it happens that there is a similar case; it is not unique, but has its counterpart; by coincidence; not come singly but in pairs;

[無度] excessive; immoderate; without restraints;

悲哀無度 carry one's grief to excess;

規求無度 covet without limit; unbounded covetousness;

荒淫無度 be vicious beyond measures; indulge in sensual excesses; excessive indulgence in lewdness; given to sexual pleasures; immeasurably dissolute;

揮霍無度 abuse money without limit; squander wantonly;

縱慾無度 indulge in carnal pleasure; oversexed; without restraint;

[無端] for no reason; unjustified; unprovoked; without cause; without reason;

無端生事 create a disturbance for no reason;

無端受責 be falsely accused and condemned;

無端侮辱 gratuitous insult;

[無法] cannot; incapable; unable;

無法比擬 beyond comparison;

無法可施 there is nothing one can do about it; unable to do anything about it;

無法可想 at the end of one's rope; no alternative; no way out; powerless; there is no help for;

無法控制 out of control;

無法理解 incomprehensible;

無法彌補 irrecoverable; irretrievable; past remedy;

無法實行 impossible of execution;

無法挽救 beyond help;

無法無天 anomy; completely lawless; defy laws human and divine; have no respect for law; lawless and godless; recklessly; run riot; run wild; totally devoid of conscience and respect for law; violate all laws, human and divine;

無法形容 beyond description; have no means of putting sth into words; impossible to describe;

無法應付 at one's wit's end; at th end of one's rope; without resources; unable to cope with;

[無方] in the wrong way; not in the proper way; not knowing how;

[無妨] doesn't matter; may as well; might as well; there's no harm;

試一試也無妨 there is no harm in having a try;

[無非] little more than; no more than; no other than; nothing but; only; simply;

[無風] airless; without air;

無風不起浪 there are no waves without wind; there is no smoke without fire; where there's smoke, there's fire;

無風的日子 airless day;

無風起浪 create problems where none exists; create trouble out of nothing; make disturbance out of nothing; make much ado about nothing; make uncalled-for trouble; start a big trouble out of nothing; stir up trouble about nothing;

無風三尺浪 there are billows three feet high even if there is no wind;

[無功] without achievements;

無功不受祿 no gains without pains;

無功而返 a wild goose chase; return without accomplishing anything;

無功受祿 get a reward without deserving it; have done nothing to deserve the favour;

勞而無功 a fruitless attempt; all one's efforts come to naught; beat the air; bite a file; exert oneself to no purpose; labour lost; labour wasted; make futile efforts; much cry and little wool; plough the sand; spend one's labour to no purpose; the cow gives a good pail of milk and then kicks it over; toil in vain; toil with no gain; work fruitlessly; work hard but to no avail;

[無辜] guiltless; innocent; the innocent;

哀矜無辜 pardon the innocent;

累及無辜 compromise the guiltless; involve the innocent; make the innocent suffer; the trouble involves innocent people;

枉殺無辜 kill an innocent person unjustly;

省釋無辜 release the innocent;

株連無辜 involve the innocent in a criminal case;

[無故] for no reason; uncalled for; without cause; without reason;

無故遲到 late without cause;

無故缺席 absent without excuse;

無故生有 make trouble out of nothing;

[無怪] no wonder; not to be wondered at;

[無關] have nothing to do with; no concern; no relationship; unconcerned;

無關成本 irrelated cost;

無關大局 a side issue; have no bearing on the general situation; have no effect on the overall situation; insignificant; not to affect the general situation; not to matter very much; of little account;

無關宏旨 a matter of no consequence; insignificant; of no consideration; of no great importance; of no significance; unimportant;

無關緊要 count for little; insignificant; nothing serious; of no great importance; of no significance; unimportant;

無關輕重 not of great importance;

無關痛痒 care for nothing; completely indifferent to; not important at all; of no concern; of no consequence;

無關重要的人物 a cog in the machine; a man of little account; a man of no account; a mere cipher; a small potato; cipher in algorism; mere circumstance; no account; poor circumstance; remote circumstance;

相互無關 independent of each other;

[無光] (1) aphotic; (2) loss of prestige;

無光帶 aphotic zone;

無光區 aphotic region;

面上無光 feel ashamed; lose face; loss of prestige;

[無過] free from mistakes;

但求無過 hope only to be free from mistakes; seek only to avoid a flaw; seek only to escape blame;

人孰無過 every man has his faults; every man has the defects of his qualities; every man is subject to error; he is lifeless that is faultless; no man is infallible; no man lives without a fault; nobody is without faults; none found without fault; there is no man but has his faults; there is no man without faults; there is none without a fault; to err is human;

[無害] do no harm to; harmless; innocuous; innoxious;

[無憾] without regret;

死而無憾 die having nothing to regret; die without regret;

[無核] nuclear-free;

無核化 nonnuclearization;

無核區 nuclear-free zone;

[無後] heirless; without posterity;

無後顧之憂 with the rear secure; without fear of an attack from the rear;

[無花果] fig;

無花果樹 fig;

~無花果樹葉 fig leaf;

[無話] nothing chatted;

無話不談 chat with sb without reserve; in each other's confidence; keep no secrets from each other; tell one another everything;

無話可答 at a loss for words; have no fitting reply to make; have no words to answer; have nothing to say in reply;

無話可說 can say nothing more; cannot think of anything to say; find nothing to say; have nothing to say; there is nothing one can say;

無話則短，有話則長 if nothing more happens they story will be short, if events come, it will be long;

[無患] free from danger;

安全無患 free from danger;

有備無患 be prepared against want; have a second string to one's bow; preparedness averts peril; preparedness prevents calamity; readiness is all; store is no sore; when one is well prepared there will be no disaster; where there is precaution, there will be no danger; with all precautions taken, one is safe;

W

[無火] fireless;

無火不生煙 everything has its seed; no smoke without fire; nothing comes from nothing; where there's smoke, there's fire;

無火不生煙，無風不起浪 there is no smoke without fire and there are no waves without wind;

無火煮食 fireless cooking;

[無稽] absurd; fantastic; groundless; unfounded; wild;

無稽之談 a cock-and-bull story; a false tale; a fishy story; a tale of a tub; absurd view; baseless gossip; Canterbury tale; clotted nonsense; cooked-up story; fable; fabrication; fantastic talk; fiction; groundless statement; groundless utterances; rumours; sheer nonsense; traveller's tale; unfounded talk; wild talks;

荒誕無稽 absurd; absurd and groundless; fantastic; incredible; preposterous;

荒唐無稽 frivolous and unfounded; most absurd; out of thin air;

[無機] inorganic;

無機分析 inorganic analysis;

無機化學 inorganic chemistry;

[無疾而終] die a natural death; die in one's sleep; die without a sickness; die without any illness; die without known cause;

[無幾] (1) almost the same; hardly any; little; not many; not much; very few; very little; (2) not long afterwards; shortly;

寥寥無幾 very few;

所差無幾 almost alike; not much difference;

所剩無幾 there is very little left;

相差無幾 almost the same;

[無際] boundless;

碧野無際 the green grassland stretches to the horizon;

瀰望無際 the boundless horizon;

一望無際 a boundless expanse of; an uninterrupted stretch of; command an extensive view; spread out far beyond the horizon; stretch to the horizon; wide stretches of;

[無堅不摧] all-conquering; capable of destroying any stronghold; carry all before one; nothing is indestructible; overrun all fortifications;

[無間] (1) not keeping anything from each other; very close to each other; (2) continuously; without interruption; (3) make no distinction;

無間可乘 without any chance to seize hold of;

[無疆] boundless; limitless;

萬壽無疆 a long, long life; long live forever; many happy returns of the day to eternity; may you attain boundless longevity; wish you a long life;

[無界] unbounded;

無界量 unbounded quantity;

[無可] beyond; without;

無可比敵 without rival;

無可比擬 beyond compare; beyond comparison; inapproachable; incomparable; like all nature; matchless; out of comparison; out of all comparison; pass compare, unmatchable; unparalleled; without compare;

無可辯駁 beyond all dispute; incontrovertible; indisputable; irrefutable; unanswerable; unchallengeable;

無可補救 beyond remedy; irremediable; irreparable; past remedy;

無可疵議 nothing to object to;

無可抵賴 cannot possibly be denied; undeniable;

無可非難 above reproach; beyond challenge; not blameworthy; without rebuke;

無可非議 above reproach; beyond challenge; blameless; irreproachable; not blameworthy; reproachless; unimpeachable; unobjectionable; unquestionable; without rebuke;

無可奉告 have nothing to say; no

comment;
無可估量 above measure; beyond measure; out of measure;
無可厚非 give no cause for criticism; no ground for blame; not altogether inexcusable; there is nothing to be said against it;
無可諱言 beyond all question; beyond doubt; indisputable; past dispute; there's no denying the fact; there's no hiding the fact;
無可稽考 unverifiable;
無可救藥 beyond the power of medicine; hopeless; incorrigible; incurable; past hope; past remedy;
無可理喻 above reason; not to be reasoned with;
無可彌補 beyond retrieve; past remedy;
無可名狀 indescribable; nondescript;
無可奈何 against one's will; at the end of one's resources; have no alternative; have no choice; have no way out; have to; helpless; hopeless; powerless; reluctant; willy-nilly;
無可匹敵 have no like; have no equal; peerless; unapproachable; unique; without a rival;
無可適從 at a loss what to do; irresolute; not know what course to take;
無可推諉 admit of no excuse;
無可挽回 beyond any help; beyond redemption; irredeemable; irretrievable; it can't be helped; past redemption; past saving; the die is cast; there is no help for it; too far gone; without redemption;
無可挽救 beyond retrieve; irreparable; past retrieve;
無可限量 beyond measure; infinite; know no measure; without measure;
無可責難 blameless; not be censured;
無可爭辯 admit of no dispute; beyond all question; beyond dispute; incontestable; indisputable; irrefutable; past dispute; unarguable; undeniable; undisputable; unimpeachable; unquestionable; without dispute; without question;
無可爭議 beyond controversy; indisputable;
無可指責 above reproach; beyond reproach; blameless; irreproachable; no ground for blame; unexceptionable; unimpeachable;
無可置疑 above suspicion; beyond dispute; beyond doubt; beyond suspicion; cannot be doubted; out of dispute; pass dispute; there is no doubt;
無可訾議 above criticism; unimpeachable;

[無孔] no openings;
無孔不入 all-pervasive; always have an eye on the main chance; always trying to penetrate in; enter all possible openings; get in by every opening; have a finger in every pie; intervene everywhere; let no opportunity slip by; lose no chance; penetrate everywhere; poke into every nook and corner; seize every opportunity; work in everywhere;
無孔不鑽 there is no place one does not try to penetrate; worm one's way into every crevice;

[無愧] feel no qualms; have a clear conscience; worthy of;
無愧色 without any expression of shame;
無愧於人 free from shame before anyone; have nothing to be ashamed of before anybody;
無愧於心 have a clear conscience;
當之無愧 deserving; fully desrve an honour; merit the reward; worthy of; worthy of the name;
俯仰無愧 feel not disgraceful in looking down and up — having a clear conscience;
捫心無愧 feel no qualms upon self-examination; feel that one has not done anything wrong; have a good conscience; one's heart is in the right place;
受之無愧 deserve; merit; worthy of;
問心無愧 examine oneself and find nothing to be ashamed of; feel a twinge of conscience; feel guilty; feel no qualms about; free from any compunction; have a clear conscience; have a guilty conscience; have nothing to be ashamed of; have nothing on one's conscience; have sth on one's conscience; peace of conscience; with a clear conscience;

~問心無愧，高枕無憂 a good conscience is a constant feast; a good conscience is a soft pillow;
於心無愧 feel no compunction; have a good conscience; have nothing on one's conscience;

[無賴] (1) blackguardly; rascally; scoundrelly; (2) cad; crook; rascal; villain;
無賴漢 cad;
無賴之徒 group of ruffians; shiftless person; vagabond;
百般無賴 by all crooked means; use all rascally means;
耍無賴 act shamelessly; deliberately dishonest; perverse; unreasonable;
一旦成無賴，永遠是無賴 once a cad, always a cad;

[無淚] tearless;
乾哭無淚 howl without tears; wail a few times without shedding tears;
欲哭無淚 one feels like weeping but has no tears; one wants to cry but has not tears;

[無理] unjustifiable; unreasonable;
無理取鬧 deliberately provocative; find fault with sb for no reason whatsoever; frivolous quibbling; have tantrums without cause; make trouble and create a scene; make trouble groundlessly; make trouble out of nothing; make trouble without a cause; pick a quarrel about nothing; unprovoked quarrel; unreasonable altercation; unreasonable quarrelling; utter nonsense and make trouble; wilfully make trouble;
無理式 irrational expression;
無理要求 unjustifiable demands;
無理指責 accuse unjustifiably; groundless charges; unwarranted accusations;
無理阻撓 unreasonable obstruction;
橫蠻無理 arrogant and high-handed; become high-handed in one's behaviour towards; truculent and unreasonable;

[無禮] churlish; indignity; rude; uncourteous; ungracious;
無禮的 impolite; impudent;
無禮舉動 incivility;
傲慢無禮 contumelious; discourteous; insolent; presumptuous;
別對我無禮 don't you sass me;
放肆無禮 guilty of a liberty;
真是無禮 what a cheek;

[無力] (1) feel weak; lack strength; (2) cannot afford; incapable; powerless; too poor to do sth; unable;
無力償付 insolvent;
渾身無力 feel weak all over;
四肢無力 feel weak in one's limbs;

[無良] no good; without principle; without virtue;

[無兩] matchless; unique; without match;

[無量] boundless; immeasurable; limitless; measureless;

[無聊] (1) bored; in extreme depression; indifferent and uninteresting; listless; (2) nonsensical; senseless; silly; stupid; uninteresting;
無聊苟且 careless; idle and sluggish; remiss;
無聊賴 disappointed and discouraged;
無聊之談 silly talk; talk all the time about nonsense;
感到無聊 feel bored;
極其無聊 in infinite boredom;
閒得無聊 be plagued with too much leisure; find time hand heavy on one's hands; suffer from ennui; twiddle one's thumbs;
閒極無聊 find time hang heavy on one's hands;

[無路] come to a dead end;
無路開路，遇水搭橋 open up roads and bridge rivers;
無路可走 at one's wits' end; at the end of one's rope; come to a dead end; helpless; no way out; nowhere to turn;
走投無路 at the end of one's rope; be driven from pillar to post; be driven into a corner; be driven to desperation; be driven to the wall; be locked in the horns of a dilemma; between the hammer and the anvil; between the upper and nether millstone; can find no way out; come to a dead end; come to the end of one's tether; drive sb to the last shifts; drive sb to the wall; feel oneself concerned; find oneself cornered; from pillar to post; go down a dead alley; go to the wall; have no one to turn to; have no way out; have no way to turn for help; in a

tight corner; in an impasse; land in an impasse; not know which way to turn;
~逼得走投無路 left sb no way out;
~船頭上跑馬一走投無路 riding a horse on the bow of a ship — have nowhere to go;

[無論] (1) no matter what; regardless of; whatever; (2) let alone; not to mention the fact that; to say nothing of;
無論好壞 hail, rain or shine; rain or shine;
無論晴雨 hail, rain or shine;
無論如何 any day; any how; any old how; any way; anyhow; anything like; anywise; as it may; at all costs; at all events; at all hazards; at all risks; at any cost; at any price; at any rate; at any risk; at any sacrifice; be that as it may; by all means; by all possible means; by any manner of means; by any means; come what may; cost what it may; for all the world; for any consideration or reason; for any sake; for anything; for love or money; for the life of me; for the soul of me; for worlds; happen what may; however; however it may be; however it may be; howsoever; in any case; in any circumstances; in any cost; in any event; in any sake; in any sort; in any way; in any wise; in no circumstances; in one way or another; leastwise; no matter how; no matter what happens; on all accounts; on any account; on any terms; on every account; on your life; rain or shine; regardless; right or wrong; sink or swim; under all circumstances; under any circumstances; whatever happens; whatever might happen; whether or not;

[無米] without rice;
無米之炊 cook a meal without rice; make bricks without straw;
無米作炊 cook a meal without rice; make a silk purse out of a sow's ear; make bricks without straw; make omelettes without breaking eggs; make sth without the things needed;

[無名] (1) nameless; (2) unknown; (3) indefinable; indescribable;
無名士 anonym; anonymous person;
無名鼠輩 a pack of worthless rats;
無名小卒 a man of no mark; a mere cipher; a mere cipher; a nameless member of the crowd; a nobody; a nothing; a person of no importance; a small potato; an unimportant person; nonentity; scratch; small fry;
無名業火 irrepressible anger;
無名英雄 anonymous hero; obscure hero; unknown hero; unknown soldier; unsung hero;
無名之輩 nameless nothings;
無名指 ring finger;
榜上無名 fail in an examination; one's name is not among those of the successful on the published list;

[無明火] anger; fury; wrath;
無明火起 flare up for no reason at all;

[無奈] cannot help but; have no alternative; have no choice;
出於無奈 as it cannot be helped; no other course was open to sb; only because one can do no better; out of sheer necessity; there being no alternative;
迫於無奈 be compelled against one's will;

[無能] incapable; incompetent; inefficient; without talent;
無能的人 duffer;
無能為力 beyond one's power; can do nothing about it; can't do anything about it; down and out; incapable of action; lacking the ability for the task at hand; not in a position to; out of one's capability; powerless; unable to help;
無能之輩 no-mark;
腐敗無能 corrupt and incompetent;
譾陋無能 shallowly experienced and incapable;
軟弱無能 weak and incompetent;
庸懦無能 indolent, timid and incapable;

[無尿] anuria;
無尿症 absent urine output; oligoanuria;
結石性無尿 calculous anuria;
腎性無尿 renal hermaturia;

[無朋] incomparable; matchless; peerless;

[無期] no definite term; with no end in sight;
無期徒刑 life imprisonment;

[無奇不有] pits might fly; there is no lack of strange things; there is nothing too strange in the world;

W

[無前] invincible; unmatched; unprecedented;

[無情] callous; devoid of emotions; devoid of feelings; heartless; inexorable; merciless; ruthless;

無情的 callous;

無情無緒 bored; listless and indifferent;

無情無義 show ingratitude for favours; show ingratitude for kindness received;

薄倖無情 inconstant in love;

淡漠無情 indifferent and merciless; sternly cool and unmoved;

冷酷無情 icy indifference;

鐵面無情 inexorable; just and stern; relentless; unmoved by personal appeals;

轉面無情 turn against a friend and show him no mercy;

[無窮] boundless; endless; inexhaustible; infinite; infinitude; infinity; interminable; limitless;

無窮大 infinity;

~ 無窮大符號 infinity-sign;

~ 負無窮大 minus infinity; negative infinity;

~ 極性無窮大 polar infinity;

~ 潛無窮大 potential infinity;

~ 實無窮大 actual infinity;

~ 正無窮大 plus infinity; positive infinity;

無窮無盡 a world of; boundless; endless; inexhaustible; interminable; unfailing; world without end;

無窮小 infinitesimal;

其樂無窮 find it a delight; have endless pleasure in some artistic pursuit; have infinite joy in doing sth worthwhile; the joy is boundless; there is no end of happiness in it; what joy it is to...;

其味無窮 a favour that lingers long in the mind; a lasting pleasant taste; an after-taste that lingers long in the mind; an overtone that lingers long in the mind; have a boundless good flavour; highly delightful; its relish is inexhaustible; its relish is perpetual; its taste is unexhausted; much is left for people to think for a long time; so rich in taste that the more one eats it, the more one likes it; so tasty as to leave a pleasant awareness of it long afterwards;

[無求] need no help;

無求到處人緣好，不飲由他酒價高 if you do not ask their help, all men are good-natured; if you don't drink, the price of wine is of no interest; if you do not beg a favour, men everywhere will appear good-natured; if you do not want to drink, it matters not should the wine too dear;

無求於人 be one's own master; independent; need no help from others;

[無權] have no right;

無權過問 have no voice in sth; no right to butt in; not within one's jurisdiction;

無權無勇 have neither fighting skill nor courage;

[無缺] intact; undamaged;

[無人] (1) unmanned; (2) depopulated; uninhabited; unmanned;

無人不曉 all the world knows; be known to all;

無人不知 be known to all;

無人地帶 no-man's-land;

無人過問 nobody cares about it; nobody's business; not to be attended to by anybody; unclaimed; unwanted;

無人問津 abegging; be left without anybody to care for; go begging; have no bidders; no one shows any interest in; nobody cares to ask about; nobody is interested in; there isn't any buyers;

無人之境 no man's land;

~ 如入無人之境 as if entering no man's land — breaking all resistance; as if there were no one in sight; like entering an unpeopled land — meeting no resistance;

目中無人 care for nobody; consider everyone beneath one's notice; contemptuous of others; haughty; have no respect for anyone; look down on everyone else; look down one's nose at everybody; on the high horse; overweening; snooty; supercilious; too big for one's shoes; too big for one's trousers; with one's nose in the air;

旁若無人 act as if no one is around; arrogantly; have no regard for others;

眼中無人 arrogant; haughty; having no respect for anyone; too big for one's boots;

[無任] extremely; immensely;
無任感荷 be very much obliged; feel very much indebted;
無任感激 deeply grateful; feel most grateful;
無任歡迎 most welcome;

[無日] (1) not a single day; (2) soon;

[無傷] doesn't matter; no harm;
無傷大體 cannot spoil the whole situation; do no harm to the main side of things; have very little ill effect on the main aspect of things; it does not hurt the important essentials;
無傷大雅 immaterial; involving no major principle; it doesn't matter; no serious harm is done; not to affect things as a whole; not to matter much; permissible in polite society;

[無上] highest; paramount; supreme;
無上光榮 matchless honour; the highest honour;
無上權力 supreme power;
無上無下 regardless of above or below;
至高無上 above everything else; crowning; most lofty; paramount; supreme; the highest; the most exalted; the supreme; unrivalled;

[無涉] have nothing to do with; no business; no concern; not involved;

[無神論] atheism;
無神論者 atheist;

[無聲] noiseless; silent;
無聲地哭泣 cry silently;
無聲電影 silent move;
無聲無息 be buried in oblivion; be completely unknown; inglorious; obscure; soundless and colourless;
無聲無臭 completely unknown; obscure; unknown;
寂靜無聲 silent;
靜寂無聲 a perfect silence prevails; there is a dead calm;
悄然無聲 quiet and silent;

[無師自通] acquire a skill without being taught; learn without a teacher; self-taught;

[無事] nothing;
無事不登三寶殿 never to to see sb without a reason; never go to the temple for nothing; no one comes to the Hall of the Trinity without a reason; would not go to sb's place except on business;
無事可做 there is no more to be done;
無事空忙 busy oneself with nothing; faff; faff about; faff around;
無事忙 a busybody; busy for nothing; busy idleness; make much ado about nothing;
無事生非 create problems where none exists; create troubles without cause; deliberately provocative; make trouble out of nothing; make uncalled-for touble; start trouble when things are quiet; stir up trouble unnecessary;
無事張皇 much ado about nothing; much cry and little weal; scared about nothing;
無事自擾 bark at the moon; get into a stew about nothing; make a fuss about nothing; make much ado about nothing;
若無其事 as if nothing had happened; nonchalant; without compunction;
閒來無事 free and at leisure; unoccupied and have nothing to do;
相安無事 at peace with each other;
行若無事 behave as if nothing had happened; go about calmly as if nothing had happened;
行所無事 maintain perfect composure; unruffled;
裝作無事 pretend that nothing happened;

[無視] brush aside; consider as unimportant; defy; disregard; have no high opinion of; ignore; pay no attention to;
無視法令 ignore a decree;
無視法律 defy the law;
無視警告 disregard a caution;
無視原則 disregard a rule;

[無數] (1) countless; infinity; innumberable; myriad; numerous; uncounted; (2) an unknown number of; not know for certain; uncertain;
無數的 countless; zillion;
心中無數 not to know for certain; not to know one's own mind; not too sure; without clear aims;
胸中無數 feel unsure of sth; have no figures in one's head; have no idea as to how things stand; not to know what's what;

[無霜] frostless;

[無雙] matchless; peerless; unique; unparalleled; unrivaled;
無雙國士 a man of superior talent;
並世無雙 foremost; peerless;
國士無雙 a state scholar of no equal;

[無私] disinterested; self-forgetful; selfless; unselfish;
無私的 altruistic;
無私無慮 free from care; happy-go-lucky;
無私有弊 being in an awkward position, one who has no corrupt practices is liable to be under suspicion;
秉公無私 handle affairs justly;
大公無私 give no thought to self; impartial; impartial and act without thought of self; selfless; unselfish;
鐵面無私 just and stern; impartial and incorruptible; integrity and justice; not to spare anyone's sensibilities; strict and impartial; strictly impartial;
~ 鐵面無私的人 impartial man;
~ 包公審案—鐵面無私 Magistrate Bao trying a case — a face as impartial as cast iron;
直正無私 exactly straight and impartial;

[無損] cannot harm; intact;
完好無損 in good shape;
有益無損 can only do good, not harm;
於己無損 it doesn't hurt oneself;

[無所] all things;
無所不包 all-embracing; all-encompassing; all-inclusive; everything is contained therein; include all things; nothing is left out;
無所不會，無所不能 can do anything; there is nothing one cannot do and nothing one is not able to do;
無所不能 all-powerful; almighty; capable of doing anything; omnipotent;
無所不談 say one's say; talk about everything under the sun;
無所不通 there is no feat of which one is not capable; there is nothing one does not understand;
無所不為 commit all manner of crimes; do all kinds of bad things; do all manner of evil; do every evil imaginable; ready to do anything; stop at nothing;
無所不用其極 employ the meanest of tricks; go all lengths; go all the way; go to any extreme; go to any lengths; go to extremes in every measure; go to extremes on every count; leave no stone unturned; move hell; pursue everything to its brutal end; resort to every conceivable means; stop at nothing; use every trick up one's sleeve;
無所不有 have all; omnifarious;
無所不在 omnipresence; ubiquitous;
無所不知 have infinite knowledge; know every profession; know everything; there is nothing which one does not know; omniscience; understand every subject;
無所不至 by every possible means; capable of anything; in every conceivable way; omnipresent; penetrate everywhere; spare no pains to; stop at nothing; ubiquitous;

[無他] (1) for no other reason than; nothing else; (2) dedicated; loyal; (3) in good health; safe;

[無頭案] case without any clues; unsolved mystery;

[無往] wherever one goes;
無往不利 be benefited in every way; ever successful; everything prospers with him; go smoothly everywhere; lucky in every endeavour; meet with success without a hitch wherever one goes; succeed wherever one goes; successful in whatever one does;
無往不在 omnipresent; present everywhere;

[無望] despair of; hopeless; without hope;
無望之福 unexpected luck;

[無微不至] be shown lavishly; considerate in every way; down to the very last detail; hand and foot; in every possible way; lavish every care on; meticulous; to the last atom; very thoughtful; without any detail not taken care of;

[無為] inaction; inactivity; let things take their own course;
無為而治 govern by doing nothing that goes against nature;

[無味] (1) tasteless; unpalatable; (2) dull; insipid; uninteresting;
淡而無味 flat and tasteless; milk and water; insipid; tasteless; wishy-washy;

枯燥無味 dry as dust;
食之無味 find it tasteless; have a nasty taste;
~食之無味，棄之可惜 hardly worth eating but not bad enough to throw away;

[無畏] dauntless; fearless; unafraid; unscared; without fear;
大無畏 dauntless; fearless; indomitable;

[無謂] meaningless; pointless; senseless;

[無…無…] neither...nor...;
無盡無休 boundless; continuous; endless; incessant; limitless;
無咎無譽 have neither fault to find with nor praise to bestow on;
無了無休 ceaseless; continuous; endless; on and on; without stopping;
無時無地 every minute and everywhere;
無始無邊 vastly expansive and everlasting;
無影無形 immaterial; impalpable; incorporeal; without a trace; without form or substance;

[無誤] correct; right; verified and found correct;
核查無誤 check and find correct;
準確無誤 unerring accuracy;

[無暇] have no time; too busy; without leisure;
無暇抽身 be occupied; be tied up;
無暇顧及 have no time to attend to the matter;
無暇後顧 have no time to look after things one has left behind;
無暇及此 have no time for this;
無暇兼顧 too busy to attend to other things;
無暇他顧 have no time to attend to other things;

[無瑕] perfect; without blemish; without defect;
無瑕可謫 flawless;
純潔無瑕 as pure as a lily;
淳潔無瑕 pure and flawless;
完美無瑕 as pure as the driven snow;

[無限] an infinite of; boundless; immeasurable; infinite; infinitude; infinity; limitless; unlimited;
無限哀愁 be extremely grieved;
無限哀傷 be extremely grieved; grief-stricken;
無限哀痛 boundless grief;
無限公司 unlimited company;
無限期 for an indefinite time; indefinite duration; indefinitely;
無限上綱 elevate minor mistakes to the level of principles; exaggerate the mistakes of others to the maximum; raise the matter up and above the level of principle; ultimate escalation of charges; unwarrantedly raise a matter to the level of principle;
直到無限 to infinity;

[無線] cordless; wireless;
無線電 radio; wireless;
~無線電波 radio wave;
~無線電傳真 radioautogram;
~無線電廣播 radio broadcasting;
~無線電技術 radiotechnics;
~無線電人員 radioman;
~無線電台 radio station;
~無線電通訊 telecommunication;
~導波無線電 guided-wave radio;
~航空無線電 aeroradio;
~機載無線電 airborne radio;
無線電話 cordless phone;
無線電鑽 cordless drill;

[無效] in vain; ineffective; invalid; null and void; nullity; of no avail; of no effect; to no effect; useless;
無效技術合同 invalid contract of technology;
無效投資 invalid investment;
無效專利 invalidated patent;
抗議無效 protest in vain;
勸之無效 try in vain to persuade sb;
使無效 deactivate;

[無懈可擊] above reproach; airtight; flawless; hard to fault; impregnable; invulnerable; leave no room for criticism; no flaw; no one can find any fault with; nothing to object to; unable to find any chinks in sb's armour; unassailable; unexceptionable; unimpeachable; watertight; with no chink in one's armour; with no ground for blame; with no weakness to exploit;

[無心] (1) in no mood; not in the mood for; (2) inadvertently; unintentionally; unwittingly;
無心戀戰 have no desire to continue fighting; have no heart for further

fighting;
無心學習 have no heart for study;
無心之失 inadvertent mistake;
無心之言 throwaway lines;
有嘴無心 say what one does not mean;
雲出無心 an inadvertent act; clouds arise without design; sth done without consideration;

[無信] devoid of faith; faithless;
好利無信 prefer benefits at the expense of faith;
言而無信 break one's word; eat one's words; fail to carry out one's promise; fail to keep faith; fail to keep one's word; fail to live up to one's promise; go back on one's word; one's words are not dependable;

[無形] imperceptibly; intangible; invisible; virtually; without taking a form;
無形產權 intangible property;
無形貿易 invisible trade;
無形收入 invisible income;
無形支出 invisible expenditure;
無形中 imperceptibly; invisibly; unknowingly; virtually;
無形資產 intangible assets;

[無須] need not; not necessary; not have to; unnecessary;
無須考慮 nned not take into consideration;
無須細説 it's unnecessary to go into details;

[無涯] boundless; endless; limitless;
一望無涯 boundless; stretch far off into the distance and out of sight; stretching beyond the horizon;

[無煙] smoke-free; smokeless;
無煙工業 smokeless industry;
無煙環境 some-free environment;
無煙區 smoke-free zone;

[無言] have nothing to say;
無言可答 at a loss for word; can say no more and be silent; have no word to answer; have not a word to say in return; nothing to say in reply; speechless with embarrassment;
無言可諱 undeniable;
無言以對 have nothing to say in reply;
低頭無言 bow and be silent; lower one's head and say nothing;
俯首無言 bend one's head in silence;
窘口無言 distressed mouth said nothing;
蔑然無言 not uttering a word;
羞愧無言 be abashed into silence;
啞口無言 be left without an argument; be reduced to silence; be rendered speechless; become speechless as a dumb person; dumb-founded; have nothing to say for oneself; inarticulate; put sb to silence; reduce sb to silence; remain dumb; silent as a dumb month; speechless; strike dumb; tongue-tied;
~駁得啞口無言 argue sb down; jump down sb's throat; leave sb flat; make scores off sb; put sb to silence; reduce sb to silence; shut up;
~吃驚得啞口無言 dumb with astonishment;
~嚇得啞口無言 be struck dumb with horror;

[無顏] have no face to;
無顏見江東父老 have no face to go back home to see one's elders; too ashamed to go back home to see one's elders;
無顏見人 fly from the face of men; have no face to show to any man; not to have the face to appear in public; too ashamed to face anyone;

[無厭] insatiable; never tire of;
貪得無厭 grasping miser; an avaricious man; as greedy as wolf; avaricious; flay a flint; greedy of gain; insatiable of gain; insatiably greedy; one's greed knows no bounds;

[無恙] feel well; in good health; safe; safe and sound; well;

[無業] (1) unemployed; (2) without property;
無業遊民 hobo; vagrant;

[無依] have nobody to rely on;
無依無靠 have no one to rely on;
孑立無依 stand alone with no one to rely on;

[無疑] beyond doubt; undoubtedly; unquestionably;

[無以] cannot be;
無以復加 cannot be surpassed; extremely; in the extreme; in the highest degree; incapable of further increase; not to be surpassed; the best of its kind; the most that can be; to the utmost; utterly; utmost;
無以為報 unable to make any recompense; unable to repay a kindness;

無以為答 unable to answer;
無以為對 do not know how to reply;
無以為繼 hard put to find a sequel;
無以為力 difficult to be of help;
無以為生 have nothing to live on; indigent;
無以自解 cannot extricate oneself from; unable to explain oneself away; unable to give an excuse;
無以自遣 have no way to amuse oneself; hav no way to cheer oneself up; have nothing to divert oneself with; need but do not have some diversion;

[無益] no good; unprofitable; useless; without benefit;
後悔無益 cry over spilled milk; repentance is of no avail;
悔之無益 repentance is of no avail; there is no point in repenting;
空勞無益 labour in vain; make a futile effort; work to no avail;
勤有功，嬉無益 diligence has its reward, but nothing is gained by indolence;
徒悔無益 it is no use repenting of what is done; mere regret is of no use; there's no use crying over spilt milk;
徒勞無益 get nothing for one's pains;
於事無益 it will do no good;

[無異] as good as; not different from; tantamount to; the same as;
無異議 unanimous; without a dissenting voice;

[無意] (1) have no intention; have no interest in; not be inclined to; (2) accidentally; inadvertently; unwittingly;
無意識 automatic; unconscious;
無意於此 not in the vein for it; not interested in that; not keen on it;
無意之中 accidentally; by chance; unaware; unintentionally; unwittingly;
無意中 accidentally; by accident; by chance; unexpectedly; unintentionally;

[無因] (1) without cause; without reason; (2) in no position to; no way to; unable to;

[無庸] need not; no need to; unnecessary;
無庸多言 need scarcely say;
無庸諱言 frank; no need for reticence;
無庸細述 there is no need to go into details; this needn't be related in detail;
無庸置喙 brook no intervention; not allow others to butt in; not be allowed to meddle in;
無庸置疑 admit of no doubt; doubtless; unquestionable;
無庸贅述 it's unnecessary to go into details;

[無用] of no use; otiose; useless;
無用的人 dead duck; dead head; dead loss; dead wood; no-hoper; useless person;
無用鼠輩 just a bunch of softies;
無用武之地 lack scope for their abilities;
無用之才 dead head; dead loss; deadhead; useless person;
空說無用 empty boasts are useless; there's no use flapping about it;
哭也無用 crying is of no avail;
老而無用 old and unfit for anything; outgrow one's usefulness;
全然無用 all to no avail;

[無憂] free from care;
無憂無慮 a free heart; carefree; careless; clear of worry; free from care; freedom from care; high, wide, and handsome; light of heart; light-hearted; lightsome; limpid; on wings; without a worry and care in the world; without sorrow and anxiety;
~無憂無慮的 carefree;
無憂無慮的人 happy-go-lucky person;
高枕無憂 lay aside all anxiety and rest content; rest easy; shake up the pillow and have a good sleep; sit back and relax; sit pretty; sleep peacefully without anxiety; sleep quietly without care; sleep secure; sleep soundly without any worries; without worry;
後顧無憂 free from care;

[無由] have no way of; in no position to; no way to; not in a position to do sth; unable to;

[無有] nothing and something;
無有其匹 matchless; peerless; without equal;
從無到有 develop from nothing; from nonexistence to pass into existence; grow out of nothing; start from scratch;

[無欲則剛] one can be austere if one has no selfish desires;

[無緣] (1) no chance; no opportunity; (2)

without lot; without luck; (3) no way to; unable to;
無緣無故 for no reason at all; for nothing at all; gratuitous; uncalled-for; unprovoked; without cause; without reason; without sake;

[無遠弗屆] no place is too far away to be reached;

[無怨] without enmity
無怨無仇 have no enmity against sb;
勞而無怨 one lays tasks without repining;
死而無怨 die happy; die without a grudge; go to one's death without resentment; harbour no resentment down in the dark depths of the Nine Springs; lay down one's life with no regret;
雖死無怨 although I die I shall not repent; even though I die it will be without regret; I should feel no resentment if I had to die for; If I die now I shall have no regrets; though we die we will not have thoughts of revenge in our hearts;

[無韻詩] blank verse;

[無知] ignorant; not know A from B; not know a great A from a bull's foot;
無知便是福 ignorance is bliss;
無知的人 ignoramus; ignorant person;
無知妄説 ignorant and idle chatter; ignorant nonsense; ignorant twaddle;
無知無識 devoid of the most common knowledge;
無知之徒 ignorant fellow;
鄙陋無知 shallow and ignorant;
部份無知 partial ignorance;
充滿無知 be steeped in ignorance;
出於無知 out of ignorance;
狂妄無知 conceited and ignorant;
蒙昧無知 stupid and ignorant;
懵懵無知 quite ignorant;
年幼無知 ignorance for being young;
完全無知 absolute ignorance; complete ignorance;

[無中生有] baseless; beget sth out of nothing; churn out cock-and-bull stories; come out of thin air; create groundless rumours; create sth out of nothing; fabricate rumours; fabricate rumours out of thin air; fabricated; fictitious; frame up; groundless; invent; make out of the whole cloth; make sth out of nothing; manufacture out of thin air; out of clear sky; out of the empty air; out of thin air; produce sth where nothing should be; pure invention; purely fictitious; sheer fabrication; unfounded; utterly false;
無中不能生有 from nothing, nothing can come; nothing comes of nothing; nothing comes out of the sack but what was in it; of nothing comes nothing; there came nothing out of the sack but what was in it; there come nought out of the sack but what was there;

[無主] confused;
六神無主 be confused; be perplexed; be struck all of a heap; in a state of utter stupefaction; lose one's presence of mind;

[無足為奇] no wonder that...; not to be wondered at;

[無罪] guiltless; innocent; not guilty;
無罪判決 acquittal;
無罪釋放 set a person free with a verdict of "not guilty";
宣判無罪 acquittal;

百無 not one out of a hundred;
別無 have no...but;
不無 not without;
毫無 by no means; devoid of; not in the least; without the least;
家無 a family cannot;
絕無 absolutely not;
目無 show no respect to...;
南無 be converted to the dharma;
人無 a person cannot;
身無 have not one's own;
手無 without in one's hands;
萬無 absolutely not; never; not the least;
胸無 nothing inside oneself;
虛無 emptiness; nihility; nothingness; void;
一無 not in the least;
有無 have and have-not;

wu

【蜈】 centipede;

[蜈蚣] centipede;
蜈蚣草 centipede grass;

wu

【蕪】 (1) luxuriant growth of weeds; (2) decayed or rotten vegetation; (3)

confused; in disorder; mixed up; (4) neglected, as land; waste;
［蕪鄙］ unsystematic and meagre;
［蕪駁］ confused; disorderly; mixed-up;
［蕪詞］ superfluous words;
［蕪累］ mixed-up and superfluous;
［蕪俚］ coarse and vulgar;
［蕪雜］ in a jumble; miscellaneous; mixed and disorderly;
蕪雜之詞 ambiguous words;

繁蕪 loaded with unnecessary words; wordy;
荒蕪 (be left) abandoned; (lie) waste;
平蕪 open grassland;

wu

【鼯】 flying squirrel;
［鼯鼠］ flying squirrel;

wu³

wu

【五】 (1) fifth; five; (2) Chinese musical notation;
［五八］ five and eight;
五行八作 different trades and callings; small trademen of various kinds; various small tradesmen;
［五彩］ (1) the five colours of blue, yellow, red, white and black; (2) colourful; multicoloured;
五彩斑斕 a riot of colour; an assemblage of colours; blazing with colour; colourful; in amazing colours; multicoloured; pavonian; pavonine;
五彩繽紛 a riot of colour; blazing with colour; colourful; multicoloured;
五彩碎紙 confetti;
~撒五彩碎紙 throw confetti;
［五分］ five;
五分錢 five cents;
五分制 five points scale;
五分鐘 five minutes;
~五分鐘熱度 by fits and starts; short-lived enthusiasm; the basin is but a blaze;
［五更］ fifth watch of the night;
［五穀］ five grains;
五穀不分 cannot tell corn from turnips; cannot tell wheat from beans – ignorant of common things; not to know pulse from corn; not to know the difference between the five grains; unable to distinguish one kind of grain from another;
五穀豐登 a bumper grain harvest; a golden harvest; an abundant harvest of all food crops; good harvests; the crops are abundant;
［五官］ (1) the five sense organs – ears, eyes, lips, nose and tongue; (2) facial features;
五官不正 irregular features; one's features are not proper;
五官端正 have regular features; well-featured;
［五花］ (1) streaky; (2) streaky pork;
五花八門 a motley of variety of; all kinds of; all sorts and kinds; all sorts of; in many different ways; many and manifold; multifarious; of a wide variety; rich in variety;
五花大綁 tie sb neck and heels; tie sb's hands behind his back with a rope that is looped round his neck;
五花肉 streaky pork;
［五金］ (1) the five metals; (2) alloy; hardware; metals in general;
五金店 hardware store;
［五里霧中］ all at sea; be lost in mystery; be tossed on an ocean of doubts; completely at a loss; in a fog; utter bewilderment;
如墮五里霧中 as if lost in a thick fog; be tossed on an ocean of doubts; utterly mystified;
在五里霧中 in a haze;
墜入五里霧中 be plunged into a dense fog; be tossed on an ocean of doubts; completely lost at sea;
［五六］ five and six;
説五道六 make thoughtless comments;
挑五嫌六 pick and choose;
王五趙六 any man in the street;
［五倫］ five human relationships;
五倫觀念 the notion of the five cardinal relationships (in Chinese culture);
［五內］ five viscera – heart, lungs, liver, kidneys, and spleen;
五內沸然 become feverish and restless;
五內俱焚 be rent with grief; be stricken with grief and mortification; feel extremely upset with sorrow;
五內俱裂 as if one's bowels have been cut

through; feel one's five internal organs torn with pain;
五內如焚 grief-stricken; one's heart is rent with grief; one's heart is torn by anxiety; very anxious;
深銘五內 profoundly grateful;
[五日京兆] constant shift of office; holding office only for a brief period; not expecting to remain long in office;
[五三] five and three;
五局三勝制 best of five games; three out of five sets;
[五色] five colours;
五色斑爛 riot of colours;
五色椒 red pepper;
五色無主 become confused and turn pale;
目迷五色 be dazzled by a riot of colours; be bewildered by a complicated situation;
[五十] fifty;
五十步笑百步 one who retreats fifty paces mocks one who retreats a hundred — different in degrees but the same in essence; Satan reproves sin; the frying-pan said to the kettle: Avaunt, black brows; the pot calling the kettle black; the pot calls the kettle black;
~以五十步笑一百步 the pot calls the kettle black; those who retreat fifty paces are to laugh at those who retreat a hundred paces;
五光十色 all sorts of colours; bright with many colours; in fanciful colours; kaleidoscopic; motley colours; multicoloured; multifarious; of all kinds; of great variety; parismatic; resplendent with variegated colouration;
[五世其昌] may the family prosper five generations running; may you be blessed with many children and grandchildren; may you prosper for give generations;
[五體] the five body constituents — tendon, vessel, muscle, hair and skin, bone;
五體投地 admire sb from the bottom of one's heart; kneel at the feet of; prostrate oneself in admiration; prostrate oneself on the ground; throw oneself down at sb's feet;
[五味] the five flavours — sweet, sour, bitter, pungent, and salty;
[五絃琴] banjo;
[五線譜] musical score using the staff notation; staff;
[五香] a kind of blended spice used in Chinese cooking;
[五月] (1) May; (2) fifth month of the lunar calendar;
五月節 Dragon Boat Festival;
[五嶽] Five Great Mountains;
五嶽名山 the Five Great Mountains;

第五 fifth;
二百五 (1) idiot; rash person; scatterbrain; (2) smatter;
禮拜五 Friday;
破五 fifth of the first lunar month (shops did not start doing business until after that day);
十五 (1) fifteen; (2) ten and five;
星期五 Friday;
一毛五 fifteen cents;
一退六二五 deny all responsibility; evade all responsibility;

wu

【午】 (1) high noon; midday; noon; (2) a surname;
[午安] good afternoon;
[午餐] lunch; luncheon;
午餐便當 packed lunch;
午餐館 lunch counter;
午餐櫃枱 lunch counter;
午餐盒飯 lunch box;
午餐券 luncheon voucher;
午餐肉 luncheon meat;
午餐時間 lunch break; lunch hour; lunchtime;
午餐休息時間 lunch break;
午餐飲料 lunchtime drink;
午餐約會 lunch date;
吃午餐 eat lunch; have lunch; lunch;
~請人出去吃午餐 take sb out to lunch;
~外出吃午餐 go out for lunch; go out to lunch;
~休息吃午餐 break for lunch;
~一起吃午餐 do lunch;
工作午餐 working lunch;
盒裝午餐 box lunch; packed lunch;
簡便午餐 light lunch;
沒有免費的舉止 there's no free lunch;
商務午餐 business lunch;

~談商務午餐 power lunch;
星期天午餐 Sunday lunch;
學校午餐 school lunch;
早午餐 brunch;
自備午餐 packed lunch;
自助午餐 lunch buffet;
~半自助午餐 semi lunch buffet;
做午餐 make lunch;

[午飯] midday meal; lunch;
午飯高峰時間 lunchtime rush;
吃午飯 have lunch;
~留下來吃午飯 stay for lunch;
有四道菜的午飯 a four-course lunch;

[午後] afternoon;
[午覺] afternoon nap; noontime snooze;
[午前] before noon; forenoon;
[午睡] afternoon nap; noontime snooze;
[午休] afternoon nap; midday rest; noon break; noontime rest; take a nap after lunch;
[午宴] lunch; luncheon;
歡迎午宴 welcoming lunch;

[午夜] midnight;
午夜十二點 12 midnight;

傍午 near noontime; shortly before noon;
端午 Dragon Boat Festival (the fifth day of the fifth lunar month);
過午 afternoon;
上午 forenoon; morning;
亭午 noon; midday;
庭午 (1) noon; (2) the bright moon in the sky;
下午 afternoon;
嚮午 midday; noon; toward noon;
正午 high noon; noon;
中午 high noon; midday; noon; noonday;
卓午 midnoon;
子午 meridian;

wu

【伍】 (1) military unit of five soldiers; (2) a surname; (3) associate with a person; (4) five;

隊伍 (1) army; troops; (2) contingent; ranks;
行伍 the ranks;
落伍 drop behind; fall behind the ranks; strangle;
配伍 compatibility of medicines;
入伍 join the army;
退伍 leave the army; retire from active military service;
為伍 associate with;

wu

【仵】 opposing; wrong;

[仵作] coroner; post-mortem examiner;

wu

【忤】 (1) disobedient; recalcitrant; stubbornly defiant; uncongenial; (2) blunder; mistake; wrong;

[忤逆] (1) recalcitrant; stubborn defiance; (2) disobedient to one's parents;
[忤視] look at with a jaundiced eye; look defiantly at;
[忤物] at oods with others; cannot get along with people; disagree with others;

wu

【迕】 (1) meet; (2) oppose;

[迕逆] (1) go against one's superiors; (2) delinquent in filial piety;
[迕意] oppose one's will;

wu

【武】 (1) force; military; (2) connected with boxing skill, swordsplay; (3) fierce; valiant; (4) fight; force; (5) a surname;

[武備] armaments and military provisions; defense preparation;
[武打] martial arts;
[武德] soldierly virtues;
[武斷] arbitrary decision; assertive;
武斷行事 execute business dogmatically;
武斷專橫 act arbitrarily;
脾氣武斷 of dogmatic temper;
遇事武斷 dogmatize on things;

[武夫] person of great physical strength;
一介武夫 rough-neck; warrior;

[武官] military attaché; military officer;
空軍武官 air attaché;
使館陸軍武官 military attaché;

[武力] (1) force; (2) military force; military might;
武力干涉 interfere through the use of force;
武力解決 settle differences by force; solution through the use of force;
武力威脅 threat of force;
武力鎮壓 armed suppression;
使用武力 betake oneself to arms;
訴諸武力 appeal to arms; go to arms; resort to the use of force;
通過武力 by force;

[武林] circle of boxers;
[武器] armament; armature; arms; weaponry; weapons;
武器化 weaponization;
武器交易 arms deal; weapons deal;
武器試驗 weapon test;
~武器試驗場 weapon proving ground;
暗藏武器 conceal weapons;
常規武器 conventional weapons;
導彈武器 guided missile armature; missile armament;
發射武器 fire a weapon;
反潛武器 antisubmarine weapon;
反魚雷武器 anti-torpedo armature;
放下武器 ground arms; lay down arms; throw down one's weapon;
輔助武器 backup armature;
攻擊性武器 offensive weapon;
航空武器 air armament;
核武器 nuclear weapon; nuke;
~戰略核武器 strategic nuclear weapon;
揮舞武器 brandish a weapon;
火箭武器 rocket armament;
進攻性武器 attack armature;
空戰武器 air-to-air armature;
攜帶武器 bear arms; carry arms;
佩帶武器 carry side arms;
輕武器 small arms;
殺傷武器 antipersonnel weapon;
生化武器 biochemical weapon;
生物武器 biological weapons;
使用武器 use a weapon;
隨身武器 side arms;
一種武器 a weapon;
原子武器 atomic weapon;
遠射武器 standoff weapon;
致命武器 deadly weapon; lethal weapon;
重武器 heavy armament; heavy weapons;
[武士] knight; warrior;
武士俑 figurine of warrior;
[武術] art of defence; chivalry; martial arts;
武俠片 swordsmen film;
武俠小說 martial art stories;
[武藝] fighting skills;
武藝超群 extremely skilful in martial arts;
武藝出眾 one's fighting skill is far above that of common men; one's military arts excel all;
武藝高強 excel in martial arts; high skilled in military drill;
[武裝] (1) arm; armed; (2) military uniform;
武裝部隊 armed forces;
武裝衝突 armed clash; armed conflict; open hostilities;
武裝反抗 up in arms;
武裝分子 armed force;
武裝干涉 intervene by arms;
武裝集團 army body;
武裝力量 armed forces;
~武裝力量建設 armed forces build-up;
武裝起義 rise in arms;
武裝組織 armed groups;
重新武裝 rearm;
全身武裝 be armed from top to toe;

比武 demonstrate fighting skills in a tournament; joust;
動武 come to blows; resort to forces; start a fight; use force;
黷武 bellicose; militaristic; warlike;
繼武 follow close on sb's heels;
練武 do weapon practice; practise martial arts;
尚武 emphasize military affairs; set great store by martial qualities;
神武 intelligent and courageous; wise and powerful;
威武 might; mighty; power; powerful;
玄武 (1) (of Taoism) God of the Northern Sky; (2) tortoise;
演武 practise traditional martial arts;
英武 of soldierly bearing; valiant;
勇武 brave; valiant;
用武 display one's abilities or talents; resort to force;
踵武 follow in sb's footsteps; imitate;

wu

【侮】 bully; disgrace; humiliate; insult;
[侮罵] insult with words;
[侮慢] haughty and rude; slight; treat disrespectfully;
[侮蔑] despise; disgrace; scorn; slight;
[侮弄] make a fool of;
[侮辱] humiliate; humiliation; insult; put sb to shame; subject sb to indignities;
當眾侮辱 offer an affront to; open insult; put an affront upon a person;
甘受侮辱 sit down under insults;
各種侮辱 all sorts of indignities;
極端侮辱 crowning indignity; final indignity; ultimate indignity;
忍受侮辱 pocket the affront;
受到侮辱 be affronted by; suffer an

affront;
~覺得受到侮辱 feel affronted;
[侮上] arrogant to one's superior;

欺侮 browbeat; bully; humiliate; insult; play the bully; ridicule; treat sb high-handedly;
輕侮 insult; contempt; scorn;
外侮 external aggression; foreign aggression;
狎侮 impolite to; show improper intimacy with; treat with disrespect;
禦侮 resist foreign aggression;

wu
【牾】 (1) oppose; (2) gore;

牴牾 conflict; contradict;

wu
【娬】 attractive; lovely;
[娬媚] very attractive;

wu
【摀】 (1) conceal; cover; hide; (2) put into an air-tight container;
[摀蓋] (1) cover up; hide; keep secret; (2) disguise; masquerade;

wu
【舞】 (1) dance; prance; (2) move about as in a dance; (3) dance with sth in one's hands; (4) brandish; wave; wield;
[舞伴] dancing partner;
[舞弊] embezzlement; engage in embezzlement; fraudulent practices; malpractice; misconduct;
舞弊營私 indulge in malpractices and obtain private advantages;
徇私舞弊 indulge in malpractices for the benefit of relatives or friends;
營私舞弊 practise corruption for selfish ends;
[舞步] dance steps; steps;
一套舞步 a dance routine;
[舞場] ballroom; dance hall;
[舞池] dance floor; dancing floor;
[舞蹈] (1) dancing; (2) dance;
舞蹈病 chorea;
~敬禮舞蹈病 chorea salutante;
~偏身舞蹈病 chorea dimidiata;
~妊娠性舞蹈病 chorea gravidarum;
~癱瘓性舞蹈病 chorea mollis;
舞蹈家 dancer;
舞蹈教師 dancing master;
舞蹈狂 choromania;
舞蹈演員 dancer; hoofer;
舞蹈音樂 dance music;
舞蹈症 chorea;
急性舞蹈症 acute chorea;
老年性舞蹈症 senile chorea;
偏側舞蹈症 hemilateral chorea;
偏身舞蹈症 chorea dimidiata;
偏癱後舞蹈症 posthemiplegic chorea;
癱瘓性舞蹈症 paralytic chorea;
跳躍性舞蹈症 dancing chorea;
先天性舞蹈症 chorea;
心臟型舞蹈症 chorea cordis;
夜發性舞蹈症 chorea nocturna;
古典舞蹈 classical dance;
民間舞蹈 folk dance;
排練舞蹈 rehearse for a dance;
[舞動] brandish; wave;
[舞歌] dance song;
[舞會] ball; dancing party;
參加舞會 go to a dancing party;
化裝舞會 fancy dress ball; masked ball; masquerade ball;
假面舞會 masked ball;
舉行舞會 give a dance;
組織舞會 organize dances;
[舞姬] dancing girl;
[舞技] dancing skills;
[舞劇] dance drama;
舞劇片 ballet film;
舞劇團 dance drama troupe;
舞劇院 ballet theatre; theatre of dance drama;
[舞男] gigolo;
[舞弄] brandish; wave; wield;
[舞女] dance-hostess; dancing girl;
[舞曲] dance music;
創作舞曲 compose dance music;
兩步舞曲 two-step;
演奏舞曲 play dances;
[舞獅] lion dance;
[舞術] art of dancing;
[舞台] arena; stage;
舞台工作人員 stage hand;
舞台後 offstage;
舞台技師 stage-technologist;
~主任舞台技師 stage-technologist-in-charge;
舞台監督 stage manager;
舞台經驗 stage experience;
舞台劇 stage play;

舞台兩側 wings;
舞台美術 scenic ornamental painting;
舞台前部 downstage; proscenium;
舞台設計 stage design; stage set;
舞台效果 stage effect;
舞台藝術 stagecraft; theatrical art;
舞台照明 stage illumination;
舞台指示 stage direction;
舞台裝置 stage setting;
搬上舞台 be presented on the stage; present to the stage; stage;
~重新搬上舞台 restaging;
競技場式舞台 arena-type stage;
上舞台 come on stage;
旋轉舞台 revolving stage;
走上舞台 go on stage;

[舞廳] ballroom; dance hall;

[舞文] fiddle at writing;
舞文弄法 juggle with the law; pervert the law by playing with legal phraseology;
舞文弄墨 confuse facts by means of writing; engage in phrase-mongering; fiddle at writing; juggle with words; play on words; play with the pen; show off literary skill; spread oneself; write in a showy style;
~舞文弄墨，搖唇鼓舌 word-mongering, tongue-wagging;

[舞榭] halls for the performance of dances;
舞榭歌臺 dance halls and song-filled pavilions; entertainment setups;

芭蕾舞 ballet;
伴舞 dancing partner;
編舞 (1) choreographer; (2) choreography;
抃舞 cheer and dance; make merry;
冰舞 dancing on skates;
草裙舞 Hawaiian dance; hula-hula;
茶舞 tea dance;
單人舞 solo dance;
獨舞 solo dance;
方舞 square dance;
飛舞 dance in the air; flutter;
鋼管舞 pole dancing;
歌舞 song and dance;
鼓舞 brace; embolden; fortify; gladden; hearten; impulse; infuse; inspire; kindle; nerve; support; sustain;
紅綢舞 red silk dance;
呼拉舞 hula;
狐步舞 foxtrot;
華爾滋舞 waltz;
揮舞 brandish; wave; wield;
集體舞 group dancing;
交際舞 ballroom dancing; social dance; social dancing;
肯肯舞 cancan;
兩步舞 two-step;
龍舞 dragon dance;
扭擺舞 gump 'n' grind; twist;
扭臂舞 gump 'n' grind;
飄舞 dance in the wind;
起舞 (1) rise and dance; (2) be excited with joy;
森巴舞 samba;
扇舞 fan dance;
蛇舞 snake dance;
獅子舞 lion dance;
雙人舞 a dance for two persons;
四人舞 dance for four people;
太陽舞 sun dance;
踢踏舞 step dance; tap dance;
踢舞 tittup;
跳舞 boogie; dance; shake a leg; toe and heel;
土風舞 country dancing; folk dance;
脱衣舞 strip tease;
掀舞 churning and pounding;
艷舞 enticing dances; striptease; voluptuous;
秧歌舞 yangko dance (in China);
腰鼓舞 drum dance; waist drum dance;
搖擺舞 rock and roll;
佾舞 (1) a dance to celebrate Confucius' birthday; (2) rows of ceremonial dancers;
戰舞 war dance;
柱舞 pole dance;
桌上舞 table dance;

wu

【憮】 disappointed; regretful;
[憮然] disappointedly; regretfully;

wu

【廡】 (1) corridor; hallway; (2) (of vegetation) dense or luxuriant;

wu

【鵡】 parrot;

鸚鵡 parrot;

wu⁴

wu

【兀】 (1) cut off the feet; (2) high and flat on the top; (3) this; (4) ignorant-looking;
[兀立] stand upright;

［兀自］ still;
兀自一人 all alone by oneself;
［兀坐］ sit upright;

涅兀 unstable; unsteady;
突兀 (1) abrupt; sudden; unexpected; (2) lofty towering;

wu
【勿】 do not; never; not;
［勿論］ let alone; regardless of;
格殺勿論 capture and summarily execute; kill on the spot with the authority of the law; kill with lawful authority; no matter if killed;
［勿念］ do not worry;
［勿藥］ recover from illness;
勿藥之喜 the pleasure of taking no more drugs;
得沾勿藥 happily recovered from illness; recover from illness in good time;
喜沾勿藥 no more medicine is required; one will recover soon from illness;
早沾勿藥 get well very soon; wish sb a speedy recovery; wish sb an early recovery from illness;

wu
【戊】 fifth of the ten celestial stems;
［戊夜］ predawn hours;

wu
【阢】 apprehensive; uneasy;
［阢隉］ intranquil; jittery; uneasy; unpeaceful;

wu
【物】 (1) matter; thing; (2) content; substance;
［物必有偶］ every jack has his jill; everything has a counterpart;
［物產］ natural resources; produce; products;
［物腐蟲生］ germs grow in decayed things; ruin befalls only on those who have weaknesses; worms breed in decaying matter;
［物阜］ products abound;
物阜民豐 products abound and the people live in plenty;
物阜民康 goods are in plentiful supply and the people are happy; goods overflow and the people are happy;
民康物阜 goods overflow and the people are happy; people are healthy and thing plentiful;
［物故］ dead; deceased; die; pass away;
物故身亡 pass away;
［物候學］ phenology;
［物華］ (1) essence of things; (2) beautiful scene;
物華天寶 good products from the earth are nature's treasures;
［物換星移］ change of the seasons; changes in worldly affairs; things change with the passing of years;
［物極必反］ a thing negates itself when developed to the extreme; a thing turns into its opposite if pushed too far; as soon as a thing reaches its extremity, it reverses its course; change comes on at the heels of fortune; extremities last not always; fortune is like glass it breaks when it is brightest; no extreme will hold long; once a certain limit is reached, a change in the opposite direction is inevitable; the last drop makes the cup run over; things always reverse themselves after reaching an extreme; things go in the opposite direction when they become too extreme; things turn into their opposites when they reach the extreme; things which have reached their extremes turn into their opposites; things will develop in the opposite direction when they become extreme; when a thing reaches its limit it turns round; when sth reaches its limit there is bound to be a reaction;
［物價］ commodity prices; prices;
物價昂貴 exorbitant price;
物價變化 price change;
物價波動 price fluctuation;
物價補貼 subsidies for commodity prices;
物價改革 price reform;
物價局 bureau of price;
物價控制 price control; price fixing;
物價猛漲 soaring prices;
物價偏高 prices are rather high;
物價上漲指數 index of price rising;
物價太高 prices are too high;
～抱怨物價太高 complain about high prices;

物價穩定 price stability; stability of commodity prices;
物價指數 price index;
~零售物價指數 index of retail prices;
物價總指數 general price index;
高昂的物價 alpine prices;
哄抬物價 whoop up the price;
降低物價 bring down the price;
提高物價 mark up prices;
調節物價 regulate prices;
穩定物價 stabilize prices;
壓低物價 force down the price;

[物件] articles; things;
小物件 doohickey;

[物盡其用] let all things serve their proper purpose; make the best use of everything; the utility of things should be exhausted; top material resources to the full; turn everything to good account;

[物競天擇] natural selection; survival of the fittest;

[物鏡] objective;
多透鏡物鏡 poly-lens objective;
黏合物鏡 cemented objective;
去象差物鏡 anastigmatic objective;
相物鏡 phase objective;
消色差物鏡 achromatic objective;

[物理] (1) innate laws of things; (2) physics;
物理變化 physical changes;
物理力學 physical mechanics;
物理量 physical quantity;
物理學 physics;
~半導體物理學 semiconductive physics;
~超聲物理學 ultrasonic physics;
~磁泡物理學 bubble physics;
~大氣物理學 atmospheric physics;
高層大氣物理學 aeronomy;
~等離子體物理學 plasma physics;
~低溫物理學 low temperature physics;
~地殼構造物理學 tectonophysics;
~地球物理學 geophysics;
採礦地球物理學 mining geophysics;
海洋地球物理學 marine geophysics;
陸上地球物理學 terrestrial geophysics;
探測地球物理學 exploration geophysics;
天文地球物理學 astrogeophysics;
~電物理學 electrophysics;
~電真空物理學 electro-vacuum physics;
~高能物理學 high energy physics;
~固體物理學 solid state physics;
~核子物理學 nuclear physics;
~化學物理學 chemical physics;
~航空物理學 aerophysics;
~激光物理學 laser physics;
~近代物理學 modern physics;
~經典物理學 classical physics;
~理論物理學 theoretical physics;
~粒子物理學 particle physics;
~量子物理學 quantum physics;
~生物物理學 biophysics;
~實驗物理學 experimental physics;
~太陽物理學 solar physics;
~天體物理學 astrophysics;
~統計物理學 statistical physics;
~相對論物理學 relativistic physics;
~應用物理學 applied physics;
~原子核物理學 physics of the atomic nucleus;
~原子物理學 atomic physics;
~雲物理學 cloud physics;
物理治療法 physiotherapy; physical therapy;
物理治療師 physical therapist; physiotherapist;
高分子物理 polymer physics;
化學物理 chemical physics; chemisophysics;
數學物理 mathematical physics;

[物離鄉貴] commodity commands a higher price where it is not grown;

[物料] materials and supplies;

[物流] logistics;

[物莫如新，友莫如故] everything is good when new, but friendship is good when old;

[物品] article; goods;
擺放物品 house goods;
貴重物品 valuable article; valuables;
易爛物品 perishable article;

[物色] choose; look for; scout for; seek out;
物色人才 look for qualified persons; seek out talented persons;

[物傷其類] all beings grieve for their fellow beings; everyone feels for his fellow creatures; like feels for like; like mourns over the death of like;

[物體] body; substance; object;

[物外] beyond the physical world;
超然物外 above worldly considerations; hold aloof from the world; stay away

from the scene of contention;
游心物外 let the mind soar free from the material things;

[物望] object of popular admiration;

[物我兩忘] become unaware of both the self and the outside world;

[物業] property;
物業管理 property management;
物業註冊 property registration;
~物業註冊宗數 number of property registration;
~住宅物業註冊 residential property registration;
海外物業 overseas properties;

[物以類聚] all things of one species come together; birds of a feather flock together; like attracts like; like begets like; like draws like; like draws to like; people of similar taste and habits like to associate with one another; things of one kind come together;
物以類聚，人以群分 birds of a feather flock together; things of a kind come together; people of a mind fall into the same group; things of one species come together; different kinds of people form different groups;

[物以稀為貴] a thing is valued if it is rare; a thing is valued in proportion to its rarity; objects are valued because of their rarity; the rarer it is, the more it is worth; the worth of a thing is best known by the want of it; when a thing is scarce, it is precious;

[物議] public censure; public criticisms;
物議沸騰 popular criticisms are boiling;
免遭物議 so as not to incur criticism by the masses; so as to avoid public censure;
有招物議 incur criticism by the masses; invite public criticism; make a public censure;

[物慾] craving for material things; material desires; worldly desires;

[物證] material evidence;

[物質] material; matter; substance;
物質報酬 material reward;
物質波 matter wave;
物質財富 material wealth;
物質詞 physical word;
物質刺激 material incentive;
物質回報 material rewards;
物質建設 material development;
物質獎勵 material reward;
物質結構 material construction;
物質利益 material benefit;
物質名詞 material noun;
物質生活 material affair; material life; physical life;
物質市場 materials market;
物質文化 material culture;
物質文明 material civilization;
物質享受 creature comforts;
物質意義 physical meaning;
物質主義 materialism;
暗物質 dark matter; dark substance;
反物質 antimatter;
非結晶物質 amorphous substance;
非生物物質 abiotic substance;
碱性物質 alkaline substance;
抗爆物質 antidetonating substance;
親兩性物質 amphoipathic substance;

[物種] species;
物種屏障 species barrier;
物種學 speciology;
同源物種 allied species;

[物主] owner;
物主代詞 possessive pronoun;
物主形容詞 possessive adjective;

[物資] goods and materials; supplies;
積壓物資 stockpiled goods;
一堆物資 a heap of materials;

愛物 (1) cherished object; (2) love all creatures;
傲物 haughty; insolent; overbearing; rude;
百物 all things;
寶物 treasure;
爆炸物 explosive;
杯中物 the thing in the cup — wine; alcoholic drinks;
博物 natural science;
財物 belongings; property;
參照物 reference;
產物 outcome; product; result;
長物 anything that may be spared; surplus;
沉澱物 precipitate; sediment;
沉積物 deposit; sediment;
池中物 man of mediocre abilities;
寵物 animal companion; pet; pet animal;
出版物 publication;
儲藏物 hoardings;
儲物 storage;

W

醇化物 alcoholate;
刺激物 stimulant; stimulus;
大人物 great personage; important person;
代謝物 metabolite;
等價物 equivalent; objects of equal value;
地物 surface features;
動物 beast; animal; zoon;
毒物 poison; poisonous substance;
讀物 reading material;
睹物 see things;
對立物 antithesis; opposite;
二硫化物 bisulphide;
二氧化物 dioxide;
發物 stimulating food, such as mutton, fish, shrimps, etc.;
反射物 reflector;
廢物 dreck; dud; garbage; good-for-nothing; rubbish; trash; waste material; waste substance; waster;
分泌物 secretion;
風物 scenery;
福物 sacrificial wine and meat;
氟化物 fluoride;
高聚物 high polymer;
公物 public property;
汞化物 mercuride;
供物 offerings;
購物 shop;
古物 ancient objects; antiquities; archaeology; curio;
穀物 cereal; grain;
怪物 (1) eccentric person; (2) monster; monstrosity;
鬼物 ghost; spirit;
洪積物 diluvium;
喉異物 foreign body of larynx;
化合物 chemical compound;
穢物 filth;
混合物 mixture compound;
貨物 cargo; commodity; goods; merchandize; stock of goods;
及物 transitive;
見物 see things;
僭建物 illegal structure;
建築物 building; structure;
景物 scenery;
靜物 still life;
舊物 (1) original territory of the nation; (2) things left behind by the ancestors, esp. decrees and regulations and cultural relics;
聚合物 polymer;
刊物 journal; periodical; publication;
殼狀物 hoose; husk;
可燃物 combustibles;
礦物 mineral;
冷凝物 condensate;
禮物 gift; present;
獵獲物 bag;
獵物 bag; capture; chase; prey;
磷化物 phosphide;
硫化物 sulphide;
鹵化物 halide; halogenide;
絡合物 complex compound;
氯化物 chloride;
媒介物 intermediate; intermedium;
名物 name and description of a thing;
橈萬物 scatter things here and there;
內寄生物 endoparasite;
釀熱物 ferment material;
凝結物 coagulum;
農作物 agricultural products; crop; plant;
濃縮物 concentrate;
棄物 discarded useless things; trash;
器物 artifact; implement; instrument; tool; utensils;
氫化物 hydride;
氫氧化物 hydroxide;
氰化物 cyanide;
情物 love token;
殼物 shellish in general;
人物 (1) character; (2) figure; personage;
三氧化物 trioxide;
砷化物 arsenical; arsenide;
神物 (1) phenomenon; prodigy; wonder; (2) deity; immortal; supernatural being;
滲出物 ooze;
生物 (1) animate object; living things; (2) biology; (3) organism;
生長物 product; resultant;
失物 lost article; lost property;
什物 articles for daily use; odds and ends;
食物 ailment; eatable; edible; food; foodstuff; provision;
實物 (1) material object; (2) entity; matter;
事物 object; thing;
飾物 (1) articles for personal adornment; (2) decoration ornaments;
書物 books and other things concerned with books;
庶物 all the things of the universe;
水合物 hydrate;
水化物 hydrate;
隨葬物 burial articles; funeral objects;
縮合物 condensation compound;

碳化物 carbide;
糖化物 saccharide;
銻化物 stibnide;
天物 products of nature;
同化物 assimilator;
同系物 homologue;
土物 local product;
外寄生物 ectoparasite;
外物 material comfort;
玩物 plaything; toy;
萬物 all things on earth; all things under the sun; everything in the world;
翫物 toys;
唯物 materialistic;
微生物 microbe; micro-organism;
文物 cultural relic; historical relic;
污染物 contaminant; pollutant;
污物 ordure;
無機物 inorganic substance; inorganic matter;
無生物 inanimate object; nonliving matter;
無物 devoid of content;
忤物 at odds with others; cannot get along with people; disagree with others;
小人物 nobody unimportant person;
信物 authenticating object; token;
性玩物 sex object;
溴化物 bromide;
壓倉物 ballast;
衍生物 derivative;
掩蔽物 screen;
陽物 penis;
氧化物 oxide;
妖物 evil spirit; monster;
藥物 drugs; medicament; medicine; pharmaceuticals;
一物 one thing;
衣物 clothing and other articles of daily use;
遺物 relics of the deceased; remains;
易燃物 combustibles; inflammables;
異物 (1) extremely valuable object; rare treasure; (2) peculiar thing; strange thing; uncommon thing; (3) the dead;
英物 outstanding figure;
尤物 (1) uncommon person; (2) rare beauty; woman of extraordinary beauty;
雜物 miscellaneous items; odds and ends;
宰物 able to manage affairs;
贓物 (1) bribes; (2) booty; loot; plunder; spoils; stolen goods;
髒物 foul;
造物 Nature; the divine force that create the universe;
長物 belongings; property;
障礙物 barrier; entanglement; obstacle;
遮蔽物 defilade;
遮蓋物 cover;
珍物 (1) treasures; valuables; (2) delicacies;
證物 exhibit;
織物 fabric; textiles;
植物 flora; plant; vegetation;
贅物 sth superfluous; sth useless;
濁物 blockhead; bloody fool; idiot;
作物 (1) crop; cropper; (2) literary composition;

wu

【悟】 awake to; become aware of; comprehend; realize;

［悟禪］ come to understand the principle of Chan;

［悟道］ awake to truth;

［悟性］ comprehension; the power of understanding;

參悟 understand from meditation;
徹悟 come to a complete awakening;
澈悟 realize completely; understand thoroughly;
頓悟 epiphany; insight;
悔悟 awake from sin; realize one's error and show repentance; repent;
會悟 realize a truth;
解悟 come to understand; realize;
憬悟 come to see the truth; wake up to reality;
覺悟 (1) awareness; consciousness; understanding; (2) become aware of; become politically awakened; come to understand;
領悟 comprehend; grasp; understand;
神悟 marvelously quick understanding;
率悟 quick in understanding; realize quickly;
曉悟 realize (truth, mistake, etc.);
省悟 come to realize the truth, error, etc.; wake up to reality;
惺悟 awake to the truth; realize;
醒悟 come to realize the truth, error, etc.; wake up to reality;
玄悟 profound understanding of an abstruse theory;
穎悟 (of a teenager) bright; clever;

wu

【務】 (1) must; necessary; sure to; (2) affairs; business; duty; (3) attend to; be engaged in; devote one's efforts to; strive after;

［務本］ attend to fundamentals;
［務必］ be sure to; by all means; must;
［務農］ be engaged in agriculture;
［務期必克］ sure to win;
［務求］ strive for;
［務實］ deal with concrete matters relating to work;
務實派 group of doing concrete matters;
務實作風 practical style of work;
崇本務實 do things in a solid manner;
［務使］ ensure; make sure;
［務希］ please be sure to;
務希見諒 earnestly hoping that you will forgive me; I sincerely hope you'll excuse me;
［務正］ attend to one's proper duties;

報務 work concerning telegraphing and radio operation;
本務 one's real duty;
財務 financial affairs;
常務 day-to-day business; routine;
乘務 service;
黨務 Party affairs; Party work;
防務 defence; matters pertaining to defence;
服務 give service to; serve;
港務 port administrative affairs;
公務 official business; public affairs;
關務 customs matters;
國務 affairs of the state; national affairs;
航務 navigational matters;
會務 club affairs; committee affairs;
急務 urgent task;
家務 domestic service; household chores; household duties; housework;
教務 educational administration;
警務 police affairs; police service; policing;
劇務 (1) stage management; (2) stage manager;
軍務 military affairs; military task;
勞務 labour service; personal service; physical labour;
內務 home affairs; internal affairs;
票務 ticketing;
僑務 affairs concerning nationals living abroad;
勤務 (1) duty; service; (2) odd-jobman;
任務 assignment; duties; job; mission; responsibility; task;
商務 business affairs; commercial affairs;
時務 current affairs; trend of the times;
世務 worldly affairs;
事物 (1) general affairs; (2) routine; work;
樞務 state affairs; the duty of the premier;
庶務 (1) business matters; general affairs; (2) person in charge of business matters;
稅務 affairs pertaining to taxation; tax administration;
俗務 chores; everyday matters; worldly cares;
碎務 chores;
瑣務 trifling matters;
特務 spy; secret agent; special task;
外務 (1) external affairs; foreign affairs; (2) matters outside one's job;
細務 trifling matters;
校務 administrative affairs of a school or college;
洋務 foreign affairs; foreign business;
要務 important business; urgent business;
業務 business activities; official functions; professional work; vocational work;
醫務 medical matters; medical service;
義務 (1) duty; obligations; (2) voluntary; volunteer;
雜務 chores; miscellaneous duties; odd jobs; sundry duties;
債務 borrowing; debt; liability; obligation; the amount due;
賬務 accounts in general; affairs concerning accounts;
政務 affairs of the government; government administration; government affairs;
職務 duty; function; job; post;
篆務 official affair;
總務 (1) general affairs; (2) person in charge of general affairs;

wu

【晤】 interview; meet; see; see face to face;
［晤對］ meet face to face;
［晤面］ meet; see; see each other;
［晤商］ discuss in an interview; face-to-face negotiation;
［晤談］ converse; have a talk; interview; meet and talk;
［晤言］ meet and talk;

會晤 meet;
面晤 meet;

wu

【惡】 abhor; detest; dislike; hate; loathe;
［惡從膽生］ a spell of wrath rises from one's heart;
［惡惡］ hate evil;

[惡嫌] abhor; detest; hate; loathe;
好惡 likes and dislikes;
交惡 become enemies; fall foul of each other;
可惡 detestable; hateful;
痛惡 bitterly detest; hate bitterly;
嫌惡 detest; loathe;
羞惡 feel ashamed and disgusted about one's own or sb else's wrong doing;
厭惡 be disgusted with; detest; loathe;
憎惡 abominate; bitterly detest;

wu

【嫵】 (1) beautiful; charming; (2) name of a star;

wu

【塢】 (1) castle; entrenchment; fortified building; low wall around a village for defense; (2) a structure which slants to a lower centre on all sides — as a shipyard;

[塢區] dockland;

船塢 dock; shipyard;
浮船塢 floating (dry) dock;
花塢 sunken flowerbed;
山塢 col;

wu

【寤】 awake from a sound sleep;

[寤寐] awake or asleep;
寤寐不忘 not to forget it sleeping or upon awakening;
寤寐籌思 take counsel of one's pillow;

[寤生] give birth to a baby while asleep;

wu

【誤】 (1) error; mistake; (2) fail to seize the right moment; miss; (3) harm; injure; suffer; (4) by accident; by mistake;

[誤報] misreport; report incorrectly;

[誤筆] a slip of the pen;

[誤差] error; misalignment;
誤差極大 miss by a mile;
安全誤差 error on the safe side;
不規則誤差 abnormal error;
測量誤差 measuring error;
陳化誤差 aging error;
初始誤差 initial error;
加速角誤差 acceleration misalignment;
角度誤差 angular misalignment;
絕對誤差 absolute error;
零誤差 zero-error;
人為誤差 human error;
容許誤差 admissible error;
騷動誤差 agitation error;
捨入誤差 rounding error;
相對誤差 relative error;

[誤傳] transmit incorrectly;

[誤導] mislead;

[誤點] behind schedule; behind time; late; overdue;

[誤犯] offend unintentionally;

[誤國] cause harm to national causes; damage national interests; mismanage national affairs;
誤國殃民 injure the country and bring calamity to the people; obstruct national affairs and bring woe to the masses;

[誤會] get one's wires crossed; misunderstanding; misapprehend; misapprehension; misconstrue; mistake; misunderstand;
澄清誤會 clear up a misunderstanding;
存有誤會 under an illusion;
糾正誤會 correct a misunderstanding;
消除誤會 clear the air; clear up misapprehension; dispel the misapprehensions;
一場誤會 a misunderstanding;
引起誤會 give rise to misunderstanding;

[誤記] record incorrectly;

[誤解] get sb wrong; misconceive; misconstrue; misinterpret; misread; mistake; misunderstand; misunderstanding; spell sb back; take amiss;
避免誤解 avert misconceptions;
產生誤解 produce misunderstanding;
完全誤解 get hold of the wrong end of the stick;
消除誤解 clear the air; remove misunderstanding;
引起誤解 cause misapprehension;
有一點誤解 a bit of a myth;

[誤期] behind schedule; fail to meet the deadline;

[誤人] harm people;
誤人不淺 do people great harm;
誤人誤己 harm both others and oneself;

[誤認] identify incorrectly;

[誤殺] (1) unintentional homicide; (2) kill a person by mistake;
[誤傷] accidentally injure; hurt by mistake;
[誤時] behind time;
[誤事] bungle matters;
[誤算] miscalculate; miscount;
[誤為] mistake one thing for another;
[誤信] believe what is unreliable; misplace one's confidence;
[誤譯] misinterpret; misinterpretation; mistranslate; mistranslation;
[誤引] misquote;
[誤用] misuse;

筆誤 a slip of the pen; make a mistake in writing;
遲誤 delay; procrastinate;
舛誤 error; mishap;
錯誤 error; mistake; mistaken; wrong;
耽誤 delay; hold;
訛誤 error (in a text);
詿誤 affect adversely; be involved in trouble and therefore be punished or suffer;
罣誤 affect adversely; be involved in trouble and therefore be punished or suffer;
勘誤 correct errors in printing;
口誤 slip of the tongue;
謬誤 falsehood; mistake;
失誤 fault; miss; muff;
脫誤 omissions and errors;
違誤 disobey orders and cause delay;
無誤 without error;
延誤 fail because of procrastination; incur loss through delay;
貽誤 affect adversely; bungle; cause delay or hindrance;
正誤 correct (typographical) errors;
坐誤 let slip (a golden opportunity);

wu

【鎢】 tungsten; wolfram;
[鎢絲燈] tungsten lamp;

wu

【霧】 (1) fog; mist; vapour; (2) fine spray;
[霧鬢雲鬟] beautiful tresses of a woman;
[霧燈] fog lamp; fog light;
[霧合] gather together like the mist;
[霧化] atomization;
霧化器 atomizer;
~玻璃霧化器 glass atomizer;
~機械霧化器 mechanical atomizer;
~空氣霧化器 air atomizer;
~噴射霧化器 blast atomizer; jet atominer;
~氣流霧化器 airstream atomizer;
~氣壓霧化器 pneumatic atomizer;
~石墨霧化器 graphite atomizer;
~懸滴霧化器 hanging-drop atomizer;
超聲波霧化 ultrasonic atomization;
惰性氣體霧化 inert gas atomizer;
機械霧化 mechanical atomization;
靜電霧化 electrostatic atomization;
均勻霧化 uniform atomizing;
起始霧化 initial atomizer;
氣壓霧化 air atomization;
燃料霧化 fuel atomization;
使霧化 atomize;
水霧化 water atomization;
推進劑霧化 propellant atomization;
液膜霧化 liquid-sheet atomizer;
油霧化 oil atomization;
[霧氣] fog; mist;
結滿霧氣 mist up;
[霧散] disperse like mist;
霧消雲散 the fog lifts and the clouds disperse;
[霧水] dew;
除去霧水 defog;
一頭霧水 in bewilderment; in confusion;

薄霧 haze; mist; reek;
塵霧 dust fog; fume;
大霧 dense fog;
防霧 antifogging;
海霧 sea fog; sea smoke;
離子霧 ion-atmosphere;
迷霧 (1) anything that misleads people; (2) dense fog;
濃霧 dense fog; smog; smoke;
噴霧 atomization; mist spray; spray;
平流霧 advective fog;
起霧 mist up;
五里霧 thick fog;
霧凇霧 rime fog;
下霧 foggy; mist;
雪霧 snow and mist;
煙霧 mist; smog; smoke fog; smoke; vapour;
妖霧 fogs spread by demons (in mythology);
一層霧 a veil of mist;
雲霧 clouds and mist; mist;

wu

【騖】 (1) rush; speed; (2) uninhibited; unrestrained;

[騖外] depart from one's proper role;

[騖遠] impractically ambitious; overambitious;

旁騖 inattentive; seeking sth other than one's profession, work, etc.;

外騖 not concentrate (on any one thing);

wu

【鶩】 duck;

[鶩舲] small boat;

xi¹

xi

【兮】 adjunct;

xi

【西】 (1) west; western; (2) foreign; occidental; the West; Western;

[西北] (1) northwest; (2) northwest China;
西北風 northwest wind;
喝西北風 drink the northwest wind — have nothing to eat; feed on the winter's northwestern wind — suffer from cold and hunger; live on air;

[西部片] cowboy film; Wild West movie;

[西菜] Western-style food;

[西窗剪燭] happy reunion of friends chatting together late into the night;

[西方] (1) west; westward; (2) Occident; West; (3) Western Paradise;
西方淨土 happy land in the west; heavenly paradise;
西方人 occidental; Westerners;
西方語言 Occidental languages;

[西風] west wind; westerly; westerly wind;
西風帶 westerlies;
~ 極地西風帶 polar westerlies;
~ 盛行西風帶 prevailing westerlies;
~ 溫帶西風帶 temperate westerlies;
~ 中緯度西風帶 middle-latitude westerlies;
~ 最大緯向西風帶 maximum zonal westerlies;
西風落葉 the west wind and fallen leaves — an autumn scene;
西風蕭瑟 moan of the west wind;

[西服] Western-style clothes;

[西瓜] watermelon;
西瓜皮 watermelon rind;
西瓜瓤 watermelon flesh;
西瓜子 watermelon seed;

[西紅柿] tomato;
西紅柿醬 tomato sauce;

[西化] Occidentalize; Westernize;

[西畫] Western painting;

[西曆] (1) Gregorian calendar; (2) Christian era;

[西米] sago;

[西式] Western style;

[西天] Western heaven;
上西天 go to the Western Paradise; kick the bucket;
~ 送上西天 send sb to heaven;

[西屋] west wing;

[西席] private tutor; teacher;

[西行] go west; travel westward;

[西學] Western learning;

[西諺] Western proverb;

[西洋] West; Western;
西洋菜 watercress;
西洋鏡 (1) peep show; (2) hanky-panky; trickery;
西洋李 greengage;
西洋人 occidental;

[西域] Western Regions;

[西元] Gregorian calendar;

[西樂] Western music;

[西藏] Tibet; Xizang;
西藏文化 culture of Tibet;
西藏舞 Tibetan dance;

[西裝] louge suit; Western-style clothes;
西裝袋 garment bag;

東西 (1) east and west; (2) from east to west; (3) (used for human beings or animals) creature; thing; (4) thing;
歸西 die; pass away;
日平西 dusk; sundown;
中西 Chinese and Western;

xi

【吸】 (1) breathe in; draw; inhale; (2) absorb; imbibe; suck in; suck up;

[吸塵機] vacuum cleaner;
真空吸塵機 vacuum cleaner;

[吸蟲] fluke;
腸吸蟲 intestinal fluke;
肺吸蟲 lung fluke;
肝吸蟲 liver fluke;
血吸蟲 blood fluke;
~ 雌血吸蟲 female schistosoma;
~ 雄血吸蟲 male schistosoma;

[吸毒] be on drugs; become addicted to narcotics; do drugs; drug abuse; drug taking; drug use; smoke opium; take drugs; use drugs;
吸毒成癮 be addicted to drugs; be hooked on drugs; dependent on drugs; get hooked on drugs;
~ 吸毒成癮的人 drug addict;
吸毒販毒 drug abuse; drug trafflicking;
吸毒鬼 dopehead;
吸毒過量 drug overdose;

吸毒問題 drug problem;
吸毒者 drug addict; drug user; druggie;
吸了毒的 bombed;
嘗試吸毒 experiment with drugs;
經常吸毒 on drugs;

[吸附] adsorp; sorption;
吸附劑 sorbent;
~ 螯合吸附劑 chelate sorbent;
吸附膜 sorption film;
吸附提取 sorption extraction;
吸附作用 adsorptive action;
催化吸附 catalyzed sorption;
動態吸附 dynamic adsorption;
多層吸附 multilayer sorption;
分子吸附 molecular adsorption;
化學吸附 chemical adsorption;
活性吸附 activated adsorption;
交換吸附 exchange adsorption;
接觸吸附 contact adsorption;
競爭吸附 competitive adsorption;
離解吸附 dissociation adsorption;
黏土吸附 clay adsorption;
平衡吸附 equilibrium adsorption;
氣體吸附 gas adsorption;
色譜吸附 chromatographic adsorption;
炭吸附 char adsorption;
陽極吸附 anodic adsorption;
原子吸附 atomic adsorption;
置換吸附 displacement adsorption;

[吸管] drinking straw;
一根吸管 a straw;

[吸光] absorptance;
吸光百分率 percent absorption;
吸光測定法 absorptiometry;
吸光度 absorptance;

[吸量管] pipette;

[吸濾器] suction filter;

[吸墨] ink-absorbing;
吸墨性能 ink absorption;
吸墨紙 blotter; blotting paper;

[吸能器] power absorber;

[吸盤] sucker; sucking disc;
腹吸盤 ventral sucker;
肛吸盤 anal sucker;
後吸盤 posterior sucker;
口吸盤 oral sucker;
前吸盤 anterior sucker;

[吸氣] breathe in; inhale;
吸氣劑 getter;
~ 鋇鈦吸氣劑 batalum getter;
~ 塊狀吸氣劑 bulk getter;
~ 丸式吸氣劑 pellet getter;
吸氣瓶 aspirator bottle;
吸氣裝置 breathing apparatus;

[吸器] haustorium;
反足吸器 antipodal haustorium;
合點吸器 chalazal haustorium;
胚囊吸器 embryo sac haustorium;

[吸槍] aspirator gun; suction gun; suction pistol;

[吸取] absorb; assimilate; draw; drink in; suck up;
吸取教訓 draw a lesson;
吸取精華 absort the quintessence;
吸取能量 absorb energy;
吸取水份 absort water;

[吸熱] absorption of heat;
吸熱板 absorber plate;
吸熱層 heat absorbing coating;
吸熱反應 endothermic reaction;
吸熱分解 endothermic decomposition;
吸熱過程 endothermic process;
吸熱化合物 endothermic compound;
吸熱劑 heat absorbent;
吸熱面 heat-absorbng surface;
吸熱器 heat absorber; heat dump; heat sink; thermal absorber;
吸熱性 heat absorptivity;

[吸入] inhale;
吸入空氣 inhale air;

[吸聲] sound absorption;
吸聲板 acoustic board; panel absorber;
吸聲材料 acoustic absorbent; sound-absorbing material;
吸聲建築 acoustic construction;
吸聲能力 sound-absorbing power;
吸聲器 acoustic absorbent; sound absorption;
~ 板式吸聲器 panel absorber;
~ 多孔吸聲器 porous absorber;
吸聲毯 sound-absorbing blanket; sound absorbent quilt;
吸聲體 absorber;
~ 空間吸聲體 functional absorber; suspended absorber;
吸聲系數 acoustical absorptivity;
吸聲織物 acoustextile;
播音室吸聲 studio absorption;
觀眾吸聲 audience absorption;

[吸收] (1) absorb; assimilate; assimilation; draw; imbibe; soak up; suck up; take up; (2) enlist; recruit;

吸收比 absorptance;
吸收比色計 absorptiometer;
吸收測量學 absorptiometry;
吸收牀 absorbent bed;
吸收功率 power absorption;
吸收劑 absorbent; absorber;
~ 薄膜吸收劑 film absorber;
~ 二氧化碳吸收劑 carbon-dioxide absorbent;
~ 放射性吸收劑 radioactivity absorber;
~ 粉狀吸收劑 powdered absorbent;
~ 浮動吸收劑 floating absorbent;
~ 極性吸收劑 polar absorbent;
~ 塊狀吸收劑 lump absorbent;
~ 油吸收劑 oil absorber;
~ 中性吸收劑 neutral absorbent;
~ 中子吸收劑 neutron absorber;
~ 紫外線吸收劑 ultraviolet absorbent;
吸收率 absorptance; absorption; absorptivity;
~ 發光表面吸收率 luminous surface absorptivity;
~ 副射表面吸率 radiant surface absorptivity;
吸收能力 absorbing ability; absorptance; absorptivity;
吸收器 absorber;
~ 衝擊壓力吸收器 shock pressure absorber; surge absorber;
~ 電弧吸收器 arc absorber;
~ 二氧化碳吸收器 carbon-dioxide absorber;
~ 輻射吸收器 radiation absorber;
~ 干擾吸收器 interference absorber;
~ 慣性吸收器 inertia absorber;
~ 脈衝吸收器 pulse absorber;
~ 噴啉吸收器 spray absorber;
~ 聲流吸收器 sound stream absorber;
~ 數字吸收器 digit absorber;
~ 湍流接觸吸收器 turbulent contact absorber;
~ 渦輪氣體吸收器 turbine gas absorber;
~ 懸掛吸收器 suspended absorber;
~ 中性吸收器 neutral absorber;
吸收熱量 absorb heat;
吸收食物 assimilate food;
吸收水份 suck up moisture;
吸收思想 imbibe ideas;
吸收塔 absorber;
~ 高壓吸收塔 high-pressure absorber;
~ 硫醇吸收塔 mercaptan absorber;
吸收體 absorbent; absorber;
~ 紅外線吸收體 infrared absorber;
~ 寄生吸收體 parasitic absorber;
~ 完全吸收體 perfect absorber;
~ 紫外線吸收體 ultraviolet absorber;
吸收外資 absorb foreign capital;
吸收系數 absorptance; absorption;
吸收性 absorptivity;
吸收養份 absorb nourishment;
吸收知識 absorb knowledge;
吸收裝置 absorption apparatus;
表面吸收 face absorption;
超熱吸收 epithermal absorption;
窗口吸收 window absorption;
等效聲吸收 equivalent sound absorption;
等效吸收 equivalent absorption;
低層大氣壓吸收 low-layer absorption;
電子吸收 orption of electrons;
房間聲吸收 room absorption;
光化吸收 actinic absorption;
極光吸收 auroral absorption;
抗張強度吸收 tensile strength absorption;
內吸收 enteral absorption;
全吸收 total absorption;
熱吸收 thermal absorption;
雙光子吸收 two-photon absorption;
水蒸氣吸收 ater avpour absorption;
鬆弛型吸收 relaxation type absorption;
微量光吸收 low optical absorption;
諧振吸收 resonance absorption;
油珠吸收 absorption by drops;
有害吸收 unwanted absorption;
真吸收 true absorption;

[吸水] absorb water;
吸水力 water-absorbing power;
吸水率 water absorption;
吸水性 water absorption;
吸水紙 absorbent paper;

[吸吮] absorb; suck; suckle;

[吸血] suck blood;
吸血鬼 bloodsucker; vampire;

[吸煙] have a smoke; smoke; smoking;
吸煙服 smoking jacket;
吸煙室 smoking room;
吸煙者 smoker;
~ 不吸煙者 nonsmoker;
被動吸煙 passive smoking;
反吸煙 anti-smoking;
~ 反吸煙活動 anti-smoking campaign;
禁止吸煙 no smoking; smoking is forbidden; smoking is prohibited;
膩煩別人吸煙 hate smoking by other

people;

[吸引] appeal to; attract; attraction; charm; draw to; fascinate;

吸引力 drawing power; lure; pulling power;

~有吸引力 attractive; charming;

吸引人 attract people;

吸引外資 absorb foreign funds; attract foreign investment;

磁吸引 magnetic attraction;

電磁吸引 electromagnetic attraction;

靜電吸引 electrostatic attraction;

局部吸引 local attraction;

毛管吸引 capillary attraction;

性吸引 sexual attraction;

[吸脹作用] imbibition

[吸着] sorption;

吸着劑 sorbent;

~非離子吸着劑 non-ionic sorbent;

~選擇性吸着劑 selective sorbent;

呼吸 breathe; respire;

解吸 release the absorbed gas or solute;

空吸 suction;

深呼吸 breathe deeply;

吮吸 suck;

xi

【希】 (1) desire; expect; hope; long; wish; (2) precious; rare; scarce; strange; (3) come to a stop gradually; (4) a surname;

[希罕] (1) rare; scarce; uncommon; (2) care; cherish; value as a rarity; (3) rare thing; rarity;

[希冀] desire; wish for;

[希慕] desirous of; long for;

[希奇] (1) rare; strange; uncommon; (2) appreciate; attach importance to; value;

[希企] hope for; hope to;

[希榮] aspire for the glory of high office;

[希圖] hope and scheme for;

[希望] care; desire; expect; expectation; have a yen for; hope; look forward to; want; wish;

希望落空 fail to attain one's hope;

抱有希望 have hope; hold out hope;

充滿希望 full of hope;

大有希望 bid fair; full of hope; full of promise; give great promise; promise high hopes; show great promise; stand a chance; there is great hope for;

帶來希望 give hope; offer hope;

放棄希望 abandon hope; give up hope; lose hope;

實現希望 realize one's hope;

唯一希望 the only hope;

我倒希望 I'd like to believe that;

一線希望 a beam of hope; a blue bore; a flash of hope; a gleam of hope; a glimmer of hope; a ray of hope; a silver lining; a thread of hope;

~抱一線希望 hope against hope;

~還有一線希望 all is not lost;

衷心希望 sincerely hope;

[希微] extremely little; very little;

[希有] very rare;

[希旨] cater to the wishes of a superior;

xi

【扱】 collect; gather;

[扱引高賢] gather men of wisdom;

xi

【析】 (1) break apart; divide; rip apart; separate; split; (2) analyse; explain; interpret; (3) a surname;

[析骨] break apart a skeleton;

[析疑] clarify a doubt; explain a doubt;

[析義] clear up doubts; clear up a doubtful point; dispel doubts; resolve doubts;

辨析 differentiate and analyse; discriminate;

電滲析 electro-dialysis;

分析 analyse;

解析 analyse;

離析 (1) analyse; (2) disintegrate; disperse; separate from one another;

縷析 analyse in detail;

剖析 analyse; dissect;

xi

【恓】 frightened and worried;

[恓惶] frightened and worried; vexed; worried;

[恓恓] lonely; lonesome;

xi

【唏】 grieve; sob with sorrow; weep with sorrow;

[唏嘘] sigh; sob;

唏噓長歎 draw a long sigh;

噓唏 sob;

xi

【奚】 (1) how; what; where; why; (2) a surname;

［奚落］ gibe; jeer at; laugh at; make a fool of; scoff at; taunt;

奚落一番 make sarcastic remarks against sb; scoff at sb; take a dig at sb;

［奚幸］ vexed; worried;

xi

【栖】 same as 棲；

xi

【悉】 (1) all; entirely; (2) be informed of; know; learn;

［悉皆］ altogether; entirely; without exception;

［悉力］ with all one's strength; with might and main;

［悉數］ all; enumerate in full detail; every single one; the entire sum;

悉數奉還 return all that has been borrowed; return all that has been taken away;

悉數歸公 the entire amount is confiscated to the public;

［悉聽］ follow one's order;

悉聽尊便 according to your preference; do just as you please; you can suit yourself about;

悉聽尊命 I will do everthing as you order;

［悉心］ devote all one's attention; take the utmost care; with concentrated effort; with one's whole heart;

悉心研究 devote oneself to the study of sth;

備悉 know the whole story; learn completely;

得悉 hear of; learn about;

洞悉 know clearly; understand thoroughly;

獲悉 learn of an event;

驚悉 be shocked to learn;

據悉 by report; it is reported;

聆悉 hear; learn;

深悉 fully aware; know thoroughly;

審悉 be familiar with; know sth or sb well;

熟悉 acquaint oneself with; at home in; at home with; be acquainted with; be apprised of; conversant with; familiar to sb; familiar with; familiarize oneself with; get in with; great on; have an intimate knowledge of; have...at one's fingertips; in with; know...from A to Z; know...like a book; know...like the back of one's hand; know sth or sb well; very familiar with;

探悉 ascertain; find out; learn;

孅悉 intelligent and knowledgeable of every detail;

纖悉 detailed; exhaustive; familiar with every detail of; know thoroughly;

詳悉 detailed and thorough; know clearly;

欣悉 delighted to learn; glad to learn; happy to learn;

知悉 aware of; be informed of; know; learn of;

xi

【晞】 (1) dry; dry in the sun; (2) sunshine at daybreak;

xi

【淅】 (1) wash rice; water for washing rice; (2) a river in Henan;

［淅瀝］ patter;

雨聲淅瀝 monotonous sounds of rain pattering down; patter of the rain;

［淅米］ wash rice;

［淅淅］ the sound of the mild wind;

淅淅瀝瀝 continuous patter of raindrops;

淅淅秋風 soughing of the autumn breeze;

xi

【烯】 (1) colour of fire; (2) alkene;

苯乙烯 styrene;

丁二烯 butadiene;

丁烯 butane;

聚丙烯 polypropylene;

聚氯乙烯 polyvinyl chloride (PVC);

聚乙烯 polyethylene; polythene;

乙烯 ethylene;

xi

【欷】 sigh; sob;

［欷歔］ sigh; sob;

欷歔流涕 shed tears; sigh and sob;

歔欷 sob;

xi

【硒】 selenium;

xi

【晰】 clear; distinct;

明晰 clear; distinct;

清晰 distinct; lucid;

xi

【棲】 (1) perch; rest; settle; stay; (2) the

place one stays; (3) (now rare) bed;
[棲泊] come to anchor; stay temporarily;
[棲遲] sojourn; travel and rest;
[棲處] stay at a place; (2) an bode;
[棲居] dwell; live;
[棲身] dwell; live; stay;
[棲宿] rest for the night;
[棲息] perch; rest; stay;
棲息地 habitat;
[棲棲] anxious; jittery; jumpy;
棲棲遑遑 anxious; jumpy; nervous;
[棲止] settle at a place;

xi

【犀】 (1) sharp-edged and hard; (2) rhinocero;
[犀兵] sharp weapons;
[犀角] rhinoceros horn;
[犀利] incisive; sharp; trenchant;
目光犀利 look sharply at; one's eyesight is sharp;
[犀牛] rhinocero;
[犀錢] coin made of rhinoceros horn;
[犀照] very discerning;

靈犀 (often derogatory) tacit understanding (or comprehension);
毛犀 Coelodonta antiquitatis;
披毛犀 Coelodonta antiquitatis;
無角犀 acerathere;

xi

【稀】 (1) rare; scarce; uncommon; (2) scattered; sparse; (3) thin; watery;
[稀薄] rare; rarefied; thin; wishy-washy;
變得稀薄 thin out;
[稀飯] congee; gruel; porridge;
熬稀飯 cook rice gruel;
吃稀飯 eat porridge;
[稀罕] (1) rare; rarity; scarce; (2) care;
[稀客] rare visitor;
[稀爛] (1) completely mashed; pulpy; (2) broken to bits; smashed to pieces; smashed to smithereens;
扯得稀爛 be torn to shreds;
打個稀爛 beat ... into a pulp;
稀巴爛 be completed smashed;
~砸個稀巴爛 crush into tiny broken pieces — completely crushed; smash to smithereens;
[稀破] ruptured; tattered; torn;
[稀奇] (1) rare; strange; (2) care;
稀奇古怪 bizarre; odd; out of the way; outlandish; quaint; strange and eccentric;
[稀缺] scarce;
稀缺商品 deficient article;
[稀少] few; few and far between; little; rare; scarce; sparse;
人口稀少 have a sparse population;
人煙稀少 be sparsely populated;
[稀世] extremely precious; extremely rare;
稀世珍本 a rare book in the world;
稀世之才 supramundane power of intellect;
稀世之珍 a rare gem of the age; an extremely rare treasure;
[稀釋] dilute; dilution; thinning;
稀釋劑 thinner;
~塗料稀釋劑 paint thinner;
連續稀釋 serial dilution;
流出物稀釋 effluent dilution;
燃料稀釋 fuel dilution;
雙重稀釋 double dilution;
酸液稀釋 acid dilution;
油被燃料稀釋 dilution thinning;
[稀疏] dispersed; few and far between; few and scattered; scattered; sparse; thin;
稀疏的鬍鬚 spare beard;
稀疏的頭髮 sparse hair; thin hair;
稀疏零落 sparse and scattered;
樹林稀疏 the trees are sparse;
[稀鬆] (1) loose; poor; sloppy; (2) trivial; unimportant; (3) indifferent; not interested;
[稀稀拉拉] diffuse and flat; few and far between; few and scattered; sparse; thin; thinly scattered;
[稀稀落落] sparse; thinly scattered;
[稀有] one in a million; rare; uncommon; unusual;
稀有金屬 rare metal;

古稀 seventy years of age;
拉稀 have diarrhea; have loose bowels; suffer from diarrhoea;
糖稀 thin malt sugar;
依稀 dimly; vaguely;

xi

【腊】 (1) dried meat; (2) extremely; very;

xi

【溪】 brook; mountain stream;

［溪谷］ canyon; dale; gorge; valley;

［溪澗］ brook; mountain stream;

［溪流］ brook; mountain stream; stream; ravine stream;

水聲汩汩的溪流 burbling brook;

［溪水］ water of a mountain stream;

［溪蟹］ river crab;

山溪 mountain stream;

小溪 small stream;

X

xi

【傒】 (1) expect; wait for; (2) narrow path; short cut;

［傒待］ expect; look forward to;

［傒徑］ narrow path; shortcut; snap course;

xi

【晳】 (1) fair skin; white; (2) differentiate; discriminate; distinguish;

白晳 fair-skinned; light-complexioned;

xi

【僖】 (1) joy; joyful; (2) a surname;

xi

【熙】 (1) bright; bright and brilliant; sunny; (2) booming; flourishing; prosperous; (3) gay; merry; peaceful and happy;

［熙朝人瑞］ a glorious dynasty and a prosperous people;

［熙春］ spring; springtime;

［熙洽］ peaceful and prosperous;

［熙熙］ peaceful and happy;

熙熙而來 coming in large crowds;

熙熙攘攘 alive with; bustle with activity; coming and going busily; coming and going in groups; hustle and bustle; push and jostle each other;

［熙笑］ laugh happily;

［熙怡］ amiable and cordial;

xi

【蜥】 lizard;

［蜥蜴］ lizard;

巨蜥 Varanus salvtator;

蛇蜥 Ophisaurus gracilis;

鬣蜥 agama;

xi

【豨】 hog; pig;

xi

【嘻】 (1) interjection of grief or surprise; (2) laughing happily;

［嘻和］ affable; cordial; friendly;

［嘻嘻］ laughing happily;

嘻嘻哈哈 giggling; laughing and joking; laughing and talking happily; mirthful; run on; tittering with joy;

［嘻笑］ giggle; laugh merrily; titter;

嘻笑顏開 wild with joy;

笑嘻嘻 smiling broadly;

噫嘻 expressing grief; sighing;

xi

【嬉】 frolic; have fun; play; sport;

［嬉淚］ tears of joy;

［嬉鬧］ frolic; romp;

［嬉弄］ rollicksome;

［嬉皮］ grinning;

嬉皮賴臉 a slobbering appearance; grinning cheekily; shameless;

嬉皮笑臉 behave in a noisy, gay and boisterous manner; grinning and smiling; grinning cheekily; grinning mischievously; smiling and grimacing; with a cunning smile; with an oily smile;

［嬉水］ paddle;

嬉水池 paddling pool; wading pool;

［嬉戲］ frolic; have jun; make merry; play; romp; sport;

［嬉笑］ laughing and playing; mischievous smile; playful; playsome;

嬉笑怒罵 making fun of and cursing angrily – write freely;

嬉笑自若 laughing and playing just as if one were in one's own home;

［嬉游曲］ divertisement; play; sport;

xi

【膝】 knee;

［膝部］ knee;

膝部手術 knee operation;

［膝蓋］ knee; prayer bones;

［膝下］ children;

膝下承歡 please one's parents by living with them;

膝下兒女 children surrounding parents'

knees – children living with their parents;
膝下猶虛 have no children; still childless;

抱膝 with one's arms about one's knees;
促膝 sit close together; sit knee to knee;
護膝 kneecap; kneepad;
牛膝 the root of bidentate achyranthes (Achyranthes bidentata);
盤膝 cross one's legs;
屈膝 bend one's knees; drop on one's knees; fall on one's knees; give in; go down on one's knees; kneel down; knuckle down; succumb;

xi
【熹】 (1) dawn; faint sunlight; (2) giving out faint light;
[熹微] dim; pale;

xi
【羲】 Fu Xi 伏羲, a legendary ruler who introduced houses;

xi
【樨】 cassia tree;

草木樨 sweet clover;
木樨 (1) egg beaten and then cooked; (2) sweet-scented osmanthus;

xi
【禧】 auspiciousness; blessings; happiness;

xi
【蟋】 cricket;
[蟋蟀] cricket;
蟋蟀草 yard grass;
蟋蟀嘎嘎 crickets chirp; crickets chirrup; crickets creak;

xi
【谿】 (1) gorge; valley; (2) brook; creek; stream;
[谿谷] river valley;
[谿壑] mountain valley; ravine;
[谿澗] mountain brook;

勃谿 family quarrel;

xi
【徯】 brawl; quarrel; squabble;

xi
【蹊】 (1) footpath; path; (2) trample; tread;
[蹊徑] narrow path; path; way;
獨闢蹊徑 develop a new style of one's own; open a new road for oneself;
[蹊蹺] extraordinary; queer; strange;
事有蹊蹺 smell a rat in the matter; some mystery underlies this affair;
[蹊隧] path; trail;
[蹊要] strategic point on a path;

xi
【醯】 acid; pickle; vinegar;

xi
【曦】 sunlight; sunshine;
[曦光] sunlight; sunshine;

晨曦 first rays of the morning sun;

xi
【巇】 (1) crack; (2) hazardous;
[巇險] (1) steep and difficult to ascend; (2) full of danger and hardship;

xi
【犧】 (1) beast of a uniform colour for sacrifice; sacrifice; (2) give up;
[犧犧惶惶] troubled; vexed;
[犧牲] do sth at the expense of; sacrifice;
犧牲車馬，保存將帥 sacrifice the pawns to save the generals; save the queen by sacrificing the knights;
犧牲品 sacrificial lamb;
~時尚犧牲品 fashion victim; style victim;
犧牲生命 lay down one's life;
犧牲者 victim;
部份犧牲 partial sacrifice;
願為犧牲 willing to sacrifice for;
壯烈犧牲 die as a martyr;
自我犧牲 self-sacrifice;

xi
【鼷】 house mouse;
[鼷鹿] traguild;
[鼷鼠] house mouse;
[鼷穴] mousehole;

xi
【蠵】 a kind of large-sized turtle;
[蠵龜] loggerhead turtle;

xi
【鸂】 a kind of water bird resembling the mandarin duck;

xi
【觿】 a bodkin made of ivory, horn, etc.

used for undoing knots;

xi²

xi

【昔】 (1) ancient; bygone; formerly; former times; of old; the past; (2) evening; night; (3) the end;

[昔酒] old wine; vintage wine;

[昔年] bygone years; former years; past years;

[昔人] ancient people;

[昔日] in former days;

昔日的輝煌 splendours of another age;

昔日威風，掃地以盡 one's former arrogance has been trampled into the dust for good; one's past arrogance has been swept into oblivion;

[昔時] in former days; in the olden days;

[昔歲] last year;

[昔昔] every night;

[昔賢] ancient sages;

[昔者] before; formerly; in ancient times; in former times;

疇昔 in former times;

古昔 in ancient times;

今昔 the present and the past; today and yesterday;

奶昔 milk shake;

平昔 in the past;

夙昔 (1) in the past; past times; (2) day and night;

素昔 ordinarily; regularly; so far; usually;

宿昔 (1) days gone by; the past; (2) long-standing;

往昔 in the former times; in the past;

憶昔 recall the bygone days with nostalgia; recollect the past;

在昔 formerly; in former times; once upon a time;

xi

【席】 (1) mat; (2) place; seat; take a seat; (3) banquet; feast; dinner; (4) rely on; (5) a surname;

[席不暇暖] before the chair upon which one sits has become warm; constantly on the go; constantly on the move; in a tearing hurry; not to sit long enough to warm the seat; on the trot;

[席次] seating arrangement; the order of seats;

[席地] on the ground;

席地而坐 sit down on the floor; sit on the ground;

幕天席地 have the sky for curtains and the earth for a mat — everywhere is a good place to settle down;

[席豐履厚] crack a tidy crust; make a comfortable income;

[席捲] take away everything;

席捲而去 abscond bag and baggage; leave nothing behind; make a clean sweep and decamp; make off with everything that one can lay hands on; take everything away;

席捲而逃 abscond, lock, stock and barrel;

席捲全國 sweep over the country;

席捲全球 sweep across the globe;

席捲天下 absorb the whole world like the rolling up of a mat; carry the world before one; conquer the whole country; roll up the empire like a mat;

[席帽] straw hat;

[席票] food ticket;

[席上] (1) scholars; the learned; (2) on the dining table;

[席位] seat;

保住席位 hold onto a seat; keep a seat;

邊緣席位 marginal seat;

得到一個席位 gain a seat;

失去一個席位 lose a seat;

一個席位 a seat;

贏得一個席位 win a seat;

擁有席位 hold a seat;

[席珍待聘] arranging one's rarities while waiting for official employment; person of capability awaiting employment;

[席子] mat; matting;

被告席 dock; defendant's seat;

避席 leave one's seat;

餐席 cover;

草席 grassmat; straw mat;

出席 attend; be present;

割席 break up an old friendship;

貴賓席 seats for distinguished guests;

還席 give a return banquet;

即席 extemporaneous; impromptu; off the cuff; offhand;

酒席 feast;

就席 be seated at table;

炕席 kang mat;

離席 leave the table or a meeting;
涼席 summer sleeping mat (made of bamboo, etc.);
列席 attend a meeting in the capacity of an observer;
流水席 dinner served separately as the guests arrive in succession;
蘆席 mat made of thin bamboo strips;
篾蓆 mat made of thin bamboo strips;
旁聽席 public gallery; visitors' seats;
蒲席 cattail mat; rush mat;
起席 leave a dinner party;
全席 full-course dinner;
缺席 absent; absent from a meeting; in absentia;
衽席 sleeping mat;
入席 take one's seat at a table for a meal;
軟席 soft seat or berth;
上席 the top of the table;
首席 (1) seat of honour; (2) chief; the highest-positioned; the highest-ranking; the senior;
素席 vegetarian feast;
逃席 leave a feast without permission;
退席 leave a banquet or a meeting;
葦席 reed mat;
西席 private tutor; teacher;
筵席 (1) seats arranged at a banquet; (2) banquet; feast; (3) mat for sitting on;
宴席 banquet; feast;
議席 seat in a legislative assembly; seat in parliament;
茵席 cushion; mat;
原告席 prosecutor's (or plaintiff's) seat;
擇席 be unable to sleep well in a new place;
枕席 (1) the pillow and the mat — bedding; (2) mat used to cover a pillow; pillow mat;
爭席 contend for a seat;
正席 table of honour in a grand feast;
證人席 witness box; witness stand;
主賓席 seat for the guest of honour;
主席 chair; chairman; chairperson; president;
坐席 (1) attend a banquet; (2) take one's seat at a banquet table;

xi

【息】 (1) breath; (2) news; tidings; (3) cease; end; stop; (4) rest; (5) grow; multiply; (6) interest;

[息謗] silence slanders;
[息兵] end hostilities; stop fighting;
[息火] put out a fire;
[息禍] bring disasters to an end;
[息肩] be relieved of a responsibility; put down one's burden;
[息交] have no intercourse with the world;
息交絕游 break off intercourse with the world; go into seclusion; have no intercourse with society; keep oneself to oneself; shut oneself up;
[息怒] let one's anger cool off;
[息肉] polyp;
息肉病 polyposis;
~幼年型息肉病 juvenile polyposis;
癌性息肉 carcinopolypus;
鼻息肉 nasal polyp;
耳息肉 aural polyp; otopolyus;
宮頸息肉 cervical polyp;
喉息肉 laryngeal polyp;
後鼻孔息肉 choanal polyp;
囊性息肉 cystic polyp;
青少年息肉 juvenile polyp;
炎性息肉 inflammatory polyp;
幼年性息肉 juvenile polyp;
增生性息肉 hyperplastic polyp;
直腸息肉 polyp of rectum;

安息 (1) go to sleep; rest; (2) rest in peace;
本息 capital and interest;
鼻息 breath;
屏息 catch one's breath; hold one's breath;
不息 without cease;
拆息 short-term interest;
出息 future; promise; prospects;
喘息 (1) breather; breathing spell; (2) gasp for breath; pant;
低息 low interest;
惵息 holding breath from fear;
定息 fixed interest;
付息 pay the interest;
姑息 appease; be over lenient toward; indulge;
股息 dividend; stock dividend;
減息 reduce interest on loans;
將息 recuperate; rest;
利息 interest;
脈息 pulse;
年息 annual interest;
平息 (1) calm down; come to an end; quiet down; subside; (2) put down; stamp out; suppress;
棲息 perch; rest; roost; stay;
起息 (1) get up in the morning and retire in the night; (2) start bearing interest;
氣息 (1) breath; (2) flavour; smell;
憩息 have a rest; pause for rest; rest; take a rest;

欠息 debit interest;
全息 hologram;
雀息 remain quiet; remain silent;
日息 daily interest;
入息 income;
弱息 my child;
稍息 stand at ease;
生息 (1) exist; live; (2) multiply; propagate;
聲息 (1) information; (2) noise; sound;
衰息 come to a halt;
瞬息 in a wink; in the twinkling of an eye;
蘇息 (1) rest; (2) come back to life; revive;
太息 heave a deep sigh; lament; sigh;
歎息 (1) lament; sigh in lamentation; (2) exclaim; (3) sigh;
愓息 pant from fear;
調息 regulate one's breath;
停息 cease; stop;
微息 weak and feeble;
無息 interest-free (loan);
棲息 perch; rest; stay;
消息 (1) information; news; (2) news; tidings;
歇息 (1) go to bed; put up for the night; (2) have a rest;
信息 (1) information; (2) information; message; news;
休息 have a rest; rest;
訊息 information; message; messaging; news; tidings;
奄息 stop for rest;
一息 have a breath; respiration;
遊息 play and rest;
月息 monthly interest;
懾息 hold one's breath in fear;
止息 cease; stop;
窒息 smother; stifle; suffocate;
孳息 (1) grow; (2) interest;
滋息 bear interest;
子息 (1) interest; profits from capital investment; (2) male offspring; son;
作息 work and rest;

xi

【惜】 (1) care for tenderly; cherish; have a high opinion of sth; show fondness for; show love for; value highly; (2) grudge; spare; (3) feel sorry for sb; have pity on sb; pity; regret; sympathize;

［惜別］ hate to see sb go; reluctant to part; unwilling to part;
惜別會 farewell party;
惜別之情 the feeling of reluctance to part;
握手惜別 grasp a person's hand in farewell;

［惜福］ make sparing use of one's wealth; refrain from leading an excessively comfortable life;

［惜力］ contribute one's labour reluctantly; not do one's best; sparing of one's energy;

［惜售］ reluctant to sell out;

愛惜 (1) cherish; hold sth dear; make good use of; make the best use of sth; prize; treasure sth; use sparingly; value; (2) miserly; niggardly; stingy;
不惜 (1) not hesitate (to do sth); (2) not spare; not stint;
悼惜 deplore; lament;
顧惜 love and take good care of; treasure;
可惜 it's a pity; it's too bad;
憐惜 feel tender and protection toward; have pity for; sympathize with; take pity on;
吝惜 grudge; spare; stint;
體惜 understand and sympathize with;
痛惜 deeply regret; deplore;
惋惜 feel sorry for sb or about sth; have pity for;
珍惜 cherish; treasure; treasure and avoid wasting; value;
軫惜 have pity on; mourn with deep regret;

xi

xi

【習】 (1) exercise; practise; review; (2) get accustomed to; used to; (3) custom; habit; usual practice; (4) a surname;

［習兵］ (1) train troops; (2) versed in the art of war;

［習得］ acquisition;
語言習得 language acquisition;
~第二語言習得 second language acquisition;
~兒童語言習得 child language acquisition;

［習定］ enter into meditation and get rid of desires;

［習非］ accustomed to wrongdoing;
習非成是 accept what is wrong as right when one grows accustomed to it; get used to what is wrong and regard it as right; through practice the erroneous becomes correct; what becomes

customary is accepted as right;

[習慣] (1) accustomed to; inured to; used to; (2) convention; custom; groove; habit; usual practice;

習慣成自然 custom reconciles us to everything; custom is second nature; habit is a second nature; habit makes things natural; once a use, forever a custom; once you form a habit, it comes natural to you;

習慣使然 by force of habit; from force of habit;

習慣勢力 force of habit;

習慣性 (1) inertia; (2) habitual;

習慣用語 language of habitual use;

習慣於 accustom sb to sth; accustom sb to the habits of; be accustomed to; be in the habit of doing sth; be inured to; be used to; be wont to; feel at home in;

不習慣 unaccustomed;

成為習慣 become a habit;

~不習慣一個人生活 be not used to living on one's own;

改變習慣 change one's habits;

改掉習慣 get out of a habit;

個人習慣 personal habits;

購物習慣 buying habits;

好習慣 good habit;

壞習慣 bad habit; nasty habit;

~改掉壞習慣 break a habit; kick a habit;

戒除習慣 kick the habit;

良好習慣 desirable habits;

~養成良好習慣 develop desirable habits;

令人討厭的習慣 unfortunate habit;

收視習慣 viewing habits;

衛生習慣 hygienic habit; sanitary habit;

消費習慣 spending habits;

養成習慣 acquire a habit; cultivate a habit; develop a habit; fall into the habit of; form a habit; get into a habit; nuture a habit;

飲酒習慣 drinking habits;

飲食習慣 eating habits;

閱讀習慣 reading habit;

早起的習慣 the habit of getting up early;

[習見] commonly seen;

[習氣] bad custom; bad habit; bad practice;

官僚習氣 bureaucratic habits;

養成不良習氣 form a bad habit;

沾染習氣 be corrupted by prevailing bad practices;

[習染] (1) contract a bad habit; fall into a bad habit; (2) bad habit;

[習尚] (1) common practice; honoured custom; (2) fashion;

[習熟] familiar with; understand;

[習俗] convention; custom; habitude; practice;

習俗移人 habit and custom can change one's nature;

不拘習俗 free from old customs and habits;

傳統習俗 tradition;

~根據傳統習俗 by tradition;

民間習俗 folk custom;

狃於習俗 be bound by custom;

社會習俗 social conventions;

外國習俗 alien customs;

鄉村習俗 rural customs;

囿於習俗 constrained by convention; constrained by custom;

[習題] examples; exercises;

[習習] (1) breezy; refreshing; (2) flying; lively;

[習性] appetence; dispositions; habit; habitual nature; mannerism; temperament;

[習焉不察] too accustomed to sth to call it in question;

[習以為常] a matter of common practice; become a force of habit; become accustomed to sth; become proficient at sth; fall into a habit; get accustomed to; used to;

[習藝] learn a skill; learn a trade;

[習用] habitually use; use as a habit;

[習與性成] habit becomes second nature; habit makes things natural; long practice becomes second nature;

[習語] idiom;

個人習語 idiolect;

~個人習語歧義 idiolectal ambiguity;

[習字] do exercises in calligraphy; learn calligraphy; practise penmanship;

習字帖 copybook;

[習作] (1) do exercises in composition; (2) exercise in composition;

諳習 be skilled in; be versed in; familiar with;

補習 take lessons after school or work; tutorial;

傳習 pass on and learn knowledge and skill;

惡習 bad habits; cacoethes; evil practices; pernicious habits;

復習 brush up; dust off; get up; go over; look

over; look through; review; review lessons learned; revise; run over;

固習 deep-rooted habit; inveterate habit;
痼習 deep-rooted habit; inveterate habit;
積習 deep-rooted habits; long-standing practice; old habits;
見習 be on probation; learn on the job;
講習 lecture and study;
教習 teacher;
練習 drill; exercise; practise;
陋習 bad habits; corrupt customs;
染習 contract bad babits;
實習 externship; field trip; fieldwork; internship; practice;
熟習 have the knack of; learn by heart; practised in; skilful at; skilled in; well versed in;
誦習 learn by recitation;
玩習 learn and practise;
溫習 review one's lessons; revise;
閑習 familiar with; well versed in;
嫻習 adept at; skilled in;
選習 study;
學習 emulate; study;
研習 examine and study; learning; research and study;
演習 drill; dry run; dummy run; exercise; manoeuvre; practice;
肄習 practise;
預習 (1) prepare lessons before class; (2) rehearse;
自習 learn and practice by oneself;

xi

【媳】 daughter-in-law;
［媳婦］ (1) daughter-in-law; son's wife; (2) wife of a relative of the younger generation;
兒媳婦 daughter-in-law;
娶個媳婦過繼個兒 get a daughter-in-law and lose a son;
娶媳婦兒 (1) take a wife; (2) get a daughter-in-law;
孫媳婦 granddaughter-in-law; grandson's wife;
討媳婦 get a wife for one's son;
姪媳婦 one's nephew's wife; the wife of brother's son;
弟媳 younger brother's wife;
童養媳 little girl raised in the family of her future husband; child bride;

xi

【熄】 (1) extinguish; put out; (2) destroy; obliterate; quash;
［熄燈］ put out the light; switch off the light; turn off the light;
［熄滅］ cut off; die out; extinct; extinguish; go out; put out; quench;
火熄滅 a fire goes out;

xi

【蓆】 straw mat;
［蓆子］ straw mat;
一領蓆 a mattress;

xi

【裼】 (1) take off one's top garment; (2) (in ancient China) wrapper or outer garment worn over a fur;
袒裼 take off one's jacket (or coat) and expose part of the body;

xi

【覡】 sorcerer; wizard;

xi

【錫】 (1) tin; (2) bestow;
［錫恩］ do a favour;
［錫福］ bestow happiness; bless;
［錫匠］ tinsmith;
［錫器］ tinware;
［錫紙］ silver paper; tin foil;
焊錫 soldering tin; tin solder;

xi

【檄】 summons to arms in ancient times;
［檄文］ (1) official call to arms; (2) official denunciation of the enemy;
傳檄 disseminate (or spread) an official call to arms (or official denunciation of the enemy);

xi

【隰】 (1) low, marshy land; (2) newly opened farmland; (3) a surname;

xi

【襲】 (1) assail; attack by surprise; make a surprise attack on; raid; take by surprise; (2) carry on as before; follow the pattern of; hereditary; inherit; (3) clothe in; put on; wear; (4) a set of dress; a suit of clothes; (5) double; repeated; (6) appropriate; plagiarize; (7) a surname;

[襲奪] attack by surprise; take by surprise; take over by a surprise attack;

[襲封] inherit a title from one's forefathers;

[襲擊] attack by surprise; come at; fly at sb's throat; make a raid; make a surprise attack on; raid; surprise attack;

襲擊名單 hit list;

拂曉襲擊 dawn raid;

[襲來] sweep over;

突然襲來 sweep over;

[襲取] (1) take by surprise; (2) take over;

[襲人] (1) copy; (2) assail one's nose;

襲人故智 copy an old trick;

花氣襲人 the fragrance of flowers assails one's nose;

[襲用] follow a practice; take over;

襲用古方 take over an age-old recipe;

奔襲 long-range incursion;

抄襲 crib; plagiarize;

勦襲 (1) borrow indiscriminately from other people's experience; (2) lift; plagiarize;

承襲 (1) adopt; follow (a tradition, etc.); (2) inherit;

蹈襲 follow slavishly;

急襲 launch a sudden and fierce attach;

空襲 aerial attack; air attack; air raid; make an air raid; launch an air attack;

奇襲 launch a surprise attack on; raid; surprise attack;

強襲 attack the enemy by means of an artillery barrage;

侵襲 hit; invade and attack; make a sneak attack on; make an intrusive attack on; make inroads on; smite;

世襲 hereditary; inherit;

偷襲 attack by surprise; sneak attack; sneak raid; surprise attack;

突襲 make a surprise attack;

沿襲 carry on as before; follow the tradition;

掩襲 mount a surprise attack;

夜襲 night attack; night raid;

因襲 carry on as before; copy; follow; follow conventions and traditions;

xi³

xi

【洗】 (1) bathe; clean; cleanse; clear; rinse; wash; (2) baptize; (3) kill and loot; sack; (4) develop; (5) shuffle;

[洗兵] end hostilities; stop fighting;

[洗擦] wash and scrub;

[洗車] wash a car;

洗車場 car wash;

洗車處 car wash;

洗車服務 valeting service;

[洗塵] give a welcome dinner to a visitor from afar;

洗塵接風 give a banquet of welcome for a visitor from afar; give a dinner of welcome to a friend on his return from travel; invite a visitor to a feast upon his arrival;

設饌洗塵 set out food and give a welcome dinner;

[洗滌] absterge; clean; cleanse; rinse; wash;

洗滌標籤 care label;

洗滌劑 abstergent; detergent; washingup liquid;

~ 複配洗滌劑 built detergent;

~ 抗生物洗滌劑 bioresistant detergent;

~ 兩性洗滌劑 ampholytic detergent;

~ 通用洗滌劑 all-purpose detergent;

~ 陰離子洗滌劑 anion detergent;

洗滌瓶 wash bottle;

~ 氣體洗滌瓶 wash-bottle for gases;

洗滌器 scrubber;

~ 多效洗滌器 multiwash scrubber;

~ 機械洗滌器 mechanical washer scrubber scrubber;

洗滌設備 washing appliance;

蒸汽洗滌 steam clean;

[洗耳] clean one's ears;

洗耳恭聽 bend an ear; clean one's ears; cock one's ears to listen; one is all ears; listen respectfully; prick up one's ears; strain one's ears to listen; with open ears;

鑿壞而遁，洗耳不聽 wash one's ear and refuse to listen;

[洗髮] have hair washed; shampoo;

洗髮粉 shampoo powder;

洗髮膏 paste shampoo;

洗髮劑 shampoo;

~ 塊狀洗髮劑 cake shampoo;

~ 一小袋洗髮劑 a sachet of shampoo;

洗髮水 shampoo;

洗髮液 liquid shampoo;

[洗垢求瘢] find fault with sb on purpose; pick

holes in;

[洗甲] end hostilities; have a truce;

[洗腳] wash one's feet;

[洗劫] loot; pillage; plunder; ransack; sack; sack everything;

洗劫一空 be robbed of everything one has; rifle;

[洗潔精] detergent;

[洗淨] abstersion; wash sth until it's clean;

洗淨劑 abstersive;

[洗禮] (1) baptism; be baptize; (2) severe test;

病牀洗禮 clinic baptism;

接受洗禮 accept baptism;

舉行洗禮 baptize;

臨終洗禮 clinic baptism;

受洗禮 be baptized;

再洗禮 anabaptism;

[洗臉] wash one's face;

[洗練] elegant; polished; refined; succinct; terse;

[洗面] wash one's face;

眼淚洗面 one's face is bathed in tears; tears rain down one's cheeks; wash one's face with tears; with tears all over one's face;

以淚洗面 cry with abandon; one's face is bathed in tears; tears bathe the cheeks; wash one's face with tears — weep bitterly;

[洗腦] brainwash; brainwashing; indoctrinate; indoctrination;

進行洗腦 brainwash;

[洗片機] film-developing machine;

[洗錢] launder money; money laundering;

[洗清] redress; wash away;

洗不清 unable to vindicate oneself;

[洗腎] dialysis;

洗腎機 dialyzer;

[洗手] (1) wash one's hands; (2) stop doing evil and reform oneself; (3) wash one's hands of sth;

洗手不幹 clear one's skirts; hang up one's axe; never to do such a thing again; quit committing crimes; through with; throw up; wash one's hand of it once and for all; wash one's hands of the matter; wash one's hands of the whole affair;

洗手間 cloakroom; commode; lavatory; rest room; toilet; washroom; water closet;

~女洗手間 ladies' cloakroom; the ladies;

[洗漱] wash one's face and rinse one's mouth;

洗漱用品 toiletries;

[洗刷] (1) scrub; wash and brush; (2) clear oneself of; vindicate oneself; wash off;

洗刷地板 scrub the floor;

洗刷污迹 wash the dirty marks off;

[洗頭] have one's hair washed; shampoo; wash one's hair;

[洗碗] wash the dishes;

洗碗布 dishcloth; dishrag;

洗碗工 dishwasher;

洗碗機 dishwasher;

洗碗盤 dishpan;

洗碗水 dishwater;

[洗胃] gastric lavage;

[洗心] cleanse one's heart;

洗心滌慮 cleanse one's heart and order one's behaviour; cleanse the heart from sin; make a thorough reformation; purify the heart and do away with cares; reform oneself thoroughly; repent genuinely; start life anew;

洗心革面 amend one's life; 戈 change one's heart and reform; cleanse one's heart and order one's behaviour; cleanse the heart from sin; reform oneself thoroughly; start life anew; turn over a new leaf;

滌慮洗心 sweep away anxieties and wash the heart;

革面洗心 reform oneself thoroughly; turn over a new leaf;

~革面洗心，重新做人 reform oneself inside out and start life anew; repent genuinely and make a fresh start;

[洗雪] clear sb of a false charge; redress a wrong; right a wrong; wipe out a disgrace;

[洗衣] do one's washing; wash clothes;

洗衣槽 laundry chute;

洗衣袋 laundry bag;

洗衣店 laundry;

~自助洗衣店 launderette;

洗衣房 laundry;

洗衣粉 soap powder; washing powder;

洗衣工 laundryman;

洗衣機 laundry machine; washer; washing machine;

~烘乾洗衣機 washer-dryer;
~一台洗衣機 a washing machine;
洗衣筐 laundry basket;
洗衣女工 washerwoman;
洗衣盆 washtub;
洗衣日 washday; washing day;
洗衣裳 wash clothes;
洗衣液包 liquitab;

［洗印］ film processing;
洗印車間 film laboratory;
洗印機 film processor;
黑白洗印機 black and white film processor;

［洗澡］ bathe; have a bath; take a bath; wash;
洗澡間 bathroom;

［洗盞更酌］ throw away the dregs from the wine-cup and fill it once more to the brim; wash the glass and change the liquor—continue drinking;

［洗濯］ cleanse; launder; wash;

筆洗 small tray for washing brushes;
擦洗 clean; rinse; scrub; scrubbing;
拆洗 (1) strip and clean; (2) unpick and wash;
沖洗 (1) develop (a film); (2) rinse; wash;
乾洗 dry-clean;
盥洗 wash one's hand and face;
湔洗 clear sb of a false charge; redress a wrong; wash clean;
漿洗 wash and starch;
浸洗 soak through and wash;
淋洗 drip-wash;
領洗 be baptised;
漂洗 potch; rinse;
清洗 (1) clean; cleaning; rinse; wash; wash clean; (2) comb out; eliminate; get rid of; purge; weed out;
施洗 baptize;
受洗 be baptized; receive baptism;
梳洗 clean up; comb one's hair and wash up; wash and dress;
刷洗 brushing; clean; scrub; wash out;
涮洗 rinse;
酸洗 pickle;
血洗 slaughter sanguinary;
用手洗 handwash;

xi

【枲】 male nettle-hemp;

［枲麻］ male hemp;

xi

【徙】 (1) migrate; move from one place to another; move one's abode; shift; (2) be exiled;

［徙邊］ move prisoners to the border areas;

［徙貫］ move one's residence to another place;

［徙居］ change one's residence; migrate; move house;
徙居內地 move up-country;

［徙任］ be transferred to another post; change to another post;

［徙善］ change for the better; reform;

［徙移］ migrate; move;

［徙倚］ indecision; irresolution; linger in hesitation;

［徙義］ change one's course toward what is right;

［徙宅忘妻］ one's living place is moved, but his wife is not taken along—extreme forgetfulness;

流徙 drift about; float about;
遷徙 migrate; move;

xi

【喜】 (1) delighted; happy; joyful; pleased; (2) happy event; joyful thing; occasion for celebration; (3) pregnancy; (4) fond of; have inclination for; like; love;

［喜愛］ fond of; keen on; have an inclination for; keen on; like; love;
不喜愛 not down sb's alley; not up sb's alley;
~我不喜愛集郵 stamp-collecting is not up my alley;
逗人喜愛 crack sb up; get a laugh from a person;
非常喜愛 think the world of sb;
深受顧客喜愛 win warm praise from customers;
深受喜愛 go down a treat;

［喜報］ bulletin of glad tidings;

［喜不自勝］ be delighted beyond measure; be overwhelmed with joy; be pleased beyond one's expectations; be transported with joy; beside oneself with joy; happy beyond words; in pleased surprise; joy beyond all

expectations; unable to contain oneself for joy; with unexpected joy;

[喜沖沖] be filled with gayety; in a joyful mood; joyful and gay; look exhilarated;

[喜出] be overjoyed;

喜出非分 be overjoyed;

喜出望外 be overcome with unexpected joy; delighted with one's unexpected good fortune; joy over unexpected good luck; overjoyed; pleasantly surprised; pleased beyond one's expectations; unexpected joy;

[喜從天降] a gift from the gods; a sudden unexpected happy event; an unexpected gladness; an unexpected piece of good fortune; can hardly believe one's good fortune; heaven-sent fortune; one's happiness seems to have dropped from the heavens; one's happiness is so unexpected as though it has dropped down from Heaven;

[喜房] bridal chamber;

[喜好] be interested in; be taken up with; death on; delight in; fond of; given to; go in for; great on; have a fancy for; have a liking for; have a predilection for; have a preference for; have a taste for; have a zest in; have an interest in; have one's heart in; interest oneself in; keen on; like; love; revel in; show an interest in; take a fancy to; take an interest in; take delight in; take pleasure in; take to;

喜好相同 have the same tastes; share a taste;

[喜歡] (1) fond of; keen on; like; love; prefer; (2) be filled with joy; delighted; elated; happy;

暗自喜歡 keep the joy to oneself;

不喜歡 dislike; distaste;

很喜歡 have a weakness for sth;

開始喜歡 cotton to; sth grows on sb;

討人喜歡 charming; cute; delightful; likeable; personable; pretty;

~討人喜歡的人 adorable creature; pleaser; real peach; sweetie;

[喜見於面] a face lit up with pleasure; not disguise one's gladness; visibly pleased;

[喜酒] (1) wine drunk at a wedding feast; (2) wedding feast;

[喜劇] comedy;

喜劇節目 comedy show;

喜劇連續劇 comedy series;

喜劇演員 comedian; comedy actor;

~女喜劇演員 comedienne;

喜劇作家 comdy writer;

打鬧喜劇 slapstick;

怪誕喜劇 screwball comedy;

輕喜劇 light comedy;

情境喜劇 sitcom; situation comedy;

音樂喜劇 musical comedy;

[喜樂] (1) gladness; great pleasure; joy; (2) give a zest to one's joy;

[喜娘] maid of honour;

[喜怒] happiness and anger;

喜怒哀樂 happiness, anger, grief and joy — the gamut of human feeling; happy or angry, sad or joyous; joy and anger, pleasure and sorrow; joy, anger, sorrow and happiness; joys and sorrows;

喜怒不形於色 expressionless; poker-faced; show no emotion; with a deadpan face;

喜怒無常 be given to capricious moods; capricious; changing quickly between pleasure and anger; having an unpredictable temper; moody; subject to changing moods; temperamental;

[喜氣] happy expression or atmosphere;

喜氣洋洋 a joyful atmosphere; a festive mood; a cheerful look; alight with happiness; all smiles; be filled with gaiety; burst with happiness; burst with joy; ebullition of joy; full of joy; in a lively outburst of happiness; jubilant all over; on cloud nine; radiance; radiant with joy; seethe with joy; with a jubilant atmosphere;

~臉上喜氣洋洋 one's face is alight with hap

喜氣洋溢 a joyful expression spreads all over the face; be overflowing with happiness;

[喜慶] (1) happy; joyous; jubilant; (2) auspicious occasions; happy events; happy occasions; (3) celebrate;

喜慶的日子 red-letter day;

婚喪喜慶 weddings and funerals;

[喜鵲] magpie;
喜鵲報喜 the magpie forcasts good news;
喜鵲喳喳叫 a magpie chatters;
[喜人] gratifying; satisfactory;
[喜容] happy look;
[喜色] happy expression; joyful look;
面有喜色 complacent look; wear a happy expression;
喜形於色 a face lit up with pleasure; a happy expression in one's countenance; appear merry; beam with delight; beam with happiness; have an expression of delight; light up with pleasure; look happy; look very pleased; one's face is lit up; visibly pleased;
喜盈於色 radiant with joy;
[喜上加喜] two happy events come one after the other; two happy events succeed one another;
[喜事] (1) happy event; joyous occasion; (2) wedding;
辦喜事 host a party on a joyous occasion; manage a wedding; organize a wedding; prepare for a happy occasion;
人逢喜事精神爽 a merry heart makes a cheerful countenance; joy puts heart into a man; on festive occasions one is in good spirits; people are in high spirits when involved in happy events; the heart's mirth does make the face fair; the joy of the heart makes the face merry;
~人逢喜事精神爽，春風得意馬蹄疾 the heart's mirth does make a cheerful countenance; the joy of the heart fairly colours the face; the joy of the heart makes a fair colour; the merry heart makes a fair face and a good complexion;
一樁喜事 a happy event;
[喜帖] wedding invitation;
[喜聞樂見] delighted to hear and see; like to hear and see; love to see and hear; receive with pleasure;
[喜信] good news; happy tidings;
[喜雪] seasonable snow; timely snow;
[喜訊] glad tidings; good news; happy news;
喜訊頻傳 glad tidings come one after the other; good news keeps pouring in; the happy news come one after another;
[喜筵] wedding feast;
[喜洋洋] beaming with joy; radiant;
[喜憂] pleasure and melancholy;
半喜半憂 half in pleasure and half in melancholy;
忽喜忽憂 fluctuate between hopes and fears;
時喜時憂 now gay, now gloomy;
轉喜為憂 laugh on the other side of one's face; laugh on the wrong side of one's face; sing on the wrong side of one's mouth;
[喜雨] seasonable rain; timely rainfall; welcome fall of rain;
普降喜雨 a seasonable fall of rain over a wide area; a widespread fall of seasonable rain;
[喜悅] delightful; happy; joyful; joyous;
喜悅之情 feeling of joy;
感到無比喜悅 feel a heavenly joy;
濃濃的喜悅 undiluted joy;
一陣喜悅 a wave of joy;
[喜滋滋] feeling pleased; filled with joy; joyful; looking pleased;

暗喜 feel secretly delighted; feel secretly happy;
報喜 announce good news; report success;
悲喜 joy and sorrow; sad and funny;
衝喜 save a patient's life by giving him a wedding to counteract bad luck;
大喜 great rejoicing;
道喜 congratulate sb on a happy occasion;
恭喜 congrats; congratulate; congratulation;
害喜 feel morning sickness of pregnant woman; pregnant;
賀喜 congratulate sb on a happy occasion;
歡喜 (1) delighted; happy; joyful; (2) delight in; fond of; like;
驚喜 pleasantly surprised;
可喜 gratifying heartening;
空喜 windy joy;
狂喜 be ravished with joy; rejoice with wild excitement; wild with joy;
雙喜 double happiness;
同喜 (in answer to sb's congratulations) thanks, the same to you;
欣喜 delighted; enjoyable; glad; gratifying; happy; joyful;
幸喜 fortunately; luckily;

有喜 be pregnant;

xi

【葸】 (1) scared; timid; (2) displeased look; not pleasant;

畏葸 be afraid; be timid;

xi

【屣】 sandals; shoes;

敝屣 worn-out shoes; worthless thing;

xi

【蓰】 (1) a variety of grass; (2) five times of anything; fivefold;

倍蓰 several times (between twofold to ninefold);

xi

【諰】 (1) speak frankly; (2) apprehensive;

[諰諰] afraid; apprehensive; fearful;

xi

【蟢】 a kind of long-bodied and long-legged spider;

xi

【璽】 (1) seal of an emperor; (2) formal seal of a state; national emblem;

xi⁴

xi

【夕】 (1) dusk; sunset; (2) evening; night; (3) oblique; slant; (4) a surname;

[夕暉] slanting rays of the setting sun;

[夕煙] evening mist;

[夕陽] the setting sun;

夕陽返照 the glow of setting sun; the sunset glow;

夕陽如血 the setting sun is as red as blood;

夕陽西下 the sun sets in the west;

[夕照] evening glow; glow of the setting sun;

除夕 New Year's Eve;

旦夕 in a short while; this morning or evening;

七夕 the seventh evening of the seventh moon (when according to legend the Cowherd and the Girl Weaver meet in Heaven);

前夕 eve;

朝夕 (1) a very short time; (2) day and night; morning and evening;

xi

【卌】 (1) forty; (2) fortieth;

xi

【汐】 nighttide; the flow of the tide at night;

xi

【系】 (1) connection; system; (2) department; faculty; (3) genealogy; lineage; (4) clique; party line; (5) bear on; relate to; (6) be concerned; feel anxious; (7) be; (8) a surname;

[系列] (1) a line of sth; (2) row; series;

系列報導 serial reports;

系列產品 series products;

系列片 film series;

反應系列 reaction series;

生態系列 ecological series;

同系列 homologous series;

一系列 a series of; a train of;

[系譜] family tree; genealogy; lineage;

[系數] coefficient;

系數比較 coefficient comparison;

安全系數 assurance coefficient; safety factor;

變位系數 addendum coefficient;

傳聲系數 acoustic transmission coefficient;

活度系數 activity coefficient;

降聲系數 acoustical reduction coefficient;

均衡系數 balanced coefficient;

~不均衡系數 unbalanced coefficient;

黏着系數 adhesion coefficient;

聲反射系數 acoustic reflection coefficient;

聲透射系數 acoustical transmission; coefficient;

聲相位系數 acoustic phase; coefficient;

酸度系數 acidity coefficient;

調節系數 accommodation coefficient;

吸音系數 acoustic absorption coefficient;

[系統] system;

系統安全 system safety;

~系統安全工程師 system safety engineer;

~系統安全危害分析 system safety hazard analysis;

系統安裝費 system installation fee;

系統操作員 system operator;

系統測試時間 system test time;

系統程序 system programme;

~系統程序庫 system library;

~系統程序設計 system programming;
~系統程序語言 system programming language;
~系統程序員 system programmer;
系統錯誤 systematic error;
系統動力學 system dynamics;
系統方法 systems approach;
系統仿真 systematic simulation;
系統分析 system analysis;
~系統分析員 system analyst;
系統風險 systematic risk;
系統工程 system engineering;
~系統工程理論 theory of systems engineering;
~系統工程師 system engineer
系統管理 system management;
~系統管理程序 programmes of system management;
~系統管理員 system administrator;
系統規劃 system planning;
系統化 systematize;
~系統化程序設計 systematic programming;
系統環境仿真 system environmental simulation;
系統恢復 system recovery;
~系統恢復時間 system recovery time;
系統集成 system on chip;
系統監查 system audit;
系統開發 systems development;
系統科學 systematic science;
~系統科學方法 systematic scientific method;
系統可靠性 system reliability;
系統領導 systematic leadership;
系統盤 system disk;
系統偏差 system deviation;
系統評價 system evaluation;
系統軟件 systems software;
系統設計 system design;
~系統設計員 system designer;
系統生態學 systematic ecology;
系統試驗 system testing;
系統協調 system coordination;
系統性 systematization;
系統有效性 system effectiveness;
系統語法 systemic grammar;
系統語言學 systemic linguistics;
系統運行 system running;
系統綜合分析 comprehensive analysis of system;
辦公系統 office system;
採用系統 adopt a system;
大系統 mega-system;
~大系統理論 theory of large scale system;
單向系統 uni-directional system;
電力系統 power system;
對稱系統 symmetric system;
~非對稱系統 asymmetric system;
多語系統 multilingual system;
翻譯系統 translation system;
防火系統 fire-prevention system;
分系統 subsystem;
~表示分系統 indication subsystem;
~控制分系統 control subsystem;
封閉性系統 closed system;
呼吸系統 breathing system;
開發系統 develop a system;
排水系統 drainage system;
神經系統 nervous system;
生態系統 ecological system;
鐵路系統 railway system;
通訊系統 communication system;
消化系統 digestive system;
一個系統 a system;
一套系統 a system;
郵電系統 postal system;
子系統 subsystem;
~子系統安全分析 subsystem safety analysis;
~耦合子系統 coupled subsystems;
~正規子系統 normal subsystem;
~指令子系統 command subsystem;
組織系統 organizational channels;

[系綜] ensemble;
廣義系綜 generalized ensemble;
原子核系綜 nuclear ensemble;
正則系綜 canonical ensemble;

[系族] family lineage; genealogy;

奧陶系 Ordovician Period;
白堊系 Cretaceous System;
嫡系 (1) direct line of descendants; (2) closest ties of relationship; one's own clique;
第三系 Tertiary Period;
第四系 Quaternary Period;
二疊系 Permian system;
翻譯系 translation department;
放射系 radiating system;
父系 (1) paternal line; the father's side of the family; (2) patriarchal;
根系 root system;
河外星系 extra-galactic nebula;
河系 river system; water system;

恒星系 galaxy; stellar system;
泌尿系 urological system
母系 (1) maternal side; (2) matriarchal;
派系 clique; faction; grouping;
旁系 collateral;
傍系 indirect blood relatives;
品系 strain;
譜系 pedigree;
區系 fauna;
三疊系 Triassic System;
山系 mountain system;
石碳系 Carboniferous Period;
世系 bloodline; family tree; genealogy; pedigree; stock;
水系 hydrographic net; river system;
太陽系 solar system;
體系 setup; system;
星系 galaxy;
姓系 family line;
岩系 rock formation; rock series;
音系 phonetic system;
銀河系 the Galaxy; the Milky Way system;
語系 language family;
圓系 system of circles;
雲系 cloud system;
直系 direct line relative;
職系 grade;
子系 offspring; posterity;

xi

【矽】 silicon;

［矽土］ silica;

xi

【肸】 (1) dispersed; spread out; (2) laughing; smiling; (3) flourishing;

xi

【穸】 (1) grave; tomb; (2) dead of night;

窀穸 grave; tomb;

xi

【係】 (1) bind; (2) consequences; relationship; (3) to be; (4) a surname;

［係獲］ capture;

［係數］ coefficient;

關係 (1) affect; concern; have to do with; (2) bearing; impact; significance; (3) because of; since; (4) credentials showing membership in or connection with an organization; (5) relation; relationship;

xi

【盻】 look in anger;

xi

【郤】 (1) an area in the ancient state of Jin; (2) crack; hollow; (3) a surname;

［郤地］ vacant area; vacant lot;

xi

【細】 (1) slender; slim; thin; (2) fine; in small particles; (3) thin and soft; (4) delicate; exquisite; fine; precise; (5) careful; (6) minute; (7) detailed; petty; trifling;

［細胞］ cell;
細胞板 cell plate;
細胞壁 cell wall;
細胞變態 cytomorphosis;
細胞併合 cell fusion;
細胞發生 cytogenesis;
細胞反應 cell effect;
細胞分化 cell differentiation;
細胞分裂 cell division;
細胞感應性 irritability of cell;
細胞肛 cytopyge;
細胞工程 cell engineering;
細胞過多 hypercellularity;
細胞過少 hypocellularity;
細胞核 cell nucleus;
細胞化學 cytochemistry;
細胞混合 cytomixis;
細胞集合 cell aggregation;
細胞減少 cyhtoreduction;
細胞結構 cellularity;
細胞口 cytostome;
細胞膜 cell membrane;
細胞內運動 intracellular movement;
細胞培養 cell culture;
細胞破裂 plasmatorrhexis;
細胞器 cellular organelle; organelle;
~亞細胞器 subcellular organelle;
~自主性細胞器 autonomous organelle;
細胞色素 cytochrome;
細胞生理學 cytophysiology;
細胞生物學 cytobiology;
細胞死亡 cell death;
細胞體 cell body;
細胞外消化 extracellular digestion;
細胞形態學 cytomorphology;
細胞學 cytology;
細胞液 cell sap;
細胞遺傳學 cytogenetics;

細胞運動 cytoplasmic movement;
細胞增殖 cell multiplication;
細胞張力 cell turgidity;
細胞質 cytoplasm;
細胞組織 cellular tissuee;
癌細胞 cancer cell;
白細胞 leucocyte; white blood cell;
~白細胞增多 leucocytosis;
分佈性白細胞增多 distributive leucocytosis;
相對白細胞增多 relative leucocytosis;
消化性白細胞增多 digestive leucocytosis;
~多核白細胞 multinuclear leucocyte;
~顆粒白細胞 granular leucocyte;
~嗜鹼白細胞 basophilic leucocyte;
~嗜酸白細胞 acidophile leucocyte;
扁平細胞 pavement cell;
單核細胞 uninuclear cell;
單細胞 unicellular;
感覺細胞 seensory cell;
幹細胞 stem cell;
紅細胞 erythrocyte; red blood cell;
卵細胞 egg cell; ovum;
蜜腺細胞 nectarous cell;
母細胞 mother cell;
胚細胞 blastocyte;
人造細胞 artificial cell;
攝物細胞 athrocyte;
神經細胞 nerve cell;
生殖細胞 generative cell; reproductive cell;
體細胞 somatic cell;
網狀細胞 reticulocyte;
無核細胞 akaryote;
性細胞 sex cell;
血細胞 haematocyte; haemocyte;
營養細胞 vegetative cell;
游動細胞 zoogonidium;
原始細胞 initial;
~精子器原始細胞 antheridial initial;
~射線原始細胞 ray initial;
~形成層原始細胞 cambial initial;
脂肪細胞 adipose cell;
滋養細胞 nutrient cell;
子細胞 daughter cell;

[細查] investigate thoroughly;

[細察] examine thoroughly; observe carefully; observe in detail;
細察究竟 examine the outcome minutely;
細察來意 judge the motive of one's coming;

[細長] long and thin; slender; tall and slender; tenuous;

[細大不捐] pay attention to the main aspects as well as to the minor ones; reject nothing, big or small;

[細讀] perusal; peruse; read carefully;
細讀文件 peruse a document;

[細度] fineness;
成品細度 finish fineness;
集料細度 fineness of aggregate;
水泥細度 cement fineness;

[細兒] young son;

[細工] fine and delicate work;

[細活] fine and delicate work;

[細講] state in detail;

[細嚼慢咽] chew carefully and swallow slowly; take one's time in eating;

[細節] details; minor points; minutiae; partifulars; specific; trifles;
細節安排 arrangement of particulars;
細節描寫 description of details;
不顧細節 disregard the particulars;
彩色細節 colour detail;
黑白細節 black-and-white detail;
具體細節 concrete details; exact details;
設計細節 design details;
提供細節 give particulars;
圖像細節 image detail;
詳情細節 detailed particulars;
主要的細節 essential details;

[細謹] overcautious about small points in etiquette;

[細究] examine into details;

[細君] one's wife;

[細菌] bacteria; germs;
細菌病 bacteriosis;
~細菌病毒 bacteriovirus;
細菌毒血症 bacteriotoxemia;
細菌鏡檢法 bacterioscopy;
細菌恐怖 bacteriophobia;
細菌療法 bacteriotherapy;
細菌武器 bacteriological weapon;
細菌學 bacteriology;
~細菌學家 bacteriologist;
~定量細菌學 quantitative bacteriology;
~工業細菌學 industrial bacteriology;
~公共衛生細菌學 public health bacteriology;
~鑒定細菌學 determinative bacteriology;
~乳品細菌學 dairy bacteriology;

~ 食品細菌學 food bacteriology;
~ 獸醫細菌學 veterinary bacteriology;
~ 衛生細菌學 sanitary bacteriology;
~ 醫學細菌學 medical bacteriology;
細菌營養 bacteriotrophy;
細菌戰 bacteriological warfare;
變形細菌 transmuted bug;
產色細菌 chromogenic bacteria;
大腸型細菌 coliform bacteria;
發光細菌 photogenetic bacteria;
發酵性細菌 zymogeneous bacteria;
非產氣細菌 anaerogenic bacteria;
浮游細菌 bacterioplankton;
腐敗細菌 putrefactive bacteria;
腐生細菌 metatrophic bacteria;
共生細菌 symbiotic bacteria;
寄生細菌 parasitic bacterium;
甲烷細菌 methane bacteria;
抗酸細菌 acid fast bacteria;
硫細菌 sulphur bacteria;
耐氧細菌 aerotolerant bacteria;
人造細菌 artificial bacteria;
嗜酸細菌 acidophilic bacteria;
嗜溫性細菌 mesophilic bacteria;
水生細菌 water bacteria;
鐵細菌 iron bacteria;
土壤細菌 soil bacteria;
硝化細菌 nitrate bacteria;
需氧細菌 aerobic bacteria;
厭氧細菌 anaerobic bacteria;
易溶性細菌 lyso-sensitive bacteria;
真細菌 true bacteria;

[細看] examine in detail; look at carefully;
定睛細看 give sb a good look; give sth a good look;
[細粒岩] fine-grained rock;
[細流] (1) small creek; (2) trickle;
涓涓細流 trickle;
一股細流 a trickle;
[細路] narrow path;
[細論] discuss in detail; elaborate;
[細密] (1) fine; fine and closely woven; close; (2) detailed; meticulous;
細密的部署 detailed arrangements;
細密的分析 detailed analysis;
紋理細密 have a fine grain;
針腳細密 the stitches are close;
質地細密 fine-grained; of close texture;
[細民] commoners; the masses; the people;
[細目] detailed items;
[細嫩] delicate; fair and tender; tender;
[細膩] (1) fine and smooth; (2) exquisite; minute;
感情細膩 sensitive;
[細巧] dainty; delicate; delicate and ingenious; exquisite; fine and delicate;
[細情] details of a matter;
[細軟] jewelry, expensive clothing and other valuables;
[細潤] fine and glossy;
[細弱] slender and weak; slim and fragile; thin and delicate;
[細聲] very low voice;
細聲細氣 in a soft voice; soft-spoken;
[細事] matters of little significance; trifles; trifling matters;
[細水] small stream;
細水長流 a small stream flows far; do sth little by little without cessation; economize to avoid running short; go about sth little by little without a let-up; make the reserves last a long period; plan on a long-term basis; practise frugality to avoid running short; resources can last a long time if consumed slowly;
[細説] give a detailed account; state in detail;
細説本末 recount the development from the beginning;
細説端詳 give a full and detailed account; give full particulars; relate all this in elaborate detail;
細説詳情 relate all this in elaborate detail;
[細絲] fine thread;
[細談] talk in detail;
[細聽] listen attentively;
側耳細聽 incline the head and listen attentively; prick up one's ears;
[細微] fine; minute; slight; subtle; tiny;
細微差別 fine distinction; subtle difference;
細微末節 details; side issues; trivial details;
細微之至 minute to the extreme;
[細味] think over carefully;
細味其言 ponder his words;
[細問] question in detail;
[細務] trifling matters;
毛舉細務 bring up trifling matters; enumerate all the details; talk about little things;

[細細] (1) very low; (2) very light; (3) very fine; (4) fine and delicate;

[細想] deliberate; deliberation; give careful thought to; ponder; think over sth carefully;

細想一下 think over;

[細小] little; petty; tiny; very small;

[細心] attentive; careful; cautious; circumpspective;

細心揣摩 think of it carefully;

辦事很細心 careful at work;

工作很細心 careful with one's work;

很細心 it is thoughtful of sth;

[細行] one's behaviour in trivial matters;

細行不矜 not attend to trifle matters;

[細腰] (1) slender waist; (2) slim-waisted wasp;

細腰削肩 with an ell-like figure and narrow, sloping shoulders;

[細雨] drizzle; fine rain;

細雨霏霏 a light drizzle; a light rain starts falling;

細雨紛紛 a steady fall of drizzling rain;

細雨蒙蒙 continuous drizzling;

細雨斜風 drizzle and slanting breeze;

毛毛細雨 drizzle; drizzling rain; mizzle;

牛毛細雨 drizzle; fine drizzling rain; mizzle;

斜風細雨 light wind and drizzling rain;

[細語] low and tender talk; pillow talk;

耳邊細語 whisper in one's ear;

[細則] by-laws; detailed rules and regulations;

[細針密縷] delicate and fine needlework; in fine, close stitches — in a meticulous way;

[細枝] slender twig; twiggery;

細枝末節 minor details; nonessentials; small branches — petty matters of no importance; trifles;

[細緻] (1) exquisite; fine and delicate; (2) careful; careful and thorough; meticulous; painstaking;

細緻周到 meticulous and attending to minute details in everything;

工作細緻 careful with one's work;

[細字] characters of very small size; fine print;

[細作] secret agent; spy;

把細 careful; cautious; mindful;

備細 all the details of; in detail;

粗細 the rough and the refined;

單細 delicate; slender;

底細 exact details; ins and outs;

繁細 excessively minute; overloaded with details;

工細 exquisite; skillful;

過細 meticulous; very careful;

加細 refine; refinement;

奸細 enemy agent; spy;

精細 fine; meticulous;

巨細 big and small;

苛細 harsh and loaded down with trivial details;

毛細 capillary;

瑣細 (1) frivolous; petty; trifling; (2) troublesome;

微細 tiny; very thin;

纖細 fine; slender; slim; tenuous; very thin;

詳細 at great length; at large; detailed; extensive; in great detail; in full; minute;

心細 careful; cautious;

嚴細 strict and careful;

奘細 thick and thin;

仔細 (1) attentive; careful; (2) economical; careful; frugal; look out;

xi

【翕】 (1) close; fold; (2) draw together; gather;

[翕合] join together; put together;

[翕忽] agile; nimble; swift;

[翕然] entirely harmonious; peace and stability; uniform;

[翕翼] fold wings;

[翕張] open and close alternately;

xi

【舄】 shoes; slippers;

xi

【隙】 (1) crack; crevice; fissure; (2) complaint; dislike; dispute; grudge; (3) leisure; spare time; (4) loophole; opportunity; (5) important corridor; important passageway;

[隙地] open space; unoccupied place;

冰隙 crevasse;

乘隙 take advantage of a loophole; turn sb's mistake to one's own account;

仇隙 bitter quarrel; feud;

縫隙 chink; crack; cranny; crevice; slit;

間隙 (1) gap; space; (2) interval of time;

空隙 (1) interval; (2) gap; space;

孔隙 hole; pore; small opening;
裂隙 chasm; crack; crevice; fissure; fracture;
伺隙 wait for an opportunity;
罅隙 crack; loose seam;
嫌隙 dislike born out of mutual resentment or suspicion; enmity;
有隙 harbour a grudge;
餘隙 clearance;

xi

【禊】 semi-annual exorcism performed at water's edge in ancient times;

xi

【潟】 saline land;
［潟湖］ lagoon;

xi

【歙】 inhale; suck;

xi

【戲】 (1) play; sport; (2) have fun; jest; joke; make fun of; (3) drama; play; show;
［戲班］ dramatic troupe; theatrical company; theatrical troupe;
［戲筆］ poem written at will;
［戲詞］ actor's lines;
［戲法］ conjuring; jugglery; juggling; magic; sleight of hand; tricks;
戲法人人會變，各有巧妙不同 everyone can do tricks, but not all tricks are the same; magicians are many, but each has his own tricks;
變戲法 conjure; conjuring; juggle; manipulate by trickery; perform sleight of hand;
［戲館子］ playhouse; theatre;
［戲劇］ (1) drama; play; theatre; (2) scenario; script;
戲劇衝突 dramatic conflict;
戲劇翻譯 drama translation;
戲劇工作人員 theatrical workers;
戲劇化 dramatize;
戲劇界 dramatic circles; theatrical circles;
戲劇老師 dreama teacher;
戲劇式反語 dramatic irony;
戲劇學校 drama school;
戲劇演出 performance;
邊緣戲劇 fringe theatre;
改編成戲劇 dramatize;
荒誕派戲劇 absurd theatre;
實驗戲劇 fringe theatre;
［戲迷］ drama fan; theatre fan; theatre goer;
［戲目］ theatrical programme;
［戲弄］ dupe; hoodwink; kid; make fun of; play a practical joke on; play tricks on; poke fun at; tease;
［戲票］ theatre ticket; ticket for a play;
免費戲票 complimentary ticket;
［戲曲］ drama; play; theatrical composition; traditional opera;
［戲耍］ make fun of; play tricks on; tease;
［戲水］ play in water; play with water;
［戲臺］ stage;
［戲文］ drama; theatrical writing;
［戲嬉］ merrymaking; play;
［戲謔］ banter; crack jokes; jest; joke; pleasantry; witticism;
［戲言］ jest; joke; say sth for fun; witticism;
君無戲言 the king's words are to be taken seriously;
［戲院］ movie house; theatre;
［戲中有戲］ there are shows within the show;
［戲裝］ theatrical costume;
［戲子］ actor; actress; dramatic player;
［戲作家］ dramatist;

敖戲 frolic; make merry; play; rollick; romp;
把戲 (1) acrobatics; (2) cheap trick; game; scheme; trick;
百戲 acrobatics (in ancient times);
扮戲 (1) make up; (2) perform on stage; play a role in a play; play the part of;
本戲 a whole series of an opera (as contrasted to highlights from an opera);
蹦蹦兒戲 the original from a pingjiu;
採茶戲 local opera popular in Jianxi, Hubei, Guangxi, and Anhui Provinces;
唱戲 act in an opera;
嘲戲 make fun of; poke fun at;
大戲 (1) Beijing opera; (2) full-scale drama;
地方戲 local drama; local opera;
獨腳戲 one-person show;
獨角戲 one-person show;
對臺戲 rival show;
兒戲 trifling matter;
鬼把戲 (1) dirty trick; sinister plot; (2) trick;
好戲 (1) good play; (2) great fun;
猴戲 monkey show;
花燈戲 a kind of local opera, popular in Yunnan and Sichuan provinces;
花鼓戲 flower-drum opera, popular in Hunan,

Hubei, Jiangxi, and Anhui provinces;
滑稽戲 farce;
京戲 Beijing opera;
看戲 see a movie;
傀儡戲 puppet play; puppet show;
梨園戲 a variety of Fujian opera;
柳子戲 a branch of Shandong local operas;
馬戲 circus;
木偶戲 puppet play; puppet show;
南戲 a kind of local classical opera in South China;
鬧戲 farce;
排戲 rehearse a performance; rehearse a play;
配戲 play a supporting role;
皮影戲 leather-sil-houette show; shadow play;
前戲 foreplay;
球戲 ball game;
耍戲 make a fool of sb;
調戲 assail with obscenities; flirt with women; indecent assault; molest; play the make on; take liberties with;
聽戲 go to the opera;
文明戲 modern drama;
文戲 Chinese operas characterized by singing and acting;
武戲 Chinese operas characterized by acrobatic fighting;
嬉戲 frolic; have jun; make merry; play; romp; sport;
險戲 dangerous;
現代戲 modern opera, drama, etc.;
小戲 operetta;
諧戲 jest; joke;
演戲 (1) act in a play; put on a play; (2) playact; pretend;
夜戲 evening performance; night show;
一場戲 a play;
一齣戲 a play;
一幕戲 an act;
一台戲 a theatrical performance;
淫戲 (1) sexual intercourse; (2) pornographic shows;
影戲 leather-sil-houette show; shadow play;
遊戲 (1) game; recreation; (2) play;
藏戲 Zang opera;
折子戲 lighlights from operas;
重頭戲 (1) opera difficult to act or sing; (2) important task;
壯戲 Zhuang opera;
做戲 (1) act in a play; (2) playact; put on a show;

xi

【餼】 (1) present as a gift; (2) animals; animals for sacrifice; (3) grains; rice; (4) animal feeds; fodder; provision;

[餼羊] sheep for sacrifices;

xi

【繫】 connect; fasten; join; link; tie;

[繫絆] bridle; hinder;
[繫泊] moor a boat;
[繫詞] copula;
繫詞性動詞 copulative verb;
繫詞性複合詞 copulative compound;
繫詞性連詞 copulative conjunction;
[繫掛] be concerned about; many worries;
[繫懷] have one's heart drawn by;
[繫戀] inextricably in love with; reluctant to leave;
[繫留] moor;
[繫馬] tie up a horse;
[繫念] have constantly on one's mind;
[繫囚] be imprisoned;
[繫腰] girdle; waistband;
[繫獄] be imprisoned; imprison;

逮繫 arrest and detain;
聯繫 communicate with; contact; contact with; connection; forge links with; get in touch with; get into touch with; get on to; in touch; keep in contact with; keep in touch with; keep links with; keep touch with; keep up with; maintain links with; mainties with; make contact; make contact with;
維繫 hold together; maintain;

xia¹

xia

【瞎】 (1) blind; blindly; (2) aimlessly; foolishly; groundlessly; heedless; reckless;

[瞎編] fabricate; make up;
[瞎猜] a shot in the dark; guess blindly; guess groundlessly; guess wildly; guess without ground; make a random guess; make a wild guess;
[瞎扯] chat aimlessly; speak nonsense; talk recklessly; talk rubbish; tell lies; waffle;
[瞎闖] make rash moves; make reckless; move ahead without a set purpose;

[瞎吹] brag; make wild boasts;
瞎吹牛 throw the bull;
[瞎搞] do a thing without any method;
瞎搞一通 act without a plan; make a mess of;
[瞎話] hooey; lies; nonsensical remark; untruth;
[瞎賴] put blame on others without the slightest justification;
[瞎聊] chat idly; converse at random; jaw; talk nonsense;
[瞎忙] bustle without plan or purpose; busy for nothing; busy with; mess about;
[瞎矇] calculate roughly;
[瞎鬧] (1) act senselessly; make nonsense; mess about; (2) fool around; mischievous;
瞎鬧一氣 kick up a row; make a row; raise hell; raise the mischief;
[瞎弄] throw into confusion; throw into disorder;
[瞎捧] heap praises on sb blindly;
[瞎碰亂闖] strike out at random;
[瞎說] blab; bullshit; speak groundlessly; talk irresponsibly; talk nonsense; talk rubbish;
瞎說八道 make reckless utterances; talk nonsense; talk through one's hat; tell lies;
瞎說的人 blab; blabber;
瞎說一頓 nonsensical talk; talk about sth useless; talk nonsense;
胡吹瞎說 brag groundlessly; drivel irresponsibly;
[瞎眼] blind;
[瞎謅] make up wild stories; speak groundlessly; talk irresponsibly; waffle;
[瞎抓] do things without a plan; go about sth in a haphazard way;
瞎抓亂碰 go about one's work blindly and haphazardly;
[瞎子] blind man; blind person;
瞎子吃蒼蠅一眼不見為淨 the blind eat many a fly;
瞎子戴眼鏡一多餘 a blind person wearing glasses — all for show;
瞎子點燈白費蠟 as useless as a blind man lighting a candle; it is like lighting a lamp for a blind man — absolutely useless; just as a blind man is wasting a candle by lighting it; like lighting a candle for a blind man — a sheer waste;
瞎子害眼睛一沒治了 a blind person hurts his eyes — incurable;
瞎子見錢眼也開 money will open a blind man's eyes; on seeing money, even a blind man would have his eyes wide open;
瞎子看戲，人笑亦笑 a blind man sees the show — follow others in laughter;
瞎子摸象 the blind man feels an elephant — take a part for the whole;
瞎子摸魚 like a blind man groping for fish — act blindly; like blind man trying to catch fish with his bare hands;
瞎子拿書供人讀 a blind man takes a book, which only others can read;
睜眼瞎子 a man who can neither read nor write; a man unable to write or read; illiterate person

抓瞎 be at a loss what to do; be in a rush and muddle;

xia

【蝦】 shrimp;
[蝦乾] dried prawn;
[蝦蛄] mantis shrimp;
[蝦醬] shrimp paste; shrimp sauce;
[蝦塊] prawn cubes;
[蝦米] dried shrimps;
[蝦皮] dried small shrimps;
[蝦片] prawn slices; shrimp cracker;
[蝦仁] shrimp meat;
[蝦油] shrimp sauce;
[蝦子] shrimp eggs; shrimp roe;

螯蝦 crayfish;
大蝦 prawn;
對蝦 shrimps;prawn;
河蝦 river prawn; shrimp;
磷蝦 euphausiid; krill;
糠蝦 mysid;
龍蝦 lobster;
鹵蝦 a kind of food made from shrimps, salt, etc.;
毛蝦 shrimp;
明蝦 prawn;

青蝦 freshwater shrimp;
魚蝦 fish and shrimps;

xia²

xia

【匣】 (1) case; small box; (2) cage;
[匣子] casket; small box; small case;
黑匣子 black box; flight recorder;
話匣子 (1) gramophone; (2) radio receiving set; (3) chatterbox;

暗匣 camera obscura;
彈匣 magazine;
鏡匣 dressing case; wooden case with a looking glass and other toilet articles;
聲匣 voice box;

xia

【狎】 show disrespect; show familiarity; show intimacy;
[狎而敬之] intimate but respectful;
[狎妓] indulge in dallying with prostitutes; visit a brothel;
狎妓冶遊 intimate with prostitutes and frequent brothels;
[狎近] very familiar; very intimate;
[狎客] (1) disrespectful person; impolite person; rude person; (2) a prostitute's customer;
[狎昵] improperly familiar with; very familiar; very intimate;
[狎弄] impolite to; rude to; show improper familiarity with;
[狎翫] show disrespect from familiarity;
[狎侮] impolite to; show improper intimacy with; treat with disrespect;
[狎邪] (1) indulge in vice; visit a brothel; (2) improper;

玩狎 (1) dally with; (2) play with frivolously;

xia

【俠】 (1) person dedicated to helping the poor and weak; (2) chivalry; (3) a surname;
[俠盜] robber dedicated to the cause of justice;
[俠骨] chivalrous spirit;
俠骨心腸 chivalrous frame of mind;
[俠客] chivalrous expert; person adept in martial arts and having a strong sense of justice and ready to help the weak; swordsman;
[俠烈] chivalrous;
[俠氣] chivalry;
[俠義] chivalrous; strong sense of justice;

豪俠 gallant; gallant man;
劍俠 knight-errant; swordsman who champions the cause of the down-trodden;
遊俠 person adept in martial arts and given to chivalrous conduct;

xia

【柙】 (1) pen for wild beasts, especially the fierce ones; (2) case for sword; scabbard;

xia

【洽】 (1) diffuse; spread; (2) agreement; harmony; (3) negotiate;
[洽辦] handle an assignment through negotiation;
[洽博] of wide experience and knowledge;
[洽化] diffuse virtuous influence;
[洽商] discuss;
[洽談] consult together; discuss together;
[洽聞] learned; of wide knowledge; widely read;
[洽議] meet and discuss sth;

xia

【峽】 (1) gorge; strait; (2) isthmus; (3) narrow;
[峽谷] canyon; chasm; gorge; gulch; trench;
大峽谷 grand canyon;
箱形峽谷 box canyon;
[峽口] narrow;
[峽灣] sea lock;

地峽 isthmus;
海峽 channel; strait;
山峽 gorge;

xia

【狹】 (1) narrow; (2) narrow and limited; parochial;
[狹隘] (1) narrow; (2) narrow-minded; parochial;
狹隘的觀點 parochial point of view;
見地狹隘 narrow in outlook;
心胸狹隘 narrow-minded;
[狹長] long and narrow;

［狹陋］ narrow and dingy;

［狹路］ narrow path; narrow road;

狹路相逢 come into unavoidable confrontation; meet in a narrow path — inevitable revenge; run into each other on a narrow path — be squeezed into an ever-shrinking domain;

［狹小］ narrow and small;

狹小的 cramped;

~狹小的空間 narrow space;

襟度狹小 narrow-minded;

氣量狹小 narrow-minded;

心地狹小 small-minded;

眼光狹小 shortsighted;

［狹義］ narrow sense;

狹義語境 micro-context;

［狹窄］ (1) cramped; narrow; (2) narrow and limited;

狹窄的 cramped;

~狹窄的山道 narrow mountain path;

心地狹窄 narrow-minded;

心胸狹窄 narrow-minded;

胸懷狹窄 narrow-minded;

褊狹 cramped; narrow;

寬狹 breadth; width;

xia

【暇】 free time; leisure; spare time;

［暇景］ leisure hours; spare time;

［暇刻］ free moment;

［暇日］ days of leisure; free days; leisure; spare time;

［暇時］ at leisure; at one's leisure; in one's leisure time; spare time;

［暇逸］ idle; relax; relaxation;

［暇豫］ leisurely; relaxation; relaxed;

不暇 be too busy (to do sth); have no time (for sth);

空暇 free time; spare time;

無暇 be too busy; have no time;

閒暇 leisure;

餘暇 leisure; leisure time; spare time;

xia

【瑕】 (1) flaw in a piece of jade; (2) defect; flaw; shortcoming;

［瑕病］ blemish; flaw;

［瑕疵］ blemish; defect; flaw; moil;

瑕疵污垢 besmear sb's reputation;

［瑕隙］ loophole;

抵瑕蹈隙 attack sb's weak points; exploit the shortcomings of others; point out sb's flaws;

［瑕瑜］ good and bad points; virtues and flaws;

瑕瑜互見 every white has its black and every sweet its sour; have both correct and mistaken aspects; have both merits and defects; have both strong and weak points; have defects as well as merits; see both its good and bad points;

瑕瑜俱見 see both its good and bad points;

瑾瑜匿瑕 flaws hidden in a beautiful gem — even in the most beautiful gem there are flaws;

瑕不掩瑜 defects cannot belittle virtues; one flaw cannot mar the jade — small defects cannot obscure great virtues; one flws cannot obscure the splendour of the jade — the defects cannot obscure the virtues; the flaws do not detract from the jade's essential beauty — blemishes do not detract from a man's greatness;

xia

【遐】 (1) distant; far; (2) lasting; long; (3) advanced in years; (4) die down; vanish; (5) abandon; cast off;

［遐布］ spread far and wide;

［遐邇］ far and near;

遐邇皆知 know to all; well-known far and ear;

遐邇聞名 enjoy widespread renown; well-known far and near;

遐邇一體 both the near and the distant are treated alike;

［遐方］ distant places;

［遐福］ great happiness; lasting blessings; lasting happiness;

［遐軌］ long-established models of conduct;

［遐荒］ distant and out-of-the-way places;

［遐蹟］ matters and stories of ancient people;

［遐舉］ go on a distant journey;

［遐齡］ advanced age; longevity; long life;

［遐棄］ (1) cast away; reject; shun; (2) desert one's post;

［遐思］ wild and fanciful thoughts;

［遐眺］ stretch one's sight as far as it can reach;

［遐想］ be lost in wild and fanciful thoughts;

daydream; reverie;
[遐心] (1) thought of keeping aloof; (2) wish to abandon; (3) desire to live in retirement;
[遐祉] lasting blessings; lasting happiness;
[遐志] lofty ambition; lofty aspiration;
[遐終] forever;

xia
【舝】 linchpin;

xia
【轄】 (1) linchpin; (2) administer; govern; manage; (3) noise of wheels;
[轄境] area under one's jurisdiction;
[轄下] under the jurisdiction of;
[轄治] administer; govern; rule;

管轄 administer; control over; exercise; have jurisdiction over;
統轄 control over; exercise; govern;
直轄 directly under the jurisdiction of;

xia
【霞】 evening glow; morning glow; rosy clouds;
[霞光] rays of morning or evening sunlight; sunglow;
霞光四射 the sky is suffused with a rosy light;
霞光萬道 a myriad of sun rays;
[霞霧滿天] the sky is covered with mist — it is foggy;

彩霞 pink clouds; rosy clouds;
錦霞 rosetinted clouds;
曉霞 rosy clouds at daybreak;
晚霞 sunset clouds; sunset glow; the evening glow;
煙霞 mist and clouds in the twilight; mists and rosy clouds in the twilight;
雲霞 rosy clouds;
早霞 morning glow; rosy clouds of dawn; rosy dawn;
朝霞 morning glow; rosy clouds of dawn; rosy dawn;

xia
【黠】 (1) clever; shrewd; smart; (2) artful; crafty; cunning; wily;
[黠慧] clever; shrewd; smart;
[黠吏] crafty officials;
[黠鼠] (1) cunning rat; (2) cunning person;
[黠智] clever; crafty; shrewd; smart;

鬼黠 crafty; sly;
慧黠 clever and artful; shrewd;
狡黠 crafty; cunning;

xia⁴
xia
【下】 (1) below; down; under; (2) lower; inferior; (3) latter; next; second; (4) down; downward; (5) under; (6) alight; descend; get off; (7) fall; (8) deliver; issue; (9) go to; (10) exit; (11) cast; put in; (12) dismantle; take away; take off; (13) form; (14) apply; use; (15) give birth to; lay; (16) capture; take; (17) give in; yield; (18) finish; leave off; (19) less than; (20) a mouthful;

[下巴] (1) lower jaw; (2) chin;
下巴掛鈴鐺—想（響）到哪説到哪兒 a bell hanging on the chin — speaking whatever occurs to one;
下巴伸出 jut jaw;
下巴窩 dimple in the chin;
揉擦下巴 rub jaw;
雙下巴 double chin;
脱下巴 dislocated jaw;
向後縮的下巴 receding chin;
向後削的下巴 retreating chin;
[下拜] bow;
躬身下拜 bend the knee in obeisance; bow with the body slightly bent, as a sign of respect;
[下班] clock off; come off work; go off work; knock off; leave office; off duty;
按時上下班 keep good working hours;
五點下班 knock off at five;
早點下班 knock off early;
[下輩] next generation; younger generation of a family;
下輩子 life after death; the life to come; the next incarnation; the next life;
[下筆] begin to write; put pen to paper; start writing;
下筆成篇 have literary acumen; write a composition in a stream; write like an angel;
下筆成章 have a ready pen; have literary acumen; whatever one writes turns

into a fine essay; write like an angel; write quickly and skilfully;

下筆快 write with ease;

下筆立就 write off without hesitation; write with ease and forthwith completed;

下筆千言 thousands of words flow from one's pen; write quickly; write with amazing speed;

下筆千言，離題萬里 a thousand words from the pen in a stream, but ten thousand li away from the theme — write fast and at length but not to the point; long-winded and irrelevant; write quickly but stray from the theme;

下筆如有神 write as if with a magic pen; write like an angel; write quickly and powerfully;

[下邊] (1) as follows; following; (2) below; under;

[下膊] lower arm;

[下不來] (1) cannot get down; (2) embarrassed;

[下不去] cause sb to lose face; go against; harass;

[下不為例] just for once; not to be made a precedent; not to be repeated; not to be taken as a precedent; this does not constitute a precedent;

[下部] (1) lower part; (2) private parts;

[下策] bad measure; bad plan; bad policy; bad strategy; stupid move; unwise decision;

[下層] (1) lower layer; lower stratum; (2) low-ranking;

下層階級 lower class;

下層社會 lower orders; underclass;

[下場] (1) exit; go off stage; leave the playing field; take one's exit; (2) take an examination; (3) end; fate;

好下場 good ending;

[下車] (1) get off; get out of a car; (2) take up new office;

下車伊始 as soon as one alights from official carriage — on arrival; immediately on arrival at a new post; the moment one alights from the official carriage — the moment one takes up one's official post; the moment one arrives at a post of appointment;

讓人下車 put sb off;

中途下車 break the journey;

[下沉] (1) sink; submerge; subside; (2) cave in; sink; subside;

[下廚] go to the kitchen; prepare food;

[下船] debark; disembark; go ashore;

[下牀] get up;

跳下牀 jump out of bed;

[下垂] droop; hang down; sag;

[下次] next; next time;

下次吧 take a rain check;

[下存] remain after deduction;

[下達] make known to lower levels; transmit to lower levels;

下達命令 issue an order; issue commands;

下達任務 assign a task;

下達指示 give instructions;

口頭下達 give verbal instructions;

書面下達 issue written instructions;

[下代] descendant; next generation;

[下蛋] lay eggs;

[下等] (1) inferior; low-grade; (2) depraved; mean;

[下跌] drop; fall; plummet; slide;

[下毒] poison; put poison into sth;

下毒手 lay murderous hands on; lay violent hands on sb; resort to violent treachery; strike a vicious blow;

[下顎] lower jaw;

下顎骨 lower jaw bone; mandible;

下顎骨折 mandibular;

下顎脱位 dislocation of the lower jaw;

[下凡] descend to earth from heaven;

[下飯] go along with rice;

[下方] (1) south and west; (2) below; under; (3) the earth;

[下房] servant's quarters;

[下放] transfer to a lower level;

[下風] (1) at a disadvantage; in an inferior position; (2) leeward;

甘拜下風 acknowledge defeat; acknowledge the corn; admit defeat; admit oneself beaten; admit that sb has gained the upper hand; bow to sb's superiority; concede defeat willingly; confess oneself beaten; give in; give sb best; lower one's sail; lower one's flag; show the white feather; strike one's flag; throw in one's hand; throw in the towel; toss in the towel; willing

to take an inferior position;
佔下風 at a disadvantage;

[下崗] go off sentry duty;

[下跪] go down on one's knees; kneel down;

[下海] (1) go to sea; put out to sea; (2) go fishing on the sea; (3) become professional actors or actresses; (4) turn professional;
下海工作 go to sea;
下海經商 plunge into the private business;

[下懷] one's concern; one's desire; one's heart's desire;
正中對手下懷 play into sb's hands

[下回] next time;
下回分解 it will be told in the next chapter; to be continued in the next chapter;
~且聽下回分解 be analyzed and explained below; no such effort will be made for the present;

[下貨] ship goods; unload goods;

[下級] (1) lower levels; (2) subordinates;

[下嫁] marry someone beneath her station;

[下賤] base; cheap; degrading; low; mean;

[下江] downstream;

[下降] come down; decline; decrease; descend; downgrade; droop; drop; fall; fall off; go down;
略有下降 decline slightly;
數量的下降 drop in quantity;
突然下降 go down rapidly;
徒然下降 decline sharply;
穩步下降 go down steadily;
物價在下降 prices are falling;
質量的下降 fall in quality;
逐月下降 decline monthly;

[下腳] (1) get a foothold; make a short stay; plant one's foot; (2) residual raw materials; scraps;

[下酒] (1) go with wine; (2) go well with wine;
下酒菜 a dish that goes with wine;

[下課] come off from class; dismiss class; finish class; get out of class;
下課鈴 recess bell;

[下款] (1) name of the donor; (2) signature at the end of a letter; signature in a scroll;

[下來] alight; come down; come from a higher place; go among the masses;
安定下來 quiet down;
~局勢安定下來 the situation has settled down;
安靜下來 calm down; pipe down; quiet down;
扳下來 pull off;
背下來 learn by heart;
~把…背下來 repeat...by heart; repeat...from memory;
從出租汽車下來 alight from a taxi;
掉下來 drop down; get down;
蹲下來 squat down;
滾下來 dislodge; roll down;
滑下來 slide down;
冷靜下來 calm down; cool down; cool off; simmer down; sober down;
留下來 hand over; stop behind; wait behind;
~留下來吃晚飯 stay for dinner;
慢慢停下來 stop slowly;
慢下來 slow down;
平靜下來 calm down;
撕下來 tear off;
塌下來 cave in; collapse; fall down;
~塌下心來 keep one's mind on sth;
跳下來 jump down;
遺傳下來 hand down by heredity;
鎮靜下來 become calm; calm down; collect; compose oneself; cool it; gather up one's sense; keep calm; keep cool; keep one's shirt on; simmer down; stay calm;

[下淚] shed tears;
黯然下淚 grieve to the shedding of tears;

[下聯] second line of a couplet;

[下列] as follows; following; listed below;

[下令] give orders; order;

[下流] (1) lower reaches of a river; (2) flow down; (3) downstream; (4) dirty; low; low-down; mean; nasty; near the bone; obscene; off colour; scurrilous;
下流勾當 base acts; despicable tricks;
下流話 dirty language; foul language; lewd comments; obscene language; obscenities;
~滿口下流話 make the air blue;
下流笑話 blue jokes; dirty jokes;
舉止下流 have a coarse manner;

[下樓] descend the stairs; go downstairs;

[下略] what follows is omitted;

[下落] (1) whereabouts; (2) drop; fall;

下落不明 among the missing; one's whereabouts is a mystery;
自由下落 free fall;

［下馬］ (1) dismount from a horse; get down from a horse; (2) abandon; discontinue; drop;
下馬威 a head-on blow at the first encounter; instant severity; prompt reprisals; severity shown by an official on assuming office; the severity of a newly-appointed official;
滾鞍下馬 alight from one's horse; slip out of the saddle; turn quickly upon one's saddle and dismount;
拉下馬 unseat;

［下面］ (1) below; under; underneath; (2) following; next; (3) lower level; (4) men at the lower levels;

［下麵］ cook noodles;

［下女］ maid;

［下品］ inferior; low-grade;
下品貨 low-quality goods;

［下聘］ present betrothal gifts;

［下棋］ have a game of chess; play chess;

［下潛］ dive;

［下情］ conditions at the lower levels; feelings of the masses; the opinions of the masses;
下情上達 conditions at the lower levels be made known to the higher levels; make the situation at the lower levels known to the higher authorities; make the situation below known to those above; notify the superior of the circumstance of the inferiors; report the feelings of the common people to the higher authorities; report the state of affairs to the higher level;

［下去］ (1) descend; go down; (2) continue; go on;
按下去 press down;
滑落下去 slide off;
混不下去 can no longer permit oneself to drift along; cannot get by; cannot stay on the job any longer; difficult for one to keep on going; no longer able to carry on as before; no longer able to muddle along;
活不下去 lack the means, strength to live on;
説不下去 (1) unable to continue one's speech; (2) not acceptable to one's sense of propriety;

［下人］ servant;

［下山］ go down a hill; go down a mountain; go downhill;
下山容易上山難 going downhill is easy, going uphill is difficult; it is easier to walk downhill than uphill;
奔下山 run down the hill;

［下身］ (1) lower part of the body; (2) loin; private parts; privates; (3) trousers;

［下剩］ be left;

［下士］ corporal;

［下世］ die; pass away;

［下室］ bedroom;

［下手］ (1) put one's hand to; set about; set to; start; start doing sth; (2) commit a crime; (3) assistant; helper; inferior attendant;
滾油鍋裏撿金子—難下手 picking gold out from a pot of boiling oil — difficult to put one's hand into;
急於下手 eager to set to sth;
沒有機會下手 there is no chance to set about;
伺機下手 wait for the opportunity to set about;
無從下手 have no way of doing sth; not know how to start;
先下手為強 he who strikes first gains the advantage; he who strikes first prevails; it's always advantageous to make the first move; offence is the best defence; the best defence is offence; the early bird gets the worm; the first blow is half the battle; to take the initiative is to gain the upper hand; whoever strikes the first blow has the advantage;
~先下手為強，後下手遭殃 he who strikes first prevails, he who strikes late fails;

［下首］ right-hand seat;

［下書］ deliver a letter;
下書人 messenger;

［下屬］ minion; subordinate;

［下水］ (1) be launched; enter the water; (2) launch a boat; (3) fall into evil ways; take to evildoing; (4) downriver; downstream;

下水道 drain; foul water sewer; sewer;
~合流下水道 combined sewer;
~總下水道 common sewer;
下水管 drain;
下水禮 the ceremony of launching a ship;

[下榻] put up; stay; take up abode;

[下台] (1) get off stage; step down from the stage or platform; (2) extricate oneself from a position; fall out of power; go out of power; leave office; out of power; relieve from office; resign; resign one's right;
趕下台 outcast; throw out; turn out; unhorse;
下不了台 on the spot; put sb to a nonplus; cannot find a way out of embarrassing situation; unable to back down with good grace; unable to extricate oneself from an awkward position; unable to find a way out of an embarassing situation; unable to get off the spot;
要求下台 call for sb's scalp;

[下堂] be divorced by one's husband; leave one's husband;

[下體] (1) loin; lower part of the body; (2) private parts; privates;
下體護身 jockstrap;

[下田] cultivate the land; work on farmland;

[下帖] send an invitation;

[下同] similarly hereinafter; the same below;

[下頭] (1) as follows; (2) below; under;

[下位關係] hyponymy;

[下位義項] hyponym;

[下文] (1) what flows in the passage; (2) outcome; sequel; what follows;

[下問] learn from one's inferior;
不恥下問 ask for advice from those beneath oneself; modest enough to consult one's inferiors; not consider it beneath one's dignity to learn something from one's subordinates by asking about it; not feel ashamed to ask and learn from one's subordinates; not feel ashamed to consult his inferiors; not feel ashamed to seek advice from those beneath his station in life; not to mind seeking advice from the rank and file; stoop to ask advice from the common run of people;

[下無怨骨，上無怨人] no one, whether dead or living, will have any cause to complain;

[下午] afternoon;
下午茶 afternoon tea;
下午場 matinee;
下午好 good afternoon;
每天下午 every afternoon;
明天下午 tomorrow afternoon;
整個下午 all afternoon; all the afternoon;

[下霧] foggy; mist;

[下限] floor level; lower limit; prescribed minimum;

[下陷] cave in; sag; sink; undercut;

[下鄉] go to the countryside; rusticate;

[下行] traveling away from the starting point of a line;
下行車 the down train;

[下旋] backspin; underspin;

[下雪] snow;

[下學] leave for home after school;

[下旬] last ten days of a month;

[下嚥] swallow;

[下野] be forced to relinquish power; resign from official posts; retire from the political arena;

[下游] downstream;
甘居下游 be resigned to a state of lagging behind; be resigned to backwardness; be resigned to being backward; rest content with lagging behind;
河的下游 lower reaches of a river;

[下愚] fool; imbecile;

[下雨] rain;
下雨天 rainy day;
天要下雨，娘好嫁人 if it threatens to rain or your mother wishes to remarry, there is no way to stop them;
下起雨來 it starts to rain;
在下雨 it's raining;

[下獄] imprison; put behind bars; put into prison; send to jail; throw into prison;

[下月] next month;

[下載] download;
可下載 downloadable;

[下葬] bury; committal;

[下肢] lower limbs;

[下指] cataphora;

[下種] sow seed;

[下逐客令] ask an unwelcome guest to leave; order guest unceremoniously to get out; show sb the door; throw out a guest after he has overstayed his welcome;
[下注] put stake; stake a wager; wager;
[下箸] start eating;
[下粧] remove stage makeup and costume;
[下罪] convict;
[下作] (1) low; nasty; vulgar; (2) gluttonous; greedy;
[下座] inferior seat;

X

安下 retire for rest;
暗下 secretly;
擺下 (1) put down; (2) arrange;
卑下 base; humble; low; mean;
筆底下 ability to write;
筆下 (1) ability to write; (2) the wording and purport of what one writes;
陛下 His (or Her) Majesty; Your Majesty;
不下 (1) as good as; on a par with; (2) as many as; no less than;
部下 (1) subordinate; (2) troops under one's command;
扯下 tear down;
城下 under the city wall;
吃不下 not feel like eating; unable to eat any more;
打下 (1) capture; take; (2) lay a foundation;
帶下 morbid leucorrhoea;
當下 at once; immediately; instantly;
刀下 under the knife;
倒下 fall down;
低下 humble; low;
底下 below; beneath; under;
地下 (1) subterranean; underground; (2) secret; underground;
殿下 His (or Her) Highness; Your Highness;
掉下 (1) fall; (2) drop;
定下 fix; set;
丟下 lay aside; leave behind; throw down;
放下 lay down; put down;
垓下 Gaixia, in Anhui Province;
高下 relative superiority or inferiority;
閣下 His (or Her) Excellency; Your Excellency;
攻下 capture; overcome; take;
跪下 drop to one's knees; kneel;
麾下 (1) commander; your Excellency; (2) those under one's command;
記下 keep a record of; make a minute of; make a note of; minute down; take notes of;
腳下 under one's feet;
節下 festival; holiday;
刻下 at present; at the moment;
拉下 haul down;
林下 in the country;
留下 stay behind; wait behind;
樓下 downstairs;
落下 fall down;
門下 (1) hanger-on of an aristocrat; (2) disciple; pupil;
名下 belonging or related to sb; under sb's name;
目下 at present; now;
年下 lunar New Year holidays;
取下 take down;
泉下 nether world; world of the dead;
扔下 abandon; leave behind; put aside; throw down;
日下 at present;
容不下 unable to accommodate; unable to contain; unable to hold; unable to take in;
如下 as below; as follows;
閃下 leave behind;
上下 (1) high and low; old and young; ruler and subjects; senior and junior; superior and inferior; (2) above and below; from top to bottom; up and down; (3) go up and come down; go up and down; (4) about; more or less;
舍下 at present; at the moment;
身底下 (1) under the body; (2) the place where one is living;
省下 save money;
剩下 be left over; remain;
賸下 be left over; leave behind;
時下 at present; at the moment; in these days; nowadays; of the moment;
收下 accept; receive;
手底下 (1) at hand; (2) at the hands of sb; (3) one's financial condition at the moment; (4) under; under the leadership of;
手下 (1) at hand; (2) under the leadership of; under; (3) at the hands of sb; (4) one's financial condition the moment;
屬下 subordinates;
樹下 under the tree;
水下 submerged; under water;
睡下 lie down;
私下 in private; in secret; privately; under the rose;
撕下 tear down;
臺下 off the stage;
淌下 shed;

躺下 lie down;
天底下 (1) at hand; (2) at the hands of sb; (3) one's financial condition at the moment; (4) under; under the leadership of;
天下 (1) domination; rule; (2) hand under heaven; the world or China;
停下 shut down; stop;
投下 (1) drop; throw down; (2) invest in;
脱下 drop; shed; take off;
王天下 rule over the empire;
往下 downward;
穩下 calm down;
膝下 (1) (in letters) address to one's parents; (2) children;
轄下 under the jurisdiction of;
現下 (1) at present; now;
鄉下 country; countryside; village;
向下 down; downward;
脅下 the armpit; under the ribs;
卸下 disboard; unsnatch;
形而下 phenomenal; physical;
簷下 under the eaves;
眼底下 (1) at the moment; (2) right before one's eyes;
眼下 at present; at the moment; now;
腋下 armpit; under the arm;
一下 (1) once; one time; (2) all at once; all of a sudden; in a short while;
遺下 leave behind;
以下 (1) below; under; (2) the following;
意下 (1) in one's heart; in one's mind; (2) idea; opinion;
於下 as follows; below;
餘下 remaining;
宇下 under the roof;
雨下 downpour; storm;
月下 under the moon;
在下 I; my humble self;
摘下 pick off;
之下 under;
直下 deteriorate steadily;
擲下 please hand...to me;
住不下 cannot accommodate;
足下 you;
坐下 sit down;

xia

【夏】 (1) summer; (2) a surname;

［夏蟲語冰］ a summer insect discusses ice－one who talks of what he knows nothing about;
夏蟲不可語冰 don't speak of ice to insects that live only one summer; don't talk of ice to a butterfly;

［夏冬］ summer and winter;
夏出冬蟄 come out in summer and sleep in winter;
夏葛冬裘 linen in summer and fur dress in winter; right things come at the right time; wear coarse clothes in summer and fur in winter;
夏爐冬扇 stoves in summer and fans in winter － out of reason;
夏衫冬裘 wear thin garments in summer and furs in winter;
夏食冬蟄 eat in summer and sleep in winter;

［夏侯］ a surname;

［夏季］ summer; summertime; the summer season;

［夏枯草］ bugle; bugleweed;

［夏曆］ lunar calendar;

［夏糧］ summer grain crops;

［夏令］ (1) summer; summertime; (2) summer weather;
夏令時間 daylight saving time; summer time;
夏令營 summer camp;

［夏眠］ aestivation;
夏眠場所 estivaculum;

［夏末］ late summer;
夏末初秋 it is the end of summer, just turning into autumn;

［夏去秋來］ autumn succeeds summer; summer lengthens into autumn;

［夏日］ (1) summer days; (2) the summer sun;
夏日可畏 oppressive summer sun; the summer sun is to be dreaded;
夏日炎炎 summer days are very hot;
酷熱難受的夏日 sweltering summer days;

［夏收］ summer harvest;
夏收夏種 summer harvesting and sowing;
夏收作物 summer crops;

［夏天］ summer; summer days;
明年夏天 next summer;

［夏蚊成雷］ mosquitoes are humming round in summer;

［夏衣］ summer clothing; summer wear;

［夏雨雨人］ the summer rain soothes people － a timely help to the masses;

［夏蟄］ aestivation;
夏蟄動物 aestivator;

［夏至］ June solstice; summer solstice;
夏至點 summer solstice;
［夏裝］ summer clothes; summer dress;
半夏 tuber of pinellia;
初夏 early summer;
春夏 spring and summer;
華夏 ancient name for China;
苦夏 lose appetite and weight in summer;
立夏 Beginning of Summer (7th solar term);
三夏 the three summer jobs (planning, harvesting and field management);
盛夏 high summer; midsummer; the height of summer;
消夏 spend the summer at leisure; take a summer holiday;
歇夏 stop working during the dog days;
炎夏 hot summer; summer at its hottest;
一夏 a summer season;
中夏 China;
仲夏 second month of summer;
諸夏 various Chinese kingdoms;

xia

【廈】 edifice; tall building;
［廈門］ Xiamen, in Fujian;

噶廈 former Tibetan local government;

xia

【暇】 leisure; spare time;

xia

【嚇】 frighten; intimidate; scare; startle; threaten;
［嚇出來］ scare out;
［嚇掉了魂］ be scared out of one's wits; be scared stiff;
［嚇唬］ browbeat; frighten; intimidate; scare;
［嚇跑］ scare away; scare off;
［嚇人］ frightening; terrifying;
嚇人一跳 give sb a scare; give sb a start; take sb aback;
扒了皮的癩蛤蟆—活着討厭，死了還嚇人 a skinned toad – disgusting while alive, dreadful when dead;

驚嚇 frighten; scare;

xia

【罅】 cleft; crack; fissure; flaw; rift;
［罅漏］ (1) crack; leak; seam; (2) defect; deficiency; fault; flaw; loophole; omission; shortcoming;
［罅隙］ chink; crack; loose seam; rift;
石罅 crack in rock;
云罅 rift in the clouds;

xian¹

xian

【仙】 (1) celestial being; fairy; god; immortal; (2) divine;
［仙才］ genius;
［仙丹］ cure-all; divine pill; elixir of life; panacea;
仙丹花 red ixora;
仙丹妙藥 elixir of life; elixir vitae; miracle drug;
［仙風］ divine bearing;
仙風道骨 divine bearing; divine post; one's outstanding behaviour like that of immortals; sage-like type;
仙風逸骨 have an elegant bearing;
［仙公］ (1) male immortal; (2) venerable old man;
［仙姑］ (1) fairy godmother; female celestial; female immortal; (2) sorceress; (3) woman Daoist;
［仙鶴］ red-crowned crane;
［仙境］ (1) fairyland; land of the divine; paradise; wonderland; (2) place of exquisite natural beauty;
如入仙境 as if one were in a fairyland;
［仙居］ divine abode;
［仙女］ fairy; fairy maiden; female celestial; woman of divine beauty;
［仙禽］ crane;
［仙人］ (1) celestial being; immortal; (2) very beautiful woman;
仙人果 prickly pear;
仙人掌 cactus;
~仙人掌螟 cactoblastis;
~仙人掌素 cactin;
［仙山］ a mountain inhabited by the immortals;
仙山瓊閣 a jewelled palace in elfland's hills; a jewelled palace on the mountain of the immortals;
［仙逝］ die; pass away;
［仙術］ magic arts;
［仙桃］ divine peach;
［仙童］ fairy messenger boy;
［仙鄉］ fairyland;

[仙真] Daoist god; immortal;
[仙姿] fairylike look;
仙姿玉質 divine countenance and gem quality;
[仙子] (1) fairy maiden; female celestial; (2) celestial being; fairy; immortal;

八仙 Eight Immortals;
狐仙 fairy fox;
秋水仙 autumn crocus; meadow saffron;
神仙 celestial being; immortal; supernatural being;
水仙 Chinese sacred lily; daffodial; dilly;
天仙 beauty; fairy;
威霧仙 root of Chinese clematis;
修仙 try to make and then take pills of immortality and cultivate oneself to become an immortal;
謫仙 an immortal living among mortals; genius; prodigy;

xian

【先】 (1) first; foremost; (2) before; earlier; in advance; (3) ancestors; elder generations; (4) the deceased; the late; (5) before; earlier on; (6) a surname;
[先輩] ancestors; elder generations; members of a former generation; the senior generation; the seniors;
革命先輩 the old generation of revolutionaries;
[先慈] my late mother;
[先達] elder leaders;
[先導] (1) forerunner; guide; precursor; (2) lead the way; (3) mentor; teacher;
[先到灶頭先得食] first come, first served; he that runs fastest gets the ring; if you arrive early, you get ahead of others; it's the early bird that catches the worm; the early bird catches the worm; those ho are first at the fire will get their dinner first;
[先帝] late emperor;
[先睹為快] all eagerness to see it; consider it a pleasure to be among the first to read it;
[先端] tip of sth;
[先發] attack first;
先發制敵 ahead of the enemy; anticipate the enemy; steal a march on a rival;
先發制人 attack first in order to cripple the opponent's defenses; beat to the draw; catch the ball before the bound; dominate the enemy by striking first; draw the first blood; fire the first shot; forestall the enemy; gain mastery by striking first; get the drop on; get the jump on; get the upper hand by taking the initiative; preemptive; steal a march on; strike the first blow; take the ball before the bound; take the initiative;
先發制人的攻擊 preemptive attack;
[先鋒] forerunner; harbinger; pioneer; trailblazer; van; vanguard;
先鋒隊 vanguard;
打先鋒 fight in the van; lead the van; lead the way; pioneer;
急先鋒 daring vanguard;
開路先鋒 pathbreaker; pioneer; trailblazer;
[先夫] my late husband;
[先河] anything that is advocated earlier; beginning of sth; forerunner; harbinger;
[先後] (1) early or late; order; priority; (2) one after another; successively;
先後緩急 in the order of urgency;
不先不後 just at the right time; not a bit earlier or later;
承先啟後 be the heir to ancient sages and the teacher of posterity; carry on the past heritage and open up the future; inherit the past and usher in the future; serve as a link between past and future;
~承先啟後，繼往開來 carry forward our revolutionary cause and develop it; carry forward the revolutionary cause pioneered by our predecessors and forge ahead into the future;
先打後拉 first attack and then cajole;
先到後走 the first to arrive and the last to leave;
先到先得 first come, first served;
先敬羅衣後敬人 a smart coat is a good letter of introduction; good clothes open all doors;
先禮後兵 a gentleman first and a soldier second; courteous before the use of force; courtesy before the use of

force; take strong measures only after courteous ones fail; try fair means before resorting to force; try the effect of politeness before resorting to force;
先斬後奏 act first and report afterwards; do things first and ask for approval afterwards; execute the criminal first and report to the emperor afterwards;
先縱後擒 give line and scope;
知所先後 know what should precede and what should follow;

[先見] foreknowledge; foresight;
先見之明 a long head; able to anticipate; able to predict; ability to foresee; farsightedness; foresight; prescience; prevision; prophetic vision; second sight; show foresight; the ability to discern what is coming;
~有先見之明 foresighted; have a long head; have foresight; prescient; provident; see beyond one's nose; take long views;

[先進] advanced;
先進班組 advanced group;
先進個人 advanced individual;
先進國 advanced nations; civilized nations; developed powers;
先進技術 advanced techniques; advanced technology;
~引進先進技術 introduce advanced technology;
先進社會 an advanced society;
先進設備 advanced equipment;

[先決] prerequisite;
先決條件 postulate; precondition; prerequisite;

[先覺] one who becomes awakened earlier in politics and social reforms; prophet;

[先君] my late husband;

[先例] former example; precedent; previous case taken as an example;
按照先例 in the light of precedents;
古無先例 unprecedented in history;

[先烈] martyr;
革命先烈 revolutionary martyrs;

[先民] ancients; the former men;

[先母] my late mother;

[先期] before the appointed time; beforehand; earlier on; in advance;

[先前] before; previously;

[先遣] be sent in advance; detaching; send in advance;
先遣人員 advance agent; advance man;

[先趨] forerunner; predecessor;

[先驅] ancestor; foregoer; forerunner; harbinger; pioneer; precursor; predecessor; progenitor; vanguard;
哲學界的先驅 philosophical ancestor;

[先人] (1) ancestors; forebears; forefathers; previous generations; (2) my late father;
先人後己 put other people's interest above one's own; put others before oneself; serve the others first;

[先入] (1) first impressions; (2) preconception;
先入為主 first impressions are half the battle; first impressions are most lasting; first impressions are strongest; formulate preconceived ideas; preconceived ideas keep a strong hold; prejudiced; prejudices die hard;
先入之見 bias; preconceived ideas; preconception; prejudice;

[先生] (1) teacher; (2) gentleman; mister; sir; (3) doctor;
好好先生 a jolly good fellow; a man who is always polite and never says no; a regular brick; a regular fellow; a regular guy; a yes-man; a person who offers no resistance; duck soup; goody-goody; Mr good;
小先生 pupil teacher;
一位先生 a gentleman;

[先聲] harbinger; herald; first signs;
先聲奪人 demoralize one's opponent by a show of strength; forestall one's opponent by a show of strength; overawe others by displaying one's strength; with an impressive start;

[先聖] (1) Confucius; (2) ancient sages;

[先師] (1) teachers of the older generations; (2) Confucius;

[先史] prehistoric;

[先世] ancestors; forebears; forefathers;

[先室] my late wife;

[先天] (1) congenital; inborn; innate; (2) a priori; innate; natural physical endowments;
先天不足 a weak natural physical endowment; an inadequate natural

endowment; be born with a feeble constitution; congenitally deficient; inborn eeficiency; inherited weakness; suffer from an inherent shortage;
先天缺陷 the birth defect;

[先頭] (1) ahead; in advance; in front; (2) before; formerly; in the past; previously;
先頭部隊 vanguard;

[先王] (1) late emperor; (2) ancient sage sovereigns;

[先賢] ancient saints and sages; scholars of the past; wise men;
步武先賢 tread in the footsteps of ancient worthies;

[先行] (1) go ahead of the rest; start off before the others; (2) beforehand;
先行詞 antecedent;
先行經濟指數 anticipated economic index;
先行句 antecedent clause;
先行篇 prequel;
先行權 right of way;
~有先行權 have right of way;
先行通知 notify in advance;
先行同化 anticipatory assimilation;
先行異化 anticipatory dissimilation;
先行意義 anticipatory meaning;
先行者 forerunner;
先行知照 give a previous notice; notify beforehand;
先行主語 anticipatory subject;

[先緒] ancestral heritage;

[先嚴] my deceased father;

[先驗] a priori;
先驗哲學 transcendental philosophy;

[先要] first essentials;

[先於] antedate;

[先澤] benefit from one's ancestor;

[先兆] foreboding; harbinger; indication; omen; portent; sign;

[先哲] great thinker of the past; sage;
先哲前賢 ancient philosophers and worthies; the great thinkers of the past; the wise men of the past;

[先正] (1) wise men of the past; (2) wise ministers of the past;

[先知] (1) person of foresight; (2) clairvoyant; prophet;
先知先覺 person of foresight;
女先知 prophetess;
僞先知 false prophet;
未卜先知 foresee; have foreknowledge; know without seeking divination; prophet;

[先子] (1) deceased father; (2) ancestor;

比先 formerly;
當先 at the head; in the front ranks; in the van;
儘先 giving first priority to;
領先 go into the lead; in the lead; lead; take the lead;
起先 at first; in the beginning;
搶先 beat sb to it; compete to be the first; do sth before others have a chance to; rush ahead; try to be the first to do sth; try to beat others in performing sth;
事先 beforehand; in advance;
首先 above all; above all else; as a starter; at first; at the beginning; beyond all else; beyond all things; come first; first; first and foremost; first of all; first off; for one thing...for another; in the first place; in the first instance; primary; the first thing; the very first; to begin with; to start with;
率先 take the lead in doing sth; the first to do sth;
優先 have priority; take precedence;
預先 beforehand; in advance;
原先 (1) former; original; (2) in the beginning; in the very beginning;
在先 ahead; at that time; before; beforehand; formerly; in front; in the past;
早先 before; in the past; previously; some time ago;
占先 occupy before others; preempt;
佔先 get ahead of; take precedence; take the lead;
爭先 try to be the first to do sth;
祖先 ancestors; forebears; forefathers; progenitors;
最先 (1) earliest; first; foremost; (2) at first; in the beginning;

xian

【祆】 Ormazd, supreme deity in Zoroastrianism;

[祆教] Zoroastrianism;

xian

【掀】 (1) lift with the hands; raise; (2) cause; expose; stir; stir up;

[掀動] lift; raise; set in motion; start; stir up;

tilt;

[掀翻] throw;

[掀開] cause; open; uncover; unveil;

[掀起] (1) lift; raise; stir up; (2) cause to surge; surge;

掀起波濤 raise waves;

掀起蓋子 lift the lid;

掀起面紗 raise the veil;

[掀騰] overturn; stir;

[掀天] (1) rise to the sky; (2) reach the heaven;

掀天動地 world-shaking;

掀天揭地 earthshaking; turn the whole world upside down; turn the world bottomside up; world-shaking;

掀天事業 awe-inspiring achievement;

[掀舞] churning and pounding;

xian

【酰】 acly;

[酰胺] amide;

酰胺分解 amidolysis;

酰胺黑 amido black;

丁酰胺 butyric acid amide;

甲酰胺 methane amide;

檸檬酰胺 citric amide;

肉桂酰胺 cinnamic amide;

乙酰胺 acetic amide; acid amide;

xian

【銛】 keen-edged; sharp;

xian

【暹】 rise (said of the sun);

xian

【鮮】 (1) fresh; new; (2) attractive; bright; bright-coloured; (3) delicious; tasty;

[鮮翠] fresh and green;

[鮮果] fresh fruit;

鮮果盤 fresh fruit platter;

[鮮紅] bright red; scarlet;

[鮮花] flowers; fresh flowers;

鮮花插在牛糞上 a woman married to a vulgar husband; stick a lovely flower in a dunghill;

鮮花怒放 the flowers are bursting into full bloom; the flowers are now blooming in all their splendour;

鮮花盛開 the blossoms open in all their glory; the flowers bloom luxuriantly;

一把鮮花 a bunch of flowers; a sheaf of flowers;

一朵鮮花 a flower;

~一朵鮮花插在牛糞上 a fresh flower on a heap of cow-dung — a pretty girl is married to a stupid husband;

一簇鮮花 a bunch of flowers; a cluster of flowers;

一束鮮花 a bouquet of flowers; a bunch of flowers; a sheaf of flowers;

[鮮活] fresh and lively;

[鮮麗] effulgent; fresh-looking and beautiful; resplendent;

[鮮亮] bright and shining;

[鮮美] delicious; fresh and delicious; tasty;

鮮美可口 delicious; palatable; tasty;

[鮮明] (1) bright; bright-coloured; (2) clear-cut; crystal-clear; distinct; distinctive;

鮮明有力 distinct and forceful;

節奏鮮明 with strongly accentged rhythms;

色彩鮮明 bright-coloured;

主題鮮明 have a distincttheme;

[鮮嫩] delicacy; fresh and tender;

[鮮皮] fresh hide;

[鮮肉] fresh meat;

[鮮食] (1) fresh food; (2) eat fresh food;

[鮮味] fresh flavour;

[鮮新] bright and new; fresh; refreshing;

[鮮血] blood; fresh blood;

鮮血迸流 the blood is flowing in streams; the fresh blood flows out;

鮮血濺飛 the red blood flows;

鮮血淋漓 drench with blood; drip with blood; fresh blood is streaming out; the blood oozes out;

口吐鮮血 blood gushes from one's mouth; spit blood;

[鮮艷] bright-coloured; brilliance; gaily-coloured; resplendent;

鮮艷奪目 attractively bright-coloured; dazzlingly beautiful; resplendent; splendour blinds the eyes;

鮮艷可愛 beautiful and lovable — as a flower;

[鮮衣] new clothes;

鮮衣美食 new clothes and delicious food — extravagant living;

[鮮魚] fresh fish;

白鮮 shaggy-fruited dittany;

保鮮 guard against spoilage of food; maintain refeshness; retain freshness;

海鮮 seafood;

活鮮 fresh aquatic food;
淺鮮 insignificant; slight;
時鮮 (1) in season; (2) seasonable delicacies;
新鮮 (1) fresh; (2) new; novel; original; strange;
魚鮮 fish and shellfish as food; seafood;

xian

【孅】 delicate; fine; slender; small; thin;
[孅介] a small bit; tiny;
[孅弱] delicate; frail; weak;
[孅手] delicate hands of a woman;
[孅悉] intelligent and knowledgeable of every detail;

xian

【躚】 turn round and round;
[躚躚] dance; turn round and round; twirl;

翩躚 (of dancing) lightly; trippingly;
蹁躚 whirling about (in dancing);

xian

【纖】 delicate; fine; minute; slender; tiny;
[纖塵] fine dust;
纖塵不染 as clean as a whistle; as neat as a new pin; free from dust; not soiled by a particle of dust; maintain one's original pure character; maintain one's personal integrity; spotlessly clean; there is not a speck of dust;
[纖疵] slight error;
纖疵不較 slight errors deserve no attention;
[纖兒] immature children;
[纖毫] every small detail; extremely minute; minute; tiny parts of things; tiny things; very little;
[纖介] minute; very small;
[纖巧] dainty; delicate; fine;
纖巧別緻 delicate and particular;
[纖人] fragile person;
[纖柔] delicate and soft;
[纖弱] delicate; fragile; slim and fragile; thin and weak;
[纖手] delicate hands;
纖手細腰 tender hands and slender waist;
[纖瘦] delicate and slender;
[纖絲] fibril;
[纖維] fibre;
纖維板 fibreboard;
纖維蛋白 fibrin;
~纖維蛋白原 fibrinogen;
纖維分解 cellulosis;
纖維弧菌素 cellvibriocin;
纖維素 cellulose; fibre;
~纖維素塑料 cellulosic plastics;
~纖維素塗料 cellulosic varnish;
~半纖維素 semicellulose;
~動物纖維素 animal cellulose;
~鹼纖維素 alkali cellulose; soda cellulose;
~水合纖維素 hydrate cellulose;
~天然纖維素 native cellulose;
~再生纖維素 regenerated cellulose;
~真菌纖維素 fungus cellulose;
~植物纖維素 plant cellulose;
短纖維 (1) short staple; (2) staple fibre;
風乾纖維 air dry fibre;
弓狀纖維 arcuate fibre;
合成纖維 diamars;
肌原纖維 muscular fibril; muscle fibril; myofibril;
膠原纖維 collagen fibre;
聚光纖維 light focusing fibre;
聯合纖維 association fibre;
陶瓷纖維 ceramic fibre;
網狀纖維 reticular fibre;
[纖悉] detailed; exhaustive; familiar with every detail of; know thoroughly;
纖悉無遺 no detail escapes notice;
[纖細] fine; slender; slim; tenuous; very thin;
[纖纖] (1) delicate; fine; minute; slender; (2) sharp;
纖纖細故 detail; trivial events;
纖纖玉手 fine and slim hands of a young woman;
[纖小] fine; tenuous;
[纖妍] slim and pretty;
[纖腰] slender waist;
纖腰秀項 have a slender waist and a beautiful neck;
[纖玉] delicate jade — a woman's delicate hands;

化纖 chemical fibre;

xian²
xian

【弦】 (1) bowstring; chord; string; (2) strings of a musical instrument; (3) spring; (4) first quarter of a lunar month;

［弦歌］ (1) sing with stringed accompaniment; (2) means of education;
弦歌不輟 the schooling goes on without interruption; the sound of music and singing never ends;
［弦琴］ stringed instrument;
手搖弦琴 hurdy-gurdy;
［弦誦］ chant;
［弦索］ strings of an instrument;
弦索笙歌 string struments; the flute and singing;
［弦線］ strings of a musical instrument;
［弦音］ music from a stringed instrument;
［弦月］ crescent moon;
［弦樂］ string music;
弦樂隊 string orchestra;
弦樂器 stringed instrument;
弦樂三重奏 string trio;
弦樂四重奏 string quartet;
弦樂五重奏 string quintet;
［弦柱］ neck of a stringed instrument;

單弦 story-telling to musical accompaniment;
底弦 bottom chord;
定弦 tune a stringed instrument;
斷弦 wife's death;
反餘弦 inverse sine;
弓弦 bowstring;
公弦 common chord;
固定弦 constant chord;
管弦 pipes and strings;
和弦 chord;
箭弦 arrows and bowstrings;
老弦 the thicker inner string on the huqin;
里弦 the thicker inner string on the huqin;
琴弦 string (of a musical instrument);
三弦 sanxian, a three-stringed plucked instrument;
上弦 first quarter of the moon;
絲弦 (1) a kind of local opera in Hebei Province; (2) silk string for a musical instrument;
外弦 the thinner outer string on the huqin;
下弦 last (or third) quarter (of the moon);
心弦 heartstrings; the heart's cord;
續弦 remarry after the death of one's wife; the second wife married after the death of one's wife;
葉弦 blade chord;
餘弦 cosine;
正弦 sine;
子弦 very fine silk string for musical instruments;

xian
【咸】 all; completely; fully; together; wholly;
［咸信］ generally believed that;

xian
【啣】 vulgar form of 銜；

xian
【絃】 same as 弦；

xian
【舷】 bulwarks of a ship; the gunnel; the gunwale;
［舷邊］ gunwale;
［舷窗］ porthole; scuttle;
［舷燈］ sidelight;
［舷弧］ curve of a deck line;
［舷門］ gangway on a ship for passengers;
［舷梯］ accommodation ladder; gangway ladder;

船舷 side of a ship (or boat);
干舷 freeboard;
右舷 starboard;
左舷 port;

xian
【閑】 (1) bar; barrier; fence; (2) defend; (3) big; (4) accustomed to; familiar with; well-versed in; (5) same as 閒；(6) laws; regulations; (7) stable;
［閑常］ ordinary; usually;
［閑漢］ bum; idler; vagrant;
［閑靜］ peaceful and calm in mind;
［閑居］ lead a quiet life; lead a retired life;
［閑媚］ quiet and charming;
［閑書］ books for killing time;
［閑要］ amuse oneself; kill time;
［閑習］ familiar with; well versed in;

xian
【閒】 (1) calm; placid; quiet; tranquil; (2) idle; not busy; unoccupied; (3) lying idle; not in use; unoccupied; (4) free time; leisure; spare time;
［閒不住］ always keep oneself busy; refuse to stay idle;
［閒步］ roam at leisure; stroll without a destination;
［閒扯］ chat; engage in chitchat; shoot the

breeze; shoot the bull;

[閒蕩] bugger about; loaf about; mooch about; mooch around; saunter; stroll;

[閒地] public land; waste land;

[閒飯] eat one's food in idleness;

吃閒飯 lead an idle life; live in idleness; loafer; sponger;

~不吃閒飯 not be an idler;

[閒房] vacant room;

[閒逛] loiter; poke around; putz around; saunter; stroll;

在街上閒逛 walk the streets;

[閒漢] bum; jobless person; vagrant;

[閒話] (1) chat; chitchat; digression; (2) complaint; (3) gossip; (4) chat about;

閒話當年 chat about bygone days;

閒話古今 talk casually about the past and present;

閒話少説 cut the cackle; let's get back to the subject; save your breath to cool your porridge;

閒話少説，言歸正傳 enough of this digression, and back to the true story; enough of this digression, let's return to our story; put aside all idle talk and tell only the true story; return from a digression;

閒話休提 return from the digression;

傳閒話 give tongue to gossip;

扯閒話 talk gossip;

講閒話 dig dirt about sb;

甩閒話 complain; grumble;

説閒話 gossip; make idle talk; make unfavourable comments; talk behind sb's back;

[閒混] futz; idle about; idle away;

整天閒混 futz around all day;

[閒靜] quiet; undisturbed;

[閒居] lead an idle life; stay at home idle;

[閒空] free time; leisure; spare time;

[閒聊] bull session; chat; chew the rag; chinwag; gossip; have a chat with; natter; schmooze;

閒聊瑣事 have a good gossip on trivial matters;

愛閒聊 chatty;

[閒民] the unemployed;

[閒氣] anger about trifles; needless anger;

鬭閒氣 quarrel with trifles;

爭閒氣 argue over trifles;

[閒錢] idle money; spare cash; spare money;

[閒人] (1) idlers; persons with nothing to do; unoccupied person; (2) persons not concerned;

閒人免進 admittance to staff only; loungers are not permitted to enter; no admittance; no admittance except on business; no admittance to outsiders; no entrance; off limits to all unauthorized persons; out of bounds to nonauthorized personnel;

閒人莫入 loiterers keep away; no entrance except on business;

[閒散] at a loose end; free and at leisure; idle; unoccupied; unused; with no important tasks at hand; with nothing to do;

閒散人員 idle people;

閒散資金 idle fund;

投閒置散 occupy an insignificant position; put in an idle position; stay idle; throw on the scrap heap;

[閒時] leisure; spare time;

閒時不燒香，急時抱佛腳 when all is well you do not burn incense, but when in trouble, you clasp Buddha's feet;

[閒事] (1) a matter that does not concern one; other people's business; (2) unimportant matter;

管閒事 poke one's nose into others' business;

~愛管閒事 have a finger in every pie; have an oar in every man's boat; like to poke one's nose into other people's business; love meddling in other people's affairs; meddlesome; meddling; nosy; officious; pushing;

~愛管閒事的人 back-seat driver; fleabag; meddler; meddlesome person; snooper; stickybeak; stirrer;

~多管閒事 have an oar in veryman's boat; poke one's nose in everyman's affairs; poke one's nose in everyman's business; put one's finger in many pies; stick one's nose into what isn't one's business;

~好管閒事 enjoy having one's finger in every pie; fond of meddling in other man's business; have an oar in very man's boat; like poke and pry; meddlesome; pose one's nose in other people's affairs;

~好管閒事的人 buttinsky; Mr buttinsky;
~莫管閒事 don't meddle in others' business; mind your own business;
~少管閒事 mind one's own affairs; mind one's own business;

[閒適] leisurely and comfortable; quiet and comfortable;

[閒書] books for killing time; light readings;

[閒談] chat; chinwag; chit-chat; confabulate; engage in chitchat; small talk;
飯後閒談 sit around gossiping after dinner;

[閒田] public land; vacant field; waste land;

[閒暇] leisure; unoccupied;
閒暇無事 at leisure and unoccupied;

[閒笑] pleasant chatter;

[閒邪存誠] restrain vicious and foster sincere habits;

[閒心] free, unburdened mind; leisurely mood; peaceful mood;

[閒雅] easy; elegant; graceful; refined;

[閒言] (1) gossip; idle talk; (2) balder-dash;
閒言閒語 gossips; sarcastic complaints; sarcastic remarks;
~招來閒言閒語 set tongues wagging;

[閒燕] peace and quiet;

[閒逸] carefree; leisurely;
閒情逸緻 in a leisurely and carefree mood; peaceful and comfortable mood;

[閒語] (1) personal talk; (2) gossips; sarcastic remarks;

[閒雲野鶴] (1) a recluse with no fixed abode; a recluse with no fixed occupation; a wild stock or floating clouds; the quietness and comfortableness of a secluded life; (2) as free as a bird; carefree;

[閒雜] without fixed duties;
閒雜人等 (1) idlers; loafers; (2) unconcerned persons;
閒雜人員 miscellaneous personnel; people without fixed duties;

[閒在] idle; quiet and comfortable;

[閒職] an official post with very little to do;

[閒置] leave unused; let sth lie idle; set aside;
閒置不用 lay aside; leave unused; put away; put to one side; shlve;

[閒坐] sit at leisure; sit idle;

安閒 enjoying leisure; leisurely; peaceful and carefree; relaxation;
罷閒 out of work;
幫閒 hang on to and serve the rich and powerful by literary hack work;
得閒 at leisure; free; have leisure;
等閒 (1) aimless; thoughtlessly; (2) (treat) lightly; ordinary; umimportant;
冬閒 slack winter season;
防閒 guard against and restrict;
賦閒 unemployed;
空閒 (1) free; idle; (2) free time; leisure; spare time;
農閒 slack farming season;
清閒 at leisure; have all the time one needs; have plenty of leisure; idle;
輕閒 at leisure;
偷閒 avail oneself of a leisure moment; snatch a moment of leisure; steal a moment of leisure;
退閒 be free from office duties; be retired;
消閒 kill the leisure time; kill time; pass time idly;
蕭閒 (1) at ease; leisurely; (2) desolate; lonely;
歇閒 rest;
休閒 arder; ease; leasure; lie fallow; relaxation;
幽閒 (1) gentle and serene; (2) leisurely and carefree;
悠閒 leisurely; leisurely and carefree; unhurried; unrestrained;
優閒 carefree; free and content; leisure;
餘閒 leisure; spare time;
踰閒 break decorum; break moral conventions;

xian

【嫌】 (1) suspect; suspicion; (2) enmity; grudge; ill will; (3) complain; complain of; detest; dislike; object; reject;

[嫌猜] dislike and suspicion;

[嫌疵] criticize; dislike;

[嫌忌] dissatisfied with what others do; reject; suspect;

[嫌怕] afraid of;

[嫌棄] abandon; cold-shoulder; dislike and avoid; give up in disgust; reject;

[嫌惡] detest; disgust; loathe; sick of;

[嫌隙] dislike born out of mutual resentment; enmity; feeling of animosity; grudge; ill will; old grudge; suspicion born out of dislike;

嫌隙冰消 an ill-will melts like ice;
[嫌厭] dislike; loathe;
[嫌疑] suspect; suspicion;
嫌疑犯 suspect;
嫌疑分子 marked man; suspected person;
嫌疑人 suspect;
~主要嫌疑人 prime suspect;
嫌疑行為 suspicious conduct;
避免嫌疑 save oneself from suspicion;
貪污嫌疑 suspicion of corruption;
[嫌怨] grudge; enmity; resentment;
[嫌憎] dislike; dislike and avoid; hate;

避嫌 avoid arousing suspicion; avoid being suspected; avoid doing anything that may arouse suspicion; avoid suspicion;
猜嫌 suspicious and jealous;
惹嫌 incur hatred; provoke dislike;
稍嫌 slightly more or less than the ideal state;
涉嫌 be involved in a crime; be suspected of being involved; come under suspicion; inviting suspicion; suspect;
釋嫌 (1) dispel suspicion; (2) dispel ill feeling;
討嫌 annoying; disagreeable; incur dislike;
微嫌 slight animosity;
惡嫌 abhor; detest; hate; loathe;
挾嫌 bear a grudge; harbour resentment;

xian
【銜】 (1) hold in the mouth; (2) bear; cherish; harbour; (3) rank; title;
[銜恩] cherish gratitude;
[銜恨] bear a grudge; harbour resentment;
[銜華佩實] bear both flowers and fruits — a good essay which has solid substance and beautiful sentences; blossom and bear fruit — a writing rich in substance and graceful in style;
[銜環] repay with gratitude;
銜環結草 repay a kindness;
銜環相報 like the wounded bird, who is saved by a kind preserver;
銜環以報 repay with gratitude;
[銜接] adjoin; connect; dovetail; join; lie next to; link up;
銜接學位 top-up degree;
[銜枚] with a gag in the mouth;
銜枚疾走 hastening with mouth gags; marsh swiftly with a gag in the mouth;
[銜命] act according to a directive; follow an order;
[銜泣] sob;
[銜冤] have a simmering sense of injustice; have no chance of airing one's grievances; nurse a bitter sense of wrong;
銜冤而死 die with a simmering sense of injustice; die with one's name uncleared; with a bitter sense of wrong and die;
銜冤負屈 suffer an unjust grievance;
銜冤去世 pass away in grievance;

官銜 official title;
軍銜 military rank;
領銜 head the list of signers (of a document);
授銜 confer sb the title of;
台銜 your rank;
頭銜 official title of a person;
虛銜 nominal title;
學銜 academic rank;
職銜 post and rank; the official title of a person;

xian
【嫺】 (1) gracious; refined; (2) skilled; skillful;
[嫺靜] demure; gentle and refined; quiet and refined;
[嫺熟] adept in; consummate; expert; skilled in;
[嫺習] adept at; skilled in;
嫺習文藝 familiar with literature and the arts; skilled in literature and arts; well-read;
嫺習武藝 skilled in martial arts;
[嫺雅] cultured; elegant; polished; refined;
嫺雅斯文 quiet and gentle;
風度嫺雅 agreeable in manner;
高尚嫺雅 grace; noble and refined;
態度嫺雅 have refined manners;

xian
【賢】 (1) able; talented; versatile; (2) good; virtuous; worthy; (3) admire; esteem; praise; (4) able and virtuous person; worthy person;
[賢才] capable and virtuous person;
賢才君子 virtuous and talent person;
簡擢賢才 select and promote a person with preeminent ability;
湮滯賢才 restrain a talent — a talent hampered in a low position;
援拔賢才 recommend a talent;

[賢達] prominent personage; the social elite; wise and virtuous; worthy;
[賢德] good and honest virtue; good conduct; virtuous;
[賢惠] good and wise; virtuous and intelligent;
[賢慧] wifely;
[賢荊] my dear wife;
[賢勞] work industriously for the public;
[賢良] (1) able and virtuous; (2) person of talents and vritue;
妒賢嫉良 envy the virtuous and wise;
[賢明] capable and virtuous; sagacious; wise and able;
[賢母] wise mother;
[賢能] able and virtuous personage; talented and virtuous;
賢能統治 meritocracy;
辟召賢能 summon worthies and talents to court;
妒賢嫉能 envious of the worthy and able; envy someone better or abler than oneself; envy the good and be jealous of men of ability; jealous and envious of capable men;
嫉賢妒能 jealous of capable people;
薦賢任能 recommend and employ the capable and deserving;
任賢用能 use the wise and employ the capable;
推賢讓能 cede to the worthy and yield the post to the able; recommend the worthy and give away to the able; select the virtuous and give place to the talented;
選賢舉能 appoint the good and able men to office; pick out and promote talents; recruit and utilize talented people; select the good and the capable for public service;
選賢任能 select and appoint talented, capable people;
[賢妻] (1) good wife; (2) my dear wife;
賢妻良母 a clever wife and wise mother; a dutiful wife and loving mother; a good wife and loving mother; an understanding wife and loving mother;
[賢人] person of virtue; worthy man;
[賢士] distinguished men; person of high moral standing;
廣納賢士 send far and wide to invite men of ability;
敬賢禮士 respect wisdom and revere scholarship; treat able men and scholars with the greatest courtesy;
輕賢慢士 despise worthies; value lightly wise men and be arrogant toward one's officers;
[賢淑] virtuous and understanding;
[賢彥] virtuous person;
[賢愚] the wise and the stupid;
[賢哲] person outstanding in virtue and learning; wise and able person;
[賢者] men of talents and virtue; the good; the virtuous;
賢者多勞 a good man is always wanted for everything; the able and virtuous are always busy;

舉賢 promote men of ability;
前賢 people of virtue of the older generations;
群賢 a host of wise men; all the wise men;
讓賢 relinquish one's post in favour of sb better qualified; yeild one's position to a better qualified person;
尚賢 exaltation of the virtuous;
聖賢 sages and men of virtue; saints;
時賢 contemporary men of ability and integrity; social leaders of the time; the great scholars of the period;
昔賢 ancient sages;
先賢 ancient saints and sages; scholars of the past; wise men;
鄉賢 respected village scholars;
選賢 appoint good people;

xian

【諴】 (1) in agreement; in harmony; (2) honest; sincere;

xian

【癇】 epilepsy;

xian

【鹹】 briny; salted; saltish; salty;
[鹹菜] pickled vegetables; pickles; salted vegetables;
[鹹肉] bacon; salted meat;
[鹹澀] salty and bitter;
[鹹水] saline water; salt water;
鹹水魚 salt-water fish;
[鹹酸] salty and sour;
[鹹味] saline taste; saltiness;

[鹹魚] salted fish;

xian³

xian

【洗】 a surname;

xian

【蜆】 corbicula leana, a variety of bivalves;

xian

【跣】 barefooted;

[跣子] slippers;

[跣足] barefooted;

xian

【銑】 (1) shiny metal; (2) pig iron;

[銑牀] miller; milling machine;
- 端面銑牀 face miller;
- 鼓形銑牀 drum miller;
- 卧式銑牀 horizontal miller;

[銑工] miller;

[銑鐵] cast iron; pig iron;

[銑削] milling;
- 成形銑削 form milling;
- 連續銑削 continuous milling;
- 斜面銑削 angular milling;

xian

【險】 (1) a place difficult of access; defile; difficult; narrow pass; obstructed; strategic pass; (2) danger; dangerous; risk; (3) cunning; mean and crafty; sinister; vicious; (4) almost; by a hair's breadth; by inches; nearly; within an ace of;

[險隘] dangerous; defile; strategic; strategic pass;

[險地] a place difficult of access; dangerous situation; perilous position;

[險惡] (1) dangerous; ominous; perilous; precarious; (2) devious; diabolic; evil; malicious; mean; sinister; treacherous; vicious; wicked;
- 病情險惡 dangerously ill;
- 處境險惡 in a dangerous situation;
- 居心險惡 of a malicious disposition; vicious in one's motives;
- 用心險惡 have evil motives; have sinister intentions;

[險峰] perilous peak;
- 翻越險峰 cross a perilous peak;
- 攀登險鋒 scale the perilous peak;

[險工] dangerous task;

[險固] strategic and impregnable;

[險境] dangerous situation; precarious position;
- 處於險境 on a razor edge;
- 身處險境 in danger;
- 脱離險境 out of danger;

[險峻] dangerous and steep; precipitous; scarry;

[險情] dangerous case; dangerous omen;
- 控制險情 control the dangerous circumstances;
- 排除險情 remove the dangerous condition;
- 遭遇險情 meet with dangers;

[險區] danger zone;

[險勝] edge out; narrow victory; nose out; win by a narrow margin; win by a neck; win by a whisker;
- 險勝的 close-run;

[險灘] dangerous shoal; rapids;

[險戲] dangerous;

[險象] dangerous sign on phenomenon;
- 險象環生 beset with danger; dangers lurking on all sides; incessant crises; incessant occurrence of crises; signs of danger appearing everywhere;
- 險象頻生 dangerous images appear instantly;

[險些] almost; narrowly; nearly;
- 險些兒 a close shave; a narrow shave; all but; fail by a hair's breadth; nearly; stop short of; within a hair of; with a hair's breadth of; with an ace of;

[險要] strategically located and difficult of access;

[險易] (1) difficult and easy; (2) disturbance and peace;

[險語] sensational remark;

[險詐] sinister and crafty; treacherous; treachery;

[險寨雄關] strategic pass; strategic stockade and impregnable pass;

[險兆] evil omen;

[險症] crucial symptoms; dangerous illness; serious disease; severe illness;
- 險症要用猛藥醫 desperate diseases must have desperate cures; desperate diseases require desperate remedies;

[險中弄險] take a dangerous step along a

dangerous direction;
［險阻］ dangerous; dangerous and difficult; difficult; hazardous; precarious;

隘險 of great strategic value;
保險 (1) be bound to; guarantee; sure; (2) insurance;
出險 (1) get out of danger; (2) be threatened; in danger;
陡險 steep and dangerous;
風險 danger; hazard; risk;
好險 near thing;
火險 (1) fire insurance; (2) fire danger;
奸險 malicious; wicked and crafty; treacherous;
艱險 difficult and dangerous; hardships and dangers;
驚險 alarmingly dangerous; breathtaking; thrilling;
冒險 at the risk of; brave; risk; run risks; risk one's life; risk one's neck; take a chance; take a risk; take chances; take the risk of; venture; venture on;
排險 remove danger;
憑險 by relying on the terrain which is strategically located and difficult of success;
搶險 go to the rescue hurriedly; rush to deal with an emergency; rush to meet an emergency;
山險 a place strategically located and difficult of access;
涉險 adventure; be engaged in an adventure;
壽險 life insurance;
水險 marine insurance;

探險 explore; make explorations; venture into the unknown;

天險 natural barrio; natural defence;
脫險 bring through; escape danger; out of danger; out of the woods;
危險 danger; dangerous; perilous; risky;
巇險 (1) steep and difficult to ascend; (2) full of danger and hardship;
心險 crafty and evil-minded;
行險 embark on a dangerous task; take great risks;
凶險 dangerous;
兇險 critical; extremely dangerous;
要險 be concerned with one's honour;
陰險 crafty; cunning; deceitful; insidious; sinister; treacherous;
遇險 in danger; in distress; meet with a mishap; meet with danger;

xian
【嶮】 lofty; precipitous; steep;
［嶮巇］ (of mountain path) dangerous and difficult;

xian
【鮮】 few; rare; seldom;
［鮮乏］ scarce;
［鮮民］ (1) orphan; (2) underprivileged people;
［鮮少］ few; rare;
鮮少難得 very few and hard to get;
［鮮為人知］ rarely known by the people;
［鮮有］ rare; seldom to have;

xian
【獮】 (1) autumn hunting; (2) hunt; kill;

xian
【燹】 (1) fires set off by troops or shells; (2) outdoor fire;

兵燹 fire, havoc, turmoil caused by war;

xian
【蘚】 lichen; moss;
［蘚斑］ patches of lichen;
［蘚類］ moss;
［蘚苔］ lichen; moss;

水蘚 sphagnum;
苔蘚 moss;

xian
【顯】 (1) apparent; clear; evident; manifest; obvious; (2) display; expose; make known; manifest; show; (3) famed; illustrious and influential; prominent; renowned; reputed; well-known;
［顯白］ (1) make clear; show; (2) clear; evident;
［顯擺］ reveal; show off;
［顯比］ simile;
［顯出］ appear; exhibit; express; give evidence; show;
顯出…樣子 assume an air of; give oneself airs; have an air of; put on an air of;
［顯達］ achieve prominence in officialdom; attain high office; illustrious and influential;
［顯得］ appear; look; seem;
［顯官］ high official;
［顯貴］ bigwigs; eminent personages;

出身顯貴 born into the purple;

[顯赫] celebrated; eminent; glorious; illustrious; impressive; mighty; outstanding; powerful; prominent; renowned;

顯赫一時 glorious for a time; once almighty; once mighty; quite spectacularly;

地位顯赫 in a prominent position;

~ 地位顯赫的人 a person of exalted altitude;

聲勢顯赫 have a powerful influence;

[顯化] clear;

[顯豁] conspicuous; evident; obviously clear;

[顯見] apparent; it is evident that; obvious; self-evident;

顯而易見 apparently; as plain as print; as plain as the nose on one's nose; clear as day; crystal clear; easy to see; evidently; obviously; see with great ease; stand out in bold relief; stick like a sore thumb; stick out a mile; tells its own tale; very plain and obvious;

[顯爵] high government position;

[顯考] my late father;

[顯老] look old;

不顯老 bear one's age well;

[顯靈] a ghost making its presence or power felt;

[顯露] appear; become visible; flowering; manifest itself; unveil;

顯露頭角 make one's mark; show one's promise;

顯露原形 betray the cloven foot; show its original shape; show its real form;

[顯明] clear; distinct; manifest; marked; obvious; remarkable;

顯明性翻譯 overt translation;

[顯目] conspicuous; showy;

[顯弄] flaunt; show off;

[顯親] (1) glorify one's parents; (2) powerful relatives;

顯親揚名 bring glory to one's parents and become celebrated; glorify one's parents and become famous;

[顯然] apparent; clearly; evidently; it is evident that; obviously; visible;

[顯示] bespeak; demonstrate; indicate; presentation; reveal; show;

顯示地址 explicit address;

顯示卡 display card;

顯示屏 monitor;

顯示器 display; displayer; monitor;

~ 圖像顯示器 graphic display;

~ 液體顯示器 liquid crystal diode monitor;

~ 陰極射線管顯示器 cathode ray tube monitor;

顯示區 display space;

顯示軟件 software for display;

顯示終端 video terminal;

報警顯示 alarm display;

單色顯示 monochrome display;

附加顯示 additional display;

無聲顯示 aural-null presentation;

尋址顯示 addressed display;

有聲顯示 aural presentation;

指向標顯示 beacon presentation;

[顯微] show the minute points;

顯微結構 microstructure;

~ 典型顯微結構 typical microstructure;

顯微鏡 microscope;

~ 顯微鏡檢查 microscopic examination;

~ 電子顯微鏡 electron microscope;

~ 離心顯微鏡 centrifuge microscope;

~ 裂隙燈顯微鏡 slit lamp biomicroscope;

~ 偏振光顯微鏡 polarizing microscope;

~ 雙目顯微鏡 binocular microscope;

顯微手術 microsurgery;

顯微術 microscopy;

~ 電子顯微術 electron microscopy;

~ 化學顯微術 chemical microscopy;

顯微外科 microsurgery;

顯微組織 microstructure;

~ 非平衡顯微組織 non-equilibrium microstructure;

~ 晶團顯微組織 colony microstructure;

[顯顯] bright and brilliant; illustrious;

[顯現] appear; manifest oneself; reveal oneself; show; visualize;

[顯像管] kinescope;

全玻璃式顯像管 all-glass kinescope;

投影顯像管 projection kinescope;

[顯性] (1) dominance; (2) transparent;

顯性詞 transparent word;

獨親顯性 antithetical dominance;

交替顯性 alternating dominance;

總顯性 aggregate dominance;

[顯學] practical learning;

[顯眼] conspicuous; eye-catching; in plain sight; showy; striking;

[顯揚] (1) acclaim; cite; commend; praise; (2) celebrated; famous;

[顯要] (1) powerful and influential; (2) bigwigs; important personage; influential figure; notables; VIPs;
顯要人物 dignitary;

[顯耀] (1) well known for one's fame or power; (2) show off;

[顯影] developing; development;
顯影液 developer;
~彩色顯影液 colour developer;

[顯章] clarify; make clear; state with honesty;

[顯著] clear; evident; eye-catching; marked; notable; outstanding; pronounced; remarkable; striking;
顯著的 conspicuous;
顯著特徵 marked feature;

表顯 display; express;
重顯 rendition;
大顯 to full play;
漸顯 fade in;
明顯 clear; obvious;
淺顯 apparent; easily understandable; easy to read and understand; obvious; plain;
清顯 honoured official positions;
榮顯 honour and high position;
彰顯 manifest; obvious; show forth;
昭顯 eminent; evident; famous; prominent;
尊顯 honorable; noble; of high position; respectable; venerable;

xian

【獫】 dog with a long snout or muzzle;

[獫狁] Xianyun, an ancient nationality in China;

xian⁴

xian

【見】 (1) appear; manifest; visible; (2) introduce;

xian

【限】 (1) boundary; limit; (2) limit; restrict; set a limit;

[限定] define; determine; determiner; fix; limit; prescribe a limit to; restrict; specification; specify;
限定詞 determiner;
~規定限定詞 regular determiner;
~後位限定詞 postdeterminer;
~名詞限定詞 noun determiner;
~前位限定詞 predeterminer;
限定動詞 finitive;
限定複合詞 determinative compound;
限定性 defining;
~限定性關係從句 defining relative clause;
~限定性形容詞從句 defining adjectival clause;
超出限定 exceed a limit;
詞形限定 morphological specification;
句法限定 syntactic specification;

[限度] limits; measures; tethers;
超出限度 go over a limit; overstep the limit;
超過限度 go beyond the limit;
超過正常限度 overstep the normal limit; push the envelop;
達到限度 reach the limitation;
法定限度 legal limit;
凡事都有限度 everything has its limit;
設定限度 set a lmit;
驗收限度 acceptance limit;
振幅限度 amplitude limit;
最大限度 the maximum limit;
最低限度 the lowest limit;
最高限度 the highest limit;
最小限度 the minimum limit;

[限額] limit; limitation; norm; quota;
限額制度 quota system;
撥款限額 appropriation limitation;
超出限額 overshoot;
貸款限額 loan ceiling;
債務限額 debt limitation;
最高限額 cap;

[限幅] limiting;
飽和限幅 saturation limiting;
截止限幅 cutoff limiting;
雙向限幅 double limiting;

[限價] price control;

[限量] limit the quantity of; set bounds to;
限量版 limited edition;

[限令] order sb to do sth within a certain time;

[限期] (1) set a time limit; within a definite time; (2) deadline; time limit;
限期報到 report for duty by the prescribed time;
限期提前 the deadline has been advanced;
限期已滿 the time limit has been reached;
趕上限期 meet a deadline;
延長限期 extend the time limit;
有限期 have a deadline;

[限時] fix the time; set a deadline; set a time limit; set the time;

[限於] confined to; due to; limited to; owing to the limitation of;

限於篇幅 as space is limited;

[限制] confine; constraint; cramp; limit; place restrictions on; restraint; restrict; restriction; shut down on;

限制附加語 restrictive adjunct;
限制器 limitator; limiter; restrictor;
~超速限制器 overspeed limiter;
~電壓限制器 voltage limitator;
~積分限制器 integral restrictor;
~加速度限制器 acceleration restrictor;
限制生產 put restrictions on production;
限制數量 limit to a number or amount;
限制性代碼 restricted code;
限制性翻譯 restricted translation;
限制性關係詞 restrictive relative;
限制性關係從句 restrictive relative clause;
限制性述謂結構 qualifying predication;
限制性同位 restrictive apposition;
~限制性同位語 restrictive appositive;
限制性形容詞 restrictive adjective;
限制性修飾詞 restrictive modifier;
限制言論自由 gag;
限制主義 restrictionism;
動態限制 dynamic constraint;
高度限制 height limit;
供水限制 restriction on water supply;
積極限制 active restraint;
交叉限制 crossing restriction;
進口限制 a limitation on imports;
淨空限制 clearance limitation;
軍備限制 arms limitation;
開支限制 spending limit;
貿易限制 restriction of trade;
模限制 mode confinement;
年齡限制 age limit;
頻帶限制 band limitation;
取消限制 life control; remove restrictions;
任期限制 term limits;
設備限制 equipment constraint;
時間限制 time limit;
受限制 have restrictions;
速度限制 speed limit;
同現限制 co-occurrence restriction;
信貸限制 credit restriction;
嚴格限制 strict limit;
語境限制 contextual restriction;
預算限制 budget constraint; budget restraint;
重量限制 weight limit;
自願限制 voluntary restraint;

程限 (1) formula; form; (2) time or place limit;
大限 day of one's doom;
戶限 threshold;
緩限 extend the time limit; put off the deadline;
極限 (1) extremity; limit; maximum; ultimate limit; (2) limit;
界限 (1) ambit; boundary; demarcation line; dividing line; (2) end; limit;
局限 confine; limit; localization;
寬限 extend a time limit; grace;
門限 threshold;
年限 age limit; fixed number of years;
期限 deadline; time limit;
權限 jurisdiction; limits of authority;
容限 allowance; tolerance;
上限 superior limit; top limit; upper limit;
昇限 ceiling;
時限 deadline; time limit;
蝕限 eclipse limit;
為限 not to exceed; serve as a limit; within the limit of;
無限 an infinite of; boundless; immeasurable; infinite; infinitude; infinity; limitless; unlimited;
下限 floor level; lower limit; prescribed minimum;
象限 quadrant;
依限 within the time limit;
有限 (1) finite; limited; (2) not many; only a few;
逾限 exceed the limit; go beyond the bounds; go beyond the limits;
遠限 distant time limit;
越限 exceed the time limit;
展現 extend the deadline; extend a time limit;
制限 (1) confine; limit; restrict; (2) bound; limit; confines;

xian

【峴】 (1) a mountain in Hubei; (2) steep hill;

xian

【現】 (1) current; existing; now; present; (2) do sth in time of need; extempore; (3) available; on hand; ready; (4) cash; ready money; (5) appear; emerge; reveal; show;

[現編] extemporize;
現編現唱 make up a song as one sings;
[現場] (1) scene; (2) on the spot; site; spot; work field;
現場辦公 handle official business on the spot;
現場表演 life performance; live show; perform live;
現場採訪 spot coverage; talk show;
現場參觀 field trip;
現場抽查 spot check;
現場服務 field services;
現場顧問 field adviser;
現場會 on the spot meeting;
現場教學 on the spot instruction;
現場考試 examination on the spot;
現場錄音 location sound recording;
現場試驗 field test;
現場研究 field research;
現場治療 on-the-spot treatment;
保護現場 keep the scene intact;
奔赴現場 rush to the scene;
奔向現場 hasten to the spot;
工作現場 worksite;
來到現場 come to the spot;
破壞現場 destroy the scene;
清查現場 check the scene out;
施工現場 worksite
試驗現場 testing ground;
視察現場 inspect the scene;
[現成] at hand; ready; ready-made; off the peg; off the rack;
現成的 off-the-peg; off-the-rack; off-the-shelf;
現成衣服 ready-made clothes;
吃現成 reap the profit;
撿現成 get an uneared gain;
[現鈔] hard cash;
[現出] display; reveal;
現出原形 come out in one's true colours;
[現存] available; existing; extant; in stock; on hand;
[現代] (1) contemporary age; modern times; present age; (2) contemporary; current; modern; present;
現代病 modern disease;
現代的 contemporary; modern-day; present-day;
~最現代的 cutting-edge; leading-edge;
最現代的科技 leading-edge technology;
現代管理理論 modern management theory;
現代化 modernization; modernize;
~現代化建設 modernization construction;
~現代化戰爭 modernized war;
~現代化住宅 modern dwelling;
~實現現代化 achieve modernization;
現代教育 modern education;
現代劇 modern play;
現代迷信 modern superstituion;
現代派 modernism; modernist school;
現代生活 contemporary living;
現代詩 contemporary poetry;
現代史 contemporary history;
現代舞 modern dance;
~現代舞劇 modern dance drama;
現代性 modernity;
現代音樂 contemporary music;
現代主義 modernism;
~後現代主義 postmodernism;
現代作戰理論 modern war theory;
現代作戰模擬 modern war simulation;
現代作戰戰略 modern war strategy;
後現代 postmodern;
[現付] cash payment;
[現貨] goods on hand; spot goods; stock goods;
現貨供應 can be purchased off the shelf; off-the-shelf;
現貨價格 spot price;
現貨交易 spot transaction;
現貨市場 spot market;
[現價] current price; present price; ruling price;
[現金] (1) cash; hard cash; ready money; spot cash; (2) cash reserve in a bank;
現金報酬 cash reward; monetary reward;
現金短缺 run out of cash;
現金管理 cash control;
現金交易 cash transaction;
現金流轉 cash flow;
現金收入 cash receipts;
現金預算 cash budget;
現金預支 cash advance;
現金餘額 cash balance;
現金賬 cash account; money account;
~零用現金賬 petty cash account;
現金賬戶 cash account;
現金折扣 cash discount;
現金支出 out-of-pocket expenses;
現金支付 payment in cash;

~用現金支付［的］ cash-in-hand;
不用現金 cashless;
電子現金 e-cash; electronic cash;
付現金 pay cash;
活動現金 free cash;
急需現金 need cash badly;
即付現金 sharp cash;
接受現金 receive cash;
淨現金 net cash;
可用現金 available cash;
零用現金 petty cash;
吸收現金 absorb cash;
閒置現金 idle cash;

［現今］ at present; now; nowadays; these days;

［現局］ present situation;

［現款］ cash; ready money;

［現期］ current;

［現錢］ cash; ready money;

［現任］ (1) at present hold the office of; (2) currently in office; incumbent; present;
現任牧師 incumbent priest;
現任者 incumbent;
現任總統 incumbent president;

［現生］ present incarnation; present life;

［現時］ at present; now;

［現實］ (1) actuality; reality; things as they are; (2) actual; practical; pragmatic; real;
現實點 get real;
現實化 actualization;
現實人 real person;
現實人道主義 realistic humanitarianism;
現實生活 actual life; real life;
現實問題 real-life problems;
現實意義 realism;
現實主義 realism;
~超現實主義 super realism;
~革命現實主義 revolutionary realism;
~批判現實主義 critical realism;
~新現實主義 new realism;
悲慘的現實 unhappy reality;
當前的現實 realities of the day;
反映現實 mirror reality;
可怕的現實 gruesome reality;
客觀現實 objective reality;
面對現實 face the reality; face to face with reality; realistic;
逃避現實 escape from reality;
~逃避現實的人 ostrich;
脫離現實 be divorced from reality; unrealistic;
無視現實 shut one's eyes to facts;
虛擬現實 visual reality;
嚴酷的現實 facts of life;
正視現實 look at the facts in the face;

［現世］ (1) the world nowadays; this life; this-worldly; (2) be disgraced; bring shame on oneself; lose face;
現世現報 get punished quickly for the evil one has just done; retribution in one's own lifetime;
活現世 it's disgraceful;

［現勢］ current situation; present situation;

［現下］ at present; now;

［現…現…］
現吃現做 cook for immediate consumption; freshly prepared as ordered;
現買現賣 sell sth right after it is bought; straight cash deal;
現學現教 learn while one teaches;
現用現買 buy as one needs for the day; buy for immediate use;

［現象］ appearance; phenomenon;
現象學 phenomenonology;
不規則現象 irregularity;
常見的現象 common phenomenon;
磁現象 magnetic phenomenon;
均衡現象 balanced phenomenon;
~不均衡現象 unbalanced phenomenon;
可喜的現象 gratifying phenomenon;
老化現象 ageing phenomenon;
類似的現象 similar phenomenon;
歷史現象 historical phenomenon;
黏附現象 adhesion phenomenon;
社會現象 social phenomenon;
雙語現象 bilingualism;
~個人雙語現象 individual bilingualism;
吸附現象 adsorption phenomenon;
再現象 reconstructed image;
暫時現象 transient phenomenon;
自然現象 natural phenomenon;

［現銷］ sale by real cash; sale for cash;

［現形］ betray oneself; reveal one's true features; show one's true colours;

［現行］ (1) currently in effect; existing; in force; in operation; presently effective; (2) active;
現行標準 current standards;
現行法律 violate the laws in effect;
現行犯 an offender caught re-handed;
現行政策 current policies;

［現眼］ be embarrassed; cut a sorry figure; lose

face; make a scene; make a spectacle of oneself;

[現役] active duty; active service;
[現銀] ready cash;
[現有] existing; have on hand; now available;
[現在] at once; at present; at the moment; for the moment; immediately; now; nowadays; of the moment; presently; right now;
現在分詞 present participle;
現在幾點 can you tell me the time; have you the right time; how goes the enemy; what do you make the time; what is the time; what o'clock is it; what time is it now;
現在進行式 present continuous tense;
現在時 present tense;
~ 編年史中的現在時 annalistic present;
~ 格言中的現在時 aphoristic present;
~ 歷史現在時 historic present; historical present tense;
現在式 present;
~ 反覆現在式 iterative present;
現在完成進行式 present perfect continuous tense;
現在完成時 present perfect tense;
現在完成式 present perfect;
從現在起 from now on;
直到現在 down to this time; until now; up to now;

[現職] current post; present employment; present job;
[現狀] current situation; existing state of affairs; present situation; status; things as they are;
安於現狀 be reconciled to the situation; be satisfied with the existing state of affairs; come to terms with one's existence; come to terms with one's situation; content with things as they are; stick in the mud; take things as they are; take things as they come;
~ 安於現狀者 happy camper;
保持現狀 defend the status quo; leave the matter as it is;
改變現狀 change the status quo;
滿於現狀 be content with things as they are; be satisfied with the present situation;
世界現狀 current world state of affairs;
維持現狀 maintain the present condition; maintain the status quo; preserve the status quo;

表現 acquit oneself; comport; display; express; manifest; show; show off;
呈現 appear; emerge; present;
重現 reappear; rendition;
出現 appear; appear on the scene; arise; come along; come on the scene; emerge; enter on the scene;
兌現 (1) cash a cheque; pay cash; redemption; (2) fulfil; honour a commitment; make good a promise; make real; realize;
發現 discover; discovery; find;
浮現 appear before one's eyes; drift; emerge; occur; raise;
復現 cash; pay in cash;
共現 co-occurrence;
活現 appear vividly; come alive;
閃現 flash; flicker; flash before one; glint;
實現 accomplish; achieve; attain; bring about; come true; complete; difficult of accomplishment; easy of accomplishment; enforce; fruition; materialize; realize;
體現 embody; give expression to; incarnate; reflect;
貼現 discount;
顯現 appear; manifest oneself; reveal oneself; show; visualize;
隱現 (1) appear indistinctly; (2) in and out;
涌現 come to the fore; emerge in large numbers; spring up;
湧現 crop up; emerge;
再貼現 rediscount;
再現 be reproduced; playback; reappear; recover; recur; rendition;
展現 develop; emerge; present before one's eyes; unfold before one's eyes; yield up;

xian

【莧】 amaranth;
[莧菜] amaranth;

馬齒莧 purslane;

xian

【陷】 (1) pitfall; trap; (2) get stuck; get bogged down; (3) cave in; sink; (4) frame; frame up; (5) be captured; fall; (6) defect; deficiency;
[陷敵] (1) crash into the enemy position; (2) fall into the enemy's hands;

[陷害] caluminiate; frame up; make a false charge against; plot a frame-up; set up; snare; trap;
[陷阱] booby trap; deadfall; gin; pit; pitfall; snare; trap;
[陷坑] (1) snare; trap; (2) cave; hollow;
[陷落] (1) sink; submerge; (2) be lost to the enemy;
[陷沒] (1) sink; submerge; (2) be captured by the enemy;
[陷溺] be drowned; sink; submerge;
[陷人於罪] frame sb; up; incriminate sb;
[陷入] be caught in; be entrapped; enmeshed; fall into; get bogged down in; land oneself in; mire oneself in; sink into;
陷入包圍 be besieged by; be encircled by;
陷入沉思 deep in meditation; lost in thought;
陷入重圍 find oneself tightly encircled;
陷入法網 be caught in meshes of the law;
陷入僵局 come to a deadlock; reach an impasse;
陷入窘境 fall into difficult circumstances; get into a hobble; get into an awkward position; in a tight corner;
陷入絕境 at bay; be drawn into a hopeless situation; bring to bay; get into extreme difficulty; have one's back to the wall; out on a limb; with one's back to the wall;
陷入絕望 be sunk in despair;
陷入苦境 be cornered; get into hot water; in a pickle; land in a predicament; tie oneself in knots;
陷入困境 be cornered; between the horns of a dilemma; fall into dire straits; find oneself in a tight corner; find oneself in the mire; get into a mess; get into hot water; get into scrapes; get into trouble; have a wolf by the ears; in a cart; in a hole; in a jam; in a tight corner; in hot water; in Queer Streets; in the soup; land in a predicament; land oneself in a fix; on the horns of a dilemma; put in a tight spot; put to the push; stick to the mire;
陷入羅網 be caught in a net; fall into a snare;
陷入魔掌 fall into the devil's hand;
陷入泥坑 get down hopeless in a quagmire;
陷入泥淖 mire oneself in a swamp;
陷入貧困 sink into poverty;
陷入圈套 fall into a trap; get trapped into;
陷入危機 beset with a crisis; deep in crisis;
[陷身] land oneself in;
陷身囹圄 be confined to jail; behind prison bars; put in jail;
[陷於] be caught in; fall into; land oneself in; sink into;
陷於被動 be thrown into passivity; fall into passive position;
陷於重圍 be closely besieged by the enemy;
陷於孤立 find oneself isolated;
陷於絕境 be driven to the last ditch; in extremity; like a rat in a hole; no hope for escape; stand at bay; surrender oneself to despair; turn to bay;
陷於困境 fall into dire straits; find oneself in a tight corner; land oneself in a fix;
陷於魔掌 fall into the devils's hand;
陷於泥沼 get bogged down in the mud;
陷於死地 be drive to desperation; be entrapped into a fatal position;
[陷陣] break enemy ranks; take an enemy position;

凹陷 (1) depressed; hollow; sunken; (2) cave in; sink;
拗陷 depression;
崩陷 cave in; collapse; fall in; sink; subside;
沉陷 (1) cave in; sink; (2) settlement;
攻陷 capture; storm;
構陷 frame a case against sb; make a false charge against sb;
淪陷 be occupied by the enemy; fall into enemy hands; flood; submerge;
氣陷 air pocket;
缺陷 blemish; defect; drawback; fault; flaw;
失陷 fall; fall into enemy hands; fall to the enemy;
塌陷 cave in; collapse; sink; subside;
窪陷 low-lying; sunken;
誣陷 frame a case against; frame sb; frame sb up; incriminate falsely; make false charge against sb;
下陷 cave in; sag; sink; undercut;

xian
【羨】 (1) covet; (2) envy;

［羨財］ covet wealth;
［羨慕］ (1) covet; (2) envy;
羨慕的 envious;
出於羨慕 out of envy;
令人羨慕 enviable;
［羨歎］ praise;

稱羨 envy; express one's admiration;
歎羨 sigh in admiration;
欣羨 admire;
歆羨 admire;
豔羨 admire; envy;

X

xian
【腺】 gland;
［腺癌］ glandular cancer;
汗腺癌 syringocarcinoma;
甲狀腺癌 thyroid carcinoma;
淋巴腺癌 cancer of the lymph glands;
黏液腺癌 mucinous adenocarcinoma;
前列腺癌 cancer of the prostate gland;
腎腺癌 adenocarcinoma of kidney;
息肉樣腺癌 polypoid adenocarcinoma;
［腺病］ adenopathy;
［腺垂體］ adenohypophysis;
［腺瘤］ adenoma; glandular tumour;
單形性腺瘤 monomorphic adenoma;
膽管腺瘤 bile duct adenoma;
濾泡性腺瘤 follicular adenoma;
膜性腺瘤 membranous adenoma;
皮質腺瘤 cortical adenomas;
腎腺瘤 adenomas of kidney;
脂肪腺瘤 lipoadenoma;
［腺肉瘤］ adenosarcoma;
［腺體］ gland;
［腺炎］ adenitis;
包皮腺炎 tysonitis;
腸腺炎 enteradenitis;
耳下腺炎 mumps;
汗腺炎 hydradenitis;
淚腺炎 dacryoadenitis;
腮腺炎 parotiditis;
唾液腺炎 sialadenitis;
胃腺炎 gastradenitis;
胰腺炎 pancreatitis;
陰道腺炎 adenosis vaginae;
硬化性腺炎 scleradenitis;
［腺硬化］ adenosclerosis;
［腺增大］ hyperadenosis;
［腺周炎］ periadenitis;

扁桃腺 tonsil;
臭腺 scent gland;
毒腺 poison gland;
耳下腺 parotid gland;
汗腺 apocrine sweat gland; sweat gland;
頜下腺 salivary gland;
甲狀腺 thyroid gland;
淚腺 lachrymal gland;
淋巴腺 lymph node (or gland);
蜜腺 nectar;
內分泌腺 endocrine gland;
前列腺 prostate (gland);
乳腺 mammary gland;
腮腺 parotid gland;
舌下腺 sublingual gland;
生殖腺 sebaceous gland;
絲腺 silk gland;
松果腺 pineal body;
腎上腺 adrenal; adrenal gland;
胃腺 gastric gland;
無管腺 ductless gland;
性腺 sexual gland;
胸腺 thymus gland;
胰腺 pancreas;
增殖腺 adenoids;

xian
【線】 (1) string; thread; wire; (2) line; (3) made of cotton thread; (4) line; route; (5) boundary; demarcation line; (6) brink; verge;
［線段］ line segment;
［線對］ pair;
控制線對 control pair;
塞繩線對 cord pair;
［線匯］ congruence;
代數線匯 algebraic congruence;
共焦線匯 confocal congruences;
迷向線匯 isotropic congruence;
雙曲性線匯 hyperbolic congruence;
四面線匯 tetrahedral congruence;
特殊線匯 special congruence;
線性線匯 linear line congruence;
直紋線匯 rectilinear congruence;
［線路］ circuit; line;
線路板 circuit board;
［線圈］ coil;
電樞線圈 armature coil;
副線圈 secondary coil;
工作線圈 actuating coil;
空心線圈 aircore coil;

吸收線圈 absorbing coil;
折狀線圈 accordion coil;

［線人］ informer; nark; stool pigeon;
警方線人 police informer;

［線衫］ T-shirt;

［線上］ online;
線上資料處理 online data processing;
線上資訊 online information;

［線索］ clue; lead; thread;
查找線索 trace a clue;
發現線索 discover a clue;
留下線索 leave a clue;
一條線索 a clue;
重要線索 important clues;
追查線索 follow up a clue;

［線毯］ cotton blanket;

［線條］ (1) lines in drawing; (2) figure; lines;
線條畫 line drawing;
線條均稱 in drawing;

［線性］ linearity;
線性變化 linear change;
線性思維 linear thinking;
非線性 nonlinearity;
~互補非線性 complementary nonlinearity;
~幾何非線性 geometric nonlinearity;
~間隙非線性 backlash nonlinearity;
~組合非線性 nonlinearity;
校驗線性 checking linearity;
掃描線性 deflection linearity;
振幅線性 amplitude linearity;

［線裝本］ thread-bound edition;

暗線 foreshadowing;
邊線 foul line; sideline;
補給線 supply line;
佈線 wiring;
踩線 step on line;
槽線 trough line;
測地線 geodesic;
側線 (1) lateral line; (2) siding;
拆線 take out stitches;
串線 wrong number;
垂線 perpendicular line; vertical line;
磁力線 magnetic line of force;
搭線 (1) make contact; (2) act as a go-between; act as a matchmaker;
單行線 one-way road;
單線 (1) single line; (2) single track;
導火線 (1) a small incident that touches off a big one; direct cause of an event; (2) (blasting) fuse;
導線 (1) conductor; (2) traverse;
等高線 contour;
等力線 line of force;
等量雨線 isohyet;
等溫線 isotherm;
等壓線 isobar;
底線 bottom line;
地平線 horizon;
地線 ground wire;
電報線 telegraphic line;
電力線 electric line of force; power line;
電線 electric cable; wire;
釣線 fishing line;
吊線 plumb line;
渡線 crossover;
短截線 stub;
短線 goods in short supply;
斷線 (1) break off relations with; (2) lose continuity in tradition or accomplishments; (3) disconnection;
供電線 power supply line;
法線 normal;
髮際線 hairline;
分界線 boundary; line of demarcation;
分水線 water-shed;
防線 line of defence;
封鎖線 blockade line;
鋒線 frontal line;
復線 multiple track;
幹線 artery; main line; trunk line;
高潮線 high-water mark (line);
高壓線 high tension wire;
割線 secant;
股線 plied yarn;
管線 general term for pipes, tubes, wires, cables, etc.;
光線 light; luminous beam; ray; ray of light;
國防線 national defence line;
國境線 boundary line;
海岸線 coastline;
海防線 coastal front;
航海線 boundary line of territorial waters;
航線 air route; airline; airway; itinerary; navigation route; route; way;
橫道線 (pedestrians') street crossing;
紅外線 infrared ray;
弧線 arc;
畫線 draw a line;
環行線 belt line;
回歸線 tropic;
火線 (1) battle (on firing, front) line; (2) live

wire;
飢餓線 on the verge of starvation;
基線 base line; datum lines;
基準線 datum line;
極線 polar line;
漸近線 asymptote;
交通線 communication lines;
接地線 earth wire; ground wire;
接線 wiring;
界線 (1) demarcation line; (2) boundary; bounds;
金線 gold thread;
經線 (1) meridian (line); (2) warp;
警戒線 cordon; security line;
褲線 creases (of trousers);
力線 line of force;
流水線 assembly line;
流線 streamline;
路線 (1) line; (2) itinerary; route;
裸線 bare wire;
麻線 faxen thread; linen thread;
毛線 knitting wool;
棉線 cotton; cotton thread;
瞄準線 sight line;
明線 open wire; open-wire line;
墨線 (1) line made by a carpener's ink marker; (2) line in a carpenter's ink marker;
母線 (1) bus; bus bar; (2) generator; genratrix;
內線 back door; inner line;
拋物線 parabola;
皮線 rubber-sheathed wire;
平行線 parallel lines;
漆包線 enamel insulated wire;
鉛垂線 plumb line;
牽線 (1) control from behind the scenes; pull strings; pull wires; use indirect influence to gain one's ends; (2) act as go-between;
前線 front; front line;
切線 tangent; tangent line;
曲線 curve;
全線 all fronts; entire length; whole line;
熱線 (1) heat ray; (2) hot line;
絨線 (1) floss for embroidery; (2) knitting wool;
軟線 flexible cord;
撒線 let out the string of a kite;
散兵線 skirmish line;
紗包線 cotton-covered wire;
紗線 yarn;
視線 (1) eyesight; (2) line of sight; (3) line of vision;
生命線 lifeblood; lifeline;
輸電線 transmission line;
水線 waterline;
絲包線 insulated wire (with silk winding);
絲線 silk thread;
膛線 rifling;
天線 aerial; antenna;
跳接線 jump cables; jump leads;
鐵線 wire;
汀線 beach line;
外線 (1) exterior lines; (2) outside connections;
緯線 (1) parallel; (2) weft;
無線 wireless;
絃線 cord; thread;
斜線 oblique line;
虛線 (1) dotted line or line of dashes; (2) imaginary line;
旋輪線 cycloid;
雪線 snow line;
牙線 dental floss;
壓線 line ball;
延長線 extension (or extended) line;
沿線 along the line;
眼線 (1) eyeliner; (2) police informer;
羊腸線 catgut (suture);
一段線 a length of wire;
一根線 a line; a thread;
一條線 a line;
一線 (1) a beam; a flash; a gleam; a glimmer; a ray; a thread; (2) a beam of; a flash of; a gleam of; a glimmer of; a ray of; a thread of;
引火線 fuse;
引線 (1) sewing needle; (2) go-between; (3) fuse;
影線 hatching;
有線 wired;
在線 online;
佔線 the line is busy;
戰線 battle front; front;
折線 broken line;
針線 (1) needle and thread; (2) needlework;
陣線 alignment; front; ranks;
支線 branch line;
直線 (1) straight line; (2) sharp; steep;
中垂線 perpendicular bisector;
中心線 centre line;
中線 (1) central line; centre line; median line; (2) halfway line;
載重線 load line; load waterline;
終點線 finishing line; finishing tape;
軸線 (1) axis; (2) spool cotton; spool thread;
專線 (1) line for special use; (2) special railway line;
專用線 special railway line;
裝配線 assembly lines;

裝卸線 loading-unloading siding;
子午線 meridian (line);
紫外線 ultraviolet ray;
自動線 transfer machine;
總線 bus;
作業線 production line;

xian
【憲】 (1) constitution; statute; (2) intelligent;
[憲兵] military police; military policemen;
[憲法] charter; constitution;
憲法草案 draft constitution;
憲法條文 constitutional provision;
頒布憲法 promulgate a constitution;
國家憲法 national constitution;
修改憲法 amend the constitution;
[憲綱] legal provision;
[憲令] laws and ordinances;
[憲網] arm of law; net of justice;
[憲威] official prestige;
[憲憲] complacent;
[憲則] laws and instituions;
[憲章] charter;
[憲政] constitutional government; constitutional rule; constitutionalism;
[憲制] constitutional; constitutional government;

立憲 constitutionalism; establish the constitutional system;
違憲 unconstitutional; violation of the constitution;
彝憲 laws; regulations;
制憲 draw up a national constitution;

xian
【縣】 county; prefecture;
[縣丞] assistant magistrate;
[縣城] county town;
[縣官] county magistrate;
[縣令] county magistrate;
[縣試] county examination;
[縣署] county office;
[縣學] county school;
[縣長] county magistrate;
[縣志] county chronicle;

知縣 county magistrate;
自治縣 autonomous county;

xian
【餡】 any kind of stuffing for dumplings;
[餡餅] meat pie; pasty; pie; tart;
百果餡餅 mince pie;
菜肉餡餅 pot pie;
凝乳餡餅 curd tart;
蘋果餡餅 apple tart;
水果餡餅 fruit pie;
羊肉餡餅 braxy pie;
小餡餅 turnover;
~蘋果小餡餅 apple turnover;
一塊餡餅 a piece of pie; a slice of pie;
油煎餡餅 fried pie;
油炸餡餅 fritter;
豬肉餡餅 pork pie;
[餡兒] stuffing;
露餡兒 give oneself away; give the game away; let the cat out of the bag; spill the beans;
[餡糕] patty;

夾餡 stuffed pastry;
露餡 give oneself away;
肉餡 meat stuffing;

xian
【𧏙】 half-grown bean;

xian
【獻】 (1) dedicate; donate; forward; offer; present; (2) display; put on; show; stage; (3) cater to; curry favour; flatter;
[獻寶] (1) present a treasure; (2) offer a valuable piece of advice; (2) display what one cherishes; show off what one treasures;
[獻曝] offer my humble gift or advice;
[獻策] make suggestions; offer advice;
[獻醜] show my poor skill; that's the best I can do;
獻醜獻醜 please do not laugh at my performance;
顯能獻醜 show off and manifest what one is unfit for;
[獻詞] congratulatory message; dedication; dedication speech;
[獻花] lay a wreath; present bouquets; present flowers;
[獻技] display one's feat; stage a performance of special skills;

［獻計］ make suggestions; offer advice; present a scheme for adoption;
獻計獻策 come up with new and better ways to do things; suggest ways and means;
［獻金］ (1) contribute money; (2) money contributed;
［獻酒］ offer wine;
［獻可替否］ persuade sb to do good and dissuade him/her from doing evil;
［獻禮］ (1) present a gift; (2) ceremony of offering presents;
［獻媚］ (1) act coquettishly; (2) act obsequiously; curry favour with; flatter; make up to; toady; try to ingratiate oneself with;
獻媚求寵 insinuate oneself into sb's favour;
獻媚討好 fawn on and curry favoaur with; toady and get advantage from; win favour in the eyes of;
［獻旗］ present a banner;
［獻身］ devote oneself to; give one's life for; offer oneself to a cause;
獻身工作 devote oneself to one's work;
獻身社會 dedicate oneself to public services; offer oneself to social work;
為國獻身 give up one's life for one's country;
為事業獻身 sacrifice oneself for one's career;
［獻歲］ beginning of a new year;
［獻血］ donate blood;
［獻藝］ (1) demonstrate one's talents; exhibit one's skill; (2) appear on stage for a performance;

呈獻 respectfully present;
奉獻 offer as a tribute; present with respect;
貢獻 contribute; contribution; dedicate; devote;
祭獻 sacrifice;
敬獻 offer respectfully; present politely;
捐獻 contribute; donate; present;
文獻 document; literature;
酌獻 honour a deity with wine;

xian
【霰】 sleet; snow and rain;
［霰彈］ canister shot; case shot;
霰彈槍子彈 huckshot;
霰彈筒 canister;
［霰石］ aragonite;

xiang1
xiang
【相】 (1) each other; mutually; one another; reciprocal; (2) see for oneself; (3) substance; (4) a surname;
［相愛］ love each other;
相親相愛 be kind to each other and love each other;
永遠相愛 love each other with an undying affection;
［相安］ live in peace with each other;
相安無事 at peace with each other; live harmoniously in peace; live in peace with each other; live together peacefully;
［相伴］ accompany sb; be a companion of each other; together;
［相幫］ aid; help;
［相報］ serve in return;
怒顏相報 return sb an angry look;
以軀相報 I ought to use this body of mine to serve you only;
怨怨相報 hatred begets hatred;
［相比］ compare with each other; match;
相比之下，方見其長 gain by contrast;
與上年相比 year on year;
［相並］ abreast; side by side;
［相差］ differ;
相差甚微 the difference is negligible; the difference is slight;
相差無幾 about equal; almost the same; little difference; not much difference; somewhat on a par; there is hardly any difference between; without much difference;
相差懸殊 a wide difference; different distantly and extremely; differ greatly;
［相成］ (1) complement each other; (2) complementary in action;
［相稱］ a good assortment; a good match for; commensurate to; commensurate with; comport with; fit each other; match each other; match with; proportional to; proportionate to; symmetrical;
相稱的 commensurate;
不相稱 ill-matched; out of proportion; unbecoming; unsuited;
容貌與年齡相稱 look one's age;

與場合相稱 suitable to the occasion;

[相持] be locked in a stalemate; refuse to budge;

相持不下 at a deadlock; at a stalemate; be locked in a stalemate; come to a deadlock; deadlocked; each refuses to yield; each sticks to his own stand;

兩軍相持 the two armies maintain their ground;

[相處] get along with; get on; live together; spend time together;

相處得很好 at peace with sb; fit in well with sb; get along well with sb; get on well with sb; hit it off with sb; live in amity; live in harmony; live in peace; relate to; on friendly terms; on good terms;

不好相處 difficult to get along with;

慈和相處 live on friendly terms;

和睦相處 keep in with; live in amity; live together in a friendly way; live in harmony; live side by side peacefully and friendly; live together in peace; live together in unity; on friendly terms; smoke the calumet together; smoke the pipe of peace together;

難以相處 hard to get along with;

難與相處 difficult to get along with; hard to get along with sb;

[相傳] (1) according to legend; it is said that; tradition has it that; (2) be handed down from generation to generation;

[相打] have a fight;

[相待] treat a person;

赤心相待 treat sb with all sincerity;

士別三日，刮目相待 a scholar who has been away three days must be looked at with new eyes; after a scholar's absence of three days, one will see in him a man changed for the better;

以誠相待 rank with; give sb a fair shake;

以禮相待 treat sb or people with courtesy;

[相當] (1) about; considerably; fairly; quite; rather; somewhat; to a great extent; very; (2) balance; correspond to; equivalent; match; (3) appropriate; fit; suitable;

得失相當 break even; half loss, half gain; gains and losses balance each other; the gains offset the losses;

個頭相當 of about the same height;

供求相當 supply balances the demand;

[相得] friendly; harmonious;

相得益彰 benefit by associating together; bring out the best in each other; bring out the best of each other through cooperation and coordination; complement each other; each complements the other; each gains in appearance from the presence of the other; each improves by association with the other; each shining more brilliantly in the other's company;

[相等] equal; equal in amount; equal in number; equivalent; parity; the same;

相等的 coequal;

[相抵] balance; cancel each other; counterbalance; neutralize; offset;

[相鬥] fight against each other;

兩虎相鬥 a fight between two big powers; a struggle between two tigers;

[相對] (1) face to face; opposite; (2) relative; (3) comparatively; corresponding; relatively;

相對而泣 look into each other's eyes and weep; mingle tears;

相對而坐 sit face to face; sit opposite to each other;

相對而言 relatively speaking;

相對論 relativity; relativity theory; theory of relativity;

~ 相對論電動力學 relativistic electrodynamics;

~ 相對論力學 relativistic mechanics;

~ 相對論量子理論 relativistic quantum theory;

~ 相對論量子力學 relativistic quantum mechanics;

~ 相對論流體力學 relativistic dydromechanics;

~ 相對論物理學 relativistic physics;

~ 廣義對相論 general theory of relativity;

~ 狹義相對論 special theory of relativity;

相對默然 face each other in silence;

相對同義詞 relative synonym;

相對無言 fall silent with each other; look at one another but make no remarks; sit facing each other in silence; sit opposite to each other in silence;

相對性 relativity;

~ 相對性反義詞 contrary;

~ 相對性原理 relativity principle;

相對最高級 relative superlative;

[相煩] trouble sb with requests;

[相反] by contrast; contradictory; contrary; contrary to; go contrary to; in contrast to; in contrast with; in opposition to; on the contrary; opposed to each other; opposite; quite the contrary; run contrary to; to the contrary;
相反詞 antonym;
相反的 contrary;
相反地 contrariwise;
相反相成 both contrary and complementary to each other; both opposite and complementary to each other; oppose each other and yet also complement each other;
完全相反 complete opposites;
正好相反 the exact opposite of;
正相反 the other way around; the other way round;
~ 正相反的 antithetical;

[相仿] alike; similar;
年齡相仿 alike in age;

[相逢] come across; come face to face with each other; meet by chance; meet each other;
相逢恨晚 regret not having met earlier; regret that the meeting has not taken place sooner; regret to have not met sb before; regret to have seen each other too late;
恨不相逢未嫁時 regret meeting a true lover only after one's marriage; what a pity that we didn't meet before you and I were married;
萍水相逢 chance acquaintance; meet by chance; strangers meeting by chance like patches of drifting duckweed; meet by chance; meet casually; ships that pass in the night;
無奇不成書，無緣不相逢 there is no true fairy-story without a miracle, and no meeting without predestination;

[相扶] support each other;
兩瞽相扶 two blind men support each other – neither one will lead;

[相符] agree; agree with; conform to; correspond to; match; tally with;
與…相符 comport with; conform to; tie in with;

[相輔] complement each other;
相輔而行 coordinate; go together;
相輔相成 complement each other; exist side by side and play a part together; inseparably interconnected; reciprocate and complement;

[相干] (1) be concerned with; connected; have to do with; related; (2) coherent;
相干性 coherence; mutual coherence;
~ 橫向相干性 transverse coherence;
~ 空間相干性 space coherence;
~ 時間相干性 temporal coherence;
~ 瞬時相干性 transient coherence;
~ 相位相干性 phase coherence;
不相干 beside the point; have nothing to do with; irrelevant; not relate to;
~ 毫不相干 have nothing to do with; have nothing to say to; irrelevant;
與我甚麼相干 what concern is it of mine;

[相告] pass information; tell;
盡情相告 make a clean breast of things to sb; unbosom oneself to sb;
傾誠相告 outpour one's heart;

[相隔] apart; at a distance of; be separated by;
相隔多年 after an interval of many years;
相隔千里 a long way away from each other;
相隔千山萬水 be separated by numerous rivers and mountains;
相隔天涯 as far apart as heaven and earth;

[相顧] look at each other;
相顧而笑 they both laugh, looking into each other's eyes;
相顧失色 change colour, looking at each other; look at each other in dismay; look at each other in fear;
相顧一笑 smile at each other knowingly;

[相關] bound up with; connected; correlation; dependence; interrelated; related;
相關成本 related cost;
相關程序 relative programme;
相關分析法 method of relative analysis;
相關關係預測 forecasting of relevance;
相關計 correlometer;
相關器 correlator;
~ 電荷相關器 charge correlator;
~ 光相關器 optical correlator;
~ 快速相關器 high-speed correlator;
~ 模擬相關器 analogue correlator;
~ 圖象相關器 image correlator;
相關圖 correlatograph; correlogram;

~ 實驗相關圖 experimental correlogram;
相關性 correlation;
彼此相關 relative to each other;
典型相關 canonical correlation;
疊合相關 coincidental correlation;
二項相關 binomial correlation;
各不相關 each looks after himself; independent;
函數相關 functional dependence;
交叉相關 cross correlation;
漠不相關 entirely unrelated; of no consequence;
曲線相關 curvilinear correlation;
數據相關 data correlation;
統計相關 statistical dependence;
息息相關 be closely bound up; breathe the same breath; closely linked; vitally interrelated;
線性相關 linear dependence;
循環相關 circular correlation;
直接相關 direct correlation;
自相關 auto correlation;

[相規以善] persuade sb to take the good path;

[相好] (1) on familiar terms; on intimate terms; (2) good friend; intimate friend; (3) have an affair with; (4) lover; mistress; sweetheart;

[相合] agree with; conform to; fit;

[相互] each other; mutual; one another mutually; reciprocal;
相互幫助 help each other;
相互包庇 shield each other;
相互猜疑 suspicious of each other;
相互吹捧 flatter each other; sing one another's praises;
相互詞 reciprocal term;
相互代詞 reciprocal pronoun;
相互抵消 cancel out each other;
相互動詞 reciprocal verb;
相互攻擊 accuse each other;
相互關係 correlation; mutual relation; reciprocal relation;
相互關心 reciprocal consideration;
相互敬愛 mutually respect each other;
相互理解 have mutual understanding;
~ 加強相互理解 enhancement of mutual understanding;
相互利用 make use of each other;
相互諒解 mutual understanding; understand one another;
相互傾軋 do each other down; get locked in strife; jostle against each other; scramble;
相互為用 interact; interplay;
相互信任 mutual trust;
相互需求 reciprocal demands;
相互厭惡 be disgusted with each other;
相互依存 interdependent;
相互依賴 depend on each other;
相互影響 influence each other; interact;
相互擁抱 embrace each other; throw themselves into each other's arms;
相互支持 support each other;
相互作用 interact; interplay; mutual action;
~ 相互作用分析 interaction analysis;
~ 相互作用功能 interactional function;
~ 相互作用時間 interactive time;
~ 宿主病毒相互作用 host-virus interaction;

[相護] shield each other;
官官相護 all bureaucrats shield each other; at court one hand will quash the other; bureaucrats shield one another; government officials protect the rights and reputation of their fellow officers; officials shield one another; one hand washes the other and both the face;

[相會] (1) meet; meet each other; meet together; (2) tryst;
鵲橋相會 meet each other across the Milky Way;

[相繼] in succession; one after another;
相繼不絕 continue uninterruptedly; in succession; one after another;
相繼而來 arrive in succession; come one after the other;
相繼而起 one event treads close on another;
相繼死亡 die off; die one after another;

[相加] add together;

[相煎太急] bitter against each other; internal struggle; press sb too hard; torment sb too hard;

[相見] meet in person;
相見恨晚 regret we didn't meet sooner;
傾誠相見 a genuine meeting of minds; cardinal to each other; frank to each other; heart-to-heart; make a clean breast of each other;
以誠相見 shoot square with; shoot straight with;

[相間] alternate with; spaced in-between;

[相將而去] go off supporting each other;

[相交] (1) intersect; (2) associate with; friends; make friends with;
相交線 intersecting lines;
相交有年 have been friends for years;
互不相交 mutually exclusive;
兩線相交 intersection of two lines;
以利相交，利盡而疏 a friendship that is based on money will dissolve when money runs low;

[相較] compare with each other;

[相接] connect with; join; meet;
短兵相接 a close-quarter fighting; come to close quarters; engage in hand-to-hand fight; fight at close quarters; fight hand to hand with; fight hilt to hilt; hand-to-hand fighting; in close combat; war to the knife;
目光相接 meet one's eye;
踵趾相接 follow the footsteps;

[相近] alike; almost identical with; approximate; close; contiguity; resemble; similar;
相近的 contiguous;
相近聯想 association by contiguity;

[相敬] respect each other;
相敬如賓 respect each other as if the other were a guest; respect each other like treating guests;
~如賓之敬 respect as a guest;
相敬相愛 be deeply attached to each other very intimately; love and respect each other; love each other deeply; mutual respect and affection;

[相救] help out of difficulty; rescue;

[相聚] assemble; get together; meet together; meet up;
相聚一堂 get together;

[相距] apart; at a distance of; away from;
相距不遠 not far from one another;

[相看] (1) look at each other; (2) appraise each other;
刮目相看 have a completely new appraisal of sb; hold sb in greater esteem; hold sb in high esteem; keep eyes polished; look at sb with new eyes; make the town sit up and take notice; regard sb with special esteem; set a higher value on sb; see sb in a new light; sit up and take notice; treat sb with increased respect;
冷眼相看 look at coldly; look coldly upon;
另眼相看 (1) look at sb with quite different eyes; pay special regard to; regard sb with special respect; regard with special attention; (2) look at sb in a different light; see sb in a new light; treat sb with special consideration; view a person in quite a different light than one does the rest of the people; view sb in a new, more favourable light;

[相賴] depend on each other;

[相聯] association;
相聯處理機 associative processor;
相聯存儲理論 associative memory system;
相聯語言 associative language;

[相連] connected; joined; linked; linked together;

[相鄰] adjacent; adjoin;
相鄰臂 adjacent arm;
相鄰的 contiguous;

[相罵] abuse each other; revile each other;

[相瞞] not tell sb the truth;
實不相瞞 tell you honestly; to tell you the truth;

[相謀] work together;
各不相謀 each works his own way;

[相陪] be accompanied by; in the company of;

[相配] match up; match well; mesh with;

[相碰] bump against; collide with;

[相撲] sumo; wrestle with each other;
相撲手 sumo wrestler;

[相切條件] condition for tangency;

[相親] size up a perspective spouse;
相親相愛 deeply attached to each other; kind to each other and love each other; love each other; love one another;

[相求] ask for a favour; beg; entreat;
同氣相求 like attracts like; like draws to like; people of the same tastes and habits like to be together;

[相去] differ;
相去不遠 nearby; not far from each other; very close;
相去天涯 as far apart as the sky and the sea;
相去天淵 as far apart as the sky and the

sea;

相去無幾 little difference; pretty much the same; the difference is insignificant; there is not much difference; very nearly the same;

[相覷] look at each other;

[相勸] offer advice; persuade;

[相讓] make concessions;

各不相讓 each refuses to give in to the other; each trying to outdo the other; neither being ready to give way; neither is willing to give ground;

[相擾] bother; disturb;

[相容] compatible;

相容性 compatibility;

~ 程序相容性 programme compatibility;

~ 結構相容性 structural compatibility;

不相容 incompatible;

~ 毫不相容 utterly incompatible with;

[相如] resemble each other;

[相濡以沫] help each other when both are in humble circumstances; mutual help and relief in time of poverty;

以沫相濡 use one's meagre resources to help another in time of need;

[相若] alike; similar;

[相善] on friendly terms; on good terms;

[相商] confer; consult; consult with; exchange views; talk over with;

[相生相剋] mutual production and destruction; mutual promotion and restraint;

[相時而動] adapt oneself to circumstances; wait for the proper moment for action;

[相識] (1) be acquainted with each other; know each other; (2) acquaintance;

相識滿天下，知心能幾人 one's acquaintances may fill the world, but one's real friends can be but few;

不打不相識 by scratching and biting, cats and dogs come together; friends are often made after a fight; from an exchange of blows friendship grows; it takes a fight for people to get to know each other; no discord, no concord; out of blows friendship grows;

老相識 old acquaintance;

似曾相識 seem to have met before;

素不相識 complete strangers to; have never met before; have never seen before; strangers to each other; total strangers;

[相視] look at each other;

相視而笑 smile at each other;

相視莫逆 underrupted friends;

[相率] leading one another; one after another; together;

[相思] (1) in love with each other; lovesickness; miss each other; pine for each other; yearning between lovers; (2) acacia;

相思病 lovesickness;

~ 害相思病 lovelorn; lovesick;

相思病無藥醫 no herb will cure love; where love is in the case, the doctor is an ass;

相思樹 acacia;

~ 草原相思樹 prairie acacia;

單相思 one-sided love; unrequited love;

兩地相思 long for each other in different places; longing of parted lovers;

[相似] a perfect model of; akin to; alike in; all over; analogous to; bear a striking likeness to; bear a strong resemblance to; bear analogy to; like; likeness; more or less the same; resemble; similitude; take after; the very image of; there are striking resemblances between A and B;

相似處 analogy;

相似詞 synonymous phrase;

相似聯想 association by similarity;

相似形 similar figures;

相似性 similarity;

~ 動態相似性 dynamic similarity;

~ 幾何相似性 geometrical similarity;

~ 流變相似性 rheological similarity;

~ 系統相似性 system similarity;

相似字 synonym;

結構相似 structural similitude;

類型相似 typological similarity;

水動力相似 hydrodynamic similitude;

應力相似 stress mimilitude;

運動相似 kinematic similitude;

[相隨] (1) follow; (2) accompany;

銜尾相隨 follow one after another; in one line, one after another; march in single file; one close behind another; walk one after the other;

[相談] converse; talk together;

[相提並論] be mentioned in the same breath with; be regarded as being in the same category; hold a candle to; hold a stick to; mention in the same breath; name in the same day; place on a par with; put on a par with; speak of in the same breath; speak of two things in the same breath; treat as comparable;

[相通] be interlinked; communicate with each other;

[相同] alike; equal; identical; parity; similar; the same;

大不相同 entirely and totally different; quite a different pair of shoes;

各不相同 differ from one another; diverse from each other; have nothing in common with each other;

~各不相同的意見 wide divergence of opinion;

~性格各不相同 differ in disposition; of different temperaments;

毫不相同 as like as an apple to an oyster;

[相投] agree with each other; compatible; congenial;

意氣相投 congenial;

針芥相投 a magnet attracts needles and mustard seeds stick to amber; magnet point and minute filings attracted to each other;

志趣相投 like-minded; people of similar purpose and interest;

[相托] entrust;

[相望] look at each other;

隔岸相望 face each other across the river; see each other from either bank;

[相違] (1) differ; disagree; (2) be separated; part;

[相維] support each other;

[相位] phase;

相位分佈 phase distribution;

相位模糊 phase ambiguity;

相位調整 phasing;

~軌道電路相位調整 track circuit phasing;

~掃描相位調整 phasing of the scan;

~聲道相位調整 channel phasing;

反饋相位 back feed phase;

基帶相位 baseband phase;

天線相位 antenna phase;

載波相位 carrier phase;

[相惡] mutual inhibition;

[相習成風] customs are formed by practice; usages arise from common practice;

[相像] alike; likeness; resemble; similar;

長得十分相像 look very much alike;

[相向] face each other; opposite direction;

拔刀相向 draw one's sword against; draw upon sb; pull a knife on sb;

倒戈相向 attack one's own men; become a turncoat; revolt against constituted authority; turn one's force against one's master;

惡眼相向 cast an evil eye on sb;

反顏相向 look with a turned countenance;

怒目相向 flash fire; gaze upon with animosity; glare at; glare defiance at each other; glower at; look daggers at; stare angrily;

[相信] be convinced of; believe; believe in; credence; have faith in;

相信真理 believe in truth;

相信直覺 have faith in intuition;

不相信 disbelief; disbelieve; incredulity; incredulous;

錯誤地相信 believe erroneously;

固執地相信 believe obstinately;

很難相信 it is hard to believe that...;

荒謬地相信 believe irrationally;

絕對相信 be absolutely convinced;

普遍相信 there is a widespread conviction that;

殊難相信 hardly credible; very difficult to believe;

完全相信 believe thoroughly;

一般人都相信 it is generally believed that;

[相形] by comparison;

相形見絀 appear deficient in comparison; be outshone; compare unfavourably with; found to be inferior by comparison; inferior by comparison; pale by comparison; prove definitely inferior; put to shame; seem pallid by comparison; throw sth in the shade;

~使相形見絀 overshadow;

相形之下 by comparison; by contrast; in comparison with; when compared;

[相須] depend on each other;

[相續] (1) inherit; (2) continue one after another;

[相沿] hand down; pass down from generation

to generation without change;
相沿成習 become a custom through long usage; become common practice through long usage;
相沿已久 have been so far a long time; have come down for a long time;

[相邀] invite;

[相依] correlative with; depend on each other; interdependent;
相依為命 all in all together; be bound by a common destiny; depend on each other for survival; keep alive by relying on each other; make a living by depending on each other; mutually depending on each other for living; rely upon each other for life; share their life together; stick together and help each other in difficulties;
輔車相依 as close as the jowls and the jaws; as dependent on each other as the jowls and the jawbone; rely on one another as cheek and jowl; the cheekbones and the jaws are mutually dependent;

[相宜] appropriate; fitting; proper; suitable;

[相異] alien; diversity;

[相迎] greet; welcome;
伏道相迎 kneel in the road to welcome;
降階相迎 go down the steps to meet sb;
下階相迎 go down the steps to meet;

[相映] contrast with; form a contrast; set each other off;
相映成趣 contrast finely with each other; form a delightful contrast; form an amusing contrast; form an interesting contrast; gain by contrast;

[相應] (1) corresponding; relevant; (2) act in responses; work in concert with;
相應不理 disregard another's request;
表裏相應 coordinated attack;
手口相應 action and words are in correspondence;

[相友] be friends together;

[相與] (1) get along with sb; (2) together; with each other;
相與大笑 have a good laugh together;
相與愕然 stare at each other in surprise;
相與偕老 cast in one's lot with a partner for life;
以誠相與 honest with;

[相遇] approach; encounter; meet; meet each other; rendezvous;

[相約] make an appointment; reach an agreement;

[相贈] give a present; present a gift;
傾囊相贈 empty one's purse to give to sb; give to sb all the money in one's purse;

[相爭] argue vehemently; fight each other over sth; quarrel;

[相知] (1) be well acquainted with each other; know each other well; (2) bosom friends; close friends; great friends;
相知恨晚 it is much to be regretted that we have not met earlier; regret that one has not got to know sb sooner;
相知有素 have known each other long;

[相中] settle on; take a fancy;

[相助] help; help each other;
拔刀相助 draw a sword and render help; help another for the sake of justice; take up the cudgels against an injustice;
緩急相助 help each other in case of need;
解囊相助 help sb generously with money; loose the purse strings – assist financially; put one's hand in one's pocket;
傾囊相助 empty one's purse to help; exhaust all one has to help; give all one's all to help; give generous financial assistance; give one's all to help sb; offer all one has to help sb;

[相撞] bump against; collide; collide with each other; smash together; strike;
側面相撞 side-on collision;
迎面相撞 head-on crash;
正面相撞 head-on collision; head-on crash; head-on smash;

[相左] (1) fail to meet each other; (2) at odds with each other; conflict with each other; differ; disagree; fail to agree;

互相 mutual; each other; hand in glove with;
兩相 both parties; both sides;

xiang
【香】 (1) aromatic; balmy; fragrant; sweet-smelling; (2) appetizing; delicious; tasty; (3) with good appetite; with relish; (4) soundly; (5) popular; wel-

come; (6) perfume; spice; (7) balm; incense; joss spice; stick;

[香檳] champagne; champers;
香檳酒 champagne;
~香檳酒瓶 champagne bottle;
~玫瑰香檳酒 pink champagne;
~蘋果香檳酒 champagne cider;
~甜香檳酒 sweet champagne;
~無泡香檳酒 still champagne;
~一瓶香檳酒 a bottle of champagne;
精美香檳 fine champagne;

[香菜] coriander; parsley;

[香腸] banger; sausage;
香腸肉卷 sausage roll;
德國香腸 German sausage;
肝泥香腸 liver sausage;
絞肉香腸 minced sausage;
烤香腸 grilled sausage;
薩拉米香腸 salami;
生香腸 fresh sausage;
熟香腸 cooked sausage;
小牛肉香腸 veal sausage;
羊肉香腸 mutton sausage;
一根香腸 a sausage;
炸香腸 fried sausage;
早餐香腸 breakfast sausage;
豬肉香腸 pork sausage;

[香臭] fragrance and stench;
香臭不辨，敵我不分 unable to distinguish fragrance from stench or ourselves from the enemy;
香臭不分 can't tell stench from perfume;

[香袋] sachet; small perfumed bag;

[香稻] rice;

[香斗] incense pot;

[香芳濃郁] give off a rich perfume;

[香粉] cosmetic powder; face powder;
搏香弄粉 apply a lot of make-up; doll up oneself;

[香風拂拂] the winds waft waves of fragrance;

[香馥馥] fragrant; sweet-smelling;

[香菇] mushroom;

[香瓜] cantaloupe; muskmelon;

[香閨] lady's chamber;

[香花] (1) fragrant flowers; (2) writings or works that are beneficial to the people;
香花毒草 fragrant flowers and poisonous weeds;
香花供養 offering sacrifice with fragrant flowers;

[香灰] incense ashes;

[香火] (1) joss sticks and candles burning at a temple; (2) oath; vow;
香火不絕 endless stream of pilgrims;
香火弟兄 sworn brothers;
香火情 sworn love between man and woman;
香火甚盛 attract a large number of pilgrims; have many worshippers;

[香蕉] banana;
香蕉船 banana split;
香蕉粉 bananina;
香蕉共和國 banana republic;
香蕉皮 banana peel; banana peeling; banana skin;
~踩香蕉皮 slip on banana skins;
~扒香蕉皮 peel a banana;
香蕉樹 banana;
香蕉水 banana oil;
香蕉油 banana oil;
過熟的香蕉 overripe banana;
一串香蕉 a bunch of bananas; a hand of bananas;
一個香蕉 a banana;

[香界] Buddhist temples;

[香精] attar; essence; perfume;
香精油 essential oil; floral attar;
複合香精 compound essence;
馥奇香精 fougere perfume;
合成香精 synthetic attar;
玫瑰香精 rose attar;
人造香精 artificial essence;
乳油香精 cream essence;
食用香精 flavouring essence;
香囊香精 sachet perfume;
想像型香精 fancy perfumes;

[香菌] champignon;

[香客] pilgrim; visitors to sacred places;

[香蠟] candles and incense;

[香料] balm; flavouring; perfume; spice;
香料架 spice rack;
合成香料 synthetic perfume;
~半合成香料 semisynthetic perfume;
食用香料 flavouring;
~合成食用香料 synthetic flavouring;
~人造食用香料 artificial flavouring;
~天然食用香料 natural flavouring;
天然香料 natural perfume;
藥用香料 medicinal perfume;
皂用香料 soap perfume;

[香爐] incense burner; thurible;
[香茅] citronella; lemon grass;
香茅基 citronellyl;
香茅醛 citronella;
香茅油 citronella;
[香囊] sachet;
[香噴噴] (1) sweet-smelling; (2) appetizing; savoury;
[香片] (1) scented tea; (2) jasmine tea;
[香氣] aroma; fragrance; pleasant odour; sweet smell;
香氣芬馥 give off a rare fragrance;
香氣撲鼻 a sweet smell assails the nostrils; a sweet smell greets us; feel a sharp aroma; fragrance strikes the nose; the scent of sth reaches one's nose;
香氣四溢 suffuse an exquisite fragrance all around;
飽滿香氣 full aroma;
持久香氣 durable aroma;
一陣香氣 a waft of perfume;
[香芹] sheep's-parsley;
[香水] cologne; fragrance; perfume; scent; toilet water; wash;
香水廠 perfumery;
香水店 perfumery;
香水調制 perfumery;
化妝香水 beauty water;
噴香水 spray perfume;
洒香水 spray perfume;
一瓶香水 a bottle of perfume;
[香甜] (1) delicious; fragrant and sweet; luscious; sweet; (2) soundly;
香甜酒 bumbo;
[香筒] incense holder;
[香味] odour; smell; spiciness; sweet smell;
香味很淡 flat aroma;
純真香味 fine aroma;
[香消玉殞] a beauty passes away; the fragrance is gone and the jade is fallen－the death of a pretty woman;
[香煙] (1) cigarette; ciggy; coffin nail; fag; (2) incense smoke;
香煙盒 cigarette case;
香煙繚繞 the smoke of incense rises in volutes;
香煙裊裊 curl up in the air like smoke;
香煙煙嘴 cigarette holder;
薄荷香煙 mentholated cigarette;
帶濾嘴香煙 filter cigarette;
免稅香煙 duty-free cigarettes;
圓形香煙 round cigarette;
一包香煙 a pack of cigarettes; a packet of cigarettes;
一條香煙 a carton of cigarettes;
一筒香煙 a tin of cigarettes;
一枝香煙 a burn; a cigarette; a fag; a gasper;
走私香煙 contraband cigarettes;
[香艷] (1) flowery; of boudoir; (2) sexy;
尋香探艷 seek for fragrance and visit beauties;
[香油] sesame oil;
[香皂] perfumed soap; scented soap; toilet soap;
[香脂] (1) face cream; (2) balm; balsam;
香脂傣杉 balsam;
加拿大香脂 fir balsam;
禾木香脂 acaroid balsam;
[香珠] rosary of sandalwood;
[香燭] joss sticks and candles;
香燭紙馬 incense, candle and shoe-shaped paper;

安息香 (1) benzoin; (2) benzoresin; (3) styrax benzoin;
百里香 thyme;
沉香 agalloch eaglewood;
吃香 be much sought after; find favour with sb; very popular; well-liked;
醇香 fragrant; rich;
大茴香 anise; star anise;
丁香 (1) clove; (2) lilac;
芳香 aromatic; fragrant; sweet fragrance;
焚香 burn incense;
廣木香 costusroot;
花香 fragrance of a flower;
茴香 fennel;
藿香 wrinkled giant hyssop;
降香 Acronychia pedunculata;
進香 go on a pilgrimage to a temple;
留蘭香 spearmint;
龍腦香 borneo camphor; borneol;
龍涎香 ambergris;
木香 (1) Aristolochia debilis; (2) Aucklandia lappa; (3) banksia rose;
拈香 burn joss sticks; offer incense;
盤香 incense coil;
噴香 delicious; fragrant;
奇南香 agalloch eaglewood;

伽南香 agalloch eaglewood;
清香 delicate and fresh fragrance; delicate fragrance; faint scent; mild fragrance; pleasant smell; refreshing fragrance;
乳香 frankincense;
瑞香 winter daphne;
上香 go to a temple to pray; offer incense;
燒香 burn incense; burn joss sticks;
麝香 musk;
書香 having literary or intellectual fame;
松香 colophony; rosin;
檀香 sandalwood; white sandalwood;
甜香 sweet and fragrant;
蚊香 mosquito-repellent incense;
五香 (1) spices; (2) the five spices (prickly ash, star aniseed, cinnamon, clove and fennel);
線香 slender stick of incense;
心香 devotion; piety; sincerity;
馨香 (1) fragrance; (2) smell of burning incense;
行香 hold or participate in a prayer service at a temple;
薰香 fragrance; perfume;
夜來香 evening primrose; night willow herb;
異香 rare fragrance; unusuality sweet smell;
幽香 delicate fragrance;
餘香 lingering fragrance;
鬱金香 tulip;
芸香 strong-scented herb; rue;
炷香 (1) burn incense; (2) a stick of incense;
紫丁香 lilac;

xiang
【廂】 (1) side room; wing of a building; (2) vicinity or outskirts of a city;
［廂房］ side room;
百葉廂 thermometer screen;
包廂 box in a theatre;
壁廂 side;
車廂 railroad car; railway carriage;
城廂 the city proper and areas just outside its gates;
關廂 neighbourhood outside of a city gate;
機廂 engine room;
兩廂 (1) both sides; (2) wing-room on either side of a one-side of a one-storey house;

xiang
【湘】 (1) short for Xiangjiang River; (2) name for Hunan;
［湘劇］ Hunan opera;
［湘竹］ speckled bamboo;

xiang
【鄉】 (1) country; countryside; rural area; (2) home town; home village; native place; (3) township;
［鄉巴佬］ boor; bumpkin; churl; country bumpkin; country cousin; hayseed; hick; redneck; rustic; yokel;
鄉巴佬酒吧 redneck bar;
［鄉愁］ homesickness;
［鄉村］ country; countryside; rural area; village;
鄉村的 bucolic; countrified;
鄉村地區 rural area;
鄉村婦女 countrywoman;
鄉村俱樂部 country club;
鄉村舞 country dancing;
鄉村音樂 country music;
~ 鄉村音樂歌手 country singer;
鄉村宅第 country seat;
［鄉黨］ local communities;
［鄉關］ one's hometown; one's native place;
［鄉貫］ one's hometown; one's native place;
［鄉國］ one's fatherland; one's native place;
［鄉戶］ village population; village resident;
［鄉宦］ the village gentry holding official positions;
［鄉間］ in the countryside; in the rural area;
鄉間別墅 country house;
鄉間宅第 country house;
［鄉井］ one's hometown; one's native plae;
［鄉居］ live in the countryside;
［鄉聚］ hamlet; village;
［鄉老］ country elder;
［鄉里］ (1) home village; (2) fellow villager;
［鄉裏鄉氣］ countrified; foolish and clumsy; rustic; stupid-looking;
［鄉鄰］ persons from the same rural neighbourhood;
［鄉民］ countryfolk; villager;
［鄉僻］ far from town; out-of-the-way;
［鄉親］ (1) fellow villagers; (2) local people; villagers;
［鄉曲］ a place far from town; an outof-the-way place; remote and out-of-the-way rural areas;
［鄉人］ (1) villagers; (2) persons from the same village;
［鄉紳］ country gentlemen; squires; the country

gentry;
鄉豪劣紳 village bullies and local tyrants;
[鄉思] homesickness; nostalgia;
鄉思纏綿 be tormented by nostalgia;
纏綿鄉思 be tormented by homesickedness;
[鄉談] local dialects; native dialects;
[鄉土] (1) one's homevillage; one's native soil; (2) local; of one's native land;
本鄉本土 one's homeland;
鄉土風味 local flavour;
鄉土觀念 provincialism;
鄉土文學 native literature;
[鄉下] countryside; rural area; village;
鄉下的 country;
鄉下老 country bumpkin;
鄉下人 countryfolk; countryman; country person; rustic; villager;
鄉下女人 countrywoman;
搬遷到鄉下 move to the countryside;
住在鄉下 live in the country;
[鄉賢] respected village scholars;
[鄉校] village school;
[鄉學] village school;
[鄉野] pastoral; rural;
跋涉鄉野 trudge through the countryside;
[鄉音] local accent; one's native accent;
鄉音難改 local accent can hardly alter;
[鄉勇] local militia; village militiamen;
[鄉愚] stupid rustics;
[鄉愿] hypocrite;
[鄉長] township head;
[鄉鎮] (1) villages and towns; (2) small towns;
鄉鎮企業 rural and township enterprises; town and village enterprises; township enterprises; township industries;
~ 鄉鎮企業集團 township enterprise group;
~ 鄉鎮企業經濟學 economics of two and village enterprises;
~ 發展鄉鎮企業 develop township industries;
鄉鎮經濟 village and town economy;

阿鄉 bumpkin; country bumpkin; rustic; yokel;
敝鄉 our village;
城鄉 city and countryside; town and country; urban and rural;
故鄉 one's birthland; one's birthplace; one's hometown; one's native place;
懷鄉 homesick;
還鄉 return to one's native place;
回鄉 return to one's home village;
家鄉 homeland; homeplace; hometown; native place;
老鄉 fellow townsman; fellow villager;
離鄉 leave one's native place;
夢鄉 dreamland; slumberland;
山鄉 mountain area;
水鄉 region of rivers and lakes;
睡鄉 (1) dreamland; the land of Nod; (2) state of being asleep;
思鄉 homesick; think of one's home;
四鄉 outskirts; suburbs;
他鄉 a place far away form home; alien land; other lands;
同鄉 countryman; fellow provincial; fellow townsman; fellow villager; homeboy; home girl; homey;
外鄉 another part of the country; some other place;
下鄉 go to the countryside; rusticate;
仙鄉 fairyland;
異鄉 away from one's home; foreign community; foreign land; strange land;
游鄉 (1) parade sb through the village; (2) solicit customers through the village;
梓鄉 one's hometown; one's native place;
醉鄉 paradise of drunkenness; the dazed state in which a drinker finds himself;

xiang

【箱】 box; chest; trunk;
[箱蓋] case cover; cover;
控制器箱蓋 controller cover;
離合器箱蓋 clutch housing cover;
軸箱蓋 axle box cover; box cover;
[箱子] box; case; chest; trunk;
打開箱子 unpack a suitcase;
大箱子 chest; trunk;
一套箱子 a nest of boxes;

暗箱 (1) anything shaped like a box; (2) box; case; trunk; (3) camera obscura;
百寶箱 jewel box; jewel case;
板條箱 crate;
保健箱 medical kit;
保潔箱 litter-bin;
保險箱 safe; strongbox;
變速箱 gearcase;
冰箱 ice box; freezer; frig; fridge; icebox; refrigerater;
沉箱 caisson;

齒輪箱 gearbox;
傳動箱 transmission case;
牀頭箱 headstock;
彈藥箱 ammunition chest; cartridge box;
電冰箱 freezer; fridge; refrigerator;
風箱 bellows;
蜂箱 beehive; hive;
副油箱 (1) auxiliary tank; (2) drop tank;
烘箱 oven;
貨箱 container;
集裝箱 container;
檢舉箱 box for accusation letters;
接線箱 junction box;
鏡箱 woman's dressing case;
開箱 open sb's boxes;
烤箱 oven;
垃圾箱 dustbin; garbage can;
連管箱 header;
柳條箱 wicker suitcase (or trunk);
冷藏箱 fridge; refrigerator;
煤箱 coal hod; coal scuttle;
木箱 wooden box;
皮箱 leather suitcase; leather trunk;
票箱 ballot box;
汽油箱 gasoline tank; petrol tank;
錢箱 cash box;
砂箱 sandbox;
水箱 cistern; water tank;
手提箱 suitcase;
藤箱 rattan case;
提箱 suitcase;
添箱 give presents to a bride;
跳箱 (1) box horse; (2) box horse jump;
投票箱 ballot box;
信箱 letterbox; mailbox; main slot; mailbox; postbox;
藥箱 medical kit; medicine chest;
一滿箱 trunkful;
一箱 (1) a boxful; (2) a box of; a case of; a chest of; a crate of;
衣箱 suitcase; trunk;
意見箱 suggestion box;
銀箱 cash box;
油箱 fuel tank; petrol tank;
郵箱 letterbox; mail drop; mailbox; postbox;
枕頭箱 jewel case;
裝箱 box; pack in a box;
紙板箱 cardboard case or box; carton;
子彈箱 cartridge box;
軸承箱 bearing box;
軸箱 axle box;

xiang

【緗】 light-yellow silk;
［緗色］ pale yellow;

xiang

【薌】 (1) smell of rice-grains; (2) aromatic; pleasant smell; spicy; (3) incense used for fumigation;

xiang

【襄】 (1) assist; help; (2) accomplish; achieve; complete; (3) raise; rise; (4) high; (5) undress; (6) thoroughbred horse; (7) a surname;
［襄辦］ act as deputy; deputy manager; help manage;
［襄理］ (1) assistant manager; (2) help manage;
［襄助］ assist; help;

xiang

【纕】 wear;

xiang

【鑲】 (1) fill in; inlay; mount; set; (2) border; edge; hem; (3) name of an ancient weapon;
［鑲板］ panel; paneling;
鑲板釘 panel pin;
［鑲邊］ edge; hem;
［鑲進去］ set sth in;
［鑲嵌］ fill in; inlay; inset; mount; set;
金漆鑲嵌 gold-inlaid lacquer ware;
［鑲入物］ inlay;
［鑲牙］ crown a tooth; fill in an artificial tooth; have a tooth filled;

xiang

【驤】 (1) horse with the right hind leg white; (2) uplift; (3) galloping with a raised head;
［驤首］ raise the head proudly;
［驤騰］ advance with determination; gallop forward;

xiang²

xiang

【庠】 school;
［庠生］ student of a prefectural county school;
［庠序］ school;
庠序之數 public education;

縣庠 county school;

xiang

【降】 (1) submit to; surrender; (2) bring to terms; conquer; subjugate;

［降伏］ (1) bring to terms; conquer; subdue; vanquish; (2) bring in; tame;

降龍伏虎 subdue the dragon and tame the tiger — overcome powerful adversaries; subdue wild animals;

［降服］ surrender; yield;

［降旗］ flag of surrender;

［降順］ surrender and give allegiance to; yield and pledge allegiance to;

［降妖］ subjugate evil spirits;

降妖伏魔 overcome all evil spirits; vanquish demons and monsters;

歸降 surrender;

納降 accept the enemy's surrender;

乞降 beg to surrender;

請降 beg to surrender;

勸降 induce to capitulate;

受降 accept a surrender;

投降 capitulate; surrender;

誘降 lure into surrender;

詐降 lure into surrender;

招降 summon sb to surrender;

xiang

【祥】 auspicious; favourable; propitious;

［祥麟］ legendary horse-like animal;

［祥瑞］ auspicious sign; propitious omen;

［祥雲］ auspicious clouds;

［祥兆］ good omen; propitious sign;

安祥 composed; peaceful; serene; undisturbed;

不祥 ill omen; inauspicious; ominous; unlucky;

慈祥 amicable; kind;

發祥 occur; prospered; rise;

禨祥 pray to the gods for blessing;

吉祥 auspicious; lucky; propitious;

祺祥 auspicious; fortunate; lucky; propitious;

瑞祥 auspiciousness; good fortune; good luck; good omen;

妖祥 bad and good omens;

禎祥 good omen; lucky omen;

xiang

【翔】 circle in the air; soar;

［翔步］ pace about in the room; walk with slow, regular steps;

［翔貴］ great rise in prices;

［翔集］ gather the essence from many sources;

［翔盡］ detailed and complete;

［翔實］ detailed and accurate; full and accurate;

［翔羊不去］ hover around;

［翔泳］ birds and fish;

翱翔 fly about; hover; soar; take wing; wheel in the air;

飛翔 circle in the air; hover;

滑翔 glide;

回翔 circle round; wheel;

xiang

【詳】 (1) complete; detailed; minute; (2) details; particulars; (3) know clearly; know the details;

［詳檢］ thorough check;

［詳解］ detailed annotation; explain in detail;

［詳盡］ at large; backwards and forwards; detailed; exhaustive; thorough;

詳盡透徹 in a comprehensive and penetrating way;

詳盡無遺 exhaustive; in minute detail; thorough;

［詳密］ detailed and comprehensive; elaborate; meticulous;

［詳明］ complete and explicit; detailed and very clear; full and clear;

［詳盤細查］ subject sb to a searching cross-examination;

［詳情］ detailed information; ins and outs; particulars;

詳情後報 details to follow;

詳情細節 the details of a story;

不知詳情 not know the details;

獲得詳情 obtain detailed information;

［詳實］ full and accurate;

［詳述］ cover the waterfront; dilate; discuss; expatiate; explain;

詳述本末 tell the whole story from beginning to end;

［詳談］ go into details; talk out;

［詳悉］ detailed and thorough; know clearly;

［詳細］ at great length; at large; detailed; extensive; in great detail; in full; minute;

詳細地 in detail;

詳細審計 detailed audit;

詳細說明 explain at some length;

詳細討論 discuss in detail;

詳細敘述 go into detail;
詳詳細細 in every detail and particular;

安詳 composed; serene;
不詳 (1) not in detail; (2) not quite clear;
端詳 examine; look sb up and down; scrutinize;
內詳 name and address of sender enclosed;
周詳 complete; comprehensive;

xiang3

xiang

【享】 (1) enjoy; receive; (2) offer; (3) entertain;

[享福] enjoy a happy life; have a blessing; live in ease and comfort;
羨人享福 in envy of the happiness of others;
有福同享 share each other's fortunes; share prosperity with;
~ 有福同享，有禍同當 for better or for worse; go through thick and thin together; happiness and joy we shall share in common and loyally help each other in suffering; share bliss and misfortune together; share happiness as well as trouble; share joys and sorrows; share weal and woe; stick together through thick and thin; we will cast our lot together, all or none;

[享樂] indulge in creature comforts; lead a life of pleasure;
享樂度時 spend one's time enjoying oneself;
享樂思想 hedonism; pleasure-seeking;
享樂主義 hedonism;
~ 享樂主義者 hedonist;
盡情享樂 enjoy oneself to heart's content;
追求享樂 pursue pleasure;
縱情享樂 glut oneself with pleasures;

[享年] die at the age of;

[享受] delectation; enjoy; indulge oneself in;
享受榮華富貴 enjoy high position and great wealth;
享受人生 enjoy life;
享受天倫之樂 enjoy family happiness;
愛享受 be a lover of pleasure;
感官享受 pleasure of the senses;
盡情享受 luxuriate;
視覺享受 visual enjoyment;
貪圖享受 seek ease and comfort;
物質享受 material comforts;

[享用] enjoy; enjoy the use of;

[享有] enjoy; have in possession; possess;
享有佳譽 enjoy a high reputation;
享有盛名 enjoy high reputation;
享有盛譽 gain a high repute;
享有特權 enjoy privilege;

[享譽] enjoy a reputation;
享譽國際 of international stature;
享譽全國 gain national fame; of national stature;
享譽全球 of world stature; world known;
~ 享譽全球的音樂家 musician of world stature;

安享 enjoy; live in ease and comfort;
分享 have a share in; partake of; share; sharing;
共享 enjoy together; share; sharing;
坐享 sit idle and enjoy;

xiang

【想】 (1) think; (2) consider; suppose; think; (3) expect; hope; (4) desire; feel like; wanna; want to; would like to; (5) miss; remember with longing;

[想必] most probably; presumably; probably;

[想不通] be not convinced; beyond comprehension; cannot figure it out; cannot figure out why; incomprehensible; remain unconvinced;

[想出] come up with; dope out; enter; excogitate; think; think out;

[想到] call to mind; hit upon an idea; remember; think of;
馬上想到 spring to sb's mind;
沒想到 not to expect;
誰想到 who would have thought;
突然想到 pop into one's head; pop into one's mind;
想得到 expect; imagine; think;

[想法] idea; notion; opinion; thinking; view; way of looking at sth; what one has in mind;
想法子 devise means; think of a scheme;
不科學的想法 unscientific ideas;
不切實的想法 airy-fairy notion;
交換想法 exchange opinions;
內心的想法 inner voice;
說出想法 utter an idea;

[想家] homesick; nostalgic;

[想見] gather; imagine; infer; visualize;

[想開] look at the bright side;

想開點 look at the bright side;

想得開 look on the bright side of things; not to take to heart; take sth philosophically; try to look on the bright side of things;

想不開 take a matter to heart; take some misfortune too seriously; take things too hard; unable to take a resigned attitude;

~老想不開 cannot put sth out of one's mind; keep on worrying;

[想來] in my conjecture; in my guess; it may be assumed that; presumably; suppose; think of;

想來想去 consider carefully and at length; think back and forth to oneself; think it over and over again; turn sth over and over in one's mind;

[想念] ache for; cherish the memory of; give thought to; long to see again; miss; remember with longing;

[想起] call to mind; occur; recall; remember; think of;

想起來 look back;

想不起 beyond recollection; past recollection;

~想不起來 cannot remember; unable to call to mind;

[想入非非] a flight of fancy; aim at the moon; allow one's fancy to run wild; aspire after the impossible; build castles in the air; cast beyond the moon; entertain a wild hope; fantasy; far-fetched imagination; full of whims; give free play to one's imagination; give full rein to one's imagination; give loose rein to one's fancy; give to speculation; go off into wild flights of fancy; harbour fantastic ideas; harbour improper thoughts; have a maggot in one's head; have bees in one's head; have one's head full of bees; have one's head in the clouds; have strange fancies; have strange whims; in cloudland; in the clouds; indulge in dreams; indulge in fantasy; indulge in wishful thinking; let one's imagination run riot; let one's imagination run wild; level at the moon; nourish wild ideas; off one's trolley; one's head is full of bees; one's imagination runs away with one; stretch of imagination; wishful thinking;

[想死] (1) get tired of life; long for death; (2) dying for; long very much for;

[想通] become convinced; come round; straighten out one's thinking;

[想頭] (1) idea; notion; thought; (2) expectation; hope; (3) thinking;

[想望] (1) desire; expect; hope; long for; (2) admire; look up to;

想望風采 anxious to see your appearance and bearing; wish to see your pleasant face;

[想想] think about;

想想看 think about it;

~先想想看 think over sth first;

好好想想 think sth through;

停下來想想 pause for thought;

想一想 pause to think;

[想像] (1) conceive; dream; fancy; imagine; think; visualize; (2) imagination;

想像功能 imaginative function;

想像力 imagination; imaginative power;

~充滿想像力 full of imagination;

~發揮想像力 use one's imagination;

~非凡的想像力 great imagination;

~豐富的想像力 fertile imagination; good imagination;

~缺乏想像力 lack of imagination;

~生動的想像力 vivid imagination;

~有想像力 have imagination;

~展現想像力 display imagination; show imagination;

想像跳躍 imaginative leap; leap of imagination;

[想要] feel like; intend; want to; wish;

誰想要… who wants...

[想着] keep in mind; miss; think of;

暗想 foster an idea; muse; nurse an idea; nurture an idea; ponder; secret thoughts; think in secret; turn over in one's mind;

巴想 await anxiously; hope anxiously;

不管你怎樣想 any way you slice it;

不想 have no heart to do sth; have no stomach for;

猜想 guess; imagine; suppose; suspect; think;
暢想 give free rein to one's imagination; give the reins to one's thoughts; pamper imagination;
痴想 illusions; wishful thinking;
浮想 thoughts flashing across one's mind;
感想 impressions; reflections; thoughts;
構想 (1) compose; conceive; visualize; (2) blueprint; concept; idea; proposition;
懷想 think about sb with affections; yearn for;
幻想 fancy; fantasy; illusion; make belief; square the circle;
回想 (1) recall; recollect; think back; (2) anamnesis;
假想 (1) hypothesis; imagination; make-believe; phantom; supposition; (2) fictitious; hypothetical; imaginary;
渴想 hope earnestly; long for;
空想 daydream; fancy; fantasy; hope in vain; idle dream;
理想 aspiration; ideal;
聯想 associate; association; connect in the mind;
料想 expect; presume; think;
夢想 (1) dream of; pipe dream; woolgathering; (2) earnest wish; fond dream;
緬想 recall; think of;
冥想 deep thoughts; medicate; think deeply;
默想 contemplate; ruminate;
奢想 think wishfully; wishful thinking;
涉想 think about;
設想 (1) assume; conceive; envisage; imagine; (2) idea; rough plan; scheme; tentative idea; tentative plan;
試想 considering that; just think; think it over;
思想 (1) consider; think; (2) idea; ideology; (3) thinking; thought;
所想 think;
推想 (1) guess; imagination; (2) imagine; reckon;
妄想 absurd pursuit; daydream; delusion; forlorn hope; kink; vain hope; wishful thinking;
我倒想 I'd like to think that;
細想 deliberate; deliberation; give careful thought to; ponder; think over sth carefully;
遐想 be lost in wild and fanciful thoughts; daydream; reverie;
心想 expect; figure; think;
休想 can whistle for; don't imagine that it's possible; stop dreaming;
虛想 imagine; mere wish;
玄想 fancy; fantasy; illusion;
懸想 fantasize; illusion;
逸想 idealistic thoughts; thoughts that are not worldly;
意想 expect; imagine;
又一想 on second thought; on second thoughts;
欲想 desires for wealth and women;
預想 anticipate; expect;
再一想 on second thought; on second thoughts;
追想 recall; remember nostalgically; reminisce;
着想 consider; for the sake of; take into consideration;

xiang

【餉】 (1) pay; provisions for military or police; (2) entertain with food; feast; present food as gift;

[餉賓] entertain guests with food;
[餉饋] soldier's rations;
[餉錢] soldier's pay;
[餉項] soldier's pay; army funds;
[餉遺] donate; present as a gift;
[餉銀] soldier's pay;

發餉 issue pay;
關餉 get one's pay;
軍餉 (of soldier, policeman) get one's pay;
扣餉 deduct pay;
糧餉 rations for the army;
領餉 receive one's pay;
薪餉 soldier's pay and rations;
月餉 monthly pay;

xiang

【鯗】 dried and salted fish;

白鯗 a kind of preserved fish;
鰻鯗 dried eel;

xiang

【響】 (1) echo; noise; sound; (2) make a sound; ring; sound; (3) loud; noisy;

[響徹] resound through; reverberate through;
響徹九霄 echo to the sky;
響徹四方 resound in all directions;
響徹雲霄 echo to the skies; make the welkin ring; rend the air; rend the skies; rend the welkin; resound through the skies;

[響噹噹] (1) loud; noisy; (2) famous; outstanding; up to the mark;
鑼在本山敲不響，隔山敲打響噹噹 a prophet is not without honour save in his own country; a prophet is without honour in his own country; never

a prophet was valued in his native country;

[響亮] (1) loud and clear; resonant; resounding; sonorous; vibrant; (2) straightforward;

[響鈴] bell;

[響馬] mounted highwaymen;
公路響馬 highwayman;

[響聲] noise; sound; echo;
沙沙的響聲 rustling sould;

[響尾蛇] crotalid; rattlesnake; sidewinder;
響尾蛇毒 crotaline;

[響應] answer; echo in support; respond;
得到響應 meet with a response;
熱心地響應 respond heartily to;
聞風響應 hear the news and rise up in response;
迅速地響應 quickly respond to;

打響 (1) begin to exchange fire; open fire; start shooting; (2) get off to a good start; make a good start; win initial success;
發響 make a sound;
反響 echo; repercussion;
轟響 thunder;
回響 echo; resound;
混響 reverberation;
交響 symphonic;
巨響 loud crash;
絕響 anything (e.g. art, skill) lost to the modern world; lost music;
鳴響 peal; tingle;
山響 deafening; rattling; thunderous;
聲響 noise; sound;
雙響 firecracker that detonates twice; double-bang firecracker;
嗣響 succeed to one's forefather's business;
音響 acoustics; sound;
影響 affect; exert an influence on; have influence on; have influence over; influence; interfere with; produce an impact on; under the influence of;

xiang

【饗】 (1) banquet; dine and wine guests; give a big party; (2) sacrificial ceremony;

[饗宴] feast;

xiang⁴

xiang

【向】 (1) direction; trend; (2) face; turn towards; (3) favour; partial to; side with; (4) always; all along; (5) until now; (6) a surname;

[向背] support or oppose;
人心向背 the feelings of the people; whether the people are for or against; whether the public attitude for or against; who commands popular sympathy; with whom popular sympathy lies;

[向地性] geotropism;

[向光性] phototropism;

[向後] (1) backward; towards the back; turn around; (2) in the future;
向後轉 about turn; about-face;
準備向後 action rear;

[向來] all along; always; heretofore; hitherto; until now;
向來如此 it has always been so;

[向理不向人] side with whoever is right; stand by what is right, not by a particular person;

[向例] according to custom;

[向量] vector;
向量角 vectorial angle;
向量徑 radius vector;
伴隨向量 adjoint vector;
活動向量 activity vector;
解析向量 analytic vector;
面積向量 area vector;

[向明] (1) toward daybreak; (2) bright side of a house;

[向慕] admire sb;

[向氣性] aerotropism;

[向前] ahead; forward; go forward; onward;
向前看 look ahead;
~向前看的 forword-looking;
向前移動 move onwards;
衝向前 rush ahead;
奮勇向前 forge ahead;
跑向前 run forward;
趲馬向前 urge on a horse;
準備向前 action front;

[向熱性] thermotropism;
負向熱性 negative thermotropism;
正向熱性 positive thermotropism;

[向日] (1) sunward; (2) in former days; in the past;
向日葵 sunflower;
~具柄向日葵 prairie sunflower;

向日性 heliotropism;
[向榮] on the road to prosperity;
[向上] (1) up; upward; (2) make progress; strive upward; try to improve oneself;
向上爬 ambitious; careerist; climb to the upper echelon of society; climb up the social ladder; intent on personal advancement; office seeker; social climber;
引體向上 chin-up;
[向食性] sitotropism;
[向濕性] hygrotropism;
[向水性] hydrotropism;
[向外] (1) turn outward; (2) upwards of;
[向晚] toward the evening;
[向往] be attracted toward; look forward to; yearn for;
[向無此例] there is no precedent for this;
[向下] down; downward;
此端向下 bottom;
[向心力] centripetal force;
[向性] tropism;
向性運動 tropic movement;
負向性 negative tropism;
正向性 positive tropism;
[向學] inclined to study; determine to study;
勵志向學 stimulate oneself to study;
[向陽] facing the sunny side;
[向右] towards the right;
[向隅] disappointed for having missed the opportunity; feel left out; miss the opportunity; stand in a corner;
向隅而泣 be left to bewail despairingly in the cold; be left to grieve in the cold; weep all alone in a corner; weep in a corner and bewail one's sad fate;
[向者] in the past;
[向左] towards the left;
向左轉 left turn;
奔向 rush towards;
測向 finding;
單向 one-way; unidirectional;
定向 bearing; clearly determined goal; directional; orientation; predetermined orientation;
動向 tendency; trend;
反向 (1) opposite direction; (2) back; backward; counter; reversal; reverse;
方向 direction; orientation;
風向 (1) wind direction; (2) turn of events;
負向 negative orientation;
歸向 incline to; turn towards;
橫向 crosswise; horizontal;
徑向 radial;
流向 afflux;
邁向 march toward;
面向 (1) face; turn in the direction of; turn one's face to; (2) be geared to the needs of; cater to;
內向 introvert; introversion;
逆向 backward; reverse;
偏向 be partial to; erroneous tendency;
傾向 be inclined to support one side rather than the other; deviation; inclination; leaning; proclivity; proneness; propensity; tend to; tendency; trend;
趨向 (1) direction; tendency; trend; (2) incline to; tend to;
取向 orientation;
去向 the direction in which sb or sth has gone;
趣向 aptitude; personal inclination;
全向 isotropic; omnidirection;
山向 the direction which a grave faces;
雙向 bidirectional; bilateral; double-direction; two-way;
四向 towards all directions;
通向 lead to;
外向 extroversion; outgoing;
相向 face each other; face to face; opposite direction;
性向 disposition;
一向 (1) earlier on; lately; (2) all along; consistently; for always; (3) hitherto; up to now;
意向 inclination; intention; purpose;
正向 positive;
指向 direct; point to; directional;
志向 ambition; aspiration; ideal;
軸向 axial;
轉向 change directions; change one's political position; diversion; steering; sway; swing; turn; turn around; turn in the direction of; turn round;
縱向 (1) from south to north; (2) vertical;
走向 (1) the run; the trend; (2) head for; move toward; on the way for;

xiang

【巷】 lane; alley;
[巷道] (1) tunnel; (2) alley; back street; lane;
[巷口] entrance to a lane;
[巷陌] streets and lanes;

[巷尾] end of a lane;
[巷議] local gossips; local rumours;
[巷戰] combat in street; house to house fighting; street battle; street fighting;
[巷子] lane; alley;
狹窄的巷子 narrow lane;

陋巷 mean alley;
閭巷 alley; lane;

xiang

【相】 (1) appearance; countenance; facial features; looks; (2) bearing; posture; (3) examine; look at and appraise; read; study; (4) photograph; (5) phase; (6) assist;
[相變] phase change;
[相冊] photo album;
[相法] physiognomy;
[相府] prime minister's residence;
[相公] (1) premier; (2) young gentleman;
[相國] prime minister;
[相機] (1) watch for an opportunity; (2) camera;
相機處宜 act on one's own discretion;
相機而動 bide one's time; see what can be done; wait for an opportunity to act; wait for the right time for action;
相機而行 act as the circumstances direct;
相機行事 act according to the circumstances; act as circumstances dictate; act as the occasion demands; act when the time is opportune; do as one sees fit; take care of the matter as change offers itself; watch for an opportunity for action; watch for the proper moment for action;
端穩相機 hold the camera steady;
傻瓜相機 autofocus camera;
數碼相機 digital camera;
~ 電腦數碼相機 computerized digital camera;
八百萬像素相機 eight megapixel camera;
[相架] frame;
立式相架 stand-up frame;
[相角] photo corner;
[相貌] appearance; countenance; face; facial features; looks;
相貌端正 have regular features;
相貌魁偉 person of stately and prepossessing appearance;
相貌平平 bland in appearance; not to be much to look at; singularly plain;
相貌堂堂 a commanding appearance; handsome and highly esteemed; have a dignified appearance; have a majestic bearing; of splendid appearance;
相貌猥瑣 have a trifling appearance;
appearance;
獰醜相貌 having a repulsive ugly appearance;
[相面] practice physiognomy; tell sb's fortune by reading his face;
相面先生 fortune teller;
[相命] fortune telling;
[相女配夫] study your own daughter properly when finding her a husband;
[相片] photo; photograph; photoprint; pix; print;
即印相片 instant print;
洗相片 develop a photo;
一張相片 a photograph;
[相人] practise physiognomy;
[相聲] comic dialogue; crosstalk; mimic;
單口相聲 monologue comic talk;
單人相聲 stand-up;
~ 單人相聲演員 stand-up;
對口相聲 crosstalking; stand-up;
説相聲 perform a comic dialogue;
[相時而動] adapt oneself to the circumstances; come up at the proper moment; wait for the right time to take action; watch for the proper moment for action;
[相士] (1) fortune teller; (2) appraise a person's latent ability;
[相手術] palmistry;
[相術] physiognomy;
[相紙] photographic paper; printing paper;
彩色相紙 colour paper;

拜相 be appointed prime minister;
扮相 appearance of an actor or actress in costume and makeup;
本相 real, original appearance or character;
變相 covert; in disguised form;
儐相 (1) best man of a bridegroom; (2) bride's maid;
丞相 prime minister;
吃相 table manner;
單項 monophase; single phase;

多項 heterogeneous;
惡相 evil countenance;
怪相 grimace;
寒酸相 miserable and shabby;
季相 aspect; aspection; seasonal aspect;
假相 false appearance;
將相 generals and ministers of state; military and political leaders;
均相 homogeneous phase;
看相 practice physiognomy;
可憐相 pitiable look;
老相 old for one's age;
兩相 both parties; both sides;
亮相 (1) make a stage pose; strike a pose on the stage; (2) declare one's position; state one's views;
陸相 land facies;
賣相 (1) exterior; the outward appearance; the packaging; (2) appearance; looks;
面相 facial looks;
奴才相 servile behaviour; servility;
皮相 skin-deep; superficial;
破相 face marred by a scar;
窮相 an appearance indicating poverty;
三相 three-phase;
上相 come out well in a photograph; photogenic;
食相 phase of an eclipse;
實相 truth;
識相 know how to avoid embarrassment; know when to yield with grace; sensible; tactful;
手相 palmistry;
首相 prime minister;
形相 appearance; facial look;
凶相 ferocious features; fierce look;
岩相 lithofacies;
洋相 biff; make an exhibition of oneself; pratfall;
一張相 a photograph; a picture;
印相 printing;
月相 phase of the moon;
宰相 prime minister;
賊相 criminal looks;
長相 features; looks;
照相 (1) take a photo; take a picture; take photographs; take photos; take pictures; (2) have one's picture taken;
真相 actual state of affairs; naked truth; real situation; truth;
裝相 behave affectedly;

xiang

【象】 (1) elephant; (2) image; portrait; snapshot; (3) outward appearance of sth; phenomenon; (4) ivory;

[象鼻] elephant's trunk;

[象齒焚身] an elephant is killed because of its ivory — warning against hoarding wealth; the tusk of an elephant causes its death; wealth brings woe;

[象鳥] elephant bird;

[象棋] chess;
國際象棋 chess;
~國際象棋棋盤 chessboard;
~國際象棋棋子 chessman;
~下國際象棋 play chess;
下象棋 play chess;
下一盤象棋 have a game of chess;
一副象棋 a set of chess;
一盤象棋 a game of chess;
中國象棋 Chinese chess;

[象散] astigmatism;
象散測定儀 astigmatometer;
象散器 astigmatizer;
電子光學象散 electron-optical astigmatism;
反常象散 against-the-rule astigmatism;
潛在象散 latent astigmatism;

[象限] quadrant;

[象胥] interpreter or translator in ancient China;

[象牙] elephant's tusk; ivory;
鼠口不出象牙 a filthy mouth can't utter decent language; no ivory will come of a rat's mouth;
象牙雕刻 ivory carving;
象牙黑 abaiser;
象牙畫舫 gayly decorated ivory pleasure boat;
象牙龍舟 ivory dragon boat;
象牙塔 ivory tower;
象牙通花扇 ivory fan;

[象譯] graphic translation;

[象徵] (1) symbolize; (2) symbol;
象徵性 as a token; symbol; token;
~象徵性的 ceremonial;
~象徵性語言 figurative language;
象徵主義 symbolism;
和平的象徵 symbol of peace;
力量的象徵 emblem of strength;
權力的象徵 symbol of power;
身分象徵 symbol of identity;

表象 idea;
病象 symptom of a disease;

抽象 abstract; abstracting; abstraction;
大象 elephant;
對象 (1) object; target; (2) boyfriend; girlfriend; match; prospective spouse;
構象 conformation;
怪象 strange phenomenon;
海象 morse; walrus;
旱象 signs of drought;
好象 be like; seem;
幻象 mirage; phantom;
渾象 celestial globe;
活象 look exactly like;
跡象 indications; marks; signs;
假象 (1) false appearance; false impression; (2) false form; false image;
景象 picture; scene; sight;
鏡像 mirror image;
脈象 pulse condition; type of pulse;
毛象 mammoth;
米相 rice weevil;
氣象 (1) atmosphere scene; (2) meteorological phenomena; (3) meteorology;
乾象 celestial phenomena;
示象 aspect;
天象 astronomical phenomena; celestial phenomena;
萬象 all manifestations of nature; every phenomenon on earth;
險象 dangerous sign or phenomenon;
現象 appearance; phenomenon;
心象 mental image;
星象 astrology;
形象 figure; form; image;
懸象 celestial phenomena;
血象 blood picture; hemogram;
一群象 a drove of elephants; a herd of elephants;
一頭象 an elephant;
異象 strange phenomena;
意象 concept; idea; image; imagery;
印象 impression; mental image;
徵象 sign; straw in the wind; symptom;

xiang

【項】 (1) back of the neck; nape; (2) sum of money; (3) article; class; item; kind; matter; (4) term; (5) a surname;

[項背] nape; person's neck and back;
項背相望 one after another in close succession;

[項鏈] chain; necklace;
短項鏈 choker;
金項鏈 gold necklace;
珊瑚項鏈 coral necklace;
一串項鏈 a necklace;
一條項鏈 a necklace;
摘下項鏈 take off one's necklace;
珍珠項鏈 pearl necklace;
鑽石項鏈 diamond necklace;

[項目] item; project;
項目貸款 project financing;
項目法人 project entity;
項目符號 bullet point;
項目負責人 project leader;
項目工程師 project engineer;
項目經理 project manager;
項目評估 project appraisal;
項目融資 project finance;
項目設計 project design;
項目實體 project entity;
項目招標 project bidding;
項目整體風險 total project risk;
項目綜合管理 general project management of;
項目綜合評價 synthetic project evaluation;
非常項目 abnormal item;
個人項目 individual event;
工程項目 engineering project;
化工項目 chemical project;
援助項目 aid project;
緩建項目 postpone a construction project;
徑賽項目 track events;
討論項目 item for discussion;
內容項目 content item;
田徑項目 track and field events;
田賽項目 field events;
團體項目 team event;
營業項目 business items;
應計項目 accrued items;
運動項目 sports event;
增列項目 additional item;
正式項目 title event;
支出項目 item of expenditure;

[項圈] collar; necklace;
狗項圈 dog collar;

[項式] nomial;
單項式 monomial;
多項式 polynomial;
~多項式的次數 degree of polynomial;
~伴隨多項式 adjoint polynomial;
~不可約多項式 irreducible polynomial;
~對稱多項式 symmetrical polynomial;
~仿射多項式 affine polynomial;

~齊次多項式 homogeneous polynomial
~無偏差多項式 affectless polynomial;
二項式 binomial;
三項式 trinomial;
[項莊舞劍，意在沛公] kiss the baby for the nurse's sake – with ulterior motives;

長項 forte;
常數項 constant term;
出項 expenses; item of expenditure;
詞項 lexical item;
存項 balance; credit balance;
單項 individual event;
多項 multinominal; multiple; polynomial;
二項 binary; binomial;
後項 last term; second term;
進項 income; receipts;
頸項 nape of the neck; neck; scruff of the neck;
款項 (1) a sum of money; fund; (2) section of an article in a legal document;
內項 inner term;
前項 antecedent; preceding article;
強項 forte; strong; unyielding;
弱項 weak spot; yielding;
三項 three-term;
事項 item; matter;
説項 ask leniency or special consideration; intercede for sb; put in a good word for sb; try to persuade;
同類項 like terms;
外項 extreme;
餉項 soldier's pay; army funds;
要項 key item; key point;
已知項 known terms;
義項 semantic item;
用項 expenditures; items of expenditure;
雜項 miscellaneous items; sundry;
債項 the amount due;
賬項 accounting item;
中項 mean;
中心項 central term;
逐項 member by member; term by term;
專項 special item;
最小項 lowest term;

xiang

【像】 (1) appearance; image; (2) imitate; (3) like; resemble; take after; (4) as; as if; as it were; as though; no more...than; not...any more than; so to speak; the way; what; (5) like; such as;

[像差] aberration;
像差計 aberrometer;
單色像差 monochromatic aberration;
第二級像差 secondary aberration;
第一級像差 primary aberration;
電子光學像差 electron-optical aberration;
高次像差 higher aberration;
光線像差 ray aberration;
光學像差 optical aberration;
橫像差 lateral aberration;
慧形像差 coma aberration;
幾何像差 geometrical aberration;
孔徑像差 aperture aberration;
偏轉像差 deflection aberration;
距離像差 distantial aberration;
色像差 chromatic aberration; colour aberration;
透鏡像差 lens aberration;
消色像差 achromatic aberration;
主縱像差 principal longitudinal aberration;
縱向像差 longitudinal aberration;
[像話] appeal to reason;
這才像話 now that's the way to talk; now you are talking;
真不像話 what a carry-on;
[像貌] person's looks;
像貌非凡 a distinguished appearance;
像模像樣 (1) look respectable; with an air of importance; (2) with all sincerity;
[像片] photograph;
航攝像片 aerial photo;
[像是] look like; seem;
[像素] pixel;
百萬像素 megapixel;
[像樣] decent; presentable; proper in appearance; sound; up to the mark;
不像樣 improper behaviour;
像像樣樣 decently;

不像 unlike;
成像 formation of image; imagery;
倒像 inverted image;
雕像 effigy; monument; statue;
佛像 figure of Buddha; image of Buddha;
負像 negative image;
好像 appear; as if; as it were; look; look as if; look like; seem; seemingly;
畫像 (1) draw a portrait; portray; (2) portrait; portrayal;
幻像 ghost; mental image; mirage; phantom; vision;

繪像 draw portraits;
活像 a model of sb; an exact replica of sb; bear a strong resemblance to sb; favour sb; have a look of sb; have a strong resemblance to sb; look as if indeed; look exactly like sb; remarkably alike; resemble sb; show a strong resemblance to sb; take a strong resemblance to; take after sb; the double of sb; the living image of sb; the spit and image of; the very image of sb; the very picture of sb;
蠟像 wax figure; waxwork;
錄像 video; videotape;
泥像 clay statuette;
偶像 heartthrob; idol; image;
人像 figure; portrait; image;
攝像 (1) make a video recording; (2) shoot pictures;
神像 (1) image of a dead person; (2) idol; the statue of a god;
聲像 sound image;
獅身人面像 sphinx;
石膏像 plaster statue;
石像 stone statue;
視像 video;
四不像 hodge-podge of sth that resembles nothing; neither fish, flesh, fowl, nor good red herring; neither fish nor fowl; nondescript;
塑像 (1) make an idol; (2) plastic figure; statue;
銅像 bronze image; bronze statue;
圖像 image; imagery; picture;
相像 alike; similar;
想像 (1) conceive of; dream; fancy; imagine; think; visualize; (2) imagination;
小像 portrait;
肖像 likeness of a person; portrait;
繡像 (1) embroidered portraits; (2) exquisitely drawn portrait;
虛像 virtual image;
學不像 try to imitate in vain;
遺像 portrait of a dead person;
音像 audio and video;
影像 image;
映像 image; map;
造像 make a portrait; make a statue; make an image;
鑄像 erect a metal statue;
自畫像 self-portrait;

xiang

【橡】 chestnut oak; acorn; oak;

［橡蟲］ oak worm;

［橡膠］ rubber;
橡膠老化 ageing of rubber;
橡膠樹 rubber tree;
橡膠靴 rubber boot;
~長筒橡膠靴 gumboot;
橡膠園 rubber plantation;
灌注橡膠 castable rubber;
通用橡膠 all-purpose rubber;

［橡皮］ (1) eraser; (2) rubber;
橡皮擦 rubber; eraser;
橡皮船 rubber dinghy;
橡皮減震 rubber shock absorption;
橡皮筋 elastic band; rubber band;
橡皮泥 play dough;
橡皮糖 chewing-gum; chewy candy; gumdrop;
橡皮艇 rubber dinghy;
橡皮圖章 rubber stamp;
人造橡皮 ameripol;

［橡樹］ oak;

xiang

【曏】 (1) a period of time; (2) once upon a time;

［曏者］ once upon a time;

xiang

【嚮】 (1) direct; guide; lead; (2) be inclined toward; lean toward;

［嚮晨］ toward dawn;

［嚮導］ docent; guide;
當嚮導 act as a guide;

［嚮邇］ approach;

［嚮晦］ toward dusk;

［嚮明］ toward dawn;

［嚮往］ aspire; long; look forward to;
嚮往自由 yearn for freedom;

［嚮午］ toward noon;

xiao¹

xiao

【枵】 empty;

［枵薄］ thin and flimsy;

［枵腹］ empty stomach;
枵腹從公 attend to the office on an empty stomach; do one's duty even with an empty stomach; serve others without salary;
枵腹而睡 go to bed with an empty stomach;

［枵耗］ waste;

［枵厚］ thin and thick;

［枵木］ dried-up tree trunk;
［枵然］ big;

xiao

【宵】 dark; evening; night;
［宵半］ midnight;
［宵會］ night meeting;
［宵禁］ curfew;
解除宵禁 lift a curfew;
撤消宵禁 lift a curfew;
實行宵禁 impose a curfew;
［宵類］ thieves and rascals;
［宵魄］ the moon;
［宵人］ mean person;
［宵小］ evildoers; gangsters and the like; thieves; thieves and rascals;
［宵行］ travel by night;
［宵夜］ midnight snack;
［宵中］ midnight;
［宵燭］ glowworm;

春宵 spring night;
良宵 happy evening;
深宵 deep in the night;
通宵 all night; the whole night; throughout the night;
夜宵 midnight snack;
元宵 fifteenth night of the first lunar month;
中宵 middle of the night; midnight;

xiao

【消】 (1) die out; disappear; vanish; (2) allay; alleviate; dispel; disperse; eliminate; extinguish; quench; remove; (3) pass the time in a leisurely way; while away the time; (4) need; take;
［消波］ wave suppression;
消波裝置 wave suppression arrangement;
［消沉］ dejected; depressed; downhearted; low-hearted; low-spirited;
［消愁］ allay cares; dispel worries;
消愁解悶 banish boredom; chase one's gloom away; disencumber one's mind of care; dispel depression; divert oneself from boredom; drown care; end all care; quench sorrow and dissipate worry; relieve the loneliness and grief;
消愁破悶 dispel melancholy and break the thrall of boredom;
把酒消愁 drown one's worries in drink; take to drinking to forget one's sorrows;
將酒消愁 drown one's worries in drink; take to drinking to forget one's sorrows;
酒消百愁 all anxieties are drowned in the cup;
［消除］ cancel; cancellation; cancelling; clear up; dispel; eliminate; elimination; get rid of; remove; stamp out; wipe;
消除弊端 remedy a drawback;
消除不滿情緒 remove dissatisfaction;
消除分歧 eliminate differences; iron out differences;
消除隔閡 remove misunderstanding;
消除顧慮 dispel misgivings;
消除困難 remove difficulties;
消除歧義 disambiguation;
消除器 absorber; eliminator; eraser;
~火花消除器 spark absorber;
~輪跡消除器 wheelmark eliminator; wheelmark eraser;
~調制消除器 modulation eliminator;
消除危險 eliminate danger;
消除污染 abatement of pollution;
消除誤會 clear up a misunderstanding; dispel misunderstanding; remove misunderstanding;
消除嫌疑 clear up suspicion;
消除疑慮 dispel one's misgivings;
消除隱患 remove a hidden danger;
消除障礙 remove obstacles;
消除疾病 eradicate a disease;
消除皺紋 smooth away wrinkles;
消除自卑感 eliminate the sense of inferiority;
對角線消除 diagonal wipe;
回波消除 echo cancellation;
激波消除 shock wave cancellation;
漂移消除 drift cancellation;
失真消除 distortion elimination;
水平消除 horizontal wipe;
瞬變消除 transient elimination;
誤差消除 error cancelling;
消煙除塵 eliminate smoke and dust;
噪音消除 noise cancellation;
阻尼消除 damping elimination;
［消磁］ degauss; degaussing; demagnetization; demagnetize;
消磁電纜 degaussing cable;
消磁能力 erasing ability;

消磁器 demagnetizer; eraser; magnetic eraser;
~ 磁帶消磁器 magnetic tape eraser;
~ 磁頭消磁器 head demagnetizer; head eraser;
~ 整體消磁器 bulk eraser;
消磁頭 erasing head;
消磁線圈 anti-magetized coil;
人工消磁 manual degaussing;
自動消磁 automatic degaussing;

[消毒] (1) discontaminate; disinfect; disinfection; pasteurize; sterilization; sterilize; (2) degassing; (3) eliminate pernicious influence; wipe out pernicious influence;
消毒劑 disinfectant;
~ 空氣消毒劑 aerosol disinfectant;
消毒器 disinfector; sterilizer;
~ 電器消毒器 electric sterilizer;
~ 自動消毒器 automatic sterilizer;
低溫消毒 cold sterilization;
地面消毒 ground disinfection;
廢水消毒 wastewater disinfection;
進行消毒 carry out disinfection;
空氣消毒 air sterilization;
區域消毒 locality disinfection;
食物消毒 food sterilization;
同時消毒 concurrent disinfection;
土壤消毒 soil disinfection;
溴消毒 bromine disinfection;
用酒精消毒 disinfect with alcohol;
煮沸消毒 sterilize by boiling;

[消防] fire control; firefighting;
消防查察車 firefighting inspection car;
消防車 fire engine; fire truck;
~ 幫浦消防車 pump firefighting truck;
~ 化學消防車 chemical firefighting truck;
~ 泡沫消防車 foam firefighting truck;
~ 水庫消防車 reservoir firefighting truck;
~ 水塔消防車 water tower firefighting truck;
~ 水箱消防車 water tank firefighting truck;
~ 雲梯消防車 aerial ladder firefighting truck;
消防船 fireboat;
消防隊 fire brigade; fire department; fire service;
~ 消防隊隊長 fire chief;
消防喉 fire hose;
~ 消防喉轆 fire hose reel;
消防後勤車 firefighting logistic truck;
消防警備車 fire guard car;
消防龍頭 fire hydrant;
消防勤務車 firefighting service car;
消防栓 fire hydrant;
消防署 fire department; fire service;
~ 消防署署長 fire chief;
消防通道 fire exit;
消防演習 fire drill;
消防員 firefighter; fireman;
消防站 fire house; fire station;

[消費] consume;
消費本位 consumption standard;
消費部門 consuming sector;
消費產品 consumption products;
消費超前 consumption ahead of time;
消費潮流 consumption tide;
消費城市 consumer city;
消費道德 consumption moral;
消費抵制 consumer sales resistance;
消費動機 motive of the consumer;
消費方式 consumption pattern;
消費個性 personality of the consumer;
消費構成 structure of consumption;
消費合作 consumptive cooperation;
消費基金 consumption fund;
消費技術 consumption technology;
消費結構 consumption structure;
消費經濟學 economics of consumption;
消費決策 consumption policy;
消費率 consumption rate;
消費品 articles of consumption; consumables; consumer goods; consumption goods;
~ 消費品工業 consumer industry;
~ 消費品市場 consumer goods market;
~ 耐用消費品 consumer durables; durable goods;
消費傾向 propensity to consumption;
消費趨勢 consumption trend;
消費社會 consumer society; consumption society;
消費市場 consumer market;
消費水平 consumption level; consumption standard;
消費稅 consumer tax;
消費態度 attitude of the consumer;
消費統計 statistics of consumption;
消費物價指數 consumer price index;
~ 一般消費物價指數 general consumer

price index;
消費心理 consumer psychology;
消費行為 consumer behaviour;
消費需要 consumer needs;
消費者 consumer;
~ 消費者權益 consumer rights and interests;
~ 消費者市場 consumer market;
~ 消費者調查 consumer research;
~ 消費者團體 consumer group;
~ 消費者文化 consumer culture;
~ 消費者協會 association of consumers;
~ 消費者信心 consumer confidence;
~ 消費者行為 consumer behaviour;
~ 消費者主權 consumer authority;
消費知覺 perception of consumer;
消費主義 consumerism;
消費資料 consumer information;
白色消費 white consumption;
表面消費 apparent consumption;
超前消費 overconsuming;
高消費 upscale;
國內消費 domestic consumption;
基本消費 basic consumption;
集體消費 collective consumption;
家庭消費 household consumption;
軟性消費 soft consumption;
炫耀性消費 conspicuous consumption;
直接消費 direct consumption;
自發消費 autonomous consumption;

[消光] extinction; light extinction;
波狀消光 oscillatory extinction;
初級消光 primary extinction; undulatory extinction; wavy extinction;
斜消光 inclined extinction; oblique extinction;

[消耗] (1) consume; exhaust; expend; use up; (2) deplete;
消耗精力 consume one's energy;
消耗能源 consume the sources of energy;
消耗石油 consume petroleum;
消耗體力 consume one's strength;
消耗戰 war of attrition;
低消耗 low consumption;
空氣消耗 air consumption;
能量消耗 consumption of energy;
燃料消耗 fuel consumption;
日常消耗 current consumption;
陽極消耗 anode consumption;
原料消耗 consumption of raw materials;

[消化] (1) digest; digestion; (2) absorb mentally;
消化不良 bad digestion; dyspepsia; indigestion;
~ 闌尾炎性消化不良 appendicular dyspepsia;
~ 酸性消化不良 acid dyspepsia;
消化道 alimentary canal; alimentary tract;
消化劑 digestant;
消化力 digestion;
消化道出血 alimentary canal haemorrhage;
消化力 digestion;
消化良好 eupepsia;
消化器官 digestive organs;
消化正常 eupepsia;
消化液 digestive juice;
鹼性消化 alkaline digestion;
人工消化 artificial digestion;
酸性消化 acid digestion;
細菌消化 bacterial digestion;
需氧消化 aerobic digestion;
厭氧消化 anaerobic digestion;

[消魂] be held spellbound;

[消極] (1) negative; (2) inactive; passive; pessimistic;
消極悲觀 remain passive and pessimistic;
消極詞匯 passive vocabulary;
消極怠工 slack in work; work to rule;
消極抵抗 passive resistance;
消極修辭 immovable rhetoric;
消極因素 negative factor;
消極影嚮 negative influence;
消極語言 consumer language; passive language;
~ 消極語言知識 passive language knowledge;

[消減] abate; decrease; diminish; lessen; reduce;

[消解] clear up; dispel;

[消弭] avert; bring to an end; prevent; put an end to; terminate;
消弭禍患 soothe catastrophes;
消弭水患 prevent flood disasters;
消弭宿怨 bring an old grudge to an end;

[消滅] (1) die out; pass away; perish; (2) abolish; annihilate; destroy; eliminate; eradicate; exterminate; wipe out;
消滅赤字 wipe out deficits;
消滅特權 abolish privileges;
消滅天花 terminate smallpox;
消滅蚊蠅 wipe out mosquitoes and flies;

消滅文盲 wipe out illiteracy;
自行消滅 die out of itself;

[消磨] (1) fritter away; sap; wear down; (2) idle away; while away;
消磨精力 fritter away one's energy;
消磨時間 while way the time; while the time away;
消磨時間 kill time; pass the time;
消磨時日 count one's thumbs; while away the time;
消磨歲月 fill up the time; spend the time; while away the tedious hours; while away the time;
消磨志氣 sap one's will;

[消氣] allay one's anger;

[消遣] (1) divert oneself; while away the time; (2) diversions; pastimes; recreation;

[消郤] eliminate; get rid of;

[消溶] melt;

[消融] melt;

[消散] (1) dissipate; scatter and disappear; slake; vanish; (2) elimination;
煙消雲散 be dispersed; be dissipated; be gone; blow over; come to smoke; disappear completely; disappear in a flash; end in smoke; melt away; melt into air; pass away like a breath of wind; turn to dust and ashes; vanish into smoke; vanish into thin air; vanish like mist and smoke;

[消色器] colourkiller;

[消聲器] muffler;
集筒式消聲器 concentric cylinder muffler;
排氣消聲器 exhaust muffler;
氣管消聲器 gas-pipe muffler;

[消失] die away; die out; disappear; disappearance; dissipation; dissolve; fade away; vanish;
消失不見 vanish from sight;
消失在黑暗中 fade into darkness;
消失在雨中 disappear in the rain;
暗中消失 be lost in the darkness;
迅速消失 disappear rapidly;
突然消失 disappear suddenly;
逐漸消失 die away; fade out; peter out;

[消逝] die away; elapse; fade away; vanish;

[消釋] clear up; dispel;
消釋疑慮 dispel misgivings; free sb from doubts and misgivings;

[消受] (1) enjoy; (2) bear; endure;
沒福消受 unable to enjoy; not to have the luck to enjoy;
無福消受 not have the luck to enjoy; unable to take advantage of;

[消瘦] emaciated; emaciation; lose flesh; lose weight; skinny; wasted;
消瘦病 pine;
~ 營養不良性消瘦病 nutritional marasmus;
逐漸消瘦 waste away;
老年性消瘦 geromarasmus;
面容消瘦 look emaciated;

[消暑] relieve summer heat; take a summer holiday;
消暑止渴 relieve summer heat and quench thirst;

[消損] (1) wear and tear; (2) wear down; wear off;

[消退] degrade; fade away; vanish gradually;

[消亡] (1) demise; die out; extinct; perish; wither; wither away; (2) subduction;

[消息] (1) info; information; news; (2) news; tidings;
消息閉塞 little information;
消息傳得很快 news spreads fast; news travels fast;
消息傳開 news spreads;
消息來源 source of news;
消息靈通 well-informed;
~ 消息靈通人士 informed sources; those in the know; well-informed circles; well-formed sources;
暗通消息 send a secret message;
爆炸性消息 explosive news; shocking news;
不幸的消息 dire news; terrible news;
公佈消息 publish the news;
官方消息 official news;
~ 半官方消息 semi-official information;
廣播消息 radio news;
好消息 good news;
~ 好消息是…壞消息是 the good news is...the bad news is...;
~ 沒有消息就是好消息 no news is good news;
花邊消息 tit bit;
壞消息 bad news; heavy news;
假消息 disinformation;
可靠消息 reliable news;
令人振奮的消息 cheering news;
散佈消息 spread the news;

透露消息 disclose the news;
探聽消息 fish for information;
提供消息 give information;
聽到消息 hear the news;
透消息 let out a secret; reveal news;
小道消息 grapevine news;
~ 別聽小道消息 don't heed the hearsay;
洩露消息 break the news; transpire information;
新消息 latest information; latest news;
杳無消息 have no news of sth; have not heard from sb;
一條消息 a bit of news; a piece of news;
一則消息 a piece of news;
有消息 have some news;
最新消息 hot news; latest news; spot news;

X

[消夏] relieve summer heat;

[消閒] kill time; pass time idly;
消閒解悶 distract the mind; relieve boredom;

[消歇] become extinct; fade away; stop; subside;

[消炎] dephlogisticate; diminish inflammation; reduce inflammation;
消炎的 anti-inflammatory;

[消夜] have a midnight snack; midnight snack;

[消音] deaden a sound; sound deadening;
消音器 deadener; muffler; silencer;
~ 發動機消音器 jet silencer;
~ 感應消音器 induction silencer;
~ 毛氈消音器 felt deadener;

[消隱] blanking;
標題消隱 caption blanking;
不對稱消隱 asymmetric blanking;
場消隱 field blanking;
垂直消隱 vertical blanking;
地區消隱 zone blanking;
方位消隱 azimuth blanking;
複合消隱 mixed blanking;
高速消隱 high-speed blanking;
行消隱 line blanking;
回掃消隱 return trace; blanking;
逆程消隱 flyback blanking; retrace blanking;
色同步消隱 burst blanking;
束消隱 beam current blanking;
圖像消隱 picture blanking;
有效消隱 efficient blanking;
噪音消隱 noise blanking;
最後消隱 final blanking;

[消災] forestall calamities; prevent calamities;
消災降福 bring good luck and ward off calamities; prevent calamities and bring happiness;
延年消災 make sb live longer and keep him out of danger;

[消長] growth and decline; rise and fall; ups and downs; vicissitudes; wane and wax;

[消震] shock absorption;
消震器 shock absorber;
~ 聲響消震器 acoustic shock absorber;

[消腫] remove a swelling;
消腫藥 discutient;

冰消 deglaciate;
撤消 cancel; rescind;
吃不消 be too much for sb to do sth; more than one can bear; unable to stand;
打消 dispel; get rid of; give up; remove;
抵消 cancel out; counteract; counterbalance; kill; neutralize; offset; set-off;
對消 cancel out each other; offset;
花消 (1) cost; expense; (2) commissions; taxes and levies;
取消 abandon; abolish; abrogate; annul; be cleared of; be edged out by; call off; cancel; cancellation; cross out; deprive sb of; discard; dispense with; do away with; liquidate; negate; nullify; obliterate; off; put an end to; reject; relinquish; remove; renounce; repeal; repudiate; rescind; revoke; scrap; strip of; write off;
只消 have only to; just; need only; only;
祇消 all one has to do is; you only need to;

xiao

【梟】 (1) owl; (2) smuggler of contrabands; (3) brave and unscrupulous;

[梟哺] reformed son;

[梟匪] smuggler of contraband;

[梟將] brave general;

[梟盧] gamble with dice;

[梟亂] cause turmoil; confuse;

[梟鳥] owl;

[梟示] display the head of a decapitated person;

[梟首] decapitate a person and hang his head on a pole;
梟首示眾 expose a cut-off head to public

view as a warning to;

[梟雄] fierce, ambitious man;

梟雄之姿 carriage of a villain;

鹽梟 salt smuggler;

xiao

【逍】 (1) loiter; wander in a leisurely manner; (2) at ease; free and unfettered; leisurely and carefree; take one's ease;

[逍遙] free and unfettered; leisurely; loiter about; unhurried; saunter about; wander about in leisure;

逍遙法外 at large; beyond the arm of the law; get off scot-free; go unpunished; on the loose; remain at large; remain out of the law's reach;

逍遙一生 free and unfettered the whole life; saunter through life;

逍遙自在 at one's ease; at peace with the world and oneself; carefree; enjoy a free and leisurely life; enjoy leisure without restraint; enjoy oneself; in a state of blissful abstraction; free and easy; free and unfettered; jaunty; leisurely and carefree; take life easy;

xiao

【硝】 (1) niter; saltpetre; (2) tan leather;

[硝煙] smoke of gunpowder;

硝煙彌漫 a cloud of smoke floats over the battlefield;

火硝 nitre; saltpetre;

砒硝 mirabilite;

皮硝 mirabilite;

xiao

【綃】 (1) fabric made of raw silk; (2) raw silk;

[綃鈔] hair kerchief;

[綃頭] silk hood for binding the hair;

xiao

【銷】 (1) melt; (2) annul; cancel; dispel; vanish; (3) market; sell; (4) expend; spend; (5) crude iron; pig iron;

[銷案] close a legal case;

[銷耗] (1) expenditure; (2) cost; spend;

[銷毀] destroy;

[銷魂] carried away; enraptured; feel transported; transported;

銷魂奪魄 be overwhelmed by one's passion; fascinating; feel transported;

銷魂蝕骨 go into ecstasies;

銷魂蝕魄 be overwhelmed by one's passion; feel transported;

銷魂醉魄 bewitch the mind and intoxicate the senses;

黯然銷魂 be plunged in grief; dumb with grief; grief-stricken; sorrow at parting; sorrow-stricken; sorrowful; very gloomy;

[銷貨] merchandise sales;

[銷金] (1) lavish wealth; (2) be decorated with gold; gilt;

銷金窟 brothel;

銷金嵌玉 be covered with gold leaf and encrusted with brilliant stones;

銷金紙 gilt paper;

[銷量] sales; sales volume;

銷量驟降 sales slump;

銷量猛增 sales soar;

銷量下降 sales drop; sales fall; sales go down;

出口銷量 export sales;

零售銷量 high-street sales; retail sales;

年銷量 annual sales;

全球銷量 worldwide sales;

[銷路] market; sale; outlet;

銷路不暢 have a poor market;

銷路不好 find no market; find no sale; there is a poor market;

銷路好 find a good market; have a good sale; there is a good market;

銷路很差 there is a very poor market;

銷路很廣 have a great sale;

銷路很好 find a good market; have a good sale; sell well;

銷路狹窄 there is a narrow market;

銷路循環 market cycle;

銷路一般 have a moderate sale;

打開銷路 open up a market;

很有銷路 find a ready sale;

無銷路 find no market; find no sale;

有銷路 have an outlet;

~沒有銷路 fall flat on the market; find no market;

[銷聲匿跡] abscond quietly; cease all public activities; cease to show one's face; disappear from the scene; efface oneself; fall into the shade; go into hiding; go to Jericho; go where the

woodbine twineth; hide goings-on; hide oneself; in complete hiding; keep out of the way; keep silent and lie low; vanish without leaving any trace behind;

[銷售] market; sale; sell; sell goods; selling;
銷售包裝 consumer package; sales package;
銷售部門 sales department;
銷售處 point of sale;
銷售代理 sales agency;
~ 銷售代理人 sale agent;
銷售隊伍 sales force;
銷售額 sales figures;
銷售管理員 sales supervisor;
銷售技巧 salesmanship;
銷售技術 sales technique;
銷售計劃 plan for sale promotion;
銷售記錄 record of sales;
銷售會計 sales accounting;
銷售量 sales volume;
銷售路貨 sale of goods afloat;
銷售能力 sales ability;
銷售期貨 forward sale;
銷售潛力 sales potential;
銷售確認書 sales confirmation;
銷售數字 sales figures;
銷售税 sales tax;
銷售體系 sales system;
銷售網 sales network;
~ 銷售網點 sales outlet;
增加銷售網點 increase the sales outlets;
銷售限期 sell-by date;
銷售現貨 spot sale;
銷售信息系統 marketing information system;
銷售學 marketing;
~ 出口銷售學 export marketing;
~ 基本銷售學 basic marketing;
銷售業績 sales performance;
銷售業務 sales operation;
銷售優勢 sales advantage;
銷售預測 sales forecast;
銷售預算 sales budget;
銷售指標 sales target;
銷售總額 grass sales;
抽佣銷售 slae on commission basis;
大規模銷售 mass marketing;
單邊銷售 straight sale;
單面銷售 straight sale;
定額銷售 sale as per quota;
高效銷售 efficient distribution;
共同銷售 cooperative marketing;
估計銷售 estimated sale;
計劃推銷 planned selling;
間接銷售 indirect sale;
交叉銷售 cross-selling;
零星銷售 retail selling;
憑產地銷售 sale as per origin;
憑規格銷售 sale as per specifications;
憑貨樣銷售 sale by sample;
區外銷售 extraterritorial sale;
直接銷售 direct sale;

[銷行] be marketed; be sold; sell;

[銷賬] cancel debts;

包銷 exclusive sales; have exclusive selling rights;
報銷 (1) present a bill of expenses; (2) hand in a list of expended articles; (3) strike out; wipe out;
本銷 domestic sale; local sale;
插銷 (1) bolt; (2) plug;
產銷 produce and market;
暢銷 best seller; command a ready sale; command a good sale; enjoy a huge circulation; find a ready market; go like hot cakes; go off like hot cakes; have a good sale; have a ready market; have a ready sale; in good demand; in great demand; in great request; meet with a good sale; meet with a ready sale; sell like hot cakes; sell well; well-received;
撤銷 cancel; rescind; revoke;
承銷 underwrite;
沖銷 strike a balance;
傳銷 pyramid selling;
促銷 promote the sale; promotion; sales promotion;
代銷 act as a commission agent; sell goods on a commission basis;
吊銷 revoke; withdraw;
定銷 fix the quotas for marketing;
兜銷 find customers for trade; hawk;
返銷 resell grain to the place of production;
訪銷 sales promotion;
分銷 distribute;
供銷 supply and market;
勾銷 cancel; expunge; liquidate; strike out; wipe out; write off;
購銷 buying and selling; purchase and sale;
核銷 cancel after verification;
寄銷 consignment sale;

經銷 deal in; distribute; sell; sell on commission;
競銷 compete for the market;
開銷 expenditure; expense; pay expenses;
內銷 domestic sale; sell in the home market;
俏銷 in great demand; sell well;
傾銷 cutthroat sale; dump; dumping;
賒銷 charge sales; sell on credit;
試銷 place goods on trial sale; trial sale;
統銷 state monopoly for marketing;
推銷 market; merchandise; peddle; promote sales; sales promotion; selling;
脱銷 out of stock; sold out;
外銷 export sales; export trade; for export;
現銷 sale by real cash; sale for cash;
行銷 on sale; sell;
營銷 marketing;
硬銷 hard sell;
運銷 transport goods to other places for sale;
展銷 exhibit and sale;
直銷 direct sale;
滯銷 dull of sale; sales slump; unmarketable; unsaleable;
注銷 annul; be written off; cancel; make void; nullify;
柱銷 pin;

xiao

【霄】 (1) clouds; (2) heaven; sky; (3) night; (4) dissolve; exhaust;

[霄漢] firmament; heavens; sky;
 氣沖霄漢 fearless; have a noble revolutionary spirit and great enthusiasm; one's spirits soaring to the firmament;

[霄壤] heaven and earth;
 霄壤之別 a world of difference; as different as heaven and earth; as far apart as heaven and earth; poles apart; worlds apart;

[霄外] beyond the sky;

重霄 the highest heavens;
九重霄 the highest heavens;
青霄 azure sky; blue sky;
雲霄 the skies;

xiao

【蕭】 (1) desolate; lonely; quiet; (2) respectful; reverent; (3) a surname;

[蕭晨] autumn morning;

[蕭斧] sharp axe;

[蕭規曹隨] follow the established rules; move in a rut; tread in sb's footsteps;

[蕭牆] screen wall facing the gate of a Chinese house;
 蕭牆禍起 there will be trouble in the family; trouble arises within one's own doors; trouble breaks out at home;
 蕭牆之禍 internal strife; trouble arising at home; trouble behind the screen wall — trouble at home; trouble from within; trouble within the home;
 禍起蕭牆 there is internal strife afoot; troubles arises behind the walls of the home — trouble arises within the family; trouble breaks out at home;

[蕭然] (1) deserted; desolate; lonely; (2) disorderly; in commotion;
 蕭然物外 untrammeled by worldly affairs;
 環堵蕭然 in a cold, bare room;
 滿目蕭然 a melancholy and solitary aspect as far as the eyes can see;

[蕭颯] bleak; cool and soothing winds of autumn; desolate;

[蕭散] uninhibited and carefree;

[蕭瑟] (1) rustle in the air; sough; (2) bleak; deserted; desolate;

[蕭森] desolate; dreary and desolate; lonely;

[蕭疏] (1) bleak; desolate; (2) sparse but graceful; thinly scattered;

[蕭索] bleak and chilly; chilly; deserted; desolate; lonely;
 滿目蕭索 a melancholy and solitary aspect as far as the eyes can see;

[蕭條] (1) bleak; deserted; desolate; (2) depression; doldrums; in the doldrums; slack; sluggish; slump;
 蕭條期 slack time;
 百業蕭條 all business languishes;
 大蕭條 great depression;
 輕度蕭條 mild depression;
 全面蕭條 full-blown depression;
 商業蕭條 business depression;
 身後蕭條 die without leaving progeny behind; without money after one's death; without progeny after one's death;
 市況蕭條 business is slow; the market is depressed;

[蕭閒] (1) at ease; leisurely; (2) desolate; lonely;

[蕭蕭] (1) neigh; whinny; (2) sough; whistle;

xiao

【鴞】 owl;

鵂鴞 owl and the like;
雕鴞 bubobubo;Tulata scutulata;
鷹鴞 ninox scul;

xiao

【簫】 flute; pipe; wind instrument;
［簫笛］ flute;
吹簫弄笛 play the flute;
［簫鼓］ piping and drumming;
［簫管］ panpipe and double flute;
洞簫 vertical bamboo flute;

xiao

【瀟】 sound of beating rain and whistling wind;
［瀟灑］ casual and elegant; dashing and refined; elegant and unconventional; natural and unrestrained;
瀟灑不群 light-hearted and uncommon;
瀟灑自如 casual and elegant; natural and unrestrained; with an easy grace;
風流瀟灑 gay and light-hearted; graceful but not showy;
［瀟瀟］ (1) whistling and pattering; (2) drizzly;

xiao

【囂】 (1) clamour; din; hubbub; noise; (2) haughty; proud;
［囂謗］ be slandered by others;
［囂塵］ (1) noise and dust; (2) noisy, dusty world;
［囂浮］ (1) frivolous; (2) noisy world;
［囂競］ run after fame and wealth boisterously;
［囂然］ (1) sad; (2) hungry;
［囂囂］ (1) confusing; resound; (2) detached and self-contented;
［囂張］ aggressive; arrogant; bossy; haughty; rampant; unbridled;
囂張一時 rampage for a time; run rampant for a time; unbridled; very noisy for a time;
塵囂 hubbub; uproar;
煩囂 noisy and annoying;
叫囂 clamour; raise a hue and cry;
喧囂 clamour; hullabaloo; noisy;

xiao

【驍】 (1) brave; valiant; (2) fine horse;
［驍悍］ brave and fierce;
［驍將］ valiant general;
將驍兵鋭 the leaders are full of spirit and the men full of energy;
［驍騎］ brave and fierce cavalry;
驍騎悍將 brave cavalry led by a valiant general;
［驍衛］ imperial guards;
［驍驍］ valiant;
［驍雄］ capable and ambitious;
［驍勇］ brave; valiant;
驍勇善戰 brave and skilful in warfare;

xiao

【蠨】 teraguatha, a kind of spider with long legs;
［蠨蛸滿室］ the rooms are filled with cobwebs;

xiao³

xiao

【小】 (1) little; minor; small; tiny; (2) for a short time; for a while; (3) junior; young; (4) humble; lowly; mean; (5) light; petty; slight; trivial; unimportant;
［小巴］ minibus;
［小半］ less than half; the lesser part; the smaller half; the smaller part;
［小包］ packet;
［小報］ newssheet; small newspaper;
通俗小報 tabloid;
［小本］ small capital;
小本經營 do business in a small way; do business with little capital; go in for sth in a small way; run with a small capital;
小本生意 small business;
［小便］ apple and pip; burn the grass; dicky-diddle; do; drain one's radiator; drain one's snake; empty one's bladder; evacuate the bladder; go tap a kidney; have a leak; have a quickie; have a run off; life his leg; make number one; make salt water; make water; micturate; pass urine; pass water; pee; piddle; pie and mash; piss; plant a sweet pea; point Percy at the porcelain; pump ship; retire; scatter; see a man about a dog; see one's aunt; shake hands with an old friend; shake the

dew off the lily; shoot a lion; spend a penny; take a leak; take a quickie; tap a keg; tinkle; urinate; water the lawn; water the stock; whiz;
小便槽 urinal;
小便混濁 cloudy urine;
小便困難 have trouble urinating;
小便盆 urinal;
~男小便盆 urinal;
小便失禁 aconuresis; incontinence of urine;
驗小便 urine test;

[小別] brief separation; part for a short while;
小別勝新婚 a brief parting is as sweet as a honeymoon;

[小病] ailment; indisposition; minor ailment; minor illness;

[小步] stroll;
小步急跑 scurry; scuttle;
小步舞曲 minuet;

[小財] humble fortune;
發小財 make a humble fortune;

[小菜] (1) pickled vegetables; (2) common dishes; plain dishes; side dishes; (3) easy job;
小菜一碟 a piece of cake;

[小產] miscarriage;

[小腸] small bowels; small intestines;
小腸灌腸 small bowel enema;
小腸結腸炎 enterocolitis;
~出血性小腸結腸炎 haemorrhagic enterocolitis;
~壞死性小腸結腸炎 necrotizing enterocolitis;
~局限性小腸結腸炎 regional enterocolitis;
小腸氣 hernia;
小腸虛寒 asthenia-cold of small intestine;
小腸炎 enteritis; inflammation of the small intestine;

[小車] cart;
狗拉小車 dogcart;

[小城] small town; town;
歷史悠久的小城 a town steeped in history;

[小吃] (1) eats; refreshments; snacks; (2) cold dish; made dish;
小吃部 refreshments room;
小吃店 snack bar;
小吃館 small restaurant; eatery;
吃小吃 eat a snack;
開胃小吃 appetizer;
雜錦小吃 assorted appetizers;

[小丑] (1) buffoon; clown; knave; (2) contemptible wretch;
逗樂小丑 jester;
跳梁小丑 buffoon; clown; clumsy mischief-doer; contemptible scoundrel; little rascal; petty burglar;

[小醜] (1) mean person; (2) petty thief;
小醜跳梁 a contemptible wretch making trouble; petty criminals on the rampage;

[小船] boat; skiff;
狹長小船 narrow boat;
一隻小船 a small boat;

[小蔥] spring onion;
小蔥拌豆腐，一清二白 as plain as a dish of white bean curd and green scallions; clearcut; complete innocent; explicit;

[小錯] slide; slip; small mistake;
小錯不改，大錯即來 small mistakes left uncorrected will lead to bigger ones;

[小刀] knife; pocket knife; small sword;
摺疊式小刀 penknife;

[小島] islet;

[小道] branch; pass; passageway; path; pathway; trail; walkway;
小道理 minor principle;
小道消息 hearsay; rumour; the grapevine; the grapevine gossip;
小道新聞 grapevine news;
花園小道 garden path;
盤山小道 winding mountain path;
石子小道 gravel path;
一條小道 a path;

[小笛] whistle;
六孔小笛 penny whistle;

[小滴] droplet;

[小弟] (1) little brother; (2) little boy;

[小店] (1) inn; lodging house; (2) small store;
野村小店 little inn in a village;

[小調] (1) ditty; popular tune; (2) minor;

[小洞] small leak;
小洞不補，大洞叫苦 a little leak neglected, in time will sink a ship; a little neglect may breed great mischief; a small leak will sink a great ship; for want of a nail the shoe is lost, for want of a shoe the horse is lost, for want of

a horse the rider is lost;

[小兒] (1) child; infant; children; (2) my son;
小兒科 paediatrics;
小兒麻痺症 infantile paralysis; polio;

[小販] badger; hawker; pedlar; stall holder; trucker; vendor;

[小費] gratuity; tips;

[小斧] hatchet;

[小婦] (1) concubine; (2) young woman;

[小腹] lower abdomen;

[小狗] little dog; pup; puppy; young dog;
小狗狺吠 puppy yelps;
丁點大的小狗 tiny little puppy;
可愛的小狗 darling little dog;
一窩小狗 a litter of pups;
一隻小狗 a puppy;

[小姑] one's husband's younger sister; sister-in-law;
小姑獨處 girl not yet betrothed; remain a spinster; young unmarried woman; young woman living alone;

[小鼓] side drum; snare drum;

[小鬼] buster; little devil; mischievous child; imp;

[小國] small country;

[小過] (1) minor mistake; (2) minor demerit;

[小孩] ankle-biter; child; kid; kiddie; kiddy; moppet; nipper; small child;
小孩子 ankle-biter; child; kid; kiddy; small child;
剛學走路的小孩 toddler;
任性的小孩 capricious child;
淘氣的小孩 naughty child;
討厭的小孩 brattish child;
有禮貌的小孩 well-mannered child;

[小號] (1) trumpet; (2) small size;
小號手 trumpeter;

[小河] brook; rivulet;

[小戶] (1) small family; (2) poor, humble family;
小戶人家 a poor, humble family;

[小謊] fib;
撒小謊 fib;

[小惠] small favour;
好行小惠 take pleasure in making small favours;

[小雞] chick;
小雞咯咯 chickens cluck;
小雞嘰嘰叫 a chick cheeps; a chick peeps; a chick pips, a chick pules;
一窩小雞 a brood of chickens;

[小家子] vulgar, lower-class person;
小家子氣 appearing nervous in public – characteristic of people of low birth;

[小將] young general;

[小結] (1) brief summary; interim summary; (2) summarize briefly;

[小節] small matter; trifles;
不拘小節 defy trivial conventions; neglect minor points of conduct; not bother about small matters; not stick at trifles;
拘泥小節 punctilious;

[小姐] miss; young lady;
大小姐 little madam;
漂亮的小姐 bonny lass;
世界小姐 Miss World;
最上鏡小姐 Miss Photogenic;

[小解] make water; pass water; urinate;

[小徑] cart track; path;
山間小徑 defile;
山嶇小徑 precipitous and narrow path;
自然小徑 nature trail;
一條小徑 a path;

[小楷] regular script;

[小看] belittle; disdain; look down on; make light of; slight; think little of; treat lightly;

[小康] comparatively well off; fairly well-off; snug; well-to-do;
小康家庭 well-off family;
小康社會 well-to-do society;
小康生活 well-off;
小康水平 comparatively well-off level;
~達到小康水平 attain the well-off standard;
小康之家 a comfortable family; a family with a modest competence;

[小考] quiz; test;

[小量] a little; a small amount; a speck;
少量的水 a small amount of water;

[小路] cart track; passageway; path; pathway; trail; walkway;
抄小路 across lots;
偏僻小路 byway;
一條小路 a path;

[小賣] peddle;
小賣部 snack counter;
小賣店 store;
~一家小賣店 a store;

[小麥] wheat;

青稈小麥 bluestem wheat;
無芒小麥 beardless wheat;
有芒小麥 awned wheat;
圓錐小麥 duckbill wheat;

[小貓] kitten; kitty;
小貓喵喵叫 a kitten mews;
一窩小貓 a litter of kittens;
一隻小貓 a kitten;

[小妹] (1) little sister; (2) little girl; (3) young female servant;

[小米] millet;

[小民] commoner;
昇斗小民 the peck and hamper people; the poor people; those who live from hand to mouth;

[小名] one's childhood name;

[小腦] cerebellum;

[小鳥] birdie; dickey; dicky; a little bird;
小鳥依人 as a little bird rests upon a man — a timid and lovable little woman; lovely and pliant like a little bird;
一群小鳥 a flock of little birds;
依人小鳥 dolly bird;

[小牛] calf;
小牛皮 calfskin;
小牛胴體 calf carcass;
小牛咩咩叫 a calf baas; a calf bleats;
小牛肉 veal;
一頭小牛 a calf;

[小女] my daughter;

[小品] (1) inferior; low-grade; (2) short creation;
小品詞 particle;
小品文 essay; feuilleton;

[小妻] concubine;

[小氣] (1) cheese-paring; close; mean; niggardly; parsimonious; stingy; tight; (2) narrow-minded; petty; small;
小氣鬼 cheapskate; miser; niggard; penny pincher; scraper; scrooge;

[小錢] small sum of money;
小錢不去，大錢不來 if a little money does not go out, great money will not come in;
一點點小錢 peanuts;

[小瞧] look down on;

[小橋] foot bridge; small bridge;

[小巧] elfin; small and exquisite;
小巧的 dinky;
小巧玲瓏 dainty and cute; little and dainty; small and exquisite; small and pretty;

[小丘] hill; hillock;

[小曲] ditty; popular tune;

[小人] (1) base person; mean person; vile character; villain; (2) person of low position;
小人得勢 the tail wags the dog;
小人得志 a small man having greatness thrust upon him; a small man intoicated by success; villains holding sway;
小人國 Lilliput; Land of Pygmies;
小人無大志 little things amuse little minds;
小人物 blighter; cipher; cog in the machine; nobody; nonentity; small fry; small potato; unimportant person;
小人乍富，難免有禍 set a beggar on horseback and he'll ride to the devil;
卑鄙小人 louse;
濫伍小人 go about with low-down people;
市道小人 small-time trader;
先小人，後君子 specify terms clearly at first and use a good deal of courtesy later;
以小人之心，度君子之腹 gauge the heart of a gentleman with one's own mean measure; like a dwarf plumbing the heart of a giant with his midget sounding rod; like the knave who uses his own yardstick to measure the motives of upright men; measure the mind of an upright man by the yardstick of a knave; measure the stature of great men by the yardstick of small men; with the heart of the mean trying to estimate what's in the heart of the great;
遠小人 keep away from mean persons;

[小舌] lingula; uvula;

[小聲] lower one's voice; speak low;

[小食] refreshments; snacks;

[小時] hour;
小時候 as a child; during one's childhood; in childhood;
小時了了 clever and understanding when young; intelligent as a child;
小時偷針，大時偷金 he that steals an egg will steal a nag; he that ill steal a pin

will steal a better thing; he that will steal an egg will steal an ox;
安培小時 ampere-hour;
好幾個小時 for hours on end;
僅僅幾個小時 a matter of hours;
每小時 every hour;
~每小時都有的 by the hour; from hour to hour;
一個半小時 an hour and a half;
一個小時 an hour;
一天二十四小時 all hours;
學分小時 credit hour;
燭光小時 candle hour;

[小事] minor matter; petty thing; small matter; trifle; trivial matter;
小事聰明，大事糊塗 penny wise and pound foolish;
小事大訓 reprimand severely for minor matters; take like a Dutch uncle;
小事糊塗，大事精細 pay no heed to trifles, but be serious with big things;
小事拘謹，大事混沌 strain at a gnat and swallow a camel;
小事注意，大事自成 take care of the pence, and the pounds will take care themselves;
小事做不來，大事又不做 disdain minor assignments while being unequal to major ones;

[小試] make a casual trial;
小試鋒芒 display only part of one's talent; make a casual demonstration of one's capability;
小試牛刀 display only a small part of one's talent; make a casual demonstration of one's capability; show sth of one's ability; try one's hand at;
小試身手 exhibit part of one's skill; flex one's muscles;

[小視] belittle; despise; feel contempt for sth; look down upon;

[小叔] brother-in-law;

[小樹] sapling;

[小鼠] mouse;
叢林小鼠 jungle mouse;
關節小鼠 joint mouse;

[小數] decimal; decimal fraction;
小數點 decimal point;
集合小數 packed decimal;
同位小數 similar decimals;
無盡小數 infinite decimal; non-terminating decimal; unlimited decimal;
循環小數 circulating decimal; periodic decimal; recurring decimal; repeating decimal;
有盡小數 finite decimal; terminating decimal;

[小睡] beauty sleep; catnap; catch some Z's; forty winks; lie down; nap;
飯後小睡 postprandial nap;
日間小睡 power nap;

[小説] fiction; novel; story;
小説家 novelist;
愛情小説 love novel;
報告小説 documentary novel; reportage novel;
長篇小説 novel;
純文學小説 literary novel;
短篇小説 short story;
方言小説 dialectic novel;
諷刺小説 satirica;
記實小説 document novel;
科幻小説 science fiction;
科學幻想小説 science fiction;
垃圾小説 trashy novel;
歷史小説 historical novel;
連載小説 serial story;
廉價小説 dime novel;
冒險小説 novel of adventures; adventure story;
色情小説 sensation novel;
深受歡迎的小説 much affected novel;
睡前小説 bedtime story;
懸疑兇殺小説 whodunnit;
一本小説 a novel;
一部小説 a novel;
優秀的小説 a dilly of a novel;
章回小説 serial novel;
偵探小説 detective novel; detective story;
中篇小説 novelette;

[小題大做] a fuss about a trifle; a hair to make a tether of; a long harvest about a little corn; a storm in a tea cup; a tempest in a teapot; break a fly on the wheel; crush a butterfly on the wheel; fettle; fuss; great cry and little wool; make a big thing out of sth; make a fuss about a trifling matter; make a fuss over a trifling matter; make a long harvest about a little corn; make a meal of; make a mountain out of a molehill; make heavy weather of sth; make much of a little matter; make much of a trifle; much ado about nothing; raise a great fuss about trifles; stir a storm in a teacup; strain at a gnat; use a sledge-hammer on a gnat; too much of a little matter;

[小體] corpuscle;
骨小體 bone corpuscle;
關節小體 articular corpuscle;
環層小體 lamellar corpuscle;
球狀小體 bulbus corpuscle;
生殖小體 genital corpuscle;
牙骨質小體 cementum corpuscle;
柱狀小體 cylindrical corpuscle;

[小艇] skiff; small boat;

[小童] child;

[小偷] burglar; petty thief; pilferer; sneak thief; thief;
小偷小摸 petty pilferage; pick and steal; picking and stealing; pilfering;
一伙小偷 a mob of thieves;
捉拿小偷 apprehend a thief;

[小腿] lower leg; shank;
小腿過短 microcnemia;
小腿脛 lower part of the leg;
小腿痙攣 scelotyrbe;
小腿痛 scelalgia;

[小巫] minor magician;
小巫見大巫 be dwarfed; like a minor magician in the presence of a great one — appear far inferior in comparison; like a small sorcerer in the presence of a great one — feel dwarfed; no comparison between; one cannot be compared to the other; pale into insignificance by comparison; the moon is not seen where the sun shines; when the sun shines, the light of stars is not seen; when the sun shines, the moon has nought to do;

[小屋] cottage; hut; little house;
單層小屋 bungalow;
舒適的小屋 cosy little house;

[小溪] brook; creek; small stream; streamlet;

[小像] portrait;

[小歇] breath;

[小寫] lower-case letter;
小寫字母 lower-case letters;
小寫字體 lower case;

[小心] careful; cautious; pay attention to; take care;
小心的 chary;
小心燈火 careful of the light;
小心對付 manage;
小心火燭 beware of fire; careful about fires; guard against fire;
小心謹慎 buck one's ideas up; careful; cautious; circumspect; discreet; discretion; gingerly; prudent; with great care;
小心輕放 handle with care;
小心提防 look over one's shoulder;
小心為妙 one cannot be too careful;
小心行事 act cautiously; handle matters carefully; play it cozy;
小心眼兒 (1) extremely sensitive; narrow-minded; petty-minded; (2) miser; narrow-minded person; petty-minded person; stingy person;
小心翼翼 cautiously; in a gingerly fashion; play it safe; tiptoe; tread on eggs; very carefully; very gingerly; very scrupulous; very timidly; warily; wary; watchful and reverent; with caution; with great care; with kid-gloves; with the greatest care; with the greatest circumspection;
小心做事 do sth with care;
不小心 carelessly;
過馬路很小心 very careful when crossing the street;
加倍小心 make assurance doubly sure;
賠小心 make apologies;

[小星] concubine;

[小型] compact type; midget; miniature; minitype; pocketsize; small-scale; small-sized;
小型報紙 tabloid;
小型電腦 minicomputer;
小型公共汽車 minibus;
~小型化 miniaturization;
~小型化設計 miniaturization design;
小型企業 small enterprise;

[小休] short rest;
小休時間 comfort break;

[小學] (1) elementary school; grade school; high school; primary school; (2) philological studies;
小學生 primary school pupil; schoolchild;

小學校長 schoolmaster;
初級小學 lower primary school;
附屬小學 attached primary school;
高級小學 higher primary school;
一所小學 a junior school;

[小牙] denticle;
小牙症 microdontia;

[小鴨] duckling;
醜小鴨 ugly duckling;

[小羊] lamb;

[小引] foreword; introductory note;

[小影] (1) photograph; portrait; (2) shadow;

[小於] smaller than;

[小魚] fry;

[小雨] light rain; sprinkle;
下小雨 drizzle;
下着小雨 it's sprinkling;
一陣小雨 a spatter of rain;

[小月] thirty-day month;

[小賬] gratuity; tip;
不收小賬 no gratuities accepted;

[小照] portrait; small-size photo;

[小鎮] small town;
濱海小鎮 seaside town;
工業小鎮 industrial town;
歷史小鎮 historic town;
外地小鎮 provincial town;
一個小鎮 a small town;

[小指] little finger;

[小豬] piglet;
一窩小豬 a litter of piglets;

[小住] sojourn;

[小傳] brief biography;

[小篆] small-seal script;

[小桌] small table;
備用小桌 occasional table;
輕便小桌 occasional table;

[小子] buster; chap; pipsqueak;
傲慢無禮的小子 whippersnapper;
半大小子 boy in puberty;
好小子 attaboy;
混小子 little brat; little rascal;
窮小子 poor bum;
傻小子 silly boy; young fool;
小小子 little boy;

[小字] small character;
小字報 small-character poster;

[小組] group;
小組翻譯 group translation;
小組討論 group discussion;
小組委員會 subcommittee;
翻譯小組 translation team;
戲劇小組 drama club;

矮小 low; low and small; short and slight; short and small; short-statured; undersized;
愛小 go after petty advantages; greedy for small gains; keen on gaining petty advantages;
本小 small capital;
褊小 narrow; petty; small;
初小 lower primary school;
從小 as a child; from childhood;
大小 (1) big or small; (2) the degree of seniority; (3) adults and children; (4) bulk; dimension; magnitude; scale; size; volume;
膽小 chicken-hearted; chicken-livered; cowardice; cowardliness; cowardly; timid;
短小 short; short and small; small;
多小 many and few;
放小 tone down;
附小 attached primary school;
高小 higher primary school;
關小 turn down;
極小 minimum;
家小 wife and children;
較小 less; lesser;
嬌小 small and delicate;
口小 young;
老小 grown-ups and children; one's family;
量小 small mind;
渺小 insignificant; negligible; paltry; tiny;
藐小 insignificant; negligible; paltry; tiny;
脾過小 microsplenia;
妻小 wife and children;
器小 small vessel;
人小 small person;
弱小 weak and small;
瘦小 thin and small;
縮小 contract; lessen; narrow; reduce; shrink;
貪小 greedy for small gains or profits;
完小 elementary school; primary school;
微小 little; small; tiny;
細小 tiny; trivial; very small;
狹小 narrow and small;
纖小 fine; tenuous;
宵小 evildoers; gangsters and the like; thieves; thieves and rascals;
些小 (1) a bit; a little; (2) a small amount;
么小 diminutive; minute; puny;
幼小 young and small;
窄小 narrow and small;
中小 small and medium-sized;

足過小 micropodia;
最小 the least; the minimum; the smallest;
做小 be sb's concubine;

xiao
【筱】 (1) little slender bamboo; (2) little; small;
［筱妻］ concubine;

xiao
【曉】 (1) dawn; daybreak; (2) know; understand; (3) explain; let sb know; tell;
［曉暢］ (1) have a good command of; master; (2) clear and fluent; clear and smooth;
［曉得］ aware of; know;
天曉得 God knows; Heaven knows;
［曉光］ twilight;
［曉會］ realize;
［曉嵐］ morning mist;
［曉人］ (1) explain; tell; (2) reasonable person;
［曉色］ scene in the early morning;
［曉示］ explain; notify; tell explicitly;
曉示民眾 announce to the common people; instruct the public;
［曉事］ understanding and experienced;
［曉市］ morning market;
［曉悟］ realize; realize the truth; understand;
［曉霞］ rosy clouds at daybreak;
［曉行夜宿］ go one's way by the light of the sun and rest by night; start at dawn and stop at dusk; start early and halt late; travel at dawn and stop for rest at night; travel during the day and sleep at night;
［曉諭］ explain; give explicit instructions; tell;
曉諭天下 explain to the public; proclaim throughout the world;

報曉 a harbinger of dawn; announce the arrival of dawn; herald the break of day;
薄曉 around sunrise; dawn;
洞曉 have a clear knowledge of; know sth thoroughly;
分曉 (1) outcome; solution; (2) understand clearly; (3) reason;
拂曉 before dawn; break of day;
揭曉 announce; announce the results; make known; publish;
破曉 dawn; daybreak; first light;
侵曉 dawn; daybreak; early morning;
清曉 dawn; daybreak;
通曉 drench; familiar with; have a good knowledge; thoroughly understand; understand;
易曉 clear and intelligible; easy to understand;
知曉 aware of; know; learn of; understand;

xiao
【篠】 (1) a variety of bamboo with thin and short stems; (2) bamboo basket;

xiao
【謏】 (1) little; small; (2) induce;
［謏才］ limited talent;
［謏聞］ known only to a small circle;

xiao⁴
xiao
【孝】 (1) filial piety; (2) mourn; mourning;
［孝愛］ filial love;
［孝慈］ filial piety and parental tenderness;
［孝道］ principle of filial piety;
［孝悌］ dutiful son and respectful to one's elder brothers;
［孝服］ (1) mourning dress; (2) mourning period;
［孝家］ person in mourning;
［孝謹］ show filial piety for one's parents with great care;
［孝敬］ give presents to; piety; show filial respect for;
［孝男］ bereaved son;
［孝女］ bereaved daughter;
［孝順］ show filial obedience;
［孝思］ heart of filial piety;
孝思不匱 forever filial;
［孝悌］ filial piety and fraternal duty;
孝悌忠信 loyalty and filial piety;
［孝心］ filial piety; love and devotion to one's parents; love toward one's parents;
一片孝心 show one's filial piety;
［孝行］ filial conduct;
［孝養］ serve one's parents with all material needs;
［孝衣］ mourning dress;
［孝義］ devotion to one's parents and loyalty to one's friends;
［孝友］ filial piety and brotherly love;
［孝子］ (1) devoted child; dutiful son; submissive and obedient son; (2) bereaved son;

X

孝子節婦 filial sons and virtuous widows;
孝子賢孫 dutiful son; filial offspring; filial progeny; filial sons and good grandsons; pious scion; true son; worthy sons;
久病牀前無孝子 a dutiful son is never found at the bedside of one who is long ill;

不孝 infilial;
穿孝 in mourning; put into mourning; wear mourning clothes;
帶孝 in mourning; in the mourning; wear mourning for a parent or relative;
戴孝 in mourning;
吊孝 pay a condolence call;
掛孝 wear mourning clothes;
守孝 observe mourning for one's parent;
脱孝 pass the period of mourning;
謝孝 visit and thank friends for their presence at a funeral;
愚孝 blind devotion to one's parents;
至孝 extremely filial;
忠孝 loyalty and filial piety;
重孝 deep mourning;

X

xiao
【肖】 alike; like; resemble; similar;
［肖似］ look very much alike;
［肖像］ likeness of a person; portrait;
肖像畫 portrait painting;
［肖子］ filial son;

逼肖 resemble closely;
畢肖 bear a striking resemblance to;
不肖 unworthy;

xiao
【哮】 (1) breathe with difficulty; gasp; pant; (2) howl; roar;
［哮喘］ (1) asthma; (2) wheeze;
哮喘病 asthma;
~變應性哮喘病 allergic asthma;
~哮喘病發作 access of asthma;
過敏性哮喘 allergic asthma;
花粉性哮喘 pollen asthma;
痙攣性哮喘 spasmodic asthma;
特應性哮喘 atopic asthma;
外源性哮喘 extrinsic asthma;
心痛性哮喘 cardiac asthma;
心性哮喘 cardiac asthma;
心源性哮喘 cardiac asthma;
隱源性哮喘 cryptogenic asthma;
支氣管哮喘 bronchial asthma;
職業性哮喘 occupational asthma;

咆哮 roar; thunder;

xiao
【效】 (1) effect; (2) follow; follow the example of; imitate; mimic; (3) devote to; render a service to; (4) offer;
［效誠］ faithful; sincere;
［效法］ follow the example of; follow the lead of; imitate; model oneself on; learn from; take sb as a model;
［效仿］ follow the example of; imitate;
［效果］ (1) effect; effectiveness; result; (2) sound effects;
效果賓語 effected object;
效果間接賓語 effected indirect object;
效果良好 get favourable results; to good purpose;
效果審計 effectiveness audit;
效果狀語從句 adverbial clause of effect;
貶低…的效果 play down the effect of sth;
固着效果 anchor effect;
廣告效果 advertising effectiveness;
毫無效果 to no purpose;
教學效果 result of teaching;
累積效果 accumulative effect;
配置效果 allocative effect;
特殊效果 special effect;
音響效果 acoustic effect; sound effects;
［效勞］ bear a hand; can I help you; do sb a favour; give a hand; I am at your service; lend a hand; render service; what can I do for you; work for;
甘願效勞 exert oneself voluntarily in the service of another; glad to do sth for sb; glad to offer one's services; render readily a service to sb; serve willingly;
樂於效勞 glad to offer one's services;
為國效勞 render one's services to the country; serve one's country;
效犬馬之勞 at sb's beck and call; render humble services; serve one's master faithfully;
自願效勞 volunteer one's service;
［效力］ (1) render a service to; serve; (2) effect; efficacy; potence; (3) avail; effect; force;
發生效力 do the trick;

具有同等效力 equally authentic;

[效率] effect; effectiveness; efficiency; productivity;
效率很高 highly efficient;
成本效率 cost effectiveness;
低效率 low efficiency;
分配效率 allocative efficiency;
工作效率 work efficiency;
光行差效率 aberration effect;
降低效率 lower efficiency;
教學效率 teaching efficiency;
絕對熱效率 absolute heating effect;
絕熱效率 adiabatic efficiency;
勞動效率 labour efficiency;
能源效率 energy efficiency;
熱效率 thermal efficiency;
生產效率 production efficiency;
提高效率 improve efficiency; increase efficiency; raise efficiency;
天線效率 aerial efficiency;
投資效率 investment efficiency;
增進效率 develop efficiency;
總效率 aggregate efficiency;

[效命] (1) obey orders; (2) go all out to serve sb regardless of the consequence; pursue an end at the cost of one's life;
效命疆場 defend the territory of one's country bravely; ready to lay down one's life on the battlefield; serve on the battlefield;
為國效命 pursue the country's end regardless of one's own life;

[效能] effect; efficacy; efficiency; potency;

[效顰] blindly imitate with ludicrous effect;
效顰學步 copy servilely; play the ape;

[效死] ready to give one's life for a cause; render one's service at the risk of losing one's life;
效死疆場 die on the frontier; seek death or glory on the battlefield;
效死相報 I will pledge my life to repay you; I will reward your mercy with my service and I will not fear to die;

[效驗] desired result; efficacy; intended effect;

[效益] achievements; beneficial result; benefit; effectiveness;
效益成本比率 benefit-cost ratio;
效益工資 wage based on benefits;
效益現值 present value of benefits;
效益最優原理 optimal effect principle;
增進效益 increase economic returns;

[效應] action; effect; influence;
效應器 effector;
儲孔效應 hole storage effect;
衝穿效應 punch-through effect;
磁效應 magnetic effect;
~ 生物磁效應 biomagnetic effect;
後體效應 afterbody effect;
怪峰效應 ghosting effect;
鄰界效應 adjacency effect;
熱效應 heating effect;
順位效應 cis-effect;
溫室效應 greenhouse effect;

[效用] effectiveness; utility; usefulness;
比較效用 comparative utility;
基數效用 cardinal utility;
絕對效用 absolute utility;
實際效用 actual utility;

[效尤] follow a bad example;
以儆效尤 as a warning to others; in order to warn against bad examples; so as to deter anyone from committing the same crime; warn others against following a bad example; warn others against making the same mistake;
尤而效之 imitate in the wrongdoings;

[效忠] allegiance; devote oneself heart and soul to; loyal to; pledge allegiance; pledge loyalty to;

報效 render service to repay sb's kindness;
成效 effect; result;
等效 equivalent effect;
仿效 follow the example of; imitate;
肥效 fertilizer efficiency;
工效 work efficiency;
功效 effect; efficacy;
後效 (1) after-effect; (2) future performance;
見效 become effective; produce the desired effect;
療效 curative effect;
奇效 with miraculous efficacy;
神效 magical effect; marvelous effect; miraculous effect; wondrous efficacy;
生效 become effective; come into effect; come into force; come into operation; effective; enter into force; go into effect; take effect; valid;
失效 (1) cease to be effective; lose effectiveness; lose efficacy; (2) be no longer in force; become invalid; fall into abeyance; go into abeyance;
時效 (1) effectiveness for a given period of time;

(2) ageing;
實效 actual effect; substantial results;
收效 bear fruit; get the desired result; produce effects; prove effective; yield results;
殊效 marked efficacy; special efficacy;
速效 quick results; speedy relief;
特效 specialficacy; specially good effect;
投效 offer one's service to sb;
罔效 in vain; ineffective; to no avail;
無效 in vain; ineffective; invalid; null and void; nullity; of no avil; of no effect; to no effect; useless;
有效 effective; efficacious;
增效 (1) increase efficiency; (2) synergy;
奏效 effective; efficacious; get the desired result; have the intended effect; prove effective; successful;

xiao

【校】 college; school; university;
［校車］ school bus;
［校董］ (1) member of the board of trustees of a school; (2) director of a school;
［校隊］ school team;
［校風］ school spirit; school tradition; the prevailing atmosphere of a school;
［校服］ school clothes; school uniform;
穿着校服 wear one's school uniform;
一套校服 a school uniform;
［校歌］ college song; school song;
［校規］ school regulations;
違反校規 violate school regulations;
制定校規 establish school regulations;
遵守校規 abide by school regulations; follow school rules;
［校花］ campus queen; queen of the college; school belle;
［校徽］ school badge; school emblem;
［校際］ inter-academic; inter-collegiate; inter-school; inter-scholastic;
校際比賽 inter-school competition;
校際合作 inter-school cooperation;
校際活動 inter-school activity;
校際交流 inter-collegiate exchange;
［校刊］ school calendar; school magazine;
［校曆］ college almanac; school calendar;
［校名］ school name;
［校內］ inside the school; within the school;
［校旗］ school flag;
［校慶］ anniversary celebrations of a school;
［校舍］ school building; school premise;
［校外］ after-school;
校外活動 after-school activities;
［校訓］ school motto;
［校醫］ school doctor;
［校友］ alum; alumnus; old boy;
校友會 alumni association;
男女校友 alumni;
男校友 alumnus; old boy;
女校友 alumna; old girl;
［校園］ campus; school yard;
校園歌曲 campus songs;
校園文化 campus culture;
重返校園 back to school;
大學校園 university campus;
［校長］ (1) head teacher; headmaster; principal; schoolmaster; (2) chancellor; president; (3) vice-chancellor;
校長負責制 principal responsibility system;
校長職務 headship;
大學校長 chancellor; president; vice-chancellor;
代理校長 acting principal;
副校長 vice-president;
～大學副校長 vice-president;
男校長 headmaster;
女校長 headmistress;
一任校長 serve as a principal once;
中學校長 head; principal;
小學校長 schoolmaster;
［校址］ location of a school;

本校 our school;
敝校 our school;
大校 (1) senior captain; (2) senior colonel;
分校 branch campus;
復校 reactivate a school; reactivation of a school;
幹校 cadre school;
高校 college; institution of higher education;
軍校 military academy; military school;
留校 (1) stay at school during vacation; (2) retain to work in a college after graduation;
民校 school run by the local people;
母校 alma mater;
全校 the whole school;
日校 day school;
上校 captain; colonel; group captain;
少校 lieutenant commander; major; squadron leader;

鄉校 village school;
學校 educational institution; school;
夜校 evening school; night school;
院校 colleges and universities;
中校 command; lieutenant colonel; wing commander;

xiao

【笑】 cachinnate; cackle; chortle; chuckle; crack one's face; deride; giggle; grin; guffaw; have them rolling in the aisle; horselaugh; knock them in the aisles; laugh; laugh one's head off; laugh up one's sleeve at; lay them in the aisles; mock; ridicule; roar; rock them in the aisles; roll them in the aisles; simper at; smile; smirk at; snicker; taunt; titter;

[笑柄] butt; joke; laughing-stock; mocking-stock; standing joke; stock joke;
成為笑柄 butt of a joke;
免貽笑柄 so as not to leave a handle for ridicule;
時常提起的笑柄 standing joke;

[笑不可遏] cannot stop laughing; in an uncontrollable fit of laughter; roll with laughter;

[笑哈哈] laugh heartily; laughingly; with a laugh;

[笑呵呵] cheerful and gay; happy and gay;
面上笑呵呵，心裏毒蛇窩 have a face wreathed in smiles and a heart filled with gall;

[笑話] gag; jest; joke;
笑話百出 make many ridiculous mistakes;
笑話沒有人笑 a joke falls flat;
行內笑話 in-joke;
好笑的笑話 funny joke; good joke;
~ 不好笑的笑話 bad joke; terrible joke;
黃色笑話 naughty joke;
簡直是笑話 that's a laugh;
講笑話 break a jest; crack a joke; tell a joke; tell funny stories; tell jokes;
可別笑話 please do not laugh at my gift;
老掉牙的笑話 old joke;
令人反感的笑話 cruel joke; sick joke;
鬧笑話 make a fool of oneself; make a funny mistake; make a stupid mistake; pull a boner;
~ 鬧出笑話 make a fool of oneself; pull a boner;
惹人笑話 get laughed at; make a laughing-stock of oneself;
說笑話 crack a joke; jest;
下流笑話 smutty jokes;

[笑匠] comedian;

[笑劇] farce; opera bouffe;

[笑裏藏刀] betray with a kiss; cloak and dagger; conceal a knife in one's smile; conceal a sword in a smile; hide a dagger in a smile; there is a hidden dagger behind his smiling face; velvet paws hide sharp claws;

[笑臉] smiling face;
笑臉陪話 smile sheepishly and coax sb;
笑臉相迎 give sb a welcoming look; give the glad eye; greet sb with a broad smile; meet sb with a smiling face; receive sb with a smiling countenance; salute sb with a smile; smile one's welcome; welcome sb with a beaming face; welcome sb with smiles;
人無笑臉休開店 a person without a pleasant face should not open a shop; a person without a smiling face should not open a shop;
嘻皮笑臉 laughing in a frolicsome manner;
一副笑臉 a smiling face;

[笑料] jape; jest; joke; laughing stock; ribtickler;

[笑罵] deride; deride and taunt; mock and berate;
笑罵由他 let others say what they like;
笑罵由人 let others say what they like; let them talk and criticize all they like;

[笑貌] smiling expression; smiling face;

[笑眯眯] all smiles; beaming; smilingly; with a smile on one's face;
笑眯了眼 all smiles; grin all over;

[笑面虎] friendly-looking villain; a tiger with a smiling face—treacherous fellow; wolf in sheep's clothing;

[笑納] accept kindly;
尚希笑納 hope you will graciously accept;

[笑破不笑補] better a clout than a hole out;

[笑氣] laughing gas;

[笑容] smile; smiling expression;
笑容可掬 affable smile; all smiles; radiant with smiles; show pleasant smiles;

smile broadly; the face beams with a broad smile; with a charming smile;

笑容滿面 a face radiating with smiles; a smile lit up one's face; all smiles; grin from ear to ear; have a broad smile on one's face; with a beaming face; with a face all smiles;

不露笑容 keep a straight face; keep one's countenance;

臉帶笑容 a smile is on one's face;

臉堆笑容 one's face is wreathed with smiles;

臉浮笑容 one's face breaks into a smile;

一絲笑容 a little smile; a smile; a smile lights up one's face;

［笑聲］ laugh; laughter; sound of laughter;

笑聲鼎沸 bubble with laughter;

笑聲爽朗 burst out in peals of laughter;

笑聲洋溢 bursts of laughter keep floating out;

刺耳的笑聲 raucous laughter;

嗤嗤笑聲 peals of laughter;

一陣笑聲 a burst of laughter; a peal of laughter; a ripple of laughter; an outburst of laughter;

預先錄製的笑聲 canned laughter;

［笑談］ comic stories; laughing stock; object of ridicule;

［笑紋］ laughter lines;

［笑窩］ dimple;

［笑嘻嘻］ all smiles; grinning; look very happy; smiling broadly;

［笑顏］ crack one's face; smiling face;

笑顏常開 beam with smiles at all times;

［笑靨］ (1) dimple; (2) smiling face;

［笑一笑］ cheese; give a smile; say cheese;

笑一笑，十年少；愁一愁，白了頭 an ounce of mirth is worth a pound of sorrow; smiles make one young, worries make one aged;

［笑意］ smile;

一絲笑意 a faint smile; a ghost of a smile; a mere trace of a smile;

［笑吟吟］ smile happily;

［笑影］ smiling expression;

［笑語］ talk and smile;

笑語連天 talk and laugh merrily and incessantly;

笑語輕盈 chatter merrily; smile at each other as they whisper; talk and laugh merrily and lightheartedly; talk cheerfully;

笑語喧嘩 uproarious talk and laughter;

笑語盈盈 chatter merrily; smiling at each other as they whisper; talk and laugh merrily and lightheartedly; talk cheerfully;

［笑逐顏開］ a smile creeps across one's face; all smile; be wreathed in smiles; beam with pleasure; beam with smiles; give a broad smile; laugh cheerfully; one's face is beaming with smiles of joy; with a cheery smile;

暗笑 chuckle; laugh behind sb's back; laugh in one's heart; laugh in one's sleeve; laugh up one's sleeve; snicker; snigger;

鄙笑 jeer; mock; ridicule; scoff at; taunt;

慘笑 smile wanly;

諂笑 smile ingratiatingly;

嘲笑 banter; chaff; deride; flout at; hold sb up to mockery; hold sth up to mockery; jeer; jeer at; jest; jibe; joke; laugh at; make a butt of; make a mockery of; make mock of sb; mock; poke fun at; rally; ridicule; scoff at; scorn; sneer at; twist;

嗤笑 laugh at; sneer at;

痴笑 giggle; laugh foolishly;

癡笑 giggle; titter;

恥笑 mock; sneer at;

大笑 guffaw; laughter;

逗人笑 crack sb up;

發笑 laugh;

非笑 ridicule; sneer at;

乾笑 hollow laugh; laugh a hollow laugh;

格格笑 cackle;

憨笑 simper; smile fatuously;

含笑 grin; have a smile on one's face; smilingly; wearing a smile; with a smile;

好笑 funny; laughable; ridiculous;

譁笑 roar with laughter; uproarious laughter;

歡笑 hilarity; laugh heartily; laughter; mirth;

譏笑 deride; jeer; ridicule; sneer at;

奸笑 smile in a sinister way;

見笑 (1) arouse ridicule; (2) laugh at;

可笑 funny; laughable; ludicrous; ridiculous;

哭笑 cry and laugh;

苦笑 bitter smile; forced smile; produce a forced smile; wry smile;

狂笑 laugh boisterously; laugh wildly; roars of laughter; wild laugh;

冷笑 grin with dissatisfaction, helplessness, etc.; laugh grimly; sardonic grin; sneer;

賣笑 be forced to earn a living by prostitution or singing;
瞇着眼笑 smile at someone through half-closed eyes;
獰笑 grin hideously;
賠笑 smile apologetically;
竊笑 laugh in one's sleeve;
取笑 make fun of; ridicule;
傻笑 giggle; laugh foolishly;
訕笑 deride; mock;
哂笑 laugh at with contempt;
失笑 cannot hlep laughing; laugh in spite of oneself;
耍笑 (1) have fun; joke; (2) make fun of; play a joke on sb;
説笑 chat and laugh; kid; joke; talk and laugh;
談笑 obtain talk and laugh cheerfully;
騰笑 arouse laughter; seething; steaming;
調笑 make fun of; tease;
偷笑 chuckle;
玩笑 jest; joke;
微笑 smile;
熙笑 laugh happily;
嘻笑 laugh merrily;
嬉笑 be laughing and playing;
閒笑 pleasant chatter;
笑一笑 cheese; give a smile; say cheese;
言笑 talk and laugh;
一笑 a grin; a smile;
貽笑 make a laughingstock of oneself;

xiao

【傚】 copy; emulate; imitate; model after; pattern after;
［傚尤］ follow the example of a wrongdoer;

xiao

【酵】 leaven; yeast;
［酵母］ barm; leaven; yeast; zymase;
酵母精 yeast extract;
丙酮酵母 acetone yeast;
管底酵母 bottom yeast;
混合酵母 compound barm;
尖頭酵母 apiculate yeast;
酒精酵母 alcohol yeast;
［酵素］ enzyme;
［酵學］ zymetology; zymology;

xiao

【嘯】 (1) whistle; (2) cry or shout in a sustained voice; howl;
［嘯傲］ talk and behave in a carefree manner;
［嘯波］ whistler waves;
［嘯聚］ band together; gang up;
嘯聚山林 call each other and form a gang in the forest; go to the greenwood;
［嘯鳴］ (1) scream; (2) whistle;
［嘯聲］ sqeak; squeal; whistle;

海嘯 seismic sea wave; tsunami;
呼嘯 scream; whistle;

xie1

xie

【些】 a few; a little; a small number; a small quantity; some;
［些兒］ (1) a little while; (2) a little bit;
［些個］ a little;
［些微］ a bit; a little; slightly; thimbleful;
［些小］ a bit; a little;
［些些］ a little;
［些許］ a few; a little; a modicum;
［些子］ a little;

好些 a good deal of; quite a lot;
某些 a few; certain; some;
那些 those;
哪些 what; which; who;
險些 narrowly; nearly;
一些 a few; a little; a number of; an amount of; certain; some;
有些 (1) a few; some; (2) rather; somewhat;
這些 these;

xie

【歇】 (1) have a rest; rest; (2) knock off; (3) go to bed; sleep;
［歇班］ have time off; off duty;
［歇泊］ lie at anchor;
［歇處］ place to stay for the night;
［歇頂］ bald; get a bit thin on top; get bald as one gets older;
［歇乏］ rest after toiling;
［歇伏］ stop work during the dog days; take a vacation in summer;
［歇工］ knock off; stop work;
［歇後語］ end-clipper;
［歇會兒］ come up for air; rest a while;
［歇肩］ remove the load from one's shoulder for a rest;
［歇腳］ rest the feet after walking; stop on the way for a rest;
［歇涼］ enjoy the cool in some shade; relax in a

cool place;
[歇馬] (1) dismount and take a rest; (2) stop working;
[歇氣] stop for a threather or a rest;
[歇晌] take a midday nap or rest;
[歇斯底里] hysteria;
[歇宿] lodge; make an overnight stop; put up for the night; spend the night; stay for the night;
歇一宿 stay for the night;
[歇腿兒] (1) rest one's feet after a long walk; (2) rest at a place; stay at an inn;
[歇息] (1) have a rest; (2) go to bed; put up for the night; stay at an inn;
[歇閒] rest;
[歇晌兒] rest after lunch;
[歇歇兒] take a little rest; take an afternoon nap;
歇一歇 take a break; take a rest;
[歇心] peaceful and carefree; relaxed;
[歇業] close a business; go out of business;
關店歇業 close up shop and stop business; put up the shutters;
[歇嘴] shut up; stop talking;

安歇 (1) go to bed; (2) retire for the night; take a rest;
間歇 blank; dwell; intermission;
衰歇 tend to end because of decline;
宿歇 pass the night and rest;
停歇 (1) close down; stop doing business; (2) cease; stop; (3) stop for a rest;
消歇 become extinct; fade away; stop; subside;
小歇 breath;
休歇 (1) stop for rest; take a rest; (2) take a nap;

xie

【蝎】 scorpion;
[蝎貝] scorpion shell;
[蝎毒] scorpion venom;
[蝎子] scorpion;

蛇蝎 snakes and scorpions;

xie

【蠍】 scorpion;
[蠍虎] gecko; house lizard;
[蠍子] scorpion;

xie²

xie

【邪】 (1) depraved; evil; heretical; mean; vicious; wicked; (2) abnormal; irregular;
[邪財] ill-gotten gains; ill-gotten wealth;
[邪蕩] dissolute; obscene;
[邪道] depraved life; evil ways; heterodoxy; vice;
歪門邪道 crooked ways; dishonest practices;
[邪惡] canker; evil; turpitude; vicious; wicked;
邪惡的 baneful;
除邪驅惡 remove noxious influences and get rid of evil;
[邪法] black magic; witchcraft;
[邪計] conspiracy; evil schemes;
[邪教] cult; heathendom; heresy; paganism; perverse religious sects;
[邪譎] evil and dishonest; wicked and crafty;
[邪路] debauchery; evil ways; vice; wrong path;
引向邪路 be led into wrong path; lead astray;
走上邪路 follow the wrong track; go astray; take to evil ways;
[邪謀] evil scheme; conspiracy;
[邪媚] fawning; obsequiousness;
[邪謬] absurd; corrupt; evil;
[邪魔] demons; devils; evil spirits;
邪魔外道 crooked ways; heterodox;
[邪念] evil intentions; evil thoughts; wicked ideas;
[邪佞] evil person; mean person;
[邪僻] abnormal; heterodox;
[邪氣] (1) evil look; perversity; (2) evil influence; perverse trend;
[邪曲] crooked; wicked;
[邪術] demonic magic; sorcery; voodooism;
[邪説] fallacy; heresy; heretical ideas;
邪説暴行 depraved speech and tyrannous actions;
左道邪説 heresy; heretical ideas;
[邪祟] evil doing; evil things;
[邪偽] deceitful; false;
[邪心] bad intentions; evil intentions; evil thoughts; wicked ideas;
[邪行] evil deeds; wicked conduct;
[邪淫] lewdness; licentiousness; lustful;

辟邪 (1) exorcise evil spirits; ward off evils; (2) a fabulous animal with two horns;

不信邪 not believe in heresy; refuse to be misled by fallacies;
氛邪 evil air;
風邪 ailment asid due to cold or exposure;
奸邪 (1) crafty and evil; treacherous; (2) crafty and evil person
祛邪 eliminate evil;
驅邪 drive out evil spirits;
狎邪 (1) indulge in vice; visit a brothel; (2) improper;
壓邪 repress evil influences;
妖邪 monstrous; strange; weird; wicked;
正邪 the good and the evil;
中邪 be bewitched;

xie

【協】 (1) agree; agreement; (2) bring into harmony; common; coordinate; joint; united; (3) aid; assist; help;

[協辦] do sth jointly;

[協定] agreement;
協定關稅 agreed tariff;
協定貿易 agreement trade;
協定書 protocol;
~ 附加協定書 additional protocol;
~ 貿易協定書 trade protocol;
~ 最後協定書 final protocol;
協定稅率 conventional tariff;
保障協定 safeguard an agreement;
賠償協定 reparations agreement;
草簽協定 initial an agreement;
存貨協定 stocking agreement;
貸款協定 credit agreement; loan agreement;
訂立協定 enter into an agreement;
多邊協定 multilateral agreement;
附屬協定 collateral agreement;
恪守協定 stick to an agreement;
關稅協定 tariff agreement;
國際協定 international agreement;
海關協定 customs agreement;
海運協定 martime agreement;
和平協定 peace agreement;
合作協定 cooperation agreement;
~ 科學技術合作協定 agreement on scientific and technical cooperation;
~ 文化合作協定 agreement on cultural cooperation;
貨幣協定 monetary agreement;
貨易協定 truck agreement;
交換協定 exchange agreement;
價格協定 price agreement;
金融協定 financial agreement;
經濟援助協定 agreement on economic aid;
君子協定 gentleman's agreement;
口頭協定 verbal agreement;
臨時協定 provisional agreement; temporary agreement;
履行協定 fulfil an agreement;
臨時協定 provisional agreement;
貿易協定 trade agreement;
~ 互惠貿易協定 reciprocal trade agreement;
~ 民間貿易協定 non-governmental trade agreement;
~ 雙邊貿易協定 bilateral trade agreement;
~ 政府間貿易協定 inter-governmental trade agreement;
~ 政府貿易協定 government trade agreement;
~ 自由貿易協定 free trade agreement;
秘密協定 undisclosed agreement;
配額協定 quota agreement;
清算協定 clearing agreement;
區域協定 regional agreement;
商品協定 commodity agreement;
~ 國際商品協定 international commodity agreement;
書面協定 written agreement;
雙邊協定 bilateral agreement;
破壞協定 violate an agreement;
撕毀協定 tear up an agreement;
試行協定 pilot agreement;
雙邊協定 bilateral agreement;
停火協定 ceasefire agreement;
停戰協定 ceasefire agreement;
維護協定 maintain an agreement;
委托協定 consignment agreement;
行政協定 executive agreement;
移交協定 devolution agreement;
易貨協定 barter agreement;
意向協定 intention agreement;
永久性協定 permanent agreement;
友好協定 amicable agreement;
運費協定 rate agreement;
正式協定 formal agreement;
支付協定 payment agreement;
~ 雙邊支付協定 bilateral payment agreement;
追索權協定 recourse agreement;
遵守協定 abide by the agreement; observe an agreement;

[協方差] covariance;

複協方差 complex covariance;
廣義協方差 general covariance;
規範協方差 gauge covariance;
環境協方差 environmental covariance;
落後協方差 lag covariance;
偏協方差 partial covariance;
樣本協方差 sample covariance;
正定協方差 positive definiteness covariance;
總體協方差 population covariance;

[協防] help to defend a place;

[協和] harmonize; harmony;

[協會] association; institute; society;
出版工作者協會 publishers association;
登山協會 mountaineering association;
翻譯工作者協會 translators association;
翻譯協會 translation association;
房地產業協會 real estate association;
婦女協會 women's guild;
廣告協會 advertising association;
國際交流協會 international exchange association;
集郵協會 philately association;
家禽業協會 poultry industry association;
教育國際交流協會 education association for international exchange;
進出口企業協會 import and export enterprises association;
科學技術協會 association of science and technology;
科學探險協會 scientific expedition association;
旅遊協會 tourism association;
律師協會 bar association;
皮革工業協會 leather industry association;
企業管理協會 enterprises management association;
企業家協會 enterprenuers association;
期刊協會 periodicals association;
攝影家協會 phtographers association;
書法家協會 calligraphers association;
私營企業協會 private enterprises association;
外商投資企業協會 foreign enterprises association;
舞蹈家協會 dancers association;
戲劇家協會 dramatists association;
鄉鎮企業協會 rural and township enterprises association;
消費者協會 consumers association;
新聞工作者協會 journalists association;
野生動物保護協會 wildlife protection association;
藝術家協會 artists association;
音樂家協會 musicians association;
友好協會 friendship association;
雜技家協會 acrobats association;
質量管理協會 quality control association;
作家協會 writers association;

[協理] (1) assist in the management of; (2) assistant manager;
協理副校長 associate pro-vice-chancellor;

[協力] exert together; in cooperation with; join in a common effort; unite efforts; work in concert;
協力進攻 launch a joint assault;
協力同心 all of one mind; cooperate with one heart; make concerted efforts; of one heart; unite together in a common effort; with one heart; work as one man; work in full cooperation and with unity of purpose;
齊心協力 work together with one heart;
同心協力 all of one mind; cooperate with one heart; make concerted efforts; of one heart; unite together in a common effort; with one heart; work as one man; work in full cooperation and with unity of purpose;

[協商] bargaining; consult; consult with each other; discuss; negotiate; negotiation; talk things over;
協商對話 consultation and dialogue; consultation and discussion;
協商價格 negotiated price;
協商一致 reach unanimity through consultation;
共同協商 hold a mutual consultation;
關稅協商 tariff bargaining;
教育協商 educational bargaining;

[協調] adjust; bring about full coordination; bring into line; bring to harmony; cohere with; concert; coordinate; coordination; harmonize; integrate;
協調策略 corordination tactics;
~大協調策略 grand coordination tactics;
協調發展 coordinate the development;
協調人 coordinator;
協調委員會 coordination committee;
協調員 coordinator;
~合作協調員 cooperative coordinator;

不協調 mismatch;
感應協調 inductive coordination;
工作協調 work in unity;
破壞協調 spoil the harmony;
射擊協調 fire coordination;
身心協調 mind-body coordination;
稅收協調 tax coordination;
運動協調 motor coordination;
運價協調 tariff coordination;
支出協調 coordination of expenditures;
周期協調 periodic coordination;

[協同] cooperate with; coordination; join others in an undertaking; synergism; teamwork; work in coordination with; work with others;
協同動作 concerted action;
協同開發環境 cooperative development environment;
協同論 synergetics;
協同作用 synergism; synergy;
協同作戰 fight in coordination;
人機協同 man-machine coordination;
時間上的協同 time coordination;

[協議] (1) agree on; (2) agreement; deal; treaty; (3) discuss; negotiate;
協議範圍 scope of agreement;
協議工資 agreement wage;
協議離婚 divorce by consent;
協議利益 benefit of agreement;
協議書 agreement;
~海損協議書 average agreement;
協議數據單元 protocol data unit;
協議稅則 bargaining tariff;
協議條款 terms of an agreement;
包銷協議 exclusive sale agreement;
承包協議 contractor's agreement;
初步協議 preliminary agreement;
船員協議 crew agreement;
達成協議 arrive at an agreement; clinch a deal; close a deal; come to an agreement; conclude a deal; conclude an agreement; cut a deal; do a deal; make an agreement; reach a deal; reach an agreement; strike a deal;
擔保協議 security agreement;
締結協議 enter into an agreement;
訂立協議 conclude an agreement;
廢止協議 annul an agreement;
恪守協議 adhere to the agreement;
工資和工時協議 pay-and-hours agreement;
工資協議 wage agreement;
和平協議 peace deal; peace agreement;
金融協議 financial agreement;
口頭協議 oral agreement; patrol agreement; verbal agreement;
臨時協議 temporary agreement;
貿易協議 trade agreement;
簽訂協議 sign an agreement;
簽署協議 sign a deal;
商定協議 negotiate an agreement;
書面協議 written agreement;
談成協議 negotiate a deal;
特許協議 concession agreement;
庭外和解協議 out-of-court settlement;
違背協議 go back on an agreement; renege on an agreement;
違反協議 breach an agreement; violate an agreement;
選擇權協議 option agreement;
一項協議 an agreement;
有協議 have an agreement;
正式協議 formal agreement;
~非正式協議 informal agreement;
政治協議 political deal;
執行協議 carry on an agreement;
最後協議 final agreement;
遵守協議 hold to an agreement; honour an agreement; keep an agreement; stick to an agreement;

[協約] agreement; alliance;

[協助] assist; give assistance; help; help mutually; provide help;
大力協助 provide great help;

[協奏曲] concerto;

[協作] collaborate; collaboration; cooperate with; cooperation; joint efforts; work in coordination with;
協作精神 the spirit of cooperation;
協作能力 collaboration skills;
協作站 cooperative station;
協作中心 cooperation centre;
分工協作 share out the work and cooperate with one another; work in cooperation with a due division of labour;
互相協作 cooperate with each other;
跨校協作 inter-school collaboration;
商業協作 commercial coordination;
損害協作 impair the coordination;

貧協 poor and lower-middle peasants'

association;
調協 (1) harmonious; (2) mediate;
妥協 come to terms; compromise;

xie

【挾】 (1) clasp under the arm; hold sth under the arm; (2) bosom; embrace; (3) blackmail; coerce; exhort; force sb to submit to one's will; hold sb as a hostage; (4) harbour;

[挾持] hold sb under duress;

[挾仇] harbour an old wrong or bitter resentment; nurse an enmity;

[挾帶] (1) carry under one's arms; (2) smuggle;

[挾貴] presume upon one's blue blood;
挾貴自重 proud of being in high position;

[挾恨] bear a grudge; harbour hatred;
挾恨尋仇 harbour hatred and seek for vengeance;

[挾擊] attack from the flank; outflank;

[挾勢] presume upon one's influence; take advantage of one's power;

[挾嫌] bear a grudge; harbour resentment;
挾嫌報復 bear resentment against sb and retaliate; take revenge on the ground of a secret enmity;

[挾義誅伐] condemn sb in the name of justice;

[挾制] force sb to do one's bidding; take advantage of sb's weakness to enforce obedience;

要挾 coerce; threaten;

xie

【脅】 (1) flank; (2) force; threaten with force; (3) shrink; shrug shoulders;

[脅持] hold sb by violence;

[脅從] be forced to join;

[脅肩] shrug the shoulders;

[脅迫] coerce; coercion; threaten with force;
脅迫的 coercive;
橫遭脅迫 be unduly influenced by;

[脅下] armpit; under the ribs;

[脅制] coerce; control with threat of force;

威脅 menace; threaten;
誘脅 lure by promise of gain and threaten;

xie

【偕】 accompany; in the company of; together; together with;

[偕老] grow old together as man and wife; husband and wife grow old together;
偕老同歡 live happily together ever afterwards; live to old age together;

[偕同] along with; be accompanied by; in the company of;

xie

【斜】 diagonal; inclined; leaning; oblique; slanting; sloping;

[斜槽] chute;

[斜度] degree of inclination;

[斜槓] forward slash;

[斜暉] slanting beams of the setting sun;

[斜頸] torticollis;
假性斜頸 spurious torticollis;
間歇性斜頸 intermittent torticollis;
精神性斜頸 mental torticollis;
痙攣性斜頸 spasmodic torticollis;
迷路性斜頸 labyrinthine torticollis;
神經源性斜頸 neurogenic torticollis;

[斜路] evil way; wrong course; wrong path;

[斜睨] despise; look askance; look down on;
橫目斜睨 cross the eyes and look askance; leer; leer at;

[斜坡] inclination; incluine; slope; steep incline;
邊緣地斜坡 borderland slope;
大陸斜坡 continental slope;
路堤斜坡 embankment slope;

[斜視] askance; cast a sidelong glance; cockeyed; look awry; look sideways; skew; skew-eyed; slant; slant; squint-eyed; strabismus
斜視的 wall-eyed;
假性斜視 pseudostrabismus;
間歇性斜視 intermittent strabismus;
麻痺性斜視 paralytic strabismus;
目不斜視 not look sideways; look neither right nor left; refuse to be distracted;
內斜視 cross-eye;
~內斜視的 cross-eyed;
潛伏性斜視 latent strabismus;
調節性斜視 accommodative strabismus;
周期性斜視 cyclic strabismus;

[斜躺] recline;

[斜體字] italics;

［斜紋］ twill;
斜紋的 cross-grained;
花紋斜紋 figured twills;
破斜紋 broken twill;
山形斜紋 feather twills;
［斜線］ oblique line;
斜線符號 oblique;
斜線號 solidus;
斜線球 cross shot; diagonal shot;
~ 斜線球路 cross course;
［斜眼］ (1) strabismust; (2) cross-eye; squint-eye; (3) cross-eyed;sloe-eyed; squint-eyed;
斜眼偷看 see sb out of the corner of one's eye;
斜眼一瞟 look askance at; throw sb a sidelong glance;
［斜陽］ declining sun; setting sun;

背斜 anticline;
乜斜 glance sideways;
偏斜 deviation;
攲斜 incline; lurch; slant;
傾斜 dip; incline; lean; slant; slope; tilt; tilting;
歪斜 askew; aslant; crooked;

xie
【絜】 (1) ascertain; assess; measure; (2) regulate; restrain;

xie
【勰】 harmonious;

xie
【鞋】 footwear; shoes;
［鞋拔］ shoe lifter; shoehorn;
［鞋幫］ sides of a shoe; upper;
皮鞋幫 leather uppers;
［鞋撐］ shoe tree;
［鞋帶］ bootlace; shoelace; shoestring;
鞋帶鬆了 one's shoelaces are undonep
解開鞋帶 untie one's shoelaces;
繫鞋帶 tie one's laces; tie one's shoe;
~ 俯下身去繫鞋帶 bend to tie one's shoelace;
［鞋底］ sole of a shoe;
鞋底魚 four-lined tongue-sole;
［鞋店］ shoeshop; shoe store;
［鞋墊］ insole; shoe pad;
［鞋釘］ shoe nail;
［鞋跟］ heel of a shoe;
［鞋盒］ shoebox;
［鞋匠］ archer; cobbler; shoemaker;
［鞋扣子］ shoe buckle;
［鞋面］ instep; upper; vamp;
［鞋舌］ shoe flap; tongue;
［鞋刷］ shoe brush;
［鞋童］ shoeshine boy;
［鞋襪］ shoes and socks;
［鞋眼］ eyelet;
［鞋油］ shoe polish;
［鞋子］ shoes;
擦鞋子 clean one's shoes; polish one's shoes;
穿上鞋子 put one's shoes on;
穿着鞋子 wear shoes;
蹬掉鞋子 kick one's shoes off;
結實笨重的鞋子 clodhopper;
脱下鞋子 slip one's shoes off; take one's shoes off;
一雙鞋子 a pair of shoes;

便鞋 cloth shoes; playshoes; sandal; slippers;
冰鞋 skating boots;
補鞋 mend shoes; repair shoes;
布拖鞋 cloth slipper;
布鞋 cloth shoes;
草鞋 straw sandals;
擦鞋 shoeshine;
船鞋 deck shoes;
帶式鞋 T-strap shoe;
釘鞋 spikes;
冬鞋 winter shoes;
高跟鞋 high-heeled shoes;
高腰鞋 ankle boot;
厚底鞋 platform shoes;
戶外用鞋 outdoor footwear;
滑雪鞋 ski boots;
膠鞋 rubber shoes;
涼鞋 foothold; sandal;
露趾鞋 open-toed shoes;
慢跑鞋 logging shoes;
棉鞋 cotton-padded shoes;
男式鞋 men's shoes;
牛津鞋 oxfords;
女鞋 woman's shoe;
跑鞋 running shoes; track shoes;
皮鞋 leather shoe;
破鞋 loose woman; wanton;
淺口式鞋 court shoe; pump;
球鞋 gym shoes; sneakers; tennis shoes;
毯鞋 felt shoes;
靸鞋 (1) slippers; (2) strong cloth shoes;

上鞋 sole a shoe;
緔鞋 sole a shoe;
舌式鞋 slip-on; loafer;
雙帶式拖鞋 cross-band slipper;
雙色鞋 two-tone shoes;
素頭式鞋 plain toe shoe;
套鞋 galoshes; overshoes;
鐵鞋 skate;
拖鞋 slippers;
脱鞋 remove shoes; take off shoes;
外耳式鞋 casual shoe; lace-up;
蛇皮鞋 snakeskin shoes;
繫帶的鞋 lace-up shoes;
修鞋 mend shoes; repair the shoes;
繡鞋 embroidered shoes;
雪鞋 snowshoes;
一雙鞋 a pair of shoes;
一隻鞋 a shoe;
油鞋 waterproof shoes;
雨鞋 galoshes; rubber boots;
氈鞋 felt shoes;

xie

【諧】 (1) congruous; harmonious; in accord; in harmony; (2) come to an agreement; settle; (3) funny; humorous; jest; joke;

[諧波] harmonic;
電流諧波 current harmonics;
複合諧波 combined harmonic;
晶體諧波 crystal harmonic;
聽覺諧波 aural harmonic;
萬散諧波 discrete harmonic;

[諧附] compromise and follow;
[諧和] accord; agreement; concordant; harmonious; harmony;
[諧價] negotiate the price;
[諧劇] farce;
[諧美] harmonious and graceful;
[諧偶] harmonious couple;
[諧趣] fun; humour; pleasantry;
[諧戲] jest; joke;
[諧星] comedian;
[諧謔] banter; jest; pleasantry; wisecrack;
諧謔曲 scherzo;
語帶諧謔 speak somewhat jokingly;
[諧易] humorous and easy-going;
[諧振] resonance;
諧振器 resonator;
~ 蝶式諧振器 butterfly resonator;
~ 空腔諧振器 cavity resonator;
電流諧振 current resonance;
動態諧振 dynamic resonance;
雙峰諧振 double-hump resonance;
天線諧振 antenna resonance;
振幅諧振 amplitude resonance;

和諧 (1) melodious; tuneful; (2) harmonious;
詼諧 humorous; jocular;
俳諧 comic; satiric;
失諧 detune;
調諧 (1) harmonious; (2) resonate; syntonize; tune; tuning;
莊諧 sobriety with humour;

xie

【擷】 collect; gather; pick;
[擷采] cull; gather; pick;
[擷芳] pick flowers;

採擷 (1) pick; pluck; (2) gather;

xie

【攜】 (1) carry; take; take along; (2) help; hold sb by the hand; lead; take sb by the hand;
[攜抱] carry in one's arms;
[攜帶] carry; carry with oneself; take along;
攜帶方便 easy to carry about;
便於攜帶 easy to carry;
[攜眷] take one's family along;
攜眷同行 travel with one's family;
[攜手] (1) hand in hand; hold each other's hand; (2) cooperate;
攜手並進 advance hand in hand; join hands and advance together; march forward hand in hand;
攜手同行 go hand in hand; walk with arms linked;
[攜同] bring along;
[攜幼] take one's young children along;
[攜贓而逃] escape with one's booty; get away with one's booty;
[攜杖而行] walk with a cane; walk with a stick;

提攜 (1) lead a child by the hand; (2) guide and support;

xie

【纈】 (1) tie a knot; (2) silk with patterns or designs woven into it;

xie3
xie

【血】 (1) blood; blood relationship; (2) menses;

［血淋淋］ (1) bloody; dripping with blood; (2) bloody;

［血暈］ bruise;

xie

【寫】 (1) write; (2) compose; (3) depict; describe; (4) draw; paint; sketch;

［寫本］ copy; hand-copied book; hand-written copy; transcript;

［寫出］ draw up; write out;

［寫法］ style of writing;

［寫稿］ contribute to a magazine; write for a magazine;

［寫入］ write in;

［寫生］ draw from nature; paint from life; sketch;
寫生簿 sketchpad;
寫生畫 sketch;
外出寫生 go out sketching;

［寫詩］ compose a poem;
寫詩作畫 compose poetry and paint; write poems and do paintings;
寫詩作文 write poems and essays;

［寫實］ write realistically;
寫實主義 realism;

［寫手］ hack;

［寫書］ write a book;

［寫算］ write and be good at figures;
能寫會算 be able to write and use the abacus;
能寫善算 be able to write and be good at figures;

［寫信］ compose a letter; write a letter;
用中文寫信 write a letter in Chinese;

［寫意］ freehand brushwork in traditional Chinese painting; make an impressionistic portrayal;
寫意畫 ideal painting;

［寫照］ description; image; representation; portrayal;

［寫真］ (1) draw a portrait; portrait a person; (2) portrait; (3) describe sth as it is;

［寫字］ practise calligraphy; practise penmanship; write; writing;
寫字檯 desk;
寫字員 scribe;
揮筆寫字 drive a pen;

［寫作］ pen and ink; pencraft; penmanship; writing;
寫作風格 style of writing;
~ 雜亂無章的寫作風格 amorphous style of writing;

編寫 (1) compile; (2) compose; write;
採寫 write after interviewing;
草寫 running hand;
抄寫 copy; transcribe;
大寫 (1) capitalization; capitalize; (2) capital form of a Chinese numeral;
複寫 duplicate; make carbon copies; reproduce;
改寫 adapt; rewrite;
蓋寫 overwrite;
簡寫 simplified form of Chinese characters;
描寫 depict; describe; portray; represent;
摹寫 (1) copy; imitate; (2) describe; depict;
默寫 write from memory;
拼寫 spell; transliterate;
譜寫 compose;
繕寫 copy; write out;
手寫 take notes by oneself;
書寫 write; writing;
抒寫 describe; express; write of;
速寫 (1) sketch; (2) literary sketch;
縮寫 (1) abbreviate; abbreviation; (2) abridge;
淘寫 pour out one's heart;
特寫 (1) feature article; (2) close-up;
謄寫 copy out; transcribe;
填寫 fill in; write;
聽寫 dictate;
小寫 lowercase letter;
撰寫 author; write;

xie4
xie

【卸】 (1) discharge; unload; (2) remove; strip; (3) get rid of shirk;

［卸車］ unload from a vehicle;

［卸除］ get rid of; remove;

［卸貨］ unload goods;

［卸肩］ lay down responsibilities;

［卸任］ be relieved of one's office;

［卸下］ disboard; unsnatch;

［卸壓］ decompress; decompression.

［卸載］ break the bulk; disembark; download cargoes; dump; load-off; relief; unload;

［卸責］ shirk the responsibility;

［卸妝］ remove make-up and ornaments;

拆卸 disassemble; dismantle; dismantling; dismounting;
交卸 hand over the duties of office to one's successor;
推卸 shirk responsibility;
脱卸 shake off; shirk responsibility;
裝卸 (1) load and unload; (2) assemble and dissemble;

xie

【洩】 (1) discharge; let out; (2) drain; ejaculate; leak; reveal; (3) disperse; give vent to; scatter; vent;

[洩底] disclose a secret;
[洩憤] give vent to one's anger;
洩私憤 give vent to personal spite; vent personal spite;
[洩恨] give one's grudge; give vent to one's resentment; vent one's anger;
[洩勁] discouraged; disheartened; slacken one's efforts;
[洩漏] disclose; divulge; give away; leak; leak out; leakage; let out; make known; reveal;
煤氣洩漏 gas leak;
水洩漏 water leak;
通地洩漏 earth leakage;
外洩漏 external leakage;
油洩漏 oil leak;
真空洩漏 vacuum leak;
自然洩漏 natural leak;
[洩露] disclose; divulge; leak out; reveal;
洩露機密 leakage of confidential information;
洩露秘密 break the secret; disclose the secret to; glow the gab; blow the gaff; leak out the secret; let on; let out the secret;
[洩氣] (1) lose strength; (2) disappointing; discouraging;
氣可鼓而不可洩 morale should be boosted, not dampened;
[洩涕] come to tears; cry;
[洩瀉] diarrhoea; have loose bowels;

發洩 give vent to; let off; let out;
漏洩 leak;
排洩 (1) drain; (2) excrete; let off;
傾洩 fall in torrents;
宣洩 (1) drain; lead off; (2) get sth off one's chest; reveal one's pent-up feelings;
早洩 premature ejaculation;

xie

【屑】 (1) bits; chips; crumbs; odds and ends; trifles; (2) care; mind;

[屑屑] trifling; trivial;
[屑意] care; mind;
[屑子] crumbs;

不屑 disdain to do sth; feel it beneath one's dignity to do sth;
銼屑 filings;
煤屑 coal dust; coal splinters;
木屑 bits of wood;
碎屑 bits; chippings; fragments; parings; scraps;
瑣屑 trifling;
鐵屑 iron filings; metal filings;
頭屑 dandruff;
岩屑 rock fragments; rock waste;
玉屑 (1) broken jade; (2) snow; (3) exquisite writing;
紙屑 scraps of paper;

xie

【械】 (1) weapons; (2) implements; machinery; (3) fetters; shackles; (4) arrest and put in prison;

[械彈] weapons and ammunition;
[械鬥] fight with weapons between groups of people; scuffle;
[械繫] shackle a prisoner;
[械用] implements;

機械 (1) machine; machinery; (2) inflexible; mechanical; rigid;
繳械 (1) disarm; (2) lay down one's arms; surrender one's weapons;
軍械 armament; armature; arms; ordnance;
器械 (1) appliance; instrument; apparatus; machinery; (2) military weapons; weaponry;
槍械 firearms; weapons;
藥械 insecticide-spreading instruments;

xie

【渫】 eliminate; remove;

xie

【絏】 (1) reins; ropes for leading animals; (2) bind; fetters;

xie

【楔】 (1) wedge; (2) gatepost;

［楔緊］ wedge it tight;
［楔平］ wedge even;
［楔破］ cleave with a wedge;
［楔石］ keystone;
［楔形］ wedge-shaped;
楔形文字 arrow character; cuneiform; sphenogram;
［楔正］ wedge up;
［楔住］ put a wedge in to fasten;
［楔子］ (1) wedge; (2) foreword; preface; prologue;

xie
【解】 a surname;

xie
【榭】 arbour; kiosk; pavilion;

水榭 waterside pavilion;
舞榭 hall for the performance of dances;

xie
【懈】 inattentive; negligent; relaxed; remiss;
［懈弛］ relax;
［懈怠］ remiss; slack; sluggish;
［懈慢］ neglectful; negligent;
［懈氣］ slacken one's efforts;
［懈意］ inactivity; indolence;

不懈 unremitting; untiring;
鬆懈 (1) inattentive; slack; (2) loose; relax; slacken;

xie
【廨】 government building; public office;
［廨宇］ government office building;

xie
【澥】 (1) blocked stream; stop the flow of water; (2) another name of 渤海;

xie
【獬】 (1) Pekingese dog; (2) mythical animal which was supposed to know the difference between right and wrong;

xie
【燮】 blend; harmonize; harmonious;
［燮和］ harmonize; living in harmony;
［燮理］ adapt; adjust; harmonize; well-regulated;
燮理陰陽 adjust the dual power of negative and positive principles;
［燮友］ gentle; good-natured;

xie
【褻】 (1) underwear; (2) dirty; filthy; (3) intimate; (4) look down upon; slight; (5) acquainted with; familiar;
［褻臣］ intimate courtier;
［褻瀆］ abuse; blasphemy; disrespectful; insult; profane; slight;
褻瀆神明 blasphemy;
［褻服］ underclothing;
［褻近］ intimate with;
［褻慢］ show disrespect; treat sb with contempt;
［褻器］ chamber pot;
［褻玩］ treat with disrespect because of over-intimacy;
［褻狎］ close and unduly intimate;
褻狎輕佻 intimate with and act frivolously;
［褻衣］ underwear; undies;
［褻尊］ condescend; deign to;

猥褻 act indecently towards a woman; obscene; salacious;
淫褻 act indecently towards a woman;

xie
【謝】 (1) thank; (2) apologize; make an apology; (3) decline; (4) fade; wither; (5) a surname;
［謝病］ decline office on account of ill health;
［謝忱］ sincere gratitude; thankfulness;
［謝詞］ thank-you speech;
［謝恩］ express thanks for great favours; thank sb for his favour;
千恩萬謝 a thousand thanks; many thanks; be eternally indebted; give a thousand thanks; profuse gratitude; very profuse in one's thanks;
［謝過］ apologize for having done sth wrong;
［謝函］ thank-you letter;
［謝候］ express thanks and compliments;
［謝絕］ close one's doors; decline; deny oneself to; refuse;
謝絕參觀 decline all social parties; inspection declined; no visitors allowed; not open to visitors; visitors not admitted;
謝絕入場 no admission;

X

[謝客] decline to see visitors;
[謝老] resign from office on account of age;
[謝禮] (1) return present; (2) honorarium;
[謝領] accept with thanks;
[謝媒] reward a matchmaker;
[謝幕] acknowledge the applause; answer a curtain call; curtain call; respond to a curtain call;
[謝卻] decline; politely refuse;
[謝師宴] dinner party given by graduating students in honour to their teachers;
[謝世] die; leave the world; pass away;
[謝帖] letter of thanks; note of thanks; thank-you note;
[謝孝] visit and thank friends present at a funeral;
[謝謝] (1) thank you; thanks; (2) thanks for your payment;
謝謝你 thank you;
謝了又謝 thank again and again;
[謝信] thank-you letter;
[謝意] appreciation; gratitude; thankfulness;
表達謝意 express one's gratitude;
表示謝意 express one's thanks;
謹致謝意 please accept my sincere thanks;
聊表謝意 just a token of gratitude; just to show my appreciation;
深深的謝意 profound thanks;
先致謝意 thank you in advance; thank you in anticipation;
預致謝意 thank you in advance;
[謝罪] apologize; apologize for an offence; offer an apology;
謝罪禮 peace offering;
謝罪請宥 acknowledge a fault and beg for forgiveness;
當眾謝罪 apologize in public;

拜謝 express one's thanks; humbly thank;
璧謝 decline a gift with thanks;
不謝 it's my pleasure; not at all;
不用謝 anytime; no problem; that's all right;
稱謝 express one's thanks; thank;
酬謝 thank sb with a gift;
辭謝 decline politely; decline with thanks; reject with thanks;
答謝 acknowledge; express appreciation; reciprocate;
代謝 (1) supersession; (2) metabolize;
道謝 express one's thanks; thank;
凋謝 (1) with and fall; wither away; (2) die of old age;
多謝 grateful to sb; many thanks; much obliged; thank; thank you; thankful to sb; thanks a lot;
感謝 grateful; thank;
面謝 thank in person;
鳴謝 express one's thanks formally;
申謝 acknowledge one's indebtedness; express one's gratitude; extend one's thanks;
衰謝 old and desolate; wither and fall; wither away;
遜謝 decline humbly and modestly;
推謝 decline an offer on some pretext;
婉謝 decline with great gentleness and courtesy; politely decline; refuse with than
萎謝 fade; wither;
揖謝 bow in thanks;
致謝 convey thanks; express one's thanks; extend thanks to; offer thanks; thank;
踵謝 thank in person;

xie

【邂】 chance to meet; meet by chance; meet without prior engagement;
[邂逅] meet accidentally; meet by chance; meet unexpectedly;
邂逅相逢 an unexpected encounter; chance to meet sb; come across; meet sb by chance; meet sb unexpectedly; run into;
邂逅相遇 chance meeting; come across one another accidentally; come on by chance; encounter; meet by chance; run into sb; ships that pass in the night; unexpected encounter;

xie

【薤】 allium bakeri;

xie

【瀉】 (1) flow swiftly; pour out; rush down; (2) diarrhea; have diarrhoea; have loose bowels;
[瀉出] leak out; spurt out;
[瀉地] cover the whole ground;
水銀瀉地 split quicksilver covering the whole ground;
~ 如水銀瀉地 flow about in all directions; like split quicksilver covering the whole ground;
銀川瀉地 a bright moon lights up the ground; the moon casts its silver sheen

upon the ground; the silvery moonlight cascades to the ground;
月光瀉地 the silvery moonlight cascades to the ground;
[瀉肚] diarrhoea; have diarrhoea; have loose bowels;
[瀉痢] diarrhoea;
[瀉水] drain off water;
[瀉藥] cathartica; laxatives; purgatives;

奔瀉 pour down; rush down;
補瀉 reinforcing and reducing methods;
催瀉 purgation;
腹瀉 diarrhoea; have lose bowels;
流瀉 emit;
傾瀉 come down in torrents; flood; flow out; pour down; rush down;
水瀉 watery diarrhoea;
吐瀉 vomiting and diarrhoea; vomiting and purging;
洩瀉 have diarrhoea; have loose bowels;
止瀉 stop diarrhoea;

xie

【蟹】 crab;
[蟹粉] crab meat; minced crab meat;
[蟹黃] crab spawn; ovary and digestive glands of a crab;
[蟹柳] crab stick;
蟹柳釀蕃茄 crab stick stuffed in tomato;
[蟹箝] nippers of a crab; pincers of a crab;
[蟹肉] crab meat;
[蟹行] go sideways; move laterally;
[蟹爪] crab's claws;

扁塔蟹 flat-topped crab;
大閘蟹 Shanghai hairy crab;
鬼蟹 ghost crab;
海蟹 sea crab;
河蟹 river crab;
寄居蟹 hermit crab; soldier crab;
鋸緣青蟹 mud crab;
藍蟹 blue crab;
陸地蟹 land crab;
馬尾蟹 horse hair crab;
毛蟹 hairy crab;
沒腳蟹 a crab without legs; in a flurry — a supportless person;
面具蟹 mask crab;
螃蟹 crab;
青梭子蟹 blue swimming crab;
青蟹 blue crab;
軟殼蟹 soft-shelled crab;
沙蟹 ghost crab; sand crab;
食草蟹 shore crab;
梭子蟹 swimming crab;
太平洋大蟹 dungeness crab;
溪蟹 stream crab;
雪花蟹 queen crab;
椰子蟹 coconut crab;
一隻蟹 a crab;
硬殼蟹 hard-shelled crab;

xie

【瀣】 mist; vapour;

沆瀣 evening mist;

xie

【躞】 (1) proceeding; walking; (2) axis;
[躞蹀] proceeding; sidle along in mincing steps; walking;

蹀躞 (1) walk in small steps; (2) pace about;

xin¹

xin

【心】 (1) heart; (2) feeling; mind; (3) centre; core; (4) conscience; moral nature;
[心愛] fond of; love; sb dear to one's heart; sth dear to one's heart; treasure; treasured;
心愛的人 one's beloved; loved one;
~最心愛的人 light of sb's life;
[心安] calmness of emotion; carefree; peace of mind;
心安即福 peace of mind is a blessing;
心安理得 feel at ease and justified; feel no qualm; happy and at peace; have an easy conscience; peace of conscience; with mind at rest and conscience clear;
心安神閒 one's heart is at rest and one's spirit at ease; the mind is at peace and free from anxiety;
[心包炎] pericarditis;
癌性心包炎 carcinomatous pericarditis;
病毒性心包炎 viral pericarditis;
出血性心包炎 haemorrhagic pericarditis;
創傷性心包炎 traumatic pericarditis;
風濕性心包炎 rheumatic pericarditis;
積膿性心包炎 purulent pericarditis;
積水性心包炎 pericarditis with effusion;
局限性心包炎 localized pericarditis;

黏連性心包炎 adhesive pericarditis;
尿毒症心包炎 uremic pericarditis;
膿氣性心包炎 pyopneumopericardium;
膿性心包炎 pyopericarditis;
滲出性心包炎 pericarditis with effusion;
特發性心包炎 idiopathic pericarditis;
細菌性心包炎 bacterial pericarditis;
心肌心包炎 myopericarditis;
心內膜心包炎 endopericarditis;
腫瘤性心包炎 neoplastic pericarditis;

[心病] (1) anxiety; worry; (2) secret trouble; sore point; (3) heart disease; mental disorder;
心病還須心藥醫 no herb will cure love; no doctor can cure love-sickness; where love is in the case, the doctor is an ass;
白天見鬼一心病 seeing ghosts in the daytime — have secret troubles;

[心搏] heartbeat;
心搏過速 tachyrhythmia;
心搏失調 cardiataxia;
心搏停頓 cardiac standstill;
心搏停止 asystolia;
心搏徐緩 bradycardia;

[心不由主] cannot control one's mind; lose mental control; lose self-control; unable to control one's mind;

[心不在焉] absence of mind; absent-minded; in an absent way; in brown study; in the clouds; inattentive; jump the track; nobody home; one's heart is no longer in it; one's mind is not in it; one's mind is occupied with other things; one's wits go woolgathering; out to lunch; preoccupied with sth else; with an abstracted air; with one's mind wandering; with one's thoughts elsewhere; woolgathering;
心不在焉的 absent-minded; abstracted;
心不在焉地 absently;

[心裁] conception; idea; mental plan;
別出心裁 adopt an original approach; create sth that is uncommon to all; different from the usual pattern; have an unconventional idea; ingenious; original; think out sth different; try to be different;
獨出心裁 create new styles; original; show originality; out of one's own head; out of the way; unique in one's planning and design;
自出心裁 make a new departure; think up an idea of one's own;

[心腸] (1) heart; intention; (2) mood; state of mind;
心腸好 have a good heart; have a kind heart;
心腸軟 have a soft heart; soft-hearted;
~心腸軟的 tender-hearted;
心腸軟的人 bleeding heart; softie;
好心腸 good-hearted;
菩薩心腸 great kind heart; have a heart of gold; kind-hearted and merciful;
軟心腸 soft-hearted;
蛇蝎心腸 have a murderous heart;
鐵石心腸 a cold heart; a heart of flint; a heart of steel; a heart of stone; an unfeeling heart; as hard as a flint; as hard as a stone; dead to all feelings; drop millstones; flint-hearted; hard-hearted; have a heart as hard as stone; have a heart as hard as iron; have a heart of stone; iron-hearted; sweep millstones;
~一副鐵石心腸 have a heart of stone;
硬心腸 a heart of stone; hard-hearted;

[心潮] surging thoughts and emotions; tidal surge of emotions;
心潮翻滾 one's mind is confused and excited; one's mind is in a tumult; one's mind is racing; thoughts tumble through one's mind like tides;
心潮激蕩 thought surging in one's mind;
心潮澎湃 feel an upsurge of emotion; full of excitement; one's mind is flooded with memories; one's thoughts surge like the tide;
心潮起伏 one's heart seem to rise and fall like the waves; one's hopes rise and ebb; the tide in one's heart rises and falls;

[心馳] deep longing;
心馳神往 have a deep longing for; one's thoughts fly to;
身在心馳 the body is present but the spirit is far away;

[心慈] kind; kind-hearted; soft-hearted;
心慈面軟 kind heart and soft countenance; tender-hearted and unable to turn down others' requests;

心慈手辣 have a hand of iron but a heart of gold;
心慈手軟 faint of heart and hesitant in action; faint-hearted and hesitant in action; kind-hearted and irresolute; show mercy to sb; soft-hearted;

[心粗] careless; thoughtless;
心粗氣浮 not sober and cool-headed;

[心存魏闕] undying loyalty to one's own country while living on a strange land;

[心膽] (1) heart and gallbladder; (2) courage; guts; will and courage;
心膽俱裂 be frightened out of one's wits; strike terror into the hearts of; terror-stricken;
寒人心膽 make one's blood cold;

[心得] what one has learned from work, study, practice, etc.;

[心底] heart; innermost being;
從心底 deep down;

[心地] character; conscience; mind; moral nature; true nature;
心地光明 clear conscience; upright;
心地善良 good-natured; have a heart of gold; kind-hearted; one's heart is in the right place;
心地狹窄 have a heart that is very narrow; have a mean heart; narrow-minded; not of a generous disposition;

[心電] electrocardio;
心電場 cardiac electric field; cardioelectric field;
心電圖 cardiogram; electrocardiogram;
~振動心電圖 vibro cardiogram;
心電學 elecyrocardiology;

[心動] (1) palpitation of the heart; (2) become interested in sth;
心動描記器 cardiograph;
心動圖 cardiogram;
見錢心動 be tempted by money;
怦然心動 eager with excitement; palpitate with excitement;

[心毒] evil heart; wicked heart;
心毒口辣 vicious with a sharp, quick tongue;
心毒手辣 callous and cruel; cold-blooded; merciless at heart and in deeds; vicious and ruthless;
貌慧心毒 bear the semblance of an angel and the heart of a devil;

[心多] over-suspicious;

[心煩] annoyed; fretful; perturbed; piqued; upset; vexed;
心煩技癢 itchy and restless; the desire to display that in which one excels;
心煩意亂 be climbing up the walls; be crawling up the walls; confused and worried; confused in mind; distracted; get hot under the collar; get on sb's nerves; have a troubled breast; in an emotional turmoil; off one's top; perturbed; set sb's nerves on edge; terribly upset; with troubled and distorted thoughts;
使人心煩 nagging; niggling;

[心房] atrium; auricle;
心房刀 atriotome;
心房肥大 atriomegaly;
心房分離 atrial dissociation;
心房梗死 atrial infarction;
心房擴大 dilation of heart;
心房起搏 atrial pacing;
心房切開術 atriotomy;
心房收縮 atrial systole;
心房停頓 atrial standstill;
心房增大 atrial enlargement;
原始心房 primitive atrium;

[心肥大] cardiomegaly;

[心扉] (1) door of one's heart; (2) way of thinking;
封閉心扉 close one's mind to;
敞開心扉 open one's heart to;

[心肺] heart and lung;
狼心狗肺 as cruel as a wolf; brutal and cold-blooded; completely without conscience; cruel and unscrupulous; ferocious and diabolical in nature; ferocious and rapacious; heartless and ungrateful; rapacious as a wolf and savage as a cur; the heart of a beast; wicked-hearted; with the heart of a wolf;
沒心沒肺 inattentive; wanting in care;

[心服] acknowledge one's defeat sincerely; admire sincerely and willingly; have one's heart won; geninuely convinced;
心服口服 admit sb's superiority with sincerity; fully convinced; genuinely convinced; sincerely convinced;
令人心服 carry conviction;

[心浮] flighty and impatient; restless and

fretful; unsettled and short-tempered; unstable;

心浮氣燥 unsettled and short-tempered;

[心腹] (1) bosom friend; confidant; henchman; reliable agent; trusted subordinate; (2) faith; loyalty;

心腹大患 mortal malady;

心腹話 confidential talk;

心腹朋友 bosom friend; sworn friend; very intimate friend;

心腹人 confidant; trusted subordinate;

心腹事 innermost secrets;

心腹之患 mortal malady; the threat from within;

心腹之交 bosom friend; very intimate friend;

披露心腹 disclose a secret; tell one's innermost thoughts;

推心置腹 confide in sb; lay bare one's heart; open one's heart to; pour out all one's inmost feeling; put every trust in; repose full confidence in sb;

[心肝] (1) conscience; (2) darling; honey; sweetheart;

心肝寶貝 all in all to sb; darling; one's most beloved person; one's most beloved thing; one's sweet; sweetheart; the person that one loves most;

沒心肝 heartless; ungrateful;

剖心露肝 bare one's heart; open one's heart to sb;

全無心肝 absolutely ungrateful; completely without scruples; dead to all feeling; totally heartless; totally unconscionable;

痛徹心肝 cut sb to the heart — a deep grief;

抓心撓肝 upset; worry;

[心高] ambitious;

心高氣傲 proud and arrogant;

心高志大 have high ambitions;

[心廣體胖] a clear conscience contributes to physical well-being; a liberal mind and a well-nourished body; carefree and contented; fit and happy; hale and hearty; liberal in mind and stout of body; of wide girth and ample heart;

[心寒] be bitterly disappointed;

心寒齒冷 bitterly disappointed; cast a chill over one; chill the heart;

心寒膽怯 shuddering and fearful; trepidation;

心寒毛豎 the heart shudders and the hair stands on end;

令人心寒 cast a chill over one;

[心狠] callous; flinty; hard-hearted; heartless; unfeeling;

心狠手辣 hard-hearted and cruel; cruel and evil; wicked and merciless;

[心紅似火] one's heart is as red as fire;

[心花怒放] brimming with joy; burst with joy; cheer the cockles of one's heart; delight the cockles of one's heart; elated; feel exuberantly happy; gladden the cockles of one's heart; highly delighted; in an extremely happy mood; one's heart melts away; one's heart sings with joy; rejoice the cockles of one's heart; wild with joy;

[心懷] (1) cherish; entertain; harbour; (2) intention; purpose; (3) mood; state of mind;

心懷不軌 harbour dark designs; have evil intentions;

心懷不滿 be filled with resentment; feel discontented; harbour quiet resentment; nurse a grievance; store up resentment;

心懷不平 feel aggrieved; have a grievance against;

心懷不善 cherish evil thoughts; harbour ill intent;

心懷仇恨 nurse hatred in one's heart;

心懷敵意 have an enmity against; hostile to;

心懷惡意 have designs on; have evil intentions towards;

心懷二意 harbour disloyal sentiments; have two faces;

心懷鬼胎 conceive mischief; entertain dark schemes; have evil intentions; have sinister motives; have ulterior motives; with misgivings in one's heart;

心懷叵測 cherish evil designs; entertain rebellious schemes; harbour dark designs; harbour evil intentions; have an ax to grind; have an evil intent towards; have some dirty tricks up one's sleeve; nurse evil intentions;

[心慌] (1) flustered; get alarmed; nervous; panicky; shaken and perturbed; (2) palpitate;

心慌意亂 alarmed and nervous; all in a fluster; all in the wind; be confused and uncertain as to what to do; fall into a flutter; lose one's balance; lose one's presence of mind; lose one's wits totally; mentally confused; nervous and flustered; one's mind is in a tumult; shaken and perturbed;

[心灰] disheartened;

心灰意懶 a broken spirit; discouraged; disheartened; dispirited; downcast and disappointed; downhearted; extremely discouraged; feel disheartened; lose heart; one's heart dies within one; out of heart;

心灰意冷 dispirited; downhearted; feel discouraged and hopeless; pessimistic and dejected;

意冷心灰 discouraged; disheartened; dispirited; downhearted; greatly discouraged;

[心回意轉] a change of heart; alter one's mind; change one's mind; change one's views; come around; repent; start a new life;

[心肌] cardiac muscle;

心肌病 cardiomyopathy; disease of the heart muscle;

~產後心肌病 postpartum cardiomyopathy;

~充血性心肌病 congestive cardimyopathy;

肥厚性心肌病 hypertrophic cardiomyopathy;

繼發性心肌病 secondary cardiomyopathy;

~缺血性心肌病 ischemic cardiomyopathy;

~特發性心肌病 idiopathic cardiomyopathy;

~特異性心肌病 specific heart muscle disease;

~限制性心肌病 restrictive cardiomyopathy;

原發性心肌病 primary cardiomyopathy;

中毒性心肌病 toxic cardiomyopathy;

心肌挫傷 myocardial contusion;

心肌斷裂 fragmentation of myocardium;

心肌梗塞 myocardial infarction;

~急性心肌梗塞 acute myocardial infarction;

心肌梗死 myocardial infarction;

~急性心肌梗死 acute myocardial infarction;

心肌功能不全 myocardial insufficiency;

心肌功能喪失 myocardial stunning;

心肌心包炎 myopericarditis;

心肌炎 myocarditis;

~白喉性心肌炎 diphtheritic myocarditis;

~病毒性心肌炎 viral myocarditis;

~風濕性心肌炎 rheumatic myocarditis;

~過敏性心肌炎 hypersensitivity myocarditis;

~急性心肌炎 acute myocarditis;

~慢性心肌炎 chronic myocarditis;

~肉芽腫性心肌炎 granuomatous myocarditis;

~特發性心肌炎 idiopathic myocarditis;

~細菌性心肌炎 bacterial myocarditis;

~原蟲性心肌炎 protozoal myocarditis;

~中毒性心肌炎 toxic myocarditis;

[心機] craftiness; scheming; thinking;

白費心機 a sheer waste of brains; fail in one's designs; make plans to no avail; rack one's brains in vain; scheme in vain;

白用心機 fail in one's designs; scheme in vain;

費盡心機 beat one's brains about; cudgel one's brains; exert one's powers of thought to the utmost; exhaust all mental efforts; exhaust one's abilities; rack one's brains; rack one's wits; ransack; take great pains to; tax one's ingenuity;

徒費心機 hatch plots in vain; rack one's brains in vain; scheme to no avail; waste one's contrivances;

枉費心機 cudgel one's brain in vain;

[心急] impatient; short-tempered;

心急火燎 burning with impatience; in a nervous state;

心急口快 impatient and outspoken; outspoken;

心急情切 impatience and eagerness;

心急如焚 burning with anxiety; one's heart is torn with anxiety;

心急如火 afire with impatience; burn with impatience; one's mind is tense with a great sense of urgency;

心急水不開 a watched pot is long in

boiling; a watched pot never boils;
心急腿慢 the more impatient, the slower the movement;

[心疾] (1) illness caused by deep worries; (2) mental ailment;

[心計] calculation; designs of the mind; planning; scheming;
心計毒辣 one's clever schemes are poisonous and cruel;
工於心計 adept at scheming; calculating;
計上心來 a new idea flashes across one's mind; a plan comes into one's mind; a stratagem comes to mind; an idea comes across one's mind; bethink oneself of a good plan; concoct a plan; have a brainwave; hit upon an idea; one thinks out a plan; strike out a plan; stumble on a plot;
煞費心計 beat one's brains;

[心悸] palpitation of the heart;

[心跡] innermost feelings; real intentions;
表白心跡 bare one's true intentions; unbosom oneself; unburden one's heart;
表明心跡 lay bare one's true feeling; show clearly one's mind;
剖白心跡 lay bare one's true feelings; lay one's heart bare;

[心堅] one's heart is firm;
心堅如石 one's heart is as constant as stones; one's heart is firm as a rock;
心堅石穿 when one's heart is single-minded even rocks are riven; with a strong will power, nothing is impossible;

[心匠] a welding of ideas into plans;

[心交] close friend;

[心焦] anxious; impatient; very eager; vexed; worried;

[心絞痛] angina pectoris;
心絞痛恐怖 anginophobia;
~不穩定型心絞痛 unstable angina pectoris;
~遞增型心絞痛 crescendo angina;
~典型性心絞痛 typical angina;
~假心絞痛 pseudoangina;

[心勁] (1) idea; thought; (2) analytic ability;

[心驚] tremble with fear;
心驚膽戰 all of a jump; be deeply alrmed; quake with fear; shake with fright; tremble with fright;
心驚肉跳 be filled with apprehension; feel nervous and apprehensive; have one's heart in one's mouth; have the jitters to palpitate with aniety and fear; jumpy; make one's flesh creep; nervous and feel creepy and shivery; one's heart leaps into one's throat; sudder with fear; tremble with fear; trepidation;
膽顫心驚 one's heart beats with fear; strike terror into the heart of; tremble with fright;
膽戰心驚 be mortally frightened; be prostrated with fear; be terror-stricken; funky; in constant dread; in holy terror; in terror; nervous and jumpy; one's heart beats with fear; strike terror into the heart of; tremble with fear;
肉顫心驚 feel nervous and creepy;

[心旌] fluttering heart; unsettled state of mind;

[心靜] a mind free of worries and cares; calm;
心靜自然涼 so long as one keeps calm, one doesn't feel the heat too much;

[心境] frame of mind; mental state; mood; state of mind;
心境安寧 have a peaceful mind; have peace of mind;
心境不佳 in a bad mood;

[心淨] at ease; be cleared of worries;

[心坎] (1) bottom of one's heart; heart's chord; (2) bosom; dear to the heart;
從心坎裏 from the privacy of one's thoughts;

[心肯] acceptance in the heart; inner approval; inner assent;

[心孔] intellectual capacity;

[心口] (1) bosom; pit of the stomach; solar plexus; (2) one's utterance and what he really thinks;
心口不一 speak contrary to one's thought; speak one way and think another;
心口如一 faithful to one's words; frank and unreserved; honest and straightforward; say what one thinks; speak from the heart; speak one's mind; the mouth agrees with the mind; what one says is indeed what one thinks;

[心寬] carefree; feeling at peace with the world; not lend oneself to worry and

anxiety; open-minded; optimistic;
心寬體胖 broad-mindedness brings health; laught and grow fat; laughter will make one fat; liberal mind brings health; when the mind is at ease, the body becomes fat; when the mind is enlarged, the body is at ease;

[心曠神怡] carefree and happy; feel on top of the world; feel way above par; free of mind and happy of heart; of good cheer; refresh and gladden sb's heart; relax and happy;

[心虧] guilty conscience;
心虧理怯 have a guilty conscience and an unjust case;

[心勞] feel tired;
心勞力拙 feel tired in mind and exhausted in strength;
心勞日拙 fare worse and worse for all one's scheming; go from bad to worse for all one's pains; make tiring and useless pretentions;

[心理] mentality; mind; psychology;
心理保健 mental health;
心理變態 psychopathology;
心理病態 mental abnormality;
心理不平衡 have an unbalanced mentality;
心理測驗 mental test;
心理發展 mental development;
心理分析 psychoanalysis;
心理輔導 psychological counseling;
心理價值 psychological value;
心理健康 mental health;
心理能力 mental ability;
心理年齡 mental age; psychological age;
心理失常 aberration;
心理素質 psychological diathesis;
心理衛生 mental hygiene;
~運動心理衛生 athletic psychological hygience;
心理文化 psychoculture;
心理問題 psychological problem;
心理學 psychology;
~心理學家 psychologist;
臨牀心理學家 clinical psychologist;
~心理學系統觀 systems approach to psychology;
~比較心理學 comparative psychology;
~變態心理學 abnormal psychology;
~病態心理學 abnormal psychology;
~超心理學 parapsychology;
~成人心理學 adult psychology;
~大眾心理學 pop psychology;
~動物心理學 zoopsychology;
~動作心理學 act psychology;
~個人心理學 personal psychology;
超個人心理學 transpersonal psychology;
~教育心理學 psychology of education;
~能動心理學 activist psychology;
~社會心理學 social psychology;
比較社會心理學 comparative social psychology;
~圖書心理學 biliopsychology;
~應用心理學 applied psychology;
~職業心理學 occupational psychology;
心理訓練 psychological training;
心理壓力 psychological pressure;
心理要素 psychological factor;
心理醫生 head shrinker; psychiatrist;
心理因素 psychological factor;
心理優勢 psychological advantage;
心理語言學 psycholinguistics;
心理戰 psychological warfare; psywar; war of nerves;
心理障礙 mental disorder;
心理診斷 psychodiaghnosis;
心理治療 psychotherapy;
心理主語 psychological subject;
心理咨詢 psychological advice;
心理作用 imaginary perception; mental reaction;
矛盾心理 ambivalence;

[心裏] at heart; in mind; in the heart;
心裏暗笑 laugh in one's sleeve;
心裏悲痛 sore at heart;
心裏別扭 feel all wrong;
心裏不安 not feel at ease;
心裏沉重 weight heavily on one's heart;
心裏打鼓 feel diffident; have butterflies in the stomach;
心裏發毛 feel nervous; feel scared; panic-stricken;
心裏發悶 feel constriction in the area of the heart;
心裏煩悶 sick at heart;
心裏害怕 afraid at heart;
心裏很不安寧 feel rather worried;
心裏話 one's innermost thoughts and feelings;
~講心裏話 bare one's heart; open one's mind;
~說心裏話 speak one's mind;

心裏明白 clear in one's mind;
心裏難過 one's heart is filled with pain;
心裏盤算 turn things over in one's mind;
心裏拋不開 cannot put it out of one's mind;
心裏七上八下 agitated; perturbed;
心裏踏實 feel at ease;
心裏一怔 one's heart misses a beat;
心裏有鬼 be up for some trick; have a bellyful of tricks; have an ulterior object in view;
心裏有數 aware of sth without speaking out; know very well in one's heart;
心裏鬱悶 feel blue; feel depressed; feel low;
心裏越怕鬼越來 the more afraid you are, the more likely the devil is to come;
心裏扎根 strike roots in one's heart; take deep roots in the heart of sb; take root in one's self;
別往心裏去 hope you don't mind; just forget it; not take…to heart; think nothing of it;
放在心裏 keep in mind; bear in mind;
看在心裏 make a mental note of;

[心力] mental and physical efforts; mental power;
心力不足 cardianeuria;
心力計 cardiometer;
心力交瘁 both the mind and strength are worn out; mentally and physically exhausted; physically and mentally tired; tire oneself out both mentally and physically;
心力衰竭 cardiac failure; heart failure;
~充血性心力衰竭 congestive heart failure;
~收縮性心力衰竭 systolic heart failure;
竭盡心力 exert one's heart and strength to the utmost; exhaust one's mental abilities; put one's body and soul into a task; with all one's mind and energy; work to the best of one's ability;
極盡心力 put one's body and soul into a task; work to the best of one's ability;

[心連心] heart linked to heart; of one mind with; one's heart beats with the heart of sb;
聯了親，心連心 if you are related, your hearts are together;

[心靈] (1) clear; intelligent; quick-witted; (2) heart; mental; mind; spirit; spiritual; soul;
心靈感應 telepathy;
心靈美 beautification of mind;
心靈深處 the abyss of one's mind;
心靈手敏 clever in mind and quick of action;
心靈手巧 clear and deft; quick-witted and nimble-fingered; the mind is clever as the hands are numble;
心靈主義 mentalism;
福至心靈 when fortune comes, one's mind is alert — luck brings wisdom; when good luck comes, one has good ideas; when luck come it brings astuteness;

[心領] (1) understand without verbal exchange; understanding; (2) appreciate;
心領神會 appreciate sb's thought; enter into; know without being told; mental conception; readily take a hint; secret understanding; take the hint; understand tacitly;

[心路] (1) process of thinking; scheme; wit; (2) mindedness; tolerance;

[心亂] confused and perturbed;
心亂如麻 extremely confused and disturbed; have one's mind all in a tangle; have one's mind as confused as a tangled hemp; in a stew; off the hooks; terribly upset; utterly confused and disconcerted;
眼花心亂 one's eyes are not clear and one's heart confused;

[心滿意足] complacent; contented; feel very pleased with; fully contented; fully satisfied; in the pride of one's heart; perfectly content; rest satisfied; solid satisfaction; to one's heart's content; very contented;

[心迷] be confused of mind; puzzled;

[心苗] decisions; ideas; intentions; opinions;

[心明] one's mind is clear;
心明如鏡 one's mind is as clear as a mirror;
心明眼亮 able to see everything clearly and correctly; see and think clearly; sharp-eyed and clearheaded; with one's mind clear and eyes sharp;

[心律] rhythm of the heart;
心律不齊 arrhythmia;

心律過緩 bradyrhythmia;
心律失常 arrhythmia;
~慢性心律失常 chronic arrhythmia;
~青年期心律失常 juvenile arrhythmia;
~永久性心律失常 perpetual arrhtythmia;

［心慕手追］ imitate laboriously; what one's heart admires the hands follow;

［心目］ inward eye; mental view; mind; mind's eye;
心目中 (1) in one's eye; in one's heart; in one's mental view; in one's mind; in one's mind's eye; (2) in one's memory;
~心目中最主要的 uppermost in one's mind;
奪人心目 grasp one's heart and dazzle one's eyes;
養目潤心 please the eye and gladden the heart — good to see or hear;
以娛心目 amuse oneself;

［心內膜］ endocardium;
心內膜病 endocardiopathy;
心內膜心包炎 endopericarditis;
心內膜炎 endocarditis;
~膿毒性心內膜炎 septic endocarditis;
心內膜硬化 endocardial sclerosis;

［心皮］ carpel; carpellum;
心皮柄 carpophore;
心皮化 carpellody;
心皮序列 carpellotaxy;
瓣狀心皮 valve carpel;
單心皮 solitary carpel;
假瓣心皮 pseudovalve carpel;
結實心皮 solid carpel;
~半結實心皮 semi-solid carpel;

［心平氣和］ become gentle with; calmly and relaxedly; even-tempered and goodhumoured; in a calm mood; in a placid mood; in cold blood; in one's sober senses; of a peaceful disposition; peace of mind; without losing one's temper;

［心氣］ (1) intention; motive; (2) frame of mind; state of mind; (3) ambition; aspiration;

［心虔意誠］ with pious wishes;

［心竅］ very b capacity for clear thinking;
心竅玲瓏 very bright-minded;
財迷心竅 be obsessed by a lust for wealth;
鬼迷心竅 be obsessed; be possessed;
迷了心竅 be captivated by; be obsessed with; be possessed with; under an obsession of;
錢迷心竅 be blinded by lust for gain;
權迷心竅 be obsessed by a lust for power; power-happy;

［心情］ feeling tone; frame of mind; mood; state of mind;
心情暗淡 dismal mood;
心情悲傷 in a sorrowful mood;
心情不佳 feel out of one's plate; in bad mood; in low spirits;
心情暢快 have ease of mind;
心情沉悶 feel depressed;
心情沉重 heavy heart; one's heart sinks; with a heavy heart;
心情複雜 mixed emotions; mixed feelings;
心情好 chirpy; in a good mood;
心情歡暢 be filled with joy; in high spirits;
心情豁達 in an open-minded frame of mind; liberal in affection;
心情激動 excited; thrilled;
心情激憤 be filled with indignation;
心情緊張 nervous;
心情舒暢 a mind at ease; ease of mind; enjoy ease of mind; feel happy; good-humoured; have one's mind at ease; in good humour; in a merry mood;
心情紊亂 affective disroders;
心情壓抑 feel constrained;
心情愉快 have a light heart; in a cheerful frame of mind; in a good mood;
心情愉悦 in a cheerful frame of mind; in a good mood;
心情沮喪 depressed;
昂奮的心情 buoyant spirit;
改變心情 change one's mood;
好心情 a good mood;
沒有心情 in no mood for sth;
愉快的心情 beatific state of mind;

［心曲］ (1) heart; innermost being; mind; (2) sth weighing on one's mind;
亂人心曲 disturb the complexities of the mental processes;

［心去人難留］ when one's heart is gone, it is difficult to keep his body;

［心如］ one's heart is like…;
心如冰炭 heartless and cold as ince;
心如潮湧 one's thoughts surge like the

tide;

心如刀刺 feel as if a knife were piercing one's heart; feel as if one's heart were pierced by daggers; feel as though a knife were sticking into one's heart;

心如刀割 feel as if a knife were piercing one's heart; feel as if one's heart were stabbed by a knife; feel as though a knife has been plunged into one's heart; feel greatly distressed like one's heart usffers a knife cut; like a dagger cuts deep into one's heart; one's heart contracts in pain as if stabbed by a knife; one's heart feels as if transfixed with a dagger;

X

心如刀割，淚如雨下 one's heart breaks and one's tears cascade;

心如刀絞 feel as if a knife were being twisted in one's heart;

心如刀扎 one's heart seems pierced with a knife;

心如滾潮 like tossing waves in one's heart; one's mind is in a tumult;

心如火焚 burning with impatience; one's heart is afire; torn by anxiety;

心如古井 call forth no response in sb's breast; one's heart is as tranquil as an old well;

心如金石堅 the heart is as constant as metals and stones are durable;

心如纍塊 be weighed down by anxious cares;

心如蛇蝎 have the heart of a devil; one's heart is as poisonous as any viper or scorpion;

心如石沉 one's heart sinks like a stone;

心如死灰 one's heart is like dead ashes — utterly dispirited;

心如鐵石 have a heart of stone; keep one's heart as hard as the nether millstone; one's heart is like iron or stone; with a steelcold heart;

心如懸旌 one's heart flutters like a pennant in the wind;

心如懸鐘 the heart is like a hanging bell;

心如針扎 feel as if needles were pricking one's heart; feel greatly distressed as though one's heart pricks;

心如止水 a mind tranquil as still water; one's mind settles as still water; the heart is like still water;

[心軟] kind-hearted; soft-hearted; tender-hearted;

趁人心軟 impose upon a person's kindness;

口兇心軟 one's bark is worse than one's bite;

[心善] kind heart; kind-hearted;

心善面冷 has a heart of gold although one seldom smiles;

形醜心善 have a rough look but a good heart;

[心上] at heart; in one's heart; in one's mind; in the heart;

心上人 lover; sweetheart;

別把它放在心上 don't give it another thought;

掛在心上 bear in mind; have on one's mind; have sth at heart; keep sth in mind;

[心神] mood; state of mind;

心神不安 feel perturbed; feel uneasy; fidgety; have the fidgets; ill at ease; not to feel easy in one's mind; suffer from the fidgets;

心神不定 a confused state of mind; a restless mood; agitated; an unstable mood; anxious and preoccupied; distracted; feel restless; have no peace of mind; ill at ease; in a state of discomposure; indisposed; out of sorts; wandering in thought;

心神不羈 difficult to concentrate one's mind on sth; with one's mind running wild;

心神顛倒 go off into raptures; utterly confused;

心神恍惚 ill at ease and full of dread; in a trance; perturned in mind;

蕩人心神 play havoc with one's feelings;

[心聲] aspirations; heartfelt wishes; intentions; the heart's desire; thinking; thoughts;

言為心聲 as a man's heart is, so does he speak; as the inner life is, so will be the language; one's words reflect one's thinking; speech is the picture of the mind; speech is the voice of one's heart; what the heart thinks the tongue speaks; words are echoes of the heart; words are the voice of the mind; words express what is in the heart;

一吐心聲 unbosom;

[心盛] enthusiastic; in high spirits;

[心實] honest; truthful;

[心事] a load on one's mind; secrets in one's mind; sth weighing on one's mind; worry;

心事重重 be cumbered with care; be laden with anxiety; be preoccupied by some troubles; be weighed down with care; gloomy with worry; sth weighs heavily on one's mind; there are too many problems on one's mind; with a heavy heart;

説明心事 disclose one's mind;

吐露心事 pour out one's heart;

一樁心事 a matter on one's mind;

~了卻一樁心事 take a load off one's mind;

一宗心事 a matter that worries one;

有心事 have a weight on one's mind;

[心室] ventricle;

心室肥大 ventricular hypertrophy;

心室功能 ventricular function;

單心室 single ventricle;

右心室 right ventricle;

左心室 left ventricle;

[心手] mind and hand;

心手相應 as the mind wills, the hand responds; at one's finger's end; mind and hand in accord;

得心應手 (1) in a masterly way; what the heart wishes one's hand accomplish; with facility; with high proficiency; (2) handy; serviceable;

[心術] designs; intentions; schemes;

心術不正 be corrupted at heart; harbour evil intentions; lack of sincerity; not have one's heart in the right place; one's intention is not right;

[心思] (1) ideas; intelligence; thoughts; (2) thinking; thoughts; (3) mood; state of mind;

費心思 mental exertion;

~白費心思 bother one's head for nothing; make futile efforts; rack one's brains in vain;

花心思 exertion;

挖空心思 rack one's brains;

剜空心思 exhaust one's wits;

想心思 contemplate; ponder;

一門心思 have one's heart set on;

用心思 do a lot of thinking; think hard;

再運心思 reconsider;

[心死] abandoned; heartless; in a state of stupour;

哀莫大於心死 despair is the greatest sorrow; he begins to die that quits his desires; no sorrow is greater than despair; nothing gives greater cause for sorrow than despair; nothing gives so much cause for sorrow as the death of one's heart; nothing is more lamentable than a dead heart; the greatest pity is the death of the human heart; there is no poverty like the poverty of spirit; there is nothing worse than apathy; tine heart, tine all;

[心酸] feel sad; grief-stricken; grieved; heartsick; heartsore; sadden;

令人心酸 cause sb's heart to ache; make sb want to cry out of pity;

[心算] do sums in one's head; mental arithmetic;

心算能力 ability of mental arithmetic;

[心髓] innermost beings; innermost feelings;

[心碎] broken heart; heartbreak; heart-broken;

令人心碎 break a person's heart; break sb's heartstrings; break the heartstrings of sb; heart-breaking; heart-rending; tear sb's heart;

[心態] mentality;

[心疼] (1) love dearly; (2) feel sorry; make one's heart ache; one's heart bleeds;

[心田] (1) one's heart; (2) one's disposition; one's intentions;

[心恬氣和] a pleasant peaceful frame of mind;

[心跳] (1) heartbeat; (2) palpitation of the heart caused by fear or anxiety;

氣吁心跳 out of breath and with a fast-beating heart;

[心痛] (1) cardiac pain; (2) feel the pangs of the heart;

心痛徹背 chest pain radiating to the back;

心痛如絞 have an excruciating pain in the chest;

心痛欲碎 one's heart is breaking and aches so badly with sorrow;

令人心痛 heartrending;

[心投意合] hit it off perfectly; in perfect agreement; in rapport; of the same opinion;

[心頭] (1) intentions; the heart; the mind; (2) the hearts of animals;

心頭恨 ranking hatred;
心頭火起 angry; flare up in anger; infuriated; one's heart burns; one's mind is inflamed with passion;
心頭肉 the apple of one's eye; sb dear to the heart; sth dear to the heart;
心頭石落 as if a heavy stone has been removed from the pit of one's stomach;
心頭小鹿 one's heart beats wildly; one's heart goes pit-a-pat; with a throbbing heart;
喜在心頭 feel joyous; feel jubilant;
~笑在臉上，喜在心頭 with a smile on one's face and joy in one's heart;
湧向心頭 crowd on one's mind; rise in the mind; well up in one's mind;

[心為形役] the heart is being put to toil by the body;

[心窩] (1) in one's heart; (2) region between the ribs;

[心無二用] one cannot keep one's mind on two things at the same time; one can't do two things at once; one should concentrate one's attention on one thing at a time; one's mind could not work on two things together; the mind cannot be devoted to two things at one time;

[心細] careful; cautious;
才大心細 have a great talent and an attentive mind;

[心下垂] cardiophtosia;

[心弦] heartstrings; the heart's cord;
觸動心弦 touch a string; touch sb on a tender string; touch the right chord; tug at sb's heart; tug at sb's heartstrings;
動人心弦 deeply moving; pull at sb's heartstrings; rouse one's tender emotions; stir up one's inmost feelings; strike a chord in the heart of sb; strike a deep chord in the heart of sb; touch sb's feeling; touch the right chord; tug at one's heartstrings;
扣人心弦 carry one away; cliff-hanging; grip the hearts of sb; heartthrilling; play on sb's heartstrings; pull at sb's heartstrings; soul-stirring; thrilling; touch one's feelings; touch sb to the heart; tug at one's heartstrings;
~扣人心弦的 gripping;

[心險] crafty and evil-minded;

[心香] devotion; piety; sincerity;

[心想] expect; figure; think;

[心象] mental image;

[心心] mind acts on mind;
心心念念 anxiously longing for; keep in mind always; keep thinking about; remember always;
心心相連 be closely attached to each other; be linked in their hearts;
心心相印 a complete meeting of minds; all of one mind; both of the same mind; have identical feelings and views; have mutual affinity; hearts and feelings find a perfect response; in complete rapport; in mutual understanding; in perfect harmony with; kindred spirits; mind acts on mind; mutually attached to each other; share the feelings of; share the same feelings; the communion of heart with heart; their love is reciprocal;
將心比心 compare one's feelings with another's; feel for others; have to see things through other people's eyes; judge other person's feeling by one's own;
以心傳心，不立文字 the Buddhist dharma is taught through the mind, not through the written word;
以心換心 confidence begets confidence;

[心性] constitution of the mind; disposition; temperament;
明心見性 familiar with sb's disposition; find one's true self; understand the mind and see the disposition;

[心胸] ambition; aspiration; breadth of mind; capacity for tolerance;
心胸開闊 capacious;
~心胸開闊的人 person of capacious mind;
心胸豁達 broad-minded; with a great heart;
心胸開闊 broad-minded; unprejudiced;
心胸狹窄 narrow-minded; small-minded; intolerant;
開拓心胸 broaden one's mind;

[心秀] intelligent without seeming so;

[心虛] (1) afraid of being found out; have a guilty conscience; with a guilty conscience; (2) diffident; lacking in self-confidence;

心虛膽怯 apprehensive and cowardly; have a guilty conscience;

理虧心虛 feel apprehensive because one is in the wrong;

做賊心虛 a guilty conscience is a self-accuser; a guilty conscience feels continual fear; a guilty conscience is evermore suspicious and full of fear; a guilty conscience is a self-accuser; a guilty conscience is ever more suspicious and full of fear; have a guilty conscience; he that has a great nose thinks everybody is speaking of it; have a guilty conscience;

[心許] acclaim without words; tacit acceptance; tact approval;

心許目成 convey love by exchanging longing glances;

[心緒] mood; state of mind;

心緒不寧 flutter; in a disturbed state of mind; in a flutter; in a state of agitation; one's state of mind is not at ease;

心緒沸騰 one's heart is in a tumult;

心緒煩亂 emotionally upset; in an emotional turmoil;

心緒繚亂 in a confused state of mind;

[心懸兩地] one's mind is concerned within two places; have worries at two places at the same time;

[心血] painstaking care; painstaking efforts;

心血管學 cardiovasology;

心血來潮 a whim; be prompted by a sudden impulse; be seized by a whim; have a brainstorm; hit upon a sudden idea; in an impulsive moment; on the spur of the moment;

~心血來潮，忘乎所以 be carried away by a sudden impulse; be carried away by one's whims and act recklessly; forget oneself in a moment of excitement; forget oneself in an impulsive moment; lose one's head in a moment of excitement;

~心血來潮的決定 spur-of-the-moment decision;

~一時心血來潮 on a whim; on impulse;

費盡心血 expend all one's energies; with much ado;

[心學] study of the mind;

[心炎] carditis;

風濕性心炎 rheumatic carditis;

鏈球菌性心炎 streptococcal carditis;

全心炎 pancarditis;

疣性心炎 verrucous carditis;

[心眼兒] (1) heart; mind; (2) intention; (3) cleverness; intelligence; (4) unfounded doubts; unnecessary misgivings;

心眼兒多 full of unnecessary misgivings; oversensitive; too much attention to details;

心眼兒好 generous; generous and kindhearted; good-natured; kindhearted;

壞心眼兒 evil intention; ill will;

沒心眼兒 candid; careless; frank; lack of calculation; mindless;

耍心眼兒 exercise one's wits for personal gain; lip service; mere empty talk; pull a shrewd trick; show off one's joking talent; slick talker; sweet-talk; talk glibly; very crafty;

一個心眼兒 (1) devotedly; have one's heart set on sth; (2) of one mind;

直心眼兒 frank; open; straightforward;

[心眼活泛] have a supple mind; quick-witted;

[心癢] itching heart;

心癢難搔 itch in the heart but unable to scratch it — too happy to know what to do;

[心漾] one's heart aroused by desires;

[心藥] psychological treatment;

[心儀] admire in the heart;

心儀其人 admire a particular person;

[心意] (1) kindly feelings; regard; (2) decision; idea; intention; opinion; purpose;

半心半意 half-hearted; lukewarm; not with all one's heart;

~半心半意的 faint-hearted; half-hearted;

心意卡 greeting card;

合心意 be satisfied with sth;

回心轉意 change one's mind; change one's views; come around; come round; correct one's thinking and attitude; have a change of heart; repent;

假心假意 hypocritical show of friendship; pretend to;

全心全意 body and soul; complete devotion; have one's heart and soul;

heart and soul; put one's heart and soul into; unstinted support; up to the handle; wholeheartedly; with all one's heart; with all one's heart and soul; with heart and hand; with wholehearted devotion;

三心兩意 (1) change one's mind constantly; have two minds; hesitating; in two minds; infirm of purpose; irresolute; of two minds; play the field; undecided; vacillating; (2) half-hearted;

~三心兩意的 fickle;

輸心服意 follow with sincere willingness;

一點心意 a small token of one's appreciation; a small way of showing one's love for sb; a token of one's regard;

一片心意 a small token of our hearts;

以表心意 express one's feeling; in order to prove one's sincerity;

重要的是心意 it is the thought that counts;

[心譯] mental translation;

[心音] cardiac sound;

心音聽診器 cardiophone;

心音圖 cardiophonogram;

[心硬] callous; stony-hearted; unfeeling;

[心影] impression; mental image;

[心餘力拙] bite of more than one can chew; more than willing but lacking the power to; the spirit is willing, but the flesh is weak; unable to do what one wants very much to do;

[心猿意馬] a heart like a capering monkey and a mind like a galloping horse — restless; capricious; fanciful and fickle; perturbed; restless and whimsical; scatter-brained; unsettled in mind; wavering in purpose; with the heart of an ape and the mind of a horse — in a restless and jumpy mood;

意馬心猿 difficult to concentrate one's mind on sth; fanciful and fickle; in a restless and jumpy mood; indecisive; restless and whimsical; the heart of an ape and the mind of a horse; unsettled in mind; wavering;

[心願] aspiration; cherished desire; one's heart's desire;

心願力違 the spirit is willing, but the flesh is weak;

以遂心願 in order to answer one's expectation; in order to crown one's wishes;

[心臟] (1) cardiac; (2) heart; (3) ticker;

心臟病 cardiac disease; heart disease; heart problem; heart trouble;

~心臟病發作 heart attack;

~心臟病學 cardiology;

心臟病學家 cardiologist;

~心臟病醫生 cardiologist;

~風濕性心臟病 rheumatic heart disease;

~老年性心臟病 presbycardia;

~缺血性心臟病 ischemic heart disease;

心臟穿刺術 cardiocentesis;

心臟搭橋手術 bypass operation; bypass surgery;

心臟肥大 athlete's heart; cardiomegaly;

心臟鏡 cardioscope;

心臟擴大 cardiac enlargement;

心臟擴張 dilatation of the heart;

心臟起搏 cardiac pacing;

~心臟起搏器 cardiac pacemaker;

心臟切開術 cardiotomy;

心臟手術 cardiac surgery; heart operation;

心臟衰竭 cardiac failure; heart failure;

~充血性心臟衰竭 congestive failure;

心臟停搏 cardiac arrest;

心臟下垂 cardioptosis;

心臟線 cardioid;

心臟休克 cardiac shock;

心臟修補術 cardiorrhaphy;

心臟炎 carditis;

~風濕性心臟炎 rheumatic carditis;

心臟意外 cardiac accident;

心臟增大 cardiac enlargement;

人造心臟 artificial heart;

[心窄] narrow-minded;

[心照] have an understanding; understand without being told;

心照不宣 have a tacit understanding; tacit agreement; tacit understanding; take wordless counsel;

[心折] admire without reservations; have one's heart won;

[心正不怕邪] if the heart is upright, there need not be any apprehension of depravity;

[心知] consciousness; intelligence; the mind;

[心直口快] frank and outspoken; frank and sincere; frank by nature with a ready tongue; honest and outspoken; speak one's mind freely; wear one's heart on one's sleeve;

[心志] fortitude; will power;

[心智] abilities and powers of the mind; mentality;

[心中] at heart; in one's heart; in one's mind; in the heart; in the mind;

心中暗喜 be secretly pleased; rejoice in one's heart; secretly feel pleased;

心中不服 a lack of hearty support; mutinous in one's heart;

心中狐疑 with one's stomach heaving with torturing doubts;

心中懷怒 nourish anger in one's heart;

心中納悶 be grieved and disappointed;

心中盤算 debate in one's mind; debate with oneself;

心中丘壑 obstinate to one's own ideas;

心中無數 not know for certain; not know one's own mind; not too sure; without clear aims;

心中抑鬱 one's mind is depressed;

心中有鬼 have a bellyful of tricks; have sth to hide; have ulterior designs;

心中有愧 feel ashamed; have a guilty conscience; have sth on one's conscience;

心中有數 feel sure of; have a clear idea about; have a good idea of how things stand; have a pretty good idea of; know at heart; know fairly well; know one's own mind; know the score; know what's what;

[心軸] mandrel;

定徑心軸 fixed mandrel;

空心心軸 hollow mandrel;

錐形心軸 conical mandrel;

自動脹開心軸 automatic expanding mandrel;

[心醉] be charmed; be enchanted; be fascinated;

心醉神迷 be thrown into ecstacies; in an ecstasy of delight; in ecstasies over;

愛國心 patriotic feeling; patriotism;

安心 (1) feel at ease; have peace of mind; (2) keep one's mind on sth;

靶心 bull's eye;

背心 sleeveless garment;

本心 conscience; true intention;

筆心 (1) pencil lead; (2) refill;

褊心 narrow-minded and impatient;

變心 cease to be faithful; cease to love one's spouse; jilt a lover;

冰心 (1) chaste; virtuous; (2) not enthusiastic; somewhat indifferent;

波心 (1) centre of a water-ring; (2) heart of a trouble;

操心 (1) be concerned over; take pains; trouble about; worry about; (2) rack one's brains;

趁心 be gratified; find sth satisfactory;

稱心 be gratified or satisfied;

成心 intentionally; on purpose; with deliberate intent;

誠心 sincere desire; wholehearted;

吃心 become suspicious; oversensitive;

痴心 infatuation;

癡心 (1) blind love; blind passion; infatuation; (2) silly wish;

赤心 genuine sincerity; loyalty; sincere; sincere heart; wholehearted devotion;

春心 a desire for love; a longing for love; thoughts of love;

刺心 pierce the heart;

磁心 magnetic core;

從心 follow one's wishes;

粗心 careless; thoughtless;

醋心 belching of acid from stomach;

存心 accidentally-on-purpose; cherish certain intentions; deliberately; intentionally; on purpose;

寸心 (1) at heart; in the heart; in the mind; (2) feelings;

歹心 evil intent;

丹心 loyal heart; loyalty;

擔心 entertain apprehension of; feel anxious; have apprehensions for; under the apprehension; worry;

當心 (1) attention; be careful; beware; heads up; look out; mind; see that; take care; watch one's step; watch out; (2) in the centre;

燈心 lampwick; wick;

地心 the earth's core;

點心 dessert; dim sum; light refreshments; pastry;

定心 centre;

動心 be aroused; be moved;

多心 oversensitive; suspicious;

噁心 disgusting; feel like vomiting; feel nausea; feel sick; nauseating; repulsive; sicchasia; turn sick;

二心 disloyalty; half-heartedness;

貳心 rebellious mind;
芳心 heart of a young lady;
放心 at ease; breathe easy; feel relieved; free from cares; have one's heart at ease; put one's heart at ease; rest assured; rest one's heart; set one's mind at rest;
費心 (1) give a lot of care; take a lot of trouble; (2) may I trouble you (to do sth);
分心 (1) divert one's attention; (2) give attention to sth else;
負心 desert one's love or lover; fail to be loyal to one's love;
腹心 (1) belly and the heart; (2) true thoughts and feelings; (3) reliable agent; trusted subordinate;
甘心 (1) be willing; readily; (2) be reconciled to; resign oneself to;
公心 (1) fair-mindedness; (2) selflessness;
攻心 attempt to demoralize sb; make a psychological attack; try to persuade an offender to confess;
掛心 anxious for; be concerned about; keep in mind;
關心 be concerned about; be concerned for; be concerned with; be interested in; care about; care for; concern oneself about; concern oneself with; display deep concern for; display one's concern for; express great concern for; express one's concern for; feel concerned about; feel concerned for; give first place to; have a concern for; have a thought for; have...at heart; have ...in one's heart; make over; make the most of; show concern for; show consideration for; show one's concern for; solicitous for; surround sb with love and care; take...to one's heart; think of; thoughtful about;
歸心 submit to the authority of another;
果心 fruit pith;
寒心 (1) be bitterly disappointed; (2) afraid; fearful; feel the blood running cold;
好心 good intention;
核心 centre; core; crux; heart; kernel; nucleus;
黑心 black heart; evil mind;
狠心 cruel-hearted; heartless;
恒心 constancy of purpose; perseverance;
橫心 become desperate; steel one's heart;
紅心 loyal heart;
湖心 middle of a lake;
歡心 favour; liking; love;
灰心 disappointed; discouraged; disheartened; lose heart;
會心 come to understand without explanation;
慧心 clear, alert mind;
蕙心 pure heart;
禍心 evil intent; evil intention; malice;
機心 (1) machination; (2) movement;
雞心 (1) heart-shaped; (2) heart-shaped pendant;
嫉妒心 jealousy;
忌妒心 jealousy;
夾心 with filling;
奸心 cunning mind;
江心 the middle of a river;
匠心 craftsmanship; ingenuity; inventiveness; originality;
交心 lay one's heart bare; open hearts to each other; open one's heart to;
焦心 feel terribly worried;
腳心 arch of the foot;
戒心 alertness; vigilance; wariness;
進取心 enterprising spirit;
盡心 do sth with all one's heart; put one's heart and soul into; with all one's heart;
經心 careful; conscientious; mindful;
精心 elaborately; meticulous; painstaking;
驚心 heart-stirring;
揪心 (1) anxious; worried; (2) agonizing; heartrending;
居心 harbour evil intention;
決心 all set; bent on; bent upon; bound; decide; determination; determine; determined; from a resolution; make a resolution; make up one's mind; out to; pass a resolution; resolve; resolved; set on; set oneself to; set one's heart on; set one's mind on; take a resolution;
軍心 morale of the troops; soldiers' morale;
開心 feel happy; full of glee; get a kick; in high glee; make joy; rejoice; take joy;
可心 likeable; satisfying; to the liking of; to the satisfaction of;
空心 (1) hollow; (2) become hollow; (3) on an empty stomach;
口心 the mouth and the mind;
苦心 pains; trouble taken;
寬心 at ease; feel at rest; feel free from anxiety; feel relieved; find relief; relaxed; set one's mind at ease;
虧心 go against conscience; have a guilty conscience;
勞心 work with one's mind;
離心 centrifugal;
憐憫心 sympathy;
良心 conscience;

兩條心 in fundamental disagreement; not of one mind;
兩心 affection for each other; (2) disloyalty;
留心 be careful; take care;
滿心 have one's heart filled with sth;
眉心 between the eyebrows;
昧心 against one's conscience;
捫心 examine one's conscience; feel one's heart by hand;
盟心 swear mutual devotion;
民心 common aspiration of the people; popular feelings; popular sentiments; popular support;
銘心 always remember; imprint on one's mind;
耐心 patience;
鬧心 be agitated; irritate; restless; upset;
內心 (1) heart; innermost being; (2) incentre;
泥心 sand core;
嘔心 exert one's utmost effort; take great pains;
旁心 excentre;
偏心 (1) bias; partial; partiality; (2) eccentric;
平心 calmly;
婆心 kind heart;
欺心 disregard the dictates of one's own conscience;
齊心 of one heart; of one mind;
虔心 piety; sincere reverence;
潛心 devote oneself to sth; do sth with great concentration; have a quiet concentrated mind;
愜心 contented; pleased; satisfied; satisfactory;
琴心 the emotional appeal through lute playing;
清心 (1) carefree; (2) free one's mind of worries;
傾心 (1) admire; fall for; fall in love with; lose one's heart to; (2) cordial; heart-to-heart; intimate and candid; warm and sincere;
輕心 negligent;
情心 compassion;
球心 centre of a sphere;
屈心 have a guilty conscience;
悛心 repentant heart;
熱心 ardent; avid; eager; earnest; enthusiastic; warmhearted;
人心 human emotion; human feeling; human heart; human will; morale; popular feeling; public peeling; the will of the people;
仁心 charity; kindheartedness; kindness;
忍心 hardhearted; have the heart to; merciless; steel one's heart; unfeeling;
如心 contented; gratified; pleased; satisfied;
蕊心 stamens and pistils;
散心 carefree; direct oneself from cares for relaxation; drive away one's cares; ease up; enjoy a diversion; let one's mind relax; relieve boredom;
砂心 moulding sand core;
善心 compassionate heart; kind heart; benevolence; good intention; kindhearted; kindness; mercy;
傷心 break one's heart; broken-hearted; grieved; hurt one's feelings; sad;
賞心 please the heart;
燒心 (1) heartburn; (2) turn yellow at the heart;
身心 body and mind;
深心 deep in one's heart;
生心 disloyal to;
省心 save worry;
實心 (1) honest; sincere; (2) in a serious manner; (3) solid;
豕心 avaricious; greedy;
事業心 devotion to one's work;
收心 (1) bring one's mind back from; concentrate on more serious things; get into the frame of mind for work; (2) have a change of heart;
手心 (1) palm of the hand; (2) control; in the hands of sb;
舒心 agreeable; pleasant;
淑心 pure heart;
爽心 cheerful; gratified; pleased; satisfied;
水心 centre of a stream;
順心 gratifying; satisfactory;
私心 selfish motives; selfishness;
死心 drop the idea forever; give up the idea forever; give up one's hope for good; have no more illusions about the matter; think no more of sth;
鬆心 carefree;
素心 (1) simple and honest; (2) one's conscience;
酸心 (1) heartbroken; grieved; sad; (2) heartburn;
遂心 after one's own heart; fulfil one's desire; have one's own way; have one's will; to one's liking;
他心 dishonesty; insincerity; treachery; unfaithfulness;
塌心 set one's mind at ease; settle down to sth;
貪心 avarice; avarious; greed; greedy; insatiable; voracious;
談心 have a heart-to-heart talk; serious and intimate discussion;
溏心 with a soft yolk;
掏心 from the bottom of one's heart;
提心 have one's heart in one's mouth;
甜心 sweetheart;

貼心 close; intimate;

鐵心 (1) iron core; (2) have a heart of iron;

同情心 sympathy;

同心 (1) be united at heart; be united in common purpose; with one heart; (2) concentric; homocentric;

童心 childish heart; childishness; childlike innocence;

痛心 distressed; grieved; heartbroken; very sorry;

偷心 steal sb's heart;

歪心 crooked mind; evil mind; twisted mind;

外心 (1) unfaithful intention; (2) circumcentre;

違心 against one's will; contrary to one's convictions;

唯心 idealistic;

窩心 feel irritated; feel vexed;

無心 (1) in no mood; not in the mood for; (2) inadvertently; unintentionally; unwittingly;

悉心 devote all one's attention; take the utmost care; with concentrated effort; with one's whole heart;

洗心 cleanse one's heart;

細心 attentive; careful; cautious; circumpspective;

遐心 (1) the thought of keeping aloof; (2) the wish to abandon; (3) the desire to live in retirement;

閒心 free, unburdened mind; leisurely mood;

小心 careful; cautious; take care;

孝心 filial piety; love and devotion to one's parents; the love toward parents;

歇心 peaceful and carefree; relaxed mood;

邪心 bad intentions; evil intentions; evil thoughts; wicked ideas;

心連心 heart linked to heart; of one mind with; one's heart beats with the heart of sb;

信心 faith; confidence;

形心 centre of figure; centroid;

型心 core;

雄心 great ambition; lofty aspiration;

修心 cultivate one's mind;

虛榮心 vanity;

虛心 modest; open-minded; with an open mind;

懸心 concerned about sb;

血心 loyalty; sincerity;

薰心 becloud the mind;

岩心 core;

養心 cultivate mental calm; nourish the mind;

野心 (1) ambition; wild ambition; (2) greediness;

頁心 type page;

一條心 at one; of one heart and one mind; of one mind;

一心 (1) heart and soul; wholeheartedly; (2) at one; of one mind;

疑心 (1) doubt; suspect; suspicion; (2) suspect doubt;

異心 dishonesty; disloyalty; infidelity; insincerity; treachery;

慇心 feel for;

淫心 immoral thoughts; sexual desire;

用心 attentively; diligently; with concentrated attention; exercise caution; pay attention; take care;

憂心 anxiety; worry;

遊心 think deep into sth;

有心 (1) have a mind to; have the intention of; intend to; set one's mind on; (2) deliberately; purposely;

玉心 a heart as pure as jade;

欲心 one's desires;

愿心 reward that a superstitious person promises to offer to God;

圓心 centre of a circle;

在心 attentive; feel concerned; keep in mind; mind;

髒心 dirty mind; impure heart;

糟心 (1) annoyed; dejected; vexed; (2) unlucky; (3) get into a mess;

責任心 sense of responsibility;

賊心 crooked mind; wicked and suspicious mind; wicked heart; evil designs; evil intentions;

扎心 heartbreaking;

齋心 purify the mind;

宅心 intention;

張心 worry oneself with requests;

掌心 centre of the palm;

蔗心 centre stem of the cane;

真心 actual intention; from the bottom of one's heart; heartfelt; sincere; real intention; true intention; wholehearted;

枕心 pillow;

知心 (1) intimate; understanding; (2) bosom friend;

至心 the most sincere heart;

忮心 jealousy;

中心 centre; core; crux; epicenter; heart; hub; kernel;

忠心 devotion; faithfulness; loyalty; sincerity;

衷心 cordial; heartfelt; sincere; wholehearted;

重心 (1) core; focus; heart; key point; (2) centre of gravity;

軸心 (1) axle centre; (2) axis;

珠心 nucellus;
注心 concentrate attention; focus attention;
專心 be absorbed; concentrate one's attention;
轉心 harbour evil thoughts; hold evil thoughts in the mind;
壯心 great aspiration; lofty ideal;
自尊心 self-respect;
足心 the sole of the foot;
醉心 be bent on; be enamoured of; be enamoured with; be engrossed in; be infatuated with; be intoxicated with;

xin

【辛】 (1) acrid; bitter; hot; pungent; (2) hard; laborious; toilsome; (3) suffering; (4) a surname;

[辛臭] acrid and stinking;

[辛楚] sad; sorrowful;

[辛苦] hard; laborious; toilsome;
辛苦賺來的錢 hard-earned money;
白賠辛苦 knock at a deaf man's labour;
白費辛苦 expend labour for nothing;
白辛苦 get nothing for one's pain;
~白辛苦一場 it is labour lost;
備嚐辛苦 undergo all kinds of hardships;
不辭辛苦 not shirk from toil and hardship; not shirk hardships; put oneself out of the way; spare no pains; take the trouble to; work tirelessly;
含辛茹苦 bear bitter hardships; drink a bitter cup; endure all kinds of hardships; endure suffering; put up with hardships; suffer untold hardship; undergo all sorts of hardships and deprivations;
千辛萬苦 all kinds of hardships; all kinds of trials and tribulations; all kinds of untold hardships; go through thick and thin; go through untold hardships; innumerable hardships; innumerable trials and tribulations; labouriously; numberless sufferings and hardships; set one's shoulders to the wheel; severe toil; spare no pains; suffer all conceivable hardships; untold hardships;
茹苦含辛 bear bitter hardships; drink the bitter cup; endure all possible hardships; put up with hardships; undergo all possible hardships;
萬苦千辛 face innumerable difficulties; set one's shoulders to the wheel; spare no pains;
辛辛苦苦 at great pains to; laboriously; take all the trouble to; take great pains to; with great efforts; with so much toil; work laboriously;

[辛辣] acerbity; acridity; bitter; hot; peppery and acrid; pungent;

[辛勞] great care; great effort; pains; toil;
備嚐辛勞 have experienced hardships and difficulties;
不辭辛勞 not shirk from toil and hardship; not shirk hardships; put oneself out of the way; spare no pains; take the trouble to; work tirelessly;

[辛勤] diligent; hardworking; industrious; with one's shoulder to the collar;
辛勤勞動 labour assiduously; work hard;

[辛酸] bitter; hardships; miserable; sad; the bitters of life;
辛酸往事 sad memories;
飽嚐辛酸 go through the mill; pass through the mill; taste to the full the bitterness of life;
備嚐辛酸 drain the cup of bitterness to the dregs; experience all the sufferings; have a rough time;
嚐盡辛酸 drink to the lees; have experienced all the hardships of;
歷盡辛酸 drink the cup of bitterness to the dregs;

[辛味] acrid taste;

悲辛 grieved; sad;
艱辛 hardships;

xin

【忻】 delight; happy; joy;

[忻忻] pleased and satisfied;
忻忻得意 beam with pleasure; delighted; pleased;

xin

【昕】 dawn; daybreak;

[昕夕從公] attend to public duties morning and evening; devote oneself to official duties day and night;

xin

【欣】 delighted; glad; happy; joyful;

[欣忭] happy; joyous;

[欣戴] support gladly;

[欣敬] pay glad homage to;

[欣快] euphoria;
[欣然] joyfully; with good grace; with pleasure;
欣然從命 comply with sb's wish joyfully; obey an order with pleasure; obey without reluctance;
欣然接受 accept readily; accept with pleasure; take sth in good part;
欣然領諾 accept with enthusiasm; consent joyfully;
欣然命筆 gladly set pen to paper; happy to start writing; in one's happiness to pen the following lines; write down as inspiration dictates;
欣然同意 agree readily; consent cheerfully; consent gladly;
欣然應承 jump at; promise without hesitation;
欣然允諾 consent readily;
欣然自得 proud and self-satisfied;
[欣賞] admire; appreciate; enjoy;
自我欣賞 self-appreciation;
[欣慰] comforted; contented; delighted; gratified; relieved; satisfied;
令人欣慰 heartwarming;
值得欣慰 a cause for pride;
[欣悉] delighted to learn; glad to learn; happy to learn;
[欣喜] delighted; enjoyable; glad; gratifying; happy; joyful;
欣喜雀躍 dance for joy; dance with joy; excitedly jump into the air; jump up and down with joy;
欣喜若狂 an ecstasy of joy; as happy as a lark; be intoxicated with joy; beside oneself with joy; delirious with delight; ecstasize; exult; fly into raptures; go mad with joy; go wild with joy; in a transport of delight; in a transport of joy; in raptures; jubilantly happy; jump out of one's skin; leap out of one's skin; leap with joy;
[欣羡] admire; envy;
[欣欣] glad;
欣欣然 complacent; happy; joyful;
欣欣向榮 a living atmosphere; an invigorating atmosphere; flourishing; full of life and vigour; in a hopeful and cheerful mood; on the up; prosperous; rapidly moving towards prosperity; thriving;
[欣幸] joyful and thankful; rapture;
[欣悦] delighted; glad; happy; joyous;
歡欣 (1) happy; (2) flourishing; thriving;

xin

【芯】 pith of rushes;
[芯撐] chaplet;
單面芯撐 stem chaplet;
管子芯撐 stalk-pipe chaplet;
螺旋芯撐 spring chaplet;
螺旋形芯撐 radiator chaplet;
雙面芯撐 double-head chaplet;
陀螺形芯撐 diabolo type chaplet;
[芯片] microchip;
芯片產業 microchip industry;

鉛筆芯 lead in a pencil;
玉米芯 cob; corncob;

xin

【炘】 (1) brilliant and bright; (2) scorch; scorching hot;

xin

【莘】 (1) long; (2) numerous; (3) a kind of plant;
[莘莘] many; numerous;
莘莘學子 students in large numbers;

xin

【訢】 delight; happy; joy;
[訢然] happy; very pleased;
[訢訢] joyfully;

xin

【新】 (1) brand-new; fresh; new; newly; novel; renewed; (2) beginning; starting; (3) modern; recent; (4) newly-wed; recently married;
[新版] new edition;
[新辦] newly established;
[新編] (1) newly compiled; (2) newly organized;
[新兵] new recruits; raw recruits; recruits;
新兵訓練營 boot camp;
一批新兵 a batch of recruits;
[新潮] new wave; new fashioned;
新潮的 groovy; modist;
新潮流 new trend;
[新陳] the new and the old;
新陳代謝 (1) metabolism; (2) assimilation of the new and excretion of the old;

bringing in new blood; the coming of the new and giving way of the old; the new superseding the old; the replacement of the old with the new; the transition from the old order of things to the new;
~新陳代謝的 metabolic;
~新陳代謝綜合症 metabolic syndrome;
~使發生新陳代謝 metabolize;
推陳出新 bring forth sth new from the old; bring forth the new through the old; evolve new things from the old; find sth new in what is old; the old is thrown out and the new is ushered in; the new emerges out of the old; weed out the old to let the new emerge; weed through the old to bring forth the new; weed through the old to create the new; weed through the old to let the new grow;

[新愁] fresh sorrows;

[新春] (1) early spring; (2) Lunar New Year;
新春快樂 Happy Lunar New Year;
喜迎新春 joyously see in the lunar New Year;

[新詞] neologism;
新詞創造 coinage;
短語新詞 phrasal neologism;

[新法] (1) new method; new technique; (2) new laws;

[新房] (1) bridal chamber; bridal room; (2) new house;

[新婦] bride;

[新故] the new and the old;
送故迎新 (1) bid farewell to those departing and greet the arrival of newcomers; (2) send off the old year and usher in the new;
吐故納新 exhale the old and inhale the new; get rid of the stale and take in the fresh;
溫故知新 by restudying the old one learns sth new; gain new insights through restudying old material; gain new knowledge by reviewing the old; keep cherishing one's old knowledge so as to continually acquiring new; know what is new by keeping fresh in one's mind what one is already familiar with; learn the new by restudying the old; recalling the past helps one to know the present; review what one has learned and know what is new; understand the present by reviewing the past;
厭故喜新 dislike the old and be fond of the new;

[新寡] be newly divorced;
文君新寡 newly widowed woman;

[新官] new broom;
新官上任 take a new official post;
新官上任三把火 a new broom sweeps clean; a new official applies strict measures; new brooms sweep clean;

[新貴] newly appointed official;

[新歡] new lover; new sweetheart;
另結新歡 throw sb over for sb else;

[新婚] newly married;
新婚不如遠別 a night after absence is better than a wedding night; reunion after long separation is better than a wedding night;
新婚夫婦 newly married couple; newly-married; newlyweds;
~一對新婚夫婦 a newly-wedded couple;
新婚燕爾 happy wedding; newly married;
新婚之夜 wedding night;
燕爾新婚 conjugal bliss; happy wedding; joy of new marriage; marital happiness; newly married;

[新交] new acquaintance; new friend;
新交故知 new acquaintances and old friends — new and old friends;

[新教] protestantism;

[新近] freshly; in recent times; lately; newly; recently;
新近隱喻 recent metaphor;

[新進] (1) new employees of an organization; (2) novice;

[新舊] the new and the old;
新舊交替 the new replaces the old; the transition from the old to the new;
半新不舊 half-new; neither new or shabby; no longer new;
褒舊貶新 glorify the old and belittle the new;
得新厭舊 disdain the old when one gets the new;
翻舊如新 repair sth old and make it as good as new;
舊的不去，新的不來 the new should replace the old; without discarding the

old, there would be no coming of the new;
舊瓶新酒 new wine in old bottles — new content in old form;
舊識新交 friends, old and new; old friends and new acquaintances;
舊雨新知 old friends and new acquaintances; one's old and new friends;
舊知新交 friends old and new; old friends and new acquaintances;
舊字新義 an old word in a new sense;
棄舊憐新 be tired of the old and fascinated by the new; fickle in one's affection; prefer new to old acquaintances; reject the old and love the new; turn the back on one lover and go with another;
棄舊圖新 abandon sth old for sth new; change and start afresh; give up sth whose freshness has been worn off for sth novel; reject the old for the new; renounce one's past and start with a clean slate; start afresh; turn over a new leaf;
棄舊迎新 change the new for the old; reject the old and welcome the new; replace the old with the new;
去舊布新 eliminate the old to make way for the new;
去舊更新 do away with the old and change it for the new;
送舊迎新 ring out the Old Year and ring in the New Year; see off the old and welcome the new; speed the old guest and welcome the new; usher out the parting guest and welcome in the new one;
喜新厭舊 abandon the old for the new; fond of the new and tired of the old; like the new and dislike the old; love the new and loathe the old; off with the old love and on with the new; refect the old and crave for the new; tired of the old and fascinated by the new; turn one's back on one lover to go with another;
新不如舊 the new is not so good as the old;
新瓶裝舊酒 a new bottled filled with old wine; a superficial change; old stuff with a new label; old wine in new bottles;
修舊如新 repair sth old and make it as good as new;
厭舊喜新 dislike the old and take a delight in the new; reject the old and crave for the new; tired of the old and fascinated by the new;
整舊如新 restore sth to its original shape and appearance;

[新居] new home; new residence;
搬入新居 move in; move to a new house;

[新郎] bridegroom;
準新郎 bridegroom-to-be; would-be bridegroom;

[新老交替] succession of the new to the old;

[新曆] Gregorian calendar; solar calendar;

[新貌] new look;

[新苗] young shoots; young sprouts;

[新民] improve the people;

[新年] New Year;
新年除夕 New Year's Eve;
新年快樂 Happy New Year;
新年之始 turn of the year;
鳴鐘迎接新年 ring in the new year;

[新娘] bride;
新娘禮服 bridal gown;
新娘面紗 bridal veil;
新娘親友團 bridal party;
新娘套房 bridal suite;
大齡新娘 mature bride;
未來的新娘 bride-to-be;
準新娘 bride-to-be; would-be bride;

[新派] modern school; new school;

[新奇] new; newfangled; novel; strange;
趨新獵奇 hunt for novelty;

[新區] newly developed area;

[新曲] new musical composition; new song; new tune;

[新人] (1) new hands; (2) bride; (3) new love; (4) person with modern thoughts;
新人輩出 more and more people of a new type will come to the fore;
新人新事 new people and new things; new personalities and new deeds;
一代新人 a new generation of people;

[新任] newly appointed; newly sworn-in;

[新生] (1) newborn; (2) new student; (3) new life; rebirth; regeneration;
新生力事 new force; new rising force; newly emerging force;
新生事物 new things; newly emerging

things;
大學新生 entrant;
一年級新生 fresher;
[新詩] new poetry;
新體詩 new poetry;
[新式] modern; of a new model; of a new style;
新式拼法 new spelling;
[新手] green hand; greenhorn; new hand; novice; raw recruit;
[新書] new book;
新書目錄 accession catalogue, accession list;
新書預告 announcement of forthcoming books;
[新歲] beginning of a new year;
[新聞] news;
新聞辦公室 press office;
新聞報導 news coverage; newspaper report; reportage;
~攝影新聞報導 photojournalism;
新聞編輯 (1) news editing; (2) news editor;
~新聞編輯室 newsroom;
新聞播音員 news caster; newsreader;
新聞採訪 news-gathering;
新聞炒作 gonzo journalism;
新聞櫥窗 newsphoto display case;
新聞傳播學 news communication studies;
新聞電視學 journalistic television;
新聞電訊 dispatch;
新聞短片 newsreel;
新聞發佈 news release;
~新聞發佈會 news briefing; news conference; press conference;
舉行新聞發佈會 give a news briefing;
~新聞發佈官 briefing officer; press officer;
新聞發言人 news spokesman; spokesman;
新聞法規 journalistic rules;
新聞反饋 news feedback;
新聞翻譯 journalistic translation; news translation;
新聞分析 news analysis;
~新聞分析員 news analyst;
新聞封鎖 news blackout;
新聞稿 news release; press release;
新聞工作者 journalist; journo;
~自由新聞工作者 freelance journalist;
新聞公報 press communique;
新聞管理學 science of news management;
新聞廣播 news broadcasting; newscast;
~新聞廣播學 news broadcasting science;
~新聞廣播員 newscaster;
新聞記者 correspondent; journalist; newsman; newspaperman; reporter;
~新聞記者席 press gallery;
~美術新聞記者 artist reporter;
~女新聞記者 newspaperwoman; newswoman;
新聞價值 news value; news worthiness;
新聞檢查 press censorship;
新聞簡報 bulletin;
新聞結構 news structure;
新聞界 circle of journalists; press circles;
新聞快訊 newsflash;
新聞立體化 stereo-journalism;
新聞媒體 mass media; news media;
新聞美學 journalistic aesthetics;
新聞秘書 press secretary;
新聞人格化 journalistic personification;
新聞人物 newsmakers; person of the hour; people in the limelight; people in the news;
新聞社 news agency;
新聞攝影機 newsreel camera;
新聞攝影記者 cameraman;
新聞事業 journalism;
新聞司 department of information;
新聞特寫 news features;
新聞提要 news headlines; news round-up;
新聞通報 press handout;
新聞透明度 news transparency;
新聞網絡 news group;
新聞文化學 science of journalistic culture;
新聞文體 journalese;
新聞現場感 on-the-spot journalism;
新聞心理學 psychology of journalism;
新聞信息 news information;
新聞信札 news letter;
新聞學 journalism;
新聞影片 newsreel;
新聞雜誌 newsmagazine;
新聞照片 news picture;
新聞紙 newsprint;
新聞中心 press centre;
新聞主體 news body;
新聞組 newsgroup;
新聞自由 freedom of press; press freedom;
爆炸新聞 unexpected news;
本地新聞 local news;
~本地新聞部 city desk;

~本地新聞記者 city editor;
標題新聞 banner headline;
財經新聞 financial news;
~財經新聞部 city desk;
大新聞 big news;
地區新聞 regional news;
獨家新聞 exclusive news;
發布新聞 release news;
罐頭新聞 canned news;
國際新聞 international news;
國際新聞廣播 world news broadcast;
國內新聞 home news; national news;
~國內新聞廣播 home news broadcast;
國外新聞 foreign news;
花邊新聞 box news;
假新聞 canard;
內幕新聞 inside dope; inside story;
趣味小新聞 factoid;
軟新聞 soft news;
頭版新聞 front page news;
頭條新聞 lead story; top news; top-line news;
小道新聞 grapevine news;
一則新聞 a piece of news; an item of news;

[新禧] happy new year;

[新鮮] (1) fresh; (2) new; novel; original; (3) strange;
新鮮經驗 fresh experience; new experience;
新鮮感 novelty;
~新鮮感消失 the novelty wears off;
不新鮮 stale;
試新嘗鮮 have a taste of what is just in season;

[新星] new star; nova; rising star;
矮新星 dwarf nova;
超新星 supernova;
樂壇新星 rising star in the world of music;

[新興] burgeoning; new and developing; newly developing; rising;
新興城市 boom town;
新興工業 sunrise industry;
新興勢力 forces in the ascendance; rising forces;

[新型] late model; new pattern; new type;

[新秀] promising young person; up-and-coming youngster;

[新學] new learning;

[新異] the new and the different;
求新立異 on the lookout for whatever is novel;

[新穎] new; new and original; novel; originality;

[新月] (1) new moon; (2) crescent moon;
新月形 crescentiform;
赤道下新月 sub-equatorial crescent;
黃新月 yellow crescent;
眉如新月 one's eyebrow is like the crescent moon; one's eyebrows are curved like the sickle of the new moon;
一彎新月 a new crescent moon; a new moon;

[新增] newly increased;
新增城市人口 newly-born population of a city;
新增國民收入 sum of newly-gained national income;

[新知] (1) new friends; (2) new knowledge; new learning;

[新制] new system;

[新著] new work;

嘗新 taste a new delicacy;
重新 (1) again; (2) afresh; anew;
創新 blaze new trails; bring forth new ideas; innovate;
從新 afresh; anew;
簇新 brand new;
鼎新 innovate;
翻新 make over; recondition; renovate; retrofit;
復新 make anew; make to look as new;
革新 innovate; innovation;
更新 renew; renewal; renovate; replace; update;
履新 take or asume one's new office or post;
納新 take in the fresh;
清新 crisp; delightfully fresh; fresh; pure and fresh; refreshing;
全新 brand new;
日新 daily renewal;
如新 brand as if it were new;
時新 stylish; trendy;
刷新 (1) freshen; refurbish; renovate; (2) break;
維新 make political reform; reform;
鮮新 bright and new; fresh; refreshing;
一新 a fresh look; a new look;
迎新 (1) see the New Year in; welcome the arrival of the New Year; (2) welcome the new arrivals;
嶄新 brand-new; completely new;

湛新 brand-new;
知新 know sth new;
自新 make a fresh start; make a new person out of oneself; self-renewal; turn over a new leaf;
最新 latest; most up-to-date; newest;

xin

【歆】 (1) (of gods) accept offerings, etc.; (2) admire; submit to willingly; (3) move; quicken;
［歆慕］ cherish;
［歆羡］ admire; envy;
［歆艷］ admire; envy;

xin

【鋅】 zinc;
［鋅版］ zinc plate;

一層鋅 a coat of zinc;

xin

【薪】 (1) faggot; firewood; fuel; (2) pay; salary;
［薪俸］ pay; salary; wages;
［薪工］ pay; wages;
［薪火］ (1) torch; (2) torch of learning passed from master to pupil;
薪盡火傳 as one piece of fuel is consumed, the flame passes to another — the touch of learning is passed on from teacher to student and from generation to generation;
［薪給］ pay; salary; wages;
［薪金］ pay; salary; wages;
薪金税 payroll tax;
固定薪金 fixed salary;
應計薪金 accrued salary;
預支薪金 prepaid salary;
［薪水］ earnings; pay; salary; wages;
薪水低的 low-paid;
基本薪水 basic salary;
一份薪水 a salary;
賺薪水 earn a salary; get a salary; receive a salary;
［薪餉］ soldier's pay and rations;
［薪資］ pay; salary; wages;

半薪 half one's salary;
抽薪 take out the firewood;
低薪 low-paid;
底薪 base salary; basic salary;
發薪 pay salary; pay wage;
乾薪 draw wages without working; salary drawn for a sinecure; unemployed salary;
工薪 wages;
加薪 salary increase;
年薪 yearly salary;
起薪 starting salary;
欠薪 back pay; overdue wages;
樵薪 gather firewood; gather fuel;
日薪 day wage;
停薪 stop payment to an employee;
月薪 monthly pay; monthly salary;
週薪 weekly salary;

xin

【馨】 strong and pervasive fragrance;
［馨香］ (1) aroma; fragrance; (2) smell of burning incense;
馨香禱祝 burn incense and pray to the gods — earnestly pray for sth; sincerely wish;
馨香馥鬱 very fragrant;
馨香萬世 one's fragrance is handed down to myriad generations;

清馨 delicate fragrance; faint scent;
紫馨 jasmine;

xin

【鑫】 good profit;

xin²

xin

【尋】 beg; entreat;
［尋死］ (1) attempt suicide; try to commit suicide; (2) commit suicide;
尋死覓活 attempt suicide repeatedly; seek one's own death; threaten sb with death; threaten to kill oneself; try to commit uicide; want to end one's own life;

侵尋 gradually; little by little;
搜尋 look for; search for; seek; seek and find;
找尋 look for; search for; seek;
抓尋 look for; search for;
追尋 pursue; search; seek; track down;

xin⁴

xin

【囟】 skull; top of the human head;

xin

【芯】 central part of an object;

X

[芯子] (1) fuse; wick; (2) forked tongue of a snake;

xin

【信】 (1) true; (2) confidence; faith; honesty; trust; truthfulness; (3) believe; trust; (4) believe in; profess faith in; (5) aimless; at random; at will; easy; free; without a plan; (6) pledge; sign; token; credentials; evidence; (7) letter; mail; (8) information; message; news; word;

[信筆] write as fancy dictates; write freely without hesitation; write without much thought;
信筆塗鴉 clumsy in penmanship; write carelessly; write rough and ready;
信筆寫來 write down one's ideas as they come to mind;
信筆直書 write freely as fancy dictates; write freely without too much hesitation;

[信標] beacon;
信標系統 beaconage;
超聲波信標 supersonic wave beacon;
船艦信標 ship beacon;
燈光信標 electric beacon;
地面信標 ground beacon;
定向信標 directive beacon;
跟蹤信標 tracking beacon;
工作信標 operational beacon;
歸航信標 home beacon; homing beacon;
航路信標 beaconing;
航線信標 airway beacon;
航向信標 course beacon;
進場信標 approach marker beacon;
~盲目進場信標 blind approach beacon;
雷達安全信標 radar safety beacon;
閃光信標 oscillating beacon;
聲納信標 sonar beacon;
識別信標 identification beacon;
雙向信標 two-course beacon;
微波信標 microwave beacon;
無線電信標 radio beacon;
~對話無線電信標 talking radio beacon;
~旋轉無線電信標 rotation radio beacon;
音響無線電信標 aural radio beacon;
應答器信標 responder beacon;
障礙物信標 obstruction beacon;
指向信標 direction-giving beacon;
中繼信標 relay beacon;
自動求救信標 automatic rescue beacon;

[信步] stroll; stroll aimlessly; take a leisurely walk; walk aimlessly; wander;
信步來到 come to a place in aimlessly wandering;
信步閒踱 roam about without definite objective; take a leisurely walk; walk about aimlessly;
信步閒遊 roam about without definitive objective; walk aimlessly;
閒庭信步 stroll idly in a courtyard;

[信差] carrier; postman;

[信從] listen to; trust and comply with; trust and follow;

[信貸] credit;
信貸標準 credit standards;
信貸部 lending department;
~零售信貸部 retail landing department;
信貸法 credit laws;
信貸風險 credit risk;
~信貸風險管理 management of the creditable adventure;
信貸機構 credit agency;
信貸價值 credit worthiness;
信貸緊縮 credit crunch;
信貸擴大 credit expansion;
信貸期 credit period;
信貸市場 credit market;
信貸條件 credit terms;
信貸限制 credit restriction;
信貸協議 credit agreement;
信貸資金 credit funds;
擺動信貸 swing credit;
承兑信貸 acceptance credit;
凍結信貸 frozen credit;
短期信貸 consumer credit;
分期付款信貸 instalment credit;
季節性信貸 seasonal loan;
取得信貸 get credit; obtain credit;
收緊信貸 credit squeeze; tighten credit;
賒購信貸 credit account;
使用信貸 use credit;
消費信貸 consumer credit;

[信得過] can be believed; credible;
信不過 have no trust in; incredible; mistrust;

[信而有證] borne out by evidence;

[信封] envelope; mailer;
標準信封 standard-size envelope;
拆開信封 slit an envelope open;
貼有郵票的回郵信封 stamped addressed

envelope;

[信奉] believe in; embrace;

[信服] admire; be convinced; believe in; completely accept; trust;
令人信服的 cogent;

[信稿] draft of a letter;

[信鴿] carrier pigeon; homing pigeon;

[信管] fuse;

[信函] letter;

[信號] signal; signaling;
信號燈 lights;
~交通信號燈 stop light; traffic lights;
信號旗 code flag; signal flag;
信號員 signalman;
~閉塞信號員 block signalman;
~霧信號員 fog signalman;
信號系统 signal system;
~第二信號系统 second signal system;
~第一信號系统 first signal system;
安全信號 safety signal;
報警信號 alarm signal;
報時信號 time signal;
傳輸信號 carry a signal;
錯誤信號 wrong signal;
發出信號 emit a signal; give a signal; send out a signal;
發射信號 transmit signals;
發送信號 send out a signal;
呼救信號 SOS;
見到信號 catch the signal;
接收信號 pick up a signal; receive a signal;
警告信號 warning signal;
雷達信號 radar signal;
求救信號 distress signal;
昇起信號 hoist the signal; raise the signal;
聲音信號 sound signal;
視覺信號 visual signal;
數字信號 digital signal;
雙向信號 both-way signaling;
危險信號 danger signal;
無線電信號 radio signal;
煙霧信號 smoke signal;
自動信號 signaling;

[信及豚魚] one's sincerity can move even the lowest creatures; one's sincerity moves even the sucking pigs and fish;

[信箋] letter paper; writing paper;

[信件] letter; mail; missive;
信件格 pigeonhole;
大批信件 large number of letters;
電腦編印信件 computer-generated letter;
私人信件 personal letter;
投遞信件 deliver mail;
雪片般飛來的信件 avalanche of letters;
一批信件 a batch of letters; a crop of letters;
一扎信件 a sheaf of letters;

[信教] profess a religion; religious;

[信靠] trust;

[信口雌黃] criticize freely without careful thought; free with one's tongue; lie in one's throat; make deceitful statements; make irresponsible remarks; make unfounded charges; talk sheer nonsense; wag one's tongue too freely;
信口雌黃，一派胡説 irresponsible talk; this is sheer nonsense;

[信口胡說] babble; barefaced falsehood; let out a stream of lies; sheer nonsense; speak thoughtlessly; talk recklessly; tattle;

[信口開河] aimless talk; brag irresponsibly; have a loose tongue; irresponsible chat; let one's tongue run away with one; lie in one's teeth; lie in one's throat; loosen one's tongue; loosen up; open one's mouth wide; rambling blether; run off at the mouth; say whatever comes to one's mind; shoot at the mouth; shoot off; shoot off one's mouth; shoot one's mouth off; speak without measuring one's words; talk at random; talk drivel; talk in a loose kind of way; talk irresponsibly; talk off the top of one's head; talk recklessly; talk through one's hat; talk without forethought; unbridle the tongue; wag one's tongue too freely;
信口開河的人 big mouth; blabbermouth;
信口開河，胡說八道 speak at random and talk nonsense; talk at random and utter sheer nonsense;

[信賴] come and go upon; count on; have faith in; trust;

[信馬由疆] be easily influenced by the circumstances of the moment; give free rein to; have no fixed opinion; ride with lax reins—let things take their natural course;

[信念] belief; conviction; faith; persuasion;
不變的信念 abiding faith;
堅定信念 impregnable belief;
堅守信念 follow the courage of one's opinions; have the courage of one's convictions;
雙重信念 doublethink;
[信女] female believer;
[信皮] envelope;
[信片] postcard;
[信任] be credited with; believe; believe in; bring sb into one's confidence; confide in; credence; give credit; have confidence in; have faith in; have trust in; trust; trust in;
博取信任 win sb's confidence;
不信任 distrust; have no confidence in; have no faith in; mistrust; not believe in;
獲得信任 gain credence;
[信賞必罰] due rewards and punishments will be meted out without fail; there should be due rewards and punishments;
[信實] honest; reliable; trustworthy;
[信史] authentic history; faithful historical account; true history;
[信使] courier; messenger; messenger boy;
信使往還 exchange of correspondence and emissaries;
[信士] (1) believer; follower of a religion; (2) honest person;
[信誓] faithful oaths; faithful pledges;
信誓旦旦 give sb one's firm and solemn promise; pledge in all sincerity and seriousness; sincere pledge; solemn vow; take an oath devoutly; vow solemnly;
[信手] at random; conveniently; without a previous plan;
信手拈來 get at random; get without effort; have word at one's fingertips and write with facility; pick at random; pick with facility and ease; take at random; take without much forethought;
[信守] abide by; honour; keep; stand by;
信守不渝 unswervingly faithful;
信守諾言 as good as one's word; keep a promise; regardful of one's promises; stick to one's promise;
信守協議 abide by an agreement;
[信天翁] albatross;
[信條] article of creed; article of faith; belief; creed; credo; dogma; precept; tenet;
[信筒] letter box; mailbox; pillar box; postbox;
[信徒] adherent; believer; devotee; disciple; follower;
[信托] trust;
信托財產 trust property;
信托關係 fiduciary relation;
信托基金 trust fund;
信托款項 trust money;
信托人 truster;
~被信托人 trustee;
信托聲明書 declaration of trust;
信托投資 trust and invest;
~信托投資公司 trust and investment corporation;
信托文件 trust instrument;
信托協定 trust agreement;
信托銀行 trust bank;
信托帳戶 trust account;
信托證 trust deed;
信托資產 trust asset;
保密信托 blind trust;
成立信托 create a trust; set up a trust;
公益信托 charitable trust;
固定信托 fixed trust;
靈活信托 flexible trust;
年金信托 annuity trust;
商業信托 business;
受益信托 benefit trust;
投資信托 investment trust;
遺囑信托 testamentary trust;
[信託] confide; entrust; trust;
信託公司 trust company;
[信望] prestige;
[信物] authenticating object; keepsake; pledge; token of promise;
[信息] information; message; news;
信息安全性 information security;
信息包 information package;
信息爆炸 information explosion;
信息產業 information industry;
~新信息產業 new information industries;
信息超載 information overload;
信息成本 information cost;
信息城市 information city;
信息處理 information processing;
~信息處理管理 information processing management;

~信息處理器 information processor;
~信息處理系統 information processing system;
~信息處理中心 information processing centre;
~信息處理終端 information processing terminal;
~中文信息處理 Chinese information processing;
信息傳播 information propaganda;
信息傳遞 communication;
信息動力 information drive;
信息都市 information city;
信息發佈會 information conference;
信息發送 messaging;
信息翻譯 information translation;
信息反饋 information feedback;
~信息反饋系統 information feedback system;
信息仿生學 information bionics;
信息分析 information analysis;
~信息分析中心 information analysis centre;
信息服務 information service;
~信息服務公司 information service company;
~信息服務業 information service industry;
信息負荷 information load;
信息港 information port; infoport;
信息高速公路 information superhighway;
信息革命 information revolution;
信息工業 information industry;
信息公司 information company;
信息功能 informative function;
信息管理 information management;
~信息管理服務 information management service;
~信息管理系統 information management system;
~信息管理現代化 information management modernization;
~信息管理自動化 information management automation;
信息含量 information content;
信息核心 information focus;
信息化 informationize;
~信息化社會 informationized society;
信息環境 information environment;
信息機構 information organization;
信息技術 information technology;
~信息技術革命 information technological revolution;
信息價值 value of information;
信息檢索 information retrieval;
~信息檢索技術 information retrieval technique;
~信息檢索系統 information retrieval system;
~信息檢索網絡 information retrieval network;
~信息檢索語言 information retrieval language;
~信息檢索中心 information retrieval centre;
信息交換 information exchange; information interchange;
~信息交換台 information message exchange board;
~信息交換網絡 infoswitch;
信息交際 informative communication;
信息交流 information exchange;
信息交易所 information exchange;
信息結構 information structure;
信息經紀人 information broker;
信息經紀市場 information broker market;
信息經濟 information economy;
~信息經濟學 information economics;
信息科學 information science;
信息空隙 information gap;
信息庫 information bank;
信息類型 information type;
信息量 information volume;
~平均信息量 entropy;
相對平均信息量 relative entropy;
相關平均信息量 joint entropy;
信息靈通 well-informed;
信息流 information flow;
~信息流程 information flow;
~信息流控制 information flow control;
~信息流通 information circulation;
信息論 information theory;
信息民主 information democracy;
信息內容 information content;
信息能力 information ability;
信息平台 launch pad;
信息圈 information circle;
信息社會 information society;
信息時代 information age;
信息市場 information market;
信息速率 information rate;
信息提取 information extraction;
~信息提取能力 information extraction ability;

信息通信網 information communication network;
信息通訊公司 infocom;
信息完整性 information integrity;
信息網 information network;
信息文獻 informative text;
信息污染 information pollution;
信息系統 information system;
~信息系統工程 information system engineering;
~電子信息系統 electronic messaging system;
信息銷售網絡 information and marketing network;
信息效率 information efficiency;
信息需求量 quantity of information requirement;
信息學 informatics;
~神經信息學 neuroinformatics;
信息壓縮 information compression;
信息研究 information research;
信息意識 information consciousness;
信息用戶 information user;
信息預測 information prediction;
信息源 information resources;
信息載體 information media;
信息戰 infowar;
信息障礙 information obstacle;
信息政策 information policy;
信息中介公司 infomediary;
信息中心 information centre;
信息資源 information resources;
信息咨詢 information consultancy;
~信息咨詢業 information and consultant industry;
信息總線結構 information bus architecture;
信息組織 information organization;
包含信息 contain information;
報警信息 alarm message;
背景信息 background information;
補充信息 supplementary information;
超信息 exformation;
傳遞信息 transmit information;
傳播信息 diffuse information; disseminate information;
打探信息 look for information; seek information;
發佈信息 release news;
發送信息 send a message;
封鎖信息 suppress information;
管理信息 administration information;
獲取信息 get information; receive information;
緊急信息 urgent message;
會計信息 accounting information;
收到信息 get a message; receive a message;
收集信息 collect information; gather information;
搜集信息 gather information;
提供信息 give information; provide information;
通知信息 broadcast message;
新聞信息 news information;
一條信息 a piece of information; an item of information;
異常信息 abnormal information;
有信息 have information;
重要信息 important message;
字母信息 alphabetic information;
自動信息 automatic message;

[信箱] letterbox; mailbox; main slot; postbox;
信箱號碼 box number;
留言信箱 voice mail;
郵政信箱 post office box;
語音信箱 voice mail;

[信心] confidence; faith;
信心百倍 be filled with boundless confidence; brim with confidence; full of confidence; with unbounded confidence;
信心危機 crisis of confidence;
重振信心 restore one's confidence;
動搖信心 shake sb's confidence;
恢復信心 restore one's confidence;
積聚信心 muster up confidence;
激發信心 spire confidence;
堅定的信心 unfaltering confidence;
企業信心 business confidence;
缺少信心 lack confidence; lack of confidence;
增強信心 boost confidence;

[信仰] belief; believe in; conviction; faith;
信仰療法 faith healing;
信仰自由 freedom of faith; liberty of belief;
背棄信仰 break one's faith;
始終不渝的信仰 abiding faith;
動搖信仰 shake sb's belief;
改變信仰 alter one's belief;
民間信仰 folk beliefs;
忠於信仰 keep faith;

[信以為然] accept a statement as true; believe sth to be so;
[信以為真] accept sth as true; take in; take sth as gospel; take sth for gospel truth; take sth to be true;
[信疑] belief and doubt;
將信將疑 in a half-and-half state of belief and doubt; half believe; half believing, half doubting; half seriously and half sceptically;
且信且疑 half-believing and half-doubting;
[信義] faith; good faith; honesty;
信義素著 always righteous and true;
不顧信義 guilty of bad faith;
[信譯] faithful translation;
[信用] credit; trustworthiness;
信用差距 credibility gap;
信用等級 credit rating;
信用額 credit limit;
信用管理 credit management;
信用好 have a good credit;
信用卡 credit card; smart card;
~信用卡服務 credit card services;
~信用卡號碼 credit card number;
~信用卡捐款 credit card donation;
~一張信用卡 a credit card;
信用可靠的 creditworthy;
信用評級 credit rating;
信用條款 credit terms;
信用透支 credit facilities;
信用債券 debenture bond;
信用賬戶 charge account; credit account;
信用昭著 one's credit is evident; one's credit is well-known;
信用政策 credit policy;
信用證 letter of credit;
~信用證結算 settlement with a letter of credit;
~信用證條件 credit terms;
~信用證有效期 expiry date of a letter of credit; validity of a letter of credit;
~信用證制度 letter of credit system;
~保兑信用證 confirmed letter of credit;
不保兑信用證 unconfirmed letter of credit;
~不可轉讓信用證 non-transferable letter of credit;
~償付信用證 reimbursement credit;
~承兑信用證 banker's acceptance letter of credit;
~從屬信用證 ancillary credit;
~當地信用證 local credit;
~對背信用證 back to back letter of credit;
~對開信用證 reciprocal letter of credit;
~附屬信用證 auxiliary credit;
~跟單信用證 documentary letter of credit;
~光票信用證 clean letter of credit;
~即期信用證 sight letter of credit;
遲付即期信用證 deferred sight letter of credit;
~開出信出證 issuance of letter of credit;
~可分割信用證 divisible letter of credit;
不可分割信用證 non-divisible letter of credit;
~可轉讓信用證 assignable credit;
~循環信用證 revolving letter of credit;
不循環信用證 fixed letter of credit;
~議付信用證 negotiable letter of credit;
公開議付信用證 general negotiable letter of credit;
指定議付信用證 restricted negotiable letter of credit;
~預支信用證 anticipatory letter of credit;
~展延信用證 extended letter of credit;
信用狀 letter of credit;
~保兑信用狀 confirmed letter of credit;
~保證信用狀 stand-up letter of credit;
~不保兑信用狀 confirmed letter of credit;
~不可轉讓信用狀 unassignable letter of credit;
~公開信用狀 open credit;
~還款信用狀 reimbursement letter of credit;
~即期信用狀 sight letter of credit;
~可取消信用狀 revocable letter of credit;
~流動信用狀 negotiable letter of credit;
~旅行信用狀 traveller's letter of credit;
~憑轉信用狀 back-to-back letter of credit;
~普通信用狀 general credit;
~商業跟單信用狀 commercial documentary letter of credit;
~商業信用狀 commercial letter of credit;
~循環信用狀 revolving credit;
~銀行信用狀 bank credit;
~原始信用狀 original letter of credit;
~遠期信用狀 time letter of credit;
承兑信用 acceptance credit;
改良信用 amelioration credit;

國際信用 international confidence;
講信用 keep a promise; keep one's word;
~ 不講信用 not keep one's word;
沒有信用 have no credit;
農業信用 agricultural credit;
失去信用 lose one's credit;
守信用 abide by one's promise; abide by one's word; act up to one's promise; be as good as one's word; deliver the goods; fit one's deeds to one's words; fulfil one's promise; honour one's words; keep one's promise; keep one's word; live up to what one promises; mean what one says; redeem one's promise; stand to one's promise; true to one's word;
~ 不守信用 back out; back out of one's promise; break faith with sb; break one's promise; break one's word; fail to keep a promise; fail to make good one's promise; foreswear oneself; forsake oneself; go back from one's word; go back on one's word; go back upon one's word; not to keep one's word; worse than one's word;
以昭信用 show good faith;
預支信用 anticipatory credit;
賬面信用 book credit;

［信譽］ credit; credit and reputation; prestige; reputation;
信譽不好 have a bad credit;
信譽卓著 enjoy a good reputation;
信譽廣告 prestige advertising;
信譽好 have a good credit;
信譽掃地 be discredited; discredit sb completely; sweep every bit of sb's credit into the dust; one's credit reaches rock bottom;
保持信譽 keep up one's credit;
降低信譽 lower credit;
喪失信譽 lose one's credit;
損害信譽 impair credit;
挽回信譽 redeem the reputation;
重視信譽 attached importance to reputation;

［信源］ information source; message source;

［信札］ letter;
信札往來 exchange of correspondence;

［信紙］ letter paper; notepaper; writing paper;
信紙大小 letter-size;
印有抬頭的信紙 letterhead;

保價信 insured letter;
報信 inform; notify; report news;
背信 a breach of faith; break one's promise; break one's words; faithless;
拆信 open a letter;
長信 long letter;
誠信 faith; good faith;
寵信 favour and trust;
電信 telecommunications;
篤信 a devout believer in; believe truly; sincerely believe in;
讀信 read a letter;
短信 note; short letter;
發信 post a letter;
封信 seal up a letter;
覆信 write a letter in reply;
感謝信 letter of thanks;
公開信 open letter;
掛號信 registered letter;
航空信 airmail; airmail letter;
賀信 congratulatory letter; letter of congratulation;
黑信 anonymous letter from a hostile pen; poison-pen letter;
回信 (1) letter in reply; (2) verbal message in reply; (3) answer a letter; reply to a letter; write back;
寄信 mail a letter; post a letter; send a letter;
家信 letter to or from one's family;
堅信 be firmly convinced; confident of; firmly believe;
檢舉信 letter of accusation;
介紹信 letter of introduction;
可信 credible; dependable;
恐嚇信 black-mailing letter; threatening letter;
口信 message; oral message; word;
快信 express letter;
來信 (1) letter received; (2) incoming letter;
迷信 have blind faith in; superstition;
匿名信 anonymous letter;
平信 ordinary mail; surface mail;
憑信 believe; trust;
棄信 discard faith;
虔信 piety;
淺信 weak faith;
親信 right-hand man; trusted associate; trusted follower; trusted supporter; close associates; confidants; cronies; intimate; one's own men; protege;
輕信 credulity; easily believe; easily place trust in; gullible; lightly believe; lightly put faith in; readily believe; readily place trust in;

take for granted;
取信 enjoy the trust of;
確信 be convinced; certitude; confident; firmly believe; sure;
然信 pledge to keep a promise;
深信 be deeply convinced; believe strongly; deep faith; firmly believe;
失信 break one's promise; break one's word; go back on one's word;
收信 get a letter; receive a letter;
書信 correspondence; letters; missive; written messages;
爽信 fail to keep a promise;
私信 personal letter;
送信 carry letters; deliver a message; deliver letters; send letters;
探信 make inquiries;
聽信 (1) wait for information; (2) believe; believe what one hears; listen to and believe;
通信 communicate by letter; correspond; telecommunication;
威信 cachet; popular trust; prestige;
慰問信 letter of consolation;
無信 devoid of faith; faithless;
誤信 believe what is unreliable; misplace one's confidence;
喜信 good news; happy tidings;
咸信 generally believed that;
相信 be convinced of; believe; believe in; credence; have faith in;
寫信 compose a letter; letter writing; write; write letters;
謝信 thank-you letter;
凶信 bad news;
唁信 condolatory letter;
一疊信 a wad of letters;
一封信 a letter;
一捆信 a bundle of letters;
一批信 a batch of letters;
疑信 belief and doubt;
音信 mail; message; news;
引信 detonator; fuse;
印信 official seal;
有信 keep one's promise;
證明信 certificate;
置信 believe;
忠信 faithful and honest;
資信 credit;
自信 believe in oneself; self-confident;

xin

【焮】 (1) burn; cauterize; heat; (2) "heat" in Chinese medicine;
［焮天］ fire burning fiercely;

xin

【釁】 (1) anoint with blood in worship; (2) anoint the body; (3) rift between people;
［釁端］ cause of a fight; controversial issue; dispute;
［釁起蕭牆］ internal strife; trouble breaks out at home; troubles come up within the screen of the court — there is internal strife afoot;
［釁面吞炭］ smear one's face in disguise and eat charcoal — in order to seek for vengeance;
［釁隙］ a rift between different groups of people;

xing¹
xing

【星】 (1) star; (2) heavenly body; (3) spark; (4) bit; droplet; particle; (5) movie star; (6) by night; nocturnal; (7) a surname;
［星辰］ heavenly bodies; stars;
［星塵］ stardust;
［星馳］ travel very fast like a shooting star;
［星等］ magnitude;
絕對星等 absolute magnitude;
視星等 apparent magnitude;
［星斗］ heavenly bodies; stars;
［星光］ starlight; starshine;
星光燦爛 be spangled with stars; star-studded gathering; star-spangled; the stars are very brilliant;
［星漢］ Milky Way; stars;
［星號］ asterisk;
［星河］ Milky Way;
［星火］ (1) small fire; spark; spot fire; (2) meteor; shooting star; (3) very urgent matter;
星火燎原 a little spark makes a great fire; a little spark can cause conflagration; a single spark can start a prairie fire; a spark causes a prairie fire; a spark neglected burns the house; a spark of fire may burn the whole forest;
急如星火 no delay; extremely pressing;

X

in hot haste; most urgent; of great urgency; requiring lightning action; whip and spur; with spur and yard;

[星際] interplanetary; interstellar;
星際旅行 interstellar travel; space travel;

[星家] astrologist;

[星空] starlit sky; starry sky;
翹首星空 lift up one's eyes to the starry sky; look up at the starry sky;

[星列] arrayed like stars;

[星羅棋布] dotted around like stars in the sky and scattered like the pieces on a chessboard; scattered about in every direction; scattered all over like stars in the sky or chessmen on the chessboard; spread all over the place; spread out like stars and chess piece; star-studded;
星羅棋布，遍地開花 spread and blossom out everywhere;

[星眸] bright eyes; starry eyes;

[星期] (1) week; (2) weekday;
星期二 Tuesday;
星期六 Saturday;
星期日 Sunday;
~ 星期日報 Sunday newspaper;
~ 星期日司機 Sunday driver;
~ 下星期日 next Sunday;
~ 一個星期日 a Sunday;
星期三 Wednesday;
星期四 Thursday;
星期天 Sunday;
~ 上個星期天 last Sunday;
星期五 Friday;
~ 便裝星期五 casual Friday; dress-down Friday;
星期一 Monday;
本星期 this week;
後星期 the week after next;
前星期 the week before last;
上星期 last week;
下星期 next week;
一個多星期 over a week;
一個星期 a week;
一星期 a week;
整個星期 all week;

[星球] celestial body; heavenly body; planet; star;
星球大戰 star war;

[星散] scattered about like the stars;

[星速] hurriedly; without delay;

[星探] talent scout in the movie industry;

[星體] celestial body; heavenly body;

[星團] constellation; star cluster;
昂星團 Pleiades;
畢星團 Hyades;
超星團 supercluster;
球狀星團 globular star cluster;
疏散星團 open star cluster;

[星系] galaxy;
星系團 cluster of galaxies;
棒旋星系 barred spiral galaxy;
不規則星系 irregular galaxy;
超星系 supergalaxy;
河外星系 external galaxy;
紅外星系 infrared galaxy;
活動星系 active galaxy;
類星星系 quasi-stellar galaxy;
三重星系 triple galaxy;
射電星系 radio galaxy;
雙重星系 binary galaxy;
橢圓星系 elliptical galaxy;
旋渦星系 spiral galaxy;
致密星系 compact galaxy;
總星系 metagalaxy;

[星象] configurations of the stars;
星象館 planetarium;
星象家 astrologer;
星象學 astrometry;

[星星] fires of heaven; heavenly fires; stars;
星星點點 bits and pieces; fragmentary; tiny spots;
星星之火 sparks of fire;
星星之火，可以燎原 a little spark can cause a conflagration; a single spark can cause a conflagration; a single spark can start a prairie fire; from a little spark may burst a mighty flame;
閃亮的星星 twinkling stars;
一群星星 a cluster of stars;
一簇星星 a cluster of stars;

[星形] star-polygon;

[星學] (1) astronomy; (2) astrology;

[星夜] starlit night; starry night;
星夜啟程 set out by starlight; set out in great haste;

[星移斗轉] change in the positions of the stars; change of the seasons; flow of time; passage of time;

[星移物換] aspects of things have changed; change of the seasons; things change with the passing of the years; things have changed;

[星月] moon and stars;

星月交輝 the moon and stars shine brightly; the stars and moon vie with each other in brightness;

戴月披星 get up by starlight and not to down tools till the moon rises; go to work before dawn and come home after dark;

披星戴月 with the stars as cloak and the moon as hat; work from dawn till dark;

[星雲] nebula;

星雲假說 nebula hypothesis;

星雲群 stellar nebula;

暗星雲 dark nebula;

寶瓶座耳輪星雲 Helical nebula in Aquarius;

變光星雲 variable nebula;

不規則星雲 irregular nebula;

塵埃星雲 dust nebula;

發射星雲 emission nebula;

反射星雲 reflection nebula;

河外星雲 extragalactic nebula;

狐狸座啞鈴星雲 Dumbbell nebula in Vulpecula;

亮星雲 luminous nebula;

獵戶座大星雲 great nebula in Orion;

獵戶座馬頭星雲 Horse-Head nebula in Orion;

彌漫亮星雲 bright diffuse nebula;

彌漫星雲 diffuse nebula;

氣體星雲 gaseous nebula;

天琴座環狀星雲 Ring nebula in Lyra;

橢圓星雲 elliptical nebula;

仙女座星雲 Andromeda nebula;

星落雲散 separate and disperse quickly; suffer a crushing defeat;

銀河星雲 galactic nebula;

行星狀星雲 planetary nebula;

漩渦星雲 spiral nebula;

~三角座漩渦星雲 Triangulum Spiral;

雲寒星淡 the clouds are chilly and the stars are without lustre;

[星族] stellar population;

[星座] constellation;

北天星座 northern constellations;

黃道星座 zodiacal constellations;

南天星座 southern constellations;

矮星 dwarf;

暗伴星 dark companion;

暗星 dark star;

拜星 worship famous stars blindly;

白矮星 white dwarf;

伴星 companion star;

北斗星 Big Dipper;

北極星 North Star;

孛星 comet;

奔星 meteor; shooting star;

變星 variable star;

超巨星 supergiant star;

超新星 supernova;

辰星 (1) morning star; (2) planet Mercury;

晨星 (1) stars at dawn; (2) morning star;

大行星 major planet;

戥星 sliding weight on a small steelyard;

繁星 array of stars; clusters of stars;

福星 lucky star; mascot;

歌星 singing star; star singer;

海王星 Neptune;

海星 sea star; starfish;

恒星 fixed star; star;

紅外星 infrared star;

紅星 red star;

彗星 comet;

昏星 evening star;

火流星 bolide; fireball;

火星 (1) flake; spark; sparkle; spunk; (2) Mars;

金星 stars; Venus;

救星 emancipator; liberator; saviour; white knight;

巨星 giant; giant star; megastar;

聚星 multiple star;

侃星 (1) chatterbox; (2) great boaster;

剋星 jinx-hex; one's natural enemy;

客星 nova;

老人星 Canopus;

類地行星 terrestrial planet;

類木行星 Jovian planet;

零星 (1) fragmentary; odd; piecemeal; (2) a few; a little; a small amount; (3) scattered; sporadic;

流星 falling star; meteor; shooting star;

明星 celebrity; star;

冥王星 Pluto;

木星 Jupiter;

內行星 interior planet;

牛郎星 Altair;

棋星 chess star;

啟明星 Venus;

牽牛星 Altair;

球星 athletic star;

群星 (1) the myriads of stars; (2) a galaxy of stars;
日星 the sun and the stars;
掃帚星 comet;
疏星 sparse stars;
雙星 binary star; double star;
水流星 water meteors;
水星 Mercury;
太白星 Venus;
坍縮星 collapsar;
天郎星 Sirius;
天南星 Arisaema consanguineum;
天王星 Uranus;
童星 child star; underage film star;
土星 Saturn;
衛星 (1) satellite; the moon; (2) artificial satellite; man-made satellite;
五角星 five-pointed star;
小行星 minor planet;
小星 concubine;
諧星 comedian;
新星 new star; nova; rising star;
行星 planet;
掩星 occultation;
一顆星 a star;
影星 film star; movie star;
游星 wandering star;
隕星 meteorite;
災星 bad luck; disaster;
早行星 early star;
暫星 nova;
賊星 meteor;
占星 cast a horoscope; divine by astrology;
鎮星 Saturn;
織女星 Vega;
智多星 mastermind; resourceful person;
中子星 neutron star;
眾星 myriad of stars;
主星 primary;
追星 chase after pop stars;

xing

【惺】 (1) clever; intelligent; wise; (2) indecisive; wavering;

［惺忪］ one's eyes are not yet fully open after waking up;
醉眼惺忪 have one's eyes blurred with drinking;

［惺悟前愆］ become conscious of past faults;

［惺惺］ (1) alert; awake; clear-headed; (2) clever; intelligent; wise;
惺惺惜惺惺 clever people like clever people; the intelligent ones sympathize with their own kind when they suffer; the wise appreciate one another;
惺惺作態 be affected; have affected manners; simulate;
假惺惺 hypocritically; keep up the face; put on a show of affability; shed crocodile tears;

xing

【猩】 (1) red; scarlet; (2) yellow-haired ape;

［猩紅］ bloodred; scarlet;
猩紅熱 scarlatina; scarlet fever;
布帛猩紅 cloth scarlet;
花猩紅 perylene scarlet;
紙猩紅 paper scarlet;

［猩色］ scarlet;

［猩猩］ chimpanzee; orangutan;
大猩猩 gorilla;
黑猩猩 chimpanzee;

xing

【腥】 (1) raw fish; raw meat; (2) having the smell of fish, seafood, etc.;

［腥臭］ stench; stinking smell as of rotten fish;

［腥德］ debauchery; dissipated ways; evil conduct;

［腥氣］ smelly;

［腥聞］ notoriety; scandalous acts;

葷腥 (1) meat; (2) fish;
血腥 reek of blood;

xing

【興】 (1) become flourish; popular; prosper; rise; thrive; (2) happen; occur; take place; (3) encourage; promote; (4) begin; establish; initiate; launch; open; start;

［興辦］ establish; found; initiate; set up;

［興邦］ rejuvenate a country;
多難興邦 deep distress resurrects a nation; much distress regenerates a nation;

［興兵］ mobilize troops; open hostilities; send an army; start war;
興兵動武 start hostilities;

［興廢］ rise or fall;
興廢存亡 reestablish what has been abolished;

［興奮］ excited; exciting; exhilaration; hectic; stimulated; sweep off one's foot;

興奮劑 (1) agonist; analeptic; excitant; pick-me-up; stimulant; (2) shot in the arm;
~ 抗興奮劑 contrastimulant;
興奮若狂 crazy with excitement;
興奮性 excitability;
興奮藥丸 pep pill;
非常興奮 on cloud nine; very excited;
很興奮 keyed up;
十分興奮 in a whirl; stoked; very excited;
一陣興奮 a buzz of excitement; a flurry of excitement; a ripple of excitement; a surge of excitement;

[興復] restore; revive;

[興革] initiate what is good to the people and get rid of what is harmful; reform;

[興工] start construction;

[興國] revigorate the country;
興國安邦 make the country prosperous and stable; rejuvenate and stabilize a country;
科教興國 revigorate the country through science and education;

[興家] make one's family prosper;
興家立業 make one's family prosper and establish a competency;
興家猶如針挑土，敗家好似水推舟 money comes like earth scooped up with a needle and it goes like sand washed away by water;
白手興家 become rich from scratch; build up from nothing; build up one's fortune from scratch; from rags to riches; lift oneself by one's own bootstraps; rise from poverty; rise in life by one's own efforts; run up from a shoestring; self-made; start empty-handed start from scratch; start on a shoestring;
~ 白手興家的人 self-made man;

[興建] build; construct; establish;

[興利] promote what is beneficial;
興利除弊 initiate the useful and abolish the harmful; make a profit and get rid of past abuses; promote what is beneficial and abolish what is harmful;
興利除害 start the good practices and weed out harmful ones;
興利庫容 utilizable capacity;

[興隆] brisk; flourishing; prosperous; thriving; vigorous;
生意興隆 do a roaring trade;

[興滅] revive the extinguished;
興滅繼絕 restore a fallen dynasty; restore a fallen state; revive the extinguished states and restore families whose lines of succession have been cut off — rise from the ashes;
興滅舉廢 revive what has been abolished;

[興起] gain power; grow up; on the upgrade; rise; spring up;

[興戎] mobilize troops; open hostilities;

[興盛] flourishing; prosperous; thriving; up in the ascendant; vigorous;

[興師] dispatch troops; mobilize troops; send an army;
興師動眾 mobilize troops about and stir up the people — drag in many people; muster large forces — employ a tremendous amount of manpower;
興師討伐 mobilize and send troops to suppress; mobilize the armed forces and send a punitive expedition against; mobilize troops and punish;
興師問罪 denounce sb publicly for his crimes; go with an army to punish sb; mobilize troops to chastise rebels; send a punitive force;

[興時] fashionable; popular at the moment;

[興衰] rise and decline; vicissitudes;

[興訟] commence litigation; start a lawsuit;

[興騰] become increasingly prosperous; gain vigour;

[興替] rise and fall; ups and downs; vicissitudes; waxing and waning;

[興亡] prosperity and adversity; rise and fall;

[興旺] boom; flourishing; palmy; prosperous; roaring; thriving;
興旺發達 flourish; get on very well; on one's legs; prosper; thrive;

[興修] build; start construction;

[興許] maybe; perhaps;

[興學] build schools; promote learning;

[興作] (1) gain power; rise; (2) build; construct; establish; found;

勃興 grow vigorously; rise suddenly;
不興 (1) out of fashion; (2) impermissible;
大興 go in for sth on a big scale;
復興 resurge; revive;
時興 fashionable; popular;

新興 new and developing;
振興 cause to prosper; develop vigorously;
中興 resurge;

xing
【騂】 (1) red; (2) brown; (3) harmonious; well-arranged;

xing²
xing
【刑】 corporal punishment; penalty; punishment; torture;

[刑場] execution ground; place of execution;
[刑典] criminal code; penal code;
[刑法] corporal punishment; criminal law; torture;
刑法典 penal code;
違反刑法 commit a criminal offence;
[刑罰] criminal penalty; penalty; punishment;
刑罰學 penology;
~刑罰學家 penologist;
嚴厲刑罰 stiff penalties;
[刑警] criminal police;
[刑具] implements of punishment; instruments of torture;
[刑律] criminal law;
[刑滿] expiration of the imprisonment;
刑滿釋放 be released after serving a sentence; be released upon completion of a sentence;
[刑期] prison term; term of imprisonment; term of penalty;
[刑事] criminal; penal;
刑事案 criminal case;
~刑事案件 criminal case;
刑事處分 criminal sanctions;
刑事犯 criminal; criminal suspect;
刑事司法學 study of criminal judicature;
刑事訴訟 criminal suit;
刑事損害 criminal damage;
刑事學 criminology;
~刑事學家 criminologist;
刑事責任 criminal responsibility; responsibility for a crime;
刑事追究 criminal sanctions;
[刑訊] inquisition by torture;

鞭刑 flogging;
笞刑 flogging; whipping;
處刑 condemn; sentence;
從刑 accessory punishment;
大刑 cruel punishment;
電刑 electric instruments of torture;
動刑 apply corporal punishment;
毒刑 cruel corporal punishment;
非刑 brutal torture;
服刑 be executed; imprisonment; serve a sentence;
宮刑 castration;
緩刑 conditional condemnation; imprisonment with a suspension of sentence; suspended sentence;
極刑 capital punishment;
減刑 abatement from penalty; abatement of penalty; commutation; commute a sentence; mitigate a sentence; reduce a penalty;
絞刑 death by hanging;
酷刑 brutal corporal punishment; cruel torture; savage torture;
臨刑 just before execution;
流刑 penalty of banishing the criminals to do forced labour in a remote place;
免刑 exempt from punishment;
墨刑 tattooing the face as a punishment;
判刑 pass a sentence; sentence;
輕刑 light punishment;
肉刑 corporeal punishment;
上刑 apply the third degree; put sb to torture; torture;
慎刑 mete out punishments carefully;
受刑 be punished; be tortured;
贖刑 buy freedom from punishment;
私刑 illegal punishment;
死刑 capital punishment; death penalty; death sentence;
逃刑 escape the sentence;
徒刑 imprisonment; prison sentence;
行刑 carry out a death sentence; execute;
嚴刑 cruel torture; severe punishment;
劓刑 cutting off the nose as a punishment;
用刑 torture;
重刑 heavy penalty; severe punishment;
主刑 principal penalty;
從刑 accessory punishment;
罪刑 penalty; punishment;

xing
【行】 (1) go on foot; walk; (2) go; move; travel; (3) makeshift; temporary; (4) current; prevail; (5) act; carry out; do; perform; work; (6) behaviour; conduct; (7) all right; O.K.; (8) able;

capable; competent; (9) path; road;
[行板] andante;
[行不通] (1) block; unable to pass; (2) end in a blind alley; get nowhere; unworkable; won't do; won't work; (3) impracticable; impractical; not feasible; of no avail; prove infeasible in practice;
行得通 practicable; will do; will work;
[行不行] will it do; would it be all right;
[行不由徑] consistently follow the correct path; do not take shortcuts; follow the proper rules; not take an evil way;
[行步] go;
行步如飛 go like a streak; go like blazes;
[行車] drive;
行車安全 road safety; traffic safety;
~注意行車安全 drive with caution;
行車道 carriageway;
行車通道 access road;
安全行車 drive with caution;
[行成於思] a deed is accomplished through taking thought; success depends on forethought;
[行程] distance of run; flight; itinerary; journey; length of travel; route of travel;
附加行程 additional travel;
後退行程 backward travel;
壓縮行程 compression travel;
預定行程 itinerary;
[行船] navigate; sail a boat; steer a boat;
[行刺] assassinate; assassination;
[行踏] frequent; walk;
[行動] (1) get about; move about; (2) act; take action; (3) actions; behaviour; conduct; operation;
行動不便 have difficulty getting about; tied by the leg;
行動方案 action point;
行動果斷 act decisively;
行動緩慢 slow-moving; move slowly; slow in action;
~行動緩慢的人 plodder;
行動畫派 action painting;
行動計劃 plan of action;
行動敏捷 be agile in one's movement; move quickly;
行動起來 go into action;
行動勝於空話 actions speak louder than words;
行動委員會 action committee;
行動小組 action group;
行動一致 act in concert; act in unison;
行動自如 move reely; move without impairment;
行動自由 freedom of action; freedom of movement;
~限制行動自由 restrict the freedom of action;
採取行動 begin to act; take action;
防空行動 air defence action;
奉命行動 act pursuant to the orders;
共同行動 go hand in hand with;
見諸行動 translate into action;
緊急行動 urgent action;
開始行動 make a move;
立即行動 act immediately; act now; make a rapid action;
請即行動 act now;
推遲行動 delay an action;
無行動 inaction;
一致行動 concerted action;
~採取一致行動 take concerted action;
正義行動 act of justice;
直接行動 direct action;
[行都] temporary capital;
[行而不果] undecided in one's course of action;
[行販] hawker; pedler; vender;
[行房] have sexual intercourse; have sexual relations with one's legal spouse; sleep together;
[行宮] abode of an emperor on a tour;
[行好] act charitably; charitable; do good; merciful; perform charitable deeds; practise charitable deeds; show kindness to;
[行賄] bribe; grease sb's fist; grease sb's hand; grease the fist of sb; grease the hand of sb; offer a bribe; oil sb's fist; oil sb's hand; oil the fist of sb oil the hand of sb; payola; resort to bribery;
行賄受賄 offering or accepting bribes;
行賄詐騙 bribery and swindling;
向人行賄 bribe sb; cross sb's palm; grease sb's palm; oil sb's fist; oil sb's hand; oil sb's palm; tickle sb's palm;
[行貨] (1) trade; (2) use bribery methods;
[行賈] traveling businessman;

［行姦］ commit adultery;

［行將］ about to; imminent; just going to; on the verge of;
行將就緒 about to be in order; about to be ready;
行將入木 dying; getting closer and closer to the coffin — fast approaching death; have one foot in the grave; nearing death; not long for this world; one's days are numbered;

［行劫］ commit robbery; loot; rob;
企圖行劫 attempted robbery;

［行經］ (1) go by; pass; pass by; pass through; (2) a little friend has come; fall off the roof; feeling that way; feeling unwell; have a visitor; have her rags on; have her run on; have it on; have the flags flying; her relations have come; I have friends to stay; ill; in the period; indisposed; little sister is here; menstruate; my auntie has come to stay; my cousins have come; my friend has come; on the rag; she's got painters in; she's visiting Red Bank; sick; the captain has come; the captain is at home; the cardinal has come; the flag is up; the flag of defiance is out; the red flag is up; the red rag is on; the visitors with the red hair have come;

［行徑］ acts; behaviour; conduct; disgraceful behaviour;
卑鄙行徑 sordid conduct;
卑劣行徑 base conduct; dishonourable behaviour;
惡劣行徑 disgusting conduct;
可惡的行徑 abhorrent conduct;

［行軍］ march;
行軍牀 camp bed;
長途行軍 route march;

［行客］ traveller;

［行了］ it's alright; it's settled;

［行樂］ indulge in pleasures; make merry; play; seek amusement; seek pleasure;
行樂及時 enjoy at the right time; enjoy pleasure in good time; live while we may; make merry while one can;

［行禮］ give a salute; make a salute; salute;
躬身行禮 bend;
舉手行禮 raise one's hand in solute;
屈膝行禮 bow a courtesy; drop a courtesy;
做此官來行此禮 observe the customs of the place; when in Rome, do as the Romans do;

［行李］ baggage; luggage;
行李車廂 baggage car;
行李負責人 baggage master;
行李寄存處 baggage room; left luggage office;
行李架 luggage rack;
行李收發員 baggage man;
行李提領處 baggage reclaim;
行李箱 boot; trunk;
行李員 bellboy; bellhop;
超重行李 excess luggage;
打點行李 pack up;
寄存行李 left luggage;
檢查行李 check the baggage;
拿行李 take one's luggage;
~幫人拿行李 help sb with his luggage;
收拾行李 pack up;
手提行李 hand luggage;
無人認領的行李 abandoned baggage; unclaimed baggage;
一件行李 a piece of baggage; a piece of luggage;

［行獵］ go hunting; hunt;

［行路］ travel; walk on the road;
行路人 passers-by;

［行旅］ persons going on a long journey; travellers; wayfarers;

［行囊］ travelling bag; wallet;

［行年］ at the age of;

［行騙］ cheat; deceive; practise deception; practice fraud; swindle;

［行期］ date of departure;
行期未定 the date of departure is not yet fixed;

［行乞］ beggar; beg; beg alms; beg one's bread; panhandle;
行乞的人 mendicant;

［行篋］ travelling suitcase;

［行竊］ commit theft; steal;

［行人］ passer-by; pedestrian;
行人道 sidewalks of a street;

［行色］ circumstances of departure;
行色匆匆 bustle about packing one's luggage; in a hurry to depart; in a hurry to go on a trip; in a hurry to leave; in a rush getting ready for a

journey; pressed for time on a journey; set out on one's journey in a great hurry;
以壯行色 enable sb to depart in style; provide for a proper style of travelling;

[行善] do charitable work; do good deeds; do good works; show mercy;
行善如登，行惡如崩 following virtue is like climbing a hill while following evil is like slipping down a precipice;
行善最樂 take pleasure in doing good;
暗中行善 do good by stealth;
千日行善，善猶不足；一日行惡，惡自有餘 doing good for a thousand days is still not enough, but doing ill for one day will be too much;

[行商] itinerant merchant; itinerant trader; pedlar; travelling salesman;

[行賞] reward the meritorious;
照功行賞 decide on awards on basis of merit; reward one according to his merit;

[行書] running script;

[行屍走肉] dead-alive person; lump of clay; lump of earth; utterly worthless person; walking corpse;

[行時] (1) all the rage; fashionable; in vogue; (2) in the ascendant;

[行使] employ; exercise; perform; wield;

[行駛] go; ply; travel;
超速行駛 drive over the speed limit;
緩慢行駛 poke along;

[行事] (1) act; handle matters; (2) behaviour; conduct;
行事動詞 performative verb;
行事分析 performative analysis;
行事功能 performative function;
行事話語 performative;
按規則行事 go by the rulebook; play the game;
按計行事 act upon a plan; adhere to a plan;
背後行事 go behind sb's back;
見機行事 act according to circumstances; act as circumstances dictate; act as the occasion demands; act on seeing an opportunity; adapt oneself to circumstances; do as one sees fit; play to the score; profit by the occasion; see one's chance and act; use one's own judgment and do what one deemed best;
小心行事 act cautiously; handle matters carefully; play it cozy;
因時行事，各當其宜 in the morning mountains, in the evening fountains; in the morning the heights, in the evening the depths; the morning to the mountain, the evening to the fountain;

[行書] action-script; cursive handwriting; running script;

[行述] brief biography of a deceased person;

[行為] act; action; behaviour; conduct; deed;
行為奔放 conduct oneself unconventionally; licentious in conduct;
行為本分 behave oneself decently;
行為表現 performance;
行為不當 ill-behaved;
行為不檢點 depart from correct conduct;
行為動詞 activity verb;
行為反射 behaviour reflex;
行為方式 behaviour pattern;
行為高尚 act nobly;
行為規範 behavioural norm;
行為可恥 act ignobly;
行為科學 behaviour science;
~行為科學方法 behavioural sciences approach;
行為美 behaviour beautification;
行為名詞 action noun;
行為模式 behavioural model;
行為目標 behavioural objective;
行為矯正 behaviour modification;
行為失常 go mental;
行為失控 discontrol;
行為無禮 ill-mannered;
行為形態 formation of behaviour;
行為異常 behavioural abnormality;
行為越軌 go off the rails;
行為障礙 behaviour disorder;
行為正當 act rightly;
行為治療 behaviour therapy;
行為主義 behaviourism;
~行為主義理論 behaviourist theory;
~行為主義心理學 behaviourist psychology;
~行為主義語言學 behaviourist linguistcs;
行為準則 code of conduct;
保留行為 retention behaviour;

卑鄙的行為 a base action; meanness;
~容忍卑鄙的行為 brook meanness;
~制止卑鄙的行為 obstruct a base action;
標準行為 criterion behaviour;
不正當的行為 impropriety;
粗魯的行為 rude action;
敵對行為 act of hostility;
定向行為 orientation behaviour;
定型行為 stereotyped behaviour;
短期行為 short-termism;
對稱行為 symmetrical behaviour;
改正行為 correcting behaviour;
古怪行為 cranky behaviour; eccentric behaviour; erratic behaviour; odd behaviour; strange behaviour;
怪誕行為 antics;
化學行為 chemical behaviour;
集體行為 collective behaviour;
交配行為 mating behaviour;
欺騙行為 imposture;
遷移行為 migratory behaviour;
取食行為 trophic behaviour;
權宜行為 expediency behaviour;
群體行為 group behaviour;
群眾行為 crowd behaviour;
認知行為 cognitive behaviour;
攝食行為 ingestive behaviour;
生殖行為 reproductive behaviour;
探究行為 exploratory behaviour;
討厭的行為 bratty beghaviour;
逃避行為 escape behaviour;
條件行為 conditioned behaviour;
完善行為 consummatroy behaviour;
猥褻行為 obscene acts; indecent acts;
下流行為 immodest behaviour;
相關行為 correlation behaviour;
性行為 sexual behaviour;
厭惡行為 aversive behaviour;
有目的的行為 purposive behaviour;
有組織行為 organization behaviour;
愚蠢行為 an act of folly;
欲求行為 appetitive behaviour;
異常行為 abnormal behaviour;
越軌行為 impermissible behaviour;
真空行為 vacuum behaviour;
智能行為 intelligent behaviour;
組織行為 organization behaviour;

[行文] (1) style of writing; (2) send an official communication to other organizations;
行文尖刻 wield a caustic pen;
行文流暢 read smoothly;

[行俠] chivalrous;
行俠好義 chivalrous and fond of doing good deeds;
行俠仗義 have a strong sense of justice and ready to help the weak;

[行險] embark on a dangerous task; take great risks;

[行銷] on sale; sell;
行銷全國 on sale throughout the country;

[行星] planet;
行星學 planetology
大行星 major planet; principal planet;
導航行星 navigational planets;
九大行星 nine principal planets;
類地行星 terrestrial planet;
類木行星 Jovian planet;
內行星 inferior planet; inner planet;
人造行星 artificial planet;
外行星 outer planet; superior planet;
小行星 asteroid; minor planet; planetoid;
~小行星帶 asteroidal belt;

[行刑] carry out a death sentence; execute;
行刑場 execution ground;
行刑隊 firing squad;
行刑人 executioner;

[行兇] commit killing; commit murder; commit physical assault; do violence;
行兇犯法 break the law and commit crimes;
行兇作惡 break the law and commit evils;

[行醫] practise medicine;
行醫濟世 practise medicine to save people;
行醫天下 travel around practising medicine;

[行吟] wander while reciting poems;
行吟詩人 minstrel;

[行雲] floating clouds;
行雲流水 like floating clouds and flowing water — natural and smooth;
妙歌行雲 the melodious singing lingers in the air;
輕如行雲 as light as a cloud;
響遏行雲 so sonorous it stops the passing clouds;

[行運] be favoured by good luck; have everything going one's way;

[行詐] cheat; deceive; swindle;

[行政] administer; administration; government;

行政安全 administrative safety;
行政案件 administrative case;
行政處罰 administrative punishment;
行政法規 administrative regulations;
行政法律責任 administrative legal liability;
行政法庭 administrative tribunal;
行政干預 administrative interference;
行政功能 administrative function;
行政管理 administrative management;
~行政管理體系 administrative management system;
~加強行政管理 strengthen administrative management;
行政機關 administrative organizations;
行政監督 administrative supervision;
行政拘留 administrative detention;
行政舉措 administrative measure;
行政決策 administrative decision-making;
行政立法 administrative legislation;
行政領導學 science of administrative leadership;
行政目標管理 administrative objective management;
行政區 administrative region;
~特別行政區 special administrative region;
行政人員 administrator;
行政生態分析 administrative ecological analysis;
行政手段 administrative means; administrative measure;
行政訴訟 administrative lawsuit;
行政網絡 administrative network;
行政文獻 administrative text;
行政效率 administration efficiency;
行政信息 administrative information;
行政責任 administrative responsibility;
行政執法 executive law enforcement;
行政制裁 administrative sanction;
行政中心 administrative centre;

[行止] (1) whereabouts of a person; (2) behaviour; conduct;
行止不定 one's movements are highly uncertain;
行止不檢 dissolute in conduct;
行止不明 one's whereabouts are unknown;
行止無定 there is no telling where sb is;
行止有虧 one's conduct has some shortcomings;

[行舟] sail a boat;
借水行舟 borrow water to sail one's boat;

[行裝] (1) luggage; (2) outfit for a journey;

[行狀] brief biographical sketch of a deceased person;

[行資] travelling expenses;

[行蹤] tracks of a person; whereabouts of a person;
行蹤不定 movement very uncertain; uncertain whereabouts;
行蹤不明 one's whereabouts are unknown;
行蹤詭秘 mysterious movements; secret in one's movement and trace; surreptitious in one's movements;
行蹤飄忽 no definite date of coming and going;
行蹤無定 have no fixed abode; with an uncertain place of lodging;

[行走] go on foot; run; walk;
空間行走 space walk;

頒行 issue for enforcement; make public and put into practice; promulgate and enforce;
暴行 atrocity; outrage; savage act; violent act;
卑行 of the lower generation;
詖行 evil behaviour or conduct;
濱行 on the point of going;
瀕行 about to leave; upon leaving;
並行 (1) parallel; (2) walk side by side; (3) do two or more things at the same time;
跛行 have a limp; lameness; limp; walk lamely; walk with a limp;
不行 (1) out of the question; (2) be dying; (3) no good; not work; (4) not good; (5) awfully; extremely;
步行 go on foot; walk;
操行 (1) behaviour of a student; conduct of a student; (2) disgusting; shameful;
暢行 pass unimpeded;
出行 go on a long journey;
辭行 say goodbye before setting out on a journey; take one's leave;
此行 this trip;
代行 act on sb's behalf;
倒行 (1) go against the trend; (2) retroactive;
道行 religious or moral attainments
德行 (1) moral conduct; moral integrity; (2) disgusting; shameful;
東行 eastbound;
獨行 (1) walk alone; (2) insist on one's own

ways in doing things;
斷行 categorically carry out;
惡行 evil conduct; immoral conduct;
發行 distribute; issue; publish; put on sale;
仿行 do in accordance with; follow; pattern after;
放行 let sb pass;
飛行 flight; flying;
風行 in fashion; in vogue; popular;
奉行 pursue;
躬行 do sth in person;
孤行 be bent on having one's own way; cling obstinately to one's course;
航行 navigate by air or by water;
橫行 be on a rampage; run amuck; run wild;
划行 paddle; row;
滑行 coast; freewheel; freewheeling; slide;
環行 go in a ring; make a circuit;
穢行 abominable behaviour;
紀行 travel notes;
餞行 give a farewell dinner;
進行 (1) carry out; undertake; (2) advance; march;
舉行 come off; conduct; give; go off; hold; pass off; stage; take place;
開行 strart a vehicle;
刊行 print and publish;
可行 doable; feasible; practicable; workable;
苦行 ascetic practices;
力行 do sth persistently; try hard to practise;
例行 routine;
厲行 make great efforts to carry out; strictly enforce;
臨行 before leaving; on departure;
另行 do, act, etc. separately or at some other time;
流行 fashionable; prevalent; popular;
旅行 journey; travel;
履行 make great efforts to carry out; practise; rigorously enforce; strictly carry out; strictly enforce;
難行 difficult to move;
逆行 go in the opposite direction;
爬行 crawl; creep;
漂行 float;
品行 behaviour; conduct;
平行 (1) of equal rank; of the same level; on an equal footing; (2) simultaneous;
跂行 (1) go on foot; walk; (2) creep; move;
琦行 admirable conduct;
起行 set out; start on a journey;
啟行 set out; start on a journey;
潛行 (1) move under water; (2) move stealthily;
強行 break; by force; force; jam;
全武行 brawl; free-for-all;
逡行 shrink;
繞行 (1) detour; (2) orbit; revolve around sth;
人行 pedestrian;
善行 charity; philanthropic act;
上行 (1) go up; (2) sail upriver;
蛇行 (1) move like a snake; take a zigzag course; (2) crawl; creep along;
攝行 hold an office in an acting capacity;
盛行 current; in vogue; prevail; prevalent;
施行 (1) apply; come into force; execute; go into effect; put in force; (2) act; carry out; enforce; implement; perform; put sth in practice;
時行 fashionable; popular;
實行 bring into effect; carry into effect; carry out; implement; practise; put into action; put into effect; put into practice;
駛行 go; run; sail;
試行 put into trial use; trial implementation; try out;
獸行 beastly conduct; brutal act;
淑行 virtuous conduct;
順行 direct motion;
肆行 act at the dictate of one's own will without any thought for others; act recklessly; indulge;
送行 (1) see sb off; (2) give a send-off party;
素行 one's true disposition;
隨行 accompany; go along; go together; in company with;
體行 embody in one's own actions;
通行 (1) go through; pass through; travel through; (2) current; general;
同行 travel together;
徒行 go on foot; hike; walk;
推行 carry out; implement; implementation; practise; promote; pursue; put into practice;
拖行 tow;
西行 go west; travel westward;
細行 one's behaviour in trivial matters;
無行 villainous; wicked;
下行 (1) go down; (2) sail downriver; sail downstream; (3) (of a document) to be issued to the lower levels;
先行 beforehand; commander of an advance unit; in advance; start off before the others;
現行 (1) currently in effect; existing; in force; in operation; presently effective; (2) active;
宵行 travel by night;

銷行 be on sale; sell;
孝行 filial conduct;
邪行 evil deeds;
偕行 go together with;
蟹行 go sideways; move laterally;
行不行 will it do; would it be all right;
性行 character; nature and conduct;
修行 practise Buddhism or Daosim;
巡行 go the rounds; make a circuit of;
循行 make rounds of inspection;
徇行 make rounds of inspection;
言行 statements and actions; words and deeds;
雁行 (1) walk like flying wild geese, one afer another; (2) brothers;
洋行 foreign business firm;
也行 all right; that will do too;
一行 a group of travelling together; party;
易行 easy to do; easy to practise;
義行 act of justice; chivalrous act;
懿行 (1) virtuous deed; (2) woman's virtuous conduct;
吟行 traveling minstrel;
淫行 licentious conduct;
銀行 bank; banking house;
印行 print and distribute; publish;
庸行 regular course of action;
游行 (1) roam; wander; (2) march; parade;
遊行 (1) parade; (2) demonstrate; demonstration; march;
紆行 proceed through a winding and twisting path;
預行 apply beforehand; put in force beforehand;
遠行 a journey to a distant place; go on a long journey; travel to a distant place;
運行 in motion; move;
趲行 hurry in a journey; travel hurriedly;
暫行 for the time being; provisional; temporary;
真行 good;
知行 knowledge and action;
執行 carry out; enforce; execute; implement;
志行 principle and conduct; purpose and behaviour;
自行 (1) by oneself; individually; personally; (2) of one's own accord; of oneself; voluntarily;
罪行 atrocities; crime; criminal acts; guilt; offences;
遵行 act in accordance with; act on; follow; put into practice;
左行 (1) from left to right; (2) keep to the left;

xing

【形】 (1) appearance; figure; form; shape; (2) body; entity; (3) appear; look; (4) compare; contrast; (5) complexion; (6) contour; terrain;

[形便] advantages offered by terrain;

[形成] form; produce as a result; take shape;
形成層 cambium;
~創傷形成層 wound cambium;
~次生形成層 secondary cambium;
~疊生形成層 stratified cambium;
~副形成層 accessory cambium;
~繼生形成層 successive cambium;
~木栓形成層 cork cambium;
~束間形成層 interfascicular cambium;
~束中形成層 fascicular cambium;
~維管形成層 vascular cambium;
形成風氣 become a common practice;
形成僵局 come to a deadlock;
概念形成 concept formation;
開始形成 begin to take shape;

[形單影隻] all alone; be left along with only one's own shadow; extremely lonely; single and alone; single shadow; solitary; solitary form,

[形而上] metaphysical; noumenal;
形而上學 metaphysics;

[形而下] phenomenal; physical;

[形合式] hypotaxis;

[形骸] one's body; one's skeleton;
自忘形骸 beyond oneself;

[形穢] vulgar appearance;
心邪形穢 when the mind is filthy, the appearance will not be any better;
自慚形穢 feel ashamed of one's ungainly appearance; feel inferior to others; feel put to shame by sb; have a sense of inferiority; humble oneself; look small; think small beer of oneself;

[形跡] (1) movements and expression; (2) formality;
形跡可疑 look suspicious; of doubtful aspect; of suspicious appearance and behaviour; one's movements are supicious; shady-looking; suspicious-looking;
不露形跡 betray nothing in one's expression and movements;

[形浪意骸] given to sensual pleasures;

[形類詞] form class word;

[形貌] appearance of a person; countenance;

[形容] (1) appearance; countenance; form; shape; (2) describe;
形容悲戚 one's face is ravaged with grief;
形容詞 adjective;
~形容詞補語 adjective complement;
~形容詞從句 adjectival clause;
~形容詞分詞 adjectival participle;
~形容詞分詞從句 adjectival participle clause;
~形容詞化 adjectivization;
~形容詞化名詞 adjectival noun;
~形容詞結構 adjectival structure;
~形容詞謂語 adjectival predicate;
~形容詞物主代詞 adjectival possessive pronoun;
~形容詞性 adjectival;
~形容詞性從句 adjectival clause;
~形容詞性化 adjectivization;
~形容詞修飾詞 adjective modifier;
~形容詞組 adjective group;
~比較級形容詞 comparative degree adjective;
~動詞形容詞 verbal adjective;
~動態形容詞 dynamic adjective;
~動作形容詞 dynamic adjective;
~分詞形容詞 participial adjective;
~附着形容詞 adherent adjective;
~複合形容詞 compound adjective;
~個別形容詞 distributive adjective;
~固有形容詞 inherent adjective;
~非固有形容詞 non-inherent adjective;
~關係形容詞 relative adjective;
~可分等形容詞 gradable adjective;
~兩極形容詞 bipolar adjective;
~名詞化形容詞 adjectival noun;
~名詞派生形容詞 denominal adjective;
~年齡形容詞 age adjective;
~派生形容詞 derived adjective;
~強化形容詞 intensifying adjective;
~原級形容詞 positive degree adjective;
~指示形容詞 demonstrative adjective;
~最高級形容詞 superlative degree adjective;
形容盡致 accurate and detailed description;
形容句 adjectival sentence;
形容枯槁 emaciated, dried appearance; haggard; look haggard;
形容憔悴 looking wan; thin and pallid; withered-looking;
形容猥瑣 frivolous portrayal;
形容消瘦 gaunt and thin; look thin;

[形神] body and spirit;

[形式] form; format; formation; layout; modality; shape;
形式比較級 formal comparative;
形式賓詞 formal object;
形式程度 degree of formality;
形式詞 form word;
形式對等 formal equivalence;
形式對應 formal correspondence;
形式活潑 lively in form;
形式結構障礙 formal structural obstruction;
形式量表 scale of formality;
形式普遍現象 formal universal;
形式上 for formality's sake; formal; in form; nominally;
形式系統 formal system;
形式性程度 degree of formality;
形式意義 formal meaning;
形式語段 formal text;
形式增補 formal expansion;
形式種類 formal class;
形式主義 formalism;
形式主語 formal subject;
地址形式 address format;
動詞形式 form of a verb;
堆集形式 accumulative formations;
分析形式 analytic form;
改變形式 change form;
規範形式 canonical form;
基本形式 base form;
基礎形式 base form;
簡單形式 simple form;
交替形式 alternative form;
絕對形式 absolute form;
卡片形式 card format;
流於形式 become a mere formality;
邏輯形式 logical form;
區域形式 area format;
縮醛形成 acetal formation;
徒具形式 mere formality;
徒有形式 mere formality;
注重形式 lay stress on form;

[形勢] (1) contour; terrain; topographical features; (2) landscape; situation; circumstances;
形勢逼人 reality is a compelling force; the compelling force of circumstances; the situation demands immediate action; the situation is pressing; the situation spurs us on;

形勢不妙 the situation is rather bad;
形勢大好 the situation is excellent;
形勢倒轉 for the tables to be turned; the tide turns; turn the table;
形勢好轉 the situation takes a favourable turn;
形勢喜人 the situation is gratifying;
形勢險要 strategically important terrain;
抱怨形勢 grumble over the situation;
當前形勢 current situation;
分析形勢 analyze a situation; size up a situation;
估計形勢 size up a situation;
觀察形勢 examine the situation; observe the situation;
觀望形勢 see which way the wind is blowing; wait for the cat to jump;
國際形勢 international situation;
國內形勢 domestic situation;
控制形勢 dominate the situation;
目前形勢 present situation;
扭轉形勢 reverse a situation;
迫於形勢 under the pressure of events; under the stress of circumstances;
全國形勢 national situation;
認清形勢 realize the situation;
社會形勢 social landscape;
適應形勢 adapt to the situation;
外交形勢 diplomatic situation;
形格勢禁 be forced to stop doing sth according to circumstances; be obstructed by conditions and prohibited by circumstances;
政治形勢 political landscape;
總的形勢 general situation;

[形似] formal resemblance; look like; resemble; similar in form;

[形態] appearance; form; pattern; shape; state;
形態變化 morphological change;
形態分析 morphology;
形態構成 form construction;
形態美 formal beauty;
形態心理學 configurationism;
形態學 morphology;
~晶體形態學 crystal morphology;
~年齡形態學 age morphology;
~派生形態學 derivational morphology;
~人類形態學 human morphology;
~社會形態學 social morphology;
~細胞形態學 cellular morphology;
~植物形態學 plant morphology;
形態要素 formative;

[形體] (1) body; physique; shape; (2) form and structure;

[形相] appearance; countenance; facial look; form;
窮形盡相 appear in all one's ugliness; cut a contemptible figure; describe in minute, vivid detail;

[形象] figure; form; image; visualization; vivid;
形象良好 have a good image;
形象思維 think in terms of images;
擺脱形象 lose an image; shed an image;
創造形象 create an image;
低端品牌形象 downmarket image;
典型形象 model personalities; typical character; typical image;
反面形象 negative image;
改變形象 change one's image;
改善形象 improve one's image;
乾淨的形象 clean-cut image;
高端品牌形象 upmarket image;
公共形象 public image;
好的形象 good image;
壞的形象 bad image;
健康的形象 wholesome image;
破壞形象 damage one's image;
樹立形象 cultivate one's image;
損害形象 tarnish an image;
擁有形象 have an image;
正面形象 positive image;

[形銷骨立] as lean as a rake; one's figure is wearing to the bones; worn to a shadow;

[形形色色] a great variety and diversity; all brands of; different hues of; diverse; every description; every shade and hue; in all their manifestations; many varieties; of all descriptions; of all forms; of all hues; of all kinds; of all shades; of all shades and colours; of all stripes; of assorted types; of different sorts; of every description; of every hue; of various forms; this, that, and the other;

[形影] form and shadow;
形影不離 be always together; be never apart; follow each other like form and shadow; hand-in-hand; hunt in couples; inseparable as body and

shadow; keep each other's company all the time; not separate for a moment; stick like glue;
形影相吊 body and shadow comforting each other — extremely lonely; sad and solitary;
形影相隨 as close as form and shadow; follow like a shadow; follow sb wherever he goes; go hand in hand; inseparable; intimate; keep close at sb's side; never to leave each other's side;
~影形相隨 as the shadow following the substance;
藏形匿影 conceal one's identity; go into hiding; hide from public notice; stay in concealment;

[形質] form and substance;

[形狀] appearance; conformation; form; likeness; shape;
各種形狀 every shape and size;
詭狀殊形 fantastic shapes and strange forms; grotesque shapes;
平面形狀 two-dimensional shape;
奇形怪狀 bizarre in appearance; fantastic shape; grotesque appearance; grotesque in appearance; grotesque in form; grotesque in shape; of odd shape; outlandish; peculiar; queer; sth curiously shaped; strange sights; strange-looking;
妖形怪狀 grotesque;

[形蹤] (1) traces of a person; whereabouts of a person; (2) behaviour of a person;
形蹤不定 have no fixed residence; wander here and there unpredictably;
形蹤詭秘 of dubious background;

鞍形 saddle;
八邊形 octagon;
半形 half angle;
邊形 number of sides of a polygon;
變形 become deformed; change shape; deform; deformation; out of shape; transfigure; transshape;
彪形 tall and big;
波形 waveform;
長方形 rectangle;
成形 form; shaping; take shape;
雛形 embryonic form;
詞形 morphology;
單形 simplex;
地形 terrain; topography;
丁字形 T-shaped;
定形 (1) set; (2) board;
隊形 formation;
多邊形 polygon;
多角形 polygon;
方形 square;
仿形 profile modeling;
放射形 radiation;
弓形 (1) segment of a circle; (2) arched; bow-shaped; curved;
工字形 I-shaped;
拱形 arch;
勾股形 right triangle;
構形 configuration;
骨畸形 bone malformation;
弧形 arc;
花形 floral pattern;
環形 annular; ringlike;
畸形 abnormal; deformity; lopsided; malformation;
矯形 orthopaedy; plastic;
框形 frame;
矩形 rectangle;
口形 degree of lip-rounding
菱形 rhomb; rhombic; rhombus;
流形 manifold;
六邊形 hexagon;
籠形 cage-shaped;
馬鞍形 shape of a saddle;
馬蹄形 shape of a hoof; U-shaped;
內接形 inscribed figure;
披針形 lanceolate;
七邊形 heptagon; septangle; septilateral;
情形 circumstances; condition; general condition; situation; state of affairs;
穹形 arch; arched; dome-shaped; ault; vaulted;
球形 ball-shaped; globular; spherical;
全等形 congruent figures;
三邊形 triangle;
三角形 triangle;
三稜形 triangular prism;
三面形 trihedral;
傘形 umbrella type;
扇形 (1) fan-shaped; (2) sector;
蛇形 snake-like;
十邊形 decagon;
四邊形 quadrilateral;
梯形 (1) ladder-shaped; (2) trapezium;
體形 bodily form; body shape; build; external physical appearance; physique;
條形 linear leaf;

同形 homotype;
筒形 shape of a tube or ball;
圖形 contour; figure; graph; outline; sketch;
橢圓形 ellipse;
外切形 circumscribed figure;
外形 appearance; external form;
忘形 be carried away; beside oneself; get carried away; have one's head turned;
無形 imperceptibly; intangible; invisible; virtually; without taking a form;
五邊形 pentagon;
顯形 betray oneself; reveal one's feature;
現形 betray oneself; reveal one's true features; show one's true colours;
線形 long and narrow;
相似形 similar figures;
相形 by comparison; make a comparison;
楔形 wedge-shaped;
星形 star-polygon;
異形 strange form; strange shape;
隱形 invisible;
有形 concrete; tangible; visible;
原形 original form; original shape; primary form; true shape under the disguise;
圓形 circular; round; spherical;
整形 orthopedics;
正多邊形 regular polygon;
正方形 square;
正三角形 regular triangle;
錐形 cone; taper;
字形 font; form of a character;

xing
【邢】 (1) name of an ancient state during the Spring and Autumn Period; (2) a surname;

xing
【型】 (1) earthen mould for casting; (2) model; pattern; standard; (3) law; stature; (4) fashion; style; type;
[型板] template;
[型號] marker; model; model number; type; marking;

矮型 dwarf;
表現型 phenol-type;
超薄型 super slim;
超微型 superminiature;
成型 take shape;
大型 large-scale;
典型 archetype; example; model; type; typical case; typical example;
定型 finalize the design; stereotype; take shape;
髮型 coiffure; hairdo; hairstyle;
構型 configuration;
機型 (1) type; (2) model;
劑型 form of a drug;
句型 sentence pattern;
巨型 colossal; giant; heavy; huge; large;
孔型 pass;
類型 cut; form; mold; type;
臉型 cast of one's face;
流線型 streamline;
模型 (1) model; mock-up; pattern; (2) model set; mould pattern;
輕型 light; light-duty;
砂型 sand mould;
生態型 ecotype;
體型 build; external physical appearance; type of build;
外型 appearance; contour; external form; outline; profile;
微型 mini-; miniature;
小型 compact type; midget; miniature; minitype; pocketsize; small-scale; small-sized;
新型 late model; new pattern; new type;
血型 blood group; blood type;
牙型 tooth form;
葉型 leaf type;
乙型 Grade B; Type B;
異型 aerofoil; wing section;
音型 figure;
原型 ancestor; prototype;
造型 model; modeling; mould; mould-making;
紙型 paper matrix; paper mould;
中型 medium-sized; middle-sized;
重型 heavy; heavy-duty; heavy type;
轉型 crossover;
鑄型 casting mould;

xing
【陘】 deep valley; defile; gorge;

xing
【硎】 grindstone; whetstone;

xing
【鉶】 a kind of receptacle for food in ancient times;

xing
【餳】 (1) malt sugar or syrup; (2) sticky; (3) dull eyesight; poor eyesight;

xing³
xing
【省】 (1) examine oneself critically; intro-

X

spect; reflect; (2) visit; (3) aware; become conscious; know; understand;
［省察］ examine one's thoughts and conduct; examine oneself critically; introspect;
［省會］ (1) exhort; instruct; (2) know; understand;
［省親］ pay a visit to one's parents or elders;
［省事］ clever and understanding; conscious;
［省視］ examine carefully; inspect; survey; visit;
［省問］ ask about; send one's respects to;
［省悟］ awakening; realize;

反省 make a self-examination;
歸省 go home for a visit; go home to pay respects to one's parents;
猛省 realize suddenly;
內省 introspect;
深省 come to realize one's error etc. fully;

xing
【惺】 awake from ignorance; become aware of;
［惺悟］ awake to the truth; realize;

xing
【醒】 (1) come to; recover from; regain consciousness; sober up; (2) awake; be roused; wake up; (3) clear in mind; cool in mind;
［醒得了］ wake up in time;
［醒盹兒］ shake off drowsiness; wake up from a nap;
［醒豁］ clear; explicit;
［醒酒］ dispel the effects of alcohol; sober up from drunkenness;
［醒覺］ awake; wake;
［醒來］ wake up;
［醒目］ attract attention; catch the eye; eye-catching; striking;
［醒腦］ refreshment; restoring consciousness;
［醒脾］ (1) amuse oneself; entertain; refresh one's mind; (2) make fun of;
［醒神］ induce resuscitation;
［醒獅］ awakened lion;
［醒悟］ awakening; come to realize the truth; wake up to reality;
［醒醒］ wake up; wakey-wakey;
［醒眼］ attract attention; catch the eye; refreshing;

復醒 wake up again;
喚醒 awaken; wake up;
叫醒 wake up;
驚醒 (1) wake up with a start; (2) awaken; cause to wake up; rouse suddenly from sleep;
警醒 be on the alert; sleep lightly;
覺醒 (1) awake; awaken; awakening; (2) a waking state;
猛醒 realize suddenly;
夢醒 awake from a dream;
清醒 (1) clear-headed; sane; sober; (2) come round; come to; come to one's senses; recover consciousness; regain consciousness;
深醒 come to realize one's error, etc. fully;
睡醒 wake up from sleep;
甦醒 come back to life; come to; revive;
蘇醒 awake; come to; come round; regain consciousness; revive;
提醒 remind; warn;
醉醒 regain presence of mind after getting drunk; sober up;

xing
【擤】 blow one's nose;
［擤鼻涕］ blow one's nose;

xing⁴
xing
【行】 behaviour; conduct;
［行成於思］ a goal is achieved through thinking carefully; success depends on forethought;
［行誼］ conduct and virtues;
［行狀］ brief biography of the deceased;

xing
【杏】 (1) apricot; (2) apricot kernels; (3) apricot flowers;
［杏兒］ apricot;
［杏核］ stone of an apricot;
［杏紅］ apricot pink;
［杏花］ apricot blossoms;
［杏黃］ apricot yellow;
［杏臉］ beautiful face of a woman;
杏臉生春 have a cheerful look;
［杏林］ medical profession;
杏林春滿 in praise of one's high medical skill;
［杏面］ beautiful face of a girl;
［杏脯］ dried apricot meat; preserved apricot meat;

[杏仁] (1) almond; (2) apricot kernel;
杏仁餅 apricot cake;
~蛋白杏仁餅 macaroon;
杏仁茶 almond dessert;
杏仁粉 almond powder;
杏仁精 apricot essence;
杏仁露 syrup of almonds;
杏仁色 almond;
杏仁糖 praline;
杏仁油 almond oil;
苦杏仁 armeniaca amara;
甜杏仁 armeniaca dulcis;
[杏實] apricot fruit;
[杏樹] apricot; apricot tree;
[杏壇] teaching profession;
[杏桃] prune and peach trees;
杏桃如畫，垂柳如絲 with prune and peach trees like a painting and drooping willows like silken threads;
[杏眼] apricot-like eyes;
杏眼柳腰 apricot-like eyes and soft waistline of a beauty;
杏眼桃腮 almond-shaped eyes and peachred cheeks; large eyes and rosy cheeks;
杏眼秀眉 with almond-shaped eyes and long eyebrows;
杏眼圓睜 with eyes distended with fury;
柳眉杏眼 graceful eyebrows and large eyes;
桃腮杏眼 peach-red cheeks and almond-shaped eyes; rosy cheeks and almond eyes;
[杏月] second month of the lunar calendar;
[杏子] apricot fruit;
杏子酒 abricotine;

山杏 armeniaca ansu;
銀杏 ginkgo;

xing
【姓】 (1) family name; surname; (2) clan; family; people;
[姓名] full name of a person; name; surname and personal names;
姓名牌 name tag; nameplate;
改名換姓 change one's name and surname; change one's surname and given name;
更名改姓 assume a false name; change one's whole name; conceal one's real name;
更姓改名 change one's name; change one's surname and given name;
互通姓名 introduce to each other; tell one's name to the other;
埋名隱姓 conceal one's name and surname; conceal one's real name; keep one's identity hidden;
行不更名，坐不改姓 whether I travel or stay at home I do not change my name;
有名有姓 of verifiable identity;
真名實姓 real name; right name;
坐不改姓，行不更名 whether travelling or staying at home, one does not change one's name;
[姓譜] genealogy;
[姓氏] family name; surname;
[姓系] family line;

百姓 common people;
敝姓 my family name;
大姓 (1) surname of an aristocratic family; (2) popular surname;
復姓 resume the original family name;
複姓 compound surname; two-character surname;
貴姓 your family name; your last name; your surname;
雙姓 compound name; two-syllable surname;
俗姓 the secular surname of a Buddhist monk;
同姓 of the same surname;
外姓 not of the same surname;
異姓 those with different surnames;
種姓 cast;
子姓 descendants; offspring;
尊姓 your name;

xing
【幸】 (1) good fortune; good luck; (2) rejoice; (3) fortunately; luckily; (4) I hope; I trust; pray; (5) favour; (6) a surname;
[幸存] survive;
[幸得] fortunately; thanks to;
[幸而] fortunately; luckily; thanks to;
[幸福] bliss; happiness; well-being;
幸福美滿 happiness without alloy;
家庭幸福 domestic happiness;
追求幸福 seek happiness;
[幸好] fortunately; just as well; luckily;

[幸虧] as luck would have it; but for; fortunately; luckily; thanks to;

[幸免] escape by sheer luck; have a narrow escape;

幸免一死 escape death by sheer good luck;

幸免於難 a close shave; a narrow shave; a narrow squeak; a near squeak; escape by the skin of one's teeth; escape death by a hair's breadth; escape death by sheer luck;

[幸事] blessing; fortune;

[幸未] fortunately, it's not;

幸未成災 fortunately it does not cause a disaster;

[幸喜] fortunately; luckily;

[幸有] fortunate to have;

[幸運] (1) good fortune; good luck; jam on it; (2) felicity; fortunate; lucky;

幸運草 four-leaf clover;

幸運兒 fortune's favourite; lucky beggar; lucky fellow; lucky guy;

幸運之神 Lady Luck; goddess of fortune;

你真幸運 lucky you;

祝你幸運 may good luck attend you;

嬖幸 be favoured by the ruler;

薄幸 fickle; inconstant in love;

不幸 adversity; misfortune; sad; unfortunate;

寵幸 favour sb;

恩幸 royal favour;

慶幸 congratulate oneself; rejoice oneself;

榮幸 be honoured; have the honour of;

是幸 be much obliged;

天幸 close shave; providential escape;

萬幸 by sheer luck; fortunately; most lucky; very fortunate; very lucky;

為幸 it would be fortunate;

奚幸 vexed; worried;

喜幸 feel delighted; happy;

欣幸 glad and thankful; joyful and thankful; rapture;

巡幸 (of an emperor) go on an inspection tour;

xing

【性】 (1) character; disposition; nature; nature of a person; temper; (2) property; quality; (3) sex;

[性愛] sexual love;

性愛的 amatory;

自由性愛 free love;

[性暴] irascible; hot-tempered;

[性本能] sexual instinct;

[性變態] parasexuality; perversion; sex perversion;

性變態者 pervert;

[性別] sex; sexual distinction; sexuality;

性別改變 sex change;

性別角色 gender role; roles of different genders;

性別決定 sex determination;

性別扭曲的人 gender-bender;

性別偏見 gender bias; sexism;

性別平等 gender equality;

性別歧視 sexual discrimination;

~性別歧視者 sexist;

性別政治 sexual politics;

跨性別 transgender;

異體性別 heterogametic sex;

[性病] venereal disease;

[性剝削] sexploitation;

[性殘善疑] suspicious and cruel;

[性衝動] sex drive; sex impulse; sexual drive; sexual impulse;

[性道德] sex ethics;

[性犯罪] sexual offence;

[性感] sex appeal; sexy;

性感的 dishy; sexy;

~性感的人 cracker; hottie; sexually attractive person; sexy person;

~十分性感的 luscious;

性感迷人的身體 luscious body;

性感明星 sex sirens; sexy stars;

性感偶像 sex symbol;

[性高潮] climax; come; come off; cum; orgasm;

[性格] character; disposition; nature; personality; temperament;

性格奔放 possess a bold and unrestrained character;

性格不合 incompatibility of temperament;

性格分析 character analysis;

~性格分析學 characterology;

性格開朗 have a bright and cheerful disposition;

性格內向 introverted;

性格輕浮 have a frivolous disposition;

性格特徵 personality traits;

性格特別的人 quite a character;

性格外向 extroverted;

性格溫和 gentle;

性格演員 character actor;
性格直爽 forthright in character;
暴露性格 reveal one's character;
大方的性格 bounteous nature;
刻薄的性格 acrid disposition;
內向性格 introversion;
外向性格 extroversion; extrovert personality; outgoing personality;
中向性格 ambiversion;
專橫的性格 dominant personality;

[性關係] have sex; love affair; sexual relationship;
發生性關係 sleep together;
亂搞性關係 put oneself about;

[性急] hot-tempered; impatient; impetuous; impulsive; short-tempered;
性急的人 hothead;

[性交] act of love; action; amorous congress; amorous rites; aphrodisia; approach; art of pleasure; balling; bonk; caress; carnal acquaintance; carnal connection; carnal engagement; carnal enjoyment; carnal knowledge; carnal relations; carnalize; coitus; compress; concubitus; congress; conjugal relations; conjugal rites; conjugal visit; conjugate; connection; consummation; conversation; copulate; copulation; crouch with; deed of kind; do a kindness to; do it; do some good for oneself; do the chores; effect intromission; enjoy a woman; familiar with; federate; fix her plumbing; foraminate; foregather; fruit that made men wise; funch; game; get it on; get one's leg over; go all the way with sb; go the limit; go the whole route; go to bed with; gratification; grease the wheel; greens; have a bit; have one's will of a woman; have relations; improper intercourse; in Abraham's bosom; in bed; intercourse; intimate with; jump; keeping company; larks in the night; last favours; lewd infusion; lie with; life one's leg; light the lamp; love life; lovemaking; make it; make love; make somconc; make out; make time with; marital duty; matinee; meaningful relationships; night work; nookie; on the make; pareunia; perform; play; play at in-and-out; play doctor; please; pluck; possess carnally; rites of love; scale; score; screw the arse off; see; service; sex experience; sexual intercourse; sexual intimacy; sleep together; switch; the bee is in the hive; the facts of life; tie the true lover's knot; union; venereal act; what Eve did with Adam; work;
性交恐怖 coitophobia;
安全性交 safe sex;

[性教育] sex education; sexual education;

[性解放] sexual liberation;

[性禁忌] sex taboo;

[性開放] sexually open;
性開放的人 swinger;

[性冷感] frigidity;

[性涼] cool in nature; coo-natured;

[性烈] fiery disposition; fierce tempered;
性烈如火 a passion like fierce fire;

[性靈] natural disposition and intelligence;

[性命] one's life;
性命難保 can hardly keep oneself alive; one's life will be difficult to save;
保全性命 save one's own life; save one's skin;
保住性命 save one's carcass;
身家性命 one's life and family possessions;

[性能] function; nature; performance; property;
性能測試 performance test;
性能評價 performance evaluation;
性能穩定 stable performance;
車削性能 turning ability;
防腐性能 antiseptic property;
防污性能 antifouling property;
防震性能 anti-shock performance;
飛機性能 aeroplane performance;
高性能 high-performance;
~高性能電腦 high-performance computer;
~高性能汽車 high-performance car;
合格性能 acceptable performance;
豁出性命 risk one's life;
起飛性能 take-off ability;
設計性能 design performance;
速度性能 speed ability;

[性虐待狂] sadism;

[性癖] idiosyncrasy; one's peculiar likes and dislikes;

[性器官] genitals; reproductive organs; sexual organs;

[性氣] disposition; personality; temperament;

[性侵犯者] sex offender;

[性情] disposition; temper; temperament;
性情暴躁 have an irascible temperament; short-tempered;
性情剛烈 obstinate;
性情乖戾 perverse in temperament; sullen in nature;
性情急躁 ardent in temper;
性情平和 even-tempered; have a calm temper;
性情柔順 of a yielding disposition;
性情溫和 have a sweet temper; moderate in temper; of a gentle nature; with a gentle nature;
性情溫柔 amiable disposition; have a gentle disposition; have a sweet temper; moderate in temper of very benign nature;
性情相投的人 soul mate;
豪邁性情 magnanimous disposition;
陶冶性情 mould one's temperament; shape one's spirit;
性靜情逸 quiet and easy disposition;
怡情養性 contribute to one's inner tranquility; contribute to one's peace of mind;
怡情悅性 cheer the heart and please the feelings; cheerful; feel easy and happy; happy; joyful; please one's mind and delight one's spirit; relaxed and happy;

[性取向] sex orientation; sexual orientation;

[性騷擾] sexual harassment;

[性生活] sex life; sexual life;

[性特徵] sexual characteristics;

[性玩物] sex object;

[性無能] impotent;

[性腺] sex gland;
性腺病 gonadopathy;
性腺發生 gonadogenesis;
~ 性腺發生不全 gonadal dysgenesis;
性腺發育不全 gonadal dysgenesis;

[性向] disposition;

[性行為] hanky-panky; rumpy pumpy; sex instinct act; sexual behaviour;
不安全的性行為 unsafe sex;
發生性行為 have sex;
婚前性行為 premarital; sex before marriage;
婚外性行為 sex outside marriage;

[性學] sexology;

[性慾] concupiscence; libido; sexual appetite; sexual desire; sexual urge;
性慾衝動 sexual impulse;
性慾倒錯 paraphilia;
性慾發生 erotogenesis;
性慾高潮 orgasm;
性慾過強的 oversexed;
性慾過盛的 oversexed;
性慾減退 hyposexuality;
性慾異常 sexopathy;
性慾障礙 sexual desire disorder;
同性性慾 homoerotism;
幼兒性慾 infantile sexuality;

[性早熟] sexual precocity;
神經源性性早熟 neurogenic precocious puberty;
特發性性早熟 idiopathic precocious puberty;
同性性早熟 isosexual precocious puberty;
真性性早熟 true precocious puberty;

[性質] character; characteristic; nature; property; quality;
性質形容詞 qualitative adjective;
話語性質 tenor of discourse;
交替性質 alternating property;
刷光性質 brushing property;
軸承性質 bearing property;

[性知識] sex knowledge;

[性週期] sexual cycle;

[性狀] character;
性狀穩定 stabilization of characteristics;
度量性狀 metrical character;
分歧性狀 divergent character;
副性狀 accessory character;
獲得性狀 acquired character;
鑒別性狀 diagnostic character;
母體性狀 maternal character;
農藝性狀 agronomical character;
人為性狀 artificial character;
數量性狀 quantitative character;
顯性性狀 dominating character;
遺傳性狀 hereditary character;
隱性性狀 recessive; recessive character;
栽培性狀 cultivated character;
中間性狀 intermediate character;

[性子] (1) disposition; temper; (2) potency; strength;
性子過急 too quick on the trigger;
暴性子 hot temper; irascible temper;
逞性子 wayward;
火性子 hot-tempered;
急性子 (1) of impatient disposition; short-tempered; (2) impetuous person;
~急性子，慢手腳 quick-tempered but slow in action;
鬧性子 go into a temper;
使性子 indulge in one's temper; lose one's temper;
直性子 (1) downright; forthright; straightforward; (2) straightforward person;
左性子 pigheaded; stubborn; wilful;

癌性 cancerous;
拗性 obstinacy; recalcitrance; stubbornness;
傲性 proud temperament;
爆性 hot-tempered; quick-tempered;
背日性 apheliotropism;
本性 instincts; one's natural character; the real nature;
必然性 certainty; inevitability;
必要性 necessity;
變性 (1) denature; (2) degenerate; retrogress;
變異性 variability;
變應性 allergy;
表面性 superficiality;
秉性 natural disposition; natural instincts; nature;
稟性 natural instincts; natural disposition; natural temperament;
不育性 sterility;
殘酷性 ruthlessness;
長期性 protracted nature;
徹底性 thoroughness;
成性 become sb's second nature; by nature;
持久性 durability; endurance;
抽象性 abstractness;
傳導性 conductivity;
傳染性 infectiousness;
傳熱性 heat-transfer;
傳音性 sound conductibility;
創造性 creativeness; creativity;
純潔性 purity;
雌性 female;
磁性 magnetic; magnetism;
脆弱性 fragility;
脆性 brittleness; embrittlement;
代表性 representative; typical;
單色性 monochromaticity;
導電性 electric conductivity;
導性 conductivity;
地方性 local characteristics;
典型性 typicalness;
定性 (1) determine the nature of an offence; (2) determine the chemical composition of a substance; (3) qualitative;
動搖性 vacillation;
鬥爭性 fighting spirit;
獨創性 originality;
獨立性 independence; independent character;
獨特性 distinctiveness; uniqueness;
毒性 poisonness; toxicity;
對稱性 symmetry;
對抗性 antagonism;
多樣性 diversification;
多義性 polysemy;
多元性 pluralism;
墮性 inertia; inertness; sluggishness;
耳性 remembrance;
二重性 dual character; duality;
二象性 dual property; duality;
惡性 lethal; malignant; pernicious; vicious;
方向性 directivity;
放射性 radioactivity;
風濕性 rheumatoid;
否定性 negativity;
服務性 service;
複雜性 complexity;
腐蝕性 corrosiveness;
賦性 inborn nature;
改性 modified;
蓋然性 probability;
概括性 generality;
乾性 dry; dryness;
綱領性 programmatic;
感性 perception; perceptual;
感夜性 nyctinasty;
剛性 rigidity;
革命性 revolutionary character;
個性 (1) individual character; personality; (2) particularity; specific property;
根性 natural instincts; nature;
共性 general character; generality;
慣性 inertance; inertia; sluggishness; the force of inertia;
規律性 regularity;
過敏性 allergic; allergy;
海洋性 maritime;
合成性 complexity;

合法性 legitimacy;
合理性 rationality;
換性 transsexual;
揮發性 volativity;
毀滅性 crushing; destructive;
慧性 intelligence;
或然性 probability;
活性 activated; active; activity;
火敏性 photosensitiveness;
火性 hot temper;
機動性 mobility; fluidity;
及物動詞 transitive verb;
集體性 collectivity;
急性 acute;
極性 polar; polarity;
技術性 of a technical nature;
季節性 seasonal;
寄生性 parasitical nature;
記性 memory;
繼承性 heredity;
碱性 alkalinity; basicity;
見性 see the Buddha-like nature;
建設性 constructive;
間歇性 intermission; intermittence;
階級性 class nature;
經常性 constancy; regularity;
精確性 correctness;
警覺性 alertness; vigilance;
警惕性 vigilance;
局限性 limitations;
決定性 decisiveness;
均一性 homogeneity;
抗病性 disease resistance;
抗磁性 diamagnetism;
抗寒性 cold-resistance;
抗旱性 drought resistance;
抗水性 water-resistance;
抗藥性 drug-resistance;
科學性 scientific spirit;
可達性 accessibility;
可靠性 reliability;
可能性 possibility;
可逆性 reversibility;
可燃性 combustibility;
可數性 countability;
可塑性 plasticity;
可譯性 translatability;
可約性 reducibility;
可知性 knowability;
客觀性 objectivity;
狂熱性 fanaticism;
理性 rational; reason; sense;
歷史性 of historic significance;
連貫性 coherence; continuity;
連續性 continuity;
良性 benign;
兩重性 dual nature; duality;
兩面性 dual character;
兩性 (1) both sexes; (2) amphiprotic;
烈性 (1) spirited; (2) strong; violent;
劣根性 deep-rooted bad habits;
靈活性 flexibility; mobility;
靈性 intelligence;
流動性 mobility; fluidity;
流行性 epidemic;
掠奪性 predatoriness;
濾過性 filterability;
邏輯性 logicality;
慢性 (1) chronic; (2) phlegmatic temperament;
酶性 enzymic;
盲動性 rashness in action;
盲目性 blindness;
免疫性 immunity;
母性 maternal instinct;
目的性 aim; purpose;
慕光性 phototaxis;
耐病性 disease tolerance;
耐寒性 cold-resistance;
耐旱性 drought hardiness;
耐久性 durability; endurance;
耐磨性 wearability;
耐熱性 heat-resistance;
耐水性 water-resistance;
耐酸性 acid-resistance;
耐性 endurance; patience;
耐蔭性 shade tolerance;
耐雨性 rain fastness;
耐振性 vibration strength;
男性 (1) male; male sex; (2) man;
內在性 immanency;
能動性 dynamic role; initiative;
能育性 fertility;
恰當性 appropriateness;
撓性 flexibility;
黏結性 cohesiveness;
黏性 stickness; viscidity;
牛性 stubbornness;
奴性 servility; slavishness;
女性 (1) fair sex; fairer sex; female; female sex; weaker sex; (2) woman;
偶然性 contingency; fortuity;
排他性 exclusiveness;
派性 cliquism; factionalism; ripper; tribalism;
膨脹性 expansibility;

脾性 disposition; temperament;
癖性 habitual tendency; natural inclination; proclivity; propensity;
片面性 one-sidedness;
品性 moral character;
破壞性 destructiveness;
迫切性 urgency;
普遍性 universality;
氣性 disposition; temperament;
遷移性 migration;
親和性 compatibility;
傾向性 tendentiousness;
區域性 regional;
趨光性 phototaxis;
趨熱性 thermotaxis;
趨藥性 chemotaixs;
去磁性 demagnetization;
群眾性 of a mass character;
染色性 dyeability;
熱脆性 hot-shortness;
人性 (1) human nature; humanity; (2) reason;
忍性 forcibly restrain one's temper;
任性 capricious; headstrong; intractable; self-willed; unrestrained; wayward; wilful;
韌性 (1) tenacity; (2) ductility; toughness;
溶混性 miscibility;
柔性 femininity; flexibility; gentleness; pliancy; softness;
軟性 bland; gentle; light; mild; soft;
繕性 cultivate one's nature;
煽動性 instigation;
社會性 sociality;
伸縮性 elasticity; flexibility;
神秘性 mysteriousness; mystery;
滲透性 permeability;
生性 (1) affinity; by nature; natural disposition; nature; (2) aloof; unfriendly;
時間性 timeliness;
適應性 adaptability;
實踐性 practicality;
試探性 exploratory;
收縮性 contractibility;
獸性 barbarity; brutish nature;
淑性 gentle disposition;
屬性 attribute; property;
率性 (1) one's natural disposition; (2) act according to the dictates of one's conscience;
爽性 may just as well;
水溶性 solubility;
水性 (1) unpredictable temperament; (2) water condition;
順磁性 paramagnetism;
瞬時性 instantaneity;
思想性 ideological content;
死性 having a one-track mind; inflexible; obstinate; stiff; stubborn;
塑性 plasticity;
酸性 acidity;
索性 may just as well; simply;
彈性 elasticity; flexibility; resilience; spring;
特殊性 particularity;
特性 character; characteristics; distinctive features; peculiarities; properties; trait;
天性 natural disposition; natural instincts; natural temperaments; nature;
鐵磁性 ferromagnetism;
通性 common characteristics; general character;
同步性 synchronism;
同性 (1) of the same sex; (2) of the same character; (3) isomorphism;
同一性 identity;
統一性 unity;
透熱性 diathermancy;
透視性 perspectivity;
妥協性 tendency towards compromise;
凸性 convexity;
外在性 externalism;
完整性 completeness; integrity;
忘性 absent-mindedness; forgetfulness;
威脅性 menace;
危害性 harmfulness; perniciousness;
危險性 danger; peril;
穩定性 stability;
無性 asexual;
悟性 comprehension; understanding;
物質性 materiality;
吸濕性 hygroscopicity;
習性 appetence; dispositions; habit; habitual nature; mannerism; temperament;
系統性 systematism;
戲劇性 theatricality;
先天性 congenital nature; innateness;
顯性 (1) dominance; (2) transparent;
限制性 restrictive;
線性 linearity;
現實性 actuality; realizability;
相對性 relativity;
相干性 coherence; coherency;
向地性 geotropism;
向光性 phototropism;
向熱性 thermotropism;
向日性 heliotropism;
向溶性 solubility;

向食性 sitotropism;
向濕性 hygrotropism;
向水性 hydrotropism;
向性 tropism;
象徵性 symbolic;
心性 constitution of the mind; disposition; temperament;
雄性 male;
旋光性 optical rotation;
選擇性 selectivity;
血性 courage and uprightness; strong sense of righteousness;
學術性 of academic nature;
亞急性 subacute;
延續性 continuity;
延性 ductivity;
延展性 ductility; extensibility;
陽性 (1) positive; (2) male sex;
養性 discipline one's temperament;
藥性 property of a medicine;
野性 jungle instincts; unruliness; untamed; wild nature;
一般性 generality;
一致性 community;
依賴性 dependence;
異性 (1) of the other sex; opposite sex; (2) of a different nature;
藝術性 artistry;
陰性 (1) negative; (2) female; feminine gender;
隱性 opaque; recessiveness;
因果性 causality;
硬性 hard; hard-and-fast; inflexible; rigid; stiff;
永久性 eternity; perpetuity;
優越性 superiority;
由性 act at will;
育性 fertility;
預見性 farsightedness;
賊性 (1) crafty disposition; (2) evil mind;
戰鬥性 militancy;
真實性 authenticity; truthfulness;
真性 (1) the natural property; (2) one's natural disposition;
正確性 correction;
正義性 sense of justice;
知性 intellect;
直性 forthright; outspoken; straightforward;
中性 (1) neutral; (2) neuter gender;
中毒性 toxic;
重要性 importance; significance;
周期性 cyclicity; periodicity;
主動性 initiative;
準確性 accuracy;
拙性 clumsy; slow-witted; stupidity;
資性 one's disposition;
恣性 unrestrained behaviour;
自發性 spontaneity;
自覺性 consciousness;
組織性 sense of organization;
縱性 do as one pleases;

xing

【倖】 (1) fortunate; good fortune; good luck; lucky; (2) dote on; spoil;

［倖存］ survive by good luck;
倖存者 survivor;
~唯一倖存者 sole survivor;

［倖得］ obtain by luck;

［倖進］ attain by luck; be promoted by luck;

［倖免］ escape by luck; survive luckily;

僥倖 lucky;

xing

【荇】 nymphoides peltala;

［荇菜］ duckweed;

xing

【悻】 angry; enraged; indignant;

［悻然］ angry; resentful;

［悻悻］ angry; resentful;
悻悻而去 go away disapprovingly; leave in a huff;
悻悻然 angry; enraged; huffish;

［悻直］ bluff; blunt; brusque;

xing

【莕】 nymphoides peltala;

［莕菜］ kind of water plant;

xing

【興】 desire to do sth; excitement; interest; mood to do sth;

［興沖沖］ do sth with joy and expedition; excited;

［興高采烈］ above oneself; as jolly as a sandboy; blithe; boisterous; buoyant; cheerful; cheery; effervescence; elated; elated and overjoyed; excited; exhilarated; expansive; exultant; feel one's oats; full of beans; full of spirits and elated; go into raptures; have a hectic time; in a bright humour; in buoyant spirits; in exuberant spirits; in good form; in good spirits; in great delight; in great spirits; in high glee; in high spirits; in one's altitudes; in the pride of one's heart; joyful bustle; jubilant; on the high ropes; on top of the world; on wings; sparkling with joy; tails up; with great gusto; with rapturous joy;

[興會] a fit of enthusiasm;
興會淋漓 showing much interest and enthusiasm;

[興盡悲來] feeling of sadness follows a bout of pleasure; he who laughs on Friday will weep on Sunday;

[興起] aroused; excited;

[興趣] eagerness; interest; taste; willingness;
興趣盎然 burning with enthusiasm; unflagging interest;
興趣相投 find each other congenial; have similar tastes and interests;
出於興趣 as a matter of interest;
感興趣 be interested in; have a strong stomach;
~不感興趣 incurious, indifferent; not interested in; uninterested;
不感興趣的東西 not one's cup of tea;
~對音樂感興趣 be interested in music;
勾起興趣 tickle sb's fancy;
激發興趣 whip up interest;
滿腔興趣 with absorbed interest;
沒興趣 have no stomach for;
強烈的興趣 passionate interest;
無興趣 disinterest;
~無興趣的 disinterested;
學術興趣 academic interest;

[興頭] enthusiasm; keen interest;
興頭上 at the height of one's enthusiasm; be carried away with sth;

[興味] enjoyability; interest;
興味盎然 with keen interest;
興味索然 barren of interest; bored stiff; cut and dried; dull and boring; lose all interest in sth; not to show a spark of interest; uninterested;
興味相投 have similar tastes and interests;

[興致] eagerness; interest; mood to enjoy; willingness;
興致盎然 full of zest;
興致勃勃 a flow of spirits; in a big way; full of enthusiasm; in a good humour; in high feather; in high spirits; in the best of spirits; of good cheer; tails up; with exhilaration;
興致索然 in an ill humour; out of spirits;

敗興 dampen one's enthusiasm; dampen one's interest; disappointed; frustrated; lessen one's pleasure;
勃興 grow vigorously; rise suddenly;
乘興 while one is in high spirits;
高興 be glad to; be willing to; glad; happy;
豪興 keen interest; overflowing spirits;
即興 impromptu;
盡興 enjoy to one's heart's content;
酒興 mood to drink;
掃興 disappointing; frustrated;
詩興 urge for poetic creation;
雅興 aesthetic mood; refined interest;
意興 interest; mood to do sth;
游興 interest in going on an excursion;
餘興 (1) lingering interest; (2) entertainment after a gathering;
助興 liven things up;

xiong¹
xiong

【凶】 (1) bad; evil; inauspicious; (2) crop failure; famine; (3) unfortunate; unlucky; (4) fierce; ferocious; (5) fearful; fearsome; terrible; (6) act of violence; murder; (7) excessive; very;

[凶暴] fierce and brutal;

[凶殘] bloodthirsty; fierce and cruel; merciless; savage and cruel;

[凶惡] brutish; fearful; ferocious;
窮凶極惡 act outrageously and ferociously; atrocious; devilish; diabolic; enormity; extreme ferocity; extremely evil; extremely vicious; extremely violent and wicked; ferocious; fierce and malicious; frantic; fiendish brutes; in a vicious and unrestrained way; infernal; most brutal; most vicious; nefarious; notoriously vicious; of the blackest dye; of the deepest dye; outrageous; Satanic; savage in the extreme; sinister in the extreme; truculent; unscrupulous and vicious; utterly evil; utterly ferocious; utterly malignant and ferocious; villainous without any redeeming feature; wickedness and

evil carried to the utmost possible degree; with the look of a fiendish brute;
生性凶惡 ferocious by nature;
相貌凶惡 have ferocious looks;
[凶犯] murderer;
[凶服] mourning dress;
[凶悍] fierce and tough;
凶悍的人 hardass;
[凶耗] death notice; bad news;
[凶狠] fierce and malicious;
[凶橫] fierce and arrogant;
凶橫直追 bludgeon one's way deep into;
[凶吉] portentous and propitious;
逢凶化吉 fall on one's legs; land on one's feet; luck out; misfortunes turn into blessings; turn calamities into blessing; turn ill luck into good;
~逢凶化吉，遇難呈祥 if anything untoward happens, one's bad luck will turn into good;
化凶為吉 change the portentous into the propitious;
凶多吉少 be fraught with grim possibilities; bode ill rather than well; more ominous than propitious; promise more evil than good;
[凶具] casket; coffin;
[凶禮] funeral rite;
[凶猛] ferocious; violent;
[凶夢] bad dream; nightmare;
[凶年] year of famine; year of misfortune;
凶年惡歲 lean years; time of dearth;
[凶氣] fearsome air of a person;
[凶器] lethal weapon;
[凶殺] homicide; murder;
[凶煞] evil spirit that causes illness, death, etc;
[凶神] demon; evil spirit;
凶神惡煞 devil; fiend;
[凶事] unlucky incidents;
[凶手] murderer; assassin;
[凶死] death by violence;
[凶徒] evildoer; villain;
[凶險] dangerous;
[凶相] ferocious features; fierce looks;
[凶信] bad news;
[凶焰] aggressive arrogance; ferocity;
[凶宅] haunted house;
[凶兆] bad omen;

幫凶 assist in a crime;
避凶 avoid impending trouble; flee from evil;
逞凶 act violently; act with murderous intent;
吉凶 good or ill luck;
行凶 commit physical assault; do violence;
元凶 arch criminal; prime culprit;
正凶 principal murderer;

xiong
【兄】 (1) elder brother; (2) courteous form of address between men;

[兄弟] bro; brothers;
兄弟姐妹 brothers and sisters;
兄弟如手足 brothers are like hands and feet;
兄弟鬩牆 brothers fight among themselves — internal strife; brothers fight at home; discord between brothers; internal dispute; internal quarrel;
兄弟鬩於牆，外禦其侮 brother quarrelling at home join forces against attacks from without; internal disunity dissolves at the threat of external invasion;
兄弟之邦 fraternal countries;
把兄弟 sworn brothers;
胞兄弟 brothers by the same parents;
表兄弟 cousins;
~親房表兄弟 first cousins;
~遠房表兄弟 second cousins;
稱兄道弟 address each other as brothers; address each other in great familiarity; call cousins with; call each other brothers; fraternize with; on intimate terms;
乾兄弟 nominal brothers;
呼兄喚弟 address each other as brothers; call each other brothers;
結義兄弟 sworn brothers;
孔懷兄弟 great fraternal sympathy;
兩兄弟 two brothers;
盟兄弟 sworn brothers not linked by kinship;
奶兄弟 foster brother;
難兄難弟 noble pair of brothers; one as good as the other;
排行中間的兄弟 middle brother;
契兄弟 sworn brothers;
親兄弟 blood brothers; brothers born of the same parents;
~親兄弟，明算帳 clear reckoning makes

long friends; even among brothers, accounts should be settled without ambiguity; even brothers keep careful accounts; even reckoning makes long friends; financial matters should be settled clearly even between brothers; short accounts make long friends;

堂兄弟 cousins;

~ 親房堂兄弟 first cousins;

~ 遠房堂兄弟 second cousins;

兄友弟恭 show love and respect as good brothers should; the elder brother should be kind, the younger respectful;

宜兄宜弟 affectionate brothers;

異父母兄弟 half brother;

異母兄弟 brothers born of different mothers; half brothers;

姻兄弟 cousin-in-law;

[兄嫂] one's elder brother and his wife;

[兄台] you;

[兄長] elder brother;

胞兄 blood elder brother;

表兄 cousin; elder male cousin; first cousin;

從兄 elder male cousin;

弟兄 brothers;

父兄 (1) father and elder brothers; (2) head of a family;

老兄 brother; man; mate; old chap; old cock; partner;

內兄 brother-in-law; wife's elder brother;

仁兄 my dear friend;

如兄 elder sworn brother;

師兄 (1) one's senior fellow apprentice; (2) son of one's master; (3) father's apprentice;

弒兄 commit fratricide; fratricide;

堂兄 elder male cousin;

xiong

【兇】 (1) cruel; ferocious; fierce; violent; (2) inhuman; truculent;

[兇暴] cruel and violent;

[兇惡] evil; ferocious; malignant; wicked;

[兇犯] criminal; murderer;

[兇漢] gangster; hoodlum; violent person;

[兇悍] ferocious; fierce; savage; truculent;

[兇狠] fierce;

[兇猛] ferocious; fierce;

[兇器] murderous weapon;

暗藏兇器 conceal a dangerous weapon;

[兇殺] homicide; manslaughter; murder;

兇殺科 homicide;

[兇神惡煞] fiends; fierce demon and devils;

[兇手] assassin; killer; murderer;

女兇手 murderess;

[兇險] cruel and mean;

[兇相] ferocious features; fierce look;

[兇兇] clamorous; noisy;

幫兇 accessary; accomplice;

行兇 commit killing; commit murder; commit physical assault; do violence;

疑兇 suspected murderer;

元兇 crime culprit;

xiong

【匈】 (1) bosom; breast; thorax; (2) clamour;

xiong

【洶】 (1) restless; tumultuous; turbulent; unquiet; (2) clamorous; noisy; uproarious;

[洶動] disturbed; restless; unquiet;

[洶洶] (1) sound of roaring waves; (2) truculent; violent; (3) agitated; tumultuous;

[洶湧] insurge; rage; tempestuous; turbulent;

洶湧急流 flashy flow;

洶湧澎湃 rise in a surging tide; rise in tempestuous waves; roll irresistibly onward; run mountains high; surge forward; surging; surging forward like a torrential tide;

xiong

【恟】 (1) afraid; frightened; (2) noisy;

[恟懼] afraid; frightened;

[恟恟] tumultuous;

xiong

【胸】 (1) bosom; breast; bust; chest; thorax; (2) heart; mind;

[胸部] bosom; breast; bust; chest; thorax;

胸部大的 chesty;

豐滿的胸部 ample bosom;

胸部豐滿的 stacked;

[胸腹] chest and belly;

[胸骨] breastbone; sternum;

[胸花] boutonniere;

[胸懷] ambition; aspiration; breast; heart; mind;

胸懷大志 aim high; cherish high aspirations in one's mind; cherish high

ideals; cherish lofty designs in one's bosom; entertain great ambitions; fly a high pitch; fly at high game; fly at higher game; fly high; have lofty aspirations; hitch one's wagon to a star; think big;
胸懷寬廣 broad-minded; large-minded; have largeness of mind;
胸懷磊落 frank; harbour no evil thought; honest; open-hearted and upright;
胸懷全局 have the overall situation in mind; keep the whole situation in mind;
胸懷若谷 one's broad-mindedness is vast as the ocean;
胸懷世界 bear the whole world in mind; one's heart embraces the whole world;
胸懷坦白 a free heart; frank and open; largeness of mind; open-hearted;
胸懷韜略 one's bosom hides a strategy;
胸懷狹窄 narrow-minded; narrow-mindedness; small-minded;
敞胸露懷 bare the breast; frank; open-minded;

[胸肌] chest muscle; pectorals;
胸肌病 pectoral myopathy;
~深部胸肌病 deep pectoral myopathy;

[胸襟] breadth of mind; mind;
胸襟豁達 broad-minded; have a large breadth of mind; have largeness of mind; open-minded;
胸襟開闊 broad-minded; large-minded; liberal in outlook; unprejudiced;
胸襟遠大 breadth of mind;
揪住胸襟 seize sb by the jacket;

[胸口] (1) middle of the chest; (2) pit in the upper part of the stomach;

[胸毛] chest hair;

[胸膜] pleurae;
胸膜炎 pleurisy; pleuritis;
出血性胸膜炎 hemorrhagic pleuritis;
~肥厚性胸膜炎 pachypleuritis;
~化膿性胸膜炎 suppurative pleuritis;
假胸膜炎 pseudomeningitis;
結核性胸膜炎 tuberculous pleuritis;
局限性胸膜炎 circumscribed pleurisy;
~狼瘡性胸膜炎 lupus pleuritis;
彌漫性胸膜炎 diffuse pleurisy;
黏連性胸膜炎 adhesive pleurisy;
尿毒症性胸膜炎 uremic pleuritis;
滲出性胸膜炎 exudative pleurisy;
硬結性胸膜炎 indurative pleurisy;
增生性胸膜炎 proliferating pleurisy;

[胸脯] chest;
腆着胸脯 stick out one's chest;

[胸膛] breast; chest;
怒滿胸膛 one's breast is filled with anger;
挺起胸膛 stand straight in gesture of self-confidence; stick out one's chest;

[胸痛] have a pain in the chest;
流行性胸痛 epidemic pleurodynia;

[胸圍] (1) bust; chest measurement; (2) bra;

[胸無] nothing inside oneself;
胸無點墨 be unable to read or write; ignorant; illiterate; unlearned; unlettered;
胸無宿物 nothing is concealed in a straightforward person's mind;

[胸衣] corselette;
緊身胸衣 bustier; corset;
貼身胸衣 camisole;

[胸宇] one's ambition; one's aspiration;

[胸章] badge;

[胸罩] bra; brassiere; breast shield; bust bodice;
無肩帶胸罩 strapless bra;
運動胸罩 sports bra;

[胸針] brooch;

[胸肢] thoracic appendage;

扁平胸 flat chest;
捶胸 thump one's chest;
低胸 low-cut;
龜胸 pigeon-breast;
護胸 chest plate; chest protector;
雞胸 chicken breast;
隆胸 breast implant;
麻痺胸 paralytic chest;
袜胸 stomacher;
膿胸 pyothorax;
劈胸 right against the chest;
平胸 flat chest;
氣胸 (1) pneumothorax; (2) pneumothorax;
酥胸 soft and smooth skin of a woman's breast;
挺胸 square one's shoulders; throw out one's chest; thrust out one's chest;
心胸 (1) breadth of mind; capacity for tolerance; (2) ambition; aspiration;
血胸 haemothorax;

xiong

【詾】 (1) argue loudly; (2) litigation; (3)

disorders; miseries;
[詾詾] (1) argue loudly; (2) noisy;

xiong²
xiong

【雄】 (1) male; masculine; virile; (2) grand; imposing; (3) mighty; powerful; (4) with great power and influence; (5) triumph; victory; win; (6) scold others with insulting words; (7) a surname;

[雄辯] convincing argument; eloquence; forceful presentation of one's points in a debate;
雄辯高談 a vigorous debate and high talk;
雄辯是銀，沉默是金 speech is silver while silence is gold;
雄辯滔滔 argue eloquently;

[雄兵] crack troops; powerful army;

[雄才] great talent; remarkable ability and wisdom;
雄才大略 bold and capable; extremely capable; great talent and bold vision; rare gifts and bold strategy;

[雄大] great and mighty;

[雄飛] strive for bigger and better things;
雄飛突進 soar up bravely and advance suddenly;

[雄風] awe-inspiring air; gallant and stately manner;

[雄蜂] drone;

[雄關] impregnable pass;

[雄豪] (1) heroes; powerful people; (2) ambitious and warlike; martial;

[雄厚] abundant; ample; considerable; plentiful; rich; solid; substantial; tremendous;

[雄渾] forceful; grand; grandiose; powerful; vigorous and firm;

[雄雞] cock; male chicken;

[雄健] energetic; powerful; robust; strapping; very healthy; vigorous; virile and energetic;

[雄糾糾] gallantly; imposing; looking brave and resolute; valiantly;
雄糾糾，氣昂昂 full of mettle; valiant and spirited; valiantly and spiritedly;

[雄貓] tomcat;
雄貓哀叫 a tomcat howls; a tomcat yowls;

[雄氣] gallant disposition; heroic disposition;

[雄勝] strategic pass;

[雄師] powerful army; crack troop;

[雄視] dominate;
雄視一方 cut a conspicuous figure in a place;

[雄圖] ambitious scheme; grandiose plan; great ambition; great aspiration;
雄圖大略 great design and big plan;
雄圖大業 grandiose and noble enterprise; great cause;

[雄威] grand and powerful;

[雄偉] grand; grandeur; imposing; magnificent; majestic; stately;
雄偉氣魄 with the great boldness and vision;
雄偉壯麗 grand; magnificent; sublime;

[雄文] great works; profound and powerful writing;

[雄心] great ambition; lofty aspiration;
雄心勃勃 ambitious; messianic; with breathless eagerness to; with determination and ardour;
雄心不死 refuse to give up one's ambition;
雄心未死 an undying ambition; not willing to give up; still full of ambition;
雄心壯志 great and lofty aspirations; great ideals and lofty aspirations; high ambitions; high aspiring mind; high hopes and great ambitions; lofty ambitions; lofty aspirations and high aims; lofty ideals and high aspirations; magnificent and heroic aims;
~ 樹雄心，立壯志 aim high and have lofty ambitions; foster lofty ideals, set high goals;
樹立雄心 set up lofty aspirations;

[雄蕊] stamen;
不育雄蕊 sterile stamen;
單強雄蕊 monodynamous stamen;
單體雄蕊 monadelphous stamen;
多體雄蕊 polyadelphous stamens;
具備雄蕊 perfect stamen;
四體雄蕊 tetradelphous stamen;

[雄性] male;
雄性激素 androgen male hormone;

[雄壯] full of power and grandeur; magnificent; majestic; powerful;

powerful in momentum; powerful in strength and impetus; strong; virile;
威武雄壯 full of power and grandeur;
[雄姿] brave appearance; dashing look; heroic bearing; heroic posture; look of audacity and prowess; majestic appearance; manly form;
雄姿英發 cut a bold and successful figure; take a heroic posture;

稱雄 hold sway over a region; rule a district byu force or power;
雌雄 male and female;
奸雄 arch-careerist; master of political intrigues;
兩雄 two strong forces;
去雄 castrate; emasculate; emasculation;
群雄 group of warlords;
梟雄 fierce and ambitious person;
驍雄 capable and ambitious;
英雄 great man; hero;
爭雄 contend for hegemony; contend for supremacy; struggle for supremacy;

xiong
【熊】 (1) bear; (2) shine brightly; (3) a surname;
[熊抱] bearbug;
[熊蜂] bumblebee;
[熊貓] bearcat; panda;
大熊貓 Ailuropoda; giant panda;
[熊皮] bearskin;
熊皮高帽 bearskin;
[熊市] bear market;
熊市的 bearish;
[熊熊] ablaze; bright and brilliant; flaming; flaming and glorious; raging; shining;
熊熊烈火 blazing fire; raging fire; raging flames;
[熊腰虎背] with a bear's loin and a tiger's back;
[熊掌] bear's paws;

白熊 polar bear; white bear;
北極熊 polar bear;
貂熊 glutton;
大灰熊 grizzly bear;
大熊 bear;
洞熊 cave bear;
狗熊 black bear;
海熊 fur seal; ursine seal;
黑熊 black bear;
浣熊 coon; raccoon;
馬熊 brown bear;
貓熊 panda;
樹熊 koala; wallaby;
玩具熊 teddy bear;
棕熊 brown bear;

xiong⁴
xiong
【敻】 (1) aim high; seek; (2) pre-eminent; superior;
[敻古] a long, long time ago; in ancient times;
[敻絕] peerless; second to none;
[敻敻] long;

幽敻 profound;

xiu¹
xiu
【休】 (1) cease; stop; (2) rest; (3) happiness; joy; weal;
[休兵] (1) cease fire; stop fighting; (2) armistice; truce;
[休耕] fallow; lie fallow;
[休怪] (1) stop blaming; (2) stop wondering;
[休會] adjourn a meeting;
[休假] (1) go on a vacation; have a holiday; take a vacation; (2) on leave; take a leave;
休假日 day off;
休假一天 take a day off;
得到休假 get a vacation;
回家休假 go home on furlough;
結束休假 finish one's holiday;
推遲休假 postpone one's leave;
[休克] shock;
休克療法 shock therapy;
創傷性休克 traumatic shock;
過敏性休克 anaphylactic shock;
繼發性休克 secondary shock;
膿毒性休克 septic shock;
神經源性休克 neurogenic shock;
術後休克 postoperative shock;
外傷性休克 traumatic shock;
心性休克 cardiac shock;
心源性休克 cardiogenic shock;
性休克 shock;
中毒性休克 toxic shock;
[休老] retire owing to old age;
[休眠] dormancy; quiescence;

休眠期 resting period;
二次休眠 secondary dormancy;
內部休眠 internal dormancy;
強行休眠 imposed dormancy;
強制休眠 forced dormancy;
生理休眠 physiological dormancy;
失水休眠 anabiosis;
誘導休眠 induced dormancy;
種子休眠 seed dormancy;

[休妻] divorce one's wife;

[休戚] favourable and unfavourable experiences; for better and worse; joys and sorrows; weal and woe;
休戚相關 be bound together by common interests; be bound together in a common cause; of close concern to each other; feel for others' woes; identify oneself heart and soul with; seemingly contradictory things closely related; share each other's joy and sorrow; share good and bad luck; share joys and sorrows with each other; share weal and woe; solidarity;
休戚相關，患難與共 be bound by a common cause and go through thick and thin together;
休戚與共 go through thick and thin together; share each other's weal and woe; share joy and sorrow; share weal and woe; share the same fate; stand together through thick and thin; throw in one's lot with;

[休賽季節] close season;

[休書] divorce announcement letter;
一紙休書 a divorce paper;

[休憩] have a rest; rest;

[休提] do not mention;

[休庭] adjourn;

[休息] have a break; have a rest; rest; rest from work; take a break; take a rest;
休息片刻 come up for air; take a momentary rest;
休息日 day off;
休息室 chill room;
休息時間 break; coffee break;
休息五分鐘 have a five-minute break;
休息一下 have a rest; take a break;
~好好休息一下 have a good slack;
幕間休息 intermission;
卧牀休息 rest in bed;

[休閒] arder; ease; leisure; lie fallow; relaxation;
休閒服 casual wear; sports wear;
休閒業 leisure industry;
休閒中心 leisure centre;

[休想] can whistle for; don't imagine that it's possible; stop dreaming;

[休歇] (1) stop for rest; take a rest; (2) take a nap;

[休休] (1) good at heart; (2) quiet and serene;

[休學] suspend one's schooling without losing one's status as a student; suspension of schooling; temporary absence from school;

[休養] convalesce; recuperate;
休養生息 lick one's wounds; recuperate and multiply; rehabilitate; rest and build up one's strength; rehabilitation;
休養院 rest home; sanatorium;
~幹部休養院 sanatorium for officials;

[休業] (1) be closed down; suspend business; suspension of business; (2) come to an end of a short-term course;

[休戰] armistice; cease-fire; cessation of hostilities; stop fighting; truce;

[休止] cease; cessation; stop;
休止符 rest;
無休無止 ceaseless; endless; on and on; without cessation; without end;
無止無休 tireless; without cessation;

罷休 cease; give up; let the matter drop; stop;
半休 work half day;
彪休 angry; wrathful;
病休 sick leave; take a sick leave;
補休 take deferred holidays;
不休 ceaselessly; endlessly;
調休 work on one's day off in exchange for a day off on one's work day;
干休 bring to an end; give up;
甘休 willingly to give up; willing to stop;
公休 general holiday;
輪休 (1) have holidays by turns; (2) rotation farming;
全休 complete rest;
退休 retire;
午休 afternoon nap; midday rest; noon break; noontime rest; take a nap after lunch;
小休 short rest;
中休 have a break;

xiu

【庥】 protect; shade; shelter;

xiu

【修】 (1) adorn; decorate; (2) mend; repair; (3) compile; edit; write; (4) cultivate; study; (5) build; construct; (6) cut; prune; sharpen; trim; (7) long; tall and slender; (8) revisionism;

［修版］ retouching;
修版工 retoucher;

［修錶匠］ watchmaker;

［修補］ (1) fettle; mend; patch up; repair; revamp; (2) mending; patching; repatching;
修補工 mender;
表面修補 skin patching;
小修小補 running repairs;
修修補補 patch up; tinker;

［修長］ slender; slim; tall and thin;
修長補短 cut off from the long to add to the short; make up a deficiency by a surplus;

［修船廠］ boatyard;

［修辭］ diction; figure of speech; rhetoric;
修辭格 figure; figure of speech;
~技巧修辭格 technical figure;
修辭功能 rhetorical function;
修辭結構 rhetorical structure;
修辭問句 rhetorical question;
修辭性疑問句 rhetorical interrogation;
修辭學 stylistics;
動態修辭 dynamic rhetoric;
矛盾修辭 oxymoron;

［修道］ cultivate oneself according to a religious doctrine;
修道士 friar;
修道院 (1) abbey monastery; (2) cloister; convent; nunnery;
~修道院迴廊 cloister;
~修道院院長 abbot;
女修道院院長 abbot;
~大修道院 abbey;
~女修道院 convent; nunnery;
女修道院學校 convent school;
女修道院長 abbess;

［修德］ cultivate one's virtue;
修德行善 strive after virtue and practise good deeds;

［修訂］ amend; amendment; reformulate; revise;
修訂版 revised edition;

［修短不齊］ uneven in length;

［修髮］ trim one's hair;

［修福］ do good deeds in order to win blessings;
修福修壽 cultivate happiness and longevity;

［修復］ (1) make as good as new; renovate; repair; restore; (2) repair;
修復舊觀 restore it to original shape and appearance;
重組修復 recombination repair;
切補修復 excision repair;
生物修復 biological repair;

［修改］ alter; amend; correct; emend; modification; modify; revise;
修改稿 revised draft;
解析修改 analytic modification;
全面修改 comprehensive amendments;
直方圖修改 modification;

［修蓋］ build; construct;

［修函］ write a letter;

［修好］ (1) fence-mending; foster cordial relations between states; (2) do good works;
修好措施 fence-mending measures;
修好對話 fence-mending talks;
修好訪問 fence-mending trip;
捐嫌修好 be reconciled; make up with sb;

［修和］ conciliate and unite;

［修剪］ clip; cut; prune; shave; trim;

［修建］ build; construct; erect; repair and build;
修建機場 build an airport;
修建碼頭 construct a wharf;
修建橋樑 construct a bridge;

［修腳］ pedicure;
修腳刀 pedicure knife;
修腳工 pedicurist;

［修久］ a very long time;

［修舊利廢］ repair and utilize old or discarded things; repair old equipment and make use of waste materials; repair the old and put the waste to use;

［修理］ fix; mend; overhaul; patch up; put to rights; repair; revamp;
修理工 fittermender; repairman;
~電視機修理工 television repairman;
修理機器 repair a machine;
半年修理 biannual repair;
海損修理 average repair;

開始修理 commence the repairs;
臨時修理 casual repair;
破損修理 breakdown repair;
完成修理 complete repairs;

[修煉] practise asceticism;

[修路] build roads; road repairing;
修路工 road mender;

[修面] shave one's face;
修面刷 shaving brush;

[修名] good reputation; high prestige;

[修明] enlightened and orderly;

[修睦] cultivate friendship with neighbours;
修睦講信 foster harmonious relations and carry out one's promises;

[修墓] renovate ancestral graves;

[修女] nun; sister;
當修女 take the veil;

[修配] repair and supply replacements;

[修葺] renovate; repair;
修葺一新 be completely renovated; take on a new look after renovation;

[修橋] build bridges;
修橋補路 be enthusiastic in promoting public welfare; build bridges and repair roads;
修橋鋪路 build roads and bridges; deeds of merit;

[修容] make up one's features;
修容院 beauty parlour;

[修傘匠] umbrella renovator;

[修繕] betterment; refurbish; renovate; repair;

[修身] cultivate one's moral character; cultivate oneself; practise moral culture;
修身齊家 cultivate one's moral character and manage the family's affairs well; cultivate one's moral character and put one's family affairs in order; cultivate oneself and put family in order;
修身止謗 correct one's own ways in order to stop gossip; stop slander by correcting one's own ways;
修身自省 look after one's conduct by self-examination;
淨心修身 cleanse one's heart and order one's behaviour;
清心修身 cleanse one's heart and temper one's behaviour;

[修士] brother; friar; monk;

[修飾] (1) adorn; decorate; embellish; (2) beautify; doll up; take care of one's appearance;
修飾成分 adjunct;
~修飾成分結構 adjunctival;
修飾詞 modifier;
~並列修飾詞 coordinate modifier;
~從屬修飾詞 subordinate modifier;
~後置修飾詞 postmodifier;
~前置修飾詞 premodifier;
修飾關係 attribution;
修飾規則 rule of attribution;
修飾形容詞 adherent adjective;
修飾性 figurative;
~修飾性辭格 rhetorical figure;
~修飾性副詞 adverb as adjunct;
修飾言語 modified speech;
修飾語 modifier;
~名詞修飾語 adnominal;
修飾轉移 transferred epithet;
不加修飾 natural; without polishing;

[修書] (1) compile a book; (2) write a letter;

[修文] develop culture and education;
修文偃武 improve learning and hide the sword;

[修鞋] mend shoes; repair shoes;

[修心] cultivate one's mind;
修心篤行 become pure in heart and good in behaviour;
修心養性 cultivate one's mind and improve one's character; cultivate one's original nature; enjoy obscurity for the sake of self-improvement;

[修行] (1) practise Buddhism; (2) practise Daoism;
修行出家 strive for virtue and leave the home – become a monk;
經明行修 good both in character and in scholarship;

[修學] study;

[修養] (1) accomplishment; mastery; training; (2) self-cultivation;
修養精神 form one's mind;
有修養的 cultivated; well-bred;

[修業] go to school; pursue academic studies; study at school;
修業年限 length of schooling;
進德修業 education in character and knowledge;

[修造] repair and build;

[修真] cultivate the true self;

修真養靜 achieve true peace of mind;
修真養性 engage in self-cultivation; nourish one's true nature;

［修整］ (1) recondition; repair and maintain; (2) prune; trim;
修整器 trimmer;
~煤堆修整器 coal pile trimmer;
邊坡修整 trimming of slope;
火腿修整 ham trimming;
路肩修整 trimming of shoulder;

［修正］ amend; correct; correction; revise; update;
修正案 amendment;
~提出修正案 bring an amendment; introduce an amendment; make an amendment; move an amendment; put forward an amendment;
修正錯誤 correct mistakes;
修正器 corrector; modifier;
~測音修正器 acoustic corrector;
~距離修正器 range corrector;
~色彩載波修正器 colour carrier modifier;
修正液 correction fluid;
修正主義 revisionism;
彈道修正 ballistic correction;
角度修正 angular correction;
口頭修正 oral amendment;
音測修正 acoustic correction;
有待修正 subject to correction;
準線修正 alignment correction;

［修竹］ tall bamboo;
修竹參差 long and short bamboos mixed together;
修竹茂林 tall bamboos and thick forest;
翠叢修竹 verdant grove of bamboo;
茂林修竹 deep woods and tall bamboos; flourishing woods and tall bamboo bushes — an agreeable environment; thick forest and tall bamboos;

［修築］ build; construct; put up;

包修 guarantee the repair of sth;
保修 give a service warranty; repair under warranty;
報修 request repairs;
必修 take a required course;
編修 compile; edit;
補修 study for a second time courses one has flunked;
重修 (1) rebuild; renovate; (2) retake a course after failing to pass examination;
翻修 rebuild;
返修 refit;
房修 home repair; house repair;
回修 return sth for repairs;
檢修 examine and repair; overhaul; overhauling; recondition; service;
進修 engage in advanced studies; further one's education; further one's learning; further one's studies; study; take a refresher course;
快修 quick service;
培修 repair;
潛修 cultivate oneself in quiet privacy;
搶修 do rush repairs; make urgent repairs on; race against time in making a repair job; rush to repair; rush-repair;
清修 lead a life of few wants and ambitions;
繕修 mend; repair;
失修 disrepair; fall into disrepair; in a dilapidated state; in bad repair; in disrepair; wanting in repair;
歲修 annual repairs;
維修 keep in good repair; maintain; maintenance; service; upkeep;
興修 build; start construction;
選修 take as an elective course;
研修 research and study;
整修 condition; put in order; rebuild; recondition; renovate; repair; reramp; restore; touch up;
主修 (1) major in; specialize in; (2) responsible for the repair of;
專修 major in; specialize in;
裝修 (1) decorate and repair; equip; fit up; refurbish; spruce up; (2) fixtures; trims; (3) renovation worker;
自修 (1) review one's lessons by oneself; self-study; (2) educate oneself; study on one's own; teach oneself;
纂修 compile; edit; prepare;

xiu

【羞】 (1) bashful; shy; (2) disgrace; insult; shame; (3) abashed; ashamed;

［羞慚］ abashed; ashamed; humiliated; mortified;
羞慚滿面 be overwhelmed with shame; shamefaced; the flush of shame spreads over one's face;
羞慚無地 almost too ashamed to show one's face;
感到羞慚 be abashed; feel abashed;

［羞恥］ (1) sense of shame; (2) ashamed;

shame;
羞恥之心 sense of shame;
人無羞恥，百事可為 if a man is dead to shame, he can do all sorts of evils;

[羞答答] bashful coy; shy;
羞不敢答 too ashamed to attempt to reply;
羞羞答答 bashful; coy; shamefaced; shy;

[羞刀難入鞘] a drawn sword cannot be put back into the scabbard; a thing once begun will not be put off until done; once it is started, go through with it; over shoes, over boots; what is done cannot be undone;

[羞憤] ashamed and angry; ashamed and resentful;
羞憤成疾 shame and rage alternately take possession of one till one falls ill;
羞憤交加 be overwhelmed with shame and rage; be torn between rage and shame;
羞恨交加 shame and resentment mingle; with mingled shame and resentment;

[羞愧] abashed; ashamed; disgraced; morified; shamed;
抱慚含羞 be overcome by shame;
羞愧不安 feel ashamed and be ill at ease;
羞愧難當 embarrassed beyond words; feel terribly ashamed;
羞愧難言 be ashamed beyond words;
感到羞愧 be abashed; feel abashed; stand abashed;

[羞赧] blush because of shyness;

[羞惱] humiliated and indignant;
羞惱成怒 become angry from shame;
又羞又惱 be overwhelmed with shame and vexation; with shame and annoyance;

[羞怩] bashful; embarrassed;

[羞怯] abash; diffidence; sheepish; shy; shy and nervous; timid;
羞怯陳言 narrate shyly and nervously;

[羞人] feel ashamed; feel embarrassed;
羞人答答 abashed; ashamed; bashful about; flush with embarrassment; very shy;

[羞辱] (1) dishonour; humiliation; shame; (2) humiliate; put sb to shame; subject sb to indignities;
當眾羞辱 humiliate sb in public; offer an affront to sb in public;

[羞澀] bashful; embarrassed; shy;
羞澀阮囊 embarrassingly short of money; lacking sufficient funds to meet necessary expenses; short of cash; utterly broke; with no money in the purse;

[羞惡] ashamed of evil deeds;
羞惡之心 feeling of shame; moral sense; sense of shame;

帶羞 look bashful; look shy;
害羞 bashful; shy;
含羞 bashfully; be overcome by shyness; shy; with a shy look;
嬌羞 bashful; blushing; coy; shy;
沒羞 unabashed; unblushing;
怕羞 bashful; blushing; coy; shy;
識羞 feel ashamed;
遮羞 conceal one's disgrace; cover one's nakedness; cover up one's embarrassment; hush up a scandal;

xiu

【脩】 (1) same as 修; (2) dried meat; (3) salary for a teacher in ancient times; (4) a surname;

[脩金] salary presented to a teacher;

束脩 private tutor's remuneration;

xiu

【貅】 a fierce and courageous soldier; a kind of animal like a tiger;

貔貅 (1) mythical wild animal; (2) bold and powerful troops;

xiu

【髹】 (1) a kind of dark-red paint; (2) paint or lacquer;

xiu

【鵂】 owl;

鵋鵂 owl;

xiu

【饈】 (1) eat a meal; (2) offer; offer as tribute; (3) dainty; delicacy; delicious food;

珍饈 delicacies;

xiu³
xiu

【朽】 (1) decay; decayed; rot; rotten; (2) aged; old and useless;
[朽敗] decayed and rotten;
[朽腐] rotten; rotting;
[朽骨] decaying bones;
[朽壞] decay; decayed; rot; rotten;
[朽爛] decayed and rotten;
[朽邁] old and useless; old and weak; senile;
[朽木] (1) decayed trees; rotten trees; rotten wood; (2) good-for-nothing; hopeless person;
朽木不可雕也 a useless person cannot be made good; a useless piece of furniture; decayed wood cannot be carved; ill flesh never made good broo; one cannot carve in rotten wood; one cannot make a silk purse out of a sow's ear; rotten wood cannot be carved;
朽木糞土 decayed wood or manure; rotten wood and dirt; useless stuff; useless things; worthless person;

不朽 immortal;
腐朽 (1) decayed; rotten; (2) decadent; degenerate;
枯朽 withered and rotten;
老朽 old and useless;
衰朽 decrepit; feeble and decaying;

xiu

【宿】 night;
[宿夕] (1) single night; (2) short period of time;

通宿 all night; the whole night;

xiu⁴
xiu

【秀】 (1) put forth new ears; put forth new flowers; (2) beautiful; delicate; elegant; fine; graceful; (3) brilliant; competent; excellent; outstanding;
[秀拔] fine style of calligraphy;
[秀才] (1) county graduate; (2) scholar; skilful writer; (3) fine talent;
秀才不出門，全知天下事 a scholar does not step outside his gate, yet he knows all the happenings under the sun; a scholar, without going out, can know the affairs in the world; without going outdoor the scholar knows all the wide world's affairs;
秀才人情紙半張 a gift costs a scholar no more than a half sheet of paper;
秀才談書，屠夫談豬 talk shop; the scholar speaks of books, and the butcher talks about swine — each speaks of his own occupation;
秀才遇著兵，有理講不清 impossible for scholars to reason with soldiers;
秀才造反，三年不成 scholars stage a rebellion without result even if they try for three years;
酸秀才 impractical old scholar; pedantic scholar; priggish pedant;
[秀出] distinguished; outstanding;
秀出班行 a notch above others; among the select best; distinguished from one's kind;
[秀頂] bald head; bald-headed;
[秀而不實] flowering but fruitless; put forth flowers but bear no fruit;
[秀發] (1) blooming; (2) fine-looking; good-looking; handsome;
[秀麗] beautiful; elegant; fine; graceful; handsome; pretty;
[秀眉] long hairs in the eyebrows of an aged person;
秀眉大眼 big eyes and slender eyebrows; fine eyebrows and large eyes;
明眸秀眉 clear-eyes with a winning look; the enticing glances of a beauty; the fond gazing of a beauty;
杏眼秀眉 with almond-shaped eyes and long eyebrows;
[秀美] beautiful; elegant; fine; graceful;
[秀媚] elegant and graceful;
秀而不媚，清而不寒 charming but not coquettish, with a clarity of complexion but not coldness;
[秀氣] (1) delicate; elegant; fine; (2) refined; urbane; (3) delicate and well-made;
[秀色] one's beauty;
秀色可餐 a beauty to feast one's eyes on; beautiful enough to feast the eyes; so pretty that one would like to eat it up;
秀色迷人 be ravished by the beauty of sb;

［秀外慧中］ beautiful and intelligent; pretty and intelligent;
［秀雅］ beautiful and refined; fine; graceful;
［秀異］ outstanding; striking;

閨秀 (1) young lady; (2) graceful girls; lady writer; literary woman; woman with literary talent;
娟秀 graceful; pretty;
俊秀 handsome and refined; pretty;
內秀 seemingly rough, but intelligent;
奇秀 wonderfully beautiful;
清秀 delicate and pretty; delicate-looking; good-looking; well-shaped; with clear-cut features;
韶秀 delicate and pretty; good-looking and handsome;
挺秀 elegant and prominent; straight and graceful; tall and graceful;
心秀 intelligent without seeming so;
新秀 promising young person; up-and-coming youngster;
軒秀 distinguished; eminent; prominent;
逸秀 talents above the average;
穎秀 outstandingly talented;
優秀 excellent; fine; foremost; outstanding; remarkable; splendid;
擢秀 (1) luxuriant; (2) gifted; talented;

xiu

【岫】 (1) cave; cavern; (2) mountain peak;

遠岫 distant hill or mountain;

xiu

【臭】 (1) odours; smells; (2) smell;
［臭腺］ scent glands;

xiu

【宿】 constellation; asterism;

星宿 constellation;

xiu

【袖】 (1) sleeve; (2) hide things up one's sleeves; put things in one's sleeves; tuck inside one's sleeve;
［袖標］ armband;
［袖口］ wristband; cuff;
［袖扣］ cuff link;
［袖孔］ armhole;
［袖套］ oversleeves;
［袖章］ armband;
［袖珍］ pocket; pocket-size;
袖珍本 pocket book; pocket edition;
袖珍電視機 mini television;
袖珍電台 pocket radiophone;
袖珍計算機 pocket computer;
袖珍計算器 pocket calculator;
［袖子］ sleeve;
大衣的袖子 arms of the coat;
捲起袖子 roll up one's sleeves;
一隻袖子 a sleeve;

拂袖 give a flick of one's sleeve;
領袖 leader;
攘袖 roll up one's sleeves;
衫袖 sleeves;
套袖 oversleeve;
衣袖 sleeve;
罩袖 oversleeve;

xiu

【嗅】 scent; smell; sniff;
［嗅覺］ olfactory sensation; sense of smell;
嗅覺不靈 have a bad nose for; have a poor sense of smell;
嗅覺不全 merosmia;
嗅覺倒錯 parosmia;
嗅覺過敏 hyperosphresia;
嗅覺減退 hyposmia;
嗅覺缺乏 anosmia;
嗅覺缺失 anosmia;
嗅覺喪失 anosmia;
嗅覺異常 allotriosmia;
嗅覺障礙 dysosmia;
嗅覺正常 euosmia;

xiu

【溴】 bromine;
［溴水］ bromine water;

xiu

【繡】 (1) embroider; (2) embroidery;
［繡工］ embroidery;
［繡花］ do embroidery; embroider; embroidery;
繡花工 embroider;
繡花針 embroidery needle;
繡花枕頭 (1) pillow with an embroidered case; (2) outwardly attractive but worthless person;
繡花枕頭，虛有其表 pillow with an embroidered case looks impressive but lacks real worth; beauty is but skin-deep; many a fine dish has nothing on

it; outwardly attractive but worthless person;

［繡畫］ embroidered picture;

［繡球］ ball of rolled silk;

［繡像］ (1) embroidered portraits; (2) exquisitely drawn portrait;

［繡鞋］ embroidered shoes;

［繡針］ embroidery needle;

尖如繡針 as sharp as a needle;

抽繡 punchwork;

刺繡 embroider; embroidery;

錦繡 brocade;

絨繡 woolen embroidery;

十字繡 cross-stitch embroidery;

xiu

【銹】 rust;

［銹病］ rust;

黑銹病 black rust;

疱狀銹病 blister rust;

茶銹 tea stain;

防銹 antirust;

生銹 get rusty;

鐵銹 rust;

一層銹 a flake of rust;

xu¹

xu

【吁】 sigh;

［吁吁］ pant; puff; sound of panting;

喘吁吁 puff and blow;

氣吁吁 gasp for breath; pant;

xu

【戌】 eleventh of the terrestrial branches;

［戌時］ period of the day from 7 p.m. to 9 p.m.;

［戌月］ ninth month of the lunar year;

屈戌 staple;

xu

【盱】 (1) open one's eyes wide; (2) anxious; uneasy; worried;

［盱衡］ (1) look with one's eyes wide open; (2) make a general survey;

盱衡當世 have open eyes and know what is going on; have the knowledge of the time;

盱衡厲色 gaze in stern countenance;

盱衡人物 open eyes on people and things;

［盱盱］ (1) stare with eyes wide open; (2) proud and haughty;

xu

【胥】 (1) all; mutually; together; (2) wait for; (3) assist; serve in an advisory role; (4) inspect; survey; (5) keep away from; separated; (6) final particle — all; (7) store; (8) a variety of official ranks through ancient dynasties; (9) a surname;

［胥賴］ thoroughly depend on;

［胥吏］ petty official;

xu

【訏】 (1) boast; brag; (2) big; great; (3) sigh;

xu

【虛】 (1) emptiness; empty; hollow; unoccupied; void; (2) diffident; timid; (3) in vain; (4) false; (5) humble; modest; (6) in poor health; weak; (7) guiding principles; theory;

［虛謗］ accuse groundlessly;

［虛報］ false declaration; make a false report; report untruthfully;

虛報冒領 fraudulent applications and claims; make a fraudulent application and claim;

［虛薄］ poor in ability;

［虛詞］ empty word; form word; function word; structural word;

［虛誕］ fantastic; preposterous; unreal;

［虛度］ dream away; fritter away; let slip idly by; pass time fruitlessly; spend time in vain; waste time;

虛度光陰 fiddle about; fool away time; fritter away one's time; idle away time; loaf away time; loiter one's time away; misspend one's time; squander one's time; waste one's time;

虛度年華 idle away one's time; pass the years in vain; spend one's days vainly; spend vainly the best of one's days; waste one's life;

虛度韶光 loiter away one's glorious youth; vainly live through one's prime;

虛度時光 idle away one's time; lose time by idleness; spend the hour idly;

虛度一生 dream away one's life; dream

out one's life; dream through one's life; idle away one's life; loaf through life; pass one's life in vain;
芳華虛度 idle away one's youth; youth pases away in vain;
年華虛度 have spent one's best years without any achievements;
[虛發] shoot without hitting the target;
彈無虛發 each shot is on target; every shot told; no shot is wasted; not a single shot missed its target;
[虛浮] empty; impractical; superficial; unsubstantial; vain;
[虛構] dream out; dream up; fabricate; fictitious; fictive; frame; invent; make up; trump up;
虛構的情節 made-up story;
虛構的人物 fictitious;
虛構世界 fictive world;
虛構性話語 fictional discourse;
向壁虛構 fabricate; gross fabrication; make up out of one's head;
[虛寒] deficiency cold;
[虛耗] expend to no avail; fritter away; waste;
虛耗公帑 waste public funds;
[虛話] empty talk; lie; unfounded statement;
[虛懷] humble; open-minded;
虛懷若谷 extremely open-minded; free from pride and prejudices; in a receptive mood; modest and open-minded;
[虛幻] illusory; imaginary; unreal; visionary;
[虛晃] deceptive movement; feint;
身體虛晃 body feint;
手臂虛晃 arm feint;
[虛己] humble; open-minded;
虛己下問 humble oneself and make enquiry;
虛己以聽 listen to advice with an open mind; listen to criticisms attentively;
[虛假] dishonest; false; insincere; sham; unreal;
弄虛作假 employ trickery; fraud and deception; gerrymander; invent stories; practise fraud; resort to deceit; trick;
[虛價] nominal price;
[虛驕] unfounded pride;
[虛驚] false alarm; nervous fear;
飽受虛驚 suffer from nervous fears;
一場虛驚 a false alarm;
[虛空] empty; hollow; vacant space; void;
[虛誇] boastful; bombastic; brag; exaggerative;
[虛禮] empty forms; mere courtesy;
[虛利] nominal profit;
[虛糜] spend to no avail; waste;
虛靡光陰 idle away one's time; waste time;
[虛名] bubble reputation; empty reputation; false reputation; undeserved reputation;
虛名無實 a reputation of no substance; have an empty reputation;
蝸角虛名 strive for an empty reputation;
浪得虛名 have unearned reputation;
徒負虛名 enjoy an undeserved reputation; have a name unworthy of it;
徒具虛名 exist only in name; have an undeserved reputation;
徒有虛名 enjoy undeserved fame; vainly possessing an empty name;
~徒有虛名，並無實學 enjoy a reputation unwarranted by any real learning;
[虛擬] (1) fictitious; invented; (2) assume; suppositional;
虛擬磁盤 virtual disc;
虛擬地址 virtual address;
虛擬動詞 subjunctive verb;
虛擬內存 virtual memory;
虛擬現實技術 virtual reality technique;
虛擬語氣 subjunctive mood;
虛擬式 subjunctive form;
虛擬專用網 virtual private network;
虛擬作業 dummy activity;
[虛盤] offer without engagement;
[虛榮] empty glory; vainglory; vainglorious; vanity;
虛榮心 vainglory; vanity;
愛慕虛榮 be vain; be vainglorious;
愛虛榮 vainglorious;
[虛弱] (1) debilitated; debility; in poor health; weak; (2) feeble; flabby; weak;
虛弱無能 miserably flabby; weak and powerless;
兵力虛弱 weak in military strength;
國力虛弱 have a weak national strength;
身體虛弱 in poor health;
使虛弱 debilitate;
體質虛弱 have a delicate constitution;
[虛設] exist in name only;

形同虛設 exist in name only; nothing but an empty shell; perform practically no function;

[虛聲] (1) bluff; make a deceptive show of power; (2) empty reputation; undeserved reputation;

虛聲恫嚇 bluff; bluster; scare sb by an empty threat;

[虛實] (1) false or true; (2) actual situation;

實中有虛，虛中有實 have imagination in reality and reality in imagination;

虛不掩實 false appearances can never cover up facts;

虛虛實實 a mixture of truth and deceit; feints and ambushes; in appearance or in fact; interweave truth with fiction; the truth mingles with the false;

虛中有實，實中有虛 provide for the real in the unreal and for the unreal in the real;

[虛數] imaginary number;

純虛數 pure imaginary number;

共軛虛數 conjugate imaginary number;

[虛談] empty talk; impractical suggestions;

[虛頭] false statement; lie;

[虛妄] fabricated; invented; preposterously fantastic; unfounded;

[虛偽] false; hypocritical; insincere; sham; spurious;

虛偽的 cheesy;

虛偽賬戶 fictitious account;

詐巧虛偽 cunning and hypocritic;

[虛文] (1) dead letter; rules and regulations that have become a dead letter; (2) empty forms; mere formalities; impractical formalities;

虛文浮禮 conventionalities; mere formalities;

虛文縟節 empty forms; rituals;

[虛無] emptiness; nihility; nothingness; void;

虛無縹緲 entirely unreal; illusive; floating and intangible; illusory; in the clouds; in the misty void; nothing to hold on; purely imaginary; shapeless and elusive; utterly visionary; vague with nothing in it; with no reality whatsoever;

虛無妄想 nihilism;

虛無主義 nihilism;

~虛無主義者 nihilist;

[虛銜] nominal title;

[虛線] (1) dotted line; (2) imaginary line;

[虛想] imagine; mere wish;

[虛心] modest; open-minded; with an open mind;

虛心好學 modest and eager to learn;

虛心求教 ready to listen to advice; willing to take advice;

虛心聽取 listen patiently; listen with an open mind;

虛心下氣 humble and meek;

[虛徐] leisurely;

[虛言] (1) false remarks; unfounded statements; (2) empty talk; meaningless words; platitude;

[虛譽] buble reputation; false fame;

[虛造] fabricate; invent;

鄉壁虛造 create out of nothing;

向壁虛造 create out of nothing; fabricate; make up out of one's head; trump up;

嚮壁虛造 fabricate out of nothing;

[虛詐] falsehood and trickery;

[虛字] empty word; form word; function word;

乘虛 catch sb napping; take advantage of a weak point;

膽虛 jittery; nervous; scared;

空虛 aeriality; emptiness; hollow; inanity; void;

脾虛 asthenia of the spleen;

氣虛 deficiency of vital energy;

謙虛 (1) humble; modest; self-effacing; unassuming; (2) make modest remarks;

潛虛 live in seclusion;

清虛 high and mild; refined and nonaggressive;

太虛 the great void; the universe;

務虛 discuss political and ideological guidelines;

心虛 (1) afraid of being found out; guilty conscience; with a guilty conscience; (2) diffident; lacking in self-confidence;

玄虛 (1) cunning and evil schemes; deceitful tricks; (2) empty and without substance; mystery;

懸虛 hard to believe; incredible;

血虛 blood deficiency;

陽虛 lack of vital energy;

盈虛 fullness and emptiness; ups and downs; waxing and waning;

庸虛 mediocre and incapable;

玉虛 fairyland;

子虛 (1) emptiness; nothingness; (2) fiction;

紫虛 firmament; sky;

xu

【須】 (1) have to; must; need; (2) await; wait for; (3) probably; (4) moment; while; (5) a surname;

［須待］ (1) have to wait until; (2) expect; look forward to;

［須當］ must;

［須得］ must have; should have;

［須留］ stay a while; wait a moment;

［須索］ (1) blackmail; extort; (2) must;

［須要］ have to; must;

［須臾］ instant; short moment; short while;
- 須臾之間 in a flash; in a little while; in an instant; in the twinkling of an eye;

［須知］ (1) have to know; it must be understood that; one should know that; should know; (2) note; notice; points for attention;
- 須知盤中粟，粒粒皆辛苦 one should know that every single grain on the plate is the fruit of hard work;

必須 have to; must;
斯須 very short moment;
無須 need not;
務須 be sure to; must;
些須 a few; a little;

xu

【欻】 suddenly;

xu

【需】 (1) demand; need; require; want; (2) expenses; necessaries; needs; provisions; (3) delay; hesitation;

［需款］ in need of money; need money;

［需求］ demand; need; requirement;
- 需求不足 lack of demand;
- 需求很大 in great demand; much in demand;
- 需求激增 surge in demand;
- 需求價格 demand price;
- 需求上升 demand increases; demand rises;
- 需求下降 demand falls;
- 跟上需求 keep pace with demand; keep up with demand;
- 工藝需求 arts demand;
- 國內需求 domestic demand;
- 降低需求 reduce demand;
- 絕對需求 absolute demand;
- 滿足需求 cope with demand; meet a need; meet demand;
- 實際需求 actual demand;
- 世界需求 world demand;
- 提升需求 increase demand;
- 推動需求 boost demand;
- 消費需求 consumer demand;
- 追加需求 additional demand;
- 總需求 aggregate demand;
- ~累積總需求 aggregate demand;

［需氧］ aerobian;
- 需氧菌 aerobe;
- 需氧生活 aerobiosis;
- 需氧生物 aerobian; aerobiont;
- 需氧微生物 aeromicrobe;
- 需氧性 aerobism;

［需要］ demand; entail; need; require; want;
- 需要層次論 requirement level theory;
- 需要量 requirement;
- ~材料需要量 material requirement;
- ~年度需要量 annual requirement;
- ~實際需要量 actual requirement;
- ~預計需要量 anticipated requirement;
- 需要乃發明之母 necessity is the mother of invention;
- 需要品 essentials; necessities;
- 需要預測 demand forecasting;
- 不需要 have no use for;
- 超越性需要 metaneed;
- 出於需要 out of necessity;
- 符合需要 fit the bill;
- 基本需要 basic needs;
- 經濟需要 economic necessity;
- 滿足需要 meet a demand;
- 如有需要 if it is necessary; if need be;
- 市場需要 needs of the market;
- 實際需要 actual demand; physical demand; practical necessity;
- 特殊需要 special needs;
- 政治需要 political necessity; political needs;

必需 essential; indispensable;
產需 supply and demand;
供需 supply and demand;
急需 (1) badly in need of; (2) urgent need;
軍需 military supplies;
內需 domestic demand;
如需 if you need to;
所需 needs; requirements;
毋需 do not need;

X

xu

【嘘】 (1) breathe out slowly; (2) utter a sigh; (3) burn; come into contact with sth; scald; (4) hush; sh; shush;

［嘘氣］ blow; send out breath from the mouth;

［嘘聲］ breathe out slowly; catcall;

嘘聲四起 hiss and boo everywhere; resound with catcalls; wave of hisses all round;

［嘘唏］ sob;

嘘唏搖頭 shake one's head with a deep sigh;

［嘘嘘］ snore;

喘嘘嘘 puff and blow;

［嘘音］ hush;

吹嘘 boast; lavish praise on oneself or others;

唏嘘 sob;

xu

【墟】 (1) high mound; (2) ancient town; ghost town; (3) wild, waste land; (4) periodic marketplace; (5) destruction; ruins;

［墟里］ small village;

［墟墓］ neglected burial grounds;

［墟市］ the fair grounds of a village;

xu

【嬃】 term of address for elder sisters in the state of Zhu in ancient China;

xu

【歔】 (1) exhale from the nose; (2) sob;

［歔欷］ sniffle; sob;

歔欷嘆息 sob and sign with sniffing;

［歔吸］ draw; suck;

xu

【繻】 (1) fine gauze; (2) pieces of silk used as credentials;

xu

【鬚】 (1) beard; whiskers; (2) awn;

［鬚眉］ (1) beard and eyebrows; (2) men;

鬚眉交白 white with age;

［鬚髮］ beard and hair;

鬚髮皆白 have white hair and beard;

［鬚根］ fine rootlets of plants;

［鬚後水］ aftershave;

［鬚生］ bearded character;

［鬚髯如戟］ stroll; walk leisurely;

［鬚子］ (1) tassel; (2) palpus;

刮個鬚子 have a shave;

刮鬚子 shave;

觸鬚 corris;

鬍鬚 beard; beard and moustache; moustache;

虎鬚 tiger's whiskers;

花鬚 pistil; stamen;

假鬚 false beard;

鯨鬚 baleen; whalebone;

捲鬚 tendril;

虬鬚 curly beard;

拈鬚 finger one's beard; stroke one's beard;

剃鬚 shave;

蓄鬚 grow a beard;

髭鬚 moustaches and beards;

xu²

xu

【徐】 (1) calm; composed; gently; slowly; (2) a surname;

［徐步］ stroll; walk leisurely; walk slowly;

徐步而行 walk with slow steps;

徐步緩行 amble along;

［徐緩］ slow; unhurriedly;

［徐來］ gently blow;

［徐娘半老］ in her middle age; past her prime;

徐娘半老，風韻猶存 a charming woman in middle age; the woman in her forties is still attractive, despite her age; the woman in her thirty-forties still retains a great deal of charm;

［徐圖殲擊］ wipe out the enemy troops at our convenience;

［徐徐］ (1) calm; gently; relaxed and dignified; (2) slowly;

徐徐而來 come with relaxed and dignified steps;

xu³

xu

【昫】 warmth of the rising sun;

xu

【栩】 (1) a species of oak; (2) glad; pleased;

［栩栩］ lively; vivid;

栩栩然 very glad and pleased;

栩栩如生 as vivid as life; both vivid and lively; come alive; instinct with life; to the life; to the quick; true to life; true to nature;

栩栩自得 self-complacent; well-pleased; well-satisfied;

xu

【許】 (1) commend; praise; (2) allow; approve; permit; promise; (3) maybe; perhaps; possibly; (4) place; (5) be betrothed; promise to marry; (6) expect; (7) a little more than; about; (8) a surname;

[許多] a big percentage of; a crowd of; a flock of; a good deal of; a good few of; a great deal of; a great many; a heap of; a host of; a hundred and one; a large amount of; a large body of; a large number of; a large quantity of; a lot; a lot of; a mass of; a number of; a pile of; a power of; a sight of; a store of; a thousand and one; a wealth of; a world of; all manner of; an army of; bags of; heaps of; hundreds of; in profusion; lots and lots of; lots of; many; many in number; much; no end of; not a few; numbers of; numerous; plenty; plenty of; quite a few; stacks of; thousands of; volumes of;
許多次 many's the time;
許多的書 a great number of books;
許多孩子 many a child;
許多天 many's the day;
許許多多 a great many; lots and lots of;
~許許多多的孩子 a great many children;

[許嫁] betroth a daughter;

[許久] for a long time; for ages; for quite some time;

[許可] allow; approve; clearance; consent; give permission; licence; licensing; permit;
許可證 licence; permit;
~許可證持有人 licensee;
~許可證貿易 licensing trade;
~出口許可證 export permit;
~臨時許可證 provisional licence;
~停車許可證 parking permit;
~總許可證 blanket licence;
出口許可 licensing of export;
官方許可 official permission;
獲得許可 obtain permission; receive permission;
請求許可 ask for permission; request permission;
入口許可 licensing of import;
書面許可 written permission;
特別許可 special permission;

[許諾] give one's word; make a promise; promise;
作出許諾 make a promise;

[許配] affiance; be affianced to; be betrothed to; betroth one's daughter to;

[許是] maybe; perhaps;

[許願] make a vow to a god;
許願要還 a promise needs to be carried out;
燒香許願 burn incense to make a wish;

[許字] betroth a girl;

不許 (1) must not; not allow; (2) cannot;
稱許 commend; praise;
何許 what place; where;
或許 likely; maybe; might; perhaps; possible; would;
幾許 how many; how much;
嘉許 approve; commend;
獎許 acclaim; praise;
默許 acquiesce in; tacitly consent to;
期許 be expected to; expect to;
認許 acknowledge; approve;
容許 (1) allow; (2) tolerate; (3) perhaps; possibly;
若許 like this; thus;
稍許 a bit; a little;
少許 a few; a little; a modicum;
特許 chartered; concession; franchise; special permission;
推許 approve; esteem and commend; praise;
些許 a few; a little; a modicum;
心許 acclaim without words; tacit acceptance; tact approval;
興許 maybe; perhaps;
邪許 call out in one voice; yell in unison;
也許 maybe; perhaps; probably;
應許 (1) agree; promise; (2) allow;
允許 allow; consent; give permission; grant; permit;
稱許 praise; speak favourably of;
讚許 commend; deserve of high praise; give a high appraisal to; loud in the praise of; make sb a compliment; meet sb's approbation; pay high tribute to; praise; praise sb a compliment; praise sb up to the skies; set a high value on; sing sb's praiscs; sing the praise of; speak highly of; speak favourably of; win high priase;

准許 allow; approve; permit;
自許 conceited; pretentious; regard oneself as;

xu
【湑】 luxuriant; rich;

xu
【煦】 (1) warm and cosy; (2) favours; good graces; kind and gracious; kindness;
［煦伏］ grace of raising and educating;
煦伏之恩 grace to warm and cover;
［煦煦］ (1) benevolent; gracious; kind; (2) balmy; warm and fine;
［煦日］ (1) warm sun; (2) warm and fine day;

xu
【詡】 (1) boast; brag; exaggerate; (2) common; make widely known; popular; (3) (now rare) clever and brave; (4) (now rare) harmonious;
［詡詡］ (1) lively; vivid; (2) boast; brag; (3) harmonious;

自詡 boast; praise oneself;

xu
【鄦】 an ancient state in present-day Henan;

xu
【諝】 (1) sagacity; wisdom; (2) clever idea; stratagem;

xu⁴
xu
【旭】 (1) brilliance of the rising sun; (2) rising sun; (3) complacent; smug;
［旭日］ rising sun;
旭日初昇 early in the morning; rising like the early morning sun — in the ascendant; the sun is rising;
旭日東昇 the red sun rises in the east;
［旭旭］ (1) complacent; smug; (2) uproarious;

朝旭 rising sun;

xu
【序】 (1) foreward; introduction; preface; (2) order sequence; sequence of things;
［序跋］ preface and postscript;
［序列］ (1) array; order; succession; (2) number sequence; sequence; sequencing;
序列號 serial number;
~一個序列號 a serial number;
序列化規則 sequencing rules;
遞增序列 increasing sequence;
多重序列 multiple sequence;
機械序列 machine sequencing;
無界序列 unbounded sequence;
無限序列 infinite sequence;
線形序列 linear sequence;
有限序列 finite sequence;
有界序列 bounded sequence;
［序論］ introduction;
［序幕］ curtain raiser; prelude; prologue;
［序目］ preface and contents;
［序曲］ introduction; overture; prelude;
［序數］ ordinal; ordinal number;
序數詞 ordinal;
不可分解序數 indecomposable ordinal;
非極限序數 non-limit ordinal;
可構造序數 constructive ordinal;
容許序數 admissible ordinal;
［序文］ foreword; preface;
［序言］ foreword; preface; introduction;
［序奏］ prelude;

按姓氏筆劃為序 list in the order of the number of strokes in surnames;
按序 according to the order of sequence; in sequence;
程序 course; order; procedure; proceeding; process; programme; routine; sequence;
詞序 word order;
次序 arrangement; order; sequence; succession;
代序 in lieu of a preface;
倒序 inverted; reverse;
工序 procedure; production processes; working procedure;
花序 inflorescence;
脈序 venation;
逆序 inversion;
排序 ordering;
愆序 unseasonable heat or cold;
時序 seasons; times;
順序 (1) plain sequence; sequence; succession; (2) according to right order; in proper order; in turn;
庠序 school;
循序 follow in proper sequence; in proper order; in proper sequence; proceed in good order; proceed step by step;
雁序 brothers;

語序　word order;
秩序　(1) order; sequence; (2) arrangement;
自序　(1) author's foreword; author's preface; (2) autobiographic note;

xu

【卹】 (1) help; pity; relieve; (2) commiseration; considerate; sympathy;
［卹病］ show sympathy for the sick;
［卹孤］ relieve orphans;
［卹金］ compensation; pension for a disabled person or the family of the deceased; relief payment;
死亡卹金　death benefit;
［卹款］ indemnity for a lost life;
［卹老］ relieve the aged;
［卹民］ mindful of the people's hardships;
［卹貧］ give relief to the poor;
［卹然］ astonished; startled;
［卹養金］ pension;
［卹政］ benevolent government;

不卹　disregard;
撫卹　comfort and compensate a bereaved family;
贍卹　contribute money to charity;
體卹　considerate of and sympathize with; favour; show solicitude for; understand and sympathize with;
軫卹　pity deeply;
賑卹　relieve the distressed;
拯卹　save and help;

xu

【洫】 ditch; moat;

xu

【畜】 (1) raise; rear; (2) a surname;
［畜產］ animal products; livestock products;
畜產品　animal by-products;
［畜欄］ corral;
［畜牧］ animal husbandry; livestock industry; raise livestock; rear livestock;
畜牧場　grazing ground; livestock farm; range;
畜牧工人　stockman;
畜牧師　husbandian;
~高級畜牧師　senior husbandian;
畜牧學　animal husbandry; zootechny;
畜牧業　animal husbandry; stock farming;
［畜棚］ arn;
［畜養］ keep; raise; rear;

愛畜　pet;
家畜　cattle; domestic animal; farm livestock; livestock;
六畜　the six domestic animals (pig, ox, goat, horse, fowl and dog);
牧畜　animal husbandry; livestock breeding;
牲畜　domestic animals; livestock;
獸畜　beast;

xu

【敍】 (1) chat; talk; (2) describe; express; narrate; recount; tell; (3) arrange in order; (4) assess; appraise; evaluate; rate;
［敍別］ have a farewell talk; say goodbye to each other;
［敍功］ assess merits;
敍功行賞　go over the records and decide on awards;
［敍舊］ talk about the old days;
［敍情］ bare one's heart;
［敍事］ narrate; recount;
敍事結構　narrative structure;
敍事詩　narrative poem;
敍事文　narrative prose;
［敍實］ factual;
敍實動詞　factual verb;
敍實性　factuality;
［敍述］ give an account of; narrate; narration; render an account of;
敍述事情的經過　give an account of the event;
敍述文　narrative text;
敍述者　narrator;
［敍説］ narrate; tell;
［敍談］ chat; chit-chat; get together and chat; talk together;
［敍文］ preface;
［敍言］ foreword; preface;
［敍用］ appoint; assign sb to a post; employ;

插敍　narration interspersed with flashbacks;
暢敍　converse cheerfully; talk to one's heart's content;
倒敍　flashback; narrate from the end;
記敍　narrate;
鋪敍　elaborate; narrate in detail;
銓敍　grade qualifications and select officials;
追敍　recount; relate;
自敍　(1) author's preface; (2) autobiographical note;

xu

【勗】 encourage; stimulate;

［勗勉］ encourage; prompt; urge;

xu

【酗】 lose temper when drunk;

［酗酒］ alcohol abuse; alcoholism; drink deep; drink hard; drink heavily; drink like a fish; have excessive drinking; hit the bottle; indulge in excessive drinking; on the drink; take to drinking;

酗酒滋事 get drunk and create a disturbance;

酗酒者 dipsomaniac;

開始酗酒 hit the bottle;

［酗訟］ accuse each other for getting drunk;

xu

【絮】 (1) cotton wadding; (2) fluffy; wooly; (3) cotton-like object; (4) wad with cotton; (5) long-winded;

［絮叨］ chatter; gabby; garrulous; long-winded; tiresomely talkative; wordy;

絮叨鬼 prattler;

［絮煩］ (1) long-winded; talkative; windy; wordy; (2) bored; tired of; weary;

［絮聒］ (1) chatter; windy and tiresome; (2) bother sb; importune incessantly; trouble sb;

絮聒不休 annoyingly talkative; chatter; din; din in one's ears;

［絮棉］ cotton for wadding;

［絮絮］ continuous and garrulous;

絮絮不休 ceaseless chatter; jabber continuously; long-winded; talk rapidly and trivially;

絮絮叨叨 babble; harp on; hum about; repeat over and over again;

［絮語］ garrulous; incessantly chatter; wordy;

敗絮 waste cotton — a dry and useless thing;

叨絮 longwinded;

飛絮 floating catkins;

聒絮 keep talking noisily;

花絮 interesting sidelights; tidbits;

柳絮 catkin;

棉絮 (1) cotton fibre; (2) cotton wadding;

吐絮 opening of bolls;

xu

【慉】 bring up; raise;

［慉結］ depressed; melancholy;

xu

【緒】 (1) end of a thread; (2) clue; (3) beginning; (4) mental state; (5) leftovers; remains; remnants;

［緒論］ foreword; introduction; preface;

［緒言］ foreword; introduction; preamble; preface;

［緒業］ business; calling;

［緒餘］ remnants; surplus;

別緒 sorrow of parting;

愁緒 feeling of sadness; gloomy mood; skein of sorrow;

端緒 clue; inkling;

就緒 in order; ready;

情緒 (1) feeling; mood; morale; sentiments; spirit; (2) depression; moodiness; sullenness;

思緒 (1) one's thinking; train of thought; (2) feeling; mood;

頭緒 clue; lead; main threads;

先緒 ancestral heritage;

心緒 mood; state of mind;

意緒 (1) threads of thoughts; (2) mood; state of mind;

肇緒 beginning;

xu

【蓄】 (1) collect; reserve; save up; store; (2) cultivate; grow; (3) entertain; harbour; (4) expect; wait;

［蓄財］ store up wealth;

［蓄髮］ grow long hair;

［蓄恨］ long pent-up hatred;

［蓄洪］ store floodwater;

蓄洪防旱 store floodwater for use against a drought;

蓄洪工程 flood storage work;

［蓄積］ accumulate; save up; store up;

［蓄謀］ premeditate; secret plan;

蓄謀叛變 harbour plans for an insurrection;

蓄謀迫害 harbour a design of persecuting sb;

蓄謀已久 have deliberately planned over a long period of time; have plotted for a long time; keep on plotting for a long time;

［蓄念］ long-conceived idea;

蓄念已久 have long entertained such ideas;

[蓄妾] concubinage;
[蓄鋭] husband one's strength and store up energy;
[蓄水] store water;
蓄水層 aquifer;
蓄水池 reservoir;
[蓄養] raise;
[蓄疑] harbour suspicion;
[蓄意] deliberate; harbour certain intentions; premediated;
蓄意報復 harbor thoughts of revenge;
蓄意不良 harbour evil designs;
蓄意出錯 make mistakes purposely;
蓄意攻擊 make a calculated attack;
蓄意抗命 defy orders intentionally;
蓄意謀殺 commit a premeditated murder;
蓄意疏忽 neglect sth wilfully;
蓄意挑釁 premediated provocation;
蓄意行騙 practise deliberate deception;
蓄意已久 hope for a long time; long hoped for;
蓄意製造 concoct deliberately; create deliberately; engineer deliberately; fabricate deliberately;
[蓄怨] harbour animosity; harbour ill will;
[蓄志] long-cherished ambition;
蓄志遠大 aspire after greatness; have an earnest ambition for sth high and great;

儲蓄 deposit; save;
含蓄 (1) contain; embody; (2) implicit; suggestive rather than explicit; veiled; (3) reserved; restrained;
積蓄 accumulate; lay up a purse; put aside; salt away; save; save up;
攔蓄 retain;
私蓄 private savings;
餘蓄 personal savings;
蘊蓄 contain beneath the surface; latent;
貯蓄 hoard; store up;

xu

【漵】 (1) edge of river; waterside; (2) a river in Hunan;

xu

【續】 (1) continuous; successive; (2) continue; extend; join; (3) add; supply more;
[續版] reprint of a book;
[續編] sequel;
[續貂] add to sth good with sth bad;
[續訂] renew one's subscription;
[續後] afterward; later;
[續集] sequel;
[續借] renew;
[續命湯] decoction to stimulate a dying person; life-saver;
[續母] stepmother;
[續絃] remarry;
續絃之喜 happy occasion of marrying a second wife;
[續續] continuously; incessantly; successively;
[續約] renew a contract;

持續 continuance; continuation; continued; sustained;
待續 be continued;
後續 follow-on; follow-up;
繼續 carry on; continue; continue to; continue up; continue with; get on with; go ahead with; go on; keep at; keep on doing sth; keep on with; last; proceed to; proceed with;
接續 continue; follow;
絕續 die out or survive;
連續 again and again; at a stretch; consecutive; continual; continuance; continuation; continue; continuously; for ...running; in a row; in succession; last; nonstop; on end; one after another; repeated; running; stretch; successively; without a break; without a let-up; without a stop;
陸續 in succession; one after another;
手續 formalities; procedures; processes; routines;
相續 (1) inherit; (2) continue one after another;
延續 be continued; continue; go on; last;

xuan¹
xuan

【宣】 (1) announce; declare; proclaim; (2) circulate; propagate; (3) drain; lead off; (4) a surname;
[宣佈] announce; declare; proclaim;
宣佈獨立 declare independence;
宣佈戒嚴 declare martial law;
宣佈無效 declare sth invalid;
宣佈作廢 declare invalid;
當眾宣佈 announce publicly;
[宣稱] allege; assert; declare; profess; pronounce;

[宣傳] conduct propaganda; give publicity to; plug; promote; propagate; publicize;
宣傳車 promotion car;
宣傳費 publicity expense;
宣傳工具 mass communications; mass media;
宣傳畫 poster;
宣傳活動 propaganda exercise;
宣傳機器 propaganda machine;
宣傳品 promotion material; propaganda material;
宣傳員 press agent; publicist;
宣傳運動 propaganda campaign;
宣傳戰 propaganda war;
宣傳者 propagator;
大力宣傳 conduct vigorous propaganda;
大事宣傳 a whoop and a holler; ballyhoo; give great publicity; hype; play up;
廣為宣傳 give a great deal of publicity;
政治宣傳 political propaganda;

[宣導] guide by creating a better understanding;

[宣讀] read off in public; read out in public;

[宣撫] pacify by propaganda;

[宣告] announce; declare; proclaim; pronounce;
宣告破產 declare bankruptcy; go bankrupt;
宣告無效 declare null and void;
宣告員 announcer;

[宣講] deliver a speech; explain and publicize; orate; preach; read and explain;

[宣令] issue an order;

[宣募] (1) recruit; (2) collect;

[宣判] announce the verdict; pronounce judgement;

[宣示] announce; declare; make publicly known;
宣示一二 vie sb some inkling of;

[宣誓] make a pledge; make a vow; swear an oath; take an oath;
宣誓公證人 commissioner for oaths;
宣誓就職 be sworn in; swearing-in; take the oath of office;
宣誓人 affiant;
宣誓書 affidavit; written oath;
~立宣誓書 make an affidavit; sign an affidavit; swear an affidavit;
宣誓效忠 swear allegiance and pledge eternal loyalty to; take an oath of fealty;
舉手宣誓 hold up one's hand and take a solemn oath;

[宣威] extend one's power;

[宣言] declaration; manifesto;

[宣揚] advertise; advocate; propagate; publicise; publicise and exalt;

[宣淫] engage in lascivious activities in public;

[宣戰] declaration of war; declare war; hang out the red flag; proclaim war;
不宣而戰 open hostilities without declaring war; start an undeclared war;

[宣召] summon to imperial court;

[宣紙] rice paper;

xuan

【軒】 (1) high; lofty; (2) door; window; (3) small room with windows; (4) balcony; porch; (5) room; studio;

[軒昂] dignified; high; imposing; lofty;
軒昂氣宇 dignified; exalted; manly;

[軒朗] open; wide;

[軒闊] generous; open-minded;

[軒然] (1) delighted; smiling; (2) lofty; towering;
軒然大波 big, crushing wave; big dispute; great disturbance; mighty uproar; violent wave;
軒然自得 delighted and satisfied; hold head high; self-pleased;

[軒爽] bright and airy;

[軒秀] distinguished; eminent; prominent;

[軒軒] (1) complacent; (2) outstanding;
軒軒自得 delighted and satisfied with oneself;

[軒豁] open; wide;

[軒輊] (1) good or bad; (2) high or low;
不分軒輊 equal; equally matched; on a par;
無分軒輊 a draw or tie; equal; make no difference between the high and low chariots; well-matched;

xuan

【喧】 clamour; noisy; talk noisily;

[喧賓奪主] a boisterous guest usurps the place of the host; a gatecrasher supplanting the host; a minor issue taking precedence over a major one; a presumptuous guest usurps the host's role; a reversal of the order of host and guest; a talkative guest usurping the place of the host; steal the show; the sauce is better than the fish; the secondary supersedes the primary; the wrangling guest robs the place of the host;

[喧嘩] confused noise; hubbub; kerfuffle; uproar;
一片喧嘩 a babel of sounds;

[喧鬧] bustle; din; hoopla; noise and excitement; racket; rag;
喧鬧的 boisterous;
喧鬧聲 din; hubbub;
高聲喧鬧 raise the roof;

[喧嚷] clamour; din; hubbub; racket;

[喧擾] noise and disturbance; tumult;

[喧騰] hubbub; noise and excitement; uproar;
一片喧騰 a hubbub of voices;

[喧天] fill the air with noise; make a deafening sound;
喧天震地 great ovation;

[喧囂] (1) hurly-burly; noisy; (2) clamour; din; hullabaloo;
喧囂不已 clamour without stopping; incessant vociferation; repeated outcry; the clamour is incessant;
喧囂鼓噪 make a clamour; make outcries; stir up a commotion;
喧囂一時 bluster for a time; create a stir; kick up a terrific racket for a while; make a din for a time; make a lot of noise for a time; raise a hue and cry for a while; vociferous for a time;

xuan

【揎】 (1) pull up the sleeves and show the arms; (2) fight with bare hands;

[揎擊] hit with bare fists;

[揎拳] pull up the sleeves and get ready to fight;

xuan

【暄】 (1) comfortable and genial; warm; (2) fluffy; soft;

[暄風] spring breeze;

[暄寒] talk;

[暄涼] greetings to one another;

[暄暖] warm and comfortable;

[暄騰] fluffy; soft;

[暄妍] warm weather and captivating scenery;

xuan

【萱】 daylily;

[萱草] daylily; tawny daylily;
萱草忘憂 a son is a comfort to the mother;

[萱堂] one's mother;

xuan

【瑄】 ornamental piece of jade;

xuan

【諼】 (1) deceive; (2) forget;

[諼草] daylily;

xuan

【讀】 bawl; shout;

[讀呼滿道] shouting fills the roads;

xuan

【翾】 flit; fly;

[翾翾] flitting; flying sprightly;

xuan²

xuan

【玄】 (1) black; dark; (2) far and obscure; mystic; occult; (3) abstruse and subtle; deep and profound; (4) incredible; unreliable; (5) silent and meditative; (6) a surname;

[玄奧] (1) abstruse and subtle; difficult to comprehend; (2) mysteries; profundities;

[玄服] dark dress;

[玄黃] (1) heaven and earth; (2) dark yellow;
玄黃翻覆 overthrow of heaven and earth;

[玄機] profound and mysterious truth; profound theory;

[玄理] profound theory;

[玄妙] abstruse and subtle; mysterious; profound;
玄妙莫測 difficult to guess or comprehend;

[玄默] taciturn and meditative;

[玄謀] subtle and profound scheme;

[玄青] deep black;

[玄孫] great-great-grandson;
玄孫女 great-great-granddaughter;

[玄武岩] basalt;

[玄悟] profound understanding of an abstruse theory;

[玄想] fancy; fantasy; illusion;

[玄虛] (1) cunning and evil schemes; deceitful tricks; (2) empty and without

substance; mystery;
故弄玄虛 cast a mist before sb's eyes; deliberately mystifying; deliberately to make things look mysterious; kick up a cloud of dust; make a mystery of; mystifying; play dishonest juggling tricks; use intrigues and tricks;
故作玄虛 make a mystery of;
[玄學] metaphysics;
[玄遠] profound and lasting;
[玄月] ninth month in the lunar calendar;
[玄之又玄] mystery of mysteries — extremely mysterious and abstruse; the most mysterious of the mysterious;
[玄著] abstruse writings;

xuan

【旋】 (1) circle; revolve; spin; (2) come back; return; turn back; (3) a moment; a very short while; soon; (4) urinate;
[旋兒] circle;
[旋風] whirlwind;
旋風式的 whirlwind;
[旋即] forthwith; immediately afterwards;
[旋里] return to one's hometown;
[旋律] canto; melody;
優美的旋律 lilt; tuneful melody;
主旋律 leitmotif;
[旋輪線] cycloid;
長輻旋輪線 prolate cycloid;
短輻旋輪線 curtate cycloid;
圓內旋輪線 hypocycloid;
~四尖圓內旋輪線 hypocycloid of four cusps;
圓外旋輪線 epicycloid;
[旋鈕] knob;
粗調旋鈕 coarse adjustment knob;
微調旋鈕 fine adjustment knob;
[旋繞] curl up; drift about; move in an orbit; orbit; revolve around; wind around;
[旋塞] cock;
閉鎖旋塞 closing cock;
放氣旋塞 blast cock;
放洩旋塞 blow-off cock;
轉換旋塞 changeover cock;
[旋踵] very short time;
旋踵即逝 disappear in the twinkling of an eye; vanish before one has time turn round;
不旋踵 in less time than it takes to turn one's heels;
[旋轉] revolve; rotate; rotation; spin; turn round and round;
旋轉餐廳 revolving restaurant;
旋轉門 circulating door; revolving door;
旋轉面 surface of revolution;
旋轉器 rotator;
~鐵氧體旋轉器 ferrite rotator;
旋轉乾坤 earth-shaking; effect a drastic change in the established order of a country; make the heavens turn backwards — able to turn the tide of world events; turn heaven into earth and vice versa;
旋轉體 solid of rotation;
旋轉軸 axis of rotation;
旋轉自如 rotate freely; revolve freely;
單足旋轉 pirouette;
角旋轉 angular rotation;
絕對旋轉 absolute rotation;
快速旋轉 gyrate;
天旋地轉 feel one's head swim; the heavens and earth go round; they sky and earth are spinning round; very dizzy;
[旋子] spinor;
反變旋子 contravariant spinor;
共變旋子 covariant spinor;
共軛旋子 conjugate spinor;

側旋 sidespin;
反氣旋 anticyclone;
迴旋 (1) circle round; (2) have room for manoeuvre;
凱旋 return in triumph; with flying colours;
螺旋 (1) helix; spiral; (2) screw;
盤旋 (1) circle around; hover; wheel; (2) linger; stay; tarry;
氣旋 cyclone;
上旋 top spin;
渦旋 vortex;
斡旋 mediate;
下旋 backspin; underspin;
周旋 (1) have social intercourse with; socialize; (2) contend with; deal with;

xuan

【漩】 whirlpool;
[漩渦] (1) whirlpool; (2) dispute; quarrel;
感情的漩渦 whirlpool of emotion;
捲入漩渦 get involved in a conflict;

泡漩 water current with rough waves and whirlpools;

xuan

【璇】 (1) fine jade; (2) name of a constellation;

［璇璣］ the four stars in the bowl of the Big Dipper;

xuan

【縣】 same as 懸 , hang;

xuan

【璿】 fine jade;

［璿宮］ gem-studded chamber;

［璿圖］ nation; state;

xuan

【懸】 (1) hang; suspend; (2) outstanding; in suspension; unresolved; unsettled; (3) be concerned for; feel anxious; solicitous; (4) imagine; (5) far apart; (6) dangerous;

［懸案］ (1) pending criminal case; unsettled law case; (2) outstanding issue; unsettled question;

懸案未結 the case is being suspended; the case is still not settled;

［懸臂］ cantilever;

懸臂梁 cantilever;

［懸垂］ hang down;

倒懸垂 inverted hang;

［懸斷］ judge without any sufficient basis;

［懸浮］ suspend;

懸浮火車 aerotrain;

懸浮列車 aerotrain;

懸浮物質 suspended matter;

膠體懸浮 colloidal suspension;

［懸隔］ (1) inaccessible; remote; (2) be separated by a great distance;

［懸掛］ hang; suspend;

懸腸掛肚 cause extreme worry and distress; harbour deep concern for sth;

［懸河］ (1) pour continually; (2) speak eloquently;

懸河瀉水 one's eloquence may be compared to a fast-flowing river; one's words pour forth like rushing water; one's words pour from one's lips like refreshing water from a mountain spring;

［懸壺］ practise medicine;

懸壺濟世 practise medicine in order to help people;

懸壺行醫 practise medicine;

懸壺之慶 birthday of a male;

［懸絕］ completely different;

［懸空］ (1) hang in the air; suspend in midair; (2) be divorced from reality;

［懸鏈］ catenary;

懸鏈曲面 catenoid;

懸鏈線 catenary;

~ 變形懸鏈線 transformed catenary;

~ 單懸鏈線 single catenary;

~ 等阻懸鏈線 catenary of equal resistance;

~ 球面懸鏈線 spherical catenary;

~ 雙重懸鏈線 compound catenary;

~ 雙曲懸鏈線 hyperbolic catenary;

~ 橢圓懸鏈線 elliptic catenary;

懸鏈作用 catenary action;

［懸梁］ (1) hang oneself from a beam; (2) overbeam;

懸梁自盡 commit suicide by hanging oneself from a beam; hang oneself;

［懸念］ (1) be concerned about; cliffhanger; miss; suspense; (2) audience involvement;

［懸旗］ hang a flag; hoist a flag;

［懸賞］ post a reward; offer a reward;

懸賞緝拿 offer a reward for the capture of sb; set a price on sb's head;

［懸殊］ differ by a wide margin; great disparity; very different; wide gap;

［懸索橋］ suspension bridge;

［懸談］ make a rambling talk;

［懸梯］ hanging ladder;

［懸駝就石］ put the cart before the horse; put the incidental before the fundamental; put the trivial above the important; reverse the order of importance;

［懸望］ hope with misgivings; long for anxiously; look forward eagerly;

［懸想］ conjecture; fancy; imagine; speculate;

［懸象］ celestial phenomena;

［懸心］ concerned about sb;

懸心吊膽 be filled with anxiety as well as fear; in a constant state of suspense; in a state of anxious suspense; on the tenterhooks;

［懸虛］ hard to believe; incredible;

unbelievable;

[懸崖] beetling cliffs; cliff; crag; hanger; overhanging cliff; precipice; rock cliff; scarp; steep cliff;
懸崖絕壁 sheer precipices and overhanging rocks; steep precipices and cliffs;
懸崖勒馬 desist from doing sth before it is too late; draw up sharp on the brink of catastrophe; halt before the abyss; pull back before it is too late; pull back right away from the brink of the abyss; rein in at the brink of the precipice — wake up and escape disaster at the last moment; rein in one's horse on the brink of a precipice; stop on the edge of the precipice and not to go any farther; stop one's horse on coming to the precipice; ward off disaster at the critical moment; withdraw sharply from imminent disaster;
懸崖峭壁 cliffs and precipices; dangerously steep mountains; precipitous rock faces and sheer cliffs; sheer precipice and overhanging rocks;
懸崖深谷 high cliffs and deep gullies;

[懸疑] suspense;

[懸雍垂] lingula; uvula;

逋懸 a long overdue rent; arrears;

垂懸 hanging;

倒懸 (1) be hung by the feet; (2) in a dire situation;

虛懸 imagine; invent;

xuan³

xuan

【選】 (1) choose; pick; select; (2) elect; (3) anthology; selection;

[選拔] choose; select; select from candidates;
選拔委員會 selection committee;

[選本] anthology; selected works;

[選材] select suitable material;

[選出] elect; pick out; select;

[選詞] select a word group;
選詞法 method of selecting word groups;
~ 合意選詞法 acceptable alternative method;

[選答題] multiple choice;

[選單] menu;
下拉式選單 drop-down menu; pull-down menu;

[選定] decide on a selection; designate;
撤銷選定 deselect; deselection;

[選讀] (1) selected readings; (2) elect a course;

[選段] selection;

[選購] purchase on selection;

[選集] anthology; selected works; selected writings; selections;

[選間] in a short time;

[選舉] election; elect; vote;
選舉法 election law; electoral law;
選舉候選人 election candidate;
選舉活動 election campaign; electoral campaign;
選舉結果 election results;
選舉年 election year;
選舉權 right to vote;
~ 被選舉權 right to stand for election;
選舉人 voter;
選舉勝利 election victory;
選舉失敗 election defeat;
選舉舞弊 ballot rigging;
選舉學 psephology;
選舉制 electoral system;
~ 選舉制度 electoral system;
補缺選舉 by-election;
操縱選舉 ballot rigging;
差額選舉 multi-candidate election;
當地選舉 local election;
等額選舉 single-candidate election;
地方選舉 local election;
地區選舉 regional election;
多黨選舉 multiparty election;
國會選舉 congressional election;
間接選舉 indirect election;
進行選舉 conduct an election;
聯邦選舉 federal election;
臨時選舉 snap election;
領導人選舉 leadership election;
民主選舉 democratic election;
舉行選舉 call an election; have an election; hold an election;
市長選舉 mayoral election;
議會選舉 parliamentary election;
直接選舉 direct election;
總統選舉 presidential election;
~ 總統選舉活動 presidential campaign;

[選料] choice of materials;
選料講究 high quality materials;
選料考究 choice material;

[選美] beauty pageant;

選美比賽 beauty contest; beauty pageant;
選美大會 beauty pageant;
選美會 beauty contest;
選美王后 beauty queen;

[選民] (1) elector; voter; (2) constituency; electorate;
選民榜 list of eligible voters;
選民登記 registration of voters;
~選民登記冊 poll register;
選民名冊 electoral register;
選民區 constituency;
選民證 voters' card;
全體選民 electorate;
游離選民 floating voter;

[選派] designate; nominate; select;

[選票] ballot; ballot paper;
地方選區選票 geographical constituency ballot paper;
拉選票 canvass;
撈取選票 angle for votes;
郵寄選票 postal vote;

[選區] constituency; electoral district; electoral ward;
選區選民 constituent;
地方選區 geographical constituency;

[選取] choose; select;

[選人] choose people;
選人唯賢 choose none but the best;

[選任] choose and appoint;

[選手] competitor; contestant; player;
標槍選手 javelin throwing player;
棒球選手 baseball player;
防守型選手 defensive player;
高爾夫球選手 golfer;
攻擊型選手 aggressive player; attacking player;
國際象棋選手 chess player;
籃球選手 basketball player;
鏈球選手 hammer throwing player;
摩托車選手 racing motorcyclist;
排球選手 volleyball player;
乒乓球選手 table tennis player;
汽車賽選手 automobile racer;
鉛球選手 shot putting player;
橋牌選手 bridge player;
手球選手 handball player;
水球選手 water polo player;
鐵餅選手 discus throwing player;
網球選手 tennis player;
圍棋選手 go player;
象棋選手 Chinese chess player;
一批選手 a team of players;
羽毛球選手 badminton player;
種子選手 seeded player;
自行車選手 racing cyclist;
足球選手 football player;

[選習] study;

[選賢] appoint good people;
選賢圖治 select highly capable people who will be put in office to administer the country;

[選修課] elective course;

[選用] select and appoint to a post;

[選閱] review and select;

[選擇] choice; choose; option; select; selection;
選擇標準 selection criteria;
選擇並列連詞 alternative coordinator;
選擇的自由 freedom of choice;
選擇電管 selectrode;
選擇對策原則 countermeasure selection principle;
選擇格式 alternative pattern;
選擇過程 selection procedure; selection process;
選擇關係 choice relation;
選擇器 chooser; selector;
~記發器選擇器 register chooser;
~節目選擇器 programme chooser;
~吸收選擇器 absorbing selector;
~振幅選擇器 amplitude selector;
選擇題 multiple-choice question;
選擇問句 alternative question;
選擇性 selectivity;
~符合選擇性 coincidence selectivity;
~有效選擇性 effective selectivity;
選擇疑問句 alternative interrogation;
別無選擇 have no choice;
~別無選擇時 if it comes to the push; if push comes to shove; when push comes to shove;
代碼選擇 code selection;
典範選擇 canonical choice;
定向選擇 consecutive selection;
分時選擇 time-sharing option;
輻度選擇 amplitude selection;
進行選擇 make one's option;
面臨選擇 be faced with a choice;
人工選擇 artificial selection;
任務選擇 task option;
認知選擇 cognitive selection;
適應選擇 adaptive selection;
隨機選擇 random selection;

無意識選擇 unconscious selection;
性選擇 sexual selection;
樣板選擇 copy choice;
硬件選擇 hardware select;
有選擇 have a choice;
~沒有選擇 have no choice;
職業選擇 career choice; occupational choice; vocational choice;
自動選擇 automatic select;
最後選擇 final selection;
作出選擇 make a choice; make a selection;

［選址］ site selection;
選址原則 site selection principles;

編選 compile; select and edit;
補選 by-election;
採選 select and purchase;
初選 initial separation; original selection; primary election;
磁選 magnetic separation;
大選 general election;
當選 be elected;
風選 select by winnowing;
浮選 select by flotation;
複選 (1) election by delegates; indirect election; (2) run-off; (3) semi-final;
改選 re-elect;
乾選 dry separation;
賄選 get elected by bribery; practise bribery at an election;
揀選 choose; pick out; select; sort;
精選 carefully choose; cherrypick; pick out the best; select carefully;
競選 a candidate for; campaign for; enter into an election contest; have one's hat in the ring; put up for; run against sb for; run for; stand for; start for; throw one's hat into the ring; toss one's hat into the ring;
遴選 choose; select; select sb for a post;
落選 fail to be chosen; fail to be elected; lose an election;
民選 be elected by people;
票選 elect by ballot;
聘選 engage and select;
評選 appraise and elect; choose through public appraisal; discuss and elect;
普選 general election; universal suffrage;
銓選 select officials after evaluating qualifications;
人選 candidates; choice of persons; the person selected;
任選 optional;
入選 be chosen; be selected;
篩選 dressing by screening; screen; sift; sieving;
上選 the choicest;
詩選 collection of poems; poetry anthology;
濕選 wet separation;
水選 select seeds or ores with water;
穗選 select seeds ear by ear;
特選 carefully chosen; hand-picked;
提選 choose; select;
挑選 choose; pick; pick out; select; single out; take one's pick of;
推選 choose; elect;
文選 literary selections; selected works;
膺選 be elected;
預選 preliminary election;
中選 be chosen; be selected;
自選 free; optional;

xuan

【癬】 ringworm; tetter;

［癬疥］ skin disease;

白癬 ringworm;
發癬 tinea capitis;
花斑癬 tinea versicolour;
黃癬 favus;
甲癬 onychomycosis; ringworm of the nails;
腳癬 athlete's foot; ringworm of the foot;
疥癬 mange;
牛皮癬 psoriasis;
蛇皮癬 pityriasis;
手癬 tinea manuum;
體癬 ringworm of the body; tinea corporis;
頭癬 tinea capitis;
頑癬 stubborn dermatitis;
足癬 tinea of the foot; tinea pedis;

xuan⁴
xuan

【炫】 (1) bright; dazzling; shining; (2) display; flaunt; show off;

［炫怪］ try to attract others' attention by sensationalism;

［炫惑］ dazzle and confuse;

［炫目］ dazzle the eyes;

［炫能］ show off one's ability;
自炫其能 show off one's ability;

［炫示］ display; show off;

［炫俗］ flaunt; show off;

［炫炫］ dazzling; sparkling;

［炫耀］ flash it away; flaunt; make a display of; show off;
炫耀武力 make a show of force;
武力炫耀 arrogance of power;
［炫鬻］ flaunt; show off;

xuan
【眩】 (1) confused vision; dizzy; giddy; (2) bewildered; confuse; dazzled;
［眩巴］ blink;
眩巴眼兒 wink one's eyes in quick succession;
［眩眼］ wink;
眩眼間 a very short time; in the twinkling of an eye;
［眩暈］ vertigo;
變壓性眩暈 alternobaric vertigo;
創傷後眩暈 post-traumatic vertigo;
假眩暈 pseudovertigo;
流行性眩暈 epidemic vertigo;
麻痺性眩暈 paralytic vertigo;
迷路性眩暈 labyrinthine vertigo;
器質性眩暈 organic vertigo;
剩留性眩暈 residual vertigo;
外周性眩暈 peripheral vertigo;
胃病性眩暈 stomachal vertigo;
胃性眩暈 gastric vertigo;
壓力性眩暈 pressure vertigo;
眼病性眩暈 ocular vertigo;
夜發性眩暈 nocturnal vertigo;
原發性眩暈 primary vertigo;
陣發性眩暈 paroxysmal vertigo;
直立性眩暈 vertical vertigo;
中毒性眩暈 toxic vertigo;
自發性眩暈 essential vertigo;
卒中性眩暈 apoplectic vertigo;
壓力性眩暈 pressure vertigo;
眼病性眩暈 ocular vertigo;

昏眩 dizzy; giddy;
瞑眩 dizziness, as a side effect of drugs;
目眩 dazzled; dizzy;

xuan
【衒】 (1) boast; brag; show off; (2) recommend oneself;
［衒露］ show off one's talent;
［衒弄］ flaunt; pedantic; show off;
［衒女］ girl who flaunts her beauty all around;
［衒俏］ show off one's charms; try to be cute;
［衒士］ boastful scholar;
［衒耀］ boast; brag; flaunt; show off;
［衒異］ show off one's talents;
衒異露才 show off and expose ability;

xuan
【渲】 colour with paint;
［渲染］ (1) apply colours to a drawing; colour with paint; (2) exaggerate; make exaggerated additions in a story to play up; pile it on; play up;
不加渲染 make no exaggeration; not ply up;
大加渲染 embroidery;
過度渲染 overblown;

xuan
【絢】 adorned and stylish; bright and brilliant;
［絢爛］ bright and brilliant; glittering; gorgeous; luscious; splendid;
［絢麗］ florid; gorgeous; magnificent;
［絢練］ brilliant with lighting and colours; flashing;

xuan
【鉉】 device for carrying a tripod;

xuan
【鏇】 (1) a kind of wine-heater; (2) a kind of metal tray; (3) pare with a knife;

xue¹
xue
【削】 (1) cut; pare; shave; whittle; (2) deprive;
［削壁］ cliff; precipice;
削壁深壑 steep peaks and deep ravines;
［削波］ clipping;
正向削波 positive clipping;
［削薄］ (of hair) thin out;
削薄剪子 thinning scissors;
［削除］ omit; strike out; take out;
［削奪］ deprive sb of sth; take sth by force;
［削髮］ shave one's head;
削髮剪子 haircutting scissors;
削髮披緇 shave one's head and become a monk;
削髮為僧 make oneself a shaveling; shave one's head and be a monk;
削髮修行 tonsure one's head and enter the religious life;
［削蹟］ conceal oneself from the world; lead a recluse life;
［削籍］ dismiss an official from a government

post;

［削價］ cut prices; lower the price;

［削肩］ sloping shoulders;

細腰削肩 with an ell-like figure and narrow, sloping shoulders;

［削減］ curtail; cut down; reduce; slash; whittle down;

大幅削減 slash;

［削平］ (1) pare; smooth; (2) conquer; put down; suppress;

［削弱］ abate; cripple; devitalize; enfeeble; put a brake on; sap; weaken;

削弱敵人的力量 weak the enemy;

［削鐵如泥］ the sword would cut clean through iron as though it were mud;

［削正］ ask sb to examine and improve a script;

［削職］ deprive a person of a position;

［削足適履］ act in a Procrustean manner; an impractical solution of a problem; cut the feet to fit the shoes; main the facts to fit a procrustean bed; make fit the Procrustean bed; place on the Procrustean bed; stretch on the Procrustean bed; stretch the facts to fit a Procrustean bed; trim the toes to fit the shoes; use an unreasonable and impractical method; whittle down the feet to fit the shoes;

筆削 correct one's writing mistakes;

剝削 exploit;

車削 turning;

斧削 make corrections;

刮削 scrap;

滾削 hobbing;

減削 cut down; reduce;

朘削 (1) exploit; (2) cut down; reduce;

砍削 chop back;

拉削 broaching;

切削 cutting;

刪削 cut out; delete; erase; expunge; remove; strike out;

瘦削 angular; gaunt; slim; very thin;

銑削 milling;

xue

【靴】 boot;

［靴帶］ bootlace;

［靴底］ soles of boots;

［靴鞋店］ bootery;

［靴子］ boots;

防毒靴 gas-protection boot;

掛靴 retire from a football team;

膠靴 galoshes; high rubber overshoes; rubber boot;

馬靴 riding boots;

傘兵靴 jump boot;

雨靴 rubber boots;

毡靴 felt boots;

xue

【薛】 (1) a kind of marsh grass; (2) name of an ancient state in present-day Shandong; (3) a surname;

xue²

xue

【穴】 (1) cave; den; hole; (2) grave; (3) acupuncture point;

［穴居］ cave-dwelling; live in caves;

穴居野處 dwell in caves in the wilds; live in the wilds and dwell in caves;

凹穴 hollow;

冰穴 ice cave;

巢穴 den; hideout; lair; nest;

地穴 abra;

洞穴 burrow; cave; cavern;

耳穴 ear acupuncture point;

匪穴 bandits' lair;

虎穴 tiger's cave; tiger's den;

會穴 crossing point;

窖穴 storage pit;

結穴 last few sentences of an article;

空穴 hole;

孔穴 cavity; hole;

墓穴 coffin pit; grave; monument; open grave; tomb; vault;

氣穴 airlock; air pocket;

壽穴 graveyard built before one dies;

太陽穴 temples;

鼷穴 mousehole;

巖穴 cave; cavern;

蟻穴 ants' nest;

xue

【踅】 hang about; loiter around;

［踅溜風］ cyclone; whirlwind;

［踅身］ turn around; turn the body;

［踅探］ peep; spy; watch and investigate stealthily;

［踅轉］ rotate; turn; whirl;

xue

【學】 (1) learn; study; (2) imitate; mimic; (3) knowledge; learning; (4) branch of learning; subject of study; (5) college; school;

［學伴兒］ school companion;

［學報］ journal; academic journal;
 大學學報 college journal;

［學不躐等］ learn without skipping necessary steps; learning should proceed step by step;

［學不完］ have an endless amount to learn;

［學不嫌老］ one is never too old to learn;

［學不像］ try to imitate in vain;

［學不厭］ learn with indefatigable zeal; tireless in learning;
 學而不厭 have an insatiable desire to learn; insatiable in learning; learn without satiety; never tired of studying; study tirelessly;
 ~學而不厭，誨人不倦 insatiable in learning and tireless in teaching;

［學步］ learn to walk;
 學步車 baby walker;
 學步邯鄲 imitate others slavishly and lose one's own originality;

［學潮］ campus commotion; student strike; student unrest;

［學懂學通］ understand and have a good grasp of;

［學額］ student quota;

［學而時習之，不亦説乎］ is it not a pleasure, having learned sth, to try it out at due intervals;

［學而優則仕］ a good scholar will make an official; excellence in scholarship leads to officialdom; he who excels in learning can be an official; officialdom is the natural outlet for good scholars;

［學而知之］ wisdom obtained by studies;

［學閥］ academic clique; scholar-tyrant;

［學非所用］ one does not do that which one has learned; what one learns does not fit him for a certain job;

［學費］ tuition; tuition fee;
 交學費 (1) pay tuition; (2) learn by experience; pay a price for one's errors;

［學分］ credit;
 學分制 credit system;
 學分轉換 credit transfer;

［學風］ style of study;

［學府］ institution of higher education; seat of learning;

［學富五車］ one's mind conceals more knowledge than that can be contained in the five cartloads of books; wealthy in knowledge;
 學富五車，才高八斗 universal genius;

［學館］ school;

［學海］ sea of learning;

［學好］ emulate good; learn from good examples;
 學好千日不足，學壞一日有餘 an ill weed gros apace; ill weeds grow apace; to learn what is good, a thousand days are not sufficient; learn what is evil, an hour is too long;
 學好三年，學壞三天 an evil lesson is soon learned; that which is evil is soon learned;
 學好學通 study hard to grasp the essence;
 學壞容易學好難 it is easier to fall than to rise; that which is evil is soon learned;

［學會］ (1) learn; master; succeed in learning; (2) institute; learned society; society;
 電子學會 electronics society;
 法學會 law society;
 翻譯學會 translation society;
 方言學 dialectology;
 核學會 nuclear science society;
 計算機學會 computer science society;
 機械工程學會 society of mechanical engineering;
 建築學會 civil engineering society;
 教育學會 education society;
 會計學會 accounting society;
 林學會 forestry society;
 氣象學會 meteorology society;
 鐵道學會 railway society;
 統計學會 statistics society;
 衛生統計學會 society of hygienic statistics;
 物理學會 physics society;
 信息學會 information society;
 醫學會 medical society;
 造紙學會 paper-making society;
 製冷學會 refrigeration society;
 中醫藥學會 traditional Chinese medicine

society;

[學籍] one's name on the school roll; one's status as a student;
保留學籍 retain one's status as a student;
取消學籍 be struck off the school roll;

[學級] classes and grades in school;

[學家] specialist or scholar of a field or discipline;
地理學家 geographer;
地質學家 geologist;
動物學家 zoologist;
法學家 jurist;
海洋學家 oceanographer;
化學家 chemist;
經濟學家 economist;
考古學家 archaeologist;
科學家 scientist;
昆蟲學家 entomologist;
歷史學家 historian;
鳥類學家 ornithologist;
農學家 agriculturalist;
氣象學家 meteorologist;
人類學家 anthropologist;
生理學家 physiologist;
生態學家 ecologist;
生物學家 biologist;
水利學家 hydraulician;
天文學家 astronomer;
物理學家 physicist;
心理學家 psychologist;
語法學家 grammarian;
語言學家 linguist;
植物學家 botanist;

[學界] academic circles; educational circles;

[學究] pedagogue; pedant; egghead;
老學究 old pedant;

[學科] branch of learning; course; discipline; subject;
學科評估 curriculum judgement;
學科文化 disciplinary culture;
學科研究 disciplinary studies;
~多學科研究 multi-disciplinary studies;
交叉學科 cross discipline;
跨學科 interdiscipline;
~跨學科方法 interdisciplinary method;

[學理] theory;

[學歷] academic credentials; educational background;
基本學歷 initial qualification;

[學力] academic attainments; educational level; scholarship; scholastic ability;

[學齡] school age;
學齡兒童 school-age child;
學齡前兒童 children below school age;

[學名] (1) scientific name; (2) a name given to one on beginning school life;

[學年] academic year; school year;
學年考試 year-end examination;

[學派] school; school of thought;
古典學派 classical school;

[學期] school term; semester; term; term-time;
春季學期 spring term;
秋季學期 autumn term; fall term;
下學期 coming term; next semester;

[學前] pre-primary; preschool education;
學前班 infant school;
學前兒童 pre-primary children;
學前教育 infant school education; preschool education;
學前年齡 preschool age;

[學人] scholar;

[學舌] (1) mechanically repeat other people's words; mimic; parrot; (2) gossip; loosetongued;

[學舍] school building;

[學生] (1) pupil; student; (2) disciple; follower;
學生班長 monitor;
學生餐 school meal;
學生代表 student representative;
~男學生代表 head boy;
~女學生代表 head girl;
學生貸款 student loan;
學生會 student association; student union;
學生人數 student population;
學生時代 one's student days;
學生頭 (of hairstyle) student's haircut;
學生消息 student news;
學生運動 student movement;
成人學生 mature student;
大齡學生 mature student;
大學生 college student; colleger;
二年級學生 second-year student; sophomore;
法科學生 law student;
翻譯學生 translation student;
老師寵愛的學生 teacher's pet;
明星學生 star student;
男學生 schoolboy;
女學生 girl student;
普通智力的學生 students of average intelligence;
全日制學生 full-time student;

全體學生 student body;
三好學生 triple-A student;
三年級學生 third-year student, junior;
四年級學生 fourth-year student; senior;
特殊學生 exceptional student;
小學生 primary school student;
夜校學生 evening student;
一班學生 a class of students;
一隊學生 a group of students;
一名學生 a student;
一年級學生 first-year student; freshman;
一組學生 a group of students;
優秀學生 outstanding student;
~優秀學生名單 dean's list;
中等學生 average student;
中途退學學生 drop-out student;
中學生 middle school student; secondary school student;
走讀學生 day pupil;

[學時] class hour; period;

[學識] academic attainments; erudition; knowledge; learning; scholarly attainments; scholarship;
學識過人 excel in knowledge;
學識淺薄 have little learning;
學識淺陋 have meagre knowledge;
學識淹博 be learned; be well-read;
學識淵博 have a large stock of information; have great learning; learned; one's learning is profound and immense;
~學識淵博的人 a person of great learning;
有學無識 know a great deal of books but lack insight and discrimination;

[學士] (1) scholar; (2) holder of the bachelor's degree;
學士學位 bachelor's degree; first degree;
理學士 bachelor of science;
名譽學士 honorary degree;
神學士 bachelor of divinity;
文學士 B.A.; bachelor of arts; bachelor of letters; Litt.B.;
醫學士 bachelor of medicine;

[學塾] old-style private school;

[學術] academic; intellectual; learning; science;
學術報告 academic report;
學術地位 academic position; academic standing;
學術獨立 intellectual autonomy;
學術翻譯 academic translation;
學術風氣 academic atmosphere;
學術講座 academic forum;
學術交流 academic exchange;
學術界 academia; academic circles; academic community; academic world;
學術論文 research paper; thesis;
學術委員會 academic committee;
學術研究 academic research;
學術英語 English for Academic Purposes;
學術職稱 academic title;
學術自由 academic freedom;
不學無術 have neither learning nor skill; ignorant and incompetent; without learning and without skill;

[學說] doctrine; theory;

[學堂] school;

[學童] schoolchild; schoolchildren;
男學童 schoolboy;
女學童 schoolgirl;
一群學童 a crowd of schoolchildren; a troop of schoolchildren;

[學徒] apprentice; student; trainee;
學徒督察 inspector of apprentices;
學徒工作 apprenticeship;
學徒年限 apprenticeship;
學徒期` apprenticeship;
學徒制 apprenticeship;
翻譯學徒 apprentice translator;

[學位] academic degree; degree;
學位論文 thesis;
學位文憑 diploma;
學位證書 degree's diploma;
博士學位 doctor's degree;
初級學位 first degree;
副學士學位 associate degree;
高級學位 advanced degree; higher degree;
攻讀學位 do one's degree;
名譽學位 honorary degree;
榮譽學位 honorary degree; honours degree;
授予學位 confer a degree; grant a degree;
雙優學位 double first;
校外學位 external degree;
學士學位 first degree;
研究生學位 graduate degree;

[學問] erudition; knowledge; learning; scholarship;
學問高深 of considerable learning;
學問淵博的人 erudite scholar; living

dictionary; person of great learning; walking dictionary; walking encyclopaedia;
搬弄學問 show off one's erudition;
有學問 erudite; learned; lettered;
增進學問 advance in knowledge;
做學問 do research; engage in scholarship;

[學習] emulate; learn; study;
學習成果 learning outcomes;
學習成效 learning effectiveness;
學習詞典 learner's dictionary;
學習活動 learning activities;
學習機會 learning opportunities;
學習階段 learning stage;
學習經歷 learning experience;
學習目標 learning objective;
學習內容 learning materials;
學習評估 learning assessment;
學習曲線 learning curve;
學習社群 learning community;
學習跳級 academic acceleration;
學習文化 learn to read and write;
學習障礙 learning difficulties; learning disability;
學習者 learner;
學習重點 learning objectives;
學習資源 learning resources;
伴隨學習 concomitant learning;
程序學習 programmed learning;
從經驗中學習 learn from experience;
遞進學習 learn progressively;
獨立學習 independent study;
發奮學習 put all one's energies into one's studies; stimulate oneself to study;
分科學習 compartmental learning;
服務學習 service learning;
附加學習 accretion learning;
概念學習 concept learning;
共同學習 cooperative learning;
好好學習 study hard;
迴避學習 avoidance learning;
機械學習 rote learning;
繼續學習 continued learning;
加強學習 accentuation learning;
簡括學習 abridged learning;
課堂學習 classroom learning;
連鎖學習 chain learning;
聯想學習 associative learning;
努力學習 study hard;
情感性學習 affective learning; appreciative learning;
情境學習 contextual learning;
勤奮學習 assiduous learning;
認知學習 cognitive learning;
善於學習 good at learning;
同化學習 assimilative learning;
喜歡學習 like learning;
厭惡學習 have an allergy to studying;
在學習 be at one's desk;
終身學習 lifelong learning;

[學銜] academic rank;

[學校] school; educational institution;
學校操場 school playground;
學校場地 campus;
學校紀律 school discipline;
學校假期 school holidays;
學校建築 school architecture;
~學校建築物 school building;
學校課程 school curriculum;
學校禮堂 school hall;
學校歷史 history of a school;
學校上課日 school day;
學校生活 school life;
學校午餐 school lunch;
學校語法 school grammar;
學校作業 school assignment;
半工半讀學校 part-work and part-study school;
辦學校 set up schools;
殘疾人學校 school for the disabled;
成人學校 adult school;
慈善學校 charity school;
電機製造學校 electrical machinery school;
電器製造學校 electrical appliances manufacturing school;
獨立學校 independent school;
二部制學校 two-shift school;
翻譯學校 translation school;
附屬學校 affiliated school;
高等學校 institution of higher education;
課後留在學校 stay after school;
工讀學校 reform school;
工業學校 technical school;
工藝學校 polytechnic school;
公立學校 public school;
廣播電視學校 broadcast television school;
貴族學校 school for privileged students;
國立學校 national school;
海軍學校 naval academy;
函授學校 correspondence school;
航空工業學校 aeronautical engineering school;

護士學校 nursing school;
化學工業學校 chemical engineering school;
技術學校 technology school;
~中等技術學校 secondary technical school;
寄宿學校 boarding school;
繼續學校 continuation school;
假日學校 vacation school;
教會學校 missionary school; parochial school;
教區學校 parochial school;
精修學校 finishing school;
進修學校 continuation school;
軍事學校 military academy; military school;
空軍軍官學校 air force academy;
礦業學校 mining school;
理工科學校 institute;
立案學校 accredited school;
聾啞學校 blind and dumb school; school for deaf-mutes;
盲人學校 school for the blind;
美術學校 art school; final arts school;
免費學校 free school;
民辦學校 school run by the local people; school set up by the local people;
模範學校 model school;
氣象學校 meteorological school;
森林工業學校 forestry school;
商業學校 commercial school;
社團學校 corporation school;
省立學校 provincial school;
師範學校 normal school; teachers' training school;
~幼兒師範學校 school for kindergarten teachers;
十年一貫制學校 compound school of ten-year system;
石油地質學校 petroleum geological school;
實驗學校 experimental school;
市立學校 city school; municipal school;
視察學校 inspect a school; make an inspection in a school;
水產航海學校 fishery and navigation school;
水產技術學校 marine products technical school;
水上流動學校 waterborne school;
私立學校 independent school; private school;
寺院學校 monastic school;
速成學校 short-term secondary school;
特殊學校 special school;
體育學校 school of physical education; sports school;
~業餘體育學校 spare-time sports school;
鐵路技術學校 railway engineering school;
土木建築學校 civil engineering school;
衛生學校 health school;
文法學校 grammar school;
文科學校 liberal arts school;
文明學校 civilized school;
縣立學校 district school;
舞蹈學校 dancing academy; school of dancing;
戲曲學校 opera school;
巡迴學校 mobile school;
冶金機械學校 school of metallurgical machinery;
業餘學校 spare-time school;
一所學校 a school;
藝術學校 arts and crafts school;
~業餘藝術學校 amateur arts school;
音樂學校 music conservatory;
預科學校 six form college;
帳篷學校 tent school;
正規學校 regular school;
職業學校 trade school; vocational school;
~中等職業學校 secondary vocational school;
中等學校 secondary school;
中小學校 primary and secondary schools;
中專學校 technical secondary school;
重點學校 key school;
主日學校 Sunday school;
專業學校 vocational school;
~中等專業學校 secondary vocational school;
子弟學校 self-established school;
~員工子弟學校 self-established school;
走讀學校 day school;

［學養］ learning and cultivation;

［學樣］ imitate sb's example;

［學業］ one's studies; school work;
學業成績 scholastic achievements; scholastic attainment;
學業壓力 pressure from study;

［學以致用］ learn in order to practise; make study serve the practical purpose; make use of what one has learned; study for the sake of application; study sth in

order to apply it;

［學藝］(1) sciences and arts; (2) learn a trade;

［學友］fellow student; schoolmate;

［學員］mentee; student; trainee;

［學院］academy; college; conservatory; faculty; institute; school;

學院主義 academicism;
財經學院 college of finance and economics;
初級學院 junior college;
船舶學院 college of shipping;
大學學院 university college;
地質學院 college of geology;
電影學院 college of cinema;
對外貿易學院 college of foreign trade;
法學院 college of law; faculty of law;
紡織學院 college of textile engineering;
飛行學院 training college for pilots;
鋼鐵學院 college of iron and steel engineering;
高級學院 senior college;
工程學院 college of engineering;
~ 電訊工程學院 college of telecommunications engineering;
~ 建築工程學院 college of architectural engineering;
工學院 engineering institute; technical college; college of engineering;
工業學院 college of industry;
工藝美術學院 institute of arts and crafts;
公安學院 public security institute;
公立學院 public college;
公路學院 college of highway;
廣播學院 radio broadcasting institute;
國際關係學院 college of international relations;
國際政治學院 institute of international politics;
海洋學院 college of oceanography; oceanology college;
海運學院 college of mercantile marine; institute of marine transport; mercantile marine institute;
函授學院 correspondence college; correspondence institute;
航空學院 aviation institute; college of aeronautical engineering;
化工學院 college of chemical engineering;
教會學院 Christian college;
教派學院 sectarian college;
教師培訓學院 teacher training college;
教育學院 college of education;
進修學院 college of further education; continuing education;
經濟學院 institute of economics;
礦冶學院 college of mining and metallurgy;
礦業學院 college of mining technology; mining institute;
理科學院 college of science;
理學院 college of science;
林學院 college of forestry; forestry college;
美術學院 academy of fine arts; fine arts academy;
民族學院 institute for nationalities;
農學院 agricultural institute; college of agriculture;
農業機械學院 college of agricultural machinery;
普通學院 general college;
認可學院 accredited college;
商學院 business college; college of commerce; school of business;
社會學院 college of sociology;
社區學院 community college;
神學院 divinity college; theological college; theological seminary;
師範學院 college of preceptors; normal college; pedagogical institute; teacher-training college; teachers' college; training college;
石油學院 college of petroleum; petroleum institute;
市立學院 municipal college;
獸醫學院 veterinary college;
暑期學院 summer institute;
水產學院 collage of marine products;
水利電力學院 college of water conservancy and electric power;
私立學院 endowed college; private college;
體育學院 college of physical education; physical culture institute;
鐵道學院 college of railway;
土壤學院 college of soil sciences;
外國語學院 college of foreign languages; institute of foreign languages;
外交學院 institute of diplomacy;
外貿學院 college of foreign trade; institute of foreign trade;
外語學院 college of foreign languages;

school of foreign languages;
衛星學院 satellite college;
文科學院 liberal arts college;
文理學院 college of arts and science; college of letters and science;
文學院 college of liberal arts; college of literature; faculty of arts;
舞蹈學院 college of dancing;
戲劇學院 college of drama; drama institute;
鄉村學院 village college;
醫學院 faculty of medicine; medical college;
藝術學院 academy of fine arts; school of fine arts;
音樂學院 conservatory of music; faculty of music; music conservatory; school of music;
郵電學院 college of post and telecommunications;
語言學院 language institute;
政法學院 college of political science and law;
職業培訓學院 training college;
職業學院 vocational college;
~ 單科職業學院 monovocational college;
州立學院 state college;
住宿學院 residential college;
專科學院 cluster college;
專上學院 higher education institution;
~ 自資專上學院 self-financed higher education institution;
專業學院 professional college;

[學長] mentor; one's senior at school;
學長計劃 mentorship programme;

[學者] learned person; learned person; person of learning; scholar;
有成就的學者 accomplished scholar;

[學制] (1) educational system; school system; (2) length of schooling;

[學子] student;

癌學 cancerology; oncology;
辦學 run a school;
孢粉學 palynology;
飽學 erudite; learned; scholarly; well-learned; well-versed; widely-read;
貝殼學 conchology;
兵學 military science;
冰川學 glaciology;
病毒學 virology;
病理學 pathology;
病原學 aetiology;
博物館學 museology;
博學 erudite; extensive study; knowledgeable; learned; well-read; wellversed; wide range of studies or learning;
才學 erudition; scholarship; talent and learning;
測繪學 surveying; topography;
測量學 surveying;
測震學 seismometry;
產科學 obstetrics;
超聲學 ultrasonics;
初學 begin to learn;
輟學 discontinue one's studies; leave off one's study; stop schooling;
詞典學 lexicography;
詞法學 morphology;
詞匯學 lexicology;
詞義學 semantics;
詞源學 etymology;
磁學 magnetics; magnetism;
村學 village school;
大學 (1) college; uni; university; (2) *The Great Learning*;
代數學 algebra;
彈道學 ballistics;
道學 (1) Neo-Confucianism; (2) affectedly moral;
低溫學 cryogenics;
地層學 stratigraphy;
地理學 geography;
地貌學 geomorphology;
地名學 toponomy;
地熱學 geothermics;
地史學 historical geology;
地溫學 study of ground temperature;
地文學 physical geography; physiography;
地形學 topography;
地衣學 lichenology;
地震學 seismology;
地志學 topology;
地質學 geology;
電磁學 electromagnetics;
電工學 electrical engineering;
電化學 lector-chemistry;
電學 electricity (as a science);
電子學 electronics;
冬學 study groups organized by peasants to learn to read and write in winter slack season;
動電學 electrokinetics;
動力學 dynamics; kinetics;
動物學 zoology;
督學 educational inspector; inspector of schools;

毒理學 toxicology;
篤學 devoted to study; diligent in study; studious;
兒科學 paediatrics;
耳病學 otiatrics;
耳科學 otology;
發生學 embryology;
法理學 jurisprudence;
法位學 tagmemics;
法學 jurisprudence; science of law;
法醫學 medical jurisprudence;
翻譯學 translatology;
方言學 dialectology;
仿生學 bionics;
放學 classes are over;
分類學 taxology;
佛學 Buddhism;
符號學 semiotics;
復學 resume one's interrupted studies;
輻射學 radiology;
副語言學 paralinguistics;
婦科學 gynaecology;
耕作學 agronomics;
工程學 engineering;
工學 engineering;
工藝學 technology;
公學 public school;
骨學 osteology;
古生物學 palaeontology;
古植物學 paleobotany;
光化學 photochemistry;
光譜學 spectroscopy;
光學 optics;
國學 studies of Chinese ancient civilization;
海洋學 oceanography;
漢學 (1) the Han school of classical philology; (2) Sinology;
好學 bookish; diligent; educated; fond of learning; learned; scholarly; studious;
航海學 navigation;
航空學 aeronautics; aviation;
核醫學 nuclear medicine;
核子學 nucleonics;
和聲學 harmonics;
喉科學 laryngology;
後學 pupil of younger age; scholar of younger age;
湖沼學 limnology;
化學 chemistry;
火山學 volcanology;
幾何學 geometry;
畸形學 teratology;
機械學 mechanics;
積分學 integral calculus;
計量學 metrology;
寄生蟲學 parasitology;
家學 knowledge passed on from generation to generation in a family; knowledge transmitted from father to son;
家政學 domestic science; home economics; household arts;
假道學 (1) hypocrite; (2) sanctimonious person;
建築學 architecture;
講學 discourse on an academic subject; give lectures;
校勘學 textual criticism;
教學 (1) education; teaching; (2) teaching and studying; (3) teacher and student;
教育學 pedagogy;
解剖學 anatomy;
金石學 epigraphy; study of inscription ancient bronzes and stone tablets;
金相學 metallography;
晶體學 crystallography;
經濟學 economics;
經學 study of Confucian classics;
精神病學 psychiatry;
靜電學 electrostatics;
靜力學 statics;
就學 (1) go to study with a private tutor; (2) go to school;
舊學 old Chinese learning;
蕨類學 pteridology
絕學 ancient learning lost to the modern world;
軍事學 military science;
開學 school opens; term begins;
考古學 archaeology;
科學 science; scientific knowledge;
口腔學 stomatology;
礦物學 mineralogy;
昆蟲學 entomology; insectology;
賴學 cut class; play traunt;
類型學 typology;
理學 (1) science; (2) idealist school of Confucian philosophy;
力學 mechanics;
林學 forestry;
臨牀學 clinical medicine;
流行病學 epidemiology;
留學 study abroad;
倫理學 ethics;
論理學 logic;
邏輯學 logic;
買貨學 buyology;

霉菌學 mycology;
酶化學 zymochemistry;
酶學 enzymology;
美學 aesthetics;
蒙學 old-style private school;
泌尿學 urology;
免疫學 immunology;
民俗學 folklore;
民族學 ethnology;
名學 logic;
銘刻學 epigraphy;
目錄學 bibliography;
腦科學 brain science; encephalic;
內分泌學 endocrinology;
內科學 internal medicine;
鳥類學 ornithology;
農學 agronomy;
農藝學 agronomy;
胚胎學 embryology;
皮膚病學 dermatology;
品學 character and scholarship;
樸學 down-to-earth learning;
氣候學 climatology;
氣象學 meteorology;
淺學 shallow learning; superficial learning;
勤學 study diligently;
求學 (1) attend school; go to college; go to school; receive education; study; (2) pursue one's studies; seek knowledge;
曲學 heretical school;
軀體學 somatology;
勸學 exhortation to study; urge sb to study hard;
熱電學 pyroelectricity;
熱工學 heat engineering;
熱化學 thermo-chemistry;
熱力學 thermodynamics;
人類學 anthropology;
人種學 ethnology;
儒學 the teachings of Confucius;
入學 (1) start school; (2) admission; enrol; enter a school; entrance; register;
蠕蟲學 helminthology;
三角學 trigonometry;
森林學 forestry;
上學 at school; attend school; go to school;
社會學 sociology;
神經病學 neurology;
神學 theology;
生理學 physiology;
生態學 ecology;
生物學 biology;
生藥學 pharmacognosy;
昇學 enter a higher school;
聲能學 sonics;
聲學 acoustics; phonics;
聲韻學 phonology;
失學 be deprived of education; be obliged to discontinue one's studies; lack formal education; unable to go to school;
詩學 poetics;
實學 real learning; sound scholarship;
碩學 erudite scholar;
史料學 science of historical data;
史前學 prehistory;
史學 (1) history; (2) historiography;
視學 educational inspector; inspection;
獸醫學 veterinary medicine;
書志學 bibliography;
塾學 family school;
數學 mathematics;
術語學 terminology;
水力學 hydraulics;
水聲學 marine acoustics;
水文學 hydrology;
俗學 secular studies;
宿學 erudite; well-learned;
算學 (1) mathematics; (2) arithmetic;
所學 what is learned;
胎生學 embryology;
苔蘚學 bryology;
逃學 bunk off; cut class; escape school; hooky; play hookey; play hooky; play truant; skip school; skive; truancy; truant;
陶瓷學 ceramics;
天氣學 synoptic meteorology;
天文學 astronomy;
停學 drop out of school; rusticate; stop going to school; suspend sb from school;
同學 (1) classmate of sb; schoolmate of sb; in the same class; in the same school; (2) classmate; condisciple; fellow student; school chum; schoolmate;
統計學 statistics;
圖書館學 library science;
土壤學 soil science;
土質學 soil science;
退學 discontinue one's schooling; drop out; drop out of school; leave school; withdraw from a school;
拓撲學 topology;
外科學 surgery;
晚學 your pupil;
為學 engage in studies;
微分學 differential calculus;

微積分學 infinitesimal calculus;
微生物學 microbiology;
僞科學 pseudoscience;
衛生學 hygienics;
文學 literature;
文藝學 study of literature and its law of development;
文字學 philology;
物候學 phenology;
物理學 physics;
西學 Western learning;
細胞學 cytology;
細菌學 bacteriology;
戲劇學 dramaturgy;
下學 leave for home after school;
顯學 well-known theory;
縣學 county school;
鄉學 village school;
向學 be determined to learn; be inclined to study;
小學 (1) elementary school; grade school; high school; primary school; (2) philological studies;
酵學 zymetology; zymology;
心病學 cardiology;
心理學 phychology;
心學 study of the mind;
新文學 new vernacular literature;
新學 new learning;
星學 (1) astronomy; (2) astrology;
星占學 astrology;
興學 build schools; promote learning;
形而上學 metaphysics;
形態學 morphology;
性學 sexology;
休學 suspend one's schooling without losing one's status as a student; suspension of schooling; temporary absence from school;
修辭學 rhetoric;
修學 study;
畜牧學 animal husbandry;
玄學 metaphysics;
血管學 angiology;
訓詁學 critical interpretation of ancient texts;
牙科學 dentistry;
岩石學 petrology;
岩性學 lithology;
眼科學 ophthalmology;
藥劑學 pharmaceutics; pharmacy;
藥理學 pharmacology;
藥物學 materia medica;
冶金學 metallurgy;
夜大學 evening university;
醫學 medical science; medicine;
遺傳學 genetics;
蟻學 myrmecology;
義學 free private school; free school;
音位學 phonemics;
音響學 acoustics;
音系學 phonology;
音韻學 phonology;
印章學 sigillography;
營養學 nutriology;
優生學 eugenics;
游學 study in some other place or abroad;
遊學 study abroad;
魚類學 ichthyology;
魚族學 ichthyography;
宇宙學 cosmography;
語法學 grammar;
語符學 glossematics;
語文學 philology;
語言學 linguistics;
語義學 semantics;
語音學 phonetics;
語源學 etymology;
園藝學 horticulture;
月面學 selenography;
運籌學 operations research;
運動學 kinematics;
隕石學 meteoritics;
韻律學 prosody;
在學 at school;
造船學 shipbuilding;
造林學 silviculture;
藻類學 algology;
戰略學 science of strategy;
戰術學 science of tactics;
戰役學 science of campaigns;
哲學 philosophy;
真菌學 mycology;
診斷學 diagnostics;
正學 orthodox learning;
植物學 botany;
指紋學 dactylography;
志學 dedicate oneself to the pursuit of learning;
治療學 therapeutics;
治學 devote oneself to learning; do scholarly research; make a study of subjects; pursue one's studies; study;
製圖學 cartography;
中小學 primary and secondary schools;
中學 (1) high school; middle school; secondary school; senior school; (2) Chinese learning;

中藥學 traditional Chinese pharmacology;
中醫學 traditional Chinese medicine;
鐘學 campanology;
腫瘤學 oncology;
竺學 study of Buddhism;
助學 develop education;
轉學 transfer to another school;
自學 self-learning; self-study; self-taught; study independently; study on one's own; teach oneself;
組織學 histology;

xue

【鷽】 tanager;

xue³

xue

【雪】 (1) snow; (2) avenge; clean; wipe away; wipe out;

［雪白］ snow-white; snowy white;

［雪暴］ blizzard; snowstorm;

［雪崩］ snowslide; avalanche of snow;
雪崩學家 avalanchologist;
板狀雪崩 slab avalanche; windslab avalanche;
吹積雪崩 drift avalanche;
電子雪崩 electron avalanche;
放電雪崩 discharge avalanche;
粉狀雪崩 powder avalanche;
關閉雪崩 turn-off avalanche;
滑移雪崩 slip avalanche;
混合雪崩 mixed avalanche;
塊狀雪崩 ground avalanche;
離子雪崩 ion avalanche;
聲子雪崩 phonon avalanche;

［雪車］ sledge;

［雪恥］ avenge an insult; wipe out a humiliation or disgrace;
雪恥報仇 blot out a disgrace and avenge a grievance; wipe out a disgrace and avenge a grievance;
報仇雪恥 avenge a wrong and wipe out a humiliation; pay old scores; pay off old scores; settle an old score; take revenge and wipe out a disgrace; take revenge for an insult; wipe off old scores; wipe out an old score;

［雪地］ snowfield;
雪地冰天 all covered in ice and snow; frozen land; land of snow and ice; world of ice and snow;
雪地車 snowmobile;
雪地靴 moon boot;

［雪堆］ snowbank; snowdrift;

［雪膚］ snow-white skin;
雪膚花貌 skin as white as snow and complexion as beautiful as flowers;

［雪恨］ avenge; take vengeance;
報仇雪恨 avenge a grievance; avenge oneself; get even with a hated enemy; glut one's revenge; hurt sb in return for a wrong; pay off old scores; take revenge and redress hatred;

［雪花］ snowflakes;
雪花飛舞 snowflakes are dancing in the air; snowflakes are whirling; snowflakes dance in hazy mist; the falling snow whirls and drifts as if in a dance;
雪花膏 vanishing cream;
雪花飄飄 snow is falling;
一陣雪花 a flurry of snow;

［雪肌］ snow-white skin;

［雪茄］ cigar;
雪茄煙 cigar;
~白雪茄煙 white cigar;
黑雪茄 black cigar;
小雪茄 cigarillo;
一支雪茄 a cigar;

［雪景］ landscape of snow; snow scene;

［雪裏探梅］ seek plum blossoms among snowdrifts;

［雪亮］ bright as snow; shiny;

［雪泥鴻爪］ a swan's footprints found on snow and mud — constant departure and reunion of friends;

［雪片］ snowflake;
雪片飛來 pour in like snowflakes;

［雪撬］ sleigh;
雪撬鈴 sleigh bells;
狗拉雪撬 dog sled;
運木雪撬 logging sleigh;

［雪球］ snowball;
滾雪球 snowball;

［雪人］ snowman;

［雪山］ snow-capped mountain;

［雪上加霜］ add frost to snow; add to the misfortunes of a man who is already unfortunate; heap calamities on someone who is already oppressed; calamities come in succession; disasters pile up one another; it never rains but it

pours; misfortune never comes singly;
[雪松] cedar;
雪松木 cedarwood;
[雪條] flavoured popsicle; ice lolly;
[雪霧] snow and mist;
[雪線] snow line;
[雪消冰解] ice and snow melt;
[雪鞋] snowshoes;
[雪中送炭] give help to one in need; give timely assistance; help a person in distress; offer fuel in snowy weather; provide sb with fuel in snowy weather; send a present of firewood in cold weather; send charcoal in snowy weather — provide timely help; timely assistance; yeoman's service;

白雪 snow; white snow;
冰雪 ice and snow;
初雪 first snow;
大雪 (1) heavy snow; (2) Great Snow;
風雪 snowstorm; wind and storm;
滑雪 ski; skiing;
積雪 accumulated snow;
湔雪 redress a grievance; right a wrong;
降雪 snow;
粒雪 firn;
融雪 snow melt;
瑞雪 auspicious snow; timely snow;
掃雪 sweep away the snow;
賞雪 enjoy snow scenes;
申雪 vindicate sb from a wrong;
霜雪 (1) frost and snow; (2) snowwhite;
洗雪 clear sb of a false charge; redress a wrong; right a wrong; wipe out a disgrace;
喜雪 seasonable snow; timely snow;
下雪 snow;
小雪 (1) Slight Snow; (2) slight snow;
一層雪 a blanket of snow; a cloak of snow; a layer of snow; a mantle of snow;
一場雪 a fall of snow;
一點雪 a bit of snow; a sprinkling of snow;
一堆雪 a bank of snow; a mass of snow;
雨雪 a fall of snow;
澡雪 clean; cleanse; purify;
昭雪 exonerate; redress a wrong; redress an injustice; rehabilitate;
陣雪 snow shower;

xue

【鱈】 cod;
[鱈魚] cod; codfish;
鱈魚鬆 fibered codfish;

牙鱈 whiting;

xue⁴
xue

【血】 (1) blood; (2) blood relationship; related by blood;
[血癌] leukaemia;
[血案] bloody incident; murder case;
血案如山 with a long list of bloody crimes;
[血斑] blood stains;
[血本] principal; original capital;
血本無歸 no return of hard-earned captial;
[血崩] menorrhagia;
血崩症 metrorrhagia;
[血塵] blood dust; haemoconia;
血塵病 haemoconiosis;
[血沉] erythrocytic sedimentation rate;
[血蟲] bloodworm;
[血點] blood splashes; blood spots; drops of blood;
[血毒症] blood poisoning;
[血管] blood vessel;
血管肺 vascular lung;
血管梗塞 infarct;
血管痙攣症 vascular spasm;
血管瘤 angioma; hemangioma; vascular tumour;
~ 癌樣血管瘤 canceroderm;
~ 單純性血管瘤 hemangioma simplex;
~ 肥大性血管瘤 hypertrophic angioma;
~ 老年性血管瘤 senile angiomas;
~ 硬化性血管瘤 sclerosing hemangioma;
血管收縮劑 angiotonics;
血管癱瘓 vasoparesis;
血管痛 angialgia;
血管學 angiography; angiology;
血管炎 angiitis;
~ 變應性血管炎 hypersensitivity angiitis;
~ 大腦血管炎 cerebral vasculitis;
~ 過敏性血管炎 hypersensitivity vasculitis;
~ 壞死性血管炎 necrotizing angiitis;
~ 結節性血管炎 nodular vasculitis;
~ 皮膚血管炎 angiodermatitis;
~ 青斑血管炎 livedo vasculitis;
~ 全血管炎 panangiitis;
~ 系統性血管炎 systemic vasculitis;
~ 血栓性血管炎 thromboangiitis;

血管硬化 angiosclerosis; sclerosis vascularis;
血管張力 angiotasis;
血管照相術 angiography;
毛細血管 blood capillary;
人造血管 artificial blood vessel;
微血管 capillaries;
一根血管 a vein;

[血海] a sea of blood;
血海深仇 blood debt; huge debt in blood; intense and deep-seated hatred;
血海冤仇 blood feud;

[血汗] blood and sweat; sweat and toil;
血汗工廠 sweatshop;
血汗錢 hard-earned money; money earned by hard toil;
血汗所得 be earned by the sweat and blood of sb;
榨乾血汗 wring every ounce of sweat and blood out of sb;

[血紅] as red as blood; blood red; scarlet;
血紅蛋白 haemoglobin;
~不穩定血紅蛋白 unstable hemoglobins;
血紅素 heme;

[血蹟] bloodstain;
血蹟斑斑 all covered with bloodstains; be besmeared with blood; blood-soaked; bloodstained;

[血漿] blood plasma;

[血口噴人] attack sb with most malicious words; curse and slander; make false accusations against others; make unfounded and malicious attacks upon sb; smite with the tongue; slander venomously;

[血庫] blood bank;
一個血庫 a blood bank;

[血塊] blood clot;
白色血塊 white clot;

[血虧] anaemia;
血虧閉經 amenorrhoea due to deficiency of blood;

[血淚] blood and tears; extreme sorrow;
血淚斑斑 full of blood and tears; with spots of tears and blood;
血淚仇 vengeful feelings nurtured by blood and tears;
血淚史 heart-rending story; sad story;

[血量] blood volume;

[血淋淋] (1) bloody; (2) naked facts;

[血流] the blood flows;
血流成河 blood flows in rivers; blood is flowing over the ground like water; shed blood like water;
血流成渠 blood fills the water courses; blood flows in streams; the ground is covered with streams of blood;
血流漂杵 blood flows so as to float a pestle; great massacre;
血流如注 a stream of blood; bleed like a pig; bleed like a struck hog; bleed profusely; blood streaming down; shed blood like water; the blood gushes in torrents;
皮破血流 get bumped and bruised; run into bumps and bruises;
頭破血流 be beaten; be crushed; head broken and bleeding; one's head covered with bumps and bruises; run into bumps and bruises; seriously injured;
~打得頭破血流 be badly battered; be badly trounced; beat sb black and blue; maul and cut up;

[血路] blood vessel;

[血淥淥] blood dripping all around; sanguinary;

[血脈] (1) large and small blood vessels; (2) blood relationship;
血脈流通 blood circulation;

[血尿] blood urine; bloody urine; haematuria; urina cruenta;
地方性血尿 endemic haematuria;
功能性血尿 functional haematuria;
假血尿 pseudohaematuria;
尿道性血尿 urethral haematuria;
肉眼血尿 gross haematuria;
特發性血尿 essential haematuria;
原發性血尿 primary haematuria;
自發性血尿 essential haematuria;

[血凝反應] haemagglutination;
被動血凝反應 passive haemagglutination;
間接血凝反應 indirect haemagglutination;
冷血凝反應 cold haemagglutination;

[血盆大口] large and fierce-looking mouth;

[血氣] (1) disposition; (2) animal spirits; sap; vigour; (3) courage and uprightness;
血氣方剛 easily excited; full of animal spirits; full of sap; full of vigour and vitality; full of vim and vigour; hot-tempered; in one's raw youth; in one's

salad days; in the green;
血氣虛弱 frail; weak constitution;
血氣之勇 brute courage; foolhardiness;

[血親] blood relation; blood relatives; consanquinity;
血親關係 consanguinity;

[血清] serum;
血清白蛋白 serum albumin;
血清病 serum disease;
血清漿液 blood serum; serum;
血清球蛋白 serum globulin;
血清學 serology;
抗毒血清 antitoxic serum;
抗霍亂血清 anticholera serum;
淋巴血清 lymph serum;
妊娠血清 pregnancy serum;

[血球] blood cells; blood corpuscle; corpuscle;
白血球 white blood cell; white blood corpuscle;
紅血球 red blood cell; red blood corpuscle;

[血肉] flesh and blood;
血肉橫飛 blood and flesh fly in every direction;
血肉模糊 be badly mutilated;
血肉相連 as close as flesh and blood; be linked by flesh-and-blood ties; be related by flesh and blood; bone of the bone and flesh of the flesh; flesh of its flesh and blood of its blood; link together as flesh and blood; maintain flesh-and-blood ties; ties of flesh and blood;
血肉相連，休戚與共 flesh and blood relationship; with common joys and sorrows;
血肉之親 blood relationship;
血肉之軀 flesh and blood; human body;
有血有肉 full of life; full of vivid details; lifelike; true to life; vivid;

[血書] letter written in one's own blood;

[血栓] thrombus;
血栓切除 thrombectomy;
血栓形成 thrombosis;
~產後血栓形成 puerperal thrombosis;
血栓性血管炎 thromboangiitis;
血栓症 thrombosis;
鞍狀血栓 saddle embolism;
蒼白血栓 pale thrombus;
傳播性血栓 propagated thrombus;
創傷性血栓 traumatic thrombus;
機化血栓 organized thrombus;
寄生蟲性血栓 parasitic thrombus;
原發血栓 primary thrombus;

[血水] (1) blood; (2) bloodstained water;
血濃於水 blood is thicker than water;

[血絲蟲] filaria;
血絲蟲病 filariasis;

[血糖] blood sugar;
低血糖 hypoglycemia;
~低血糖症 hypoglycemia;
餐後性低血糖症 postprandial hypoglycemia; reactive hypoglycemia;
反應性低血糖症 reactive hypoglycemia;
營養性低血糖症 alimentary hypoglycemia;

[血統] ancestry; blood lineage; blood relationship; lineage; pedigree;
貴族血統 of blue blood;
母系血統 matrilinear strain;
中國血統 of Chinese ancestry; of Chinese origin;
一半中國血統一半英國血統 be half Chinese and half English;

[血污] blood-smeared; bloodstained;

[血小板] blood platelet; thrombocyte;
血小板減少症 thrombocytopenia;
血小板溶解 thrombocytolysis;
巨血小板 giant platelet;

[血心] loyalty; sincerity;

[血腥] bloody; sanguinary;
血腥錢 blood money;
血雨腥風 a foul wind and a rain of blood;

[血型] blood group; blood type;
A 型 Group A;
B 型 Group B;
O 型 Group O;

[血性] strong sense of righteousness;

[血胸] hemothorax;

[血虛] blood deficiency;
血虛不孕 sterility due to deficiency of blood;

[血壓] blood pressure;
血壓低 low blood pressure;
血壓高 high blood pressure;
低血壓 low blood pressure;
~直立性低血壓 orthostatic hypotension;
高血壓 high blood pressure; hypertension;
不穩定型高血壓 labile hypertension;
惡性高血壓 malignant hypertension;
~急進性高血壓 accelerated hypertension;
~繼發性高血壓 secondary hypertension;

~假高血壓 pseudohypertension;
腎形高血壓 renal hypertension;
~腎血管性高血壓 renovascular hypertension;
特發性高血壓 idiopathic hypertension;
原發性高血壓 primary hypertension;
症狀性高血壓 symptomatic hypertension;
自發性高血壓 essential hypertension;
降低血壓 bring high blood pressure down;
量血壓 take one's blood pressure;
正常血壓 orthoarteriotony;

[血液] blood;
血液病 blood disease;
血液凝固 blood coagulation;
血液透析 haemodialysis;
血液學 haematology;
血液循環 blood circulation;
淨化血液 purify the blood;

[血友病] bleeder disease; haemophilia;
典型血友病 classical haemophilia;
假血友病 pseudohaemophilia;

[血緣] blood relationship; consanguinity; ties of blood;

[血債] debt of blood;
血債累累 a record of sanguinary crimes; have a mountain of blood debts; heavy blooddebts;
血債血還 blood demands blood; blood for blood; blood must atone for blood; blood will have blood; debts of blood must be paid in blood; demand blood for blood; make sb pay blood for blood; the blood debts must be repaid in kind; the debt in blood must be repaid with blood;
償還血債 pay blood debt;
一筆血債 a debt of blood;

[血戰] bloody battle;
血戰到底 fight to the bitter end; fight to the finish; fight to the last drop of one's blood;

[血腫] haematoma;
搏動性血腫 pulsating haematoma;
實質性血腫 parenchymatous haematoma;

[血中毒] blood poisoning;

[血脂] blood lipoids;

敗血 poisonous blood;
鼻出血 nasal phemorrhage; nosebleed; pistaxie;
鼻血 nasal haemorrhage; nosebleed;
碧血 blood shed in a just cause;
便血 have blood in one's stool;
補血 enrich the blood;
查血 have a blood test;
腸出血 enterorrhagia;
充血 become bloodshot; congestion; engorgement; hyperaemia;
出血 (1) plunk down; shed blood; (2) pay a large sum of money for sth; (3) bleeding; hemorrhage;
大出血 massive haemorrhage;
喋血 bloodbath; bloodshed;
動脈血 arterial blood;
多血 hyperemia;
耳出血 otorrhagia;
放血 bloodletting;
肺充血 pulmonary congestion;
肺出血 pulmonary haemorrhage;
肝血 liver-blood;
高氧血 leonectic blood;
膏血 people's fat and blood;
狗血 dog's blood;
骨出血 osteorrhagia;
骨血 flesh and blood;
喉出血 laryngorrhagia;
換血 bring in new blood; overhaul personnel;
活血 invigorate the circulation of blood;
雞血 chicken's blood;
經血 menses; menstruation;
捐血 donate blood;
咳血 cough up blood;
欬血 cough up blood;
冷血 cold-blooded; cold-bloodedness;
流血 bleed; shed blood;
咯血 cough up blood;
沬血 blood flowing in one's face; a bleeding face;
腦充血 encephalemia;
腦出血 cerebral haemorrhage;
腦貧血 cerebral anaemia;
腦溢血 cerebral apoplexy; cerebral haemorrhage;
內出血 internal haemorrhage;
尿血 blood in the urine; haematuria;
牛血 ox blood;
衄血 bleed from five sense organs;
嘔血 haematemesis;
脾充血 splenemphraxis;
脾出血 splenorrhagia;
貧血 anaemia;
泣血 weep blood;
潛血 occult blood;
潛隱血 occult blood;
全血 whole blood;

熱血 fervent; fiery-spirited; hot-blooded; righteous ardour; warm blood; zealous;
溶血 haemolysis;
歃血 smear the blood of a sacrifice on the mouth;
腎充血 nephrohaemia;
腎出血 nephrorrhagia;
失血 lose blood;
嗜血 bloodsucking; bloodthirsty;
輸血 (1) blood transfusion; (2) give aid and support;
溲血 haematuria;
胎盤血 placental blood;
吐血 spit blood; spit out blood; vomit blood;
外出血 external haemorrhage;
胃出血 bleeding from the stomach; gastrorrhagia;
溫血 warm-blooded;
吸血 suck blood;
鮮血 blood;
獻血 donate blood;
心血 painstaking care; painstaking efforts;
咽部充血 congested throat;
驗血 blood test;
一滴血 a drop of blood;
一塊血 a clot of blood;
一灘血 a pool of blood;
齦出血 ulorrhagia;
飲血 (1) weep in deep sorrow; (2) drink blood;
隱血 occult blood;
淤血 extravasated blood;
瘀血 blood stasis; hematoma;
浴血 bathed in blood;
止血 stanch bleeding; stop bleeding;
豬血 pig's blood;

xue

【雪】 (1) snow-white; snowy; (2) avenge; wipe out grievances;
［雪白］ snow-white; snowy;
［雪恥］ avenge an insult; wipe out a shame;
雪恥復國 wipe out national shame and recover the fatherland;
［雪恨］ avenge one's grudge;
［雪亮］ bright as snow; shiny;
［雪冤］ clear oneself of a false charge; redress a wrong; vindicate oneself; wipe out grievances;

xue

【謔】 banter; crack a job; tease;
［謔而不虐］ joke without hurting anyone; tease without embarrassing;
［謔近於虐］ joke in order to wound;
［謔浪笑敖］ with scornful words and jeering smiles;
調謔 crack a joke; tease;
戲謔 banter; make fun of; tease;
諧謔 banter;

xun¹

xun

【焄】 (1) rising flames; (2) aroma;

xun

【熏】 mild; warm;
［熏陶］ edify; nurture;
［熏天］ becloud the sky;
勢焰熏天 one's fury beclouds the sky; one's power dominates the world like a flame reddening the sky; very influential and powerful;
［熏夕］ dusk; evening time;
［熏熏］ delighted; pleased;

xun

【窨】 add aroma to tea by mixing it with jasmine;

xun

【勳】 achievements; honours; merits; meritorious services;
［勳功］ meritorious services;
［勳績］ meritorious services; outstanding contributions;
［勳爵］ a rank conferred in recognition of merits;
［勳勞］ meritorious services; outstanding contributions;
［勳位］ rank;
［勳業］ meritorious services and great achievements;
［勳章］ decoration; medal of honour;
功勳 exploit; meritorious service;
奇勳 distinguished service; outstanding contribution;
授勳 confer orders or medals;
殊勳 meritorious service; outstanding merit;
元勳 founding father;

xun

【壎】 an ancient Chinese wind instrument;

xun

【獯】 a northern barbarian tribe in ancient

China;

xun

【薰】 (1) becloud; cauterize; embalm; perform; smoke; (2) hot; warm; (3) coumarouna odorata;

［薰風］ warm wind from the south;
薰風習習 the south wind blows gently;

［薰爐］ brazier;

［薰沐］ burn incense and take a bath;

［薰然］ amiably; gently; warmly;

［薰染］ be influenced and contaminated by one's surroundings;

［薰陶］ edify; mould a person's character through the influence of education;

［薰香］ fragrance; perfume;

［薰心］ becloud the mind;

xun

【曛】 (1) dusk; sunset; twilight; (2) dim glow of the setting sun;

［曛黑］ dusky;

［曛黃］ dusk; sunset;

［曛日］ setting sun;

xun

【燻】 (1) fumigate; smoke; (2) mild; warm;

［燻風］ southerly winds;
燻風習習 southerly winds are pleasant; warm breeze;
燻風徐來 fresh warm breezes play leisurely on...;

［燻黑］ blacken by smoke;

［燻烘］ fumigate;

［燻爐］ brazier;

［燻沐］ bathe and apply perfume;

［燻染］ influence;

［燻肉］ bacon; smoke meat;

［燻死］ suffocate to death;

［燻魚］ smoke fish; smoked fish;

［燻製］ fumigate; smoke; smoking;
控制燻製 controlled smoking;
冷法燻製 cold smoking;
熱燻製 hot smoking;

xun

【纁】 light red;

［纁裳］ light red dress;

xun

【醺】 drunk; intoxicated; tipsy;

［醺醺］ inebriated; tipsy; under the influence of liquor;
醺醺大醉 irrecoverably drunk;
醉醺醺 drunk; sottish; tipsy;

xun²

xun

【旬】 (1) period of ten days; (2) period of ten years; (3) throughout; widespread; (4) inspect; tour;

［旬報］ ten-day report;

［旬刊］ ten-day periodical;

［旬年］ (1) full year; (2) ten years;

［旬日］ ten days;

［旬歲］ whole year;

［旬月］ (1) whole month; (2) ten months;

初旬 first ten days of a month;
兼旬 twenty days;
上旬 first ten days of the month;
中旬 second ten days of the month;
下旬 last ten days of the month;

xun

【巡】 (1) cruise; go on circuit; inspect; make one's rounds; patrol; (2) round of drinks; (3) cop; policeman;

［巡按］ governor of a province;

［巡杯］ toast with the guests around the table;

［巡邊守疆］ proceed on a tour of inspection of the frontiers;

［巡查］ go on a tour of inspection; make one's rounds; patrol and investigate;
加強巡查 step up inspection work;

［巡察］ make an investigation;
巡察員 inspector;
~步行巡察員 walking inspector;
~車站巡察員 station inspector;
~調車巡察員 shunting inspector;
~工廠巡察員 works inspector;

［巡防］ (1) patrolman; watchman; (2) patrol;

［巡撫］ provincial governor;

［巡航］ cruise;
巡航導彈 cruise missile;
大氣層巡航 aerocruise;

［巡迴］ go the rounds; make a circuit of; tour;
巡迴報告 report tour;
巡迴大使 roving ambassador; ambassador-at-large;
巡迴演出 performing tour;
巡迴醫療 go round visiting patients; make a tour to visit the patients; make the rounds visiting patients;

巡迴展覽 mobile exhibition;
[巡警] (1) patrolman; policeman; (2) inspect; patrol;
[巡禮] (1) pilgrimage to a holyland; (2) inspection tour;
[巡邏] make the inspection rounds; patrol;
巡邏車 squad car;
巡邏隊 patrol;
巡邏警車 patrol car;
巡邏艇 patrol boat;
反潛巡邏 antisubmarine patrol;
近岸巡邏 inshore patrol;
[巡視] make an inspection tour;
巡視員 counsel; inspector;
~助理巡視員 assistant counsel; assistant inspector;
[巡私緝盜] patrol against thieves and smugglers;
[巡行] make the rounds of inspection;
[巡洋艦] cruiser;
導彈巡洋艦 guided missile cruiser;
反潛巡洋艦 antisubmarine cruiser;
防空巡洋艦 anticraft cruiser;
核動力巡洋艦 nuclear-powered cruiser;
教練巡洋艦 training cruiser;
輕型巡洋艦 light cruiser;
遠程巡洋艦 long distance cruiser;
重型巡洋艦 heavy cruiser;
[巡夜] make nightly patrols;
[巡閱] inspect; make the rounds of inspection;

出巡 (1) royal progress; (2) go out on an inspection tour; tour of inspection;
逡巡 hang back; hesitate to move forward;
梭巡 move around to watch and guard; patrol;

xun
【徇】 (1) pervading; (2) profit;
[徇情] act wrongly out of personal considerations; practise favouritism;
徇情枉法 bend the law for the benefit of friends or relatives; twist the law to suit one's own purposes;
法不徇情 the law knows no kindness; the law protises no favouritism; the law will never give in to personal considerations;
[徇私] profit
徇私偏袒 have partiality for sb; partial to and side with; show favouritism to sb;
徇私枉法 bend the law for the benefit of relatives; tailor the law to suit one's selfish ends; twist the law to suit one's own purpose;
徇私舞弊 do wrong to serve one's friends or relatives; play favouritism and commit irregularities;

xun
【洵】 certain; real; true;
[洵屬] certainly; truly;

xun
【峋】 irregular stretches of mountains;

嶙峋 (1) jagged; rugged; (2) bony; thin;

xun
【紃】 cord; silk ribbon;

xun
【郇】 (1) an ancient state in present-day Shanxi; (2) a surname;

xun
【荀】 (1) an ancient state; (2) a kind of herb; (3) a surname;

xun
【珣】 kind of jade;

xun
【尋】 (1) look for; search; seek; (2) measure of length;
[尋寶] hunt for treasure; treasure hunt;
[尋查] search for;
[尋常] common; commonplace; ordinary; routine; usual;
不尋常 extraordinary; out of the ordinary; uncommon; unusual;
非比尋常 not of the common run; out of the ordinary; unusual;
異乎尋常 abnormal; beyond the common; bizarre; extraordinary; out of the common; out of the ordinary; out of the way; thundering; unconventional; unusual;
[尋芳] (1) go on a picnic for viewing flowers; (2) seek carnal pleasure;
尋芳客 patron of brothels;
尋芳踏翠 take a walk across the flowers and grass;
[尋訪] look for; make inquiries about; try to locate;
[尋根] in search of things related to one's ancestors; seek roots;

尋根究底 come down to bedrock; examine into the bottom; get down to bedrock; get to the bottom of; get to the roots of; have the why and the wherefore; inquire deeply into; investigate thoroughly; search to the bottom;
尋根索源 inquire into the root of the matter; make a thorough investigation into; probe to the bottom of;
尋根問底 come down to bedrock; get down to bedrock; make a thorough investigation; probe deeply;

[尋機] look for an opportunity;
[尋究] try insistently to find out;
[尋樂] look for distractions; seek amusement; seek pleasure;
[尋盟] restate old treaties and renew friendly relations with other countries;
[尋覓] look for; seek;
[尋摸] look for; seek;
[尋求] explore; pursue; seek; go in quest of;
[尋事] pick a quarrel; seek a quarrel; stir up trouble;
尋事惹非 find fault and make trouble make trouble; seek a quarrel;
尋事生非 make trouble; provoke mischief; seek a quarrel; stir up trouble;

[尋思] consider; meditate; ponder; reflect; think sth over;
尋思一計 cudgel one's brains for a ruse;
低頭尋思 bend one's head and try hard to remember; lower one's head in thought; with bowed head in deep thought;
肚裏尋思 think within oneself;

[尋俗] ordinary;
[尋索] explore; seek;
[尋味] chew sth over; ruminate; think over;
[尋釁] pick a quarrel; provoke;
尋釁滋事 seek a quarrel and challenge a fight; try to pick a quarrel;
找喳尋釁 fasten a quarrel upon sb; pick a quarrel with sb;

[尋幽] visit places;
尋幽覽勝 visit places of scenic beauty;
踏勝尋幽 choose places of scenic beauty;

[尋找] cast about for; explore; forage for; go in quest of; in search of; look for; search; search for; seek; seek for; try to find;
尋找無著 nowhere to be found; unknown whereabouts;

[尋趾] address; addressing;
重覆尋趾 repetitive addressing;
短縮尋趾 abbreviated addressing;
固有尋趾 inherent addressing;
間接尋趾 indirect addressing;
絕對尋趾 absolute addressing;
累加尋趾 accumulator addressing;
延遲尋趾 deferred addressing;
隱式尋趾 implied addressing;
字母尋趾 alphabetic addressing;

翻尋 rummage; try to find;
搜尋 search for; seek;
英尋 fathom;
找尋 look for; search for; seek;
抓尋 look for; search for;
追尋 pursue; search; seek; track down;

xun

【循】 (1) abide by; comply with; follow; (2) postpone; procrastinate; (3) in orderly fashion; (4) inspect;

[循便] be guided by expediency in performing tasks; take advantage of expediency;
[循常] common; ordinary; usual;
[循分] act according to one's duty; fulfill one's obligations;
[循規] follow the conventional rules;
循規蹈矩 accord with the custom and law; behave in a fit and proper way; by rule and line; conform to rules; follow the conventional rules and regulations; follow the custom or law; go round like a horse in a mill; hew to the line; in the traces; keep to the straight and narrow path; law-abiding; obey the rules and regulations; observe all rules and regulations; observe due decorum; not to step out of bounds; stick to convention; toe the line in all sincerity; walk the chalk;
無規可循 have no rules to follow;

[循環] circulate; come round in order; cycle; cycling; move in a cycle;
循環按鈕 cycle button;
循環泵 circulator;
~氣體循環泵 gas circulator;
~洗滌液循環泵 detergent circulator;
循環不息 in a cyclical recurrent manner;

in interminable succession; move in endless cycles;
循環的 cyclic;
循環對立 cyclic opposition;
循環基金 revolving fund;
循環論證 argue in a circle; reason in a circle; vicious circle;
循環器 circulator;
~光學循環器 optical circulator;
~寬波帶循環器 broadband circulator;
~三通路循環器 three-terminal circulator;
~水循環器 water circulator;
~四通路循環器 four-terminal circulator;
~微波循環器 microwave circulator;
~自鎖循環器 latching circulator;
循環賽 round robin; round-robin series;
~小組循環賽 group round robin;
循環往復 go and return in following a circle; move in cycles; repeat in endless cycles;
循環系統 circulatory system;
超循環 hypercycle;
催化劑循環 catalyst circulation;
大循環 systemic circulation;
定向循環 constant circulation;
對流循環 convectional circulation;
惡性循環 vicious circle; vicious cycle; vicious spiral;
放氣循環 bleed cycle;
肺循環 pulmonary circulation;
冠狀循環 coronary circulation;
空氣循環 air circulation;
累加循環 accumulation cycle;
連續循環 continuous circulation;
詮釋循環 hermeneutic circle;
熱循環 thermal cycling;
實際循環 actual cycle;
雙循環 double circulation;
酸液循環 acid circulation;
體循環 systemic circulation;
溫濕循環 temperature-humidity cycling;
吸收循環 absorption cycle;
小循環 pulmonary circulation;
血液循環 blood circulation;
鹽水循環 brine circulation;
營養物循環 nutrient cycling;
應變循環 strain cycling;
再循環 recycle;
自動工作循環 automatic work cycle;

[循理] in accordance with reason;

[循吏] square and benevolent official;

[循例] according to rules; in accordance with precedents;

[循俗] follow customs and traditions;

[循行] make rounds of inspection;

[循序] follow in proper sequence; in proper order; in proper sequence; proceed in good order; proceed step by step;
循序漸進 advance gradually in due order; advance in regular order; advance one step at a time; by gradations; by intervals; by regular steps; by stages; follow in order and advance step by step; follow in proper sequence and make steady progress; gradual improvement; proceed in an orderly way and step by step; step by step;

[循循善誘] good at giving methodical and patient guidance; lead one gradually into good practices; teach with skill and patience; lead sb gradually and patiently on the right path;

因循 carry on as before; continue in the same old rut;
遵循 abide by; adhere to; follow;

xun

【詢】 (1) ask; inquire; (2) deliberate and plan; (3) honestly; truly;

[詢察] investigate and inquire;

[詢價] enquiry;
詢價人 inquirer;
特定詢價 specific enquiry;
一般詢價 general enquiry;
專門詢價 specific enquiry;

[詢問] ask about; debrief; inquire; inquiry; interrogation; make inquiries;
詢問處 information desk;
詢問器 interrogator;
~編碼詢問器 coded interrogator;
~車站詢問器 station interrogator;
~船隻詢問器 shipboard interrogator;
~機載詢問器 airborne interrogator;
~顯示數據詢問器 video data interrogator;
~小功率詢問器 low-power interrogator;
車站詢問 station interrogation;
定向詢問 directional interrogation;
多頻詢問 multiple-frequency interrogation;
鍵盤詢問 keyboard inquiry;

連續詢問 continuous interrogation;
手動詢問 manual interrogation;
無規則詢問 random interrogation;
遠程詢問 remote inquiry;

查詢 inquire about;
探詢 inquire about; make cautious enquiries about; try to sound out;
庭詢 court hearing;
責詢 interpellate;
偵詢 examine a suspect;
徵詢 consult; hold consultation with; probe; seek advice; seek the opinion of; solicit opinions;
質詢 address inquiries to; ask for an explanation; interpellate;
咨詢 consult with; seek advice from;
諮詢 consult; enquire and consult; hold counsel with; seek advice from;

xun
【潯】 (1) steep bank by the stream; (2) name of Jiujiang in Jiangxi;

江潯 river bank;

xun
【撏】 pick; pluck; take;

xun
【蕁】 urtica;
［蕁麻］ nettle; stinging nettle;
蕁麻疹 nettle rash;

xun
【鱘】 sturgeon;

白鱘 Chinese paddlefish;

xun⁴
xun
【汛】 (1) sprinkle; (2) flood; abundant water; (3) menstruation;
［汛城］ guard a city;
［汛期］ flood season;

潮汛 spring tide;
春汛 (1) spring flood; (2) spring fishing season;
冬汛 winter fishing season;
防汛 food prevention;
伏汛 summer flood;
淩汛 winter wind;
秋汛 autumn flood;
桃汛 spring flood;
魚汛 fishing season;

xun
【迅】 fast; sudden; swift;
［迅風］ gale;
［迅急］ speedy; swift; very fast;
［迅疾］ impetuous; quick; rapid; speedy; swift;
［迅即］ at once; immediately;
迅即出發 march off on the instant;
迅即處理 take immediate action on;
迅即動身 set off immediately;
［迅捷］ agile; fast; quick; speedy; swift;
［迅雷］ a sudden clap of thunder;
迅雷不及掩耳 as sudden as lightning; as swift as a sudden clap of thunder; hit sb like a thunderbolt; with lightning speed;
［迅流］ rapid stream;
［迅猛］ swift and violent;
迅猛興起 develop rapidly and vigorously;
［迅速］ by leaps and bounds; prompt; quick; rapid; speedy; swift;
迅速地 in leaps and bounds; like the wind; quickly; rapidly;
迅速發展 expand by leaps and bounds;
迅速回答 make a prompt reply;
迅速離開 speed away;
迅速離去 make a rapid departure;
迅速行動 prompt on the job;
動作迅速 swift in motion;
反應迅速 swift in response;
判斷迅速 swift with judgement;
［迅走］ go fast; hurry on;

奮迅 enthusiastic and swift;

xun
【徇】 (1) display; show; (2) issue orders in the army; (3) comply with; follow; give in to; submit to; (4) quick; (5) die for a cause;
［徇難］ die for a just cause; die for one's country;
［徇首］ show the head of a decapitated offender to warn against repetition of the offense;
［徇行］ make rounds of inspection;
［徇義］ follow the cause of righteousness even at the expense of one's life;

xun

X

【殉】 (1) die for a cause; sacrifice one's life for; (2) be buried alive with the dead;

［殉財］ die of desire for wealth;
貪夫殉財 die of an inordinate desire for wealth; the greedy die in search of wealth;

［殉道］ a martyr for religion; die a martyr's death; die for the right cause; die in the cause of justice;
殉道精神 martyrdom;
殉道者 martyr;

［殉國］ die a martyr's death; die for one's country; die for one's motherland; give one's life for one's country;

［殉教］ die for a religious cause;

［殉節］ die to protect one's virtue for the sake of honour;

［殉利］ die for money;

［殉名］ win fame at the expense of one's life;

［殉難］ die for a cause; die for one's country; martyrdom;

［殉情］ die for love;

［殉葬］ be buried alive with the dead;
殉葬奴隸 immolated slaves;
殉葬品 sacrificial objects;

［殉職］ die at one's post; die in line of duty; die on one's job;
以身殉職 die at one's post; die on one's duties; give one's life in the course of performing one's duty;

xun

【訊】 (1) ask; inquire; question; (2) information; news; (3) interrogate; put on trial; question in court;

［訊辦］ prosecute; put on trial and convict;

［訊斷］ hand down a judgement;

［訊檢］ interrogate the defendant and examine the pertinent evidence;

［訊聽］ make inquiries;

［訊問］ (1) interrogate; question; (2) correspondence;
同意接受訊問 agree to submit to questioning;

［訊息］ information; message; news; tidings;
本來訊息 original message;
多媒體訊息 multimedia message;

傳訊 summon for interrogation;
電訊 (1) telephone dispatch; (2) radio communication signals;
候訊 await court trial;
簡訊 news in brief;
零訊 odd scraps of news;
審訊 inquest; interrogate; try;
死訊 news of sb's death;
提訊 bring before the court; bring sb up for trial;
停訊 stop court proceedings;
通訊 (1) communication; correspondence; (2) news dispatch; news report; newsletter;
聞訊 hear the news; learn of the news;
問訊 (1) ask; inquire; (2) send one's regards to;
喜訊 glad tidings; good news; happy news;
刑訊 try by torture;
音訊 mail; message; news; tidings;
資訊 information;

xun

【訓】 (1) admonish; exhort; instruct; lecture; teach; train; (2) example; model;

［訓斥］ dress down; dressing-down; rebuke; reprimand;
一頓訓斥 a dressing down;

［訓詞］ admonition; instructions;

［訓導］ teach and guide;

［訓迪］ teach and enlighten;

［訓詁］ gloss;
訓詁學 classical Chinese semantics;

［訓話］ exhort; lecture;

［訓練］ coach; discipline; drill; train; training;
訓練班 training class;
訓練部隊 train troops;
訓練場地 training ground;
訓練得不好 out of training;
訓練得好 in training;
訓練法 training;
~ 循環訓練法 circuit training;
訓練量 volume of exercise;
訓練有素 be trained with regularity; be well-trained;
翻譯訓練 translation training;
高級訓練 advanced training;
積極訓練 active discipline;
基本訓練 basic training;
加緊訓練 intensify the training;
加強訓練 accentuation training;
接受訓練 take one's training;
進行訓練 perform a drill;
課堂訓練 academic training;
缺乏訓練 lack training;

賽前訓練 spring training;
適應性訓練 acclimatization training;
投入訓練 go into training;
形式訓練 formal discipline;
循環訓練 do circuits;
直接訓練 direct discipline;
智力訓練 mental discipline;
最優訓練 optimization;

[訓令] instructions from a superior office;
[訓蒙] teach young boys and girls; tutor children;
[訓勉] encourage; exhort;
[訓示] (1) admonish; (2) instructions;
違反訓示 violate instructions;
[訓育] educate and train;
[訓諭] instruct;
[訓政] political tutelage;

古訓 ancient maxims; old saw;
集訓 assemble for training;
家訓 parental precept;
教訓 (1) lesson; moral; (2) chide; educate; give sb a talking; lecture sb; teach sb a lesson;
軍訓 military training;
輪訓 train personnel in rotation;
培訓 cultivate; train;
請訓 ask the emperor for instructions before taking up an official appointment;
師訓 teacher education;
受訓 receive training;
校訓 school motto;
遺訓 teachings of the deceased;
彝訓 regular exhortations;
整訓 train and consolidate troops;

xun

【巽】 (1) bland; mild; submissive; subservient; (2) fifth of the Eight Diagrams;

xun

【馴】 (1) tame and docile; (2) tame;

[馴服] docile; tame; tractable;
馴服的 docile;
[馴化] domesticate; acclimatize;
風土馴化 acclimation;
[馴獸師] animal trainer; handler; tamer;

xun

【遜】 (1) abdicate; (2) humble; modest; (3) inferior to; not as good as; (4) a surname;

[遜讓] surrender to another; yield;
[遜色] inferior; not as good as;
大為遜色 not in the same street with; throw sb into the shade;
毫不遜色 with the best of them;
毫無遜色 by no means inferior; not a halfpenny the worse;
[遜順] humble and yielding; respectfully obedient;
謙卑遜順 humble and retiring;
[遜王] abdicated king;
[遜位] abdicate;
[遜謝] decline humbly and modestly;

不遜 impertinent; rude;
謙遜 modest; unassuming;

xun

【蕈】 (1) mushroom; fungus; (2) mildew; mould;

毒蕈 poisonous fungus; toadstool;
毒蠅蕈 poisonous fungus;
多孔蕈 a kind of mushroom or fungus;
松蕈 pine mushroom;
香蕈 champignon;
羊肚蕈 morel;

ya¹

ya

【丫】 (1) crotch; fork; (2) crotched; forked; ramified;

［丫鬟］ female slave; servant girl; slave girl;
丫鬟抱小孩—別人的 a baby held by a servant girl — sb else's;

［丫頭］ (1) girl; (2) slave girl;
黃毛丫頭 a chit of a girl; a saucy miss; a silly little girl; a slip of a girl; a prig of a girl; a witless young girl; a young girl;
～黃毛丫頭十八變 a girl changes all the time before reaching womanhood;
傻丫頭 minx;
死丫頭 hussy; you elfish girl; you naughty girl;
小丫頭 (1) little girl; (2) young housemaid;
野丫頭 tomboy;

［丫枝］ crotch; forked branch;

枝丫 branch; twig;

ya

【呀】 creaking sound;

［呀然失驚］ be taken unaware and become quite frightened;

［呀呀學語］ the baby is learning to talk;

啊呀 aya;
哎呀 ah; aiya; blast it; by Jove; damn; damned it; dear me; jeez; my eyes; my God; my word; oh; oh, dear; oh, my; oof; whoa; yahoo;
唉呀 dear me; my god; oh;
吧呀 (1) big-mouthed (2) quarrel;
咿呀 (1) creak; squrak; (2) babble; prattle;

ya

【押】 (1) give as security; mortgage; pawn; (2) detain; detain in custody; imprison; take into custody; (3) escort; (4) signature; mark in lieu of signature; sign; stamp;

［押當］ (1) pawn sth; (2) small pawnshop;

［押抵］ give sth as a security for payment of a debt; mortgage;

［押定］ sign an agreement;

［押號］ sign; stamp;

［押匯］ documentary bill;
出口押匯 outward documentary bill;
進口押匯 inward documentary bill;

［押貨］ (1) mortgage goods; (2) escort a shipment of goods from one place to another;

［押解］ escort; send away under escort;
押解出境 deport under escort;

［押金］ cash pledge; deposit;
付押金 give a deposit;
留下押金 leave a deposit;
收回押金 get back a deposit;
收押金 collect a deposit;

［押款］ mortgage; obtain loans against security;

［押送］ send a person to prison; send to another place under escort;
押送犯人 escort a criminal; send a criminal away under escort;

［押歲錢］ money given to children by elders on the Lunar New Year's Eve;

［押尾］ (1) after; last; (2) sign at the end of a document;

［押運］ escort goods in transportation;
押運貨物 transport goods under guard;
押運人 supercargo;

［押韻］ rhyme;
押韻翻譯 rhymed translation;

［押質］ mortgage; pawn;

［押住］ detain in custody;

抵押 collateral; collateralize; hock; hold in pledge; hypothecate; mortgage; pawn; pledge;
典押 mortgage; pawn;
關押 lock up; put in prison;
管押 keep in custody; take sb into custody;
花押 signature on documents, contracts, etc;
畫押 make one's cross; sign;
羈押 detain; take into custody;
寄押 leave sth as security for a loan;
拘押 take into custody;
看押 detain; take into custody;
扣押 (1) detain; hold in custody; (2) distrain;
簽押 autograph; sign;
收押 detain; take into custody;
退押 return deposits to tenants in the land reform;
在押 in custody; in prison;
質押 assign sth as security under an arrangement; mortgage;
作押 mortgage; offer sth as a pledge;

ya

【椏】 forked branch of a tree;

[椏杈] (1) crotch; fork; (2) crotched; forked;
[椏枝] forking branch;

枝椏 branch; twig;

ya

【鴉】 (1) crow; raven; (2) opium;
[鴉巢生鳳] a phoenix from a crow's nest—an ugly mother gives birth to a pretty daughter;
[鴉鳴鵲噪] full of confused voices;
[鴉默悄聲] remain silent;
[鴉片] opium; opium plant;
鴉片成癮 the opium habit is formed;
鴉片斗 opium cup;
鴉片鬼 opium sot;
鴉片屎 opium ashes;
鴉片煙 opium; opium drug;
鴉片煙館 opium den;
鴉片煙筒 opium pipe;
[鴉青] reddish blue;
[鴉雀] crows and sparrows;
鴉雀無聲 all is quiet; dead silent; in perfect silence; no birds sing; not a bird's cheep is to be heard; not a sound can be heard; not even a crow or sparrow can be heard; silence reigns; so quiet that not a single voice can be heard;
鴉飛雀亂 utter disorder;
鴉默雀靜 as silent as the grave; death-like silence; even crows and sparrows hold peace and keep silence;
[鴉色] reddish blue;
[鴉知反哺] the crow knows to disgorge its food in order to feed its parents;
[鴉嘴] crow's bill;
鴉嘴帽 cap;

渡鴉 raven;
寒鴉 jackdaw;
老鴉 crow;
山鴉 chough;
松鴉 jay;
塗鴉 (1) scribble; poor calligraphy; write badly; (2) graffiti;
烏鴉 crow; raven;

ya

【鴨】 duck;
[鴨背] duck's back;
像水過鴨背 like water off a duck's back;
[鴨蛋] duck's egg;
鴨蛋臉兒 oval face;
鹹鴨蛋 salted duck eggs;
[鴨公] drake;
[鴨黃] duckling;
[鴨腳] duck's feet;
[鴨叫] quacks of a duck;
[鴨梨] Hebei pear;
[鴨群] flock of ducks;
[鴨絨] down on a duck's abdomen;
鴨絨被 duck's down quilt;
鴨絨背心 duck's down waistcoat;
[鴨舌帽] cap with a visor; flat cap;
[鴨掌] duck's web;
[鴨珍兒] duck's gizzard;
[鴨子] duck;
鴨子呱呱叫 a duck quacks;
鴨子嘎嘎 ducks quack;
打鴨子上架 drive a duck onto a perch;
一對鴨子 a brace of ducks;
[鴨嘴] duck's bill;
鴨嘴筆 drawing pen;
鴨嘴龍 duck-billed dinosaur;
鴨嘴獸 platypus;

八寶鴨 duck dish with various nuts and seeds;
板鴨 pressed salted duck;
北京填鴨 Beijing duck;
鳳頭鴨 tufted duck;
公鴨 drake;
家鴨 duck;
烤鴨 roast duck;
綠頭鴨 mallard;
水鴨 teal;
填鴨 force-fed duck;
小鴨 duckling;
野鴨 mallard;
一群鴨 a flock of ducks;
針尾鴨 pintail;

ya

【壓】 (1) press; weigh down; (2) control; keep under control; put down; quell; (3) crush; (4) intimidate; repress; (5) approach; getting near; (6) excel; surpass others; (7) pigeonhole; shelve; (8) risk on sth; stake;
[壓扁] crush; flatten by pressure;
[壓出] extrusion;
壓出機 extruder;

~ 多頭壓出機 multi-head extruder;
~ 冷進料壓出機 cold feed extruder;
~ 斜角壓出機 angular head extruder;
~ 液壓式壓出機 hydraulic pressure extruder;

［壓倒］ excel; overpower; overwhelm; surpass; win;
壓倒對方 prevail against one's opponent;
壓倒性勝利 landslide victory; overwhelming victory;
壓倒一切的 all-conquering; overriding;

［壓低］ abate; bring down; depress; lower; reduce;
壓低吵鬧聲 hold down the noise;
壓低價格 bring down the price; force prices down;
壓低噪門 lower one's voice; speak under one's breath;
壓低聲音 lower one's voice;

［壓服］ bring sb to one's knees; coerce; compel sb to submit; force sb to submit; overpower; subjugate; suppress;
壓服私慾 restrain passion;
壓而不服 coercion will never result in convincing sb;

［壓感］ pressure-sensitive;
壓感電傳紙 pressure-sensitive telex paper;
壓感複寫打印紙 pressure-sensitive copying paper;

［壓根兒］ altogether; completely; entirely; totally;

［壓壞］ damaged by high pressure;

［壓擠］ extrude;

［壓價］ demand a lower price; force prices down;
被壓價 be gazundered;

［壓肩迭背］ press breast to back and shoulder to shoulder;

［壓緊］ compress; make sth tight by applying high pressure;

［壓驚］ becalm sb's nerves after a shock; quiet a frightened child;
壓驚辟邪 allay fear and ward off evil influences;

［壓境］ approach the border; mass on the border; press on to the border;

［壓卷］ writing that surpasses all the others;

［壓捆機］ baler;
撿拾壓捆機 field baler;
~ 頂喂式撿拾壓捆機 top-opening baler;
~ 捲壓式撿拾壓捆機 rotary baler;
~ 側喂式撿拾壓捆機 side-opening baler;
~ 直流型撿拾壓捆機 straight-through baler;
~ 自動撿拾壓捆機 automatic pickup baler; pick-up baler;
莖稿壓捆機 straw baler;

［壓力］ (1) exert force by pressure; pressure; tension; (2) overwhelming force; pressure;
壓力鍋 pressure cooker;
壓力很大 under a lot of strain;
壓力計 manometer;
~ 絕對壓力計 absolute manometer;
~ 無液壓力計 aneroid manometer;
~ 自動平衡壓力計 automatic balance; manometer;
壓力太大 the strain is too much for sb;
壓力團體 pressure group;
擺脱壓力 get rid of stress;
沉重的壓力 incubus;
承受壓力 under stress;
處理壓力 cope with pressure;
大氣壓力 atmospheric pressure;
附加壓力 additional pressure;
感到壓力 feel the stress;
減輕壓力 ease off the pressure; reduce stress;
精神壓力 mental pressure;
絕對壓力 absolute pressure;
軍事壓力 military pressure;
橋台壓力 abutment pressure;
屈服於壓力 give in to pressure;
施加壓力 twist sb's arm;
外部壓力 outside pressure;
外交壓力 diplomatic pressure;
學業壓力 pressure from study;
應付壓力 meet the pressure;
輿論壓力 coercion of public opinion;
主動壓力 active pressure;
作用壓力 actuating pressure;

［壓路車］ road-roller; roller;

［壓路機］ roller;
蒸汽壓路機 steamroller;

［壓派］ ride roughshod over;

［壓平］ crush; even; flatten; smash;

［壓迫］ force; oppress; press hard; repress; ride on sb's back;
反抗壓迫 struggle against oppression;
受壓迫 suffer oppression;

消滅壓迫 abolish oppression;

[壓破] broken by high pressure;

[壓氣] (1) calm sb's anger; (2) compress;
壓氣機 compressor;

[壓強] intensity of pressure; pressure;

[壓人] overwhelm others;
以勢壓人 oppress people by force; overwhelm others by one's power; overwhelm people with one's power;

[壓死] (1) crush to death; (2) die after being hit by a car;
被壓死 be crashed to death;

[壓碎] crush to pieces;

[壓縮] compaction; compress; compression; condense; cut down; reduce;
壓縮比 compression ratio;
壓縮衝程 compression stroke;
壓縮點火 compression ignition;
壓縮機 compressor;
~氨氣壓縮機 ammonia compressor;
~空氣壓縮機 air-boost compressor;
~膜式壓縮機 diaphragm-type compressor;
~容積式壓縮機 displacement compressor;
~振幅壓縮機 amplitude compressor;
~製冷壓縮機 cold compressor;
壓縮開銷 draw in one's expenditure;
壓縮開支 curtail expenses; cut down expenses;
壓縮空氣 compressed air;
壓縮氣體 compressed gas;
壓縮物 compressor;
壓縮性 compressibility;
~表面壓縮性 surface compressibility;
~粉末壓縮性 compressibility of a powder;
壓縮儀 compressometer;
大大壓縮 reduce greatly;
黑度壓縮 black compression;
絕熱壓縮 adiabatic compression;
頻帶壓縮 band width compression;
曲線型壓縮 curve-pattern compaction;
區域壓縮 band compression;
通道壓縮 channel compression;
再壓縮 recompression;
~絕熱再壓縮 adiabatic recompression;
~流動再壓縮 flow recompression;
~射流再壓縮 jet recompression;
增量壓縮 incremental compaction;
逐漸壓縮 gradually reduce;
自動音量壓縮 automatic volume compression;

[壓條機] plodder;
肥皂壓條機 soap plodder;
真空壓條機 vacuum plodder;

[壓邪] repress evil influences;

[壓抑] (1) constrain; curb; depress; hold back; inhibit; repress; suppress; (2) oppressive; stifling;
精神壓抑 be depressed in spirit;
心情壓抑 feel constrained;
性壓抑 sexual repression;

[壓軋] squeeze;
壓軋機 squeezer;
~鱷式壓軋機 alligator squeezer; crocodile squeezer;

[壓榨] (1) extort; oppress; squeeze; (2) extract by applying high pressure;
壓榨機 squeezer;
~檸檬壓榨機 lemon squeezer;
~人力壓榨機 hand squeezer;

[壓制] clampdown; inhibit; overbear; restrain; stifle; subject; suppress;
壓制不同意見 stifle different opinions; stifle opposite opinions;
壓制怒氣 check one's anger;
壓制怨氣 contain a feeling of resentment;

[壓住] detain; keep down; put down by force; suppress;
壓住陣腳 hold the line; keep the troops in battle array;
壓不住 unable to exercise control over a group of people due to lack of personal ability;
壓得住 (1) have the ability to undertake a task; (2) keep down;

按壓 check; hold back; press; restrain;
逼壓 oppress;
層壓 lamination;
超高壓 (1) superhigh pressure; (2) extrahigh voltage;
衝壓 punch; stamp;
大氣壓 atmospheric pressure;
低氣壓 depression; low pressure;
低壓 (1) low pressure; (2) depression; (3) low tension; low voltage; (4) minimum pressure;
電壓 voltage;
鍛壓 forge and press;
風壓 wind pressure;
高氣壓 high pressure;
高血壓 high blood pressure; hypertension;

高壓 (1) high pressure; (2) high tension; high voltage; (3) maximum pressure;
黑壓壓 a dense mass of;
積壓 keep long in stock; overstock;
擠壓 extrude;
減壓 decompress; pressure reduction; reduce presssue; relax the pressure;
降壓 step down;
扣壓 pigeonhole; withhold;
脈壓 pulse pressure;
模壓 mould pressing;
偏壓 bias; bias voltage;
欺壓 bully and oppress; cheat and oppress; high-handed behaviour; push around; ride roughshod over;
汽壓 steam pressure; vapour pressure;
氣壓 air pressure; atmospheric pressure; barometric pressure; pressure;
強壓 oppress and crush;
揿壓 press down; push down;
熱壓 hot pressing;
滲透壓 osmotic pressure;
昇壓 boost; step up;
收縮壓 systolic pressure;
舒張壓 diastolic pressure;
水壓 hydraulic pressure;
彈壓 quell; suppress;
特壓 extra pressure;
調壓 pressure regulation;
卸壓 decompress; decompression.
血壓 blood pressure;
眼內壓 intraocular pressure;
眼壓 intraocular pressure; intraocular tension;
液壓 hydraulic pressure;
抑壓 coerce; curb; restrain;
油壓 oil pressure;
增壓 pressurization;
掌上壓 press-up;
鎮壓 (1) put down; suppress; (2) execute;
指壓 acupressure;
制壓 (1) overpower; overwhelm; suppress; (2) neutralize;
重壓 heavy load; great pressure; weight;
鑽壓 bit pressure; bit weight;

ya²
ya

【牙】 (1) teeth; (2) ivory; (3) tooth-like thing;

［牙白口清］ able to speak articulately;

［牙本質］ dentin;
功能性牙本質 functional dentin;
繼發性牙本質 secondary dentin;
原發性牙本質 primary dentin;

［牙病］ dental disease;

［牙槽］ socket of the tooth;
牙槽出血 odontorrhagia;
牙槽骨髓炎 alveolar osteomyelitis;
牙槽膿漏 pyorrhoea;
牙槽膿腫 alveolar abscess;
牙槽炎 alveolar; alveolitis;

［牙齒］ gnashers; tooth;
牙齒保健 dental health;
牙齒打戰 make sb's teeth chatter;
牙齒護理 dental care;
牙齒侵蝕症 dental erosion;
牙齒咬合不正 malocclusion;
牙齒問題 dental problems;
愛護牙齒 take good care of one's teeth;
保護牙齒 preserve one's teeth; take care of one's teeth;
掉牙齒 lose a tooth;
伶牙俐齒 fluent; have a silver tongue; silver-tongued; very good at speaking and talking;
露出牙齒 show one's teeth;
一個牙齒 a tooth;
一顆牙齒 a tooth;
一排牙齒 a row of teeth;
張牙露齒 show one's teeth;

［牙牀］ gum;

［牙雕］ ivory carving;
牙雕玉飾 ivory carvings and jade ornaments;

［牙發生］ odontogenesis;
牙發生不全 odotogenesis imperfecta;
牙發育不良 hypodontia;

［牙粉］ tooth powder;

［牙縫兒］ space between the teeth;

［牙膏］ toothpaste;
擠牙膏 squeeze tooth paste out from the tube;
一管牙膏 a tube of toothpaste;

［牙根］ base of the teeth;
牙根發酸 put sb's teeth on edge; set sb's teeth on edge;

［牙垢］ tartar on the teeth;

［牙骨質］ cement; cementum; crusta petrosa; tooth bone;
牙骨質破壞 cementoclasia;
牙骨質細胞 cementocyte;
細胞性牙骨質 cellular cementum;

［牙關］ mandibular joint;
牙關緊閉 lockjaw; with jaws shut tight;
牙關緊鎖症 trismus;
咬緊牙關 bite the bullet; carry a stiff upper lip; clench one's jaws; endure with dogged will; grit one's teeth; keep a stiff upper lip; set one's teeth;
［牙慧］ stale expression;
［牙尖］ dental cusp;
［牙科］ dentistry;
牙科保健員 dental hygienist;
牙科護士 dental nurse;
牙科學 dentistry;
牙科醫生 dental surgeon; dentist;
牙科診所 dental clinic; the dentist; the dentist's;
牙科助手 dental hygienist;
牙科專家 odontologist;
［牙列不齊］ malalignment;
［牙婆］ procuress;
［牙籤］ toothpick;
牙籤盒 toothpick holder;
［牙肉收縮］ gingival recession;
［牙神經痛］ odontoneuralgia;
［牙石］ tartar;
［牙刷］ toothbrush;
一把牙刷 a toothbrush;
［牙鬆］ looseness of the tooth;
［牙髓］ dental pulp;
牙髓炎 pulpitis;
~ 開放性牙髓炎 open pulpitis;
~ 細菌性牙髓炎 anachoretic pulpitis;
~ 增生性牙髓炎 hyperplastic pulpitis;
壞死性牙髓 necrotic pulp;
壞死牙髓 dead pulp;
［牙挺］ elevator;
［牙痛］ toothache;
航空牙痛 aero-odontodynia;
減輕牙痛 ease toothache;
陣發性牙痛 grinding toothache;
［牙脱落］ exfoliation;
［牙線］ dental floss;
［牙型］ tooth form;
［牙牙］ babble;
牙牙學語 babble; babble out one's first speech sounds; begin to babble; learn to speak;
［牙炎］ odontitis;
［牙癢］ gnash one's teeth;
恨得牙癢 gnash one's teeth with hatred;
［牙搖動］ vacillation of the tooth;
［牙醫］ dentist;
牙醫業 dentistry;
牙醫助手 hygienist;
看牙醫 go to the dentist;
矯形牙醫 orthodontist;
［牙移位］ tooth migration;
病理性牙移位 pathologic tooth wandering;
［牙齦］ gum;
牙齦紅腫 redness and swelling of the gum;
牙齦口炎 gingivostomatitis;
牙齦裂 gingival cleft;
牙齦瘤 epulides;
~ 肉芽腫性牙齦瘤 epulis granulomatosa;
牙齦膿腫 gumblil; parulis;
牙齦炎 gingivitis;
［牙釉質］ enamel; encaustum;
［牙折裂］ odontoclasis;
［牙質］ dentine;
［牙周病］ periodontal disease; periodontosis;
［牙周炎］ periodontitis;
邊緣性牙周炎 marginal periodontitis;
成人牙周炎 adult periodontitis;
單純性牙周炎 simple periodontitis;
化膿性牙周炎 purulent periodontitis;
急進性牙周炎 rapidly progressive periodontitis;
青春期前牙周炎 prepubertal periodontitis;
青少年型牙周炎 juvenile periodontitis;
齦牙周炎 gingivoperiodontitis;

聱牙 hard to read;
拔牙 extract a tooth; pull out a tooth;
板牙 screw die; threading die;
鮑牙 bucktooth;
補牙 fill a tooth; have a tooth stopped; stop a tooth;
槽牙 front tooth; molar;
蟲牙 carious tooth;
出牙 dentia; teethe; teething; tooth eruption;
大板牙 protruding tooth; snag;
大牙 (1) molar; (2) front tooth; (3) one's teeth;
倒牙 set one's teeth on edge;
掉牙 a tooth drops off;
毒牙 poison fang;
佛牙 tooth relic of the Buddha;
敢開牙 dare to ask a high price;
恒牙 permanent tooth;

後牙 back teeth;
虎牙 canine tooth;
換牙 grow permanent teeth;
假牙 artificial tooth; dentures; false tooth; store teeth;
尖牙 fang;
狼牙 (1) wolf's fang; (2) cryptotaeneous cinquefoil;
獠牙 long sharp, protruding tooth;
門牙 front tooth; incisor;
磨牙 (1) argue endlessly; talk nonsense; (2) idle away time; kill time; (3) crack sth between the teeth; grind one's teeth; grit one's teeth;
奶牙 baby teeth; milk teeth;
前牙 front teeth;
犬牙 (1) canine tooth; (2) fang (of a dog);
人造牙 artificial tooth;
乳牙 baby tooth; milk tooth;
塞牙 food stuck between the teeth;
刷牙 brush one's teeth;
托牙 denture;
鑲牙 crown a tooth; fill in an artificial tooth; have a tooth filled;
榫牙 tenon;
象牙 elephant's tusk; ivory;
小牙 denticle;
咬牙 (1) grind one's teeth; (2) grit one's teeth;
一顆牙 a tooth;
月牙 crescent moon;
長牙 cut a tooth; cut one's teeth; cut teeth; grow teeth;
爪牙 talons and fangs;
智牙 wisdom tooth;
蛀牙 tooth decay;
齜牙 open the mouth and show the teeth;

ya

【芽】 bud; shoot; sprout;
［芽胞］ gemma;
［芽菜］ bean sprouts;
［芽豆］ sprouted broad bean;
［芽兒］ bud; shoot; sprout;

不定芽 adventitious bud;
側芽 lateral bud;
抽芽 bud; sprout;
出芽 (1) budding; germinate; put forth buds; sprout; (2) budding; gemmation; prolification;
催芽 accelerate the germination of seeds;
頂芽 apical bud; terminal bud;
豆芽 beansprout;
發芽 bud; germinate; sprout;
繁殖芽 brood bud;
副芽 accessory bud;
冠芽 crown bud;
果芽 fruit bud;
花芽 blossom bud; flower bud;
黃豆芽 soya bean sprout;
活芽 active bud;
綠豆芽 mug bean sprout;
麥芽 malt;
萌芽 germinate; sprout;
嫩芽 burgeen; peel; tender shoot;
胚芽 plumule;
潛伏芽 latent bud; resting bud;
肉芽 granulation;
新芽 (1) sprout; (2) maiden work of a young man;
休眠芽 dormant bud; resting bud;
腋芽 axillary bud;
幼芽 bud; young shoot;
再生芽 regeneration bud;
肢芽 appendage bud;
茁芽 sprout;
總芽 end bud;

ya

【枒】 (1) coconut tree; (2) felloes of a wheel; (3) disorderly growth of twigs;
［枒杈］ crotches;
枒杈結網 build a web on a forked branch;

ya

【蚜】 aphid; plant louse;
［蚜蟲］ aphid; aphis; greenfly; plant louse;
蚜蟲採集器 aphidozer;
蚜蟲專家 aphidologist;

菜蚜 vegetable aphid;
赤楊綿蚜 woolly alder aphid;
高梁蚜 aoliang aphid;
麥蚜 wheat aphid;
棉蚜 cotton aphid;
綿蚜 woolly aphid;
桃蚜 green peach aphid;
癭蚜 gall aphid;

ya

【崖】 (1) cliff; precipice; (2) brink; verge; (3) forbidding; high and steep; precipitous;
［崖岸］ haughty;
［崖壁］ precipice;
［崖谷］ valley between precipices;

［崖略］ outline;
［崖鹽］ rock salt;
［崖燕］ cliff swallow;

冰崖 glacial cliff;
巉崖 crag;
斷層崖 fault cliff; fault scarp;
斷線崖 fault-line cliff; fault-line scarp;
海崖 sea cliff;
浪蝕崖 wave-cut cliff;
峭崖 vertical cliff;
山崖 cliff;
視覺崖 visual cliff;
懸崖 beetling cliffs; cliff; crag; hanger; overhanging cliff; precipice; rock cliff; scarp; steep cliff;
雲崖 high cliff;

ya
【涯】 (1) bank; water's edge; water front; (2) limit; (3) faraway places;
［涯岸］ edge; limit;
［涯際］ edge; limit;

生涯 career; profession;
天涯 end of the world; remotest corner of the earth;
無涯 boundless; endless; limitless;

ya
【衙】 (1) government office; (2) congregate; gather; meet; (3) (in Tang Dynasty) front hall of the palace; (4) a surname;
［衙集］ assemble; gather together;
［衙吏］ government clerk;
［衙門］ yamen;
［衙署］ government office;
［衙役］ yamen runner;

官衙 government office;

ya³
ya
【亞】 a pronunciation of 亞；

ya
【啞】 (1) dumb; mute; (2) hoarse; husky;
［啞巴］ dumb person; mute;
啞巴吃黃蓮一有苦說不出 like a dumb person tasting bitter herbs — unable to express one's discomfort; one has to suffer in silence;
啞巴吃黃蓮一有口難言 when a dumb person eats gentian, he tastes the bitterness inside;
啞巴吃餃子一心裏有數 when a dumb person eats dumplings, he knows what is what;
啞巴虧 one's grievances which are unable to speak out;
啞巴夢見媽，說不出的苦 like a dumb person dreaming of his mother — unable to voice one's distress;
［啞劇］ dumb show; mime; pantomime; mummery;
啞劇演員 mummer;
［啞鈴］ dumb-bell; weights;
啞鈴操 dumb-bell exercises;
［啞謎］ puzzling remark; riddle;
打啞謎 propose a riddle; talk in riddles;
解啞謎 explain a riddle; solve a riddle;
［啞然］ (1) silent; (2) describing of the sound of laughter;
啞然失笑 a faint laugh escapes sb; can't help laughing; chuckle to oneself; guffaw; laugh involuntarily; unable to stifle a laugh;
啞然無聲 mute; silence reigns; soundless;
［啞子］ dumb person; mute;
啞子吃黃蓮 like a dumb person eating a bitter plant — be a silent victim;

聾啞 deaf and dumb; deaf-mute;
吵啞 hoarse; husky; raucous;
嘶啞 hoarse;
喑啞 dumb; mute;
瘖啞 dumb; mute;

ya
【雅】 (1) elegant; graceful; (2) polished; refined; sophisticated; (3) correct; proper; (4) frequently; much; often; usually; (5) acquaintance; friendship;
［雅愛］ your help; your patronage;
［雅步］ leisurely and graceful steps;
［雅詞］ elegant diction;
［雅淡］ simple and elegant;
［雅故］ (1) old friend; (2) usually;
［雅觀］ graceful and elegant in appearance; in good taste; nice appearance; nicelooking; refined;
不雅觀 bad form; do not look nice

or proper; offensive to the eye; unbecoming; ungraceful;
~姿態不雅觀 one's gestures are ungraceful;

[雅號] your gracious name;

[雅懷] generous heart; refined taste and disposition;

[雅誨] your esteemed opinion;

[雅集] gathering of men of letters;

[雅鑒] for your perusal;

[雅教] your honoured advice;

[雅量] (1) broad-mindedness; generosity; magnanimity; (2) great capacity for drinking;
雅量不小 show much clemency and conciliation;
有雅量 have generosity;

[雅氣] elegant; tasteful;
佈置得雅氣 be decorated with much taste;
穿得雅氣 be tastefully dressed in an elegant style;
樣式雅氣 be graceful in style;
顯得雅氣 show an elegance;

[雅趣] elegant tastes; refined pleasure; refined tastes;

[雅人深致] a refined pleasure of poetic minds; a sophisticated person with profound thoughts; the mind of a refined man is far-reaching — producing effects that extend far;

[雅士] person of refined tastes; refined scholar;

[雅事] refined activities of the intelligentsia;

[雅俗] the refined and the vulgar; the sophisticated and the simple-minded;
雅俗共賞 appeal to all; appeal to both the sophisticated and the simple-minded; appeal to highbrows and lowbrows; be admired by scholars and laymen alike; be enjoyed by both the educated and the common people; both the refined and the vulgar can take pleasure in; everyone can enjoy; for the enjoyment of both the educated and the common; highbrows and lowbrows alike can enjoy; suit all tastes; suit both refined and popular tastes; the uneducated as well as the educated can appreciate it;
雅而不俗，恭而不倨 delicacy without fastidiousness, respect without arrogance;
一雅一俗 one is elegant, the other is vulgar;

[雅素] (1) personal background; (2) old friendship; (3) virtue in simplicity;

[雅玩] refined pastimes of the intelligentsia;

[雅望] your extraordinary reputation;
雅望非常 a person of elegant appearance and courteous manner;

[雅興] aesthetic mood; refined interest;
雅興不淺 have a really keen interest in sth; really in an aesthetic mood;
無此雅興 in no mood for such things; not to be in such a poetic mood;

[雅馴] elegant;
文不雅馴 the writing is not polished;

[雅言] (1) honest advice; well-intentioned criticism; (2) things one often talks about;

[雅意] your kind offer; your kindness;
雅意心領 I appreciate your kindness but must decline the offer;

[雅游] easy to get along with people;

[雅正] (1) correct; standard; (2) graceful and upright; honest; righteous; upright; (3) would you kindly point out my inadequacies;

[雅致] elegant; refined; tasteful;
雅致的 elegant;
~雅致的裝束 clothes with elegance;
擺設雅致 be tastefully furnished;
陳設得雅致 be furnished with great elegance;
辭吐雅致 refined conversation;
裝束雅致 show good taste in clothes;

[雅座] private room; comfortable seats;

博雅 erudition; learned and accomplished; well-informed and refined;
大雅 elegant; refined;
淡雅 quiet and elegant; simple but elegant;
典雅 elegant; refined;
風雅 literary pursuits;
高雅 elegant and of good taste; noble and graceful;
古雅 of classic beauty and elegant taste;
精雅 elegant; graceful; neat and refined; refined;
清雅 quiet and elegant; refined;
儒雅 learned and refined;
素雅 quiet and in good taste; simple but elegant;
溫雅 gentle and cultivated; refined;

文雅 cultured; gentle; refined;
閒雅 easy; elegant; graceful; refined;
嫻雅 elegant; refined;
秀雅 beautiful and refined;
淹雅 deep and refined;
幽雅 chaste and elegant; quiet and tastefully laid out;
優雅 (1) elegant; (2) graceful;
藻雅 elegant; fine; graceful;

ya⁴

ya

【亞】 (1) inferior; second; (2) Asia;
［亞軍］ runner-up; second place;
獲得亞軍 get a second; win second place;
［亞聖］ the Lesser Sage — Mencius;

阿摩尼亞 ammonia;

ya

【軋】 crush; grind;
［軋花］ cotton ginning;
軋花廠 cotton ginning mill;
軋花機 gin;
~鋸齒軋花機 saw gin;
~刷式軋花機 brush cotton gin;
凹凸軋花 embossing;
［軋傷］ run over and injure;
［軋碎］ break; crush; crush to pieces;
［軋軋］ creaking sound of a machine in operation;

傾軋 engage in factional strife; engage in internal strife; fight for power; in-fighting; jostle against one another; jostle with one another;
壓軋 squeeze;

ya

【迓】 go out to receive; receive; welcome;

迎迓 meet; welcome;

ya

【訝】 (1) be surprised; express surprise; surprise; (2) (now rare) same as 迓;

怪訝 amazed; astonished; surprised;
惊訝 amazed; astonished; surprised;

ya

【婭】 mutual address between one's sons-in-law;

姻婭 relations by marriage;

ya

【揠】 pull up; tug upward;
［揠苗助長］ help the rice shoots grow by pulling them up; spoil things by excessive enthusiasm;

ya⁵

ya

【呀】 (1) gape; (2) particle used after a phrase for emphasis, surprise, etc.;

yan¹

yan

【奄】 (1) bathe; drown; soak; (2) remain; (3) castrated man; castrate;
［奄留］ stay longer than intended;
［奄息］ stop for rest;
［奄奄］ weak breathing;
奄奄待斃 hang by a thread; on the point of dying;
奄奄一息 at one's last gasp; barely breathing; dying; on the verge of death;

yan

【咽】 gullet; larynx; pharynx; throat;
［咽白喉］ pharyngeal diphtheria;
［咽扁桃體］ pharyngeal tonsil;
［咽部充血］ congested throat;
［咽惡性腫瘤］ malignant tumour of the pharynx;
［咽喉］ (1) larynx; throat; (2) narrow, throat-like passage of strategic importance;
咽喉痛 sore throat;
壞疽性咽喉痛 ulcerated sore throat;
鏈球菌性咽喉痛 streptococcal sore throat;
濾泡性咽喉痛 spotted sore throat;
膿毒性咽喉痛 septic sore throat;
咽喉腫痛 swelling and pain in the throat;
［咽後膿腫］ retropharyngeal abscess;
［咽良性腫瘤］ benign tumour of the pharynx;
［咽痛］ pharyngalgia;
［咽頭］ pharynx; throat;
［咽峽炎］ angina;
［咽炎］ pharyngitis;
白喉性咽炎 diphtheritic pharyngitis;
肥大性咽炎 hypertrophic pharyngitis;
壞疽性咽炎 gangrenous pharyngitis;
急性咽炎 acute pharyngitis;
口瘡性咽炎 aphthous pharyngitis;

鏈球菌性咽炎 streptococcal pharyngitis;
慢性咽炎 chronic pharyngitis;
膜性咽炎 membranous pharyngitis;
泡狀咽炎 vesicular pharyngitis;
疱疹性咽炎 pharyngitis herpetica;
鼠疫性咽炎 plague pharyngitis;
萎縮性咽炎 atrophic pharyngitis;

yan

【殷】 dark red;

［殷紅］ blackish red; dark red;

yan

【胭】 (1) cosmetics; (2) throat;

［胭粉］ rouge and face powder;
胭粉小説 love stories; novels featuring romantic plots;

［胭脂］ blusher; cochineal; rouge;
胭脂紅 carmine;
胭脂虎 shrew; virago;
胭脂樹 annatto;

yan

【淹】 (1) drown; flood; soak; steep in; submerge; (2) delay; procrastinate; (3) stay; stranded;

［淹敗］ be routed; damaged by water;

［淹博］ erudite; wide;
淹博學問 deep and wide in learning; have a wide knowledge;

［淹纏］ delay; drag along; linger a long time;

［淹沈］ (1) bed-ridden for a long time; (2) procrastinate;

［淹遲］ dilatory; slow;
淹遲其行 delay one's departure;

［淹貫］ well-versed; widely-read;
淹貫群書 thoroughly familiar with all books;

［淹煎］ vexed; worried;

［淹踐］ abuse; trample down; use roughly;

［淹留］ stay for a long period;

［淹沒］ drown; flood; inundate; submerge;
被洪水淹沒 be inundated with flood;

［淹溺］ drowning;

［淹識］ erudition; profundity;
淹識時事 well-informed of current events;

［淹死］ be drowned;
淹死在洪水中 get drowned in the deluge;
容易淹死 drown easily;

［淹宿］ overnight;

［淹通］ be thoroughly acquainted with; well-versed;

［淹雅］ deep and refined;
淹雅華美 cultured and beautiful;
淹雅之士 deeply cultured and refined scholar;

［淹月］ for a whole month;

［淹潤］ amiable but timid; intimate but shy;

［淹滯］ talented persons holding inferior posts;

水淹 in flood;
滯淹 remain at a standstill;

yan

【湮】 (1) bury in oblivion; fall into oblivion; (2) block; clog up; stop; (3) long;

［湮沈］ have no chance to rise in the world;

［湮蓋］ inundate;

［湮滅］ annihilate; bury; bury in oblivion; destroy;
湮滅無聞 lose in oblivion;

［湮沒］ be buried; bury; fall in oblivion; forgotten; neglected;
湮沒不彰 fall into the shade;
湮沒無聞 be buried in oblivion; be entirely forgotten; fall into oblivion; fall into obscurity; pass into oblivion; remain obscure; remain unknown; sink into oblivion; vanish and be forgotten;

［湮遠］ very long in time;

yan

【焉】 (1) how; when; why; (2) it; (3) there; (4) and so; so that; (5) final particle indicating numerous senses;

［焉得］ how can one be;

［焉敢］ how dare;

［焉用］ why is it necessary to use;

［焉有］ how could there be such;

［焉知］ how could one know;
焉知非福 how could you know it is not a blessing;

yan

【崦】 a mountain in Gansu;

yan

【腌】 dirty; filthy; unclean;

［腌菜］ pickled vegetables; pickles;

yan

【菸】 tobacco leaf;

［菸草］ tobacco;

［菸葉］ tobacco leaves;

yan

【煙】 (1) fumes; smoke; (2) mist; vapour; (3) be irritated by smoke; (4) cigarette; tobacco; (5) opium; (6) a surname;

[煙靄] mist and clouds;

[煙波] lakes; mist and ripples; mist-covered waters;
煙波浩渺 a vast expanse of misty, rolling waters; a wide expanse of mist-covered waters; mists and waves stretch far into the distance; the wide expanse of misty waters;

[煙草] baccy; tobacco;
烤煙草 toast tobacco;
無煙煙草 smokeless tobacco;
種煙草 grow tobacco;

[煙囪] chimney;
煙囪工業 smokestack industry;
煙囪冒煙 the chimney smokes;
打掃煙囪 clean a chimney; sweep a chimney;
林立的煙囪 a forest of chimneys;
大煙囪 smokestack
一個煙囪 a chimney;

[煙袋] smoking pipe;
水煙袋 narghile; water pipe;

[煙蒂] cigarette butt; cigarette end; dog-end; fag end;

[煙斗] pipe;
煙斗通條 pipe cleaner;
抽煙斗 smoke a pipe;
和平煙斗 peace pipe; pipe of peace;

[煙鬼] heavy smoker; opium smoker;

[煙海] as huge and vast as mists over the sea;
浩如煙海 as vast as the open sea; as vast as the smoke and sea;
如墮煙海 all at sea; as if lost in a fog; as if lost on a misty sea; be lost in the clouds; completely at a loss; lose one's bearing; lose oneself in the clouds;

[煙盒] cigarette case;

[煙花] (1) fireworks; (2) a mist of flowers－beautiful scenery of spring flowers; (3) fanfare; prosperity;
煙花表演 pyrotechnics;
煙花粉黛 courtesans; singsong girls;
煙花粉柳 the prostitutes;
煙花柳巷 red-light district;
煙花門巷 brothels; houses of ill fame; red-light district;
放煙花 set off fireworks;

[煙灰] cigarette ash; tobacco ash;
煙灰碟 ashtray;
煙灰缸 ashtray;
～一個煙灰缸 an ashtray;

[煙火] (1) kitchen smoke; (2) cooked food; (3) signal beacon; (4) fireworks;
煙火表演 fireworks display;
不食人間煙火 not eat cooked food; otherworldly;
不食煙火 live on fruits; stop eating cooked food;
放煙火 let off fireworks;
小心煙火 caution against smoke and fire;
煙消火滅 come to an end; disappear; the smoke drifts away, the fire goes out; vanish;
嚴禁煙火 smoking or lighting fire strictly forbidden;

[煙酒] tobacco and alcohol;
煙酒不沾 touch neither tobacco nor alcohol;
煙酒税 wine and tobacco tax;

[煙具] smoking set;

[煙帽] cowl;

[煙煤] bitumite;
低級煙煤 low rank bitumite;
褐性煙煤 lignite bitumite;
中級煙煤 medium rank bitumite;

[煙苗] opium poppy;

[煙幕] screening smoke; smoke curtain; smoke screen; veil;
煙幕彈 smoke bomb;
放煙幕 put up the smoke screen;

[煙農] tobacoo grower;

[煙圈] puff;

[煙視媚行] give a swift glance and fawn; look and move slowly;

[煙絲] cut tobacco; pipe tobacco;

[煙頭] cigarette butt; cigarette end; dog-end; unfinished cigarette;
撿煙頭 gather cigarette butts;
扔煙頭 throw away a cigarette butt;

[煙囪] chimney; funnel; smoke pipe; stovepipe; ventilation pipe;
煙囪管帽 chimney pot;
煙囪清掃工 chimney sweep;
複式煙囪 multiple chimney;
高煙囪 chimney-stalk;

鐵煙囪 iron plate chimney;
通風煙囪 air chimney;
總煙囪 chimney-stack;
煙囪 chimney;

[煙味] smell of smoke;
聞到煙味 smell smoke;

[煙霧] mist; smog; smoke; vapour;
煙霧彈 smoke bomb;
煙霧警報器 smoke alarm; smoke detector;
煙霧彌漫 be enveloped in mist; be permeated with thick fog and smoke; full of smoke; heavy with smoke; smoke-laden; smoky; smudgy; vapoury;
煙霧騰騰 be filled with steam and smoke; hazy with smoke; smoke-laden;
煙霧信號 smoke signal;
刺激性煙霧 irritating smog;
袋濾器煙霧 bag hose fume;
電子煙霧 electrosmog;
副產煙霧 by-product fume;
光化煙霧 photochemical smog;
濃重的煙霧 heavy smog;
穩靜煙霧 calm smog;
煙籠霧罩 be enveloped in mist;
氧化劑煙霧 oxidant smog;
一層煙霧 a veil of smoke;
一團煙霧 a cloud of smoke;
引起煙霧 cause a fog;
有毒煙霧 toxic smog;
瘴煙毒霧 clouds of pestilential vapour; miasmal clouds;
致命煙霧 killer smog;

[煙霞] mist and clouds in the twilight; mists and rosy clouds in the twilight;

[煙葉] tobacco leaf;

[煙癮] (1) tobacco addiction; (2) crave for tobacco;

[煙油] tobacco tar;

[煙雨] misty rain;
煙雨莽蒼 vast blur of mist and rain;
煙雨濛濛 the fine rain is drizzling in the misty weather;
煙雨山影 the mists veil the distant mountains in rainy weather;
瘴雨蠻煙 pestilential rain and unhealthy mist;

[煙雲] (1) mists and clouds; (2) passing scene;
煙雲過眼 as transient as a fleeting cloud;
過眼煙雲 as transient as a fleeting cloud; like floating smoke and passing clouds; passing scene;
渺若煙雲 as vague as mist;

[煙柱] column of smoke;
一道煙柱 a column of smoke;

安全型煙 low-tar cigarette;
板煙 (of tobacco) plug;
鼻煙 snuff;
炊煙 smoke from kitchen chimneys;
抽煙 smoke; smoke a cigarette;
大煙 opium;
風煙 smoke that spreads with the wind;
烽煙 beacon; beacon-fire;
旱煙 tobacco;
湖煙 mist on a lake;
嚼煙 chewing tobacco;
戒煙 abstain from smoking; break off smoking; cut out smoking; cut out tobacco; drop smoking; give up smoking; hold off from smoking; keep away from smoking; keep away from tobacco; lay aside the habit of smoking; lay off smoking; refrain from smoking; stay off cigarettes; stop smoking; swear off tobacco; through with smoking; wean oneself from smoking;
禁煙 ban opium-smoking and the opium trade;
捲煙 (1) cigarette; (2) cigar;
烤煙 flue-cured tobacco;
狼煙 smoke signal;
煤煙 (1) smoke from burning coal; (2) soot;
濃煙 dense smoke; smoke smudge;
排煙 discharge smoke;
青煙 light smoke;
輕煙 smoke;
讓煙 offer sb a cigarette;
人煙 signs of human habitation;
曬煙 sun-cured tobacco;
水煙 shredded tobacco for water pipes;
外國煙 imported cigarettes;
無煙 smoke-free; smokeless;
吸二手煙 passive smoking;
吸煙 smoke;
夕煙 evening mist;
香煙 (1) cigarette; ciggy; coffin nail; fag; (2) incense smoke;
硝煙 smoke of gunpowder;
一袋煙 a pouch of tobacco;
一股煙 a trail of smoke;
一口煙 a puff of a cigarette; a suck of smoke;
一溜煙 in a flash; in an instant; run away swiftly; speed off; vanish like smoke;
一縷煙 a curl of smoke; a trail of smoke; a wisp of

smoke;
一陣煙 a burst of smoke;
油煙 lampblack;
雲煙 clouds and fog; clouds and mist;
紙煙 cigarette;

yan
【嫣】 beautiful; captivating; charming; fascinating; handsome; lovely;
［嫣紅］ bright red; rich crimson;
［嫣然］ beautiful; merrily; sweet;
嫣然一笑 captivating smile; give a bewitching smile; give a captivating smile; give a charming smile; give a sweet smile; give a winsome smile;

yan
【鄢】 (1) an ancient state in present-day Henan; (2) a surname;

yan
【醃】 pickle; salt;
［醃菜］ pickled vegetables; pickles;
一瓶醃菜 a jar of pickles;
［醃肉］ salted meat; salted pork;
［醃泡］ marinate;
醃泡汁 marinade;
［醃魚］ salted fish;
［醃製］ curing;
大量醃製 bulk curing;
家庭醃製 domestic curing;
桶中醃製 barrel curing;
真空醃製 vacuum curing;
裝箱醃製 box curing; tierce curing;

yan
【蔫】 (1) (of plants) fade; wither; (2) ennui; listless; spiritless; (3) calm and quiet; expressionless;
［蔫甘］ amiable and mild;
［蔫了］ finished; withered;
［蔫土匪］ deceitful hypocrite; honest-faced crook;

yan
【燕】 a state in present-day Hebei during the Period of the Warring States;

yan
【閼】 formal wife of the chieftain of Xiongnu in the Han Dynasty;

yan
【閹】 (1) castrate; (2) eunuch;
［閹割］ castrate; neuter; spay;
被閹割 neutered;
~被閹割的公貓 neutered tomcat;
彈性閹割 elastration;
［閹雞］ capon;
［閹牛］ bull stag; bullock; ox;
小閹牛 bullock;
［閹奴］ eunuch;
［閹人］ castrated person; eunuch;
［閹寺］ eunuch;
［閹羊］ wether;

天閹 naturally important person;

yan
【懨】 (1) in poor health; sickly; (2) peaceful; tranquil;
［懨懨］ (1) in poor health; sickly; (2) content; peaceful;

yan
【臙】 cosmetics; face-powder; rouge;
［臙脂紅］ carmine;
［臙脂虎］ shrew;

yan²
yan
【妍】 (1) attractive; beautiful; charming; cute; good-looking; pretty; (2) coquettish; seductive;
［妍麗］ attractive; beautiful; charming;
［妍皮］ beautiful skin;
妍皮不裹痴骨 beautiful in appearance and clever in mind;

爭妍 contend in beauty;

yan
【言】 (1) speech; words; (2) express; mean; say; speak; talk; (3) dialect; language; tongue; (4) character; word; (5) a surname;
［言必有信］ as good as one's word;
言必信，行必果 always be true in word and resolute in deed; promises must be kept and action must be resolute; promises must be kept and actions resolutely taken; what is said must be done, and what is done must be carried to a result;
［言必有中］ hit the point whenever one speaks; whenever one says sth one hits the mark; whenever one speaks, one

speaks to the point;

[言不及義] indulge in gossip without touching anything serious; make idle talk; never say anything serious; talk frivolously;

[言不應點] break one's word; not keep one's word;

[言出法隨] enforce the regulations to the letter; the order, once given, will be strictly enforced;

[言出身證] vouch one's words with one's deeds;

[言傳] explain in words;

言傳身教 instruct sb not only in words, but also by deeds; set up example for others with both precept and practice; teach by personal example as well as by verbal instruction; teach by percept and example;

[言詞] diction; expressions; one's words; statements; what one says; words;

言詞辯論 verbal argument of litigants at a court of law;

言詞不雅 use vulgar language;

言詞鋒利 speak daggers;

言詞懇切 sincere in what one says; speak in an earnest tone;

言詞激烈 speak with indignation;

言詞尖鋭 use sharp words;

言詞謹慎 prudent in utterance;

言詞情景 situation of utterance;

言詞閃爍 incoherent speech; jumping from one subject to another;

言詞速度 rate of utterance;

言詞婉轉 speak tactfully; use gentle words;

言詞犀利 speak daggers;

言詞意義 utterance meaning;

得體的言詞 befitting words;

拙於言詞 clumsy in expressing oneself; inarticulate;

[言動] words and conduct; speech and behaviour;

言動不苟 careful words and practice; prudent in speech and behaviour;

[言對] (1) converse; meet and talk; (2) coupling of words;

[言官] imperial censor;

[言歸於好] be reconciled; become reconciled; bury the hatchet; bury the tomahwak; heal the breach; kiss and be friends; maintain amicable relations hereafter; make friends again; make it up with sb; make one's peace with sb; make peace with; make sb's peace with; make up a quarrel; on good terms again; put up the sword; reconcile; resume friendship; shake and be friends; sink a feud; smoke the pipe of peace; square oneself with; start with a clean slate;

[言歸正傳] and now to be serious; come back to our story; come to business; get down to business; hark back to the subject; jesting apart; jesting aside; joking apart; joking aside; keep to the record; lead the conversation to serious things; let's resume the narration; resume the thread of one's discourse; return from the digress; return to one's muttons; return to the subject; return to the topic of discussion; revert to the original topic of conversation;

[言過其實] boast; bombastic; brag; come it strong; draw the long bow; exaggerate; give a false colour; go it strong; hyperbolize; inflated; make a mountain out of a molehill; overshoot the truth; overstate; overstate the fact; pile on the agony; pull the long bow; strain the truth; stretch a point; stretch the facts; turn geese into swans;

[言和] become reconciled; bury the hatchet; make peace;

[言及] mention; talk about; touch on;

[言簡意賅] brief and to the point; compendious; comprise the matter in few words; concise and comprehensive; give the essentials in simple language; impart a deep meaning with only a few words; terse but comprehensive; terse in language and comprehensive in meaning;

[言教] give verbal directions; teach by precept; teach by word of mouth; teach by words;

言教不如身教 example is better than precept; teaching by words is not as good as teaching with deeds;

[言盡於此] have no more to say; have nothing

more to say;

[言路] channels through which criticisms and suggestions may be communicated to the leadership;

堵塞言路 stifle criticisms and suggestions;

廣開言路 provide wide opportunities for airing views;

[言論] speech; views;

言論自由 freedom of expression; freedom of speech;

~保障言論自由 guarantee freedom of speech;

發表言論 express one's opinion; state one's views;

[言明] declare; make a statement; state clearly;

[言莫難喻] beyond description;

[言人人殊] different people, different version; different people give different views; each person offers a different version; each person tells a different story; every person differs in his statement; everybody has a different story; everyone gives a different version;

[言色] words and countenance;

察言觀色 examine a person's language and observe his countenance; watch a person's every mood;

[言事若神] foresee with divine accuracy; foretell like a prophet; foretell things accurately;

[言談] conversation; words and speech;

言談粗俗 speak in a harsh tone;

言談舉止 speech and deportment;

言談微中 one's speech is subtle;

言談之間 during a conversation; from the way sb talks;

羞於言談 coy of speech;

[言聽計從] act at sb's beck and call; act upon whatever sb says; always follow sb's advice; always listen to sb's words and accept his advice; believe and act upon whatever sb suggests; have an unquestioning faith in sb; have full confidence in sb; have implicit faith in sb; jump through a hoop for sb; listen to every word sb says; listen to sb's words and follow his counsels; readily listen to sb's advice and accept it; take sb's advice and adopt his plan; trust sb completely;

[言外] between the lines; beyond the words spoken;

言外有意 more is meant than meets the ear;

言外之意 ideas not expressed in words; implication; implied meaning; meaning between the lines; meaning beyond the literal words; real meaning; what is actually meant;

妙在言外 the beauty lies beyond the mere wording;

[言笑] talk and laugh;

言笑自若 completely at ease; go on talking and laughing as if nothing had happened; natural and calm; talk and laugh imperturbably; undisturbed;

[言行] statements and actions; words and deeds;

言行不符 deeds not matching words; one does not do what one preaches; words and acts do not correspond; words do not correspond with deeds;

言行不檢點 let oneself loose;

言行不一 actions repugnant to one's words; one does not do what on preaches; one's actions are not in keeping with one's promises; one's acts belie one's words; one's conduct disagress with one's words; one's conduct is at variance with one's words; one's deeds do not match one's words; one's deeds do not square with one's words; one's doings belie one's commitments; one's words and deeds are at complete variance; one's words are at variance with one's deeds; one's words are not matched by deeds; say one thing do another; talk one way and behave another; words and actions do not match; words and deeds contradict each other; what one does belies one's commitments;

言行過分 overstep the mark;

言行謹慎 mind one's Ps and Qs;

言行若一 live up to one's words;

言行失檢 blot one's copybook; indiscretion;

言行相悖 practise against what one preaches;

言行相顧 practise what one preaches;

言行信篤 faithful in word and deed;
言行一致 act in accordance with one's words; actions matching words; as good as one's word; deeds accord with words; fit one's deeds to one's words; live up to one's words; match one's deeds with one's words; match word to deed; match words with deeds; one's actions accord with one's words; one's actions are in keeping with one's promises; one's deeds and words are in accord; one's deeds and consistent with one's words; one's words correspond with one's actions; square one's words with one's conduct; stand by one's word; suit one's actions to one's words; the deeds suit the words; the deeds match the words;
察其言，觀其行 check what he says against what he does; examine his words and watch his deeds; observe his speech and behaviour;
嘉言懿行 fine words and lofty deeds; wise words and noble deeds;
踐言實行 fulfil a promise and put into operation;
謹言慎行 be careful as to one's words or behaviour; be cautious with one's words and actions; be cautious with one's words and deeds; be discreet in word and deed; be prudent in making statements and careful in personal conducts; mind one's Ps and Qs; speak and act cautiously; watch your step and mind what you are saying;
行不顧言 act differently from what one says; not to act according to one's words; not to practise what one preaches; say one thing but to do sth else;
行過於言 better than one's words;
言不顧行 speeches are not in accordance with action;
言不及行 words are not equal to practice;
言不踐行 words are not equal to practice;
言出即行 no sooner said than done;
言浮於行 one's practice does not meet one's words; speak above one's abilities; words float above practice;
言清行濁 one's words are nice, but one's actions are dirty; one's words are pure, but one's actions are vile; one's words are sweet, but one's actions are dirty;
言信行果 truthful in speech and firm in action; promises must be kept and actions resolutely taken; true to one's word and firm in one's actions; trustworthy in word and resolute in action;
坐言起行 no sooner said than done;

［言猶在耳］ while the words are still ringing in one's ears;

［言語］ speech;
言語 speech; spoken language; words;
言語變體 speech variety;
言語病理學 speech pathology;
言語重複 analogia;
言語粗鄙 coarse in speech;
言語粗俗 coarse and vulgar in speech;
言語粗野 expressions are coarse and wild;
言語錯誤 speech error;
言語得體的 well-spoken;
言語風格 speech style;
言語技能 speech repertoire;
言語結構 verbal construction;
言語節奏 speech rhythm;
言語缺陷 speech defect;
言語連續體 speech continuum;
言語情境 speech situation;
言語社團 speech community;
言語失調 speech disorder;
言語事件 speech event;
言語速度 rate of speech;
言語無味 insipid talk; keep on jawing;
言語行為 speech act;
~言語行為分類法 speech act classification;
~言語行為理論 speech act theory;
~表達性言語行為 expressive speech act;
~表述性言語行為 locutionary act;
~陳述性言語行為 indicative speech act;
~成事性言語行為 perlocutionary act;
~間接言語行為 indirect speech act;
言語學 philology;
言語閱讀 speech reading;
言語障礙 speech impediment;
言語治療 speech therapy;
言語綜合 speech synthesis;
標準言語 standard speech;
不言不語 keep silent; utter not a single word;
常規言語 formulaic speech;
粗言惡語 dirty words; four-letter words;

the rough side of the tongue;
訛言訛語 erroneous and irresponsible talk;
風言風語 groundless, satiric remarks; groundless talk; slanderous gossip; unfounded rumours;
寡言少語 reticent; taciturn;
~寡言少語的人 man of few words; person of few words;
罕言寡語 quiet and unexpressive;
豪言壯語 heroic pledge; heroic utterance; splendid vow; brave words;
後言不接前語 having no connection with the previous conversation; speak incoherently;
花言巧語 a lot of artful talk; banana oil; blandishments; do a snow job; fair words; fine and deceiving words; fine rhetoric; fine words; flannelmouthed; flowery words and cunning statements; honeyed words; make a sophisticated speech; mouth fair words; plausible; pretty words; seductive speech; sweet chatter; sweet talk; talk clever stuff; use specious excuses; wiles;
簡潔的言語 brief speech;
酒言酒語 speak under the influence of drink; words uttered under the influence of liquor;
誑言妄語 wild talks and lies;
冷言冷語 cold remarks; cold words; cool remarks; cynicism; ironic remarks; mocking words; sarcastic comments; sarcastic remarks; shafts of ridicule;
七言八語 all offering different opinions; all sorts of opinion; all talking in confusion;
千言萬語 a great deal of talk; innumerable words; a host of words; a torrent of words; many many words in one's heart; there's much one wants to say; thousands and thousands of words;
~千言萬語，歸到一句話 in a word; in brief; in short;
~千言萬語，湧上心頭 thousands of words well up in one's heart;
柔言蜜語 speak in a melting voice;
三言兩語 a couple of words; a word or two; in a few words; in one or two words;
生硬的言語 blunt speech;
甜言蜜語 blarney; coax with delusive promise; fine-sounding words; glib talk; honeyed words; honey-lipped; honey-mouthed; honey-sweet words; honey-tongued; oily tongue; smooth-tongued; soft words; sugarplum; sugary words; sweet talk; sweet words and honeyed phrases; tidbits;
~甜言蜜語的人 cooer;
~吃蜂蜜，説好話—甜言蜜語 sweet words and honeyed phrases;
溫言軟語 with mild and affectionate words;
言三語四 crticize without much thinking;
言多語失 one is liable to make a slip of the tongue, if one talks a great deal;
言來語去 argue; talk back and forth; talk over and over again;
真言實語 tell the truth; what one says is true;
隻言片語 a few isolated words and phrases; a few words; a single word; a word or two; just a few words;
自言自語 say to oneself; soliloquize; speak to oneself; talk to oneself; think aloud; think out loud;

[言責] responsibility of offering advice;

[言者] speaker;

言者無心，聽者有意 a careless word may be important information to an attentive listener; a casual remark sounds deliberate to a suspicious listener;
言者無意，聽者有心 a pair of good ears will drain dry a hundred tongues; one pair of ears draws dry a hundred tongues;
言者無罪，聞者足戒 blame not the critic, heed what he says; blame not the speaker but be warned by his words; do not blame the one who speaks but heed what you hear; don't blame the speaker but take his words as a worning; it is not the one who speaks who is culpable; it is up to the one who listens to exercise due caution;
言者諄諄，聽者藐藐 the speaker is earnest bu the hearer is casual; the speaker talks with great earnestness, but the audience pays little attention; the words are earnest but they fall on deaf ears;

[言之] state;

言之不詳 be stated too briefly;

言之成理 present in a reasonable way; say sth with solid judgement; sound reasonable; speak in a rational and convincing way; speak on the strength of reason; stand to reason; talk sense; well-reasoned; what one says makes sense;

言之過甚 exaggerated statement; go too far; put it strong;

言之過早 it's too early to say; make a premature statement; premature to say; speak too soon; still too early to say;

言之可恥 it is disgraceful to speak of it;

言之歷歷，如在眼前 give a glowing account;

言之無文，行而不遠 non-elegant words will not become popular;

言之無物 an empty talk; devoid of substance; hot air; make an inane remark; mere verbiage; talk endlessly with no substance at all;

言之無心 often says things one does not mean;

言之有據 speak in good authority; speak on good grounds;

言之有理 hold water; it stands to reason; speak in a rational and convincing way;

言之有物 have substance in a speech;

言之有信 honour one's own words;

言之中肯 the cap fits; the remark is to the point;

言之鑿鑿 say sth with certainty; say with definite evidence;

慨乎言之 say it with a sigh;

廣而言之 in a general sense; speaking generally;

換言之 in other words;

極而言之 talk in extreme terms;

簡言之 all things considered; briefly; by and large; first and last; in a few words; in a nutshell; in a word; in brief; in fine; in sum; in short; in the lump; make a long story short; on the whole; take it all in all; the long and short of it;

~簡而言之 briefly speaking; for shortness's sake; in a few words; in a nutshell; in brief; in short; make a long story short; to put it in a nutshell; to sum up;

要而言之 to put it briefly; to sum up;

易言之 in other words;

總而言之 all things considered; at any rate; by and large; cut a long story short; first and last; in a few words; in a nutshell; in a word; in brief; in fine; in one word; in short; in sum; in the lump; make a long story short; on the whole; put it briefly; take it all in all; taking one thing with another; the long and the short of it; to make a long story short; to sum up;

[言重] speak so seriously and strongly as to embarrass sb;

言重九鼎 one's word carries the weight of nine tripods — weighty advice;

[言狀] describe;

八言 poem of eight-character lines;

謗言 defamatory remark; libel; slander;

辟言 go away because of an offensive statement;

弁言 foreward; preface;

不言 keep silent; without saying;

讒言 malicious talk;

昌言 speak without reservation;

常言 saying;

倡言 initiate; propose;

重言 repeat a character;

出言 speak;

傳言 (1) hearsay; rumour; (2) pass a message;

make a statement; speak;

待言 need to say;

讜言 proper words;

導言 introduction;

鼎言 weighty advice;

斷言 affirm; allege; assert categorically; aver; declare; say with certainty; state with certainty;

惡言 abusive words; vicious remarks;

發言 speech; statement;

煩言 complaints;

方言 dialect;

廢言 dismiss sb's statement as untrue;

附言 postscript;

甘言 honeyed words;

敢言 (1) speak out; (2) vocal;

格言 maxim; motto;

好言 nice words;

胡言 rave; talk nonsense;

謊言 a bit of fiddle; bunk; categorical inaccuracy; cover story; distort facts; embroider the truth; erroneous report; eyewash; fabrication; fib; fiddle-faddle; flannel; forked-tongue; humbug; lie; falsehood; misinform; mispresent the facts; plausible denial; porky; prevaricate; selective facts; story; strain; stretch; swing the lamp; tale of a tub; tall tale; terminological inexactitude; yenta;

諱言 dare not or would not speak up;
諫言 remonstration to the emperor;
進言 give a word of advice; offer suggestions;
開言 begin to speak; start to talk;
空言 empty talk; impractical words;
狂言 boastful talk; bragging; crazy remarks; crazy talk; incoherent talk; nonsense; ravings; wild language;
讕言 calumny; slander;
濫言 talk nonsense;
立言 expound one's ideas in writing;
例言 introductory remarks; notes on the use of a book;
留言 leave a message; leave one's comments;
流言 gossip; rumour;
美言 put in a good word for sb;
妙言 witty remark;
名言 famous maxim; well-known saying;
難言 feel embarrassed to mention;
諾言 promise;
片言 a few words; a phrase or two; just a few words;
棄言 (1) break one's word; unable to keep one's promise; (2) words which have become obsolete and no longer in circulation;
前言 (1) foreword; introduction; preamble; preface; (2) previous remarks; (3) the words of past thinkers;
巧言 smooth words;
輕言 speak lightly; speak without thinking;
人言 (1) human speech; (2) public opinion;
善言 well-intentioned advice;
奢言 extravagant talk;
申言 state reasons;
慎言 speak cautiously;
聲言 claim; declare;
失言 improper remark; make an indiscreet remark; make improper utterances; put one's foot in one's mouth; say what should not be said; slip of the tongue;
食言 break one's promise; break one's word; eat one's own words; fink out; go back on one's word;
碩言 boastful talk; grand words;
誓言 oath; pledge;
訟言 announce; declare; speak in public;
託言 make excuses;
婉言 gentle words; speak tenderly; tactful expressions;
萬言 ten thousand words;
妄言 talk nonsense; tell lies; wild talk;
危言 alarmist talk;
文言 classical Chinese;
無言 have nothing to say;
晤言 meet and talk;
戲言 casual remark; joke;
閒言 (1) gossip; idle talk; (2) balder-dash;
虛言 (1) false remarks; unfounded statements; (2) impty talk; meaningless words; platitude;
序言 foreword; preface;
敍言 foreword; preface;
緒言 foreword; introduction; preface;
宣言 declaration; manifesto;
佯言 lie; tell a lie;
揚言 declare;
妖言 fallacy; heresy;
謠言 groundless allegation; rumour;
藥言 sincere admonitions;
一言 a word;
遺言 words of the deceased;
異言 dissenting words;
逸言 extravagant talk;
引言 foreword; introduction;
庸言 commonplace words;
莠言 bad words; dirty words;
迂言 absurd statement; impractical remarks;
諛言 flattering words; flattery;
語言 language;
預言 foretell; predict; prediction; prophecy;
寓言 allegory; fable;
怨言 complaint; grumble;
約言 pledge; promise;
譖言 calumny; slander;
贈言 words of advice given to a friend at parting;
箴言 admonition; maxim;
枕邊言 pillow talk;
諍言 frank admonition;
證言 testimony;
知言 (1) words of wisdom; (2) know the true meaning of one's words;
直言 speak bluntly; state outright;
質言 honest talk; plain talk;
至言 (1) words of the utmost importance; (2) the most virtuous utterances;
忠言 earnest suggestion; sincere advice;
墜言 slip of the tongue;

贅言 unnecessarhy words;
縱言 continue an informal and free conversation;

yan

【岩】 (1) large rock; (2) cliff; crag; (3) mountain;

[岩岸] rocky coast;
[岩壁] (1) dyke; (2) cliff;
[岩層] ground; rock formation; rock stratum;
不穩定岩層 bad ground;
未開發岩層 virgin ground;
[岩牀] sill;
[岩洞] cave; cavern; grotto;
[岩蓋] laccolite; laccolith;
[岩基] batholith;
[岩架] ledge;
[岩漿] magma;
[岩頸] neck; plug;
[岩居穴處] dwell in mountain caves;
[岩脈] rock vein;
[岩石] crag; rock;
岩石學 petrology;
堅硬岩石 solid rock;
年代久遠的岩石 ancient rocks;
一層岩石 a layer of rock;
[岩鹽] rock salt;
[岩樣] rock sample;
[岩株] stock;

安山岩 andesite;
石灰岩 limestone;
白雲岩 dolomite;
斑岩 porphyry;
板岩 slate;
碧玄岩 basanite;
變質岩 metamorphic rock;
冰磧岩 tillite;
巉岩 dangerously steep rock; precipitous rock;
成層岩 stratified rock;
成岩 diagenesis;
沉積岩 sedimentary rock;
粉砂岩 siltstone;
風成岩 aeolian rock;
橄欖岩 peridotite;
黑曜岩 obsidian;
花崗岩 granite;
煌斑岩 lamprophyre;
輝長岩 gabbro;
輝綠岩 diabase;
混合岩 migmatite;
火成岩 aqueous rock;
火山岩 volcanic;
基性岩 basic rock;
基岩 bedrock;
角岩 hornstone;
角礫岩 breccia;
角頁岩 hornfels;
流紋岩 rhyolite;
泥灰岩 marlstone;
泥沙岩 siltstone;
泥岩 mudstone;
黏土岩 clay rock;
凝灰岩 tuff;
攀岩 climbing;
噴出岩 extrusive rock;
片麻岩 gneiss;
片岩 schist;
千枚岩 phyllite;
溶岩 lava; magma; molten rock;
砂板岩 sandy slate;
砂岩 sandstone;
砂質岩 arenaceous rock;
閃長岩 diorite;
生物岩 biogenic rock;
石炭岩 limestone;
石英岩 quartzite;
酸性岩 acid rock;
碎屑岩 clastic rock;
透水岩 permeable rock;
圍岩 country rock; surrounding rock;
偉晶岩 pegmatite;
細砂岩 fine sand layer;
玄武岩 basalt;
岩漿岩 magmatic rock;
鹽岩 rock salt;
頁岩 shale;
葉岩 shale;
硬吵岩 graywacke;
油頁岩 oil shale;
鑿岩 drilling;
珍珠岩 pearlite;
正長岩 syenite;
中性岩 intermediate rock;

yan

【延】 (1) extend; lengthen; prolong; prolongate; protract; spread; (2) defer; delay; postpone; procrastinate; (3) engage; invite; send for;

[延長] extend; lengthen; prolong; prolongate; protract;
延長服役期 have an extension of enlistment;

延長線 extension lead;
[延遲] be delayed; defer; delay; hold over; postpone; put off; retard;
延遲付款 tardy in one's payment;
延遲器 delayer;
延遲作用 delayed application;
高度延遲 altitude delay;
孔徑延遲 aperture delay;
模擬延遲 analogue delay;
聲延遲 acoustic delay;
信標延遲 beacon delay;
[延宕] procrastinate; slow in taking action;
[延擱] (1) procrastinate; (2) neglect;
[延緩] defer; delay; postpone; put off;
延緩衰老 prevent premature senility;
[延會] postpone a meeting; put off a meeting;
[延見] give an audience to sb; grant an interview with sb;
[延接] receive guests;
[延津之合] reunion after parting;
[延頸舉踵] crane one's neck and stand on tiptoe;
[延口殘喘] draw a few more wretched breaths;
[延攬] recurit talented people;
[延蔓] spread like a vine;
[延納] employ talents;
延納賢才 receive and be kind to talents;
[延聘] employ; engage; invite the service of;
[延期] (1) be postponed; defer; delay; lay over; postpone; put off; put over; (2) extend;
延期付款 delay payment;
延期啟程 put off one's departure;
延期簽證 have one's visa extended;
延期審判 postpone the hearing;
延期支付 deferred payment;
需要延期 need an extension;
[延請] extend an invitation to; invite;
[延入] invite to enter;
[延伸] elongate; extend; stretch;
延伸到海邊 extend as far as the sea;
向四周延伸 extend around;
[延時] time-delay;
[延眺] crane the neck to look;
[延拓] continuation;
跳變延拓 jump continuation;
同構延拓 continuation of isomorphisms;
[延誤] delay; fail because of procrastination; hold-up; incur loss through delay;
延誤時機 miss an opportunity because of a delay;
延誤時間 lose time;
延誤診治 delay the diagnosis and treatment;
避免延誤 avoid delay; save delay;
發生延誤 involve a delay;
埋怨延誤 complain of the delay;
造成延誤 cause a delay;
[延續] be continued; continue; go on; last;
延續至今 continue into the present;
[延譽] make sb's good name widely known;

挨延 delay; procrastinate; put off;
遲延 delay; drag on; postpone; retard;
苟延 linger on;
廣延 extension;
呼延 surname;
稽延 postpone; put off;
拉延 expand; pull;
曼延 stretching;
蔓延 extend; spread;
綿延 continue far and long; stretch long and unbroken;
遷延 defer; delay; procrastinate;
伸延 elongate; extend; stretch;
順延 postpone; put off;
推延 postpone; put off;
拖延 defer; delay; drag on; postpone; procrastinate; put off; put over; stall for time;
外延 extension;
宛延 long and winding; meander;
暫延 adjourn temporarily; postpone tentatively to;
招延 recruit;
周延 distribution;

yan

【沿】 (1) along; follow; go along; (2) continue; hand down; (3) continuous; successive;
[沿岸] along the bank; along the coast; alongshore; coastal; littoral; offshore;
沿岸流 alongshore currents;
沿岸行駛 coast along the shore; hug the shore;
沿岸巡邏 patrol the shore;
[沿邊] along the edge;
沿邊開放 open border areas to the outside world;
[沿波討源] follow up the stream and seek the

source; make a thorough investigation of a thing;

［沿道兒］ all along the road;

［沿革］ course of change and development; evolution;

［沿海］ along the coast; coastal; inshore; littoral; offshore;

沿海地區 coastal area; coastal region; litoral;

沿海航行 skirt the coast;

沿海開放城市 coastal open cities;

沿海貿易 coasting trade;

沿海一帶 along the coastal region;

［沿河］ along the river;

［沿江］ along the river;

沿江開放 open river areas to the outside world;

［沿街］ along the street;

沿街道路 frontage road;

沿街叫賣 hawk one's wares in the streets; loudly announce goods for sale along the streets; peddle;

沿街乞討 beg from door to door;

沿街小販 walk;

［沿例］ follow a precedent;

［沿路］ along the road; along the way; on the roadside; on the way;

沿路走 go along the road;

［沿門托鉢］ beg alms from door to door; beg for alms from house to house; beg from house to house with a bowl in hand; live a mendicant monk;

［沿途］ on the way; throughout the journey;

沿途宣傳 propaganda on the way;

［沿襲］ carry on as before; follow the tradition;

沿襲陳規 follow convention;

沿襲古老習俗 adhere to ancient customs;

世代沿襲 come down through generations;

［沿線］ along the line;

在鐵路沿線 along the railway;

［沿用］ continue following the old practices; continue to use;

沿用常規 follow conventional lines;

［沿著］ follow; go along;

邊沿 edge; fringe;

窗沿 windowsill;

牀沿 edge of a bed;

炕沿 edge of a heatable brick bed;

前沿 forward position;

相沿 hand down; pass down from generation to generation without change;

yan

【炎】 (1) burning hot; scorching; sultry; (2) blaze; flame; flare; (3) inflammation;

［炎方］ south;

［炎風］ northeast wind;

［炎附寒棄］ cleave to influential and wealthy persons and discard poor and unimportant ones;

［炎涼］ (1) change in temperature; hot and cold; (2) change in attitude toward persons; snobbishness;

炎涼世態 the aspect of worldly affairs, now hot and now cold;

世態炎涼 the aspect of worldly affairs, now hot and now cold;

［炎熱］ blazing; burning hot; scorching; very hot;

炎熱的 blistering; hot;

~ 十分炎熱的 steaming hot;

忍受炎熱 bear sultry heat; stand sultry heat;

［炎暑］ dog days of summer; hot summer; summer at its hottest; sweltering summer days;

［炎天］ dog days; hot day;

［炎威］ oppressively imposing;

［炎夏］ hot summer; summer at its hottest;

炎夏烈日 scorching sun in hot summer days;

炎夏盛暑 a broiling heat of summer permeates the air;

炎夏永晝 endless summer days;

［炎炎］ (1) blazing; scorching; sweltering; very hot; (2) awe-inspiring; impressive and imposing;

［炎陽］ scorching sun;

［炎症］ inflammation;

發生炎症 be inflamed;

急性炎症 acute inflammation;

減輕炎症 reduce inflammation;

控制炎症 control inflammation;

慢性炎症 chronic inflammation;

消除炎症 diminish inflammation;

引起炎症 cause inflammation;

［炎腫］ inflammation with swelling;

鼻竇炎 nasosinusitis;
鼻炎 rhinitis;
扁桃體炎 tonsillitis;
腸結腸炎 enterocolitis;
腸神經炎 enteroneuritis;
腸系膜炎 mesenteritis;
腸炎 enteritis;
腸周炎 perienteritis;
唇炎 cheilitis; inflammation of the lips;
大腦炎 cerebritis; encephalitis;
膽管炎 cholangitis;
膽囊炎 cholecystitis;
動脉炎 arteritis;
耳血管炎 angiotitis;
耳炎 otitis;
發炎 inflame; inflammation;
肺腸炎 pneumoenteritis;
肺炎 pneumonia;
附睪炎 epididymitis;
腹膜炎 peritonitis;
肝炎 hepatitis;
睪丸炎 orchitis;
巩膜炎 scleritis;
骨關節炎 osteoarthritis;
骨靜脈炎 inflammation of the veins of a bone; osteophlebitis;
骨膜炎 periostitis;
骨軟骨關節炎 osteochondroarthritis;
骨軟骨炎 osteochondrosis;
骨髓炎 osteomyelitis;
骨性關節炎 osteoarthritis;
骨炎 inflammation of the bone; osteitis;
鼓膜炎 tympanitis;
冠周炎 pericoronitis;
關節炎 arthritis;
黑皮炎 melanodermatitis;
虹膜炎 iritis;
喉氣管炎 laryngotracheitis;
喉炎 laryngitis;
骺炎 epiphysitis;
滑膜炎 synovitis;
肌炎 infammation of a muscle; myositis;
脊膜脊髓炎 meningomyelitis;
脊膜炎 spinal meningitis;
脊髓炎 myelitis;
甲溝炎 paronychia;
肩關節炎 inflammation of the shoulder joint; omarthritis;
瞼角炎 blepharitis angularis;
瞼腺炎 sty;
瞼炎 palpebritis;
瞼緣炎 blepharitis;
腱鞘炎 tenosynovitis;
腱炎 tendinitis;
結膜炎 conjunctivitis;
靜脉炎 phlebitis;
抗炎 anti-inflammatory;
口角炎 perleche;
口炎 stomatitis;
闌尾炎 appendicitis;
肋膜炎 pleurisy;
淚腺炎 dacryoadenitis;
顱骨炎 cranitis;
卵巢炎 ovaritis;
脉管炎 vasculitis;
盲腸炎 appendicitis;
腦脊髓炎 encephalomyelitis;
腦膜炎 meningitis;
腦炎 encephalitis;
黏膜炎 mucositis;
尿道炎 urethritis;
女陰炎 vulvitis;
膀胱炎 cystitis;
盆腔炎 pelvic infection;
皮炎 dermatitis;
氣管炎 tracheitis;
前列腺炎 prostatitis;
前庭炎 vestibulitis;
乳腺炎 mastitis;
腮腺炎 parotitis;
舌炎 glossitis;
舌周炎 periglossitis;
神經炎 neuritis;
腎膀胱炎 nephrocystitis;
腎炎 nephritis;
腎盂腎炎 pyelonephritis;
腎盂炎 pyelitis;
食管炎 esophagitis;
視網膜炎 retinitis;
輸精管炎 deferentitis;
輸卵管炎 salpingitis;
輸尿管炎 urethritis;
外陰炎 vulvitis;
胃肝炎 gastrohepatitis;
胃十二指腸炎 gastroduodenitis;
胃炎 gastritis;
腺炎 adenitis;
腺周炎 periadenitis;
消炎 dephlogisticate; diminish inflammation; reduce inflammation;
心包炎 pericarditis;
心肌炎 myocarditis;
心內膜炎 endocarditis;
心炎 carditis;

胸膜炎 pleurishy;
牙髓炎 pulpitis;
牙齦炎 gingivitis;
牙炎 odontitis;
牙周炎 periodontitis;
咽喉炎 pharyngitis;
咽峽炎 angina;
咽炎 pharyngitis;
眼炎 ophthalmia;
胰腺炎 pancreatitis;
齦牙周炎 gingival periodontitis;
齦炎 gingivitis;
陰道炎 vaginitis;
疣性皮炎 verrucous dermatitis;
疣狀皮炎 verrucose dermatitis;
支氣管炎 bronchitis;
趾炎 dactylitis; inflammation of a toe;
膣炎 vaginal inflammation;
直腸炎 proctitis; redtitis;
中耳炎 otitis media;
主動脈炎 aortitis;
子宮頸炎 cervicitis;
子宮炎 uteritis;
縱隔炎 mediastinitis;

yan

【研】 (1) examine; go to the very source; investigate; research; search into carefully; study; (2) consider; deliberate; discuss; (3) grind; powder;

[研究] examine; go to the very source of; look into; research; study; study and research;
研究班 tutorial class;
研究成果 research findings;
研究部門 research department;
研究範圍 area of research;
研究費 research fund;
研究工作 research work;
研究計劃 research project;
研究結論 research conclusions;
研究經費 research funding; research grant;
研究開發 research and development;
研究科學 study science;
研究領域 area of research; field of research;
研究生 graduate student; research student;
~ 研究生院 grad school; graduate school;
研究實習員 research assistant;
研究所 research institute;
研究題目 research topic;
研究小組 research team;
研究員 research fellow; researcher;
~ 二等研究員 by-fellow;
~ 副研究員 associate research fellow; associate researcher;
~ 助理研究員 assistant researcher;
研究院 academy; research institute;
研究中心 research centre;
研究助理 research assistant;
從事研究 go in for the study;
單調乏味的研究 plodding research;
調查研究 investigate and study;
獨立研究 independent research;
發展研究 promote research;
翻譯研究 translation studies;
高級研究 advanced studies;
基礎研究 basic research;
進行研究 carry out research; conduct research;
開創性研究 pioneering research;
開始研究 begin one's study;
科學研究 scientific research;
歷史研究 historical research;
潛心研究 bury oneself in one's study;
深入研究 devote a deep study to;
文化研究 cultural studies;
悉心研究 devote oneself to the study of sth;
學術研究 academic research;
一項研究 a piece of research;
醫學研究 medical research;
應用研究 application study;
指導研究 direct study;
中止研究 give up the study of...;
宗教研究 religious studies;

[研磨] (1) grind; pestle; (2) abrade; polish; (3) lapping;
磨料研磨 abrasive lapping;
外圓研磨 cylindrical lapping;
壓緊研磨 cramp lapping;

[研求] examine into; explore; research and examine; study;

[研碎] grind to pieces;

[研討] deliberate; discuss;
研討會 seminar; symposium; workshop;
~ 投資研討會 investment seminar;
~ 專題研討會 symposium;

[研習] examine and study; learning; research and study;
研習會 seminar; workshop;

專題研習 project learning;
[研修] research and study;
[研製] develop; manufacture; prepare;
研製工作 development work;

調研 investigation and study;
科研 scientific research;
鑽研 study intensively;

yan
【焰】 a pronunciation of 焰;

yan
【揅】 (1) grind; powder; rub fine; (2) study thoroughly;
[揅經] study the classics;

yan
【筵】 (1) bamboo mat; (2) banquet; feast;
[筵席] (1) seats arranged at a banquet; (2) banquet; feast; (3) a mat for sitting on;
大擺筵席 make a feast; spread a feast;
肆筵疫席 entertain guests; set the table for guests;

綺筵 magnificent feast;
瓊筵 elaborate feast; luxurious dinner; sumptuous banquet;
盛筵 grand banquet; nosh-up; splendid meal; sumptuous dinner;
壽筵 birthday feast;
喜筵 wedding feast;

yan
【綖】 a hat's hanging flap in ancient times;

yan
【蜒】 dragonfly;

yan
【閻】 (1) gate of a lane; (2) a surname;
[閻君] King of Hell;
[閻羅] Yama, the King of Hades;
閻羅王 King of Hell;
去見閻羅王 meet your maker;
[閻王] (1) King of Hell; Yama; (2) extremely cruel and violent person;
閻王殿 Palace of Hell; Palace of the King of Hell;
閻王好見，小鬼難纏 better speak to the master than the man;
閻王好見，小鬼難當 the lackeys are even more difficult to deal with;
閻王下帖子—真要命 drive sb to his death; like the King of Hell dispatching invitation cards;
閻王爺的告示—鬼話連篇 ghostly words; like the King of Hell putting up a proclamation; pack of lies;
閻王帳 shark's loan; usurious loan;
活閻王 devil incarnate; tyrannical ruler;
見閻王 die; kick the bucket;

閭閻 common people; district inhabited by the common people;

yan
【檐】 (1) brim; (2) cornice; eaves of a house;
[檐溝] eaves gutters;
[檐子] eaves;

矮檐 low eave;
重檐 double-eaved roof;
房檐 eaves;
飛檐 overhanging eaves; upturned eaves;
廊檐 eaves of a veranda;
帽檐 brim of a hat;
屋檐 eaves;
斜挑檐 raking cornice;

yan
【顏】 (1) countenance; face; (2) prestige; reputation; (3) colours; dyes; (4) a surname;
[顏厚] (1) brazen; thick-skinned; unblushing; (2) shame-faced;
[顏料] colour; dyestuff; pigment;
顏料盒 paintbox;
複合顏料 composite pigment;
活性顏料 active pigment;
水彩顏料 watercolour;
酸性顏料 acid pigment;
調顏料 mix paints;
塗顏料 lay paint on;
一管顏料 a tube of paint;
一盒顏料 a box of paints;
製造顏料 make paints;
[顏貌] features; looks;
[顏面] (1) countenance; face; (2) face; honour; prestige;
顏面掃地 be thoroughly discredited; lose face altogether;
~覺得顏面掃地 feel publicly disgraced;
保全顏面 save face;
大失顏面 be utterly disgraced; make one lose face very badly;

［顏色］ (1) colour; hue; pigment; (2) countenance; facial expression;
顏色詞 colour term;
顏色很美 have beautiful coloration;
顏色淺 light in colour;
顏色形容詞 colour adjective;
顏色學 chromatics;
~顏色學家 chromatist;
顏色自若 calm in facial expression; composed in countenance;
暗淡的顏色 dim colour; dull colour; pale colour;
辨別顏色 distinguish between colours;
給顏色看 let sb have a taste of one's strength; show sb a thing or two;
加深顏色 darken the colour heighten the colour;
五顏六色 all the colours of the rainbow; of variegated colours; riotous with colour; varicoloured;

汗顏 blush with shame; feel deeply ashamed;
紅顏 beautiful woman; beauty;
厚顏 brazen; cheeky; thick-skinned;
歡顏 happy appearance; happy looks;
霽顏 calm down after a fit of anger;
開顏 beam; smile;
赧顏 be shamefaced; blush;
破顏 break into a smile;
強顏 (1) force a smile; (2) shameless;
秋顏 fading beauty;
容顏 facial appearance; looks;
弱顏 bashful;
盛顏 one's look in the prime of one's life;
衰顏 face of an old person;
靦顏 bashful; shy; timid;
童顏 ruddy complexion and hoary head;
溫顏 happy and agreeable look;
無顏 have no face to;
笑顏 smiling face;
怡顏 pleasant look; smiling;
玉顏 fair complexion;
朱顏 (1) beautiful face of a young lady; (2) beautiful face of a youth;
駐顏 preserve a youthful complexion; retaining youthful looks;

yan

【簷】 (1) eaves of a house; (2) edge of anything sloping downward;

［簷篷］ canopy;
懸臂式簷篷 cantilevered canopy;

［簷前］ front of the eaves;

［簷下］ under the eaves;

yan

【嚴】 (1) grave; grim; inclement; inexorable; relentless; rigid; rigorous; severe; solemn; stern; (2) reverence; (3) tight; (4) father; (5) a surname;

［嚴辦］ deal with severely; punish with severity; take a severe disciplinary measure against;
依法嚴辦 punish with severity according to law;

［嚴懲］ punish severely;
嚴懲不貸 punish mercilessly; punish severely without mercy; punish with severity; punish without leniency; severely punish;
嚴懲吸毒 lay a heavy penalty on drug taking;
嚴懲罪犯 impose a grave penalty on an offender;
按法嚴懲 mete out severe punishment according to the law;
得到嚴懲 bear a sad punishment;
給予嚴懲 administer stiff punishment;
受到嚴懲 be drastically punished;
逃脱嚴懲 escape grievous penalty;
需要嚴懲 demand severe discipline;

［嚴詞］ in stern words; in strong terms;
嚴詞反駁 give a strongly-worded refutation;
嚴詞拒絕 give a stern rebuff; refuse sternly; repudiate with stern words;
嚴詞譴責 condemn sternly; denounce in strong terms; fulminate against; make a stern denunciation of;
嚴詞申斥 give sb a lick with the rough side of one's tongue; rebuke in stern words;
嚴詞彈劾 condemn in strong terms; impeach in strong terms;
嚴詞痛斥 come down on sb like a load of bricks;
嚴詞責備 read the riot act;
嚴詞指責 rant;

［嚴慈］ father and mother;

［嚴冬］ arduous winter; severe winter; very cold winter;
嚴冬酷暑 in freezing winter or sweltering summer; through hot summer and

bitter winter;
嚴冬臘月 in harsh winter; in the dead of winter; it's now the twelfth month, the very middle of a bitterly cold winter;

[嚴防] guard carefully; remain vigilant; strictly on guard against; take strict precautions against;
嚴防火災 take strict precautions against fire;
嚴防洩密 exercise extreme caution of telling secrets;

[嚴父] (1) stern father; (2) my father;
嚴父慈母 a stern father and a compassionate mother; a severe father and a kind mother;

[嚴格] hard on sb; keep a strict hand on sb; rigid; rigorous; severe; stern to sb; strict; strict with sb; stringent;
嚴格判斷 severe in judgement;
嚴格說來 in the strict sense of the world; strictly speaking;

[嚴寒] bitter cold; killing freeze; freezing cold; severe cold;
嚴寒酷暑 bitter cold or torrid heat; in freezing winter and in sultry summer; on freezing winter days or broiling days in summer;

[嚴戢吏弊] put a stop to official abuses;

[嚴謹] (1) careful; cautious; not given to rashness; (2) rigorous; strict; (3) compact; well-knit;
方法嚴謹 adopt a rigorous approach;
說話嚴謹 cautious in speaking; exact in the use of words;
態度嚴謹 assume a studied attitude;
文風嚴謹 have a severe style of writing;

[嚴禁] clampdown; forbid strictly; prohibit strictly;
嚴禁吸煙 smoking is strictly prohibited;
嚴禁煙火 smoking and lighting fires strictly forbidden;

[嚴緊] close; rigorous; strict; tight;

[嚴究不貸] offender will be strictly prosecuted;

[嚴君] (1) stern father; (2) stern king;

[嚴竣] austere; grim; rigorous; severe; stern;
嚴竣考驗 severe test;

[嚴苛] harsh;

[嚴刻] exacting; harsh;

[嚴酷] (1) bitter; inclement; grim; harsh; severe; (2) cruel; ruthless;
嚴而不酷 strict but not stern;

[嚴冷] severe cold;

[嚴厲] ruthless; severe; stern; stringent;
嚴厲懲罰 have sb's hide;
嚴厲處理 handle without gloves;
嚴厲的 draconian;
嚴厲申斥 skin sb alive;
嚴厲制裁 apply severe sanctions; severe punishment;

[嚴令] order strictly; strict order;
嚴密 accurate; close; exact; narrow; precise; rigid; rigorous; strict; tidy; tight;
嚴密防範 take strict precautions against;
嚴密防守 guard carefully;
嚴密防衛 tight defense;
嚴密封鎖 impose a tight blockade;
嚴密關注 watch with the deepest concern;
嚴密監視 keep close watch over; put under close surveillance;
嚴密看守 keep watch and ward;
嚴密注視 closely follow; keep a sharp look-out;

[嚴明] strict and impartial;
紀律嚴明 observe strict discipline;
軍紀嚴明 maintain severe military discipline;

[嚴命] (1) strict order; (2) order from one's father;

[嚴判] severe judgment;

[嚴親] father;

[嚴師] severe teacher; stern teacher; strict teacher;
嚴師出高徒 a strict teacher produces outstanding students; capable are pupils trained by strict masters;
嚴師畏友 a severe teacher and an esteemed friend; a stern teacher and a friend of high moral character;

[嚴飭] order strictly;

[嚴守] strictly abide; strictly observe;
嚴守崗位 keep the post;
嚴守合同 abide staunchly by a contract;
嚴守規則 toe the line;
嚴守秘密 maintain strict secrecy;
嚴守諾言 unswervingly faithful to one's promise;
嚴守時間 as punctual as the clock;
嚴守時刻 punctual to the minute;
嚴守陣地 uphold the position;

嚴守中立 adhere to neutrality; observe stiff neutrality; remain a neutral strictly;

[嚴絲合縫] dovetail; fit together perfectly; join tightly;

[嚴肅] (1) earnest; grave; gravitas; serious; solemn; (2) serious-looking; (3) enforce;

嚴肅批評 criticize with sharp words;

嚴肅認真 serious and conscientious; strict and conscientious; with the attitude of being serious and conscientious;

嚴肅文學 serious literature;

嚴肅音樂 classical music; heavy music;

表情嚴肅 have a serious mien;

[嚴細] strict and careful;

[嚴刑] cruel torture; severe punishments;

嚴刑逼供 extort a confession from sb by torture; extract confession by torture; interrogate sb under torture to exact a confession;

嚴刑竣法 draconian laws; harsh laws and severe punishments; severe punishment under strict laws;

嚴刑拷打 beat up cruelly; subject sb to severe torture; torture sb cruelly;

[嚴嚴地] closely; tightly;

[嚴以律己] exercise strict self-discipline; strict with oneself;

嚴以律己，寬以待人 forgive others but not yourself; forgive others often, yourself never; pardon all but thyself; strict with oneself and broad-minded towards others;

[嚴陣以待] be prepared to meet the challenge; in combat readiness; in full array; in full battle array; ready in full battle array; remain in combat readiness; stand ready in battle array; wait in full battle array;

[嚴整] in neat formation; well-disciplined;

[嚴正] rigorous; serious and principled; solemn and just; stern; strictly correct;

持身嚴正 very exacting with regard to one's personal conduct;

義正辭嚴 fairness in principle and severity in speech; in categorical terms; in no uncertain terms; solemn and just; speak sternly out of a sense of justice; speak with the force of justice;

[嚴重] critical; grave; serious; severe;

嚴重錯誤 serious error;

~發現嚴重錯誤 detect a serious error;

~犯嚴重錯誤 make a bad mistake;

嚴重打擊 hard knock;

~受到嚴重打擊 get a hard knock;

嚴重犯罪 commit a grave crime;

嚴重分歧 serious fissure in a party;

嚴重後果 serious consequences;

嚴重事故 nasty accident;

~避免嚴重事故 avoid a nasty accident;

嚴重違法 violate the law grossly;

形勢嚴重 grave situation;

[嚴妝] in formal attire;

[嚴裝] dress neatly and properly;

從嚴 on the strict side;

家嚴 my father;

解嚴 declare martial law ended; life a curfew;

戒嚴 be placed under martial law; cordon off an area; enforce martial law; impose a curfew;

謹嚴 careful and precise;

妻管嚴 henpecked;

綦嚴 very severe; very stringent;

森嚴 (1) forbidding; stern; (2) close; tight;

挺嚴 rather stiff; very strict;

威嚴 dignified; dignity; majestic; prestige;

先嚴 my deceased father;

莊嚴 solemn; stately;

嘴嚴 able to keep a secret; capable of keeping secrets; cautious about speech; discreet in speech;

尊嚴 dignified; dignity; sanctity;

yan

【巖】 (1) crag; rock; (2) cave;

[巖洞] mountain cave;

[巖居穴處] (1) live in mountain caves; (2) live in seclusion;

[巖穴] cave; cavern;

yan

【鹽】 (1) salt; (2) envy;

[鹽盒] salt cellar;

[鹽井] salt mine; salt well;

[鹽水] brine; saltwater;

鹽水消毒 disinfect with saltwater;

飽和鹽水 saturated brine;

充氧鹽水 ammoniacal brine;

廢鹽水 depleted brine;

黃瓜鹽水 cucumber brine;

浸漬鹽水 immersion brine;

冷卻鹽水 refrigerated brine;
冷卻用鹽水 cooling brine;
濃鹽水 strong brine;
淡鹽水 light salt brine;
天然鹽水 natural brine;
脱汞鹽水 mercury-depleted brine;
稀鹽水 weak brine;
增濃鹽水 fortifying brine;
製冷鹽水 refrigerating brine;
注射鹽水 pumping brine;

胺鹽 amine salt;
熬鹽 make salt by boiling sea water;
池鹽 lake salt;
赤血鹽 potassium ferricyanide; red prussiate of potash;
醋酸鹽 acetate;
大鹽 crude salt;
碘鹽 iodate;
複鹽 double salt;
硅酸鹽 silicate;
海鹽 sea salt;
湖鹽 lake salt;
黃血鹽 yellow prussiate of potash;
磺酸鹽 sulphonate;
鉀鹽 sylvite;
鹼式鹽 basic salt;
椒鹽 spiced salt;
精鹽 refined salt; table salt;
井鹽 well salt;
礦鹽 halite; rock salt;
磷酸鹽 phosphate;
硫酸鹽 sulphate;
絡鹽 complex salt;
硼酸鹽 borate;
榷鹽 levy salt taxes;
食鹽 salt; table salt;
酸式鹽 acid salt;
鉈鹽 thallium salt;
鉭酸鹽 tantalite;
碳酸鹽 carbonate;
銻酸鹽 stibate; stibiate;
鐵鹽 molysite;
脱鹽 desalinate;
無機鹽 inorganic salts;
硝酸鹽 nitrate;
瀉鹽 Epsoms salts;
岩鹽 halite; rock salt;
一匙鹽 a spoon of salt;
一撮鹽 a pinch of salt;
一袋鹽 a bag of salt;
一瓦罐鹽 a clay jar of salt;

營養鹽 nutrient salt;
原鹽 crude salt;
在傷口上抹鹽 rub salt into the wound;
正鹽 normal salt;
中式鹽 neutral salt;
中性鹽 neutral salt;
重氮鹽 diazonium salt;

yan³

yan

【沇】 flowing and engulfing; overflowing and brimming;

yan

【奄】 (1) cover; overspread; surround; (2) abruptly; all of a sudden; rapidly; suddenly; (3) a surname;

［奄忽］ abrutpy; quickly; suddenly;
［奄有］ put under one's control;

yan

【兗】 one of the states in ancient times;

yan

【衍】 (1) develop; overflow; spread out; (2) ample; plenty and abundant; (3) level; plain and even; (4) lake; marsh; (5) slope; (6) redundant; superfluous; (7) bamboo box; (8) a surname;

［衍變］ develop; develop and change; evolve;
［衍射］ diffract; diffraction;
衍射光柵 diffraction grating;
衍射條紋 diffraction fringe;
超聲波光學衍射 ultrasonic light diffraction;
縫隙衍射 diffraction by slit;
晶體衍射 crystal diffraction;
近焦衍射 microscopic diffraction;
聲的衍射 sonic diffraction;
遠焦衍射 telescopic diffraction;
［衍生］ derive from;
衍生物 derivative;
［衍文］ interpolations; redundancies owing to misprinting;
［衍衍］ walk fast;
衍衍清泉 flowing is the clear spring;
［衍繹］ elaborate; expound;

奧衍 deep; profound;
蕃衍 increase gradually in number or quantity; multiply;
繁衍 multiply;
敷衍 expound; go through the motions; narrate

and elaborate; perfunctory; skimp; whitewash;
平衍 open and flat;
篋衍 bamboo box;
沃衍 fertile area;
孳衍 multiply;

yan

【弇】 (1) narrow-necked container; (2) cover; (3) profound;

［弇陋］ have meagre knowledge;

yan

【偃】 (1) fall on one's back; lay down; lie on one's back; (2) earthern bank; embankment; (3) at rest; cease; desist; lay off; stop; suppress; (4) a surname;

［偃兵］ stop a military action;

［偃蹇］ (1) arrogant; (2) sit idle on the pretext of being ill;

［偃仆］ fall down flat; fall on one's back;

［偃鼠］ mole;

［偃臥］ lie on one's back;

［偃月］ crescent moon;

yan

【掩】 (1) conceal; cover; cover up; hide; (2) close; shut; (3) get squeezed while shutting a door, lid, etc.; (4) catch by surprise; launch a surprise attack; take by surprise;

［掩鼻］ cover one's nose;
掩鼻而嚐 hold one's breath while eating;
掩鼻而過 cover the nose and hurry away; cover the nose and pass by; hold one's nose and pass by; pass by holding one's nose;

［掩蔽］ conceal; cover; hide; masking; screen; shelter; take cover;
反向掩蔽 backward masking;
利用掩蔽 take cover;
射束掩蔽 beam masking;
聲掩蔽 audio masking;
找到掩蔽 find cover;

［掩不住］ cannot shut out; unable to cover; unable to hide;

［掩藏］ conceal; hide;

［掩耳］ plug one's ears;
掩耳不聞 close one's ear to; turn a deaf ear to;
掩耳盜鈴 bury one's head in the sand; close up one's own ears and steal a bell; run away from one's own shadow; stuff the ears when stealing a bell — self-deceit; the cat shuts its eyes when stealing cream; the cat shuts its eyes while it steals cream;

［掩蓋］ blanket; cloak; conceal; cover; cover up; enshroud; shroud;
掩蓋本領 blanket power;
掩蓋錯誤 cover up one's fault;
掩蓋行蹤 cover up one's tracks;
掩蓋真相 cover up the facts;
掩蓋罪行 maks one's guilt;

［掩護］ (1) cover; screen; shield; (2) camouflage;

［掩擊］ mount a surprise attack; waylay;

［掩卷］ close books; stop reading;

［掩口］ cover one's mouth with one's hand;
掩口而笑 hide one's smile; laugh in secret; put one's hand to one's mouth to hide one's laughter;

［掩埋］ bury; entomb;

［掩門］ close the door; shut the door;

［掩面］ cover one's face;
掩面哀泣 cover one's face and cry sadly;
掩面大哭 cover up one's face and begin to weep; bide one's face and sob bitterly;
掩面而泣 cover one's face and weep; put one's finger in one's eye;
掩面失色 cover one's eyes and turn pale;
掩面嗚咽 bury one's face in one's hands and begin to weep;
掩面遮羞 hide one's shame by screening one's face;
雙手掩面 bury one's face in one's hands;

［掩目捕雀］ catch birds with one's eyes closed; self-deceit;

［掩泣］ cover one's face and weep; weep silently;

［掩殺］ attack by surprise; make a surprise attack; pounce on;

［掩上］ shut;

［掩飾］ (1) camouflage; cloak; conceal; cover up; cover-up; gloss over; put a good face on; (2) deception;
掩飾驚恐 hide one's fear;
掩飾自己過失 cover one's mistakes;
毫不掩飾 make no bones about; make no secret of; not mince words; totally undisguised; undisguisedly;

［掩襲］ mount a surprise attack;

［掩眼法］ camouflage; cover-up;
［掩隱］ hide away;
［掩映］ set off;

虛掩 leave the door unlocked or unlatched;
遮掩 (1) cover; envelop; (2) conceal; hide;

yan

【眼】 (1) eye; (2) glance; look; (3) aperture; opening; orifice; small hole; tiny hole; (4) key point;
［眼癌］ eye cancer;
［眼巴巴］ (1) with steady gaze; (2) anxiously; eagerly; expectantly; (3) helplessly;
［眼白］ white of the eye;
［眼波］ bright-eyed; eyesight; fluid glance; vision;
［眼不見］ what eyes do not see;
眼不見為淨 out of sight, out of mind; what eyes do not see is regarded as clean; what the eye doesn't see, the heart doesn't grieve over; what the eye sees not, the heart rues not;
眼不見，心不煩 one who avoids seeing trouble does not have to worry about trouble; what the eye doesn't see the heart doesn't grieve over;
眼不見，心不想 far from eye, far from heart; out of sight, out of mind;
［眼岔］ mistake one for another;
［眼饞］ covet; envious;
眼饞饞 watch enviously;
眼饞肚飽 the eye is bigger than the belly;
［眼眵］ gum;
［眼穿］ await anxiously; expect eagerly;
［眼大心肥］ proud and arrogant;
［眼袋］ under-eye bags;
割眼袋 have one's under-eye bags removed;
［眼底］ (1) right before one's eyes; (2) at present;
盡收眼底 have a panoramic view;
［眼兒］ (1) eye; (2) orifice; tiny hole;
［眼福］ a feast to the eye; delight to the eye; joy to the eye; the good fortune of seeing sth rare or beautiful;
眼福不淺 lucky enough to see; not a shallow delight to the eye;
飽享眼福 enjoy the sight to one's great satisfaction; feast one's eyes on;
飽眼福 feast one's eyes on;
～大飽眼福 feast one's eyes; glut one's eyes;
～一飽眼福 enjoy watching sth to the full; feast one's eyes on sth; feed one's sight; glut one's eyes;
［眼高手低］ conceited but incompetent; fastidious but incompetent; have grandiose aims but puny abilities; have great aims but poor ability; have high ambition but low ability; have high standards but little ability; have sharp eyes but clumsy hands; high in aim but lowrate in execution; one's ability doesn't match one's high goal; pursue an aim far beyond one's reach;
［眼高心傲］ have a haughty look and a proud heart;
［眼觀鼻，鼻觀心］ sit quietly without looking sideways;
［眼觀六路］ keep one's eyes over;
眼觀六路，耳聽八方 have sharp eyes and keen ears; keep one's eyes and ears open — extraordinarily alert; observant and alert;
［眼光］ (1) eye; foresight; insight; sight; vision; (2) the way of looking at things; view;
眼光短淺 short-sighted;
眼光寬廣 bread of view;
眼光敏銳 have sharp eyes;
眼光銳利 have an eye in one's head;
眼光遠大 far-sighted; have a broad vision;
非難的眼光 disapproving eye;
老眼光 old views; old ways of looking at things; out-dated views;
敏銳的眼光 acute eyesight;
同情的眼光 sympathetic eye;
有眼光 have good taste;
～有眼光的 clear-sighted; discerning;
［眼黑］ avarice; greedy;
［眼紅］ (1) covet; envious; jealous; (2) angry; furious; (3) red-eyed;
［眼花］ dim of sight; dizzy; giddy; have blurred vision; have dim eyesight;
眼花兒 apple of one's eye; darling;
眼花繚亂 be dazzled; bedazzlement; dazzle one's eyes; in a daze; see things in a blur;
眼花心亂 one's eyes are not clear and one's heart confused;

老眼昏花 dim-sighted from old age;
目眩眼花 dazed and blurred;
頭昏眼花 cutting out paper dolls; dazed; dizzy; feel dizzy and with eyesight dimmed; light-headed; mentally confused; one's head begins to swim and one's eyes were misted; punck-drunk; see stars; slap-happy; with head giddy and eyes dazzled

[眼肌] eye muscles;
眼肌病 ocular myopathy;
眼肌癱瘓 ophtalmoplegia;
眼肌炎 ophthalmomyositis;

[眼積水] hydrophthalmos;
全眼積水 hydrophthalmos totalis;

[眼疾] (1) eye ailment; eye disease; eye trouble; (2) keen-eyed;
眼疾手快 sharp eyes and agile hands;
眼疾嘴快 keen-eyed and quick-witted; quick of eye and deft of beak;

[眼尖] quick of sight; sharp-eyed;

[眼瞼] eyelid;
眼瞼功能不全 insufficiency of the eyelids;
眼瞼痙攣 blepharospasm;
眼瞼下垂 ptosis;
眼瞼炎 blepharitis;
~邊緣性眼瞼炎 blear eye;

[眼見] what one sees;
眼見為實 seeing is believing; what you see is true;

[眼角] corner of the eye;
眼角含情 gaze at sb with tenderness;

[眼睫毛] eyelashes;

[眼界] outlook; one's field of vision;
眼界高 have one's standard set high;
大開眼界 eye-opener; eye-opening; feed one's sight on; get an eyeful; have an eyeful; widen one's horizon;
廣開眼界 broaden one's field of vision; one's field of vision is vastly enlarged; widen one's horizon;
開闊眼界 broaden one's outlook; broaden one's horizons; widen one's field of vision;
開眼界 enrich one's experience; see the world; widen one's horizon; widen one's vision;
~開開眼界 broaden one's vision;

[眼鏡] eyeglass; eyewear; glasses; spectacles;
眼鏡盒 case for glasses; glasses case; spectacle case;
眼鏡猴 tarsier;
眼鏡腳 spectacle side;
眼鏡鏈 spectacle-string;
眼鏡鋪子 optician's shop;
眼鏡框 spectacle frame;
眼鏡橋 spectacle bridge;
眼鏡蛇 cobra;
眼鏡王蛇 king cobra;
眼鏡熊 spectacled bear;
保護眼鏡 protective spectacles;
變色眼鏡 chameleon;
戴眼鏡 wear spectacles;
~戴上眼鏡 put on one's glasses;
~戴眼鏡的 bespectacled;
戴着眼鏡找眼鏡 had it been a bear it would have bitten you;
單片眼鏡 eyeglass; monocle;
防毒眼鏡 gas-protection goggles;
防護眼鏡 protective goggles;
黑眼鏡 sunglasses;
夾鼻眼鏡 pince-nez;
金邊眼鏡 gold-rimmed glasses;
近視眼鏡 glasses for the short-sighted;
老花眼鏡 presbyopic glasses;
配眼鏡 have one's eyesight tested for glasses;
散光眼鏡 glasses for the astigmatic;
雙光眼鏡 bifocal glasses; bifocals;
太陽眼鏡 dark glasses;
望遠式眼鏡 telescopic spectacles;
無框眼鏡 rimless glasses;
一副眼鏡 a pair of glasses; a pair of spectacles;
隱形眼鏡 contact lens;
~戴隱形眼鏡 wear contact lens;
有色眼鏡 tinted glasses;
遠視眼鏡 glasses for the far-sighted;
摘下眼鏡 take off one's glasses;

[眼睛] eye;
眼睛凹陷 hollow-eyed;
眼睛熬紅 one's eyes are bloodshot from lack of sleep;
眼睛白瞪 roll one's eyes in fury;
眼睛朝下看 throw one's eyes to the ground;
眼睛充血 one's eyes became bloodshot;
眼睛發定 with staring eyes;
眼睛翻白 turn up the whites of one's eyes;
眼睛紅紅 with bloodshot eyes;
眼睛尖 have all one's eyes about one;
眼睛檢查 eye examination; eye test;
~全面眼睛檢 comprehensive eye

examination;
眼睛哭紅 one's eyes are red from crying;
眼睛哭腫 cry one's eyes out;
眼睛冒火 be in an angry mood; one's eyes flash fire;
眼睛眯縫 laugh till one's eyes are slits;
眼睛疲勞 eyestrain;
眼睛凸出的 bugeyed;
眼睛向上翻 turn up one's eyes;
眼睛向下 cast one's sights on the masses;
眼睛雪亮 have a discerning eye;
眼睛一瞬 a twinkling of the eye; in the twinkling of an eye;
眼睛長在頭頂上 be too haughty; have one's eyes at the top of one's head;
愛護眼睛 protect one's eyes;
擦亮眼睛 become more clear-sighted; heighten one's viligance; keep one's eyes skinned; keep one's eyes wide open; on the outlook; remove the scales from one's eyes; sharpen one's vigilance; wide the dust from one's eyes;
擦眼睛 wipe one's eyes;
瞪大眼睛 open one's eyes wide;
~瞪大眼睛的 goggle-eyed;
~瞪大眼睛看 goggle;
瞪眼睛 goggle one's eyes; with dilated eyes;
~氣得瞪眼睛 roll one's eyes in fury;
垂下眼睛 cast one's eyes down; lower one's eyes;
發亮的眼睛 beamy eyes;
費眼睛 try one's eyes;
火眼金睛 penetrating insight; piercing eye;
哭腫了眼睛 cry one's eyes out;
藍眼睛 blue eyes;
累眼睛 weary one's eyes;
瞇起一隻眼睛 narrow one's eye;
眯眼睛 narrow one's eyes;
瞇上眼睛 close one's eyes;
揉眼睛 rub one's eyes;
挖眼睛 gouge out eyes;
捣上眼睛 cover up one's eyes;
一雙美麗的眼睛 lovely eyes;
一雙眼睛 a pair of eyes;
一隻眼睛 an eye;
眨眼睛 bat; blink; blink one's eyes;
~眨一下眼睛 bat an eye; give sb a wink; wink;
睜大眼睛 open one's eyes wide;
睜開眼睛 open one's eyes;

[眼看] (1) imminent; in a moment; soon; (2) see sth happening; (3) look on passively; watch helplessly;

[眼科] ophthalmology;
眼科學 ophthalmology;
眼科醫生 eye doctor; oculist; ophthalmologist;
眼科醫師 oculist;
眼科醫院 hospital of ophthalmology;

[眼孔] eyelet; orifice;

[眼庫] eye bank;

[眼寬人熟] sociable;

[眼眶] (1) eye socket; orbit; (2) rim of the eye;
眼眶凹陷 sunken eyes;

[眼淚] eyedrops; tears; waterwork;
眼淚包 be easily reduced to tears;
眼淚鼻涕 shed streams of tears and mucus; the waterworks begin to play; weeping and sniffling;
眼淚涔涔 drip with tears; in a flood of tears; one's eyes water;
眼淚橫流 stream with tears;
眼淚哭乾 cry until one has no more tears to shed; weep until one's tears run dry;
眼淚滿眶 the tears are filling one's eyes;
眼淚迷蒙 one's eyes are dim with tears; one's eyes are misted with tears;
眼淚如雨 one's tears fall like rain;
眼淚上湧 tears come into one's eyes; tears rise to one's eyes; tears start to one's eyes; the tears gush to one's eyes;
眼淚簌簌 one's tears fall fast; tears streaming down;
眼淚汪汪 eyes brimming with tears; full of tears; having eyes damp with tears; in tears; one's eyes are moist with tears; one's eyes drown in tears; one's eyes is filled with tears; one's eyes swim in tears; tears well up in one's eyes; with eyes swimming in tears; with tearful eyes;
眼淚洗面 one's face is bathed in tears; tears rain down one's cheeks; wash one's face with tears; with tears all over one's face;
眼淚笑出 laugh till one's tears come;
眼淚淹面 be bathed in tears;
眼淚盈眶 one's eyes fill with tears; tears fill the eyes; tears gush from one's eyes; tears spring into one's eyes;

tears standing in the eyes; tears suffuse one's eyes;
眼淚湧湧 dash the tears from one's eyes;
眼淚欲滴 tears are very near to one's eyes; tears well from one's eyes; tears well up in one's eyes;
眼淚直淌 burst into a flood of tears; tears are welling from one's eyes;
白流眼淚 waste one's tears;
憋住眼淚 fight back tears;
擦乾眼淚 wipe one's eyes;
感動得流眼淚 be softened into tears;
含着眼淚 have tears in one's eyes; in tears; with tears in one's eyes;
揩眼淚 wipe away tears;
哭乾眼淚 cry until one has no more tears to shed;
流眼淚 shed tears;
流下辛酸的眼淚 weep bitter tears;
流下眼淚 reduce sb to tears;
抹去眼淚 wipe away one's tears;
忍不住掉眼淚 cannot restrain one's tears;
忍住眼淚 choke down one's tears; fight back tears; keep back one's tears;
淌眼淚 pipe one's tears; shed tears;
淌眼淚 in tears; shed tears;
~淌眼抹淚 cry; weep;
笑出眼淚 laugh till one cries; laugh till the tears come; laugh till the tears roll down one's cheeks;
辛酸的眼淚 bitter tears;
一滴眼淚 a drop of tear; a tear;
一眶眼淚 tearful;
一陣眼淚 a burst of tears;

[眼力] (1) eyesight; vision; (2) discerning ability; discrimination; judgment; power of judgment;
眼力不錯 have good taste and good eyes;
眼力差 have poor eyesight;
眼力過人 person of excellent judgement;
好眼力 have good eyesight;
訓練眼力 train one's eye;
有眼力 have a discerning eye;

[眼裏] in one's eyes; within one's vision;
不在眼裏 beneath one's notice; have no respect for; show one's contempt for; snap one's fingers at; think nothing of; treat with disdain;
~不放在眼裏 beneath one's notice; make light of sth; not consider sth worthy of one's attention;
看在眼裏 notice sth out of the corner of one's eye; watch sth with the tail of one's eye;
~看在眼裏，記在心裏 bear in mind what one sees; see and heed;

[眼簾] iris;
進入眼簾 meet one's eyes;
垂下眼簾 one's eyes sink;
躍入眼簾 leap out at;
映入眼簾 catch one's eye; greet one's eye; strike one's eye;

[眼亮] clear-sighted; sharp-sighted;

[眼眉] brow;
直眉瞪眼 be stupefied; fume; in a daze; look angry; stare blankly; stare in anger;

[眼明] sharp-eyed;
眼明手快 clearly discerning, swift-handed; nimble; one's eye is clear and one's hand swift; quick of eye and deft of hand; see things clearly and act speedily; sharp of sight and quick of hand; sharp-eyed and quick-moving;
眼明心亮 see and think clearly; sharp-eyed and clear-headed;
氣平眼明 an even temper makes for a clear sight;
嘴閉眼明 keep the mouth shut and the eyes open;

[眼目] (1) eyes; (2) serve as the eye of another; spy;
迷人眼目 confuse the eyes of the people; fool people; pull the wool over sb's eyes; throw dust in sb's eyes;
眼豎目橫 stare in anger or contempt;
以娛眼目 please the eye;

[眼泡] upper eyelid;
腫眼泡 bags under one's eyes;

[眼皮] eyelids;
眼皮底下 under one's eyes; under the nose of sb;
眼皮打架 cannot keep one's eyes open;
眼皮直跳 one's eyes keep twitching;
錯翻眼皮 turn a wrong eyelid;
單眼皮 single-fold eyelid;
哭腫眼皮 cry one's eyes out;
上眼皮 upper eyelid;
雙眼皮 double-fold eyelid;
下眼皮 lower eyelid;

[眼前] (1) before one's eyes; (2) at present; at the moment; now;

禍在眼前 misfortune is before one's very eyes;
近在眼前 at hand; imminent; right before one's eyes; right here under one's nose;
~ 近在眼前卻又遙不可及 so near and yet so far;
眼面前的事 daily things; everyday events;

[眼球] bulb of the eye; eyeball;
眼球突出 proptosis;
~ 搏動性眼球突出 pulsating exophthalmos;
眼球炎 ophthalmitis;
~ 全眼球炎 panophthalmitis;
大眼球 macrophthalmia;

[眼圈] eye socket; rim of the eye;
黑眼圈 dark circles under one's eyes;

[眼熱] covet; envious;

[眼如水杏] one's eyes are like almonds swimming in water;

[眼色] a cue given with the eyes; a hint given with the eyes; expression of one's eyes; meaningful glance; wink;
遞眼色 dart a meaning look at sb; hint with the eyes; tip sb the wink; wink at sb;
丟眼色 give a hint with the eyes; give sb a wink; tip sb the wink; wink at sb;
~ 丟個眼色 give a hint with the eyes; tip sb the wink;
看眼色 ready to take hint;
沒眼色 inconsiderate; unable to see the fitness of things;
施以眼色 give sb the wink; shoot at sb a meaning glance; shoot sb a warning glance;
使眼色 say sth with eyes; shoot sb a warning glance;

[眼神] (1) expression in one's eyes; gleams of the eyes; light; (2) eyesight;
眼神不濟 have poor eyesight;
咄咄迫人的眼神 withering look;
一絲失望的眼神 a flicker of disappointment;

[眼生] look unfamiliar; unfamiliar by sight;

[眼屎] gum in the eyes; secretions of the eyes;

[眼手] hands and eyes;
眼到手到 take down notes while reading;
眼快手疾 quick of eye and deft of hand;

[眼熟] look familiar; seem to know; seemingly familiar by sight;

[眼跳] twitching of the eyelid;
眼跳心驚 nervous apprehension;

[眼同] together with;

[眼痛] eye strain;

[眼窩] eye socket; orbit;

[眼下] at present; at the moment; currently; for the moment; now;

[眼線] (1) eyeliner; (2) police informer;
眼線筆 eyeliner pencil;
眼線液 eyeliner;

[眼壓] intraocular pressure; intraocular tension;
眼壓計 tonometer;
正常眼壓 normal intraocular tension;

[眼炎] ophthalmia;
觸染性眼炎 contagious ophthalmia;
傳染性眼炎 infectious ophthalmia;
春季眼炎 spring ophthalmia;
感光眼炎 photophthalmia;
結節性眼炎 ophthalmia nodosa;
卡他性眼炎 catarrhal ophthalmia;
顆粒性眼炎 granular ophthalmia;
淋病性眼炎 gonorrheal ophthalmia;
膿性眼炎 ophthalmoblennorrhea;
泡性眼炎 phlyctenular ophthalmia;
皮膚眼炎 dermato-ophthalmitis;
濕疹性眼炎 ophthalmia eczematosa;
銅屑眼炎 chalkitis;
新生兒眼炎 adenologaditis;
周期性眼炎 periodic ophthalmia;
轉移性眼炎 metastatic ophthalmia;

[眼藥] eye ointment; eyedrops;
眼藥膏 eye ointment;
~ 上眼藥膏 apply eye ointment to the eyes;
眼藥水 eyedrops; eyewash; eyewater;
~ 點眼藥水 put drops in the eyes;

[眼翳] mist;

[眼影] eye shadow;
眼影粉 eye shadow powder;

[眼暈] (1) halo; (2) feel dizzy;
青光眼暈 glaucomatous halo;
覺得眼暈 feel dizzy;

[眼罩] blind pack; blinder; blinker; eye patch; eyeshade;

[眼震] nystagmus;
擺動性眼震 pendular nystagmus;
繼發性眼震 secondary nystagmus;
假眼震 pseudonystagmus;
迷路性眼震 labyrinthine nystagmus;

弱視性眼震 amblyopic nystagmus;
視動性眼震 opticokinetic nystagmus;
隨意性眼震 voluntary nystagmus;
眼病性眼震 ocular nystagmus;
隱性眼震 latent nystagmus;
振動性眼震 vibratory nystagmus;
自發性眼震 spontaneous nystagmus;

[眼睜睜] (1) in broad daylight; openly; publicly; right before one's eyes; (2) unfeelingly; watch helplessly; (3) attentive; watchful;

[眼中釘] a thorn in the flesh; eyesore;
眼中釘—拔掉了才舒坦 thorn in one's flesh;
眼中釘，肉中刺 thorn in one's flesh;
拔除眼中釘 pull out the thorn in one's flesh;
拔去眼中釘 pull out the sting in one's eye; remove a person one hates most;

[眼中人] loved one; person after one's heart;

[眼珠] eyeball;
有眼無珠 as blind as a bat; eyes and no eyes; have eyes but fail to see; have eyes without eyeballs – have eyes but see not; have two slits for eyes but cannot see; lack discerning power;

礙眼 (1) inconvenience; stand in the way; (2) eyesore; offend the eye; unpleasant to look at; unpleasant to the eye;
凹眼 (1) sunken eyes; (2) celophthalmia;
昂眼 bungeye;
巴白眼 (1) whites of the eyes; (2) contemptuous look; supercilious look; (3) contempt; disdain;
板眼 (1) measure in traditional Chinese music; (2) orderliness;
背眼 where one cannot easily be seen;
閉眼 close one's eyes;
碧眼 blue-eyed;
鼻子眼 nostril;
刺眼 (1) dazzling; (2) offending to the eye; unpleasant to look at;
打眼 (1) attract attention; catch the eye; (2) beautiful; good-looking; (3) drill; punch a hole;
單眼 simple eye;
擋眼 obstruct one's view;
瞪眼 (1) open one's eyes wide; stare; (2) get angry with sb; glower and glare at sb;
電眼 (1) electric eye; magic eye; (2) tuning eye;
鬥眼 cross-eyed;
獨眼 one-eyed;
對眼 (1) cross-eye; internal strabismus; (2) to one's liking; to one's taste;
二五眼 (1) inferior ability; inferior quality; (2) incompetent person;
放眼 take a broad view;
飛眼 make eyes; ogle;
複眼 compound eye;
乾瞪眼 look on in despair; stand by anxiously, unable to help;
溝眼 opening of sewers;
過眼 look over;
害眼 have eye trouble;
紅眼 (1) bloodshot eye; pinkeye; (2) jealous of sb; (3) become infuriated; see red;
花眼 presbyopia;
晃眼 dazzlingly bright;
慧眼 discerning eye; insight;
火眼 pink eye;
雞眼 corn; clavus;
假眼 ocular prosthesis;
節骨眼 critical juncture; vital link;
近視眼 myopia;
巨眼 macrophthalmia;
開眼 add to one's experience; broaden one's mind; broaden one's view; enrich one's experience; open one's eyes; open one's mental horizon; see new things; see the world; widen one's horizons; widen one's view;
孔眼 eyelet;
扣眼 buttonhole;
睞著眼 blinking one's eyes;
老花眼 presbyopia;
老視眼 presbyopia;
淚眼 tearful eyes;
冷眼 (1) unemotional, objective attitude; (2) indifferent reception;
兩眼 one's eyes;
龍眼 longan;
滿眼 (1) have one's eyes filled with; (2) meet the eye on every side;
猫眼 cat's eye;
卯眼 mortise;
眉眼 eye and brow; features; looks;
媚眼 seductive eyes;
蒙眼 blindfold;
砲眼 (1) porthole; (2) blasthole; borehole;
礮眼 (1) embrasure; (2) borehole; dynamite hole;
屁眼 butthole;
起眼 attract attention; striking;

氣眼 (1) air hole; (2) gas hole;
千里眼 (1) far-sighted person; (2) field glasses;
槍眼 (1) loophole; (2) bullet hole;
親眼 personally; with one's own eyes;
青光眼 glaucoma;
青眼 favour; good graces;
覷著眼 narrow one's eyes and gaze at sth with great attention;
泉眼 mouth of a spring;
人造眼 visilog;
肉眼 naked eye;
入眼 agreeable to look at; pleasing to the eye; to one's liking;
鋭眼 keen-sighted; sharp-eyed;
沙眼 trachoma;
砂眼 sand holes;
傻眼 be dumbfounded; be stunned;
霎眼 wink;
上眼 worth looking at;
實心眼 have a one-track mind;
勢利眼 snob; snobbish;
手眼 artifice; trick;
鼠眼 (1) small, protruding eyes; (2) lack of foresight;
豎眼 angry looks;
雙眼 eyes;
睡眼 sleepy eyes;
順眼 pleasing to the eye;
死心眼 obstinate; stubborn;
榫眼 mortise;
鎖眼 work buttonholes;
挑眼 fastidious;
偷眼 steal a glance;
網眼 mesh;
顯眼 conspicuous; showy;
現眼 lose face; make a fool of oneself;
小心眼 narrow-minded;
斜眼 (1) strabismus; (2) cross-eyed; (3) cross-eyed person;
心眼 (1) heart; mind; (2) intention; (3) tolerance;
虛字眼 form word; function word;
芽眼 eye;
腰眼 either side of the small of the back;
耀眼 dazzling;
賊眼 furtive glance; shifty eyes;
扎眼 dazzling; garish; loud; offending to the eye;
眨眼 twinkle; wink;
招眼 attractive;
針眼 (1) eye of a needle; (2) pinprick;
直心眼 frank; straightforward;
轉眼 in an instant; in the twinkling of an eye;
着眼 consider in a certain aspect; see from the angle of;
字眼 choice of words; diction; wording;
走眼 midjudge; mistake;
醉眼 eyes showing the effects of drink;

yan
【鄢】 a county in Henan;

yan
【揜】 (1) rob; take by force; (2) conceal; cover up; (3) shut;

yan
【渰】 (of clouds) form; rise;

yan
【琰】 glitter of gems;

yan
【演】 (1) develop; evolve; (2) elaborate; expound; (3) act; perform; play; (4) exercise; practise;

[演變] develop; develop and change; evolve;
社會的演變 social evolution;

[演播] broadcast; telecast;
演播室 broadcast studio; studio;
~ 播出演播室 broadcast studio;
~ 彩色電視演播室 colour television studio;
~ 特技演播室 effects studio;

[演唱] sing in a performance;
演唱歌曲 give song recitals;
演唱技巧 vocal techniques;

[演出] perform a play; put on a play; put on a show; show;
演出單位 producer;
演出隊 performance troupe;
~ 業餘演出隊 amateur performance troupe;
演出很精彩 splendid performance;
演出節目 items on the programme;
演出經理 impresario;
演出戲劇 give dramatic entertainment;
演出雜技 give an acrobatic performance;
演出者 performer;
演出主辦人 impresario;
乏味的演出 uninspiring performance;
告別演出 farewell performance; swansong;
~ 做告別演出 give a farewell performance;
觀摩演出 festival; performance before fellow artists for the purpose of discussion and emulation;

精彩的演出 stellar performance;
令人激動的演出 electrifying performance;
領銜演出 head the cast;
首次演出 debut; first performance; première;
巡迴演出 make a travelling show; tour;
一場演出 a show;
主持演出 host a show;

[演化] develop and change; evolution; evolve;
演化論 theory of evolution;
生物演化 organic evolution;
跳躍演化 salutatory evolution;
直向演化 orthogenesis;

[演技] acting abilities; acting skill;

[演講] address; deliever a speech; give a lecture; make a speech; lecture; oration; speech;
演講比賽 oratorical contest; speaking contest;
演講稿撰寫人 speechwriter;
演講術 oratory;
演講廳 lecture hall; lyceum;
演講者 speaker;
~ 特邀演講者 guest speaker;
~ 席後演講者 after-dinner speaker;
長篇演講 disquisition;
發表演講 deliver an address; give a speech;
公開演講 give a public address; make a public lecture;
即席演講 impromptu speech;
令人信服的演講 convincing speech;
聽演講 attend a lecture;
巡迴演講 lecture tour;
一次演講 a talk;
作演講 deliver a lecture; give a lecture;

[演練] drill;

[演示] demonstrate; demonstration;
幻燈片演示 slide demonstration;
實物演示 visual demonstration;

[演説] deliver a speech; give a speech; make an address;
演説家 orator;
精彩演説 able speech;
首次演説 maiden speech;
聽演説 attend a lecture;

[演算] calculus; calculation; do exercises in mathematics; mathematical exercises;
概率演算 calculus of probability;
觀測演算 calculus of observations;
進行演算 perform calculation;
命題演算 propositional calculus;
求導演算 derivation calculus;
張量演算 tensor calculus;
自然推理演算 calculus of nature inference;

[演替] succession;
演替頂級群落 climax community;
演替頂極 climax;
演替環境 successional habitat;
演替系列 succession spectrum;
演替原理 principle of succession;
不規則演替 anomalous succession;
人為演替 anthropogenic succession;
生物演替 biotic succession;
異發演替 allogenetic succession;
自發演替 autogenic succession;
自然地理演替 physiographic succession;
自養演替 autotrophic succession;

[演武] practise martial arts;

[演習] drill; dry run; dummy run; exercise; manoeuvre; practice;
聯合演習 have a joint maneuver;
實彈演習 practise with live ammunition;
消防演習 get a fire drill;
野外演習 have a field exercise;

[演戲] (1) act in a play; put on a play; (2) act; playact; pretend;

[演義] historical novel; historical romance;

[演繹] deduce; inference;
演繹法 deductive method;
演繹推理 deductive reasoning;

[演員] actor; actress; brother of the buskin; performer;
演員表 cast;
演員休息室 green room;
扮演男主角的演員 leading man;
扮演女主角的演員 leading lady;
當演員 go on the boards; tread the boards;
電影演員 screen actor; movie actor;
趕角演員 quick-change artist;
歌劇演員 operatic artist;
明星演員 star actor;
男演員 actor;
~ 偶像男演員 matinee idol;
~ 一個男演員 an actor;
女演員 actress;
~ 一個女演員 an actress;
~ 一群女演員 a bevy of actresses;
跑龍套演員 walk-on;
配角演員 minor role actor;

全體演員 cast;
挑選演員 casting; choose the cast;
舞蹈演員 dancer;
舞台演員 stage performer;
性格演員 character actor;
一班演員 a troupe of actors;
一流演員 top-notch actor;
一群演員 a troupe of actors;
雜技演員 acrobat;
主要演員 featured players;
專業演員 professional actor;
做演員 on the boards;

[演奏] give a performance; perform; play a musical instrument;
演奏會 concert; recital;
~巡迴演奏會 concert tour;
演奏台 bandstand;
演奏音樂 play music;
演奏樂器 play an instrument;

搬演 act; perform;
扮演 act; act sb; act the part of sb; be dressed up to represent sb; carry off one's role of sb; dress up as sb; interpret the role of sb; in the character of sb; make oneself up as sb; play sb; play the role of sb; take on the role of sb;
編演 write and stage a play;
表演 (1) perform; play; (2) demonstrate;
操演 demonstrate; drill;
重演 (1) put on an old play, etc; (2) recur; repeat;
串演 act the role of; play the role of;
導演 (1) direct; (2) director; film director; screen director; stage director;
調演 transfer a theatrical troupe;
公演 perform in public;
合演 put on joint performances;
會演 put on joint performances;
匯演 put on joint performances;
講演 give a lecture; lecture; make a speech;
開演 begin;
排演 rehearse;
上演 perform; put on the stage;
飾演 act the part of; play; play the role of;
試演 put on a trial performance;
天演 evolution;
推演 deduce; infer;
義演 benefit performance; charity performance; charity show;
預演 preview; preview show; rehearsal; walk through;
主演 play the lead; play the lead role; play the leading role in a play; star in a motion picture;

yan
【蝘】 (1) a variety of cicada; (2) gecko;
[蝘蜓] gecko;

yan
【黶】 bluish black;
[黶黮] dark;

yan
【甗】 earthenware vessel;

yan
【儼】 (1) majestic; solemn; respectable; (2) as if; like;
[儼然] (1) dignified; solemn; stern; (2) arranged in neat order; (3) just like;
儼然一色 exactly the same in colour; of just the same colour;
[儼如] just like;
[儼若] just like;

yan
【鼴】 mole;
[鼴鼠] mole;

針鼴 echidna; spiny anteater;

yan
【巘】 hilltop; mountain; peak;

yan
【魘】 nightmare;
[魘夢] paranoia;

夢魘 nightmare;

yan
【黶】 black mole;

yan4

yan
【咽】 gulp; swallow;
[咽氣] breathe one's last; die;
[咽下去] gulp down; swallow;

yan
【彥】 (1) accomplished; (2) elegant; (3) handsome; outstanding; (4) erudite scholar; learned; person of ability and virtue;
[彥會] gathering of distinguished personalities;
[彥士] refined and accomplished scholar;

yan

【唁】 condole with sympathy for the bereaved;

［唁電］ condolatory telegram; message of condolence; telegram of condolence;

［唁函］ letter of condolence; message of condolence;

［唁信］ condolatory letter;

電唁 send a message of condolence by telegram;
吊唁 condole; offer one's condolences; pay last respects to;
慰唁 condole with sb;

yan

【宴】 (1) entertain at a banquet; feast; (2) comfort; ease; leisurely;

［宴安］ feel happy and contented; live in idle comfort;
宴安鴆毒 live in easy comfort and suffer its poisonous effect; seeking pleasure is like drinking poisoned wine; voluptuous comfort is poison;

［宴會］ banquet; dinner party; feast;
宴會廳 banquet hall;
大宴會 big banquet;
答謝宴會 reciprocal banquet;
歡迎宴會 welcoming banquet;
舉行宴會 hold a dinner party;

［宴居］ lead a leisurely life;

［宴樂］ gather together;

［宴請］ entertain;
宴請貴賓 entertain the distinguished guests;

［宴席］ banquet; feast;

［宴饗］ give a great dinner;

［宴飲］ dine and wine; feast;
宴飲方酣 the banquet is at its height;

［宴遊］ leisure trip;

便宴 informal dinner;
赴宴 attend a banquet;
國宴 state banquet;
歡宴 entertain at a banquet on some happy occasion;
婚宴 wedding banquet;
家宴 family dinner;
設宴 give a banquet; give a dinner party; throw a banquet;
盛宴 grand banquet; sumptuous feast;
晚宴 evening dinner;
午宴 lunch; luncheon;
饗宴 feast;
謝師宴 a dinner party given by graduating students in honour of their teachers;
邀宴 (1) invite to a feast; (2) invitation to a dinner party;
御宴 royal feast;

yan

【晏】 (1) clear; (2) evening; late; (3) peaceful; quiet; (4) a surname;

［晏寂］ very quiet and silent;

［晏駕］ death of an emperor;

［晏起］ get up late;

［晏寢］ sit up late;

［晏然］ peaceful and easy; quiet and comfortable;

［晏如］ peaceful and easy;

［晏晏］ mild and tender;

yan

【堰】 bank of earth; dike; embankment; levee; weir;

［堰塞湖］ barrier lake;

［堰洲］ barrier;

埂堰 earth dike;
曲線堰 curved-sided weir;
收縮堰 contracted weir;
塘堰 small reservoir;
圍堰 cofferdam;
溢流堰 downflow weir;
溢水堰 flush weir;

yan

【焰】 (1) blaze; blazing; flame; (2) brilliant; glowing;

［焰火］ fireworks;

［焰色］ flame;
焰色反應 flame reaction;

［焰焰］ blazing;

敵焰 enemy's arrogance;
光焰 flare; radiance;
火焰 flame;
烈焰 roaring flame;
內焰 inner flame;
砲口焰 muzzle flash;
氣焰 arrogance; bluster; hauteur; overweening arrogance;
勢焰 arrogance and power;

外層焰 outer flame;
外焰 outer flame;
兇焰 aggressive arrogance; fearsome air;
氧化焰 oxidizing flame;

yan
【硯】 inkslab; inkstone;
[硯弟] junior classmate;
[硯耕] plough the field of the inkslab—live by writing;
[硯盒] case for an inkslab;
[硯臺] inkslab; inkstone;
[硯瓦] inkslab;
[硯兄] elder classmate;
硯兄硯弟 classmates; schoolmates;
[硯友] classmates; fellow students;

端硯 a kind of high-quality inkslab made in Duanxi, Guangdong Province;

yan
【雁】 wild goose;
[雁帛] correspondence; letters;
[雁封] letters; written messages;
[雁戶] transient resident;
[雁行] (1) walk like flying wild geese, one after another; (2) brothers;
雁行成行 wild geese fly in formation;
雁行折翼 a break in a row of flying geese — the death of a brother;
[雁序] brothers;
雁序之情 brotherly affection;
[雁杳魚沈] lose contact; without news or letters;
[雁影分飛] separation of brothers;
[雁陣] wild geese formation;
雁陣掠空 wild geese in arrow — head formation winged through the azure sky;
雁陣南飛 a flock of wild geese flows south in a V formation;
[雁足] correspondence; letters;
雁足傳書 (1) epistle; (2) bring a letter; bring a message;

白雁 white wild goose;
大雁 wild goose;
豆雁 bean goose;
鴻雁 swan goose;
鵲雁 magpie goose;
頭雁 leading wild goose;
雪雁 snow goose;
一群雁 a flock of wild geese;

yan
【焱】 same as 焰 , flames;

yan
【厭】 (1) be disgusted with; detest; dislike; hate; (2) be bored with; be tired of; get tired of; (3) satisfied; surfeited;
[厭煩] bored; boredom; dislike; fed up with; sick of; wearied; vexed;
感到厭煩 be bored; get bored;
~ 感到厭煩的 cheesed off;
令人厭煩 boring;
~ 令人厭煩的人 crashing bore;
[厭恨] hate; loathe;
[厭倦] boredom; ennui; lassitude; tired of; weary of;
厭倦的 cheesed off;
厭倦人生 weary of life;
[厭棄] detest and reject; get rid of; give up; loathe; reject;
[厭食] apocleisis; lack of appetite;
厭食的 anorexic;
厭食症 anorexia;
~ 神經性厭食症 anorexia nervosa;
[厭世] (1) disgusted with the world; pessimistic; world-weary; (2) die; pass away; (3) misanthropy;
厭世的 world-weary;
厭世嫉俗 become disgusted with life;
厭世主義 cynicism; pessimism;
悲觀厭世 pessimism and world-weariness;
[厭惡] abhor; abominate; antipathy; detest; disgusted with; dislike; have an abhorrence of; hold sb in abhorrence; hold sth in abhorrence; hold sth in abomination; loathe; repugnance;
厭惡的 antipathetic;
厭惡和尚，恨及袈裟 those who dislike monks also hate monkish vestments;
厭惡賭博 abhorrent of gambling;
令人厭惡 disgusting; loathsome;
~ 令人厭惡的 grotty; gruesome;
招人厭惡 incur odium;
[厭戰] demoralized by war; tired of war; war-weary; weary of war;

不厭 not mind doing sth; not object to; not tire of;

會厭 epiglottis;
生厭 become bored; become tired of sth;
討厭 abhorrent of; adverse to; allergitic to; antipathetic to; averse to; bad news; be annoyed with; be annoyed at; be browned-off with; be disgusted at; be disgusted by; be disgusted with; be fed up with; bore; detest; disagreeable; disgusting; dislike; hate; have a dislike for; have a distaste for; have a horror of; have an aversion to; have no time for; have no use for; hold sth in abomination; indisposed; loathe; nasty; pain in the neck; nuisance; repugnant to; sick of; take a dislike to; tired of; trouble; troublesome;

yan
【鴈】 (1) same as 雁 , wild goose; (2) same as 贗 , bogus, forged;

yan
【燕】 (1) swallow; (2) comfort; ease; (3) enjoy; feast;
[燕安] comfort; ease; peace;
[燕八哥] starling;
[燕巢於幕] the swallow makes its nest on a tent — insecure;
[燕出] go out in secrecy;
[燕妒鶯慚] make the gaudy swallows and orioles pale with envy; snatch a master's favours from a rival;
[燕頷虎頸] swallow's beak and a tiger's head — a noble look; dignified appearance;
[燕好] very fond of each other;
[燕賀] offer congratulations on the completion of a new residence;
[燕剪] swallow's tail in the shape of scissors;
[燕居] live at ease; live at leisure;
[燕雀兒] finch;
五雀六燕 about the same; six of one and half a dozen of the other;
[燕樂] (1) entertain; please; (2) popular music;
[燕侶] husband and wife; married couple;
燕侶鶯儔 devoted couple; happily married couple;
[燕麥] oat;
燕麥餅 oat cake;
燕麥片 oatmeal;
燕麥粥 gruel; porridge;
[燕女] delight in women;
[燕寢] place for rest;
[燕雀] bramble finch;
燕雀安知鴻鵠之志 how can a common fellow read the mind of a great man; what can a swallow know of the aims of a swan goose;
燕雀處堂 swallows and sparrows nesting in the hall, unmindful of the spreading blaze — oblivious of imminent danger in the comfort of an easy life;
燕雀相賀 offer congratulations on the completion of a new residence;
[燕然勒石] engrave military merits on a stone;
[燕瘦環肥] women attractive in their own ways;
[燕婉] friendly; genial;
燕婉之歡 harmonious happiness between husband and wife;
燕婉之求 demand for an ideal husband; seek an ideal husband;
[燕尾] forked tail; swallow tail;
燕尾服 swallow-tailed coat; tailcoat;
[燕窩] bird's nest;
[燕燕於飛] deeply attached to each other;
[燕翼] help; support;
燕翼貽謀 hand down a good plan to posterity;
[燕飲] feast;
[燕遊] make pleasure trips;
[燕魚] Spanish mackerel;
[燕語] soft chirping of swallows;
[燕子] swallow;
燕子銜泥空費力，乳燕羽豐各自飛 the swallow that builds its nest is wasting its energy, for when the little swallows' wings grow strong, they will fly away;
一群燕子 a flock of swallows;

飛燕 flying swallows;
海燕 petrel;
灰沙燕 sand martin;
家燕 swallow;
金絲燕 esculent swift;
乳燕 young swallows;
土燕 general term for pratincole;
閒燕 peace and quiet;
崖燕 cliff swallow;
鶯燕 orioles and swallows;
雨燕 swift;

yan

【諺】 adage; aphorism; proverb; saying;
［諺文］ Korean alphabet;
［諺語］ adage; proverb; saying;

古諺 old saying;
農諺 farmer's proverb; farmer's saying;

yan

【鴳】 a species of quail;

yan

【嚥】 gulp; swallow;
［嚥氣］ breathe one's last; die;
［嚥下困難］ dysphagia;

yan

【鷃】 quail;
［鷃雀］ quails and sparrows;

yan

【贗】 bogus; counterfeit; fake; forged; sham; spurious;
［贗本］ fake; imitation; phony; sham;
［贗幣］ counterfeit coin;
［贗品］ counterfeit; fake; forgery; imitation; sham;

yan

【饜】 (1) full-stomached; satiated; (2) take plentifully of;
［饜食］ eat to repletion;
［饜事］ busy; plenty to do;
［饜飫］ eat to repletion; glut;
［饜足］ satiated; surfeited;

yan

【驗】 (1) analyze; check; examine; test; (2) produce an effect; produce the expected result; prove effective; (3) prove; verify;
［驗鈔器］ detect counterfeit money machine;
［驗電器］ electroscope;
電容驗電器 condensing electroscope;
金箔驗電器 gold-leaf electroscope;
自動記錄驗電器 automatic-recording electroscope;
［驗方］ effective medical prescriptions;
［驗光師］ optician;
［驗貨］ examine goods;
［驗看］ examine; take a close look;
［驗勘］ inspect; investigate;
［驗明］ ascertain by a test; ascertain by an examination;
驗明正身 identify; make a positive identification of a criminal before execution;
［驗尿］ urine test;
［驗傷］ examine an injury;
［驗屍］ (1) autopsy; postmortem examination; (2) identification of a corpse;
驗屍報告 autopsy report;
驗屍官 coroner;
［驗收］ check and accept; check before acceptance; check upon delivery;
驗收檢驗 acceptance inspection;
到貨驗收 inspection of incoming merchandise;
進行驗收 carry out an acceptance inspection;
［驗算］ check computations;
驗算公式 check formula;
做驗算 make a checking calculation;
［驗血］ blood test;
［驗證］ confirm by evidence; test and verify;
驗證功能
有待驗證 remain to be tested; attest function;

按驗 investigate the evidence of a case;
案驗 investigate the evidence of a case;
參驗 compare and verify; investigate and check;
測驗 test;
查驗 check; examine;
抽驗 spot-test; test sample;
點驗 check; examine item by item;
化驗 perform a laboratory test;
檢驗 checkout; check-up; examine; inspect; inspection; survey; test; verify;
校驗 check; proof; test; verify;
經驗 experience; go through;
勘驗 inquest;
考驗 test; try;
靈驗 (1) efficacious; (2) (of a prediction) accurate; right;
奇驗 (1) unusual efficacy; (2) uncanny accuracy;
實驗 do an experiment; experiment; make a test;
試驗 experiment; test;
體驗 experience firsthand; firsthand experience; learn through one's personal experience; learn through practice;
先驗 a priori;
效驗 desired result; intended effect;
應驗 be confirmed; come true;

占驗 confirmation of an oracle;
徵驗 verify;
證驗 verify;
左驗 witness;

yan
【讌】 banquet; feast;
[讌服] everyday dress; informal dress;
[讌饗] banquet; feast;
[讌飲] banquet; feast;

yan
【艷】 (1) colourful; gaudy; gorgeous; (2) amorous; (3) admire; envy; (4) beautiful and captivating; (5) radiant; (6) plump; voluptuous;
[艷稱] famed for her beauty;
[艷福] good fortune in love affairs;
艷福不淺 have a lot of good fortune in love affairs;
飛來艷福 unexpected romantic affair with a beauty;
[艷歌] love song;
[艷紅] bright-red;
[艷絕] extremely beautiful;
[艷麗] bright-coloured and beautiful; captivating; charming; gorgeous; magnificent; radiantly beautiful;
艷麗多彩 pretty and colourful;
艷麗奪目 of dazzling beauty;
[艷色] beauty of a woman;
[艷射] dazzling;
[艷詩] love poem in a flowery style;
艷詩濃詞 love poem in a flowery style;
[艷史] amorous adventures; love affairs; romantic adventures;
[艷事] erotic affairs; romantic adventures;
[艷舞] enticing dances; striptease; voluptuous;
[艷羨] admire; envy; long for;
[艷陽] sunny spring weather;
艷陽天 bright spring day; bright sunny skies; charming bright springtime;
[艷遇] encounter with a beautiful woman; one's affair; one's romantic history;
[艷姿] beautiful appearance; charming looks; enticing looks;
[艷裝] gaudy dress;
艷裝華服 gorgeously dressed; make up one's face heavily and dress gaudily; make up one's face heavily and wear gaudy clothes;

哀艷 sad and beautiful; sad but flowery; sadly touching;
浮艷 ostentatious; showy but unsubstantial;
紅艷艷 brilliant red;
嬌艷 delicate and charming; tender and beautiful;
濃艷 bright-coloured; rich and gaudy;
鮮艷 bright-coloured; gaily-coloured;
香艷 (1) flowery; (2) sexy;
歆艷 admire; envy;
妖艷 pretty and coquettish;
淫艷 seductive;
冶艷 pretty and coquettish;

yan
【鹽】 (1) salt; (2) envy;

yan
【釅】 strong;

yan
【讞】 judge at a court of law;
[讞牘] records of criminal cases;
[讞讞其德] upright is one's virtue;
[讞獄] sentence;

yan
【灩】 inundating; overflowing;

yang¹

yang
【央】 (1) entreat; request; (2) central; centre; middle; (3) end; finish;
[央告] ask earnestly; beg; beseech;
東央西告 plead from one for another;
[央請] make a request;
[央求] beg; entreat; implore; plead;
央求寬恕 beseech for forgiveness;
[央託] entrust; request;
[央央] (1) bright; (2) jangling;

中央 (1) centre; middle; (2) central authorities;

yang
【泱】 (1) great; profound; (2) (of clouds) turbulent;
[泱漭] (1) expansive and boundless; (2) gloomy;
泱漭無際 vast without limit;
[泱泱] (1) vast; (2) broad and deep; great; magnificent;
泱泱大風 impressive manner of a great

country;
泱泱大國 great country; great and proud country;
泱泱海洋 boundless and bottomless ocean;

yang
【殃】 (1) calamity; disaster; misfortune; (2) bring disaster to;
[殃禍] disasters and calamities;
[殃及] bring disaster to;
殃及池魚 bring disaster to the fish in the moat;
殃及無辜 bring disaster to the innocent; involve the innocent in the trouble; shoot at a pigeon and kill a crow; trouble involves the innocent people;
[殃民] bring disaster to the people; wrong and suppress the people;
殃民禍國 injure the masses and bring disaster to the country;

禍殃 calamity; catastrophe; disaster;
災殃 calamity; disaster; suffering;
遭殃 suffer disaster;

yang
【秧】 (1) rice seedling; (2) fish-fry; (3) (now rare) cultivate;
[秧歌] yangko;
秧歌舞 yangko dance;
[秧苗] rice seedling; rice shoot;
[秧田] rice seedling bed;
[秧子] seedling;

拔秧 pull up seedlings;
撥秧 pull up seedlings;
菜秧 vegetable sprout;
插秧 transplant rice seedlings;
稻秧 rice seedlings;
花秧 flower sapling;
拉秧 uproot plants;
撓秧 weed rice fields and loosen the soil around the seedlings;
蒔秧 transplant rice seedlings;
樹秧 sapling;
魚秧 fingerling;
育秧 raise rice seedlings;

yang
【鞅】 (1) halter; martingale; (2) horse;
[鞅斷車停] the halter breaks and the carriage stops;
[鞅掌] overburdened; weariness;
鞅掌無寧 harassed without rest; so busy as to have no leisure to tidy oneself up;

yang
【鴦】 female mandarin duck;

yang²
yang
【羊】 (1) goat; sheep; (2) a surname;
[羊腸] bowel of a sheep;
羊腸鳥道 meandering footpath; narrow winding trail;
羊腸小道 path full of twists and turns; meandering footpath; narrow winding trail; small winding path; winding narrow path; zigzag path;
[羊齒] ferns;
[羊毫] writing brush made of wool;
[羊狠狼貪] exploit and oppress the people;
[羊角] (1) cleat; ram's horns; (2) cyclone; whirlwind;
羊角辮 (of hairstyle) bunches; ram's horns;
羊角錘 claw hammer;
羊角瘋 epilepsy;
~ 抽羊角瘋 have an attack of epilepsy;
~ 發羊角瘋 have an attack of epilepsy;
[羊叫] bleating of a sheep;
[羊欄] sheepfold;
[羊毛] wool;
羊毛出在羊身上 after all, the wool still comes from the sheep's back — in the long run, whatever you're given, you pay for; without a sheep, there can be no wool;
羊毛袋 wool sack;
羊毛的 fleecy;
羊毛衫 woolen sweater;
~ 高圓領羊毛衫 polo-neck sweater;
~ 開襟羊毛衫 cardi; cardigan;
羊毛衣 woolen wear;
羊毛脂 lanolin;
剪羊毛 shear a sheep;
~ 剪羊毛的人 shearer;
羔羊毛 lambswool;
[羊膜] amnion;
羊膜穿刺術 amniocentesis;
羊膜腔 amniotic cavity;
羊膜細胞 amniotic cell;
[羊排] lamb chop; mutton chop;

烤羊排 grilled lamb chop;

[羊皮] sheepskin;

羊皮革 buckskin;

羊皮紙 parchment; sheepskin;

~仿羊皮紙 artificial parchment;

~假羊皮紙 imitation parchment;

~美術羊皮紙 art parchment;

~紗管羊皮紙 spooling parchment;

~塗蠟羊皮紙 waxed parchment;

~植物羊皮紙 vegetable parchment;

狼披羊皮 wolf in sheep's skin; the wolf puts on a sheep's skin;

扒羊皮 skin a sheep;

披着羊皮吃羊 eat sheep on a sheep's clothing;

[羊圈] sheepfold; sheep pen;

[羊群] flock of sheep;

羊群裏頭出駱駝 stand out like a camel in a flock of sheep;

虎入羊群 as tigers among a flock of sheep;

[羊肉] mutton;

羊肉不曾吃，空惹一身羶 miss the goat meat and just get the smell of the goat;

涮羊肉 mutton cooked in a chafing pot;

一大塊羊肉 a junk of mutton;

[羊水] amnion fluid; amniotic fluid;

羊水破了 sb's waters break;

[羊頭] sheep's head;

掛羊頭賣狗肉 hang out a sheep's head when what one is selling is dog's meat; hanging up a sheep's head and selling dog meat; he cries wine, and sells vinegar; offer chaff for grain; sell a pig in a poke; sell dog-meat as mutton; sell dog meat under the label of a sheep's head; sell horsemeat as beefsteak; swindle others by making false claims;

[羊癲風] have an attack of epilepsy;

[羊叫] baa; bleat;

[羊脂] suet;

羊脂玉 white jade;

粗毛羊 coarse-wooled sheep;

大角羊 bighorn sheep;

帶頭羊 bellwether;

羔羊 kid; lamb;

公羊 ram;

羯羊 wether;

羚羊 antelope; gazelle;

綿羊 sheep;

母羊 ewe;

牧羊 shepherd; tend sheep;

奶羊 milch goat;

牛羊 oxen and sheep;

盤羊 argali;

山羊 (1) goat; (2) buck;

石羊 bharal; blue sheep;

灘羊 a kind of sheep raised in Ningxia and Gansu;

替罪羊 scapegoat;

頭羊 bellwether;

餼羊 sheep for sacrifices;

岩羊 bharal; blue sheep;

閹羊 wether;

一大群羊 a mob of sheep;

一群羊 a bunch of sheep; a flock of sheep;

一頭羊 a sheep;

一隻羊 a sheep;

羱羊 ibex;

豬羊 pigs and sheep;

紫羚羊 bongo;

yang

【佯】 (1) feign; pretend; sham; (2) deceitful; false; feigning;

[佯病] pretend to be ill;

[佯攻] feign attack; make a feint;

[佯狂] feign madness; feigned madness;

[佯死] feign death; pretend to be dead;

[佯言] lies; tell a lie;

[佯裝] feign; pretend; sham;

佯裝熟睡 pretend to be asleep;

[佯醉假癲] make a false show of drunkenness and insanity;

[佯作] bogus;

佯作不見 close one's eyes to; feign blindness; look through one's fingers at; pretned to be blind; turn a blind eye to;

佯作不知 affect ignorance; dissimulate; feign ignorance; pretend not to know;

佯作惶恐 feign the greatest astonishment;

佯作震惊 pretend a great surprise;

倘佯 wander about unhurriedly;

yang

【徉】 (1) roam; stray; unsettled; (2) hesitating; unsettled;

徜徉 wander about unhurriedly;

yang

【洋】 (1) vast; (2) ocean; (3) foreign; Occidental; Western; (4) modern; (5) imported;

［洋場惡少］ juvenile delinquent; rich young bully in a metropolis;

［洋葱］ onion;
- 洋葱皮 onion skin;
- 洋葱湯 onion soup;
- 洋葱頭 onion bulb;
- 紅皮洋葱 red onion;
- 嫩洋葱 green onion;
- 一畦洋葱 a bed of onions;

［洋房］ foreign-style house; Western-style house;

［洋服］ Occidental dress; Western-style clothes;

［洋行］ foreign business firm;

［洋化］ be Westernized;
- 洋化教育 Westernized education;

［洋灰］ cement;

［洋貨］ foreign goods; imported products;

［洋涇濱］ pidgin;
- 洋涇濱英語 pidgin English;
- 洋涇濱語 pidgin;
- ~洋涇濱語化 pidginization;
- ~洋涇濱語形式 pidginized form;

［洋酒］ imported wine and spirits;

［洋蠟］ candle;

［洋流］ marine current;

［洋樓］ Western-style building;

［洋爐］ Western stove;

［洋面］ sea surface;

［洋奴］ flunkey of the Occident; slave of a foreign master;
- 洋奴思想 slavish mentality to foreign things;

［洋氣］ foreigh style;
- 穿得洋氣 be dressed in foreign style;
- 顯得洋氣 have a foreign style;
- 洋裏洋氣 exotic flavour; in a pompously foreign style; in an ostentatiously foreign style; outlandish;

［洋槍］ rifle;

［洋人］ foreigner; Westerner;

［洋文］ foreign language;

［洋務］ foreign affairs; foreign business;

［洋相］ biff; make an exhibition of oneself; pratfall;
- 大出洋相 cut a poor figure; cut a sorry figure; make a bad show; make a ridiculous figure; make an exhibition of oneself

［洋洋］ (1) full of water; (2) extensive; great; vast; (3) elated; in high spirits;
- 洋洋大觀 an impressive array of exhibits; extensive view; grand; fine spectacle; grandiose; imposing; impressive; magnificent; most majestic sight; spectacular;
- 洋洋大篇 a flood of ink; a magnificent piece of writing;
- 洋洋得意 crow over; elated; immensely proud; in high spirits; jubilant; proud and happy; very pleased with oneself; walk on air; well-contented;
- 洋洋灑灑 copious and fluent; of great length; voluminous;
- 洋洋萬言 a flood of words; run to ten thousand words; very lengthy;
- 洋洋自得 be pleased with oneself; complacent; feel oneself highly flattered; proud and pleased with oneself; self-satisfied;
- 懶洋洋 anguid; listless;
- 喜氣洋洋 bursting with joy;
- 喜洋洋 beaming with joy; radiant;

［洋溢］ be filled; be fraught with; be permeated with; brim with;
- 才氣洋溢 brilliant intelligence;
- 熱情洋溢 brim with enthusiasm;

［洋中］ foreign and Chinese;
- 洋為中用 adapt foreign things for Chinese use; adapt foreign things to Chinese needs; make foreign things serve China;

［洋裝］ (1) Western dress; (2) Western binding;

- 北冰洋 Arctic Ocean;
- 重洋 seas and oceans;
- 崇洋 worship foreign things;
- 出洋 go abroad;
- 海洋 seas and oceans;
- 懶洋洋 indolent; languid; languor; lethargy; listless;
- 留洋 study abroad;
- 外洋 foreign country;
- 汪洋 boundless; vast;
- 西洋 West; Western;
- 喜洋洋 beaming with joy; radiant;
- 現洋 silver dollar;
- 銀洋 silver dollar;

遠洋 (1) ocean; (2) oceanic;

yang

【昜】 bright; glorious;

yang

【烊】 melt; smelt;

[烊金] molten metal;

yang

【揚】 (1) raise; (2) throw up and scatter; winnow; (3) make known; spread; (4) get excited; stir; (5) a surname;

[揚鞭] raise the whip;

揚鞭摧馬 flourish the whip to urge on the horse; urge one's horse on with a whip; whip one's horse on;

催馬揚鞭 flourish the whip to urge on the horse; urge one's horse on with a whip; whip one's horse on; whip one's horse up to a swift trot;

[揚波] swelling of waves;

[揚長] in a stalking manner; swaggeringly;

揚長避短 adopt sb's good points and avoid his shortcomings; enhancement of strong points and elimination of weaknesses; give play to one's strong points and avoid one's shortcomings;

揚長而去 sail out of the room; stalk off; stride away with the head in the air; stride away without looking back; strut off; swagger off;

[揚塵] raise dust;

東海揚塵 unpredictability of world affairs;

[揚帆] hoist the sails; set sail;

揚帆過海 sail across the seas;

[揚穀去糠] winnow chaff from grain;

[揚厲] show a dauntless spirit;

[揚名] become famous; become known; have one's name up; make a name for oneself;

揚名海外 make their reputations abroad;

揚名天下 become known throughout the country; become world-famous; enjoy tremendous popularity in the world; make a noise in the world;

揚名於世 become famous throughout the country; become world-famous; raise one's name to the world;

立身揚名 gain fame and position;

顯身揚名 make a glorious name for oneself; show one's mettle and make a name;

[揚起] elevate; kick up;

[揚棄] discard; renounce;

[揚琴] dulcimer;

[揚榷] expound briefly;

揚榷古今 make a cursory review of the past and the present;

[揚善] spread others' good deeds;

[揚聲] (1) raise one's voice; (2) boast prestige;

揚聲器 loudspeaker; speaker;

~薄帶揚聲器 band loudspeaker;

~低聲揚聲器 base loudspeaker;

~電容揚聲器 capacitive speaker;

~鋁膜揚聲器 aluminium speaker;

~舌簧揚聲器 armature loudspeaker;

~室內揚聲器 cabinet speaker;

~雙極揚聲器 bipolar loudspeaker;

~雙向揚聲器 bidirectional loudspeaker;

~同軸揚聲器 coaxial speaker;

[揚湯止沸] try to stop water from boiling by scooping it up and pouring it back—an ineffectual remedy; try to stop water from boiling by skimming it off and pouring it back;

[揚威] attain eminence; show one's great authority;

耀武揚威 a warlike gesture; bluff and bluster; brandish one's swords; exhibit military prowess; flaunt one's prowess; in triumph; make a big show of one's strength; make a show of force; mount the high horse; parade military prowess; presume upon one's power to intimidate others; rattle the sabre; ride the high horse; sabre-rattling; show military prowess; show off one's power; show off one's strength; show one's might; show one's prowess; swagger about and brandish one's weapons; swagger before others; with much pomp and glory and display of might;

[揚言] declare in public; exaggerate; pass the word that; spread words; threaten;

公然揚言 spread words in public;

[揚揚] complacently; triumphantly;

揚揚得意 smug and complacent;

揚揚自得 complacent; look like that cat that ate the canary; proud and pleased

with oneself; very pleased with oneself;
沸沸揚揚 bubbling with nose;
紛紛揚揚 fluttering about;
意氣揚揚 elated; in high spirits;

昂揚 high-spirited;
褒揚 commend; praise;
表揚 commend; praise;
播揚 broadcast; propagate; spread;
簸揚 winnow;
不揚 ugly;
闡揚 expound and propagate;
傳揚 spread;
導揚 advocate; preach;
發揚 (1) carry forward; development; (2) make full use of;
飛揚 float; fly upward;
弘揚 propagate;
宏揚 disseminate;
激揚 (1) drive evil and usher in good; (2) boost; encourage; inspiring;
飄揚 flutter; wave;
聲揚 advocate; make public;
頌揚 extol; sing the praises of sb;
顯揚 (1) praise; (2) be renowned;
宣揚 advocate; play up; propagate;
抑揚 rising and falling;
鷹揚 outstanding; powerful;
悠揚 melodious; rising and falling;
游揚 extol; praise;
揄揚 priase;
遠揚 one's reputation is known far and wide;
贊揚 commend; exalt; extol; glorify; praise;
讚揚 a pat on the back; commend; full marks to sb; glorify; pat sb on the back; pay a tribute to; praise; speak highly of;
張揚 make widely known; publicize;

yang

【陽】 (1) sun; (2) male; masculine; (3) south of a hill; (4) north of a river; (5) bright; brilliant; (6) male genital; (7) in relief; (8) open; overt; (9) positive; (10) a surname;

[陽春] springtime;
陽春白雪 caviar to the general;
陽春麵 cooked noodles without any dressing;
小陽春 (1) Indian summer; warm weather in late autumn; (2) balmy weather in the tenth lunar month;
有腳陽春 far-reaching benevolence;

[陽剛] strong in character;

[陽溝] open ditch;

[陽關道] broad road; thoroughfare;
你走你的陽關道，我過我的獨木橋 you may walk along fortune's wide road but I would choose the risky plank of insecurity — you look after your own concern and leave me to my own affairs; you take the open road, I'll cross the log bridge — you go your way, I'll go mine;
陽關大道 bright future; broad highway; even highway; right way;

[陽光] sunbeam; sunlight; sunshine;
陽光燦爛 bright sunshine; the sun is resplendent; the sun is shining brightly; the sun shines bright;
陽光刺眼 the eyes are affected by the sunlight;
陽光和煦 genial sunshine;
陽光明媚 sunny; the sun is shining brightly; the sun shines gaily;
~陽光明媚的 sun-kissed;
陽光普照 sunlight floods the earth; the sun illuminates every corner of the land; the sun is shining over all the earth; the sunlight shines on the whole world;
陽光照耀 the sun is shining;
不要接觸陽光 keep out of the sun;
春日陽光 spring sunshine;
反射陽光 flash back the sunlight;
沐浴陽光 bathe oneself in the sun;
午後陽光 afternoon sun; afternoon sunshine;
一抹陽光 a ray of sunshine;
一束陽光 a beam of sunlight; a shaft of sunlight;
遮擋陽光 fend off the sun; keep off the sun;

[陽和] balmy; warm;

[陽極] anode; positive pole;
陽極保護 anode protection;
陽極飽和 anode saturation;

[陽具] dick; jigger; joystick; kidney-wiper; middle leg; mole; nudger; padlock; tadger; tail; third leg; three-piece suit; tinkler; todger; wanger; weapon; wee man; wick; wille; willy; winkie; winky; yard; John Thomas; Mr Sausage;

necessaries; one's old fellow; one's peter; one's sexing-piece; the corey; the dangler; the donger; the male reproductive organ; the Percy; the short arm;

［陽離子］ cation;
陽離子發生物 cationgen;
陽離子劑 cationics;
陽離子交換劑 cationite;
陽離子移變 cationotropy;
二價陽離子 bivalent cation;
類陽離子 cationoid;
絡陽離子 complex cation;
水合陽離子 hydrated cation;
四價陽離子 quadrivalent cation;
填隙陽離子 intersititial cation;
酰基陽離子 acylkum cation;
有機陽離子 organic cation;

［陽曆］ Gregorian calendar; solar calendar;

［陽平］ second tone;

［陽傘］ parasol; sunshade; umbrella;
一把陽傘 a sunshade;

［陽世］ the world of the living;

［陽台］ (1) balcony; veranda; (2) trysting place;
陽台隔板 partition between two balconies;
後陽台 back balcony;
一個陽台 a balcony;
正面陽台 front balcony;

［陽痿］ impotence;
次陽痿 secondary impotence;
功能性陽痿 functional impotence;
花燭夜陽痿 wedding night impotence;
繼發性陽痿 secondary impotence;
精神性陽痿 psychic impotence;
內分泌性陽痿 endocrine impotence;
器質性陽痿 organic impotence;
神經源性陽痿 neurogenic impotence;
糖尿病性陽痿 diabetic impotence;
原發性陽痿 primary impotence;

［陽物］ penis;

［陽性］ (1) positive; (2) male sex;
陽性反應 positive reaction;
假陽性 false positive;

［陽月］ tenth month in the lunar calendar;

殘陽 setting sun;
朝陽 face the sun;
重陽 Double Ninth Festival;
端陽 Dragon Boat Festival;
還陽 revive after death;
驕陽 blazing sun;
青陽 springtime;
山陽 sunny side of a mountain;
太陽 (1) sun; (2) sunlight; sunshine;
頹陽 setting sun;
夕陽 setting sun;
向陽 face the sun;
斜陽 setting sun;
炎陽 scorching sun;
艷陽 bright sun;
億陽 aeon;
陰陽 male and female; positive and negative;
朝陽 the morning sun; the rising sun;
遮陽 sunshade;
壯陽 stimulate male virility;

yang

【楊】 (1) poplar; (2) willow; (3) a surname;

［楊花］ poplar blossoms; poplar filaments;

［楊柳］ willow;
楊柳成行 lined with rows of willows;
楊柳低垂 willow branches hanging downward;
楊柳婆娑 the willows dance in the breeze;

［楊梅］ arbutus;

［楊桃］ carambola; star fruit;

白楊 white poplar;
赤楊 alnus japonica;
大葉楊 Chinese white poplar;
毒膚楊 poison oak;
胡楊 diversiform-leaved poplar;
黃楊 Chinese littleleaf box;
青楊 cathay poplar;
水楊 catkin willow;
響楊 Chinese white poplar;

yang

【煬】 (1) blazing fire; roaring; (2) put before the fire;

yang

【瘍】 infections; skin diseases;

潰瘍 ulcer;

yang

【颺】 (1) blown about by the wind; (2) blow away; fly away; (3) scatter; spread;

輕颺 flutter; stream;

yang³

yang

【仰】 (1) face upward; look up; (2) admire;

adore; look up to; respect; revere; (3) depend on; rely on; (4) swallow;

[仰不愧天] feel no shame before God;

[仰毒] swallow poison; take poison;

[仰俯] look up and stoop down;

仰俯之間 between looking up and stooping down;

仰取俯拾 taking from above and picking from below;

仰事俯畜 support one's family; support one's parents and feed one's wife and children; support parents as well as wife and children;

[仰給] depend on;

仰給於人 depend on others for support;

[仰賴] dependant on; look to; rely on;

[仰面] faceup; upturned face;

仰面朝天 fall flat on one's back; lie on one's back; with one's face towards the sky;

仰面大笑 look up and begin to laugh loud; throw up one's head and laugh;

仰面跌足 stamp on the ground with iritation and in perplexity;

仰面獰笑 head high, one laughs ominously;

仰面求人 spy one's face and implore sb;

[仰慕] admire; admire and respect; adore; look up to; regard with admiration;

[仰攀] (1) climb up; (2) climb socially;

仰攀高貴 scramble up to high and nobles;

[仰起] fling;

仰起頭 lift up one's head;

[仰求] dependent on sb; turn to sb for help;

[仰食於人] depend on another person for living;

[仰首伸眉] with one's chin up and eyebrows dancing — look of exultation;

[仰天] look up to heaven;

仰天長歎 cast one's eyes up to the sky and sigh deeply; lift up one's eyes and sigh; look to the heavens and draw a sigh; look up to heaven and sigh heavily; look up to the sky and keep heaving deep sighs; sigh deeply; sigh, gazing towards heaven;

仰天長嘯 cry into the air; make a long wheezing noise in the open air; make a long whistle into the air;

仰天垂淚 gaze up at the sky and let the tears roll down one's cheeks;

仰天大笑 laugh sardonically; lean back and laugh; look up to the sky and laugh; throw back one's head to laugh long and loud;

仰天呼冤 cry to heaven for vengeance;

仰天望月 look up at the moon;

仰天興歎 look up to the sky and draw a sigh;

[仰望] look up at; rely on;

[仰臥] lie on the back;

仰臥起坐 sit-up;

~ 做二十個仰臥起坐 do twenty sit-ups;

[仰泳] backstroke;

[仰仗] rely on;

仰仗權威 depend on power and influence;

仰仗人勢 rely on others' influence;

仰仗他人 rely on others;

[仰止] admiration;

俯仰 bending of the head; lifting of the head; simple action; simple move;

景仰 admire and respect; hold in deep respect; respect and admire;

敬仰 revere; venerate;

久仰 be pleased to meet you;

欽仰 esteem; revere;

素仰 have always admired; have always looked up to;

信仰 belief; believe; faith;

讚仰 regard with admiration and respect;

瞻仰 look at with reverence;

宗仰 hold in esteem;

鑽仰 seek the truth and stick to it;

yang

【氧】 oxygen;

[氧化] oxidation; oxidize;

氧化劑 oxidizer; oxidizing agent;

氧化鎂 magnesia;

~ 輕質煅燒氧化鎂 light-burned magnesia;

~ 重質氧化鎂 heavy-burned magnesia; heavy-calcined

氧化物 oxidate; oxide;

~ 超氧化物 hyperoxide; superoxide;

~ 過氧化物 peroxide;

~ 碱性氧化物 bais oxide;

~ 抗氧化物 antioxidant;

~ 兩性氫氧化物 amphoteric hydroxide;

~ 兩性氧化物 amphoteric oxide;

~ 氫氧化物 hydroxide;

~酸性氧化物 acid oxide; acidic oxide;
氧化焰 oxidizing flame;
氧化作用 oxygenation;
電解氧化 electrolytic oxidation;
加速氧化 accelerated oxidation;
空氣氧化 air oxidation;
生物氧化 biological oxidation;
需氧氧化 aerobic oxidation;
陽極氧化 anodic oxidation;
自動氧化 auto-oxidation;

[氧氣] oxygen;
氧氣面罩 oxygen mask;
氧氣帳 oxygen tent;
產生氧氣 produce oxygen;
吸進氧氣 breathe in oxygen;

臭氧 ozone;
輸氧 perform oxygen therapy;
脱氧 deoxidate; deoxidize;

yang

【鞅】 halter; martingale;
[鞅鞅] discontentedly;
[鞅掌] all-bustled; overburdened; weariness;
鞅掌無寧 harassed without rest;

yang

【養】 (1) keep; provide for; support; (2) breed; bring up; grow; keep; raise; rear; (3) give birth to; (4) adoptive; (5) cultivate; educate; form; (6) convalesce; recuperate one's health; (7) keep in good repair; maintain; (8) a surname;
[養兵] maintain an army; maintain and train soldiers;
養兵千日，用兵一時 a thousand days the country nurtures its soldiers and all for one day's battle; armies are to be maintained for years but used on a single day; maintain an army for a thousand days to use it for an hour; maintain soldiers a thousand days for one hour's service; train troops for a thousand days and use them in an emergency;
養兵自守 keep the army in condition and devote all one's energies to defense;
[養病] convalesce; nurse a disease; recuperate; take rest and nourishment to regain one's health;
[養成] cultivate; develop; discipline and train;
養成習慣 accustom oneself to; cultivate habits;
[養兒] bring up children;
養兒防老 bring up children for one's old age; raise children for one's old age; raise children to provide against old age; raise sons as insurance against the insecurity of old age; raise sons to provide for one's old age; rear children against old age;
養兒育女 bring up children; rear children;
[養分] nutrient;
養分過多 eutrophication; excessive fertilization;
[養蜂] engage in apiculture; keep bees; raise bees;
養蜂場 apiary; bee yard; beehouse;
養蜂人 beekeeper; beemaster;
養蜂業 apiculture business; beekeeping;
[養父] adoptive father; foster father;
養父母 adoptive parents; foster parents;
[養漢] woman having extramarital affairs;
[養護] (1) conserve; maintain; (2) curing;
養護公路 maintain public highways;
經常養護 constant maintenance;
年度養護 annual maintenance;
橋梁養護 bridge maintenance;
特別養護 extraordinary maintenance;
[養花] grow flower;
[養晦] live in retirement and wait for an opportunity to stage a comeback;
養晦藏拙 conceal oneself and prevent one's foolishness from being exposed;
養晦待時 dwell in retirement waiting for an opportunity; retire and hide awaiting an opportunity;
養晦守拙 keep growing in spirit while keeping away from public life;
養晦韜光 conceal one's talents; hide one's light under a bushel;
遵時養晦 bide one's time during a period of ill luck; dwell in retirement, waiting for the appropriate time to come; live in seclusion and wait for a better chance;
遵養時晦 live in retirement and wait for the right time for a comeback in public life;
[養活] (1) feed; keep; support; (2) bring up; raise;
養活父母 provide support to one's

parents;
養活家室 maintain one's family;
養活自己 earn one's own living;
要靠別人養活 need others' support for livelihood;

[養雞] raise chickens;

[養家] support one's family;
養家糊口 earn the family's living; sustain a family;
養家活口 earn bread for one's family; earn the family's living; feed and clothe one's family; keep the family supplied with provisions; provide food and clothes for one's family; provide for one's life and family; support one's family;
幫助養家 contribute to the family support;

[養靜] flee from the a busy and noisy place to cultivate mental calm;

[養口] support one's family;

[養老] (1) provide for the aged; (2) live out one's life in retirement;
養老保險 aged insurance;
養老基金 pension fund;
養老金 annuity; old-age pension;
~養老金計劃 pension plan; pension scheme;
~社會保險型養老金 social security-type pensions;
~一筆養老金 a pension;
養老送終 nourish one's parent in his old age and bury his dead body; serve parents while living and give proper burial after death;
養老院 almshouse; asylum for the aged; home for the aged; nursing home; old people's home; rest home;
慈幼養老 kind to the young and care for the old;
靠兒女養老 be provided for in one's old age by one's children;

[養料] nourishment; nutriment;
提供養料 supply nutrients;
需要養料 need nutrients;

[養路] road maintenance;
養路工 linesman;

[養母] adoptive mother; foster mother;

[養娘] (1) maid; (2) wet nurse; (3) foster mother;

[養女] adopted daughter; foster daughter;

[養親] support and serve parents;

[養傷] heal one's wounds; nurse one's injuries;

[養身] keep one's body fit; nourish one's body;
養身涵心 take good care of one's health;

[養神] have mental relaxation; repose; rest to attain mental tranquility;
養神閉目 conserve one's energy by closing the eyes; refresh oneself;
閉目養神 close one's eyes for a rest; close the eyes and give the mind a brief rest;

[養生] keep in good condition; keep in good health; nourishing of life; preserve one's health;
養生送死 nourish the living and bury the dead; birth and funeral – the events of life;
養生飲食 macrobiotic diet;
養生葬死 nourish the living and bury the dead;
養生之道 rules of physical and mental health; the way to keep fit; the way to maintain good health;

[養望] cultivate one's reputation;

[養心] cultivate mental calm; nourish the mind;
養心守拙 keep to one's primitive simplicity;
養心怡神 refresh one's spirit by keeping quiet;

[養性] discipline one's temperament;
養性守拙 enjoy obscurity and simplicity;
養性修身 cultivate one's moral character and behave ethically;
清心養性 purify one's heart and cultivate one's moral character;
守心養性 cultivate one's mind and preserve its original good nature;

[養魚] breed fish; fish farming; engage in pisciculture;
養魚場 fish farm; fishery;
養魚缸 aquarium;

[養育] breeding; bring up; parenting; raise and educate; raising; rear;
養育之恩 love and care given to one from childhood;
養育子女 bring up one's children; rear children;
扶植養育 groom and foster;

[養真] discipline one's temperament;

［養殖］ breed; cultivation; culture;
養殖海帶 cultivate kelp;
養殖業 fish farming;
養殖珍珠 cultivate pearls;
海水養殖 marine acquaculture;
水產養殖 aquaculture;
~水產養殖場 aquafarm;
［養珠］ cultured pearls;
［養子］ (1) adopted son; adoptive son; foster child; foster son; (2) bear a child; bring up a child;
收為養子 adopt a child;
［養尊處優］ do oneself proud; do oneself well; eat the fat of the land; enjoy high position and live in ease and comfort; enjoy wealth and honour; lead a comfortable life; like a cow in a clover-field; live a comfortable, luxurious life; live a quiet and leisurely; live at ease and in comfort; live high off the hog; live in clover; live in luxury; live in the lap of luxury; live like a lord; live like a prince; live like pigs in clover; live on the fat of the land; molly-coddle oneself; play the wanton; provide for oneself and live comfortably; revel in a high position and indulge in comfort;

保養 (1) take good care of one's health; (2) keep in good repair; maintain;
抱養 adopt a child;
補養 take nourishing food to build up one's health;
哺養 feed; rear;
放養 put in a suitable place to breed;
奉養 support and wait upon;
扶養 bring up; foster;
撫養 bring up; foster;
供養 provide for one's parents; provide for the need of one's parents; support;
涵養 ability to control oneself; conserve; self-restraint;
護養 (1) cultivate; nurse; (2) maintain;
豢養 feed; keep;
給養 provisions; victuals;
寄養 entrust one's child to the care of sb;
家養 domestic; tame;
將養 recuperate; rest;
嬌養 pamper; spoil;
教養 (1) bring up; educate; train; (2) breeding; culture; education; upbringing;
靜養 convalesce; have a good rest to recuperate; have a rest-cure; rest quietly to recuperate;
圈養 rear livestock in pens;
療養 convalesce; recuperate;
領養 adopt;
培養 (1) foster; train; (2) culture;
棄養 die; pass away;
榮養 support one's parents;
贍養 provide for; support;
生養 give birth to;
收養 adopt; take in and bring up;
飼養 raise; rear;
素養 accomplishment; attainment;
所養 be provided for;
調養 recuperate;
罔養 hesitate; unable to make a decision;
餵養 feed; keep; raise; rear;
孝養 serve one's parents with all material needs;
休養 convalesce; recuperate;
修養 (1) accomplishment; training; (2) self-cultivation;
蓄養 rasie;
學養 learning and cultivation;
馴養 raise and train;
怡養 enjoy good health and live a happy life;
頤養 keep fit; take care of oneself;
迎養 support one's parents by taking them to one's own home;
營養 nourishment; nutrition;
終養 resign from one's office to care for one's parents at home;
滋養 nourish; nourishment;
縱養 spoil a child;

yang
【瀁】 (1) water in motion; (2) move a boat or sth in water; (3) rapid; ripple; wave; (4) overflow; (5) a river in Shaanxi;

yang
【癢】 (1) itch; tickle; (2) itchy;
［癢處］ the place where it itches;
搔到癢處 say sth right to the point; scratch at the place that itches — touch the exact point; scratch where it itches — hit the nail on the head;
［癢癢］ itch; tickle; ticklish;

yang⁴
yang
【怏】 discontented; disheartened; dispirited;

[怏然] discontent; unhappy;
[怏怏] disgruntled; sullen;
怏怏不樂 cheerless; disconsolate; discontented and unhappy; far from feeling comfortable; feel sad and gloomy; get the blues; greatly disappointed; have a fit of the blues; have the blues; in low spirits; in poor spirits; in the blues; morose; out of spirits;
怏怏度日 mope time away;
怏怏而別 march off somewhat discontentedly;
怏怏而出 withdraw sulkily;
怏怏而返 return home in a very melancholy mood;
怏怏而歸 come back quite crestfallen; go home sadly;
[怏悒] discontent; melancholy; sad;
[怏鬱] gloom; melancholy; pensive;

yang
【恙】 (1) disease; (2) worry;

貴恙 your illness;
微恙 slight illness;
無恙 in good health; safe and sound;

yang
【煬】 (1) blazing fire; (2) put before the fire;

yang
【漾】 (1) ripple; (2) be tossed about lightly; brim over; overflow; (3) throw up; vomit;
[漾波] ripples;
[漾奶] throw up milk; vomit milk from repletion;
[漾漾] rippling;
[漾舟] enjoy boating;

蕩漾 ripple; undulate;

yang
【樣】 (1) appearances; looks; (2) form; mode; pattern; shape; style; (3) model; pattern; sample; (4) kind; sort; type; variety;
[樣板] (1) sample plate; (2) template; (3) example; model; prototype;
當做樣板 serve as a model;
仿形樣板 copying template;
角度樣板 angular template;
凸輪樣板 cam template;
[樣本] sample; specimen;
充足樣本 adequate sample;
附加樣本 additive samples;
真實樣本 authentic specimen;
[樣兒] appearance;
一個樣兒 alike; in the same manner; of the same sort;
[樣方] quadrat;
覆蓋樣方 cover quadrat;
計數樣方 count quadrat;
空樣方 empty quadrat;
普查樣方 census quadrat;
[樣品] exponent; prototype; sample; specimen;
參考樣品 reference sample;
考古學樣品 archaeological specimen;
空氣樣品 air sample;
商業樣品 commercial sample;
示範樣品 pilot sample;
[樣式] form; model; pattern; style; type;
過時樣式 out-of-date model;
流行樣式 latest mode;
最新樣式 latest model;
[樣樣] all; each and every; every kind;
樣樣兒 every sort; every variety;
樣樣皆通，樣樣稀鬆 a little of everything, and nothing at all; a little of everything is nothing in the main; Jack of all trades, and master of none; to know everything is to know nothing;
樣樣喜歡 like everything;
樣樣照辦 follow sb in every detail;
樣樣宗宗 diversified; of all sorts; varied;
[樣張] specimen sheet;
相片樣張 proof;
[樣子] (1) appearances; looks; shapes; (2) air; manner; (3) model; pattern; sample; (4) likelihood; tendency;
擺樣子 do sth for show; for appearance's sake; put on for appearance's sake;
~擺出無知的樣子 put on an air of ignorance;
~擺出學者的樣子 pose as a scholar;
~擺出一副恩人的樣子 assume a patronizing attitude;
~非擺樣子 not for show;
~為了擺樣子 for show;
~衹是擺樣子 only for show;
得意的樣子 triumphant airs;

一副無辜的樣子 a look of innocence;
這個樣子 that's sb all over;
~我就是這個樣子 that's me all over;
裝樣子 do sth for appearance sake; put on an act;
做樣子 empty gestures; go through the motion of doing sth; make fashion; pretend to do sth;

榜樣 example; model;
變樣 change in design;
別樣 another; of a different kind;
採樣 sample;
抽樣 sample;
打樣 (1) draw a design; (2) make a proof;
大樣 (1) full-page proof; (2) detail drawing;
底樣 a copy for the record;
多樣 diversified; manifold; of various kinds or forms; various;
放樣 loft;
紅樣 proof sheet;
花樣 (1) pattern; variety; (2) trick;
貨樣 sample goods;
校樣 proof sheet;
礦樣 sample ore;
兩樣 different;
毛樣 galley proof;
模樣 (1) appearance; look; (2) about; approximately;
那樣 in that way; like that; of that kind; so; such;
哪樣 (1) what kind of; (2) any kind of;
清樣 final proof; foundry proof;
取樣 sample;
砂樣 drilling mud cuttings;
時樣 latest fashion;
式樣 model; tyle; type;
試樣 test sample;
死樣 doltish; stupid and dull; wooden;
同樣 (1) as...as; equal; same; similar; (2) in the same way; likewise; similarly;
圖樣 blueprint; design; drawing; mould; pattern;
像樣 (1) decent; presentable; (2) up to the mark;
小樣 galley proof;
鞋樣 outline of sole; shoe pattern;
學樣 imitate sb's example;
岩樣 (1) rock specimen; (2) core sample;
一樣 (1) alike; as...as ever; as good as; exactly the same; the same; (2) a kind of; a type of;
異樣 (1) different; (2) peculiar; unusual;
原樣 original sample; original shape;
怎樣 how;
展樣 (1) stately; (2) broad-minded;
照樣 after a pattern;
這樣 like this;
字樣 (1) model of written characters; (2) printed or written words;
走樣 (1) deviate from the original; get out of shape; go out of form; lose shape; out of shape; (2) different from what is expected;

yang

【養】 support one's parents;

yao¹

yao

【么】 (1) insignificant; small; tiny; (2) youngest son or daughter of a family; (3) one; (4) alone; lone; (5) a surname;

［么兒］ youngest son;

［么妹］ youngest sister;

［么麼］ diminutive; minute; tiny;
么麼小醜 despicable wretch; petty skunk;

［么小］ diminutive; minute; puny;

yao

【夭】 freshlooking; tender; young;

［夭桃］ beautiful peach;
夭桃穠李 beautiful peach and plum blossoms;
翠柳夭桃 willows of tender green and pink flowering peach trees;

yao

【吆】 cry; shout;

［吆喝］ (1) cry; shout; (2) hawk;

yao

【妖】 (1) demon; evil spirit; ghost; goblin; monster; phantom; (2) evil and fraudulent; (3) bewitching; seductive;

［妖道］ black magic; witchcraft;

［妖風］ evil wind; noxious trend; ruined trend;
妖風毒霧 evil wind and miasma;

［妖怪］ bogy; demon; evil spirit; goblin; monster;
興妖作怪 conjure up a host of demons to make mischief; invoke a host of demons to make trouble; make trouble; raise the devil; stir up trouble;

［妖精］ (1) demon; evil spirit; (2) alluring woman;
小妖精 coquettish young girl; goblin; gremlin; hobgoblin;

［妖媚］ bewitching; seductively charming;

[妖魔] demon; evil spirit; jinn;
妖魔鬼怪 all the forces of evil; demons and ghosts; evil spirits of all kinds; ghosts and monsters; monsters of every description;
妖魔亂舞 evil spirits of all kinds dance in riotous revelry;
[妖孽] (1) unlucky omens; (2) person or event associated with evil or misfortune; (3) evildoer;
[妖女] fairy enchantress;
[妖氣] (1) bewitching dressing; (2) evil phenomenon;
妖裏妖氣 lascivious air; seductive and bewitching; seductive;
[妖嬈] enchanting; fascinating;
[妖人] evil enchanter; sorcerer;
[妖書] magical books;
[妖術] black art; sorcery; witchcraft;
[妖物] evil spirit; monster;
[妖祥] bad and good omens;
[妖邪] monstrous; strange; weird; wicked;
[妖言] absurd statements; heresies; fallacies;
妖言惑眾 arouse people with wild talks; cheat people with sensational speeches; deceive people with fabulous stories; delude people with strange legends; spread fallacies to deceive people; spread wild rumours to mislead the people; wild rumours mislead the masses;
[妖艷] foxy; pretty and coquettish; tarty;
妖艷迷人的女子 foxy lady;
看起來太妖艷 look too tarty;
[妖冶] bewitchingly pretty; pretty and coquettish; seductive; seductive charms;
妖冶女子 femme fatale;
[妖異] abnormal omens;
[妖由人興] supernatural things are created by men;
[妖災] calamities and prodigious things;

女妖 enchantress;

yao
【要】 (1) ask; claim; demand; make a claim; request; (2) blackmail; coerce; force; threaten; (3) invite; request the presence of; (4) make an arrangement; (5) a surname;
[要擊] ambush midway; intercept an enemy;
[要盟] impose an alliance on another state by threat of force;
[要錢] ask for money;
逼人要錢 press a person for money;
[要求] appeal for; ask; bate an ace; beseech; call on; call sth down; claim; crave; demand; entreat; implore; make a request; make an appeal; plead; request; require; requirement; solicit;
要求高的 demanding;
要求者 claimant;
答應要求 acede to a demand; accede to a request;
反要求 counterclaim; counterdemand;
附帶權利要求 accessory claim;
附帶要求 attendant claim;
合法要求 legal claim;
滿足要求 meet a requirement;
難以實現的要求 tall order;
賠償要求 compensation claim;
普遍要求 popular demand;
信息要求 information requirements;
一點要求 a requirement;
再三要求 importune;
戰爭賠償要求 war-damage claim;
準確度要求 accuracy requirement;
[要挾] blackmail; coerce; put pressure on; threaten;
[要約] enter into an agreement;

yao
【祅】 (1) calamity due to terrestrial disturbances; (2) bizarre;

yao
【腰】 (1) midriff; waist; (2) kidneys; (3) pocket; (4) middle of sth;
[腰包] billfold; bum bag; money belt; pocket; purse; wallet;
搜腰包 search sb's pockets; search sb for money and valuables;
掏腰包 dig into one's purse; foot a bill; meet a bill; pay out of one's own pocket; produce one's purse; untie one's purse strings;
~不肯掏腰包 unwilling to spend money;
~自掏腰包 pay out of one's own pocket;
填滿腰包 line one's pockets;
[腰部] lumbar;
腰部疼痛 pain in the lumbar region;

[腰纏] money one carries when travelling;
腰纏萬貫 have ten thousand pieces of silver stored in one's girdle;
[腰帶] belt; girdle; waistband;
吊襪束腰帶 garter belt; suspender belt;
放鬆腰帶 loosen one's waistband;
褲腰帶 trouser belt;
寬腰帶 cummerbund;
勒緊腰帶 tighten one's waistband;
繫着腰帶 wear a waistband;
[腰刀] sabre-like knife;
[腰桿子] back; backing;
腰桿子不硬 have no strong backing;
腰桿子硬 have strong backing;
挺起腰桿子 straighten one's back;
[腰骨] pelvic bones;
[腰果] cashew; cashew nut;
腰果樹 cashew;
[腰肌勞損] strain of lumbar muscles;
[腰如纖柳] her slender waist is supple as an osier;
[腰身] waist;
腰身很胖 have no waist;
腰身纖細 have a slender waist;
[腰痛] lumbago;
一陣腰痛 a stab of lumbago;
[腰腿] nimbleness of one's waist and legs;
腰酸腿疼 aching back and legs;
[腰圍] (1) girth; waist; (2) girdle;
量腰圍 measure sb's waist;
[腰圓] kidney-shaped; oval-shaped;
膀大腰圓 beefy; hefty; hulky; husky; stout;
膀闊腰圓 beefy; broad-shouldered and solidly-built; hefty; husky; stout;
[腰斬] chop in two at the waist;
[腰子] kidneys;
仗腰子 back up sb;

半中腰 halfway; middle;
抱腰 assist; help; lend support to;
叉腰 rest the arms on the hips; stand with arms akimbo;
扠腰 stand with arms akimbo;
撐腰 back up; support;
楚腰 slender waist;
當腰 middle wait;
等腰 isosceles;
蜂腰 wasp waist;
哈腰 (1) bend one's back; stoop; (2) bow;
絝腰 trousers waist;
褲腰 trousers waist;
攔腰 by the waist; round the middle;
懶腰 stretch;
柳腰 slender waist;
攣腰 crooked back;
毛腰 arch one's back;
山腰 half way up the mountain;
伸腰 straighten one's back; straighten oneself up;
彎腰 bend one's back;
細腰 (1) slender waist; (2) slim-waisted wasp;
繫腰 girdle; waistband;
纖腰 slender waist;
折腰 bow;
中腰 middle part of the side;
豬腰 pig kidney;

yao

【葽】 (1) polygala japonica; (2) dense or luxuriant growth of grass or weeds;

yao

【徼】 (1) pray for; (2) hide; shade;
[徼福] pray for blessings;
[徼名] seek fame;

yao

【邀】 (1) ask; invite; request; (2) seek; solicit; (3) intercept; (4) measure; weigh;
[邀寵] (1) make oneself liked by a superior; (2) try to win the spouse's love;
邀寵圖賞 try to please sb so as to win his favour and be rewarded;
[邀功] take credit for someone else's achievements;
邀功請賞 take credit and seek rewards for someone else's achievements;
邀功圖賞 seek credit for another's accomplishment;
[邀集] call together; invite to a gathering; invite to meet together;
[邀擊] intercept and attack; waylay and attack;
[邀截] intercept;
[邀勒] force sb to stay;
[邀留] invite to stop over;
[邀請] invite;
邀請函 invitation card; invitation letter;
發出邀請 send an invitation;
個人邀請 personal invitation;
獲得邀請 have an invitation;

接受邀請 accept an invitation;
拒絕邀請 decline an invitation; refuse an invitation; turn down an invitation;
收到邀請 get an invitation; receive an invitation;
晚宴邀請 dinner invitation;
午宴邀請 lunch invitation;
正式邀請 formal invitation; official invitation;

［邀賞］ try to please sb so as to find favour with him and be rewarded;
［邀宴］ (1) invite to a feast; (2) invitation to a dinner party;
［邀遊］ invite sb for an outing;
［邀約］ (1) invitation; (2) make an appointment;

柬邀 send a written invitation;
特邀 invite specially;
相邀 invite;
應邀 at sb's invitation; on invitation;
招邀 invite; request sb to come;

yao²

yao

【爻】 strokes in diagrams for divination;
［爻辭］ explanations of diagrams for divination;
［爻書］ intertwined scripts;
［爻象］ diagrams for divination;

yao

【肴】 cooked food; dishes;
［肴亂］ confuse; mislead;

yao

【姚】 (1) elegant; good-looking; handsome; (2) a surname;
［姚黃魏紫］ fascinating yellow and lofty purple;

yao

【洮】 a river in Gansu;

yao

【崤】 a mountain in Henan;

yao

【淆】 confused and disorderly; mixed;
［淆亂］ confuse; mislead;
淆亂視聽 confuse and muddle the truth; mislead the public;
［淆雜］ miscellaneous; mixed;

yao

【陶】 as in 臯陶, a person in ancient China;
［陶陶］ delighted; happy;

yao

【堯】 (1) a legendary sage king in ancient China; (2) eminent; high; lofty; (3) a surname;
［堯堯］ lofty; sublime;

yao

【殽】 (1) confusion; disorder; mess; (2) dishes;
［殽核］ dishes and fruit;
［殽亂］ confused; disorderly; messy;
［殽雜］ disorderly; messy;

yao

【軺】 a kind of light carriage;

yao

【搖】 (1) rock; shake; wag; wave; (2) shake; sway; wobble; (3) row; scull; (4) agitate; annoy; incite;
［搖擺］ oscillate; rock; sway; swing; swing to and fro; vacillate;
搖擺不定 play pendulum; swing like a pendulum; tremble in the balance; vacillation and wavering; wave;
搖擺舞 rock-and-roll;
搖擺音樂 swing music;
大搖大擺 astrut; come swaggeringly; roister; swagger;
東搖西擺 totter along;
隨着音樂搖擺 swing to the music;
向兩邊搖擺 sway from side to side;
左右搖擺 vacillate to the left and right;
［搖臂］ rocker arm;
地輪搖臂 bogie rocker arm;
制動搖臂 brake rocker arm;
［搖船］ row a boat;
［搖盪］ rock; sway; swing; wobble;
［搖動］ rock; shake; sway; swing; wave;
搖動用具 shaking appliance;
前後搖動 rock back and forth;
在風中搖動 rock in the wind;
左右搖動 rock from side to side;
［搖桿］ rocker;
排氣搖桿 exhaust rocker;
曲柄搖桿 crank rocker;
［搖滾］ rock-and-roll;
搖滾吉他 rock guitar;

Y

搖滾舞 rock-and-roll dance;
搖滾樂 hard rock; rock music; rock'n'roll;
~迷幻搖滾樂 acid rock;

[搖撼] give a violent shake to; rock; shake to the root or foundation; shake violently;

[搖晃] quake; rock; shake; sway; swing to and fro; unsteady;
搖晃瓶子 shake the bottle;
東搖西晃 faltering; roll oneself from side to side;
前後搖晃 sway back and forth;
在風中搖晃 shake in the wind;
左右搖晃 roll from side to side;

[搖籃] cradle;
搖籃曲 cradle song; lullaby; nursery song;

[搖鈴] ring the bell;

[搖馬] rocking horse;

[搖錢樹] cash cow; legendary tree that sheds coins when shaken—a ready source of money; milch cow; money-maker; money-spinner; money tree;
勤是搖錢樹，儉是聚寶盆 industry is fortune's right hand, and frugality one's left hand;

[搖舌] talk glibly;

[搖手] (1) handle; (2) shake one's hand in admonition or disapproval; wave one's hand;

[搖首] shake one's head in disapproval;

[搖頭] shake one's head;
搖頭擺手 wag one's head and wave one's hand; toss one's head and tail;
搖頭擺尾 shake the head and wag the tail;
搖頭晃腦 nod one's head – assume an air of self-approbation;
搖頭太息 shake one's head and heave a deep sigh; shake the head and utter a deep sigh;

[搖尾] wag the tail;
搖尾狗 trundle-tail;
搖尾乞憐 wag one's tail to seek pity;

[搖搖] shakily; shaky;
搖搖擺擺 go swaying; reeling and swaggering – proud bearing in walking; swagger; swing;
搖搖晃晃 faltering; tottering; shaky; vacillating and staggering; wobbly;
搖搖頭 shake one's head;
搖搖欲墜 crumbling; groggy; hang by a thread; nod to its fall; on the ropes; on the verge of collapse; precarious; ramshackle; shake as if about to fall; shaky; toppling; totter to its fall; tottering; tumble-down; wobbly;

[搖曳] flicker; shaking; sway; wavering gently;
搖曳不定 gutter;
搖曳多姿 shake slightly in many carriages;
翠竹搖曳 green bamboos sway in the breeze;
輕輕搖曳 sway gently;

[搖椅] rocking chair;

動搖 shake; waver;
扶搖 whirlwind;
猛搖 shake; wrench;
飄搖 drift about in the wind; totter;
招搖 act ostentatiously; attract undue publicity; swagger with full pomp;

yao

【傜】 compulsory labour service;

[傜賦] compulsory labour and land tax;

[傜糧] food provisions for forced labourers;

[傜役] conscript labour; corvee;

yao

【猺】 (1) jackal; (2) a tribe in Guangdong, Guangxi, and Yunnan;

青猺 masked civet;

yao

【瑤】 (1) precious jade; (2) clean, pure and white; (3) precious; treasurable; valuable;

[瑤碧] agate with a greenish lustre;

[瑤池] fairyland;
駕返瑤池 mourn for the death of a woman;

[瑤華] (1) blossoms as white and pure as jade; (2) precious; treasurable;

[瑤箋] your letter;

[瑤圃] fairyland;

[瑤臺] (1) tower-like building; (2) beautiful terrace;

[瑤英] most precious kind of jade;

瓊瑤 precious jade;

yao

【遙】 distant; far; remote;

[遙測] telemetering; telemetry;
遙測計 telemeter;
~電流遙測計 current telemeter;
~模擬遙測計 analog telemeter;
~正比遙測計 direct relation telemeter;
遙測天線 telemetry antenna;
遙測資料 telemetry data;
連續遙測 continuous telemetering;
聲學遙測 acoustic telemetry;
位置自動遙測 automatic position telemetering;
載波遙測 carrier telemetering;
自適應遙測 adaptive telemetry;

[遙感] remote sensing;
遙感技術 remote sensing techniques;
遙感衛星 remote-sensing satellite;
多波段遙感 multi-band remote sensing;
機載遙感 airborne remote sensing;
微波遙感 microwave remote sensing;

[遙隔] far-off;

[遙見] see at a distance;

[遙控] distant control; remote control; telecontrol;
遙控板 remote control panel;
遙控器 remote control; remote controller;
遙控設備 remote control equipment;
~安全遙控設備 safety remote control equipment;
遙控裝置 remote-control arrangement;
電子遙控 electronic telecontrol;
繼電遙控 all-relay telecontrol;

[遙臨] approach from afar;

[遙望] look at a distant place; look into the distance; take a distant look;

[遙遙] a long way off; far away;
遙遙領先 enjoy a commanding lead; far ahead; way ahead;
遙遙無期 at a far distant date; in the indefinite future; not within the foreseeable future; put off to the indefinite future; till doomsday;
遙遙相對 face each other across a distance; stand far apart facing each other; stand opposite each other at a distance;

[遙夜] long night;

[遙影] distant shadow;

[遙遠] distant; far and remote; faraway; remote;
遙遠地 from afar;

逍遙 carefree; free and unfettered;

yao

【銚】 (1) a kind of farm tool; (2) a surname;

yao

【嶢】 (of mountains) high; tall;

[嶢嶢] (1) towering; (2) upright;

yao

【窰】 (1) brick furnace; kiln; (2) pottery; (3) coal shaft; (4) cave; (5) brothel;

[窰洞] (1) cave dwelling; (2) opening of a kiln;
地坑式窰洞 underground cave dwelling;
獨立式窰洞 individual cave dwelling;
靠山窰洞 cave dwelling against a mountain;
靠崖式窰洞 cave dwelling against a scarp;
土坯拱窰洞 arched cave dwelling built of sun-dried mud brick;
下沉式窰洞 underground cave dwelling;
沿溝窰洞 sunken cave dwelling along a ditch;
磚石窰洞 brick cave dwelling;

[窰口] arched entrance of a cave dwelling;

[窰臉] front of a cave dwelling;

[窰子] (1) brothel; (2) prostitute;

瓷窰 kiln;
煤窰 coalpit;
炭窰 charcoal kiln;
瓦窰 brickkiln;
磚窰 brickkiln;

yao

【餚】 dishes and food;

[餚饌] sumptuous courses at a meal;

菜餚 cooked dishes;
佳餚 delicacies;
酒餚 wine and delicacies;

yao

【謠】 (1) ballad; folk song; song; (2) rumour;

[謠傳] hearsay; rumour;

[謠誦詬詠] it only needs one puff of rumour to blow up a gale; concoct all sorts of rumours;

[謠俗] folklore;

[謠言] groundless allegation; rumour;
謠言傳開 a rumour spreads;
謠言紛傳 rumour is about;

謠言紛紜 alive with rumours; rumours and gossip are everywhere; rumours are flourishing; there are many rumours going the rounds;
謠言惑眾 delude the people with rumours; lying rumours lead astray the people; wild rumours mislead the masses;
謠言流傳 a rumour goes around; a rumour circulates;
謠言滿天飛 all sorts of rumours are going the rounds;
謠言四起 rumours are rife;
否認謠言 deny a rumour;
編造謠言 cook up a story and spread it around; start a rumour;
傳播謠言 spread a rumour;
散佈謠言 spread a rumour;
證實謠言 confirm a rumour;

［謠諑］ calumny; rumour; slander;
謠諑紛紜 there are many rumours going the rounds;

風謠 folk rhyme; folk song;
歌謠 ballad; ditty; folk song; nursery rhyme; rustic song;
民謠 folk rhyme; folk song;
闢謠 deny a rumour; refute slanders;
俗謠 popular songs;
童謠 children's folk rhyme;
造謠 cook up a story and spread it around; start a rumour;

yao

【繇】 (1) same as 傜, labour service; (2) luxuriant;

［繇賦］ compulsory labour and land tax;
繇役百姓 force the masses to labour for the government;

yao

【鰩】 nautilus; ray;

yao³

yao

【夭】 (1) die young; (2) repress; suppress; (3) fresh-looking; tender; young;

［夭遏］ prevent; stop;
［夭昏］ die young;
［夭壽］ die young;
［夭亡］ die young;
［夭折］ (1) die young; (2) come to a premature end;
中途夭折 wither on the vine;

yao

【杳】 (1) distant and out of sight; (2) deep and expansive; (3) quiet; silent;

［杳眇］ distant and indistinguishable;
［杳冥］ deep, dark and obscure;
［杳然］ lonely; quiet and silent;
杳然無蹤 leave without a trace;
［杳杳無蹤］ gone without leaving a trace; leave without a trace;
［杳遠］ far distance;

yao

【殀】 (1) die young; (2) be wronged;

yao

【咬】 (1) bite; sink one's teeth into; snap at; (2) bite; grip; (3) bark; (4) incriminate another person when blamed or interrogated; (5) articulate; pronounce; (6) nitpicking;

［咬扯］ give vent by angry talking;
［咬定］ insist;
一口咬定 assert categorically; cling to one's view; insist emphatically; insist on saying sth; state categorically; stick to one's statement; stick to what one says; stubbornly assert that; the arbitrary assertion that;
［咬破］ (1) bite through; break with one's teeth; (2) make a thorough remark about sth;
［咬人］ bite;
會叫的狗不咬人 barking dogs seldom bite; great barkers are no biters;
［咬舌］ have a lisp; lisp; speak imperfectly; speak with a lisp;
［咬牙］ (1) grit one's teeth; (2) grind one's teech;
咬牙切齒 clench one's teeth; gnash one's teeth; grind one's teeth; set one's teeth;
［咬住］ (1) bite into; grip with one's teeth; (2) grip; refuse to let go of; seize; take firm hold of;
［咬字］ enunciate;
咬字清楚 enunciate clearly; have clear articulation; pronounce every word clearly;

反咬 against one's accuser;

yao

【窈】 (1) deep; obscure; secluded; (2) tranquil;

［窈冥］ (1) dusky; obscure; (2) deep; mysterious; profound;

［窈窕］ (1) attractive and charming; gentle and graceful; quiet and modest; (2) far and deep; secluded;

窈窕淑女 modest and refined maiden; quiet and modest maiden; slender, graceful girl;

［窈窈］ (1) dusky; obscure; (2) far and deep; profound;

yao

【舀】 ladle out water;

［舀水勺］ baler;

［舀湯］ ladle out soup;

［舀子］ dipper; ladle; scoop;

yao

【窅】 (1) far and deep; mysterious; (2) sad;

［窅眇］ deep; far and deep;

［窅冥］ (1) far and deep; obscure and mysterious; (2) sunken eyes;

［窅然］ sad; touched;

［窅窅］ (1) sombre; (2) deep;

yao

【齩】 bite;

yao⁴

yao

【要】 (1) essential; important; necessary; (2) ask for; desire; want; wish; (3) ask sb to do sth; (4) want to; wish to; (5) it is necessary; must; ought to; should; (6) be going to; shall; will; (7) need; take; (8) might; must; (9) if; in case; suppose;

［要隘］ key point; strategic pass;

［要便］ often; usually;

［要不］ if not; or; or else; otherwise;

［要不要］ would you like to have;

［要衝］ communication centre; communication hub; key place; strategic position;

［要道］ thoroughfare;

［要得］ desirable; fine; good;

要得到 sweat out;

要不得 intolerable; no good; not be tolerated; objectionable; unacceptable;

［要地］ important place; strategic point;

［要點］ alpha and omega; essentials; gist; key points; main points;

要點歸納如下 the main points may be summarized as follows;

概括要點 outline the essentials;

基本要點 nuts and bolts;

講授要點 teach the essentials;

明確要點 keep the essentials in view;

學習要點 learn the essentials;

總結要點 sum up the main points;

［要端］ essentials; main points;

［要犯］ important criminal; most-wanted criminal;

［要飯］ beg alms;

要飯的 beggar;

［要港］ important port; key port;

［要害］ (1) crucial points; vital parts; (2) key point; strategic point;

打中要害 deal a blow at the heart; drive the nail; hit home; hit on the vital spot; hit squarely on the chin; hit the mark; hit the nail on the head; hit the right nail on the head; hit where it really hurts; strike home; touch sb to the quick;

迴避要害 parry the crucial issue;

擊中要害 cut to the quick; have hit at the nub of; hit close to home; hit home; hit sb where it hurts; hit sb's vital point; hit the point; shoot home; strike at the root of; strike home; touch sb's tender spot;

抓住要害 take up a vital part;

［要好］ (1) befriend; close friends; on good terms; (2) desire to excel; eager to improve oneself; try hard to make progress; (3) in love with;

［要謊］ ask a price higher than the real cost of commodities;

［要價］ ask a price; charge; offer;

要價昂貴 ask a heavy price;

［要件］ (1) important document; (2) important condition;

［要津］ key post;

位居要津 hold a key post; hold a sensitive position; occupy a key position;

［要緊］ (1) essential; important; (2) critical; matter; serious;

不要緊 it doesn't matter; no matter;

［要勁］ make strenuous efforts;

［要訣］ key to success in doing sth;

[要口] important checkpoint;
[要括] summarize;
[要領] essentials; gist; important points; main points;
不得要領 miss the point;
不切要領 off the point; pointless;
領會要領 see the main points;
掌握要領 gain the essentials; seize the essentials;
[要路] (1) main route; thoroughfare; (2) eminent position;
[要略] (1) important plan; (2) outline; summary; synopsis;
[要麼] or;
要麼…要麼 either...or; have the alternative of;
[要眇] (1) attractive; (2) engaging; significance and abstrusity;
[要命] (1) nuisance; (2) awfully; extremely; (3) too much to endure; (4) drive sb to death;
笨得要命 as stupid as an owl; as stupid as they make them;
長得要命 as long as one's arm;
煩得要命 bored to death;
渴得要命 extremely thirsty; have a spark in one's throat;
恨得要命 burning with inveterate hatred;
冷得要命 be damn cold;
怕得要命 fear intensely; go in mortal fear of; in mortal fear; mortally fear;
嚇得要命 be frightened out of one's life; bring sb's heart into his mouth; frighten the hell out of sb; frighten the living daylights out of sb; frighten the pants off sb; frighten the shit out of sb; make sb's heart leap out of his mouth; scare the hell out of sb; scare the living daylights out of sb; scare the pants off sb; scare the shit out of sb;
想得要命 miss sb very much; want to do or get sth very badly;
兇得要命 fiendish;
[要目] main items; principal points;
[要強] aggressive; eager to be at the top; strive to excel;
[要人] biggie; big gun; big shot; heavyweight; man of the moment; prominent figure; very important person (VIP);
要人善忘 person of importance easily forgets;
當地要人 local notable;
小地方的要人 a big fish in a little pond;
[要塞] citadel; fort; fortress; strategic point; stronghold;
[要是] if; in case; suppose;
要不是 but for; but that; if it had not been for; if it wasn't for; if it were not for;
[要事] important matter; urgent business;
另有要事 have another fish to fry;
[要死] to death;
要死要活 desperate;
病得要死 sick into death;
煩得要死 be plagued to death;
怕得要死 be frightened out of one's wits; be frightened to death; be scared to death; half dead with fear;
~怕得要死，恨得要命 beside oneself with fright and hatred; fear and hate to the utmost; mortally fear and bitterly hate;
嚇得要死 be frightened to death;
笑得要死 die with laughter; laugh oneself to death;
[要素] chief factors; chief ingredients; essentials; essential facts; key elements;
成功要素 essentials to success;
基本要素 basic essentials;
經濟要素 economic factors;
生活要素 factor in living;
[要圖] important plan; urgent task;
[要聞] front-page story; headlines; important news items;
[要我說] if I had my way;
[要務] important business; urgent business;
[要險] be concerned with one's honour;
[要項] key item; key point;
[要言不煩] give the essentials in simple language; in brief and without any tedious words; pithy; succinct; terse;
[要義] alpha and omega; essentials; key points; main themes;
科學要義 the alpha and omega of science;
[要因] essential factor; important cause;
[要員] big hitter; high-ranking officials; high-up; higher-up; important officials; top brass;
軍事要員 military top brass;
[要之] in a nutshell; in short; to sum up;
[要知] the person who wishes to know;

要知河深淺，須問過河人 the person who has waded through water knows it best;
要知前方路，須問過來人 he who wishes to know the road ahead must ask those who have trodden it; if you wish to know the road ahead, inquire of those who have travelled it;
要知水深淺，須問過來人 the person who has waded through the river knows it best;
要知心腹事，但聽口中言 if you wish to kno a man's thoughts, you need only to listen to his conversation;

[要職] important post;
竊居要職 occupy a high post unjustly; usurp a high post;
身居要職 hold an important position; occupy an important position;

[要旨] essential ideas; gist; key points; main ideas; the whole point of sth;
計劃的要旨 keystone of the plan;

必要 indispensable; necessary;
不要 do not;
衝要 strategically important places;
次要 less important; minor; secondary; subordinate;
撮要 make an abstract;
大要 outline; main points;
扼要 brief and to the point;
概要 essentials; outline;
綱要 (1) outline; sketch; (2) compendium; essentials;
機要 confidential;
輯要 abstract; summary;
紀要 summary of minutes;
簡要 brief; concise and to the point;
將要 be going to; will;
緊要 critical; vital;
訣要 knack; secret of success; tricks of the trade;
切要 essential; indispensable;
首要 of the first importance;
樞要 central administrative department;
提要 make an abstract;
顯要 important personage; powerful and influential;
險要 strategically located and difficult of access;
須要 have to; must;
需要 need; want;
摘要 make a summary;
祇要 provided; so long as;
至要 most important;
重要 important; significant;
主要 main; principal;

yao
【葯】 (1) angelica; (2) same as 約, to wrap up; (3) simplified form of 藥;

yao
【樂】 delight in; fond of; like; love;
[樂群] fond of company and learning from one's friends;

yao
【曜】 (1) daylight; sunshine; (2) glisten; shine;
[曜靈] sun;

yao
【燿】 same as 耀, shine brilliantly;

yao
【藥】 (1) drug; medicine; remedy; (2) cure with medicine; (3) kill with poison;
[藥杯] medicine glass;
[藥餅] cake of medicine;
[藥補] herbal diet;
藥補不如食補 a diet cures more than the doctors; a kitchen physic is the best physic;
[藥材] medicinal materials;
[藥草] medicinal herbs;
[藥廠] pharmaceutical factory;
[藥單] prescription;
[藥到病除] act like a charm; as the medicine takes effect, the symptoms lessen;
[藥典] pharmacopeia;
[藥店] chemist's shop; drugstore; pharmacy; the chemist's;
[藥方] prescription;
開藥方 make a prescription; prescribe medicine; write out a prescription;
[藥房] chemist's shop; dispensary; drugstore; pharmacy;
藥房主任 head of pharmacy;
[藥費] expenses for medicine;
藥費昂貴 medicine is expensive;
交付藥費 pay the expenses of medicine;
[藥粉] medicinal powder;
[藥膏] ointment; salve; unguent;
配製藥膏 make up an ointment;
塗藥膏 apply an ointment;
一管藥膏 a tube of ointment;

[藥劑] drug; medicament; medicine; remedy;
藥劑師 chemist; dispensing chemist; druggist; pharmacist;
藥劑學 pharmaceutics; pharmacy;
[藥酒] medicinal liquor;
[藥力] efficacy of a drug;
藥力發作 the drug is taking effect;
[藥理學] pharmacology;
[藥量] dosage;
[藥籠中物] talents in reserve;
[藥片] pill; tablet;
[藥品] drugs; pharmaceutical products;
配製藥品 prepare medicines;
[藥瓶] medicine bottle;
[藥鋪] dispensary; druggist's store; herbal medicine shop;
[藥散] medicinal powder;
[藥商] chemist; drug dealer;
[藥師] chemist; druggist; pharmacist;
主管藥師 pharmacist-in-charge;
主任藥師 chief pharmacist;
~副主任藥師 deputy chief pharmacist;
[藥石] (1) medicines and stone needles for acupuncture; (2) sincere admonitions;
藥石罔效 all kinds of medicine are unavailing; all medical treatment has failed; all medicines have failed to effect a cure; all medicines are tried and found useless; medicines produce no effect; no drugs are of any avail; pass treatment;
藥石之言 sincere admonitions;
[藥水] (1) liquid medicine; medicinal liquid; (2) lotion;
眼藥水 eye drops;
一瓶藥水 a bottle of liquid medicine;
[藥糖] lozenge;
[藥丸] pill medicine;
藥丸盒 pill-box;
[藥物] drugs; medicament; medicine; pharmaceuticals;
藥物過敏 drug allergy;
藥物檢驗 drug test;
藥物中毒 drug poisoning;
管制藥物 controlled substance;
缺乏藥物 lack medical supplies;
注射藥物 injectable drugs;
[藥箱] medical kit; medicine chest;
[藥性] nature of a drug; property of a medicine;
[藥言] sincere admonitions;
藥言可取 sincere admonitions are acceptable;
[藥用] for medical use;
[藥油] medical oil;
抹點藥油 apply some medical oil;
[藥皂] medicated soap;

安眠藥 sleeping pill;
安胎藥 a medicine for stabilizing fetus to prevent from abortion or miscarriage;
熬藥 decoct medicinal herbs;
白藥 white medicinal powder;
鼻藥 nose drops;
表藥 medicine administered to bring out the cold;
補藥 tonic;
擦藥 apply ointment;
採藥 gather medicinal herbs;
草藥 medicinal herbs;
搽藥 rub on some external medicine;
成藥 patent medicine;
舂藥 pound medicinal herbs in a mortar;
春藥 love potion; philter; aphrodisiac;
催情藥 philter;
打藥 cathartic;
彈藥 ammunition;
毒藥 poison; toxicant;
防暑藥 heat-stroke preventive;
服藥 take medicine;
膏藥 plaster;
國藥 traditional Chinese medicine;
焊藥 solder; welding flux;
花藥 anther;
火藥 gunpowder;
急救藥 first-aid medicine;
煎藥 decoct medicinal herbs;
解表藥 diaphoretic;
解毒藥 antidote;
酒藥 yeast for brewing rice wine;
苦藥 acrid drug;
良藥 effective medicine; good medicine;
涼藥 medicine of a cold nature;
麻藥 anaesthetic;
蒙藥 anaesthetic; narcotic;
猛藥 strong cure;
迷幻藥 hallucinogenic;
妙藥 miraculous cure; panacea;
抹藥 apply ointment to the affected area;
內服藥 medicine for oral administration;
凝血藥 coagulant;
農藥 agricultural chemical; pesticide;

配藥 make up a prescription;
熱藥 medicine of a hot nature;
乳藥 take poison;
入藥 be used as medicine;
殺蟲藥 insecticide; pesticide;
山藥 Chinese yam;
上藥 apply ointment to the affected area;
芍藥 Chinese herbaceous peony;
生藥 crude drug;
聖藥 effective medicine;
施藥 dispense medicine free of charge;
試藥 reagent;
鼠藥 rat poison;
司藥 chemist; pharmacist;
湯藥 decoction of medicinal ingredients;
投藥 medicate;
特效藥 effective cure; specific drug;
土藥 home-made opium;
丸藥 pill of Chinese medicine;
萬靈藥 cure-all; panacea; wonder drug;
外敷藥 medicine for external application;
勿藥 recover from illness;
西藥 Western medicine;
下藥 (1) prescribe a medicine; (2) put in poison;
仙藥 elixir;
顯影藥 developer;
消炎藥 antiphlogistic;
瀉藥 cathartic; laxative;
心藥 sychological treatment;
眼藥 eye ointment; eyedrops; medicament for the eyes;
一錠藥 a tablet;
一服藥 a dose of medicine;
一粒藥 a pill; a tablet;
一片藥 a pill;
一帖藥 a dose of herbal medicine;
一丸藥 a pill;
一味藥 one of the ingredients is a medicinal herb;
一種藥 a kind of medicine;
醫藥 medicine;
引藥 supplementary dose;
炸藥 explosive;
止瀉藥 antidiarrheal;
止血藥 haemostatic;
製藥 pharmacy;
中草藥 Chinese herbal medicine;
中藥 traditional Chinese medicine;
抓藥 fill a prescription;
裝藥 filling; powder charge;
佐藥 adjuvant;
坐藥 suppository;

yao
【颻】 waving and drifting with the wind;

yao
【耀】 (1) dazzle; shine; (2) boast of; show off; (3) credit; honour;
［耀光］ sparkle; sparkling;
［耀目］ dazzle;
［耀眼］ dazzling;
耀眼增光 dazzling;
［耀耀］ bright;

炳耀 bright and luminous;
光耀 (1) brilliance; brilliant light; (2) glorious; honourable;
誇耀 brag about; show off;
榮耀 glorious;
閃耀 glitter; shine;
顯耀 (1) be well-known for one's fame or power; (2) show off;
炫耀 (1) beam; dazzle; (2) make a display of; show off;
照耀 illuminate; shine;

yao
【躍】 bound; jump; leap; spring; vault;
［躍動］ in lively motion; move actively;
［躍過］ vault over;
躍過圍欄 vault over the fence;
［躍進］ (1) leap forward; (2) make rapid progress;
［躍馬］ give the horse its head; let a horse gallop;
橫刀躍馬 gallop ahead with one's sword drawn;
［躍起］ jump up; leap up;
［躍躍欲試］ eager to have a try;

跳躍 bound; jump; leap;

yao
【鷂】 hawk; sparrow hawk;
［鷂鷹］ hawk; sparrow hawk;
［鷂魚］ ray;
［鷂子］ (1) sparrow hawk; (2) kite;

yao
【鑰】 key; lock;
［鑰匙］ key; unlocking key;
鑰匙保管員 keyholder;
鑰匙兒 key ring;
鑰匙卡 key card;

鑰匙孔 keyhole;
鑰匙鏈 keychain;
鑰匙圈 key ring;
房門鑰匙 door key;
萬能鑰匙 master key; passkey; skeleton key;
一把鑰匙 a bunch of keys; a key;
一把鑰匙開一把鎖 open different locks with different keys — use different methods to deal with different people; use the right key to open the lock;
一串鑰匙 a bunch of keys; a string of keys;

ye¹

ye

【耶】 Jesus;

ye

【掖】 (1) conceal; hide; (2) squeeze in; stuff; (3) fold; roll up;

［掖進去］ stuff sth with;
［掖掖蓋蓋］ clandestinely; stealthily;

藏掖 try to cover up;

ye

【噎】 (1) choke with food; (2) choke off;

ye²

ye

【邪】 (1) answer in unison; (2) same as 耶, an ending particle;

［邪呼］ answer in unison;
［邪許］ call out in one voice; yell in unison;

ye

【耶】 phrase-final particle for a question;

ye

【琊】 used in 琅琊, ancient name of the eastern portion of Shandong;

ye

【揶】 jeer at; play a joke on; ridicule;

［揶揄］ deride; jeer at; play a joke on; ridicule; taunt; tease;

ye

【椰】 coconut; coconut palm; coconut tree;

［椰菜］ savoy;
花椰菜 cabbage; cauliflower;
［椰雕］ coconut carving;
［椰林］ coconut forest;
一片椰林 a grove of coconut;
［椰肉］ coconut meat;
［椰樹］ coco; coconut palm; coconut tree;
［椰油］ coconut butter; coconut oil;
［椰子］ (1) coconut palm; (2) coconut;
椰子餅 coconut cake;
~蛋白椰子餅 macaroon;
椰子樹 cocoa palm; coconut tree;
椰子糖 coconut candies;
椰子汁 coconut milk;
［椰棕］ coconut fibre;

棗椰 date palm;

ye

【爺】 (1) grandfather; (2) father; (3) master; sir; (4) god;

［爺娘］ father and mother;
打爺罵娘 unfilial;
［爺爺］ (1) grandfather; grandpa; (2) sir;
老爺爺 great-grandfather;

阿爺 dad; daddy; pa; papa;
包爺 (1) person who undertakes a lawsuit; (2) go-between in business who receives a cut of the profit;
大爺 (1) uncle; grandpa; (2) gluttonous idler; (3) lazy, arrogant and wilful man;
佛爺 Buddha;
姑爺 son-in-law;
侃爺 big talker;
老太爺 (1) old gentleman; (2) your father;
老天爺 heavens;
老爺 grandfather;
姥爺 maternal grandpa; maternal grandfather;
少爺 (1) young master of the house; (2) your son;
師爺 private assistant in a local yamen;
太爺 great-grandfather;
王爺 his royal highness;
灶王爺 kitchen god;

ye³

ye

【也】 also; among the number; and; and neither; and so; as; as well; as well as; either; equally; like; likewise; neither; neither...nor; no less; no more; no more...than; nor; not...any more than; not...either;not only...but also; or; same; so; too; vice versa;

［也罷］ never mind;

也罷…也罷 or; or not; whether...or;
[也好] all well and good; it may not be a bad idea; may be well; that is fine;
[也就] and then;
[也就是說] consequently; in other words; namely; that is; that is to say;
[也是] also the same;
[也未可知] maybe; perhaps;
[也行] all right; that will do too;
[也許] maybe; perhaps; probably;
[也有] (1) there are in addition; (2) there are others;

ye
【冶】 (1) fuse metal; smelt metal; (2) fascinating; seductively dressed or made up;
[冶工] blacksmith;
[冶金] metallurgy;
冶金學 metallurgy;
~化學冶金學 chemical metallurgy;
~火法冶金學 dry metallurgy;
~有色冶金學 copper metallurgy;
汞齊冶金 amalgam metallurgy;
細菌冶金 bacteria metallurgy;
氧化冶金 chlorine metallurgy;
[冶煉] smelt;
冶煉廠 smeltery;
[冶容] (1) seductive looks; (2) wear seductive make-up;
冶容誨淫 a bewitching countenance invites lewdness; seductive looks incite to wantonness; dress prettily invites adultery;
[冶艷] beautiful; charms; pretty and coquettish;
[冶業倡倏] loose women picked up by men; prosititues and courtesans; women of easy virtue;
[冶游] frequent brothels; visit prostitutes;

陶冶 (1) make pottery and smelt metal; (2) exert a favourable influence on;
妖冶 pretty and coquettish;

ye
【野】 (1) countryside; fields; open country; wilderness; (2) boundary; limit; (3) not in power; out of office; (4) barbarous; rude; uncultivated; undomesticated; untamed; wild; (5) rough; rude; (6) abandoned; unrestrained; unruly;
[野菜] edible wild vegetables;
[野餐] go on a picnic; picnic;
野餐地點 picnic place; picnic site; picnic spot;
野餐區 picnic area;
野餐提籃 picnic basket; picnic hamper;
野餐者 picnicker;
野餐桌 picnic table;
去野餐 go on a picnic;
一次野餐 a picnic;
[野草] weed;
野草叢生 be choked with weeds; be overgrown with weeds;
野草閒花 girls to be picked up; loose women picked up by men; promiscuous women; prostitutes and courtesans; women of easy virtue;
拔除野草 pluck out weeds; root up weeds;
拔野草 pull up weeds;
除盡野草 extirpate weeds;
除去野草 weed out weeds;
掘野草 dig up the weeds;
長滿野草 be overgrown with weeds;
[野炊] cook a meal in the open;
[野服] simple dress;
[野狗] pie-dog; pye-dog; stray dog; wild dog;
野狗逐食 like mongrels fighting over garge;
[野合] illicit connection; illicit copulation;
[野花] (1) wild flowers; (2) harlot;
野花閒草 girls to be picked up; loose women picked up by men; prostitutes and courtesans; women of easy virtue;
家花不如野花香 extramarital relationships are more pleasurable; the harlot is more charming than one's own wife;
遍地野花 wild flowers blossom everywhere;
[野火] bush fire; prairie fire; twitchfire; wild fire;
[野雞] (1) pheasant; (2) street walker; unlicensed prostitute;
打野雞 visit low-class brothels;
[野老] aged peasant; aged rustic; old man;
[野驢] onager;
[野馬] bronco; jughead; mustang fury horse; uncontrolled person; wild horse;

騎野馬 ride the bronco;

[野蠻] (1) barbarous; brutal; cruel; uncivilized; (2) brutal; rough; rude; unreasonable;
野蠻的 brutal;
野蠻人 barbarians; savages;
野蠻事件 brutality;
野蠻行為 brutality;

[野貓] (1) alley cat; serval; wild cat; (2) badger;

[野牛] bison; wild ox;

[野禽] wild fowl;

[野犬] wild dog;

[野人] barbarian; rustic; savage; wild man;
野人獻曝 a countryman offers the heat of the sun as a present; present sunshine to a king; trivial contribution;

[野生] uncultivated; undomesticated; wild;
野生動物 undomesticated animals; wild animals; wildlife;
~野生動物絕種 extinction of wild animals;
~保護野生動物 protect wild life;
野生性 wildness;
野生植物 agrarian plants; undomesticated plants; wild plants;

[野史] privately compiled history; unofficial history;

[野獸] brute; wild animal; wild beast;
野獸派 fauvism;
捕獵野獸 hunt a wild beast;
馴服野獸 tame a wild beast;
一群野獸 a pride of animals;
追趕野獸 chase a wild beast;
追蹤野獸 trace a wild beast;

[野兔] hare;
一隻野兔 a hair;

[野外] field; open country; outdoors;
野外旅行 excursion; outing;
野外實習 conduct fieldwork;
野外演習 have a field exercise;
野外運動 field sports;
睡在野外 sleep in the open country;
在野外 in the open;

[野味] game; venison;

[野心] (1) ambition; wild ambition; (2) greediness;
野心勃勃 a flight of ambition; be obsessed with ambition; be overweeningly ambitious; burn with an ambition; full of ambition; indulge oneself in ambition; lust for;
野心不死 cling to one's ambitious designs; one's personal ambitions unsatisfied;
野心家 adventurist; ambitious schemer; careerist; man of ambition;
狼子野心 a cruel person with wild ambitions; a person greedy and cruel and full of wild ambitions; a person who will stop at nothing to satisfy his wild ambitions; a wicked monster; a wild ambition; a wolf with a savage heart; a wolfish ambition; a wolfish nature; an ambitious wolf cub; diabolical ambitions; savage like a wolf in disposition; the ambition of a wolf cub; the devouring ambition of a careerist; wolfish ambition;
領土野心 territorial ambition;
政治野心 political ambition;

[野性] jungle instincts; unruliness; untamed; wild nature;
野性難改 wild nature cannot be changed easily;
野性難馴 untamable;

[野鴨] wild duck;
一群野鴨 a flock of wild ducks;

[野營] camping; outdoor camping;
野營車 camper; camper van;
野營活動 camping;
結束野營 break up a camp;
去野營 go camping;

[野戰] field operations;
野戰部隊 combat troops; field forces;
野戰軍 field army;
野戰醫院 field hospital;

[野豬] boar;

蔽野 cover the whole field;
遍野 scatter over the wilderness;
草野 (1) among the people; (2) non-governmental;
朝野 (1) the court and the commonalty; (2) the government and the public;
粗野 boorish; rough; uncouth;
村野 villages and fields;
分野 dividing line;
荒野 the wilds; wilderness;
郊野 countryside; outskirts;
狂野 violent and rough;
曠野 wilderness;
平野 open country outside a city;

清野 clear the fields;
丘野 rural country;
撒野 act boorishly; act wantonly; act wildly; behave atrociously; behave rudely; run wild;
山野 mountain villages and the remote wilderness;
識野 field of awareness;
視野 field of vision;
疏野 impolite; rude;
四野 surrounding country;
田野 field; open country;
沃野 fertile land;
下野 be forced to relinquish power; resign from official posts; retire from the political arena;
鄉野 pastoral; rural;
原野 open country;
越野 cross-country;
在野 not be in office;
朝野 the government and the people;

ye4

ye

【曳】 drag; haul; tow; tug;

［曳網］ seine;
底層曳網 ground seine;
地曳網 beach seine; haul seine;
無兜曳網 bagless beach seine;

［曳足而行］ walk with a shuffling gait;

拖曳 drag and pull;
搖曳 flicker; sway;

ye

【夜】 (1) evening; night; (2) dark; darkness; (3) night trip; night traveling;

［夜班］ graveyard shift; night duty; night shift; night work;
上夜班 go on night shift; graveyard shift; work on a night shift;
~上夜班的人 night shift;
下夜班 off night duty;
值夜班 on night duty;

［夜半］ dead of night; midnight;
夜半更深 late at night;
夜半破門 break into sb's house at midnight;
夜半敲門 beat upon sb's gate in the middle of the night;

［夜不成眠］ lie awake all night; remain awake till daybreak; sleep refuses to come; unable to sleep at night;

［夜不交睫］ never sleep a wink at night;

［夜餐］ midnight meal; night snack;

［夜娼］ night walker;

［夜長夢多］ a long delay may give rise to many a hitch; a long delay means many hitches; a long night gives rise to many dreams; a long night is fraught with dreams; delay always brings danger; there is many a slip between the cup and the lip;
路必有彎，夜長夢多 a long lane has its twists and turns and a long night is fraught with dreams;

［夜場］ evening show; night show;

［夜車］ (1) night train; (2) burn the midnight oil; study late at night;
開夜車 burn the midnight oil; consume the midnight oil; put in extra time at night; sit up deep into the night; sit up late; stay late at work; stay up late; stay up until midnight; turn night into day; work deep into the night; work far into the night; work late into the night; work overtime at night;

［夜燈］ nightlight;
小夜燈 nightlight;

［夜度娘］ prostitute;

［夜蛾撲火］ a moth flying into the fire; a moth throwing itself into a flame; bring destruction upon oneself; flirt with death; seek one's own doom;

［夜分］ midnight;

［夜工］ night job; night work;

［夜光］ moonlight;
夜光棒 lightstick;
夜光雲 noctilucent cloud;

［夜航］ night flight;

［夜壺］ chamber pot;

［夜活］ night work;

［夜間］ at night; in the night-time; night; night-time;

［夜景］ night scenes; nightscape;

［夜靜］ the dead of night; the still of the night;
夜靜更深 the dead hours of the night; in the still of night; the dead of night;

［夜課］ night classes;

［夜來香］ evening primrose; night willow herb;

[夜闌] in the dead of night; late at night;
夜闌人靜 all is quiet in the dead of night; deep in the night; in the dead of night; in the still of night;
[夜裏] at night; night-time;
在夜裏 in the night;
[夜涼如水] chilling autumn night;
[夜漏] in the night-time;
[夜盲] night blindness;
夜盲症 night blindness;
~先天性夜盲症 congenital night blindness;
[夜貓子] (1) owl; (2) person who enjoys night life; nighthawk;
[夜幕] cope of night; curtain of night; gathering darkness;
夜幕降臨 evening closes in; night has fallen; the night screen has hung down;
[夜尿] nocturnal enuresis;
[夜勤] night duty; night shift; night work;
[夜曲] nocturne;
小夜曲 serenade;
[夜色] dim light of night;
夜色黯然 the night is getting dark;
夜色蒼茫 twilight at dusk;
夜色沉沉 the night is dark;
夜色漸濃 the night grows blacker; the night is pressing up;
夜色降臨 night falls;
夜色闌珊 in the hushed stillness of night; in the quiet of night;
夜色籠罩 be enveloped in darkness;
夜色茫茫 night resumes its reign;
夜色漆黑 the night is pitch dark;
趁着夜色 by moonlight; by starlight;
[夜深] in the dead of night; late at night;
夜深漏殘 in the dead of night;
夜深人靜 at the dead of night; in the dead hours of the night; in the quiet of the night; in the stillness of the night; the night is dark and silent;
夜深人靜不眠時 in the still watches of the night;
[夜市] night fair; night market;
逛夜市 visit night markets;
[夜嗽] nocturnal cough;
[夜臺] grave;
[夜晚] dark hours; in the night; night;
夜晚天光 skylight;
夜晚的寂靜 the still of the night; stillness of the night;
趁着夜晚 by night;
每個夜晚 at night; every night;
萬籟俱寂的夜晚 in the still of the night;
星光照耀的夜晚 starlit night;
[夜望鏡] snooperscope;
[夜襲] night attack; night raid;
[夜戲] evening performance; night show;
[夜宵] night snack;
吃夜宵 have a midnight snack;
[夜校] evening class; evening school; night school;
上夜校 attend evening classes;
[夜夜] every night; night after night;
[夜鶯] nightingale;
夜鶯啾啾叫 a nightingale jugs;
[夜鷹] goatsucker; nighthawk; nightjar;
[夜月靜明] the night is still and the moon is at its full;
[夜住曉行] resting at night and travelling by day;
[夜總會] nightclub;
夜總會區 clubland;
泡夜總會 clubbing;
[夜作] night work;
打夜作 work overtime at night;

暗夜 dark night;
熬夜 burn the midnight oil; far into the night; keep up; sit up; sit up late at night; sit up deep into the night; sit up far into the night; stay up; stay up all night; stay up late; stop up; up for; wait up; work late into the night; work until deep into the night;
白夜 white night;
半夜 (1) half of the night; (2) in the middle of the night; midnight;
丙夜 midnight;
查夜 go the rounds at night;
長夜 long night;
徹夜 all night long; all through the night;
除夜 New Year's Eve;
隔夜 of the previous night;
過夜 (1) pass the night; stay overnight; (2) of the previous night;
寒夜 chilly night; cold night;
黑夜 blind man's holiday; dark night; night;
後半夜 second half of the night; small hours;
極夜 polar night;
今夜 this evening; tonight;

連夜 that very night; the same night;
漏夜 midnight; the dead of night;
年夜 Lunar New Year's Eve;
起夜 get up in the night to urinate;
前半夜 first half of the night;
前夜 eve; the night before last;
清夜 in the stillness of night;
晴夜 clear night;
日夜 day and night; round the clock;
入夜 at nightfall;
上半夜 before midnight;
上夜 on night duty;
深夜 deep in the night; in the small hours of the morning; late at night;
守夜 keep night watch; keep watch at night; spend the night on watch;
刷夜 spend the night outside with shady characters;
夙夜 day and night; morning and night;
宿夜 morning and night;
歲夜 New Year's Eve;
通夜 all night; the whole night;
午夜 midnight;
戊夜 predawn hours;
下半夜 time after midnight;
宵夜 midnight snack;
消夜 midnight snack;
星夜 starlit night; starry night;
巡夜 go on night patrol;
遙夜 long night;
一夜 one evening;
夤夜 at the dead of night; deep in the night; in the depth of the night;
永夜 a long night;
元夜 night of the fifteenth of the first lunar month;
月夜 moonlit night;
整夜 all night long; the whole night; throughout the night;
值夜 on duty for the night;
中夜 midnight;
終夜 all night long; the whole night;
晝夜 day and night; round the clock;
子夜 midnight;

ye

【咽】 choke; speak in a choked vocie; weep in a choked voice;

［咽嗚］ sob;
咽嗚抽泣 be seized with convulsive sobbing;
咽嗚啼哭 cry and sob softly;
咽咽嗚嗚 break out into sobs;

悲咽 grieve and sob;
鼻咽 nasopharynx;
哽咽 choke with sobs;
喉咽 laryngopharynx;
淒咽 (of voice) low and sad; sob while speaking;
舌咽 glossopharyngeum;
嗚咽 (1) sob; whimper; (2) make mournful sounds;
幽咽 (1) whimpering; (2) murmuring;

ye

【拽】 (1) drag; pull; (2) drag after; trail;

ye

【頁】 (1) leaf; sheet of paper; (2) page;

［頁邊］ margin;
［頁次］ page number;
［頁腳］ footer;
［頁碼］ page number;
頁碼編定 pagination;
頁碼標注 pagination;
［頁眉］ header;
［頁面］ page;
頁面頂端 top of the page;
［頁式］ page;
頁式印刷機 page printer;
頁式閱讀機 page reader;
［頁尾］ footer;
［頁岩］ shale;
瀝青頁岩 bituminous shale;
泥質頁岩 argillaceous shale;
燭煤頁岩 cannel shale;

版權頁 copyright page;
冊頁 album of paintings or calligraphy;
插頁 insert; inset;
襯頁 end-paper;
對頁 facing page; opposite page;
扉頁 title page;
附頁 attached sheet;
合頁 hinge;
後頁 backpage;
畫頁 page with illustration; plate;
活頁 loose-leaf;
空白頁 blank page;
配頁 gather;
篇頁 articles and pages;
前頁 front matter;
缺頁 missing page;
首頁 first page; title page;
書名頁 title page;

書頁 page;
網頁 website;
折頁 fold;

ye
【射】 a pronunciation of 射, as in 僕射;

ye
【掖】 (1) extend a helping hand; support another; (2) armpits; (3) by the side; side; (4) side-apartments in the palace;
［掖門］ small side door of the palace;

扶掖 help support;
宮掖 palace chambers;
獎掖 reward and promote;
誘掖 guide and help;

ye
【液】 fluid; juices; liquid;
［液化］ liquate; liquefaction; liquefy;
液化空氣 liquefied air;
液化器 liquefier;
~空氣液化器 air liquefier;
液化石油氣 liquefied petroleum gas;
液化天然氣 liquefied natural gas;
液化沼氣 liquid marsh gas;
級聯液化 cascade liquefaction;
明膠液化 gelatin liquefaction;
氣體液化 gas liquefaction;
［液晶］ liquid crystal;
液晶電視 LCD colour television;
液晶顯示 liquid crystal display;
~液晶顯示屏 liquid crystal display panel;
~液晶顯示器 liquid crystal display device;
［液體］ liquid;
液體比重計 hydrometer;
液體打火機 liquid lighter;
液體動力學 hydrodynamics;
液體灌裝機 liquid filter;
液體火箭 liquid rocket;
液體吸氣計 absorptionmeter;
締合液體 associated liquid;
散裝液體 bulk liquids;
霧化液體 atomized liquid;
［液壓器］ hydraulic press;

補液 fluid infusion;
腸液 intestinal juice;
定影液 fixing bath;
毒液 venom;
廢液 waste liquid;
汗液 perspiration; sweat;
焊液 soldering fluid; welding fluid;
滑液 synovia;
漿液 size;
津液 (1) body fluid; (2) saliva;
浸漬液 maceration extract;
浸液 infusion;
精液 come; cum; semen; seminal fluid;
淚液 tear;
淋巴液 lymph;
濾液 filtrate;
母液 mother liquor; mother solution;
腦脊液 cerebrospinal fluid;
黏液 mucus;
尿液 urina; urine;
強鹹液 aqueous alkali;
染液 dye liquor;
溶液 solution;
乳化液 emulsion;
乳液 emulsion;
乳濁液 emulsion;
乳狀液 emulsion;
神經液 neurohumour;
滲出液 ooze;
輸液 infuse;
漱液 gargarism;
水溶液 aqueous solution;
提取液 extract;
體液 body fluid;
銅氨液 cuprammonia;
唾液 saliva;
胃液 gastric juice;
消化液 digestive juice;
懸濁液 turbid liquid;
血液 blood;
胰液 pancreatic juice;
雲液 (1) wine; (2) name for mica;
真溶液 real solution;
汁液 juice;
組織液 tissue fluid;

ye
【腋】 armpit;
［腋毛］ armpit hair;
［腋窩］ armpit;
［腋下］ armpit; under the arm;

肘腋 elbow and armpit;

ye
【業】 (1) industry; line of business; trade;

(2) job; occupation; profession; (3) course of study; (4) cause; enterprise; (5) estate; property; (6) engage in; (7) already; (8) action; deed; karma;

[業戶] owner of property;

[業荒於嬉] distraction deprives work of excellence;

業精於勤荒於嬉 a fertile field, when neglected, will produce nothing but weeds and thorns; the progress of studies comes from hard work and is retarded by frivolities;

[業績] feat; track record;

業績不佳 underperform;

業績審計 performance audit;

[業界] industry;

業界巨頭 caption of industry;

[業精於勤] a subject is mastered through diligent study; efficiency comes from diligence; rich knowledge and great ability come from diligence; the essential of work is diligence; the progress of studies comes from hard work;

[業權] proprietorship;

[業師] one's teacher;

[業務] business activities; official functions; professional work; vocational work;

業務尖子 professional backbone;

業務能力 professional ability; professional proficiency;

業務性質 professional quality;

業務賬戶 activity account;

保險業務 insurance business;

不談業務 sink a shop;

純業務 net business;

代理業務 agency business;

貸款業務 money-lending business;

埋頭業務 engross oneself in vocational work;

批發業務 wholesale business;

日常業務 day-to-day business;

外匯業務 foreign exchange business;

信托業務 fiduciary business;

學習業務 pursue one's vocational study;

鑽研業務 study diligently one's profession;

租船業務 charter business;

[業醫] practise medicine;

[業餘] (1) after-hours; sparetime; (2) amateur;

業餘愛好的 amateurish; Corinthian;

業餘愛好者 amateur;

業餘畫家 amateur painter;

業餘兼職工作 after-hours job;

業餘上課 attend classes after working hours;

業餘行為 amateurism;

業餘演出 amateur performance;

[業主] property owner; proprietor;

獨資業主 personal proprietor;

女業主 proprietress;

小業主 petty proprietor;

罷業 go on strike; shopkeepers' strike; strike;

霸業 accomplishments of obtaining the dominant position;

報業 business of the press;

本業 (1) agriculture; farming; (2) original occupation;

畢業 finish school; graduate;

閉業 wind up one's business;

捕鯨業 whale-fishery;

採礦業 mining industry;

產業 estate; property;

常業 career occupation;

創業 do pioneering work; set up business; start an undertaking; start up in business;

從業 get a job; take up an occupation;

大業 great cause; great undertaking;

待業 awaiting assignment to a job; awaiting employment; wait for employment;

電影業 film industry;

伐木業 lumbering;

復業 re-establish a business; resume or return to business;

副業 auxiliary occupation; side-line occupation; subsidiary occupation;

工商業 industry and commerce;

工業 industry;

功業 achievements; exploits;

行業 biz; branch of a trade; calling; industry; line of business; line of work; profession; trade;

宏業 great achievement;

基業 base; foundation;

鴻業 achievements of a ruler;

家業 family property;

結業 complete a course; wind up one's studies;

就業 get a job; obtain employment;

開業 (1) go into operation; open for business; set up shop; start business; (2) open a private practice;

課業 lessons; school-work;
礦業 mining industry;
立業 start one's career;
林業 forestry;
牧業 animal husbandry; livestock farming;
釀酒業 win-making industry;
農業 agriculture; farming;
企業 business; enterprise;
請業 ask questions concerning lessons;
輕工業 light industry;
商業 business; commerce; trade;
生業 means of livelihood; profession;
失業 at an idle end; at leisure; at loose ends; in dry dock; jobless; on the beach; on the dole; out of a job; out of bread; out of employment; out of work; fall out of employment; go on the dole; have no work; lose one's employment; lose one's job; lose one's work; unemployed; unemployment;
實業 industry and commerce;
始業 begin;
事業 (1) cause; undertaking; (2) enterprise;
手工業 handicraft industry;
守業 safeguard one's heritage;
受業 be taught; your student;
授業 teach; tutor;
水產業 aquatic products industry;
嗣業 inherit a business; inherit a fortune;
素業 former profession; former vocation;
宿業 karma;
糖業 sugar industry;
停業 (1) close down; stop doing business; (2) stop doing business temporarily;
同業 (1) same trade or business; (2) person of the same trade or business;
為業 as a means of livelihood;
偉業 exploit; great cause;
無業 (1) unemployed; (2) without property;
物業 property;
歇業 close a business; go out of business;
休業 (1) be closed down; suspend business; suspension of business; (2) come to an end of a short-term course;
修理業 repairing trades;
修業 study at school;
緒業 business; calling;
畜產業 livestock products industry;
畜牧業 animal husbandry; livestock farming;
學業 one's studies; school work;
勳業 meritorious service and great achievement;
鹽業 salt industry;
養蠶業 sericulture;
養蜂業 apiculture;
養禽業 poultry industry;
養魚業 fishery;
遺業 business left behind by one's ancestors;
肄業 study in school or at college;
淫業 profession of prostitution;
飲食業 catering trade;
營業 do business;
魚業 fishery;
漁業 fishery;
運輸業 transport service;
在業 employed;
擇業 choose an occupation;
造船業 ship-building;
造紙業 paper-making industry;
製造業 manufacturing industry;
正業 regular occupation;
執業 (1) engage in a profession or trade; (2) vocation or trade;
職業 occupation; profession; vocation;
紙業 paper enterprise; paper industry;
置業 buy a house;
重工業 heavy industry;
專業 (1) specialized subject; (2) specialized trade or profession;
轉業 be transferred to another job;
卒業 graduate;
祖業 (1) undertaking of one's ancestors; (2) estate handed down from one's ancestors;
作業 school assignment;

ye

【葉】 (1) foliage; leaf; (2) leaf-like thing; (3) leaf; page; (4) part of a historical period; (5) a surname;

［葉柄］ petiole;
［葉黃素］ xanthophyll;
［葉綠素］ chlorophyll;
［葉綠體］ chloroplast;
［葉輪］ impeller;
封閉式葉輪 closed impeller;
離心式葉輪 centrifugal impeller;
氣動葉輪 air impeller;
［葉落］ leaves fall;
葉落歸根 an apple does not fall far from the apple tree; the fruit falls near the branch; the leaves always fall toward the root;
葉落知秋 one falling leaf is indicative of the coming of autumn; the falling leaves announce the approach of

autumn;
風舞葉落 the wind blows and the leaves fall to the ground;

[葉脈] vein;
葉脈序 leaf venation;

[葉片] (1) blade; leaf blade; (2) van;
葉片排列 blade arrangement;
葉片裝置 blading;
~衝動式葉片裝置 impulse blading;
~倒車葉片裝置 back blading;
~反動式葉片裝置 reaction blading;
~渦輪機葉片裝置 turbine blading;
~正車葉片裝置 ahead blading;
安裝葉片 blading;
不扭曲葉片 non-warped blade;
插入式葉片 inserted blade;
長葉片 linear leaf;
衝擊式葉片 impulse section blade;
重疊葉片 overlapped blades;
導向葉片 guide blade; guide vane;
等截面葉片 uniform-section blade;
動葉片 rotor blades;
反作用葉片 reactance blade; reaction blade;
分離葉片 separate blade;
分流葉片 split blade;
風機葉片 fan blade;
渦輪葉片 turbine;
~燃氣渦輪葉片 gas-turbine blade;
後曲葉片 backward curve blade;
後彎葉片 sweptback blade;
徑向葉片 radial blade;
靜葉片 stator blade;
可調葉片 adjustable blade; adjustable vane;
螺旋槳葉片 propeller blade;
螺旋葉片 helical blade;
離心葉片 centrifuge blade;
末級葉片 exhaust stage blade; last stage blade;
扭葉片 warped blade;
扭轉葉片 twist blades;
平葉片 flat blade;
強制渦流葉片 forced vortex blade;
鎖緊葉片 loacking blade;
調頻葉片 frequency-modulating blade;
~不調頻葉片 unturned blade;
推料葉片 pusher blade;
削短葉片 shortened blade;
圓頭葉片 round-nosed blade;
整體葉片 integral blade;
直立彎葉片 vertical curved blade;
直葉片 prismatic blade;
~徑向直葉片 straight radial blade;
鑄造葉片 cast blade;
轉動葉片 moving blade; rotating blade;
錐形葉片 taper blade;
自由渦流葉片 free vortex blade;

[葉柵] cascade; cascade of blades; vane cascade;
導向葉柵 blade cascade;
渦流環葉柵 vortex-ring cascade;
壓氣機葉柵 compressor cascade;

[葉舌] ligule;

[葉酸] folic acid;

[葉型] leaf type;

[葉子] leaf;
開始長出葉子 come into leaf; in leaf;
一片葉子 a leaf;

抱莖葉 amplexicaul leaf;
孢子葉 sporophyll;
敗葉 fallen leaves;
捕蟲葉 insect-catching leaf;
殘葉 fallen leaves;
草葉 grass;
茶葉 tea; tea leaves;
齒狀葉 serrate leaf;
匙形葉 spatulate leaf;
初葉 (1) early years of a century; (2) primordial leaf;
單葉 simple leaf;
對生葉 opposite leaf;
肺葉 lobe of the lung;
複葉 compound leaf;
肝葉 hepatic lobes;
肝右葉 right lobe of the liver;
肝左葉 left lobe of the liver;
合葉 hinge;
荷葉 lotus leaf;
紅三葉 red clover;
紅葉 red autumn leaf; red leaf;
互生葉 intergrowth leaf;
急尖葉 acute leaf;
箭頭形葉 sagittate leaf;
漸尖葉 acuminate leaf;
槳葉 paddle;
闊葉 broad-leaved;
蔞葉 betel-peper;
卵圓形葉 ovate leaf;
輪生葉 verticillate leaves;
落葉 (1) fallen leaves; (2) deciduous leaf;
末葉 last years;
嫩葉 tender leaves;

披針形葉 lancolate leaf;
胚葉 germinal layer;
桑葉 mulberry leaves;
十字形對生葉 decussate leaf;
樹葉 foliage; leaves of a tree;
霜葉 leaves turning white;
雙生葉 binate leaf;
桐葉 leaves of a paulownia;
托葉 stipule;
完全葉 complete leaf;
無柄葉 sessile leaf;
線形葉 linear leaf;
菸葉 tobacco leaf;
煙葉 tobacco leaf;
一葉 a leaf;
圓頭葉 obtuse leaf;
掌狀葉 digitate leaf;
針葉 conifer;
枝葉 (1) branches and leaves; (2) minor details; non-essentials;
中葉 middle period;
子葉 cotyledon;

ye

【曄】 (1) bright; radiant; (2) prosperous; thriving;

[曄然] prosperous; thriving;
[曄曄] prosperous; thriving;

ye

【謁】 call on; have an audience with; pay one's respects to; see a superior;

[謁告] ask for leave of absence;
[謁歸] go home on leave;
[謁見] call on; have an audience with; see a superior;
[謁禁] ban on visitors;
[謁片] calling card; visiting card;
[謁舍] guest house; hostel;

拜謁 (1) call to pay respect; pay a formal visit; (2) pay homage;
參謁 (1) pay one's respects to; (2) pay homage to;
晉謁 call on sb; have an audience with;
請謁 ask for an audience;
趨謁 go and see a senior;
詣謁 pay a visit to sb;

ye

【鄴】 (1) ancient name for a part of present-day Henan; (2) a surname;

ye

【燁】 blazing; glorious; splendid;

ye

【擪】 press with a finger;

ye

【靨】 dimples in the face;

[靨子] mole on the cheek;

酒靨 dimple;
笑靨 (1) dimple; (2) smiling face;

yi¹

yi

【一】 (1) one; (2) same; uniform; union; (3) alone; single; (4) all; throughout; whole; (5) concentrated; wholehearted; (6) each; every; per; (7) a; an; the; (8) as soon as; once;

[一把] a bunch of; a bundle of; a handful of; a pair of; a wisp of;

一把勁 one's energies;
~鼓一把勁 marshal one's energies; put on a spurt;
一把抓 (1) authoritarian; dictatorial; grasp all the authority; grasp all the power; take everything into one's own hands; (2) fail to put first things first; try to tackle all problems at once regardless of their relative importance;
撈一把 gain some advantage; make a hand of; profiteer; rake in profit; reap some profit;
~大撈一把 reap fabulous profits;
倒打一把 blame others while one is at fault oneself; bring a completely false accusation against; falsely accuse one's critic; lay the blame on others while oneself is at fault; make false charge; make unfounded counter charges; put the blame on one's victim; recriminate; trump up a countercharge against one's accuser;
拉他一把 give sb a helping hand; help sb;
抓一把 take a handful;

[一百] one hundred;

一百八十度轉彎 a 180-degree turn; do an about-turn; make a 180-degree about-face; make a turn of 180 degrees; make an about-turn;
一百週年 centenary; centennial;

百不得一 not one out of a hundred is acceptable;
百不失一 there is not a single miss in a hundred tries;
百裏挑一 a person in a thousand; cream of the crop; one among many; one in a hundred; one in a thousand; pick one out of a hundred;
~百裏挑一的人物 sb is only one among many;
百中無一 not one in a hundred;
懲一儆百 make an example of sb; punish one as a warning to a hundred; punish one to warn a hundred;
教一儆百 teach one person by punishment to warn a hundred;
人一己百 if others succeed by making one ounce of effort, I will make a hundred times as much effort;
殺一儆百 execute one as a warning to a hundred; execute one to warn a hundred; kill sb as a warning to others; put one person to death as a warning to hundreds of others;
一了百了 all troubles end when the main trouble ends; death ends all one's trouble; the solution of one problem leads to the solution of all other problems;
一樹百獲 there are many advantages in fostering people of ability; to encourage the talented will be rewarded manifold;
一順百順 nothing succeeds like success;
一死百了 death pays all scores; death quits all scores; death squares all accounts;
一以抵百 a match for a hundred men; able to withstand a hundred men;
以一當百 everyone is worth a hundred; one will be worth a hundred;
以一奉百 with one working to provide for a hundred;
以一警百 punish one as a warning to the others; punish one to caution a hundred; punish one to warn many;

[一敗] a defeat;
一敗如水 be defeated completely; sustain a crushing defeat;
一敗塗地 a complete debacle; a complete failure; a complete fiasco; a crushing defeat; a dead failure; a total loss; an overwhelming defeat; be completely destroyed; be routed; be ruined completely; beat hollow; bite the dust; bite the ground; collapse completely; done to the wide; done to the world; down and out; fail completely; fall to the ground; get the worst of it; hunt grass; ignominious defeat; play checkmate with; put to rout; suffer a crashing defeat;

[一班] (1) a class; a group; a squad; a troupe; (2) a class of; a group of; a squad of; a troupe of;

[一斑] a speck; a spot; a tiny part;
得窺一斑 able to see a segment of a whole;
窺豹一斑 have only a limited view; see a segment of a whole; see one ringed spot on a leopard;
窺一斑而知全豹 from a part one may divine the whole; from his foot you may know Hercules;

[一般] (1) as a rule; common; generally; usually; (2) just like; same as;
一般詞 general word;
~一般詞匯 general lexicon;
一般化 vague generalization;
一般見識 bother oneself arguing with; hold the same kind of view; lower oneself to the same level as sb;
一般來説 generally speaking;
一般理論 the general theory of employment, interest and money;
一般條款 general administrative clauses;
一般系統理論 general system theory;
一般性 common quality; generality;
~一般性詞典 general dictionary;
~一般性翻譯 general translation;
一般性翻譯理論 general translation theory;
~一般性同義詞 general synonym;
~一般性文獻 general text;
~一般性文摘 general abstract;
~一般性知識 general knowledge;

[一板] mechanical;
一板三眼 work in a mechanical way and refuse to make appropriate adaptations;
一板一眼 following a prescribed pattern; in good order and well arranged; in regular sequence; methodically;

scrupulous and methodical; step by step;

[一瓣] a segment of; a petal of; a section of; a slice of;

[一半] half; in part; moiety; one half;

一半天 in a day or two;

多一半 (1) most; most likely; probably; (2) the greater part;

一鱗半爪 fragments; odd bits; odds and ends; scrapes of;

一星半點 a tiny bit; a very small amount; just a little; slightest;

一言半語 a word or two;

一知半解 a smack of knowledge; a smattering of knowledge; half knowledge; half-baked knowledge; have only a smattering; incomplete comprehension; know only superficially; tyro and smatterer;

用去一半 spend half of it;

[一幫] (1) a band; a clique; a gang; a group; a mob; (2) a band of; a clique of; a gang of; a group of; a mob of;

[一鎊] a pound;

[一包] (1) a bale; a box; a bundle; a pack; a package; a packet; a parcel; a sack; (2) a bale of; a box of; a bundle of; a pack of; a package of; a packet of; a parcel of; a sack of;

[一抱] an armful of;

[一報還一報] like for like; measure for measure; requite like for like;

[一杯] a cup of; a glass of; a mug of; a tankard of;

一杯在手，萬事全丟 forget everything when a cup of wine is in one's hand;

倒一杯 fill a cup of;

分一杯羹 have a finger in the pie; have a share; take a share of the spoils;

喝一杯 drink a cup of; have a cup of; have a drink; take a cup of; wet one's whistle;

~去喝一杯 go for a drink;

再來一杯 the same again;

[一倍] double;

比…多一倍 as many again as; as much again as;

長一倍 as long again as;

大一倍 as big again as; as large again as;

~比…大一倍 as large again as;

[一輩] a generation;

一輩子 a lifetime; all one's life; as long as one lives; man and boy; one's whole lifetime; throughout one's life;

~一輩子的朋友 lifelong friend;

~白活一輩子 (1) dishonour one's white hair; (2) pass one's life in vain;

老一輩 older generation;

[一本] (1) a book; a copy; a reel; a volume; (2) a book of; a copy of; a reel of; a volume of;

一本萬利 a small investment brings a ten-thousand-fold profit; make a ten-thousand-fold profit; gain enormous profit out of small capital investment; make big profits with a small capital;

一本正經 in a serious manner; in all seriousness; in dead earnest; in downright earnest; in sad earnest; keep a straight face; poker-faced; priggery; priggish; prim and proper; prudish; with feigned impartiality; with the utmost gravity;

[一鼻子灰] be rebuffed; meet frustration; meet humiliation; meet rejection; run into a stone wall;

抹一鼻子灰 get rebuffed when trying to please; meet with a rebuff; suffer a snub;

碰一鼻子灰 be sent off with a flea in one's ear; be snubbed; cold shoulder; get rebuffed; knock one's nose into ashes; meet with a rebuff; singe one's feathers; suffer a snub;

~鍋膛裏吹火—碰一鼻子灰 blow at the fire in a stove; get rejected; get snubbed; have one's nose smudged with ashes;

[一筆] (1) a debt of; a sum of; (2) one stroke;

一筆勾銷 abolish at one stroke; cancel; clean the slate; liquidate; out to the bone; pass the sponge over; reject offhand; score out; settle an account once and for all; undo sth by a single stroke; wipe off the slate; wipe out; write off at one stroke;

一筆抹殺 be gainsaid; blot out at one stroke; completely deny; condemn out of hand; cut to the bone; go to naught; obliterate; reject offhand; totally negate; write off wholesale; write off with one stroke of the pen;

[一碧萬頃] boundless; vast; watery blue reaching far beyond the horizon;

[一壁] at the same time; simultaneously;

[一邊] (1) one side; (2) aside; beside; by the side; on one side;

一邊倒 enjoy overwhelming superiority; fall on one side; lean to one side; side with sb without reservation;

~一邊倒的 lopsided;

向一邊地 crabwise;

[一遍] once; one time;

[一變] change;

搖身一變 by a sudden metamorphosis; change one's identity; give oneself a shake and change into another form; suddenly change; take a different form with a shake; up to the trick of a volte-face; with a twist of the body, one makes a sudden change;

[一表非俗] a person of uncommon appearance and very noble in his looks; unlike the common run of men;

[一併] all; along with all the others; at the same time; in the lump; together with; wholly;

[一波] a ripple; a wave;

一波不興 no bubble comes up; there is not a ripple on the water;

一波方平，一波又起 a new wave arises when the previous one has barely subsided; one storm has scarcely subsided when another breaks out; one woe goes, another comes;

一波三折 a series of frustrations; full of twists and turns; full of ups and downs; hit one snag after another; meet repeated difficulties; striking one snag afer another; suffer one setback after another; with turns and twists; with ups and downs;

一波未平，一波又起 before one squabble is over the next one crops up; catastrophes follow one another; hardly has one wave subsided when another rises — one trouble follows another; it never rains but it pours; misfortunes never come alone; one event succeeds another;

[一步] a single step; a step;

一步不讓 fight every inch of the way; not to yield a step;

一步步 step by step;

一步登天 a meteoric rise to fame; a sudden rise in life; fast advancement in one's career; have a meteoric rise; have a sudden success; reach Heavens at a single bound — have a meteoric rise; reach the sky in a single bound — attain the highest level in one step;

一步三回頭 with every step one looks back three times;

一步一顛 one's head nodding with every stride; stagger along;

一步一個腳印 every step leaves its print — work steadily and make solid progress; leave one's foot-mark with every step; one step leaves one foot-mark — do things in a down-to-earth manner;

一步一鬼 a suspicious heart will see imaginary ghosts;

一步一看 take one step and look around before taking another;

一步一趨 follow in sb's footsteps; follow others at every step; follow suit blindly;

比人領先一步 keep one step ahead of sb; stay one step ahead of sb;

不尋常的一步 unusual step;

第一步 the first step;

積極的一步 positive step;

進一步 go deeper into; take a step forward; take further steps; to better;

前所未有的一步 unprecedented step;

搶先一步 steal a march on sb;

退一步，進兩步 a step backward today will mean two steps forward in the days to come;

~退一步說 even if that is so; even so;

~退一步想 on second thoughts;

下一步 the next step;

向前邁前的一步 a step forward;

朝正確方向邁出的一步 a step in the right direction;

走錯一步 one false move; one false step;

~走錯一步路 make a wrong move;

走一步 take a step;

~走一步看一步 do as one sees fit; take one step and look around before taking another — proceed without a long-range plan;

［一部］ a volume of; a work of;
一部分 a part; a portion; partial; partially;
［一餐］ a meal;
美味的一餐 a delicious meal;
［一冊］ a copy of;
人手一冊 everybody has a copy; in everybody's hand;
［一層］ (1) one floor; one story; (2) a stratum; (3) a bed of; a blanket of; a cloak of; a coat of; a curtain of; a deck of; a film of; a flake of; a floor; a floor of; a layer; a layer of; a level of; a line of; a mantle of; a ring of; a story; a story of; a veil of;
一層樓 a storey;
～欲窮千里目，更上一層樓 ascend another storey to see a thousand miles further; if you want to have a more distant view, go up another storey.
一層一層地 in layers;
［一刬］ one and all; without exception;
［一場］ (1) a performance; (2) a bout of; a game of;
痛哭一場 give free vent to one's sorrow with many tears and loud laments; have a good cry;
［一唱三歎］ one sings and the other three joins in; sing or write with affected pathos;
［一朝天子一朝臣］ a new chief brings in new aides; a new dynasty uses new ministers; every emperor has a cabinet composed of his own favourites; every new sovereign brings his own courtiers—a new chief brings in new aides;
［一車］ a load of;
［一臣不事二主］ a man cannot serve two masters;
［一塵不染］ as clean as a new pin; free from dust; not be soiled by a speck of dust; not be stained by a speck of dust; spotlessly clean; there is not a speck of dust; remain uncontaminated; spotless;
［一成］ ten percent;
一成不變 conservative; fixed and unchangeable; hard and fast; immutable and frozen; inflexible; invariable; it is unchanging and unchangeable; move in a rut; run in a groove; set in one's ways; unalterable; unchangeable;
一成一旅 narrow in territory and scanty in troops; weak in force;
［一程］ a short distance;
［一匙］ a spoon; a spoonful of;
［一籌］ a tally;
一籌莫展 at one's wit's end; at the end of one's rope; at the end of one's tether; can find no way out; find oneself in the mire; helpless; in a completely hopeless position; in an impasse; not have a feather to fly with; not knowing what to do; nothing can be done; stick oneself in the mire; up a gum tree; with one's finger in one's mouth;
更勝一籌 better by one tally;
技高一籌 more skilful;
較勝一籌 a little better; better by one degree;
聊勝一籌 slightly better;
略勝一籌 a cut above; a notch above; a stroke above; just a little better; keep one step ahead of; one-up one sb; slightly better; slightly superior to;
稍勝一籌 a cut above; a notch above; just a little better; just a shade better; slightly better; slightly superior to;
稍遜一籌 a cut below; slightly inferior to;
勝人一籌 a stroke above; one-up on sb;
［一觸即潰］ be easily put to rout; be routed at the first encounter; collapse at the first encounter;
［一串］ a bunch of; a cluster of; a rope of; a strand of; a string of;
［一詞］ a word;
一詞多義 polysemy;
不贊一詞 keep silent; make no comment;
不置一詞 lay out not a single word; not to utter a comment;
各執一詞 cling to one's own interpretation; each holds to his own statement; each one has his own words; each sticks to his own version;
［一次］ (1) once; one time; (2) a liner;
一次不成例 once is no rule;
一次被咬，下次膽小 once bitten twice shy;
一次性 one-off;
有一次 on one occasion; once;
［一叢］ a clump of; a patch of; a thicket; a tuft

of; a tussock of;

[一蹴而就] accomplish in one move; accomplish one's aim in one move; at a heat; at one stroke; expect results overnight; gain success in one step; reach at a single leap; reach the goal in one step; succeed in doing sth at the first try; win an easy success; with one bound;

[一簇] a bunch of; a clump of; a cluster of; a group of; a tuft of; a wisp of;

[一撮] a handful of; a pinch of;

一小撮 a handful of;

[一打] a dozen;

一打一拉 alternate hard an soft tactics; hit and cajole by turns; strike and stroke alternately; use the stick and the carrot;

[一代] a generation; a generation of;

下一代 younger generation;

[一袋] a bag of; a pouch of; a sack of;

一小袋 a sachet of;

[一帶] area; surroundings;

一帶而過 glance off; make a casual remark in passing;

[一擔] a load of; two baskets of; two buckets of;

[一旦] (1) as soon as; in case; once; whenever; (2) someday; (3) a day;

毀於一旦 be destroyed in a moment; be destroyed in one day; be wiped out in a day;

[一黨] one party;

一黨制 single-party system;

一黨專政 one-party dictatorship;

[一檔] first gear;

[一刀] a cut of;

一刀兩斷 break apart with one stroke; break off all relations with; break with.. once and for all; cut into two at one stroke of the knife; give sb the gate; make a clean break with; part grass rags with; sever at one blow; sever at one stroke; sever relations by one stroke; through with;

一刀切 allow no flexibility; cut it even at one stroke — make it rigidly uniform; impose uniformity; make it a hard-and-fast rule; simply ask all areas to do the same thing at the same time;

[一道] (1) alongside; on the same path; side by side; together; (2) a; one; (3) a beam of; a coat of; a flash of; a line of; a shaft of; a streak of; a trail of;

[一得] a good idea;

一得一失 a gain here, a loss there; gain in one thing and lose in another;

一得之功 a minor success; an occasional success;

一得之愚 my humble opinion;

[一燈如豆] the light of a rapeseed oil lamp is as small as a pea;

[一等] first-class; first-rate; top-grade; top-notch;

低人一等 a cut below others; a grade lower than others; inferior to others;

高人一等 a cut above other people;

加人一等 a cut above most people; a cut above others; a notch above the others;

罪加一等 doubly guilty;

[一滴] a blob; a drop;

[一點] (1) a few; a little; a little bit; in a way; partial; small amount; some; to some extent; (2) a bit of; a dash of; a modicum of; a morsel of; a piece of; a speck of; a sprinkling of; a stroke of; a trifle of; a whiff of; an ounce of; (3) a point;

一點不假 absolutely true; on the dead; true as I stand here; upon my word;

一點點 dust; pick; tad;

一點兒 a bit; a bit of; a little; a morsel of; a shade; a streak of; a trifle; a whit; faintly; slightly; something;

~ 差一點兒 not good enough; not quite up to the mark; slightly inferior to; within a hair of; within an ace of; within an inch of;

一點也不 not a jot; not a jot or tittle; not an iota; not by a jugful; not one iota; not one jot or tittle;

~ 一點也不難 no sweat;

~ 一點也不在乎 not care a brass button; not care a button; not care a jot;

一點一滴 bit by bit; every bit; every drop; every little bit;

一點一點地 bit by bit; by bits; inch by inch;

攻其一點，不及其餘 attack sb for a particular fault without taking other

things into account; attack sb for a single fault without considering his other aspects; pounce on one point and ignore all others; seize upon one point and ignore the overall picture;
關於那一點 on that score;

[一吊] a string of;

[一碟] a dish of; a plate of;

[一疊] a heap of; a pile of; a sheaf of; a wad of;

[一丁點兒] a wee bit;

[一定] (1) fixed; regular; specified; (2) certain; given; particular; (3) bound to; certainly; must; surely; necessarily; (4) due; fair; proper;
一定是 it must be so;
一定有鬼 there is sth fishy;
一定之規 a fixed pattern; a set rule; one's own way;

[一錠] a tablet of; an ingot of;

[一丟點兒] just a tiny bit;

[一丟就忘] out of sight, out of mind;

[一冬] one winter season;

[一動] (1) a jerk; a jolt; a move; move once; (2) at every turn; easily; frequently;
一動不動 keep one's body unmoved; not move a muscle; not move an inch; not stir; perfectly still;
~一動不動地站着 stand still; stand stockstill;
一動不如一靜 better rue sit than rue flit; better sit and rue than flit and rue; moving is not as good as staying put; to stay put is better than to move;
一動兒 easily; frequently;

[一棟] a building; a house;

[一斗] hodful;

[一讀] first reading;

[一睹為快] enjoy the pleasure of sb's acquaintance; glad to see sb;

[一度] (1) at one time; for a time; once; (2) on one occasion;

[一端] (1) one end; (2) one respect; one side of the matter;
舉其一端 for instance; just to mention one example;

[一段] (1) one paragraph; one passage; one stanza; (2) a chunk of; a leg of; a length of; a period of; a piece of; a section of; a streak of;

[一堆] a bank of; a bundle of; a crop of; a crowd of; a group of; a heap of; a host of; a mass of; a mountain of; a pile of; a ruck of; a tumble of;

[一隊] (1) a contingent; a detachment; (2) a body of; a caravan of; a column of; a fleet of; a flotilla of; a group of; a team of; a train of; a platoon of;

[一對] a brace; a couple; a pair;
一對一 mano a mano; one-for-one; one-to-one;
~一對一對等詞 one-to-one equivalent;
~一對一對應 one-to-one correspondence;
一對一對應詞 one-to-one correspondent;
~一對一翻譯 one-to-one translation;

[一墩] a cluster of;

[一頓] (1) a pause; (2) a fit of; a meal of;
抽打一頓 give sb a belting;
大罵一頓 break into a torrent of abuse;
亂吹一頓 brazen-faced braggarts;
亂打一頓 lash out at;
痛打一頓 give sb a good beating; give sb a sound thrashing; lash out at sb;
揍一頓 beat; give a sound beating;
~痛揍一頓 give sb a thorough beating;

[一…多…] one...many...;
一專多能 become expert in one field while at the same time possessing all-round knowledge and ability; expert in one thing and good at many; master many skills while specializing in one;

[一二] a few; a little;
一二三五六一沒事 one, two, three, five and six; – nothing goes amiss;
粗知一二 have a rough idea about; know a little; know sth about;
但知其一，不知其二 have only a partial understanding of a situation;
得一望二 have an insatiable desire to acquire more;
獨一無二 in a class by itself; one and only one; second to none; singular; solitary; the only one in existence; the only one of its kind; the original without copies; unique; unmatched; unparalleled;
合二而一 combine two into one; two combining into one;
略知一二 have a rough idea; have a smattering of it; know just a little;
數一數二 among the best; at the top of the

ladder; count as one of the very best; top-notch; one of the best; the first or second;

說二不一 a person of word; keep one's promise; stand by one's word;

說一不二 as good as one's word; mean what one says; stand by one's word;

說一是一，說二是二 to say one it is one and to say two it is two; whatever one says goes;

一不做，二不休 a thing once begun will not be put off until done; as well be hanged for a sheep as for a lamb; carry the thing through, whatever the consequences; go any length; go to great lengths; go to all lengths; go the whole hog; in for a penny, in for a pound; over shoes, over boots;

一大二公 large in size and collective in nature; larger in size and having a higher degree of public ownership;

一而二，二而一 exactly the same thing;

一分為二 a whole divides into two; bisect; divide one into two; one divides into two; rend in two; split into two;

一就是一，二就是二 one is just one and two just two;

一平二調 equaliterianism and indiscriminate transfer of resources;

一僕難侍二主 no man can serve two masters;

一窮二白 backward both economically and culturally; grinding poverty; poor and blank; poor and culturally blank; poverty and blankness;

一石二鳥 kill two birds with one stone;

一是一二是二 carefully;

有一必有二 never twice without three times;

有一無二 the one and only; the only one of its kind; unique; unmatched; unparallelled;

知其一，不知其二 aware of one aspect and be ignorant of the other; have a one-sided view; have only a partial understanding of a situation; know only a part of the story; know only one aspect of a thing;

~祇知其一，不知其二 aware of only one aspect and ignorant of the other; one cannot see the wood for the trees;

祇見其一，不見其二 see only one side of the matter and overlook the other;

[一發] a round of; an outbreak of; even; together;

一發難收 once started it can hardly stop;

[一番] (1) a dose of; a lot of; a piece of; (2) once;

[一帆風順] be coming up roses; bon voyage; go like a dinner of broth; go on smoothly without a hitch; good innings; pan out; plain sailing; roses all the way; sail before the wind; smooth sailing; without a hitch;

祝你一帆風順 all the best;

[一反] a reversal of; contrary to;

一反常態 act out of one's character; act out of one's normal behaviour; contrary to one's moral behaviour; contrary to one's usual practice; contrary to the way sb usually behaves; depart from one's normal behaviour; go into a flat spin; not to be one's usual self; reverse one's previous stand;

[一方] (1) a party; one side; (2) a region; an area; (3) a cubic meter of; a piece of; a square of;

一方受災，八方支援 when one place is hit by a disaster, help streams in from all over the country;

一方之寄 a responsible government position which carries considerable authority;

各霸一方 each lorded it over a district;

天各一方 each in a different corner of the world; far apart; far away from each other; live far apart from each other; we are each in a different quarter;

雄霸一方 hold a part of the country and exercise undisputed authority; rule by force in a region — as a feudal lord; take forcible possession of a territory;

在道義的一方 on the side of the angels;

在善的一方 on the side of the angels;

[一分錢] a cent;

一分錢一分貨 get what one pays for; give value for value; nothing for nothing; nothing for nothing and every little for a halfpenny; the higher the price, the better is the quality of the merchandise;

一分錢也不能減 not bate a penny of it;

[一份] (1) a part; a portion; a share; (2) a copy of; a helping of; a list of; a piece of; a portion of; a slice of;

一小份 spice;

[一服] a dose of;

[一幅] a piece of;

[一副] (1) a pair; a set; (2) a look of; a pack of; a pair of; a set of;

[一概] all; totally; without exception;

一概而論 lump together; lump under one head; make sweeping generalizations; take in the lump; treat different matters as the same;

一概其餘 draw inferences about other cases from one instance;

[一缸] a jar of; a vat of;

[一格] a specimen;

聊備一格 may serve as a specimen;

[一個] (1) a; an; one; (2) a piece of; a word of;

一個巴掌拍不響 one hand alone cannot clap – it takes two to make a quarrel; one cannot clap with one hand;

一個巴掌遮不住太陽 one cannot shut off the sunlight with one hand;

一個半 one and a half;

一個唱紅臉一個唱白臉 one plays the gentleman and the other the villain;

一個釘子一個眼 give tit for tat;

一個個 (1) one by one; (2) each and every one;

一個夠 to one's heart's content;

一個和尚挑水吃，兩個和尚扛水吃，三個和尚沒水吃 everybody's business is nobody's business; one boy helping, a pretty good boy; two boys, half a boy; three boys, no boy;

一個將軍一個令 new lords, new laws;

一個接一個 back-to-back; one by one;

一個籬笆三個樁，一個好漢三個幫 a fence needs the support of three stakes, an able fellow needs the help of three other people; no flying without wings;

一個蘿蔔一個坑 one radish, one hole – each has his own task, and there is nobody to spare;

一個人 a person;

~每一個人 all and sundry; everyone;

一個碗不響，兩個碗叮噹 it takes two to make a quarrel;

好一個 what a;

~好一個天才 what a genius he is;

~好一個偽君子 what a hypocrite;

另一個 another;

每四個中有一個 one of out every four;

四個中有一個 one in five;

[一根] a bar of; a blade of; a branch of; a leaf of; a piece of; a stick of;

[一共] all told; altogether; in all; the total amount;

[一骨碌] get up hastily;

[一古腦兒] completely; lock, stock and barrel; neck and crop; root and branch; the devil and all;

[一股] (1) a strand; a streak; (2) a blast of; a burst of; a gang of; a gust of; a horde of; a jet of; a puff of; a skein of; a spurt of; a stream of; a trickle of; a whiff of; (3) full of;

一股腦兒 all in one package; altogether; completely; neck and crop; root and branch; stock and barrel; the devil and all; the whole lot altogether;

[一鼓] at one stroke;

一鼓而殲 annihilate at one stroke; finish off at one blow;

一鼓而下 be conquered without difficulty; conquer in an overpowering attack;

一鼓聚殲 wipe out all at one stroke;

一鼓可得 gain in one beat of the drum;

一鼓作氣 at a dash; at one fling; brace oneself; get sth done in one tremendous effort; in a row; in one sustained effort; make a vigorous effort; pluck up courage with the first drum; press on without letup;

[一掛] a braid of; a string of;

[一管] a tube of;

[一貫] all along; consistent; from beginning to end; persistent; unswerving;

一貫作風 the consistent way of doing things;

一貫作業 integrated operation;

[一罐] a jar of; a jug of;

[一鍋] a boiler of; a cauldron of; a pan of; a pot of;

[一國] one country;

一國兩制 one country, two systems;

一國三公 a state with three rulers – too many leaders in a country;

[一過就忘] out of sight, out of mind; pass as a

watch in the night;

[一行] (1) a line; a row; a single file; (2) a line of; a row of;
一行不專，飯碗難端 a man of many trades begs his bread on Sundays;
在一行，怨一行 every one finds fault with his own trade;

[一好] what is good;
一好百好，一丑百丑 what is good is all good and what is bad is all bad;
一好遮百醜 for one good deed a hundred ill deeds should be overlooked;

[一盒] a box of; a case of; a casket of; a tin of;

[一泓清碧] a pond of clear water; a pool with lucid water;

[一哄] in a hubbub;
一哄而出 rush noisily out;
一哄而起 be aroused to precipitate action; be brought about in a rush; rush headlong into mass action;
一哄而散 break up in an uproar; disperse in a hubbub; stampede;

[一呼] call; shout;
一呼百諾 have hundreds at one's neck and call; one command draws a hundred answers; one's summons are answered by a hundred voices;
~ 堂上一呼，天下百諾 a call in the court is responded by many;
一呼百應 a hundred responses to a call;
一呼即來 come like a dog at a whistle;
袒臂一呼 wave one's arm and shout;

[一忽兒] a little while; in a moment;

[一壺] a kettle of; a pot of;
一壺千金 things that are ordinarily worthless become very valuable when they are needed;
一壺水 a kettle of water; a pot of water;

[一花獨放不是春] a single flower is not spring; one swallow does not make a summer; spring does not arrive with the blossoming of a single flower;

[一環] one link;
一環扣一環 all linked with one another; closely linked;
一環一報 an eye for an eye; tit for tat;
一環折，全鏈斷 with one link broken, the whole chain is broken;

[一晃兒] (1) flash; pass in a flash; (2) in a short period; in an instant;

[一揮而就] dash off in a flash; finish at one go; finish writing an article very quickly; just a flourish of the pen and it's done; write out with one stroke of the pen;

[一回] (1) chapter; (2) once; one time; (3) occasion; round;
一回生，二回熟 awkward at first, but easy afterwards; difficult at first but easy later on; difficult the first time, easy the second; first meeting, strangers; second meeting, old friends; first time awkward, second time skilful; first time strangers, second time friends; ill at ease the first time, at home the second; soon get to know each other; strangers at the first meeting, but friends at the second; the first time strangers, the second time acquaintances;
一回事 (1) one and the same thing; (2) a matter; one thing;
~ 另一回事 another matter;
說是一回事，做是另一回事 to say is one thing, to practise is another;
每一回 at every turn;
祇此一回 once and for all; only this time and no more;

[一會兒] (1) a little while; a short while; in a jiffy; in a moment; presently; (2) now..., now...; one moment...the next...;
一會兒…過一會兒 one moment...the next;
一會兒見 see you later;
待一會兒 just a little while; moments later;
等一會 wait for a while;
~ 稍等一會 hang on; hold on
站一會兒 stand for a little while;

[一伙] a band of; a gang of; a group of; a mob of; a pack of;

[一擊] a blow;
當頭一擊 one for sb's nob;
致命一擊 coup de grace;

[一級] one-level;

[一己] oneself; self;
一己私利 one's own selfish interests;
一己為私 be motivated purely by self-interest; pursue one's own ends;
一己之見 one's private judgement;
一己之私 one's own selfish interests;

one's private ends;

[一計] one tactic;
一計不成，又生一計 when one tactic fails, they fall back on another;
心生一計 a good idea occurs to sb; a scheme comes to one's mind; hit upon idea;

[一劑] a dose of; a whiff of;

[一家] the same family;
一家打墻，兩家好看 one family builds a wall, two families enjoy it;
一家老少 all members of the family; everyone in one's house, young and old, the whole family, old and young;
一家三代 three generations from the same family;
一家數口 three are several members in one's family;
一家同心，糞土成金 when all members of a family are of the same mind, all things become possible;
一家團圓 one's family is reunited;
一家兄弟 belong to the same family;
一家之計在於和，一生之計在於勤 harmony should be the policy of the family, diligence that of the individual;
一家之言 a distinctive doctrine; a school of thought; an authority in a certain field; an original system of thought;
~成一家之言 create a philosophy of one's own;
一家之長 boss of the house;
一家之主 boss of a family; boss of a household; good man of the house; man of the house; head of the family; master of the house; paterfamilias;
獨此一家 the only authentic brand;
哪一家 which one;
衹此一家 this is the only shop of its kind;
~衹此一家，別無分店 the one and only store, no branch office; this is the only shop and there is no any other branch elsewhere;
自成一家 create a school of one's own; develop a style of one's own; strike out a new line for oneself; strike sth new; unique in one's style;

[一肩] shoulder;
一肩擔載 assume full responsibility;
一肩行李，兩袖清風 possess nothing but one's personal belongings;

[一見] a single glance;
一見為快 enjoy the pleasure of sb's acquaintance; glad to see sb;
百聞不如一見 a thousand words of hearsay are not worth a single glance at the reality; better seeing once than hearing a hundred times; hearsays are no substitutes for seeing with one's own eyes; it is better to see sth once than hear about it a hundred times; seeing for oneself is a hundred times better than hearing from others; seeing for oneself is better than all hearsays; seeing is believing; there is nothing like seeing for oneself; to see is to believe; to see it once is better than to hear a hundred times;

[一件] a piece of; a stick of; a work of; an article of;

[一箭] one arrow;
一箭雙雕 achieve two things at one stroke; accomplish two objects by one effort; answer a double purpose; catch two pigeons with one bean; hit two hawks with one arrow; kill two birds with one stone; shoot two hawks with one arrow;
一箭之地 a bowshot; a short distance; a stone's throw;
一箭之遙 a bow's cast; a bow-shot; at a stone's throw;
一箭中鵠 shoot and hit with the first arrow;

[一江如練] the river lies as smooth as silk;

[一將功成萬骨枯] a general builds his success on ten thousand bleaching bones; a single general's reputation is made out of ten thousand corpses; a single general achieves fame on the rotting bones of ten thousand; it's the blood of the rank and file that has won the general's promotion; one general achieves renown over the dead bodies of ten thousand soldiers; the achievements of a general cost many lives; the blood of the soldier makes the glory of the general;

[一交] a fall;

[一腳] (1) a kick; (2) take part in sth;

一腳高，一腳低 up-and-down;
一腳踢翻 knock sb down with one's foot; send sb sprawling with one kick; shoot up a foot to send sb sprawling;
一腳踢開 kick aside; kick away; kick out; spurn away;

[一覺醒來] wake up after a sound sleep;

[一節] a length of; a passage of; a section of;

[一截] a length of; a section of;

[一介不取] not to take a single penny unrightfully;

[一斤] one catty;

[一經] as soon as; immediately after; once;

[一竟全功] accomplish the whole task at one stroke; bring work to completion;

[一…就] as soon as; directly; no sooner have...than; once; the moment;
一叫就到 answer to a call in a flash;
一抓就靈 once sb is grasped...all problems can be solved;

[一局] a game of; a round of;

[一舉] at a blow; at a brush; at one stroke; at one fell swoop; at the first try; with one action;
一舉成功 succeed in one stroke;
一舉摧毀 shatter; smash with one blow;
一舉得男 get a son as one's first child;
一舉多得 achieve many things at one stroke; answer multiple purpose; kill two birds with one stone;
一舉兩得 achieve two things at one stroke; answer a double purpose; attain two objectives by a single move; catch two piegeons with one bean; dual gain; kill two birds with one stone; kill two flies with one slap; serve two ends;
一舉十觴 toss off bumper after bumper;
一舉消滅 annihilate...at one stroke; deal...the coup de grace;
一舉一動 all one's proceedings; any move; each and every move; every act; every act and every move; every movement and every action; every particular gesture; whole behaviour;
多此一舉 bring owls to Athens; burn daylight; carry coals to Newcastle; carry owls to Athens; carry salt to Dysart and puddings to Tranent; carry water to the river; fan the breezes; gild refined; knock at an open door; make an unnecessary move; perform unnecessary labour; send owls to Athens; thrash over old straw; uncalled-for; water one's grass after a good rain;
~ 井邊賣水—多此一舉 sell water by the side of a well – make an unnecessary move;

[一句] a line of; a word of;
一句感激的話 a word of thanks;
東一句，西一句 talk incoherently;
熱一句，冷一句 fling hot words and cold words alternately;
天一句，地一句 speak incoherently;

[一捲] (1) a reel; (2) a coil of; a reel of; a roll of; a spool of;

[一絕] a special skill; a unique accomplishment; a unique talent;

[一看] at a glance;
一看便知 readily see; see at a glance;
一看二幫 first to observe, and second to give help; observe and help;
一看就懂 be apprehended at a glance; learn by merely reading it once over; see at a glance; see with half an eye;
乍眼一看 at first appearance; at first sight;

[一棵] (1) a head of cabbage; a tree; (2) a head of; a tuft of;

[一顆] a piece of;
一顆老鼠屎，敗壞一鍋湯 one crop of a turd mars a whole pot of porridge; one drop of poison infects the whole tun of wine; one ill weed mars a whole pot of pottage; one wicked weed spoils a whole mess of porridge; the rotten apple injures its neighbours;
一顆子彈 a bullet;

[一客] a helping of; a portion of;
一客冰淇淋 an ice-cream;
一客不煩二主 a guest should not have to trouble two hosts; a single guest does not require to lodgings; one guest should not bother two hosts; one should not impose on two patrons;

[一刻] a moment; a quarter; a short while; an instant;
一刻不離 not to leave sb for a single moment;
一刻千金 every minute is precious; one moment is worth a thousand pieces of gold; time is priceless; value every

minute;

一刻鐘 a quarter of an hour; fifteen minutes;

最後一刻 the last moment;

[一孔土窯] a cave;

[一口] (1) flatly; readily; with certainty; promise without hesitation; (2) pure; (3) a bite; a mouthful; (4) a draught of; a morsel of; a mouthful of; a nip of; a sip of; a whiff of;

一口吃不成個胖子 you cannot build up your constitution on one mouthful; you cannot get fat on one mouthful — you must keep at it;

一口啐臉 spit in sb's face;

一口回絕 flatly refuse;

一口氣 a breath; at a breath; at a stretch; at a whack; at one fling; at one go; at one sitting; in one breath; right off the reel; straight off the reed; without a break; without stopping;

~一口氣背出 reel off;

~吹一口氣 give a puff;

~緩一口氣 gather a breath; get a breathing space; take a breather;

鬆一口氣 breathing spell; breathe more easily; for a deep relief; relax;

~透一口氣 catch a breath; have a breathing spell;

~吸入一口氣 indrawn breath;

~吸一口氣 take a breath;

~爭一口氣 strive for a vindication;

佛繞一炷香，人爭一口氣 Buddha needs incense, and a man needs self-respect;

~最後一口氣 sb's last gasp;

一口一聲 without interruption;

嚐一口 take a taste of;

喝一口 drink a mouthful of sth; take a drink;

如出一口 all say the same thing; everyone says so; in one voice; unanimously; with one voice;

一小口 toothful;

~咬了一小口 take a nibble of sth;

[一扣] (1) a ninety-percent discount; (2) button up;

[一塊] (1) a block; a piece; a lot; (2) a block of; a cake of; a chunk of; a handful of; a loaf of; a lump of; a piece of; a plot of; a sheet of; a slab of; a slice of; a tablet of; an area of;

一塊兒 (1) at the same place; (2) altogether;

一塊兒走 come along;

一塊肥肉落到狗嘴裏 a tender fillet of lamb snapped up by the jaws of a cur;

[一筐] a basket of; a crate of; a hamper of;

[一夔已足] one able person is enough for the job;

[一捆] a bale of; a bundle of; a head of; a sheaf of; a truss of; a wisp of;

[一來] (1) on the one hand; (2) as soon as sb arrives;

一來二去 in the course of frequent contact; in the course of time;

一來二往 in the course of contacts;

一來一往 back and forth; in and out;

[一籃] a basket of; a hamper of;

一籃子 a basket of;

[一攬子] package; wholesale;

[一懶生百邪] idleness is the mother of all sin; idleness is the root of all evil;

[一覽] bird's-eye view; general survey;

一覽表 chart; compendium; data sheet; general table; list; listings; schedule; table; table-look-up;

~賬戶一覽表 account chart;

一覽無餘 a panoramic view; a single glance takes in all; command the whole view of; cover all at one glance; in full view; take in everything at one glance; unobstructed;

一覽在目 bird's-eye view; commanding view;

[一浪高過一浪] each surging is higher than the previous one; in surging tides; one wave is higher than the other; surge ahead with increasing vigour; surge wave upon wave;

[一勞永逸] efficacious forever; for good; for good and all; for keeps; get sth done once and for all; hold good for all times; make a great effort to accomplish sth once and for all; once and away; once and for all; put things right once and for all; win everlasting ease with one great effort;

一勞永逸地 for altogether;

[一類] (1) of the same category; of the same class; of the same species; (2) a

category of; a kind of; a sort of; a type of;

[一愣] taken aback;

[一力] do all one can; do one's best;

一力成全 do one's best to help; spare no effort in helping sb to accomplish sth;

[一粒] a grain of;

一粒耗子屎，壞掉一鍋粥 for every fruit consumed by a rat a hundred are spoiled; one bit of rat's dung ruins the whole basin of porridge; one crop of a turd mars a whole pot of porridge;

[一櫪兩騾] a man having two women at the same time;

[一連] at a stretch; in a row; in succession; running;

一連幾天 for days on end;

一連數載 for years in succession; for years on end;

[一連串] a chain of; a round of; a series of; a streak of; a string of; a succession of; a train of; a volley of;

[一臉] one's face;

一臉惡霸相，十足流氓腔 acting the tyrant and talking gangster language; hundred per cent tyrant's features and gangster's logic;

一臉橫肉 look ugly and ferocious; with grim face;

一臉死相 have the seal for death on one's face;

一臉兇相 a fierce look on one's face;

[一兩] one and two;

一掰兩開 break a cake open with one's hands;

一式兩份 in duplicate; with a duplicate copy;

一葉兩豆 be prevented from knowing the truth by some artful person;

[一列] a column; a row;

[一令] a ream of;

[一溜兒] (1) a row; (2) neighbourhood; vicinity;

[一流] (1) first-rate; (2) of the same class;

一流服務 first-class service;

一流設備 first-class equipment;

一流水平 first-class standard;

一流質量 first-class quality;

超一流 supreme;

第一流 top-notch;

~第一流的公司 top-notch company;

[一綹] a lock of; a skein of; a tuft of; a wisp of;

[一龍九種] a dragon has nine kinds of offsprings;

[一簍] a basket of; a crate of;

[一爐] a batch of; a cast of;

[一路] (1) all the way; throughout the journey; (2) of the same kind; (3) go the same way; take the same route;

一路保重 look after yourself on the journey; take good care of yourself on the way;

一路貨色 be tarred with the same brush; be tarred with the same stick; brids of a feather; cut from the same cloth; of the same brand; of the same ilk; of the same kind; of the same mould, of the same stock, of the same stripe; the same sort of stuff; tweedledum and tweedledee;

一路領先 lead from the beginning; take the lead to the end;

一路平安 a good journey; all the best; bon voyage; have a good trip; I wish you a safe journey; may you be safe throughout the journey;

一路上 on the way;

一路上很順利 everything is all right on the way;

一路順風 a pleasant journey; all the best; bon voyage; may a favourable wind send you safely home;

[一縷] a curl of; a strand of; a stream of; a trail of; a wisp of;

[一律] (1) alike; same; uniform; (2) all; without exception; (3) equally; uniformly;

千篇一律 a set form for all cases; a set method for different cases; a set mould for everything that comes up; a thousand pieces of the same tune; all harping on the same theme with slight variations; all in the same key; apply a set rule to everything; dead level; dull; follow a fixed pattern; follow a stereotyped pattern; follow the same pattern; harp on the same subject; harp on the same theme; have a set form for all cases; invariably; monotonous; repeat each other; repetitious; same;

stereotyped; unvaried; without changes;
~千篇一律的 cookie cutter;

[一輪] a round of;

[一羅] a gross of;

[一落] a heap of; a pile of; a stack of;
一落千丈 a calamitous decline; a disastrous decline; a drastic decline; a great drop; a precipitate drop; a ruinous decline; a sudden decline; a terrific drop; decline drastically; fall off to beat the band; have a sudden fall; make a sudden steep plunge; nose-dive; sink drastically; suffer a disastrous decline;

[一碼事] the same thing;
另一碼事 another pair of shoes;

[一脈] of the same origin;
一脈相承 a true disciple of; be imbued with the same spirit; come down from the same origin; in direct line of descent; in the same strain;
一脈相傳 derived from the same origin;
一脈相通 be intimately tied up with; kindred to;

[一毛] (1) a hair; (2) ten cents; (3) an insignificant thing;
一毛不拔 as close as a clam; as mean as a miser; as tight as a drum; close-fisted; not give a cent; not lift a finger; not stir a finger; not turn a finger; refuse to contribute a single cent; stingy; too stingy to pull out a hair; unwilling to give up even a hair; unwilling to sacrifice even a single hair;

[一枚] a coin;

[一門] (1) a course in a curriculum; (2) a branch of; a piece of; (3) one source;
政出一門 political leadership comes from one source;

[一面] (1) one aspect; one section; one side; (2) at the same time; simultaneously;
一面倒 excessively dependent on sth or sb;
~一面倒比賽 a one-sided game;
一面砌墻兩面光 a wall built by a family is enjoyed by two families;
一面如舊 become intimate friends at the first meeting; feel like old friends at the first meeting;
一面之詞 a one-sided statement; a one-sided story; an account given by one party only; the statement of only one of the parties;
一面之交 a casual acquaintance; a nodding acquaintance; a passing acquaintance; be casually acquainted; have a bowing acquaintance; have a nodding acquaintance; have a speaking acquaintance; have met only once;
一面之緣 happen to have met sb once; the pleasure of having met once;
~有一面之緣 happen to have met once;
獨當一面 assume responsibility for a certain sector; manage on one's own; shoulder responsibility alone; take charge as chief; take charge of a department; the boss of a section; the head of one department; undertake the task alone;
好的一面 the upside;
另一面 the other side;
~請看這一頁的另一面 please read the other side of the page;
網開一面 give lenient treatment to sb; give sb a way out; leave one side of the net open — give the wrongdoer a way out; let sb slip through the net; purposely leave loopholes for an escape from the law; put sb in the way of escaping;

[一瞑不視] close one's eyes and die; dead; die;

[一命] a life;
一命抵一命 demand a life for a life;
一命歸陰 die;
一命嗚呼 breathe one's last; breathe out one's life; die; fall lifeless; give up the ghost; have had one's chips; kick the bucket; peg out; pop off; pop one's clogs; snuff it; turn up one's toes;

[一抹] a faint trace of sth;

[一木難支] a single post cannot bear the burden; a single post cannot support a mansion; how can you support your mansion with one log; it is difficult to support sth single-handed;

[一年] a year; one year;
一年半載 a year or so; in about a year; six months to a year; six to twelve months;
一年到頭 all the year round; at all seasons; in season and out of season;

the whole year round; the whole year through; throughout the year; year in and year out; year-round;
一年復始 at the start of the new year;
一年生 annual;
一年四季 all the year round; at all seasons of the year; the four seasons of the year; throughout the four seasons of the year; throughout the year;
一年一度 annual; once a year; yearly;
一年之計在於春 April and May are the keys of year; make your plans for the year in spring; spring is the best time to do the year's work; the whole year's work depends on a good start in spring; the work for the year is best begun in the spring;
待了一年 stay for a year;
輝煌的一年 banner year;

[一念] one thought;
一念之差 a false step; a momentary slip with serious consequences; a wrong decision made in a moment of weakness; a wrong thought on the spur of the moment;
一念之誠 one sincere thought;

[一怒而去] go away in a temper; leave in anger;

[一排] a block of; a line of; a range of; a rank of; a row of; a screen of; an array of;
一排又一排 row upon row;

[一派] (1) a faction; a group; a school; (2) a pack of;
一派大好 the situation is excellent;

[一盤] a coil of; a dish of; a game of; a plate of; a reel of;
一盤散沙 a dish of loose sand; a heap of loose sand; a plate of loose sand; a sheet of loose sand; disunited; in a state of disunity;

[一旁] by the side of; on the sideline; one side;

[一砲而紅] become famous all at once; have a meteoric rise to fame; runaway success;

[一盆] (1) a basin; a bowl; a plate; a pot; a tray; a tub; (2) a basin of; a bowl of; a plate of; a pot of; a tray of; a tub of;
一盆火 a pot of fire;
~明是一盆火，暗是一把刀 make a show of great warmth while stabbing sb in the back;

[一蓬] a clump of;

[一捧] a double handful of;

[一批] (1) a batch; a shipment; an array; (2) a batch of; a body of; a consort of; a crop of; a galaxy of; a group of; a muster of; a number of; a party of; a set of; a stock of; a supply of; an array of; an assortment of;

[一匹] a bolt of; a roll of;

[一篇] (1) a chapter; a literary article; (2) a piece of; a sheet of;

[一偏] one-sided;
一偏之見 a one-sided view;

[一片] (1) a petal; (2) a blanket of; a blaze of; a body of; a flood of; a mass of; a scene of; a sea of; a sheet of; a slice of; a stretch of; a tract of; an area of; an expanse of;
一片嘴，兩片舌 double-talk;
打成一片 at one with; be fused with; be unified as one; become a harmonious whole; become integrated with; become one with; form an indivisible whole; identify oneself with; integrate oneself with; merge with; one with; unify as one;
一小片 sippet;

[一瞥] a glimpse; a quick glance; looksee;
驚鴻一瞥 barely to catch a glimpse of a passing beauty;
情意脈脈的一瞥 an amorous glance;

[一貧如洗] abject poverty; as poor as a church mouse; as poor as Job; at low-water mark; bare of money; destitute; down and out; down on one's uppers; extremely poor; hard up; in a poorhouse; in utter destitution; not a feather to fly with; not have a shot in one's locker; not have a shirt on one's back; not have two halfpennies to rub together; not to have a shirt to one's back; penniless; sit on the Penniless Bench;

[一品] the highest rank in officialdom in ancient China;
一品當朝 a first rank court official; first rank in the imperial court;
一品夫人 the wife of a highest-ranking

official in ancient China;
一品紅 Christmas flower;

[一平如鏡] as flat as a mirror;

[一瓶] a bottle of; a flask of;
一瓶子不響，半瓶子晃蕩 shallow streams make most din; shallow waters make the greatest sound; the half-filled bottle sloshes, the full bottle remains still — the dabbles in knowledge chatters away, the wise man stays silent;

[一期] a class of; a period of; a phase of; a term of; an issue of;

[一齊] at the same time; in unison; simultaneously; together;
一齊動手 get to work altogether;

[一起] (1) all together; in company; in the same place; together; (2) a case of;
一起一伏 heave; move up and down; rise and fall regularly;
合在一起 put together;
混在一起 intermingle;
連在一起 join together;

[一氣] (1) at a stretch; at one go; without a break; without stop; (2) hand in glove; of the same gang; (3) a fit; a spell; (4) get angry;
一氣呵成 accomplish sth without any interruption; accomplish sth without any letup; carry sth through without stopping; complete in one breath; form a coherent whole; get sth done at a dash; get sth done at a heat; get sth done at a stretch; get sth done at one go; make smooth reading;
一氣之下 in a fit of anger; in a huff;
胡吹一氣 boast outrageously; bosh; talk big and irresponsibly; tell tall stories;
亂轟一氣 blast away indiscriminately;
亂講一氣 make irresponsible remarks; speak indiscreetly;

[一千] a thousand; chiliad;
一千塊 one thousand dollars;

[一塹之虧，一智之長] a fall into the pit, a gain in your wit;
吃一塹，長一智 a fall into the pit, a gain in your wit; adversity is a great schoolmaster; adversity is the school of wisdom; each time one takes a loss, one gains knowledge; experience bought by suffering teaches wisdom; experience is the mother of wisdom; experience must be bought; experience teaches; learn from experience;

[一槍未發，滴血未流] not fire a single shot or shed a drop of blood;

[一腔無明] be overwhelmed with unspeakable grief;

[一鍬挖不出一口井] a tree will not fall at one blow; an oak is not felled at one chop;

[一切] all; every; everything;
一切從簡 dispense with all unnecessary formalities;
一切就緒 all is in order; everything is ready;
一切落空 a complete failure;
一切如常 everything is the same as usual; things are as usual;
一切如舊 everything is as of old; everything remains unchanged;
一切如愿 all is going just as one wishes; everything is as one wishes; may all go well;
一切正常 all's well;
不顧一切 desperately; neck or nothing; neck or nought; regardless of all consequences; stop at nothing;
藐視一切 despise everything;
目空一切 as proud as Lucifer; consider everybody and everything beneath one's notice; full of oneself; look down on everyone else; with one's nose in the air;
獻出一切 give one's all for sb/sth;
蟻視一切 regard everything with contempt;
這一切 the whole thing;

[一傾積愫] acquaint you fully with my deep feeling; pour out one's heart to sb;

[一秋] one autumnal season;

[一曲] a song;
再奏一曲 encore;

[一去] go; leave;
一去不返 go for good and all; gone forever;
一去不復返 gone for ever; gone with the wind; leave for good; once gone, never come back;
一去不回 leave for good;

[一圈] a circle; a lap; a round; one round;
最後一圈 last lap;

[一拳] a blow;

一拳一腳 with a blow of one's fist and a kick from one's foot;

打一拳 throw a punch;

［一犬吠影，百犬吠聲］ a dog that barks at random makes all the street bark in earnest; like dogs, when one barks all bark; one barking dog sets all the street a-barking; one dog barks at a shadow and the pack barks at the noise; one dog bark at sth and the rest bark at him—credulous; when one dog barks at a shadow all the others join in—slavishly echo others;

［一群］ a bevy of; a circle of; a clump of; a cluster of; a company of; a congregation of; a crowd of; a drift of; a drove of; a flight of; a flock of; a gaggle of; a galaxy of; a gang of; a group of; a herd of; a horde of; a host of; a huddle of; a mob of; a multitude of; a pack of; a party of; a pride of; a rabble of; a school of; a shoal of; a swarm of; a throng of; a troop of; a troupe of; an array of;

一小群 packet;

［一人］ one man; one person;

一人把關，萬夫莫敵 if one man guards the pass, ten thousand are unable to get through; one man can hold out against ten thousand;

一人班 do the whole task;

一人不抵二人智 a man's wisdom cannot comete with that of two; two heads are better than one;

一人吵不起架 it takes two to make a quarrel;

一人傳十，十人傳百 flow lip to lip; go from mouth to mouth; pass the news from person to person;

一人傳虛，萬人傳實 fling dirt enough and some will stick; one man tells an idle story and it becomes fact in the mouths of ten thousand;

一人倒下，萬人起來 thousands will take the place of one who has fallen; when one falls, thousands more will rise;

一人得道，雞犬昇天 when a man attains the Way, even his pets ascend to heaven — when a man gets to the top, all his friends and relations get there with him; when a man becomes powerful, those near him ride on his coattails to success — unashamed nepotism;

一人頂兩 one can do the work of two; one can do the work of two persons put together;

一人獨吞 not to share gain with others;

一人計短，二人計長 two heads are better than one;

一人困難，人人相助 if someone is in difficulty, everybody is ready to help; one is helped by others when one is in difficulties; when sb is in difficulties, all the rest help out;

一人難稱百人心 all complain; it is hard to please all parties; no piper can please all ears; one man can hardly meet the wishes of everybody; you cannot please everyone;

一人難如千人意 it is hard to meet the wishes of everybody; one person can hardly meet the wishes of everybody;

一人拼命，萬夫莫當 none can stop a person who defies death; ten thousand men are no match for one desperado;

一人一票 one man, one vote;

一人一遭，天公地道 turn about is fair play;

一人之交 on as close terms as one man; very intimate relations;

一人之下，萬人之上 he has only one over him and millions under him;

一人智不如兩人議 four eyes see better than two;

一人做事一人當 a man must bear the consequences of his own acts; if a man does wrong, he alone must take the blame; hold oneself solely responsible for what one has done; one must bear the consequences of one's own acts; one should answer for what one does oneself; when one performs a deed, one should bear its consequence;

家有千口，主事一人 a family has many tongues but only one master;

空無一人 there's nobody;

~街上空無一人 the street is deserted;

［一任］ (1) allow; (2) a term of service; a tenure; a tour;

［一仍］ as ever; still;

一仍舊章 follow the beaten path; follow the old routine; get into a rut; let things remain the same; move in a squirrel cage; stick to the old practice;

[一日] one day; such a day;

一日不見，如隔三秋 a day apart is like three years;

一日夫妻百日恩 a day together as husband and wife means endless devotion the rest of your life; one night of love is worth a hundred of friendship;

一日官司十日打 fight a lawsuit for one day and it will go on for ten;

一日千里 advance very rapidly; at a tremendous pace; by leaps and bounds; with giant strides;

一日三餐 can three meals a day; have three meals every day;

一日三秋 a day seems as long as three years; one day seems like three years;

一日數起 several happenings in one day;

一日為師，終身為父 he who teaches me for one day is my father for life;

一日為師，終身為師 he who teaches me for one day is my teacher for life;

一日游 day trip; one-day tour;

一日之長 a little bit more capable than others;

一日之計在於晨 an hour in the morning is worth two in the evening; morning hours are the best time of the day to work; some work in the morning may trimly be done, that all the day after may hardly be won; the whole day's work depends on a good start in the morning;

一日之雅 a day's acquaintance; the pleasure of a day spent together; the pleasure of knowing sb;

數十年如一日 with perseverance and consistency;

有朝一日 if by chance; if there'll be one day when; one day; should the day come when; some day; some day in the future; some time or other; sometime;

終有一日 one day there will happen;

[一榮俱榮] honour one and you honour them all;

一榮俱榮，一損俱損 be bound together for good or ill;

[一如] just like;

一如既往 as always; as before; just as in the past;

一如其名 as its name implies;

一如尊命 it shall be as you wish;

[一三] one and three;

舉一反三 draw inferences about other cases from one instance; infer other things from one fact; from one example you may judge of the whole; just mention on example which serves for the rest;

舉一反三，觸類旁通 from one judge of the rest; from one learn all; single out one thing and bring out its bearings; the single item will suffice to typify all the rest;

[一掃而空] clear away; clear off; get rid of sth lock, stock and barrel; make a clean sweep of; sweep all aside; sweep away; wipe out;

[一色] (1) of one colour; of the same colour; (2) of the same type; uniform;

[一山] one mountain;

一山不能藏二虎 a great man can brook no rival; when Greek meets Greek then comes the tug of war;

[一善] one good deed;

一善遮百惡 charity covers a multitude of sins;

日行一善 do one good deed a day;

[一晌] a short moment;

[一身] (1) all over the body; the whole body; (2) suit; (3) all alone; concerning one person only; single person;

一身臭汗 stink with perspiration;

一身臭名 earn a very bad name for oneself;

一身擔當 face everything oneself;

一身二任 hold two posts simultaneously;

一身縞素 be dressed in mourning white;

一身裹裘 be wrapped in furs from top to toe;

一身煥然 be arrayed in finery from head to foot;

一身冷汗 a cold sweat; be bathed in cold and clammy perspiration; cold sweat breaks out all over one's body; in a cold sweat; wet with cold sweat;

一身兩役 hold two jobs at the same time;

serve in a dual capacity;
一身綾羅 be dressed in silks and satins;
一身輕 free-hearted;
~無債一身輕 happy is the person who owes nothing; out of debt, out of danger; when the debts are paid, the body feels light;
一身榮耀 be loaded with honours;
一身臊 have one's goodwill taken for ill intent;
一身是病 be afflicted by several ailments; be burdened with illness; full of infirmities;
一身是膽 absolutely fearless; be filled with courage; brave all through; every inch a hero; full of courage; have plenty of guts; know no fear; the very embodiment of valour; the whole body is one mass of courage; very brave;
一身是汗 be steeped in sweat; in a complete sweat; sweaty all over;
一身是債 be burdened down with debts; deep in debt; head over heels in debt; up to one's neck in debt;
一身素裹 be dressed all in white;
一身銅臭 covetous; the whole body smells of copper;
一身痛重 general pain and heaviness;
一身衣服 a suit of clothes;
一身臃腫 be heavily padded;
一身重孝 in full mourning;
萃於一身 be embodied in sb;
孑然一身 living alone;
無官一身輕 feel light all over the body after being removed from the office; far from court, far from care; one feels carefree when he is relieved of official duties; out of office, out of care;

[一神] monotheistic;
一神教 monotheism; monotheistic religions;
一神論 monotheism;
~一神論者 monotheist;

[一生] all one's life; from the womb to the tomb; lifetime; throughout one's life;
一生待明日，萬事成蹉跎 tomorrow never comes;
一生坎坷 a lifetime of frustrations; have bad luck all one's life;
一生潦倒 a failure all one's life; remain poor all one's life;
一生飄蕩 drive hither and thither all one's life;
一生清貧 in poverty from birth to death;
一生受用 enjoy the benefit all one's life;
一生辛勞 a life of hardship; labour uphill all one's life;
一生一世 from the cradle to the grave; in all one's born days; one's whole life;
九死一生 close shave; narrow escape from death; narrow squeak; survive all perils;
了此一生 end this life;
終其一生 throughout one's life;

[一聲] say a word; utter a word;
一聲不吭 as mute as a fish; as mute as a statue; as mute as a stone; keep one's mouth shut; say neither ba nor bum; say nothing; without a murmur; without saying a word;
一聲不響 as dumb as a fish; as mute as a mouse; not to say a word; not to utter a sound; without many words;
一聲長歎 draw a deep sigh; heave a long sigh; let out a long heavy sigh;
一聲長嘯，群山齊應 give a long, loud halloo which is echoed by all the hills;
一聲春雷 a clap of spring thunder; a spring thunderstorm;
一聲號令 issue an order;
一聲叫喊 a call; a cry;
一聲令下 as soon as the order is given; at the first call;
一聲砲響 as the sound of a bomb rent the air; the report of a cannon; the salvoes of;
一聲槍響 a shot;
夠了請說一聲 say when;
嚎叫一聲 give a howl;
哼了一聲 give a snort of contempt;
砰的一聲 with a bang; with a bump; with a thump;
呀然一聲 fling open with a creaking sound;
祗要你說一聲 just say the word;

[一十] (1) one and ten; (2) ten;
一傳十，十傳百 get round very quickly; spread far and wide; spread from mouth to mouth; spread like wildfire; travel fast;
一目十行 learn ten lines at a glance; read ten lines of writing with one single glance;

一曝十寒 blow hot and cold; by fits and snatches; by fits and starts; do sth by fits and starts; work hard for one day and do nothing for ten;
一以當十 one fights against ten;
一以抵十 one fights against ten; pit one against ten;
以十當一 pit ten against one;
以一當十 pit one against ten;
以一抵十 one is able to resist ten; one is good for ten;
因一推十 deduce ten from one; take one to generalize the ten;
知一不知十 know only one aspect of a thing and be ignorant of the whole situation;

[一時] (1) for a moment; for a short while; momentary; temporary; (2) a period of time; (3) accidentally;
一時半刻 a little while; a short time;
一時衝動 act on impulse; be seized with a sudden impulse; momentary impulse; on the spur of the moment;
一時得逞 have one's way for a time; succeed for a time;
一時得勢 get the upper hand for a while; in the ascendent for a short while;
一時苟安 gain temporary ease;
一時糊塗 be temporarily confused; in a thoughtless moment; lose one's head for the moment;
一時激動 flicker; touch;
一時疏忽 a momentary oversight; an oversight;
一時忘情 forget oneself;
一時忘形 for a time beside oneself with joy;
一時一個樣 at one time, this way; at another time, some other way;
一時一刻 for a single moment;
一時一事 a short period or a single incident; a single act or a short period of one's life;
一時瑜亮 two equally talented contemporaries;
一時之計 makeshift; temporary measures;
一時之苦，終身受惠 an hour to suffer, a lifetime to live;
一時之快 a moment' comfort; temporary relief;
一時之怒 a temporary annoyance; in a momentary burst of anger;
彼一時，此一時 circumstances alter cases; the conditions are different;
此一時，彼一時 circumstances have changed with the passage of time; this is one situation and that was another; times have changed;
得逞一時 have one's way for a time; succeed for a time;
鼓噪一時 make a great to-do about sth for a time;
冠絕一時 the best for a time;
橫行一時 run amuck at for a certain time; run wild for a time;
名冠一時 overtop the age; well-known in one's time;
名噪一時 make a noise in the world;
千載一時 a golden opportunity; a rare chance; a time of a thousand years; a very rare chance; an extremely rare opportunity; once in a lifetime; once in a thousand years;
祇顧一時 take a short view;

[一世] (1) an age; an epoch; (2) a lifetime;
一世之雄 a champion of the generation; a hero of the age; the outstanding person of the age;
不可一世 be extremely arrogant;
~自以為不可一世 swagger like a conquering hero;
度過一世 live out one's days;

[一事] belong to the same organization;
一事成，事事成 nothing succeeds like success;
一事當前 at every turn; when any issue arises; whenever sth crops up;
一事通，百事鬆 success in one thing makes success in other things easier;
一事無成 accomplish nothing; achieve nothing; come to naught; fail to achieve anything; get nowhere; have nothing accomplished; not a thing accomplished; with one's finger in one's mouth;
多一事不如少一事 avoid trouble whenever possible; don't meet trouble halfway; it's better to save trouble; let things slide whenever possible; one upset less is preferable to one upset more; the less trouble the better;
經一事，長一智 by every affair a person transacts,

~不經一事，不長一智 one can't gain knowledge without practice; experience is the mother of wisdom; in doing, one learns; one learns from experience; wisdom comes from experience;

[一視同仁] be treated the same; be treated without distinction; extend the same treatment to all; give equal treatment to everything; give the devil its due; impartial; no respecter of persons; not make chalk of one and cheese of the other; treat all on the same footing; treat all with the same kindness; treat equally without discrimination; without discrimination;

[一手] (1) good at; proficiency; skill; (2) move; trick; (3) all alone; all by oneself; single-handed;

一手包辦 (1) be entirely handled by sb; be manipulated by sb single-handedly; do sth all by oneself; keep everything in one's own hands; single-handedly; take everything on oneself; undertake sth alone; (2) arbitrary; dictatorial;

一手策劃 engineer single-handed;

一手次牌 a poor hand

~有一手次牌 have a poor hand;

一手得來，一手失去 lose on the swings what one makes on the roundabout;

一手好棋 a game at chess;

~下一手好棋 play a good game at chess;

一手好牌 a good hand;

~有一手好牌 have a good hand;

一手好手藝 good craftsmanship; master of the craft;

~有一手好手藝 sb is a master of one's craft;

一手好字 good handwriting; write a good hand;

~寫一手好字 write a beautiful hand;

一手交錢，一手交貨 cash on delivery; give me the cash, and I will give you the goods; transaction in cash; with one hand I take the money, with the other I release the goods;

一手難抓兩頭鰻 he that hunts two hares often loses both; if you run after two hares, you will catch neither;

一手砲製 concoct sth single-handed;

一手擎天 hold up the sky with one hand; lift up the sky with one hand; prop up the sky with a single hand;

一手挑起 be all started by sb;

一手挑起爭端 the dispute was all started by sb;

一手養大 be brought up by sb;

一手一足 one hand and one foot;

一手硬一手軟 promote one thing and neglect another thing at the same time;

一手栽培 bring sb up single-handed; raise sb all by oneself;

一手造成 be fomented single-handedly by; solely responsible for;

一手遮天 hide the truth from the masses; hoodwink the public; pull the wool over the eye of the public;

一手之寬 handbreadth;

插上一手 get one's finger into the pie; have a hand in; poke one's nose into;

留一手 have a card up one's sleeve; hold back a trick or two in teaching a skill; keep sth in reverse;

~留了一手 have sth in reserve; hold back a trick or two;

~留有一手 have a card up one's sleeve;

露一手 make an exhibition of one's abilities; show off; show off one's skill;

有一手兒 have remarkable skill;

[一束] (1) a bob; a bunch; a head; a taft; (2) a beam of; a bouquet of; a bunch of; a bundle of; a cluster of; a hank of;

[一雙] (1) a couple; a pair; braces; dual; twain; (2) a pair of;

[一瞬] a flash; an instant; in an instant; the twinkling of an eye;

一瞬即逝 disappear in a flash; vanish in a flash;

[一順兒] alike; in the same direction;

[一説] (1) according to one theory; (2) a brief explanation;

一説曹操，曹操就到 speak of angels, and you will hear their wings; speak of the devil and he will appear; to mention the wolf's name is to see the same;

一説就做 suit the action to the words;

[一絲] a breath of; a flicker of;

一絲不差 exactly the same; not a bit of difference; without the least difference;

一絲不錯 all correct; all true;

一絲不苟 conscientious and meticulous; dot the i's and cross the t's; neglect no detail; in a careful and thoroughgoing way; meticulous; no detail is overlooked; not be the least bit negligent; scrupulous about every detail; with the greatest care;
一絲不掛 as naked as a worm; as naked as one was born; as naked as one's mother bore one; buck baked; completely naked; completely nude; have not a stitch on; have nothing on; in a state of nature; in nature's garb; in one's birthday suit; in one's skin; in the altogether; in the nude; naked; naked as a jaybird; not have a rag to one's back; not have a stitch on; nude; stark naked; starkers; strip to the buff; unclothed; wearing one's birthday clothes; without a shred of clothing on; without a stitch of clothing;
一絲一毫 a shred of; a tiny bit; a trace of; an atom of; an iota; the least; the slightest; the smallest scrap of;

［一宿］ overnight stay; one night;
一宿風流 one-night stand;

［一算］ calculate; count;
掐指一算 calculate; count;
屈指一算 reckon on one's fingers;

［一所］ a measure word;

［一塌刮子］ all; altogether; completely; entirely; in all;

［一榻橫陳］ lay crosswise on the bed; lie in bed;

［一胎率］ one-child ratio;

［一灘］ (1) a puddle of water; a smudge; a stain; (2) a pool of; a puddle of;

［一堂］ (1) in the same hall; under the same roof; (2) a period of; a set of;
聚首一堂 gather together;

［一趟］ (1) a ride; a trip; (2) a row of;
白跑一趟 make a fruitless trip; make a futile trip;
頭一趟 for the first time;

［一套］ (1) a set; a suit; (2) a pack of; a set of; an article of;
別跟我來這一套 don't give me that;
不吃這一套 not to allow oneself to be pushed around; not to take sth lying down;
還是那一套 same old excuse; same old story;
老一套 old practice; old ways; outmoded; the beaten track; the old set of practices; the same old story; the same old stuff; the same old thing; trite;
另搞一套 do what suits oneself; go one's own way;
明一套，暗一套 act one way in the open and another in secret; double-dealing;
~明裏一套，暗裏一套 act one way in the open and another way in secret;
陽一套，陰一套 act one way in public and another in private; carry fire in one hand and water in another; feign compliance while acting in opposition;
陰一套，陽一套 act one way in public and another in private; be engaged in double-dealing;
嘴上一套，心裏一套 carry fire in one hand and water in the other;

［一體］ (1) organic whole; (2) all people concerned; to a man;
一體化 integration; unify;
~一體化信息服務 universal information service;
一體兩面論 the double-aspect theory;
集於一體 all rolled into one;
結為一體 become one flesh;
融成一體 merge into an organic whole;
自成一體 have a style of one's own;

［一天］ (1) a day; (2) one day; (3) all day long; from morning till night; the whole day;
一天到晚 all day; all day long; as the day is long; from dawn to dusk; from morning till night; the whole day;
一天星斗 a sky sown with stars; a star-studded sky; the sky is covered with stars; the sky is full of stars;
一天一次 once a day;
一天雲霧散 all the clouds and mist in the day are over;
酷熱的一天 a roasting hot day;
過一天，算一天 drift through life; live from day to day; muddle along with no thought of tomorrow; while away the days;
每隔一天 on alternate days;
下周這一天 a week from today; a week today; today week;
有一天 one day; someday;

~總有一天 one day; one fine day; one of these days; some day; sometime or other; sooner or later;

[一條] a bar of; a carton of; a loaf of; a pair of; a piece of;

[一跳] a jump;

嚇了一跳 be taken aback; jump out of one's skin; leap out of one's skin; strike terror into; throw a scare into;

[一貼] (1) glue; paste; (2) a piece of;

[一帖] a dose of;

[一通] know one thing;

一通百通 by knowing one method you will know all; grasp this one thing and you will grasp everything; sort this one thing out and you will sort out all the rest;

亂打一通 shower blows on;

[一同] at the same time and place; in the company of; together; together with;

[一桶] a barrel of; a bucket of; a drum of; a pail of;

[一統] integrate; unify; unitary; unite;

一統江山 territories under one sovereign;

一統天下 bring the whole empire under one's rule; bring the whole world under one's domination; unify the whole country;

[一頭] (1) a head; (2) a bulb of; a head of;

[一吐] get it off one's chest;

一吐為快 glad to get it off one's chest;

[一團] a ball of; a cloud of; a lump of; a mass of;

一團和氣 amicable; an easy-going atmosphere; full of goodwill toward one another; harmonious; harmony all round; keep on good terms; keep on the right side of everyone; maintain harmony all round; unprincipled peace;

一團漆黑 an utter failure; completely in the dark; entirely ignorant of; one mass of black with no distinguishable objects; pitch-dark; utterly hopeless;

一團糟 a chaotic state; a complete mess; a glorious muddle; a holy mess; balls-up; chaos; go haywire; in a hopeless mess; in a terrible mess; make a mess of; mess;

~弄得一團糟 make a mess of;

抱成一團 gang up; hang together; hold together to form a clique;

搓作一團 roll into a ball;

慌作一團 be struck all of a heap; be thrown into utter confusion; crouch with fear; in a flutter; in great excitement;

擠作一團 huddle together;

亂成一團 a scene of chaos; in a disorderly situation; in great confusion;

亂作一團 become a scene of chaos; in great confusion;

捏成一團 crush up;

扭作一團 the two are grappling with each other;

揪作一團 twist up into a lump;

蜷成一團 (1) hunch; (2) round;

揉成一團 roll into a mass by kneading;

縮成一團 be huddled up; cuddle up in a heap; curl up; huddle oneself up; roll oneself into a ball; shrink up;

縮作一團 cuddle up in a heap; curl up into a ball; huddle oneself up; roll oneself into a ball; shrink into oneself;

[一退六二五] deny all responsibility; evade all responsibility;

[一碗] a bowl of;

[一萬] (1) ten thousand; (2) one and ten thousand;

掛一漏萬 for one thing cited, then thousand may have been left out; think of one and omit ten thousand;

以一持萬 grasp the key point; take a coat by the collar; take a net by the headrope;

自一推萬 draw deduction from one to thousands;

[一汪] a pool of; a puddle of;

[一網打盡] capture all at once; capture in one net; catch all at one swoop; catch all in one draft; catch all in one dragnet; catch the whole lot in a dragnet; make a clean sweep; round up at one swoop; round up the whole gang at one fell swoop; take all at one haul of the net;

[一望] a single glance;

一望而知 it needs no ghost to tell us; it is written all over one's face; know all at a single glance; see with half an eye;

一望無際 a boundless expanse of; an uninterrupted stretch of; command an

extensive view; stretch to the horizon; wide stretches of;

一望無涯 boundless; stretch far off into the distance and out of sight; stretching beyond the horizon;

~八十歲的老太婆打哈欠——一望無涯(牙) an eighty-year-old granny yawning — no teeth to be seen;

一望無垠 stretch as far as the eye can see; stretch beyond the horizon; interminable; unbounded; vast in extent;

[一味] (1) blindly; habitually; invariably; (2) ingredient;

一味孤行 go one's own way;

一味蠻幹 act rashly and arbitrarily; persist in acting blindly;

一味遷就 make endless concessions; make one concession after another;

一味撒謊 lie like a gas meter;

一味退讓 retreat constantly;

一味拖延 procrastinate;

一味迎合 go all the way to meet;

一味指責 blindly censure; invariably blame;

[一位] a; one;

一位述謂結構 one-place predicate;

哪一位 who is it;

[一文] a single cent;

一文不化 not pay a single cent; without spending a cent;

一文不名 as poor as a church mouse; at low-water mark; broke to the world; flat broke; have no money; not a feather to fly with; not a shirt to one's back; not a shot in the locker; not have a penny to one's name; not have a shilling in the world; not have a shot in one's locker; penniless; without a penny to one's name;

一文不值 not worth a bean; not worth a cent; not worth a copper; not worth a damn; not worth a farthing; not worth a fillip; not worth a penny; not worth a stiver; not worth a whoop; not worth a plugged nickel; not worth anything; not worth the paper on which it is written; of no earthly use; of no use whatsoever; worthless;

一文錢難倒英雄漢 a hero may be utterly embarrassed by the want of a single cash;

一文一武 one military and the other civil;

不名一文 broke; have not a bean; not a shot in one's locker; not have a sausage; on the rocks; penniless; stony-broke; without a penny to one's name;

[一窩] (1) a family; a nest; a nestful; (2) a brood of; a litter of;

一窩蜂 like a swarm of bees; swarm;

一窩蜂吹 cancel the whole thing; dismiss altogether;

[一無] not in the least;

一無長物 have no superfluous possessions; have only bare necessities at home — no savings;

一無結果 nothing comes of it;

一無僅存 nothing is saved;

一無可取 count for nothing; good for nothing; have nothing to recommend one; not to be good for anything; worthless;

一無可疑 not a shadow of doubt;

一無例外 none is an exception; without exception;

一無是處 a bundle of negatives; absolutely without merit; can never get anything right; completely wrong; devoid of any merit; good for nothing; have no saving grace; have nothing worthy of praise; in dark colours; never get anything right; nothing is right; there is not a single merit; without a single virtue;

~一無是處的人 a waste of space;

一無所長 a Jack of all trades; a Jack of all trades and master of none; have no special skill; have nothing going for one; without any skill;

一無所成 accomplish nothing; come to no practical result; end up in smoke; have accomplished nothing; have nothing to show for all one's efforts; shoe the goslings; with one's finger in one's mouth; without any success;

一無所得 can find nothing; nothing is gained; nowhere;

一無所獲 empty-handed; gain nothing; gainless; make no gains at all;

一無所能 can do nothing; incapable of doing anything;

一無所求 for nothing;
一無所有 as bare as the palm of one's hand; have nothing at all; not to have a penny to bless oneself with; not to have a stiver; not to have a thing to one's name; not to own a thing in the world; own nothing at all; walk on one's shoestrings;
一無所知 absolutely ignorant of; have no idea of; in the dark; know little or nothing about; know neither buff nor style; know nothing about; know nothing at all about sth; not have the least inkling of; not to have the least inkling of; not to know anything about;
~ 一無所知的 clueless;
一無相識 there is not a single person one knows;
一無怨言 never utter a word of complaint; no complaint ever pases one's lips; without a word of complaint;

[一誤而誤] commit one mistake after another; keep on making mistakes; make things worse by repeated delays; one error leads to another;

[一物] one thing;
一物降一物 everything has its superior; there is always one thing to conquer another;

[一夕數驚] in constant fear;

[一息] have a breath; respiration;
一息尚存 a spark of life remains; as long as one is alive; as long as one lives; so long as one has a breath left; so long as there is still breath left in one; there is still one breath remaining; till one's last gasp;
一息奄奄 in the last gasp;
奄奄一息 dying;

[一下] (1) once; one time; (2) all at once; all of a sudden; in a short while;
一下子 all at one; at a blow; at a clap; at a single blow; at a single stroke; at a single sweep; at a sitting; at a whack; at one blow; at one fell; at one scoop; at one sitting; at one stroke; at one swoop; holus-bolus; in a tick; in one whack; overnight; with a scoop;
捶了一下 give sb a thump;
東一下，西一下 act aimlessly;
拍了一下 give sb a clap; give sb a pat;
親一下 give sb a kiss;
偷吻一下 steal a kiss;

[一夏] a summer season;

[一線] (1) a beam; a flash; a gleam; a glimmer; a ray; a thread; (2) a beam of; a flash of; a gleam of; a glimmer of; a ray of; a thread of;
日長一線 daytime gradually lengthens after the winter solstice;

[一箱] (1) a boxful; (2) a box of; a case of; a chest of; a crate of;

[一向] (1) earlier on; lately; (2) all along; consistently; for always; (3) hitherto; up to now;

[一笑] a grin; a smile;
一笑頓釋 bring sb round with a laugh;
一笑而去 leave with a smile;
一笑千金 a smile is worth a thousand pieces of gold; an enchanting smile;
一笑傾城 a singel smile would overthrow a city;
一笑置之 carry off with a laugh; chuckle at; chuckle over sth; dismiss with a laugh; dismiss with a smile; dispose of sth with a smile; laugh away; laugh off; laugh off as a joke; laugh out of corut; pass the thing off with a laugh; smile at; smile away; with a sneer;
一笑作答 answer only by a smile;
淡然一笑 a watery smile;
點頭一笑 nod with a smile;
付之一笑 afford to laugh at; carry off with a laugh; dismiss with a laugh; laugh and forget about it; laugh away; laugh off;
回眸一笑 give a smile, glancing back prettily; look back and flash a smile at sb; look back at sb with a smile;
會心的一笑 a knowing smile;
冷冷一笑 a wintry smile; give a bleak smile; give a sneering laugh;
聊博一笑 just for your entertainment;
勉強一笑 crack a smile;
調皮的一笑 puckish grin;
置之一笑 carry off with a laugh; laugh out of court;

[一些] a few; a little; a number of; an amount of; certain; some;

[一心] (1) heart and soul; wholeheartedly; (2)

at one; of one mind;

一心不能二用 a man cannot spin and reel at the same time; a man cannot whistle and drink at the same time; no man can do two things at once;

一心二用 keep one eye on;

一心為公 be utterly devoted to public interests; set one's heart on the common good; wholehearted devotion to the public interest;

一心向往 give all one's heart to; give one's heart completely to;

一心一德 at one; of one heart and one mind; wholeheartedly and faithfully; with united will;

一心一意 at one; be bent on; have one's heart in sth; heart and soul; intent on; of one heart and mind; one-minded; put one's whole heart into; single-hearted; single-minded; singleness of purpose; undivided attention; wholeheartedly; with all one's heart and mind; with body and soul; with one heart and one mind; with wholehearted devotion;

人居兩地，情發一心 people may be physically separated, but their spirits meet;

上下一心 of one heart and mind;

萬眾一心 all for one and one for all; all have one heart; all of one heart; all unite in one purpose; millions of people unite as one man; unite as one; with one heart and one mind;

［一新］ a fresh look; a new look;

煥然一新 acquire a completely new outlook; have a bright and new look; look brand-new; look fresh and bright; spick and span; take a new turn; take on an altogether new aspect;

油飾一新 freshly painted;

［一行］ a group travelling together; party;

一行百效 one makes a start, others will follow suit;

［一巡］ a helping of; a round of;

［一言］ a word;

一言蔽之 in a few words; in a nutshell; in a word; in short; sum up in a word;

~一言以蔽之 in a nutshell; in a word; in short; to make a long story short; to sum up;

一言不答 answer only by a smile;

一言不發 button up one's mouth; have nothing to say for oneself; keep one's mouth tight shut; not a word is said; not to breathe a word; not to say a word; not to utter; say nothing; without saying a word;

一言不合 a single jarring note in conversation;

~一言不合，拔刀相向 a word and a blow;

一言不留 not leave a word;

一言不洩 not breathe a syllable about;

一言道破 lay bare its secret with one remark;

一言既出，駟馬難追 a word spoken is an arrow let fly; a word spoken is past recalling; better the foot slip than the tongue trip;

一言九鼎 solemn promise;

一言難盡 difficult to embody in a single sentence; difficult to put in a nutshell; it is a long story; it is hard to explain in a few words; that is a long, long story;

一言喪邦 bring disaster to the nation by a mere word;

一言堂 one person alone has the say; what I say goes;

一言為定 a bargain is a bargain; a promise is a promise; call it a call; call it a deal count it as settled; it's a whack; it is agreed; reach a verbal agreement; sth is settled; that's a bargain; that's a deal; that's a whack;

一言未了 before one finishes speaking;

一言興邦 flourish the state by a mere word;

一言一行 a word and an action; each word and act; every word and deed; in all that one says and does;

一言一語 every word and phrase;

一言作譬 have a parable for explaining sth;

［一眼］ a glance;

一眼便知 can see it with half an eye; can tell at a glance;

一眼看穿 see through at a glance; see through with a discerning eye;

一眼看去 (1) take a sweeping look; (2) at first glance;

一眼看中 become infatuated with sb at

first sight;
瞅了一眼 take a look at;
看了一眼 give sth or sb a look; throw one's eye on;
瞥了一眼 cast a look at; catch a momentary glance; have a quick peek at; peek; snatch a momentary glance; take a peek into;
瞥之一眼 cast a look at; catch a momentary glance; snatch a momentary glance;
偷看一眼 cast a furtive glance; peek; sneak a glance; sneak a look; sneak a peek; steal a glance; steal a look; take a furtive glance;

[一燕不成夏] one swallow does not make a summer;

[一氧化碳] carbon monoxide;

[一樣] (1) alike; as...as ever; as good as; exactly the same; the same; (2) a kind of; a type of;
彼此一樣 it makes no difference;
都一樣 same difference;
跟新的一樣 as good as new; like new;
和別人一樣 same as anyone else;
你也一樣 same to you;
同平時不一樣 not one's usual self;
同平時一樣 as always; as usual;
我也一樣 me too; same here;
也是一樣 more of the same;
一模一樣 be a copy of sb; look identical;

[一頁] (1) one page; (2) a leaf of; a piece of; a sheet of;
翻開新的一頁 turn over a new leaf;
前一頁 previous page;
下一頁 next page;
~翻到下一頁 turn over the page;

[一夜] one evening;
一夜好覺 a good night's sleep;
一夜情 one-night stand;
一夜之間變成百萬富翁 become a millionaire overnight;
停留一夜 stop overnight;
輾轉反側的一夜 have a rough night;
整整一夜 all night long;

[一葉] a leaf;
一葉蘭 pleione;
一葉偏舟 a skiff; a small boat; a small rowboat; a tiny boat;
一葉障目 covering one's eyes with a leaf; see no further than one's nose;
~一葉障目，不見泰山 a leaf before the eye shuts out Mount Taishan — have one's view of the important overshadowed by the trivial; one cloud is enough to eclipse the sun;
一葉知秋 a small sign can indicate a great trend; a straw shows which way the wind blows; it is a straw in the wind; one falling leaf is indicative of the coming of autumn; the falling of one leaf heards the autumn;

[一一] each; each one; everyone; in turn; all and sundry; one after another; one by one;
一一告別 bid farewell to all, one after another; say goodbye to everyone;
一一檢查 examine one by one;
一一如命 act according to sb's wish; everything has been done as ordered; everything is as you wish; it shall be as you wish;
來一殺一，來兩殺雙 come one I kill one; come two, I kill a pair;
買一送一 buy one get one free;
恕不一一 I am sorry I cannot go into details;
一晃一晃 sway;
一龍一豬 one is very capable, while the other is extremely incompetent;
一撇一捺 one stroke to the left and another to the right;
一瘸一拐 dot and carry one; dot and go one; dot-and-go-one; limp; limpingly; walk jerkily and unevenly;
一山一石 each mount and crag;
一五一十 a blow-by-blow account; enumerating on and on; in detail; in good order and with nothing missing; systematically and in full detail; the whole story;
一蟹不如一蟹 each one is inferior to the last; go from bad to worse; worse and worse;
有一說一 come clean; speak the bold truth; tell the whole truth;
~有一說一有二說二 call a spade a spade;

[一衣帶水] a narrow strip of water; a narrow water course; a strip of water; be connected by a stream; be joined by a strip of water; be separated by a mere strip of water; be separated by a

scarcely perceptible creek; be separated only by a strip of water;

[一以貫之] one principle runs through it all; one unity pervading all things;

[一意] (1) with complete devotion; (2) stubbornly;

一意孤行 act arbitrarily; be bent on having one's own way; cling obstinately to one's course; dead set on having one's own way; do one's own thing; do sth against the advice of others; go one's own way; have one's own way; hell-bent on having one's own way; insist on having one's own way; persist in one's course; persist in wilfully and arbitrarily; self-assertion; self-opinionated; self-willed; take one's own course; wheel and deal; wilfully cling to one's own course;

專心一意 be bound up in; undivided attention;

[一飲而盡] at one gulp; drain the cup with one gulp; drink at a draught; drink it off; drink the whole in a draft; drink up; empty one's glass; empty one's cup in one gulp; fetch off; gulp down a drink; toss off the cup;

[一應] all; everything;

一應俱全 available in all varieties; complete in all varieties; complete in every line; complete with everything; from soup to nuts; lack for nothing; there is a full line of;

[一擁] rush;

一擁而入 swarm in;

一擁而上 come forth with a rush; rush up in a crowd; throw oneself forward;

[一隅] a corner;

一隅三反 deduce by analogy; draw inferences from one instance; judge the whole from one sample;

一隅之地 a small plot of land;

一隅之見 a glance from a corner;

退據一隅 withdraw into a corner;

[一雨] a rainfall;

一雨成秋 a sudden shower turns the lingering heat into the brisk cool air of autumn; after a rainfall the weather turns cool as if it were autumn;

一雨成災 one rainfall creates a blood;

[一語] a remark;

一語成讖 a saying turns out to be a prophecy; the prophecy has unfortunately come true;

一語道破 betray sb/sth in a statement; clear up the matter in a single sentence; get to the heart of the matter in a few words; hit the mark with a single comment; hit the nail on the head; lay bare the truth with one penetrating remark; puncture a fallacy with one remark;

一語到題 come to the point;

一語擊中 hit with one vivid expression; the word goes right to the heart of the matter;

一語驚四座 one's remark gives everyone there a surprise;

一語破的 hit the exact point with a word; hit the mark with a single comment; hit the nail on the head; hit the target with one remark;

一遇風浪 in moments of stress; whenever a storm blows up;

[一元復始] the beginning has come again; the restart of the first; the spring has come again; the year returns to its beginning; with the beginning of another year;

[一元化] centralized; unified;

一元化體制 unified system;

[一元論] monism;

[一員] a member of;

一員大將 an able general;

一員悍將 a brave warrior;

[一躍] jump; take a leap;

一躍成名 spring into fame;

一躍而過 jump...at one bound; leap over...at one bound; take a leap over;

一躍而起 get up with a jump; jump to one's feet; jump up all of a sudden; nip-up;

[一月] (1) January; (2) first month of the lunar year; (3) one month;

百星不如一月 the moon is better than one hundred stars — quality is more important than quantity;

月復一月 month after month;

[一扎] a bundle of; a sheaf of;

[一再] again and again; over and over; repeatedly; time and again;

一再蹉跎 let one opportunity after another

slip away;
一再宣稱 declare time and again;
一再展緩 be postponed again and again;
一不可再 once is forgivable, twice is not;
~ 可一不可再 just for once; once is enough; once is forgivable, not twice;
一錯再錯 repeat an error; repeat one's mistakes;
一多再多 more and yet more;
一而再，再而三 again and again; happen repeatedly; more than once; more than one occasion; over and over; over and over again; repeatedly; time and again; try again and again despite failure; twenty and twenty times;
一讓再讓 make one concession after another;
一忍再忍 bear and forbear;
一拖再拖 postpone again and again;
一誤再誤 commit one mistake after another; continue making errors; go further along the erroneous path; keep on making mistakes; make one error after another; make things worse by repeated delays; one error leads to another; put off again;

[一遭] the first time;
一遭生，二遭熟 strangers at first meeting become familiar at the next;
祇此一遭 for once in one's life; only once;
~ 祇此一遭，下不為例 only this time and no more;

[一早] early in the morning;

[一則] (1) one item; (2) a piece of; an item of; (3) on the one hand;
一則以喜，一則以悲 feel both joy and sorrow;
一則以喜，一則以懼 feel both joy and fear; feel pleased yet fearful;

[一站式] one-stop;
一站式商店 one-stop store;

[一張] a piece of; a sheet of; a slip of;
一張一弛 (1) off and on; (2) alternate tension with relaxation; labour and rest; tense and relax; tense up and relax alternately; tension alternating with relaxation; tension and lull; work and play;

[一章] a chapter;

[一朝] (1) in one day; (2) once;
一朝被蛇咬，三年怕井繩 a burnt child dreads the fire; once bitten by a snake, one shies at a coiled rope for the next three years; the scalded dog fears cold water;
一朝覆亡 collapse in one short day;
一朝千古 die suddenly;
一朝情義斷，樣樣不順眼 faults are thick where love is thin;
一朝人落泊，愛情生翼飛 when poverty comes in at the door, love flies out at the window;
一朝一夕 a short duration of time; a short period of time; a single day; in a morning and an evening; in one day; in one morning; overnight;
一朝有事 should anything happen some day;
一朝之忿 a sudden outburst of anger;
學善三年，學惡一朝 an ill weed grows apace; ill weeds grow apace;

[一轍] of the same track;
如出一轍 almost the same; coincide with; cut from the same cloth; exactly the same as; follow the same pattern; follow the same track with; identical; originate from the same source; run in the same groove; very similar;
同出一轍 come from the same place; cut from the same cloth; of an identical nature; originate from the same source;

[一着] a move;
一着不慎，滿盤皆輸 a chain is no stronger than its weakest link; a false step may lose the whole game; a single careless move and the entire game is lost; a single careless move spoils the entire game; one careless move and the whole game is lost; one careless move loses the whole game; one false move may lose the game;
棋高一着 a stroke above; one too many for; one up on; outmatch one's opponent; superior in stratagem; superior to one's opponent;
祇因一着錯，滿盤俱是輸 a single false move loses the game;
走錯一着，全盤皆輸 a trip in one point would have spoiled all;

[一針見血] exactly right; go right to the

heart of the matter; hit the nail on the head; incisively; make a pointed remark; pierce to the truth with a single pertinent remark; pointedly; put one's finger on the weak spot; reveal the heart of the matter in a few words; straight from the shoulder; straight to the heart of the matter; to the point; touch sb on the raw;

[一枕黃粱] a fond dream; a pipe dream; a vain dream;

[一陣] (1) a burst; a fit; a peal; a puff; (2) a bout of; a burst of; a clap of; a fit of; a flurry of; a gale of; a gust of; a hail of; a roar of; a round of; a spasm of; a spate of; a spatter of; a spell of; a squall of; a storm of; a sudden gust of; a torrent of; a volley of; a waft of;
一陣一陣的 in waves; occasionally; wave after wave;
一陣子 a period of time; a spell; for a while;
~ 前一陣子 earlier on; early on;
哄笑一陣 burst into a peal of laughter;
熱一陣又冷一陣 in alternate bursts of hot and cold;

[一隻] a; an; one;
一隻耳朵進，一隻耳朵出 go in one ear and out the other; in at one ear and out at the other;
一隻耗子搞壞一鍋湯 a little coloquintida spoils all the broth;
一隻爛桃壞滿筐 a rotten apple injures its neighbours;
一隻手拍不響 it takes two to make a quarrel;
一隻碗不響，兩隻碗叮噹 it takes two to make a quarrel;
一隻嘴唇兩張皮，翻來覆去全是你 your tongue is a double-edged sword;

[一支] a contingent of;

[一枝] a piece of; a stick of;
一枝獨秀 outshine others;
一枝之棲 a minor position; a shelter;

[一直] (1) all along; all the time; all the way; all the while; all through; always; as ever; as the day is long; constantly; continuously; ever since; from...till now; hold; keep; on end; till; to this day; until; used to be; (2) go straight forward;

[一紙] a document;
一紙千斤 a mere sheet of paper weighs more than a thousand catties;

[一至] to such extent;
一至於此 come even to such a pass; come to such an extreme;

[一致] consistent; identical; in accordance with; one and all; showing no difference; unanimous; with one accord;
一致關係 agreement; concord;
一致性 concord; uniformity;
~ 尺寸一致性 dimensional uniformity;
~ 離散一致性 discrete uniformity;
~ 一致性測試 conformance test;
表裏一致 honest and sincere;
動作一致 act in uniformity; keep strokes;
看法一致 go along with; go with sb; see eye to eye;
齊心一致 uniform and one-hearted;
人稱一致 person concord;
學用一致 integrate study with application;
與…一致 comport with;

[一種] (1) one kind; one species; one type; (2) a kind of; a sort of; a type of;
一種義務 an obligation;
哪一種 which one;

[一周] (1) a circle; a cycle; a revolution; (2) a week;
繞場一周 go round the stadium; march around the arena; victory lap;

[一株] a tree;

[一柱] a column of;
一柱擎天 one pillar supporting the sky — shouldering the heavy responsibility of high office;

[一桌] (1) tableful; (2) a table of;

[一子] a bundle of; a hank of;
一子皈依，九祖昇天 a son prepared to serve the Buddha to the end will let nine sinful ancestors to Heaven ascend;

[一自] since;

[一字] a character; a single word; a word; every character; every word; one character; one word;
一字褒貶 one word clearly expressing praise or censure — a strict, deliberate

choice of words; praise or criticize with a single word;
一字不差 in so many words; not a word is mistaken;
一字不錯 every word is correct; not a single error in the characters;
一字不漏 not drop a letter; not miss even a word; without missing a single word;
一字不識 be absolutely illiterate; cannot read or write; completely illiterate; not know A from B; not know a B from a battledore; not know a B from a bull's foot; not know a single character; not know the simplest character; unable to recognize a single written character;
一字不爽 exact to the world; word for word;
一字不提 not breathe a single word about; not mention a word about;
一字長蛇陣 a long line; a single-line battle array; a single-line formation;
一字千金 a single word is worth a thousand pieces of gold; each word worths a thousand pieces of gold;
一字千鈞 one word weighs a thousand kilograms;
一字腿 the splits;
~扒一字腿 do the splits;
一字一板 in a deliberate way; unhurriedly and clearly;
一字一句 every single word or phrase;
一字一淚 a teardrop for every word;
一字之褒 a word of commendation;
一字之貶 a word of censure;
一字之差 a difference of only a single word; the difference is only one word; the difference lies in a single word;

[一總] (1) all told; altogether; in all; (2) all;

[一組] (1) a batch; a group; a parcel; a piece; a set; (2) a group of; a set of;
四人一組 foursome;

[一嘴] put in a word;
插一嘴 chip in; interpose;

[一醉方休] get good and drunk;

抱一 stick to one principle;
不一 differ; vary;
純一 simple; single;
單一 single; unitary;
單打一 (1) concentrate on one thing only (2) have a one-track mind;
第一 first; first and foremost; for starters; foremost; primary; the first;
二合一 two in one;
二一 two and one;
封一 front cover;
劃一 standardized; uniform;
混一 amalgamate;
均一 even; homogeneous; uniform;
平一 suppress (a rebellion) and unify;
如一 identical; uniform;
什一 one tenth;
素一 simple and honest;
同一 identical; same;
統一 integrate; unify; unified; unitary; unite;
萬一 (1) a very small percentage; one ten-thousandth (2) contingency; eventually; if by any chance; just in case;
唯一 only; sole;
惟一 only; sole; the only kind; the only one; unique;
星期一 Monday;
之一 one in...;
逐一 one by one;
專一 concentrated; single-minded;

yi

【伊】 (1) he; she; (2) a surname;

[伊始] beginning;

[伊於胡底] what will happen; when it will stop; where it will all end; where it will lead to;

木乃伊 mummy;

yi

【衣】 (1) apparel; attire; dress; garments; clothes; clothing; (2) coating; covering; (3) a surname;

[衣包] canvas bag;

[衣被] clothing and bedding;
衣被群生 clothe and shelter the poor — spread all-round benefits to the people;

[衣鉢] teaching handed down from a master to his pupil;
衣鉢相傳 inherit the legacy of; inherit the priestly robe and dish from generation to generation; one's mantle descends to sb; one's mantle falls on sb;
衣鉢真傳 the keeper of true teachings; the real recipient of the mantle and the bowl — one has been initiated into the mysteries of any section;

true teachings handed down from the master;
承繼衣鉢 inherit the mantle of;

［衣不蔽體］ be dressed in rags; have nothing but rags on one's back; have scarcely a rag to one's back; not have a rag to one's back; not have a shirt to one's back; not have a stitch to one's back; wear rags; wear shabby clothes;

［衣不解帶］ not undress;

［衣不如新，人不如舊］ new clothes are best, and so are old acquaintances; with clothes the new are best, with friends the old are best;

［衣櫥］ dresser; wardrobe;

［衣服］ clothes; clothing; dress; duds;
衣服合身 the coat fits well;
衣服架 clothes rack;
衣服是新的好，朋友是舊的好 with clothes the new are best, with friends the old are best;
薄的衣服 light clothing;
補衣服 mend clothes; patch clothes; patch up a garment;
穿好衣服 get dressed;
穿上衣服 put one's clothes on;
穿衣服 wear clothes;
~沒穿衣服 have no clothes on;
定做衣服 custom-made clothes;
二手衣服 second-hand clothes;
乾淨的衣服 clean clothes;
很多衣服 many clothes;
換衣服 change one's clothes;
緊身衣服 tight-fitting clothes;
舊衣服 cast-offs; hand-me down;
寬鬆衣服 loose-fitting clothes;
晾衣服 dry clothes; put the washing out;
烙衣服 iron clothes;
攞起衣服 tuck up the skirt of a garment;
普通的衣服 ordinary clothes;
日常的衣服 everyday clothes;
曬衣服 hang out clothes;
時髦的衣服 fashionable clothes; trendy clothes;
試衣服 try on a dress;
收拾衣服 pack up clothes;
脱掉衣服 peel off clothes; take off one's clothes; undress;
脱光衣服 strip off clothes;
脱去衣服 undo a dress;
脱衣服 disrobe; get undressed; take off one's clothes;
脱下衣服 remove one's clothes; take off one's clothes;
洗衣服 do the washing; wash one's clothes;
休閒衣服 casual clothes;
一包衣服 a bundle of clothes; a pack of clothes;
一層衣服 a layer of clothing;
一堆衣服 a heap of clothes;
一件衣服 a dress; a piece of clothing; an article of clothing; an item of clothing;
一筐衣服 a hamper of clothes;
一套衣服 a suit;
一種衣服 a kind of clothes;
摺衣服 fold clothes;
熨衣服 do the ironing; iron clothes;
最好的衣服 one's best clothes;
最漂亮的衣服 one's best bib and tucker;
做衣服 have a dress made; make a dress;

［衣冠］ dress; hat and clothes;
衣冠不整 like sth the cat has brought in; not properly dressed; one's cap and robe are not in proper order; sloppily dressed;
衣冠楚楚 dapper; dressed like a gentleman; immaculately dressed; in full feather; in smart clothes; put on the ritz; very neatly and stylishly dressed;
~衣冠楚楚的 well-groomed;
衣冠禽獸 a beast in human attire; a beast in human clothing; a brute of a man; a dressed-up beast; a gentleman in appearance but a beast in conduct; a wolf in sheep's clothing;
衣冠文物 civilization and culture;
衣冠梟獍 a beast in human attire; a brute;
衣冠整齊 neatly dressed;
衣冠冢 a tomb containing personal effects of the deceased;
優孟衣冠 act on the stage; imitate other people; pass fake imitations for genuine;

［衣櫃］ commode; wardrobe;
大衣櫃 wardrobe;
~單門大衣櫃 single-door wardrobe;
~三門大衣櫃 three-door wardrobe;
~雙門大衣櫃 double-door wardrobe;
嵌入式衣櫃 built-in wardrobe; fitted wardrobe;
小衣櫃 clothes cabinet;

[衣架] coat hanger;
衣架棍 rail;
曬衣架 airer for clothes;
[衣襟] front of a garment;
淚濕衣襟 wet the front part of one's garment with tears; tears bedew one's coat; tears stain one's clothes;
淚沾衣襟 tears bedew one's coat; tears wet the jacket;
[衣錦] embroidered clothes; silken robes;
衣錦還鄉 glorious homecoming after having won high honours and social recognition; go back home in embroidered clothes; go home loaded with honours; return home after making good; return home in glory; return to one's hometown in glory; return to one's hometown in silken robes;
衣錦榮歸 return covered with honours to one's home; return home with high honours;
衣錦食肉 wear silk and eat flesh – wallow in luxury;
衣錦夜行 parade beautifully dressed at night – go without due appreciation; parade beautifully dressed in the dark; wearing embroidered robes, one strolls by night;
衣錦晝行 act for show; parade beautifully dressed in broad daylight; walk in embroidered clothes in daytime;
[衣殼] capsid;
多面體衣殼 polyhedral capsid;
內衣衣殼 inner capsid;
絲狀衣殼 filamentous capsid;
[衣褲] suit;
運動衣褲 sweatsuit;
[衣履] clothes and shoes;
衣履敝穿 slovenly dressed;
衣敝履穿 in ragged clothes and worn-out shoes; out at heels; out at elbows;
[衣料] cloth;
一塊衣料 a piece of cloth;
[衣領] collar;
[衣帽] hats and coats;
衣帽架 coatstand; hall stand; hall tree; hat tree;
衣帽間 checkroom; cloakroom; coat check; coatroom; locker room;
[衣莫如新，人莫如故] everything is good when new, but friends when old; new clothes and old friends are best;
[衣若懸鶉] bedraggled dress like a beggar's;
[衣衫] clothes; dress;
衣衫襤褸 be clad in rags; be clothed in ragged garments; be dressed in tatters; down at the heels; in rags; like sth the cat has brought in; one's clothes are hanging in ribbons; out at heels; out at the elbows; shabby in dress;
祇敬衣衫不敬人 the clothes, not the people, are respected;
[衣裳] clothes; clothing; garments;
穿衣裳 put on clothes;
馬靠鞍裝，人靠衣裳 fine feathers make fine birds; the tailor makes the man;
人靠衣裳馬靠鞍 clothes make a man just as a saddle makes a horse; fine feathers make fine birds; nine tailors make a man; the tailor makes the man;
人在衣裳馬在鞍 clothes make the man; fair feathers make fair fowls; fine feathers make fine birds;
涮衣裳 rinse clothes;
[衣食] food and clothing; what one lives on;
衣食不周 cannot feed or clothe oneself properly; hardly able to keep body and soul together; have not enough in the belly and on the back; not to have enough for food and clothing; not to have proper clothing nor enough to eat; too poor to feed and clothe oneself well; wanting in food and clothing; with insufficient food and clothing;
衣食豐足 have plenty of food and clothing;
衣食父母 those on whom one's livelihood depends;
衣食住行 clothing, food, shelter and means of travel, the four basic needs of everybody; food; clothing, shelter and transportation, basic necessities of life;
衣食足而後知禮義 if men have wealth, they are able to be courteous; wealth enables men to be courteous; well fed, well bred;
敝衣惡食 having a very low standard of living;
粗衣淡食 coarse clothes and simple food; rough clothes and simple fare;

粗衣簡食 rough clothes and simple fare;
惡衣惡食 coarse clothing and simple food; coarse food and clothing; poor clothing and poor food;
豐衣足食 have adequate food and clothes; have ample food and clothing; have enough to eat and wear; well provided with food and clothing; well-clad and well-fed; well-fed and well-clothed;
減衣縮食 more economical; practise austerity; scant oneself in food and clothes; scrimp on food and clothing;
節衣縮食 economize food and clothing; live frugally; more economical; practise austerity; save on food and clothing; scant oneself in food and clothes;
解衣推食 doff one's own garments to cloth sb else and give him the food from one's own place — treat sb with great kindness; off one's own coat and food — treat sb sincerely;
賴衣賴食 depend on others for a living;
靡衣偷食 ignobly lead an extravagant life; live in luxurious extravagance;
暖衣飽食 warm clothing and well-fed; well-fed and clothed;
施衣布食 give food and clothing to the needy;
縮衣節食 economize; economize food and clothing; economize on clothing and food; practise austerity; reduce expenses on clothing and food;
推食解衣 do anything one possibly can to help; give food and clothing to the needy; help one in need; offer one's own clothes and food to help others; put off one's own clothes and offer one's own food to others; show kindness to others;
推衣解食 share happiness and woe with one's followers;
宵衣肝食 diligent in discharging official duties; dress before dawn and wait until dusk for dinner; get up before dawn and eat late — busy with state affairs; get up early and take one's meal late;
衣單食薄 thinly clad, badly fed;
衣暖食飽 be warmly clothed and well fed;
衣溫食飽 be warmly clothed and well fed; in good keep; well fed and clothed;

[衣飾] clothes and ornaments;
[衣物] clothing and other articles of daily use;
衣物間 locker room;
衣物籃 clothes basket;
保暖衣物 warm clothing;
一堆衣物 a bundle of clothes;
[衣香鬢影] ladies in smart clothes; women in rich attire;
[衣箱] suitcase; trunk;
[衣袖] sleeve;
淚濕衣袖 wet one's sleeve with tears;
[衣裝] (1) dress; (2) clothes and luggage;
佛要金裝，人要衣裝 fine clothes make the man; fine feathers make fine birds; fine tailors make a man; the tailor makes the man;
人憑衣裝馬憑鞍 clothes make a man just as a saddle makes a horse; fine feathers make fine birds;
人要衣裝 the tailor makes the man;
~人要衣裝，佛要金裝 apparel makes the man; fine clothes make the man; fine feathers make fine birds;
[衣着] apparel; attire; clothing; dress; headgear and footwear;
衣着得體 be suitably dressed;
衣着過時的 frumpy;
衣着古板的 frumpy;
衣着合宜 be suitably dressed;
衣着華麗 be loudly dressed;
衣着儉樸 dress simply;
衣着講究 in smart clothes;
衣着樸素 be plainly dressed;
衣着入時 dress neatly, quite in accord with the time of year;
衣着時髦 be dressed up;
衣着素雅 be tastefully dressed in a simple style;
衣着艷麗 in one's colourful dress;
衣着整潔 be neatly attired; be neatly dressed;
講究衣着 care much about dress;
~不講究衣着 not think much about dress;

白衣 (1) white clothes; (2) clothes of the common people; (3) commoner;
百結衣 ragged clothing;
百衲衣 (1) monk's ragged robe, made of patches (2) ragged clothing;
胞衣 afterbirth;
避彈衣 bulletproof garments;

便衣 (1) civilian clothes; plain clothes (2) plain-clothesman;
布衣 (1) cloth gown (2) common people;
裁衣 cut cloth for making dress;
采衣 bright garments; colourful garments;
衩衣 woman's gown with slits on the sides;
腸衣 casing (for sausages);
氅衣 (1) coat; outer garment; (2) costume of a Daoist priest;
晨衣 dressing gown; morning gown;
襯衣 shirt; under-clothes;
成衣 (1) ready-made clothes (2) tailoring;
鶉衣 ragged clothes;
粗衣 coarse clothing;
大衣 overcoat;
單衣 unlined jacket;
蝶衣 wings of a butterfly;
冬衣 winter coat;
法衣 garments worn by a Buddhist monk or Daoiot priest at a religious ceremony;
風衣 windbreaker; windcheater; wind coat;
葛衣 ko-hemp cloth;
更衣 (1) change one's clothes (2) wash one's hands; go to toilet;
估衣 second-hand clothes;
掛衣 coat; coating;
寒衣 winter clothing;
號衣 livery or army uniform;
浣衣 wash clothes;
箭衣 archer's dress;
錦衣 embroidered dress;
柩衣 pall;
救生衣 life jacket;
寬衣 take off your coat;
晾衣 sun clothes;
撩衣 hold up the lower part of a garment;
毛衣 sweater; woolen sweater; woolly;
棉衣 cotton-padded clothes;
冥衣 paper clothing burned for use of the dead;
內衣 undergarment; underclothes; underdress; underlinen; underwaist; underwear; undies; unmentionables;
砲衣 gun cover;
礮衣 canvas covering of an artillery piece; gun cover;
披衣 throw on gown;
皮衣 (1) fur clothing (2) leather clothing;
破衣 duds;
潛水衣 diving suit;
寢衣 bedclothes; sleeping gown;
青衣 (1) black clothes (2) maid (3) the demure middle-aged or young female character type in Chinese operas;
囚衣 convict's clothes; prisoner's garb;
球衣 sports shirt; sweat shirt;
缺衣 short of clothes;
絨衣 sweater shirt;
曬衣 dry clothes in the sun;
僧衣 kasaya, a patchwork outer vestment worn by a Buddhist monk;
上衣 jacket; upper outer garment;
試衣 fitting;
壽衣 grave-clothes; shroud;
書衣 book jacket;
睡衣 bathrobe; nightclothes; nightgown; nighty; sleeping gown; nightclothes; nightwear; pajamas;
素衣 (1) plain clothes; (2) white mourning dress;
蓑衣 straw or palmbark rain cape;
胎衣 (of humans) afterbirth;
苔衣 moss;
袒衣 dress in a hurry with part of the flesh showing;
糖衣 sugar-coat;
燙衣 iron clothes;
鐵衣 (1) armour; (2) iron rust;
脱衣 remove one's clothing; take off one's clothes;
外衣 (1) jacket; outer garment (2) appearance; semblance;
韋衣 (1) hunting clothes; (2) simple clothes;
衛生衣 sweatshirt;
洗衣 do one's washing; wash clothes;
戲衣 stage costume;
夏衣 summer clothing; summer-wear;
鮮衣 new clothes;
線衣 cotton knitwear;
孝衣 mourning dress;
胸衣 corselette;
褻衣 underwear; undies;
血衣 blood-stained garment; clothes covered with gore;
游泳衣 bathing costume; swimming costume; swimsuit;
雨衣 raincoat;
浴衣 bathrobe;
罩衣 dustcoat; overall;

yi

【依】 (1) depend on; lean to; rely on; (2) comply with; consent; follow; yield to; (3) according to; in the light of; judging by; (4) forgive; tolerant;
［依傍］ (1) depend on; rely on; (2) emulate;

imitate; model after; pattern after;

[依次] in order; in proper order; in proper sequence; one by one; successively;

依次遞補 fill in order of established precedence; fill vacancies in order of precedence; fill vacancies in proper order;

依次發言 speak in turn;

依次更替 successive replacement;

依次就座 go to one's seat in due order; sit in order of seniority; take seats in proper order;

依次入座 go to one's seat in due order; take seats in proper order;

[依從] comply with; follow; listen to; submit to; yield to;

依從父母 obedient to one's parents;

不得不依從 have to comply;

[依存] depend on sb or sth of existence; interdependent;

依存語法 dependency grammar;

相互依存 dependent on each other; interdependent;

[依戴] rely on and look up to sb;

[依法] according to law; by operation of law; in conformity with legal provisions;

依法辦案 handle a case in accordance with the law;

依法辦理 handle in accordance with law;

依法懲辦 bring to justice; deal with in accordance with the law; punish according to law; punish in accordance with the law;

依法懲處 keep sb in line by punishment; punish in accordance with the law;

依法處理 be dealt with according to the law;

依法從事 deal with according to the law; settle according to the law;

依法逮捕 arrest in the name of the law;

依法究辦 investigate and deal with according to law;

依法扣押 practise a legal attachment;

依法論處 punish according to the law;

有法必依 abide by the laws; ensure that the laws are strictly observed;

[依附] (1) adjoin; attach oneself to; become an appendage to; depend on; (2) submit to;

依附權貴 attach oneself to bigwigs; depend on influential powers;

[依歸] reliance and resort;

無所依歸 have no one to depend on and nowhere to live;

[依計而行] act according to the plan; take a share in the scheme;

[依舊] as before; as usual; in the usual manner; in the usual way; still;

依舊故我 I am just as before;

風韻依舊 as charming as before; look still attractive; one's majesty and charm still remain;

[依據] (1) according to; in the light of; judging by; on the basis of; (2) basis; foundation;

依據不足 be based on insufficient grounds;

依據科學 rest on a scientific basis;

沒有依據 have no basis;

無所依據 nothing to base on; nothing to prove;

有事實依據 have factual evidence;

[依靠] (1) depend on; rely on; (2) backing; sb to fall back on; support;

依靠救濟 go on relief; on relief;

生活有依靠 have one's livelihood assured;

無依無靠 all alone in the world; be left forlorn and without a protector; completely helpless; have no one to depend on; have no one to turn to; have nothing to depend on; helpless; high and dry; with no one to rely on; with no one to turn to; with nothing to support one;

[依賴] dependence; dependency; dependent on; rely on;

依賴別人 dependent on others;

依賴關係 base oneself on one's social relationships; rely on one's powerful relations;

依賴性 dependence; the habit of relying on others;

~應力依賴性 stress dependence;

依賴於人 depend on others; lean on sb;

擺脱依賴 shake off dependence on;

不再依賴 end one's dependence on;

常態依賴 normal dependency;

互相依賴 interdependent;

可以依賴 reliable;

相互依賴 correlative dependence; depend on each other; have mutual dependence;

尋求依賴 seek support;

［依戀］ feel attachment to sb; feel reluctant to part with; reluctant to leave;

依戀父母 feel attached to one's parents;

無所依戀 nothing to be reluctant to leave;

［依流平進］ arrange in order of seniority; be promoted according to status;

［依慕］ adore;

［依憑］ depend on; rely on;

［依然］ as...as ever; as before; as usual; nonetheless; remain the same; still;

依然故我 I am just the same as before; I am still my same old self; I am very much my old self; I remain the same as before; my circumstances have not changed much; one is still very much the same old self;

依然如故 none the better for it; non the worse; remain as before; remain one's same old self; remain the same as before; remain unchanged;

依然有效 remain valid; still hold good;

風采依然 one's elegance remains as before;

［依實］ according to fact; confess truthfully;

依實招供 confess the truth at court;

［依勢淩人］ insult people by presuming on one's power;

［依順］ obedient;

百依百順 all obedience; docile and obedient; eat out of sb's hand; feed out of sb's hand; obey sb implicitly; on a string;

千依百順 a nose of wax with sb; all obedience; all things to sb; agree with sb about everything; as yielding as wax; assent to every order; at sb's beck and call; compliant; comply all the time with the dictates of sb; dance to sb's pipe; do the bidding of sb; docile and obedient; like wax in sb's hands; on a string; serve sb hand and foot; subservient; subservient to sb's every wish; wax in sb's hands;

［依隨］ comply with; follow;

［依托］ (1) depend on; rely on; (2) backing; prop; support;

［依偎］ cuddle up; lean close to snuggle up to; snuggle;

［依違］ admit and deny;

依違不定 undecided;

依違兩可 equivocal in one's attitude; have no definite conviction of one's own; shilly-shally; sit on the fence; swim between two waters; unable to make up one's mind; undecided; yea and nay;

［依稀］ dimly; vaguely; uncertain; unclear;

依稀記得 remember vaguely;

依稀可見 dimly visible;

［依限］ within the time limit;

［依依］ reluctant to part;

依依不捨 a sense of reluctance to part from sb; cannot bear to leave; cannot bear to part; cannot tear oneself away from; feelings of regret at parting; have a great attachment to; have a strong attachment to; have an invincible attachment to; reluctant to leave; reluctant to part; unwilling to part from; unwilling to part with;

依依惜別 be distressed at parting; bid an affectionate adieu to sb; part reluctantly from;

［依約］ (1) by agreement; in accordance with the promise; (2) follow conventions and traditions; (3) indistinct; obscure;

［依允］ comply with;

［依仗］ (1) sb to fall back on; (2) count on; rely on;

依仗權勢 count on one's powerful connections; rely on authority and power; rely on one's power and position;

無所依仗 have nothing to rely upon;

［依照］ according to; in compliance with; in the light of;

依照慣例 according to custom;

依照習俗 in obedience to a custom;

依照先例 in the light of precedents;

跛依 slanting; unbalanced;

皈依 believe devoutly in Buddhism or some other religion;

歸依 believe devoutly in Buddhism or some other religion;

憑依 base oneself on; rely on;

偎依 lean close to;

無依 have nobody to rely on;

相依 be interdependent; depend on each other;

依依 reluctant to part;

yi

【咿】 a form used to represent a sound;

［咿唔］ recite or intone in reading;

［咿呀］ (1) creak; squeak; (2) babble; prattle;
咿呀語 babbling;

yi

【猗】 (1) an exclamation indicating admiration; (2) adverbial particle;

［猗靡］ flow and flutter with the wind;

［猗猗］ splendid and flourishing;

［猗與］ an exclamation indicating admiration;

yi

【壹】 elaborate form of 一;

yi

【揖】 (1) bow with one's hands folded in one's front; (2) defer to; yield politely;

［揖拜］ make a bow with the folding in front;
深揖長拜 bow deeply and salute extensively;

［揖別］ bid adieu;

［揖客］ greet a guest;

［揖讓］ (1) courtesy between the host and his guests; (2) abdicate; give up a position for a better man;

［揖謝］ bow in thanks;

羅圈兒揖 circular bow to all sides;
作揖 make a bow with hands clasped in front;

yi

【欹】 (1) fierce dog; (2) interjection of pleasure;

［欹歟盛哉］ what a grand occasion; what a grand sight;

yi

【漪】 ripples;

［漪瀾］ ripples;
漪瀾蕩漾 the green water shimmers in the soft breeze; the surface of the lake ripples;

［漪漣］ cat's kin;

漣漪 ripples;

yi

【禕】 excellent;

yi

【銥】 iridium;

yi

【噫】 alas;

yi

【繄】 (1) phrase-initial particle; (2) a verb functioning like the verb "to be"; (3) alas;

yi

【醫】 (1) doctor; physician; surgeon; (2) medical science; medical service; medicine; (3) cure; treat;

［醫病］ cure a disease; treat a patient;

［醫卜星相］ doctors, fortune-tellers and astrologers; medicine, fortune-telling, astrology and phrenology;

［醫道］ art of healing; medical knowledge; medical science; medical skill; physician's skill; skill of a doctor;

［醫德］ medical ethics;
醫德高尚 a doctor with lofty medical ethics;
違反醫德 against medical ethics; violate medical ethics;

［醫方］ medical prescription;

［醫官］ medical official;

［醫館］ hospital;

［醫護］ health care;
醫護保險 health insurance;
醫護人員 health-care professionals;

［醫家］ skilled doctor;

［醫科］ department of medicine;
醫科大學 medical university;
醫科學生 medic; medical student; medico;

［醫理］ principles of medical science;

［醫療］ cure a disease; medical treatment; treat a disease;
醫療保健 health care;
醫療保險 medical insurance;
~醫療保險基金 medical insurance fund;
醫療隊 medical team;
~田間醫療隊 medical station in the fields;
~巡迴醫療隊 mobile medical team;
醫療服務 medical services;
醫療艇 medical ship;
醫療網 medical and health network;
醫療信息系統 medical information system;
醫療援助 medical assistance;
醫療證明 medical certificate;

醫療質量 quality of medical care;
醫療中心 health centre;
半費醫療 semi-paid medical care;
補助性醫療 complementary medicine;
公費醫療 free medical serve;
減費醫療 discount medical care;
接受醫療 be medically treated;
勞保醫療 labour-protection medical care;
免費醫療 free medical care;

自費醫療 private medicine; self-paid medical care;

[醫林] medical circles; medical faculty;

[醫生] doc; doctor; medic; medical doctor; medical practitioner; medico; physician; surgeon;
醫生醫病，不能醫命 a doctor can cure diseases but cannot alter fate;
本區醫生 local doctor;
泌尿科醫生 urologist;
鼻科醫生 rhinologist;
病理科醫生 pathologist;
產科醫生 obstetrician;
赤腳醫生 barefoot doctor;
初級醫生 junior doctor;
傳染病醫生 doctor for infectious diseases;
兒科醫生 paediatrician;
耳鼻喉醫生 ear-nose-throat doctor;
飛行醫生 flying doctor;
婦科醫生 gynaecologist;
骨科醫生 orthopedist;
喉科醫生 laryngologist;
會診醫生 consulting physician;
家庭醫生 family doctor;
江湖醫生 quack; quack physician;
結核病醫生 doctor for tuberculosis;
精神科醫生 psychiatrist;
看醫生 consult a doctor; see a doctor; visit a doctor;
理療科醫生 physiotherapist;
臨牀醫生 clinician;
冒牌醫生 quack;
腦科醫生 brain specialist;
內科醫生 physician;
內科住院醫生 house physician;
女醫生 lady doctor;
皮膚科醫生 dermatologist;
普通科醫生 general practitioner;
矯形外科醫生 orthopedic surgeon;
請教醫生 consult a physician;
請醫生 call a doctor; send for a doctor;
救護醫生 ambulance doctor;
~男救護醫生 ambulance man;
~女救護醫生 ambulance woman;
去請醫生 call in a doctor; go and fetch a doctor; go for a doctor;
全科醫生 general practitioner;
神經科醫生 nerve specialist;
實習醫生 houseman intern; intern;
外科醫生 surgeon;
外科住院醫生 house surgeon;
小兒科醫生 paediatrician;
協助醫生 assist a physician;
心臟科醫生 heart specialist;
心臟外科醫生 cardiac surgeon;
牙科醫生 dental surgeon; dentist;
眼科醫生 eye-doctor; oculist;
一隊醫生 a team of doctors;
一名醫生 a doctor;
醫院醫生 hospital doctor;
營養醫生 dietician;
針刺醫生 acupuncture doctor;
針灸科醫生 acupuncture and moxibustion doctor;
整形外科醫生 plastic surgeon;
諮詢醫生 ask a doctor; consult a doctor;
值班醫生 doctor on duty;
腫瘤科醫生 oncologist;
主任醫生 chief doctor; chief physician;
主治醫生 attending doctor; doctor in charge; physician in charge; surgeon in charge;
住院醫生 resident physician;
專科醫生 specialist;

[醫師] doctor; physician; surgeon;
臨牀醫師 clinician;
主任醫師 chief physician;
~副主任醫師 deputy chief physician;
主治醫師 doctor-in-charge;

[醫書] medical books;

[醫術] art of healing; medical skills;
醫術不高 lack in medical skills;
醫術高 know the art of medicine;
精通醫術 have superb medical skill;
提高醫術 improve one's medical skills;
研究醫術 study the art of medicine;
運用醫術 exercise one's medical skills;

[醫務] medical matters;
醫務部 department of medical administration;
~醫務部主任 head of the department of medical administration;

醫務工作者 medical worker;
醫務人員 health professional; medical personnel;
醫務所 clinic;

[醫學] medical science; medicine;
醫學博士 doctor of medicine;
醫學仿生學 medical bionics;
醫學界 medical profession;
醫學倫理學 medical ethics;
醫學院 college of medicine; medical school;
傳統醫學 traditional medicine;
法醫學 forensic medicine;
工業醫學 industrial medicine;
航空醫學 aeromedicine;
環境醫學 environmental medicine;
基礎醫學 preclinical medicine;
精通醫學 have a profound knowledge of medicine;
軍事醫學 military medicine;
空間醫學 aerospace medicine;
老年醫學 geriatric medicine;
臨牀醫學 clinical medicine;
潛水醫學 diving medicine;
社會醫學 social medicine;
身心醫學 psychosomatic medicine;
實驗醫學 experimental medicine;
現代醫學 modern medicine;
心理醫學 psychic medicine;
宇航醫學 aerospace medicine;
宇宙醫學 space medicine;
預防醫學 preventive medicine;
整體醫學 holistic medicine;
正統醫學 conventional medicine; orthodox medicine;

[醫藥] healing drugs; medicines;
醫藥費 hospital bill; medical bill; medical expenses;
醫藥罔效 incurable with medicine; medical aid has been useless;
缺醫少藥 short of doctors and medicine; have few trained doctors and very little medicine; the shortage of doctors and medicine;

[醫院] hospital;
按摩醫院 massage hospital;
產科醫院 maternity hospital;
傳染病醫院 hospital for infectious diseases;
創辦醫院 institute a hospital;
兒童醫院 children's hospital;
婦產科醫院 obstetrics and gynaecology hospital;
婦科醫院 gynaecology and obstetrics hospital;
附屬醫院 affiliated hospital;
隔離醫院 isolation hospital;
工廠醫院 plant hospital;
骨科醫院 osteologic hospital;
管理醫院 operate a hospital;
後方醫院 base hospital;
教學醫院 teaching hospital;
開辦醫院 run a hospital;
口腔醫院 stomatological hospital;
陸軍醫院 army medical hospital;
痲瘋醫院 leprosy hospital;
人民醫院 people's hospital;
善終醫院 hospice;
實習醫院 training hospital;
鄉村小醫院 cottage hospital;
心血管病醫院 cardiovascular diseases hospital;
胸科醫院 thoratic diseases hospital;
牙科醫院 dental hospital;
一家醫院 a hospital;
一所醫院 a hospital;
針灸醫院 acupuncture hospital;
整形外科醫院 plastic surgery hospital;
中醫醫院 hospital of Chinese medicine;
腫瘤醫院 tumour hospital;
住進醫院 be admitted to hospital; go into a hospital;
綜合醫院 general hospital;

[醫治] cure; give medical treatment; heal; treat;
醫治病人 give medical treatment to a patient; treat a patient;
醫治無效 fail to respond to any medical treatment; treatment is of no avail;
醫治有效 the treatment worked well;
得到醫治 obtain medical treatment;

法醫 legal medical expert;
國醫 (1) traditional Chinese medical science (2) doctor of traditional Chinese medicine;
就醫 go to a doctor; seek medical advice;
軍醫 medical officer; military surgeon;
良醫 good doctor;
名醫 famous doctor;
群醫 doctors;
儒醫 a physician of traditional Chinese medicine who used to be a scholar;
神醫 highly skilled doctor; miracle-working

doctor;

施醫 give free medical service;
世醫 doctor of traditional Chinese medicine known for generations;
獸醫 vet; veterinarian; veterinary surgeon;
太醫 imperial physician;
巫醫 witch doctor;
西醫 (1) Western medicine; (2) doctor trained in Western medicine;
校醫 school doctor;
新醫 Western medicine;
行醫 practice medicine;
牙醫 dentist;
業醫 practise medicine;
庸醫 quack; charlatan;
御醫 imperial physician;
中醫 (1) doctor of traditional Chinese medicine; practitioner of Chinese medicine; (2) traditional Chinese medicine science;

yi
【黟】 (1) ebony; (2) black; dark;

yi
【鷖】 (1) gull; (2) dark blue; (3) phoenix;

yi²

yi
【匜】 washbasin;

yi
【夷】 (1) safe; smooth; (2) raze; (3) eliminate; execute; exterminate; kill; wipe out; (4) a name for ancient tribes in the east; (5) foreign country; foreigner; (6) at ease; peaceful; (7) big; great; (8) classes; grades; (9) a surname;
［夷狄］ eastern barbarians in ancient China;
南夷北狄 barbarous tribes on the south and the north of ancient China;
［夷簡］ simple life;
［夷滅］ wipe out;
［夷由］ hesitating; undecided;
［夷族］ extermination of an entire family;

鄙夷 despise; look down upon; scorn;
凌夷 decline;
陵夷 decline;
芟夷 (1) eliminate; wipe out; (2) mow (grass);
辛夷 flower bud of lily magnolia;

yi
【圯】 bank; bridge;

yi
【沂】 four rivers originating in Shandong;

yi
【迆】 meandering; winding;
［迆邐］ meandering; tortuous; winding;

yi
【宜】 (1) appropriate; fitting; good; proper; right; suitable; (2) had better; ought to; should; (3) matter; (4) fit; put in order; suit; (5) a surname;
［宜男］ prolific of male children;
［宜然］ suitable;
［宜人］ agreeable; delightful; pleasant;
宜人的 balmy; congenial;
風景宜人 the scenery is lovely;
氣候宜人 the weather is agreeable;
［宜於］ good for; suitable for;

yi
【怡】 (1) cheerful; happy; joyful; (2) harmony; on good terms; (3) a surname;
［怡蕩］ find pleasure in wanton ways;
［怡和］ delightful harmony; on very pleasant terms;
［怡樂］ pleasures;
［怡然］ contented; happy; pleasant and contented; satisfied and happy;
怡然自得 feel a glow of happiness; find one's inner peace; happy and contented; happy and pleased with oneself; in a pleasurable glow of satisfaction;
怡然自樂 contented and happy;
［怡色］ look cheerful; look pleased; pleasant look;
［怡神］ inspire peace and harmony in one's mind;
怡神下氣 speak mildly and pleasantly; with a subdued and soft voice;
賞景怡神 enjoy the landscape to one's satisfaction;
養心怡神 refresh one's spirit by keeping quiet;
［怡聲］ pleasing voice that is soft and tender;
［怡顏］ pleasant look; smiling;
怡顏悅色 cheerful countenance and contented appearance;
［怡養］ enjoy good health and live a happy life;
［怡怡］ harmonious;
［怡悅］ find joy in; take delight in;

yi

【咦】 hey; well; why;

yi

【姨】 (1) aunt; one's mother's sisters; (2) one's wife's sisters; sisters-in-law;

[姨表] cousinship; maternal cousins;

[姨父] husband of a maternal aunt; uncle;

[姨姐] one's wife's elder sister;

姨姐妹 sisters on one's mother's side;

[姨媽] aunt; maternal aunt;

[姨妹] younger sisters of one's wife;

[姨母] aunt; maternal aunt;

[姨娘] concubine of one's father;

[姨婆] grandaunt;

[姨兄] elder cousin on one's mother's side;

姨兄弟 male cousins on one's mother's side;

[姨丈] uncle;

yi

【洟】 nasal mucus; snivel;

[洟涕] nasal mucus; snivel;

yi

【胰】 pancreas;

[胰島素] insulin; pancreatin;

胰島素 insulin;

~ 胰島素酶 insulinase;

~ 牛胰島素 bovine insulin;

~ 球蛋白鋅胰島素 globin zinc insulin;

~ 組朊胰島素 histone insulin;

[胰腺炎] pancreatitis;

急性胰腺炎 acute pancreatitis;

結石性胰腺炎 calcareous pancreatitis;

慢性胰腺炎 chronic pancreatitis;

yi

【眙】 as in 盱眙 , name of a county;

yi

【荑】 (1) mow; (2) weed;

yi

【貤】 move; remove; turn;

yi

【痍】 bruise; sore; wound;

yi

【迻】 transfer; translate;

[迻錄] copy by hand; make a transcript of; transcribe;

[迻譯] translate;

yi

【移】 (1) move; remove; shift; (2) affect; alter; change; influence; (3) convey; forward; transfer; transmit; transplant;

[移步] move one's steps; walk;

[移船就岸] come of one's own accord; make progress easier; move one's boat to get ashore;

[移動] change; move; shift;

移動電話 mobile telephone;

~ 移動電話系統 mobile telephone system;

移動商務 m-commerce; mobile commerce;

移動數據通信網 mobile data communication network;

移動用戶識別碼 mobile identification number;

移動桌椅 move about the desks and chairs;

飛速移動 hurtle;

緩慢移動 crawl; poke along;

前後移動 move to and fro;

上下移動 move up and down;

向右移動 move to the right;

向左移動 move to the left;

左右移動 move from side to side;

[移換] change;

[移禍] shift trouble to another; shirk one's reponsibility by incriminating another person;

[移交] (1) handover; transfer; turn over; (2) deliver into sb's custody; hand over one's job to a successor;

移交權力 transfer power;

移交責任 transfer responsibility;

[移居] migrate; move one's residence; move to another place for settlement;

移居各處 move around; shift about;

移居國外 emigrate from one's own country; emigrate to a foreign country;

移召海外 migrate overseas;

大移居 diaspora;

[移開] move away;

[移苗] transplant seedlings;

[移民] (1) emigrate; immigrate; migrate; (2) emigrant; immigrant; migrant;

移民局 the immigration office;

移民入境 immigration;

移民限額 immigration quota;

移民政策 immigration policy;
非法移民 illegal immigrant;
技術移民 immigrants with skills;
接納移民 admit immigrants; take in immigrants;
禁止移民 ban immigrants from;
經濟移民 economic migrant;
同化移民 assimilate immigrants;
限制移民 limit immigrants;

[移挪] use money for a purpose not originally intended;
[移棲] migrancy; migrate;
[移情作用] empathy;
[移沙造田] create farmland by removing sand drifts;
[移山] move mountains;
移山倒海 conquer and transform nature; remove mountains; remove mountains and drain seas; very capable; very resourceful;
移山填溝 remove hills and fill gullies;
移山填海 move mountains and fill up seas;
移山易河 move mountains and change the courses of rivers;
移山造田 move hills to build up fields; remove hills to build up farmland;
移山治河 level the mountains and harness the rivers;
移山治水 move mountains and tame rivers;

[移時] a brief period of time; a little while;
[移書] write a letter to sb;
[移位] shift;
迴圈移位 cyclic shift;

[移徙] move and settle in an undeveloped place;
[移星換斗] change the positions of stars; extremely powerful;
[移易] alter; change;
[移譯] translate;
[移用] embezzle; misappropriate;
[移玉] may I request your company at;
[移植] (1) transplant; transplantation; (2) graft;
胚胎移植 embryo transplantation;
皮膚移植 skin graft;
器官移植 transplantation of organs;
受精卵移植 transplantation of fertilized eggs;
葉綠體移植 chloroplast transplantation;
自體移植 autoplastic transplantation;

[移置] move to another place;
[移住] change one's place of dwelling; move and settle down in another land;
[移轉] transfer;

yi

【蛇】 (1) complacent; (2) pretend cordiality;

[蛇蛇] calmy; leisurely;

yi

【眱】 stare at someone for a long time without talking;

yi

【貽】 (1) give to; make a gift of sth; present to; (2) bequeath; hand down; leave behind; pass on to;

[貽貝] mussel;
[貽害] bring trouble to another; leave a legacy of trouble;
貽害後世 entail woe on the later generations;
貽害學生 mislead young students;
貽害無窮 entail no end of trouble; entail untold troubles; involve endless trouble;

[貽患] bring disaster;
養虎貽患 breed up a crow and he will tear out your eyes; cherish a viper in one's bosom; nourish a snake in one's bosom; nourish a tiger to be a source of trouble in the future; nourish a raven and it will scratch out your eyes; to rear a tiger is to court calamity; warm a snake in one's bosom;
衍溢貽患 overflowing brings calamity;

[貽累] implicate another;
[貽誤] affect adversely; bungle; cause hindrance;
貽誤大局 disrupt the general plan;
貽誤工作 affect the work adversely; make the work suffer;
貽誤青年 mislead young people;
貽誤戰機 bungle the chance of winning a battle; forfeit a chance for combat; hinder military operations; spoil the opportunity to win a battle;
貽誤終身 bring evil upon one's whole life; incur the ridicule of experts;

[貽笑] make a laughing stock of oneself;

貽笑大方 be laughed at by experts; be laughed at by those who know; become a laughing stock of the learned people; expose oneself to ridicule; give an expert cause for laughter; incur the ridicule of experts; make a laughing stock of oneself in front of experts;
貽笑後人 give the youngsters cause for laughter;
貽笑千古 a laughing stock down the centuries; a laughing stock through the ages;
貽笑天下 be laughed at in the world;
貽笑萬世 make oneself a laughing stock for generations to come;

[貽贈] leave sth to posterity; present;
[貽遺] hand down;

yi

【詒】 (1) words as gift usually given at parting; (2) hand down to posterity;

yi

【飴】 (1) syrup; (2) delicious; tasty; (3) delicacies; (4) give as a gift; present;
[飴糖] malt sugar;
飴糖果 barley candy; barley sugar;

高梁飴 sorghum candy; sweets made of sorghum syrup;

yi

【疑】 (1) disbelieve; doubt; suspect; (2) call into question; doubt; doubtful; dubious; question; skeptical; uncertain; (3) incomprehensible; mysterious; questionable; strange; (4) dummy; false; sham;
[疑案] (1) disputed case; doubtful case; puzzling case; uncertain case; unsettled case; (2) mystery;
[疑謗] suspected and slandered;
[疑兵] deceptive deployment of troops;
疑兵計 deceive the enemy by sham deployment; deceptive military deployment;
[疑猜] conjecture; guess; suspect;
[疑點] dubious points; questionable points;
無合理疑點 beyond reasonable doubt;
[疑竇] doubt; suspicion;
疑竇全消 all doubts are removed;
疑竇頓生 a doubt arises;
頓生疑竇 feel suspicious suddenly;
啟人疑竇 arouse sb's suspicion;
消除疑竇 remove a doubt;
[疑犯] criminal suspect;
[疑古] skeptical of antiquity;
[疑惑] doubt; feel uncertain; not be convinced; suspect;
疑惑不解 completely bewildered; feel puzzled; have doubts;
疑惑不決 hang in doubt; hesitating and unable to settle a question;
[疑忌] suspicious and jealous;
[疑懼] apprehend; misgive; suspicious and fearful;
疑懼頓消 lose all fears and doubts;
疑懼橫生 apprehension arising on every hand — a feeling of suspicion and fear;
[疑慮] anxiety; apprehension; doubts; misgivings;
疑慮不決 suspicious and irresolute; suspicious and unable to decide;
疑慮重重 suspicion and mistrust;
疑慮頓消 one's suspicions are allayed;
心中充滿疑慮 one's heart is full of misgivings;
一絲疑慮 a niggle of doubt;
[疑難] (1) difficult; knotty; (2) problem; puzzle; question;
疑難百出 difficulties crop up everywhere;
疑難重重 be filled with puzzles and perplexities;
疑難雜症 difficult and complicated cases of illness;
[疑似] seemingly certain but at the same time uncertain; suspected to be;
[疑團] a maze of suspicion; clogging suspicion; doubts and suspicions;
疑團冰釋 a doubt has been eliminated; a doubt has been removed; be cleared of doubt; all doubts are resolved; suspicions have been dissolved completely;
疑團重重 dark shadows of doubt lurk in one's mind;
疑團頓消 all doubt is soon set at rest; the puzzle in one's mind is suddenly solved;
疑團盡釋 all the suspicions are cleared

up;

疑團莫釋 cannot dissipate one's doubts; dark shadows of doubt lurking in one's mind; doubts and suspicions cannot be cleared up;

滿腹疑團 full of dounts and suspicions;

心起疑團 asrouse one's supicion;

[疑問] doubt; problem; query; question;

疑問代名詞 interrogative pronoun;

疑問副詞 interrogative adverb;

疑問號 question mark;

疑問句 interrogative sentence;

~ 陳述疑問句 declarative question;

~ 反意疑問句 disjunctive question; tag question;

~ 否問疑問句 negative question;

~ 附加疑問句 question tag;

~ 感歎疑問句 exclamatory question;

~ 間接疑問句 indirect question;

~ 具體疑問句 specific question;

~ 傾向性疑問句 conducive question;

~ 特殊疑問句 special question;

~ 選擇疑問句 alternative question;

~ 間接選擇疑問句 indirect alternative interrogation;

~ 一般疑問句 general question;

毫無疑問 beyond all doubts;

解答疑問 answer a question;

提出疑問 raise a question;

有疑問 have a question;

[疑心] (1) doubt; suspect; suspicion; (2) suspect doubt;

疑心生暗鬼 a suspicious heart will see imaginary ghosts; he that has a great nose thinks everybody is speaking of it; suspicion creates fantastic fears;

疑心重 too ready to suspect;

疑心自誤 make one's own mistakes for being suspicious;

起疑心 cast doubt on; have doubts about;

讓人疑心 arouse doubts;

有些疑心 a little doubtful;

[疑信] belief and doubt;

疑信參半 half in belief and half in doubt; half-believing and half-doubting; in a half-and-half state of belief and doubt; not quite sure − half in doubt;

[疑行無成] hesitation leads up to failure;

[疑兇] suspected murderer;

[疑意] doubt in mind;

[疑義] doubt; dubious interpretation; dubious point;

[疑影] a shadow of suspicion; harbour suspicions;

[疑雲] misgivings or suspicion clouding one's mind;

疑雲消散 the misgivings are dispelled;

[疑則勿任，任則勿疑] don't appoint a man if you suspect him and don't suspect him if you appoint him;

[疑陣] a deceptive battle array to mislead the enemy;

猜疑 harbour suspicions; have misgivings; suspect; suspicious;

遲疑 hesitate;

存疑 unanswered question; leave a question open;

多疑 oversensitive; suspicious;

犯疑 suspicious;

狐疑 doubt; suspicion;

懷疑 call into question; doubt; have a suspicion that; suspect; suspicious about; suspicious of; there is reason to suspect;

解疑 disambiguation;

驚疑 surprised and bewildered;

可疑 doubtful; dubious; questionable; suspicious;

起疑 become suspicious; begin to suspect; smell a rat; suspect;

怯疑 timid and vacillating;

袪疑 dispel doubt;

闕疑 leave the question open; unsettled point;

然疑 between believing and suspecting;

生疑 become suspicious; suspicious;

釋疑 clear up doubts; dispel doubts; resolve a doubt; settle uncertainties;

無疑 beyond doubt; undoubtedly; unquestionably;

析疑 clarify a doubt; explain a doubt;

嫌疑 suspect; suspicion;

信疑 belief and doubt;

蓄疑 harbour suspicion;

懸疑 suspense;

猶疑 hesitate;

質疑 call into question; query; question;

置疑 doubt;

yi

【儀】 (1) appearance; demeanour; deportment; looks; manners; (2) ceremonies; rites; (3) gift; present; (4) appa-

ratus; instrument; (5) a surname;

[儀表] (1) appearance; bearing; deportment; (2) apparatus; instrument; instrumentation; meter;
儀表板 dashboard; instrument panel;
儀表不凡 cut a fine figure; handsome looks; imposing appearance;
儀表大方 poised and graceful;
儀表堂堂 dignified in appearance; impressive-looking; noble and dignified;
飛機儀表 aircraft instrument;
工業測量儀表 industrial instrumentation;
航空儀表 aeronautical instrument; airborne instrument;
計量儀表 measuring instrumentation;
手提儀表 portable appliance;
萬能儀表 all-purpose instrument;
自動平衡儀表 automatic balance instrument;

[儀範] (1) demeanour; (2) model of conduct;

[儀器] apparatus; appliance; instrument;
儀器顯示 instrument shows;
儀器元件 instrument package;
安裝儀器 install an instrument;
高空儀器 aerological instrument;
航空儀器 aeronautical instrument;
化學儀器 chemical apparatus;
精密儀器 precision instrument;
~一套精密儀器 a gang of precision instruments;
設計儀器 design an apparatus;
生產儀器 produce instruments;
聲學儀器 acoustic instrument;
物理儀器 physical apparatus;
先進儀器 advanced equipment;
一套儀器 a set of apparatus;

[儀容] appearance; looks;
儀容不整 untidy in one's appearance;
儀容端好 regular correct manners and conduct;
儀容端莊 one's demeanor is upright;

[儀式] ceremony; function; rite;
儀式語言 ritual language;
頒獎儀式 awards ceremony;
畢業儀式 graduation ceremony;
參加儀式 attend a ceremony;
出席儀式 present at a ceremony;
奠基儀式 foundation stone laying ceremony;
歡迎儀式 welcoming ceremony;
簡單的儀式 simple ceremony;
結婚儀式 wedding ceremony;
舉行儀式 hold a ceremony;
授獎儀式 prize-awarding ceremony;
下水儀式 launching ceremony;
主持儀式 conduct a ceremony; perform a ceremony;
宗教儀式 religious ceremony; religious rites;

[儀態] bearing; demeanour; deportment;
儀態端莊 an air of dignity;
儀態高貴 have a noble bearing;
儀態萬千 appear in all her glory; charming poises and exquisite bearing; distinguished air of elegance and coquetry; incomparably graceful; regal bearing;
儀態威嚴 have a dignified bearing; possess a dignified bearing;
儀態優雅 have a graceful deportment;

[儀仗] flags and weapons carried by a guard of honour;
儀仗隊 a guard of honour; honour guard;
~檢閱儀仗隊 inspect the guard of honour;

八分儀 octant;
殯儀 undertaking;
覿儀 presents offered at a meeting;
測程儀 log;
測距儀 range finder;
測量儀 survey instrument;
測深儀 depth sounder; fathometer;
測斜儀 inclinometer;
赤道儀 equatorial telescope;
磁力儀 magnetometer;
奠儀 gift of money made on the occasion of a funeral;
電導儀 conductivity gauge;
地磁儀 magnetometer;
地動儀 seismograph as invented by the Chinese scientist Zhang Heng in A.D. 132;
地球儀 terrestrial globe;
地震儀 seismograph; seismometer;
定向儀 direction finder;
二儀 heaven and earth;
方位儀 azimuth compass;
菲儀 my small gift; my unworthy gift;
風向儀 anemoscope;
豐儀 elegant demeanor;

賻儀 gift to a bereaved family;
干涉儀 interferometer;
渾天儀 (1) armillary sphere; (2) celestial globe;
渾儀 armillary sphere;
計程儀 log;
積分儀 integrator;
極譜儀 polargraph;
簡儀 abridged armilla;
經緯儀 theodolite; transit;
禮儀 etiquette; protocol; rite;
量日儀 heliometer;
量圖儀 map measurer;
六分儀 sextant;
羅盤儀 compass;
平板儀 plane table;
七政儀 orrery;
傾斜儀 inclinometer;
求積儀 planimeter;
熱象儀 thermal imaging system;
日冕儀 coronagraph;
攝譜儀 spectrograph;
聲譜儀 sound spectrograph;
視距儀 tachemeter;
淑儀 rank of court ladies in ancient China;
水平儀 level;
水準儀 surveyor's level; levelling instrument;
司儀 master of ceremonies;
縮放儀 pantograph;
探空儀 sounding device;
探傷儀 flaw detector;
探魚儀 fish detector; fish-finder;
天頂儀 zenith telescope;
天球儀 celestial globe;
天文儀 astroscope;
天象儀 planemeter;
土儀 gift of native product;
陀螺儀 gyro; gyroscope;
威儀 dignity of demeanour; impressive and dignified manner; majesty;
象限儀 quadrant;
心儀 admire in the heart;
旋光儀 optical rotator;
夜視儀 night-vision device;
玉儀 (1) complexion as smooth as jade; (2) jade-ornamented instrument for observing heavenly bodies;
葬儀 burial rites; furneral rites;
芝儀 your noble face;
質譜儀 mass spectrograph; mass spectrometer;
贄儀 ceremonial presents; presents of homage;
重力儀 gravimeter; gravity meter;
中星儀 meridian instrument; transit instrument;
子午儀 meridian instrument;
照准儀 alidade;
准直儀 collimator;

yi

【遺】 (1) lose; miss; (2) sth lost; (3) omit; slip over; (4) forget; (5) keep back; leave behind; leave over; (6) leftovers; remnants; (7) abandon; desert; (8) bequeath; hand down; leave behind at one's death; legacy; (9) emission; (10) urinate;

［遺愛］ the benevolence left behind by a dead person;
甘棠遺愛 sweet memories left behind by a popular official after his retirement; the memory left behind by a virtuous and capable official;

［遺筆］ writings of a deceased person;

［遺策］ (1) mistake; wrong move; (2) a plan left behind by the dead;

［遺產］ heritage; inheritance; legacy;
遺產繼承人 legatee;
遺產税 death duty; estate duty;
教育遺產 educational heritage;
精神遺產 intellectual legacy;
歷史遺產 historical heritage; historical legacy; legacy of history;
民族遺產 national legacy;
文化遺產 cultural heritage;
奪取遺產 seize an inheritance;

［遺臭］ infamy;
遺臭萬年 a bad reputation that will be long remembered; an everlasting shame; be covered with odium for thousands of years to come; be cursed by posterity; be condemned by posterity; be discredited forever; be reviled for thousands of years; go down in history as a byword of infamy; hand down a bad name for myriads of years; leave a bad name for thousands of years to come; leave a bad name forever; leave a foul reputation for myriad years; leave a name that stinks through the ages; leave a stench for all time; live in history as a byword of infamy; one's

name will be anathema for all time; one's name will stink through the ages; remain forever infamous;

[遺傳] hereditary; inherit; inheritance;

遺傳變數 genetic variance;
遺傳變異 heritable variation;
~遺傳變異性 variability of heredity;
遺傳病 hereditary disease; heredopathia;
遺傳參數 genetic parameter;
遺傳傳染 heredoinfection;
遺傳工程 genetic engineering;
~遺傳工程設計 genetic engineering project;
~遺傳工程實驗 genetic engineering experiment;
遺傳獲得量 genetic advance; genetic gain;
遺傳基本規律 fundamental laws of heredity;
遺傳疾病 genetic disease;
遺傳結構 genetic structure;
遺傳膠質 genetic glue;
遺傳進展 genetic advance; genetic gain;
遺傳力 heritability;
遺傳密碼 genetic code;
遺傳畸形 genetic abnormality, genetic freak;
遺傳器官 organ for inheritance;
遺傳缺陷 genetic defect;
遺傳生態學 genecology;
遺傳適應性 genetic adaptation;
遺傳死亡 genetic death;
遺傳特性 hereditary trait;
遺傳物質 substance of heredity;
遺傳相關 genetic correlation;
遺傳性阻礙 genetic block;
遺傳學 genetics;
~遺傳學家 geneticist;
~遺傳學説 theory of heredity;
~計算機遺傳學 computer genetics;
~群體遺傳學 colony genetics;
~染色體遺傳學 chromosome genetics;
~生統遺傳學 biometrical genetics;
~細胞遺傳學 cytogenetics;
~形式遺傳學 formal genetics;
遺傳性 genetic;
~遺傳性載體 genetic carrier;
~遺傳性阻礙 genetic block;
遺傳移植技術 genetic transplantation technique;
遺傳信息 genetic information;
遺傳異常 genetic abnormality; genetic freak;
遺傳因數 genetic factor;
遺傳因子 gene; genetic factor;
遺傳影響 genetic implication;
遺傳雜種 genetic hybrid;
遺傳指令 genetic command;
遺傳組分 genetic component;
遺傳組合 genetic composition;
遺傳咨詢 genetic consulting;
伴性遺傳 sex-linked inheritance;
從性遺傳 sex-influenced inheritance;
返體遺傳 atavism;
返祖遺傳 atavism;
隔代遺傳 atavism;
混合遺傳 blending heredity;
交替遺傳 alternative inheritance;
毛色遺傳 colour inheritance;
母體遺傳 parental heredity;
旁親遺傳 collateral inheritance;
融合遺傳 blending heredity;
數量遺傳 quantitative heredity;
雙線遺傳 amphilinear heredity;
限性遺傳 sex-limited inheritance;
隱性遺傳 recessive inheritance;
直接遺傳 immediate heredity;

[遺大投艱] shoulder a heavy and difficult responsibility;

[遺毒] evil influence of some old practice;

[遺風] remains of a former dynasty;

遺風餘烈 customs and influences handed down from last generations;

[遺腹子] posthumous child;

[遺稿] posthumous manuscripts;

[遺孤] orphan;

[遺骸] corpse; remains;

[遺害] cause troubles;

遺害無窮 cause endless troubles to future generations; entail calamities for years to come; entail untold troubles; leave endless troubles;

[遺憾] feel sorry; pity; regret; sorry;

遺憾終生 rue it bitterly all one's life;
表示遺憾 express one's regret;
毫無遺憾 have no regrets;
深表遺憾 express deep regret at;
死無遺憾 die without regret;
無所遺憾 have no regrets;
真遺憾 it is a great pity; it is a shame; what a shame;

終身遺憾 one's lifelong regret;

[遺恨] feel sorry; regret; regrettable;

遺恨綿綿 have a lasting remorse;

遺恨終身 regret sth all one's life;

竟成遺恨 our fondest hope turns into an everlasting regret;

[遺患] bring trouble in the future;

遺患無窮 sow the seeds of trouble in the future;

養癰遺患 a carbuncle neglected becomes the bane of your life – leaving evil unchecked spells ruin; neglecting a carbuncle will cause trouble – tolerate evil brings disaster; the submitting to one wrong brings on another;

[遺禍] leave behind disaster and cause suffering to people;

[遺跡] historical remains; relics;

歷史遺跡 historical ruins;

遺跡江湖 go away from home and roam about the world;

[遺計] drawback; loophole; mistake;

[遺教] teachings left by the deceased;

[遺精] nocturnal emission;

[遺老] (1) old adherents of the past dynasty; old diehards; old fogy; (2) ministers of the preceding dynasty;

遺老遺少 antediluvian survivals; diehards old and young; old fogies and young diehards; the leftovers from the former dynasty; the old and young men of the past dynasty;

[遺烈] achievements of one's forefathers;

[遺留] hand down; leave behind; leave over;

遺留數據 legacy data;

遺留物 carry-over;

[遺漏] leave out; miss; omission; omit; oversight;

有許多遺漏 have numerous omissions;

[遺落] (1) lose; (2) carefree;

[遺民] (1) adherents of a former dynasty; (2) survivors of a great upheaval;

[遺命] injunctions of a dead person;

[遺墨] calligraphy or paintings by a dead person;

[遺棄] abandon; cast away; cast off; forsake; throw-out;

遺棄情人 jilt one's lover;

不合法遺棄 malicious abandonment;

[遺缺] vacancy;

[遺容] (1) remains; (2) portrait of the deceased;

遺容面模 death mask;

[遺失] lose;

遺失不補 not reissued if lost;

[遺書] (1) posthumous papers; (2) a letter left by one immediately before death;

[遺俗] old custom; traditional practices;

[遺體] (1) corpse; remains; (2) one's body;

[遺忘] forget; neglect;

遺忘了 be ancient history;

遺忘症 amnesia;

被徹底遺忘 be utterly forgotten;

被遺忘 pass into silence;

近事遺忘 ecmnesia;

[遺聞] hearsay that is handed down;

[遺物] relics of the deceased; remains;

古代遺物 relic of ancient days;

[遺下] leave behind;

[遺孀] widow;

[遺像] portrait of a dead person;

[遺訓] teachings of the deceased;

[遺言] last testament; last words; words of the deceased;

[遺業] business left behind by one's ancestors;

[遺願] last wish; unfulfilled wish of the deceased;

臨終遺願 dying wish; final wish; last wish;

遵照死者遺願 respect the last wish of the deceased;

[遺澤] the benevolence left behind by a dead person;

遺澤在民 beneficence left behind to the masses;

[遺贈] bequeath; bequest; legacy;

多餘遺贈 residual legacy;

根據遺贈 by bequest;

金錢遺贈 pecuniary legacy;

累積遺贈 cumulative legacy;

普通遺贈 general legacy;

指定遺贈 specific legacy;

指示遺贈 demonstrative legacy;

[遺照] portrait of the deceased;

[遺址] the old site of a building or city which no longer exists; ruins;

典型遺址 type site; type station;

文化遺址 historical culture sites;

［遺志］ behest of a dying person; unfulfilled wish;
繼承先烈遺志 carry out the behest of the martyrs;
［遺珠］ talented person out of employment;
遺珠之恨 regrets for being unable to employ all the talents;
［遺囑］ (1) will of a dead person; (2) instructions of a dying person;
毀掉遺囑 destroy a will;
可變更的遺囑 ambulatory will;
立遺囑 draw up a will; make a testament; make a will;
簽認遺囑 acknowledge a will;
生前遺囑 living will;
寫遺囑 write a will;
~改寫遺囑 rewrite one's will;
［遺著］ posthumous work;

補遺 addenda; appendix; supplement;
夢遺 nocturnal emission; wet dream;
拾遺 appropriate lost property;
餉遺 donate; present as a gift;
貽遺 hand down;

yi

【頤】 (1) keep fit; nourish; rear; take care of oneself; (2) cheeks; (3) a surname;
［頤神］ have a mental relaxation; rest one's mind;
［頤養］ keep fit; nourish; recuperate; take care of oneself;
［頤指］ signify one's intentions by twisting the cheeks;
頤指氣使 bossy to others; come to quarter-deck over sb; give orders by moving one's chin or by snorting; insufferably arrogant; order people about as one fancies; order people about by gestures; order sb about;

夥頤 many;
期頤 centenarian; hundred-year-old person;

yi

【簃】 small house attached to a pavilion;

yi

【彝】 (1) goblet; wine vessel; (2) laws; regulations; (3) constant; regular; (4) ceremonial vessels;
［彝倫］ cardinal human relationships;
［彝憲］ laws; regulations;
［彝訓］ regular exhortations;

yi³

yi

【乙】 (1) second of the ten Celestial Stems; (2) one; (3) someone; (4) ancient surname;
［乙胺］ aminoethane; ethylamine;
［乙苯］ ethylbenzene;
［乙醇］ alcohol; ethanol; ethyl alcohol;
［乙等］ Grade B; second grade;
［乙基］ ethyl;
［乙醚］ ether;
［乙腦］ type B meningitis;
［乙醛］ acetaldehyde;
［乙炔］ acetylene; ethyne;
［乙酸］ acetic acid; ethanoic acid;
乙酸鋇 barium acetate;
乙酸苯胺 aniline acetate;
乙酸鈣 calcium acetate; lime acetate;
乙酸鉻 chromium acetate;
乙酸汞 mercury acetate;
乙酸鋁 aluminium acetate;
乙酸嗎啡 morphine acetate;
乙酸錳 manganese;
乙酸鈉 sodium acetate;
乙酸鎳 nickelous acetate;
乙酸鉛 lead acetate;
乙酸鈽 acerous acetate;
乙酸鐵 ferric acetate;
乙酸銅 cupric acetate;
乙酸戊酯 amyl acetate;
乙酸銀 silver acetate;
［乙烷］ ethane;
［乙烯］ ethane; ethylene;
［乙酰］ acethyl;
乙酰胺 acetylamine;
乙酰氨基 acetylamino;
乙酰化 acetylate;
~乙酰化作用 acetylation;
乙酰氯 acetylchloride;
［乙型］ Grade B; Type B;
乙型肝炎 hepatitis B; serum hepatitis;

甲乙 A and B;

yi

【已】 (1) cease; stop; (2) come to an end; complete; finish; (3) already; (4) ex-

cessive; too much;
[已定] already fixed; already settled;
[已故] the deceased; the late;
[已婚] married;
[已經] already; before; by; enough; no longer; past; since;
[已滿] (1) already full; (2) already expired;
[已然] already so;
[已往] before; in the past; previously;
[已知] known;
已知數 know number;
已知信息 known information;

yi

【以】 (1) by means of; take; use; (2) according to; (3) because of; (4) in order to; so as to;
[以暴易暴] displace violence with violence; replace evil with evil; replace one tyranny by another;
[以備] ready for;
以備不測 make ready for accidents;
以備不時之需 against a rainy day; for emergency needs;
以備不虞 be prepared for any contingency; be prepared for unforeseen danger; in order to guard against contingencies; in order to provide for emergency; provide against any contingency; provide against the time of need; so as to provide against contingencies;
以備萬一 be prepared for the unlikely; be prepared for the worse; prepare against all eventualities; provide against any contingency;
[以便] (1) for the purpose of; in order that; in order to; so as to; so that; to the effect that; with the aim of; (2) for the convenience of;
[以冰致蠅] attract flies with ice; teach a pig to play on a flute;
[以博一粲] for your entertainment; in exchange for laughter; in order to merit a smile; just for your amusement; provoke a smile;
[以此] for this reason; on this account;
以此類推 deduce the rest from this; the rest can be deduced accordingly; the rest can be done in the same manner;
以此例彼 compare one thing to another;
以此為鑒 take this as a warning;
以此為戒 hold it up as an awful example; take this as a lesson;
以此為例 this is to be regarded as a rule;
以此為憑 this will serve as a proof; this will serve as certification;
以此為質 take this as the standard;
以此為最 this is considered to be the best; this one is the best;
[以次] (1) in due order; in proper order; in turn; (2) the following;
以次充好 sell seconds at best quality prices;
以次傳遞 pass it on to the next;
以次各章 following chapters;
[以待] wait for;
以待時機 bide one's time; wait for an opportunity;
拭目以待 wait and see;
虛位以待 a vacant seat awaits sb; leave a seat vacant for sb; save a seat for sb;
虛席以待 leave a seat vacant for sb; reserve a seat for sb;
虛左以待 leave the seat of honour for sb; reserve the honoured post for sb;
[以盜捕盜] set a thief to catch another thief;
[以德報德] recompense kindness with kindness; return good for good; one good turn deserves another;
以德報德，以怨報怨 like for like;
[以德報怨] repay evil with good; repay injury with kindness; return good for evil; requite evil with good; requite ingratitude with kindness;
[以毒攻毒] attack one villain with another; combat poison with poison; counteract one toxin with another; cure a poisoned patient with poison; fight evil with evil; fight fire with fire; fight poison with poison; like cures like; set a thief to catch a thief; take a hair of the dog that bit you; use poison as an antidote for poison; vanquish an opponent by the same means as he used; use poison as an antidote to poison;
[以多為勝] crush an enemy by numerical superiority;
[以訛傳訛] be wrongly informed; circulate erroneous reports; convey incorrectly

what is already incorrect; propagate an error; spread a falsehood; spread an error; spread false information; spread false news; transmit incorrectly an erroneous message;

[以惡報惡] answer a person according to his demerits; evil got, evil spent; return what one takes;

[以惡抗惡] oppose evil with evil;

[以豐補欠] have high yield areas help low yield areas; make up for a crop failure with a bumper harvest; make up for poor harvest in years of rich harvest; store up in fat years to make up for lean ones;

[以工代幹] appoint a worker as an official;

[以故] therefore;

[以管窺天] look at the sky through a tube;

[以還] since;

[以後] (1) after; afterward; from then on; hereafter; later; later on; since then; subsequent to; (2) at a later date;

從今以後 from now on; from this day on;

早飯以後 after breakfast;

[以火攻火] fight fire with fire;

[以及] along with; and; as well as; including;

[以介眉壽] best wishes for long life; many happy returns of the day;

[以來] since;

從古以來 from of old till now; from time immemorial;

有史以來 since the beginning of recorded history; since the dawn of history; throughout history; within the memory of men;

自古以來 ab antiquo; down the ages; down through the ages; from ancient times to the present; from everlasting; from the old; from time immemorial; since ancient times; since remotest times; since time immemorial;

[以蠡測海] measure the ocean with a dipper — have a shallow understanding of a person or subject; measure the sea with an oyster shell — make an appraisal in the light of limited knowledge;

[以禮] according to propriety; in a civil way; with courtesy; with respect;

以禮培話 speak to sb with all courtesy;

以禮相待 pay due attention to; receive sb with courtesy; treat sb with due respect;

以禮相爭 argue with sb in a civil way;

以禮治軍 discipline the army according to propriety;

[以鄰為壑] profit oneself at the expense of others;

[以卵擊石] fight a hopeless battle; hurl eggs against a stone; kick against the pricks; like an egg dashing itself against a rock — bound to be defeated; like an egg knocking itself against a stone; like an egg trying to crush a stone — grossly overestimate one's own strength; like hurling an egg at a rock; smash stones with eggs; strike an egg on a rock; throw an egg against a rock — court defeat by fighting against overwhelming odds; throw an egg at a stone;

[以貌取人] evaluate people on the basis of appearance; judge a person by his appearance; judge people by outward appearance; judge people solely by their appearance; select people by their looks;

以貌取人，失之子羽 a fair face may be a foul bargain;

不可以貌取人 must not judge by appearances;

勿以貌取人 do not judge a man by his look; don't judge people by appearances; it is not the gay coat that makes the gentleman; it is not the hood that makes the monk; there is no trusting to appearance;

[以免] in order to avoid; lest; so as not to;

[以內] including; less than; within; within the limits of;

[以偏概全] take the part for the whole;

[以其人之道還治其人之身] answer in kind; beat sb at his own game; beat sb at his own weapon; challenge sb at his own weapon; deal with a man as he deals with you; dose sb with his own physic; fight sb at his own weapon; give it back to sb; give sb a dose of his own medicine; give sb a taste of his own medicine; pay in kind; pay back in kind; pay sb back in his own coin; pay sb back in the same coin; repay in kind; reply in kind; requite like for like; return in kind; return like for like; serve sb with the same sauce; serve the same sauce to sb; treat sb in the same way he treats others; treat sb with a dose of his own medicine;

[以前] ago; before; ex-; former; formerly; in the past; old; once; previous; prior to; since; used to be;

很久很久以前 light years ago;

很久以前 a long time ago; long ago; since the year dot; time out of mind;

[以勤補拙] amend stupidity by diligence; make up for lack of natural talent by hard work; make up for stupidity by diligence;

[以求] in an attempt to; in order to;

以求免去 deprecate;

以求一逞 in a bid for success; in order to attain the end; in the hope of realizing one's ambition;

[以上] above; and upwards; in excess of; more than; or above; over; upwards of;

在一般水平以上 above the average;

[以少擊眾] fight against longer odds;

[以身] in one's own person; personally;

以身試法 dare to violate the law; defy the law; test the law in one's own person;

以身相許 have a sexual relation with the beloved willingly; pledge to marry sb;

以身許國 dedicate oneself to the country's cause;

以身殉職 die at one's post; die on one's duties; give one's life in the course of performing one's duty;

以身作則 hit the nail on the head; live what one teaches; make oneself an example; make oneself serve as an example to others; play an exemplary role; practise what one preaches; set an example for others to follow; set oneself up as an example;

[以升量石] a little man cannot understand the ways of a true gentleman;

[以石投水] get along well with each other; like throwing stones into the water;

[以食愈饑，以學愈愚] the cure of hunger is food, that of ignorance is study;

[以手加額] exhibit gratification; fold one's hands upon one's forehead; place one's hand over one's forehead;

[以售其奸] achieve his treacherous purpose; in order to carry out an evil plot;

[以水救水] aggravate the situation instead of checking it; encourage an evil doer; fight the flood with water;

[以湯止沸] stir the soup to stop it from boiling — a temporary redress;

[以外] (1) except; in addition; other than; (2) beyond; outside; without;

[以往] before; formerly; in the past; previously;

以往鑒來 draw lessons from history in order to avoid such happenings in the future; take the past experiences as guides for the future;

以往況今 compare the present with the past;

長此以往 if things continue this way; if things go on like this;

[以為] believe; consider;

竊以為 in my humble opinion;

自以為是 believe sth to be correct; consider oneself always in the right; have a firm belief in one's on opinions; opinionated; regard oneself as infallible; self-opinionated; self-righteous; stuck-up; think oneself right;

~自以為是的 cocksure;

[以文會友] associate by means of literature; gather friends together for literary activities; make friends by one's writing; meet friends on literary grounds;

[以文興商] commerce flourishes with civilization;

[以我為主] keep the initiative in our own hands; take ourselves as the dominant factor;

[以物易物] barter; exchange of goods; exchange of one commodity for another; trade one thing against another;

[以下] below; less than; no more than; under;

在一般水平以下 below the average;

[以血洗血] blood must atone for blood; blood will have blood; demand blood for blood; slaughter for slaughter; the blood debt must be repaid in kind;

[以迅雷不及掩耳之勢] with lightning speed in a whirlwind drive; with the suddenness of a thunderbolt;

[以牙還牙] a tooth for a tooth; an eye for an eye; answer blows with blows; fight fire with fire; give as good as one gets; like for like; repay evil with evil; return blow for blow; return like for like; tit for tat; tooth for tooth;

以牙還牙，以眼還眼 an eye for an eye and a tooth for a tooth; eye for eye, tooth for tooth; measure for measure; meet force by force; serve sb with the same sauce; serve the same sauce to sb;

[以眼還眼] an eye for an eye;

[以夷制夷] play both ends against the middle; play off one power against another; play one barbarian state against another; use barbarous people to subjugate their own races;

[以怨報德] bite the hand that feeds one; recompense good with evil; requite benefit with injuries; requite kindness with ingratitude; requite love with hate; return evil for good;

[以怨報怨] requite injury for injury;

[以債養債] borrow money to pay debts;

[以直報怨] justice in return for injustice; repay injustice with justice;

[以至] (1) down to; until; up to; (2) so...that...; to such an extent as to;

[以致] as a result; consequently; so that; with the result that;

[以智勝智] diamond cut diamond;

[以珠彈雀] employ pearls to strike birds; get sth at too dear a cost; give much to get little; make big investment for small returns; shoot sparrows with pearls; the gram is not worth the candle;

[以…著稱] be known as; be noted for;

[以資] as a means of;

以資參考 provide for reference;

以資鼓勵 as an encouragement; by way of encouragement; for the sake of encouragement;

以資彌補 make up a shortage; make up the deficit;

以資證明 this is to certify that;

[以…自居] regard oneself as...;

報以 return with;
何以 how; why;
加以 in addition; moreover;
借以 for the purpose of; so as to;
可以 (1) can; may; (2) passable; pretty good; (3) awful;
賴以 depend on; rely on;
難以 difficult to; hard to;
是以 therefore; hence;
數以 the number is counted by;
所以 as a result; so; therefore;
無以 cannot be;
用以 (1) use sth to achieve an end; (2) in order to; so as to;
予以 give; grant;
足以 enough to; sufficient to;

yi

【矣】 (1) final particle denoting a perfect tense; (2) auxiliary denoting determination; (3) same as 哉 or 乎 in usage;

yi

【迆】 (1) proceed in a winding way; (2) connected; joined;

[迆邐] (1) joined together; (2) meandering; winding;

[迆靡] connected; joined;

[迆涎] extend continuously;

yi

【迤】 same as 迆;

yi

【苡】 coix agrestis, a kind of plant whose grains are used as food or medicine;

[苡米] seed of Job's tears;

[苡仁] seed of Job's tears;

yi

【釔】 yttrium;

yi

【倚】 (1) lean against; lean on; rest on; (2) count on; depend on; rely on; (3) biased; partial;

[倚傍] emulate; pattern after;

[倚薄] (1) gather together; (2) come one after

another;
[倚伏] causally related;
[倚負] depend on; rely on;
[倚靠] (1) count on; rely on; (2) lean against; (3) support;
[倚賴] depend on; rely on;
[倚馬可待] have a ready pen;
[倚門] lean against the door;
倚門而立 lean by the door;
倚門而望 lean against the doorpost, craning one's neck; watch anxiously from the doorway for sb's return;
[倚恃] depend on; rely on;
[倚勢] rely on one's position; rely on one's power;
倚勢淩人 rely on one's position to treat others with contumely and injustice; throw one's weight around;
倚勢謀利 use one's influence to gain profit;
倚勢欺人 insult people by presuming on one's power; take advantage of one's position to bully people;
倚勢壓人 use one's power to oppress others; throw one's weight;
倚勢仗貴 misuse one's power and influence;
[倚托] depend on; rely on;
[倚偎] cuddle;
倚紅偎翠 cuddle to the red and lean towards the green — frequent brothels;
[倚仗] count on; presume on; rely on;
倚仗財勢 presume on one's wealth and power;
倚仗官勢 rely on an official and take advantage of his influence;
倚仗權勢 count on one's powerful connections; rely on one's power and position;
倚仗他人過活 depend on others for a living;
[倚重] entrust a person with heavy responsibility; rely heavily on sb's service;
[倚裝待發] learn against the luggage, one is ready to start on a journey;

跛倚 biased; partial; prejudiced;
徙倚 indecision; irresolution; linger in hesitation;

yi

【扆】 screen;

yi

【猗】 gentle, soft and pliant;

yi

【椅】 (1) bench; chair; (2) idesia polycarpa;
[椅背] back of a chair;
[椅子] chair;
一把椅子 a chair;
一個椅子 a chair;
一張椅子 a chair;
摺椅子 fold a chair;
[椅座] seat;
曲面椅座 contoured seat;

背椅 chair with a back;
長椅 bench;
扶手椅 armchair;
靠椅 armchair;
輪椅 wheelchair;
圈椅 round-backed chair;
睡椅 reclining chair;
躺椅 chaise longue; deckchair;
藤椅 cane chair; rattan chair;
籐椅 rattan armchair;
搖椅 rocking chair;
折椅 collapsible chair;
摺椅 folding chair;
竹椅 bamboo chair;
轉椅 revolving chair; swivel chair;
轉椅 revolving chair; swivel chair;
桌椅 tables and chairs;
座椅 seat;

yi

【釔】 illinium;

yi

【旖】 (1) romantic; tender; (2) attractive; charming; graceful; lovely; (3) fluttering of flags;
[旖旎] charming and gentle; graceful;
旖旎風光 charming sight; exquisite scenery; lovely scenes; romantic sight;

yi

【踦】 (1) pierce; (2) touch;

yi

【檥】 moor a boat to the bank;

yi

【蟻】 ant;
[蟻巢] ant nest;
[蟻動] move like ants;
[蟻封] ant hill;

Y

[蟻附] swarm over;
[蟻合] swarm to a place from all sides;
[蟻結] band together;
[蟻聚] swarm to a place from all sides;
[蟻寇] petty robber;
蟻寇成群 petty robbers form into groups;
[蟻潰] disperse like ants;
蟻潰四方 scattering like ants in all directions;
[蟻民] we, the people;
[蟻慕] long for; yearn for;
[蟻丘] ant hill;
[蟻視] despise;
蟻視一切 regard everything with contempt;
[蟻王] queen ant;
[蟻穴] ants' nest;
[蟻學] myrmecology;

白蟻 termite; white ant;
螞蟻 ant;

yi
【艤】 moor a boat to the bank;

yi
【顗】 quiet; solemn; tranquil;

yi
【轙】 (1) rings on the yokes; (2) wait;

yi⁴
yi
【弋】 (1) catch; take; (2) shoot with arrow and bow;
[弋獲] catch;
[弋獵] hunt;
[弋取] catch;

yi
【刈】 mow; reap;
[刈草機] mower; mowing machine;
[刈割寬度] width of cut;

yi
【肊】 (1) same as 臆 ; (2) breastbone;

yi
【亦】 also; too;
[亦步亦趨] ape sb at every step; dance after sb's pipe; dance after sb's whistle; dance to sb's music; dance to sb's pipe; dance to sb's tune; follow in sb's footsteps; follow sb's walking; follow the example of another person at each move; perform to sb's baton; slavish imitation;
[亦發] (1) all the more; (2) simply;
[亦即] i.e.; namely; that is; viz.;
[亦且] and also; as well;
[亦然] also; similarly; too;

yi
【屹】 (of a mountain) rise high; stand erect; stand majestic;
[屹立] stand erect; stand towering like a giant;
屹立不動 immovable; stand rock-firm; stand rock-still;
昂然屹立 stand like a towering mountain;
[屹然] majestic; towering;
屹然不動 as firm as a rock; stand firm and erect; stand rock-firm;

yi
【衣】 clothe; dress; wear;
[衣被] (1) cover; (2) do sb a favour;
衣被蒼生 clothe and shelter the poor;

估衣 second-hand clothes;

yi
【佚】 (1) comfort; idleness; (2) err; (3) a surname;

yi
【役】 (1) guard the frontier; labour; military service; service; (2) dispatch; work on official duties; (3) employ as a servant; servant; use as a servant; (4) do; undertake;
[役夫] labourer; servant;
[役齡] enlistment age;
[役馬] workhorse;
[役使] employ as a servant; enslave; make sb work; use; work;
[役屬] control; master;
[役損] weaken from fatigue;
[役役] (1) belabour; overwork; (2) servile;
[役於人] serve others;

兵役 military service;
差役 (1) corvée; (2) bailiff in a feudal yamen;
服役 (1) be on active service; enlist in the army; (2) do corvée labour;
賦役 taxes and corvée;
工役 (1) labourer working on a public project; (2) manual worker;

緩役 deferment of service;
拘役 a prison term, shorter than a set term of imprisonment;
苦役 hard labour; penal servitude;
勞役 (1) corvée; (2) force labour; penal servitude;
免役 exempt from service;
奴役 enslave;
僕役 domestic servant;
使役 use livestock;
戍役 garrison duty;
退役 retire or be released from military service;
現役 active; active duty; active service; on active service;
衙役 yamen runner;
徭役 corvée;
于役 serve in the army;
預備役 reserve duty;
戰役 battle; campaign;

yi

【抑】 (1) curb; press down; repress; (2) force to; restrain; (3) bend; bow; (4) either; else; or; or if; still; then; (5) but; (6) alas; oh;

[抑挫] curb;
[抑遏] coerce; curb; restrain; suppress;
[抑拱] invert;
平緩抑拱 flat invert;
隧道抑拱 tunnel invert;
[抑或] or; or else;
[抑菌] bacteriostasis; bacteriostatic;
抑菌劑 bacteriostat;
抑菌作用 bacteriostasis; bacteristatic action;
[抑勒] repress and restrain;
[抑且] besides; moreover; or;
[抑首] lower one's head;
[抑損] (1) reduce; (2) modest;
[抑壓] coerce; curb; restrain;
[抑揚] modulate; rise and fall;
抑揚頓挫 cadence; intonation; modulation in tone;
抑揚格 iambic;
[抑抑] cautious and grave;
[抑鬱] depressed; depression; despondent; gloomy; sad and melancholy;
抑鬱不樂 in the blues; melancholy; sad and sorry; suffer from spleen;
抑鬱不平 feel disgruntled;
抑鬱成疾 fall ill from depression; so disheartened that one falls sick;
抑鬱症 depression;
~抑鬱症患者 depressive;
~產後抑鬱症 postnatal depression;
感到抑鬱 suffer from spleen;
精神抑鬱 be depressed in spirits; mental depression;
抗抑鬱 antidepression;
~抗抑鬱藥 antidepressant;
面色抑鬱 have a gloomy look; have a melancholy facial expression;
心情抑鬱 feel depressed;
心中抑鬱 one's mind is depressed;
[抑止] check; choke; control; restrain; suppress;
[抑制] check; containment; control; curb; inhibition; rejection; repress; restrain; suppression;
抑制程式 containment procedure;
抑制衝動 inhibit one's impulses;
抑制感情 hold back one's emotions;
抑制激情 curb one's passions;
抑制劑 depressant; inhibitor;
~變構抑制劑 allosteric inhibitor;
~陽極抑制劑 anodic inhibitor;
~陰極抑制劑 cathodic inhibitor;
抑制能力 inhibiting ability;
抑制怒氣 check one's anger; put a curb to one's anger;
抑制器 suppressor;
~電弧抑制器 arc suppressor;
~負阻管抑制器 dynatron suppressor;
~回波抑制器 echo suppressor;
抑制情緒 repress one's emotion;
抑制情慾 curb one's passions;
抑制慾望 put a curb on one's desire;
抑制作用 inhibition; repression;
背景抑制 background suppression;
併發抑制 concurrent inhibition;
腐蝕抑制 corrosion inhibition;
共態抑制 common-mode rejection;
共相抑制 inphase rejection;
基因抑制 gene suppression;
接觸抑制 contact inhibition;
空氣抑制 air inhibition;
條件性抑制 conditioned inhibition;
調幅抑制 amplitude-modulation rejection;
渦流抑制 eddy-current confinement;
先天抑制 congenital inhibition;
載波抑制 carrier suppression;
雜波抑制 clutter suppression;

自我抑制 be inhibited;

貶抑 belittle; devalue;
遏抑 keep down; suppress;
勒抑 (1) extort and suppress; (2) force sb to reduce the price;
壓抑 (1) constrain; depress; (2) oppressive; stifling;

yi

【邑】 (1) city; town; (2) county; (3) state; (4) same as 悒;
［邑豪］ village bully;
［邑落］ (1) hamlet; (2) tribe;
［邑廟］ district temple;
［邑人］ people of the same county;
［邑紳］ gentry;
［邑庠］ county school;
［邑邑］ depressed;
［邑宰］ county magistrate;
［邑尊］ county magistrate;

采邑 benefice; fief;
封邑 manor estate granted by a monarch;

yi

【杙】 (1) boundary mark; fence; (2) tiny wooden post;

yi

【佾】 row of dancers;
［佾生］ boy dancers;
［佾舞］ (1) dance to celebrate Confucius' birthday; (2) rows of ceremonial dancers;

yi

【易】 (1) easy; (2) amiable; lenient; (3) change; (4) barter; exchange; (5) a surname;
［易地］ in another person's shoes;
易地而處 empathise with others; in another person's shoes; look at a matter from another person's viewpoint;
易地皆然 it is the same everywhere;
［易發難制］ it is easier to start sth than to stop it;
［易拉罐］ fliptop can; pop-top can; pull-top can; ring-pull can;
［易爛］ perishable;
易爛物品 perishable article;
［易名］ change one's name;
［易怒］ irascible; prone to anger;
易怒的 hair-trigger; irascible;
［易燃］ combustible; inflammable;
易燃物 combustibles; inflammables;
［易人］ change a person;
［易如］ as easy as;
易如反掌 as easy as ABC; as easy as child's play; as easy as damn it; as easy as falling off a log; as easy as turning one's palm over; as easy as turning over one's hand; as easy as winking;
~易如反掌的事情 cakewalk;
易如破竹 as easy as to cleave a bamboo with a sharp knife;
易如探囊取物 as easy as taking a thing out of one's pocket;
易如沃雪 as easy as the melting of snow;
易如指掌 as easy as pointing at a palm;
［易事］ easy matter;
誠非易事 by no means easy;
［易手］ change hands;
［易俗］ change customs; change practices;
［易位］ translocation;
不等易位 unequal translocation;
簡單易位 simple translocation;
連續易位 tandem translocation;
平衡易位 balanced translocation;
相互易位 reciprocal translocation;
~非相互易位 non-reciprocal translocation;
［易曉］ clear and intelligible; easy to understand;
［易行］ easy to do; easy to practise;
［易學難精］ easy to learn but difficult to master;
［易於］ apt to; easily;
［易主］ change masters; change owners;
［易子而食］ exchange children for eating;

辟易 retreat;
變易 change; vary;
改易 change; transform;
更易 alter; change;
好容易 do sth with great difficulty;
和易 gentle; mild;
簡易 (1) simple and easy; (2) simply constructed; simply equipped;
交易 business; trade;
貿易 trade;

平易 (1) amiable; unassuming; (2) (of a piece of writing) easy; plain;
淺易 simple and easy;
輕易 easy; lightly; rashly;
容易 (1) apt; likely; (2) easy; simple;
移易 alter; change;

yi
【泆】 (1) dissipated and licentious; libertine; (2) flooding; overflowing;

yi
【奕】 (1) abundant; grand; great; (2) elegant; good-looking; gorgeous; (3) anxious; worried; unsettled; (4) in good order; in sequence;
[奕奕] (1) gorgeous; grand and graceful; (2) anxious; unsettled;

yi
【弈】 "go" game;
[弈棋] "go" game;

yi
【疫】 epidemic; plague; pestilence;
[疫病] blight; epidemic disease;
菜豆疫病 bean blight;
豆莢疫病 pod blight;
灰疫病 gray blight;
莖疫病 cane blight; stem blight;
麥粒疫病 kernel blight;
疱疫病 blister blight;
細菌疫病 bacterial blight;
線狀疫病 thread blight;
[疫苗] vaccine;
接種疫苗 be vaccinated; take vaccination;
[疫源] epidemic focus;
[疫症] epidemic;
疫症學 epidemiology;

避疫 escape from epidemics;
畜疫 epidemic disease of domestic animals;
防疫 epidemic prevention;
媾疫 breeding paralysis; covering disease;
虎疫 cholera;
檢疫 quarantine;
口蹄疫 foot-and-mouth disease;
免疫 immunity;
時疫 epidemic;
獸疫 animal diseases;
鼠疫 pestilence; plague;
瘟疫 pest pestilence; plague;

yi
【羿】 a legendary archer;

yi
【昳】 bright;
[昳麗] radiantly beautiful;

yi
【栧】 (1) rowing-sweep; (2) instrument for correcting a bow;

yi
【射】 a pronunciation of 射 ;

yi
【浥】 moist; wet;
[浥濕] moist; wet;
[浥浥] moist;
[浥潤] moist; wet;

yi
【益】 (1) advantage; benefit; beneficial; profit; (2) add to; augment; increase; (3) all the more; in a higher degree; increasingly; to a greater extent; more;
[益蟲] beneficial insects;
保護益蟲 protect beneficial insects;
[益處] advantages; benefit; good; profit;
得到益處 obtain an advantage;
沒得到甚麼益處 gain little advantage;
[益多] more and more;
[益發] all the more; ever more; increasingly; more and more;
益發困難 increasingly difficult;
[益加] all the more; ever more; increasingly; more and more;
[益母草] motherwort;
[益鳥] beneficial birds; insectivorous birds;
[益氣] stimulate the vital forces;
益氣補神 beneficial to one's humour and vivify one's spirit; stimulate the vital forces;
益氣補血 build up one's vital energy and nourish the blood;
益氣強心 invigorate one's vital energy and reinforce the heart;
[益壽] lengthen one's life;
延年益壽 extend one's years; lengthen one's life; prolong life; promise longevity;
[益胃] reinforce one's stomach; tonify one's stomach;

［益友］ beneficial friends; helping friends; useful friends;
成為益友 become one's helpful friend;
交益友 make a worthy friend;
良師益友 one's good teacher and friend;
［益智］ (1) grow in intelligence; (2) longan;

裨益 advantage; benefit;
補益 benefit; help;
純益 net profit;
得益 benefit; profit;
公益 public good; public welfare;
獲益 benefit;
教益 benefit obtained after being instructed; enlightenment;
進益 improvement; progress;
利益 benefit; interest;
請益 ask for advice; ask for instructions;
權益 rights and interests;
饒益 surplus; abundance; wealthy;
日益 day by day; increasingly;
收益 gains; income;
受益 benefit from; profit by;
損益 (1) gains and losses; profit and loss; (2) increase and decrease;
無益 useless; unprofitable;
效益 beneficial result; benefit;
有益 beneficial; useful;
愈益 increasingly; more and more;
增益 gain;

yi
【悒】 troubled in the mind; unhappy;
［悒憤］ resent; unhappy with anger;
［悒悶］ depressed; low-spirited;
［悒怏］ dejected; depressed; grieved; sad; unhappy;
悒怏不已 remains depressed;
［悒悒］ depressed; grieved; sad; unhappy; worried;
悒悒不樂 dejected and dispirited; depressed and unhappy; fee depressed; feel sad and gloomy; with a very downhearted spirit;
［悒鬱］ desolate; melancholy; unhappy;

憂悒 anxious; worried;
郁悒 dejected; depressed;

yi
【挹】 (1) decant liquids; (2) retreat; (3) make place for another;
［挹注］ draw from one to make up the deficits in another; supplement;

獎挹 reward and promote;

yi
【異】 (1) different; (2) extraordinary; peculiar; strange; uncommon; unusual; (3) foreign; unfamiliar; unknown; (4) marvel; surprise; wonder; (5) another; other; (6) separate;
［異邦］ foreign country;
淹久異邦 be long delayed in a foreign country;
［異稟］ extraordinary endowments; extraordinary talent;
［異步］ asynchronous;
異步發電機 asynchronous generator;
異步操作 asynchronous operation;
異步傳輸 asynchronous transmission;
~異步傳輸模式 asynchronous transfer mode;
異步計算機 asynchronous computer;
異步振子 non-synchronous vibrator;
［異才］ genius; unusual talent;
［異彩］ extraordinary splendour;
大放異彩 cut a conspicuous figure;
［異常］ abnormal; abnormality; anomaly; exception; extraordinary; preternatural; singular; strange; unusual;
異常的 aberrant; anomalous;
異常集中 abnormal concentration;
異常現象 anomaly;
傳播異常 propagation anomaly;
地磁異常 magnetic anomaly;
地球化學異常 geochemical anomaly;
發現異常 note abnormalities; observe sth unusual;
負異常 negative anomaly;
光學性異常 optical anomaly;
舉止異常 behave strangely;
氣候異常 climatic anomaly;
局部異常 local anomaly;
染色體異常 chromosomal anomaly;
神色異常 not one's usual self;
數據異常 data exception;
先天性異常 congenital anomaly;
行為異常 behavioral abnormality;
正異常 positive anomaly;
重力異常 gravity anomaly;

指數溢出異常 exponent overflow exception;

[異代] different age; different era;

[異道] (1) different path; different route; (2) different viewpoints;

[異等] (1) remarkable; unusual; (2) different grade;

[異地] foreign land; strange land;
異地辦學 run a school in another area;
異地結算 settle between different areas;

[異動] change; reshuffle;

[異讀] variant pronunciations;

[異端] heresy; heterodoxy; strange doctrines;
異端邪說 heresy; heretical beliefs; heterodox doctrines; heterodoxy; unorthodox opinions;

[異方殊俗] different customs in alien countries;

[異服] outlandish costume; strange clothing;

[異構] isomery;
異構化 isomerization;
~催化異構化 catalytic isomerization;
~鹼法異構化 alkali isomerization;
異構酶 isomerase;
~磷酸葡糖異構酶 glucose phosphate isomerase;
~葡萄糖異構酶 glucose isomerase;
異構體 isomer;
~互變異構體 dynamic isomer;
~構象異構體 conformational isomer;
~末端異構體 end isomer;
~同分異構體 isomeride;
官能異構 function isomerism;
光學異構 optical isomerism;
互變異構 tautomerism;
幾何異構 geometric isomerism;
鏈異構 chain isomerism;
順反異構 cis-trans isomerism;
同分異構 isomerism;
旋光異構 optical isomerism
側鏈異構 side isomery;

[異國] foreign country; foreign land;
異國情調 exotic; exotic atmosphere; exotic touch;
身死異國 die in an alien land;

[異化] (1) alienation; (2) dissimilation;
異化作用 catabolism;
局部異化 partial dissimilation;
鄰接異化 juxtapositional dissimilation;
~非鄰接異化 incontiguous dissimilation;
逆異化 regressive dissimilation;
順異化 progressive dissimilation;

[異己] alien; dissident;
擯斥異己 dismiss those who hold different opinions; reject dissidents;
打擊異己 crack down on the dissident;
排除異己 discriminate against those who hold different views;
誅鋤異己 destroy those who hold different views; eliminate those who hold different views; liquidate dissenters; wipe out dissenters;

[異教] cult; heathenism; paganism;
異教的 heterodox;
異教徒 heathen; pagan;

[異客] stranger;

[異類] (1) those of a different class; (2) non-human; (3) aliens;

[異名] different name;

[異能] extraordinary talents; genius;

[異曲同工] achieve the same goal with different means; achieve the same result cleverly in two different approaches; different songs are sung with the same excellence; different tunes rendered with equal skill — different in approach but equally satisfactory in result; express the same meaning in two different sentences; the same meaning expressed in different words; the same result achieved by different methods;

[異趣] difference of tastes and interests;

[異人] (1) extraordinary person; idiosyncratic person; (2) stranger;

[異日] (1) another day; some other day; (2) bygone days; former days;

[異時] past time;

[異事] (1) peculiar affair; (2) different matter; (3) be engaged in different occupations;

[異數] (1) different rank; (2) courteous reception; unusual favour;

[異說] (1) heresies; (2) different interpretation; different theory;

[異俗] (1) different custom; (2) bad custom;

[異態] strange bearing; strange manner;

[異體] (1) variant form; (2) not belong to the same body;

異體受精 cross-fertilization;
異體字 a variant form of a Chinese character;

[異同] (1) differences and similarities; (2) inconsistent;
文化異同 cultural differences;

[異味] (1) rare delicacy; (2) peculiar smell;
發出異味 give off a peculiar smell;
聞到異味 smell a strange smell;

[異文] alternate script;

[異聞] (1) strange story; strange tale; unusual news; (2) different report;

[異物] (1) extremely valuable object; rare treasure; (2) peculiar thing; strange thing; uncommon thing; (3) dead;

[異鄉] away from one's home; foreign community; foreign land; strange land;
異鄉孤客 stranger in a foreign land;
異鄉人 stranger;
客愁異鄉 be alienated in a strange land longing for one's homeland;
身死異鄉 die in a strange place;

[異香] rare fragrance; unusually sweet smell;
異香不散 the air was filled with various fragrances;
異香異氣 unusual kind of pleasant smell;
滿室異香 the house is filled with a rare fragrance;

[異想天開] a flight of fancy; a stretch of the imagination; ask for the moon; come out with most fantastic ideas; cry for the moon; expect wonders; fanciful; fanciful ideas; get fancy ideas into one's head; give loose to the fancy; given rein to fancy; have a maggot in one's head; have bats in the belfry; have bees in the brain; have bees in the head; have fantastic notions; have one's head full of bees; indulge in the wildest fantasy; indulge one's fancy; lend wings to one's imagination; let one's imagination run away with one; one's head is full of bees; vagarious; whimsical; wild hopes; wish for the moon; wishful thinking;

[異象] strange phenomena;

[異心] dishonesty; disloyalty; infidelity; insincerity; treachery;

[異形] strange form; strange shape;

[異性] (1) of the opposite sex; of the other sex; (2) of a different nature;
異性齒 heterodont teeth;
異性戀 heterosexuality;
異性朋友 friend of the other sex;
異性相吸 there is a natural attraction between sexes;
各向異性 anisotropy;
~磁感應各向異性 induced magnetic anisotropy;
~磁各向異性 magnetic anisotropy;
~光學各向異性 optical anisotropy;
~介電各向異性 dielectric anisotropy;
~交換各向異性 exchange anisotropy;
~晶態各向異性 crystalline anisotropy;
~晶體各向異性 crystal anisotropy;
~流動各向異性 streaming anisotropy;
~鐵磁各向異性 ferromagnetic anisotropy;
~應力各向異性 stress anisotropy;
~折射各向異性 refraction anisotropy;

[異姓] those with different surnames;

[異言] dissenting words;
並無異言 raise no objection;

[異樣] (1) difference; (2) peculiar; strange; unusual;

[異議] dissent; objections;
異議範圍 scope of opposition;
異議費 opposition fee;
表示異議 express one's dissent; show one's dissent; voice one's dissent;
持異議 dissent in opinion;
~持異議者 dissenter;
~獨持異議 alone hold a different opinion; the only one to dissent;
~力持異議 raise a strong objection;
毫無異議 have not the slightest objection;
沒有異議 have no dissent; raise no objection;
提出異議 demur; make an objection; raise an objection; voice an objection;
~正式提出異議 lodge an objection;
引起異議 arouse dissent;
有異議 have an objection;

[異域] (1) alien land; foreign land; strange land; (2) place far away from home; (3) some other place;
葬身異域 be buried in a foreign country; die in a foreign country;

[異兆] strange omen;

[異質] of a different nature; of a different

quality;
[異志] disloyal heart;
[異族] different clan;
辨異 distinguish differences between things;
變異 mutation; variation;
差異 difference; discrepancy; disparity; divergence; diversity; variance;
詫異 be astonished; be surprised;
乖異 odd; unconventional;
瑰異 preeminent;
詭異 strange;
駭異 astonished; shocked;
驚異 amazed; astonished; surprised;
離異 divorce;
立異 take an uncommon stand;
奇異 queer; strange;
歧異 difference; different;
神異 gods and spirits; magical; miraculous;
特異 (1) distinctive; peculiar; (2) excellent; superfine;
無異 not different from; the same as;
新異 novel; strange;
穎異 (1) extraordinarily intelligent; (2) new and original;
優異 excellent; outstanding;
尤異 outstanding;
珍異 rare;
卓異 outstanding; remarkable; unusual;

yi
【翌】 immediately following in time; next; tomorrow;
[翌年] next year;
[翌日] following day; next day; tomorrow;
中秋節翌日 the day following the Mid-Autumn Festival;
[翌朝] tomorrow morning;

yi
【翊】 (1) flying; (2) assist; help; (3) respectful;
[翊戴] assist and support a ruler;
[翊翊] respectful;

yi
【腋】 a pronunciation of 腋;

yi
【軼】 (1) excel; surpass; (2) go loose; scattered;
[軼材] outstanding talents;
[軼倫] outstanding; surpass one's contemporaries;
[軼群] excel the rest;
[軼詩] scattered poems;
[軼事] anecdote;
[軼蕩] unrestrained;
[軼聞] anecdote;

yi
【逸】 (1) ease; idleness; leisure; (2) escape; flee; run away; (3) exceed; go beyond; go to excess; (4) live in retirement; rustic; (5) lost; (6) let go; let loose; (7) error; fault; mistake; (8) excel all others; outstanding; superior;
[逸才] outstanding talent;
[逸出] effusion; overshoot;
逸出常軌 against the regular practice; depart from the normal practice; get off the beaten track; go off at a tangent; not common; not regular; run off the track;
逸出題外 digress from the main subject; travel out of the subject;
逸出正道 err from the path of duty;
[逸度] elegant air; refined manner;
[逸話] anecdote;
[逸居] comfortably lodged; live in idleness; live in retirement;
逸居偃息 live in luxurious idleness; loll in the lap of luxury;
[逸口] make an indiscreet remark;
[逸樂] comfort and pleasure; enjoyment of an easy life;
[逸漏] escape;
[逸民] hermit; recluse;
[逸品] superior piece of artistic work;
[逸氣] out-of-this-world air; outstanding disposition;
[逸囚] set prisoners free;
[逸趣橫生] full of wit and humour; replete with humour; replete with refined interest; witty and humorous;
[逸群] head and shoulders above others; outstanding;
[逸聲] decadent music;
[逸士] (1) person of great virtue; (2) scholar retiring from the world;
[逸事] anecdote;

[逸文] ancient writings no longer extant;
[逸聞] anecdote;
逸聞軼事 anecdote;
[逸暇] leisure; spare time;
[逸想] idealistic thoughts; thoughts that are not worldly;
[逸興] refined interest; refined taste;
[逸秀] talents above the average;
[逸言] extravagant talk;
[逸逸] decently and in good order;
[逸豫] enjoy oneself; live in idleness;
逸豫亡身 overindulgence leads to ruin;
[逸欲] idleness and lust;
[逸志] easy-going habit;
[逸足] fleet-footed; walking very fast;

安逸 ease and comfort; easy; easy and comfortable; leisurely and comfortable;
超逸 free and natural; unconventionally graceful;
勞逸 labour and rest;
飄逸 elegant; graceful;
遒逸 forceful and moving;
散逸 carefree; dissipation;
逃逸 break loose and get away; escape; runaway;
暇逸 idle; relax; relaxation;
閑逸 carefree; leisurely;
隱逸 be a hermit; live in seclusion; withdraw from society and live in solitude;
愉逸 happy and leisurely;
縱逸 dissolute; uninhibited; unrestrained;

yi

【意】 (1) idea; meaning; thought; (2) desire; inclination; intention; wish; (3) anticipate; expect; (4) hint; suggestion;
[意表] expectations; what one expects;
出人意表 beyond all expectations; beyond one's expectation; come as a surprise; contrary to one's expectations; exceeding all expectations; to one's surprise;
[意到筆隨] the pen follows where the mind reaches; write with ease;
[意符] ideograph;
意符同義詞 ideographic synonym;
意符文字 ideographic writing;
[意合式] parataxis;
[意會] sense; understand by insight;
祇可意會，不可言傳 can always be felt and understand, but never described; can be apprehended but not expressed; can be apprehended by the heart but not expressed by the mouth; can be subtly appreciated, but not put into words; can only be sensed, but not explained in words; only to be sensed, but not explained in words; only to be sensed, not explained; the meaning can be figured out but cannot be put into words;
[意簡言賅] a few simple ideas succinctly expressed;
[意見] (1) advice; idea; opinion; point; proposal; suggestion; view; (2) comment; complaint; criticism; different opinions; objection; different opinions;
意見分歧 be divided in opinion; differ in opinion; differ in views; disagree; dissent; diverge in views; have a difference of opinion; opinions are divided;
意見溝通 communication;
意見書 written opinions;
意見相左 at variance; disagree in opinion; fail to agree; have different opinions; hold different views;
意見箱 suggestion box;
意見一致 agree; have identical views; of one mind; see eye to eye with sb;
意見有分歧 be divided in opinion; conflict with each other; disagree in opinion;
意見自由 freedom of expression;
寶貴意見 valuable suggestions;
表達意見 express one's views;
~自由表達意見 express one's view freely;
表明意見 explain one's idea;
採納意見 adopt an idea;
發表意見 express one's view; utter one's opinion;
~大膽發表意見 adventure one's opinion;
~公開發表意見 air one's view;
~即席發表意見 deliver an offhand opinion;
反對意見 counterview;
改變意見 change one's view;
各種意見 varied opinions; variety of opinions;
堅持意見 abound in one's own sense; hold to one's view; stick to one's view;

交換意見 exchange views;
接受意見 accept an opinion;
鬧意見 feel resentful because sth is not to one's liking; sulk;
取得一致意見 arrive at an agreement;
搜集意見 gather opinions;
提出意見 offer one's opinion; present one's view;
提供意見 give suggestions;
提意見 make comments;
聽取意見 receive complaints;
同意各自保留不同意見 agree to differ; agree to disagree;
完全贊成這個意見 be all in favour of the idea;
寫出意見 write one's opinion;
修正意見 revise one's view;
一點意見 a bit of advice; an idea;
徵求意見 request the consent of;
專家的意見 expert opinion;
轉達意見 forward a view;

[意匠] (1) creativity; ingenuity; (2) artistic conception; novel design;

[意境] artistic conception; frame of mind; mood; prospect;
意境深遠 have profound artistic conception; magnificently conceived;

[意料] expect; anticipate;
意料之外 contrary to expectation; in a way different from what is expected; unexpectedly;
意料之中 as expected; in accordance with expectations;
出乎意料 beyond expectation; contrary to one's expectations; cup the climax; exceed one's expectations; out of a clear sky; out of nowhere; outside of expectation; to one's amazement; to one's surprise; unexpectedly;
出人意料 come as a surprise; exceed all expectation; surpass anticipation;

[意念] idea; thought;
意念飄忽 flight of ideas;

[意氣] (1) heart; will and spirit; (2) disposition; temperament; (3) emotion; personal feelings;
意氣衝天 high-spirited;
意氣風發 be fired with boundless enthusiasm; boundless enthusiasm; daring and energetic; full of high spirits; full of pep; high-spirited and vigorous; in high and vigorous spirits; in high feather; in high spirits; on one's mettle;
意氣沮喪 crestfallen; depressed; disappointed; discouraged; disheartened; dispirited; in low spirits; utterly disheartened;
意氣相投 alike in temperament; congenial; congenial with each other; find each other congenial; have the same likes and dislikes; of a congenial temper; of similar tastes and inclinations; of the same cast of mind; share the same aspirations and have the same temperament;
意氣消沉 a cup too low; demoralized; depressed; depression; despondent; down in the dumps; downhearted; have a fit of blues; have the blues; in a blue funk; in low spirits; in poor spirits; in the doldrums; in the dumps; melancholy; out of spirits;
意氣軒昂 high-blown;
意氣揚揚 elated; in high spirits; jauntily; perk; triumphant;
意氣用事 abandon oneself to emotions; act on impulse; be influenced by sentiment in handling things; be swayed by personal feelings; give way to one's feelings; unable to set hold of oneself;
意氣之爭 dispute caused by personal feelings; dispute due to personal feelings; quarrel over a matter of emotion;
意氣自得 easy and dignified;
鬧意氣 act on impulse without consideration; pick quarrels;
失去意氣 downcast;

[意趣] charm; interest and charm;

[意識] awareness; consciousness;
意識到 awake to; aware; aware of; conscious of; realize;
意識療法 consciousness therapy;
意識流 stream of consciousness;
意識提高 consciousness raising;
意識形態 ideology;
不良意識 undesirable messages;
超越意識 transcent consciousness;
共同意識 general consciousness;
集體意識 collective consciousness; group consciousness;

客觀意識 objective consciousness;
潛意識 subconsciousness;
雙重意識 double consciousness;
文化意識 cultural awareness;
下意識 subconscious;
戰術意識 tactical awareness; tactical consciousness;
職務意識 post consciousness;
自意識 self-awareness;

[意思] (1) idea; meaning; (2) desire; opinion; wish; (3) token of affection; (4) look like; seem;
意思意思 serve as a token;
別誤會我的意思 don't get me wrong;
不好意思 (1) ashamed; diffident; feel embarassed; feel shy; ill at ease; (2) find it embarrassing to do sth;
夠意思 really sth; terrific;
理解意思 grasp the meaning; understand the meaning;
沒意思 (1) bored; (2) have no fun; poor fun; uninterested;
沒有領會意思 miss the point;
你是甚麼意思 what do you mean;
我就是這個意思 that's what I mean;
我知道你的意思 I know what you mean;
小意思 (1) little keepsake; slight token of regard; small gift; (2) little matter; mere trifle; trifle;
一種意思 a meaning;
意裏意思 speak hesitatingly and indistinctly;
有意思 good fun;
這是甚麼意思 what's that supposed to mean;
知道意思 know the meaning;

[意態] air; appearance; bearing; manner;

[意圖] intent; intention; purpose;
暗示意圖 drops hints of sb's designs;
表明意圖 express one's intention; make known one's intention;
第二個意圖 second intention;
第一個意圖 first intention;
改變意圖 change one's intention;
透露意圖 reveal one's intention;
隱瞞意圖 disguise one's intention;

[意外] (1) unforeseen; unexpected; (2) accident; mishap; surprise;
意外保險 accident insurance;
意外重逢 extrordinary meeting;
意外的 accidental; unexpected; unhoped-for;
~易遭遇意外的 accident prone;
意外地發現 be surprised to find that;
意外事故 accident; unexpected accident; unforeseen event;
意外收獲 unexpected gains;
意外損傷 accidental damage;
意外死亡 accidental death;
出人意外 beyond all expectations; beyond one's expectation; come as a surprise; contrary to one's expectations; exceeding all expectations; to one's surprise;
~完全出人意外 be totally unexpected;
出於意外 against one's expectation; contrary to expectation; out of one's reckoning;
感到意外 be taken by surprise;
有點意外 a bit of a shock;
造成意外 cause an accident;

[意味] (1) implication; meaning; significance; (2) flavour; impression; touch; (3) portend;
意味深長 express volumes; expressive; full of meaning; hold profound implications; of profound significance; pregnant with meaning; profound in meaning; profound sense; speak volumes; tell volumes;

[意謂] it seems to say;

[意下] (1) in one's heart; in one's mind; (2) idea; opinion;
意下如何 what do you think;

[意想] expect; imagine;
意想不到 beyond expectation; never think of it; unexpected; unlooked-for;
~意想不到的事 a turn-up for the books;

[意向] inclination; intention; purpose;
意向不明 one's intentions are not clear;
意向從屬連詞 subordinator of preference;
意向書 letter of intent; statement of intention;
意向狀語從句 adverbial clause of preference;
購買意向 buying intention;
投資意向 investment intention;

[意象] concept; idea; image; imagery;
意象修辭 imagery rhetoric;
意象主義 imagism;

[意興] enthusiasm; interest; mood to do sth;
意興勃勃 highly enthusiastic;

意興闌珊 feel dispirited; one's interest is worn-out; with flagging interest;
意興索然 enthusiasm wanes; have not the least interest; no longer be interested in;

［意緒］(1) threads of thoughts; (2) mood; state of mind;

［意義］(1) meaning; purport; sense; (2) importance; significance;
意義成分分析 componential analysis;
意義單位 semanteme;
意義關係 meaning relation;
意義假設 meaning postulate;
意義矛盾 contradiction;
意義內包 meaning inclusion;
意義排斥 meaning exclusion;
意義潛勢 meaning potential;
意義區分 differentiation of meaning;
意義限制 meaning constraint;
意義轉移 transfer of meaning;
比喻意義 figurative meaning;
貶低…的意義 play down the significance of sth;
標準意義 normal meaning;
表層意義 surface meaning;
表情意義 expressive meaning;
表述意義 locutionary meaning;
詞匯意義 lexical meaning;
刺激意義 stimulus meaning;
次要意義 secondary meaning;
次意義 secondary sense;
多重意義 multiple meaning;
反映意義 reflected meaning;
方位意義 locative meaning;
風格意義 stylistic meaning;
概念意義 conceptual meaning;
感情意義 emotive meaning;
功能意義 functional meaning; functional significance;
關係意義 relational meaning;
核心意義 core meaning;
換喻性意義 metonymical meaning;
基本意義 essential meaning;
幾何意義 geometric significance;
交際意義 communicative meaning;
教育意義 educational meaning; pedagogical meaning;
結構意義 structural meaning;
句子意義 sentence meaning;
科技意義 scientific and technological meaning;
口語意義 colloquial meaning;
聯想意義 associative meaning;
沒意義 (1) bored; (2) uninteresting;
命題意義 propositional meaning;
模糊意義 fuzzy meaning;
內涵意義 connotative meaning;
內在意義 intrinsic meaning;
派生意義 derivative meaning; derived meaning;
普通意義 accepted meaning;
情感意義 affective meaning;
情景意義 situational meaning;
區別性意義 differential meaning;
上下文意義 co-textual meaning;
社會意義 social meaning;
深遠意義 far-reaching significance;
生態意義 ecological significance;
實際意義 practical significance;
實質意義 material meaning;
外延意義 denotative meaning;
現實意義 current significance;
形式意義 formal meaning;
營養意義 nutritional significance;
引伸意義 extensional meaning;
語境意義 contextual meaning;
語言學意義 linguistic meaning;
~微語言學意義 microlinguistic meaning;
預定意義 prospective significance;
中心意義 central meaning;
總體意義 total meaning;

［意譯］free translation; liberal translation; paraphrase; sense translation; sense-for-sense translation;

［意淫］mental adultery;

［意猶未盡］not have given full expression to one's views;

［意有所寓］allegoric;

［意欲］desire; volition;
意欲功能 conative function;

［意愿］aspiration; inclination; desire; wish;
意愿動詞 volitional verb;

［意在筆先］the idea seems to run ahead of the brush; whatever one wishes to say, the pen follows; work out the plot before putting pen to papers;

［意在言外］have a meaning beyond the mere words; more is meant than meets the ear; the meaning is implied; the real meaning is not expressed but implied;

［意旨］intention; will; wish;

迎意承旨 pander to sb's wish; scratch sb where it itches;

[意志] volition; will; will power;

意志薄弱 as weak as water; feeble-minded; have a weak will; infirm; infirm of purpose; weak of purpose; weak-willed;

~意志薄弱的 weak-willed;

~意志薄弱的時刻 weak moment;

意志的較量 battle of wills; clash of wills;

意志的考驗 test of will;

意志堅定 inform of purpose; steady in one's purpose; strong will; strong-minded;

意志堅強的 strong-willed;

意志力 effort of will; willpower;

~缺乏意志力 lack the will;

~有很強的意志力 have a strong will;

~有意志力 have the will;

意志消沉 dejected; demoralized; depressed; despondent; low-spirited; pessimistic;

鍛鍊意志 steel one's will;

鋼鐵般的意志 iron will; will of iron;

堅強意志 nerves of steel;

磨練意志 anneal the will;

先意承志 do everything to please one's parents; do things before one's superior asks one to do them;

運用意志 exercise one's will;

自由意志 free will;

[意中] anticipated; expected;

意中人 a bit of jam; the person of one's heart; the person one is in love with;

意中之事 sth that is expected;

本意 original intention; real meaning;

筆意 charm of stroke; flow of thought in writing;

鄙意 my humble opinion;

表意 ideographic;

不過意 be sorry; feel apologetic;

不意 unawareness; unexpectedly; unpreparedness;

誠意 good faith; sincerity;

傳意 communicative;

創意 initiative;

春意 (1) beginning of spring; spring is in the air; (2) thoughts of love;

醋意 jealousy;

措意 be careful; look out;

達意 express one's ideas;

大意 (1) general effect; general idea; gist; main idea; (2) careless; inattentive; negligent;

歹意 evil intention; malice;

得意 complacent; pleased with oneself; very proud of oneself;

敵意 enmity; hostility;

惡意 ill will; vicious intention;

反意 disjunctive;

公意 public will;

故意 by design; by intention; deliberately; go out of one's way; intentionally of set purpose; on purpose; willfully;

害意 interfere with the sense;

寒意 chill in the air;

好意 good intention; kindness;

合意 to one's liking; to one's taste;

厚意 kind thought; kindness;

會意 (1) knowing; understanding; (2) associative compounds;

加意 with close attention; with special care;

假意 deliberately; hypocrisy; insincerity; intentionally;

介意 mind; take offence;

盡意 express all one intends to express;

經意 be careful; take care;

敬意 respect; tribute;

酒意 tipsy feeling;

倦意 drowsiness;

決意 be determined; have one's mind made up;

可意 gratifying; satisfactory;

刻意 painstakingly; sedulously;

快意 pleased; satisfied;

來意 one's purpose in coming;

樂意 be ready to; be willing to; happy; pleased;

立意 be determined; approach; conception; make up one's mind;

留意 alive to; careful; keep an eye on; keep one's eyes open; look out;

綠意 green;

滿意 be satisfied; satisfied;

美意 good intention; kindness;

民意 popular will; will of the people;

命意 (1) assign subject (of essay, painting, etc.); (2) implication;

起意 conceive a design;

歉意 apology; regret;

愜意 be pleased; be satisfied;

情意 affection; tender regards;

任意 at will; wantonly;

如意 as one wishes; satisfied;

鋭意 determined and dauntless;

善意 good intention; goodwill;

深意 profound meaning;

神意 divine will; will of God;
生意 (1) life and vitality; tendency to grow; (2) business; business deal; trade;
盛意 generosity; great kindness;
失意 be disappointed; be frustrated;
詩意 poetic quality or flavour;
示意 give a sign; hint;
適意 agreeable; enjoyable;
授意 incite sb to do sth;
抒意 express thoughts or ideas;
攄意 give expression to one's feelings;
率意 (1) act on the spur of the moment; follow one's inclination; (2) with all one's sincerity;
睡意 drowsiness; sleepiness;
肆意 at will; recklessly; wantonly; wilfully; without any restraint;
隨意 as one pleases; at will;
遂意 fulfil one's desire; to one's liking;
他意 another intention;
特意 for a special purpose; specially;
天意 God's will; will of Heaven;
同意 access; accede to; accession; agree; agreement; agree to; agree with; approve; approve of; assent to; assentation; by agreement; come along; comply with; concur; consent; consent to; cotton to; fall in with; go along with; go with; hold with; in agreement with; in favour of; say amen to; see eye to eye with; see with;
玩意 (1) plaything; toy; (2) gadget; stuff; thing;
微意 token of gratitude;
無意 (1) have no intention; have no interest in; not be inclined to; (2) accidentally; inadvertently; unwittingly;
迕意 oppose one's will;
笑意 smile;
寫意 freehand brushwork in traditional Chinese painting; make an impressionistic portrayal;
屑意 care; mind;
懈意 inactivity; indolence;
謝意 appreciation; gratitude; thankfulness;
心意 (1) kindly feelings; regard; (2) decisions; ideas; intentions; opinions; purposes;
蓄意 deliberate; harbour certain intentions; premeditated;
雅意 your kind offer; your kindness;
一意 (1) with complete devotion; (2) stubbornly;
疑意 doubt in mind;
用意 idea; intention; meaning; purpose;
有意 (1) be inclined to; be interested; have a mind to; show interest; (2) deliberately; intentionally; purposely;
愚意 my humble opinion;
語意 semantics;
寓意 allegoric meaning; implied meaning; import; message; moral;
原意 (1) original meaning; (2) original intentions;
愿意 like; ready; want; willing; wish; would give the world to;
願意 (1) willing; (2) like; want;
悦意 (1) agreeableness; pleasantness; (2) expression of happiness;
在意 care about; mind; take notice of; take to heart;
真意 true intent and real meaning;
執意 be bent on; be determined to; insist on;
旨意 (1) decree; order; (2) intention; will;
至意 best and sincerest intention;
致意 convey one's best regards; convey one's best wishes; give one's regards; present one's compliments; salutation; salute; send one's greeting;
中意 agreeable; catch the fancy of; satisfied; suit one's fancy; to one's liking;
誅意 criticize sb not because of what he has done but because of his motive for doing it;
主意 (1) idea; plan; suggestion; (2) decision; definite view;
屬意 fix one's mind on sb; have a preference for;
注意 care about; careful; have an eye on; look out; mindful of; notice; on the look-out; on the watch; pay attention to; show application; take care; take note of; watch; watch one's step; watch out;
着意 act with care and effort; pay attention to; take pains;
濁意 muddy idea;
恣意 reckless; unbridled; unscrupulous; wilful;
醉意 signs or feeling of getting drunk;
怍意 ashamed; feel ashamed;

yi

【溢】 (1) brim over; flow over; overflow; spill; (2) excessive;

［溢出］ brim over; flow over; overflow; spill over;
- 溢出檢驗 overflow check;
- 定點溢出 fixed overflow;
- 階碼溢出 characteristic overflow;
- 滿得溢出 full to overflowing;
- 運算溢出 arithmetic overflow;

［溢洪道］ spillway;

測流式溢洪道 lateral flow spillway;
跌水式溢洪道 drop spillway;
直井式溢洪道 shaft spillway;

[溢價] at a premium;
[溢漫] brim over; flow over; spill;
[溢美] praise excessively;
溢美之詞 exaggerated praises;
溢美之言 words of fulsome praise;
[溢目] crowd one's sight; too numerous to be fully seen;
[溢惡] excessively abusive;
[溢於言表] find vent in words; one's feeling shows between the lines; with sentiments overflowing all too evidently;
[溢譽] excessive praises; flatter; praise excessively;

充溢 full to the brim; overflowing;
耳溢 otorrhea;
滿溢 spill over;
漫溢 brim over; flood; overflow;
噴溢 gush out; pour out;
湓溢 overflow;
飄溢 float and brim with;
闐溢 fill to the brim;
洋溢 be filled with; brim with;
盈溢 brim over;
漲溢 overflow;

Y

yi

【義】 (1) just; justice; righteous; righteousness; (2) charity; chivalry; generosity; philanthropy; (3) human ties; relationship; (4) adopted; adoptive; (5) connotation; meaning; significance; (6) artificial; false; unreal; (7) a surname;

[義兵] (1) troops of justice; (2) volunteers;
[義薄雲天] one's high morality reaching up to the clouds;
[義不容辭] a compelling obligation; a responsibility one cannot relinquish; act from a strong sense of duty; an inescapable duty; an obligation one cannot decline; duty-bound not to refuse; incumbent upon one to; moral obligation prohibits declination of the call;
[義齒] artificial teeth;
[義弟] younger foster brother;
[義方] principle of justice;
[義憤] moral indignation; righteous anger; righteous indignation;
義憤激昂 be aroused to righteous indignation;
義憤填膺 afire with noble indignation; be filled with righteous indignation; boiling over with indignation; feel indignant at the injustice;
激於義憤 be moved to action by righteous indignation; be roused to righteous indignation; be stirred by righteous indignation; be urged by public spiritedness;
[義風] prevailing sense of justice;
[義父] adopted father; foster father;
[義工] (1) volunteer services; (2) volunteer worker;
義工活動 volunteer services;
[義結金蘭] adopt each other as sworn brothers; become sworn brothers; become true confederates and blood brothers; enter into a masonic bond with each other; swear eternal friendship; take an oath of brotherhood;
[義舉] act of charity; chivalrous deed;
共襄義舉 let everybody help to promote this worthy undertaking;
[義軍] troops of justice;
[義理] argumentation; principles; reason;
義理昭著 principles of righteousness are evident;
[義利] duty and interest;
捨利取義 give up an interest to faithfulness; sacrifice profit to duty;
重義輕利 value justice above material gains;
[義例] outline of a book;
[義賣] charity bazaar; charity sale;
義賣市場 charity bazaar;
舊雜貨義賣 jumble sale;
[義門] family noted for righteousness;
[義民] people with a deep sense of justice;
[義母] adoptive mother; foster mother;
[義女] adopted daughter; foster daughter;
[義僕] faithful servant;
[義旗] banner of justice; flag of the troops of

justice;

[義氣] code of brotherhood; personal loyalty;
義氣相投 one's temper and nature are in accord with sb;
講義氣 loyal to one's friend;
賣賣義氣 show one's loyalty to one's friends;
重義氣 particular about loyalty to friends;

[義犬] faithful dog; loyal dog;

[義人] righteous person;

[義乳] falsies;

[義賽] benefit match;

[義師] righteous army; troops of justice;

[義士] righteous person;

[義手] artificial hand;

[義塾] private school charging no tuition;

[義素] sememe;
義素層 sememic stratum;

[義務] duty; obligation;
義務工 do voluntary service;
義務工作 volunteer work;
義務服務 voluntary service;
義務教育 compulsory education; mandatory education;
義務勞動 voluntary labour;
不可推卸的義務 compelling obligation;
法律義務 legal obligation;
解除義務 relieve from obligations;
盡義務 do one's duty; fulfil one's obligation; perform one's duty;
履行義務 discharge oneself of one's duty;
~停止履行義務 abrogate one's obligation;
平衡權利與義務 strike a balance between rights and obligations;
契約義務 conventional obligations;
有法律上的義務 be legally obliged;
有義務 under a general obligation to;

[義項] semantic item;

[義行] act of justice; chivalrous act;

[義兄] elder foster brother;

[義學] free private school; free school;

[義演] benefit performance; charity performance; charity show;

[義勇] voluntary and courageous;
義勇軍 army of volunteers;

[義戰] holy war; war for justice;

[義肢] artificial limbs;

[義子] adopted child; foster son;

[義足] artificial leg;

奧義 profound meaning; subtle meaning;
褒義 appreciative meaning; commendatory sense; complimentary sense;
背義 renounce honour;
本義 literal sense; original meaning;
貶義 derogatory sense;
不義 injustice;
詞義 word meaning;
大義 cardinal principles of righteousness;
道義 moral principles; morality and justice;
定義 define; definition;
多義 polysemous;
恩義 gratitude; spiritual debt;
反義 antonymous;
公義 justice;
廣義 (1) broad sense; wide sense; (2) generalized;
含義 implication; import; meaning; message; sense;
涵義 connotation; implication; meaning;
假借義 figurative sense;
講義 handout; lecture notes; teaching materials;
教義 credo;
就義 be executed for championing a just cause; die a martyr;
名義 (1) name; (2) in name;
歧義 ambiguity; ambiguous words; different interpretations; different meanings; equivocal; sth open to interpretations; various interpretations;
起義 insurrection; revolt; uprising;
情義 ties of friendship, comradeship, etc;
取義 die for a cause of justice and righteousness;
仁義 kind-heartedness and justice;
尚義 love uprightness;
失義 loss of rectitude;
實義 full;
釋義 explain the meaning of words, phrases, etc.;
守義 maintain one's integrity;
首義 be the first to rise in revolt;
同義 synonymous;
文義 (1) literary content; (2) thought or idea expressed in writing;
析義 clear up doubts; clear up a doubtful point; dispel doubts; resolve doubts;
徙義 change one's course toward what is right;
俠義 have a sense of justice or righteousness and ready to help the poor and the weak;
狹義 narrow sense;
孝義 devotion to one's parents and loyalty to one's friends;
信義 faith; good faith;

徇義 follow the cause of righteousness even at the expense of one's life;
演義 historical novel; historical romance;
要義 essential points;
疑義 doubt; doubtful point;
意義 meaning; significance;
引申義 extended meaning;
音義 pronunciation and meaning of text;
語義 meaning suggested by the words;
仗義 rely on a sense of justice;
正義 (1) just; justice; righteous; (2) (of a language or writing) correct sense; proper sense;
忠義 (1) faithful and virtuous; (2) people of loyalty and virtue;
主義 doctrine; -ism;
轉義 figurative sense; transferred meaning;
字義 literal meaning;
遵義 stand up for righteousness;

Y

yi

【肄】 (1) learn; practise; study; (2) toil; work hard; (3) leftovers; remnants; (4) fresh twigs;
［肄習］ practise;
［肄業］ learn; study; study at college; study in school;
肄業證書 transcript;

yi

【裔】 (1) descendants; posterity; (2) hem of a garment; (3) remote regions; (4) (now rare) general name for the northern barbarians; (5) a surname;
［裔夷］ frontier tribes;
［裔裔］ (1) walk; (2) cascade down;
［裔冑］ remote descendants;

後裔 descendant; offspring;
苗裔 progeny; descendants;

yi

【詣】 (1) arrive; go to a place; reach; (2) call on; visit; (3) achievements; attainments;
［詣門］ visit sb;
［詣謁］ pay a visit to sb;
詣謁台端 pay you a call;

造詣 attainments;

yi

【蜴】 lizard;

yi

【億】 a hundred million;
［億萬］ billion; hundreds of millions; millions upon millions;
億萬富翁 billionaire;
~女億萬富翁 billionaires;
億萬年 aeon;
億萬人民 hundreds of millions of people;
億萬斯年 eternity; for aeons; for billions of years; time without end;
［億陽］ aeon;
［億兆］ (1) astronomical in number; countless; numberless; (2) the masses; the people;

yi

【毅】 endurance; firm; fortitude; resolute;
［毅力］ determination; indomitability; perseverance; stamina; will; willpower;
有堅強的毅力 have a determined will; have much willpower;
［毅然］ courageously; firmly; resolutely; with determination;
毅然決然 determinedly; in a determined manner; resolutely and firmly; wilfully; with firm determination; without the least hesitation;
毅然做出決定 make a decision decisively;
［毅勇］ firm courage; fortitude;
［毅志］ ambition; determination;

沉毅 calm; composed;
剛毅 resolute and steadfast;
堅毅 firm and persistent; with unswerving determination;

yi

【誼】 (1) friendship; (2) same as 義;
［誼不容辭］ the principle of friendship will not admit of a refusal;

交誼 friendly relations; friendship;
聯誼 friendship ties;
戚誼 ties between relatives;
情誼 friendly feeling; friendship;
世誼 friendship spanning two or more generations;
友誼 friendship;

yi

【熠】 bright and brilliant; luminous;
［熠燿］ (1) bright and luminous; (2) firefly; glow-worm;

［熠熠］ bright; bright and luminous; glistening;

yi

【瘞】 bury;

yi

【黖】 black;

yi

【劓】 cut off the nose;

［劓刑］ cut off sb's nose as a punishment;

yi

【憶】 bear in mind; recall; recollect; remember;

［憶及］ call to mind; recollect; remember;

［憶舊］ recall the bygone days with nostalgia; recollect the past;

［憶苦］ recall one's sufferings;

憶苦思甜 call to mind one's past sufferings and think over the source of the present happiness; contrast past bitterness with today's happiness; recall past bitterness in contrast with today's happiness; recall past miseries and speak of present happiness;

［憶念］ nostalgic memory; recollection;

［憶起］ call to mind; recall; remember;

憶起舊事 recollect old scenes;

憶起往事 bring recollections to one's mind;

［憶昔］ recall the bygone days with nostalgia; recollect the past;

回憶 call to mind; come back; dredge up; recollect; what is called to mind;

記憶 memory; recall; remember;

追憶 recall; recollect;

yi

【縊】 hang; strangle;

［縊痕］ constriction;

近端縊痕 subterminal constriction;

近中縊痕 submedian constriction;

［縊頸］ hang oneself;

［縊殺］ hang; strangle to death;

［縊死］ hang oneself;

自縊 hang oneself;

yi

【嶧】 peaks rising one upon another;

yi

【懌】 delighted; glad; happy; pleased;

［懌悦］ delighted; glad; happy; pleased;

yi

【噎】 cloudy; dim; obscure;

yi

【殪】 (1) die; (2) kill;

yi

【翳】 (1) conceal; screen; (2) haziness of objects due to a weakened vision; (3) chariot cover; (4) film over a diseased eye;

［翳滅］ disappear;

［翳翳］ dim; hazy; obscure; vague;

［翳障］ ocular; scale;

yi

【翼】 (1) wings; (2) flank; (3) fins; (4) assist; help; (5) protect;

［翼庇］ patronize; protect;

［翼側］ flank;

翼側攻擊 flank attack;

［翼戴］ assist and support;

［翼護］ shelter and protect;

［翼梁］ spar;

連續翼梁 continuous spar;

彎曲翼梁 cambered spar;

組合翼梁 composite spar;

［翼卵］ patronize; protect;

翼卵之恩 gratitude of rearing;

［翼日］ next day;

［翼翼］ (1) careful; cautiously; (2) flourishing; prosperous; thriving; vigorous; (3) numerous;

鼻翼 wings of the nose;

比翼 fly wing to wing;

蟬翼 cicada's wings;

機翼 wing of an aircraft;

戢翼 (of a bird) fold its wings;

襟翼 wing flap;

兩翼 (1) both wings (2) both flanks;

卵翼 cover with wings as in brooding; shield;

蚋翼 wings of a gnat — very tiny things;

翕翼 fold wings;

燕翼 help; support;

右翼 right wing;

左翼 left wing;

yi

【臆】 (1) one's chest; (2) subjectively;

［臆測］ conjecture; guess; surmise;

［臆斷］ arbitrary judgment; assume; draw a conclusion from conjecture; suppose;
［臆度］ conjecture; guess; surmise;
［臆見］ personal notions; personal opinions; subjective views;
［臆説］ assumption; hypothesis; supposition;
［臆造］ concoct; fabricate; make up;

腷臆 unhappy; worried;
胸臆 one's feelings; thought;

yi
【斁】 dislike; tired; weary of;

yi
【薏】 (1) heart of a lotus seed; (2) seeds of Job's tears;
［薏米］ seeds of Job's tears;
［薏苡］ Job's tears;
薏苡明珠 accuse sb falsely of taking a bribe;
薏苡之謗 be accused of corruption;

yi
【鎰】 ancient unit of weight;

yi
【繹】 (1) draw silk; (2) continuous; uninterrupted; (3) deduce; infer;
［繹如］ continuous;
［繹思］ think of sth continuously;
［繹味］ seek out the meaning;
［繹繹］ (1) galloping; (2) successive;

絡繹 in an endless stream;
衍繹 elaborate; expound;
演繹 deduction;

yi
【藝】 art; craft; dexterity; skill;
［藝妓］ geisha; geisha girl;
［藝林］ artistic circles;
［藝齡］ length of sb's artistic career;
［藝名］ professional name; stage name;
［藝能］ art; artistic skill; skill;
［藝人］ actor; artist; entertainer; performing artist; professional player;
街頭藝人 street entertainer;
吸引人群的藝人 crowd puller;
專業藝人 artiste;
［藝術］ art;
藝術本能 art instinct;
藝術才華 artistry;
藝術成就 artistic achievement; artistic merit;
藝術電影 arty film;
藝術方法 method in literature and art;
藝術歌曲 art song;
藝術館 art centre;
~ 群眾藝術館 mass art centre;
藝術技巧 artistry;
藝術家 artist;
~ 二流藝術家 second-rate artist;
~ 當代一流的藝術家 first-rate artist of the day;
~ 電影藝術家 motion picture artist;
~ 概念派藝術家 conceptual artist;
~ 恐怖藝術家 hunk artist;
~ 偉大的藝術家 great artist;
~ 舞蹈藝術家 dancing artist;
~ 一個藝術家 an artist;
~ 一群藝術家 a colony of artists;
~ 有成就的藝術家 accomplished artist;
~ 著名的藝術家 distinguished artist;
~ 卓越的藝術家 eminent artist;
藝術鑒賞 virtuosity;
藝術教育 art education;
藝術節 arts festival;
藝術界 artistic circles; world of art;
藝術借鑒 reference in art;
藝術空間 art space;
藝術誇張 artistic exaggeration;
藝術流派 genre; school;
藝術品 artware; work of art;
~ 普遍性藝術品 universal artwork;
~ 一件藝術品 a work of art;
藝術生涯 artistic career;
藝術術語 artistic term;
藝術水平 artistic level;
藝術天才 artistic talent; gift for art;
藝術細胞 art cell;
藝術效果 artistic effects;
藝術形式 art form;
藝術性 artistic quality; artistry;
~ 藝術性翻譯 artistic translation;
藝術珍品 rare art treasures;
藝術指導 art director; artistic guidance;
藝術總監 art director;
藝術作風 style in art;
藝術作品 artwork;
表演藝術 performing arts;
抽象派藝術 abstract art;
懂藝術 arty;
翻譯藝術 art of translation;
民族藝術 national arts;

社交藝術 art of socializing;
為藝術而藝術 art for art's sake;
舞台藝術 theatre arts;
喜歡藝術 have a great taste for art; have an artistic taste;
戲劇藝術 dramatic arts;

[藝壇] art circle;

[藝徒] art apprentice;

[藝文] literature and fine arts;

[藝苑] art and literary circles; realm of art and literature;

才藝 talent and skill;
材藝 ability and art;
船藝 boatmanship; seamanship;
工藝 (1) craft; handicraft; (2) technology;
花藝 floriculture;
技藝 artistry; skill;
絕藝 consummate art or skill;
賣藝 make a living as a performer;
農藝 agriculture;
七藝 the seven liberal arts: arithmetic, geometry, astronomy, music, grammar, rhetoric, and logic;
棋藝 one's skill in playing chess;
球藝 ball game skills; skills in playing a ball game;
曲藝 balladry; ballad-singing and story-telling; musical arts;
色藝 beauty and accomplishments;
手工藝 handicraft art;
手藝 (1) craftsmanship; workmanship; (2) handicraft; trade;
玩藝兒 (1) thing; (2) plaything; toy;
文藝 belles-lettres; literature and art;
無藝 (1) having no norms; lawless; (2) limitless;
武藝 fighting skills;
習藝 learn a skill; learn a trade;
獻藝 (1) demonstrate one's talents; exhibit one's skill; (2) appear on stage for performances;
學藝 (1) sciences and arts; (2) learn a trade;
遊藝 entertainment; recreation;
園藝 horticulture;
制藝 eight-part essay;
作藝 give a performance; perform; put on a performance;

yi

【議】 (1) opinion; view; (2) argue; debate; discuss; exchange views on; negotiate; talk over; (3) comment; criticize;

[議案] bill; motion; proposal; recommendation;
表決議案 take a vote on a motion;
反對議案 against a bill raise objection to a bill;
放棄議案 abandon a bill;
擱置議案 lay aside a bill; shelve a bill;
扣壓議案 burke a bill;
起草議案 draw up a bill;
提出議案 present a bill;
通過議案 adopt a bill; approve an act;
修改議案 modify a motion;
一項議案 a bill;
贊成議案 for a bill;

[議場] assembly hall;

[議程] agenda;
安排議程 prepare the agenda;
臨時議程 provisional agenda;
確定議程 settle the agenda;
審定議程 approved agenda;

[議定] arrive at a decision after discussion;
議定書 agreement; protocol;
~銀行議定書 banking agreement;

[議訂] negotiate;

[議購] purchase on negotiation;

[議和] conduct peace negotiations; make peace; negotiate peace;

[議會] assembly; congress; council; parliament;
議會法案 act of parliament;
議會政治 parliamentary politics;
解散議會 dissolve parliament;
區議會 district council;
入選議會 be elected o parliament;
市議會 city council;
懸峙議會 hung parliament;
召開議會 summon parliament;
鎮議會 town council;

[議價] (1) negotiate a price; (2) negotiated price;
議價糧 negotiated price grain;
議價能力 ability to bargain;
議價油 negotiated price oil;
個別議價 individual bargaining;
集體議價 collective bargaining;

[議決] decide at a meeting; pass a resolution; resolve after deliberation;

[議論] comment; discuss; talk;
議論不休 carry on endless discussions;
議論紛紛 be widely discussed; give rise to much discussion; raise a babel

of criticism of; say to one another; tongues are wagging;
議論風生 create a lively atmosphere by one's talk; the convivial evening gives rise to a warm discussion of many subjects;
議論龐雜 numerous and jumbled views;
議論文 argumentative writing;
崇論宏議 an exalted discussion and extensive statement; a great essay or lofty exposition of point of view;
大發議論 speak at great length; talk a lot;
引起很多議論 provoke much discussion;

[議親] negotiate a marriage;

[議事] discuss official business;
議事規則 point of order;
議事日程 agenda; order of the day;
~議事日程表 order paper;
議事廳 assembly hall;

[議題] a subject under discussion; a topic for discussion;
改變議題 change the subject under discussion;
結束議題 drop the subject under discussion;
社會議題 social issues;
爭議性議題 controversial issues;

[議席] seat in a legislative assembly; seat in parliament;

[議員] member of a legislative assembly;
當選為議員 be elected to Parliament;
後座議員 back bencher;
男議員 assembly man;
女議員 assembly woman;
區議員 district councilor;

[議院] congress; legislative assembly; parliament;
下議院 the Lower House;

[議長] speaker of a legislative body;
副議長 vice-president;

謗議 criticize; libel; slander;
駁議 dispute; refute;
倡議 propose;
成議 come to an agreement;
芻議 my humble opinion;
動議 motion;
非議 censure; reproach;
附議 second a motion; support a proposal;
復議 reconsider a decision;
腹議 criticize in one's mind;
公議 hold a public discussion;
瞽議 groundless statements; wild talks;
和議 peace negotiations;
橫議 extreme views; far-fetched arguments; radical statements;
緩議 defer the discussion;
會議 conference; meeting;
計議 confer; consult; deliberate;
建議 proposal; propose; suggest; suggestion;
較議 dispute; refute;
決議 resolution;
抗議 protest;
另議 be discussed separately;
面議 discuss personally;
擬議 draft; draw up; proposal; recommendation;
評議 appraise sth through discussion;
清議 political criticism by scholars;
商議 discuss; exchange views on;
審議 consider; deliberate;
思議 imaginable; thinkable;
俗議 popular opinion;
提議 motion; proposal; propose; suggest;
廷議 court discussion; court meeting; discussion at imperial court;
庭議 court meeting;
物議 criticism from the people;
洽議 meet and discuss sth;
巷議 local gossips; local rumours;
協議 (1) agree on; (2) agreement; deal; treaty; (3) discuss; negotiate;
異議 dissent; objection;
惲議 deliberate; discuss;
再議 discuss sth later; talk about sth again;
爭議 argue; dispute; engage in a controversy;
眾議 public opinions;
酌議 consider and discuss;
諮議 (1) confer; discuss; (2) government consultants;
訾議 censure; criticize; discuss the failings of others; impeach; unfavourable criticism;

yi

【譯】 interpret; translate; translation;

[譯本] translated text; translation;
英譯本 English translation;

[譯筆] style of a translation;
譯筆流暢 the translation reads smoothly;

[譯成] put into; render into; translate into; turn into;
譯成各種文字 translate into all tongues;

[譯出] translate from;
譯出語 source language;

[譯法] translation method;
順譯法 translation in regular sequence;
[譯稿] translated manuscript;
校訂譯稿 revise a translated manuscript;
[譯後] post-translation;
譯後編輯 post-editing; post-translation editing;
[譯碼] decoding; interpretation; transcode;
譯碼器 decoder;
~ 代數譯碼器 algebraic decoder;
~ 反饋譯碼器 feedback decoder;
~ 級聯譯碼器 cascaded decoder;
~ 運算譯碼器 operation decoder;
~ 紙帶譯碼器 paper tape decoder;
重合譯碼 coincidence decoding;
故障譯碼 syndrome decoding;
混合譯碼 hybrid decoding;
排列譯碼 permutation decoding;
最佳譯碼 optimal decoding;
[譯名] translated name;
譯名規範化 standardization of terminology;
[譯評] translation criticism;
譯評人 translation critic;
[譯前] pre-translation;
譯前編輯 pre-editing; pre-translation editing;
[譯入] translate into;
譯入語 target language;
[譯社] translation agency;
[譯審] translation vetter;
副譯審 associate translation vetter;
[譯述] translate freely;
[譯文] translated text; translation;
譯文詞滙 target lexis;
譯文流暢 the translation reads smoothly;
譯文輸出 output;
譯文輸入 input;
譯文語法 target grammar;
得體的譯文 happy translation;
地道的譯文 idiomatic translation;
典範譯文 model translation;
流暢的譯文 smooth translation;
正確的譯文 correct translation;
忠實的譯文 close translation;
[譯音] transliteration;
[譯語] target language;
[譯員] translator; interpreter;
譯員訓練 translator training;
包工譯員 contracted translator;
高級譯員 senior translator;
公司譯員 company translator;
官方譯員 official translator;
雙語譯員 bilingual translator;
[譯者] translator;
譯者注 translator's note;
[譯著] translation;

筆譯 translate in writing; written translation;
編譯 editor and translator; translate and edit;
重譯 retranslate;
撮譯 summary translation;
翻譯 translate; translation; translator;
合譯 co-translate; co-translation;
佳譯 good translation;
借譯 loan translation;
今譯 modern translation; modern-language translation;
口譯 interpret; oral interpretation;
欠譯 under-translation;
通譯 interpret; interpreter; translate; translator;
迻譯 translate;
移譯 translate;
意譯 free translation;
音譯 transliterate;
摘譯 select passages and translate them;
直譯 literal translation; word-for-word translation;

yi
【鐿】 ytterbium;

yi
【鷁】 a fabulous sea bird;
[鷁首] bow of a boat;

yi
【囈】 talk in sleep;
[囈語] (1) talk in one's sleep; (2) crazy talk; ravings;
心理學囈語 psychobabble;

夢囈 (1) rigmarole; (2) somniloquy;

yi
【懿】 (1) exemplary; fine; good; virtuous; (2) chaste; modest;
[懿德] (1) fine virtue; (2) woman's meritorious character;
[懿範] a fine example of womanly virtue;
[懿親] close relatives;
[懿行] (1) virtuous deed; (2) woman's virtuous conduct;

yi

【驛】 courier station;
［驛車］ courier cart;
［驛道］ courier route; post road;
［驛館］ courier hostel; courier station; post house;
［驛路］ courier road; post road;
［驛馬］ courier horse; posthorse; relay;
［驛騎］ posthorse;
［驛使］ courier;
［驛亭］ courier station; post house;
［驛站］ coaching inn; courier station; post house;

yin¹
yin

【因】 (1) cause; reason; (2) as a result of; because of; by reason of; for; on account of; since; (3) carry on; follow; (4) according to; in accordance with; in the light of; on the basis of;
［因病］ because of illness; due to illness;
因病請假 absent on sick leave; ask for sick leave;
因病身故 die for an illness;
因病下藥 apply medicine according to indications;
［因材施教］ educate sb according to his natural ability; suit teaching to the aptitude of the pupil; suit the instruction to the student's level; teach students according to their aptitude; teach students in accordance with their aptitude;
因材施教的教育 progressive education;
因材施教法 individualized, method of instruction;
［因財失義］ gain money and lose one's friend; gain wealth at the expense of justice;
［因此］ because of this; consequently; for that reason; hence; on that account; so; therefore; thus;
［因而］ and so; as a result; therefore; thus; with the result that;
［因革］ course of change and development; evolution; successive changes;
［因公］ on business; on duty;
因公出差 away on official business; go on a public errand; take an official trip;
因公廢私 neglect the private affairs because of public business;
因公負傷 be wounded in the line of duty;
因公受獎 be rewarded for one's official duties;
因公外出 away on business;
因公犧牲 die while on duty;
因公殉職 die in an accident while on duty; die in the course of performing one's duty;
［因故］ for this reason;
［因何］ for what reason; why;
［因果］ (1) cause and effect; chain of cause and effect; (2) karma; preordained fate;
因果報應 as a man sows, so let him reap; retributive justice;
因果並列連詞 cause-and-effect coordinator;
因果副詞 adverb of cause and result;
因果關係 causal relation; causality; causation; cause-effect relation;
～因果關係的 causal;
～間接因果關係 indirect causation;
因果性 causality; causation;
倒果為因 reverse cause and effect; take the effect for the cause;
倒因為果 reverse cause and effect; take the cause for the effect;
顛倒因果 invert cause and effect;
宏觀因果 macroscopic causality;
互為因果 interact as both cause and effect; reciprocal causation;
混淆因果 confuse cause and effect;
微觀因果 microscopic causality;
以果為因 take the effect for the cause;
以因為果 take the cause for the effect;
由因推果 from the cause to the effect;
［因恐］ for fear of; lest;
［因明］ Indian classical logic; science of logic;
［因難見巧］ display masterly artistry as a result of the degree of difficulty;
［因人］ (1) depend on others; (2) vary with each individual;
因人成事 accomplish sth by help of others; achieve sth with the help of others; depend on others for success in one's work; rely upon others in accomplishing sth;
因人而異 differ from person to person; vary from person to person; vary with different individuals; vary with each

individual;
因人設事 create a job in order to accommodate a person;

[因是] because of this;

[因勢利導] give guidance according to the situation; guide a matter along its course of development; guide a matter in the light of its general trend; guide action according to circumstances; improve the occasion;

[因素] elements; factors;
因素比較 factor comparison;
因素分析法 method of factor analysis;
不可比因素 non-comparable factors;
長期因素 long-term factors;
短期因素 short-term factors;
多種因素 a combination of circumstances; a set of circumstances;
環境因素 environmental factors;
基本因素 fundamental factors;
技術性因素 technical factors;
進化的因素 evolutionary factors;
強有力的因素 powerful factors;
燃耗因素 burnup factor;
人的因素 human factors;
生物因素 biotic factor;
體積因素 bulk factor;
未知因素 unknown factors;
已知因素 known factors;
質量因素 quality factors;
重大因素 vital factors;
主導因素 governing factors;
主要因素 chief elements; principal factor;
最大因素 main factor;

[因為] after; as; as a result of; at; because; because of; by; by dint of; by reason of; by right of; by virtue of; due to; failing; for; from; in; in consequence of; in consideration of; in default of; in right of; in that; in the absence of; in view of; in virtue of; inasmuch as; of; on; on account of; on the ground of; on the ground that; on the score of; out of; over; owing to; seeing that; since; thanks to; that; through; wanting; what with; with;

[因襲] carry on as before; copy; follow; follow conventions and traditions;
因襲陳規 follow outmoded rules;
因襲前人 follow in the footsteps of one's predecessors;
因襲相沿 be handed down by traditions;

[因循] carry on as before; continue in the same old rut;
因循苟且 follow routines without thinking about improvement;
因循舊習 gentility;
因循老例 follow the old routine;
因循守舊 cling conservatively to the old system; follow the beaten path; follow the beaten track; get into a groove; get into a rut; live in the past; lockstep; move in a rut; stick to old routine; stick to old ways; traditionalism;
因循延誤 procrastinate until it is too late; sit back and allow the situation to deteriorate;
因循坐誤 fail to grasp the opportunity and let the situation pass by; procrastinate and allow the situation to deteriorate; sit back until it is too late;

[因噎廢食] give up eating for fear of choking — refrain from doing sth necessary for fear of a slight risk; refuse to eat for fear of choking; give up a good cause because of a slight mishap; throw away the apple because of the core; throw the baby out with the bathwater;

[因由] cause; origin; reason;

[因緣] (1) cause; principal and subsidiary causes; (2) predestined relationship;

[因之] because of that; on this account;

[因致] so as to cause;

[因子] divisor; factor;
因子定理 factor theorem;
因子分解 factorization;
~典範因子分解 canonical factorization;
~多項式因子分解 factorization of polynomial;
~譜因子分解 spectral factorization;
餘因子 cofactor;
充氣因子 aeration factor;
代數餘因子 algebraic cofactor;
複素因子 complex divisor;
離心因子 acentric factor;
臨界素因子 critical prime divisor;
偶然因子 accidental factor;
縮減餘因子 reduced cofactor;
微分因子 differential divisor;
吸收因子 absorption factor;

餘因子 complementary divisor;
正規餘因子 normalized cofactor;
病因 the cause of a disease; the origin of a disease;
成因 cause of formation; contributing factor; origin;
蓋因 it is because;
歸因 ascribe to; attribute to;
海洛因 heroin; scag; skag; skank;
基因 gene;
近因 immediate cause;
咖啡因 caffeine;
可卡因 cocaine; coke;
內因 internal cause;
孽因 sinful cause;
起因 as a result of; causation; cause; origin;
前因 antecedent; cause;
死因 cause of death;
外因 external cause;
無因 (1) without cause; without reason; (2) in no position to; no way to; unable to;
要因 essential factor; important cause;
有因 there is a reason for it;
誘因 incentive; inducement; remote cause;
原因 account; at the back of sth; cause; reason;
緣因 cause;
遠因 remote causes;
只因 for the simple reason that; only because;
主因 major cause; principal cause;
茲因 now because;
罪因 cause of a crime;

yin

【姻】 (1) marriage; (2) relation by marriage; (3) one's husband's family;
[姻伯] uncle by marriage;
[姻家] (1) families of the married couple; (2) elders of the families of the married couple;
[姻母] aunt by marriage;
[姻戚] relatives by marriage;
[姻親] relatives by marriage;
姻親關係 relationship by marriage;
[姻婭] in-laws; relatives by marriage;
[姻緣] marriage;
姻緣前定 a couple's conjugal fate is prearranged;
姻緣天定 marriages are made in heaven;
露水姻緣 casual affair;
美滿姻緣 conjugal felicity; a happy marriage;
婚姻 marriage; matrimony;
聯姻 connections through marriages; unite by marriage;

yin

【音】 (1) sound; voice; (2) information; news; tidings; (3) accent; tone;
[音標] phonetic symbols; phonetic transcription;
音標文字 phonetic alphabet;
國際音標 international phonetic alphabet;
注上音標 mark with phonetic symbols;
[音波] sound waves;
[音步] foot;
音步翻譯 metrical translation;
[音叉] tuning fork;
[音長] tonal length;
[音程] interval;
[音塵] traces; whereabouts;
[音調] pitch; tone; tune;
音調不準 out of tune;
音調符號 circumflex;
音調尖 have a shrill tone;
唱錯音調 sing a wrong note;
降低音調 lower the tone;
提高音調 raise the tone;
悅耳的音調 dulcet tones;
[音渡] juncture;
閉音渡 close juncture;
雙杠音渡 double bar juncture;
雙交叉音渡 double cross juncture;
[音符] musical note; note;
八分音符 eighth note; quaver;
二分音符 half note; mimim;
二全音符 breve;
三連音符 triplet;
三十二分音符 demi-semi-quaver; thirty-second note;
十六分音符 semi-quaver; sixteenth note;
四分音符 crotchet; quarter note;
[音高] pitch; tonal height;
絕對音高 absolute pitch;
[音階] gamut; musical scale; scale;
半音階 chromatic scale; semitone;
~半音階和聲 chromatic harmonies;
大音階 major scale;
全音階 diatonic scale;
小音階 minor scale;

自然音階 diatonic scale;

[音節] syllable;

音節詞 syllable;

~三音節詞 trisyllable;

音節文字 syllabic writing;

閉音節 close syllable;

單音節 monosyllabic;

~單音節詞 monosyllabic word;

~單音節性 monosyllabism;

~單音節語 monosyllabic language;

多音節 polysyllabic;

~多音節詞 polysyllabic word;

開音節 open syllable;

六音節的 hexasyllabic;

雙音節 dissyllable;

重讀音節 stressed syllable;

~非重讀音節 unstressed syllable;

自由音節 free syllable;

[音量] sound volume; volume;

音量大 give great volume;

[音律] temperament; tone system;

[音名] musical alphabet;

[音頻] audio frequency;

音頻存取單元 audio access unit;

音頻複製 audio dubbing;

音頻格式 audio format;

音頻緩衝器 audio buffer;

音頻混疊 audioanalysis filter bank;

音頻混合器 audio mixer;

音頻輸出 audio out;

音頻輸入 audio in;

[音容] (1) voice and countenance; (2) likeness of the deceased;

音容宛在 as if the person were in the flesh; as if the person were still alive; can see sb's smile and hear his voice today as clearly as if he were standing before us; one's voice and appearance seem to be still with us; voice and facial expression of the deceased are still vividly remembered;

音容笑貌 (1) one's voice and expression; (2) the likeness of one's laughing face;

[音色] timbre; tone colour;

音色不同 have different timbres;

音色美 have a beautiful tone;

外吐音色 egressive-click timbre;

言語音色 speech timbre;

震動音色 percussive timbre;

[音詩] tone poem;

[音書] correspondence; information; letters; news;

音書斷絕 news and letters are broken off;

[音速] speed of sound;

[音素] phoneme;

音素翻譯 phonemic translation;

[音位] phoneme;

音位變體 allophone;

音位學 phonemics;

~生成音位學 generative phonemics;

~音段音位學 segmental phonemics;

~自主音位學 autonomous phonemics;

詞源音位 etymological phoneme;

複合音位 compound phoneme;

同化音位 assimilatory phoneme;

相關音位 correlative phoneme;

重音音位 accentual phoneme;

[音系學] phonology;

詞級音系學 word-level phonology;

生成音系學 generative phonology;

[音響] acoustics; audio; sound;

音響公司 audio supplies company;

音響設備 audio supplies; sound installation;

音響系統 sound system;

音響效果 sound effects;

個人音響 personal stereo;

組合音響 hi-fi stereo system;

[音像] audio and video;

音像世界 audio-video world;

音像市場 tape market;

音像作品 audio-video works;

[音效卡] sound card;

[音問] news and letters;

音問兩絕 news and letters are disconnected;

常通音問 keep up correspondence; maintain friendly intercourse by letter;

久疏音問 have been negligent in correspondence;

[音信] mail; messages; news;

互通音信 communicate with each other;

迄無音信 have received no information so far;

杳無音信 completely not heard from; have never been heard of since; no tidings have been heard for a long time;

[音訊] mail; messages; news; tidings;

互通音訊 communicate with each other;

[音義] pronunciation and meaning;

[音譯] transliteration;

音譯詞 transliterate;

部份音譯 partial transliteration;

[音域] compass; range;

[音樂] music;

音樂愛好者 music lover;
音樂比賽 musical competition;
音樂茶座 music café;
音樂大師 virtuoso;
音樂電視 music TV;
音樂行家 musical adept;
音樂行業 music business;
音樂盒 music box;
音樂會 concert; musical recital;
~音樂會表演 concert performance;
~音樂會門票 concert ticket;
~慈善音樂會 charity concert;
~告別音樂會 farewell concert;
~古典音樂會 classical concert;
~管絃音樂會 orchestral concert;
~戶外音樂會 outdoor concert;
~舉辦音樂會 put on a concert; stage a concert;
~舉行音樂會 concertize; do a concert; give a concert;
~爵士音樂會 jazz concert;
~流行音樂會 pop concert;
~露天音樂會 open-air concert;
~漫步音樂會 prom; promenade concert;
~去聽音樂會 attend a concert; go to a concert;
~室內音樂會 indoor concert;
~現場音樂會 live concert;
~逍遙音樂會 prom; promenade concert;
~搖滾音樂會 rock concert;
~一場音樂會 a concert;
~周年音樂會 annual concert;
音樂家 musician;
~業餘音樂家 amateur musician;
~優秀音樂家 consummate musician;
~專業音樂家 professional musician;
音樂劇 musical;
音樂療法 music therapy;
音樂門鈴 musical doorbell;
音樂迷 music-lover;
音樂廳 concert hall; lyceum;
音樂晚會 musical soiree;
音樂系 department of music;
音樂學 musicology;
音樂學校 music school;
音樂學院 academy of music; conservatory; conservatory of music;
音樂演奏技巧 musicianship;
音樂指揮 musical director;
音樂專欄 music column;
愛好音樂 like music;
背景音樂 background music; piped music;
標題音樂 programme music;
~無標題音樂 absolute music;
不懂音樂 have no ear for music;
唱片音樂 canned music;
襯托音樂 background music;
吹奏音樂 brass band music;
純音樂 absolute music;
電子音樂 electronic music;
獨立音樂 indie music;
歌劇音樂 operatic music;
古典音樂 classical music;
~古典音樂曲目 classical repertoire;
廣東音樂 Guangdong music;
黑人音樂 soul music;
教堂音樂 church music;
爵士音樂 jazz;
流行音樂 pop music;
~電子流行音樂 electronica;
民間音樂 folk music;
民族音樂 national music;
幕間音樂 interlude music;
偶然音樂 aleatoric music;
氣氛音樂 mood music;
輕音樂 light music;
情調音樂 mood music;
山地音樂 country music;
室內樂 chamber music;
抒情音樂 sentimental music;
聽音樂 listen to music;
舞蹈音樂 dance music;
嘻哈音樂 hip-hop music;
喜愛音樂 love music;
戲劇音樂 theatrical music;
現場音樂 live music;
現代音樂 modern music;
鄉村音樂 country music;
效果音樂 effect music;
演奏音樂 make music; play music;
嚴肅音樂 serious music; solemn music;
搖擺音樂 rock music;
一段音樂 a piece of music;
庸俗音樂 vulgar music;
主題音樂 theme music;
中古音樂 medieval music;
宗教音樂 sacred music;

[音韻] rhyme;

音韻學 phonology;

[音障] sound barrier;

突破音障 break the sound barrier;

[音質] acoustic fidelity; tone quality;

八音 every sound of music;
半音 semitone;
鼻音 nasal sounds;
標音 notation;
播音 be on the air; broadcast;
擦音 fricative;
顫音 trill;
串音 crosstalk;
低音 bass; low pitch;
定音 set the tone;
讀音 pronunciation;
發音 articulate; get one's tongue round;
梵音 chanting of the Buddhist scriptures;
泛音 overtone;
福音 (1) gospel; (2) glad tidings; good news;
輔音 consonant;
高音 (1) high pitch; (2) top;
觀音 Goddess of Mercy; Guanyin;
國音 standard Chinese pronunciation approved by the government;
鼾音 sonorous rale;
喉音 guttural sound;
話音 (1) one's voice in speech; (2) implication; tone;
回音 (1) echo; (2) reply; response; (3) turn;
惠音 your esteemed letter;
基音 fundamental tone;
佳音 favourable reply; good tidings; welcome news;
靜音 mute;
口音 (1) voice; (2) accent;
連音 sandhi;
錄音 film recording; recording; sound recording;
落音 just come to a pause;
配音 dubbing;
拼音 phonetic transcription;
清音 voiceless sound;
跫音 footsteps; sound of steps;
瓊音 clear and crisp sound;
全音 whole tone;
塞擦音 affricate;
塞音 plosive;
嗓音 one's voice;
賞音 appreciate music;
聲音 sound; voice;
嗣音 continue one's messages;
調音 tune;
同音 homophone;
土音 local accent; local pronunciation;
弦音 music from a stringed instrument;
鄉音 local accent; one's native accent;
消音 deaden a sound; sound deadening;
諧音 harmonics;
心音 cardiac sound;
噓音 hush;
譯音 transliteration;
餘音 lingering sound;
語音 (1) speech sounds; (2) pronunciation;
玉音 (1) your letter; (2) valuable words; (3) imperial decrees; (4) jade-like music – beautiful sound;
元音 vowel;
樂音 musical sound;
雜音 (1) noise; (2) murmur; (3) static;
噪音 din; noise; unpleasant noise;
正音 correct pronunciation;
知音 (1) a friend keenly appreciative of one's talents; bosom friend; (2) one who is versed in music;
中音 alto; tenor;
重音 (1) stress; accent; (2) accent;
注音 transcribe;
囀音 warble tone; wobble;
濁音 (1) voiced sound; (2) dullness;
子音 consonant;
走音 clinker;

yin

【殷】 (1) abundant; flourishing; prosperous; rich; thriving; (2) ardent; eager; (3) civil; courteous; hospitable; polite; (4) a surname;

[殷富] prosperous; rich; wealth; well-off;

[殷鑒] setback which serves as a warning to others;
殷鑒不遠 the lessons of history are close at hand;

[殷切] ardent; eager;
殷切期待 expect earnestly;
殷切期望 expect earnestly;

[殷勤] courteous; eagerly attentive; polite; solicitous;
殷勤備至 all attention;
殷勤侍奉 wait on sb hand and foot;
殷勤待客 attentive to one's guests;
殷勤相待 entertain sb with great attention; treat sb with the greatest honour;
殷勤周到 treat sb with great consideration;
百般殷勤 courtesy expressed in numerous ways;
獻殷勤 do everything to please; flatter;

Y

ingratiate; make oneself liked; pay one's addresses; pay one's attentions; show sb excessive attentions;
~大獻殷勤 dance attendance on sb; do everything to please sb; do one's utmost to please and woo; pay one's addresses to sb; serve sb hand and foot;

[殷商] prosperous merchant;
[殷盛] abundant; flourishing; prosperous; thriving;
[殷實] prosperous; substantial; well-off;
殷實人家 well-off families;
~出身殷實人家 come from a well-off family;
家道殷實 of a well-to-do family;
[殷殷] (1) abundant; prosperous; rich; thriving; (2) civil; courteous; polite; (3) mournful; sad; sorrowful;
殷殷垂誡 admonish sincerely;
殷殷垂問 inquire about anxiously;
殷殷屯屯 well-off;

殷憂 deep sorrow; great worries;
情殷 with warm regard;
朱殷 dark-red;

yin

【氤】 spirit of harmony;
[氤氳] (of mist) dense; enshrouding; thick;

yin

【茵】 (1) carpet; cushion; mat; (2) skimmia japonica; (3) artemisia capillaris;
[茵陳] oriental wormwood;
[茵席] cushion; mat;

yin

【陰】 (1) cloudy; dark; overcast; (2) shade; (3) hidden; secret; (4) negative; (5) female; feminine; (6) north side of a hill; (7) south side of a river; (8) back side; (9) moon; (10) reproductive organs of both sexes; (11) hell; Hades; (12) cunning and crafty; (13) injure another in a clandestine manner; (14) time; (15) a surname;
[陰暗] dark; dim; gloomy; overcast;
[陰兵] women soldiers;
[陰部] cunt; fanny; fud; front bottom; front passage; grumble and grunt; hole; little man in the boat; minge; mole-catcher; mott; muff; pussy; quim; slit; slot; sluice; tenuc; the private parts; twam; twammy; twat; twim; twot; vilva winker; yoni;
陰部潰瘍 pudendal ulcer;
陰部裂 pudendal fissure;
陰部疝 pudendal hernia;
女性陰部 fanny;
[陰沉] cloudy; gloomy; overcast; sombre;
今天天氣很陰沉 it's very heavy today;
陰陰沉沉 dreary; dusky; gloomy;
[陰唇] labia; lips of the vulva;
陰唇連合 comissura labiorum pudendi;
陰唇隆起 labial swelling;
陰唇疝 labial hernia;
小陰唇 nympha;
[陰道] (1) vagina; (2) shaded road;
陰道襞 vaginal fold;
直腸陰道襞 rectovaginal fold;
陰道病 vaginosis;
細菌性陰道病 bacterial vaginosis;
陰道出血 vaginal haemorrhage;
陰道乾燥 colpoxerosis;
陰道隔 vaginal septum;
~直腸陰道隔 rectovaginal septum;
陰道肌層 tunica muscularis vaginae;
~陰道肌層炎 myocolpitis;
陰道積膿 pyocolpos;
陰道積氣 aerocolpos;
陰道積水 hydrocolpos;
陰道積血 hematocolpos;
陰道痙攣 colpospasm;
陰道口 vaginal orifice;
陰道擴張 colpectasia;
陰道瘻 vaginal fistula;
~直腸陰道瘻 rectovaginal fistula;
陰道膀胱炎 colpocystitis;
陰道旁炎 paravaginitis;
陰道腔 vaginal canal;
陰道疝 vaginal hernia;
直腸陰道疝 rectovaginal hernia;
陰道痛 colpodynia; vaginal pain;
陰道脱垂 colpoptosis;
陰道狹窄 colpostenosis;
陰道炎 vaginal inflammation; vaginitis;
~白喉性陰道炎 diphtheritic vaginitis;
滴蟲性陰道炎 trichomonas vaginitis;
~肥厚性陰道炎 pachyvaginitis;
宮頸陰道炎 cervicovaginitis;
顆粒狀陰道炎 granular vaginitis;
老年性陰道炎 senile vaginitis;

~霉菌性陰道炎 colpitis mycotica;
黏連性陰道炎 adhesive vaginitis;
~外珠菌陰道炎 candidal vaginitis;
氣腫性陰道炎 colpitis emphysematosa;
~脱屑性陰道炎 desquamative inflammatory vaginitis;
外陰陰道炎 vulvovaginitis;
萎縮性陰道炎 atrophic vaginitis;
陰道周圍炎 pericolpitis;

[陰德] a good deed to the doer's credit in the next world; one's unpublicized good deed;

[陰地] (1) agraveyard; (2) a place where sunshine cannot reach;
陰地植物 shade plant;

[陰蒂] clitoris;
陰蒂包皮 preputium clitoridis;
陰蒂肥大 clitorimegaly;
陰蒂體 corpus clitoridis;
陰蒂頭 glans clitoridis;
陰蒂炎 clitoritis;
巨陰蒂 megaloclitoris;

[陰電] negative electricity;

[陰毒] cunning; insidious; meaning; sinister;

[陰風] (1) chilly winds; (2) evil winds; ill winds; sinister winds;
陰風森森 dark, chilly and exceptionally gloomy;
陰風習習 a chilly breeze blows about sb;
刮陰風 stir up an ill wind; stir up evil gusts;
煽陰風 fan up an evil wind; secretly stir up trouble;
~煽陰風，點鬼火 fan the winds of evil and spread the fires of turmoil — foment trouble; fan up evil winds and flames;

[陰伏] (1) one's sins unknown to others; (2) ambush secretly;

[陰府] Hades; netherworld;

[陰乾] dry in the shade;

[陰功] a good deed to the doer's credit in the next world; one's unpublicized good deeds;
陰功積德 accumulate deeds of charity; accumulate merits; cast one's bread upon the waters; do good by stealth; do good deeds in secret; do good things without the knowledge of others; gain merit in the next world; merit divine grace;

[陰溝] (1) covered drain; culvert; sewer; (2) vagina;
陰溝裏翻船 fail miserably in a very easy task;

[陰寒] cold and humid;

[陰核] clitoris;

[陰戶] female reproductive organ; vagina;

[陰晦] dark; dismal; shady;

[陰魂] soul; spirit; the spirits of the dead;
陰魂不散 haunting spectre; the ghost does not go away; the haunting ghost of sb remains at large; the soul refuses to leave;

[陰極] cathode; negative pole;
儲備式陰極 dispenser cathode;
電弧陰極 arc cathode;
複合陰極 complex cathode;
輔助陰極 auxiliary cathode;
覆蓋陰極 covered cathode;
活化陰極 activated cathode;
集射陰極 beam cathode;
加導體陰極 adconductor cathode;
擴散陰極 diffusion cathode;
碳化陰極 carbonized cathode;

[陰間] Hades; the shades; the underworld;

[陰莖] dick; penis; prick; putz; willy;
陰莖包皮 prepuce;
陰莖背 dorsum penis;
陰莖勃起 penile tumescence;
~夜間陰莖勃起 nocturnal penile tumescence;
陰莖出血 phallorrhagia;
陰莖大的 well-endowed; well-hung;
陰莖反射 penis reflex;
陰莖根 radix penis;
陰莖腳 crus penis;
陰莖頸 cervix glandis;
陰莖裂 penischisis;
陰莖球 bulb of penis;
陰莖痛 phallalgia;
陰莖頭 head of penis;
~陰莖頭包皮炎 balanoposthitis;
~陰莖頭炎 balanitis;
糜爛性陰莖頭炎 erosive balanitis;
糖尿病性陰莖頭炎 diabetic balanitis;
陰莖退縮 phallocrypsis;
陰莖彎曲 phallocampsis;
陰莖炎 penitis;
陰莖異常勃起 priapism;
~繼發性陰莖異常勃起 secondary

priapism;
陰莖腫 phalloncus;
假陰莖 dildo;
巨陰莖 macrophallus;
軟垂的陰莖 flaccid penis;
小陰莖 microphallus;

［陰冷］ (1) gloomy and cold; raw; (2) glum; sombre;
陰冷陰冷 gloomy and cold;

［陰曆］ lunar calendar;
陰曆年 the Chinese Lunar New Year;

［陰涼］ (1) shady and cool; (2) cool place; shade;
陰涼處 a shaded, cool place;

［陰靈］ the spirits of the deceased;

［陰霾］ haze; thin mist;
陰霾密布 dense clouds darken the sky; the sky is covered with haze;

［陰毛］ feathers; pubic hair; pubes; pubis; short hairs; short-and-curlies; turf;

［陰門］ vaginal orifice;

［陰謀］ conspiracy; frame-up; plot; scheme;
陰謀詭計 conspiracies and plots; dark schemes and tricks; dishonest scheme; hanky-panky; intrigues and conspiracies; plots and tricks; schemes and intrigues; tricks and schemes; underhand methods;
陰謀家 conspirator;
陰謀小集團 cabal;
參與陰謀 take part in a conspiracy;
策劃陰謀 brew a plot; contrive a conspiracy;
搞陰謀 conspire;
揭露陰謀 uncover a conspiracy; unmask a conspiracy;
捲入一個陰謀 get entangled in a scheme;
破獲陰謀 uncover a plot;

［陰囊］ scrotum;
陰囊瘤 oscheoma;
陰囊隆起 scrotal swelling;
陰囊疝 scrotal hernia;
陰囊水腫 hydrocele;
陰囊炎 oscheitis;
陰囊腫大 oscheocele;
陰痿 impotence;

［陰人］ woman;

［陰日］ overcast day;

［陰森］ frightful; ghastly; gloomy; gruesome;
陰森可怖 ghastly and blood-curdling;
陰森可怕 ghastly and blood-curdling;
陰森森 gloomy; ominous; weird;
陰氣森森 atmosphere of austere gloominess;

［陰室］ (1) one's bedroom; one's private quarter; (2) an underground cellar for storage of ice;

［陰私］ privacy; private affairs; shameful secrets;

［陰司］ netherworld;

［陰天］ cloudy day; overcast sky;
陰天的 overcast;

［陰惡］ undiscovered evil deed;

［陰險］ crafty; cunning; deceitful; insidious; sinister; treacherous;
陰險毒辣 insidious and deadly; sinister and ruthless;
陰險狡猾 insidious and crafty; treacherous and cunning;
~陰險狡猾的人 viper;
奸詐陰險 deceitful and designing;
居心陰險 of a malicious disposition;
為人陰險 treacherous;

［陰性］ (1) negative; (2) female; feminine gender;
陰性反應 negative reaction;

［陰陽］ male and female; positive and negative;
陰陽怪氣 cynical; deliberately ambiguous; eccentric; enigmatic; queer;
陰陽家 astrologer; geomancer; sorcerer;
陰陽人 hermaphrodite;
陽奉陰違 agree outwardly but disagree inwardly; comply in public but oppose in private; comply in public while opposing in private; feign compliance while acting in opposition; obey in public but disobey in private; overtly agree but covertly oppose; passive resistence; pretend compliance; pretend to obey;

［陰翳］ dark; gloomy; shady;

［陰影］ cloud; shade; shadow;
擺脱陰影 lay the ghost of sth;
管頸陰影 neck shadow;
快速陰影 fast shadow;
落後陰影 lagging shadow;
微弱陰影 feeble shadow;
消除陰影 lift the shadow;

［陰雨］ cloudy and rainy; overcast and rainy;
陰雨晦冥 it is a gloomy day and raining

continuously;
陰雨連綿 a run of wet weather; cloudy and drizzly for days on end; there is an unbroken spell of wet weather;
陰雨天 cloudy and rainy;
[陰鬱] depressed; dismal; dreariment; gloomy;
陰鬱的 cheerless; gloomy;
感到陰鬱 feel gloomy;
減輕陰鬱 lighten the gloom;
看起來陰鬱 look dismal;
驅除陰鬱 dispel the gloom;
[陰雲] dark clouds; rain clouds;
陰雲蔽日 dark clouds hide the sun;
陰雲蔽月 dark clouds cover the moon;
陰雲低垂 the sky is dark and lowery;
陰雲密布 dark clouds are gathering; the sky is covered with dark clouds; the sky is overcast;
天空佈滿陰雲 the sky is overcast with dark clouds;
[陰詐] crafty; cunning; deceitful;
[陰宅] graveyard;
[陰鷙] sinister and ruthless;

碑陰 back of a stone tablet;
背陰 in the shade; obscurity;
寸陰 very short time;
分陰 moment;
光陰 sands of time; time;
諒陰 (1) imperial mourning; (2) mourning shed;
女陰 cunnus; vulva;
太陰 (1) moon; (2) lunar;
舔陰 cunnilingus;
外陰 vulva;

yin
【湮】 (1) bury; (2) block; (3) long in time;
[湮沈] have no chance to rise in the world;
[湮蓋] inundate;
[湮滅] bury; destroy;
[湮沒] be buried; bury;
湮沒不彰 fall into the shade;
湮沒無聞 pass into oblivion; remain obscure; remain unknown;
[湮遠] very long in time;

yin
【喑】 (1) lose one's voice; (2) keep silent;
[喑聾] deaf and mute; deaf mute;
[喑啞] dumb; mute; unable to talk;

yin
【愔】 composed; peaceful; serene;
[愔愔] quiet and pleasant;

yin
【絪】 cloudy; foggy; misty;
[絪縕] dense; enshrouding; thick;

yin
【慇】 (1) mournful; sorrowful; (2) regardful; respectful;
[慇懃] eagerly attentive; solicitous;
[慇心] feel for;
[慇慇] melancholy; mournful; sad; sorrowful;
[慇憂] deep grief; distress; sorrow;

yin
【蔭】 shade;
[蔭蔽] conceal; cover;
蔭蔽集結 concentrate under cover;

yin
【瘖】 dumb; mute;
[瘖啞] dumb; mute;

yin
【禋】 (1) worship with sincerity and reverence; (2) offer sacrifices to the Heaven;

yin
【銦】 indium;

yin
【譠】 respectful; venerable;

yin
【闉】 (1) bent; curved; (2) gate of the city wall;

yin²

yin
【吟】 (1) chant; intone; recite; sing; (2) moan; sigh; (3) cry of certain animals;
[吟唱] chant; sing;
[吟哦] chant; recite poetry with a cadence;
[吟客] poet;
[吟詩] hum verse; recite poems;
吟詩詠懷 compose poems to express one's feelings; express one's feelings by verse;
吟詩作對 chant poetry and write couplets;
吟詩作畫 chant poetry and paint pictures; write and sing poems or to draw;
[吟誦] chant; intone; recite;
[吟壇] poetic circles;

[吟味] recite with appreciation; recite with relish;

[吟嘯] (1) sing in freedom; whistle in freedom; (2) lament; sigh;

吟嘯扼腕 wring one's hands and lament;

吟嘯自若 whistle or shout in freedom;

吟嘯自娛 amuse oneself with loud singing;

[吟行] travelling minstrel;

[吟詠] chant; intone a verse; recite with a cadence;

沉吟 meditate in silence; mutter to oneself; unable to make up one's mind;

歌吟 sing;

蛩吟 chirps of crickets;

呻吟 groan; moan;

笑吟吟 smiling happily;

行吟 wander while reciting poems;

猿吟 monkey's cry;

Y

yin

【垠】 (1) bank of a stream; (2) boundary; limit;

yin

【狺】 snarling of dogs;

[狺狺] yelp;

狺狺狂吠 bark frenziedly;

yin

【寅】 (1) third of the twelve Earthly Branches; (2) colleague; fellow officer; (3) horary sign;

[寅吃卯糧] anticipate one's income; draw one's pay in advance; eat next year's food;

[寅時] period of the day from 3 a.m. to 5 a.m.;

[寅誼] friendship between colleagues;

[寅憂夕惕] on tenderhooks from morning till evening;

[寅月] first month of the lunar calendar;

yin

【夤】 (1) hold sb in respectful awe; (2) deep;

[夤夜] at the dead of night; deep in the night; in the depth of the night;

夤夜登程 set off late at night; set out in the depth of the night; start off on a journey at the dead of night;

[夤緣] make use of one's connections to climb; try to advance one's career by currying favour with important people;

夤緣際會 ride the crest of good luck;

夤緣求寵 worm oneself into sb's favour;

yin

【淫】 (1) excessive; (2) dissolute; lascivious; lewd; libidinous; licentious; loose; wanton; (3) obscene; pornographic; (4) debauch; seduce; tempt;

[淫奔] elope; elopement;

[淫辭] obscene expressions; wanton language;

[淫蕩] lascivious; lewd; licentious; loose in morals; lustful; profligate;

淫蕩的 lascivious; licentious; lubricious; wanton;

~淫蕩的人 libertine;

[淫放] give free vein to one's passion;

[淫靡] extravagant;

[淫風] dissoluteness and debauchery that prevail; libidinous practices; wanton customs;

[淫婦] cocotte; immoral woman; scarlet woman; slag; slapper; whore;

[淫鬼] demon of lust;

[淫棍] immoral man; lewd man; womanizer;

[淫畫] obscene pictures; pornographic pictures;

[淫穢] bawdy; dirty; filthy; obscene; pornographic; salacious;

淫穢出版物 pornographic publication;

淫穢歌曲 lewd songs;

淫穢錄相帶 obscene videocassette;

淫穢書刊 pornography;

淫穢物品 pornographic goods;

淫穢語言 indecent words; obscene language;

淫穢照片 obscene photo;

[淫徑] depraved courses;

[淫樂] carnal pleasures; give free rein to sexual desire; wantonness;

[淫亂] debauchery; licentious; promiscuous;

集體淫亂 gang-bang;

[淫糜] extravagant;

[淫目] lascivious looks;

[淫念] carnal desires; lust;

[淫巧] clever in improper ways; lewdly suave;

[淫辱] violate a woman;

[淫色] lust;

[淫聲] lewd songs;

[淫視] come-hither look; lascivious looks; make sheep's eyes;
[淫書] obscene books;
[淫談] obscene talks;
[淫娃] depraved girl;
淫娃蕩子 fast women and lewd men;
[淫威] abuse of power; despotic power;
濫施淫威 indiscriminate abuse of power;
[淫猥] filth; indecent; obscene; pornographic;
[淫戲] (1) sexual intercourse; (2) pornographic shows;
[淫褻] act indecently towards a woman;
[淫心] immoral thoughts; sexual desire;
[淫行] licentious conduct;
[淫謔] obscene jesting;
[淫艷] seductive;
[淫業] prostitution;
[淫泆] debauchery; wantonness;
[淫雨] excessive rain; incessant rain;
淫雨成災 excessive rains become a calamity;
淫雨綿綿 it's raining excessively;
[淫慾] carnality; lust; sexual desire; wanton desires;
淫慾過度 abandon oneself to passion; excessive indulgence in the pursuit of pleasures;

荒淫 debauched; dissolute; licentious;
姦淫 (1) adultery; illicit sexual relations; (2) rape; seduce;
賣淫 accost; cruise; fast life; get the rent; have apartments to let; hustling; Mrs. Warren's profession; on the battle; on the game; on the stroll; prostitute oneself; prostitution; see company; sit for company; sit at show windows; social service; street of shame; street of sin; streetwalking; the oldest profession; the social evil; the trade; vice; walk the streets;
侵淫 gradually;
手淫 do-it-yourself; fluff one's duff; hand job; jack off; jerk off; masturbation; play with oneself; wank;
邪淫 lewdness; licentiousness; lustful;
宣淫 engage in lascivious activities in public;
意淫 mental adultery;
滯淫 (1) remain at a standstill; (2) stagnation;
縱淫 abandon oneself to carnal desire; debauched; dissolute;

yin
【鄞】 a county in Zhejiang;

yin
【銀】 (1) silver; (2) relating to currency; relating to money; wealth; (3) silver-coloured; silvery;
[銀白] colour of silver; silvery; silvery white;
[銀杯] silver cup;
[銀本位] silver standard;
銀本位貨幣 silver currency;
銀本位制 silver standard;
[銀幣] silver; silver coin;
[銀蟾] moon;
[銀鯧] silvery pomfret;
[銀道] galactic equator;
銀道坐標 galactic coordinates;
[銀盾] silver plague;
[銀耳] white fungus;
[銀髮] silver hair;
[銀粉] silvery powder;
[銀釭] lamp;
[銀根] money supply;
銀根緊 money is tight;
銀根鬆 money is easy;
[銀漢] Milky Way;
[銀行] bank; banking house;
銀行辦事員 bank clerk;
銀行本票 cashier's cheque;
銀行承兑匯票 banker's acceptances;
銀行存款結餘 bank balance;
銀行存折 bank book; passbook;
銀行分行 branch bank;
銀行服務 banking; banking service;
~電話銀行服務 telephone banking;
銀行管理 bank management;
銀行匯票 bank draft; banker's draft; discount market;
銀行家 banker;
~投資銀行家 investment banker;
銀行假日 bank holiday;
銀行結單 bank statement;
銀行經理 bank manager;
銀行利率 bank rate;
銀行票據 bank money;
銀行收付處 service station;
銀行手續費 bank charge;
銀行團 consortium;
銀行信貸 bank credit;
銀行休業 banking holiday;
銀行業 banking;

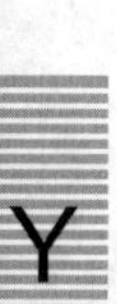

銀行業務 banking;
~電子銀行業務 electronic banking;
~工業銀行業務 industrial banking;
~境外銀行業務 offshore banking;
~連鎖銀行業務 chain banking;
~投資銀行業務 investment banking;
~網上銀行業務 internet banking; online banking;
~小額銀行業務 retail banking;
~信托銀行業務 trust banking;
~野貓銀行業務 wildcat banking;
~中央銀行業務 central banking;
銀行營業時間 banking hours;
銀行帳戶 bank account;
~一個銀行帳戶 a bank account;
銀行支行 subbranch bank;
保兑銀行 confirming bank;
保證銀行 confirming bank;
~支付保證銀行 certifying bank;
本地銀行 local bank;
邊緣銀行 fringe bank;
參考銀行 reference bank;
償付銀行 reimbursing bank;
承兑銀行 accepting bank;
~票據承兑銀行 acceptance bank;
儲備銀行 reserve bank;
儲蓄信貸銀行 commercial bank;
儲蓄銀行 deposit bank; savings bank;
~保證儲蓄銀行 guaranty savings bank;
~互助儲蓄銀行 mutual savings bank;
~郵局儲蓄銀行 post office savings bank;
代收銀行 associate banker of collection; collecting bank;
貸款銀行 loan bank;
抵押銀行 mortgage bank;
地方銀行 district bank; local bank;
發行貨幣銀行 bank of issue;
發證銀行 licensing bank;
付還銀行 reimbursing bank;
付款銀行 paying bank;
工業銀行 industrial bank;
購票銀行 negotiating bank;
管理銀行 manage a bank;
國家銀行 national bank; state bank;
國內銀行 domestic bank;
國外銀行 overseas bank;
國有化銀行 nationalized bank;
合股銀行 joint stock bank;
匯兑銀行 exchange bank;
結算銀行 settling bank;
借方銀行 debt bank;
進出口銀行 export-import bank;
開發銀行 bank for reconstruction and development; development bank;
~近海開發銀行 offshore bank;
開匯銀行 issuing bank;
開業銀行 operating bank;
開證銀行 issuing bank; opening bank;
~委托開證銀行 requesting bank;
跨國銀行 multinational bank;
勞工銀行 operatives bank;
聯號銀行 allied banks;
聯屬銀行 affiliated bank;
聯營銀行 affiliated bank; associated bank;
農業銀行 agricultural bank;
清算銀行 clearing bank;
商業銀行 commercial bank; merchant bank;
~國有商業銀行 state-owned commercial bank;
省銀行 provincial bank;
實業銀行 industrial bank;
市銀行 city bank;
收款銀行 due bank;
受票銀行 drawee bank;
受托銀行 consigned banker of collection; trustee bank;
私營銀行 private bank;
特許銀行 chartered bank;
貼現銀行 discount bank;
通知銀行 advising bank; notifying bank;
投資銀行 investment bank;
土地銀行 soil bank;
外國銀行 foreign bank;
外匯銀行 foreign exchange bank;
~指定外匯銀行 appointed foreign exchange bank;
往來銀行 corresponding bank;
無人銀行 self-service bank;
鄉村銀行 country bank;
信貸銀行 credit bank;
~長期信貸銀行 long-term credit bank;
信托儲蓄銀行 trustee savings bank;
信托銀行 trust bank;
野雞銀行 wildcat bank;
業務聯繫銀行 corresponding bank;
一家銀行 a bank;
議付銀行 negotiating bank; negotiation bank;
指定銀行 designated bank;
中央銀行 banker's bank; central bank;
專業銀行 specialized bank;
轉證銀行 transmitting bank;
準備銀行 reserve bank;

［銀號］ banking house;
［銀核］ galactic nucleus;
［銀河］ galaxy; Milky Way;
銀河系 Milky Way Galaxy;
~銀河系中心 galactic centre;
［銀紅］ pale rose colour;
［銀狐］ silver fox;
［銀黃］ silver and gold;
［銀潢］ Milky Way;
［銀婚］ silver anniversary; silver wedding;
銀婚紀念 silver wedding anniversary;
［銀貨兩訖］ the goods are delivered and the bill is cleared;
［銀極］ galactic pole;
北銀極 north galactic pole;
南銀極 south galactic pole;
［銀獎］ silver award;
［銀匠］ silversmith;
［銀庫］ treasury;
［銀礦］ silver; silver mine; silver ore;
脆銀礦 black silver;
淡紅銀礦 light ruby silver;
輝銀礦 vitreous silver;
［銀兩］ silver;
［銀幕］ projection screen; screen;
銀幕外 off-screen;
大銀幕 big screen;
將…的生平事蹟搬上銀幕 have one's life story told in film;
寬銀幕 wide-screen;
~寬銀幕變形鏡頭 wide-screen adjustable lens;
~寬銀幕電影 wide-screen film;
上銀幕 be screened in a film;
［銀鷗］ herring gull;
［銀牌］ silver medal;
［銀盤］ (1) silver dish; (2) moon; (3) galactic disc;
［銀票］ banknote;
［銀瓶］ silver pot; silver vase;
［銀器］ silverware;
擦銀器 rub up the silver;
［銀錢］ money; wealth;
［銀色］ silvery;
［銀兔］ moon;
［銀箱］ cash box;
［銀屑病］ psoriasis;
剝脱性銀屑病 exfoliative psoriasis;
盤狀銀屑病 discoid psoriasis;
脂溢性銀屑病 seborrhiasis;
［銀杏］ gingko;
［銀洋］ silver dollar;
［銀魚］ silverfish; whitebait;
油炸銀魚 deep-fried whitebait;
［銀暈］ galactic halo;
［銀朱］ vermilion;
［銀竹］ heavy rain;
［銀燭］ bright candle;
［銀子］ silver;
一錠銀子 a small ingot of silver;

白銀 silver;
金銀 gold and silver;
首銀 silver jewellery;
收銀 collect money;
水銀 mercury;
現銀 ready cash;
餉銀 soldier's pay;
乙酸銀 silver acetate;
足銀 sterling silver;

yin
【齗】 (1) gums of the teeth; (2) dispute;

yin
【霪】 rain heavily for a long time;
［霪雨］ excessive rain; incessant rain;
霪雨綿綿 heavy continuous rain; it keeps drizzling for days on end;

yin
【齦】 gum of the teeth;
［齦壁］ gingival wall;
［齦出血］ ulorrhagia;
［齦瘤］ epulis;
新生兒齦瘤 epulis of newborn;
［齦膿腫］ parulis;
［齦牙周炎］ gingivoperiodontitis;
［齦炎］ gingivitis;
剝脱性齦炎 desquamative gingivitis;
出血性齦炎 haemorrhagic gingivitis;
壞血病性齦炎 scorbutic gingivitis;
鏈球菌性齦炎 streptococcal gingivitis;
疱疹性齦炎 haerpetic gingivitis;
妊娠性齦炎 pregnancy gingivitis;
妊娠齦炎 gingivitis gravidarum;

yin³

yin
【尹】 (1) govern; rule; (2) a surname;

yin
【引】 (1) draw; stretch; (2) guide; lead; (3)

introduce; (4) retire; (5) leave; (6) attract; lure; (7) cause; make; (8) cite; quote; (9) unit of length;

[引爆] detonate; detonation;
引爆裝置 detonator;

[引避] (1) yield one's place; (2) avoid;
引避賢路 retire and give room to better men;

[引出] draw forth; extract; elicit; lead to;
引出教訓 draw a moral from;
引出結論 lead up to a conclusion;

[引導] guide; lead; pilot;
引導按鈕 call-on button;
引導詞 introducer;
引導冠詞 introductory article;
引導性寫作 guided writing;

[引得] index;

[引逗] entice; lure; seduce; tantalize; tease;

[引渡] extradite;

[引發] initiate; touch off; trigger;
引而不發 draw the bow but not to release the arrow — show people what to do without doing it for them; draw the bow without shooting;

[引弓] draw the bow;
引弓待發 have one's finger on the trigger; have the arrow in place and the bow drawn; hold oneself ready for action;

[引航] pilotage;
出口引航 outward pilotage;
進口引航 inward pilotage;
雷達引航 radar pilotage;
自由引航 free pilotage;

[引號] inverted comma; quotation mark; speech mark;
單引號 single quotation marks;
雙引號 double quotation marks;

[引火] ignite; kindle a fire; light;
引火燒身 criticize oneself so as to get criticism from others; draw fire against oneself — make self-criticism to encourage criticism from others; draw the fire upon oneself — bring trouble to oneself; get oneself into trouble;
引火物 firelighter; kindling;

[引疾] take illness as a reason for resignation;
引疾求退 implore resignation under pretext of illness;

[引見] introduce; present;

[引薦] recommend;

[引進] (1) recommend; (2) bring in; import; importation; introduce from elsewhere;

[引頸] crane one's neck to look forward;
引頸長鳴 stretch one's neck and utter a cry;
引頸而盼 crane one's neck to wait;
引頸而望 crane one's neck to watch for; stretch the neck to look;
引頸就戮 bare one's neck to the word; crane one's neck to be executed; extend one's neck for the final stroke; meet one's death without resistance; stick one's neck out to have one's head chopped off; stretch the neck to be beheaded;
引頸企足 raise one's head and stand on tiptop — eagerly looking forward to;
引頸自刎 commit suicide by slashing one's own neck; cut one's throat in suicide;

[引鏡自照] have a mirror brought and look at oneself; take a mirror to look at oneself;

[引咎] hold oneself responsible for a serious mistake; take the blame; take the blame on oneself;
引咎辭職 take the blame to oneself and resign;
引咎自責 bear the blame and reproach oneself; blame oneself; lay the blame on oneself; take the blame upon oneself;

[引決] commit suicide;
引決自裁 commit suicide;

[引理] lemma;
逼近引理 approximation lemma;
基本引理 fundamental lemma;

[引力] attracting force; attraction; gravitation; gravitational attraction;
引力場 gravitational field;
引力範圍 gravisphere;
引力微子 gravitino;
地球引力 earth attraction; gravitational attraction;
地心引力 terrestrial attraction;
電磁引力 electromagnetic attraction;
電引力 electric attraction;
分子間引力 intermolecular attraction;
分子引力 molecular attraction;
核引力 nuclear attraction;
化學引力 chemical attraction;

靜電引力 electrostatic attraction;
偶極引力 dipole attraction;
人造引力 artificial gravity;
統計引力 statistical attraction;
萬有引力 universal gravitation universe attraction;
~萬有引力定律 law of universal gravitation;
月球的引力 gravitational pull of the Moon;

[引領] crane one's neck to look into the distance; eagerly look forward to sth; stretch the neck in order to have a better look;
引領而望 crane one's neck for a look; crane one's neck to look forward; stretch out one's neck and look after;
望風引領 gaze at the wind and stretch out the neck – anxiously expecting sb;

[引路] approach; approach road; guide; lead the way;
在前面引路 lead on;

[引滿] (1) draw a bow to the full; (2) fill the cup to the brim;

[引起] arise from; arise out of; arouse; bring about; bring down the house; bring on; bring to; call forth; cause; create; engender; evoke; give rise to; induce; kick up; lead to; lead up to; produce; set off; stir up; touch off; trigger;
引起爆炸 result in an explosion; set off an explosion;
引起大笑 give provocation to laughter;
引起敵對行動 lead hostilities;
引起公憤 arouse popular indignation; arouse public indignation; arouse public wrath; incur public wrath; stir up public indignation; touch off public indignation;
引起公眾騷動 provoke public disorder;
引起公眾注意 arouse public attraction;
引起共鳴 arouse sympathy; ring the bell; strike a sympathetic chord;
引起哄動 cause a sensation; create a stir; make a stir;
引起哄堂大笑 set off a roar of laughter;
引起懷疑 arouse suspicion; give rise to suspicion;
引起警覺 arouse vigilance;
引起驚恐 cause fright;
引起連鎖反應 set off a chain reaction;
引起麻煩 cause trouble; give rise to trouble;
引起騷亂 raise a disturbance;
引起世界矚目 arouse worldwide attention;
引起誤解 lead to misunderstanding;
引起興趣 attract interest;
引起嚴重後果 lead to grave consequences;
引起議論 cause to talk;
引起戰爭 lead to a war; lead up to a war;
引起讚賞 attract appreciation;
引起者 causer;
引起爭論 start an argument; touch off a controversy;
引起注意 attract attention; attract sb's attention; attractive; bring to sb's attention; call attention; catch sb's eye; draw attention; excite attention;

[引擎] engine;
引擎發生故障 the engine has gone wrong;
引擎蓋 bonnet; hood;
發動引擎 start the engine;

[引燃] ignite;
引燃管 ignitron;
~氣冷引燃管 air cooled ignitron;
~水冷引燃管 water cooled ignitron;

[引人] induce sb;
引人發笑 induce sb to laugh; make sb laugh; provocative of mirth;
引人入彀 induce sb to fall in with one's plans; lead people into a snare;
引人入勝 absorbing; alluring; attractive; bewitching; enchanting; engrossing; fascinating; interesting and entertaining; open up a new view; ravishing; tempting;
~引人入勝的故事 compelling story; page turner;
引人上鈎 bring sb to the lure; dangle a tempting bait to hook sb; rope sb in;
引人注目 attract sb's attention; attract the gaze of people; become the centre of attention; catch the eye; conspicuous; eye-catching; notable; noticeable; remarkable; spectacular; strike the eye; striking;
引人注意 absorb sb's attention; arrest the mind; arrest the attention; attract notice; bring to sb's attention; bring to sb's notice; draw attention; strike the

mind; in the limelight;

[引入] call; draw into; introduce; lead into;
引入歧途 be led astray; lead sb astray; lead sb off the right path; lead sb onto a wrong way; lead sb up the garden path; mislead; misleading;
引入圈套 ensnare; lure sb into a trap;
引入正途 set sb on the right path;

[引申] expound; extend in meaning;
引申詞義 extend the meaning of a word;
引申新詞 derived neologism;
引申意義 derived meaning;
詞義引申 extension of meaning;

[引述] quote;
錯誤引述 misquote;
間接引述 indirect discourse; indirect speech; reported speech;

[引水] draw water;
引水工程 diversion works;
引水灌田 channel water into the fields; chanel water to irrigate the fields;
引水上山 draw water up a hill; lead the water up to the hills;
鑿山引水 punch holes into the mountains on both sides of the gully to lead the water out;

[引退] resign; retire from office;
避嫌引退 withdraw from a post to avoid suspicion;
抽身引退 leave one's work and resign; retire from active public life; withdraw from one's post;
負咎引退 bear the consequence and tender one's resignation;
及時引退 take a timely leave;
全部引退 retire altogether;

[引文] quotation; quoted passage;
核實引文 verify a quotation;

[引歉] step away from a delicate case in order to avoid others' suspicion;
引歉辭退 withdraw from one's post to avoid suspicion;

[引線] (1) sewing needle; (2) go-between; (3) fuse;
引線搭橋 act as a pimp; bring sb into contact with sb;
穿針引線 put thread into a ne3edle; thread a needle;
鏇中引線 pull a thread of silk from a mass of loss – bring order from chaos;

[引信] fuse;
複合式引信 combination fuse;
震動引信 concussion fuse;
自炸引信 autodestructive fuse;

[引言] foreword; introduction; preamble; preface;

[引藥] supplementary dose;

[引以為…] regard sth as...;
引以為傲 take pride in;
引以為恥 regard it as a disgrace; think it a shame;
引以為憾 deem it regrettable;
引以為豪 enough to make oneself proud;
引以為鑒 take warning from;
引以為戒 draw a lesson from; learn a lesson from; serve as a warning; take it as an object lesson; take warning from;
引以為例 cite as an example;
引以為榮 cite as an honour; count it an honour; consider it an honour; deem it an honour; esteem it an honour; regard it as an honour; take it as a great honour;
引以為慰 take comfort in sth;

[引用] (1) cite; quote; (2) appoint; recommend;
錯誤引用 misquote;

[引誘] accost; attract; cajole; entice; induce; lead on; lure; persuade; seduce; tempt;

[引語] citation; quotation;
引語形式 citation form;
分裂引語 broken quotation;
間接引語 indirect discourse; indirect quotation; indirect speech; reported speech;
直接引語 direct quotation;

[引證] adduce; cite as proof or evidence; quote;

[引致] bring about; bring forth;

[引子] introduction; introductory music;

[引座員] usher;
男引座員 usher;
女引座員 usherette;

辟引 appoint to office; summon to court;
標引 index;
稱引 quote;
導引 guide; lead;
逗引 tease;
發引 carry out the coffin upon burial;
勾引 entice; seduce; tempt;
汲引 promote;

薦引 propose sb for a post; recommend;
逆引 (of dictionary-compiling) inverse; reverse;
牽引 (1) drag; haul; involve; pulling; tow; (2) draw; traction;
市引 unit of length;
索引 index;
挽引 pull with force;
誤引 misquote;
吸引 appeal to; attract; attraction; charm; draw to; fascinate;
小引 foreword; introductory note;
誘引 lure; seduce;
援引 (1) cite; quote; (2) recommend or appoint one's friends or appoint one's friends or favourites;
摘引 quote;
招引 attract; induce;
徵引 cite; quote;
指引 guide; show;
轉引 quote from a secondary source;
擢引 pick and promote;

yin

【蚓】 earthworm;
[蚓蜥] amphisbaena;

yin

【飲】 (1) drink; (2) drinks; (3) swallow; (4) keep in the heart; nurse; (5) be hit;
[飲冰] cool oneself down by gulping ice water;
飲冰茹檗 drink ice water and eat the stump – the hard life of a widow;
[飲茶] drink tea;
飲茶進點 have tea and snacks;
飲茶聊天 talk over a cup of tea;
[飲醇自醉] win others' support with one's virtue;
[飲彈] be hit by a bullet;
飲彈畢命 die of a bullet shot; die of hit by bullet;
飲彈身亡 be killed by a bullet;
[飲風餐露] feed on wind and dew; live a primitive and hard life; take in wind and eat dew–a hard life of a monk or nun;
[飲恨] (1) harbour a grudge; nurse a grievance; swallow grievances; (2) be defeated in a contest;
飲恨而終 die with a deep regret; die with a grievance in one's heart;
飲恨吞聲 endure insults and injuries; harbour hatred in the heart; swallow one's resentment and choke back one's sobs;
飲恨終身 harbour hatred all one's life;
[飲餞] give a farewell party to a friend;
[飲盡] drain; drink off;
[飲酒] belt down; bend an elbow; crook one's little finger; crook the elbow; drink liquor; drink wine; drinking; go on the batter; go on the spree; hit the bottle; imbibe; juice; life one's elbow; lift one's little finger; moisten one's clay; on the batter; raise an elbow; throw one's little finger; tip one's elbow; turn up one's little finger; wet; wet one's clay; wet one's whistle; wood up;
飲酒不多 drink a little
飲酒賦詩 drink and write poems;
飲酒過度 drink far too much; drink heavily; drink to excess;
飲酒過量 drink beyond one's capacity; over the limit;
飲酒解愁 drink sorrow down; drown one's sorrows in wine;
飲酒賞花 drink wine and look at the flowers;
飲酒賞樂 feast and enjoy music;
飲酒適度 temperate in drinking;
飲酒誤事 liquor causes delay in one's business;
飲酒作樂 drink and amuse oneself; drink wine and make merry; enjoy oneself drinking; give oneself up to dissipation, spending days and nights in drinking and music; wine and music are the order of the day;
飲酒作詩 compose poems while drinking wine;
沉湎於飲酒 abandon oneself to drinking;
從不飲酒 never touch liquor;
滴酒不飲 taste no drop of wine;
孤酒難飲 hard to drink alone;
酒隨量飲 drink according to one's capacity;
未成年飲酒 underage drinking;
[飲料] beverage; bevvy; drink;
飲料工業 beverage industry;
飲料瓶 carafe;
冰飲料 cold beverage;
充氣果汁飲料 carbonated fruit beverage;

充氣人造果味飲料 carbonated nonalcoholic beverage;
充氣飲料 carbonated beverage; effervescent beverages;
~不充氣飲料 still beverage;
刺激性飲料 stimulating beverage;
非酒飲料 non-alcoholic beverage;
果汁飲料 fruit juice beverage;
喝飲料 have drinks;
混合飲料 mixed drinks;
酒精飲料 alcoholic beverage; alcoholic drinks;
咖啡飲料 coffee beverage;
可可飲料 cocoa drink;
烈性飲料 ardent drink;
冷飲料 cold drinks;
檸檬飲料 lemon beverage;
配製飲料 synthetic beverage;
啤酒類飲料 beer-like beverage;
清涼飲料 cool drinks; cooling beverages;
釀造飲料 brewed beverages;
熱飲料 hot drinks;
乳製飲料 milk beverage;
軟飲料 soft drink;
酸橙飲料 limeade;
酸乳飲料 sour milk beverage;
提神飲料 cordial drink; refreshing drink;
有氣飲料 fizzy drink;
煮泡飲料 brewing beverages;

[飲泣] weep in deep sorrow; weep in silence;
飲泣吞聲 dare not shed tears and cry out; gulp down tears; sob and endure pains silently; swallow one's tears; weep silent tears;
含悲飲泣 sob pitifully; weep pitiful tears;

[飲器] drinking vessel;

[飲刃而死] suicide; take one's own life by means of a sword;

[飲食] diet; drink and eat; eatables and drinkables; food and drink;
暴飲暴食 eat and drink excessively; eat and drink too much at one meal; guzzle;
飲食不進 can neither eat nor drink; refuse food;
飲食服務 serve food and drinks for money;
~承辦飲食服務 catering;
飲食療法 dietetic therapy; dietotherapy; food therapy;
飲食男女 food, drink, and sex — man's natural instincts;
飲食失調 have unbalanced food;
~飲食失調症 bulimia; eating disorder;
習慣性飲食失調症 bulimia nervosa;
飲食攤 food stall;
飲食衛生 dietetic hygiene;
飲食無度 excessive eating and drinking;
飲食無味 have no appetite for food or drink;
飲食學 dietetics;
~飲食學家 dietitian;
飲食業 catering trade; food catering; restaurant business;
飲食有度 abstemious; abstemious diet; temperate in eating and drinking;
不進飲食 refuse food and drinks;
不思飲食 have no desire to eat;
均衡飲食 balanced diet;
清淡飲食 bland diet;
少量飲食 a bit and a sup;
痛風飲食 gouty diet;

[飲水] (1) drinking water; (2) drink water;
飲水不忘挖井人 don't forget the well-diggers when you drink from this well; when you drink the water, think of those who dig the well;
飲水當思挖井人 let every man praise the bridge he goes over; let every man speak well of the bridge that carries him over;
飲水過多 hyperposia;
飲水過少 hypoposia;
飲水機 water cooler;
飲水器 drinking equipment;
~噴泉式飲水器 drinking fountain;
飲水思源 cast no dirt into the well that hath given you water; gratitude for the source of benefit; let every man praise the bridge he goes over; let every man speak well of the bridge that carries him over; never cast dirt into that fountain of which thou hast sometimes drink; remember past kindness; remember the source of one's blessings; when drinking water, think of its source — never to forget where one's happiness comes from; when one drinks water, one must not forget where it comes from — bear in mind where happiness comes from;
啜菽飲水 a dutiful son to one's parents even in poverty; have a simple diet;

poor but filial;

[飲血] (1) weep in deep sorrow; (2) drink blood;
茹毛飲血 eat raw meat and drink blood — live the life of a savage;
[飲用] drink;
飲用水 drinking water; potable water;
免費飲用 drinking is free;
適於飲用 suitable for drinking;
[飲譽] enjoy popularity; have good reputation;
飲譽南北 enjoy popularity north and south;
[飲醉] get drunk;

餐飲 food and drink;
暢飲 drink one's fill;
谷飲 live like a hermit;
酣飲 drink to the full;
豪飲 drink to the limit of one's capacity; winebibbing;
狂飲 binge; on the piss;
冷飲 cold drink;
熱飲 hot drink;
肆飲 indulge in drinking;
痰飲 phlegm-retention disease;
痛飲 drink one's full; drink to one's heart's content;
饗飲 enjoy offered food and drink;
宴飲 dine and wine; feast;
燕飲 feast;
讌飲 banquet; feast;
縱飲 drink uninhibitedly; indulge in drinking;

yin

【靷】 the leather belts that connect a cart with the horse;

yin

【隱】 (1) concealed; hidden from view; mysterious; (2) dormant; latent; (3) dark; obscure; (4) live like a hermit; retire; (5) grievous; painful; (6) destitute; poor; (7) a surname;
[隱報] deceptive reporting;
[隱比] metaphor;
[隱蔽] conceal oneself; cover up; hide; seek cover; shelter; take cover;
[隱藏] conceal; go into hiding; hide; remain under cover; stash away;
隱藏處 cache; hide; hideaway; hide-out; hiding place;
隱藏缺陷 conceal defects;
隱藏色 cryptic colouration;
隱藏物 cache;
隱藏罪犯 conceal an offender;
[隱惻] commiseration; sympathy;
[隱遁] live in seclusion; retire from public life;
[隱伏] lie concealed; lie low;
[隱含] implication;
隱含性翻譯 covert translation;
隱含性行事話語 implicit performative;
[隱患] hidden dangers; hidden troubles; latent dangers; lurking perils;
發現隱患 scent a hidden danger;
構成隱患 constitute a latent danger;
減少隱患 lessen the hidden dangers;
檢查隱患 try to find out the hidden troubles;
消除隱患 nip any trouble in the bud; remove a hidden peril;
造成隱患 cause a hidden trouble;
[隱晦] ambiguous; obscure; vague; veiled;
隱晦曲折 ambiguous and devious; obscure and veiled; veiled and roundabout;
隱晦言詞 obliquity;
[隱諱] avoid mentioning; cover up;
毫不隱諱 outspokenly; with great candour; without any reservation;
[隱几而躺] fall asleep leaning over the table; lean on a table and sleep;
[隱疾] unmentionable disease;
[隱晶結構] aphanatic texture;
[隱居] hermit; live in seclusion; retire from public life; withdraw from society and live in solitude;
隱居不出 make oneself scarce; seclude oneself from society; withdraw from society and live in solitude;
隱居處 hermitage;
隱居的 cloistered;
隱居多年 spend many years in retirement;
隱居田園 dwell in one's native place in seclusion;
隱居在家 live in seclusion of one's own home;
隱居者 recluse;
韜晦隱居 hide one's light and live in seclusion;
[隱瞞] conceal; cover up; hide; hide the truth; hold back;
隱瞞出身 conceal one's birth;
隱瞞錯誤 cover up one's mistake;

隱瞞觀點 keep one's opinion from being known;
隱瞞意圖 conceal one's intent;
隱瞞真相 conceal the truth; hide the truth; suppress the truth;
不敢隱瞞 dare not conceal the truth;
意圖隱瞞 cover-up;

[隱秘] (1) conceal; hide; (2) secret;
隱秘不説 not disclose a secret;

[隱名] conceal one's name; remain anonymous;

[隱沒] conceal oneself; disappear gradually; fade; hide;

[隱匿] conceal; cover; go into hiding; hide; lie low;
隱匿的 cloistered;
隱匿行蹤 cover up one's track; make oneself invisible;

[隱情] secret;
其中必有隱情 there must be sth behind it;

[隱忍] bear insults; bear patiently; bottom up one's resentment; forbear;
隱忍不言 forbear from speaking;

[隱士] anchorite; hermit; recluse;
隱士住處 hermitage;
女隱士 anchoress;

[隱私] (1) conceal; hide; (2) secrets;
隱私權 right to privacy;
揭人隱私 expose another person's secrets; expose sb's shameful secret;

[隱慝] hidden crime; some secret wickedness; unrevealed guilt;

[隱聽] eavesdrop;

[隱痛] hidden sorrow;

[隱退] go and live in seclusion; reclusion; resign; retire; retire from political life;

[隱微] (1) invisible; latent; (2) profound;

[隱現] (1) appear indistinctly; (2) in and out;
忽隱忽現 flicker; go in and out; in and out;
若隱若現 appear indistinctly; discernible at one moment and gone the next; half-hidden; indistinct; loom; partly hidden partly visible;
時現時隱 come and go;
時隱時現 flickering; now appearing, now disappearing;

[隱形] invisible;
隱形飛機 invisible aircraft;
隱形人 invisible man;
隱形設計 stealth design;
隱形失業 disguised unemployment; hidden unemployment;
隱形眼鏡 contact lens;
保持隱形 remain undetected;

[隱性] opaque; recessiveness;
隱性採訪 covert coverage;
隱性詞 opaque word;
隱性收入 disguised income;

[隱逸] recluse; retired person;

[隱隱] faint; indistinct; unclear;
隱隱出現 loom up;
隱隱約約 dimly; faintly; indistinct; loom up;
隱隱作痛 feel a dull pain;

[隱憂] hidden worries; lurking dangers;

[隱語] enigmatic language; insinuating language; parables; riddles;

[隱喻] metaphor;
隱喻對等 metaphorical equivalent;
隱喻歧義 metaphorical ambiguity;
隱喻性新詞語 metaphorical neologism;
隱喻意義 metaphorical meaning;
本來隱喻 original metaphor;
標準隱喻 standard metaphor; stock metaphor;
陳腐隱喻 cliché metaphor;
創造性隱喻 creative metaphor;
單一隱喻 simplex metaphor;
古怪隱喻 bizarre metaphor;
合成隱喻 complex metaphor;
混雜隱喻 mixed metaphor;
僵化隱喻 dead metaphor;
生動的隱喻 racy metaphor;

[隱約] faint; indistinct; obscure;
隱約出現 loom in sight;
隱約可見 can be seen dimly; faintly visible;
隱約其詞 beat about the bush; speak in equivocal terms; use ambiguous language;
隱約顯示 adumbrate;

[隱者] hermit; recluse;

[隱衷] feelings one wishes to keep to oneself; hidden and unspoken feelings;

豹隱 lead the life of a hermit; live in retirement;
惻隱 compassion; pity;
過癮 enjoy oneself to the full;
漸隱 fade out;
樵隱 recluse who leads a woodcutter's life;

容隱 hide; not reveal; try to cover up;
上癮 get into the habit (of doing sth);
市隱 hermit in a city;
索隱 expose sth hidden;
探隱 make research into secret facts;
逃隱 flee into seclusion;
退隱 retire from public life;
消隱 blanking;
煙癮 craving for tobacco;
掩隱 hide away;

yin
【檃】 (1) straighten bent wood; (2) adjust; correct;

yin
【癮】 (1) addiction; habitual craving; (2) strong interest;
[癮頭] addiction; strong interest;
癮頭大 have a strong craving;
癮頭足 have a strong craving;

yin⁴
yin
【印】 (1) chop; seal; stamp; (2) imprint; mark; (3) engrave; print; (4) conform; (5) a surname;
[印本] printed copy; printed book;
抽印本 offprint;
鉛印本 stereotype edition;
試印本 trial edition;
縮印本 edition reprinted in a reduced format;
套印本 chromatograph edition;
預印本 preprint;
[印次] impression; printing;
[印發] print and distribute;
[印盒] seal box;
[印花] (1) printing; (2) revenue stamp;
印花布 printed calico;
印花稅 stamp duty;
~ 免印花稅 no stamp duty;
印花紙 blotting paper; calico paper;
底色印花 blotch printing;
棉布印花 calico printing;
模版印花 block printing;
燒花印花 burn-out printing;
塗料印花 coat printing;
網版印花 screen printing;
[印片] film printing; printing;
印片機 film-printing machine;
[印譜] collection of imprints of seals by famous engravers;
[印簽] signature;
[印刷] print;
印刷廠 printing house;
印刷錯誤 misprint;
印刷電路 printed circuit;
~ 印刷電路板 printed circuit board;
印刷工 printer;
印刷機 printing press;
~ 凹版印刷機 intaglio press;
~ 二回轉印刷機 two-revolution press;
~ 輪轉印刷機 rotary press;
~ 平台印刷機 flat-bed press;
~ 平壓式印刷機 platen press;
~ 凸版印刷機 relief press;
印刷精美 be beautifully printed;
印刷磨損 press batter;
印刷片 printing film;
~ 彩色印刷片 colour printing film;
印刷品 printed matter;
印刷術 art of printing;
凹版印刷 intaglio printing;
凹凸印刷 die stamping; embossing;
報紙印刷 newspaper printing;
彩色印刷 multicolour printing;
磁性印刷 magnetic printing;
大印量印刷 long run;
單面印刷 be printed on one side;
第一次印刷 first impression;
非法印刷 make unlicensed printing;
活版印刷 movable type printing;
靜電印刷 xerography;
孔版印刷 stencil printing;
刻版印刷 block printing;
臘版印刷 mimeography;
美術印刷 fine arts printing;
平版印刷 planography;
軟管印刷 soft tube printing;
手搖印刷 hand press printing;
書籍印刷 book printing;
絲網印刷 screen printing; silk screen printing;
特種印刷 special printing;
貼花印刷 decal printing;
鐵皮印刷 steel plate printing;
凸版印刷 relief printing;
網點印刷 halftone;
小印量印刷 short run;
[印數] print run;
[印台] ink pad; stamp pad;
[印相] printing;

印相器 printer;

[印象] impression; mental image;
印象派 impressionism;
~印象派畫家 impressionist; impressionist painter;
~印象派作曲家 impressionist;
產生印象 create an impression;
持久的印象 lasting impression;
錯誤的印象 false impression; mistaken impression;
第一印象 first impression; immediate impression; initial impression;
~第一印象很重要 first impressions count;
負面印象 negative impression;
給人印象 give an impression;
獲得印象 get an impression;
良好的印象 favourable impression;
留下印象 make an impression;
模糊的印象 vague impression;
清晰的印象 clear impression; vivid impression;
深刻的印象 deep impression;
突出的印象 outstanding impression;
總的印象 general impression;
最初的印象 first impression;
得到印象 gain an impression;
加深印象 deepen the impression;
深刻的印象 deep impression; strong impression;
鮮明的印象 distinct impression;
造成印象 create an impression; produce an impression;
正面印象 positive impression;
總體印象 general impression; overall impression;

[印行] publish;

[印章] seal; signet; stamp;

[印證] confirm; corroborate; prove; verify;
有待印證 yet to be confirmed;

拜印 be appointed to a public office;
板印 print with engraved blocks;
編印 compile and print; publish;
補印 reprint;
彩印 colour printing;
重印 reprint;
抽印 offprint;
打印 chop; print; printing; stamp;
大印 seal; seal of power;
翻印 reprint; reproduce;
封印 seal;
付印 (1) go to press; send to the press; (2) turn over to the printing shop;
複印 copy; copying; duplicate; photocopy; xerox;
蓋印 affix one's seal;
鋼印 (1) steel seal; embossing seal; (2) embossed stamp;
古印 ancient seal;
官印 official seal;
火漆印 seal;
火印 a mark burned on bamboo or woodern articles; brand;
膠印 offset; offset printing;
腳印 footmark; footprint; track;
刊印 set up and print;
列印 mimeograph; print; put a seal on; stamp;
烙印 brand; sear; stigma;
摹印 a style of characters or letter on ancient seals; copy and print;
排印 set up type and print;
鉛印 letter press printing; stereotype;
簽印 put a seal on; sign;
鈐印 put a stamp on;
石印 lithographic printing; lithography;
手印 (1) impression of the hand; (2) fingerprint; thumb print;
刷印 print;
帥印 seal of the commander-in-chief;
水印 watermark;
縮印 reprinting books in a reduced format;
拓印 monotype; rubbing;
套印 chromatography;
洗印 develop and print; process;
血印 bloodstain;
壓印 press;
影印 photomechanical printing; photo-offset process;
用印 affix an official seal to a document;
油印 mimeograph;
摘印 take away the official seal;
掌印 keep the seal; be in power;
指印 fingerprint;
爪印 nail mark; print; trace;
足印 footmsark; footprint;

yin
【胤】 long successions of descendants; posterity;

yin
【陰】 shaded by trees;

yin
【飲】 make animals drink;

［飲馬］ water a horse;
飲馬投錢 pay even for a horse's drink of water – extreme honesty;
［飲人以和］ treat others with kindness;

yin

【廕】 harbour; protect; shelter;
［廕庇］ harbour; protect; shelter;

yin

【窨】 cellar; underground storeroom;
［窨井］ inspection well;
［窨室］ cellar; vault;

yin

【蔭】 (1) shade; shade of trees; (2) protect; shelter; (3) with the support of;
［蔭庇］ patronize; protect; protect the younger generation or descendants;
［蔭涼］ shady and cool;
路上沒有蔭涼 the road offers no shade;
［蔭翳］ in the shade of a luxuriant growth of trees;
［蔭鬱］ heavily shaded by trees;

庇蔭 (1) give shade; (2) shield;

yin

【憖】 (1) willing; (2) cautious;
［憖憖］ careful; overcautious;

ying¹
ying

【英】 (1) flower; leaf; petal; (2) distinguished; outstanding; prominent; surpassing; (3) hero; outstanding person; (4) fine; handsome; (5) Britain; (6) English; (7) a surname;
［英拔］ distinguished; outstanding; prominent; surpassing;
［英鎊］ pound; sterling; sterling pound;
英鎊符號 pound sign;
英鎊結存 sterling balance;
英鎊區 sterling area;
英鎊債券 sterling bounds;
英鎊支付協定 sterling agreement;
記賬英鎊 clearing sterling;
可轉讓英鎊 transferable sterling;
歐洲英鎊 Euro-pound;
［英才］ gifted person; person of outstanding ability; the able and the clever;
添聘英才 employ additional talents;
［英尺］ foot;
［英寸］ inch;
立方英寸 cubic inch;
平方英寸 square inch;
線性英寸 linear inch;
圓英寸 circular inch;
［英斷］ intelligent decision;
［英發］ intelligent and energetic;
［英豪］ hero; outstanding figure;
［英華］ (1) luxuriant beauty; (2) fame; glory; honour;
英華煥發 beauty and adornment are displayed externally;
含英咀華 containing the cream of the literary tradition; enjoy the beauty of words; relish the joys of literature; study and relish the beauties of literature;
［英魂］ spirits of the war dead;
［英傑］ (1) brilliant; eminently talented; (2) handsome and energetic; handsome and spirited; smart; (3) great man; hero;
［英俊］ handsome; smart;
英俊的 good-looking; handsome;
［英里］ land mile; mile;
噸英里 ton mile;
法定英里 statute mile;
航空英里 aeronautical mile;
空英里 air mile;
實測英里 measured mile;
線英里 wired mile;
信道英里 channel miles;
［英烈］ brave; heroic; valiant;
［英靈］ noble spirit; spirit of a martyr; spirit of the brave departed;
［英髦］ men of ability;
［英明］ brilliant; intelligent; perspicacious; sagacious; wise;
英明果斷 wise and resolute;
英明決策 brilliant policies of decisive and fundamental importance; wise policy;
英明遠見 sagacity and farsightedness; wisdom and foresight;
［英名］ fame; glory; illustrious name; renown;
英名掃地 have one's great fame tarnished or soiled;
英名遠揚 establish one's illustrious name;
［英年］ years of youthful vigour;
［英氣］ bravery; heroic spirit; noble spirit;
英氣勃勃 full of animated courage; with martial spirit;

Y

[英挺] distinguished; outstanding; prominent;
[英偉] great;
[英文] English;
英文報 English newspaper;
[英武] brave and strong; gallant; valiant; valorous;
[英物] outstanding figure;
[英雄] great man; hero;
英雄輩出 give birth to a multitude of heroes; heroes are coming forward in multitudes; productive of heroes;
英雄本色 true colour of a hero;
英雄崇拜 hero worship;
英雄兒女 young heroes and heroines;
英雄豪傑 heroes; outstanding figures;
英雄好漢 good brave fellows; heroes;
英雄美人 ideal combination of a hero and a beauty;
英雄末路 the end of a hero;
英雄難過美人關 a hero cannot get out of the influence of a woman; heroes are always attached to beauties;
英雄氣短 a hero has lost his might;
英雄氣短，兒女情長 the ambition of a hero may be of a short duration, the affection of lovers, however, last long;
英雄氣慨 gallant mettle; heroic spirit; heroism;
英雄人物 heroic figure;
英雄識英雄 like knows like;
英雄所見略同 great minds think alike; good wits jump; great wits jump together; heroes have similar views;
英雄無用武之地 a hero with no place to display his prowess — have no scope for the exercise of one's abilities; an able person with no scope for displaying his abilities;
英雄造時勢 heroes decide the course of history; heroes make issues;
英雄壯志 heroic aspiration;
超級英雄 superhero;
逞英雄 play the hero; pose as a hero;
傳奇英雄 swashbuckling hero;
當代英雄 heroes of the day;
反英雄 antihero;
古代英雄 heroes of antiquity;
慧眼識英雄 discerning eyes can tell greatness from mediocrity;
民族英雄 national hero;
女英雄 heroine;

人民英雄 the people's heroes;
時勢造英雄 great times make great people;
無名英雄 unnamed heroes; unsung heroes;
戰鬥英雄 combat hero;
[英英] (1) bright; brilliant; (2) resounding;
[英勇] brave; courageous; gallant; heroic; valiant; valorous;
英勇不屈 heroic and indomitable; heroically and unyieldingly; show unyielding heroism;
英勇奮斗 fight courageously; heroic struggle; struggle valiantly;
英勇奮戰 fight bravely; put up a fearless fight;
英勇就義 die a heroic death; die with one's head high; face execution bravely; give one's life heroically;
英勇善戰 bold and able to fight; brave and skilful in battle; heroic and combatworthy;
英勇無比 unrivalled in bravery;
英勇無敵 no one can withstand;
英勇無雙 unequalled heroism; unrivalled bravery;
英勇犧牲 die heroically; give up one's life heroically; heroic sacrifice;
英勇行為 heroics;
英勇戰斗 figh heroically; put up a heroic fight;
英勇卓絕 extremely brave;
表現得英勇 display gallantry;

[英語] English;
英語講得好 speak perfect English;
英語教學 English Language Teaching;
標準英語 King's English; Queen's English; Standard English;
~ 次標準英語 substandard English;
~ 非標準英語 non-standard English;
純正英語 pure English; Queen's English;
當代英語 contemporary English; current English;
地道英語 idiomatic English;
古代英語 old English;
古英語 old English;
黑人英語 Black English;
基本英語 basic English;
基礎英語 basic English;
講英語 speak English;
~ 講英語的人 Anglophone;

教英語 teach English;
近代英語 modern English;
精通英語 have a masterly command of English;
科技英語 English for Science and Technology
口頭英語 conversational English; spoken English;
口語英語 colloquial English;
美國英語 AmerEnglish; American English;
~ 標準美國英語 Standard American English;
日常英語 everyday English;
商業英語 business English;
書面英語 written English;
世界英語 World English;
通曉英語 acquire command of English;
一點英語 a bit of English;
譯成英語 translate into English;
英國英語 British English;
~ 標準英國英語 Standard British English;
正規英語 formal English;
正式英語 formal English;
~ 非正式英語 informal English;

[英姿] dashing appearance; heroic bearing; heroic posture; bright and valiant look;
英姿煥發 dashing and spirited; heroic bearing; of dignified bearing;
英姿颯爽 bright and brave; mighty in spirit and heroic bearing; valiant and heroic in bearing;

仇英 Anglophobia;
笏石英 sceptre-quartz;
精英 (1) cream; essence; quintessence; (2) elite; person of an outstanding ability;
蒲公英 dandelion;
群英 a large number of brilliant minds;
石英 quartz;
瑤英 the most precious kind of jade;
玉英 (1) jade of best quality; (2) cactus flowers;
紫石英 amethyst;
紫雲英 Chinese milk vetch;

ying
【瑛】 (1) glitter of jade; (2) a transparent piece of jade;

ying
【罃】 long-necked bottle;

ying
【嬰】 baby; bundle of joy; infant; suckling;

[嬰兒] babe; baby; bundle of joy;
嬰兒安全警報器 baby alarm;
嬰兒車 baby carriage; buggy; perambulator; pram;
~ 手推嬰兒車 baby carriage;
~ 推嬰兒車 push a pram;
~ 摺疊式輕便嬰兒車 buggy;
嬰兒牀 cot; crib;
嬰兒猝死 cot death;
嬰兒奶粉 baby milk;
嬰兒期 babyhood;
嬰兒推車 baby carriage;
嬰兒似的 babyish;
嬰兒裝 baby clothes;
懷抱中的嬰兒 infant in arms;
連體嬰兒 conjoined twins;
試管嬰兒 test-tube baby;
一個嬰兒 a baby;

[嬰孩] baby; bundle of joy; infant;
嬰孩時代 babyhood;

[嬰疾] catch an illness; fall sick;

女嬰 baby girl;
溺嬰 drown a newly-born baby;
棄嬰 foundling;

ying
【應】 need; ought to; should;
[應辦] that should be handled;
[應當] duty-bound; naturally; ought to; should;
[應得] deserved; due;
應得的 well-deserved;
~ 應得的勝利 well-deserved victory;
咎有應得 deserve blame; deserve reproof of; open to censure;
罪有應得 a proper punishment for one's bad behaviour; deserve one's punishment; get one's just deserts; serve sb right; the punishment is well deserved; the punishment fits the crime; well-deserved punishment; worthy of punishment;

[應份] part of one's job;
[應否] should or should not;
[應付] payable;
應付賬款 payable account;
窮於應付 at a loss to cope with the situation; hard put to cope with the situation;
挺身應付 desperate;

[應該] behoove; belong; bound to; deserve; do well; due; expected to; have no business to; incumbent on; it is time that; it is time to; merit; might; must; ought to; owe; right; shall; should; supposed to; up to; want; well;
應該是吧 I guess so; I suppose so;

[應力] strain; stress;
黏附應力 adhesive stress;
實際應力 actual stress;
外加應力 applied stress;
許用應力 admissible stress;
作用應力 applied stress;

[應收] receivable;
應收賬款 receivable account;

[應須] duty-bound; ought to; should;

[應有] deserved; due; proper;
應有的 well-earned;
~應有的休息 well-earned rest;
應有盡有 be provided with all one needs; have all that is necessary; have all the things one desires; have everything that one expects to find; have everything that one could wish for; nothing is wanting; there is everything that should be there; whatever needed is available;

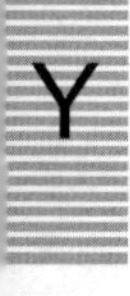

報應 come home to roost; judgment; retribution;
本應 should have been so anyway;
策應 act in concept with each other;
酬應 have social intercourse with; social intercourse;
答應 (1) answer; reply; respond; (2) accede to; agree; comply with; promise;
對應 correspondence;
反應 reaction; response;
感應 (1) interaction; reaction; response; (2) irritability; (3) induction;
供應 accommodate; supply;
呼應 act in cooperation with each other; echo; work in concert with;
理應 ought to; should;
內應 planted agent;
適應 accommodate oneself to; accustom oneself to; adapt to; adjust; become seasoned to; come to terms with; fit; make adjustment to; season oneself to; suit; tune in to;
順應 adjust to changes; comply with; conform to;
肆應 good at dealing with varied matters properly;
相應 (1) corresponding; relevant; (2) act in responses; work in concert with;
響應 answer; echo in support; respond;
效應 action; effect; influence;
一應 all; everything;
照應 (1) look after; take care of; (2) correlate;

ying
【膺】 (1) breast of a person; (2) bear; receive;

[膺懲] send a punitive expedition against; send armed forces to suppress;
[膺任] be appointed to an office;
[膺選] be elected;

服膺 (1) bear in mind; (2) feel deeply convinced;

ying
【罌】 jar with a small mouth;

[罌粟] opium poppy;
罌粟花 poppy flowers;

ying
【攖】 (1) irritate; offend; (2) disturb; stir up;

[攖病] be attacked by disease;
[攖其鋒] blunt the thrust;

ying
【櫻】 (1) cherry; (2) oriental cherry;

[櫻貝] sea shell;
[櫻草] primrose;
[櫻唇] small, beautiful mouth of a woman;
櫻唇皓齒 cherry lips and gleaming teeth;
檀口櫻唇 red lips of a pretty girl; small and reddish mouth of a woman;

[櫻花] oriental cherry; sakura;
[櫻桃] cherry;
櫻桃紅 cerise;
櫻桃酒 kirsch;
櫻桃木 cherry; cherrywood;
櫻桃樹 cherry tree;
櫻桃小口 small cherry-like mouth;
櫻桃園 cherry orchard;
茶蔗櫻桃 ground cherry;
糖衣櫻桃 glace cherry;
甜櫻桃 cluke cherry; sweet cherry; whiteheart cherry;
一串櫻桃 a bunch of cherries;
月桂櫻桃 cherry-laurel;

ying

【瓔】 necklace of precious stones;

［瓔珞］ necklace of jade and pearls;

ying

【鶯】 greenfinch; oriole; warbler;

［鶯歌］ songs of the oriole;

鶯歌燕鳴 the melodious call of the golden orioles and the twittering of the swallows;

鶯歌燕舞 a scene of prosperity; orioles sing and swallows dart — the joys of spring;

［鶯谷］ talented but remaining in obscurity;

［鶯花］ orioles and flowers of spring;

［鶯簧］ the melodious warble of the oriole;

［鶯遷］ be promoted; move into a new residence;

［鶯燕］ orioles and swallows;

鶯燕滿堂 the hall is full of orioles and swallows — a multitude of dancing and sing-song girls;

鶯妒燕嗔 snatch a master's favours from a rival;

鶯聲燕語 her voice is pleasant like those of nightingales and swallows; the birdlike sound of a woman's voice; the pleasant effect of a woman's speech;

鶯啼燕語 orioles sing and swallows chatter;

鶯鶯燕燕 a crowd of women chattering together pleasantly; orioles and swallows — a bevy of young girls;

鶯囀燕鳴 orioles and swallows are twittering;

鶯囀燕語 one's voice is as beautiful as the flute-like notes of the orioles or the early chirping of the swallows;

縫葉鶯 tailor-bird;
黃鶯 oriole;
鷦鶯 wren warbler;
柳鶯 willow warbler;
夜鶯 nightingale;

ying

【纓】 (1) chin strap for holding a hat; (2) tassel; (3) leaves of turnips;

［纓冠］ put on a hat hastily;

［纓絡］ ornamental fringes on a garment;

長纓 long rope, string, etc;
請纓 request a cord from the emperor (to bind the enemy); volunteer for military service;

ying

【鷹】 eagle; falcon; hawk;

［鷹翔高空，非雨即風］ when eagles soar high, there's either wind or rain;

［鷹架］ scaffold;

［鷹派］ hawks;

［鷹犬］ (1) falcons and hounds; (2) hired thug; lackey;

鷹犬爪牙 falcons and dogs, talons and teeth — lackeys;

［鷹視］ fierce look;

鷹視狼步 a wicked and fierce person; look at things like hawks and run like wolves;

［鷹揚］ outstanding; powerful;

［鷹鸇］ hawks and vultures;

鷹鼻鷂眼 hawk-nosed and vulture-eyed — avaricious look;

鷹瞵鶚視 look at sb fiercely; look at sth fiercely;

［鷹爪］ talons of a falcon;

［鷹嘴豆］ chickpea; garbanzo;

蒼鷹 goshawk;
老鷹 black-eared kite; eagle; hawk;
獵鷹 falcon;
貓頭鷹 owl;
雀鷹 sparrow hawk;
山鷹 eagle;
小鷹 eaglet;
鷂鷹 sparrow-hawk;
夜鷹 goatsucker; nightjar;
魚鷹 (1) cormorant; (2) fish hawk; osprey; sea eagle;
戰鷹 fighting eagle;

ying

【鸚】 parrot;

［鸚哥］ parrot;

［鸚鵡］ parrot;

鸚鵡嘎嘎 parrots squawk;

鸚鵡學舌 imitate another person's words like a parrot; repeat what others say; parrot;

鳳頭鸚鵡 cockatoo;
虎皮鸚鵡 hudgie;
葵花鸚鵡 cockatoo;
一隻鸚鵡 a parrot;

ying²
ying

【迎】 (1) go to meet; greet; welcome; (2) meet face to face; move towards;

[迎賓] receive guests;
迎賓館 guest house;
迎賓員 greeter;
倒屣迎賓 greet a visitor with the shoes on back to front; meet friends with one's sandals upturned; put on slippers hurriedly to extend welcome; put one's shoes the wrong way in receiving one's guests; rush out in haste to receive the guests; welcome sb with the greatest deference;
治席迎賓 give a banquet in honour of the guests;

[迎晨] at dawn; at daybreak;
[迎春] greet the New Year;
迎春花 winter jasmine;
[迎敵] engage the enemy forces; meet the enemy in battle;
[迎風] (1) against the wind; facing the wind; windward; (2) down the wind; with the wind;
迎風翱翔 ride on the wind;
迎風而行 go up the wind; have the wind in one's face;
迎風飛舞 dancing in the wind;
迎風飛翔 cleave the air; fly against the wind;
迎風航行 sail close to the wind; sail near the wind;
迎風前進 haul to the wind;
迎風流淚 suffer from watering eyes when one is in the wind;
迎風冒雪 brave the wind and snow; face the wind and go striding through the snow;
迎風面 windward side;
迎風飄舞 whirl about in the wind;
迎風飄揚 flutter in the breeze; wave in the wind;
迎風搖曳 bending before the wind;
迎風招展 flutter in the wind; fly in the wind;
迎風展翅 flap the wings into the wind;
[迎合] cater to; pander to; play up to;
迎合潮流 go with the current of the times;
迎合人意 fall in with the wishes of other persons; scratch a person where he itches;
迎合時尚 pander to the trend of the times;
[迎候] await the arrival of; go out to await; greet;
迎候客人 await the arrival of one's guest;
[迎虎於門] meet a tiger at the door; meet trouble half-way;
[迎擊] intercept; meet and attack an advancing enemy; meet head-on;
[迎見] receive visitors;
[迎接] greet; meet; receive; welcome;
迎接大駕 come to fetch your Majesty;
[迎面] face to face; head-on; in one's face; right against one's face in the opposite direction;
迎面碰上 meet head-on;
迎面撲來 spray into one's face;
迎面相擊 strike head-on;
[迎難而上] advance against difficulties; grasp the nettle; press ahead in face of difficulties;
[迎年] (1) pray for a rich harvest; (2) welcome the arrival of the New Year;
[迎親] go to the bride's home to escort her back to wedding;
迎親送友 usher in and out the guests and relatives;
[迎娶] (of a man) marry;
[迎刃而解] be easily put in order; be easily solved; be readily solved;
[迎人] meet sb with;
善氣迎人 give sb a welcoming look; give sb the glad eye; meet sb with a smiling face; receive sb with a smiling countenance; smile one's welcome;
[迎上來] come onward;
[迎送] greet and see off;
迎來送往 welcome and send off; welcome and speed the parting of guests;
迎來迎送 welcome visitors and see them off;
[迎頭] directly; head-on;
迎頭而上 meet it head-on;
迎頭趕上 catch up forthwith; come up from behind; try hard to catch up;
迎頭痛擊 a hard knock at the head; a head-on hammer-blow; deal a severe blow; deal head-on blows; give a good hiding; give sb a bad knock on the head; knock sb on the head; make a

in one's heart of hearts;
雪窗螢火 study by the light of reflected snow or glow-worms;

[螢石] fluorite;

ying

【營】 (1) camp; military barracks; (2) battalion; (3) administer; handle; manage;

[營地] camping ground; campsite;
冰川營地 glacier camp;
臨時營地 encampment;
旅途營地 approach camp;
適應性營地 acclimatization camp;

[營販] manage sale business;

[營房] barracks;

[營工] do paid labour;
營工度日 live only selling one's labour power;

[營火] campfire; firelight; watch fire;
營火會 campfire gathering;

[營建] construct;

[營救] rescue; succour;
營救行動 rescue attempt;

[營利] engage in making profit; make money; seek profits;
營名營利 strive for fame and wealth;

[營亂] perplexed;

[營盤] military camp; barracks;

[營求] seek;

[營生] earn a living; make a living;

[營私] feather one's nest; seek private gain;
營私舞弊 engage in fraud for selfish ends; engage in fraudulent and unlawful practices for one's own benefit; indulge in malpractices for private advantages; practise graft;
營私自肥 feather one's nest; plan private interest and enrich oneself;
結幫營私 band together to seek selfish interests; gang up to pursue selfish interests;
結黨營私 band together for selfish purposes; engage in factional activities in pursuit of personal gains; form a clique for private interests; form a clique to serve one's own selfish interests; form a party for selfish purposes; form clique to pursue one's own selfish interests; form self-seeking clique; gang up to pursue one's own interest; gang up together for selfish benefits; knock together a clique to pursue one's own interests; set up a coterie in pursuit of selfish interests;
植黨營私 form a clique for selfish purposes; set up a clique for one's own selfish interests;

[營銷] marketing;
營銷經理 marketing manager;
比較營銷 comparative marketing;
伏擊式營銷 ambush marketing;
直接營銷 direct marketing;

[營養] nourishment; nutriment; nutrition;
營養不良 athrepsia; athrepsy; dystrophy; innutrition; malnourished; malnutrition; poorly nourished; undernourishment
~營養不良性潰瘍 trophic ulcer;
~營養不良性水腫 alimentary oedema;
營養不良性萎縮 metatrophy;
營養不良性消瘦病 nutritional marasmus;
~創傷後營養不良 wound dystrophy;
~惡性營養不良 malignant malnutrition;
全身營養不良 pantatrophia;
痛性營養不良 algodystrophy;
~脂質營養不良 lipodystrophy;
營養不足 oligotrophy;
營養豐富 highly nutritious; very nourishing;
營養過度 hypernutrition;
~營養過度病 hyperalimentosis;
營養過緩 bradytrophia;
營養過少 oligotrophy;
營養過剩 excess nutrient;
營養價值 nutritional value; nutritive value;
營養良好 eutrophia; well nourished;
營養平衡 nutritive equilibrium;
營養缺乏病 deficiency disease; deprivation disease;
營養缺乏症 deficiency disease; deprivation disease;
營養神經性潰瘍 trophoneurotic ulcer;
營養神經性萎縮 trophoneurotic atrophy;
營養食品 nutriment;
營養素 nutrient;
~礦質營養素 mineral nutrient;
~生物營養素 biological nutrient;
營養體 nutrient body; trophozoite; vegetative organ;
營養物 nutrient; nutriment;
~水溶性營養物 water soluble nutrients;

~ 無菌營養物 sterile nutrient;
~ 藻類營養物 algal nutrient;
營養性病變 trophic lesion;
營養需求 nutritional requirement;
營養學 nutriology;
~ 營養學家 dietician;
營養異常 anomalotrophy;
營養飲食 nutraceutical diet;
營養障礙 dystrophia;
營養專家 nutrition expert;
動物式營養 holozoic nutrition;
腐生營養 saprophytic nutrition;
寄生營養 parasitic nutrition;
全動型營養 holozoic nutrition;
全植型營養 holophytic nutrition;
缺乏營養 lack nutritions;
礦質營養 mineral nutrition;
吸收營養 absorption of nourishment;
增加營養 have additional nutrients;
植物式營養 holophytic nutrition;
自養營養 autotrophic nutrition;

[營業] do business; engage in business;
營業本領 business acumen;
營業部主任 sales officer;
營業成本 operating cost;
營業額 business turnover; business volume; turnover;
~ 年營業額 annual business turnover;
營業時間 business hours; opening hours;
~ 開始營業時間 opening time;
~ 停止停止營業 closing time;
營業稅 business tax;
開始營業 begin doing business; open business;
停止營業 close a business; close up a shop; shut up a business; shut up a shop;
暫停營業 be temporarily close;
~ 餐廳新春期間暫停營業 the restaurant will be close for the Lunar New Year holidays;

[營營] hustle and bustle about;

[營運] service;
營運費用 running costs;
營運資金 working capital;

[營長] battalion commander;

[營帳] tent sheet;

[營治] construct;

安營 camp; encamp; pitch a camp;
拔營 break camp; strike camp;
兵營 barracks; military camp;
大本營 (1) base camp; home base; nerve centre; (2) general headquarters;
代營 manage a business on sb's behalf;
獨營 individual management; sole management;
隔離營 detention camp;
公營 publicly-operated; publicly-owned;
國營 state-operated; state-run;
合營 jointly-operated; jointly-owned;
集中營 concentration camp;
加強營 reinforced battalion;
經營 deal in; be engaged in trade; engage in trade; go into business; go into trade; manage; operate; run; trade in;
軍營 barracks; military camp;
老營 (1) bandits' den; (2) barracks;
聯營 joint operation;
露營 camp out; encamp;
民營 run by private citizens;
難民營 refugee camp;
青年營 youth camp;
設營 encamp; quarter;
舍營 billet;
私營 privately-operated; privately-owned;
宿營 take up quarters;
偷營 make a surprise attack on an enemy camp;
夏令營 summer camp;
行營 field headquarters;
野營 bivouac; camp;
運營 be in motion and do business;
紮營 encamp; pitch a tent of camp;
陣營 camp;
怔營 seized with terror; terrified;
專營 monopoly;
鑽營 curry favour with sb for personal gains;

ying

【瀅】 bright and clear; clear water; glossy;

ying

【瀛】 (1) ocean; sea; (2) within the lake;

[瀛海] ocean; sea;

[瀛寰] globe; the world over;

ying

【蠅】 fly;

[蠅糞點玉] a little of a fly's speck will smear the purity of jade — a slight flaw will blemish a good person;

[蠅量級] flyweight;

[蠅拍] flyflap; flyswatter;

[蠅頭] small as the head of a fly; tiny;
蠅頭微利 a profit as small as the head of a

fly – petty profits; petty gains;
蠅頭小楷 very small characters;
[蠅蠅] crawling; wriggling;
[蠅子] fly;

蒼蠅 fly;
萃萃蠅 tsetse fly;
狗蠅 dog louse fly;
家蠅 housefly;
綠豆蠅 a kind of fly;
麻蠅 a kind of fly;
馬蠅 horse botfly;
牛皮蠅 gadfly;
牛蠅 gadfly;
沙蠅 sand fly;

ying
【瀠】 tiny stream;

ying
【嬴】 (1) win; (2) gains; profits; surplus;
[嬴得] win;
[嬴家] winner;
大嬴家 big score;
[嬴利] gains; profits;
[嬴錢] win money by gambling;
[嬴餘] profit; surplus;

ying³

ying
【郢】 name of the capital of the state of Chu during the Spring and Autumn Period;
[郢書燕說] distorted interpretation; give strained interpretations and draw far-fetched analysis to misinterpret the original meaning;

ying
【景】 image; reflection; shadow;
[景從] follow like a shadow;
[景附] follow closely;

ying
【影】 (1) image; reflection; shadow; (2) sign; trace; vague impression; (3) photograph; picture; (4) film; movie;
[影調] tone;
[影集] photograph album;
[影迷] cinephile; film buff; film fan; movie fan;
一群影迷 a throng of film fans;
[影片] film; movie; picture;
影片發行 film distribution; film hiring; film letting out; film renting;
影片公司 film corporation;
影片加工 film adaptation;
影片結構 film composition;
彩色影片 colour film;
出演影片 appear in a film; appear in a movie;
大成本影片 big-budget movie;
導演影片 direct a movie;
低成本影片 low-budget movie;
發行影片 release a film;
放映影片 run a picture; screen a movie; show a movie;
非常刺激的影片 nail-biter;
黑白影片 black-and-white film;
黃色影片 yellow film;
剪輯影片 edit a film;
叫座的影片 box-office film;
經典影片 classic movie;
巨資拍攝的影片 blockbuster;
色情影片 blue movies;
審查影片 censor a film;
無聲影片 silent film;
攝製影片 turn out a movie;
性感影片 sexy movie;
藝術影片 art cinema;
有聲影片 sound film;
戰爭影片 bang bang;
主演影片 star in a movie;
[影評] film review;
影評人士 film critic;
[影射] allude to; hint at; innuendo; insinuate;
[影視] film and television;
影視點播 video on demand;
影視界 film and TV circles;
影視旅遊城 film-TV tourist zone;
影視文化 film and TV culture;
影視演員 film and TV actors and actresses;
影視音響產品 video and sound equipments;
影視之星 videostar;
[影壇] filmdom; movie circles;
[影線] hatching;
交叉影線 cross-hatching;
[影響] affect; exert an influence on; have influence on; have influence over; influence; interfere with; produce an impact on; under the influence of;
影響發展 interfere with the development;

Y

影響健康 affect one's health;
影響進程 influence the course;
影響力 coat-tails;
貶低…的影響 depreciate the influence of;
不良的影響 abjective influence;
產生影響 exert an influence; produce an influence;
持久的影響 lasting influence;
大氣影響 atmospheric influence;
發揮影響 wield influence;
壞的影響 bad influence;
極大的影響 great influence;
積極的影響 positive influence;
減輕影響 weaken the effect;
間接的影響 indirect influence;
間接地影響 affect indirectly;
擴大影響 widen one's influence;
強大的影響 powerful influence; strong influence;
人為影響 anthropogenic influence;
深遠的影響 deep influence; profound influence;
生物影響 biotic influence;
施加影響 exercise influence; wield influence;
受到影響 yield to the influence of;
淡化影響 cool off the effect;
消極的影響 negative influence;
相當大的影響 considerable influence;
相互影響 cross-fertilization; cross-fertilize;
削弱影響 reduce the influence; weaken the influence;
壓縮性影響 compressibility influence;
嚴重影響 great influence;
~受到嚴重影響 take a hit;
有影響 have influence on;
直接的影響 direct influence;
重要的影響 important influence; major influence; significant influence;

[影像] image;
黃色影像 yellow image;
青色影像 cyan image;

[影星] film star; movie star;

[影印] photocopy;
影印本 copy; photocopy;
~直接影印本 photostat copy;
影印文件 photocopy a document;

[影影綽綽] dimly; indistinct; shadowy; vaguely;

[影院] cinema; movie theatre;
藝術影院 art house;

[影展] (1) photo exhibition; (2) movie festival;

[影子] (1) reflection; shadow; (2) sign; trace; vague impression;
影子價格 shadow price;
影子內閣 shadow cabinet;
長長的影子 long shadow;
身正不怕影子斜 a clean conscience laughs at false accusations; a righteous person fears no criticisms;
投下影子 cast a shadow; throw a shadow;

[影蹤] trace;
影蹤全無 not a trace remained;
杳無影蹤 go without leaving a trace; vanish;

暗影 (1) image; shadow; (2) umbra;
半影 penumbra;
背影 sight of sb's back;
播影 telecast;
搏影 fight the shadow;
彩影 colour movie;
倒影 inverted image or reflection in water;
電影 film; motion picture;
定影 fix;
合影 group photo; have a group photo taken;
黑影 shadow;
後影 shape of a person or thing as seen from the back;
幻影 unreal image;
剪影 make a paper-cut silhouette; outline; sketch;
留影 take a photo or have a picture taken as a souvenir;
泡影 bubble; visionary hope, plan, etc;
人影兒 (1) figure; trace of a person's presence; (2) shadow of a human figure;
射影 point of intersection;
攝影 (1) take a photograph; (2) shoot a film;
身影 figure; form; silhouette;
書影 printed matter that indicates the type form or partial content of books and periodicals;
縮影 epitome; miniature;
投影 project; projection;
息影 retire from public life;
顯影 develop;
小影 small-sized photograph;
笑影 smiling expression;
心影 mental image;
陰影 shadow;
造影 radiography;
正投影 orthogonal projection;

蹤影 trace; sign;

ying

【潁】 a river and a place in Anhui;

ying

【穎】 (1) distinguished; outstanding; remarkable; talented; (2) sharp point of an awl; (3) point of a writing brush; (4) awn of a grain; top part of a grain;

[穎慧] bright; clever; intelligent;

[穎脱] distinguish oneself in performance;

[穎悟] bright; clever; very bright;

[穎秀] outstandingly talented;

[穎異] extraordinarily intelligent; new and original;

[穎哲] clever and wise;

聰穎 bright; clever; intelligent;

新穎 new and original; novel;

ying

【癭】 (1) reddish swelling on the neck; (2) gnarl;

[癭病] goiter;

[癭蟲] gall insect;

蟲癭 gall;

ying4

ying

【迎】 meet a visitor in person;

ying

【映】 (1) mirror; reflect; reflection shine; (2) project;

[映襯] relieve against; set off;

[映奪] catch the eyes; dazzle the eyes;

[映日] bright sunlight;

[映入] map into;

映入眼簾 come into sight; come into view; greet the eye; leap to the eyes; meet the eye; strike the eye;

[映山紅] azaleas;

[映射] (1) cast light upon; shine upon; (2) mapping;

伴隨映射 adjoint mapping;

保積映射 area-preserving mapping;

仿射映射 affine mapping;

解析映射 analytic mapping;

[映像] image; map;

[映眼] dazzling; glaring;

[映月] study by moonlight;

[映照] cast light on; shine upon;

襯映 serve as a foil; set off;

反映 (1) make known; report; (2) mirror; reflect;

放映 on show; show a film;

輝映 emit and reflect light;

上映 run; show a film;

試映 give a preview;

掩映 set off one another;

ying

【硬】 (1) firm; hard; solid; stiff; (2) strong; (3) obstinate; (4) by force; forcibly; (5) good; (6) able;

[硬斑] induration;

硬斑病 morphea;

[硬搬] copy everything mechanically; transplant mechanically;

[硬邦邦] very hard; very stiff;

[硬幣] coins; hard currency; hard money;

變造硬幣 altered coin;

低值硬幣 minor coin;

發行硬幣 issue coins;

金屬硬幣 metallic coin;

拋硬幣 flip a coin; toss a coin;

收集硬幣 collect coins;

受損硬幣 damaged coin;

損傷硬幣 mutilated coin;

偽造硬幣 counterfeit coins;

[硬度] hardness; solidity;

鈣硬度 calcium hardness;

磨損硬度 abrasive hardness;

球壓硬度 ball-indentation hardness;

視硬度 apparent hardness;

[硬漢] dauntless man; man of fortitude; man of iron;

[硬化] harden; hardening; sclerosis; solidify; stiffen;

硬化病 sclerosis;

~ 系統性硬化病 systemic sclerosis;

表面硬化 case hardening;

分散硬化 cluster hardening;

瀝青硬化 asphalt hardening;

內臟硬化 splanchnosclerosis;

脾硬化 splenokeratosis;

滲碳硬化 carbon case hardening;

腎小球硬化 glomerulosclerosis;

腎血管硬化 nephroangiosclerosis;

腎硬化 nephrosclerosis;
時效硬化 age hardening;
系統性硬化 systemic sclerosis;
小動脈硬化 arteriolar sclerosis;
心內膜硬化 endocardial sclerosis;
血管硬化 angiosclerosis; sclerosis vascularis;
遇冷硬化 harden by being cooled;
自身硬化 harden by itself;

[硬話] big talk; defiant talk;

[硬件] hardware;
硬件安全裝置 hardware security device;
硬件參考平台 hardware reference;
硬件程序 hardware programme;
硬件語言 hardware language;
硬件資源 hardware resource;
浮點硬件 floating point hardware;
計算機硬件 computer hardware;
雙倍精度硬件 double-precision hardware;
相容硬件 compatible hardware;

[硬結] calluse;
硬結的 calloused;

[硬來] do sth forcibly;

[硬朗] hale and hearty; sturdy and strong;
身體仍然硬朗 one's body is still going strong;

[硬木] hardwood;

[硬盤] hard-disk;

[硬碰硬] (1) confront the tough with toughness; diamond cut diamond; (2) extremely inflexible;

[硬皮] callus;
硬皮病 scleroderma;
~局限性硬皮病 circumscribed scleroderma;
~彌漫性硬皮病 diffuse scleroderma;
~全身性硬皮病 generalized scleroderma;
硬皮書 hardback; hardcover;
硬皮症 scleroderma;
~新生兒硬皮症 sclerema neonatorum;
~脂肪性硬皮症 sclerema adiposum;

[硬拼] fight desperately; fight recklessly;

[硬是] (1) actually; really; (2) just; simply;

[硬說] assert; insist on saying; stand on one's views;

[硬糖] boiled sweet;

[硬體] hardware;

[硬挺] (1) endure with all one's will; endure with one's best; hold out with all one's might; put up with all one's might; stick out; (2) rigid; stiff;

[硬土] hard soil;

[硬銷] hard sell;

[硬性] hard; hard-and-fast; inflexible; rigid; stiff;
硬性規定 hard-and-fast rules; rigid and inflexible ruling; rigid regulations;

[硬要] demand insistently;

[硬譯] stilted translation;

[硬仗] all-out battle; fierce battle; formidable task; tough battle;
打硬仗 fight a hard battle;

[硬掙] serviceable;

焙硬 bake;
繃硬 hard as a stone; stiff as a board;
根兒硬 be backed up; have connections; have strong support;
過得硬 able to stand all tests; become truly proficient in sth; have a good mastery of; have superb skill;
過硬 able to pass the stiffest test; have a perfect mastery of sth; really up to the mark;
堅硬 hard; solid;
僵硬 (1) inflexible; rigid; (2) stiff;
頸僵硬 stiff neck;
臉硬 flinty; ruthless;
強硬 (1) flinty; hard; stiff; strong; tough; (2) defiant; truculent; unyielding;
軟硬 gentle or harsh; soft or hard;
生硬 arbitrary; awkward; inflexible; rigid; stiff;
瘦硬 fine and forceful;
死硬 (1) die-hard; very obstinate; (2) rigid; stiff;

ying

【媵】 (1) maid who accompanies a bride to her new home; (2) concubine; (3) present as a gift;

ying

【應】 (1) answer; echo; react to; respond; (2) comply with; grant; (3) cope with; deal with; (4) a surname;

[應變] adapt oneself to changes; meet an emergency; strain
應變措施 emergency measure;
應變能力 adaptability;
陳脆應變 age embrittlement strain;
沉着應變 meet the danger calmly;
絕熱應變 adiabatic strain;
均勻應變 affine strain;
臨機應變 act according to what the

circumstances dictate;
隨機應變 do as the circumstances require; rise to the occasion;

[應承] agree to do sth; consent; promise;
應承履約 promise to carry out an agreement;
點頭應承 respond by a nod;

[應酬] (1) engage in social activities; have social intercourse; treat with courtesy; (2) treat with courtesy;
應酬功能 phatic function;
應酬信件 courtesy letters;
應酬性談話 phatic communion;
不善應酬 unskilled in social dealings;
忙於應酬 busy with social activities;
善於應酬 skilful in social dealings;

[應答] answer; answer back; reply; respond;
應答燈 answer lamp;
應答如流 answer as quickly as the flowing of water; answer the question without any hitch; answer with a readiness equal to the flowing of water; give answers quickly and fluently; give fluent replies; reply readily and fluently; one's replies flow like a stream; quick at repartee;
應答設備 answering machine;
應答時間 answering time;
應答信號 answer back;
機智的應答 repartee;
齊聲應答 reply in unison;

[應典] fulfil a promise;

[應對] answer; reply;
應對衝突 deal with conflicts;
應對如流 answer questions fluently; answer the questions without any hitch; give fluent replies;

[應付] (1) cope with; deal with; handle; (2) do sth perfunctorily;
應付裕如 all there; cope with successfully; equal to the occasion; handle with ease; meet with abundant means; rise to the occasion;
應付自如 able to handle people and situations successfully; handle a situation with ease;
難於應付 difficult to deal with;
容易應付 easy to deal with;

[應和] echo; work in concert with;

[應急] meet an contingency; meet an emergency; meet an urgent need;
應急燈 emergency light;
應急對策 expedient;
應急法寶 an ace in the hole;
應急措施 emergency measure; exigencies;
應急計劃 contingency;
應急妙計 keep an ace up one's sleeve;
應急錢 mad money;

[應計] accrued;
應計股利 accrued dividend;
應計期票息 accrued interest on notes payable;
應計債券息 accrued interest on bonds;

[應接] receive;
應接不暇 too busy to attend to; too numerous to take in; there are more than one can attend to;

[應景] do sth for the occasion;
應景詩 occasional verses;

[應考] sit for an examination; take an examination;

[應門] (1) gatekeeper; (2) answer the door;
應門而出 answer the door;
留神應門 be alert in answering the door;
無人應門 there is no answer;

[應募] (1) subscribe; (2) answer a draft call;

[應諾] agree to do sth; promise; undertake;

[應聘] accept an offer of employment;

[應聲] at the sound of;
應聲蟲 echo; mouthpiece; parrot; stooge; yesman;
應聲而倒 fall as soon as the bang is heard; fall at the report of;

[應時] (1) in season; seasonable; (2) at once; immediately;
應時輟景 meet the requirements of the times; seasonable and timely;
應時當令 fashionable; in season; seasonable and timely;
應時對景 fashionable and adapt to the environment;
應時而動 act according to circumstances;
應時而至 come at a most opportune moment; come in time;
應時水果 fruits of the season;
不再應時 out of season;
正應時 in season;

[應市] be offered for sale; go on the market; put on the market;

[應世] know how to deal with social affairs and people;

[應試] sit for an examination; take an examination;
應試未中 sit for an examination but fail to pass;
到場應試 present oneself for an examination;
[應手] smoothly; without a hitch;
[應許] assent; promise;
滿應滿許 promise anything and everything;
[應驗] be confirmed; be fulfilled; come true;
[應邀] at sb's invitation; on invitation;
應邀出席 invite to attend; present by invitation;
應邀而來 come by request;
應邀訪問 visit upon invitation;
應邀外出 be asked out;
[應用] (1) application; apply; make use of; use; utilize; (2) for practical application;
應用程序 application programme;
~應用程序包 application programme package;
應用對比語言學 applied contrastive linguistics;
應用翻譯理論 applied translation theory;
應用構造程序 application builder;
應用技術 application technology;
~應用技術衛星 application technology satyllite;
應用開發人員 application developer;
應用開發系統 application development system;
應用科學 applied science;
應用控制語言 application control language;
應用軟件 application software;
~應用軟件工程 application software engineering;
應用生成器 application generator;
應用式語言 applicative language;
應用文 practical writing;
應用型人才 trained talent;
應用語言學 applied linguistics;
得到應用 come into use;
計算機應用 computer application;
經濟應用 economic application;
空虛應用 vacuous application;
[應允] allow; assent; consent; permit;
應允和解 give assent to a reconciliation;
[應運] in response to the needs of the times;
應運而生 arise at the historic moment; be born in response to the needs of the times; come with the tide of fashion; emerge as the times demand; rise in response to the proper time and conditions;
[應戰] (1) meet an enemy attack; (2) accept a challenge;
沈着應戰 accept a challenge composedly; meet the attack calmly;
出征應戰 go out to meet the enemy;
倉促應戰 rashly accept battle;
準備應戰 prepare for an attack;
[應召] respond to a call; respond to summons;
應召女郎 call girl;
應召入伍 be drafted for military service;
[應診] see patients; take in and treat patients;
[應徵] (1) be recruited; enlist; (2) answer to calls; respond to a call for contributions;
應徵入伍 be called to the colours; be drafted into the army; be recruited into the army;
免於應徵 be exempted from conscription;

暗適應 dark adaptation;
報應 retribution;
策應 support by coordinated action; act in concert with each other;
承應 promise;
酬應 have social intercourse with;
磁感應 magnetic induction;
磁效應 magnetic effect;
答應 (1) answer; reply; (2) consent; promise;
對應 correspond;
反應 react; reaction; respond; response;
副反應 by-reaction;
感應 (1) interaction; response; (2) induction;
供應 supply;
核反應 nuclear reaction;
互感應 mutual-induction;
互應 mutual-induction;
接應 (1) come to one's aid; reinforce; (2) supply;
救應 aid and support; reinforce;
內應 planted agent;
順應 adjust to changing circumstances; conform to;
相應 act in responses; corresponding; relevant; work in correct;
響應 answer; respond;
效應 effect;

照應 coordinate; correlate; look after; take care for;
自感應 self-induction;
支應 (1) attend to; wait on; (2) cope with; deal with;

yong¹

yong
【邕】 (1) harmonious; peaceful; (2) (now rare) cultivate plants; (3) short for Yongning 邕寧 , a county in Guangxi;
[邕邕] harmonious; peaceful;

yong
【庸】 (1) common; commonplace; mediocre; (2) inferior; second-rate; (3) need;
[庸闇] ignorant; stupidity;
[庸才] mediocre person; mediocrity;
[庸夫] common people;
庸夫凡卒 common labourers; ordinary people;
庸夫俗子 mediocre people and laymen; philistines;
[庸碌] common; mediocre; mediocre and unambitious;
庸碌無能 inferior and incapable; mediocre and incompetent;
庸庸碌碌 common and unremarkable; commonplace; mediocre and unambitious;
[庸民] common people; masses;
[庸人] deadhead; dead loss; mediocre person;
庸人多福 simple people are the happiest;
庸人自擾 excessive anxiety; fuss about nothing only to trouble oneself; much ado about nothing; unnecessary worry; worry about imaginary troubles; worry about troubles of one's own imagination;
[庸俗] low; philistine; vulgar;
庸俗化 vulgarization;
庸俗無聊 meaningless; vulgar and silly;
庸俗下流 vulgar and mean;
[庸行] regular course of action;
[庸虛] mediocre and incapable;
[庸言] cliche; commonplace; platitude; trite remark;
庸言庸行 commonplace words and deeds; ordinary and common words and acts;
[庸醫] charlatan; quack; quack doctor;
庸醫殺人 a quack kills people;
[庸中佼佼] giant among dwarfs;

凡庸 common-place; mediocre;
附庸 (1) appendage; (2) dependency; vassal state;
昏庸 fatuous; muddle-headed;
平庸 commonplace; indifferent; mediocre ordinary;
妄庸 very common and somewhat conceited;
無庸 need not;
毋庸 need not;
中庸 (1) mediocre; (2) golden mean;

yong
【傭】 a pronunciation of 傭;
雇傭 employ; hire;

yong
【雍】 (1) harmony; (2) block up; obstruct; (3) a surname;
[雍和] harmony;
[雍睦] friendly; harmonious;
[雍穆] harmonious;
雍穆不爭 free from discord and disagreement; harmonious without dispute;
[雍容] natural, graceful and poised;
雍容大雅 display poise and refinement;
雍容爾雅 display poise and refinement; have an easy manner; natural, graceful and poised;
雍容華貴 dignified and graceful; elegant and poised;
雍容其德 courteousness is one's virtue;
雍容雅步 peaceful and mild steps;
雍容自得 in the peace of mind; poised;
風度雍容 elegant and poised; have a dignified bearing;
進止雍容 dignified in carriage;
[雍雍] harmonious; peaceful;
[雍閼] block; obstruct;

yong
【慵】 idle; indolent; lazy;
[慵惰] idle; inactive; indolent; lazy;
[慵困] tired and sleepy;
[慵懶] languor;

yong
【鄘】 an ancient state in present-day Henan;

yong
【墉】 fortified wall; wall;

yong
【擁】 a pronunciation of 擁;

yong
【臃】 a pronunciation of 臃;
［臃腫］ (1) too fat to move; (2) overstaffed;
臃腫的 corpulent;
穿得臃腫 be cumbersomely dressed;
機構臃腫 be overstaffed;
一身臃腫 be heavily padded;

yong
【雝】 harmonious; peaceful;

yong
【廱】 (1) harmonious; (2) imperial university or academy;
［廱廱］ harmonious;

yong
【灉】 (1) flowing back of flooding waters; (2) a river in Shandong;

yong
【饔】 (1) eat cooked food; (2) breakfast; (3) slaughter animals;
［饔飧］ breakfast and supper;
饔飧不繼 discontinuation of supper after breakfast;

yong
【癰】 carbuncle;
［癰瘍］ large carbuncle;
［癰腫］ carbuncle;

yong²
yong
【庸】 a pronunciation of 庸；

yong
【喁】 (1) harmony of sounds; (2) state of a fish putting its mouth above the water surface;
［喁喁］ (1) everyone looking up to sb; (2) in whispers;
喁喁待哺 waiting with open mouth to be fed;
喁喁私語 bill and coo; talk in whispers;

yong
【傭】 (1) hire; hire a servant; (2) domestic helper; servant;
［傭兵］ mercenaries;
［傭工］ hired labourer; servant;
［傭人］ servant;
女傭人 maidservant;
［傭作］ be hired to do sth;
女傭 handmaiden;

yong
【慵】 a pronunciation of 慵；

yong
【墉】 a pronunciation of 墉；

yong
【鏞】

yong
【顒】 (1) severe; (2) great; large;
［顒望］ eager for; hoping anxiously;
［顒顒］ (1) admiring; (2) turbulent; (3) dignity; solemn;

yong³
yong
【永】 always; eternal; everlasting; forever; long in time; permanent;
［永安］ perpetual peace;
［永別］ be parted by death; die; part for good; part forever; part never to meet again;
［永不］ never; never ever; will never;
永不變色 will never change colour;
永不變心 remain loyal till one's dying day; never cease to be faithful;
永不稱霸 never seek hegemony;
永不掉隊 never drop behind;
永不翻身 subjugated forever;
永不分離 never be separated;
永不後悔 never look back;
永不回頭 never take the road back;
永不褪色 will never fade;
永不忘懷 cherish in one's memories as long as one lives;
永不敘用 never be employed again;
永不要說永不 never say never;
［永存］ eternal; lasting forever; live for ever and ever; remain forever;
永存不泯 everlasting; immortal;
浩氣永存 one's noble spirit is imperishable;
［永古］ time immemorial;
［永固］ remain secure forever;
［永恒］ eternal; everlasting; perpetual;
永恒不滅 eternal and indestructible;
永恒運動 perpetual motion;

[永久] constant; durable; endless; enduring; everlasting; for good; forever; lasting; long-lasting; permanent; perpetual; unchanging; unending;
永久地 for altogether; permanently;
永久地址 permanent address;
永久和平 everlasting peace; permanent peace;
永久相傳 handed down forever;
永久賬戶 permanent account;
[永訣] be separated by death; gone forever; part forever;
[永命] long life; longevity;
[永慕] remember forever;
[永年] long life; longevity;
[永日] all the day; long day;
[永生] (1) immortal; (2) eternal life;
永生不死 live eternally;
永生永世 for ever and ever; generation after generation; world without end;
獲得永生 be immortalized;
許諾永生 promise eternal life;
[永矢弗諼] swear never to forget;
[永世] (1) eternity; forever; (2) whole lifetime;
永世不忘 remember sth for life; will bear sth in mind for life; will never forget sth;
永世不朽 everlasting; last forever;
永世長存 live for ever and ever;
永世難忘 never forget sth for the rest of one's life;
永世無窮 perpetual and inexhaustible;
[永逝] gone forever;
[永夜] a long night;
[永遠] always; eternally; ever; for always; for evermore; forever; perpetually;
永遠不忘 will never dismiss sth from one's mind;
永遠屹立 stand throughout eternity;

雋永 meaningful;

yong
【甬】 (1) a measure of capacity; (2) alternative name of Ningbo;
[甬道] (1) paved path leading to a main hall or a tomb; (2) corridor;

yong
【泳】 (1) swim; (2) dive;
[泳道] lane;
[泳褲] bathing trunks; swimming trunks;
一條泳褲 a pair of bathing trunks; a pair of swimming trunks;
[泳衣] cozzie; swimsuit;
[泳裝] bathing suit; cozzie;

背泳 backstroke;
側泳 sidestroke;
電泳 electrophoresis;
蝶泳 butterfly; butterfly stroke;
冬泳 winter swimming;
海豚泳 dolphin butterfly; dolphin fishtail;
裸泳 skinny-dipping;
爬泳 crawl; over-arm stroke;
潛泳 underwater swimming;
蛙泳 breaststroke;
翔泳 birds and fish;
仰泳 backstroke;
游泳 swim; swimming;
自由泳 (1) crawl; (2) free-style stroke;

yong
【俑】 wooden figures of men and women buried with the dead;

兵馬俑 wooden or clay figures of warriors and horses buried with the dead;
木俑 wooden figurine buried with the dead;
泥俑 clay figure buried with the dead;
陶俑 pottery figurine;
武士俑 warrior figure;
作俑 originate a wicked practice;

yong
【勇】 (1) bold; brave; courageous; fearless; intrepid; valiant; (2) conscript; soldier;
[勇不可擋] too courageous to be met with; too valiant for anyone to face;
[勇而無謀] brave but not astute; brave but without plans; brave but without stratagem; valiant but imprudent;
[勇敢] bold; brave; courageous; gallant; heroic; valiant;
勇敢不屈的 stout-hearted;
勇敢的 dauntless; gutsy;
~勇敢的行為 bravery;
勇敢剛毅的人 heart of oak;
勇敢沉著 brave and steady;
勇敢善戰 brave and resourceful in battle; courageous and skilful in battle;
勇敢無匹 unrivalled in bravery;

勇敢自衛 brave in defense;
沉着勇敢 have calm courage;
非常勇敢 lion-hearted;
機智勇敢 brave and resourceful;
生性勇敢 brave by nature; have courage in one's blood;

[勇悍] brave and fierce;

[勇將] fearless general;

[勇決] brave and resolute; decisive; determined;

[勇猛] bold and powerful; brave and fierce; full of valour and vigour;
勇猛果斷 bold and resolute; brave and decisive;
勇猛果敢 bold and decisive;
勇猛前進 march boldly forward;
勇猛如虎 as bold as a lion;
勇猛如獅 as brave as a lion;
勇猛善戰 brave and resourceful in battle;
勇猛無比 one's valour is unparalleled; unrivaled in bravery;

[勇氣] bravery; courage; fearlessness; gallantry; guts; heroism; intrepidity; nerve; prowess;
勇氣倍增 one's courage redoubled;
鼓起勇氣 call up one's courage; keep up one's courage; pick up one's courage; pluck up one's heart; take one's heart;
鼓足勇氣 boost one's courage; muster up courage; pluck up one's courage; screw up one's courage; summon up one's courage;
恢復勇氣 regain one's nerve;
沒勇氣的 chicken;
缺乏勇氣 lack courage;
失去勇氣 lose one's courage; lose one's nerve;
無畏的勇氣 unflinching courage;
需要勇氣 call for boldness; need courage; require fearlessness;
有勇氣 have courage;
~有勇氣的 gritty;

[勇士] brave and strong person; warrior;
勇士不怕死 a brave person does not evade death;

[勇退] withdraw courageously;

[勇武] brave; daring; intrepid; valiant;
勇武過人 surpass others in valour;

[勇於] bold in; brave in; have the courage to;
勇於創新 brave in making innovations; have the courage to bring forth new ideas;
勇於負責 brave in shouldering responsibilities;
勇於改過 bold enough to mend one's ways; bold in correcting one's mistakes;
勇於實踐，大膽創新 bold in puting things into practice and blazing new trails;

[勇者不懼] bravery admits of no fear; the courageous are free from fear;

逞勇 act recklessly;
大勇 (1) great courage; (2) courageous people;
奮勇 bravely; courageously;
尚勇 esteem valour;
神勇 extraordinarily brave;
鄉勇 local militia; village militiamen;
驍勇 brave; valiant;
義勇 voluntary and courageous;
毅勇 firm courage; fortitude;
英勇 brave; heroic;
遊勇 stragglers and disbanded soldiers;
智勇 intelligent and brave;
鷙勇 fierce and brave;
忠勇 loyal and brave; loyal and courageous;

yong
【涌】 gush out; pour out; rise; spring; surge;

[涌波] bore;

[涌潮] sea bore;

[涌出] gush out; pour out;
涌出鮮血 gush with blood;

[涌進] overflow; pour in;

[涌浪] surge; swell;

[涌泉] bubbling fountain; fountain;
涌泉潺潺 bubbling of the spring;

[涌上] rush; stream; upwell;
涌上心頭 upwell in one's mind;

[涌現] come to the fore; emerge in large numbers; spring up;

[涌至] arrive like a flood;

yong
【湧】 (1) gush out; pour out; well out; (2) rise; surge;

[湧出] spring out; well out;
大量湧出 gush;

[湧進] swarm into; sweep into;

[湧來] roll in;
捐款紛紛湧來 donation came rolling in;

[湧泉] fountain; spring;
思若湧泉 one's though is like the bubbling spring;
[湧入] inflow; inrush; rush in;
大量湧入 influx;
突然湧入 irruption;
[湧上來] (1) well up; (2) come in a sweep;
湧上心來 come up in the mind like a ground swell;
[湧現] crop up; emerge;
[湧至] arrive like a flood;

溢湧 gush; surge;
洶湧 tempestuous; turbulent;

yong
【詠】 (1) chant; hum; sing; (2) chirping of birds;
[詠唱] chant;
[詠古] write poems on ancient subjects;
[詠桑寓柳] express one's hidden sentiments and feelings by means of gentle allusions and ambiguous phrases;
[詠詩] chant poems;
[詠歎] chant; intone; sing;
詠歎調 arias;
[詠贊] praise; sing the praises of;

歌詠 singing;
觴詠 chant poems while drinking;

yong
【蛹】 chrysalis; pupa;
[蛹化] pupation;
[蛹臥] live in seclusion;

蠶蛹 silkworm chrysalis;

yong
【踴】 (1) jump; leap; (2) rise; (3) cut off one's feet as a form of punishment; (4) happy;
[踴躍] (1) jump; leap; (2) eagerly; enthusiastically;
踴躍歡呼 leap and cheer;
踴躍投票 cast one's vote actively;
踴躍爭先 vie with one another for the first place;
踴躍支援 fall over one another to give support to;

yong
【壅】 block up; obstruct; stop;
[壅蔽] conceal; cover;
[壅隔] block up; obstruct; stop the flow of;
[壅塞] block up; clogged up; congested; jamed;

yong
【擁】 (1) embrace; hold in one's arms; (2) gather around; (3) swarm; throng; (4) support; (5) have; possess;
[擁抱] cuddle; embrace; hold in one's arms; hug;
擁抱親吻 hugs and kisses;
擁抱一下 give sb a cuddle;
親切的擁抱 affectionate embrace;
左擁右抱 have a woman in each arm; have several mistresses at the same time;
[擁鼻] hold one's nose;
[擁戴] support a leader;
[擁護] advocate; back; endorse; support; uphold;
擁護改革 supporter of a cause of reform;
擁護真理 stand up for the truth;
擁護政策 espouse a policy;
衷心擁護 give wholehearted support; support wholeheartedly;
[擁擠] crowded; packed; push and squeeze;
擁擠喧囂 hustle and bustle;
過度擁擠 overcrowding;
交通很擁擠 the traffic is very heavy;
相當擁擠 be filled to overflowing;
[擁立] set up a ruler and declare allegiance to him;
[擁入] crowd into;
[擁上來] come in a swarm;
擁上心來 well up;
[擁有] be armed with; come into possession of; come into sb's possession; conquer; get possession of sth have; hold; in possession of; in the possesion of; occupy; of; own; possess;
擁有大量財產 own an extensive property;
擁有權力 be possessed of power;
擁有者 possessor;
部份擁有 have part ownership;
共同擁有 jointly own;
全資擁有 wholly own;

簇擁 cluster round;
蜂擁 flock; swarm;

yong

【臃】 (1) swell; swelling; (2) fat and clumsy;

[臃腫] (1) fat and clumsy; too fat to move; (2) overstaffed;
臃腫重疊 overstaffed and overlapping;

yong⁴

yong

【用】 (1) apply; employ; use; (2) spend; (3) expenses; (4) use; usefulness; (5) need; (6) drink; eat; take;

[用兵] command troops; make use of troops; manipulate troops; resort to arms; use military forces;
用兵神速 marvellously quick in moving troops;
不得不用兵 have no alternative but resort to arms;
善於用兵 be well versed in the art of war;

[用不完] cannot be used up; too many or too much for use;

[用不着] (1) it is not worth while to; there is no need to; (2) have no use for;

[用餐] dine; have one's meal;
用餐者 diner;
外出用餐 dine out;

[用場] application; use;
沒用場 useless;
派不上用場 have no use;
派上用場 put to application;
有點用場 of some help;
有用場 useful;

[用處] good; use;
有些用處 of some use;
有用處 useful;
~大有用處 of great use;
~沒有多大用處 of little avail;
~沒有用處 of little use;

[用詞] read; verbal; wording;
用詞不當 inappropriate choice of words; incorrect wording; impropriety;
用詞精當 masterly choice of words; precise and appropriate wording;

[用得着] (1) find sth useful; need; serve the desired purpose; (2) there is need to;

[用地] land for a specific use;
用地佈局 land use distribution;

[用電] use electricity;
用電量 electricity consumption;
用電需求 electricity demand;
限制用電 brownout;

[用度] expenditure; expense;

[用法] use; usage;
用法簡便 easy to use;
一般用法 common usage;

[用飯] eat a meal; have a meal; take a meal;

[用費] cost; expense;

[用功] diligent; hard-working; studious;
用功學習 apply oneself to studies;
不用功 not hard-working;
讀書用功 diligent at one's lessons; study hard;
臨時用功 mug up;
埋頭用功 be buried in study;

[用光] exhaust; max out; run out of; use up;
用光錢 max out money;

[用戶] consumer; customer; subscriber; user;
用戶安全 user safety;
用戶操作語言 user operated language;
用戶成本 user cost;
用戶代理 user agent;
用戶電視服務 user TV service;
用戶服務 user service;
用戶工程 user engineering;
~用戶工程師 customer engineer;
用戶工作區 user interface;
用戶公用網 common user network;
用戶功能 user function;
用戶減少 consumers decrease;
用戶交換系統 customer switching system;
用戶接口管理 user interface manager;
~用戶接口管理系統 user interface management system;
用戶經濟價值 economic value to customers;
用戶聯機設備 user kit;
用戶模型 user model;
用戶區 user area;
用戶群 user group;
用戶設備 user set;
用戶設計 user design;
用戶信息 user information;
~用戶信息控制 customer information control;
~用戶信息網 user information network;
用戶業務 user service;
用戶增加 increase in the number of consumers;
用戶終端 user terminal;

~用戶終端業務 teleservices;
用戶狀態 user mode;
當前用戶 active user;
分時用戶 time-sharing user;
高用量用戶 memory hog;
擴大用戶 extend one's service;
系統用戶 system user;
運輸用戶 transport user;
終端用戶 end user;
最終用戶 end user;

[用計] employ schemes; use tricks;

[用盡] exhaust; use up;
用盡存貨 use up one's stock;
用盡方法 by hook or by crook; employ all means; exhaust one's wits; go to all lengths; resort to every means; use every possible means;
用盡全力 exert oneself to the utmost; make one's best exertions;
用盡心機 exhaust every power of the mind; exhaust one's abilities; leave no stones unturned;
用盡一切辦法 employ all available means; exhaust every means; use every possible effort;

[用勁] exet oneself; put forth one's strength;

[用具] apparatus; appliance; implement; tool;
安全用具 safety appliance;
辦公用具 office appliance;
廚房用具 kitchen ware;
機械用具 mechanical appliances;
潛水用具 diving appliances;
書寫用具 writing utensils;
搖動用具 shaking appliance;

[用力] exert oneself; lay out one's strength; make an effort; put forth one's strength;
用力動作 movement of strength;
用力過度 exert oneself strenuously; make strenuous efforts;
用力舉 lift with much effort;
用力拉 pull with an effort;
用力推 push hard;

[用命] obey orders;

[用品] articles for use;
防護用品 protecting appliance;
化裝用品 cosmetics;
急救用品 first-aid appliance;
家庭用品 goods for domestic use; houseware;
日常用品 daily necessities;
生活用品 articles for daily use;
衛生用品 sanitary articles;
文化用品 stationary goods;

[用錢] spend money;
用錢很大方 generous with money;
用錢如水 spend money like water;

[用情] appeal to emotion; feel serious about a love affair;
用情不專 frivolous in affairs of the heart;

[用人] (1) servant; (2) employ people;
用人不當 not choose the right person for the job; use wrong people for a job;
用人不疑，疑人不用 if you use a person, don't suspect him; if you suspect a person, don't use him;
用人得當 make proper use of personnel;
善於用人 know how to choose the right person for the right job;

[用膳] have one's meals;

[用事] (1) act; handle things; manage things; (2) in power;
感情用事 abandon oneself to emotion; act according to one's sentiment; act impetuously; allow emotions to sway one's judgment; be swayed by emotions; do sth in an emotional manner; give oneself over to blind emotions; give way to one's feelings; let emotions hold sway;
意氣用事 be swayed by personal feelings;

[用特函達] hence this letter;

[用途] use;
用途廣泛 have many uses;
多用途 multi-purpose;
~多用途的 all-purpose;
~多用途室 utility room;

[用完即扔] throwaway;

[用武] (1) display one's abilities; (2) resort to force; use force;
用武之地 a place to display one's abilities;
~沒有用武之地 outlive its usefulness;

[用賢] employ people of wisdom and virtue;
用賢任能 appoint the noble and talent for the important post; use the capable and employ the skilled;

[用心] attentively; diligently; with concentrated attention; exercise caution; pay attention; take care;
用心不良 ill-intentioned;
用心狠毒 with vicious intent;

用心竭力 attentively and diligently; exhaust one's brain and energy;
用心良苦 for all one's pains; lay oneself out;
用心思索 do some hard thinking; think hard;
用心聽 listen with concentration;
用心學習 attentive to one's studies;
用心險惡 have vicious ulterior motives; with malicious intent;
別有用心 have a hidden purpose; have an axe to grind; have ulterior motives;
無所用心 give one's thought to nothing; not to give serious thought to anything; remain idle; show one's concern to nothing; without applying one's mind to anything good;
做事情很用心 very careful in doing anything;

[用刑] torture;

[用以] (1) use sth to achieve an end; (2) in order to; so as to;

[用意] idea; intention; meaning; purpose;
用意何在 just what are you up to; what is the motive; what is your intention;

[用語] (1) choice of words; wording; (2) phraseology; terminology;
法律用語 legal language;
廣告用語 advertising language;
家庭用語 familial language;
金融用語 financial language;
科學用語 scientific words;
口語用語 oral language; spoken language;
禮貌用語 term of courtesy;
日常用語 everyday sentences;
書面用語 written language;
通俗用語 popular language;
醫學用語 medical language;
藝術用語 art terms;
用語粗俗 employ vulgar terms;

[用之不竭] in endless supply; inexhaustible; never be used up;

[用字] wording;

愛用 love to use; prefer to use;
搬用 apply indiscriminately; copy mechanically;
備用 alternate; in reserve; reserve; spare;
柄用 be held in esteem by the monarch and given authority;
撥用 appropriate; set apart for a specific use;
不用 (1) need not; (2) disuse; (3) have no intention to become;
採用 adopt; employ; use;
拆用 strip sth integrated and use the pieces separately;
常用 in common use;
抄用 plagiarize;
代用 substitute;
待用 inactive; standby;
盜用 embezzle; usurp;
得用 capable; competent;
調用 transfer under a unified plan;
頂用 fit for use; of help; of use; serve the purpose;
動用 draw on; employ; put to use;
反作用 counter-action; reaction;
費用 charge; cost; expense; fare; fee; outlay; tip; tuition;
敷用 apply;
服用 take medicine;
副作用 side effect; by-effect;
公用 communal; for public use;
共用 common; sharing;
功用 function; role;
管用 alive and well; effective;
慣用 consistently use; habitually practice;
罕用 seldom used;
合用 (1) fit for use; meet the requirement; (2) share sth;
活用 make flexible use of;
急用 urgently need;
家用 (1) domestic; household; (2) domestic money; family expenses; housekeeping money; (3) home application;
交用 turn over for use;
節用 economize expenses;
借用 (1) borrow; have the loan of; (2) use sth for another purpose;
禁用 forbidden;
軍用 for military use;
可用 available; usable;
濫用 abuse; use indiscriminately;
利用 avail oneself of; cash in on; exploit; find a use for sth; make the most of; make use of; play on; play up to; play upon; put to use; seize on; seize upon; take advantage of; trade on; trade upon; turn to account; utilize; use; utilization;
連用 use consecutively; use together;
兩用 dual purpose;
零用 pocket money; spend money in small sums;
留用 continue to employ; keep on;
錄用 employ; engage; give a post to sb; take on; take sb on the staff;

妙用 magical effect;
民用 civil; for civil use;
耐用 durable;
農用 agricultural use;
挪用 (1) divert funds; (2) embezzle; misappropriate;
聘用 be hired on contract; employ; engage;
起用 (1) raise up; (2) reinstate a dismissed official; reinstate a retired official;
啟用 start using an official seal, etc.;
任用 appoint; assign sb to a post;
日用 daily expenses; of daily use;
肉用 carnal; table;
擅用 appropriate; take and use as one's own; use without permission;
商用 commercial use;
省用 economize; save;
施用 employ; use;
食用 be used for food; edible;
實用 functional; practical;
使用 apply; employ; make use of; resort to; use;
試用 (1) be on probation; (2) test; try out;
適用 suitable for use;
受用 (1) enjoy; enjoyable; (2) comfortable; feel good;
私用 (1) for personal use; (2) illegal use;
所用 chosen; what is used;
他用 another use;
套用 apply mechanically; use indiscriminately;
通用 (1) in common use; (2) interchangeable;
外用 for external application; for external use;
無用 of no use; useless;
誤用 misuse;
習用 habitually use;
襲用 adopt sth that has been used in the past;
享用 use sth to one's satisfaction (materially or spiritually);
效用 effectiveness; usefulness;
械用 implements;
信用 (1) credit; trustworthiness; (2) credit;
敘用 appoint (an official); employ;
選用 select and apply;
焉用 why is it necessary to use;
沿用 continue following the old practices; continue to use;
藥用 for medical use;
移用 embezzle; misappropriate;
引用 (1) appoint; recommend; (2) cite; quote;
飲用 drink;
應用 apply; use;
有用 beneficial; practical; serviceable; useful;
語用 pragmatic;
御用 be for the use of a ruler; serving as a tool;
援用 cite; quote;
運用 apply; employ; exercise; make use of; put to use; utilize;
甄用 employ by an examination;
徵用 commandeer; take over for use;
支用 disburse;
致用 attain practical use; for practical purposes;
陟用 promote to a higher position;
置用 buy for use;
中用 effective; useful;
重用 put sb in a important position;
專用 be for a special use;
擢用 promote to a post;
自用 (1) be for private use; (2) self-willed;
租用 rent; hire; take on lease;
作用 (1) act on; action; function; (2) effect;

yong

【佣】 commission;

［佣金］ commission;
佣金代理人 commission agent;
佣金率 rate of commission;
代購佣金 buying commission;
代理人佣金 agent's commission;
代銷佣金 selling commission;
遞加佣金 commission on a sliding scale;
追加佣金 overriding commission;

you¹

you

【攸】 (1) distant; far; (2) fast; fleeting; (3) concern; (4) a surname;

［攸關］ concern;
利害攸關 a matter of gains and losses; be closely related to sb's interest; concern sb's vital interests; have a stake in;
人命攸關 a matter of life and death;
生死攸關 of life and death; of vital importance;
~ 生死攸關的問題 a matter of life and death; a matter of life or death;
性命攸關 a matter of life and death; life-or-death; of vital importance;
顏面攸關 have to do with one's face;

［攸歸］ be charged properly;
咎有攸歸 the blame is put on the proper one; the fault is charged to the proper person;
責有攸歸 the responsibility should lie where it belongs;
罪有攸歸 responsibility for crime can be

traced;

[攸然] joyfully; leisurely;

[攸攸] (1) distant; far; (2) deep;

you

【幽】 (1) deep and remote; lonely; secluded; solitary; (2) dark; gloomy; obscure; (3) hidden; secret; (4) quiet; tranquil; (5) confine; imprison; (6) of the netherworld;

[幽暗] dim; gloomy;

[幽閉] (1) put under house arrest; (2) confine oneself indoors;

幽閉恐懼感 claustrophobia;

[幽獨] lonely; solitary;

[幽房] secluded inner room;

[幽憤] hidden resentment; resent; sulky;

[幽谷] deep and secluded valley; dingle;

[幽會] lover's rendezvous; tryst;

[幽魂] ghost;

[幽寂] secluded and lonely; secluded and solitary;

[幽界] Hades; the underworld;

[幽禁] (1) put under house arrest; (2) imprison; keep under detention;

[幽靜] peaceful; placid; quiet and secluded; serene;

幽靜雅致 retired and quiet;

[幽居] live away from society; live in seclusion;

[幽靈] apparition; ghost; spirit;

[幽流] subterranean flow of water;

[幽美] pathetically beautiful;

[幽眇] sophisticated;

[幽明] the world of the living and that of the dead;

幽明異路 the dead and the living are in different roads;

[幽冥] (1) netherworld; (2) dark; gloomy;

[幽默] humorous;

幽默風趣 have a fine sense of humour;

幽默感 sense of humour;

~很有幽默感 have a good sense of humour;

幽默文學 humorous literature;

幽默作家 humourist;

病態幽默 black humour; morbid humour; sick humour;

風趣幽默 have a fine sense of humour;

富於幽默 have a lot of humour;

黑色幽默 black humour;

黑幽默 black humour;

[幽棲] live away from society;

[幽期] (1) contemplated time for retirement; (2) appointment for a secret meeting;

[幽情] pensive mood; exquisite feelings;

發思古之幽情 muse over things of the remote past; nostalgia for the past;

[幽囚] cast in prison; confine; imprison; shut up;

幽囚終身 be imprisoned for life;

[幽趣] delightful serenity of seclusion;

[幽人] hermit; recluse;

[幽深] deep and quiet; deep and serene;

[幽思] (1) meditate; ponder; (2) thoughts on remote things;

情發幽思 muse over remote things;

[幽邃] deep and quiet; profound; unfathomable;

[幽婉] profound and complicated;

[幽微] faint; obscure; weak;

[幽閒] (1) gentle and serene; (2) leisurely and carefree;

[幽嫻貞靜] elegant and graceful; retired and modest;

[幽香] delicate fragrance;

一縷幽香 a stream of perfume; a wave of indescribably sweet perfume;

[幽雅] chaste and elegant; quiet and tastefully laid out;

[幽咽] whimpering;

[幽影] looming; mirage;

[幽幽] (1) dim; faint; (2) deep; distant; faraway; looming in the distance;

幽幽啜泣 sob quietly;

[幽怨] hidden bitterness;

清幽 quiet and beautiful; quiet and secluded; secluded and charming;

尋幽 visit places;

you

【悠】 (1) extensive; far; long; remote in time or space; vast; (2) meditative; pensive; sad; (3) gentle; leisurely; slow; soft; (4) swing;

[悠闇] far and dim;

[悠長] long; long-drawn-out;

[悠蕩] sway; swing;

[悠動] swing;
[悠忽] idle away the time; lazy and idle;
[悠久] age-old; long; long in time; long-standing;
歷史悠久 have a long history; rich in history;
文化悠久 have a civilization of long standing;
[悠緬] distant; far;
[悠邈] distant; far;
[悠謬] absurd; preposterous;
[悠然] (1) carefree and leisurely; in a leisurely manner; (2) distant; far away; long;
悠然而逝 go off pretty easy; past and gone;
悠然散步 stroll leisurely;
悠然神往 one's thoughts turn to distant things;
悠然自得 act in a leisurely, contented manner; carefree and content; complacently; contentedly take one's ease;
過得很悠然 pass one's days in carefree leisure;
[悠閒] leisurely; leisurely and carefree; unhurried; unrestrained;
悠閒逸樂 live in idleness;
悠閒自在 leisurely and carefree;
生活得悠閒 lead a life of leisure;
[悠揚] melodious; rising and falling;
琴韻悠揚 sweet music is being played on the lute;
[悠悠] (1) long; long-drawn-out; remote; (2) leisurely; unhurried;
悠悠長夜 the nights seems to drag;
悠悠蕩蕩 drift gently; float about;
悠悠忽忽 in a trance; loiter;
悠悠揚揚 soft and ringing;
悠悠自得 carefree and content;
悠悠自在 at leisure and easy-going;
悠哉悠哉 carefree; free from restraint;
[悠遠] distant; far; long ago; long time ago;
[悠著] take things easy;

顫悠 shake; quiver;
忽悠 flicker;
晃悠 shake from side to side; stagger;
慢悠悠 sluggishly; unhurriedly;
飄悠 float or drift slowly;
轉悠 (1) dark; dim; (2) turn;

you
【麀】 doe; female deer;
[麀鹿] doe; female deer;

you
【憂】 (1) worried; worry; (2) anxiety; sad; sorrow;
[憂愁] agony; anguish; depressed; grief; melancholy; misery; mournful; remorse; sad; sadness; woe; worried;
感到憂愁 feel depressed;
很憂愁 be very depressed;
滿臉憂愁 sad appearance;
驅散憂愁 dispel one's feelings of sorrow;
消憂解愁 allay grief; relieve sb from anxiety;
[憂憤] grieved and indignant; worried and indignant;
憂憤欲絕 one's sorrows make one wish to die;
[憂患] distress; hardship; misery; suffering; trouble; worry;
憂患餘生 a person who has known adversity and sorrow; a survivor of many disasters; survive countless distresses and worries; the remainder of one's life after a disaster;
飽經憂患 be no stranger to sorrow; have gone through a good deal of misery; have gone through great misery; have suffered untold tribulations;
備嚐憂患 have undergone much worry and hardships;
內憂外患 anxiety arising from within and trouble coming from without; domestic and foreign problems; domestic trouble and foreign invasion; internal and external troubles; internal disturbance and foreign aggression; internal revolt and foreign invasion;
[憂疾成病] ill with anxiety and melancholy;
[憂煎] in agonies of worry;
[憂懼] anxious and fearful; worried and apprehensive;
憂懼萬狀 extremely anxious and fearful;
[憂苦以終] distressed to death;
[憂勞] worries and toil;
憂勞成疾 fall sick with grievance and toil; lose one's health because of care;
宵旰憂勞 busy with state affairs; labour incessantly on duties;

[憂樂] joys and sorrows;
憂樂共享 share joys and sorrows;
憂樂相共 share worries and blessings;
先憂後樂 grieve first and rejoice afterwards; first labour, later enjoy;

[憂慮] anxious; apprehensive; concerned; worried;
憂慮成疾 get sick from worry; the anxiety makes one ill; worry brings on an illness;
憂慮重重 sick at heart;
憂慮而死 worry oneself to death;
憂慮傷身 care injures the health;
憂慮萬分 extremely worried; sweat blood;
充滿憂慮 full of anxiety;
非常憂慮 be desperately anxious; feel strong anxiety for sth;
令人憂慮 alarming;
拋掉憂慮 cast care aside;
深感憂慮 be very worried; feel extremely anxious;
神色憂慮 wear an expression of worry;
消除憂慮 allay apprehensions; hush one's anxiety;
引起憂慮 cause anxiety;

[憂悶] depressed; feeling low; grieved; suffer mental agonies; weighed down with cares; worried;

[憂慼] distressed; sad and worried; weighted down with sorrow;
憂慼相關 mutually affected by each other's woes; mutually afflicted;

[憂容] sad look; worried look;

[憂傷] distressed; laden with grief; weighed down with sorrow; worried and grieved;
憂傷而死 die of a broken; die of sorrow;
憂傷令人老 grief ages us;
感到憂傷 feel sad and worried;
克制憂傷 control one's grief; get over one's distress;
滿心憂慮 one's heart is full of grief;
驅散憂傷 chase away one's grief;
無比憂傷 eat one's heart out;
陷入憂傷 sink into melancholy;

[憂思] pensive;
憂思未艾 worry continuously;

[憂喜] sadness and joy;
憂喜參半 half downcast and half glad;
憂喜交集 bitter sweet; have mixed feelings of joy and grief; sadness and joy mingle;
轉憂為喜 change from sorrow to joy;

[憂心] anxiety; worry;
憂心忡忡 anxiety-ridden; be oppressed by tormenting anxieties; care-laden; care-ridden; deeply grieved in one's heart; full of anxiety; have a heart loaded with worry; have kittens; heavy-hearted; in dismay; laden with anxiety; sick at heart; weigh down with anxieties; worry a great lot; worry to death;
憂心烈烈 burn with sorrow;
憂心如焚 anxiety gnaws at one's heart; be killed by grief; burning with anxiety; deeply worried; devour one's heart; eat one's heart out; eat out one's heart; in a stew; sorrow-stricken; very anxious; worry oneself to death;
憂心如煎 his heart burns with melancholy so that the pain is like that of boiling oil in him;

[憂形於色] draw a long face; look dismal and unhappy; make a long face; pull a long face; put on a long face; sadness is manifested on the countenance; wear a long face; wear a sad expression; wear a worried expression;

[憂悒] anxious; cheerless; dejected; depressed; despondent; melancholy; worried;
憂悒不歡 anxious and unrest without joy; joyless; upset;

[憂鬱] dejected; heavy-hearted; melancholy;
憂鬱不樂 anxious and uneasy without joy;
憂鬱成疾 become sick from grief; get sick from her worry; ill with anxiety and melancholy;
憂鬱的 lugubrious;
憂鬱而死 die of grief;
憂鬱寡歡 anxious and unrest without joy; as melancholy as a cat;
憂鬱症 hypochondria; melancholia;
感到憂鬱 suffer melancholy;
抗憂鬱 anti-anxiety;
驅散憂鬱 dissipate melancholy;
憂憂鬱鬱 in the dumps; low-spirited; melancholy;

[百憂] all sorrows; all worries;

擔憂 anxious; worry;
丁憂 be in mourning for one's parent's death;

分憂 help sb to tide over a difficulty; share sb's sorrows, worries, etc.;
殷憂 great worry;
慇憂 deep grief; distress; sorrow;
隱憂 secret worry;
幽憂 distressed; laden with grief; weighed down with sorrow;
宅憂 in mourning;
湛憂 deep worry;
軫憂 worried and grieved;

you

【優】 (1) excellent; good; (2) abundant; plenty; (3) actor; actress;

[優待] favourable treatment; give preferential treatment;
優待客人 give courteous treatment to one's guests;
優待券 privilege ticket;

[優等] excellent; first-rate; high grade; high quality; high-class; top line; top quality;

[優點] advantages; merits; strong points; virtue;
優點和缺點 strengths and weaknesses;
發揮自己的優點 bring out one's strong points;
有很多優點 have many good qualities;

[優厚] favourable; liberal; munificent;
優厚待遇 excellent pay and conditions; liberal wages and benefits;
工資優厚 have a good salary;

[優化] optimize;
優化程序 optimized programme;
優化勞動組合 optimize the organization of labour;
優化算法 optimizing algorithm;
優化組合 optimized composition;

[優惠] favourable; preference; preferential;
優惠待遇 preferential treatment;
優惠幅度 margin of preference;
優惠國 favoured nation;
優惠價 preferential price;
優惠價格 preferential price;
優惠利率 prime rate;
優惠條款 favourable terms;
優惠政策 preferential policy;
~ 實行優惠政策 launch a preferential policy;
財政優惠 financial preference;
費用優惠 expense preference;
特價優惠 special offer;
享受優惠 enjoy privileges;
消費者優惠 consumer preference;

[優禮] special kindness;

[優良] excellent; fine; good;
質量優良 superior in quality;

[優劣] good and bad;
優劣不分 no discrimination between good and bad;
分出優劣 separate the sheep from the goats; separate the wheat from the chaff;
扶優去劣 develop the good and eliminate the bad;
難分優劣 very hard to tell which is better;
棄劣取優 reject what is bad and absorb what is good;

[優伶] (1) actor; (2) actress;

[優美] (1) exquisite; fine; graceful; (2) fine; good; graceful; pure poetry; sheer poetry; wonderful;
優美自如 with an easy grace;
步態優美 walk with grace;
身材優美 have a figure of great beauty; possess a good figure;
舞姿優美 dance with much grace;

[優缺] excellent vacancy;

[優人] actor;

[優容] treat with leniency; treat with magnanimity;

[優柔] (1) leisurely; (2) gentle; mild; (3) weak in character;
優柔寡斷 flabby; haw and gee about; incapable of taking a strong decision; indecisive; infirm of purpose; irresolute; irresolute and hesitant; peaceable and easy-going but lacking the strength of making quick decisions; pusillanimous; pussyfoot; shillyshally; spineless; undecided; vacillating; weak and irresolute; weak-kneed; weak-minded; wishy-washy; yea and nay;
~ 優柔寡斷的人 weak-minded person;

[優生] eugenics;
優生學 eugenics;
優生優育 give a good birth and good care;

[優勝] superior; winning;
優勝獎 winning prize;
優勝劣敗 the survival of the fittest; the weakest goes to the wall;

優勝者 champion; winner;
佔優勝 win a triumph;

[優勢] dominant position; goodness; predominance; preponderance; superiority; supremacy; vigour;
優勢地位 position of strength;
優勢方言 dominant dialect;
優勢種 dominant; dominant species;
~ 恒存優勢種 constant dominant;
~ 生態優勢種 ecological dominant;
~ 穩定優勢種 permanent dominant;
~ 暫時優勢種 temporary dominant;
保持優勢 hold on to one's favourable position; keep on top;
材料優勢 material advantage;
處於優勢 in a strong position;
具有優勢 enjoy an advantage; have an advantage;
絕對優勢 definite advantage;
人力優勢 man advantage;
失去優勢 lose ground;
位置優勢 position advantage;
異核優勢 heterocaryotic vigour;
贏得優勢 win an advantage;
雜種優勢 heterotic vigour; hybrid vigour;
佔優勢 gain the ascendancy over; get the ascendancy over; have the ascendancy over; in the ascendant; obtain the ascendancy over; preponderate;
爭奪優勢 carry out a struggle for superiority;

[優為] good at sth;

[優先] have priority; preferential; take precedence;
優先股 preferred stock;
優先權 priority;
~ 優先權申請 priority application;
~ 給予優先權 accord priority;
~ 極限優先權 limit priority;
~ 假定優先權 assumed priority;
~ 絕對優先權 absolute priority;
~ 強制優先權 forced priority;
~ 中斷優先權 interrupt priority;
~ 作業優先權 job priority;
優先選擇 choose in preference;
優先債權 prior charge;
優先照顧 give preference to sb;

[優閒] carefree; free and content; leisure;
優閒自得 one is contented with his leisure; with abundant leisure one is contented;

[優秀] excellent; fine; foremost; outstanding; remarkable; splendid;
優秀的 excellent;
優秀生 excellent student;
優秀份子 the elite;
品格優秀 display good moral qualities; sound in character;
最優秀 of the first water;

[優選法] optimum seeking method;

[優雅] elegant; graceful;
優雅的 courtly;

[優異] excellent; outstanding; remarkable;

[優優] (1) amiable; gentle; (2) ample;

[優游] (1) carefree; leisurely and carefree; (2) indecisive;
優游處之 take things easy; treat sth with ease;
優游林下 live in the countryside leisurely and happily after retirement;
優游歲月 live in leisure through the months and years; pass one's days in carefree leisure;
優游自得 completely free and at ease;
優游自在 comfortable and at ease; leisurely and carefree;
優游卒歲 pass the year in pleasure;
優哉游哉 leisurely and carefree; leisurely and unhurried; living a life of ease and leisure;
~ 優哉游哉的生活 beer and skittles;

[優裕] affluent; comfortable; excellent; wealthy; well-to-do;
環境優裕 live in clover;
生活優裕 lead a rich life; live in affluence; well-to-do;

[優越] outstanding superior;
優越感 sense of superiority;
優越性 superiority;
無比優越 superior beyond comparison;

[優質] high grade; high quality;
優質產品 high quality products;
優質的 pukka;
優質服務 high-quality service;
優質高產 good quality and high output;
優質名牌產品 high-quality brand-name products;
優質牛肉 high-grade beef;
優質食品 pukka food;
優質優價 good articles fetch high prices;

倡優 (1) prostitute; (2) actress; entertainer;

musician;
創優 create excellence;
從優 give as generously as possible;
名優 (1) famous actor or actress; (2) famous and of excellent quality;
女優 actress;
俳優 variety artist;
全優 all-round excellence;
特優 excellent; extraordinary;
最優 best fit;

you
【櫌】 (1) draw earth over newly-sown grain; (2) a kind of hoe;

you²
you
【尤】 (1) outstanding; special; (2) articulously; especially; particularly; (3) error; fault; mistake; (4) blame; (5) a surname;
[尤其] above all; especially; in particular; particularly;
尤其強調 stress in particular;
尤其是 above all; especially; particularly; to crown all;
尤其喜歡 have a special liking for;
尤其憎恨 have a special hatred for;
尤其重要 even more important;
[尤人] blame others;
[尤甚] (1) more than; worse than; (2) especially so; particularly so;
[尤物] (1) uncommon person; (2) rare beauty; woman of extraordinary beauty;

愆尤 fault; mistake; offence;
效尤 knowingly follow the example of a wrong-doer;
怨尤 grudge; resentment;
罪尤 fault; offence;

you
【由】 (1) cause; reason; (2) because of; due to; (3) by; through; (4) follow; obey; (5) from; (6) a surname;
[由表及裏] from the exterior to the interior; proceed from outward appearance to inner essence; proceed from the outside to the inside; proceed from the surface to what lies behind; through the outside into the inside;
[由此] from this; therefore; therefrom; thus;
由此觀之 judging from this; looking at the matter from this viewpoint;
由此及彼 proceed from one point to another; proceed from the one to the other;
由此看來 by this token; in view of this; judging from this;
由此可見 that proves; this shows; thus it can be seen that;
由此可知 from this it can be seen that; hence one can see that; thus it is clear that;
由此類推 by parity of reasoning; on the analogy of this;
由此前往 go from here;
[由打] since;
[由來] (1) origin; (2) cause; reason; (3) so far; up to now;
由來已久 deep-rooted; deep-seated; have a long history; have been like this for a long time; have been going on for a long time; have been so far quite some time; it is not just today that; long-standing; of long standing; time-honoured;
[由你] as you like; as you please; whatever you say;
[由是] from this; hence;
由是觀之 looking at it from this point of view;
由是可觀 one can see therefore;
[由他去罷] leave him alone;
[由頭] cause; pretext; reason;
由頭到尾 from A to Z; from the beginning to the end;
[由性] act at will;
[由由] (1) contented; (2) hesitate; remain undecided;
[由於] as; as a result of; because of; by virtue of; considering; due to; for; for-as-much-as; in consequence of; in consideration of; in that; in the light of; in view of; in virtue of; inasmuch as; on account of; owing to; seeing that; since; take into consideration; thanks to; through; with; with a view to;
[由衷] from the bottom of one's heart; heartfelt; sincere;
由衷一笑 laugh heartily;
由衷之言 a talk straight from the heart;

sincere words; words spoken from the bottom of one's heart; words uttered in sincerity; words which come from the bottom of one's heart;

言不由衷 insincere in one's speech; not speaking one's mind; not say frankly what one thinks; not say what one thinks in one's mind; not speak honestly; not talk from the bottom of one's heart; say what one does not mean; speak affectedly; speak with one's tongue in one's cheek; speak without sincerity; talk insincerely; the words do not come from the heart;

[由…轉交] care of (c/o);

[由…組成] be composed of; be made from; be made of; be made up of; consist of;

案由 brief; main points of a case; summary;
不由 can't help; cannot but;
根由 cause; origin;
經由 by way of; via;
來由 cause; reason;
理由 account; argument; ground; justification; reason;
情由 cause; facts and reasons; reason; the hows and whys;
事由 (1) main content (of a document); (2) the origin of an incident;
率由 act according to; follow;
無由 have no way of; in no position to; no way to; not in a position to do sth; unable to;
夷由 hesitating; undecided;
因由 reason; cause; origin;
原由 cause; reason;
緣由 cause; reason;
摘由 extract the main content of a document;
自由 free; freedom; liberty; unrestrained;
蹤由 origin and development;

you

【油】 (1) fat; grease; oil; (2) apply tung oil or paint; (3) be stained with oil or grease; (4) glib; oily;

[油餅] fried salty pancakes;
糖油餅 deep-fried cakes with sugar;

[油布] oilcloth;

[油彩] greasepaint; paint;
擦去油彩 scrub off the paint;
抹掉油彩 rub off the paint;

[油菜] (1) rape; (2) Chinese cabbage;
歐洲油菜 oilseed rape;

[油船] oil carrier; oil tanker; tanker;
大型油船 king-size tanker;
冷凍油船 refrigerated tanker;
輕油油船 clean tanker;
重油油船 dirty tanker;

[油燈] oil lamp;

[油膏] ointment;
花香油膏 flower ointment;
燒傷油膏 burn ointment;
水銀藍油膏 blue ointment;

[油罐] oil tank;
圓柱形油罐 cylindrical oil tank;

[油滑] foxy; sauve and crafty; sleeky; slippery; slippery and sly;
這個人很油滑 this person is foxy;

[油畫] canvas; oil painting;
油畫布 canvas;
油畫畫布 canvas;
畫油畫 paint in oils;
一幀油畫 an oil painting;

[油灰] putty;
油灰刀 putty knife;

[油跡] greasy spots; oil stains;

[油井] oil well;
打油井 drill an oil well;

[油庫] oil depot; oil tank; tank farm;

[油亮] glossy; shiny;

[油綠] dark green;

[油輪] oil tanker; tanker;
巨型油輪 large crude carrier; monster tanker;
~超級巨型油輪 ultra large crude carrier;
一般油輪 an oil tanker; a tanker;
遠洋油輪 ocean-going overseas tanker; ocean-going tanker;

[油門] accelerator; gas pedal;
踩盡油門 press the pedal to the metal; push the pedal to the metal; put the pedal to the metal;
踩油門 step on the accelerator; step on the gas;

[油墨] ink; printing ink;
苯胺油墨 aniline ink;
玻璃紙油墨 cellophane ink;
封面油墨 book binder's ink;

[油膩] fatty; greasy; oily;
油膩的飯菜 greasy food;
洗掉油膩 get the grease off;

[油瓶] oil bottle;
八個油瓶，四個蓋兒一缺這少那 eight

oil bottles with only four tops — insufficient; nothing matches;

[油漆] (1) oil colour; paint; (2) cover with paint; paint;
油漆工 oil painter; painter;
油漆匠 oil painter; painter;
油漆桶 paint bucket;
油漆未乾 fresh paint; mind the fresh paint; wet paint;
刮掉油漆 scrape off the paint;
黃油漆 yellow paint;
藍油漆 blue paint;
塗上油漆 varnish with lacquer;
一層油漆 a coat of paint; a layer of paint;

[油然] (1) involuntarily; spontaneously; (2) copious; densely; luxuriant; profusely;
油然而生 arise spontaneously; rise of itself; well up in one's heart;

[油水] profit;
油水不大 cannot afford much; not very profitable;
油水不相融 water repels oil;
很有油水 quite profitable;
撈油水 line one's pockets with squeeze; on the take; reap some profit;

[油田] oil field;
高產油田 barreler;
開發油田 develop oil fields;

[油條] deep-fried dough sticks;
老油條 cunning person; old campaigner; old soldier; slippery person; wily old bird;
炸油條 fry twisted dough-strips;

[油桶] oil drum;

[油頭] sleek hair;
油頭粉面 heavily made up; sleek-haired and creamy-faced;
油頭滑腦 flippant; frivolous and tricky; oily; shifty-looking; slick;
粉面油頭 powder the face and anoint the head; the fair sex; the ladies;
俏大姐的油頭一輸 (梳) 得光光的 the sleek hair of a cutie — have lost everything through gambling;

[油汪汪] oily;

[油箱] fuel tank; petrol tank;
油箱蓋 petrol tank cap;
油箱門 gas cap; petrol cap;

[油壓] oil pressure;

[油印本] mimeographed booklet;

[油印機] mimeograph;

[油炸] deep fry;

[油脂] fat;
動物油脂 animal fat; tallow;

[油嘴] (1) glib-tongued; oil-tongued; (2) glib talker;
油嘴滑舌 flattering tongue; glib; glib-tongued; have a well-oiled tongue; mealy-mouthed; oily-mouthed; slimy-tongued; smooth tongue; smooth-tongued;
油嘴子 glib-tongued person; slick talker;

熬油 (1) waste lamp oil by staying up at night; (2) extract oil by heating;
阿尼林油 aniline oil;
桉油 eucalyptus;
柏油 asphalt; pitch; tar;
板油 leaf fat; leaf lard;
蓖麻油 castor oil;
薄荷油 peppermint oil;
擦油 apply pomade; coat with oil; oil; polish;
採油 extract oil;
菜油 rape oil; rapeseed oil;
菜子油 rape oil; rapeseed oil;
茶油 tea oil; tea-seed oil;
搽油 apply ointment;
柴油 diesel oil;
吃油 guzzle;
船用油 bunker oil;
臭油 tar;
打油 buy oil in small amounts;
大油 lard;
燈油 lamp-oil; kerosene;
丁香油 clove oil;
錠子油 lubricant; lubricating oil;
動物油 animal oil;
豆油 soya-bean oil;
髮油 hair oil;
浮油 floating oil on the water surface;
甘油 glycerin;
橄欖油 olive oil;
膏油 add lubricating oil;
光油 varnish;
哈什螞油 the dried oviduct fat of the forest frog;
焊油 soldering paste;
蠔油 oyster sauce;
黑油油 jet-black; shiny black;
花生油 peanut oil;
滑潤油 lubricant;
獾油 badger fat (for treating burns);
黃油 (1) butter; (2) grease;
揮發油 volatile oil;

葷油 lard;
機器油 lubricant; lubricating oil;
機油 engine oil;
加油 (1) come on; get a move on; get going; play up; speed it up; stick it; (2) gas up; pump gas; (3) go; hip, hip, hooray; up;
薑草油 ginger grass oil;
醬油 soy sauce;
焦油 tar;
鯨油 whale oil;
揩油 abuse a privilege; profit at sb's expense; take advantage of sb;
揩油 (1) find pickings; get petty advantages at the expense of other people; get what one wants by taking it without permission or by trickery; make some outside gains; scrounge; (2) take advantage of a woman;
糠油 oil abstracted from bran;
礦物油 mineral oil;
葵花油 sunflower oil;
辣醬油 pungent sauce;
煉油 (1) refine oil; (2) extract oil by heat; (3) heat edible oil;
鹵蝦油 thin juice made from shrimps, salt, etc;
麻油 sesame oil;
煤黑油 coal tar;
煤焦油 coal tar;
煤油 kerosene; paraffin;
棉籽油 cottonseed oil;
木焦油 wood tar;
奶油 cream;
凝析油 condensate;
牛油 beef tallow; butter;
皮鞋油 shoe cream; shoe polish;
撇油 skim;
貧油 be poor in oil resources;
汽提油 stripped oil;
汽油 gas; gasoline; petrol;
氣油 gas; gasoline; petrol;
清涼油 balm for treating minor ailments such as headaches;
輕油 light oil;
燃料油 fuel oil;
燃油 fuel oil;
溶性油 soluble oil;
潤滑油 lubricating oil;
上油 apply lubricant; replenish lubricating oil;
生髮油 hair oil;
生油 unboiled oil;
石蠟油 paraffin oil;
石腦油 naphtha;
石油 petroleum; oil;
食用油 cooking oil; edible oil;
食油 cooking oil; edible oil;
松焦油 pine tar;
松節油 turpentine (oil);
松香油 retinal; rosin oil;
酥油 butter;
素油 vegetable oil;
溚油 tar oil;
檀香油 sandalwood oil;
炭油 coal tar;
桐油 tung oil;
頭油 hair oil;
萬金油 (1) balm for treating minor ailments such as headaches; (2) Jack of all trades and master of none;
蝦油 shrimp sauce;
香精油 essential oil;
香茅油 citronella oil;
香油 sesame oil;
鞋油 shoe polish;
亞麻油 linseed oil;
煙油 tobacco tar;
洋油 imported oil; kerosene;
藥油 medical oil;
椰油 coconut oil;
頁岩油 shale oil;
一層油 a film of oil;
一滴油 a drop of oil;
一桶油 a drum of oil;
印油 stamp-pad ink;
硬脂油 stearine oil;
魚肝油 cod-liver oil;
魚油 fish oil;
原油 crude oil;
渣油 residual oil; residuum;
榨油 extract oil;
樟腦油 camphor oil;
芝麻油 sesame oil;
脂油 leaf fat;
植物油 vegetable oil;
中油 middle distillate;
重油 heavy oil;
豬油 lard;
注油 oil; grease; inject fuel;
棕櫚油 palm oil;

you

【疣】 papule; wart;

扁平疣 flat wart; plane wart; verruca plana; verruca plana juvenills;
出血性疣 haemorrhagic wart;
單純疣 common wart;

皮膚疣 thymian;
普通疣 common wart;
青年疣 juvenile wart;
軟骨疣 chondrophyte;
暫時性疣 fugitive wart;
珍珠疣 molluscum contagiosum;
脂溢性疣 seborrheic wart;
足底疣 plantar wart;

[疣病] verrucuosis;
[疣性皮炎] verrucous dermatitis;
[疣狀皮炎] verrucous dermatitis;

臀疣 monkey's ischial callosities; monkey's seat pads;
贅疣 (1) anything superfluous or useless; (2) wart;

you

【斿】 (1) swim; (2) rove about freely; (3) dabble in;

you

【蚰】 millipede;

you

【游】 (1) drift; float; swim; waft; (2) tour; travel; (3) part of a river; reaches; (4) associate with; (5) a surname;

[游伴] travel companion;
[游標] vernier;
重疊游標 folded vernier;
複游標 double vernier;
順游標 direct vernier;
線性游標 linear vernier;
[游程] lap;
一趟游程 do a lap; run a lap; swim a lap;
[游船] pleasure-boat;
[游蕩] gad about; gad around; loaf; loaf about; loiter; on the gad; wander;
游蕩無度 dissipated without a limit;
東游西蕩 fool around;
漫無目的的游蕩 aimless wanderings;
[游動] go from place to place; move about;
[游蜂浪蝶] dissipated young sets who take a fancy to lewdness;
[游逛] stroll about;
東游西逛 mooch about; mooch around; moon about; moon around; stroll about;
[游擊] guerrilla attack; guerrilla warfare;
游擊隊員 guerilla;
游擊營銷 guerrilla marketing;
游擊園藝 guerrilla gardening;
游擊戰 guerrilla war; guerrilla warfare;
打游擊 (1) fight as a guerrilla; (2) live at no fixed place; work at no fixed place;
~善於打游擊 good at guerrilla warfare;
~上山打游擊 join the guerrillas in the mountains; wage guerrilla warfare in the mountains;
[游記] travel notes; travelogue;
[游街] parade sb through the streets;
游街示眾 lead a criminal through the streets to show him up before the public; parade sb through the streets to expose him before the public;
[游覽] go sight-seeing; tour; visit;
[游樂] amuse oneself; play;
游樂場 amusement arcade;
[游歷] tour; travel; travel for pleasure;
[游離基] free radical;
[游龍] playing, dancing dragon;
嬌如游龍 as graceful as a dragon in swimming;
矯若游龍 as active as a speedy dragon; as nimble as a squirrel; as powerful as a flying dragon; as strong and brave as a lion;
驚鴻游龍 have the grace of a startled swan or swimming dragon;
[游民] idle people; idlers; vagabond; vagrant;
[游牧] move about in search of pasture; nomadic; rove around as a nomad;
游牧部落 ambulatory tribe;
游牧民族 nomadic people;
游牧生活 nomadic life;
[游目騁懷] let the eye take in the landscape and please the spirit; let the eye travel over the great scene and let fancy free; rejoice one's eyes and heart;
[游憩] stroll about or have a rest;
[游人] sightseer; tourist; visitor;
游人如鯽 a multitude of visitors;
游人止步 no visitors; out of bounds;
[游士] free-lancing scholar;
[游手好閒] eat the bread of idleness; fool; idle about; in the street; keep one's hands in one's pockets; live in idleness; loaf about; loaf around; loitering about and doing nothing; mess around doing nothing; not to do a stitch of work; on the loaf; rogue; shilly-shally; squander

one's time;
游手好閒的人 dawdler; layabout; loafer;

[游水] swim;

[游説] drum up support; go about selling an idea; go about drumming up support for an idea; go canvassing; lobby;
游説團 lobby;
到處游説 canvass everywhere;
四出游説 barnstorm; go around making speeches; go here and there to sell an idea;

[游絲] gossamer; hairspring;
定長游絲 timed hairspring;
平游絲 flat hairspring;
右旋游絲 right hairspring;

[游談] (1) canvass; go canvassing; (2) play and talk;

[游艇] launch; pleasure-boat; yacht;
沿海游艇 coastal yacht;
一艘游艇 a yacht;

[游玩] (1) amuse oneself; play; (2) go sight-seeing; stroll about;
去海邊游玩 go on a visit to the seaside;

[游戲] (1) game; recreation; (2) play;
游戲人間 play through life; treat life as merely playing games;
創造性游戲 creative play;
教學游戲 academic games; didactical game;
問答游戲 question-and-answer game;
想像游戲 imaginative play;
語言游戲 language play;

[游俠] person adept in martial arts and given to chivalrous conduct; traveling swordsman;

[游星] wandering star;

[游行] demonstration; march; parade;
游行示威 hold a procession in demonstration; march through the streets in demonstrations; parades and demonstrations;

[游學] study in some other place;

[游揚] extol; praise;

[游移] vacillate; waver; wobble;
游移不定 hesitating; inability to make up one's mind; keep on vacillating; shilly-shally; undecided; vacillate; wavering;
游移兩可 undecided;
游移其詞 hesitate in words;

[游藝] entertainment; recreation;
游藝會 amusement gathering;

[游戈] cruise; patrol;

[游泳] bathe; bathing; swim; swimming;
游泳比賽 swimming competition; swimming contest;
游泳池 swimming pool;
~室內游泳池 indoor swimming pool;
~室外游泳池 outdoor swimming pool;
~無邊際游泳池 infinity pool;
游泳鏡 swimming goggles;
游泳褲 bathing trunks; swim trunks; swimming trunks;
~男式游泳褲 trunks;
游泳帽 bathing cap;
游泳生物 nekton;
游泳衣 bathing suit; swimming suit;
~單件式游泳衣 one-piece bathing suit;
游泳者 bather;
長距離游泳 distance swimming;
渡峽游泳 channel swimming;
花樣游泳 synchronized swimming;
禁止游泳 no swimming allowed;
競技游泳 competitive swimming;
逆水游泳 swim against the current;
去游泳 go swimming;

[游資] floating capital; floating money; hot money; idle capital; idle fund; idle money;
國際游資 hot money from abroad;
吸引游資 absorb idle money; absorb inactive money;

[游子] wandering son;
海外游子 people residing abroad;

春游 spring outing;
浮游 (1) go on a pleasure trip; roam; (2) swim;
宦游 leave home and take up government employments;
回游 migrate;
洄游 migrate;
倦游 weary of wondering and sight-seeing;
浪游 roam for pleasure;
漫游 go on a pleasure trip; knock around; roam; rove; wander; wanderings;
漂游 float; wander;
辱游 indebted to a friend for one's friendship;
上游 upper reaches;
溯游 go upstream;
下游 lower reaches;
雅游 easy to get along with people;

冶游 frequent brothels; visit prostitutes;
優游 (1) carefree; leisurely and carefree; (2) indecisive;
雲游 roam about; travel without a destination; wander about;
中游 middle reaches;
周游 journey round; make a tour in search of adventures; travel round;

you

【猶】 (1) just as; like; (2) still; while; yet; (3) a surname;

[猶可] still all right;
[猶然] (1) just as; just like; (2) still;
[猶如] as if; just as; like;
[猶若] equivalent to; just like; tantamount to;
[猶言在耳] ring in one's ears;
[猶疑] hesitate;
[猶有可為] still retrievable;
[猶豫] hesitate; irresolute; undecided;
猶豫不定 have two minds; in twenty minds; in two minds; irresolute;
猶豫不決 a lack of decision; cross-bench mind; dither; dubious; hang a leg; hang fire; hedge off; hesitate; hesitate as to what cause to adopt; in a quandary; in twenty minds; in two minds; inability to make up one's mind; indecision; indetermination; irresolutely; of two minds; poise; remain undecided; shilly-shally; sit on the fence; unable to reach a decision; vacillate; waver; willy-nilly; wobble; yea and nay;
猶豫寡斷 doubtful and has few decisions;
打消猶豫 overcome one's hesitation;
動搖猶豫 irresolute and wavering;
毫不猶疑 every time; straight away; straight off; unhesitatingly; without the least hesitation

you

【郵】 (1) post office; (2) postal; (3) deliver mail, letters; (4) wayside station; (5) hut; lodge;

[郵包] parcel; postal parcel;
郵包區 zone;
[郵差] mail carrier; mailman; postie; postman;
[郵車] mail van; postal van;
[郵船] liner; ocean liner;
定期郵船 packet boat;
[郵戳] postmark;
在信封上蓋郵戳 postmark a letter;
[郵袋] mailbag; postbag;
[郵遞] (1) mailing; send by post; (2) postal delivery;
郵遞員 mail carrier; mailman; postie; postman;
航空郵遞 airmail;
免費郵遞 freepost;
特快郵遞 express mail;
[郵電] post and telecommunications;
郵電局 post and telecommunication office;
郵電人員 postal clerk;
郵電通訊 post and telecommunications;
~ 郵電通訊網 post and telecommunication network;
[郵費] postage; postal charges;
[郵購] buy by mail; mail-order;
郵購處 postal purchasing agency; postal purchasing centre;
郵購服務 postal purchase service;
郵購目錄 mail order catalogue;
[郵匯] remit by post;
郵匯業務 money-order business;
國際郵匯 international money order;
國內郵匯 domestic money order;
兌現郵匯 cash a postal order;
[郵寄] mail; mailing; post; send by post;
郵寄包裹 send a package by post;
郵寄廣告 mailshot;
郵寄名單 mailing list;
郵寄信件 send a letter by post; take a letter to post;
郵寄資料 mailshot;
掛號郵寄 recorded delivery; send by registered post;
海上郵寄 send through the sea mail;
航空郵寄 send by airmail;
[郵簡] stamped envelope;
[郵件] mail; post; postal matter;
郵件袋 mailbag;
郵件分揀處 sorting office;
郵件炸彈 letter bomb;
郵件轉寄 forward one's mail;
查看郵件 check one's mail;
處理郵件 handle the mail;
電子郵件 electronic mail; email;
~ 查看電子郵件 check one's emails;
~ 發電子郵件 send an email;
~ 回覆電子郵件 answer an email; reply to an email;

~刪除電子郵件 delete an email;
~收到電子郵件 get an email; receive an email;
~寫電子郵件 write an email;
~一大堆電子郵件 a blizzard of emails;
~閱讀電子郵件 read an email;
~轉發電子郵件 forward an email;
掛號郵件 certified mail;
國際郵件 international mail;
航空郵件 aerogramme; airmail;
垃圾郵件 junk mail;
聯郵郵件 union mail;
陸路郵件 surface mail;
普通郵件 snail mail;
收到郵件 get the mail;
水路郵件 surface mail;
蝸牛郵件 snail mail;

[郵局] post office;
郵局職員 post clerk;
經過郵局 go by the post office;

[郵票] postal stamp; stamp;
郵票目錄 stamp catalogue;
郵票鉗 stamp tongs;
郵票市場 stamp market;
航空郵票 air mail stamp;
紀念郵票 commemorative stamp;
缺損郵票 spoilt stamp;
特種郵票 special stamp;
一套郵票 a set of stamps;
一張郵票 a stamp;
珍貴郵票 rare stamp;
注銷郵票 cancelled stamp;
作廢郵票 invalid stamp;

[郵筒] letter box; mailbox; mail slot; pillar box; postbox;
把信投進郵筒 drop a letter into a mailbox;

[郵箱] letter box; mail drop; mailbox; postbox;

[郵政] postal service;
郵政編碼 postcode; zip code;
郵政儲金 postal savings;
郵政儲蓄 post saving;
郵政匯款 postal remittance;
郵政匯票 postal order;
郵政局 post and telecommunication office; post office;
~郵政局長 postmaster;
女郵政局長 postmistress;
郵政快件 express mail;
郵政人員 postal worker;
郵政信箱 post office box;
郵政業務 postal service;
郵政支局 branch post office;
郵政總局 general post office;

[郵資] postage;
郵資標準 postal tariff;
郵資機 franking machine; postage meter;
郵資免付 postage fee;
郵資已付 postage paid; postpaid;
包裹郵資 parcel postage;
付足郵資 pay the right postage;
附加郵資 surcharge;
掛號郵資 additional postage for registration;
國際郵資 international postage;
國內郵資 inland postage;
國外郵資 overseas postage;
欠郵資 postage due;

電郵 email;
付郵 post; mail;
海郵 by sea; sea mail;
集郵 collect stamps; stamp collecting;
軍郵 army post; army postal service;
快郵 express mail;
內郵 internal mail;
通郵 be accessible by postal communication;
投郵 mail; send a letter by mail;
鄉郵 run rural postal service;

you

【猷】 (1) plan; programme; scheme; (2) path; way; (3) draw; paint; (4) like; similar to; (5) (now rare) opening particle;

you

【遊】 (1) roam; saunter; travel; (2) befriend; make friends; study under; (3) freely wield;

[遊伴] travel companion;

[遊船] cruiser; pleasure boat; yacht;
大型遊船 cruise liner;

[遊觀] travel and see the sights;

[遊魂] homeless spirit;

[遊記] travelogue;

[遊客] tourist; traveller;
遊客止步 no trespassing;
擠滿遊客 swarm with tourists;
一群群遊客 swarms of tourists;

[遊逛] roam about; stroll;

[遊覽] (1) sightseeing; tour; visit; (2) read extensively;
遊覽車 tour bus; tourist coach;

~大型遊覽車 charabanc;
遊覽艇 pleasure cruiser;
乘船遊覽 cruise;
有導遊的遊覽 guided tour;
坐船遊覽 enjoy a boat ride;

[遊樂] entertainment; make merry; seek pleasure;
遊樂場 amusement park; funfair;
~露天遊樂場 funfair;
饜於遊樂 satiated with pleasure;

[遊歷] (1) travel; (2) travel abroad for study;
遊歷四方的人 cosmopolitan;

[遊獵] (1) travel here and there for hunting; (2) dabble in;

[遊輪] cruise;
大型遊輪 cruise ship;

[遊民] idle wanderer; vagabond; vagrant;

[遊牧] move about; rove around;

[遊禽] natatorial bird;

[遊手好閒] bum around; idle about; piss about; piss around; schlep;
遊手好閒者 idler;

[遊艇] pleasure boat; yacht;
遊艇會 yacht club;
大遊艇 cabin cruiser;

[遊息] play and rest;

[遊戲] play;
遊戲機 recreational machine;
遊戲節目卡 game card;
遊戲人間 live for fun; take nothing serious in life;
遊戲時間 playtime;
參加遊戲 attend a game;
電子遊戲 electronic games; video game;
摸彩遊戲 lucky dip;
搶座位遊戲 musical chairs;
跳背遊戲 leapfrog;
投環遊戲 quoit;
玩遊戲 play a game;
做遊戲 play games;

[遊狎] befriend and be intimate with;

[遊俠] roving gallant;

[遊心] think deep into sth;

[遊行] (1) parade; (2) demonstrate; demonstration; march;
遊行人士 demonstrant; demonstrator; marcher;
遊行示威 protest march;
~遊行示威者 marcher;
遊行者 demonstrant; demonstrator; marcher;
~一群遊行者 a troop of demonstrants; a troop of marchers;
舉行遊行 hold a parade;
抗議遊行 protest march;
群眾遊行 mass demonstration;
勝利遊行 victory parade;
政治遊行 political parade;
組織遊行 organize a parade;

[遊學] study abroad;

[遊藝會] carnival;

敖遊 travel idly; wander idly;
遨遊 stroll; travel;
暢遊 (1) enjoy a sightseeing tour; (2) have a good swim;
宸遊 emperor on tour;
出遊 go on a sightseeing tour;
串遊 saunter; stroll;
春遊 have a spring outing; spring outing;
導遊 conduct a sightseeing tour; guidebook;
交遊 keep company; make friends;
郊遊 excursion; go for an outing;
旅遊 tour; tourism;
夢遊 nightwalking; sleepwalking;
般遊 play without being conscious of the time;
神遊 feel as if one were visiting a place; make a mental travel; tour a place by imagination;
宴遊 leisure trip;
燕遊 make pleasure trips;
邀遊 invite sb for an outing;
娛遊 travel for pleasure;
遠遊 travel far away;
壯遊 (1) exciting trip; great tour; splendid tour; (2) take a long trip for ambitious project;

you

【鈾】 uranium;

[鈾礦] uranium ore;
瀝青油礦 pitchblende;

you

【楢】 quercus glandulifera;

you

【魷】 squid;

[魷魚] squid;
魷魚乾 dried squid;
炒魷魚 (1) fry squid; (2) be dismissed; be fired; be kicked out; be sacked;

you

【蝣】 mayfly;

蜉蝣 mayfly;

you

【蕕】 caryopteris divaricata, a water plant;

you

【輶】 (1) light; (2) light carriage;

[輶車] light carriage;

[輶軒] light carriage for an imperial emissary;

you

【繇】 same as 由 , through, via, by way of;

you³

you

【友】 (1) friend; (2) friendly; (3) fraternal love; fraternity; (4) befriend;

[友愛] fraternal love; friendly affection; friendship;
友愛互助 fraternal cooperation;
互助友愛 help each other out of fraternal love;
團結友愛 be united fraternally;

[友邦] ally; friendly nation;

[友儕] peers;
友儕衝突 conflicts between peers;
友儕認同 peer recognition;
友儕壓力 peer pressure;

[友黨] friendly party;

[友敵] frenemy;

[友好] (1) close friend; friend; (2) amicable; amity; buddy-buddy; congenial; friendly;
友好的 amicable; chummy;
友好關係 entente;
~ 保持友好關係 keep friends with;
友好合作 the friendly relations and cooperation;
友好接待 receive cordially;
友好人士 friendly personage;
友好往來 exchange of friendly visits; friendly intercourse;
友好相處 keep in with; live on friendly terms with;
友好協會 friendship association;
表示友好 offer friendship;
不甚友好 standoffish;
不友好的 churlish;
態度友好 have a friendly attitude;

[友軍] friendly forces;

[友朋] companions; friends;

[友情] fraternal love; friendly sentiments; friendship;
表達友情 express one's friendly sentiments;
斷絕友情 renounce friendship;
離間友情 alienate affection between friends;
削弱友情 weaken friendship;
珍惜友情 treasure friendship;

[友人] friend;

[友善] amicable; friendly;
友善的 affable;

[友誼] companionship; friendship;
友誼比賽 friendly competition;
友誼賽 friendly; friendly match;
友誼為重 set store by friendship; value friendship above all;
持久的友誼 abiding friendship; enduring friendship; lasting friendship;
背棄友誼 violate friendship;
表達友誼 show one's friendship to;
持久的友誼 abiding friendship;
斷絕友誼 break off a friendship;
毀掉友誼 blast friendships;
獲得友誼 acquire the friendship of;
建立友誼 build friendships;
損害友誼 impair the friendship;
需要友誼 need friendship;
一生的友誼 lifelong friendship;
贏得友誼 win the friendship of;
永恒的友誼 durable friendship; perpetual friendship;
珍貴的友誼 precious friendship;
真正的友誼 proven friendship; real friendship;

筆友 pen pal;
敝友 my friend;
炒友 profiteer; speculator;
敵友 enemies and friends;
賭友 gambling companions;
飯友 dinner companion;
工友 (1) fellow worker; (2) manual worker;
故友 deceased friend;
好友 boon companion;
教友 coreligionist;
酒友 drinking companion; fellow lovers of the cup;
良友 beneficial friend; good friend;
盟友 (1) sworn friends; (2) ally;

密友 boon companion; bosom friend; close friend; confidant; crony; fast friend; intimate friend;
幕友 private assistant;
男朋友 boyfriend;
難友 fellow sufferer;
女朋友 girlfriend;
女友 (1) girlfriend; (2) female friend;
朋友 (1) buddy; chum; friend; (2) boyfriend or girlfriend;
票友 amateur performer of Beijing opera;
棋友 chess friend; fellow chess player;
契友 bosom friend; close friend;
親友 relatives and friends; kith and kin;
師友 a person one can resort to for advise;
詩友 friend in poetry;
室友 room-mate;
素友 old friend;
損友 bad company; injurious friend;
探友 visit friends;
悌友 kind to friends; show fraternal love for friends;
亡友 deceased friend;
畏友 esteemed friend; friend of stern moral integrity; respectable friend;
相友 be friends together;
孝友 filial piety and fraternal love;
小朋友 children; little child;
校友 alumnus or alumna;
燮友 gentle; good-natured;
學友 fellow student; schoolmate;
硯友 classmate;
益友 friend and mentor;
獄友 cellmate;
擇友 choose friends;
戰友 comrade-in-arms;
諍友 friend who gives forthright admonition;
知友 close friend; intimate friend;
執友 bosom friend;
至友 close friend; the closest friend;
摯友 bosom friend; intimate friend;

you

【有】 (1) have; possess; (2) exist; there is; (3) as...as; (4) one; some;

[有礙] a hindrance to; detrimental; get in way of; harmful; obstruct;
有礙發展 arrest the development;
有礙觀瞻 an eyesore; leave a bad impression to the beholder, offend the eye; repugnant to the eye; unsightly;
有礙健康 detrimental to health; harmful to health;
有礙交通 hinder traffic;
有礙進步 bar progress;
有礙團結 detrimental to unity; harmful to unity;

[有案可稽] be documented; can be checked against file; on file; on record; verifiable;

[有病] ill; sick; unwell;

[有才] gifted; talented;
有才無德 have ability but no moral character;
有才無命 gifted but out of luck;
有才之士 person of talent;

[有產階級] owner class; propertied class;

[有償] compensated with money;
有償服務 repayable service;
有償新聞 pay news;

[有待] await; remain;
有待發現 remain to be discovered;
有待分曉 hang in the balance;
有待改進 there is still room for improvement;
有待解決 remain to be solved;
有待調查 await investigation;
有待完善 be left to be desired;
有待修理 stand in need of repairs;
有待研究 await being studied;
有待印證 have yet to be confirmed;

[有道] (1) learned and virtuous; (2) lawful; reasonable; right;
有道之財方可取，無道之錢莫強求 if money can be acquired with propriety, then acquire, but let not unjust wealth be sought for with violence;
盜亦有道 robbers also have their code of conduct; thieves have their code of honour;
質正有道 present to the scholars for advice and criticism;

[有德] righteous; virtuous;
有德無過 virtuous and without fault;

[有的] some;
有的是 a lot of; have plenty of; plentiful; there is no lack of;
有的放矢 shoot the arrow at the target; with a definite object in view; with a well-defined objective in mind;

[有底] know the true character of a matter;

心中有底 know what is what;

[有點兒] a bit; a little; rather; some; somewhat; sort of;

有點兒懷疑 have a kind of suspicion;

[有毒] noxious; poisonous; venomous;

有毒物質 poisonous substance;

有毒煙霧 noxious fumes;

[有耳] have ears;

隔墻有耳 pitchers have ears; walls have ears;

[有方] in the right way; with the proper method;

教導有方 be skilful in teaching and providing guidance;

教子有方 have a fine method of schooling one's children;

領導有方 exercise good leadership;

[有份兒] have a share; participate in;

[有鳳] a phoenix exists;

有鳳來儀 a phoenix comes with grace to rest;

有鳳求凰 go about looking for a mate; make a proposal;

[有夫] have a husband;

羅敷有夫 married woman;

[有感] comment on sth;

有感而發 make a comment out of personal feeling;

[有功] have performed meritorious service; have rendered great service;

有功必賞 give the credit that a person deserves;

~有功必賞，有罪必罰 merit must be rewarded and offences punished;

有功不居 disclaim all achievements;

有功不賞 leave meritorious service unrewarded;

有功不賞，有勞不錄 merit goes unrewarded and distinguished service uncited;

不求有功，但求無過 dare not hope for grat accomplishment, but hope only to be free from mistakes; not to hope to distinguish oneself, but seek only to avoid blame;

[有關] as regard to; be connected with; bear on; concern; get in with; have a bearing on; have a finger in the pie; have relation to sth; have relations with; have sth to do with; in connection with; in relation to; in the way of; involve; it's a concern of; relate to; relative to; with regard to;

有關部門 the department concerned;

有關當局 the authorities concerned;

有關方面 interested parties; the parties concerned;

有關各方 all parties concerned;

有關雙方 both parties concerned;

與此事有關 be concerned in this affair;

[有鬼] there is sth fishy;

心中有鬼 have a bellyful of tricks; have sth to hide; have ulterior designs;

[有害] detrimental; harmful; pernicious;

有害的 baneful; deleterious;

有害健康 detrimental to one's health; do harm to one's health;

有害無益 bring nothing but harm to; do harm rather than good; not helpful but harmful; worse than useless;

對人有害 pernicious to people;

對社會有害 pernicious to the society;

對心臟有害 bad for one's heart;

[有後] have offspring;

[有機] (1) there is an opportunity; (2) organic;

有機分析 organic analysis;

有機化學 organic chemistry;

有機可乘 have loopholes to exploit; there is a crack to wedge oneself into; there is a loophole that can be used; there is an opportunity to be seized; there is an opportunity to take advantage of;

有機酸 organic acid;

[有積] have digestive disorders;

有積無虞 store is no sore;

[有家難奔] have a home but be unable to go;

[有鑒於此] because of this; in view of this;

[有獎] premium;

有獎儲蓄 premium savings deposit;

有獎公債 premium savings bonds;

有獎銷售 prize-giving sales;

[有教無類] everyone can get an education, whoever; make no social distinctions in teaching; proper education levels all social classes; provide education for all people without discrimination; with education there is no distinction between classes or races;

[有界] bounded;

有界量 bounded quantity;

[有勁] (1) potent; strong; (2) amusing; interesting; (3) full of gusto;

[有救] capable of being saved; still hopeful;

[有空] at leisure; at one's leisure; have time;

[有孔蟲] foraminifera;

[有口] speak;

有口皆碑 be praised by all; be universally acclaimed; enjoy great popularity among the people; win universal praise;

有口難辯 find it hard to vindicate oneself; hard to explain;

有口難分 find it difficult to vindicate oneself;

有口難言 cannot bring oneself to mention sth; dare not speak out; find it hard to bring up a matter;

有口無心 not really mean what one says; one's bark is worse than one's bite; say what one does not mean; sharp in tongue but not malicious in mind; sharp-tongued but not malicious;

[有愧] devious;

當之有愧 I find myself not up to the honour accorded me;

良心有愧 conscience-stricken; guilty conscience;

內心有愧 have a guilty conscience;

受之有愧 accepting sth is embarrassing; I am not worthy of sth; receive sth with shame;

問心有愧 feel a twinge of conscience; feel a twinge of remorse; feel guilty; have a guilty conscience; have sth on one's conscience; pangs of conscience for;

心中有愧 feel ashamed; have a guilty conscience; have sth on one's conscience;

於心有愧 ashamed in the heart; feel ashamed; have a guilty conscience; have sth on one's conscience;

[有賴] depend on; rest on;

[有勞] have troubled;

有勞等候 I am sorry to have kept you waiting; I am sorry I kept you waiting;

有勞無逸 all work and no play;

有勞有逸 alternate work with rest;

有勞遠迎 I deeply appreciate your kindness in coming so far to meet me;

[有理] in the right; justified; logical; reasonable;

有理分式 rational fraction;

有理式 rational expression;

有理走遍天下，無理寸步難行 if you are in the right, you can travel anywhere in the world, if you are in the wrong, it's hard to move an inch; with justice on your side, you can go anywhere; without it, you can't take a step;

有理無情 disregard personal feelings;

公説公有理，婆説婆有理 both parties claim to be in the right; each of the two quarreling parties insists that it is right; each says he is right; the Old Man says he is right, the Old Lady says she is right — hard to judge; there is much to be said on both sides; wranglers never want words;

[有禮] civil; courteous; polite; well-mannered;

彬彬有禮 courteous; genial; gentility; refined and courteous; urbane; well-mannered; with a good grace;

謙恭有禮 modest and polite;

[有利] advantageous; beneficial; conducive; favourable; helpful; profitable;

有利必有弊 advantages are inevitably accompanied by disadvantages; any advantage must be accompanied with some disadvantage; everything has its advantages as well as disadvantages; good always goes together with evil; no fire without smoke; no good without its mixture of evil; no garden without its weeds; nothing is perfect; there is no fire without smoke; where there are advantages there are also disadvantages;

有利地位 advantageous position;

~處於有利地位 sitting in the catbird seat;

有利皆圖 draw water to one mill;

有利可圖 bring grist to the mill; have good prospects of gain; profitable; stand to gain; there is money in it; there is profit to be derived; there is profit to be made;

有利無弊 have everything to gain and nothing to lose; have nothing to lose but everything to gain;

有利無害 gain everything and lose nothing;

有利有弊 have both advantages and disadvantages; there are advantages and disadvantages;

[有力] energetic; forceful; powerful; strong; vigorous;
有力出力 let those with strength contribute strength;
孔武有力 full of power and energy; have great physical strength and courage; very strong;

[有臉] (1) honourable; proud; respectable; (2) favoured; loved;

[有零] odd;

[有名] (1) celebrated; distinguished; famous; illustrious; noted; renowned; well-known; (2) one's name is on the list;
榜上有名 one's name is on the list of successful candidates;

[有目共賞] appeal to all alike; evoke the admiration of the beholders; evoke the appreciation of the beholders; have universal appeal;

[有目無珠] as blind as a bat;

[有奶便是娘] he that serves God for money will serve the devil for better wages; obey anyone who feeds one; lick the hand that throws one a few crumbs; submit oneself to anyone ho feeds one; submit to whoever feeds one; whoever suckles me is my mother;

[有難同當] join in with sb to take a risk;

[有年] for years;

[有氣] angry; furious; indignant;
有氣無力 breath is present but vigour is absent; faint; feeble; listless; slack; weak; wearily;

[有錢] be made of money; in the money; rich; wealthy; well-off; well-to-do;
有錢出錢 let those with money contribute money; those with money should contribute money;
有錢出錢，有力出力 those with money can give money and those with strength can give strength;
有錢的 loaded; well-heeled; well-off;
有錢階層 moneyed classes;
有錢就花 money burns a hole in one's pocket;
有錢男子漢，無錢漢子難 money alone makes a hero; money makes the man;
有錢人 haves; old money; rich; wealthy;
~有錢人的氣派 a patina of wealth;
~巴結有錢人 court favour from the rich; fawn on the rich;
有錢使得鬼推磨 a golden key opens every door; if you have money, you can make the devil push a millstone for you; money can work miracles; money makes the mare go; money talks; money will do anything; with money, one can make the devil turn the millstone;
有錢一條龍，無錢一條蟲 with money, one is a dragon; without it, one is a worm;
有錢有勢 be possessed of wealth and power; have money and power; rich and influential; rich and powerful;
~有錢有勢的人 nob;
非常有錢 loaded; stinking rich;

[有情] be affected by love; have a tender feeling for one of the opposite sex;
有情人終成眷屬 all shall be well, Jeck shall have Jill; the lovers finally get married;
有情有義 have affection and faith;
天若有情天亦老 if heaven has emotions, it would grow old too;

[有窮] exhaustible; have a limit; have an end;

[有求] seek help;
有求必應 all requests will be granted; ask, and it shall be given you; give response to every prayer; grant whatever is requested; grant whenever asked; never to say no to any request; respond to every plea;
有求於人 have to look to others for help;

[有趣] amusing; interesting; fascinating;
有趣的 diverting;
~有趣的影片 diverting film;
胖白有趣 plump; stout;
這很有趣 this beats cockfighting; that's amusing; that's exciting; that's fascinating; that's funny; that's interesting;

[有去] there is departure;
有去無還 gone never to return; would never come out alive;
有去無回 once one leaves one's home, one has little chance of returning;

[有權] entitle;

[有染] have an affair with;
和 ... 有染 have an affair with sb;

[有人] (1) some people; somebody; someone; (2) there is sb there;

[有如] as if; as though; just like; like;

[有辱] bring dishonour to;

有辱家門 scandal to the family;

有辱門楣 be a disgrace to one's family; be a disgrace to the house;

有辱聲名 bring into discredit;

有辱斯文 be a disgrace to the educated class;

有辱祖宗 besmirch the fair fame of one's forefathers;

[有色] coloured;

[有啥吃啥] eat whatever is available;

[有啥説啥] come out with what one thinks; say what one has to say; speak one's mind;

[有傷] destructive to; harmful to;

有傷大雅 offend against good taste; offensive to good taste;

有傷風化 an offence against decency; corrupt manners and customs; destructive to the morals; harmful to public morals; harmful to society's morals;

有傷感情 hurt one's feelings;

有傷和氣 impair friendship;

有傷國體 discredit one's country; harmful to national prestige; tarnish the honour of one's country;

有傷體面 lower one's dignity;

[有身] pregnant;

[有神] (1) full of spirit; (2) miraculous;

有神論 theism;

[有生] birth; in one's remaining years;

有生必有死 as a man lives, so shall he die; dying is as natural as living; he that is once born, once must die;

有生力量 effective force; effective strength;

有生以來 even since one's birth; in all one's born days;

有生之年 in one's remaining years; the rest of one's life;

[有聲] having sound;

有聲讀物 talking books;

有聲有色 dramatically; full of sound and colour; tone and colour;

有聲資料 sound archives;

[有失] lose; there is a loss of;

有失觀瞻 lose one's dignity; make an ill appearance;

有失國體 tarnish the honour of one's country;

有失和氣 fail to keep on good terms;

有失檢點 careless about; indiscreet in;

有失身份 beneath one's dignity; lose caste;

有失體面 beneath one's dignity; lose face;

有失體統 disgraceful; drop a brick; scandalous; unbecoming;

有失無得 no gain at all but only loss; no gain but loss;

[有詩為證] a poem testifies that; there is a poem to prove the point;

[有時] at times; betimes; every so often; sometimes;

有時候 at times; by fits and starts; every now and then; every now and again; from one moment to the next; from time to time; now and then; now...now...; now...then...; occasionally; sometimes;

物各有時 everything is good in its season;

[有事] (1) be engaged; busy; occupied; (2) if sth happens; get into trouble; meet with an accident; when problems crop up;

有事來找我 come to me if you are in difficulty;

有事羈身 be detained by some business;

我現在有事 I have a matter to attend to now;

[有恃無恐] be emboldened by the support; fear nothing with sb at his back; feel reassured and emboldened; have sth secure to rely on; secure in the knowledge that one has strong backing; with someone's backing, one does not fear anything;

[有守] adhere to principles; have moral fortitude;

有守有為 act according to principles; can act and maintain certain principles; have moral integrity and be promising; uphold principles;

[有數] know how things stand;

肚裏有數 have a pretty good idea; know in one's heart; know very well in one's mind; know what's what;

心中有數 know what's what;

胸中有數 feel sure of sth; have a good idea of how things stand; have a head for figures; know quite well how things stand; know the true state of affairs;

[有司] official;

[有素] have a solid foundation;

[有損] hurt; impair;

有損大雅 offend against good taste;

有損健康 impair one's health;

有損名譽 compromise one's reputation;

有損權威性 hurt one's authority;

有損威嚴 impair one's dignity;

有損友誼 inimical to friendship;

有損尊嚴 hurt one's dignity;

[有所] somewhat; to some extent;

有所補益 of some benefit; of some help;

有所不及 there are things where one cannot compare with another;

有所不為 there are certain things that a man of principle will not stoop to;

有所不為然後可以有為 refrain from doing some things in order to be able to do other things; you must leave some things undone if you want to get others done;

有所不知 there are things which one does not know; unaware of sth;

有所成就 get sb somewhere; get somewhere; get there;

有所改進 improve to some extent;

有所顧忌 have certain scruples about;

有所顧慮 have scruples;

有所借鑒 have certain experience to draw on;

有所了解 have gained some understanding;

有所收斂 restrain oneself;

有所提高 embody some improvements;

有所選擇 be allowed a choice;

有所隱諱 there are things concealed and unspoken of;

有所轉變 have some changes;

有所長進 make a modest advance;

有所追求 after sth;

有所遵循 for general guidance; have sth to go by;

[有條] in good order;

有條不紊 everything in good order and well arranged; in a businesslike manner; in a methodical way; in a systematic fashion; in an orderly way; in apple-pie order; in good order; in good order and well arranged; in good shape; methodical; orderly; systematic; with regularity and thoroughness; without any confusion;

井井有條 be arranged in good order; in an orderly manner and in proper sequence; in apple-pie order; in good order; in perfect order; shipshape; systematically and in an orderly way;

[有頭有臉兒] (1) honoured; respected; (2) presentable;

[有托而逃] shirk responsibility under an excuse;

[有望] hopeful; promising;

[有為] capable of great achievements; promising;

有為有守 can act and maintain certain principles;

發奮有為 proving one's worth; with firm resolve to succeed;

奮發有為 enthusiastic and press on; resolve to do some great things;

年輕有為 young and promising;

[有聞必錄] note down all one has heard without discrimination; put in record all that is heard; record everything one has heard; record whatever one hears; record whatsoever has been heard;

[有無] have and have-not;

忽有忽無 suddenly appear and disappear;

互通有無 each making up what the other lacks; each supplying what the other needs; help supply each other's needs; meet each other's needs; mutual help to make up what the other lacks;

可有可無 be as well without it as with it; dispensable; inessential; may or may not be needed; might just as well not have existed; not essential; not indispensable; of no consequence;

若有若無 intangible; vague;

以有易無 barter; exchange what one has for what one has not; trade what one has in abundance for what one does not have;

有勝於無 a bit is better than nothing;

[有喜] expecting; pregnant;

[有隙] harbour a grudge;

有隙可乘 have some openings to exploit; there is a crack to get in by; there is a crack to squeeze through; there is a loophole to exploit;

[有閒階級] leisure class;

[有限] a little; finite; limited; not much; restricted;

有限公司 limited company;

有限國際招標 limited international bidding;

有限詢價 limited inquiry;

有限招標 limited tenders;

有限責任 limited liability;

財力有限 be financially limited;

範圍有限 be limited in scope;

名額有限 the number of people allowed is limited;

能力有限 be limited in one's ability;

數量有限 be limited in number;

[有線] wired;

有線電視 cable television;

~有線電視台 cable television station;

~有線電視線路 cable television line;

有線廣播 wire broadcasting;

[有向圖] digraph;

對稱有向圖 symmetric digraph;

無圈有向圖 acyclic digraph;

線有向圖 line digraph;

自補有向圖 self-complement digraph;

自逆有向圖 self-converse digraph;

[有效] effective; valid;

有效票 valid ticket;

有效期 (1) term of validity; (2) self-life of perishable goods;

有效投資 effective investing;

有效性 effectiveness;

~有效性測試 validation test;

~操縱有效性 control effectiveness;

~生物有效性 biological effectiveness;

有效需求 effective demand;

不再有效 no longer effective; no longer in force;

繼續有效 continue to be in effect;

完全有效 in full force;

行之有效 prove effective in practice;

依然有效 still in effect;

[有些] (1) a few; some; (2) rather; somewhat;

有些不妥 rather amiss;

有些過份 go a bit too far;

[有心] (1) have a mind to; have the intention of; intend to; set one's mind on; (2) deliberately; purposely;

有心情 in the vein for;

有心人 person who sets his mind on doing sth useful; person with high aspirations and determination;

有心無力 more than willing but lacking power; the spirit is willing but the flesh is weak;

有心胸 ambitious; have eyesight aiming high and far; independent-minded;

有心眼兒 shrewd; vigilant;

[有信] keep one's promise;

言而有信 as good as one's word; carry out one's word to fruition; faithful in word; true to one's word; keep a promise inviolate; make good one's promises;

[有形] concrete; tangible; visible;

有形產權 visible property;

有形固定資產 visible fixed assets;

有形貿易 visible trade;

有形資產 physical assets; tangible assets;

[有氧] aerobic;

有氧健身鞋 aerobic shoes;

有氧健身舞 aerobic dance;

[有益] beneficial; profitable; useful;

有益處 advantageous; beneficial; conducive; profitable; useful;

有益無損 can only do good, not harm; have profit but no loss; it is altogether advantageous;

有益於健康 good for one's health;

鍛煉對你有益 exercise is good for you;

對身心有益 have a happy effect both mentally and physically;

[有意] (1) be inclined to; be interested; have a mind to; show interest; (2) deliberately; intentionally; purposely;

有意搗亂 make trouble by deliberate intention;

有意刁難 deliberately make things difficult for sb; make things difficult for sb on purpose;

有意見 have reservations; have sth to say;

有意破壞 destroy...on purpose;

有意識 consciously; knowingly; purposely; wittingly;

有意說謊 tell a deliberate lie;

有意思 (1) meaningful; significantly; (2) enjoyable; exciting; interesting;

有意無意之間 by accident or design;

consciously or unconsciously; semi-conscious; wittingly or unwittingly;
有意歪曲 distort deliberately;
有意義的 meaningful; significant;
有意栽花花不發，無心插柳柳成蔭 follow love, and it will flee thee; flee love, and it will follow thee;

[有因] there is a reason for it;

[有癮] be addicted to; have formed a habit;

[有勇無謀] as bold as a blind Bayard; bold yet unskilful; boldness without contrivances; brave but not resourceful; brave but without stratey; courageous but not resourceful; foolhardy; have more guts than brains; have valour but lack strategy; more brave than wise; though brave, one lacks wisdom and tact; very brave but not very clever; with only courage and no strategy;

[有勇有謀] courageous and intelligent;

[有用] beneficial; practical; serviceable; useful;
極為有用 extremely useful;
沒有用 useless;
~抱怨沒有用 it's no use complaining;

[有餘] (1) have a surplus; have enough and to spare; (2) odd;
綽綽有餘 enough and to spare; have more than enough; more than enough to meet the needs; more than sufficient;
綽然有餘 with great saving of space;
心有餘而力不足 more than willing but lacking the power to; one is willing, yet unable; one's ability falls short of one's wishes; one's mind is willing, but the body is weak; the spirit is willing, but the flesh is weak; willing but lacking the power to do; willing but unable;
~八十老公挑擔子—心有餘而力不足 an eighty-year-old man using a carrying pole – the spirit is willing, but the flesh is not up to it;
游刃有餘 more than equal to a task; handle butcher's cleaver skilfully – do a job with skill and ease; handle a cleaver with skill; highly competent;
自足有餘 more than self-sufficient;

[有冤] when there are grievances;
有冤報冤 eye for eye; tooth for tooth;
~有冤報冤，有仇報仇 if there are grievances, revenge; if there are animosities, take vengeance; measure for measure;
有冤難伸 find no redress for one's grievances;
有冤伸冤 any injustice provokes an outcry;
~有冤伸冤，有苦訴苦 those who have been wronged stand up and demand that their wrongs be redressed and those who have been made to suffer speak out against those responsible for their suffering;
有冤無處伸 have no one to complain of one's injustice;

[有緣] linked by ties of fate;
有緣千里來相會 though born a thousand miles apart, souls which are one shall meet;
~有緣千里來相會，無緣對面不相逢 no distance can separate what heaven unites, or unite what heaven separates;
有緣千里相逢 though born a thousand miles apart, souls which are one will meet;

[有孕] expecting; pregnant;

[有增] keep growing;
有增無減 increase steadily; grow more frequent; never to reduce but increase; there is increase but no decrease;
有增無已 continue to increase; keep growing; mount without a stop; on the increase;

[有章可循] have rules and regulations to go by; have rules to follow;

[有志] aspire;
有志不在年高 one's will does not depend on how old one is;
有志一同 of the same ink;
有志者 aspirant;
~有志者事竟成 a person who has a settled purpose will surely succeed; a wilful person will have his way; determination will lead to success; nothing is impossible to a willing heart; success goes to the determined; the person who has a firm resolve will surely succeed; to him that wills, ways are not wanting; ways are not wanting to any body who hath a mind; where

there is a will there is a way; will will have will, though will woe win;
有志之士 person of high ambitions; person of noble aspirations; person with lofty ideals;
[有治人無治法] good laws without capable law enforcers are useless;
[有種] have guts;
[有主] what is primary;
有主有次 a distinction should be made between what is primary and what is secondary;
有主有從 a distinction should be made between what is primary and what is secondary;
物各有主 everything has its owner;
[有助於] conduce to; conducive to; contribute to;
有助於健康 make for good health;
[有罪] culpability; guilty;
有罪的 culpable;

保有 have; posses; own;
備有 have; be equipped with;
別有 have a special;
持有 hold;
大有 be of great;
富有 be full of; be rich in; rich; wealthy;
賦有 be endowed with some gift;
公有 publicly-owned;
固有 innate; intrinsic;
國有 belong to the state; be nationalized;
還有 (1) there is still some left; (2) furthermore; in addition;
含有 contain;
罕有 rare;
懷有 cherish; harbour; owe;
具有 be provided with; posses;
領有 posses; own;
沒有 (1) not have; there is not; without; (2) not so...as; (3) less than;
莫須有 fabricated; groundless;
確有 there is indeed;
少有 exceptional; rare; scarce; seldom;
設有 come complete with;
私有 private; privately-owned;
所有 own; possess;
特有 peculiar; characterize;
萬有 all creation; all things under the sun;
罔有 have not;
唯有 only;
惟有 alone; only;
未有 can never be; have never been; have never had;
烏有 naught; nothing;
無有 nothing and something;
希有 very rare;
稀有 rare; uncommon;
鮮有 rare; seldom to have;
現有 existing; have on hand; now available;
享有 enjoy (rights, prestige, etc);
幸有 fortunate to have;
焉有 how could there be such;
奄有 put under one's control;
也有 (1) there are in addition; (2) there are others;
應有 deserved; due; proper;
擁有 be armed with; come into possession of; come into sb's possession; conquer; get possession of sth; hold; in possession of; in the possession of; occupy; of; own; possess;
遇有 in case of; in the event of;
原有 original;
占有 take possession of;
佔有 (1) have; own; possess; (2) hold; occupy; (3) have; own;
只有 (1) alone; only; (2) have to;
祇有 alone; have nothing but; only;
專有 exclusive;
縱有 even if there is; even though there is;

you
【酉】 (1) tenth of the twelve Terrestrial Branches; (2) 5:00 p.m. - 7:00 p.m.;
[酉時] period of the day from 5 p.m. to 7 p.m.;

you
【卣】 (in ancient China) Chinese chalice; container for wine;

you
【莠】 (1) foxtail; (2) bad; detestable; ugly; undesirable; vicious;
[莠民] outlaws; wicked people; villains;
[莠言] bad words; dirty words;

良莠 the good and the bad;

you
【銪】 europium;

you
【牖】 (1) window; (2) educate; enlighten; guide;

［牖戶］ window and door;
［牖民］ educate the people; guide the people;
［牖中窺日］ peep at the sun through the window – limited outlook and experience;

戶牖 door; door and windows;

you
【槱】 ancient rite of building fires in worship;

you
【黝】 black; bluish black; dark;
［黝黑］ dark; swarthy;
［黝黝］ dark; gloomy;
黑黝黝 (1) shiny black; (2) stroll; walk about;

you⁴
you
【又】 (1) again; also; in addition to; (2) and; (3) furthermore; moreover;
［又稱］ (1) also called; also known as; (2) say further that;
［又及］ P.S. (postscript)
［又來了］ how typical; there you go again;
［又名］ alias; alternate name;
［又是］ (1) again; (2) also; (3) still another; (4) the same as;
［又說］ add;
又說又笑 talk and laugh at the same time;
［又要］ make additional demands;
又要馬兒跑得好，又要馬兒不吃草 eat one's cake and have it; expect the horse to run fast but not let it graze; have one's cake and eat it; wanting a horse to run fast yet unwilling to let it graze;
［又…又…］ and; but also;
又氣又愧 feel angry and ashamed;
又瘦又笨 lanky;
又瘦又乏 lean and weakly;
又喜又懼 feel both joy and fear; feel pleased yet fearful;
又髒又臭 dirty and smelly;

you
【右】 (1) right; right side; (2) the Right; (3) aid; assist; (4) emphasize;
［右臂］ (1) right arm; (2) important helper; right-hand man;
［右邊］ on the right; right-hand side; right side;
靠右邊走 keep to the right;
［右側］ offside;
［右面］ right-hand side; right side;
［右手］ right hand;
右手定則 right-hand rule;
［右腿］ right leg;
右腿向前舉 right leg forwards;
［右翼］ right-wing;
右翼人士 right-winger;
右翼示威者 rightist demonstrators;
右翼政黨 right-wing party;

權右 big wigs; highly-placed personalities; top dogs;
向右 towards the right;
左右 (1) about; around (2) control; influence; master; (3) retinue; those in close attendance; (4) the left and right sides;

you
【幼】 (1) under age; young; (2) child; young;
［幼蟲］ larva;
［幼鵝］ gosling;
［幼兒］ child; infant; nestling;
幼兒教育 child education;
幼兒園 kindergarten; nursery school; preschool;
~幼兒園學童 preschooler;
~單班幼兒園 one-class kindergarten;
~多班幼兒園 multi-class kindergarten;
［幼苗］ plant; sapling; seedling; tender seedling;
［幼嫩］ delicate; young and tender;
［幼年］ childhood; infancy;
幼年河 young river;
幼年喪父 lose one's father when one is still a small child;
幼年喪母 lose one's mother in early childhood;
幼年失學 be deprived of schooling in one's childhood;
幼年型息肉病 juvenile polyposis;
幼年性反射 juvenile reflex;
幼年性息肉 juvenile polyp;
［幼女］ young girl;
［幼犬］ pup;
［幼弱］ young and delicate;
［幼童］ young child;
［幼小］ young and small;
［幼學壯行］ learn in youth and act in

adulthood; learn while young and practise when strong;
[幼芽] plumules; young buds;
[幼稚] childish; naive; puerile;
幼稚可愛 naïve and lovely;
幼稚可笑 childish and ignorant; derisive; ridiculously childish;
幼稚無知 childish ignorance; young and ignorant;
幼稚園 kindergarten;
~幼稚園教育 kindergarten education;
[幼子] youngest son;

婦幼 women and children;
老幼 young and old;
年幼 under age; young;
攜幼 take one's young children along;
長幼 seniority among family members; young and old;
自幼 since childhood;

you
【有】 same as 又;

you
【佑】 aid; bless; help; protect;
[佑助] aid; assist; help;

保佑 bless and protect;
庇佑 bless; prosper;

you
【侑】 (1) help; (2) urge to eat or drink; (3) repay other's kindness;
[侑觴] urge one to drink more wine during the banquet;

you
【囿】 (1) animal farm; enclosure; park; (2) hampered; limited;
[囿於一隅] be restricted to a narrow confine; limited in the knowledge of a narrow corner; unable to see widely enough;

拘囿 adhere to rigidly; rigidly restrain;
園囿 garden; park or zoo;

you
【宥】 forgive; lenient; pardon;
[宥過] excuse a mistake;
[宥免] remit an offense;
[宥恕] excuse; forgive; pardon;
[宥罪] forgive an offense; pardon a crime;

寬宥 excuse; forgive;
原宥 excuse; forgive;

you
【柚】 (1) grapefruit; pumelo; shaddock; (2) teak; teak tree;
[柚木] (1) teak; teak tree; (2) teak; teakwood;
[柚皮] shaddock ped;
[柚子] grapefruit; pomelo; shaddock;

西柚 grapefruit;

you
【祐】 divine help;
[祐助] divine help;

you
【蚴】 larva;
[蚴蟲] larva;

毛蚴 caterpillar larva;
囊尾蚴 cysticercous cercaria;
囊蚴 bladder larva; encysted cercaria;
尾蚴 cercaria;
原尾蚴 procercoid;

you
【莠】 a pronunciation of 莠;

you
【釉】 glaze;
[釉工] glazer;
[釉陶] china; glazed pottery;
褐斑釉陶 brown china;
[釉質] enamel;

瓷釉 porcelain glaze;
色釉 colour glaze;

you
【誘】 (1) guide; induce; lead; (2) allure; captivate; decoy; entice; lure; seduce; tempt;
[誘兵] pretend to flee;
誘兵不追 not press the troop that pretend to flee;
[誘捕] entrap; entrapment; lure a criminal out of hiding and arrest him; put a pinch of salt on sb's tail; trap;
[誘導] guide; induce; induction; lead;
誘導價格 leading price;
誘導物 inducer;
誘導性問題 leading question;

成花誘導 floral induction;
接合誘導 cross induction;
胚誘導 embryonal induction;
同性誘導 assimilative induction;

[誘敵] induce the enemy;
誘敵前進 lead the enemy to advance;
誘敵深入 lure the enemy in deep;

[誘餌] bait; decoy;
充當誘餌 act as a decoy;
投誘餌 cast a bait; ground bait;

[誘發] bring out; cause to happen; induce; induction;
神經性誘發 neural induction;

[誘供] induce a person to make a confession; trap a person into a confession;

[誘拐] abduct; carry off by fraud; entice; kidnap; seduce;
誘拐兒童 abduct a child;

[誘惑] (1) entice; lure; seduce; tempt; (2) allure; attract; fascinate;
誘惑人心 tempt the hearts of the people;
誘惑力 drawing power; lure; pulling power;
不受誘惑 resist temptation;
擋不住誘惑 fall before the temptation; succumb to temptation;
抵制誘惑 resist temptation;
頂住誘惑 withstand temptation;
面對誘惑 face temptations;
受誘惑 fall before the temptation;

[誘姦] entice into unlawful sexual intercourse; seduce;

[誘騙] beguile; cajole; induce by deceit; inveigle; trap; trick;
兒童誘騙 grooming;

[誘人] attract;
誘人的 enticing; tempting;
誘人犯法 induce others to break the law;
誘人犯罪 induce others to break the law;
誘人騙局 make a feint to fool sb;
誘人入彀 use a trick to make sb do sth;
誘人為惡 seduce others to evil;
誘人作惡 attempt others to do wrong; seduce others to evil;

[誘殺] lure to destruction; trap and kill;

[誘逃] induce sb to run away from home;

[誘降] lure into surrender;

[誘脅] cajole and coerce alternatively; tempt and threaten;

[誘掖] guide and encourage; lead and help;
誘掖後進 help and encourage the younger generation;

[誘因] incentive; inducement; remote cause;
經濟誘因 financial inducements;

[誘引] lure; seduce;

[誘致] attain an objective by means of temptation;

[誘走] toll off;

利誘 lure by promise of gain;
勸誘 induce; prevail upon; talk sb into;
煽誘 agitate; incite;
引誘 accost; attract; entice; lure; seduce;

you

【鼬】 weasel;

[鼬鼠] weasel;

艾鼬 polecat;
白鼬 stoat;
臭鼬 skunk;
短尾鼬 stoat;
黃鼬 yellow weasel;
青鼬 weasel;

yu¹

yu

【迂】 (1) circuitous; indirect; roundabout; winding; (2) clinging to outworn rules and ideas; hackneyed; impractical; old-fashioned; pedantic; stale; trite; unrealistic; (3) make a detour; (4) absurd; preposterous;

[迂誕] absurd; preposterous;
迂道 detour;
迂道過訪 break one's journey to call on sb; go thither by a roundabout way;

[迂腐] hackneyed; pedantry; stale; stubborn adherence to outworn rules and ideas; trite;
迂腐見解 hackneyed opinions;
腦筋迂腐 be pedantically minded;

[迂緩] dilatory; slow in movement; sluggish;

[迂迴] circuitous; roundabout; tortuous;
迂迴其詞 approach a subject in a roundabout way; beat about the bush;
迂迴前進 advance by a roundabout route; advance in roundabout ways; roundabout ways of advance;
迂迴曲折 have many turns and curves; in

a roundabout way; in zigzags; ins and outs; not straightforward; outs and ins; tortuous and devious; twists and turns; ups and downs;
迂迴說法所有格 periphrastic genitive;
迂迴戰術 flanking tactics;
迂迴助動詞 periphrastic auxiliary;
[迂見] absurd view; impractical opinion;
[迂久] for a long time;
[迂闊] high-sounding and impracticable; unrealistic;
迂闊之論 impracticable and vague statement; impractical views;
[迂陋] hackneyed; stale;
[迂路] detour;
[迂論] impractical argument; unrealistic statement;
[迂氣] indifference to practicality; indifference to reality;
[迂曲] circuitous; tortuous; twisted; winding;
[迂儒] impractical scholar; pedant;
迂儒之論 pedantic views; the views of a scholar behind the times;
[迂言] absurd statement; impractical remarks;
[迂遠] (1) impractical; unrealistic; (2) long and twisty;
迂遠而闊 impracticable and inapplicable;
[迂直] impractical and artless;
[迂拙] impractical and clumsy; impractical and foolish;
迂拙之道 impractical and stupid doctrine;

yu

【紆】 (1) bend; distort; meander; spiral; twist; wind; (2) a knot in one's heart; melancholy;
[紆緩] dilatory; slow;
[紆迴] circuitous; roundabout; winding;
[紆青拖紫] trailing in green and purple — the dresses and ornaments of high officials in ancient times;
[紆曲] (1) twists and turns; wind; (2) insinuating;
紆曲求寵 insinuate oneself into sb's favour;
[紆體] bend one's body; bow down; crouch;
[紆行] proceed through a winding and twisting path;
[紆徐] walk slowly;
[紆餘] wind and twist;
[紆鬱] melancholy; sad;

縈紆 circuitous; tortuous;

yu

【淤】 (1) become silted up; (2) silt;
[淤積] clog up; deposit; silt up; siltation;
[淤泥] mire; sludge; slush;
淤泥灘 mud flat;
積滿淤泥 become filled with silt;
[淤塞] be choked with silt; silt up;
[淤血] blood clot;
[淤閼] blocked by silt; choked by silt;
[淤鬱] blocked; silted;
[淤滯] be retarded by silt; choked; clogged; silt up;
[淤濁] muddy and turbid;
淤濁不清 muddy and unclear;

放淤 warp;

yu

【瘀】 haematoma;
[瘀膿] pus;
[瘀青] bruise;
[瘀傷] bruise; contusion;
[瘀血] blood stasis;

yu²

yu

【于】 (1) particle in literary use: in, at, by; (2) go; proceed; take;
[于歸] girl entering into matrimony;
[于今] (1) since; up to the present; (2) nowadays;
[于思] long and thick beard and mustache;
[于役] serve in the army;

單于 chief of the Xiongnu in ancient China;

yu

【予】 I; me
[予取予求] demand everything; make endless demands for; make endless exorbitant demands; make repeated demands of sb;
[予智自雄] conceited;

yu

【余】 (1) I; me; (2) a surname;

yu

【妤】 handsome and fair;

yu

【於】 (1) at; in; on; (2) for; to; (3) from; (4) that; (5) a surname;

[於此] here; in this place;

[於後] afterwards; as follows;

[於今] at present; now; since; up to the present;
於今為烈 it is now more serious;

[於人] to others;
嫁禍於人 bring trouble to others; bring evil on another maliciously; lay one's own fault at sb else's door; put one's misfortunes onto other people's shoulders; put the blame on sb else; shift the blame on sb; shift the blame on to others; transfer the evil to another; transfer the evil to others;
嫁罪於人 cast the blame on others; lay the blame on a person;

[於思] full of beard; rich in whiskers;

[於世] in the society; in the world;
見稱於世 be well spoken of; well-known;
見知於世 be recognized by society;

[於是] as a result; consequently; hence; so; then; thereafter; thereupon; thus;

[於下] as follows; below;

[於願已足] have nothing left to wish for;

安於 be content with; be satisfied with; feel contented in;
便於 be convenient for; be easy to;
瀕於 on the brink of;
不下於 (1) as many as; no less than; (2) as good as; not inferior to; on a par with;
不亞於 as good as; not second to;
長於 good at;
沉溺於 abandon oneself to; be given over to; give oneself over to; indulge in; wallow;
出於 proceed from; start from;
處於 in a certain condition;
錞於 a bronze musical instrument in ancient China;
次於 next to sth in order or importance;
大於 above and beyond; bigger than; larger than;
耽於 addict; indulge in;
等於 (1) equal to; equivalent to; (2) amount to; be tantamount to;
定於 due to; scheduled to;
對於 at; for; in regard to; to; toward;
富於 rich in;
甘於 ready to; willing to;
敢於 dare to; have the courage to;
關於 about; apropos of; as concerns; as far as ...goes; as far as ... is concerned; as for; as regards; as to; as touching; concerning; in connection with; in reference to; in regard to; with relation to; in respect to; in the matter of; on; on the subject of; regarding; relating to; relative to; respecting; when it comes to; with reference to; with regard to; with relation to; with respect to;
歸功於 attribute the success to; be attributed to sth; be credited with sth; credit sth to sb; give the credit to; owe to;
歸於 (1) be attributed to; belong to; (2) end in; result in;
過於 excessively; too;
基於 because of; by reason of; considering; due to; in consideration of; in view of; on account of; seeing that;
急於 all eagerness; anxious; burning to; impatient; itch for; long for;
寄望於 build one's hopes upon; fasten one's hopes on; lay one's hopes on; pin one's hopes on; place one's hopes on; rest one's hope on;
見於 refer to; see;
鑑於 inasmuch as;
鑒於 as; because of; by reason of; considering; for; for as much as; inasmuch as; in consideration of; in the light of; in view of; now that; on account of; owing to; seeing that; since; take into account; with a view to;
介於 between;
近於 bordering on; little short of;
居於 be in a certain position;
苦於 (1) suffer from; (2) be more bitter than;
懶於 not enthusiastic about sth; too lazy to do sth;
樂於 glad to; happy to;
利於 beneficial to; good for;
埋首於 be engrossed in; hammer away at; immerse oneself in;
忙於 hasten; hurry;
昧於 blind to;
免於 avert; avoid;
莫過於 nothing is more...than;
難於 difficult to;
溺於 be addicted to;
期於 expect; look forward to;

巧於 a good hand at; an expert at;
趨於 tend;
取決於 be decided by; depend on; depend upon; dependent on; dependent upon; hang on; hang upon; hinge on; it's up to; lie on; rest with ride on; turn on;
善於 adept in; good at;
懾於 be awed by;
甚於 exceed; surpass;
勝於 better than; outstrip;
適於 fit; suitable for;
屬於 belong to; part of;
死於 die as a result of;
位於 be located; be situated;
先於 antedate;
限於 be confined to; be limited to;
陷於 be caught in; fall into; land oneself in; sink into;
小於 be smaller than;
宜於 good for; suitable for;
易於 apt to; easily;
勇於 be bold in; be brave in;
由於 as; as a result of; be due to; because of; by virtue of; considering; due to; for; for-as-much-as; in consequence of; in consideration of; in that; in the light of; in view of; in virtue of; inasmuch as; on account of; owing to; seeing that; since; take...into account; take sth into consideration; thanks to; through; with; with a view to;
有助於 conduce to; contribute to;
寓於 contain; imply;
源於 be derived from; begin; derive from; originate from; originate in; rise in; start; stem from;
在於 (1) lie in; rest with; (2) be determined by; depend on;
止於 stop at; this far and no further;
至於 as for; as to; go so far as to;
置於 place in; put in;
忠於 faithful to; loyal to;
終於 at last; finally;

yu
【盂】 (1) basin; jar; (2) hunting party;
[盂鉢真傳] inherited teachings of a Buddhist master;
[盂方水方] if the basin is square, the water in it would also be square;
[盂蘭盆會] Ghost Festival;

鉢盂 alms bowl;
腎盂 renal pelvis;
痰盂 cuspidor; spittoon;

yu
【臾】 (1) a little while; a moment; a short time; an instant; (2) a surname;

yu
【俞】 (1) answer affirmatively; (2) make a boat by hollowing the leg; (3) a surname;
[俞允] approve; consent;

yu
【禺】 a mountain in Zhejiang;

yu
【竽】 a kind of musical instrument with thirty-six reeds;

yu
【娛】 (1) amuse; entertain; give pleasure to; (2) amusement; joy; pleasure;
[娛樂] amusement; entertainment; recreation;
娛樂場所 entertainment establishments;
~夜間娛樂場所 night spot;
娛樂工業 entertainment industry;
娛樂行業 entertainment business;
娛樂活動 recreational activities;
娛樂價值 enterainment value;
娛樂界 entertainment world;
娛樂片 entertainment film;
娛樂室 chill room; rec room; recreation room;
娛樂性行業 show business;
娛樂業 entertainment business; entertainment industry;
娛樂中心 leisure centre; recreational centre;
[娛目] please the eye;
[娛親] please one's parents;
[娛人] make sb happy;
[娛遊] travel for pleasure;
[娛悅] (1) please sb; (2) pleased;

歡娛 happy; joy and pleasure;
文娛 cultural recreation; entertainment;
自娛 amuse oneself;

yu
【舁】 carry; lift; raise;

yu
【雩】 sacrifice for the god of rain; pray for rain;

[雩祭] ritual in praying for rain;

yu

【魚】 (1) fish; (2) a surname;
[魚白] (1) silver-gray; (2) fish sperm; milt;
[魚幫水，水幫魚] help one another;
[魚餅] fishcake;
[魚叉] harpoon;
[魚場] fishery;
[魚沉雁杳] hear of sb no more; not hear from sb at all;
[魚池] fishpond;
[魚翅] shark's fin;
[魚大水小] a big fish in shallow water—a ponderous apparatus without sufficient resources for maintenance;

[魚店] fishmonger's;
[魚肚] fish maws used as food;
魚肚白 silver-gray;
[魚餌] bait; ground bait;
[魚販] fishmonger;
[魚放三日臭，久住招人嫌] fish and company smell in three days;
[魚粉] fish meal;
[魚腹] fish belly;
葬身魚腹 be swept to a watery grave; become food for fish — be drowned; feed the fish; get drowned; go to Davy Jone's locker; in Davy's locker;
[魚竿] fishing rod;
[魚肝油] cod-liver oil;
[魚缸] fish jar; fish tank; fishbowl;
[魚鈎] angle; fishhook;
[魚骨] fishbones;
剔魚骨 bone a fish;
[魚貫] in a column; in procession; in single file; one following the other; proceed one by one;
魚貫而出 file out;
魚貫而入 enter in single file; file in; stream into;
魚貫而行 follow one after another; proceed like a school of fish, one after the other; walk in Indian file; walk one after the other;
[魚膠] isinglass;
塊狀魚膠 cake isinglass;
片狀魚膠 leaf isinglass;
[魚具] fishing tackle;
[魚籃] creel;
[魚爛而亡] fall because of internal strife;
[魚雷] torpedo;
操縱魚雷 operate a torpedo;
反魚雷 anti-torpedo;
~反魚雷武器 anti-torpedo armature;
火箭推動魚雷 rocket-assisted torpedo;
空投魚雷 aerial torpedo;
音響魚雷 acoustic torpedo;
有線制導魚雷 wire-guided torpedo;
[魚類] fish;
魚類學 ichthyology;
魚類資源 fish stocks;
魚類種類 fish species;
攀鱸屬魚類 anabas;
鰤屬魚類 amberjack;
鯷科魚類 anchovy;
養殖魚類 farmed fish;
[魚鱗] scales of a fish;
[魚龍] ichthyosaur;
魚龍混雜 dragons and fish jumble together — good and bad people are mixed up;
[魚簍] creel;
[魚露] fish sauce;
[魚目混珠] mix the genuine with the fictitious; palm sth off; pass fish eyes for pearls; pass off the sham as the genuine;
[魚盤] fish plate;
[魚片] fish fillet; slices of fish meat;
[魚群] shoal of fish;
[魚肉] (1) fish and meat; (2) victims of oppression; (3) bully; oppress;
魚肉百姓 oppress the people cruelly;
魚肉餅 fish cake;
魚肉人民 make fish and flesh of the people — prey upon the people; victimize the people;
魚肉團兒 fish ball;
魚肉丸子 minced fish balls;
魚肉鄉里 victimize the village people;
自相魚肉 prey on one another;
[魚商] fishmonger;
[魚食] fish food;
[魚市] fish market;
[魚水] fish and water;
魚水和諧 agree like fish and water — marital harmony;
魚水情深 as close as fish and water;
魚水相依 be related to each other like fish

and water; depend on each other like fish and water;
魚水之情 relations like fish to water; the relation between fish and water;

[魚湯] fish stew;
熬魚湯 cook fish stew;

[魚塘] fish pond;

[魚條] fish finger; fish stick;

[魚頭] (1) fish's head; (2) difficult part of a job;

[魚網] net;
一張魚網 a net;

[魚尾] fish tail;
魚尾板 fishplate;
~ 角型魚尾板 angle fishplate;
~ 平面魚尾板 flat fishplate;
~ 曲柄魚尾板 cranked fishplate;
~ 外側魚尾板 outer fishplate;
~ 異型魚尾板 various shaped fishplate;
魚尾紋 crow's feet;

[魚蝦] fish and shrimps;

[魚腥味] fishy smell;

[魚雁] epistles; letters;
魚雁往來 incoming and outgoing of epistolary correspondence; keep up correspondence with each other;
魚雁鮮通 seldom write to one another;

[魚業] fishery;
鮑魚業 abalone fishery;
國內魚業 domestic fishery;
海洋魚業 offshore fishery;
沿岸魚業 shore fishery;
沿海魚業 coastal fishery;

[魚游釜中] like fish swimming in a cooking pot — in imminent peril;

[魚魚雅雅] possessing an air of dignity;

[魚與熊掌，不可兼得] unable to make up one's mind as to which of two desirable things to choose;

[魚躍] dive; fish jump; fish dive;
魚躍救球 make a diving save;
魚躍龍門 a fish leaping over the dragon gate — have passed a competitive examination;
魚躍水面 the fish leapt out of the water;

[魚找魚，蝦找蝦] like attracts like; like draws to like;

[魚質龍文] dragon in outward appearance but fish in essence—inferior thing with an impressive appearance;

[魚族學] ichthyography;

[魚子] roe; spawn;
魚子醬 caviar;

八帶魚 octopus;
八爪魚 octopus;
白姑魚 white Chinese croaker;
白鱗魚 Chinese herring;
白魚 whitefish;
鮑魚 abalone;
鼊魚 frogfish;
比目魚 flounders;
鯿魚 bream;
捕魚 catch fish; fish;
鮊魚 whitefish;
曹白魚 Chinese herring;
草魚 grass carp; herb carp;
鯧魚 pomfret;
成魚 adult fish;
刺魚 stickleback;
池魚 fish in the pond;
大黃魚 large yellow croaker;
大麻哈魚 dog salmon;
大頭魚 general term for cod;
大魚 big fish;
帶魚 hairtail;
丹鳳魚 phoenix;
淡水魚 freshwater fish;
燈籠魚 lantern fish;
釣魚 go fishing;
杜父魚 (1) cottiusculus gonnez; (2) mesocotus haitej;
蠹魚 silverfish;
盾皮魚 placodermi;
多骨魚 bony fish;
鵝頭魚 goose-head;
顎針魚 needlefish;
鱷魚 alligator; crocodile;
鱷魚 crocodile;
翻車魚 moonfish; sunfish;
翻鰓魚 open-gill;
飛魚 flying fish;
鯡魚 herring;
肺魚 dipnoan;
鳳尾魚 long-tailed anchovy;
鰒魚 abalone;
鱤魚 elopichthys bambusa;
狗魚 pike;
觀賞魚 ornamental fish;
鮭魚 trout;
桂魚 mandarin fish;
海魚 sea fish;

鱖魚 Chinese perch;
河魚 river fish;
黑魚 snakehead; snake-headed fish;
很小的魚 tiddler;
紅娘魚 red gurnard; sea robin;
紅魚 red snapper;
魟魚 skate;
後肛魚 post-anal fish;
鱟魚 king crab;
蝴蝶魚 butterfly fish;
虎頭魚 lionhead;
皇帶魚 oarfish;
黃姑魚 spotted maigre;
黃花魚 yellow croaker;
黃魚 yellow croaker;
喙魚 billfish;
活魚 live fish;
鯽魚 crucian carp;
加級魚 red porgy;
甲魚 fresh-water turtoise;
鰹魚 striped tuna;
劍魚 swordfish;
金槍魚 albacore; bluefin tuna; tuna;
金線魚 golden thread; red coat;
金魚 goldfish;
棘冠星魚 acanthaster;
青魚 black carp;
鯨魚 whale;
鏡魚 butterfish; silvery pomfret;
鋸鱗魚 big-eyed soldierfish;
孔雀魚 guppy;
快魚 Chinese herring;
鱠魚 Chinese herring;
鯉魚 carp;
鰱魚 silver carp;
鐮魚 Moorish idol;
鯪魚 dace;
柳穿魚 linaria vulgaris;
隆頭魚 wrasse;
龍睛魚 telescope goldfish;
龍頭魚 Bombay duck; bumbalo;
鱸魚 bass; perch;
馬鮫魚 Spanish mackerel;
猫魚 small fish as cat's food;
矛尾魚 latimeria;
梅童魚 baby croaker;
明太魚 stock fish;
墨斗魚 cuttlefish; inkfish;
墨魚 cuttlefish; inkfish; squid;
木魚 wooden drum;
胖頭魚 bighead; variegated carp;
鯰魚 catfish;
牛舌魚 tongue sole; tonguefish;
牛尾魚 flathead;
培養魚 breed fish;
偏口魚 flatfish;
平魚 common pomfret;
旗魚 sailfish;
槍魚 marlin;
親魚 parent fish;
青鱗魚 herring;
青魚 black carp;
鯨魚 whale;
秋刀魚 saury;
驅魚 drive the fish;
熱帶魚 tropical fish;
柔魚 squid;
絨球魚 pompom;
如魚 like a fish;
軟骨魚 chondrichthyes;
三文魚 salmon;
沙丁魚 sardine;
沙魚 shark;
鯊魚 shark;
鱔魚 eel;
深海魚 abyssal fish;
神仙魚 angelfish;
虱目魚 milkfish;
石斑魚 garoupa;
石首魚 croaker;
鰣魚 hilsa herring;
食蚊魚 wickerfish;
水泡魚 bubble;
梭魚 barracuda; mullet;
梭子魚 barracuda;
鮐魚 chub mackerel;
彈塗魚 mudskipper;
塘魚 pond fish;
桃花魚 minnow;
鰷魚 hemiculter leucisculus;
頭鱸魚 silver-spotted grunt;
土鯪魚 dace;
團魚 soft-shelled turtle;
蛙蛙魚 giant salamander;
蛙魚 toadfish;
鯇魚 grass carp; herb carp;
網魚 net fish;
望天魚 celestial telescope;
文昌魚 lancelet;
烏魚 snakehead;
無顎魚 jawless fish;
武昌魚 blunt-snout bream;
鮮魚 fresh fish;
鹹水魚 saltwater fish;

鹹魚 salted fish;
香梭魚 red barracuda;
香魚 sweetfish;
鮝魚 dired fish;
小黃魚 small yellow croaker;
小魚 fry;
新翼魚 eusthenopteron;
鱈魚 cod;
燻魚 smoked fish;
鱘魚 sturgeon;
燕魚 Spanish mackerel;
楊枝魚 pipefish;
養魚 keep fish;
一大群魚 a shoal of fish;
一碟魚 a plate of fish;
一塊魚 a steak;
一筐魚 a basket of fish; a crate of fish;
一盤魚 a plate of fish;
一群魚 a school of fish; a shoal of fish;
一條魚 a fish;
一尾魚 a fish;
衣魚 bookworm; fish moth; silverfish;
銀漢魚 silverside;
銀魚 silverfish;
鸚嘴魚 parrot fish;
硬骨魚 osteichthyes;
鱅魚 bighead; variegated carp;
鱿魚 squid;
玉筋魚 sand lance;
元魚 soft-shelled turtle;
圓燕魚 platax orbicularis;
鼋魚 soft-shelled turtle;
章魚 octopus;
珍珠鱗魚 pearl-scale;
紙魚 fish moth; silverfish;
竹筴魚 horse mackerel; saurel;
抓到魚 catch a fish; land a fish;
總鰭魚 crossopterygii;

yu
【愉】 contented; happy; joyful; pleased;
[愉快] cheerful; delectable; delighted; enjoyable; gay; happy; joyful; merry; pleasurable;
非常愉快 as cheerful as a lark;
感到愉快 feel pleasure;
生活愉快 live a merry life;
玩得愉快 have a good time;
心情愉快 have a merry heart;
[愉樂] pleasant and joyful;
[愉色] cheerful expression; pleased look;
[愉逸] happy and leisurely;
[愉悅] cheerful; delighted; glad; joyful;

歡愉 happy; joyful;
婉愉 at ease; harmonious; relaxed;

yu
【渝】 (1) change one's mind; (2) another name of Chongqing; (3) another name of Jialing River in Sichuan;

yu
【腴】 (1) fat; (2) plump and soft; (3) fertile; (4) intestines of dogs and hogs; (5) rich;

豐腴 full and round; well-developed;
膏腴 fertile;

yu
【萸】 dogwood;

山茱萸 fruit of medicinal cornel;
食茱萸 ailanthus prickly ash;
吳茱萸 evodia ruta ecarpa;
茱萸 fruit of medicinal cornel;

yu
【隅】 (1) corner; nook; (2) angle; (3) out-of-the-way place; recess;
[隅反] assess by inference;
[隅目] (1) angry eyes; (2) furious;
[隅中] approaching noontime;

負隅 with one's back to a terrain that is strategically located and difficult of access;
向隅 be disappointed for having missed the opportunity; stand in a corner;

yu
【嵎】 (1) corner of a hill; (2) curved place in the mountains; (3) strategic point in the mountains;

yu
【揄】 (1) draw out; scoop out; (2) praise; show the merits of; (3) hang;
[揄揚] praise; recommend;

揶揄 deride; ridicule;

yu
【楰】 name of a plant;

yu
【畬】 land cultivated for some time;

yu

【隃】 (1) exceed; (2) a county in Shaanxi during the Han Dynasty;

yu

【愚】 (1) foolish; silly; stupid; unintelligent; unwise; (2) I; (3) cheat; deceivee; fool; make a fool of;

［愚呆］ blockheaded; dull; slow to learn; unintelligent;

［愚笨］ clumsy; foolish; imbecile; stupid;
愚笨的 crass;
~愚笨的人 dullard;
愚笨固執的 bull-headed;

［愚不可及］ abysmal ignorance; could not be more foolish; crass stupidity; hopelessly stupid; most foolish; the height of folly;

［愚痴］ feeblemindedness; imbecility;

［愚蠢］ as nutty as a fruitcake; chuckle-headed; dull; foolish; silly; stupid;
愚蠢的 clownish; cornball;
~愚蠢的人 putz; stupid creature; stupid person;
愚蠢無藥治 folly is an incurable disease; nothing can be done about fools;
非常愚蠢 as thick as two short planks; very stupid;
行為愚蠢 behave silly;

［愚獃］ fatuous; idiotic; moronic;

［愚鈍］ dull; dull-witted; slow-witted; stupid;
愚鈍的 lumpish;

［愚公移山］ determined effort can move a mountain;

［愚見］ my humble opinion;
愚見所及 as far as my humble opinion goes;

［愚陋］ stupid and vulgar;

［愚魯］ dull; stupid;

［愚昧］ benighted; fatuous; ignorant;
愚昧落後 ignorant and backward;
愚昧無知 benighted; foolishness and ignorance; ignorant and backward; lumpen; not know beans; stupid and ignorant; unenlightened;

［愚蒙］ ignorant; stupid; unenlightened;

［愚氓］ fool;

［愚民］ (1) ignorant masses; (2) keep people in ignorance; prevent people from knowing the truth;
愚民政策 obscurantism; obscurantist policy;

［愚弄］ bamboozle; deceive; dupe; hanky-panky; hoodwink; make a fool of; string along; play the fool with;
受到愚弄 be fooled;

［愚懦］ stupid and cowardly;

［愚氣］ (1) futile anger; (2) foolish; silly-looking;

［愚人］ fool; simpleton;
愚人節 All Fools' Day;

［愚頑］ ignorant and stubborn; stupid and obstinate;
蠢笨愚頑 stupid and stubborn;

［愚妄］ ignorant but self-important; stupid and rash; stupid but conceited;

［愚孝］ blind devotion to one's parents;

［愚意］ my humble opinion;

［愚者千慮，必有一得］ a fool may give a wise man counsel; a fool may sometimes speak to the purpose; a fool's bolt may sometimes hit the mark; even a fool may hit on a good idea; even a fool may sometimes have a good idea; even a fool occasionally hits on a good idea; even a fool sometimes speaks a wise word; even a fool sometimes speak to the purpose; even fools sometimes speak shrewdly; sometimes a fool gives good counsel; sometimes a fool may speak a word in season; sometimes a fool may speak to purpose;

［愚者一德］ a lucky hit by a fool;

［愚直］ stupidly honest;

［愚忠］ blind devotion to one's lord;

［愚拙］ stupid and clumsy;

痴愚 moronity;
上愚 the most stupid;
受愚 be duped; be fooled; be tricked;
下愚 fool; imbecile;
賢愚 the wise and the stupid;
鄉愚 stupid rustics;
智愚 the wise and the foolish;
朱愚 ignorant; stupid;

yu

【榆】 elm;

［榆景］ old age;

［榆木］ elm;
［榆樹］ elm;

大葉榆 mon elm;
地榆 garden burnet;
光葉榆 smooth-leaved elm;
紅榆 red elm;
榔榆 ulmus parvifolia;
美國榆 white elm;
栓皮榆 cork elm;
硬葉榆 cedar elm;

yu

【瑜】 (1) fine and flawless piece of jade; a perfect gem; (2) lustre of gems; (3) excellence; virtue; (4) yoga;

［瑜不掩瑕］ the merits do not outweigh the defects;
［瑜伽］ yoga;
瑜伽師 yogi;

yu

【虞】 (1) anxieties; fears; worries; (2) anticipate; expect; (3) cheat; deceive; (4) a legendary dynasty; (5) a state in the Spring and Autumn Period; (6) a surname;

［虞美人］ corn poppy;

不虞 (1) be unexpected; (2) contingency; eventuality; not worry about;

yu

【逾】 (1) exceed; go beyond; more than; over; pass over; (2) added; even more; (3) transgress;

［逾常］ out of the ordinary; unusual;
［逾額］ pass over the allotted number;
［逾分］ (1) excessive; over; undue; (2) transgress; (3) exorbitant;
［逾格］ as an exception;
［逾過］ exceed; pass over;
［逾恒］ go beyond the regular practice;
［逾節］ exceed the limit;
［逾邁］ pass away;
［逾期］ exceed the time limit; overdue;
逾期賬款 overdue account;
［逾墻］ climb over a wall;
逾墻鑽隙 (1) fishing boat; (2) have illicit relations with sb;
［逾權越限］ go beyond one's authority — transgress one's jurisdiction;
［逾日］ pass a day;
［逾閒蕩檢］ licentious in conduct;
［逾限］ exceed the limit; go beyond the bounds; go beyond the limits;
［逾譯］ over-translation;
［逾月］ pass over the month;
［逾越］ exceed; go beyond; pass;
逾越雷池 overstep the limitations;

yu

【漁】 (1) fishing; (2) take sth one is not entitled to; (3) pursue; seek;

［漁產］ aquatic products;
［漁場］ fishing ground;
［漁船］ fishing boat; fishing vessel;
平底小漁船 dory;
拖網漁船 trawler;
［漁村］ fishing village;
［漁夫］ fisher; fisherman;
［漁港］ fishing port;
［漁歌］ fisherman's song;
［漁火］ lights on fishing boats;
［漁獲］ fishery harvesting;
［漁具］ fishing outfit;
［漁郎］ fisherman;
［漁利］ (1) profit at others' expense; reap unfair gains; (2) easy gains; spoils;
從中漁利 take advantage of a situation to benefit oneself;
坐收漁利 profit from others' conflict; sit idle and take in a profit;
［漁民］ fisherfolk; fisherman; fishing population;
［漁區］ fishing area;
［漁人］ fisherman;
漁人得利 make capital out of a strife; profit at others' expense; when two parties quarrel, a third party benefits; the third party gets the profit;
收漁人之利 profit at others' expense; profit from others' conflict;
［漁色］ seek carnal pleasure;
漁色之徒 fellow of excessive lust;
［漁網］ fishing net;
［漁業］ fishery; fishery industry; fishing; fishing industry;
［漁舟］ fishing boat;

侵漁 seize; take by force;

Y

yu

【與】 same as 歟;

yu

【窬】 (1) hole in the wall; small door or window; (2) climb over a wall;

［窬墻窺視］ make a hole through a wall and peep through;

穿窬 cut through or climb over a wall to steal;

yu

【褕】 (1) beautiful dress; (2) loose garment;

［褕衣］ pretty dress;

yu

【諛】 flatter; toady;

［諛辭］ flattery; flattering words;

［諛言］ flattering words; flattery;

諂諛 fawn on; flatter;

阿諛 curry favour with; flatter;

yu

【餘】 (1) remaining; the remainder; the rest; (2) excess; more than; over; overplus; surplus; (3) after; beyond; (4) balance; (5) complement of a number;

［餘波］ aftermath; aftershock; afterwind; repercussion;

餘波蕩漾 the effect is till being felt;

餘波未平 the trouble is not yet over; there are still aftermaths;

［餘黨］ remnants of an outlawed faction;

［餘地］ alternative; leeway; margin; room; spare space; latitude;

不留餘地 leave no ground; leave no leeway; not to leave room for later compromise;

留有餘地 allow for unforeseen circumstances; all for unpredictable circumstances and needs; leave plenty of scope for; leave adequate leeway;

有改進的餘地 there is room for improvement;

［餘毒］ pernicious influence; pernicious vestige; residual poison;

消除餘毒 efface the pernicious influence;

［餘額］ (1) vacancies yet to be filled; (2) remaining sum; surplus;

保留餘額 obligated balance;

撥款餘額 appropriation balance;

不動戶餘額 unclaimed balance;

存折餘額 pass book balance;

對銷餘額 contra balance;

可動用餘額 available balance;

平均每日餘額 average daily balance;

平均托收餘額 average collected balance;

未分配餘額 unappropriated balance; unencumbered balance;

未清償餘額 unliquidated balance;

未清餘額 outstanding balance; unpaid balance;

未用餘額 unexpended balance;

現金餘額 cash balance;

~實際現金餘額 real cash balance;

應付餘額 payable balance;

賬面餘額 balance on account;

［餘忿未平］ anger not yet appeased;

［餘風］ influence left by a person;

［餘割］ cosecant;

反餘割 arc cosecant;

雙曲餘割 hyperbolic cosecant;

~反雙曲餘割 cosech hyperbolic cosecant;

［餘晷］ spare time;

［餘輝］ afterglow; persistence;

長餘輝 long afterglow;

短餘輝 short afterglow;

~超短餘輝 extra-short afterglow; ultrashort afterglow;

中餘輝 medium afterglow;

［餘悸］ lingering fear;

心有餘悸 have a lingering fear; one's heart still fluttering with fear; shudder in retrospect; sufficient alarm; there is still a certain trepidation; with unforgotten trepidation;

猶有餘悸 even now one is scared;

［餘燼］ (1) ashes; embers; (2) defeated and dispersed troops;

發光的餘燼 glowing embers;

劫後餘燼 signs of disaster;

［餘款］ favourable balance; remaining funds;

［餘利］ net profit; profit;

［餘力］ strength to spare;

不遺餘力 do one's level best; do one's utmost; exert every possible force; go to all lengths; leave all avenue unexplored; leave no stone unturned; make an all-out effort; make every endeavour; make the best of; move

heaven and earth; shoot the works; spare no effort; spare no pains; to the best of one's ability; to the utmost of one's power; unsparing in one's efforts; with all one's might; without sparing any effort;
行有餘力 have extra resources;
[餘糧] surplus grain;
[餘論] (1) unfinished comments; (2) epilogue;
[餘年] one's remaining years; the remaining years of one's life;
[餘孽] leftover evils; remaining evil elements; surviving supporters of an evil cause;
[餘怒] one's remaining anger;
餘怒不息 one's remaining anger is not yet quieted;
餘怒未消 feel the lingering anger;
[餘錢] spare money; surplus funds;
[餘切] cotangent;
餘切真數 natural cotangent;
反餘切 arc cotangent; inverse cotangent;
雙曲餘切 hyperbolic cotangent;
~反雙曲餘切 arch-hyperbolic cotangent;
[餘熱] waste heat;
餘熱回收率 recovery rate;
餘熱資源 waste heat resource;
[餘生] (1) one's remaining years; the remainder of one's life; the rest of one's life; (2) survival;
度過餘生 end one's life;
鋒鏑餘生 a narrow escape from cannon and fire; barely escape from disaster of war with one's life;
歡度餘生 live in happiness of the rest of one's life;
劫後餘生 a survivor of a disaster; survival of a disaster; brand from the burning; life after surviving a disaster; lucky survivor from a holocaust;
以終餘生 live out the rest of one's life;
[餘矢] coversine;
[餘味] aftertaste; agreeable aftertaste; pleasant impression; remaining taste;
餘味無窮 leave a lasting and pleasant impression;
[餘暇] free time; leisure; leisure time; spare time;
允分利用餘暇 employ one's leisure;
沒有餘暇 have no time to spare;
[餘下] remaining;
[餘閒] leisure; spare time;
[餘香] lingering fragrance;
[餘興] (1) lingering interest; (2) entertainment after a meeting or a dinner party;
[餘弦] cosine;
餘弦定理 law of cosines;
餘弦積分 integral cosine;
餘弦真數 natural cosine;
對數餘弦 logarithmic cosine;
反餘弦 arc cosine; inverse cosine;
方向餘弦 direction cosine;
上昇餘弦 raised cosine;
雙曲餘弦 hyperbolic cosine;
~反雙曲餘弦 arc-hyperbolic cosine;
[餘音] lingering sound;
餘音繚繞 the music lingers in the air;
餘音裊裊 the music lingers in the air long after the performance ends;
餘音繞梁 the prolonged vibration of the sound; the song has stopped but the voice remains; the thrilling voice keeps reverberating in the air after the vocalist has stopped singing; the tune lingers in the room;
餘音繞梁，三日不絕 the melody lingers in the room for three days; the music lingers for three days in the house; the sweet musical echo remains whirling around the house rafters for three days;
餘勇可賈 with one's strength not exhausted; with strength yet to spare;
[餘裕] ample; enough and to spare;
綽有餘裕 enough and to spare; more than enough to meet the needs;
[餘震] aftershock;

殘餘 remains; survivals;
廚餘 food waste; kitchen scraps;
多餘 (1) superfluous; surplus; (2) more than what is due; unnecessary;
富餘 have enough and to spare; have more than needed;
工餘 after hours; leisure after work;
公餘 sparetime;
結餘 balance; cash surplus;
淨餘 remainder; surplus;
課餘 after class; after school;
寬餘 (1) broad-mined and happy; (2) comfortably off; well-to-do;
其餘 the remainder; the others;

冗餘 redundance; redundancy;
三十餘 thirty-odd;
剩餘 left overt; remain;
賸餘 leave in surplus; remnants;
所餘 leftovers; remnant; what is left; what remains;
同餘 congruence;
唾餘 opinions of little importance; remarks;
無餘 nothing is left;
緒餘 remnants; surplus;
業餘 (1) amateur; (2) sparetime;
盈餘 profit; surplus;
贏餘 profit; surplus;
有餘 (1) have a surplus; have enough and to spare; (2) odd;
紆餘 winding and twisting;

yu
【覦】 a strong desire for possession; covet;
覬覦 covet;

yu
【踰】 (1) same as 逾 ; (2) excessively; overly;
[踰分] go beyond one's proper position;
[踰封] cross the national boundary;
[踰年] following year;
[踰閑] break decorum; break moral conventions;
[踰越] go beyond; transgress;
穿踰 cut through or climb over a wall;

yu
【輿】 (1) carriage; chariot; (2) chair; sedan; (3) area; territory; (4) carry; transport;
[輿地] earth; land;
輿地之學 study of geography;
[輿論] public opinion;
輿論導向 orientation in public opinion;
~ 輿論導向專家 spin doctor;
輿論沸騰 general opinion is in a very diturbed state;
輿論工具 instrument of public opinions;
輿論嘩然 public opinion is seething with indignation; there is a public outcry;
輿論監督 supervision by public opinions; supervisory function of public opinion;
輿論界 press circles; publicity; the media;
輿論引導者 opinion-maker;
輿論政治 consensus politics;
大造輿論 make a big fanfare; whip up public opinion;
國際輿論 world opinion;
控制輿論 control public opinion;
煽動輿論 stir up public opinion;
世界輿論 world opinion;
引導輿論 guide public opinion;
製造輿論 create public opinion;
觸犯輿論 offend public opinion;
左右輿論 influence public opinion;
[輿馬俱備] carriage and horses are available;
[輿情] public feeling; public sentiment;
輿情憤激 popular feeling is in fury;
輿情激昂 popular feeling is in a fury;
洞察輿情 know public sentiment well;

堪輿 geomantic omen;
權輿 (1) bud; germinate; shoot; sprout; (2) begin; start;

yu
【歟】 final particle indicating doubt, exclamation, surprise, etc.;

yu
【璵】 beautiful jade; fine jade;

yu
【旟】 (1) military flag; (2) fluttering of flags;

yu
【轝】 same as 輿 ;

yu³
yu
【予】 give;
[予以] give; grant;
予以便利 offer convenience to sb;
予以表揚 commend sb; give praise to;
予以否定 offer a negation;
予以鼓勵 give encouragement;
予以好評 offer appreciative criticism;
予以解釋 throw some light on;
予以肯定 make an affirmation;
予以賠償 give compensation;

不予 deny; not give; not grant; refuse;
賜予 bestow; grant;
賦予 endow; entrust; give;
給予 give; offer; render;
寄予 (1) place (hope, etc) on; (2) express; show;
免予 excuse sb from; exempt;
授予 award; confer;

贈予 grant;
准予 approve; grant;

yu

【宇】 (1) eaves; (2) house; roof; (3) appearance; countenance; look; (4) space; universe;

［宇稱］ parity;
宇稱守恆定律 law of parity conservation;

［宇航］ astronautical; space travel;
宇航員 astronaut; spaceman;
~ 女宇航員 astronautess;
宇航學 space aeronautics;

［宇量］ generosity; tolerance;

［宇內］ in the country; in the world;

［宇下］ under the roof;

［宇宙］ cosmos; universe;
宇宙保險單 astropolicy;
宇宙塵 cosmic dust;
宇宙大戰 cosmic war;
宇宙飛船 spacecraft;
宇宙飛行 space flight;
~ 宇宙飛行器 astrovehicle;
~ 宇宙飛行站 space station;
宇宙工廠 cosmic factory;
宇宙航空學 astronautics;
宇宙航行 astronavigation;
宇宙化學 cosmochemistry;
宇宙環境 cosmic environment; space environment;
宇宙空間 aerospace; astrospace; cosmic space;
宇宙論 cosmism; cosmology;
~ 宇宙論者 cosmologist;
~ 大爆炸宇宙論 Big Bang theory;
~ 穩恒態宇宙論 Steady State theory;
~ 振動宇宙論 Oscillation theory;
宇宙模型 cosmological model;
宇宙年 cosmic year;
宇宙起源 cosmogony; origin of the Universe;
宇宙人 cosmic man;
宇宙射線 cosmic ray;
宇宙生態學 cosmecotogy;
宇宙生物學 cosmobiology;
宇宙通信 cosmic communication;
宇宙萬物 cosmic inventory; the myriad things in the universe;
宇宙物理學 cosmophysics;
宇宙學 cosmology;
宇宙醫學 cosmic medicine;
宇宙儀 cosmosphere;
宇宙語言 cosmic language;
宇宙戰略 cosmic strategy;
宇宙之謎 riddle of the universe;
閉宇宙 closed universe;
大宇宙 macrocosmos;
島宇宙 island universe;
多元宇宙 multiverse;
靜止宇宙 static universe;
開宇宙 open universe;

杜宇 cuckoo;
寰宇 the earth; the whole world;
眉宇 forehead;
廟宇 temple;
氣宇 bearing; dignified and inspiring looks; the manner of a person's carriage; tolerance;
器宇 appearance; bearing; deportment;
神宇 expression and appearance; look;
天宇 (1) heavens; sky; (2) land under heaven; the whole world;
屋宇 building; house;
廨宇 government office building;
胸宇 one's ambition; one's aspiration;
玉宇 residence of the immortals; universe;
御宇 reign of an emperor over the nation;
院宇 house and the yard;

yu

【羽】 (1) feathers; plumes; (2) wings of a bird;

［羽化］ (1) ascend to heaven and become immortal; (2) die;
羽化登仙 ascend and become an immortal; die; take flight to the land of the immortal;

［羽量級］ feather-weight;

［羽毛］ down; feathers; plumes;
羽毛頂點 feather tip;
羽毛豐滿 full-fledged; the feather is in its length — mature;
羽毛畫 feather patchwork;
羽毛球 (1) badminton; (2) shuttlecock;
~ 打羽毛球 play badminton;
~ 塑膠羽毛球 plastic shuttle;
羽毛球場 badminton court;
羽毛球拍 badminton racket;
羽毛圈 crown of feathers;
羽毛扇 feather fan;
羽毛未豐 inexperienced; immature; unfledged; young and immature;
愛惜羽毛 (1) meticulous about one's

appearance; (2) protective of one's public image;
拔去羽毛 unplume;
全身羽毛 plumage;
一根羽毛 a feather;
沾濕羽毛 ruffle feathers;
長羽毛 feather out; fledge;
[羽扇] feather fan;
[羽檄交馳] interchanging of urgent despatches;

黨羽 members of a gang;
翟羽 pheasant feathers;
覆羽 covert;
換羽 moult;
鎩羽 (1) shed feathers; (2) crestfallen; defeated; discouraged; disheartened;
脱羽 moult;

Y

yu

【雨】 rain; rainy; wet;
[雨暴] rainstorm;
[雨布] waterproof cloth;
[雨滴] raindrop;
[雨點] raindrop;
密如雨點 as thick as hail; as thick as raindrops;
[雨後送傘] after dinner, mustard; give sb an umbrella after the rain is over;
[雨霽] the rain is over;
[雨季] monsoon; rainy season; wet season;
[雨具] things for wet weather;
[雨立] stand in the rain;
[雨量] rainfall;
雨量器 rain gauge;
雨量充足 the rainfall is plentiful;
雨量計 rain gauge;
單點雨量 point rainfall;
地形雨量 orographic rainfall;
年降雨量 annual rainfall;
一般雨量 general rainfall;
有效雨量 effective rainfall;
[雨林] rain forest;
赤道雨林 equatorial rain forest;
季雨林 monsoon forest; seasonal rain forest;
~常綠季雨林 evergreen seasonal rain forest;
熱帶雨林 tropical rain forest;
~保護熱帶雨林 protect the tropical forest;
溫帶雨林 temperate rain forest;
[雨淋] wet by the rain;
雨淋日曬 exposure to the elements; the hardship of outdoor work; wear and tear of the weather; wet by the rain and burnt by the sun;
日曝雨淋 be exposed to all kinds of weather; be exposed to rain and to the heat of the sun;
日曬雨淋 be exposed to the sun and rain; be exposed to the inclemency of the elements; be exposed to the elements; sun-scorched and rain-drenched;
[雨露] (1) rain and dew; (2) benevolence; bounty; favours; favours and kindness; grace;
雨露之恩 gracious favours;
恩同雨露 one's grace is like rain and dew;
[雨帽] rain cap; rain hat;
[雨棚] rainshed;
車站雨棚 station awning;
站台雨棚 platform awning;
[雨泣] tears falling down like rain;
[雨區] rain area;
[雨日] rainy day;
[雨傘] brolly; umbrella;
男式雨傘 men's umbrella;
女式雨傘 women's umbrella;
晴帶雨傘，飽帶乾糧 though the sun shines, leave not your cloak at home;
一把雨傘 an umbrella;
[雨聲] sound of rain;
噼噼啪啪的雨聲 the pitter-patter of raindrops;
[雨水] rain; rainfall; rainwater;
雨水不調 the rainfall is unfavourable;
雨水充足 have plentiful rain;
雨水槽 guttering;
雨水道 storm drain;
雨水管 drainpipe; storm drain;
雨水桶 water butt;
大量的雨水 an affluence of rain;
一大桶雨水 a tubful of rain;
[雨絲] drifting rain; fine rain;
[雨天] rainy day;
雨天裏 in the wet;
雨天挑稻草—越挑越重 carrying loads of rice straws in rain — the farther you go, the heavier they become;
[雨下] downpour; storm;

彈如雨下 a storm of bullets;
汗如雨下 sweat profusely; the sweat runs down like rain-drops;
淚如雨下 a banquet of brine; an inundation of tears; burst into a flood of tears; in a flood of tears; one's eyes rain tears; one's tears fall like rain; one's tears flow fast; shed a flood of tears; tears trickle down like rain;
拳如雨下 a storm of blows; blows fall fast and thick; lay into; rain blows upon; strike sb repeatedly with one's fist;

[雨鞋] rainshoes; rubber boots;

[雨衣] mackintosh; raincoat; waterproof;
連帽薄雨衣 cagoule;

[雨雲] nimbus; rain clouds;
雨散雲收 the rain stops and the sky clears up;

[雨珠] raindrop;

暴風雨 rainstorm; storm;
暴雨 rainstorm; torrential rain;
避雨 find shelter against rain; take shelter from rain;
春雨 spring rains;
大雨 heavy rain; hale water; soaker;
擋雨 keep off the rain; shelter oneself from the rain;
地形雨 orographic rain;
凍雨 sleet;
對流雨 convective rain;
多雨 rainy;
躲雨 find shelter from the rain; get out of the rain; run for cover; run for shelter; take cover from rain;
俄雨 shower;
風雨 trials and hardships; wind and wind;
穀雨 Grain Rain (6th solar term);
過雲雨 shower;
豪雨 heavy rain;
黃梅雨 intermittent drizzles;
及時雨 timely rain;
季雨 monsoon rain;
降雨 rain;
舊雨 old friend or customer;
苦雨 continuous rain;
雷雨 thunderstorm;
雷陣雨 thunder shower;
淋雨 be exposed to the rain; get wet in the rain;
霖雨 continuous heavy rain;
流星雨 meteoric shower;
落雨 rain;
毛毛雨 drizzle;
冒雨 braving the rain; in spite of the rain;
梅雨 plum rains;
霉雨 intermittent drizzles;
牛毛雨 drizzle;
祈雨 pray for rain;
晴雨 rain or shine;
請雨 pray for rain;
求雨 pray for rain;
如雨 like rain;
山雨 mountain rain;
賞雨 enjoy rainy scenes;
潲雨 (1) rain slanted by wind; (2) get wet by the slanting rain;
時雨 (1) timely rains; (2) culture and education;
絲雨 drizzle; misty rain;
酸雨 acid rain;
天雨 it rains;
透雨 soaking rain;
微雨 drizzle;
喜雨 a welcome fall of rain; seasonable rain; timely rainfall;
細雨 drizzle; fine rain;
下個不停的雨 steady rain;
下雨 rain;
小雨 light rain; sprinkle;
煙雨 misty rain;
一場雨 a cloudburst; a rain shower;
一滴雨 a drop of rain;
一點雨 a bit of rain; a sprinkling of rain;
一雨 a rainfall;
一陣雨 a shower;
陰雨 overcast and rainy;
淫雨 excessive rains; incessant rains;
霪雨 excessive rain;
遇雨 be caught in the rain;
雲雨 have sexual intercourse; make love;
陣雨 shower;
阻雨 be held back by rain;
驟雨 sudden rainstorm;

yu
【禹】 Yu, the legendary founder of the Xia Dynasty;

yu
【圄】 jail; prison;

囹圄 jail; prison;

yu
【庾】 (1) stack of grain; (2) ancient measure of capacity; (3) a surname;

yu

【敔】 ancient musical instrument;

yu

【傴】 hunchbacked;

［傴僂］ with one's back bent;

yu

【瑀】 jade-like stone;

yu

【與】 (1) give; impart; offer; (2) against; with; (3) and; together with; with;

［與奪］ give and take;

［與共］ share sth with;

存亡與共 throw in one's lot with;

［與虎］ with the tiger;

與虎謀皮 ask a tiger for its hide － request sb to act against his own interests; borrow the skin from a tiger － impossible;

與虎同眠 lie down with the tiger;

［與會］ take part in a meeting;

與會者 conventioneer;

［與君一席話，勝讀十年書］ to have a conversation with you is better than ten years of study; to have a talk with you is better than ten years' more study of books;

聽君一席話，勝讀十年書 I profit more from one consultation with you than from ten years of reading;

［與年俱衰］ decline with advancing years;

［與人］ with people;

與人方便 give help to others; give people convenience; make things easy for others;

~與人方便，自己方便 by aiming for the good of others, you will get your own; he who helps others helps himself;

與人為敵 make an enemy of sb; set oneself against;

與人為難 make it hot for sb; make things difficult for sb;

與人為善 be aimed at helping people; help others out of goodwill; with good intentions towards others; well-intentioned; well-meaning;

與人為忤 bear no ill will against anybody; live in harmony with other people;

與人無忤 bear no ill will against anybody; have no discord with others; live in harmony with other people;

與人消災 save sb from disaster;

與人有隙 have a grudge against sb; have a quarrel with sb;

［與日］ with time;

與日俱輝 the glory of...will shine on as long as the sun continues to shine;

與日俱增 constantly on the increase; grow in time; grow with each passing day; grow with time; increase with each passing day; multiply daily; multiply with every passing day; on the increase; rise daily;

［與少望奢］ expect much for little;

［與時俱進］ change with the times; keep abreast of the times; keep abreast with the times; keep pace with the progress of the times; keep up with the times; move with the times; progress with the times;

必須與時俱進 must move with the times;

［與世…］ out of the times; with the world;

與世不合 out of sympathy with the times;

與世長辭 be gathered to one's fathers; be gone forever; breathe one's last breath; depart from the world forever; depart from the world for good; die; go the way of all flesh; go the way of the earth; go the way of nature; go over to the great majority; join the great majority; pass away; pass beyond the veil; sleep with one's fathers;

與世長存 survive forever;

與世浮沉 do just as everybody does; drift with the current of the times; follow the trend; go with the stream; go with the tide; rise and sink with the rest of the world; swim with the tide;

與世隔絕 be isolated from the rest of the world; cut off from the outside world; cut off from the rest of the world; isolate oneself from the world; live in solitude; out of touch with world news; retire into one's shell; sequester oneself from the world; sequester oneself from society; shut off from the world; shut oneself into one's shell; withdraw into one's shell;

與世訣別 bid adieu to the world; say goodbye to the world;

與世推移 change with the times;

與世無怨 bear no hatred against anybody;

與世無爭 have nothing to compete for with others; hold oneself aloof from the world; in harmony with the rest of the world; on good terms with the world; stand aloof from worldly success;

與世偃仰 rise and fall with the rest of the world; tag along with the trend of the times;

[與歲俱長] grow with one's years;

[與題無關] beside the question; extraneous to the question; extraneous to the subject;

[與我無涉] have nothing to do with me; none of my business;

[與物無忤] at peace with the world; have offended no one;

[與…相比] alongside of; as against; as compared with; at the side of; beside; by comparison with; by contrast with; by the side of; compared to; compared with; in comparison with; in comparison to; in contrast to; in contrast with; in proportion to; in relation to;

[與…相反] run cross to;

[與…相符] answer to; be compatible with; be in agreement with; be in conformity with; be in harmony with; be on a par with; be on all fours with; be parallel to; conform to; consonant; consonant to; equal; in concert with;

[與…相鄰] border on;

[與…一致] accord with; bring into accord; in accord with; with one accord;

參與 a party to; have a hand in; involvement; join; partake; participate in; participation; pitch in; take part;

付與 (1) take out; (2) give; (3) pay;

給與 give, grant, pay; render; show;

讓與 cede; surrender;

容與 (1) at ease with oneself; carefree; (2) act under no constraint; give free rein to;

施與 bestow; grant;

授與 award; confer; endow; give; grant;

相與 (1) deal with sb; get along with sb; (2) together; with each other;

猗與 an exclamation indicating admiration;

贈與 donate; favour; gift; grant; present;

yu

【語】 (1) language; speech; tongue; (2) say; speak; talk; (3) proverb; saying; set phrase;

[語病] (1) faulty wording; illogical use of words; (2) difficulty in speaking caused by vocal defects;

[語不離宗] talk shop;

[語顫] fremitus;

觸覺語顫 tactile fremitus;

[語詞] phrases; words;

語詞變體 allolog;

[語調] intonation;

語調單位 tone unit;

語調上昇 intonation rises;

語調下降 intonation falls;

語調語言 language of intonation;

對比語調 contrastive intonation;

均勻語調 even intonation;

上昇語調 rising intonation;

悅耳的語調 amiable tone of voice;

[語段] text;

語段層次 textual level;

語段定向性 text-directedness;

語段對等 textual equivalence;

語段分析 text analysis;

語段功能 textual function;

語段關連性 intertextuality;

語段類別 text category;

語段類型 text typology;

語段語言學 text linguistics;

語段真空 textual vacuum;

呼語語段 vocative text;

口語語段 colloquial text; spoken text;

描述語段 descriptive text;

[語法] grammar; syntax;

語法變化 grammatical change;

語法詞 grammatical word;

~語法詞素 grammatical morpheme;

語法錯亂 agrammatism;

語法單位 grammatical unit;

語法對等詞 grammatical equivalent;

語法範疇 grammatical category;

語法翻譯 grammatical translation;

~語法翻譯法 grammar translation method;

語法分析 grammatical analysis;

~語法分析器 syntactic parser;

語法功能 grammatical function;

語法慣用法 grammatical usage;

語法規則 grammatical rule;

語法化 grammaticalization;
語法結構 grammatical structure;
語法能力 grammatical competence;
語法歧義 grammatical ambiguity;
語法手段 grammatical device;
語法同義詞 grammatical synonym;
語法形式 grammatical form;
語法項 grammatical item;
語法學家 grammarian;
語法意義 grammatical meaning;
語法主語 grammatical subject;
語法轉換 grammatical shift;
語法自然性 grammatical naturalness;
比較語法 comparative grammar;
補充語法 remedial grammar;
參考語法 reference grammar;
層次語法 stratificational grammar;
成分結構語法 constituent structure grammar;
詞匯語法 lexicogrammar;
範疇語法 category grammar;
概念語法 notional grammar;
格語法 case grammar;
功能語法 functional grammar;
關係語法 relational grammar;
觀念語法 notional grammar;
規定語法 prescriptive grammar;
規範語法 normative grammar;
國際語法 interlingua approach;
交際語法 communicative grammar;
教學語法 pedagogical grammar;
結構語法 structural grammar;
結構主義語法 structuralist grammar;
空間語法 space grammar;
歷史語法 historical grammar;
連接語法 connective grammar;
臨時語法 interim grammar;
描寫語法 descriptive grammer;
深層語法 deep grammar;
學習語法 learn grammar;
學校語法 school grammar;
研究語法 study grammer;
轉換生成語法 transformational generative grammar;
轉換語法 transformational grammar;

[語符學] glossematics;

[語感] linguistic feeling; linguistic sense;

[語匯] vocabulary;

[語際] interlingual;
語際比譯 interlingual transposition;
語際錯誤 interlingual error;
語際翻譯 interlingual translation;
語際交際 interlingual communication;
語際可譯性 intertranslatability;
語際同義詞 interlingual synonym;
語際轉移 interlingual transfer;

[語境] context;
語境重造 contextual re-creation;
語境翻譯 contextual translation;
語境覺識 context-consciousness;
語境論 contextual theory;
語境敏感語法 context-sensitive grammar;
語境填詞法 contextually appropriate method;
語境意義 contextual meaning;
語境因素 contextual factor;
語境制約語法 context-restricted grammar;
語境自由語法 context-free grammar;
廣義語境 macro-context;
環境語境 context of situation;
交際語境 communicative context;

[語句] phrases; sentences;
覓索語句 strive for phrases and sentences;

[語料] language data;
語料庫 corpus;

[語錄] quotations; recorded utterances;

[語內] intralingual;
語內比譯 intralingual transposition;
語內錯誤 intralingual error;
語內翻譯 intralingual translation;
語內交際 intralingual communication;
語內同義詞 intralingual synonym;

[語氣] (1) manner of speaking; tone; tone of voice; (2) mood;
語氣傲慢 talk in a lofty manner;
語氣詞 particle;
~加強語氣詞 intensive particle;
語氣深沉 speak in a deep tone;
語氣陰沉 speak in a dismal tone;
語氣友好 have a friendly tone;
語氣愉快 talk in a cheerful manner;
陳述語氣 indicative mood;
發端語氣 inchoative mood;
反覆語氣 frequentative mood;
高人一等的語氣 patronizing tone;
懷疑語氣 dubitative mood;
禁止語氣 prohibitive mood;
祈使語氣 imperative mood;
祈願語氣 optative mood;
勸告語氣 cohortative mood;
讓步語氣 concessive mood;

條件式語氣 conditional mood;
虛擬語氣 subjunctive mood;
願望語氣 desiderative mood;

[語塞] hesitate to make a response; tongue-tied; unable to respond;

[語素] morpheme;
語素變體 allomorph;
複數語素 plural morpheme;
互補語素 complementary morpheme;
基本語素 base morpheme;
名詞化語素 nominalization morpheme;
強調語素 emphatic morpheme;
替換語素 replacive morpheme;
添加語素 additive morpheme;

[語態] voice;
被動語態 passive voice;
~動作被動語態 actional passive;
反身語態 reflexive voice;
主動語態 active voice;

[語體] type of writing;
語體文 vernacular writing;

[語文] language;
語文水平 language proficiency;
語文學 philology;
~比較語文學 comparative philology;

[語無倫次] babble in one's statement; babble like an idiot; go off at score; ramble in one's statement; speak incoherently; use indecent language; want of order in one's speech;

[語系] language family;
拉丁語系 Latin family of languages;
漢藏語系 Han-Tibetan language family;
印歐語系 Indo-European languages;

[語序] word order;
倒裝語序 inverted order;
自然語序 natural order;

[語言] language; lingo; speech;
語言變化 language change; linguistic change;
語言變體 variety of language;
語言變異 language variation;
語言不安全感 linguistic insecurity;
語言不可譯性 linguistic untranslatability;
語言不清 alalia; inability to speak clearly;
語言測試 language testing;
語言層次 linguistic level;
語言成分 linguistic feature;
語言處理 language treatment;
語言粗俗 one's language is vulgar;
語言單位 linguistic unit;
語言當地化 naturalization;
語言地理學 linguistic map;
語言調查 language survey;
語言翻譯程序 language translator;
語言分化 linguistic divergence;
語言分類法 classification of languages;
語言分析 linguistic analysis;
語言風格 language style;
語言符號 linguistic sign;
語言功能 language function;
~語言功能論 functional theory of language;
語言規範 linguistic norm;
~語言規範化 standardization of language; standardization of speech;
語言規劃 language planning;
語言規則 language rules;
語言環境 linguistic context;
語言技巧 language skills;
語言交際 verbal communication;
語言教師 language teacher;
語言教學 language pedagogy; language teaching;
語言接觸 language contact;
語言距離 linguistic distance;
語言科學 linguistic science;
語言類型 language typology;
~語言類型學 language typology;
語言美 beautification of language;
~語言美學 linguistic aesthetics;
語言模式 language model;
~語言模式化 language modelization;
語言能力 linguistic ability; linguistic competence;
~語言能力喪失 language loss;
語言普遍現象 language universal;
語言求同 convergence;
語言歧義 linguistic ambiguity;
語言人類學 linguistic anthropology;
語言實驗室 language laboratory;
語言釋義 linguistic paraphrase;
語言水平 language proficiency;
語言素質 language aptitude;
~語言素質測驗 language aptitude test;
語言態度 language attitude;
語言統一 unification of language;
語言同義詞 linguistic synonym;
語言維持性 language maintenance;
語言文化功能 metalingual function;
語言文化移入 acculturation;
語言文學 language and literature;
~中國語言文學 Chinese language and

literature;
語言無味 drab language; insipid in language;
語言習得 language acquisition;
~語言習得裝置 language acquisition device;
~第二語言習得 second language acquisition;
語言相對性 linguistic relativity;
語言信息處理 language information processing;
語言信息結構 language information structure;
語言行為 performance;
語言性歧視 language discrimination;
語言學 linguistics; philology;
~語言學方法 linguistic method;
~語言學家 linguist;
~語言學派 linguistic school;
~機械主義語言學派 mechanistic linguistics;
~結構主義語言學派 structuralistic linguistic school;
~比較歷史語言學 comparative historical linguistics;
~比較語言學 comparative linguistics; comparativistics;
~傳統語言學 traditional linguistics;
~地理語言學 geographical linguistics;
~動態語言學 dynamic linguistics;
~對比語言學 contrastive linguistics;
~分類語言學 taxonomic linguistics;
~功能語言學 functional linguistics;
~共時語言學 synchronic linguistics;
~國際語言學 interlinguistics;
~計算語言學 computational linguistics;
~教學語言學 educational linguistics;
~結構語言學 structural linguistics;
~靜態語言學 static linguistics;
~理論語言學 theoretical linguistics;
~歷時語言學 diachronic linguistics;
~歷史比較語言學 historical and comparative linguistics;
~歷史語言學 historical linguistics;
~描寫語言學 descriptive linguistics;
~內部語言學 internal linguistics;
~普通語言學 general linguistics;
~區別語言學 areal linguistics;
~區域語言學 area linguistics; areal linguistics;
~社會語言學 sociolinguistics;
~宏觀社會語言學 macro-sociolinguistics;

~實用語言學 practical linguistics;
~數理語言學 mathematical linguistics;
~數量語言學 quantitative linguistics;
~算法語言學 algorithmic linguistics;
~統計語言學 statistical linguistics;
~外部語言學 external linguistics;
~演變語言學 evolutionary linguistics;
~應用語言學 applied linguistics;
~章句語言學 text linguistics;
語言學習 language learning;
~語言學習者 language learner;
語言藝術 language arts;
語言意義 linguistic meaning;
語言優勢 language dominance;
語言運用 linguistic performance;
~語言運用分析 linguistic performance analysis;
~語言運用目標 linguistic performance objective;
~語言運用語法 linguistic performance grammar;
語言增補 language enrichment;
語言障礙 efect of speech; lalopathy; language barrier;
語言哲學 linguistic philosophy;
語言政策 linhguistic philosophy;
語言知識 language knowledge;
~積極語言知識 active language knowledge;
語言治療 speech therapy;
語言忠貞性 language loyalty;
語言轉換 language shift;
語言自我感 language ego;
標題式語言 block language;
表層語言 adstratum;
初級語言 low-level language;
初始語言 original language;
大眾語言 popular language;
代數語言 algebraic language;
當代語言 present-day language;
地區語言 regional language;
地址語言 address language;
第二語言 second language;
第一語言 first language;
東方語言 Oriental languages;
動物語言 animal language;
多數人語言 majority language;
法定語言 official language;
分析語言 analytic language;
輔助語言 auxiliary language;
副語言 paralanguage;
~副語言特徵 paralinguistic feature;

~副語言學 paralinguistics;
高級語言 high-level language; superior language;
~超高級語言 very high-level language;
個人語言 personal language;
共同語言 common language; wavelength;
~沒有共同語言 be on a different wavelength;
~有共同語言 be on the same wavelength; speak the same language;
古代語言 ancient language;
官方語言 official language;
活語言 living language;
計劃語言 planned language;
加添語言 additional language;
僵化語言 frozen language;
教學媒介語言 medium of instruction;
接觸語言 contact language;
接受者語言 receptor language;
絕對語言 absolute language;
客廳語言 anteroom language;
目標語言 target language;
親密語言 intimate language;
親屬語言 related language;
聲調語言 tone language;
算法語言 algorithmic language;
套式語言 conventionalized speech;
通用語言 all-purpose language;
外表性語言 externalized language;
外國語言 foreign languages;
西方語言 Occidental languages;
現代語言 modern languages;
學習語言 learn a language;
元語言 metalanguage;
~元語言學分析 metalinguistic analysis;
原始語言 primitive language;
掌握語言 master a language;
正式語言 formal language;
~半正式語言 semi-formal language;
中級語言 intermediate language;

[語意] semantics;
語意雙關 words with a double meaning;

[語義] semantics;
語義變化 semantic change;
~語義變化詞 ambivalent word;
語義表達 semantic representation;
語義標記 semantic marker;
語義層 semantic layer;
~語義層次 semantic level;
語義場 semantic field;
~語義場理論 theory of semantic field;
~語義場論 field theory;
語義成分 semantic component;
語義創造性 semantic creativity;
語義對比 semantic contrastiveness;
語義對等 semantic equivalence;
~語義對等詞 semantic equivalent;
語義對立 semantic opposition;
語義對應 semantic correspondence;
語義翻譯 semantic translation;
語義範圍 semantic domain;
語義分析 semantic analysis;
語義記憶 semantic memory;
語義緊縮 semantic condensation;
語義空隙 semantic gap;
語義類別 semantic class;
語義描寫 semantic description;
語義區分 semantic differential;
語義三角 semantic triangle;
語義所指 semantic referential;
語義特徵 semantic feature;
語義學 semantics;
~詞匯語義學 lexical semantics;
~代數語義學 algebraic semantics;
~解釋語義學 interpretative semantics;
~結構語義學 structural semantics;
~理解語義學 interpretive semantics;
~普通語義學 general semantics;
~親緣語義學 kinship semantics;
~生成語義學 generative semantics;
語義習得 semantic acquisition;
語義限定 semantic specification;
語義限制 semantic constraint;
語義項 semantic item;
語義新詞 semantic neologism;
語義異常 semantic anomaly;
語義意義 semantic meaning;
語義語法 semantic grammar;
語義域 semantic area;
語義原則 semanticism;
語義增補 semantic expansion;
語義轉換 semantic shift;

[語音] (1) speech sounds; (2) pronunciation;
語音報警器 voice alarm;
語音處理 speech processing;
語音對等詞 phonetic equivalent;
語音翻譯 phonological translation;
語音合成 speech synthesis;
~語音合成處理器 voice synthesis processor;
~語音合成存儲器 voice synthesis memory;
~語音合成器 speech synthesizer;
語音和諧 euphony;

語音控制器 voice controller;
語音識別 speech recognition;
~ 語音識別系統 speech recognition system;
語音輸入 speech input;
語音學 phonetics;
~ 比較語音學 comparative phonetics;
~ 發音語音學 articulatory phonetics;
~ 聲學語音學 acoustic phonetics;
~ 聽覺語音學 auditory phonetics;
~ 自主語音學 autonomous phonetics;
語音震顫 vocal fremitus;
語音注音法 phonetic script;

[語用] pragmatic;
語用錯誤 pragmatic error;
語用對等 pragmatic equivalence;
語用對應 pragmatic correspondence;
語用翻譯 pragmatic translation;
語用功能 pragmatic function;
語用歧義 pragmatic ambiguity;
語用前題 pragmatic presupposition;
語用學 pragmatics;
語用意義 pragmatic meaning;
語用準確性 pragmatic accuracy;

[語域] register;
語域分析 register analysis;
官式語域 official register;

[語源學] etymology;

[語重心長] meaningful; say in all earnestness; say with deep feeling; sincere words and earnest wishes;

[語助詞] auxiliary; expletive; grammatical particle;

[語族] language family;

[語子] morph;
廣義語子 extended morph;
基本語子 primary morph;
交替語子 alternation morph;
併合語子 portmanteau morph;
虛語子 empty morph;

阿富汗語 Afghan (language);
阿拉伯語 Arabic (language);
阿姆哈拉語 Amharic (language);
愛爾蘭語 Irish (language);
按語 comment; note;
案語 comment; note;
暗語 code word;
巴斯克語 Basque (language);
跋語 postscript;
班巴拉語 Bambara (language);
班圖語 Bantu (language);
保加利亞語 Bulgarian (language);
本國語 mother tongue; native language;
本族語 mother tongue; native language;
編插語 agglomerating language;
標語 poster; slogan;
標準語 standard speech;
表語 predicative;
賓語 object;
冰島語 Icelandic (language);
波蘭語 Polish (language);
波利尼西亞語 Polynesian (language);
不丹語 Bhutanese (language);
不語 without uttering a word;
補語 complement;
插入語 parenthesis;
朝鮮語 Korean (language);
讖語 a prophecy to be fulfilled;
成語 idiom; set phrase;
詞語 terms; words and expressions;
丹麥語 Danish (language);
德語 German (language);
燈語 lamp signal;
低層語 basilect;
定語 attribute;
短語 phrase;
斷語 conclusion; judgment;
多語 multilingual;
俄語 Russian (language);
兒語 baby talk;
耳語 whisper; whisper in sb's ear; whispering;
法語 French (language);
反語 antiphrasis; irony;
菲律賓語 Tagalog;
飛語 gossip; rumours;
蜚語 gossip; rumours;
分析語 analytical language;
芬蘭語 Finnish (language);
佛蘭芒語 Flemish (language);
附加語 adjunct; tag;
告語 inform; let know; tell;
孤立語 isolating language;
古語 (1) archaism; (2) old saying;
國語 (1) national language; (2) Chinese national language;
漢語 Chinese (language);
漢藏語 Sino-Tibetan;
行業語 cant; jargon;
豪薩語 Hausa (language);
豪語 brave words;
荷蘭語 Dutch (language);
呼喚語 call;

呼語 direct address; vocative expression;
華語 Chinese (language);
話語 speech; spoken language;
穢語 dirty words; obscene language;
混合語 mixed language;
寄語 send words;
柬埔寨語 Kampuchean (language);
減弱語 downtoner;
膠着語 agglutinative language;
結束語 concluding remarks;
結語 concluding remarks;
捷克語 Czech (language);
敬語 (1) honorifics; (2) respectful speech;
禁忌語 taboo;
克里奧爾語 Creole (language);
克丘亞語 Quechua (language);
口頭語 pet phrase;
口語 (1) spoken language (2) slandering words;
誑語 falsehood; lie;
拉丁語 Latin (language);
浪語 nonsensical joke;
老撾語 Laotian (language);
仂語 phrase;
俚語 slang;
例語 example phrase; example word; illustrative phrase;
聯加語 conjunct;
略語 abbreviation; shortening;
羅馬尼亞語 Romanian (language);
馬耳他語 Maltese (language);
馬爾加什語 Malagasy (language);
馬拉提語 Marathi (language);
馬拉維語 Malawi (language);
馬來語 Malay (language);
馬來亞語 Malay (language);
馬其頓語 Macedonian (language);
馬雅語 Mayan (language);
曼丁哥語 Mande; Mandingo (language);
媒介語 intermediary language;
蒙古語 Mongol (language);
孟加拉語 Bengali (language);
夢語 sleep-talking;
謎語 conundrum; riddle;
密語 cryptolalia;
緬甸語 Burmese (language);
妙語 witty remark;
母語 (1) mother tongue; (2) parent language;
目的語 target language;
目語 communicate with the eyes;
尼泊爾語 Nepali (language);
黏着語 agglutinative language;
鳥語 bird call;
挪威語 Norwegian (language);
排他語 exclusive;
批語 (1) remarks on a piece of writing; (2) comments and instructions;
片語 phrase;
評語 comment; remark;
葡萄牙語 Portuguese (language);
普什圖語 Pushtu (language);
旗語 flag signal; semaphore;
綺語 (1) sexual talk; (2) literary pieces concerning love and sex;
箝語 restrict freedom of speech;
強調語 emphasizer;
強化語 intensifier;
悄語 speak softly; talk in a low voice; whisper;
親密語 intimate speech;
屈折語 inflectional language;
日語 Japanese (language);
軟語 gentle words;
薩摩亞語 Samoan (language);
僧伽羅語 Sinhalese (language);
身勢語 kinesics;
失語 aphasia;
市語 business jargon; trader's slang;
世界語 Esperanto;
手勢語 sign language;
手語 sign language;
書面語 written language;
熟語 idiom; idiomatic phrase;
術語 technical term; terminology;
雙賓語 double objects;
雙關語 pun;
雙語 bilingual;
私語 whisper;
斯拉夫語 Slavic (language);
斯洛伐克語 Slovak (language);
斯洛文語 Slovene (language);
斯瓦希里語 Swahili (language);
廋語 puzzle; riddle; enigma;
俗語 common saying; folk adage;
縮語 abbreviation;
他加祿語 Tagalog (language);
泰盧固語 Telugu (language);
泰米爾語 Tamil (language);
泰語 Thai (language);
套語 polite formula;
通古斯語 Tungus (language);
同行語 cant; jargon;
同位語 appositive;
土爾其語 Turkish (language);
土庫曼語 Turkoman (language);
土語 local dialect;

外國語 foreign language;
外加語 disjunct;
外來語 foreign word; word of foreign origin;
外位語 extra-positional word;
外語 foreign language;
妄語 wild talk;
謂語 predicate;
烏爾都語 Urdu (language);
西班牙語 Spanish (language);
希伯來語 Hebrew (language);
希臘語 Greek (language);
習語 idiom;
細語 low and tender talk; pillow talk;
閒語 (1) personal talk; (2) gossips; sarcastic remarks;
險語 sensational remark;
笑語 talking and smiling;
歇後語 end-clippers;
匈牙利語 Hungarian (language);
修飾語 modifier;
絮語 garrulity; garrulous;
言語 speech; spoken language;
諺語 proverb; saying;
燕語 soft chirping of swallows;
諺語 adage; proverb; saying;
一語 a remark;
意大利語 Italian (language);
譯語 target language;
囈語 (1) talk in one's sleep; (2) crazy talks; ravings;
引語 quotation;
隱語 enigmatic language; insinuating language;
印地語 Hindi (language);
印度尼西亞語 Indonesian (language);
英語 English (language);
用語 (1) phraseology; term; (2) choice of words;
源語 source language;
越南語 Vietnamese (language);
粵語 Cantonese dialect;
韻語 rhythmical language;
贊語 words of praise;
讚語 praise; words of praise;
藏語 Tibetan (language);
詐語 lie;
譫語 delirious speech;
咒語 incantation;
主語 subject;
狀語 adverbial; adverbial modifier;
綜合語 synthetic language;
祖魯語 Zulu (language);

yu

【窳】 (1) coarse; crude; of inferior quality; (2) lazy; (3) fragile; weak; (4) bad; mean;
[窳敗] corrupt; rot;
[窳惰] lazy and dissipated; weak and indolent;
[窳楛] coarse and fragile;
[窳劣] bad; of inferior quality; poor;
[窳陋] coarse; crude; inferior;
[窳民] idle and lazy people;

yu

【鋙】 (1) discordant; disharmonious; (2) a kind of musical instrument;

yu

【嶼】 island; islet;
島嶼 islands; islands and islets;

yu

【齬】 disagreement; discord;

yu⁴

yu

【玉】 (1) jade; (2) beautiful; handsome; pure; (3) your; (4) a surname;
[玉杯] jade cup;
玉杯象箸 jade cups and ivory chopsticks — luxury;
[玉臂] girl's arms; pretty woman's arms;
[玉鬢] white hair;
[玉帛] (1) gems and silk; jade objects and silk fabrics; (2) friendship;
[玉步] (1) one's footsteps; (2) the footsteps of a pretty girl;
[玉慘花愁] (1) cry; (2) sad;
[玉塵紛飛] a great fall of snow; a great snowfall; the snow flakes are falling thick and fast;
[玉成] contribute to the success of sth;
玉成其事 assist sb in attaining a goal; bring it off finally; bring the matter to a successful end; help make a success of it; help to bring to a successful conclusion; help to complete a thing;
鼎力玉成 help accomplish this small task with your great power;
[玉釧] jade bracelet;
[玉帶] jade belt;
[玉殿金闕] temple of luxury and beauty;
[玉雕] jade carving; jade sculpture;

玉雕工人 jade carver;

[玉鉤] (1) crescent moon; new moon; (2) jade hook;

[玉骨冰肌] bones of jade and flesh of ice—purity of character;

[玉壺] (1) jade wine cup; (2) honest and virtuous; (3) jade hourglass;

玉壺買春 buy wine;

[玉環] (1) jade rings; (2) moon;

[玉皇大帝] the Jade Emperor;

[玉肌] pure, snow-white skin of a woman;

玉肌雪膚 pure, snow-white flesh of a woman;

[玉尖] (1) tapering fingers of a beautiful woman; (2) mountain peaks;

[玉減香消] become emaciated;

[玉漿] good wine;

[玉潔冰清] as pure as jade and as clean as ice; pure and noble; pure as jade and chaste as ice;

[玉昆金友] your brothers;

[玉蘭] magnolia;

[玉粒] (1) grains; (2) grains of jade;

玉粒滿倉 the barn is full of pearly grains;

[玉樓] (1) fairyland; paradise; (2) jade tower;

玉樓赴召 die young;

[玉漏] jade hourglass;

[玉露] (1) dewdrops; (2) the best green tea;

玉露晶瑩 the grass is all bespangled with dewdrops;

玉露如霜 the pearly dew looks like frost;

玉露如珠 the dewdrops are as bright as pearls;

[玉輪] moon;

[玉貌] (1) face of a pretty girl; fair face; (2) one's face;

[玉米] corn; Indian corn; maize; mealie;

玉米餅 corn-cake;

玉米淀粉 cornstarch;

玉米粉 cornflour; cornstarch;

~粗玉米粉 cornmeal;

玉米花 popcorn;

~爆玉米花 popcorn;

~加糖玉米花 sugared popped corn;

玉米煎餅 corn chip;

玉米漿 maize jelly;

玉米粒 shelled corn;

玉米麵 cornflour; maize flour;

~玉米麵包 corn bread;

玉米片 cornflake;

~炸玉米片 corn chip;

玉米芯 corncob;

玉米摘穗機 corn picker;

玉米粥 maize gruel;

掰玉米 break off corncobs;

白玉米 white maize;

超甜玉米 super-sweet corn;

黃玉米 yellow maize;

黃質玉米 true maize;

臘質種玉米 waxy corn;

日光紅玉米 sun-red corn;

整粒玉米 whole kernel corn;

種玉米 grow corn;

[玉女] (1) young and beautiful girl; (2) one's daughter; (3) angel in the fairyland; (4) golden girl;

[玉佩] jade pendants on a girdle;

[玉器] jade articles;

[玉全] help accomplish sth;

[玉人] (1) beautiful woman; (2) lapidary;

玉人香消 the fragrance of a beauty has diminished — death of a beautiful woman;

[玉容] beautiful face;

玉容花貌 fair face and elegant form; beautiful and charming;

[玉潤珠圓] (said of a singing voice) smooth and soft;

[玉山傾倒] get drunk and collapse on the ground;

[玉山傾頹] get dead drunk and fall fast asleep;

[玉石] jade;

玉石不分 make no distinctions between the jade and the stone — not distinguish the good from the bad; thread and thrum;

玉石俱焚 jade and stones burn together;

炫玉賈石 carry high-sounding but misleading names; sell stones as jade;

[玉食] dainties; delicacies;

玉食錦衣 sumptuous food and luxurious clothing;

[玉手纖纖] slender hands of a pretty young woman;

玉奴纖手 slender fingers of a girl;

[玉樹] (1) young person with talent and good looks; (2) locust tree;

銀山玉樹 silver-clad hills and jade-like trees;

芝蘭玉樹 children of a prominent family; orchids and jade trees — symbols of young men's good conduct;

[玉碎] broken jade;

玉碎香埋 death of a woman;

玉碎珠沉 death of a beauty;

[玉體] (1) your esteemed health; your person; yourself; (2) nude body of a girl;

玉體橫陳 the beautiful nude body lying in full view;

玉體違和 sorry to learn that you are indisposed;

[玉兔] (1) jade hare in the moon; (2) moon;

玉兔東昇 the moon rises in the east;

[玉腕] wrist and forearm of a beautiful woman;

[玉璽] imperial seal;

[玉匣] (1) jade box for jewels; (2) coffin for emperors in the Han Dynasty;

[玉纖秀美] the fingers of a beauty are graceful;

[玉蕭] jade flute;

[玉屑] (1) broken jade; (2) snow; (3) exquisite writing;

[玉心] a heart as pure as jade;

玉心皎潔 a pure heart is unsullied;

[玉虛] fairyland;

[玉顏] fair complexion;

[玉燕投懷] wish one will give birth to a good child;

[玉豔] a complexion as smooth as jade;

[玉液瓊漿] good wine; top-quality wine;

[玉儀] (1) a complexion as smooth as jade; (2) a jade-ornamented instrument for observing heavenly bodies;

[玉音] (1) your letter; (2) valuable words; (3) imperial decrees; (4) jade-like music — beautiful sound;

[玉英] (1) jade of best quality; (2) cactus flowers;

[玉饗瓊醴] valuable food and wine;

[玉宇] (1) universe; (2) beautiful palace;

玉宇澄清 the sky is crystal-clear;

[玉殞香消] death of a beauty; death of a young lady;

[玉簪] jade hairpin;

[玉展] for your perusal;

[玉照] your photograph; your portrait;

[玉趾] your footsteps;

玉趾光臨 the approach of your footsteps;

[玉鐲] jade bracelet;

白玉 white jade;

碧玉 jasper;

璧玉 round piece of jade;

瑹玉 lustrous jade;

翠玉 blue jade;

剛玉 corundum;

漢白玉 white marble;

黃玉 topaz;

金玉 gold and jade; treasures;

軟玉 (1) nephrite; (2) bean curd;

晚香玉 tuberose;

瑋玉 rare treasure;

纖玉 delicate jade — a woman's delicate hands;

移玉 may I request your company;

硬玉 jadeite;

藻玉 multicoloured jade;

珠玉 (1) beautifully written verses; (2) elegant in appearance;

yu

【聿】 (1) writing instrument; (2) initial particle; (3) agile and quick; nimble;

[聿皇] fleet and nimble;

[聿越] excel; surpass;

[聿至] arrive suddenly;

yu

【育】 (1) breed; give birth to; produce; (2) bring up; nourish; nurse; raise; (3) educate;

[育才] cultivate talents; educate men of ability;

[育德] cultivate one's virtue;

[育肥] fatten;

[育兒] child rearing;

育兒假 parental leave;

[育孤] rear orphans;

[育花] cultivate flowers;

[育齡] childbearing age;

育齡期 childbearing period;

[育苗] grow seedlings;

育苗助長 cultivate the young shoots and help them thrive;

[育民] educate the people;

[育樹] cultivate trees;

[育嬰堂] foundling hospital; orphanage;

[育種] breeding;

育種栽培 breeding cultivation;

單倍體育種 monadic breeding;
定向育種 directive breeding;
混合育種 do mass breeding;
雜交育種 do cross-breeding;

保育 take good care of small children;
哺育 (1) feed; (2) foster; nurture;
不育 acyesis; infertility; sterility;
採育 fell timber and cultivate new trees;
德育 moral education;
發育 develop; grow;
繁育 breed;
肥育 fatten;
孵育 incubation;
撫育 foster; nurture;
杭育 heave ho; yo-heave-ho;
教育 educate; education; teach;
節育 practise birth control;
絕育 sterilize;
美育 art education;
培育 cultivate; foster;
生育 bear; give birth to;
飼育 raise; rear;
燾育 nurse all the things on earth;
體育 physical education;
選育 breed;
訓育 moral teachings;
養育 bring up; raise; rear;
孕育 breed; be pregnant with;
智育 intellectual education;
瀦育 periodical water-logging;
滋育 multiply; reproduce in large numbers;
自育 self-fertile;

yu
【芋】 taro;
［芋頭］ (1) taro; (2) sweet potato;

姜芋 canna edulis;
菊芋 (1) Jerusalem artichoke; (2) tuber of Jerusalem artichoke;
魔芋 konjak bean curd;
竹芋 arrowroot;

yu
【谷】 a surname;

yu
【汩】 fleeting; rapid;
［汩流］ rapids;

yu
【雨】 pour down; rain down;
［雨淚］ tears pouring down like rain;
［雨雪］ fall of snow;

yu
【昱】 (1) brightness; dazzling; light; sunshine; (2) tomorrow;
［昱昱］ dazzling;

yu
【禺】 monkey;

yu
【郁】 (1) adorned; beautiful; refined; (2) a surname;
［郁馥］ aromatic; fragrant;
［郁李］ prune;
［郁烈］ permeated with strong aroma;
［郁穆］ harmonious and refined;
［郁郁］ (1) beautifully adorned; ornamented; (2) diffusing of aroma; (3) flourishing; luxuriant; (4) elegant; refined;

yu
【峪】 ravine; valley;

yu
【浴】 (1) bath; bathe; (2) wash;
［浴場］ bathing beach; outdoor bathing place;
海水浴場 sea-water baths;
［浴池］ bath pool;
［浴德］ cultivate one's virtue;
浴德澡身 bathe one's body in virtue;
［浴佛］ bathe Buddha's image;
浴佛節 Buddha Bathing Festival;
［浴缸］ bathtub;
［浴巾］ bath towel; facecloth; washcloth;
［浴盆］ bath; bathtub;
固定浴盆 built-in bathtub;
坐浴盆 bidet;
［浴日］ (1) bright sunrise; (2) great distinction; great exploits;
［浴室］ bath; bathroom;
浴室間 bathroom stall;
公共浴室 public bath;
配套浴室 en suite;
一間浴室 a bathroom;
［浴刷］ body friction brush;
［浴堂］ bathhouse; public bath;
［浴血］ bathed in blood; bloody;
浴血奮戰 fight a bloody battle; fight hard, bloody battles;
浴血苦戰 at bay in a fierce battle; fight a bloody battle;
［浴衣］ bathrobe;

Y

牀浴 bed bath;
紡絲浴 spinning bath;
風浴 wind bath;
淴浴 bathe; have a bath;
冷水浴 cold bath;
淋浴 shower; shower bath;
沐浴 (1) have a bath; take a bath; (2) bathe; immerse; (3) ablutions; bath;
熱水浴 hot bath;
日光浴 sunbath;
沙浴 sand bath;
砂浴 sand bath;
溫水浴 warm bath;
藥浴 dip;
油浴 oil bath;
蒸氣浴 steam bath;

Y

yu

【彧】 refined, learned and accomplished;

yu

【域】 (1) domain; region; territory; (2) live; stay;

[域名] domain name;
域名搶註 cybersquatter;
~ 域名搶註者 cybersquatter;

[域內] intra-domain;

[域外] foreign country; beyond the frontier; outside China;

邦域 national territory;
地域 (1) area; district; region; (2) place; room; space;
海域 maritime space; sea area;
疆域 territory;
境域 (1) circumstance; condition; (2) area; state;
絕域 remote place;
空域 airspace;
鄰域 neighbourhood;
領域 (1) domain; territory; (2) realm; sphere;
流域 catchment area; drainage basin; watershed;
區域 district; area; region;
識域 field of awareness;
視域 field of vision;
殊域 strange lands;
數域 number field;
水域 water area;
外域 foreign lands;
西域 Western Regions;
異域 foreign lands;
意識域 sphere of consciousness;
音域 compass; range;
畛域 boundary;

yu

【尉】 in 尉遲 , a surname;

yu

【御】 (1) drive; drive a chariot; (2) imperial; (3) keep out; resist;

[御寶] imperial seal; seal of the emperor;

[御筆] handwriting of the emperor;

[御賜] bestowed by the emperor;

[御夫有術] very skilful in keeping one's husband on leash;

[御甲] strip off one's armour;
棄戈御甲 lay down one's weapon and strip off one's armour;

[御駕] (1) imperial carriage; (2) emperor;
御駕親征 the emperor personally leads his soldiers in a military operation;

[御林軍] palace guard;

[御女] (1) court ladies; court women; (2) have sexual intercourse with a woman;

[御批] comments made by the emperor;

[御妻] control one's wife;

[御前] in the presence of the emperor;
御前演出 command performance;

[御容] portrait of the emperor;

[御膳] imperial cuisine;

[御世] rule the world;

[御事] manage affairs;

[御宴] royal feast;

[御醫] imperial physician;

[御用] (1) employed by the emperor; for the use of an emperor; (2) in the pay of;
御用文人 hack writer; hired scribbler; a scribe in pay;

[御宇] reign of an emperor over the nation;

[御旨] imperial decree;

yu

【欲】 (1) desire; longing; (2) desire; want; wish; (3) about to; just going to; on the point of;

[欲愛] love inspired by desire; passion-love;

[欲罷不能] can't help carrying on; cannot refrain from going on; try to stop but cannot; unable to stop even though one wants to; wanting to stop but unable to do so;

[欲不可從] desire must be kept under control;

[欲待] intend to; want to;

[欲蓋彌彰] the harder one tries to conceal a

thing, the more it attracts attention; the more concealed, the more conspicuous; the more one quibbles, the more one is exposed; the more one tries to cover up one's fault, the more it is exposed to public view; the more one tries to cover up, the more one exposes oneself; the more one tries to hide, the more one is exposed; try to cover sth up only to make it more conspicuous;

[欲海難填] one's desires are insatiable;

[欲壑難填] avarice knows no bounds; desire hath no rest; greed is a valley that can never be filled; it is impossible to set limits to a man's desires; much would have more; no man is content with his lot; the covetous are never satisfied; the more he gets, the more he wants; there is no limit to avarice;

[欲火] the fire of desire — sexual desire;

[欲加之罪，何患無詞] a staff is quickly found to beat a dog with; any stick will do to beat a dog with; he who has a mind to beat his dog will easily find his stick; if one is out to condemn sb, one can always trump up a charge; if you want a pretence to hip a dog, say that he ate the frying-pan; it is easy to find a stick to beat a dog;

[欲念] desire; drive;

[欲巧反拙] try to be clever but turn out the contrary;

[欲擒故縱] allow sb more latitude first to keep a tighter rein on him afterwards; give somebody line; leave sb at large the better to apprehend him; let sb off in order to catch him; play cat and mouse with;

[欲取姑與] give in order to take; make concessions for the sake of future gains; in order to take, one must first give;

[欲速則不達] fool's haste is no speed; haste brings no success; haste does not bring success; haste makes waste; haste trips over its own heels; the farthest way about is the nearest way home; the longest way round is the shortest way home; the more haste, the less speed; too swift arrives as tardy as too slow;

[欲望] desire; long for; longing; lust;

[欲想] desire for wealth and women;

[欲心] one's desires;

[欲行又止] start to walk, then stop;

[欲言又止] about to speak, but say nothing; bite one's lip; hold back the words which spring to one's lips; swallow back the words on the tip of one's tongue; wish to speak but not do so on second thought;

[欲要] desire; want;

[欲願] desire; wish;

[欲障] desires that pose as one's obstacles to salvation;

饕欲 avarice; greed;
寡欲 have few desires;
亟欲 very anxious to do sth;
獸欲 animal desire; beastly appetites; beastly pleasure; bestial urge; brutal appetite; carnal desire;
俗欲 worldly thoughts;
所欲 what one desires;
逸欲 idleness and lust;
意欲 desire; volition;
恣欲 give rein to lust;

yu

【雩】 rainbow;

yu

【喻】 (1) explain; inform; instruct; make clear; tell the meaning of; (2) know; understand; (3) analogy; compare; liken; (4) a surname;

[喻之以理] reason with sb; try to make sb see reason;

暗喻 metaphor;
比喻 analogy; figure of speech; metaphor; simile;
諷喻 allegory; parable;
換喻 metonymy;
明喻 simile;
譬喻 analogy; figure of speech; metaphor; simile;
訓喻 instruct; teach;
隱喻 metaphor;
直喻 simile;
轉喻 metonymy;

yu

【寓】 (1) dwell; live temporarily; reside; sojourn; (2) residence; (3) contain; imply;

［寓兵於農］ make soldiers do the work of farmers as in times of peace; put soldiers on farm work;

［寓公］ a person of wealth living as an exile;

［寓教於娛］ make entertainment a medium of education;

［寓居］ live; make one's home in;

［寓目］ gaze; look over; stare;

［寓所］ abode; dwelling; place of residence; residence;

第二寓所 second home;

［寓託］ imply;

［寓言］ allegory; fable; parable;

寓言故事 allegoric tale;

～一則寓言故事 an allegory;

寓言家 fabulist;

寓言詩 allegoric poem;

寓言中的人物 allegorical character;

［寓意］ allegoric meaning; implied meaning; import; message; moral;

寓意深刻 contain a profound message; have a profound message; pregnant with meaning;

寓意深邃 have a profound message; pregnant with profundities;

［寓於］ contain; imply;

寓於…之中 inhabit;

敝寓 my residence;

公寓 (1) apartment; flat; (2) lodging house;

寄寓 live away from home;

yu

【馭】 (1) drive; (2) control; govern; rule; (3) driver;

［馭手］ (1) driver of a military pack train; (2) soldier in charge of pack animals;

駕馭 (1) drive; (2) control; master; tame;

yu

【棫】 thorny shrub with yellow flowers and dark fruit;

yu

【矞】 (1) bright and brilliant; charming; (2) nature bursting into life; (3) clouds of many colours;

［矞皇］ (1) bright and beautiful; (2) name of a deity;

［矞矞］ nature bursting into life;

［矞雲］ clouds of many colours;

yu

【飫】 (1) glutted; surfeited; (2) confer; grant; (3) feast; (4) drink to repletion; eat to repletion;

［飫甘饜肥］ be delicately nurtured; enjoy delicate food; feed on the fat of the land;

yu

【愈】 (1) heal; recover from illness; (2) even more; more and more; the more...the more; to a greater degree;

［愈合］ heal;

［愈加］ all the more; even more; further; increasingly; more and more;

［愈甚］ become intense; intenser;

［愈益］ increasingly; more and more;

愈益嚴重 aggravation;

［愈愈］ become greater; wax more and more;

愈多愈好 the more the better;

愈快愈好 the sooner the better;

愈來愈糟 change for the worse; get worse and worse; go from bad to worse;

愈老愈健 become more firm as one grows old;

愈氣愈惱 aggravate;

愈陷愈深 get bogged down deeper and deeper; plunge deeper and deeper;

愈演愈烈 become ever more violent; become increasingly fierce; grow in intensity;

愈早愈好 the sooner the better;

愈戰愈強 grow in strength in fighting; grow stronger and stronger through fighting;

愈治愈糟 grow worse with the treatment;

病愈 recover from an illness;

yu

【毓】 (1) bring up; nurse; nurture; rear; (2) grow;

yu

【煜】 (1) bright and brilliant; (2) blazes; flames; (3) illuminate; shine;

［煜煜］ bright and shining;

yu

【裕】 (1) abundant; plentiful; (2) tolerant; (3) generous; magnanimous; (4) slowly; take time;

［裕國］ enrich the nation;

裕國裕民 enrich the state and the people;

［裕如］ effortlessly; with ease;

［裕裕］ at peace with the world; take it easy;

充裕 abundant; ample; plentiful;

豐裕 in plenty; well-off; well provided for;

富裕 prosperous; well-off; well-to-do;

寬裕 comfortably off; well-off; well-to-do;

饒裕 abundance; affluence;

優裕 abundant; affluent; well-to-do;

餘裕 ample; enough and to spare;

yu

【遇】 (1) come across; encounter; meet; run into; (2) receive; treat; (3) chance; luck; opportunity; (4) win confidence of sb; (5) match with; rival; (6) a surname;

［遇便］ at one's convenience;

［遇刺］ be attacked by an assassin;

遇刺身死 be assassinated;

［遇到］ come across; encounter; meet; run into;

遇到厄運 meet with a harsh fate;

遇到困難 come up against difficulties; fall into difficulties;

遇到冷眼 meet with disfavour;

遇到矛盾 fall into contradictions;

遇到危險 face a danger;

遇到險境 be placed in a perilous situation;

遇到障礙 encounter obstacles;

遇到知己 find a bosom friend;

遇到阻力 meet obstructions;

［遇敵］ encounter the enemy;

［遇害］ be assassinated; be murdered;

［遇合］ (1) meet and get along well; (2) meeting of minds;

遇合有緣 the meeting is destined;

［遇見］ bump into; come across; meet; run into;

偶然遇見 accidentally meet; meet sb by accident;

［遇救］ be rescued; be saved;

［遇難而退］ flinch from a difficulty;

［遇難］ (1) die in an accident; get killed in an accident; (2) be murdered;

遇難身亡 be killed in an accident;

［遇人不淑］ be married to a bad husband; ill matched in marriage;

［遇時］ catch the right opportunity; ride at the crest of one's fortune;

［遇事］ when anything comes up; when anything crops up;

遇事不慌 unruffled whatever happens;

遇事不怒 never get angry whatever happens;

遇事樂觀 look through rose-coloured glasses;

遇事生風 make a mountain out of a molehill; sow discord whenever possible; stir up trouble;

［遇險］ in danger; in distress; meet with a mishap; meet with danger;

［遇有］ in case of; in the event of;

［遇雨］ be caught in the rain;

遇雨順延 subject to postponement in case of rain;

［遇着］ encounter; meet;

寵遇 treat as a favourite;

待遇 (1) deal; treat; treatment; (2) salary;

機遇 favourable circumstances; opportunity;

際遇 favourable or unfavourable turns in life; spells of good or bad fortune;

景遇 circumstances; one's lot;

境遇 circumstances; one's lot;

冷遇 cold reception; cold shoulder;

禮遇 courteous reception;

奇遇 pleasant encounter;

巧遇 chance encounter;

外遇 paramour;

相遇 meet;

艷遇 encounter with a beautiful woman;

優遇 give special treatment;

遭遇 encounter; meet with;

值遇 come across; meet with;

yu

【預】 (1) beforehand; in advance; (2) make ready; prepare; reserve; (3) take part in;

［預報］ advance notice; announcement; forecast; forecasting; prediction;

預報不準 the forecast is inaccurate;

預報員 forecaster;

地震預報 earthquake forecast;

航空預報 airways forecast;

農業氣象預報 agrometeorological forecasting;
氣候預報 climatological forecast;
區域預報 area forecast; district forecast;
日預報 daily forecast;
天氣預報 weather forecast;
~ 天氣預報員 weather forecaster;
災情預報 forecast natural calamities;

[預備] get ready beforehand; prepare in advance;
預備功課 prepare one's lessons;
預備會議 preparatory meeting;
預備考試 prepare for a test; prepare oneself for an examination;
預備期 probationary period;
預備役 reserve duty; reserve service;
~ 預備役部隊 reserve duty force;
~ 預備役軍官 reserve duty officer;
~ 預備役訓練 reserve duty training;

[預卜] augur; foretell; predict;
預卜吉凶 try to predict good or bad fortune;

[預測] calculate; forecast; make a forecast; predict; prediction;
預測方法 forecasting methodology;
預測分析方法 prediction analysis method;
預測技術 forecasting technique;
預測控制 predictive control;
預測理論 prediction theory;
預測器 predictor;
預測學 forecasting studies;
預測者 forecaster;
預測指標 predictor;
預測終端系統 forecasting terminal system;
環境預測 environmental forecasting;
經濟預測 economic forecasting; economic prediction;
企業預測 business forecast;
商情預測 business forecast; business forecasting;
生產預測 product forecast;
收成預測 crop forecast;
水紋預測 hydrological forecasting;
現金預測 cash forecast;
銷售預測 marketing forecasting;

[預產期] estimated date of childbirth;

[預抵期] estimated time of arrival;

[預定] (1) fix in advance; predetermine; schedule; (2) reserve;
預定計劃 plan ahead;

[預訂] book; place an order; subscribe; subscribe in advance;
預訂房間 book in;
預訂一空 be booked up;
超額預訂 overbook;
重複預訂 double-book; double-booking;
打電話預訂 book by phone;
可預訂的 bookable;
取消預訂 cancel reservations;

[預斷] prejudge;

[預防] forestall; guard against; make provision against; nip in the bud; prepare against; prevent; prevent beforehand; take precautions against;
預防措施 preventative measures; preventive measures;
預防犯罪 prevention of crimes;
預防火災 take precautions against fires;
預防勝於治療 prevention is better than cure;
預防事故 prevention of accidents; provide against accidents;
預防性維護 preventive maintenance;
預防意外 provide against accidents;
預防注射 preventive inoculation;

[預付] pay in advance; prepayment;
預付貸款 payment in advance;
預付利息 prepaid interest;
預付税款 prepayment of taxes;
預付資本 advanced capital;
承兑預付 prepayment of acceptance;
運費預付 prepayment of freight charges;

[預感] (1) forebode; foreboding; have a premonition; hunch; (2) premonition; presentiment;
不祥的預感 ominous presentiment;
我早有預感 I have a hunch;

[預告] (1) announce in advance; herald; (2) advance notice;
預告按鈕 advance button;
預告片 trailer;

[預購] purchase in advance;

[預計] calculate in advance; estimate; expect;
預計錯誤 out in the calculation;
按照預計 according to expectation;
超過預計 exceed the estimates;
根據預計 on estimation;
難以預計 difficult to calculate;
通過預計 by estimate;
無法預計 beyond calculation;

[預見] anticipate; envision; foresee; predict; see beforehand; see beyond;
預見力 second sight;
無法預見 unforeseeable; unforeseen;
[預科] preparatory course; prior course;
[預料] anticipate; augur; bargain for; expect; predict; surmise;
出乎人們預料 beyond expectation;
可以預料 it is possible to predict;
難以預料 it is difficult to predict;
如所預料 according to expectation; as was expected;
無法預料 it is impossible to anticipate;
[預留] keep sth in reserve; put aside for later use;
[預錄] canned;
預錄笑聲 canned laughter;
預錄音樂 canned music;
[預謀] plan beforehand; plan in advance; premeditate; scheme beforehand;
預謀暗殺 premeditate murder;
預謀反叛 preconcert a revolt;
預謀事件 got-up affair;
[預期] anticipate; estimate; expect;
預期從句 prospective clause;
預期錯誤 anticipation error;
預期定述 anticipated identification;
預期會計 forward accounting;
超出預期 exceed the expectation; surpass the expectation;
低於預期 below expectations;
高於預期 above expectations;
[預熱] preheating;
預熱器 preheater;
~鼓風預熱器 blast preheater;
~焦炭預熱器 coke preheater;
~空氣預熱器 air preheater;
高頻預熱 electronic preheating; high-frequency preheating; preheating by dielectric losses; radio frequency preheating;
局部預熱 local preheating;
[預賽] preliminary competition;
參加預賽 enter a preliminary contest;
[預示] forebode; forecast; foresee; foretell; predict; presage; prognostic of; prognosticate; prophesize; prophetic of;
預示未來 presage for the future;
[預售] advance booking; open to booking;
[預算] budget; calculate in advance; estimate;
預算本體 main budget;
預算赤字 budget deficit;
預算的 budgetary;
預算法 budget law;
預算開支 budgetary expenditure;
預算控制 budget control;
預算收入 budgetary revenue;
預算提案 budget proposal;
預算委員會 budget committee;
預算盈餘 budget surplus;
預算賬戶 budget account;
預算政策 budgetary policy;
編制預算 make a budget; prepare a budget;
本期預算 current budget;
標準預算 standard budget;
表決預算 vote on a budget;
補充預算 supplementary budget;
財務預算 financial budget;
財政預算 fiscal budget;
長期預算 long-range budget;
超出預算 overspend one's budget;
城市預算 city budget;
赤字預算 deficit budget; red-letter budget;
持續預算 perpetual budget;
初步預算 preliminary budget;
純預算 net budget;
單一預算 single budget;
低預算 low budget;
短期預算 short-range budget;
方案預算 programme budget;
費用預算 expense budget;
附屬預算 annexed budget;
複式預算 multiple budget;
購貨預算 purchasing budget;
固定預算 fixed budget;
滾計預算 rolling budget;
國防預算 defence budget; national defence budget;
國家經濟預算 nations' economic budget;
國家預算 national budget; state budget;
國民經濟預算 national economic budget;
核定預算 approved budget; final budget;
黑字預算 black-letter budget;
績效預算 performance budget;
家庭預算 family budget; household budget;
減少預算 cut down the budget;
教育預算 educational budget;
緊縮預算 austerity budget; tight budget;
靜態預算 static budget;
軍事預算 military budget;

聯邦預算 federal budget;
臨時預算 interim budget; provisional budget;
年度預算 annual budget; yearly budget;
派定預算 imposed budget;
龐大預算 big hudget; large budget;
平衡預算 balance the budget;
普通預算 ordinary budget;
人工預算 labour budget;
商品預算 merchandise budget;
社會預算 social budget;
生產預算 production budget;
實物預算 physical budget;
時間預算 time budget;
市政預算 municipal budget;
削減預算 budget cut;
歲出預算 annual expenditure budget; appropriation budget;
歲入預算 annual revenues budget; revenue budget;
攤派預算 assessed budget;
彈性預算 flexible budget;
提出預算 submit a budget;
投資預算 investment budget;
通過預算 pass a budget;
統一預算 unified budget;
外匯預算 exchange budget; foreign exchange budget;
現金預算 cash budget;
項目預算 project budget;
銷售預算 sales budget;
小額預算 small budget;
行政預算 administrative budget;
修訂預算 revise the budget;
延續預算 continuous budget;
業務預算 operating budget;
永久預算 constant budget;
有預算 have a budget;
月度預算 monthly budget;
責任預算 responsibility budget;
增加預算 increase the budget;
暫定預算 tentative budget;
整數預算 lump-sum budget;
正常預算 normal budget; regular budget;
州預算 state budget;
周預算 monthly budget;
追加預算 additional budget; supplementary budget;
資本預算 capital budget;
總體預算 overall budget;
總預算 general budget; gross budget; ledger budget; master budget;
最初預算 initial budget;
做預算 make a budget;

[預聞] interfere with; participate in;

[預習] (1) prepare lessons before class; (2) rehearse;

[預先] beforehand; in advance;
預先警告 warning in advance;

[預想] anticipate; expect;

[預選] preliminary selection; preselect; preselection;
預選器 preselector;
~步進式預選器 stepping preselector;
~第二預選器 second preselector;
~第一預選器 first preselector;
~中繼預選器 relay preselector;
參加預選 hold a primary election;
脈衝預選 impulse preselection;
頻道預選 channel preselection;

[預言] (1) foretell; predict; prophesy; (2) forecast; prognostication; prophecy; prediction;
預言家 fortuneteller; prophet;
做出預言 make a practice of foretelling;

[預演] preview; preview show; rehearsal; walk through;
預演一部戲 rehearse a play;

[預約] (1) make an appointment; (2) order; subscribe;
預約簿 appointment book;
預約看病 have an appointment with one's doctor;
預約面試 seek an interview with an appointment;
預約日期 booking date;
預約時間 booking time;
取消預約 cancel an appointment;

[預展] preview of an exhibition; private view;
內部預展 sneak preview;

[預兆] harbinger; foregleam; foreshadow; foretaste; omen; presage; sign;
吉祥的預兆 happy omen;
災禍的預兆 a boding of disaster;

[預支] advance; draw in advance;
預支薪水 advance sb his / her wage; draw one's salary in advance;

[預知] foreknowledge; know beforehand; know in advance; precognition;
預知如何行動 foreknow what to do;

[預制] prefabricated;
預制言語 prefabricated speech;

預制語言 prefabricated language;
[預祝] congratulate beforehand;

干預 intervene; meddle;

yu
【鈺】 hard variety of gold;

yu
【嫗】 old woman;
[嫗鱗魨] queen triggerfish;

老嫗 old woman;

yu
【獄】 (1) jail; prison; (2) case; lawsuit;
[獄犯] convict;
[獄警] prison police;
[獄吏] jailer; prison officer;
[獄首] wardsman;
[獄訟] lawsuit;
[獄友] cellmate;
[獄卒] prison guard; turnkey;

犴獄 prison;
犴獄 prison;
出獄 be discharged from prison; be released from prison;
地獄 hell; inferno; the lower world; the nether netherworld;
典獄 prison warder;
斷獄 settle a lawsuit;
活地獄 hell on earth;
監獄 bucket and pail; clink; cooler; hard site; jail; penitentiary; pokey; poky; prison; slammer;
劫獄 break inbto a jail and rescue a prisoner;
牢獄 jail; prison;
煉獄 purgatory;
入獄 be sent to jail; put in prison;
訟獄 lawsuit; litigation;
文字獄 literary inquisition;
繫獄 be imprisoned; imprison;
下獄 send to jail; put into prison;
讞獄 sentence;
鬻獄 accept bribes from litigants;
冤獄 unjust charge;
越獄 escape from prison;
造獄 (1) start litigation; (2) extraordinary criminal code;
折獄 decide a lawsuit;

yu
【瘉】 (1) cured; healed; (2) ill; sick;

yu
【與】 participate in; take part in;
[與會] participate in a conference;
[與聞] have a participant's knowledge of; let into; participate in the affair;

參與 a party to; have a hand in; involvement; join; partake; participate in; participation; pitch in; take part in;

yu
【語】 admonish; inform; tell;
[語人] tell others;

言語 answer; speak; talk;

yu
【蜮】 tortoise-like creature;

yu
【慾】 (1) desire; greed; passion; (2) lust; (3) appetite;
[慾海] sea of passions;
慾海無邊 greed knows no bounds;
[慾火] passion; the fire of lust;
慾火焚身 the fire of lust is so hot that it consumes the body;
慾火如焚 burning desire; one's heart is tortured by lusts; the insatiable lust of youth is blazing within like a fire;
[慾令智昏] greed can benumb reason;
[慾念] craving; desire; longing;
[慾望] craving; desire; longing; urge;
刺激慾望 stimulate the desire;
充滿慾望 be filled with lust;
滿足慾望 slake a craving; slake a desire;
強烈慾望 compulsion;
引起慾望 arouse desire;

禁慾 suppress sensual desire for enjoyment;
情慾 sexual passion; lust;
求知慾 thirst for knowledge;
肉慾 carnal desire;
色慾 sexual desire;
食慾 appetite;
嗜慾 pleasure-seeking desire;
獸慾 animal desire;
私慾 selfish desire;
物慾 material desire;
性慾 sexual desire;
縱慾 indulge in sensual pleasure;

yu
【蔚】 (1) a county in Hebei; (2) a surname;

yu

【禦】 guard against; take precautions against;

[禦敵] guard against the enemy;

[禦寒] protect oneself from cold; take precautions against cold;

禦寒充饑 allay hunger and resist cold; keep out the cold and stop hunger;

[禦寇] guard against bandits; guard against the insults of foreign powers; take precautions against invaders;

[禦侮] resist foreign aggression;

抵禦 resist; withstand;
防禦 defend;
駕禦 (1) drive; (2) control; tame;
抗禦 resist and defend;

yu

【諭】 (1) inform or notify by a directive; (2) command; decree; edict; instruction;

[諭示] notify by an edict;

[諭知] notify by a directive;

[諭旨] imperial edict;

鈞諭 your instruction;
上諭 imperial edict;
手諭 personal written instruction of a senior;
曉諭 give explicit instructions;
訓諭 instruct; teach;

yu

【豫】 (1) at ease; comfort; (2) same as 預 ; (3) excursion; travel; trip; (4) cheat; lie; (5) one of the nine political divisions in ancient China; (6) a surname; (7) short for Henan; (8) delighted; happy; pleased;

猶豫 hesitant; irresolute;

yu

【遹】 (1) comply with; follow; (2) avoid; shun; (3) bad; perverse; (4) a surname;

yu

【閾】 (1) doorsil; threshold; (2) separated; (3) confined;

視閾 visual threshold;
聽閾 threshold of audibility;
痛閾 threshold of pain;

yu

【隩】 (1) bend of a stream; cove; (2) warm; (3) inhabitable land;

yu

【馭】 flitting; flying rapidly;

yu

【燠】 warm;

yu

【蕷】 Chinese yam;

yu

【癒】 cured; healed;

yu

【魊】 a fabulous creature;

yu

【鴥】 myna;

鴝鴥 myna;

yu

【譽】 (1) fame; glory; honour; reputation; (2) eulogize; praise;

稱譽 acclaim; sing the praises of;
馳譽 be known far and wide; famous;
干譽 seek for higher reputation;
過譽 overpraise;
毀譽 praise or blame;
美譽 good name; good reputation;
名譽 fame; reputation;
榮譽 glory; honour;
商譽 goodwill;
聲譽 fame; reputation;
盛譽 great fame; high reputation;
享譽 enjoy a reputation;
信譽 credit; reputation;
虛譽 bubble reputation; false fame;
延譽 make sb's good name widely known;
溢譽 excessive praises; flatter; praise excessively;
飲譽 enjoy popularity; have a good reputation;
讚譽 commend; praise;
終譽 everlasting name; immortality; long-lasting fame;

yu

【鬻】 (1) sell; vend; (2) bring up; (3) childish; young;

[鬻爵] sell ranks;

賣官鬻爵 raise money by selling official

titles; sell government posts and titles; sell offices and barter ranks; sell official posts for a consideration; sell ranks and titles;

［鬻文］ write for pay;

鬻文為生 earn bread by writing; make a living by writing; make a living with one's pen; take writing as one's means of living;

［鬻獄］ accept bribes from litigants;

［鬻子］ (1) merchant; trader; (2) young child; (3) sell one's own children;

炫鬻 flaunt; show off;

yu

【鷸】 sandpiper; snipe;

［鷸蚌相爭］ the fight between the snipe and the clam;

鷸蚌相爭，漁人得利 as neither the snipe nor the clam would give way in fighting, a fisherman comes and catches them both; if a snipe and a clam are locked in fight, it is only to the advantage of the fisherman; if two parties fight, a third party will benefit; two dogs strive for a bone, and the third runs away with it; when shepherds quarrel, the wolf has a winning game; when the snipe and the clam are locked in fight, it is the fisherman who stands to benefit;

紅腳鷸 redshank;

丘鷸 woodcock;

山鷸 woodcock;

田鷸 snipe;

yu

【鬱】 (1) tulip; (2) plum; (3) held in check; pent-up; stagnant; (4) strongly fragrant; (5) luxuriant; (6) depressed; gloomy; (7) a surname;

［鬱勃］ lushly; luxuriantly;

［鬱沉沉］ dejected; depressed; despondent; low-spirited;

［鬱積］ pent-up; smolder;

［鬱結］ suffer from pent-up feelings;

［鬱金香］ tulip;

［鬱悶］ depressed; gloomy; have pent-up emotions;

［鬱陶］ anxiously; melancholy; pensive; sad;

［鬱悒］ dejected; depressed; melancholy;

［鬱燠］ (1) blazing; burning hot; scorching; (2) melancholy;

［鬱鬱］ (1) lush; luxuriant; (2) depressed; gloomy; melancholy; (3) strongly fragrant; (4) elegant; refined;

鬱鬱不樂 a cup too low; dejected; depressed; despondent; disconsolate; down in the dumps; down in the mouth; downhearted; have a fit of blues; have the blues; in a dismal mood; in the doldrums; jobless; look blue; out of spirits; sing the blues; sulky; sullen;

鬱鬱成疾 fall ill of unhappiness;

鬱鬱蔥蔥 wild profusion of vegetation; green and luxuriant; it grows greener and fresher; lush; luxuriantly green;

鬱鬱而死 die of grief;

鬱鬱寡歡 feel low; get the hump; heavy-hearted; in low spirits; in poor spirits; melancholy; mope; one's spirits droop; out of humour;

悲鬱 sad and vexed;

蒼鬱 verdant and luxuriant;

沉鬱 depressed; gloomy;

葱鬱 luxuriantly green; verdant;

馥鬱 heavy perfume; strong fragrance;

濃鬱 rich; strong;

氣鬱 obstruction of the circulation of vital energy;

蓊鬱 lush; luxuriant;

抑鬱 depressed; despondent;

憂鬱 dejected; melancholy;

yu

【籲】 appeal; ask; beseech; implore; request; urge;

［籲請］ beseech; request; urge;

［籲求］ implore; urge;

［籲天］ appeal to God;

呼籲 appeal; call on;

yuan¹

yuan

【寃】 (1) grievance; injustice; oppression; wrong; (2) animosity; enmity; feud; hatred; (3) kid; pull sb's leg; (4) bad

Y

luck; disadvantage; (5) waste money; (6) make false accusations;

[冤案] injustice; unjust case; wronged case;

[冤仇] enmity; feud;

冤仇宜解不宜結 better to get rid of an enmity than keep it alive; if enmity is not settled amicably threre is no end to it;

消除冤仇 work off rancor;

[冤大頭] a person deceived on account of his generosity;

[冤鬼] wronged soul;

[冤魂] the ghost of a murdered person;

冤魂不散 the ghost of the wronged never takes a rest;

[冤家] enemy; foe;

冤家對頭 bitter enemy; deep-seated antagonist; opponent and foe;

冤家路窄 enemies are bound to meet on a narrow road — one cannot avoid one's enemy; enemies are fated to meet; enemies are likely to meet each other; enemies will meet in a narrow alley — confrontation inevitable; the road is narrow for enemies — opponents always meet; the road of the enemies is narrow;

冤家宜解不宜結 better to get rid of an enmity than keep it alive; if enmity is not settled amicably there is no end to it;

俏冤家 pretty but naughty lover;

賊無冤家，但偷便家 opportunity makes the thief; the hole calls the thief;

[冤假錯案] cases in which people are unjustly charged;

[冤親] one's enemies and relatives;

[冤情] details of a grievance;

[冤屈] (1) treat unjustly; wrong; (2) injustice; wrongful treatment;

喊冤叫屈 call for redressing grievance; complain loudly about an alleged injustice; cry out about one's grievances; cry out for justice;

鳴冤叫屈 complain about an injustice; complain and call for redress; complain loudly about an alleged injustice; complain of discrimination; cry for redress of a wrong; cry out for justice; make bitter complaints; voice grievances;

受到冤屈 suffer a wrong;

[冤枉] (1) treat unjustly; wrong; (2) not repay the effort; not worthwhile;

冤枉好人 blacken a good man's name; wrong a good man; wrong an innocent person;

冤枉路 unnecessary long way;

~走冤枉路 go the long way;

冤枉錢 not get one's money's worth; pay for a dead horse; waste money;

~花冤枉錢 not get one's money's worth; pay for a dead horse; waste money;

受冤枉 suffer a wrong;

[冤有頭，債有主] a wrong has a source, a loan has a lender; a wrong has its instigator, and a debt has its lender; every grievance has its insurer and every debt its debtor; every herring should hang by its own head; every injustice has its perpetrator, every debt has its debtor; every wrong has its cause, every debt has its debtor; no debts without creditors, no hatred without cause; one's hatred is directed against one's enemy only, and the creditor will collect the debt only from the debtor;

[冤獄] miscariage of justice; unjust verdict;

[冤冤相報] each revenges the other; reprisal breeds reprisal;

沉冤 gross injustice; unrighted wrong;

含冤 suffer a wrong;

呼冤 call for justice;

申冤 (1) redress an injustice; right a wrong; (2) appeal for redress of a wrong;

訴冤 complain about grievances; state injustice;

銜冤 have a simmering sense of injustice; have no chance of airing one's grievances; nurse a bitter sense of wrong;

雪冤 clear sb of a false charge; redress a wrong;

有冤 when there are grievances;

yuan

【淵】 (1) abyss; deep pool; deep waters; gulf; (2) deep; erudite; profound; (3) a surname;

[淵博] broad and profound; erudite;

學識淵博 wide and thorough scholarship;

[淵沖] deep but open-minded;
[淵富] rich and variegated;
[淵廣] broad and extensive;
[淵海] (1) deep pool and big ocean; (2) broad and profound;
[淵默] profound and silent;
[淵泉] deep springs;
[淵然而靜] profound and still;
[淵深] deep; erudite; profound;
[淵識] erudite and sophisticated; well versed in learning and rich in experience;
淵識博學 erudite; profound knowledge and extensive learning; well-read;
[淵玄] deep; profound;
[淵淵] (1) deep and still; (2) sound of drums;
[淵源] origin; source;
家學淵源 have the deep influence of a scholarly family;
追溯淵源 trace back the origin of…;
[淵遠] deep; profound;
[淵詣] deep meaning; profound meaning;

鼻淵 nasosinusitis;
深淵 abyss;
天淵 high heaven and deep sea; poles apart;

yuan
【鳶】 (1) hawk; kite (a bird); (2) kite (a toy);

紙鳶 kite;

yuan
【鴛】 male of the mandarin duck;
[鴛盟] pledge between lovers;
[鴛鴦] mandarin ducks;
鴛鴦戲水 mandarin ducks playing in the water — affectionate couple making love joyfully;
亂點鴛鴦 cause an exchange of partners by mistake between two couples engaged to marry;
野鴛鴦 illicit lovers;

yuan
【鵷】 legendary phoenix;

yuan²
yuan
【元】 (1) beginning; first; primary; (2) chief; principal; (3) basic; fundamental; (4) component; unit; (5) unit of currency; (6) a surname;

[元寶] gold ingot;
[元春] New Year;
[元旦] New Year's Day;
[元惡] chief criminal; principal culprit;
元惡大憝 chief criminal and great enemy;
[元件] component; element; part;
元件數目 number of components;
~減少元件數目 reduce the number of components;
操作元件 executive component;
超導元件 superconducting component;
電路元件 circuit component;
電子元件 electronic component;
~微電子元件 microelectronic element;
分立元件 discreet component; discreet component part;
兩用元件 dual component;
內接元件 intraconnection element;
平衡元件 equalizing component;
聲耦元件 acoustic coupling element;
適應元件 adaptive element;
外接元件 outward element;
微型元件 microelement;
有源元件 active element;
[元老] doyen; senior statesmen;
三朝元老 a senior stateman of three rulers in succession;
[元龍高臥] negligent in attending to one's guests;
[元配] first wife;
[元氣] strength; vigour; vitality;
元氣大傷 one's constitution is greatly undermined; sap one's vitality;
元氣十足 vigorousness;
元氣旺盛 full of vitality; thriving;
補元氣 tone up the vitality;
大傷元氣 knock the stuffing out of; sap one's vitality; take the stuffing out of; undermine one's constitution;
恢復元氣 rebuild one's physical constitution; regain one's vigour;
有傷元氣 debilitate the constitution;
[元青] deep black;
元青布 black cloth;
[元首] (1) chief executive; head of a state; ruler; (2) beginning;
國家元首 head of state;
名義元首 titular head;
[元帥] marshal; supreme commander;
海軍元帥 Admiral of the Fleet;
空軍元帥 Marshal of Air Force;

Y

陸軍元帥 field marshal;

[元素] element;

元素分析 elemental analysis;
元素符號 symbol of element;
鉑族元素 platinum family element;
超導元素 superconducting element;
超環元素 transplutonium;
超鈾元素 transuranium element;
放射性元素 radioactive element;
副族元素 subgroup element;
過渡元素 transition element;
活性元素 active element;
金屬元素 metallic element;
~半金屬元素 semimetallic element;
~非金屬元素 non-metallic element;
鑭系元素 lanthanide series;
類似元素 analogous element;
稀土元素 rare-earth element;
稀有元素 rare element;
執行元素 action element;
重元素 heavy elements;
主族元素 main group element;

[元宵] Lantern Festival; night of the fifteenth of the first lunar month;

[元兇] crime culprit;

[元夜] night of the fifteenth of the first lunar month;

[元音] vowel;

暗元音 dark vowel;
半元音 semi-vowel;
閉音節元音 checked vowel;
閉元音 closed vowel;
複雜元音 complex vowel;
後元音 back vowel;
基本元音 basic vowel;
連接性元音 connecting vowel;
前元音 front vowel;
雙元音 diphthong;
中元音 central vowel;

[元魚] soft-shelled turtle;

[元月] (1) first month of the lunar year; (2) January;

變元 argument;
單元 unit;
多元 mutli-; plural;
二元 binary; dual;
復元 as good as new;
改元 change the designation of an imperial reign; change the title of a reign;
公元 Christian era;
紀元 (1) beginning of an era; (2) epoch; era;
加元 buck; Canadian dollar;
解元 the scholar who won the first place in provincial imperial examinations;
金元 American dollar;
歷元 epoch;
美元 American dollar; buck; U.S. dollar;
乾元 beginning of heaven's creation;
日元 yen;
三元 top three candidates at the three levels of civil service examinations in imperial China;
上元 fifteenth of the first lunar month;
銅元 silver dollar;
西元 Gregorian calendar;
狀元 (1) the very best; (2) first in the highest imperial examination;

yuan

【沅】 a river flowing through Hunan;

yuan

【芫】 daphne genkwa,

[芫荽] coriander; parsley;

yuan

【苑】 a surname;

yuan

【爰】 accordingly; therefore; thereupon;

[爰爰] slow and cautious;

[爰至今日] down to the present day;

yuan

【原】 (1) original; primary; (2) beginning; origin; source; (3) raw; unprocessed; (4) excuse; pardon; (5) open country; plain; (6) graveyard; (7) a surname;

[原版] original edition; original negative;

[原本] (1) master copy; original manuscript; (2) copy of the first edition; (3) original text; (4) formerly; originally;

原原本本 as exact as it is; chapter and verse; from beginning to end; from first to last; from the very beginning to the end; give chapter and verse for; in detail from very beginning; tell the real story; the whole story; without omitting a single circumstance;

[原產地] country of origin; source area;

[原點] origin;

程序原點 programme origin;
天線原點 antenna origin;
坐標原點 grid origin;

[原封] intact; with the seal unbroken;
原封不動 conserve intact; keep intact; keep sth in its totality; leave intact; maintain unchanged in its original state; preserve intact; remain in its entirety; remain untouched; take over sum and substance; untouched;
原封退回 return to the sender a parcel or letter unopened; the gift or letter is returned to sb unopened;

[原稿] manuscript; master copy; original manuscript;
親筆原稿 original holograph manuscript;
謄寫原稿 copy the manuscript;
修改原稿 polish the manuscripts;
一份原稿 a manuscript;
整理原稿 digest the manuscript;

[原告] complainant; plaintiff;

[原故] cause; reason;
推原其故 analyze the cause; infer from premises; trace back to a cause;

[原核] pronucleus;
雌性原核 female pronucleus;
精子原核 sperm pronucleus;
靜止原核 stationary pronucleus;
雄原核 male pronucleus;
游走原核 wandering pronucleus;

[原基] rudiment;
腦原基 brain rudiment;
中腸原基 mesentron rudiment;

[原籍] a native of; ancestral home; native home; native place; original domicile;

[原價] (1) original price; (2) production cost;

[原件] original copy;

[原來] (1) former; in the first place; originally; (2) so; turn out to be;
原來如此 I see; I understand; it explains the matter; so that is how it is; so that is how matters stand; that accounts for it; that accounts for the milk in the coconut;

[原理] axiom; principle; tenet; theory;
抽象原理 abstract principle;
翻譯原理 translation principle;
輻角原理 argument principle;
基本原理 basic principle; fundamental principle;
絕熱原理 adiabatic principle;
科學原理 principles of science;
普遍原理 general principles;
設計原理 principle of programme design;
審計原理 auditing principle;

[原諒] excuse; forgive; pardon;
不可原諒 inexcusable;
不能原諒 unforgivable; unpardonable;

[原料] crude materials; raw materials; rough materials;
原料短缺 there is a lack of raw materials;
供應原料 supply raw material;
加工原料 process raw material;

[原煤] raw coal;
一層原煤 a layer of raw coal;

[原配] one's first wife;

[原色] (1) beige; (2) primary; (3) primary colours;
原色嗶嘰 beige serge;
原色毛紗 beige yarn;
發送原色 transmission primaries;
接收機原色 receiver primaries;

[原生質] protoplasm;

[原始] (1) firsthand; original; (2) origin; source; (3) backward; primitive;
原始本能 primitive instinct;
原始檔案 primary files;
原始美 pristine beauty;
原始人 primitive; primitive person;
原始森林 virgin forest;
原始社會 primitive society;
原始資料 first-hand data; primary sources; raw data;

[原素] element;
子原素 daughter element;

[原委] all the details; whole story;
盡悉原委 know all the details of the matter; know the whole story of the affair;
窮原竟委 come to the root of the matter; get to the bottom of sth; get to the bottom of the matter; get to the root of things so as to gain a complete knowledge of them; go behind sth; go to the heart of sth; inquire into the utmost details; investigate thoroughly; make a thorough inquiry into sth; make an exhaustive inquiry into sth; run sth to earth; trace sth to its source to find out what it is all about;
事情原委 the beginning and the end of a matter;
事有原委 this happens with reason;
説明原委 explain why and how;

[原文] original; original text;

原文讀者 reader of the original;

[原先] (1) former; original; (2) in the beginning; in the very beginning;

[原形] original form; original shape; primary form; true shape under the disguise;

保持原形 hold its shape; retain its shape;
暴露原形 betray oneself;
動詞原形 root form of the verb;
恢復原形 resume the normal shape;

[原型] ancestor; prototype;

原型範疇 prototypic category;
原型複合詞 primary compound;
原型器官 ancestral organ;
原型語言 ancestral language;

[原樣] original sample; original shape;

[原野] field; open country; plain;

穿過原野 through the fields;
平坦的原野 smooth plains;

[原意] (1) original meaning; (2) original intentions;

改變原意 change one's intention;
解釋原意 explain the original meaning;
領會原意 perceive the original meaning;
探索原意 extract the net meaning;
歪曲原意 extort the meaning;
誤解原意 mistake what sth means;
掩飾原意 disguise one's meaning;

[原因] account; at the back of sth; cause; reason;

原因從屬連詞 subordinator of reason;
原因介詞 preposition of reason;
原因連詞 casual conjunction;
原因狀語 adverbial of cause;
~ 原因狀語從句 adverbial clause of reason;
並存原因 concurrent cause;
常見原因 common cause;
出於安全原因 for security reasons;
出於個人原因 for personal reasons;
出於某種原因 for some unknown reason;
調查原因 investigate the cause;
非機遇原因 assignable cause;
根本原因 fundamental cause; root cause; underlying cause;
合理原因 valid reason;
間接原因 indirect cause;
內在原因 immanent cause;
偶然原因 chance cause; occasional cause;
確定原因 determine the cause; establish the cause; identify the cause;
說明原因 give a reason;
想出原因 think of a reason;
形式原因 formal cause;
由於同樣的原因 by the same token;
由於種種原因 for one reason or another;
找出原因 discover the cause; find the cause;
正當原因 legitimate reason;
知道原因 see a reason;
直接原因 direct cause; immediate cause; proximate cause; real reason;
重要原因 leading cause; major cause; major reason;
主要原因 chief cause; chief reason; main cause; primary cause;

[原由] cause; reason;

[原油] crude;

原油裂解 crack crude;
輕原油 light crude;
石臘基原油 paraffin-base crude;
脫氣原油 degassed crude;
右旋原油 dextrorotary crudes;

[原有] original;

[原則] principle;

原則上同意 agree in principle;
原則問題 a matter of principle;
背離原則 deviate from one's principles;
背棄原則 desert one's principles;
比較原則 principle of comparison;
出賣原則 barter away principles;
道德原則 moral principles;
放棄原則 abandon one's principles;
合作原則 co-operative principle;
互補原則 complementarism;
基本原則 basic principle; fundamental principle;
堅持原則 adhere to one's principle; stick to one's principles;
堅持自己的原則 stick to one's principles;
堅守原則 uphold principles;
違背原則 betray one's principles;
無原則 unprincipled;
有原則 have principles;
有自己的原則 have one's limits;
政治原則 political principles;
指導原則 guiding principle; guideline;
主導原則 guiding principles;
主要原則 main principles;
自發原則 automatic principle;
宗教原則 religious principles;

[原職] former post;

[原址] former address;

[原主] legal owner; original owner;
復歸原主 restore to its owner; return to the original owner;
物歸原主 restore sth to its rightful owner; return a thing to its rightful owner; revert the things lost to the original owner;

[原著] original; original work;
參考原著 refer to the original;
閱讀原著 read the original;
忠於原著 keep strictly to the original;

[原子] atom; atomic;
原子筆 ball-point pen;
原子變化 atomic change;
原子彈 atom bomb; atomic bomb;
~原子彈狂 atomania;
原子動力船 atomic ship;
原子訛詐 atomic blackmail;
原子反應 atomic reaction;
原子反應堆 atomic pile;
原子分裂 atomic fussion;
原子輻射 atomic radiation;
原子館 atomarium;
原子核 atomic nucleus;
~原子核反應堆 nuclear reactor;
原子轟炸機 atom bomber;
原子化 atomization;
原子結構 atomic structure;
原子量 atomic weight;
原子論 atomistics; atomology;
原子能 atomic energy;
~原子能發電站 atomic power plant;
原子砲 atomic artillery;
原子時代 atomic age;
原子説 atomic theory;
原子突襲 atomic action;
原子武器 atomy;
原子襲擊 atomic attack; atomic strike;
原子效應 atomic effect;
原子性 atomicity;
原子序數 atomic number;
原子學 atomics; atomism;
~原子學家 atomist;
原子醫學 atomedics;
原子鐘 atomic clock;
帶電原子 charged atom;
電離原子 ionized atom;
二價原子 bivalent atom;
複合原子 compound atom;
活化原子 activated atom;
基態原子 ground state atom;
靜型原子 static atom;
克原子 gram atom;
裂變原子 fissionable atom;
平方原子 squared atom;
強子原子 hadronic atom;
橋原子 bridge atom;
受主原子 acceptor atom;
束縛原子 bound atom;
四價原子 qeuadrivalent atom;
穩定原子 stationary atom;
移位原子 displaced atom;
雜環原子 heterocyclic atom;
雜原子 hetero atom;
雜質原子 impurity atom;
子系原子 daughter atom;
自由原子 free atom;

[原罪] original sin;

[原作] original work;
原作風格 style of the original;
歪曲原作 take liberties with the original work;

冰原 ice field;
病原 (1) cause of disease; pathogeny; (2) pathogen;
草原 grassland; prairie;
復原 (1) recover from an illness; (2) rehabilitate;
高原 highland; plateau;
還原 return to the original condition;
荒原 wasteland; wilderness;
膠原 collagen;
抗原 antigen;
燎原 set the prairie ablaze;
莽原 wilderness overgrown with grass;
酶原 fermentogen; zymogen;
平原 flatlands; plain;
神經原 neuron;
苔原 tundra;
糖原 glycogen;
雪原 snowfield;
中原 central plains;
準平原 quasiplain;

yuan

【員】 (1) member of an organization; (2) person engaged in some field of activity; (3) outer limits of land;

[員工] personnel; staff; staff member;

扳道員 pointsman; switchman;
辦事員 office worker;
保管員 storekeeper; storeman;

保健員 health worker;
保育員 child-care worker;
報幕員 announcer;
報務員 radio operator; telegraph operator; telegraphist;
編目員 cataloguer;
兵員 soldiers; troops;
病員 patient; sick personnel;
播音員 announcer;
捕狗員 dog warden; dogcatcher;
簿記員 bookkeeper;
裁員 cut down the number of persons employed;
採購員 purchasing agent; purchasing representative;
參議員 senator;
測量員 surveyor;
查票員 ticket examiner;
查賬員 account examiner;
抄寫員 copyist;
超員 exceed the set number;
成員 member;
承審員 judicial officer;
乘務員 attendant on a train;
出納員 cashier; teller;
船員 crew;
炊事員 cook;
從事員 shop employee;
打字員 typist;
大員 high-ranking official;
擔架員 stetcher-bearer;
黨員 party member;
店員 shop assistant;
調查員 investigator;
調度員 controller; dispatcher;
諜報員 intelligence agent;
動員 arouse; mobilize;
隊員 team member;
發令員 starter;
發行員 publisher;
翻譯員 translator;
飛行員 aviator; pilot;
放映員 projectionist;
服務員 attendant;
幅員 size of the country;
復原 (1) restore; (2) demobilize;
輔導員 assistant;
高級譯員 senior translator;
閣員 member of the cabinet;
公務員 civil servant;
故事員 story-teller;
僱員 employee;
官員 officer; official;
觀察員 observer;
管理員 administrative personnel; manager;
廣播員 broadcaster; radio announcer;
櫃員 counter clerk;
海員 mariner; sailor; seaman;
化驗員 laboratory technician;
話務員 telephone operator;
劃圖員 designer;
會員 member;
繪圖員 cartographer; draftsman;
擠奶員 milker;
擊球員 batsman; batter;
稽查員 customs officer;
記分員 marker; scorekeeper;
記工員 workpoint recorder;
技術員 technician;
駕駛員 driver; pilot;
監察員 supervisor;
減員 deplete numbers;
檢票員 inspector;
檢驗員 inspector;
檢疫員 quarantine officer;
講解員 guide;
接生員 midwife;
交通員 liaison man;
糾察員 picket;
校對員 proofreader;
教導員 political instructor;
教練員 coach; instructor;
教養員 nursery instructor;
教員 instructor; teacher;
教職員 teaching and administrative staff;
解說員 announcer; commentator; narrator;
警衛員 bodyguard;
警員 police constable; policeman;
救生員 lifeguard; lifesaver;
軍械員 armourer;
考勤員 time keeper;
科員 section member;
雷達員 radar operator;
聯絡員 liaison man;
列車員 attendant on a train;
領港員 harbour pilot;
領航員 navigator; pilot;
領水員 navigator; pilot;
錄音員 recordist;
輪機員 engineer;
滿員 (1) at full strength; (2) all seats taken;
盟員 member of an alliance;
密碼員 cryptographer;
描圖員 tracer;
描寫員 describer;

擬題員 item writer;
女推銷員 saleswoman;
女郵遞員 postwoman;
跑壘員 base runner;
陪審員 juror; juryman;
評論員 commentator;
情報員 intelligence agent;
潛水員 diver; frogman;
勤務員 (1) odd-jobber; (2) servant;
勤雜員 odd-jobber;
球員 ballplayer;
人員 personnel; staff;
冗員 redundant personnel;
曬圖員 blueprinter;
傷病員 the sick and wounded;
傷員 wounded personnel;
社員 (1) member of a society; (2) commune member;
審計員 auditor;
審判員 judge; judicial officer;
事務員 office clerk;
實驗員 laboratory technician;
稅務員 tax collector;
收款員 cashier;
收票員 ticket collector;
守場員 fielder;
守壘員 baseman;
守門員 goalkeeper;
售貨員 shop assistant;
售票員 conductor; ticket seller;
書記員 clerk;
屬員 officials under a superior official;
速記員 stenographer;
司令員 commander; commanding officer;
司泵員 pump man; pumper;
司線員 linesman;
飼養員 poultry raiser;
送貨員 delivery man;
隨員 (1) retinue; suite; (2) attache;
特派員 delegate; emissary;
謄寫員 copyist;
通信員 messenger;
通訊員 correspondent;
統計員 statistician;
投遞員 mailman; postman;
團員 member of a delegation;
推銷員 salesman;
委員 committee member;
衛生員 health worker; medical orderly;
文員 clerk; pen pusher;
鄉郵員 rural postman;
協理員 political assistant;
宣傳員 propagandist;
學員 mentee; student; trainee;
巡邊員 linesman;
研究員 researcher;
演員 actor; actress; performer;
驗收員 accepter;
要員 important official;
議員 member of a legislative assembly;
譯電員 cryptographer; decoder;
譯員 (1) translator; (2) interpreter;
營業員 shop employee;
引水員 pilot;
郵遞員 mailman; postman;
宇航員 astronaut; spaceman;
運動員 sportsman;
丈量員 surveyor;
戰鬥員 fighter;
偵察員 scout;
職員 functionary; office worker; staff; staff member;
指導員 political instructor;
值班員 person on duty;
植保員 plant protector;
製圖員 cartographer; draftsman;
仲裁員 arbitrator;
眾議員 representative;
專員 commissioner;
總動員 general mobilization;

yuan
【袁】 (1) graceful look of a flowing robe; (2) a surname;

yuan
【湲】 (of water) flowing;

潺湲 lowing slowly;

yuan
【援】 (1) lead; (2) take hold of; pull by hand; (3) cite; quote; (4) aid; help; reinforce; rescue;
[援案] in accordance with a precedent; quote a precedent;
[援筆] take up a pen to write;
援筆疾書 take up a brush and write quickly;
援筆直書 take up a pen and write quickly;
[援兵] reinforcements;
[援隊] support unit;
[援救] come to the aid of; deliver from danger; rescue; save;

[援據] adduce as proof; cite as proof;

[援軍] reinforcements; relief troops;

[援例] cite a precedent; follow a precedent; invoke a precedent;
無例可援 have no precedent to go by; there is no precedent to quote;
有例可援 there is a precedent to quote;

[援手] (1) aid; extend a helping hand; rescue; save; (2) helper;

[援外] (1) cite; quote; (2) appoint or recommend one's friends or favourites; (3) foreign aid;

[援引] cite a precedent as proof;
援引經典 quote from classics and canons;
援引條款 quote an article;
援引先例 quote a precedent;
大量援引 quote extensively;
援經引典 quote from classics and canons;

[援用] cite; invoke; quote;
援用成例 cite a precedent;

[援照] according to; adduce; cite;

[援助] aid; help; support;
援助人員 aid worker;
援助項目 aid project;
財政援助 financial support;
償還性援助 refundable assistance;
垂直援助 vertical assistance;
道義援助 moral support;
給與援助 give assistance to; lend one's aid to; render assistance to;
官方援助 public assistance;
及時援助 prompt aid;
技術援助 technical assistance;
精神援助 spiritual support;
緊急援助 bail out; emergency aid;
雙邊援助 bilateral assistance;
調整性援助 adjustment assistance;
外來援助 external assistance;
無償援助 non-reimbursable assistance;
物質援助 material support;
業務援助 operational assistance;
優惠性援助 concessionary assistance;

奧援 ally; moral or material support; powerful backer;
馳援 rush to the rescue;
打援 attack enemy reinforcements;
後援 backing; backup force; reinforcements; support;
經援 economic aid;
救援 come to sb's help; rescue;
軍援 military aid;
攀援 (1) climb; (2) climb up through pull;
乞援 ask for help; beg for aid;
請援 ask for help;
求援 ask for help; seek relief;
聲援 express support for; support;
受援 receive aid;
外援 external assistance; foreign aid; outside help;
無援 helpless;
應援 make a move to reinforce;
增援 reinforce;
支援 assist; support;
阻援 hold off enemy reinforcements;

Y

yuan

【園】 (1) area of land for growing plants; (2) place for public recreation;

[園地] (1) garden plot; (2) field; scope;
讀者園地 readers' corner;
文學園地 scope of literary creation;

[園丁] gardener;
園丁鳥 gardener bird;
當園丁 work as a gardener;

[園林] garden; park;
園林工人 park gardener;
園林建築師 landscape architect;
假山園林 rock garden; rockery;
中國園林 landscape park of China;

[園陵] emperor's mausoleum; emperor's tomb;

[園廬] gardens and houses;

[園圃] garden; nursery garden; orchard; plantation; vegetable garden;
園圃棚 potting shed;

[園田] vegetable garden;

[園藝] garden husbandry; gardening; horticulture;
園藝工人 gardener;
園藝活 gardening;
園藝家 horticulturist;
園藝商店 garden centre;
園藝手套 garden gloves;
園藝學 landscape gardening;
~園藝學家 landscape gardener;
園藝業 landscape gardening;
園藝專欄 gardening column;
園藝作物 garden crop;
愛好園藝 be interested in landscape gardening; found of gardening;
擅長園藝 have a green thumb; have green fingers;

［園遊會］ garden party;
［園主］ owner of a garden;
［園子］ garden;
菜園 vegetable farm;
茶園 (1) tea planation; (2) a place where tea and soft drinks are served; tea garden;
動物園 zoo;
公園 park; public garden;
故園 hometown; native place;
果木園 orchard;
果園 orchard;
花園 garden;
家園 home; homeland;
醬園 sauce and pickle shop;
樂園 amusement park; paradise;
梨園 (1) theatre; (2) theatrical circles;
陵園 cemetery;
蘋果園 apple orchard;
葡萄園 grapery; vineyard;
桑園 mulberry field;
田園 fields and gardens;
庭園 flower garden;
校園 campus; school yard;
幼兒園 kindergarten;
幼稚園 kindergarten;
御花園 imperial garden;
宅園 private garden;
竹園 bamboo plantation;

yuan

【圓】 (1) circular; round; spherical; (2) circle; (3) satisfactory; (4) complete; justify; make plausible; (5) monetary unit; (6) coin of fixed value and weight;
［圓場］ help to effect a compromise; mediate;
打個圓場 explain and smooth the matter over; help settle a quarrel;
打圓場 do peacemaking; ease a situation; help effect a compromise; help settle a quarrel; mediate a dispute; proffer one's good offices; smooth out a dispute; smooth things over;
［圓成］ complete a piece of work; help sb to attain his aim;
［圓櫈］ round stool;
［圓頂］ dome; round top;
圓頂帽 peaked cap with a high crown;
［圓度］ roundness;
稜圓度 prismatic roundness;
平均圓度 average roundness;
［圓方］ the round and the square;
方趾圓顱 a creature with rectangular feet and a round head — a human being;
枘圓鑿方 a square peg in a round hole; incompatible; not fitting; unsuited to each other;
外圓內方 round outside but square inside — outwardly gentle but inwardly stern; smooth and easy-going in manners but highly principled in daily life; smooth on the surface, firm at heart;
圓顱方趾 round skull and square toes — a human being;
智圓行方 have a good disposition and an upright character; know all around and act straight; round in disposition, square in action;
［圓規］ pencil compass;
［圓號］ French horn; horn;
［圓乎乎］ round and full;
［圓弧］ arc;
［圓滑］ diplomatic; slick and sly; smooth and evasive; tactful;
圓滑的人 smooth article; smoothie; sophisticated person;
圓滑的手段 tactful means;
説話圓滑 have a smooth tongue;
［圓環］ rotary; traffic circle;
［圓活］ (1) clever and active; energetic; flexible; nimble; quick-minded; (2) a rich and round voice;
［圓寂］ die; pass away;
［圓徑］ diameter;
［圓鋸］ circular saw;
電動圓鋸 buzz saw;
［圓塊］ lump;
圓塊的 lumpy;
~布滿圓塊的 lumpy;
~有圓塊的 lumpy;
［圓臉］ round face;
［圓滿］ (1) perfect; satisfactory; (2) complete;
圓滿成功 complete success;
圓滿結束 bring to a happy ending; bring to a successful close; come to a happy termination; end in a satisfactory way; round off;
圓滿解決 be brought to a satisfactory settlement; be settled satisfactorily;
達到圓滿 come to perfection;
功德圓滿 come to a successful end;

Y

結局圓滿 come to a happy ending; have a successful end;

[圓夢] interpret a dream;

[圓盤] disc;

開孔圓盤 apertured disc;

窩眼圓盤 alveolar disc;

陽極圓盤 anode disc;

遮光圓盤 blanking disc;

[圓球] ball; globe; sphere;

[圓圈] circle; ring;

[圓全] (1) complete; satisfactory; (2) help sb succeed;

[圓潤] mellow and full;

[圓石] cobble; cobblestone;

[圓熟] dexterous; proficient; skilled; skilful;

[圓通] accommodating; capable of adapting oneself to circumstances; flexible;

[圓筒] cylinder;

[圓頭] (of hairstyle) round cut;

圓頭刀 palette knife;

[圓舞曲] waltz;

[圓系] system of circles;

[圓心] centre of a circle;

圓心角 central angle;

[圓形] circular; round; spherical;

[圓圓] round;

圓圓胖胖的 chubby;

[圓月] (1) full moon; (2) drink together in the moonlight on Mid-Autumn Festival;

一輪圓月 the full moon is round like a chariot wheel;

[圓潤] mellow and full;

[圓周] circumference;

圓周角 angle of circumference;

圓周率 the ratio of the circumference of a circle to its diameter;

單位圓周 unit circumference;

等圓周 equal circumference;

滾動圓周 rolling circumference;

平均油罐圓周 average tank circumference;

[圓珠] ball; ballpoint;

[圓柱] circular column; cylinder;

圓柱對稱 cylindrosymmetry;

圓柱晶 cylindrulite;

圓柱面 cylindrical surface;

圓柱體 cylinder;

~圓柱體的 cylindrical;

~存取圓柱體 access cylinder;

[圓錐] cone;

圓錐面 circular conical surface;

定心圓錐 centring cone;

共軸圓錐 coaxial cone;

基圓錐 base cone;

外切圓錐 circumscribed cone;

[圓桌] round table;

圓桌會談 round-table talks;

圓桌會議 round-table conference; round-table meeting;

[圓鑿方枘] a square head and a round socket; a square peg in a round hole; at variance with each other; incompatible; like a square tenon for a round mortise;

半圓 semicircle;

扁圓 oblate;

長圓 oval;

大圓 great circle;

點圓 point circle;

方圓 (1) circumference; (2) neighbourhood;

輔助圓 auxiliary circle;

桂圓 longan;

滾圓 round as a ball;

渾圓 perfectly round;

內接圓 inscribed circle;

內切圓 inscribed circle;

團圓 reunion;

外接圓 circumcircle;

外切圓 circumcircle;

小圓 small circle;

鴨蛋圓 oval;

銀圓 silver dollar;

正交圓 orthogonal circles;

yuan

【源】 (1) fountainhead; source; (2) cause; source;

[源本] origin of an event;

拔本塞源 abandon the source; clear up source and restore purity; despise the source; extirpate the root of an evil;

追本窮源 examine to the bottom; get to the bottom of; get to the root of the matter; go into a matter thoroughly; go to the heart of the matter; inquire deeply into; investigate into the origins; trace back to the beginning; trace to its source;

追本溯源 get to the root of the matter; trace to sth's source;

[源流] (1) origin and development; source

and course; (2) all the details; full particulars; the whole story;
窮源溯流 trace to the very source of sth;
源清流清 a clear stream comes from a pure source; if a stream is clear, it is because the source is clear;
源遠流長 a distant source and a long stream — long-standing and well established;
~中國文化源遠流長 the source of the Chinese culture is distant and its course long;

[源碼] source code;

[源泉] fountain; fountainhead; original source; source; wellspring;
知識的源泉 well of knowledge;

[源頭] fountainhead; head; headstream; headwater; source of a stream;
源頭減廢 reduction of waste at source;

[源文] source text;
源文詞匯 source lexis;
源文語法 source grammar;

[源語] source language;
源語背景 source language setting;
源語傳統 source language tradition;
源語讀者 source language reader;
源語對應 source language correspondence;
源語分析 source language analysis;
源語干擾 source language interference;
源語規範 source language norm;
源語文化 source language culture;
源語文獻 source language text;
~源語文獻層次 source language text level;
源語作者 source language writer;

[源於] be derived from; begin; derive from; originate from; rise in; start; stem from;

[源源] continuously; in a steady stream;
源源本本 from beginning to end; the whole story; without omissions;
源源不絕 a constant torrent of; an uninterrupted flow of; come forth endlessly; continually; flow like water; in a steady stream;
源源而來 come in an endless flow; come incessantly like a stream; incessantly; keep pouring in; keep rolling in; pour; pour in incessantly;
源源而至 come in an endless flow;
源源接濟 continue to supply;

本源 origin; ultimate; source;
病源 cause of a disease;
兵源 manpower resources;
波源 wave source;
財源 bankroll; financial resources;
詞源 etymology;
氮源 origin of nitrogen;
導源 derive; originate;
電源 power source; power supply;
發源 originate; rise;
肥源 source of manure;
輻射源 radiant;
根源 origin; root; source;
光源 illuminant; light source;
河源 source of a river;
貨源 source of goods; supply of goods;
來源 origin; originate; source; stem from;
能源 energy resources;
起源 origin; originate from;
泉源 (1) fountainhead; springhead; wellspring; (2) source;
熱源 heat source;
聲源 source of sound;
水源 (1) source of a river; (2) source of water;
溯源 trace to the source;
無源 passive;
有源 active;
淵源 origin; source;
源源 continuously; in a steady stream;
震源 focus;
中子源 neutron source;
資源 natural resources; resources;

yuan

【猿】 ape; gibbon;

[猿臂] (1) ape's arms; (2) long arms;
輕舒猿臂 shoot up one's powerful arm; with a dexterous turn of the arm;

[猿號] ape's call; gibbon's howls;

[猿猴] ape; apes and monkeys;

[猿類] anthropoid;

[猿人] ape; ape-man; anthropoid ape; gorilla;

[猿聲] gibbon's howls;
猿聲悲啼 monkeys cry out in anguish;

[猿啼] gibbon's howl;
猿啼虎嘯 monkeys cry and tigers roar;

[猿吟] monkey's cry;

長臂猿 gibbon;
類人猿 anthropoid; ape;
人猿 anthropoid; ape;

yuan
【緣】 (1) cause; reason; (2) brink; edge; (3) predestined relationship; (4) along;
[緣邊] border; edge; hem; margin;
[緣法] (1) follow the old laws; (2) abide by the law;
緣法而治 rule in accordance with established practices;
[緣分] (1) lot or luck by which people are brought together; (2) destiny as conditioned by one's past; predestined relationship; relationship by fate;
[緣故] cause; reason;
由於天氣的緣故 on account of the weather;
由於這個緣故 for this cause;
[緣何] why;
[緣木求魚] a complete waste of time; climb a tree to catch a fish – a fruitless approach; fish in the air; get blood from a stone; get blood from a turnip; it is very hard to shave an egg; milk the bull, milk the pigeon; utterly impossible; wring water from a flint;
[緣起] (1) genesis; origin; (2) account of the founding of an institution; (3) account of the beginning of a project; (4) foreword; preface;
[緣飾] embellish with words;
[緣因] cause;
[緣由] cause; reason; the whys and wherefores;
凡事皆有緣由 there is no effect without cause;

邊緣 (1) border; edge; verge; (2) borderline; marginal;
地緣 geo-;
化緣 beg alms;
機緣 lucky chance;
絕緣 (1) insulate; (2) be cut off from;
良緣 happy match;
路緣 curb; kerb;
攀緣 (1) climb; (2) climb up through pull;
人緣 popularity; relations with people;
投緣 agreeable; congenial;
無緣 have not had the luck;
血緣 blood relationship; ties of blood;
因緣 (1) principal and subsidiary causes; (2) predestined relationship;
姻緣 the happy fate which brings lovers together;

yuan
【蝯】 same as 猿 , monkey;

yuan
【螈】 (1) diemctylus pyrrhogaster; (2) a kind of silkworm;

yuan
【轅】 (1) shafts; (2) magistrate's office; (3) a surname;
[轅馬] shaft horse;

車轅 shaft of a cart, etc;
駕轅 be hitched up;
行轅 field headquarters;

yuan
【黿】 soft-shelled turtle;
[黿魚] a kind of large turtle; soft-shelled turtle;

yuan³
yuan
【遠】 (1) distant; far; remote; (2) deep; profound; (3) keep at a distance; keep away;
[遠避] keep at a distance; keep far away from;
遠避高蹈 keep away from and go on a long journey; lead a hermit's life far away from the mundane world;
[遠別] (1) separate fro a journey to a distant land; (2) part for a long time;
[遠播] spread far and wide;
[遠程] long-distance; long-range; remote;
遠程處理 teleprocessing;
遠程導彈 long-range missile;
遠程電化教育 tele-education;
遠程火箭 long-range rocket;
遠程計劃 long-range plan;
遠程監控 telemonitoring;
遠程控制台 remote console;
遠程通信 telecommunication;
~遠程通信會議 telecommunication conference;
遠程網絡 internet;
遠程信息 remote message;
~遠程信息處理 remote message processing;
~遠程信息學 telematics;
遠程站 remote station;
遠程終端 remote terminal;

[遠處] afar off; distant; in the distance;
自遠處 from afar;

[遠大] ambitious; broad; long-range; very promising;
理想遠大 have a high ideal;
目光遠大 set one's sights high; take a broad view of matter;
前途遠大 have a bright future; have a great future;
眼光遠大 farsighted; have a broad vision;

[遠道] a long way; afar; distant; faraway;
遠道傳聞 a rumour originated from a distance;
遠道而來 come a long way; come from afar;
遠道來訪 come from afar for a visit to; visit from afar;

[遠方] distant place; remote place;
遠方來鴻 a letter from afar;
來自遠方 come from a remote part of the earth; from afar;

[遠房] distantly related;
遠房親戚 distant relative; remote kinsfolk;

[遠非] far from; not anywhere near; not nearly; nowhere near;
遠非如此 far from being so; far from it;
遠非昔比 a far cry from the past;

[遠隔] distant; far; far apart; remote;
遠隔重洋 be separated by many seas; be separated by seas and oceans; be separated by vast oceans;
遠隔千里 be separated by a great distance; be separated by thousands of miles; thousands of kilometers away from;

[遠古] ancient times; remote antiquity;
遠古時代 remote antiquity;
~在遠古時代 in remote antiquity;

[遠見] breath of vision; far-sighted view; foresight; prescience;
遠見卓識 a long head; a long sight; acute and far-sighted mind; breath of vision; far-sightedness; foresight and sagacity; sagacity;
有遠見 far-sighted; have foresight;
~沒有遠見 lack foresight;

[遠郊] outer suburbs; outskirts;

[遠近] (1) far and near; remote or close; (2) distance;
遠近聞名 known far and near; known far and wide; known to all, far and wide; widely known;
見遠不見近 much water runs by the mill than the miller knows not of;
近悅遠來 the near one pleases and the far one comes — to do one's utmost to satisfy people near and far;
漫遊遠近 roam over;
捨近求遠 forgo what is close at hand seek what is far afield; go for the abstruse and forget the obvious; go round the sun to meet the moon; reject what is near at hand and seek for what is far away; seek greener pastures elsewhere;
言近指遠 express far-reaching meaning in simple words; simple in language but profound in meaning; simple words but deep meaning; some simple words carry a profound meaning;
由近及遠 from the close to the distant; from the near to the remote;
由遠而近 come closer and closer; draw near; from the remote to the near;
遠交近攻 befriend the distant enemy while attacking the nearer one; befriend the distant states while attacking those nearby; keep friendly relations with distant states and attack the near ones; make friends with distant countries and attack the neighbouring ones;
遠遠近近 far and near; far and wide;
自遠而近 approach from a distance; from far to near;

[遠景] (1) distant view; long-range perspective; vista; (2) future; prospect; (3) long shot;
遠景規劃 great and farsighted plan; long-term plan;
遠景研究 advanced research;
規劃遠景 plan one's future;

[遠鏡] telescope;

[遠距] long distance;
遠距離 long-distance;
~遠距離教學 long-distance education;

[遠離] aloof; far away;
遠離塵囂 far from the madding crowd;
遠離家鄉 far away from one's native village;
遠離俗界 aloof from the crowd;

[遠路無輕擔] a light load is heavy to carry far; a straw is heavy in a long journey;

light burdens, long borne, grow heavy;

[遠慮] advance planning; worry and plan far ahead;

計深慮遠 a far-sighted plan that goes deep into the most probable changes in the years to come; the plan is deep-laid in terms of the distant future;

人無遠慮，必有近憂 he lives unsafely that looks too near on things; if a man is not far-sighted he is bound to encounter difficulties in the near future; if one has no long-term considerations, he can hardly avoid troubles every now and then; those who do not plan for the future will find trouble at their doorstep; unpreparedness spells failure;

[遠略] (1) great plan for the future; (2) accomplish great achievements in a distant place;

[遠謀] plan far ahead;

[遠年] long ago;

[遠念] show concern for a dear one during separation;

[遠期] at a specified future date; forward;

遠期交易 forward; futures;

遠期外匯業務 forward exchange;

[遠親] distant relatives; remote kinsfolk;

遠親不如近鄰 a close neighbour means more than a distant relative; a distant relative is not as good as a near neighbour; a near neighbour is better than a far-dwelling kinsman; a relative far away is not as helpful as a neighbour close by; a relative far off is less helpful than a neighbour close by; an afar off relative is not as helpful as a near neighbour; better is a neighbour that is near than a brother far off; distant relatives are not as helpful as close neighbours; distant relatives are of less account than near neighbour;

遠親交配 outbreeding;

遠親近鄰 distant relatives and next-door neighours;

遠親近戚 both distant relations and near relatives — all connections;

富在深山有遠親 every one is kin to the rich man; rich folk have many friends; the rich never want for kindred;

關係親近的遠親 kissing cousin;

[遠識] forward-looking;

[遠視] (1) hypermetropia; hyperopia; (2) look from a distance; (3) far-sighted; long-sighted;

遠視散光 hypermetropic astigmatism;

~單純遠視散光 simple hyperopic astigmatism;

遠視眼 far-sighted; hypermetropia; hyperopia;

曲度遠視 curvature hyperopia;

相對遠視 relative hyperopia;

隱性遠視 latent hyperopia;

[遠水] distant water;

遠水不解近渴 distant waters cannot quench present thirst — the aid is too slow in coming to be of any help; while the grass grows the horse starves;

遠水不救近火 distant water will not put out a fire close at hand — a slow remedy cannot meet an urgency; distant waters are powerless against near fires; water far away is not of much use in putting out a fire nearby; water from afar cannot quench a nearby fire; while the grass grows the horse starves;

[遠送] see one off far;

恕不遠送 excuse me for not accompanying you farther;

[遠眺] take a distant look; view distant places;

極目遠眺 gaze into the distance; look far into the distance; strain one's eyes to look at the distance;

騁目遠眺 scan distant horizons;

倚欄遠眺 lean against the railing to see in the distance; lean on the parapet and gaze into the distance;

[遠圖] plan far ahead; plan for the future;

[遠限] distant time limit;

[遠行] go on a long journey; journey to a distant place; travel to a distant place;

凜於遠行 afraid of going on a long journey;

[遠洋] (1) ocean; (2) distant seas;

遠洋帶 pelagic zone;

遠洋貨輪 ocean-going freighter;

遠洋客輪 ocean liner;

遠洋輪 seagoing ship;

遠洋生物 pelagic organism;

[遠揚] one's reputation is known far and

wide;
臭名遠揚 notoriety;
聞風遠揚 flee far away in getting wind of sth; run away on hearing the news;

[遠因] remote causes;

[遠遊] travel far away;

[遠征] expedition;
遠征隊 expedition;
遠征軍 expeditionary force;
參加遠征 join an expedition;

[遠矚] look far ahead; take a look at faraway places;

[遠走] go far away;
遠走高飛 flee far away; fly far and high; fly high and go away; go far away; off to distant parts; slip away to distant place; take it on the lam; take wing;
遠走他鄉 off to a place far away from home; travel to distant parts;
驚避遠走 hide from fear and go far away;

[遠足] excursion; hike; hiking; outing; pleasure trip on foot; walking tour;
遠足鞋 hiking boots;
林間遠足 hike in the woods;

[遠族] remote clan; one's distant relatives;

[遠祖] one's remote ancestors;

邊遠 far from the centre; outlying; remote;
長遠 long-range; long-term;
弘遠 far and wide;
迴遠 far; faraway;
久遠 far back; remote;
路遠 great distance;
偏遠 faraway; remote;
深遠 deep and far; far-reaching; profound and lasting;
疏遠 distant; estrange; not in close touch;
跳遠 long jump;
騖遠 overambitious;
遙遠 distant; faraway; remote;
以遠 beyond;
永遠 always; ever; forever;
悠遠 (1) long time ago; (2) distant; far off; remote;

yuan⁴
yuan

【怨】 (1) enmity; hatred; ill will; resentment; (2) blame; complain;

[怨仇] old enemy;

[怨毒] enmity; hatred; malice;

[怨誹] blame; murmur against;

[怨憤] discontent and indignation;

[怨府] object of general indignation;

[怨恨] enmity; grudges; hate; ill will; resentment;
恨天怨地 utter maledictions against the whole world;
懷怨匿恨 entertain a secret grudge;
激起怨恨 awake the resentment; rouse resentment;
訴怨吐恨 complain of one's untold misery and pour out one's wrath;
消除怨恨 allay resentment; settle a grudge;
招怨恨 incur hatred;

[怨家] adversary; foe; old enemy;

[怨結] pent-up hatred;

[怨命] blame one's fate;

[怨慕] be dissatisfied and full of earnest desire;

[怨女] old spinster;
怨女曠夫 a grieving maid and a desolate man; a spinster and an unmarried man; a woman without husband and a man without a wife;

[怨偶] unhappy couple; unharmonious couple;
一對怨偶 an ill-matched couple;

[怨氣] complaints; grievances; resentment;
怨氣衝天 one's resentment mounts to heaven; one's wrath rises to the sky;
充滿怨氣 be filled with anger; be filled with spleen;
發洩怨氣 give vent to one's grievance; vent one's resentment;
有一肚子怨氣 full of complaints;

[怨曲] blues;
節奏怨曲 rhythm and blues;

[怨色] resentful look;

[怨聲] cries of discontent;
怨聲不絕 complain always; complain unceasingly;
怨聲遍地 complaints arose all throughout the country;
怨聲載道 complaints are heard everywhere; complaints rise all round; grumblings are heard all over; murmurs of discontent fill the streets; swamp with complaints; voices of discontent are heard everywhere;

[怨歎] sigh with bitterness;

[怨天] blame Heaven;

怨天尤命 curse one's stars; quarrel with Providence; repine against Providence and at one's fate; repine at Heaven and lay the blame on fate;

怨天尤人 blame everyone and everything but oneself; blame fate or other people; blame god and man; blame Heaven and other people; complain about natural conditions and other people; discontented with one's lot; grumble against Heaven and lay the blame upon other people; murmur against Heaven and blame other people; show resentment at Heaven and lay the blame on man;

[怨望] grudges; resentment;

[怨言] complaint; grumble;

從不發怨言 never utter a word of complaint;

發出怨言 voice a complaint;

沒有怨言 have no complaints to make;

有一肚子怨言 have a lot of complain about...;

[怨艾] grudges; resentment;

自怨自艾 blame and censure oneself; complain about oneself; full of remorse; regret one's past mistakes and try to do better in the future; repent and redress one's errors; self-reproach; trail at fate;

[怨尤] grudges; resentment;

哀怨 plaintive; sad; tragic;
抱怨 complain; grumble; murmur against;
仇怨 enmity; hatred; hostility;
恩怨 feeling of gratitude; grievances;
含怨 bear a grudge; carry a grudge;
積怨 accumulated rancor; piled-up grievances;
結怨 contract enmity; incur hatred;
埋怨 blame; complain; grumble;
民怨 popular discontent;
宿怨 old grudge; old scores;
嫌怨 grudge; resentment;
憎怨 bear a grudge against;
招怨 incur animosity;

yuan

【苑】 (1) garden; park; (2) gathering place;

[苑囿] garden; park;

禁苑 imperial garden;
林苑 imperial hunting ground;
鹿苑 deer park;
藝苑 art and literary circles;

yuan

【院】 (1) courtyard; yard; (2) designation for certain government and public offices; (3) college; (4) hospital;

[院落] compound; courtyard;

[院墻] wall that surrounds a house;

[院士] academician;

[院校] colleges and universities;

院校合作 inter-institutional collaboration;

院校評審 institutional accreditation;

高等院校 institutions of higher learning;

藝術院校 art academy;

[院宇] house and the yard;

[院長] college head; dean; president;

副院長 associate dean; vice-dean; vice-president;

~學院副院長 associate dean;

學院院長 college head; faculty dean; director;

研究院院長 dean of the graduate school;

醫院院長 director; president;

[院子] compound; courtyard; yard;

保育院 nursery school;
病院 specialized hospital;
博物院 museum;
參議院 senate;
產院 maternity hospital;
場院 threshing ground;
出院 leave hospital;
傳染病院 hospital for infectious diseases;
大院 compound; courtyard;
電影院 cinema; movie theatre
法院 court; court of justice;
瘋人院 lunatic asylum; mad-house;
歌劇院 opera house;
孤兒院 orphanage;
國務院 (1) state council; (2) state department;
後院 backyard;
話劇院 theatre;
妓院 brothel;
檢察院 procuratorate;
精神病院 psychiatric hospital;
敬老院 home of respect for the aged;
劇院 (1) theatre; (2) troupe;
科學院 academy of sciences;
療養院 convalescent hospital; sanatorium;
美容院 beauty parlour; beauty shop;
前院 front courtyard;

入院 be admitted to hospital;
僧院 Buddhist temple;
上議院 upper house;
上院 upper house;
設計院 designing institute;
書院 academy of classical learning;
四合院 quadrangle;
寺院 monastery; temple;
庭院 courtyard;
衛生院 public health centre;
戲院 theatre;
下議院 lower house;
下院 lower house;
休養院 rest home; sanatorium;
修道院 convent; monastery;
學院 college; institute;
研究院 (1) graduate school; (2) research institute;
醫院 hospital;
議院 legislative assembly;
影院 cinema; movie theatre;
宅院 house;
眾議院 house of representatives;
住院 be hospitalized; be in hospital;

yuan

【媛】 (1) beautiful woman; beauty; (2) miss; young lady;

嬋媛 lovely;

yuan

【掾】 general term referring to public officials in ancient China;

yuan

【瑗】 (1) huge ring of fine jade; (2) name of a kind of jade;

yuan

【愿】 (1) desire; hope; wish; (2) ready; willing; (3) vow;

[愿共勉之] let us encourage each other in our endeavours;
[愿心] reward that a superstitious person promises to offer to God;
[愿意] like; ready; want; willing; wish; would give the world to;
[愿者不難] all things are easy that are done willingly; what we do willingly is easy;

鄉愿 hypocrite;

yuan

【遠】 avoid; keep away from; keep at a distance; shun;

yuan

【願】 (1) desirous of; willing; (2) ambition; anything one wishes; aspiration; (3) vow; (4) think;

[願海] profound wish;
[願望] aspiration; desire; wish;
願望單 wish list;
願望實現 get one's wish; sb's wish comes true;
願望思維 wishful thinking;
共同願望 collective wishes;
~ 人民的共同願望 collective wishes of the people;
滿足願望 fulfil one's wish; grant one's wish;
死亡願望 death wish;
[願意] (1) willing; (2) like; want;
不管願意不願意 like it or not; willy-nilly;
不願意 (1) loathe; not willing; (2) be indisposed; feel indisposed; indisposition; loathe; not want to;
如果你願意 if you like;

本願 one's real wish;
不願 reluctant; unwilling;
償願 fulfil one's wish;
初願 one's original wish;
但願 if only;
發願 express one's desire;
甘願 readily; willingly;
宏願 at aspirations; noble ambition;
寧願 prefer; would rather;
情願 prefer; would rather;
請願 present a petition;
如願 achieve what one wishes;
誓願 pledge;
夙願 long-cherished wish;
宿願 long-cherished wish;
遂願 fulfil one's desire;
心願 aspiration; wish;
許個願 make a wish;
許願 (1) make a vow; (2) promise sb a reward;
遺願 unfulfilled wish of the deceased;
意願 aspiration; wish;
志願 aspiration; ideal; wish;
祝願 wish;
自願 of one's own accord; voluntary;

yue¹

yue

【曰】 say (an archai usage);

yue

【約】 (1) appointment; arrange; date; engagement; rendezvous; (2) ask in advance; invite in advance; (3) agreement; appointment; (4) bind; restrain; restrict; (5) economical; frugal; poor; (6) brief; simple; (7) about; approximately; around; estimated; (8) vague;

[約定] agree on; agree to; appoint; arrange;
約定地點 appointed place;
約定價格 strike price;
約定時間 appointed time;
約定俗成 accepted through common practice; conventional; established by usage; generally accepted and well-established; prescriptive; sanctioned by popular usage;
按照約定 by a preconcerted arrangement;
根據約定 according to a preconcerted agreement;

[約法] (1) provisional constitution; (2) bind with rules;
約法三章 (1) agree on a three-point law — make a few simple rules to be observed by all concerned; (2) verbal agreement;

[約會] appointment; date; engagement;
安排約會 arrange for an engagement; fix an appointment;
跟人約會 make an appointment with sb;
推遲約會 put off an engagement;
有約會 have a date;
遵守約會 keep a date;

[約見] make an appointment to meet sb;

[約盟] agreement; alliance; covenant; sworn compact;

[約莫] about; approximately; or so; roughly;

[約期] (1) appoint a time; date of appointment; fix a date; (2) time limit of a contract;

[約請] ask; invite;

[約束] bind; constraint; cramp; keep within bounds; repress; restrain;
約束自己的思想 restrain one's mind;
擺脱約束 break restraints; get rid of restraints;
不受約束 jump the traces; kick over the traces;
服從約束 submit to restraint;
互不約束 free from each other;
受到約束 suffer restraints;
雙側約束 bilateral constraint;
需要約束 need restraint;
軸向約束 axial constraint;
主動約束 active constraint;
自我約束 self-discipline;

[約數] (1) estimated number; (2) exact divisor;

[約同] agree to do sth together; make an appointment;

[約言] one's word; pledge; promises;
約言之 cut a long story short; in a few words; in a word; in brief; in short; make a long story short;

暗約 secret treaty;
背約 break an agreement; fail to keep one's promise; to back on one's word;
草約 draft agreement; draft treaty; protocol;
成約 treaty;
綽約 graceful;
大約 (1) about; approximately; in the region of ; somewhere about; (2) probably;
締約 conclude a treaty; sign a treaty;
訂約 conclude a treaty; enter into an agreement;
負約 break one's promise;
赴約 keep an appointment;
稿約 notice to contributors;
公約 (1) convention; pact; (2) joint pledge;
規約 stipulations of an agreement;
函約 make an appointment;
和約 peace treaty;
毀約 break one's promise;
集約 intensive;
儉約 economical; thrifty;
簡約 brief; concise; sketchy; terse;
踐約 keep an appointment;
節約 economize; practise thrift;
解約 cancel a contract; terminate an agreement;
舊約 Old Testament;
履約 honour an agreement; keep an appointment;
盟約 treaty of alliance;
密約 secret agreement;
破約 break one's promise;
契約 contract; deed;
如約 according to appointment;
商約 commercial treaty;
失約 fail to keep an appointment;
誓約 pledge; solemn promise;
守約 keep one's promise;
爽約 break an appointment;

特約 engage by special arrangement;
條約 pact; treaty;
婉約 graceful and restrained;
違約 break a contract; break off an engagement; violate a treaty;
相約 make an appointment; reach an agreement;
協約 agreement;
邀約 invite;
隱約 faint; indistinct;
預約 make an appointment;
制約 condition; restrict;
租約 lease;

yue4

yue

【月】 (1) moon; (2) month; (3) monthly; (4) full-moon shaped; round;

[月白] bluish white; very pale blue;
月白風清 the moon is bright and the air serene; the moon is bright and the wind cool; the moon is pale and the breeze is refreshing; the moon is white and the winds mild;
月白江清 the moonlight falls white upon the clear water of the river;

[月半] fifteenth day of a month;

[月報] (1) monthly report; (2) monthly journal;

[月表] monthly chronology;

[月餅] moon cake;
冰皮月餅 snowy moon cake;
一塊月餅 a moon cake;
中秋月餅 moon cake for Mid-autumn Festival;

[月初] beginning of a month;

[月旦] appraise people;
月旦春秋 make comments about the good or the evil of a character;

[月淡星稀] the moon grows pale and the stars dwindle;

[月底] end of a month;

[月度] monthly;

[月費] monthly expenses;

[月份] month;
冬季月份 winter months;
二月份 February;

[月宮] legendary palace on the moon;

[月光] moonbeam; moonlight; moonshine;
月光泛影 the moon casts its bright reflection in the water; the moon illuminates the water into a bright sheet of light;
月光花 large moonflower;
月光皎潔 the moon shines bright;
月光如水 a flood of translucent moonlight; the moonlight is clear as water; the moonlight shines like water; watery moonbeams;
月光升起 the moon comes up; the moon rises;
月光石 moonstone;
月光下 in the moonlight;
月光照耀 the moon shines;
一道月光 moonbeam;
一縷月光 a streak of moonlight;
一片月光 a flood of moonlight;

[月桂] bay; laurel;
月桂果 bayberry;
月桂樹 bay tree; laurel; sweetwood;
月桂葉 bay leaf;

[月華] brightness of the moon; moonlight;
月華如水 a flood of translucent moonlight; watery moonbeams;
月華如晝 it is a bright moonlit night; the moon is bright as day; the moon is like day for brightness; the moon makes the night as bright as day;
月華似水 the moon casts its silver sheen upon the ground;

[月季票] season ticket;

[月結單] monthly statement;

[月經] beno; bloody Mary; blue days; courses; cramps; discharge; domestic afflictions; effluvium; the flowers; her time; holy week; little friend; menses; menstrual flow; menstruation; monthlies; monthly courses; mother-nature; periods; problem days; roses; show; terms; the curse; the female complaint; the female disorder; the female problem; the female trouble; the flowers; the illness; the thing; wallflower week;
月經閉止 absence of menses; amenorrhoea;
月經病 emmeniopathy;
月經不調 irregular menses; irregular menstruation; menoxenia;
月經布 sanitary napkin;
月經過多 excessive menstruation; hypermenorrhoea;

月經過頻 epimenorrhoea;
~月經過頻過多 epimenorrihagia;
月經過少 hypomenorrhoea; scanty menstrual flow;
月經減少 relative amenorrhoea;
月經來潮 menstruate; menstruation;
月經淋漓 menostaxis;
月經流出 menorrhoea;
月經頻多 menometrorrhagia;
月經頻發 polymenia;
月經頻少 polyhypomenorrhoea;
月經期 menstrual cycle; menstrual period; period;
~月經期口出血 stomatomenia;
月經失調 menstrual disorder;
月經停止 amenorrhoea; cessation of menses;
月經痛 period pain;
月經稀發 oligomenorrhoea;
月經稀少 infrequent menstruation;
月經障礙 paramenia;
月經周期 menstrual cycle;
臭味月經 bromomenorrhoea;
假月經 pseudomenstruation;
無卵性月經 nonovulational menstruation;
無排卵性月經 nonovulational menstruation;
異位月經 vicarious menstruation;
隱性月經 cryptomenorrhoea;
正常月經 eumenorrhoea;

[月刊] monthly; monthly magazine;
半明刊 fortnightly;
雙月刊 bimonthly;
一本明刊 a monthly;

[月老] matchmaker; the old man under the moon—the god who unites people in marriage;
當月老 play cupid;

[月曆] monthly calendar;
雙月曆 bimonthly calendar;

[月亮] moon; parish lantern;
月亮出來了 the moon came up;
月亮出現 the moon appears; the moon comes up;
月亮落下了 the moon set;
月亮升上天空 the moon rises into the sky;
河裏撈月亮—白費勁 fishing for the moon in the river — a vain effort;
金色的月亮 yellow moon;
銀色的月亮 silver moon;

[月輪] moon;

[月落] the moon goes down;
月落西沉 the moon sinks westward;
月落霜寒 the moon goes down and the frosty night is cold;
月落星沉 the moon is down and the stars have set;
月落星稀 the moon is sinking and the stars are fading;

[月滿則虧，水滿則溢] the moon waxes only to wane, water brims only to overflow;

[月杪] end of a month;

[月面] lunar surface;
月面溝紋 rill;
月面環形山 lunar crater;
月面圖 lunar map;
月面圓穀 lunar circus;

[月明] the moon is bright;
月明風清 the moon is bright and the breeze is light;
月明如晝 the moon is shining as bright as day;
月明星朗 a bright moon and shining stars — a fine night; the moon and stars shine brilliantly;
月明星稀 the moon is bright and the stars are few; with a clear moon and few stars;

[月末] end of a month;

[月面學] selenography;

[月披銀妝] the moon comes out mantled in silver;

[月票] (1) monthly pass; (2) monthly ticket;
出示月票 present one's monthly ticket;

[月球] the moon;
月球表面 lunar surface;
月球的 lunar;
月球天平動 lunar libration; libration of the moon;
飛向月球 fly to the moon;

[月日] month and day;
某月某日 in such a month and on such a day;

[月色] moonlight;
月色澄清 clear moonlight;
月色輝映 the moon is shining in the clear sky;
月色昏黃 faint moonlight;
月色漸暗 the moon gets darker and darker;
月色晶瑩 the moon is as clear as crystal;
月色滿街 the moonlight floods the streets;

月色滿天，霜華遍地 it is a moonlit night, and hoar-frost covers the ground;
月色朦朧 the light of the moon is misted; the moon is obscured;
月色朦朧，星辰昏暗 the moon is dimmed by clouds and the stars are darkened;
月色迷朦 the moon dons a fuzzy cloak;
月色明朗 the moon is bright; the moon shines clear and bright;
月色清白 the moon is white and clear;
月色清寒 clear, cold moonlight;
月色無光 the moon is dimmed;
月色盈庭 the courtyard is flooded by moonlight;
湖光月色 the shimmering moonlight on the lake;
滿庭月色 the courtyard is flooded by moonlight;

[月蝕] eclipse of the moon; lunar eclipse;
半影月蝕 penumbral lunar eclipse;
看到月蝕 see the moon in eclipse;

[月臺] railway platform;

[月頭] beginning of a month;

[月吐銀輝] the moon begins to shed its silvery light; the moon casts its silver sheen;

[月彎如鈎] the moon is curved like a hook;

[月望] fifteenth day of a lunar month;

[月息] monthly interest;

[月夕花朝] moonlit evening and flowery morning — a pleasant day coupled with a fine landscape;

[月下] under the moon;
月下花前 under the moon and before the flowers;
月下老人 matchmaker; the Old Man of the Moon — the god who unites persons in marriage;
月下漫步 have a walk by moonlight; roam in the moonlight;

[月相] phases of the moon;

[月薪] monthly pay; monthly salary;

[月夜] moonlit night;

[月盈則虧，水滿則溢] the moon perfects itself only to wane, and water fills only to overflow; the moon waxes only to wane, water brims only to overflow;

[月盈則食] moon begins to wane the moment it becomes full; the moon waxes and wanes;

[月影花痕] shadow of the moon and flowers;

[月暈] halo of the moon;
月暈而風 a halo round the moon indicates the rising of the wind; the haloed moon foretells a gale is imminent;
月暈而風，礎潤而雨 a halo round the moon means wind, a damp plinth means rain;

[月雲] moon and clouds;
鏤月裁雲 engrave the moon and cut out clouds — a skilled work of art or literature;
落月停雲 waning moon and standing cloud — think of old friends;

[月震] moonquake;

[月中] middle of a month;
月中人 the man in the moon;

[月終] end of a month;

[月墜花折] the moon drops the flower break — death of a beauty;

八月 (1) August; (2) eighth month of the lunar year;
包月 monthly payment;
出月 next month;
大月 (1) solar month of thirty-one days; (2) lunar month of thirty days;
淡月 slack month;
當月 that very month; the same month;
冬月 eleventh month of the lunar year;
蛾眉月 crescent moon;
二月 (1) February; (2) second month of the lunar year;
風月 (1) wind and moon; (2) love affairs;
恒星月 sidereal month;
季月 last month of a season;
霽月 unclouded moon;
皎月 bright moon;
九月 (1) September; (2) ninth month of the lunar year;
虧月 waning moon;
臘月 twelfth month of the lunar year;
累月 month after month;
曆月 calendar month;
臨月 month when childbirth is due;
六月 (1) June; (2) sixth month of the lunar year;
滿月 full moon;
蜜月 honeymoon;
明月 bright moon;
品月 pale blue;
七月 (1) July; (2) seventh month of the lunar year;

全月 the whole month;
日月 life; livelihood;
閏月 intercalary month in the lunar calendar; leap month;
三月 (1) March; (2) third month of the lunar year;
賞月 enjoy looking at the moon;
十二月 (1) December; (2) twelfth month of the lunar year;
十一月 (1) November; (2) eleventh month of the lunar year;
十月 (1) October; (2) tenth month of the lunar year;
朔望月 lunar month;
朔月 new moon;
四月 (1) April; (2) fourth month of the lunar year;
歲月 years;
跳月 moon dance;
凸月 gibbous moon;
玩月 enjoy looking at the moon;
旺月 busy month;
望月 full moon;
五月 (1) May; (2) fifth month of the lunar year;
小月 (1) solar month of thirty days; (2) lunar month of twenty-nine days;
新月 (1) crescent; (2) new moon;
一個月 a month;
一月 (1) January; (2) first month of the lunar year;
盈月 waxing moon;
元月 (1) first month; (2) first lunar month;
匝月 full month;
齋月 month of fast;
正月 first month of the lunar year;
逐月 month by month;
足月 born after the normal period of gestation;

yue

【戉】 same as 鉞 , a large axe;

yue

【刖】 cut off the feet as a punishment;

yue

【岳】 (1) great mountain; high mountain; (2) one's wife's parents; (3) a surname;

［岳父］ one's father-in-law; one's wife's father;

［岳母］ one's mother-in-law; one's wife's mother;

山岳 lofty mountain;

yue

【悦】 (1) contented; glad; happy; pleased; (2) delight; gratify; please;

［悦從］ follow willingly;

［悦耳］ agreeable to the ear; musical; pleasing to the ear; sweet-sounding;
悦耳的 mellifluous;
悦耳動聽 listenable; lush; pleasant to the ear; please the ears; sweet-sounding;
悦耳易記的 catchy;
~ 悦耳易記的歌曲 catchy song;

［悦服］ heartily admire; submit willingly;

［悦口］ palatable; savory; tasty;

［悦樂］ pleasure;

［悦目］ good-looking; pleasant to the eye; pleasing to the eye;
賞心悦目 a feast for the eye; a perfect delight to the eye; cheerful and pleasing to the eye; find the scenery pleasing to both the eye and the mind; flatter the heart and please the eye; gladden the eyes and heart; gladden the heart and please the eye; let the eye take in the landscape and please the spirit; pleasant to look at; pleasant to the eye;
爽心悦目 entertaining; refreshing to the heart and pleasing to the eye;

［悦人］ delightful; pleasant; pleasing;

［悦色］ happy look;
好諛悦色 regard flattery as pleasure and cherish lust as desire;
和顏悦色 amiable manner; benign countenance; be all smiles and sweetness; be outwardly all friendliness and kindness; with a kind and pleasant countenance;
歡容悦色 a bright face; a joyous and lively countenance;
喜顏悦色 gladsome countenance;

［悦心］ cheer; gladden;

［悦意］ (1) agreeableness; pleasantness; (2) expression of happiness;

［悦豫］ delighted; happy; pleased;

［悦澤］ gorgeous; pleasantly bright;

愛悦 love;
抃悦 cheer;
喜悦 happy; joyous;

愉悦 cheerful; delighted;

yue
【軏】 crossbar at the end of the poles of a cart;

yue
【越】 (1) climb over; get over; go across; jump over; skip; (2) exceed; go beyond; transgress; (3) at a high pitch; (4) even more; the more; (5) an ancient state; (6) a surname;

[越窗而入] leap in through the window;

[越次] disregard the proper order;

[越冬] live through the winter; overwintering;

[越法] illegal; transgress the law; unlawful;

[越發] all the more; even more; the more;

[越房躐屋] make one's way into a house over walls and roofs;

[越分] go beyond one's proper position;

[越軌] exceeds the bounds; go beyond what is proper; overstep; transgress;
越軌行為 aberrant behaviour; deviant behaviour; impermissible behaviour; transgression;
從來不越軌 never get off the track;

[越過] cross; negotiate; surmount;
越過範圍 overstep the limits;
越過極限 exceed the maximum;
越過界線 step over the line;
越過雲層 fly over the clouds;
越過障礙 surmount obstacles;

[越級] skip grades in promotion;
越級提昇 promote sb more than one grade at a time;

[越界] cross the border; go beyond the boundary; overstep the boundary; transgress the bounds; trespass;

[越境] encroah upon the territory of an adjacent country;

[越禮] go beyond the bounds of propriety;

[越年] the following year;

[越期] pass the deadline; pass the time limit;

[越墻] climb over a wall; scale a wall;
越墻而逃 escape by climbing over the wall;

[越權] act beyond one's authority; act without authorization; exceed one's power or authority;
越權行事 act beyond one's authority; overstep one's authority;

[越日] following day;

[越位] offside;
沒有越位 online;

[越限] exceed the time limit;

[越野] cross-country;
越野車 all-terrain vehicle; off-road vehicle;
越野跑 cross-country running;
越野賽跑 cross-country race;

[越獄] break jail; break prison; escape from prison; jailbreak;
越獄而逃 break from a prison and abscond; escape from prison;

[越…越…] increasingly more; more and more; steadily more;
越多越好 the more the better;
~人越多越好 the more the merrier;
越多越要 the more one has, the more one wants;
越快越好 the faster the better; the quicker the better; the sooner the better;
越來越多 a growing number;
~越來越多的人 a growing number of people;
越來越好 become better and better; become better with each passing day; get better and better;
越來越糟 get worse and worse; go further and far worse; take extra trouble and find oneself in a worse position than before;
越描越黑 the more one tries to cover up a scandal, the more it stinks;
越陷越深 be bogged down deeper and deeper; become more and more unpopular; sink deeper and deeper;
越想越氣 the more one thinks of it, the angrier one grows; the more one thinks about it, the madder one gets;
越早越好 the earlier, the better;
越戰越強 grow ever stronger with fighting; grow from strength to strength in fighting; grow stronger with the fighting; the more one fights the stronger one grows;
越戰越勇 one's courage mounts as the battle progresses;
越走越遠 go farther down; go further and further down;

[越俎代庖] do on behalf of another sth not

in one's own line duty; exceed one's functions and meddle in others' affairs; go beyond one's duties; meddle with another's affairs; poach on sb's preserve; poach on sb's territory; take another's job into one's own hands;

超越 surmount; surpass; transcend;
穿越 cut across; pass through;
飛越 fly over;
橫越 overstep; traverse;
僭越 overstep one's authority;
跨越 leap over; stride across;
侵越 infringe upon;
清越 clear and melodious;
騰越 jump over;
優越 advantageous; outstanding; superior;
逾越 exceed; go beyond; pass;
聿越 excel; surpass;
卓越 excellent; outstanding; remarkable;

yue

【粵】 (1) Guangdong Province; (2) Cantonese; (3) opening particle;
［粵菜］ Cantonese food;
［粵劇］ Cantonese opera;
［粵考］ examine;
［粵犬吠雪］ things rarely seen are regarded as strange beings;
［粵人］ Cantonese;
［粵語］ Cantonese dialect;

yue

【葯】 a pronunciation of 葯 ;

yue

【鉞】 large axe;
［鉞石］ axe stone;
斧鉞 large, axe-shaped weapon in ancient times;

yue

【説】 same as 悦 , delight, please;

yue

【樂】 (1) music; (2) a surname;
［樂池］ orchestra pit;
［樂典］ musicological book;
［樂段］ period;
華彩樂段 cadenza;
結束樂段 coda;
［樂隊］ band; orchestra;
樂隊隊員 bandsman;
樂隊開始演奏 the band played up;
樂隊領班 bandleader;
樂隊領銜者 frontman;
樂隊人員 orchestra;
樂隊席 orchestra pit; orchestra seat; orchestra stall;
樂隊指揮 conductor; musical director;
單人樂隊 one-man band;
獨立樂隊 indie band;
管弦樂隊 orchestra;
管樂隊 band;
交響樂隊 symphony orchestra;
軍樂隊 military band;
流行樂隊 pop group;
室內樂隊 chamber orchestra;
銅管樂隊 brass band;
弦樂隊 string orchestra;
小樂隊 combo;
搖滾樂隊 rock band; rock group;
一個樂隊 a band; an orchestra;
助演樂隊 support band;
［樂句］ phrase;
［樂劇］ music drama;
［樂理］ music theory; musicology;
［樂譜］ music book; music score; musical notation; score sheet;
樂譜夾 music case;
樂譜架 music stand;
活頁樂譜 sheet music;
一篇樂譜 a piece of music; a sheet of music;
［樂器］ musical instrument;
樂器組 section;
~ 節奏樂器組 rhythm section; section;
撥絃樂器 plucked instruments;
打擊樂器 percussion instruments;
弓絃樂器 bowed stringed instruments;
管樂器 wind instruments;
簧樂器 reed instrument;
鍵盤樂器 keyboard instruments;
木管樂器 wood-wind instruments;
銅管樂器 brass-wind instruments;
演奏樂器 play an instrument;
一件樂器 a musical instrument;
中國樂器 Chinese musical instruments;
［樂曲］ musical composition; piece of music;
創作樂曲 compose music;
譜寫樂曲 write music;
一首樂曲 a piece of music;
［樂師］ musician;
［樂壇］ music circles;

[樂團] (1) philharmonic society; (2) philharmonic orchestra;
步操樂團 marching band;
交響樂團 symphony orchestra;
民族樂團 national music orchestra;
中央樂團 Central Philharmonic Society;
[樂章] movement;
第二樂章 second movement;
第三樂章 third movement;
第四樂章 fourth movement;
第一樂章 first movement;

哀樂 dirge; funeral march; funeral music; lament; music of lament;
愛樂 philharmonic;
吹打樂 ensemble of wind and percussion instruments;
吹奏樂 band music; wind music;
打擊樂 percussion music;
鼓樂 strains of music accompanied by drumbeats;
管弦樂 orchestral music;
管樂 wind instrument music;
國樂 traditional Chinese music;
交響樂 symphony;
爵士樂 jazz;
軍樂 martial music; military music;
民樂 folk music;
配樂 dub in background music; incidental music;
器樂 instrumental music;
輕音樂 light music;
聲樂 vocal music;
室內樂 chamber music;
絲竹樂 ensemble of traditional stringed and woodwind instruments;
西樂 Western music;
絃樂 stringed instrument music;
搖滾樂 rock and roll; rock music; rock'n'roll;
音樂 music;
奏樂 play music; strike up a tune;
作樂 (1) compose; write music; (2) play music;

yue

【閱】 (1) go over; read; (2) examine; inspect; observe; review; (3) experience; pass through;
[閱報] read newspapers;
[閱畢] after reading;
[閱兵] inspect troops; review troops;
閱兵典禮 dress parade;
[閱操] watch a military drill;
[閱讀] read; reading;
閱讀法 reading approach;
閱讀過緩 bradylexia;
閱讀架 bookrest;
閱讀器 reader;
~ 標記閱讀器 badge reader;
閱讀速度 reading speed;
閱讀徐緩 bradylexia;
閱讀障礙 reading disorder;
閱讀作業 reading assignment;
課外閱讀 extracurricular reading;
快速閱讀 speed reading;
仔細閱讀 pore over; read carefully;
自動閱讀 automatic reading;
[閱卷] go over examination papers; grade examination papers;
[閱覽] read;
閱覽室 reading room;
開架閱覽 open access;
[閱歷] (1) see, hear or do for oneself; (2) experience;
閱歷豐富 has seen a great deal of life;
閱歷艱辛 have a rough time;
閱歷淺 be little experienced in one's life;
閱歷深 be much experienced in one's life;
豐富的閱歷 a vast amount of experience;
[閱時] last a period of time;
[閱世] experience the ways of life; see the world;
閱世漸深 gain more and more experience of life;
閱世頗深 be deeply experienced in worldly affairs;

參閱 consult; refer to;
查閱 consult; look up;
傳閱 circulate for perusal; pass round for perusal;
訂閱 subscribe to a publication;
翻閱 browse; flick through; flip through; glance over; leaf through; look over; read over;
檢閱 (1) review; (2) look over;
校閱 read and revise;
批閱 read and amend; read over; read over and give comments;
披閱 open and read;
評閱 read and appraise;
圈閱 read and circle;
賞閱 read and appreciate;
審閱 check and approve;
索閱 ask for a publication for reference;
選閱 review and select;

巡閱 inspect; make the rounds of inspection;
贈閱 publication given free by the publisher;

yue
【樾】 shade of trees;

yue
【嶽】 high mountain; lofty summit; peak;

yue
【龠】 (1) a kind of flute; (2) a kind of measuring vessel;

yue
【藥】 a pronunciation of 藥;

yue
【瀹】 (1) cook or boil with soup; (2) soak; wash; (3) harness;

yue
【躍】 bound; jump; leap; spring;
[躍步] galloping;
[躍動] in lively motion; move actively;
[躍過] jump across; leap over;
躍過柵欄 jump up over the fence;
躍過籬笆 leap over a fence;
躍過障礙物 take a leap over an obstacle;
[躍進] (1) leap forward; make a leap; (2) make rapid progress;
[躍馬] give the horse its head; let a horse gallop;
躍馬飛馳 leap on a horse and ride swiftly;
躍馬橫車 (of a chess game) jump the horse over and drive the chariot crosswise;
躍馬橫刀 spur the horse and level the swords — take a challenging position;
[躍起] jump up; leap up;
[躍遷] transition;
[躍然] appear vividly;
躍然紙上 full of life; show forth in one's writing; stand vividly revealed in the pages; stand vividly revealed on the paper; vivid;
[躍昇] zoom;
[躍躍欲試] anxious to have a try; eager to have a try; impatient to have a try; itch for a try; itch to have a go;

忭躍 great joy; leap with joy; tremendous pleasure;
飛躍 (1) leap; (2) develop by leaps and bounds;
歡躍 dance for joy;
活躍 active; dynamic; enliven; invigorate;
雀躍 jump for joy;
騰躍 (1) active; lively; prance; (2) skyrocket;
跳躍 caper; dance; hop; jump; leap;
一躍 jump; take a leap;
踴躍 (1) jump; leap; (2) eagerly; enthusiastically;
魚躍 fish dive;

yue
【禴】 a kind of annual sacrifice;

yue
【籥】 (1) a short flute or pipe used in ancient China; (2) key;

yue
【鑰】 (1) key; (2) lock;

yun¹
yun
【暈】 (1) faint; giddy and dizzy; (2) do things without purpose; (3) faint; swoon; (4) halo;
[暈車] carsickness;
暈車的 carsick;
[暈船] have seasickness; seasickness;
[暈倒] faint and fall; fall in a faint; pass out; swoon;
[暈過去] faint; pass out;
[暈機] airsickness; have airsickness;
暈機病 airsickness;
暈機的 airsick;
[暈厥] faint; syncope;
抽搐性暈厥 convulsive syncope;
咳嗽暈厥 cough syncope;
心性暈厥 cardiac syncope;
[暈頭] (1) blockhead; (2) feel dizzy;
暈頭巴腦 feel dizzy and giddy;
暈頭轉向 all of a heap; confused and disoriented; in a regular tizzy; lose one's bearing; out of one's bearing;
[暈暈忽忽] (1) dizzy; giddy; (2) confused in mind; muddle-headed;

發暈 faint; feel dizzy; feel giddy;
光暈 aureole;
紅暈 blush; flush;
日暈 solar halo;
乳暈 areola mammae;
山暈 mountain sickness;
頭暈 dizzy; giddy;
眩暈 dizziness; feel dizzy;
血暈 bruise;
眼暈 feel dizzy;

Y

銀暈 galactic halo;
月暈 lunar halo;

yun
【氳】 atmosphere of harmony; spirit of harmony; spirit of prosperity; spirit of vigour;

氤氳 (of mist) enshrouding;

yun
【贇】 agreeable; fine; pleasant;

yun²
yun
【云】 say; speak;
［云何］ how; why;
［云云］ and so forth; and so on; so and so;
人云亦云 echo the views of others; follow another's lead in voicing opinions; follow what others have said; parrot the words of others; parrot what others say; repeat others' ideas; repeat what others say; repeat word for word what others say; say what everybody says;
~八哥兒的嘴巴一人云亦云 a myna's tongue — echo the views of others;
如是云云 thus and thus;

yun
【匀】 (1) even; smooth; (2) divide evenly; even up; (3) spare;
［匀稱］ balanced; even; harmonious; symmetrical; well-balanced; well-proportioned;
［匀出］ share sth; spare sth;
［匀分］ divide equally; share and share alike;
［匀和］ evenly distributed;
［匀臉］ powder and paint one's face evenly;
［匀實］ even; uniform;
［匀圓］ evenly round;
［匀整］ even and orderly; neat;

拌匀 mix thoroughly; mix well;
均匀 even; well-distributed;
調匀 mix well; stir even;

yun
【昀】 (1) dawn; daybreak; sunrise; (2) sunshine;

yun
【芸】 (1) rue; (2) same as 耘, weed;
［芸編］ books;
［芸草］ rue; strong-scented herb;
［芸窗］ study;
［芸豆］ kidney bean;
［芸臺］ imperial library;
［芸香］ rue;
［芸芸］ many; numerous;
芸芸眾生 all mortal beings; common herd; people of the world;

yun
【紜】 busy; confusing; disorderly;
［紜紜］ diverse and confused; numerous and disorderly;

紛紜 diverse and confused;

yun
【耘】 weed;
［耘草］ remove weeds; weed;
［耘鋤］ hoe;
［耘田］ weed rice fields;
耘人之田 manage business on behalf of others;

耕耘 cultivate; plough and weed;
夏耘 summer hoeing;

yun
【雲】 (1) clag; cloud; (2) a cloud of; a large number of; (3) short for Yunnan Province; (4) a surname;
［雲彩］ clouds illuminated by the rising or setting sun;
［雲層］ layers of clouds;
高雲層 altostratus;
［雲帶］ cloud band;
［雲滴］ cloud droplet;
［雲底］ cloud base;
［雲頂］ cloud top;
［雲端］ in the clouds;
［雲朵］ cloud mass;
［雲光］ sky;
陸照雲光 land sky;
水照雲光 water sky;
雪照雲光 snow sky;
［雲海］ a sea of clouds;
［雲漢］ Milky Way;
［雲鬢］ the beautiful hairdo of an attractive woman;
［雲集］ come together in crowds; congregate; converge; flock together; gather;

Y

[雲際] in the clouds;
[雲景] cloudscape;
[雲譎波詭] bewilderingly changeable; changing kaleidoscopically; fast and unexpected changes; sudden and perplexing changes; unpredictable, ever-changing nature of things;
[雲開] the clouds disperse;
雲開見日 the clouds disperse and the sun appears; the clouds lift and the sun comes out;
雲開日出 the sun scatters the clouds;
[雲量] cloudage; cloudiness;
[雲羅] dense clouds;
[雲冪] ceiling;
[雲杪] distant and high;
[雲母] mica;
雲母屏風 a mother-of-pearl screen;
脆雲母 brittle mica;
黑雲母 black mica;
人造雲母 artificial mica;
石棉雲母 abstestos mica;
[雲泥] couds and mud — great difference in social standing;
雲泥異路 as different as cloud from mud — wide differences between noble and base classes;
雲泥之別 clouds and mud — great difference in social standing;
[雲片] cloud sheet;
[雲起龍驤] (1) rise up in time of social upheavals; (2) rise of great heroes;
[雲氣] thin, floating clouds;
[雲區] cloud-land;
[雲雀] meadow lark; skylark;
雲雀囀鳴 a lark warbles;
[雲擾] confused; disorderly; disturbance;
[雲日] clouds and light; clouds and the sun;
撥雲見日 redress wrong and restore justice; remove the cloud of suspicion; sweep away the dark clouds and bring sb the light;
干雲蔽日 tower into the clouds and cover up the sun;
乾雲蔽日 tall woods cover the sun;
[雲杉] spruce;
白雲杉 white spruce;
垂枝雲杉 weeping spruce;
黑雲杉 black spruce;
藍葉雲杉 blue spruce;

銀白雲杉 silver fur spruce;
[雲散] disperse like clouds;
雲散日現 the clouds roll away and the sun comes out;
雲散天青 the clouds soon disperse and the sky becomes clear;
雲散煙消 disappear as if by evaporating;
[雲石] marble;
[雲屬] cloud genera;
[雲梯] aerial ladder; scaling ladder;
雲梯消防車 an aerial ladder fire engine;
[雲天] clouds and sky—high above;
雲天高誼 great kindness and friendship;
觀雲知天 watch the clouds and know signs in the sky;
[雲頭] in the clouds;
[雲圖] cloud atlas; cloud chart;
衛星雲圖 satellite cloud picture;
[雲團] cloud cluster;
[雲霧] clouds and mist;
黑雲迷霧 dark clouds and heavy fog;
拿雲握霧 extremely capable;
濃雲密霧 dense mist and clouds;
如坐雲霧 as if sitting in the clouds and mists; confused; muddled;
騰雲駕霧 fly up to the cloudy regions; mount the clouds and ride the mist; ride on the mists and clouds;
雲屯霧集 gather together like clouds — multitude;
雲繞霧罩 be shrouded in mist and clouds;
雲消霧散 the clouds disperse and the fog lifts; the clouds melt and the mists disperse; the troubles are over;
雲遮霧障 be lost in mist and clouds;
[雲系] cloud system;
[雲霞] rosy clouds;
雲蒸霞蔚 radiant, colourful and flourishing; the rosy clouds are slowly rising;
[雲霄] the skies;
高入雲霄 reach towards the sky; rise up in the clouds; stand out against the sky; tower high above the level of the clouds;
聳入雲霄 prick toward the sky; reach into the clouds; reach towards the sky; tower into the clouds; tower to the skies;
直上雲霄 soar straight up into the sky;
[雲簫] a kind of panpipe;

[雲煙] clouds and mist; clouds and smog;
雲煙過眼 clouds and smoke that float past the eyes; things having no lasting value;

[雲液] (1) wine; (2) mica;

[雲游] roam about; travel without a destination; wander about;
雲游天下 roam about the world;

[雲雨] (1) grace and favour; (2) make love; sexual intercourse;
雲雨巫山 the couple is enraptured with love;
翻雲覆雨 (1) blow hot and cold; change attitudes constantly; (2) have sexual intercourse;
~翻手為雲，覆手為雨 blow hot and cold; change and change about; chop and change; play fast and loose;
呼雲喚雨 (1) command the clouds and rains; (2) control the forces of nature;
巫山雲雨 (1) rendezvous between two lovers; (2) have sexual intercourse;
雲收雨散 (1) dispersion; separation; (2) the end of sexual intercourse;
雲消雨歇 the rain is over and the clouds have scattered;
雲行雨施 benevolent to the people;

[雲月] clouds and moon;
餐雲臥月 hardships of travel; poverty-stricken;
烘雲托月 paint clouds to set off the moon; prominence through contrast; provide a foil to set off a character in a literary work; set off the moon by painting the clouds around it; use contrast effect to set off the object in literary or artistic works;
輕雲淡月 light clouds and glimmering moon;

[雲章] the emperor's handwriting;

白雲 white clouds;
波狀雲 undulates; wave cloud;
彩雲 morning glow; roseate clouds; rosy clouds;
殘雲 last clouds;
層雲 stratus;
愁雲 cloud of sorrow; depressing clouds; heavy clouds;
稠雲 dense clouds;
穿雲 break through the clouds;
淡積雲 cumulus humilis;
低雲 low cloud;
地形雲 orographic cloud;
電荷雲 charge cloud;
多雲 cloudy;
風雲 wind and cloud;
浮雲 floating clouds;
高層雲 altostratus;
高積雲 altocumulus;
高雲 altostratus; high clouds;
河外星雲 extragalactic nebula;
恒星雲 star cloud;
火燒雲 resplendent sunset;
積雨雲 cumulonimbus;
積雲 cumulus;
捲層雲 cirrostratus;
捲積雲 cirrocumulus;
捲雲 cirrus;
浪雲 billow cloud;
雷雨雲 thundercloud;
凌雲 reach the clouds; soar to the skies;
密雲 cloudy;
蘑菇雲 mushroom cloud;
暮雲 evening clouds;
濃積雲 cumulus congestus;
青雲 (1) high official position; (2) retirement; (3) sky;
卿雲 propitious clouds bringing well-being to all;
慶雲 auspicious clouds;
人造雲 cloudier;
如雲 like clouds;
入雲 into the clouds;
瑞雲 auspicious clouds;
梢雲 auspicious clouds;
酸雲 acid cloud;
天雲 heaven and clouds;
彤雲 (1) red cloud; (2) dark cloud;
微雲 thin cloud;
烏雲 black clouds; dark clouds;
祥雲 auspicious clouds;
星雲 nebula;
行雲 floating clouds;
煙雲 (1) mists and clouds; (2) passing scene;
一層雲 a layer of clouds; a veil of clouds;
一朵雲 a cloud;
一堆雲 a bank of clouds;
疑雲 suspicion clouding one's mind;
陰雲 dark cloud;
雨層雲 nimbostratus;
雨雲 nimbus;
矞雲 clouds of many colours;
原子雲 atomic cloud;

月雲 moon and clouds;
狀雲 dog-shaped clouds;
戰雲 war cloud;
陣雲 dense clouds;
直展雲 cloud with vertical development;
中雲 medium cloud;

yun
【筠】 skin of the bamboo;

竹筠 bamboo;

yun
【蕓】 rape, also known as 油菜 ;

yun³
yun
【允】 (1) allow; consent; grant; permit; (2) appropriate; fair; just; proper; (3) faithful; loyal; sincere; truly;
[允差] franchise;
[允從] comply with; consent to; follow one's advice; promise to follow one's advice;
[允當] appropriate; fit; proper; suitable;
[允諾] consent; promise; undertake;
點頭允諾 nod in acceptance; nod in acquiescence; nod in agreement;
兌現允諾 fulfil one's promise;
欣然允諾 consent readily;
遵守允諾 meet one's promise;
[允洽] fair; proper; well settled;
[允許] allow; consent; give permission; grant; permit;
允許差誤 allowable error;
允許破例 grant exception;
允許值 permissible value;
不允許 not allow;
口頭允許 permit verbally;
請求允許 ask for permission;
如果時間允許 if time permits;
如果天氣允許 weather permitting;
如果條件允許 if the situation permits it;
書面允許 give a written permission;
[允執厥中] fair to all;
[允准] approve; consent; grant;

答允 undertake;
公允 even-handed; fair and equitable;
慨允 permit generously; promise generously;
平允 fair and just;
率允 promise at random; promise carelessly;
應允 (1) assent; consent; (2) allow; permit;
中允 fair; fair-minded; impartial; just;

yun
【狁】 a barbarian tribe to the north in ancient times;

yun
【隕】 (1) fall from the sky or outer space; (2) die;
[隕落] (1) fall from the sky or outer space; (2) die; pass away;
[隕滅] (1) fall from outer space and burn up; (2) meet one's death; perish;
[隕命] die;
[隕石] meteorite;
隕石雨 meteor shower;
[隕涕] tears falling;
[隕鐵] meteoric iron;
[隕星] meteor; meteorite;
隕星坑 meteorite crater;
隕星學 meteortics;
隕星雨 meteor shower;
[隕越] (1) topple and fall down; (2) fulfil one's duties improperly;

yun
【殞】 (1) die; perish; (2) same as 隕 , fall;
[殞落] fall;
[殞滅] annihilate; exterminate; meet one's death; perish; wipe out;
[殞命] die; meet one's death; perish;
[殞沒] die; perish;
[殞石] meteorite;

yun⁴
yun
【孕】 conceive; get pregnant;
[孕婦] pregnant woman;
孕婦裝 maternity clothes;
[孕期] gestation; pregnancy;
[孕育] be pregnant with; breed; foster; nourish; nurse; nurture;
孕育劑 inoculant;
~ 二次孕育劑 post inoculant;
~ 碳基孕育劑 carbon-based inoculant;
~ 硅基孕育劑 silicon-based inoculant;

包孕 contain; embody; include;
避孕 contraception;
宮外孕 extrauterine pregnancy;
懷孕 pregnant;
身孕 pregnancy;

受孕 become pregnant;
有孕 be expecting;

yun
【惲】 (1) consider; deliberate; plan; (2) a surname;
[惲謀] plan; scheme;
[惲議] deliberate; discuss;

yun
【鄆】 (1) an ancient town in Shandong; (2) a surname;

yun
【慍】 angry; displeased; indignant; irritated; vexed;
[慍懟] resent;
[慍恨] indignation; rancour; resentment;
[慍怒] angry; chagrin; displeased; inwardly angry; irritated;
[慍容] angry appearance; displeased look; face of resentment;
[慍色] angry appearance; displeased look; gloomy countenance; irritated look;
面有慍色 pull a long face;

yun
【暈】 (1) halo; mist; vapours; (2) feel dazzled; feel dizzy; feel faint; feel giddy;
暈車 (1) bussick; (2) carsick; (3) trainsick;
暈船 seasick;
暈飛機 airsick;

yun
【韵】 (1) rhyme; (2) harmony;

yun
【運】 (1) motion; move; movement; revolve; (2) carry; ship; transport; (3) make use of; use; utilize; (4) fortune; luck;
[運搬] move; transport;
[運筆] wield the brush; wield the pen;
運筆如飛 quick in writing;
[運籌] map out strategy; planning and management;
運籌帷幄 devise strategies within a command tent; work out plans;
~ 運籌帷幄之中，決勝千里之外 contrive strategic plans in the headquarters and win victory in a battle a thousand li away; sit within a command tent and devise strategies that will assure victory a thousand li away; work out splendid plans to win victories in battles a thousand miles away;
運籌學 operational research;
拙於運籌 play one’s cards badly;
[運單] bill of lading;
[運道] (1) fortune; luck; (2) a road for grain transportation;
[運動] (1) motion; movement; (2) athletics; exercise; physical exercise; sports; (3) campaign; drive; movement; social movement; (4) lobby;
運動比賽學 agonistics;
運動病 motion sickness;
運動不能 akinesia;
~ 運動不能症 akinesia;
運動場 gymnasium; playground; sports arena; stadium;
運動場地 sports field; sports ground;
運動遲緩 bradykinesia;
運動倒錯 parakinesia;
運動隊 sports team;
運動服 leisurewear; sports clothing;
運動服裝 sportswear;
運動感 kinaesthesia;
~ 運動感覺 kinaesthetic sense;
運動功能減退 hypocinesia;
運動功能亢進 hypercinesia;
運動過度 acrocinesis; acrokinesia; hypercinesia;
運動過緩 bradycinesia;
運動過強 hypermotility;
運動後疲乏 postactivation exhaustion;
運動會 athletic meet; games; sports meet;
~ 奧林匹克運動會 Olympic Games;
~ 大學校際運動會 inter-university sports;
~ 露天運動會 outdoor games;
~ 全國運動會 national games;
~ 田徑運動會 track meet; track-and-field sports;
~ 學校運動會 school sports;
運動計劃 plan of campaign;
運動家 athlete; sportsman;
~ 天才運動家 gifted athlete;
運動減弱 hypomotility;
運動減少 hypokinesia;
運動健將 master of sports;
運動交際心理 athletic communication psychology;
運動精神 sportsmanship;
運動能力 (1) athletic ability; (2) kinetism;
運動貧乏 poverty of movement;

運動衫 sports shirt;
~長袖運動衫 sweatshirt;
運動傷病 sports injury;
運動失調 parakinesia;
運動使人健康 exercise is promotive of health;
運動痛 kinesalgia;
運動項目 sport; sporting event;
~競爭性運動項目 competitive sport;
運動鞋 running shoes; sneakers;
~高幫運動鞋 high-tops;
~膠底運動鞋 sneaker;
~一對運動鞋 a pair of sneakers;
~一雙運動鞋 a pair of sneakers;
運動心理衛生 athletic psychological hygiene;
運動學 kinematics;
~流變運動學 rheological kinematics;
~流體運動學 hydrokinematics;
~平面運動學 plane kinematics;
~相對論運動學 relativistic kinematics;
運動員 athlete; player; sportsman; sportsperson; sportswoman;
~登山運動員 mountaineer;
~短跑運動員 sprinter;
~二級運動員 second-class sportsman;
~帆板運動員 windsurfer;
~滑雪運動員 skier;
~擊劍運動員 fencer;
~舉重運動員 weightlifter;
~老練運動員 veteran player;
~明星運動員 star player;
~女運動員 sportswoman;
~全能運動員 all-around athlete; all-round sportsman; all-rounder;
~拳擊運動員 boxer;
~柔道運動員 judoist;
~賽車運動員 go-carting player;
~賽艇運動員 rowing player;
~三級運動員 third-class sportsman;
~射擊運動員 shooting player;
~射箭運動員 archer;
~摔跤運動員 wrestler;
~速滑運動員 speed skater;
~體操運動員 gymnast;
~田徑運動員 track-and-field athlete;
~跳高運動員 high jumper;
~跳水運動員 diver;
~跳遠運動員 longer jumper;
~業餘運動員 amateur athlete;
~一個運動員 an athlete;
~一級運動員 top-grade sportsman;
~一名運動員 an athlete;
~一群運動員 a crowd of players;
~優秀運動員 ace player; top-notch player;
~游泳運動員 swimmer;
~職業運動員 professional athlete;
~半職業運動員 semi-professional athlete;
運動障礙 dyskinesia; dyspraxia;
運動正常 eukinesia;
變速運動 variable motion;
冰上運動 ice sport;
不對稱運動 asymmetric motion;
不結盟運動 non-aligned movement;
大量運動 plenty of exercise;
登山運動 mountaineering;
墊上運動 mat exercise;
冬季運動 winter sport;
發起運動 launch a campaign; mount a campaign;
帆板運動 windsurfing;
帆船運動 yachting;
反向運動 adversive movement;
分子運動 molecular motion;
輔助運動 accessory movement;
改革運動 reform movement;
搞運動 start a campaign;
個人運動 individual sport;
國際性運動 international campaign;
航空運動 aviation sports;
划船運動 rowing;
划艇運動 canoeing;
滑雪運動 skiing;
戶外運動 outdoor sport;
機械運動 mechanical movement;
極限運動 extreme sport;
擊劍運動 fencing;
技巧運動 acrobatic gymnastics;
加速運動 accelerate motion;
角諧運動 angular harmonic motion;
節約運動 movement towards economizing;
經常運動 take regular exercise;
劇烈運動 strenuous exercise; violent exercise; vigorous exercise;
~做劇烈運動 take vigorous exercise;
舉重運動 weightlifting;
絕對運動 absolute motion; absolute movement;
開展運動 conduct a campaign; run a campaign; wage a campaign;
領導運動 lead a campaign; spearhead a campaign;
馬球運動 polo;

馬術運動 equestrian sports;
摩托車運動 motorcycling;
募捐運動 campaign for contributions;
輕微運動 light exercise;
球類運動 ball games; ball sport;
~ 非球類運動 non-ball sport;
曲線運動 curvilinear motion;
全國性運動 national campaign; nationwide campaign;
全球運動 global campaign;
全世界運動 worldwide campaign;
拳擊運動 boxing;
缺乏運動 lack exercise; short of exercise;
熱身運動 warm-up exercises;
熱運動 thermal motion;
柔道運動 judo;
賽車運動 go-carting;
賽艇運動 rowing;
上下運動 move up and down;
掃盲運動 anti-illiteracy campaign;
射擊運動 shooting;
射箭運動 arching;
身體接觸類運動 contact sport;
十項全能運動 decathlon;
十項運動 decathlon;
室內運動 indoor sport;
適量運動 moderate exercise;
摔跤運動 wrestling;
水上運動 aquatic sports; marine sports; water sports;
速滑運動員 speed skating;
體操運動 gymnastics exercise;
體育運動 sports;
~ 參加體育運動 be engaged in athletics;
~ 進行體育運動 perform physical exercises;
田徑運動 athletic sports; track and field athletics;
~ 田徑運動員 track and field athlete;
跳高運動 high jump;
跳傘運動 parachuting;
跳水運動 diving;
跳遠運動 longer jump;
外表運動 apparent motion;
往復運動 advance and return movement; alternate motion;
危險的運動 dangerous sports;
五項運動 pentathlon;
夏季運動 summer sports;
相對運動 relative motion;
一場運動 a campaign;
圓周運動 circular motion;
勻變速運動 uniformly varying motion;
勻加速運動 uniformly accelerated motion;
勻減速運動 uniformly decelerated motion;
勻速運動 uniform motion;
政治運動 political campaign;
直線運動 rectilinear motion;
職業運動 professional sport;
周日運動 diurnal motion;
自然運動 natural exercise;
自行車運動 cycling;
做運動 do exercise; take exercise;

[運費] carriage; fare; freight; freight charges; transportation expenses;
運費待收 freight to be collected;
運費到付 freight payable at destination;
運費單 bill of lading;
運費付訖 carriage paid; freight paid;
運費免收 freight absorption;
運費未付 carriage forward;
運費已付 carriage paid; freight paid;
運費預付 freight prepaid;
比例運費 pro rata freight;
航空運費 air freight;
填載運費 distress freight;
預付運費 advance freight charge;
增列運費 additional freight;

[運河] canal;
運河船 canal boat;

[運會] international situations; trends of the time;

[運貨] transport goods;
運貨車廂 freight car;
運貨飛機 aerovan;
運貨量 volume of freight;
公路運貨 the movement of goods by road;
免費運貨 free delivery;

[運價表] tariff;
分段運價表 sectional tariff;
國內運價表 internal tariff;
過境運價表 transit tariff;
聯運價表 combined tariff; joint tariff;
統一運價表 standard tariff;

[運馬] carry horses;
運馬棚車 horse trailer; horsebox;
運馬拖車 horse trailer; horsebox;

[運煤] transport coal;
運煤工人 coalman;

[運命] destiny; fate; fortune;

[運泥車] mover;

[運牛車] cattle truck;

[運氣] fortune; luck;
運氣不好 in bad luck; luckless;
運氣好 in luck; luck out;
~ 運氣好的話 with a bit of luck;
~ 有些人就是運氣好 some people have all the luck;
運氣問題 a matter of luck;
好運氣 good fortune;
沒有運氣 have no luck; not have any luck; not have much luck;
沒這樣的運氣 no such luck;
碰運氣 chance one's luck; depend upon luck; pot luck; stand one's chance; take a chance; try one's luck;
~ 碰碰運氣 chance one's luck; take a chance; try one's fortune; try one's luck;
全憑運氣 pure luck; sheer luck;
試一試運氣 try one's luck;
一點運氣 a piece of luck; a stroke of luck;
一份運氣 a piece of luck;

[運球] dribble;
變向運球 change-of-direction dribble;
空中運球 air dribble;
兩次運球 double; dribble;
埋頭運球 head-down dribble;
抬頭運球 head-up dribble;
延緩運球 delayed dribble;

[運輸] carriage; traffic; transport; transportation;
運輸包裝 transport package;
運輸車 transporter;
運輸船 transport boat; transport ship; transporter;
運輸代理人 shipping agent;
運輸費 transport charge; carriage;
運輸工具 means of delivery; means of transportation;
運輸公司 carrier;
~ 跨國運輸公司 international carrier;
運輸機 freighter; transport plane;
~ 超高音速運輸機 hypersonic transport plane;
~ 超音速運輸機 supersonic transport plane;
~ 短程運輸機 short-range transport plane;
~ 可改裝運輸機 convertible transport plane;
~ 跨音速運輸機 transonic transport plane;
~ 亞音速運輸機 subsonic transport plane;
~ 遠程運輸機 long-range transport;
大宗運輸 aggregate traffic;
對流運輸 cross-haul traffic;
公路運輸 highway transport;
海上運輸 sea transport;
航空運輸 air transport;
集體運輸 mass transit;
陸路運輸 overland transit;
內河運輸 inland transport;
市郊運輸 commuting traffic;
水上運輸 water transport;
鐵路運輸 railway transport;
中轉運輸 traffic in transit;

[運數] fate; fortune; luck;

[運水] transport water;
運水船 water tanker;

[運送] consignment; convey; ship; transport;
運送物 consignment;

[運算] arithmetic; operation;
運算器 arithmetic-logic unit;
並行運算 parallel arithmetic;
部份運算 partial arithmetic;
串行運算 serial arithmetic;
單字長運算 single length arithmetic;
定點運算 fixed-point arithmetic;
多倍長度運算 multilength arithmetic;
多倍精度運算 multiprecision arithmetic;
多重運算 multiple arithmetic;
二進制運算 binary arithmetic; binary operation;
浮點運算 floating point operation;
機器運算 machine arithmetic;
階運算 exponent arithmetic;
絕對值運算 signed magnitude arithmetic;
邏輯運算 logical operation;
內部運算 internal arithmetic;
逆運算 inverse operation;
數學運算 mathematical operation;
雙字長運算 double word length arithmetic;
四則運算 four fundamental operations;
算術運算 arithmetic operation;
外部運算 external arithmetic;
完點運算 fixed point operation;
位運算 bit arithmetic;
小數運算 decimal arithmetic;

[運行] in motion; move; run;
運行過程 operational procedure;
~ 在運行過程中 on the fly;
運行情況 operational aspect;
運行軟件 runtime software;
運行時間 running time;

運行域 execution domain;
運行周期 period of runtime;
安全運行 running safely;

[運營] (1) put into operation; (2) in operation;
運營成本 operation cost;
運營條件 operating conditions;

[運用] apply; employ; exercise; make use of; put to use; utilize;
運用才能 utilize one's abilities;
運用常識 exercise one's common sense;
運用機敏 exercise one's tact;
運用判斷力 exercise one's judgement;
運用權力 exercise one's power; use one's power; wield one's authority;
運用忍耐力 exercise one's patience;
運用想像力 exercise one's imagination;
運用意志力 exercise one's willpower;
運用之妙，存乎一心 ingenuity in applying tactics depends on hard thinking; ingenuity in varying tactics depends on mother wit;
運用資本 working capital;
運用自如 grasp and apply skilfully; handle with great skill and perfect ease; have a perfect mastery of; use with facility;

[運載] carry;
運載方法 means of delivery;
運載工具 carrier;
運載火箭 carrier rocket;
運載貨物 carry a cargo;
運載技術 delivery technique;

[運轉] (1) revolve; turn round; (2) operate; run; travel; work;
運轉能力 running ability;
運轉速度 operational speed;
運轉周期 cycle of operation;
運轉自如 go slick; run slick;
安全運轉 safe operation;
時來運轉 fortune is smiling; time has moved in one's favour;
正常運轉 operate properly;

[運作] running;
順暢運作 smooth running;

搬運 carry; transport;
包運 transport;
背運 unlucky;
駁運 transport by lighter;
財運 luck in making money;
漕運 transport grain by boat to the capital;
承運 undertake to transport;
晨運 morning calisthenics; morning exercises;
儲運 storage and transport;
倒運 out of luck;
盜運 illegal transport;
調運 allocate and transport;
厄運 adversity; misfortune;
惡運 bad luck; ill luck; misfortune;
噩運 bad luck;
販運 transport goods for sale;
工運 labour movement;
海運 ocean carriage; ocean shipping; sea transportation; transport by sea;
航運 shipping; transportation by water;
好運 a piece of luck; a stroke of luck; good luck;
河運 river transport;
紅運 good luck;
護運 ship sth under guard;
鴻運 good luck;
貨運 freight transport;
集運 gather together and transport;
交運 have a spell of good fortune;
禁運 embargo;
客運 passenger transport;
空運 air transport;
快運 express;
聯運 through traffic; through transport;
陸運 transport by car or train;
霉運 bad luck;
民運 civil transport;
命運 (1) destiny; fate; lot; (2) course of development;
農運 peasant movement;
盤運 carry; transport;
起運 start shipment;
啟運 start shipment;
氣運 destiny; fate;
搶運 race against time in sending out materials; rush delivery of goods;
清運 clean up and take away;
榷運 tax on transportation;
時運 fortune; luck;
輸運 transport; transportation;
水運 ship; transport by boat;
順運 with a lucky chance;
私運 smuggle;
偷運 secretly transport;
頹運 declining fortune;
托運 consign for shipment;
託運 consign; consign for shipment;
旺運 spell of good luck;
幸運 fortunate; good luck; lucky;

押運 escort in transportation;
應運 in response to the needs of the times;
載運 convey by a means of transport;
轉運 (1) convey; forward; transfer; tranship; transport; (2) have a change of luck; have a turn of luck; luck turns in one's favour;
裝運 load and transport;
撞大運 try one's luck;
走運 by good luck; devil's luck; fall on one's feet; have fortune on one's side; have good luck; have one's moments; in luck; land on one's feet; luck is on one's side; luck of the devil; luck out; lucky; lucky sb; on the gravy train; one's luck is in; play big luck; strike luck; touch luck; you never know your luck; what a stroke of luck;

yun
【熨】 iron clothes;
[熨斗] iron;
電熨斗 electric iron;
[熨平] iron;
[熨衣板] ironing board;

yun
【緼】 (1) loose hemp; old yarn; (2) chaotic; confused;
[緼袍] coarse clothing;
絪緼 (of mist) enshrouding;

yun
【醞】 (1) brew; ferment; (2) deliberate on; (3) wine;
[醞藉] cultivated and refined;
[醞釀] (1) brew; ferment; (2) begin to form;
醞釀起義 ferment an uprising;
醞釀騷亂 brew mischief; ferment trouble;
醞釀陰謀 brew a plot;
醞釀作亂 ferment trouble;

yun
【韻】 (1) harmony of sound; musical sound; sweet tone; (2) rhymes; (3) elegant; polished; refined; sophisticated; (4) vowels;
[韻腳] rhyme;
[韻律] prosody;
韻律意義 prosodic meaning;
[韻詩] rhymed poetry;
無韻詩 blank verse;
[韻事] (1) literary or artistic pursuits, ofen with pretense to good taste and refinement; (2) romantic affair;
風流韻事 love affair; romantic affair; romance;
[韻味] aroma; lasting appeal; lingering charm;
[韻文] literary composition in rhyme; rhymed composition; verse;
韻文翻譯 metrical translation;
[韻語] (1) rhymed sentences; (2) refined remark;
步韻 rhyme;
詞韻 rhyme of prose-poetry;
次韻 use the rhyme sequence of a poem;
疊韻 rhyming binomes;
豐韻 charming appearance or carriage; graceful poise;
風韻 charm; graceful bearing;
氣韻 artistic conception; tone of a work;
神韻 romantic charm;
詩韻 rhyme in poetry;
押韻 rhyme;
音韻 rhyme;
餘韻 lingering charm;
字韻 rhyme of a character;

yun
【轀】 (1) collect; gather; (2) have in store; hold in store; store; (3) deep; profound; (4) sultry; sweltering;

yun
【蘊】 accumulate; contain;
[蘊藏] contain; have in store; hold in store;
蘊藏巨大潛力 have enormous potentialities;
[蘊含] contain; include;
[蘊涵] (1) contain; (2) implication;
互蘊涵 mutual implication;
實質蘊涵 material implication;
形式蘊涵 formal implication;
嚴格蘊涵 strict implication;
[蘊藉] cultured and restrained; refined and cultivated; temperate and refined;
風流蘊藉 graceful but not showy; urbanely charming;
[蘊結] pent-up; restrained;
[蘊蓄] have in store; latent; lie hidden and undeveloped;
[蘊蘊] sultry; sweltering;
底蘊 details; inner secret;

za¹

za

【匝】 circle; encompass; make a revolution round;
［匝道橋］ ramp;
［匝地］ all over the ground; everywhere;
［匝月］ full month;

密密匝匝 dense; thick;
密匝匝 dense; thick;

za

【咂】 sip; suck; take in food with the tongue;
［咂乾］ suck dry;
［咂摸］ meditate on; ponder; think over;
［咂嘴］ click the tongue; make clicks of praise;
咂嘴弄舌 make clicks of admiration; purse one's lips; smack one's lips;

za

【拶】 press; squeeze;
［拶指］ finger-squeezing torture;

za

【紮】 bind; fasten; tie;
［紮好］ bind together; tie up;
［紮緊］ fasten securely; tighten;
［紮營］ encamp; pitch tents;

包紮 bind up; dress; pack; pack up; wrap up;
結紮 ligate;
捆紮 bundle up; tie up;
屯紮 be stationed; encamp;

za²

za

【砸】 (1) break; crash and break; knock; pound; smash; squash; stamp; (2) bungled; fail; fall through; (3) beat to a pulp; mash;
［砸鍋］ break up a relationship;
［砸爛］ crush to a mash;
［砸了］ (1) knock and break; (2) bungle; busted; fail;
［砸傷］ be injured by a crashing object;
［砸死］ be crushed to death;
［砸碎］ break into pieces; shatter; smash;

za

【雜】 (1) miscellaneous; mixed; sundry; (2) blend; mingle; mix; (3) medley; motley; (4) petty and numerous;
［雜八湊兒］ collection of varied things; motley of different things; odds and ends;
［雜布］ coarse cloth;
［雜草］ hogweed; rank grass; weed;
雜草叢生 be overgrown with weeds; the weeds run riot; weeds spring up;
拔除雜草 pull up weeds; weed out the rank grass;
除盡雜草 extirpate weeds; pull up weeds by the roots;
除雜草 clear away weeds; weed;
多年生雜草 perennial weed;
根除雜草 pull up weeds;
水生雜草 aquatic weed;
有害雜草 injurious weed;
［雜處］ live together;
五方雜處 have a mixed population; inhabited by people from all regions; where people from all regions congregate;
［雜湊］ knock together; odds and ends;
［雜沓］ confused; disorderly;
［雜費］ (1) incidental expenses; incidentals; (2) miscellaneous fees; sundry charges; sundry fees;
雜費賬 petty expenses account;
［雜感］ (1) rambling observations; random thoughts; (2) a type of literature recording random thoughts;
［雜工］ backman; handyman;
［雜燴］ (1) hotchpotch; mixed stew; (2) combo; hotchpotch; medley; miscellany; mixture;
吃雜燴 have hotchpotch;
大雜燴 hotch potch; mishmash;
做雜燴 prepare hotchpotch;
［雜婚］ intermarriage;
［雜活］ odd jobs;
［雜貨］ groceries; sundry goods;
雜貨店 corner drugstore; general store; grocery; grocery store; sundry store;
~ 廉價雜貨店 dime store;
~ 食品雜貨店 grocery;
雜貨商 sundriesman;
日用雜貨 various household supplies;
食品雜貨 grocery;
［雜技］ acrobatics;
雜技般的 acrobatic;

雜技表演 acrobatic performance;
雜技團 acrobatic troupe;
雜技晚會 soiree acrobatics;
雜技演員 acrobat;
表演雜技 do acrobatics; perform acrobatics;

[雜記] (1) jottings; notes; (2) miscellanies;

[雜交] cross breeding; crossing; hybridization;
雜交分子 hybrid molecule;
雜交結合力 crossability;
雜交物種 hybrid species;
分子雜交 molecular hybridization;
複合雜交 composite crossing;
混精雜交 heterosperminous hybridization;
嫁接雜交 graft hybridization;
逆代雜交 backcross;
強迫雜交 compulsory crossing;
人工雜交 artificial crossing; artificial hybridization;
屬間雜交 intergeneric hybridization;
無性雜交 asexual hybridization;
相反雜交 reciprocal crossing;
營養雜交 vegetative hybridization;
有性雜交 sexual hybridization;
遠緣雜交 distant hybridization;
種間雜交 intervarietal crossing;

[雜居] live together;

[雜劇] comedy; farce; variety show;

[雜勞] chronic disease of the elderly people;

[雜糧] coarse cereals;

[雜亂] confused and disorderly; disorder; hugger-mugger; in a jumble; in a muddle; jumbled; mixed and disorderly; mussiness;
雜亂不堪 all in a jumble; all in tumble; in unbearable confusion;
雜亂無章 all in a mess; all in a muddle; all in confusion; all in tumble; any old how; anyway; chaotic; confused and disorderly; disorderly; disorderly and unsystematic; disorganized; every which way; hurrah's nest; in a great mess; in a state of confusion; in complete shambles; in the rough; in utter confusion; in utter disorder; motley; out of joint; out of order; out of trim; rough-and-tumble; welter; without order or logical connection; without pattern or order;
很雜亂 in a jumble; in a mess;
雜而不亂 mixed but not confused;

[雜念] distracting thoughts;
雜念重重 be preoccupied by distracting thoughts;
滿腦子雜念 be preoccupied with distracting thoughts;
排除雜念 banish distracting thoughts; dismiss distracting thoughts;
有雜念 have distracting thoughts;

[雜牌] less known and inferior brand;
雜牌產品 inferior products;
雜牌貨 goods of an inferior and less known brand;
雜牌軍 troops of miscellaneous brands;

[雜品] groceries; sundry goods;

[雜評] short commentary;

[雜然] all; unanimously;

[雜色] motley; variegated;

[雜耍] juggle; juggler's feats; variety show;
雜耍表演者 juggler;
玩雜耍 juggle; perform acrobatics;
~玩雜耍的人 juggler;

[雜稅] irregular taxes; miscellaneous taxes;

[雜談] chat; rambling talk; random talk; tittle-tattle;

[雜文] essay;

[雜務] chores; miscellaneous duties; odd jobs; sundry duties;
雜務羈身 be detained by odd jobs; be fully occupied with sundry duties;
雜務工 dogsbody;
處理雜務 handle sundry duties;
幹雜務 do odd jobs;
家庭雜務 chore;

[雜物] miscellaneous items; odds and ends;
雜物間 lumber room;
雜物室 box room;
雜物箱 glove compartment;
零星雜物 odds and ends;

[雜項] miscellaneous items; sundry;
雜項費用 miscellaneous expenses;

[雜音] (1) noise; (2) murmur; (3) static;
心臟雜音 heart murmur;

[雜質] impurity;
除去雜質 remove impurities;
含有雜質 contain impurities;
兩性雜質 amphoteric impurity;
清除雜質 eliminate impurity;
受主雜質 acceptor impurity;
陽極雜質 anodic impurity;

[雜誌] journal; magazine; periodical;
辦雜誌 run a magazine;
編輯雜誌 edit a magazine;
創辦雜誌 found a magazine;
電子雜誌 e-zine;
訂閱雜誌 subscribe to a magazine;
翻翻雜誌 look through a magazine;
翻雜誌 flick through the pages of a magazine; thumb through the pages of a magazine;
黃色雜誌 naughty magazine;
瀏覽雜誌 skim through a magazine;
色情雜誌 raunchy magazine;
停訂雜誌 discontinue one's subscription to a magazine;
網絡雜誌 webzine;
文藝雜誌 literary magazine;
續訂雜誌 renew one's subscription to a magazine;
一本雜誌 a magazine;
一疊雜誌 a stack of magazines;
一捆雜誌 a bundle of magazines;
預訂雜誌 subscribe to a magazine;

[雜種] (1) crossbreed; hybrid; (2) bastard; son of a bitch;
雜種動物 crossbreed;
雜種狗 mongrel dog; mutt;
雜種後代 descendent of hybrid; offspring of hybrid;
雜種羊 cross-bred sheep;
雜種優勢 heterosis;
單性雜種 unisexual hybrid;
定型雜種 constant hybrid;
反交雜種 reciprocal hybrid;
狗雜種 cocksucker;
居間雜種 intermediate hybrid;
兩性雜種 bisexual hybrid;
雙核雜種 dikaryotic hybrid;
衍生雜種 derivative hybrid;
遠緣雜種 distant hybrid;

駁雜 heterogeneous; mixed;
嘈雜 clamorous; full of confused noises; noisy and confused;
摻雜 mingle; mix;
羼雜 mingle; mix;
叢雜 motley;
錯雜 jumbled; mixed;
打雜 do odds and ends; fix up odds and ends; serve as a handyman;
繁雜 many and various; miscellaneous;
複雜 complex; complicated;
混雜 mingle; mix;
雞雜 chicken giblets;
夾雜 be mingled with; be mixed up with;
間雜 be intermingled; be mixed;
苛雜 exorbitant taxes and levies;
拉雜 ill-organized; rambling;
亂雜 confused; mixed and disorderly;
猱雜 noisily and cynically;
龐雜 in a cumbersome jumble; multifarious and disorderly; numerous and jumbled;
勤雜 odd job;
秋雜 autumn sundries;
冗雜 confused; disorderly; lengthy and jumbled; many and diverse; miscellaneous; mixed up;
揉雜 mixed-up;
沓雜 confused; crowded and mixed;
猥雜 numerous and varied;
蕪雜 in a jumble; miscellaneous; mixed and disorderly;
閒雜 without a fixed job;
淆雜 mingle; mix;
殽雜 disorderly; messy;

za⁵
za

【臢】 dirty; filthy;

zai¹
zai

【災】 (1) calamity; disaster; (2) adversity; personal misfortune;

[災變] catastrophe; disaster;
初等災變 elementary catastrophe;
紅外災變 infrared catastrophe;
極化災變 polarizability catastrophe;
紫外災變 ultraviolet catastrophe;

[災害] calamities; damages; disasters; fatalities;
災害經濟學 economics of catastrophe;
災害救濟 calamity relief;
災害社會學 sociology of calamity;
災害學 calamitics;
防止災害 prevent disasters;
自然災害 natural calamity;

[災患] calamities; disasters;
屢經災患 suffer calamity after calamity;

[災荒] famine caused by floods or droughts;
鬧災荒 suffer from famine;
引起災荒 cause famine;

[災禍] calamities; catastrophes; disasters;
災禍臨頭 a great disaster is befalling; a

great disaster is imminent;
避開災禍 avert disaster;
接二連三的災禍 a chapter of accidents;
幸災樂禍 chuckle at sb's discomfiture; crow over; delight in the misfortunes of others; derive pleasure from others' misfortune; exult at the misfortune of others; exult in the misfortune of others; exult over the misfortune of others; exult when another meets with mischance; glad when other people are in difficulties; gloat over others' misfortune; laugh at others' troubles; make game of others' calamities; make merry over another's mishap; mock at others' woes; rejoice in the misfortunes of others; Roman holiday; schadenfreude; take pleasure in the calamity of others; take pleasure from the misfortune of others;
引災惹禍 court disaster; invite trouble;
災梨禍棗 book which is poorly written and not worth reading;
災連禍結 succession of disasters;
招致災禍 court disaster; invite disaster;

[災黎] refugees created by disasters;
災黎遍野 the land is filled with disaster-stricken refugees;
遍地災黎 famine-stricken people are found everywhere;
存慰災黎 visit and console the calamity-stricken people;

[災民] victims of a natural calamity;

[災難] calamity; catastrophe; disaster; suffering;
災難深重 bitterest suffering; calamity-ridden; disaster-ridden; woe-stricken;
災難性後果 disastrous consequences;
避開災難 avert a calamity;
避免災難 averta a calamity;
大災難 holocaust;
帶來災難 bring disaster;
多災多難 always dogged by misfortunes; be dogged by bad luck; be dogged with misfortunes and mishaps; be plagued by frequent ills; calamitous; come upon a series of misfortunes; ill-starred; suffer a chapter of accidents;
躲災避難 avoid the coming trouble; escape with one's life and hide from danger; hide somewhere until the evil is past;
防止災難 against any misfortune;
民族災難 national disaster;
三災八難 have one trouble after another; suffer from one ailment after another; numerous adversities and calamities; various illnesses and ailments;
一場災難 a disaster;
一災生百難 of one ill comes many;
戰爭災難 war calamity;
招致災難 court disaster; invite disaster;

[災情] condition of a disaster;
災情勘查車 disaster perambulator car;
災情嚴重 losses caused by the disaster are serious;

[災區] disaster area; distress area;
支援災區 provide relief to disaster-stricken areas;

[災殃] calamity; disaster; suffering;

雹災 disaster caused by hail;
成災 cause disaster;
蟲災 plague of insects;
防災 take precautions against natural calamities;
飛災 unexpected disaster;
風災 disaster caused by a windstorm;
旱災 drought;
洪災 flood;
蝗災 plague of locusts;
回祿之災 fire disaster;
火災 fire;
救災 provide disaster relief;
澇災 damage caused by waterlogging;
鬧災 suffer from natural disasters;
受災 be hit by a natural adversity;
水災 flood;
天災 natural disaster;
消災 remove ill fortune;
妖災 calamities and prodigious things;
遭災 by hit by a natural calamity; encounter disaster;
招災 bring disasters upon oneself; invite disasters;
賑災 relieve the people in stricken areas;
震災 disaster caused by an earthquake;

zai

【哉】 phrase-final particle expressing emotions;

zai

【栽】 (1) grow; plant; (2) insert; plant; stick; (3) assist; care; (4) force sth on

sb; impose; (5) fail; fall; tumble;
［栽倒］ fall down;
［栽跟頭］ come a cropper; fall over; suffer a setback; trip up; tumble;
［栽排］ make arrangements for;
［栽培］ (1) plant and cultivate; tend; (2) educate; foster; train; (3) give special favour; receive special favour;
栽培群落 agrium;
栽培人才 cultivate and nourish talent;
暖房栽培 hothouse cultivation;
人工栽培 artificial cultivation;
無土栽培 soilless cultivation;
［栽贓］ (1) plant stolen goods on sb; (2) fabricate a charge against sb; frame sb;
栽贓嫁禍 fabricate a charge against sb; plant stolen goods on sb and put the blame the sb;
栽贓誣害 incriminate sb with planted evidence; place stolen goods on sb to implicate him; plant a stolen article with sb else in order to frame him;
［栽植］ plant; raise; transplant;
［栽種］ grow; plant;
［栽子］ seedlings; young plants;

輪栽 crop rotation;
盆栽 pot culture;
移栽 transplant;

zai
【菑】 same as 災, calamity; disaster, misfortune;

zai³
zai
【宰】 (1) butcher; kill; slaughter; (2) govern; preside; rule; (3) a surname;
［宰輔］ premier; prime minister;
宰輔之量 the capacity to serve as prime minister;
宰輔之職 the office of a premier;
［宰割］ invade; oppress and exploit;
［宰木］ trees around a grave;
［宰牛］ slaughter a cow;
［宰肉］ chop meat; cut up meat;
［宰殺］ butcher; kill; slaughter;
［宰物］ able to manage affairs;
［宰相］ prime minister;
宰相肚裏能撐船 a prime minister's heart is big enough to pole a boat in — a great person should be large-minded; a prime minister's mind should be broad enough for poling a boat — a great man is broad-minded and magnanimous; eagles catch no flies;
宰相之才 talent with the ability to rule the country;
宰相之器 potentialities to be a prime minister;
［宰制］ dominate; rule;

挨宰 be done for; be ripped off;
屠宰 butcher; slaughter;
主宰 dominate; dictate;

zai
【崽】 (1) son; (2) whelp; young animal;
［崽子］ bastard; son of a bitch; whelp;
狼崽子 greedy and cold-blooded; ingrate;

西崽 man servant;

zai
【載】 year;

半載 half a year; six months;

zai⁴
zai
【再】 (1) again; once more; repeated; (2) before; further; still; then; (3) come back; return;
［再拜］ bow twice;
［再版］ (1) second edition; (2) reprint; second impression;
［再不］ never again; or; or else;
再也不 never again;
［再次］ once again; once more; second time;
［再度］ once again; once more; second time;
再度當選 be re-elected;
再度流行 come back;
［再發］ have a relapse;
［再犯］ (1) repeat an offense; (2) second-time offender;
再犯不赦 repeated offenders are unpardonable;
［再會］ goodbye; see you again;
［再婚］ marry again; remarriage; remarry;
［再加］ besides; in addition; on top of that;
［再嫁］ remarry;
［再見］ adieu; adios; bye; bye-bye; cheerio;

Z

ciao; good day to you; goodbye; have a nice day; laters; see you; see you again; see you around; so long;

[再來] (1) come again; stop back; (2) request for a repetition;
重新再來 all over again; back to square one;
過一會再來 stop back;

[再起] (1) recur; revive; rise again; stage a comeback; (2) assume public office again;
東山再起 back on the rails; bob up like a cork; make a comeback; return to a previous stage; rise from one's ashes; stage a comeback;

[再熱] reheat;

[再三] again and again; over and over again; repeatedly; time and again;
再三拜謝 bow many times and thank someone again and again;
再三煩擾 in one's wool;
再三考慮 consider over and over;
再三思維 give a matter careful thought; ponder carefully over; think it over again and again;
再三推辭 decline again and again;
再三挽留 press sb to stay; repeatedly urge sb to stay;
再三再四 again and again; many and many times; over and over again; repeatedly; time after time; time again; time and time again; twenty and twenty times;
再三斟酌 consider carefully again and again;
再三囑咐 bid again and again; bid time after time; din into sb's ear; exhort again and again; exhort time after time; tell again and again; tell time after time;
至再至三 repeatedly; twice and thrice;

[再生] (1) second so-and-so; (2) regenerate; regeneration;
再生父母 one's great benefactor; one's second parents;
再生器 actifier; regenerator;
~ 脈衝再生器 impulse regenerator;
~ 數字再生器 digital regenerator;
再生之德 the grace of rebirth — one's grateful acknowledgement;
再生資源 renewable resources;
再生作用 palingenesis;
白土再生 clay regeneration;
化學再生 chemical regeneration;
人工再生 artificial regeneration;
新性再生 cenogenetic regeneration;
資源再生 resource regeneration;

[再世] rebirth;
華陀再世 rebirth of the great doctor Hua Tuo;

[再說] (1) put off (2) besides; furthermore; what is more; (3) please repeat;
再說一遍 didn't catch it; didn't quite hear; I beg your pardon; miss; repeat; say it again;

[再思而後行] second thoughts are best;

[再現] be reproduced; playback; reappear; recover; recur; rendition;
彩色再現 chromatic rendition; colour rendition;
灰度再現 gray-scale rendition;

[再議] discuss sth later; talk about sth again;

[再再] again and again; repeatedly; time and again;
再接再勵 advance from strength to strength; continue to exert oneself; forge ahead in disregard of obstructions; make persistent efforts; redouble one's efforts; work ceaselessly and unremitting; with ever-renewed efforts; with reanimated courage;

[再造] born a second time; give sb a new lease on life;
恩同再造 a favour tantamount to giving sb a new lease of life; as merciful as if one had rebuilt sb's character; one's goodness has made sb a new person;

[再則] besides; moreover;

[再者] besides; by way of a postscript; furthermore; in addition; moreover;

[再作馮婦] back to the salt mines; do sth which one has done before; take on a risky, difficult job again; take one's old job again;

不再 not any more; no longer;
一再 again and again; over and over; repeatedly; time and again;

zai

【在】 (1) at; in; on; up to; (2) alive; exist;

living; present; (3) join or belong to an organization; member of an organization; (4) consist in; depend on; rest with;

[在案] (1) on record; (2) on the police record;

[在幫] member of a secret society;

[在場] on the scene; on the spot; present;
不在場 absent from the scene;
當時沒人在場 no one was on the scene at the time;

[在處] everywhere;

[在此] here;
在此情況下 in the circumstances; under the circumstances;
在此一舉 depend upon this one movement; hang upon this single action;
志不在此 have an ambition for things beyond what is presently available;

[在公] (1) as part of one's duty; (2) for the sake of the public; officially;

[在行] an expert at sth; in the know; in the trade; know sth well; know the A to Z of sth; know the ropes; professional;
很在行 up one's alley;

[在後] as follows; behind; later;

[在乎] (1) care; care about; mind; take to heart; (2) consist in; depend on; lie in; rest with;
不在乎 not care;
~不在乎地 airily;
~毫不在乎 completely unperturbed; like it's going out of style; make nothing of; not care a bean; not care a bit; not care a cuss; not care a hang; not care a pin; not care a row of beans; not care a stiver; not care a snap; not care at all; not give a damn; not give a snap; not mind at all; think little of; without the slightest compunction;
~滿不在乎 as if nothing has happened; give no heed; make nothing of; not care a curse; not care a pin; not care a rap; not care a rush; not care in the least; not give a damn; not give a rush for; not worry at all; totally unconcerned;
滿不在乎的 cavalier; devil-may-care;
對名利滿不在乎 not care in the least about one's fame and gain;
裝作滿不在乎 pretend not to worry at all;

[在即] imminent; near at hand; shortly; soon;
成功在即 the success is in sight;
考試在即 the examination is near at hand;
完工在即 will complete the work soon;

[在家] (1) at home; in; (2) remain a layman;
在家辦公的人 homeworker;
在家不會迎賓客，出外方知少主人 if one does not receive guests at home, one will meet with few hosts abroad;
在家出家 practise Buddhism at home;
在家靠父母，出門靠朋友 one depends upon one's parents at home and upon one's friends abroad; at home one relies on one's parents and outside on one's friends;
在家納福 enjoy the blessings of life at home;
在家千日好 dry bread at home is better than roast meat abroad; home is home be it never so homely; home is home though it be never so homely;
~在家千日好，出門一朝難 east or west, home is best; it is good to stay at home a year and hard to be away from home an hour; there is no place like home;
在家人 layman;
不在家 out;

[在假] on leave;

[在劫難逃] if you are doomed, you are doomed; impossible to escape one's doom; there is no escape from one's fate; what is destine cannot be avoided;

[在疚] in mourning;

[在理] reasonable; right; sensible;
說的話在理 reasonable statement;
要求在理 reasonable in one's demand;

[在內] consist in; include; inclusive; inside;

[在前] ahead; before; beforehand; in front;

[在上] on high;
高高在上 be far removed from the masses and reality; consider oneself superior; high up in the air; hold oneself aloft from the masses; live in the clouds; remote from masses; ride the high horse; set oneself high above the masses; sit high up in the clouds; sit up high in a leading position; sit up on high; stand high above the masses; stand upon one's pantofles; very lofty;

[在室] (said of girls) still unmarried;

[在世] above ground; alive; in this world; living;

[在事] hold a position; in charge of;

[在所] will;
在所不辭 will not decline under all circumstances; will not flinch; will not hesitate to; will not refuse under any circumstances;
在所不計 irrespective of;
在所不究 forgivable; will not be prosecuted;
在所不免 inevitable; natural; unavoidable;
在所不惜 regardless of the cost; will never balk at; will not grudge;
在所難免 can hardly be avoided; impossible to be avoided; scarcely avoidable; unavoidable;

[在逃] at large; on the loose; on the run;

[在外] excluding; not including; outside;
在外地主 absentee landlord;
在外房東 absentee landlord;
在外用餐 dine out;
淹卹在外 live in exile;

[在望] (1) in sight; in view; visible; (2) in the offing;
和平在望 peace is in sight;
勝利在望 victory is in view;

[在位] in power; in the position; on the throne; reign;
在其位，謀其政 being at the post, one will worry about any matter concerned therewith;

[在握] in one's hands; under one's control; within one's grasp;
大權在握 get one's hands on power; hold real power in one's hand;
勝券在握 have the game in one's hand;
勝利在握 success is within one's grasp;
智珠在握 hold the pearl of wisdom — cope with all matters with schemes and strategies;

[在昔] formerly; in former times; once upon a time;

[在下] I; my humble self;

[在先] ahead; at that time; before; beforehand; formerly; in the past;
有例在先 there are precedents for that;
有言在先 forewarn; let sth be clearly understood; make sth clear beforehand;
有約在先 have a previous engagement;

[在線] online;
在線翻譯 online translation;
~ 在線翻譯系統 online translation system;
在線實時處理 online real time processing;

[在鄉隨鄉] do in Rome as the Romans do; in a strange land, do as the natives do; when in Rome, do as the Romans do;

[在心] attentive; feel concerned; keep in mind; mind;
懷恨在心 be full of rancour against sb; bear sb a grudge; bear sb a spite; cherish a secret resentment against; entertain a feeling against; harbour a grudge against; harbour resentment in one's heart; have a spite against; have resentment rankling on one's mind; nurse rancour against;
永記在心 remain forever in one's heart and spirit;

[在學] at school;

[在押] being imprisoned; under detention;

[在…言…] from the perspective of;
在官言官 from the strictly official point of view;
在商言商 to a businessman, profit comes first;

[在野] (1) hold no official position; out of power; (2) in opposition;
在野黨 opposition party;

[在意] care about; mind; take notice of; take to heart;
在意分數 take one's marks to heart;
在意錢 care about money;
別在意 forget it;
不在意 (1) could not care less; not care; not care a damn; pay no attention to; (2) careless; negligent;
~ 不在意的 blithe;
毫不在意 not care a bit; not care a dump; not care a rap; not care a whoop;
沒在意 not notice sth / sb;

[在於] (1) consist in; lie in; rest with; (2) be determined by; depend on;

[在在] everywhere; in all aspects;
在在皆是 can be seen everywhere;

[在職] at one's post; hold a position; in-service; on the job;
在職短期課程 in-service short course;

Z

在職教育 in-service education;
~ 在職教育工作者 in-service educator;
在職進修 in-service education; in-service training; on-the-job training;
在職考取的學位 in-service degree;
在職培訓 in-service training; on-the-job training;
~ 在職培訓課程 in-service development course;
在職期間 during one's tenure of office;
在職學習 in-service learning;
在職訓練 in-service training;
在職研究生 on-the job research student;
在職語文進修課程 in-service language improvement course;

[在座] present;

不在 be away;
存在 exist; existence;
好在 fortunately; luckily;
何在 where;
健在 still living and in good health;
內在 inherent; internal;
潛在 latent; potential;
實在 (1) real; true; (2) dependable; honest;
所在 cation; place;
外在 external; extrinsic;
閒在 idle; quiet and comfortable;
現在 at once; at present; at the moment; for the moment; immediately; now; nowadays; of the moment; presently; right now;
早在 as far back as;
站在 standing;
正在 in course of; in process of;
旨在 with the intention of;
自在 free; unrestrained;

zai

【載】 (1) be loaded with; carry; load; (2) publish; record; (3) fill; (4) all over the road; everywhere along the way; (5) and; as well as; at the same time;

[載波] carrier;
副載波 subcarrier;
~ 伴音副載波 audio subcarrier;
~ 彩色副載波 colour subcarrier;
~ 色度副載波 chrominance subcarrier;

[載道] (1) fill the streets; (2) convey principles;
頌聲載道 praises all along the way;
文以載道 writings are for conveying truth;

[載福] enjoy happiness; receive blessings;

[載荷] load; loading;
單位載荷 specific loading;
動力載荷 dynamic loading;
加速載荷 accelerating load;
吸收載荷 absorption load;
有效載荷 payload;
~ 容量有效載荷 capacity payload;
~ 設計有效載荷 design payload;
~ 實驗有效載荷 experimental payload;
最大載荷 payload;

[載貨] carry cargo; carry freight; carry goods;
載貨搭客 carry goods and passengers;

[載籍] books;

[載酒問字] studious and inquisitive;

[載客] carry passengers;

[載量] carrying capacity;
安全載量 safety carrying capacity;

[載流子] carrier;
多數載流子 majority carrier;
少數載流子 minority carrier;

[載明] record clearly;

[載人] manned;
載人飛船 manned spacecraft;
載人航天器 manned space vehicle;
載人空間站 manned space station;

[載體] carrier;
催化載體 catalytic carrier;
電荷載體 charge carrier;
電子載體 electron carrier;
活化載體 activated carrier;
晶片載體 chip carrier;
鏈鎖載體 chain carrier;
數據載體 data carrier;
陶瓷載體 ceramic carrier;
遺傳性載體 genetic carrier;
遺傳載體 genetic carrier;

[載譽歸來] come back winning high praise; return home winning high praise;

[載運] carry; transport;

[載…載…] sometimes...sometimes...;
載馳載驅 darting and dashing;
載飛載止 flying awhile, alighting to rest awhile;
載笑載言 talk and laugh at the same time;
載舟覆舟 the water that bears the boat is the same that swallows it;
~ 水可載舟，亦可覆舟 fire and water are good servants, but bad masters; one knife cuts both my bread and my fingers; the same knife cuts bread and fingers; the water that bears the boat is

the same that swallows it;
~水能載舟，亦能覆舟 the same knife cuts bread and fingers; the water that bears the boat is the same that swallows it;

[載重] carrying capacity;

半載 half load;
駁載 barge transport;
承載 bear the weight of;
搭載 carry;
登載 carry; publish;
附載 take subsidiary notes;
負載 load; loading;
過載 overload;
貨載 transport a cargo;
記載 account; record; write down;
刊載 publish;
連載 publish in instalments;
滿載 fully loaded with; loaded to capacity;
馱載 carry a load on the back;
壓載 ship's ballast;
運載 deliver;
重載 freight; heavy-duty;
轉載 (1) transfer; transport; (2) reprint;
裝載 load;

Z

zan¹

zan

【簪】 (1) hair clip; (2) hairpin for women; (3) stick in the hair; wear;

[簪花] stick a flower on one's cap; wear a flower;
簪花妙筆 graceful style of handwriting;
簪花弄媚 wearing flowers in the hair and making eyes at sb;

[簪子] woman's hairpin;

玉簪 jade hairpin;

zan²

zan

【咱】 (1) we; (2) I; me

[咱們] we; you and I;

zan³

zan

【拶】 torture device in ancient China;

[拶子] sticks for squeezing a person's fingers;

zan

【昝】 a surname;

zan

【揝】 save money;

[揝錢] save money; save up;

zan

【攢】 accumulate; hoard; save;

[攢錢] hoard money; save money;

積攢 save bit by bit;

zan

【趲】 (1) hasten; hurry; rush through; (2) urge; (3) save money;

[趲程] hurry in a journey;
[趲路] hurry in a journey; journey hurriedly;
[趲行] hurry in a journey; travel hurriedly;
[趲造] build with haste;
[趲足] savings;

zan⁴

zan

【贊】 (1) aid; assist; back; help; support; (2) commend; eulogize; exalt; extol; glorify; praise;

[贊成] accede; agree on; agree to; agree with; all for; approve of; assent; be reconciled to; comply; concur; consent to; endorse; favour; give sth a nod; go all the way with sb; go along with sb; hold with; in agreement with; in favour of; see eye to eye with sb; subscribe to;
贊成票 affirmative vote;
~互投贊成票 logrolling;
不贊成 take a dim view of;
舉手贊成 approve sth with a show of hands;
拍手贊成 clap one's hands in approval;
全部投票贊成 all the votes are in the affirmative;
雙手贊成 all for it; raise both hands in approval; support fully;

[贊理] help manage;
[贊美] exalt; extol; glorify; praise;
[贊佩] admire; esteem;
[贊賞] admire; commend; extol; praise;
[贊頌] extol; eulogize; praise; sing the praises of;
[贊歎] exclaim in praise; gasp with admiration;
[贊同] agree with; approve of; be all for; consent to; countenance; endorse; go along with;
暗示贊同 imply assent;

得到贊同 win acceptance with;
點頭贊同 nod in approval; nod in consent;
恕我不能贊同 I beg to disagree;
完全贊同 all for;

[贊許] approve of;
[贊揚] commend; exalt; extol; glorify; praise;
[贊語] praises; words of praise;
[贊助] donate money; patronize; sponsor; support;
贊助計劃 supporting programme;
贊助人 patron; sponsor;
~女贊助人 patroness;
贊助者 backer;
提供贊助 provide assistance;

參贊 counsellor;

zan

【暫】 a pronunciation of 暫;

短暫 brief; of short duration;

zan

【鏨】 (1) chisel; chiseling; (2) carve; chisel; engrave;

[鏨刀] chisel; graver;
[鏨子] chisel;
[鏨字] engrave characters;

扁頭鏨 bolt chisel;
扁鏨 firmer chisel;
角鏨 cold chisel;
冷鏨 bench chisel; cold chisel;
套柄鏨 cocket chisel;
中心鏨 centre chisel;

zan

【酇】 (1) a community of a hundred families during the Zhou Dynasty; (2) a feudal state in the Han Dynasty;

zan

【讚】 (1) applaud; commend; eulogize; laud; praise; (2) same as 贊;

[讚詞] words of praise;
[讚歌] song of praise;
[讚禮] master of ceremonies;
[讚美] compliment; eulogize; extol; glorify; laud; praise;
讚美不盡 appreciate sth without stopping; beyond praise;
讚美詩 canticle;
極大的讚美 great compliment;
接受讚美 accept a compliment;
求讚美 fish for compliments;

[讚佩] admire; esteem; think highly of;
[讚賞] admire; appreciate; commend; praise;
擊節讚賞 clap and applaud; clap one's hands in admiration; clap the hands in applause;
深受讚賞 be received with much appreciation;

[讚頌] eulogize; extol; sing the praises of;
[讚歎] gasp in admiration; highly praise;
讚歎不已 praise again and again; sing sb's praise without ceasing;
讚歎太息 praise and sigh with admiration;
博得觀眾的讚歎 evoke the admiration of the audience;
發出讚歎 utter admiration;

[讚許] commend; give a high appraisal to; loud in the praise of; make sb a compliment; pay high tribute to; praise; praise sb a compliment; praise sb up to the skies; set a high value on; sing sb's praises; sing the praise of; speak highly of; speak favourably of;
獲得讚許 win approval;
贏得讚許 call forth commendation;
值得讚許 deserve approval;

[讚揚] commend; full marks to sb; glorify; pat sb on the back; pay a tribute to; praise; speak highly of;
讚揚性形容詞 commendatory adjective;
大加讚揚 lavish praise on; praise highly;
受到高度讚揚 be highly commended;
值得讚揚[的] creditable;

[讚仰] regard with admiration and respect;
[讚語] praise; words of praise;
[讚譽] commend; praise;
表現值得讚譽 creditable performance;
最高讚譽 highest compliment;

稱讚 acclaim; commend; commendation; compliment; pat sb on the back; praise; slap sb on the back;
誇讚 acclaim; praise; speak highly of;
評讚 estimate and praise;
盛讚 pay a high compliment to; profusely praise;
頌讚 acclaim; praise;
詠讚 sing the praises of;

zang¹

zang

【牂】 ewe;

［牂雲］ dog-shaped clouds;

［牂牂］ dense; thick;

zang

【贓】 (1) bribe; (2) booty; loot; plunder; stolen goods;

［贓官］ corrupt official;
酷吏贓官 cruel and greedy officials;

［贓款］ money acquired illicitly;

［贓埋］ accuse falsely; malign; slander;

［贓否］ pass judgement on people;
贓否人物 pass judgement on people;

［贓品］ booty; loot; plunder; stolen goods;

［贓物］ booty; loot; plunder; spoils; stolen goods;
藏起贓物 hide the booty;
買賣贓物 buy and sell spoils;
沒收贓物 confiscate the spoils;
轉移贓物 transfer spoils;

分贓 divide the spoils; share the booty; share the loot;
起贓 recover stolen articles; scrumming; track down and recover stolen goods;
貪贓 take bribes; practise graft;
退贓 give up ill-gotten gains;
窩贓 harbour stolen goods;
銷贓 dispose of stolen goods;
栽贓 bring a false charge against sb; frame sb;
賊贓 booty; spoils; stolen goods;
追贓 make sb disgorge the spoils; recover what has been stolen;

zang

【髒】 dirty; filthy;

［髒土］ dirty soil;

［髒痕］ streak of dirt;
一道髒痕 a streak of dirt;

［髒物］ foul;

［髒心］ dirty mind; impure heart;
髒心爛肺 dirty in character;

［髒字］ dirty word; obscene word; swearword;

骯髒 (1) dirty; filthy; (2) base; despicable;

zang

【臢】 dirty; filthy;

zang³

zang

【駔】 (1) strong horse; swift horse; (2) horse broker;

［駔儈］ broker;
駔儈佣金 broker's commission;

zang⁴

zang

【奘】 large; powerful; stout; thick;

［奘粗］ stout; thick;

［奘細］ thick and thin;

zang

【葬】 bury;

［葬地］ burial ground; grave;

［葬禮］ funeral service; funeral rites; obsequies;

［葬埋］ bury;

［葬身］ be buried;
葬身火海 be engulfed in a sea of flames;
葬身火窟 be buried in flames; become food for flames;
葬身異域 be buried in a foreign country; die in a foreign country;
葬身魚腹 be drowned; be swept to a watery grave; become food for fish; feed the fish; get drowned;
葬身之地 burial ground; come to a bad end;
~死無葬身之地 come to a bad end; die a graveless death; die and go unburied; die without a burial place;

［葬送］ bury; ruin; spell an end to;
葬送前途 ruin one's future;

［葬儀］ burial rites; funeral rites;

安葬 bury the dead; lay to rest;
殯葬 funeral and interment; hold a funeral procession and bury the dead;
國葬 state funeral;
海葬 sea burial;
火葬 cremate; cremation;
埋葬 bury; entomb;
墓葬 grave;
陪葬 be buried with the dead;
遷葬 move sb's grave to another place;
喪葬 conduct the funeral and handle the burial;
收葬 bury the dead;
送葬 attend a burial ceremony; take part in a funeral procession;
水葬 water burial;
隨葬 be buried with the dead;
天葬 celestial burial;
土葬 burial in the ground;
下葬 bury; committal;

Z

殉葬 be buried alive with the dead;

zang

【藏】 (1) depository; storage; storing place; warehouse; (2) Buddhist or Daoist scriptures; (3) Tibet;

[藏府] storage; warehouse;

[藏藍] reddish-blue colour;

[藏文] Tibetan language;

[藏語] Tibetan;

[藏族] Tibetan nationality;

寶藏 precious deposits;

道藏 Daoist sutra;

庫藏 warehouse;

釋藏 Buddhist sutra;

zang

【臟】 entrails; viscera;

[臟腑] (1) entrails; viscera; (2) one's integrity;

五臟六腑 entrails; internal organs of the body; viscera; vital organs of the human body;

[臟器] internal organs of the body; viscera;

[臟燥] hysteria;

脺臟 pancreas;

肺臟 lung;

肝臟 liver;

內臟 internal organs of the body; viscera;

脾臟 spleen;

腎臟 kidney;

心臟 (1) heart; (2) centre;

zao[1]

zao

【遭】 (1) incur; meet with; suffer; (2) (measure-word) round; (3) (measure-word) a time; a turn;

[遭變] be hit by a great misfortune; have an accident;

[遭到] encounter; meet with; suffer;

遭到反對 meet with opposition;

遭到拒絕 be turned down; meet with refusal;

遭到冷遇 meet with disfavour;

遭到失敗 suffer defeat;

遭到嚴重破壞 be seriously damaged;

[遭厄] meet with disaster;

[遭兒] (1) occasion; time; (2) complete turn; full circle;

[遭逢] (1) come across; encounter; meet with; (2) vicissitudes in one's life;

遭逢不幸 suffer misfortune;

遭逢際會 suffer a crisis;

遭逢盛世 live in prosperous times;

[遭害] be assassinated; be killed; be murdered;

[遭際] circumstances; one's lot in life;

[遭家不造] be bereaved of a parent; be bereaved of parents;

[遭劫] meet with disaster;

[遭難] meet with death; meet with difficulty; meet with misfortune;

[遭受] be subjected to; suffer; sustain;

遭受剥削 suffer exploitation;

遭受侮辱 be subjected to indignity;

遭受壓迫 be subjected to oppression;

遭受拆磨 be subjected to torture;

[遭殃] meet with disaster; meet with misfortune; set in the neck; suffer; suffer disaster;

[遭遇] (1) encounter; experience; meet with; run up against; (2) vicissitudes in one's life;

遭遇不幸 have hard luck; meet with misfortune;

遭遇敵人 encounter an enemy;

不幸遭遇 hard-luck story;

[遭災] by hit by a natural calamity; encounter disaster;

[遭罪] endure hardships; endure tortures; have a hard time; suffer;

周遭 about; around; round;

zao

【糟】 (1) distiller's grains; grains; be pickled with grain or in wine; (2) decayed; poor; rotten; spoiled; (3) in a mess; in a wretched state;

[糟糕] alas; damn it; good God; good gracious; good heavens; goodness gracious; great guns; hard lines; how terrible; my God; too bad; what a mess; what bad luck;

糟糕透頂 rotten all the way through; rotten to the core; worse than nothing;

更糟糕的是 to add insult to injury; to crown it all; to top it all;

[糟害] damage; make havoc of;

Z

[糟毀] damage by rough treatment;
[糟踐] (1) debase; degrade; ruin; waste; (2) insult; libel;
[糟糠] (1) distillers' grains; poor men's foodstuffs; (2) the wife one married in poverty;
糟糠夫妻 bread-and-cheese marriage; love in a cottage;
糟糠之妻 the wife one married in poverty; the woman married to a man before he became prosperous;
糟糠之妻不下堂 a wife who has shared her husband's hard lot must never be cast aside; a wife who shared poverty may not be divorced in time of comfort;
[糟爛] decayed; rotten; spoiled;
[糟了] alas; too bad;
[糟粕] (1) dregs of wine; (2) dregs; refuse; sth of little value;
去其糟粕，取其精華 discard the crude and select the refined;
[糟錢兒] fifthy lucre;
[糟擾] thanks for your hospitality;
[糟蹋] (1) debase; degrade; ruin; spoil; waste; (2) affront; insult; ravage; trample on; violate;
糟蹋糧食 waste grain;
[糟透了] how terrible; it is beastly bad; too bad; what a mess; what an awful nuisance;
[糟心] (1) annoyed; dejected; vexed; (2) unlucky; (3) get into a mess;

懊糟 upset; vexed;
搞糟 make a mess of; mess up;
酒糟 distillers' grains;
酵糟 fermented glutinous rice;
亂糟糟 (1) chaotic; in a mess; (2) confused; perturbed;
弄糟 make a mess of; spoil;
一團糟 in a mess;

zao
【蹧】 ruin; spoil;
[蹧蹋] ruin; spoil;

zao²
zao
【鑿】 (1) bore; chisel; wood-boring instrument; (2) bore through; chisel; pierce through; (3) actual; authentic; conclusive; indisputable; real; true; (4) polish rice; (5) forced interpretation;
[鑿洞] bore a hole; drill a hole;
[鑿井] dig a well; drill a well; sink a well;
[鑿開] bore through; cut open;
[鑿空] far-fetched; forced;
[鑿枘] incompatible;
鑿圓枘方 incompatible; like a square peg in a round hole; not fitting; unsuited to each other;
[鑿氣] obstinate; stubborn;
[鑿岩] rock drilling;
鑿岩工 rock driller;
[鑿鑿] certain; true; verified;
鑿鑿可據 certain and reliable;
言之鑿鑿 say sth with certainty;
[鑿子] chisel;

扁尖鑿 cape chisel;
穿鑿 give a far-fetched interpretation; read too much into sth;
雕刻鑿 carving chisel;
橫切鑿 cross cut chisel;
角鑿 corner chisel;
開鑿 cut (a canal, etc.);
冷鑿 bench chisel;
木工鑿 carpenter's flat chisel;
平鑿 chipping chisel;
確鑿 accurate; authentic; based on truth; beyond doubt; conclusive; ironclad; irrefutable; precise; reliable; sound;
枘鑿 cannot see eye to eye; incompatible;
十字頭鑿 cross mouthed chisel;
填隙鑿 caulking chisel;
彎鑿 bent chisel;

zao³
zao
【早】 (1) morning; (2) ago; as early as; before; for a long time; long ago; (3) beforehand; early; in advance; premature; previous; (4) good morning;
[早安] good morning;
[早班] morning shift;
[早餐] breakfast; brekkie;
早餐麥片 breakfast cereals;
早餐枱 breakfast bar;
美式早餐 American breakfast;
談商務的早餐 power breakfast;

一頓早餐 a breakfast;
英式早餐 English breakfast;

[早操] morning calisthenics; morning exercises;

[早產] premature birth;

[早場] morning show;

[早潮] morning tides;

[早車] morning train;

[早晨] dawn; daybreak; early morning; morning;
在早晨 in the morning;

[早春] early spring;

[早到] arrive ahead of time; arrive early;
早到遲走 get to work early and leave late;

[早點] (1) breakfast; (2) sooner;
早點兒 earlier; sooner;

[早飯] breakfast;
早飯以後 after breakfast;

[早慧] clever in one's childhood; early bloomer;
早慧早衰 soon ripe, soon rotten;

[早婚] early marriage; get married at an early age; marry too early; marry young;
早婚早育 marry early and have children early;

[早計] early planning;

[早間] morning;

[早就] long since;

[早戀] fall in love at an early age; puppy love;

[早年] (1) one's early years; (2) in bygone years; many years ago; years ago;
早年夭折 die an early death;

[早期] early phase; early stage;
早期階段 initial stage;

[早起] (1) early to rise; get up early; (2) early in the morning;
早起三光，晚起三慌 the person who does not rise early never does a good day's work;
早起三朝當一工 an hour in the morning before breakfast is worth two all the rest of the day; to get up early for three mornings is equal to one day in time;
早起三朝當一天 to get up early for three mornings is equal to one day of time;
早起晚睡 early to rise and late to bed;

[早日] at an early date; early; soon;

[早上] early in the morning; early morning; morning;
早上好 good morning;
早上四點 four o'clock in the morning;
第二天早上 following morning; next morning;
今天早上 this morning;
明天早上 tomorrow morning;
星期一早上 Monday morning;
昨天早上 yesterday morning;

[早晌] morning;

[早時] in former times;

[早世] die young;
早世殞命 die an early death;

[早市] morning market;

[早逝] early death;

[早熟] (1) ripen early; (2) reach puberty early; (3) precocious;
早熟早爛 soon ripe, soon rotten;
熟得早，老得早 soon ripe, soon rotten;

[早衰] early ageing; premature senility;

[早霜] early frost;

[早睡] sleep early;
早睡早起 early to bed and early to rise; go to bed early and rise early; go to bed with the lamb, and rise with lark; keep early hours;

[早歲] in one's youth; one's early years;

[早退] leave early;

[早晚] (1) morning and evening; (2) sooner or later; (3) time; (4) some day; some time in the future;
從早到晚 early and late; from dawn till dusk; from morning till night; from sun to sun; from sun up to sundown;
趕早不趕晚 the earlier the better;
沒早沒晚 without regard to time of day;
早出晚歸 go off in the early morning, not return till late at night; go out early and come back at dusk; go out early and return late; go out in the morning and return in the evening; go to work early and come home late;

[早霞] rosy clouds of dawn; rosy dawn;
早霞不出門，晚霞行千里 a rainbow in the morning is the shepherd's warning; a rainbow at night is the shepherd's delight; an evening red and morning gray will set the traveller on his way; evening red and morning gray help the traveller on his way;
早霞主雨，晚霞主晴 rosy morning clouds

Z

indicate rain, and a rosy sunset means fine weather;

[早先] before; in the past; previously; some time ago;
早先申請 previous application;

[早些天] a few days earlier;

[早洩] premature ejaculation;

[早在] as far back as;

[早早兒] as early as possible; well in advance;

[早…早…] early...early...;
早起早睡 keep early hours;
早眠早起 go to bed early and get up early the next morning; keep good hours;

[早則] (1) fortunately; (2) already;

趁早 as early as possible; seize the opportunity;
遲早 early or late; first or last; sooner or later;
過早 premature; untimely;
及早 as soon as possible; seize the opportunity;
絕早 extremely early;
明早 tomorrow morning;
起早 rise early;
侵早 early morning;
清早 dawn; early in the morning; early morning;
提早 shift to an earlier time;
一大早 early in the morning;
一清早 early in the morning;
一早 early in the morning;

zao

【蚤】 flea; louse;

虼蚤 flea;
狗蚤 dog flea;
沙蚤 sandhopper;
水蚤 water flea;
跳蚤 flea;

zao

【棗】 (1) jujube; (2) a surname;

[棗本] book; volume;

[棗核] date stone;

[棗紅] bordeaux; purplish red;
阿果棗紅 algol bordeaux;
鉻印染棗紅 chrome printing bordeaux;
亮棗紅 brilliant bordeaux;
偏鉻棗紅 metachrome bordeaux;
酸性棗紅 acid bordeaux;
顏料棗紅 pigment bordeaux;
重氮淺棗紅 diazo light bordeaux;
重氮鹽棗紅 diazol bordeaux;

[棗木] jujube;

[棗泥] jujube paste;

[棗樹] date tree; jujube; jujube tree;

[棗子] date;

海棗 date; date palm;
黑棗 date-plum persimmon;
蜜棗 candied date; preserved date;
軟棗 dateplum persimmon;
沙棗 narrow-leaved oleaster;
酸棗 wild jujube;
烏棗 black jujube; smoked jujube;
椰棗 date plum;

zao

【澡】 bathe; wash;

[澡缸] tub;
熱水澡缸 hot tub;

[澡盆] bathtub;
澡盆塞子 bath plug;
木製澡盆 wooden bathtub;

[澡身] take a bath;
澡身浴德 develop one's moral being and lead a virtuous life;

[澡塘] common bathing pool; public baths;

[澡堂] bath; bathhouse; public baths;

[澡雪] clean; cleanse; purify;

擦澡 rub oneself down with a wet towel; take a sponge bath;
搓澡 give a rubdown with a demp towel;
洗澡 take a bath;

zao

【繅】 a kind of silk;

zao

【藻】 (1) beautiful; elegant; gorgeous; magnificent; splendid; (2) alga; pondweed; (3) diction; language; wording;

[藻翰] (1) beautiful feather; (2) elegant writing;
藻翰滿紙 elegant phrases and sentences are written all over the paper;

[藻繪] elegance; magnificence; splendour;

[藻類] alga;
藻類學 algology; phycology;
淡水藻類 freshwater alga;
短生藻類 ephemeral alga;
多核藻類 coenocytic;
浮游藻類 floating alga;
寄生藻類 parasitic alga;

經濟藻類 economic alga;
鈣性藻類 calcareous alga;
珊瑚藻類 coralline alga;
嗜冷藻類 cryophilic alga;
嗜氣性藻類 aerophilic alga;
水生藻類 hydrobiontic alga;
土壤藻類 soil-inhabiting alga;
有毒藻類 poisonous alga;

[藻麗] beautiful; splendid;

[藻煤] boghead coal;

[藻飾] (1) embellishments in writing; (2) polish writings;
藻飾其非 gloss over one's faults with flowery words;

[藻雅] elegant; fine; graceful;
藻雅芬芳 refined and fragrant;

[藻玉] multicoloured jade;

擒藻 write in a flowery style;
辭藻 flowery language; ornate diction; rhetoric;
海藻 marine alga; seaweed;
狢藻 waterbugtrap;
紅藻 red alga;
藍綠藻 blue-green alga;
藍藻 blue-green alga;
狸藻 bladderwort;
綠藻 green alga;
品藻 appraise;
山藻 smooth and flowery literary style;
水藻 alga;
團藻 volvox;
文藻 decorative embellishments of writing;

zao⁴

zao

【皂】 soap;

[皂白] black and white; right and wrong;
不分皂白 indiscriminately; make no distinction between right and wrong; make no inquiries about the circumstances; unable to distinguish black from white; unable to distinguish right from wrong;

[皂粉] laundry soap; powdered soap; soap powder;

肥皂 soap;
檀香皂 sandal soap;
香皂 perfumed soap; toilet soap;
藥皂 medicated soap;

zao

【阜】 (1) black; (2) menial labour;

[阜白] (1) black and white; (2) right and wrong;
阜白不分 fail to distinguish between right and wrong;

zao

【造】 (1) build; create; make; (2) cook up; invent; make up; manufacture; (3) educate; (4) arrive at; go to; reach; (5) crop;

[造幣廠] mint;

[造成] (1) bring about; cause; cause to happen; create; effect; engender; give rise to; result in; (2) build up; complete; compose;
造成混亂 cause confusion;
造成假象 create a false impression; put up a facade;
造成聲勢 build up momentum;

[造船] build a ship; shipbuilding;
造船廠 boatyard; dockyard; shipbuilding yard; shipyard;
造船公司 shipbuilder;
造船業 shipbuilding industry;

[造次] hasty; hurried; impetuous; in a hurry; in urgency and haste; rash;
造次顛沛 a moment of haste and plight; wander about in hurry and in misery;
造次行事 act rashly;
造次之間 in a moment of haste; in one's hurry;
不敢造次 dare not act rashly; not venture;

[造端] begin; originate;

[造反] rebel; revolt; rise up against;

[造訪] call on; pay a visit;

[造福] benefit; bring benefit to;
造福人類 benefit mankind; promote the well-being of mankind;
造福人民 bring genuine happiness to the people;
造福人群 do good deeds to benefit mankind;
為民造福 bring benefits to the people;

[造府] call on; call on sb at his home; pay a visit;
造府拜謁 call at your house to pay respects; pay a formal visit at your house;

Z

[造化] (1) Heaven; (2) Mother Nature; (3) the Creator; (4) one's good fortune; one's good luck;
造化弄人 a sport of fate; the god of destiny makes fools of the people;
有造化 be born under a lucky star; lucky;

[造價] building cost;
造價昂貴 involve great expense;

[造酒] brew alcoholic beverages;
造酒廠 a brewery;

[造就] (1) bring up; educate; train; (2) achievements; attainments;
造就人才 make useful citizens through education; train qualified personnel;

[造句] make a sentence;

[造林] afforestation;
造林法 afforestation;
~人工造林法 artificial afforestation;
~天然造林法 natural afforestation;
造林學 silviculture;
重新造林 re-afforestation; reforestation;
國家造林 national afforestation;
農業造林 reclamative afforestation;

[造命] (1) master of other people's fate; (2) convert one's misfortune into fortune;

[造孽] do evil things;
造孽作惡 commit crime and do evil;

[造勢] media hype; spin;
造勢者 a spinner;

[造物] Heaven; the Creator;
造物主 the Creator;

[造像] make a portrait; make a statue; make an image;

[造型] (1) modelling; mold-making; (2) model; mold;
造型車間 make-up department;
造型工 moulder;
造型美觀 handsome appearance;
造型藝術 formative arts; plastic arts;
造型優美 be beautifully shaped;

[造謠] cook up a story and spread it around; start a rumour;
造謠惑眾 confuse people with lies; frabricate rumours to mislead people; spread rumours to confuse people;
造謠生事 cause trouble by false stories; cause trouble by rumour-mongering; spread rumours to create trouble; start a rumour to create trouble; stir up trouble by rumour-mongering;
造謠誣蔑 lies and calumnies; make stories and hurl venmous shafts at; rumour-mongering and mud-slinging; rumours and slanders; spread lies and slanders; spread rumours and sling mud;
造謠陷害 fabricate rumours and trump up charges against sb;
造謠中傷 fabricate rumours to slander people; hurt sb by calumnious fabrication; make up stories to defame others; mud-slinging; slander sb without the slightest excuse; spread rumours to injure others' reputation;
造謠作祟 rumours and tricks;
背後造謠 start rumours behind sb's back;
平空造謠 spread unfounded rumours; start a rumour gratuitously;

[造渣] slagging;
碳化物造渣 carbide slagging;
氧化造渣 fluoride slagging;

[造詣] (1) attainments; (2) call on; visit;
造詣頗深 be steeped in; well up in;

[造獄] (1) start litigation; (2) extraordinary criminal code;

[造紙] make paper; papermaking;
造紙廠 paper mill;
造紙術 papermaking technology;

[造字] coin words; coinage;

[造作] (1) make; (2) affectations; artificial; pretentious; unnatural;
不造作[的] artless;

編造 (1) compile; work out; (2) concoct; cook up; fabricate; invent; make up;
變造 fabricate; forge;
承造 build; make;
重造 recreation;
創造 bring about; create; produce;
打造 forge;
締造 create; found;
鍛造 forge;
仿造 be modelled on; copy; counterfeit;
改造 reform; remake; remould; transform;
構造 build; construction; structure;
假造 (1) counterfeit; forge; (2) fabricate; invent;
建造 build; construct; make;
兩造 both parties in a lawsuit;
釀造 brew; make;
捏造 concoct; fabricate; trump;
人造 artificial; man-made;
深造 pursue advanced studies;

生造 coin;
塑造 (1) model; mould; (2) portray;
偽造 fabricate; forge;
修造 make as well as repair;
虛造 cook up; fabricate;
臆造 fabricate; make up;
營造 build; construct;
再造 born a second time; give sb a new lease of life;
趲造 build with haste;
肇造 first establish; found;
鑄造 cast; found;

zao
【灶】 the same as 竈;

zao
【竈】 (1) kitchen; (2) cooking stove;
[竈間] kitchen;
[竈君] God of the Kitchen;
[竈台] top of a kitchen range;
[竈頭] kitchen place;

病竈 focus of infection;
大竈 (1) brick kitchen range; (2) ordinary mess;
電竈 electric cooking stove;
祭竈 offer sacrifices to the kitchen god;
爐竈 kitchen range;
小竈 special mess;
掌竈 chef;
中竈 medium mess;

zao
【慥】 kind-hearted; sincere;
[慥慥] earnest and wholehearted; honest and sincere;

zao
【噪】 (1) chirp; (2) confusion of voices; noisy;
[噪聒] be noisy; make loud, confused noise;
[噪聲] buzz; din; noise;
噪聲不定性 noise ambiguity;
噪聲計 sound-level meter;
噪聲控制 noise abatement; noise control;
噪聲污染 noise pollution;
[噪音] din; noise; unpleasant noise;
噪音標準 noise standard;
噪音分析器 sonic noise analyzer;
噪音控制 noise abatement; noise control;
噪音污染 noise pollution;
噪音指數 the figure of noise;
白澡音 white noise;
環境噪音 ambient noise;
降低噪音 reduce noise;
空傳噪音 airborne noise;
平息噪音 subside noise;
消除噪音 abate the noise;
抑制噪音 suppress noise;
振幅噪音 amplitude noise;

聒噪 clamorous; noisy;
呼噪 make loud, confused noise;

zao
【燥】 (1) arid; dry; parched; (2) impatient; restless;
[燥熱] hot and dry;
[燥濕] hot and moist;

鼻燥 dry nose;
乾燥 (1) arid; dry; (2) boring; dull;
高燥 high and dry;
枯燥 dull and dry; monotonous; uninteresting;

zao
【譟】 (1) noise of a crowd; (2) abuse; slander;

鼓譟 clamour; make an uproar;

zao
【躁】 (1) hot-tempered; irritable; (2) restless; uneasy;
[躁動] move restlessly;
[躁喝] very thirsty;
[躁急] restless; uneasy;
[躁烈] burning;
[躁熱] dry and hot;

煩躁 agitated; fidgety; in a fret; irritable;
浮躁 flighty and rash; impetuous; impulsive;
急躁 (1) irascrible; irritable; (2) impetuous; rash;
焦躁 impatient; restless with anxiety;
莽躁 sudden;

ze²

ze
【咋】 (1) bite; gnaw; (2) loud noise;
[咋舌] be left breathless; be left speechless; bite one's tongue;

ze
【則】 (1) criterion; law; norm; regulation; rule; standard; (2) a particle indicating consequence; (3) numerary

particle; (4) but; however; (5) follow; imitate;

［則度］ regulations; rules;

［則例］ precedent; set rule;

［則聲］ make a sound; utter a word;

多則…少則 not more than; and not less than

法則 law; rule;

否則 if not; or else; otherwise;

規則 (1) regulation; rule; (2) regular;

或則 either…or; or;

簡則 general rules and regulations;

然則 but; but then; in that case; then;

實則 actually; in fact;

守則 regulations; rules;

稅則 customs tariff; tax regulations;

雖則 although; though;

遂則 afterwards; and then;

通則 general rule;

細則 detailed rules and regulations;

憲則 laws and instituions;

一則 (1) one item; (2) a piece of; an item of; (3) on the one hand;

原則 principle;

再則 besides; moreover;

章則 rules and regulations;

準則 criterion; norm; standard;

總則 general principles; general rules;

ze

【迮】 (1) pressing; urgent; (2) helter-skelter; hurried;

ze

【窄】 a pronunciation of 窄;

ze

【笮】 (1) narrow; pressing; (2) boards laid across rafters; (3) arrow bag;

ze

【責】 (1) duty; responsibility; (2) demand; require; strict with; (3) blame; censure; reprimand; reproach; upbraid; (4) call sb to account; question closely; (5) punish;

［責備］ blame; chide; reprimand; reproach; reprove; take sb to task; upbraid;

百般責備 load sb with all manners of reproaches;

良心責備 have a guilty conscience; have compunctions; one's own conscience rebukes one; prickings of conscience;

嚴加責備 haul a person over the coals;

［責貶］ fault-finding;

［責成］ charge one with a duty; enjoin; instruct;

［責打］ punish by beating; punish by flogging; punish by lashing;

［責罰］ penalty; punish; punishment;

［責分］ one's duty; one's share of responsibility;

［責怪］ blame;

［責己］ blame oneself; hold oneself responsible;

責己嚴，責人寬 strict with oneself and lenient towards others;

［責令］ charge; instruct; order;

［責罵］ blame; chastise; dress down; dressing-down; rebuke; scold; upbraid;

給人一頓責罵 give sb a ticking off;

嚴厲責罵 castigate; castigation;

一頓責罵 a dressing;

［責難］ blame; censure;

［責全］ demand perfection in others; expect others to do a flawless job;

［責人］ blame others;

責人先責己 do not complain about other people if you are as bad as they are;

責人嚴而律己寬 severe with others and lenient towards oneself; the pot calling the kettle black;

恕己責人 lenient to oneself and severe on others;

［責任］ duty; responsibility;

責任保險 liability insurance;

責任編輯 executive editor;

責任範圍 limitation of liability;

責任感 calling; responsibility; sense of responsibility;

責任會計 responsibility accounting;

責任險 liability insurance;

責任在於 the onus is on sb to do sth;

責任中心制 responsibility-centered system;

責任重大 have a grave responsibility;

責任制 accountability; responsibility system;

~目標責任制 target responsibility system;

~全面責任制 overall responsibility system;

責任終止 cesser of liability;

保兑責任 confirmed engagement;
不可推卸的責任 compelling obligation;
財政責任 fiscal responsibility;
承擔責任 accept the blame; assume responsibility; bear the blame; shoulder the blame; shoulder the responsibility; take on responsibility; take the blame;
撤回責任 relinquish one's responsibility;
負法律責任 bear legal liability;
負起責任 assume the responsibility; keep one's end up; keep up one's end;
個人責任 personal responsibility;
公民責任 civic responsibilities;
共同責任 corporate responsibility;
貨幣責任 dollar responsibility;
集體責任 collective responsibility;
肩負責任 shoulder responsibility;
解除責任 dissolve the duty;
連帶責任 joint responsibility;
履行責任 exercise responsibility;
民事責任 civil responsibility;
全面責任 overall responsibility;
雙方都有責任 it takes two to tangle;
逃避責任 escape the duty; evade a responsibility; flee responsibility; shirk responsibility;
~逃避責任的方法 cop-out;
~逃避責任的藉口 cop-out;
推諉責任 abandon one's duty; pass the buck;
推卸責任 abdicate responsibility; dodge one's responsibility; shift responsibility onto others; shirk one's responsibility;
刑事責任 criminal liability; responsibility for a crime;
一份責任 a share of responsibility;
有限責任 limited liability;
有責任 as in duty bound; in duty bound;
直接責任 direct responsibility;
轉移責任 divert one's responsibility;
最終責任 ultimate responsibility;

[責善] exhort sb to practise good deeds;
[責望] blame and complain when sb fails to accomplish a difficult task;
[責問] blame and demand an explanation; call sb to account;
[責無旁貸] a responsibility one cannot relinquish; a responsibility one cannot shirk; an inescapable duty; cannot shift the responsibility to others; duty-bound; one's unshirkable responsibility; the buck stops here; there is no shirking the responsibility;
[責詢] interpellate;

貶責 reprimand; reproach;
叱責 rebuke; scold;
斥責 denounce; reprimand;
負責 in charge of; responsible for;
呵責 give sb a dressing-down; scold sb severely;
咎責 responsibility for an offence;
苛責 excoriate; reproach severely;
譴責 condemn; denounce;
權責 right and duty;
塞責 perform one's duty
文責 author's responsibility;
言責 responsibility of offering advice;
杖責 punish by caning;
職責 duty; obligation; responsibility;
指責 accuse; censure; criticize; reprove;
專責 specific responsibility;
罪責 responsibility for an offence;

ze
【舴】 small boat;
[舴艋] small boat;

ze
【嘖】 (1) compete for a chance to speak; (2) a click of the tongue; (3) interjection of approval or admiration; (4) argue; dispute;
[嘖嘖] (1) a click of the tongue; (2) remarks;
嘖嘖稱善 praise with a click of the tongue;
嘖嘖稱羨 click the tongue in admiration;
嘖嘖歎賞 profuse in one's praise;

ze
【幘】 headdress; turban;

ze
【擇】 choose; pick out; select;
[擇不開] (1) cannot be separated; (2) inseparable;
[擇地] choose a site;
[擇對] select a mate; select a spouse;
[擇肥而噬] select the fat ones and eat them — select rich people for extortion;
[擇吉] pick an auspicious day;
擇吉開張 choose a lucky day to open a business; choose an auspicious day to

Z

start a business;

[擇交] choose friends; select friends;

[擇鄰] select neighbours;

[擇木] choose a master; choose a perch;

擇木而處 select trees on which they roost — find out who is the best and serve;

良禽擇木 a fine bird chooses a tree to nestle in — choose a master to serve; good birds select their roosts; the prudent bird selects its tree;

[擇偶] select a mate; select a spouse;

[擇佩] choose a spouse;

[擇期] select a good day;

[擇親] make marriage arrangements for one's children;

[擇人而事] (1) choose the virtuous to serve; (2) find the right man to marry;

[擇日] choose a good day;

擇日成親 choose a lucky day for the wedding; select the wedding day;

擇日起程 choose a day on which to set out; choose an auspicious day and set off; fix a departure date;

[擇食] select one's food;

饑不擇食 a hungry person is not choosy about his food; a hungry person is not picky and choosy; a hungry person will eat anything given him; all food is delicious to the starving; beggars cannot be choosers; beggars must not be choosers; hunger finds no fault with the cookery; hunger gives relish to any food; hunger has always a good cook; hunger is the best sauce; hunger sweetens beans; hungry dogs will eat dirty puddings; hungry people are not particular about their food; nothing comes amiss to a hungry man; nothing is unwelcome to the hungry; the best sauce is hunger; when hungry, one takes any food that is ready;

~饑不擇食，寒不擇衣 when one is hungry, one eats what there is; when one is cold, one wears what one has;

[擇席] choosy about the bed;

[擇婿] choose a good husband for one's daughter;

擇婿嫁女 choose a worthy husband for one's daughter;

[擇選] choose; select;

[擇業] choose an occupation;

[擇友] choose friends;

別擇 distinguish and choose;

採擇 select and adopt;

抉擇 choose;

選擇 choose; select;

ze

【澤】 (1) pool; pond; (2) damp; moist; (3) brilliance; gloss; lustre; (4) favour; grace; kindness; (5) benefit; enrich;

[澤被] extend benefit;

澤被天下 benefits spread to all people; spread all-round benefit to the people;

澤被萬世 one's graces reach down to many generations; the good grace will be felt for countless generations to come;

[澤國] (1) a land that abounds in rivers and lakes; marsh; swamp; (2) inundated areas;

盡成澤國 a whole area becomes submerged; all the land is inundated;

[澤民] benefit the people;

澤民億兆 benefit myriads of people;

[澤袍] comrades in arms;

草澤 (1) grassy marsh; swamp; (2) among the people; rustic origin;

恩澤 bounties bestowed by a monarch;

芳澤 fragrance of a woman;

光澤 brilliance; burnish; gloss; lustre; sheen; shine;

涸澤 dried-up lake; dry up a lake;

湖澤 lakes and marshes;

沮澤 marsh; swamps;

脉澤 maser;

袍澤 fellow officers;

潤澤 lubricate; moist; moisten; smooth;

色澤 colour; colour and lustre; hue; tinge; tint;

手澤 hand-writing left by one's forefathers;

塗澤 gloss over; whitewash;

渥澤 great kindness; profound benefaction;

先澤 benefits from one's ancestors;

香澤 (1) hair oil; (2) fragrance; sweet smell;

遺澤 the benevolence left behind by a dead person;

瑩澤 transparent and shiny;

悦澤 gorgeous; pleasantly bright;

沼澤 marsh; swamp;

ze

【簀】 (1) bamboo bed mat; (2) be densely collected together;

ze

【賾】 abstruse; deep; profound;

ze⁴

ze

【仄】 (1) oblique; (2) of the three tones other than the even tone; (3) narrow; (4) uneasy;

［仄聲］ oblique tones;

［仄仄］ narrow;

逼仄 cramped; narrow;

平仄 level and oblique tones;

歉仄 uneasy due to regretfulness;

ze

【昃】 after noon; afternoon;

zei²

zei

【賊】 (1) bandit; burglar; robber; thief; (2) enemy; rebel; traitor; (3) harm; (4) kill; (5) clever; crafty; cunning; deceitful; furtive; wicked; (6) extremely;

［賊兵］ enemy troops; rebel soldiers;

［賊巢］ thieves' den;

［賊船］ pirate ship;

［賊黨］ gang of bandits; group of traitors; rebel factions;

［賊盜］ brigands; thieves and robbers;

［賊匪］ bandits; rebels;

［賊鬼］ cunning and crafty;

賊鬼溜滑 crafty; dishonest;

［賊害］ cause harm to another;

［賊將］ general of the enemy troops; rebel general;

［賊寇］ bandits; rebels;

［賊人］ corned beef; robber; thief;

賊人膽虛 have a guilty conscience; the evil-doers are always timid;

［賊頭］ bandit leader; chief robber;

賊頭賊腦 act suspiciously; behave stealthily like a thief; every inch of sb a thief; furtive; have a mean look; thief-like; villainous-looking;

［賊徒］ thieves;

［賊相］ criminal looks;

［賊心］ crooked mind; wicked and suspicious mind; wicked heart; evil designs; evil intentions;

賊心不死 not give up one's gangster designs; refuse to give up one's evil designs;

［賊性］ (1) crafty disposition; (2) evil mind;

賊性不改 a thief cannot change his nature;

賊性難改 the nature of an evil man is incorrigible;

［賊眼］ furtive glance; shifty eyes;

賊眼覞覷 one's shifty eyes squinted right and left;

賊眼一溜 cast a furtive look at sth;

賊眉賊眼 have a shifty look; roguish looks;

［賊贓］ booty; spoils; stolen goods;

［賊子］ traitor;

叛臣賊子 traitors to the country;

笨賊 stupid burglar;

大眼賊 ground squirrel; suslik;

盜賊 bandits; robbers;

飛賊 (1) cat burglar; (2) air marauder;

工賊 blackleg; scab;

慣賊 hardened thief;

國賊 traitor;

海賊 sea poacher;

家賊 thief in the family;

奸賊 conspirator; traitor;

馬賊 mounted gangsters;

賣國賊 traitor;

蟊賊 pest;

民賊 traitor to the people;

木賊 scouring rush;

戕賊 injure; undermine;

槍烏賊 squid;

擒賊 catch a thief;

認賊 take a thief as;

書賊 biblioklept;

土賊 bandit;

烏賊 cuttlefish; inkfish;

竊賊 burglar; thief;

一群賊 a pack of thieves;

一日為賊，終生是賊 once a thief, always a thief;

捉賊 catch thieves;

作賊 be a thief;

zen¹

zen

【譖】 a pronunciation of 譖;

zen³
zen

【怎】 how; what; why;
［怎得］ (1) how could; (2) how;
［怎的］ how; what; why;
［怎麼］ how; what; why;
怎麼辦 what is to be done;
怎麼回事 what is the blow;
怎麼見得 how so;
怎麼說呢 shall we say;
怎麼樣 how is it;
~ 不怎麼樣 not up to much; so-so; very indifferent;
怎麼也不行 it is out of the question;
怎麼做 how to do sth;
~ 教你怎麼做 show you the ropes;
不怎麼 not particularly; not very;
［怎奈］ but alas; except that;
［怎能］ how can;
［怎樣］ how; in what way;
不讓怎樣 one way or another; one way or the other;
那又怎樣 so what;
你覺得怎樣 what do you say;

Z

zen⁴
zen

【譖】 charge falsely; slander;
［譖人］ slander others;
［譖言］ slanderous remarks;

zeng¹
zeng

【曾】 (1) relationship between great-grand-children and great-grandparents; (2) a surname;
［曾孫］ one's great-grandson;
曾孫女 one's great-granddaughter;
［曾祖］ one's great-grandfather;
曾祖母 one's great-grandmother;

zeng

【增】 add; add to; enlarge; gain; grow; increase;
［增白劑］ brightener; whitener;
耐漂增白劑 bleach-stable brightener;
熒光增白劑 fluorescent brightener; optical brightener;
［增兵減灶］ bring in reinforcements while reducing cooking-stoves;
［增補］ add to; augment; enlargement; increase and supplement; supplement;
增補本 enlarged edition;
增補從句 supplementing clause;
增補性狀語 supplementive adverbial;
詞匯增補 lexical expansion;
句法增補 syntactic expansion;
［增產］ increase production;
增產保收 increase the production and ensure a good harvest;
增產幅度 amount of increase in production;
增產節約 increase the production and practise economy; strive for an increased production and economy;
增產增收 increase the production and the revenue;
［增稠］ thickening;
增稠器 thickener;
~ 聚合增稠器 polymeric thickener;
~ 旋風增稠器 cyclone thickener;
~ 漲流增稠器 dilatant thickener;
剪切增稠 shear thickening;
膠乳增稠 latex thickening;
重力增稠 gravity thickening;
［增大］ amplify; enlargement; magnify;
［增訂］ revise and enlarge;
增訂本 revised and enlarged edition;
增訂條款 additional article;
［增多］ add to; grow in number; increase;
［增光］ add lustre to; add to the prestige of; do credit to; glorify;
為國增光 do credit to one's country;
為家庭增光 cast lustre on one's family;
［增廣］ advance; enlarge; widen; widen one's knowledge;
［增加］ add; add to; augment; build up; enlarge; exceed; extend; get a raise in; go up; have a rise in; increase; jump; on the increase; put on; raise;
增加百分之十 increase by 10%;
增加開支 loosen the purse-strings;
不斷增加 on the increase;
略有增加 slight increase;
自動增加 autonomous increase;
［增減］ increases and decreases;
［增進］ advance; enhance; further; promote; upstep;
增進食慾 whet one's appetite;
增進相互了解 further mutual understanding;

[增刊] supplement;
彩色增刊 colour supplement;
[增量] increment;
角增量 angular increment;
年增量 annual increment;
平均增量 average increment;
字節增量 byte increment;
[增強] boost; enhance; enhancement; heighten; reinforcement; strengthen;
增強劑 enhancer;
增強凝聚力 increase cohesion;
增強器 intensifier;
~ 電光象增強器 electron-optical image intensifier;
~ 火花增強器 spark intensifier;
~ 級聯式象增強器 cascade image intensifier;
增強體質 build up one's health;
增強信心 heighten one's confidence;
增強勇氣 raise one's spirits;
增強語 amplifier;
輪廓增強 edge enhancement;
石棉增強 asbestos reinforcement;
數字光電增強 digital photo enhancement;
數字增強 digital enhancement;
圖像增強 image enhancement;
信號增強 signal enhancement;
[增生] hyperplasia;
增生性息肉 hyperplastic polyp;
骨質增生 hyperplasia;
結腸黏膜增生 colonic mucosal hyperplasia;
顱骨增生 hyperostosis cranli;
內皮增生 endotheliosis;
前列腺增生 prostatic hyperplasia;
胸腺髓質增生 thymic medullary hyperplasia;
牙骨質增生 cement hyperplasia;
疣狀增生 verrucous hyperplasia;
[增塑劑] plasticizer;
催化增塑劑 catalytic plasticizer;
抑菌增塑劑 bacteriostatic plasticizer;
[增損] profits and losses;
[增添] add; add to; increase; supplement;
增添光彩 add lustre to; add to the prestige of; do credit to;
增添力量 gain in strength;
增添收入 supplement one's income;
增添新意 add new meaning to;
[增效] (1) increase efficiency; (2) synergy;
增效作用 building action;
[增壓] pressurization;
增壓艙 pressurized cabin;
增壓器 supercharger;
~ 差動增壓器 differential supercharger;
~ 高空增壓器 altitude supercharger;
~ 離心式增壓器 centrifugal supercharger;
化學增壓 chemical pressurization;
燃料箱增壓 tank pressurization;
油箱增壓 fuel-tank pressurization;
[增益] (1) augment; increase; profit; (2) gain;
絕對增益 absolute gain;
聲頻增益 audio gain;
天線增益 aerial gain;
[增譯法] amplification method;
[增援] reinforce; reinforcement;
要求增援 call for reinforcements;
[增增] numerous;
[增長] grow; increase; increases and advances; rise;
增長才幹 develop qualities; enhance abilities and talents; enhance one's abilities;
高速增長 alpine increase;
明顯增長 rise appreciably;
穩步增長 increase steadily;
指數增長 exponential increase;
載荷增長 load increase;
[增值] appreciation; increase the value; increment;
增值稅 added value tax;
~ 增值稅發票 bills of added value tax;
重估增值 appraisal increment;
[增殖] proliferation;
細胞增殖 cell proliferation;

倍增 multiply; redouble;
遞增 increase by degrees; increase progressively;
激增 increase sharply; shoot up;
新增 newly increased;
有增 keep growing;

zeng

【憎】 abhor; abominate; detest; hate; loathe;
[憎妒] bear a jealous hatred for;
[憎恨] detest; hate; hold a grudge against; odium;
[憎嫉] feel a jealous hatred for;
[憎惡] abhor; abominate; animosity; animus; detest; loathe;
自我憎惡 self-abhorrence;

［憎嫌］ dislike; hate;
［憎怨］ bear a grudge against; feel bitterness for;

愛憎 love and hate; one's likes and dislikes;
可憎 disgusting; hateful;
所憎 what the people hate;
嫌憎 dislike and avoid; hate;

zeng
【熷】 arrow attached to a silk cord for shooting birds;

zeng
【繒】 silk; silk fabrics;
［繒網］ lift net;

zeng⁴
zeng
【甑】 earthenware for cooking;
［甑中生塵］ in an extremely poor condition; so poor that dust has collected in one's cooking pot;
［甑子］ rice steamer;

zeng
【贈】 give as a present; present as a gift;
［贈本］ presentation copy;
［贈別］ wish sb well in parting;
［贈給］ bestow; confer; donate; give; present;
［贈金］ cash gift; give a cash gift;
［贈券］ gift coupon;
［贈刊］ supplement;
星期天贈刊 Sunday supplement;
［贈款］ grant; largess;
［贈禮］ gift; present;
贈禮便條 compliment slip;
［贈票］ free ticket;
［贈品］ complimentary gift; gift; giveaway; present;
［贈券］ complimentary ticket;
［贈送］ give as a present; present as a gift;
贈送儀式 presentation ceremony;
接受贈送 receive a gift;
拒絕贈送 refuse a gift;
免費贈送的 complimentary;
［贈言］ words of advice;
［贈與］ donate; favour; gift; grant; present;
免稅贈與 exempt gift;
相互贈與 mutual gift;
應稅贈與 taxable gift;
［贈予］ grant;
［贈閱］ given free by the publisher;
贈閱本 complimentary copy;

賻贈 present a gift to a bereaved family;
回贈 give a gift in return;
惠贈 so kind as to give;
婚贈 nuptial gift;
謹贈 with the compliments of;
敬贈 offer respectfully;
捐贈 contribute; donate;
餽贈 give as a present; make a present of sth; present a gift;
饋贈 give as a present;
腆贈 costly presents; rich gifts;
相贈 give a present; present a gift;
貽贈 leave sth to posterity; present;
遺贈 bequeath; bequest; legacy;
轉贈 give sth that has been given to one as a persent;
追贈 confer posthumously;

zha¹
zha
【扎】 (1) prick; run a needle into; stick a needle into; (2) get into; plunge;
［扎彩］ hang up festoons;
［扎根］ take root;
［扎實］ solid; strong; sturdy;
扎扎實實 in a down-to-earth manner; in a well-grounded way; solid; sturdy; work conscientiously;
［扎手］ (1) prick the hand; (2) difficult to handle; thorny;
扎手舞腳 make exaggerated gestures;
［扎心］ heartbreaking;
［扎眼］ (1) dazzling; offending to the eye; (2) offensively conspicuous;
［扎營］ encamp; pitch a tent or camp;

安扎 camp; settle down;
綁扎 (1) bind up; wrap up; (2) bundle up; pack; tie up;
屯扎 station;
一扎 a bundle of; a sheaf of;
掙扎 struggle;
駐扎 be stationed;

zha
【查】 a surname;

zha
【抯】 stiff and erect;

zha

【渣】 (1) dregs; residue; sediment; (2) broken bits;

［渣滓］ dregs; dross; residue; sediment;
社會渣滓 scum;

殘渣 dregs; residual;
沉渣 dregs; sediment;
出渣 slag tap;
豆渣 bean dregs;
廢渣 waste residue;
浮渣 dross;
鋼渣 dross;
礦渣 slag;
爐渣 cinder; slag;
麻渣 dregs of linseeds or sesame seeds;
煤渣 cinder; clinker; coal cinders; coal slag;
奶渣 cottage cheese;
人渣 scum;
炭渣 cinder;
藥渣 dregs of a decoction;
油渣 (1) dregs of fat; (2) oil residue;
造渣 slag formation; slag making;
蔗渣 bagasse;

zha

【楂】 (1) a species of hawthorn; (2) wooden raft;

山楂 (1) hawthorn; (2) haw;

zha²

zha

【扎】 strive; struggle;

［扎掙］ strive; struggle;
扎掙不住 cannot keep up; cannot maintain; struggle in vain;

［扎營］ encamp; pitch a camp; pitch a tent;

馬扎 campstool; folding stool;
掙扎 struggle;

zha

【札】 (1) thin pieces of wood used for writing in ancient China (2) letter;

［札記］ reading notes;

筆札 (1) stationery; (2) writings;
簡札 brief letter;
來札 your letter;
手札 personal letter;
書札 correspondence; letters;
信札 letters;

zha

【軋】 roll;

粗軋 rough;
滾軋 roll;
精軋 finish rolling;
冷軋 cold-roll;
熱軋 hot-roll;

zha

【炸】 deep-fry; fry in oil;

［炸雞］ fried chicken; fry chicken;

［炸醬］ fried bean sauce;

zha

【紮】 (1) bind; fasten; tie; (2) post; station; stop;

［紮門］ stand guard at a gate;

［紮營］ encamp; pitch tents; station troops;

zha

【閘】 (1) floodgate; sluice gate; (2) dam up water; (3) brake; (4) switch;

［閘板］ (1) sluice; (2) wooden panel protecting the window;

［閘車］ brake;

［閘口］ floodgate; sluice;

［閘門］ floodgate;
打開閘門 open the floodgate;

［閘瓦］ brake shoe;
合成閘瓦 composition brake shoe;
金剛石閘瓦 diamond brake shoe;
鑄鐵閘瓦 cast iron brake shoe;

車閘 brake;
船閘 shop lock;
電閘 electric brake; electric switch;
風閘 pneumatic brake;
涵閘 culvert and sluice;
腳閘 back-pedalling brake;
手閘 handbrake;
水閘 sluice; water gate;
跳閘 tripping;
魚閘 fish lock;
總閘 main switch;

zha

【劄】 (1) brief note; letter; (2) directive;

［劄記］ reading notes;

zha

【鍘】 hay knife;

Z

［鍘草機］ chaff cutter; hay cutter;
［鍘刀］ fodder chopper;

zha³

zha

【眨】 blink; wink;
［眨巴］ blink;
眨巴眼兒 wink one's eyes in quick succession;
［眨眼］ twinkle; wink; very short time;
眨眼反應 blink response;
眨眼過頻 palpebration;
眨眼間 a very short time; in the twinkling of an eye;
殺人不眨眼 hard-hearted;
一眨眼 in a wink;
~一眨眼工夫 in a twinkling; in a wink; in the twinkling of an eye; on the instant;

zha⁴

zha

【乍】 (1) at first; for the first time; (2) abruptly; suddenly; unexpectedly; (3) extend; spread;
［乍到］ (1) arrive at some place unexpectedly and suddenly; (2) have just arrived at some place;
新來乍到 newcomer; newly arrived;
［乍富］ from rags to riches; sudden wealth;
［乍見］ (1) meet for the first time; (2) see suddenly;
［乍猛的］ abruptly; suddenly;
［乍然］ abruptly; unexpectedly;
［乍聞］ learn suddenly sth for the first time;
［乍乍的］ just now;

zha

【吒】 (1) shout with anger; (2) smack in eating;

zha

【咋】 all of a sudden; suddenly;

zha

【柵】 bamboo fence;
［柵欄］ bar; fence; gate; palisade; railing;
車站柵欄 station fence;
防雪柵欄 snow fence;
固定柵欄 fixed fence;
活動柵欄 portable fence;
木柵欄 board fence;
鐵絲柵欄 wire fence;
一根柵欄 a bar;
［柵塘］ fenced-off pond;
光柵 (1) grating; (2) raster;
欄柵 balustrade; barrier; railing;
葉柵 cascade; cascade of blades; vane cascade;

zha

【炸】 (1) burst; explode; (2) blast; blow up; bomb; (3) flare up; fly into a rage; get mad; (4) disperse boisterously; flee in terror;
［炸彈］ bomb;
炸彈爆炸 a bomb explodes; a bomb goes off; bomb blast; bomb explosion;
炸彈恐嚇 bomb scare;
~虛假炸彈恐嚇 bomb hoax;
炸彈恐慌 bomb scare;
炸彈威脅 bomb threat;
炸彈襲擊 bomb attack; bombing;
包裹炸彈 parcel bomb;
釘子炸彈 nail bomb;
定時炸彈 time bomb;
放置炸彈 plant a bomb;
航空炸彈 aerobomb;
集束炸彈 cluster bomb;
汽車炸彈 car bomb;
扔炸彈 drop a bomb;
深水炸彈 depth bomb; depth charge;
投擲炸彈 throw a bomb;
土製炸彈 homemade bomb;
未爆炸彈 unexploded bomb;
一顆炸彈 a bomb;
一批炸彈 a stick of bombs;
引爆炸彈 detonate a bomb; set off a bomb;
郵包炸彈 parcel bomb;
郵件炸彈 letter bomb; parcel bomb;
運送炸彈 transport bombs;
智能炸彈 smart bomb;
子母炸彈 cluster bomb;
自殺性炸彈 suicide bomb;
［炸毀］ blast; blow up; destroy by bombing;
［炸裂］ break by explosion;
［炸傷］ be injured in bombing;
［炸死］ kill by bombing;
［炸藥］ dynamite; explosive;
甘油炸藥 dynamite;
高級炸藥 high explosive;
合格炸藥 acceptable explosive;
可塑炸藥 plastic explosive;
烈性炸藥 atomite; high explosive;

組合炸藥 composite explosive;

爆炸 blast; blow up; burst; detonate; explode; explosion;
轟炸 bomb; bombardment; bombing;
煎炸 frying;
油炸 deep fry;

zha
【痄】 scrofulous swellings and sores;

zha
【蚱】 grasshopper; locust;
[蚱蜢] grasshopper; locust;
一隻蚱蜢 a grasshopper;

zha
【詐】 (1) cheat; feign; lie; pretend; swindle; (2) bluff sb into giving information; trick into; (3) suddenly; unexpectedly;
[詐敗] feign defeat;
詐敗而退 retreat as if one was worsted;
詐敗佯輸 feign defeat;
佯輸詐敗 pretend to be defeated;
[詐病] feign illness; malinger; pretend to be ill;
[詐財] cheat for money;
[詐稱] state falsely; tell a lie;
[詐唬] bluff; bluster;
[詐婚] cheat by using marriage as a bait;
[詐騙] chicanery; con trick; jiggery-pokery; swindle;
詐騙錢財 defraud of money; obtain money by fraud;
詐騙為生 make one's living by lying and imposture;
金融詐騙 financial swindle;
識破詐騙 see through the swindle;
[詐欺] cheating; deception; fraud; imposture;
詐欺斂財 obtain money under false pretences;
[詐術] cheating; chicanery; fraud; guile;
[詐死] fake death; feign death; play dead; pretend to be dead;
[詐偽] artful; cunning; deceitful; falsehood;
[詐降] fake surrender; feign surrender; pretend to surrender;
[詐語] fabrication; falsehood; lie;

鄙詐 deceitful; despicably untruthful;
變詐 cunning means;
刁詐 crafty; knavish;
訛詐 blackmail; extort under false pretences; intimidate;
詭詐 crafty; cunning;
奸詐 crafty; deceitful; fraudulent; on the crook; treacherous;
狡詐 crafty; cunning;
譎詐 crafty; cunning;
欺詐 cheat; swindle;
敲詐 blackmail; extort; practise extortion; racketeer;
巧詐 artful; ingenious fraud; tricky;
權詐 crafty; fraudulent; treacherous;
險詐 sinister and crafty;
行詐 cheat; deceive; swindle;
虛詐 falsehood and trickery;
陰詐 crafty; cunning; deceitful;

zha
【搾】 extract; press for juice; squeeze; wring;
[搾出] squeeze out;
[搾果機] juicer;
[搾汁] liquidize;
搾汁機 blender; liquidizer;

zha
【榨】 press for juice; squeeze ;
[榨菜] hot pickled mustard tuber;
[榨取] (1) exploit; extort; rob; (2) extract; press for juice; squeeze;
[榨油] extract oil;

壓榨 (1) press; squeeze; (2) oppress and exploit;

zha
【蜡】 year-end sacrifice of the Zhou Dynasty;
[蜡月] twelfth lunar month;

zhai¹
zhai
【摘】 (1) pick; pluck; take off; (2) choose; make extracts from; select; (3) jot down; (4) expose; unveil;
[摘編] extract and compile;
[摘抄] (1) extract; make extracts; take passages; (2) excerpts; extracts;
[摘除] excise;
[摘花] pluck flowers;
[摘記] (1) jot down; take notes; (2) excerpt; extract;

［摘奸發伏］ expose conspiracies and secrets; point out the treacherous people and expose their hidden crimes; reveal treason and disclose a secret;
［摘借］ ask for a loan; borrow;
［摘句］ make quotations; quote;
摘句成章 put sentences together in a composition; stud a composition with picked up phrases;
［摘錄］ (1) excerpt; extract; make extracts; take passages; (2) excerpt; extract;
［摘取］ pick; select; take;
［摘下］ pick off;
摘下帽子 take off one's hat;
［摘選］ select;
［摘要］ abstract; digest; summary;
摘要賬戶 abstract account;
報告摘要 summary of reports;
報紙摘要 abstract of the newspaper;
成果摘要 summary of results;
合同摘要 abstract of contract;
商情摘要 business condition digest;
寫摘要 write a précis;
做摘要 write an abstract;
［摘譯］ select and translate;
［摘引］ quote;
［摘印］ take away the official seal;
［摘由］ key extracts;

攀摘 pick from trees;
搶摘 seize the fruits;
文摘 digest; abstract;
指摘 blame; censure; criticize; pick faults and criticize; point out the faults of others;

zhai

【齋】 (1) vegetarian diet; vegetarian meal; (2) abstain from meat; fast; (3) give alms to a monk; (4) building; room; study;
［齋飯］ vegetarian food;
［齋戒］ abstain from meat; fast;
齋戒沐浴 fast and ablution; fast and take a bath before a religious observance; make one's ablution; perform one's ablution;
［齋期］ fast days;
［齋舍］ (1) room for fasting; (2) study; (3) school;
［齋堂］ dining room in a Buddhist temple;
［齋心］ purify the mind;
［齋月］ the month of fast;

長齋 permanent abstention from meat;
吃齋 (1) abstain from eating meat; (2) (of monks) have meals;
時齋 keep vegetarian fast;
封齋 Ramadan;
開齋 (1) resume a meat diet; (2) come to the end of Ramadan;
施齋 give food to monks or nuns;
書齋 study;

zhai²

zhai

【宅】 dwelling; house; residence;
［宅邸］ abode; hotel; residence;
［宅地］ croft; toft;
［宅第］ big house; mansion;
豪華宅第 stately home;
［宅門］ gate of a house;
［宅舍］ dwelling;
［宅心］ intention;
宅心仁厚 of a kindly disposition; settle the mind with benevolence and honesty;
［宅憂］ in mourning;
［宅園］ private garden;
［宅院］ house; house with a courtyard;
［宅子］ house; residence;

卜宅 (1) choose a residence; (2) choose a tomb site;
本宅 one's own residence;
豪宅 luxury property;
家宅 family dwelling;
窟宅 den; lair;
坤宅 bride's family;
內宅 inner chambers for women folk;
乾宅 bridegroom's home called during a wedding;
凶宅 haunted house;
陰宅 graveyard;
住宅 dwelling; residence;
綴宅 physical human body;

zhai

【翟】 a surname;

zhai

【擇】 a pronunciation of 擇；

zhai³
zhai

【窄】 (1) contracted; narrow; tight; (2) mean; narrow-minded;

[窄道] narrow path;

[窄縫] narrow slit;

[窄門] narrow door;

[窄巷] narrow lane;

[窄小] narrow and small;

背窄 have a narrow back;
寬窄 size; width;
狹窄 (1) cramped; narrow; (2) narrow and limited;
心窄 narrow-minded;

zhai⁴
zhai

【砦】 military outpost; stockade;

鹿砦 abates;
樁砦 post obstacles;

zhai

【債】 debt; obligation;

[債多不愁] when there are too many debts, one stops worrying about them;

[債額] amount of debt;

[債戶] debtor;

[債家] creditor;

[債款] loan;
外國債款 external borrowings;

[債權] claim; creditor's rights; outstanding claims;
債權國 creditor nation;
債權人 claimant; claimer; creditor; debtee;
~部份擔保債權人 partially secured creditor;
~擔保充分的債權人 full secured creditor;
~破產債權人 creditor of bankruptcy;
~欺詐性債權人 fraudulent creditor;
~無擔保債權人 unsecured creditor;
~優先債權人 preferential creditor;
~正當債權人 bona fide creditor;
不良債權 bad claim;
貨幣債權 money claim;
統一債權 equalization claim;
轉讓債權 assigned claim;

[債券] bond; debenture;
債券持有人 bond holder;
債券發行市場 bond floatation market;
債券還本 bond refunding;
債券投資 bond investment;
債券賬戶 debenture account;
不兌換債券 irredeemable bonds;
產業債券 industrial bond;
長期債券 long-term bond;
金融債券 bank debenture;
垃圾債券 junk bond;
信用債券 debenture;
以繳債券 bond subscriptions;
應付債券 bond payable;

[債台高築] a mountain of debts; accumulate high debts; be immersed in debt; become debt-ridden; deep in debt; heavily in debt; over head and ears in debt; run heavily into debt; up to one's ears in debt; up to one's neck in debt;
債台高築的 debt-ridden;

[債務] borrowing; debt; liability; obligation; the amount due;
債務纏身 be embarrassed by debts; be involved in debt;
債務減免 debt relief;
債務累累 be burdened with debts; be saddled with debts;
債務人 debtor;
~破產債務人 bankruptcy debtor;
~失踪債務人 absence debtor;
~雜項債務人 sundry debtors;
擺脱債務 extricate oneself from debt; go out of debt; rid oneself of debt;
保證債務 guaranteed debt; surety obligation;
償付債務 meet a debt;
償還債務 pay back the debt;
到期債務 matured liability;
短期債務 current liabilities; stopgap borrowing;
高額債務 heavy debts;
勾銷債務 cancel a debt; write off a debt;
國內債務 internal debts;
還清債務 clear a debt; clear one's debts;
即期債務 demand debt;
積欠債務 amass debts; run up debts;
減少債務 reduce a debt;
了結債務 wipe off a debt;
免去債務 forgive sb a debt;
企業債務 enterprise debt;
豁免債務 release a debt;
完全債務 perfect obligation;
未清償債務 outstanding debt;

unliquidated obligation; unpaid debt;
無息債務 passive debt;
選擇債務 alternative obligation;
一筆債務 a debt;
銀行債務 bank debt;
賬面債務 book debts;
中期債務 intermediate debt;

［債項］ amount due;
［債主］ creditor; debtee;

背債 be burdened with debts; be saddled with debts; in debt;
逼債 press for payment of debts;
避債 avoid creditors;
償債 pay a debt;
催債 dun sb for payment of debt; press for payment of debt;
抵債 pay a debt by labour; pay a debt in kind;
賭債 gambling debt;
躲債 avoid a creditor;
惡債 odious debts;
放債 lend money for interest;
負債 in debt; incur debts; indebtedness; liability;
公債 government bonds; government loans; public loans; state loans;
國債 government loan; national debt;
還債 pay off a debt; repay a debt; settle a debt;
借債 borrow money; raise a loan;
舊債 long-standing debts; old debts;
舉債 borrow money; raise debts;
賴債 bilk one's creditors; repudiate a debt;
內債 internal debt;
錢債 debt;
欠債 behind with; fall into debt; get into debt; in debt; in debt to; in deficit; in hock; in hock to sb; in the hole; in sb's debt; in the red; into sb; owe a debt; owe sb money for; run into debt; run into debt to sb;
收債 collect a debt;
宿債 long overdue debt;
逃債 dodge a creditor; run away from the creditor;
討債 ask for the payment of a debt; demand the repayment of a loan;
外債 external debt; foreign debt;
血債 a debt of blood;
一筆債 a debt;
一大堆債 a mountain of debt;

zhai

【寨】 stockade;

［寨主］ leader;
［寨子］ stockaded village;

拔寨 (1) break camp; (2) capture; storm;
村寨 stockade village;
山寨 fortified mountain village; mountain fastness;

zhai

【瘵】 (1) disease; illness; tuberculosis; (2) distress;

zhan¹

zhan

【占】 (1) divine; divine by casting lots; practise divination; (2) observe; (3) a surname;

［占卜］ divine; practise divination;
占卜吉凶 divine fortune or misfortune;
［占斷］ find out by practising divination;
占斷吉凶 cast lots through divine means; find out good or bad luck by divination;
［占卦］ divination; divine by the Eight Diagrams; tell by divination;
占卦算命 divine one's fortune;
占卦問卜 consult the oracle; inquire about by divination;
［占課］ divine by tossing coins; the art of divination;
［占夢］ interpret a dream;
［占念］ a divination that comes true;
［占頭］ bad omen;
［占星］ cast a horoscope; divine by astrology;
占星術 astrology;
占星學 astrology;
［占驗］ confirmation of an oracle;

星占 cast a horoscope; divine by astrology;

zhan

【沾】 (1) moisten; wet; (2) be stained with; contaminate; stain; tinge; (3) touch; (4) get sth out of association with sb or sth;

［沾邊］ (1) touch on only lightly; (2) close to what it should be; relevant;
根本不沾邊 completely irrelevant;
［沾唇］ touch the tips;
酒不沾唇 never touch wine; not to touch a drop of wine;
［沾光］ benefit from association with sb or sth;

從中沾光 derive the full benefit from sth;
直接沾光 benefit sb directly;

［沾寒］ catch cold; suffer from a cold;

［沾洽］ be moistened by copious rain;

［沾親帶故］ be related somehow or other; have ties of kinship or friendship; with blood or marital relationship;

［沾染］ be contaminated by; be infected with; be steeped in; be tainted with; become addicted to;

沾染惡習 be tainted with bad habits; slide into bad habits;
沾染世俗 be corrupted by worldly ways;
沾染習氣 be corrupted by prevailing bad practices;
容易沾染 become easily infected by;

［沾濕］ (1) damp; make wet; moisten; wet; (2) imbued with;

［沾手］ (1) touch with one's hand; (2) have a hand in;

［沾水］ soak in water;

［沾污］ contaminate; pollute;

［沾潤］ (1) moisten; wet; (2) harvest benefits from the side;

［沾沾自喜］ complacent over; feel complacent; hug oneself on; hug oneself with delight; hug oneself with joy; pat oneself on the back; play the peacock; pleased with oneself; priggish; self-complacent; self-contented; smug; smug and complacent;

［沾漬］ be imbued with; soak in;

均沾 share equally;

zhan

【呫】 whisper;

zhan

【旃】 (1) flag with a bent staff; (2) auxiliary particle; (3) woolen fabrics; (4) a surname;

zhan

【覘】 inspect; investigate secretly; observe; peep; see; spy; spy on;

［覘國］ inspect and survey conditions within a nation;

［覘候］ look out for; spy on;

zhan

【詹】 (1) talk too much; verbosity; (2) reach; (3) a surname; (4) (now rare) divine; (5) look up; oversee; select;

［詹詹］ argumentative; quarrelsome;

zhan

【霑】 (1) be soaked; become damp; become wet; imbue with; moisten; (2) drunk; imbibed; (3) bestow favours;

［霑恩］ be granted special favours; indebted to;

［霑沐］ receive favours;

［霑染］ (1) get affected by a communicable disease; (2) gain a small advantage;

［霑衣］ soaked through the clothing;

［霑醉］ dead drunk;

zhan

【氈】 (1) felt; (2) blanket;

［氈帽］ felt cap;

［氈幕］ felt tent;

［氈頭筆］ felt-tip pen;

［氈鞋］ felt shoes;

［氈子］ felt;

毛氈 felt;
吸音氈 baffle blanket;
細氈 fine felt;
油毛氈 asphalt felt;
油氈 asphalt felt;

zhan

【邅】 very difficult to proceed;

迍邅 move forward with difficulty; unable to achieve one's ambition;

zhan

【瞻】 (1) look at; look forward; look up; (2) regard respectfully; regard with reverence;

［瞻顧］ look ahead and behind; wait and see;

瞻前顧後 look ahead into the future and back into the past — weigh one's steps by thinking of consequences; look before and behind; look fore and aft — take into account both past experience and the situation that may possibly arise in the future; look round the corner; peer ahead and look behind — over-cautious and indecisive;

［瞻念］ look to; think of;

瞻念前途 think of the future;
瞻念前途，不寒而慄 shudder at the thought of the future;

Z

[瞻視] behold; look;
[瞻望] (1) look far ahead; look forward; (2) look up to;
瞻望未來 look into the future;
[瞻仰] (1) look at with reverence; pay respects to; (2) look up to;
瞻仰遺容 pay one's respects to the remains of sb; pay respects to sb's remains;
瞻仰尊顏 look up to sb's face with reverence;

觀瞻 the scene and the impression sth leaves on people;

zhan
【譫】 delirious;
[譫妄] delirium;
焦慮性譫妄 anxious delirium;
慢性酒精性譫妄 chronic alcoholic delirium;
中毒性譫妄 toxic delirium;

zhan
【饘】 thick congee or porridge;
[饘粥糲食] bread and water diet; plain and coarse food; the poorest and most meagre food;

zhan
【鱣】 eel;

zhan
【鸇】 a kind of bird of prey;

zhan³

zhan
【展】 (1) extend; spread out; stretch; unfold; unroll; (2) give free play to; (3) postpone; prolong; (4) exhibition; (5) a surname;
[展拜] visit;
[展布] (1) expound; (2) display one's talents;
[展翅] fly; get ready for flight; open out the wings; spread the wings;
展翅翱翔 soar on the wings;
展翅飛翔 spread its wings to fly;
展翅高飛 soar to great heights; spread the wings and soar high;
有翅難展 unable to make use of one's ability;
[展出] exhibit; put on display; on show;
展出物 exhibit;
公開展出 exhibit before the public;
[展緩] (1) postpone; put off; (2) extend the deadline; extend the time limit;
[展技] demonstrate one's ability to the fullest extent;
[展卷] open a scroll;
[展開] (1) amplify; decoil; develop; open up; spread; spread out; unfold; (2) carry out; develop; launch;
展開翅膀 stretch open wings;
展開法 expansion method;
展開書信 unfold a letter;
展開討論 set off a discussion;
[展寬] stretch; stretching;
展寬器 stretcher;
~脈衝展寬器 pulse stretcher;
白展寬 white stretch;
視頻展寬 video stretching;
同步展寬 sync stretching;
[展覽] display; exhibit; exhibition; put on display; show;
展覽公司 exhibition company;
展覽會 exhibition; expo; fair;
~廣告展覽會 advertising exhibition;
~皮革展覽會 leather fair;
~商品展覽會 commodity fair;
~學校展覽會 school exhibition;
~一個展覽會 an exhibition;
展覽日期 exhibition period;
籌備展覽 arrange an exhibition;
航空展覽 aeroshow;
流動藝術展覽 artmobile;
汽車展覽 motor show;
時裝展覽 fashion show;
書法展覽 Chinese calligraphy exhibition;
書籍展覽 book exhibition;
圖書展覽 book exhibition;
巡迴展覽 travelling exhibition;
[展墓] visit a grave;
[展品] exhibit; item on display;
[展期] (1) be postponed; be put off; extend the deadline; extend the time limit; postpone; renewal; (2) extended insurance;
[展示] display; exhibit; lay bare; open up before one's eyes; reveal; show;
展示會 a trade show; an exhibition;
[展縮] flexible;
[展望] (1) look into the distance; (2) envisage; envision; look ahead; look into the

future; outlook;
展望未來 look forward to the future;
經濟展望 business outlook;
[展限] extend the deadline; extend the time limit;
[展現] develop; emerge; present before one's eyes; unfold before one's eyes; yield up;
展現眼前 be unfolded before sb's eyes;
[展銷] exhibit and sell;
展銷會 commodities fair; sales exhibition;
[展樣] (1) stately; (2) broad-minded;

參展 participate in an exhibition;
大展 spread the wings;
發展 (1) develop; expand; (2) admit; recruit;
花展 flower show;
畫展 art exhibition;
匯展 collective exhibition;
進展 evolve; make headway; make progress; march;
菊展 chrysanthemum exhibition;
開展 launch; unfold;
擴展 expand;
平展 open and flat;
鋪展 spread out;
親展 (1) meet in person; (2) to be opened by the addressee only;
商展 trade fair;
伸展 extend; spread; spread out; stretch; stretching;
施展 display;
書展 book fair;
舒展 (1) extend; unfold; (2) be at easy; feel comfortable;
影展 (1) photo exhibition; (2) movie festival;
玉展 for your perusal;
預展 preview of an exhibition; private view;
招展 flutter; sway; wave;

zhan

【斬】 (1) chop; cut; (2) behead; kill;
[斬釘截鐵] act with determination and courage; categorical; directly; in a firm tone; implacably; resolute and decisive; with curt finality; with decision and dispatch; without mincing words;
[斬斷] chop off; cleave;
斬斷魔爪 chop off the octopus arms; trim the claws of;
斬斷青絲 shave off one's hair to enter monastery;
斬斷情絲 cut off the threads of love;
[斬伐] (1) conquer; subjugate; (2) behead; execute; (3) fell trees; prune;
[斬獲] cause enemy troops heavy casualties and material loss; score a victory on the battlefield;
[斬將] behead enemy generals;
斬將搴旗 behead enemy generals and capture their flags;
搴旗斬將 pull up enemy flags and behead enemy generals on the battlefield;
[斬盡殺絕] exterminate once and for all; kill all; massacre to the last man; wipe out the whole lot;
[斬決] carry out an execution by beheading the criminal;
[斬肉刀] chopper;
[斬首] behead; decapitate; guillotine;
斬首示眾 behead a criminal and exhibit the severed head to the public as a warning to would-be offenders; cut off sb's head to display to the public; expose a cut-off head to public view as a warning;
[斬妖] exorcise evil spirits;

擒斬 capture and behead;
腰斬 cut sth in half;
斫斬 chop; cut; hew;

zhan

【琖】 jade wine cup; jage chalice;

zhan

【盞】 (1) small cup; small shallow container; (2) numerical adjunct;

把盞 hold cup in hand;
燈盞 oil lamp;
酒盞 small wine cup;

zhan

【搌】 (1) bind; (2) mop; wipe;
[搌布] dish towel; dishcloth; mopping cloth;

zhan

【嶄】 (1) high and steep; towering; (2) fine; swell; (3) new; novel;
[嶄然] (1) completely changed; (2) high and steep;
[嶄新] brand-new; completely new;
嶄新的制服 brand-new tunic suit;

Z

［嶄巖］ rough and steep;

zhan

【輾】 (1) toss about in bed; (2) pass through many hands or places;

［輾側不寐］ toss and turn in bed, unable to sleep;

［輾轉］ (1) roll about; toss about in bed; (2) pass through many hands or places;
輾轉不安 toss about and feel uneasy;
輾轉反側 have a sleepless night; toss about in bed; toss all night; toss and tumble; toss and turn restlessly; toss from side to side; turn backward and forward;
輾轉流傳 pass through many hands; spread from place to place;
輾轉難忘 cannot forget; keep thinking in one's mind; revolving sth over and over in the mind; unable to forget it;
輾轉思維 rack one's brains; turn sth over in one's mind;
輾轉相告 pass from mouth to mouth;

zhan⁴

zhan

【占】 occupy;

［占領］ occupy;

［占據］ occupy by force; occupy illegally;

［占先］ occupy before others; preempt;

［占有］ take possession of;

zhan

【佔】 occupy; seize; take by force; usurp;

［佔據］ hold; occupy; take over; take possession of; usurp;
佔據有利地形 occupy an advantage point;

［佔領］ capture; hold; occupy; seize;
佔領區 occupied area;

［佔先］ get ahead of; take precedence; take the lead;

［佔有］ (1) have; own; possess; (2) hold; occupy; (3) have; own;
佔有不動產 hold estate;
佔有財產 get possession of the property;
非法佔有 take illegal possession of sth;

霸佔 occupy forcibly; seize;
獨佔 have sth all to oneself; monopolize;
攻佔 attack and occupy; storm and capture;
進佔 attack and occupy;
強佔 occupy forcibly; seize;
搶佔 race to control;
侵佔 invade and occupy;
圈佔 draw a circle on the ground and occupy;
吞佔 take possession of sth illegally;
襲佔 capture a place by a surprise attack;

zhan

【站】 (1) on one's feet; stand; stand up; step; take a stand; (2) halt; stop; (3) station; stop; (4) station for rending certain services;

［站班］ on duty; stand guard;

［站得高，看得遠］ far-sighted; from the most commanding height and with the greatest vision; have the vantage ground from which to see far ahead; have vision; stand high and gaze far; stand on a vantage point and have a far-sighted view;

［站定］ stand still;

［站隊］ line up; queue up; stand in line;
站隊買票 line up to buy tickets;

［站崗］ be on sentry duty; stand guard; stand sentry;
站崗放哨 keep guard and stand sentry; stand guard; stand sentinel;

［站立］ on one's feet; stand;
足尖站立 stand on tiptoe;

［站排］ line up;

［站台］ platform; station;
出發站台 departure platform;
到達站台 arrival platform;

［站位］ positioning;

［站穩］ (1) come to a stop; (2) stand firm; take a firm stand;
站穩腳跟 get a firm foothold; stand fast; stand firm; take a firm stand;

［站在］ standing;
站在那裏 standing there;
站在一旁說風涼話 make irresponsible and carping comments from the side-lines; make sarcastic remarks from the side-lines;

［站長］ head of a station;

［站住］ (1) halt; stop; (2) keep one's feet; stand firmly on one's feet; (3) hold water; tenable;
站住腳 (1) halt; stop; (2) consolidate one's position; hold one's ground;
站不住 (1) unable to keep standing; (2)

disputable; full of loopholes;
~站不住腳 cannot hold one's ground; cannot hold water; cannot stand up; have not a leg to stand on; invalid; lame; on thin ice; unable to hold one's position; unable to stand on one's feet; untenable;
站得住 (1) able to hold one's position; able to stand; (2) irrefutable; sound;
~站得住腳 able to stand on one's feet; hang together; hold water; tenable; valid;

保健站 health station;
邊防站 frontier station;
變電站 transformer substation;
兵站 army service station; military depot;
補給站 supply depot;
不停站 buses whistling past a bus stop;
菜站 wholesale vegetable market;
車站 station; stop;
抽水站 pumping station;
到達站 destination;
電車站 trolley-bus stop;
電灌站 electric pumping station;
電力站 electric power station;
發電站 power station;
防疫站 epidemic prevention station;
肥育站 fattening station;
服務站 neighbourhood service centre;
供應站 supply centre;
觀通站 observation and communication post;
廣播站 broadcasting station;
航空站 air station;
航天站 space-port;
換裝站 transhipment station;
回收站 collection depot;
火電站 thermal power station;
火車站 railway station;
貨運站 freight terminal;
急救站 first-aid station;
加油站 filling station; gas station; petrol station;
檢查站 check-point;
檢疫站 quarantine station;
救護站 first-aid station;
空間站 space station;
雷達站 radar station;
聯絡站 liaison station;
糧站 grain distribution station;
排灌站 irrigation and drainage pumping station;
配給站 ration centre;
氣象站 meteorological station;
始發站 station of departure;
實驗站 experiment centre;
收購站 purchasing station;
收音站 radio station;
獸醫站 veterinary station;
水文站 hydrometric station;
投票站 polling station;
推銷站 sales promotion centre;
網站 web;
衛生站 clinic; health station;
消防站 fire station;
銷售站 sales place;
信號站 signal station;
星際站 interplanetary station;
修配站 repair station;
宣傳站 propaganda station;
驗收站 check-and-acceptance centre;
揚水站 pumping station;
醫療站 health centre; medical station;
驛站 coaching inn; courier station; post house;
雨量站 precipitation station; rainfall station;
診療站 clinic;
徵兵站 drafting centre;
中繼站 relay station;
中轉站 transfer station;
終點站 terminus;
終站 terminal station; terminal stop;
轉運站 transfer post;

zhan

【棧】 (1) inn; storehouse; tavern; warehouse; (2) a road made along a cliff; (3) (now rare) pen; stable; (4) a surname;

[棧單] warrant;
[棧豆] fodder;
[棧房] (1) storehouse; warehouse; (2) inn;
[棧主] innkeeper;
[棧租] godown charge; godown rent; storage;

行棧 broker's storehouse;
貨棧 warehouse;
客棧 hostel; inn;
戀棧 be unwilling to leave one's official post;
糧棧 grain depot;

zhan

【湛】 (1) dewy; (2) deep; profound; (3) a surname; (4) same as 沈；

[湛碧] jade-like colour like deep water;
[湛恩] deep favour; deep kindness; great

kindness;
[湛靜] profound quiet;
[湛藍] azure; azure blue; dark blue;
[湛然] (1) calm; quiet; tranquil; (2) transparent;
[湛新] brand-new;
[湛憂] deep worry;
[湛湛] (1) dewy; (2) deep; profound;

澄湛 clear; transparent;
精湛 consummate; exquisite;
清湛 clear; limpid;
深湛 profound and thorough;

zhan

【綻】 (1) crack; ripped seam; (2) defect; flaw;
[綻裂] rip; split;
[綻露] reveal a matter;

開綻 come unsewn;
破綻 (1) burst seam; (2) flaw; weak point;

zhan

【暫】 (1) for a short time; not lasting; of short duration; temporarily; (2) for the moment; for the time being; temporary; (3) abruptly; suddenly;
[暫別] a short separation; part for a short time;
[暫定] arranged for the time being; provisional; tentative;
暫定計劃 tentative plan;
[暫擱] abeyance; hold in abeyance; keep in abeyance; leave in abeyance;
[暫候] wait for a short time;
[暫緩] defer; hold for a while; postpone for a while; put off;
暫緩處死 suspend execution;
暫緩答覆 defer making a reply;
暫緩決定 put off making a decision;
[暫借] borrow for a short time;
[暫留] stay for a short time;
[暫且] for the moment; for the time being;
[暫缺] left vacant for the time being; out of stock for the time being;
[暫時] at the moment; for the moment; for the present; for the time being; temporary; transient; yet;
暫時現象 transient phenomenon;
暫時需要 temporary needs;
[暫停] (1) adjourn; at pause; be in abeyance; make a pause; stop temporarily; suspend; (2) time-out;
暫停付款 suspend payment;
暫停工作 suspend work temporarily;
暫停鍵 pause button;
暫停一會 come up for air;
[暫行] for the time being; provisional; temporary;
暫行法 provisional laws;
暫行規定 interim provisions; temporary provisions;
[暫延] adjourn temporarily; postpone tentatively to;
[暫住] lodge temporarily at; stay for a while;

短暫 brief; momentary; of short duration; transient;

zhan

【戰】 (1) battle; fighting; war; (2) contend; contest; fight; (3) shiver; shudder; tremble; (4) a surname;
對陣戰 pitched battle;
海戰 naval battle; sea battle;
空戰 air battle;
陸戰 land battle;
[戰敗] (1) be defeated; be vanished; lose a battle; suffer a defeat; (2) beat; defeat; vanquish;
戰敗國 defeated belligerent; defeated nation;
戰敗一方 defeated belligerent;
[戰報] battlefield report; war bulletin; war communique;
[戰備] combat readiness; war preparations;
[戰場] battlefield; battlefront; battleground;
[戰船] man-of-war; war vessel; warship;
[戰刀] sabre;
[戰地] battlefield; battleground;
戰地服裝 battledress;
戰地記者 war correspondent;
[戰抖] shiver; shudder; tremble;
[戰鬥] (1) battle; combat; fight; (2) fighting; militant;
戰鬥疲勞症 combat fatigue;
戰鬥機 battle plane; combat aircraft; fighter plane;
~戰鬥機部隊 fighter arm;
戰鬥經驗 experience of combat;

戰鬥力 combat effectiveness; combat strength; fighting capacity;
戰鬥人員 combatant;
不分勝負的戰鬥 drawn battle;
短兵相接的戰鬥 hand-to-hand combat;
奮勇戰鬥 act a good part;
艱難的戰鬥 uphill battle;
投入戰鬥 come into action; go into action; go into battle;
殊死戰鬥 mortal combat;
一場戰鬥 a battle;

[戰端] beginning of a war;
重起戰端 renew hostilities; war breaks out again;

[戰犯] war criminal;
懲處戰犯 try a war criminal;
甲級戰犯 A-class war criminals;
審判戰犯 try a war criminal;

[戰俘] captive; prisoners of war;
交換戰俘 exchange prisoners of war;
釋放戰俘 liberate prisoners of war;

[戰斧] battleaxe;

[戰歌] battle song; fighting song;

[戰功] battle achievements; meritorious military service; military exploits;
戰功彪炳 the meritorious military service being very illustrious;
戰功顯赫 one's meritorious military service is illustrious; shining with exploits;

[戰鼓] battle drums; war drums;

[戰國] Warring States;

[戰果] combat success; military achievements; results of battle; victory; war results;
戰果輝煌 achieve splendid results on the battlefield; brilliant combat performance; win a brilliant military victory;

[戰壕] trench; entrenchment;

[戰和] war or peace;
不戰不和 no war, no peace;

[戰後] after the war; postwar;
戰後餘殃 aftermath of war;

[戰患] disaster of war;

[戰火] flames of war;
戰火紛飛 flames of war raging everywhere; war-ridden;
戰火考驗 be tested in the raging flames of war;
戰火連天 the flames of war rage across the land;
戰火蔓延 the flames of war are spreading;
戰火彌漫 flames of war are filling the air;

[戰禍] disaster of war;

[戰機] opportunity for combat;

[戰績] battle achievements; combat gains; military exploits; military successes;
戰績輝煌 extraordinary battle achievements;

[戰艦] battleship; warship;

[戰局] war situation;

[戰況] progress of a battle; situation on the battlefield; the war situation;
戰況報導 war news;

[戰慄] shiver; shudder; tremble;
渾身戰慄 all of a tremble;
戰戰慄慄 tremble with fear; shuddering with fright;

[戰利品] booty; captured equipment; loot; spoils of war; war trophies;

[戰亂] chaos and social upheavals brought about by war; chaos caused by war;

[戰略] strategy;
戰略產業 strategic industry;
戰略導彈部隊 strategic missile forces;
戰略規劃 strategic plan;
戰略核力量 strategic nuclear forces;
戰略核武器 strategic nuclear weapons;
戰略家 strategist;
~紙上談兵的戰略家 closet strategist;
戰略經營 strategic management;
戰略決策 strategic decision-making;
戰略力量 strategic forces;
戰略情報 strategic information;
戰略學 science of strategy;
戰略重點 strategic emphasis; strategic focus;
戰略資源 strategic resources;
改變戰略 improve one's strategy;
核戰略 nuclear strategy;
周邊戰略 peripheral strategy;

[戰馬] battle steed; charger; war-horse;

[戰歿] be killed in action; die in battle;

[戰前] antebellum; before the war; prewar;
戰前歲月 antebellum years;
戰前談判 antebellum negotiations;

[戰勤] civilian war service;

[戰區] battle zone; theatre of operations; theatre of war; war zone;

[戰勝] defeat; overcome; triumph over;

戰勝敵人 win a victory over the enemy;
戰勝對手 defeat one's opponent;
戰勝國 victorious nation;
戰勝困難 surmount difficulties;
不戰而勝 conquer without a single fight; defeat sb without a fight; win hands down;
連戰連勝 victorious in battle after battle; win a series of victories;
屢戰屢勝 fight repeatedly and win every battle; score one victory after another; win every battle; win victory after victory;
三戰兩勝 the best of three games; win two out of three games;
一戰而勝 gain the victory by a single blow;
戰之能勝 able to win when one fights;

[戰時] wartime;

[戰史] annals of war; war history;

[戰士] (1) man; soldier; (2) champion; combatant; fighter; warrior;
自由戰士 freedom fighter;

[戰事] clashes; fighting; hostilities; war;
戰事突起 hostilities break out;

[戰書] letter of challenge; written declaration of war;
下戰書 deliver a challenge in writing;

[戰術] art of war; military tactics;
戰術家 tactician;
戰術意識 tactical consciousness;
變換戰術 change tactics;
缺乏戰術 lack in tactics;
閃電戰術 blitz tactics;
滲透戰術 infiltration tactics;
游擊戰術 guerrilla tactics; partisan tactics;

[戰死] be killed in action; die in battle;
戰死沙場 be killed in battle; bite the dust; die in battle; lay down one's life on the battlefield;

[戰線] battlefront; battle line;
擴大戰線 widen the battlefront;

[戰役] battle; campaign;
具有歷史意義的戰役 historic battle;
重大戰役 great battle;
重要戰役 important battle; major battle;
著名戰役 famous battle;

[戰友] battle companion; brother-in-arms; comrade-in-arms;
同甘共苦的戰友 comrades-in arms sharing weal and woe; fellow fighters through thick and thin;

[戰雲] war cloud;
戰雲彌漫 war clouds hang over the horizon; war is imminent;
戰雲密布 gathering war clouds;

[戰戰兢兢] apprehensive and careful; cautiously; gingerly; in fear and trembling; run scared; trembling with fear; trembling with fright; trembling with terror; very cautious; with caution; with the most meticulous care; with trepidation;

[戰陣] deployment of troops;

[戰爭] conflagration; war; warfare;
戰爭爆發 outbreak of war; war breaks out;
戰爭浩劫 devastating war;
戰爭基金 war chest;
戰爭經濟學 economics of war;
戰爭狂人 warmaniac; war-monger;
戰爭疲勞症 battle fatigue;
戰爭片 military film; war film;
戰爭史 annals of war;
戰爭狀態 state of war;
戰爭罪行 war crime;
~粉飾戰爭罪行 whitewash war crimes;
按鈕戰爭 push-button warfare;
參加戰爭 fight in a war;
常規戰爭 conventional war;
電子戰爭 electronic warfare;
發動戰爭 make war; start a war; unleash a war; wage war;
防止戰爭 avert war; avoid war; prevent war;
輻射戰爭 radiological warfare;
國內戰爭 civil war;
核戰爭 nuclear war;
~全面核戰爭 all-cut nuclear war;
化學戰爭 chemical warfare;
假戰爭 phoney war;
經濟戰爭 economic warfare;
局部戰爭 local war;
侵略戰爭 aggressive warfare; war of aggression;
全面戰爭 all-embracing war; all-out war; full-scale war;
全球戰爭 global war;
人民戰爭 people's war;
現代戰爭 modern war;
消滅戰爭 eradicate war;
引起戰爭 bring on a war;

有限戰爭 limited war;
正規戰爭 regular warfare;
正義戰爭 just war;

鏖戰 fight a pitched battle; fight hard;
百戰 fight a hundred battles;
白刃戰 hand-to-hand combat;
備戰 (1) prepare for war; (2) be prepared against war;
筆戰 paper battle; paper warfare; polemic writing; written polemics;
搏戰 box; combat; engage in hand-to-hand combat;
不戰 without fighting;
參戰 enter a war; go to war; take part in a war;
持久戰 protracted war;
初戰 initial battle;
催化戰 catalytic war;
打戰 shiver; tremble;
地道戰 tunnel warfare;
地雷戰 mine warfare;
督戰 supervise operations;
惡戰 fierce battle; hard fighting;
防禦戰 defensive warfare;
奮戰 fight bravely;
攻擊戰 attack; offensive;
攻堅戰 storming of heavily fortified positions;
攻心戰 psychological attack;
觀戰 (1) watch others fight; (2) watch sports games and liven things up;
海戰 naval battle; sea warfare;
酣戰 be engaged in a fierce battle;
寒戰 shiver;
壕塹戰 trench warfare;
好戰 bellicose; warlike;
會戰 (1) meet for a decisive battle; (2) join in a battle;
混戰 confused fight; melee; tangled warfare;
機動戰 mobile warfare;
激戰 fight seriously;
殲滅戰 war of annihilation;
交手戰 hand-to-hand fight;
交戰 at war; be engaged in fight; deliver battle; do battle; wage war;
狙擊戰 sniping action;
決戰 decisive war;
開戰 open hostilities;
抗戰 war of resistance against aggression;
坑道戰 tunnel warfare;
空戰 air action; air battle; air-to-air battle; air-to-air combat;
苦戰 hard struggle; wage an arduous struggle;
冷戰 cold war;
力戰 fight hard;
連戰 successive battles;
臨戰 just before going into war;
論戰 controversy; debate; polemic;
貿易戰 trade war;
耐戰 able to continue fighting for a long time;
內戰 civil war;
搦戰 challenge to fight;
砲戰 artillery action;
礮戰 artillery action;
破擊戰 sabotage operations;
破襲戰 sabotage operations;
棋戰 chess battle; game of chess; fight it out in chess;
前哨戰 skirmish;
槍戰 exchange of fire; firefight; gun battle; gunfight; shoot-out;
請戰 ask for a battle assignment;
求戰 (1) seek battle; (2) ask for a battle assignment;
雀戰 play a game of mahjong;
肉搏戰 hand-to-hand fight;
熱戰 hot war;
閃電戰 lightning war;
閃擊戰 lightning war;
善戰 good at fighting in battle;
商戰 commercial war; trade war;
舌戰 argue heatedly; debate with verbal confrontation; have a verbal battle with;
神經戰 war of nerves;
聖戰 holy war; sacred war;
生物戰 biological warfare;
實戰 actual combat;
水戰 naval battle;
死戰 battle to the last; desperate fight; fight to the death; life-and-death battle;
殊死戰 last-ditch battle;
速決戰 war of quick decision;
挑戰 (1) challenge to battle; (2) challenge to a contest;
停戰 armistice; break off the action; cessation of hostilities; truce;
統戰 united front;
外匯戰 exchange war;
細菌戰 bacteriological warfare;
消耗戰 war of attrition;
巷戰 combat in street; house to house fighting; street battle; street fighting;
心理戰 psychological warfare;
休戰 cease fire; truce;
序戰 initial battle;

Z

宣戰 declaration of war; declare war; hang out the red flag; proclaim war;
血戰 bloody battle;
厭戰 be weary of war;
野戰 field operations;
夜戰 night fighting;
義戰 war for moral principles;
迎戰 meet an approaching enemy head-on;
應戰 (1) meet an enemy attack; (2) accept a challenge;
游擊戰 guerrilla warfare;
運動戰 mobile warfare;
遭遇戰 contact battle;
陣地戰 positional warfare;
征戰 go on an expedition;
正規戰 regular warfare;
助戰 (1) assist in fighting; (2) bolster sb's morale;
轉戰 fight in one place after another;
阻擊戰 blocking action;
總體戰 general warfare;
作戰 conduct operations; do battle; fight; fight against; go to battle; make war;

Z

zhan
【蹔】 same as 暫;

zhan
【蘸】 (1) dip into sauce; (2) (of a woman) marry again;
[蘸筆] dip a writing brush in ink;
蘸筆疾書 dip a brush in ink and write swiftly;
[蘸火] quenching;
[蘸濕] dip;

zhang¹
zhang
【張】 (1) extend; open; spread; stretch; (2) exaggerate; (3) look; (4) opening of a new shop; (5) display; set out; (6) leaf; sheet; (7) a surname;
[張本] (1) anticipatory action; (2) anticipatory remark;
[張弛] fast and loose; tension and relaxation;
久張則馳，久習則實慣 a bow long bent grows weak;
有張有弛 there are tension and relaxation;
張而不弛 not get to extremes;
[張大] exaggerate; magnify; publicize widely;
張大其詞 exaggerate; lay it on thick; make exaggerated statements; overstate;
張大其事 publicize a matter;
[張燈結彩] be decked out and hung with lanterns; be decorated with festive lanterns and bunting; be festooned with lights and streamers; hang lanterns and festoons; hang up lanterns and coloured buntings; hang out lanterns and put up decorations; hang up lanterns and silk festoons;
[張帆] carry a sail; hoist a sail; lift a sail; press of canvas; press of sail;
張帆待航 set sail;
[張弓] draw the bow;
張弓搭箭 attach arrow to bow; fit the arrow to the bowstring; stretch bow and fix arrow; with bows drawn and arrows set;
張弓滿月 draw the bow to its full extent; one's bow arched like a full moon;
[張挂] decorate; hang up;
[張冠李戴] attribute sth to the wrong person; confuse one thing with another; get the wrong end of the stick; get the wrong sow by the ear; have the wrong sow by the ear; mistake one thing for another; the name does not correspond to the actuality;
[張皇] alarmed; flurried; flustered; scared;
張皇敗露 fail for being scared out of wits; spoil an affair by nervousness;
張皇失措 be frightened and at a loss what to do; be scared out of one's senses; be scared out of one's seven senses; be scared out of one's wits; be seized with panic; be struck with panic; fall into a flutter; get into a panic; in a flurry of alarm; lose composure; lose mental control; lose one's head; lose one's presence of mind; panic-stricken; panic-struck; panicky;
[張開] expand; extend; open; spread; stretch open;
張開手 open one's hand;
[張口] open mouth;
張口病 grape;
張口結舌 agape and tongue-tied; at a loss for words; gape with astonishment; gape with wonder; in open-mouthed astonishment; one's tongue glues itself to the roof of one's mouth; see a wolf;

with open mouth;
張口凝視 stare with open mouth;
張口傾聽 listen with parted lips;
張口吐舌 hang one's tongue out in astonishment; stick out one's tongue in amazement;
張口欲言 on the point of speaking; open one's mouth to speak;
張口咋舌 click one's tongue in surprise;
飯來張口 eat a ready-cooked meal; those who eat but don't work;

[張狂] abandon oneself to pleasure; dissipate without inhibition; flippant and impudent;

[張李] anybody;
説張道李 gossip about this or that person;
張三李四 any man in the street; anybody;
~怪張三，怨李四 go around blaming everybody;

[張力] tensile strength; tension;
張力不等 heterotonia;
張力過低 hypotonia;
張力過高 hypertonia;
張力過強 hypertonus;
張力減退 hypotonus;
張力缺乏 abirritation;
張力缺失 atonia;
張力失常 dystonia;
張力異常 paratonia;
張力正常 normotonia;
表面張力 surface tension;
附着張力 adhesion tension;
黏合張力 adhesive tension;
雙向張力 biaxial tension;
水氣張力 aqueous vapour;

[張量] tensor;
締合張量 associated tensor;
反對稱張量 antisymmetrical tensor;
加速度張量 acceleration tensor;
絕對張量 absolute tensor;

[張羅] (1) raise funds; raise money; scare up; (2) get busy about; take care of;
張羅佈網 lay a trap to lure;
張羅顧客 attend the customers;
張羅人才 (1) net talent; (2) set a snare for talent;
四出張羅 try to get sth in all dircctions from all sources;

[張目] (1) open one's eyes wide; (2) boost sb's arrogance; help publicize an unworthy cause;
助敵張目 inflate the arrogance of the enemy;

[張手] open one's hands;

[張貼] paste up; placard; plaster; post; post up; put up;
張貼佈告 put up a notice;
禁止張貼 post no notices;

[張望] (1) peep through a crack; (2) look about; look around; look into the distance;
東張西望 gaze around; gaze right and left; glance this way and that look all round; peer around; peer in all directions;
~出洞的老鼠—東張西望 a rat just out of its hole — peering around;
四下張望 look round;
~驚慌地四下張望 look around in alarm;
探頭張望 crane one's neck and look around;

[張心] worry oneself with requests;

[張眼] open one's eyes;

[張揚] make public; make widely know; publicize;
四處張揚 spread sth all over the place;

[張嘴] (1) open one's mouth; (2) ask for a favour; ask for a loan;
七張八嘴 at sixes and sevens; in a state of disagreement;

擘張 draw a bow;
鴟張 stretched wings of an owl — oppressors;
重張 re-open;
出張 (of mahjong) discard a tile;
分張 say goodbye;
更張 adjust the strings of a musical instrument;
乖張 eccentric and unreasonable; odd and intractable;
關張 close down;
慌張 flurried; flustered;
緊張 a bundle of nerves; be strung up; be tensed up; key up; nervous; strained; tense; tension; tonus;
開張 (1) begin doing business; open a business; (2) first transaction of a day's business; (3) wide and magnificent;
誇張 (1) exaggerate; overstate; (2) hyperole; (3) give prominence to; stress;
擴張 dilation; enlarge; expand; extend; extension; spread;
廓張 enlarge; expand;

皮張 hide; pelt;
鋪張 extravagant;
掞張 smooth but untruthful; suave but exaggerating;
伸張 promote; uphold;
聲張 disclose; make public;
弛張 tension and relaxation;
舒張 relaxation;
翕張 close and open; furl and unfurl;
囂張 aggressive; arrogant; bossy; haughty; pushy; rampant; unbridled;
樣張 specimen page; specimen sheet;
一張 a piece of; a sheet of; a slip of;
印張 a unit for printing paper;
紙張 paper;
輈張 (1) flurried; (2) insolent;
侜張 cheat; deceive;
主張 advocate; assertion; maintain; opinion; position; proposal; proposition; view;

zhang

【章】 (1) chapter; piece of writing; section; (2) organized body; stature; system; (3) order; (4) regulation; rule; (5) emblem; seal; stamp; (6) make clear; make known; (7) example; pattern; (8) a surname;

［章程］ articles of association; constitution; regulations; rules; statutes;
廢除章程 abolish a rule;
否決章程 vote down a rule;
捍衛章程 defend the constitution;
頒布章程 promulgate regulations;
批准章程 ratify a constitution;
起草章程 draft a constitution;
實施章程 enforce the rule;
違反章程 break a rule;
無視章程 disregard the rule;
宣傳章程 publicize the rule;
執行章程 carry out rules;
制定章程 lay down a rule;
遵守章程 follow rules;

［章動］ nutation;
傾角章動 nutation of inclination;
太陽章動 solar nutation;
月球章動 lunar nutation;
自由章動 free nutation;

［章法］ (1) art of composition; presentation of ideas in a piece of writing; (2) methodicalness; orderly ways;

［章皇］ anxious, agitated and not knowing what to do;

［章回體］ a type of traditional Chinese novels with captions for each chapter;

［章節］ chapters and sections;

［章句］ proper division into chapters and sentences;
雕章琢句 polish a composition; write in ornate style;
斷章摘句 lift a sentence out of context; quote isolated passages; quote truncated passages and sentences out of context; take words and phrases out of context;
堆句砌章 pile up phrases and allusions; pile up sentences;
鈎章棘句 complicated and abstruse writing; intricate and obscure passage;
搜章摘句 search for chapters and pick sentences;
尋章摘句 cull phrases but not meaning; labour over the wording in a pointless manner; write in cliche without originality;
引章摘句 quote remarkable passages and cull model sentences;
綴句成章 put sentences together in composition;

［章臺］ brothel; house of ill fame;

［章魚］ octopus;

［章則］ rules and regulations;

［章章］ clear; evident;

報章 (1) newspaper; (2) reply letter; return mail;
臂章 (1) armband; (2) shoulder emblem;
辭章 (1) poetry and prose; prose and verse; (2) art of writing;
黨章 party constitution;
典章 decrees and regulations; institutions;
蓋章 affix one's seal;
公章 common seal; official seal;
規章 regulations; rules;
華章 your magnificent writing;
徽章 badge; insignia;
會章 (1) constitution of an association; (2) emblem of an association;
肩章 (1) shoulder loop; (2) epaulet;
急就章 hurriedly-written essay;
紀念章 souvenir badge;
簡章 general regulations;
獎章 decoration; medal;
爵章 badges of nobility conferred on noblemen

in Mongolia, Tibet and Mohammedan districts after the birth of the Republic;
領章 collar badge; collar insignia;
篇章 sections and chapters; writings;
詩章 (1) poem; (2) inspiring story;
綬章 cordon;
私章 personal seal; signet;
圖章 seal; stamp;
團章 league constitution;
王章 royal institution;
違章 break rules and regulations;
文章 (1) article; essay; (2) writings; (3) hidden meaning; implied meaning;
紋章 coat of arms; crest;
顯章 clarify; make clear; state with honesty;
憲章 charter;
橡皮章 rubber-stamp;
胸章 badge;
袖章 armband;
勛章 decoration; medal;
牙章 ivory seal;
印章 seal; stamp;
豫章 camphor tree;
樂章 movement;
照章 act in accordance with the regulations;
證章 badge;
周章 be cared; effort; trouble;
奏章 memorial to the throne;

zhang
【彰】 (1) clear; evident; obvious; (2) colourful; ornamental; (3) display; make known; manifest;
［彰明］ clarify; expound; manifest;
彰明較著 already so obvious; as clear as crystal; be easily seen; be known to everyone; conspicuous; extremely obvious and ostensible; very obvious;
彰明昭著 be known to everyone; easily seen; very clearly shown;
［彰顯］ manifest; obvious; show forth;
［彰彰］ evident; famous; well-known;
彰彰明甚 very clear; well-known and evident;
彰彰若是 as clear as that;
彰彰在目 clear for all to see;

表彰 commend; honour;
昭彰 clear; manifest;

zhang
【漳】 (1) a river in Fujian; (2) a river in Henan;

zhang
【獐】 river deer; roe deer;
［獐子］ river deer;

zhang
【鄣】 an ancient state in today's Shandong;

zhang
【樟】 camphor tree;
［樟木］ (1) camphor tree; (2) wood of a camphor tree;
樟木箱 camphorwood trunk;
［樟腦］ camphor;
樟腦球 camphor ball;
［樟樹］ camphor tree;

zhang
【璋】 ancient jade ornament used in state ceremonies;

圭璋 (1) high-quality jade; (2) noble character;
弄璋 give birth to a boy;

zhang
【蟑】 cockroach; roach;
［蟑螂］ bug; cockroach; roach;

zhang³
zhang
【長】 (1) elder; older; senior; (2) eldest; oldest; (3) chairman; chief; commander; head; leader; (4) grow; (5) begin to grow; (6) enhance; increase; (7) appear; become; look;
［長輩］ elder members of a family; senior family members;
尊敬長輩 respect for senior family members;
［長成］ (1) grow to adulthood; (2) grow into;
［長瘡］ form a boil;
［長出］ come into bud; come into leaf; send forth;
［長大］ attain adulthood; be brought up; grow; grow up; mature;
長大成人 be grown to adulthood; become a grown-up; come to man's estate;
長大成熟 cut one's eye-teeth;
［長房］ eldest branch;
［長官］ senior officer;
［長進］ make progress;
不長進 good-for-nothing; without improvement or progress;
～了不長進 cannot make any progress;

Z

~了無長進 have made no progress in the least;

[長老] (1) elders; elders of a Buddhist monastery; (2) reverent address for a monk;

[長毛] (1) get hairy; grow feather; grow hair; (2) mouldy;

[長男] eldest son;

[長女] eldest daughter;

[長胖] become fat; flesh out; flesh up; gain flesh; gain weight; get fat; get flesh; make flesh; pick up flesh; put on flesh; put on weight;

[長上] elders and superiors;

[長入] evolve; grow into;

[長孫] (1) eldest grandson; (2) a surname;

[長媳] wife of one's eldest son;

[長相] appearances; features; looks;

長相像 a close resemblance between sb; a precise counterpart of; as like as peas; be a copy of; be alike; be an edition of; be the picture of; be the image of; bear close resemblance to; in the likeness of; in the similitude of; look alike; resemble; similar in appearance; take after; the spit and image of;

[長兄] one's eldest brother;

[長牙] cut a tooth; cut one's teeth; cut teeth; grow teeth;

[長幼] seniority among family members; young and old;

長幼有序 respect for seniority;

家中長幼 senior and junior family members;

敬長撫幼 respect for elders and care for youngsters;

[長者] (1) elder; senior; (2) person of virtue; venerable elder;

有長者風 have the ways of a venerable elder;

[長子] one's eldest son; one's firstborn;

長子繼承制 primogeniture;

長子代父 the elder brother must take his father's place;

班長 (1) class monitor; (2) squad leader; (3) team leader;

部長 commissioner; head of a department; minister;

參謀長 chief of staff;

廠長 factory director; factory manager;

場長 head of a farm;

成長 (1) grow to maturity; (2) grow up;

處長 head of a department; section chief;

船長 captain; skipper;

次長 under-secretary; vice-minister;

村長 village head;

段長 head of a section;

隊長 (1) group leader; team leader; (2) caption;

工長 foreman; section chief;

耆長 elders;

股長 section chief;

官長 (1) government official; (2) officer;

行長 president of a bank;

護士長 head nurse;

會長 president of an association;

機長 aircraft commander;

家長 (1) head of a family; paterfamilias; patriarch; (2) parents;

檢察長 chief procurator;

見長 grow perceptibly;

艦長 caption of a warship;

教務長 register;

教長 dean;

局長 director-general; head of a department;

軍長 army commander;

科長 section chief;

理事長 president of a council;

連長 company commander;

列車長 head of a train crew;

旅長 brigade commander;

秘書長 secretary-general;

年長 older in age;

排長 platoon leader;

親長 one's elderly relatives;

酋長 (1) chief of a tribe; (2) sheik;

區長 administrative chief; district head;

社長 president;

審判長 presiding judge;

生長 (1) grow; (2) be brought up; grow up;

省長 governor of a province;

師長 (1) teacher; (2) division commander;

市長 mayor;

首長 leading cadre; senior officer;

署長 administrator;

水手長 boatswain;

司務長 (1) mess officer; (2) company quartermaster;

司長 head of a department;

所長 bureau chief; head of an institute;

廳長 head of a department under a provincial government;

庭長　presiding judge;
徒長　grow excessively;
團長　(1) regimental commander; (2) head of a delegation, troupe, etc.;
外長　foreign minister; minister of foreign affairs;
委員長　chairman of a committee;
縣長　county magistrate;
鄉長　administrative chief of a town;
消長　growth and decline; rise and fall; ups and downs; vicissitudes; wane and wax;
校長　(1) head teacher; headmaster; principal; schoolmaster; (2) chancellor; president; vice-chancellor;
兄長　elder brother;
學長　mentor; one's senior at school;
議長　speaker of a legislative body;
營長　battalion commander;
院長　director of a hospital, museum, institute, faculty, etc.;
增長　grow; increase; rise;
站長　head of a station;
助長　foster;
茁長　flourish; thrive;
滋長　develop; grow;
總長　cabinet minister;
族長　clan elder; head of a clan;
組長　group leader;
尊長　elders and betters; one's elders or superiors;

zhang

【掌】　(1) palm of the hand; (2) slap with one's hand; smack; strike with the palm of the hand; (3) control; in charge of; supervise; wield; (4) the bottom of certain animals' feet; (5) shoe sole or heel; (6) horseshoes; (7) a surname;

[掌舵]　(1) at the helm; operate the rudder; steer a boat; take the tiller; (2) person in charge;

[掌故]　(1) historical anecdotes; (2) national institutions;

[掌摑]　slap; slapping;
開心掌摑　happy slapping;

[掌管]　administer; in charge of; manage; supervise; take charge of;
掌管財務　hold the purse-strings;
掌管一切事務　take care of everything;

[掌櫃]　manager of a shop; shopkeeper;

[掌理]　manage; supervise; take charge of;

[掌權]　exercise control; in power; wield power;

[掌上壓]　press-up;

[掌聲]　applause; clapping; the sound of clapping;
掌聲爆發　applause bursts out;
掌聲雷動　a round of applause; a storm of applause set the rafters ringing; applaud to the echo; burst into thunderous applause; the applause is deafening; the applause raises the roof; thunderous applause;
爆發出掌聲　burst into applause;
博得掌聲　draw forth applause;
零星的掌聲　a smattering of applause;
熱烈的掌聲　tumultuous applause;
一陣稀疏的掌聲　a spatter of applause;
一陣掌聲　a burst of applause; a crash of applause; a peal of applause; a round of applause;

[掌紋]　hand lines; palm prints;

[掌握]　grasp; in one's grasp; know well; master; within one's power;
掌握分寸　act properly; behave oneself; exercise sound judgement; handle appropriately;
掌握局勢　have the situation under control; have the situation well in hand;
掌握要領　grasp the essentials;
掌握政權　hold the control of political power;
掌握之中　have...in one's pocket; in one's hands; in sb's clutches; lie at sb's mercy; under the control of; within one's grasp;
掌握主動權　have the initiative in one's hands;
掌握自己命運的人　a mater of one's own destiny;

[掌心]　centre of the palm;
孫悟空跳不出如來佛的掌心　like the Monkey King who cannot jump out from Buddha's palm;

[掌印]　in power; keep the seal;

[掌政]　head a government;

[掌嘴]　slap sb in the face;

巴掌　(1) palm of the hand; (2) slap;
抃掌　clap one's hands;
鼓掌　applaud; clap one's hands; handclap;
擊掌　clap one's hands;
腳掌　sole of the foot;

魔掌 devil's clutches; evil hands;
拍掌 applaud; clap one's hands;
手掌 palm;
熊掌 bear's paws;
鴨掌 duck's web;
鞅掌 overburdened; weariness;
指掌 fingers and palms;
執掌 in control of; manage; superintend; take full charge of; wield;
職掌 (1) in charge of; (2) charges; duties;

zhang
【漲】 go up; rise;
[漲潮] flood tide;
漲潮力 tide raising force;
[漲跌] price fluctuation;
[漲風] upward trend of commodity prices;
[漲幅] rate of increase;
[漲回] rises and corrections;
大漲小回 take big leaps with small corrections;
~ 樓價大漲小回 property prices take big leaps with small corrections;
[漲價] appreciation; raise prices; rise in price;
變相漲價 disguised increase in prices; raise prices by deceptive means;
亂漲價 arbitrary price hikes;
[漲落] fluctuate; rise and fall;
大漲大落 fluctuate violently; sharp changes; violent fluctuations;

暴漲 rise suddenly and sharply;
飛漲 rise sharply; soar;
高漲 run high; upsurge;
激漲 rise; run high;
看漲 be expected to rise;
猛漲 break through; leap;
上漲 go up; rise;
昇漲 go up; rise;
驟漲 rise suddenly;

zhang⁴
zhang
【丈】 (1) measure (land); (2) elder; senior; (3) form of address for certain male relatives by marriage; (4) unit of length;
[丈夫] one's hubby; one's husband; one's worse half;
丈夫氣慨 manliness; manly;
丈夫有淚不輕彈，只因未到傷心處 a man does not easily shed tears until his heart is broken; men only weep when deeply hurt;
大丈夫 man; real man; true man;
~ 大丈夫敢做敢當 a gentleman bears responsibility for all the serious consequences of his deeds;
~ 大丈夫拿得起放得下 a man can take temporary setbacks;
~ 大丈夫能屈能伸 a great man knows when to yield and when not; a real man is able to stoop or stand up; a true man can either stoop or stand;
~ 大丈夫輸得起 a man of substance is able to rise after a fall;
~ 大丈夫説話算話 a true man never goes back on his word;
怕老婆的丈夫 henpecked husband;
女中丈夫 masculine woman;
未來的丈夫 future husband;
無毒不丈夫 a real man lacks not in venom; one who is not ruthless is not a truly great man; ruthlessness is the mark of a truly great man;
[丈量] measure; survey;
[丈母娘] mother-in-law; one's wife's mother;
老丈人 father-in-law; one's wife's father;

姑丈 husband of one's father's sister; uncle;
姐丈 brother-in-law; elder sister's husband;
萬丈 bottomless; lofty;
姨丈 husband of one's maternal aunt; uncle;
岳丈 father-in-law; wife's father;

zhang
【仗】 (1) weaponry; (2) hold a weapon; (3) depend on; lean upon; rely on; (4) battle; war;
[仗劍而出] come out resting hand on sword;
[仗馬寒蟬] as mute as a mouse; maintain a discreet silence;
[仗氣] rely on emotion;
[仗恃] rely on an advantage;
[仗勢] take advantage of one's power or connection with influential people;
仗勢霸道 misuse one's power and influence in order to intimidate and coerce the weak;
仗勢欺人 abuse one's power and bully the people; bully others because one has power; bully people on the strength

of one's powerful connections; bully the weak on one's power; make use of sb's position to bully others; pull one's rank on others; rely on sb else's power to bully people; take advantage of one's own power to bully people; take one's position to lord it over and insult people; throw one's weight about; trust to one's power and insult people;

仗勢倚財 presume on one's power and rely upon his own wealth; rely on one's wealth and power;

仗勢疏財 despise wealth and stand for justice; distribute wealth in a good cause; donate money for worthy causes; generous in aiding needy people; give money to righteous cause; help the needy and look lightly on wealth; spend on a good cause;

恃強仗勢 trust to one's violence and depend on one's influence;

狗仗人勢 an underling gets haughty on the strength of an influential relative; like a dog counting on its master's backing — bully others because of one's master power and position; like a dog taking advantage of its master's power — play the bully with the backing of a powerful person; taking advantage of one's connection with a powerful person;

依官仗勢 count on one's powerful connections; rely on one's power and position; rely on power and authority of officials; rely on the powerful; rely upon an official and take advantage of his influence; take advantage of one's position and power;

倚財仗勢 presume on one's power and rely upon one's wealth; rely on one's wealth and power;

倚親仗勢 rely on one's powerful relatives;

[仗義] rely on a sense of justice;

仗義疏財 think little of one's fortune in one's enthusiasm for charity;

仗義行仁 love deeds and help those who are in need;

仗義勇為 help a lame dog over a stile;

仗義執言 speak boldly in defense of justice; speak in accordance with justice; speak out from a sense of justice; speak out to uphold justice; speak straightforwardly for justice;

疏不仗義 distribute wealth and act righteously; give generously; indifferent to wealth but concerned about virtue;

疏財仗義 distribute wealth and act righteously;

[仗着] take advantage of;

仗着本事 rely on one's own ability;

爆仗 crackers; firecrackers;

敗仗 defeat; lose a battle;

打仗 fight; fight a battle; go to war; make war;

開仗 make war; open hostilities;

砲仗 firecracker;

礮仗 firecracker;

憑仗 depend on; rely on;

勝仗 victorious battle; victory;

死仗 tough battle;

仰仗 look to sb for backing; rely on;

依仗 count on; rely on;

儀仗 flags and weapons carried by a guard of honour;

倚仗 count on; rely on;

硬仗 formidable task; tough battle;

zhang

【杖】 (1) cane; staff; stick; (2) beat with a cane; flog with a stick; (3) (now rare) mourning staff; (4) presume on;

[杖擊] hit with a cane;

[杖莫如信] there is nothing like sincerity to trust to;

[杖責] punish by caning;

禪杖 Buddhist monk's staff;

拐杖 walking stick;

魔杖 magic wand;

手杖 walk stick;

雪杖 ski stick;

zhang

【長】 remainder; surplus;

[長物] belongings; property;

zhang

【帳】 (1) canopy; curtain; (2) tent; (3) scroll;

[帳頂] top of a mosquito net;

[帳幔] tent;

[帳幕] tent;

[帳篷] big top; cabana; tent;
帳篷學校 tent school;
登山用帳篷 alpine tent;
雙人帳篷 two-person tent;
一頂帳篷 a tent;
[帳子] (1) bed-curtain; (2) mosquito net;

幔帳 curtain; screen;
昇帳 summon the generals to the tent for discussion;
蚊帳 mosquito net;
營帳 tent;

zhang
【脹】 (1) full-stomached; glutted; (2) swelling of skin; (3) expand;
[脹飽] fullness of the stomach from overeating;
[脹大] swell;
[脹滿] full; glutted; inflated;
[脹悶] tightness of the stomach;

發脹 (1) sell; (2) feel distended;
膨脹 expand; inflate; swell;
腫脹 (1) swell; (2) oedema and abdominal distension;

zhang
【幛】 a scroll of silk mounted with appropriate wording sent as a gift for wedding, funeral, etc.;

賀幛 sheet of red silk for congratulation purposes;
壽幛 sheet of red silk for birthday congratulation;
挽幛 sheet of red silk for funerals;
喜幛 sheet of red silk for wedding;

zhang
【漲】 expand; swell;
[漲潮] flow;
[漲水] swell; swell of a river;
[漲縮] swell and shrink;
[漲溢] overflow;

zhang
【障】 (1) hinder; obstruct; (2) barrier; screen; (3) dyke; embankment; (4) defend; guard; shield; (5) guarantee;
[障礙] (1) barrier; hurdle; obstacle; obstruction; (2) handicap; malfunction;
障礙物 hindrance; obstacle; obstruction;
表達障礙 presentation obstruction;
發育障礙 developmental disorders;
功能性障礙 functional disorder;
聽覺障礙 hearing disorder;
無形障礙 glass ceiling;
心身障礙 psychosomatic disorder;
學習障礙 learning disorder;
運用障礙 dyspraxia;
[障蔽] block; obstruct; screen; shut out;
[障眼法] (1) legerdemain; (2) cover-up; camouflage;
[障子] screen;

白內障 cataract;
保障 bulwark; ensure; guarantee; protect; safeguard;
蔽障 obstacle in the mind to understanding; obstacle to faith;
頂障 ceiling;
風障 wind-break;
故障 accident; blunder; breakdown; bug; conk; defect; do not work; do not work properly; failure; fault; hitch; inaction; ineffective; malfunction; out of gear; out of order; sth wrong; stoppage; trouble;
花障 hedge-row with flowers;
路障 roadblock;
綠內障 glaucoma;
魔障 demon; evil spirit;
內障 cataract;
孽障 vile spawn; evil creature;
排障 fault-removing;
屏障 protective screen;
熱障 heat barrier;
聲障 sound barrier;
翳障 ocular; scale;
音障 sound barrier;
欲障 desires that pose as one's obstacles to salvation;
智障 intellectual disability;

zhang
【嶂】 mountain barrier; precipitous mountain;
[嶂谷] narrow gorge;

疊嶂 peaks rising one higher than another;

zhang
【賬】 (1) account; (2) account books; (3) debts; (4) bill; credit; loan;
[賬本] account book;
[賬簿] account book; accounts;

[賬單] bill; check; reckoning; statement of account;
開賬單 ask for the bill;
一張賬單 a bill;

[賬房] (1) accountant's office; cashier's office; (2) accountant; cashier; teller; treasurer;

[賬戶] bank account;
賬戶裏有錢 there's money in one's account;
擺動賬戶 swing account;
保險賬戶 underwriting account;
不動產賬戶 immovable account;
成本賬戶 cost account;
儲蓄賬戶 savings account;
貸款賬戶 loan account;
擔保賬戶 assigned account;
對開賬戶 back-to-back account;
對應賬戶 corresponding account;
負債賬戶 liability account;
輔助賬戶 auxiliary account;
個人賬戶 single account;
共同賬戶 common account;
紅利賬戶 bonus account;
換算賬戶 conversion account;
混合賬戶 combined account; mixed account;
活期儲蓄賬戶 current savings account;
活期存款賬戶 current deposit account;
活期賬戶 checking account;
基金賬戶 fund account;
~一般基金賬戶 general fund account;
集合賬戶 collective account;
交易賬戶 transaction account;
結算賬戶 clearance account;
進口收入賬戶 import credit account;
進口支出賬戶 import debit account;
居民賬戶 resident account;
~非居民賬戶 non-resident account;
開賬戶 open an account;
可靠賬戶 reliable account;
空頭賬戶 bear account;
虧損賬戶 deficit account;
利潤賬戶 profit account;
利息賬戶 interest account;
聯行賬戶 inter-bank account;
臨時賬戶 provisional account;
流水賬戶 running account;
名義賬戶 nominal accounts;
拋空賬戶 short account;
清算賬戶 clearance account;
商業賬戶 commercial account;
社團賬戶 society account;
私人賬戶 private account;
提款賬戶 drawing account;
調整賬戶 adjusting account;
停滯賬戶 sleeping account;
往來賬戶 book account; current account;
現金賬戶 cash account; money account;
虛偽賬戶 fictitious account;
業務賬戶 activity account;
一個賬戶 an account;
永久賬戶 permanent account;
預算賬戶 budget account;
增殖賬戶 accretion account;
摘要賬戶 abstract account;
債券賬戶 debenture account;
政府賬戶 overnment account;
證券賬戶 securities account;
支票賬戶 cheque account;
主要賬戶 principal account;
資本賬戶 capital account;

[賬款] credit; funds on account; value in account;
過期賬款 past due account;
應付賬款 payable account;
應收賬款 receivable account;
逾期賬款 overdue account;

[賬面] book; account;
賬面價值 book value;
賬面損失 book loss;

[賬目] account; items of an account;
賬目不清 account not in order;
賬目混亂 confused account;
結餘賬目 balance account;
借方賬目 debtor account;
開支賬目 expenditure account;
票據賬目 bills account;
清理賬目 adjust the accounts;
整理賬目 adject account;

[賬務] accounts in general; affairs concerning accounts;

[賬項] accounting item;

查賬 check account;
出賬 item of expenditure;
呆賬 bad debts;
倒賬 (1) bad debts; failure to collect payment; (2) refuse to pay loans under various excuses;
抵賬 pay a debt in kind;
放賬 lend money for interest;
費用賬 expense account;
付賬 pay a bill;

掛賬 charge to one's account;
過賬 transfer items;
花賬 padded accounts;
還賬 pay one's debt; repay a debt;
會賬 pay a bill;
混賬 bastard; scoundrel; son of a bitch;
記賬 (1) keep accounts; (2) charge to an account;
假賬 false accounts;
交賬 (1) hand over the accounts; (2) account for;
結賬 balance the books; close accounts; close the book; settle accounts; square accounts;
舊賬 old debts; long-standing debts;
開賬 (1) make out a bill; (2) pay the bill;
開支賬 expense account;
拉賬 be in debt; run into debt;
賴賬 (1) repudiate a debt; (2) go back on one's word;
爛賬 (1) mess accounts; (2) bad debts;
老賬 long-standing debts;
流水賬 current account; day-to-day account; journal account;
賣賬 buy;
盤賬 check accounts;
賠賬 pay for the loss of cash or goods entrusted to one;
簽賬 spending;
清賬 square an account;
讓賬 insist on footing the bill; want to pay a bill for another;
認賬 acknowledge a debt;
入賬 enter into the account book;
煞賬 make out a statement;
上賬 enter sth in an account;
賒賬 buy or sell on credit;
收入賬 receiving account;
收益賬 income account;
損益賬 profit and loss account;
算一算賬 do one's sums; work out accounts;
算賬 (1) balance accounts; balance the books; cast accounts; do accounts; make out bills; work out accounts; (2) pay the bill; (3) get even with sb; settle accounts with sb; square accounts with sb;
搪賬 evade paying debts;
討賬 ask for payment; demand the payment of a debt;
外賬 overdue bill;
細賬 itemized account;
現金賬 money account;
銷賬 cancel from an account;
小賬 gratuity; tip;
押賬 leave sth as security for a loan;
要賬 demand payment of a debt;
雜費賬 petty expenses account;
折賬 pay a debt in kind;
轉賬 transfer accounts;
總賬 general ledger;
做賬 keep accounts;

zhang

【瘴】 miasma;

［瘴地］ miasmal place;

［瘴氣］ miasma; pestilential vapour;

zhao[1]

zhao

【招】 (1) beckon with one's hand; summon; wave one's hand; (2) enlist; raise; recruit; (3) attract; cause; effect; incite; incur; invite; (4) notice; poster; signboard; (5) entice; induce; provoke; tease; (6) admit; confess; (7) device; move; trick; (8) infect;

［招安］ offer amnesty and enlistment to rebels;

［招標］ call for tender; invite bid; invite tenders;
招標條件 tender conditions;
招標通知 tender notice;
招標文件 bidding documents;
招標制 system of public bidding;
出口招標 export tender;
公開招標 open bidding;
~非公開招標 closed bidding; sealed bid;
進口招標 import tender;

［招兵］ raise troops; recruit soldiers;
招兵買馬 conscript men for soldier and buy horses — expand a fighting force; enlist followers; gather together a following of mercenaries; hire men and buy horses — raise an army; prepare for war;
招兵聚將 summon troops;

［招打］ invite a spanking;

［招待］ entertain; receive; serve; welcome;
招待不周 not be attentive enough to guests;
招待會 reception;
招待甚殷 offer cordial hospitality;
招待室 reception room;
招待所 guest house;
招待員 receptionist;
女招待 hostess;

［招風］ attract too much attention and invite

trouble; catch the wind; look for trouble; provoke mischief;
招風耳 protruding ears;
招風惹草 get oneself into trouble;
招風惹雨 attract too much attention and invite trouble; stir up trouble;
惹草招風 stir grass and bring wind — get oneself into trouble;

[招福] welcome and invite blessings;

[招撫] call to surrender; offer amnesty and enlistment to rebels; pacify;

[招附] call the enemy to join one's own side;

[招工] employ workers; hire workers; recruit; recruit workers;

[招供] confess one's crime;
逼人招供 press sb into confession;

[招股] call for capital; solicit shareholders;

[招呼] (1) call; (2) greet; hail; say hello to; (3) notify; tell; (4) take care of;
打招呼 (1) greet sb; say hello; tip one's hat; (2) give a previous notice; inform; notify in advance; remind; warn; (3) let sb know; notify;
~打個招呼 in salutation; make one's salutation; salute sb;
~點頭打招呼 greet sb with a nod; nod to sb in greeting;
~和藹地打招呼 greet affably;
~互相打招呼 exchange greetings;
~親切地打招呼 greet cordially;
點頭招呼 nod to sb as a greeting;

[招回] recall;

[招魂] call back the spirit of the dead;
招魂送鬼 search for the lost soul or send the departed's spirit off;
招魂引魄 summon the spirits;
揚幡招魂 fly a funeral banner to summon sb's soul — try to revive what is obsolete;

[招禍] court disasters; invite troubles;
招禍臨身 bring misery on oneself; call down calamity upon oneself;

[招集] gather together;

[招忌] bring upon oneself envy; invite jealousy;
名高招忌 great winds blow on high hills;

[招嫉] bring upon oneself envy; invite jealousy;

[招架] defend; hold one's own; resist; ward off blows; withstand;
招架不住 cannot sustain the blows; no match for sb; not to be able to hold one's own; unable to defend; unable to hold off; unable to hold on; unable to hold one's ground against; unable to parry; unable to resist; unable to stand up to; unable to ward off;

[招咎] invite troubles;

[招考] admit by examination; give public notice of entrance examination;

[招徠] canvass; solicit business;
招徠顧客 solicit customers;
好貨無需招徠 good wine needs no bush;
以廣招徠 in order to promote patronage; so as to attract more customers; with a view to promoting sales;

[招攬] canvass; solicit customers;
招攬生意 canvass business order; drum up trade; extend business by securing new customers;

[招冷] catch cold;

[招領] announce the finding of lost property;

[招門納婿] bring a son-in-law into one's house; have the groom move into one's house after the marriage; take a husband;

[招募] (1) enlist; recruit; (2) solicit;
招募入伍 enlist sb for the army;
四出招募 beat up for; go about to enlist into the army;

[招牌] shop sign; signboard;
金字招牌 a signboard in gold characters — a vainglorious title; gold-lettered signboard; gilded placard;
理髮店招牌 barber pole;

[招聘] advertise for vacancies; employ; give public notice of a vacancy to be filled; invite applications for a job; recruit;

[招親] (1) have the groom move into one's house after the marriage; take a husband; (2) marry into and live with one's bride's family;

[招權納賄] abuse one's power and take bribes; seize power and accept bribes;

[招惹] (1) bring upon oneself; cause; court; incur; provoke; (2) provoke; tease;
招惹生非 stir up trouble;
招惹是非 bring trouble on oneself; cause misunderstanding; find oneself in trouble; provoke dispute; stir up

Z

trouble; wake a sleeping dog;

[招認] confess one's crime; plead guilty;

[招商] canvass business; invite outside investment;

招商引資 canvass business and induce investment;

[招生] enroll new students; recruit students;

招生辦公室 admission office;

招生制度 admission system; enrolment system;

[招式] movements in martial art;

一招一式 every gesture and motion;

[招事] bring trouble on oneself; invite trouble;

[招收] recruit; take in;

[招手] beckon with the hand; wave one's hand;

招手致意 wave back in acknowledgement; wave in acknowledgement; wave one's greetings;

[招數] (1) move in chess; (2) movement in Chinese martial art; (3) device; scheme; trick;

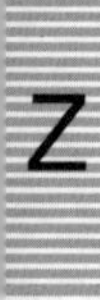

[招說] (1) annoying; (2) acknowledge; confess;

[招貼] bill; notice; placard; poster;

禁止招貼 post no bills;

[招賢] solicit the service of the virtuous and capable;

招賢舉能 enlist able and upright men; enlist people of ability and uprightness;

招賢納士 invite to one's die men of wisdom and valour; like to meet all celebrated scholars; receive all good fellows from everywhere; seek for scholars and men of correct behaviour; seek out able men and receive them; welcome wise counsellors and bold warriors;

[招降] call for surrender; summon sb to surrender;

招降納叛 assemble a coterie of undesirable elements; draw deserters and traitors into one's service; recruit deserters and accept mutineers; recruit deserters and traitors; recruit turncoats and renegades;

招降納叛，結黨營私 draw deserters and traitors into one's service and form cliques in pursuit of one's on selfish interests; enlist deserters and renegades and form cliques to serve one's own selfish interests; recruit capitulationists and turncoats and form a clique for selfish purposes; recruit turncoats, take in renegades and set up a clique for selfih interests;

招降納順 welcome the submissive and receive the favourable;

[招笑兒] funny; hilarious; incite laughter; incur ridicule;

[招延] recruit;

[招眼] attractive; conspicuous; in limelight; make oneself conspicuous;

招眼毒 cause jealousy;

[招邀] invite; request sb to come;

[招搖] act ostentatiously; attract undue publicity; swagger with full pomp;

招搖過市 behave ostentatiously; cut a dash; cut a wide swath; show off; swagger about; swagger around town; swagger down the streets; swagger through the streets;

招搖撞騙 bluff and deceive; deceive and beguile; swagger and swindle; swindle and bluff; swindle under false pretences; try every trick to mislead the public;

舉止招搖 have flashing manners;

[招引] attract; cause; incur; induce; invite;

招蜂引蝶 act like a habitual flirt; attract the attention of the elegant young idlers; flirt with men; make passes to men without discrimination;

[招怨] incur animosity; incur grudges; incur odium; inspire hate;

招怨惹恨 cause hatred; sow seeds of hatred;

招怨樹敵 arouse a nest of hornets; arouse animosity and incite opposition; arouse hornets' nest; inspire animosity and make enemy;

[招災] bring disasters upon oneself; invite disasters;

招災惹禍 bring evil and provoke woe; court disasters; invite troubles; shoot one's neck;

財多招災 wealth invites danger;

[招展] flutter; sway; wave;

[招之即來] on call at any hour;

招之則來，麾之則去 have sb at one's beck and call;

［招致］ (1) recruit; scout about for; (2) bring about; cause; incur; induce; invite; lead to; result in;

［招贅］ have the groom live with one's family after the marriage; take in a son-in-law to bear bride's family name;

［招租］ advertise for tenants; for rent; let;

［招罪］ bring sth bad upon oneself;

拔招 (in a chess game) rescind a false move;

高招 brilliant idea; clever move;

花招 (1) flourish; showy movement in Chinese martial art; (2) game; gimmick; hocus-pocus; legerdemain; sleight of hand trick;

絕招 (1) unique skill; (2) unexpected stratagem;

市招 shop sign; signboard;

自招 confess;

zhao

【昭】 (1) bright; luminous; (2) clear; obvious; (3) eminent; prominent; (4) display; make open; show; (5) a surname;

［昭代］ enlightened age;

［昭明］ (1) clear; evident; (2) become bright;

［昭然］ clear and obvious; evident; very clear;

昭然若揭 abundantly clear; as clear as crystal; as clear as day; as clear as daylight; as clear as noonday; as clear as the sun at noonday; as plain as the nose on one's face; be completely bared there and then; clear as crystal; clear as daylight;

［昭示］ declare publicly; make clear to all;

昭示全國 declare to the whole nation;

［昭蘇］ come to; wake up;

［昭顯］ eminent; evident; famous; prominent;

［昭雪］ exonerate; redress a wrong; redress an injustice; rehabilitate;

明冤昭雪 get one's wrongs put right; right a wrong;

平冤昭雪 rehabilitate sb; right a wrong;

昭冤雪恨 one's injuries are washed away; the person wronged has been rehabilitated; the wrong has been righted;

［昭耀］ bright and brilliant; shining;

［昭彰］ clear; evident; manifest; obvious; prominent;

眾目昭彰 be seen clearly by everyone; clear to all;

［昭昭］ clear and evident; known to all;

昭昭在目 clear in the people's eyes;

［昭著］ clear; evident; famous; obvious;

zhao

【釗】 encourage;

zhao

【朝】 (1) early morning; morning; (2) day;

［朝貴］ powerful courtiers;

［朝後］ face backward;

［朝暉］ morning light; morning sunlight;

［朝露］ ephemeral; morning dew; transitory;

浮雲朝露 life is as short as passing clouds and morning dew;

危如朝露 in imminent danger as the morning dew; vanishing soon after the sun shines on it;

［朝暮］ morning and evening;

朝村暮郭 stay in the village at dawn and in the city at night;

朝打暮罵 be beaten by day and misused by night;

朝齏暮鹽 lead a hard life; live in poverty; serve slated vegetables in the morning and only salt in the evening — poor living;

朝來暮往 come in the morning and go in the evening — frequency of visits;

朝往暮返 go in the morning and return in the evening;

朝秦暮楚 change one's loyalty frequently; fickle; inconstant; play fast and loose; quick to shift sides;

朝三暮四 always changing one's mind; blow hot and cold; capricious; change one's mind frequently; changeable, chop and change; keep changing one's mind; not know one's own mind; play fast and loose; shift and veer; unreliable;

朝生暮死 an ephemeral existence; be born in the morning and die at night — the brevity of life; from the cradle to the grave is but a day's journey;

朝思暮盼 long for sth day and night;

朝思暮想 on one's mind day and night; think about sb from dawn to dusk; yearn day and night;

朝朝暮暮 day and night; every morning

Z

and evening; for days and days;

[朝氣] exuberance and aggressiveness; fresh spirit; vigour; vitality; youthful spirit;

朝氣蓬勃 bubble over with life; fresh and vigorous; full of vigour and vitality; full of vitality; full of youthful spirit; imbued with vitality; lusty; spirited; teem with life and vitality; vigorous;

[朝前] face forward;

[朝日] morning sun; rising sun;

[朝天] (1) go to court; (2) face upward;

[朝夕] (1) daily; day and night; from morning to night; morning and evening; (2) a very short time;

朝夕不安 can find no peace or rest day and night;

朝夕不暇 busy day and night; be occupied all day long;

朝夕夢想 dream day and night of;

朝夕難保 in imminent danger of death; may die at any time;

朝夕相處 be closely associated; together from morning to night;

花朝月夕 beautiful days and nights with moon and flowers; delightful weather and beautiful prospects;

朝不保夕 in constant fear; live in constant fear for one's livelihood; may fall at any moment; not to know at dawn what may happen by dusk — in a precarious state;

朝不慮夕 be preoccupied with the current crisis; in a precarious state; in the morning one does not know what will happen in the evening; live in constant fear for one's doom; unable to plan out one's day;

朝不謀夕 be preoccupied with the current crisis; fail to plan even for the immediate future; not know in the morning what may happen in the evening — in a precarious state; unable to plan one's day;

朝餐夕宿 take one's meals by day and sleep at night;

朝發夕至 set off in the morning and arrive in the evening — good communications; start at dawn and arrive at dusk — a day's journey; start at daybreak and arrive at sunset — a short distance;

朝詈夕楚 beat and abuse sb morning and night;

朝令夕改 issue an order at dawn and rescind it at dusk — make frequent changes in policies; issue an order in the morning and cancel it in the evening — inconstant in policy; the law is not the same at morning and at night;

朝乾夕惕 (1) diligent and alert from morning till night; (2) diligence in one's work;

朝聞夕改 quick reform of one's faults; rapid amendment;

朝饔夕飧 breakfast in the morning and dinner in the evening — said of one who has nothing to do but eating;

只爭朝夕 race against time; seize every minute; seize the day and seize the hour; seize the day; seize the hour, seize time by the forelock;

[朝霞] morning glow; rosy clouds of dawn; rosy dawn;

朝霞滿天 the rosy colour of dawn spreads all over the sky;

朝霞滿天，金光燦爛 the sky turns bright with the golden rays of the sun;

朝霞映湖 the glory of the morning is mirrored in the lake;

朝霞主雨，晚霞主晴 red sky at night, shepherd's delight; red sky in the morning, shepherd's warning; rosy morning clouds indicate rain, and a rosy sunset means fine weather;

[朝旭] rising sun;

[朝陽] morning sun; rising sun;

朝陽工業 sunrise industry;

朝陽鳴鳳 outspoken admonitions;

鳳鳴朝陽 phoenix singing in morning sun — a good omen for the country; the male phoenix sings facing the sun — an auspicious sign;

[朝野] the government and the people;

[朝政] affairs of the state;

今朝 now; the present;

一朝 (1) in one day; (2) once;

zhao

【著】 (1) bear; take; (2) method; plan;

[著風] expose to wind;

[著慌] anxious; jittery; worried;

[著急] anxious; worried;
[著涼] catch cold;
[著忙] anxious; nervous; panicky;
[著數] (1) move in chess; (2) movement in Chinese martial art; (3) device; trick;

zhao²
zhao

【着】 (1) touch; (2) be affected by; feel; (3) burn; light; (4) fall asleep;
[着慌] be thrown into a panic; become flustered; get alarmed;
[着火] (1) be captivated; be fascinated; (2) catch fire; inflame; kindle; on fire;
紙容易着火 paper catches fire easily;
[着急] feel anxious; worry;
着急要走 anxious to go;
別着急 be easy; don't hurry; easy does it; please calm down; take it easy; take your time;
不着急 in no hurry; take your time;
~不用着急 there's no hurry;
乾着急 be anxious but unable to do anything;
[着涼] catch a chill; catch cold;
[着迷] be captivated; be enchanted; be fascinated;
着迷的 enraptured;
看着了迷 have one's eyes glued on; unable to keep one's eyes off;
[着魔] be bewitched; be possessed;
[着眼] direct one's attention to; eye with attention; have sth in mind;
着眼點 a starting point; the point to watch;
大處着眼 far-sighted; keep the general goal in sight; pay attention to the important points;

zhao³
zhao

【爪】 (1) claw; talon; (2) nail;
[爪蹄獸] chalicothere;
[爪士] lackeys; retainers;
[爪牙] lackeys; underlings;
爪牙官 lackeys of a ruthless ruler;
張牙舞爪 bare fangs and brandish claws – make threatening gestures; bare one's fangs and open one's claws – make threatening gestures like a beast of prey; bare one's teeth; indulge in sabre rattling; put out a claw; sabre rattling; show one's claws; show one's fangs and claws; with bared fangs; with one's fangs bared and one's claws sticking out;
[爪印] nail mark; print; trace;

步爪 ambulatory claw;
端爪 apical claw;
顎爪 jaw claw;
附爪 accessory claw;
跗爪 tarsal claw;
鴻爪 traces left over by past events;
角質爪 horny claw;
鱗爪 (1) scales and nails; (2) small bits;
魔爪 claws; tentacles;
鎖爪 locking claw;
鐵爪 iron claw;
網爪 web claw;
蟹爪 crab claw;
中爪 median claw;

zhao

【找】 (1) find; look for; search for; seek; (2) call on; want to see; (3) give change;
[找遍] search everywhere;
[找病] ask for trouble; look for trouble;
[找補] make up a deficiency;
[找碴] carp; cavil;
找碴挑錯 look for excuse or occasion for a quarrel or fight; pick fault with;
[找到] find; seek out;
找不到 look in vain; search in vain;
[找換] give change;
[找平] make level;
[找齊] (1) even up; make equal; (2) make up a deficiency;
[找錢] give change;
少找錢 shortchange;
[找人] look for sb;
找人短處 pick a hole in sb's coat;
找錯了人 come to the wrong shop;
找對了人 come to the right shop;
[找事] (1) look for a job; seek employment; (2) look for trouble; pick a quarrel;
[找死] court death; invite death; seek death;
[找頭] change;
[找由頭兒] search for the origin of sth;
[找尋] look for; search for; seek;
東找西尋 look for sb/sth in all directions;

查找 search out;
尋找 cast about for; explore; forage for; go in quest of; in search of; look for; search; search for; seek; seek for; try to find;
自找 ask for it; suffer from one's own action;

zhao

【沼】 lake; marsh; pond; pool;
［沼地］ marshland;
［沼氣］ methane;
沼氣爆炸 explosion of firedamp;
散發沼氣 give off methane;
生成沼氣 form methane;
［沼澤］ bog; marsh; moor; swamp;
沼澤地 marsh; quagmire;
~ 沼澤地帶 fen; fenland;
~ 一塊沼澤地 a marsh;
草本沼澤 herbaceous swamp;
草甸沼澤 meadow moor;
淡水沼澤 freshwater swamp;
低位沼澤 low moor;
富養沼澤 eutrophic swamp;
紅樹林沼澤 mangrove swamp;
藺草沼澤 rush-swamp;
泥炭沼澤 peat moor;
禾草沼澤 grass moor;
陷入沼澤 become bogged in the swamp;
沿海沼澤 marine swamp;
走過沼澤 go through the swamp;

潮沼 tidal marsh;
池沼 pond; pool;
顫沼 quaking bog;
高沼 moor;
泥沼 quagmire; swamp;
鹽沼 salt marsh;

zhao⁴
zhao

【召】 (1) call together; call up; convene; summon; (2) cause; invite;
［召鬼驅鬼］ call in Beelzebub to cast out Satan;
召鬼容易驅鬼難 it is easier to raise the devil than to lay him;
［召喚］ call; summon;
緊急召喚 urgent call;
［召回］ recall;
召回大使 recall the ambassador;
［召禍］ cause trouble; court disaster;
［召集］ call together; convene; draw together;
召集大會 convene an assembly;
召集人 convener;
立刻召集 summon immediately;
［召見］ call in; summon;
分別召見 summon sb separately;
公開召見 summon sb on a public occasion;
［召開］ convene; convoke;
召開會議 call a meeting; convene a meeting;
提前召開 covene before the due date;
［召募］ enlist; recruit;
［召租］ for rent;

感召 impel; move and inspire;
號召 appeal; call; draw;
宣召 summon to imperial court;
徵召 (1) call up; enlist; (2) appoint to an official position;

zhao

【兆】 (1) sign; (2) omen; (3) trillion; (4) begin; (5) a surname;
［兆民］ masses; people;
［兆頭］ omen; portent; sign;
［兆域］ grave;
［兆周］ megacycle;

惡兆 bad omen; evil boding; ill omen;
吉兆 auspicious sign; good omen;
夢兆 dream omen;
前兆 forerunner; forewarning; harbinger; omen; premonition;
瑞兆 propitious portent;
先兆 foreboding; harbinger; indication; omen; portent; sign;
險兆 evil omen;
祥兆 good omen; propitious sign;
凶兆 boding of evil; ill omen;
異兆 strange omen;
億兆 (1) astronomical in number; countless; numberless; (2) masses; people;
預兆 omen; presage;
朕兆 omen; portent; sign;
徵兆 omen; portent; sign;

zhao

【炤】 interchangeable with 照 , shine;

zhao

【笊】 bamboo skimmer;
［笊籬］ bamboo wicker; wire strainer;

Z

zhao

【棹】 (1) oar; scull; (2) boat;

［棹進］ row the boat forward;

zhao

【詔】 (1) announce; proclaim; (2) coach; instruct; teach and direct; (3) edict; imperial decree; mandate;

［詔告］ proclaim;

［詔令］ imperial edict;

［詔命］ imperial edict;

［詔書］ imperial edict;

［詔諭］ imperial instructions;

手詔 order of a ruler in his personal writing;

zhao

【旐】 embroidered pennant;

zhao

【照】 (1) illuminate; light up; shine; (2) mirror; reflect; (3) photograph; take a picture; (4) photograph; picture; (5) certificate; licence; permit; (6) look after; take care of; (7) notify; proclaim; (8) contrast; (9) understand; (10) in the direction of; towards; (11) according to; in accordance with; (12) a surname;

［照搬］ copy; indiscriminately imitate;

［照辦］ act accordingly; act in accordance with; act upon; comply with; follow;

［照本宣科］ echo what the books say; read item by item from the text; report a speech verbatim;

［照常］ as usual;

照常辦公 business as usual; the office is open as usual;

照常營業 the business is carried on as usual;

［照抄］ (1) copy word for word; (2) imitate indiscriminately;

照抄照搬 copy mechanically; copy sth by rote; simply copy sth down and transmit it;

［照度］ illumination;

環境照度 ambient illumination;

孔徑照度 aperture illumination;

平均照度 average illumination;

［照拂］ attend to; care for; look after;

［照付］ pay the full amount according to the price tag;

［照顧］ attend to; care; care for; give consideration to; look after; make allowances for; minister to; see to; show consideration for; take care of; tend;

照顧病人 attend to a patient;

照顧不周 didn't look after you well enough;

照顧全局 consider the situation as a whole; take the whole into account;

照顧學生 care for the students;

照顧自己 look after oneself;

~有能力照顧自己 be capable of looking after oneself;

百般照顧 show sb every consideration;

照前顧後 examine what is coming and reflect on the consequences;

［照管］ look after; in charge of; tend;

照管花園 tend the garden;

［照護］ attend; look after; nurse; tend;

［照會］ (1) present a note to a government; (2) diplomatic memorandum; diplomatic note;

抗議照會 note of protest;

［照價］ according to the set price;

照價賠償 compensate according to the cost; pay the full price for;

［照鏡自憐］ sympathize with oneself in the mirror;

［照舊］ as before; as of old; as usual;

［照看］ attend to; keep an eye on; look after;

照看孩子 look after the children;

［照理說］ logically;

［照例］ as a rule; as per usual; as usual; follow precedents; follow usual practices; usually;

照例遲到 late as per usual;

［照亮］ light up;

光照亮 light shines;

［照料］ attend to; look after; mind; take care of; tend;

照料事情 take care of things;

精心照料 take precious good care of;

悉心照料 coddle; take the utmost care of sb;

妥為保藏 under lock and key;

［照臨］ illuminate; light up; shine on;

［照面］ come face to face; meet;

打個照面 come face to face with sb; meet

face to face with sb; meet sb face to face; run into sb;
互不照面 avoid each other;

[照明] illumination; lighting;
照明車 floodlight truck;
~ 火場照明車 fire site illuminating car;
照明彈 flare;
照明架 lighting rig;
照明器 illuminator; luminaire;
~ 照明器械 illuminating apparatus;
~ 靶子照明器 target illuminator;
~ 不透明照明器 opaque illuminator;
~ 單色照明器 monochromatic illuminator;
~ 防爆照明器 explosion-proof luminaire;
~ 廣角型照明器 wide-angle luminaire;
~ 熒光照明器 fluorescent luminaire;
~ 圓形照明器 circular luminaire;
照明強度 illumination intensity;
照明設備 illuminating equipment; lighting installation;
照明師 lighting electrician;
照明裝置 illuminator;
安全照明 emergy lighting; safety lighting;
~ 安全照明裝置 safety lighting fitting;
背景照明 background lighting;
反向照明 antidromic illumination;
環境照明 ambient illumination; ambient lighting;
人工照明 artificial illumination;
室內照明 ambient lighting;
天線照明 antenna illumination;
用電燈照明 be lighted with electric light;

[照排] phototype setting;
照排機 phototypesetter;
照排設備 phototypesetting equipment;
照排系統 phototypesetting system;

[照片] photo; photograph; pic; picture; print; snapshot;
照片沒照好 the photo does not come out;
照片歪了 the photo is crooked;
彩色照片 colour photograph; colour print;
~ 即取彩色照片 take-away colour print;
低調照片 low-key photograph;
集成照片 photo-montage;
面部照片 mugshot;
微粒照片 microdot;
顯微照片 micrograph;
~ 電子顯微照片 electron micrograph;
~ 掃描顯微照片 scanning micrograph;
一張照片 a photograph;

[照射] (1) shine upon; (2) exposure;
本底照射 background exposure;
急性照射 acute exposure;
容許照射 allowable exposure;

[照說] as a rule;

[照算] (1) charge accordingly; (2) charge without deduction;

[照相] (1) take a photo; take a picture; take photographs; take photos; take pictures; (2) have one's picture taken;
照相暗箱 camera obscura;
照相簿 photo album;
照相館 photo studio;
照相機 camera;
~ 照相機架 camera mount; camera stand;
~ 測速照相機 speed camera;
~ 低角照相機 small-angle camera;
~ 電子照相機 electronic camera;
~ 反射式照相機 reflecting camera;
~ 分色照相機 three-colour camera;
~ 高溫照相機 high-temperature camera;
~ 觀察照相機 view camera;
~ 航空照相機 aerocamera;
~ 盒式照相機 box camera;
~ 即拍即印照相機 instamatic camera;
~ 即印照相機 instant camera;
~ 記者照相機 press camera;
~ 立體照相機 stereocamera;
~ 全景照相機 panoramic camera;
~ 掃描照相機 scanning camera; sweep camera;
~ 數碼照相機 digicam;
~ 數字照相機 digicam;
~ 通用照相機 all-round camera;
~ 透射照相機 transmission camera;
~ 微顯照相機 microscope camera;
~ 小型照相機 miniature camera;
~ 袖珍照相機 compact camera;
~ 一架照相機 a camera;
~ 折合式照相機 folding camera;
~ 中子照相機 neutron camera;
照相啦 look at the birdie; watch the birdie;
照相學 photography;
~ 天體照相學 astrophotography;
照相儀 photoheliograph;
~ 太陽單色光照相儀 spectroheliograph;
~ 天體照相儀 astrograph;
雙筒天體照相儀 double astrograph;
擺好姿勢照相 pose for a photo;
不喜歡照相的 camera-shy;

航空照相 aerial photography;
回擺照相 oscillation photograph;
體視照相 stereoscopic photograph;
透射照相 transmission photography;

[照樣] (1) after a pattern or model; (2) all the same; as before; in the same old way;

[照妖鏡] demondetector; monster-revealing mirror;

[照耀] enlighten; illuminate; radiate; shine;

[照應] (1) look after; take care of; (2) correlate;
照應範圍 anaphoric island;
照應域 anaphoric island;
後照應 cataphora;
~ 後照應所指 cataphoric reference;
互相照應 coordinate with each other;

[照章] act in accordance with the regulations;
照章辦理 manage according to rules;
照章辦事 act according to the rules; act on the principle of; carry on according to rules and regulations; do everything by rule; go by the book; go by the rules; proceed according to regulations; work in accordance with established rules;

[照直說] speak frankly; talk bluntly;

[照准] (1) aim; (2) request granted;
礙難照准 cannot approve; find it difficult to comply;

按照 according as; according to; after; agreeable to; agreeably to; along; as; at; be based on; be scheduled; by; by any measure; considering; follow; from; in; in accordance with; in compliance with; in conformity to; in conformity with; in line with; in proportion as; in proportion to; in pursuance of; in the light of; on; on its merits; on the basis of; on the principle of; pursuant to; the way; to; under;
比照 according to; contrast; in the light of;
彩照 colour photo;
參照 consult; refer to;
殘照 evening glow; setting sun;
查照 note;
車照 vehicle licence;
對照 compare with; contrast with;
反照 reflect; reflection of light;
仿照 follow; imitate;
輻照 irradiation;
關照 (1) look after; (2) notify by word of mouth;
光照 illuminate;
護照 passport;
劇照 stage photo; still;
快照 snapshot;
落照 glow of the setting sun;
拍照 take a photo;
牌照 licence plate; licence tag;
憑照 certificate; licence;
普照 illuminate all places;
日照 sunshine;
夕照 evening glow;
戲照 photo of a person in stage costume;
小照 small-sized photo;
寫照 portrayal;
心照 have a tacit understanding;
依照 according to; in compliance with; in the light of;
遺照 portrait of the deceased;
映照 cast light upon; shine upon;
玉照 one's photograph; one's portrait;
授照 according to;
知照 inform; notify; tell;
執照 licence; permit;
燭照 illuminare; light up;
遵照 act in accordance with; obey;

zhao

【罩】 (1) coop; cover; wrap; (2) casing; cover; hood; shade; (3) cloak; mantle;

[罩不住] unable to control a situation;

[罩單] drop cloth;

[罩袍] dust-gown; dust-ruobe;
白色罩袍 surplice;

[罩棚] canvas covering over a court;

[罩篷] canopy;

[罩衫] dustcoat; overall;

[罩袖] oversleeves; sleevelets;

[罩衣] dustcoat;
大襟兒罩衣 dustcoat with buttons on the right;
對襟兒罩衣 dustcoat with buttons down the front;

[罩子] casing; cover; hood; shade;

牀罩 bedspread; counterpane;
燈罩 lampshade;
機罩 bonnet;
口罩 mask;
鏈罩 chain cover; chain guard;
籠罩 envelop; shroud;
面罩 face guard;
奶罩 bra; brassiere;
袍罩 long gown worn over a robe;

Z

乳罩 bra; brassiere;
紗罩 (1) gauge covering; (2) mantle;
外罩 duystcoat; outer garment; overall
胸罩 bra; brassiere;
眼罩 (1) eyeshade; (2) blinkers;

zhao
【肇】 (1) begin; commence; start; (2) cause; (3) devise; found; (4) adjust; make right;
[肇端] beginning; start;
[肇國] found a nation;
[肇禍] cause an accident; cause trouble;
[肇基] do the spadework; lay the foundation; pave the way;
[肇建] found;
[肇亂] cause trouble; create a disturbance; create disorder; create rebellion; create upheaval;
[肇始] begin; commence; initiate; start;
[肇事] cause trouble; create a disturbance; stir up disturbances; stir up trouble;
肇事生非 make trouble;
肇事作亂 create an incident;
[肇訟] go to law;
[肇歲] beginning of a new year;
[肇緒] beginning;
[肇造] first establish; found;

zhao
【趙】 (1) an ancient feudal state; (2) a surname;

zhao
【曌】 same as 照 ;

zhao
【櫂】 (1) oar; paddle; row; (2) paddle; row; (3) general name for boat;
[櫂船] row a boat;
[櫂歌] boat song;

zhe[1]
zhe
【折】 (1) fall head over heels; roll over; turn over; turn upside down; (2) pour all out; pour back and forth between two containers;
[折餅] toss about in bed;
[折疊] collapsible; folding;
折疊船 folding boat;
折疊牀 folding bed;
折疊刀 folding knife;
折疊凳 folding stool;
折疊帆布牀 foldaway cot;
折疊機 folding machine;
折疊剪 folding scissors;
折疊門 folding door;
折疊傘 folding umbrella;
折疊天線 collapsible aerial; collapsible antenna;
折疊衣服 fold up the clothes;
折疊椅 folding chair;
折疊桌 folding table;
[折根頭] fall head over heels; somersault;
向後折根頭 turn backward somersaults;
向前折根頭 turn forward somersaults;
在草地上折根頭 turn a somersault on the lawn;
[折扣] discount;
不折不扣 (1) a hundred per cent; to the letter; (2) out-and-out; without reservation;
打折扣 (1) at a discount; give a discount; sell at a discount; (2) fall short of a promise; fall short of a requirement;
七折八扣 not pay the full amount; with various deductions;
[折籮] collect the leftovers of a banquet in a basket;
[折騰] toss about; turn from side to side;
折騰頭髮 fiddle about with one's hair;
幾經折騰 after much toing and froing;
來回折騰 toss about; toss to and fro;
疼得折騰 toss oneself about in pain;
瞎折騰 fool around; mess about;
整夜折騰 toss about all night;
[折罪] atonement for crime;
立功折罪 recognition of good deeds as atonement for sb's crime;

zhe
【螫】 (1) poisonous insect; (2) scorpion; (3) sting;
[螫針] sting; stinger;

zhe
【遮】 (1) conceal; cover; hide; screen; shade; shield; shut out; (2) block; intercept; obstruct; (3) cover up;
[遮板] curtain board; sunshade;
[遮蔽] block; cover; conceal; hide from view; obstruct; screen;
遮蔽物 cover; shelter;

遮天蔽日 blot up the sky and cover the sun; cover all the sky;

[遮藏] conceal; cover up; hide;

[遮醜] hide one's shame;

遮醜布 G-string;

[遮擋] fend; keep out; shelter from;

遮擋風寒 keep off the cold;

遮擋風沙 keep the sand in check;

遮擋風雨 shelter sb from the weather;

遮擋光線 shut out the light;

遮擋入口 conceal the entrance;

遮擋陽光 keep the sun off;

[遮斷] block from view; block off; obstruct;

[遮風] shield from wind;

遮風擋雨 keep out wind and rain;

[遮蓋] (1) cover; overspread; (2) conceal; cover over; cover up; hide;

遮蓋醜聞 hush up a scandal;

遮蓋事實 cover the facts; keep back the facts;

遮蓋下體 cover up one's private parts;

遮蓋真相 conceal the truth; withhold the truth;

被雪遮蓋 be blocked by snow;

遮天蓋地 blot out the sky and hide the earth;

遮頭蓋面 act stealthily; cover one's head and face;

遮遮蓋蓋 conceal an unpleasant sight; prevent sb from knowing;

[遮光] block light;

遮光罩 lens hood;

[遮截] block; shut off; stop;

[遮攔] block; conceal; cover; fend off; hinder; impede; obstruct;

[遮臉] cover one's face;

以手遮臉 veil one's face with one's hand;

[遮路] block the road;

[遮瞞] hide the truth; lie in order to conceal the truth;

[遮面] cover one's face; shade one's face;

[遮篷] awning;

[遮羞] conceal one's disgrace; cover one's nakedness; cover up one's embarrassment; hush up a scandal;

[遮眼法] camouflage;

[遮掩] camouflage; conceal; cover; cover up; envelop; hide; overspread;

東掩西遮 hide and cover from place to place;

遮遮掩掩 try to cover up; dodging and dissembling; in a somewhat disguised manner;

[遮陽] protect from the sunlight;

遮陽板 sunshading board;

遮陽帽 pith helmet;

遮陽傘 parasol;

~大遮陽傘 parasol; sunshade;

[遮陰布] codpiece;

[遮蔭] shade;

[遮止] stop sb's progress;

[遮住] block; cover; obstruct;

遮不住 cannot be concealed; unable to cover up;

zhe²
zhe

【折】 (1) break; snap; (2) lose; suffer the loss of; (3) bend; twist; (4) change direction; turn back; (5) be convinced; be filled with admiration; (6) amount to; convert into; (7) discount; rebate; (8) fold; (9) a surname;

[折半] give fifty per cent discount; reduce a price by half; reduce by half; reduce to half; sell at half price;

[折北] be defeated;

[折衝] repulse the enemy; subdue the enemy; ward off the enemy;

折衝御侮 repel foreign aggression;

折衝尊俎 engage in diplomatic negotiations; out-manoeuvre the enemy over glasses and wine; win by superior diplomacy;

[折抵] set off against;

[折疊] fold;

折疊牀 folding bed;

折疊傘 folding umbrella;

折疊椅 folding chair;

便於折疊 fold easily;

[折斷] break; break asunder; break off; rive; snap;

折斷腿 break one's leg;

[折服] (1) bring into submission; subdue; submit; (2) acknowledge the superiority of others; be convinced; be filled with admiration;

傾心折服 submit cordially; submit with admiration;

衷心折服 admire from the heart;

[折福] reduce blessings in one's later life because of excessive easy living;
[折光] refract light; refracted light;
[折合] amount to; convert into; equivalent to;
[折回] turn back;
[折價] (1) equivalent to; (2) allowance;
折價出售 sell at cut-rate prices;
折價換購 trade-in;
折價賠償 pay compensation at the market price;
折價退賠 pay compensation at the market price;
以舊換新交易的折價 trade-in allowance;
[折箭] break an arrow;
折箭為盟 break an arrow as vow to keep one's promise;
折箭為誓 a vow is taken with the breaking of an arrow;
[折節] (1) act obsequiously; (2) change the habit of living;
折節讀書 take a sudden liking to studying;
折節下交 extend one's acquaintance among inferiors; humble oneself in making acquaintances;
[折舊] depreciation;
折舊估算 depreciation appraisal;
折舊換新 trade in an old thing for a new one;
折舊基金 depreciation fund;
非常折舊 abnormal depreciation;
慣例折舊 conventional depreciation;
加速折舊 accelerated depreciation;
賬面折舊 book depreciation;
綜合折舊 composite depreciation;
[折扣] abatement; allowance; discount; rebate;
折扣店 outlet store;
打折扣 give a discount;
額外折扣 discount;
銀行折扣 bank discount;
預付折扣 anticipated discount;
總合折扣 aggregate discount;
[折開] take asunder;
[折賣] sell one's property;
[折門] accordion door; folding door;
[折磨] cause physical or mental suffering; submit to an ordeal; torment; trials and afflictions;
折磨至死 torment sb to death;
備受折磨 be bitterly afflicted; prey up on sb;
~身心備受折磨 be bitterly afflicted both in body and spirit;
免除折磨 be released from torture;
受良心的折磨 be tormented with the stings of conscience;
受折磨 in torment;
受疾病的折磨 be tortured with a disease;
為煩惱所折磨 be beleaguered with annoyance;
自我折磨 self-torture;
[折讓] discounts and allowances;
[折辱] humiliate; insult;
[折扇] folding fan;
[折射] refract; refraction;
折射定律 law of refraction;
折射法 refraction method;
折射計 refractometer;
折射率 index of refraction; refractive index;
折射望遠鏡 refracting telescope;
雙折射 birefringence;
~電場致雙折射 electric birefringence;
~電光雙折射 electrooptical birefringence;
~分子雙折射 molecular birefringence;
~負雙折射 negative birefringence;
~光學雙折射 optical birefringence;
~晶狀雙折射 crystalline birefringence;
~離子致雙折射 ionic birefringence;
~流動雙折射 flow birefringence; streaming birefringence;
~取向雙折射 orientation birefringence;
~特性雙折射 intrinsic birefringence;
~形狀雙折射 form birefringence;
~應變雙折射 strain birefringence;
~應力雙折射 stress birefringence;
~圓偏振雙折射 allogyric birefringence;
~圓振雙折射 circular birefringence;
~正雙折射 positive birefringence;
[折實] reckon the actual amount after a discount;
[折算] convert; equivalent to;
[折損] damage;
[折頭] discount rate;
[折腰] bow; humble oneself;
不為五斗米折腰 cannot make curtesies for the salary of five bushels of rice;
摧眉折腰 bow and scrape; bow unctuously; lower one's brows and bow respectfully;
[折獄] decide a lawsuit;

[折枝] (1) massage; (2) snap a twig;
[折衷] compromise;
折衷主義 eclecticism;
[折子] folding notebook;
折子戲 highlights from operas; selected scenes;
[折足覆餗] not equal to the task; without the required ability to undertake a given task;

拗折 break by twisting;
八折 twenty per cent discount;
百折 repeated setbacks;
波折 obstacles; obstructions; setbacks; twists and turns;
摧折 (1) break; snap; (2) frustrate; reverse; setback; subdue;
存折 bank book; deposit book; passbook;
挫折 blow; frustration; reverse; setback; subdue;
對折 fifty per cent discount;
骨折 fracture;
撓折 force to yield;
磨折 cause physical or mental suffering;
磬折 humpbacked;
攀折 pull down and break off;
曲折 (1) circuitous; curving; intricate; tortuous; ups and downs; winding; zigzag; (2) complications; intricacy; not smooth; not straightforward;
屈折 flexion; inflection;
心折 admire without reservations; have one's heart won;
夭折 (1) die young; (2) come to a premature end;
周折 complicated course of development; complication; setbacks; troublesome course of development; twists and turns;
轉折 (1) a turn in the course of events; complications; twists and turns; (2) transition;
奏折 memorial to the throne;

zhe

【哲】 (1) sagacious; wisdom; wise; (2) philosopher; sage; thinker; wise man;
[哲理] philosophical principle; philosophical theory;
哲理詮釋學 philosophical hermeneutics;
哲理詩 philosophic poetry;
尋求哲理 seek philosophy;
[哲人] philosopher; sage;
哲人其萎 passing away of a wise man; the philosopher is dying;
[哲學] philosophy;
哲學範疇 field of philosophy;
哲學家 philosopher;
哲學理論 theory of philosophy;
哲學文獻 philosophical text;
超驗哲學 transcendentalism;
純理論哲學 academic philosophy;
純哲學 pure philosophy;
道德哲學 moral philosophy;
煩瑣哲學 scholasticism;
古代哲學 ancient philosophy;
古怪哲學 cranky philosophy;
教育哲學 educational philosophy;
經濟哲學 economic philosophy;
經院哲學 scholastic philosophy; scholasticism;
數理哲學 mathematical philosophy;
思辯哲學 speculative philosophy;
語言哲學 linguistic philosophy;
自然哲學 natural philosophy;

睿哲 divinely wise; sagacious;
先哲 great thinker of the past; sage;
賢哲 wise and able person;

zhe

【蜇】 (1) jellyfish; (2) sting;

海蜇 jellyfish;
蛇蜇 anguine lizard;

zhe

【摺】 (1) fold; plait; (2) curved and winding; (3) pull and break; (4) folder;
[摺尺] folding ruler;
[摺牀] folding bed;
[摺刀] folding knife; pocket knife;
[摺櫈] campstool;
[摺疊] fold up; plait together;
摺疊牀 camp bed; folding bed;
摺疊刀 penknife;
摺疊傘 telescopic umbrella;
摺疊椅子 collapsible chair; folding chair;
摺疊桌 folding table;
可摺疊的 collapsible;
[摺兒] fold;
[摺痕] crease; fold; line made by folding;
[摺角] dog-ear; make a dog-ear;
[摺門] folding door;
[摺面桌] pembroke table;
[摺傘] folding umbrella;
[摺扇] folding fan;

Z

[摺椅] folding chair;
輕便扶手摺椅 director's chair;
輕便摺椅 lounger;
日光摺椅 lounger;
[摺子] piece of paper folded into pages;
[摺奏] memorial submitted to the emperor;

zhe
【輒】 (1) sides of a chariot; (2) arbitrary; dictatorial; (3) in that case; then; (4) always; every time;
[輒然] still;

動輒 at every turn; easily;

zhe
【慴】 fearful; frightened; terrified;

zhe
【磔】 (1) dismember a human being; (2) downward stroke sliding to the right in Chinese calligraphy;

zhe
【褶】 (1) riding clothes; (2) fold; pleated;
[褶邊] frill;
[褶層] fold;
[褶痕] crease; fold;
[褶襇] pleat;
多道褶襇 accordion pleat;
手風琴式褶襇 accordion pleat;
[褶曲] fold;
不定形褶曲 amoeboid fold;
盆地褶曲 basin fold;
協調褶曲 accordant fold;
[褶裙] pleated skirt;
百褶裙 skirt with accordion pleats;
對褶裙 box pleat skirt;
腰褶裙 full skirt gathered around the waist;
[褶皺] (1) fold; (2) wrinkle;
褶皺山 fold mountain; folded mountain;
不對稱褶皺 asymmetrical fold;
彎曲褶皺 buckle fold;
箱狀褶皺 box fold;
[褶子] (1) pleats; (2) folds; (3) wrinkles;

打褶 pleat;

zhe
【謫】 (1) blame; censure; reproach; (2) penalize; punish; (3) one's fault; (4) banish to a distant place; exile;
[謫奸] punish the wicked;
謫奸發伏 condemn the wicked and disclose secrets; expose the wiles of treacherous men;
[謫居] live in exile;
[謫戍] be exiled to the border;
謫戍邊陲 be banished to the frontiers;
[謫仙] immortal living among mortals; genius; prodigy;
[謫降] (1) demote and exile to the frontier; (2) descend to the earth;

貶謫 banish a high official from the court; demote and exile;

zhe
【轍】 ruts; wheel tracks;
[轍叉] frog;
夾緊轍叉 clamp frog;
鋭角轍叉 acute frog;
中心轍叉 centre frogs;
[轍亂旗靡] chariots in disorder and banners drooping; crisscross chariot tracks and drooping banners;

車轍 rut;
覆轍 track of an overturned cart;
改轍 change one's course of action;
軌轍 rut;
合轍 (1) in agreement; (2) in rhyme;
涸轍 in dire poverty;
沒轍 at one's wits' end; can find no way out; have no way out; have no solution;

zhe
【懾】 awe-struck; fearful;
[懾服] submit because of fear; yield from fear;
[懾息] hold one's breath in fear;
[懾慴] lose one's courage in fear;

zhe³
zhe
【者】 (1) he who; those who; (2) adverbial;

愛國者 patriot;
愛好者 fan;
悲觀主義者 pessimist;
筆者 author; writer;
編者 compiler; editor;
表演者 performer;

儐者 receptionist;
參觀者 visitor;
參加者 attendant;
操縱者 controller;
倡導者 initiator;
持分者 stakeholder;
重婚者 bigamist;
從者 followers;
崇拜者 worshipper;
出版者 publisher;
傳播者 spreader;
帶菌者 carrier;
貸款者 creditor;
得獎者 prize-winner;
帝國主義者 imperialist;
獨裁者 dictator;
獨唱者 soloist;
獨奏者 soloist;
讀者 reader;
黷武主義者 militarist;
多元論者 pluralist;
發行者 publisher;
分裂主義者 splittist;
分散主義者 decentralist;
風頭主義者 seeker after the limelight;
復仇主義者 revanchist;
改編者 reviser;
感傷主義者 sentimentalist;
告密者 informer;
革命者 revolutionary;
工作者 worker;
功利主義者 utilitarian;
瞽者 blind person;
觀光者 sightseer;
國際主義者 internationalist;
捍衛者 defender;
和平主義者 pacifist;
後者 the latter;
患者 patient; sufferer;
懷疑主義者 sceptic;
閽者 gatekeeper; janitor;
或者 maybe; or; perhaps;
機會主義者 opportunist;
機械論者 mechanist;
集體主義者 collectivist;
極端主義者 extremist;
極權主義者 totalitarian;
記者 correspondent; reporter;
繼承者 inheritor;
建設者 builder; constructor;
校訂者 checker; reviser; verifier;
教條主義者 dogmatist;
劫持者 hijacker;
經驗主義者 empiricist;
勞動者 labourer; worker;
老者 old person;
領唱者 leading singer;
領導者 leader;
流浪者 tramp; vagrant;
流亡者 exile;
掠奪者 plunderer;
冒險主義者 adventurist;
民主主義者 democrat;
民族主義者 nationalist;
目擊者 eye-witness;
旁觀者 onlooker; spectator;
平均主義者 egalitarian; equalitarian;
前者 the former;
強者 the strong;
人道主義者 humanist;
弱者 the weak;
社會主義者 socialist;
設計者 designer;
生產者 producer;
勝利者 victor; winner;
失敗主義者 defeatist;
失業者 the unemployed;
實用主義者 pragmatist;
實在論者 realist;
實證主義者 positivist;
使者 emissary; envoy;
世界主義者 cosmopolitan;
侍者 attendant; servant;
首倡者 initiator;
受害者 sufferer; victim;
唆使者 abettor; instigator;
死者 the dead; the deceased;
宿命論者 fatalist;
逃亡者 person who flees from home;
挑撥者 instigator;
同謀者 accomplice; conspirator;
同情者 sympathizer;
統治者 ruler;
投降主義者 capitulationist;
托荒者 pathbreaker; pioneer;
唯美主義者 aesthete;
唯我主義者 solipsist;
唯物主義者 materialist;
唯心主義者 idealist;
違法者 law-breaker;
尾隨者 tailer;
偽善者 hypocrite;
未來主義者 futurist;
衛道者 apologist;

無產者 proletarian;
無神論者 atheist;
犧牲者 victim;
吸毒者 drug addict;
先驅者 forerunner; pioneer;
先行者 forerunner;
現實主義者 realist;
相對主義者 relativist;
享樂主義者 hedonist;
象徵主義者 symbolist;
消費者 consumer;
行為主義者 behaviourist;
形式主義者 formalist;
幸存者 survivor;
修正主義者 revisionist;
虛無主義者 nihilist;
學者 person of learning; scholar;
馴獸者 animal tamer;
演唱者 singer;
演奏者 performer;
厭世者 pessimist;
譯者 translator;
擁護者 supporter; upholder;
優勝者 champion; winner;
有產者 person of property;
躁狂者 maniac;
再者 besides; furthermore; moreover;
佔領者 occupant;
長者 (1) elder; senior; (2) venerable elder;
肇事者 troublemaker;
折中主義者 eclectic;
陣亡者 person killed in action;
執行者 executor;
殖民主義者 colonialist;
種族主義者 racist;
主觀主義者 subjectivist;
追隨者 adherent; follower;
著者 author;
自由主義者 liberalist;
宗派主義者 sectarian;
作者 author; writer;

zhe

【啫】 jelly;
［啫喱］ jelly;
啫喱糖 jelly candies;
~ 彩虹啫喱糖 rainbow jelly candies;
~ 三色啫喱糖 tri-colour jelly candies;

zhe

【赭】 (1) red; (2) hematite; (3) ocher;

zhe

【鍺】 germanium;

zhe⁴

zhe

【柘】 (1) thorny tree; (2) sugarcane;
［柘彈］ a slingshot made of the tree;
［柘漿］ sugarcane juice;
［柘榴］ the pomegranate;

zhe

【浙】 (1) Zhejiang; (2) a river;

zhe

【這】 (1) this; (2) now;
［這般］ like this; so; such;
這般光景 such a pitiable state of affairs; such a sad condition;
［這邊］ here; this side;
［這次］ current; present; this time;
［這兒］ (1) here; (2) now; then;
［這等］ like this; such;
［這番］ all this;
［這個］ (1) this; this one; (2) this;
［這會兒］ at this moment; now;
［這件］ this piece;
［這裏］ here; this place; where we are;
這裏有鬼 I smell a rat; sth fishy is going on; there is some dirty work going on here; there is sth fishy about it;
［這麼］ this;
這麼一來 as a result; as a result of that; consequently; in this way;
說是這麼說 that is what we say;
［這那］ this and that;
說這說那 say this and this;
問這問那 ask about this and that;
這山望着那山高 always think the grass is greener on the other side; it is always the other mountain that looks higher; never happy where one is; the apples on the other side of the wall are the sweetest; the grass always looks greener on the other side of the fence; the grass is always greener on the other hill;

zhe

【蔗】 sugarcane;
［蔗根］ root of the sugar-cane;
［蔗農］ sugarcane grower;
［蔗肉］ flesh of the cane;
［蔗糖］ cane sugar; sugar from cane; table

sugar;
[蔗心] centre stem of a cane;
[蔗汁] cane juice; sugarcane juice;

甘蔗 sugarcane;

zhe

【鷓】 partridge;
[鷓鴣] partridge;
鷓鴣媒 decoy partridge;
鷓鴣啼 crowing of the partridge;

zhe5
zhe

【着】 adverbial particle;

本着 in conformity with; in line with;
跟着 immediately; right away;
歸着 put in order; tidy up;
接着 (1) catch; (2) carry on; follow; in a row; in succession; on end;
緊着 hurry; speed;
隨着 along with; follow in the wake of;
為着 for; in order to;
向着 (1) face; turn towards; (2) be partial to;
沿着 along;

zhei4
zhei

【這】 this or that;
[這個] this one;
[這年] in that particular year; in that year; in this year;
[這天] on this particular day;

zhen1
zhen

【珍】 (1) treasures; valuables; (2) precious; rare; valuable; (3) dainties; delicacies;
[珍愛] love dearly; treasure; value; very fond of;
[珍寶] gem; jewellery; treasure;
發現珍寶 find rare treasures;
歷史珍寶 precious historical treasures;
稀世珍寶 rare treasures;
[珍本] rare book; rare edition;
[珍藏] consider valuable and collcct appropriately; treasure up;
珍藏密斂 hide in a very safe place; keep in a very safe place;
珍藏品 collector's item;
[珍怪] rarities; strange happenings;
[珍貴] precious; rare; valuable;
珍貴古玩 precious antiques;
珍貴手稿 rare manuscript;
非常珍貴 of great rarity;
十分珍貴 like gold dust;
時間珍貴 time is precious;
[珍品] curio; delicacies; gem; precious objects; treasures; valuables;
陶瓷珍品 ceramic treasures;
[珍奇] rare; rare and precious;
[珍禽] rare bird;
珍禽異獸 precious birds and rare animals; rare birds and animals; rare fowls and strange animals;
[珍賞] highly value and appreciate;
[珍視] cherish; have a high opinion of; prize; treasure; value;
珍視建議 value one's advice;
珍視友誼 value one's friendship;
[珍玩] cruios of great value; rare curios;
[珍味] rare delicacies;
[珍聞] fillers; news titbits; valuable information;
[珍物] (1) treasures; valuables; (2) delicacies;
[珍稀] rare;
珍稀動物 rare animal;
珍稀植物 rare plant;
[珍惜] cherish; treasure; treasure and avoid wasting; value;
珍惜分陰 every moment counts; improve every moment; treasure every moment;
[珍饈] ambrosia; dainties; delicacies;
異果珍饈 rare fruits and delicacies; strange fruit and fine dishes;
[珍餚異饌] all dainty meats and fine dishes; ambrosia;
[珍異] rare; rare and precious;
[珍重] (1) hold dear; set great store; treasure; value highly; (2) take good care of yourself;
[珍珠] gem; pearls;
珍珠雞 guinea fowl;
珍珠米 Indian corn; maize;
珍珠母 mother-of-pearl; nacre;
珍珠色的 pearly;
珍珠似的 pearly;
人工養殖的珍珠 cultured pearl;
人造珍珠 imitation peral;

一串珍珠 a rope of-pearls; a strand of pearls; a string of pearls;
一顆珍珠 a pearl;

八珍 eight delicacies;
家珍 family heirloom;
奇珍 curio; rare treasure; rarity;
袖珍 pocket; pocket-size;

zhen

【貞】 (1) chastity of a woman; (2) pure; virtuous; (3) correctly firm; incorruptible; (4) dedication; devotion; loyal; (5) divine; inquire by divination;

[貞白] chastity; integrity;

[貞操] (1) chastity; purity and chastity; virginity; (2) loyalty; moral integrity;
出賣貞操 sell one's chastity;
毀損貞操 spoil one's chastity;
失去貞操 lose one's chastity;
維護貞操 defend one's chastity;

[貞而不諒] firm but not stubborn;

[貞婦] chaste woman;

[貞固] stick to righteousness and virtue;

[貞節] (1) chastity; purity; virtue; (2) tenacity to hold on to one's integrity;
貞節無瑕 there is not a speck on the honour;

[貞潔] chaste and pure; chaste and undefiled; chastity; virtuous;
貞潔的 chaste;

[貞烈] ready to die to preserve one's chastity;
九烈三貞 have a sharp sense of honour;
三貞九烈 have a sharp sense of honour; ready to die to preserve one's chastity; women who die in defence of their honour;

[貞木] (1) hardwood; (2) symbolic of people of rectitude;

[貞女] chaste girl; virgin;
貞女不事二夫 a chaste woman never remarries;

[貞人] person of high moral standing and integrity;

[貞士] person of integrity; person of virtue;

[貞淑] pure and chaste;

堅貞 consistently faithful;
童貞 chastity; virginity;
忠貞 faithful and unwavering; loyal and steadfast;

zhen

【胗】 (1) same as 疹; (2) same as 肫;

[胗兒] gizzard of a fowl;

[胗肝兒] gizzard and liver;

雞胗 chicken's gizzard;
鴨胗 duck's gizzard;

zhen

【真】 (1) actual; factual; genuine; real; substantial; true; (2) indeed; really; truly; (3) clearly; (4) a surname;

[真愛] true love;

[真棒] excellent;

[真誠] earnest; genuine; honest; sincere; true;
真誠對待 deal honestly with;
真誠合作 cooperate sincerely;
真誠悔過 repent sincerely;
真誠實意 with the utmost sincerity and cordiality;
真誠無私 sincere and selfless;
真誠相見 genuine meeting of minds; talk from the heart with nothing concealed;
不真誠的 disingenuous;
缺乏真誠 lack sincerity;
真真誠誠 with all one's heart; with all one's heart and soul;

[真的] true;
說真的 no kidding;

[真諦] essence; true essence; true meaning;

[真個] indeed; really; truly;

[真箇] actually; really;
真箇銷魂 really captivating;

[真話] true statements; truth;
講真話 speak the truth;
說真話 speak the truth; tell the truth;
笑談之中有真話 there's many a true word spoken in jest;

[真蹟] authentic works;

[真假] genuine and sham; real and fake; true and false;
真假莫辨 cannot distinguish whether sth is genuine or fake; cannot tell whether sth is true or false; not to know the real from the false; not to know whether sth is true or not;
半真半假 half genuine and half forged; half-genuine, half-sham; partly true, partly false;
辨別真假 distinguish the true from the false;

假談真打 prate about peace while making attacks;
假戲真做 do sth seriously after starting it as a ruse;
弄假成真 fulfil what is promised as a joke; pretence may become reality; say in fun what is fulfilled in earnest; what is make-believe has become reality; what is said in fun is fulfilled in earnest;
棄假歸真 give up falsehood and return to truth; turn from what is false to what is true;
似真還假 falsely true;
以假攙真 adulaterate; mix up truth with falsehood;
以假充真 pass fake imitations for genuine; pass for genuine; pass off the false as genuine;
以假亂真 create confusion by passing off the spurious as genuine; mix the false with the true; mix the spurious with the genuine; palm off falsehood as truth; pass off a fake as genuine;
真真假假 a mixture of truth and falsehood; both real and sham; some feature being real and others sham; the true blended with the false; truth mingled with falsehood; truth mixed with falsehood;

[真金不怕火] a genuine article can stand any test; a good anvil does not fear the hammer; an honest person does not fear detection; an honest person does not fear the light; pure gold fears no fire; sth genuine can stand any test; true blue will never stain; true gold fears no fire—a person of integrity can stand severest tests; true gold does not fear fire; truth fears not the flames of slander and injustice;

[真空] vacuum;
真空包裝 vacuum packaging;
真空管 vacuum tube;
真空瓶 vacuum bottle;
真空吸塵機 vacuum cleaner;
粗真空 coarse vacuum;
低真空 black vacuum;
乾真空 dry vacuum;
極限真空 highest attained vacuum;
局部真空 partial vacuum;
絕對真空 absolute vacuum; complete vacuum;
填補真空 fill a vacuum;

[真菌] fungus;
真菌學 mycology;
抗真菌[的] anti-fungal;

[真理] (1) truth; (2) righteousness;
真理必勝 truth will prevail;
真理面前，人人平等 everyone is equal before the truth;
背離真理 depart from the truth;
堅持真理 uphold the truth;
絕對真理 absolute truth; gospel truth;
普遍真理 universal truth;
違背真理 entruth upon the truth;
相對真理 relative truth;
尋求真理 seek truth;
一點點真理 a shred of truth
追求真理 aspire after truth; follow truth;

[真皮] (1) dermis; (2) genuine leather;

[真品] genuine article;

[真巧] what a coincidence;

[真切] clear; distinct; vivid;
看得真切 have a clear view of sth;
聽得真切 hear distinctly;

[真情] (1) actual happenings; actual state of affairs; facts; real situation; truth; (2) real sentiments; true feelings;
真情流露 reveal true sentiments;
真情實感 real feelings;
真情實話 round unvarnished tale;
真情實意 genuine affection; real sentiments;
流露真情 reveal one's true feelings;
傾訴真情 open one's heart to sb;
掩飾真情 mask one's sentiments;

[真詮] correct explanation; correct meaning;

[真確] (1) authentic; real true; (2) clear; distinct;
千真萬確 a tested truth; absolutely true; as big as life; as I live by bread; as large as life; as sure as a gun; as sure as death; as sure as eggs is eggs; as sure as fate; as sure as I am alive; as sure as life; as sure as nails; as sure as one lives; I can say it for certain; I know it for a certainty; indisputable; it is a dead certainty; it is only too true; quite certain; real and true; sure enough; that's only too true; the honest truth; upon my word; very real;

~ 千真萬確的事實 absolute fact;
~ 千真萬確地 really and truly;

[真人] (1) immortal; (2) real person;
真人不露相 a person of substance does not like to show off;
真人不露相，深山出駿馬 fairest gems lie deepest; true merit does not advertise itself;
真人面前不說假 before a really honest man, he will not tell lies; don't lie before a sincere person;
真人真事 actual person and event; real people and real events; the characters are real and the story is true;

[真善美] the true, the good and the beautiful; truth, goodness and beauty;

[真實] authentic; factual; real; true;
真實的 true;
~ 不真實的 mendacious; untrue;
真實可信 genuine and believable;
真實條件從句 real conditional;
真實性 authenticity; realness; truth; truthfulness; verisimilitude;
真實原則 reality principle;
不真實 inveracity; mendacity; untruthfulness;
~ 聽起來不真實 not ring true; ring hollow;
貨真價實 excellent goods at reasonable prices; genuine goods and fixed prices;

[真率] frank and honest; straightforward; unaffected;

[真偽] true and false;
真偽莫辨 cannot distinguish between real and false; cannot distinguish whether sth is true or false; unable to tell the true from the false;
不辨真偽 fail to distinguish between truth and falsehood; unable to distinguish the genuine from the imitation; unable to tell the true from the false;
明辨真偽 can tell true from false;
難辨真偽 hard to distinguish between the true and false;
去偽存真 discard the false and retain the true; discard what is false and keep what is genuine; disentangle truth from falsehood; eliminate the false and retain the true; remove the false and retain the true; rid the fake and retain the genuine; sift the true from the false; winnow truth from falsehood;

[真相] actual state of affairs; naked truth; real situation; truth;
真相大白 come out in the wash; the actual state of affairs has made clear; the case is entirely cleared up; the cat is out of the bag; the facts are clear now; the lid is off of sth; the murder is out; the true facts have been brought into daylight; the truth is out; the truth has been revealed; the whole affair is now out in the open; the whole truth has been brought into daylight; with the lid off;
查明真相 ascertain the truth; find out the truth;
迴避真相 avoid the truth;
獲知真相 arrive at the truth;
看清真相 remove the scales from sb's eyes;
了解真相 know the truth;
目睹真相 see the true facts with one's own eyes;
弄清真相 find out the truth; get at the truth; get to the truth;
揭露真相 reveal the truth; uncover the truth;
全部真相 full truth; whole truth;
推斷真相 reason out the truth;
歪曲真相 distort the truth;
掩蓋真相 cover up the facts;
知道真相 learn the truth;

[真心] actual intention; from the bottom of one's heart; heartfelt; sincere; real intention; true intention; wholehearted;
真心誠意 have one's heart in the right place; in earnest; in good faith; with all one's heart;
真心好意 good intentions;
真心話 sincere talks; words from the bottom of one's heart;
真心悔改 sincerely repent and earnestly reform oneself;
真心善意 open and true-hearted; sincerely and with good intentions; with sincerity and good intentions;
真心實意 genuinely and sincerely; in earnest; in good faith; sincerely; truly and wholeheartedly; with one's whole heart;
真心相愛 love sb heart and soul;
真心真意 from the bottom of one's heart;

have a sincere desire; heartfelt; honest; wholehearted; with all one's soul;
一片真心 a true heart; from the bottom of one's heart; in all sincerity; straight from one's heart; true heart;
[真行] good;
[真性] (1) natural property; (2) natural disposition;
[真意] true intent and real meaning;
[真正] (1) actual; precise; real; (2) genuine;
真正主語 real subject;
[真知] genuine knowledge; true knowledge;
真知灼見 correct and penetrating judgement; incisive judgement; profound insight; real knowledge and deep insight;
[真摯] cordial; genuine; sincere; true;
[真珠] natural pearl;

葆真 safeguard one's divine nature – untarnished by all desires, etc.;
逼真 (1) lifelike; realistic; true to life; true to nature; (2) clearly; distinctly;
傳真 (1) portraiture; (2) facsimile; fax;
純真 pure; sincere;
當真 (1) take seriously; (2) really; true;
仿真 emulate; simulate;
高保真 high fidelity;
歸真 return to one's original purity;
果真 as expected; really; sure enough;
亂真 (1) look genuine; (2) spurious;
清真 Islamic; Moslem;
認真 (1) earnest; conscientious; serious; (2) take seriously; take to heart;
失真 (1) differ from the original; (2) distort;
率真 forthright and sincere;
天真 innocent; naïve;
仙真 (1) Daoist god; (2) immortal;
寫真 (1) draw a portrait; portrait a person; (2) portrait; (3) describe sth as it is;
修真 cultivate the true self;
養真 discipline one's temperament;

zhen

【砧】 (1) anvil; (2) torture instrument;
[砧板] chopping block;
[砧子] hammer block; anvil;

鍛砧 smith anvil;
台砧 bench anvil;
鐵砧 anvil;

zhen

【針】 (1) needle; pin; probe; (2) stitch; (3) anything like a needle; (4) injection; shot; (5) acupuncture;
[針鼻兒] eye of a needle;
[針砭] (1) ancient form of acupuncture; (2) admonition; point out sb's errors and offer salutary advice; remonstrance;
苦語針砭 point out sb's errors and offer salutary advice with faithful words;
[針插] (1) pin cushion; (2) stick into sth with a pin;
針插不進，水潑不進 impenetrable and watertight;
[針吹] needle blow;
[針刺] acupuncture;
針刺療法 acupuncture therapy;
[針對] (1) aim directly at; be aimed at; be directed against; counter; point at; (2) in accordance with; in connection with; in the light of;
[針法] stitching;
十字針法 cross-stitch;
[針鋒] point of a needle;
針鋒相對 a Roland for an Oliver; blow for blow; contrast sharply with; give tit for tat; measure for measure; sharply opposed to each other; stand in sharp opposition; tit for tat;
[針管] syringe;
[針盒] sewing kit;
[針尖] pinpoint; point of a needle;
針尖對麥芒 a pin against an awe; diamond cut diamond;
[針灸] acupuncture; acupuncture and moxibustion;
針灸麻醉 acupuncture analgesia;
針灸穴位 acupuncture point;
針灸醫生 acupuncturist;
針灸治療 acupuncture treatment;
進行針灸 apply acupuncture;
[針式] pin-type;
針式打印機 pin-type printer;
[針無兩頭利] it is impossible for a man to do two things at once; there is no needle with both ends pointed;
[針頭] pinhead;
針頭線腦 a sewing kit; needle and thread; odds and ends needed for sewing;

[針線] (1) needle and thread; (2) needlework;
針線盒 sewing kit;
針線活 needlework;
飛針走線 do needlework very skilfully; do skilful needlework; sew quickly; use the needle with great speed;
一針一線 a single needle or a piece of thread; so much as a needle or thread; stitch by stitch;

[針眼] sty;
長針眼 have a sty;

[針葉] conifer;
針葉林 conifer forest;
針葉樹 conifer;

[針織] knitting;
針織廠 knitting mill;
針織品 knit goods; knitting; knitwear;
~ 針織品商店 knitwear shop;

繃針 pin;
避雷針 lightning rod;
錶針 watch hand;
別針 (1) pin; safety pin; (2) brooch;
插針 stick in a pin;
唱針 gramophone needle; stylus;
穿針 thread a needle;
磁針 magnetic needle;
刺針 lance;
打針 give or have an injection;
大頭針 pin;
耳針 ear acupuncture;
髮針 hairpin;
方針 guiding principle; policy;
防疫針 inoculation;
分針 minute hand;
縫衣針 sewing needle;
鉤針 crochet hook;
骨針 spicule;
迴形針 paper clip;
帽針 hatpin;
秒針 second hand;
強心針 cardiotonic injection;
曲別針 paper clip;
紉針 thread a needle;
時針 hour hand;
試針 experimental injection;
松針 pine needle;
探針 probe;
綉花針 embroidery needle;
胸針 brooch;
一包針 a paper of pins;
一根針 a needle;
扎針 give an acupuncture treatment;
螫針 sting; stinger;
織針 knitting needle;
指南針 compass;
指針 (1) guide; manual; (2) arrow; index; indication needle; (3) hands of a clock;
撞針 firing pin;
總方針 general policy; general principle;

zhen

【偵】 (1) detect; investigate; scout; spy; (2) detective; scout; spy;

[偵查] investigate a crime;
偵查案件 investigate the case;
偵查結果 result of the investigation;
偵查罪行 investigate the crime;
進行偵查 carry out investigations;
有待偵查 await investigation;

[偵察] reconnoiter; scout; surveillance;
偵察部隊 scouting forces;
偵察敵情 gather intelligence about the enemy;
偵察機 reconnaissance plane; scouting aeroplane;
~ 遠程偵察機 long-range reconnaissance aeroplane;
偵察衛星 reconnaissance satellite;
低空偵察 low-altitude surveillance;
火力偵察 reconnaissance by firing;
空中偵察 aerial reconnaissance; high altitude surveillance;
四處偵察 have a scout round;

[偵緝] track down and arrest;

[偵碼機] cellular phone read system;

[偵破] bust a crime; clear up a case; crack a criminal case; solve a case;

[偵探] (1) do detective work; gumshoe; investigate; (2) detective; spy;
偵探工作 gum-shoeing;
偵探片 detective film;
偵探小說 detective story;
便衣偵探 plain clothes detective;
僱用偵探 employ a detective;
私家偵探 private detective; private eye; private investigator;
私人偵探 private detective; private eye; private investigator;
業餘偵探 amateur detective;

[偵聽] intercept; monitor;
偵聽器 detectaphone;

[偵詢] examine a suspect;

zhen
【斟】 (1) fill a cup with; pour into a cup; (2) consider;
[斟茶] fill a cup with tea;
[斟酒] pour wine into a cup;
[斟滿] fill a cup to the brim;
[斟酌] (1) fill a cup with wine; (2) consider; deliberate; think over; weigh and consider;
斟酌得失 weigh the pros and cons carefully;
斟酌盡善 consider the best plan; consult about the most perfect way to do sth;
斟酌利弊 weigh the advantages and disadvantages;
斟酌勘酌 think the matter over;
費斟酌 exhaust one's mind to think;
有待斟酌 wait pending further consideration;
斟句酌意 study intensively a sentence and elicit its meaning;
斟字酌句 deliberate over the choice of words and the construction of sentences; go over one's wording carefully; refine on the words; refine upon the wording to write in ornate style; weigh each sentence and each word; weigh one's words;

zhen
【楨】 (1) sturdy wood; (2) posts at ends of walls;
[楨幹] backbone; core member;

zhen
【椹】 block; chopping board;
[椹板] chopping board;

zhen
【榛】 hazelnut;
[榛雞] hazel hen;
[榛仁] kernel of the hazelnut;
[榛實] hazelnut;
[榛榛] be overgrown with wild plants;
[榛子] hazelnut;

zhen
【甄】 (1) discern; discriminate; distinguish; examine; (2) potter's wheel; (3) make pottery ware; (4) grade by examinations; (5) make clear; (6) a surname;
[甄拔] select talent by a competitive examination;
甄拔人才 select people of talent;
[甄別] grade by an examination; screen;
甄別考試 screening examination;
[甄審] screen and select candidates;
[甄汰] eliminate by an examination;
[甄陶] mold clay;
[甄選] select talented people;
[甄用] employ by an examination;

zhen
【禎】 (1) auspicious; good omen; (2) a surname;
[禎祥] good omen; lucky omen;

zhen
【蓁】 (1) wild pepper; (2) luxuriant;
[蓁蓁] (1) dense; thick; (2) overgrown;

zhen
【箴】 (1) needle; probe; (2) admonish; exhort; warn;
[箴砭] stone probes;
[箴銘] admonitions carved on a stone;
[箴規] admonitions; exhort;
[箴諫] admonish; caution against; exhort;
[箴石] stone probes;
[箴言] admonitions; exhortations; maxims;

zhen
【禛】 be blessed because of one's sincerity;

zhen
【臻】 (1) best; utmost; (2) arrive at; reach;

zhen
【鍼】 same as 針, a needle;

zhen³

zhen
【枕】 (1) pillow; (2) rest the head on; (3) block;
[枕伴] bed fellow; pillow companion;
[枕邊人] wife;
[枕邊言] pillow talk;
[枕戈] rest on one's arms;
枕戈待旦 lie on one's arms; lie with one's head pillowed on a spear, waiting for day to break; maintain combat readiness; make a pillow of one's spear waiting for daybreak — battle-ready; rest on one's arms; sleep on one's arms;
枕戈待敵 lie with one's head pillowed on a spear, awaiting the enemy; stand by;
枕戈待命 all set to start the battle; await

Z

eagerly the order for;
枕戈寢甲 pillow on a weapon and sleep on an armour — toil of war;
枕戈以待 mentally alert and ready; ready at all times; rest on one's arms;
[枕巾] pillow cover;
[枕衾] pillow and quilt;
共枕同衾 share the same pillow and sleep in the same quilt — married;
淚沾枕衾 the pillow is wet with tears;
同衾共枕 share the same quilt and the same pillow;
枕冷衾寒 loneliness in bed; pillow and cold quilt — lonely with no bedfellow; the pillow and the bed are cold — sleeping alone;
[枕木] railway sleeper; sleeper; tie;
防腐枕木 antiseptic wooden sleeper;
桿材枕木 pole tie;
失效枕木 defective sleeper;
四分枕木 quarter tie;
鐵道枕木 railroad tie;
轉轍枕木 crossing sleeper;
[枕石漱流] have no interest in worldly things; live in seclusion;
[枕套] pillowcase; pillowslip;
[枕頭] pillow;
枕頭假 duvet day;
枕頭套 pillow case;
枕頭戰 pillow fight;
開枕頭會 have a private talk between husband and wife;
[枕席] (1) bedding; the pillow and the mat; (2) pillow mat;
枕席不安 cannot sleep peacefully; cares disturb one's sleep; toss about in bed;
枕席之間 while in bed;
枕席自荐 willing to become sb's wife;

安枕 sleep in peace;
高枕 shake up the pillow;
軌枕 sleeper; tie;
靠枕 back cushion;
落枕 (1) stiff neck; (2) one's head touching the pillow;
衾枕 quilts and pillows;

zhen
【疹】 eruption; rashes;
[疹病] exanthema;
[疹子] carbuncles; measles;
出疹子 suffer from measles;

斑疹 macula;
風疹 nettle rash; urticarial;
汗疹 prickly heat;
紅疹 erythema;
痲疹 measles;
疱疹 (1) bleb; (2) herpes;
皮疹 rash;
丘疹 papule;
濕疹 eczema;
藥疹 drug rash;

zhen
【畛】 (1) footpaths between fields; (2) boundary; limit;
[畛域] boundary;
不分畛域 make no distinctions; there is no discrimination against the boundary;

zhen
【紾】 (1) turns; twists; (2) switch;
[紾臂] twist the arm;

zhen
【診】 (1) diagnose; examine; (2) report; tell;
[診病] diagnose a disease;
[診察] examine a patient;
[診斷] diagnose; diagnosis; diagnostic;
診斷程序 diagnotor;
診斷學 diagnostics;
~ 超聲診斷學 ultrasonic diagnostics;
~ 等離子體診斷學 plasma diagnostics;
診斷專家 diagnostician;
病理診斷 pathological diagnosis;
錯誤診斷 error diagnostic;
鑒別診斷 differential diagnosis;
臨牀診斷 clinical diagnosis;
品性診斷 character diagnosis;
早期診斷 early diagnosis;
[診候] examine and diagnose; treat a patient;
[診療] make a diagnosis and give treatment;
診療室 consulting room; doctor's consultation room;
診療所 polyclinic;
~ 兒童診療所 children's polyclinic;
診療院 sanatorium;
~ 兒童診療院 children's sanatorium;
[診脈] feel sb's pulse; take sb's pulse;
[診切] examine a person's pulse;
[診視] examine;
[診所] clinic;
聯合診所 polyclinic;
流動診所 ambulatory clinic;

[診症] consultation;
診症室 consulting room;
[診治] make a diagnosis and give treatment;
給病人診治 give medical treatment to a patient;
有效診治 effective treatment;

按診 pressing;
出診 make a house call; pay a home visit; visit a patient at home;
初診 pay the first visit;
觸診 palpate;
覆診 consult further with a doctor;
候診 wait for one's turn to see a doctor; wait to see the doctor;
會診 consultation of doctors;
急診 emergency call; emergency treatment;
開診 begin to treat patients;
叩診 percuss;
脈診 diagnose by felling the pulse;
門診 outpatient service;
捫診 palpate;
切診 feel the pulse and palpate;
確診 diagnose; form a correct diagnosis on a disease; make a definite diagnosis;
施診 give free medical treatment;
聽診 auscultate;
望診 observe the patient's complexion, etc.;
聞診 diagnose through auscultation and olfaction;
問診 diagnose through interrogation;
巡診 make a round of visits;
應診 take in and treat patients;

zhen

【軫】 (1) wooden bumper at the rear of a cart; (2) deeply; very much; (3) a surname;
[軫悼] mourn with deep grief;
[軫懷] sorrowfully cherish the memory of sb;
[軫慕] remember with deep emotion;
[軫念] remember with deep emotion; sorrowfully cherish the memory of sb; think anxiously about;
軫念時艱 bear in mind the troubles of the country;
[軫宿] one of the twenty-eight constellations;
[軫惜] have pity on; mourn with deep regret;
[軫卹] pity deeply;
[軫憂] worried and grieved;
[軫軫] grand; magnificent; majestic;

zhen

【稹】 (1) circumspect; (2) (of roots) entwined;

zhen

【縝】 close; fine; minute;
[縝紛] numerous;
[縝密] careful; deliberate; meticulous;
[縝緻] fine and delicate;

zhen

【鬒】 dark, glossy hair;

zhen⁴

zhen

【振】 (1) flap; shake; (2) arouse to action; brace up; raise; rise; rise with force and spirit; (3) pull up; relieve; save; (4) restore order;
[振拔] extricate oneself from a predicament and brace oneself up to action;
[振筆] wield the brush;
振筆疾書 move the brush and write swiftly; write rapidly; write with flying strokes;
振筆直書 take up the brush and write vigorously; wield the brush furiously;
[振臂] raise one's arms;
振臂高呼 raise one's arm and shout;
振臂一呼 arouse to action; raise one's arm and cry for action — issue a call for action; sound the trumpet call of action;
[振兵] rally the troops;
[振怖] alarm;
[振翅] flap wings; flutter;
振翅翺翔 soar with wings flapping;
振翅高飛 flap the wings and soar high into the sky; flutter and soar high;
[振盪] (1) vibration; (2) oscillation;
振盪器 oscillator; vibrator;
~多諧振盪器 multivibrator;
~截止多諧振盪器 biased multivibrator;
~平衡多諧振盪器 balanced multivibrator;
~自激多諧振盪器 astatic multivibrator;
自振盪 auto-oscillation;
~斷續自振盪 interrupted auto-oscillation;
~對稱自振盪 symmetric auto-oscillation;
~不對稱自振盪 non-symmetric autooscillation;
~寄生自振盪 parasitic auto-oscillation;

Z

[振動] motion; vibrate; vibration; vibratory motion;
振動理論 vibration theory;
振動能力 vibration ability;
振動器 vibrator;
~電動振動器 electrodynamic vibrator;
~電振動器 electric vibrator;
~混凝土振動器 concrete vibrator;
~強制振動器 forced vibrator;
固有振動 natural vibration;
橫振動 transverse vibration;
聲振動 acoustic vibration;
受迫振動 forced vibration;
彎曲振動 bending vibration;
諧振動 harmonic motion;
原子振動 atomic vibration;
縱振動 longitudinal vibration;
阻尼振動 damped oscillation;
自動振動 autovibration;
[振靡] awaken the weak and enervated;
[振奮] be inspired with enthusiasm; rise with force and spirit; rouse oneself; uplifting;
振奮精神 heighten one's fighting spirit; inspire enthusiasm;
振奮人心 encouraging; exciting; fill people with enthusiasm; heartening; heart-stirring; inspire people; inspire popular morale; inspiring; invigorating;
振奮士氣 boost the morale of the troops;
精神振奮 uplifted;
群情振奮 everyone is excited;
[振幅] amplitude;
振幅調制 amplitude modulation;
[振古] from ancient times;
[振濟] give aid to the distressed; relieve the distressed;
[振救] help; relieve;
[振鈴] ring a bell;
[振起] get aroused; rise and meet a challenge; stir up;
[振刷] arouse oneself; rise;
[振威] extend one's imposing prestige; inspire awe;
[振興] cause to prosper; develop vigorously; promote; re-energize;
振興教育 vitalize education;
[振衣] shake one's clothing;
[振纓] become an official; rise to officialdom;
[振振有詞] say plausibly; speak forcefully; speak plausibly and at length; speak plausibly and volubly; talk fluently and loudly;
[振作] arouse oneself; bestir oneself; brace up; display vigour; exert oneself; pull oneself together;
振作精神 bestir oneself; brace oneself; brace up; cheer up; raise steam; summon up one's energy;
振作起來 cheer up;
振作士氣 boost the morale; bring up the morale;
振作有為 bestir oneself to be promising; stimulate the mind to do sth;
重新振作 pull oneself together;

不振 dejected and apathetic; in low spirits;
重振 reorganize;
共振 resonance;
諧振 resonance;

zhen

【朕】 (1) the royal "we"; (2) auguries; omens; portents; signs;
[朕兆] omens; portents; signs;

zhen

【陣】 (1) a row of troops; the army; (2) battle; battle array; fight at the front; go to war; (3) front; position; (4) a period of time;
[陣地] battle field; position;
陣地戰 pitched battle; trench warfare;
撤離陣地 evacuate a position;
防禦陣地 defensive position;
鞏固陣地 consolidate a position;
堅守陣地 hold one's ground;
進攻陣地 attack position;
人在陣地在 fight to the death in defence of one's position; hold one's position at all costs;
[陣風] gusty wind;
中等陣風 moderately gusty wind;
[陣腳] (1) front line; (2) circumstances; position; situation;
亂了陣腳 break one's stride; keep sb off their stride; knock sb off stride; put sb off their stride; throw sb off stride;
[陣列] array;
磁心陣列 core array;
疊代陣列 iterations array;

二極管陣列 diode array;
放大器陣列 amplifier array;
檢測器陣列 detector array;
平衡陣列 balanced array;
數據陣列 data array;
位錯陣列 dislocation array;

[陣歿] be killed in action; die on the battlefield;

[陣前] on the battlefield;

[陣容] (1) battle array; battle formation; (2) cast; line-up;
陣容強大 grand cast; strong line-up;
陣容整齊 have a well-balanced line-up;

[陣勢] battle array; order of battle;
擺開陣勢 draw up troops for battle; put in battle array;

[陣亡] be killed in action; fall in action; fall in battle;
陣亡將士 the war dead;

[陣線] alignment; front; line of battle;

[陣雪] snow shower;

[陣營] camp; encampment;
在同一陣營 in the same camp;
政治陣營 political camp;

[陣雨] occasional drizzle; passing shower; rain shower; shower; shower of rain;
大陣雨 heavy shower;
雷陣雨 thunder shower;
氣團陣雨 air-mass shower;
一場陣雨 a shower;

[陣雲] dense clouds;

[陣陣] at intervals; by fits and starts; intermittently; now and again; repeatedly; spasmodically;

[陣子] a period of; a spell of;
那陣子 at that time;
前陣子 some days ago;

擺陣 deploy troops;
敗陣 be beaten in a contest; be defeated on the battlefield;
出陣 (1) go forth into battle; (2) take part in an athletic contest;
敵陣 enemy position;
點陣 lattice;
對陣 confront each other;
叫陣 challenge the opponent to a fight;
矩陣 matrix;
列陣 array; in battle array;
臨陣 before going to a battle;
迷魂陣 maze; scheme to bewitch sb; trap;
怯陣 (1) battle-shy; (2) stage fright;
上陣 (1) go into battle; (2) pitch into the work;
蚊陣 swarms of mosquitoes;
雁陣 wild geese formation;
一陣 (1) a burst; a fit; a peal; a puff; (2) a bout of; a burst of; a clap of; a fit of; a flurry of; a gale of; a gust of; a hail of; a roar of; a round of; a spasm of; a spate of; a spatter of; a spell of; a squall of; a storm of; a sudden gust of; a torrent of; a volley of; a waft of;
疑陣 a deceptive battle array to mislead the enemy;
戰陣 deployment of troops;
助陣 cheer for a contestant;

zhen
【陳】 tactical deployment of troops;

zhen
【酖】 poisonous wine;
[酖毒] poisoned wine;

zhen
【揕】 stab; strike; thrust;

zhen
【瑱】 press; weigh;

zhen
【賑】 (1) give aid to the distressed; relieve the distressed; (2) prosperous; rich; wealthy;

[賑饑] feed the hungry; relieve famine;

[賑濟] aid; relieve;
賑濟難民 provide relief for refugees;
賑濟貧民 dispense alms for the poor;
賑濟災民 aid the victims of natural calamities; relieve the people in stricken areas;
出錢賑濟 give money in alms;

[賑捐] contribute to relief funds;

[賑款] relief funds;

[賑糧] relief food;

[賑貧] relieve the poor;

[賑卹] relieve the distressed;

[賑災] relieve the people in stricken areas;

放賑 give famine relief;
施賑 give to the poor;

zhen
【震】 (1) shake; shock; tremble; vibrate; (2) deeply astonished; greatly excited;

[震波] earthquake wave; seismic wave;
[震顫] quiver; shake; shudder; tremble; tremor;
震顫病 trembles;
震顫麻痺 shaking palsy;
汞毒性震顫 tremor mercurialis;
家族性震顫 familial tremor;
咳嗽性震顫 tussive fremitus;
流行性震顫 epidemic tremor;
偏身震顫 hemitremor;
語音震顫 vocal fremitus;
[震悼] be shocked and grieved;
[震蕩] shake; shock; shock waves; tremor; vibrate;
腦震盪 concuss; concussion;
[震動] chatter; quake; shake; shock; vibrate;
震動全國 reverberate throughout the nation;
震動人心 make a great impact on people;
劇烈震動 judder;
震天動地 earth-shaking; rend the air; shake heaven and earth; world-shaking;
[震幅] amplitude of an earthquake;
[震駭] greatly shocked; greatly terrified; stunned;
[震撼] shake; shock; vibrate;
震撼人心 have a great impact on; soul-stirring; stirring; thrilling;
震撼世界 shake the whole world;
震撼天地 shake the skies and land;
震天憾地 rock the earth; shake the skies and land; world-shaking;
[震級] magnitude;
震級表 magnitude scale;
[震驚] alarm; astonish; consternation; in a state of shock; shock;
震驚朝野 alarm the court, officials, and common people;
震驚世界 make a stir all over the world;
震驚中外 shock the country and the whole world;
大為震驚 be much shaken; be terribly shocked; have a fit; have a thousand fits; in a state of shock; in deep shock; throw a fit; throw a thousand fits;
非常震驚 come as a shock;
感到震驚 get a shock; have a shock;
故作震驚 pretend to be shocked; with a show of dismay;
令人震驚 nasty shock;
深感震驚 complete shock; total shock;
[震懼] in trepidation; terrified;
[震恐] be shocked;
[震怒] convulsive rage; enraged; furious; greatly infuriated; rage; wrath;
大為震怒 become furious; fly into a rage; foam at the mouth;
[震慴] be frightened;
[震群] earthquake swarm;
[震懾] awe; frighten;
震懾四海 hold the four seas in awe;
[震霆] loud thunderclap; sudden peal of thunder;
[震央] epicentre;
[震源] focus; hypocenter;
震源距 focal distance;
震源深度 depth of focus;
[震災] disaster caused by an earthquake;
[震中] epicenter;
震中距 epicentral distance;
震中區 epicentral area;

爆震 detonate;
避震 shock absorption;
地震 earthquake;
發震 occurrence of earthquake;
防震 (1) take precautions against earthquakes; (2) shockproof;
海震 seaquake;
激震 shock;
減震 shock absorption;
抗震 take antiseismic measures;
前震 foreshock;
強震 strong shock;
弱震 weak shock;
聲震 sonic boom;
威震 inspire awe;
微震 (1) slight shock; (2) microseism;
消震 shock absorption;
星震 starquake;
眼震 nystagmus;
餘震 aftershock;
月震 moonquake;
主震 main shock;

zhen

【鴆】 (1) a kind of venomous bird; (2) poisoned wine;
[鴆毒] (1) poison; venom; (2) harm by devious means; slander;
[鴆酒] poisoned wine;

[鴆媒] libel; slander;

zhen

【鎮】 (1) keep down; press down; put down; quell; subdue; suppress; (2) calm; tranquil; (3) town; (4) guard; (5) garrison post; (6) cool with cold water or ice;

[鎮暴] riot control;

[鎮定] calm; composed; cool; self-composed;
鎮定的 composed; phlegmatic;
鎮定自若 in possession of oneself; perfectly calm and collected; remain clam and ease;
保持鎮定 keep cool;
沈着鎮定 presence of mind; sedate;
故作鎮定 be whistling in the dark;
強自鎮定 do one's best to keep a calm exterior; force oneself to keep one's cool;
神色鎮定 composure and presence;
依然鎮定 remain calm;

[鎮服] conquer; subdue;

[鎮撫] suppress and pacify;

[鎮靜] calm; cool; compose oneself; composed; unruffled;
鎮靜劑 depressant; sedative; tranquilizer;
鎮靜藥 downer;
保持鎮靜 hang loose; hold one's nerve; keep cool; keep face; keep one's calm; keep one's cool; keep one's countenance; keep one's hair on; keep one's head; keep one's shirt on; keep one's nerve; keep one's wig on; keep one's wool on; remain calm; stay loose;
~ 混亂中保持鎮靜 keep calm amid confusion;
沉着鎮靜 philosophic calm;
故作鎮靜 affect composure; feign composure; keep a stiff upper lip; pretend to be calm for a certain purpose; put on a show of calmness; stimulate composure with sth in mind; try to hide one's dismay;
假作鎮靜 pretend to be calm;
強作鎮靜 make an effort to appear composed; strive to maintain an appearance of calm; try hard to keep one's composure;
情緒鎮靜 in a calm mood;
依然鎮靜 remain calm;

[鎮日] all day long; the whole day;

[鎮守] garrison; guard;

[鎮痛] (1) abirritate; ease pain; (2) analgesia;
鎮痛劑 abirritant; anodyne; painkiller;
安定鎮痛 neuroleptoanalgesia;

[鎮壓] clampdown; crush down; crush out; crush up; put down; repress; suppress;
鎮壓叛亂 put down a rebel;
軍事鎮壓 military repression;
種族鎮靜 racial repressions;

[鎮紙] paperweight;

[鎮子] market town; town;

冰鎮 iced;
城鎮 cities and towns;
村鎮 villages and small towns;
藩鎮 military governor;
古鎮 ancient town;
集鎮 market town; town;
市鎮 market towns; small towns; towns;
鄉鎮 (1) villages and towns; (2) small towns;
小鎮 small town;
重鎮 (1) important city; key position; place of strategic importance; (2) key figure;
坐鎮 personally take charge of an operation, garrison duty, etc.;

zheng1

zheng

【丁】 sound;

[丁丁] clang;

zheng

【正】 first month of the lunar calendar;

[正場] gala show;

[正旦] lunar New Year's Day;

[正割] secant;

[正切] tangent;
正切定理 law of tangents;
反雙曲正切 arc-hyperbolic tangent;
反正切 arc tangent;

[正矢] versine;

[正月] first month of the lunar year; first moon;

新正 New Year;

zheng

【征】 (1) journey far away; (2) attack; conquer; reduce to submission; (3) collect taxes; levy taxes; (4) snatch;

take; (5) a surname;

[征伐] battle; on the warpath; punitive military action;

[征服] conquer; conquest; subjugate;

征服者 conqueror;

~外來征服者 alien conqueror;

征服自然 conquer nature; conquest of nature;

[征斂] levy and collect taxes;

[征馬] (1) war horse; (2) traveller's horse;

[征收] levy and collect taxes;

征收機關 government revenue collecting offices;

[征討] go on a punitive expedition; quell; subjugate;

[征途] journey;

[征戰] go on an expedition;

南征北戰 fight battles throughout the length and breadth of the country; fight north and south;

能征慣戰 used to war or fighting;

[征誅] send out a punitive expedition;

出征 go on an expedition; go out to battle;

從征 go on an expedition; go out to battle;

親征 go on an expedition by the emperor himself; go out to battle by the emperor himself;

遠征 go on an expedition;

zheng

【爭】 (1) contend; strive; struggle; (2) argue; dispute; fight; quarrel; (3) lack; short of;

[爭霸] contend for hegemony; scramble for supremacy;

爭霸世界 contend for world domination;

爭霸戰 fight for hegemony; power struggle; struggle for power;

[爭辯] altercation; argue; debate; dispute;

愛爭辯的 disputatious;

不可爭辯 indisputable;

無可爭辯 beyond debate; beyond dispute;

[爭標] rival each other for a trophy;

[爭產] fight for inheritance;

[爭吵] altercate; altercation; bandy; brawl; bunfight; face-off; quarrel; squabble; wrangle;

爭吵不休 become entangled in endless quarrels; bicker endlessly;

避免爭吵 abstain from quarreling; avoid a quarrel; avoid a scene;

發生爭吵 a quarrel breaks out;

高聲爭吵 noisy quarrel;

激烈的爭吵 acrimonious quarrel;

平息爭吵 patch up a quarrel;

情侶間的爭吵 lovers' quarrel;

挑起爭吵 provoke a quarrel;

為錢爭吵 squabble over money;

[爭寵] compete for sb's favour;

爭寵奪愛 snatch sb's favours from a rival;

爭寵求榮 strive for a superior's favour and for high honours;

[爭鬥] conflict; contend; struggle;

明爭暗鬥 fight both with open and secret means; naked and hidden struggle; open quarrels and secret wrangles; overt and covert struggle;

爭妍鬥艷 compete with each other for beauty of looks; contend in beauty and fascination; vie with sb in beauty;

[爭端] cause of dispute; dispute;

邊界爭端 border dispute;

長期爭端 long-running dispute;

解決爭端 resolve a dispute; settle a dispute;

領土爭端 territorial dispute;

內部爭端 domestic dispute;

挑起爭端 provoke a controversy;

調解爭端 pour oil on troubled water;

嚴重爭端 series dispute;

引起爭端 lead to a dispute;

[爭奪] contend for; fight for; scramble for; struggle for; vie with sb for sth;

爭奪食物 scramble for food;

爭奪市場 contend for markets; seize markets;

爭奪戰 battle over a city;

你爭我奪 vie with each other;

爭城奪地 conquer cities and capture territories by force of arms;

爭分奪秒 against time; battle against time; every minute is to be contested; make every minute and second count; outpace time; race against time; seize every minute; seize the seconds; work against time;

[爭功] contend for credit;

[爭光] win glory;

為國爭光 a credit to one's country; bring credit to one's country; reflect credit on one's country; struggle for the glory of the country; win honour for the country;

[爭衡] scramble for advantage; vie for superiority;

[爭競] compete; vie;

[爭論] altercate; altercation; contention; controversy; debate; dispute; passage at arms; passage of arms;

爭論不休 argue ceaselessly; enter into endless arguments; have an endless debate; keep on arguing;

愛爭論的 disputatious;

跟人爭論 have an argument with sb;

激烈的爭論 acrimonious dispute;

盲目爭論 argue in the dark;

挑起爭論 open up argument;

為小事而爭論 contend about trifles;

引起許多爭論 give rise to much controversy;

爭長論短 dispute with sb on minor issues; haggle about trifles; quarrel over trifles; squabble; wrangle for an ass's shadom;

[爭鳴] contend;

[爭氣] (1) strive to excel; try to win credit for; (2) intelligent; sensible;

不爭氣 disappointing; fail to live up to expectations; let sb down;

為家庭爭氣 bring credit to the family;

[爭強] struggle for supremacy;

爭強鬥勝 desire to excel over others; fight for the leading role;

[爭取] compete for; fight for; strive for; try to get; win over;

爭取時間 (1) try to avoid the waste of time; (2) stall for time;

爭取主動 contend for the initiative; take the initiative; try to gain the initiative;

努力爭取 make a long arm for;

[爭勝] struggle for the supper hand;

[爭訟] dispute through a lawsuit;

[爭席] contend for a seat;

[爭先] try to be the first to do sth;

爭先發言 try to hve the floor before others;

爭先恐後 fall over each other; fall over one another; in a mad rush to be the first; make a headlong rush; rush on to the front; rush to get ahead of others; strive to be the first and fear to lag behind; vie with each other in doing sth;

[爭雄] contend for hegemony; contend for supremacy; struggle for supremacy;

[爭議] argue; dispute; engage in a controversy;

爭議當事人 disputing parties;

避免爭議 avoid a dispute; avoid controversy;

稅收爭議 tax dispute;

無可爭議 beyond controversy; beyond dispute;

引起爭議 [的] contentious;

有爭議 in dispute;

~有爭議的 disputable;

招致爭議 court dispute;

[爭執] argue; contest; dispute; refuse to give in;

爭執不下 each holds his ground; each sticks to his guns; each sticks to his own stand; neither can convince the other;

家庭爭執 family quarrel;

仲裁爭執 arbitrate a dispute;

[爭嘴] (1) fight for food; (2) argue in self-defense;

鬥爭 combat; conflict; fight; struggle;

紛爭 dispute; wrangle;

核戰爭 nuclear war;

競爭 compete;

抗爭 refuse to comply with; resist; strive against;

力爭 (1) do all one can to; strive by every means to; (2) argue strongly; debate vigorously;

論爭 argument; debate;

內爭 internal strife;

拼爭 struggle for;

廷爭 debate at court in the emperor's presence;

相爭 argue vehemently; fight each other over sth; quarrel;

戰爭 conflagration; war; warfare;

政爭 political strife;

zheng
【貞】 a pronunciation of 貞 ;

zheng
【烝】 (1) rise, as steam; (2) many; numerous; (3) lewdness among the older generation; (4) same as 蒸 , steam;

[烝黎] the masses; the people;

[烝民] the masses; the people;

[烝烝] (1) rising and flourishing; (2) sincere and filial;

zheng

【崢】 (1) lofty; (2) distinguished; noble; outstanding; (3) dangerous; perilous; steep; (4) harsh; rigorous; severe;

[崢嶸] (1) lofty and steep; (2) distinguished; extraordinary; outstanding;

崢嶸歲月 eventful years; the most uncommon years and months of one's life;

崢嶸軒峻 in perfect condition and undiminished splendour;

zheng

【掙】 (1) struggle; (2) earn;

[掙命] fight for one's life;

[掙錢] earn money; make money;

掙錢養家的人 breadwinner;

[掙扎] struggle;

奮力掙扎 struggle with all one's might;

瘋狂掙扎 frenzied and desperate kicks;

Z

zheng

【猙】 fierce-looking; hideous; repulsive;

[猙獰] fierce-looking; hideous; repulsive;

猙獰面目 brutish features; diabolical face; forbidding countenance; grim visage; repulsive physiognomy;

面容猙獰 have a ferocious look;

zheng

【楨】 a pronunciation of 楨;

zheng

【睜】 open the eyes;

[睜眼] open the eyes;

睜眼不管 look on with folded arms;

睜一隻眼，閉一隻眼 pretend not to see; purposely overlook; turn a blind eye to sth; wink at sth;

睖睜 be in a daze; stare blankly;

zheng

【鉦】 a kind of gong;

[鉦鼓] gongs and drums;

zheng

【筝】 (1) a kind of string instrument; (2) kite;

風筝 kite;

古筝 twenty-one-string plucked instrument;

zheng

【蒸】 (1) evaporate; (2) steam; (3) crowded;

[蒸餅] steamed cake;

[蒸發] atmid(o)-; evaporate; evaporation; evaporization;

蒸發測定器 atmometer;

蒸發計 atmidometer;

~陶瓷蒸發計 clay atmometer;

蒸發冷卻 transpiration cooling;

蒸發量測定法 atmometry;

蒸發器 evaporator;

~補償蒸發器 evaporator;

~多效蒸發器 compound evaporator;

~離心蒸發器 centrifugal evaporator;

~旋管蒸發器 coil evaporator;

~原料蒸發器 feed evaporator;

蒸發學 atmology;

蒸發岩 evaporate;

分批蒸發 batch vaporization;

防止蒸發 avoid evaporating;

附加蒸發 additional vaporization;

空氣中蒸發 air evaporation;

離子束蒸發 ion beam evaporation;

平衡蒸發 equilibrium evaporization;

強制循環蒸發 forced circulation evaporation;

閃急蒸發 flash evaporation;

[蒸飯] steam rice;

蒸沙成飯 cook sand with the hope of turning it into rice — a hopeless task;

[蒸鍋] boiler; steamer;

雙層蒸鍋 double boiler;

[蒸餾] distill; distillation;

蒸餾廠 distillery;

蒸餾釜 distillery;

蒸餾器 alembic; distiller;

~氨蒸餾器 ammonia distiller;

~船用蒸餾器 marine distiller;

蒸餾設施 distillation plant;

蒸餾室 distillery;

蒸餾水 distilled water;

蒸餾塔 distillation tower;

常壓蒸餾 atmospheric distillation;

防腐蒸餾 aseptic distillation;

分解蒸餾 fractional distillation;

分析蒸餾 analytical distillation;

共沸蒸餾 azeotropic distillation;

酒精蒸餾 alcohol distillation;

[蒸籠] bamboo steamer;

[蒸民] common people;

[蒸氣] steam; vapour;

蒸氣房 steam room;
蒸氣機 steam engine;
蒸氣計 atmidometer;
蒸汽霧 steam fog;
飽和蒸氣 saturated steam;
~未飽和蒸氣 unsaturated steam;
產生蒸氣 generate steam;
常壓蒸氣 atmospheric steam;
大氣水蒸氣 atmospheric water vapour;
額外蒸氣 blead steam;
放出蒸氣 blow off steam;
汽油蒸氣 gasoline vapour;
殺菌蒸氣 bactericidal vapour;
水蒸氣 steam; vapour; water vapour;
酸性蒸氣 acid vapour;
霧化蒸氣 atomization;
積聚蒸氣 gather steam;

[蒸散] evapotranspiration;

[蒸暑] steaming heat of summer;

[蒸騰] transpiration;
蒸騰作用 transpiration;
角質層蒸騰 transpiration;
皮孔蒸騰 lenticular transpiration;
氣孔蒸騰 stomatal transpiration;
相對蒸騰 relative transpiration;

[蒸鬱] the rising of steam;

[蒸蒸日上] become more and more flourishing; become more prosperous every day; continually on the rise; getting more and more prosperous; in the ascendant; more and more thriving; on the upgrade; on the upswing; thrive with each passing day; thriving;
生產蒸蒸日上 production is on the upswing;

[蒸煮] cook; cooking;
蒸煮器 cooker;
~電力蒸煮器 electric cooker;
~分批蒸煮器 batch cooker;
~加壓蒸煮器 pressure cooker;
~飼料蒸煮器 feed cooker;
~蒸氣蒸煮器 steam cooker;
常壓蒸煮 atmospheric cooking;
分段蒸煮 stage cooking;
乾熱蒸煮 air cooking;
擠壓蒸煮 extrusion cooking;
加壓蒸煮 pressure cooking;
酸法蒸煮 acid cooking;
太陽能蒸煮 solar cooking;
蒸氣蒸煮 steam cooking;
清蒸 steam in clear soup;
燻蒸 stifling; suffocating;

zheng

【徵】 (1) go on a long journey; (2) go on an expedition; (3) call to arms; conscript; recruit; (4) collect; impose; (5) ask for; enquire; request; solicit; (6) evidence; proof; (7) sign;

[徵兵] call-up; conscription; draft;
徵兵局 draft board;
徵兵卡 draft card;
徵兵制 conscription system;

[徵答] solicit answers to questions;

[徵調] call up; requisition;

[徵發] collect; levy;

[徵伐] go on a punitive expedition;

[徵稿] solicit contributions;

[徵歌] summon singers to perform;
徵歌選色 pursue sensory pleasure;

[徵購] requisition by purchase;

[徵候] indications; signs; symptoms;

[徵婚] advertize for life partner; marriage advertising; marriage-seeking;
徵婚廣告 marriage advertisement;
徵婚啟事 lonely-hearts advertisement;

[徵集] (1) collect; (2) call up; draft; recruit;

[徵斂] collect taxes;
苛徵暴斂 extort heavy taxes and levies;

[徵糧] impose grain levies; requisitioning of grain;

[徵募] conscript; enlist; hire; recruit;

[徵聘] advertise for; give public notice of vacancies to be filled; invite applications for jobs;

[徵求] ask for; seek; solicit;
徵求會員 recruit members;
徵求意見 ask for opinions; solicit views on;

[徵實] verify;

[徵收] collect; impose; levy;

[徵稅] levy tax; tax collection; taxation;

[徵文] solicit articles or essays;

[徵象] sign; straw in the wind; symptom;

[徵詢] ask advice of; consult; hold consultation with; probe; seek the opinion of; solicit opinions;

[徵驗] verify;

[徵引] cite; quote;

繁徵博引 quote from many sources;
廣徵博引 quote and prove fully;
旁徵博引 load one's pages with references; quote copiously from many sources; quote extensively; quote right and left; well documented; well provided with supporting material;
詳徵博引 quote extensively and in detail;

[徵用] take over for use;

[徵召] (1) call up; conscript; draft; enlist; (2) appoint to an official position;
徵召令 call-up;
徵召入伍 enlist in the army;

[徵兆] omen; symptom;

表徵 superficial characteristics; surface features;
病徵 symptom of a disease;
緩徵 postpone the imposition of a tax;
開徵 begin to collect taxes;
秋徵 collect the agricultural tax in kind after the autumn harvest;
夏徵 collect the agricultural tax in kind after the summer harvest;
象徵 signify; symbol; symbolize; token;
應徵 respond to the call of conscription and be recruited;

Z

zheng

【諍】 (1) admonish; criticize sb's faults frankly; expostulate; remonstrate; (2) same as 爭, dispute;

[諍訟] fight a legal battle; lawsuit;

[諍友] a friend who does not hesitate to remonstrate;
諍友嚴師 a friend who will give forthright admonition and a teacher who is strict with the students;

zheng

【錚】 (1) clang of metal; (2) gongs;

[錚錚] clang; clank;
亮錚錚 glittering; shining;

zheng

【癥】 disease; illness; obstruction of the bowels;

[癥結] (1) basic problem; bottleneck; crucial reason; crux; difficult point; (2) obstruction of the bowels;
癥結所在 the crux of; where the trouble lies;
問題的癥結 crux of the matter;

zheng³

zheng

【拯】 (1) deliver; rescue; save; (2) lift up; raise;

[拯救] deliver; deliverance; rescue; save;
拯焚救溺 put out a fire and save people from drowning — lift the masses from woe;

[拯溺] assist the weak;
拯溺扶危 assist the weak and oppressed; deliver the people from extreme sufferings;
拯溺救焚 put out a fire and save people from drowning — lift the masses from woe;

[拯卹] save and help;

zheng

【整】 (1) complete; entire; intact; whole; (2) in good order; neat; orderly; systematic; tidy; (3) put in order; rectify; tidy; (4) adjust; make ready; mend; repair; (5) make sb suffer; punish; (6) do; make;

[整版] devote a full page to; full page;
整版廣告 full-page advert;

[整倍] multiple;

[整備] make ready;

[整飭] (1) consolidate; rectify; straighten out; (2) in good order; neat; tidy;
整飭戎行 preserve order and discipline in the army;

[整除] exact division; exactly divisible;

[整頓] consolidate; put sth in good order; readjust; rectify; reorganize;
整頓部署 straighten out the lines;
整頓改造 be reorganized and transformed; put to order and reform;
整頓紀律 strengthen discipline;

[整風] rectification of incorrect style of work;
整風運動 rectification campaign; rectification movement;
開門整風 open-door rectification;

[整改] rectify and reform;

[整個] all; entire; total; whole;
整個國家 whole nation;
整個來說 by and large; generally speaking; on the whole;
整個上午 whole morning;
整個社會 whole society;

整個世界 whole world;
整個早上 all the morning;
整個裝置 complete appliance;

[整合] (1) conformity; (2) integrate; unite;
不整合 unconformity;
~複合不整合 composite unconformity;
~化學不整合 chemical unconformity;
~混合不整合 blended unconformity;
~角度不整合 angular unconformity;

[整潔] clean and tidy; natty; neat; neat and clean; prim; shipshape; spruce;
打扮整潔 brush up;

[整塊] the whole piece;

[整理] adjust; arrange; put in order; regulate; sort out; straighten out; straighten up;
整理東西 pack away things;
整理計劃 get one's plan into shape;
整理思想 put one's ideas in order;
整理思緒 marshal one's thoughts;
整理行裝 pack; pack one's things for a journey;
整理賬目 straighten out the accounts;

[整列] (1) form neat lines; (2) whole column; whole row;

[整流] (1) commutation; (2) rectification; resistance rectification;
整流波紋 commutator ripple;
整流器 commutator; rectifier;
~整流器片 commutator segment;
~半波整流器 half-wave rectifier; single-way rectifier;
~半導體整流器 semiconductor rectifier;
~點接觸整流器 point-contact rectifier;
~換向整流器 rectifier commutator;
~可控硅整流器 silicon-controlled rectifier;
~裂環整流器 split ring commutator;
~平均整流器 averaging rectifier;
~通風式整流器 ventilated commutator;
~硒整流器 selenium rectifier;
~蓄電池整流器 accumulator rectifier;
~鍺整流器 germanium rectifier;
整流罩 cowling;
半波整流 single-wave rectification;
發電機整流 generator commutation;
過整流 over commutation;
無電花整流 sparkless commutation;
直線整流 straight-line commutation;

[整路] repair a road;

[整年] all the year round; the whole year; throughout the year;

[整批] batch;

[整齊] (1) in good order; neat; orderly; shipshape; snug; taut; tidy; well-arranged; (2) even; regular; well-balanced;
整齊劃一 neat and uniform; uniform;
整齊清潔 clear and tidy;
不整齊 irregular;
穿著整齊 be dressed up to the nines; be neatly dressed;
十分整齊 be very neatly arranged;

[整日] all day long; the whole day;
整日整夜 whole day and night;

[整容] perform face-lifting;
整容手術 plastic surgery;
整容外科 plastic surgery;
~整容外科手術 cosmetic surgery; plastic surgery;
整容醫生 plastic surgeon;

[整數] integer; integral number; round number; round sum; whole number;
代數整數 algebraic integer;
二進制整數 binary integer;
負整數 negative integer;
例外整數 exceptional integers;
同餘整數 congruent integers;
正整數 positive integer;

[整肅] (1) rigid; stern; strict; (2) purge;
整肅綱紀 screw up discipline;

[整套] a complete set of; a package of; a whole set;

[整體] ensemble; entirety; whole;
整體的 holistic;
整體規劃 overall planning;
整體架構 overall framework;
整體思維 organism thinking;
整體性翻譯 holistic translation;
整體語 holophrase;
一個整體 a whole;
有機的整體 organic whole;

[整天] all day; all day long; the whole day;
整天操勞 work day in and day out;
整天無所事事 idle away all day;
一整天 all day;
~煩了一整天 niggle sb all day;
~忙了一整天 busy all day; on the go the whole day long;
~睡了一整天 sleep all through the day;

[整屋] repair a house;

[整形] orthopedics;
整型手術 cosmetic surgery; plastic

operation; plastic surgery;
整形外科 orthopaedics; plastic surgery;
~ 整形外科病房 orthopaedic ward;
~ 整形外科醫生 orthopaedic surgeon; orthopedist;

[整修] condition; put in order; rebuild; recondition; renovate; repair; revamp; restore; touch up;
整修路面 put a road in decent order;

[整夜] all night; the whole night; throughout the night;
一整夜 the whole night;

[整衣] adjust one's clothes;
整衣冠 adjust one's hat and dress;

[整整] a good; clear; exactly; fair; full; good; if a day; long; round; solid; throughout; to a day; whole;
整整齊齊 be arranged to a nicety; in apple-pie order; in perfect order; shipshape; very neat and orderly;

[整治] (1) adjust and repair; fix; renovate; repair; set in order; (2) dredge a river; (3) fix; punish;

[整裝] dress up; get one's things ready;
整裝出發 get ready to set off; get things together in preparation for the journey;
整裝待發 all packed up and ready to go; be fully equipped for a journey; pack up and ready to go; ready to start; wait for the order to start;
整裝待命 be prepared to await further instructions; get everything ready and await orders; ready for orders; stand by waiting for orders;
整裝就道 dress up and prepare for one's journey;

挨整 be punished; be straightened out; be subjected to criticism and punishment; be victimized politically;
重整 reform;
工整 carefully and neatly done;
平整 flatten; level;
齊整 neat; uniform;
調整 adjust; adjustment; regulate; setting; trim; tune-up;
完整 complete; entire; intact; integrated; undamaged; whole;
休整 rest and reorganize;
修整 (1) repair and maintain; (2) prune; trim;
嚴整 in neat formation;
勻整 even and orderly; neat and well spaced;

zheng⁴
zheng

【正】 (1) honest and virtuous; straight; straightforward and unbending; upright; (2) main; situated in the middle; (3) punctually; sharp; (4) obverse; right; (5) honest; (6) appropriate; correct; proper; right; (7) not contaminated; pure; (8) chief; main; principal; (9) person in charge; person in command; (10) regular; (11) positive; (12) rectify; set right; (13) exactly; just; (14) a surname;

[正本] (1) reserved copy; (2) original;
正本清源 attack a problem at its root – reform thoroughly; effect radical reform; radical reform; reform from the bottom; reform radically; thoroughly overhaul;

[正常] average; common; normal; regular; usual;
正常的 normal;
~ 低於正常的 subnormal;
低於正常的溫度 subnormal temperatures;
正常狀態 normality;
不正常 abnormal; abnormality; irregular;
~ 有點不正常 have a cog loose;
恢復正常 back to normal; return to normal;
完全正常 perfectly normal;

[正大] aboveboard; honest; just and fair; upright;
正大光明 fair and frank; fair and square; just and honourable; just and open; open and above-board; open as the day; square and honest; upright and open-minded;
~ 正大光明的 dinkum;
~ 為人正大光明 just and honorable;
光明正大 above board; above board and straightforward; entirely above board; fair and square; frank and righteous; just and honourable; on the square; open and above board; openly and honestly; plain dealing; sporting; upright;

[正當] just the time for; just when;
正當其時 at the opportune moment; high

time; in the nick of time; just at that time;
正當中 right in the middle;
[正當] (1) appropriate; correctitude; justifiable; legistimate; proper; rightful; (2) just at that time; just when; right at that time;
正當理由 proper reasons;
正當途徑 appropriate means; proper ways;
不正當 devious; dishonest; illegitimate; improper; on the crook;
[正道] correct path; proper way; right course; right track; right way;
背離正道 depart from the right path; turn aside from the path of rectitude;
反歸正道 correct ways of life; return to orthodox church;
離開正道 wander from the right path;
偏離正道 leave the path of righteousness;
走正道 follow the correct path;
[正法] (1) proper law; (2) execute;
[正反] positive and negative;
正反握 combined grip;
[正犯] principal criminal;
[正方] (1) adjust to the right course; (2) square;
正方體 cube;
正方形 square;
[正負] plus-minus; positive and negative;
負負得正 two negatives make a positive; two negatives make an affirmative;
[正骨] bonesetting; set a bone;
正骨術 bonesetting;
正骨醫生 bonesetter;
[正規] normal; regular; standard;
正規編制 regular structure;
正規兵團 regular armies;
正規部隊 regular unit;
正規化 normalization;
~非正規化 casualization;
正規軍 regular army; regular forces;
正規性 normality;
~可遞正規性 transitive normality;
~弱正規性 weak normality;
~完全正規性 complete normality;
正規學校 normal school; regular school;
[正軌] right track;
納回正軌 return to the right track;
走上正軌 get onto the right path; set on the correct path;
[正好] exactly; exactly right; just enough; just in time; just right;
[正號] plus sign;
[正貨] (1) hard currency; legal tender; (2) genuine and excellent;
[正經] (1) decent; honest; respectable; (2) proper; serious; (3) standard; (4) indeed; really; truly;
正經八百 earnest; in all seriousness; serious;
不正經 not serious;
~老不正經 old but still licentious;
假正經 pretend to be serious;
~假裝正經 assume an air of modesty; assume the guise of a person of integrity; feign a correct posture; pose as a person of high morals; pretend to be a cultivated person; pretend to be a saint; put on the appearance of honesty;
正正經經 in earnest;
[正理] correct principles; valid reasons;
[正路] correct path; right course; straight path;
正路不走走斜路 leave the correct track for the wrong one; turn from the right road and take the wrong one — give up an honest life for a dishonest one;
[正論] reasonable opinion; sound statement;
[正門] front door; front gate; main entrance;
[正面] (1) front; frontage; obverse side; right side; (3) positive; (4) directly; openly;
正面的 frontal; full face;
正面攻擊 frontal attack;
正面全裸的 full frontal;
[正名] rectification of name;
正名責實 call a thing by its right name;
[正拍] forehand;
正拍扣球 forehand smash;
正拍握拍法 forehand groundstroke;
[正派] decency; decent; honest; upright; virtuous;
正派人 straight shooter;
天性正派 have the instincts of a gentleman;
作風正派 honest and upright in one's way;
[正碰] direct impact; head-on collision;
[正片] feature film; positive;
彩色正片 colour positive;

彩色透明正片 positive colour transparency;
分色正片 separation positive;
複製正片 dupe positive;
有聲正片 sound positive;

[正品] certified goods; certified products; quality goods;

[正妻] one's legal wife;

[正氣] healthy atmosphere; righteousness;
正氣凜然 awe-inspiring; righteous;
正氣上昇 a healthy atmosphere prevails;
昂昂正氣 air of nobility and righteousness;
浩然正氣 awe-inspiring righteousness;
天地有正氣 there is justice in heaven and on earth;

[正巧] (1) as it happens; chance to; happen to; it happens that; (2) in the nick of time; just at the right time; just in time;
正巧趕到 arrive in the nick of time;

[正確] accurate; appropriate; correct; proper; right;
正確性 accuracy; correctness;
觀察正確 accurate in one's observation;
絕對正確 absolutely correct;
完全正確 right on the money;

[正人先正己] he is not fit to command others that cannot command himself; he that would command must serve; he who laughs at crooked men should need walk very straight; know your own faults before blaming others for theirs; physician, heal thyself; sweep before your own door;

[正如] exactly as; just as;

[正色] (1) pure colours; (2) stern and serious facial expression;
正色厲聲 with a severe countenance and a harsh voice;

[正身] one's real person; one's real self;

[正式] formal; official; regular;
正式翻譯 formal translation;
正式合同 formal contract; official contract;
正式團體 formal group;
正式文體 formal level of speech;
正式文獻 formal text;
正式新詞 formal neologism;
正式言語 formal speech;
正式英語 formal English;
正式語言 formal language;
正式語域 official register;
非正式 informal; unofficial;

[正史] history books written in biographical style; official history;

[正是] exactly so; yes;

[正事] one's proper business;
正事要緊 business before pleasure;
談正事 talk business;

[正室] (1) one's legal wife; (2) one's male heir;

[正視] face squarely; face up to; look at sth without bias; look squarely at; look straight in the eye;
正視困難 face difficulties squarely; face up to difficulties;
正視危機 face the crisis squarely;
正視現實 face reality squarely; look reality in the face;
不忍正視 hate the sight of; heartbreaking to look at;

[正手] forehand;
正手抽球 forehand drive;
正手攔球 forehand volley;
正手握拍法 forehand grip;
正手遠抽 forehand long drive;

[正數] positive number;

[正題] (1) subject of a talk; (2) thesis;
不離正題 stick to one's text;
偏離正題 get off the track; wander from the main subject;

[正體] (1) standardized form of Chinese character; (2) regular script; (3) block letter;
正體字 block letter;

[正廳] (1) main hall; (2) stalls in a theatre;
正廳後座 pit;
正廳前座 stalls;
正廳入口 entrance to the auditorium;

[正統] authorized; orthodox;
正統觀點 orthodox view;
正統觀念 orthodoxy;
正統派 orthodox school;

[正途] proper course; proper way;
不循正途 not follow the correct path; stray from the path of duty;

[正文] main body; text;

[正午] high noon; noon;
地方正午 local noon;
分區正午 zone noon;

平正午 mean noon;
日過正午 the sun is past the zenith;
月球正午 lunar noon;

[正誤] correct mistakes;

[正席] table of honour in a grand feast;

[正向] positive;
正向強化 positive reinforcement;
正向轉移 positive transfer;

[正邪] good and evil;
正邪相爭 struggle between the vital energy and the pathogenic factor;
改邪歸正 abandon the depraved way of life and return to the path of virtue; break away from evil ways and return to a virtuous way; forsake heresy and return to the truth; give up an evil way of life and reform oneself; give up evil and return to good; give up one's evil ways and return to the right path; give up vice and return to virtue; go straight; square it; stop doing evil and reform oneself; straight up; turn over a new leaf; on the straight;
~改邪歸正的人 poacher turned gamekeeper;
棄邪歸正 alter from bad to good; break away from the evil and return to the virtuous way; change from bad to good; correct one's conduct; forsake heresy and return to the right way; give up one's evil ways and return to the path of righteousness; give up vice and return to virtue; leave false ways and come back to the true ones; mend one's way; reject evil ways and start on the right track; stop doing evil and reform oneself;
去邪歸正 break away from the evil and return to the virtuous way; forsake heresy and return to the right way; give up evil ways and return to the right; reject evil ways and start on the right track; stop doing evil and reform oneself;
捨正從邪 deflect from the right cause;

[正學] orthodox learning;

[正弦] sine;
正弦一餘弦定理 sine-cosine law;
正弦定理 law of sines;
正弦對數 logarithmic sine;
正弦真數 natural sine;
反正弦 arc sine; inverse sine;
積分正弦 integral sine;
三階正弦 sine of the third order;
雙曲正弦 hyperbolic sine;

[正要] about to; on the point of;
正要走出去 on the point of leaving;

[正業] proper duties; regular occupation;
不務正業 (1) not engage in honest work; (2) ignore one's proper occupation; not attend to one's proper duties;
~不務正業的人 layabout; wastrel;

[正義] justice; righteous;
正義感 sense of justice; sense of what is right;
~有正義感 with a feeling for justice;
正義之師 army dedicated to a just cause; army fighting for a just cause;
背離正義 deviate from justice;
崇尚正義 uphold justice;
伸張正義 promote justice;

[正音] correct pronunciation;
正音法 orthoepy;

[正在] in course of; in process of; in the midst of;

[正直] candid and fair; fair-minded; honest; rectitude; straight-forward and unbiased; up and up; upright; upright and honest;
正直的人 straight arrow;
誠實正直 clean-living;

[正值] it happened just when; just at that time;

[正中] right in the centre; right in the middle;
正中奸計 fall right into the villain's trap;
正中下懷 after sb's heart; exactly what one wants; fit in exactly with one's wishes; hit one's fancy; just hit the spot; play into sb's hands; suit one's book; touch the spot;
正中要害 hit the nail on the head; hit the right nail; to the point;

[正字] correct character; correct writing; standard form of Chinese character;
正字法 orthography;
~正字法詞 orthographic word;

[正宗] (1) orthodox school; (2) traditional;

板正 regular upright;
辯正 distinguish right from wrong;
秉正 just; upright;
撥正 correct; set right;
駁正 correct by argument;

補正 supplement and correct;
呈正 present one's writings to others for criticisms, corrections, etc;
純正 (1) pure; unadulterated; (2) appropriate; proper;
訂正 correct; revise;
端正 (1) regular; upright; (2) correct; proper; rectify;
反正 (1) come over from the enemy's side; (2) anyway; in any case;
方正 (1) upright and foursquare; (2) righteous; upright;
斧正 make corrections;
改正 amend; correct;
剛正 honourable and principled; upright;
更正 make corrections;
公正 (1) fair; fair and square; fair-minded; impartial; just; righteous; (2) a surname;
歸正 mend one's ways; reform oneself;
矯正 put right; rectify;
校正 proofread and correct; rectify;
教正 advise and correct;
糾正 correct; redress;
就正 solicit comments;
勘正 proofread and correct;
匡正 correct; rectify;
立正 stand at attention;
廉正 honest and upright;
修正 (1) correct; revise; (2) mutilate; revise;
嚴正 solemn and just;
真正 (1) genuine; true; (2) indeed; really;
指正 (1) point out mistakes so that they can be corrected; (2) make comments or criticisms;

zheng

【政】 (1) political affairs; politics; (2) government; (3) administration;

[政變] coup; coup d'etat;
政變企圖 coup attempt;
政變失敗 failed coup;
軍事政變 coup d'etat;
武裝政變 putsch;

[政柄] political power; regime; reins of government;

[政策] policy;
政策的變化 change in policy;
政策法學說 policy jurisprudence;
政策經濟評價 economic evaluation of policy;
政策科學 policy science;
政策連續性 continuity of the policy;
政策市 policy market;
政策性投資 investment by policy;
政策性銀行 policy-oriented bank;
政策制定者 policymaker;
對外政策 foreign policy;
反通貨膨脹政策 anti-inflation policy;
反托拉斯政策 antitrust policy;
高壓政策 high-handed policy;
會計政策 accounting policy;
農業政策 agricultural policy;
傾斜政策 preferential policy;
上有政策，下有對策 the higher authorities have policies, the localities have their counter-measures;
外交政策 foreign policy;
~外交政策顧問 foreign policy advisor;
優惠政策 preferential policy;
總政策 general policy;

[政黨] political party;
政黨候選人 party candidate;
政黨領袖 party leader;
政黨主席 party chairman;
加入政黨 accede to a party;
執政黨 ruling party;

[政敵] political adversary; political opponent; political rival;

[政法] politics and law;
政法學院 institute of political science and law;

[政府] government;
政府部門 government department;
政府部長 government minister;
政府官員 government official;
政府機構 government agency; government institution; government organization;
~政府機構改革 government institutional restructuring;
推進政府機構改革 restructure government institutions;
~非政府機構 non-governmental organizations;
政府機關 government apparatus;
政府開支 government spending;
政府審計 government audit;
政府職能 government functions;
本屆政府 incumbent;
促請政府 call on the government;
大政府 big government;
地方政府 local government;
顛覆政府 subvert the government;

管理政府 run a government;
建立政府 establish a government;
軍政府 junta;
看守政府 caretaker government;
傀儡政府 puppet government; puppet regime;
聯邦政府 federal government;
聯合政府 coalition government;
臨時政府 interim government; provisional government;
流亡政府 government in exile;
抨擊政府 attack a government;
區政府 district government;
人民政府 people's government;
省政府 provincial government;
市政府 municipal government;
推翻政府 overthrow the government; overturn the government;
偽政府 bogus government;
無政府 anarchy;
~無政府的 anarchic;
~無政府主義 anarchism;
無政府主義者 anarch; anarchist;
縣政府 county government;
鄉政府 township government;
選舉政府 elect a government;
右翼政府 right-wing government;
政黨政府 party government;
鎮政府 town government;
支持政府 support the government;
中央政府 central government;
自治政府 self-government;
組成政府 form a government;
左翼政府 left-wing government;

[政綱] political programme;

[政績] achievements in one's official career; administrative achievements;
政績斐然 the achievements of one's official career are remarkable;

[政簡刑清] little government work and few criminal cases;

[政見] political views; politics;
發表政見 manifestation;

[政教] the state and the church;
政教分離 the separation of religion from politics; the separation of the church from the state;
政教合一 the unification of the state and the church;

[政界] government circles; political circles; the political arena;
進入政界 enter politics; go in politics;

[政局] political scene; political situation;

[政客] plo; politician; politico;
精明圓通的政客 adroit politican;
老奸巨猾的政客 wily politician;
善變的政客 political acrobat;
一群政客 a knot of politicians;
油滑的政客 slick politico;

[政況] political situations;

[政令] government order;

[政略] government policy;

[政論] political commentary;
政論家 political commentator;
政論文 political prose;

[政企] government and enterprise;
政企不分 a mixture of government administration and enterprise management;
政企分開 separate the functions of government from those of enterprises;

[政權] political power; political regime; regime; reins of government;
政權更替 regime change;
政權形態 polity;
把持政權 have the control of political power;
放棄政權 resign one's political power;
現政權 present regime;
行使政權 wield political power;
運用政權 exercise one's political power;

[政事] government affairs;

[政壇] political arena;
踏入政壇 enter politics;

[政體] form of government; polity; system of government;
君主政體 monarchy;
民主政體 democracy;

[政委] political commissar;

[政務] affairs of the government; government administration; government affairs;
政務官 administrative officer;

[政爭] political strife;

[政制] government hierarchy; political system;
政制發展 institutional development;

[政治] (1) political affairs; politics; (2) government administration;
政治安定 political stability;
政治抱負 political aspirations;
政治報告 political report;
政治避難 political asylum;

政治變革 political transformation;
政治才幹 political acumen;
政治參與 political participation;
政治地理 political geography;
~ 政治地理學 political geography;
政治顛覆 political subversion;
政治多元化 political pluralization;
~ 政治多元化主義 political pluralism;
政治犯 political prisoner; political offender; prisoner of conscience;
政治共同體 political community;
政治活動 politicking; political activities; political campaign;
政治機器 political machine;
政治家 politician; statesman;
~ 傑出的政治家 conspicuous statesman;
政治糾紛 political dispute;
政治經濟學 political economy;
政治就是這樣 that's politics;
政治局 political bureau;
~ 政治局常務委員會委員 member of the standing committee of the political bureau;
~ 政治局委員 member of the political bureau;
~ 政治局候補委員 alternate member of the political bureau;
政治課 political course;
政治立場 political stand;
政治聯繫 political affiliation;
政治路線 political line;
政治民主化 political democratization;
政治難民 political refugee;
政治庇護 political asylum;
政治評論員 political commentator;
政治取向 political orientation;
政治權力 political power;
~ 積聚政治權力 amass political power;
政治權利 political rights;
~ 剥奪政治權利 deprive sb of his political rights;
政治上不正確 politically incorrect;
政治上的變化 political change;
政治上正確 politically correct;
政治生態 political ecology;
政治生涯 one's political life;
政治實體 body politic; political entity;
政治史 political history;
政治事務 political affairs;
政治體制改革 reform a country's political structure;
政治透明度 political transparency;
政治文化 political culture;
政治舞台 political arena;
政治系統 political system;
政治獻媚 political toadyism;
政治行動 political action;
政治宣言 political declaration;
政治生態 political ecology;
政治洗腦 political brainwashing;
政治宣傳 political propaganda;
政治學 political science; politics; political integration;
~ 地理政治學 geopolitics;
~ 地緣政治學 geopolitics;
政治優勢 political advantage;
政治正確性 political correctness;
政治制度 political institution; political system;
政治自由 political liberty;
不過問政治 leave politics alone;
不問政治 shun politics;
獨裁政治 autocracy;
非政治的 apolitical;
搞政治 play politics;
寡頭政治 oligarchy;
~ 寡頭政治家 oligarch;
官僚政治 bureaucracy;
金權政治 money politics;
軍人政治 stratocracy;
民主政治 democracy;
清明政治 clean politics;
強權政治 power politics;
~ 搞強權政治 practise power politics;
熱衷於政治 an absorption with politics;
涉獵政治 dabble in politics;
神權政治 theocracy;
武力政治 power politics;
現實政治 realpolitik;
鑽研政治 delve in politics;
爭論政治 argue about politics;
政黨政治 party politics;

霸政 hegemonism; oligarchy; rule by force;
暴政 despotic rule; tyranny;
弊政 maladministration; misrule;
柄政 take the reins of government;
秉政 hold political power;
財政 finance;
參政 participate in government and political affairs; take part in government; take part in politics;
朝政 the political situation and power of an imperial government;

從政 become a government official; enter politics; go into politics;
當政 hold political power; in office; in power;
德政 benevolent rule;
地政 administrative affairs of the utilization and requisition of land;
法政 law and politics;
復政 regain power;
干政 interfere in politics;
戶政 administration concerning residents and residency;
荒政 neglect affairs of the state;
惠政 benevolent rule or administration;
家政 home economics; household management;
簡政 streamline administration;
建政 establish political power;
軍政 (1) army and government; (2) military and politics; (3) military administration;
苛政 harsh government; tyranny;
涖政 administer the government;
廉政 incorrupt government;
民政 civil administration;
內政 home affairs; internal affairs;
虐政 tyrannical government;
親政 taken over the administration of government upon coming of age;
勤政 assiduous in government affairs;
仁政 benevolent government;
攝政 act as regent;
失政 misrule a nation;
施政 administer political administration; administrate; administration; execute government orders; govern;
時政 current politics;
市政 municipal administration;
聽政 administer; govern; hold court; rule;
為政 in government administration;
憲政 constitutional government; constitutional rule; constitutionalism;
行政 administration;
恤政 benevolent government;
訓政 political tutelage;
郵政 postal service;
掌政 head a government;
朝政 affairs of the state;
知政 administer the government; handle state affairs;
執政 at the helm of the state; hold power; hold the reins of the government; in office; in power;
主政 head the administration; person in charge;
專政 dictatorship;
咨政 political advisor;
資政 political advisor;

zheng

【症】 (1) ailment; disease; (2) symptoms or manifestations of a disease;

［症候］ (1) disease; (2) symptom;
症候群 syndrome;

［症狀］ symptom;
症狀療法 symptomic treatment;
症狀性貧血 symptomatic anaemia;
症狀學 semiology;
臨牀症狀 clinic symptom;
明顯症狀 manifest symptoms;
前驅症狀 predrome; premonitory symptom;
全身症狀 constitutional symptom;
晚期症狀 termal symptom;
早期症狀 early symptom;
主要症狀 cardinal sympton;
自覺症狀 subjective symptom;

癌症 cancer;
敗血症 septicaemia;
崩症 menorrhagia of the uterus;
併發症 complication;
病症 disease; illness;
不育症 barrenness; sterility;
呆小症 cretinism;
多毛症 hypertrichosis;
多尿症 polyuria;
疳症 infantile malnutrition;
乾眼症 xerophthalmia;
官能症 functional disease;
寒症 symptoms caused by cold factors;
合併症 complication;
紅視症 aerythropsia;
後遺症 (1) sequelae; (2) negative influence;
黃視症 xanthopsia;
急腹症 acute abdominal disease;
急症 actue disease; emergency;
健忘症 amnesia;
禁忌症 contraindition;
巨人症 gigantism;
絕症 fatal disease; incurable disease; terminal disease;
戀物症 fetishism;
痳症 gonorrhea;
聾症 deafness;
夢行症 sleepwalking; somnambulism;
夢游症 sleepwalking; somnambulism;
尿崩症 diabetes insipidus;

尿毒症 uraemia;
尿少症 oliguria;
怯症 (1) impotent; (2) fear and nervousness caused by poor health;
失眠症 insomnia;
失識症 agnosia; inability to recognize objects by use of the senses;
失寫症 agraphia;
失語症 aphasia;
適應症 indication;
死症 fatal disease; incurable disease;
貪食症 bulimia;
頑症 chronic and stubborn disease; persistent ailment;
痿症 flaccid paralysis;
狹心病 angina pectoris;
險症 crucial symptoms; dangerous illness; serious disease; severe illness;
眩暈症 dizziness; vertigo;
血崩症 metrorrhagia;
血毒症 blood poisoning;
炎症 inflammation;
眼乾症 xerophthalmia;
夜尿症 enuresis;
疫症 epidemic;
抑鬱症 depression;
診症 consultation;
自閉症 autism;

zheng
【掙】 (1) struggle to get free; try to throw off; (2) earn; make;
[掙揣] strive hard;
[掙飯吃] earn a living;
[掙命] struggle to save one's life;
[掙錢] earn money; make money;
掙錢糊口 earn one's crust;
掙錢養家 earn money to support one's family;
[掙少花多] live beyond one's income; live beyond one's means; live beyond one's salary;
掙得多，花得快 the more money one earns, the more one spends;
[掙脱] get rid of; shake off; struggle to free oneself;

zheng
【幀】 (1) numerary adjunct; (2) one of a pair;
裝幀 binding and layout;

zheng
【証】 certificate; certify; evidence; proof;

zheng
【鄭】 (1) earnest; formal; serious; solemn; (2) a surname;
[鄭聲] immoral ballads;
[鄭重] (1) earnest; important; serious; solemn; (2) careful; cautious;
鄭重承諾 give one's solemn promise;
鄭重其事 act with due care and respect; in earnest; serious and earnest; take the matter seiously; with gravity;
鄭重聲明 tell the world; solemnly declare;
態度鄭重 serious in one's attitude;

zheng
【證】 (1) demonstrate; prove; (2) evidence; proof; testimony; (3) card; certificate; (4) disease; illness;
[證詞] evidence; testimony;
駁回證詞 rebut evidence;
提供證詞 give testimony;
[證法] demonstration;
間接證法 indirect demonstration;
解析證法 analytic demonstration;
直接證法 direct demonstration;
[證婚] chief witness at a wedding ceremony;
[證件] certificate; credentials; papers;
出示證件 show one's credentials;
持有證件 hold a certificate;
海關證件 custom papers;
偽造證件 forge certificates;
[證據] evidence; proof; testimony; witness;
證據力 probative value;
證據確鑿 irrefutable evidence; the evidence is certain;
證據確鑿，鐵案如山 with conclusive irrefutable evidence;
查賬證據 accounting evidence;
充分證據 good evidence;
傳聞證據 hearsay evidence;
活生生的證據 living proof;
科學證據 scientific proof;
間接證據 circumstantial evidence;
沒有絲毫證據 not a scrap of evidence; not a shred of evidence;
明顯的證據 clear evidence;
確鑿的證據 hard evidence;
實驗證據 empirical evidence;
提出證據 offer testimony;
提供證據 give evidence;

銷毀證據 destroy evidence;
新的證據 fresh evidence;
一項證據 a piece of evidence;
醫學證據 medical evidence;
有力的證據 strong evidence;
有證據 there is proof;
掌握證據 hold proofs;

[證明] a witness to; attest to; attestation; bear out; bear witness; certification; certify; confirm; corroborate; demonstrate; evidence of; give proof of; prove; testify;
證明書 certificate; testimonial;
~保險證明書 insurance certificate;
~出口證明書 export certificate;
~健康證明書 health certificate;
~鑒定證明書 assay certificate;
~身分證明書 identity certificate;
~審計證明書 audit certificate;
~死亡證明書 death certificate;
~衛生證明書 sanitary certificate;
~驗收證明書 acceptance certificate;
證明文件 certificate; testimonial; supporting document; supporting paper;
充分證明 speak volumes about; speak volumes for;
出口證明 export certification;
存在性證明 existence proof;
檢驗證明 certificate of proof;
健康證明 health certification;
醫生證明 medical certification;
運輸證明 certificate of carriage;
在職證明 incumbency certification;
質量證明 quality certification;

[證券] bond; negotiable securities; security;
證券持有人 fund holder;
證券發行市場 securities primary market;
證券公司 security company; stock broker company;
證券交易市場 securities second market;
證券交易税 securities exchange tax;
遊戲交易所 arena of the bears and bulls; bourse; stock exchange;
證券期貨文易 future transaction;
證券市場 security market; stock market;
~中短期證券市場 short and medium term securities market;
證券收益率 rate of return;
證券投資 portfolio investment;
證券違約風險 default risk;
證券現貨交易 spot cash transaction;
證券賬戶 securities account;
證券轉讓證 transfer deed;
長期證券 long-term security;
短期證券 short-term security;
公司證券 corporation securities;
可轉換證券 convertible security;
買賣證券 play the market;
外國證券 foreign security;
優先證券 senior security;
有價證券 security;

[證人] witness;
重要證人 material witness;
專家證人 expert witness;

[證實] affirm; authenticate; confirm; confirmation; corroborate; corroboration; demonstrate; prove; verify;
被證實 be attested to;
官方證實 official confirmation;
有待證實 remain to be confirmed;

[證書] certificate; certification; credential;
產權證書 certificate of title;
高級證書 senior certificate;
化驗證書 analysis certificate;
檢定證書 verification certificate;
交貨證書 delivery certificate;
教師證書 teacher's certificate;
就業證書 work certificate;
投資證書 investment certificate;
委任證書 certificate of appointment;
學歷證書 academic certificate;
債券證書 bonded certificate;
職業證書 vocational certificate;
專業證書 professional certificate;

[證物] exhibit;

[證言] testimony;

[證驗] (1) verify; (2) efficacy; real results;

案證 evidence of a case;
保證 assure; ensure; give sb one's word; guarantee; pledge; pass sb one's word; pledge sb one's word; warranty;
辨證 discriminate;
辯證 dialectical; discriminate and verify;
表證 illness that has not attacked the vital organs of the human body;
查證 investigate and verify; check and testify;
對證 check; verify;
反證 counter-evidence; disproof;
否證 falsify;

工作證 employee's card;
公證 notarization;
合格證 certificate of inspection;
記者證 press card;
駕駛證 driving licence;
見證 (1) witness; (2) evidence; testimony;
結婚證 marriage certificate;
借書證 library card;
舉證 adduce; put to the proof;
考證 do textual research; make textual criticisms;
例證 example; illustration;
論證 (1) demonstration; proof; (2) grounds of argument;
明證 case in point; clear proof; evidence; token;
旁證 circumstantial evidence; collateral evidence; side witness;
憑證 evidence; proof;
簽證 visa;
求證 look for evidence; try to prove;
球證 referee; umpire;
詮證 explain correct meaning of the text point by point;
確證 conclusive evidence; confirmation; convincing proof; definite evidence; ironclad proof; solid evidence;
人證 testimony given by a witness;
認證 attestation; authentication;
身份證 identity card;
實證 authentic proof;
順證 serious case that improves steadily;
死亡證 death certificate;
搜查證 search warrant;
鐵證 ironclad proof; irrefutable evidence;
通行證 pass; permit;
為證 serve as evidence; serve as proof;
偽證 false witness; perjury;
誣證 perjury; give false testimony;
物證 material evidence;
顯證 clear proof;
許可證 licence; permit;
學生證 student's identity card;
驗收證 check-and-acceptance certificate;
驗證 confirm by evidence; test and verify;
引證 cite as evidence; quote as proof;
印證 confirm; verify;
指證 produce evidence; prove;
罪證 evidence of a crime; proof of one's guilt;
左證 supporting evidence;
佐證 proof;
作證 bear witness; give evidence; testify;

Z

zhi¹
zhi

【之】 (1) someone; (2) that; these; this; those; (3) arrive at; go to; leave for; (4) winding; zigzag;

［之安］ peace;
恬愉之安 the peace of comfort;

［之寶］ the treasure of;
寶中之寶 the treasure of treasures;
視為之寶 regard as the most valuable treasure;
無價之寶 invaluable asset; priceless treasure;

［之輩］ run of people;
庸碌之輩 ordinary class of person;
庸庸之輩 common run of men;

［之筆］ brush;
如椽之筆 masterly writing; one's big writing brush is like a rafter; powerful pen;
神來之筆 delicate touch; inspired passage; stroke of genius;

［之賓］ guest;
入幕之賓 constant friend; frequent and welcomed guest;

［之濱］ territory;
率土之濱 all this land; all within the boundaries; within the territory of a state;

［之才］ a person of; a talent of;
八斗之才 a person of great talent; a person with exceptional ability; a talent of talents; gifted; myriad-minded; of many gifts; scintillate with wit;
跨灶之才 capability of bestriding the kitchen-range; excel one's father in knowledge and ability;
經國之才 be skilled in managing public affairs; statesmanship;
經世之才 great ability to rule the country;
可造之才 person suitable for training; promising young person;
命世之才 born talent; one who is destined to govern;
王佐之才 have the capabilities of a prime minister;

［之差］ difference;
一髮之差 a hair's breadth;

［之長］ be skilled at; superiority;
矮中之長 a giant among dwarfs; a Triton

among the minnows;
取人之長 suck a person's brains;
~取人之長，補己之短 overcome one's shortcoming by learning from other's strong points;
一技之長 a single skill; professional skill; proficiency in a particular line; skilful in one field; speciality; what one is skilled at speciality;
爭一日之長 strive for only temporary superiority;

[之忱] sincerity;
獻曝之忱 prove one's honesty; sincerity of offering the warmth of the sun to sb;

[之仇] hatred;
貿首之仇 bitter hatred; inveterate hatred; so full of hatred that each wants to get the other's head;

[之處] place;
所到之處 wherever one goes;

[之道] means; way;
糊口之道 means to live by;
邪枉之道 crooked path;
瑩拂之道 principle of purity;
中庸之道 middle course; middle of the road; the doctrine of the mean; the golden mean;

[之德] kindness;
曹丘之德 kindness of recommendation;
好生之德 take pleasure in the welfare of living things; the virtue in sparing animal life;

[之的] target;
眾矢之的 a common target for scorn; a target for all; a target for attack; a target of public censure; a target of public criticism; become a target for all; under attack on all sides;
眾視之的 the observed of all observers;

[之地] place;
必爭之地 a hotly contested spot; a place of strategic importance;
不毛之地 arid land; bare land; barren land; desert;
不食之地 place of no farming;
彈丸之地 a bit of land; a place as small as a pellet; a small clod of earth; a tiny place; small bit of land; small holding; tiny area;
立錐之地 a speck of land;
~貧無立錐之地 as poor as Lazarus; in extreme poverty; so poor as to have no room to stick an awl on; utterly destitute;
容身之地 place to stay;
容膝之地 place just big enough to get the knees in; a tiny spot;
一矢之地 bow-shot; short distance;
一席之地 space for one person; tiny space;

[之惡] evil;
桀紂之惡 the devil is not so black as he is painted;

[之恩] favour;
跪乳之恩 filial piety;
沐人之恩 bask in sb's favour;

[之風] trend;
不正之風 evil winds; malpractices; unhealthy tendency; unsound tendencies; unwholesome tendencies; wrong ways of doing things;
~政界種種不正之風 abusive practices in politics;

[之福] happiness;
齊人之福 have a concubine; have more than one wife; the happiness of having two wives;
如天之福 as good as the blessing of Heaven;

[之歌] elegy; song;
蒿里之歌 funeral scrolls of elegies written on the death of a friend;

[之隔] be separated by; separation;
一墻之隔 be separated only by a wall; partition by a wall;
一山之隔 be separated only by a mountain;
一水之隔 be separated only by a river;
一息之隔 a heartbeat away;

[之功] achievement;
貪天之功 arrogate to oneself the merits of others; claim credit for other people's achievements; lay claim to what one has done nothing to deserve; take credit for what is accomplished naturally;
~貪天之功據為己有 appropriate to oneself the meritorious services of others; arrogate to oneself the credit of others; credit other people's achievements to oneself; take credit for the

achievements of others; take the credit of other people's achievements for oneself;
一簣之功 the effort that brings about the final success; the last basket of earth that helps in building mound;

[之國] country;
萬乘之國 a state with ten thousand chariots — a big country;

[之好] union;
朱陳之好 the union of two families;

[之合] match;
天作之合 heaven-made match; match blessed by God; match by Heaven; union made by heaven;

[之後] after; after this; afterwards; later;

[之華] celebration;
唐棣之華 celebrate a brother's reunion;

[之禍] disaster;
飛來之禍 unexpected trouble;
焚如之禍 the woe of fire destruction;

[之計] plan;
緩兵之計 a plot to gain time in order to complete defense; a stratagem to gain a respite; a stratagem to stall off immediate attack by the enemy; a trick to gain time; measures to stave off an attack; stalling tactics;
為今之計 a plan for the present juncture; have a plan for the present;

[之急] urgency;
當務之急 crying obligation; most pressing demand of the day; pressing matter of the moment; task of top priority; urgent matter; urgent task; urgent task on hand;

[之鯽] silver carp;
過江之鯽 as numerous as a school of silver carps moving down a stream;

[之家] family;
世祿之家 family of hereditary emoluments;
數口之家 family of several mouths; small family;
五口之家 family of five;

[之間] among; between;
彈指之間 at the snap of a finger; in a flash; in a moment; in a short moment; in a twinkling of an eye; in an instant; instantly;
俯仰之間 in a flash; in a short span; in a twinkling; in an instant; in the twinkling of an eye;
顧指之間 the moment of glancing back and moving a finger — instantly;
眉睫之間 in close proximity;
去取之間 between taking and leaving;
霎時之間 for a moment; in a wink; momentarily;
斯須之間 in an instant;
絲忽之間 in the briefest space of time; instantly;
一霎之間 in the twinkling of an eye;
一瞬之間 in a flash; in an instant; in the twinkling of an eye;
指顧之間 before you turn your back; in a short while;
仲伯之間 there is no choice between the two;
轉眼之間 as swift as a wink; before you can say Jack Robinson; before you know where you are; in a flash; in a jiffy; in a trice; in a twinkling; in a wink; in an instant; in jig time; in no time; in the turn of a hand; in the twinkling of an eye; on the instant;

[之見] view;
塵俗之見 commonplace view;
管窺之見 limited outlook; one's narrow views; the view through a tube; what has been seen through a tube;
井蛙之見 narrow view; tunnel vision;
先入之見 preconception;
一孔之見 glimpses of the truth; limited view; narrow view; peephole view; short-sighted; tunnel vision; very limited outlook;
庸腐之見 simple and stale point of view;

[之鑒] lesson;
覆車之鑒 examples to take warning from; object lesson; precedents from which to take warning;

[之交] acquaintance; friends;
八拜之交 sworn brother; sworn sister;
筆墨之交 literary friends;
管鮑之交 a friendship as close as gold and stone; David and Jonathan — good friendship; the friendship of Guan Zhong and Bao Shuya — like the friendship of Damon and Pythias;
患難之交 brothers in misfortune; companions in adversity; fellow

victims; fellowship in misfortune; foul weather friends; friends in adversity; friends in adversity; tested friends;
金蘭之交 bosom friends; intimate friendship; sworn brothers;
萍水之交 brief acquaintance; short acquaintance; incidental acquaintance;
契臂之交 sworn friends;
雲霞之交 high-minded friendship;
再世之交 friendship of the second generation;
總角之交 childhood chum; childhood friend; friend since childhood;

[之階] stepping-stone;
進身之階 stepping-stone;

[之京] equal;
莫與之京 have no equal; nothing is comparable;

[之敬] renumeration;
不腆之敬 small gift;
修羊之敬 private tutor's remuneration;
脩羊之敬 emoluments for a teacher;

[之客] guest;
不速之客 casual visitor; chance-comer; crasher; gate-crasher; guest who drops in by chance; uninvited guest;

[之口] mouth;
防民之口，甚於防川 to stop the mouth of the people is more difficult than stopping a river;

[之哭] tear;
秦庭之哭 beg in tears for assistance in desperation;

[之樂] joy of sth;
桑中之樂 illicit love;
于飛之樂 happiness of a married couple deeply in love;

[之淚] tear;
一掬同情之淚 cannot help shedding tears of sympathy; shed tears of sympathy;

[之類] and so forth; and so on; and the like; and what not;

[之力] efforts;
吹灰之力 just a small effort; the effort needed to blow away a speck of dust; the least effort;
~不費吹灰之力 able to do it on one's head; as easy as blowing off dust; as easy as falling off a log; just a small effort; no skin off sb's nose; with minimum effort; without the least effort;
助一臂之力 bear a hand; lend a hand; lend a helping hand;

[之量] capacity;
兼人之量 able to drink twice as much as another; have the capacity of two persons;

[之靈] spirit;
在天之靈 go ghost; the spirit of the deceased;

[之流] and his like;

[之路] road; way;
必經之路 the only way which must be passed;
必由之路 the only way; the road one must follow or take;
自新之路 the chance to turn over a new leaf; the opportunity to begin all over again; the road to a new life;
走必由之路 take the only route which must be passed;

[之慮] anxiety;
踐冰之慮 apprehensive; dangerous;

[之論] view;
目睫之論 superficial view;
折中之論 impartial in one's opinion;
誅心之論 exposure of sb's ulterior motives; penetrating criticism;

[之貉] jackal;
一丘之貉 all tarred with the same brush; be tarred with the same stick; badgers of the same mound; birds of a feather; both of a hair; brigands of the same stripe; evil persons of the same type; jackals from the same hillock; nothing to choose between them; of the same batch; out from the same cloth; out of the same cloth; people of the same ilk; tigers from the same den;

[之美] (1) beauty; (2) credit; good point;
掠人之美 claim credit due to others; reap where one has not sown; rob other's good point;

[之妙] subtlety;
深得其中之妙 fully appreciate its subtlety; have got the trick of it;

[之明] knowledge;
自知之明 a correct self-assessment; have a clear estimation of oneself; know one's limitation; know one's place; know oneself; self-knowledge;

Z

~ 無自知之明 ignorance of one's limited capabilities; lack of self-knowledge;
~ 有自知之明 know one's limits; know one's place; know oneself; see ourselves as others see us;
人貴有自知之明 it is important to know one's own limitations; self-knowledge is wisdom;

［之末］ end;
強弩之末 a spent arrow; a spent force; a strong force that has been exhausted; an arrow at the end of its flight; at the end of an arrow's flight; exhausted; powerless; spent; the arrow from a strong bow becomes weak after flying its distance;
錐刀之末 negligible profits; small gains;

［之謀］ plan;
忽忽之謀 ill-conceived plan;

［之木］ tree;
無本之木 tree without roots;

［之難］ danger;
急人之難 eager to help those in need; help people in danger;

［之內］ in; included; including; inside; within;
眉睫之內 in close proximity;
在步行距離之內 within walking distance;

［之年］ in the age of;
垂暮之年 in declining years; in old age;
垂髫之年 young childhood;
大有之年 abundant year; bumper year; good year for crops;
篤老之年 venerable age; very old age;
耳順之年 sixty years of age;
花甲之年 sixty years of age;
老耄之年 senile age;
破瓜之年 (of a girl) sixteen years of age;
衰暮之年 advanced in years;

［之鳥］ bird;
驚弓之鳥 a bird startled by the mere twang of a bowstring – a badly frightened person; a bird that starts at the sight of a bow – a once-bitten person; a bow-shy bird – nervously alert; a burnt child dreads the fire; a scalded cat dreads cold water; burned child fears fire;
傷弓之鳥 a bird that starts at the sight of a bow – a badly frightened person; a bird which has been hurt by an arrow – a once-bitten person; the bird that has been injured by the bow – the person who learns to be cautious from having his finger burnt once;

［之癖］ excessive fondness;
盤龍之癖 excessive fondness of gambling;

［之戚］ bereavement;
鼓盆之戚 be bereaved of one's wife;

［之契］ deed;
金蘭之契 close and intimate friendship; sworn brothers;

［之氣］ spirit;
浩然之氣 liberal mind; moral force; natural greatness of soul; noble spirit; one's vital spirit; spirit of fearlessness; the Great Spirit;

［之前］ ago; before; before this; prior to;
臨睡之前 last thing at night;

［之犬］ dog;
喪家之犬 a dog without its master; a homelsss cur; a homeless dog; a lost pup; a stray cur; a stray dog;
~ 如喪家之犬 like a dog with the tail between the legs; like a dog without its master;

［之強］ ace of aces;
強中之強 ace of aces; the strongest of the strong;
~ 強中自有強中手 a tough's tough; among the strong, there's always a stronger; diamond cut diamond; even among the very foremost, there is one who leads the way; however strong you are, there is always someone stronger; no matter how strong a person is, there will be always another stronger than he/she;
~ 強中自有強中手，能人背後有能人 for every able person there is always one still abler; however strong you are, there is always someone stronger;

［之情］ feeling;
烏鳥之情 filial piety;

［之請］ request;
不情之請 my presumptuous request;

［之囚］ prisoner;
階下之囚 captive; prisoner;

［之秋］ autumn;
孟春之秋 beginning of the first month of spring;

［之軀］ body;
七尺之軀 body of seven feet in height;

manly body; virile body;
萬金之軀 one's priceless self;

[之辱] humiliation;
胯下之辱 crawl between another's legs – drain the cup of humiliation;

[之三] the third; three;
四分之三 three-quarter;

[之上] above; on; over;

[之舌] tongue;
不爛之舌 glib tongue;
如簧之舌 glib tongue;

[之聲] (1) noise; (2) voice; (3) talk;
炫耳之聲 talks that brighten the ears;

[之食] food;
嗟來之食 food handed out on contempt; sth rudely offered;
硯田之食 earn a living by writing;

[之士] person;
鶴鳴之士 scholar widely admired for both virtue and learning;
鴻博之士 person of extensive learning;
捷才之士 scholar of nimble wits;
曠遠之士 profound scholar; scholar with an open mind;
熊虎之士 brave warrior;
衒學之士 pedantic scholar;
有識之士 far-sighted personages; knowledgeable people; people with a discerning eye; person of insight; person with breadth of vision;

[之世] period;
熙和之世 period of prosperity and peace;

[之事] affair; matter;
涯分之事 affair of one's duty;
常有之事 commonplace matter; matter of frequent occurrence;

[之數] amount;
箋箋之數 insignificant amount of money;

[之水] water;
無源之水 water without a source;
~無源之水，無本之水 like water without a source and a tree without roots – things without foundation;

[之説] remark;
謬悠之説 fallacy; unreasonable remarks;

[之談] talk;
不根之談 mere talk; unfounded statements;

[之痛] pain;
剝膚之痛 pain of being skinned;

[之徒] fellow; gangster;
不逞之徒 bad man; cornerman; desperado; disgruntled elements; gangster; hooligan; lawless gang; people disaffected to the government; plug-ugly; rascal; reckless fellow; rogue; scamp; unruly; vagabond;
游食之徒 people without definite profession; vagrant;

[之外] besides; beyond; except; in addition;
除此之外 apart from; as well as; aside from; besides this; excepting this; in addition; in addition to; not including; on top of; over and above; with the exception of;

[之王] king;
百獸之王 king of all animals – the lion; monarch of all beasts;
獸中之王 king of beasts – the lion;
無冕之王 uncrowned king;

[之望] respect;
山斗之望 be respected by all;

[之危] perilous situation;
趁人之危 take advantage of another's perilous state;

[之文] article;
臆撰之文 original essay;

[之物] things;
身外之物 external things; worldly goods;
倘來之物 illegal gain; sth coming through an improper channel; sth that comes to hand unexpectedly; undeserved gain; unexpected gain; windfall;

[之錫] reward;
百朋之錫 handsome reward; very expensive gift;

[之喜] happiness;
夢熊之喜 compliment on the birth of a boy; prognostic from a dream;
弄瓦之喜 give birth to a baby girl; pleasure of having a girl born;
弄璋之喜 give birth to a boy; pleasure of having a son born;
雙瓦之喜 give births to twin girls;
雙璋之喜 give births to twin boys;
湯餅之喜 feast on the third day after a child's birth;
宴爾之喜 bliss of the newlyweds; joy of giving a feast in entertainment;

[之暇] leisure;
公餘之暇 after the business hour; in the

intervals of public duties; leisure after offcial duties; leisure from public duties;

[之下] under;
乍聽之下 at first hearing;

[之嫌] suspicion;
李下之嫌 be found in a suspicious position; be suspected of a theft; under suspicion of stealing;

[之鄉] a land of;
魚米之鄉 district where fish and rice are abundant; land flowing with milk and honey; land of agriculture and dishery; land of fish and rice; land of plenty; natural granary; region abundant in fish and rice; region teeming with fish and rice; rich district with plenty of fish and rice; town known for its abundance of fish and rice;
~產自魚米之鄉 be produced in a land abundant in rice and fish;

[之心] heart;
防人之心不可無 the cat is a good friend but it scratches;

[之性] disposition;
虺蜴之性 poisonous and sneaking; the disposition of a lizard;

[之幸] fortune;
邀天之幸 very lucky;

[之虛] shadow;
虛中之虛 shadow of a shadow;

[之選] choice;
干城之選 a capable general who can be trusted with the defense of the country;
空群之選 person of great ability; pick of the best;

[之學] learning; teaching;
黃老之學 the learning of Emperor Huang and Lao Zi;

[之雅] pleasure;
同寅之雅 pleasure of being colleagues in office;

[之言] talk;
背口之言 talk behind one's back;
阿好之言 statement to please one side;
汗漫之言 words spoken in a roundabout way;
媒妁之言 words of a matchmaker;
無徵之言 baseless talk; unfounded assertion;

[之腋] piece;
一狐之腋 a piece under the forelegs of the fox — a precious thing; the best part of sth;

[之一] one in...; one out of...;
七分之一 one out of seven; seventh;
萬分之一 dimi; one out of ten thousand;

[之意] meaning;
話外之意 idea not expressed in words; implied meaning; more is meant than meets the ear; the meaning between the lines; what is actually meant;
獻芹之意 it is only a small gift — self-depreciatory phrase in giving a present;

[之音] sound;
弦外之音 connotations; implied meaning; implication; insinuation; mental reservation; overtones;

[之憂] trouble; worry;
采薪之憂 worry about gathering firewood — ill health;
內顧之憂 family troubles; internal distresses; worry for domestic troubles;

[之友] friend;
面交之友 know each other by chance;

[之魚] fish;
離水之魚 fish out of water;

[之冤] wrong accusation;
不白之冤 a case of being wrongly accused; an innocence incapable of being vindicated; an unrighted wrong; be wronged; to be pronounced guilty without being able to disprove the guilt; suffer wrong; unredressed injustice; unrighted wrong;
覆盆之冤 dark injustice; irredeemable wrong; wrong that can never be righted;

[之願] wish;
向平之願 marriages of one's sons and daughters;

[之災] calamity; disaster;
回祿之災 fire disaster;
無妄之災 undeserved catastrophe; unexpected calamity;

[之症] disease;
不治之症 disease without remedy; fatal disease; fatal sickness; incurable malady;

[之爭] battle; struggle;

蠻觸之爭 a worthless death struggle over a trifling matter;

[之知] knowledge;

挈瓶之知 petty cleverness; trivial knowledge;

[之直] straight;

如箭之直 as straight as an arrow;

如矢之直 straight as an arrow;

[之姿] paragon;

絕世之姿 paragon of beauty;

[之中] among; in; in the midst of;

百忙之中 despite many claims on one's time; in the midst of pressing affairs; in the thick of things; while fully engaged;

冥冥之中 in the unseen world;

掌握之中 have sth in one's pocket; in one's hands; in sb's clutches; lie at sb's mercy; under the control of; within one's grasp;

[之助] assistance;

指臂之助 mutual assistance; the assistance of finger and forearm;

[之子] (1) bride; (2) son;

之子於歸 marriage of a girl; the bride goes to her new home; the maiden goes to her future home;

螟蛉之子 adopted son; son by adoption;

[之字路] zigzag course; zigzag road;

[之卒] troops;

瓦合之卒 rabble troops;

[之尊] royalty;

九五之尊 imperial throne; position of an emperor; royal position;

[之作] work;

必傳之作 work that will certainly go down to posterity;

反之 on the contrary; otherwise;

兼之 besides; moreover;

總之 in a word; in short;

zhi

【支】 (1) prop up; put up; (2) prick up; raise; (3) protrude; raise; (4) bear; support; sustain; (5) put sb off; send away; (6) defray; disburse; draw money; pay; (7) branch; offshoot; subdivision; (8) measure-word; (9) count; (10) the twelve Earthly Branches; (11) a surname;

[支部] branch;

[支撐] bracing; crutch; prop up; support; sustain; timbering;

支撐動作 movement of support;

支撐門面 keep up appearance; maintain the front show;

大量支撐 heavy bracing;

倒十字支撐 cross handstand;

導洞支撐 gallery timbering;

底斜支撐 bottom lateral bracing;

剛性支撐 rigid bracing;

橫向支撐 lateral bracing;

框架支撐 cruciform bracing;

拉力支撐 tension bracing;

菱形支撐 diamond bracing;

密閉支撐 close timbering;

前沿支撐 advance timbering;

橋支撐 bridge bracing;

下弦支撐 lower chord bracing;

小爐支撐 port bracing;

斜側支撐 diagonal side bracing;

柱間支撐 column bracing;

[支持] at sb's back; at the back of sb; backing; bear; buttress; countenance; for; hold out; stand up for; sustain;

支持理論 support theory;

支持率 approval rating;

支持軟件 support software;

支持者 backer; camp follower; follower; supporter; sympathizer;

~忠實支持者 loyal supporter;

暗中支持 give secret support to;

表示支持 in sympathy with sth;

撤回表持 withdraw support;

大力的支持 strong support;

鼎力支持 powerful support;

動員支持 mobilize support;

獨力支持 support single-handedly;

給予支持 give support;

公眾支持 popular support; public support;

毫無保留的支持 all-out support;

後勤支持 logistic support;

獲得支持 have support;

極大的支持 massive support;

積極支持 active support;

全力支持 give full support to;

~給予全力支持 give sb one's unqualified support;

全心全力的支持 whole-hearted support;

完全支持 all for;

一貫的支持 unfailing support;

一致的支持 unanimous support;
增加支持 build up support;
爭取支持 drum up support; rally support;

[支出] (1) disburse; expend; pay; (2) disbursement; expenditure; outlay;
支出總額 aggregate spending;
財政支出 expenditure;
赤字支出 deficit spending;
額外支出 additional outlay;
國防支出 expenditure on national defence;
累計支出 accumulated outlay;
臨時支出 contingent outlay;
實際支出 actual outlay;
投資支出 investment spending;
應計支出 accrued expenditure;
預算支出 budgetary outlay;
追加支出 additional expenditure;
總支出 total expenditure;

[支絀] insufficient; not enough;
左支右絀 at the end of one's tether; find it hard to cover expenses; find it hard to cover expenses; hard-pressed for money; have too many problems to cope with; in financial straits; in straitened circumstances; not to have enough money to cover the expenses; unable to cope with a situation; unable to tackle one problem without aggravating another;

[支點] fulcrum; point of support;
杠桿支點 lever fulcrum;
控制桿支點 control lever fulcrum;

[支店] branch store;

[支隊] department;
防暴支隊 riot police department;

[支付] pay; payment;
支付地點 place of payment;
支付方式 mode of payment;
支付工具 means of payment;
支付貨幣 currency of payment;
支付票據 bill of payment;
支付時間 time of payment;
支付條件 terms of payment;
國外支付 foreign payment;
貨到支付 delivery on arrival;
津貼支付 allowance payment;
實物支付 payment in kind;
息票支付 coupon payments;
現金支付 cash payment;
逾期支付 back payment;

[支架] bolster; cantilever; support; timbering;
垛式支架 cog timbering;
輔助支架 auxiliary support;
固定支架 fixed bolster;
夾固支架 clamping support;
交叉支架 arm support;
臨時支架 false timbering;
前探支架 cantilever timbering;
人字形支架 herringbone timbering;

[支離] be broken up;
支離破碎 all broken up; be reduced to fragments; breaks and cracks; broken up into fragments; cracks and breaches; fallen apart; in pieces; fragmented; incoherent; reduced to fragments; torn to pieces;
支離散亂 all jumbled up;

[支流] (1) affluent; tributary of a river; (2) minor aspects; non-essentials;
一條支流 a branch of a river; an affluent of a river;
再匯合支流 anabranch;

[支配] (1) allocate; arrange; budget; (2) control; dominate; govern;
支配關係 government;
~動詞支配關係 verbal government;
~強支配關係 strong government;
~弱支配關係 weak government;
~雙重支配關係 double government;
~體詞支配關係 adsubstantival government;
受人支配 under sb's sway;
聽人支配 resign oneself to another's control;

[支票] cheque;
支票簿 chequebook;
~支票簿新聞 chequebook journalism;
~一本支票簿 a chequebook;
支票戶 cheque account;
~計息支票戶 interest-bearing cheque account;
~銀行支票戶 bank cheque account;
支票賬戶 cheque account;
保付支票 certified cheque; marked cheque;
不可轉讓支票 non-negotiable cheque; not negotiable cheque;
不能兑現支票 dishonoured cheque;
重發支票 duplicate cheque;
到期支票 matured cheque;
兑現支票 cash a cheque;

~ 部份兌現支票 split cheque;
~ 未兌現支票 outstanding cheque;
付持票人支票 bearer cheque;
個人支票 personal cheque;
更改支票 altered cheque;
股利支票 dividend cheque;
國庫支票 public cheque;
過期支票 overdue cheque; stale cheque;
橫線支票 crossed cheque;
劃線支票 crossed cheque;
~ 普通劃線支票 general crossed cheque;
~ 未劃線支票 uncrossed cheque;
~ 無記名劃線支票 open crossed cheque;
匯款支票 remittance cheque;
即期支票 sight cheque;
記名支票 order cheque;
~ 不記名支票 bearer cheque;
交換中支票 clearing cheque;
結算支票 clearing house cheque;
拒付支票 rejected cheque;
開支票 draw a cheque; write a cheque;
可背書支票 endorsable cheque;
空白支票 blank cheque;
空頭支票 bad cheque; dishonoured cheque; dud cheque; rubber cheque;
來人支票 bearer cheque;
聯行支票 inter-bank cheque;
旅行支票 international cheque; traveller's cheque;
清算支票 settlement cheque;
缺點支票 lame cheque;
抬頭支票 order cheque;
通融支票 kiting cheque;
退還支票 returned cheque;
托收支票 uncollected cheque;
未付支票 outstanding cheque;
未注日期支票 undated cheque;
無法交付的支票 unendorsed cheque;
無效支票 dead cheque;
小額支票 slender cheque; small cheque;
限額支票 limited cheque;
~ 無限額支票 unlimited cheque;
巡迴支票 circular cheque;
一張支票 a cheque;
已付支票 paid cheque;
銀行支票 banker's cheque; cashier's cheque;
遠期支票 post-dated cheque;
注銷支票 cancelled cheque;
轉手支票 third party cheque;
作廢支票 voided cheque;

[支氣管] bronchial tubes; bronchus;
支氣管癌 bronchogenic carcinoma;
支氣管病 bronchopathy; disease of the bronchial tubes;
支氣管出血 bronchorrhagia;
支氣管痙攣 bronchospasm;
支氣管擴張 bronchiectasis;
~ 支氣管擴張藥 bronchodilator;
~ 支氣管擴張症 bronchiectasis;
支氣管囊腫 brochocele;
支氣管氣喘 bronchial asthma;
支氣管切開術 bronchotomy;
支氣管哮喘 bronchial asthma;
支氣管炎 bronchitis; inflammation of the bronchial tubes;
~ 出血性支氣管炎 haemorrhagic bronchitis;
~ 急性支氣管炎 acute bronchitis;
~ 寄生蟲性支氣管炎 parasitic bronchitis;
~ 慢性支氣管炎 chronic bronchitis;
~ 膜性支氣管炎 membranous bronchitis;
~ 蠕蟲性支氣管炎 verminous bronchitis;
~ 滲出性支氣管炎 exudative bronchitis;
小支氣管 bronchus;

[支取] draw money;

[支吾] equivocate; hum and haw; prevaricate;
支吾了事 hurry through a work carelessly; put through a business carelessly;
支吾其詞 equivocate; hum and haw; make an ambiguous statement; mince matters; mince one's words; prevaricate; quibble; speak evasively; try to avoid giving a definite answer;
支吾搪塞 evade the issue; hedge and dodge; hum and haw; parry a question; quibble;
支支吾吾 equivocate; falter; hum and haw; speak with hesitation;
左支右吾 equivocate; prevaricate;

[支線] branch line;

[支用] disburse;

[支援] aid; assist; back; help; hold up; support;
支援部隊 support unit;
支援服務 support system;
~ 校本支援服務 in-school support system;
支援災區 give aid to the disaster areas;
技術支援 technical support;

[支柱] column; mainstay; pillar; prop; stanchion; strut; support;
支柱產業 pillar industry; support industry;
~ 振興支柱產業 invigorate pillar

industries;
機翼支柱 aerofoil strut;
精神支柱 anchor; anchorage;
~信仰的精神支柱 anchor of one's faith;
~宗教是他的精神支柱 religion is his anchorage;
坑道支柱 pit prop;
空心金屬支柱 hollow prop;
梁支柱 beam stanchion;
磨擦支柱 friction prop;
天篷支柱 awning stanchion;
斜支柱 raking prop; diagonal stanchion;
弦桿支柱 boom support;
液壓支柱 hydraulic prop;
組合支柱 built-up stanchion;
作用支柱 actuating strut;

[支座] support;
橋梁支座 bridge support;
球形支座 beaded support;
雙向支座 bilateral support;
制動器支座 brake support;

超支 overspend;
墊支 advance expenditure; give an advance;
分支 branch;
借支 ask for an advance on one's pay; obtain an advance on one's salary;
開支 (1) expenditure; expenses; pay expenses; spend; spending; (2) get the pay; pay wages;
旁支 collateral branch;
日支 daily expenditure; daily expenses;
收支 income and expenses; revenue and expenditure;
透支 cash advance; make an overdraft; overdraw; take out an overdraft;
一支 a contingent of;
預支 draw money; get one's pay in advance;
總支 general branch;

zhi

【氏】 an ancient barbarian tribe to the west;

zhi

【卮】 container for holding wine; goblet with handles;

漏卮 (1) leaky wine vessel; (2) unfavourable balance of international payments;

zhi

【汁】 fluid; juice; sap;

[汁液] juice; sap;
白汁 white sauce;
菠蘿汁 pineapple juice;
殘汁 dregs;
橙汁 orange juice;
膽汁 bile;
毒汁 venom;
番茄汁 tomato juice;
果汁 fruit juice; juice;
橘汁 orange juice;
橘子汁 orange juice;
墨汁 prepared Chinese ink;
牛肉汁 beef extract;
蘋果汁 apple juice;
葡萄汁 grape juice;
肉汁 gravy; meat juice;
乳汁 milk;
西紅柿汁 tomato juice;
椰子汁 coconut milk;

zhi

【枝】 (1) branch; twig; (2) limbs; (3) branch off; (4) measure-word;

[枝幹] trunk and branches;
共枝別幹 learn from the same master but start one's own school;

[枝根] ramose roots;

[枝節] (1) minor matters; (2) complication; knottiness;
枝節叢生 branches and knots sprout luxuriantly; troubles arise here and there;
枝節橫生 branch forth; bring up unexpected trouble; create side issues; deliberately complicate an issue;
別生枝節 have new complications;
節外生枝 bring about extra complications; bring up unnecessary ramifications; cause complications; complicate matters; create side issues; deliberately complicate an issue; give rise to other contingencies; inject side issues; new problems crop up unexpectedly; proliferate issues and problems; raise obstacles; side issues crop up unexpectedly;
枝枝節節 complexity and diversity; complications; minor issues; digressive;

[枝解] dismemberment;

[枝蔓] branches and tendrils; complicated and

confused;

枝辭蔓語 lengthy and confused talk;

[枝條] twig;

一根枝條 a stick;

[枝頭] on the branch;

[枝葉] (1) branches and leaves; (2) minor details; nonessentials;

枝葉繁茂 in leafy profusion; with luxuriant foliage and branches;

枝葉扶疏 both the branches and leaves spread out; the branches and leaves are luxuriant but well-spaced; with branches profusely covered with leaves;

殘枝敗葉 the decaying branches and withered leaves;

殘枝落葉 the decaying branches and fallen leaves;

粗枝大葉 be done in broad strokes; crude and careless; crude and perfunctory; crude and sketchy; in a cursory fashion; slapdash; slipshod; sketchy; sloppy;

枯枝敗葉 dead twigs and withered leaves;

枯枝落葉 dry branches and fallen leaves;

金枝玉葉 illustrious descendants; of royal stock; the offspring of a high official;

瓊枝玉葉 descendants of the royal family; royal posterity;

柔枝嫩葉 supple twigs and tender leaves;

有枝添葉 add details of story; deliberately embellish the facts;

有枝有葉 addition to the truth;

枝繁葉茂 with luxuriant foliage — have many children and grandchildren;

[枝子] branch; twig;

側枝 lateral branch;

分枝 tree branch;

瘋枝 a branch that bears no fruit;

橄欖枝 olive branch;

桂枝 cassia twig;

果枝 (1) fruit branch; fruit-bearing shoot; (2) boll-bearing branch;

荔枝 litchi;

蘖枝 tiller;

駢枝 (1) double finger or toe; (2) superfluous;

樹枝 branch; twig;

修枝 prune;

壓枝 layer;

整枝 prune; train;

zhi

【知】 (1) aware of; know; realize; (2) inform; notify; tell; (3) knowledge; (4) administer; in charge of;

[知兵] be well versed in military arts;

[知賓] receptionist;

[知恥] have a sense of shame;

知恥近乎勇 feeling of shame is close to bravery; knowing shame is akin to courage;

毫不知恥 have the impudence to; lose all sense of shame;

恬不知恥 brazen-faced; shameless; unashamed;

[知道] aware of; know; realize; understand;

不知道 don't know; dunno; search me;

~ 我一點都不知道 that's news for me;

~ 我一直都不知道 I never knew that;

東西好不好，吃了才知道 the proof of the pudding is in the eating;

誰知道 (1) who knows; (2) who would have thought;

天知道 God knows;

無法知道 there's no telling;

想知道 wonder;

要知道 after all;

[知底] in the know; know the inside story;

[知非] know one's mistakes;

知非之年 fifty years of age;

[知府] magistrate of a prefecture;

[知更鳥] redbreast; robin;

[知過] realize one's mistake;

知過必改 always correct an error when one becomes aware of it; if a mistake is found, then correct it;

知過改過 acknowledge one's faults and correct them;

[知會] notify officially;

[知己] (1) intimate; understanding; (2) alter ego; bosom friend; confidant; soul mate; (3) know oneself;

知己友人 a friend who knows one well;

知己知彼 estimate correctly one's own strength as well as that of one's opponent; know yourself as well as the opponent;

知己知彼，百戰百勝 know one's own strength and the enemy's is the sure way to victory; knowing one's own situation and that of the enemy

guarantees victory in every battle; knowing yourself and knowing the enemy, in a hundred battles there will be a hundred victories; one who knows his own strength and that of the enemy is invincible in battle;
酒逢知己千杯少，話不投機半句多 if you drink with a bosom friend, a thousand cups are too few, and if you argue with a man, half a sentence is too much;
明於知彼，暗於知己 good at knowing others, but poor at knowing oneself; understand others but not oneself;
明於知己，暗於知彼 good at knowing oneself and poor at knowing others; good at knowing oneself but poor at knowing one's enemy;
謬托知己 claim sb to be one's bosom friend who is actually not;
女性知己 confidante;
視為知己 look upon sb as one's best friend; treat sb as a bosom friend;
士為知己者死 a gentleman is ready to die for his bosom friends; the scholar dies for his bosom friend;
~士為知己者死，女為悦己者容 a gentleman will die for the patron who recognizes his worth, a girl will doll herself up for the man who loves her;
叨在知己 being fortunate to be your intimate friend; I put you to shame by being your intimate friend;
引為知己 admit sb into one's confidence; regard sb as a bosom friend; take sb into confidence;
知彼知己 know both sides; know others and know oneself; know the enemy and know yourself; know yourself as well as the enemy;

[知交] bosom friend; intimate friend;
知交有年 be intimated with for years; on intimate terms with a person for years;

[知津] know the ford; know the way;

[知盡能索] knowledge exhausted and energy finished;

[知覺] (1) consciousness; (2) perception;
知覺分析 perceptual analysis;
知覺過敏 hyperesthesia;
知覺神經 sensory nerves;
知覺力 perceptivity;
超感知覺 extrasensory perception;
後知後覺 those who learn in later generation;
恢復知覺 recover consciousness; regain consciousness;
深度知覺 depth perception;
失去知覺 lose consciousness;
形狀知覺 form and shape perception;

[知客] person in charge of reception at ceremonies;

[知禮] know the rules of propriety; say and act in proper manners;

[知了] cicada;

[知名] celebrated; famous; noted; well-known;
知名度 awareness; celebrity; recognition;
~國際知名度 international recognition;
~國內知名度 national recognition;
知名人士 big name; celebrated people; celebrity; famous name; famous person; noted personage; outstanding character; outstanding personality; people of distinction; person of mark; person of note; person of renown; public figure; well-known personage;
~社會知名人士 public figure;
知名作家 famous writer;

[知命] resign to fate;
知命安身 be contended with one's lot and the position he is in;
知命之年 fifty years of age;
達天知命 aware that all things depend upon the will of God;
畏天知命 stand in awe of Heaven and resign to fate;

[知難] in the face of difficulties;
知難而進 advance in the face of difficulties; go forward despite difficulties; keep advancing in defiance of difficulties; press ahead in the face of difficulties; press forward in spite of difficulties; take the bull by the horns; weather a point;
知難而退 beat a retreat in the face of difficulties; retreat rather than to court failure; shrink back from difficulties; withdraw after learning of the difficulties;
知難行易 it is easier to do a thing than to know the why;

[知其不可而為之] do sth even though one knows it is impossible to succeed; know the trends cannot be turned back and still want to do it;

[知其然不知其所以然] know that sth is so but not why is so; know the hows but not the whys;

[知情] in the know; know the facts of a case or the details of an incident;

知情不報 conceal what one knows of a case; fail to report the truth;

知情不舉 conceal what one knows of a case;

知情達理 reasonable; sensible;

知情人 insider; those in the know;

知情識趣 have the grace to do sth;

[知趣] have a sense of propriety; know how to behave in a delicate situation; sensible; tactful;

[知人] know people;

知人論世 he can size up people by his simple devices and is so alive to the changes about him that he proves to be a good commentator on the current situation;

知人善任 discover able people and put them at suitable posts; horses for courses; know how to judge and use people; know one's subordinate and make good use of them;

知人知面不知心 a fair face may hide a foul heart; appearances are deceitful; cats hide their claws; in knowing a man, you may know his face, but not his heart; it is impossible to judge a man's heart from his face; one may know a person for a long time without understanding his true nature;

知人之長 sensible of others' merits;

知人之明 ability to appreciate a person's character and capability; keen insight into a person's character;

觀相知人 study a person's physiognomy reveals his/her character;

[知事] magistrate of a county;

[知識] (1) information; know-how; knowledge; learning; science; (2) intellectual;

知識爆炸 knowledge explosion;

知識編譯 knowledge compilation;

知識產權 intellectual property;

~知識產權法 intellectual property law;

~保護知識產權 protection of intellectual property;

知識產業 intellectual industry;

知識範疇 knowledge domain;

知識分子 intellectuals; intelligentsia;

~鄙視知識份子 despise intellectuals;

知識工程 knowledge engineering;

~知識工程學 knowledge engineering;

知識構成 knowledge composition;

知識化 knowledgization;

知識獲取 knowledge acquisition;

知識結構 structure of knowledge;

知識界 intelligentsia; intellectual circle;

知識庫 knowledge bank;

知識老化 ageing of knowledge;

知識論 epistemology;

知識密集型 knowledge intensive;

~知識密集型工業 knowledge intensive industry;

~知識密集型經濟 knowledge intensive economy

~知識密集型企業 knowledge intensive enterprise;

~知識密集型學習 knowledge intensive learning;

知識青年 educated youth; young intellectuals;

知識淵博 a store of learning; erudite; have a wide range of knowledge; learned;

保健知識 health knowledge;

背景知識 background knowledge;

傳播知識 distribute knowledge;

遞加知識 cumulative knowledge;

獲得知識 acquire knowledge; gain knowledge; get knowledge;

基本知識 basic knowledge; the ABC of sth;

基礎知識 basic knowledge;

技術知識 technical know-how;

積累知識 accumulate knowledge;

局部知識 local knowledge;

擴展知識 broaden one's knowledge; expand one's knowledge;

累積的知識 cumulative knowledge;

理性知識 conceptual knowledge;

賣弄知識 flash one's knowledge;

沒有知識 ignorant; illiterate;

全局知識 global knowledge;

實驗知識 experimental knowledge;

書本知識 book learning;

吸收知識 absorb knowledge;

先驗知識 a priori knowledge;

性知識 facts of life;

學到知識 acquire knowledge;

一般知識 general knowledge;
增長知識 improve one's knowledge; increase one's knowledge;
增進知識 advancement of knowledge; increase one's knowledge;
專業知識 expert knowledge; specialist;

[知書識禮] well-educated and a model of propriety;

[知悉] aware of; be informed of; know; learn of;

[知縣] county magistrate;

[知曉] aware of; know; learn of; understand;
誰個不知，那個不曉 there is not a person who does not know;
無從知曉 have no way of finding out about it;
業已知曉 gave knowledge of the matter;

[知心] (1) intimate; understanding; (2) bosom friend;
知心話 heart-to-heart talk; intimate words;
知心換命 stick together through thick and thin;
知心朋友 bosom friend; intimate friend;
知心人 bosom friend;

[知新] know sth new;

[知行] knowledge and action;
知行合一 knowledge and action should go hand in hand;
行易知難 it is easier done than said; to do is easier than to know; to know how is easier than to know why;
知易行難 it is easier said than done; it is easier to know a thing than to do it;

[知性] intellect;

[知言] (1) words of wisdom; (2) know the true meaning of one's words;
知言知人 to know the force of words is to know men;

[知音] (1) a friend keenly appreciative of one's talents; bosom friend; (2) one who is versed in music;
知音難覓 it is difficult to find an understanding friend;
知音識趣 friends on fully understanding and harmonious terms with each other;

[知友] close friend; intimate friend;

[知遇] have found a patron or superior appreciative of one's ability;
知遇之恩 gratitude for receiving help and encouragement by a superior;

[知照] inform; notify; tell;

[知者不言，言者不知] those who know much talk little; those who know little talk much;

[知政] administer the government; handle state affairs;

[知止] know where to stop;

[知足] content with one's lot;
知足不辱 being contented with one's lot, one will not be disgraced by others for it; he who is contented with his lot will not be humiliated; to be always contented means a lifetime without disgrace;
知足常樂 a contented mind is a perpetual feast; a man who is contented will be happy; content is happiness; content is more than a kingdom; contentment brings happiness; enough is as good as a feast; happiness lies in contentment; he who is contented is always happy; where content is, there is a feast; who is contented enjoys;
知足無求 one who is contented with what he has had asks for nothing more;
不知足 greedy; insatiable;
要知足 count one's blessings;

不知 all at sea; beyond sb; have no idea of; ignorant of; in the dark; it beats me; know nothing about; not aware of; not have a clue; not hear about; not know; the last person to know; without the knowledge of;
超知 gifted and talented; unusually intelligent;
飭知 inform a subordinate;
得知 be informed of;
感知 sense perception;
告知 inform; notify;
故知 old friend;
獲知 learn;
良知 intuitive knowledge;
明知 be fully aware; know perfectly well;
前知 foretell the future;
親知 with real personal knowledge;
情知 be fully aware; know perfectly well;
求知 seek knowledge;
確知 know for sure;
稔知 know sb quite well;
認知 cognition;
深知 know thoroughly; realize fully;
示知 inform; notify;

受知 be appreciated and well-treated by a superior;
熟知 know very well;
説知 inform; let sb know; notify;
素知 have known for some time;
所知 what one knows;
通知 dispatch a notice; give notice; inform of; let one know; make sth known; notify; send a circular; send sb the news;
未知 unknown;
聞知 hear; know from others; learn;
無知 ignorant; not know A from B; not know a great A from a bull's foot;
先知 (1) person of foresight; (2) prophet;
相知 (1) be well acquainted with each other; know each other well; (2) bosom friends; close friends; great friends;
心知 consciousness; intelligence; the mind;
新知 (1) new friends; (2) new knowledge; new learning;
須知 (1) have to know; it must be understood that; one should know that; should know; (2) note; notice; points for attention;
焉知 how could one know;
要知 person who wishes to know;
已知 known;
預知 foreknowledge; know beforehand; know in advance; precognition;
諭知 notify by a directive;
真知 genuine knowledge; true knowledge;
致知 extend one's knowledge;
周知 generally known; public knowledge;
週知 known to all; make known to all;
自知 know oneself;

zhi

【肢】 (1) limbs of a person; (2) legs of an animal; (3) wings or feet of a bird;

[肢病] acropathy;
肢病理學 acropathology;

[肢帶] limb girdle;

[肢骨] bones of one's limbs;
肢骨痛 acrostealgia;

[肢解] dismember; pull sb limb from limb; tear sb limb from limb;
肢解尸體 tear a body apart;

[肢體] (1) limbs; (2) limbs and trunk; the body;
肢體語言 body language;

[肢痛] melagra;
肢痛病 acromelalgia;
肢痛症 acrodynia;

[肢腫症] acroedema;

附肢 appendage;
胳肢 tickle sb;
後肢 hindquarters;
鋏肢 chelophora;
假肢 artificial limb;
截肢 amputate;
前肢 forelegs; forelimbs;
上肢 upper limbs;
四肢 arms and legs; four limbs;
下肢 lower limbs;
胸肢 thoracic appendage;
義肢 artificial limb;

zhi

【芝】 (1) a kind of purplish fungus symbolizing nobility; (2) a kind of fragrant herb; (3) a surname;

[芝艾俱焚] iris and artemisia are burnt together — the honourable and lowly perish together; the good perishes with the bad;

[芝焚蕙歎] like mourns over the death of like; the orchid sighs at the burning of the iris — sympathize with one's kind;

[芝蘭] orchid;
芝蘭氣味 noble friendship;
芝蘭之室 a room full of fragrant orchids;
~如入芝蘭之室 like entering a room full of fragrant orchids — benefit from associating with people of a noble character;

[芝麻] (1) sesame; (2) sesame seed;
芝麻醬 sesame butter; sesame paste;
芝麻開花 like sesame flowers shooting up high and higher;
芝麻開花節節高 a sesame stalk puts forth blossoms notch by notch, higher and higher; like sesame in bloom, each flower grows higher than the last; rise joint by joint like sesame flowers on the stem; shoot up higher and higher like sesame flowers;
芝麻油 sesame oil;
抓了芝麻，丟了西瓜 run after the less important things, forgetting the important ones; strain at a gnat and swallow a camel;
~撿了芝麻，丟了西瓜—因小失大 drop

a watermelon to pick up a sesame seed — concentrate on minor matters to the neglect of major ones; let the plough stand to catch a mouse; pick up the sesame seeds but overlook the watermelons — mindful of small matters to the neglect of large ones;
細揀芝麻，疏丟西瓜 penny wise and pound foolish;

[芝眉] dignified eyebrows;

[芝士] cheese;
藍紋芝士 blue cheese;
軟芝士 soft cheese;
硬芝士 hard cheese;

[芝儀] your noble face;

靈芝 glossy ganoderma;
紫芝 a kind of gill fungus;

zhi
【祗】 (1) respect; revere; (2) same as 祇, only;

zhi
【胝】 calluses on hands or feet;

zhi
【脂】 (1) fat; grease; (2) rouge; (3) a surname;

[脂蛋白] lipoprotein;
高密度脂蛋白 high-density lipoprotein;
~極高密度脂蛋白 very high-density lipoprotein;
血清脂蛋白 serum lipoprotein;

[脂肪] fat;
脂肪變 fatty change;
脂肪代謝 lipometabolism;
脂肪蛋白 lipoprotein;
脂肪發生 adipogenesis;
脂肪分解 lipophagy;
脂肪過多 hyperliposis;
~脂肪過多症 lipomatosis;
脂肪過少 hypoliposis;
脂肪壞死 adiponecrosis;
脂肪減少 lipopenia;
脂肪痢 steatorrhea;
脂肪粒 fat granule;
脂肪瘤 adipose tumour; fatty tumour;
脂肪缺乏病 fat-deficiency disease;
脂肪肉瘤 liposarcoma;
脂肪疝 fat hernia;
脂肪生成 lipogenesis;
脂肪水腫 lipedema;
脂肪酸 fatty acid;
脂肪痛 adiposalgia;
脂肪突出 adipocele;
脂肪細胞 adipose cell;
脂肪增多 lipotrophy;
脂肪增生 lipohypertrophy;
脂肪組織 adipose tissue;
飽和脂肪 saturated fat;
抽脂肪 liposuction;
食用脂肪 edible fat;
脫色脂肪 bleached fat;
直腸脂肪 bung fat;

[脂粉] cosmetics; rouge and face powder;
脂粉不染 wear no make-up;
脂粉場中 among pretty ladies;
脂粉氣的 feminine; poncy; sissy;
擦脂抹粉 paint rouge and power;
搽脂抹粉 apply cosmetics; paint and powder one's face; paint and powder oneself; rub on the rouge and daub the paint;
施脂粉 apply cosmetics; wear makeup;
塗脂抹粉 apply cosmetics; apply facial makeup; apply power and paint; deck oneself out; deck up; make up; paint and powder oneself;
~為自己塗脂抹粉 try to whitewash oneself;
庸脂俗粉 ordinary oil and common powder — commonplace woman;

[脂膏] wealth;
脂膏不潤 being put in the grease it does not get glossy — incorruptible official;
民脂民膏 fat of the people; flesh and blood of the people; hard-won possessions of the people; people's lifeblood; wealth produced by the people with blood and sweat;

[脂類] lipid;
被膜脂瘤 capsulare lipoma;
衍生脂類 derived lipid;
貯存脂類 depot lipid;

[脂瘤] lipoma;
頸部環形脂瘤 annulare colli lipoma;
樹脂狀脂瘤 arborescens lipoma;

[脂酶] lipase;
胃脂脂酶 gastric lipase;
胰脂脂酶 pancreatic lipase;
植物脂酶 vegetable lipase;

[脂油] lard;

採脂 tap resin;

抽脂 liposuction;
低脂 low-fat;
耳脂 earwax;
高脂 fatty;
絳脂 rufin;
礦脂 petrolatum; vaseline;
磷脂 phophatide;
凝脂 solidified lard;
瓊脂 agar-agar;
乳脂 butterfat;
軟脂 palmitin;
潤滑脂 lubricating grease;
樹脂 resin;
松脂 pine resin; rosin;
塗脂 apply powder;
脱脂 defat; degrease;
香脂 (1) face cream; (2) balm; balsam;
血脂 blood lipoids;
胭脂 rouge;
羊毛脂 lanolin;
硬脂 stearin; tristearin;
油脂 fat; oil;

zhi

【隻】 (1) alone; one of a pair; one only; single; (2) measure-word; (3) odd;

［隻句］ brief note; single sentence;

［隻立］ stand alone;

［隻日］ odd days of a lunar month;

［隻身］ all by oneself; alone; by oneself;
隻身獨往 go there alone;
隻身赴敵 go alone to fight the enemy;
隻身幸免 sole survivor;
隻身在外 away from home all by oneself;

［隻手］ single-handed;
隻手不能遮天 one hand cannot cover the sky;

［隻眼］ (1) one-eyed; (2) fresh view; original idea;
別具隻眼 have an original view;

［隻影］ all alone; all by oneself;

［隻字］ brief note; single character; single word;
隻字不訛 every word of it is true;
隻字不談 say nothing about;
隻字不提 keep silent about; make no mention of; not a word is said about; not a word slips from one's mouth about; not breathe a word about sth; not drop a word; there is no mention at all of;
隻字不吐 clam up;
隻字片語 just a few words; short note;
隻字片紙 fragments of writing; just a short note; very brief note;
片紙隻字 brief note; just a short note;

zhi

【梔】 gardenia; jasmine;

［梔子］ gardenia; jasmine;

zhi

【搘】 lean on; prop up; support;

［搘拄］ prop; support;

zhi

【蜘】 spider;

［蜘蛛］ spider;
蜘蛛網 cobweb; spider's web;
蜘蛛學 arachnology; araneology;
~ 蜘蛛學家 araneologist;
蜘蛛中毒 arachnidism;
大蜘蛛 big spider;

zhi

【織】 knit; weave;

［織補］ darn; mend;

［織布］ weave cloth; weaving;
織布廠 weaving mill;
織布機 loom;

［織畫］ woven pictures;

［織機］ loom;
傳動帶織機 belting loom;
毛毯織機 blanket loom;
手工織機 hand loom;

［織錦］ brocade; silk brocade;
織錦廠 brocade mill;
風景織錦 silk-woven landscape;

［織麻］ weave linen;

［織襪］ knit socks; knit stockings;

［織網］ spin a web;

［織烏］ the sun;

［織物］ fabric; textiles;

［織針］ knitting needle;

編織 (1) knit; knitting; weaving and bralding; (2) fabricate;
促織 cricket;
紡織 spin and weave;
耕織 farming and weaving;
交織 (1) interweave; (2) mingle;
羅織 frame up;
組織 form; organization; organize;

zhi²

zhi

【治】 when pronounced as a verb;

zhi

【直】 (1) straight; straighten; (2) from top to bottom; longitudinal; vertical; (3) fair; just; unbiased; upright; upright and honest; (4) frank; outspoken; straightforward; (5) directly; first-hand; (6) continuously; (7) vertical stroke; (8) just; merely; only; simply;

［直筆］ unprejudiced writing; write in an unprejudiced way;
直筆而書 write according to facts;

［直播］ (1) direct seeding; (2) direct broadcast; live broadcast; live telecast;

［直撥］ direct dialing service;

［直…才］ it...not until...that; not...until; not until...do;

［直腸］ rectum;
直腸癌 cancer of the rectum; rectal cancer;
直腸出血 hemoproctia;
直腸反射 rectal reflex;
直腸痙攣 proctospasm;
直腸擴張 proctectasia;
直腸麻痺 paralysis of the anus; proctoparalysis;
直腸切除 proctectomy; surgical resection of the rectum;
直腸失禁 rectal incontinence;
直腸痛 pain at the anus; pain in the rectum; rectalgia;
直腸息肉 polyp of rectum;
直腸性便秘 proctogenous constipation;
直腸炎 inflammation of the rectum; proctitis;
潰瘍性直腸炎 ulcerative proctitis;
直腸直肚 frank; outspoken; straightforward;
直腸周圍炎 inflammation around the rectum; paraproctitis;
巨直腸 megarectum;

［直陳］ describe truthfully; state frankly;

［直達］ go non-stop to; through;
直達車 nonstop express; through train;

［直待］ go on waiting;

［直搗黃龍］ follow in hot pursuit right up to the enemy headquarters; march to the enemy's heartland; press forward to the enemy's capital; smash the enemy lair; sotrm the enemy's den;

［直到］ (1) till; until; (2) up to;

［直道］ (1) straight path; (2) talk candidly;
直道事人 serve a person with the right path;

［直瞪瞪］ stare blankly;

［直供不諱］ give the truth without reserve;

［直觀］ intuitive; object; visual;
直觀編輯 visual editing;
直觀教學 object teaching;
直觀預測 intuitive forecasting;

［直哼哼］ groan with pain;

［直話］ frank speech; outspoken remarks;

［直己］ devote oneself to justice;

［直減率］ lapse rate;
幹絕熱直減率 dry adiabatic lapse rate;
濕絕熱直減率 wet adiabatic lapse rate;
溫度直減率 lapse rate of temperature;

［直諫］ admonish without reserve;

［直角］ right angle;
直角形 rectangular;
~雙直角形 birectangular;

［直接］ direct; directness; firsthand; immediate;
直接標價 direct quotation;
直接賓語 direct object;
直接成本 direct cost;
直接成分分析法 immediate constituent analysis;
直接詞匯對等 direct terminological equivalence;
直接對等 direct equivalence;
直接法 direct method;
直接翻譯 direct translation;
直接教學法 direct method;
直接税 direct tax;
直接引語 direct speech;

［直截］ blunt; flat and plain; point-blank; simple and direct; straightforward;
直截了當 bluntly; by the string rather than the bow; cold turkey; come down to brass nails; come from the shoulder; come straight to the point; decisive; downright; flat; flat and plain; flat-footed; forthright; get down to brass nails; get down to brass tacks; in explicit terms; in no uncertain terms; in straightforward terms; outright; outspoken; plump; pointblank; say

without mincing words; simple and direct; straight from the shoulder; straightforward; up and down; without any beating about the bush; without circumlocution; without further ado; with preamble; without preliminaries;
直截了當地說 put it baldly;

[直徑] (1) diameter; (2) straight path;
共軛直徑 conjugate diameters;
角直徑 angular diameter;
近似直徑 approximate diameter;
平均直徑 average diameter;
天線直徑 antenna diameter;
原子直徑 atomic diameter;

[直覺] hunch; intuition;
直覺告訴我 my hunch is that;

[直立] stand erect;
豎直立 stand erect on one's hands;

[直諒] honest and understanding;

[直溜] straight;
直溜溜 straight;

[直流電] direct current;

[直前] go straightforward;
奮勇直前 screw up one's courage and push forward;
勇往直前 advance bravely; advance courageously; drive fearlessly forward; go boldly ahead; go bravely ahead; go bravely forward; go forward courageously; go forward fearlessly; go forward without hesitation; forge ahead dauntlessly; forge ahead valiantly; march fearlessly onward; march forward courageously; stride bravely forward; take one's courage in both hands;

[直情徑行] act heedlessly; go one's own way;

[直嚷嚷] groan with pain;

[直入] go right in;
單刀直入 a cold turkey; by the string rather than the bow; come directly to the point; come right to the point; come straight to the point; cut the cackle and come to the horses; make a direct attack on subject; point-blank; speak without beating about the bush; without preamble; without preliminaries;

[直上] rise quickly;
扶搖直上 be promoted quickly in official career; be successful in one's career; get up the social ladder quickly; on the rapid rise; rise directly to a high position;

[直射] collineation;

[直升機] copter; helicopter;
直升機機場 heliport;
直升機停機坪 helicopter pad;
救護直升機 helicopter aerial ambulance;
武裝直升機 gunship;
消防直升機 fire-fighting helicopter;

[直視] look steadily at;
瞠目直視 wild-eyed with surprise;

[直書] write straightforwardly;
肆筆直書 let go the pen and write as on thinks;

[直屬] under the direct control of;

[直率] candid; frank; outspoken; straightforward;
不夠直率 lacking in frankness;
為人直率 frank with sb;

[直爽] candid; forthright; frank; straightforward;

[直説] say out;

[直挺挺] bolt upright; stiff; straight;

[直通] lead directly to; reach directly;

[直系] direct line relative;
直系的 lineal;
直系後代 lineal descendants;
直系親屬 direct relation;

[直轄] directly under the jurisdiction of;

[直下] deteriorate steadily;
急轉直下 go into a precipitous decline; rapid deterioration of a situation; sudden change for the worse; sudden turn for the worse; take a sudden decisive turn; turn abruptly towards a new vista;

[直線] (1) straight line; (2) sharp; steep;
直線管理 line management;
直線經理 line manager;
直線球 straight ball;

[直銷] direct sale;
直銷員 door-to-door salesman;

[直形鍋] stewing pan;

[直言] frank remarks; speak bluntly; state outright;
直言賈禍 be persecuted for one's frank criticism; be punished for having voiced one's critical opinions; frankness in speech causes trouble;

straight talk brings trouble;
直言勸諫 use blunt words to remonstrate;
直言無諱 outspoken in one's remarks; speak one's mind out;
直言無隱 give sb a bit of one's mind; speak one's mind; tell the truth without reservation;
直言相告 lay one's cards on the table;
持愛直言 crasping your love for me, I take leave to speak without reservation;
恕我直言 excuse me for speaking bluntly; to put it bluntly;

[直譯] literal translation; word-for-word translation;
直譯詞 teral translation word;
半直譯 semi-literal translation;

[直喻] simile;

[直指] point;
直指詞 pointer word;

[直至] till; until; up to;

筆直 as straight as an arrow; hold upright; in a beeline; perfectly straight;
秉直 (1) frank and honest; (2) adhere to correct principles;
垂直 perpendicular; vertical;
剛直 upright and outspoken;
耿直 fair and just; honest and frank; integrity; straight forward; upright;
鯁直 honest and frank;
憨直 honest and straightforward; honest and upright;
簡直 actually; all right; almost; almost exactly; at all; borders on; complete; downright; enough; fairly; hardly; literally; little short of; might as well; nothing but; nothing less than; nothing short of; scarcely; sheer; simply; so...as to; so much so that; so...that; such...as to; such...that; to the point of; veritable;
僵直 rigidity; stiff;
徑直 directly; straightaway;
梏直 straightforward in disposition;
樸直 honest and straightforward; simple and honest;
鉛直 plumb; vertical;
強直 rigid;
峭直 severe; stern;
曲直 right and wrong;
伸直 straighten; stretch out;
率直 blunt; candid; candour; frank; honest; straight; straightforward; unreserved;
爽直 candid; forthright; frank; outspoken; straightforward;
坦直 straightforward;
挺直 erect; straight and upright;
悻直 bluff; blunt; brusque;
一直 (1) all along; all the time; all the way; all the while; all through; always; as ever; as the day is long; constantly; continuously; ever since; from...till; hold; keep; on end; till; to this day; until; used to be; (2) go straight forward;
迂直 impractical and artless;
愚直 stupidly honest;
正直 candid and fair; fair-minded; honest; rectitude; straight-forward and unbiased; up and up; upright; upright and honest;
質直 simple and honest; solid and straightforward;
忠直 faithful and upright; straightforward;
戇直 blunt and tactless; simple and honest; simple and upright;
嘴直 speak frankly; speak out without reservation;

zhi

【姪】 (1) nephew; niece; (2) I; me;

[姪兒] nephew;

[姪婦] wife of one's nephew;

[姪女] niece; one's brother's daughter;
姪女婿 one's niece's husband;

[姪孫] grandnephew; one's brother's grandson;
姪孫女 grandniece; one's brother's granddaughter;

[姪子] nephew; one's brother's son;

表姪 son of a male cousin;
內姪 wife's nephew;
子姪 sons and nephews;

zhi

【指】 (1) finger; (2) direct; point; (3) indicate; mean; refer to; (4) number of people; (5) intentions; (6) main theme; (7) hope; (8) depend on;

[指板] finger-board;

[指標] index; index arm; index sign; indicator; norm; quota; target;
純指標 net indicator;
軟指標 soft target;
完成指標 hit the target;
線性指標 linear indicator;

主要經濟指標 main economic indicators;

[指斥] denounce; reprove;

[指出] a sign of; lay one's finger on; point out; show clearly;
指出錯誤 point out faults;
指出缺點 point out sb's shortcomings;
必須指出 it must be pointed out;
最新報告指出 according to a new report;

[指導] conduct; direct; guidance; guide; instruct; supervise;
指導教授 supervisor;
指導人 supervisor;
指導委員會 guiding committee;
指導員 counselor; supervisor;
~就業指導員 employment counselor; guidance counselor;
多謝指導 thank you for your advice;

[指點] advise; give directions; give pointers; instruct; show how; teach;
指點迷津 Ariadne's thread; point out the right way to sb when he goes astray; show sb how to get on the right path;
指指點點 (1) gesticulating; (2) indicate; point; point out;

[指定] allocate; appoint; assign;
指定產品 appointed products;
指定代理 agency by appointment;
指定用途補助金 indicated grants;

[指法] fingering;

[指腹為婚] prenatal betrothal;

[指骨] bones of fingers;
指骨過短 brachyphalangia;
指骨缺失 ectrophalangia;
指骨頭 head of phalanx of fingers;
指骨炎 phalangitis;

[指顧間] in a short while;
指顧間事 happen very soon; in a matter of moments; in no time at all;

[指歸] main theme;

[指痕] fingermark;

[指環] ring;
鑲玉指環 a ring inlaid with a gem;

[指揮] (1) command; conduct; direct; (2) commander; director; (3) conductor;
指揮棒 baton;
指揮部 command post; headquarters;
~最高指揮部 high command;
指揮艙 command module;
指揮官 commandant; commander; commanding officer;
~副指揮官 second-in-command;
指揮交通 direct traffic;
指揮若定 direct a battle steadily; direct with perfect ease; give competent leadership; perfectly calm and collected in commanding the army;
男指揮 drum major;
女指揮 conductress; directress; drum majorette; majorette;
親自坐陣指揮 assume personal command;
瞎指揮 blind direction; blindly order others about; give arbitrary directions; give blind directions; issue confused orders; mess things up by giving wrong orders; order about arbitrarily;
總指揮 commander-in-chief;

[指雞罵狗] abuse one over the shoulder of another; make oblique accusations; point at one thing and abuse another; point at the chicken and curse the dog; scold a person indirectly;

[指甲] fingernail;
指甲草 balsamine;
指甲刀 nail clipper;
指甲銼 nail file;
指甲肥大 onychauxis;
~單純指甲肥大 hyperonychia;
指甲過小 micronychia;
指甲剪 nail clippers; nail scissors;
指甲砂銼 emery board;
指甲刷 nailbrush;
指甲修護師 manicurist;
指甲營養不良 onychodystrophy;
指甲硬化 scleronychia;
指甲油 fingernail polish; nail polish;
~抹指甲油 paint one's nail;
灰指甲 onychomycosis;
剪下的指甲 nail parings;
巨指甲 megalonychia;
弄斷指甲 break one's nail;
染指甲 paint fingernails;
手指甲 finger nail;
修指甲 manicure;
咬指甲 bit one's nails; chew one's nails;

[指跡] fingermark;

[指尖] fingertip;

[指間襞] interdigital fold;

[指間潰瘍] ulcus interdigitale;

[指教] direction and guidance; give advice; give comments;
敬請指教 humbly request your advice;

please give me your advice;

[指節] knuckle;

[指痙攣] dactylospasm;

[指靠] count on; depend on; look to;

[指控] accuse; allegation; charge;

承認指控 admit a charge;

否認指控 deny a charge;

面臨指控 face charges;

未經證實的指控 unproven allegations;

刑事指控 criminal charge;

嚴重指控 serious charge;

重罪指控 felony charge;

[指擴張] digital dilation;

[指令] (1) direct; instruct; order; (2) directive; instruction; order; (3) command; instruction;

指令按鈕 command push button;

指令常數 instruction constant;

指令格式 instruction format;

指令時間 instruction time;

指令系統 instruction system;

指令性計劃 mandatory planning;

指令性文摘 indicative abstract;

指令語言 command language;

比較指令 comparison order;

編碼指令 code order;

初始指令 origin directive;

分支指令 branch order;

基本指令 basic instruction;

絕對指令 absolute instruction; absolute order;

算術指令 arithmetical instruction;

條件指令 conditional order;

優先指令 advantage instruction;

有效指令 actual instruction;

[指路] point the way;

指路標 finger post; guidepost; signpost;

指路明燈 a beacon lighting up one's way forward; the beacon light;

指路牌 finger post; fingerboard; guidepost; road delineator; signpost;

[指鹿為馬] call a stag a horse; call white black; distort facts; talk black into white;

[指迷] give advice; give guidance; indicate the way; show the way;

[指名] mention by name; name; single out by name;

指名道姓 identify by name the person; mention sb's name; name names;

指名辱罵 call a person names; insult someone by using bad names;

[指明] demonstrate; indicate clearly; point out; show clearly; single out;

指明出路 point the way out;

指明原因 demonstrate the cause;

[指模] fingerprint;

指模學 dactylography;

[指南] fingerpost; guide; guidebook; how-to; manual;

指南車 southward pointing cart;

指南針 compass;

旅行指南 guidebook;

入門指南 primer;

用法指南 instruction manual;

用戶指南 user manual;

[指派] appoint; assign; designate; name;

[指認] identify from a group;

[指日] in a few days; in a matter of days;

指日高陞 get promoted soon;

指日可成 can finish in a few days; can perform the deed in a day;

指日可待 able to count for the days; can be expected soon; close at hand; in the near future; just around the corner; point and day and await for it;

指日可數 the days...are numbered;

指日為誓 swear by the sun;

[指桑] point at the lime tree

指桑道槐 name the lime tree but really mean the acacia — hidden allusions and innuendoes;

指桑罵槐 a veiled abuse; abuse a person by ostensibly pointing to someone else; abuse one over the shoulder of another; curse one thing while pointing to another; make oblique accusations; mock the locust on behalf of the mulberry tree; scold the locust while pointing at the mulberry;

[指使] incite; instigate; put sb up to sth;

暗中指使 work the ropes;

背後有人指使 be instigated by sb behind;

目指氣使 give order by look or glance — bossy to others; order people about by gesture;

受人指使 act at sb's instigation;

[指示] (1) indicate; point; (2) instruct; (3) directive; instruction; (4) direction; presentation; reading;

指示詞 deixis;

~地點指示詞 place deixis;
~話語指示詞 discourse deixis;
指示代詞 demonstrative pronoun;
指示燈 signal;
~轉向指示燈 turn signal;
指示劑 indicator;
指示量 indicatrix;
~漫射指示量 diffusion indicatrix;
~球面散射指示量 spherical indicatrix of scattering;
指示器 detector; indicator; pointer;
~方位指示器 bearing pointer;
~合格指示器 accepted indicator;
~加速度指示器 acceleration indicator;
~接觸指示器 contact pointer;
~絕對壓力指示器 absolute pressure indicator;
~目標命中指示器 on-target detector;
~偏心度指示器 eccentricity detector;
~數據指示器 data pointer;
指示物 indicator;
指示線 indicatrix;
~光學指示線 optical indicatrix;
~曲率指示線 curvature indicatrix;
指示形容詞 demonstrative adjective;
指示意義 deictic meaning;
指示語 indicator;
指示者 indicator;
差頻指示 beat frequency indication;
發出指示 give instructions;
返回指示 back indication;
接受指示 take instructions;
明確指示 specific instructions;
日曆指示 calendar indication;
書面指示 written instructions;
一項指示 an instruction;
異常指示 abnormal indication;
止損指示 stop-loss order;
遵守指示 observe instructions;

[指數] exponent; index; index number;
指數化 indexation;
~價格指數化 indexation of prices;
股票指數 share index; stock index;
股市指數 stock market index;
結晶指收 crystalline indices;
金融指數 financial index;
晶體指數 crystal indices;
絕熱指數 adiabatic exponent; adiabatic index;
老化指數 ageing index;
臨界指數 critical exponent;
磨耗指數 resistance index;
磨蝕指數 abrasion index;
生活費指數 cost of living index;
收斂指數 convergence exponent;
微分指數 differential exponent;
物價指數 commodity price index;
虛指數 imaginary exponent;
狀形指數 form exponent;
綜合指數 composite index;

[指算] (1) count by fingers; (2) use of the abacus;

[指頭] finger;
十個指頭有長短 even the ten fingers cannot be of equal length — men are not all perfect; fingers are unequal in length — you can't expect everybody to be the same;

[指望] (1) count on; look forward to; look to; (2) hope; prospect;
空指望 forlorn hope; vain hope;

[指紋] dactylogram; fingerprint;
指紋法 dactylography;
指紋鑒定法 dactyloscopy;
指紋結構 dactylotype;
指紋譜 dactylogram;
指紋學 dactylography;

[指向] direct to; point to;

[指壓] acupressure;

[指要] essential points; theme;

[指引] guide; index; point the way; show;
指引卡 guide card;
指引性信息 indexical information;
課程指引 curriculum guide;

[指印] fingerprint;

[指責] accuse; animadvert; censure; charge; chide; condemn; criticize; disparage; find fault with; finger-pointing;
指責應受指責的 lay the blame at the right door; lay the blame on the right shoulder;
受良心的指責 be afflicted with a conscience;
受指責 get the blame;
無可指責的 blameless;
嚴加指責 flay; scold;

[指摘] blame; censure; criticize; pick faults and criticize; point out the faults of others;
信人雌黃的指摘 airy censure;

[指掌] fingers and palms;
了如指掌 be conversant with; have sth at

one's fingertips; know like the back of one's hand; know sth like a book; know sth thoroughly;
瞭如指掌 know the alpha and omega of sth; know thoroughly;
~對事情瞭如指掌 know the alpha and omega of things;
惜指失掌 spoil the ship for a ha'p'orth of tar; stint a finger onely to lose the whole hand — try to save a little only to lose a lot;
易如指掌 a piece of cake; as easy as ABC; as easy as child's play; as easy as damn it; as easy as falling off a log; as easy as pie; as easy as shelling peas; as easy as turning one's palm over; as easy as winking; at a hand's turn;

［指針］ (1) guide; manual; (2) arrow; index; indication needle; (3) hands of a clock;
單頭指針 single-headed arrow;
風向指針 wind arrow;
航道指針 course arrow;
一根指針 a hand;

［指正］ (1) point out mistakes so that they can be corrected; (2) make a comment or criticism;

［指證］ produce evidence; prove;

暗指 give a hint; hint; imply; innuendo; insinuate;
大拇指 thumb;
大指 thumb;
二拇指 forefinger; index finger;
髮指 boil with anger; bristle with anger;
泛指 be used in a general sense; make a general reference; refer to sth in general;
將指 (1) middle finger; (2) big toe;
腳指 toe;
戒指 ring;
蘭花指 orchid-shaped fingers;
拇指 (1) thumb; (2) big toe;
屈指 count on one's fingers;
染指 take a share of sth one is not entitled to;
食指 forefinger; index finger;
手指 finger;
彈指 a short moment;
特指 refer in particular to;
無名指 ring finger;
五指 five fingers;
小拇指 little finger;
中指 middle finger;

zhi

【值】 (1) value; valuable; (2) deserve; worth; worthy of; (3) happen to; (4) on duty; on the shift; take one's turn at sth;

［值班］ on duty; on the shift; on watch;
值班者 watchkeeper;

［值得］ be worthy of; deserve; worth;
值得考慮 worth considering;
值得同情 deserve sympathy;
值得玩味 worth pondering; worth ruminating over;
值得一看的 be well worth a visit; watchable;
不值得的 unworthy;

［值錢］ costly; expensive; valuable;

［值勤］ on duty;
值勤表 duty roster; roster; rota;
值勤人員 personnel on duty;

［值日］ on duty for the day; one's turn to be on duty;

保值 hedge appreciation; preserve the value of sth;
比值 specific value; ratio;
幣值 currency value;
貶值 (1) devaluate; devalue; fall in value; go down in value; (2) depreciate;
不值 not worth;
插值 interpolation;
產值 output value;
初值 initial value;
當值 on duty;
調值 tone pitch;
二值 two-valued;
峰值 peak value;
根值 root-value;
估值 appraisement; value of assessment;
極值 extreme; extremum;
計值 evaluation;
價值 (1) value; (2) worth;
淨值 net value; net worth;
絕對值 absolute value;
輪值 be on duty in turns;
面值 (1) face value; par value; (2) denomination;
恰值 just at the time of;
熱值 calorific value;
色值 colour value;
昇值 appreciate; go up in value; increase in value; rise in value;
時值 duration value;

適值 coincidentally; happen by coincidence; happen exactly when; just when;
數值 figure; magnitude; numerical number; numerical value; value;
酸值 acid value;
現值 current value;
音值 value;
正值 it happened just when; just at that time;
增值 appreciate; rise in value;
主值 basic magnitude; principal value;
中值 mean;
總值 total price; total value;

zhi

【執】 (1) grasp; hold; seize; (2) direct; execute; take charge of; (3) arrest; detain; (4) maintain; persist in; stick to; uphold;

［執筆］ do the actual writing; write;
倩人執筆 ask sb to write on one's behalf; ghostwrite;

［執鞭］ act as a coach driver for sb;
執鞭隨鐙 hold sb's whip and follow his stirrup; hold the whip and walk by the stirrups of sb's saddles;

［執法］ enforce the law; execute the law; law enforcement;
執法必嚴 laws already enacted must be enforced to the letter; strict in enforcing the law;
執法犯法 break laws while in charge of their enforcement; the law-enforcement personal are found guilty of law-breaking activities;
執法如山 adhere to legal principles without fear; be firm as a rock in administering justice; uphold the law strictly; enforce the law strictly; vigorous enforcement of laws;
執法人員 law enforcer;
執法相繩 observe the law and measure with a plumb-line;

［執紼］ attend a funeral;
執紼送殯 attend a funeral; hold a staff wrapped in white paper in the funeral procession;

［執教］ teacher;

［執經問難］ students holding the classics and making inquiries;

［執柯］ matchmaker;
執柯作伐 arrange the match; engage an agent; matchmaker;

［執禮］ observe the formalities; stick to etiquette;
執禮甚恭 treat sb with great respect;

［執迷不悟］ adhere to one's foolish way without awakening; adhere to one's wrong course without awaking; obstinately refuse to listen to reason; obstinately stick to a wrong course; persist in one's wrong course; perverse; refuse to come to one's senses; refuse to admit one's error; refuse to mend one's way; refuse to realize one's error; stick with wrong ideas;

［執拍］ hold the racket;
執拍手 racket hand;

［執拗］ pig-headed; recalcitrant; stubborn; wilful;

［執事］ deacon;
女執事 deaconess;

［執手］ hold hands;
執手同行 walk together;
執手同游 saunter holding each other's hand;
執手為禮 shake hands;

［執委會］ executive committee;

［執行］ carry out; enforce; execute; implement;
執行程序 executive programme;
執行範圍 scope of execution;
執行功能 performing function;
執行官 executive officer;
~首席執行官 chief executive officer;
執行機構 actuator;
執行紀律 enforce the discipline;
執行秘書 executive secretary;
執行任務 carry out a task; perform a mission;
執行系統 executive system;
執行長 chief executive officer;
執行者 enforcer; executor;
程序執行 programme execution;
獲准執行 get the green light; receive the all clear;
解釋執行 interpretive execution;
拒不執行 refuse to carry out; refuse to execute; refuse to implement; refuse to perform;
強令執行 arbitarily give orders to carry out sth;
強制執行 compulsory execution;

停止執行 halting execution;
逐步執行 step execution;

[執業] (1) engage in a profession or trade; (2) vocation or trade;
執業律師 legal practitioner; practising lawyer;
執業醫生 medical practitioner; practising doctor;

[執意] be bent on; be determined to; insist on;
執意不從 obstinately refuse to yield;

[執友] bosom friend;

[執掌] in control of; manage; superintend; take full charge of; wield;

[執照] license; permit;
執照持有人 licensee;
執照費 license fee;
出示執照 show one's license;
吊銷執照 revoke a license;
發執照 grant a license;
獲得執照 get a license;
駕駛執照 driver's license; driving license;
扣執照 forfeit a license;
臨時執照 temporary license;
領執照 take out a license;
配給執照 distribution license;
申請執照 apply for a license;
授予執照 award a license;
營業執照 business license;

[執政] at the helm of the state; hold power; hold the reins of the government; in office; in power;
執政黨 the party in power; the ruling party;
開始執政 come into power;

[執中] follow the middle road; impartial; keep to the golden mean;

[執着] inflexible; persist in; punctilious; rigid;
如此執着 so insistent;

存執 counterfoil; stub;
父執 friends of father's generation;
固執 obstinate; persist in; stick to; stubborn;
回執 (1) short note acknowledging receipt of sth; (2) receipt;
堅執 insist strongly;
拘執 rigidly adhere to;
爭執 disagree; dispute;

zhi

【植】 (1) grow; plant; (2) erect; establish; set up;

[植被] vegetation; vegetation cover;
植被圖 vegetation chart;
植被型 vegetation form; vegetation type;
草本植被 herbosa;
沉水植被 submerged vegetation;
地面植被 ground vegetation;
浮現植被 emerging vegetation;
荒漠植被 desert vegetation;
本本植被 lignose;
沼澤植被 swamp vegetation;
自然植被 natural vegetation;

[植耳而聽] prick up one's ears to listen—listen attentively;

[植立] erect; set up;

[植樹] plant trees;
植樹還林 afforestation;
植樹運動 afforestation campaign;
~義務植樹運動 voluntary afforestation campaign;

[植物] plant; vegetation;
植物半球 vegetative hemisphere;
植物分類學 phytotaxonomy; systematic botany;
植物構造學 structural botany;
植物極 plant pole;
植物激素 plant hormone;
植物界 the plant world;
植物開花 a plant flowers;
植物區系 flora;
~北極高山植物區系 arctalpine flora;
~淡水植物區系 fresh-water flora;
~異源植物區系 allogenous flora;
植物群 flora;
植物人狀態 vegetative state;
植物生理學 plant physiology;
植物生長 a plant grows;
植物學 botany;
~古植物學 palaeobotany;
植物岩 phytolith;
~非可燃性植物岩 acaustophytolith;
植物油 vegetable oil;
~一桶植物油 a pipe of vegetable oil;
植物園 botanical garden;
白蘞屬植物 ampelopsis;
伴人植物 synanthropic plant;
被子植物 angiosperm;
草本植物 herb; herbaceous plant; herbage;
~常綠草本植物 evergreen herbage;
~多年生草本植物 perennial herb;
~高草本植物 altoherbosa;
~海生草本植物 marine herb;

~鋪地草本植物 carpet herb;
草屬植物 grass; weed;
~牛舌草屬植物 anchusa;
草原植物 psilophyte;
常綠植物 evergreen plant;
常見植物 common plant;
沉水植物 submerged plant;
蟲媒植物 entomophilous plant;
葱屬植物 allium;
單細胞植物 unicellular plant;
單子葉植物 monocotyledon;
當歸屬植物 angelica;
頂生植物 acrogen;
動物形植物 zoophyte;
豆科植物 legume;
短生植物 ephemeral plant;
~春季短生植物 vernal ephemeral plant;
多年生植物 perennial;
芳香植物 scent plant;
附生植物 air plant;
~半附生植物 hemiepiphyte;
~樹上附生植物 epiphyte arboricosa;
高山植物 alpine; alpine plant;
古老植物 relic plant;
旱生植物 xerophilous plant;
濶葉植物 broadleaved plant;
寄生植物 parasite plant;
寄主植物 host plant;
近親植物 close relative plant;
蕨類植物 fern; pteridophyta;
開花植物 anthophorous plant;
兩棲植物 amphiphyte;
鱗莖植物 bulb plant;
陸生植物 terrestrial;
綠生植物 greenery;
蔓生植物 overgrowth; trailing plant;
蜜腺植物 nectarous plant;
木本植物 ligneous plant;
木材植物 xylplant;
內長植物 endogenous plant;
攀緣植物 climbing plant;
培育植物 cultivate plants;
盆栽植物 pot plant; potted plant;
氣生植物 aerial plant;
纖維植物 fibrous plant;
染料植物 dye plant;
熱帶植物 tropical plant;
肉莖植物 stem succulent;
森林植物 forestry growth;
砂土植物 silicicola;
食蟲植物 insectivorous plant;
食菌植物 fungivorous plant;
雙子葉植物 dicotyledon;
水底植物 benthophyte;
水生植物 aquatic plant;
獸煤植物 zoophilous plant;
土著植物 indigenous plant;
外來植物 exotic plant;
外長植物 exogenous plant;
維管植物 vascular plant;
無葉植物 aphyllous plant;
稀有植物 rare plant;
喜氮植物 nitrophilous plant;
喜鈣植物 calciphilous plant;
喜鹼植物 alkaline plant;
喜砂植物 psammophilous plant;
喜濕植物 hygrophilous plant;
喜溫植物 thermophilous plant;
喜鹽植物 halophilous plant;
喜蟻植物 ant plant;
喜雨植物 ombrophile;
先鋒植物 pioneer;
嫌風植物 anemophobe;
嫌鈣植物 calciphobous plant;
嫌寒植物 frigofuge;
嫌鹼植物 basifuge;
嫌酸植物 oxyphobe;
嫌雪植物 chionophobous plant;
嫌鹽植物 halophobe;
嫌雨植物 ombrophobe;
顯花植物 phanerogamia;
鄉土植物 indigenous plant;
陽性植物 light-demanding plant;
藥用植物 medical plant;
野生植物 wild plant;
一年生植物 annual;
~蕨類一年生植物 pteridotherophyte;
~水生一年生植物 hydrotherophyte;
一種植物 a kind of plant;
異域植物 exotic plant;
隱花植物 cryptogamia;
隱芽植物 cryptophyte;
陰地植物 shade plant;
陰性植物 shade-demanding plant;
優勢植物 dominant plant;
有花植物 flowering plant;
油料植物 oil plant; oil-pressing plant;
園藝植物 garden plant;
雜交植物 hybrid plants;
~培育雜交植物 cultivating hybrid plants;
栽培植物 cultivated plant;
沼生植物 helophyte;
針葉植物 conifer;
指向植物 compass plant;

中溫植物 mesotherm;
種子植物 seed plant;
自養植物 autophyte;

裁植 planting;
春植 plant in spring;
定植 field planting;
扶植 foster; groom sb to be; prop up;
密植 close planting;
培植 cultivate; culture; foster; educate; foster; raise; train;
手植 plant personally;
移植 (1) transplant; (2) graft;
栽植 plant; transplant;
再植 replant;
種植 grow; plant;

zhi

【殖】 (1) breed; grow in abundance; multiply; prosper; (2) colonize;

[殖民] colonize; establish a colony; settle people in a less developed area;
殖民地 colony;
~ 殖民地居民 colonial; colonist;
殖民政策 colonial policy;
殖民主義 colonialism;
~ 殖民主義者 colonialist;
~ 新殖民主義 neocolonialism;

繁殖 breed; propagate; reproduce;
貨殖 engage in trade;
墾殖 reclaim and cultivate wasteland; reclaim land and live on it; reclaim wasteland and go in for production;
生殖 engender; generate; procreation; reproduction;
養殖 breed;
增殖 (1) hyperplasia; multiplication; (2) reproduce;
滋殖 reproduce in large numbers;

zhi

【跖】 (1) sole of the foot; (2) name of a notorious robber;

[跖狗吠堯] everyone is for his master; side with the wicked and hate the wise;

zhi

【摭】 collect; pick up from the ground; take up;

[摭採] collect;
[摭取] (1) collect; pick up; take; (2) plagiarize;
[摭拾] collect; pick;
摭拾群言 collect views from various sources;
摭拾遺文 make random quotes from obsolete writings;

zhi

【質】 (1) character; disposition; nature; temperament; (2) quality; (3) matters; substances; (4) plain; simple; (5) question; (6) pledge; (7) mortgage; pawn;

[質壁分離] plasmolysis;
初始質壁分離 incipient plasmolysis;
臨界質壁分離 critical plasmolysis;
明顯質壁分離 evident plasmolysis;
[質變] change in substance;
[質成] ask a third party to arbitrate a dispute;
[質地] quality; texture;
質地堅韌 strong but pliable in texture;
質地精良 excellent in quality; of best quality;
質地考究 superior in quality;
質地細密 fine-grained; of a close texture;
質地優良 excellent in quality; fine quality; superior quality;
[質點] particle;
[質對] check; verify;
[質光] mass luminosity;
質光關係 mass-luminosity relation;
[質粒] plasmid;
質粒嵌合體 plasmid chimera;
[質量] (1) mass; (2) quality;
質量保證 quality assurance;
質量差的 piss-poor;
質量詞 quality word;
質量第一 quality first;
質量工程 quality engineering;
質量管理 quality management;
質量好 have quality;
質量監督 quality surveillance;
質量鑒定 appraisal of quality;
質量控制 quality control;
質量評比 quality appraisal;
質量審核 quality audit;
質量數 mass number;
質量信息 quality information;
質量要求 quality requirements;
質量因素 quality factor;
質量中心 centre of mass;
保證質量 guarantee of quality;
肥育質量 feeding quality;

感官質量 aesthetic quality;
量少質差 lacking in quantity and quality;
臨界質量 critical mass;
劣等質量 bottom quality;
洗煉質量 affining quality;

[質料] quality; raw material;

[質明] dawn; daybreak;

[質樸] plain; simple and unadorned; unaffected;
質樸無華 simple and artless; unsophisticated;
剛健質樸 vigorous and simple;
談話質樸 speak with simplicity;
為人誠懇質樸 honest and unaffected;

[質讓] admonish bluntly;

[質數] prime number;

[質素] quality;
質素評估 quality assessment;
~翻譯質素評估 translation quality assessment;
翻譯質素 translation quality;

[質體] plast;
原生質體 protoplast;

[質問] call to account; interrogate; query; question;
質問證人 interrogate the witness;
一連串的質問 a battery of questions;

[質詢] address inquiries to; ask for an explanation; interpellate;
議會質詢 parliamentary inquiry;

[質言] honest talk; plain talk;
質言之 in other words; in short; put it bluntly; to put it in plain language;

[質疑] call into question; query; question;
質疑問難 raise doubts and difficult questions for discussion;
提出質疑 raise a query;

[質直] simple and honest; solid and straightforward;
質直好義 upright and righteous;

[質子] proton;
質子化 protonize;
蛻變質子 disintegration proton;
反衝質子 recoil proton;
核質子 nuclear proton;
水合質子 hydrated proton;
陰質子 negative proton;

zhi

【縶】 (1) bind; connect; tie; (2) imprison; (3) bridle;

[縶維] retain;

zhi

【蟄】 hibernate;

[蟄蟲] dormant insects; hibernating insects; torpid insects;

[蟄伏] (1) hibernate; (2) lie low;

[蟄居] live in seclusion;

[蟄雷] first spring thunder;

[蟄蟄] in a cluster; in a swarm;

zhi

【擲】 cast; throw;

[擲地] throw to the ground;
擲地有聲 extremely elegant and valuable;

[擲還] return sth to me;

[擲交] hand over;

[擲球] throw;
裁判擲球 referee throw;
正手擲球 forehand throw;

[擲下] please hand it to me;

zhi

【職】 (1) duty; job; (2) office; post;

[職別] level of position; official rank;

[職稱] professional ranks and titles;
職稱改革 reform in professional titles;
職稱評定 evaluation of professional titles;
專業職稱 professional title;

[職等] grade of position; official rank;

[職分] (1) duty; (2) official post; position;

[職工] (1) staff and workers; staff members; (2) labour; workers;
職工福利 employee welfare;
~職工福利資金 employee welfare fund;
職工會 labour union;
初級職工 junior staff;
輔助職工 auxiliary staff;
固定駐地職工 stationary staff;
合同職工 contract workers;
技術職工 technical staff;
寄宿職工 lodged staff;
解僱職工 discharge employees;
精減職工 cut down labour force; reduce the number of staff and workers;
臨時職工 short-term worker;
流動職工 mobile staff;
留宿職工 accommodated staff;
外勤職工 outdoor staff;
運營職工 operational staff;
在職職工 active staff;
正式職工 regular staff;

Z

[職官] one's official position and duties;

[職能] function;

職能地位 functional status;

擴大職能 extend functions;

社會職能 social function;

政府職能 government functions;

[職權] authority of office; function and power; powers of office;

職權範圍 limits of one's functions and powers; terms of reference;

超越職權 exceed one's power;

濫用職權 abuse one's power;

利用職權 abuse prerogatives; exploit one's office; take advantage of one's position and power;

行使職權 exercise one's functions and powers;

有職無權 be a figurehead; have a nominal appointment; hold a position without the authority that goes with it; hold the post but not the power;

有職有權 be entrusted with the responsibility and authority that should go with one's post; exercise the functions and powers that go with a post; exercise the power that goes with one's post; have authority commensurate with one's posts; hold both the post and the authority;

[職任] one's position in an office;

[職守] duty; post;

安於職守 stay at one's post;

各安職守 each minds his own business; stay at their posts;

克盡職守 strictly observe one's duty;

曠離職守 desert one's post;

擅離職守 absence without leave; desert one's duties;

疏於職守 negligent of one's duties;

玩弄職守 negligence; neglect one's duties;

玩忽職守 derelict in one's duties; dereliction; negligence of duty; remiss; remissness;

忠於職守 be devoted in one's duty;

[職位] position; post;

職位共享 job-sharing;

部級職位 ministerial post;

獲得職位 get a duty;

接受職位 accept the post;

免除職位 depose;

穩定的職位 steady job;

[職務] duty; function; job; post;

職務津貼 duty allowance;

職務評估 job evaluation;

職務意識 post consciousness;

保留職務 retain the post;

代行職務 fill the breach; step into the breach;

放棄職務 throw up one's job;

履行職務 perform a job;

~履行職務能力 job performing ability;

實際職務 active duty;

謝絕職務 decline a duty;

終身職務 permanent job;

[職系] grade;

一般職系 general grades;

[職銜] post and rank; the official title of a person;

[職業] calling; career; occupation; profession; vocation;

職業安定 have security of employment;

職業保障 job security;

職業病 occupational disease;

職業大學 vocational college;

職業道德 professional ethics;

~職業道德教育 professional ethics education;

職業翻譯員 professional translator;

職業輔導 occupational guidance;

職業婦女 career women;

職業顧問 career counselor; careers advisor; careers officer;

職業技能 job skill;

職業技術 professional skills;

~職業技術教育 professional technical education;

~職業技術學校 vocational technical school;

~職業技術中學 vocational technical high school;

職業教育 occupational education;

職業介紹所 employment agency;

職業流動 professional floating;

職業女性 career woman;

職業前途教育 livelihood education;

職業社會學 occupational sociology;

職業心理學 occupational psychology;

職業性翻譯 professional translation;

職業性犯罪 occupational crime commitment;

職業選擇 job selection;

職業學校 vocational school;
職業訓練 job training; occupational training; vocational training;
職業治療 occupational therapy;
職業中學 vocational high school;
職業中毒 occupational poisoning;
改變職業 change one's occupation;
固定職業 fixed occupation; regular occupation;
~無固定職業 have no fixed occupation;
~有固定職業 have a regular occupation;
選擇職業 choose a profession;
自謀職業 find a job by oneself;

[職員] functionary; office worker; staff member;
職員宿舍 staff quarters;
白領職員 white-collar employee;
教職員 teaching and administrative staff;
增加職員 augment the staff;

[職責] duty; obligation; responsibility;
職責所在 duty-bound;
安全職責 safety responsibilities;
翻譯職責 translation task;
解除職責 dissolve the responsibilities;
履行職責 do one's duty;
勤於職責 apply oneself to one's duty in business;
一項職責 a duty;

[職掌] (1) in charge of; (2) charges; duties;
[職志] lifework; mission;

罷職 dismiss; remove from office;
本職 one's job;
貶職 demote;
撤職 be dismissed from office; be removed from office; dismiss sb from his post; remove sb from office;
稱職 come up to the scratch; competent; fill a post with credit; worth one's salt;
褫職 deprive sb of his post; remove sb from office;
辭職 hand in one's resignation; quit office; resign; send in one's jacket; send in one's papers; stand down; submit one's resignation;
到職 arrive at one's post;
調職 be transferred to another post;
瀆職 dereliction of duty; malfeasance;
復職 reinstate an official to the former position; reinstate sb in one's former office; reinstatement; resume one's post;
高職 high position;
革職 be discharged from office; deprive sb of his post;
公職 public employment; public office;
供職 hold office;
官職 government post; official position;
兼職 hold two or more posts concurrently;
解職 dismiss from office; relieve sb of his post;
盡職 fulfill one's duty;
就職 accede to an office; assume office; come into office; enter upon office; get into office; go into office; take office;
厥職 its; their;
軍職 official post in the army;
曠職 be absent from duty without leave;
浪職 neglect one's duty;
離職 (1) leave office; resign; (2) leave one's job temporarily;
留職 retain one's post;
免職 be dismissed from one's post; remove sb from office;
溺職 dereliction; negligence of duty;
去職 no longer hold the post; quit office;
任職 hold a post; take office;
聖職 holy post;
失職 delinquent; dereliction of one's duty; neglect one's duty; negligence of duty; negligent in the performance of duties;
守職 stick to one's duty;
授職 confer a rank; give an official job to;
曠職 dereliction of duty;
述職 report on one's work;
順職 dutiful; live up to one's duty;
天職 natural duty;
停職 suspend sb from his duties; suspend sb from office; suspension;
退職 resign from office;
文職 civil post;
武職 position of a military officer;
閒職 official post with very little to do; sinecure;
現職 present post;
削職 deprive a person of a position;
殉職 die at one's post; die in line of duty; die on one's job;
要職 important post;
在職 be at one's post; be on the job;
正職 principal post;
專職 (1) sole duty; specific duty; (2) full-time;

zhi

【躕】 falter; hesitate;
[躕躅] (1) faltering; hesitant; (2) azalea;

zhi

【蹠】 (1) step on; tread on; (2) sole of the foot;

［蹠骨］ metatarsal bones;

zhi

【躑】 falter; hesitate;

［躑躅］ loiter around; walk to and fro;

躑躅而行 shuffle along; stagger; uncertain whether to advance or retire; walk with a mincing step; walk with a shuffling gait;

躑躅街頭 on the pavement; tramp the streets; wander about the streets;

zhi³

zhi

【止】 (1) cease; desist; still; stop; (2) till; to; (3) only;

［止謗］ stop libels; stop slanders;

止謗莫若自修 nothing stops gossip as correcting one's own way;

［止步］ go no further; halt; stand still; stop;

止步不前 cease to advance; go no further; halt; make no headway; stand still;

游客止步 no visitors;

［止付］ stop payment;

［止戈為武］ military forces are to be used only for the maintenance of peace and order;

［止汗］ check sweating;

止汗藥 antihidrotic;

［止境］ end; limit; terminal point;

無止境 have no boundary; have no limits; know no end;

~ 漫無止境 know no bounds; limitless; on and on; without limit;

~ 學無止境 knowledge has no limit; knowledge is infinite; learning is an endless process; there is no end to learning; there is no limit to knowledge;

~ 永無止境 know no end; of no bounds; world without end;

［止咳］ relieve a cough; stop coughing;

止咳糖 cough drop; cough lozenge; cough sweet;

止咳糖漿 cough syrup; linctus;

止咳藥水 cough medicine; cough mixture; cough syrup;

［止渴］ assuage thirst; quench thirst;

止渴生津 quench thirst and help produce saliva;

止渴消勞 relieve thirst and fatigue;

生津止渴 help produce saliva and slake thirst;

望梅止渴 console oneself with false hopes; feed on fantasy; the sight of plums quenches one's thirst – imagined satisfaction;

飲鴆止渴 drink poison to quench thirst – seek temporary relief regardless of the disastrous consequence; quench a thirst with poison – a supposed remedy having the opposite effect; stop thirst by drinking poison – temporary relief which results in disaster;

［止怒］ stop anger;

［止熱］ abort a fever;

［止水］ stagnant water; still water;

止水不波 still water does not have ripples;

心如止水 a mind tranquil as still water; one's mind settles as still water; the heart is like still water;

［止痛］ assuage pain; kill pain; relieve pain; stop pain;

止痛藥 analgesic; painkiller;

［止息］ cease; stop;

［止瀉］ stop diarrhea;

止瀉藥 antidiarrheal;

［止血］ stanch bleeding; stop bleeding;

止血藥 styptic;

［止癢］ alleviate itching; relieve itching; stop itching;

［止於］ stop at; this far and no further;

止於至善 arrive at supreme goodness;

［止住］ bring to a stop; desist; halt; stop;

不止 (1) incessantly; without end; (2) exceed; more than; not limited to;

底止 end; limit;

遏止 check; hold back; stop;

防止 avoid; forestall; guard against; prevent;

廢止 abolish; annul; put an end to;

何止 far more than; not only;

截止 close; end;

禁止 ban; bar; clamp down on; debar; forbid; lay an embargo on; lay ban on; place a check on; place sth under a ban; prohibit; proscribe; put sth under ban; put the lid on; under ban; under embargo;

靜止 at a standstill; motionless; static;
舉止 bearing; demeanour; front; habit; manner; mien;
涖止 arrive; present;
棲止 dwell; settle at a place; sojourn; stay;
豈止 much more than; not at all limited to;
起止 beginning and end; start-stop;
勸止 advise sb not to; dissuade sb from;
容止 appearance and manner; looks and carriage;
逝止 going and staying;
衰止 dye out;
停止 at a halt; at a standstill; at an end; bring an end to; bring to a halt; bring to a standstill; call a halt; call off; cease; close; come off it; come to a conclusion; come to a halt; come to a standstill; come to an end; conclusion; cry a halt; desist; end; fall calm; grind to a halt; halt; make an end of; pause; put an end to; stop; suspend; terminate; wind up;
為止 till; up to;
限止 limit; restrict;
行止 (1) whereabouts; (2) behaviour; conduct;
休止 cease; stop;
仰止 admiration;
抑止 check; restrain;
遮止 stop sb's progress;
知止 know where to stop;
制止 check; prevent;
中止 discontinue; suspend;
終止 (1) end; stop; (2) terminate; (3) cadence;
阻止 block; debar; hold back; prevent; prohibit; proscribe; stop;

zhi

【只】 (1) merely; only; (2) but; yet;
［只得］ be obliged to; have to; there is no alternative;
［只顧］ (1) care about only; (2) please do not hesitate to;
［只管］ as you wish; please do not hesitate to;
［只好］ have to; the next best thing to do is to; the only alternative is to;
［只見］ (1) see only; (2) behold;
［只可］ can only;
［只怕］ afraid of only one thing;
［只是］ (1) but; yet; (2) just; merely; only;
［只消］ have only to; just; need only; only;
［只要］ (1) want only; (2) all one has to do is to;
［只因］ for the simple reason that; only because;
［只有］ (1) alone; only; (2) have to;

不只 not merely; not only;
僅只 only;

zhi

【旨】 (1) intention; objective; purpose; will; (2) imperial decree; (3) beautiful; excellent; good; (4) delicious; pleasant to the palate; tasty;
［旨甘］ dainties; delicacies;
［旨歸］ (1) principle; (2) objective;
［旨酒］ good wine;
［旨趣］ objectives; purports;
［旨意］ (1) decree; order; (2) intention; will;
［旨在］ with the intention of;

奧旨 main theme;
本旨 real intention; real meaning;
大旨 general idea; main points;
法旨 God's decree;
甘旨 delicacies;
弘旨 main theme of an article;
宏旨 leading idea of an article; main theme;
聖旨 imperial directive; imperial edict; imperial will;
希旨 cater to the wishes of a superior;
要旨 gist; main idea;
意旨 intention; wish;
諭旨 imperial edict;
主旨 gist; substance;
宗旨 aim; purpose;

zhi

【址】 foundation; land on which to build a house; location;

按址 according to the address;
廠址 factory site;
地址 address; location; site;
廢址 abandoned site;
故址 site of an ancient monument, etc.;
會址 (1) site of an association; (2) site of a conference or meeting;
校址 the location of a school;
舊址 old address;
新址 new address;
網址 website address;
遺址 relics; ruins;
原址 former address;
住址 home address;

Z

zhi

【沚】 sandy islet in a stream; small sandbank;

zhi

【阯】 address; site;

zhi

【芷】 angelica;

白芷 root of Dahurian angelica;

zhi

【咫】 (1) ancient measure of length; (2) near;

［咫尺］ very close;

咫尺天涯 so near and yet so far;

咫尺之間 only a short distance; very close;

近在咫尺 a very short distance away; but a few feet from here; close at hand; right under the nose of sb; well within reach;

~近在咫尺，遠若山河 near each other as we are, we are as far apart as if separated by hills and rivers;

zhi

【祉】 blessedness; blessings; happiness; welfare;

［祉祿］ happiness and wealth;

zhi

【祇】 just; merely; only;

［祇得］ be obliged to; have no alternative but; have to;

［祇顧］ (1) be absorbed in; (2) merely; only care for; simply;

［祇管］ (1) by all means; not hesitate to; (2) just; merely;

［祇好］ be forced to; have no other alternative but; have to;

祇好作罷 be forced to give up; have to be dropped;

［祇怕］ afraid of only one thing;

［祇是］ (1) just; merely; only; (2) simply;

［祇消］ all one has to do is; you only need to;

［祇要］ all; any; as long as; as soon as; at all; but; enough; if; if...but; if only; in so far as; just; on condition that; once; only; provided; provided that; simply; so; so far as; so long as; so much as; so that; the moment; what; when; where; while;

祇要功夫深，鐵杵磨成針 constant dropping wears the stone; constant grinding can turn an iron rod into a needle — perseverance spells success; if you work at it hard enough, you can grind an iron rod into a needle — the future becomes the present if you fight for it; with time and patience the leaf of the mulberry becomes satin;

祇要人手多，牌樓搬過河 many hands make light work;

祇要有水，何患無魚 there is as good fish in the sea as ever comes out of it;

［祇有］ alone; have nothing but; only;

祇有船靠岸，哪有岸靠船 if the hill will not come to Mohammed, Mohammed will go to the hill; if the mountain will not come to Mohammed, Mohammed must go to the mountain;

祇有錯買，沒有錯賣 it is the buyer, not the seller, that errs; the buyer needs a hundred eyes, the seller not one;

祇有天知道 God alone knows; goodness knows; heaven knows;

祇有招架之功，並無還手之力 can only parry sb's blows without being able to hit back; only able to defend oneself but unable to hit back; with strength enough only for defence but not to hit back;

［祇知其然，不知其所以然］ know only that sth is so but not why it is so; know only the hows but not the whys; know only what is done but not why it is done;

zhi

【指】 same as 旨；

zhi

【枳】 (1) bramble; (2) a variety of orange with very thick skin;

［枳橙］ citrange;

［枳落］ thorn hedge;

［枳維］ maintain a relationship;

zhi

【紙】 paper;

［紙板］ cardboard;

紙板盒 cardboard box; cartoon;

紙板圖樣 cardboard cut-out;

紙板屋區 cardboard city;

一層紙板 a thickness of cardboard;

[紙包不住火] a secret cannot be kept forever; fire cannot be wrapped in paper; murder will out; paper cannot wrap up a fire; truth will out;

[紙背] back of the paper;

力透紙背 one's vigour penetrates to the back of the paper;

[紙幣] banknote; paper money;

假紙幣 funny money;

[紙薄] as thin as paper;

官情紙薄 human feelings of sympathy are as thin as paper in officialdom;

[紙盒] carton; paper box;

單層紙盒 single-layer carton;

硬紙盒 carton;

折疊紙盒 lock carton;

[紙花] paper flowers;

[紙婚] first wedding anniversary; paper wedding;

[紙漿] paper pulp; pulp;

化學紙漿 chemical pulp;

慢煮紙漿 low boiled pulp;

濃紙漿 thick pulp;

生紙漿 raw pulp;

稀薄紙漿 lapped pulp;

[紙巾] tissue;

厚紙巾 paper towel;

一盒紙巾 a box of tissue;

[紙牌] playing cards;

[紙錢] nether banknotes;

燒紙錢 burn nether banknotes;

[紙片] scraps of paper;

一張紙片 a scrap of paper;

[紙傘] oilpaper umbrella;

[紙扇] paper fan;

[紙上] on paper;

紙上談兵 academic talks; armchair strategy; empty talks; engage in idle theorizing; fight only on paper; impractical schemes; indulge in empty talk; make plans without reality; mere paper talk; use empty words;

躍然紙上 full of life; vivid;

[紙條] slip of paper;

一張紙條 a slip of paper;

[紙屑] scraps of paper;

五彩紙屑 confetti;

[紙煙] cigarette;

[紙業] paper enterprise; paper industry;

[紙張] paper; sheets of paper; stationery;

一疊紙張 a heap of paper;

[紙醉金迷] given to sensual pleasures; indulge in a wanton life; lead a voluptuous life; live in luxury;

紙醉金迷，聲色犬馬 wallow in the fleshpots;

靶紙 target sheet;
白報紙 newsprint;
板紙 board; paperboard;
包裝紙 wrapping paper;
報紙 (1) newspaper; (2) newsprint;
玻璃紙 cellophane wrapper;
捕蠅紙 flypaper;
布紋紙 wove paper;
蚕紙 paper with silkworm eggs;
蒼蠅紙 flypaper;
草紙 (1) rough straw papery; (2) toilet paper;
襯紙 interleaving paper; slip sheet;
打字紙 typing paper;
道林紙 mechanical pulp-free printing paper;
電報紙 telegraph form;
電子紙 electronic paper;
方格紙 squared paper;
放大紙 enlarging paper;
仿紙 sheets with printed letters for children to practise calligraphy;
廢紙 waste paper;
複寫紙 carbon paper;
複印紙 uplicating paper;
感光紙 sensitive paper;
稿紙 draft paper;
隔音紙 sound insulating paper;
公文紙 paper for copying documents;
橫格紙 lined paper;
活頁紙 paper for a loose-leaf notebook;
火紙 touch paper;
糊壁紙 wall paper;
糊墻紙 wall paper;
剪紙 paper-cut; scissor-cut;
捲煙紙 cigarette paper;
拷貝紙 copy paper;
繪圖紙 drawing paper;
蠟光紙 glazed paper;
蠟紙 stencil;
濾紙 filter paper;
馬糞紙 strawboard;
綿紙 tissue paper;
面巾紙 face tissue;
描圖紙 tracing paper;
描寫紙 tracing paper;

敏化紙 sensitized paper;
牛皮紙 kraft paper;
皮紙 tough paper;
契紙 contract; deed;
墻紙 wall paper;
輕磅紙 light-weight paper;
曬圖紙 blueprint paper;
色紙 coloured paper;
砂紙 abrasive paper; sand paper;
燒紙 paper made to resemble money and burned as an offering to the dead;
石印紙 lithographic paper;
試紙 test paper;
手紙 toilet paper;
透明紙 cellophane; cellophane paper;
圖畫紙 drawing paper;
圖紙 blueprint; drawing;
土紙 handmade paper;
衛生紙 toilet paper;
吸墨紙 blotting paper;
錫紙 tin foil; silver paper;
顯影紙 developing-out paper;
相紙 photographic paper;
新聞紙 (1) newspaper; (2) newsprint;
信紙 letter paper; writing paper;
羊皮紙 parchment;
一刀紙 one hundred sheets of paper;
一捆捆紙 bundles of paper;
一捆紙 a bale of paper;
一令紙 a ream of paper;
一張紙 a piece of paper; a sheet of paper;
印刷紙 printing paper;
油紙 oilpaper;
有光紙 glazed paper;
造紙 papermaking;
折紙 paper folding;
鎮紙 paperweight;
製圖紙 drawing paper;
皺紋紙 crepe paper;
竹紙 paper made from young bamboo;
狀紙 plaint; written complaint;
字典紙 bible paper;
字紙 wastepaper with characters written on it;

zhi

【趾】 (1) toe; (2) foot; (3) footprints; tracks;

［趾高氣揚］ above oneself; arrogant; as proud as a peacock; as proud as Punch; be bloated with arrogance; carry one's head high; cocky; crow over; drag oneself up; draw oneself up; get a swelled head; give oneself airs and swagger about; high and mighty; hold one's head high; in all one's splendour; lift one's head high; on one's high horse; on stilts; proud as a peacock; proud as a stack on fire; puff one's chest out; put on an elated look; put on the ritz; raise the horn; ride one's high horse; step high and look proud; swagger about and give oneself airs; with one's head in the air;

［趾骨］ phalanx of the foot;
趾骨過短 brachyphalangia;
趾骨炎 phalangitis;

［趾關節］ digital joints;

［趾甲］ toenail;
趾甲過小 micronychia;
趾甲硬化 scleronychia;
巨趾甲 megalonychia;

［趾尖］ tiptoe;

［趾間］ interdigital;
趾間襞 interdigital fold;
趾間潰瘍 interdigital ulcer;
趾間皮炎 interdigital dermatitis;

［趾痙攣］ dactylospasm;

［趾裂］ toe crack;

［趾膿腫］ toe abscess;

［趾水腫］ dactyledema;

［趾脫落］ dactylolysis;
自發性趾脫落 dactylolysis spontanea;

［趾彎曲］ clinodactyly;

［趾炎］ dactylitis; inflammation of a toe;

腳趾 toe;
蹼趾 webbed toe;

zhi

【軹】 ends of an axle;

zhi

【黹】 embroidery; needlework;

針黹 needle work;

zhi

【酯】 ester;

聚酯 polyester;
醛酯 aldehydoester;

zhi

【徵】 one of the five musical notes in Chinese scale;

zhi4
zhi

【至】 (1) arrive at; reach; (2) till; to; until; (3) extremely; most; very;

[至寶] most precious asset; most valuable treasure;
奉若至寶 revere sth as a priceless treasure; treat sth as one's most valuable treasure; value sth highly;
如獲至寶 as if a precious jewel has fallen into one's hands; as if one has found a treasure; as if one has obtained an extremely valued treasure; like acquiring a rare treasure; receive sth like a godsend; rejoice over a windfall; seem to have hit the jackpot;

[至材] extremely gifted; extremely talented;

[至誠] complete sincerity; sincere; the greatest sincerity;
至誠高節 person of supreme sincerity and nobility;
至誠格天 sincerity moves heaven;
至誠所至，金石為開 no difficulty is insurmountable if on sets one's mind on it;
一片至誠 a true heart; candid; in all sincerity; open-hearted;

[至遲] at the latest; no later than;

[至此] (1) arrive here; come here; (2) have come this far; have developed to this point;

[至大] extremely large; greatest;
至大至剛 exceedingly great and exceedingly strong; the greatest and most unbending;

[至當不移] most suitable and not subject to change;

[至德] the highest virtue;

[至多] all; at best; at most; maximum; no more than; the most;

[至公] absolutely just; absolutely unbiased;
至公無私 absolute justice and no prejudice;

[至好] (1) simply wonderful and fabulous; the best; (2) closest friend; great friend;

[至急] extremely urgent; most urgent;

[至極] extremely; the most; to the utmost degree;

[至交] alterego; one's best friend; one's closest friend; one's most intimate friend;
至交契友 an intimate and congenial friend; bosom friend;

[至今] so far; to this day; until now; up to now; up to the present time; yet;

[至靠] most dependable friend;

[至樂] extremely happy and jubilant;

[至親] one's close kin; one's close kinsman; one's very close relative;
至親友好 one's close relations and dear friends; one's close relatives and good friends;

[至情] the most genuine feeling;

[至人] (1) person of virtue; sage; saint; (2) perfect person;
至人無己 a sage is selfless;
至人無夢 a virtuous man seldom has dreams;

[至仁] highest degree of kindness and magnanimity;

[至日] winter and summer solstices;

[至如] as to; with regard to;

[至若] as to; come to; with regard to;

[至善] the highest level of virtue; the supreme good;
至善至美 it is perfection itself;
臻於至善 at one's best;

[至上] (1) highest; supreme; (2) come first;

[至少] at any rate; at least; on any account; the least;

[至聖] Confucius;
至聖先師 Confucius;
至聖至明 most sagacious and intelligent;

[至死] till death; to the last; unto death;
至死不變 stick to one's course until the end of one's days; unswerving till death; will not change even unto death;
至死不改 refuse to change to the very end;
至死不屈 die game; not yield till death;
至死不悟 hold on to one's wrong belief till death; incorrigibly stubborn; never to repent even at death's door; not to repent even unto death;
至死不渝 never to change even unto death; remain faithful until death; remain unswerving until death;
至死方休 be released only by death; not stop until death;

至死無大事 nothing is dreadful to a person who is willing to die;
奮戰至死 fight to the death;
[至孝] extremely filial;
[至心] the most sincere heart;
[至言] (1) words of the utmost importance; (2) the most virtuous utterances;
[至要] imperative; the most important;
是為至要 which is very important;
[至友] (1) close friend; (2) closest friend;
[至意] the best and sincerest intention;
[至於] as for; as regards; as to; go as far as; with regard to; with respect to;
不至於 go so far as to; may not be as...as one might...; unlikely;
[至尊] the most august;
北至 summer solstice;
備至 in every possible way; to the utmost;
冬至 Winter Solstice;
分至 tropic;
及至 (1) leading to; so...as to; so that; (2) consequently; hence;
截至 by; up to;
乃至 and even;
甚至 as...as; enough; even; far from; go so far as to; if anything; if not more; in fact; indeed; nay; nor yet; not a; not a single; not once; not one; not to say; or more; reflexive pronoun; so...that; so far from; so much so that; such...that; the comparative; the superlative; very; yews;
俟至 wait until;
沓至 come one after another without stop;
夏至 June solstice; Summer Solstice;
一至 to such extent;
以至 (1) down to; up to; (2) to such an extent as to;
涌至 arrive like a flood;
湧至 arrive like a flood;
聿至 arrive suddenly;
直至 (1) till; until; (2) up to;
踵至 arrive just behind; arrive upon the heels of another;
周至 attentive and satisfactory; considerate; thoughtful;
驟至 arrive suddenly; come without warning;

zhi

【志】 (1) ambition; aspiration; desire; ideal; (2) determination; purpose; will; (3) keep in mind; (4) annals; records; (5) mark; sign;
[志操] ambition and moral fortitude;
[志酬意滿] have one's wish fulfilled and rest satisfied;
[志大] ambitious;
志大才疏 ambitious but incompetent; have great ambition but little talent; have high ambition but no real ability; have high aspirations but little ability; high in aim but low-rate in execution;
才疏志大 have great ambition but little talent; bitch one's wagon to a star; inspire more than one can achieve; one's ability falling short of one's aspiration;
[志得意滿] complacent; fully contented;
[志怪] record the weird, occult and mysterious;
[志堅如鋼] have a will of steel; have an iron will; with a will as strong as steel;
[志節] one's ambition and moral fortitude;
[志略] (1) ambition and talent; (2) record the general outline; (3) annal; sketch; synopsis;
[志氣] ambition; aspiration; will;
志氣軒昂 aim high in life;
很有志氣 full of ambition;
沒志氣 without ambition;
人憑志氣，虎仗其威 men rely on their will and tigers on their strength;
長他人志氣，滅自己威風 boost the enemy's moral and dampen one's own spirit; laud the spirit of the enemy and belittle that of our own; puff up the enemy's moral and lower one's own;
長志氣 enhance the spirit; fortify the high resolve; fortify the will;
[志趣] aspiration and interest; inclination;
志趣相投 after one's own heart; congenial; congenial to; congenial with; find each other congenial; friends of similar purpose and interests; have similar aspiration and interest; have the same aspirations and interests; hit it off; like-minded; of like mind;
~志趣相投的人 like-minded people;
[志士] honest patriot; person of high ambitions; person of ideals and integrity; person of purpose and virtue;

志士仁人 kind and upright men; people of purpose and virtues; people who are actuated by high ideals; people who have high ideals; people with lofty ideals;

[志同道合] cherish the same ideals and follow the same path; have a common goal; hit if off well together; in the same camp; of one mind; share the same ambition and purpose; share the same view; two minds with but a single thought;

[志向] ambition; aspiration; ideal;
志向遠大 one's aspiration is far-reaching;
~ 志向遠大的人 person of vaulting ambition;
實現志向 fulfil one's ambition;

[志行] principle and conduct; purpose and behaviour;

[志學] dedicate oneself to the pursuit of learning;

[志願] (1) aspiration; ideal; wish; (2) do sth of one's own free will; volunteer; voluntarily;
志願工作 voluntary work;
志願社團 voluntary association;
志願者 volunteer;

大志 great ambition; lofty aspiration;
得志 attain one's ambition; have a successful career;
鬥志 fighting spirit; will to fight;
篤志 earnestly resolve to;
方志 local chronicles;
弘志 great ambition;
惑志 doubt; suspicion;
立志 be determined; resolve;
墓志 epigraph; inscription on the memorial tablet within a tomb;
奇志 lofty aspirations;
鋭志 determination; earnest intention; sharp will; spirit of enterprise;
喪志 destroy the mind; lose one's ambition; lose one's determination;
伸志 have one's ambition fulfilled;
神志 consciousness; senses;
矢志 swear that one will never change;
肆志 be puffed up with pride;
夙志 long-cherished ambition;
素志 long-cherished ambition;
宿志 long-cherished ambition;
他志 other ambitions; other ideas;
同志 comrade;
遐志 lofty ambition; lofty aspiration;
縣志 county chronicle;
心志 ambition; fortitude; will; will power;
蓄志 have had an ambition for a long time;
遺志 unfulfilled wish;
意志 will;
遠志 great and far-reaching ambition;
異志 disloyal heart;
逸志 easy-going habit;
意志 volition; will; will power;
毅志 ambition; determination;
有志 aspire;
職志 life work;
壯志 great ambition; great aspirations; lofty ideal;

zhi

【忮】 dislike; jealous;

[忮求] greedy for sth; jealous and greedy;
不忮不求 generous to others and lacking greediness; neither jealous nor greedy;

[忮心] jealousy;

zhi

【豸】 reptiles without feet;

蟲豸 insects;
獬豸 legendary animal;

zhi

【制】 (1) establish; institute; set up; (2) formulate; work out; (3) control; overpower; prevail; restrict; (4) system;

[制幣] standard currency;

[制裁] punish; sanction;
道德制裁 moral sanction;
法律制裁 legal sanctions;
經濟制裁 economic sanctions;
貿易制裁 trade sanctions;
強制性制裁 compulsory sanction;
取消制裁 lift sanctions;
實施制裁 impose sanctions;
實行制裁 impose sanctions upon;
予以制裁 mete out punishment to sb;

[制導] guidance;
波速制導 beam guidance;
全程制導 all-way guidance;
全慣性制導 all-inertial guidance;
聲學制導 acoustic guidance;
主動制導 active guidance;

[制定] draft; draw up; enact; establish;

Z

formulate; institute; lay down; set up; work out;
制定法令 draft laws and decrees;
制定法律 draw up laws;
制定規章 lay down rules and regulations;
制定計劃 make a plan;
制定政策 formulate policies;

[制動] apply the brake; brake;
制動燈 brake light;
制動距離 braking distance;
制動器 arresting gear; brake;
~差動制動器 differential brake;
~複動制動器 double-acting brake;
~副制動器 auxiliary brake;
~均壓制動器 counter pressure brake;
~空氣制動器 air brake;
~盤式制動器 disc brake;
~配重制動器 counter weight brake;
~皮帶制動器 belt brake;
~平衡制動器 balanced brake;
~汽車制動器 automotive brake;
~氣力制動器 atmospheric brake;
~氣壓制動器 air pressure brake;
~吸收制動器 absorption brake;
~錐形制動器 conic brake;
~自動制動器 automatic brake;
制動液 brake fluid;
大氣制動 aero-braking;
階段制動 graduated application;
緊急制動 emergency application;

[制度] institution; system;
制度化教育 institutionalized education;
制度性術語 institutional term;
制度性文獻 institutional text;
法律制度 legal institutions; legal system;
封建制度 feudalism;
規章制度 rules and regulations;
教育制度 system of education;
奴隸制度 slavery;
政治制度 political institution;
綜合制度 comprehensive system;

[制服] (1) bring under control; conquer; overcome; prevail over; put down; quell; subdue; surmount; (2) uniform;
制服敵人 subdue an enemy;
穿着制服 be in uniform;
一套制服 a uniform;

[制海權] command of the sea; naval supremacy;

[制衡] check and balance;
制衡的 countervailing;
制衡原理 the principle of checks and balances;

[制空權] air domination; air supremacy; control of the air;

[制錢] coins officially designated for circulation;

[制勝] be victorious; prevail; triumph; win;
克敵制勝 defeat the enemy and win victory; gain mastery over the enemy; vanquish the enemy; win victory over the enemy;

[制式] regular; regulation;

[制限] (1) confine; limit; restrict; (2) bound; limit; confines;

[制憲] draw up a national constitution;
制憲會議 constituent assembly;

[制壓] (1) overpower; overwhelm; suppress; (2) neutralize;

[制宜] make measures to suit different conditions;
因地制宜 act according to the circumstances; act in accordance with the circumstances; adapt to local conditions; adopt measures suiting local conditions; do sth in line with local conditions; do the right thing at the right place; do what is appropriate according to the regional circumstances; do what is suitable to the environment; hinge on local conditions; suit measures to local conditions; take appropriate measures in accordance with local conditions; take measures suited to local conditions;
因人制宜 suit measures to different people; treatment chosen according to the variability of physique of an individual;
因時制宜 act according to the circumstances; act according to the time; act in accordance with the times; do the right thing at the right time; do what is appropriate according to the circumstances; do what is suitable to the occasion; in a manner suitable to the time; take measures suited to the time;
因事制宜 circumstances alter cases; do what is suitable to the occasion; suit measures to different things;

[制約] condition; constraint; restraint; restriction;
倒行制約 retroactive inhibition;
功能制約 functional constraint;
共軛制約 conjugate constraint;
交叉制約 cross-over constraint;
內包制約 inclusion constraint;
施事制約 agent constraint;
順行制約 proactive inhibition;
循環制約 cyclic constraint;
[制止] check; curb; face down; prevent; put an end to; stop;
[制作] formulate;

百分制 hundred-mark system;
幣制 currency system;
編制 (1) weave braid; (2) draw up; work out;
兵役制 system of military service;
兵制 military system;
裁制 curtail; restrict;
代議制 representative system of government;
單位制 system of unit;
抵制 (1) boycott; (2) resist;
帝制 imperial system; monarchy;
定制 customized; have sth made to order;
扼制 check; choke; control; keep under control by force;
遏制 keep down; suppress;
二部制 two-shift system;
二進制 binary system;
法制 legal system;
父權制 patriarchy;
改制 reform a system;
工役制 requirement system of labourers working on public projects;
公有制 public ownership;
公制 metric system;
官制 bureaucratic establishment;
管制 (1) control; (2) put under surveillance;
國會制 parliamentarism;
國有制 state ownership system;
合議制 collegiate system;
機制 (1) machine-made; machine-processed; (2) mechanism;
建制 organizational system;
節制 (1) abstinence; abstinency; chasten; check; control; moderate in; (2) command; control;
舊制 old system;
君主制 monarchy;
郡縣制 the system of prefectures and counties;
克制 control; exercise restraint;
控制 be brought under control; bridle; bring under control; command; contain; containment; control; curb; dominate; gain control of; get command of; get under control; govern; have command over; have control of; have control over; have under control; in control of; in the hands of; keep one's hands on; keep under control; lead sb by the nose; reign; take control of; under sb's thumb; under the control of;
聯邦制 federal system;
兩黨制 two-party system;
兩院制 two-chamber system;
輪班制 system of working in shifts;
美制 American system;
米制 metric system;
秒制 second system;
母權制 matriarchy;
募兵制 mercenary system;
奴隸制 slave-owning system;
配給制 ration system;
牽制 check; contain; curb; hold at bay; manacle; pin down; restrain; tie down; tie up;
鉗制 contain; hold fast; hold tight; immobilize; keep under control with force; pin down; tie down;
箝制 force; pin down; use pressure upon;
強制 compel; force;
全日制 full-time;
三班制 system of working in three shifts;
三熟制 triple-cropping system;
十進制 decimal system;
私有制 private ownership;
守制 remain in mourning for one's parent;
受制 (1) under the control of; (2) endure hardship, etc.;
稅制 tax system;
所有制 system of ownership;
淘汰制 elimination system;
體制 set-up; structure; system; system of organization;
調制 modulation;
統制 control; govern;
五分制 five-grade marking system;
限制 confine; constraint; cramp; limit; place restrictions on; restraint; restrict; restriction; shut down on;
憲制 constitutional government;
挾制 force sb into submission by taking advantage of his/her weakness;
脅制 coerce;
新制 new system;

形制 shape and structure;
學分制 credit system;
學制 (1) education system; (2) length of schooling;
壓制 (1) stifle; suppress; (2) press;
一院制 one-chamber legislature;
一長制 system of one-man leadership;
抑制 control; inhibition; restrain;
議會制 parliamentarism;
預制 prefabricated;
宰制 dominate; rule;
責任制 system of job responsibility;
徵兵制 university military service;
政制 government hierarchy; political system;
專制 (1) autocratic; despotic; tyrannical; (2) autocracy;
自制 self-control; self-discipline; self-restraint;

zhi

【治】 (1) administer; control; govern; manage; rule; (2) harness; regulate; (3) peace; order; (4) cure; treat; (5) control; wipe out; (6) punish; (7) research; study; (8) a surname;

[治安] peace and order of a nation; public order; public security;
治安很差的 tough;
~治安很差的地區 tough area;
治安機關 law-enforcement agencies;
長治久安 long period of stability;
破壞治安 breach of the peace;
擾亂治安 disturb public order;
維持治安 maintain public order;

[治辦] successful discharge of duties;

[治本] deal with a trouble at the source; effect a permanent cure; get at the root; get at the root of a problem; provide fundamental solutions to the problems; take radical measures; treat a matter thoroughly;
治本之道 the right thing to do to get to the root of the problem;

[治標] cope with the symptoms only; provide temporary solutions to the problems; take stopgap measures;
治標不治本 cure the symptoms, not the disease; palliatives;

[治兵] direct military affairs; lead troops;

[治病] cure the sickness; treat an ailment; treat a disease;
治病救人 cure the sickness and save the patient; help sb mend his ways to save him; set a person right;
治病強身 cure diseases and improve health;
藥苦治病，甜言誤人 bitter medicine is curative, honey words are misleading;

[治功] achievement of managing national affairs;

[治躬] cultivate oneself;

[治國] administer a country; govern a nation; manage state affairs; rule a country;
治國安邦 administer state affairs well and ensure national securtiy;
治國安民 run the country well and give the people peace and securtiy;
治國之才 talent fitted to administer a country; statemanship;
以法治國 genuine rule of law; running the country according to law;

[治洪] flood control;

[治家] manage a household; regulate a family;

[治經] study classics;

[治軍] direct military affairs; direct troops;

[治理] (1) administer; govern; manage; put in order; (2) bring under control; harness; regulate;
治理國家 administer a country; run a country;
治理整頓 harness and rectify; improvement and rectification;

[治療] cure; remedy; treat;
治療見效 respond well to treatment;
治療要求 therapeutic needs;
治療師 healer; therapist;
~職業治療師 occupational therapist;
癌症治療 cancer treatment;
不孕症治療 infertility treatment;
及時治療 give timely treatment;
~得到及時治療 receive timely treatment;
接受治療 get treatment; have medical treatment; receive treatment;
精心治療 give meticulous treatment;
經過治療 undergo treatment;
康復治療 rehabilitation therapy;
驅蟲治療 anthelmintic treatment;
群體治療 group therapy;
入院治療 hospital treatment;
需要治療 need treatment; require treatment;
整體治療 holistic treatment;

住院治療 be hospitalized;

[治亂] order and disorder; peace and upheaval;

治亂興亡 rise and fall of a nation;

治亂之道 proper way of government;

從亂到治 move from chaos to order;

[治平] govern nation and bring peace to the world;

[治戎] use military forces;

[治權] power of a government;

[治喪] funeral service; make funeral arrangements; manage a funeral; take care of the funeral rites;

[治生] make a living;

[治世] times of peace and prosperity;

[治事] transact business;

[治術] the ways and means of a good government;

[治水] prevent floods by water control; regulate rivers and watercourses; river control; tame a river;

治水改土 bring the water under control and improve the soil;

[治絲益棼] make confusion worse confounded; make matters worse; sort out silk threads improperly only to tangle them further — do sth which only makes matters worse;

[治學] devote oneself to learning; do scholarly research; make a study of subjects; pursue one's studies; study;

治學嚴謹 careful and exact scholarship; meticulour scholarship;

[治愈] cure; healing; mend;

治愈疾病 cure a disease;

治愈率 cure rate;

~提高治愈率 improve the cure rate;

無法治愈 incurable;

[治裝] purchase things necessary for a long journey;

[治罪] bring to justice; punish sb for a crime;

包治 guarantee a cure;

懲治 mete out punishment to; punish;

處治 punish;

德治 rule of virtue;

耳治 hear;

法治 govern by law; rule by law;

防治 prevent and cure;

根治 bring under permanent control; cure once and for all; effect a radical cure; fundamental solution;

救治 treat and cure;

涖治 exercise the administration of a government;

吏治 workstyle and achievement of officials;

窮治 manage a matter by first examining into it thoroughly;

人治 rule by man; rule of man;

三明治 butty; sandwich; sarnie;

省治 provincial capital;

食治 food therapy;

調治 recuperate under medical treatment;

統治 (1) dominate; rule; (2) control; govern;

文治 civil administration;

轄治 govern; rule;

縣治 county jurisdiction;

醫治 cure; give medical treatment;

營治 construct;

診治 make a diagnosis and give treatment;

整治 (1) renovate; (2) punish;

政治 political affairs; politics;

郅治 extremely well-governed;

州治 district government; state government;

自治 autonomy; self-government;

zhi

【炙】 (1) broil; burn; cauterize; heat; roast; toast; (2) roast meat;

[炙背] expose the back to the sun;

[炙炒] broil;

[炙乾] dry by applying heat;

[炙火] warm at a fire;

炙手可熱 hot enough to scald one's hands; so hot that it burns one's hand;

焦炙 extremely anxious;

親炙 be personally tutored;

zhi

【帙】 book casing; book wrapper;

卷帙 books; works;

zhi

【峙】 stand erect like a mountain;

zhi

【致】 (1) convey; deliver; present; send; transmit; (2) devote; (3) bring about; incur; occasion; result in; (4) delicate; fine; (5) manner or style that engages attention or arouses interest;

[致哀] express one's condolences; pay one's respects;

[致癌] cancer-causing; carcinogenic;
致癌的 carcinogenic;
致癌物 cancer-causing agent; carcinogen; carcinogenic substance;
~ 大氣致癌物 atmospheric carcinogen;
~ 化學致癌物 chemical carcinogen;
~ 環境致癌物 environmental carcinogen;
~ 潛在致癌物 potential carcinogen;
~ 誘變致癌物 mutagenic carcinogen;
~ 有機致癌物 organic carcinogen;
致癌物質 carcinogenic substance;
致癌作用 carcinogenic action; carcinogenesis;

[致辭] address; deliver a speech; make a speech;

[致電] send a telegram;

[致富] achieve prosperity; acquire wealth; become prosperous; become rich;
不以正道致富 get rich by devious ways;
發財致富 amass great fortunes; enrich; get rich; make one's fortune; make one's pile;
發家致富 build up family fortunes; enrich one's family; enrich oneself; make one's family's fortune;
徒手致富 start out empty-handed and become rich later;
由窮致富 from rags to riches;

[致果] achieve victory; attain results;

[致函] write to;

[致賀] congratulate; extend congratulations; offer one's congratulations;

[致候] send one's regards;

[致敬] pay homage; pay one's respects to; pay tribute to; salute;

[致禮] salutation;
抱拳致禮 express salutations with folded hands; salute with hands folded and raised in front of one's face;

[致力] take special aim at;
致力於 apply oneself to; dedicate oneself to; devote oneself to; engage oneself in; work for;

[致命] (1) causing death; deadly; fatal; lethal; mortal; vital; (2) sacrifice one's life;
致命打擊 deadly blow; fatal blow; lethal blow; mortal blow;
致命弱點 Achilles heel; fatal weakness; heel of Achilles;
致命傷 (1) mortal wound; (2) weak point; vulnerability;
致命事故 fatal accident;
致命一擊 death blow;

[致身] dedicate one's life to;

[致使] bring about; cause; result in;

[致書] send a letter;

[致死] cause death; deadly; lethal; result in death;
致死劑量 lethal dosage; lethal dose;
致死量 lethal dosage; lethal dose;
~ 最小致死量 minimal lethal dose; minimum lethal dose;
單相致死 monophasic lethal;
多相致死 polyphasic lethal;
配子致死 gametic lethal;
平衡致死 balanced lethal;
意外致死 misadventure;

[致送] give; send;
致送紀念品 give sb a souvenir;

[致謝] convey thanks; express one's thanks; extend thanks to; offer thanks; thank;
致謝信 thank-you letter;
向…致謝 a vote of thanks to sb;

[致意] convey one's best regards; convey one's best wishes; give one's regards; present one's compliments; salutation; salute; send one's greeting; with the compliments of;
致意便條 compliment slip;
抱拳致意 salute with hands folded and raised in front of one's face;
點頭致意 nod a greeting; nod in acknowledgement; nod in salutation;
揮帽致意 salute by raising one's hat;
揮手致意 wave greetings to; wave to sb in acknowledgement;
舉杯致意 raise one's glasses in salute;
向人致意 give sb's compliments to; make sb's compliments to; pay one's compliments to; present one's compliments to; send sb's compliments to;
招手致意 wave back in acknowledgement; wave in acknowledgement; wave one's greetings;

[致用] attain practical use; for practical purposes;

[致知] extend one's knowledge;

大致 (1) on the whole; (2) approximately; more or less; roughly;
導致 account for; bring about; bring on; cause; end in; end up in; give rise to; lead to; lead up to; result in;
風致 (1) charming appearance and behaviour; (2) charm and wit; special flavour;
工致 neat and refined;
羅致 collect; enlist the services of; gather together; recruit; secure sb in one's employment;
密致 fine and close;
情致 appeal; temperament and interest;
遂致 consequently; subsequently; thereupon;
所致 as a result of; be caused by; result from; the result of;
興致 eagerness; interest; mood to enjoy; willingness;
雅致 elegant; refined;
一致 consistent; identical; in accordance with; one and all; showing no difference; unanimous; with one accord;
以致 as a result; so that;
引致 cause; give rise to;
誘致 attain an objective by means of temptation;
招致 (1) enlist the services of; recruit; (2) bring about; cause; result in;
轉致 convey through another person;

zhi

【郅】 (1) extremely; very; (2) a surname;
［郅隆］ extremely flourishing; extremely prosperous;
［郅治］ extremely well-governed;
臻於郅治 secure peace and prosperity;

zhi

【秩】 (1) order; orderly; (2) official salaries; (3) decade;
［秩祿］ official salaries;
［秩滿］ completion of the tenure of a public rest;
［秩然］ neat; orderly;
秩然有序 neat and well-arranged; orderly; shipshape;
［秩序］ (1) order; sequence; (2) arrangement;
秩序大亂 in total disorder;
秩序井然 in apple-pie order;
公共秩序 public order;
社會秩序 social order;
~擾亂社會秩序 upset social order;

zhi

【桎】 (1) fetters; shackles; (2) suffocate;
［桎梏］ shackles;
桎梏生靈 fetter and handcuff living beings;
擺脱桎梏 throw off the shackles;
衝破桎梏 break through the shackles;
忍受桎梏 bear the yoke;

zhi

【陟】 (1) ascend; mount; (2) advance; elevate; proceed; promote; (3) (now rare) male horse;
［陟罰］ promote and demote; reward and punish;
［陟級］ be promoted in rank;
［陟降］ promote and demote;
［陟用］ promote to a higher position;

zhi

【痔】 haemorrihoids; piles;
［痔瘡］ haemorrhoids; piles;
［痔核］ blind piles;
［痔漏］ anal fistula;
［痔切除］ haemorrhoidectomy;

內痔 internal piles;
外痔 external piles;
血痔 bleeding piles;

zhi

【窒】 block; obstruct; stop up; stuff up;
［窒礙］ obstacle; have obstacles; obstructed;
［窒悶］ badly ventilated; closed; stuffy;
［窒塞］ block; obstruct; stop up;
［窒息］ smother; stifle; suffocate;
窒息而死 die by suffocation;
窒息作用 asphyxiant action;
幾乎窒息 be almost stifled;
［窒慾］ restrain one's lusts;

zhi

【畤】 place for worshipping the heaven, the earth, and the five sage kings in ancient times;

zhi

【紩】 sew;

zhi

【智】 (1) capable; intelligent; talented; (2) wisdom; (3) prudence; (4) a surname;
［智藏官在］ the wise are left to live in obscurity while the corrupt hold office;

[智鬥] vie in wisdom;
智鬥力敵 a battle of wits and a contest of strength;
智鬥舌戰 argue heatedly; engage in a battle of words and match wits; have a verbal battle with sb;

[智多星] mastermind; resourceful person;

[智慧] intelligence; wisdom; wit;
智慧絕頂 extremely intelligent;
多想出智慧 much thinking yields wisdom;
缺乏智慧 lack wisdom;

[智庫] think tank;

[智力] gray matter; intellect; intelligence; mentality;
智力測驗 intelligence test;
智力差異 intellectual difference;
智力超群 tower above the rest in vigour and height of intellect;
智力常數 intelligence constant;
智力發展 intellectual development;
智力分佈 intelligence distribution;
智力扶貧 help the poor with intelligence;
智力工程 intelligence engineering;
智力過人 extremely intelligent;
智力結構 intelligence structure;
智力競賽 intelligence competition;
~智力競賽機 intelligence competition machine;
智力開發 intellectual development;
智力類型 types of intellect;
智力年齡 intelligence age; mental age;
智力衰退 intellectual deterioration;
智力投資 intelligence investment;
智力引進 import of intelligence;
智力資源 intelligence resources;
抽象智力 abstract intelligence;
鬥智鬥力 fight a battle of wits and a contest of strength;
兒童智力 children's intelligence;
社會智力 social intelligence;
訓練智力 train the intellect;
一般智力 general intelligence;
增強智力 increase intelligence;

[智慮] wisdom;
竭智盡慮 devote one's mental resources to the full;

[智略] intelligence and tact; wisdom and resourcefulness;

[智謀] (1) cleverness; (2) resourcefulness; (3) strategy; tactics;
智小謀大 have too little wisdom to undertake great things;
足智多謀 able and resourceful; full of wrinkle; have one's wits about one; ingenuity; resourceful; shifty; wise and full of stratagems; wise and resourceful; with all one's wits about one;

[智囊] brain truster; brainpower; wise person;
智囊機構 brain making organization;
智囊技術 think tank technique;
智囊流失 brain drain;
智囊人物 think-tanker;
智囊團 brain trust; think tank;
智囊文化 brain trust culture;
智囊中心 think centre;

[智能] brain power; intellect; intellectual ability; intelligence; knowledge and ability; mind;
智能辦公系統 intelligent office system;
智能報盜電話 intelligent alarm telephone;
智能測驗 aptitude test;
智能管理 intelligent administration;
智能卡 smart card;
智能打印機 intelligent printer;
智能犯罪 intelligence crime;
智能分佈系統 distributed intelligence system;
智能複印機 intelligent copier;
智能工作站 intelligent workstation;
智能機器 intelligent machine;
~智能機器人 intelligent robot;
智能計算機 intelligent computer;
智能教育 intelligent education;
智能控制 intellectual control;
~智能控制器 intellectual controller;
~智能控制系統 intelligent control system;
智能軟件 intelligence software;
智能設備 intelligent device;
智能設計 intelligent design;
智能武器 intelligent weapons;
智能型 intelligence;
~智能型辦公室 intelligence office building;
~智能型信息 intelligent messaging;
智能循環 intelligence circulation;
智能儀器 intelligent instruments;
智能印刷機 intelligent printer;
智能終端 intelligence terminal;
機器智能 machine intelligence;

Z

人工智能 artificial intelligence;
智盡能索 at one's wits' end; at the end of one's rope; on one's beam ends;

[智巧] brains and tact;

[智窮] at one's wits' end;
智窮才盡 at one's wits' end; at the end of one's rope; at the end of one's row; at the end of one's resources; at the end of one's tether; come to the end of one's rope; come to the end of one's tether; get to the end of one's tether, reach the end of one's tether; run to the end of one's rope;
智窮計竭 at a loss for a good plan; at one's wits' end;

[智取] outwit; take by strategy;
祇可智取，不可強攻 the only way to take the enemy position is by strategy, not by forceful attack;
祇可智取，不可力敵 must use guile to overcome sth instead of strength; must use strategy instead of force;

[智商] intelligence quotient (IQ);

[智勝] outflank; outfox; outsmart;

[智士] intellect; brainpower;

[智識] knowledge;

[智術] strategem; trickery;

[智牙] wisdom tooth;

[智勇] intelligent and brave;
智勇過人 wiser and bolder than most others;
智勇兼備 combining the qualities of intelligence and bravery; intelligent and brave;
智勇雙絕 exceptionally brave and resourceful;
智勇雙全 both intelligent and courageous; brave and resourceful; combine wisdom with courage; have both skill and dash; intelligent and courageous; wise and courageous; with both mettle and wisdom; with courage and brains combined;

[智愚] the wise and the foolish;
大智若愚 a great intelligent person looks dull; a person of great wisdom often appears slow-witted; a mastermind looks like a fool; great wisdom takes the looks of folly; smooth water runs deep; still waters run deep; the greatest wisdom is like foolishness; the wisest person is often stupid-looking;

[智育] intellectual development; intellectual education;

[智障] intellectual disability;
智障人士 persons with intellectual disabilities;

[智者] sage; wise person;
智者不上兩回當 it is a silly fish that is caught twice with the same bait; the wise will not be fooled twice;
智者改過愚者頑 a wise person changes his mind, a fool never;
智者貴於乘時 the wise person takes the occasion when it serves;
智者樂水 the wise person finds pleasure in streams; the wise person takes pleasure in water;
智者千慮，必有一失 a good marksman may miss; even Homer sometimes nods; even the wise are not free from error; every man has a fool in his sleeve; it is a wise man that never makes mistakes; no man is wise at all times; the best workman sometimes blunders; the wisest man, in a thousand schemes, must make at least one mistake; the wisest man may be overseen;
智者善聽 the wise person is always a good listener;
智者知人 an intelligent person understands others;

才智 ability and wisdom;
低智 below-normal intelligence;
鬥智 battle of wits;
故智 old stratagem;
機智 quick-witted; resourceful;
急智 nimbleness of mind in dealing with emergencies; quick-wittedness;
集智 collective wisdom;
理智 intellect; reason;
明智 sensible; wise;
睿智 wise and far-sighted;
弱智 weak intelligence;
上智 the most intelligent; the wisest;
神智 intelligence; mental ability;
術智 clever and skilful;
黠智 clever; crafty; shrewd; smart;
心智 mentality; the abilities and powers of the mind;
益智 (1) grow in intelligence; (2) longan;

zhi

【痣】 birthmarks; moles; nevus;

色痣 pigmented mole;
胎痣 birthmark;

zhi

【蛭】 leech;

肺蛭 lung fluke;
肝蛭 liver fluke;
水蛭 leech;

zhi

【彘】 hog; pig; swine;

zhi

【稚】 childish; delicate; immature; small; young; young and tender;

[稚蚕] young silkworm;
[稚齒] (1) children; (2) toddlers; (3) young people;
[稚齡] tender age;
[稚女] young girls;
[稚氣] childishness; innocence of a child;
稚氣青年 immature youth;
稚氣舉止 delicate manner;
稚氣猶存 still possess the innocence of childhood;
極為稚氣 extremely childish;
顯得稚氣 look childish;
[稚弱] tender and delicate;
[稚態] pedomorphism;
[稚子] child;

幼稚 (1) young; (2) childish; naïve;

zhi

【置】 (1) place; put; (2) establish; install; set up; (3) buy; procure; purchase;

[置辦] buy; procure; purchase; secure;
置辦家具 buy furniture;
[置備] purchase;
[置辯] argue; defend; explain; rebut; refute;
[置辭] choice of words;
[置後] postpone;
[置換] replacement; substitution;
置換反應 substitution reaction;
金屬置換 metal replacement;
陽離子置換 cation replacement;
直接置換 direct replacement;
[置酒] give a feast; throw a banquet;
置酒款待 give a feast to entertain sb;
[置若罔聞] disregard completely; give no heed to; ignore completely; keep no heed to; keep quiet on; leave sth out of consideration; let slide like water off a duck's back; pay no attention to; pay no heed to; remain indifferent to; seal one's ears to; shut one's ears to; stop one's ears to; take no heed of; take no notice of; treat sth with indifference; turn a deaf ear to;
[置身] place oneself; stay;
置身度外 indifferent; keep oneself from getting involved;
置身局外 keep aloof from; keep out of; not be drawn into; refrain from getting involved; remain aloof from;
置身其間 be involved; put oneself in the midst of;
置身事外 detach oneself from; have nothing to do with; keep out of the business; keep out of the affair; not to get involved in; refuse to be drawn into the matter; remain aloof from the affair; stay aloof from the affair; stay away from an affair;
[置信] believe; confide;
[置業] buy a house or flat;
置業者 house buyer;
~ 首次置業者 first-time buyer;
[置疑] doubt;
無容置疑 admit of no doubt; it is no question; undoubted;
[置用] buy for use;
[置於] place in; put in;

安置 arrange; arrange for; arrange suitable posts for; find a place for; have a good rest; help settle down; put in a proper place; settle;
不置 incessantly;
佈置 (1) arrange; decorate; (2) assign; make arrangements for;
處置 (1) deal with; dispose of; handle; manage; (2) punish;
措置 handle; manage;
倒置 anastrophe; inversion; invert; pend; place upside down; reversing;
放置 lay aside; lay up;
廢置 put aside as useless;
擱置 abeyance; fall into abeyance; hold in abeyance; in abeyance; keep in abeyance;

lay aside; lay on the shelf; leave in abeyance; pigeonhole; shelve;
購置 purchase;
歸置 clear away; put in order; tidy up;
後置 postposition;
恝置 neglect; take things coolly; treat with indifference;
留置 leave;
排置 put in good order;
內置 built-in; `
配置 allocate; configuration; configure; deploy; dispose;
偏置 offset; offsetting;
棄置 cast aside; discard; throw aside;
前置 prepose;
設置 (1) establish; found; put up; set up; (2) fit; install;
添置 acquire; add to one's possessions; purchase additionally; put in extra furniture;
位置 (1) location; place; seat; site; (2) place; position;
閒置 lay aside; leave unused; let sth lie idle; set aside;
移置 move to another place;
裝置 (1) apparatus; appliance; assembly; attachment; device; equipment; installation; rig; rigging; (2) equip with; fit; furnish with; install; mount; plant;

zhi

【輊】 low rear of a chariot;

zhi

【雉】 (1) pheasant; (2) a unit of a volume measure in ancient China;
[雉雞] pheasant;

虹雉 monal;
角雉 tragopan;

zhi

【寘】 (1) place; put; (2) discard; (3) cause; make; (4) full;

zhi

【滯】 at a standstill; blocked; impeded; sluggish; stagnant; stationary;
[滯伏] (1) lie hidden; (2) lack ambition;
[滯固] inflexible; obstinate;
[滯後] delay; file over; lag; lagging;
滯後電路 lagging circuit;
滯後裝置 lagging device;
定時滯後 constant time lag;
燃燒滯後 combustion lag;
相位滯後 lagging phase;
增長滯後 building-up lag;
[滯積] pile up;
滯積不銷 overstocked and unsaleable;
[滯累] burden of the temporal world;
[滯留] (1) be detained; be held up; (2) remain at a standstill;
氣體滯留 gas hold-up;
溶劑滯留 solvent hold-up;
液體滯留 liquid hold-up;
總滯留 total hold-up;
[滯悶] have pent-up feeling;
[滯泥] adhere too closely; stubborn and inflexible;
滯滯泥泥 sticky in doing things; stubborn and not agile;
[滯胃] indigestion; lie heavy on sb's stomach; lie heavy on the stomach;
[滯銷] dull of sale; sales slump; unmarketable; unsaleable;
滯銷貨 poor-selling products; unmarketable products; unsaleable goods;
滯銷品 unsaleable article;
[滯淹] remain at a standstill;
[滯淫] (1) remain at a standstill; (2) stagnation;
[滯運] adversity; bad fortune;
[滯住] detained; impeded; stopped;

板滯 dull; stiff;
沉滯 move sluggishly; stagnate;
遲滯 (1) slow-moving; sluggish; (2) delaying action;
磁滯 magnetic hysteresis;
呆滯 (1) dull; inert; lifeless; (2) dull; idle; slack; sluggish; stagnant;
凝滯 move sluggishly;
濡滯 procrastinate; slow;
停滯 at a standstill; be held up; bog down; stagnate; stagnation;
淹滯 talented persons holding inferior posts;
淤滯 be retarded by silt; choked; clogged; silt up;
阻滯 blocked; impeded; obstructed; retardant;

zhi

【製】 (1) create; make; manufacture; produce; (2) compose literary work; (3) cut out garments and make them; (4)

Z

fashion; form; model; pattern;

[製版] make a printing plate;

[製備] preparation;
玻璃製備 glass preparation;
電解製備 electrolytic preparation;
委托製備 custom preparation;
原圖製備 art work preparation;

[製幣] coin;
製幣廠 mint;

[製成] be made from; manufacture;
製成品 finished products; products;

[製訂] draw up; evolve; formulate; map out; work out;

[製法] method of making sth;

[製革] tanning;
製革工 furworker; tanner;
製革工廠 tannery;

[製漿] pulping;
製漿工 masher;

[製冷] refrigeration;
製冷劑 refrigerant;
製冷系統 refrigerating system;

[製模] mould;
製模工 moulder;

[製片] producer;
製片廠 movie studio;
~製片廠經理 studio manager;
製片費用 cost price; net cost;
製片顧問 adviser; consultant;
製片人 producer;
製片主任 executive producer;

[製品] manufactured items; products;
豆製品 bean products;
泡沫製品 foam article;
肉製品 meat products;
乳製品 dairy products; milk product;
~乳製品廠 creamery;
~乳製品商店 creamery;
手工製品 handmade article;
鐵製品 ironwork;
竹製品 bamboo articles; bamboo ware;

[製糖] refine sugar;
製糖廠 sugar refinery;

[製圖] cartograph; make charts; make maps;
製圖法 chartography;
製圖家 chartographer;
製圖學 cartography;
~計算機製圖學 computer cartography;
製圖員 cartographer; draughtsman;
大比例尺製圖 large scaled cartography;
地植物學製圖 geobotanical cartography;

[製靴] bootmaking;
製靴工 bootmaker;

[製藥] pharmacy;
製藥廠 pharmaceutical factory;

[製造] (1) make; manufacture; produce; (2) create; fabricate; engineer;
製造廠 manufactory;
製造商 manufacturer;
製造武器 make weapons;
製造業 the manufacturing business; the manufacturing industry;
製造者 maker;
~機器製造者 machine maker;
~奶油製造者 butter maker;
~天線製造者 antenna maker;
粗製濫造 cobble up; crudely made; manufacture in a rough and slip-shod way; rough-and-tumble; turn out rough and slipshod products;
國內製造 home manufacture;
互換性製造 interchangeable manufacturing;
奶油製造 butter manufacture;

[製作] fabricate; make; manufacture;
製作人 producer;
精心製作 elaboration;

焙製 cure sth by drying it over a fire;
編製 compile; draw up;
採製 collect and process;
創製 create; formulate; institute;
訂製 customize;
仿製 be modeled on; copy;
縫製 sew;
複製 copy; copying; duplicate; replication; reproduce;
改製 customize;
光製 finish;
繪製 draw;
監製 supervise the manufacture of;
精製 make with extra care; refine;
煉製 refine;
秘製 made from secret formulas;
砲製 concoct; cook up;
攝製 produce;
特製 manufacture for a special purpose;
提製 distil; extract; obtain through refining;
調製 modulate;
土製 crudely manufactured;
燻製 fumigate; smoke; smoking;
研製 (1) manufacture; prepare; (2) prepare

medicinal powder by pestling;
預製 prefabricate;
自製 made by oneself; self-made; self-manufactured;

zhi
【誌】 (1) put down; record; write down; (2) a record;
［誌哀］ indicate mourning; condole;
［誌悼］ condole;
［誌賀］ send sth as a token of congratulation;
［誌銘］ epitaph;
［誌念］ send sth as a souvenir;
［誌慶］ offer congratulations;
［誌喜］ offer congratulations;

碑誌 inscriptions on a tablet;
標誌 indicate; mark; sign; symbol; symbolize;
墓誌 inscriptions on the memorial tablet within a tomb;
日誌 daily journal;
網誌 blog; weblog;
縣誌 county annals;
鄉土誌 local records;
雜誌 (1) magazine; (2) notes; records;

zhi
【疐】 fall; stumble; suffer a fall; trip;

zhi
【銍】 sickle;

zhi
【幟】 (1) flag; pennant; pennon; (2) mark; sign;

旗幟 (1) banner; flag; (2) colours; stand;

zhi
【摯】 (1) earnest; sincere; (2) a surname;
［摯友］ boon companion; bosom friend; intimate friend; trusted friend;
摯友良朋 intimate friends and good companions;

誠摯 cordial; sincere;
懇摯 earnest and sincere;
深摯 profound and sincere;
真摯 cordial; sincere;

zhi
【緻】 close; delicate; dense; fine;
［緻密］ (1) close; delicate; fine; (2) appropriate; careful;

精緻 exquisite; fine;
細緻 careful; meticulous;

zhi
【質】 (1) pawn; (2) hostage; pledge;
［質庫］ pawnshop;
［質權］ pledge;
［質押］ assign sth as a security under an arrangement; mortgage;

白質 white matter;
本質 essence; essential characteristics; essential qualities; innate character; intrinsic quality; nature;
變質 (1) deteriorate; go bad; (2) metamorphism;
材質 quality of a material;
齒質 dentine;
單質 simple substance;
蛋白質 protein;
地質 geology;
電解質 electrolyte;
電介質 dielectric;
對質 confront in court;
腐殖質 humus;
灰質 gray matter;
蕙質 good and pure quality of a person;
基質 substratum;
繭質 cocoon quality;
角質 cutin;
介質 medium;
界質 medium;
劣質 inferior; of low quality; of poor quality;
流質 liquid diet;
煤質 medium;
內質 endoplasm;
皮質 cortex;
品質 (1) character; quality; (2) quality;
樸質 natural; simple and unadorned;
氣質 (1) disposition; temperament; (2) makings; qualities;
殼質 chitin;
人質 hostage;
溶質 solute;
弱質 tender constitution;
神經質 nervousness;
實質 essence; substance;
水解質 hydrolyte;
水質 water quality;
素質 (1) quality; (2) diathesis;
體質 constitution; physique;
土質 soil property; soil texture;
物質 (1) matter; substance; (2) material;

形質 form and substance;
性質 character; characteristic; nature; property; quality;
牙質 (1) made of ivory; (2) dentine;
音質 (1) tone quality; (2) acoustic fidelity;
優質 high grade; top quality;
有機質 organic matter;
釉質 enamel;
雜質 (1) impurity; (2) foreign matter;
資質 intelligence; natural endowments;

zhi

【膣】 vagina;
［膣炎］ vaginal inflammation;

zhi

【懥】 angry; enraged; indignant; resentful;

zhi

【贄】 (1) presents given at first meeting; (2) gifts to a superior;
［贄見］ bring gifts along and request an audience;
贄見禮 presents offered at calling on sb;
［贄敬］ gifts presented to teachers or masters;
［贄儀］ ceremonial presents; presents of homage;

zhi

【識】 (1) record; remember; (2) mark; sign;

zhi

【騭】 (1) stallion; (2) go up; rise; (3) predestined;

zhi

【鷙】 (1) birds of prey; (2) cruel; fierce; violent;
［鷙猛］ cruel; fierce; ruthless;
［鷙鳥］ birds of prey;
［鷙勇］ fierce and brave;

zhi

【躓】 (1) stumble; trip; (2) be frustrated; suffer a setback;
［躓頓］ stumble and stop;
［躓蹶］ stumble and fall;
躓蹶不起 stumble and unable to rise;

zhi

【鑕】 a kind of guillotine in ancient China;
斧鑕 executioner's block and cleaver;

zhong¹

zhong

【中】 (1) centre; middle; (2) China; Chinese; Sino-; (3) among; between; in; mid-; middle; within; (4) intermediate; medium; (5) halfway between two extremes; mean; (6) intermediary; (7) fit for; good for; (8) in the course of; in the process of;
［中班］ (1) middle class in a kindergarten; (2) middle shift; swing shift;
［中飽］ batten on money entrusted to one's care; embezzle; line one's own pockets; pocket money to which one has no claim; squeeze;
中飽私囊 batten on money entrusted to one's care; embezzle; embezzle public funds; fill one's pocket with public funds; line one's pockets with other people's money;
［中波］ medium wave;
［中材］ person of ordinary talent;
［中菜］ Chinese dishes; Chinese meal;
［中餐］ (1) midday meal; (2) Chinese food; Chinese meal;
［中草藥］ Chinese herbal medicine; Chinese medicinal herb;
［中策］ second best plan;
［中層］ middle-level;
中層管理 middle-level management;
［中產］ middle class;
中產階級 bourgeois; middle class;
［中常］ average;
［中場］ midfield;
中場休息 half-time; intermission;
踢中場 play in midfield;
［中程］ intermediate range; medium range;
中程飛彈 intermediate range missile; medium-range missile;
［中輟］ give up halfway; stop in the middle of sth;
［中道］ halfway;
中道而廢 abandon halfway; give up before finishing; wither on the vine;
中道而棄 give up halfway;
中道而行 follow the middle course;
中道而止 stop halfway;
［中等］ (1) secondary; (2) medium; moderate;
［中點］ centre mark; middle point; midpoint;
中點標誌 centre mark;
［中斷］ break off; discontinue; interrupt; interruption; pull the plug; severance;

suspend;
中斷比賽 break off the match;
中斷交通 suspend traffic;
中斷聯繫 break contact;
中斷應答 acknowledge interrupt;
中斷友誼 renounce friendship;
電流中斷 current interruption;
電路中斷 circuit interruption;
服務中斷 service interruption;
交通中斷 interruption of communication;
禁止中斷 disabled interruption;
內部中斷 internal interruption;
偶然中斷 contingency interruption;
允許中斷 enable interruption;
周期性中斷 cycled interruption;
自動中斷 automatic interruption;

[中耳] middle ear;
中耳炎 otitis media;
~航空性中耳炎 aerotitis media;
~急性化膿性中耳炎 acute suppurative otitis media;
~急性卡他性中耳炎 acute catarrhal otitis media;
~結核性中耳炎 tuberculosis otitis media;
~慢性化膿性中耳炎 chronic suppurative otitis media;
~慢性卡他性中耳炎 chronic catarrhal otitis media; chronic suppurative otitis media;
~黏連性中耳炎 adhesive otitis media;
~氣壓性中耳炎 barootitis media;

[中飯] lunch;
早中飯 brunch;

[中分] (of hairstyle) centre parting;

[中鋒] centre; centre forward;
中鋒策應 centre-pivot play;

[中耕] intertill;
中耕機 cultivator;
~稻田中耕機 field cultivator;
~分組式中耕機 gang cultivator;
~火焰中耕機 flame cultivator;
~窄行中耕機 narrow-row cultivator;
~鑿形中耕機 chisel cultivator;

[中古] medieval; medieval times; Middle Ages;
中古英語 middle English;

[中國] (1) China; (2) Cathay; (3) Middle Kingdom;
中國人 Chinaman; Chinese; Chink; Chinkie; Chinky; cufflink;
中國式英語 Chinese English; Chinglish;
中國問題專家 China expert;
中國專家 Chinese expert;

[中和] (1) balance out; neutralize; (2) justice and peace;
中和作用 neutralization;

[中華] China; Chinese nation; Chinese people;
中華文化 Chinese traditional culture;
振興中華 rejuvenate China; the rejuvenation of the Chinese nation;

[中悔] change one's mind in middle course;

[中火] medium heat;

[中級] intermediate; middle rank;
中級班 intermediate class;
中級程度 intermediate level;
中級語言 intermediate language;

[中繼] relay; trunking;
中繼法 trunking;
~迂迴中繼法 alternative trunking;
中繼線 trunk;
~空層中繼線 dead lever trunk;
~空號中繼線 dead line trunk; dead number trunk;
~雙向中繼線 both-way trunk;
中繼站 relay station;
有線中繼 wired trunking;
直通中繼 straightforward trunking;

[中堅] hard core; nucleus; spark plug;
中堅分子 backbone elements; the hard core; the salt of the earth; those playing the backbone role; those who are the backbone of;
~教會的中堅分子 pillar of the church;
中堅人物 key personnel;

[中間] (1) among; between; (2) in the centre; in the middle; (3) intermediate; interspace; middle;
中間層 mesosphere;
中間產品 intermediate; intermediate products;
~石油化學中間產品 petrochemical intermediate;
中間產物 intermediate;
~複製中間產物 replicative intermediate;
~瞬時中間產物 transient intermediate;
中間匯率 medial rate;
中間階級 middle class;
中間路線 middle-of-the-road;
中間名 middle name;
中間派 fence-sitter; middle-of-the-roader; neutral faction; straddler;
~中間派的 centrist;

Z

中間偏右 right-of-centre;
中間偏左 left-of-centre;
中間人 (1) broker; (2) go-between; mediator;
中間體 intermediate;
~苯炔中間體 benzyne intermediate;
~關鍵中間體 key intermediate;
~化學中間體 chemical intermediate;
~染料中間體 dyestuff intermediate;
中間突破 break through at the centre; break through in the middle; make a breakthrough in the middle;
在馬路中間 in the middle of the road;

[中將] (1) lieutenant general; (2) vice-admiral;
空軍中將 air marshal;

[中膠層] mesogloea;

[中介] intermediary; medium;
中介世界 mediated world;
中介系統 intermediary system;
中介組織 intermediary organization; mediated organization;

[中距] mid-range;

[中絕] perish before reaching a conclusion; stop midway;

[中看] good to look at;
中看不中吃 good to look at but rotten inside; look nice but do not taste nice; pleasant to the eye but not agreeable to the palate;
中看不中用 all is not gold that glitters; cheap and nasty; pleasant to the eye but of no use;

[中肯] to the purpose;
言不中肯 not to speak to the point;

[中空如鼓] hollow as a drum;

[中饋] unmarried;
中饋乏人 have no one to cook one's food — have no wife;
中饋猶虛 one is not married yet; still unmarried;

[中欄] intermediate hurdles;
400米中欄 400-metre intermediate hurdles;

[中立] neither on one side nor the other; neutral; neutrality;
中立地位 neutrality;
中立國 neutral nation;
中立領土 neutral territory;
中立區 neutral zone;
中立水域 neutral waters;
保持中立 adhere to neutrality; maintain neutrality; remain neutral; sit on the fence; sit on the hedge;
恪守中立 observe a strict neutrality;
守中立 keep away from disputes; maintain neutrality;

[中量級] middle weight;

[中流] (1) middle of the stream; (2) average; middle;
中流砥柱 a pillar rock in midstream; a tower of strength; mainstay; stand firm as a rock in mid-stream; the chief cornerstone;
中流換馬 change horses in midstream; swap horses in the middle of a stream;

[中路] (1) middle of the road; (2) mediocre;

[中落] sudden fall of one's family fortune; decline;

[中腦] mesencephalon; midbrain;
中腦炎 mesencephalitis;

[中年] midlife; middle age; middle-aged;
中年發福 middle-aged spread;
中年危機 midlife crisis;
中年之後 autumn of one's life;
過了中年 come to one's autumn;
人到中年 be over the hill;

[中農] middle peasant;
富裕中農 well-to-do middle peasant;
老中農 old middle peasant;
上中農 upper middle peasant;
下中農 lower middle peasant;
~貧下中農 poor and lower middle peasant;
新中農 new middle peasant;

[中期] medium term; middle period; mid-term;
中期投資 medium-term investments;

[中秋] mid-autumn;
中秋節 Mid-autumn Festival;
月到中秋分外明 the harvest moon is exceptionally bright; the mid-autumn moon is exceptionally bright;

[中區] (1) central; central area; (2) midcourt;

[中圈] centre circle;
中圈跳球 tip-off;

[中權] (1) main army; (2) central administration;

[中人] agent; go-between; intermediary; mediator; middleman;
勾欄中人 prostitute;

[中山狼] perfidious person;

[中山裝] Chinese tunic suit;

[中燒] burning inside one's heart;

仇火中燒 flames of hatred blazes in one's heart; one's heart is aflame with hatred;

妒火中燒 be consumed with envy; burn with envy; burn with jealousy; green with envy; jealousy ran red-hot through sb;

饑火中燒 acute hunger; burning desire for food;

怒火中燒 be burning with anger; be seething with anger; flames of wrath leap in one's breast; fury burns in one's heart; in hot blood; make sb's blood boil; one's anger smoulders; one's blood is up; simmer with rage; the anger in one's heart flares up;

如火中燒 all burnt up; like a fire burning in one's heart; very angry;

[中式] Chinese style; Chinese way;

[中士] (1) petty officer second-class; (2) sergeant;

[中世] Middle Ages;

中世紀 Middle Ages;

~中世紀語言學 medieval linguistics;

[中樞] centre; centrum; main centre; pivot;

中樞療法 centrotherapy;

中樞神經素 centronervin;

中樞性幻覺 centrophose;

勃起中樞 erection centre;

反射中樞 reflex centre;

呼氣中樞 expiratory centre;

記憶中樞 memory centre;

加速中樞 accelerating centre;

減壓中樞 depressor centre;

聯合中樞 association centre;

射精中樞 ejaculation centre;

神經中樞 nerve centre;

吞咽中樞 deglutition centre;

運動中樞 motor centre;

[中堂] a large scroll of painting hung vertically in the parlour;

[中庭] atrium;

[中停] interrupt; stop in the middle; suspend;

[中聽] agreeable to the hearer; pleasant to the ear;

不中聽 not worth listening;

[中途] halfway; midway; on the way;

中途變卦 change one's mind in middle course;

中途換馬 change horses halfway; change horses in midstream;

中途停留 stopover;

中途停業 terminate operations before scheduled expiration;

中途退場 leave before the meeting is over; march out in the middle of a meeting;

中途夭折 come to a premature end; die on the vine; wither on the vine;

中途站 staging post;

[中土] (1) Cathay; China; (2) Central Plains;

[中外] at home and abroad; China and foreign countries; Chinese and foreign; in China and abroad;

中外合資 Sino-foreign joint venture;

~中外合資經營企事 Sino-foreign joint venture enterprise;

~中外合資企業 Sino-foreign joint venture;

中外聞名 be known at home and abroad; be known both in China and abroad;

馳名中外 be popular both at home and abroad;

外強中乾 fierce of visage and faint of heart; outward strength but inner weakness; outwardly strong but inwardly weak; strong on the surface, but actually weak; strong in appearance but weak inside; strong without but feeble within;

外為中用 make foreign things serve China;

信孚中外 enjoy the confidence both of foreigners and of one's own people;

譽滿中外 enjoy high reputation at home and abroad;

昭信中外 inspire confidence and faith within and without the nation; show good faith to the nation and abroad;

[中位] (1) median; (2) central;

中位數 the median;

中位限定詞 central determiner;

[中尉] (1) lieutenant junior grade; (2) first lieutenant;

空軍中尉 flying officer;

陸軍中尉 lieutenant;

[中文] Chinese; Chinese language;

中文系 Department of Chinese;

[中午] high noon; midday; noon; noonday;

中午十二點 noon;

[中西] Chinese and Western;
中西合璧 a combination of Chinese and Western elements;
中西文化 Chinese and Western cultures;
學貫中西 have a thorough knowledge of both Western and Chinese learnings;

[中夏] China;

[中項] mean;
等比中項 geometric mean;
等差中項 arithmetic mean;

[中宵] middle of the night; midnight;

[中小] small and medium-sized;
中小企業 small and medium-sized enterprises;
中小型企業 small and medium-sized enterprises;

[中校] (1) commander; (2) lieutenant colonel;
海軍中交 commander;
空軍中校 wing commander;

[中心] centre; core; crux; epicenter; heart; hub; kernel;
中心杯 centerpiece;
中心詞 head word;
中心地域 heartland;
中心對稱 centrosymmetry;
中心球 entrosphere;
~巨型中心球 giant centrosphere;
中心人物 central figure; key figure;
中心如焚 burning with passion; the heart seems to be burning;
中心思想 central idea; gist;
中心線 centerline;
中心鞘 centrortheca;
中心性 centrality;
中心意義 central meaning;
中心質 centroplasm;
~中心質體 centroplast;
翻譯中心 translation centre;
活性中心 active centre;
金融中心 financial centre;
漫無中心 ramble;
聲中心 acoustic centre;
體育中心 athletic centre;
研究中心 research centre;
引力中心 attracting centre;
娛樂中心 recreation centre;
鎮中心 town centre;

[中興] come back to activity; rise after decline; resurgent; resurgence; revival; reviving;

[中型] medium-sized; middle-sized; midsize;
中型公共汽車 van;
中型公司 middle-sized company;

[中性] neuter; neutral;
中性的 neuter;
中性過去時 neutral preterite tense;
中性反應 neutral reaction;
中性現在時 neutral present tense;

[中學] (1) high school; middle school; secondary school; (2) Chinese learning;
中學生 secondary school students;
中學校長 principal;
初級中學 intermediate school; junior high school; junior middle school;
附屬中學 affiliated secondary school; attached middle school;
高級中學 senior high school; senior middle school;
公立中學 public school;
技術中學 technical school;
農業中學 agricultural middle school;
上中學 be in high school;
實驗中學 experimental middle school;
速成中學 short-term secondary school;
文法中學 grammar school;
一所中學 a high school;
重點中學 key middle school;
綜合中學 comp; comprehensive school;

[中旬] middle-part of a month;

[中亞] Central Asia;

[中央] (1) centre; middle; (2) central authorities;
中央處理器 central processing unit (CPU);
中央集權 centralization of authority;
中央控制台 central control desk;

[中腰] middle part of the side;
半中腰 halfway; middle;

[中藥] traditional Chinese medicine;
中藥店 Chinese drugstore;
一服中藥 a dose of Chinese medicine;
一劑中藥 a dose of Chinese herbal medicine;
一種中藥 a type of Chinese medicine;

[中葉] middle period;

[中夜] midnight;

[中衣] underclothing; underwear;

[中醫] (1) traditional Chinese medical science; (2) doctor of traditional Chinese medicine; practitioner of Chinese medicine;

中醫學院 institute of traditional Chinese medicine;
看中醫 see a doctor of Chinese medicine;

[中音] alto; tenor;
中音部 alto;
中音歌手 alto;
男中音 tenor;
女中音 mezzo-soprano;
~女中音歌手 mezzo-soprano;
上次中音 countertenor;

[中游] middle reaches;
甘居中游 be content to stay mediocre; be content with the second-best; be resigned to mediocrity; resign oneself to a state of mediocrity;

[中原] Central China; Central Plains;
中原文化 culture of Central China;
中原逐鹿 bid for state power; fight among rivals for the throne;
牧馬中原 become master of the country;

[中正] fair; impartial; just; not prejudiced; unbiased;

[中止] break off; discontinue; interrupt; let-up; suspend;

[中值] mean;
中值定理 theorem of mean;

[中指] middle finger;

[中轉] change trains;
中轉站 transfer station;

[中子] neutron;
中子彈 neutron bomb;
中子星 neutron star;
超熱中子 above-thermal neutron;
慢化中子 degraded neutron;
微中子 neutrino;
下代中子 daughter neutron;

暗中 (1) in darkness; in the dark; (2) behind someone's back; clandestinely; hidden secretly; in secret; on the sly; privately; surreptitiously;
便中 at one's convenience;
猜中 figure answer out; guess right;
尺中 cubital;
初中 junior middle school;
從中 from among; out of; therefrom;
打中 hit; hit the mark; hit the target;
當中 (1) in the centre; in the middle; (2) among;
釜中 in a pot;
附中 attached middle school;
高中 senior middle school;
個中 therein;
彀中 shooting range;
紅中 (mahjong) red dragon tile;
話中 in one's words;
慧中 intelligent inside;
集中 centralize; concentrate; concentrated;
擊中 hit the target;
就中 among;
居中 (1) be placed in the middle; in the middle; (2) mediate between parties;
看中 settle on; take a fancy;
空中 in the air; in the sky;
郎中 (1) doctor; physician trained in herbal medicine; (2) ancient official title;
囊中 in the bag;
內中 in; inside;
年中 mid-year; middle of the year;
其中 among; in; among them; among which; among whom; in; in it; in the midst; in which; of them; of those; of which; therein; within;
期中 interim; midsemester; midterm;
切中 hit the mark;
熱中 (1) pursue with fervor; (2) be fond of;
人中 philtrum;
日中 midday; noon;
適中 (1) adequate; appropriate; just right; moderate; (2) well situated;
手中 in the hands of;
庭中 in the yard;
投中 score a basket; shoot the ball in;
途中 en route; on passage; on the way;
甕中 in a jar;
無形中 invisibly; virtually;
相中 settle on; take a fancy;
宵中 midnight;
心中 at heart; in one's heart; in one's mind; in the heart; in the mind;
洋中 foreign and Chinese;
意中 anticipated; expected;
隅中 approaching noontime;
月中 middle of a month;
折中 compromise;
震中 epicenter;
正當中 right in the middle;
正中 centre; middle;
之中 among; in; in the midst of;
執中 follow the middle road; impartial; keep to the golden mean;

zhong

【忪】 (1) agitated; (2) frightened;

怔忪 alarmed and panicky; terrified;

zhong

【忠】 (1) devoted; honest; (2) constant; faithful; loyal; patriotic; sincere;

[忠臣] official loyal to his sovereign;
忠臣不怕死 a loyal servant of the state does not fear death;
忠臣不事二主 a loyal subject never serves two kings;
忠臣烈士 righteous governors and those who die for their country;

[忠忱] faithfulness; loyalty;

[忠誠] faithful; loyal; truthful;
忠誠的人 loyalist;
忠誠卡 loyalty card;
忠誠可靠 both loyal and trustworthy;
忠誠老實 honest and faithful;
不忠誠 disroyal;
無限忠誠 unmeasured loyalty;
顯示忠誠 show fidelity towards;
相互忠誠 mutual fidelity;

[忠告] honest advice; sincere advice; sincere counsel;
一個忠告 a piece of advice; a word of advice;

[忠厚] honest and tolerant; kind and big-hearted; sincere and kindly;
忠厚老實 upright and honest;
忠厚仁德 loyal, generous, kindly and virtuous;
忠厚質樸 simple and honest; unsophisticated;

[忠君] loyal to the throne;
忠君愛國 patriotic and loyal to the throne;

[忠良] (1) faithful and honest; (2) virtuous person;
顯忠遂良 promote the loyal and good people;

[忠烈] loyal till death; martyrdom; patriotism;
忠烈祠 martyrs' shrine;
一門忠烈 all the members of a family died as martyrs;

[忠實] faithful; reliable; true;
忠實可靠 as true as steel; loyal and reliable; on the up and up; reliable; unfailing;

[忠恕] magnanimity;
忠恕之道 principle of benevolence and loyalty; the doctrine of loyalty and consideration for others;

[忠順] loyal and obedient;

[忠孝] loyalty and filial piety;
忠孝節義 loyalty, filial piety, chastity and righteousness;
忠孝雙全 both loyal to one's country and filial to one's parents; both loyalty and filial piety are attained; complete in fidelity and filial piety;
忠孝之道 the teachings of loyalty and filial piety;
移孝為忠 substitute filial piety with loyalty to the country;

[忠心] devotion; faithfulness; loyalty; sincerity;
忠心報國 repay one's country withy loyalty; work for the country heart and soul;
忠心赤膽 whole-hearted devotion;
忠心耿耿 faithful and conscientiously; infinitely loyal; loyal and devoted; loyal, faithful and true; most faithful and true; single-hearted; single-minded; staunch and steadfast; unswerving loyalty;
忠心為國 true and loyal to the state;
赤膽忠心 ardent loyalty; loyalty; true devotion; utter devotion; wholehearted dedication;
耿耿忠心 be dedicated heart and soul; dogged adherence to;

[忠信] faithful and honest;

[忠言] earnest advice; sincere advice;
忠言逆耳 faithful words grate upon the ear; good advice jars on the ear; honest advice is hard to accept; truth seldom sounds pleasant;
不納忠言 deaf to honest words;
一句忠言 a bit of advice; a few words of advice; a piece of advice;

[忠義] (1) faithful and virtuous; (2) people of loyalty and virtue;

[忠勇] loyal and brave; loyal and courageous;

[忠於] devoted to; faithful to; loyal to; true to;
忠於國家 faithful to one's fatherland;
忠於職守 be devoted to one's duty; faithful in the discharge of one's duties;

[忠貞] faithful and true; loyal and steadfast;
忠貞不二 be always true to sb; be steady in one's allegiance; show great and unchanging loyalty;

忠貞不屈 staunch and indomitable;
忠貞不渝 stalwart; true to the core; unswerving in one's loyalty;
忠貞如一 loyal from first to last;
忠貞之士 person of loyalty;

[忠直] faithful and upright; straightforward;

不忠 be unfaithful to; infidelity; two-time;
盡忠 (1) serve the country faithfully; (2) die for the country;
朴忠 faithful; honest; loyal;
效忠 allegiance; devote oneself heart and soul to; loyal to; pledge allegiance; pledge loyalty to;
愚忠 blind devotion to one's lord;

zhong
【盅】 small cup;

茶盅 tea cup;
酒盅 wine cup;

zhong
【衷】 (1) heartfelt; inner feelings; sincere; (2) good and virtuous; (3) appropriate; befitting; proper; propriety; (4) undergarments; (5) a surname;

[衷腸] innermost feelings; sincere words; words right from one's heart;

[衷懷] inner feelings;
互吐衷懷 open out to each other;

[衷款] sincerity;

[衷情] feelings in one's heart; heartfelt emotion; inner feelings;
互訴衷情 recount each other with their inner feelings; they open their hearts to each other;

[衷曲] heartfelt emotion; inner feelings; the voice of one's heart; words from the bottom of one's heart;
不露衷曲 keep one's counsel; not reveal one's inner feelings;
一敘衷曲 have a hearty talk;

[衷心] cordial; heartfelt; sincere; wholehearted;
衷心愛戴 love sb from the bottom of one's heart; love wholeheartedly; love with all one's heart;
衷心的 heartfelt;
衷心感謝 express one's sincere thanks to; thank sincerely; thank sb from the bottom of one's heart;
衷心滿意 be sincerely satisfied with;
衷心擁護 give wholehearted support; support wholeheartedly;
衷心折服 admire from the heart;
衷心祝願 congratulate sb heartily; sincerely wish;

[衷衣] underwear;

初衷 original intention;
苦衷 difficulties that one is reluctant to discuss;
熱衷 (1) hanker after; (2) be fond of;
隱衷 feelings one is reluctant to disclose;
由衷 from the bottom of one's heart; sincere;
折衷 compromise;

zhong
【終】 (1) come to an end; end; conclude; conclusion; finish; (2) death; end; (3) after all; at last; eventually; finally; in the end; in the long run; (4) all; entire; whole;

[終場] conclusion of a matter; end of a game; end of a performance; end of a show; finale;

[終點] (1) destination; finishing point; terminal point; (2) finish;
終點裁判員 judge at the finishing line;
終點帶 finishing tape;
終點線 (1) finishing line; (2) tape;
終點站 terminal;

[終端] terminal;
終端處理機 terminal handler;
終端機 terminal computer;
終端局 terminal port;
終端器 terminal unit; termination;
~可移動終端器 movable termination;
~匹配終端器 matched termination;
~無反射終端器 non-reflecting termination;
終端用戶 end user;
短路終端 short-circuit termination;
激光器終端 laser termination;
智能終端 intelligence terminal;

[終伏] end of summer;

[終古] (1) for a long time; forever; (2) in ancient times; through all antiquity;
終古紅顏多薄命 since old times, beautiful women have suffered a harsh life;

[終歸] after all; at last; be bound to; eventually; finally; in the end;

[終極] end; finality;

[終結] conclusion; end; finality; termination;
終結體 terminate aspect;
[終竟] (1) after all; finally; in the end; in the long run; (2) come to an end; end;
[終究] after all; eventually; in the end;
[終久] after all; eventually; in the end; in the long run;
[終局] end; outcome;
[終老] throughout one's life; until death;
[終了] be finished; close; complete; conclude; end; end up; terminate;
[終年] (1) the age at which one dies; (2) all the year round; the whole year; throughout the year;
終年累月 for months and years on end; month after month and year after year;
[終篇] finish writing an article;
[終曲] finale;
[終日] all day long; from morning till night; throughout the day;
不可終日 (1) be anxious throughout the day; (2) be in a desperate situation;
[終身] all one's life; lifelong; whole life;
終身伴侶 lifelong companion;
終身不嫁 lead apes in hell; remain unmarried all one's life;
終身不忘 keep in memory throughout one's life span;
終身大事 important affair of a final settlement in life; main affair of one's life; marriage;
終身的 lifelong;
終身服務 life service;
終身僱傭 permanent employment;
終身會員 life member;
終身教育 lifelong education;
終身事業 lifelong career; one's lifework;
終身受僱 life employment;
終身遺憾 one's lifelong regret;
終身有靠 can depend on sb all one's life;
終身之恨 lifelong sorrow; one's eternal remorse;
終身之交 lifelong friends;
終身職 lifetime job; office for life;
終身制 lifelong tenure; system of life tenure;
悔恨終身 have a secret regret for life; nurse a secret regret all one's life; regret all one's life;
私定終身 pledge to marry without the permission of parents;
[終生] all one's life; the whole life; throughout one's life;
終生難忘 never to forget in one's life;
終生學習 learning for life; life-long learning;
終生遺憾 repent forever;
抱憾終生 harbour a lifetime remorse; have a remorse of a lifetime; have a secret regret for life; regret sth to the end of one's days;
抱恨終生 bitterly lament the nonfulfilment of one's mission; cherish hatred all one's life; feel remorse for the rest of one's life; harbour an eternal sorrow; regret all one's life; regret forever; regret sth to the end of one's days; with a feeling of bitter frustration;
獨身終生 pass one's life unmarried; remain single all one's life;
感恩終生 grateful to sb as long as one lives;
齎恨終身 die without realizing one's ambitions;
[終食] duration of a meal;
[終始] from beginning to end;
[終歲] the whole year; throughout the year;
[終天] (1) all day long; from morning till night; (2) all one's life; forever;
終天年 live up one's allotted life span;
終天之恨 eternal regret; lifelong regret;
終天之慕 lifelong respect;
抱恨終天 bitterly lament the non-fulfilment of one's mission; cherish hatred all one's life; feel remorse for the rest of one's life; harbour an eternal sorrow; regret all one's life; regret forever; regret sth to the end of one's days; with a feeling of bitter frustration;
含眼終天 die unavenged;
[終須] have to in the end; there is no escaping of it sooner or later; unavoidable in the long run;
[終養] resign from one's office to care for one's parents at home;
[終夜] all night long; the whole night through; throughout the night;
[終於] at last; end in; eventually; finally; in the end; result in; ultimately;

[終譽] everlasting name; immortality; long-lasting fame;
[終站] terminal station; terminal stop;
[終朝] (1) the whole morning; (2) the whole day; throughout the day;
[終止] (1) close; come to an end; end; stop; suspend; (2) abrogation; annulment; termination;
終止符 full stop; period; stop character;
終止合同 termination of contract;
終止日 date of termination;
鏈終止 chain termination;
雙分子終止 bimolecular termination;

病終 die of disease;
告終 come to an end; end up;
臨終 on one's deathbed;
年終 the end of the year;
善終 die a natural death; die in one's bed; hospice care;
始終 all along; first, midst, and last; from beginning to end; from start to finish; remain; throughout;
飾終 funeral rites;
送終 attend upon a dying parent or other senior member of one's family; prepare for the burial of one's parents;
月終 end of a month;
最終 final; ultimate;

zhong
【鍾】 (1) a kind of wine container; (2) accumulate; concentrate; converge; (3) a surname;
[鍾愛] cherish; dote on; love deeply;
[鍾靈毓秀] a place endowed with the fine spirits of the universe; this well-endowed region has brought forward men of talent;
[鍾情] deeply in love; fall in love;
情之所鍾 the drift of passion; when the love is concentrated on;
一見鍾情 fall in love at first sight; fall in love with sb the first time one sets one's eyes on sb; love at first sight; take a shine to sb; take an instant fancy to;

龍鍾 decrepit; senile;
所鍾 love;

zhong
【螽】 katydid;
[螽花] spikelet;
[螽斯] katydid;

zhong
【鐘】 (1) bell; (2) clock; (3) time as measured in hours and minutes; (4) handless cup; (5) a surname;
[鐘擺] clock pendulum; pendulum;
[鐘錶] clocks and watches; timepieces;
鐘錶匠 clockologist;
鐘錶鋪 watchmaker's shop;
鐘錶學 horology;
[鐘點] (1) a time for sth to be done or to happen; (2) hours;
[鐘鼎文] bronze inscriptions; inscriptions on bronze bells and tripods;
[鐘兒] bell;
[鐘鼓] bells and drums;
鐘鼓齊鳴 bells and drums sound simultaneously;
晨鐘暮鼓 the morning bell and the evening drum — timely exhortations to virtue and purity;
暮鼓晨鐘 daily call to religious life; the evening drum and the morning bell;
[鐘樓] (1) bell tower; (2) clock tower;
[鐘面] clock face; face of a clock;
[鐘鳴鼎食] enjoy affluence; live an extravagant life;
鐘鳴鼎食之家 a family of great wealth; rich and noble families;
鐘鳴漏盡 in one's declining years;
[鐘乳] stalactite;
鐘乳洞 stalactite grotto;
鐘乳石 stalactite;
[鐘聲] sound of tolling a bell; toll of a bell;
鐘聲滴答 a clock ticks;
[鐘頭] hour;
[鐘學] campanology;

擺鐘 pendulum clock;
壁鐘 wall cloth;
標準鐘 chronometer clock;
底料鐘 bottom;
電鐘 electric clock;
吊鐘 fuchsia;
分鐘 minute;
掛鐘 wall clock;
洪鐘 large bell;

花鐘 floral clock;
加料鐘 charging bell;
晶體鐘 crystal clock;
警鐘 alarm bell;
看鐘 glance at the clock; look at the clock;
曆鐘 calendar clock;
龍鐘 decrepit; senile;
濾鐘 filter bell;
鳴鐘 toll;
鬧鐘 alarm clock;
排鐘 chimes;
氣體鐘 air clock;
氣壓鐘 atmospheric clock;
潛水鐘 diving bell;
敲鐘 toll a bell;
燃料鐘 fuel bell;
喪鐘 death knell; funeral bell;
生物鐘 biological clock;
石英鐘 atomic clock;
時鐘 clock; time bell;
水壓鐘 hydrostatic bell;
陶鐘 pottery vessel for wine;
天文鐘 astronomical clock;
霧鐘 fog bell;
壓力鐘 pressure bell;
一口鐘 (1) a bell; (2) a mantle;
一座鐘 a clock;
原子鐘 atomic clock;
中音鐘 tenor bell;
重力鐘 gravity clock;
子母鐘 synchronized clocks;
自鳴鐘 chime clock; striking clock;
座鐘 desk clock;

zhong³

zhong

【冢】 (1) high grave; tomb; (2) peak; summit; (3) eldest; (4) great; prime; supreme;

［冢婦］ eldest daughter-in-law;
［冢君］ ancient term for a sovereign;
［冢宰］ prime minister;
［冢子］ (1) eldest son; (2) crown prince;

叢冢 group of graves;
土冢 grave mound;
義冢 burial ground for the destitute;

zhong

【塚】 grave; high tomb; mound;

［塚中枯骨］ rotten bones in the graveyard;

zhong

【腫】 boil; swell; swelling;

［腫大］ swell up;
［腫毒］ swelling; tumour;
［腫塊］ bump;
［腫瘤］ tumour;

腫瘤病 oncosis;
腫瘤切除術 lumpectomy;
腫瘤學 oncology;
癌樣腫瘤 cancerous tumour; cancroid tumour;
惡性腫瘤 malignant tumour;
睪丸腫瘤 orchiocele;
喉惡性腫瘤 malignant tumour of larynx;
喉良性腫瘤 benign tumour of larynx;
良性腫瘤 benign tumour;
囊性腫瘤 cystoma;
腦腫瘤 brain tumour;
脾腫瘤 splenoma;
咽惡性腫瘤 malignant tumour of pharynx;
咽良性腫瘤 benign tumour of pharynx;

［腫痛］ swollen and inflamed;
［腫脹］ swell; swelling;

淋病性腫脹 blennorrhagic swelling;
暫時性腫脹 fugitive swelling;

癌腫 malignant tumour;
肺膿腫 lung abscess; suppuration of the lung;
肺氣腫 emphysema; pneumonectasis; pulmonary emphysema;
肺水腫 oedema pulmonary; pulmonary oedema;
肝膿腫 liver abscess;
骨囊腫 bone cyst;
紅腫 red and swollen;
喉膿腫 laryngeal abscess;
瞼水腫 hydrohlepharon;
腱鞘腫 onkinocele;
囊腫 cyst;
腦膿腫 abscess;
膿腫 abscess;
氣腫 emphysema;
青腫 bruised and swollen;
舌腫 glossoncus;
腎膿腫 kidney abscess;
水腫 edema;
消腫 remove a swelling;
血腫 haematoma;
炎腫 inflammation with swelling;
齦膿腫 parulis;
臃腫 (1) too fat to move; (2) overstaffed;
癰腫 carbuncle;

Z

臃腫 (1) fat and clumsy; too fat to move; (2) overstaffed;
趾膿腫 toe abscess;
趾水腫 dactyledema;
足水腫 pododema;

zhong

【種】 (1) genus; kind; sort; species; (2) races; (3) seeds; (4) descendants; posterity; (5) breed; strain; (6) grit; guts;

[種別] classification;
[種肥] seed manure;
[種類] class; kind; sort; type; variety;
 種類名詞 species noun;
[種落] tribe;
[種馬] stallion; studhorse;
 種馬場 stud farm;
[種苗] sprout;
[種皮] seed coat;
[種群] population;
 馴化種群 domestic population;
 動物種群 animal population;
 繁殖種群 breeding population;
 野化種群 feral population;
[種種] a variety of; all kinds of; all sorts of;
 種種籍口 various excuses;
 種種原因 a variety of reasons;
[種子] germ; seed;
 改良種子 improved seed;
 混雜種子 foreign seeds;
 一把種子 a handful of seeds;
 脂肪種子 fatty seed;
[種族] population; race; tribe;
 種族背景 ethnic background;
 種族衝突 racial conflict;
 種族仇恨 enthnic animosity;
 ~減輕種族仇恨 alleviate ethnic animosity;
 種族的 ethnic;
 種族革命 racial revolution;
 種族隔離 apartheid; racial segregation;
 種族關係 race relations;
 種族滅絕 genocide;
 種族偏見 racial prejudice; racism;
 種族平等 racial equality;
 種族歧視 colour bar; racial discrimination;
 種族清洗 ethnic cleansing;
 種族語意翻譯 ethno-semantic translation;
 種族中心主義 ethnocentrism;
 種族主義 racialism; racism;
 ~種族主義者 racist;

白種 white race;
備種 make preparations for sowing;
兵種 arm of the services;
播種 plant seeds; seed; seeding; sow;
傳種 propagate; reproduce;
純種 full blood; pedigree; purebred;
多種 diversified; many and various; multiple; various;
工種 branch of work; kind of work; profession; type of work in production;
花種 flower seed;
絕種 become extinct; die out;
菌種 type culture;
謬種 error; fallacy;
那種 that kind;
偶見種 rare species;
品種 (1) breed; cultivated varieties; (2) assortment; variety;
人種 ethnic group; human species; race;
撒種 sow seeds;
特種 particular kind; of a special kind; special type;
同種 of the same race;
物種 species;
下種 sow seed;
一種 (1) one kind; one species; one type; (2) a kind of; a sort of; a type of;
有種 have guts;
育種 breeding;
雜種 (1) crossbreed; hybrid; (2) bastard; son of a bitch;
栽種 grow; plant;

zhong

【踵】 (1) heel; (2) call in person; (3) follow close behind;

[踵見] call reapeatedly in person;
[踵決肘見] down at the heels and elbows — tattered dress; out at the heels and the elbows;
[踵門] call at another's house in person;
 踵門拜別 personally pay a farewell call;
 踵門道謝 call in person to express one's thanks;
 踵門求見 call on sb at his abode; seek an interview at sb's house;
[踵事增華] carry on a predecessor's task and make a greater success of it; follow a precedent and add to its excellence;

take over and carry forward;
[踵武] carry on the work of one's predecessors;
[踵謝] thank in person;
[踵至] arrive just behind; arrive upon the heels of another;

繼踵 follow close on sb's heels;
接踵 follow close behind; follow on sb's heels;
旋踵 in a moment; in an instant; in no time;

zhong⁴
zhong
【中】 (1) fit exactly hit; (2) be hit by; fall into;
[中標] win the bidding;
中標合同 contract awarded;
[中彩] win a lottery prize; win a prize at a lottery;
[中吃] good to eat; tasty;
[中彈] be struck by a bullet; get shot;
[中的] hit the bull's-eye; hit the mark; hit the nail on the head; hit the right point; hit the target;
[中第] pass the civil examinations;
[中毒] be poisoned; intoxication; poison; poisoning; toxicosis;
中毒性痙攣 toxic spasm;
中毒性水腫 toxic oedema;
中毒性萎縮 toxic atrophy;
病理性中毒 pathological intoxication;
臭氧中毒 ozone intoxication;
放射性中毒 radioactive poisoning;
汞中毒 mercury intoxication;
急性中毒 acute poisoning;
酒精中毒 alcohol intoxication; alcohol poisoning;
慢性中毒 chronic intoxication; chronic poisoning;
煤氣中毒 gas poisoning;
膿毒中毒 septic intoxication;
鉛中毒 lead poisoning;
妊娠中毒 gestosis;
食物中毒 food intoxication; food poisoning;
水中毒 water intoxication;
酸中毒 oxyosis;
銅中毒 copper poisoning;
外因性中毒 exogenic toxicosis;
外源性中毒 exogenic toxicosis;
職業中毒 occupational poisoning;
自體中毒 autoxemia;
[中風] apoplexy; paralytic stroke; stroke; suffer from a stroke of paralysis;
中風發作 apoplectic fit;
假中風 pseudoapoplexy;
一陣中風 a fit of apoplexy;
[中伏] be ambushed;
[中寒] be attacked by cold; catch cold;
[中計] be taken in; be trapped; be victimized by a scheme; fall into a trap; walk into a trap;
[中獎] get the prize; win a prize;
[中節] (1) in rhythm; (2) proper and just;
[中酒] drunk; intoxicated;
[中舉] pass the provincial civil service examination;
[中看] good to look at;
[中肯] appropriate; fair; pertinent; relevant; to the point;
[中理] reasonable;
[中籤] be chosen by lot;
[中傷] cast aspersions on sb; defamation; defame; hurt sb insidiously; malign; slander; vilify;
背後中傷 back-stabbing; calumniate sb behind one's back; rip up the back; stab sb in the back;
~背後中傷的人 back-stabber;
惡語中傷 attack with vicious words; calumniate; cast aspersions on sb; do sb dirt; malign sb viciously; say malicious remark to hurt sb; slander with malicious language; speak ill of sb; use abusive words to hurt others; use bad language to insult people;
~惡意中傷對手 hurt one's opponent with vicious slanders;
~互相惡意中傷 speak ill of each other;
[中暑] have a sunstroke; heat exhaustion; heatstroke;
[中聽] pleasant to the ear;
[中邪] be bewitched;
[中選] be chosen; be selected; win an election;
[中意] agreeable; catch the fancy of; satisfied; suit one's fancy; to one's liking;
不中意 not to one's liking;
[中用] serviceable; useful;
不中用 good for nothing; no good; not

worth one's salt; of no use; thumbs down; to no purpose; unfit for anything; useless;
~最不中用 not of the least use;

卒中 apoplexy; be seized with apoplexy;
打中 hit; hit the target;
擊中 hit; hit the target;
看中 be satisfied with; take a fancy to;
命中 hit the target;
切中 hit the mark;
相中 settle on; take a fancy to;
正中 be just what one hopes for;

zhong
【仲】 (1) second month in a season; (2) second in order of birth; (3) intermediate; middle; (4) a surname;
[仲裁] arbitrate;
仲裁裁決 arbitral decision; arbitration award;
仲裁程序 arbitration procedure;
仲裁法 arbitration law;
~仲裁法規 arbitration statute;
~仲裁法庭 arbitration tribunal;
~仲裁法院 arbitration court;
仲裁費 arbitration fee;
仲裁規則 rules for arbitration;
仲裁機構 arbitral agency;
仲裁人 arbitrator;
仲裁試驗 referee test;
仲裁書 arbitration award;
仲裁條款 arbitration clause;
仲裁委員會 appeal committee; arbitration committee;
仲裁協議 arbitral agreement;
臨時仲裁 ad hoc arbitration;
商業仲裁 commercial arbitration;
提交仲裁 submission to arbitration;
[仲春] middle of spring; midspring;
[仲冬] middle of winter; midwinter;
[仲尼] another name of Confucius;
[仲秋] middle of autumn; midautumn;
[仲夏] middle of summer; midsummer;
仲夏日 Midsummer Day;
[仲子] one's second son;

伯仲 be much the same;
杜仲 the bark of eucommia;
昆仲 elder and younger brothers;

zhong
【重】 (1) weigh; weight; (2) heavy; weighty; (3) deep; grave; serious; severe; (4) important; significant; (5) attach importance to; emphasize; lay stress on; value; (6) discreet;
[重辦] severely punish; take severe action against;
[重寶] treasure of much value;
[重兵] a large number of troops; massive forces;
重兵把關 the pass is heavily guarded;
重兵壓境 massive forces have been deployed along the border;
派駐重兵 station massive forces;
[重病] serious disease; serious illness;
重病在牀 be confined to one's bed with a serious illness;
患重病 contract a serious illness;
[重臣] important official of the emperor;
[重懲] chastise severely; punish severely;
[重酬] handsome reward; substantial reward;
[重創] (1) serious wound; (2) inflict a serious blow on; inflict heavy losses on; maul heavily;
身受重創 severely wounded;
[重大] grave; great; important; serious; significant; weighty;
重大案件 important case;
重大貢獻 major contribution;
重大突破 quantum jump;
重大消息 grave news;
重大責任 heavy responsibility;
[重擔] difficult task; heavy burden; heavy load; heavy responsibility;
擔重擔 bear a heavy burden; carry the ball;
挑重擔 should heavy loads; take on a heavy job;
~甘挑重擔 ready to take on heavy responsibilites; take the heaviest burden on oneself;
~搶挑重擔 rush to shoulder heavy responsibilities; vie with each other for difficult task;
~勇挑重擔 bravely shoulder the difficult tasks; ready to shoulder heavy tasks; take on the heavy job with determination; take up the heavy burden with courage;
~爭挑重擔 rush to carry the heaviest load; step forward and to be first to

carry heavy loads; vie with each other for the hardest job;
卸下重擔 be relieved of the heavy burden;

[重地] important place; restricted area;

[重典] severe provisions;
律以重典 punish severely by law;

[重點] emphasis; focal point; stress;
重點訪問 focused interview;
重點工程 key project; major project;
~重點工程項目 key engineering project;
重點學校 key school;
重點中學 key middle school;
工作重點 focal point of the work;
突出重點 stress the main point;
學習重點 learning objectives;
抓不住重點 not see the forest for the trees; not see the wood for the trees;

[重罰] fine heavily; heavy fine; punish severely; severe punishment;

[重犯] important criminal;

[重負] heavy burden; heavy load; heavy responsibility;
重負載 heavy load;
分擔重負 share the burden;
加以重負 load down;
如釋重負 as if a heavy weight has been lifted from one's mind; as if a load has been lifted; as if relieved of a heavy load; feel a sense of relief; feel as if a big load has been taken off one's mind; feel as if released from a big burden; feel greatly relieved; heave a sigh of relief;
釋去重負 be relieved of a heavy burden;

[重活] heavy work;

[重價] high price;

[重力] force of gravity; gravitational force; gravity; gravity force; power of gravity; pull of gravity;
重力法 gravitational method;
重力計 gravimeter;
~激光絕對重力計 laser absolute gravimeter;
~無定向重力計 astatized gravimeter;
重力儀 gravimeter;
~靜力重力儀 static gravimeter;
~氣體重力儀 gas gravimeter;
~彈簧重力儀 spring gravimeter;
重力異常 gravity anomaly;
標準重力 normal gravity;
假重力 virtual gravity;
絕對重力 absolute gravity;
模擬重力 simulated gravity;
人造重力 artificial gravity;

[重利] (1) high interest rate; (2) value material gain; (3) huge profit;

[重量] heft; scale; weight;
重量分析 gravimetric analysis;
重量級 heavy weight;
到岸重量 arrived weight;
額外重量 additional weight;
減輕重量 lessen the weight; reduce the weight;
絕對重量 absolute weight;
確認重量 ascertained weight;

[重名] (1) fame; (2) attach importance to fame; value fame;

[重砲] heavy artillery; heavy guns;
野戰重砲 field heavy artillery;

[重任] heavy responsibility; important mission; important office; important post; important task;
被委以重任 be given an important task;
擔負重任 take on heavy responsibilities; undertake an important business;
肩負重任 shoulder the burden of heavy responsibilities;
堪當重任 can fill a position of great responsibility; capable of shouldering important tasks; have broad shoulders;
堪負重任 have broad shoulders — able to shoulder heavy responsibilities;
身負重任 be charged with important tasks; shoulder an important task;
身肩重任 bear a heavy burden; shoulder heavy responsibilities;
委以重任 entrust sb with an important task;
膺此重任 hold such a post of great responsibility;
御下重任 get the world off one's back;

[重商主義] mercantilism;

[重傷] serious injury; severe wound;
重傷風 severe cold;
身負重傷 be badly wounded; be seriously injured;

[重賞] reward generously;
重賞之下必有勇夫 a good paymaster never wants workmen; by offering an ample reward some brave men are sure to be secured; generous rewards rouse one to heroism; one may be brought if

the price is high enough; when a high reward is offered, brave fellows are bound to come forward;

[重視] attach importance to; cherish; consider important; make much account of; pay attention to; take account of; take into account; take sth seriously; think highly of; think the world of; value;

不重視 make light account of; make light of; make little account of; not hold of much account; of little account;

過份重視 overemphasize;

極為重視 hold sth in great account; hold sth of much account; make the most of;

[重水] heavy water;

[重頭戲] a play involving much singing and action; an opera difficult to act or sing;

[重托] great trust;

[重心] (1) core; focus; heart; key point; (2) centre of gravity;

重心坐標 areal coordinates;

[重刑] heavy penalty; severe punishment;

[重型] heavy; heavy-duty; heavy type;

[重壓] heavy load; great pressure; weight;

[重要] important; major; significant; vital;

重要的是 the point is;

重要關頭 critical point; crucial moment; important juncture;

重要人物 great figure; important figure;

重要事實 material facts;

重要問題 important issue; important question;

重要性 importance; significance;

~貶低…的重要性 belittle the importance of...;

~淡化事件的重要性 play down the importance of sth;

~當地的重要性 local importance;

~全國的重要性 national importance;

~失去重要性 lose its importance;

~實際的重要性 practical importance;

重要約會 heavy date;

不重要 amount to little; not amount to a hill of beans; not amount to a row of pins; not amount to much; of little account; of little amount; of no account;

次等重要 of secondary importance;

格外重要 particular importance;

極其重要的 all-important; of crucial importance;

每秒鐘都很重要 every second counts;

每一分錢都很重要 every penny counts;

認為自己很重要 think that the world revolves around one;

日趨重要 increase in importance;

同等重要 equal importance;

相當重要 considerable importance; enormous importance; great importance;

相對重要 relative importance;

尤為重要 of prime importance;

至關重要 critical importance; crucial importance; of primary importance; vital importance;

至為重要 of paramount importance; of the utmost importance;

最為重要 of primary importance;

[重義輕貲] love generous deeds and look lightly upon money; value justice above material gains;

[重音] (1) stress; accent; (2) accent;

次重音 secondary accent;

第一重音 primary stress;

對比重音 contrastive stress;

鈍重音 grave accent;

含糊的重音 slurred accent;

加重重音 stress accent;

尖重音 acute accent;

力重音 dynamic accent;

量重音 quantitative accent;

邏輯重音 logical stress;

形態重音 morphological accent;

音高重音 pitch accent;

樂調重音 musical accent;

樂音重音 chromatic accent;

質重音 qualitative accent;

中間重音 medial accent;

主重音 primary accent; primary stress;

[重用] put sb in an important position;

重用人材 put people of ability and learning in important positions;

[重油] heavy oil;

[重載] heavy load; heavy-duty; freight;

[重責] (1) important responsibility; (2) flog severely; scold severely;

[重杖] flog severely;

[重鎮] (1) important city; key position; place of strategic importance; (2) key figure;

[重罪] felony; grave crime; heavy offence;

重罪犯 felon;

愛重 love and respect;
寶重 treasure; value;
保重 take care of oneself;
笨重 cumbersome; heavy;
比重 (1) proportion; (2) specific gravity;
並重 lay equal stress on;
慘重 disastrous; grievous; heavy; serious;
側重 lay particular emphasis on; put special emphasis on;
超重 (1) overload; (2) overweight;
沉重 (1) heavy; (2) critical; serious;
吃重 arduous; bear; strenuous;
持重 cautious; prudent;
粗重 (1) loud and jarring; (2) big and heavy; (3) thick and heavy; (4) heavy; strenuous;
繁重 heavy; strenuous;
負重 carry a heavy load on one's back;
貴重 precious; valuable;
過重 overweight;
荷重 load; weight;
加重 (1) increase the weight of; (2) make or become more serious;
借重 enlist sb's help; rely on for support;
淨重 net weight;
敬重 deeply respect; esteem;
舉重 weight lifting;
看重 attach importance to; regard as important;
空重 empty weight;
口重 (1) salty; (2) fond of salty food;
隆重 grand; solemn;
毛重 gross weight;
凝重 dignified; imposing;
濃重 dense; strong; thick;
皮重 tare;
偏重 lay particular stress on;
器重 have a high opinion of sb; think highly of;
輕重 (1) weight; (2) degree of seriousness; (3) propriety;
容重 unit weight;
深重 extremely serious; very grave;
慎重 careful; prudent;
失重 weightlessness; zero gravity;
體重 body weight;
推重 have a high regard for; hold in esteem;
危重 critical; grave;
穩重 dignified; prudent; steady;
嚴重 critical; grave; serious; severe;
言重 speak so seriously and strongly as to embarrass sb;
倚重 entrust a person with heavy responsibility; reply heavily on sb's service;
載重 carrying capacity;
珍重 (1) highly value; hold dear; set great store; treasure; (2) take good care of yourself;
鄭重 (1) serious; solemn; (2) careful; cautious;
注重 emphasize; lay emphasis on; pay special attention to;
莊重 grave; serious; solemn;
着重 emphasize; stress;
輜重 (1) lugguage; (2) military supplies;
自重 conduct oneself with dignity;
尊重 esteem; respect;

zhong

【眾】 (1) many; numerous; (2) the crowd; the multitude; the people; (3) all;

[眾多] multitudinous; numerous;

[眾寡] the few and the many;

眾寡不敵 be hopelessly outnumbered; fight against hopeless odds; the few are no match for the many; the few cannot fight the many; there is no contending against odds;

眾寡懸殊 against great odds; the disparity of numerical strength is too great;

敵眾我寡 against heavy odds; be outnumbered by the enemy;

以眾暴寡 bully the minority;

[眾口] what people say;

眾口紛紜 everybody talking at once;

眾口交謫 be censured by everybody;

眾口難調 it is difficult to cater for all tastes; it is difficult to cook it to suit everyone's taste; it is difficult to make everyone feel satisfied; it is hard to please all; no dish pleases all plates alike; no dish suits all tastes; tastes differe;

眾口如一 all agree in saying; everyone says so; with one voice;

眾口爍金 if you throw mud enough, some of it will stick; people's gossip is enough to melt metals; public clamour can confound right and wrong; public clamour can melt metals; the voice of many people confuse right with wrong; when all men say you are an ass, it is time to bray;

眾口相傳 spread from mouth to mouth;

眾口一詞 all agree in saying; all tell the same story; everyone says so; in the same story; say of one accord; speak with one voice; unanimously; with one voice;

[眾目] what people see;
眾目共睹 what every eye sees; what everyone can see;
眾目睽睽 in the face of the world; in the full blaze of publicity; in the full glare of publicity; under the public gaze; under the watchful eyes of the people; with a crowd of people watching; with everybody watching;
眾目所見 be seen by all; what every eye sees; what everyone can see;
眾目昭彰 be seen clearly by everyone; clear to all;

[眾怒] anger of the masses; public wrath;
眾怒難犯 an aroused public is hard to tackle with; hard to stand the united wrath of the masses; it is dangerous to antagonize the masses; it is dangerous to incur the anger of the masses; it is difficult to go against the anger of all; one cannot afford to incur public wrath; the anger of a crowd is difficult to opoose; the ire of the multitude is difficult to oppose;
惹犯眾怒 arouse a nest of hornets;

[眾人] all people; everybody; many people; the multitude;
眾人拾柴火焰高 great things may be done by mass effort; the fire burns high when everybody adds wood to it — more people mean greater power; there is strength in numbers; when everybody adds fuel the flames rise high — more people, more strength;
眾人眼睛是杆秤 everyone has eyes; public opinion is objective;
眾人一條心，黃土變成金 if we are all of one heart and one mind, we can change clay into gold;

[眾生] all living creatures; all sentient beings;
普救眾生 save all living beings from calamities;

[眾望] people's expectations; popular confidence;
眾望所歸 command public respect and support; enjoy popular confidence; stand high in popular favour; the object of public esteem; the people's hope is centered on;
不孚眾望 fail to live up to the public expectations; fall short of people's expectations; not popular with the people;
名孚眾望 prestige commands popularity;
深孚眾望 enjoy great popularity; enjoy high prestige;
有負眾望 fail to live up to people's expectations; fall short of public expectations;

[眾星] myriad of stars;
眾星拱斗 all stars turn towards the North Star;
眾星拱月 a myriad of stars surrounding the moon — a host of lesser lights around the leading one; all the stars twinkle around the bright moon;
眾星捧月 a myriad of stars surround the moon; all the famous stars drawing a circle of admirers around him or her; all the stars bend towards the moon; many people cluster around the one whom they respect;

[眾議] public opinions;
眾議紛紜 public opinions are divergent;
獨排眾議 hold one's own opinion against that of the majority;
力排眾議 do one's utmost to hold one's opinion against that of the majority; override all objections; prevail over all dissenting views; refute the consensus and present a new plan;

[眾志成城] collective purposes form a fortress; our wills unite like a fortress; union is strength; unity of purpose is a formidable force; unity of will is an impregnable citadel;

[眾醉獨醒] all are besotted except one who remains sober;

出眾 exceptional; out of the ordinary; outstanding;
大眾 the masses; the people; the public;
當眾 before the public; in front of everybody; in public; in the presence of all; openly;
公眾 the public;
觀眾 audience; spectator;
惑眾 delude or confuse people;
聚眾 gather a crowd;
民眾 the common people; the masses of the people; the populace;
群眾 the common people; the general public; the masses;

示眾 exhibit to the public; expose publicly; put before the public; show to the public;
恃眾 presume on numbers; take advantage of superiority in numbers;
庶眾 the common people; the commoners; the masses; the multitude;
率眾 lead a crowd; lead a large group of people;
隨眾 follow the crowd;
聽眾 audience; listeners;
徒眾 crowd; gang; croup of followers;
萬眾 millions of people; multitude;

zhong

【種】 (1) cultivate; grow; plant; sow; (2) vaccinate;

[種菜] grow vegetables;
[種德] accumulate virtuous deeds; cultivate virtues;
[種地] cultivate the land; do farm work; farm; go in for farming; till land;
[種痘] vaccinate;
[種…得…] one gets what one plants;
種瓜得瓜 as a man sows, so shall he reap; every man is the son of his own works; planting squash, you get squash;
~種瓜得瓜，種豆得豆 as a man sows, so he shall reap; as they sow, so let them reap; as you sow you shall mow; for whatsoever a man soweth, that shall be also reap; one reaps what he sows; plant melons and get melons; reap as what one has sown; sow beans and get beans; you must reap what you have sown;
種麥得麥 as a man sows, so shall he reap;
[種花] cultivate flowers; grow flowers;
種花養鳥 plant flowers and keep birds;
種花植木 grow flowers and plant trees; plant flowers and trees;
[種禍] sow the seeds of calamity;
[種樹] plant trees;
栽花種樹 cultivate flowers and trees; grow flowers and plant trees;
[種田] farm; till;
種田的 farmer;
種田人 farmer;
[種植] cultivate; grow; plant; planting; raise;
種植戶 grower;
混合種植 mixed planting;
田邊種植 field border planting;

備種 make preparations for sowing;
補種 replant; resow;
點種 dibble;
複種 multiple cropping;
耕種 cultivate; plough and sow; till; work on the farm;
間種 intercrop;
接種 have an inoculation; inoculate;
連種 continuous cropping;
輪種 alternation of crops; crop rotation;
搶種 rush-plant;
秋種 autumn sowing;
試種 plant experimentally;
套種 interplant;
夏種 summer planting;
引種 introduce a fine variety;
栽種 grow; plant;

zhou¹

zhou

【州】 (1) administrative district in ancient China; (2) county; (3) state; (4) islet; sand bar; (5) a surname;

[州官] county magistrate;
祇許州官放火，不許百姓點燈 one man may steal a horse while another may not look over a hedge; the magistrates are free to burn down houses, while the common people are forbidden even to light lamps; the magistrate may burn down houses but the ordinary people cannot even light their lamps; the powerful can do what they want, the weak are not allowed to do anything;
[州花] state flower;
[州際] interstate;
[州長] commissioner; governor of a state;
州長職位 governorship;
副州長 vice-governor;
[州治] district government; state government;

自治州 autonomous prefecture;

zhou

【舟】 boat; ship; vessel;

[舟車] (1) vessels and vehicles; (2) journey;
舟車勞頓 exhausted from a long travel; fatigued by a long journey; travel-worn;
[舟楫] ship; vessel;
[舟人] boatman;

[舟子] boatman;
泛舟 go boating;
飛舟 swift boat;
浮舟 pontoon;
樺皮舟 birch bark;
龍舟 dragon boat;
扁舟 skiff; small boat;
輕舟 light boat; small boat;

zhou

【周】 (1) circumference; periphery; (2) circuit; make a circuit; move in a circular course; (3) all around; all over; everywhere; (4) attentive; thoughtful; (5) week; (6) cycle; (7) aid; provide for; relieve; (8) a surname;

[周報] weekly;
[周邊] pheriphery;
周邊廣告 ambient advertising;
周邊戰略 peripheral strategy;
[周波] cycle;
[周長] circumference; perimeter;
[周打魚] fish chowder;
周打魚湯 fish chowder;
[周到] attentive and satisfactory; considerate; thoughtful;
待客周到 keep a good house;
[周而復始] come full circle; go round and begin again; go round and round; make a circle and start again from the beginning; move in circles; repeat the process again and again;
[周忌] first anniversary of a person's death;
[周濟] give alms; help out the needy; help the poor with money; relieve;
[周界] circumference; perimeter;
[周徑] diameter;
[周刊] weekly; weekly magazine;
三周刊 triweekly;
雙周刊 fortnightly; biweekly;
[周流] circulate; go round; travel all over;
周流不息 flowing round without stopping;
[周密] attentive to every detail; careful; thorough;
周密考慮 think over carefully;
[周末] weekend;
周末愉快 have a good weekend;
去度周末 go on a weekend;
[周年] anniversary; full year;
周年紀念 anniversary; jubilee;
~ 結婚周年紀念 wedding anniversary;
~ 金婚周年紀念 gold wedding anniversary;
~ 六十周年紀念 diamond jubilee;
~ 五十周年紀念 golden jubilee;
~ 銀婚周年紀念 silver wedding anniversary;
[周期] circle; cycle; period; round; revolution;
周期表 periodic table;
周期性 periodicity;
~ 長周期性 long periodicity;
~ 環境周期性 environmental periodicity;
~ 內源周期性 endogenous periodicity;
~ 潛周期性 hidden periodicity;
~ 有條件周期性 conditional periodicity;
差拍周期 beat cycle;
馴化周期 acclimation period;
繁殖周期 breeding cycle;
工作周期 action cycle;
光周期 photoperiod;
~ 臨界光週期 critical photoperiod;
退火周期 annealing cycle;
吸附周期 adsorption cycle;
應答周期 acknowledge cycle;
有效場周期 active field period;
[周親] closest relatives;
[周全] (1) aid; help; (2) complete with all that is desired; comprehensive; thorough;
八面周全 please all the parties; satisfactory to every detail;
[周日] (1) weekday; (2) diurnal;
周日圈 diurnal circle;
周日運動 diurnal motion;
[周身] all over the body; whole body;
周身打量 look sb over from head to foot; stare sb up and down; survey sb from top to toe;
周身端詳 eye sb from head to toe;
[周歲] one full year of life; the first anniversary;
[周天] a complete circle of 360 degrees;
[周圍] about; around; on every side; round vicinity; surroundings;
周圍地區 surrounding area;
周圍環境 surrounding circumstances;
周圍炎 periarthritis;
~ 闌尾周圍炎 periappendicitis;
~ 膽囊周圍炎 perichlecystitis;
~ 陰道周圍炎 pericolpitis;
~ 直腸周圍炎 paraproctitis;
注流周圍 stream circumference;

Z

[周詳] complete and detailed; comprehensive;
[周旋] (1) circle round; (2) attend to friends; attend to guests; go about; have social intercourse with; mix with other people; socialize; (3) contend with; deal with; fight;
周旋到底 fight to the bitter end; have it out to the finish;
虛與周旋 act diplomatically with sb;
[周延] distribution;
[周遊] journey round; make a tour in search of adventures; travel round;
周遊列國 roam the various states; tour the various countries; travel far and wide; travel through all the kingdom; travel to many countries;
周遊世界 go on a world tour; make a tour round the world; tour the world; travel round the world;
[周遭] about; around; round;
[周章] (1) be confused; be scared; (2) effort; trouble;
大費周章 make much ado; take great pains;
煞費周章 spare no effort; take great pains; with much ado;
[周折] complicated course of development; complication; setbacks; troublesome course of development; twists and turns;
一番周折 a good deal of bother;
[周正] properly in place; regular; upright;
[周知] generally known; public knowledge;
如所周知 as everybody knows; as is known to all; as is well known;
眾所周知 as everyone knows; as is known to all; as is well known; every barber knows that; everybody knows that; it is common knowledge that; it is known to all that; it is well known that; known by everyone; on record; to a proverb; universally known; widely known;
[周至] attentive and satisfactory; considerate; thoughtful;
[周轉] (1) turnover; (2) have enough to meet the need;
周轉不靈 in financial straits; not have the sufficient funds to meet all the needs; not have enough cash to answer needs;
周轉資金 circulating fund; revolving fund; working fund;
[周咨博訪] inquire around and visit everywhere;

每周 weekly;
千周 kilocycle;
三周 three weeks;
四周 all around;
一周 (1) a circle; a cycle; a revolution; (2) a week;
圓周 circumference;
兆周 megacycle;

zhou

【洲】 (1) island in a river; (2) continent;
[洲汀] island in a river;
[洲際] intercontinental;
洲際貿易 intercontinental trade;
[洲嶼] island in a river;
[洲沚] island in a river;
[洲渚] island in a river;

綠洲 oasis;
三角洲 delta;
沙洲 sandbank; shoal;
汀洲 sand shoal;

zhou

【啁】 chirping of a bird;
[啁噍] wren-likebird;
[啁啾] chirp; twitter; warble;
[啁哳] twitter;

zhou

【粥】 congee; porridge; rice gruel;
[粥杯] porridger;
[粥飯] porridge and rice;
一粥一飯 a bowl of congee or rice;
~一粥一飯，當思來之不易 in taking a mouthful of congee or rice, you should bear in mind that its production is not easy;
[粥碗] porringer;
[粥粥] (1) chuckchuck sound; (2) weak;
粥粥無能 weak and incompetent;

熬粥 cook congee;
大米粥 rice porridge;
喝粥 eat porridge;
臘八粥 laba porridge;
綠豆粥 mung bean porridge;
小豆粥 red bean porridge;

一鍋粥 a cauldron of gruel; a pot of porridge; all in a muddle; complete mess;

zhou

【週】 (1) period; week; (2) cycle; revolution;

［週報］ weekly newspaper;

［週到］ considerate; thoughtful;

［週會］ weekly meeting;

雙週會 biweekly meeting;

［週刊］ weekly periodical;

［週末］ weekend;

［週年］ full year; anniversary;

週年紀念 commemoration of an anniversary;

［週期］ cycle; period;

［週歲］ full year;

［週薪］ weekly salary;

［週知］ be known to all; make known to all;

本週 this week;

上週 last week;

zhou

【輈】 shaft of a cart;

［輈張］ (1) flurried; (2) insolent;

zhou

【賙】 aid; give; relieve;

［賙濟］ relieve the needy;

zhou

【盩】 mountain recess; turn of a mountain range;

zhou

【鵃】 a kind of pigeon;

鶻鵃 a kind of pigeon;

zhou²

zhou

【妯】 sisters-in-law; wives of one's brothers;

［妯娌］ sisters-in-law; wives of one's brothers;

zhou

【舳】 stern of a ship;

［舳艫］ rectangular boat;

舳艫千里 formation of ships extending over a thousand miles;

zhou

【軸】 (1) axis; axle; pivot; (2) scroll;

［軸承］ bearing;

可調軸承 adjustable bearing;

空氣靜力軸承 aerostatic bearing;

瑪瑙軸承 agate bearing;

支承軸承 backup bearing;

支撐軸承 axial bearing;

主軸承 base bearing;

［軸心］ axis;

［軸子］ axis; axle; pivot;

長軸 major axis;

超軸 over haulage;

車軸 axle;

地軸 earth's axis;

短軸 minor axis;

共軛軸 conjugate axis;

共軸 coaxial;

橫截軸 transverse axis;

極軸 polar axis;

主軸 principal axis;

zhou³

zhou

【肘】 (1) elbow; (2) catch one by the elbow;

［肘關節］ elbow joint;

［肘節］ toggle;

［肘腋］ close by; near at hand;

肘腋之患 disturbances coming from those closest;

［肘子］ (1) pig's knuckle; (2) elbow;

後肘子 hind knuckle;

醬肘子 spiced pork shoulder;

肐膊肘子 elbow;

前肘子 fore knuckle;

臂肘 elbow;

翻肘 turn over the elbows;

拐肘 elbow;

掣肘 hinder; retard;

zhou

【帚】 besom; broom;

zhou⁴

zhou

【咒】 (1) incantation; (2) curse; damn; swear;

［咒罵］ abuse; call names; curse; invective; revile; swear at;

百般咒罵 abuse in every possible way; heap abuse;

連聲咒罵 a stream of invective;

切齒咒罵 grind out an oath;

一陣咒罵 a hail of curse;
[咒人] curse people;
[咒語] abracadabra; curses; imprecation; incantation;
唸咒語 incantation;
[咒願] pledge; oath;
[咒詛] curse; swear at;

賭咒 take an oath;
符咒 amulets; charms;
魔咒 magic spell;
唸咒 chant incantation; intone charms;
詛咒 curse; swear;

zhou
【宙】 eternity; infinite time; time without beginning or end;
[宙合] all embracing; all encompassing;

宇宙 (1) universe; (2) cosmos;

zhou
【紂】 (1) tyrant; (2) crupper of a saddle;

zhou
【冑】 helmet;
[冑甲] helmet and armour;

貴冑 descendants of nobles;
甲冑 armour;

zhou
【晝】 (1) day; daylight; daytime; (2) a surname;
[晝分] high noon;
[晝晦] dim sunshine;
[晝夢] day dreaming;
[晝寢] asleep during the day; take a nap;
晝寢廢時 taking a nap is a waste of time;
[晝日] day; daytime;
[晝夜] day and night; round the clock;
晝夜不停 for 24 hours at a stretch; night and day; round the clock;
晝夜不息 day and night without rest; going on day and night without stopping;
晝夜倒班 work in shifts round the clock;
晝夜兼程 travel day and night with all possible speed;
晝夜平分 equinox;
卜晝卜夜 day and night without cease; indulge in debauchery day and night;
不分晝夜 both day and night; both by day and by night;
不捨晝夜 day and night; regardless of day and night; work day and night;
炫晝縞夜 illuminate day and night;
夜出晝伏 appear by night and hide by day;
夜行晝伏 march by night and conceal oneself by day;
晝長夜短 the days are long and the nights short;
晝短夜長 days are short and nights long;
晝伏夜出 hide by day and come out by night; hide in the daytime and come out at night; lie low in daytime and act at night;
晝伏夜行 conceal oneself by day and march by night;
晝行夜宿 travel by day and rest by night;

白晝 daytime;
極晝 polar day;

zhou
【甃】 (1) brick wall of a wall; (2) build a well; (3) construct with bricks;

zhou
【皺】 (1) contract; crease; crumple; fold; wrinkle; (2) creases; folds; rumples; wrinkles;
[皺巴巴] creased; crumpled; wrinkled;
皺皺巴巴 creasy; crumpled; full of creases; not smooth; shrivelled;
[皺襞舌] lingua plicata;
[皺波] ripples;
[皺裂舌] wrinkled tongue;
[皺眉] frown; knit one's brows;
皺眉蹙額 draw the bros together into wrinkles; frown; knit one's brows; with knitted brows; wrinkle one's brows;
皺眉頭 contract one's brows; frown; knit one's brows;
[皺縮舌] wrinkled tongue;
[皺胃] abomasum;
皺胃氣脹 abomasal bloat;
皺胃失張力 abomasal atony;
皺胃炎 abomasitis;
[皺紋] creases; folds; lines; ruffles; rumples; wrinkles;
皺紋紙 crepe paper;

滿臉皺紋 have many lines on one's face;
起皺紋 furrow;
一道皺紋 a wrinkle;

褶皺 (1) fold; (2) wrinkle;

zhou
【縐】 (1) crape; crepe; (2) creased; crinkled; wrinkled;
[縐布] crape; crepe;
[縐紗] crepe silk;
[縐紋] creases; crinkles; folds; wrinkles;
[縐紙] crepe paper; twisting paper;

zhou
【籀】 (1) large seal in calligraphy; (2) deduce;
[籀書] majuscule seal script;
[籀文] style of calligraphy current in the Zhou Dynasty;

zhu¹
zhu
【朱】 (1) bright red; red; vermilion; (2) cinnabar; (3) a surname;
[朱筆] writing brush dipped in red link;
[朱唇] red lips;
朱唇皓齒 red lips and white teeth; rosy lips and ivory white teeth;
玉面朱唇 a beautiful and fashionable woman;
[朱邸] residence of a nobleman;
[朱頂鳥] redpoll;
[朱古力] chocolate;
[朱紅] bright red; scarlet; vermilion;
仿朱紅 imitation vermilion;
鎘朱紅 cadmium vermilion;
偶氮朱紅 azo vermilion;
水銀朱紅 quicksilver vermilion;
油朱紅 oil vermilion;
[朱黃] red and yellow;
[朱欄玉砌] with walls of jasper and pillars and balustrades of ruby;
[朱樓] houses of the wealthy and influential;
朱樓畫棟 red balconies and brightly coloured pillars;
朱樓瓊室 vermilion pavilions and splendid mansions;
[朱輪華轂] red and ornate carriages used by noblemen in ancient times;
[朱門] red-lacquered doors of wealthy homes; rich and influential families; vermilion gates;
朱門酒肉臭 behind the red gate wine overflows and meat rots;
[朱甍碧瓦] green tiles and crimson roofs;
[朱墨] (1) red and black; (2) ink made of cinnabar;
朱墨爛然 with profuse comments written in red;
[朱批] writing remarks in red with a brush;
[朱漆] red lacquer; red paint;
[朱雀] rosefinch;
[朱砂] cinnabar;
[朱文] characters on a seal carved in relief;
[朱顏] (1) beautiful face of a young lady; (2) beautiful face of a youth;
朱顏鶴髮 hale aged man; the hair is snow white but the face is that of a young person;
[朱衣] red robe worn by the emeperor during summer;
[朱殷] dark-red;
[朱愚] ignorant; stupid;
[朱垣碧甍] red walls and green tiles;

銀朱 vermilion;

zhu
【侏】 (1) short; (2) dwarf; pigmy;
[侏儒] crile; dwarf; midget;

zhu
【洙】 a river in Shandong;

zhu
【邾】 an ancient state in present-day Shandong;

zhu
【株】 (1) numerary auxiliary for counting trees; (2) roots that grow above ground;
[株幹] trunk of a tree;
[株金] capital;
[株連] implicate; involve others in a criminal case;
株連九族 implicate the nine generations of a family;
株連全家 bring the whole family a lot of trouble;
[株戮] be executed for a crime committed by one's relatives or friends;

Z

［株蔓］ involve people in a crime;
［株守］ hold on stubbornly to a silly idea; take no action but wish that sth would come one's way;

病株 diseased or infected plant;
菌株 strain;
母株 mother plant;
幼株 seedling;
岩株 stock;
一株 a tree;

zhu

【珠】 (1) pearl; (2) bead; (3) pupil of the eye; (4) a surname;
［珠蚌］ pearl oyster;
［珠寶］ gems; jewellery; pearls and jade;
珠寶商 jeweller;
珠寶箱 treasure chest;
珠寶鐘錶店 jeweller's;
假珠寶 sham jewellery;
人造珠寶 costume jewellery;
一件珠寶 a piece of jewellery;
一批珠寶 a trove of jewels;
［珠箔］ curtain of pearls; screen of beads;
［珠翠］ pearls and jades;
［珠兒］ beads;
［珠光寶氣］ be adorned with brilliant jewels and pearls; be richly bejewelled; bedecked with jewels;
［珠光體］ pearlite;
殘餘珠光體 residual pearlite;
精細珠光體 fine pearlite;
球狀珠光體 globular pearlite;
［珠汗］ beads of perspiration;
［珠喉］ smooth and sweet voice of a vocalist;
［珠戶］ pearl divers;
［珠還］ return a valuable thing;
珠還合浦 return a valuable thing to its rightful owner;
合浦珠還 recover a thing which has been lost; things lost are regained;
［珠璣］ exquisite wording of a piece of writing; gems; graceful writings; pearls;
［珠雞］ guinea fowl;
［珠淚］ tears;
珠淚滾滾 one's tears fall like pearls and beans; the tears pour down one's cheeks; the tears run from one's eyes in torrents;
珠淚簌簌 big tears trickle down from one's eyes; one's tears fall like pearls; tears trickle down one's cheeks; the tears run down one's face like water dropping through a sieve;
珠淚盈眶 tears like pearls fill the eyes;
［珠履］ shoes with pearls as ornament;
［珠聯璧合］ excellent combination; excellent match; happy combination; perfect pair; strings of pearls and girdles of jade;
［珠簾］ bead curtains;
［珠母］ pearl oyster;
［珠算］ calculation with an abacus; operation on the abacus; reckoning by the abacus;
［珠胎］ (1) abnormal growth caused by a little grain of sand in an oyster; (2) human embryo in a woman's body;
珠胎暗結 a human embryo is formed in the woman's body; pregnant;
［珠玉］ (1) beautifully written verses; (2) elegant and state in appearance;
［珠圓玉潤］ elegant and polished; round and pearls and smooth as jade;
［珠子］ (1) pearls; (2) beads;
一顆珠子 a pearl;

蚌珠 pearl;
寶珠 precious jewel;
串珠 string of beads;
電珠 small bulb;
耳珠 tragus;
鋼珠 steel ball;
滾珠 steel ball;
汗珠 beads of perspiration; beads of sweat;
淚珠 beads of sorrow; teardrops;
連珠 (1) chain of pearls; (2) in rapid succession;
露水珠 dewdrops;
露珠 beads of dew; dewdrops;
明珠 bright pearl; jewel;
唸珠 beads; rosary;
胚珠 ovule;
蕊珠 (1) palace of gods; (2) one of the Daoist scriptures;
數珠 beads;
水珠 drop of water;
香珠 rosary of sandalwood;
眼珠 eyeball;
養珠 cultured pearls;
夜明珠 legendary luminous pearl;

遺珠 talented person out of employment;
雨珠 raindrop;
圓珠 ball; ballpoint;
珍珠 gem; pearl;
真珠 natural; pearl;

zhu

【茱】 dogwood;
［茱萸］ dogwood;

zhu

【硃】 (1) vermilion; (2) imperial;
［硃筆］ vermilion writing brush;
［硃批］ imperial rescript;
［硃砂］ cinnabar;
硃砂痣 red mole;
［硃諭］ imperial decree;

zhu

【蛛】 spider;
［蛛絲］ cobweb; gossamer; spider's thread;
蛛絲馬跡 traces and hues;
［蛛網］ cobweb; spider's web;
密如蛛網 as fine as a spider's web — the meshes of the law;

紅蜘蛛 red spider;
麥蜘蛛 red spider;
蜘蛛 spider;

zhu

【誅】 (1) execute; kill; put a criminal to death; (2) punish; (3) exterminate; weed out;
［誅除］ eliminate; eradicate; root out;
［誅戮］ kill; put to death; slaughter;
［誅論］ sentence to death;
［誅滅］ eliminate; eradicate;
天誅地滅 be destroyed by heaven and earth; stand condemned by God;
［誅奸］ punish the traitorous;
［誅求］ blackmail; demand booty; demand greedily; exact; exploit; make endless exorbitant demands;
誅求無厭 make incessant, excessive demands;
誅求無已 make endless demands;
［誅夷］ launch a punitive campaign against barbarians;
［誅意］ criticize sb not because of what he has done but because of his motive for doing it;

zhu

【銖】 (1) ancient unit of weight; (2) blunt; dull; obtuse; (3) a surname;
［銖鈍］ dull knives and spears;
［銖兩］ minute; small; tiny;
銖兩悉稱 exactly equal in weight; have the same weight; match in every small detail;
［銖衣］ extremely ligh-weight garment;
［銖錙必較］ stand on weight and measure;

zhu

【諸】 (1) all; various; (2) a surname;
［諸般］ all kinds; all sorts;
［諸多］ a good deal of; a lot of; many; numerous;
諸多不便 great inconvenience; in many ways inonvenient; quite a lot of trouble; rather inconvenient;
［諸父］ one's father's brothers; paternal uncles;
［諸葛］ a surname;
［諸公］ all the gentlemen;
諸公同好 people of the same taste; people who have the same taste;
［諸姑］ one's father's sisters;
諸姑姐妹 all the ladies;
［諸行百藝］ every trade and profession;
［諸侯］ feudal princes;
諸侯爭霸 the princes vie for supremacy;
［諸季］ all one's younger brothers;
［諸舅］ all one's maternal uncles;
［諸君］ you gentlemen;
［諸母］ one's father's concubine;
［諸如］ like; such as;
諸如此類 all the rest of it; and all that; and everything of the sort; and such; and the like; and what not; blah, blah, blah, or the like; so on and so forth; such matters as this; such things like that; things like that; things of that sort; various things like that; yada yada, yada;
諸如此類，不勝枚舉 such instances are too numerou to mention; things like these defy enumeration;
諸如此類，不一而足 and so forth and so on; and so on and so forth; and so on and so on;
［諸色］ different kinds;
諸色人等 different kinds of people; motley crowd;

Z

［諸生］ all the students;
［諸位］ all of you; everybody; ladies and gentlemen;
［諸夏］ the various Chinese kingdoms;

公諸 make public;
訴諸 appeal to; resort to;

zhu

【豬】 (1) hog; pig; swine; (2) pig-headed person;
［豬八戒］ pigsy;
豬八戒吃人參果—不知啥滋味 pigsy eating ginseng fruit – no flavour;
豬八戒倒打一耙 make unfounded counter-charges; put the blame on one's victim;
［豬婆龍］ giant sea turtle; giant tortoise;
［豬場］ pig farm; piggery;
［豬肚］ pork's tripe;
［豬肝］ pork's liver;
豬肝色 liver-coloured;
［豬骨頭］ pigbone;
［豬叫］ a pig grunts; a pig squeals; grunting of hogs;
［豬欄］ pigpen; pigsty;
［豬玀］ pig; swine;
［豬排］ pork chop;
烤豬排 grilled pork chop;
［豬皮］ hogskin; pigskin;
炸豬皮 pork rinds;
［豬圈］ hogpen; pigpen; pigsty;
［豬肉］ pork;
凍豬肉 frozen pork;
剁碎豬肉 chopped pork;
醬豬肉 spiced pork;
生豬肉 raw pork;
~一大塊生豬肉 a large gobbet of pork;
熟豬肉 cooked pork;
鹹豬肉 bacon;
一大塊豬肉 a large cut of pork;
［豬舌］ pig's tongue;
［豬舍］ pig house;
［豬食］ pig feed;
［豬蹄］ pig's feet; trotter;
［豬頭］ pig's head;
［豬腿］ (1) pig's legs; (2) ham; legmeat of the hog;
［豬尾］ pig's tail;
［豬瘟］ hog cholera; swine fever;
［豬血］ pig's blood;
［豬羊］ pigs and sheep;
殺豬宰羊 butcher pigs and sheep; kill pigs and sheep;
［豬腰］ pig kidney;
［豬油］ lard;
顆料狀豬油 grainy lard;
混合豬油 compound lard;
精製豬油 prepared lard;
優質豬油 prime lard;
［豬仔］ piglet; porkling;
［豬肘］ pork shoulder;
醬豬肘 spiced pork leg;

蠢豬 idiot; stupid swine;
肥育豬 fattening pig;
肥豬 lardass; porker;
海豬 dolphin;
豪豬 porcupine;
河豬 river hog;
箭豬 porcupine;
江豬 black finless porpoise;
毛豬 live pig;
如豬 like a pig;
生豬 live pig;
死豬 dead pig;
小豬 piglet;
野豬 wild boar;
一口豬 a pig;
一頭豬 a pig;
雜種豬 cross-bred pig;

zhu

【瀦】 pond; pool;
［瀦留］ retention;
［瀦育］ periodical water-logging;

zhu

【櫫】 post; stalk; stick; wooden peg;

zhu²

zhu

【朮】 podophyllum versipelle;
［朮酒］ medicinal wine;

白朮 rhizome of large-headed atratylodes;
蒼朮 rhizome of Chinese atractylodes;

zhu

【竹】 (1) bamboo; (2) a surname;
［竹板］ bamboo clappers;
竹板平雕 bamboo board with shallow carving;

[竹苞松茂] firm as the roots of a clump of bamboos and luxuriant as the pine tree — the fit proportion of architecture; symbolizing prosperity of family;
[竹帛] (1) bamboo tablets and textiles; (2) books;
垂名竹帛 names handed down in history;
[竹菜] edible plant;
[竹笛] bamboo flute;
[竹雕] bamboo carving;
[竹釘] bamboo peg;
[竹筏] bamboo raft;
[竹竿] bamboo cane; bamboo pole;
[竹槓] bamboo carrying pole;
[竹根青] bamboo green colour;
[竹工] bamboo works;
[竹罐] bamboo jar;
[竹雞] bamboo partridge;
[竹簡] bamboo slips;
秦墓竹簡 bamboo slips in the graves of the Qin Dynasty;
[竹匠] bamboo worker;
[竹節] bamboo joint;
[竹徑] bamboo path;
[竹刻] bamboo carving; bamboo engraving;
[竹筐] bamboo basket; bamboo crate;
[竹籃] bamboo basket;
竹籃子打水一場空 as futile as drawing water with a bamboo basket — achieve nothing; catch the wind with a net; draw water with a sieve; draw water with a bamboo basket — a useless effort; ladle water with a wicker basket — all in vain; pour water into a sieve;
[竹簾] bamboo curtain; bamboo screen;
竹簾畫 bamboo-curtain painting;
[竹林] bamboo forest; bamboo grove;
竹林之遊 association with learned scholars;
[竹籠] bamboo cage;
[竹馬] bamboo hobbyhorse; hobbyhorse;
竹馬青梅 companion in youth;
竹馬之好 companion in youth;
竹馬之交 friendship in youth;
騎竹馬 ride a bamboo hobbyhorse;
[竹幕] bamboo curtain;
[竹排] bamboo raft;
[竹片] split bamboos;
竹片詩雕 bamboo veneer with Chinese calligraphy in poetic verse;
竹片線雕 bamboo veneer with fine "thread carving";
[竹器] bamboo ware;
[竹青] bamboo bark;
[竹實] bamboo seed;
[竹鼠] bamboo rat;
[竹絲] bamboo splint;
竹絲玩具 toy made of bamboo filament;
[竹筍] bamboo shoot; bamboo sprout;
[竹榻] bamboo couch;
[竹胎] bamboo shoot;
[竹梯] bamboo ladder;
[竹亭] bamboo pavilion;
[竹筒] bamboo tube;
竹筒倒豆子 hold nothing back; make a clean breast of sth; pour beans out of a bamboo tube — withhold nothing;
[竹頭木屑] seemingly unimportant but useful things;
[竹葉青] (1) green bamboo snake; (2) bamboo-leaf-green liquor;
[竹椅] bamboo chair;
[竹園] bamboo plantation;
[竹杖] bamboo staff;
芒鞋竹杖 straw sandals and bamboo stick;
[竹枝詞] ancient folk songs with love as their main theme;
[竹汁] bamboo juice;
[竹紙] bamboo paper;
[竹子] bamboo pole;
一根竹子 a bamboo stick;
一蓬竹子 a clump of bamboo;

斑竹 mottled bamboo;
爆竹 banger; firecracker;
成竹 know what to do;
淡竹 henon bamboo;
簞竹 a variety of giant bamboo;
腐竹 dried bean milk cream in tight rolls;
黑竹 black bamboo;
箭竹 sinarundinaria nitida;
空竹 diabolo;
苦竹 bitter bamboo;
綦竹 green bamboo;
破竹 irresistible force;
琴竹 mallet;
箬竹 indocalamus;
石竹 carnation;

絲竹 traditional string and wind instruments;
天竹 nandina;
文竹 asparagus fern;
烏竹 black bamboo;
湘竹 mottled bamboo; speckled bamboo;
修竹 bamboo; tall bamboo;
銀竹 heavy rain;
紫竹 black bamboo;

zhu

【竺】 (1) ancient name of India; (2) a surname;
[竺經] Buddhist scripture;
[竺學] study of Buddhism;

zhu

【逐】 (1) chase; follow; pursue; (2) banish; drive off; drive out; exile; expel; (3) gradually; little by little; one by one;
[逐北] pursue the vanquished troops;
[逐波而去] be carried away by waves; go over the waves;
[逐步] gradually; proceed orderly; step by step;
[逐臣] banished subject; vassal in exile;
[逐臭] rim after filth;
逐臭之夫 a fellow who pursues rancidness;
[逐出] chase sb out of; drive out; eject; expel; kick out; oust; propel;
逐出門外 drive out of the door;
[逐次] each time; gradually; in succession; on each of the occasions; successive;
[逐點] point by point;
[逐電] go as quickly as a flash of lightning;
[逐個] one by one;
[逐漸] by degrees; gradually; little by little;
[逐客] exile;
逐客令 order the guests to leave;
[逐利] pursue material gains;
[逐鹿] bid for state power; chase the deer — fight for the throne; seek an office; vie for power; vie for the throne;
逐鹿中原 chase the deer on the Central Plains — try to seize control of the empire; fight among rivals for the throne;
[逐末] pursue trivial things;
[逐年] annually; with each passing year; year after year; year by year;
逐年逐月 month by month and year by year;
[逐日] daily; day after day; day by day; every day;
逐日追風 chase the sun and drive the wind;
[逐勝] pursue enemy troops in retreat;
[逐勢] strive for power and influence;
[逐條] article by article; item by item; point by point;
逐條逐句 article by article and sentence by sentence;
[逐兔先得] the leader in the hunt gets the quarry;
[逐退] drive back; repulse;
[逐項] member by member; term by term;
逐項驗收 check item by item before acceptance;
[逐一] detail by detail; one by one;
逐一解決 settle one by one; solve one after another;
逐一逐二 arrange in order; take up one by one;
[逐月] month by month; monthly;
[逐字] verbatim; word by word; word for word;
逐字翻譯 metaphrase;
逐字逐句 word by word and sentence by sentence; word for word; literal; verbatim;

奔逐 chase; run after;
斥逐 (1) dismiss from office; expel; (2) dismiss from presence;
放逐 banish; exile; send into exile;
角逐 compete; contend; enter into rivalry; juggle for; tussle;
驅逐 banish; chase; deport; drive off; drive out; drive out of; eject; evict; expel; extradite; get rid of; oust;
追逐 (1) chase; pursue; run after; (2) quest; seek;

zhu

【舳】 stern of a ship;
[舳艫] rectangular boat;
舳艫千里 formation of ships extending over a thousand miles;

zhu

【筑】 a kind of ancient string instrument;

zhu

【築】 (1) build; construct; (2) house; room;

［築路］ build roads;
［築墻］ build walls;
［築室道謀］ ask every passerby how to build one's house; house built by the wayside is either too high or too low;
築室道謀，莫衷一是 too much consulting confounds;
［築壇］ build an altar;
［築堤］ bild a dyke; build an embankment;
［築土］ build an earth-fill structure;

構築 build; construct;
建築 (1) build; construct; erect; (2) building; edifice; structure;
澆築 pour;
修築 build; construct;

zhu
【燭】 (1) candle; (2) illuminate; light up; shine upon; (3) watt;
［燭察］ have an insight into; see and understand clearly;
［燭光］ candlelight; candlepower;
燭光暗淡 the candle burned dim;
燭光如豆 the candlelight are burning low, as small as little peas;
半球形燭光 hemispherical candlepower;
標稱燭光 nominal candlepower;
射束燭光 beam candlepower;
視燭光 apparent candlepower;
微弱的燭光 dim light of a candle;
［燭花］ snuff;
燭花報喜 the hopping wick announces happy news;
［燭架］ candlestand; candlestick;
［燭燼月沉］ the candlelights go out and the moon sinks in the sky;
［燭淚］ guttering of a candle;
燭淚熒然 the guttering of a candle is bright;
［燭籠］ lantern;
［燭台］ candlestick;
分支燭台 candelabra;
［燭芯］ candlewick;
燭芯紗 candlewick;
［燭幽索隱］ like a candle lighting up the dark, leaving nothing hidden;
［燭照］ illuminate; light up;
燭照人心 illuminate a person's heart with a candle;
［燭燭］ brightly; brilliantly;

秉燭 by the candlelight;
炳燭 by the bright candlelight;
殘燭 expiring candle;
花燭 fancy candles lit in the bridal chamber at wedding;
火燭 things that may cause a fire;
蠟燭 candle;
燃燭 light a candle;
香燭 joss sticks and candles;
宵燭 glow-worm;
銀燭 bright candle;

zhu
【躅】 falter; hesitate;

躑躅 loiter around; walk to and fro;

zhu³
zhu
【主】 (1) host; (2) chief; host; leader; master; owner; (3) party concerned; person concerned; (4) Jesus Christ; God; Lord; (5) Allah; (6) chief; main; primary; principal; (7) in charge of; manage; take charge of; (8) in favour of; (9) stand for; (10) officiate at; (11) indicate; signify;
［主辦］ auspices; direct; hold; host; sponsor;
主辦單位 host unit;
主辦國 host country;
主辦者 promoter;
［主筆］ chief commentator; chief editor; editor-in-chief;
［主編］ chief editor; editor-in-chief;
主編職位 editorship;
副主編 associate managing editor; deputy managing editor;
［主賓］ guest of honour;
主賓席 head table;
［主播］ presenter;
［主持］ direct; manage; take charge of;
主持辯論 chair a debate;
主持公道 uphold justice;
主持人 chairperson; host; presenter; quizmaster;
~女主持人 chairwoman; hostess;
~著名的主持人 well-known presenter;
主持一切 play the master;
主持正義 stand for righteousness;

Z

[主菜] main course; principal dish;
一道主菜 a main course;
[主場] home court; home ground;
主場比賽 home gam;
主客場比賽 home and away games;
[主唱] lead singer;
樂隊主唱 leader singer of a band;
[主詞] subject;
代詞主詞 pronoun subject;
[主次] primary and secondary;
主次不分 confuse the minor and nonessential things with the major and essential ones; confuse the primary with secondary; make no distinction between the major...and the minor one;
主次顛倒 reverse the order of importance;
主次分明 make a distinction between the important and lesser one;
[主從] principal and subordinate;
主從關係 subordination;
主從句 main clause;
[主導] (1) dominant; guiding; leading; (2) leading factor;
主導產業 prime mover industry;
主導詞 dominant word;
主導同義詞 synonymic dominant;
[主動] of one's own accord; take the initiative;
主動分詞性結構 active participial construction;
主動靈活 take the initiative and be flexible;
主動式被動語態 active passive voice;
主動語態 active voice;
採取主動 take the initiative;
喪失主動 lose the initiative;
贏得主動 win initiative;
[主隊] home team; host team;
[主犯] leader of a racket; main culprit; prime culprit; principal criminal;
[主峰] highest peak in a mountain range; main peak of a mountain;
[主婦] hostess; housewife; mistress of the house;
家庭主婦 homemaker; housewife;
[主幹] (1) trunk; (2) main force; mainstay;
[主稿] chief writer;
[主格] subjective case;
[主根] main root; taproot;
[主攻手] ace spiker;
[主顧] client; customer;
拉主顧 solicit customers;
老主顧 regular customer;
熟主顧 frequent visitor; old customer;
[主觀] subjective;
主觀武斷 deal subjectively and arbitrarily; subjective assertion;
主觀臆斷 subjective and groundless conclusion;
主觀臆造 subjective conjecture;
[主管] (1) boss; chief; (2) take charge of;
主管機關 the authorities concerned;
主管人 person-in-charge;
主管職位 directorship;
財務主管 the person in charge of financial affairs;
[主和] advocate peace;
主和派 the doves;
[主婚] preside over a wedding ceremony;
[主機] (1) main engine; mainframe; (2) host computer;
主機板 mainboard;
主機接口 interface;
[主見] definite view; one's own judgement; one's own views; set view;
無主見 cannot make up one's mind about anything; have no opinion of one's own; indecisive;
心無主見 weak-willed;
有主見 know one's own mind;
[主講] (1) give a lecture; lecture on a topic; (2) key speaker; main speaker;
[主將] (1) chief commander; commanding general; mainstay; (2) the most important athlete in a sports team;
[主教] bishop;
大主教 archbishop;
副主教 archdeacon;
紅衣主教 cardinal;
[主角] lead; leading character; leading player; leading role; main actor; main actress; major character; protagonist;
唱主角 have a leading role in a play; hold a key role;
男主角 actor; chief actor; leading man; male lead; male title role;
~最佳男主角 best actor;
女主角 actress; female lead; leading lady;
~選定女主角 cast the female lead;
~最佳女主角 best actress;
飾演主角 cast in the lead role;

演主角 take the leading role;

[主句] main clause; principal clause;

[主考] (1) in charge of an examination; (2) chief examiner;

[主客] guest of honour;

反客為主 reverse the positions of the host and the guest; turn from guest into host; reversal of the order of host and guest; turn from a guest into a host;

客散主人寬 when the guests have left the host is at peace;

客隨主便 a guest should suit the convenience of the host; do as one's host thinks fit; the guest must accord to the host what he likes;

[主控] master control;

主控程序 master control programme;

主控開關 master switch;

主控制台 master console;

主控自動化 master control automation;

[主課] main subject; major course;

[主力] main force; main strength of an army; principal force;

主力軍 main force; principal force;

主力艦 battleship; capital ship;

[主糧] staple food grain;

[主流] (1) main current; main stream; mainline; the mother current; (2) essential aspect;

主流計算 mainstream computing;

主流教育 mainstream education;

主流領域 highways;

~非主流領域 byways;

主流政治 mainline politics;

[主謀] (1) head a conspiracy; (2) chief instigator; chief plotter; principal conspirator;

[主母] lady of the house; mistress;

[主腦] (1) centre of operation; control centre; (2) boss; chief; leader; leading light; mastermind;

[主奴] master and servant;

[主僕] master and servant;

有其主必有其僕 like master, like man; such master; such servant;

[主權] (1) sovereign rights; sovereignty; (2) right of autonomy;

主權國家 sovereign state;

主權象徵 representations of the sovereignty of the country;

主權移交 transfer of sovereignty;

國家主權 nation's sovereignty; state sovereignty;

海洋主權 maritime sovereignty;

絕對主權 absolute sovereignty;

聯合主權 conjoint sovereignty;

領土主權 territorial sovereignty;

消費者主權 consumer sovereignty;

永久主權 permanent sovereignty;

[主人] boss; host; landlord; master; owner;

主人公 (1) master; (2) hero; heroine; leading character in a novel; protagonist;

~男主人公 hero;

~女主人公 heroine;

主人翁 (1) master; (2) hero; heroine; leading character in a novel; protagonist;

北道主人 the host;

打狗看主人 in beating a dog regard must be paid to the status of its master; in beating a dog you must consider who is the owner;

盜憎主人 robbers hate the owner of lost property;

男主人 man of the house;

女主人 (1) hostess; (2) the lady of the house; the managress of the company;

盜憎主人 robbers hate the owner of lost property;

[主任] chairman; director; head; minister;

主任科員 principal staff member;

~副主任科員 principal staff member;

主任秘書 chief secretary;

班主任 class adviser; form teacher; head teacher; teacher in charge of a class;

~班主任制 system of putting a teacher in charge of each class;

車間主任 director; manager;

副主任 deputy director; vice-chairman; vice-minister;

體育指導主任 athletic director;

系主任 department chairman; department head;

~副系主任 deputy chairman;

學部主任 chairman;

研究中心主任 director of a research centre;

政治部主任 director of political department;

[主日] Sunday;

主日學校 Sunday school;

[主食] principal food; staple food;

[主使] (1) abet; incite; instigate; (2) behind-the-scene operator; mastermind; ringleader;

[主題] issue; key subject; main theme; motif; point; problem; proposition; question; subject; theme; thesis; topic;

主題詞 theme-word;

主題歌 theme song;

主題化 thematization;

主題句 topic sentence;

主題卡 subject card;

主題明確 with a clear-cut theme;

主題突出語言 topic-prominent language;

主題意義 thematic meaning;

偏離主題 digress; digression; stray from the point;

[主位] seat of the host;

[主謂] subject-predicate;

主謂詞組 subject-predicate word group;

主謂結構 subject-predicate construction;

主謂句 subject-predicate sentence;

主謂式合成詞 subject-predicate complex word;

[主席] chair; chairman; chairperson; president;

主席台 platform; rostrum;

主席團 presidium;

主席職位 chairmanship;

擔任主席 take the chair;

副主席 deputy chairman; vice-chairman; vice-president;

就任主席 take the chair;

女主席 chairwoman;

[主心骨] (1) backbone; mainstay; pillar; (2) definite view; one's own judgement;

[主刑] principal penalty;

[主修] (1) major in; specialize in; (2) responsible for the repair;

主修科目 major subject;

[主演] play the lead; play the lead role; play the leading role in a play; star in a motion picture;

聯合主演 costar;

~聯合主演明星 costar;

[主要] chief; essential; important; largely; mainly; major; primary; principal; the major part of;

主要動詞 main verb;

主要核心 main focus;

主要刊物 leading publication;

主要語言 primary language;

主要賬戶 principal account;

主要助動詞 primary auxiliary;

[主頁] homepage;

[主義] doctrine; -ism; principle;

愛國主義 patriotism;

霸權主義 hegemonism; policy of seeking hegemony;

~霸權主義者 hegemonist;

拜金主義 mammonism; money worship; worship of gold;

拜物主義 fetishism;

保護主義 protectionism;

保守主義 conservatism;

悲觀主義 pessimism;

本本主義 bookism;

本位主義 departmental egoism;

不抵抗主義 policy of non-resistance;

不合作主義 principle of non-cooperation;

懲處主義 doctrine of punishment;

抽象主義 abstractionism;

大男子主義 chauvinism; male chauvinism;

~大男子主義蠢豬 male chauvinist pig;

~大男子主義者 chauvinist;

地方主義 localism;

帝國主義 imperialism;

~封建帝國主義 feudal-imperialism;

~社會帝國主義 social-imperialism;

~資本帝國主義 capitalist-imperialism;

黷武主義 militarism;

法西斯主義 Fascism;

~反法西斯主義 anti-fascism;

~反法西斯主義者 anti-fascist;

~封建法西斯主義 feudal-fascism;

~社會法西斯主義 social-fascism;

分散主義 decentralism;

風頭主義 showing off; striving for the limelight;

封建主義 feudalism;

復仇主義 revanchism;

復古主義 doctrine of "back to the ancients";

福利主義 material benefits;

改良主義 reformism;

感傷主義 sencantilism;

個人主義 individualism;

功利主義 utilitarianism;

工聯主義 trade unionism;

工團主義 syndicalism;

公式主義 formulism;

共產主義 communism;
~共產主義制度 communist system;
共和主義 republicanism;
孤立主義 isolationism;
古典主義 classicism;
官僚主義 bureaucracy; bureaucratism;
關門主義 closed-doorism;
國粹主義 nationalism;
國際主義 internationalism;
國家主義 nationalism;
過激主義 extremism;
漢族主義 Han ethno-nationalism;
~大漢族主義 Han-chauvinism;
合法主義 legalism;
和平主義 pacifism;
懷疑主義 skepticism;
荒誕主義 absurdism;
~荒誕主義者 absurdist;
機會主義 opportunism;
極端主義 extremism;
極權主義 totalitarianism;
集權主義 totalitarianism;
~中央集權主義 centralism;
集體主義 collectivism;
家族主義 clannishness;
教條主義 dogmatism; doctrinairism;
結構主義 structuralism;
錦標主義 cups and medals mania;
禁慾主義 asceticism;
經濟主義 economism;
經驗主義 empiricism;
絕對主義 absolutism;
軍閥主義 warlordism;
軍國主義 militarism;
客觀主義 objectivism;
空談主義 idle chatter;
空想主義 utopianism;
恐怖主義 terrorism;
苦行主義 asceticism;
會計主義 accounting doctrine;
擴張主義 expansionism;
浪漫主義 romanticism;
樂觀主義 optimism;
理想主義 idealism;
利己主義 egoism;
利他主義 altruism;
~利他主義者 altruist;
歷史主義 historicism;
列寧主義 Leninism;
流寇主義 roving-rebel ideology;
馬克思主義 Marxism;
馬列主義 Marxism-Leninism;
賣國主義 national betrayal;
盲動主義 putschism;
冒險主義 adventurism;
蒙昧主義 obscurantism;
民權主義 democratism;
民生主義 principle of welfare;
民主集中主義 democratic talons;
民主主義 democratism;
民族主義 nationalism;
~大民族主義 big-nationality chauvinism; great-nation chauvinism;
命令主義 commandism;
能動主義 activism;
奴才主義 servility;
奴隸主義 slavish mentality; slavishness;
爬行主義 doctrine of trailing behind at a snail's pace;
排外主義 antiforeignism; exclusivism;
平均主義 egalitarianism; equalitarianism;
~絕對平均主義 absolute equalitarianism;
侵略主義 jingoism;
取消主義 liquidationism;
全勤主義 presenteeism;
犬儒主義 cynicism;
人本主義 humanism;
人道主義 humanitarianism;
~人道主義精神 the spirit of humanitarianism;
人文主義 humanism;
三民主義 the Three People's Principles;
僧侶主義 fideism;
沙文主義 chauvinism;
~大俄羅斯沙文主義 great-Russian chauvinism;
~大國沙文主義 great-power chauvinism;
山頭主義 mountain-stronghold mentality;
社會主義 socialism;
~社會主義改造 socialist transformation;
~社會主義建設 socialist construction;
~社會主義制度 socialist system;
~空想社會主義 utopian socialism;
神秘主義 mysticism;
失敗主義 defeatism;
實利主義 utilitarianism;
實驗主義 positivism;
實用主義 pragmatism;
實證主義 positivism;
世界主義 cosmopolitanism;
事務主義 routinism;
綏靖主義 pacifism;
逃跑主義 flightism;
調和主義 accommodationism;

conciliationism;
通貨主義 currency doctrine;
投降主義 capitulationism;
退卻主義 policy of retreat;
唯美主義 aestheticism;
唯我主義 solipsism;
唯物主義 materialism;
~辯證唯物主義 dialectical materialism;
~歷史唯物主義 historical materialism;
唯心主義 idealism;
尾巴主義 tailing behind the masses; tailism;
未來主義 futurism;
溫情主義 excessive tenderheartedness; undue leniency;
文牘主義 red-tape;
文化主義 culturalism;
無政府主義 anarchism;
現實主義 realism;
~超現實主義 surrealism;
相對主義 relativism;
享樂主義 hedonism;
象徵主義 symbolism;
小團體主義 cliquism; small-group mentality;
寫實主義 realism;
信仰主義 fideism;
形式主義 formalism;
行為主義 behaviourism;
修正主義 revisionism;
虛無主義 nihilism;
學院主義 academicism;
厭世主義 pessimism;
印象主義 impressionism;
英雄主義 heroism;
~個人英雄主義 individualistic heroism;
游擊主義 guerrilla-ism;
折衷主義 eclecticism;
折中主義 eclecticism;
殖民主義 colonialism;
~新殖民主義 neo-colonialism;
中立主義 neutralism;
種族主義 racialism; racism;
~反種族主義 anti-racism;
重商主義 mercantile doctrine; mercantilism;
主觀主義 subjectivism;
資本主義 capitalism;
~資本主義制度 capitalist system;
~官僚資本主義 bureaucrat-capitalism;
~國家資本主義 state-capitalism;
~壟斷資本主義 monopoly-capitalism;
~買辦資本主義 comprador-capitalism;
專制主義 despotism;
自然主義 naturalism;
自由主義 liberalism;
宗派主義 factionalism; sectarianism;

[主意] (1) idea; plan; suggestion; (2) decision; definite view;
變主意 change one's mind; under a change of heart;
出主意 offer good counsel;
~幫人出主意 assist sb with good counsel;
打主意 (1) evolve an idea; make a decision; think of a plan; (2) have ideas about; plan; seek; try to obtain;
~打錯主意 pray without one's beads;
~打定主意 arrive at a decision; hold firmly one's determination; make up one's mind; set one's heart on;
~另打主意 cook up new schemes; make some other plans; seek some other ways;
改變主意 backpedal; change of heart; change one's mind;
鬼主意 wicked idea; evil plan; evil plot;
好主意 good idea; that's a brilliant idea; that's a good idea; that's a marvelous idea; that's a practical idea; that's a wonderful idea; that's an excellent idea; what a capital idea;
~那是個好主意 that's a thought;
壞主意 bad idea;
沒主意 cannot make up one's mind; lose one's head;
拿主意 make a decision; make up one's mind;
~拿不定主意 cannot come to a conclusion; cannot make a decision; cannot make up one's mind;
~拿定主意 come to a conclusion; make a decision; make up one's mind;
巧主意 bright idea;
餿主意 lousy idea;
有個主意 have an idea;

[主因] major cause; principal cause;

[主語] subject of a sentence;
主語補語 subject complement;
主語層次 subjective level;
主語重譯法 reiteration of subject;
主語從句 subject clause;
主語附加語 subject adjunct;
主語生格 subject genitive;

主語突出語言 subject-prominent language;
表意主語 notional subject;
存在主語 existential subject;
地點主語 locative subject;
複合主語 compound subject;
工具主語 instrumental subject;
後提主語 postponed subject;
接受主語 recipient subject;
邏輯主語 logical subject;

[主宰] (1) decide; dictate; dominate; (2) force that controls and governs the destiny of mankind or the development of things (3) person in charge; person with supreme powers;

[主張] advocate; assertion; maintain; opinion; position; proposal; proposition; view;
主張改革 stand for change;
擅作主張 make an unilateral or arbitrary decision;
自作主張 act on one's own; decide all by oneself; decide for oneself; follow one's own bent; have one's own way of doing things; reckon without one's host; on one's own responsibility; self-assertion; take liberties; thrusting;

[主震] main shock;

[主政] head the administration; person in charge;

[主桌] head table;

[主旨] gist; purport; substance;

[主子] boss; master;

霸主 hegemon;
背主 disloyal to one's master;
賓主 guest and host;
財主 moneybag; rich man;
廠主 factory owner;
船主 shipowner;
地主 (1) landlord; landowner; (2) host;
店主 shopkeeper; storekeeper;
房主 house owner;
公主 princess;
顧主 client; customer; patron;
僱主 employer;
戶主 head of a household;
火主 source of a fire;
貨主 owner of cargo;
寄主 host of a parasite;
教主 founder of a religion;
救世主 savior;
爵主 heir apparent to a title of nobility;
君主 monarch; sovereign;
苦主 family of the victim in a murder case;
領主 feudal lord; suzerain;
買主 buyer; customer;
賣主 bargainor; seller; vendor;
沒主 (1) belong to nobody; (2) unmarried woman;
盟主 leader of an alliance;
廟主 head priest of a temple;
民主 democracy;
牧主 herd owner;
人主 king; sovereign;
入主 enter and host;
神主 memorial tablet; spirit tablet;
失主 owner of lost property;
施主 (1) alms giver; benefactor; (2) donor;
事主 victim of a crime;
受主 acceptor;
寺主 abbot;
宿主 host;
天主 God;
田主 landlord;
為主 give first place to; give priority to; mainly; the most important;
屋主 owner of a house;
無主 confused;
物主 owner;
小業主 small proprietor;
雄主 king of great talent and bold vision;
業主 property owner; proprietor;
易主 change masters; change owners;
有主 what is primary;
原主 original owner;
園主 owner of a garden;
債主 creditor; debtee;
寨主 leader;
棧主 innkeeper;
真主 Allah;
自主 act on one's own; autonomy; decide for oneself; independent; keep the initiative in one's own hands; one's own master;
作主 (1) take up the responsibility for making a decision; (2) back up; support;
做主 (1) take up the responsibility for making a decision; (2) back up; support;

zhu

【拄】 (1) post; prop; (2) lean on; (3) make sarcastic remarks; ridicule;

[拄笏看山] have a deep liking for natural charms even when occupying a high

position;
［拄杖］ crutch; staff; stick;

zhu

【渚】 sand bar in river;

zhu

【煮】 boil; cook; decoct; stew;
［煮菜］ prepare dishes; prepare food;
［煮蛋］ boil an egg;
煮蛋計時器 egg-timer;
［煮豆燃萁］ boil beans with beanstalks — internecine fight; burn beanstalks to cook beans; make a fire of beanstalks for boiling beans; make use of the stalk to cook the peas — intramural fight among brothers;
［煮飯］ cook meals; cook rice;
［煮沸］ boil heat water until it boils; bring to the boil;
［煮鶴焚琴］ cook crane for meat and burn string instruments for fuel — offence against culture;
［煮爛］ stew sth until it's tender;
［煮茗］ boil tea; infuse tea; make tea;
煮茗清談 gossip over a teacup;
［煮肉］ cook meat;
［煮熟］ cook thoroughly;
［煮鹽］ get salt by evaporation of seawater;
［煮粥］ cook congee;

水煮 water cooking;

zhu

【貯】 deposit; hoard; save up; store up;
［貯備］ hoard for future needs; store up;
貯備金 reserve funds;
［貯藏］ (1) hoard; store up; (2) deposits;
貯藏室 storage room; storeroom;
［貯存］ deposit; hoard; stockpile; store up;
貯存空間 storage space;
［貯積］ accumulate; store up;
［貯水］ store water;
貯水池 pond for storing water; reservoir;
貯水箱 cistern;
［貯蓄］ hoard; store up;

zhu

【麈】 (1) a kind of deer; (2) dust; whisk;
［麈談］ converse leisurely while holding a duster;
［麈尾］ duster;

zhu

【屬】 (1) compose; (2) direct; instruct;
［屬對］ search for a suitable sentence to match another;
［屬令］ direct; instruct;
［屬目］ gaze; look at eagerly;
［屬託］ ask sb to do sth;
［屬文］ compose a piece of prose writing;
［屬望］ centre one's hope on; look forward to;
［屬意］ fix one's mind on sb; have a preference for;
［屬垣有耳］ walls have ears — aware of eavesdroppers;
［屬者］ lately; recently;

zhu

【囑】 advise; ask another to do sth; charge; direct; enjoin; entrust; instruct;
［囑咐］ charge sb with a task; enjoin; exhort; tell;
［囑託］ entrust; request sb to do sth;
叮囑 repeatedly advise; urge again and again;
醫囑 doctor's advice;
遺囑 (1) will of a dead person; (2) instructions of a dying person;
諄囑 give repeated advice;

zhu

【矚】 gaze; stare;
［矚爵］ gaze; look steadily; observe carefully; pay attention; watch;
［矚目］ fix one's eyes on; focus one's attention upon;
舉世矚目 become the focus of world attention;
受人矚目 come into prominence; come to prominence;
［矚望］ (1) look forward to; (2) gaze at; look long and steadily upon;
矚望已久 have been eagerly looking forward to it for a long time;

zhu⁴

zhu

【宁】 (1) save; stockpile; store; (2) stand;

zhu

【住】 (1) dwell; inhabit; live; stay; (2) cease; stop;
［住不下］ cannot accommodate;
［住持］ abbot; head monk of a temple;
［住處］ accommodation; domicile; dwelling;

Z

residence; lodging; quarters;
找住處 look for accommodation;

[住房] housing; lodgings;
住房改革 housing reform;
住房緊張 housing shortage;
住房津貼 housing allowance;
住房政策 housing policy;
公共住房 public housing;
人均住房 per-capita housing;

[住戶] household; resident;

[住家] (1) live; reside in; (2) home; household; residence;

[住居] dwell; live; reside;

[住口] belt up; button it; button up; button up your lip; cut the cackle; dry up; hold your tongue; not a word; not say a word; pull in your ears; quit it out; quit your muttering; say no more; shut sb's mouth; shut up; stop sb's mouth; stop talking; stop your gab; stow your gab;

[住民] inhabitant; resident;

[住手] cut it out; hands off; stay one's hand; stop; stop it;

[住宿] get accommodation; lodge; put up; stop at; stay overnight;
住宿車 camping van;
免費住宿 rent-free accommodation;

[住所] abode; domicile; dwelling place; home; residence;
日常住所 habitual abode;
永久住所 permanent abode;
住無定所 reside in unfixed-abode;

[住校生] boarder;

[住院] be hospitalized; in hospital;
住院病人 inpatient;
住院部 inpatient department;
住院部主任 head of the inpatient department;
住院醫生 resident physician;

[住宅] dwelling; dwelling house; house; residence;
住宅單位 residential unit;
住宅房屋 dwelling house;
住宅區 residential area; settlement area; updown;
~住宅區和商業區 midtown;
~城市近郊住宅區 suburbs;
~城市遠郊住宅區 exurbs;
~高級住宅區 uptown neighbourhoods;
住宅商品化 housing commercialization;
住宅市填 dormitory town;
住宅新村 housing estate; housing development;
複式住宅 duplex;
~低密度複式住宅 low-rise duplex;
~三層複式住宅 triplex apartment;
海景住宅 sea-view apartment;
豪華住宅 luxurious residence;
花園住宅 garden residence;
~台階式花園住宅 step-garden residence;
市鎮住宅 townhouse;
四房住宅 four-bedroom apartment;

[住址] address; home address;

[住嘴] button it; button your lip; button your mouth; hold one's tongue; shut up;

按住 hold up; keep under control; press down and not let go; repress; restrain; withhold;
扒住 cling to; hold on to;
絆住 be detained; be held back; entangle; successfully hinder movement;
保住 keep; preserve; save;
抱住 hold in one's arms; hold on to;
憋住 fight back; hold back; keep down;
屏住 hold;
不住 ceaselessly; continuously;
踹住 keep the feet upon;
吃住 eat and live;
打住 bring to a halt; hold on; stop;
擋住 (1) check; halt; hamper; stop; (2) obstruct; screen; shield; (3) bar; block; stem;
盯住 keep a close watch on;
頂住 hold out against; stand up to; withstand;
釘住 nail securely;
封住 seal; seal up;
銲住 fix with solder;
記住 at the back of one's mind; bear in mind; carry sth in mind; commit to memory; fix in one's mind; get sth by heart; hold in one's head; impress on one's memory; keep at the back of one's mind; keep in mind; know sth by heart; learn by heart; make a mental note of; memorize; remember; say sth by heart;
禁不住 unable to bear; unable to endure;
禁得住 able to bear; able to endure;
揪住 grab tightly;
居住 dwell; live; make one's abode; reside; take up one's abode;
卡住 get stuck; seize;
看住 watch closely;
靠得住 dependable; reliable; trustworthy;

Z

愣住 be taken aback; become speechless because of astonishment;
瞞住 close;
迷住 bewitch; charm; enchant; fascinate;
拿住 (1) hold firmly; (2) put under arrest;
耐不住 unable to bear; unable to stand;
起住 the beginning and the end;
掐住 grasp; hold; seize;
且住 hold it; stop it;
擒住 succeed in capturing;
忍住 restrain;
塞住 block up; stop up;
煞住 hold it; stop;
拴住 (1) hold; (2) make fast; tie up;
鎖住 lock up;
同住 live together;
挽住 hold back;
圍住 be surrendered;
穩住 (1) hold back sb from intervening in one's plans; (2) make stable;
問住 unable to answer a question asked;
閒不住 always keep oneself busy; refuse to stay idle;
小住 sojourn;
楔住 put a wedge in to fasten;
押住 detain in custody;
壓住 detain; keep down; put down by force; suppress;
掩不住 cannot shut out; unable to cover; unable to hide;
咬住 (1) bite into; grip with one's teeth; (2) grip; refuse to let go of; seize; take firm hold of;
移住 change one's place of dwelling; move and settle down in another land;
站住 (1) halt; stop; (2) keep one's feet; stand firmly on one's feet; (3) hold water; tenable;
暫住 lodge temporarily at; stay for a while;
罩不住 unable to control a situation;
遮住 block; cover; obstruct;
止住 bring to a stop; desist; halt; stop;
滯住 detained; impeded; stopped;
抓住 capture; catch hold of; grasp; grip;
捉住 catch; get sb by the neck; seize;

zhu

【佇】 (1) stand; (2) expect; hope;

［佇候］ look forward to; stand and wait for a long time;
佇候佳音 look forward to hearing your good message;

［佇立］ stand a long time; stand motionless; stand still;

zhu

【助】 aid; assist; help;

［助產士］ midwife;

［助詞］ expletive;

［助教］ teaching assistant;

［助理］ (1) assist; (2) assistant;
助理編輯 assistant editor;
助理教授 assistant professor;
助理研究員 assistant research fellow;
助理員 clerk;
~查賬助理員 audit clerk;
~會記助理員 assistant accounts clerk;
技術助理 technical assistant;
科技助理 technical and scientific assistant;
特別助理 special assistant;

［助力］ assistance; help;

［助跑］ approach; run-up;
助跑距離 run-up;

［助人］ help others;
助人為快樂之本 happiness lies in rendering help to others; service begets happiness;
助人為樂 consider it a joy to help others; find it a pleasure to help others; glad to help others; take delight in helping others;
樂於助人 love to help others; obliging; ready to help others;

［助手］ aide; assistant; helper;
得力助手 right arm; right hand; right-hand man;
外交事務助手 diplomatic aide;

［助聽器］ audiphone; deaf aid; hearing aid;
電助聽器 electric hearing aid;
空氣傳導助聽器 air conduction hearing aid;
真空管助聽器 vacuum hearing air;

［助推］ boost;
助推火箭 booster rocket;
助推器 assist; booster;
~助推器拋投 booster jettisoning;
~助推器系統 booster system;
~火箭助推器 rocket assist;
~噴氣助推器 jet assist;
~起飛助推器 take-off assist;

［助威］ boost the morale of; cheer for; encourage; goad on;

［助興］ add to the amusement; add to the fun;

join in merry-making; liven things up;
助興節目 sideshow;
聊以助興 just for entertainment;

［助學］ develop education;
助學金 grant-in-aid; stipend; student grant;
捐資助學 make financial donations to help develop education;

［助戰］ (1) assist in fighting; (2) bother sb's morale;

［助長］ abet; encourage; foment; foster; give a loose rein to sth bad; indulge; nurture; promote the development of;
拔苗助長 spoil things by excessive enthusiasm; spoil things by overanxiety for quick results;

［助裝］ give money to a departing friend as travelling expenses;

［助陣］ cheer for a contestant;

［助紂為虐］ abet an ill-doer; help a tyrant to victimize his subjects; hold a candle to the devil;

幫助 assist; assistance; help;
臂助 assist; give a helping hand; help;
補助 allowance; subsidy;
扶助 help; support;
輔助 (1) assist; (2) auxiliary; subsidiary; supplementary;
互助 cooperation; help each other; mutual aid;
借助 be backed by; by; by help of; by means of; by the aid of; draw support from; have the aid of; on the strength of; through one's help; with the aid of; with the assistance of; with the help of;
救助 help sb in danger; succor;
捐助 contribute; offer;
內助 wife;
求助 resort to; seek aid; seek help; turn to sb for help;
相助 help; help each other;
襄助 assist; help;
協助 assist; give assistance; help; provide help;
醫助 assistant doctor;
佑助 aid; assist; help;
祐助 divine help;
援助 give assistance to; support;
贊助 give assistance to; support;
資助 aid financially; subsidize;
自助 help oneself; self-help;

zhu

【杼】 shuttle of a loom;

［杼柚］ loom;
杼軸其空 poverty; the looms are empty;

機杼 (1) loom; (2) conception;

zhu

【注】 (1) pour; (2) concentrate on; engross; (3) stakes (in gambling); (4) annotate; explain; (5) notes; (6) record; register;

［注定］ be destined; be doomed;
命中注定 be decreed by fate; be destined by fate; be predestined; predoom;
~命中注定的 sth is written in the stars;

［注腳］ annotation; footnote;

［注解］ (1) annotate; (2) annotations; footnotes;

［注明］ make a footnote; mark out;

［注目］ fix one's eyes on; focus one's look on; gaze at; look attentively; stare at;
注目禮 parade salute;
惹人注目 arrest sb's eye; attract attention; attract the gaze of the people; stick out like a sore thumb;
引人注目 attract the gaze of the people;

［注入］ empty into; injection; pour into;
注入式 cramming method; method of spoon feeding;
電荷注入 charge injection;
電流注入 current injection;
基極注入 base injection;
陰極注入 cathode injection;

［注射］ get a shot; inject;
注射器 syringe;
注射證明 vaccination certificate;
防疫注射 immunization inoculation;
肌肉注射 intramuscular injection;
激發注射 booster injection;
靜脈注射 intravenous injection;
皮下注射 inject hypodermically;
預防注射 protective inoculation;

［注釋］ (1) annotate; (2) annotation; footnote;
注釋性譯文 gloss translation;
一條注釋 a note;

［注視］ focus one's look on; gaze at; look attentively at; watch;
注視天空 gaze into the sky;
側目注視 give sb a sidelong glance; look at sb with a sidelong glance;
密切注視 keep a lookout; keep a weather

eye on;
嚴加注視 keep a sharp lookout;
[注疏] notes and commentaries;
[注水] water injection;
[注銷] annul; be written off; cancel; make void; nullify;
[注心] concentrate attention; focus attention;
[注意] care about; careful; have an eye on; look out; mindful of; notice; on the look-out; on the watch; pay attention to; show application; take care; take note of; watch; watch one's step; watch out;
注意力 attention;
~注意力持續時間 attention span;
~注意力時距 attention span;
~加強注意力 acuminate one's attention;
不注意 inattention;
不受人注意 fall on deaf ears; recede into the background; stand in the background; stay in the background;
不自覺注意 involuntary attention;
沒注意 fail to notice;
惹人注意 attract attention; catch sb's eye;
有意注意 voluntary attention;
自發注意 spontaneous attention;
[注音] transcribe;
[注重] attach importance to; consider to be important; emphasize; lay emphasis on; lay stress on; pay attention to;
注重實效 emphasize practical results;

備注 remarks;
垂注 show concern;
賭注 stakes;
附注 annotation;
關注 follow with interest; pay close attention to; show solicitude for;
貫注 (1) be absorbed in; concentrate on; (2) be connected in meaning or feeling;
灌注 pour into;
回注 recycle;
集注 focus;
加注 fill; refuel;
夾注 interlinear notes;
箋注 notes and commentaries;
澆注 pouring;
腳注 footnote;
眷注 take good care of;
批注 annotate and comment on;
評注 notes and commentary;
簽注 write comments on a document;
傾注 (1) empty into; pour into; stream down into; (2) concentrate on; devote; direct to; throw into;
詮注 notes and commentary;
投注 betting;
下注 put stake; stake a wager; wager;
挹注 draw from one to make up the deficits in another; supplement;
專注 be absorbed in; concentrate one's attention on; devote one's mind to;

zhu

【柱】 (1) pillar; post; (2) column-shaped object; (3) cylinder;
[柱臣] important ministers of a nation;
[柱廊] colonnade;
[柱面] cylindrical surface;
[柱塞] plunger;
反向柱塞 counter plunger;
緩衝柱塞 buffer plunger;
加速器柱塞 accelerator plunger;
[柱石] cornerstone; pillars of a nation;
[柱頭] capital; column capital; stigma;
混合式柱頭 composite capital;
伸臂柱頭 bracket capital;
斜角式柱頭 angular capital;
[柱仗而行] walk leaning on a staff; walk with the aid of a stick;
[柱子] pillar; post;
一根柱子 a pillar;

鼻柱 columna nasi;
冰柱 icicle;
砥柱 mainstay;
房柱 pillars of a house;
汞柱 mercury column;
護柱 bollard;
花柱 style;
脊柱 spinal column;
礦柱 pillar;
棱柱 prism;
立柱 stanchion;
列柱 colonnade;
門柱 doorpost;
戧柱 side support;
擎天柱 mainstay of a family;
三色柱 barber's pole;
沙柱 dust devil; sand column;
石柱 column;
水柱 water column;

台柱 (1) important actor in a troupe; (2) important person in an organization;
弦柱 neck of a string instrument;
煙柱 column of smoke;
一柱 a column of;
圓柱 column; cylinder;
支柱 column; mainstay; pillar; prop; stanchion; strut; support;

zhu
【苧】 China grass; ramie;
[苧麻] China grass; ramie;

zhu
【柷】 an ancient musical instrument;

zhu
【炷】 (1) wick of a candle; (2) stick of incense; (3) burn; cauterize;
[炷香] (1) burn incense; (2) stick of incense;

zhu
【祝】 (1) express good wishes; wish; (2) congratulate; felicitate; (3) celebrate; (4) a surname;
[祝詞] (1) congratulations; congratulatory message; congratulatory speech; (2) prayers at sacrificial rites in ancient times;
[祝典] celebration;
[祝福] benediction; blessing; wish happiness to;
祝福者 well-wisher;
[祝告] implore in prayer; invoke;
[祝好] best wishes; with best wishes;
[祝賀] congratulate; felicitate;
祝賀新年 wish sb a happy New Year;
[祝捷] celebrate a victory;
[祝酒] drink a toast; toast;
答謝祝酒 respond to the toast;
相互祝酒 exchange toasts;
[祝融] god of fire;
祝融為虐 the god of fire wrings great havoc;
祝融為災 conflagration; there is a fire accident;
[祝壽] celebrate sb's birthday; offer birthday congratulations; wish sb a happy birthday;
[祝頌] congratulate and commend; express good wishes;
[祝文] congratulatory message;
[祝願] wish;
互相祝願 exchange mutual good wishes;

禱祝 pray and express one's wishes;
廟祝 temple attendant in charge of incense and religious service;
年祝 years of jubilation;
慶祝 celebrate; congratulate;
巫祝 witch; wizard;
預祝 congratulate beforehand;
詛祝 pray to a deity;

zhu
【蛀】 (1) worms that eat wood or books; (2) bore; eat into;
[蛀齒] decayed teeth; dental caries;
[蛀蟲] borer; moth;
[蛀洞] cavity;
[蛀心蟲] borer;
[蛀牙] dental decay; tooth decay;

zhu
【紵】 linen; ramie; sackcloth;

zhu
【著】 (1) apparent; famous; marked; obvious; outstanding; (2) make known; manifest; prove; set forth; show; (3) author; write; (4) book; work;
[著稱] celebrated; famous;
[著績] well-known achievements; well-known results;
[著錄] put down in writing; record;
[著名] celebrated; famous; noted; renowned; well-known;
[著書] author a book;
著書立說 write books and establish one's theory; write books to propound one's ideas;
仰屋著書 dedicate oneself to one's writings;
[著述] (1) compile; write; (2) books; literary works; writings;
從事著述 be engaged in writing scholarly works;
[著者] author; writer;
[著作] (1) books; works; writings; (2) write;
著作等身 author with many works to his/her credit;
著作權 copyright;
~著作權保護 copyright protection;
著作權保護對象 object of copyright

Z

protection;
著作權保護期 term of copyright protection;
著作權保護體系 system of copyright protection;
~著作權登記 registration of copyright;
~著作權法 copyright law;
~著作權歸屬 ownership of copyright;
~著作權糾紛 copyright disputes;
~著作權人 copyrighter;
~著作權主體 subject of copyright;
一系列著作 a series of works;

編著 compile;
炳著 eminent; renowned;
歸著 put in order; tidy up;
合著 co-author; rite in collaboration with;
較著 conspicuous; obvious;
巨著 great work; monumental work;
論著 treatise; work;
名著 famous work; masterpiece; masterwork;
土著 original inhabitants;
顯著 notable; outstanding; striking;
遺著 posthumous work;
譯著 translated works;
原著 original work;
昭著 evident; obvious;
專著 monograph; treatise;
撰著 compose; write;
卓著 distinguished; outstanding;

zhu

【註】 (1) annotations; commentaries; footnotes; (2) list; record; register;
［註冊］ charge of registration; post; register;
註冊處 register office;
註冊入學 matriculation;
註冊商標 registered brand; registered trademark;
註冊資本 registered capital;
註冊主管員 registrar;
註冊主任 registrar;
商業註冊 commercial registration;
雙重註冊 double registration;
［註定］ destined; doomed; predestined;
［註記］ annotation; note;
［註腳］ annotation; footnote;
［註解］ (1) annotate; define; explain with notes; (2) annotations; footnotes; notes;
［註明］ explain clearly in writing; give clear indication of; make a footnote; mark out;
［註釋］ annotations; commentaries; explanatory notes; notes;
［註疏］ (1) explain; (2) explanatory notes;
［註銷］ annul; cancel; nullify; revoke; write off;

邊註 marginal note;
批註 (1) annotate and comment on; (2) annotations; annotations and commentaries; marginalia;
評註 (1) make commentary and annotation; (2) notes and commentary;
銓註 annotate;

zhu

【馵】 a horse with the near hind leg white;

zhu

【箸】 chopsticks;
［箸子］ chopsticks;

zhu

【翥】 soar; take off;

zhu

【駐】 (1) halt; stay; (2) be stationed;
［駐兵］ station troops;
［駐車］ parking;
駐車燈 parking light;
［駐地］ (1) cantonment; encampment; station; (2) seat;
［駐防］ garrison; on garrison duty;
［駐節］ be stationed in a country;
［駐軍］ garrison troops; station troops;
［駐守］ defend; garrison;
［駐外］ be stationed abroad;
駐外代辦處 representative office;
駐外代表 overseas representative;
［駐顏］ preserve a youthful complexion; retaining youthful looks;
駐顏有術 have a recipe for eternal youth;
［駐扎］ be quartered; be stationed;

常駐 permanent; resident;
進駐 enter and be stationed in; enter and garrison;
留駐 be stationed;
派駐 dispatch;

zhu

【鑄】 (1) cast metal; melt metal; (2) educate; influence; (3) a surname;
［鑄幣］ coin; coinage; coined money; mint

coins; mintage;
鑄幣廠 mint;
代用鑄幣 substitutionary coinage;
國際鑄幣 international coinage;
減色鑄幣 debased coinage;

[鑄成] cast into;
鑄成大錯 commit a howler; commit a serious mistake; make a great blunder; make a gross error; make a sad mistake; make great mistakes; miss a figure; run into great error;

[鑄錯] commit blunders;

[鑄鋼] cast steel;

[鑄工] (1) foundry work; (2) founder; foundry worker;

[鑄件] cast; casting;
杯形鑄件 cup-shaped casting;
多孔鑄件 blistered casting;
抗腐蝕鑄件 corrosion resisting casting;
耐酸鑄件 acid-proof casting;
青銅鑄件 bronze casting;
無蕊鑄件 coreless casting;
藝術鑄件 art casting;
有蕊鑄件 cored casting;
裝甲鑄件 armour casting;

[鑄劍為犁] beat the swords into ploughshares;

[鑄人] educate and influence people;

[鑄山煮海] excavate copper from mountain mine for coining and cook sea-water for salt — to develop natural resources;

[鑄鐵] cast iron; iron casting;
高級優質鑄鐵 high-duty cast-iron;
灰鑄鐵 gray cast-iron;
可鍛鑄鐵 malleable cast-iron;

[鑄銅] cast copper;

[鑄像] erect a metal statue;

[鑄造] casting; coinage; founding;
鑄造廠 foundry;
鑄造車間 foundry;
免費鑄造 gratuition coinage;
限制鑄造 limited coinage;

[鑄字] type founding; typecasting;
鑄字工廠 type foundry;
鑄字工 letterfounder;
鑄字工人 type founder;

電鑄 electroform;
澆鑄 cast; pour;
冷鑄 chill casting;
熔鑄 cast; found;
壓鑄 die-cast;

zhua[1]
zhua

【抓】 (1) catch; clutch; grab; grasp; make a snatch at; seize; snatch; take; (2) scratch; (3) arrest; catch; (4) pay special attention to; stress; (5) responsible for; take charge of; (6) attract; grip;

[抓到籃裏便是菜] all is fish that comes to net; whatever's in the basket can be used as food;

[抓斗] grab; grapple;
電動液壓式抓斗 electric-hydraulic grab;
起重機抓斗 crane grab;
三叉抓斗 three-tine grapple;
四叉抓斗 four-tine grapple;
自動抓斗 automatic grab;

[抓耳撓腮] (1) scratch one's ears; tweak one's ears and scratch one's cheeks; (2) impatient; uneasy; (3) agitated; (4) anguished; depressed;

[抓好] do a good job of; make great efforts to;

[抓痕] scratch;

[抓獲] arrest; capture; seize;

[抓尖兒] come off first; get the best portion;

[抓緊] firmly grasp; hold tight; pay close attention to;
抓緊時機行事 make hay while the sun shines;
抓而不緊，等於不抓 not to grasp firmly is not to grasp at all;

[抓舉] snatch;
單臂抓舉 one hand snatch;
箭步式抓舉 split snatch;
雙手抓舉 two-hand snatch;
下蹲式抓舉 squat snatch;

[抓空] use leisure moments;

[抓破] injure one's skin by scratching;
抓破臉 (1) hurt the face by scratching; (2) break off friendly relations;

[抓取] grab; overshot; take by grasping;

[抓權] grab power;

[抓人] arrest sb;

[抓頭] scratch the head;

[抓瞎] at a loss what to do; be thrown off balance; find oneself at a loss; in a rush and muddle; lose composure; lose one's head;

[抓尋] look for; search for;

Z

［抓癢］ scratch an itchy part;
［抓藥］ fill a prescription;
照方抓藥 act in accordance with;
［抓爪］ grasping claw;
［抓住］ capture; catch hold of; grasp; grip;
抓住不放 tackle sth on one's hand firmly and persistently;
抓住要害 take up a vital point;
緊緊抓住 hold on tight;
一把抓住 catch one by the arm; grab hold of; take hold of;

瞎抓 do things without a plan;

zhua
【撾】 beat; strike;

zhua
【髽】 bun; chignon; coil; women's head-dress in mourning;
［髽髻］ bun; chignon; coil;

zhua³
zhua
【爪】 (1) claw; talon; (2) nail;
［爪士］ lackeys; retainers;
［爪牙］ lackeys; retainers;
爪牙鷹犬 lackeys and hired ruffians;
［爪印］ nail mark; print; trace;
［爪子］ claw; paw; talon;
雞爪子 chicken's claws; chicken's feet;
鴨爪子 duck's web;
一隻爪子 a paw;

棘爪 detent; pawl;
錨爪 fluke;

zhuai³
zhuai
【跩】 waddling;

zhuai⁴
zhuai
【拽】 catch; drag; pull;
［拽象拖犀］ of great strength;
［拽子］ arm-disabled person;

zhuan¹
zhuan
【耑】 same as 專；

zhuan
【專】 (1) concentrate; focus; (2) monopolize; (3) special; specialized; (4) expert;

［專案］ special case for investigation;
專案法官 ad hoc judge;
［專才］ specialist;
［專差］ on a special errand; on a special mission; special errand; special mission;
［專長］ special skill; speciality; what one is skilled in;
發揮專長 give full play to sb's professional knowledge or skill;
學有專長 expert in a special field of study; have acquired a speciality from study; have specialized knowledge of a subject;
［專場］ special performance; show intended for a limited audience;
［專車］ special car; special train;
［專程］ special trip;
［專誠］ for a particular purpose; specially; with the exclusive purpose of;
專誠拜訪 make a special trip to call on sb; pay a special visit to sb;
［專寵］ monopolize the ruler's love;
［專此奉聞］ I write this specially to inform you that;
［專電］ news dispatch; special dispatch;
［專斷］ act arbitrarily; make an arbitrary decision;
［專訪］ special report on a special visit;
［專攻］ major in; make a speciality of; specialize in;
［專函］ letter written for a specific purpose; special letter;
［專號］ special issue;
［專橫］ arbitrary; despotic; dictatorial; domineering; tyrannical;
專橫跋扈 act arbitrarily; carry things with a high hand; despotic; imperious and despotic; ride roughshod over;
專橫的 bossy; domineering; overbearing;
～專橫的態度 high-handed manner;
［專化］ specialized;
專化特性 specialized feature;
［專家］ expert; guru; maven; past master; proficient; specialist;
專家版 professional edition;
專家程序 expert programme;
專家訪談 interview with expert;
專家顧問組 professional advisor group;

專家內閣 expert cabinet;
專家系統 expert system;
專家學者 specialists and scholars;
專家預測 forecasting by experts;
專家治國 technocracy;
專家組合 technostructure;
鼻科專家 rhinologist;
喉科專家 laryngologist;
腦科專家 brain specialist;
軟件專家 software expert;
神經病科專家 neuropathist;
心臟病專家 heart specialist;
心臟血管專家 cardiovascular specialist;
牙科專家 otologist;
一批專家 a consort of specialists;

[專精] concentrate one's efforts on;

[專刊] (1) special issue; (2) monograph;

[專科] (1) junior college education; (2) particular course of study;
專科學校 junior college;

[專款] special fund;

[專欄] column; special column;
專欄作家 columnist;
報紙專欄 newspaper column;
定期專欄 regular column;
書評專欄 book review column;

[專利] monopoly; patent;
專利持有人 patent holder;
專利代理 patent agency;
~專利代理機構 patent agency;
~專利代理人 patent agent;
專利法 patent law;
專利號 patent number;
專利技術 patent technology;
專利糾紛 patent dispute;
專利局 patent office;
專利品 patent; patent article;
專利權 monopoly; patent; patent right;
~專利權持有人 patent holder;
~專利權人 patentee;
專利申請 patent application;
~專利申請人 patent applicant;
專利事務所 patent agency;
專利文件 patent documents;
專利文獻 patent documentation;
專利許可證 patent license;
專利有效期 term of patent;
專利證書 letter patent;
專利制度 patent system;
產品專利 product patent;
附屬專利 dependent patent;
改進專利 improvement patent;
工業專利 industrial monopoly;
國家專利 national monopoly;
機密專利 secret patent;
進口專利 patent of importation;
買方專利 buyer's monopoly;
普通專利 common monopoly;
申請專利 apply for a patent;

[專力] with concentrated effort;

[專論] monograph;

[專賣] monopoly;
專賣店 monopoly shop;
專賣價格 monopoly price;
專賣局 monopoly bureau;
~國家煙草專賣局 state bureau of tobacco monopoly;
專賣權 monopoly right; patent;

[專美] attain distinction alone; monopolize all the praises;

[專門] (1) specialized; specially; (2) special field; specialty; (3) deliberately;
專門程度 degree of technicality;
專門詞語 technical word;
專門翻譯 specialized translation;
專門化 specialization;
~管理專門化 management specialization;
~語義專門化 specialization of meaning;
專門機構 special agency;
專門人才 expert; people with professional skill; professional; specialist;
專門術語 jargon; nomenclature; technical terms;
專門文獻 specialized text;
專門形容詞 technical adjective;
專門知識 expertise; specialized knowledge;

[專名] proper name; proper noun;
專名翻譯法 proper noun rendition;
專名號 roper noun mark;

[專區] prefecture;

[專權] dictatorial; grab all the power; in full power;

[專人] specially assigned person;

[專任] full-time; regular;

[專擅] act without authorization; do sth on one's own authority; do things without asking for approval; usurp authority;
專擅獨斷 act on one's own authority and come to an independent decision; usurp power and decide everything by

oneself;

[專設] ad hoc;

[專史] specific history;

[專使] special envoy;

[專署] prefectural commissioner's office;

[專題] special subject; special topic;

專題報導 report on a special topic;
專題報告 memoir;
專題調查 investigation of a special subject;
專題討論 seminar;
專題研究 monographic study;
專題演講 lecture on a special topic;

[專項] special item;

專項貸款 special-purpose loan;
專項資金 special fund;

[專心] attentive; be absorbed; concentrate one's attention; whole-hearted;

專心一意 be bound up in; undivided attention;
專心一志 concentrate one's attention on;
專心於 apply one's mind to;
專心致志 apply one's mind to; be absorbed in; be attached to sth; be bent on; be bound up in; be engrossed in; be preoccupied with; be steeped in; bend one's mind to; buckle down; bury oneself in; busy at; commit oneself to; concentrate one's attention on; deep in; devote one's attention to; devote one's mind to; devote oneself to; do sth with all one's heart; eager to; focus one's attention on; give one's mind to; have a good mind to do sth; keep one's mind on; mad for; occupy oneself with; peg away; put one's back into; put one's heart into; put one's life into; put one's mind into; put one's whole heart and soul into; set one's heart on; set one's mind to; steep oneself in; throw oneself heart and soul into; throw oneself into; with rapt attention; with single-hearted devotion;
不專心 unabsorbed;

[專修] major in; specialize in;

專修學校 special training school;

[專業] (1) discipline; special field of study; specialized subject; (2) special line; specialized trade;

專業標準 professional standard;
專業才能 professional competency;
專業廠家 specialized plant;
專業承包商 specialist contractor;
專業道德 professional ethics;
專業對口 a job suited to one's special training;
專業戶 specialized household;
專業化 professionalization; specialization;
~專業化分工 specialized division;
~專業化生產 specialized production;
~地區專業化 region specialization;
~教育專業化 educational specialization;
~生產專業化 productive specialization;
~完全專業化 complete specialization;
~早期專業化 early specialization;
專業技能 professional skill;
~專業技術職務 professional and technical posts;
專業教育 professional education;
專業精神 dedication to a job;
專業精英 professional elite;
專業考試 professional examination;
專業課 specialized course;
專業會計 professional accounting;
專業能力 professional competence;
專業判斷 professional judgment;
專業人士 professional;
~專業人士階級 professional class;
專業人員 personnel in a specific field;
專業認可 specialized accreditation;
專業文體 technical level of speech;
專業學校 college of careers; professional school;
專業訓練 professional training;
專業語言 special language;
專業知識 professional knowledge; specialized knowledge;
專業資格 professional qualification;
專業準則 professional qualification;
附屬專業 subspecialty;
一門專業 a speciality;

[專一] concentrate one's attention on; concentrated; single-minded; singleness; undivided;

專一性 specificity;
~寄主專一性 host specificity;
~絕對專一性 absolute specificity;
~區域專一性 regional specificity;
~相對專一性 relative specificity;
愛情專一 steadfast in love;

[專營] monopoly;

專營權 franchise;

[專用] be used exclusively for; for a special purpose; special use; use exclusively;

專用程序庫 private library;

專用集裝箱 specific purpose container;

專用軟件 special purpose software;

專用衛星 special satellite;

專用英語 English for Special Purposes;

專用線 siding;

~工廠專用線 factory siding;

~工業專用線 industrial siding;

~煤礦專用線 colliery siding;

[專有] exclusive;

專有出版權 exclusive publishing right;

專有技術 specialized technique;

~專有技術產權 property in know-how;

~專有技術轉讓合同 know-how transfer contract;

專有名詞 proper noun;

[專欲難成] the desire of the individual is difficult to accomplish;

[專員] assistant director; attaché; commissioner;

副專員 deputy commissioner;

經濟專員 economic attaché;

商務專員 commercial attaché;

文化專員 cultural attaché;

[專責] specific responsibility;

[專政] dictatorship;

無產階級專政 dictatorship of the proletariat;

資產階級專政 dictatorship of the bourgeoisie;

[專職] (1) sole duty; specific duty; (2) full-time;

專職教師 full-time teacher;

[專制] (1) autocratic; despotic; tyrannical; (2) autocracy;

專制獨裁 despotic dictatorship;

專制君主 autocrat;

專制統治 autocracy;

專制政體 autocracy;

專制主義 absolutism;

~開明的專制主義 enlightened absolutism;

[專著] monograph; treatise;

[專注] be absorbed in; concentrate one's attention on; devote one's mind to;

[專專] focus one's attention on;

博專 profound and specialized;

大專 universities and specialized colleges;

中專 special secondary school;

zhuan

【磚】 brick;

[磚房] brick house;

[磚石] masonry;

[磚瓦] bricks and tiles;

一磚一瓦 a brick and a tile; a single brick and tile;

冰磚 ice-cream brick;

茶磚 brick tea;

瓷磚 ceramic tile; glazed tile;

多孔磚 cellular brick; cork brick;

高爐磚 blast furnace brick;

格子磚 checker brick;

鉻美磚 chrome-magnesite brick;

鉻矽磚 chrome silica brick;

鉻磚 chromite brick;

缸磚 quarry tile;

拱磚 arch brick;

弧形磚 compass brick;

混凝土磚 concrete brick;

火泥磚 cement brick;

火磚 firebrick;

絕熱磚 cellinsulate brick;

空心磚 air brick; cavity brick; cell brick; hollow brick;

爐底磚 bottom brick;

爐腹磚 bosh brick;

爐體磚 body brick;

鋁土磚 bauxite brick;

煤渣磚 cinder brick;

煤屑磚 coal-dust brick;

煤磚 coal brick;

鎂磚 magnesia brick;

耐酸磚 acid-proof brick;

黏土磚 clay brick;

普通磚 common brick;

敲門磚 a stepping stone to success;

青磚 black brick; blue bricks;

砂磚 bath brick;

滲碳矽磚 carbonizing silica brick;

石棉磚 asbestos brick;

束磚 bonding brick;

水泥磚 cement brick;

炭磚 carbon brick;

碳化矽磚 carborundum brick;

碳矽磚 carbide brick;

陶磚 earthenware brick;

矽磚 silica brick;

胸墻磚 breast-wall brick;
窰頂磚 ceiling brick;
一層磚 a layer of bricks;
一堆磚 a heap of bricks; a pile of bricks;
一塊磚 a brick;
硬磚 clinker brick;
鑄造磚 cast brick;

zhuan

【顓】 (1) cautious; (2) dull; ignorant; stupid; (3) a surname;

[顓兵秉政] assume military responsibility and hold the political power;

[顓蒙] foolish and nescient; ignorant;

[顓頊] a legendary ruler in ancient China;

[顓顓] (1) ignorant; stupid; (2) careful; respectful;
顓顓獨居 live a lonely and ignorant life;

zhuan³
zhuan

【轉】 (1) change; take a turn; turn; (2) convey; pass on; transfer; transport; (3) indirect; roundabout; (4) roll; (5) migrate; move;

[轉背] as soon as one turns one's back; face about; turn round;

[轉變] (1) change; transform; undergo changes; (2) change; shift; turnabout;
轉變立場 shift one's stand; switch sides;
轉變態度 turnabout in attitudes;
大轉變 about-face; about-turn;
開始轉變 on the turn;

[轉播] rebroadcast; relay a broadcast; relay broadcasting; retransmit; retransmission;
轉播電台 relay station;
轉播站 relay station;
衛星轉播 satellite transmitting;
無線電轉播 wireless relay broadcasting;
無源轉播 passive retransmission;
現場轉播 field pickup;
有線轉播 rediffusion on wire; wire relay broadcasting;

[轉車] change trains or buses; transfer to another train or bus;

[轉船] change to another ship; tranship;

[轉達] communicate; convey; mediate; pass on; transmit through another person;

[轉貸] enlending;

[轉道] go by way of; make a detour;

[轉遞] send through another person;
轉遞地址 forwarding address;

[轉動] (1) revolve; rotate; turn; turn round; (2) budge; move;
反向轉動 contrarotation;
快速轉動 spin like a top;

[轉發器] transponder;
被動式轉發器 passive transponder;
加工轉發器 process transponder;
相干轉發器 coherent transponder;

[轉告] communicate; pass on; transmit;

[轉化] change; conversion; transform;
轉化率 percent conversion;
單程轉化 once-through conversion;
恒定深度轉化 constant level conversion;
生化轉化 biochemical conversion;
雙重轉化 dual conversion;
吸熱轉化 endothermic conversion;

[轉圜] (1) intercede; retrieve an undesirable development; (2) listen to advice readily;

[轉換] change; changeover; convert; conversion; switch; transform;
轉換比率 conversion ratio;
轉換成分 transformational component;
轉換規則 transformational rules;
轉換話題 change the subject of conversation; switch the conversation to another subject;
轉換鍵 switch key;
轉換器 converter;
~聲象轉換器 acoustic image converter;
~數字轉換器 digital converter;
轉換生成語法 transformational-generative grammar;
轉換語法 transformational grammar;
並行轉換 concurrent conversion;
層次轉換 level shift;
充氣轉換 charging changeover;
詞類轉換 conversion in the parts of speech;
代碼轉換 code switching;
地址轉換 address conversion;
電源轉換 power supply changeover;
翻譯轉換 translation shift;
風格轉換 style shift;
功能轉換 functional shift;
交叉轉換 overlap changeover;
句法轉換 anacoluthon;
能量直接轉換 direct energy conversion;

數字轉換 digital conversion;
算術轉換 arithmetic conversion;
天線轉換 aerial changeover;
制動轉換 brake changeover;

[轉回] return; turn back;

[轉迴] metamorphorsis; the transmigration of souls;

[轉會] transfer;
轉會費 transfer fee;
轉會名單 transfer list;

[轉機] favourable turn; turn for the better; turning point;

[轉嫁] (1) pass to; shift; transfer; (2) remarry;
轉嫁危機 shift one's burden of crisis onto others;

[轉交] deliver in care of another person; forward; pass on to; reassign; transmit;

[轉角] corner of a building; corner of a street;

[轉借] lend;

[轉矩] torque;
轉矩計 torquemeter;
~電子轉矩計 electronic torquemeter;
~晶體管轉矩計 torquemeter;
控制轉矩 controlling torque;
起步轉矩 breakaway torque;
制動轉矩 brake torque;

[轉科] (1) change one's major; (2) go to a different medical division; transfer from one department to another;

[轉口] entrepot; transit;
轉口貨物 transit goods;
轉口貿易 entrepot trade; intermediate trade;
轉口税 transit duties;

[轉臉] (1) turn one's face; (2) in a wink; in no time; in the twinkling of an eye;

[轉捩點] crunch; turning point;

[轉錄] recording; transfer;
轉錄機 re-recorder;
轉錄系統 re-recording system;

[轉輪] wheel;
大轉輪 big wheel;

[轉賣] resell; subpurchase;

[轉年] next year; the coming year; the following year;

[轉念] change one's mind; have second thoughts; reconsider and give up an idea; think better of;

[轉暖] become warm (the weather);

[轉盤] turntable;
唱機轉盤 gramophone turntable;
十字轉盤 two-way turntable;
斜角轉盤 oblique turntable;

[轉去] go back; turn and go;

[轉讓] make over; transfer the possession of;
轉讓方 assignor;
轉讓費 royalty;
轉讓權 assignment right;
不得轉讓 not transferable;
技術轉讓 technology transfer;

[轉入] change over to; shift to; switch over to;
轉入正常 return to noral;

[轉身] face about; turn round; turn the body;
小得無法轉身 there's not enough room to swing a cat;

[轉生] reincarnation; transmigration;

[轉世] transmigrate into another body;

[轉手] (1) change hands; fall into another's hands; pass on; sell what one has bought; (2) a brief period of time;
轉手變卦 change one's mind in a short moment;
轉手成空 lose all quickly;
轉手倒賣 buy sth and resell it at a profit;

[轉售] sell what one has bought;

[轉述] relate sth as told by another; report;
轉述引語 reported speech;

[轉瞬] (1) a moment; a trice; an instant; in a flash; in a twinkle; (2) turn the eyes;
轉瞬即逝 passing; vanish in a twinkle;
轉瞬之間 as quick as a wink; in a flash; in a twinkle; in a twinkling; in a wink; in the twinkling of an eye;

[轉送] (1) pass on; transmit on; (2) make a present of sth given to one;

[轉速] tachy;
轉速表 tachometer;
~半自動轉速表 aided tachometer;
~交流轉速表 A.C. tachometer;
~漏氣式轉速表 air leak tachometer;
~直流轉速表 direct current tachometer;
轉速測定法 tachometry;
轉速計 tachometer;
~電容式轉速計 capacitor tachometer;
~離心式轉速計 centrifugal tachometer;
~摩擦式轉速計 air braking tachometer;
~鐘錶式轉速計 chronometric tachometer;
轉速脈衝 tacho-pulse;

[轉題] change the subject;
轉題聯加語 transitional conjunct;
[轉頭] turn one's head;
[轉託] entrust through another person;
[轉彎] make a turn; swerve; take a turn; turn a corner; turn in another direction;
轉彎抹角 (1) beat about the bush; devious; fool round the stump; full of twists and turns; in a devious way; in a roundabout way; insinuatingly; mince; oblique; prunes and prism; twisty; talk in a roundabout way; (2) go along a zigzag course;
急轉彎 (1) dogleg; sharp bend; sharp turn; take a sudden turn; (2) make a radical change; (3) zigzag;
~路上有個急轉彎 there is a sharp bend in the road;
三彎九轉 full of twists and turns; many twists and turns;
[轉為] be turned into;
轉敗為功 turn failure into success;
轉嗔為喜 change one's initial ill-humour into a feeling of satisfaction; the anger on one's face gives way to joy;
轉怒為歡 begin to laugh instead of being angry; one's rage is turned into joy;
[轉徙] migrate from place to place; wander about;
[轉向] change directions; change one's political position; diversion; steering; sway; swing; turn; turn around; turn in the direction of; turn round;
轉向指示燈 indicator; turn signal;
~轉向指示燈開關 indicator; turn signal;
轉向裝置 steering;
~動力轉向裝置 power steering; power-assisted steering
~自動轉向裝置 power steering; power-assisted steering;
不可逆轉向 irreversible steering;
昏頭轉向 confused and dizzy; with a swirling head;
雙轉向 double steering;
[轉型] crossover;
[轉學] transfer to another school;
轉學生 transfer student;
[轉眼] in a flash; in a moment; in an instant; in the twinkling of an eye;
轉眼便忘 out of sight, out of mind;
轉眼不見 in the twinkling of an eye it ceases to exist;
轉眼成空 vanish in the twinkling of an eye;
轉眼之間 as swift as a wink; before you can say Jack Robinson; before you know where you are; in a flash; in a jiffy; in a trice; in a twinkling; in a wink; in an instant; in jig time; in no time; in the turn of a hand; in the twinkling of an eye; on the instant;
一轉眼 in a wink of an eye;
[轉頁] turn over the leaf;
[轉業] be transferred to civilian work; change one's career; change one's trade;
[轉移] (1) divert; diversion; migration; shift; transfer; (2) change; transform;
轉移詞 transferred word;
轉移目標 divert sb's attention;
轉移視線 (1) divert public attention; divert sb's attention; draw attention to some other matter; (2) divert the line of sight; turn the gaze;
轉移意義 transferred meaning;
轉移陣地 evacuate position;
安全轉移 move to safe places;
胞核轉移 nuclear migration;
詞匯轉移 lexical transfer;
負向轉移 negative transfer;
結構轉移 structural transfer;
氫轉移 hydrogen migration;
戰略轉移 strategic shift;
[轉椅] revolving chair; swivel chair;
[轉義] transferred meaning;
轉義翻譯法 trope device;
[轉喻] metonymy;
標準轉喻 stock metonymy;
[轉譯] retranslation;
[轉引] quote from a secondary source;
[轉運] (1) convey; forward; transfer; transport; trans-ship; (2) have a change of luck; have a turn of luck; luck turns in one's favour;
轉運港 transit port;
轉運口岸 entrepot;
[轉載] reprint;
[轉贈] make a present of sth given to one;
[轉輾] toss about;
轉輾不寐 toss about all night; toss about restlessly all night in one's bed;

轉輾反側 toss and turn;

［轉戰］ fight in one place after another;

轉戰南北 fight north and south;

［轉賬］ bring forward; carry forward; carry over; transfer accounts;

電子資金轉賬 electronic funds transfer;

［轉折］ (1) complications; turn in the course of events; twists and turns; (2) transition;

轉折並列連詞 transitional coordinator;

轉折詞 adversative; transitive word;

轉折從句 adversative clause;

轉折點 crossroads; turning point;

～人生轉折點 turning point in one's life;

～弗業轉折點 career crossroads;

轉折連詞 adversative conjunction;

［轉致］ convey through another person;

［轉租］ farm out; sublease; sublet;

［轉子］ rotor;

不對稱轉子 antisymetric rotor;

鼓風機轉子 blower rotor;

［轉字鎖］ combination lock;

暗轉 blackout;

扳轉 (1) turn around; (2) tip the scale; turn the tide;

承轉 pass on or forward;

倒轉 reverse; turn the other way round;

掉轉 turn round;

調轉 (1) change; switch; (2) transfer to another job;

翻轉 overturn; turn;

反轉 reverse;

好轉 improve; take a turn for the better;

回轉 turn round;

結轉 carry-over;

流轉 (1) on the move; roam; wander about; (2) the circulation of sth;

逆轉 become worse; deteriorate; kick back; reverse; set-back; take a turn for the worse;

扭轉 (1) reverse; turn back; (2) turn round;

偏轉 deflect;

婉轉 (1) mild and indirect; tactful; (2) sweet and agreeable;

旋轉 revolve; turn;

運轉 (1) revolve; turn round; (2) operate; work;

輾轉 (1) pass through many hands and places; (2) toss about in bed;

中轉 change trains;

周轉 have enough to meet the need; turnover;

zhuan

【囀】 (1) chirp; twitter; warble; (2) pleasing to the ear;

［囀喉］ pleasant voice; sweet voice;

［囀鳴聲］ tweedle; warble;

［囀音］ warble tone; wobble;

zhuan4

zhuan

【傳】 (1) commentaries on classics; (2) biography; (3) novel or story written in historical style;

［傳記］ biography; life story;

傳記小説 saga novel;

傳記作者 biographer;

聖徒傳記 hagiography;

溢美的傳記 hagiography;

［傳略］ biographical sketch; brief biography;

［傳驛］ courier station;

別傳 supplementary biography;

立傳 glorify sb by writing his/her biography;

列傳 biographies;

評傳 critical biography;

小傳 brief biography;

自傳 autobiography;

zhuan

【瑑】 engraving on a jade-tablet;

zhuan

【撰】 compose; write;

［撰次］ compile;

［撰稿］ prepare manuscripts; write;

撰稿人 writer;

～採訪撰稿人 free-lancer;

～特約撰稿人 staff writer;

～自由撰稿人 freelance writer; freelancer;

撰稿員 copywriter;

［撰錄］ make a selection;

［撰述］ compose; write;

［撰文］ compose; write;

［撰寫］ author; write;

［撰著］ compose; write;

編撰 compile;

杜撰 fabricate; make up;

zhuan

【篆】 (1) seal type; (2) seal; (3) a surname;

［篆刻］ seal cutting; stamping-seal engraving;

［篆書］ seal character; seal script;

［篆體］ seal characters;

［篆務］ official affair;

Z

[篆章] chop; seal;
[篆字] characters written in the seal type;

大篆 a style of calligraphy;
小篆 a style of calligraphy;

zhuan
【篹】 same as 撰 ;

zhuan
【賺】 (1) earn; gain; make a profit; (2) cheat; deceive;
[賺錢] make money; make a profit;
賺錢生意 paying proposition; profitable business;
賺錢養家的人 bread-winner; wage-earner;
[賺人] cheat sb;
[賺頭] profit; sth to gain;

zhuan
【轉】 revolution; revolve; rotate; turn; turn round and round;
[轉動] revolve; roll; rotate; run; turn; twirl;
[轉門] revolving door; turnstile;
[轉磨] at a loss in the face of a difficulty;
[轉圈] circle; ring; turn; whirl;
[轉石不生苔] a rolling stone gathers no moss;
轉石不生苔，轉業不聚財 a rolling stone gathers no moss; on a rolling stone no moss will stand;
[轉臺] revolving stage;
[轉檯] turntable;
[轉向] (1) get lost; lose one's bearing; lose one's way; (2) a change in one's philosophy;
[轉心] harbour evil thoughts; hold evil thoughts in the mind;
[轉一轉] take a short walk; take a turn;
[轉椅] swivel chair;

打轉 turn round and round;
公轉 revolve;
空轉 (1) (of a motor) idle; (2) turn without moving forward;
自轉 rotate;

zhuan
【饌】 (1) prepare food; (2) eat and drink; feed; provide for;
[饌具] food vessels;

盛饌 sumptuous dinner;
餚饌 sumptuous courses at a meal;

zhuang¹
zhuang
【庄】 (1) farmhouse; (2) market place; (3) banker; (4) cottage;

zhuang
【妝】 (1) adorn oneself; doll up; make up; (2) jewels for adornment; (3) disguise; pretend;
[妝扮] doll up;
[妝點] adorn; apply make-up; dress up;
[妝奩] dowry;
[妝樓] lady's private boudoir;
[妝飾] adorn; deck out; decorate; dress up;
[妝梳] comb and dress one's hair;
[妝臺] lady's dressing table;

補妝 fix one's make-up; touch up one's make-up;
化妝 apply make-up; do one's make-up; put on make up; wear make-up;
靚妝 beautiful adornments;
濃妝 heavy make-up;
梳妝 dress and make up;
眼妝 eye make-up;
卸妝 take off formal dress and ornaments; take off make-up;

zhuang
【莊】 (1) hamlet; village; (2) large farmhouse; manor house; (3) market; shop; store; (4) grave; serious; (5) august; dignified; sober; solemn; stately; (6) a surname;
[莊戶] farmer; peasant household;
[莊稼] crops; emblement;
[莊家] (in a gambling game) banker; bookmaker; marketmaker; turf account;
[莊客] tenant farmers;
[莊口] market;
[莊論] dignified statement;
[莊奴] tenant farmer;
[莊諧] sobriety with humour;
莊諧并作 combine sobriety with humour;
亦莊亦諧 serious and facetious at the same time; sometimes with real earnestness and sometimes with playful gaiety;
[莊嚴] dignified; solemn; stately;
莊嚴肅穆 an atmosphere of solemnity

and reverence prevails; in a solemn and awe-inspiring atmosphere; with a solemn silence;

[莊園] manor;
莊園大宅 country seat;
莊園的 manorial;

[莊重] grave; serious; solemn;
保持莊重 keep one's gravity;
舉止莊重 grave in manner;
神情莊重 look serious;

茶莊 tea shop;
村莊 hamlet; village;
端莊 decorum; demure; dignified; sedate;
飯莊 restaurant;
鍋莊 folk dance of the Zang;
連莊 (of mahjong) stay on as the dealer;
農莊 farmstead;
票莊 firm for exchange and transfer of money;
錢莊 banking house; money house; private bank;
山莊 country house; mountain villa;
田莊 country estate; farmhouse; farmstead;
做莊 be the banker;

zhuang
【粧】 same as 妝 ;

zhuang
【裝】 (1) adorn; attire; doll up; dress up; make up; (2) clothes; outfit; (3) stage make-up and costume; (4) disguise; feign; make believe; pretend; (5) fill in; fill up; load; pack; (6) fit; install;

[裝扮] attire; deck out; doll up; dress up;

[裝包] pack; packing;

[裝備] equip; fit out;
裝備線 assembly line;
武器裝備 ordnance;
~ 反潛武器裝備 antisubmarine ordnance;
~ 防空武器裝備 anti-aircraft ordnance;
~ 水下武器裝備 underwater ordnance;

[裝裱] mount a picture;

[裝病] feign illness; malinger; pretend sickness;
裝病者 malingerer;

[裝船] load cargoes aboard a freighter;
裝船費 loading charge;
提前裝船 advance shipment;

[裝袋] bagging;
裝袋裝置 bagging apparatus;

[裝點] deck; decorate; dress;

[裝訂] bookbinding;
裝訂成冊 bind in a volume; bind a book; bind together in book form;
裝訂工 binder;
半革裝訂 half binding;
第一版裝訂 primary binding;
機械裝訂 machine binding;
加固裝訂 reinforced binding;
臨時性裝訂 temporary binding;
皮脊裝訂 quarter binding;
全革裝訂 whole binding;
人工裝訂 hand binding;
鐵線裝訂 wire stitching;
無線裝訂 perfect binding; threadless binding;

[裝璜] decorate; decoration;
裝璜門面 create a good public impression; do sth for form's sake; do sth for the sake of appearances; do window dressing; keep up appearances; put on a good front; put up a facade;
不加裝璜 no frills;

[裝貨] load goods; loading; pack goods; shipment;
裝貨箱 crate;

[裝甲] (1) plate armour; (2) armoured;
裝甲板 plate armour;
裝甲兵部隊 cavalry;
裝甲步兵 armoured infantry;
裝甲部隊 armoured troops;
裝甲車 armoured car; tank;
裝甲飛機 armoured aeroplane;
裝甲列車 armoured train;
裝甲師 armoured division;
裝甲戰車 armoured fighting vehicle;
砲塔裝甲 turret armour;

[裝假] feign; make believe; pretend;

[裝料] charging;
分裝料 layer charging;
高壓裝料 high-pressure charging;
料籃裝料 basket charging;
人工裝料 hand charging;

[裝滿] fill; fill up;

[裝配] assemble a machine;
裝配工 fabricator; fitter;
裝配機器 assemble a machine;

[裝腔] affect certain airs; artificial; behave affectedly;
裝腔作勢 affect manners; affected; airs and graces; assume airs of importance; assume an appearance; behave affectedly; do the grand; full

of affections; give oneself airs; have a pretentious manner; indulge in histrionics; make a pretense of dignity; make grand gestures; on stilts; parade the idea that; perk oneself up; play-acting; pretend innocence; pretentious; put on; put on airs; strike a pose; strike an attitude; try to be impressive;
~ 裝腔作勢的 la-di-da;

[裝窮] feign to be poor;
裝酸哭窮 feign to be poor;

[裝傻] act dumb; feign ignorance; feign stupidity; play possum; pretend to be ignorant; pretend to be naive; pretend to be silly; pretend to be stupid; pretend not to know;
裝傻充楞 play the fool;
裝瘋賣傻 feign madness and act like an idiot; feign madenss and play the fool; feign oneself mad and act like a fool; play the fool; pretend to be crazy and stupid; pretend to be mad;
裝聾作傻 pretend to be ignorant of sth; pretend to know nothing and hear nothing;

[裝設] be equipped with; equip; install;

[裝飾] (1) adorn; decorate; embellish; ornament; set off; (2) deck; doll up; make up;
裝飾品 decorative item; adornment; ornament; ornamental item;
裝飾音 grace; grace note; ornament;
波紋裝飾 combed decoration;
車刻裝飾 engine-turned decoration;
單色裝飾 monochrome decoration;
吊懸裝飾 drop ornament;
幾何圖形裝飾 geometrical ornament;
精緻裝飾 gracious décor;
室內裝飾 interior decoration;
書邊裝飾 edge decoration;
寓言裝飾 fable decoration;

[裝束] attire; dress;
裝束入時 in fashionable dress;
裝束時髦 dress fashionably; dress in up-to-date fashion;
一種裝束 a costume;

[裝睡] feign sleep; pretend to sleep; pretend to be asleep; sham sleep;

[裝死] death mimicry; feign death; play dead; sham death;
裝死賣活 act shamelessly;

[裝蒜] affected; feign ignorance; make a pretence; pretend not to know; pretentious;
別裝蒜 come off it;

[裝箱] box; pack in a box;
裝箱費 packing charges;

[裝卸] (1) load and unload; (2) assemble and disassemble;
裝卸工 loader;
~ 碼頭裝卸工 stevedore;
裝卸區 loading place;

[裝修] (1) decorate and repair; equip; fit up; refurbish; spruce up; (2) fixtures; trims; (3) renovation worker;
品味裝修 tasteful decorations;
雅緻裝修 nicely decorated;

[裝運] load and transport; pack and transport; ship;
裝運費用 shipping expenses;
裝運時間表 shipment schedule;
遲誤裝運 delayed shipment;
定期裝運 timed shipment;
~ 不定期裝運 indefinite shipment;
分批裝運 partial shipment;
分期裝運 shipment by instalments;
即期裝運 immediate shipment;
加速裝運 expediting shipment;
近期裝運 near shipment;
盡速裝運 ship as soon as possible;
提前裝運 advancing shipment;
延期裝運 extending shipment;
遠期裝運 distant shipment; forward shipment;
中止裝運 suspending shipment;
準時裝運 punctual shipment;

[裝載] freight; loading; shipping; shipment; storage;
裝載機 loader;
~ 裝載機手 loader operator;
裝載量 carrying capacity;
~ 安全裝載量 safe carrying capacity;
裝載設備 charging appliance;
混合裝載 combined shipment;

[裝幀] binding and layout;

[裝置] (1) apparatus; appliance; assembly; attachment; device; equipment; installation; rig; rigging; (2) equip with; fit; furnish with; install; mount; plant;
爆炸裝置 explosive assembly;

並聯裝置 parallel arrangement;
船台裝置 gross assembly;
打捆裝置 binding attachment;
鍍鋅裝置 galvanizing rig;
反射裝置 reflex attachment;
反應堆裝置 reactor arrangement;
防霜凍裝置 antifrost device;
防震裝置 antiknock device;
附加裝置 additional facilities;
紅外自動裝置 automatic infrared facility;
換輥裝置 changing rig;
基片裝置 base-wafer assembly;
計程裝置 log arrangement;
計算裝置 accounting device;
加速裝置 accelerating installation;
檢驗裝置 verifying attachment;
鉸接裝置 hinge assembly;
警報裝置 alarming apparatus;
警告裝置 alarm device;
警鐘裝置 bell rigging;
進氣裝置 air-intake installation;
絕熱裝置 adiabatic apparatus;
均壓裝置 equalizer assembly;
空氣調節裝置 air conditioning apparatus;
冷卻裝置 coolant mechanism;
臨界裝置 critical assembly;
瞄準裝置 aiming mechanism;
錨定裝置 anchoring arrangement;
排水裝置 water-freeing arrangement;
皮帶傳動裝置 belt pulley attachment;
拋光裝置 buffing attachment;
氣密裝置 airtight assembly;
確認裝置 acknowledging device;
掃雷裝置 mine-sweeping arrangement;
省時裝置 time-saving device;
實驗裝置 experimental facility;
輸送裝置 conveying appliance;
天線裝置 aerial installation;
調壓裝置 pressure regulation appliance;
聽覺調整裝置 auditory adjusting apparatus;
通風裝置 ventilating arrangement;
筒夾裝置 collet attachment;
推進裝置 propulsive arrangement;
脱琉裝置 desulfurizing installation;
吸氣裝置 breathing apparatus;
消波裝置 wave suppression arrangement;
小裝置 doodah;
壓模裝置 die assembly;
陽極裝置 anode assembly;
遙控裝置 remote-control arrangement;
照相裝置 camera assembly;
裝袋裝置 bagging apparatus;
整個裝置 complete appliance;

[裝醉] pretend to be drunk;

[裝作] feign; pretend;

安裝 assemble; erect; fix; install; lay on; mount;
扮裝 make up;
包裝 pack; packaging; packing;
便裝 casual wear; everyday clothes;
拆裝 disassemble and reassemble;
春裝 spring clothing;
袋裝 in bags;
吊裝 hoist;
冬裝 winter clothing;
封裝 capsulation; encapsulation;
服裝 apparel; clothing; costume; dress; fashion; garment;
改裝 (1) change one's dress; (2) repack; (3) refit; (4) disguise oneself as;
古裝 ancient costume;
罐裝 canning;
盒裝 boxed;
紅裝 clad in red;
化裝 (1) make up; (2) disguise oneself;
假裝 disguise oneself as; dress up as; feign; pretend; simulate;
簡裝 plainly-packed;
精裝 (1) cloth-bound; hardback; hardcover; (2) skilfully-packed;
軍裝 military uniform;
鎧裝 armouring;
獵裝 hunting jacket;
露臍裝 (1) bare midriff; (2) midriff-baring shirt;
迷彩裝 camouflage uniform;
男裝 men's clothing;
女裝 women's dress;
平裝 paperback;
瓶裝 bottled;
喬裝 disguise;
輕裝 (1) light; (2) with light packs;
秋裝 autumn clothing;
戎裝 martial attire; military dress; military uniform;
散裝 bulk; in bulk;
上裝 (1) dress up; make up; (2) top;
盛裝 be dressed in one's best; dress out; dress up; in fine array; in full dress; in rich attire;
時裝 fashion; fashionable dress;
束裝 pack up;
套裝 suit;
童裝 children's wear;

偽裝 (1) feign; pretend; (2) disguise; mask;
武裝 milary equipment;
西裝 Western-style clothes;
戲裝 theatrical costume;
下裝 remove stage make-up and costume;
夏裝 summer clothing; summer wear;
卸裝 remove stage make-up and costume;
新裝 (1) new clothes; (2) new look;
行裝 outfit for a journey;
休閒裝 shell suit;
洋裝 (1) Western-style clothes; (2) Western way of book-binding;
整裝 get one's things ready;
治裝 purchase things necessary for a long journey;
中裝 traditional Chinese clothing;

zhuang

【樁】 (1) pile; post; stake; (2) numerary auxiliary for affairs or matters;

[樁錐] hammer;

zhuang⁴

zhuang

【壯】 (1) robust; strong; sturdy; vigorous; (2) make better; strengthen; (3) big; grand; great; magnificent; (4) prime of one's life;

[壯大] (1) big and strong; vigorous; (2) expand; grow in strength; strengthen;
發展壯大 develop and grow in strength; expand; go from strength to strength;

[壯膽] boost sb's courage; embolden; strengthen one's courage;
財能壯膽 wealth may strengthen one's courage;
給自己壯膽 whistle in the dark;
夜過墳場吹口哨—為自己壯膽 whistling in a dark graveyard;

[壯丁] able-bodied man;

[壯夫] able-bodied person; sturdy person;

[壯工] coolie; unskilled labourer;

[壯觀] beautiful view; breath-taking view; grand sight; great sight; impressive view; spectacular view;

[壯健] strong and healthy; sturdy;
壯健如牛 as strong as an ox;

[壯舉] courageous feat; daring act; feat; great achievement; heroic undertaking; magnificent feat;

[壯闊] grand; grandiose; magnificent; vast;

[壯麗] glorious; grand and imposing; magnificent; majestic; splendorous;

[壯烈] brave; courageous; heroic; on a grand and spectacular scale;
壯烈犧牲 die a glorious death; die a heroic death; die as a martyr; die for one's country; give one's life heroically; sacrifice one's life bravely and gloriously;

[壯美] full of grandeur; grandeur and serenity; magnificent and beautiful; splendour; sublime;

[壯年] prime of one's life;
壯年河 mature river;
壯年期 (1) prime; (2) maturity;
已過壯年 past one's prime;

[壯氣] (1) brave morale; (2) encourage a spirit; inspire enthusiasm;

[壯然] dignified-looking; forbidding;

[壯盛] healthy; strong and prosperous;

[壯士] brave person; hero; person of stout heart; warrior;
壯士斷腕 a vigorous man cut off his arm — make a quick decision as situation demands; decide promptly and opportunely; make a prompt decision at the right moment;
壯士暮年，雄心不已 an old hero still cherishes high aspirations; the heart of the hero in his old age is as stout as ever;

[壯實] robust; stocky; sturdy;
壯實的 burly;

[壯圖] ambitious attempt; attempt at sth spectacular;

[壯心] great aspiration; lofty ideal;

[壯陽] stimulate male virility;
壯陽劑 aphrodisiac;

[壯遊] (1) exciting trip; great tour; splendid tour; (2) take a long trip for ambitious project;

[壯猷] (1) great achievement; (2) great strategy;

[壯志] great ambition; great aspiration; lofty ideal;
壯志豪情 lofty ideal and sentiments; the determination and lofty ideals;
壯志淩雲 cherish high aspirations; fearless and high-hearted; soaring ambition; with soaring aspirations;

壯志未酬 die before the fulfilment of one's ambition; have one's ambition frustrated; with one's lofty aspirations unrealized;
豪情壯志 lofty sentiments and aspirations; lofty spirit and soaring determination;
未酬的壯志 thwarted ambition;
心懷壯志 cherish an ambition; harbor an ambition; nurse an ambition;

悲壯 heroic and tragic; moving and tragic; solemn and stirring; tragically heroic;
膘壯 fat and strong;
粗壯 (1) stout; sturdy; (2) thick and strong; (3) deep and resonant;
膽壯 fearless; full of courage;
肥壯 stout and strong;
復壯 rejuvenate;
豪壯 bold; daring; grand and heroic;
宏壯 great and solid;
健壯 healthy and strong; robust;
精壯 able-bodied; strong;
氣壯 strong spirit;
強壯 energetic; robust; strong; sturdy; vigorous; virile;
少壯 young and energetic; young and vigorous;
雄壯 full of power and grandeur; hale and hearty; magnificent; majestic; powerful; powerful in momentum; powerful in strength and impetus; strong; virile;
茁壯 healthy and strong; vigorous;
足壯 physically strong;

zhuang
【狀】 (1) appearance; form; look; shape; (2) describe; narrate; (3) plaint; written appeal; written complaint; (4) condition; situation; state; (5) certificate;
[狀詞] contents of an accusation;
[狀況] condition; state; state of affairs; status;
狀況非常好 in tip-top condition;
讓人不滿意的狀況 unsatisfactory situation;
營業狀況 business status;
賬務狀況 accounts status;
[狀貌] appearance; form; look;
[狀態] condition; situation; state; state of affairs; status;
狀態動詞 stative verb;
狀態連繫動詞 current linking verb;
狀態良好 in good form; in good nick; in good shape;
狀態形容詞 stative adjective;
財務狀態 financial situation; financial status;
待命狀態 armed state;
導電狀態 conduction state;
共軛狀態 conjugate action;
平衡狀態 balanced state;
設備狀態 device status;
原型狀態 archetype state;
戰爭狀態 state of war;
~處於戰爭狀態 in a state of war;
最佳狀態 in peak condition;
[狀語] adverbial modifier;
狀語賓格 adverbial accusative;
狀語從句 adverbial clause;
~持續狀語從句 adverbial clause of duration;
~距離狀語從句 adverbial clause of distance;
狀語分詞從句 adverbial participle clause;
狀語分詞短語 adverbial participle clause;
狀語連詞 adverbial conjunction;
狀語小品詞 adverbial particle;
狀語修飾詞 adverbial modifier;
比較狀語 adverbial of comparison;
比例狀語 adverbial of proportion;
必具性狀語 obligatory adverbial;
持續狀語 adverbial of duration;
地點狀語 adverbial of place;
方面狀語 adverbial of respect;
方式狀語 adverbial of manner;
結果狀語 adverbial of result;
介詞狀語 prepositional adverbial;
句子狀語 sentence adverbial;
距離狀語 adverbial of distance;
目的狀語 adverbial of purpose;
頻度狀語 adverbial of frequency;
前位狀語 preposition adverbial;
讓步狀語 adverbial of concession;
時間狀語 adverbial of time;
條件狀語 adverbial of condition;
原因狀語 adverbial of cause;
[狀元] (1) the very best; (2) the first in the highest imperial examination;
行行出狀元 every profession produces its own leading authority; every profession produces its own specialists; every trade has its master;
[狀紙] plaint; written complaint;
[狀子] plaint; written complaint;

保狀 guarantee certificate;

病狀 symptom of a disease;
慘狀 miserable condition or sight;
牒狀 documents pertaining to a lawsuit;
告狀 (1) bring a lawsuit against sb; file a suit; go to law against sb; indict; sue; (2) complain of one's grievances; lodge a complaint against sb with his superior;
供狀 deposition; written confession;
環狀 annular; ringlike;
獎狀 certificate of award; certificate of merit; citation; diploma; honourary credential; testimonial;
粒狀 graininess; granular;
鏈狀 chain;
摹狀 depict; portray;
情狀 situation; state of affairs;
球狀 sphericity;
訟狀 indictment;
訴狀 indictment; plaint; written complaint;
萬狀 (1) extremely; in the extreme; (2) all possible shapes and forms; myriad forms;
網狀 reticular;
現狀 current situation; existing state of affairs; present situation; status; things as they are;
行狀 brief biographical sketch of a deceased person;
形狀 appearance; conformation; form; likeness; shape;
性狀 shape and properties;
言狀 describe;
原狀 original state; previous condition;
症狀 symptom;
罪狀 charges in an indictment; facts about a crime;

zhuang

【撞】 (1) bump against; run into; (2) bump into; meet by chance; (3) barge; dash;
［撞車］ traffic collision;
撞車事故 automobile accident; car accident;
［撞大運］ try one's luck;
［撞倒］ knock down by a bumping;
［撞鬼］ (1) encounter a ghost; (2) run around in distraction;
［撞壞］ damage by bumping;
［撞機］ air crash;
撞機事故 air crash;
~險些發生的撞機事故 air miss;
［撞擊］ dash against; ram; strike;
［撞見］ bump into; catch sb in the act; meet by chance; meet unexpectedly; run across; run into;
［撞開］ burst open; knock away by bumping;
［撞騙］ cheat; look about for a chance to swindle; swindle;
［撞破］ (1) hurt by bumping; (2) surprise sb in an illegal act or awkward situation;
［撞人］ burst into; thrust into;
［撞入］ burst into; thrust into;
［撞傷］ contuse; injure by bumping;
［撞死］ kill by a crash;

拔撞 (1) win honour for sb; (2) back sb up; (3) boast one's moral; pump up one's courage;
衝撞 (1) bump against; collide; (2) offend;
跌撞 stumbling and bumping into things;
頂撞 argue with one's elder or superior; talk back;
防撞 crashproof;
莽撞 crude and impetuous; rash; rude;
冒撞 intrude;
猛撞 bump; cannon; collision; crash; smash;
碰撞 (1) collide; collision; crash; knock against; run foul of; run into; (2) cannon; hit; impact;
相撞 bump against; collide; collide with each other; smash together; strike;
用頭撞 nut;

zhuang

【戇】 simple-minded;
［戇直］ blunt and tactless; simple and honest; simple and upright;

zhui[1]

zhui

【隹】 general name for short-tailed birds, such as pigeons;

zhui

【追】 (1) chase after; follow; pursue; trace; (2) drive; expel; (3) look into; trace; (4) go after; seek; (5) recall; (6) posthumously; retroactively;
［追逼］ (1) pursue closely; (2) extort; press for;
［追兵］ pursuing troops; troops in pursuit;
［追捕］ chase; pursue and capture; trace and arrest;
追捕者 pursuer;
［追查］ find out; investigate; trace;
［追到］ catch up with;

[追悼] commemorate the dead; mourn over a person's death;
追悼會 memorial service;
[追放] banish;
[追封] ennoble posthumously;
[追趕] chase; chase after; pursue; quicken one's pace to catch up; run after; try to catch up with;
追趕者 pursuer;
你追我趕 chase each other; try to outdo each other; try to overtake each other;
~競賽中你追我趕 chase each other in a contest;
[追根] get to the bottom of sth;
追根究底 get to the root of; go into the whys and wherefores of sth; have the why and the wherefore; search to the bottom;
追根求源 get at the root of; go to the root of; trace back to the sources;
追根溯源 find by hand and thorough search; go to the fountain head; investigate into the origins of; trace sth to its source;
追根尋源 get to the bottom of the affair; go to the heart of the matter; make a thorough inquiry into sth; search to the bottom; trace sth to its source;
[追懷] reminiscence;
追懷故舊 bring old acquaintances to mind;
追古懷舊 recall past events with deep feeling; redolent of the past; think of the past affairs;
[追歡] pursue pleasure;
[追還] recover;
[追回] recover; retrieve;
追回贓物 confiscation or recovery of ill-gotten goods; recover stolen property;
[追悔] feel remorse; regret; repent;
追悔莫及 tardy repentance; too late for repentance; too late to repent;
[追擊] chase and attack; follow and attack; pursue and attack;
[追記] (1) postscript; record afterward; write down afterwards or from memory; (2) cite posthumously;
[追加] add to; make an addition;
追加從句 appended clause;
追加介詞 addition preposition;
追加投資 additional investment;
追加預算 additional budget;
[追薦] pray for the dead; seek blessings for the dead;
追薦亡靈 pray for blessing on the dead;
[追繳] demand the payment; press for payment afterwards;
[追剿] pursue and wipe out;
[追究] find out; investigate; investigate and punish; look into;
追究責任 be held responsible for; call to account; find out who is to blame;
概不追究 no action will be taken;
刑事追究 criminal sanctions;
[追口] back cut; falling cut; felling cut;
[追念] remember with nostalgia;
追念往事 recall early days; reminisce about the past;
[追陪] follow and keep company of an elder;
[追平] draw level;
[追窮寇] pursue the tottering foe;
[追求] aspire; court; go after; pursue; seek;
追求者 admirer;
追新求異 on the lookout for what is novel;
[追認] (1) subsequently confirm or endorse; (2) confer posthumously;
[追上] draw level;
[追身] close to the body;
追身球 close-to-the-body-shot;
[追授] award posthumously;
[追述] recount; tell about the past;
[追思] think back;
[追溯] date from; retrospect; review; run; trace back to; trace the origin of;
追溯翻譯法 retrospective method;
追溯既往 run back over the past; trace the origin of the bygone;
[追隨] follow;
追隨不捨 follow sb closely;
追隨潮流 go with the tide;
追隨者 acolyte; camp follower; disciple; follower;
[追索] (1) search for; (2) make insistent demands for payment; press for payment;
[追討] (1) dun for; (2) pursue and subdue;
[追問] examine minutely; make a detailed inquiry; question closely; question

insistently;

［追想］ recall; remember nostalgically; reminisce;

［追星］ chase after pop stars;

追星熱 fan craze;

追星少女 groupie;

追星族 celebrity worshipper;

［追敘］ (1) recount; relate; tell about the past; (2) flashback; narration of earlier episodes;

［追尋］ pursue; search; seek; track down;

［追憶］ call to memory; look back; recall; recollect; remember;

追憶往事 a trip down memory lane; a walk down memory lane;

［追影］ paint sb's likeness after his death;

［追源］ trace the origin of;

溯本追源 go back to the source; trace to the beginnings;

［追遠］ honour one's ancestors with sacrifices;

［追贈］ confer posthumously;

［追逐］ (1) chase; pursue; run after; (2) quest; seek;

追奔逐北 chase an enemy force in full retreat; give chase to a routed enemy; pursue a routed army;

追風逐電 chase the wind and lightning; with great speed;

追名逐利 crave for personal fame and gain; go after fame and money; seek fame and gain; woo fame and fortune;

［追蹤］ be on the track of; follow the trail of; pursue; trace; track;

追蹤電話 trace a call;

追蹤報導 follow-up report;

圖像追蹤 tracking;

跟追 follow the tracks of sb; shadow sb;

緊追 hot pursuit;

猛追 give a hot pursuit;

窮追 go in hot pursuit; hot on sb's trail; pursue vigorously;

尾追 be in hot pursuit; follow close behind;

zhui

【椎】 (1) bludgeon; hammer; mace; mallet; (2) beat; hammer; hit; strike; (3) vertebra;

［椎鈍］ dull-witted; stupid;

［椎骨］ vertebra;

［椎鼓］ beat a drum;

［椎擊］ strike with a mallet;

［椎魯］ dull and stupid;

［椎埋］ (1) kill sb and bury his body; (2) dig graves;

［椎牛］ kill an ox;

［椎剽］ kill and rob a person;

［椎殺］ kill with a mallet;

［椎體］ centrum;

鞍形椎體 heterocoelous centrum;

弓成椎體 perichordal centrum;

弓形椎體 arch centrum;

後凹椎體 opisthocoelous centrum;

寰椎體 atlantean centrum;

兩凹椎體 amphicoelous centrum;

兩平椎體 amphiplatyan centrum;

前凹椎體 procoelous centrum;

索成椎體 chordal centrum;

無凹椎體 acoelopus centrum;

異凹椎體 anemocoelous centrum;

［椎心泣血］ deep sorrow; excruciating pains; extreme grief;

寰椎 atlas;

脊椎 vertebra;

荐推 sacrum;

頸椎 cervical vertebra;

胸椎 thoracic vertebra;

腰椎 lumbar vertebra;

zhui

【錐】 (1) awl; (2) awl-shaped object; (3) bore; drill; make a hole; pierce; (4) cone;

［錐度］ taper;

錐度規 taper gauge;

［錐體］ cone; pyramid;

皮質錐體 cortical pyramid;

橋台錐體 abutment cone;

鈍頭錐體 blunt nosed cone;

圓錐體 circular cone;

制動錐體 brake cone;

［錐形］ cone; taper;

［錐指］ very limited outlook;

［錐子］ awl;

冰錐 icicle;

頂錐 addendum cone;

反足錐 antipodal cone;

改錐 screwdriver;

起錐 screwdriver;

肛門錐 anal cone;
寄生錐 adventive;
稜錐 pyramid;
沙錐 snipe;
受精錐 attraction cone;
絲錐 tap;
頭錐 ephalic cone;
雪崩錐 avalanche cone;
圓錐 circular cone; taper;

zhui
【騅】 piebald horse;

zhui4
zhui
【惴】 afraid; anxious; apprehensive; worried;
［惴恐］ dread; fear;
［惴慄］ alarmed and on tenterhooks; anxious and fearful;
［惴懼］ anxious and worried; in fear and trembling;
［惴惴］ afraid; apprehensive; fearful; feel apprehensive; feel uneasy; timorous;
惴惴不安 anxious and fearful; anxious and uneasy; apprehension and uneasiness; be alarmed and on tenterhooks; feel uneasy; greatly upset; live in terror and uncertainty;

zhui
【綴】 (1) combine; compose; put together; (2) mend clothes; patch up; sew; stitch; (3) decorate; stud;
［綴補］ patch up clothes;
［綴合］ join together; put together;
［綴輯］ compile and edit; compose; put words together correctly;
［綴文］ compose an essay; write a composition;
［綴宅］ physical human body;

補綴 mend; patch;
詞綴 affix;
點綴 (1) embellish; ornament; (2) use sth merely for show;
後綴 suffix;
連綴 (1) join together; put together; (2) cluster;
拼綴 join; make up;
前綴 prefix;
音綴 syllable;

zhui
【墜】 (1) drop; fall; (2) weigh down; (3) hanging object; weight;
［墜地］ (1) be born; come to this world; (2) fall; (3) failure;
［墜典］ historical books;
［墜肚］ have loose bowels;
［墜毀］ crash; fall and break;
［墜機］ plane crash;
墜機事故 airplane accident; flying accident; plane accident;
［墜樓］ fall from a building;
［墜落］ drop; fall; plunge;
墜落身亡 plunge to one's death;
［墜馬］ fall off a horse;
墜馬而亡 fall from the saddle and die on the spot;
［墜胎］ abort; abortion;
［墜言］ slip of the tongue;
［墜子］ (1) eardrops; earrings; (2) pendant;

下墜 straining; tenesmus;

zhui
【縋】 hang by a rope; let down by a rope;
［縋城］ climb down a city wall by a rope;
［縋登］ climb by a rope;

zhui
【餟】 libation;

zhui
【贅】 (1) superfluous; useless; (2) redundant; repeat; (3) follow around; (4) burdensome; (5) pawn things for money; (6) congregate; meet; (7) son-in-law who takes the place of a son in a family without heir;
［贅筆］ superfluous touch;
［贅詞］ redundance; repetitious words; superfluous words;
［贅及］ (1) add to; append to; (2) postscript;
［贅瘤］ anything superfluous or useless;
［贅述］ give unnecessary details; redundance; say more than is needed;
［贅物］ sth superfluous; sth useless;
［贅婿］ a son-in-law who lives in the home of his wife's parents;
［贅言］ say more than is needed; unnecessary words; verbosity;
不待贅言 it would be superfluous to dwell on the matter any more;
［贅疣］ (1) excrescence; wart; wen; (2)

Z

anything superfluous or useless;
[贅子] sell one's son to another as a slave;

冗贅 diffuse; verbose;
肉贅 wart;
入贅 marry into and live with one's bride's family;
招贅 have the groom live with one's family after the marriage;

zhun¹

zhun

【肫】 (1) earnest; sincere; (2) gizzard of a fowl;
[肫肫] earnest; sincere;

雞肫 chicken gizzard;
鴨肫 duck gizzard;

zhun

【迍】 difficult position; falter;
[迍邅] in a difficult situation; in a predicament; in a sorry plight; move forward with difficulty; unable to achieve one's ambition;

zhun

【窀】 pit for the coffin;
[窀穸] grave; tomb;

zhun

【諄】 earnest and patient;
[諄切] sincerely and warmly;
[諄囑] give repeated advice;
[諄諄] earnestly and tirelessly;
諄諄告誡 admonish repeatedly; earnest advice; enjoin earnestly; enjoin repeatedly; exhort tirelessly; urge repeatedly;
諄諄嘉勉 praise and encourage earnestly; urge sb to greater efforts with words of encouragement;
諄諄教誨 earnest teachings; instruct earnestly and tirelessly; inculcate;
諄諄善誘 teach and guide untiringly; teach repeatedly;
諄諄訓誨 admonish repeatedly;
諄諄囑咐 caution earnestly; give earnest advice;

zhun³

zhun

【准】 (1) allow; approve; authorize; grant; permit; (2) in accordance with; (3) equal; equivalent; (4) certainly; definitely; surely;
[准保] certainly; for sure;
[准將] brigadier general; commodore;
海軍准將 commodore;
空軍准將 air commodore;
[准尉] warrant officer;
[准許] allow; approve; permit;
[准予] approve; authorize; grant; permit;

不准 forbid; not allow; prohibit;
恩准 approved by his majesty;
核准 approval; check and approve; examine and approve; ratify;
獲准 obtain permission;
批准 accede; admit of; allow; approve; authorize; clearance; concede; endorse; give a license to; give permission; give sanction to; grant one's request; grant sb permission to; let; license; permit; ratify; sanction;
特准 special permit;
允准 approve; consent; grant;
照准 request granted;

zhun

【隼】 (1) aquiline nose; (2) falcon; hawk;

zhun

【準】 (1) even; level; (2) accurate; criterion; rule; standard; (3) aim; sight; (4) to-be; would-be; (5) quasi-;
[準保] guarantee;
[準備] (1) get ready; preparation; prepare; ready; (2) plan;
準備工作 lead-up;
準備活動 (of exercises) warming-up;
準備就緒 all set; ready to roll; the preparations are completed;
準備萬一 be prepared for an emergency; expect the worst; keep one's powder dry; prepare for the worst;
準備向後 action rear;
準備向前 action front;
重置準備 reserve for replacement;
存儲數據準備 memory data ready;
改建準備 reserve for improvement;
擴充準備 reserve for extension;
兩手準備 have two strings to one's bow; prepare oneself for eventualities;
事前準備 advance preparation;
數據終端準備 data terminal ready;

為…準備 be ready for; be set up with; get ready to; make preparations for; pave the way for; prepare for; prepare to;
預先準備 advance preparation;
增建準備 reserve for additional building;
專業準備 professional preparation;

[準成] dependable; reliable;
[準程] definite standard; norm;
[準定] definitely;
[準兒] certain; sure;
[準話] honest words;
[準期] punctually;
[準確] accurate; correct; exact; precise;
準確不爽 quite correct with no mistake;
準確度 accuracy; degree of accuracy;
準確發音 correct pronunciation; get one's tongue round;
準確填詞法 exact word method;
準確性 accuracy;
~ 翻譯準確性 accuracy in translation;
[準繩] (1) marking line; (2) criterion; standard;
[準時] at the scheduled time; on schedule; on the button; on the dot; on the minute; on the tick; on time; prompt; punctual; sharp; to the minute; to the tick; to the very moment;
準時不誤 on time;
非常準時的 as regular as clockwork; like clock;
[準式] criterion; regulation; rule;
[準頭] accuracy; judgement; standard;
[準則] criterion; formula; norm; rule; standard;
代數準則 algebraic criterion;
方式準則 maxim of manner; maxim of relevance;
幅度準則 amplitude criterion;
關係準則 maxim of relevance;
會話準則 conversational maxim;
基本設計準則 basic design criterion;
控制準則 control criterion;
明確而必然不變的準則 hard-and-fast rules;
偏移準則 deflection criterion;
社會準則 social norms;
文化準則 cultural norms;

標準 criterion; standard;
對準 (1) aim at; (2) align; alignment;
基準 criterion; standard;
校準 calibrate; calibration;
瞄準 aim; aiming; lay; sight; take aim; train;
拿不準 be still in the air;
誰能説得準 who can say;
水準 level; standard;
説準 it's settled;
作準 be valid; count;

zhuo¹

zhuo

【捉】 (1) clutch; grasp; hold; seize; (2) apprehend; arrest; capture; catch;
[捉鼻] hold in contempt;
[捉刀] ghostwrite; write an article for someone else;
捉刀人 ghostwriter;
捉刀代筆 ask sb to write in the name of another;
代人捉刀 ghostwrite for others; write sth for sb else;
倩人捉刀 employ others to write an essay in one's name; ghostwrite;
[捉虎容易放虎難] it is easier to catch a tiger than let it go—it is easier to start sth than to conclude it satisfactorily;
[捉姦] catch adultery in the act;
捉姦勒索 be blackmailed for being caught when committing adultery;
[捉襟見肘] cannot make ends meet; hard up; have to many difficulties to cope with; have too many problems to tackle; in straitened circumstances; on one's uppers; out at elbows;
[捉迷藏] (1) blindman's buff; hide-and-seek; play hide-and-seek; (2) beat the brush;
[捉摸] ascertain; fathom;
捉摸不到 play handy-dandy with sb;
捉摸不定 difficult to ascertain; elusive; freakish; unfathomable; unpredictable;
~ 捉摸不定的人 will o' the wisp;
不可捉摸 unpredictable;
[捉拿] apprehend; arrest; catch;
捉拿歸案 bring sb to justice; run down;
捉拿者 captor;
[捉弄] embarrass; have a game with sb; make fun of; play a joke on sb; tease;
百般捉弄 play a thousand tricks on sb;
[捉狹] mischievous;
捉狹鬼 mischievous fellow;
[捉妖] catch the evil spirit; exorcise;
[捉賊] catch thieves;

Z

捉賊捉贓 if you go to discover thieves, you must find the booty; in arresting a thief, you must get the stolen goods; to catch a thief you must find the stolen goods;
賊喊捉賊 a robber acting like a cop; a thief crying"stop thief"; cover oneself up by shouting with the crowd; the devil rebuking sin;
[捉住] catch; get sb by the neck; seize;
捉住要害 catch one on the hip;

把捉 grasp;
捕捉 catch; seize;
活捉 capture sb alive;
擒捉 arrest; capture; catch;

zhuo
【桌】 desk; table;
[桌布] tablecloth;
一塊桌布 a table cloth;
[桌燈] desk lamp;
[桌面] desktop; tabletop; top of a table;
桌面出版系統 desktop publishing system;
桌面電腦 desktop computer;
[桌球] table tennis;
[桌扇] desk fan;
[桌上舞] table dance;
[桌椅] tables and chairs;
桌椅板凳 tables, chairs, stools, and benches;
捶桌拍椅 pound the table and slap the chair;
更新桌椅 renew tables and chairs;
購置桌椅 purchase tables and chairs;
[桌子] desk; table;
桌子角 corner of a table;
桌子腿 table leg;
擺桌子 set the table;
擦桌子 wipe the table;
長方形桌子 oblong table;
方桌子 square table;
拍桌子 pound the table;
一套桌子 a nest of tables;
一張桌子 a desk; a table;
用拳頭猛敲桌子 bang one's fist on the table;
圓桌子 round table;

矮桌 low table;
案桌 long narrow table;
冰桌 glacier table;
餐桌 dining table;
飯桌 dining table;
方桌 square desk;
高桌 high table;
供桌 altar;
櫃桌 hutch table;
混音桌 mixing desk;
咖啡桌 coffee table;
課桌 desk;
滿桌 a tableful of;
牌桌 card table;
盤桌 tray table; tray-top table;
書桌 desk; writing desk;
野餐桌 picnic table;
藤桌 rattan table;
圍桌 cloth hanging over the sides of a table;
小桌 small table;
一桌 (1) tableful; (2) a table of;
圓桌 round table;
摺面桌 pembroke table;
主桌 top table;

zhuo
【涿】 (1) drip; soak; trickle; (2) old and current names of counties, rivers, in various places;
[涿濕] be soaked through;

zhuo
【棹】 same as 桌, table;

zhuo²

zhuo
【灼】 (1) burn; cauterize; scorch; (2) bright; brilliant; clear; luminous; (3) flowers in full bloom;
[灼艾分痛] brotherly love;
[灼骨] burn the bones;
[灼見] brilliant views; penetrating views; profound views;
[灼爛] badly burned;
[灼明] lustrous;
[灼然] crystal-clear; obvious;
[灼熱] broil; scorching hot;
[灼傷] burn;
[灼痛] burning pain;
[灼灼] (1) bright; brilliant; shining; (2) blooming;
目光灼灼 with keen, sparkling eyes;

焦灼 deeply worried; very anxious;
燒灼 burn; scorch;

zhuo

【卓】 (1) high; lofty; tall and erect; (2) brilliant; eminent; outstanding; (3) a surname;

[卓奪] your discerning decision;

[卓爾] eminent; outstanding;

卓爾不群 among the select best; be distinguished from one's kind; cap all; different from the common people; eminent; out of ten thousand; out of the common run; outstanding; preeminent; remarkable; rise above the common herd; stand above the rest; stand head and shoulders above all others; stand out among others; tower above one's contemporaries; tower above the rest; unusual and peculiar;

[卓見] brilliant ideas; excellent opinions;

[卓絕] (1) extreme; of the highest degree; (2) eminent; outstanding; peerless; prominent; unsurpassed;

卓絕千古 unmatched past or present; unprecedented;

[卓立] stand alone; stand out; stand upright;

卓立一世 stand lofty in one's age;

[卓然] brilliant; distinguished; eminent; outstanding; stately;

[卓識] sagacity; superior insight;

[卓殊] distinguished; unusual;

[卓午] midnoon;

[卓異] outstanding; remarkable; unusual;

[卓越] brilliant; excellent; foremost; outstanding; remarkable;

[卓著] distinguished; eminent; outstanding; prominent; well-known;

卓著勛勞 noted for meritorious service;

聲譽卓著 famous; widely known;

[卓卓] distinguished; outstanding;

zhuo

【拙】 (1) awkward; clumsy; (2) my;

[拙笨] awkward; clumsy; dull; stupid; unskilful;

拙嘴笨腮 slow of tongue and clumsy of utterance;

[拙筆] my calligraphy; my painting; my writing;

[拙夫] clumsy husband;

[拙稿] my poor manuscript;

[拙工] incompetent worker; poor craftsman;

[拙計] foolish scheme;

[拙見] my humble opinion;

[拙荊] my wife;

[拙口鈍辭] slow of tongue and clumsy of utterances;

[拙劣] bochy; clumsy; inferior;

拙劣手法 clumsy trick; inferior tactics;

手段拙劣 hanky-panky tactics;

手法拙劣 play a poor game; play a wretched game;

[拙實] big and strong; raw and sturdy; solidly built;

[拙性] clumsy; slow-witted; stupidity;

[拙眼] an uninformed man;

笨拙 awkward; dull;

藏拙 hide one's inadequacy by keeping quiet;

古拙 simple and unsophisticated;

眼拙 not remember if one has seen sb before;

迂拙 impractical and stupid;

愚拙 stupid and awkward;

zhuo

【斫】 chop or cut wood;

[斫斷] chop off; cut off; sever;

[斫木] chop or cut wood;

[斫殺] kill with a hatchet;

[斫頭] behead; decapitate;

[斫斬] chop; cut; hew;

zhuo

【茁】 (1) growing; sprouting; (2) strong; sturdy; vigorous;

[茁芽] sprout;

[茁長] flourish; thrive;

[茁壯] healthy and strong; sturdy; vigorous;

茁壯成長 grow healthily; grow strong and tall; steadily mature;

[茁茁] sprouting;

zhuo

【酌】 (1) drink; pour out; (2) a meal with wine; (3) consider; think over; weigh and consider;

[酌辦] handle by taking actual circumstances into consideration;

[酌裁] consider and decide;

[酌處權] discretion;

[酌定] decide according to one's judgment;

[酌奪] make a considered decision;

[酌加] make considered additions;

［酌減］ cut down according to circumstances; make considered reductions;
［酌酒］ pour wine;
酌酒吟詩 recite poetry over a glass of good wine; sip wine and write poems;
［酌量］ consider; deliberate; use one's judgement; weigh and consider;
［酌情］ act according to circumstances; take into consideration the circumstances; use one's discretion;
酌情處理 act according to one's judgement; act after full consideration of the actual situation; act at one's discretion; deal with sth on the merits of each case; depend upon circumstances; do as one thinks fit; exercise discretion in light of the circumstances; handle as one sees fit; settle a matter as one sees fit;
酌情而定 be determined by the circumstances; decide according to the circumstances; depend upon the circumstances;
［酌獻］ honour a deity with wine;
［酌議］ consider and discuss;

便酌 informal dinner;
參酌 consider a matter in accordance with; consult and deliberate over;
對酌 have a drink together;
菲酌 my humble dinner;
清酌 the wine offered to gods in worship;
商酌 consult and deliberate over; discuss and consider;
斟酌 consider; deliberate over; think over;
自酌 enjoy a cup of wine all by oneself;

zhuo

【涿】 soak;

zhuo

【啄】 peck;
［啄花鳥］ flowerpecker;
［啄木鳥］ woodpecker;
［啄食］ eat by pecking; peck;
［啄啄］ (1) cackling of hens; (2) sound of tapping at a door;

剝啄 tap;

zhuo

【棁】 (1) joist; (2) cane; club;

zhuo

【琢】 (1) carve or chisel jade; (2) improve; polish; refine;
［琢句］ sentence formation; write and polish phrases and sentences;
琢句雕詞 polish sentences and engrave phrases;
［琢磨］ (1) carve and polish; (2) improve; polish; refine;
如琢如磨 as jade is wrought by chisel and stone — slow process of education and scholarship;
［琢石］ ashlar;
表面琢石 face ashlar;
光面琢石 plane ashlar;
光細琢石 smooth ashlar;
尖琢石 pointed ashlar;
平面琢石 plane ashlar;
人字形琢石 herring-bone ashlar;

雕琢 (1) carve; sculpture; (2) write in an ornate style;

zhuo

【着】 (1) wear; (2) come into contact with; touch; (3) whereabouts; (4) send; (5) apply; use;
［着筆］ begin to write; put pen to paper;
［着處］ everywhere;
［着地］ reach the ground; touch the ground;
着地點 ground zero;
［着花］ blossom; flower;
［着力］ apply force; exert oneself; put forth effort;
着力描寫 concentrate one's efforts on depicting; take great pains to describe;
［着陸］ alight; descend to the ground; land; landing; touch down;
緊急着陸 crash landing; emergency landing;
平墜着陸 pancake landing;
強行着陸 crash landing;
軟着陸 soft landing;
三點着陸 three-point landing;
下降着陸 descending and landing;
儀表着陸 instrument landing;
硬着陸 hard landing; rough landing;
［着落］ (1) whereabouts; (2) assured source;
沒有着落 keep sb in the air;
沒着沒落 (1) anxious; unsteady; unsure; (2) unresolved; unsettled;

[着墨不多] briefly describe; sketchily paint;
[着棋] play chess;
[着人先鞭] steel a march on;
[着色] colour; dye; put colour on;
[着實] (1) indeed; really; (2) concrete and substantial; dependable;
着實不錯 very good indeed;
[着手] put one's hand to; set about; set one's hand to; start doing sth;
着手成春 cure every patient he treats; have admirable skill in curing diseases; have miraculous skill in treating the patients; sickness retires at one's touch;
[着想] consider; for the sake of; take into consideration;
為別人着想 have consideration for others;
[着眼] consider in a certain aspect; have sth in mind; see from the angle of;
[着衣] put on garments; wear clothing;
[着意] act with care and effort; pay attention to; take pains;
[着重] emphasize; stress;
着重號 mark of emphasis;

挨着 close to; get close to; next to;
抱着 embrace; hold in one's arms;
背着 carry on the back;
本着 according to; based on; in conformity with; in line with; in the light of;
猜不着 cannot guess; miss one's guess; unable to make out the right answer; unable to reach the right answer;
沉着 calm; composed; cool-headed; steady;
穿着 apparel; dress; what one wears;
蹲着 crouching; squatting;
等着 waiting;
盯着 fix one's eyes on; gaze at; glue one's eyes on; keep a close watch on; keep an eye on; stare at;
凍着 have a cold;
犯得着 it is worthwhile;
飛着 float in the air; not decided; unsolved;
附着 adhere to; stick; to;
該着 certainly. naturally; ought to;
跟着 (1) follow; in the wake of; (2) at once; right away;
夠不着 beyond one's reach; cannot reach;
懷着 be filled with; cherish; harbour;
膠着 agglutinative; reach a deadlock;
接着 (1) catch; (2) carry on; follow; go on; proceed;
瞞着 hold out on;
慢着 hold one's horses; wait a minute;
黏着 mucus; adhere; adhesion; agglutination; bond; stick together;
瞧着 (1) while looking; (2) let's see;
數不着 not count as outstanding;
順着 along; with;
隨着 along with; in pace with; in the wake of;
透着 appear; look; seem;
為着 for; in order to;
吸着 sorption;
想着 keep in mind; miss; think of;
一着 a move;
衣着 clothing;
用不着 (1) it is not worth while to; there is no need to; (2) have no use for;
用得着 (1) find sth useful; need; serve the desired purpose; (2) there is need to;
遇着 encounter; meet;
仗着 take advantage of;
執着 inflexible; rigid;
攥着 grasp; hold tight;
坐着 sitting;

zhuo
【斮】 cut; pare;
[斮趾] cut off one's toes as punishment;
[斮足] cut off one's feet as punishment;

zhuo
【椓】 (1) hammer; strike; (2) castrate;

zhuo
【焯】 (1) same as 灼, burn; (2) bright and brilliant;

zhuo
【斲】 chop; hew;
[斲雕為樸] do away with vanity and adopt unadorned simplicity; get rid of ornamentation for simplicity's sake;
[斲喪] (1) chop down completely; (2) waste one's vitality by dissipation;
斲喪身體 destroy one's body — waste one's vitality by dissipation;

zhuo
【諑】 rumour;
謠諑 slander; smear;

zhuo
【踔】 (1) go across; go beyond; (2) very far; very high;
[踔絕] (1) very high; (2) prominent;

［踔遠］ very far; very high;

zhuo

【濁】 (1) turbid; muddy; (2) corrupt; evil; tumultuous; (3) stupid and idiotic; (4) name of a constellation;

［濁才］ fool;

［濁度］ turbidity;

［濁酒］ unstrained wine;

［濁口］ foul-mouthed;

［濁浪］ muddy waves;

［濁流］ turbid stream;

［濁氣］ bad breath; foul smell;

［濁世］ (1) chaotic times; corrupted world; (2) mortal world;

［濁水］ turbid water;

清塵濁水 completely cut off from each other, with no chance to meet;

［濁物］ blockhead; bloody fool; idiot;

凡胎濁物 a common run of men; only a common person;

［濁意］ muddy idea;

［濁音］ (1) voiced sound; (2) dullness;

心濁音 cardiac dullness;

~絕對心濁音 absolute cardiac dullness;

白濁 gonorrhea;

惡澤 filthy; foul;

渾濁 muddy; turbid;

混濁 (1) muddy; turbid; (2) nubecula;

尿渾濁 cloudy urine;

清濁 (1) clear and turbid; (2) honest and dishonest;

污濁 dirty; filthy; foul; muddy;

淤濁 muddy and turbid;

zhuo

【擢】 (1) extract; pick out; pull out; select; take out; (2) promote; raise;

［擢第］ get chosen by passing an examination;

［擢髮難數］ innumerable like the hair on the head; things cannot be numbered, as the hairs on the head; too numerous to count; uncountable;

［擢昇］ advance; elevate to a higher position; promote;

［擢秀］ (1) luxuriant; (2) gifted; talented;

［擢引］ pick and promote;

［擢用］ pick and promote; promote to a post;

拔擢 select and promote the best;

zhuo

【濯】 (1) wash; (2) eliminate vices; (3) grand; magnificent; (4) a surname;

［濯錦以魚］ make the ugly beautiful;

［濯濯］ (1) bald; bare; (2) bright and brilliant; (3) fat and sleek;

洗濯 cleanse; wash;

zhuo

【繳】 harpoon;

zhuo

【鐲】 (1) a kind of bell used in the army in ancient times; (2) armlet; bracelet;

［鐲子］ armlet; bracelet;

腳鐲 anklet;

手鐲 bracelet;

腕鐲 bracelet;

玉鐲 jade bracelet;

zhuo

【鷟】 a kind of water bird;

zi¹

zi

【吱】 (1) squeak; (2) chirp; peep;

［吱聲］ make a sound; utter sth;

［吱喳］ chatter;

吱喳叫 chirrup;

［吱吱］ squeak; squeaking sounds;

吱吱叫 cheep;

吱吱喳喳 chat; chirp together; talk in confusion;

嘎吱 creak;

咯吱 creak; groan;

zi

【孜】 never weary; unwearied and diligent;

［孜孜］ diligent; hardworking; industrious;

孜孜不倦 always taking great pains over; assiduous and never tired; drive away at; indefatigably and diligently; like a beaver; peg away at; persevere in doing; work with diligence and without fatigue;

孜孜以求 assidusouly seek; diligently strive after;

zi

【咨】 (1) consult; inquire; (2) very formal official communication;

［咨訪］ ask for advice; consult;
［咨謀］ take counsel with;
［咨請］ make an official request; seek official opinions;
［咨文］ official communications between offices of equal rank;
［咨詢］ consult; inquire;
咨詢費 consulting fee;
咨詢服務 consulting service;
~ 咨詢服務公司 reference service company;
咨詢公司 consulting company;
咨詢委員會 consultative committee;
咨詢中心 consulting centre;
自咨詢 self-referentiality;
［咨政］ political advisor;

zi

【姿】 (1) appearance; looks; (2) bearing; gesture; manner; position;
［姿貌］ woman's looks;
［姿媚］ elegant and graceful manners;
［姿容］ appearance; looks;
姿容絕代 one's beauty is unparallelled;
姿容婉麗 have pretty and graceful features;
姿容秀美 good-looking; pretty;
［姿色］ beauty; charm; good looks;
［姿勢］ (1) bearing; carriage; deportment; (2) gesture; posture;
姿勢優美 have a graceful carriage;
擺姿勢 pose;
~ 擺 (好) 姿勢 strike a pose;
低姿態 in a low profile;
開始姿勢 starting position;
［姿首］ pretty face and beautiful hair;
［姿態］ (1) gesture; one's bearing or carriage; posture; (2) attitude; pose;
姿態婀娜 have a graceful carriage; have an elegant figure;
姿態控制 attitude control;
導彈姿態 missile attitude;
低姿態 low profile;
~ 保持低姿態 keep a low profile;
地心姿態 geocentric attitude;
凍僵姿態 frozen attitude;
防禦姿態 defense attitude;
飛行姿態 flight attitude;
俯衝姿態 diving attitude;
俯仰姿態 fore-and-aft attitude;
高姿態 high attitude; lofty stance; magnanimous attitude;
故作姿態 play hard to get;
滑跑姿態 ground-run attitude;
滑翔姿態 glide attitude;
極限姿態 extreme attitude;
開始姿勢 starting position;
起飛姿態 take-off attitude;
千恣百態 in different poses and with different expressions;
強迫姿態 forced attitude;
十字姿態 crucifixion attitude;
做作的姿態 agonistic poses;

多姿 varied in posture;
丰姿 agreeable manners;
風姿 charm; graceful bearing;
跪姿 kneeling position;
立姿 standing position;
瓊姿 elegant appearance; graceful appearance;
淑姿 graceful deportment; graceful manner;
天姿 natural beauty;
臥姿 prone position;
仙姿 fairylike look;
雄姿 brave appearance; dashing look; heroic bearing; heroic posture; majestic appearance; manly form;
艷姿 beautiful appearance; charming looks; enticing looks;
英姿 dashing appearance; heroic bearing; heroic posture; bright and valiant look;

zi

【茲】 (1) this; (2) at present; here; now;
［茲因］ now because...;

赫茲 hertz;
今茲 this year;
來茲 coming year;

zi

【淄】 (1) black; dark colour; (2) a river in Shandong;

zi

【孳】 (1) bear or beget in large numbers; (2) work with sustained diligence;
［孳茂］ luxuriant;
［孳生］ breed; grow and multiply; multiply; propagate;
［孳息］ (1) grow; (2) interest;
［孳衍］ grow in number; multiply;
［孳孳］ work with sustained diligence;
孳孳為利 work hard for money;

Z

zi

【滋】 (1) grow; (2) increase; multiply; (3) nourish; (4) give rise to; (5) more; (6) burst; spurt out; (7) juice; sap;

［滋補］ nourishing; nutritious; tonic;
滋補食品 nourishment; nourishing food; nutrient;
滋陰補陽 nourishment for vitality;

［滋多］ increase; multiply;

［滋蔓］ grow and spread; grow vigorously; lush; teeming;
滋蔓難圖 a weed that spreads more and more is difficult to deal with — it will be too late to deal with an enemy if he is allowed to grow in strength;

［滋茂］ lush; luxuriant; teeming;

［滋擾］ disturb peace and order; harass; make trouble; trouble;

［滋潤］ (1) enrich; freshen; (2) moist; moisten;

［滋生］ (1) breed; multiply; propagate; reproduce in large numbers; (2) cause; create; provoke;
滋生地 breeding ground;
滋生事端 cause trouble; create a disturbance; kick up a row; make a row; make trouble; raise a row;

［滋事］ cause trouble; create trouble; disturb peace;
滋事分子 troublemaker;

［滋味］ flavour; taste;
滋味無窮 the taste is everlasting;
愁滋味 taste of sorrow;
勝利的滋味 taste of victory;
失敗的滋味 taste of failure;
一種滋味 a taste;

［滋息］ bear interest;

［滋養］ (1) nourish; (2) nourishment; nutrition;
滋養品 nourishing food; nourishment; nutrient; nutritive food;

［滋育］ multiply; reproduce in large numbers;

［滋長］ develop; grow; thrive;
滋長蔓延 grow and spread;
潛滋暗長 grow and develop secretly; grow secretly and gradually; spread and grow secretly;

［滋殖］ reproduce in large numbers;

［滋滋］ pleased;
樂滋滋 contented; pleased;
美滋滋 very pleased with oneself;
甜滋滋 (1) pleasantly sweet; (2) delighted; happy;
喜滋滋 be filled with joy; feel pleased;

［滋嘴兒］ grin; smile;

繁滋 multiply profusely;

zi

【粢】 (1) rice to be offered as sacrifice; (2) grains;

zi

【菑】 (1) land under cultivation for one year; (2) weed grass;

zi

【資】 (1) capital; means; money; property; wealth; (2) charges; expenses; fees; (3) aid; assist; help; subsidize; support; (4) provide; supply; (5) natural ability; natural endowment; one's disposition; (6) qualifications; record of service; (7) trust;

［資本］ capital;
資本核定 assessment of capital;
資本化 capitalization;
~ 地租資本化 capitalization of land rents;
~ 利息資本化 capitalization of interest;
~ 收入資本化 capitalization of earnings;
資本集中 concentration of capital;
資本家 capitalist;
~ 不法資本家 law-breaking capitalist;
~ 個別資本家 individual capitalist;
~ 功能資本家 functioning capitalist;
~ 貨幣資本家 money capitalist;
~ 借貸資本家 loaning capitalist;
~ 民族資本家 national capitalist;
~ 商業資本家 merchant capitalist;
~ 生產資本家 productive capitalist;
~ 有閒資本家 idle capitalist;
資本結構 capital structure;
~ 最佳資本結構 optimal capital structure;
資本輸出 export of capital;
資本賬戶 capital account;
資本周轉 circulation of funds;
資本主義 capitalism;
~ 資本主義經濟 capitalist economy;
~ 資本主義者 capitalist;
~ 資本主義制度 capitalist system;
~ 產業資本主義 industrial capitalism;
~ 福利資本主義 welfare capitalism;
~ 國家資本主義 state capitalism;
~ 金融資本主義 financial capitalism;
~ 壟斷資本主義 monopoly capitalism;

~商業資本主義 commercial capitalism;
~自由資本主義 laissez-faire capitalism;
資本資產 capital asset;
不變資本 constant capital;
法定資本 authorized capital;
輔助資本 auxiliary capital;
固定資本 fixed capital;
~固定資本投資 investment in fixed assets;
過剩資本 circulating capital;
核定資本 assessing capital;
貨幣資本 money-capital;
~可變貨幣資本 variable money-capital;
~可用貨幣資本 available money-capital;
~潛在貨幣資本 virtual money-capital;
積累資本 accumulated capital;
借入資本 borrowed capital;
借貸資本 loan capital;
可變資本 variable capital;
流動資本 active capital; circulating capital; floating capital;
商品資本 commodity capital;
商業資本 commercial capital;
社會資本 social capital;
社會總資本 aggregate social capital;
生產資本 productive capital;
實際資本 actual capital;
實收資本 paid-in capital;
提供資本 capital financing;
無形資本 intangible capital;
現實資本 actual capital;
信貸資本 loan capital;
虛構資本 fictitious capital;
有形資本 tangible capital;
增值資本 appraisal capital;
種子資本 seed capital; seed money;
周轉資本 working capital;
專用資本 special capital;

[資財] assets; capital and goods; funds and goods; riches; wealth;

[資產] (1) means; property; real estate; (2) capital; capital fund; (3) assets;
資產倍增計劃 property doubling plan;
資產重組 asset reorganization;
資產擔保 assets cover;
資產倒賣 asset stripping;
資產負債結構 assets-debts structure;
資產紅利 asset dividend;
資產階級 bourgeoisie; capitalist class;
~民族資產階級 national bourgeoisie;
~小資產階級 petty bourgeoisie;
資產會計 assets accounting; erosion of property;
資產流失 erosion of property;
資產評估 make an appraisal of one's assets;
資產收益 asset income;
資產增值 appreciation;
不記名資產 impersonal assets;
呆滯資產 slow assets;
抵押資產 hypothecated assets;
遞耗資產 diminishing assets;
遞延資產 deferred assets;
定額資產 assets with norm;
凍定資產 frozen assets;
短期資產 short-term assets;
風險資產 risk assets;
負資產 negative equity;
公司資產 corporate assets;
固定資產 fixed assets;
~固定資產投資 fixed-asset investment;
~無形固定資產 intangible fixed assets;
國際準備資產 international reserve assets;
國外短期資產 foreign short-term assets;
國外資產 external assets;
國有資產 state-owned assets;
~國有資產流失 give state-owned assets away; loss of state-owned assets;
黃金資產 gold assets;
活動資產 active assets;
貨幣資產 monetary assets;
~非貨幣資產 non-monetary assets;
淨資產 net asset;
可疑資產 doubtful assets;
流動資產 circulating assets; current assets; floating assets; immediate assets; liquid assets;
~非流動資產 non-current assets;
免計資產 non-admitted assets;
名義資產 nominal assets;
清產核資 reappraise the stocks and assets of enterprises;
損耗資產 wasting assets;
投資資產 investment assets;
外滙資產 foreign exchange assets;
無形資產 intangible assets;
現今資產 cash assets;
虛假資產 fictitious assets;
營業資產 committed assets;
應折舊資產 depreciable assets;
運用資產 working assets;
雜項資產 miscellaneous assets;
賬面資產 ledger assets;

賬外資產 non-ledger assets;
資本資產 capital assets;
儲備資產 reserve assets;
注冊資產 registered capital;

[資敵] assist the enemy; treason;

[資斧] travelling expenses;

[資賦] one's natural endowments;

[資格] credentials; qualification;
資格證書 credential;
教師資格 teacher's qualification;
老資格 (1) seniority; (2) old-timer; senior; veteran;
~擺老資格 come play the old soldier; flaunt one's seniority; pride oneself on being a veteran; put on the airs of a veteran;
取消資格 disqualify; disqualification;
~自動取消資格 automatic disqualification;
學術資格 academic qualifications;
醫生資格 medical qualification;
有資格 capable; qualified;
正式資格 formal qualification;
職業資格 vocational qualification;
專業資格 professional qualification;

[資金] bankroll; capital; coffer; fund; grubstake;
資金不足 inadequate capital;
~資金不足的 cash-starved;
資金傳輸系統 money transfer system;
資金回收率 rate of capital return;
資金積累 accumulation of funds;
資金流動 capital movements;
資金內流 capital influx;
資金外流 capital efflux;
資金援助 financial assistance;
資金周轉 circulation of funds;
成品資金 current fund for finished product;
風險資金 risk funds;
固定資金 fixed assets;
回籠資金 recoup funds;
基建資金 capital construction fund;
積累資金 accumulate capital funds;
建設資金 funds for construction;
經營資金 operating fund;
流動資金 circulation fund; current assets; current fund;
~缺少流動資金 a shortage of circulating funds;
投資資金 money capital;
現存資金 cash on hand;
信貸資金 credit fund;
周轉資金 circulation fund;
儲備資金 current fund for procurement;
自籌資金 raise funds independently;
自有資金 owned fund;

[資力] financial strength;
資力雄厚 financially powerful; have a large capital; solid financial strength;

[資歷] credentials; qualifications and record of service;
資歷過高的 overqualified;

[資料] (1) means; (2) data; info; material;
資料處理 information processing;
資料檔 file;
資料庫 data bank; data base;
資料收集 data collection;
資料學 information science;
第二手資料 secondary source;
個人資料 personal information;
生產資料 means of production;
~輔助生產資料 auxiliary means of production;
生活資料 means of livelihood;
搜集資料 gather information;
有聲資料 sound archives;
直接資料 primary source;

[資深] senior;
資深望重 one's reputation is distinguished;

[資送] (1) send away with money provided; (2) give a dowry to a daughter on her marriage;
資送回籍 give sb money and send him home;

[資望] qualification and prestige; seniority and prestige;

[資信] credit;
資信調查 credit information;
資信可靠 creditworthy;

[資性] one's disposition;

[資訊] information;
資訊工程 information engineering;
資訊科技 information technology;
資訊自由 freedom of information;
不良資訊 undesirable information;
媒體資訊 media information;

[資優生] bright student;

[資源] natural resources; resource;
資源編輯器 resource compiler;

資源豐富 abound in natural resources; rich in natural resources;
資源共享 resource sharing;
~ 資源共享控制 resource sharing control;
資源管理 resource management;
~ 資源管理程序 resource management programme;
資源配置 resources allocation;
資源税 resource tax;
資源依賴 resources dependence;
資源再生 resource regenerating;
資源轉移 transfer of the resources;
豐富資源 ample resources;
海洋資源 marine resources;
可更新資源 renewable resources;
~ 不可更新資源 non-renewable resources;
空氣資源 air resources;
人力資源 human resources;
水產資源 aquatic resources;
水生資源 aquatic resources;
水資源 water resources;
特別資源 ad hoc resources;
天然資源 natural resources;
~ 天然資源豐富 be abundant in natural resources;
土地資源 land resources;
現今資源 cash resource;
學習資源 learning resources;
再生資源 renewable resources;
自然資源 natural resources;
~ 保護自然資源 preserve the natural resources;

[資政] political advisor;
[資質] intelligence; natural endowments;
資質平平 of middling talent; one's natural disposition is ordinary;
[資助] aid financially; patronage; provide financial assistance; subsidize;
資助人 patron; sponsor;
~ 女資助人 patroness;

筆資 fees for writing; remuneration for writing; writer's fees;
茶資 payment for tea;
籌資 financing;
川資 pay; wage;
工資 pay; remuneration; salary; wage;
耗資 consume funds;
合資 combined investment;
集資 collect funds; collect money; concentrate funds; pool resources; raise funds;
捐資 make donations;
勞資 labour and capital;
憑資 be based on; depend on; rely upon;
欠資 postage due;
僑資 overseas Chinese capital;
融資 financing;
潤資 remuneration for a writer, etc.;
師資 teacher;
天資 flair; inborn talent; intellectual capacity; natural endowments; natural gifts; talent;
投資 investment;
外資 foreign capital;
物資 goods and materials;
薪資 pay; salary; wage;
行資 travelling expenses;
以資 as a means of;
郵資 postage;
游資 floating capital; floating money; hot money; idle capital; idle fund; idle money;

zi

【貲】 (1) money; property; riches; wealth; (2) count; estimate; measure; (3) fine;
[貲財] money; valuables; wealth;
[貲郎] one who purchases a public post;

不貲 immeasurable; incalculable;

zi

【趑】 falter;
[趑趄] (1) plough one's way; walk with difficulty; (2) hesitate to advance;
趑趄不前 hang back; hesitate to act or choose one's course; hesitate to advance; hesitating whether to go forward or not; hobble along;

zi

【緇】 (1) black; (2) black silk;
[緇帶] black belt;
[緇流] Buddhist monk;
[緇素] Buddhist monks and laymen;
[緇帷] dense forest; forest overgrown with trees;

zi

【輜】 (1) curtained carriage; (2) wagon for supplies;
[輜車] (1) covered wagon; (2) baggage cart;
[輜重] (1) luggage; (2) military supplies;
輜重兵 transportation corps;
輜重車 transport vehicles;
輜重隊 transport troops; transport units;

zi

【諮】 confer; consult; enquire; take counsel;

［諮商］ counseling;

［諮文］ official communication between equals;

［諮詢］ consult; enquire and consult; hold counsel with; seek advice from;

諮詢局 advice bureau;

諮詢欄 advice column;

諮詢民意 consult the people for their opinions;

諮詢委員會 advisory committee;

諮詢制度 counseling system;

諮詢中心 advice centre;

集體諮詢 group counseling;

就業諮詢 employment counseling;

遺傳諮詢 genetic counseling;

［諮議］ (1) confer; discuss; (2) government consultants;

zi

【錙】 ancient unit of weight;

［錙介］ diminutive; minute; tiny;

［錙銖］ a small quantity; a trifle;

錙銖必較 alive to one's own interests; argue about little details; calculating and unwilling to make the smallest sacrifice; count cents and pennies; dispute over every trifle; excessively mean in one's dealings; fight over the smallest trifles; not to bate a penny of it; quibble over every penny; skin a flint; square accounts in every detail;

錙銖不爽 the accounts are exact to a cent;

錙銖計較 counting cents and pennies; miserly;

zi

【髭】 moustaches;

［髭口］ bearded mouth; man's mouth;

［髭毛兒］ bristle up; get furious;

［髭面］ hairy face; unshaven face;

［髭男］ heavily bearded man;

［髭鬚］ moustaches and beards;

zi

【鼒】 tripod tapering off towards the top;

zi

【鎡】 hoe; mattock;

［鎡基］ big hoe;

zi

【齜】 (1) open one's mouth and show the teeth; (2) uneven teeth;

［齜牙］ open one's mouth and show one's teeth;

齜牙瞪眼 gnash one's teeth and stare in anger;

齜牙咧嘴 (1) look fierce; show one's teeth; (2) contort one's face in agony; grimace in pain;

zi³

zi

【子】 (1) child; offspring; son; (2) person; (3) ancient title of respect for a learned or virtuous person; (4) egg; seed; (5) tender; young; (6) sth small and hard; (7) copper;

［子本］ principal and interest;

［子簇］ subvariety;

閉子簇 closed subvariety;

~局部閉子簇 locally closed subvariety;

不可約子簇 irreducible subvariety;

基本子簇 fundamental subvariety;

解析子簇 analytic subvariety;

真子簇 proper subvariety;

［子代］ filial generation;

［子彈］ bullet;

塑料子彈 plastic bullet;

橡膠子彈 rubber bullet;

一發子彈 a bullet; a round of cartridge;

一顆子彈 a bullet;

一粒子彈 a bullet;

一陣子彈 a hail of bullets;

裝子彈 load a gun; load a pistol;

［子道］ filial duties;

［子弟］ children; juniors; sons and younger brothers; young dependents;

子弟兵 army made up of the sons of the people;

膏粱子弟 the son of a rich and important family;

及門子弟 disciples directly taught by master;

誤人子弟 harm the younger generation; lead young people astray; mislead and cause harm to the young men;

［子房］ ovary;

［子婦］ (1) son and daughter-in-law; (2) daughter-in-law; one's son's wife;

［子宮］ uterus; womb;

子宮癌 cancer of the uterus; cancer of the womb; uterine cancer;

子宮白帶 metroleukorrhea;
子宮襞 arbor vitae uteri;
子宮病 hysteropathy; metropathy; uterine disease;
子宮出血 endometrorrhagia; metrorrhagia; uterine bleeding;
子宮發育不全 uterine hypoplasia;
子宮功能不良 dysfunction of uterus;
子宮功能不全 uterine insufficiency;
子宮環 intrauterine device;
子宮肌瘤 hysteromyoma;
子宮積水 hydrometra;
子宮積血 hematometra;
子宮絞痛 uterine colic;
子宮頸 cervix; cervix of the womb; uterine cervix;
~ 子宮頸癌 cancer of the cervix; cervical cancer;
~ 子宮頸糜爛 cervical erosion;
~ 子宮頸炎 cervicitis;
~ 外子宮頸 exocervix;
子宮痙攣 hysterospasm;
子宮口 ostium uteri;
子宮帽 cervical cap;
子宮內膜 endometrium;
~ 子宮內膜炎 endometritis;
~ 剝脱性子宮內膜炎 exfoliative endometritis;
~ 產後子宮內膜炎 puerperal endometritis;
~ 膜性子宮內膜炎 membranous endometritis;
~ 腺性子宮內膜炎 glandular endometritis;
子宮塞 vaginal pessary;
子宮疝 hysterocele;
子宮收縮 uterine contraction;
子宮痛 hysterodynia;
子宮脱垂 metroptosis; prolapse of uterus;
子宮外孕 ectopic pregnancy; extrauterine pregnancy;
子宮萎縮 metratrophia;
子宮無力 metratonia;
子宮下垂 hysteroptosia;
子宮炎 hysteritis; metritis; uteritis;
~ 產後子宮炎 lochiometritis;
~ 膿性子宮炎 pyometritis;
子宮硬化 uterosclerosis;
鞍型子宮 saddle-shaped uterus;
青春期子宮 pubescent uterus;
妊娠子宮 gravid uterus;
心形子宮 uterus cordiformis;

[子薑] young ginger;
[子金] interest from principal;
[子句] clause;
從屬子句 dependent clause;
[子規] cuckoo;
[子粒] grains; kernels; particles; seeds;
[子綿] unginned cotton;
[子民] people; subjects of a kingdom;
[子模] submodule;
閉子模 closed submodule;
容許子模 allowed submodule;
餘子模 complement submodule;
[子母] (1) mother and child; (2) principal and interest;
子母彈 cluster bomb;
[子目] subtitle;
[子女] children; offspring; sons and daughters;
成年子女 grown-up children;
獨生子女 only child;
婚生子女 children born in wedlock; legitimate children;
~ 非婚生子女 children born out of wedlock; illegitimate children;
無子女的 childless;
養子女 adoptees;
[子時] period of the day from 11 p.m. to 1 a.m.;
[子實] beans; grains; kernels; seeds;
[子式] minor;
補子式 complementary minor;
餘子式 complement minor;
主子式 principal minor;
[子嗣] male offspring; son;
[子孫] children and grandchildren; descendants; posterity; scion;
子孫後代 coming generations; future generations; the generations to come; posterity;
子孫滿堂 have many children and grandchildren;
子孫萬代 our children and future generations; our children and our children's children;
抱子弄孫 carry one's grandson in arms and dally with him;
傳子傳孫 bequeath to children and grandchildren; pass on one's skills to one's sons and grandsons;
斷子絕孫 die sonless; die without issue; may you be the last of your line; may

you die sonless; may you die without sons;
桂子蘭孫 famous posterity;
絕子絕孫 die without issue; heirless; may you be the last of your line; may you die sonless; one's posterity may be cut off;
徒子徒孫 adherents; disciples and followers; hangers-on and their spawn; successors;
炎黃子孫 all people of Chinese descent; all the children of the Yellow Emperor; the Chinese people;
貽禍子孫 entail evil on posterity;
子子孫孫 generation after generation of descendants; heirs; offspring;

[子午] meridian;
子午圈 meridian;
~磁子午圈 magnetic meridian;
~地理子午圈 geographic meridian;
~起點子午圈 zero meridian;
~下子午圈 ante meridian;
子午線 meridian;
~本初子午線 first meridian;
~標準子午線 standard meridian;
~大地子午線 geodetic meridian;
~副子午線 secondary meridian;
~基準子午線 reference meridian;
~平均子午線 mean meridian;
~天體子午線 celestial meridian;
~天文子午線 astronomical meridian; terrestrial meridian;
~虛子午線 fictitious meridian; virtual meridian;
~主子午線 principal meridian;
子午儀 meridian instrument;

[子系] offspring; posterity;

[子姓] descendants; offspring;

[子虛] (1) emptiness; nothingness; (2) fiction;
子虛烏有 fictitious; imaginary; pure imagination; sheer fiction; unreal;
事屬子虛 pure imagination; sheer fiction;

[子婿] one's daughter's husband; one's son-in-law;

[子夜] midnight;

[子葉] cotyledon;
背倚子葉 incumbent cotyledon;
出土子葉 epigeal cotyledon;
對折子葉 conduplicate cotyledon;
回折子葉 diplecolobous cotyledon;
緣倚子葉 accumbent cotyledon;

[子音] consonant;

哀子 son newly bereaved of mother;
矮子 dwarf; short person; shortie; shorty;
愛子 beloved son; favourite son;
庵子 (1) thatched hut; (2) nunnery;
鞍子 saddle;
案子 (1) counter; long table; (2) case; law case;
暗門子 unlicensed prostitute;
鏊子 griddle;
把子 (1) bundle; (2) weapons used in operas; (3) a handful; (4) gang; group;
靶子 target;
把子 handle;
白子 white chessman;
敗子 prodigal; spendthrift; wastrel;
稗子 barnyard grass; barnyard millet;
扳子 spanner; wrench;
板子 (1) board; plank; (2) birch; punishing bamboo;
班子 (1) theatrical troupe; (2) organized group;
半輩子 half a lifetime;
半吊子 (1) dabbler; smatterer; (2) tactless and impulsive person;
半子 son-in-law;
幫子 (1) outer leaf; (2) upper of a shoe;
梆子 (1) watchman's clapper; (2) wooden clappers;
膀子 (1) arm; (2) wing;
棒子 (1) club; cudgel; stick; (2) the ear of maize;
包子 steamed stuffed bun;
雹子 hail; hailstone;
孢子 spore;
胞子 spore;
刨子 plane;
鉋子 plane;
豹子 leopard; panther;
杯子 cup; glass; goblet; tumbler;
背子 basket for carrying a load on back;
被子 quilt;
輩子 all one's life; lifetime;
錛子 adze;
本子 (1) book; notebook; (2) edition;
綳子 embroidery frame; hoop;
鏰子 small coin;
筆桿子 pen-holder;
鼻子 nose;
秕子 blighted grain;
箅子 grate; grid;
鞭子 whip;
辮子 (1) pigtail; plait; (2) braid;
婊子 prostitute; whore;

别子 (1) small pin for the case of a thread-bound book; (2) pendant on a tobacco pouch;
檳子 a species of apple which is slightly sour and astringent;
餅子 pancake;
撥子 plectrum;
脖子 neck;
跛子 cripple; lame person;
步子 pace; step;
簿子 book; notebook;
才子 gifted scholar;
菜子 (1) vegetable seed; (2) rapeseed;
蠶子 silkworm seed;
䅟子 billion-dollar grass;
槽子 groove; manger; slot; trough;
艚子 freighter;
草甸子 grassy marshland;
草子 grass seed;
冊子 book; volume;
層子 straton;
叉子 fork;
茬子 tubble;
杈子 branch;
岔子 (1) accident; trouble; (2) branch road; side road;
鏟子 shovel;
腸子 intestines;
廠子 (1) factory; mill; (2) depot; yard;
場子 place where people gather for various purposes;
車子 small vehicle;
超子 hyperon;
臣子 official in feudal times;
沉子 sinker;
橙子 orange;
蟶子 razor clam;
呈子 memorial; petition;
池子 (1) pool; (2) dance floor;
匙子 spoon;
尺子 rule; ruler;
赤子 newborn baby;
翅子 shark's fin;
蟲子 insect; worm;
綢子 silk fabric;
厨子 cook;
處子 maiden; virgin;
椽子 beam; rafter;
窗格子 window lattice;
窗子 window;
牀子 machine tool;
錘子 hammer;
戳子 punch; seal; stamp;

磁子 magneton;
鑹子 ice pick;
村子 hamlet; village;
湊份子 (1) club together; get together; (2) bother sb;
醋罈子 (1) vinegar jar; (2) jealous person;
汆子 kind of kettle;
矬子 dwarf; shortie;
大伯子 one's brother-in-law; one's husband's elder brother;
大肚子 (1) pot belly; (2) pregnant; (3) big eater;
大姑子 one's sister-in-law; one's husband's elder-sister;
大舅子 one's brother-in-law; one's wife's elder brother;
大姨子 one's sister-in-law; one's wife's elder sister;
呆子 blockhead; idiot;
帶子 belt; tape;
袋子 bag; sack;
單子 monad;
膽子 courage; nerve;
撣子 duster;
擔子 (1) carrying pole and the loads on it; (2) burden; load;
蛋子 egg-shaped thing;
彈子 (1) pellet shot from a slingshot; (2) billards;
擋子 blind; fender; screen; shade;
刀子 pocket knife; small knife;
道子 line;
稻子 paddy; rice;
笛子 bamboo flute;
嫡子 one's wife's son;
弟子 disciple; student;
點子 (1) drop; (2) dot; spot; (3) beat; (4) key point; (5) idea; pointer;
電滾子 (1) motor generator; (2) electric motor;
電子 electron;
墊子 cushion; mat;
調子 (1) melody; tune; (2) tone; (3) view;
銚子 pot for decocting herbal medicine;
碟子 dish; plate;
釘子 (1) nail; (2) snag;
定子 stator;
錠子 spindle;
洞子 (1) greenhouse; (2) cave;
兜子 bag pocket;
豆子 (1) bean; pea; (2) bean-shaped object;
獨子 only son;
犢子 calf;
肚子 tripe;
對子 antithetical couplet;

墩子 block of wood or stone;
垛子 (1) buttress; (2) battlements;
馱子 load;
囮子 decoy;
娥子 moth;
兒子 son;
耳子 ears;
筏子 raft;
法子 method; way;
反質子 antiproton;
反中子 antineutron;
販子 dealer; monger;
方子 prescription;
房子 (1) building; house; (2) room;
妃子 imperial concubine;
榧子 (1) Chinese torreya; (2) Chinese torreyanut;
痱子 prickly heat;
分子 (1) numerator; (2) molecule;
份子 one's share of expenses in buying a gift for a mutual friend;
瘋子 lunatic; madman;
縫子 crack; crevice;
麩子 bran;
浮子 (1) float; (2) carburetor float;
斧子 axe; hatchet;
附子 monkshood;
蓋子 (1) cover; lid; (2) shell;
矸子 waste;
柑子 mandarin orange;
桿子 pole;
稈子 stalk;
缸子 bowl; mug;
羔子 kid; lamb;
膏子 medicinal extract;
稿子 (1) draft; sketch; (2) contribution; manuscript; (3) idea; plan;
鴿子 dove; pigeon;
閣子 small wooden house;
格子 check;
個子 build; height;
根子 (1) root; (2) source;
埂子 low bank of earth between fields;
弓子 (1) bow; (2) bow-shaped object;
公因子 common factor;
鉤子 (1) hook; (2) hook-shaped object;
姑子 nun;
孤子 orphan;
穀子 (1) millet; (2) unhusked millet;
股子 share;
骨子 frame; ribs;
瓜子 melon seed;
掛子 Chinese-style unlined upper garment;
拐子 (1) cripple; (2) swindler;
關子 climax; hinge; key;
冠子 comb; crest;
管子 pipe; tube;
館子 eating house; restaurant;
罐子 jar; pot;
光質子 photoproton;
光子 photon;
桄子 reel;
鬼點子 trick; wicked idea;
鬼子 devil;
櫃子 cupboard;
輥子 roller;
磙子 (1) stone roller; (2) roller;
棍子 rod; stick;
鍋子 (1) bowl; (2) chafing dish;
果子 (1) fruit; (2) deep-fried dough stick;
餜子 deep-fried dough stick;
孩子 child;
蚶子 blood clam;
漢子 fellow;
蒿子 Artemisia; wormwood;
毫子 silver coin;
貉子 raccoon dog;
耗子 (1) mouse; (2) rat;
合子 zygote;
盒子 (1) box; case; (2) a kind of fireworks;
核子 nucleon;
猴子 monkey;
瘊子 wart;
鬍子 (1) beard; (2) moustache;
瓠子 a kind of edible gourd;
花池子 flower bed;
花子 seed;
劃子 small rowboat;
環子 link; ring;
荒子 semifinished product;
幌子 (1) shop sign; signboard; (2) cover; pretence;
豁子 breach; opening;
伙子 company; partnership;
集子 anthology; collected works;
蟣子 nit;
激子 exciton;
繼子 adopted son;
甲子 cycle of sixty years;
夾子 (1) clip; tongs; (2) folder;
架子 (1) frame; stand; (2) framework; outline; (3) airs; (4) posture;
尖子 (1) pointed end; (2) best of its kind; (3) sudden rise in pitch;
趼子 callus;

趼子	callus;
剪子	clippers; scissors;
毽子	shuttlecock;
腱子	tendon;
嚼子	bit;
餃子	dumpling;
轎子	sedan;
節子	knot;
癤子	(1) boil; furuncle; (2) knot;
結子	knot;
介子	meson; mesotron;
芥子	mustard seed;
金子	gold;
禁子	jailer;
精子	sperm; spermatozoon;
鏡子	(1) looking glass; mirror; (2) glasses; spectacles;
舅子	one's brother-in-law; one's wife's brother;
駒子	foal;
鋦子	cramp used in mending crockery;
局子	office;
橘子	tangerine;
句子	sentence;
卷子	examination paper;
橛子	peg; wooden pin;
蹶子	hind legs;
君子	gentleman;
蝌子	tadpole;
錁子	small ingot of gold or silver;
坑子	hollow; pit;
空子	(1) gap; opening; (2) chance; opportunity;
口子	(1) hole; opening; (2) cut; tear;
扣子	(1) knot; (2) button;
褲子	pants; trousers;
快中子	fast neutron;
筷子	chopsticks;
款子	sum of money;
筐子	small basket;
框子	frame;
盔子	basin-like container;
辣子	chili; hot pepper;
癩子	person affected with favus on the head;
籃子	basket;
廊子	corridor; veranda;
浪子	loafer; prodigal;
離子	ion;
粒子	particle;
蓮子	lotus seed;
簾子	curtain; screen;
量子	quantum;
料子	(1) material for making clothes; (2) woolen fabric; (3) makings; stuff;
林子	forest; woods;
領子	collar;
瘤子	tumour;
聾子	deaf person;
籠子	(1) cage; coop; (2) basket; container;
漏子	(1) funnel; (2) flaw; loophole;
爐箅子	grate;
爐子	furnace; stove;
路子	approach; way;
麻子	(1) pockmarks; (2) person with a pockmarked face;
馬褡子	saddle-bag;
麥子	wheat;
慢中子	slow neutron;
幔子	curtain; screen;
帽子	(1) cap; hat; (2) brand; label;
梅子	plum;
猸子	crab-eating mongoose;
糜子	broom corn millet;
猛子	dive;
面子	face;
苗子	(1) seedling; young plant; (2) young successor;
抿子	small hairbrush;
明子	pine torch;
命根子	one's very life;
抹子	trowel;
末子	dust; powder;
沫子	foam; froth;
眸子	eye; pupil;
氆子	woolen fabric made in Xizang;
模子	mould; pattern;
奶子	milk;
奈子	crab apple;
男子	male; man;
攮子	dagger;
內子	my wife;
泥子	putty;
逆子	unfilial son;
碾子	stone roller;
女子	female; woman;
耙子	harrow; rake;
筢子	bamboo rake;
拍子	(1) bat; racket; (2) beat; time;
牌子	(1) plate; sign; (2) brand; trademark;
盤子	(1) plate; tray; (2) prices; quotations;
胖子	fatty;
狍子	roe deer;
袍子	gown; robe;
泡子	bulb;
配子	gamete;
盆子	basin; pot;

棚子 shack; shed;
皮鞭子 leather-thonged whip;
皮夾子 pocketbook; wallet;
皮子 (1) hide; leather; (2) fur;
痞子 riff-raff; ruffian;
片子 (1) roll of film; (2) film; movie; (3) disc;
篇子 sheet;
騙子 cheat; swindler;
票子 bank note; bill;
瓶子 bottle;
脯子 breast meat;
譜子 music score;
鋪子 shop; store;
妻子 (1) wife; (2) wife and children;
棋子 chessman;
旗子 banner; flag; pennant;
釺子 hammer drill; rock drill;
鉗子 forceps; pincers; pliers;
腔子 (1) thorax; (2) beheaded trunk;
槍桿子 barrel of a gun;
雀子 freckle;
茄子 aubergine; eggplant;
曲子 melody; song;
圈子 circle; ring;
瘸子 cripple; lame person;
裙子 skirt;
瓤子 flesh; pulp;
日子 (1) date; day; (2) time; (3) life;
熱中子 thermal neutron;
褥子 cotton-padded mattress;
孺子 child;
塞子 cork; plug;
嗓子 (1) larynx; throat; (2) voice;
嫂子 one's sister-in-law; wife of one's elder brother;
沙子 (1) grit; sand; (2) pellets; small grains;
傻子 blockhead; fool;
篩子 sieve; sifter;
色子 dice;
扇骨子 the ribs of a fan;
扇子 fan;
上輩子 (1) ancestors; (2) previous existence;
勺子 ladle; scoop;
哨子 whistle;
身子 (1) body; (2) pregnancy;
嬸子 wife of one's father's younger brother;
繩子 rope; string;
虱子 louse;
石子 cobble; cobble-stone; pebble;
釋子 monk;
瘦子 lean person;
梳子 comb;
豎子 (1) boy; lad; (2) fellow; mean fellow;
庶子 concubine's son;
刷子 brush; scrub;
水鱉子 apus;
水池子 (1) pond; pool; (2) sink;
栓子 embolus;
穗子 fringe; tassel;
松子 pinenut;
蘇子 perillaseed;
素因子 prime factor;
算子 operator;
孫子 grandson;
榫子 tenon;
梭子 (1) shuttle; (2) cartridge clip;
太子 crown prince;
攤子 (1) vendor's stand; (2) setup;
癱子 person suffering from paralysis;
罎子 earthern jar;
毯子 blanket;
探子 (1) scout; (2) thin tube;
絛子 silk braid; silk ribbon;
桃子 peach;
套子 (1) case; sheath; (2) conventional remark;
藤子 vine;
梯子 ladder; stepladder;
蹄子 hoof;
天子 emperor;
條子 (1) strip; (2) brief informal note;
帖子 card; note;
亭子 kiosk; pavilion;
梃子 frame;
桐子 seed of the tung tree;
童子 boy; lad;
頭子 boss; chief; chieftain;
禿子 baldhead;
土包子 clodhopper; country humpkin;
兔子 hare; rabbit;
團子 dumpling;
推子 hair-clippers;
腿子 henchman; lackey;
屯子 village;
托子 base; support;
駝子 humpback; hunchback;
砣子 emery wheel for cutting jade;
娃子 (1) slave; (2) baby; child;
袜子 socks; stockings;
彎子 curve; turn;
丸子 (1) ball; round mass of food; (2) bolus; pill;
腕子 wrist;
王子 king's son; prince;
網子 hairnet; net;
圍子 (1) defensive wall; (2) curtain;

帷子 curtain;
葦子 reed;
位子 place; seat;
蚊子 mosquito;
屋子 room;
杌子 foot-stool;
痦子 mole; naevus;
席子 mat;
戲報子 theatrical poster;
戲本子 script for a play or an opera;
戲館子 theatre;
戲子 actor; actress;
瞎子 blind person;
蝦子 shrimp roe;
下輩子 next life;
仙子 (1) female celestial; (2) celestial being; immortal;
弦子 three-stringed plucked instrument;
橡子 acorn;
小辮子 handle;
小冊子 booklet; pamphlet;
小肚子 lower abdomen; underbelly;
小姑子 one's sister-in-law; one's husband's younger sister;
小孩子 child;
小伙子 lad; young fellow;
小舅子 one's brother-in-law; one's wife's younger brother;
小日子 cozy and happy life of a small family;
小叔子 one's brother-in-law; one's husband's younger brother;
小姨子 one's sister-in-law; one's wife's younger sister;
小月子 one's abortion; miscarriage;
小子 (1) young people; (2) younger generation;
孝子 (1) dutiful son; (2) son in mourning;
蝎子 scorpion;
鞋拔子 shoehorn;
鞋子 shoes;
心子 centre; core;
星子 bit; particle;
性子 (1) temper; (2) potency; strength;
袖子 sleeve;
鬚子 palpus; tassel;
楦子 (1) shoe last; shoe tree; (2) hat block;
靴子 boots;
學子 student;
鴨子 duck;
牙子 (1) serrated edge; (2) middleman;
煙子 soot;
檐子 eaves;
燕子 swallow;
洋鬼子 foreign devil;
養子 foster child;
樣子 (1) appearance; shape; (2) air; manner; (3) pattern; sample;
腰桿子 (1) back; (2) backing; support;
腰子 kidney;
椰子 (1) coconut tree; (2) coconut;
葉子 leaf;
一輩子 a lifetime; all one's life;
一下子 all at once; all of a sudden; once; one time;
一陣子 a period of time; a spell;
椅子 chair;
義子 adopted son;
因子 factor;
銀子 silver;
引子 introduction;
印把子 seal of authority;
印子 (1) mark; print; trace; (2) usury;
纓子 (1) hat tassels; (2) anything shaped like tassels;
蠅子 fly;
影子 (1) reflection; shadow; (2) sign; trace;
油柑子 phyllanthus emblica;
遊子 wandering son;
幼子 youngest son;
魚子 roe;
餘因子 complementary divisor;
原子 atom;
園子 area of land for growing plants;
院子 compound; courtyard; yard;
栽子 seedling; young plant;
崽子 bastard; whelp;
鑿子 chisel;
劄子 ancient official document;
砟子 tiny fragments of stone or coal;
柵子 fence; hedge;
寨子 stockade village;
長子 eldest son;
障子 barrier;
招子 (1) bill; poster; (2) shop sign; (3) move; trick;
罩子 cover; shade;
折子 booklet used for keeping accounts, etc.;
褶子 (1) pleat; (2) crease; wrinkle; (3) wrinkle;
疹子 measles;
質子 proton;
稚子 child;
直腸子 frank; outspoken;
中子 neutron;
盅子 handleless cup;
種子 seed;
舟子 boatman;

珠子 (1) pearl; (2) bead;
竹子 bamboo;
主子 boss; master;
柱子 pillar; post;
爪子 claw; paw; talon;
錐子 awl;
桌子 table;
鐲子 bracelet;

zi
【仔】 careful;
[仔密] close-knitted; close-woven;
[仔肩] bear the burden;
[仔細] attentive; careful; punctilious; to a crumb;
仔細考慮 consider carefully;

產仔 farrow;

zi
【姊】 one's elder sister;
[姊妹] elder and younger sisters; sisters;
姊妹花 two sisters;
親姊妹 sisters born of the same parents;

zi
【籽】 seeds of plants;
[籽粒] grains of seeds;

棉籽 cottonseed;
油菜籽 rapeseed;

zi
【耔】 hoe up earth around a plant;

zi
【秭】 one trillion;

zi
【茈】 bupleurum;

zi
【梓】 (1) catalpa ovata; (2) home town; (3) make furniture; (4) carve words on woodboard; (5) (now rare) a surname;
[梓宮] coffin for an emperor;
[梓匠輪輿] carpenters and wheelwrights;
[梓里] one's home town; one's native place;
[梓器] coffin;
[梓人] architect; builder; carpenter; wood engraver;
[梓鄉] one's hometown; one's native place;
梓鄉梓里 one's native place;

桑梓 one's native place;

zi
【笫】 bed;

zi
【紫】 (1) purple; violet; (2) a surname;
[紫斑] petechia;
紫斑病 purpura;
[紫菜] laver;
[紫丁香] lilac;
[紫癜] pelioma; peliosis; purpura;
變應性紫癜 allergic purpura;
出血性紫癜 purpura haemorrhagica;
單純性紫癜 purpura simplex;
風濕性紫癜 purpura rheumatica;
過敏性紫癜 anaphylactic purpura;
精神性紫癜 psychogenic purpura;
老年性紫癜 purpura senilis;
甾體性紫癜 steroid purpura;
[紫羔] Chinese blue sheep;
[紫紅] fuchsia; purplish red;
萬紫千紅 a blaze of colour; a profusion of colour; a riot of colour; a vast display of dazzling colours; innumerable flowers of purple and red;
~萬紫千紅才是春 it is spring only when all the flowers are blooming;
[紫花地丁] Chinese violet;
[紫薑] tender shoots of ginger;
[紫膠] shellack;
紫膠片 shellack;
~脫色紫膠片 decolourized shellack;
漂白紫膠 bleached shellack; kiln-dry shellack;
石榴紫膠 garnet shellack;
[紫金] pure gold;
[紫羅蘭] violet;
[紫泥] purple ink for imprinting of seals;
[紫氣] auspicious atmosphere;
紫氣東來 the ruddy light comes from the east — a propitious omen;
[紫色] purple; violet;
淡紫色 lilac; mauve;
淺紫色 lavender;
[紫杉] yew; yew tree;
[紫檀] red sandalwood;
[紫藤] wistaria;
[紫銅] red copper;
[紫外光] ultraviolet rays;
[紫虛] firmament; sky;
[紫藥水] gentian violet;

[紫竹] black bamboo;

苯胺紫 mauve;
甲紫 gentian violet;
絳紫 dark reddish purple;
醬紫 dark reddish purple;
龍膽紫 gentian violet;
葡萄紫 dark purple;
青紫 (1) high position; (2) cyanosis;

zi
【滓】 dregs; lees; sediment;

渣滓 dregs; sediment;

zi
【訾】 (1) blame; censure; slander; (2) blemishes; faults; ill; (3) measure; (4) confine to; limit to; (5) consider; estimate; (6) meagre; poor; (7) a surname;
[訾病] find fault with;
[訾毀] defame; slander; vilify;
[訾厲] disease; illness;
[訾議] censure; criticize; discuss the failings of others; impeach; unfavourable criticism;
[訾訾] defame; slander;

zi
【訿】 same as 訾, defame, slander;

zi⁴
zi
【字】 (1) character; letter; logograph; word; (2) pronunciation; (3) form of a written or printed character; style of handwriting; (4) calligraphy; (5) receipt; written pledge; (6) be betrothed; betroth a girl;
[字典] dictionary; lexicon; thesaurus;
百科字典 encyclopedic dictionary;
查字典 consult a dictionary; look up in a dictionary; refer to a dictionary; search through a dictionary; go to a dictionary for a word;
大學字典 collegiate dictionary;
發音字典 pronunciation dictionary;
活字典 walking dictionary;
簡略字典 compendious dictionary;
簡明字典 concise dictionary;
控制字典 control dictionary;
雙語對照字典 bilingual dictionary;
一種字典 a kind of dictionary;
綜合字典 complete dictionary;
[字兒] (1) character; (2) receipt;
[字符] character;
字符比較 character comparison;
編輯字符 editing character;
佈置字符 layout character;
成幀字符 frame character;
代碼擴充字符 code extension character;
二進制編碼字符 binary coded character;
返回字符 backspace character;
格式控制字符 format effector character;
換行字符 line feed character; new line character;
間隔字符 gap character;
校驗字符 check character;
肯定字符 acknowledge character;
空轉字符 idle character;
鏈接字符 concatenation character;
命令字符 command character;
漂移字符 drifting character;
填充字符 fill character;
圖形字符 graphic character;
消除字符 clear character;
星號影像字符 asterisk picture character;
[字根] radical; root;
[字號] name of a shop;
字號鋪兒 reputable shop;
字號人物 personages and their reputation;
老字號 time-honoured brand;
~中華老字號 China's time-honoured brand;
[字盒] type mould;
[字畫] calligraphy and painting; scripts and paintings;
字畫古玩 painting, calligraphy and antiques;
[字匯] glossary; lexicon; vocabulary; wordbook;
[字蹟] handwriting; writing;
字蹟工整 neat writing; neatly lettered;
字蹟娟秀 a graceful hand; beautiful handwriting;
字蹟模糊 illegible handwriting;
[字節] byte;
百萬字節 megabyte;
千字節 kilobyte;
千兆字節 gigabyte;
萬億字節 terabyte;
兆字節 megabyte;

Z

[字句] words and expressions; writing;
字句通順 coherent and smooth writing;
堆字砌句 pile up words and phrases;
酌字斟句 choose one's words with great care; weigh one's words;
字斟句酌 choose one's words carefully; choose one's words with great care; go over one's wording; pick one's words; refine on words; weigh every word; weight one's words;
[字據] certificate; receipt; written proof;
[字裏行間] between the lines; overtone;
[字謎] riddle about a character or word;
縱橫字謎 crossword;
[字面] literal;
字面涵義 literal connotation;
字面理解 literal comprehension;
字面意義 denotative meaning; literal meaning;
字面語言 literal language;
從字面上看 on the face of;
[字模] type matrix;
[字母] character; letter; letters of alphabet;
字母表 alphabet;
字母使用 alphabetism;
字母數字 alphanumeric;
~字母數字計算機 alphanumeric computer;
字母算術 alphametic;
字母湯 alphabet soup;
字母文字 alphabetic writing;
字母學 alphabetography;
大寫字母 capital letter; capitalized letter;
交織字母 monogram;
羅馬字母 Roman alphabet;
拼音字母 phonetic alphabet;
輸入字母 input alphabets;
小寫字母 small letter;
學字母 learn one's ABC;
音節字母 syllabic alphabet;
音位字母 phonemic alphabet;
英文字母 English alphabet;
[字幕] caption; subtitle; title;
字幕編寫員 titler;
字幕頭 top title;
標題字幕 main title;
插入字幕 inlaid caption;
動畫字幕 title cartoon;
對白字幕 spoken title;
故障字幕 fault caption;
滾動字幕 roll titles;
美術字幕 art-title;
片頭字幕 credit title;
説明字幕 side title; telltale title;
特技字幕 animated caption;
外文字幕 foreign language caption;
影片字幕 film caption;
[字人] become engaged;
尚未字人 she is yet to be betrothed to sb;
[字首] prefix;
[字書] dictionary; wordbook;
[字素] grapheme;
字素變體 allograph;
[字體] form of a written or printed character; script; type; typeface;
[字條] brief note;
[字帖] copybook; model of calligraphy for practice;
[字尾] suffix;
[字形] font; form of a character;
字形學 morphology;
[字眼] character; word; diction; wording;
摳字眼兒 find fault with the choice of words; pay too much attention to the shades of meaning of words; split hairs;
挑字眼兒 find fault with the choice of words; pick bones with person;
[字樣] (1) models of Chinese characters; (2) words and phrases used in a certain context;
[字義] (1) literal meaning; (2) connotation; definition; meaning of a word;
[字譯] word translation;
[字源] etymology of a word;
[字韻] rhyme of a character;
[字正腔圓] with clear articulation and a mellow and full tune;
[字紙] paper with words written on it;
字紙簍兒 wastebasket; wastepaper basket;
[字字] every word;
字字清脆，聲聲婉轉 one's words are distinct and yet possess a continuous melody;
字字中肯 every word is to the point; every word tells;
字字珠璣 each word a gem; every phrase a gem; sparkling ideas put in writing;
[字組] block of words;
字組地址 block address;

八字 (1) character "eight"; (2) Eight Character (fortune-telling); (3) horoscope;
白字 (1) wrongly written character; (2) mispronounced character;
本字 the original form of a character;
表字 alias; courtesy name; secondary personal name;
別字 (1) wrongly written or mispronounced character; (2) alias;
草字 Chinese character written in cursive;
測字 tell fortune from the component parts of a Chinese character;
拆字 tell fortune from the component parts of a Chinese character;
赤字 deficit;
粗體字 boldfaced word;
錯別字 wrongly written or mispronounced characters;
錯字 (1) wrongly written character; (2) misprint;
打字 type; typewrite;
大字 big character;
待字 (of a girl) wait for the right man to marry;
單字 (1) individual character; (2) separate word;
點字 Braille;
疊字 reiterative locution;
丁字 T-shaped;
繁體字 traditional Chinese character;
方塊字 Chinese character;
古文字 ancient writing;
漢字 Chinese character;
好字 good handwriting;
黑體字 boldface type;
活字 letter; type;
簡化字 abbreviated character;
簡體字 simplified Chinese character;
聯綿字 Chinese words consisting of two characters, often alliterated or rhymed;
羅馬字 Roman numerals;
盲字 Braille;
美術字 art lettering; artistic calligraphy;
排字 compose; typeset;
破體字 non-standardized Chinese characters;
鉛字 letter; type;
簽字 affix one's signature;
認字 learn to read;
生字 new word;
識字 become literate; learn to read;
實字 notional word;
熟字 familiar word;
數目字 (1) figure; numeral; (2) amount; quantity;
數字 (1) digit; figure; numeral; (2) amount; quantity;
俗體字 popular form of characters;
俗字 popular form of characters;
題字 inscribe;
文字 (1) character; script; (2) written language; (3) writing;
習字 do exercises in calligraphy;
象形字 pictographic character;
小字 small letter;
楔形字 cuneiform;
寫字 write characters;
斜體字 italics;
虛字 empty word; function word;
異體字 modified character;
臟字 dirty word; swear word;
正字 correct a wrongly written character;
鑄字 cast type;

zi

【自】 (1) in person; oneself; personal; private; self; (2) certainly; natural; of course; (3) from; since; (4) a surname;

[自愛] behave like a gentleman; cherish one's good name; regard for oneself; self-love; self-respect; take care of one's health;
自愛自律 self-respect and self-discipline;
自愛自重 self-esteem and self-discipline;
不知自愛 act without self-respect;
不自愛 have no self-respect;
潔身自愛 exercise self-control so as to protect oneself from immorality; keep one's integrity and refuse to swim with the stream; lead an honest and clean life; mind one's own business in order to keep out of trouble; preserve one's purity; refuse to be contaminated by evil influence; refuse to soil one's hands;

[自傲] arrogant; self-conceited;
自傲情結 superiority complex;
居功自傲 claim credit for oneself and become arrogant;

[自拔] extricate oneself; free oneself from...;

[自白] confession; explain oneself; make a personal statement; make clear one's position; vindicate oneself;
自白書 written confession;
剖心自白 open one's heart and clear one's reputation;

[自保] self-hold; self-insurance; self-

Z

perpetuating;

[自卑] despise oneself; feel oneself inferior; self-abased; slight oneself; underestimate oneself;

自卑感 inferiority complex; sense of inferiority;

自卑情結 inferiority complex;

自卑自賤 look down on and despise oneself; self-abasement; slight and despite oneself;

[自備] provide for oneself; self-provided;

[自必] certainly; naturally; surely; unavoidably;

[自閉症] autism;

[自斃] destroy oneself; self-destruction;

[自便] as one pleases; as one wishes; at one's own convenience; suit oneself;

聽其自便 let sb act according to his convenience; let sb do as he pleases;

[自變數] argument; independent variable;

定立自變數 locator argument;

複自變數 complex argument;

虛自變數 imaginary argument;

[自裁] commit suicide; take one's own life;

[自殘] autotomy;

自殘鳩拙 feel ashamed of one's lack of creative talent;

[自察] aware of one's own behaviour; make self-examination;

[自陳] state personally;

[自稱] call oneself; claim to be; declare oneself to be; profess; style oneself;

自稱內行 call oneself an expert; claim to be an old hand;

[自持] control oneself; discipline oneself; exercise self-restraint; restrain oneself;

自恃有功 capitalize on one's achievements;

[自處] one's own position; where to place oneself;

[自此] from then on; henceforth;

[自從] ever since; from; since; since then;

[自達達人] one must be enlightened oneself before one can enlighten others;

[自大] above oneself; arrogant; cocky; conceited; egotistic; hubris; in one's altitude;

自大的 egotistical;

自大狂 egomaniac;

傲慢自大 arrogant and disdainful; overweening;

高傲自大 arrogant and self-important; be stuck up; have a big head; have a swelled head; get a swollen head; too big for one's breeches;

驕傲自大 be bloated with pride; be puffed up; be swollen with pride; cocky; conceited and arrogant; feel high and mighty; have a swelled head; get a swelled head; give oneself airs; self-important; stuck-up;

狂妄自大 arrogant and conceited; pretentious;

狂自尊大 as proud as Lucifer; self-conceited;

夜郎自大 braggadocio; ignorant and boastful; ignorant presumption; ludicrous conceit; presumptuous self-conceit; think no small beer of oneself;

~夜郎自大，利令智昏 be blinded by one's presumptuous self-conceit and overweening ambition;

自高自大 above oneself; all over oneself; an exaggerated sense of one's importance; arrogant; as vain as a peacock; assume great airs; be puffed up with wind; be stuck up; big-head; big-headed; conceited; conscious of one's importance; disgustingly self-satisfied; full of conceit; full of glory; full of vain; get above oneself; get too big for one's boots; go about with one's head in the air; have a high opinion of oneself; have an overweening opinion of oneself; high-blown; imagine oneself to be superior to others; look big; look down on all others; on high horse; pique oneself on one's abilities; self-assertive; self-important and self-exalted; stuck-up; swelled head; swollenheaded; think highly of oneself; think no small beer of oneself; too big for one's breeches; too big for one's boots; too big for one's shoes; too big for one's trousers; up stage; with one's nose in the air;

~自高自大的 bumptious;

[自當] should naturally;

自當努力 will certainly do one's best;

[自得] contented; pleased with oneself; self-

complacent; self-satisfied;
自得其樂 content with one's lot; derive pleasure from sth; enjoy oneself; find enjoyment in sth; find joy in one's own way; pleased as Punch with oneself; take delight in doing sth as a pleasurable occupation;
昂然自得 be elated; be upright and pleased with oneself; walk on air;
傲慢自得 haughty and complacent;
俯仰自得 contented and happy wherever one is;
軒軒自得 delighted and satisfied with oneself;
洋洋自得 self-satisfied;
揚揚自得 complacent; smug;
怡然自得 happy and contented;
意氣自得 easy and dignified;
雍容自得 in the peace of mind; poised;

[自頂至踵] from head to foot;

[自動] (1) of one's own accord; of one's own free will; voluntarily; (2) automatic; spontaneous;
自動包裝線 automatic packaging line;
自動報警 auto alarm;
自動曝光 automatic exposure;
自動編輯 auto edit;
自動編碼 auto coding;
~自動編碼系統 auto coding system;
~自動編碼語言 auto coding language;
自動編排系統 autopatching system;
自動標引 automatic indexing;
自動撥號 automatic dial;
~自動撥號鍵 auto dial key;
~自動撥號裝置 auto dialing unit;
自動步槍 automatic rifle;
自動測試系統 automated test system;
自動打包機 automatic packaging machine;
自動倒帶 auto rewind;
~自動倒帶控制 auto rewind control;
自動登記 automatic logging;
自動點唱機 jukebox;
自動電話 automatic telephone;
自動電梯 escalator;
自動翻譯 automatic translation;
~自動翻譯系統 automatic translation system;
自動販賣機 vending machine;
自動放像 automatic playback;
~自動放像控制 auto play control;
自動呼叫 automatic calling;
~自動呼叫系統 automatic calling system;
~自動呼叫裝置 automatic calling equipment;
自動扶梯 escalator;
自動櫃員機 automatic teller machine;
自動化 automation; automatization; automatize;
~自動化錯覺 illusions of automation;
~自動化管理系統 automatic management system;
~自動化技術工具 automatic equipment;
~自動化軟件 automated software;
~自動化霜 auto defrosting;
~自動化信息系統 automatic information system;
~半自動化 partial automation;
~編譯自動化 compiling automation;
~車間自動化 job-shop automation;
~電氣自動化 electric automatization;
~反饋自動化 feedback automation;
~分段自動化 sectional automation;
~工序自動化 process automation;
~機車自動化 locomotive automation;
~機械自動化 mechanical automation;
~靈活自動化 flexible automation;
~溜放自動化 humping automation;
~全盤自動化 all-around automation;
~全自動化 complete automatization; full automation;
~事務自動化 business automation;
~數據自動化 data automation;
~源數據自動化 source-data automation;
~信息傳遞自動化 automatization of information transmission;
~序列自動化 sequential automation;
~主控自動化 master control automation;
~裝配自動化 assembly automation;
~綜合自動化 integrated automation;
自動換擋 auto shifter;
自動恢復程序 automatic recovery programme;
自動記憶放像 automatic playback memory;
自動加載 autoload;
自動開關 an automatic switch;
自動控制 automatic control;
~自動控制系統 automatic control system;
自動快進控制 auto fast forward control;
自動亮度限制 automatic bright limiting;
自動排版 automatic typesetting;

~自動排版系統 automatic typesetting system;
自動頻率控制 automatic frequency control;
自動清零 automatic clear;
自動取款機 automatic teller;
自動軟件工程 automated softare engineering;
自動色度控制 automatic chrominance control;
~自動色度控制放大器 automatic chrominance control amplifier;
~自動色度控制檢波器 automatic chrominance control detector;
自動色度增益控制 auto colour gain control;
自動設計系統 automated design system;
自動攝影機 automatic camera;
自動生產線 automatic production line;
自動售貨機 automatic slot machine;
自動數據處理 automatic data processing;
~自動數據處理機 automatic data processing machine;
~自動數據處理系統 automatic data processing system;
~自動數據處理中心 automatic data processing centre;
自動數據交換中心 automatic data switching centre;
自動數字編碼系統 automatic digital encoding system;
自動數字交換系統 automatic digital interchange system;
自動搜索 automatic search;
自動同步開關 auto sync switch;
自動圖像傳輸 automatic picture transmission;
自動微調 automatic fine tuning;
自動性 automatism;
自動音量控制 automatic volume control;
自動語音識別系統 automatic speech recognition system;
自動質量控制 automatic quality control;
半自動 semi-automatic;
全自動 fully automatic;
~全自動編譯技術 fully automatic compiling technique;
~全自動化 automation;
~全自動洗衣機 automatic washing machine;

[自瀆] masturbation;

[自多] conceited; self-satisfied;

[自發] spontaneous; take the initiative;

[自伐] (1) abuse oneself; (2) conceited;
矜功自伐 claim credit for oneself and become arrogant; praise oneself on one's merits;

[自反] examine one's own conduct; introspect; self-examination;

[自肥] enrich oneself by misappropriating funds or material; fatten oneself; feather one's nest;
殘民自肥 fatten oneself by exploiting the people;

[自費] at one's own expense; pay one's own expenses; self-provided;
自費留學 study abroad at one's own expense;
~自費留學生 self-financed student studying abroad;
自費生 self-financed student;

[自焚] burn oneself; burn oneself to death; self-burning;

[自分] anticipate; estimate one's own ability or strength; figure;

[自封] (1) proclaim oneself; style oneself; (2) confine oneself; isolate oneself;
固步自封 continue walking in the old steps and seclude oneself; limit one's own progress; remain where one is, without desire to advance further; rest complacently on one's laurels; rest content with old practice; stand still and refuse to make progress; stick to the beaten track; unwilling to move forward;

[自奉] provide the necessities of life for oneself; treat oneself;
自奉儉約 economical in self-comforts; lead plain and simple life; live very simple; stint oneself;
自奉甚薄 live on simple fare; live very simply;
自奉甚厚 do oneself proud;
自奉甚約 lead a frugal life; live economically;
自奉優厚 do oneself proud; do oneself well;

[自負] (1) conceited; have a high opinion of oneself; think highly of oneself; (2) responsible for one's own action;
自負不淺 show oneself to be not shallow;

自負的 big-headed; bumptious;
自負盈虧 assume sole responsibility for its own profits or losses; have full responsibility for one's own profits and losses;
十分自負 be full of conceit;

[自個兒] by oneself; oneself;

[自耕農] owner-peasant;
半自耕農 semi-owner peasant;

[自供] confess;

[自顧] look after oneself;
自顧不暇 busy enough with one's own affairs; can hardly look after oneself; have trouble even in taking care of oneself; unable even to fend for oneself;
自顧自 (1) selfish; (2) mind one's business; (3) everyone for oneself;

[自豪] feel proud of; have a proper sense of pride; pride oneself on; proud of; take pride in;
引為自豪 pride oneself on; take pride in;

[自好] self-esteem; self-respect;
潔身自好 keep oneself aloof;

[自後] from now on; henceforth;

[自毀] self-destruction;
自毀長城 get rid of a capable lieutenant;
自毀前程 destroy one's own career;

[自己] one's person; oneself; self;
自己害自己 bite off one's nose; cook one's own goose; harm oneself; saw off the bough on which one is sitting; throw a stone in one's own garden; tread on one's own tail;
自己人 one of us; people on one's own side;
愛惜自己 sparing of oneself;
保養自己 take care of oneself;
出賣自己 sell oneself;
求諸自己 look to oneself;
養活自己 support oneself;
照顧自己 self-care; take care of oneself;
祇顧自己 look after number one; look out for number one;

[自給] self-contained; self-sufficient; self-supporting;
自給自足 able to support oneself; autarchy; provide enough to met one's own needs; provide for oneself; self-sufficiency; self-sufficient;
僅能自給 barely enough to support oneself;

[自家] oneself;
自家出事自家知 well may be smell fire whose gown burns;
自家的孩子背著不嫌沉 a burden of one's chice is not felt; the burden one likes is cheerfully borne;
自家掘墓自家埋 he who digs a pit for others, falls in himself; whose diggeth a pit shall fall therein;
自家人 one of us; persons within the same circle;

[自薦] introduce oneself; offer one's services; recommend oneself for a job; volunteer;
毛遂自薦 offer one's own services; offer oneself for a position;
~毛遂自薦求職 apply for a job by volunteering one's own services;

[自解] (1) self-explanation; (2) extricate oneself from;

[自矜] brag;
自矜其能 boast of oneself; bray of one's attainments;

[自今] from now on; henceforth;
自今而後 from now on;

[自盡] commit suicide; kill oneself; take one's own life;
吞金自盡 kill oneself by swallowing gold;

[自救] provide for and help oneself; rescue oneself; save oneself; self-salvation;
自救互救 self and mutual medical aid;
自救救人 save both oneself and others;

[自咎] blame oneself; rebuke oneself; self-reproach;

[自居] consider oneself to be; pose as;

[自覺] (1) aware of; (2) conscientious; of one's own free will; self-consciousness; self-realization;
自覺性 consciousness;
自覺自願 by one's own desire; conscious and willing; do sth of one's own will; on one's own initiative; voluntarily; willingly;

[自決] decide by oneself; self-determine;

[自絕] (1) alienate oneself; cut oneself off from; isolate oneself; (2) seek self-destruction;
自絕於人 alienate oneself from others; break off intercourse with others due

Z

to one's own actions; cut oneself from others;

[自控] self-control;

[自苦] give oneself unnecessary pains; look for trouble;

[自誇] boast; brag; crack oneself up; sing one's own praises;

自誇自賞 establish one's own system; indulge in self-glorification;

自誇自讚 all one's geese are swans; brag and boast oneself; plume oneself;

王婆賣瓜，自賣自誇 all one's geese are swans; every cook praises his own broth; every peddler praises his needles; nothing like leather; ring one's own bell;

[自寬] comfort oneself; self-consolation;

[自況] compare oneself with another person;

[自來] from the beginning; in the first place; originally;

自來水 running water; tap-water;

自來水筆 fountain pen;

自來水廠 waterworks;

自來水公司 water supply company;

不請自來 come in without invitation; come without being invited; gatecrash;

~不請自來的人 gatecrasher;

貨好客自來 good wine needs no bush;

酒好人自來 good wine needs no bush;

[自理] make one's own arrangements; provide for oneself; take care of oneself;

[自勵] self-excitation;

自勵勵人 encourage oneself and others;

[自立] earn one's own living; stand on one's own feet; stand on one's own legs; support oneself;

自立門戶 establish one's own school of thought; have separate kitchens; keep house; set up one's own clique;

自立生計 make one's own living;

自立為帝 assume the title of king; make oneself king;

自立一說 set forward one's own views;

自立於不敗之地 secure an invincible position;

人貴自立 every tub must stand on its own bottom; self-reliance is a virtue;

[自力] one's own efforts;

自力更生 achieve self-renewal with one's own effort; depend on one's own strength; hoe one's own row; make one's own life; make one's way in life by one's own efforts; on one's resources; paddle one's own canoe; push forward by one's own effort; put forth new life by one's own efforts; raise oneself up by one's own bootstraps; rely on one's own efforts; self-reliance; stand on one's own feet; take fate in one's own hands;

自力救濟 redress a perceived wrong by taking the law into one's own hands;

自本自力 depend on one's own resources and ability; do sth alone; with one's own capital and effort;

[自利] think of nothing but one's own gain;

[自戀] narcissism;

[自量] estimate one's own ability or strength; have a general idea of one's own abilities; make a self-assessment; measure oneself;

不自量 go beyond one's depth; not take a proper measure of oneself; overrate one's own abilities; overrate oneself;

~不知自量 do sth beyond one's ability;

~太不自量 overestimate oneself; think too much of oneself;

[自了] able to conclude sth all by oneself;

自了漢 selfish person;

[自料] anticipate; believe; figure; think;

[自憐] self-pity;

顧影自憐 admire oneself in the mirror; feel self-pity when looking at one's own shadow; look at one's image in the mirror and pity oneself; look at one's reflection and admire oneself; look at one's shadow and lament one's lot; pity oneself at the sight of one's shadow; self-affection;

[自流] artesian;

自流井 artesian well;

任其自流 leave events to take their own course; let matters slide; let things run their own course;

聽其自流 let people act freely without leadership; let things drift alone;

[自律] (1) control oneself; exercise self-control; exercise self-restraint; self-discipline; (2) autonomy;

[自滿] complacency; complacent; satisfied

with oneself; self-contented; self-satisfied;
自滿的 complacent;
自滿自欺 deceive oneself;
自滿自足 self-satisfied and self-contented;
驕傲自滿 arrogant and complacent; be inflated with pride; big with pride; conceit and self-complacency; conceited;
恬逸自滿 self-satisfied with quietness and indolence;

[自明] obvious; self-evident; self-explanatory;
不辨自明 be made clear without debate; self-evident;

[自鳴鐘] striking clock;

[自命] consider oneself; regard oneself as;
自命不凡 above oneself; conceited; consider oneself a person of no ordinary talent; consider oneself above the crowd; consider oneself an exceptional person; have a high opinion of oneself; have an unduly high opinion of oneself; on good germs with oneself; snobbery; stuck up; think too highly of oneself;
~自命不凡的 big-headed; swell-headed;
~自命不凡的態度 patronizing attitude;
自命清高 act as if one is morally better than other people; have a holier-than-thou manner;

[自然] (1) natural world; nature; (2) in the ordinary course of events; naturally; (3) naturally; of course;
自然保護 natural conservation;
~自然保護區 nature reserve; wilderness area;
自然本能 natural instincts;
自然變化 spontaneous change;
自然層次 natural level;
自然詞序 natural word-order;
自然發生 abiogenesis;
自然法 natural method;
自然規律 natural law;
自然規模 physical size;
自然界 natural world; nature;
自然科學 natural science;
自然奇觀 natural splendor;
自然數 natural number;
自然性 naturalness;
~自然性層次 level of naturalness;
~詞匯自然性 lexical naturalness;
自然語言 natural language;
自然主義 naturalism;
~自然主義語言學派 naturalistic linguistics;
變革自然 transform nature;
不自然 ill at ease;
~不自然的 contrived;
超自然 supernatural;
大自然 Mother Nature; nature;
~大自然的奧秘 mysteries of nature;
~大自然的美 beauties of nature;
改造自然 transformation of nature;
回歸自然 back to nature;
順乎自然 in the course of nature; let nature take its course;
順其自然 let nature take its course;
聽其自然 leave sb to his own devices; leave the matter as it is; leave things to chance; let it go at that; let it have its swing; let matters slide; let nature take its course; let the world slide; let the world wag as it will; let things take their own course; take the world as one finds it;
違反自然 absonant to nature;
習慣成自然 habit is second nature;

[自欺] deceive oneself; self-deceit;
自欺欺人 be hooked by one's own lies; believe one's own lies; cheat oneself and others; deceive oneself and deceive others; fool oneself as well as others; self-deceiving; whip the devil round the stump;
欺人自欺 cheat oneself and others;

[自謙] modest; self-effacing;

[自遣] amuse oneself; cheer oneself up; comfort oneself; console oneself; divert oneself from melancholy;

[自戕] abuse oneself; commit suicide; harm oneself; inflict injuries on oneself; take one's own life;

[自強] drive oneself hard; goad oneself; self-improvement; self-strengthening; strive for improvement; strive for progress;
自強不息 constantly strive to become stronger; constantly strive to strengthen oneself; continuous self-renewal; exert oneself constantly; make unremitting efforts to improve oneself;
自強自立 make earnest efforts to stand

one's feet and be independent; strive to become stronger and support oneself;

[自取] (1) ask for; invite; (2) of one's own doing;
自取滅亡 bring about one's own destruction; bring destruction on oneself; court destruction upon oneself; court one's own ruin; cut one's own throat; draw ruin upon oneself; fry in one's own grease; make nooses for one's own neck; pull down one's house about one's ears; put nooses round one's own neck; put one's head in a noose; run towards disaster; seek one's own downfall; take the road to one's doom; work one's own undoing;
自取其咎 bring blame upon oneself; bring crime upon oneself; bring misery upon oneself; have only oneself to blame; ride for a fall;
自取其辱 ask for an insult; bring discredit on oneself; bring disgrace on one's own head; invite humiliation;
禍由自取，非命非系 misfortune is sth man brings upon himself and is not necessarily determined by fate;
咎由自取 bring trouble on oneself; fly in one's own grease; get what's coming to one; have only oneself to blame; hoist with one's own petard; suffer for one's own act;

[自然] a matter of course; naturally; of course; to be sure;
自然保護 conservation of nature;
~自然保護區 natural reserve area;
自然而然 a matter of course; in the course of nature; in the ordinary course of events; natural consequences; occurring in a natural manner; of its own accord; of oneself; quite naturally;
自然地理位置 physical-geographic situation;
自然環境 natural environment;
自然界 natural world;
自然科學 natural sciences;
自然美 natural beauty;
自然人 natural person;
自然淘汰 evolution; natural selection; the survival of the fittest;
自然資源 natural resources;
~自然資源開發 natural resources exploitation;

[自任] appoint oneself to the key post; assume control personally; take personal command;

[自認] (1) believe; (2) accept adversity with resignation;
自認不諱 confess without concealment;
自認不如 acknowledge sb's superiority; consider oneself inferior to another;
自認過錯 recognize one's own error;
自認晦氣 accept bad luck without complaint; admit defeat in good grace; grin and bear it;

[自溶] autolysis; autopepsia; isophagy;
自溶作用 autolysis;

[自如] freely; smoothly; with facility;
顧盼自如 gaze round as one wishes; gaze round to one's heart's content;
進退自如 free to advance or retreat; have room for manoeuvre; proceed or step back freely;
行動自如 move freely; move without impairment;
縱擒自如 release and arrest at will — in perfect control of a situation;

[自若] calm and at ease; composed; self-possessed;
形色自若 one's countenance remains as before;

[自殺] be going without a passport; bring about one's own destruction; commit suicide; court destruction; cut one's own throat; die by one's own hand; do a Dutch act; do away with oneself; do oneself harm; do the Dutch act; douse the light; drain the cup of life; drink the waters of Lethe; Dutch act; end it all; end one's days; end one's own life; fall on one's sword; find a way out; go to Lethe; gorge out; happy dispatch; have a fatal accident; kill oneself; lay violent hands on oneself; lover's leap; make the great leap; planned termination; quaff the cup; self-destruction; self-deliverance; self-execution; self-immolation; self-

termination; self-violence; solitaire; susanside; take one's own life; take the coward's way out; take the easy way out; take the pipe; take the road of one's doom; top oneself;
自殺企圖 suicide attempt;
輔助自殺 assisted suicide;
剖腹自殺 hara-kiri;
切腹自殺 happy dispatch;
跳樓自殺 jump to death from a building;
畏罪自殺 kill oneself from fear of punishment;

[自賞] narcissistic;
孤芳自賞 a lone soul admiring his own purity; a single fragrant flower enjoys its own excellence; a solitary flower in love with its own fragrance; indulge in self-admiration; narcissistic; remain aloof from the world; think no end of oneself;

[自傷] (1) inflict injury on oneself; (2) feel sorrow for oneself; pity oneself;

[自身] oneself; self;
自身免疫 autoimmunity;
~自身免疫病 autoimmune disease;
自身難保 can hardly survive; cannot even be sure of one's own safety; hardly be able to save oneself; hard to protect one's own self; one's own life is in danger; risk one's head; unable even to fend for oneself; unable to protect oneself;

[自食] be responsible for one's own action;
自食其果 as you brew, so must you drink; as you make your bed, so you must lie int it; be caught by one's own bait; be hoisted with one's own petard; be made to pay for one's rabid evildoings; chaft in one's grease; eat one's own bitter fruit; eat the bitter fruit of one's own making; face the consequences of one's action; fret in one's grease; fry in one's grease; get what one deserves; lie in the bed one has made; melt in one's grease; reap a bitter harvest; reap the fruit of what one has sown; reap the harvest of one's misdeeds; reap the result of one's own sowing; reap what one has sown; stew in one's grease; stew in one's own juice; suffer as a result of one's actions; suffer the consequences of one's action;
自食其力 cut one's own grass; earn one's own living; earn one's salt; live by one's exertion; live by the sweat of one's brow; live on one's hump; live on by one's own toil; live on the earnings of one's own work; make a living by oneself; paddle one's own canoe; self-supporting; stand on one's own feet; stand on one's own legs; support oneself; support oneself by one's own labour;

[自恃] capitalize on; count on; presume on; self-assured for having sth or sb to rely on;
驕傲自恃 over-confidence and conceit;

[自是] (1) naturally; of course; (2) from then on; since then;

[自視] consider oneself; imagine oneself; think oneself;
自視甚高 self-important; think highly of oneself;

[自守] self-defence;
築堡自守 throw up earthworks for self-defence;

[自首] (1) confess one's crime; give oneself up to law; surrender oneself to the authorities; voluntarily surrender oneself; (2) surrender to the enemy;
自首變節 become a turncoat and surrender; make confessions and surrender; racant and turn traitor;
自首投案 give oneself up to the authorities; surrender oneself to the law;
坦白自首 surrender and confess one's crimes;
向警察自首 give oneself up to the police;

[自贖] atone for one's crime; redeem oneself;

[自述] an account in one's own words; narrate by oneself; recount by oneself;

[自署] sign one's name;

[自私] self-centred; self-seeking; selfish;
自私鬼 a lump of selfishness;
自私自利 egoistic; egotistical and self-seeking; look after one's own interest; self-centred; selfish;

[自訟] blame oneself; self-censure;

[自歎] pity oneself; regret; sigh to oneself;
自歎不如 acknowledge the superiority

of; admit with regret that one is not as good; concede that the other fellow is better qualified; consider oneself inferior to another; sigh at the idea of one's comparative unworthiness; throw in the towel; throw up the sponge;

［自同構］ automorphism;
單位自同構 unit automorphism;
對合自同構 involutive automorphism;
對偶自同構 dual automorphism;
反自同構 reciprocal automorphism;
解釋自同構 analytic automorphism;
模自同構 modular automorphism;
內自同構 inner automorphism;
逆步自同構 contragradient automorphism;
遍歷自同構 ergodic automorphism;
奇異自同構 singular automorphism;
生成自同構 generating automorphism;
同胚自同構 homeomorphism; automorphism;
外自同構 outer automorphism;
微分自同構 differential automorphism;
直積自同構 direct product automorphism;
中心自同構 central automorphism;
周期自同構 periodic automorphism;
~非周期自同構 aperiodic automorphism;
主自同構 principal automorphism;

［自同態］ endomorphism;
單一自同態 monomorphic endomorphism;
恒等自同態 identity endomorphism;
內射自同態 injective endomorphism;

［自慰］ (1) comfort oneself; console oneself; (2) onanism;
聊以自慰 comfort oneself with the thought that; find relief in; just to console oneself; lay a flattering unction to the soul; soothe oneself with a pleasant thought; whistle on one's thumb;

［自衛］ defend oneself; self-defense;
自衛反擊 fight back in self-defense; launch a counter-attack in self-defense; strike back in self-defense;
自衛還擊 launch a counterattack in self-defense;

［自刎］ commit suicide by cutting one's throat; cut one's throat;
拔劍自刎 draw one's sword to slay oneself;

［自問］ ask oneself; examine oneself; search one's own soul;
自問良心 ask one's own conscience; examine one's conscience;
自問無愧 have nothing to be ashamed of;
自問自答 ask a question and answer it oneself; think to oneself;
反躬自問 ask oneself; examine oneself; hold communion with oneself; search one's conscience; search one's heart; search one's soul; turn back and question oneself;
撫躬自問 examine one's own conscience; examine oneself; examine the question through self-reflection; hold communication with oneself; search one's heart;
捫心自問 examine oneself; introspection;

［自我］ (1) oneself; self; (2) ego;
自我暴露 self-betrayal; self-exposure; self-revealing;
自我辯解 try to justify oneself; self-justification;
自我標榜 advertise oneself; blow one's own trumpet; glorify oneself; sing one's own praises;
自我表現 demonstrate by oneself; self-expression;
自我補償 self-liquidating;
自我成才 self-accomplishment;
自我傳播 ego communication;
自我吹噓 boast smugly; boost oneself; toot one's own horn;
自我催眠 idiohypnotism;
自我導向 inner directness;
自我發展 self-development;
自我反省 examine one's own errors; introspection; search one's conscience; self-examination; self-reflection;
自我菲薄 self-abasement;
自我奮鬥 paddle one's own canoe; self-made person; strike out of oneself;
自我改造 remould oneself;
自我恭維 pat oneself on the back;
自我管理 self-management;
~自我管理能力 self-management skills;
自我毀滅 self-destruction; sign one's own death warrant;
自我檢查 introspection; self-check; self-examination;
自我檢討 self-criticism; self-examination;

自我教育 self-education;
自我接納 self-acceptance;
自我解嘲 console oneself with soothing remarks; find excuses to console oneself; lay the flattering unction to one's soul; pat oneself on the back after one's feelings have wounded;
自我介紹 introduce oneself to; make oneself known to; self-introduction;
自我克制 self-abnegation; self-control; self-denial; self-restraint; tutor oneself;
自我肯定 self-affirmation;
自我批評 criticize oneself; self-criticism;
自我評估 self-evaluation;
自我實現 self-actualization;
自我陶醉 imagine oneself to be better than one really is; indulge in daydreaming; indulge in self-delusion; indulge in the joy over one's successes; intoxicated with oneself; self-glorification;
自我提高 self-enhancement;
自我完善 improve oneself; self-integrity;
自我犧牲 self-renunciation; self-sacrifice;
自我欣賞 self-admiration; self-appreciation;
自我宣揚 blow one's own trumpet; self-advertisement;
自我訓練 self-training;
自我意識 self-consciousness;
自我約束機制 self-restraint mechanism;
自我照顧 self-care;
~自我照顧能力 skills of self-care;
自我中心 egocentric;
~自我中心性語言 egocentric speech;
~自我中心主義 ego-centrism;
自我主義 egotism;
~自我主義者 egotist;
自我作古 founder or originator of sth; pioneer; the first to do sth;
認識自我 know oneself;

[自誤] cause damage to one's own interest;
自誤誤人 compromise the interests for oneself and those of others;
疑心自誤 make one's own mistakes for being suspicious;

[自習] learn and practice by oneself;

[自新] make a fresh start; make a new person out of oneself; self-renewal; turn over a new leaf;
懺悔自新 repent and turn over a new leaf;
改過自新 become a new person; convert from a bad life to a good one; correct one's errors and make a fresh start; correct one's mistakes and turn over a new leaf; live down; mend one's ways and start anew; reform oneself; repent and reform; start with a clean slate; turn over a new leaf;
悔過自新 express one's repentance and determination to turn over a new leaf; repent and make a fresh start; repent and start anew; repent and start with a clean slate; repent and turn over a new leaf

[自信] believe in oneself; self-confident;
自信滿懷 have self-confidence; sure of oneself;
自信心 self-confidence;
充滿自信 fully of confidence;
過於自信的 cocksure;
缺乏自信 lack in confidence; lacking in confidence; unsure of oneself;
失去自信 lose one's confidence;
有自信 have confidence;
增加自信 gain confidence; gain in confidence; grow in confidence;

[自行] (1) by oneself; individually; personally; (2) of one's own accord; of oneself; voluntarily;
自行安排 arrange by oneself;
自行辦理 manage sth individually;
自行車 bicycle; bike;
~自行車道 bicycle lane; bike way;
~一條自行車道 a bicycle lane;
~自行車運動 cycling;
~飛行自行車 aerocycle;
~固定自行車 stationary bicycle;
~騎自行車 cycle; ride a bicycle;
~三輪自行車 tricycle; trike;
~雙人自行車 tandem bicycle;
~一輛自行車 a bicycle;
~偷一輛自行車 bone a bicycle;
自行到來 come of itself;
自行解決 settle a dispute by the parties concerned; settle sth by oneself;
自行其是 act as one thinks fit; act in one's own way; act wilfully; go one's own way; have one's own way; take one's own course;
自行設法 shift for oneself;
自行設計 make designs of one's own;
自行消滅 disappear spontaneously; perish

of oneself; spontaneous disappearance;

[自省] examine oneself;
反躬自省 examine oneself by self-reflection; examine oneself critically; make a self-examination;

[自修] (1) review one's lessons by oneself; self-study; (2) educate oneself; study on one's own; teach oneself;

[自許] conceited; pretentious; regard oneself as;
孤高自許 a solitary individual and go around with one's head in the air;

[自詡] boast; brag and boast; crack oneself up; praise oneself;

[自序] (1) author's foreword; author's preface; (2) autobiographic note;

[自選] free; optional;
自選動作 optional exercises;

[自學] self-learning; self-study; self-taught; study independently; study on one's own; teach oneself;
自學成才 become a useful person by self-instruction; become talented through self-study; become trained through self-education; grow up to be useful by studying on one's own;
自學輔導 study guide;
自學教材 self-teaching material;
自學考試 self-taught examination;
自學課本 self-teaching books;

[自貽伊戚] bring trouble on oneself; give oneself unnecessary trouble; harass oneself; invite trouble; torture oneself with unpleasant thoughts; upset oneself for no reason;

[自縊] hang oneself;

[自用] (1) obstinately holding to one's own view; opinionated; self-willed; (2) for private use; personal;
剛愎自用 headstrong; obstinate and adhere to one's own judgement; obstinate and self-opinionated; self-willed and conceited; set in one's ways; wayward; wrong-headed;
師心自用 act and show overconfidence in oneself; act with self-assurance; conceited; not willing to listen to advice; opinionated;

[自由] (1) freedom; liberty; (2) at ease; at home; (3) of one's own free will;
自由變化 free variation;
自由詞素 free morpheme;
自由詞組 free word group;
自由兌換貨幣 free convertible currency;
自由翻譯 liberal translation;
自由泛濫 run wild; spread unchecked;
自由放任 follow one's own inclinations; let people do what they like; let things go their own way; unrestrained self-indulgence;
自由浮動 free float;
~自由浮動的 free-floating;
~自由浮動匯率 free-floating exchange rate;
~自由浮動貨幣 free-floating currency;
自由港 free port;
自由化 liberalization;
~貿易自由化 trade liberalization;
~外匯自由化 liberalization of exchange;
自由基 free radical;
自由價格機制 free-pricing mechanism;
自由間接引語 free indirect speech;
自由教育 liberal education;
自由經濟 free economy;
自由競爭 free competition;
自由課 free period;
自由聯想 free association;
自由戀愛 freedom to choose one's spouse;
自由論者 libertarian;
自由貿易 free trade;
~自由貿易區 free trade zone;
自由民 freeman;
自由球 free kick;
自由散漫 easy-going and adverse to discipline; free and easy; go one's own way without discipline; lax in discipline; liberalistic; loose; self-indulgence; slack;
自由詩 free verse;
自由思想 liberal ideas;
自由調節 free modulation;
自由王國 the realm of freedom;
自由行動 a free hand; act on one's own; free movements;
自由形式 free form;
自由選擇 free selection; free to choose; freedom of choice; have a free choice;
自由意譯 free translation;
自由意志 free will;
自由譯法 free translation;
自由譯者 freelance translator;
自由語素 free morpheme;

自由主義 liberalism;
自由組合 independent assortment;
~自由組合規律 law of independent assortment;
自由自在 able to do anything of one's own free will; as free as the air; as free as the wind; at liberty; at one's ease; carefree; comfortable and at ease; free and easy; free and unrestrained; on the loose; one's own man; perfectly free without restraint; take one's ease; unfettered; untrammelled;
愛好自由 freedom-loving; love freedom;
不自由 without freedom;
~不自由毋寧死 give me liberty or give me death; liberty is more important than life;
充分的自由 complete freedom; total freedom;
訂約自由 freedom of contract;
妨害自由 offense against one's personal freedom;
個人自由 individual freedom; individual liberty; personal freedom;
~標榜個人自由 flaunt individual freedom;
很大的自由 great freedom;
活動自由 freedom of movement;
交通自由 freedom of communication;
人身自由 freedom of person; personal freedom; personal liberty;
通商自由 freedom of commerce;
享有自由 enjoy freedom;
新聞自由 freedom of the press;
行動自由 freedom of movements;
政治自由 political freedom; political liberty;
宗教自由 religious freedom; religious liberty;

[自幼] since childhood;
自幼到老 from infancy to old age;
自幼失怙 lose one's father when one is little; lose one's father while still very young;

[自娛] amuse oneself;
聊以自娛 just to amuse oneself; with a view to amusing oneself;

[自圓其說] explain oneself away; fill up gaps in one's theory; give a satisfactory explanation for what one has said; hustify one's argument; justify oneself; make one's statement consistent; make one's story sound plausible; make out a good case for oneself; patch up the breach oneself;

[自願] by choice; of one's own accord; of one's own free will; volunteer;
自願合作 voluntary cooperation;
出於自願 by choice; by one's own volition; of one's free will; of one's own accord; of one's own volition; on a voluntary basis;

[自在] (1) free; unrestrained; (2) at ease; comfortable;
自在的 laid-back;
不自在 feeling uneasy; feeling uncomfortable; ill at ease; uneasy;
逍遙自在 enjoy a free and leisurely life;
自由自在 carefree; comfortable and at ease;

[自贊] (1) praise oneself; (2) introduce oneself; recommend oneself;

[自責] blame oneself; self-accusation; self-approach;

[自招] confess;
自招禍殃 bring misery on oneself; call down calamity upon oneself;
自招麻煩 ask for it; ask for trouble; bring trouble on oneself; put one's neck out; stick one's neck out;
自招嫌疑 lay oneself open to suspicion;
不打自招 admit gratuitously; admit on one's own; be condemned out of one's own mouth; betray one's evil purpose through some indiscreet act or remarks; confess to a crime without being put on the grill; confess without being pressed; let the cat out of the bag without being pressed; make a confession without duress;

[自找] ask for it; suffer from one's own actions;
自找苦吃 ask for trouble;
自找麻煩 ask for it; ask for trouble; borrow trouble; bring an old house over one's head; bring on trouble; encourage trouble; look for trouble; make a rod for oneself; prepare a rod for one's back; put one's neck out; seek trouble for oneself; wake a sleeping wolf;

[自制] self-control; self-discipline; self-

restraint;
不能自制 have no control over oneself;
[自製] made by oneself; self-made; self-manufactured;
自製影片 home movie; home video;
[自治] (1) autonomy; self-government; (2) self-discipline;
自治機構 autonomous organs;
自治旗 autonomous banner;
自治區 autonomous region;
自治權 home rule;
自治縣 autonomous county;
自治鎮 borough;
~自治鎮議會 borough council;
自治洲 autonomous prefecture;
[自重] (1) be self-dignified; be self-possessed; have self-respect; (2) dead load;
保持自重 keep self-respect;
挾洋自重 rely on the support of foreigners;
擁兵自重 maintain an army and defy orders from the central government;
[自主] act on one's own; autonomy; decide for oneself; independent; keep the initiative in one's own hands; one's own master;
自主管理 self-management;
自主權 one's power to make one's own decision; right to handle one's own affairs; sovereignty of a state;
自主性 autonomy;
[自助] help oneself; self-help;
自助餐 buffet; buffet lunch;
自助餐廳 cafeteria;
自助天助 heaven helps those who help themselves;
~天助自助者 God helps those who help themselves;
自助助人 help others by helping oneself;
[自傳] autobiography;
自傳作者 autobiographer;
[自狀其過] confess one's own mistakes;
[自…自…] do sth by oneself;
自拉自唱 accompany one's own singing; do sth all by oneself; hold forth all alone in defence of one's own views or proposals; play an instrument and sing by oneself; praise one's own effort; second one's own motion; sing to one's own accompaniment;
自賣自誇 blow one's own trumpet; indulge in self-glorification; praise the goods one sells;
自斟自飲 drink with the flies; enjoy a cup of wine all by oneself;
自作自受 as you brew, so shall you drink; one must drink as one brews; be hoisted with one's own patard; bear the ill consequences of one's own acts; bring sth upon oneself; carry what one makes; chafe in one's own grease; fall into a pit of one's own digging; fry in one's own grease; get what one deserves; have only oneself to thank; lie in the bed one has made; melt in one's own grease; one reaps what he sows; pay the fiddler; reap the fruits of one's actions; reap the whirlwind of one's own sowing; reap what one sows; self do, self have; sleep in the bed one has made; stew in one's own grease; stew in one's own juice; suffer for one's own act; suffer from one's own actions; suffer the consequences of one's own actions;
~讓他自作自受 let him stew;
[自足] self-sufficient;
自足有餘 more than self-sufficient;
[自尊] (1) proper pride; self-esteem; self-respect; (2) egotistic;
自尊心 one's feelings; self-esteem; self-respect;
自尊自大 aggrandize oneself; self-important; self-respecting and self-styled;
自尊自貴 mollycoddle oneself; think one's penny silver;
[自作裁奪] consider and decide for oneself; use one's own discretion;

暗自 inwardly; secretly; to oneself;
出自 come from; originate; stem from;
獨自 alone; by oneself; one's own;
各自 by oneself; each; respective;
徑自 without consulting anyone; without leave;
竟自 actually; unexpectedly;
來自 come from; hail from;
親自 by oneself; in person; personally;
取自 after; be extracted from; be derived from; be taken from; derive from; take from;
擅自 arbitrarily; do sth without authorization; take the liberty;

尚自 still; yet;
私自 privately; without permission;
溯自 ever since;
徒自 be of no avail; in vain;
妄自 excess presumptuous;
兀自 still;
一自 since;

zi

【恣】 debauch; dissipate; do as one pleases; throw off restraint;
[恣情] abandon oneself to passion; give free rein to passion;
恣情縱意 have everything one's own way;
[恣肆] (1) licentious; self-indulgent; unrestrained; wanton; (2) forceful and unrestrained; free and natural;
[恣睢] reckless; unbridled;
恣睢暴戾 extremely cruel and despotic; gaze in anger and act violently;
[恣所欲為] do whatever one pleases to do; indulge in doing sth; let oneself loose;
[恣性] unrestrained behaviour;
[恣意] reckless; unbridled; unscrupulous; wilful;
恣意放縱 abandon oneself to passions; indulge oneself in passions;
恣意孤行 act wilfully; do as one wishes without considering others; obstinate to have one's own way;
恣意踐踏 arrogantly trample on;
恣意歪曲 distort wilfully;
恣意妄為 act as one pleases; act willfully; act without regard for any authority; behave unscrupulously; do as one pleases; run riot;
恣意行樂 allow one to act freely in pleasure-seeking; give way to unrestrained fun;
[恣欲] give rein to lust;
[恣縱] dissolute; licentious; morally unrestrained;

放恣 proud and self-indulgent; proud and undisciplined;

zi

【剚】 (1) plant on the ground; (2) stab with a knife;

zi

【牸】 (1) female animals; (2) cow;

zi

【眥】 eye sockets;
[眥裂] open one's eyes wide;
[眥目] open one's eyes wide;

睚眥 (1) angry stare; (2) small grievance;

zi

【胾】 cut meat into pieces; meat cuts; minced meat;

zi

【漬】 (1) soak; (2) dye;
[漬病] catch a disease; fall ill; get infected;
[漬痕] smear; spot; stain;
漬痕斑駁 stained and spotted;
[漬染] dye;

醋漬 pickle;
酒漬 wine stain;
浸漬 macerate; ret; soak;
咖啡漬 coffee stain;
蜜漬 candied; preserved in sugar;
血漬 blood stain;

zong¹

zong

【宗】 (1) ancestor; (2) clan; (3) faction; sect; (4) principal aim; purpose; (5) learn from; take as one's model; (6) great master; (7) a surname;
[宗臣] (1) clan officer; (2) respected minister of state;
[宗祠] ancestral hall; ancestral temple; clan hall;
宗祠祖廟 clan ancestral temples; one's family's ancestral temple;
[宗法] patriarchal clan system;
[宗國] fatherland;
[宗匠] great master;
[宗教] religion;
宗教復興 religious revival;
宗教改革 religious reform;
宗教觀 religious view of life;
宗教教育 religious education;
宗教界 religious circles; religious world;
~宗教界人士 people in religious conscience;
宗教派別 religious sect;
宗教事務 religious affairs;
宗教術語 religious term;

Z

宗教團體 faith community;
宗教文化 religious culture;
宗教信仰 religious belief;
~發誓放棄宗教信仰 abjure one's religion;
宗教儀式 religious rites;
宗教藝術 religious art;
皈依宗教 turn religious;

[宗老] elders of a clan;

[宗廟] ancestral temple of a ruling house;

[宗派] faction; sect;
宗派活動 factional activities; sectarian activities;
宗派主義 factionalism; sectarianism;

[宗親] (1) clan relatives; members of the same clan; (2) brothers by the same mother;

[宗人] people of the same clan;

[宗師] master of great learning and integrity;
一代宗師 great master;

[宗室] imperial clansmen;

[宗仰] hold in esteem;

[宗枝] branch of the same clan;

[宗旨] aim; objective; purpose;
課程宗旨 curriculum aims;

[宗主國] suzerain;

[宗主權] sovereignty;

[宗子] eldest son of one's legal wife;

[宗族] (1) clan; paternal clan; patriarchal clan; (2) clansmen;
宗族男成員 clansman;
宗族女成員 clanswoman;
宗族長 chieftain;
外戚宗族 imperial relatives by marriage;

禪宗 Zen Buddhism;
大宗 (1) a large amount; (2) staple;
歸宗 return to one's own parents;
教宗 pontiff;
卷宗 (1) folder; (2) dossier; file;
強宗 powerful clan;
疏宗 distantly related clan;
同宗 (1) clansman; (2) have common ancestry; of the same clan;
文宗 one whose writings are modeled after;
正宗 orthodox school;
祖宗 ancestry; forefathers;

zong

【棕】 palm tree;

[棕編] coir-woven articles;

[棕黑] dark brown;

[棕紅] reddish brown;

[棕櫚] palm tree;
棕櫚酸 palmitic acid;
棕櫚油 palm oil;

[棕色] brown;
棕色地塊 brownfield site;
棕色商品 brown goods;
淡棕色 pale brown;
淺棕色 light brown;
紫棕色 purple brown;

[棕熊] brown bear;

咖啡棕 coffee brown;
可可棕 cacao brown;
鐵棕 iron oxide brown;
顏料棕 pigment brown;
油棕 oil palm;

zong

【踪】 footprint; traces; tracks;

zong

【縱】 longitudinal; vertical;

[縱斷面] vertical section;

[縱隊] column;

[縱谷] longitudinal valley;

[縱貫] run lengthwise through;

[縱橫] (1) in length and breadth; the horizontal and the vertical; (2) with great ease;
縱橫捭闔 deal with friends and enemies with skill;
縱橫家 political strategist;
縱橫交錯 arrange in a crisscross pattern;
縱橫全國 overrun the entire country;
縱橫四海 overrun the four seas; overrun the whole country;
縱橫自如 capable of moving in any direction;
老淚縱橫 tears flow from aged eyes; the old man weeps bitterly; the old man's face is covered with tears;
熱淚縱橫 shed hot tears; weep bitter tears;
涕淚縱橫 with tears streaming down one's face;

[縱火] start a fire deliberately;
縱火犯 arsonist;
縱火者 arsonist; firebug;
縱火罪 fire raising;

[縱視圖] longitudinal view;

zong

【蹤】 (1) footprint; trace; track; vestige; (2) follow the tracks of; keep track of; trail;

［蹤跡］ trace; track; vestige;

來蹤去跡 traces of coming and going; traces of one's movements; traces of one's whereabouts; traces of sth's tracks;

覓蹤訪跡 follow a clue;

渺無蹤跡 disappear completely; without a trace;

尋蹤覓跡 trace out;

杳無蹤跡 disappear without a trace; unable to obtain the slightest clue to sb's whereabouts; vanish;

［蹤影］ sign; trace; vestige;

無影無蹤 disappear completely; disappear into thin air; disappear without a shadow; into thin air; melt into thin air; not a trace left; not a trace to be seen; vanish into thin air; without a trace;

～來無影，去無蹤 come without a trace and leave without a shadow;

～消失得無影無蹤 disappear into thin air; vanish into thin air;

［蹤由］ origin and development;

藏踪 conceal oneself; go into hiding;

跟踪 follow the trail of; trace;

躡踪 follow along behind sb; track;

萍踪 tracks of a wanderer;

潛踪 go out in secret;

失踪 disappear; be missing;

行踪 tracks; whereabouts;

追踪 follow the tracks of; trace;

zong

【鬃】 (1) topknot; (2) mane;

［鬃毛］ horse mane;

［鬃刷］ bristle brush;

馬鬃 horse's mane;

豬鬃 hog bristles;

zong

【騣】 mane;

zong³

zong

【傯】 (1) busy; having no leisure; urgent; (2) in straits;

［傯傯］ in a hurry;

zong

【總】 (1) assemble; collect; gather; unite; (2) put together; sum up; (3) all; complete; general; overall; total; (4) central; chief; general; principal; (5) always; be bound; be certain; be sure; ever; constantly; frequently; invariably; must; never; no matter; no matter when; no matter where; used to; whenever; wherever; will; (6) after all; anyway; at any rate; at last; eventually; however; in any event; sooner or later;

［總編］ chief editor;

總編輯 chief editor;

副總編 deputy chief editor;

［總部］ general headquarters; head office; headquarters;

［總裁］ chief executive officer; director general; president;

副總裁 vice-president;

～高級副總裁 senior vice-president;

［總稱］ general term; generic name;

［總得］ bound to; have to; must; somehow;

［總督］ governor-general; viceroy;

［總隊］ department;

邊防總隊 border guards department;

交通警察總隊 traffic police department;

武警總隊 armed police department;

消防總隊 fire brigade department;

［總額］ sum total; total amount;

［總髮］ childhood;

［總綱］ general principles;

［總共］ add up to; all together; all told; altogether; amount to; come to; count; count up to; foot up to; in all; in number; in the aggregate; knock up; number; reach a total of; sum up to; to the tune of; total; total up to;

［總管］ (1) director; manager; superintendent; supervisor; (2) supervise;

［總歸］ after all; anyhow; eventually;

［總和］ grand total; sum total; total; whole;

［總會］ (1) assemblage; collection; conglomeration; (2) bound to; inevitable; sure to happen;

［總匯］ (1) assemblage; collection; (2)

Z

confluence;
[總計] grand total; sum total; total;
部門總計 industry total;
檢查總計 control total;
[總監] chief inspector; inspector general;
[總結] (1) sum up; summarize; (2) conclusion;
總結聯加語 summative conjunct;
[總局] headquarters; head office;
[總括] sum up; summarize;
[總攬] assume overall responsibility; take on everything;
總攬大權 assume a dominant role; be in full power; have full control of the government; have overall authority;
[總理] (1) premier; prime minister; (2) president;
副總理 vice-premier;
[總量] total;
發育總量 developmental total;
回收總量 recovery total;
[總論] general discussion; introduction; summary;
[總目] general index;
[總評] general comment; overall appraisal;
[總其成] assume overall responsibility for sth and bring it to completion;
[總是] after all; always; any; as a rule; at last; be bound; be certain; be sure; commonly; constantly; ever; eventually; every; frequently; generally; have a habit of; however; invariably; keep doing sth; must; never; no matter; one; some; sooner or later; used to; usually; when; where; will; without exception; would;
幾乎總是 nearly always;
[總數] aggregate; amount; total; total amount;
[總算] (1) all things considered; in general; on the whole; (2) at last; at long last; finally; in the end; in the long run;
[總體] general; overall; total;
總體規劃 overall plan;
總體上 by and large;
總體設計 architectural design;
總體驗收 general control reception;
總體戰爭 total war;
[總統] president;
總統顧問 adviser to the president;
總統候選人 presidential candidate;
總統權力 presidential authority;
總統助理 presidential aide;
當選總統 elected president;
副總統 vice-president;
[總務] (1) general affairs; general services; (2) person in charge of general affairs;
[總線] bus;
存儲總線 memory bus;
電線總線 cable bus;
加法總線 add bus;
數據總線 data bus;
寫入總線 write bus;
中斷總線 interrupt bus;
字符總線 character bus;
[總要] must always; should always;
[總則] general principles;
[總閘] main switch;
[總之] all and all; in a word; in brief; in short; in sum; long and short of sth; the top and bottom of it;
[總值] total price; total value;
本地生產總值 gross domestic product (GDP);
[總總] abundant; numerous; teeming;

成總 (1) altogether; in all; (2) a batch; a lot;
打總 altogether;
歸總 put together; sum up;
匯總 gather; pool;
集總 lumped;
攏總 add up; all told; altogether; in all; sum up;
一總 (1) altogether; in all; (2) all;

zong4
zong

【從】 (1) attendant; entourage; servant; (2) secondary; (3) accessory; (4) deputy; vice;
[從伯] one's father's elder paternal male cousins who are older than him;
[從弟] male cousins;
[從犯] accessory;
[從父] one's father's brothers; paternal uncles;
[從官] official aide;
[從妹] younger female cousin;
[從母] maternal aunts;
[從女] niece;
[從叔] one's father's younger male cousins;
[從孫] grandsons of one's brothers;
[從刑] accessory punishment;

[從兄] male cousin;
[從者] attendant; servant;
[從子] nephew;

zong

【綜】 (1) in a nutshell; sum up; (2) in view of; take account of; (3) arrange; (4) synthetic; (5) inquire; examine into;
[綜觀] (1) general and comprehensive view; (2) view the whole situation;
[綜管] arrange all; in overall charge;
[綜合] synthesize;
綜合報導 comprehensive dispatch; summing-up report;
綜合報告 comprehensive report;
綜合測試 integrated testing;
~綜合測試系統 integrated test system;
綜合產業 comprehensive industry;
綜合大學 comprehensive university;
綜合地址 general address;
綜合發展 comprehensive development;
綜合法 synthetic approach;
綜合翻譯 composite translation;
綜合防治 comprehensive control;
綜合福利指標 composite welfare indicator;
綜合國力 comprehensive national strength; synthetic national power;
綜合計劃管理 comprehensive plan control;
綜合教學計劃 integral instructional programme;
綜合開發 comprehensive development;
綜合科目 integrated studies;
綜合利用 comprehensive utilization;
綜合生產線 integrated production line;
綜合數字網 integrated digital network;
綜合信息服務 multimessage;
綜合信息系統 comprehensive information system;
綜合性人才 comprehensive talents;
綜合型語言 synthetic language;
綜合性錯誤 global error;
綜合性動機 integrative motivation;
綜合學習 integrated learning;
綜合業務網 integrated services network;
綜合語 synthetic language;
綜合預測 integrated forecasting;
綜合症 syndrome;
~臨界綜合症 borderline syndrome;
~適應綜合症 adaptation syndrome;
綜合治理 comprehensive treatment;
[綜括] encompass all; recapitulate; sum up;
[綜覽] comprehensive survey; view generally;
[綜攬] in overall charge;
[綜理] arrange everything; in overall charge;
[綜述] sum up; summarize;
[綜綜] draw together; knit together;

錯綜 complex; intricate;
系綜 ensemble;

zong

【粽】 glutinous rice tamale;
[粽子] glutinous rice dumplings; rice tamale;

zong

【縱】 (1) from north to south; (2) release; set free; (3) indulge; let loose; (4) jump into the air; jump up; (5) although; even if;
[縱步] (1) stride; (1) bound; jump;
[縱觀] take a free, wide look; take a sweeping look;
縱觀全局 take a panoramic view of the situation;
[縱橫] (1) in length and breadth; (2) freely; with great ease;
縱橫馳騁 dash about in battlefield and carry all before one; manoeuvre freely; move about freely and quickly; sweep through the length and breadth of;
縱橫交錯 be arranged in a criss-cross pattern; criss-cross; crosswise;
縱橫千里 thousand miles in both length and breadth;
縱橫四海 move about the whole world freely; overrun the four seas;
縱橫天下 move about the whole world freely; overrun the whole world and go anywhere as one pleases;
[縱虎] let loose a tiger;
縱虎歸山 let the tiger return to the mountain — cause calamity for the future; set a tiger free — tolerate the wicked acts of evil-doers;
縱虎入室 allow a tiger into the house — bring about ruin to oneself;
縱虎為患 connive at sb's crimes;
縱虎於市 let loose a tiger on a crowd;
[縱火] commit arson; set on fire;
縱火犯 arsonist;
[縱或] even if; though;

Z

[縱酒] drink to excess;
縱酒取樂 go on at random; go on the razzle-dazzle;
縱酒宴樂 drunken orgy;
[縱覽] look far and wide; look freely and scan;
縱覽群書 read extensively;
[縱浪] (1) uninhibited; unrestrained; (2) dissolute; profligate;
[縱令] even if; even though;
[縱目] look as far as one's eyes can see;
縱目四望 gaze far into the distance; turn one's eyes in all directions and take in as much as one can in a single sweep;
[縱情] act without self-control; as much as one likes; do as one pleases; follow one's inclinations; to one's heart's content;
縱情高歌 sing loudly and without constraint;
縱情歌唱 sing heartily; sing to one's heart's content;
縱情歡呼 cheer heartily;
縱情歡樂 have one's fling; on the loose; on the spree; revel to one's heart's content;
縱情酒色 indulge oneself in wine and sensuality;
縱情狂歡 cheer as much as one likes; cheer to one's heart's content;
縱情取樂 run after pleasure and give rein to the passions;
縱情痛哭 weep one's fill;
縱情宴樂 feast and be merry to one's heart's content;
縱情逸樂 give oneself up to pleasure and unbridled licence;
縱情招毀 overindulgence leads to ruin;
[縱囚] release prisoners;
[縱然] even if; even though;
[縱容] connive at; cosset; pamper; pass over; wink at;
縱容包庇 protect and connive at; with the connivance of;
[縱身] jump; leap;
[縱聲] laugh at the top of one's voice; shout at the top of one's voice;
縱聲大笑 burst out laughing;
[縱使] even if; even though;
[縱談] speak freely; talk freely; talk without inhibition;
[縱眺] look far and wide;
[縱脱] uninhibited; unrestrained;
[縱向] (1) from south to north; (2) vertical;
縱向時間碼 longitudinal time code;
縱向一體化 vertical integration;
縱向組合關係 paradigmatic relation;
[縱性] do as one pleases;
[縱言] continue an informal and free conversation;
[縱養] spoil a child;
[縱逸] dissolute; uninhibited; unrestrained;
[縱淫] abandon oneself to carnal desire; debauched; dissolute;
[縱飲] drink uninhibitedly; indulge in drinking;
[縱有] even if there is; even though there is;
[縱慾] give way to one's carnal desires; indulge in sensual pleasures;
縱慾無度 indulge in carnal pleasure without restraint;
[縱恣] behave without restraint; give free rein to the passions; indulge;
縱恣情慾 give rein to lusts;

操縱 (1) control; get sb by the balls; get sb by the short and curlies; have sb by the balls; have sb by the short and curlies; have sb on a string; operate; (2) manipulate; rig; run the show;
放縱 allow to run wild; let sb have his own way; self-indulgent;
驕縱 arrogant and wilful; proud and ungovernable;
嬌縱 indulge; spoil;
寬縱 indulge;
擒縱 arresting and releasing;
任縱 unrestrained;
恣縱 dissolute; licentious; morally unrestrained;

zou1

zou

【陬】 (1) corner; nook; (2) foothills; (3) live together as a tribe; (4) first month of the lunar year;
[陬落] frontier village where people live together;
[陬月] first month of the lunar year;

zou

【掫】 on the night watch;

zou

【鄒】 (1) a state in the Warring States Period; (2) a surname;

［鄒纓齊紫］ what those above do, those below will imitate;

zou

【緅】 (1) bluish red; (2) light red;

zou

【諏】 (1) confer; (2) consult; seek the advice of;

［諏訪］ ask for advice; consult; seek the advice of;

［諏吉］ consult with sb for an auspicious day; pick an auspicious day;

諏吉成婚 choose a lucky day for a wedding;

zou

【鄹】 the birthplace of Confucius in today's Qufu;

zou

【謅】 jest; joke; quip; talk nonsense;

zou

【鯫】 (1) small fish; (2) small;

［鯫生］ (1) despicable fellow; (2) my humble self;

zou

【騶】 (1) official in charge of driving carriages; (2) mounted escort;

zou³

zou

【走】 (1) go on foot; walk; (2) go swiftly; move; run; (3) depart; go away; leave; (4) call on; visit; (5) from; through; (6) depart from the original; lose the original shape, flavour, etc.; (7) leak; let loose; let out;

［走板］ (1) out of tune; sing out of rhythm; (2) speak beside the point; wander from the subject;

［走筆］ write rapidly;

走筆成章 write a composition in a stream; write quickly and skilfully;

走筆疾書 write swiftly;

走筆龍蛇 swift curling style of calligraphy;

走筆如飛 be quick in writing; rotate the pen like flying;

［走避］ evade; run away from; shun;

［走遍］ travel all over an area;

走遍全國 travel all over the country; travel the length and breadth of the whole country;

走遍天下 travel all over the world; wander through the world;

［走步］ walk with the ball;

［走道］ (1) pavement; sidewalk; (2) footpath; path; (3) aisle;

走道兒 on the road; travel;

［走到頭］ walk to the end of the road;

［走地雞］ free-range chicken;

［走電］ electric power leakage;

［走調］ off-key;

走調兒 out of tune;

離腔走調 get out of tune; sing out of key;

［走動］ (1) go for a stroll; stretch one's leg; walk about; (2) visit each other;

遞歸隨機走動 recurrent random walk;

疊對數隨機走動 iterated logarithm random walk;

走不動了 have a bone in one's leg;

［走讀］ attend a day school;

走讀男生 day school boy;

走讀女生 day school girl;

走讀生 commuting student; day student; non-resident student; out-college student;

走讀學校 day school;

［走訪］ (1) have an interview with; interview; (2) go and see; pay a visit to; visit;

挨戶走訪 visit house to house;

走親訪友 call on relatives and friends; visit relatives and friends; visit with relatives and friends;

［走風］ become known; leak out; let out a secret;

［走狗］ flunkey; lackey; lap dog; running dog; servile follower; stooge; tool;

乏走狗 decrepit running dog;

［走光］ wardrobe malfunction;

［走紅］ in favour; in vogue;

［走話］ divulge secrets;

［走火］ (1) go off accidentally; (2) overstate;

走火入魔 (1) be obsessed with sth; (2) be possessed by the Devil;

［走貨］ transport goods;

［走集］ key passage; point of convergence;

［走進］ go in and out;

走進走出 go in and out;
昂然走進 go into sth proudly;

[走開] beat it; buzz off; get lost; get out of the way; go and chase oneself; sling your hook;
慌忙走開 buzz away;
快走開 buzz off;
慢慢地走開 wander away; wander off;
悄悄走開 go away quietly;
迅速走開 shoot off;

[走廊] corridor; hall; hallway; lobby; passage; passageway; veranda;
大理石走廊 marbled hallway;
過境走廊 transit corridor;
空中走廊 air corridor;

[走了] go;
走了和尚走不了廟 the monk can run away, but not the monastery; the monk may run away, but the temple remains;
走了嘴 slip of the tongue;
~說走了嘴 slip of the tongue;
得走了 must be pushing along; should be pushing along;
該走了 must be pushing along; should be pushing along;

[走漏] (1) divulge; leak out; (2) smuggling and tax evasion;
走漏風聲 allow news to leak out; divulge a secret; leak out information; leakage of information; let out a secret; let the cat out of the bag; spill the beans; the secret leaks out;
走漏天機 give away a secret;
走漏消息 divulge secrets;

[走路] go afoot; go on foot; walk;
走路不長眼睛 jaywalk;
走路當心 mind your step; watch your step;
兩條腿走路 walk on two legs; use different approaches;
拖着腳走路 scuff one's feet; scuff one's heels;

[走馬] (1) gallop one's horse; go swiftly on horseback; ride swiftly; (2) an ambling horse;
走馬燈 merry-go-round; trotting horse lamp;
走馬看花 cast a passing glance at; give a hurried and cursory glance at; skim the surface; take a brief look at; take a rapid glance;
~走馬看花的旅行 whistle-stop tour;
走馬上任 assume a post; go to one's post; go to take office; take up office; travel to a place for a new post;
走馬章台 frequent houses of ill-fame;

[走俏] brick sales;

[走獸] beast;

[走人] leave;
不改進就走人 shape up or ship out;

[走散] (1) walk away in different directions; (2) get separated from other travelers;

[走色] fade; lose colour;

[走神] lose one's concentration; zone out;

[走失] be lost; missing; wander away;

[走時] in a spell of good luck;

[走私] engage in smuggling; smuggle;
走私貨 contraband; smuggled goods;
~一批走私貨 a cargo of contraband;
走私集團 smuggling ring;
走私罪 smuggling crime;
查緝走私 prevent and counter smuggling;

[走向] (1) run; trend; (2) head for; move toward; on the way for;

[走心經] use one's brains;

[走眼] misjudge by sight; mistake;

[走樣] (1) deviate from the original; get out of shape; go out of form; lose shape; (2) different from what is expected;

[走一走] stretch one's legs; take a walk;

[走音] clinker;

[走運] by good luck; devil's luck; fall on one's feet; have fortune on one's side; have good luck; have one's moments; in luck; land on one's feet; luck is on one's side; luck of the devil; luck out; lucky; lucky sb; on the gravy train; one's luck is in; play big luck; strike luck; touch luck; you never know your luck; what a stroke of luck;
走運時期 good patch;
真走運 luck out;
走背運 suffer from a spell of bad luck;
走好運 enjoy a spell of good luck;
走黑運 have moldy luck; run into bad luck;
走紅運 be in luck; be on the crest of the wave;
走鴻運 have a spell of good luck; in luck; be on the crest of the wave;

[走着瞧] see who is right; wait and see;
[走走] take a walk; take an airing;
[走嘴] let slip an inadvertent remark; make a slip of the tongue;

敗走 flee after defeat;
搬走 move away; move out;
傍地走 run closely on the ground;
奔走 busy running about; do a job on order; run; rush about; solicit help;
撤走 withdraw;
沖走 flush away; wash out;
出走 leave; run away;
放走 let go; release; set free;
飛走 fly away; take wing;
趕走 drive away; drive sb out of the door; expel; put sb to the door; see the back of sb; send sb packing; show sb the door; throw out;
急走 hotfoot;
疾走 trot;
競走 heel-and-toe walking race;
溜走 leave stealthily; scarper; slink; slip away; slope off;
慢走 don't go yet; good-bye; stay; take care; wait a minute;
拿走 take sth;
攆走 oust; send sb about his business; send sb packing; send sb to the right-about; show sb the door;
搶走 loot; rap;
趨走 go in haste; run away;
郤走 run backward; turn away;
逃走 escape; flee; fly; make one's escape; run away; take flight; take to one's heels;
偷走 appropriate; mooch; rob; run off; walk off with;
退走 move back; retreat; withdraw;
往回走 turn back;
行走 go on foot; run; walk;
迅走 go fast; hurry on;
誘走 toll off;
遠走 go far away;
這邊走 step this way;
走一走 stretch one's legs; take a walk;

zou⁴

zou

【奏】 (1) perform; play; (2) achieve; produce; (3) present a memorial to the emperor; report to the throne;
[奏本] memorial;
[奏刀] slither a knife;
[奏功] achieve success; have the intended effect;
奏功厥偉 have attained a great merit;
以奏膚功 complete a monumental task;
[奏技] skill in performing;
[奏捷] score a success; win a battle;
[奏凱] play the song of triumph; triumph; victorious; win victory;
[奏明] memorialize to the emperor; report to the throne;
[奏鳴曲] sonata;
小奏鳴曲 sonatina;
[奏疏] memorial to the throne;
[奏效] effective; efficacious; get the desired result; have the intended effect; prove effective; successful;
完全奏效 work like a charm;
[奏樂] play music; strike up a tune;
[奏章] memorial to the thone;
[奏折] memorial to the throne;

八重奏 octet;
伴奏 accompaniment; accompany; play an accompaniment;
變奏 variation;
撥奏 pizzicato;
重奏 ensemble;
吹奏 play wind instruments;
獨奏 solo;
二重奏 duet;
合奏 ensemble;
節奏 rhythm;
連奏 legato;
六重奏 sestet; sextet;
七重奏 septet;
齊奏 play in unison;
前奏 prelude;
三重奏 trio;
申奏 make a petition; report to the throne;
四重奏 quartet;
彈奏 play an instrument;
五重奏 quintet;
序奏 preface;
演奏 give a performance; perform; play a musical instrument;
摺奏 memorial submitted to the emperor;

zou

【揍】 (1) beat; hit hard; slug; (2) break;
[揍人] slug a person;

zou

【驟】 (1) gallop; (2) sudden; swift; (3) frequent;

［驟降］ rapid fall of;

［驟雨］ sudden rainstorm;

驟雨狂風 torrential rain and a strong wind;

秋夜驟雨 rain pelts down on one late autumn night;

［驟漲］ rise suddenly;

［驟至］ arrive suddenly; come without warning;

zu[1]

zu

【租】 (1) hire; lease; rent; (2) let out; rent out; (3) rent;

［租出］ let;

［租船］ charter; boat chartering; ship chartering;

租船合同 chartering;

~ 航次租船合同 voyage chartering;

~ 統一雜貨租船合同 uniform general chartering;

租船人 charterer;

租船契約 chartering;

~ 按日租船契約 daily chartering;

~ 定期租船契約 time chartering;

租船佣金 charterage;

單程租船 single voyage charter;

來回程租船 return voyage charter;

連續租船 consecutive voyage charter;

無條件租船 bare boat charter;

［租佃］ rent out land to tenants;

租佃關係 tenancy relationship;

租佃制度 tenancy system;

［租費］ rent; royalties;

［租購］ hire purchase;

［租戶］ tenant;

長期租戶 long-lease tenant;

［租價］ rent;

［租界］ foreign concession; foreign settlement; leased territory;

［租借］ hire; lease; rent;

［租金］ rent; rent money; rental;

租金管制 rent control;

租金上漲 the rent goes up; the rent increases;

按期付租金 punctual in rental payments;

昂貴租金 high rent;

經濟租金 economic rent;

臨時租金 interim rental;

攤提租金 amortization rent;

提高租金 increase the rent; jack up the rent; put up the rent; raise the rent;

拖欠租金 fall behind with the rent; get behind on the rent;

象徵式租金 peppercorn rent;

應計租金 accrued rental;

漲租金 rise in rents;

支付租金 pay the rent;

［租賃］ hire; lease; rent;

租賃經營 lease operation;

租賃貿易 rental trade;

租賃企業 leased enterprise;

租賃業務 leasing;

財務租賃 financial lease;

經紀租賃 brokerage lease;

暫時租賃 day-to-day lease;

［租期］ lease term; tenancy;

［租售］ for rent; for sale;

［租用］ hire; lease; rent for use; take on lease;

可供出租 for hire;

［租約］ lease;

［租子］ ground rent; land rent; rent;

包租 (1) rent a house for subletting; (2) collect a fixed rent for farmland;

逼租 a press for payment of rent;

逋租 neglect the payment of the rent;

倉租 warehouse storage charges;

承租 rent;

出租 for hire; for rent; hire; hire out; let; let out; rent;

地租 ground rent; land rent; rent;

佃租 land rent;

房租 rent;

分租 sublease; sublet;

減租 reduce rent for land;

交租 pay the rent;

年租 annual rent;

收租 collect rentals; collect rents;

田租 farm rent;

學租 rent collected on school-owned land;

押租 rent deposit;

月租 monthly rent;

棧租 godown charge; godown rent; storage;

招租 for rent; let a house;

周租 weekly rent;

轉租 farm out; sublease; sublet;

zu²
zu

【足】 (1) foot; leg; (2) adequate; enough; sufficient; (3) as much as; full;
[足背] acrotarsium; dorsum of foot;
足背反射 dorsocuboidal reflex;
[足本] unabridged;
足本辭典 unabridged dictionary;
[足病] podopathy;
足病醫生 podiatrist;
[足部] leg;
足部護理 pedicure;
[足不出戶] confine oneself within doors; keep the house; keep within doors; never to go out; never to leave one's home; never to step out of door; refrain from stepping outside the house; remain quietly at home behind closed doors; stay in;
[足長] foot length;
[足赤] pure gold;
[足額] reach the quota;
[足發育不良] atelopodia;
[足發育不全] atelopodia;
[足敷] enough for;
[足跟] heel;
足跟痛 painful heel; talagia;
淋病性足跟 gonorrhoeal heel;
[足夠] ample; enough; full; sufficient;
[足過小] micropodia;
[足蹟] (1) footmarks; footprints; tracks; (2) whereabouts;
生態足蹟 ecological footprint;
[足尖] tiptoe;
足尖旋轉 pirouette;
足尖站立 stand on tiptoe;
[足見] from this it is clear that; it serves to show; one can well perceive;
[足金] pure gold; solid gold;
[足謀寡斷] resourceful but irresolute;
[足球] association football; football; footie; footy; soccer;
足球比賽 football game; football match; soccer game; soccer match;
~一場足球比賽 a football match;
足球裁判 referee;
足球隊 football team; soccer team;
~男子足球隊 men's soccer team;
~女子足球隊 women's soccer team;
足球迷 football fans; footy fans;
~一群足球迷 a crowd of football fans;
足球明星 football star;
足球鞋 football boots;
足球員 football player; footballer; soccer player;
踢足球 play football;
五人足球 five-a-side football;
英式足球 association football;
桌上足球 foosball; table football;
[足色] of standard purity; sterling;
[足食足兵] have sufficient food and enough arms; well-provided with food and armament;
[足水腫] podedema;
[足歲] actual age; real age;
[足痛] pain in the sole of the foot; pododynia;
足痛風 gouty inflammation of the great toe; podagra;
[足突] foot process;
足突病 foot process disease;
[足外翻] strephexopodia;
[足下] you;
足下垂 footdrop;
[足癬] tinea of the foot; tinea pedis;
[足心] the sole of the foot;
[足以] enough to; sufficient to;
足以糊口 enough to keep body and soul together;
足以亂真 good enough to pass for genuine;
足以守成 good enough to carry on;
足以證明 suffice to show that;
足以致命 the wound may be fatal;
足以自豪 enough for one to be proud of; enough to make oneself proud;
足以自慰 enough to console oneself;
[足音跫然] longing to have visitors;
[足銀] sterling silver;
[足印] footmark; footprint;
[足趾] toe;
足趾骨 bones of the digits of the foot;
[足資談助] serve as a good topic of conversation;
[足壯] physically strong;
[足足] as much as; full; no less than;

螯足 cheliped;
百足 centipede;
扁平足 flatfoot;

Z

跛足 crippled; crooked-foot; lame;
補足 bring up to full strength; fill a gap; make complete; make up a deficiency;
不足 (1) deficiency; drawback; inadequate; insufficient; lack; not enough; scarcity; (2) less than; (3) beneath; not deserve; not worth; (4) cannot; need not; should not; unnecessary;
插足 (1) put one's foot in; (2) participate in;
纏足 foot-binding;
長足 by leaps and bounds;
赤足 with bared feet;
充足 abundant; adequate; ample; plenty; sufficient;
湊足 get together enough;
跌足 stamp one's foot;
蹀足 stamp the feet;
鼎足 three legs of a tripod;
頓足 stamp one's foot;
顎足 jawbone; maxillped;
豐足 abundant; plentiful;
富足 abundant; plentiful; rich;
高足 your disciple; your pupil;
鼓足 go all out;
裹足 (1) bind the feet of women; (2) hesitate for fear of danger;
何足 not worth;
捷足 nimble-footed;
立足 (1) find one's niche in; have a foothold somewhere; keep a foothold; (2) base oneself on;
斂足 hold back; hold one's steps and not go forward; withdraw one's footstep;
蔓足 cirri;
滿足 contented; satisfied; satisfy;
橈足 pleopod, swimmeret;
躡足 (1) walk with light steps; (2) join; participate in;
平足 flatfoot;
蹼足 palmate foot; webfoot;
企足 stand on tiptoe;
前足 forefoot;
蹻足 (1) raise a foot; (2) very brief period;
贍足 abundant; plenty;
上足 (1) capable students; (2) superior horses;
蛇足 feet added to a snake; superfluity;
涉足 set foot in;
失足 (1) lose one's footing; slip; (2) take a wrong step in life;
十足 completely; downright; extremely; one hundred percent; out-and-out; perfect; perfectly; sheer;
實足 full; solid;
手足 (1) brothers; members; (2) hands and feet;
蹝足 slide;
天足 natural feet; unbound feet;
頭足 head and feet;
偽足 pseudopodium;
溫足 well-off; well-to-do;
跣足 barefooted;
雁足 correspondence; letters;
饜足 satiated; surfeited;
逸足 fleet-footed; walking very fast;
義足 artificial leg;
遠足 excursion; hike; hiking; outing; pleasure trip on foot; walking tour; take long hikes;
攢足 savings;
知足 content with one's lot;
斮足 cut off one's feet as punishment;
自足 self-sufficient;

zu

【卒】 (1) lackey; servant; underling; (2) soldier; (3) group of a hundred strong people; (4) suddenly; unexpectedly; urgent; (5) after all; at last; (6) complete; finish; (7) dead; die; (8) community of three hundred families; (9) (of Chinese chess) pawn ;

[卒底於成] finally achieve success;
[卒哭] end of the period of mourning;
[卒業] complete study; finish a course of study; graduate;
[卒子] (1) private; soldier; (2) pawn;

暴卒 die a violent death; die of a sudden illness; die suddenly;
兵卒 privates; soldiers;
馬前卒 cat's paw; foot soldier; pawn; willing servant;
士卒 privates; soldiers;
戍卒 garrison soldier;
小卒 private;
獄卒 prison guard; turnkey;
走卒 lackey; pawn;

zu

【族】 (1) clan; family; tribe; relatives;(2) race; (3) class; family; (4) grow in thicket;

[族居] live together as a clan;
[族類] of the same clan; of the same race;
[族譜] pedigree of a clan;

[族權] clan authority; clan power;
[族群] ethnic group;
[族人] fellow clansmen;
[族長] clan elder; head of a clan;
女族長 matriarch;

部族 tribe;
詞族 word family;
大族 family of many branches;
仡老 Gelo nationality,
貴族 aristocrat; nobility; noble; nobleman; peer; peerage;
漢族 Han nationality;
皇族 imperial family; imperial kinsmen; people of imperial lineage;
家族 clan; family;
苗族 the Miao nationality;
滅族 extermination of an entire family;
民族 nation; nationality;
旁族 collateral family;
親族 members of the same clan;
畲族 She nationality;
士族 gentry;
氏族 clan; family;
世族 aristocractic family politically influential for generations;
水族 aquatic animals;
堂族 members of the same clan;
同族 of the same clan;
外族 (1) people not of the same clan; (2) foreigner; (3) other nationality;
王族 imperial kinsmen; people of royal lineage;
望族 distinguished family; respected and influential clan;
系族 family lineage; genealogy;
星族 stellar population;
夷族 extermination of an entire family;
遺族 descendants;
異族 different race or nation;
語族 language family;
遠族 remote clan; one's distant relatives;
藏族 Tibetan nationality;
種族 race; tribe;
宗族 (1) patriarchal clan; (2) clansman;

zu

【捽】 (1) grasp; hold with hands; seize; (2) pull up; (3) contradict; go against;
[捽髮] grasp by the hair;
[捽頸] seize by the throat;

zu

【槭】 a kind of maple;
[槭樹] maple;

zu

【鏃】 arrowhead;

箭鏃 metal arrowhead;
矢鏃 metal arrowhead;

zu³

zu

【阻】 (1) block; detain; hinder; impede; obstruct; oppose; (2) separate; (3) prevent; proscribe; stop; (4) difficulty; suffer; (5) rely on; (6) strategic pass;
[阻礙] bar; block; hinder; impede; prevent;
阻礙者 hindrance;
從中阻礙 lie in the way;
[阻擋] block the way; hinder; in the way; obstruct; resist; stem; stop;
阻擋層 blocking layer;
[阻遏] check; repress; repression; stem; stop;
多價阻遏 multivalent repression;
酶阻遏 enzyme repression;
瞬時阻遏 transient repression;
組蛋白阻遏 histone repression;
[阻隔] (1) cut off; separate; (2) be isolated; be separated;
記憶阻隔 mental block;
思維阻隔 mental block;
心理阻隔 mental block;
[阻梗] hinder; impede; obstruct;
[阻擊] block; check;
[阻絕] hinder; impede; obstruct; stop up;
[阻抗] impedance;
交流阻抗 alternating current impedance;
聲阻抗 acoustic impedance;
天線阻抗 impedance;
[阻攔] bar the way; obstruct; prevent; retard; stop; tackle;
[阻力] (1) obstruction; resistance; (2) drag; force of resistance; resistance force;
變形阻力 deformation drag;
大氣阻力 atmospheric drag;
風阻力 wind resistance;
空氣阻力 air resistance;
氣動阻力 aerodynamic drag;
水阻力 water resistance;
制動阻力 brake drag;
[阻難] make it difficult; obstruct; thwart;
[阻尼] damp; damping;
阻尼減少 deattenuation;

Z

阻尼器 damper;
~ 垂桿阻尼器 hammer damper;
~ 電流阻尼器 current damper;
~ 動力阻尼器 dynamic damper;
~ 高壓阻尼器 high-tension damper;
~ 空氣阻尼器 air damper;
絕對阻尼 absolute damping;
空氣阻尼 air damping;
氣動阻尼 aerodynamic damping;
人工阻尼 artificial damping;
聲阻尼 acoustic damping;
天線阻尼 antenna damping;

[阻撓] obstruct; put a spoke in sb's wheel; stand in the way; thwart;
阻撓策略 obstructive tactics;
百般阻撓 create all sorts of obstacles;
蓄意阻撓 obstructionism;

[阻塞] block; choke; clog; jam; obstruct; stop;
阻塞作用 choking action;

[阻止] block; debar; hold back; prevent; prohibit; proscribe; stop;

[阻滯] blocked; impeded; obstructed; retardant;

磁阻 magnetic resistance;
電阻 electric resistance;
惡阻 vomiting during early pregnancy;
封阻 blockade; blockage;
遏阻 prevent; stop;
梗阻 block; hamper;
攔阻 block; hinder; hold back; obstruct;
內阻 internal resistance;
勸阻 advise against; advise sb not to; discourage sb from; dissuade sb from; talk sb out of; warn sb against;
險阻 dangerous; dangerous and difficult; difficult; hazardous; precarious;

zu

【俎】 (1) ancient sacrificial utensil; (2) a kind of chopping block used in ancient times; (3) small table; (4) a surname;

[俎豆] sacrificial stand and pot — sacrificial rites;

[俎上肉] meat on the chopping — a helpless victim;

刀俎 butcher's knife and chopping block;

zu

【祖】 (1) one's grandfather; (2) ancestors; forebears; (3) founder; originator; (4) follow the example of; imitate; (5) a surname;

[祖輩] ancestors; forebears; forefathers;
祖祖輩輩 for generations; from generation to generation;

[祖妣] one's deceased grandmother;
烝畀祖妣 present to ancestors, male and female;

[祖鞭] strive for achievements;
先着祖鞭 give a lead;

[祖產] ancestral estate;

[祖傳] be handed down from one's ancestors;
祖傳秘方 a secret prescription handed down in the family from generation to generation; a secret recipe handed down from generation to generation;

[祖代] ancestors; forbears;

[祖道] entertain a parting friend with a feast;

[祖德] virtuous deeds of one's ancestors;

[祖墳] ancestral grave;

[祖父] one's paternal grandfather;
祖父母 paternal grandparent;
高祖父 paternal great-great-grandfather;
~ 外高祖父母 maternal great-great-grandparent;
外祖父 maternal grandfather;
~ 外祖父母 maternal grandparent;
曾祖父 paternal great-grandfather;
~ 曾祖父母 paternal great-grandparent;

[祖國] homeland; mother country; motherland; one's country; one's fatherland; one's home country; one's homeland; one's motherland; one's native country; one's native land;
祖國懷抱 embrace of the motherland;
背叛祖國 betray one's country;
回歸祖國 return to the motherland;

[祖籍] ancestral home; land of one's ancestors;

[祖餞] give a farewell dinner;

[祖居] one's ancestral home;

[祖考] (1) one's deceased grandfather; (2) ancestors;

[祖廟] ancestral temple;

[祖母] one's paternal grandmother;
祖母結 granny knot;
高祖母 paternal great-great-grandmother;
外祖母 maternal grandmother;
曾祖母 paternal great-grandmother;

[祖上] ancestors; forebears; forefathers;

[祖述] hand down as if from one's ancestors;
[祖送] give a farewell luncheon;
[祖孫] ancestors and descendants; one's grandparent and grandchild;
祖孫三代 three generations;
[祖武] one's ancestral achievements; the footsteps of one's ancestors;
[祖先] ancestors; forebears; forefathers; progenitors;
祖先拜祭 ancester worship;
女祖先 ancestress;
[祖業] (1) property inherited from one's ancestors; (2) a trade or business inherited from one's ancestors;
[祖帳] give a farewell dinner;
[祖宗] ancestors; forebears; forefathers;
光宗耀祖 add lustre to one's ancestors and the family name; bring glory on one's ancestors; bring honour to one's ancestors and the family name; make one's ancestors illustrious;
老祖宗 ancestor; doyen; forefather;
列祖列宗 array of ancestors; forebears; forefathers; successive generations of ancestors;
榮宗耀祖 act lustre to the ancestors; bring glory to one's family and ancestors; bring honours to one's ancestors; glorify and illuminate the ancestors; redound to the glory of one's ancestors; reflect credit on one's forefathers; shed lustre upon one's ancestors;

拜祖 ancestor worship;
鼻祖 earliest ancestor; founder; originator;
伯祖 grandfather's elder brother; grand-uncle;
佛祖 respectful address for Buddha;
高祖 great-great-grandfather;
皇祖 imperial ancestors before the founder of the dynasty;
上祖 remote ancestors;
始祖 earliest ancestor; first ancestor;
叔祖 grandfather's younger brother; grand-uncle;
祀祖 offer sacrifices to one's ancestors; worship ancestors;
太祖 first founder of a dynasty;
遠祖 one's remote ancestor;
曾祖 great-grandfather;

zu

【組】 (1) form; organize; (2) department; group; organization; section; team; (3) set;
[組成] be composed of; be made up of; compose; consist of; constitute; form; make from; make of;
組成部分 component; component part; constituent;
防鏽劑組成 anti-rust composition;
共沸組成 azeotropic composition;
人口組成 demographic composition;
酸液組成 acid composition;
塗料組成 coating composition;
原子組成 atomic composition;
[組分] component; constituent;
玻璃組分 glass constituent;
共溶組分 consolute component;
活性組分 active constituent;
結晶組分 crystallographic component;
可燃組分 combustible constituent;
礦物組分 mineral constituent;
色素組分 colour component;
特性組分 characteristic component;
香味組分 aroma constituent;
增效組分 building component;
[組閣] form a cabinet; organize a cabinet; set up a cabinet;
[組合] association; combination; compose; constitute; make up;
組合風險 constitution's risk;
~組合風險分析 constitution's risk analysis;
組合櫃 large wall unit;
組合傢具 combination furniture; modular furniture;
組合理論 combinatorial theory;
組合邏輯 combinatorial logic;
組合式結構 combination apparatus;
組合形式 combining form;
組合性並列 combinatory coordination;
組合意義 combinatory meaning;
組合音響 hi-fi set; hi-fi stereo system;
部份組合 partial combination;
商品組合 article mix;
[組件] assembly; component; module; package;
組成代謝 anabolism;
組件設計 component design;
電纜組件 cable assembly;

後擋蓋組件 backplate assembly;
活門組件 valve assembly;
接頭組件 adapter assembly;
空氣調節組件 air-conditioning module;
起鬧組件 alarm module;
設定組件 assignment component;
手柄組件 throttle-grip assembly;
尾輪組件 tail-wheel assembly;
椅盤組件 seat pan assembly;
軸承組件 bearing assembly;
軸組件 shaft assembly;
陣列組件 array component;

[組織] constitute; form; formation; organize; organization; texture; tissue;
組織傳播 organizational communication;
組織目標 organizational target;
組織培養 tissue culture;
組織委員會 organizing committee;
組織行為 organization behaviour;
組織學 histology;
組織再生 tissue regeneration;
組織者 organizer;
慈善組織 charitable organization;
動物組織 animal tissue;
動植物組織 tissues of plants and animals;
對口組織 counterpart organization;
個人服從組織 the individual is subordinate to the organization;
功能組織 functional organization;
國際合作組織 international cooperative organizations;
肌肉組織 muscle tissue;
間質組織 interstitial tissue;
結締組織 connective tissue;
精原組織 androgonial tissue;
淋巴組織 lymphoid tissue;
鱗狀組織 flaser texture;
黏貼組織 areolar tissue;
企業組識 business organization;
纖維組織 fibrous tissue;
神經組織 nerve tissue;
鬆散組織 crumbly texture;
彈性組織 elastic tissue;
通氣組織 aerenchyma;
網狀組織 reticulum;
微觀組織 fine texture;
吸收組織 absorptive tissue;
學術研究組織 academic organization;
營養組織 alimentary tissue;
脂肪組織 adipose tissue;
諮詢組織 advisory body;
自組織 self-organization;
~自組織系統 self-organization system;

[組裝] assembly;
葉片組裝 blade assembly;

班組 class; team;
爆破組 demolition team;
編組 (1) marshalling; (2) organize into groups;
車組 vehicle crew;
重組 recombination; reorganize; restructure;
重組 recast; recombination; reorganize; restructure;
籌組 plan and organize;
詞組 phrase; word group;
分組 (1) divide into groups; (2) grouping; subgroups;
改組 reorganize; reshuffle; shake-up;
工作組 work group; work team;
歸組 grouping;
櫃組 group;
互助組 (1) mutual aid group; (2) mutual aid team;
機組 (1) set; unit; (2) aircrew; flight crew;
教研組 teaching and research group;
繞組 winding;
小組 group;
一組 (1) a batch; a group; a parcel; a piece; a set; (2) a group of; a set of;
字組 block of words;

zu

【詛】 (1) abuse; curse; imprecate; swear; (2) make a vow; swear; take an oath; vow;

[詛罵] curse and berate;
連詛帶罵 alternate invective with curses;

[詛盟] oath; vow;

[詛咒] curse; imprecate; malediction; swear; wish sb evil;
詛咒他人，應在自身 curses come home to roost;

[詛祝] pray to a deity;

zu4

zu

【駔】 fine horse; swift horse;

zuan1

zuan

【鑽】 (1) bore; dig through; drill; penetrate; pierce; (2) get into; go through; make one's way into; (3) dig into; study intensively;

[鑽狗洞] do evil; lead a wicked life; toady to

the rich;

［鑽機］ driller;

鑽機手 driller operator;

［鑽孔］ borehole; drilling;

鑽孔器 borer; perforator

定向鑽孔 directional drilling;

橫向鑽孔 cross drilling;

開拓鑽孔 development drilling;

中心鑽孔 centre drilling;

［鑽謀］ curry favour with sb in power for personal gain; seek advantage for oneself by all means; use pull to get what one wants;

［鑽牛角尖］ (1) split hairs; take unnecessary pains to study an insignificant problem; (2) get into a blind alley; get oneself into a dead end;

［鑽探］ explore; explore by drilling; investigate; prospect;

［鑽天打洞］ seize every opportunity to secure personal gains;

［鑽研］ dig into; study intensively;

［鑽仰］ seek the truth and stick to it;

［鑽營］ (1) seek advantage for oneself by all means; (2) study and scrutinize thoroughly;

到處鑽營 poke one's nose into every corner; worm one's way to every turn;

刁鑽 artful; crafty; cunning; wily;

zuan³

zuan

【簒】 bamboo basket; splint basket;

zuan

【纂】 (1) a kind of red cloth; (2) collect; compile;

［纂訂］ collect and revise;

［纂輯］ compile;

［纂修］ compile; edit; prepare;

zuan

【纘】 carry on; continue; keep up;

zuan

【鑽】 bore a hole; pierce a hole;

［鑽牀］ drilling machine;

［鑽井］ borehole; well drilling;

鑽井工 well-sinker;

鑽井平台 drilling platform;

［鑽孔］ make a hole; perforate;

［鑽子］ awl;

zuan⁴

zuan

【揝】 clench; clutch; grip; hold or seize with the hand;

zuan

【攥】 clutch; grasp; grip;

［攥着］ grasp; hold tight;

zuan

【鑽】 (1) borer; drill; grimlet; (2) diamond; jewel;

［鑽戒］ diamond ring;

［鑽具］ drilling rig; drilling tool;

［鑽石］ diamond;

鑽石婚 diamond anniversary; diamond wedding;

［鑽子］ drill; awl;

電鑽 electric drill;

風鑽 pneumatic drill;

弓鑽 bow drill;

開鑽 spud in;

空心鑽 hollow drill;

卡鑽 jamming of a drilling tool;

手鑽 hand drill;

司鑽 driller;

手搖鑽 hand drill;

台鑽 bench drill;

下鑽 run the drilling tool into the well;

zui³

zui

【嘴】 (1) gob; mouth; (2) mouth-shaped object;

［嘴巴］ cakehole; mouth;

嘴巴不饒人 fond of making sarcastic remarks; sharp-tongued;

嘴巴乾淨點 wash your mouth out;

嘴巴利害 bitter in speech; sharp-tongued;

打嘴巴 box sb in the ear; give a good talk to; take sb to task;

自打嘴巴 contradict oneself; slap one's own face;

嘟起嘴巴 pout one's lips in displeasure;

［嘴把式］ prater;

［嘴笨］ clumsy of speech; inarticulate; not skilled in talking;

［嘴邊］ at the tip of one's tongue;

話到嘴邊 on the tip of one's tongue; the word is just on one's lips; words rush

to one's lips;
話在嘴邊 on the tip of one's tongue;

[嘴饞] fond of good food; gluttonous; inclined to eat greedily;
嘴饞肚飽 greedy while the stomach is already full;

[嘴唇] lip;
嘴唇發紫 lips turn blue;
嘴唇油滑 eloquent in speech; with one's tongue in one's cheek;
薄嘴唇 thin lips;
肥厚的嘴唇 thick blubber lips;
磕破嘴唇 split one's lip;
厚嘴唇 thick lips;
撅起嘴唇 curl up ones lips; pout one's lips; pucker one's lips; purse one's lips; with pouting lips;
潤濕嘴唇 moisten one's lips;
上嘴唇 upper lip;
舔唇咂嘴 lick one's lips and smack one's tongue;
舐舐嘴唇 moisten one's lips;
舔嘴唇 lick one's lips; smack one's lips;
下嘴唇 lower lip;
咬嘴唇 bite one's lip; chew one's lip;

[嘴刁] particular about food;

[嘴兒] (1) eloquence; (2) nozzle;
順嘴兒 slip out of one's tongue; speak casually without much thought;

[嘴乖] clever and pleasant when speaking to elders; given to sweet talking; soft-spoken;
嘴乖舌巧 full of gibes and ready with one's tongue;

[嘴急] eager to eat;

[嘴尖] cutting in speech; sharp-tongued;
嘴尖皮厚 sharp-tongued and thick-skinned;
嘴尖舌快 fluent in speech; have a loose and sharp tongue;
嘴尖舌巧 gifted with a quick and sharp tongue; have a capable tongue; sharp-tongued;
嘴尖舌酸 cutting in speech; sharp-tongued;

[嘴角] corners of the mouth;
嘴角倒掛 pull down the corners of one's mouth;
嘴角掛笑 a smile plays on one's lips; the trace of a smiles appears at the corners of one's mouth;
嘴角流涎 the corners of one's mouth are drooping;

[嘴緊] close-mouthed; secretive; tight-lipped;

[嘴嚼器] trophus;
錘型嘴嚼器 maleate trophus;
鉗型嘴嚼器 torcipate trophus;
杖型嘴嚼器 virgate trophus;

[嘴快] have a loose tongue; incapable of keeping secrets; rash in speech;
嘴快心直 be outspoken; frank; jaws are quick and heart is straight; sincere; straightforward;

[嘴懶] not inclined to talk much; taciturn;

[嘴冷] rough and plain in speech;

[嘴裏] in the mouth;
嘴裏發苦 have a bitter taste in the mouth;
嘴裏念彌陀，心裏毒蛇窩 beads about the neck and the devil in the heart; crosses without and the devil within; the cross on the breast, and the devil in the heart;
嘴裏説東，心裏想西 saying one thing while one's mind is far away on sth else;
嘴裏甜甜，心裏一把鋸鋸鐮 a honey tongue, a heart of gall; honey in the mouth and poison in the heart;

[嘴臉] countenance; face; features; look;
唬起嘴臉 put on a solemn face;
看人嘴臉 depend on another; live on another's favour;

[嘴皮子] lips;
磨嘴皮子 (1) do a lot of talking; (2) blah-blah; jabber;
耍嘴皮子 (1) brag; show off one's eloquence; slick talker; talk glibly; (2) lip service; mere empty talk; play lip service; talk big;
~大耍嘴皮子 talk glibly;

[嘴貧] chatty; talkative;

[嘴強] (1) inclined to argue; (2) talk toughly;

[嘴勤] fond of talking; ready to talk;

[嘴上] on one's lips;
嘴上掛笑 a smile is clinging to one's lips;
嘴上沒毛，辦事不牢 a man too young to grow a beard is not dependable; a man with downy lips is bound to make slips; downy lip make thoughtless slips; young people cannot be trusted with important tasks because they lack experience;

[嘴舌] mouth and tongue;
搬嘴饒舌 say evil things behind one's back;
惡嘴毒舌 bad tongue; biting tongue; bitter tongue; caustic tongue; dangerous tongue; have a vicious tongue; sharp tongue; sharp-tongued; venomous tongue; wicked tongue;
鼓嘴弄舌 wag one's tongue;
浪嘴輕舌 wag one's tongue too freely;
七嘴八舌 a babel of; a hubbub of voices; a scene of noisy and confused talking; all giving tongue together; all talking at once; all talking simultaneously producing great confusion; all talking together; confused talking; everybody talking at the same time; like a rattle-box; like a talkshot; lively discussion with everybody trying to get a word in; many diverse opinions; many men, many minds; with everybody eager to put in a word;
~家有十五口—七嘴八舌 there are fifteen people in the family — all talking at once;
輕嘴薄舌 make irresponsible remarks;
調嘴學舌 carry tales; cause alienation by spreading rumours; gossip; speak ill of sb behind his back; stir up enmity; tell tales; tittle-tattle;
嘴巧舌能 clever and plausible in speech; gifted with a quick and sharp tongue; shine in conversation;
[嘴碎] garrulous; loquacious; talkative;
[嘴損] cutting in speech; sharp-tongued;
[嘴甜] honey-mouthed; ingratiating ion speech; smooth-tongued;
嘴甜心苦 talk sweetly while harbouring evil thoughts;
嘴甜心辣 a cruel heart under the cover of sugar-coated words; sweet words and a bitter heart;
[嘴頭] mouth; tongue;
嘴頭子 (1) have a ready tongue; (2) lips;
[嘴穩] able to keep a secret; discreet in speech;
[嘴嚴] able to keep a secret; capable of keeping secrets; cautious about speech; discreet in speech;
[嘴硬] (1) never say uncle; refuse to admit a mistake; stubborn and reluctant to admit mistakes or defeats; (2) talk toughly;
嘴硬心軟 firm in speech but soft in heart;
[嘴直] speak frankly; speak out without reservation;
[嘴子] (1) anything shaped like a mouth; (2) mouthpiece;
癟嘴子 teethless person;
碎嘴子 cackler; chatter; chatterbox; garrulous person; jabber; prater;

白嘴 dish without staple food to go with it;
拌嘴 bicker; quarrel; squabble; words of a sort; wrangle;
幫嘴 speak in support of a person;
閉嘴 button one's lip; close one's mouth; hold one's tongue; keep one's peace; keep one's mouth shut; shut shop; shut up; shut one's mouth; zip one's lips;
插嘴 barge in; break in; break in upon; burst in; burst in on; burst in upon; butt in; butt in with a remark; chime in; chip in; chop in; cut in; cut into; get a word in; get a word in edgeways; interpolate; interpose; interrupt; put in; put in a word; snap sb up; strike in; take up;
饞嘴 gluttonous;
吵嘴 quarrel; squabble;
打嘴 slap sb in the face;
電嘴 ignition plug; sparking plug;
頂嘴 answer back; backchat; backtalk; reply defiantly; talk back;
鬥嘴 (1) bicker; quarrel; (2) make a jok;
堵嘴 gag sb; shut sb's mouth; silence sb;
多嘴 gossipy; long-tongued; shoot off one's mouth; speak out of turn; talk out of place; talk too much;
改嘴 modify one's previous remark;
狗嘴 dog's mouth;
號嘴 mouthpiece;
鶴嘴 jumper;
還嘴 answer back; come back; retort; talk back;
回嘴 back answer; answer back; backchat; backtalk; retort;
豁嘴 (1) harelip; (2) harelipped person;
火嘴 nozzle;
忌嘴 avoid certain food; be on a diet;
尖嘴 have a caustic tongue;
緊閉着嘴 clamp jaws;
強嘴 reply defiantly; talk back;
撅嘴 pout one's lips;
誇嘴 boast; talk big;
快嘴 quick-tongued;

蠟嘴 hawfinch;
利嘴 sharp tongue;
咧嘴 grin;
零嘴 nibble between meals;
攏嘴 close one's mouth;
漏嘴 let slip a remark;
賣嘴 self-praise; show off one's skill or kind-heartedness by talking;
抿嘴 purse one's lips;
奶嘴 nipple of a feeding bottle;
鳥嘴 beak; bill;
努嘴 pout one's lips as a signal;
噴嘴 (1) atomizer; (2) jet; nozzle; spray head; spray nozzle;
撇嘴 curl one's lip; make a lip; make a mouth; make a wry mouth; make mouths; make up a lip; shoot out the lips; twitch one's mouth;
貧嘴 garrulous; loquacious;
氣嘴 valve;
搶嘴 (1) try to beat others in being the first to talk; (2) argumentative; assertive;
翹嘴 pout one's mouth;
親嘴 kiss;
繞嘴 difficult to articulate;
嚷嘴 bicker; quarrel;
撒嘴 relax the bite;
沙嘴 sandspit;
山嘴 spur;
順嘴 (1) smoothly; (2) offhandedly;
説漏了嘴 let sth slip; slip out;
説嘴 (1) boast; brag; (2) argue; quarrel;
貪嘴 gluttonous; greedy; piggish;
鐵嘴 chatterbox; good talker; talkative;
偷嘴 steal food; take food on the sly;
歪嘴 wry mouth; wry-mouthed;
圍嘴 bib;
歇嘴 shut up; stop talking;
鴉嘴 crow's beak;
鴨嘴 duck's bill;
一張嘴 (1) a mouth; a tongue; (2) whenever one speaks;
一嘴 put in a word;
油嘴 (1) glib; glib-tongued; oil-tongued; (2) glib talker;
咂嘴 make clicks; make clicks of praise;
張嘴 (1) open one's mouth; (2) ask for a loan or a favour;
掌嘴 slap sb in the slap;
爭嘴 (1) fight for food; (2) argue in self-defense;
住嘴 button it; button your lip; button your mouth; hold one's tongue; shut up;
走嘴 make a slip of the tongue;

zui4
zui

【最】 extreme; most; superlative;
[最矮] lowest; shortest;
[最長] longest;
[最初] (1) at first; at the beginning; at the outset; initial; original; (2) earliest; first;
最初申請 initial application;
最初是 start out as;
[最大] biggest; greatest; largest; maximum;
最大公約數 greatest common divisor;
最大估量詞 maximize;
次級最大 secondary maximum;
主最大 principal maximum;
[最低] least; lowest; minimum;
最低程度詞 minimizer;
最低點 nadir;
最低工資 minimum wage;
最低價 lowest price; minimum price;
最低售價 minimum selling price;
最低限度 (1) lowest limit; (2) at least;
最低限價 bottom price; minimum price; price floor;
[最短] shortest;
[最多] at most; the most; tops;
最多一小時 one hour tops;
[最高] highest; maximum; supreme; tallest; topmost; uppermost;
最高潮 climax; culmination;
最高程度詞 maximize;
最高當局 highest authorities;
最高法院 Supreme Court;
最高峰 climax; summit;
最高公因數 greatest common factor;
最高級 (1) highest; summit; (2) superlative degree;
~ 絕對最高級 absolute superlative;
最高價 highest price; maximum price; top price;
最高權力 supreme power;
最高統帥 supreme commander;
最高學府 highest seat of learning;
[最好] (1) at one's best; by far the best; do well; first-rate; the best; the most; (2) had better; it might as well;
那就最好 that is the card for it;
[最後] at last; at length; at long last; end with;

eventually; finally; in the end; last; lastly; the final; the last;
最後期限 last date; last term;
最後勝利 final victory;
最後時刻 eleventh hour;
最後條款 final articles;
最後通牒 ultimatum;
最後一刻 eleventh hour;
最後一招 one's last shift;
到了最後 at the end of the day;

[最壞] meanest; most vicious; worst;

[最惠國] most-favoured nation;
最惠國稅 most-favoured nation duties;

[最佳] best; superlative;
最佳方式 best mode;
最佳化 optimization;
~動態最佳化 dynamic optimization;
~過程最佳化 process optimization;
~系統最佳化 system optimization;
~整體最佳化 global optimization;
最佳狀態 in top condition;
~保持最佳狀態 in top condition at all times;

[最近] (1) lately; not long ago; of late; recently; (2) closest; nearest; proximate;

[最怕] fear most;

[最少] least; minimum;
最少詞匯 minimum vocabulary;

[最先] (1) earliest; first; foremost; (2) at first; in the beginning;

[最小] least; minimum; smallest;
最小的兒子 one's youngest son;
最小的女兒 one's youngest daughter;
最小公倍數 least common multiple;

[最新] latest; most up-to-date; newest;
最新發明 latest invention;
最新樣式 latest style;

[最優] best fit;
最優等品質 extra best quality;
最優化 optimization; optimize;
~最優化標準 optimal standards;
~最優化決策 optimal decision-making;
~最優化模型 optimal model;
~最優化原理 principle of optimality;
~參數最優化 parameter optimization;
~軌道最優化 trajectory optimization;
~自適應最優化 adaptive optimization;
最優控制方法 method of optimal controlling;
最優控制理論 optimizing control theory;
最優上昇 synergic ascent;
最優適應控制 adaptive control optimization;

[最終] final; last; ultimate;

zui

【晬】 (1) first birthday of a child; (2) anniversary;

zui

【罪】 (1) crime; evil; guilt; sin; vice; (2) blame; fault; (3) hardship; pain;

[罪案] case; criminal case; details of a criminal case;

[罪不重科] a crime should not be condemned twice; one should not be punished twice for the same crime;

[罪不容誅] even death cannot excuse the offence; guilty of crimes for which even capital punishment is insufficient to atone; guilty of crimes for which even death is insufficient punishment;

[罪惡] crime; evil; guilt; sin; vice;
罪惡多端 guilty of all kinds of evil; up to all kinds of evil;
罪惡勾當 criminal activities;
罪惡累累 commit innumerable crimes; long list of crimes;
罪惡滿盈 the measure of iniquity is full;
罪惡彌天 commit a great sin; one's crimes and evil deeds reach to the heavens;
罪惡深重 be steeped in crime;
罪惡滔天 commit many towering crimes; commit monstrous crimes; guilty of monstrous crimes; with crimes mounting up to the sky;
罪惡盈天 one's crimes fill the heavens;
罪惡淵藪 a hotbed of crime; a refuge for evils; a sink of inequity;
罪惡昭彰 have committed flagrant crimes;
罪大惡極 capital offense; crime of the blackest dye; criminal and wicked in the extreme; guilty of terrible crimes; guilty of the most heinous crimes; heinous crime; mortal sin; most vicious;

[罪犯] criminal; culprit; offender; perp;

[罪過] (1) fault; offence; sin; (2) thanks, but this is really more than deserve;
風流罪過 blemishes;
洗滌罪過 cleanse away sin;

Z

[罪魁] chief criminal; ringleader;
罪魁禍首 chief culprit; chief offender; ringleader;
[罪戾] crime; evil; sin;
[罪名] accusation; charge;
罪名關天 terrible crime;
莫須有罪名 trumped-up charges;
[罪孽] evil; sin; wrongdoing that brings retribution;
罪孽深重 sinful;
[罪愆] offence; sin;
[罪人] (1) guilty person; offender; sinner; (2) blame others;
罪人不孥 the wives and children of the offenders are not involved in their crimes;
[罪上加罪] add an offense on top of another; commit crime upon crime; crime added to crime; doubly guilty; give more severe punishment for repeated offences;
[罪行] atrocities; crime; criminal acts; guilt; offences;
罪行累累 commit countless crimes; have a long criminal record;
包庇罪行 cover up crimes;
不可饒恕的罪行 unpardonable offence;
法定罪行 statutory offence;
戰爭罪行 war crime;
[罪刑] penalty; punishment;
[罪愆] crime; evil; vice; wrongdoing;
[罪因] cause of a crime;
[罪尤] fault; offence;
[罪責] responsibility for an offence;
罪責難逃 cannot escape the responsibility for the offence; cannot get away with one's crimes; cannot shirk responsibility for one's crimes;
[罪證] evidence of a crime; proof of one's guilt;
罪證俱在 all the evidence of the crime is available;
罪證確鑿，鐵案如山 the evidence of these crimes is conclusive;
罪證如山 there are irrefutable proofs of heinous crimes;
[罪狀] charges in an indictment; facts about a crime;

辦罪 punish;
抱罪 conscious of guilt; feel guilty;
得罪 cause offence to sb; cross sb; displease; get across sb; give offence to sb; in Dutch with sb; in sb's bad books; in sb's black books; offend; put up sb's pecker; run foul of sb; step on sb's toes; stroke sb the wrong way;
抵罪 be punished for a crime;
定罪 convict sb of a crime; declare sb guilty;
二茬罪 suffer for a second time;
犯罪 commit a crime; commit an offence; crime; offence;
伏罪 admit one's guilt; plead guilty;
服罪 admit one's guilt; plead guilty;
功罪 merit and fault;
怪罪 blame; complain;
歸罪 impute to; incriminate; inculpate; put the blame on;
悔罪 show penitence; show repentance;
活罪 hardship; suffering;
見罪 be blamed;
開罪 displease; offend;
論罪 decide on the nature of the guilt;
免罪 exempt from punishment;
判罪 declare guilt;
賠罪 apologize; make an apology;
泣罪 weep for a criminal's evil-doing;
輕罪 minor crime; minor offense; misdemeanour;
請罪 (1) admit one's error and ask for punishment; (2) apologize; apologize humbly; appeal for leniency;
認罪 acknowledge one's fault; acknowledge one's guilt; admit one's guilt; plead guilty;
赦罪 absolve sb from guilt; forgive an offender; pardon sb;
受罪 endure hardships; have a hard time; suffer;
恕罪 forgive a mistake; forgive a sin; pardon an offense;
贖罪 atone for one's crime;
死罪 capital crime; capital offence; penalty of death;
宿罪 sins of a previous existence;
逃罪 escape punishment;
脫罪 exonerate sb from a charge;
委罪 put the blame on sb else; shift blame on to sb else;
畏罪 afraid of punishment; dread punishment for one's crime;
問罪 call a person to account; condemn; denounce; rebuke; reprimand; reprove;
無罪 innocent; not guilty;
下罪 convict;

謝罪 apologize; apologize for an offence; offer an apology;
有罪 culpability; guilty;
宥罪 forgive an offense; pardon a crime;
原罪 original sin;
遭罪 endure hardships, etc.; have a hard time; suffer;
招罪 bring sth bad upon oneself;
折罪 atonement for a crime;
治罪 punish sb;
重罪 felony; grave crime; heavy offense;

zui

【醉】 (1) drunk; intoxicated; tipsy; (2) liquor-saturated; steeped in liquor; (3) charmed; infatuated;

[醉倒] succumb to the effect of alcohol;
醉倒街頭 dead drunk in the streets;
[醉鬼] drunkard; inebriate; sot;
[醉漢] drunkard; drunken man;
醉漢口裏說真話 what soberness conceals, drunkenness reveals;
[醉酒] drunk; drunkenness;
[醉客] drunken man;
[醉朋] alcoholic; drunkard;
[醉人] get oneself drunk;
酒不醉人人自醉 if you get drunk, it is your own fault and not that of the wine; it is not the wine that intoxicates but the drinker who gets himself drunk; wine does not make a man drunk if he's not in the mood;
[醉聖] great drinker; prodigious drinker;
[醉態] drunkenness; state of being drunk;
[醉翁] old drunkard;
醉翁之意不在酒 many kiss the baby for the nurse's sake; the drinker's heart is not in the cup — have ulterior motives;
[醉臥] lie in a drunken stupor;
[醉鄉] dazed state in which a drinker finds himself; paradise of drunkenness;
[醉心] be bent on; be enamoured of; be enamoured with; be engrossed in; be infatuated with; be intoxicated with;
醉心入迷 go into ecstasies over sth;
[醉醒] regain presence of mind after getting drunk; sober up;
[醉醺醺] drunk; inebriated; sottish; tipsy; under the influence of alcohol;
醉醺醺的 hammered;
[醉言不較] not find fault with drunken talk;
[醉眼] one's eyes show the effects of drink;
醉眼朦朧 drunken and bleary-eyed; eyes growsy from drink;
醉眼惺松 sleepy-eyed from drink;
[醉意] signs or feeling of getting drunk;
略有醉意 a little intoxicated; grow tipsy; slightly muddled with liquor;

飽醉 full and drunk;
沉醉 become intoxicated; get dead drunk;
痴醉 be intoxicated;
灌醉 fuddle; inebriate; make sb drunk;
酣醉 be dead drunk;
喝醉 drunk; have a drop too much; in drink; in the sunshine; intoxicated; pissed; sottish; take a drop too much; tipsy;
酒醉 a drop too much; about gone; at rest; awash; be given to drink; be illuminated; be lit up; be lit up like a Christmas tree; be shot; blitzed; boiled; cooked; corked; corned; crapulous; creamed; crocked; decks awash; drink without limits; drown one's sorrows; drunk; elevated; embalmed; faced; feel good; fish-eyed; flustered; fly high; fricasseed; fuddle one's nose; gassed; gay; geared-up; get a bag on; get plastered; get smashed; gifted; glowing; glued; greased; groggy; half-seas over; half-under hammered; hang one on; happy; have a bag on; have a bun on; have a buzz on; have a glow on; have a nose to light candles at; have a turkey on one's back; have one over the eight; have the sun in one's eyes; high; high as a kite; in bed with one's boots on; in drink; in one's altitude; in one's cups; in the bag; in the gun; inebriated; inked; intemperate; intoxicated; jolly; jugged; juiced; juiced up; laid-out; loaded; looped; lubricated; maudlin; mellow; merry; oiled; on the grog; ossified; owl-eyed; pass-out; petrified; pickled; pie-eyed; pigeon-eyed; plastered; polluted; potted; preserved; ripped; roostered; salted; saturated; sauced; schizzed out; see double; sheliacked; shickered; shined; skunked; smashed; soaked; soak it up; steamed; stewed; stiff; stretched; tangle-footed; tangled; tanked; tie a bag on; the worse for liquor; tie one on; tight; tipsy; tired; tuned; twisted; under the influence of alcohol;

under the influence; under the table; under the weather; unsteady on one's feet; vulcanized; walking on rocky socks; wall-eyed; wasted; watch the ant races; well-bottled; with a glow on; wrecked; zonked;

爛醉 dead drunk;
麻醉 anaesthesia; narcosis;
迷醉 be fascinated by;
如醉 as if one is drunk;
陶醉 be intoxicated; be enchanted; drink in; revel in;
微醉 squiffy;
心醉 be charmed; be enchanted;
飲醉 get drunk;
霑醉 dead drunk;
裝醉 pretend to be drunk;

zui

【蕞】 tiny; very small;

［蕞爾小邦］ tiny state;

zun¹

zun

【尊】 (1) of a senior generation; senior; (2) esteem; honour; respect; revere; venerate; (3) esteemed; honorable; honoured; noble; respectable;

［尊卑］ (1) seniors and juniors; (2) superiors and inferiors;
尊卑失序 lack due regard for precedence; lack due regard for priority in place;
辭尊居卑 refuse to accept an honourable station and occupy a humble one;
男尊女卑 male superiority and female inferiority;
天尊地卑 the sky above and the earth below;

［尊稱］ (1) address sb respectfully; (2) respectful form of address;

［尊崇］ esteem; hold in reverence; revere; venerate; worship;

［尊處］ your abode;

［尊德樂道］ honour virtue and advocate moral principles;

［尊甫］ your esteemed father;

［尊府］ your home;

［尊公］ your father;

［尊貴］ honourable; respectable; respected;
紆尊降貴 condescend to simple people; deign to; loosen respect and degrade honour;

［尊駕］ you;

［尊見］ your opinion;

［尊敬］ esteem; honour; respect; revere;
不尊敬 disrespect;
獲得尊敬 command respect; gain respect;
相互尊敬 mutual respect;
贏得尊敬 command respect; earn respect; win respect;

［尊老］ (1) respect the aged people; (2) parents;
尊老愛幼 respect the aged and take good care of children; respect the old and cherish the young;
尊老敬師 respect the old and the teachers;

［尊門］ your home; your residence;

［尊命］ your order;

［尊親］ your parents;

［尊容］ your face;

［尊榮］ dignity and honour;

［尊生］ respect life;

［尊師］ respect one's teachers;
尊師愛友 respect one's teachers and love one's friends;
尊師敬長 honour teachers and respect the elders; honour the teachers and respect the elder generation; respect one's elders and teachers;
尊師重道 honour the teacher and respect his teachings;
尊師重教 respect teachers and emphasize education;

［尊堂］ your mother;

［尊翁］ your father;

［尊顯］ honorable; noble; of high position; respectable; venerable;

［尊姓］ your name;

［尊嚴］ dignity; honour; respectability;

［尊長］ elder; older person; senior;
目無尊長 show no respect to elders and superiors; with no regard for one's elders and betters;

［尊者］ one's seniors;

［尊重］ esteem; hold in reverence; honour; respect; uphold; value; venerate;

令尊 your father;
年尊 advanced in years; old;
屈尊 condescend;
天尊 supernatural being;
褻尊 condescend; deign to;
邑尊 county magistrate;

至尊 the most august;
自尊 (1) proper pride; self-esteem; self-respect; (2) egotistic;

zun
【樽】 (1) bottle; goblet; wine jar; wine vessel; (2) luxuriant vegetation;
[樽節] economize;
[樽俎] goblet; wine vessel;
樽俎折衝 break through the enemy's defences while at cups and dishes; carry on diplomatic negotiations successfully; discharge the duties of a diplomat; engage in diplomatic negotiations; outmanoeuvre the enemy over glasses of wine; talk over cups of wine;

zun
【遵】 abide by; follow; obey;
[遵辦] execute according to instructions;
[遵從] comply with; defer to; follow; obey;
[遵奉] obey; observe;
[遵陸] go by land; take a land route;
[遵命] comply with your wish; obey your command;
遵命辦理 act in compliance with instruction; execute according to instructions;
[遵守] abide by; comply with; keep; observe;
遵守合約 observe the agreement − abide by its restrictions or provisions;
嚴格遵守 rigid adherence; strict adherence;
[遵行] act in accordance with; act on; follow; put into practice;
[遵循] abide by; adhere to; follow;
[遵依] comply with; follow;
[遵義] stand up for righteousness;
[遵照] accord with; act in accordance with; comply with; conform to; follow; obey;
[遵旨] follow imperial orders;

zun³
zun
【撙】 (1) comply with; (2) economize;
[撙節] practise economy; retrench;
撙節開支 economize expenses; retrench;
[撙省] economize;

zuo¹
zuo
【作】 (1) do; (2) workshop;
[作坊] small workshop;
[作雷] bring about one's own rain;
[作弄] make a fool of; play a trick on; poke fun at; tease;
[作死] look for trouble; seek one's death; take the road to ruin;
[作酸] feel stomach acidity;
[作揖] make a bow with hands folded in front;

zuo
【嘬】 (1) kiss; (2) suck;
[嘬奶] suck milk;

zuo²
zuo
【作】
[作踐] abuse; humiliate; insult; spoil; trample; treat harshly; waste;
[作料] condiments; materials; seasoning;
[作興] (1) allowable; (2) in good spirits; (3) in vogue; (4) hold in high regard; (5) likely; perhaps;

zuo
【昨】 late; past; yesterday;
[昨兒] yesterday;
[昨非] past mistakes;
[昨天] yesterday;
昨天晚上 last evening; last night;
昨天整天 all day yesterday;
[昨晚] last night;
[昨朝] yesterday morning;

zuo
【捽】 a pronunciation of 捽;

zuo³
zuo
【左】 (1) left; left side; (2) east side; (3) queer; unorthodox; (4) erroneous; improper; incorrect; mistaken; wrong; (5) contrary; different; (6) be demoted; descend; (7) unduly stubborn; (8) a surname;
[左臂] left arm;
[左邊] left; left side; on the left;
[左側] on the left side;
[左方] on the left; to the left;
[左顧] (1) look to the left; (2) deign to call on sb;
左顧右盼 (1) cast glances about; gaze round; glance left and right;

Z

inattentive; lack of concentration; look around; look left and right; (2) flirtatious;

[左計] impractical plan;

[左見] bias; prejudice;

[左近] in the neighbourhood; in the vicinity; nearby;

[左面] left side; left-hand side;

[左撇子] left-hander;

[左遷] be demoted;

[左傾] left-leaning; progressive;

[左券] full confidence in winning; winning hand;

持左券 confident of success; have success within one's grasp; sure to win;

可操左券 certain of success; have a winning hand; have full assurance of success; sure to succeed;

如操左券 have the ball at one's feet;

穩操左券 be bound to succeed; certain of success; certain of winning; confident of success; have full assurance of success; have the game in one's hands; hold the cards in one's hands; in the bag; success is within one's grasp; sure of success; sure to win;

執左券 be sure of success; hold the left half of a contract;

[左人] compound surname;

[左史] official historian;

[左手] (1) left hand; (2) left-hand side;

左手定則 left-hand rule;

左手執拍者 left-hand player;

[左袒] be biased; be partial to; favour one side; take sides with;

[左腿] left leg;

左腿向後舉 left leg backwards;

[左行] (1) from left to right; (2) keep to the left;

[左驗] witness;

[左翼] left wing;

左翼報紙 left-wing newspaper;

左翼的 left-wing;

左翼分子 left-winger; leftie; lefty;

左翼政黨 leftist party;

[左右] (1) at hand; by one's side; left and right; nearby; (2) about or so; or thereabouts; (3) be influenced; be swayed; influence; sway;

左右刁難 deliberately create obstructions for sb;

左右逢源 able to achieve success one way or another; as wanton as a calf with two dams; butter one's bread on both sides; gain advantage from both sides; get help from all sides; have everything going one's way; have one's bread buttered on both sides; win advantage from both sides;

左右局勢 master of the situation;

左右開弓 ambidextrous; give sb a box on both ears; hit with both hands; shoot first to one side, then to the other; shoot first with one hand, then with the other; smash both wing; use both hands alternately in quick succession; use first one hand and then the other in quick succession;

左右全局 control the whole situation;

左右手 right-hand man; valuable assistant;

左右四鄰 neighbours;

左右袒 biased; partial to; take sides; unneutral;

左右為難 be stuck between a rock and a hard place; between the devil and the deep blue sea; between two fires; get into a fix; in a bind; in a box; in a dilemma; in a quandary about; in an awkward predicament; in the middle; indecisive; on the horns of a dilemma; stand at a nonplus; torn between;

~左右為難的人 piggy in the middle;

左右搖擺 like buckets in a well; play pendulum; vacillate now to the left and now to the right; waver between the left and right;

不為左右袒 refuse to take sides in a quarrel; remain strictly neutral;

蹠左蹠右 at odds with;

顧左右而言他 evade the subject under dicussion; glance right and left and wander off the point; look right and left, and talk about other matters; look the other way; steer clear of the crucial point;

忽左忽右 have it both ways;

環顧左右 look to the left and right;

左耳入，右耳出 come in at one ear and out at the other; go in one ear and out of the other;

左扶右擁 prop up on all sides;

左輔右弼 be aided on the left and

supported on the right; help from left and right; the emperor's top ministers;
左改右改 make changes over and over again;
左難右難 on the horns of a dilemma;
左勸右勸 try again and again to persuade sb;
左説右説 say sth over and over again;
左圖右史 home library; impressive personal library; large private collection of books;
左問右問 ask everybody; question and question;

[左證] supporting evidence;
[左轉] turn left;

過左 ultra-left;
閭左 (1) district inhabited by the poor; (2) the poor;
相左 (1) cross one another's way; fail to meet each other; (2) conflict with each other; disagree;
向左 towards the left;

zuo

【佐】 (1) aid; assist; second; (2) assistant;
[佐餐] be eaten together with rice; go with rice;
[佐理] assist;
[佐命] help a prince to gain the throne and establish a new dynasty;
[佐膳] side dishes;
[佐藥] adjuvant;
[佐證] evidence; proof;

輔佐 assist a ruler in governing a country;
官佐 officer;
將佐 high-ranking military officers;
僚佐 assistants in a government office;

zuo

【撮】 pinch; tuft; very small amount;
[撮子] a tuft of sth;

zuo4

zuo

【作】 (1) get up; rise; (2) compose; write; (3) do; make; (4) works; writings; (5) affect; pretend; (6) regard as; take sb or sth for; (7) act as; become; (8) feel; have;
[作案] commit a crime;
作案記錄 criminal record;
~ 保存作案記錄 keep one's criminal record;
[作罷] drop; give up; relinquish;
[作伴] keep sb company; serve as a companion for;
[作保] go bail for sb; guarantee; guarantor; sb's guarantor; sponsor sb; stand guarantee; vouch for;
從中作保 be sb's guarantor; go bail for; play the part of the sponsor;
[作弊] cheat; indulge in corrupt practices; practise fraud;
作弊老手 cardshark;
[作壁上觀] bystander; look on indifferently; onlooker; sit by and watch; stand by watching others battle; watch the fighting from the rampart; watch with detachment;
[作別] bid farewell; say goodbye; take one's leave;
[作答] answer; reply;
避不作答 decline answering a question; parry a question;
[作抵] substitute;
[作東] stand treat;
[作對] (1) act against; choose to be sb's rival; oppose; set oneself against; (2) match with another in marriage;
成心作對 purposely antagonize sb;
[作惡] (1) do evil; indulge in evildoings; (2) gloomy; melancholy; sullen;
作惡多端 be steeped in iniquity; commit all sorts of wicked actions; do all kinds of bad things; do all kinds of evil; guilty of every conceivable atrocity; indulge in all sorts of evildoing; up to all sorts of evil;
恃強作惡 rely on one's strength to do evil;
唆人作惡 instigate others to do evil things; lead man astray;
無惡不作 as wicked as possible; be addicted to all sorts of vice; capable of committing every crime under the sun; capable of the worst crime; commit all kinds of atrocities; commit all manner of crimes; do all manner of evil; do every sort of evil thing; evil doings know no limits; extremely evil; nothing is too evil for one; stop at

no evil; stop at nothing in doing evil; there is no crime of which one is not guilty;
造孽作惡 commit crime and do evil;
諸惡莫作 every form of evil cannot be done;

[作伐] act as a go-between in marriage; act as a matchmaker; matchmaker;
挽人作伐 ask sb to act as a go-between;

[作法] (1) practise magic; resort to magic arts; (2) course of action; practise; ways of doing things; (3) art of composition;
作法自斃 be caught by one's own laws; be caught by one's own device; get caught in one's own trap; get into trouble through one's own scheme; harm set, harm get; harm watch; harm catch; make a law only to all foul of it oneself; stew in one's own juice;

[作反] rebel; revolt; rise in revolt;

[作廢] cancel; declare invalid; delete; make void; nullify;

[作風] style; style of work; way;
作風惡劣 abominable behaviour; have an obnoxious style of work;
作風民主 democratic in one's style of work;
作風拖拉 dilatory work style;
作風正派 have moral integrity; honest and upright; upright in one's daily behaviour;
保持作風 keep to one's own style;
大少爺作風 behaviour typical of the spoiled son of a rich family; extravagant ways;
浮誇作風 proneness to boasting and exaggeration;
民主作風 democratic style;

[作歌] compose a song;
作歌助觴 give a song to help sb on with his wine;

[作梗] create difficulties; hinder; obstruct;
從中作梗 come between; create difficulties; hinder sb from carrying out a plan; make things difficult for sb; place obstacles in the way; put a spoke in sb's wheel;

[作工] labour; work;

[作古] die; pass away;

[作怪] act mischievously; do mischief; make trouble; mischievous; play tricks;
醜人多作怪 there is never a foul face but there is a foul fancy;

[作官] government official; hold a government post;

[作賀] offer congratulations;

[作活] work for one's living;

[作急] in a hurry; make haste;

[作計] aim at; have in mind; make haste;

[作家] author; writer;
多產作家 copious writer;
荒誕派作家 absurdist;
劇作家 dramatist; playwright;
女作家 authoress; female writer;
~著名女作家 famous female writer;
特寫作家 feature writer;
業餘作家 amateur writer;
專欄作家 columnist;
~明星專欄作家 star columnist;
專業作家 professional writer;

[作假] (1) behave affectedly; (2) counterfeit; falsify; (3) cheat; play tricks;
作假帳 manipulation of accounts;

[作價] assess the value; set a price;

[作嫁] earn a living by working for others;

[作繭] spin a cocoon;
作繭自縛 be caught in one's own trap; cocoon oneself like a silkworm; fall into a pit of one's own digging; fall into the cocoon set by oneself; fry in one's own grease; hoist oneself with one's own petard;
老蠶作繭 toil for a living in one's old age;

[作勁] help; offer assistance to;

[作就] get sth done successfully;

[作客] (1) guest; (2) sojourn in a strange place;
作客他鄉 be a visitor in another town; live in a strange place; sojourn in a strange land;

[作苦] (1) be engaged in a hard task; (2) become bitter;

[作闊] make a vain display; show off;

[作樂] enjoy; have a good time; have fun; make merry;
苦中作樂 enjoy in adversity; find joy amid hardship;
尋歡作樂 do a bit of fun; gather roses; go on a tear; go on the spree; go to town; have beer and skittles; have fun; kick up one's heels; look for

distractions; make merry; on the loose; on the on the tiles; out on the tiles; pleasure-seeking; pursue pleasure; seek pleasure; seek the joys of lovers' union; sport;
~ 尋歡作樂者 pleasure seeker;
縱歡作樂 go on the spree; have a spree;

[作亂] rebel; rise in revolt; stage an armed rebellion; start an uprising;
犯上作亂 a deluge of rebellion; be insubordinate and rebellious; create disorder against the rulers; go against one's superior and make trouble; go against one's superior and stage an armed rebellion; make revolts and offend the upper orders; rebel against authority;

[作媒] act as a go-between in marriage;

[作美] cooperate; help; make things better for sb;

[作夢] (1) dream; (2) daydream; imagine sth as in a dream;

[作難] (1) feel awkward; feel embarrassed; (2) find oneself in a predicament; find oneself in a difficult position; make things difficult for sb;

[作孽] commit a sin; do evil; do sth that causes harm to others;
作孽錢 filthy money;
天作孽，猶可違，人作孽，不可活 if disasters come from nature, sth can be done to counter them; but if they are of one's own making, one is done for; if you leap into a well, Providence is not bound to fetch you out; the evils we bring on ourselves are the hardest to bear;
自作孽 bring disaster to oneself; sow the seeds of one's own ruin;
~ 自作孽，不可活 if you leap into a well, Providence is not bound to fetch you out; the evils we bring on ourselves are the hardest to bear;

[作弄] make a fool of; play a trick on; tease;

[作嘔] (1) feel like vomiting; feel sick; nauseate; one's gorge rises; one's stomach rises; (2) disgusting; loathsome; (3) sicken;

[作陪] accompany; be invited along with the chief guest; escort; help entertain the guest of honour;

[作品] works;
作品評價 appraisal of literary works;
作品賞析 works appreciation;
作品欣賞 appreciation of literary works;
一套油畫作品 a series of oil paintings;

[作情] (1) admire sb; (2) intercede; mediate; (3) act with affected manners;

[作曲] compose; composition; set a song to music; write a song; write music;
作曲法 composition;
作曲家 composer;

[作人] (1) get along with other people; (2) behave oneself properly; pleasant in manner;

[作如是觀] view the matter in this light;

[作色] change facial expression;
憤然作色 cynical; detest the world and its ways; feel resentful and disgusted at the living reality of society;

[作善] do good turns;

[作舍道傍] difficult to succeed;

[作聲] break silence; make noise; speak;
默不作聲 abstain from speaking; as dumb as a fish; as mute as a fish; as silent as the grave; hold one's peace; hold one's tongue; keep one's mouth shut; keep quiet; keep silent; keep silence; keep still; pass over in silence; refrain from comment; remain silent; taciturn; wall of silence;

[作詩] write poems;

[作勢] assume a posture; pretend; put on airs;

[作壽] celebrate a birthday;

[作耍] (1) joke; make fun of; (2) make merry; play;

[作速] hurry up; make haste;

[作酸] jealous of;

[作祟] (1) haunt; (2) cause trouble; exercise evil influence; make mischief;
從中作祟 do mischief surreptitiously; play tricks in secret;

[作態] act pretentiously; affect; pose; strike an attitude;

[作痛] ache; cause pain; painful;

[作外] stand on ceremony;

[作王] be a king;

[作威] bossy;
作威作福 abuse one's power tyrannically;

act like a tyrant; assume great airs; bossy; domineer over; lord it over; play the tyrant; ride roughshod over others; sit on the back of; throw one's weight about; tyrannically abuse one's power;

逞志作威 intimidate people as one pleases without any scruples;

[作為] (1) action; behaviour; conduct; deed; (2) accomplish; do sth worthwhile;

大有作為 able to develop one's ability to the full; go a long way; have full scope for one's talents; have great possibilities; much can be accomplished; there is plenty of room to develop one's talents to the full;

敢作敢為 act with courage and determination; afraid of no difficulties; dare to do everything; decisive and bold in action; ready to take responsibility; take one's courage in both hands;

~敢作敢為的 ballsy;

胡作非為 act absurdly; act wildly; behave unscrupulously; break the law; commit all kinds of outrages; commit all manner of evil; commit evil acts; commit foolish acts; do all kinds of evil; do wrong; infamous conduct; misbehaviour; misconduct; misdeed; perpetrate whatever evil one pleases; play gangster; run amuck in society;

所作所為 all one's actions; the doings of; what one does; what one does and how one behaves;

無所作為 attempt nothing and accomplish nothing; in a state of inertia;

~無所作為的 supine;

有作為 capable of outstanding achievements;

有作有為 energetic and promising; person of action;

[作偽] fake; forge; make an imitation;

[作文] (1) write a composition; (2) composition;

[作物] (1) crop; cropper; (2) literary composition;

低產作物 light cropper;

高產作物 free cropper;

穀類作物 bread crop; cereal crop;

農作物 agronomic crop;

甜菜作物 beet crop;

誘餌作物 bait crop;

中耕作物 clean-cultivated crop;

[作息] work and rest;

作息習慣 work and rest routine;

作息制度 work-and-rest system;

按時作息 keep good hours; work and rest according to the time table;

出作入息 begin work at dawn and stop at dusk;

[作押] mortgage; offer sth as a pledge;

[作癢] itch;

[作業] (1) school assignments; students' homework; (2) job; operation; task; work;

作業系統 operating system;

成批作業 batch job;

帶電作業 hot-line work;

低溫作業 work at low temperature;

翻譯作業 translation assignment;

高空作業 work on high;

高溫作業 work at high temperature;

課程作業 coursework;

課堂作業 classwork;

課外作業 homework;

後備作業 background job;

家庭作業 homework;

~交家庭作業 hand in one's homework;

~歷史家庭作業 history homework;

~生物家庭作業 biology homework;

~做家庭作業 do one's homework;

鏈式作業 chain job;

判作業 mark an assignment;

水下作業 work under water;

脱機作業 off-line job;

危險性作業 hazardous work;

虛擬作業 dummy activity;

學校作業 school assignment;

[作俑] originate a wicked practice;

[作用] (1) act on; affect; (2) actions; functions; uses;

作用詞 operator;

~邏輯作用詞 logical operator;

爆破作用 blast action;

催化作用 catalytic action;

大氣作用 atmospheric action;

對抗作用 antagonistic action;

反向作用 backward acting;

防腐作用 antiseptic action;

防霧作用 antifogging action;

副作用 after-effect; by-effects; negative

effects; side effects;
蓋覆作用 coating action;
關鍵作用 central role; key role;
後作用 after-effect;
換位作用 metathesis;
積極作用 active role;
聚束作用 bunching action;
抗菌作用 antibacterial action;
抗炎作用 anrti-inflammatory action;
老化作用 ageing action;
累積作用 accumulative action;
聯合作用 associative action;
磨損作用 abrasive action;
黏結作用 cementing action;
漂白作用 bleaching action;
起決定性作用 tip the balance; turn the balance;
起作用 (1) play a part in; play a role in; serve as; (2) assert itself; become operative; operate; show effect; take effect; tell; work;
~不起作用 like water off a duck's back;
~起了不良作用 play an unwholesome role;
~傳統依然在起作用 tradition is still alive;
平衡作用 balancing action;
殺菌作用 bactericidal action;
失去作用 out of action;
雙重作用 dual role;
雙作用 double acting;
吸附作用 adsorptive action;
懸鏈作用 catenary action;
相互作用 interaction;
~大氣相互作用 atmospheric interaction;
~帶電流相互作用 charged-current interaction;
~化學相互作用 chemical interaction;
~行為相互作用 behaviour interaction;
延遲作用 delayed application;
抑菌作用 bacteriostatic action;
增效作用 building action;
直接作用 direct action;
致癌作用 carcinogenic action;
窒息作用 asphyxiant action;
重要作用 important role; major role; significant role;
阻塞作用 choking action;

[作樂] (1) compose; write music; (2) play music;

[作賊] be a thief;
作賊心虛 betray one's guilty conscience; have a guilty conscience;
誣人作賊 accuse sb of theft; falsely accuse sb of being a thief;

[作戰] conduct operations; do battle; fight; go to battle; make war;
兩棲作戰 amphibious warfare;

[作者] writer; author;
作者卡 author card;
作者署名行 byline;
作者姓名行 byline;
女作者 authoress;
無名氏作者 anonymous author;

[作證] act as a witness in court; bear witness; give evidence; testify;
可以作證 vouch for sth;
在法庭上作證 bear witness in a court; give evidence in court;

[作主] (1) decide; take the responsibility for a decision; (2) back up; support;
當家作主 master in one's own house;
自己作主 one's own master;
作不了主 cannot call one's soul on one's own; cannot decide oneself;

[作準] (1) count; valid; (2) authentic; valid;

扮作 disguise as; dress up to;
比作 compare to; liken to; take as;
操作 manipulate; manipulation; operate;
初作 first effort; maiden work;
創作 create; creation; creative work; produce;
大作 (1) your work; (2) erupt; explode;
動作 act; action; motion; movement;
發作 (1) break out; show effect; (2) flare up; have a fit of anger; lose one's temper;
耕作 cultivate; do farm work;
工作 (1) operation; performance; work; (2) job;
旱作 dry farming;
合作 between; collaborate; collaborate with; collaboration; cooperate; cooperate with; cooperation; join hands with; play ball with; work together;
畫作 painting;
佳作 excellent literary or artistic work;
間作 intercrop;
傑作 masterpiece; masterwork;
看作 be considered as; be regarded as; be thought of as; be viewed as; consider sth as; look on sth as; regard sth as; take sth as; think of sth as; view sth as;
勞作 manual labour class in school;

連作 continuous cropping;
壟作 ridge culture;
輪作 crop rotation;
擬作 work done in the manner of a certain author;
述作 compose and create; write;
瓦作 bricklayer; plasterer;
妄作 act wildly and illegally;
仵作 post-mortem examiner;
習作 do exercises in composition;
細作 secret agent; spy;
下作 (1) low; nasty; vulgar; (2) gluttonous; greedy;
協作 collaborate; collaboration; cooperate with; cooperation; joint efforts; work in coordination with;
寫作 pen and ink; pencraft; penmanship; writing;
興作 gain power; rise; (2) build; construct; establish; found;
佯作 bogus;
夜作 night shift;
傭作 be hired to do sth;
原作 original; original work;
運作 running;
造作 (1) make; (2) affectations; artificial; pretentious; unnatural;
振作 arouse oneself; bestir oneself; brace up; display vigour; exert oneself; pull oneself together;
制作 formulate;
製作 fabricate; make; manufacture;
著作 (1) books; works; writings; (2) write;
裝作 feign; pretend;
做作 affected; artificial; pretentious;

zuo

【坐】 (1) sit; take a seat; (2) ride; travel by; (3) kneel; (4) arrive at; reach; (5) have its back towards; (6) put on a fire; (7) sink; subside; (8) kick back; recoil; (9) because; owing to;

[坐標] coordinate;
坐標尺 coordinatometer;
坐標面 coordinate plane;
坐標系 coordinate system;
~ 地圖坐標系 map coordinates system;
坐標軸 coordinate axes;
笛卡兒坐標 Cartesian coordinates;
廣義坐標 generalized coordinates;
橫坐標 abscissa;
極坐標 polar coordinates;
~ 雙極坐標 bipolar coordinates;
角坐標 angular coordinates;
~ 雙角坐標 biangular coordinates;
絕對坐標 absolute coordinate;
面積坐標 area coordinates;
容許坐標 allowable coordinates;
天球坐標 celestial coordinates;
天文坐標 astronomical coordinates;
圓坐標 circle coordinates;
正交曲線坐標 curvilinear orthogonal coordinates;
直角坐標 rectangular coordinates;
重心坐標 areal coordinates; barycentric
縱坐標 ordinate;

[坐禪] sit in meditation;
坐禪悟道 sit in meditation and apprehend the doctrine of dao;

[坐車] ride a car;
坐車玩 have a joy ride;

[坐吃山空] always taking out of the meal-tub, and never putting in, soon comes to the bottom; consume without producing; sit at home eating away one's resources; sit idle and eat, and in time one's whole fortune will be used up; sit idle at home eating away a fortune as large as a mountain;

[坐次] order of the seats in a meeting or feast;

[坐大] emerge big and strong;

[坐待] sit back and wait;

[坐等] sit back and wait;
坐等時機 bide one's time; sitting and waiting for an opportunity;
坐等天明 sit and wait for daybreak;

[坐地] (1) sit on the ground; (2) do sth on the spot; on the spot;
坐地分贓 divide the loot on the spot;

[坐墊] seat cushion;
加高坐墊 booster seat;

[坐定] be seated; take a seat;

[坐而論道] sit and prattle about the general principle;

[坐骨] ischium; sciatic nerve;
坐骨的 sciatic;
坐骨結節 tuber ischiale;
坐骨疝 ischiatic hernia;
坐骨神經痛 sciatica;

[坐觀世變] sit and watch how the wind blows;

[坐館] (1) teach in a private school; (2) secretary of an official;

[坐懷不亂] not be disturbed with a woman in one's lap; wear Joseph's coat;
[坐賈] shopkeeper;
[坐井觀天] have a very limited perspective; look at the sky from the bottom of a well;
[坐困] be confined; be shut up; be walled in;
坐困愁城 be surrounded with griefs; be walled in by one's own worries; seclude oneself in the castle of grief; wallow in slough of despondency;
[坐牢] be imprisoned; be jailed; be shut behind the bars; be taken off to prison; commit a person to prison; go to prison; in jail; in prison; lay sb by the heels; put into prison; run in; send to prison;
[坐落] be located at; be situated at;
[坐山觀虎鬥] see both sides go for each other and not to involve oneself in it; sit on top of the mountain to watch the tigers fight;
[坐失] let sth slip by;
坐失良機 allow a golden opportunity to slip past; let a fine chance slip by; let a good opportunity slip by; let slip a golden opportunity; let slip an excellent opportunity; lose a good chance; miss the boat; watch a golden chance slip by;
當取不取，坐失良機 he that will not when he may, when he will he shall have nay;
坐失時機 allow an opportunity to escape; allow an opportunity to go by; allow an opportunity to lapse; allow an opportunity to pass; allow an opportunity to slip; let an opportunity slip; let slip the opportunity; let the chance fly by without moving a finger; miss the bus; suffer the occasion to slip;
[坐食] eat without toiling;
[坐視] keep hands off; sit by and watch; sit tight and look on; watching without extending a helping hand;
坐視不管 sit watching;
坐視不救 sit and look on unconcerned; sit back and watch without going to the rescue; sit idly by without lending a helping hand; sit still and not try to save; sit there and make no effort to save;
坐視不理 look on with folded arms; sit by idly and remain indifferent;
坐視無睹 sit with arms folded;
不忍坐視 cannot bear to sit and watch without doing anything; cannot bear to stand idly by;
[坐收漁利] profit from others' conflict; reap advantage from both sides without lifting a finger; reap the spoils of victory without lifting a finger; reap third-party profit; sit idle and rake in a profit;
[坐守] guard resolutely;
[坐位] (1) place to sit; seat; (2) seat; thing to sit on;
坐位數量 seating capacity;
[坐臥] sit down or sleep;
坐臥不安 in fidgets; on hot coals; on pins and needles; unable to sit down or sleep at ease;
坐臥不寧 can neither sit nor sleep at ease; feel restless; feel restless and uneasy; on tenterhooks; unable to sit down or sleep at ease;
[坐下] sit down;
重重地坐下 plop down;
[坐享] sit idle and enjoy;
坐享其成 enjoy the fruit of others' work; one beats the bush, and another catches the bird; reap where one has not sown; sit idle and enjoy the fruits of others' labour;
坐享其利 sit idle and enjoy the gains;
坐享清福 live in comfort without working;
坐享他人成果 feed on the fruits of other's labour;
[坐也不是，站也不是] feel uneasy; not to know whether to sit or stand; on edge;
[坐以待旦] quietly to wait for the day to dawn; remain awake till dawn; sit and wait for daybreak; sit and wait for the morning; sit up and wait for daybreak;
[坐着] sitting;
坐着不動 sit still;
筆直地坐着 sit up straight; sit upright;
靜靜地坐着 sit quietly;

舒服地坐着 sit comfortably;

[坐鎮] assume personal command; personally attend to garrison duty; personally take charge of;

[坐罪不貸] punish without leniency;

安坐 sit quietly;
打坐 sit in meditation;
趺坐 sit cross-legged;
獨坐 sit all by oneself;
對坐 sit opposite to each other;
蹲坐 crouch; squat on the heels;
靜坐 (1) sit quietly; (2) sit still as a form of therapy;
起坐 rise from one's seat as a form of respect;
跂坐 sit with legs hanging above the ground;
肅坐 sit erect and in silence;
徒坐 sit in leisure; sit without doing anything;
團坐 sit around in a circle;
危坐 sit rigidly;
兀坐 sit upright;
圍桌而坐 sit around the table;
閒坐 sit at leisure; sit idle;

Z

zuo

【怍】 (1) ashamed; shame; (2) blush; change colour;

[怍色] blush; colour; feel ashamed;

[怍意] be ashamed; feel ashamed;

愧怍 ashamed;

zuo

【阼】 (1) main steps; (2) throne;

zuo

【座】 (1) place; seat; (2) pedestal; stand; (3) constellation;

[座艙] cockpit;
後座艙 rear cockpit;
機頭座艙 front cockpit;
全密閉座艙 totally-enclosed cockpit;

[座次] seating order;

[座落] be located at; be situated at;

[座上客] guest of honour; honoured guest;
座上客常滿，樽中酒不空 keep a good house;

[座談] have an informal discussion;
座談會 discussion meeting; forum; informal discussion; symposium;

[座位] place; seat;
座位安排 seating arrangements; seating plan;
座位卡 place card;
座位牌 place card;
調換座位 exchange seats;
兒童座位 child seat;
後面座位 back seat;
後排座位 back seat; rear seat;
靠窗座位 window seat;
靠通道座位 aisle seat;
空座位 spare seat;
留座位 save sb a seat;
露天座位 bleachers;
汽車座位 car seat;
前排乘客座位 passenger seat;
前排座位 front seat; front-row seat;
頭等座位 first-class seat;
一排座位 a row of seats;
嬰兒座位 baby seat;
預訂座位 book a seat; reserve a seat;

[座無虛席] all seats are occupied; every seat is occupied; have a full house; have no empty seat; with every seat taken;

[座椅] seat;
加高座椅 booster seat;
彈射座椅 ejection seat; ejector seat;

[座右銘] maxim; motto; permanent reminder; precept;
銘之座右 engrave a motto on a tablet and put it on the desk so as to always look at it;

[座鐘] desk clock;

[座子] rack; stand;

鞍座 saddle;
白羊座 Aries;
半人馬座 Centaurus;
賓女座 Virgo;
寶瓶座 Aquarius;
寶座 throne;
北冕座 Corona Borealis;
波江座 Eridanus;
豺狼座 Lupus;
蒼蠅座 Musca;
插座 outlet; socket;
茶座 (1) teahouse; (2) seats in a teahouse or tea garden;
長蛇座 Hydra;
池座 stalls;
船底座 Carina;
船帆座 Vela;
船尾座 Puppis;
大犬座 Canis Major;

大熊座 Ursa Major;
帶座 show to a seat;
單座 single seat;
燈座 lamp socket;
底座 base; foundation;
雕具座 Caelum;
訂座 make a reservation; reservation;
杜鵑座 Tucana;
盾牌座 Scutum;
飛馬座 Pegasus;
飛魚座 Volans;
鳳凰座 Phoenix;
海豚座 Delphinus;
盒座 cassette holder;
後發座 Coma Berenices;
後座 back seat; backstand;
狐狸座 Vulpecula;
機座 stand;
唧筒座 Antlia;
加座 temporary extra seat;
劍魚座 Dorado;
講座 lecture; series of lectures;
叫座 appeal to the audience; draw a large audience; draw well;
金牛座 Taurus;
就座 be seated; take one's seat;
舉座 every one present;
巨爵座 Crater;
巨蛇座 Serpens;
巨蟹座 Cancer;
矩尺座 Norrrtai;
均座 your excellency;
孔雀座 Pavo;
獵戶座 Orion;
獵犬座 Canes Venatici;
六分儀座 Sextans;
樓座 seats in the gallery of a theatre;
鹿豹座 Camelopardalis;
羅盤座 Pyxis;
落座 take one's seat;
賣座 attract large numbers of customers; draw large audiences;
滿座 capacity audience; capacity house; full house;
摩羯座 Capricorn;
末座 most inferior seat at the table;
牧夫座 Bootes;
南極座 Octans;
南冕座 Corona Australis;
南三角座 Triangulum Australe;
南十字座 Crux;
南魚座 Piscis Austrinus;
砲座 gun platform;
礮座 barbette; gun platform;
麒麟座 Monoceros;
前座 front bench;
鯨魚座 Cetus;
球座 tee;
讓座 give up one's seat to sb; offer one's seat to sb; yield a seat;
入座 take one's seat;
人馬座 Centaur; Sagittarius;
三角座 Triangulum;
上座 (1) seat of honour; (2) customers begin to come into a place;
蛇夫座 Ophiuchus;
獅子座 Leo;
室女座 Virgo;
時鐘座 Horologium;
首座 head of the table; seat of honour;
雙魚座 Pisces;
雙子座 Gemini;
水蛇座 Hydrus;
四座 all the people present;
胎座 placenta;
天鵝座 Cygnus;
天鴿座 Columba;
天鶴座 Grus;
天箭座 Sagitta;
天龍座 Draco;
天爐座 Fornax;
天貓座 Lynx;
天秤座 Libra;
天琴座 Lyra;
天壇座 Ara;
天兔座 Lepus;
天蠍座 Scorpius;
天鷹座 Aquila;
網罟座 Reticulum;
望遠鏡座 Telescopium;
尾座 tailstock;
烏鴉座 Corvus;
武仙座 Hercules;
下座 inferior seat;
蠍虎座 Lacerta;
仙后座 Cassiopeia;
仙女座 Andromeda;
仙王座 Cepheus;
顯微鏡座 Microscopimn;
小馬座 Equuleus;
小犬座 Canis Minor;
小獅座 Leo.Minor;
小熊座 Ursa Minor;
星座 constellation;

雅座 comfortable seats; private room;
蝘蜓座 Chamaeleon;
椅座 seat;
英仙座 Perseus;
印第安座 Indus;
玉夫座 Sculptor;
御夫座 Auriga;
圓規座 Circinus;
在座 be present at a meeting;
枕座 pillow;
正座 sets in the stalls;
支座 support;
柱座 column base;

zuo
【柞】 oak;
［柞蠶］ tussah silkworms;
柞蠶絲 tussur silk;
［柞樹］ oak; oak tree;

zuo
【胙】 (1) sacrificial meat; (2) blessings from heaven; (3) (now rare) report;
［胙肉］ sacrificial meat;

zuo
【祚】 (1) blessing; (2) throne; (3) year;
［祚命］ heavenly blessing;

帝祚 throne;
踐祚 ascend the throne; be enthroned;

zuo
【做】 (1) make; manufacture; produce; (2) compose; write; (3) do; engage in; (4) hold a family celebration; (5) be used as; (6) form or contract a relationship; (7) be; (8) cook; prepare;
［做愛］ a bit of meat; a Donald Duck; a leg-over; a meat injection; a navel engagement; a quick snort; a quickie; a ride; at it; bill and coo; boff sb; boffing; bonk sb; bump tummies; cattle; cattle truck; cut off a slice; diddle; dip one's wick; do the business; dunk; end to end; fuck; get a bit; get a jump; get it on; get off with sb; get one's leg over; get one's oats; give it to sb; grind; have a bit; have a bit off with sb; have a jump; have a quickie; have a roll; have it with sb; have it away with sb; have it off with sb; have sex; have sexual relations; horizontal exercise; jig-a-lig; jiggady-jig; jump; make a baby; make babies; make it with; make love; mush; naughty; nookie; perform sexual intercourse; play bouncy-bouncy; play hide the sausage; poke; pole; porking; push in the truck; put-and-take; ride sb; rumpy-pumpy; rumpty-tumpty; score with; screw; screw the arse off sb; shaft; shag; shagging; slip it to sb; slip sb a fatty; slip sb a length; stuff sb; tear off a piece; thread the needle; tummy-tickling; tup with sb;
［做伴］ keep sb company;
［做菜］ do the cooking; prepare a meal;
［做出］ come to; make;
做出成績 make good;
做出貢獻 make a great contribution;
做出決定 come to a decision; make a decision;
［做錯］ make mistakes;
一做就錯 whatever one does goes wrong;
［做大］ put on airs;
［做到］ achieve; accomplish;
［做得了］ can be done;
［做東］ act as a host to sb; host sb; play the host;
［做法］ method of work; practice; way of doing or making a thing;
標準做法 standard practice;
［做飯］ cook a meal; do the cooking; prepare a meal; prepare food;
正在做飯 be in the middle of cooking a meal;
［做工］ (1) do manual work; work; (2) workmanship;
做工粗劣 of poor workmanship;
做工精美 of excellent workmanship;
做工精細 fine workmanship;
［做官］ become an official; join government service; secure oneself an official position;
朝中有人好做官 one may be recommended and put in an important position if his relatives or friends have status and power;
叫化三年懶做官 the beggar is never out of his way;
［做鬼］ get up to mischief; play an underhand

game; play tricks;

[做好] do sth well;
做不好 cannot do sth well;

[做假] cheat;
做假帳 manipulation of account;

[做絕] (1) leave no room for manoeuver; (2) do to the utmost;

[做客] guest;

[做闊] make a display of one's riches; show off one's wealth;

[做媒] matchmaking;

[做夢] (1) dream; have a dream; (2) daydream; have a pipe dream;
做夢也想不到 beyond one's wildest dreams;
在做夢 in one's dreams;
做白日夢 build castles in the air;

[做弄] make fun of; play jokes on;

[做親] become relatives by marriage;

[做情] intercede;

[做人] (1) behave; conduct oneself; (2) upright person;
做人處世 conduct oneself in society;
做人情 do sb a good turn; give sb a favour;
做人宗旨 one's middlename;
重新做人 begin one's life anew; lead a new life; make a fresh start in life; start one's life afresh; start with a new slate; turn over a new leaf;
好好做人 behave well in society;

[做聲] make a sound; speak;
不做聲 keep silent; not say a word; say nothing;

[做事] (1) act; do a deed; handle affairs; (2) have a job; work;
做事本分 hew to the line;
做事不得法 begin at the wrong end; start at the wrong end;
做事過份 go overboard;
做事敏捷 quick and efficient in one's work;
做事情 work;
做事認真 conscientious in one's work;
做事小心點 watch what one is doing;
安心做事 keep one's mind on sth;
暗中做事 do things in an underhand way;
幫人做事 lend sb a hand in doing sth;
輪班做事 take turns to do things;

[做壽] celebrate a birthday; hold a birthday party;

[做頭] advantage to be gained from some activities; expected results;

[做戲] (1) act in a play; (2) play-act; put on a show;

[做小] be sb's concubine;

[做眼] gather intelligence;

[做賬] keep accounts;
創造性做賬 creative accounting;

[做主] decide; responsible for; take charge of;

[做莊] be the banker;

[做作] affected; artificial; pretentious;
做作的 stagy;

當做 regard as; take sth as;
定做 have sth made to order;
訂做 customize;
叫做 be called; be known as;
就是想那樣做 for the sake of it;
說做 what is said and what is done;
有很多工作要做 have a lot on one's plate;

zuo

【酢】 pour wine for the host; toast for the host;

酬酢 (1) have an exchange of toasts; (2) have social intercourse with; treat with courtesy;

Z

筆劃索引 Stroke Index

1. 本索引按筆劃數由少到多順序排列。
The index is arranged in accordance with the stroke numbers increasingly.
2. 同劃數的，按起筆筆形橫〔一〕、豎〔丨〕、撇〔丿〕、點〔丶〕、折〔乛〕順序排列。
As to characters with the same stroke number, the sequence is arranged in accordance with the starting stroke of horizontal〔一〕, vertical〔丨〕, left-falling stroke〔丿〕, dot〔丶〕, and the turning stroke〔乛〕.

1 劃

一 2796
乙 2846

2 劃

〔一〕

二 605
丁 534
3103
十 2055
七 1680

〔丨〕

卜 186

〔丿〕

人 1861
入 1917
八 35
38
乃 1552
九 1198
几 1013
1042
匕 116

〔乛〕

刁 528
了 1329
1382
刀 469
力 1347
又 2946
乜 1507
1585

3 劃

〔一〕

三 1931
亍 366
于 2949
干 730
土 2352
士 2078
工 769
才 226
下 2517
寸 415
丈 3070
大 430
446
兀 2478

〔丨〕

上 1972
1973
小 2580
口 1275
山 1954
巾 1157

〔丿〕

千 1725
乞 1698
川 369
彳 330
丸 2382
久 1199
么 2774
凡 627
勺 1983
夕 2506

〔丶〕

亡 2395
丫 2718

〔乛〕

尸 2044
己 1042
已 2846
巳 2190
弓 776
子 3246
孑 1141
孓 1224
也 2786
女 1599
刃 1888
叉 258
265

4 劃

〔一〕

王 2397
井 1187
天 2278
夫 697
元 2987
云 3013
丐 729
1496
扎 3048
3049
廿 1580
木 1540
五 2473
支 3127
卅 1929
不 186
189
仄 3045
太 2235
犬 1840
友 2936
尤 2927
歹 446
592
匹 1635
1644
厄 592
巨 1216
牙 2722
屯 2364
戈 755
2852
旡 1044
比 116
互 941
切 1764
1765

〔丨〕

止 3152
少 1983
日 1894
曰 3004
中 3172
3184
內 1565
水 2159

〔丿〕

丰 678
午 2474
手 2113
牛 1589
毛 1464
壬 1886
夭 2774
2780
仁 1885
什 1986
2056
仃 535
片 1646
1648
仆 1674
仇 343
1810
仍 1893
化 953
仂 1328
斤 1158
爪 3079
3216
反 630
兮 2488
刈 2852
介 1152
父 709
713
爻 2777
今 1157
凶 2663
分 664
675
公 776
月 3005
氏 2079
3130
勿 2479
欠 1746
丹 453
匀 3013
勾 793
796
及 1030
殳 2129

〔丶〕

卞 140
之 3120
六 1409
1419
文 2436
2448
亢 1250
方 639
火 1001
斗 554
戶 943
冗 1906
心 2605

〔乛〕

尹 2887
夬 821
尺 294
325
328
弔 530
引 2887
丑 346
孔 1272

巴 36
以 2847
允 3016
予 2949
2960
毋 2457
幻 970

5 劃

〔一〕

玉 2972
刊 1245
未 2424
末 1532
示 2085
打 422
424
巧 1760
正 3103
3110
扑 1674
卉 986
扒 37
1606
扔 1893
功 784
去 1827
瓦 2374
甘 731
世 2082
古 802
本 107
札 3049
朮 3198
可 1259
1262
叵 1670
匜 3023
丙 167
左 3295
冊 2506
丕 1635
右 2946
石 459
2056
布 217
夯 882
戊 2479
犮 179
平 1660
匝 2837
戉 3008

〔丨〕

卡 1237
1723
北 99
凸 2345
占 3054
3058
且 1765
旦 459
目 1542
叮 535
甲 1072
申 1998
冉 1852
田 2291
由 2927
冊 253
只 3153
叭 37
史 2074
央 2762
兄 2664
叱 330
叼 529
叩 1279
叫 1127
另 1401
叨 470
2254
皿 1512
1525
凹 30
囚 1810
四 2190

〔丿〕

生 2020
失 2044
矢 2075
乍 3050
禾 899
仨 1928
丘 1807
仕 2085
付 714
仗 3070
代 446
仙 2524
仟 1729
仡 756
白 45
179
仔 3254
他 2229
仞 1888
斥 330
卮 3130
瓜 817
仝 2317
乏 616
乎 931
令 1393
1400
用 2918
甩 2154
肊 2852
氐 492
497
句 793
1215
匆 401
卯 1466
犯 635
外 2376
冬 542
包 74
孕 3016

〔丶〕

主 3201
市 2079
庀 1644
立 1350
玄 2687
半 65
汀 2305
汁 3130
氾 635
忉 470
宁 3208
穴 2694
它 2229
宄 846
必 122
永 2914

〔乛〕

司 2176
尻 1252
尼 1571
民 1508
弗 699
弘 919
疋 1644
出 347
奶 1552
奴 1596
加 1062
召 3080
皮 1638
弁 140
台 2232
矛 1465
母 1539
幼 2946

6 劃

〔一〕

匡 1291
玎 535
式 2086
刑 2642
刓 2382
戎 1900
扞 879
扛 1250
寺 2193
圭 842
艾 8
芀 1553
吉 1031
扣 1280
扦 1729
托 2365
考 1252
老 1322
扱 259
2491
圯 2837
地 499
扠 258
邛 1803
耳 601
共 791
朽 2674
朴 1670
1676
再 3027
臣 297
吏 1352
西 2488
亙 766
戌 2676
在 3028
有 2937
2947
百 50
179
存 413
而 597
匠 1110
夸 1285
灰 979
戍 2143
列 1384
死 2184
成 305
夷 2837
划 951

〔丨〕

此 398
乩 1013
尖 1081
劣 1385
光 835
吁 2676
早 3036
吐 2354
2355
吋 416
旯 1305
曳 2789
曲 1815
1824
同 2317
吊 530
吃 321
1032
吒 3050
因 2874
吆 2774
屹 2852
帆 623
回 982
屺 1701
至 3157
肉 1907

〔丿〕

年 1575
朱 3195
耒 1331
缶 696
氖 1553
先 2525
牝 1659
丢 542
舌 1986
竹 3198
印 2895
乒 1659
乓 1619
休 2668
伍 2475
伎 1044
伏 699
臼 1203
1210
伐 616
仳 1644
仲 3185
仵 2475
件 1094
任 1886
1888
份 676
仰 2768
仮 1031
仿 647
伉 1250
伙 1005
自 3257
伊 2827
血 2601

2706
向 2565
囟 2629
似 2193
后 926
行 882
2642
2654
舟 3190
全 1830
合 900
兆 3080
企 1699
汆 410
兇 2665
刖 3008
肌 1013
肋 1328
1332
夙 2203
危 2410
旨 3153
旬 2711
旭 2682
旮 726
犴 22
刎 2446
匈 2665
舛 376
各 761
名 1513
多 582
586
色 1942
1954

〔丶〕

冰 162
庄 3224
亦 2852
交 1112
次 398
衣 2827
2852
亥 871
充 332
妄 2403
邙 1462
羊 2763
并 164
169
米 1491
州 3190
汗 874
879
污 2454
江 1105
汕 1962
汎 637
汐 2506
汛 2715
汜 2193
池 325
汝 1915
汊 265
忖 415
忙 1461
宇 2961
守 2120
宅 3052
字 3255
安 13
礽 1894

〔乛〕

聿 2974
艮 766
弛 325
2075
收 2108
艸 250
丞 305
奸 21
1080
如 1909
奼 265
妁 2175
妃 652
好 891
895
她 2229
羽 2961
牟 1537
阢 2479
阡 1729

7 劃

〔乛〕

阨 592

〔一〕

玕 734
弄 1414
1595
玖 1199
迂 2948
形 2649
戒 1153
邢 2653
吞 2363
扶 700
技 1045
抔 1674
扼 592
拒 1217
找 3079
批 1635
芋 2975
址 3153
扯 295
走 3277
芊 1729
抄 287
芃 1632
芄 2384
芍 1983
芒 1462
芎 1803
汞 790
924
攻 787
赤 331
折 1988
3084
3085
抓 3215
坂 62
扳 58
扮 67
孝 2587
坎 1247
均 1232
坍 2238
抑 2853
抛 1622
圾 1946
投 2332
抃 141
抆 2448
坊 643
坑 1267
抗 1250
抖 555
志 3158
抉 1224
扭 1591
把 41
42
抒 2129
劫 1141
毐 6
芚 2365
克 1262
杆 733
杜 565
杠 742
材 228
村 413
杖 3071
杙 2854
杏 2654
杉 1960
巫 2454
杓 1983
杞 1701
李 1341
杈 259
266
求 1810
孛 99
車 291
1207
甫 709
匣 2515
更 766
768
束 2143
吾 2458
豆 555
酉 2945
辰 300
否 697
1644
夾 1065
1072
尨 1484
1620
豕 2076
尬 726
忒 2262
邪 2594
2786

〔丨〕

邶 100
忐 2245
步 219
卣 2945
肖 2588
旰 741
旱 879
盯 535
呈 311
貝 99
見 1095
2538
助 3210
里 1341
呆 445
吱 3240
吠 659
呃 592
呀 2718
2727
町 535
2310
足 1217
3281
男 1554
刪 1959
困 1299
吵 291
串 376
吶 1551
呂 1425
吟 2883
吩 672
別 157
吻 2446
吹 381
吸 2488
吳 2458
呎 329
吧 37
42
45
吼 926
邑 2854
囤 2364
吮 2169
岐 1687
岑 257
岌 1033
兕 2194
囫 934

〔丿〕

邦 70
牡 1538
1540
告 754
牠 2229
我 2452
廷 2308
利 1352
禿 2345
秀 2674
私 2177
迄 1710
每 1476
佞 1589
兵 164
估 798
813
何 904
佐 3297
佑 2947
佈 218
佔 3058
攸 2921
但 459
伸 1999
佃 514
佚 2852
作 3295
3297
伯 179
伶 1393

佣 2921
低 492
你 1572
侚 794
佟 2323
住 3208
位 2425
伴 67
佇 3210
佗 2370
皁 3039
身 1222
1999
皂 3039
伺 400
2193
佛 696
伽 1065
1765
役 2852
彷 647
1620
佘 1988
余 2949
希 2491
坐 3302
谷 805
2975
孚 700
妥 2371
豸 3159
含 874
岔 265
邠 159
肝 733
肚 564
566
肛 743
肘 3193
肐 756
肜 1900
甸 514
免 1496
劬 1823
狂 1292
狄 494
角 1122
1226
1419
狃 1592
狁 3016
彤 2323
卵 1430
灸 1199
刨 86
1622
系 2506

〔丶〕

言 2731
亨 915
庋 1043
庇 123
疔 535
吝 1392
冷 1334
序 2682
迒 883
辛 2623
肓 972
冶 2787
忘 2398
2404
判 1618
兑 574
灶 3041
灼 3236
弟 507
2276
汪 2394
沅 2988
沐 1546
沛 1628
沔 1497
汰 2236
沌 581
沏 1681
沚 3154
沙 1947
汨 1492
2975
汩 805
沖 334
汭 1923
汽 1708
沃 2452
沂 2837
汾 673
汲 1033
沒 1471
1533
汴 141
汶 2448
沆 883
885
沈 2014
沉 297
沁 1777
決 1224
沇 2747
忮 3159
忡 335
忤 2475
忻 2623
忪 3177
忭 141
忱 297
快 1287
忸 1591
1600
完 2382
宋 2198
宏 920
牢 1318
究 1197
1203
良 1370
初 358
社 1989
祀 2194
祁 1690
罕 878
邲 124

〔乛〕

君 1231
那 1550
1551
1564
1568
即 1032
1044
迅 2715
屁 1645
尿 1583
尾 2420
局 1210
改 726
忌 1045
孜 3240
壯 3228
妝 3224
弛 2837
2850
妍 2731
妓 1044
妣 118
妙 1506
妊 1890
妖 2774
妨 643
644
妒 565
妞 1589
妤 2950
姒 2194
劭 1985
忍 1886
努 1597
甬 2915
邰 2234
矣 2850
阱 1187
阮 1920
阯 3154
阪 62
阬 1267
防 644
朶 587
糺 1199
災 3025
巡 2711

8 劃

〔一〕

柜 1212
奉 694
玩 2384
武 2475
青 1777
玫 1472
玠 1142
1154
表 152
玦 1227
盂 2951
忝 2293
抹 1532
1533
長 275
3067
3071
卦 819
坩 734
坷 1261
坯 1636
拓 2230
2371
拔 38
坪 1665
抨 1632
芙 703
芫 2988
芸 3013
拈 1575
1580
芾 661
703
芰 1048
芣 703
苣 1218
芽 2724
芷 3154
苡 2850
芮 1923
芼 1466
花 945
芹 1773
芥 1154
芩 1774
芬 672
芡 1747
芟 1960
芝 3135
芳 643
芯 2624
2629
坦 2246
坤 1298
押 2718
抽 341
拐 820
芭 38
拖 2366
拊 710
拍 1607
1671
者 3088
拆 266
坼 295
拎 1393
抵 498
拘 1208
抱 86
拄 3207
拉 1303
1305
垃 1304
幸 2655
拌 68
1618
抿 1512
拂 124
701
拙 3237
招 3074
坡 1669
披 1626
1637
拚 1618
亞 2725
2727
拇 1540
坳 32
拗 32
1592
其 1687
取 1824
邯 876
昔 2496
苹 1666
直 3138
苺 1473
枉 2400
林 1387
枝 3130
杯 95

枒 2724
枇 1641
杪 1506
杳 2780
柄 1923
杵 362
枚 1472
析 2491
板 62
枌 673
松 2195
杭 883
枋 643
杰 1142
枕 3097
杷 1607
杼 3211
軋 726
2727
3049
東 543
或 1005
臥 2452
事 2087
刺 400
兩 1373
雨 2962
2975
郕 167
協 2595
邳 1627
矻 1284
矽 2508
奈 1553
剞 1281
1286
奔 105
111
奇 1014
1688
奄 2727
2747
來 1306
亟 1033
殀 2780
歿 1533
郙 315
妻 1681
1710
迓 2727
迍 3234
戔 1082
到 472
郅 3165

〔丨〕

叔 2129
歧 1690
肯 1266
1267
些 2593
芈 1492
1507
卓 3237
虎 939
尚 1981
盱 2676
旺 2405
具 1217
昊 896
味 2427
杲 753
果 859
昃 3045
昆 1298
咕 799
昌 274
門 1480
呵 899
1603
咂 3023
昇 2019
2033
呸 1626
昕 2623
明 1519
易 2854
昀 3013
昂 29
旻 1512
昉 647
畀 124
呫 3055
甿 1484
虯 1813
典 510
固 813
忠 3178
咀 1212
呻 2004
咒 3193
咋 3041
3050
咐 715
呱 799
呼 932
咚 543
咆 1623
呢 1564
1571
咄 588
咖 726
1237
岸 22
岩 2738
岥 703
帖 2302
2305
岬 1073
岫 2675
帙 3163
帕 1606
岭 1393
岷 1512
帔 1628
困 1232
沓 2230
囹 1393
岡 743
罔 2400

〔丿〕

非 652
卸 2601
郏 3195
迮 2475
制 3159
知 3131
氛 672
迮 3042
牧 1546
物 2479
乖 820
刮 818
和 905
911
季 1048
委 2407
2420
竺 3200
秉 167
佳 1065
侍 2093
岳 3008
佬 1327
邱 1807
供 788
793
使 2076
2094
侑 2947
例 1355
臾 2951
兒 597
版 64
岱 449
延 2738
侃 1247
侏 3195
佻 2295
佾 2854
佩 1628
侈 329
隹 3230
佼 1123
依 2831
佯 2764
併 170
佗 266
帛 179
卑 95
的 486
494
507
阜 715
卹 2683
欣 2623
近 1165
征 3103
徂 408
往 2398
2405
爬 1606
佛 701
彼 118
所 2222
舠 470
返 634
舍 1988
1989
金 1158
刹 266
1949
1952
命 1525
肴 2777
斧 710
爸 42
受 2123
爭 3104
乳 1915
采 234
237
念 1580
攽 159
忿 676
肺 660
肢 3135
肱 789
肫 3234
肸 2508
朋 1632
股 805
肪 643
647
服 701
肥 657
周 3191
邸 499
昏 993
兔 2355
狙 1209
狎 2515
狐 934
忽 934
狗 794
狒 661
咎 1203
炙 3163
迎 2902
2909

〔丶〕

冽 1385
京 1173
享 2562
店 514
夜 2789
府 709
底 497
庖 1623
疝 1962
疙 756
疚 1203
卒 3282
忞 1512
庚 767
放 648
於 2455
2950
妾 1767
盲 1462
刻 1255
1262
劾 905
育 2974
氓 1462
1484
羌 1748
券 1841
卷 1223
並 169
炬 1218
炖 581
炒 291
炘 2624
炊 382
炕 1252
炎 2740
沫 1479
1533
法 617
623
泔 734
沽 801
沭 2144
河 907

沾 3054
沮 1209
1212
1217
油 2928
泱 2762
況 1293
泂 1196
泅 1813
泗 2194
泆 2855
泊 179
1671
泝 2203
泛 637
沴 1356
泠 1393
沿 2739
泖 1466
泡 1622
1624
注 3211
泣 1710
泮 1619
沱 2370
泌 124
1492
泳 2915
泥 1571
1573
泯 1512
沸 660
泓 920
沼 3080
波 174
1669
治 3138
3162
泑 1328
怯 1767
怙 943
怵 366
怖 221
怦 1632
怗 2302
怛 422
怏 2772
怳 978
性 2656
怍 3304
怕 1606
怜 1360
1393
怩 1571
怫 659
701
怓 1560
怪 821
怡 2837
宗 3271
定 537
宕 468
宜 2837
宙 3194
官 821
空 1267
1273
帘 1360
穸 2508
宛 2386
穹 1803
宓 1492
戾 1355
肩 1082
房 645
扂 944
衫 1960
衩 266
社 3154
祆 2527
2775
祈 1690
祇 1691
3154

〔乛〕

帚 3193
屆 1154
居 1207
刷 2152
屄 113
屈 1817
弧 934
弦 2529
弨 287
承 311
孟 1488
戕 1750
牀 379
狀 3229
孤 800
孢 77
函 875
妹 1479
姑 799
妲 422
姐 1149
妯 3193
姍 1960
姓 2655
姊 1150
3254
妳 1572
妮 1572
始 2077
帑 2254
弩 1597
孥 1596
姆 1540
虱 2049
邵 1985
彔 1419
阿 1
590
阻 3283
阼 3304
附 715
陀 2370
陂 1641
1669
糾 1197
1199

9 劃

〔丶〕

洚 1111

〔一〕

耔 3254
契 1711
1767
奏 3279
春 385
珂 1257
玷 515
珊 1960
玳 451
珀 1671
珍 3091
玲 1393
珉 1512
珈 1066
玻 176
毒 558
型 2653
拭 2095
封 678
持 325
拮 1142
拷 1253
邽 842
拑 1735
拱 790
垮 1286
城 313
茉 1533
苦 1282
苯 111
苛 1257
政 3114
苿 1644
1654
若 1925
茇 40
赴 718
赳 1198
1199
茂 1467
1538
苫 1960
苜 1547
苴 261
1209
苒 1854
苗 1504
英 2897
茌 327
苻 704
荼 1585
苓 1393
苟 795
茆 1466
苑 2988
3002
苞 78
范 637
苧 3213
苾 124
拽 2791
3216
茀 704
哉 3026
茁 3237
苕 2295
茄 1765
苔 2232
2234
茅 1465
括 818
1300
垢 796
耇 796
拴 2155
拾 1992
2059
挑 2294
2299
指 3140
垓 726
拼 1654
挓 3048
挖 2373
按 22
垠 2884
拯 3108
拶 3023
3032
某 1538
甚 1988
2015
耶 2786
革 759
1035
苣 268
巷 2566
苙 1356
故 814
胡 935
剋 1264
南 1550
1555
柰 1554
柑 734
枻 2855
枯 1281
柯 1255
柄 167
170
柘 3090
柩 1203
枰 1666
查 261
3048
相 2548
2567
柙 2515
枵 2571
柚 2947
枳 3154
柷 3213
柞 3306
柎 698
柏 54
180
柝 2372
柢 499
柵 1960
3050
枸 795
1212
柳 1409
枹 704
柱 3212
柿 2098
柁 588
2370
柮 588
枷 1066
述 2144
勃 180
軌 846
剌 1305
要 2775
2781
酊 536
柬 1088
咸 2530

威 2407
歪 2375
盃 96
甭 112
研 2742
頁 2791
厚 926
砒 1637
郁 2975
砌 1711
砂 1949
泵 112
斫 3237
砍 1247
面 1498
耐 1553
要 2153
奎 1296
耷 421
郟 1072
虺 980
985
殂 408
殃 2763
殄 2294
殆 450
皆 1135
毖 124
到 1187
勁 1167
1190

〔丨〕

韭 1199
背 96
100
貞 3092
3105
虐 1601
省 2039
2653
削 2693
昧 1479
昞 1497
盹 581
是 2095
眇 1506
昺 168
眊 1468
盻 2508
則 3041
盼 1619
易 2766
眈 454
哇 2373
2375
哎 3
哄 918
924
冒 1466
映 2909
閂 2156
禺 2951
2975
哂 2014
星 2637
昳 533
2855
昨 3295
咧 1384
眗 2680
曷 909
昴 1466
昱 2975
咦 2838
昭 3077
迪 495
畎 1841
畏 2429
毗 1641
趴 1606
胃 2430
冑 3194
畋 2292
界 1154
虹 923
虼 762
虻 1484
思 2178
盅 3179
品 1657
咽 2727
2757
2791
咱 3032
囿 2947
呷 2834
哈 865
865
咯 759
1410
1439
1443
哆 586
咬 2780
咳 865
871
1238
1258
咪 1488
峙 3163
耑 569
3216
炭 2247
罘 704
峒 2323
峋 2712
迴 1196
幽 2922

〔丿〕

舂 1006
缸 743
拜 55
看 1245
1247
矩 1212
迭 533
矧 2014
氟 704
牯 806
怎 3046
垂 383
郜 755
牲 2033
牴 499
臿 263
秬 1218
秕 119
秒 1506
香 2555
种 339
秔 1173
秋 1807
科 1255
重 337
3185
竽 2951
竿 735
迤 2850
段 571
便 141
1648
俠 2515
舁 2951
叟 2201
俏 1762
俚 1341
保 78
促 408
侶 1425
俄 590
592
俐 1356
侮 2476
俗 2202
俘 703
係 2508
信 2630
皇 974
泉 1835
皈 842
侵 1768
迫 1671
禹 2963
侯 925
侷 1211
帥 2155
2175
偲 2239
俑 2915
俟 2194
俊 1235
盾 581
待 446
449
徊 961
984
徇 2712
2715
徉 2764
衍 2747
律 1428
很 914
後 927
舡 371
舢 1960
釓 726
釔 2850
俞 2951
弇 2748
剉 417
俎 3284
郤 1843
爰 2988
食 2060
2194
盆 1631
胠 1819
胚 1626
胛 1073
胙 3306
胗 3092
胝 3136
胞 77
胖 1615
1621
胐 659
胎 2232
匍 1676
矦 925
負 716
郇 2712
勉 1497
奐 970
風 679
695
狡 1123
狩 2126
狠 915
觔 1162
訇 918
朐 1823
昝 3032
怨 3001
急 1033
胤 2896
盈 2903

〔丶〕

訂 541
計 1049
訃 716
哀 1
亭 2308
亮 1377
度 566
587
弈 2855
奕 2855
庥 2670
疣 2930
彥 2757
疥 1155
疫 2855
疤 38
兗 2747
庠 2560
郊 1118
施 2049
咨 3240
姿 3241
音 2876
帝 507
斿 2931
美 1476
姜 1106
叛 1619
卷 1829
籽 3254
前 1735
酋 1813
首 2122
炳 168
炯 1196
炸 3049
3050
炮 77
炷 3213
炫 2692
炤 3080
剃 2276
為 2414
2428
洱 604
洪 920
洧 2422
洏 600
洒 1929

洌 1385
柒 1682
洟 2838
沘 398
洸 839
洩 2602
洞 545
洄 984
洙 2129
3195
洗 2501
2535
活 999
洑 704
洎 1048
洫 2683
派 1614
洽 1724
2515
洮 2255
2777
染 1852
洵 2712
洶 2665
洛 1439
洋 2765
洴 1666
洲 3192
津 1161
洳 1919
恇 1291
恃 2095
恒 915
恓 2491
恢 980
恍 978
恫 545
2312
恬 2292
恰 1724
恉 3154
恂 2665
恪 1265
恨 915
宣 2685
宧 970
宥 2947
室 2094
客 1264
突 2346
穿 369
窀 3234
冠 822
833
郎 1315
軍 1232
扁 139
1646
扃 1196
祖 1574
衲 1552
衽 1891
衿 1162
袂 1479
祛 1819
祜 944
祐 2947
祓 706
祖 3284
神 2007
祝 3213
祚 3306
祔 718
祗 3136
祕 124
祠 391
衵 283

〔乛〕

建 1098
既 1056
屍 2049
屋 2455
咫 3154
屏 167
1666
屎 2078
弭 1492
韋 2416
峒 1257
眉 1472
胥 2676
陝 1962
孩 865
疊 1163
娃 2374
姥 1327
姱 1286
姨 2838
姪 3140
姻 2876
姝 2129
姙 1891
姚 2777
姣 1118
姘 1654
姦 1082
怒 1597
架 1075
迢 2295
迦 1065
飛 653
羿 2855
臬 2503
勇 2915
怠 450
迨 451
癸 846
柔 1906
矜 823
1161
彖 2357
陋 1416
陌 1534
降 1110
2561
陔 726
限 2538
紆 2949
紅 789
921
紂 3194
紇 909
紃 2712
約 3004
紈 2385
紀 1048
紉 1891

10 劃

〔一〕

挈 1767
挈 1072
泰 2237
秦 1774
珪 842
珥 604
珙 791
琊 2786
玭 398
珠 3196
珩 916
珣 2712
珮 1628
珞 1440
班 58
素 2203
蒲 796
恚 986
栽 3026
埔 1677
捕 186
埂 768
馬 1446
振 3099
挾 2598
荊 1162
1173
茸 1902
茜 1747
趀 1963
起 1702
萸 2267
2838
茈 268
3254
草 250
茼 2323
茵 2880
茴 985
茱 3197
茯 706
茬 1887
荇 2662
荎 1836
茶 263
荀 2712
茗 1523
1525
茭 1118
茨 391
荒 972
荄 726
捎 1981
茫 1462
捍 880
捏 1584
貢 793
埋 1450
1454
莨 766
捉 3235
捆 1298
捐 1222
袁 2993
挹 2856
捌 38
茹 1914
荔 1356
茲 391
3241
挺 2310
郝 895
911
哲 3087
耄 1467
耆 1691
挫 417
捋 1328
1427
1436
挼 1601
1925
挽 2386
恐 1272
抄 1952
捃 1235
挪 1601
挶 1211
捅 2327
盍 910
埃 3
挨 4
垛 587
588
耿 768
耽 454
恥 329
莎 2221
莕 2662
荳 557
恭 789
真 3092
3093
3094
框 1292
1293
桂 849
桔 1142
1211
栲 1254
栱 791
桓 966
栖 1682
2492
桎 3165
桄 842
桐 2323
桾 1427
株 3195
栝 818
柏 1203
桁 885
916
栓 2156
桃 2256
桅 2416
格 759
校 1128
2590
核 909
栟 1556
桉 20
根 764
栩 2680
索 2225
軒 2686
軏 3009
軔 1891
彧 2976
哥 756
鬲 760
1356
豇 1106
剸 3271
栗 1356
酌 3237

配 1628
迺 1553
翅 332
匪 659
辱 1916
1919
唇 388
脣 417
厖 1462
1620
夏 1073
2523
砝 617
砸 3023
砰 1632
砧 3095
砷 2004
砭 134
砥 499
砲 1623
1624
1626
破 1671
恧 1600
原 2988
套 2261
郲 1309
烈 1385
殊 2133
殉 2716
翃 924
致 3163
晉 1167

〔丨〕

鬥 556
柴 267
桌 3236
虔 1741
眛 1479
時 2062
郢 2907
眣 533
財 229
貤 2838
眨 3050
晟 317
2040
眩 2693
眠 1494
眙 332
2838
哮 2588
晃 978
979
哺 186
哽 768
閃 1961
晌 1972
晁 289
剔 2266
晏 2758
哔 1507
趵 87
畛 3098
蚨 706
蚜 2724
蚍 1642
蚋 1923
畔 1619
蚌 73
蚣 790
蚊 2445
蚪 555
蚇 329
蚓 2891
哨 1985
骨 801
802
806
員 2991
哩 1337
1341
圃 1677
哭 1281
圄 2963
哦 590
1603
唏 2491
恩 596
盎 30
唁 2758
哼 915
哪 1551
1552
唧 1035
唉 3
唆 2221
豈 1244
1701
峽 2515
罡 744
罟 806
罝 1209
峭 1763
峴 2539
峨 590
峪 2975
峰 690
帨 2166
迴 985
峻 1235
剛 743

〔丿〕

眚 2039
甡 2004
耕 767
1174
耘 3013
耗 897
耙 43
1606
缺 1842
毧 1902
氣 1711
氤 2880
氦 873
氧 2769
氨 20
特 2262
牷 1836
牸 3271
乘 315
2039
舐 2098
适 818
秣 1534
秫 2137
秤 321
1666
租 3280
秧 2763
秩 3165
秭 3254
秘 1492
笄 1014
笑 2591
笊 3080
笫 3254
笏 944
笈 1037
笆 38
俸 695
倩 1747
倀 274
倖 2662
借 1155
值 3144
倆 1360
1377
倚 2850
俺 21
倒 470
473
俶 366
2277
修 2670
倘 2254
俱 1209
1218
倡 274
284
個 762
候 931
俳 1609
恁 1891
倕 384
倭 2451
倪 1572
俾 119
倫 1433
倜 2277
隼 3234
隻 3137
倞 1191
1378
俯 710
倍 102
倦 1223
倌 823
臬 746
1585
臭 347
2675
射 1992
2062
2792
2855
躬 790
息 2497
島 472
們 1483
1484
郫 1642
烏 2456
鬼 847
倨 1218
倔 1227
1231
師 2050
追 3230
衄 1592
1600
逈 1196
逅 931
徒 2347
徑 1190
徐 2680
殷 2728
2879
舨 65
般 60
177
1615
航 883
舫 647
瓞 533
釘 535
541
針 3095
釗 3077
釙 1676
釕 1383
拿 1550
郗 324
逃 2257
釜 711
郤 2508
爹 533
舀 1286
2781
郛 706
豻 880
豺 268
豹 87
奚 2492
鬯 285
倉 245
飣 541
飢 1014
瓴 1394
衾 1769
翁 2450
胹 600
胯 1286
胰 2838
胱 839
胴 546
胭 2728
脈 1451
1534
朓 2300
脆 412
脂 3136
胸 2665
胳 756
胼 1648
朕 3100
胺 25
狹 2515
狴 124
狽 103
狸 1337
狷 1223
狺 2884
逖 2277
狼 1315
卿 1781
桀 1142
逢 1620
迻 2838
留 1407
芻 359

〔丶〕
清 1191
訏 2676
訐 1142
訌 924
討 2259
訕 1963
訖 1721
訓 2716
託 2367
訊 2716
記 1054
訒 1891
凍 546
衰 410
2153
畝 1540
衷 3179
高 746
亳 185
席 2496
庫 1285
迹 1014
准 3234
庭 2308
座 3304
脊 1037
1043
症 3117
疳 735
疴 1257
病 170
痁 515
疸 457
疽 1209
疾 1035
痄 3051
疹 3098
痀 1209
疼 2264
疱 1625
痂 1071
疲 1641
效 2588
紊 2448
唐 2250
凋 529
旆 1630
旄 1466
1467
旂 1691
旅 1425
旃 3055
恣 391
3271
站 3058
剖 1674
1674
竝 174
旁 1620
欬 1245
1258
畜 366
2683
羒 673
羖 811
羓 38
差 259
266
267
391
恙 2773
羔 746
迸 112
拳 1835
送 2198
敉 1492
粉 674
料 1383
迷 1489
益 2855
兼 1082
朔 2175
逆 1573
烤 1253
烘 918
烙 1327
1439
烊 2766
浙 3090
浡 180
浦 1677
浭 768
涑 2205
浯 2458
酒 1199
涇 1174
涉 1993
娑 2221
消 2572
涅 1585
浬 1341
浞 3238
涓 1222
浥 2855
涔 257
浩 896
海 866
浜 71
涖 1356
浴 2975
浮 704
浼 1479
流 1401
涕 2276
浣 969
浪 1317
浸 1167
涌 2916
浚 1235
悖 102
悚 2197
悟 2483
悄 1762
悍 880
悝 1295
1341
悃 1299
悁 1223
1224
悒 2856
悔 985
恌 2295
悅 3008
悌 2276
悛 1829
宸 300
家 1066
宵 2572
宴 2758
宮 789
害 871
容 1900
窅 2781
窄 3042
3053
窆 140
剜 2381
窈 2780
宰 3027
案 24
朗 1317
扆 2851
冢 3182
扇 1960
1962
袜 1534
2375
袒 2246
袖 2675
袍 1623
被 103
1637
祧 2295
祥 2561
冥 1523
冤 2985
〔乛〕
書 2129
郡 1235
退 2361
展 3056
屑 2602
屐 1014
弰 1981
弱 1926
奘 3034
牂 3034
孫 2218
蚩 324
陞 2033
匏 1625
烝 3105
姬 1014
娠 2004
娌 1341
娉 1659
娟 1222
恕 2144
娛 2951
娥 590
娩 1497
2386
娣 507
娘 1581
娜 1551
1601
1602
娓 2422
砮 1597
脅 2598
畚 111
能 1568
蚤 3038
桑 1938
剝 78
177
陡 555
陣 3100
陛 124
陘 2653
陟 3165
除 359
院 3002
紜 3013
紘 924
純 387
紕 1637
1642
紗 1949
納 1551
紝 1891
紛 672
紙 3154
級 1036
紋 2444
紡 647
紐 1592
紓 2133
邕 2913

11 劃

〔丿〕
笵 637
〔一〕
彗 986
舂 335
球 1813
匿 1574
責 3042
現 2539
理 1341
琉 1408
琅 1316
匭 848
規 842
捧 1634
掛 819
堵 564
掫 3276
措 418
域 2976
捺 1552
掎 1043
埯 21
掩 2748
捷 1142
焉 2728
莩 114
181
掉 530
莆 711
1676
莢 1072
莽 1463
莖 1174
莫 1534
1547
莧 2542
莒 1212
莪 591
莉 1357
莠 2945
2947
莓 1474
荷 910
911
莅 1356
荼 2347
莝 418
莩 707
1652
荽 2213
荻 495
莘 2007

2624
莎 1952
2221
莞 823
830
2388
莨 1315
捵 296
莊 3224
排 1609
赦 1996
赧 1559
堆 574
推 2357
頂 536
埤 1642
捭 54
都 554
557
埠 221
掀 2527
逝 2098
捨 1988
掄 1433
採 235
授 2126
掙 3106
3118
捻 1580
1585
教 1118
1129
掏 2255
掐 1723
掬 1211
掠 1432
掂 509
掖 2786
2792
捽 3283
3295
敖 30
33
培 1627
掊 1674
1674
接 1135
執 3145
捲 1223
掞 1963
控 1274
捩 1386
掮 1741
探 2247
捫 1483
掃 1941
1942
据 1209
1218
掘 1227
掇 586
聃 454
基 1014
聆 1394
聊 1380
勘 1246
1249
娶 1827
堇 1163
靪 536
勒 1328
帶 451
菿 475
菓 860
菙 384
萆 127
菸 2728
乾 735
1741
菉 1420
1429
郴 296
梆 71
械 1156
2602
彬 160
梵 637
婪 1310
梗 768
梧 2458
梢 1981
桿 737
梏 816
1227
梃 2311
梅 1473
梔 3137
梲 3238
麥 1452
1534
桴 707
桷 1227
梓 3254
梳 2132
梯 2266
桫 2221
桶 2327
梭 2221
紮 3023
3049
救 1203
述 1815
軛 592
斬 3057
軟 1920
連 1360
[illegible] 1250
專 3216
逋 186
敕 332
敔 2964
曹 249
速 2206
副 718
區 1819
堅 1083
豉 329
2098
逗 557
票 1652
酗 2684
酖 454
3101
戚 1682
戛 1072
硎 2653
硒 2492
硃 3197
硌 764
瓠 944
匏 1623
奢 1986
盔 1295
爽 2158
逐 3200
豝 38
殍 1652
盛 317
2040
匾 140
雩 2951
2977
雪 2705
2710
鄄 1684
頃 1800
逕 1191

〔丨〕

觜 3053
眥 3271
鹵 1419
虖 934
彪 149
處 362
366
雀 1762
1844
逍 2577
堂 2250
常 278
眶 1293
唪 694
眱 2839
匙 327
2108
逞 320
晡 186
晤 2484
晨 300
眺 2300
敗 56
販 637
眵 324
眯 1488
1492
眼 2749
眸 1537
野 2787
畢 125
啫 3090
啦 1306
啞 2725
閉 125
勗 2684
問 2448
婁 1414
1425
1427
曼 1459
晧 897
晦 987
晞 2492
冕 1497
晚 2387
啄 3238
畦 1691
畤 3165
異 2856
趼 1088
趺 698
跂 1691
1722
距 1218
趾 3156
啃 1267
趿 1929
2229
略 1433
蚶 873
蛄 801
蛆 1821
蚰 2931
蚱 3051
蚯 1810
蛉 1394
蛀 3213
蛇 1988
2839
蚴 2947
唬 941
累 1329
1331
1333
唱 285
患 970
國 853
啡 656
唯 2416
2423
啤 1642
啥 1953
唸 1581
啁 3192
啐 412
啖 459
唳 1356
啜 390
啊 1
帳 3071
崧 2196
崖 2724
崎 1682
1691
崦 2728
崍 1309
罣 820
眾 3188
崑 1298
崗 744
崔 410
帷 2416
崙 1434
崤 2777
崢 3106
崩 112
崇 339
2215
崛 1227
崌 1209
崡 876
圇 1434
圈 1223
1224
1829

〔丿〕

耜 2194
缽 175
毬 1813
氫 1781
牾 2477
造 3039
甜 2292
透 2344
梨 1337

犁	1338	梟	2576	釩	627	觖	1227	康	1249	淅	2492	淥	1420
移	2838	鳥	1582	釹	1600	猛	1487	鹿	1420	淞	2196	淄	3241
動	546	健	1099	釵	267	逢	693	旌	1174	渠	1823	情	1793
笻	1803	兜	554	殺	1950	馗	1296	族	3282	涯	2725	悵	285
笨	111	皎	1123	盒	910	夠	796	旎	1572	淹	2728	悻	2662
笸	1670	假	1073	欷	2492	祭	1058	旋	2688	淶	1309	惜	2498
笛	495		1074	悉	2492			瓷	391	涿	3236	悽	1682
笙	2033		1075	欲	2976	〔丶〕		部	221	淒	1683	悼	475
笮	3042		1076	彩	234	詎	1218	章	3066	淺	1745	惝	2254
符	706	偓	2453	覓	1494	訝	2727	竟	1191	淑	2133	惕	2277
笠	1356	偉	2423	貪	2239	訥	1564	翊	2859	淖	1563	惘	2400
笥	2194	術	2145	翎	1394	許	2681	商	1967	淌	2254	悱	659
第	507	徠	1309	貧	1655	訛	590	望	2405	混	995	悸	1058
笯	1596	徙	2503	脖	180	訢	2624	袤	1468		997	惟	2416
笤	2297	徜	280	脯	711	訟	2199		1538	涸	897	惆	343
笳	1071	得	482		1676	設	1994	率	1428		910	惛	995
笞	324		486	脰	557	這	3090		2155	淮	961	惸	1803
敏	1513	徘	1609	脤	2016		3091	牽	1729	淦	741	惚	934
偌	1927	御	2976	豚	2365	訪	648	羚	1394	淪	1434	惇	580
做	3306	從	401	脛	1191	訣	1227	羝	494	淆	2777	惦	515
偃	2748		403	脞	417	訩	2666	羗	1748	淫	2884	悴	412
偕	1135		3274	脬	1622	毫	886	羞	2672	淨	1191	惓	1836
	2598	衒	2693	脲	1584	孰	2137	瓶	1666	淝	659	悾	1272
袋	452	舸	761	脗	2447	郭	852	眷	1224	淘	2258	惋	2389
偵	3096	舳	3193	脫	2367	烹	1632	粘	1580	淴	934	惙	390
條	2295		3200	脘	830	庶	2144	粗	406	涼	1372	寇	1280
倏	2144	舴	3043	彫	529	庹	2371	粕	1674	淳	388	寅	2884
脩	2673	舶	180	匐	706	麻	1444	粒	1356	液	2792	寄	1057
悠	2922	舲	1394	魚	2952	庵	20	剪	1088	淬	412	寂	1037
側	253	船	371	猜	225	庾	2963	烯	2492	淤	2949	逭	972
偶	1603	舷	2530	逛	842	痔	3165	烽	690	涪	706	宿	2205
偈	1142	舵	588	猗	592	痏	2423	郯	2241	淡	459		2674
偎	2409	敍	2683		2834	痍	2838	烷	2385	淙	406		2675
偷	2331	斜	2598		2851	疵	391	烺	1317	淀	515	窒	3165
您	1586	途	2348	凰	974	產	270	清	1781	涴	2453	窕	2300
貨	1006	釷	2355	猓	860	痊	1836	添	2290	淚	1332	密	1493
售	2126	釦	1280	猖	274	痕	914	渚	3208	深	2004	啟	1707
停	2308	釬	1731	猊	1572	袞	851	淩	1393	涮	2156	扈	944
偽	2422	釧	377	猙	3106	凔	238	淇	1691	涵	876	袱	707
	2431	釤	1961	猝	409	庸	2913	淋	1388	婆	1670	袷	1072
偏	1646	釣	531	斛	936		2914		1392	梁	1372		1145

祼 1267
視 2098
祲 1162

〔乛〕

晝 3194
逯 1420
焄 2710
尉 2431
2976
屠 2347
屜 2277
屙 590
張 3064
艴 707
強 1112
1750
1755
將 1106
1111
蛋 460
隃 2956
娬 2477
婊 156
婭 2727
婕 1142
娼 274
婢 124
婚 994
婉 2387
婦 718
婀 590
架 1071
習 2498
翌 2859
通 2312
欸 7
596
逡 1846
務 2483
參 238
256
1936
2004
陸 1419
陵 1394
陬 3276
貫 833
陳 300
3101
陴 1642
陰 2880
2896
陶 2259
2777
陷 2542
陪 1627
紺 741
紱 707
組 3285
紬 342
343
紳 2007
細 2508
絅 1196
紩 3165
絁 2052
紾 3098
絇 1823
終 3179
絃 2530
絆 68
紵 3213
紼 707
絀 366
紹 1986
巢 289

12 劃

〔一〕

貳 606
絜 1145
2599
棐 659
琵 1642
琴 1774
琶 1606
1607
琪 1694
琳 1388
琦 1694
琢 3238
琖 3057
琥 941
琨 1298
項 873
琤 303
斑 60
琰 2755
琺 623
琮 406
琯 830
琬 2389
琛 296
琚 1209
替 2277
揍 3279
款 1291
堯 2777
堪 1247
揕 3101
揶 2786
揲 1988
描 1505
堰 2758
揠 2727
揀 1088
馭 2978
馮 693
1668
項 2569
揩 1238
華 951
959
菁 1174
揹 98
萇 283
著 3078
3213
菱 1394
菴 92
萁 1694
越 3009
趄 1210
菴 20
26
萊 1309
趁 302
超 287
萋 1686
敢 737
菽 2133
賁 107
128
674
菖 274
萌 1484
菌 1235
菲 657
659
萎 2409
萸 2955
菜 237
棻 673
菔 707
菟 2356
萄 2259
2262
萏 462
菊 1211
萃 412
菩 1676
萍 1667
菹 1210
菠 177
菅 1085
堤 494
提 494
2267
場 280
283
揚 2766
揖 2834
博 181
揭 1137
喜 2503
彭 1633
揣 369
菰 801
菡 880
菇 801
揾 2450
戟 3271
菑 3027
3242
捶 384
插 260
揪 1198
搜 2200
揑 1585
煮 3208
耋 533
揄 2955
揜 2755
援 2993
逵 1296
換 971
蛩 1803
搯 3032
3287
裁 233
揞 21
報 88
揎 2687
揮 980
殼 1258
1763
1844
壺 937
壹 2834
握 2453
摒 174
揆 1296
揉 1907
惡 592
2457
2484
掾 3003
聒 818
斯 2181
期 1016
1691
欺 1684
黃 975
散 1936
1937
斮 3239
葽 2776
葚 2102
菀 2389
蕿 2007
菹 1210
戟 1043
朝 289
3077
喪 1938
1939
辜 801
棒 73
棖 318
棤 364
棱 1334
椏 2718
棋 1694
植 3146
森 1947
棼 674
焚 673
棟 554
棫 2978
椅 2851
極 1040
椓 3239
棲 1684
2492
棧 3059
椒 1118
棹 3081
3236
棵 1257
棍 851
楔 2955
椎 384
3232
棉 1495
棚 1633
棬 1830
棕 3272
棺 823
棣 508
軻 1257
軸 3193
軹 3156
軼 2859
軫 3099
軨 1394
軺 2777
惠 987
鄢 2755
惑 1008
腎 2016
掔 1731
覃 1774
2241
粟 2207
棗 3038
棘 1037
酣 873

酤 802
鄠 1224
酢 3307
酥 2201
厫 30
皕 127
硭 1463
硬 2909
硜 1267
硝 2577
硯 2759
确 1844
硫 1408
雁 2759
鼓 1686
欹 2834
厥 1227
猋 149
尞 1380
貆 1923
殖 3148
殛 1041
殘 241
裂 1386
雄 2667
雲 3013
雰 673
雯 2445
雱 283
1621
雅 2725

〔丨〕

惄 1574
紫 3254
覘 3055
虛 2676
黹 3156
敝 124
敞 284
棠 2251
牚 303
掌 3069
晴 1800
暑 2138
最 3290
晰 2492
量 1373
1378
睏 1300
貼 2302
貺 1293
貶 140
貯 3208
貽 2839
睇 508
喏 1602
1857
戢 1040
喋 533
喃 1556
喳 260
閏 1924
開 1238
閑 2530
閎 924
晶 1174
間 1085
1101
閒 1085
1101
2530
閔 1513
喇 1305
1305
喊 878
晷 848
景 1187
2907
晾 1378
晬 3291
喈 1141
跖 3148
跋 40
跚 1961
跌 533
跗 698
跑 1623
跎 2370
跛 128
185
貴 849
蛙 2373
蛭 3168
蛐 1821
1823
蛔 985
蛛 3197
蛤 760
865
蛟 1119
畯 1236
鄂 595
喁 2914
喝 899
911
喟 1297
單 268
454
1963
斝 1075
喘 376
喞 2530
唾 2372
啾 1198
嗖 2200
喉 925
喻 2977
喚 971
喨 1379
喑 2883
啼 2267
喧 2686
喀 1237
1238
喔 1603
2451
嘅 1244
喙 987
嵌 1731
幅 707
剴 1244
凱 1244
崴 2409
幀 3118
買 1450
罥 1357
帽 1468
嵎 2955
嵑 1145
崽 3027
崿 595
嵐 1310
幄 2453
幃 2417
嵋 1476
淼 1506
黑 911
912
圍 2416
骫 2423

〔丿〕

斐 659
悲 96
甥 2034
無 2458
犇 107
掰 45
掣 295
鉼 1668
智 3165
毳 412
毯 2246
氮 461
氯 1429
犄 1016
郵 2933
犉 1924
剩 2041
逶 2410
嵇 1016
稍 1981
稈 737
程 317
稌 2349
稀 2493
黍 2139
稅 2166
稂 1316
喬 1758
筐 1292
等 489
筑 3200
策 256
筒 2327
筈 818
筏 617
筌 1836
答 421
422
筋 1162
筍 2219
筊 1124
筆 119
備 103
傅 719
舄 2511
牌 1613
貸 452
順 2169
短 570
矬 417
條 2255
堡 84
傀 844
1297
傖 246
傑 1142
集 1038
焦 1118
進 1168
傚 2593
傍 73
1620
傢 1071
皓 897
皖 2388
街 1140
衖 1414
衕 2330
復 720
徨 974
循 2713
徧 1650
須 2679
雇 816
舒 2134
畬 1986
2955
鈇 698
鈣 729
鈦 2237
鉅 1218
鈍 581
鈔 289
291
鈉 1552
鈐 1742
欽 1770
鈞 1235
鈎 794
鈧 1252
鈥 1005
鈕 1592
鈀 42
翕 2511
殽 2777
番 177
624
1615
釉 2947
傘 1936
舜 2169
貂 529
創 377
380
飩 2365
飪 1891
飫 2978
飭 332
飯 637
飲 2891
2896
脹 3072
腊 1305
2493
腌 1
29
2728
腆 2294
腓 659
腴 2955
脾 1642
腋 2792
2859
腑 711
脺 412
勝 2034
2041
腔 1748
腕 2389
週 3193
逸 2859
象 2568
猢 937
欿 1247

猩 2640
猥 2423
猴 926
猶 2933
觚 802
觝 499
猱 1560
飧 2219
然 1849
貿 1468

〔丶〕

証 3118
詁 811
訶 899
評 1667
詛 3286
詐 3051
訴 2208
診 3098
詆 499
註 3214
詠 2917
詞 392
詘 1821
詔 3081
詖 127
詒 2840
就 1204
鄗 898
敦 575
580
廂 2558
裒 1674
廁 253
401
廋 2200
斌 160
痣 3168
痡 1675
痘 557
痞 1644
痙 1191
痢 1357
痤 417
痧 1952
痛 2327
痠 2210
廊 1316
廄 1206
旐 3081
粢 3242
竦 2197
童 2323
竣 1235
啻 332
棄 1721
翔 2561
羢 1903
着 3079
3091
3238
善 1963
普 1677
粧 3225
尊 3294
奠 515
孳 3241
曾 257
3046
焯 289
3239
焮 2637
焰 2743
2758
焙 104
欻 369
934
2679
焱 2759
勞 1319
1327
湊 406
湛 3059
港 745
渫 2602
湖 937
渣 3049
湘 2558
渤 182
湢 127
湮 2728
2883
減 1088
湎 1497
湜 2069
渺 1506
測 254
湯 1970
2249
溫 2434
渴 899
1261
渨 2410
渭 2431
渦 852
2451
湍 2356
湃 1615
湫 1124
1198
溲 2200
淵 2986
湟 975
渝 2955
渰 2755
湲 2993
溢 1631
渙 972
盜 475
渟 2310
渡 568
游 2931
湔 1085
滋 3242
為 844
湉 2293
渲 2693
渾 995
998
溉 729
渥 2453
湣 1513
湄 1476
湑 2682
湧 2916
愜 1767
惵 534
愊 127
惰 588
愐 1497
惻 254
慍 3017
惺 2640
2654
愒 1245
愕 595
惴 3233
愣 1337
愀 1762
愎 127
惶 974
愉 2955
愔 2883
惲 3017
慨 1244
惱 1561
寒 876
富 719
寓 2978
割 756
窖 1134
窗 377
窘 1196
甯 1586
1589
寐 1480
鄆 3017
扉 657
棨 1708
補 187
裋 2146
裌 1072
裎 319
裕 2979
裙 1848
祺 1694
裸 833
祿 1420

〔乛〕

尋 2629
2712
畫 957
閔 1480
1483
逮 446
453
犀 2493
孱 268
弼 127
費 662
粥 3192
巽 2717
疏 2134
2145
韌 1891
鄏 1476
媒 1474
媼 32
媧 2373
絮 2684
嫂 1942
媛 3003
婷 2310
媢 1479
賀 911
登 486
發 607
皴 413
矞 2978
婺 2485
敪 586
彘 3168
隋 2213
階 1140
隄 494
2270
陽 2767
隅 2955
隈 2410
陲 384
隍 1585
隆 1410
隊 575
鄉 2558
絨 1903
絓 820
結 1138
1143
絝 1285
絰 533
絏 2602
絪 2883
綖 2743
給 764
1043
絢 2693
絳 1112
絡 1327
1440
絕 1228
絞 1123
統 2326
絲 2181
幾 1016
1043

13 劃

〔一〕

瑟 1946
瑛 2899
瑚 937
瑁 1470
1480
瑞 1923
瑪 2964
瑜 2957
瑗 3003
瑳 417
瑄 2687
瑯 1317
琿 996
瑕 2516
瑋 2423
瑑 3223
瑙 1561
頑 2385
搆 797
髡 1298
肆 2194
搽 264
搭 421
搘 3137
塔 2230
搢 1171
載 3027
3031
搏 182
屛 3214
馱 588
2370
馴 2717
填 2293
蒔 691
葚 2018
葉 2794
葫 937

葳 2410
蒽 1857
趔 1386
趑 3245
葬 3034
韮 1199
葺 1722
萬 2389
葛 760
761
蒠 2506
蒚 2451
葶 595
董 545
葆 84
葩 1606
葡 1676
葱 402
蒂 508
落 1305
1327
1440
萱 2687
葵 2349
葷 995
萹 134
1647
塌 2229
搨 2231
葭 1071
損 2219
揔 597
鼓 811
葦 2423
葼 1296
葒 924
葯 2783
3010
搗 472
塢 2485
搗 2477
塊 1288
搥 384
蜇 3087
搋 369
搬 61
搯 2255
搶 1749
1755
勢 2102
登 1804
搖 2777
搿 342
搞 753
摛 325
塘 2251
搪 2252
搐 367
達 423
搓 416
搛 1085
搠 2175
搾 3051
壺 1299
塚 3182
搧 1961
彀 797
搌 3057
搦 1602
搔 1940
聘 1659
1669
聖 2043
碁 1694
戡 1247
勤 1774
蒲 1677
靴 2694
靳 1171
靸 1929
靷 2893
靶 42
募 1547
蒨 1748
敬 1192
幹 741
楔 2602
椿 387
楛 944
1284
椹 3097
椰 2786
楠 1556
禁 1162
1170
楂 3049
楚 364
楝 1368
楲 1085
楷 1245
楨 3097
3106
楊 2768
想 2562
楫 1041
楬 1147
椳 2410
楞 1334
1337
楸 1810
楩 1648
1648
楯 2169
晳 2494
嗇 1946
榆 2956
楓 690
楹 2904
楢 2935
榔 1316
概 729
楣 1476
楙 1470
椽 376
裘 1815
軾 2105
輊 3169
軥 3193
輅 1422
較 1134
軿 1668
甦 2201
逼 113
128
剽 1653
賈 811
1075
酮 2324
酰 2528
酯 3156
酪 1523
1525
酩 1327
1440
酬 344
頍 1297
蜃 2018
感 737
擘 2743
碏 1844
碍 12
碘 511
碓 576
碑 99
硼 1632
1633
碉 529
碎 2217
碚 104
碇 541
碗 2389
碌 1420
匯 987
電 515
雷 1329
零 1395
雹 78
183
頓 559
582
鼇 3057

〔丨〕

督 557
歲 2215
貲 3245
訾 3255
粲 244
虡 1220
虜 1419
1439
虞 2957
業 2792
當 463
466
468
睛 1174
睹 564
睦 1547
睞 1309
睫 1145
嗉 2209
睆 1575
睢 1210
睢 2213
睥 1645
賊 3045
賄 991
賂 1421
賅 726
睬 236
睜 3106
睠 1224
鼎 537
嗎 1448
1450
嗒 422
2230
嗜 2103
嗑 1265
嗔 296
愚 2956
遇 2979
閘 3049
閟 128
嗝 761
戥 491
嗄 1
1953
暖 1601
盟 1485
煦 2682
歇 2593
遏 595
暗 26
暄 2687
暈 3012
3017
暉 981
暇 2516
2524
黽 1513
號 888
898
照 3081
暌 1296
畸 1016
跬 1297
跨 1286
跴 236
跮 332
跐 398
跩 3216
跣 2535
跲 1072
跳 2300
跪 850
路 1421
跤 1119
跡 1058
跟 765
園 2994
蛺 1072
蛸 1982
蜆 2535
蜈 2472
蛾 591
蜓 2310
蜊 1338
1360
蜍 361
蜉 707
蜂 690
蛻 2363
畹 2389
蜋 1317
1373
蛹 2917
豊 1344
農 1592
過 852
860
嗩 2227
骭 742
嗣 2194
嗯 597
1570
嗅 2675
嘷 888
嗚 2457
嗆 1749
1756
嗡 2451
嗟 1141
嗨 865
嗤 324
嗓 1939

遄 376
署 2139
　 2146
罣 752
置 3168
罩 3083
罪 3291
蜀 2139
幌 978
嵬 2419
嵩 2196
嵯 417
圓 2995

〔丿〕

耡 361
矮 7
雉 3169
氲 3013
毽 1101
犍 1085
歃 1954
稜 1334
稞 1257
稚 3168
稗 58
稔 1887
稠 344
愁 343
筭 2211
筠 3016
筮 2104
筴 256
　 1072
筲 1982
筧 1090
筥 1212
筱 2587
筷 1289
筦 830
節 1145
筩 2324
與 2958
　 2964
　 2983
債 3053
傲 33
僅 1163
傳 372
　 3223
傴 2964
毀 986
舅 1206
鼠 2139
牒 534
傾 1267
　 1787
僂 1414
催 410
傷 1970
賃 1392
傯 3273
傺 332
傭 2913
　 2914
遑 978
躲 587
臬 1583
皐 707
鄔 2457
粵 3010
奧 33
僇 1420
頎 1694
遁 581
衙 2725
微 2410
　 2412
徯 2494
徭 2778
徬 1621
愆 1731
艄 1982
艇 2311
鈺 2983
鉦 3106
鉗 1742
鈷 811
鈳 1257
鈸 41
　 182
鉞 3010
鉏 361
　 1212
鉬 1547
鉀 1075
鈾 2935
鈿 515
鉑 182
鈴 1394
鉛 1732
鉋 92
鈰 2106
鉉 2693
鉈 2230
鉤 794
鉍 128
鈹 1644
鉯 2851
鉧 1540
弒 2103
愈 2978
逾 2957
僉 1732
會 986
　 988
　 1288
爺 2786
禽 1776
愛 8
貅 2673
貉 889
　 910
　 1535
亂 1431
飾 2105
飽 84
飼 2195
飴 2840
頒 61
頌 2199
腠 406
腩 1559
腰 2775
腼 1497
腸 282
腥 2640
腮 1930
腫 3182
腹 722
腺 2544
腳 1124
　 1230
媵 2910
腱 1101
腦 1561
詹 3055
雊 797
肄 2868
猿 2997
獏 1538
鳩 1198
猾 953
獅 2052
猺 2778
觥 790
斟 3097
解 1150
　 1156
　 2603
猻 2219
煞 1952
　 1953
鄒 3277

〔丶〕

誆 1292
試 2104
註 820
詩 2052
詰 1147
　 1722
誇 1286
詼 981
誠 319
訿 3255
誄 1332
誅 3197
詵 2007
話 959
詬 797
詮 1836
詭 848
詢 2714
詣 2868
該 726
詳 2561
詫 266
詡 2682
裏 1344
　 1360
稟 168
廈 1953
　 2524
痲 1446
痳 1389
韵 3017
痺 128
痼 816
痱 663
痴 324
痿 2423
剷 273
瘁 412
瘀 2949
痰 2241
痾 590
廉 1363
媥 61
鄘 2913
頏 885
麂 1044
麀 2923
廕 2897
旒 1408
遊 2934
裔 2868
資 3242
靖 1193
新 2624
瓿 1674
鄣 3067
歆 2629
意 2860
雍 2913
義 2866
羨 2543
豢 972
粳 1175
粮 1373
煎 1085
猷 2934
遒 1815
道 476
遂 2217
塑 2209
慈 395
煤 1474
煳 938
煙 2729
煉 1368
煩 627
煬 2768
　 2773
煜 2978
煨 2410
煌 978
煖 1601
煥 972
塋 2904
煢 1804
煒 2423
溝 794
溘 1265
滇 509
溎 850
溥 1678
溧 1357
溽 1919
滅 1507
源 2996
裟 1952
滑 952
溷 998
準 3234
溴 2675
塗 2349
滔 2255
溪 1686
　 2494
滄 246
滃 2451
溜 1401
　 1410
滂 1619
溢 2865
溯 2209
溶 1903
滓 3255
溟 1523
溺 1574
　 1584
粱 1373
滁 361
愫 2209
慌 974
慎 2017
慄 1357

愷 1244
愾 1245
愧 1297
愴 381
慉 2684
慊 1747
1767
塞 1930
1946
寘 3169
窠 1257
窟 1282
運 3017
遍 143
1650
裱 156
褂 820
褚 365
裸 1439
裼 2500
裨 129
1644
裯 345
裾 1210
裰 587
褉 2512
福 708
禋 2883
禎 3097
禍 1008
禘 509
禕 2834

〔乛〕

肅 2207
群 1846
遐 2516
殿 515
辟 128
1645
愍 1513
違 2417
裝 3225
韰 2517
媾 797
媽 1444
媳 2500
嫉 1040
嫌 2532
嫁 1076
嫦 325
勠 1420
預 2979
彙 988
隔 760
隙 2511
隕 3016
隗 2423
隘 12
綁 72
綆 768
經 1175
綃 2577
綑 1299
絹 1224
絺 325
綏 2213
綈 2270
剿 1124

14 劃

〔一〕

瑪 1448
瑱 3101
鬩 557
瑣 2227
碧 129
瑰 844
瑲 1750
瑤 2778
斠 1134
遘 798
嫠 1338
魂 996
髦 1466
髳 648
摸 1463
1527
摶 2357
摳 1275
摽 149
1652
駁 183
駃 1230
摤 295
摥 2135
蓁 3097
蒜 2212
鄢 2731
蓍 2053
蓋 730
761
910
蓐 1919
趙 3084
趧 740
蒔 2073
墓 1547
幕 1548
蓇 813
夢 1488
蓓 104
蒐 2200
蓖 129
蒼 246
蓊 2451
蒯 1287
1289
蓑 2221
蒿 885
蓆 2500
蒺 1041
蓄 2684
蒹 1086
蒲 1677
蒞 1357
蓉 1905
蒙 1485
覡 565
摟 1414
1415
搰 1384
摞 1443
摑 859
遠 2998
3003
嘉 1071
臺 2234
蒻 1927
蓀 2219
摧 411
蒸 3106
赫 911
截 1147
翥 3214
踅 332
2694
誓 2106
摭 3148
墉 2914
境 1193
摘 3051
摔 2154
塾 528
推 1844
慤 1844
壽 2127
摺 3087
摎 1198
朅 1767
摻 268
摜 834
綦 1697
聚 1218
鄞 2885
鞅 1535
靼 424
鞅 2763
2770
蓰 2506
斡 742
878
斡 2454
熙 2494
兢 1180
暇 812
蔯 302
榧 659
榛 3097
構 797
槙 745
木莽 1463
榻 2231
榾 813
榫 2220
榭 2603
槔 752
槐 961
槌 384
覡 2500
槍 1749
榴 1408
榱 411
槁 753
榔 860
榜 72
槎 265
榕 1904
榨 3051
権 1844
疐 3171
輒 3088
輔 712
輕 1789
塹 1748
輓 2389
匱 1297
歌 757
監 1085
1102
緊 1163
酵 2593
酺 1677
甄 3097
醒 319
酷 1285
酶 1476
酴 2352
酹 1333
酸 2210
碡 559
碟 534
碴 265
厭 2759
碱 1090
碩 2073
2175
碣 1148
碳 2248
磁 396
愿 3003
奩 1363
爾 604
奪 586
豨 2494
殞 3016
需 2679
塱 2407
鳶 2987
戩 1090

〔丨〕

雌 391
對 576
嘗 283
裳 283
1981
瞄 1506
嘖 3043
夥 1005
睡 2168
瞅 346
瞍 2201
賕 1815
賑 3101
賒 1986
睽 1296
墅 2146
嘟 558
嗷 31
暢 286
閨 844
聞 2445
2450
閩 1512
1513
閥 617
閤 761
910
閣 761
閡 910
嘈 249
嗽 2201
嘔 1604
1605
嘌 1653
暝 1523
1527
遏 2231
踉 1317
1373
1379
踊 1212
踞 1059
踩 588

遺 1746
鄙 122
129
蜻 1789
蜡 3051
蜥 2494
蜮 2983
蝀 544
蜨 534
蜾 860
蜴 2868
蜘 3137
蜓 2743
蜺 1572
蜧 65
蜩 2297
蜣 1750
蜷 1836
蜿 2381
蝍 1147
蜢 1487
蜬 878
嘘 2680
骰 1954
2336
骯 29
嗶 128
團 2356
嘍 1414
1417
鳴 1524
慁 998
嘀 497
嗾 2201
嘧 1494
幘 3043
嶄 3057
嶇 1821
獃 5
446
罳 2183
罰 617
幔 1459
幗 859
幛 3072
圖 2349
嶂 3072

〔丿〕

蜚 657
659
裴 1627
翡 659
舞 2477
舞 2682
製 3169
犒 1254
舔 2294
稭 1141
種 3183
3190
稱 302
303
321
毿 3194
稨 140
熏 2710
箝 1742
箍 802
箸 3214
箕 1016
箠 1145
1954
箋 1086
箎 328
算 2211
箇 764
箄 129
箑 385
筵 2743
箚 3049
箏 3106
箙 709
箔 183
管 830
箜 1272
毓 2978
僥 1126
僖 2494
僚 1380
僭 1102
牓 73
僕 1676
僑 1758
僱 816
像 2570
雋 1224
1236
僦 1206
僮 2324
僧 1947
鼻 114
魁 1296
遞 508
銜 2533
慇 2883
槃 1616
艋 1487
銂 2653
銬 1254
銠 1327
鉺 605
鋪 2945
銍 3171
銅 2324
鋁 1428
銦 2883
銖 3197
銑 2535
銛 542
銽 2528
銓 1837
鉿 910
銚 531
2779
銘 764
銘 1523
銫 1947
鉸 1126
鉩 2834
銃 341
銨 21
銀 2885
鉫 1919
貍 1338
貌 1470
餀 1757
餌 605
蝕 2073
餉 2564
餃 1126
餅 168
領 1398
膝 2209
膊 183
膈 761
膀 72
1621
1622
腿 2360
魟 918
复 2668
疑 2840
鳳 695
颱 2234
獄 2983
獐 3067
觫 2209
雒 1443
孵 698
遙 2778
貪 2884
遛 1408
1410

〔丶〕

誡 1156
誌 3171
誣 2457
語 2965
2983
誚 1763
誤 2485
誥 755
誘 2947
誨 991
誑 1293
說 2169
2172
3010
認 1891
誦 2199
誒 595
裹 860
敲 1757
豪 889
膏 752
755
塾 2137
廑 1164
麼 1446
1450
1470
1528
1537
廔 1425
腐 711
瘌 1305
瘧 1601
瘍 2768
瘟 2436
廓 1300
瘦 2128
瘉 2983
瘓 972
瘋 691
瘖 2883
塵 301
鄜 699
旗 1694
旖 2851
膂 1427
廖 1384
辣 1305
彰 3067
竭 1148
韶 1983
端 569
颯 1929
齊 1695
熠 3088
精 1180
粺 58
粹 412
粽 3275
歉 1748
槊 2176
愬 2209
熄 2500
熗 1757
熒 2904
榮 1904
滎 2904
犖 1443
熔 1904
煽 1961
漬 3271
漭 1463
漠 1535
漢 880
滿 1455
滯 3169
漆 1686
1829
漸 1085
1102
漣 1363
漕 250
漱 2146
漚 1603
1605
漂 1651
1652
1653
滷 1419
滹 934
漫 1454
1460
漯 1439
2231
滮 972
滌 495
潄 2685
漁 2957
漪 2834
漈 1059
滸 941
滾 851
漓 1338
漉 1422
漩 2688
漳 3067
滴 494
漾 2773
演 2755
滬 944
漏 1416
漲 3070
3072
滲 2018
漻 1381
慚 243
慪 1605
慳 1732
慢 1459
慥 252
3041
慟 2330

慊 1249
慵 2913
2914
憀 1380
慘 243
慣 833
搴 1732
寨 3054
寞 1535
賓 160
寡 819
窩 2452
窬 2958
窨 2710
2897
窪 2374
察 264
寧 1586
蜜 1494
寤 2485
寢 1777
寥 1380
實 2069
皸 1235
肇 3084
綮 1708
1802
褙 105
褐 910
複 723
褓 85
褕 2958
褌 1298
褊 140
褘 981
禡 1450
禛 3097
鼐 1494

〔乛〕

劃 953
961
盡 1172
暨 1059
屢 1427
鳲 2053
屣 2506
戟 709
遜 2717
隤 2360
嫣 2731
嫩 1568
嫗 2983
嫖 1652
嫦 283
嫚 1461
嫡 495
頗 1669
1670
翟 495
3052
翠 412
翣 1954
熊 2668
態 2237
凳 491
瞀 1470
1538
際 1059
障 3072
緒 2684
綾 1396
緅 3277
綺 1708
綽 390
網 2401
綱 744
緋 657
綏 1923
維 2419
綿 1495
綸 823
1434
綵 236
綬 2128
綢 345
綹 1409
綣 1841
綜 3275
綻 3060
綰 2389
綴 3233
綠 1422
1429
緇 3245

15 劃

〔一〕

慧 991
璈 31
瑾 1164
瑠 1172
璉 1363
慝 2264
靚 1193
璀 411
璁 402
瑽 402
璃 1338
1360
璇 2689
璋 3067
犛 1338
氂 1338
1466
斄 1338
奭 912
2106
輦 1580
髮 622
髯 1852
髫 2299
撓 1561
遶 1857
墳 674
撕 2183
撒 1928
1929
撢 457
駔 248
3034
3286
駛 2078
駟 2195
駙 724
駒 1210
駐 3214
駝 2370
駘 2234
撅 1224
撩 1380
1381
蔫 1575
2731
蓮 1364
蓴 389
蔌 2209
蔕 509
趣 409
1829
趟 2254
墟 2680
撲 1675
蓽 130
慕 1548
暮 1548
摹 1528
蔞 1415
蔓 1454
1461
2394
蔑 1508
蔴 1446
蔦 1583
蔔 183
186
蓬 1633
蔡 238
蔗 3090
蔟 409
撇 1654
撐 304
蕖 1823
蔻 1280
蔚 2432
2983
撮 416
418
3297
頡 1072
1149
蔣 1109
賣 1452
蓼 1383
1420
蔭 2883
2897
撫 713
撬 1758
1763
撟 1126
1134
赭 3090
撳 1777
播 178
185
撝 981
鞏 791
熱 1858
撚 1580
墩 580
嫯 31
熬 31
遨 31
撞 3230
撤 296
摯 3171
撙 3295
增 3046
撈 1318
1321
穀 812
撏 2715
墀 328
撰 3223
撥 177
蕢 674
歎 2249
鞋 2599
鞍 21
蕝 1230
鼒 3246
槥 992
椿 3228
模 1528
1539
槿 1164
樠 1454
槽 250
樞 2135
標 149
槱 2946
槭 3283
樗 2135
樓 1415
樅 401
樊 628
麩 699
麪 1503
槲 938
樟 3067
樣 2773
樛 1198
輘 1396
輛 1380
輞 2403
輗 1572
槧 1748
暫 3033
3060
輪 1434
輬 1373
輟 390
輜 3245
敷 699
遭 3035
甌 1603
1821
歐 1603
毆 1603
賢 2533
豎 2150
豌 2381
遷 1732
醋 409
醃 2731
醇 389
醉 3293
醅 1626
醊 391
醁 1422
厲 1357
慼 1686
碼 1448
磕 1258
磊 1332
憂 2923
磔 3088
磅 73
1620
磋 416
確 1844
碾 1580
鴈 2760
賚 1310
豬 3198
殣 1164

殢 2278
殤 1972
震 3101
霄 2579
霆 2310
霉 1476
霈 1630
鴉 2719
斳 3239

〔丨〕

鬧 1564
齒 329
劇 1220
獻 2680
膚 699
慮 1430
歔 934
輝 981
弊 128
幣 128
鷩 159
賞 1972
暱 1575
瞌 1257
瞋 297
暵 881
暴 92
1678
賦 724
賬 3072
賭 564
賤 1103
賜 401
賙 3193
賠 1627
瞇 1489
瞎 2513
瞑 1503
1523
1525
嘩 951
953
嘖 1630
嘻 2494
噎 2786
噁 592
嘶 2183
嘲 290
闈 1299
閭 1424
閱 3011
闐 1317
1318
數 2140
2146
2176
嘹 1381
影 2907
鄙 2571
踖 1041
踦 1044
2851
踐 1103
踧 409
踔 3239
踝 961
踢 2267
踏 2231
踟 328
踩 237
踮 514
踣 183
踒 1768
踡 1837
踠 1635
踪 3272
踠 2389
踞 1220
蝶 534
蝴 938
蛹 1556
蝘 2757
蝠 709
螟 1922
蝰 1296
蝎 2594
蝟 2433
蝸 818
2452
蝌 1258
蝮 724
蝗 978
蝯 2998
蝜 724
蝣 2935
蝤 1815
螂 1317
蝙 136
蝦 865
2514
骷 1282
嘬 369
3295
鄲 456
嘿 914
1535
噍 1119
1134
1198
嘮 1321
嘰 1016
嶢 2779
罵 1449
罷 43
45
1644
嶠 1134
嶔 1770
嶓 179
幡 624
幢 379
幟 3171
嶙 1389
嶒 258
幞 1677
嶝 491
墨 1535
默 2869
骻 1286
骶 926

〔丿〕

輩 104
耦 1604
靠 1254
稹 3099
稽 1017
1708
稷 1059
稻 479
黎 1338
稿 753
稼 1079
篋 1767
箸 1927
箱 2559
範 639
箴 3097
箯 136
篁 978
篌 926
箭 1103
篇 1647
篠 361
篆 3223
儆 1188
僵 1107
價 1077
牖 2945
儂 1594
儉 1090
儈 1289
儋 456
億 2868
儀 2841
躺 2254
鴃 1230
皚 5
鯀 1496
魄 1674
2372
皜 899
樂 1328
2783
3010
魅 1480
僻 1645
儍 1953
質 3148
3171
衚 938
德 485
徵 3107
3156
衝 335
341
慫 2197
徹 295
衛 2432
嬃 2680
艘 1940
磐 1617
盤 1616
鋪 1679
鋩 1463
鋪 1675
1678
鋙 2972
鋏 1072
銶 2264
銷 2577
鋇 105
銲 881
鋤 361
鋰 1344
鋯 755
鋌 2311
鋨 591
銼 418
鋒 692
鋅 2629
銳 1923
鋃 1317
鍋 1210
劍 1102
劊 850
1289
鄶 1289
頫 713
鄱 1670
慾 2983
虢 859
餑 179
餔 186
餖 557
餓 595
餘 2958
餒 1564
膜 1530
1535
膝 2494
遯 582
膛 2252
滕 2265
膣 3172
膠 1120
鴇 85
頠 2424
龥 1554
魷 2935
魯 1419
魴 647
穎 2909
獗 1230
獠 1381
颳 818
觭 1017
劉 1408
皺 3194

〔丶〕

請 1800
諸 3197
諏 3277
諆 1687
諑 3239
課 1265
誹 659
諉 2424
誕 462
諛 2958
誰 1998
2159
論 1434
1435
諍 3108
諗 2015
調 531
2297
諂 273
諒 1373
1380
諄 3234
誶 2218
談 2243
誼 2868
熟 2113
2137
遮 3084
廚 361
廝 2183
廣 839
廟 1507
摩 1528
麾 981
褒 78

廠 284
廛 269
廡 2478
瘩 445
瘞 2869
瘵 823
瘕 61
瘡 378
瘤 1408
瘠 1041
瘥 268
417
賡 768
慶 1802
麃 152
1623
廢 663
凜 1392
毅 2868
敵 495
適 2106
齑 1486
頦 866
1257
翔 1149
鄯 1965
養 2770
2774
鄰 1389
糊 938
糍 397
糅 1907
翦 1091
鄭 3118
瑩 2904
熠 2868
潔 1149
澆 1120
澉 741
澍 2150
澎 1632
1633
澌 2183
潢 978
潮 290
潸 1961
潭 2243
潦 1327
1381
潛 1742
潰 1297
澂 320
潲 1986
潟 2512
澥 898
潘 1615
潼 2325
澈 296
澇 1328
潯 2715
潤 1924
澗 1102
潺 269
澄 319
潑 1669
憤 676
憭 1381
1383
憯 244
憬 1188
憒 1298
憚 462
憮 2478
憍 1121
憔 1759
憧 335
憐 1363
憎 3047
憦 1327
憫 1513
寮 1381
寬 1290
寫 2601
審 2014
窰 2779
窮 1804
窳 2972
翩 1648
褡 422
褥 1920
褟 2230
褫 330
褌 1285
褵 1338
褪 2365
褦 1328
1554
鴆 3102

〔乛〕

蝨 2054
熨 3022
慰 2431
劈 1637
1644
履 1427
層 257
彈 462
2242
獎 1108
槳 1108
漿 1107
嬉 2494
嬋 268
嫺 2533
嬌 1119
駑 1596
駕 1079
勰 2599
戮 1422
翫 2394
翬 981
鄧 491
螯 1466
遹 2984
墮 588
墜 3233
隣 1389
緙 1265
緗 2560
練 1368
緘 1086
緬 1498
緲 1506
緹 2270
緝 1023
1686
緦 2183
縕 3022
緞 571
緶 143
線 2544
緱 794
緩 969
締 509
編 134
緡 1512
緯 2424
緣 2998
畿 1017
1697

16 劃

〔一〕

駮 183
璜 978
璞 1677
璟 1188
靜 1193
靛 528
璠 628
璘 1389
璣 1023
髻 1060
髭 3246
髹 2673
擖 1237
撻 2231
擭 1009
駬 605
駱 1443
駭 873
駢 1648
馳 327
撼 881
擁 1287
擂 1331
1333
蕘 1856
蕙 992
蕈 2717
蕆 273
蕨 1230
蕤 1923
蕓 3016
據 1220
擄 1419
1439
憨 873
歕 1631
蔽 129
瞢 1486
蕞 3294
蕺 1042
蕢 1298
薨 1486
蕪 2472
蕎 1759
蕉 1121
蕃 624
628
蕕 2936
擋 466
468
蕩 468
蕊 1923
蕁 2715
擓 3216
操 248
熹 2495
蔬 2135
擇 3043
3052
擐 972
薌 2560
頳 305
撿 1091
擒 1776
擔 456
462
壇 2245
擅 1965
擁 2914
2917
穀 938
擗 1645
磬 1803
薳 2424
鞘 1763
燕 2731
2760
薐 1334
薆 13
翰 881
噩 595
頤 2846
鴣 802
橈 1561
樺 961
樾 3012
橄 741
樹 2150
橫 916
917
樸 1677
橇 413
1758
橋 1759
樵 1759
橡 2571
橦 2325
樽 3295
樨 2495
橙 320
橘 1212
橢 2371
機 1017
輳 406
輻 709
轀 2436
輯 1041
輹 724
輸 2135
輶 2936
輮 1907
整 3108
賴 1310
橐 2371
甌 1603
融 1905
翮 910
頭 2336
瓢 1652
醐 938
醞 3022
醍 2270
醒 2654
鬵 131
磧 1723
磚 3219
醌 1498
2294
歷 1358
曆 1357
奮 677
憖 2897
頰 1072

遼 1381
豭 1072
殪 2869
殫 457
霖 1389
霏 657
霓 1572
霍 1009
霎 1954
霑 3055
頸 1188

〔丨〕

閺 925
冀 1059
頻 1656
餐 240
叡 1924
盧 1418
鄴 2796
憖 157
鼈 284
瞞 1454
瞟 1652
曉 2587
曄 2796
曀 2869
瞠 305
曇 2245
縣 2547
2689
鴨 2719
噤 1162
1173
閹 558
1988
閾 2984
閽 2731
閶 274
闍 995
閻 2743
闕 2731
遲 2528
曌 3084
暾 2364
曈 2325
噸 581
鴞 2580
踳 390
蹀 534
踹 369
踵 3183
踽 1212
踰 2960
嘴 3287
蹉 589
蹄 2270
蹁 1648
踴 2917
蹂 1907
遺 2434
2843
螓 1776
螞 1449
螈 2998
螄 2183
螗 2254
螃 1621
螟 1525
噱 1230
噹 466
骼 761
骸 866
器 1722
戰 3060
噪 3041
噬 2107
鴦 2763
嗳 8
12
噫 2834
嘯 2593
罹 1338
嶧 2869
嶼 2972
嶮 2536
臻 3097
默 1536
黔 1745

〔丿〕

耨 1596
憩 1723
積 1023
穆 1549
頹 2360
穄 1060
勳 2710
篝 794
篤 565
築 3200
篚 659
篹 410
篢 2213
3224
3287
篠 2587
篩 1954
篦 131
篘 342
篙 753
篑 2221
篛 1927
舉 1213
興 2640
2662
盥 834
學 2695
儔 345
儦 105
儒 1914
雔 345
儕 268
儐 161
艗 1585
翱 31
歈 2984
鴕 2371
儘 1164
劓 2869
徼 1126
1134
2776
衡 917
艙 247
錧 832
錶 156
鍺 3090
錯 419
錛 107
錡 1697
錸 1309
錢 1743
錕 1298
錫 2500
錮 816
鋼 745
銹 2676
錐 3232
錦 1164
錚 3108
錠 541
鄮 1317
鋸 1210
1221
錳 1487
錄 1422
錒 1
錙 3246
覦 2960
歙 2512
龕 21
貓 1463
墾 1267
餞 1103
餜 860
餛 997
餧 2434
餚 2779
餡 2547
館 832
餟 3233
鴒 1396
頷 881
膩 1575
膨 1634
膰 628
膧 2325
膳 1966
縢 2265
雕 529
鴟 325
穌 2201
鮒 724
鮑 94
鴝 1823
穎 2909
獨 559
獪 1289
獬 2603
鴛 2987

〔丶〕

諾 1602
諶 302
謀 1537
諜 534
謫 1556
諲 2883
諫 1103
諴 2534
諧 2600
諕 1601
2710
諟 2108
謁 2796
謂 2433
諰 2506
諤 595
謏 2587
諭 2984
諡 2108
諼 2687
諷 695
諺 2761
諮 3246
諳 21
諦 509
諠 2687
諢 998
諞 1648
1648
諱 992
諝 2682
憑 1668
憝 580
磨 1530
1536
麇 1483
廨 2603
瘼 1537
瘻 1417
1425
廩 1392
瘸 1843
瘵 3054
瘴 3074
瘺 1417
瘳 342
麈 1623
塵 3208
凝 1587
親 1770
1803
辨 143
辦 68
龍 1410
劑 1059
羸 1439
2907
壅 2917
羲 2495
糒 105
糗 1531
糢 1815
遴 1389
糖 2252
糕 753
遵 3295
導 472
480
燒 1982
燁 2796
燎 1383
1384
燋 1121
1759
燔 628
燃 1852
燉 581
582
熾 332
燐 1389
燊 2007
螢 2904
罃 2899
縈 2904
燜 1480
1484
燈 487
濩 1010
澣 970
濊 992
2434
盪 2254
澠 1513
2038

潞 1423
澧 1344
濃 1594
澡 3038
澤 3044
濁 3240
濴 2108
激 1022
澳 34
澮 1289
澹 463
2245
澥 2603
澶 269
濂 1364
澱 528
澼 1645
憧 545
憾 881
懆 252
懌 2869
懊 34
懈 2603
懍 1392
憶 2869
憲 2547
褰 1733
寰 966
寠 1221
窺 1295
冪 1494
褳 1366
褸 1428
褶 534
3088
禧 2495
禪 269
1966
禨 1027

〔乛〕

頵 1235
遲 328
壁 130
嬖 131
選 2690
隰 2895
隮 1027
嬙 1754
嬛 1807
嬝 1583
嬡 12
嬗 1966
豫 2984
氄 1906
隨 2213
隩 34
2984
險 2535
隧 2218
縝 3099
縛 709
縟 1920
緻 3171
縉 1173
縋 3233
縐 3195
縗 411
縞 754
縊 2869
縑 1087

17劃

〔一〕

璨 245
璩 1823
璫 466
璐 1423
環 966
璵 2960
璦 13
謷 32
覯 798
黿 2998
鬁 1359
鬀 3216
幫 71
擡 2234
擣 472
騁 321
騂 881
騂 2642
騃 1773
駷 6
駿 1236
薔 1755
薑 1107
趨 1821
蕹 2604
蕾 1332
邁 1454
薯 2142
蕘 918
藉 1042
1157
薤 2278
薛 2694
薇 2414
薈 992
薊 1060
薦 1104
薪 2629
薏 2870
薄 78
183
185
蕭 2579
戴 453
薜 132
薵 886
蕡 2984
螯 3084
擤 2654
擬 1572
壕 890
聱 31
螯 31
擠 1044
盩 3193
蟄 3149
縶 3149
擯 161
擦 225
擰 1588
1589
轂 813
轂 938
擱 758
聲 2034
罄 1803
擢 3240
聰 402
鄹 3277
聯 1364
懃 1776
艱 1087
鞠 1212
擎 1800
韓 878
隸 1359
櫻 305
檣 1754
櫃 1075
檔 467
469
櫛 1149
檄 2500
檢 1091
檜 850
1289
麰 1538
檎 1776
檐 2743
檀 2245
檩 1392
檥 2851
懋 1470
轅 2998
轄 2517
輾 1580
3058
擊 1025
臨 1390
蹥 2547
醛 1837
醢 871
醜 346
醨 1340
醣 2254
醚 1491
翳 2869
緊 2834
勵 1359
磽 1758
磺 978
壓 2719
礁 1121
磷 1390
1392
磴 491
磯 1027
尷 737
殭 1107
鴷 1386
殮 1369
霜 2156
霝 1396
霞 2517

〔丨〕

齔 303
鹵鹵 161
壑 912
1009
戲 934
2512
遽 1221
虧 1295
黻 709
瞥 1654
瞰 1249
瞭 1383
1384
顆 1258
瞶 850
瞧 1759
購 798
賻 724
嬰 2899
賺 3224
瞬 2171
瞳 2325
瞵 1391
瞪 491
嚆 885
嚇 912
2524
噓 2278
闉 2883
闌 1310
闃 1829
闆 65
闇 28
闊 1300
闈 2419
闋 1845
曙 2152
曖 12
嚅 1914
蹋 2231
蹈 480
蹊 2495
蹌 1750
1757
蹐 1042
蹉 416
蹋 1583
蟒 1463
螟 1446
1450
蟎 1459
螬 250
蟖 509
螳 2254
螻 1415
螺 1436
蟈 852
蟋 2495
螭 325
蟑 3067
蟀 2155
2176
骾 768
雖 2213
嚎 890
嚓 225
嚀 1588
幪 1486
幬 345
480
覬 1061
還 866
968
斁 568
2870
罽 1061
歟 367
嶺 1399
嶽 3012
嶸 1906
點 511
黜 367
黝 2946

〔丿〕

鏄 2524
矯 1126

熷 3048
鴶 819
穗 2218
黏 1580
篲 992
篺 1613
簌 2209
篳 130
簍 1416
篾 1508
簃 2846
篷 1634
簏 1424
簇 409
篰 224
簋 849
繁 628
1670
輿 2960
歟 2960
鵂 2673
優 2925
颱 674
黛 453
償 283
儡 1332
儲 365
鼾 873
皤 1670
魑 2984
邀 2776
徽 981
禦 2984
聳 2197
鵃 3193
鍥 1768
錨 1466
鍊 1369
鍼 3097
鍇 1245
鍘 3049
鍶 2184
鍋 852
鍔 595
錘 385
鍬 1758
鍾 3181
鍛 572
鍰 969
鍍 568
鍈 1479
鎡 3246
鎃 1615
鍵 1104
龠 3012
斂 1369
歛 1369
鴿 758
谿 2495
爵 1230
貔 1644
懇 1267
谿 2495
餬 938
餳 2653
餵 2434
餿 2201
餱 926
臌 813
膿 1594
臊 1940
1942
臉 1366
膾 1290
膽 457
膻 1961
臆 2869
臃 2914
2918
謄 2265
臏 2044
毚 269
鮭 845
鮪 2424
鮫 1121
鮮 2528
2536
鮟 21
獲 1010
獮 2536
颸 1221
獯 2710
獰 1588
邂 2604
繇 2780
2936
螽 3181

〔丶〕

講 1109
謊 979
謰 1366
謖 2209
謝 2603
謠 2779
謫 3277
謗 74
謎 1480
1491
謙 1733
燮 2603
謐 1494
褻 2603
襄 2560
氈 3055
邅 3055
麋 1491
麇 1491
膺 2900
應 2899
2910
癍 62
療 1381
癉 463
癌 5
癆 1321
癇 2534
癃 1412
顇 413
鵁 1121
麇 1491
齋 3052
糟 3035
糞 678
糙 249
糠 1250
糨 1112
糝 1937
馘 859
甑 3048
燦 244
燥 3041
燭 3201
燬 986
燠 34
2984
燴 992
燧 2218
營 2905
濛 1486
鴻 924
濤 2255
濫 1314
濡 1914
濬 1236
盪 469
濕 2054
濮 1677
濠 891
濟 1044
1060
瀁 2772
濱 161
濘 1570
1589
澀 1947
濯 3240
濰 2419
懥 3172
懨 2731
懦 1602
賽 1930
蹇 1092
謇 1092
竅 1291
窿 1412
鴳 2761
襇 1092
襁 1756
禮 1345

〔乛〕

臀 2365
璧 133
臂 105
131
擘 185
避 132
屨 1221
彌 1490
孺 1914
韔 287
牆 1754
蟞 1107
駑 1914
嬪 1657
翼 2869
蝨 1466
鍪 1538
隰 2500
隱 2893
績 1027
縹 1652
繃 112
113
縵 1461
縷 1428
縲 1331
總 3273
縱 3272
3275
縫 693
696
縭 1338
縴 1748
縮 2221
繆 1507
1527
1538
1549
繅 1940

18 劃

〔一〕

璿 2689
鼇 1338
攆 1580
鬆 2196
鬈 1837
鬃 3273
翹 1760
1763
擷 1149
2600
騏 1698
騎 1061
1697
騅 3233
騄 1424
擾 1857
藍 1311
藏 247
3035
攄 2136
薰 2711
舊 1206
藐 1506
薺 1061
1697
藎 1173
擻 2201
瞽 813
鼕 545
擺 54
薩 1930
壎 2710
壙 1293
擴 1301
贅 3233
贄 3172
擲 3149
燾 480
2259
罄 1803
聶 1585
聵 1298
職 3149
鞜 2232
鞨 910
鞦 1810
鞭 136
鞫 1212
鞬 1087
覲 1165
1173
藟 1332
賾 3045
檬 1486
檯 2235
檮 2259
櫃 850
檻 1104
1247
檳 161
檸 1588
櫂 3084
鵓 185

轉 3220
3224
蹔 3064
轆 1424
轇 1198
醓 813
覆 724
醪 1321
醫 2834
蹷 409
礡 185
礎 366
壓 2796
壐 2506
邇 605
燹 2536
饕 2305
殯 162
霤 1410

〔丨〕

豐 692
齕 911
覷 1829
懟 580
叢 406
斃 131
矇 1486
題 2270
蹥 2424
瞿 1221
1821
瞼 1092
瞻 3055
闖 379
闔 910
闐 2293
闒 2232
闓 1245
闑 1585
闕 1843
1845
顒 2914
曛 2711
蹟 1027
蹣 1455
1617
蹧 3036
蹚 2250
蹕 133
蹦 113
蹤 3273
蹠 3152
蹢 497
3151
蹝 1750
1757
壘 1332
蟢 2506
蟥 978
蟪 992
蟟 1383
蟲 340
蟬 269
蟠 1617
顒 1930
蟣 1044
髁 1258
髀 133
顎 595
鵑 1223
嚕 1417
1436
顓 3220
嚪 361
黠 2517
黟 2837

〔丿〕

鐔 2245
鵠 813
938
鵝 591
穡 1947
穢 992
馥 725
穠 1595
鵚 2346
魏 2434
簙 185
簧 978
簠 713
簞 528
簪 3032
3045
簣 1298
3045
簞 457
簡 1093
簦 489
鼬 2948
鼪 2038
雙 2156
軀 1822
駼 2352
魎 1377
魍 2403
歸 845
艟 2325
鎷 1449
鎮 3103
鎛 185
鎘 761
鎖 2227
鎶 2232
鎧 1245
鎢 2486
鎳 1585
鎚 385
鎩 1953
鎗 1750
鎦 1409
鎬 754
899
鎊 74
鎰 2870
鎌 1366
鎵 1072
翻 624
鵒 2984
貘 1537
邈 1506
雞 1027
饋 2513
餽 1298
餾 1410
餻 753
朦 1486
臍 1697
臏 162
龜 844
1235
1810
鯁 768
鯉 1346
鯀 851
鯑 2271
鯇 998
鯽 1061
颺 2768
颼 2201
獷 842
觴 1972
蟹 2605
獵 1386
雛 361

〔丶〕

謨 1531
謹 1165
謳 1603
謾 1455
謫 3088
謬 1527
1592
鄘 1293
癘 1359
癖 1141
1149
顏 2743
癒 2984
癖 1644
雜 3023
麐 1390
旛 627
甕 2451
糧 1373
燻 2711
燼 1173
燿 2783
鵜 2271
瀆 562
濾 1484
瀦 3198
濾 1430
鯊 1952
瀑 94
1679
濺 1104
濼 185
1443
瀏 1409
瀍 269
瀅 2906
瀉 2604
瀋 2015
竄 410
竅 1763
額 591
邃 2218
襟 1163
襠 466
襖 32
襜 268
禱 472
禰 1491
1573

〔乛〕

甓 1645
韞 3022
醬 1112
雟 2215
嬸 2015
戳 390
彝 2846
隳 982
嚮 2571
繞 1857
繖 1937
繚 1382
繢 992
繙 624
織 3137
繕 1966
繒 3048
斷 572
雝 2914

19 劃

〔一〕

鶄 2478
鵲 1185
瓊 1807
鬍 939
鬎 1306
黿 2374
騞 1011
騠 2271
騣 3273
騙 1650
騤 1296
蘙 1927
藝 2870
薑 268
繭 1094
藕 1605
藜 1340
藥 2783
3012
藤 2265
藷 2142
藩 629
蘊 3022
壞 963
鏊 32
難 1556
1559
鞲 794
鞴 105
鵲 1845
顛 509
櫝 562
麓 1424
櫟 1359
攀 1615
麴 1823
櫓 1419
櫥 361
櫚 1425
轕 761
轎 1134
蹔 3033
轍 3088
繫 1061
2513
覈 911
醭 186
1677
醮 1134
醯 2495
醱 1674
麗 1359
礙 13

願 3003
鶴 21
獺 674
蘗 3198
酃 1396
霪 2887
霧 2486

〔丨〕

齾 993
斷 2887
黼 713
鼈 159
矇 1484
1486
贈 3048
鶡 1298
嚥 2761
曝 1679
闞 1296
關 823
曠 1293
曜 2783
疇 345
蹺 1758
躇 362
蹶 1230
1231
蹽 1380
蹼 1677
蹻 1127
1758
蹯 629
蹴 409
蹲 415
581
蹭 258
蹬 492
蟶 305
蠅 2906
蠍 2594
蟾 269
蟺 1966
蟻 2851
獸 2128
巔 2852
罽 2687
羆 1644
羅 1437

〔丿〕

矱 1010
犢 562
贊 3032
穫 1010
穩 2447
籀 3195
簸 185
185
簳 741
簾 1222
簽 1734
簷 2744
簾 1366
簿 224
籥 2580
壘 2450
牘 562
邊 137
軥 925
懲 320
犨 1618
艤 2852
鏈 1369
鏗 1267
鏢 152
鏜 2250
鏝 1461
鏤 1417
鏦 402
鏟 273
鏞 2914
鏃 3283
鏇 2693
鏡 1194
鏑 497
鏹 1750
1756
鏘 1750
鏁 2227
辭 397
饃 1532
饉 1165
饅 1455
饈 2673
鵬 1634
臕 152
臘 1305
鵩 709
鵰 530
鯖 1793
鯪 1396
鯫 3277
鯤 1298
鯧 274
鯡 657
鯰 1580
鯛 530
鯨 1185
獺 2231
飂 2785

〔丶〕

譊 1561
譁 953
譚 2245
譖 3046
譙 1760
1763
識 2073
3172
譜 1678
證 3118
譎 1230
譏 1029
鶉 389
靡 1491
1492
廬 1418
贇 3013
癟 159
癡 325
龐 1621
離 1338
鶊 768
鏖 32
麒 1698
麕 1235
麑 1572
辦 70
龏 1414
韻 3022
羸 1331
旟 2960
旝 1290
甕 2451
羶 1961
羹 2564
羹 768
類 1333
爆 94
爍 2176
瀚 881
瀨 1310
瀝 1359
瀕 161
瀯 2605
瀘 1418
瀧 1412
2158
瀛 2906
瀠 2907
懵 1486
1487
懶 1313
懷 961
鵷 2987
寵 340
襤 1312
襦 1914

〔乛〕

韡 133
韠 185
疆 1108
韜 2255
騖 2486
纇 1939
歠 391
隴 1414
縫 445
韁 1108
繩 2038
繰 1940
3038
繯 969
繹 2870
繳 1126
3240
繪 993
繡 2675
邋 1305

20 劃

〔一〕

瓌 846
瓏 1413
鬐 1698
鬢 3099
鬑 1366
騮 1409
騶 3277
騷 1940
攉 2372
藿 1010
蘋 1657
1669
蘆 1418
蘧 581
蘄 1698
蘖 1585
蘅 917
蘇 2201
警 1189
藹 8
蘑 1531
藻 3038
蘛 1807
攖 2900
蘭 1392
攙 268
壤 1855
攘 1854
1855
攏 1413
1414
攔 1311
翿 482
馨 2629
顢 1455
勸 1841
鶘 939
櫪 1360
櫨 1418
櫸 1215
礬 629
麵 1503
櫬 303
轗 1247
轘 972
轙 2852
轔 1391
鶇 332
飄 1651
醵 1222
醴 1347
醲 1595
礪 1360
礫 1360
礦 1294
霰 2548

〔丨〕

鬪 557
齟 1215
齡 1396
齣 359
齠 2299
鹹 2534
獻 2547
耀 2785
黨 467
矍 1231
瞿 2900
贍 1966
懸 2689
闞 879
1247
1249
闠 993
1298
闡 273
鶡 911
曨 1413
曦 2495
躂 2232
躁 3041
躅 3201
蠖 1010
蠓 1487
蠕 1922
蠔 891
蠐 1698
蠑 1906
鶚 596
嚴 2744
嚼 1122

1231
囔 1854
1855
嚨 1413
巉 2495
巊 269
黐 2757
黥 1800

〔丿〕

犧 2495
鰲 1340
鶖 1810
籌 345
籃 1312
纂 3287
籍 1042
譽 2984
嚳 2960
覺 1135
1231
鼯 2473
犨 342
艨 1487
艦 1104
鐃 1561
鐐 1382
1384
鐧 1094
1104
鐫 1223
鐘 3181
鐠 1678
鐙 489
492
釋 2108
饒 1856
饋 1298
饌 3224
饑 1029
臙 2731
臚 1418
朧 1413
騰 2265
鰈 534
鰛 2436
鰓 1930
鰍 1810
鰒 725
鯿 139
觸 367
獼 1491

〔丶〕

譟 3041
譯 2872
譫 3056
議 2871
癥 3108
癢 2772
辮 144
競 1195
贏 2904
糯 1602
櫺 2357
爐 1418
瀟 2580
瀹 3012
瀲 1369
瀾 1312
1314
瀰 1491
懺 274
寶 85
騫 1735
豁 912
998
1010
竇 557
襪 2375
襬 55

〔乛〕

甓 134
譬 1645
驜 1585
孀 2158
孅 2529
鶩 2487
騖 3172
繻 2680
繾 1746
纁 2711
繽 161
繼 1061

21 劃

〔一〕

鬹 1586
蠢 390
瓔 2901
鬘 1455
攝 1996
驃 1653
驅 1822
騾 1438
驄 403
驂 241
蘧 1823
驀 1537
蘩 630
蘞 1366
蘚 2536
蘢 1413
蘭 1312
蘖 186
1586
蘗 1644
攜 2600
鶩 34
鷙 3172
攩 410
轂 1281
欂 185
櫺 1396
櫻 2900
欃 269
櫳 1413
欄 1312
轟 918
轞 1105
覽 1313
醺 2711
礮 1626
礦 993
覼 1438
飆 152
殲 1087
霸 44
露 1417
1424
霶 1620
霹 1638

〔丨〕

酆 693
齜 3246
齩 2781
齦 2887
齹 417
齸 1094
鬳瓜 2757
贓 3034
贐 1173
囁 1585
囀 3223
闥 2232
闤 969
闢 1645
顥 899
曩 1560
鷃 2761
躊 346
躋 1030
躍 2785
3012
罍 1331
纍 1331
蠣 1360
蠟 1306
髏 1415
鶻 813
939
囂 2580
巍 2414
巋 1296
黮 2247
黯 29

〔丿〕

穰 2927
酇 3033
籐 2266
儷 1360
顖 1760
魑 325
巇 1508
鐵 2303
鐳 1331
鐺 305
466
鐸 587
鐶 969
鐲 3240
鐮 1295
1366
鐿 2873
鷂 627
鶴 247
饘 3056
鷂 2451
鰭 1698
鰣 2074
鰥 829
鰩 2780
鰜 1088
獾 964
鷂 2785
鷗 1409

〔丶〕

護 944
譴 1746
魔 1531
鶴 1042
癩 1310
爛 1312
麝 1997
臟 2914
辯 144
礱 1413
齎 1030
贏 1439
懽 964
糲 1360
纇 1334
夔 1296
鶹 2873
鶼 1088
鶯 2901
爛 1314
灌 834
灃 693
灘 2914
懾 3088
懼 1222
竈 3041
顧 816
襯 303
襴 3012
襶 1854
鶴 891
912

〔乛〕

屬 2142
3208
羼 274
蠡 1341
1347
饗 2565
響 2564
纈 2600
續 2685
纊 1294
纏 269

22 劃

〔一〕

鬚 2680
攤 2240
攧 510
驍 2580
驊 953
驕 1121
驎 1392
覿 497
攦 1436
攢 410
3032
鰲 32
懿 2873
聽 2305
2311
韃 424
韁 1108
歡 964
權 1837
轢 1360
轡 1630
囊 1560
鷗 1603
鑒 1105
酈 1360
鷖 2837
贋 2761

霾 1450
霽 1061

〔丨〕

齬 2972
齪 391
贖 2138
矓 1413
囈 2873
饕 2255
躚 2529
躓 3172
躕 362
躑 3152
躐 1387
疊 534
囉 1436
巔 510
羇 1030

〔丿〕

鐔 2245
鑪 1418
穰 1854
籜 2372
籟 1310
籧 1823
籙 1424
籠 1413
1414
儼 2757
鼴 2757
艫 1418
鑊 1011
鑄 3214
鑑 1105
龢 911
龕 1247
糴 497
臟 3035
鰱 1366
鰹 1088
鰾 157
鱈 2706
鰻 1455
玀 1438
獵 2538

〔丶〕

讀 557
563
譾 1094
譒 2015
巒 1430
彎 2381
孿 1432
孌 1432
瓤 1854
顫 274
鷓 3091
癭 2909
癬 2692
癮 2895
聾 1413
龔 790
襲 2500
鷟 3240
饔 2914
鷩 134
鱉 157
爝 1231
灘 2241
灑 1929
竊 1768
襶 453
襴 1313

〔乛〕

鬻 2984
纑 1418

23 劃

〔一〕

鬟 969
攬 1313
驛 2874
驗 2761
蘸 3064
蘿 1438
驚 1185
蘼 1491
蘺 1341
虀 1030
攩 467
攫 1231
攢 3287
攪 754
1127
轤 1418
轢 1360
邐 1347
饜 2761
靨 2796
鷯 1382

〔丨〕

曬 1954
顯 2536
蠨 2580
蠱 813
髒 3034
髓 2215
體 2271
髑 563
邏 1438
巘 2757
巖 2746
黲 244

〔丿〕

籥 3012
籤 1735
鬚 2495
讎 346
鷦 1122
鑤 95
鑠 2176
鑕 3172
鑛 1295
鑣 152
鑞 1306
臢 3025
3034
鱝 678
鱖 851
1231
鱔 1966
鱗 1392
鱘 2715
蠭 693

〔丶〕

讌 2762
變 145
欒 1430
攣 1432
戀 1370
鷲 1207
癯 1823
癰 2914
麟 1392
齏 1030
蠲 1223
戄 1231

〔乛〕

鷸 2985
纓 2901
纖 2529
纔 234
纕 1854
2560
鷥 2184

24 劃

〔一〕

纛 482
鬢 162
驟 3280
壩 44
鼇 32
韆 1735
虆 1331
矗 369
蠹 568
鹽 2746
2762
醽 1398
釀 1582
醾 1491
魘 2757
靆 453
靂 1360
靈 1396
靄 8
蠶 243

〔丨〕

豔 2762
顰 1657
齶 596
齷 2454
齲 1827
鹼 1094
矙 1249
鷺 1424
躞 2605
蠵 2495
髕 162
囑 3208
羈 1030
鸀 2143

〔丿〕

罐 834
黌 931
鷽 2705
衢 1823
鑪 1418
鑫 2629
鱣 3056

〔丶〕

讖 303
讒 269
讓 1855
讕 1313
鸇 3056
鷹 2901
癱 2241
癲 510
贛 742
蠢 325
灞 44
灝 899
鸂 2495
襻 1619

〔乛〕

鷫 2210

25 劃

〔一〕

鬭 557
鬣 1387
攮 1560
觀 828
835
虋 1572
欖 1314
靉 13

〔丨〕

顱 1418
躡 1586
躥 410
鼉 2371
黵 459

〔丿〕

籮 1439
籩 139
籬 1341
釁 2637
贙 924
鑰 2785
3012
鑲 2560
獾 966
饞 269
鱚 2495

〔丶〕

讙 966
蠻 1455
臠 1430
廳 2307
灣 2382

〔乛〕

糶 2302
纘 3287

26 劃

〔一〕

驥 1062
驢 1425
趲 3032
韉 1088
黶 2757

〔丨〕

矚 3208
蠼 1231

〔丿〕

鑷 1586

〔丶〕

讚 3033
灤 1430

27 劃

〔一〕

驩 966
驤 2560
顴 1840
顳 1586
釅 2762

〔丨〕

鸕 1419
躪 1392
黷 563

〔丿〕

齉 1595
鑼 1439
鑽 3286
3287
鱷 596
鱸 1419

〔丶〕

讞 2762
讜 467
鑾 1430
灨 742

〔乛〕

纜 1314
1315

28 劃

鬮 1198
鑿 3036
鸚 2901
戇 3230

29 劃

〔一〕

驪 1341
鸛 835
鬱 2985

30 劃以上

鸝 1341
爨 410
鸞 1430
灩 2762
籲 2985
麤 408